W9-DAU-372

THE UNABRIDGED MARK TWAIN
Volume II

Samuel Langhorne Clemens (1835–1910), c. 1872

THE UNABRIDGED

VOLUME II

Edited by Lawrence Teacher

Running Press
Philadelphia, Pennsylvania

PRINTED IN THE UNITED STATES OF AMERICA

Canadian representatives: John Wiley & Sons Canada, Ltd.
22 Worcester Road, Rexdale, Ontario M9W 1L1

International representatives: Kaiman & Polon, Inc.
2175 Lemoine Avenue, Fort Lee, New Jersey 07024

9 8 7 6 5 4 3
Digit on the right indicates the number of this printing

Library of Congress Cataloging in Publication Data

Clemens, Samuel Langhorne, 1835–1910
Twain unabridged, vol. 2
I. Title
PZ3.C59Tw 1979 PS1302 813'.4 79-9576
ISBN 0-89471-086-9 paperback
ISBN 0-89471-087-7 library binding

Cover illustration by Charles Santore
Cover design by James Wizard Wilson
Cover calligraphy by Peter Ruge
Interior illustration by Suzanne Clee
Design by Peter John Dorman & Stuart Teacher
Research assistance by Richard Scholl

This book was typeset from first editions of Mark Twain's works. The publisher wishes to thank Lyman W. Riley, Assistant Director of Libraries for Special Collections, Van Pelt Library, University of Pennsylvania, for his help in procuring these first editions.

Typography: English Times, with Garamond, by Comp•Art, Inc., Philadelphia, Pennsylvania; composition direction by J. Richard Conklin
Printed and bound by Port City Press, Baltimore, Maryland

This book may be ordered directly from the publisher.
Please include 75 cents postage.

Try your bookstore first.

Running Press
38 South Nineteenth Street
Philadelphia, Pennsylvania 19103

EDITOR'S NOTE

This volume represents a completed journey through the best of Mark Twain's fiction. If you already own *The Unabridged Mark Twain,* this book completes your library and is the last of Twain that this house will publish.

Because so many typesetters, writers, editors, and publishers altered Twain's words, I have attempted to go back and set stories and novels exclusively from his first editions. These were the only works that came close to being approved by him. Each novel and short story is preceded by a little note containing an occasional anecdote and a brief chronology of its publication.

My pleasure in working on *The Unabridged Mark Twain 2* was greatly enhanced by the contributions of my editorial associate, Alida Becker. This book has been an especially rewarding experience for me and there is a certain sadness that I feel in running out of first-rate Twain.

LAWRENCE TEACHER
PHILADELPHIA, PA.

CONTENTS

Mark Twain's Burlesque Autobiography and First Romance *was a small volume brought out in 1871 by Sheldon and Company, publishers of* Galaxy, *a magazine to which Twain was a regular contributor. Although Twain was not happy with the book (several years later he bought the plates and had them destroyed), he did include both the autobiography and the romance in later collections of his work. "A Burlesque Biography" appeared in* The $30,000 Bequest and Other Stories, *published by Harper & Brothers in 1906.*

A Burlesque Biography

Two or three persons having at different times intimated that if I would write an autobiography they would read it when they got leisure, I yield at last to this frenzied public demand and herewith tender my history.

Ours is a noble old house, and stretches a long way back into antiquity. The earliest ancestor the Twains have any record of was a friend of the family by the name of Higgins. This was in the eleventh century, when our people were living in Aberdeen, county of Cork, England. Why it is that our long line has ever since borne the maternal name (except when one of them now and then took a playful refuge in an alias to avert foolishness), instead of Higgins, is a mystery which none of us has ever felt much desire to stir. It is a kind of vague, pretty romance, and we leave it alone. All the old families do that way.

Arthour Twain was a man of considerable note—a solicitor on the highway in William Rufus's time. At about the age of thirty he went to one of those fine old English places of resort called Newgate, to see about something, and never returned again. While there he died suddenly.

Augustus Twain seems to have made something of a stir about the year 1160. He was as full of fun as he could be, and used to take his old sabre and sharpen it up, and get in a convenient place on a dark night, and stick it through people as they went by, to see them jump. He was a born humorist. But he got to going too far with it; and the first time he was found stripping one of these parties, the authorities removed one end of him, and put it up on a nice high place on Temple

Bar, where it could contemplate the people and have a good time. He never liked any situation so much or stuck to it so long.

Then for the next two hundred years the family tree shows a succession of soldiers—noble, high-spirited fellows, who always went into battle singing, right behind the army, and always went out a-whooping, right ahead of it.

This is a scathing rebuke to old dead Froissart's poor witticism that our family tree never had but one limb to it, and that that one stuck out at right angles, and bore fruit winter and summer.

Early in the fifteenth century we have Beau Twain, called "the Scholar." He wrote a beautiful, beautiful hand. And he could imitate anybody's hand so closely that it was enough to make a person laugh his head off to see it. He had infinite sport with his talent. But by-and-by he took a contract to break stone for a road, and the roughness of the work spoiled his hand. Still, he enjoyed life all the time he was in the stone business, which, with inconsiderable intervals, was some forty-two years. In fact, he died in harness. During all those long years he gave such satisfaction that he never was through with one contract a week till the government gave him another. He was a perfect pet. And he was always a favorite with his fellow-artists, and was a conspicuous member of their benevolent secret society, called the Chain Gang. He always wore his hair short, had a preference for striped clothes, and died lamented by the government. He was a sore loss to his country. For he was so regular.

Some years later we have the illustrious John Morgan Twain. He came over to this country with Columbus in 1492 as a passenger. He appears to have been of a crusty, uncomfortable disposition. He complained of the food all the way over, and was always threatening to go ashore unless there was a change. He wanted fresh shad. Hardly a day passed over his head that he did not go idling about the ship with his nose in the air, sneering about the commander, and saying he did not believe Columbus knew where he was going to or had ever been there before. The memorable cry of "Land ho!" thrilled every heart in the ship but his. He gazed a while through a piece of smoked glass at the pencilled line lying on the distant water, and then said: "Land be hanged,—it's a raft!"

When this questionable passenger came on board the ship, he brought nothing with him but an old newspaper containing a handkerchief marked "B.G.," one cotton sock marked "L.W.C.," one woollen one marked "D.F.," and a night-shirt marked "O.M.R." And yet during the voyage he worried more about his "trunk," and gave himself more airs about it, than all the rest of the passengers put together. If the ship was "down by the head," and would not steer, he would go and move his "trunk" farther aft, and then watch the effect. If the ship was "by the stern," he would suggest to Columbus to detail some men to "shift that baggage." In storms he had to be gagged, because his wailings about his "trunk" made it impossible for the men to hear the orders. The man does not appear to have been openly charged with any gravely unbecoming thing, but it is noted in the ship's log as a "curious circumstance" that albeit he brought his baggage on board the ship in a newspaper, he took it ashore in four trunks, a queensware crate, and a couple of champagne baskets. But when he came back insinuating, in an insolent, swaggering way, that some of his things were missing, and was going to search the other passengers' baggage, it was too much, and they threw him overboard. They watched long and wonderingly for him to come up, but not even a bubble rose on the quietly ebbing tide. But while every one was most absorbed in gazing over the side, and the interest was momentarily increasing, it was observed with consternation that the vessel was adrift and the anchor-cable hanging limp from the bow. Then in the ship's dimmed and ancient log we find this quaint note:

"In time it was discouvered yt ye troblesome passenger hadde gonne downe and got ye anchor, and toke ye same and solde it to ye dam sauvages from ye interior, saying yt he hadde founde it, ye sonne of a ghun!"

Yet this ancestor had good and noble instincts, and it is with pride that we call to mind the fact that he was the first white person who ever interested himself in the work of elevating and civilizing our Indians. He built a commodious jail and put up a gallows, and to his dying day he claimed with satisfaction that he had had a more restraining and elevating influence on the Indians than any other reformer that ever labored among them. At this point the chronicle becomes less frank and chatty, and closes abruptly by saying that the old voyager went to see his gallows perform on the first white man ever hanged in America, and while there received injuries which terminated in his death.

The great-grandson of the "Reformer" flourished in sixteen hundred and something, and was known in our annals as "the old Admiral," though in history he had other titles. He was long in command of fleets of swift vessels, well armed and manned, and did great service in hurrying up merchantmen. Vessels which he followed and kept his eagle eye on, always made good fair time across the ocean. But if a ship still loitered in spite of all he could do, his indignation would grow till he could contain himself no longer—and then he would take that ship home where he lived and keep it there carefully, expecting the owners to come for it, but they never did. And he would try to get the idleness and sloth out of the sailors of that ship by compelling them to take invigorating exercise and a bath. He called it "walking a plank." All the pupils liked it. At any rate they never found any fault with it after trying it. When the owners were late coming for their ships, the Admiral always burned them, so that the insurance money should not be lost. At last this fine old tar was cut down in the fulness of his years and honors. And to her dying day, his poor heart-broken widow believed that if he had been cut down fifteen minutes sooner he might have been resuscitated.

Charles Henry Twain lived during the latter part of the seventeenth century, and was a zealous and distinguished missionary. He converted sixteen thousand South Sea islanders, and taught them that a dog-tooth necklace and a pair of spectacles was not enough clothing to come to divine service in. His poor flock loved him very, very dearly; and when his funeral was over, they got up in a body (and came out of the restaurant) with tears in their eyes, and saying, one to another, that he was a good tender missionary, and they wished they had some more of him.

Pah-go-to-wah-wah-pukketekeewis (Mighty-Hunter-with-a-Hog-Eye-Twain) adorned the middle of the eighteenth century, and aided General Braddock with all his heart to resist the oppressor Washington. It was this ancestor who fired seventeen times at our Washington from behind a tree. So far the beautiful romantic narrative in the moral story-books is correct; but when that narrative goes on to say that at the seventeenth round the awe-stricken savage said solemnly that that man was being reserved by the Great Spirit for some mighty mission, and he dared not lift his sacrilegious rifle against him again, the narrative seriously impairs the integrity of history. What he did say was:

"It ain't no (hic) use. 'At man's so drunk he can't stan' still long enough for a man to hit him. I (hic) I can't 'ford to fool away any more am'nition on him."

That was why he stopped at the seventeenth round, and it was a good, plain, matter-of-fact reason, too, and one that easily commends itself to us by the eloquent, persuasive flavor of probability there is about it.

I always enjoyed the story-book narrative, but I felt a marring misgiving that every Indian at Braddock's Defeat who fired at a soldier a couple of times (two easily grows to seventeen in a century), and missed him, jumped to the conclusion that the Great Spirit was reserving that soldier for some grand mission; and so I somehow feared that the only reason why Washington's case is remembered and the others forgotten is, that in his the prophecy came true, and in that of the others it didn't. There are not books enough on earth to contain the record of the prophecies Indians and other unauthorized parties have made; but one may carry in his overcoat-pockets the record of all the prophecies that have been fulfilled.

I will remark here, in passing, that certain ancestors of mine are so thoroughly well-known in history by their aliases, that I have not felt it to be worth while to dwell upon them, or even mention them in the order of their birth. Among these may be mentioned Richard Brinsley Twain, alias Guy Fawkes; John Wentworth Twain, alias Jack Sheppard; Ananias Twain, alias Baron Munchausen; John George Twain, alias Captain Kydd; and then there are George Francis Train, Tom Pepper, Nebuchadnezzar, and Baalam's Ass—they all belong to our family, but to a branch of it somewhat distinctly removed from the honorable direct line—in fact, a collateral branch, whose members chiefly differ from the ancient stock in that, in order to acquire the notoriety we have always yearned and hungered for, they have got into a low way of going to jail instead of getting hanged.

It is not well, when writing an autobiography, to follow your ancestry down too close to your own time—it is safest to speak only vaguely of your great-grandfather, and then skip from there to yourself, which I now do.

I was born without teeth—and there Richard III had the advantage of me; but I was born without a humpback, likewise, and there I had the advantage of him. My parents were neither very poor nor conspicuously honest.

But now a thought occurs to me. My own history would really seem so tame contrasted with that of my ancestors, that it is simply wisdom to leave it unwritten until I am hanged. If some other biographies I have read had stopped with the ancestry until a like event occurred, it would have been a felicitous thing for the reading public. How does it strike you?

THE UNABRIDGED

VOLUME II

The Tragedy of Pudd'nhead Wilson *first appeared in the* Century *magazine from December 1893 to June 1894. To promote the serialization, the* Century *printed up a pamphlet called* Pudd'nhead Wilson's Calendar, *composed of the maxims that open each chapter of the novel, and distributed it to subscribers, newstands, and bookshops. When the American Publishing Company brought out* The Tragedy of Pudd'nhead Wilson *in book form in November of 1894, it was paired with* The Comedy Those Extraordinary Twins, *which had at one time been incorporated into the novel.*

The Tragedy of
Pudd'nhead Wilson

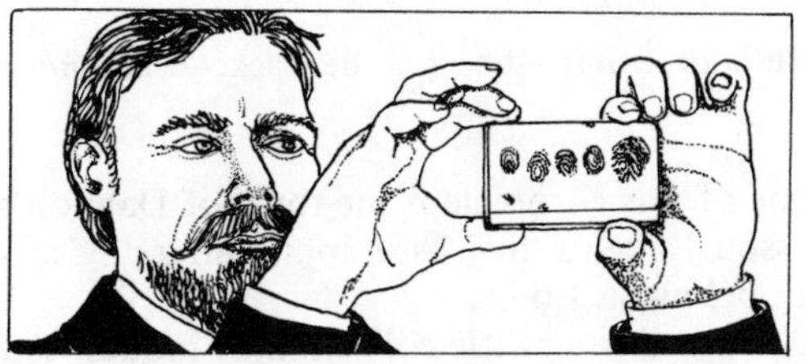

A WHISPER TO THE READER

There is no character, howsoever good and fine, but it can be destroyed by ridicule, howsoever poor and witless. Observe the ass, for instance: his character is about perfect, he is the choicest spirit among all the humbler animals, yet see what ridicule has brought him to. Instead of feeling complimented when we are called an ass, we are left in doubt.—*Pudd'nhead Wilson's Calendar.*

A person who is ignorant of legal matters is always liable to make mistakes when he tries to photograph a court scene with his pen; and so I was not willing to let the law chapters in this book go to press without first subjecting them to rigid and exhausting revision and correction by a trained barrister—if that is what they are called. These chapters are right, now, in every detail, for they were rewritten under the immediate eye of William Hicks, who studied law part of a while in southwest Missouri thirty-five years ago and then came over here to Florence for his health and is still helping for exercise and board in Macaroni Vermicelli's horse-feed shed which is up the back alley as you turn around the corner out of the Piazza del Duomo just beyond the house where that stone that Dante used to sit on six hundred years ago is let into the wall when he let on to be watching them built Giotto's campanile and yet always got tired looking as soon as Beatrice passed along on her way to get a chunk of chestnut cake to defend herself with in case of a Ghibelline outbreak before she got to school, at the same old stand where they sell the same old cake to this day and it is just as light and good as it was then, too, and this is not flattery, far from it. He was a little rusty on his law, but he rubbed up for this book, and those two or three legal chapters are right and straight, now. He told me so himself.

Given under my hand this second day of January, 1893, at the Villa Viviani, village of Settignano, three miles back of Florence, on the hills—the same certainly affording the most charming view to be found on this planet, and with it the most dream-like and enchanting sunsets to be found in any planet or even in any solar system—and given, too, in the swell room of the house, with the busts of Cerretani senators and other grandees of this line looking approvingly down upon me as they used to look down upon Dante, and mutely asking me to adopt them into my family, which I do with pleasure, for my remotest ancestors are but spring chickens compared with these robed and stately antiques, and it will be a great and satisfying lift for me, that six hundred years will.

Mark Twain.

CHAPTER I

Tell the truth or trump—but get the trick.—*Pudd'nhead Wilson's Calendar.*

The scene of this chronicle is the town of Dawson's Landing, on the Missouri side of the Mississippi, half a day's journey, per steamboat, below St. Louis.

In 1830 it was a snug little collection of modest one-and two-story frame dwellings whose whitewashed exteriors were almost concealed from sight by climbing tangles of rose-vines, honeysuckles and morning-glories. Each of these pretty homes had a garden in front fenced with white palings and opulently stocked with hollyhocks, marigolds, touch-me-nots, prince's-feathers and other old-fashioned flowers; while on the window-sills of the houses stood wooden boxes containing moss-rose plants and terra-cotta pots in which grew a breed of geranium whose spread of intensely red blossoms accented the prevailing pink tint of the rose-clad house-front like an explosion of flame. When there was room on the ledge outside of the pots and boxes for a cat, the cat was there—in sunny weather—stretched at full length, asleep and blissful, with her furry belly to the sun and a paw curved over her nose. Then that house was complete, and its contentment and peace were made manifest to the world by this symbol, whose testimony is infallible. A home without a cat—and a well-fed, well-petted and properly revered cat—may be a perfect home, perhaps, but how can it prove title?

All along the streets, on both sides, at the outer edge of the brick sidewalks, stood locust-trees with trunks protected by wooden boxing, and these furnished shade for summer and a sweet fragrance in spring when the clusters of buds came forth. The main street, one block back from the river, and running parallel with it, was the sole business street. It was six blocks long, and in each block two or three brick stores three stories high towered above interjected bunches of little frame shops. Swinging signs creaked in the wind, the street's whole length. The candy-striped pole which indicates nobility proud and ancient along the palace-bordered canals of Venice, indicated merely the humble barbershop along the main street of Dawson's Landing. On a chief corner stood a lofty unpainted pole wreathed from top to bottom with tin pots and pans and cups, the chief tinmonger's noisy notice to the world (when the wind blew) that his shop was on hand for business at that corner.

The hamlet's front was washed by the clear waters of the great river; its body stretched itself rearward up a gentle incline; its most rearward border fringed itself out and scattered its houses about the base-line of the hills; the hills rose high, inclosing the town in a half-moon curve, clothed with forests from foot to summit.

Steamboats passed up and down every hour or so. Those belonging to the little Cairo line and the little Memphis line always stopped; the big Orleans liners stopped for hails only, or to land passengers or freight; and this was the case also with the great flotilla of "transients." These latter came out of a dozen rivers—the Illinois, the Missouri, the Upper Mississippi, the Ohio, the Monongahela, the Tennessee, the Red River, the White River, and so on; and were bound every whither and stocked with every imaginable comfort or necessity which the Mississippi's communities could want, from the frosty Falls of St. Anthony down through nine climates to torrid New Orleans.

Dawson's Landing was a slaveholding town, with a rich slave-worked grain and pork country back of it. The town was sleepy and comfortable and contented. It was fifty years old, and was growing slowly—very slowly, in fact, but still it was growing.

The chief citizen was York Leicester Driscoll, about forty years old, judge of the county court. He was very proud of his old Virginian ancestry, and in his hospitalities and his rather formal and stately manners he kept up its traditions. He was fine and just and generous. To be a gentleman—a gentleman without stain or blemish—was his only religion, and to it he was always faithful. He was respected, esteemed and beloved by all the community. He was well off, and was gradually adding to his store. He and his wife were very nearly happy, but not quite, for they had no children. The longing for the treasure of a child had grown stronger and stronger as the years slipped away, but the blessing never came—and was never to come.

With this pair lived the Judge's widowed sister, Mrs. Rachel Pratt, and she also was childless—childless, and sorrowful for that reason, and not to be comforted. The women were good and commonplace people, and did their duty and had their reward in clear consciences and the community's approbation. They were Presbyterians, the Judge was a free-thinker.

Pembroke Howard, lawyer and bachelor, aged about forty, was another old Virginian grandee with proved descent from the First Families. He was a fine, brave, majestic creature, a gentleman according to the nicest requirements of the Virginia rule, a devoted Presbyterian, an authority on the "code," and a man always courteously ready to stand up before you in the field if any act or word of his had seemed doubtful or suspicious to you, and explain it with any weapon you might prefer from brad-awls to artillery. He was very popular with the people, and was the Judge's dearest friend.

Then there was Colonel Cecil Burleigh Essex, another F. F. V. of formidable caliber—however, with him we have no concern.

Percy Northumberland Driscoll, brother to the Judge, and younger than he by five years, was a married man, and had had children around his hearthstone; but they were attacked in detail by measles, croup and scarlet fever, and this had given the doctor a chance with his effective antediluvian methods; so the cradles were empty. He was a prosperous man, with a good head for speculations, and his fortune was growing. On the 1st of February, 1830, two boy babes were born in his house: one to him, the other to one of his slave girls, Roxana by name. Roxana was twenty years old. She was up and around the same day, with her hands full, for she was tending both babies.

Mrs. Percy Driscoll died within the week. Roxy remained in charge of the children. She had her own way, for Mr. Driscoll soon absorbed himself in his speculations and left her to her own devices.

In that same month of February, Dawson's Landing gained a new citizen. This was Mr. David Wilson, a young fellow of Scotch parentage. He had wandered to this remote region from his birthplace in the interior of the State of New York, to seek his fortune. He was twenty-five years old, college-bred, and had finished a post-college course in an Eastern law school a couple of years before.

He was a homely, freckled, sandy-haired young fellow, with an intelligent blue eye that had frankness and comradeship in it and a covert twinkle of a pleasant sort. But for an unfortunate remark of his, he would no doubt have entered at once upon a successful career at Dawson's Landing. But he made his fatal remark the first day he spent in the village, and it "gaged" him. He had just made the acquaintance of a group of citizens when an invisible dog began to yelp and snarl and howl and make himself very comprehensively disagreeable, whereupon young Wilson said, much as one who is thinking aloud—

"I wish I owned half of that dog."

"Why?" somebody asked.

"Because I would kill my half."

The group searched his face with curiosity, with anxiety even, but found no light there, no expression that they could read. They fell away from him as from something uncanny, and went into privacy to dicuss him. One said:

" 'Pears to be a fool."

" 'Pears?" said another. "*Is,* I reckon you better say."

"Said he wished he owned *half* of the dog, the idiot," said a third. "What did he reckon would become of the other half if he killed his half? Do you reckon he thought it would live?"

"Why, he must have thought it, unless he *is* the downrightest fool in the world; because if he hadn't thought it, he would have wanted to own the whole dog, knowing that if he killed his half and the other half died, he would be responsible for that half just the same as if he had killed that half instead of his own. Don't it look that way to you, gents?"

"Yes, it does. If he owned one half of the general dog, it would be so; if he owned one end of the dog and another person owned the other end, it would be so, just the same; particularly in the first case, because if you kill one half of a general dog, there ain't any man that can tell whose half it was, but if he owned one end of the dog, maybe he could kill his end of it and——"

"No, he couldn't either; he couldn't and not be responsible if the other end died, which it would. In my opinion the man ain't in his right mind."

"In my opinion he hain't *got* any mind."

No. 3 said: "Well, he's a lummox, anyway."

"That's what he is," said No. 4, "he's a labrick—just a Simon-pure labrick, if ever there was one."

"Yes, sir, he's a dam fool, that's the way I put him up," said No. 5. "Anybody can think different that wants to, but those are my sentiments."

"I'm with you, gentlemen," said No. 6. "Perfect jackass—yes, and it ain't going too far to say he is a pudd'nhead. If he ain't a pudd'nhead, I ain't no judge, that's all."

Mr. Wilson stood elected. The incident was told all over the town, and gravely discussed by everybody. Within a week he had lost his first name; Pudd'nhead took its place. In time he came to be liked, and well liked too; but by that time the nickname had got well stuck on, and it stayed. That first day's verdict made him a fool, and he was not able to get it set aside, or even modified. The nickname soon ceased to carry any harsh or unfriendly feeling with it, but it held its place, and was to continue to hold its place for twenty long years.

CHAPTER II

Adam was but human—this explains it all. He did not want the apple for the apple's sake, he wanted it only because it was forbidden. The mistake was in not forbidding the serpent; then he would have eaten the serpent.—*Pudd'nhead Wilson's Calendar.*

Pudd'nhead Wilson had a trifle of money when he arrived, and he bought a small house on the extreme western verge of the town. Between it and Judge Driscoll's house there was only a grassy yard, with a paling fence dividing the properties in the middle. He hired a small office down in the town and hung out a tin sign with these words on it:

DAVID WILSON.

ATTORNEY AND COUNSELOR-AT-LAW.
SURVEYING, CONVEYANCING, ETC.

But his deadly remark had ruined his chance—at least in the law. No clients came. He took down his sign, after a while, and put it up on his own house with the law features knocked out of it. It offered his services now in the humble capacities of land-surveyor and expert accountant. Now and then he got a job of surveying to do, and now and then a merchant got him to straighten out his books. With Scotch patience and pluck he resolved to live down his reputation and work his way into the legal field yet. Poor fellow, he could not foresee that it was going to take him such a weary long time to do it.

He had a rich abundance of idle time, but it never hung heavy on his hands, for he interested himself in every new thing that was born into the universe of ideas, and studied it and experimented upon it at his house. One of his pet fads was palmistry. To another one he gave no name, neither would he explain to anybody what its purpose was, but merely said it was an amusement. In fact he had found that his fads added to his reputation as a pudd'nhead; therefore he was growing chary of being too communicative about them. The fad without a name was one which dealt with people's finger-marks. He carried in his coat pocket a shallow box with grooves in it, and in the grooves strips of glass five inches long and three inches wide. Along the lower edge of each strip was pasted a slip of white paper. He asked people to pass their hands through their hair (thus collecting upon them a thin coating of the natural oil) and then make a thumb-mark on a glass strip, following it with the mark of the ball of each finger in succession. Under this row of faint grease-prints he would write a record on the strip of white paper—thus:

JOHN SMITH, *right hand—*

and add the day of the month and the year, then take Smith's left hand on another glass strip, and add name and date and the words "left hand." The strips were now returned to the grooved box, and took their place among what Wilson called his "records."

He often studied his records, examining and poring over them with absorbing interest until far into the night; but what he found there—if he found anything—he revealed to no one. Sometimes he copied on paper the involved and delicate pattern left by the ball of a finger, and then vastly enlarged it with a pantograph so that he could examine its web of curving lines with ease and convenience.

One sweltering afternoon—it was the first day of July, 1830—he was at work over a set of tangled account-books in his work-room, which looked westward over a stretch of vacant lots, when a conversation outside disturbed him. It was carried on in yells, which showed that the people engaged in it were not close together:

"Say, Roxy, how does yo' baby come on?" This from the distant voice.

"Fust-rate; how does *you* come on, Jasper?" This yell was from close by.

"Oh, I's middlin'; hain't got noth'n' to complain of. I's gwine to come a-court'n' you bimeby, Roxy."

"*You* is, you black mud-cat! Yah—yah—yah! I got somep'n' better to do den 'sociat'n' wid niggers as black as you is. Is ole Miss Cooper's Nancy done give you de mitten?" Roxy followed this sally with another discharge of care-free laughter.

"You's jealous, Roxy, dat's what's de matter wid *you,* you hussy—yah—yah—yah! Dat's de time I got you!"

"Oh, yes, *you* got me, hain't you. 'Clah to goodness if dat conceit o' yo'n strikes in, Jasper, it gwine to kill you sho'. If you b'longed to me I'd sell you down de river 'fo' you git too fur gone. Fust time I runs acrost yo' marster, I's gwine to tell him so."

This idle and aimless jabber went on and on, both parties enjoying the friendly duel and each well satisfied with his own share of the wit exchanged—for wit they considered it.

Wilson stepped to the window to observe the combatants; he could not work while their chatter continued. Over in the vacant lots was Jasper, young, coal-black and of magnificent build, sitting on a wheelbarrow in the pelting sun—at work, supposably, whereas he was in fact only preparing for it by taking an hour's rest before beginning. In front of Wilson's porch stood Roxy, with a local hand-made baby-wagon, in which sat her two charges—one at each end and facing each other. From Roxy's manner of speech, a stranger would have expected her to be black, but she was not. Only one sixteenth of her was black, and that sixteenth did not show. She was of majestic form and stature, her attitudes were imposing and statuesque, and her gestures and movements distinguished by a noble and stately grace. Her complexion was very fair, with the rosy glow of vigorous health in the cheeks, her face was full of character and expression, her eyes were brown and liquid, and she had a heavy suit of fine soft hair which was also brown, but the fact was not apparent because her head was bound about with a checkered handkerchief and the hair was concealed under it. Her face was shapely, intelligent and comely—even beautiful. She had an easy, independent carriage—when she was among her own caste—and a high and "sassy" way, withal; but of course she was meek and humble enough where white people were.

To all intents and purposes Roxy was as white as anybody, but the one sixteenth of her which was black outvoted the other fifteen parts and made her a negro. She was a slave, and salable as such. Her child was thirty-one parts white, and he, too, was a slave, and by a fiction of law and custom a negro. He had blue eyes and flaxen curls like his white comrade, but even the father of the white child was able to tell the children apart—little as he had commerce with them—by their clothes: for the white babe wore ruffled soft muslin and a coral necklace, while the other wore merely a coarse tow-linen shirt which barely reached to its knees, and no jewelry.

The white child's name was Thomas à Becket Driscoll, the other's name was Valet de Chambre: no surname—slaves hadn't the privilege. Roxana had heard that phrase somewhere, the fine sound of it had pleased her ear, and as she had supposed it was a name, she loaded it on to her darling. It soon got shortened to "Chambers," of course.

Wilson knew Roxy by sight, and when the duel of wit began to play out, he stepped outside to gather in a record or two. Jasper went to work energetically, at once, perceiving that his leisure was observed. Wilson inspected the children and asked—

"How old are they, Roxy?"

"Bofe de same age, sir—five months. Bawn de fust o' Feb'uary."

"They're handsome little chaps. One's just as handsome as the other, too."

A delighted smile exposed the girl's white teeth, and she said:

"Bless yo' soul, Misto Wilson, it's pow'ful nice o' you to say dat, 'ca'se one of 'em ain't on'y a nigger. Mighty prime little nigger, *I* al'ays says, but dat's ca'se it's mine, o' course."

"How do you tell them apart, Roxy, when they haven't any clothes on?"

Roxy laughed a laugh proportioned to her size, and said:

"Oh, *I* kin tell 'em 'part, Misto Wilson, but I bet Marse Percy couldn't, not to save his life."

Wilson chatted along for awhile, and presently got Roxy's finger-prints for his collection—right hand and left—on a couple of his glass strips; then labeled and dated them, and took the "records" of both children, and labeled and dated them also.

Two months later, on the 3d of September, he took this trio of finger-marks again. He liked to have a "series," two or three "takings" at intervals during the period of childhood, these to be followed by others at intervals of several years.

The next day—that is to say, on the 4th of September—something occurred which profoundly impressed Roxana. Mr. Driscoll missed another small sum of money—which is a way of saying that this was not a new thing, but had happened before. In truth it had happened three times before. Driscoll's patience was exhausted. He was a fairly humane man toward slaves and other animals; he was an exceedingly humane man toward the erring of his own race. Theft he could not abide, and plainly there was a thief in his house. Necessarily the thief must be one of his negroes. Sharp measures must be taken. He called his servants before him. There were three of these, besides Roxy: a man, a woman, and a boy twelve years old. They were not related. Mr. Driscoll said:

"You have all been warned before. It has done no good. This time I will teach you a lesson. I will sell the thief. Which of you is the guilty one?"

They all shuddered at the threat, for here they had a good home, and a new one was likely to be a change for the worse. The denial was general. None had stolen anything—not money, anyway—a little sugar, or cake, or honey, or something like that, that "Marse Percy wouldn't mind or miss," but not money—never a cent of money. They were eloquent in their protestations, but Mr. Driscoll was not moved by them. He answered each in turn with a stern "Name the thief!"

The truth was, all were guilty but Roxana; she suspected that the others were guilty, but she did not know them to be so. She was horrified to think how near she had come to being guilty herself; she had been saved in the nick of time by a revival in the colored Methodist Church, a fortnight before, at which time and place she "got religion." The very next day after that gracious experience, while her change of style was fresh upon her and she was vain of her purified condition, her master left a couple of dollars lying unprotected on his desk, and she happened upon that temptation when she was polishing around with a dust-rag. She looked at the money awhile with a steadily rising resentment, then she burst out with—

"Dad blame dat revival, I wisht it had 'a' be'n put off till to-morrow!"

Then she covered the tempter with a book, and another member of the kitchen cabinet got it. She made this sacrifice as a matter of religious etiquette; as a thing necessary just now, but by no means to be wrested into a precedent; no, a week or two would limber up her piety, then she would be rational again, and the next two dollars that got left out in the cold would find a comforter—and she could name the comforter.

Was she bad? Was she worse than the general run of her race? No. They had an unfair show in the battle of life, and they held it no sin to take military advantage of the enemy—in a small way; in a small way, but not in a large one. They would smouch provisions from the pantry whenever they got a chance; or a brass thimble, or a cake of wax, or an emery-bag, or a paper of needles, or a silver spoon, or a dollar bill, or small articles of clothing, or any other property of light value; and so far were they from considering such reprisals sinful, that they would go to church and shout and pray the loudest and sincerest with their plunder in their pockets. A farm smoke-house had to be kept heavily padlocked, for even the colored deacon himself could not resist a ham when Providence showed him in a dream, or otherwise, where such a thing hung lonesome and longed for some one to love. But with a hundred hanging before him the deacon would not take two—that is, on the same night. On frosty nights the humane negro prowler would warm the end of a plank and put it up under the cold claws of chickens roosting in a tree; a drowsy hen would step on to the comfortable board, softly clucking her gratitude, and the prowler would dump her into his bag, and later into his stomach, perfectly sure that in taking this trifle from the man who daily robbed him of an inestimable treasure—his liberty—he was not committing any sin that God would remember against him in the Last Great Day.

"Name the thief!"

For the fourth time Mr. Driscoll had said it, and always in the same hard tone. And now he added these words of awful import:

"I give you one minute"—he took out his watch. "If at the end of that time you have not confessed, I will not only sell all four of you, *but*—I will sell you down the river!"

It was equivalent to condemning them to hell! No Missouri negro doubted this. Roxy reeled in her tracks and the color vanished out of her face; the others dropped to their knees as if they had been shot; tears gushed from their eyes, their supplicating hands went up, and three answers came in the one instant:

"I done it!"

"I done it!"

"I done it!—have mercy, marster—Lord have mercy on us po' niggers!"

"Very good," said the master, putting up his watch, "I will sell you *here* though you don't deserve it. You ought to be sold down the river."

The culprits flung themselves prone, in an ecstasy of gratitude, and kissed his feet, declaring that they would never forget his goodness and never cease to pray for him as long as they lived. They were sincere, for like a god he had stretched forth his mighty hand and closed the gates of hell against them. He knew, himself, that he had done a noble and gracious thing, and was privately well pleased with his magnanimity; and that night he set the incident down in his diary, so that his son might read it in after years, and be thereby moved to deeds of gentleness and humanity himself.

CHAPTER III

Whoever has lived long enough to find out what life is, knows how deep a debt of gratitude we owe to Adam, the first great benefactor of our race. He brought death into the world.—*Pudd'nhead Wilson's Calendar.*

Percy Driscoll slept well the night he saved his house-minions from going down the river, but no wink of sleep visited Roxy's eyes. A profound terror had taken possession of her. Her child could grow up and be sold down the river! The thought crazed her with horror. If she dozed and lost herself for a moment, the next moment she was on her feet flying to her child's cradle to see if it was still there. Then she would gather it to her heart and pour out her love upon it in a frenzy of kisses, moaning, crying, and saying "Dey sha'n't, oh, dey *sha'n't!*—yo' po' mammy will kill you fust!"

Once, when she was tucking it back in its cradle again, the other child nestled in its sleep and attracted her attention. She went and stood over it a long time communing with herself:

"What has my po' baby done, dat he couldn't have yo' luck? He hain't done noth'n'. God was good to you; why warn't he good to him? Dey can't sell *you* down de river. I hates yo' pappy; he hain't got no heart—for niggers he hain't, anyways. I hates him, en I could kill him!" She paused awhile, thinking; then she burst into wild sobbings again, and turned away, saying, "Oh, I got to kill my chile, dey ain't no yuther way,—killin' *him* wouldn't save de chile fum goin' down de river. Oh, I got to do it, yo' po' mammy's got to kill you to save you, honey"—she gathered her baby to her bosom, now, and began to smother it with caresses—"Mammy's got to kill you—how *kin* I do it! But yo' mammy ain't gwine to desert you—no, no; *dah,* don't cry—she gwine *wid* you, she gwine to kill herself too. Come along, honey, come along wid mammy; we gwine to jump in de river, den de troubles o' dis worl' is all over—dey don't sell po' niggers down the river over *yonder.*"

She started toward the door, crooning to the child and hushing it; midway she stopped, suddenly. She had caught sight of her new Sunday gown—a cheap curtain-calico thing, a conflagration of gaudy colors and fantastic figures. She surveyed it wistfully, longingly.

"Hain't ever wore it yet," she said, "en it's jist lovely." Then she nodded her head in response to a pleasant idea, and added, "No, I ain't gwine to be fished out, wid everybody lookin' at me, in dis mis'able ole linsey-woolsey."

She put down the child and made the change. She looked in the glass and was astonished at her beauty. She resolved to make her death-toilet perfect. She took off her handkerchief-turban and dressed her glossy wealth of hair "like white folks"; she added some odds and ends of rather lurid ribbon and a spray of atrocious artificial flowers; finally she threw over her shoulders a fluffy thing called a "cloud" in that day, which was of a blazing red complexion. Then she was ready for the tomb.

She gathered up her baby once more; but when her eye fell upon its miserably short little gray tow-linen shirt and noted the contrast between its pauper shabbiness and her own volcanic irruption of infernal splendors, her mother-heart was touched, and she was ashamed.

"No, dolling, mammy ain't gwine to treat you so. De angels is gwine to 'mire you jist as much as dey does yo' mammy. Ain't gwine to have 'em putt'n' dey han's up 'fo' dey eyes en sayin' to David en Goliah en dem yuther prophets, 'Dat chile is dress' too indelicate fo' dis place.' "

By this time she had stripped off the shirt. Now she clothed the naked little creature in one of Thomas à Becket's snowy long babygowns, with its bright blue bows and dainty flummery of ruffles.

"Dah—now you's fixed." She propped the child in a chair and stood off to inspect it. Straightway her eyes began to widen with astonishment and admiration, and she clapped her hands and cried out, "Why, it do beat all!—I *never* knowed you was so lovely. Marse Tommy ain't a bit puttier—not a single bit."

She stepped over and glanced at the other infant; she flung a glance back at her own; then one more at the heir of the house. Now a strange light dawned in her eyes, and in a moment she was lost in thought. She seemed in a trance; when she came out of it she muttered, "When I 'uz a-washin' 'em in de tub, yistiddy, his own pappy asked me which of 'em was his'n."

She began to move about like one in a dream. She undressed Thomas à Becket, stripping him of everything, and put the tow-linen shirt on him. She put his coral necklace on her own child's neck. Then she placed the children side by side, and after earnest inspection she muttered—

"Now who would b'lieve clo'es could do de like o' dat? Dog my cats if it ain't all *I* kin do to tell t' other fum which, let alone his pappy."

She put her cub in Tommy's elegant cradle and said—

"You's young Marse *Tom* fum dis out, en I got to practise and git used to 'memberin' to call you dat, honey, or I 's gwine to make a mistake some time en git us bofe into trouble. Dah—now you lay still en don't fret no mo', Marse Tom—oh, thank de good Lord in heaven, you's saved, you's saved!—dey ain't no man kin ever sell mammy's po' little honey down de river now!"

She put the heir of the house in her own child's unpainted pine cradle, and said, contemplating its slumbering form uneasily—

"I 's sorry for you, honey; I 's sorry, God knows I is,—but what *kin* I do, what *could* I do? Yo' pappy would sell him to somebody, some time, en den he'd go down de river, sho', en I couldn't, couldn't, *couldn't* stan' it."

She flung herself on her bed and began to think and toss, toss and think. By and by she sat suddenly upright, for a comforting thought had flown through her worried mind—

" 'T ain't no sin—*white* folks has done it! It ain't no sin, glory to goodness it ain't no sin! *Dey 's* done it—yes, en dey was de biggest quality in de whole bilin', too—*kings!*"

She began to muse; she was trying to gather out of her memory the dim particulars of some tale she had heard some time or other. At last she said—

"Now I 's got it; now I 'member. It was dat ole nigger preacher dat tole it, de time he come over here fum Illinois en preached in de nigger church. He said dey ain't nobody kin save his own self—can't do it by faith, can't do it by works, can't do it no way at all. Free grace is de *on'y* way, en dat don't come fum nobody but jis' de Lord; en *he* kin give it to anybody he please, saint or sinner—*he* don't kyer. He do jis' as he's a mineter. He s'lect out anybody dat suit him, en put another one in his place, en make de fust one happy forever en leave t' other one to burn wid Satan. De preacher said it was jist like dey done in Englan' one time, long time ago. De queen she lef' her baby layin' aroun' one day, en went out callin'; en one o' de niggers roun' 'bout de place dat was 'mos' white, she come in en see de chile layin' aroun', en tuck en put her own chile's clo'es on de queen's chile, en put de queen's chile's clo'es on her own chile, en den lef' her own chile layin' aroun' en tuck en toted de queen's chile home to de nigger-quarter, en nobody ever foun' it out, en her chile was de king bimeby, en sole de queen's chile down de river one time when dey had to settle up de estate. Dah, now—de preacher said it his own self, en it ain't no sin, 'ca'se white folks done it. *Dey* done it—yes, *dey* done it; en not on'y jis' common white folks nuther, but de biggest quality dey is in de whole bilin'. Oh, I 's *so* glad I 'member 'bout dat!"

She got up light-hearted and happy, and went to the cradles and spent what was left of the night "practising." She would give her own child a light pat and say humbly, "Lay still, Marse Tom," then give the real Tom a pat and say with severity, "Lay *still,* Chambers!—does you want me to take somep'n' *to* you?"

As she progressed with her practice, she was surprised to see how steadily and surely the awe which had kept her tongue reverent and her manner humble toward her young master was transferring itself to her speech and manner toward the usurper, and how similarly handy she was becoming in transferring her motherly curtness of speech and peremptoriness of manner to the unlucky heir of the ancient house of Driscoll.

She took occasional rests from practising, and absorbed herself in calculating her chances.

"Dey'll sell dese niggers to-day fo' stealin' de money, den dey'll buy some mo' dat don't know de chillen—so *dat's* all right. When I takes de chillen out to git de air, de minute I 's roun' de corner I 's gwine to gaum dey mouths all roun' wid jam, den dey can't *nobody* notice dey's changed. Yes, I gwineter do dat till I 's safe, if it's a year.

"Dey ain't but one man dat I 's afeard of, en dat's dat Pudd'nhead Wilson. Dey calls him a pudd'nhead, en says he's a fool. My lan', dat man ain't no mo' fool den I is! He's de smartes' man in dis town, less'n it's Jedge Driscoll or maybe Pem Howard. Blame dat man, he worries me wid dem ornery glasses o' hisn; *I* b'lieve he's a witch. But nemmine, I 's gwine to happen aroun' dah one o' dese days en let on dat I reckon he wants to print de chillen's fingers ag'in; en if *he* don't notice dey's changed, I bound dey ain't nobody gwine to notice it, en den I 's safe, sho'. But I reckon I 'll tote along a hoss-shoe to keep off de witch-work."

The new negroes gave Roxy no trouble, of course. The master gave her none, for one of his speculations was in jeopardy, and his mind was so occupied that he hardly saw the children when he looked at them, and all Roxy had to do was to get them both into a gale of laughter when he came about; then their faces were mainly cavities exposing gums, and he was gone again before the spasm passed and the little creatures resumed a human aspect.

Within a few days the fate of the speculation became so dubious that Mr. Percy went away with his brother the Judge, to see what could be done with it. It was a land speculation as usual, and it had gotten complicated with a lawsuit. The men were gone seven weeks. Before they got back Roxy had paid her visit to Wilson, and was satisfied. Wilson took the finger-prints, labeled them with the names and with the date—October the first—put them carefully away and continued his chat with Roxy, who seemed very anxious that he should admire the great advance in flesh and beauty which the babies had made since he took their finger-prints a month before. He complimented their improvement to her contentment; and as they were without any disguise of jam or other stain, she trembled all the while and was miserably frightened lest at any moment he—

But he didn't. He discovered nothing; and she went home jubilant, and dropped all concern about the matter permanently out of her mind.

CHAPTER IV

Adam and Eve had many advantages, but the principal one was, that they escaped teething.—*Pudd'nhead Wilson's Calendar.*

There is this trouble about special providences—namely, there is so often a doubt as to which party was intended to be the beneficiary. In the case of the children, the bears and the prophet, the bears got more real satisfaction out of the episode than the prophet did, because they got the children.—*Pudd'nhead Wilson's Calendar.*

This history must henceforth accommodate itself to the change which Roxana has consummated, and call the real heir "Chambers" and the usurping little slave "Thomas à

Becket"— shortening this latter name to "Tom," for daily use, as the people about him did.

"Tom" was a bad baby, from the very beginning of his usurpation. He would cry for nothing; he would burst into storms of devilish temper without notice, and let go scream after scream and squall after squall, then climax the thing with "holding his breath"— that frightful specialty of the teething nursling, in the throes of which the creature exhausts its lungs, then is convulsed with noiseless squirmings and twistings and kickings in the effort to get its breath, while the lips turn blue and the mouth stands wide and rigid, offering for inspection one wee tooth set in the lower rim of a hoop of red gums; and when the appalling stillness has endured until one is sure the lost breath will never return, a nurse comes flying, and dashes water in the child's face, and—presto! the lungs fill, and instantly discharge a shriek, or a yell, or a howl which bursts the listening ear and surprises the owner of it into saying words which would not go well with a halo if he had one. The baby Tom would claw anybody who came within reach of his nails, and pound anybody he could reach with his rattle. He would scream for water until he got it, and then throw cup and all on the floor and scream for more. He was indulged in all his caprices, howsoever troublesome and exasperating they might be; he was allowed to eat anything he wanted, particularly things that would give him the stomach-ache.

When he got to be old enough to begin to toddle about and say broken words and get an idea of what his hands were for, he was a more consummate pest than ever. Roxy got no rest while he was awake. He would call for anything and everything he saw, simply saying "Awnt it!" (want it), which was a command. When it was brought, he said in a frenzy, and motioning it away with his hands, "Don't awnt it! don't awnt it!" and the moment it was gone he set up frantic yells of "Awnt it! awnt it! awnt it!" and Roxy had to give wings to her heels to get that thing back to him again before he could get time to carry out his intention of going into convulsions about it.

What he preferred above all other things was the tongs. This was because his "father" had forbidden him to have them lest he break windows and furniture with them. The moment Roxy's back was turned he would toddle to the presence of the tongs and say "Like it!" and cock his eye to one side to see if Roxy was observing; then, "Awnt it!" and cock his eye again; then, "Hab it!" with another furtive glance; and finally, "Take it!"—and the prize was his. The next moment the heavy implement was raised aloft; the next, there was a crash and a squall, and the cat was off on three legs to meet an engagement; Roxy would arrive just as the lamp or a window went to irremediable smash.

Tom got all the petting, Chambers got none. Tom got all the delicacies, Chambers got mush and milk, and clabber without sugar. In consequence Tom was a sickly child and Chambers wasn't. Tom was "fractious," as Roxy called it, and overbearing; Chambers was meek and docile.

With all her splendid common sense and practical every-day ability, Roxy was a doting fool of a mother. She was this toward her child—and she was also more than this: by the fiction created by herself, he was become her master; the necessity of recognizing this relation outwardly and of perfecting herself in the forms required to express the recognition, had moved her to such diligence and faithfulness in practicing these forms that this exercise soon concreted itself into habit; it became automatic and unconscious; then a natural result followed: deceptions intended solely for others gradually grew practically into self-deceptions as well; the mock reverence became real reverence, the mock obsequiousness real obsequiousness, the mock homage real homage; the little counterfeit rift of separation between imitation-slave and imitation-master widened and widened, and became an abyss, and a very real one—and on one side of it stood Roxy, the dupe of her own deceptions, and on the other stood her child, no longer a usurper to her, but her accepted and recognized master. He was her darling, her master, and her deity all in one, and in her worship of him she forgot who she was and what he had been.

In babyhood Tom cuffed and banged and scratched Chambers unrebuked, and Chambers early learned that between meekly bearing it and resenting it, the advantage all lay with the former policy. The few times that his persecutions had moved him beyond control and made him fight back had cost him very dear at headquarters; not at the hands of Roxy, for if she ever went beyond scolding him sharply for "forgitt'n' who his young marster was," she at least never extended her punishment beyond a box on the ear. No, Percy Driscoll was the person. He told Chambers that under no provocation whatever was he privileged to lift his hand against his little master. Chambers overstepped the line three times, and got three such convincing canings from the man who was his father and did n't know it, that he took Tom's cruelties in all humility after that, and made no more experiments.

Outside of the house the two boys were together all through their boyhood. Chambers was strong beyond his years, and a good fighter; strong because he was coarsely fed and hard worked about the house, and a good fighter because Tom furnished him plenty of practice—on white boys whom he hated and was afraid of. Chambers was his constant body-guard, to and from school; he was present on the playground at recess to protect his charge. He fought himself into such a formidable reputation, by and by, that Tom could have changed clothes with him, and "ridden in peace," like Sir Kay in Launcelot's armor.

He was good at games of skill, too. Tom staked him with marbles to play "keeps" with, and then took all the winnings away from him. In the winter season Chambers was on hand, in Tom's worn-out clothes, with "holy" red mittens, and "holy" shoes, and pants "holy" at the knees and seat, to drag a sled up the hill for Tom, warmly clad, to ride down on; but he never got a ride himself. He built snow men and snow fortifications under Tom's directions. He was Tom's patient target when Tom wanted to do some snowballing, but the target couldn't fire back. Chambers carried Tom's skates to the river and strapped them on him, then trotted around after him on the ice, so as to be on hand when wanted; but he wasn't ever asked to try the skates himself.

In summer the pet pastime of the boys of Dawson's Landing was to steal apples, peaches, and melons from the farmers' fruit wagons,—mainly on account of the risk they ran of getting their heads laid open with the butt of the farmer's whip. Tom was a distinguished adept at these thefts—by proxy. Chambers did his stealing, and got the peach-stones, apple-cores, and melon-rinds for his share.

Tom always made Chambers go in swimming with him, and stay by him as a protection. When Tom had had enough, he would slip out and tie knots in Chambers' shirt, dip the knots in the water to make them hard to undo, then dress himself and sit by and laugh while the naked shiverer tugged at the stubborn knots with his teeth.

Tom did his humble comrade these various ill turns partly out of native viciousness, and partly because he hated him for his superiorities of physique and pluck, and for his manifold clevernesses. Tom couldn't dive, for it gave him splitting headaches. Chambers could dive without inconvenience, and was fond of doing it. He excited so much admiration, one day, among a crowd of white boys, by throwing back somersaults from the stern of a canoe, that it wearied Tom's spirit, and at last he shoved the canoe underneath Chambers while he was in the air—so he came down on the canoe-bottom; and while he lay unconscious, several of Tom's ancient adversaries saw that their long-desired opportunity was come, and they gave the false heir such a drubbing that with Chambers's best help he was hardly able to drag himself home afterward.

When the boys were fifteen and upward, Tom was "showing off" in the river one day, when he was taken with a cramp, and shouted for help. It was a common trick with the boys— particularly if a stranger was present—to pretend a cramp and howl for help; then when the stranger came tearing hand over hand to the rescue, the howler would go on struggling and howling till he was close at hand, then replace the howl with a sarcastic smile and swim blandly away, while the town boys assailed the dupe with a volley of jeers and laughter. Tom had never tried this joke as yet, but was supposed to be trying it now, so the boys held warily back; but Chambers believed his master was in earnest, therefore he swam out, and arrived in time, unfortunately, and saved his life.

This was the last feather. Tom had managed to endure everything else but to have to remain publicly and permanently under such an obligation as this to a nigger, and to this nigger of all niggers—this was too much. He heaped insults upon Chambers for "pretending to think he was in earnest in calling for help, and said that anybody but a block-headed nigger would have known he was funning and left him alone.

Tom's enemies were in strong force here, so they came out with their opinions quite freely. They laughed at him, and called him coward, liar, sneak, and other sorts of pet names, and told him they meant to call Chambers by a new name after this, and make it common in town—"Tom Driscoll's niggerpappy,"—to signify that he had had a second birth into this life, and that Chambers was the author of his new being. Tom grew frantic under these taunts, and shouted—

"Knock their heads off, Chambers! knock their heads off! What do you stand there with your hands in your pockets for?"

Chambers expostulated, and said, "But, Marse Tom, dey's too many of 'em—dey's—"

"Do you hear me?"

"Please, Marse Tom, don't make me! Dey's so many of 'em dat———"

Tom sprang at him and drove his pocketknife into him two or three times before the boys could snatch him away and give the wounded lad a chance to escape. He was considerably hurt, but not seriously. If the blade had been a little longer his career would have ended there.

Tom had long ago taught Roxy "her place." It had been many a day now since she had ventured a caress or a fondling epithet in his quarter. Such things, from a "nigger," were repulsive to him, and she had been warned to keep her distance and remember who she was. She saw her darling gradually cease from being her son, she saw *that* detail perish utterly; all that was left was master—master, pure and simple, and it was not a gentle mastership, either. She saw herself sink from the sublime height of motherhood to the somber depths of unmodified slavery. The abyss of separation between her and her boy was complete. She was merely his chattel, now, his convenience, his dog, his cringing and helpless slave, the humble and unresisting victim of his capricious temper and vicious nature.

Sometimes she could not go to sleep, even when worn out with fatigue, because her rage boiled so high over the day's experiences with her boy. She would mumble and mutter to herself—

"He struck me, en I warn't no way to blame—struck me in de face, right before folks. En he's al'ays callin' me nigger-wench, en hussy, en all dem mean names, when I's doin' de very bes' I kin. Oh, Lord, I done so much for him—I lift'd him away up to what he is—en dis is what I git for it."

Sometimes when some outrage of peculiar offensiveness stung her to her heart, she would plan schemes of vengeance and revel in the fancied spectacle of his exposure to the world as an imposter and a slave; but in the midst of these joys fear would strike her: she had made him too strong; she could prove nothing, and—heavens, she might get sold down the river for her pains! So her schemes always went for nothing, and she laid them aside in impotent rage against the fates, and against herself for playing the fool on that fatal September day in not providing herself with a witness for use in the day when such a thing might be needed for the appeasing of her vengeance-hungry heart.

And yet the moment Tom happened to be good to her, and kind,—and this occurred every now and then,—all her sore places were healed, and she was happy; happy and proud, for this was her son, her nigger son, lording it among the whites and securely avenging their crimes against her race.

There were two grand funerals in Dawson's Landing that fall—the fall of 1845. One was that of Colonel Cecil Burleigh Essex, the other that of Percy Driscoll.

On his death-bed Driscoll set Roxy free and delivered his idolized ostensible son solemnly into the keeping of his brother, the Judge and his wife. Those childless people were glad to get him. Childless people are not difficult to please.

Judge Driscoll had gone privately to his brother, a month before, and bought Chambers. He had heard that Tom had been trying to get his father to sell the boy down the river, and he wanted to prevent the scandal—for public sentiment did not approve of that way of treating family servants for light cause or for no cause.

Percy Driscoll had worn himself out in trying to save his great speculative landed estate, and had died without succeeding. He was hardly in his grave before the boom collapsed and left his hitherto envied young devil of an heir a pauper. But that was nothing; his uncle told him he should be his heir and have all his fortune when he died; so Tom was comforted.

Roxy had no home, now; so she resolved to go around and say good-by to her friends and then clear out and see the world—that is to say, she would go chambermaiding on a steamboat, the darling ambition of her race and sex.

Her last call was on the black giant, Jasper. She found him chopping Pudd'nhead Wilson's winter provision of wood.

Wilson was chatting with him when Roxy arrived. He asked her how she could bear to go off chambermaiding and leave her boys; and chaffingly offered to copy off a series of their finger-prints, reaching up to their twelfth year, for her to remember them by; but she sobered in a moment, wondering if he suspected anything; then she said she believed she did n't want them. Wilson said to himself, "The drop of black blood in her is superstitious; she thinks there's some devilry, some witch-business about my glass mystery somewhere; she used to come here with an old horseshoe in her hand; it could have been an accident, but I doubt it."

CHAPTER V

Training is everything. The peach was once a bitter almond; cauliflower is nothing but cabbage with a college education—*Pudd'nhead Wilson's Calendar.*

Remark of Dr. Baldwin's concerning upstarts: We don't care to eat toadstools that think they are truffles.—*Pudd'nhead Wilson's Calendar.*

Mrs. York Driscoll enjoyed two years of bliss with that prize, Tom—bliss that was troubled a little at times, it is true, but bliss nevertheless; then she died, and her husband and his childless sister, Mrs. Pratt, continued the bliss-business at the old stand. Tom was petted and indulged and spoiled to his entire content—or nearly that. This went on till he was nineteen, then he was sent to Yale. He went handsomely equipped with "conditions," but otherwise he was not an object of distinction there. He remained at Yale two years, and then threw up the struggle. He came home with his manners a good deal improved; he had lost his surliness and brusqueness, and was rather pleasantly soft and smooth, now; he was furtively, and sometimes openly, ironical of speech, and given to gently touching people on the raw, but he did it with a good-natured semiconscious air that carried it off safely, and kept him from getting into trouble. He was as indolent as ever and showed no very strenuous desire to hunt up an occupation. People argued from this that he preferred to be supported by his uncle until his uncle's shoes should become vacant. He brought back one or two new habits with him, one of which he rather openly practised—tippling—but concealed another, which was gambling. It would not do to gamble where his uncle could hear of it; he knew that quite well.

Tom's Eastern polish was not popular among the young people. They could have endured it, perhaps, if Tom had stopped there; but he wore gloves, and that they couldn't stand, and wouldn't; so he was mainly without society. He brought home with him a suit of clothes of such exquisite style and cut and fashion,—Eastern fashion, city fashion,—that it filled everybody with anguish and was regarded as a peculiarly wanton affront. He enjoyed the feeling which he was exciting, and paraded the town serene and happy all day; but the young fellows set a tailor to work that night, and when Tom started out on his parade next morning he found the old deformed negro bell-ringer straddling along in his wake tricked out in a flamboyant curtain-calico exaggeration of his finery, and imitating his fancy Eastern graces as well as he could.

Tom surrendered, and after that clothed himself in the local fashion. But the dull country town was tiresome to him, since his acquaintanceship with livelier regions, and it grew daily more and more so. He began to make little trips to St. Louis for refreshment. There he found companionship to suit him, and pleasures to his taste, along with more freedom, in some particulars, than he could have at home. So, during the next two years his visits to the city grew in frequency and his tarryings there grew steadily longer in duration.

He was getting into deep waters. He was taking chances, privately, which might get him into trouble some day—in fact, *did*.

Judge Driscoll had retired from the bench and from all business activities in 1850, and had now been comfortably idle three years. He was president of the Free-thinkers' Society, and Pudd'nhead Wilson was the other member. The society's weekly discussions were now the old lawyer's main interest in life.

Pudd'nhead was still toiling in obscurity at the bottom of the ladder, under the blight of that unlucky remark which he had let fall twenty-three years before about the dog.

Judge Driscoll was his friend, and claimed that he had a mind above the average, but that was regarded as one of the Judge's whims, and it failed to modify the public opinion. Or rather, that was one of the reasons why it failed, but there was another and better one. If the Judge had stopped with bare assertion, it would have had a good deal of effect; but he made the mistake of trying to prove his position. For some years Wilson had been privately at work on a whimsical almanac, for his amusement—a calendar, with a little dab of ostensible philosophy, usually in ironical form, appended to each date; and the Judge thought that these quips and fancies of Wilson's were neatly turned and cute; so he carried a handful of them around, one day, and read them to some of the chief citizens. But irony was not for those people; their mental vision was not focussed for it. They read those playful trifles in the solidest earnest, and decided without hesitancy that if there had ever been any doubt that Dave Wilson was a pudd'nhead—which there hadn't—this revelation removed that doubt for good and all. That is just the way in this world; an enemy can partly ruin a man, but it takes a good-natured injudicious friend to complete the thing and make it perfect. After this the Judge felt tenderer than ever toward Wilson, and surer than ever that his calendar had merit.

Judge Driscoll could be a free-thinker and still hold his place in society because he was the person of most consequence in the community, and therefore could venture to go his own way and follow out his own notions. The other member of his pet organization was allowed the like liberty because he was a cipher in the estimation of the public, and nobody attached any importance to what he thought or did. He was liked, he was welcome enough all around, but he simply didn't count for anything.

The widow Cooper—affectionately called "aunt Patsy" by everybody—lived in a snug and comely cottage with her daughter Rowena, who was nineteen, romantic, amiable, and very pretty, but otherwise of no consequence. Rowena had a couple of young brothers—also of no consequence.

The widow had a large spare room which she let to a lodger, with board, when she could find one, but this room had been empty for a year now, to her sorrow. Her income was only sufficient for the family support, and she needed the lodging-money for trifling luxuries. But now, at last, on a flaming June day, she found herself happy; her tedious wait was ended; her year-worn advertisement had been answered; and not by a village applicant, oh, no!—this letter was from away off yonder in the dim great world to the North: it was from St. Louis. She sat on her porch gazing out with unseeing eyes upon the shining reaches of the mighty Mississippi, her thoughts steeped in her good fortune. Indeed it was specially good fortune, for she was to have two lodgers instead of one.

She had read the letter to the family, and Rowena had danced away to see to the cleaning and airing of the room by the slave woman Nancy, and the boys had rushed abroad in the town to spread the great news, for it was matter of public interest, and the public would wonder and not be pleased if not informed. Presently Rowena returned, all ablush with joyous excitement, and begged for a re-reading of the letter. It was framed thus:

> Honored Madam: My brother and I have seen your advertisement, by chance, and beg leave to take the room you offer. We are twenty-four years of age and twins. We are Italians by birth, but have lived long in the various countries of Europe, and several years in the United States. Our names are Luigi and Angelo Capello. You desire but one guest; but dear Madam, if you will allow us to pay for two, we will not incommode you. We shall be down Thursday.

"Italians! How romantic! Just think, ma—there's never been one in this town, and everybody will be dying to see them, and they're all *ours!* Think of that!"

"Yes, I reckon they'll make a grand stir."

"Oh, indeed they will. The whole town will be on its head! Think—they've been in Europe and everywhere! There's never been a traveler in this town before. Ma, I shouldn't wonder if they've seen kings!"

"Well, a body can't tell; but they'll make stir enough, without that."

"Yes, that's of course. Luigi—Angelo. They're lovely names; and so grand and foreign—not like Jones and Robinson and such. Thursday they are coming, and this is only Tuesday; it's a cruel long time to wait. Here comes Judge Driscoll in at the gate. He's heard about it. I'll go and open the door."

The Judge was full of congratulations and curiosity. The letter was read and discussed. Soon Justice Robinson arrived with more congratulations, and there was a new reading and a new discussion. This was the beginning. Neighbor after neighbor, of both sexes, followed, and the procession drifted in and out all day and evening and all Wednesday and Thursday. The letter was read and re-read until it was nearly worn out; everybody admired its courtly and gracious tone, and smooth and practised style, everybody was sympathetic and excited, and the Coopers were steeped in happiness all the while.

The boats were very uncertain in low water, in these primitive times. This time the Thursday boat had not arrived at ten at night—so the people had waited at the landing all day for nothing; they were driven to their homes by a heavy storm without having had a view of the illustrious foreigners.

Eleven o'clock came; and the Cooper house was the only one in the town that still had lights burning. The rain and thunder were booming yet, and the anxious family were still waiting, still hoping. At last there was a knock at the door and the family jumped to open it. Two negro men entered, each carrying a trunk, and proceeded up-stairs toward the guest-room. Then entered the twins—the handsomest, the best dressed, the most distinguished-looking pair of young fellows the West had ever seen. One was a little fairer than the other, but otherwise they were exact duplicates.

CHAPTER VI

Let us endeavor so to live that when we come to die even the undertaker will be sorry.—*Pudd'nhead Wilson's Calendar.*

Habit is habit, and not to be flung out of the window by any man, but coaxed down-stairs a step at a time.—*Pudd'nhead Wilson's Calendar.*

At breakfast in the morning the twins' charm of manner and easy and polished bearing made speedy conquest of the family's good graces. All constraint and formality quickly disappeared, and the friendliest feeling succeeded. Aunt Patsy called them by their Christian names almost from the beginning. She was full of the keenest curiosity about them, and showed it; they responded by talking about themselves, which pleased her greatly. It presently appeared that in their early youth they had known poverty and hardship. As the talk wandered along the old lady watched for the right place to drop in a question or two concerning that matter, and when she found it she said to the blond twin who was now doing the biographies in his turn while the brunette one rested—

"If it ain't asking what I ought not to ask, Mr. Angelo, how did you come to be so friendless and in such trouble when you were little? Do you mind telling? But don't if you do."

"Oh, we don't mind it at all, madam; in our case it was merely misfortune, and nobody's fault. Our parents were well to do, there in Italy, and we were their only child. We were of the old Florentine nobility"—Rowena's heart gave a great bound, her nostrils expanded, and a fine light played in her eyes—"and when the war broke out my father was on the losing side and had to fly for his life. His estates were confiscated, his personal property seized, and there we were, in Germany, strangers, friendless, and in fact paupers. My brother and I were ten years old, and well educated for that age, very studious, very fond of our books, and well grounded in the German, French, Spanish, and English languages. Also, we were marvelous musical prodigies—if you will allow me to say it, it being only the truth.

"Our father survived his misfortunes only a month, our mother soon followed him, and we were alone in the world. Our parents could have made themselves comfortable by exhibiting us as a show, and they had many and large offers; but the thought revolted their pride, and they said they would starve and die first. But what they wouldn't consent to do we had to do without the formality of consent. We were seized for the debts occasioned by their illness and their funerals, and placed among the attractions of a cheap museum in Berlin to earn the liquidation money. It took us two years to get out of that slavery. We traveled all about Germany receiving no wages, and not even our keep. We had to be exhibited for nothing, and beg our bread.

"Well, madam, the rest is not of much consequence. When we escaped from that slavery at twelve years of age, we were in some respects men. Experience had taught us some valuable things; among others, how to take care of ourselves, how to avoid and defeat sharks and sharpers, and how to conduct our own business for our own profit and without other people's help. We traveled everywhere—years and years—picking up smatterings of strange tongues, familiarizing ourselves with strange sights and strange customs, accumulating an education of a wide and varied and curious sort. It was a pleasant life. We went to Venice—to London, Paris, Russia, India, China, Japan—"

At this point Nancy the slave woman thrust her head in at the door and exclaimed:

"Ole Missus, de house is plum' jam full o' people, en dey's jes a-spi'lin' to see de gen'lmen!" She indicated the twins with a nod of her head, and tucked it back out of sight again.

It was a proud occasion for the widow, and she promised herself high satisfaction in showing off her fine foreign birds before her neighbors and friends—simple folk who had hardly ever seen a foreigner of any kind, and never one of any distinction or style. Yet her feeling was moderate indeed when contrasted with Rowena's. Rowena was in the clouds, she walked on air; this was to be the greatest day, the most romantic episode, in the colorless history of that dull country town. She was to be familiarly near the source of its glory and feel the full flood of it pour over her and about her; the other girls could only gaze and envy, not partake.

The widow was ready, Rowena was ready, so also were the foreigners.

The party moved along the hall, the twins in advance, and entered the open parlor door, whence issued a low hum of conversation. The twins took a position near the door the widow stood at Luigi's side, Rowena stood beside Angelo, and the march-past and the introductions began. The widow was all smiles and contentment. She received the procession and passed it on to Rowena.

"Good mornin', Sister Cooper"—hand-shake.

"Good morning, Brother Higgins—Count Luigi Capello, Mr. Higgins"—hand-shake, followed by a devouring stare and "I'm glad to see ye," on the part of Higgins, and a courteous inclination of the head and a pleasant "Most happy!" on the part of Count Luigi.

"Good mornin', Roweny"—hand-shake.

"Good morning, Mr. Higgins—present you to Count Angelo Capello." Hand-shake, admiring stare, "Glad to see ye,"—courteous nod, smily "Most happy!" and Higgins passes on.

None of these visitors was at ease, but, being honest people, they didn't pretend to be. None of them had ever seen a person bearing a title of nobility before, and none had been expecting to see one now, consequently the title came upon them as a kind of pile-driving surprise and caught them unprepared. A few tried to rise to the emergency, and got out an awkward "My Lord," or "Your lordship," or something of that sort, but the great majority were overwhelmed by the unaccustomed word and its dim and awful associations with gilded courts and stately ceremony and anointed kingship, so they only fumbled through the hand-shake and passed on, speechless. Now and then, as happens at all receptions everywhere, a more than ordinarily friendly soul blocked the procession and kept it waiting while he inquired how the brothers liked the village, and how long they were going to stay, and if their families were well, and dragged in the weather, and hoped it would get cooler soon, and all that sort of thing, so as to be able to say, when they got home, "I had quite a long talk with them"; but nobody did or said anything of a regrettable kind, and so the great affair went through to the end in a creditable and satisfactory fashion.

General conversation followed, and the twins drifted about from group to group, talking easily and fluently and winning approval, compelling admiration and achieving favor from all. The widow followed their conquering march with a proud eye, and every now and then Rowena said to herself with deep satisfaction, "And to think they are ours—all ours!"

There were no idle moments for mother or daughter. Eager inquiries concerning the twins were pouring into their enchanted ears all the time; each was the constant center of a group of breathless listeners; each recognized that she knew now for the first time the real meaning of that great word Glory, and perceived the stupendous value of it, and understood why men in all ages had been willing to throw away meaner happinesses, treasure, life itself, to get a taste of its sublime and supreme joy. Napoleon and all his kind stood accounted for—and justified.

When Rowena had at last done all her duty by the people in the parlor, she went up-stairs to satisfy the longings of an overflow-meeting there, for the parlor was not big enough to hold all the comers. Again she was besieged by eager questioners and again she swam in sunset seas of glory. When the forenoon was nearly gone, she recognized with a pang that this most splendid episode of her life was almost over, that nothing could prolong it, that nothing quite its equal could ever fall to her fortune again. But never mind, it was sufficient unto itself, the grand occasion had moved on an ascending scale from the start, and was a noble and memorable success. If the twins could but do some crowning act, now, to climax it, something unusual, something startling, something to concentrate upon themselves the company's loftiest admiration, something in the nature of an electric surprise—

Here a prodigious slam-banging broke out below, and everybody rushed down to see. It was the twins knocking out a classic four-handed piece on the piano, in great style. Rowena was satisfied—satisfied down to the bottom of her heart.

The young strangers were kept long at the piano. The villagers were astonished and enchanted with the magnificence of their performance, and could not bear to have them stop. All the music that they had ever heard before seemed spiritless prentice-work and barren of grace or charm when compared with these intoxicating floods of melodious sound. They realized that for once in their lives they were hearing masters.

CHAPTER VII

One of the most striking differences between a cat and a lie is that a cat has only nine lives.—*Pudd'nhead Wilson's Calendar.*

The company broke up reluctantly, and drifted toward their several homes, chatting with vivacity, and all agreeing that it would be many a long day before Dawson's Landing would see the equal of this one again. The twins had accepted several invitations while the reception was in progress, and had also volunteered to play some duets at an amateur entertainment for the benefit of a local charity. Society was eager to receive them to its bosom. Judge Driscoll had the good fortune to secure them for an immediate drive, and to be the first to display them in public. They entered his buggy with him, and were paraded down the main street, everybody flocking to the windows and sidewalks to see.

The Judge showed the strangers the new graveyard, and the jail, and where the richest man lived, and the Freemasons' hall, and the Methodist church, and the Presbyterian church, and where the Baptist church was going to be when they got some money to build it with, and showed them the town hall and the slaughter-house, and got out the independent fire company in uniform and had them put out an imaginary fire; then he let them inspect the muskets of the militia company, and poured out an exhaustless stream of enthusiasm over all these splendors, and seemed very well satisfied with the responses he got, for the twins admired his admiration, and paid him back the best they could, though they could have done better if some fifteen or sixteen hundred thousand previous experiences of this sort in various countries had not already rubbed off a considerable part of the novelty of it.

The Judge laid himself out hospitably to make them have a good time, and if there was a defect anywhere it was not his fault. He told them a good many humorous anecdotes, and always forgot the nub, but they were always able to furnish it, for these yarns were of a pretty early vintage, and they had had many a rejuvenating pull at them before. And he told them all about his several dignities, and how he had held this and that and the other place of honor or profit, and had once been to the legislature, and was now president of the Society of Freethinkers. He said the society had been in existence four years, and already had two members, and was firmly established. He would call for the brothers in the evening if they would like to attend a meeting of it.

Accordingly he called for them, and on the way he told them all about Pudd'nhead Wilson, in order that they might get a favorable impression of him in advance and be prepared to like him. This scheme succeeded—the favorable impression was achieved. Later it was confirmed and solidified when Wilson proposed that out of courtesy to the strangers the usual topics be put aside and the hour be devoted to conversation upon ordinary subjects and the cultivation of friendly relations and good-fellowship,—a proposition which was put to vote and carried.

The hour passed quickly away in lively talk, and when it was ended the lonesome and neglected Wilson was richer by two friends than he had been when it began. He invited the twins to look in at his lodgings, presently, after disposing of an intervening engagement, and they accepted with pleasure.

Toward the middle of the evening they found themselves on the road to his house. Pudd'head was at home waiting for them and putting in his time puzzling over a thing which had come under his notice that morning. The matter was this: He happened to be up very early—at dawn, in fact; and he crossed the hall which divided his cottage through the center, and entered a room to something there. The window of the room had no curtains, for that side of the house had long been unoccupied, and through this window he caught sight of something which surprised and interested him. It was a young woman—a young woman where properly no young woman belonged; for she was in Judge Driscoll's house, and in the bedroom over the Judge's private study or sitting-room. This was young Tom Dricoll's bedroom. He and the Judge, the Judge's widowed sister Mrs. Pratt and three negro servants were the only people who belonged in the house. Who, then, might this young lady be? The two houses were separated by an ordinary yard, with a low fence running back through its middle from the street in front to the lane in the rear. The distance was not great, and Wilson was able to see the girl very well, the window-shades of the room she was in being up, and the window also. The girl had on a neat and trim summer dress, patterned in broad stripes of pink and white, and her bonnet was equipped with a pink veil. She was practising steps, gaits and attitudes, apparently; she was doing the thing gracefully, and was very much absorbed in her work. Who could she be, and how came she to be in young Tom Driscoll's room?

Wilson had quickly chosen a position from which he could watch the girl without running much risk of being seen by her, and he remained there hoping she would raise her veil and betray her face. But she disappointed him. After a matter of twenty minutes she disappeared, and although he stayed at his post half an hour longer, she came no more.

Toward noon he dropped in at the Judge's and talked with Mrs. Pratt about the great event of the day, and levee of the distinguished foreigners at Aunt Patsy Cooper's. He asked after her nephew Tom, and she said he was on his way home, and that she was expecting him to arrive a little before night; and added that she and the Judge were gratified to gather from his letters that he was conducting himself very nicely and creditably—at which Wilson winked to himself privately. Wilson did not ask if there was a newcomer in the house, but he asked questions that would have brought light-throwing answers as to that matter if Mrs. Pratt had had any light to throw; so he went away satisfied that he knew of things that were going on in her house of which she herself was not aware.

He was now waiting for the twins, and still puzzling over the problem of who that girl might be, and how she happened to be in that young fellow's room at daybreak in the morning.

CHAPTER VIII

The holy passion of Friendship is of so sweet and steady and loyal and enduring a nature that it will last through a whole lifetime, if not asked to lend money.—*Pudd'nhead Wilson's Calendar.*

Consider well the proportions of things. It is better to be a young June-bug than an old bird of paradise.—*Pudd'nhead Wilson's Calendar.*

It is necessary now, to hunt up Roxy.

At the time she was set free and went away chambermaiding, she was thirty-five. She got a berth as second chambermaid on a Cincinnati boat in the New Orleans trade, the *Grand Mogul.* A couple of trips made her wonted and easy-going at the work, and infatuated her with the stir and adventure and independence of steamboat life. Then she was promoted and became head chambermaid. She was a favorite with the officers, and exceedingly proud of their joking and friendly ways with her.

During eight years she served three parts of the year on that boat, and the winters on a Vicksburg packet. But now for two months she had had rheumatism in her arms, and was obliged to let the wash-tub alone. So she resigned. But she was well fixed —rich, as she would have described it; for she had lived a steady life,and had banked four dollars every month in New Orleans as a provision for her old age. She said in the start that she had "put shoes on one bar' footed nigger to tromple on her with," and that one mistake like that was enough; she would be independent of the human race thenceforth forevermore if hard work and economy could accomplish it. When the boat touched the levee at New Orleans she bade good-by to her comrades on the *Grand Mogul* and moved her kit ashore.

But she was back in an hour. The bank had gone to smash and carried her four hundred dollars with it. She was a pauper, and homeless. Also disabled bodily, at least for the present. The officers were full of sympathy for her in her trouble, and made up a little purse for her. She resolved to go to her birthplace; she had friends there among the negroes, and the unfortunate always help the unfortunate, she was well aware of that; those lowly comrades of her youth would not let her starve.

She took the little local packet at Cairo, and now she was on the home-stretch. Time had worn away her bitterness against her son, and she was able to think of him with serenity. She put the vile side of him out of her mind, and dwelt only on recollections of his occasional acts of kindness to her. She gilded and otherwise decorated these, and made them very pleasant to contemplate. She began to long to see him. She would go and fawn upon him, slave-like—for this would have to be her attitude, of course—and maybe she would find that time had modified him, and that he would be glad to see his long-forgotten old nurse and treat her gently. That would be lovely; that would make her forget her woes and her poverty.

Her poverty! That thought inspired her to add another castle to her dream: maybe he would give her a trifle now and then—maybe a dollar, once a month, say; any little thing like that would help, oh, ever so much.

By the time she reached Dawson's Landing she was her old self again; her blues were gone, she was in high feather. She would get along, surely; there were many kitchens where the servants would share their meals with her, and also steal sugar and apples and other dainties for her to carry home—or give her a chance to pilfer them herself, which would answer just as well. And there was the church. She was a more rabid and devoted Methodist than ever, and her piety was no sham, but was strong and sincere. Yes, with plenty of creature comforts and her old place in the amen-corner in her possession again, she would be perfectly happy and at peace thenceforward to the end.

She went to Judge Driscoll's kitchen first of all. She was received there in great form and with vast enthusiasm. Her wonderful travels, and the strange countries she had seen and the adventures she had had, made her a marvel, and a heroine of romance. The negroes hung enchanted upon the great story of her experiences, interrupting her all along with eager questions, with laughter, exclamations of delight and expressions of applause; and she was obliged to confess to herself that if there was anything better in this world than steamboating, it was the glory to be got by telling about it. The audience loaded her stomach with their dinners, and then stole the pantry bare to load up her basket.

Tom was in St. Louis. The servants said he had spent the best part of his time there during the previous two years. Roxy came every day, and had many talks about the family and its affairs. Once she asked why Tom was away so much. The ostensible "Chambers" said:

"De fac' is, ole marster kin git along better when young marster's away den he kin when he's in de town; yes, en he love him better, too; so he gives him fifty dollahs a month—"

"No, is dat so? Chambers, you's a-jokin', ain't you?"

"'Clah to goodness I ain't, mammy; Marse Tom tole me so his own self. But nemmine, 't ain't enough?"

"My lan', what de reason 't ain't enough?"

"Well, I's gwine to tell you, if you gimme a chanst, mammy. De reason it ain't enough is 'ca'se Marse Tom gambles."

Roxy threw up her hands in astonishment and Chambers went on—

"Ole marster found it out, 'ca'se he had to pay two hundred dollahs for Marse Tom's gamblin' debts, en dat's true, mammy, jes as dead certain as you's bawn."

"Two—hund'd—dollahs! Why, what is you talkin' 'bout? Two—hund'd—dollahs. Sakes alive, it's 'mos' enough to buy a tol'able good second-hand nigger wid. En you ain't lyin', honey?—you wouldn't lie to yo' ole mammy?"

"It's God's own truth, jes as I tell you—two hund'd dollahs—I wisht I may never stir outen my tracks if it ain't so. En, oh, my lan', ole Marse was jes a-hoppin'! he was b'ilin' mad, I tell you! He tuck 'n' dissenhurrit him."

He licked his chops with relish after that stately word. Roxy struggled with it a moment, then gave it up and said—

"Dissen*whiched* him?"

"Dissenhurrit him."

"What's dat? What do it mean?"

"Means he bu'sted de will."

"Bu's—ted de will! He wouldn't *ever* treat him so! Take it back, you mis'able imitation nigger dat I bore in sorrow en tribbilation."

Roxy's pet castle—an occasional dollar from Tom's pocket—was tumbling to ruin before her eyes. She could not abide such a disaster as that; she couldn't endure the thought of it. Her remark amused Chambers:

"Yah-yah-yah! jes listen to dat! If I's imitation, what is you? Bofe of us is imitation *white* —dat's what we is—en pow'ful good imitation, too—yah-yah-yah!—we don't 'mount to noth'n as imitation *niggers;* en as for—"

"Shet up yo' foolin', 'fo' I knock you side de head, en tell me 'bout de will. Tell me't ain't bu'sted—do, honey, en I'll never forgit you."

"Well, *'tain't* —'ca'se dey's a new one made, en Marse Tom's all right ag'in. But what is you in sich a sweat 'bout it for, mammy? 'Tain't none o' your business I don't reckon."

"Tain't none o' my business? Whose business is it den, I'd like to know? Wuz I his mother tell he was fifteen years old, or wus n't I?—you answer me dat. En you speck I could see him turned out po'en ornery on de worl' en never care noth 'n' 'bout it? I reckon if you'd ever be'n a mother yo'self, Valet de Chambers, you wouldn't talk sich foolishness as dat."

"Well, den, ole Marse forgive him en fixed up de will ag'in—do dat satisfy you?"

Yes, she was satisfied now, and quite happy and sentimental over it. She kept coming daily, and at last she was told that Tom had come home. She began to tremble with emotion, and straightway sent to beg him to let his "po' ole nigger mammy have jes one sight of him en die for joy."

Tom was stretched at his lazy ease on a sofa when Chambers brought the petition. Time had not modified his ancient detestation of the humble drudge and protector of his boyhood; it was still bitter and uncompromising. He sat up and bent a severe gaze upon the fair face of the young fellow whose name he was unconsciously using and whose family rights he was enjoying. He maintained the gaze until the victim of it had become satisfactorily pallid with terror, then he said—

"What does the old rip want with me?"

The petition was meekly repeated.

"Who gave you permission to come and disturb me with the social attentions of niggers?"

Tom had risen. The other young man was trembling now, visibly. He saw what was coming, and bent his head sideways, and put up his left arm to shield it. Tom rained cuffs upon the head and its shield, saying no word: the victim received each blow with a beseeching "Please, Marse Tom!—oh, please,

Marse Tom!" Seven blows—then Tom said, "Face the door—march!" He followed behind with one, two, three solid kicks. The last one helped the pure-white slave over the door-sill, and he limped away mopping his eyes with his old ragged sleeve. Tom shouted after him, "Send her in!"

Then he flung himself panting on the sofa again, and rasped out the remark, "He arrived just at the right moment; I was full to the brim with bitter thinkings, and nobody to take it out of. How refreshing it was! I feel better."

Tom's mother entered now, closing the door behind her, and approached her son with all the wheedling and supplicating servilities that fear and interest can impart to the words and attitudes of the born slave. She stopped a yard from her boy and made two or three admiring exclamations over his manly stature and general handsomeness, and Tom put an arm under his head and hoisted a leg over the sofa-back in order to look properly indifferent.

"My lan', how you is growed, honey! 'Clah to goodness, I wouldn't a-knowed you, Marse Tom! 'deed I wouldn't! Look at me good; does you 'member old Roxy?—does you know yo' old nigger mammy, honey? Well now, I kin lay down en die in peace, 'ca'se I 'se seed—"

"Cut it short,—it, cut it short! What is it you want?"

"You heah dat? Jes de same old Marse Tom, al'ays so gay and funnin' wid de ole mammy. I 'uz jes as shore—"

"Cut it short, I tell you, and get along! What do you want."

This was a bitter disappointment. Roxy had for so many days nourished and fondled and petted her notion that Tom would be glad to see his old nurse, and would make her proud and happy to the marrow with a cordial word or two, that it took two rebuffs to convince her that he was not funning, and that her beautiful dream was a fond and foolish vanity, a shabby and pitiful mistake. She was hurt to the heart, and so ashamed that for a moment she did not quite know what to do or how to act. Then her breast began to heave, the tears came, and in her forlornness she was moved to try that other dream of hers—an appeal to her boy's charity; and so, upon the impulse, and without reflection, she offered her supplication:

"Oh, Marse Tom, de po' ole mammy is in sich hard luck dese days; en she's kinder crippled in de arms en can't work, en if you could gimme a dollah—on'y jes one little dol—"

Tom was on his feet so suddenly that the supplicant was startled into a jump herself.

"A dollar!—give you a dollar! I've a notion to strangle you!

Is *that* your errand here? Clear out! and be quick about it!"

Roxy backed slowly toward the door. When she was half-way he stopped, and said mournfully:

"Marse Tom, I nussed you when you was a little baby, en I raised you all by myself tell you was 'most a young man; en now you is young en rich, en I is po' en gitt'n ole, en I come heah b'lievin' dat you would he'p de ole mammy 'long down de little road dat's lef' 'twix' her en de grave, en—"

Tom relished this tune less than any that had preceded it, for it began to wake up a sort of echo in his conscience; so he interrupted and said with decision, though without asperity, that he was not in a situation to help her, and wasn't going to do it.

"Ain't you ever gwine to he'p me, Marse Tom?"

"No! Now go away and don't bother me any more."

Roxy's head was down, in an attitude of humility. But now the fires of her old wrongs flamed up in her breast and began to burn fiercely. She raised her head slowly, till it was well up, and at the same time her great frame unconsciously assumed an erect and masterful attitude, with all the majesty and grace of her vanished youth in it. She raised her finger and punctuated with it:

"You has said de word. You has had yo' chance, en you has trompled it under yo' foot. When you git another one, you'll git down on yo' knees en *beg* for it!"

A cold chill went to Tom's heart, he didn't know why; for he did not reflect that such words, from such an incongruous source, and so solemnly delivered, could not easily fail of that effect. However, he did the natural thing: he replied with bluster and mockery:

"*You'll* give me a chance—*you!* Perhaps I'd better get down on my knees now! But in case I don't—just for argument's sake—what's going to happen, pray?"

"Dis is what is gwine to happen. I's gwine as straight to yo' uncle as I kin walk, en tell him every las' thing I knows 'bout you."

Tom's cheek blenched, and she saw it. Disturbing thoughts began to chase each other through his head. "How can she know? And yet she must have found out—she looks it. I've had the will back only three months, and am already deep in debt again, and moving heaven and earth to save myself from exposure and destruction, with a reasonably fair show of getting the thing covered up if I'm let alone, and now this fiend has gone and found me out somehow or other. I wonder how much she knows? Oh, oh, oh, it's enough to break a body's heart! But I've got to humor her—there's no other way."

Then he worked up a rather sickly sample of a gay laugh and a hollow chipperness of manner, and said:

"Well, well, Roxy dear, old friends like you and me mustn't quarrel. Here's your dollar—now tell me what you know."

He held out the wild-cat bill; she stood as she was, and made no movement. It was her turn to scorn persuasive foolery, now, and she did not waste it. She said, with a grim implacability in voice and manner which made Tom almost realize that even a former slave can remember for ten minutes insults and injuries returned for compliments and flatteries received, and can also enjoy taking revenge for them when the opportunity offers:

"What does I know? I'll tell you what I knows. I knows enough to bu'st dat will to flinders—en more, mind you, *more!*"

Tom was aghast.

"More? " he said. "What do you call more? Where's there any room for more?"

Roxy laughed a mocking laugh, and said scoffingly, with a toss of her head, and her hands on her hips—

"Yes!—oh, I reckon! *Co'se* you'd like to know—wid yo' po' little ole rag dollah. What you reckon I's gwine to tell *you* for?—you ain't got no money. I's gwine to tell yo' uncle—en I'll do it dis minute, too—he'll gimme *five* dollahs for de news, en mighty glad, too."

She swung herself around disdainfully, and started away. Tom was in a panic. He seized her skirts, and implored her to wait. She turned and said, loftily—

"Look-a-heah, what 'uz it I tole you?"

"You—you—I don't remember anything. What was it you told me?"

"I tole you dat de next time I give you a chance you'd git down on yo' knees en beg for it."

Tom was stupefied for a moment. He was panting with excitement. Then he said:

"Oh, Roxy, you wouldn't require your young master to do such a horrible thing. You can't mean it."

"I'll let you know mighty quick whether I means it or not! You call me names, en as good as spit on me when I comes here po' en ornery en 'umble, to praise you for bein' growed up so fine en handsome, en tell you how I used to nuss you en tend you en watch you when you 'uz sick en hadn't no mother but me in de whole worl', en beg you to give de po' ole nigger a dollah for to git her som'n' to eat, en you call me names—*names,* dad blame you! Yassir, I gives you jes one chance mo', and dat's *now,* en it las' on'y a half a second—you hear?"

Tom slumped to his knees and began to beg, saying—

"You see I 'm begging, and it's honest begging, too! Now tell me, Roxy, tell me."

The heir of two centuries of unatoned insult and outrage looked down on him and seemed to drink in deep draughts of satisfaction. Then she said—

"Fine nice young white gen'l'man kneelin' down to a nigger-wench! I's wanted to see dat jes once befo' I's called. Now, Gabr'el, blow de hawn, I's ready . . . Git up!"

Tom did it. He said, humbly—

"Now, Roxy, don't punish me any more. I deserved what I've got, but be good and let me off with that. Don't go to uncle. Tell me—I'll give you the five dollars."

"Yes, I bet you will; en you won't stop dah, nuther. But I ain't gwine to tell you heah—"

"Good gracious, no!"

"Is you 'feared o' de ha'nted house?"

"N-no."

"Well, den, you come to de ha'nted house 'bout ten or 'leven to-night, en climb up de ladder, 'ca'se de sta'r-steps is broke down, en you'll find me. I's a-roostin' in de ha'nted house 'ca'se I can't 'ford to roos' nowhers' else." She started toward the door, but stopped and said, "Gimme de dollah bill!" He gave it to her. She examined it and said, "H'm—like enough de bank 's bu'sted." She started again, but halted again. "Has you got any whisky?"

"Yes, a little."

"Fetch it!"

He ran to his room overhead and brought down a bottle which was two-thirds full. She tilted it up and took a drink. Her eyes sparkled with satisfaction, and she tucked the bottle under her shawl, saying, "It's prime. I'll take it along."

Tom humbly held the door for her, and she marched out as grim and erect as a grenadier.

CHAPTER IX

Why is it that we rejoice at a birth and grieve at a funeral? It is because we are not the person involved.—*Pudd'nhead Wilson's Calendar.*

It is easy to find fault, if one has that disposition. There was once a man who, not being able to find any other fault with his coal, complained that there were too many prehistoric toads in it.—*Pudd'nhead Wilson's Calendar.*

Tom flung himself on the sofa, and put his throbbing head in his hands, and rested his elbows on his knees. He rocked himself back and forth and moaned.

"I've knelt to a nigger wench!" he muttered. "I thought I had struck the deepest depths of degradation before, but oh, dear, it was nothing to this . . . . Well, there is one consolation, such as it is—I've struck bottom this time; there's nothing lower."

But that was a hasty conclusion.

At ten that night he climbed the ladder in the haunted house, pale, weak and wretched. Roxy was standing in the door of one of the rooms, waiting, for she had heard him.

This was a two-story log house which had acquired the reputation a few years before of being haunted, and that was the end of its usefulness. Nobody would live in it afterward, or go near it by night, and most people even gave it a wide berth in the daytime. As it had no competition, it was called *the* haunted house. It was getting crazy and ruinous, now, from long neglect. It stood three hundred yards beyond Pudd'nhead Wilson's house, with nothing between but vacancy. It was the last house in the town at that end.

Tom followed Roxy into the room. She had a pile of clean straw in the corner for a bed, some cheap but well-kept clothing was hanging on the wall, there was a tin lantern freckling the floor with little spots of light, and there were various soap-and-candle boxes scattered about, which served for chairs. The two sat down. Roxy said—

"Now den, I'll tell you straight off, en I'll begin to k'leck de money later on; I ain't in no hurry. What does you reckon I's gwine to tell you?"

"Well, you—you—oh, Roxy, don't make it too hard for me! Come right out and tell me you've found out somehow what a shape I'm in on account of dissipation and foolishness."

"Disposition en foolishness! *No* sir, dat ain't it. Dat jist ain't nothin' at all, 'longside o' what *I* knows."

Tom stared at her, and said—

"Why, Roxy, what do you mean?"

She rose, and gloomed above him like a Fate.

"I means dis—en it's de Lord's truth. You ain't no more kin to ole Marse Driscoll den I is!—*dat's* what I means!" and her eyes flamed with triumph.

"What!"

"Yassir, en *dat* ain't all! You's a *nigger!—bawn* a nigger en a *slave!* —en you's a nigger en a slave dis minute; en if I opens my mouf ole Marse Driscoll 'll sell you down de river befo' you is two days older den what you is now!"

"It's a thundering lie, you miserable old blatherskite!"

"It ain't no lie, nuther. It's jes de truth, en nothin' *but* de truth, so he'p me. Yassir—you's my *son*—"

"You devil!"

"En dat po' boy dat you's be'n a-kickin' en a-cuffin' to-day is Percy Driscoll's son en yo' *marster*—"

"You beast!"

"En *his* name's Tom Driscoll, en *yo'* name's Valet de Chambers, en you ain't *got* no fambly name, beca'se niggers don't *have* em!"

Tom sprang up and seized a billet of wood and raised it but his mother only laughed at him and said—

"Set down, you pup! Does you think you kin skyer me? It ain't in you, nor de likes of you. I reckon you'd shoot me in de back, maybe, if you got a chance, for dat's jist yo' style— *I* knows you, throo en throo—but I don't mind gitt'n killed, beca'se all dis is down in writin' en it's in safe hands, too, en de man dat's got it knows whah to look for de right man when I gits killed. Oh, bless yo' soul, if you puts yo' mother up for as big a fool as *you* is, you's pow'ful mistaken, I kin tell you! Now den, you set still en behave yo'self; en don't you git up ag'in till I tell you!"

Tom fretted and chafed awhile in a whirlwind of disorganizing sensations and emotions, and finally said, with something like settled conviction—

"The whole thing is moonshine; now then, go ahead and do your worst; I'm done with you."

Roxy made no answer. She took the lantern and started toward the door. Tom was in a cold panic in a moment.

"Come back, come back!" he wailed. "I didn't mean it, Roxy; I take it all back, and I'll never say it again! Please come back, Roxy!"

The woman stood a moment, then she said gravely:

"Dat's one thing you's got to stop, Valet de Chambers. You can't call me *Roxy,* same as if you was my equal. Chillen don't speak to dey mammies like dat. You'll call me ma or mammy, dat's what you'll call me—leastways when dey ain't nobody aroun'. *Say* it!"

It cost Tom a struggle, but he got it out.

"Dat's all right. Don't you ever forgit it ag'in, if you knows what's good for you. Now den, you has said you wouldn't ever call it lies en moonshine ag'in. I'll tell you dis, for a warnin': if you ever does say it ag'in, it's de *las'* time you'll ever say it to me; I'll tramp as straight to de Judge as I kin walk, en tell him who you is, en *prove* it. Does you b'lieve me when I says dat?"

"Oh," groaned Tom, "I more than believe it; I *know* it."

Roxy knew her conquest was complete. She could have proved nothing to anybody, and her threat about the writings was a lie; but she knew the person she was dealing with, and had made both statements without any doubt as to the effect they would produce.

She went and sat down on her candle-box, and the pride and pomp of her victorious attitude made it a throne. She said—

"Now den, Chambers, we's gwine to talk business, en dey ain't gwine to be no mo' foolishness. In de fust place, you gits fifty dollahs a month; you's gwine to han' over half of it to yo' ma. Plank it out!"

But Tom had only six dollars in the world. He gave her that, and promised to start fair on next month's pension.

"Chambers, how much is you in debt?"

Tom shuddered, and said—

"Nearly three hundred dollars."

"How is you gwine to pay it?"

Tom groaned out—"Oh, I don't know; don't ask me such awful questions."

But she stuck to her point until she wearied a confession out of him: he had been prowling about in disguise, stealing small valuables from private houses; in fact, had made a good deal of a raid on his fellow-villagers a fortnight before, when he was supposed to be in St. Louis; but he doubted if he had sent away enough stuff to realize the required amount, and was afraid to make a further venture in the present excited state of the town. His mother approved of his conduct, and offered to help, but this frightened him. He tremblingly ventured to say that if she would retire from the town he should feel better and safer, and could hold his head higher—and was going on to make an argument, but she interrupted and surprised him pleasantly by saying she was ready; it didn't make any difference to her where she stayed, so that she got her share of the pension regularly. She said she would not go far, and would call at the haunted house once a month for her money. Then she said—

"I don't hate you so much now, but I've hated you a many a year—and anybody would. Didn't I change you off, en give you a good fambly en a good name, en made you a white gen'l'man en rich, wid store clothes on—en what did I git for it? You despised me all de time, en was al'ays sayin' mean hard things to me befo' folks, en wouldn't ever let me forgit I's a nigger—en—en—"

She fell to sobbing, and broke down. Tom said—"But you know I didn't know you were my mother; and besides—"

"Well, nemmine 'bout dat, now; let it go. I's gwine to fo'git it." Then she added fiercely, "En don't ever make me remember it ag'in, or you'll be sorry, *I* tell you."

When they were parting, Tom said, in the most persuasive way he could command—

"Ma, would you mind telling me who was my father?"

He had supposed he was asking an embarrassing question. He was mistaken. Roxy drew herself up with a proud toss of her head, and said—

"Does I mine tellin' you? No, dat I don't! You ain't got no 'casion to be shame' o' yo' father, *I* kin tell you. He wuz de highest quality in dis whole town—ole Virginny stock. Fust famblies, he wuz. Jes as good stock as de Driscolls en de Howards, de bes' day dey ever seed." She put on a little prouder air, if possible, and added impressively: "Does you 'member Cunnel Cecil Burleigh Essex, dat died de same year yo' young Marse Tom Driscoll's pappy died, en all de Masons en Odd Fellers en Churches turned out en give him de bigges' funeral dis town ever seed? Dat's de man."

Under the inspiration of her soaring complacency the departed graces of her earlier days returned to her, and her bearing took to itself a dignity and state that might have passed for queenly if her surroundings had been a little more in keeping with it.

"Dey ain't another nigger in dis town dat's as high-bawn as you is. Now den, go 'long! En jes you hold yo' head up as high as you want to—you has de right, en dat I kin swah."

CHAPTER X

All say, "How hard it is that we have to die"—a strange complaint to come from the mouths of people who have had to live.—*Pudd'nhead Wilson's Calendar.*

When angry, count four; when very angry, swear.—*Pudd'nhead Wilson's Calendar.*

Every now and then, after Tom went to bed, he had sudden wakings out of his sleep, and his first thought was, "Oh, joy, it was all a dream!" Then he laid himself heavily down again, with a groan and the muttered words, "A nigger! I am a nigger! Oh, I wish I was dead!"

He woke at dawn with one more repetition of this horror, and then he resolved to meddle no more with that treacherous sleep.

He began to think. Sufficiently bitter thinkings they were. They wandered along something after this fashion:

"Why were niggers *and* whites made? What crime did the uncreated first nigger commit that the curse of birth was decreed for him? And why is this awful difference made between white and black? . . . How hard the nigger's fate seems, this morning!—yet until last night such a thought never entered my head."

He sighed and groaned an hour or more away. Then "Chambers" came humbly in to say that breakfast was nearly ready. "Tom" blushed scarlet to see this aristocratic white youth cringe to him, a nigger, and call him "Young Marster." He said roughly—

"Get out of my sight!" and when the youth was gone, he muttered, "He has done me no harm, poor wretch, but he is an eyesore to me now, for he is Driscoll the young gentleman, and I am a—oh, I wish I was dead!"

A gigantic irruption, like that of Krakatoa a few years ago, with the accompanying earthquakes, tidal waves, and clouds of volcanic dust, changes the face of the surrounding landscape beyond recognition, bringing down the high lands, elevating the low, making fair lakes where deserts had been, and deserts where green prairies had smiled before. The tremendous catastrophe which had befallen Tom had changed his moral landscape in much the same way. Some of his low places he found lifted to ideals, some of his ideals had sunk to the valleys, and lay there with the sackcloth and ashes of pumice-stone and sulphur on their ruined heads.

For days he wandered in lonely places, thinking, thinking, thinking—trying to get his bearings. It was new work. If he met a friend, he found that the habit of a lifetime had in some mysterious way vanished—his arm hung limp, instead of involuntarily extending the hand for a shake. It was the "nigger" in him asserting its humility, and he blushed and was abashed. And the "nigger" in him was surprised when the white friend put out his hand for a shake with him. He found the "nigger" in him involuntarily giving the road, on the sidewalk, to the white rowdy and loafer. When Rowena, the dearest thing his heart knew, the idol of his secret worship, invited him in, the "nigger" in him made an embarrassed excuse and was afraid to enter and sit with the dread white folks on equal terms. The "nigger" in him went shrinking and skulking here and there and yonder, and fancying it saw suspicion and maybe detection in all faces, tones, and gestures. So strange and uncharacteristic was Tom's conduct that people noticed it, and turned to look after him when he passed on; and when he glanced back—as he could not help doing, in spite of his best resistance—and caught that puzzled expression in a person's face, it gave him a sick feeling, and he took himself out of view as quickly as he could. He presently came to have a hunted sense and a hunted look, and then he fled away to the hill-tops and the solitudes. He said to himself that the curse of Ham was upon him.

He dreaded his meals; the "nigger" in him was ashamed to sit at the white folks' table, and feared discovery all the time; and once when Judge Driscoll said, "What's the matter with you? You look as meek as a nigger," he felt as secret murderers are said to feel when the accuser says, "Thou art the man!" Tom said he was not well, and left the table.

His ostensible "aunt's" solicitudes and endearments were become a terror to him, and he avoided them.

And all the time, hatred of his ostensible "uncle" was steadily growing in his heart; for he said to himself, "He is white; and I am his chattel, his property, his goods, and he can sell me, just as he could his dog."

For as much as a week after this, Tom imagined that his character had undergone a pretty radical change. But that was because he did not know himself.

In several ways his opinions were totally changed, and would never go back to what they were before, but the main structure of his character was not changed, and could not be changed. One or two very important features of it were altered, and in time effects would result from this, if opportunity offered— effects of a quite serious nature, too. Under the influence of a great mental and moral upheaval his character and habits had taken on the appearance of complete change, but after a while with the subsidence of the storm both began to settle toward their former places. He dropped gradually back into his old frivolous and easy-going ways and conditions of feeling and manner of speech, and no familiar of his could have detected anything in him that differentiated him from the weak and careless Tom of other days.

The theft-raid which he had made upon the village turned out better than he had ventured to hope. It produced the sum necessary to pay his gaming-debts, and saved him from exposure to his uncle and another smashing of the will. He and his mother learned to like each other fairly well. She couldn't love him, as yet, because there "warn 't nothing *to* him," as she expressed it, but her nature needed something or somebody to rule over, and he was better than nothing. Her strong character and aggressive and commanding ways compelled Tom's admiration in spite of the fact that he got more illustrations of them than he needed for his comfort. However, as a rule her conversation was made up of racy tattle about the privacies of the chief families of the town (for she went harvesting among their kitchens every time she came to the village), and Tom enjoyed this. It was just in his line. She always collected her half of his pension punctually, and he was always at the haunted house to have a chat with her on these occasions. Every now and then she paid him a visit there on between-days also.

Occasionally he would run up to St. Louis for a few weeks, and at last temptation caught him again. He won a lot of money, but lost it, and with it a deal more besides, which he promised to raise as soon as possible.

For this purpose he projected a new raid on his town. He never meddled with any other town, for he was afraid to venture into houses whose ins and outs he did not know and the habits of whose households he was not acquainted with. He arrived at the haunted house in disguise on the Wednesday before the advent of the twins—after writing his aunt Pratt that he would not arrive until two days after—and lay in hiding there with his mother until toward daylight Friday morning, when he went to his uncle's house and entered by the back way with his own key, and slipped up to his room, where he could have the use of mirror and toilet articles. He had a suit of girl's clothes with him in a bundle as a disguise for his raid, and was wearing a suit of his mother's clothing, with black gloves and veil. By dawn he was tricked out for his raid, but he caught a glimpse of Pudd'nhead Wilson through the window over the way, and knew that Pudd'nhead had caught a glimpse of him. So he entertained Wilson with some airs and graces and attitudes for a while, then stepped out of sight and resumed the other disguise, and by and by went down and out the back way and started down town to reconnoiter the scene of his intended labors.

But he was ill at ease. He had changed back to Roxy's dress, with the stoop of age added to the disguise, so that Wilson would not bother himself about a humble old woman leaving a neighbor's house by the back way in the early morning, in case he was still spying. But supposing Wilson had seen him leave, and had thought it suspicious, and had also followed him? The thought made Tom cold. He gave up the raid for the day, and hurried back to the haunted house by the obscurest route he knew. His mother was gone; but she came back, by and by, with the news of the grand reception at Patsy Cooper's, and soon persuaded him that the opportunity was like a special providence, it was so inviting and perfect. So he went raiding, after all, and made a nice success of it while everybody was gone to Patsy Cooper's. Success gave him nerve and even actual intrepidity; insomuch, indeed, that after he had conveyed his harvest to his mother in a back alley, he went to the reception himself, and added several of the valuables of that house to his takings.

After this long digression we have now arrived once more at the point where Pudd'nhead Wilson, while waiting for the arrival of the twins on that same Friday evening, sat puzzling over the strange apparition of that morning—a girl in young Tom Driscoll's bedroom; fretting, and guessing, and puzzling over it, and wondering who the shameless creature might be.

CHAPTER XI

There are three infallible ways of pleasing an author, and the three form a rising scale of compliment: 1, to tell him you have read one of his books; 2, to tell him you have read all of his books; 3, to ask him to let you read the manuscript of his forthcoming book. No. 1 admits you to his respect; No. 2 admits you to his admiration; No. 3 carries you clear into his heart.—*Pudd'nhead Wilson's Calendar.*

As to the Adjective: when in doubt, strike it out.—*Pudd'nhead Wilson's Calendar.*

The twins arrived presently, and talk began. It flowed along chattily and sociably, and under its influence the new friendship gathered ease and strength. Wilson got out his Calendar, by request, and read a passage or two from it, which the twins praised quite cordially. This pleased the author so much that he complied gladly when they asked him to lend them a batch of the work to read at home. In the course of their wide travels they had found out that there are three sure ways of pleasing an author; they were now working the best of the three.

There was an interruption, now. Young Tom Driscoll appeared, and joined the party. He pretended to be seeing the distinguished strangers for the first time when they rose to shake hands; but this was only a blind, as he had already had a glimpse of them, at the reception, while robbing the house. The twins made mental note that he was smooth-faced and rather handsome, and smooth and undulatory in his movements—graceful, in fact. Angelo thought he had a good eye; Luigi thought there was something veiled and sly about it. Angelo thought he had a pleasant free-and-easy way of talking; Luigi thought it was more so than was agreeable. Angelo thought he was a sufficiently nice young man; Luigi reserved his decision. Tom's first contribution to the conversation was a question which he had put to Wilson a hundred times before. It was always cheerily and good-naturedly put, and always inflicted a little pang, for it touched a secret sore; but this time the pang was sharp, since strangers were present.

"Well, how does the law come on? Had a case yet?"

Wilson bit his lip, but answered, "No—not yet," with as much indifference as he could assume. Judge Driscoll had generously left the law feature out of the Wilson biography which he had furnished to the twins. Young Tom laughed pleasantly, and said:

"Wilson's a lawyer, gentlemen, but he doesn't practise now."

The sarcasm bit, but Wilson kept himself under control, and said without passion:

"I don't practise, it is true. It is true that I have never had a case, and have had to earn a poor living for twenty years an an expert accountant in a town where I can't get hold of a set of books to untangle as often as I should like. But it is also true that I did fit myself well for the practice of the law. By the time I was your age, Tom, I had chosen a profession, and was soon competent to enter upon it." Tom winced. "I never got a chance to try my hand at it, and I may never get a chance; and yet if I ever do get it I shall be found ready, for I have kept up my law-studies all these years."

"That's it; that's good grit! I like to see it. I've a notion to throw all my business your way. My business and your law-practice ought to make a pretty gay team, Dave," and the young fellow laughed again.

"If you will throw—" Wilson had thought of the girl in Tom's bedroom, and was going to say, "If you will throw the surreptitious and disreputable part of your business my way, it may amount to something;" but thought better of it and said, "However, this matter doesn't fit well in a general conversation."

"All right, we'll change the subject; I guess you were about to give me another dig, anyway, so I'm willing to change. How's the Awful Mystery flourishing these days? Wilson's got a scheme for driving plain window-glass out of the market by decorating it with greasy finger-marks, and getting rich by selling it at famine prices to the crowned heads over in Europe to outfit their palaces with. Fetch it out, Dave."

Wilson brought three of his glass strips, and said—

"I get the subject to pass the fingers of his right hand through his hair, so as to get a little coating of the natural oil on them, and then press the balls of them on the glass. A fine and delicate print of the lines in the skin results, and is permanent, if it doesn't come in contact with something able to rub it off. You begin, Tom."

"Why, I think you took my finger-marks once or twice before."

"Yes; but you were a little boy the last time, only about twelve years old."

"That's so. Of course I've changed entirely since then, and variety is what the crowned heads want, I guess."

He passed his fingers through his crop of short hair, and pressed them one at a time on the glass. Angelo made a print of his fingers on another glass, and Luigi followed with the third. Wilson marked the glasses with names and date, and put them away. Tom gave one of his little laughs, and said—

"I thought I wouldn't say anything, but if variety is what you are after, you have wasted a piece of glass. The hand-print of one twin is the same as the hand-print of the fellow-twin."

"Well, it's done now, and I like to have them both, anyway," said Wilson, returning to his place.

"But look here, Dave," said Tom, "you used to tell people's fortunes, too, when you took their finger-marks. Dave's just an all-round genius—a genius of the first water, gentlemen; a great scientist running to seed here in this village, a prophet with the kind of honor that prophets generally get at home—for here they don't give shucks for his scientifics, and they call his skull a notion-factory—hey, Dave, ain't it so? But never mind; he'll make his mark some day—finger-mark, you know, he-he! But really, you want to let him take a shy at your palms once; it's worth twice the price of admission or your money's returned at the door. Why, he'll read your wrinkles as easy as a book, and not only tell you fifty or sixty things that's going to happen to you, but fifty or sixty thousand that ain't. Come, Dave, show the gentlemen what an inspired Jack-at-all-science we've got in this town, and don't know it."

Wilson winced under this nagging and not very courteous chaff, and the twins suffered with him and for him. They rightly judged, now, that the best way to relieve him would be to take the thing in earnest and treat it with respect, ignoring Tom's rather overdone raillery; so Luigi said—

"We have seen something of palmistry in our wanderings, and know very well what astonishing things it can do. If it isn't a science, and one of the greatest of them, too, I don't know what its other name ought to be. In the Orient—''

Tom looked surprised and incredulous. He said—

''That juggling a science? But really, you ain't serious, are you?''

''Yes, entirely so. Four years ago we had our hands read out to us as if our palms had been covered with print.''

''Well, do you mean to say there was actually anything in it?'' asked Tom, his incredulity beginning to weaken a little.

''There was this much in it,'' said Angelo: ''what was told us of our characters was minutely exact—we could not have bettered it ourselves. Next, two or three memorable things that had happened to us were laid bare—things which no one present but ourselves could have known about.''

''Why, it's rank sorcery!'' exclaimed Tom, who was now becoming very much interested. ''And how did they make out with what was going to happen to you in the future?''

''On the whole, quite fairly,'' said Luigi. ''Two or three of the most striking things foretold have happened since; much the most striking one of all happened within that same year. Some of the minor prophecies have come true; some of the minor and some of the major ones have not been fulfilled yet, and of course may never be: still, I should be more surprised if they failed to arrive than if the didn't.''

Tom was entirely sobered, and profoundly impressed. He said, apologetically—

''Dave, I wasn't meaning to belittle that science; I was only chaffing—chattering, I reckon I'd better say. I wish you would look at their palms. Come, won't you?''

''Why certainly, if you want me to; but you know I've had no chance to become an expert, and don't claim to be one. When a past event is somewhat prominently recorded in the palm I can generally detect that, but minor ones often escape me,—not always, of course, but often,—but I haven't much confidence in myself when it comes to reading the future. I am talking as if palmistry was a daily study with me, but that is not so. I haven't examined half a dozen hands in the last half dozen years; you see, the people got to joking about it, and I stopped to let the talk die down. I'll tell you what we'll do, Count Luigi: I'll make a try at your past, and if I have any success there—no, on the whole, I'll let the future alone; that's really the affair of an expert.''

He took Luigi's hand. Tom said—

''Wait—don't look yet, Dave! Count Luigi, here's paper and pencil. Set down that thing that you said was the most striking one that was foretold to you, and happened less than a year afterward, and give it to me so I can see if Dave finds it in your hand.''

Luigi wrote a line privately, and folded up the piece of paper, and handed it to Tom, saying—

''I'll tell you when to look at it, if he finds it.''

Wilson began to study Luigi's palm, tracing life lines, heart lines, head lines, and so on, and noting carefully their relations with the cobweb of finer and more delicate marks and lines that enmeshed them on all sides; he felt the fleshy cushion at the base of the thumb, and noted its shape; he felt of the fleshy side of the hand between the wrist and the base of the little finger, and noted its shape also; he painstakingly examined the fingers, observing their form, proportions, and natural manner of disposing themselves when in repose. All this process was watched by the three spectators with absorbing interest, their heads bent together over Luigi's palm, and nobody disturbing the stillness with a word. Wilson now entered upon a close survey of the palm again, and his revelations began.

He mapped out Luigi's character and disposition, his tastes, aversions, proclivities, ambitions, and eccentricities in a way which sometimes made Luigi wince and the others laugh, but both twins declared that the chart was artistically drawn and was correct.

Next, Wilson took up Luigi's history. He proceeded cautiously and with hesitation, now, moving his finger slowly along the great lines of the palm, and now and then halting it at a ''star'' or some such landmark, and examining that neighborhood minutely. He proclaimed one or two past events, Luigi confirmed his correctness, and the search went on. Presently Wilson glanced up suddenly with a surprised expression—

''Here is record of an incident which you would perhaps not wish me to—''

''Bring it out,'' said Luigi, good-naturedly; ''I promise you it sha'n't embarrass me.''

But Wilson still hesitated, and did not seem quite to know what to do. Then he said—

''I think it is too delicate a matter to—to—I believe I would rather write it or whisper it to you, and let you decide for yourself whether you want it talked out or not.''

''That will answer,'' said Luigi; ''write it.''

Wilson wrote something on a slip of paper and handed it to Luigi, who read it to himself and said to Tom—

''Unfold your slip and read it, Mr. Driscoll.''

Tom read:

"It was prophesied that I would kill a man. It came true before the year was out."

Tom added, "Great Scott!"

Luigi handed Wilson's paper to Tom, and said—

"Now read this one."

Tom read:

"You have killed some one, but whether man, woman or child, I do not make out."

"Caesar's ghost!" commented Tom, with astonishment. "It beats anything that was ever heard of! Why, a man's own hand is his deadliest enemy! Just think of that—a man's own hand keeps a record of the deepest and fatalest secrets of his life, and is treacherously ready to expose him to any black-magic stranger that comes along. But what do you let a person look at your hand for, with that awful thing printed in it?"

"Oh," said Luigi, reposefully, "I don't mind it. I killed the man for good reasons, and I don't regret it."

"What were the reasons?"

"Well, he needed killing."

"I'll tell you why he did it, since he won't say himself," said Angelo, warmly. "He did it to save my life, that's what he did it for. So it was a noble act, and not a thing to be hid in the dark."

"So it was, so it was," said Wilson; "to do such a thing to save a brother's life is a great and fine action."

"Now come," said Luigi, "it is very pleasant to hear you say these things, but for unselfishness, or heroism, or magnanimity, the circumstances won't stand scrutiny. You overlook one detail; suppose I hadn't saved Angelo's life, what would have become of mine? If I had let the man kill him, wouldn't he have killed me, too? I saved my own life, you see."

"Yes; that is your way of talking," said Angelo, "but I know you—I don't believe you thought of yourself at all. I keep that weapon yet that Luigi killed the man with, and I'll show it to you sometime. That incident makes it interesting, and it had a history before it came into Luigi's hands which adds to its interest. It was given to Luigi by a great Indian prince, the Gaikowar of Baroda, and it had been in his family two or three centuries. It killed a good many disagreeable people who troubled that hearthstone at one time and another. It isn't much to look at, except that it isn't shaped like other knives, or dirks, or whatever it may be called—here, I'll draw it for you." He took a sheet of paper and made a rapid sketch. "There it is—a broad and murderous blade, with edges like a razor for sharpness. The devices engraved on it are the ciphers or names of its long line of possessors—I had Luigi's name added in Roman letters myself with our coat of arms, as you see. You notice what a curious handle the thing has. It is solid ivory, polished like a mirror, and is four or five inches long—round, and as thick as a large man's wrist, with the end squared off flat, for your thumb to rest on; for you grasp it, with your thumb resting on the blunt end—so—and lift it aloft and strike downward. The Gaikowar showed us how the thing was done when he gave it to Luigi, and before that night was ended Luigi had used the knife, and the Gaikowar was a man short by reason of it. The sheath is magnificently ornamented with gems of great value. You will find the sheath more worth looking at than the knife itself, of course."

Tom said to himself—

"It's lucky I came here. I would have sold that knife for a song; I supposed the jewels were glass."

"But go on; don't stop," said Wilson. "Our curiosity is up now, to hear about the homicide. Tell us about that."

"Well, briefly, the knife was to blame for that, all around. A native servant slipped into our room in the palace in the night, to kill us and steal the knife on account of the fortune incrusted on its sheath, without a doubt. Luigi had it under his pillow; we were in bed together. There was a dim night-light burning. I was asleep, but Luigi was awake, and he thought he detected a vague form nearing the bed. He slipped the knife out of the sheath and was ready, and unembarrassed by hampering bed-clothes, for the weather was hot and we hadn't any. Suddenly that native rose at the bedside, and bent over me with his right hand lifted and a dirk in it aimed at my throat; but Luigi grabbed his wrist, pulled him downward, and drove his own knife into the man's neck. That is the whole story."

Wilson and Tom drew deep breaths, and after some general chat about the tragedy, Pudd'nhead said, taking Tom's hand—

"Now, Tom, I've never had a look at your palms, as it happens; perhaps you've got some little questionable privacies that need—hel-lo!"

Tom had snatched away his hand, and was looking a good deal confused.

"Why, he's blushing!" said Luigi.

Tom darted an ugly look at him, and said sharply—

"Well, if I am, it ain't because I'm a murderer!" Luigi's dark face flushed, but before he could speak or move, Tom added with anxious haste: "Oh, I beg a thousand pardons. I didn't mean that; it was out before I thought, and I'm very, very sorry—you must forgive me!"

Wilson came to the rescue, and smoothed things down as well as he could; and in fact was entirely successful as far as the twins were concerned, for they felt sorrier for the affront put upon him by his guest's outburst of ill manners than for the insult offered to Luigi. But the success was not so pronounced with the offender. Tom tried to seem at his ease, and he went through the motions fairly well, but at bottom he felt resentful toward all the three witnesses of his exhibition; in fact, he felt so annoyed at them for having witnessed it and noticed it that he almost forgot to feel annoyed at himself for placing it before them. However, something presently happened which made him almost comfortable, and brought him nearly back to a state of charity and friendliness. This was a little spat between the twins; not much of a spat, but still a spat; and before they got far with it they were in a decided condition of irritation with each other. Tom was charmed; so pleased, indeed, that he cautiously did what he could to increase the irritation while pretending to be actuated by more respectable motives. By his help the fire got warmed up to the blazing-point, and he might have had the happiness of seeing the flames show up, in another moment, but for the interruption of a knock on the door—an interruption which fretted him as much as it gratified Wilson. Wilson opened the door.

The visitor was a good-natured, ignorant, energetic, middle-aged Irishman named John Buckstone, who was a great politician in a small way, and always took a large share in public matters of every sort. One of the town's chief excitements, just now, was over the matter of rum. There was a strong rum party and a strong anti-rum party. Buckstone was training with the rum party, and he had been sent to hunt up the twins and invite them to attend a mass-meeting of that faction. He delivered his errand, and said the clans were already gathering in the big hall over the market-house. Luigi accepted the invitation cordially, Angelo less cordially, since he disliked crowds, and did not drink the powerful intoxicants of America. In fact, he was even a teetotaler sometimes—when it was judicious to be one.

The twins left with Buckstone, and Tom Driscoll joined company with them uninvited.

In the distance one could see a long wavering line of torches drifting down the main street, and could hear the throbbing of the bass drum, the clash of cymbals, the squeaking of a fife or two, and the faint roar of remote hurrahs. The tail-end of this procession was climbing the market-house stairs when the twins arrived in its neighborhood; when they reached the hall it was full of people, torches, smoke, noise and enthusiasm. They were conducted to the platform by Buckstone—Tom Driscoll still following—and were delivered to the chairman in the midst of a prodigious explosion of welcome. When the noise had moderated a little, the chair proposed that "our illustrious guests be at once elected, by complimentary acclamation, to membership in our ever-glorious organization, the paradise of the free and the perdition of the slave."

This eloquent discharge opened the floodgates of enthusiasm again, and the election was carried with thundering unanimity. Then arose a storm of cries:

"Wet them down! Wet them down! Give them a drink!"

Glasses of whisky were handed to the twins. Luigi waved his aloft, then brought it to his lips; but Angelo set his down. There was another storm of cries:

"What's the matter with the other one?" "What is the blond one going back on us for?" "Explain! Explain!"

The chairman inquired, and then reported—

"We have made an unfortunate mistake, gentlemen. I find that the Count Angelo Cappello is opposed to our creed—is a teetotaler, in fact, and was not intending to apply for membership with us. He desires that we reconsider the vote by which he was elected. What is the pleasure of the house?"

There was a general burst of laughter, plentifully accented with whistlings and cat-calls, but the energetic use of the gavel presently restored something like order. Then a man spoke from the crowd, and said that while he was very sorry that the mistake had been made, it would not be possible to rectify it at the present meeting. According to the by-laws it must go over to the next regular meeting for action. He would not offer a motion, as none was required. He desired to apologize to the gentleman in the name of the house, and begged to assure him that as far as it might lie in the power of the Sons of Liberty, his temporary membership in the order would be made pleasant to him.

This speech was received with great applause, mixed with cries of—

"That's the talk!" "He's a good fellow, anyway, if he *is* a teetotaler!" "Drink his health!" "Give him a rouser, and no heeltaps!"

Glasses were handed around, and everybody on the platform drank Angelo's health, while the house bellowed forth in song:

For he's a jolly good fel-low,
For he's a jolly good fel-low,
For he's a jolly good fe-el-low,—
Which nobody can deny.

Tom Driscoll drank. It was his second glass, for he had drunk Angelo's the moment that Angelo had set it down. The two drinks made him very merry—almost idiotically so—and he began to take a most lively and prominent part in the proceedings, particularly in the music and cat-calls and side-remarks.

The chairman was still standing at the front, the twins at his side. The extraordinarily close resemblance of the brothers to each other suggested a witticism to Tom Driscoll, and just as the chairman began a speech he skipped forward and said with an air of tipsy confidence to the audience—

"Boys, I move that he keeps still and lets this human philopena snip you out a speech."

The descriptive aptness of the phrase caught the house, and a mighty burst of laughter followed.

Luigi's southern blood leaped to the boiling-point in a moment under the sharp humiliation of this insult delivered in the presence of four hundred strangers. It was not in the young man's nature to let the matter pass, or to delay the squaring of the account. He took a couple of strides and halted behind the unsuspecting joker. Then he drew back and delivered a kick of such titantic vigor that it lifted Tom clear over the footlights and landed him on the heads of the front row of the Sons of Liberty.

Even a sober person does not like to have a human being emptied on him when he is not doing any harm; a person who is not sober cannot endure such an attention at all. The nest of Sons of Liberty that Driscoll landed in had not a sober bird in it; in fact there was probably not an entirely sober one in the auditorium. Driscoll was promptly and indignantly flung on to the heads of Sons in the next row, and these Sons passed him on toward the rear, and then immediately began to pummel the front-row Sons who had passed him to them. This course was strictly followed by bench after bench as Driscoll traveled in his tumultuous and airy flight toward the door; so he left behind him an ever lengthening wake of raging and plunging and fighting and swearing humanity. Down went group after group of torches, and presently above the deafening clatter of the gavel, roar of angry voices, and crash of succumbing benches, rose the paralyzing cry of "FIRE!"

The fighting ceased instantly; the cursing ceased; for one distinctly defined moment there was a dead hush, a motionless calm, where the tempest had been; then with one impulse the multitude awoke to life and energy again, and went surging and struggling and swaying, this way and that, its outer edges melting away through windows and doors and gradually lessening the pressure and relieving the mass.

The fire-boys were never on hand so suddenly before; for there was no distance to go, this time, their quarters being in the rear end of the market-house. There was an engine company and a hook-and-ladder company. Half of each was composed of rummies and the other half of anti-rummies, after the moral and political share-and-share-alike fashion of the frontier town of the period. Enough anti-rummies were loafing in quarters to man the engine and the ladders. In two minutes they had their red shirts and helmets on—they never stirred officially in unofficial costume—and as the mass meeting overhead smashed through the long row of windows and poured out upon the roof of the arcade, the deliverers were ready for them with a powerful stream of water which washed some of them off the roof and nearly drowned the rest. But water was preferable to fire, and still the stampede from the windows continued, and still the pitiless drenchings assailed it until the building was empty; then the fire-boys mounted to the hall and flooded it with water enough to annihilate forty times as much fire as there was there; for a village fire-company does not often get a chance to show off, and so when it does get a chance it makes the most of it. Such citizens of that village as were of a thoughtful and judicious temperament did not insure against fire; they insured against the fire-company.

CHAPTER XII

Courage is resistance to fear, mastery of fear—not absence of fear. Except a creature be part coward it is not a compliment to say it is brave; it is merely a loose misapplication of the word. Consider the flea!—incomparably the bravest of all the creatures of God, if ignorance of fear were courage. Whether you are asleep or awake he will attack you, caring nothing for the fact that in bulk and strength you are to him as are the massed armies of the earth to a sucking child; he lives both day and night and all days and nights in the very lap of peril and the immediate presence of death, and yet is no more afraid than is the man who walks the streets of a city that was threatened by an earthquake ten centuries before. When we speak of Clive, Nelson, and Putnam as men who "didn't know what fear was," we ought always to add the flea— and put him at the head of the procession.—*Pudd'nhead Wilson's Calendar.*

Judge Driscoll was in bed and asleep by ten o'clock on Friday night, and he was up and gone a-fishing before daylight in the morning with his friend Pembroke Howard. These two had been boys together in Virginia when that State still ranked as the chief and most imposing member of the Union, and they still coupled the proud and affectionate adjective "old" with her name when they spoke of her. In Missouri a recognized superiority attached to any person who hailed from Old Virginia; and this superiority was exalted to supremacy when a person of such nativity could also prove descent from the First Families of that great commonwealth. The Howards and Driscolls were of this aristocracy. In their eyes it was a nobility. It had its unwritten laws, and they were as clearly defined and as strict as any that could be found among the printed statutes of the land. The F.F.V. was born a gentleman; his highest duty in life was to watch over that great inheritance and keep it unsmirched. He must keep his honor spotless. Those laws were his chart; his course was marked out on it; if he swerved from it by so much as half a point of the compass it meant shipwreck to his honor; that is to say, degradation from his rank as a gentleman. These laws required certain things of him which his religion might forbid: then his religion must yield—the laws could not be relaxed to accommodate religions or anything else. Honor stood first; and the laws defined what it was and wherein it differed in certain details from honor as defined by church creeds and by the social laws and customs of some of the minor divisions of the globe that had got crowded out when the sacred boundaries of Virginia were staked out.

If Judge Driscoll was the recognized first citizen of Dawson's Landing, Pembroke Howard was easily its recognized second citizen. He was called "the great lawyer"—an earned title. He and Driscoll were of the same age—a year or two past sixty.

Although Driscoll was a free-thinker and Howard a strong and determined Presbyterian, their warm intimacy suffered no impairment in consequence. They were men whose opinions were their own property and not subject to revision and amendment, suggestion or criticism, by anybody, even their friends.

The day's fishing finished, they came floating down stream in their skiff, talking national politics and other high matters, and presently met a skiff coming up from town, with a man in it who said:

"I reckon you know one of the new twins gave your nephew a kicking last night, Judge?"

"Did *what?*"

"Gave him a kicking."

The old Judge's lips paled, and his eyes began to flame. He choked with anger for a moment, then he got out what he was trying to say—

"Well—well—go on! give me the details."

The man did it. At the finish the Judge was silent a minute, turning over in his mind the shameful picture of Tom's flight over the footlights; then he said, as if musing aloud—"H'm—I don't understand it. I was asleep at home. He didn't wake me. Thought he was competent to manage his affair without my help, I reckon." His face lit up with pride and pleasure at that thought, and he said with a cheery complacency, "I like that—it's the true old blood—hey, Pembroke?"

Howard smiled an iron smile, and nodded his head approvingly. Then the news-bringer spoke again—

"But Tom beat the twin on the trial."

The Judge looked at the man wonderingly, and said—

"The trial? What trial?"

"Why, Tom had him up before Judge Robinson for assault and battery."

The old man shrank suddenly together like one who has received a death-stroke. Howard sprang for him as he sank forward in a swoon, and took him in his arms, and bedded him on his back in the boat. He sprinkled water in his face, and said to the startled visitor—

"Go, now—don't let him come to and find you here. You see what an effect your heedless speech has had; you ought to have been more considerate than to blurt out such a cruel piece of slander as that."

"I'm right down sorry I did it now, Mr. Howard, and I wouldn't have done it if I had thought: but it ain't slander; it's perfectly true, just as I told him."

He rowed away. Presently the old Judge came out of his faint and looked up piteously into the sympathetic face that was bent over him.

"Say it ain't true, Pembroke; tell me it ain't true!" he said in a weak voice.

There was nothing weak in the deep organ-tones that responded—

"You know it's a lie as well as I do, old friend. He is of the best blood of the Old Dominion."

"God bless you for saying it!" said the old gentleman, fervently. "Ah, Pembroke, it was such a blow!"

Howard stayed by his friend, and saw him home, and entered the house with him. It was dark, and past supper-time, but the Judge was not thinking of supper; he was eager to hear the slander refuted from headquarters, and as eager to have Howard hear it, too. Tom was sent for, and he came immediately. He was bruised and lame, and was not a happy-looking object. His uncle made him sit down, and said—

"We have been hearing about your adventure, Tom, with a

handsome lie added to it for embellishment. Now pulverize that lie to dust! What measures have you taken? How does the thing stand?"

Tom answered guilelessly: "It don't stand at all; it's all over. I had him up in court and beat him. Pudd'nhead Wilson defended him—first case he ever had, and lost it. The judge fined the miserable hound five dollars for the assault."

Howard and the Judge sprang to their feet with the opening sentence—why, neither knew; then they stood gazing vacantly at each other. Howard stood a moment, then sat mournfully down without saying anything. The Judge's wrath began to kindle, and he burst out—

"You cur! You scum! You vermin! Do you mean to tell me that blood of my race has suffered a blow and crawled to a court of law about it? Answer me!"

Tom's head drooped, and he answered with an eloquent silence. His uncle stared at him with a mixed expression of amazement and shame and incredulity that was sorrowful to see. At last he said—

"Which of the twins was it?"

"Count Luigi."

"You have challenged him?"

"N—no," hesitated Tom, turning pale.

"You will challenge him to-night. Howard will carry it."

Tom began to turn sick, and to show it. He turned his hat round and round in his hand, his uncle glowering blacker and blacker upon him as the heavy seconds drifted by; then at last he began to stammer, and said piteously—

"Oh, please don't ask me to do it, uncle! He is a murderous devil—I never could—I—I'm afraid of him!"

Old Driscoll's mouth opened and closed three times before he could get it to perform its office; then he stormed out—

"A coward in my family! A Driscoll a coward! Oh, what have I done to deserve this infamy!" He tottered to his secretary in the corner repeating that lament again and again in heart-breaking tones, and got out of a drawer a paper, which he slowly tore to bits scattering the bits absently in his track as he walked up and down the room, still grieving and lamenting. At last he said—

"There it is, shreds and fragments once more—my will. Once more you have forced me to disinherit you, you base son of a most noble father! Leave my sight! Go—before I spit on you!"

The young man did not tarry. Then the Judge turned to Howard:

"You will be my second, old friend?"

"Of course."

"There is pen and paper. Draft the cartel, and lose no time."

"The Count shall have it in his hands in fifteen minutes," said Howard.

Tom was very heavy-hearted. His appetite was gone with his property and his self-respect. He went out the back way and wandered down the obscure lane grieving, and wondering if any course of future conduct, however discreet and carefully perfected and watched over, could win back his uncle's favor and persuade him to reconstruct once more that generous will which had just gone to ruin before his eyes. He finally concluded that it could. He said to himself that he had accomplished this sort of triumph once already, and that what had been done once could be done again. He would set about it. He would bend every energy to the task, and he would score that triumph once more, cost what it might to his convenience, limit as it might his frivolous and liberty-loving life.

"To begin," he said to himself, "I'll square up with the proceeds of my raid, and then gambling has got to be stopped—and stopped short off. It's the worst vice I've got—from my standpoint, anyway, because it's the one he can most easily find out, through the impatience of my creditors. He thought it expensive to have to pay two hundred dollars to them for me once. Expensive—*that!* Why, it cost me the whole of his fortune—but of course he never thought of that; some people can't think of any but their own side of a case. If he had known how deep I am in, now, the will would have gone to pot without waiting for a duel to help. Three hundred dollars! It's a pile! But he'll never hear of it, I'm thankful to say. The minute I've cleared it off, I'm safe; and I'll never touch a card again. Anyway, I won't while he lives, I make oath to that. I'm entering on my last reform—I know it—yes, and I'll win; but after that, if I ever slip again I'm gone."

CHAPTER XIII

When I reflect upon the number of disagreeable people who I know have gone to a better world, I am moved to lead a different life.—*Pudd'nhead Wilson's Calendar.*

October. This is one of the peculiarly dangerous months to speculate in stocks in. The others are July, January, September, April, November, May, March, June, December, August, and February. —*Pudd'nhead Wilson's Calendar.*

Thus mournfully communing with himself Tom moped along

the lane past Pudd'nhead Wilson's house, and still on and on between fences inclosing vacant country on each hand till he neared the haunted house, then he came moping back again, with many sighs and heavy with trouble. He sorely wanted cheerful company. Rowena! His heart gave a bound at the thought, but the next thought quieted it—the detested twins would be there.

He was on the inhabited side of Wilson's house, and now as he approached it he noticed that the sitting-room was lighted. This would do; others made him feel unwelcome sometimes, but Wilson never failed in courtesy toward him, and a kindly courtesy does at least save one's feelings, even if it is not professing to stand for a welcome. Wilson heard footsteps at his threshold, then the clearing of a throat.

"It's that fickle-tempered, dissipated young goose—poor devil, he finds friends pretty scarce to-day, likely, after the disgrace of carrying a personal-assault case into a law-court."

A dejected knock. "Come in!"

Tom entered, and drooped into a chair, without saying anything. Wilson said kindly—

"Why, my boy, you look desolate. Don't take it so hard. Try and forget you have been kicked."

"Oh, dear," said Tom, wretchedly, "it's not that, Pudd'nhead—it's not that. It's a thousand times worse than that—oh, yes, a million times worse."

"Why, Tom, what do you mean? Has Rowena—"

"Flung me? No, but the old man has."

Wilson said to himself, "Aha!" and thought of the mysterious girl in the bedroom. "The Driscolls have been making discoveries!" Then he said aloud, gravely:

"Tom, there are some kinds of dissipation which—"

"Oh, shucks, this hasn't got anything to do with dissipation. He wanted me to challenge that derned Italian savage, and I wouldn't do it."

"Yes, of course he would do that," said Wilson in a meditative matter-of-course way, "but the thing that puzzled me was, why he didn't look to that last night, for one thing, and why he let you carry such a matter into a court of law at all, either before the duel or after it. It's no place for it. It was not like him. I couldn't understand it. How did it happen?"

"It happened because he didn't know anything about it. He was asleep when I got home last night."

"And you didn't wake him? Tom, is that possible?"

Tom was not getting much comfort here. He fidgeted a moment, then said:

"I didn't choose to tell him—that's all. He was going a-fishing before the dawn, with Pembroke Howard, and if I got the twins into the common calaboose—and I thought sure I could—I never dreamed of their slipping out on a paltry fine for such an outrageous offense—well, once in the calaboose they would be disgraced, and uncle wouldn't want any duels with that sort of characters, and wouldn't allow any."

"Tom, I am ashamed of you! I don't see how you could treat your good old uncle so. I am a better friend of his than you are; for if I had known the circumstances I would have kept that case out of court until I got word to him and let him have a gentleman's chance."

"You would?" exclaimed Tom, with lively surprise. "And it your first case! And you know perfectly well there never would have *been* any case if he had got that chance, don't you? And you'd have finished your days a pauper nobody, instead of being an actually launched and recognized lawyer to-day. And you would really have done that, would you?"

"Certainly."

Tom looked at him a moment or two, then shook his head sorrowfully and said—

"I believe you—upon my word I do. I don't know why I do, but I do. Pudd'nhead Wilson, I think you're the biggest fool I ever saw."

"Thank you."

"Don't mention it."

"Well, he has been requiring you to fight the Italian and you have refused. You degenerate remnant of an honorable line! I'm thoroughly ashamed of you, Tom!"

"Oh, that's nothing! I don't care for anything, now that the will's torn up again."

"Tom, tell me squarely—didn't he find any fault with you for anything but those two things—carrying the case into court and refusing to fight?"

He watched the young fellow's face narrowly, but it was entirely reposeful, and so also was the voice that answered:

"No, he didn't find any other fault with me. If he had had any to find, he would have begun yesterday, for he was just in the humor for it. He drove that jack-pair around town and showed them the sights, and when he came home he couldn't find his father's old silver watch that don't keep time and he thinks so much of, and couldn't remember what he did with it three or four days ago when he saw it last; and so when I arrived he was all in a sweat about it, and when I suggested that it probably wasn't lost but stolen, it put him in a regular passion and he said

I was a fool—which convinced me, without any trouble, that that was just what he was afraid *had* happened, himself, but did not want to believe it, because lost things stand a better chance of being found again than stolen ones."

"Whe-ew!" whistled Wilson; "score another on the list."

"Another what?"

"Another theft!"

"Theft?"

"Yes, theft. That watch isn't lost, it's stolen. There's been another raid on the town—and just the same old mysterious sort of thing that has happened once before, as you remember."

"You don't mean it!"

"It's as sure as you are born! Have you missed anything yourself?"

"No. That is, I did miss a silver pencil-case that Aunt Mary Pratt gave me last birthday—"

"You'll find it stolen—that's what you'll find."

"No, I sha'n't; for when I suggested theft about the watch and got such a rap, I went and examined my room, and the pencil-case was missing, but it was only mislaid, and I found it again."

"You are sure you missed nothing else?"

"Well, nothing of consequence. I missed a small plain gold ring worth two or three dollars, but that will turn up. I'll look again."

"In my opinion you'll not find it. There's been a raid, I tell you, Come *in!*"

Mr. Justice Robinson entered, followed by Buckstone and the town-constable, Jim Blake. They sat down, and after some wandering and aimless weather-conversation Wilson said—

"By the way, we've just added another to the list of thefts, maybe two. Judge Driscoll's old silver watch is gone, and Tom here has missed a gold ring."

"Well, it is a bad business," said the Justice, "and gets worse the further it goes. The Hankses, the Dobsons, the Pilligrews, the Ortons, the Grangers, the Hales, the Fullers, and Holcombs, in fact everybody that lives around about Patsy Cooper's has been robbed of little things like trinkets and teaspoons and such-like small valuables that are easily carried off. It's perfectly plain that the thief took advantage of the reception at Patsy Cooper's when all the neighbors were in her house and all their niggers hanging around her fence for a look at the show, to raid the vacant houses undisturbed. Patsy is miserable about it; miserable on account of the neighbors, and particularly miserable on account of her foreigners, of course; so miserable on their account that she hasn't any room to worry about her own little losses."

"It's the same old raider," said Wilson. "I suppose there isn't any doubt about that."

"Constable Blake doesn't think so."

"No, you're wrong there." said Blake; "the other times it was a man; there was plenty of signs of that, as we know, in the profession, though we never got hands on him; but this time it's a woman."

Wilson thought of the mysterious girl straight off. She was always in his mind now. But she failed him again. Blake continued:

"She's a stoop-shouldered old woman with a covered basket on her arm, in a black veil, dressed in mourning. I saw her going aboard the ferry-boat yesterday. Lives in Illinois, I reckon; but I don't care where she lives, I'm going to get her—she can make herself sure of that."

"What makes you think she's the thief?"

"Well, there ain't any other, for one thing; and for another, some of the nigger draymen that happened to be driving along saw her coming out of or going into houses, and told me so—and it just happens that they was *robbed* houses, every time."

It was granted that this was plenty good enough circumstantial evidence. A pensive silence followed, which lasted some moments, then Wilson said—

"There's one good thing, anyway. She can't either pawn or sell Count Luigi's costly Indian dagger."

"My!" said Tom, "is *that* gone?"

"Yes."

"Well, that was a haul! But why can't she pawn it or sell it?"

"Because when the twins went home from the Sons of Liberty meeting last night, news of the raid was sifting in from everywhere, and Aunt Patsy was in distress to know if they had lost anything. They found that the dagger was gone, and they notified the police and pawnbrokers everywhere. It was a great haul, yes, but the old woman won't get anything out of it, because she'll get caught."

"Did they offer a reward?" asked Buckstone.

"Yes; five hundred dollars for the knife, and five hundred more for the thief."

"What a leather-headed idea!" exclaimed the constable. "The thief da'sn't go near them, nor send anybody. Whoever goes is going to get himself nabbed, for there ain't any pawnbroker that's going to lose the chance to—"

If anybody had noticed Tom's face at that time, the gray-green color of it might have provoked curiosity; but nobody did.

He said to himself: "I'm gone! I never can square up; the rest of the plunder won't pawn or sell for half of the bill. Oh, I know it—I'm gone, I'm gone—and this time it's for good. Oh, this is awful—I don't know what to do, nor which way to turn!"

"Softly, softly," said Wilson to Blake. "I planned their scheme for them at midnight last night, and it was all finished up ship-shape by two this morning. They'll get their dagger back, and then I'll explain to you how the thing was done."

There were strong signs of a general curiosity, and Buckstone said—

"Well, you have whetted us up pretty sharp, Wilson, and I'm free to say that if you don't mind telling us in confidence—"

"Oh, I'd as soon tell as not, Buckstone, but as long as the twins and I agreed to say nothing about it, we must let it stand so. But you can take my word for it you won't be kept waiting three days. Somebody will apply for that reward pretty promptly, and I'll show you the thief and the dagger both very soon afterward."

The constable was disappointed, and also perplexed. He said—

"It may all be—yes, and I hope it will, but I'm blamed if I can see my way through it. It's too many for yours truly."

The subject seemed about talked out. Nobody seemed to have anything further to offer. After a silence the justice of the peace informed Wilson that he and Buckstone and the constable had come as a committee, on the part of the Democratic party, to ask him to run for mayor—for the little town was about to become a city and the first charter election was approaching. It was the first attention which Wilson had ever received at the hands of any party; it was a sufficiently humble one, but it was a recognition of his début into the town's life and activities at last; it was a step upward, and he was deeply gratified. He accepted, and the committee departed, followed by young Tom.

CHAPTER XIV

The true Southern watermelon is a boon apart, and not to be mentioned with commoner things. It is chief of this world's luxuries, king by the grace of God over all the fruits of the earth. When one has tasted it, he knows what the angels eat. It was not a Southern watermelon that Eve took: we know it because she repented.—*Pudd'nhead Wilson's Calendar.*

About the time that Wilson was bowing the committee out, Pembroke Howard was entering the next house to report. He found the old Judge sitting grim and straight in his chair, waiting.

"Well, Howard—the news?"

"The best in the world."

"Accepts, does he?" and the light of battle gleamed joyously in the Judge's eye.

"Accepts? Why, he jumped at it."

"Did, did he? Now that's fine—that's very fine. I like that. When is it to be?"

"Now! Straight off! To-night! An admirable fellow— admirable!"

"Admirable? He's a darling! Why, it's an honor as well as a pleasure to stand up before such a man. Come—off with you! Go and arrange everything—and give him my heartiest compliments. A rare fellow, indeed; an admirable fellow, as you have said!"

Howard hurried away, saying—

"I'll have him in the vacant stretch between Wilson's and the haunted house within the hour, and I'll bring my own pistols."

Judge Driscoll began to walk the floor in a state of pleased excitement; but presently he stopped, and began to think—began to think of Tom. Twice he moved toward the secretary, and twice he turned away again; but finally he said—

"This may be my last night in the world—I must not take the chance. He is worthless and unworthy, but it is largely my fault. He was intrusted to me by my brother on his dying bed, and I have indulged him to his hurt, instead of training him up severely, and making a man of him. I have violated my trust, and I must not add the sin of desertion to that. I have forgiven him once already, and would subject him to a long and hard trial before forgiving him again, if I could live; but I must not run that risk. No, I must restore the will. But if I survive the duel, I will hide it away, and he will not know, and I will not tell him until he reforms, and I see that his reformation is going to be permanent."

He re-drew the will, and his ostensible nephew was heir to a fortune again. As he was finishing his task, Tom, wearied with another brooding tramp, entered the house and went tiptoeing past the sitting-room door. He glanced in, and hurried on, for the sight of his uncle had nothing but terrors for him to-night. But his uncle was writing! That was unusual at this late hour. What could he be writing? A chill of anxiety settled down upon Tom's heart. Did that writing concern him? He was afraid so. He reflected that when ill luck begins, it does not come in sprinkles, but in showers. He said he would get a glimpse of that document or know the reason why. He heard some one coming, and stepped out of sight and hearing. It was Pembroke Howard. What could be hatching.

Howard said, with great satisfaction:

"Everything's right and ready. He's gone to the battle-ground with his second and the surgeon—also with his brother. I've arranged it all with Wilson—Wilson's his second. We are to have three shots apiece."

"Good! How is the moon?"

"Bright as day, nearly. Perfect, for the distance—fifteen yards. No wind—not a breath; hot and still."

"All good; all first-rate. Here, Pembroke, read this, and witness it."

Pembroke read and witnessed the will, then gave the old man's hand a hearty shake and said:

"Now that's right, York—but I knew you would do it. You couldn't leave that poor chap to fight along without means or profession, with certain defeat before him, and I knew you wouldn't, for his father's sake if not for his own."

"For his dead father's sake I couldn't, I know; for poor Percy—but you know what Percy was to me. But mind—Tom is not to know of this unless I fall to-night."

"I understand. I'll keep the secret."

The Judge put the will away, and the two started for the battle-ground. In another minute the will was in Tom's hands. His misery vanished, his feelings underwent a tremendous revulsion. He put the will carefully back in its place, and spread his mouth and swung his hat once, twice, three times around his head, in imitation of three rousing huzzas, no sound issuing from his lips. He fell to communing with himself excitedly and joyously, but every now and then he let off another volley of dumb hurrahs.

He said to himself: "I've got the fortune again, but I'll not let on that I know about it. And this time I'm going to hang on to it. I take no more risks. I'll gamble no more, I'll drink no more, because—well, because I'll not go where there is any of that sort of thing going on, again. It's the sure way, and the only sure way; I might have thought of that sooner—well, yes, if I had wanted to. But now—dear me, I've had a scare this time, and I'll take no more chances. Not a single chance more. Land! I persuaded myself this evening that I could fetch him around without any great amount of effort, but I've been getting more and more heavy-hearted and doubtful straight along, ever since. If he tells me about this thing, all right; but if he doesn't, I sha'n't, let on. I—well, I'd like to tell Pudd'nhead Wilson, but—no, I'll think about that; perhaps I won't." He whirled off another dead huzza, and said, "I'm reformed, and this time I'll stay so, sure!"

He was about to close with a final grand silent demonstration, when he suddenly recollected that Wilson had put it out of his power to pawn or sell the Indian knife, and that he was once more in awful peril of exposure by his creditors for that reason. His joy collapsed utterly, and he turned away and moped toward the door moaning and lamenting over the bitterness of his luck. He dragged himself up-stairs, and brooded in his room a long time disconsolate and forlorn, with Luigi's Indian knife for a text. At last he sighed and said:

"When I supposed these stones were glass and this ivory bone, the thing hadn't any interest for me because it hadn't any value, and couldn't help me out of my trouble. But now—why, now it is full of interest; yes, and of a sort to break a body's heart. It's a bag of gold that has turned to dirt and ashes in my hands. It could save me, and save me so easily, and yet I've got to go to ruin. It's like drowning with a life-preserver in my reach. All the hard luck comes to me, and all the good luck goes to other people—Pudd'nhead Wilson, for instance; even his career has got a sort of a little start at last, and what has he done to deserve it, I should like to know? Yes, he has opened his own road, but he isn't content with that, but must block mine. It's a sordid, selfish world, and I wish I was out of it." He allowed the light of the candle to play upon the jewels of the sheath, but the flashings and sparklings had no charm for his eye; they were only just so many pangs to his heart. "I must not say anything to Roxy about this thing," he said, "she is too daring. She would be for digging these stones out and selling them, and then—why, she would be arrested and the stones traced, and then—" The thought made him quake, and he hid the knife away, trembling all over and glancing furtively about, like a criminal who fancies that the accuser is already at hand.

Should he try to sleep? Oh, no, sleep was not for him; his trouble was too haunting, too afflicting for that. He must have somebody to mourn with. He would carry his despair to Roxy.

He had heard several distant gunshots, but that sort of thing was not uncommon, and they had made no impression upon him. He went out at the back door, and turned westward. He passed Wilson's house and proceeded along the lane, and presently saw several figures approaching Wilson's place through the vacant lots. These were the duelists returning from the fight; he thought he recognized them, but as he had no desire for white people's company, he stooped down behind the fence until they were out of his way.

Roxy was feeling fine. She said:

"Whah was you, child? Warn't you in it?"

"In what?"

"In de duel."

"Duel? Has there been a duel?"

" 'Co'se dey has. De ole Jedge has be'n havin' a duel wid one o' dem twins."

"Great Scott!" Then he added to himself: "That's what made him re-make the will; he thought he might get killed, and it softened him toward me. And that's what he and Howard were so busy about. . . . Oh dear, if the twin had only killed him, I should be out of my—"

"What is you mumblin' bout, Chambers? Whah was you? Didn't you know dey was gwyne to be a duel?"

"No, I didn't. The old man tried to get me to fight one with Count Luigi, but he didn't succeed, so I reckon he concluded to patch up the family honor himself."

He laughed at the idea, and went rambling on with a detailed account of his talk with the Judge, and how shocked and ashamed the Judge was to find that he had a coward in his family. He glanced up at last, and got a shock himself. Roxana's bosom was heaving with suppressed passion, and she was glowering down upon him with measureless contempt written in her face.

"En you refuse' to fight a man dat kicked you, 'stid o' jumpin' at de chance! En you ain't got no mo' feelin' den to come en tell me, dat fetched sich a po' low-down ornery rabbit into de worl'! Pah! it make me sick! It's de nigger in you, dat's what it is. Thirty-one parts o' you is white, en on'y one part nigger, en dat po' little one part is yo' *soul*. Tain't wuth savin'; tain't wuth totin' out on a shovel en throwin' in de gutter. You has disgraced yo' birth. What would yo' pa think o' you? It's enough to make him turn in his grave."

The last three sentences stung Tom into a fury, and he said to himself that if his father were only alive and in reach of assassination his mother would soon find that he had a very clear notion of the size of his indebtedness to that man, and was willing to pay it up in full, and would do it too, even at risk of his life; but he kept his thought to himself; that was safest in his mother's present state.

"Whatever has come o' yo' Essex blood? Dat's what I can't understan'. En it ain't on'y jist Essex blood dat's in you, not by a long sight—'deed it ain't! My great-great-great-gran'father en yo' great-great-great-great-gran'father was Ole Cap'n John Smith, de highest blood dat Ole Virginny ever turned out, en *his* great-great-gran'mother or somers along back dah, was Pocahontas de Injun queen, en her husbun' was a nigger king outen Africa— en yit here you is, a slinkin' outen a duel en disgracin' our whole line like a ornery low-down hound! Yes, it's de nigger in you!"

She sat down on her candle-box and fell into a reverie. Tom did not disturb her; he sometimes lacked prudence, but it was not in circumstances of this kind. Roxana's storm went gradually down, but it died hard, and even when it seemed to be quite gone, it would now and then break out in a distant rumble, so to speak, in the form of muttered ejaculations. One of these was, "Ain't nigger enough in him to show in his finger-nails, en dat takes mighty little—yit dey's enough to paint his soul."

Presently she muttered. "Yassir, enough to paint a whole thimbleful of 'em." At last her ramblings ceased altogether, and her countenance began to clear—a welcome sign to Tom, who had learned her moods, and knew she was on the threshold of good-humor, now. He noticed that from time to time she unconsciously carried her finger to the end of her nose. He looked close and said:

"Why, mammy, the end of your nose is skinned. How did that come?"

She sent out the sort of whole-hearted peal of laughter which God has vouchsafed in its perfection to none but the happy angels in heaven and the bruised and broken black slave on the earth, and said:

"Dad fetch dat duel, I be'n in it myself."

"Gracious! did a bullet do that?"

"Yassir, you bet it did!"

"Well, I declare! Why, how did that happen?"

"Happened dis-away. I 'uz a-sett'n' here kinder dozin' in de dark, en *che-bang!* goes a gun, right out dah. I skips along out towards t'other end o' de house to see what's gwyne on, en stops by de ole winder on de side to wards Pudd'nhead Wilson's house dat ain't got no sash in it,—but dey ain't none of 'em got any sashes, fur as dat's concerned,—en I stood dah in de dark en look out, en dar in de moonlight, right down under me 'uz one o' de twins a-cussin'— not much, but jist a-cussin' soft—'uz de brown one dat 'uz cussin', ca'se he 'uz hit in de shoulder. En Doctor Claypool he 'uz a-workin' at him, en Pudd'nhead Wilson he 'uz a-he'pin', en ole Jedge Driscoll en Pem Howard 'uz a-standin' out yonder a little piece waitin' for 'em to git ready agin. En trecky dey squared off en give de word, en *bang-bang* went de pistols, en de twin he say, 'Ouch!'—hit him on de han' dis time,—en I hear dat same bullet go *spat!* ag'in' de logs under de winder; en de nex' time dey shoot, de twin say, 'Ouch!' ag'in, en I done it too, 'ca'se de bullet glance' on his cheed-bone en skip up here en glance on de side o' de winder en whiz' right acrost my face en tuck de hide off'n my nose—why, if I'd 'a' be'n jist a inch or a inch en a half furder 't would 'a' tuck de whole nose en disfiggered me. Here's de bullet; I hunted her up."

"Did you stand there all the time?"

"Dat's a question to ask, ain't it! What else would I do? Does I git a chance to see a duel every day?"

"Why, you were right in range! Weren't you afraid?"

The woman gave a sniff of scorn.

" 'Fraid! De Smith-Pocahontases ain't 'fraid o' nothin', let alone bullets."

"They've got pluck enough, I suppose; what they lack is judgment. *I* wouldn't have stood there."

"Nobody's accusin' you!"

"Did anybody else get hurt?"

"Yes, we all got hit 'cep' de blon' twin en de doctor en de seconds. De Jedge didn't git hurt, but I hear Pudd'nhead say de bullet snip some o' his ha'r off."

" 'George!" said Tom to himself, "to come so near being out of my trouble, and miss it by an inch. Oh dear, dear, he will live to find me out and sell me to some nigger-trader yet—yes, and he would do it in a minute." Then he said aloud, in a grave tone—

"Mother, we are in an awful fix."

Roxana caught her breath with a spasm, and said—

"Chile! What you hit a body so sudden for, like dat? What's be'n en gone en happen'?"

"Well, there's one thing I didn't tell you. When I wouldn't fight, he tore up the will again, and—

Roxana's face turned a dead white, and she said—

"Now you's *done!*—done forever! Dat's de end. Bofe un us is gwyne to starve to—"

"Wait and hear me through, can't you! I reckon that when he resolved to fight, himself, he thought he might get killed and not have a chance to forgive me any more in this life, so he made the will again, and I've seen it, and it's all right. But—"

"Oh, thank goodness, den we's safe ag'in!—safe! en so what did you want to come here en talk sich dreadful—"

"Hold *on,* I tell you, and let me finish. The swag I gathered won't half square me up, and the first thing we know, my creditors—well, you know what'll happen."

Roxana dropped her chin, and told her son to leave her alone—she must think this matter out. Presently she said impressively:

"You got to go mighty keerful now, I tell you! En here's what you got to do. He didn't git killed, en if you gives him de least reason, he'll bust de will ag'in, en dat's de *las'* time, now you hear me! So—you's got to show him what you kin do in de nex' few days. You's got to be pison good, en let him see it; you got to do everything dat'll make him b'lieve in you, en you got to sweeten aroun' ole Aunt Pratt, too,—she's pow'ful strong wid de Jedge, en de bes' frien' you got. Nex', you'll go 'long away to Sent Louis, en dat'll *keep* him in yo' favor. Den you go en make a bargain wid dem people. You tell 'em he ain't gwyne to live long—en dat's de fac', too,—en tell 'em you'll pay 'em intrust, en big intrust, too,—ten per—what you call it?"

"Ten per cent, a month?"

"Dat's it. Den you take and sell yo' truck aroun', a little at a time, en pay de intrust. How long will it las'?"

"I think there's enough to pay the interest five or six months."

"Den you's all right. If he don't die in six months, dat don't make no diff'rence—Providence'll provide. You's gwyne to be safe—if you behaves." She bent an austere eye on him and added, "En you *is* gwyne to behave—does you know dat?"

He laughed and said he was going to try, anyway. She did not unbend. She said gravely:

"Tryin' ain't de thing. You's gwyne to *do* it. You ain't gwyne to steal a pin—'ca'se it ain't safe no mo'; en you ain't gwyne into no bad comp'ny—not even once, you understand; en you ain't gwyne to drink a drop—nary single drop; en you ain't gwyne to gamble one single gamble—not one! Dis ain't what you's gwyne to *try* to do, it's what you's gwyne to *do*. En I'll tell you how I knows it. Dis is how. I's gwyne to foller along to Sent Louis my own self; en you's gwyne to come to me every day o' yo life, en I'll look you over; en if you fails in one single one o' dem things—jist *one*—I take my oath I'll come straight down to dis town en tell de Jedge you's a nigger en a slave—en *prove* it!" She paused to let her words sink home. Then she added, "Chambers, does you b'lieve me when I says dat?"

Tom was sober enough now. There was no levity in his voice when he answered:

"Yes, mother, I know, now, that I am reformed—and permanently. Permanently—and beyond the reach of any human temptation.

"Den g' long home en begin!"

CHAPTER XV

Nothing so needs reforming as other people's habits.—*Pudd'nhead Wilson's Calendar.*

Behold, the fool saith, "Put not all thine eggs in the one basket"—which is but a manner of saying, "Scatter your money and your attention;" but the wise man saith, "Put all your eggs in the one basket and—WATCH THAT BASKET."—*Pudd'nhead Wilson's Calendar.*

What a time of it Dawson's Landing was having! All its life it had been asleep, but now it hardly got a chance for a nod, so swiftly did big events and crashing surprises come along in one another's wake: Friday morning, first glimpse of Real Nobility, also grand reception at Aunt Patsy Cooper's, also great robber-raid; Friday evening, dramatic kicking of the heir of the chief citizen in presence of four hundred people; Saturday morning, emergence as practising lawyer of the long-submerged Pudd'nhead Wilson; Saturday night, duel between chief citizen and titled stranger.

The people took more pride in the duel than in all the other events put together, perhaps. It was a glory to their town to have such a thing happen there. In their eyes the principals had reached the summit of human honor. Everybody paid homage to their names; their praises were in all mouths. Even the duelists' subordinates came in for a handsome share of the public approbation: wherefore Pudd'nhead Wilson was suddenly become a man of consequence. When asked to run for the mayoralty Saturday night he was risking defeat, but Sunday morning found him a made man and his success assured.

The twins were prodigiously great, now; the town took them to its bosom with enthusiasm. Day after day, and night after night, they went dining and visiting from house to house, making friends, enlarging and solidifying their popularity, and charming and surprising all with their musical prodigies, and now and then heightening the effects with samples of what they could do in other directions, out of their stock of rare and curious accomplishments. They were so pleased that they gave the regulation thirty days' notice, the required preparation for citizenship, and resolved to finish their days in this pleasant place. That was the climax. The delighted community rose as one man and applauded; and when the twins were asked to stand for seats in the forthcoming aldermanic board, and consented, the public contentment was rounded and complete.

Tom Driscoll was not happy over these things; they sunk deep, and hurt all the way down. He hated the one twin for kicking him, and the other one for being the kicker's brother.

Now and then the people wondered why nothing was heard of the raider, or of the stolen knife or the other plunder, but nobody was able to throw any light on that matter. Nearly a week had drifted by, and still the thing remained a vexed mystery.

On Saturday Constable Blake and Pudd'nhead Wilson met on the street, and Tom Driscoll joined them in time to open their conversation for them. He said to Blake—"You are not looking well, Blake; you seem to be annoyed about something. Has anything gone wrong in the detective business? I believe you fairly and justifiably claim to have a pretty good reputation in that line, isn't it so?"—which made Blake feel good, and look it; but Tom added, "for a country detective"—which made Blake feel the other way, and not only look it, but betray it in his voice—

"Yes, sir, I *have* got a reputation; and it's as good as anybody's in the profession, too, country or no country."

"Oh, I beg pardon; I didn't mean any offense. What I started out to ask was only about the old woman that raided the town—the stoop-shouldered old woman, you know, that you said you were going to catch; and I knew you would, too, because you have the reputation of never boasting, and—well, you—you've caught the old woman?"

"D——the old woman!"

"Why, sho! you don't mean to say you haven't caught her?"

"No; I haven't caught her. If anybody could have caught her, I could; but nobody couldn't, I don't care who he is."

"I am sorry, real sorry—for your sake; because, when it gets around that a detective has expressed himself so confidently, and then——"

"Don't you worry, that's all—don't you worry; and as for the town, the town needn't worry, either. She's my meat—make yourself easy about that. I'm on her track; I've got clues that——"

"That's good! Now if you could get an old veteran detective down from St. Louis to help you find what the clues mean, and where they lead to, and then——"

"I'm plenty veteran enough myself, and I don't need anybody's help. I'll have her inside of a we—inside of a month. That I'll swear to!"

Tom said carelessly—

"I suppose that will answer—yes, that will answer. But I reckon she is pretty old, and old people don't often outlive the cautious pace of the professional detective when he has got his clues together and is out on his still-hunt."

Blake's dull face flushed under this gibe, but before he could set his retort in order Tom had turned to Wilson, and was saying, with placid indifference of manner and voice—

"Who got the reward, Pudd'head?"

Wilson winced slightly, and saw that his own turn was come.

"What reward?"

"Why, the reward for the thief, and the other one for the knife."

Wilson answered—and rather uncomfortably, to judge by his hesitating fashion of delivering himself—

"Well, the—well, in fact, nobody has claimed it yet."

Tom seemed surprised.

"Why, is that so?"

Wilson showed a trifle of irritation when he replied—

"Yes, it's so. And what of it?"

"Oh, nothing. Only I thought you had struck out a new idea, and invented a scheme that was going to revolutionize the time-worn and ineffectual methods of the——" He stopped, and turned to Blake, who was happy now that another had taken his place on the gridiron: "Blake, didn't you understand him to intimate that it wouldn't be necessary for you to hunt the old woman down?"

"B'George, he said he'd have thief and swag both inside of three days—he did, by hokey! and that's just about a week ago. Why, I said at the time that no thief and no thief's pal was going to try to pawn or sell a thing where he knowed the pawnbroker could get both rewards by taking *him* into camp *with* the swag. It was the blessedest idea that ever *I* struck!"

"You'd change your mind," said Wilson, with irritated bluntness, "if you knew the entire scheme instead of only part of it."

"Well," said the constable, pensively, "I had the idea that it wouldn't work, and up to now I'm right anyway."

"Very well, then, let it stand at that, and give it a further show. It has worked at least as well as your own methods, you perceive."

The constable hadn't anything handy to hit him back with, so he discharged a discontented sniff, and said nothing.

After the night that Wilson had partly revealed his scheme at his house, Tom had tried for several days to guess out the secret of the rest of it, but had failed. Then it occurred to him to give Roxana's smarter head a chance at it. He made up a suppostitious case, and laid it before her. She thought it over, and delivered her verdict upon it. Tom said to himself, "She's hit it, sure!" He thought he would test that verdict, now, and watch Wilson's face; so he said reflectively—

"Wilson, you're not a fool—a fact of recent discovery. Whatever your scheme was, it had sense in it, Blake's opinion to the contrary notwithstanding, I don't ask you to reveal it, but I will suppose a case—a case which will answer as a starting-point for the real thing I am going to come at, and that's all I want. You offered five hundred dollars for the knife, and five hundred for the thief. We will suppose, for argument's sake, that the first reward is *advertised* and the second offered by *private letter* to pawnbrokers and——"

Blake slapped his thigh, and cried out—

"By Jackson, he's got you, Pudd'nhead! Now why couldn't I or *any* fool have thought of that?"

Wilson said to himself, "Anybody with a reasonably good head would have thought of it. I am not surprised that Blake didn't detect it; I am only surprised that Tom did. There is more to him than I supposed." He said nothing aloud, and Tom went on:

"Very well. The thief would not suspect that there was a trap, and he would bring or send the knife, and say he bought it for a song, or found it in the road, or something like that, and try to collect the reward, and be arrested—wouldn't he?"

"Yes," said Wilson.

"I think so," said Tom. "There can't be any doubt of it. Have you ever seen that knife?"

"No."

"Has any friend of yours?"

"Not that I know of."

"Well, I begin to think I understand why your scheme failed."

"What do you mean, Tom? What are you driving at?" asked Wilson, with a dawning sense of discomfort.

"Why, that there *isn't* any such knife."

"Look here, Wilson," said Blake, "Tom Driscoll's right, for a thousand dollars—if I had it."

Wilson's blood warmed a little, and he wondered if he had been played upon by those strangers; it certainly had something of that look. But what could they gain by it? He threw out that suggestion. Tom replied:

"Gain? Oh, nothing that you would value, maybe. But they are strangers making their way in a new community. Is it nothing to them to appear as pets of an Oriental prince—at no expense? Is it nothing to them to be able to dazzle this poor little town with thousand-dollar rewards—at no expense? Wilson, there isn't any such knife, or your scheme would have fetched it to light. Or if there is any such knife, they've got it yet. I believe, myself, that they've seen such a knife, for Angelo pictured it out with his pencil too swiftly and handily for him to have been inventing it, and of course I can't swear that they've never had it; but this I'll go bail for—if they had it when they came to this town, they've got it yet."

Blake said—

"It looks mighty reasonable, the way Tom puts it; it most certainly does."

Tom responded, turning to leave—

"You find the old woman, Blake, and if she can't furnish the knife, go and search the twins!"

Tom sauntered away. Wilson felt a good deal depressed. He hardly knew what to think. He was loth to withdraw his faith from the twins, and was resolved not to do it on the present indecisive evidence; but—well, he would think, and then decide how to act.

"Blake, what do you think of this matter?"

"Well, Pudd'nhead, I'm bound to say I put it the way Tom does. They hadn't the knife; or if they had it, they've got it yet."

The men parted. Wilson said to himself:

"I believe they had it; if it had been stolen, the scheme would have restored it, that is certain. And so I believe they've got it yet."

Tom had no purpose in his mind when he encountered those two men. When he began his talk he hoped to be able to gall them a little and get a trifle of malicious entertainment out of it. But when he left, he left in great spirits, for he perceived that just by pure luck and no troublesome labor he had accomplished several delightful things: he had touched both men on a raw spot and seen them squirm; he had modified Wilson's sweetness for the twins with one small bitter taste that he wouldn't be able to get out of his mouth right away; and, best of all, he had taken the hated twins down a peg with the community; for Blake would gossip around freely, after the manner of detectives, and within a week the town would be laughing at them in its sleeve for offering a gaudy reward for a bauble which they either never possessed or hadn't lost. Tom was very well satisfied with himself.

Tom's behavior at home had been perfect during the entire week. His uncle and aunt had seen nothing like it before. They could find no fault with him anywhere.

Saturday evening he said to the Judge—

"I've had something preying on my mind, uncle, and as I am going away, and might never see you again, I can't bear it any longer. I made you believe I was afraid to fight that Italian adventurer. I had to get out of it on some pretext or other, and maybe I chose badly, being taken unawares, but no honorable person could consent to meet him in the field, knowing what I knew about him."

"Indeed? What was that?"

"Count Luigi is a confessed assassin."

"Incredible!"

"It is perfectly true. Wilson detected it in his hand, by palmistry, and charged him with it, and cornered him up so close that he had to confess; but both twins begged us on their knees to keep the secret, and swore they would lead straight lives here; and it was all so pitiful that we gave our word of honor never to expose them while they kept that promise. You would have done it yourself, uncle."

"You are right, my boy; I would. A man's secret is still his own property, and sacred, when it has been surprised out of him like that. You did well, and I am proud of you." Then he added mournfully, "But I wish I could have been saved the shame of meeting an assassin on the field of honor."

"It couldn't be helped, uncle. If I had known you were going to challenge him I should have felt obliged to sacrifice my pledged word in order to stop it, but Wilson couldn't be expected to do otherwise than keep silent."

"Oh no; Wilson did right, and is in no way to blame. Tom, Tom, you have lifted a heavy load from my heart; I was stung to the very soul when I seemed to have discovered that I had a coward in my family."

"You may imagine what it cost *me* to assume such a part, uncle."

"Oh, I know it, poor boy, I know it. And I can understand how much it has cost you to remain under that unjust stigma to this time. But it is all right now, and no harm is done. You have restored my comfort of mind, and with it your own; and both of us had suffered enough."

The old man sat awhile plunged in thought; then he looked up with a satisfied light in his eye, and said: "That this assassin should have put the affront upon me of letting me meet him on the field of honor as if he were a gentleman is a matter which I will presently settle—but not now. I will not shoot him until after election. I see a way to ruin them both before; I will attend to that first. Neither of them shall be elected, that I promise. You are sure that the fact that he is an assassin has not got abroad?"

"Perfectly certain of it, sir."

"It will be a good card. I will fling a hint at it from the stump on the polling-day. It will sweep the ground from under both of them."

"There's no doubt of it. It will finish them."

"That and outside work among the voters will, to a certainty. I want you to come down here by and by and work privately among the rag-tag and bobtail. You shall spend money among them; I will furnish it."

Another point scored against the detested twins! Really it was a great day for Tom. He was encouraged to chance a parting shot, now, at the same target, and did it.

"You know that wonderful Indian knife that the twins have been making such a to-do about? Well, there's no track or trace of it yet; so the town is beginning to sneer and gossip and laugh. Half the people believe they never had any such knife, the other half believe they had it and have got it still. I've heard twenty people talking like that today."

Yes, Tom's blemishless week had restored him to the favor of his aunt and uncle.

His mother was satisfied with him, too. Privately, she believed she was coming to love him, but she did not say so. She told him to go along to St. Louis, now, and she would get ready and follow. Then she smashed her whisky bottle and said—

"Dah now! I's a-gwyne to make you walk straight as a string, Chambers, en so I's bown' you ain't gwyne to git no bad example out o' yo' mammy. I tole you you couldn't go into no bad comp'ny. Well, you's gwyne into my comp'ny, en I's gwyne to fill de bill. Now, den, trot along, trot along!"

Tom went aboard one of the big transient boats that night with his heavy satchel of miscellaneous plunder, and slept the sleep of the unjust, which is serener and sounder than the other kind, as we know by the hanging-eve history of a million rascals. But when he got up in the morning, luck was against him again: A brother-thief had robbed him while he slept, and gone ashore at some intermediate landing.

CHAPTER XVI

If you pick up a starving dog and make him prosperous, he will not bite you. This is the principal difference between a dog and a man. —*Pudd'nhead Wilson's Calendar.*

We know all about the habits of the ant, we know all about the habits of the bee, but we know nothing at all about the habits of the oyster. It seems almost certain that we have been choosing the wrong time for studying the oyster.—*Pudd'nhead Wilson's Calendar.*

When Roxana arrived, she found her son in such despair and misery that her heart was touched and her motherhood rose up strong in her. He was ruined past hope, now; his destruction would be immediate and sure, and he would be an outcast and friendless. That was reason enough for a mother to love a child; so she loved him, and told him so. It made him wince, secretly—for she was a "nigger." That he was one himself was far from reconciling him to that despised race.

Roxana poured out endearments upon him, to which he responded uncomfortably, but as well as he could. And she tried to comfort him, but that was not possible. These intimacies quickly became horrible to him, and within the hour he began to try to get up courage enough to tell her so, and require that they be discontinued or very considerably modified. But he was afraid of her; and besides, there came a lull, now, for she had begun to think. She was trying to invent a saving plan. Finally she started up, and said she had found a way out. Tom was almost suffocated by the joy of this sudden good news. Roxana said:

"Here is de plan, en she'll win, sure. I's a nigger, en nobody ain't gwyne to doubt it dat hears me talk. I's wuth six hund'd dollahs. Take en sell me, en pay off dese gamblers."

Tom was dazed. He was not sure he had heard aright. He was dumb for a moment; then he said:

"Do you mean that you would be sold into slavery to save me?"

"Ain't you my chile? En does you know anything dat a mother won't do for her chile? Dey ain't nothin a white mother won't do for her chile. Who made 'em so? De Lord done it. En who made de niggers? De Lord made 'em. In de inside, mothers is all de same. De good Lord he made 'em so. I's gwyne to be sole into slavery, en in a year you's gwyne to buy yo' ole mammy free ag'in. I'll show you how. Dat's de plan."

Tom's hopes began to rise, and his spirits along with them. He said—

"It's lovely of you, mammy—it's just—"

"Say it ag'in! En keep on sayin' it? It's all de pay a body kin want in dis worl', en it's mo'den enough. Laws bless you, honey, when I's slavin' aroun', en dey 'buses me, if I knows you's a-sayin' dat, 'way off yonder somers, it'll heal up all de sore places, en I kin stan' 'em."

"I *do* say it again, mammy, and I'll keep on saying it, too. But how am I going to sell you? You're free, you know."

"Much diff'rence dat make! White folks ain't partic'lar. De law kin sell me now if dey tell me to leave de State in six months en I don't go. You draw up a paper—bill o' sale—en put it 'way off yonder, down in de middle 'o Kaintuck somers, en sign some names to it, en say you'll sell me cheap 'ca'se you's hard up; you'll find you ain't gwyne to have no trouble. You take me up de country a piece, en sell me on a farm; dem people ain't gwyne to ask no questions if I's a bargain."

Tom forged a bill of sale and sold his mother to an Arkansas cotton-planter for a trifle over six hundred dollars. He did not want to commit this treachery, but luck threw the man in his way, and this saved him the necessity of going up country to hunt up a purchaser, with the added risk of having to answer a lot of questions, whereas this planter was so pleased with Roxy that he asked next to none at all. Besides, the planter insisted that Roxy wouldn't know where she was, at first, and that by the time she found out she would already have become contented. And Tom argued with himself that it was an immense advantage for Roxy to have a master who was so pleased with her, as this planter manifestly was. In almost no time his flowing reasonings carried him to the point of even half believing he was doing Roxy a splendid surreptitious service in selling her "down the river." And then he kept diligently saying to himself all the time: "It's for only a year. In a year I buy her free again; she'll keep that in mind, and it'll reconcile her." Yes; the little deception could do no harm, and everything would come out right and pleasant in the end, any way. By agreement, the conversation in Roxy's presence was all about the man's "upcountry" farm, and how pleasant a place it was, and how happy the slaves were there; so poor Roxy was entirely deceived; and easily, for she was not dreaming that her own son could be guilty of treason to a mother who, in voluntarily going into slavery—slavery of any kind, mild or severe, or of any duration, brief or long—was making a sacrifice for him compared with which death would have been a poor and commonplace one. She lavished tears and loving caresses upon him privately, and then went away with her owner—went away broken-hearted, and yet proud of what she was doing, and glad that it was in her power to do it.

Tom squared his accounts, and resolved to keep to the very letter of his reform, and never to put that will in jeopardy again. He had three hundred dollars left. According to his mother's plan, he was to put that safely away, and add her half of his pension to it monthly. In one year this fund would buy her free again.

For a whole week he was not able to sleep well, so much the villiany which he had played upon his trusting mother preyed upon his rag of a conscience; but after that he began to get comfortable again, and was presently able to sleep like any other miscreant.

The boat bore Roxy away from St. Louis at four in the afternoon, and she stood on the lower guard abaft the paddle-box and watched Tom through a blur of tears until he melted into the throng of people and disappeared; then she looked no more, but sat there on a coil of cable crying till far into the night. When she went to her foul steerage-bunk at last, between the clashing engines, it was not to sleep, but only to wait for the morning, and, waiting, grieve.

It had been imagined that she "would not know," and would think she was traveling up stream. She! Why, she had been steamboating for years. At dawn she got up and went listlessly and sat down on the cable-coil again. She passed many a snag whose "break" could have told her a thing to break her heart, for it showed a current moving in the same direction that the boat was going; but her thoughts were elsewhere, and she did not notice. But at last the roar of a bigger and nearer break than usual brought her out of her torpor, and she looked up, and her practised eye fell upon that tell-tale rush of water. For one moment her petrified gaze fixed itself there. Then her head dropped upon her breast, and she said—

"Oh, de good Lord God have mercy on po' sinful me—*I's sole down de river!*"

CHAPTER XVII

Even popularity can be overdone. In Rome, along at first, you are full of regrets that Michaelangelo died; but by and by you only regret that you didn't see him do it.—*Pudd'nhead Wilson's Calendar.*

July 4. Statistics show that we lose more fools on this day than in all the other days of the year put together. This proves, by the number left in stock, that one Fourth of July per year is now inadequate, the country has grown so.—*Pudd'nhead Wilson's Calendar.*

The summer weeks dragged by, and then the political campaign opened—opened in pretty warm fashion, and waxed hotter and hotter daily. The twins threw themselves into it with their whole heart, for their self-love was engaged. Their popularity, so general at first, had suffered afterward; mainly because they had been *too* popular, and so a natural reaction had followed. Besides, it had been diligently whispered around that it was curious—indeed, *very* curious—that that wonderful knife of theirs did not turn up—*if* it was so valuable, or *if* it had ever existed. And with the whisperings went chucklings and nudgings and winks, and such things have an effect. The twins considered that success in the election would reinstate them, and that defeat would work them irreparable damage. Therefore they worked hard, but not harder than Judge Driscoll and Tom worked against them in the closing days of the canvas. Tom's conduct had remained so letter-perfect during two whole months, now, that his uncle not only trusted him with money with which to persuade voters, but trusted him to go and get it himself out of the safe in the private sitting-room.

The closing speech of the campaign was made by Judge Driscoll, and he made it against both of the foreigners. It was disastrously effective. He poured out rivers of ridicule upon them, and forced the big mass-meeting to laugh and applaud. He scoffed at them as adventurers, mountebanks, side-show riff-raff, dime museum freaks; he assailed their showy titles with measureless derision; he said they were back-alley barbers disguised as nobilities, peanut pedlers masquerading as gentlemen, organ-grinders bereft of their brother monkey. At last he stopped and stood still. He waited until the place had become absolutely silent and expectant, then he delivered his deadliest shot; delivered it with ice-cold seriousness and deliberation, with a significant emphasis upon the closing words: he said he believed that the reward offered for the lost knife was humbug and buncombe, and that its owner would know where to find it whenever he should have occasion *to assassinate somebody*.

Then he stepped from the stand, leaving a startled and impressive hush behind him instead of the customary explosion of cheers and party cries.

The strange remark flew far and wide over the town and made an extraordinary sensation. Everybody was asking, "What could he mean by that?" And everybody went on asking that question, but in vain; for the Judge only said he knew what he was talking about, and stopped there; Tom said he hadn't any idea what his uncle meant, and Wilson, whenever he was asked what he thought it meant, parried the question by asking the questioner what *he* thought it meant.

Wilson was elected, the twins were defeated—crushed, in fact, and left forlorn and substantially friendless. Tom went back to St. Louis happy.

Dawson's Landing had a week of repose, now, and it needed it. But it was in an expectant state, for the air was full of rumors of a new duel. Judge Driscoll's election labors had prostated him, but it was said that as soon as he was well enough to entertain a challenge he would get one from Count Luigi.

The brother withdrew entirely from society, and nursed their humiliation in privacy. They avoided the people, and went out for exercise only late at night, when the streets were deserted.

CHAPTER XVIII

Gratitude and treachery are merely the two extremities of the same procession. You have seen all of it that is worth staying for when the band and the gaudy officials have gone by.—*Pudd'nhead Wilson's Calendar.*

Thanksgiving Day. Let all give humble, hearty, and sincere thanks, now, but the turkeys. In the island of Fiji they do not use turkeys; they use plumbers. It does not become you and me to sneer at Fiji.—*Pudd'nhead Wilson's Calendar.*

The Friday after the election was a rainy one in St. Louis. It rained all day long, and rained hard, apparently trying its best to wash that soot-blackened town white, but of course not succeeding. Toward midnight Tom Driscoll arrived at his lodgings from the theatre in the heavy downpour, and closed his umbrella and let himself in; but when he would have shut the door, he found that there was another person entering—doubtless another lodger; this person closed the door and tramped upstairs behind Tom. Tom found his door in the dark, and entered it and turned up the gas. When he faced about, lightly whistling, he saw the back of a man. The man was closing and locking his door for him. His whistle faded out and he felt uneasy. The man turned around, a wreck of shabby old clothes, sodden with rain and all a-drip, and showed a black face under an old slouch hat. Tom was frightened. He tried to order the man out, but the words refused to come, and the other man got the start. He said, in a low voice—

"Keep still—I's yo' mother!"

Tom sunk in a heap on a chair, and gasped out—

"It was mean of me, and base—I know it; but I meant it for the best, I did indeed—I can swear it."

Roxana stood awhile looking mutely down on him while he writhed in shame and went on incoherently babbling self- accusations mixed with pitiful attempts at explanation and palliation of his crime; then she seated herself and took off her hat, and her unkempt masses of long brown hair tumbled down about her shoulders.

"It ain't no fault o' yo'n dat dat ain't gray," she said sadly, noticing the hair.

"I know it, I know it! I'm a scoundrel. But I swear I meant it for the best. It was a mistake, of couse, but I thought it was for the best, I truly did."

Roxy began to cry softly, and presently words began to find their way out between her sobs. They were uttered lamentingly, rather than angrily—

"Sell a pusson down de river—*down de river!*—for de bes'! I wouldn't treat a dog so! I is all broke down en wore out, now, en so I reckon it ain't in me to storm aroun' no mo', like I used to when I 'uz trompled on en 'bused. I don't know—but maybe it's so. Leastways, I's suffered so much dat mournin' seem to come mo' handy to me now den stormin'."

These words should have touched Tom Driscoll, but if they did, that effect was obliterated by a stronger one—one which removed the heavy weight of fear which lay upon him, and gave his crushed spirit a most grateful rebound, and filled all his small soul with a deep sense of relief. But he kept prudently still, and ventured no comment. There was a voiceless interval of some duration, now, in which no sounds were heard but the beating of the rain upon the panes, the sighing and complaining of the winds, and now and then a muffled sob from Roxana. The sobs became more and more infrequent, and at last ceased. The refugee began to talk again:

"Shet down dat light a little. More. More yit. A pusson dat is hunted don't like de light. Dah—dat'll do. I kin see whah you is, en dat's enough. I's gwine to tell you de tale, en cut it jes as short as I kin, en den I'll tell you what you's got to do. Dat man dat bought me ain't a bad man; he's good enough, as planters goes; en if he could'a' had his way I'd 'a' be'n a house servant in his fambly en be'n comfortable: but his wife she was a Yank, en not right down good lookin', en she riz up agin me straight off; so den dey sent me out to de quarter 'mongst de common fiel' han's. Dat woman warn't satisfied even wid dat, but she worked up de overseer ag'in' me, she 'uz dat jealous en hateful; so de overseer he had me out befo' day in de mawnin's en worked me de whole long day as long as dey'uz any light to see by; en many's de lashin's I got 'ca'se I couldn't come up to de work o' de stronges'. Dat overseer wuz a Yank, too, outen New Englan', en anybody down South kin tell you what dat mean. *Dey* knows how to work a nigger to death, en day knows how to whale 'em, too—whale 'em till dey backs is welted like a washboard. 'Long at fust my marster say de good word for me to de overseer, but dat 'uz bad for me; for de mistis she fine it out, en arter dat I jist ketched it at every turn—dey warn't no mercy for me no mo'."

Tom's heart was fired—with fury 'against the planter's wife; and he said to himself, "But for that meddlesome fool, everything would have gone all right." He added a deep and bitter curse against her.

The expression of this sentiment was fiercely written in his face, and stood thus revealed to Roxana by a white glare of lightning which turned the somber dusk of the room into dazzling day at that moment. She was pleased—pleased and grateful; for did not that expression show that her child was capable of grieving for his mother's wrongs and of feeling resentment toward her persecutors?—a thing which she had been doubting. But her flash of happiness was only a flash, and went out again and left her spirit dark; for she said to herself, "He sole me down de river—he can't feel for a body long: dis'll pass en go." Then she took up her tale again.

" 'Bout ten days ago I 'uz sayin' to myself dat I couldn't las' many mo' weeks I 'uz so wore out wid de awful work en de lashin's, en so downhearted en misable. En I didn't care no mo', nuther—life warn't wuth noth'n' to me, if I got to go on like dat. Well, when a body is in a frame o' mine like dat, what do a body care what a body do? Dey was a little sickly nigger wench 'bout ten year ole dat 'uz good to me, en hadn't no mammy, po' thing, en I loved her en she loved me; en she come out whah I 'uz workin 'en she had a roasted tater, en tried to slip it to me,—robbin' herself, you see, 'ca'se she knowed de overseer didn't gimme enough to eat,—en he ketched her at it, en give her a lick acrost de back wid his stick, which 'uz as thick as a broom- handle, en she drop' screamin' on de groun', en squirmin' en wallerin' aroun' in de dust like a spider dat's got crippled. I couldn't stan' it. All de hell-fire dat 'uz ever in my heart flame' up, en I snatch de stick outen his han' en laid him flat. He laid dah moanin' en cussin', en all out of his head, you know, en de niggers 'uz plumb sk'yerd to death. Dey gathered roun' him to hep' him, en I jumped on his hoss en took out for de river as tight as I could go. I knowed what dey would do wid me. Soon as he got well he would start in en work me to death if marster let him; en if dey didn't do dat, they'd sell me furder down de river, en dat's de same thing. So I 'lowed to drown myself en git out o' my troubles. It 'uz gitt'n' towards dark. I 'uz at de river in two minutes. Den I see a canoe, en I says dey ain't no use to drown myself tell I got to; so I ties de hoss in de edge o' de timber en shove out down de river, keepin' in under de shelter o' de bluff bank en prayin' for de dark to shet down quick. I had a pow'ful good start, 'ca'se de big house 'uz three mile back f'om de river en on'y de work-mules to ride dah on, en on'y niggers to ide 'em, en *day* warn't gwine to hurry—dey'd gimme all de chance dey could. Befo' a body could go to de house en back it would be long pas' dark, en dey couldn't track de hoss en fine out which way I went tell mawnin', en de niggers would tell 'em all de lies dey could 'bout it.

"Well, de dark come, en I went on a-spinnin' down de river. I paddled mo'n two hours, den I warn't worried no mo', so I quit paddlin, en floated down de current, considerin' what I 'uz gwine to do if I didn't have to drown myself. I made up some plans, en floated along, turnin' 'em over in my mine. Well, when it 'uz a little pas' midnight, as I reckoned, en I had come fifteen or twenty mile, I see de lights o' a steamboat layin' at de bank, whah dey warn't no town en no woodyard, en putty soon I ketched de shape o' de chimbly-tops ag'in' de stars, en de good gracious me, I 'most jumped out o' my skin for joy! It 'uz de *Gran' Mogul*—I 'uz chambermaid on her for eight seasons in de Cincinnati en Orleans trade. I slid 'long pas'—don't see nobody stirrin' nowhah—hear 'em a-hammerin' away in de engine-room, den I knowed what de matter was—some o' de machinery's broke. I got asho' below de boat and turn' de canoe loose, den I goes 'long up, en dey 'uz jes one plank out, en I step' 'board de boat. It 'uz pow'ful hot, deckhan's en roustabouts 'uz sprawled aroun' asleep on de fo'cas'l', de second mate, Jim Bangs, he sot dah on de bitts wid his head down, asleep—'ca'se dat's de way de second mate stan' de cap'n's watch!—en de ole watchman, Billy Hatch, he 'uz a-noddin' on de companion-way;—en I knowed 'em all; 'en, lan', but dey did look good! I says to myself, I wished old marster'd come along *now* en try to take me—bless yo' heart, I's 'mong frien's, I is. So I tromped right along 'mongst 'em, en went up on de b'iler deck en 'way back aft to de ladies' cabin guard, en sot down dah in de same cheer dat I'd sot in 'mos' a hund'd million times, I reckon; en it 'uz jist home ag'in, I tell you!

"In 'bout an hour I heard de ready-bell jingle, en den de racket begin. Putty soon I hear de gong strike. 'Set her back on de outside,' I says to myself—'I reckon I knows dat music!' I hear de gong ag'in. 'Come ahead on de inside,' I says. Gong ag'in. 'Stop de outside.' Gong ag'in. 'Come ahead on de outside—now we's pinted for Sent Louis, en I's outer de woods en ain't got to drown myself at all.' I knowed de *Mogul* 'uz in de Sent Louis trade now, you see. It 'uz jes fair daylight when we passed our plantation, en I seed a gang o' niggers en white folks huntin' up en down de sho', en troublin' deyselves a good deal 'bout me; but I warn't troublin' myself none 'bout dem.

"Bout dat time Sally Jackson, dat used to be my second chambermaid en 'uz head chambermaid now, she come out on de guard, en 'uz pow'ful glad to see me, en so 'uz all de officers; en I tole 'em I'd got kidnapped en sole down de river, en dey made me up twenty dollahs en give it to me, en Sally she rigged me out wid good clo'es, en when I got here I went straight to whah you used to wuz, en den I come to dis house, en dey say you's away but 'spected back every day; so I didn't dast to go down de river to Dawson's, 'ca'se I might miss you.

"Well, las' Monday I 'uz pass'n' by one o' dem places in Fourth street whah deh sticks up runaway-nigger bills, en he'ps to ketch 'em, en I seed my marster! I 'mos' flopped down on de groun', I felt so gone. He had his back to me, en 'uz talkin' to de man en givin' him some bills—nigger-bills, I reckon, en I'se de nigger. He's offerin' a reward—dat's it. Ain't I right, don't you reckon?"

Tom had been gradually sinking into a state of ghastly terror, and he said to himself, now: "I'm lost, no matter what turn things take! This man has said to me that he thinks there was something suspicious about that sale. He said he had a letter from a passenger on the *Grand Mogul* saying that Roxy came here on that boat and that everybody on board knew all about the case; so he says that hercoming here instead of flying to a free State looks bad for me, and that if I don't find her for him, and that pretty soon, he will make trouble for me. I never believed that story; I couldn't believe she would be so dead to all motherly instincts as to come here, knowing the risk she would run of getting me into irremediable trouble. And after all, here she is! And I stupidly swore I would help him find her, thinking it was a perfectly safe thing to promise. If I venture to deliver her up, she—she—but how can I help myself? I've got to do that or pay the money, and where's the money to come from? I—I—well, I should think that if he would swear to treat her kindly hereafter—and she says, herself, that he is a good man—and if he would swear to never allow her to be overworked, or ill fed, or—"

A flash of lightning exposed Tom's pallid face, drawn and

rigid with these worrying thoughts. Roxana spoke up sharply now, and there was apprehension in her voice—

"Turn up dat light! I want to see yo' face better. Dah now—lemme look at you. Chambers, you's as white as yo' shirt! Has you seen dat man? Has he be'n to see you?"

"Ye-s."

"When?"

"Monday noon."

"Monday noon! Was he on my track?"

"He—well, he thought he was. That is, he hoped he was. This is the bill you saw." He took it out of his pocket.

"Read it to me!"

She was panting with excitement, and there was a dusky glow in her eyes that Tom could not translate with certainty, but there seemed to be something threatening about it. The handbill had the usual rude woodcut of a turbaned negro woman running, with the customary bundle on a stick over her shoulder, and the heading in bold type, "$100 REWARD." Tom read the bill aloud—at least the part that described Roxana and named the master and his St. Louis address and the address of the Fourth-street agency; but he left out the item that applicants for the reward might also apply to Mr. Thomas Driscoll.

"Gimme de bill!"

Tom had folded it and was putting it in his pocket. He felt a chilly streak creeping down his back, but said as carelessly as he could—

"The bill? Why, it isn't any use to you, you can't read it. What do you want with it?"

"Gimme de bill!" Tom gave it to her, but with a reluctance which he could not entirely disguise. "Did you read it *all* to me?"

"Certainly I did."

"Hole up yo' han' en swah to it."

Tom did it. Roxana put the bill carefully away in her pocket, with her eyes fixed upon Tom's face all the while; then she said—

"Yo's lyin'!"

"What would I want to lie about it for?"

"I don't know—but you is. Dat's my opinion, anyways. But nemmine 'bout dat. When I seed dat man I 'uz dat sk'yerd dat I could sca'cely wobble home. Den I give a nigger man a dollar for dese clo'es, en I ain't be'n in a house sence, night ner day, till now. I blacked my face en laid hid in de cellar of a ole house dat's burnt down, daytimes, en robbed de sugar hogsheads en grain sacks on de wharf, nights, to git somethin' to eat, en never dast to try to buy noth'n', en I's 'mos' starved. En I never dast to come near dis place till dis rainy night, when dey ain't no people roun' sca'cely. But to-night I be'n a-stannin' in de dark alley ever sence night come, waitin' for you to go by. En here I is."

She fell to thinking. Presently she said—

"You seed dat man at noon, las' Monday?"

"Yes."

"I seed him de middle o' dat arternoon. He hunted you up, didn't he?"

"Yes."

"Did he give you de bill dat time?"

"No, he hadn't got it printed yet."

Roxana darted a suspicious glance at him.

"Did you he'p him fix up de bill?"

Tom cursed himself for making that stupid blunder, and tried to rectify it by saying he remembered, now, that it *was* at noon Monday that the man gave him the bill. Roxana said—

"You's lyin' ag'in, sho." Then she straightened up and raised her finger:

"Now den! I's gwine to ask you a question, en I wants to know how you's gwine to git aroun' it. You knowed he 'uz arter me; en if you run off, 'stid o' stayin' here to he'p him, he'd know dey 'uz somethin' wrong 'bout dis business, en den he would inquire 'bout you, en dat would take him to yo' uncle, en yo' uncle would read de bill en see dat you be'n sellin' a free nigger down de river, en you know *him,* I reckon! He'd t'ar up de will en kick you outen de house. Now, den, you answer me dis question: hain't you tole dat man dat I would be sho' to come here, en den you would fix it so he could set a trap en ketch me?"

Tom recognized that neither lies nor arguments could help him any longer—he was in a vise, with the screw turned on, and out of it there was no budging. His face began to take on an ugly look, and presently he said, with a snarl—

"Well, what could I do? You see, yourself, that I was in his grip and couldn't get out."

Roxy scorched him with a scornful gaze awhile, then she said—

"What could you do? You could be Judas to yo' own mother to save yo' wuthless hide! Would anybody b'lieve it? No—a dog couldn't! You is de low-downest orneriest hound dat was ever pup'd into dis worl'—en I's 'sponsible for it!"—and she spat on him.

He made no effort to resent this. Roxy reflected a moment, then she said—

"Now I'll tell you what you's gwine to do. You's gwine to give dat man de money dat you's got laid up, en make him wait till you kin go to de Jedge en git de res' en buy me free agin."

"Thunder! what are you thinking of? Go and ask him for three hundred dollars and odd? What would I tell him I want with it, pray?"

Roxy's answer was delivered in a serene and level voice—

"You'll tell him you's sole me to pay yo' gamblin' debts en dat you lied to me en was a villain, en dat I 'quires you to git dat money en buy me back ag'in."

"Why, you've gone stark mad! He would tear the will to shreds in a minute—don't you know that?"

"Yes, I does."

"Then you don't believe I'm idiot enough to go to him, do you?"

"I don't b'lieve nothin' 'bout it—I *knows* you's a-goin'. I knows it 'ca'se you knows dat if you don't raise dat money I'll go to him myself, en den he'll sell *you* down de river, en you kin see how you like it!"

Tom rose, trembling and excited, and there was an evil light in his eye. He strode to the door and said he must get out of this suffocating place for a moment and clear his brain in the fresh air so that he could determine what to do. The door wouldn't open. Roxy smiled grimly, and said—

"I's got de key, honey—set down. You needn't cle'r up yo' brain none to fine out what you gwine to do—*I* knows what you's gwine to do." Tom sat down and began to pass his hands through his hair with a helpless and desperate air. Roxy said, "Is dat man in dis house?"

Tom glanced up with a surprised expression, and asked—

"What gave you such an idea?"

"You done it. Gwine out to cle'r yo' brain! In de fust place you ain't got none to cle'r, en in de second place yo' ornery eye tole on you. You's de low-downest hound dat ever—but I done tole you dat befo'. Now den, dis is Friday. You kin fix it up wid dat man, en tell him you's gwine away to git de res' o' de money, en dat you'll be back wid it nex' Tuesday, or maybe Wednesday. You understan'?"

Tom answered sullenly—

"Yes."

"En when you gits de new bill o' sale dat sells me to my own self, take en send it in de mail to Mr. Pudd'nhead Wilson, en write on de back dat he's to keep it tell I come. You understan'?"

"Yes."

"Dat's all den. Take yo' umbreller, en put on yo' hat."

"Why?"

"Beca'se you's gwine to see me home to de wharf. You see dis knife? I's toted it aroun' sence de day I seed dat man en bought dese clo'es en it. If he ketch me, I's gwine to kill myself wid it. Now start along, en go sof', en lead de way; en if you gives a sign in dis house, or if anybody comes up to you in de street, I's gwine to jam it right into you. Chambers, does you b'lieve me when I says dat?"

"It's no use to bother me with that question. I know your word's good."

"Yes, it's diff'rent from yo'n! Shet de light out en move along—here's de key."

They were not followed. Tom trembled every time a late straggler brushed by them on the street, and half expected to feel the cold steel in his back. Roxy was right at his heels and always in reach. After tramping a mile they reached a wide vacancy on the deserted wharves, and in this dark and rainy desert they parted.

As Tom trudged home his mind was full of dreary thoughts and wild plans; but at last he said to himself, wearily—

"There is but the one way out. I must follow her plan. But with a variation—I will not ask for the money and ruin myself; I will *rob* the old skinflint."

CHAPTER XIX

Few things are harder to put up with than the annoyance of a good example.—*Pudd'nhead Wilson's Calendar.*

It were not best that we should all think alike; it is difference of opinion that makes horse-races.—*Pudd'nhead Wilson's Calendar.*

Dawson's Landing was comfortably finishing its season of dull repose and waiting patiently for the duel. Count Luigi was waiting, too; but not patiently, rumor said. Sunday came, and Luigi insisted on having his challenge conveyed. Wilson carried it. Judge Driscoll declined to fight with an assassin—"that is," he added significantly, "in the field of honor."

Elsewhere, of course, he would be ready. Wilson tried to convince him that if he had been present himself when Angelo told about the homicide committed by Luigi, he would not have considered the act discreditable to Luigi; but the obstinate old man was not to be moved.

Wilson went back to his principal and reported the failure of his mission. Luigi was incensed, and asked how it could be that the old gentleman, who was by no means dull-witted, held his trifling nephew's evidence and inferences to be of more value than Wilson's. But Wilson laughed, and said—

"That is quite simple; that is easily explicable. I am not his doll—his baby—his infatuation: his nephew is. The Judge and his late wife never had any children. The Judge and his wife were past middle age when this treasure fell into their lap. One must make allowances for a parental instinct that has been starving for twenty-five or thirty years. It is famished, it is crazed with hunger by that time, and will be entirely satisfied with anything that comes handy; its taste is atrophied, it can't tell mud-cat from shad. A devil born to a young couple is measurably recognizable by them as a devil before long, but a devil adopted by an old couple is an angel to them, and remains so, through thick and thin. Tom is this old man's angel; he is infatuated with him. Tom can persuade him into things which other people can't—not all things; I don't mean that, but a good many— particularly one class of things: the things that create or abolish personal partialities or prejudices in the old man's mind. The old man liked both of you. Tom conceived a hatred for you. That was enough; it turned the old man around at once. The oldest and strongest friendship must go to the ground when one of these late-adopted darlings throws a brick at it."

"It's a curious philosophy," said Luigi.

"It ain't a philosophy at all—it's a fact. And there is something pathetic and beautiful about it, too. I think there is nothing more pathetic than to see one of these poor old childless couples taking a menagerie of yelping little worthless dogs to their hearts; and then adding some cursing and squawking parrots and a jackass-voiced macaw; and next a couple of hundred screeching songbirds, and presently some fetid guinea-pigs and rabbits, and a howling colony of cats. It is all a groping and ignorant effort to construct out of base metal and brass filings, so to speak, something to take the place of that golden treasure denied them by Nature, a child. But this is a digression. The unwritten law of this region requires you to kill Judge Driscoll on sight, and he and the community will expect that attention at your hands—though of course your own death by his bullet will answer every purpose. Look out for him! Are you heeled—that is, fixed?"

"Yes; he shall have his opportunity. If he attacks me I will respond."

As Wilson was leaving, he said—

"The Judge is still a little used up by his campaign work, and will not get out for a day or so; but when he does get out, you want to be on the alert."

About eleven at night the twins went out for exercise, and started on a long stroll in the veiled moonlight.

Tom Driscoll had landed at Hackett's Store, two miles below Dawson's, just about half an hour earlier, the only passenger for that lonely spot, and had walked up the shore road and entered Judge Driscoll's house without having encountered any one either on the road or under the roof.

He pulled down his window-blinds and lighted his candle. He laid off his coat and hat and began his preparations. He unlocked his trunk and got his suit of girl's clothes out from under the male attire in it, and laid it by. Then he blacked his face with burnt cork and put the cork in his pocket. His plan was, to slip down to his uncle's private sitting-room below, pass into the bedroom, steal the safe-key from the old gentleman's clothes, and then go back and rob the safe. He took up his candle to start. His courage and confidence were high, up to this point, but both began to waver a little, now. Suppose he should make a noise, by some accident, and get caught—say, in the act of opening the safe? Perhaps it would be well to go armed. He took the Indian knife from its hiding-place, and felt a pleasant return of his wandering courage. He slipped stealthily down the narrow stair, his hair rising and his pulses halting at the slightest creak. When he was half-way down, he was disturbed to perceive that the landing below was touched by a faint glow of light. What could that mean? Was his uncle still up? No, that was not likely; he must have left his night-taper there when he went to bed. Tom crept on down, pausing at every step to listen. He found the door standing open, and glanced in. What he saw pleased him beyond measure. His uncle was asleep on the sofa; on a small table at the head of the sofa a lamp was burning low, and by it stood the old man's small tin cash-box, closed. Near the box was a pile of bank-notes and a piece of paper covered with figures in pencil. The safe-door was not open. Evidently the sleeper had wearied himself with work upon his finances, and was taking a rest.

Tom set his candle on the stairs, and began to make his way toward the pile of notes, stooping low as he went. When he was passing his uncle, the old man stirred in his sleep, and Tom stopped instantly—stopped, and softly drew the knife from its sheath, with his heart thumping, and his eyes fastened upon his benefactor's face. After a moment or two he ventured forward again—one step—reached for his prize and seized it, dropping the knife-sheath. Then he felt the old man's strong grip upon him, and a wild cry of "Help! help!" rang in his ear. Without hesitation he drove the knife home—and was free. Some of the notes escaped from his left hand and fell in the blood on the floor. He dropped the knife and snatched them up and started to fly; transferred them to his left hand, and seized the knife again, in his fright and confusion, but remembered himself and flung it from him, as being a dangerous witness to carry away with him.

He jumped for the stair-foot, and closed the door behind him; and as he snatched his candle and fled upward, the stillness of the night was broken by the sound of urgent footsteps approaching the house. In another moment he was in his room and the twins were standing aghast over the body of the murdered man!

Tom put on his coat, buttoned his hat under it, threw on his suit of girl's clothes, dropped the veil, blew out his light, locked the room door by which he had just entered, taking the key, passed through his other door into the back hall, locked that door and kept the key, then worked his way along in the dark and descended the back stairs. He was not expecting to meet anybody, for all interest was centered in the other part of the house, now; his calculation proved correct. By the time he was passing through the backyard, Mrs. Pratt, her servants, and a dozen half-dressed neighbors had joined the twins and the dead, and accessions were still arriving at the front door.

As Tom, quaking as with a palsy, passed out at the gate, three women came flying from the house on the opposite side of the lane. They rushed by him and in at the gate, asking him what the trouble was there, but not waiting for an answer. Tom said to himself, "Those old maids waited to dress—they did the same thing the night Stevens's house burned down next door." In a few minutes he was in the haunted house. He lighted a candle and took off his girl-clothes. There was blood on him all down his left side, and his right hand was red with the stains of the blood-soaked notes which he had crushed in it; but otherwise he was free from this sort of evidence. He cleansed his hand on the straw, and cleaned most of the smut from his face. Then he burned his male and female attire to ashes, scattered the ashes, and put on a disguise proper for a tramp. He blew out his light, went below, and was soon loafing down the river road with the intent to borrow and use one of Roxy's devices. He found a canoe and paddled off down-stream, setting the canoe adrift as dawn approached, and making his way by land to the next village, where he kept out of sight till a transient steamer came along, and then took deck passage for St. Louis. He was ill at ease until Dawson's Landing was behind him; then he said to himself, "All the detectives on earth couldn't trace me now; there's not a vestige of a clue left in the world; that homicide will take its place with the permanent mysteries, and people won't get done trying to guess out the secret of it for fifty years."

In St. Louis, next morning, he read this brief telegram in the papers—dated at Dawson's Landing:

Judge Driscoll, an old and respected citizen, was assassinated here about midnight by a profligate Italian nobleman or barber on account of a quarrel growing out of the recent election. The assassin will probably be lynched.

"One of the twins!" soliloquized Tom; "how lucky! It is the knife that has done him this grace. We never know when fortune is trying to favor us. I actually cursed Pudd'nhead Wilson in my heart for putting it out of my power to sell that knife. I take it back, now."

Tom was now rich and independent. He arranged with the planter, and mailed to Wilson the new bill of sale which sold Roxana to herself; then he telegraphed his Aunt Pratt:

Have seen the awful news in the papers and am almost prostrated with grief. Shall start by packet to-day. Try to bear up till I come.

When Wilson reached the house of mourning and had gathered such details as Mrs. Pratt and the rest of the crowd could tell him, he took command as mayor, and gave orders that nothing should be touched, but everything left as it was until Justice Robinson should arrive and take the proper measures as coroner. He cleared everybody out of the room but the twins and himself. The sheriff soon arrived and took the twins away to jail. Wilson told them to keep heart, and promised to do his best in their defense when the case should come to trial. Justice Robinson came presently, and with him Constable Blake. They examined the room thoroughly. They found the knife and the sheath. Wilson noticed that there were finger-prints on the knife-handle. That pleased him, for the twins had required the earliest comers to make a scrutiny of their hands and clothes, and neither these people nor Wilson himself had found any blood-stains upon them. Could there be a possibility that the twins had spoken the truth when they said they found the man dead when they ran into the house in answer to the cry for help? He thought of that mysterious girl at once. But this was not the sort of work for a girl to be engaged in. No matter; Tom Driscoll's room must be examined.

After the coroner's jury had viewed the body and its surroundings, Wilson suggested a search up-stairs, and he went along. The jury forced an entrance to Tom's room, but found nothing, of course.

The coroner's jury found that the homicide was committed by Luigi, and that Angelo was accessory to it.

The town was bitter against the unfortunates, and for the first few days after the murder they were in constant danger of being lynched. The grand jury presently indicted Luigi for murder in the first degree, and Angelo as accessory before the fact. The twins were transferred from the city jail to the county prison to await trial.

Wilson examined the finger-marks on the knife-handle and said to himself, "Neither of the twins made those marks." Then manifestly there was another person concerned, either in his own interest or as hired assassin.

But who could it be? That, he must try to find out. The safe was not open, the cash-box was closed, and had three thousand dollars in it. Then robbery was not the motive, and revenge was. Where had the murdered man an enemy except Luigi? There was but that one person in the world with a deep grudge against him.

The mysterious girl! The girl was a great trial to Wilson. If the motive had been robbery, the girl might answer; but there wasn't any girl that would want to take this old man's life for revenge. He had no quarrels with girls; he was a gentleman.

Wilson had perfect tracings of the finger-marks of the knife-handle; and among his glass-records he had a great array of the finger-prints of women and girls, collected during the last fifteen or eighteen years, but he scanned them in vain, they successfully withstood every test; among them were no duplicates of the prints on the knife.

The presence of the knife on the stage of the murder was a worrying circumstance for Wilson. A week previously he had as good as admitted to himself that he believed Luigi had possessed such a knife, and that he still possessed it notwithstanding his pretense that it had been stolen. And now here was the knife, and with it the twins. Half the town had said the twins were humbugging when they claimed that they had lost their knife, and now these people were joyful, and said, "I told you so!"

If their finger-prints had been on the handle—but it was useless to bother any further about that; the finger-prints on the handle were *not* theirs—that he knew perfectly.

Wilson refused to suspect Tom; for first, Tom couldn't murder anybody—he hadn't character enough; secondly, if he could murder a person he wouldn't select his doting benefactor and nearest relative; thirdly, self-interest was in the way; for while the uncle lived, Tom was sure of a free support and a chance to get the destroyed will revived again, but with the uncle gone, that chance was gone, too. It was true the will had really been revived, as was now discovered, but Tom could not have been aware of it, or he would have spoken of it, in his native talky, unsecretive way. Finally, Tom was in St. Louis when the murder was done, and got the news out of the morning journals, as was shown by his telegram to his aunt. These speculations were unemphasized sensations rather than articulated thoughts, for Wilson would have laughed at the idea of seriously connecting Tom with the murder.

Wilson regarded the case of the twins as desperate—in fact, about hopeless. For he argued that if a confederate was not found, an enlightened Missouri jury would hang them, sure; if a confederate was found, that would not improve the matter, but simply furnish one more person for the sheriff to hang. Nothing could save the twins but the discovery of a person who did the murder on his sole personal account—an undertaking which had all the aspect of the impossible. Still, the person who made the finger-prints must be sought. The twins might have no case *with* him, but they certainly would have none without him.

So Wilson mooned around, thinking, thinking, guessing, guessing, day and night, and arriving nowhere. Whenever he ran across a girl or a woman he was not acquainted with, he got her finger-prints, on one pretext or another; and they always cost him a sigh when he got home, for they never tallied with the finger-marks on the knife-handle.

As to the mysterious girl, Tom swore he knew no such girl, and did not remember ever seeing a girl wearing a dress like the one described by Wilson. He admitted that he did not always lock his room, and that sometimes the servants forgot to lock the house doors; still, in his opinion the girl must have made but few visits or she would have been discovered. When Wilson tried to connect her with the stealing-raid, and thought she might have been the old woman's confederate, if not the very thief herself disguised as an old woman, Tom seemed struck, and also much interested, and said he would keep a sharp eye out for this person or persons, although he was afraid that she or they would be too smart to venture again into a town where everybody would now be on the watch for a good while to come.

Everybody was pitying Tom, he looked so quiet and sorrowful, and seemed to feel his great loss so deeply. He was playing a part, but it was not all a part. The picture of his alleged uncle, as he had last seen him, was before him in the dark pretty frequently, when he was awake, and called again in his dreams, when he was asleep. He wouldn't go into the room where the tragedy had happened. This charmed the doting Mrs. Pratt, who realized now, "as she had never done before," she said, what a sensitive and delicate nature her darling had, and how he adored his poor uncle.

CHAPTER XX

Even the clearest and most perfect circumstantial evidence is likely to be at fault, after all, and therefore ought to be received with great caution. Take the case of any pencil, sharpened by any woman: if you have witnesses, you will find she did it with a knife; but if you take simply the aspect of the pencil, you will say she did it with her teeth.—*Pudd'nhead Wilson's Calendar.*

The weeks dragged along, no friend visiting the jailed twins but their counsel and Aunt Patsy Cooper, and the day of trial came at last—the heaviest day in Wilson's life; for with all his tireless diligence he had discovered no sign or trace of the missing confederate. "Confederate" was the term he had long ago privately accepted for that person—not as being unquestionably the right term, but as being at least possibly the right one, though he was never able to understand why the twins did not vanish and escape, as the confederate had done, instead of remaining by the murdered man and getting caught there.

The court-house was crowded, of course, and would remain so to the finish, for not only in the town itself, but in the country for miles around, the trial was the one topic of conversation among the people. Mrs. Pratt, in deep mourning, and Tom with a weed on his hat, had seats near Pembroke Howard, the public prosecutor, and back of them sat a great array of friends of the family. The twins had but one friend present to keep their counsel in countenance, their poor old sorrowing landlady. She sat near Wilson, and looked her friendliest. In the "nigger corner" sat Chambers; also Roxy, with good clothes on, and her bill of sale in her pocket. It was her most precious possession, and she never parted with it, day or night. Tom had allowed her thirty-five dollars a month ever since he came into his property, and had said that he and she ought to be grateful to the twins for making them rich; but had roused such a temper in her by this speech that he did not repeat the argument afterward. She said the old Judge had treated her child a thousand times better than he deserved, and had never done her an unkindness in his life; so she hated these outlandish devils for killing him, and shouldn't ever sleep satisfied till she saw them hanged for it. She was here to watch the trial, now, and was going to lift up just one "hooraw" over it if the County Judge put her in jail a year for it. She gave her turbaned head a toss and said, "When dat verdic' comes, I's gwine to lif' dat *roof,* now, I *tell* you."

Pembroke Howard briefly sketched the State's case. He said he would show by a chain of circumstantial evidence without break or fault in it anywhere, that the principal prisoner at the bar committed the murder; that the motive was partly revenge, and partly a desire to take his own life out of jeopardy, and that his brother, by his presence, was a consenting accessory to the crime; a crime which was the basest known to the calendar of human misdeeds—assassination; that it was conceived by the blackest of hearts and consummated by the cowardliest of hands; a crime which had broken a loving sister's heart, blighted the happiness of a young nephew who was as dear as a son, brought inconsolable grief to many friends, and sorrow and loss to the whole community. The utmost penalty of the outraged law would be exacted, and upon the accused, now present at the bar, that penalty would unquestionably be executed. He would reserve further remark until his closing speech.

He was strongly moved, and so also was the whole house; Mrs. Pratt and several other women were weeping when he sat down, and many an eye that was full of hate was riveted upon the unhappy prisoners.

Witness after witness was called by the State, and questioned at length; but the cross-questioning was brief. Wilson knew they could furnish nothing valuable for his side. People were sorry for Pudd'nhead; his budding career would get hurt by this trial.

Several witnesses swore they heard Judge Driscoll say in his public speech that the twins would be able to find their lost knife again when they needed it to assassinate somebody with. This was not news, but now it was seen to have been sorrowfully prophetic, and a profound sensation quivered through the hushed court-room when those dismal words were repeated.

The public prosecutor rose and said that it was within his knowledge, through a conversation held with Judge Driscoll on the last day of his life, that counsel for the defense had brought him a challenge from the person charged at this bar with murder; that he had refused to fight with a confessed assassin—"that is, on the field of honor," but had added significantly, that he would be ready for him elsewhere. Presumably the person here charged with murder was warned that he must kill or be killed the first time he should meet Judge Driscoll. If counsel for the defense chose to let the statement stand so, he would not call him to the witness stand. Mr. Wilson said he would offer no denial. [Murmurs in the house—"It is getting worse and worse for Wilson's case."]

Mrs. Pratt testified that she heard no outcry, and did not know what woke her up, unless it was the sound of rapid footsteps approaching the front door. She jumped up and ran out in the hall just as she was, and heard the footsteps flying up the front steps and then following behind her as she ran to the sitting-room. There she found the accused standing over her murdered brother. [Here she broke down and sobbed. Sensation in the court.] Resuming, she said the persons entering behind her were Mr. Rogers and Mr. Buckstone.

Cross-examined by Wilson, she said the twins proclaimed their innocence; declared that they had been taking a walk, and had hurried to the house in response to a cry for help which was so loud and strong that they had heard it at a considerable distance; that they begged her and the gentlemen just mentioned to examine their hands and clothes—which was done, and no blood stains found.

Confirmatory evidence followed from Rogers and Buckstone.

The finding of the knife was verified, the advertisement minutely describing it and offering a reward for it was put in evidence, and its exact correspondence with that description proved. Then followed a few minor details, and the case for the State was closed.

Wilson said that he had three witnesses, the Misses Clarkson, who would testify that they met a veiled young woman leaving Judge Driscoll's premises by the back gate a few minutes after the cries for help were heard, and that their evidence, taken with certain circumstantial evidence which he would call the court's attention to, would in his opinion convince the court that there was still one person concerned in this crime who had not yet been found, and also that a stay of proceedings ought to be granted, in justice to his clients, until that person should be discovered. As it was late, he would ask leave to defer the examination of his three witnesses until the next morning.

The crowd poured out of the place and went flocking away in excited groups and couples, talking the events of the session over with vivacity and consuming interest, and everybody seemed to have had a satisfactory and enjoyable day except the accused, their counsel, and their old-lady friend. There was no cheer among these, and no substantial hope.

In parting with the twins Aunt Patsy did attempt a good-night with a gay pretense of hope and cheer in it, but broke down without finishing.

Absolutely secure as Tom considered himself to be, the opening solemnities of the trial had nevertheless oppressed him with a vague uneasiness, his being a nature sensitive to even the smallest alarms; but from the moment that the poverty and weakness of Wilson's case lay exposed to the court, he was comfortable once more, even jubilant. He left the court-room sarcastically sorry for Wilson. "The Clarksons met an unknown woman in the back lane," he said to himself—"*that* is his case! I'll give him a century to find her in—a couple of them if he likes. A woman who doesn't exist any longer, and the clothes that gave her her sex burnt up and the ashes thrown away—oh, certainly, he'll find *her* easy enough!" This reflection set him to admiring, for the hundredth time, the shrewd ingenuities by which he had insured himself against detection—more, against even suspicion.

"Nearly always in cases like this there is some little detail or other overlooked, some wee little track or trace left behind, and detection follows; but here there's not even the faintest suggestion of a trace left. No more than a bird leaves when it flies through the air—yes, through the night, you may say. The man that can track a bird through the air in the dark and find that bird is the man to track me out and find the Judge's assassin—no other need apply. And that is the job that has been laid out for poor Pudd'nhead Wilson, of all people in the world! Lord, it will be pathetically funny to see him grubbing and groping after that woman that don't exist, and the right person sitting under his very nose all the time!" The more he thought the situation over, the more the humor of it struck him. Finally he said, "I'll never let him hear the last of that woman. Every time I catch him in company, to his dying day, I'll ask him in the guileless affectionate way that used to gavel him so when I inquired how his unborn law-business was coming along, 'Got on her track yet—hey, Pudd'nhead?' " He wanted to laugh, but that would not have answered; there were people about, and he was mourning for his uncle. He made up his mind that it would be good entertainment to look in on Wilson that night and watch him worry over his barren law-case and goad him with an exasperating word or two of sympathy and commiseration now and then.

Wilson wanted no supper, he had no appetite. He got out all the finger-prints of girls and women in his collection of records and pored gloomily over them an hour or more, trying to convince himself that that troublesome girl's marks were there somewhere and had been overlooked. But it was not so. He drew back his chair, clasped his hands over his head, and gave himself up to dull and arid musings.

Tom Driscoll dropped in, an hour after dark, and said with a pleasant laugh as he took a seat—

"Hello, we've gone back to the amusements of our days of neglect and obscurity for consolation, have we?" and he took up one of the glass strips and held it against the light to inspect it. "Come, cheer up, old man; there's no use in losing your grip and going back to this child's-play merely because this big sunspot is drifting across your shiny new disk. It'll pass, and you'll be all right again,"—and he laid the glass down. "Did you think you could win always?"

"Oh, no," said Wilson, with a sigh, "I didn't expect that, but I can't believe Luigi killed your uncle, and I feel very sorry for him. It makes me blue. And you would feel as I do, Tom, if you were not prejudiced against those young fellows."

"I don't know about that," and Tom's countenence darkened, for his memory reverted to his kicking; "I owe them no good will, considering the brunette one's treatment of me that night. Prejudice or no prejudice, Pudd'nhead, I don't like them, and when they get their deserts you're not going to find me sitting on the mourner's bench."

He took up another strip of glass, and exclaimed—

"Why, here's old Roxy's label! Are you going to ornament the royal palaces with nigger paw-marks, too? By the date here, I was seven months old when this was done, and she was nursing me and her little nigger cub. There's a line straight across her thumb-print. How comes that?" and Tom held out the piece of glass to Wilson.

"That is common," said the bored man, wearily. "Scar of a cut or a scratch, usually"—and he took the strip of glass indifferently, and raised it toward the lamp.

All the blood sunk suddenly out of his face; his hand quaked, and he gazed at the polished surface before him with the glassy stare of a corpse.

"Great Heavens, what's the matter with you, Wilson? Are you going to faint?"

Tom sprang for a glass of water and offered it, but Wilson shrank shuddering from him and said—

"No, no!—take it away!" His breast was rising and falling, and he moved his head about in a dull and wandering way, like a person who has been stunned. Presently he said, "I shall feel better when I get to bed; I have been overwrought to-day; yes, and over worked for many days."

"Then I'll leave you and let you to get to your rest. Good-night, old man." But as Tom went out he couldn't deny himself a small parting gibe: "Don't take it so hard; a body can't win every time; you'll hang somebody yet."

Wilson muttered to himself, "It is no lie to say I am sorry I have to begin with you, miserable dog though you are!"

He braced himself up with a glass of cold whisky, and went to work again. He did not compare the new finger-marks unintentionally left by Tom a few minutes before on Roxy's glass with the tracings of the marks left on the knife-handle, there being no need of that (for his trained eye), but busied himself with another matter, muttering from time to time, "Idiot that I was!—Nothing but a *girl* would do me—a man in girl's clothes never occurred to me." First, he hunted out the plate containing the finger-prints made by Tom when he was twelve years old, and laid it by itself; then he brought forth the marks made by Tom's baby fingers when he was a suckling of seven months, and placed these two plates with the one containing this subject's newly (and unconsciously) made record.

"Now the series is complete," he said with satisfaction, and sat down to inspect these things and enjoy them.

But his enjoyment was brief. He stared a considerable time at the three strips, and seemed stupefied with astonishment. At last he put them down and said, "I can't make it out at all—hang it, the baby's don't tally with the others!"

He walked the floor for half an hour puzzling over his enigma, then he hunted out two other glass plates.

He sat down and puzzled over these things a good while, but kept muttering, "It's no use; I can't understand it. They don't tally right, and yet I'll swear the names and dates are right, and so of course they *ought* to tally. I never labeled one of these things carelessly in my life. There is a most extraordinary mystery here."

He was tired out, now, and his brains were beginning to clog. He said he would sleep himself fresh, and then see what he could do with this riddle. He slept through a troubled and unrestful hour, then unconsciousness began to shred away, and presently he rose drowsily to a sitting posture. "Now what was that dream?" he said, trying to recall it; "what was that dream?—it seemed to unravel that puz—"

He landed in the middle of the floor at a bound, without finishing the sentence, and ran and turned up his light and seized his "records." He took a single swift glance at them and cried out—

"It's so! Heavens, what a revelation! And for twenty-three years no man has ever suspected it!"

CHAPTER XXI

He is useless on top of the ground; he ought to be under it, inspiring the cabbages.—*Pudd'nhead Wilson's Calendar.*

April 1. This is the day upon which we are reminded of what we are on the other three hundred and sixty-four.—*Pudd'nhead Wilson's Calendar.*

Wilson put on enough clothes for business purposes and went to work under a high pressure of steam. He was awake all over. All sense of weariness had been swept away by the invigorating refreshment of the great and hopeful discovery which he had made. He made fine and accurate reproductions of a number of his "records," and then enlarged them on a scale of ten to one with his pantograph. He did these pantograph enlargements on sheets of white cardboard, and made each individual line of the bewildering maze of whorls or curves or loops which constituted the "pattern," of a "record" stand out bold and black by reinforcing it with ink. To the untrained eye the collection of delicate originals made by the human finger on the glass plates looked about alike; but when enlarged ten times they resembled the markings of a block of wood that has been sawed across the grain, and the dullest eye could detect at a glance, and at a distance of many feet, that no two of the patterns were alike. When Wilson had at last finished his tedious and difficult work, he arranged its results according to a plan in which a progressive order and sequence was a principal feature; then he added to the batch several pantograph enlargements which he had made from time to time in bygone years.

The night was spent and the day well advanced, now. By the time he had snatched a trifle of breakfast it was nine o'clock, and the court was ready to begin its sitting. He was in his place twelve minutes later with his "records."

Tom Driscoll caught a slight glimpse of the records, and nudged his nearest friend and said, with a wink, "Pudd'nhead's got a rare eye to business—thinks that as long as he can't win his case it's at least a noble good chance to advertise his palace-window decorations without any expense." Wilson was informed that his witnesses had been delayed, but would arrive presently; but he rose and said he should probably not have occasion to make use of their testimony. [An amused murmur ran through the room—"It's a clean backdown! he gives up without hitting a lick!"] Wilson continued—"I have other testimony—and better. [This compelled interest, and evoked murmurs of surprise that had a detectible ingredient of disappointment in them.] If I seem to be springing this evidence upon the court, I offer as my justification for this, that I did not discover its existence until late last night, and have been engaged in examining and classifying it ever since, until half an hour ago. I shall offer it presently; but first I wish to say a few preliminary words.

"May it please the Court, the claim given the front place, the claim most persistently urged, the claim most strenuously and I may even say aggressively and defiantly insisted upon by the prosecution, is this—that the person whose hand left the blood-stained finger-prints upon the handle of the Indian knife is the person who committed the murder." Wilson paused, during several moments, to give impressiveness to what he was about to say, and then added tranquilly, *"We grant that claim."*

It was an electrical surprise. No one was prepared for such an admission. A buzz of astonishment rose on all sides, and people were heard to intimate that the overworked lawyer had lost his mind. Even the veteran judge, accustomed as he was to legal ambushes and masked batteries in criminal procedure, was not sure that his ears were not deceiving him, and asked counsel what it was he had said. Howard's impassive face betrayed no sign, but his attitude and bearing lost something of their careless confidence for a moment. Wilson resumed:

"We not only grant that claim, but we welcome it and strongly endorse it. Leaving that matter for the present, we will now proceed to consider other points in the case which we propose to establish by evidence, and shall include that one in the chain in its proper place."

He had made up his mind to try a few hardy guesses, in mapping out his theory of the origin and motive of the murder—guesses designed to fill up gaps in it—guesses which could help if they hit, and would probably do no harm if they didn't.

"To my mind, certain circumstances of the case before the court seem to suggest a motive for the homicide quite different from the one insisted on by the State. It is my conviction that the motive was not revenge, but robbery. It has been urged that the presence of the accused brothers in that fatal room, just after notification that one of them must take the life of Judge Driscoll or lose his own the moment the parties should meet, clearly signifies that the natural instinct of self-preservation moved my clients to go there secretly and save Count Luigi by destroying his adversary.

"Then why did they stay there, after the deed was done? Mrs. Pratt had time, although she did not hear the cry for help, but woke up some moments later, to run to that room—and there she found these men standing and making no effort to escape. If they were guilty, they ought to have been running out of the house at the same time that she was running to that room. If they had had such a strong instinct toward self-preservation as to move them to kill that unarmed man, what had become of it now, when it should have been more alert than ever? Would any of us have remained there? Let us not slander our intelligence to that degree.

"Much stress has been laid upon the fact that the accused offered a very large reward for the knife with which this murder was done; that no thief came forward to claim that extraordinary reward; that the latter fact was good circumstantial evidence that the claim that the knife had been stolen was a vanity and a fraud; that these details taken in connection with the memorable and apparently prophetic speech of the deceased concerning that knife, and the final discovery of that very knife in the fatal room where no living person was found present with the slaughtered man but the owner of the knife and his brother, form an indestructible chain of evidence which fixes the crime upon those unfortunate strangers.

"But I shall presently ask to be sworn, and shall testify that there was a large reward offered for the *thief,* also; that it was offered secretly and not advertised; that this fact was indiscreetly mentioned—or at least tacitly admitted—in what was supposed to be safe circumstances, but may *not* have been. The thief may have been present himself. [Tom Driscoll had been looking at the speaker, but dropped his eyes at this point.] In that case he would retain the knife in his possession, not daring to offer it for sale, or for pledge in a pawn-show. [There was a nodding of heads among the audience by way of admission that this was not a bad stroke.] I shall prove to the satisfaction of the jury that there *was* a person in Judge Driscoll's room several minutes before the accused entered it. [This produced a strong sensation; the last drowsy-head in the court-room roused up, now, and made preparation to listen.] If it shall seem necessary, I will prove by the Misses Clarkson that they met a veiled person— ostensibly a woman—coming out of the back gate a few minutes after the cry for help was heard. This person was not a woman, but a man dressed in woman's clothes." Another sensation. Wilson had his eye on Tom when he hazarded this guess, to see what effect it would produce. He was satisfied with the result, and said to himself, "It was a success—he's hit!"

"The object of that person in that house was robbery, not murder. It is true that the safe was not open, but there was an ordinary tin cash-box on the table, with three thousand dollars in it. It is easily supposable that the thief was concealed in the house; that he knew of this box, and of its owner's habit of counting its contents and arranging his accounts at night—if he had that habit, which I do not assert, of course;—that he tried to take the box while its owner slept, but made a noise and was seized, and had to use the knife to save himself from capture; and that he fled without his booty because he heard help coming.

"I have now done with my theory, and will proceed to the evidences by which I propose to try to prove its soundness." Wilson took up several of his strips of glass. When the audience recognized these familiar mementoes of Pudd'nhead's old-time childish "puttering" and folly, the tense and funereal interest vanished out of their faces, and the house burst into volleys of relieving and refreshing laughter, and Tom chirked up and joined in the fun himself; but Wilson was apparently not disturbed. He arranged his records on the table before him, and said—

"I beg the indulgence of the court while I make a few remarks in explanation of some evidence which I am about to introduce, and which I shall presently ask to be allowed to verify under oath on the witness stand. Every human being carries with him from his cradle to his grave certain physical marks which do not change their character, and by which he can always be identified—and that without shade of doubt or question. These marks are his signature, his physiological autograph, so to speak, and this autograph can not be counterfeited, nor can he disguise it or hide it away, nor can it become illegible by the wear and mutations of time. This signature is not his face—age can change that beyond recognition; it is not his hair, for that can fall out; it is not his height, for duplicates of that exist; it is not his form, for duplicates of that exist also, whereas this signature is each man's very own—there is no duplicate of it among the swarming populations of the globe! [The audience was interested once more.]

"This autograph consists of the delicate lines or corrugations with which Nature marks the insides of the hands and the soles of the feet. If you will look at the balls of your fingers,—you that have very sharp eyesight,—you will observe that these dainty curving lines lie close together, like those that indicate the borders of oceans in maps, and that they form various clearly defined patterns, such as arches, circles, long curves, whorls, etc., and that these patterns differ on the different fingers. [Every man in the room had his hand up to the light, now, and his head canted to one side, and was minutely scrutinizing the balls of his fingers; there were whispered ejaculations of "Why, it's so—I never noticed that before!"] The patterns on the right hand are not the same as those on the left. [Ejaculations of "Why, that's so, too!"] Taken finger for finger, your patterns differ from your neighbor's. [Comparisons were made all over the house—even the judge and jury were absorbed in this curious work.] The patterns of a twin's right hand are not the same as those on his left. One twin's patterns are never the same as his fellow-twin's patterns—the jury will find that the patterns upon the finger-balls of the accused follow this rule. [An examination of the twins' hands was begun at once.] You have often heard of twins who were so exactly alike that when dressed alike their own parents could not tell them apart. Yet there was never a twin born into this world that did not carry from birth to death a sure identifier in this mysterious and marvelous natal autograph. That once known to you, his fellow-twin could never personate him and deceive you."

Wilson stopped and stood silent. Inattention dies a quick and sure death when a speaker does that. The stillness gives warning that something is coming. All palms and finger-balls went down, now, all slouching forms straightened, all heads came up, all eyes were fastened upon Wilson's face. He waited yet one, two, three moments, to let his pause complete and perfect its spell upon the house; then, when through the profound hush he could hear the ticking of the clock on the wall, he put out his hand and took the Indian knife by the blade and held it aloft where all could see the sinister spots upon its ivory handle; then he said, in a level and passionless voice—

"Upon this haft stands the assassin's natal autograph, written in the blood of that helpless and unoffending old man who loved you and whom you all loved. There is but one man in the whole earth whose hand can duplicate that crimson sign,"—he paused and raised his eyes to the pendulum swinging back and forth,—"and please God we will produce that man in this room before the clock strikes noon!"

Stunned, distraught, unconscious of its own movement, the house half rose, as if expecting to see the murderer appear at the door, and a breeze of muttered ejaculations swept the place. "Order in the court!—sit down!" This from the sheriff. He was obeyed, and quiet reigned again. Wilson stole a glance at Tom, and said to himself, "He is flying signals of distress, now; even people who despise him are pitying him; they think this is a hard ordeal for a young fellow who has lost his benefactor by so cruel a stroke—and they are right." He resumed his speech:

"For more than twenty years I have amused my compulsory leisure with collecting these curious physical signatures in this town. At my house I have hundreds upon hundreds of them. Each and every one is labelled with name and date; not labelled the next day or even the next hour, but in the very minute that the impression was taken. When I go upon the witness stand I will repeat under oath the things which I am now saying. I have the finger-prints of the court, the sheriff, and every member of the jury. There is hardly a person in this room, white or black, whose natal signature I cannot produce, and not one of them can so disguise himself that I cannot pick him out from a multitude of his fellow-creatures and unerringly identify him by his hands. And if he and I should live to be a hundred I could still do it. [The interest of the audience was steadily deepening, now.]

"I have studied some of these signatures so much that I know them as well as the bank cashier knows the autograph of his oldest customer. While I turn my back now, I beg that several persons will be so good as to pass their fingers through their hair, and then press them upon one of the panes of the window near the jury, and that among them the accused may set *their* finger-marks. Also, I beg that these experimenters, or others, will set their finger-marks upon another pane, and add again the marks of the accused, but not placing them in the same order or relation to the other signatures as before—for, by one chance in a million, a person might happen upon the right marks by pure guess-work *once,* therefore I wish to be tested twice."

He turned his back, and the two panes were quickly covered with delicately-lined oval spots, but visible only to such persons as could get a dark background for them—the foliage of a tree, outside, for instance. Then, upon call, Wilson went to the window, made his examination and said—

"This is Count Luigi's right hand; this one, three signatures below, is his left. Here is Count Angelo's right; down here is his left. Now for the other pane: here and here are his brother's." He faced about. "Am I right?"

A deafening explosion of applause was the answer. The Bench said—

"This certainly approaches the miraculous!"

Wilson turned to the window again and remarked, pointing with his finger—

"This is the signature of Mr. Justice Robinson. [Applause.] This, of Constable Blake. [Applause.] This, of John Mason, juryman. [Applause.] This, of the sheriff. [Applause.] I cannot name the others, but I have them all at home, named and dated, and could identify them all by my finger-print records."

He moved to his place through a storm of applause—which the sheriff stopped, and also made the people sit down, for they were all standing and struggling to see, of course. Court, jury, sheriff, and everybody had been too absorbed in observing Wilson's performance to attend to the audience earlier.

"Now, then," said Wilson, "I have here the natal autographs of two children—thrown up to ten times the natural size by the pantograph, so that any one who can see at all can tell the markings apart at a glance. We will call the children *A* and *B*. Here are *A's* finger-marks, taken at the age of five months. Here they are again, taken at seven months. [Tom started.] They are alike, you see. Here are *B's* at five months, and also at seven months. They, too, exactly copy each other, but the patterns are quite different from *A's,* you observe. I shall refer to these again presently, but we will turn them face down, now.

"Here, thrown up ten sizes, are the natal autographs of the two persons who are here before you accused of murdering Judge Driscoll. I made these pantograph copies last night, and will so swear when I go upon the witness stand. I ask the jury to compare them with the finger-marks of the accused upon the window panes, and tell the court if they are the same."

He passed a powerful magnifying-glass to the foreman.

One juryman after another took the cardboard and the glass and made the comparison. Then the foreman said to the judge—

"Your honor, we are all agreed that they are identical."

Wilson said to the foreman—

"Please turn that cardboard face down, and take this one, and compare it searchingly, by the magnifier, with the fatal signature upon the knife-handle, and report your finding to the court."

Again the jury made minute examinations, and again reported—

"We find them to be exactly identical, your honor."

Wilson turned toward the counsel for the prosecution, and there was a clearly recognizable note of warning in his voice when he said—

"May it please the court, the State has claimed, strenuously and persistently, that the blood-stained finger-prints upon that knife-handle were left there by the assassin of Judge Driscoll. You have heard us grant that claim, and welcome it." He turned to the jury: "Compare the finger-prints of the accused with the finger-prints left by the assassin—and report."

The comparison began. As it proceeded, all movement and all sound ceased, and the deep silence of an absorbed and waiting suspense settled upon the house; and when at last the words came—

"They do not even resemble," a thunder-crash of applause followed and the house sprang to its feet, but was quickly repressed by official force and brought to order again. Tom was altering his position every few minutes, now, but none of his changes brought repose nor any small trifle of comfort. When the house's attention was become fixed once more, Wilson said gravely, indicating the twins with a gesture—

"These men are innocent—I have no further concern with them. [Another outbreak of applause began, but was promptly checked.] We will now proceed to find the guilty. [Tom's eyes were starting from their sockets—yes, it was a cruel day for the bereaved youth, everybody thought.] We will return to the infant autographs of *A* and *B*. I will ask the jury to take these large pantograph facsimiles of *A's* marked five months and seven months. Do they tally?"

The foreman responded—

"Perfectly."

"Now examine this pantograph, taken at eight months, and also marked *A*. Does it tally with the other two?"

The surprised response was—

"No—they differ widely!"

"You are quite right. Now take these two pantographs of *B's* autograph, marked five months and seven months. Do they tally with each other?"

"Yes—perfectly."

"Take this third pantograph marked *B,* eight months. Does it tally with *B's* other two?"

"By no means!"

"Do you know how to account for those strange discrepancies? I will tell you. For a purpose unknown to us, but probably a selfish one, somebody changed those children in the cradle."

This produced a vast sensation, naturally; Roxana was astonished at this admirable guess, but not disturbed by it. To guess the exchange was one thing, to guess who did it quite another. Pudd'nhead Wilson could do wonderful things, no doubt, but he couldn't do impossible ones. Safe? She was perfectly safe. She smiled privately.

"Between the ages of seven months and eight months those children were changed in the cradle"—he made one of his effect-collecting pauses, and added—"and the person who did it is in this house!"

Roxy's pulses stood still! The house was thrilled as with an electric shock, and the people half rose as if to seek a glimpse of the person who had made that exchange. Tom was growing limp; the life seemed oozing out of him. Wilson resumed:

"*A* was put into *B's* cradle in the nursery; *B* was transferred to the kitchen and became a negro and a slave, [Sensation— confusion of angry ejaculations]—but within a quarter of an hour he will stand before you white and free! [Burst of applause, checked by the officers.] From seven months onward until now, *A* has still been a usurper, and in my finger-record he bears *B's* name. Here is his pantograph at the age of twelve. Compare it with the assassin's signature upon the knife-handle. Do they tally?"

The foreman answered—

"To the minutest detail!"

Wilson said, solemnly—

"The murderer of your friend and mine—York Driscoll of the generous hand and the kindly spirit—sits in among you. Valet de Chambre, negro and slave,—falsely called Thomas à Becket Driscoll,—make upon the window the finger-prints that will hang you!"

Tom turned his ashen face imploringly toward the speaker, made some impotent movements with his white lips, then slid limp and lifeless to the floor.

Wilson broke the awed silence with the words—

"There is no need. He has confessed."

Roxy flung herself upon her knees, covered her face with her hands, and out through her sobs the words struggled—

"De Lord have mercy on me, po' misable sinner dat I is!"

The clock struck twelve.

The court rose; the new prisoner, handcuffed, was removed.

CONCLUSION

It is often the case that the man who can't tell a lie thinks he is the best judge of one.—*Pudd'nhead Wilson's Calendar.*

October 12, the Discovery. It was wonderful to find America, but it would have been more wonderful to miss it.—*Pudd'nhead Wilson's Calendar.*

The town sat up all night to discuss the amazing events of the day and swap guesses as to when Tom's trial would begin. Troop after troop of citizens came to serenade Wilson, and require a speech, and shout themselves hoarse over every sentence that fell from his lips—for all his sentences were golden, now, all were marvelous. His long fight against hard luck and prejudice was ended; he was a made man for good.

And as each of these roaring gangs of enthusiasts marched away, some remorseful member of it was quite sure to raise his voice and say—

"And this is the man the likes of us have called a pudd'nhead for more than twenty years. He has resigned from that position, friends."

"Yes, but it isn't vacant—we're elected."

The twins were heroes of romance, now, and with rehabilitated reputations. But they were weary of Western adventure, and straightway retired to Europe.

Roxy's heart was broken. The young fellow upon whom she had inflicted twenty-three years of slavery continued the false heir's pension of thirty-five dollars a month to her, but her hurts were too deep for money to heal; the spirit in her eye was quenched, her martial bearing departed with it, and the voice of her laughter ceased in the land. In her church and its affairs she found her only solace.

The real heir suddenly found himself rich and free, but in a most embarrassing situation. He could neither read nor write, and his speech was the basest dialect of the negro quarter. His gait, his attitudes, his gestures, his bearing, his laugh—all were vulgar and uncouth; his manners were the manners of a slave. Money and fine clothes could not mend these defects or cover them up; they only made them the more glaring and the more pathetic. The poor fellow could not endure the terrors of the white man's parlor, and felt at home and at peace nowhere but in the kitchen. The family pew was a misery to him, yet he could nevermore enter into the solacing refuge of the "nigger gallery"—that was closed to him for good and all. But we cannot follow his curious fate further—that it would be a long story.

The false heir made a full confession and was sentenced to imprisonment for life. But now a complication came up. The Percy Driscoll estate was in such a crippled shape when its owner died that it could pay only sixty per cent of its great indebtedness, and was settled at that rate. But the creditors came forward, now, and complained that inasmuch as through an error for which *they* were in no way to blame the false heir was not inventoried at that time with the rest of the property, great wrong and loss had thereby been inflicted upon them. They rightly claimed that "Tom" was lawfully their property and had been so for eight years; that they had already lost sufficiently in being deprived of his services during that long period, and ought not to be required to add anything to that loss; that if he had been delivered up to them in the first place, they would have sold him and he could not have murdered Judge Driscoll; therefore it was not he that had really committed the murder, the guilt lay with the erroneous inventory. Everybody saw that there was reason in this. Everybody granted that if "Tom" were white and free it would be unquestionably right to punish him—it would be no loss to anybody; but to shut up a valuable slave for life—that was quite another matter.

As soon as the Governor understood the case, he pardoned Tom at once, and the creditors sold him down the river.

The Comedy Those Extraordinary Twins *was a story that, as Twain says, "got tangled together" with* Pudd'nhead Wilson *as his work on the novel progressed. "I pulled one of the stories out by the roots, and left the other one—a kind of literary Caesarean operation." The comedy that he had originally excised was thus given the subtitle "The Suppressed Farce" when it was published in one volume with* The Tragedy of Pudd'nhead Wilson *by the American Publishing Company in 1894.*

The Comedy
Those Extraordinary Twins

A man who is not born with the novel-writing gift has a troublesome time of it when he tries to build a novel. I know this from experience. He has no clear idea of his story; in fact he has no story. He merely has some people in his mind, and an incident or two, also a locality. He knows these people, he knows the selected locality, and he trusts that he can plunge those people into those incidents with interesting results. So he goes to work. To write a novel? No—that is a thought which comes later; in the beginning he is only proposing to tell a little tale; a very little tale; a six-page tale. But as it is a tale which he is not acquainted with, and can only find out what it is by listening as it goes along telling itself, it is more apt to go on and on and on till it spreads itself into a book. I know about this, because it has happened to me so many times.

And I have noticed another thing: that as the short tale grows into the long tale, the original intention (or motif) is apt to get abolished and find itself superseded by a quite different one. It was so in the case of a magazine sketch which I once started to write—a funny and fantastic sketch about a prince and a pauper; it presently assumed a grave cast of its own accord, and in that new shape spread itself out into a book. Much the same thing happened with "Pudd'nhead Wilson." I had a sufficiently hard time with that tale, because it changed itself from a farce to a tragedy while I was going along with it,—a most embarrassing circumstance. But what was a great deal worse was, that it was not one story, but two stories tangled together; and they obstructed and interrupted each other at every turn and created no end of confusion and annoyance. I could not offer the book for publication, for I was afraid it would unseat the reader's reason, I did not know what was the matter with it, for I had not noticed, as yet, that it was two stories in one. It took me months to make that discovery. I carried the manuscript back and forth across the Atlantic two or three times, and read it and studied over it on shipboard; and at last I saw where the difficulty lay. I had no further trouble. I pulled one of the stories out by the roots, and left the other one—a kind of literary Cæsarean operation.

Would the reader care to know something about the story which I pulled out? He has been told many a time how the born-and-trained novelist works; won't he let me round and complete his knowledge by telling him how the jack-leg does it?

Originally the story was called "Those Extraordinary Twins." I meant to make it very short. I had seen a picture of a youthful

Italian "freak"—or "freaks"—which was—or which were—on exhibition in our cities—a combination consisting of two heads and four arms joined to a single body and a single pair of legs—and I thought I would write an extravagantly fantastic little story with this freak of nature for hero—or heroes—a silly young Miss for heroine, and two old ladies and two boys for the minor parts. I lavishly elaborated these people and their doings, of course. But the tale kept spreading along, and other people got to intruding themselves and taking up more and more room with their talk and their affairs. Among them came a stranger named Pudd'nhead Wilson, and a woman named Roxana; and presently the doings of these two pushed up into prominence a young fellow named Tom Driscoll, whose proper place was away in the obscure background. Before the book was half finished those three were taking things almost entirely into their own hands and working the whole tale as a private venture of their own—a tale which they had nothing at all to do with, by rights.

When the book was finished and I came to look around to see what had become of the team I had originally started out with—Aunt Patsy Cooper, Aunt Betsy Hale, the two boys, and Rowena the light-weight heroine—they were nowhere to be seen; they had disappeared from the story some time or other. I hunted about and found them—found them stranded, idle, forgotten, and permanently useless. It was very awkward. It was awkward all around, but more particularly in the case of Rowena, because there was a lovematch on, between her and one of the twins that constituted the freak, and I had worked it up to a blistering heat and thrown in a quite dramatic love- quarrel, wherein Rowena scathingly denounced her betrothed for getting drunk, and scoffed at his explanation of how it had happened, and wouldn't listen to it, and had driven him from her in the usual "forever" way; and now here she sat crying and broken-hearted; for she had found that he had spoken only the truth; that it was not he, but the other half of the freak that had drunk the liquor that made him drunk; that her half was a prohibitionist and had never drunk a drop in his life, and although tight as a brick three days in the week, was wholly innocent of blame; and indeed, when sober, was constantly doing all he could to reform his brother, the other half, who never got any satisfaction out of drinking, anyway, because liquor never affected him. Yes, here she was, stranded with that deep injustice of hers torturing her poor torn heart.

I didn't know what to do with her. I was as sorry for her as anybody could be, but the campaign was over, the book was finished, she was side-tracked, and there was no possible way of crowding her in, anywhere. I could not leave her there, of course; it would not do. After spreading her out so, and making such a to-do over her affairs, it would be absolutely necessary to account to the reader for her. I thought and thought and studied and studied; but I arrived at nothing. I finally saw plainly that there was really no way but one—I must simply give her the grand bounce. It grieved me to do it, for after associating with her so much I had come to kind of like her after a fashion, notwithstanding she was such an ass and said such stupid, irritating things and was so nauseatingly sentimental. Still it had to be done. So at the top of Chapter XVII. I put a "Calendar" remark concerning July the Fourth, and began the chapter with this statistic:

"Rowena went out in the back yard after supper to see the fireworks and fell down the well and got drowned."

It seemed abrupt, but I thought maybe the reader wouldn't notice it, because I changed the subject right away to something else. Anyway it loosened up Rowena from where she was stuck and got her out of the way, and that was the main thing. It seemed a prompt good way of weeding out people that had got stalled, and a plenty good enough way for those others; so I hunted up the two boys and said "they went out back one night to stone the cat and fell down the well and got drowned." Next I searched around and found old Aunt Patsy Cooper and Aunt Betsy Hale where they were aground, and said "they went out back one night to visit the sick and fell down the well and got drowned." I was going to drown some of the others, but I gave up the idea, partly because I believed that if I kept that up it would arouse attention, and perhaps sympathy with those people, and partly because it was not a large well and would not hold any more anyway.

Still the story was unsatisfactory. Here was a set of new characters who were become inordinately prominent and who persisted in remaining so to the end; and back yonder was an older set who made a large noise and a great to-do for a little while and then suddenly played out utterly and fell down the well. There was a radical defect somewhere, and I must search it out and cure it.

The defect turned out to be the one already spoken of—two stories in one, a farce and a tragedy. So I pulled out the farce and left the tragedy. This left the original team in, but only as mere names, not as characters. Their prominence was wholly gone; they were not even worth drowning; so I removed that detail. Also I took those twins apart and made two separate men of them. They had no occasion to have foreign names now, but it was too much trouble to remove them all through, so I left them christened as they were and made no explanation.

The Suppressed Farce

CHAPTER I

The conglomerate twins were brought on the stage in Chapter I of the original extravaganza. Aunt Patsy Cooper has received their letter applying for board and lodging, and Rowena, her daughter, insane with joy, is begging for a hearing of it:

"Well, set down then, and be quiet a minute and don't fly around so; it fairly makes me tired to see you. It starts off so: 'HONORED MADAM—' "

"I like that, ma, don't you? It shows they're high-bred."

"Yes, I noticed that when I first read it. 'My brother and I have seen your advertisement, by chance, in a copy of your local journal——' "

"It's so beautiful and smooth, ma—don't you think so?"

"Yes, seems so to me—'and beg leave to take the room you offer. We are twenty-four years of age, and twins——' "

"Twins! How sweet! I do hope they are handsome, and I just know they are! Don't you hope they are, ma?"

"Land, I ain't particular. 'We are Italians by birth——' "

"It's so romantic! Just think—there's never been one in this town, and everybody will want to see them, and they're all *ours!* Think of that!"

"—'but have lived in the various countries of Europe, and several years in the United States.' "

"Oh, just think what wonders they've seen, ma! Won't it be good to hear them talk?"

"I reckon so; yes, I reckon so. 'Our names are Luigi and Angelo Capello——' "

"Beautiful, perfectly beautiful! Not like Jones and Robinson and those horrible names."

" 'You desire but one guest, but dear madam, if you will allow us to pay for two we will not discommode you. We will sleep together in the same bed. We have always been used to this, and prefer it.' And then he goes on to say they will be down Thursday."

"And this is Tuesday—I don't know how I'm ever going to wait, ma! The time does drag along so, and I'm so dying to see them! Which of them do you reckon is the tallest, ma?"

"How do you s'pose I can tell, child? Mostly they are the same size—twins are."

"Well then, which do you reckon is the best looking?"

"Goodness knows—I don't."

"I think Angelo is; it's the prettiest name, anyway. Don't you think it's a sweet name, ma?"

"Yes, it's well enough. I'd like both of them better if I knew the way to pronounce them—the Eyetalian way, I mean. The Missouri way and the Eyetalian way is different I judge."

"Maybe—yes. It's Luigi that writes the letter. What do you reckon is the reason Angelo didn't write it?"

"Why, how can I tell? What's the difference who writes it, so long as it's done?"

"Oh, I hope it wasn't because he is sick! You don't think he is sick, do you, ma?"

"Sick your granny; what's to make him sick?"

"Oh, there's never any telling. These foreigners with that kind of names are so delicate, and of course that kind of names are not suited to our climate—you wouldn't expect it."

[And so-on and so-on, no end. The time drags along; Thursday comes; the boat arrives in a pouring storm toward midnight.]

At last there was a knock at the door and the anxious family jumped to open it. Two negro men entered, each carrying a trunk, and proceeded up-stairs toward the guest-room. Then followed a stupefying apparition—a double-headed human creature with four arms, one body, and a single pair of legs!

It—or they, as you please—bowed with elaborate foreign formality, but the Coopers could not respond immediately; they were paralyzed. At this moment there came from the rear of the group a fervent ejaculation—"My lan'!"—followed by a crash of crockery, and the slave-wench Nancy stood petrified and staring, with a tray of wrecked tea-things at her feet. The incident broke the spell, and brought the family to consciousness. The beautiful heads of the new-comer bowed again, and one of them said with easy grace and dignity:

"I crave the honor, madam and miss, to introduce to you my brother, Count Luigi Capello," (the other head bowed) "and myself—Count Angelo; and at the same time offer sincere apologies for the lateness of our coming, which was unavoidable," and both heads bowed again.

The poor old lady was in a whirl of amazement and confusion, but she managed to stammer out:

"I'm sure I'm glad to make your acquaintance, sir—I mean, gentlemen. As for the delay, it is nothing, don't mention it. This is my daughter Rowena, sir—gentlemen. Please step into the parlor and sit down and have a bite and sup; you are dreadful wet and must be uncomfortable—both of you, I mean."

But to the old lady's relief they courteously excused themselves, saying it would be wrong to keep the family out of their beds longer; then each bowed in turn and uttered a friendly good-night, and the singular figure moved away in the wake of Rowena's small brothers, who bore candles, and disappeared up the stairs.

The widow tottered into the parlor and sank into the chair with a gasp, and Rowena followed, tongue-tied and dazed. The two sat silent in the throbbing summer heat unconscious of the million-voiced music of the mosquitoes, unconscious of the roaring gale, the lashing and thrashing of the rain along the windows and the roof, the white glare of the lightning, the tumultuous booming and bellowing of the thunder; conscious of nothing but that prodigy, that uncanny apparition that had come and gone so suddenly—that weird strange thing that was so soft-spoken and so gentle of manner and yet had shaken them up like an earthquake with the shock of its gruesome aspect. At last a cold little shudder quivered along down the widow's meager frame and she said in a weak voice:

"Ugh, it was awful—just the mere look of that phillipene!"

Rowena did not answer. Her faculties were still caked, she had not yet found her voice. Presently the widow said, a little resentfully:

"Always been *used* to sleeping together—in fact, *prefer* it. And I was thinking it was to accommodate me. I thought it was very good of them, whereas a person situated as that young man is——"

"Ma, you oughtn't to begin by getting up a prejudice against him. I'm sure he is good-hearted and means well. Both of his faces show it."

"I'm not so certain about that. The one on the left—I mean the one on *it's* left—hasn't near as good a face, in my opinion, as its brother."

"That's Luigi."

"Yes, Luigi; anyway it's the dark-skinned one; the one that was west of his brother when they stood in the door. Up to all kinds of mischief and disobedience when he was a boy, I'll be bound. I lay his mother had trouble to lay her hand on him when she wanted him. But the one on the right is as good as gold, I can see that."

"That's Angelo."

"Yes, Angelo, I reckon, though I can't tell t' other from which by their names, yet awhile. But it's the right-hand one—the blonde one. He has such kind blue eyes, and curly copper hair and fresh complexion——"

"And such a noble face!—oh, it *is* a noble face, ma, just royal, you may say! And beautiful—deary me, how beautiful! But both are that; the dark one's as beautiful as a picture. There's no such wonderful faces and handsome heads in this town—none that even begin. And such hands—especially Angelo's—so shapely and——"

"Stuff, how could you tell which they belonged to?—they had gloves on."

"Why, didn't I see them take off their hats?"

"That don't signify. They might have taken off each other's hats. Nobody could tell. There was just a wormy squirming of arms in the air—seemed to be a couple of dozen of them, all writhing at once, and it just made me dizzy to see them go."

"Why, ma, I hadn't any difficulty. There's two arms on each shoulder——"

"There, now. One arm on each shoulder belongs to each of the creatures, don't it? For a person to have two arms on one shoulder wouldn't do him any good, would it? Of course not. Each has an arm on each shoulder. Now then, you tell me which of them belongs to which, if you can. *They* don't know themselves—they just work whichever arm comes handy. Of course they do; especially if they are in a hurry and can't stop to think which belongs to which."

The mother seemed to have the rights of the argument, so the daughter abandoned the struggle. Presently the widow rose with a yawn and said:

"Poor thing. I hope it won't catch cold; it was powerful wet, just drenched, you may say. I hope it has left its boots outside, so they can be dried." Then she gave a little start, and looked perplexed. "Now I remember I heard one of them ask Joe to call him at half after seven—I think it was the one on the left—no, it was the one to the east of the other one—but I didn't hear the other one say anything. I wonder if he wants to be called too. Do you reckon it's too late to ask?"

"Why, ma, it's not necessary. Calling one is calling both. If one gets up, the other's *got* to."

"Sho, of course; I never thought of that. Well, come along, maybe we can get some sleep, but I don't know, I'm so shook up with what we've been through."

The stranger had made an impression on the boys, too. They

had a word of talk as they were getting to bed. Henry, the gentle, the humane, said:

"I feel ever so sorry for it, don't you, Joe?"

But Joe was a boy of this world, active, enterprising, and had a theatrical side to him:

"Sorry? Why, how you talk! It can't stir a step without attracting attention. It 's just grand!"

Henry said, reproachfully:

"Instead of pitying it, Joe, you talk as if——"

"Talk as if *what?* I know one thing mighty certain: if you can fix me so I can eat for two and only have to stub toes for one, I ain't going to fool away no such chance just for sentiment."

The twins were wet and tired, and they proceeded to undress without any preliminary remarks. The abundance of sleeves made the partnership-coat hard to get off, for it was like skinning a tarantula; but it came at last, after much tugging and perspiring. The mutual vest followed. Then the brothers stood up before the glass, and each took off his own cravat and collar. The collars were of the standing kind, and came high up under the ears, like the sides of a wheelbarrow, as required by the fashion of the day. The cravats were as broad as a bank bill, with fringed ends which stood far out to right and left like wings of a dragon-fly, and this also was strictly in accordance with the fashion of the time. Each cravat, as to color, was in perfect taste, so far as its owner's complexion was concerned—a delicate pink, in the case of the blonde brother, a violent scarlet in the case of the brunette—but as a combination they broke all the laws of taste known to civilization. Nothing more fiendish and irreconcilable than those shrieking and blaspheming colors could have been contrived. The wet boots gave no end of trouble—to Luigi. When they were off at last, Angelo said, with bitterness:

"I wish you wouldn't wear such tight boots, they hurt my feet."

Luigi answered with indifference:

"My friend, when I am in command of our body, I choose my apparel according to my own convenience, as I have remarked more than several times already. When you are in command, I beg you will do as you please."

Angelo was hurt, and the tears came into his eyes. There was gentle reproach in his voice, but not anger, when he replied:

"Luigi, I often consult your wishes, but you never consult mine. When I am in command I treat you as a guest; I try to make you feel at home; when you are in command you treat me as an intruder, you make me feel unwelcome. It embarrasses me cruelly in company, for I can see that people notice it and comment on it."

"Oh, damn the people," responded the brother languidly, and with the air of one who is tired of the subject.

A slight shudder shook the frame of Angelo, but he said nothing and the conversation ceased. Each buttoned his own share of the night-shirt in silence; then Luigi, with Paine's "Age of Reason" in his hand, sat down in one chair and put his feet in another and lit his pipe, while Angelo took his "Whole Duty of Man," and both began to read. Angelo presently began to cough; his coughing increased and became mixed with gaspings for breath, and he was finally obliged to make an appeal to his brother's humanity:

"Luigi, if you would only smoke a little milder tobacco, I am sure I could learn not to mind it in time, but this is so strong, and the pipe is so rank that——"

"Angelo, I wouldn't be such a baby. I have learned to smoke in a week, and the trouble is already over with me; if you would try, you could learn too, and then you would stop spoiling my comfort with your everlasting complaints."

"Ah, brother, that is a strong word—everlasting—and isn't quite fair. I only complain when I suffocate; you know I don't complain when we are in the open air."

"Well, anyway, you could learn to smoke yourself."

"But my *principles,* Luigi, you forget my principles. You would not have me do a thing which I regard as a sin?"

"Oh, bosh!"

The conversation ceased again, for Angelo was sick and discouraged and strangling; but after some time he closed his book and asked Luigi to sing "From Greenland's Icy Mountains" with him, but he would not, and when he tried to sing by himself Luigi did his best to drown his plaintive tenor with a rude and rollicking song delivered in a thundering bass.

After the singing there was silence, and neither brother was happy. Before blowing the light out Luigi swallowed half a tumbler of whiskey, and Angelo, whose sensitive organization could not endure intoxicants of any kind, took a pill to keep it from giving him the headache.

CHAPTER II

The family sat in the breakfast-room waiting for the twins to come down. The widow was quiet, the daughter was all alive with happy excitement. She said:

"Ah, they 're a boon, ma, just a boon! don't you think so?"

"Laws, I hope so, I don't know."

"Why, ma, yes you do. They're so fine and handsome, and high-bred and polite, so every way superior to our gawks here in this village; why, they'll make life different from what it was—so humdrum and commonplace, you know—oh, you may be sure they're full of accomplishments, and knowledge of the world, and all that, that will be an immense advantage to society here. Don't you think so, ma?"

"Mercy on me, how should I know, and I've hardly set eyes on them yet." After a pause she added, "They made considerable noise after they went up."

"Noise? Why, ma, they were singing! And it was beautiful, too."

"Oh, it was well enough, but too mixed-up, seemed to me."

"Now, ma, honor bright, did you ever hear 'Greenland's Icy Mountains' sung sweeter—now did you?"

"If it had been sung by itself, it would have been uncommon sweet, I don't deny it; but what they wanted to mix it up with 'Old Bob Ridley' for, I can't make out. Why, they don't go together at all. They are not of the same nature. 'Bob Ridley' is a common rackety slam-bang secular song, one of the rippingest and rantingest and noisiest there is. I am no judge of music, and I don't claim it, but in my opinion nobody can make those two songs go together right."

"Why, ma, I thought——"

"It don't make any difference what you thought, it can't be done. They tried it, and to my mind it was a failure. I never heard such a crazy uproar; seemed to me, sometimes, the roof would come off; and as for the cats—well, I've lived a many a year, and seen cats aggravated in more ways than one, but I've never seen cats take on the way they took on last night."

"Well, I don't think that that goes for anything, ma, because it is the nature of cats that any sound that is unusual——"

"Unusual! You may well call it so. Now if they are going to sing duets every night, I do hope they will both sing the same tune at the same time, for in my opinion a duet that is made up of two different tunes is a mistake; especially when the tunes ain't any kin to one another, that way."

"But, ma, I think it must be a foreign custom; and it must be right too, and the best way, because they have had every opportunity to know what is right, and it don't stand to reason that with their education they would do anything but what the highest musical authorities have sanctioned. You can't help but admit that, ma."

The argument was formidably strong; the old lady could not find any way around it; so, after thinking it over a while she gave in with a sigh of discontent, and admitted that the daughter's position was probably correct. Being vanquished, she had no mind to continue the topic at that disadvantage, and was about to seek a change when a change came of itself. A footstep was heard on the stairs, and she said:

"There—he's coming!"

"*They,* ma—you ought to say *they*—it's nearer right."

The new lodger, rather shoutingly dressed but looking superbly handsome, stepped with courtly carriage into the trim little breakfast-room and put out all his cordial arms at once, like one of those pocket-knives with a multiplicity of blades, and shook hands with the whole family simultaneously. He was so easy and pleasant and hearty that all embarrassment presently thawed away and disappeared, and a cheery feeling of friendliness and comradeship took its place. He—or preferably they—were asked to occupy the seat of honor at the foot of the table. They consented with thanks, and carved the beefsteak with one set of their hands while they distributed it at the same time with the other set.

"Will you have coffee, gentlemen, or tea?"

"Coffee for Luigi, if you please, madam, tea for me."

"Cream and sugar?"

"For me, yes, madam; Luigi takes his coffee black. Our natures differ a good deal from each other, and our tastes also."

The first time the negro girl Nancy appeared in the door and saw the two heads turned in opposite directions and both talking at once, then saw the commingling arms feed potatoes into one mouth and coffee into the other at the same time, she had to pause and pull herself out of a faintness that came over her; but after that she held her grip and was able to wait on the table with fair courage.

Conversation fell naturally into the customary grooves. It was a little jerky, at first, because none of the family could get smoothly through a sentence without a wobble in it here and a break there, caused by some new surprise in the way of attitude or gesture on the part of the twins. The weather suffered the most. The weather was all finished up and disposed of, as a subject, before the simple Missourians had gotten sufficiently wonted to the spectacle of one body feeding two heads to feel composed and reconciled in the presence of so bizarre a miracle. And even after everybody's mind became tranquilized there was still one slight distraction left: the hand that picked up a biscuit carried it to the wrong head, as often as any other way, and the wrong mouth devoured it. This was a puzzling thing, and marred the talk a little. It bothered the widow to such a degree that she presently dropped out of the conversation without knowing it, and fell to watching and guessing and talking to herself:

"Now that hand is going to take that coffee to—no, it's gone to the other mouth; I can't understand it; and now, here is the dark complected hand with a potato on its fork, I'll see what goes with it—there, the light complected head's got it, as sure as I live!" Finally Rowena said:

"Ma, what is the matter with you? Are you dreaming about something?"

The old lady came to herself and blushed; then she explained with the first random thing that came into her mind: "I saw Mr. Angelo take up Mr. Luigi's coffee, and I thought maybe he—sha'n't I give *you* a cup, Mr. Angelo?"

"Oh no, madam, I am very much obliged, but I never drink coffee, much as I would like to. You did see me take up Luigi's cup, it is true, but if you noticed, I didn't carry it to my mouth, but to his."

"Y—es, I thought you did. Did you mean to?"

"How?"

The widow was a little embarrassed again. She said:

"I don't know but what I'm foolish, and you mustn't mind; but you see, he got the coffee I was expecting to see you drink, and you got a potato that I thought he was going to get. So I thought it might be a mistake all around, and everybody getting what wasn't intended for him."

Both twins laughed and Luigi said:

"Dear madam, there wasn't any mistake. We are always helping each other that way. It is a great economy for us both; it saves time and labor. We have a system of signs which nobody can notice or understand but ourselves. If I am using both my hands and want some coffee, I make the sign and Angelo furnishes it to me; and you saw that when he needed a potato I delivered it."

"How convenient!"

"Yes, and often of the extremest value. Take the Mississippi boats, for instance. They are always over-crowded. There is table-room for only half of the passengers, therefore they have to set a second table for the second half. The stewards rush both parties, they give them no time to eat a satisfying meal, both divisions leave the table hungry. It isn't so with us. Angelo books himself for the one table, I book myself for the other. Neither of us eats anything at the other's table, but just simply works—works. Thus, you see there are four hands to feed Angelo, and the same four to feed me. Each of us eats two meals."

The old lady was dazed with admiration, and kept saying, "It is *per*fectly wonderful, perfectly wonderful!" and the boy Joe licked his chops enviously, but said nothing—at least aloud.

"Yes," continued Luigi, "our construction may have its disadvantages—in fact, *has*—but it also has its compensations, of one sort and another. Take travel, for instance. Travel is enormously expensive, in all countries; we have been obliged to do a vast deal of it—come, Angelo, don't put any more sugar in your tea, I'm just over one indigestion and don't want another right away—been obliged to do a great deal of it, as I was saying. Well, we always travel as one person, since we occupy but one seat; so we save half the fare."

"How romantic!" interjected Rowena, with effusion.

"Yes, my dear young lady, and how practical too, and economical. In Europe, beds in the hotels are not charged with the board, but separately—another saving, for we stood to our rights and paid for the one bed only. The landlords often insisted that as both of us occupied the bed we ought——"

"No, they didn't," said Angelo. "They did it only twice, and in both cases it was a double bed—a rare thing in Europe—and the double bed gave them some excuse. Be fair to the landlords; twice doesn't constitute 'often.' "

"Well, that depends—that depends. I knew a man who fell down a well twice. He said he didn't mind the first time, but he thought the second time was once too often. Have I misused that word, Mrs. Cooper?"

"To tell the truth, I was afraid you had, but it seems to look, now, like you hadn't." She stopped, and was evidently struggling with the difficult problem a moment, then she added in the tone of one who is convinced without being converted, "It seems so, but I can't somehow tell why."

Rowena thought Luigi's retort was wonderfully quick and bright, and she remarked to herself with satisfaction that there wasn't any young native of Dawson's Landing that could have risen to the occasion like that. Luigi detected the applause in her face, and expressed his pleasure and his thanks with his eyes; and so eloquently withal, that the girl was proud and pleased, and hung out the delicate sign of it on her cheeks.

Luigi went on, with animation:

"Both of us get a bath for one ticket, theater seat for one ticket, pew-rent is on the same basis, but at peep-shows we pay double."

"We have much to be thankful for," said Angelo, impressively, with a reverent light in his eye and a reminiscent tone in his voice, "we have been greatly blessed. As a rule, what one of us has lacked, the other, by the bounty of Providence, has been able to supply. My brother is hardy, I am not; he is very masculine, assertive, aggressive; I am much less so. I am subject to illness, he is never ill. I cannot abide medicines, and cannot take them, but he has no prejudice against them, and——"

"Why, goodness gracious," interrupted the widow, "when you are sick, does he take the medicine for you?"

"Always, madam."

"Why, I never heard such a thing in my life! I think it's beautiful of you."

"Oh, madam, it's nothing, don't mention it, it's really nothing at all."

"But I say it's beautiful, and I stick to it!" cried the widow, with a speaking moisture in her eye. "A well brother to take the medicine for his poor sick brother—I wish I had such a son," and she glanced reproachfully at her boys. "I declare I'll never rest till I've shook you by the hand," and she scrambled out of her chair in a fever of generous enthusiasm, and made for the twins, blind with her tears, and began to shake. The boy Joe corrected her:

"You're shaking the wrong one, ma."

This flurried her, but she made a swift change and went on shaking.

"Got the wrong one again ma," said the boy.

"Oh, shut up, can't you!" said the widow, embarrassed and irritated. "Give me *all* your hands, I want to shake them all; for I know you are both just as good as you can be."

It was a victorious thought, a master-stroke of diplomacy, though, that never occurred to her and she cared nothing for diplomacy. She shook the four hands in turn cordially, and went back to her place in a state of high and fine exaltation that made her look young and handsome.

"Indeed I owe everything to Luigi," said Angelo, affectionately. "But for him I could not have survived our boyhood days, when we were friendless and poor—ah, so poor! We lived from hand to mouth—lived on the coarse fare of unwilling charity, and for weeks and weeks together not a morsel of food passed my lips, for its character revolted me and I could not eat it. But for Luigi I should have died. He ate for us both."

"How noble!" sighed Rowena.

"Do you hear that?" said the widow, severely, to her boys.

"Let it be an example to you—I mean you, Joe."

Joe gave his head a barely perceptible disparaging toss and said: "Et for both. It ain't anything—I'd a done it."

"Hush, if you haven't got any better manners than that. You don't see the point at all. It wasn't good food."

"I don't care—it was food, and I'd 'a et it if it was rotten."

"Shame! Such language! Can't you understand? They were starving—actually starving—and he ate for both, and——"

"Shucks! you gimme a chance and I'll—"

"There, now—close your head! and don't you open it again till you're asked."

[Angelo goes on and tells how his parents the Count and Countess had to fly from Florence for political reasons, and died poor in Berlin bereft of their great property by confiscation; and how he and Luigi had to travel with a freak-show during two years and suffer semi-starvation.]

"That hateful black-bread! but I seldom ate anything during that time; that was poor Luigi's affair——"

"I'll never *Mister* him again!" cried the widow, with strong emotion, "he's Luigi to me, from this out!"

"Thank you a thousand times, madam, a thousand times! though in truth I don't deserve it."

"Ah, Luigi is always the fortunate one when honors are showering," said Angelo, plaintively, "now what have I done, Mrs. Cooper, that you leave me out? Come, you must strain a point in my favor."

"Call you Angelo? Why, certainly I will; what are you thinking of! In the case of twins, why——"

"But, ma, you're breaking up the story—do let him go on."

"You keep still, Rowena Cooper, and he can go on all the better, I reckon. One interruption don't hurt, it's two that makes the trouble."

"But you've added one, now, and that is three."

"Rowena! I will not allow you to talk back at me when you have got nothing rational to say."

CHAPTER III

[After breakfast the whole village crowded in, and there was a grand reception in honor of the twins; and at the close of it the gifted "freak" captured everybody's admiration by sitting down at the piano and knocking out a classic four-handed piece in great style. Then the Judge took it—or them—driving in his buggy and showed off his village.]

All along the streets the people crowded the windows and stared at the amazing twins. Troops of young boys flocked after the buggy, excited and yelling. At first the dogs showed no interest. They thought they merely saw three men in a buggy—a matter of no consequence; but when they found out the facts of the case, they altered their opinion pretty radically, and joined the boys, expressing their minds as they came. Other dogs got interested; indeed all the dogs. It was a spirited sight to see them coming leaping fences, tearing around corners, swarming out of every by-street and alley. The noise they made was something beyond belief—or praise. They did not seem to be moved by malice but only by prejudice, the common human prejudice against lack of conformity. If the twins turned their heads, the broke and fled in every direction, but stopped at a safe distance and faced about; and then formed and came on again as soon as the strangers showed them their back. Negroes and farmers' wives took to the woods when the buggy came upon them suddenly, and altogether the drive was pleasant and animated, and a refreshment all around.

[It was a long and lively drive. Angelo was a Methodist; Luigi was a Freethinker. The Judge was very proud of his Freethinker Society, which was flourishing along in a most prosperous way and already had two members— himself and the obscure and neglected Pudd'nhead Wilson. It was to meet that evening, and he invited Luigi to join; a thing which Luigi was glad to do, partly because it would please himself, and partly because it would gravel Angelo.]

They had now arrived at the widow's gate, and the excursion ended. The twins politely expressed their obligations for the pleasant outing which had been afforded them; to which the Judge bowed his thanks, and then said he would now go and arrange for the Freethinkers' meeting, and would call for Count Luigi in the evening.

"For you also, dear sir," he added hastily, turning to Angelo and bowing. "In addressing myself particularly to your brother, I was not meaning to leave you out. It was an unintentional rudeness, I assure you, and due wholly to accident—accident and preoccupation. I beg you to forgive me."

His quick eye had seen the sensitive blood mount into Angelo's face, betraying the wound that had been inflicted. The sting of the slight had gone deep, but the apology was so prompt, and so evidently sincere, that the hurt was almost immediately healed, and a forgiving smile testified to the kindly Judge that all was well again.

Concealed behind Angelo's modest and unassuming exterior, and unsuspected by any but his intimates, was a lofty pride, a pride of almost abnormal proportions indeed, and this rendered him ever the prey of slights; and although they were almost always imaginary ones, they hurt none the less on that account. By ill fortune Judge Driscoll had happened to touch his sorest point, *i. e.*, his conviction that his brother's presence was welcomer everywhere than his own; that he was often invited, out of mere courtesy, where only his brother was wanted, and that in a majority of cases he would not be included in an invitation if he could be left out without offence. A sensitive nature like this is necessarily subject to moods; moods which traverse the whole gamut of feeling; moods which know all the climes of emotion, from the sunny heights of joy to the black abyss of despair. At times, in his seasons of deepest depression, Angelo almost wished that he and his brother might become segregated from each other and be separate individuals, like other men. But of course as soon as his mind cleared and these diseased imaginings passed away, he shuddered at the repulsive thought, and earnestly prayed that it might visit him no more. To be separate, and as other men are! How awkward it would seem; how unendurable. What would he do with is hands, his arms? How would his legs feel? How odd, and strange, and grotesque every action, attitude, movement, gesture would be. To sleep by himself, eat by himself, walk by himself—how lonely, how unspeakably lonely! No, no, any fate but that. In every way and from every point, the idea was revolting.

This was of course natural; to have felt otherwise would have been unnatural. He had known no life but a combined one; he had been familiar with it from his birth; he was not able to conceive of any other as being agreeable, or even bearable. To him, in the privacy of his secret thoughts, all other men were monsters, deformities; and during three-fourths of his life their aspect had filled him with what promised to be an unconquerable aversion. But at eighteen his eye began to take note of female beauty; and little by little, undefined longings grew up in his heart, under whose softening influences the old stubborn aversion gradually diminished, and finally disappeared. Men were still monstrosities to him, still deformities, and in his sober moments he had no desire to be like them, but their strange and unsocial and uncanny construction was no longer offensive to him.

This had been a hard day for him, physically and mentally. He had been called in the morning before he had quite slept off the effects of the liquor which Luigi had drunk; and so, for the first half hour had had the seedy feeling, and languor, the brooding depression, the cobwebby mouth and druggy taste that come of dissipation and are so ill a preparation for bodily or intellectual activities; the long violent strain of the reception had followed; and this had been followed, in turn, by the dreary sight-seeing, the Judge's wearying explanations and laudations of the sights, and the stupefying clamor of the dogs. As a congrous conclusion, a fitting end, his feelings had been hurt, a slight had been put upon him. He would have been glad to forego dinner and betake himself to rest and sleep, but he held his peace and said no word, for he knew his brother, Luigi, was fresh, unweary, full of life, spirit, energy; he would have scoffed at the idea of wasting valuable time on a bed or a sofa, and would have refused permission.

CHAPTER IV

Rowena was dining out, Joe and Harry were belated at play, there were but three chairs and four persons that noon at the home dinner-table—the twins, the widow, and her chum, Aunt Betsy Hale. The widow soon perceived that Angelo's spirits were as low as Luigi's were high, and also that he had a jaded look. Her motherly solicitude was aroused, and she tried to get him interested in the talk and win him to a happier frame of mind, but the cloud of sadness remained on his countenance. Luigi lent his help, too. He used a form and a phrase which he was always accustomed to employ in these circumstances. He gave his brother an affectionate slap on the shoulder and said, encouragingly:

"Cheer up, the worst is yet to come!"

But this did no good. It never did. If anything it made the matter worse, as a rule, because it irritated Angelo. This made it a favorite with Luigi. By and by the widow said:

"Angelo, you are tired, you've overdone yourself; you go right to bed, after dinner, and get a good nap and a rest, then you'll be all right."

"Indeed I would give anything if I could do that, madam."

"And what's to hender, I'd like to know? Land, the room's yours to do what you please with! The idea that you can't do what you like with your own!"

"But you see, there's one prime essential—an essential of the very first importance—which isn't my own."

"What is that?"

"My body."

The old ladies looked puzzled, and Aunt Betsy Hale said:

"Why bless your heart, how is that?"

"It's my brother's."

"Your brother's! I don't quite understand. I supposed it belonged to both of you."

"So it does. But not to both at the same time."

"That is mighty curious; I don't see how it can be. I shouldn't think it could be managed that way."

"Oh, it's a good enough arrangement, and goes very well; in fact it wouldn't do to have it otherwise. I find that the teetotalers and the anti-teetotalers hire the use of the same hall for their meetings. Both parties don't use it at the same time, do they?"

"You bet they don't!" said both old ladies in a breath.

"And moreover," said Aunt Betsy, "the Freethinkers and the Baptist Bible-class use the same room over the Market-house, but you can take my word for it they don't mush up together and use it at the same time."

"Very well," said Angelo, "you understand it now. And it stands to reason that the arrangement couldn't be improved. I'll prove it to you. If our legs tried to obey two wills, how could we ever get anywhere? I would start one way, Luigi would start another, at the same moment—the result would be a standstill, wouldn't it?"

"As sure as you are born! Now ain't that wonderful! A body would never have thought of it."

"We should always be arguing and fussing and disputing over the merest trifles. We should lose worlds of time, for we couldn't go down-stairs or up, couldn't go to bed, couldn't rise, couldn't wash, couldn't dress, couldn't stand up, couldn't sit down, couldn't even cross our legs, without calling a meeting first and explaining the case and passing resolutions, and getting consent. It wouldn't ever do—now would it?"

"Do? Why, it would wear a person out in a week! Did you ever hear anything like it, Patsy Cooper?"

"Oh, you 'll find there's more than one thing about them that ain't commonplace," said the widow, with the complacent air of a person with a property-right in a novelty that is under admiring scrutiny.

"Well now, how ever do you manage it? I don't mind saying I'm suffering to know."

"He who made us," said Angelo reverently, "and with us this difficulty, also provided a way out of it. By a mysterious law of our being, each of us has utter and indisputable command of our body a week at a time, turn and turn about."

"Well, I never! Now ain't that beautiful!"

"Yes, it is beautiful and infinitely wise and just. The week ends every Saturday at midnight to the minute, to the second, to the last shade of a fraction of a second, infallibly, unerringly, and in that instant the one brother's power over the body vanishes and the other brother takes possession, asleep or awake."

"How marvelous are His ways, and past finding out!"

Luigi said: "So exactly to the instant does the change come, that during our stay in many of the great cities of the world, the public clocks were regulated by it; and as hundreds of thousands of private clocks and watches were set and corrected in accordance with the public clocks, we really furnished the standard time for the entire city."

"Don't tell me that He don't do miracles any more! Blowing down the walls of Jericho with rams' horns wa'n't as difficult, in my opinion."

"And that is not all," said Angelo. "A thing that is even more marvelous, perhaps, is the fact that the change takes note of longitude and fits itself to the meridian we are on. Luigi is in command this week. Now, if on Saturday night at a moment before midnight we could fly in an instant to a point fifteen degrees west of here, he would hold possession of the power another hour, for the change observes *local* time and no other."

Betsy Hale was deeply impressed, and said with solemnity:

"Patsy Cooper, for *de*tail it lays over the Passage of the Red Sea."

"Now, I shouldn't go as far as that," said Aunt Patsy, "but if you've a mind to say Sodom and Gomorrah, I am with you, Betsy Hale."

"I am agreeable, then, though I do think I was right, and I believe Parson Maltby would say the same. Well now, there's another thing. Suppose one of you wants to borrow the legs a minute from the one that's got them, could he let him?"

"Yes, but we hardly ever do that. There were disagreeable results, several times, and so we very seldom ask or grant the privilege, nowdays, and we never even think of such a thing unless the case is extremely urgent. Besides, a week's possession at a time seems so little that we can't bear to spare a minute of it. People who have the use of their legs all the time never think of what a blessing it is, of course. It never occurs to them; it's just their natural ordinary condition, and so it does not excite them at all. But when I wake up, on Sunday morning, and it's my week and I feel the power all through me, oh, such a wave of exultation and thanksgiving goes surging over me, and I want to shout 'I can walk! I can walk!' Madam, do you ever, at your uprising want to shout 'I can walk! I can walk'?"

"No, you poor unfortunate cretur', but I'll never get out of my bed again without *doing* it! Laws, to think I've had this unspeakable blessing all my long life and never had the grace to thank the good Lord that gave it to me!"

Tears stood in the eyes of both the old ladies and the widow said, softly:

"Betsy Hale, we have learned something, you and me."

The conversation now drifted wide, but by and by floated back once more to that admired detail, the rigid and beautiful impartiality with which the possession of power had been distributed between the twins. Aunt Betsy saw in it a far finer justice than human law exhibits in related cases. She said:

"In my opinion it ain't right now, and never has been right, the way a twin born a quarter of a minute sooner than the other one gets all the land and grandeurs and nobilities in the old countries and his brother has to go bare and be a nobody. Which of you was born first?"

Angelo's head was resting against Luigi's; weariness had overcome him, and for the past five minutes he had been peacefully sleeping. The old ladies had dropped their voices to a lulling drone, to help him steal the rest his brother wouldn't take him up-stairs to get. Luigi listened a moment to Angelo's regular breathing, then said in a voice barely audible:

"We were both born at the same time, but I am six months older than he is."

"For the land's sake!"

" 'Sh! don't wake him up; he wouldn't like my telling this. It has always been kept secret till now."

"But how in the world can it be? If you were both born at the same time, how can one of you be older than the other?"

"It is very simple, and I assure you it is true. I was born with a full crop of hair, he was as bald as an egg for six months. I could walk six months before he could make a step. I finished teething six months ahead of him. I began to take solids six months before he left the breast. I began to talk six months before he could say a word. Last, and absolutely unassailable proof, *the sutures in my skull closed six months ahead of his*. Always just that six months difference to a day. Was that accident? Nobody is going to claim that, I'm sure. It was ordained—it was law—it had its meaning, and we know what that meaning was. Now what does this overwhelming body of evidence establish? It establishes just one thing, and that thing it establishes beyond any peradventure whatever. Friends, we would not have it known for the world, and I must beg you to keep it strictly to yourselves, but the truth is, *we are no more twins than you are*."

The two old ladies were stunned, paralyzed—petrified, one may almost say—and could only sit and gaze vacantly at each other for some moments; then Aunt Betsy Hale said impressively:

"There's no getting around proof like that. I do believe it's the most amazing thing I ever heard of." She sat silent a moment or two and breathing hard with excitement, then she looked up and surveyed the strangers steadfastly a little while, and added: "Well, it does beat me, but I would have took you for twins anywhere."

"So would I, so would I," said Aunt Patsy with the emphasis of a certainty that is not impaired by any shade of doubt.

"*Any*body would—anybody in the world, I don't care who he is," said Aunt Betsy with decision.

"You won't tell," said Luigi, appealingly.

"Oh, dear no!" answered both ladies promptly, "you can trust us, don't you be afraid."

"That is good of you, and kind. Never let on; treat us always as if we were twins."

"You can depend on us," said Aunt Betsy, "but it won't be easy, because now that I know you ain't, you don't *seem* so."

Luigi muttered to himself with satisfaction: "That swindle has gone through without change of cars."

It was not very kind of him to load the poor things up with a secret like that, which would always be flying to their tongues' ends every time they heard any one speak of the strangers as twins, and would become harder and harder to hang on to with every recurrence of the temptation to tell it, while the torture of retaining it would increase with every new strain that was applied; but he never thought of that, and probably would not have worried much about it if he had.

A visitor was announced—some one to see the twins. They withdrew to the parlor, and the two old ladies began to discuss with interest the strange things which they had been listening to. When they had finished the matter to their satisfaction, and Aunt Betsy rose to go, she stopped to ask a question:

"How does things come on between Roweny and Tom Driscoll?"

"Well, about the same. He writes tolerable often, and she answers tolerable seldom."

"Where is he?"

"In St. Louis, I believe, though he's such a gad-about that a body can't be very certain of him, I reckon."

"Don't Roweny know?"

"Oh, yes, like enough. I haven't asked her lately."

"Do you know how him and the Judge are getting along now?"

"First-rate, I believe. Mrs. Pratt says so; and being right in the house, and sister to the one and aunt to t'other, of course she ought to know. She says the Judge is real fond of him when he's away, but frets when he's around and is vexed with his ways, and not sorry to have him go again. He has been gone three weeks this time—a pleasant thing for both of them, I reckon."

"Tom's ruther harum-scarum, but there ain't anything bad in him, I guess."

"Oh no, he's just young, that's all. Still, twenty-three is old, in one way. A young man ought to be earning his living by that time. If Tom were doing that, or was even trying to do it, the Judge would be a heap better satisfied with him. Tom's always going to begin, but somehow he can't seem to find just the opening he likes."

"Well now, it's partly the Judge's own fault. Promising the boy his property wasn't the way to set him earning a fortune of his own. But what do you think—is Roweny beginning to lean any towards him, or ain't she?"

Aunt Patsy had a secret in her bosom; she wanted to keep it there, but nature was too strong for her. She drew Aunt Betsy aside, and said in her most confidential and mysterious manner:

"Don't you breathe a syllable to a soul—I'm going to tell you something. In my opinion Tom Driscoll's chances were considerable better yesterday than they are today."

"Patsy Cooper, what *do* you mean?"

"It's so, as sure as you're born. I wish you could 'a' been at breakfast and seen for yourself."

"You don't mean it!"

"Well, if I'm any judge, there's a leaning—there's a leaning, sure."

"My land! Which one of 'em is it?"

"I can't say for certain, but I think it's the youngest one—Anjy."

Then there were handshakings, and congratulations, and hopes, and so on, and the old ladies parted, perfectly happy—the one in knowing something which the rest of the town didn't, and the other in having been the sole person able to furnish that knowledge.

The visitor who had called to see the twins was the Rev. Mr. Hotchkiss, pastor of the Baptist church. At the reception Angelo had told him he had lately experienced a change in his religious views, and was now desirous of becoming a Baptist, and would immediately join Mr. Hotchkiss's church. There was no time to say more, and the brief talk ended at that point. The minister was much gratified, and had dropped in for a moment, now, to invite the twins to attend his Bible-class at eight that evening. Angelo accepted, and was expecting Luigi to decline, but he did not, because he knew that the Bible-class and the Freethinkers met in the same room, and he wanted to treat his brother to the embarrassment of being caught in freethinking company.

CHAPTER V

[A long and vigorous quarrel follows, between the twins. And there is plenty to quarrel about, for Angelo was always seeking truth, and this obliged him to change and improve his religion with frequency, which wearied Luigi, and annoyed him too; for he had to be present at each new enlistment—which placed him in the false position of seeming to indorse and approve his brother's fickleness; moreover, he had to go to Angelo's prohibition meetings, and he hated them. On the other hand, when it was *his* week to command the legs he gave Angelo just cause of complaint, for he took him to circuses and horse-races and fandangoes, exposing him to all sorts of censure and criticism; and he drank, too; and whatever he drank went to Angelo's head instead of his own and made him act disgracefully. When the evening was come, the two attended the Freethinkers' meeting, where Angelo was sad and silent; then came the Bible-class and looked upon him coldly, finding him in such company. Then they went to Wilson's house, and Chapter XI of "Pudd'nhead Wilson" follows, which tells of the girl seen in Tom Driscoll's room; and closes with the kicking of Tom by Luigi at the anti-temperance mass meeting of the Sons of Liberty; with the addition of some account of Roxy's adventures as a chambermaid on a Mississippi boat. Her exchange of the children had been flippantly and farcically described in an earlier chapter.]

Next morning all the town was a-buzz with great news; Pudd'nhead Wilson had a law-case! The public astonishment was so great and the public curiosity so intense, that when the justice of the peace opened his court, the place was packed with people, and even the windows were full. Everybody was flushed and perspiring, the summer heat was almost unendurable.

Tom Driscoll had brought a charge of assault and battery against the twins. Robert Allen was retained by Driscoll, David Wilson by the defense. Tom, his native cheerfulness unannihilated by his back-breaking and bone-bruising passage across the massed heads of the Sons of Liberty the previous night, laughed his little customary laugh, and said to Wilson:

"I've kept my promise, you see: I'm throwing my business your way. Sooner than I was expecting, too."

"It's very good of you—particularly if you mean to keep it up."

"Well, I can't tell about that, yet. But we'll see. If I find you deserve it I'll take you under my protection and make your fame and fortune for you."

"I'll try to deserve it, Tom."

A jury was sworn in; then Mr. Allen said:

"We will detain your honor but a moment with this case. It is not one where any doubt of the fact of the assault can enter in. These gentlemen—the accused—kicked my client at the Market Hall last night; they kicked him with violence; with extraordinary violence; with even unprecedented violence, I may say; insomuch that he was lifted entirely off his feet and discharged into the midst of the audience. We can prove this by four hundred witnesses—we shall call but three. Mr. Harkness will take the stand."

Mr. Harkness being sworn, testified that he was chairman upon the occasion mentioned; that he was close at hand and saw the defendants in this action kick the plaintiff into the air and saw him descend among the audience.

"Take the witness," said Allen.

"Mr. Harkness," said Wilson, "you say you saw these gentlemen, my clients kick the plaintiff. Are you sure—and please remember that you are on oath—are you perfectly sure that you saw *both* of them kick him, or only one? Now be careful."

A bewildered look began to spread itself over the witness's face. He hesitated, stammered, but got out nothing. His eyes wandered to the twins and fixed themselves there with a vacant gaze.

"Please answer, Mr. Harkness, you are keeping the court waiting. It is a very simple question."

Counsel for the prosecution broke in with impatience:

"Your honor, the question is an irrelevant triviality. Necessarily they both kicked him, for they have but the one pair of legs, and both are responsible for them."

Wilson said, sarcastically:

"Will your honor permit this new witness to be sworn? He seems to possess knowledge which can be of the utmost value just at this moment—knowledge which would at once dispose of what every one must see is a very difficult question in this case. Brother Allen, will take the stand?"

"Go on with your case!" said Allen petulantly. The audience laughed, and got a warning from the court.

"Now, Mr. Harkness," said Wilson, insinuatingly, "we shall have to insist upon an answer to that question."

"I—er —well, of course I do not absolutely *know*, but in my opinion—"

"Never mind your opinion, sir—answer the question."

"I—why, I *can't* answer it."

"That will do, Mr. Harkness. Stand down."

The audience tittered, and the discomfited witness retired in a state of great embarrassment.

Mr. Wakeman took the stand and swore that he saw the twins kick the plaintiff off the platform. The defence took the witness.

"Mr. Wakeman, you have sworn that you saw these gentlemen kick the plaintiff. Do I understand you to swear that you saw them *both* do it?"

"Yes, sir,"—with decision.

"How do you know that both did it?"

"Because I *saw* them do it."

The audience laughed, and got another warning from the court.

"But by what means do you know that both, and not one, did it?"

"Well, in the first place, the insult was given to both of them equally, for they were called a pair of scissors. Of course they would both want to resent it, and so—"

"Wait! You are theorizing now. Stick to facts—counsel will attend to the arguments. Go on."

"Well, they both went over there—*that* I saw."

"Very good. Go on."

"And they both kicked him—I swear to it."

"Mr. Wakeman, was Count Luigi, here, willing to join the Sons of Liberty last night?"

"Yes, sir, he was. He did join, too, and drank a glass or two of whisky, like a man."

"Was his brother willing to join?"

"No, sir, he wasn't. He is a teetotaler, and was elected through a mistake."

"Was he given a glass of whisky?"

"Yes, sir, but of course that was another mistake, and not intentional. He wouldn't drink it. He set it down." A slight pause, then he added, casually and quite simply: "The plaintiff reached for it and hogged it."

There was a fine outburst of laughter, but as the justice was caught out himself, his reprimand was not very vigorous.

Mr. Allen jumped up and exclaimed: "I protest against these foolish irrelevancies. What have they to do with the case?"

Wilson said: "Calm yourself, brother, it was only an experiment. Now, Mr. Wakeman, if one of these gentlemen chooses to join an association and the other doesn't; and if one of them enjoys whisky and the other doesn't, but sets it aside and leaves it unprotected" (titter from the audience), "it seems to show that they have independent minds and tastes and preferences, and that one of them is able to approve of a thing at the very moment that the other is heartily disapproving of it. Doesn't it seem so to you?"

"Certainly it does. It's perfectly plain."

"Now then, it might be—I only say it might be—that one of these brothers wanted to kick the plaintiff last night, and that the other didn't want that humiliating punishment inflicted upon him in that public way and before all those people. Isn't that possible?

"Of course it is. It's more than possible. I don't believe the blonde one would kick anybody. It was the other one that——"

"Silence!" shouted the plaintiff's counsel, and went on with an angry sentence which was lost in the wave of laughter that swept the house.

"That will do, Mr. Wakemen," said Wilson, "you may stand down."

The third witness was called. He had seen the twins kick the plaintiff. Mr. Wilson took the witness.

"Mr. Rogers, you say you saw these accused gentlemen kick the plaintiff?"

"Yes, sir."

"Both of them?"

"Yes, sir."

"Which of them kicked him first?"

"Why—they—they both kicked him at the same time."

"Are you perfectly sure of that?"

"Yes, sir."

"What makes you sure of it?"

"Why, I stood right behind them, and *saw* them do it."

"How many kicks were delivered?"

"Only one."

"If two men kick, the result should be two kicks, shouldn't it?"

"Why—why—yes, as a rule."

"Then what do you think went with the other kick?"

"I—well—the fact is, I wasn't thinking of two being necessary, this time."

"What do you think now?"

"Well, I—I'm sure I don't quite know what to think, but I reckon that one of them did half of the kick and the other one did the other half."

Somebody in the crowd sung out: "It's the first sane thing that any of them has said."

The audience applauded. The judge said: "Silence! or I will clear the court."

Mr. Allen looked pleased, but Wilson did not seem disturbed. He said:

"Mr. Rogers, you have favored us with what you think and what you reckon, but as thinking and reckoning are not evidence, I will now give you a chance to come out with something positive, one way or the other, and shall require you to produce it. I will ask the accused to stand up and repeat the phenomenal kick of last night." The twins stood up. "Now, Mr. Rogers, please stand behind them."

A Voice: "No, stand in front!" (Laughter. Silenced by the court.) Another Voice: "No, give Tommy another highst!" (Laughter. Sharply rebuked by the court.)

"Now then, Mr. Rogers, two kicks shall be delivered, one after the other, and I give you my word that at least one of the two shall be delivered by one of the twins alone, without the slightest assistance from his brother. Watch sharply, for you have got to render a decision without any if's and and's in it." Rogers bent himself behind the twins with his palms just above his knees, in the modern attitude of the catcher at a base-ball match, and riveted his eyes on the pair of legs in front of him. "Are you ready, Mr. Rogers?"

"Ready, sir."

"Kick!"

The kick was launched.

"Have you got that one classified, Mr. Rogers?"

"Let me study a minute, sir."

"Take as much time as you please. Let me know when you are ready."

For as much as a minute Rogers pondered, with all eyes and a breathless interest fastened upon him. Then he gave the word: "Ready, sir."

"Kick!"

The kick that followed was an exact duplicate of the first one.

"Now then, Mr. Rogers, one of those kicks was an individual kick, not a mutual one. You will now state positively which was the mutual one."

The witness said, with a crestfallen look:

"I've got to give up. There ain't any man in the world that could tell t'other from which, sir."

"Do you still assert that last night's kick was a mutual kick?"

"Indeed I don't, sir."

"That will do, Mr. Rogers. If my brother Allen desires to address the court, your honor, very well; but as far as I am concerned I am ready to let the case be at once delivered into the hands of this intelligent jury without comment."

Mr. Justice Robinson had been in office only two months, and in that short time had not had many cases to try, of course. He had no knowledge of laws and courts except what he had picked up since he came into office. He was a sore trouble to the lawyers, for his rulings were pretty eccentric sometimes, and he stood by them with Roman simplicity and fortitude; but the people were well satisfied with him, for they saw that his intentions were always right, that he was entirely impartial, and that he usually made up in good sense what he lacked in technique, so to speak. He now perceived that there was likely to be a miscarriage of justice here, and he rose to the occasion.

"Wait a moment, gentlemen," he said, "it is plain that an assault has been committed—it is plain to anybody; but the way things are going, the guilty will certainly escape conviction. I cannot allow this. Now—"

"But, your honor!" said Wilson, interrupting him, earnestly but respectfully, "you are deciding the case yourself, whereas the jury—"

"Never mind the jury, Mr. Wilson; the jury will have a chance when there is a reasonable doubt for them to take hold of—which there isn't, so far. There is no doubt whatever that an assault has been committed. The attempt to show that both of the accused committed it has failed. Are they both to escape justice on that account? Not in this court, if I can prevent it. It appears to have been a mistake to bring the charge against them as a corporation; each should have been charged in his capacity as an individual, and—"

"But your honor!" said Wilson, "in fairness to my clients I must insist that inasmuch as the prosecution did not separate the—"

"No wrong will be done your clients, sir—they will be protected; also the public and the offended laws. Mr. Allen, you will amend your pleadings, and put one of the accused on trial at a time."

Wilson broke in: "But your honor! this is wholly unprecedented! To imperil an accused person by arbitrarily altering and widening the charge against him in order to compass his conviction when the charge as originally brought promises to fail to convict, is a thing unheard of before."

"Unheard of *where?*"

"In the courts of this or any other State."

The judge said with dignity: "I am not acquainted with the customs of other courts, and am not concerned to know what they are. I am responsible for this court, and I cannot conscientiously allow my judgment to be warped and my judicial liberty hampered by trying to conform to the caprices of other courts, be they—"

"But, your honor, the oldest and highest courts in Europe—"

"This court is not run on the European plan, Mr. Wilson; it is not run on any plan but its own. It has a plan of its own; and that plan is, to find justice for both State and accused, no matter what happens to be practice and custom in Europe or anywhere else." (Great applause.) "Silence! It has not been the custom of this court to imitate other courts; it has not been the custom of this court to take shelter behind the decisions of other courts, and we will not begin now. We will do the best we can by the light that God has given us, and while this court continues to have His approval, it will remain indifferent to what other organizations may think of it." (Applause.) "Gentlemen, I *must* have order!—quiet yourselves! Mr. Allen, you will now proceed against the prisoners one at a time. Go on with the case."

Allen was not at his ease. However, after whispering a moment with his client and with one or two other people, he rose and said:

"Your honor, I find it to be reported and believed that the accused are able to act independently in many ways, but that this independence does not extend to their legs, authority over their legs being vested exclusively in the one brother during a specific term of days, and then passing to the other brother for a like term, and so on, by regular alternation. I could call witnesses who would prove that the accused had revealed to them the existence of this extraordinary fact, and had also made known which of them was in possession of the legs yesterday—and this would of course indicate where the guilt of the assault belongs—but as this would be mere hearsay evidence, these revelations not having been made under oath—"

"Never mind about that, Mr. Allen. It may not all be hearsay. We shall see. It may at least help to put us on the right track. Call the witnesses."

"Then I will call Mr. John Buckstone, who is now present, and I beg that Mrs. Patsy Cooper may be sent for. Take the stand, Mr. Buckstone."

Buckstone took the oath, and then testified that on the previous evening the Count Angelo Cappello had protested against going to the hall, and had called all present to witness that he was going by compulsion and would not go if he could help himself. Also, that the Count Luigi had replied sharply that he would *go*, just the same, and that he, Count Luigi, would see to that, himself. Also, that upon Count Angelo's complaining about being kept on his legs so long, Count Luigi retorted with apparent surprise, '*Your* legs!—I like your impudence!' "

"*Now* we are getting at the kernel of the thing," observed the judge, with grave and earnest satisfaction. "It looks as if the Count Luigi was in possession of the battery at the time of the assault."

Nothing further was elicited from Mr. Buckstone on direct examination. Mr. Wilson took the witness.

"Mr. Buckstone, about what time was it that that conversation took place?"

"Toward nine yesterday evening, sir."

"Did you then proceed directly to the hall?"

"Yes, sir."

"How long did it take you to go there?"

"Well, we walked; and as it was from the extreme edge of town, and there was no hurry, I judge it took us about twenty minutes, maybe a trifle more."

"About what hour was the kick delivered?"

"At thirteen minutes and a half to ten."

"Admirable! You are a pattern witness, Mr. Buckstone. How did you happen to look at your watch at that particular moment?"

"I always do it when I see an assault. It's likely I shall be called as a witness, and it's a good point to have."

"It would be well if others were as thoughtful. Was anything said, between the conversation at my house and the assault, upon the detail which we are now examining into?"

"No, sir."

"If power over the mutual legs was in the possession of one brother at nine, and passed into the possession of the other one during the next thirty or forty minutes, do you think you could have detected the change?"

"By no means!"

"That is all, Mr. Buckstone."

Mrs. Patsy Cooper was called. The crowd made way for her, and she came smiling and bowing through the narrow human lane, with Betsy Hale, as escort and support, smiling and bowing in her wake, the audience breaking into welcoming cheers as the old favorites filed along. The judge did not check this kindly demonstration of homage and affection, but let it run its course unrebuked.

The old ladies stopped and shook hands with the twins with effusion, then gave the judge a friendly nod, and bustled into the seats provided for them. They immediately began to deliver a volley of eager questions at the friends around them: "What is this thing for?" "What is that thing for?" "Who is that young man that's writing at the desk? Why, I declare, it's Jack Bunce! I thought he was sick." "Which is the jury? Why, is *that* the jury? Billy Price and Job Turner, and Jack Lounsbury, and—well, I never!" "Now who would ever a'thought—"

But they were gently called to order at this point, and asked not to talk in court. Their tongues fell silent, but the radiant interest in their faces remained, and their gratitude for the blessing of a new sensation and a novel experience still beamed undimmed from their eyes. Aunt Patsy stood up and took the oath, and Mr. Allen explained the point in issue, and asked her to go on, now, in her own way, and throw as much light upon it as she could. She toyed with her reticule a moment or two, as if considering where to begin, then she said:

"Well, the way of it is this. They are Luigi's legs a week at a time, and then they are Angelo's, and he can do whatever he wants to with them."

"You are making a mistake, Aunt Patsy Cooper," said the judge. "You shouldn't state that as a *fact,* because you don't know it to *be* a fact."

"What's the reason I don't?" said Aunt Patsy, bridling a little.

"What is the reason that you do know it?"

"The best in the world—because they told me."

"That isn't a reason."

"Well, for the land's sake! Betsy Hale, do you hear that?"

"*Hear* it? I should think so," said Aunt Betsy, rising and facing the court. "Why, Judge, I was there and heard it myself. Luigi says to Angelo—no, it was Angelo said it to—"

"Come, come, Mrs. Hale, pray sit down, and—"

"Certainly, it's all right, I'm going to sit down presently, but not until I've—"

"But you *must* sit down!"

"*Must!* Well, upon my word if things ain't getting to a pretty pass when—"

The house broke into laughter, but was promptly brought to order, and meantime Mr. Allen persuaded the old lady to take her seat. Aunt Patsy continued:

"Yes, they told me that, and I know it's true. They're Luigi's legs this week, but—"

"Ah, *they* told you that, did they?" said the justice, with interest.

"Well no, I don't know that *they* told me, but that's neither here nor there. I know, without that, that at dinner yesterday, Angelo was as tired as a dog, and yet Luigi wouldn't lend him the legs to go up-stairs and take a nap with."

"Did he ask for them?"

"Let me see—it seems to me somehow, that—that—Aunt Betsy, do you remember whether he—"

"Never mind about what Aunt Betsy remembers—she is not a witness; we only want to know what you remember, yourself," said the judge.

"Well, it does seem to me that you are most cantankerously particular about a little thing, Sim Robinson. Why, when I can't remember a thing myself, I always—"

"Ah, *please* go on!"

"Now how *can* she when you keep fussing at her all the time?" said Aunt Betsy. "Why, with a person pecking at *me* that way, I should get that fuzzled and fuddled that—"

She was on her feet again, but Allen coaxed her into her seat once more, while the court squelched the mirth of the house. Then the judge said:

"Madam, do you know—do you absolutely *know,* independently of anything these gentlemen have told you—that the power over their legs passes from the one to the other regularly every week?"

"Regularly? Bless your heart, regularly ain't any name for the exactness of it! All the big cities in Europe used to set the clocks by it." (Laughter, *suppressed by the court.*)

"How do you *know?* That is the question. Please answer it plainly and squarely."

"Don't you talk to me like that, Sim Robinson—I won't have it. How do I know, indeed! How do *you* know what you know? Because somebody told you. You didn't invent it out of your own head, did you? Why, these twins are the truthfulest people in the world; and I don't think it becomes you to sit up there and throw slurs at them when they haven't been doing anything to you. And they are orphans besides—both of them. All—"

But Aunt Betsy was up again, now, and both old ladies were talking at once and with all their might; but as the house was weltering in a storm of laughter, and the judge was hammering his desk with an iron paper-weight, one could only see them talk, not hear them. At last, when quiet was restored, the court said:

"Let the ladies retire."

"But, your honor, I have the right, in the interest of my clients, to cross-exam—"

"You'll not need to exercise it, Mr. Wilson—the evidence is thrown out."

"Thrown out!" said Aunt Patsy, ruffled; "and what's it thrown out for, I'd like to know."

"And so would I, Patsy Cooper. It seems to me that if we can save these poor persecuted strangers, it is our bounden duty to stand up here and talk for them till—"

"There, there, there, *do* sit down!"

It cost some trouble and a good deal of coaxing, but they were got into their seats at last. The trial was soon ended, now. The twins themselves became witnesses in their own defense. They established the fact, upon oath, that the leg-power passed from one to the other every Saturday night at twelve o'clock, sharp. But on cross-examination their counsel would not allow them to tell whose week of power the current week was. The judge insisted upon their answering, and proposed to compel them; but even the prosecution took fright and came to the rescue then, and helped stay the sturdy jurist's revolutionary hand. So the case had to go to the jury with that important point hanging in the air. They were out an hour, and brought in this verdict:

"We the jury do find: 1, that an assault was committed, as charged; 2, that it was committed by one of the persons accused, he having been seen to do it by several credible witnesses: 3, but that his identity is so merged in his brother's that we have not been able to tell which was him. We cannot convict both, for only one is guilty. We cannot acquit both, for only one is innocent. Our verdict is that justice has been defeated by dispensation of God, and ask to be discharged from further duty."

This was read aloud in court and brought out a burst of hearty applause. The old ladies made a spring at the twins, to shake and congratulate, but were gently disengaged by Mr. Wilson and softly crowded back into their places.

The Judge rose in his little tribune, laid aside his silver-bowed spectacles, roached his gray hair up with his fingers, and said, with dignity and solemnity, and even with a certain pathos:

"In all my experience on the bench, I have not seen Justice bow her head in shame in this court until this day. You little realize what far-reaching harm has just been wrought here under the fickle forms of law. Imitation is the bane of courts—I thank God that this one is free from the contamination of that vice—and in no long time you will see the fatal work of this hour seized upon by profligate so-called guardians of justice in all the wide circumstance of this plane and perpetuated in their pernicious decisions. I wash my hands of this iniquity. I would have compelled these culprits to expose their guilt, but support failed me where I had most right to expect aid and encouragement. And I was confronted by a law made in the interest of crime, which protects the criminal from testifying against himself. Yet I had precedents of my own whereby I had set aside that law on two different occasions and thus succeeded in convicting criminals to whose crimes there were no witnesses but themselves. What have you accomplished this day? Do you realize it? You have set adrift, unadmonished, in this community, two men endowed with an awful and mysterious gift, a hidden and grisly power for evil—a power by which each in his turn may commit crime after crime of the most heinous character, and no man be able to tell which is the guilty or which the innocent party in any case of them all. Look to your homes—look to your property—look to your lives—for you have need!

"Prisoners at the bar, stand up. Through suppression of evidence, a jury of your—our—countrymen have been obliged to deliver a verdict concerning your case which stinks to heaven with the rankness of its injustice. By its terms you, the guilty one, go free with the innocent. Depart in peace, and come no more! The costs devolve upon the outraged plaintiff—another iniquity. The Court stands dissolved."

Almost everybody crowded forward to overwhelm the twins and their counsel with congratulations; but presently the two old aunties dug the duplicates out and bore them away in triumph through the hurrahing crowd, while lots of new friends carried Pudd'nhead Wilson off tavern-wards to feast him and "wet down" his great and victorious entry into the legal arena. To Wilson, so long familiar with neglect and depreciation, this strange new incense of popularity and admiration was as a fragrance blown from the fields of paradise. A happy man was Wilson.

CHAPTER VI

[A deputation came in the evening and conferred upon Wilson the welcome honor of a nomination for mayor; for the village has just been converted into a city by charter. Tom skulks out of challenging the twins. Judge Driscoll thereupon challenges Angelo, (accused by Tom of doing the kicking;) he declines, but Luigi accepts in his place against Angelo's timid protest.]

It was late Saturday night—nearing eleven.

The Judge and his second found the rest of the war party at the further end of the vacant ground, near the haunted house. Pudd'nhead Wilson advanced to meet them, and said anxiously—

"I must say a word in behalf of my principal's proxy, Count Luigi, to whom you have kindly granted the privilege of fighting my principal's battle for him. It is growing late and Count Luigi is in great trouble lest midnight shall strike before the finish."

"It is another testimony," said Howard, approvingly. "That young man is fine all through. He wishes to save his brother the sorrow of fighting on the Sabbath, and he is right; it is the right and manly feeling and does him credit. We will make all possible haste."

Wilson said—

"There is also another reason—a consideration, in fact, which deeply concerns Count Luigi himself. These twins have command of their mutual legs turn about. Count Luigi is in command, now; but at midnight, possession will pass to my principal, Count Angelo, and—well, you can foresee what will happen. He will march straight off the field, and carry Luigi with him."

"Why! sure enough!" cried the Judge, "we have heard something about that extraordinary law of their being, already—-nothing very definite, it is true, as regards dates and durations of the power, but I see it is definite enough as regards to-night. Of course we must give Luigi every chance. Omit all the ceremonial possible, gentlemen, and place us in position."

The seconds at once tossed up a coin; Howard won the choice. He placed the Judge sixty feet from the haunted house and facing it; Wilson placed the twins within fifteen feet of the house and facing the Judge—necessarily. The pistol-case was opened and the long slim tubes taken out; when the moonlight glinted from them a shiver went through Angelo. The doctor was a fool, but a thoroughly well-meaning one, with a kind heart and a sincere disposition to oblige, but along with it an absence of tact which often hurt its effectiveness. He brought his box of lint and bandages, and asked Angelo to feel and see how soft and comfortable they were. Angelo's head fell over against Luigi's in a faint, and precious time was lost in bringing him to; which provoked Luigi into expressing his mind to the doctor with a good deal of vigor and frankness. After Angelo came to he was still so weak that Luigi was obliged to drink a stiff horn of brandy to brace him up.

The seconds now stepped at once to their posts, half way between the combatants, one of them on each side of the line of fire. Wilson was to count, very deliberately, "One—two—three—fire!—stop!" and the duelists could bang away at any time they chose during that recitation, but not after the last word. Angelo grew very nervous when he saw Wilson's hand rising slowly into the air as a sign to make ready, and he leaned his head against Luigi's and said—

"O, please take me away from here, I can't stay, I know I can't!"

"What in the world are you doing? Straighten up! What's the matter with you?—*you're* in no danger—nobody's going to shoot at you. Straighten up, I tell you!"

Angelo obeyed, just in time to hear—

"One—!"

"Bang!" Just one report, and a little tuft of white hair floated slowly to the Judge's feet in the moonlight. The Judge did not swerve; he still stood erect and motionless, like a statue, with his pistol-arm hanging straight down at his side. He was reserving his fire.

"Two—!"

"Three—!"

"Fire—!"

Up came the pistol-arm instantly—Angelo dodged with the report. He said "Ouch!" and fainted again.

The doctor examined and bandaged the wound. It was of no consequence, he said—bullet through fleshy part of arm—no bones broken—the gentleman was still able to fight—let the duel proceed.

Next time Angelo jumped just as Luigi fired, which disordered his aim and caused him to cut a chip out of Howard's ear. The Judge took his time again, and when he fired Angelo jumped and got a knuckle skinned. The doctor inspected and dressed the wounds. Angelo now spoke out and said he was content with the satisfaction he had got, and if the Judge—but Luigi shut him roughly up, and asked him not to make an ass of himself; adding—

"And I want you to stop dodging. You take a great deal too prominent a part in this thing for a person who has got nothing to do with it. You should remember that you are here only by courtesy, and are without official recognition; officially you are not here at all; officially you do not even exist. To all intents and purposes you are absent from this place, and you ought for your own modesty's sake to reflect that it cannot become a person who is not present here to be taking this sort of public and indecent prominence in a matter in which he is not in the slightest degree concerned. Now, don't dodge again; the bullets are not for you, they are for me; if I want them dodged I will attend to it myself. I never saw a person act so."

Angelo saw the reasonableness of what his brother had said, and he did try to reform, but it was of no use; both pistols went off at the same instant, and he jumped once more; he got a sharp scrape along his cheek from the Judge's bullet, and so deflected Luigi's aim that his ball went wide and chipped a flake of skin from Pudd'nhead Wilson's chin. The doctor attended to the wounded.

By the terms, the duel was over. But Luigi was entirely out of patience, and begged for one more exchange of shots, insisting that he had had no fair chance, on account of his brother's indelicate behavior. Howard was opposed to granting so unusual a privilege, but the Judge took Luigi's part, and added that indeed he himself might fairly be considered entitled to another trial, because although the proxy on the other side was in no way to blame for his (the Judge's) humiliatingly resultless work, the gentleman with whom he was fighting this duel was to blame for it, since if he had played no advantages and had held his head still, his proxy would have been disposed of early. He added—

"Count Luigi's request for another exchange is another proof that he is a brave and chivalrous gentleman, and I beg that the courtesy he asks may be accorded him."

"I thank you most sincerely for this generosity, Judge Driscoll," said Luigi, with a polite bow, and moving to his place. Then he added—to Angelo, "Now hold your grip, hold your *grip*, I tell you, and I'll land him, sure!"

The men stood erect, their pitsol-arms at their sides, the two seconds stood at their official posts, the doctor stood five paces in Wilson's rear with his instruments and bandages in his hands. The deep stillness, the peaceful moonlight, the motionless figures, made an impressive picture and the impending fatal possibilities augmented this impressiveness to solemnity. Wilson's hand began to rise—slowly—slowly—higher—still higher—in another moment—

"*Boom!*"—the first stroke of midnight swung up out of the distance: Angelo was off like a deer!

"Oh, you unspeakable traitor!" wailed his brother, as they went soaring over the fence.

The others stood astonished and gazing; and so stood, watching that strange spectacle until distance dissolved it and swept it from their view. Then they rubbed their eyes like people waking out of a dream.

"Well, I've never seen anything like that before!" said the

Judge. "Wilson, I am going to confess, now, that I wasn't quite able to believe in that leg-business, and had a suspicion that it was a put-up convenience between those twins; and when Count Angelo fainted I thought I saw the whole scheme—thought it was pretext No. 1, and would be followed by others till twelve o'clock should arrive and Luigi would get off with all the credit of seeming to want to fight and yet not have to fight, after all. But I was mistaken. His pluck proved it. He's a brave fellow and did want to fight."

"There isn't any doubt about that," said Howard, and added in a grieved tone, "but what an unworthy sort of Christian that Angelo is—I hope and believe there are not many like him. It is not right to engage in a duel on the Sabbath—I could not approve of that myself; but to finish one that has been begun—that is a duty, let the day be what it may."

They strolled along, still wondering, still talking.

"It is a curious circumstance," remarked the surgeon, halting Wilson a moment to paste some more court plaster on his chin, which had gone to leaking blood again, "that in this duel neither of the parties who handled the pistols lost blood, while nearly all the persons present in the mere capacity of guests got hit. I have not heard of such a thing before. Don't you think it unusual?"

"Yes," said the Judge, "it has struck me as peculiar. Peculiar and unfortunate. I was annoyed at it, all the time. In the case of Angelo it made no great difference, because he was in a measure concerned, though not officially; but it troubled me to see the seconds compromised, and yet I knew no way to mend the matter."

"There was no way to mend it," said Howard, whose ear was being readjusted now by the doctor; "the code fixes our place, and it would not have been lawful to change it. If we could have stood at your side, or behind you, or in front of you, it—but it would not have been legitimate and the other parties would have had a just right to complain of our trying to protect ourselves from danger; infractions of the code are certainly not permissible in any case whatever."

Wilson offered no remarks. It seemed to him that there was very little place here for so much solemnity, but he judged that if a duel where nobody was in danger or got crippled but the seconds and the outsiders had nothing ridiculous about for these gentlemen, his pointing out that feature would probably not help them to see it.

He invited them in to take a nightcap, and Howard and the Judge accepted, but the doctor said he would have to go and see how Angelo's principal wound was getting on.

[It was now Sunday, and in the afternoon Angelo was to be received into the Baptist communion by immersion—a doubtful prospect, the doctor feared.]

CHAPTER VII

When the doctor arrived at Aunt Patsy Cooper's house, he found the lights going and everybody up and dressed and in a great state of solicitude and excitement. The twins were stretched on a sofa in the sitting-room, Aunt Patsy was fussing at Angelo's arm, Nancy was flying around under her commands, the two young boys were trying to keep out of the way and always getting in it, in order to see and wonder, Rowena stood apart, helpless with apprehension and emotion, and Luigi was growling in unappeasable fury over Angelo's shameful flight.

As has been reported before, the doctor was a fool—a kind-hearted and well-meaning one, but with no tact; and as he was by long odds the most learned physician in the town, and was quite well aware of it, and could talk his learning with ease and precision, and liked to show off when he had an audience, he was sometimes tempted into revealing more of a case than was good for the patient.

He examined Angelo's wound, and was really minded to say nothing for once; but Aunt Patsy was so anxious and so pressing that he allowed his caution to be overcome, and proceeded to empty himself as follows, with scientific relish—

"Without going too much into detail, madam—for you would probably not understand it anyway—I concede that great care is going to be necessary here; otherwise exudation of the aesophagus is nearly sure to ensue, and this will be followed by ossification and extradition of the maxillaris superioris, which must decompose the granular surfaces of the great infusorial ganglionic system, thus obstructing the action of the posterior varioloid arteries and precipitating compound strangulated sorosis of the valvular tissues, and ending unavoidably in the dispersion and combustion of the marsupial fluxes and the consequent embrocation of the bicuspid populo redax referendum rotulorum."

A miserable silence followed. Aunt Patsy's heart sank, the pallor of despair invaded her face, she was not able to speak; poor Rowena wrung her hands in privacy and silence, and said to herself in the bitterness of her young grief, "There is no hope—it is plain there is no hope;" the good-hearted negro wench, Nancy, paled to chocolate, then to orange, then to amber, and thought to herself with yearning sympathy and sorrow, "Po' thing, he ain' gwyne to las' throo de half o' dat;" small Henry choked up, and turned his head away to hide his rising tears, and his brother Joe said to himself, with a sense of loss, "The baptizing's busted, that's sure." Luigi was the only person who had any heart to speak. He said, a little bit sharply, to the doctor—

"Well, well, there's nothing to be gained by wasting precious time: give him a barrel of pills—I'll take them for him."

"You?" asked the doctor.

"Yes. Did you suppose he was going to take them himself?"

"Why, of course."

"Well, it's a mistake. He never took a dose of medicine in his life. He can't."

"Well, upon my word, it's the most extraordinary thing I ever heard of!"

"Oh," said Aunt Patsy, as pleased as a mother whose child is being admired and wondered at, "you'll find that there's more about them that's wonderful than their just being made in the image of God like the rest of His creatures, now you can depend on that, *I* tell you," and she wagged her complacent head like one who could reveal marvelous things if she chose.

The boy Joe began—

"Why, ma, they *ain't* made in the im——"

"You shut up, and wait till you're asked, Joe. I'll let you know when I want help. Are you looking for something, Doctor?"

The doctor asked for a few sheets of paper and a pen, and said he would write a prescription; which he did. It was one of Galen's; in fact, it was Galen's favorite, and had been slaying people for sixteen thousand years. Galen used it for everything, applied it to everything, said it would remove everything, from warts all the way through to lungs—and it generally did. Galen was still the only medical authority recognized in Missouri; his practice was the only practice known to the Missouri doctors, and his prescriptions were the only ammunition they carried when they went out for game. By and by Dr. Claypool laid down his pen and read the result of his labors aloud, carefully and deliberately, for this battery must be constructed on the premises by the family, and mistakes could occur; for he wrote a doctor's hand—the hand which from the beginning of time has been so disastrous to the apothecary and so profitable to the undertaker:

"Take of afarabocca, henbane, corpobalsamum, each two drams and a half; of cloves, opium, myrrh, cyperus, each two drams; of opobalsamum, Indian leaf, cinnamon, zedoary, ginger, coftus, coral, cassia, euphorbium, gum tragacanth, frankincense, styrax calamita, celtic, nard, spignel, hartwort, mustard, saxifrage, dill, anise, each one dram; of xylaloes, rheum ponticum, alipta moschata, castor, spikenard, galangals, opoponax, anacardium, mastich, brimstone, peony, eringo, pulp of dates, red and white hermodactyls, roses, thyme, acorns, pennyroyal, gentian, the bark of the root of mandrake, germander, valerian, bishop's weed, bay-berries, long and white pepper, xylobalsamum, carnabadium, macedonian, parsley-seeds, lovage, the seeds of rue, and sinon, of each a dram and a half; of pure gold, pure silver, pearls not perforated, the blatta byzantina, the bone of the stag's heart, of each the quantity of fourteen grains of wheat; of sapphire, emerald and jasper stones, each one dram; of hazel-nut, two drams; of pellitory of Spain, shavings of ivory, calamus odoratus, each the quantity of twenty-nine grains of wheat; of honey or sugar a sufficient quantity. Boil down and skim off."

"There," he said, "that will fix the patient; give his brother a dipperful every three-quarters of an hour——"

—"while he survives," muttered Luigi—

—"and see that the room is kept wholesomely hot, and the doors and windows closed tight. Keep Count Angelo nicely covered up with six or seven blankets, and when he is thirsty—which will be frequently—moisten a rag in the vapor of the tea-kettle and let his brother suck it. When he is hungry—which will also be frequently—he must not be humored oftener than every seven or eight hours; then toast part of a cracker until it begins to brown, and give it to his brother."

"That is all very well, as far as Angelo is concerned," said Luigi, "but what am I to eat?"

"I do not see that there is anything the matter with you," the doctor answered, "you may of course eat what you please."

"And also drink what I please, I suppose?"

"Oh, certainly—at present. When the violent and continuous perspiring has reduced your strength, I shall have to reduce your diet, of course, and also bleed you, but there is no occasion for that yet awhile." He turned to Aunt Patsy and said: "He must be put to bed, and sat up with, and tended with the greatest care, and not allowed to stir for several days and nights."

"For one, I'm sacredly thankful for that," said Luigi, "it postpones the funeral—I'm not to be drowned to-day, anyhow."

Angelo said quietly to the doctor:

"I will cheerfully submit to all your requirements, sir, up to two o'clock this afternoon, and will resume them after three, but cannot be confined to the house during that intermediate hour."

"Why, may I ask?"

"Because I have entered the Baptist communion, and by appointment am to be baptized in the river at that hour."

"Oh, insanity!—it cannot be allowed!"

Angelo answered with placid firmness—

"Nothing shall prevent it, if I am alive."

"Why, consider, my dear sir, in your condition it might prove fatal."

A tender and ecstatic smile beamed from Angelo's eyes, and he broke forth in a tone of joyous fervency—

"Ah, how blessed it would be to die for such a cause—it would be martyrdom!"

"But your brother—consider your brother; you would be risking his life, too."

"He risked mine an hour ago," responded Angelo, gloomily; "did he consider me?" A thought swept through his mind that made him shudder. "If I had not run, I might have been killed in a duel on the Sabbath day, and my soul would have been lost—lost."

"Oh, don't fret, it wasn't in any danger," said Luigi, irritably; "they wouldn't waste it for a little thing like that; there's a glass case all ready for it in the heavenly museum, and a pin to stick it up with."

Aunt Patsy was shocked, and said—

"Looy, Looy!—don't talk so, dear!"

Rowena's soft heart was pierced by Luigi's unfeeling words, and she murmured to herself, "Oh, if I but had the dear privilege of protecting and defending him with my weak voice!—but alas, this sweet boon is denied me by the cruel conventions of social intercourse."

"Get their bed ready," said Aunt Patsy to Nancy, "and shut up the windows and doors, and light their candles, and see that you drive all the mosquitoes out of their bar, and make up a good fire in their stove, and carry up some bags of hot ashes to lay to his feet——"

—"and a shovel of fire for his head, and a mustard plaster for his neck, and some gum shoes for his ears," Luigi interrupted, with temper; and added, to himself, "Damnation, I'm going to be roasted alive, I just know it!"

"Why, Looy! Do be quiet; I never saw such a fractious thing. A body would think you didn't care for your brother."

"I don't—to *that* extent, Aunt Patsy. I was glad the drowning was postponed a minute ago, but I'm not, now. No, that is all gone by: I want to be drowned."

"You'll bring a judgment on yourself just as sure as you live, if you go on like that. Why, I never heard the beat of it. Now, there,—there! you've said enough. Not another word out of you,—I won't have it!"

"But, Aunt Patsy——"

"Luigi! Didn't you hear what I told you?"

"But, Aunt Patsy, I—why, I'm not going to set my heart and lungs afloat in that pail of sewage which this criminal here has been prescri——"

"Yes, you are, too. You are going to be good, and do everything I tell you, like a dear," and she tapped his cheek affectionately with her finger. "Rowena, take the prescription and go in the kitchen and hunt up the things and lay them out for me. I'll sit up with my patient the rest of the night, Doctor; I can't trust Nancy, she couldn't make Luigi take the medicine. Of course you'll drop in again during the day. Have you got any more directions?"

"No, I believe not, Aunt Patsy. If I don't get in earlier, I'll be along by early candlelight, anyway. Meantime, don't allow him to get out of his bed."

Angelo said, with calm determination—

"I shall be baptized at two o'clock. Nothing but death shall prevent me."

The doctor said nothing aloud, but to himself he said:

"Why, this chap's got a manly side, after all! Physically he's a coward, but morally he's a lion. I'll go and tell the others about this; it will raise him a good deal in their estimation—and the public will follow their lead, of course."

Privately, Aunt Patsy applauded too, and was proud of Angelo's courage in the moral field as she was of Luigi's in the field of honor.

The boy Henry was troubled, but the boy Joe said, inaudibly, and gratefully, "We're all hunky, after all; and no postponement on account of the weather."

CHAPTER VIII

By nine o'clock the town was humming with the news of the midnight duel, and there were but two opinions about it: one, that Luigi's pluck in the field was most praiseworthy and Angelo's flight most scandalous; the other, that Angelo's courage in flying the field for conscience' sake was as fine and creditable as was Luigi's in holding the field in the face of the bullets. The one opinion was held by half of the town, the other one was maintained by the other half. The division was clean and exact, and it made two parties, an Angelo party and a Luigi party. The twins had suddenly become popular idols along with Pudd'nhead Wilson, and haloed with a glory as intense as his. The children talked the duel all the way to Sunday-school, their elders talked it all the way to church, the choir discussed it behind their red curtain, it usurped the place of pious thought in the "nigger gallery."

By noon the doctor had added the news, and spread it, that Count Angelo, in spite of his wound and all warnings and supplications, was resolute in his determination to be baptised at the hour appointed. This swept the town like wildfire, and mightily reinforced the enthusiasm of the Angelo faction, who said, "If any doubted that it was moral courage that took him from the field, what have they to say now!"

Still the excitement grew. All the morning it was traveling countrywards, toward all points of the compass; so, whereas before only the farmers and their wives were intending to come and witness the remarkable baptism, a general holiday was now proclaimed and the children and negroes admitted to the privileges of the occasion. All the farms for ten miles around were vacated, all the converging roads emptied long processions of wagons, horses and yeomanry into the town. The pack and cram of people vastly exceeded any that had ever been seen in that sleepy region before. The only thing that had ever even approached it, was the time long gone by, but never forgotten, nor even referred to without wonder and pride, when two circuses and a Fourth of July fell together. But the glory of that occasion was extinguished, now, for good. It was but a freshet to this deluge.

The great invasion massed itself on the river bank and waited hungrily for the immense event. Waited, and wondered if it would really happen, or if the twin who was not a "professor" would stand out and prevent it.

But they were not to be disappointed. Angelo was as good as his word. He came attended by an escort of honor composed of several hundred of the best citizens, all of the Angelo party; and when the immersion was finished they escorted him back home; and would even have carried him on their shoulders, but that people might think they were carrying Luigi.

Far into the night the citizens continued to discuss and wonder over the strangely-mated pair of incidents that had distinguished and exalted the past twenty-four hours above any other twenty-four in the history of their town for picturesqueness and splendid interest; and long before the lights were out and burghers asleep it had been decided on all hands that in capturing these twins Dawson's Landing had drawn a prize in the great lottery of municipal fortune.

At midnight Angelo was sleeping peacefully. His immersion had not harmed him, it had merely made him wholesomely drowsy, and he had been dead asleep many hours now. It had made Luigi drowsy, too, but he had got only brief naps, on account of his having to take the medicine every three-quarters of an hour—and Aunt Betsy Hale was there to see that he did it. When he complained and resisted, she was quietly firm with him, and said in a low voice:

"No—no, that won't do; you mustn't talk, and you mustn't retch and gag that way, either—you'll wake up your poor brother."

'Well, what of it, Aunt Betsy, he——"

" 'Sh-h! Don't make a noise, dear. You mustn't forget that your poor brother is sick and——"

"Sick, is he? Well, I wish I——"

"Sh-h-h! Will you be quiet, Luigi! Here, now, take the rest of it— don't keep me holding the dipper all night. I declare if you haven't left a good fourth of it in the bottom! Come—that's a good boy."

"Aunt Betsy, don't make me! I feel like I've swallowed a cemetery; I do, indeed. Do let me rest a little—just a little; I can't take any more of the devilish stuff now."

"Luigi! Using such language here, and him just baptised! Do you want the roof to fall on you?"

"I wish to goodness it would!"

"Why, you dreadful thing! I've a good notion to—let that blanket alone; do you want your brother to catch his death?"

"Aunt Betsy, I've *got* to have it off, I'm being roasted alive; nobody could stand it—you couldn't, yourself."

"Now, then, you're sneezing again—I just expected it."

"Because I've caught a cold in my head. I always do, when I go in the water with my clothes on. And it takes me weeks to get over it, too. I think it was a shame to serve me so."

"Luigi, you are unreasonable; you know very well they couldn't baptise him dry. I should think you would be willing to undergo a little inconvenience for your brother's sake."

"Inconvenience! Now how you talk, Aunt Betsy. I came as near as anything to getting drowned—you saw that, yourself; and do you call this inconvenience?—the room shut up as tight as a drum, and so hot the mosquitoes are trying to get out; and a cold in the head, and dying for sleep and no chance to get any on account of this infamous medicine that that assassin prescri——"

"There, you're sneezing again. I'm going down and mix some more of this truck for you, dear."

CHAPTER IX

During Monday, Tuesday and Wednesday the twins grew steadily worse; but then the doctor was summoned south to attend his mother's funeral and they got well in forty-eight hours. They appeared on the street on Friday, and were welcomed with enthusiasm by the new-born parties, the Luigi and Angelo factions. The Luigi faction carried its strength into the Democratic party, the Angelo faction entered into a combination with the Whigs. The Democrats nominated Luigi for alderman under the new city government, and the Whigs put up Angelo against him. The democrats nominated Pudd'nhead Wilson for mayor, and he was left alone in this glory, for the Whigs had no man who was willing to enter the lists against such a formidable opponent. No politician had scored such a compliment as this before in the history of the Mississippi Valley.

The political campaign in Dawson's Landing opened in a pretty warm fashion, and waxed hotter every week. Luigi's whole heart was in it, and even Angelo developed a surprising amount of interest—which was natural, because he was not merely representing Whigism, a matter of no consequence to him, but he was representing something immensely finer and greater—to wit, Reform. In him was centred the hopes of the whole reform element of the town; he was the chosen and admired champion of every clique that had a pet reform of any sort or kind at heart. He was president of the great Teetotaller's Union, its chiefest prophet and mouthpiece.

But as the canvass went on, troubles began to spring up all around—troubles for the twins, and through them for all the parties and segments and fractions of parties. Whenever Luigi had possession of the legs, he carried Angelo to balls, rum shops, Sons of Liberty parades, horse races, campaign riots, and everywhere else that could damage him with his party and the church; and when it was Angelo's week he carried Luigi diligently to all manner of moral and religious gatherings, doing his best to regain the ground he had lost before. As a result of these double performances, there was a storm blowing all the time, an ever rising storm, too—a storm of frantic criticism of the twins, and rage over their extravagant, incomprehensible conduct.

Luigi had the final chance. The legs were his for the closing week of the canvas. He led his brother a fearful dance.

But he saved his best card for the very eve of the election. There was to be a grand turn-out of the Teetotaller's Union that day, and Angelo was to march at the head of the procession and deliver a great oration afterward. Luigi drank a couple of glasses of whiskey—which steadied his nerves and clarified his mind, but made Angelo drunk. Everybody who saw the march, saw that the Champion of the Teetotallers was half seas over, and noted also that his brother, who made no hypocritical pretensions to extra temperance virtues, was dignified and sober. This eloquent fact could not be unfruitful at the end of a hot political canvass. At the mass meeting Angelo tried to make his great temperance oration but was so discommoded by hiccoughs and thickness of tongue that he had to give it up; then drowsiness overtook him and his head drooped against Luigi's and he went to sleep. Luigi apologized for him, and was going on to improve his opportunity with an appeal for a moderation of what he called "the prevailing teetotal madness," but persons in the audience began to howl and throw things at him, and then the meeting rose in wrath and chased him home.

This episode was a crusher for Angelo in another way. It destroyed his chances with Rowena. Those chances had been growing, right along, for two months. Rowena had partly confessed that she loved him, but wanted time to consider. Now the tender dream was ended, and she told him so, the moment he was sober enough to understand. She said she would never marry a man who drank.

"But I don't drink," he pleaded.

"That is nothing to the point," she said, coldly, "you get drunk, and that is worse."

[There was a long and sufficiently idiotic discussion here, which ended as reported in a previous note.]

CHAPTER X

Dawson's Landing had a week of repose, after the election, and it needed it, for the frantic and variegated nightmare which had tormented it all through the preceding week had left it limp, haggard and exhausted at the end. It got the week of repose because Angelo had the legs, and was in too subdued a condition to want to go out and mingle with an irritated community that had come to distrust and detest him because there was such a lack of harmony between his morals, which were confessedly excellent, and his methods of illustrating them, which were distinctly damnable.

The new city officers were sworn in on the following Monday—at least all but Luigi. There was a complication in his case. His election was conceded, but he could not sit in the board of aldermen without his brother, and his brother could not sit there because he was not a member. There seemed to be no way out of the difficulty but to carry the matter into the courts, so this was resolved upon. The case was set for the Monday fortnight. In due course the time arrived. In the meantime the city government had been at a stand-still, because without Luigi there was a tie in the board of aldermen, whereas with him the liquor interest—the richest in the political field—would have one majority. But the court decided that Angelo could not sit in the board with him, either in public or executive sessions, and at the same time forbade the board to deny admission to Luigi, a fairly and legally chosen alderman. The case was carried up and up from court to court, yet still the same old original decision was confirmed every time. As a result, the city government not only stood still, with its hands tied, but everything it was created to protect and care for went a steady gait toward rack and ruin. There was no way to levy a tax, so the minor officials had to resign or starve; therefore they resigned. There being no city money, the enormous legal expenses on both sides had to be defrayed by private subscription. But at last the people came to their senses, and said—

"Pudd'nhead was right, at the start—we ought to have hired the official half of that human phillipene to resign; but it's too late, now; some of us haven't got anything left to hire him with."

"Yes, we have," said another citizen, "we've got this"—and he produced a halter.

Many shouted, "That's the ticket." But others said, "No—Count Angelo is innocent; we mustn't hang him."

"Who said anything about hanging him? We are only going to hang the other one."

"Then that is all right—there is no objection to that."

So they hanged Luigi. And so ends the history of "Those Extraordinary Twins."

FINAL REMARKS

As you see, it was an extravagant sort of a tale, and had no purpose but to exhibit that monstrous "freak" in all sorts of grotesque lights. But when Roxy wandered into the tale she had to be furnished with something to do; so she changed the children in the cradle: this necessitated the invention of a reason for it; this in turn resulted in making the children prominent personages—nothing could prevent it, of course. Their career began to take a tragic aspect, and some one had to be brought in to help work the machinery; so Pudd'nhead Wilson was introduced and taken on trial. By this time the whole show was being run by the new people and in their interest, and the original show was become side-tracked and forgotten; the twin-monster and the heroine and the lads and the old ladies had dwindled to inconsequentialities and were merely in the way. Their story was one story, the new people's story was another story, and there was no connection between them, no interdependence, no kinship. It is not practicable or rational to try to tell two stories at the same time; so I dug out the farce and left the tragedy.

The reader already knew how the expert works; he knows now how the other kind do it.

MARK TWAIN.

"The Awful German Language" was an appendix to an illustrated volume of European travel sketches called A Tramp Abroad *that was brought out by the American Publishing Company in 1880 in an attempt to repeat the success of* The Innocents Abroad. *Although* A Tramp Abroad *accomplished this commercial aim, it was, unlike its predecessor, a very uneven performance.*

The Awful German Language

A little learning makes the whole world kin.—Proverbs xxxii, 7.

I went often to look at the collection of curiosities in Heidelberg Castle, and one day I surprised the keeper of it with my German. I spoke entirely in that language. He was greatly interested; and after I had talked awhile he said my German was very rare, possibly a "unique;" and wanted to add it to his museum.

If he had known what it had cost me to acquire my art, he would also have known that it would break any collector to buy it. Harris and I had been hard at work on our German during several weeks at that time, and although we had made good progress, it had been accomplished under great difficulty and annoyance, for three of our teachers had died in the meantime. A person who has not studied German can form no idea of what a perplexing language it is.

Surely there is not another language that is so slip-shod and systemless, and so slippery and elusive to the grasp. One is washed about in it, hither and hither, in the most helpless way; and when at last he thinks he has captured a rule which offers firm ground to take a rest on amid the general rage and turmoil of the ten parts of speech, he turns over the page and reads, "Let the pupil make careful note of the following *exceptions*." He runs his eye down and finds that there are more exceptions to the rule than instances of it. So overboard he goes again, to hunt for another Ararat and find another quicksand. Such has been, and continues to be, my experience. Every time I think I have got one of these four confusing "cases" where I am master of it, a seemingly insignificant preposition intrudes itself into my sentence, clothed with an awful and unsuspected power, and crumbles the ground from under me. For instance, my book inquires after a certain bird—(it is always inquiring after things which are of no sort of consequence to anybody): "Where is the bird?" Now the answer to this question,—according to the book,—is that the bird is waiting in the blacksmith shop on account of the rain. Of course no bird would do that, but then you must stick to the book. Very well, I begin to cipher out the German for that answer. I begin at the wrong end, necessarily, for that is the German idea. I say to myself, "*Regen*, (rain,) is masculine—or maybe it is feminine—or possibly neuter—it is too much trouble to look, now. Therefore, it is either *der* (the) Regen, or *die* (the) Regen, or *das* (the) Regen, according to which gender it may turn out to be when I look. In the interest of science, I will cipher it out on the hypothesis that it is masculine. Very well—then *the* rain is *der* Regen, if it is simply in the quiescent state of being *mentioned*, without enlargement or discussion—Nominative case; but if this rain is lying around, in a kind of a general way on the ground, it is then definitely located, it is *doing something*—that is, *resting*, (which is one of the German grammar's ideas of doing something,) and this throws the rain into the Dative case, and makes it *dem* Regen. However, this rain is not resting, but is doing something *actively*,—it is falling,—to interfere with the bird, likely,—and this indicates *movement*, which has the effect of sliding it into the Accusative case and changing *dem* Regen into *den* Regen." Having completed the grammatical horoscope of this matter, I answer up confidently and state in German that the bird is staying in the blacksmith shop "wegen (on account of) *den* Regen." Then the teacher lets me softly down with the remark that whenever the word "wegen" drops into a sentence, it *always* throws that subject into the *Genitive* case, regardless of consequences—and that therefore this bird staid in the blacksmith shop "wegen *des* Regens."

N.B. I was informed, later, by a higher authority, that there was an "exception" which permits one to say "wegen *den* Regen" in certain peculiar and complex circumstances, but that this exception is not extended to anything *but* rain.

There are ten parts of speech, and they are all troublesome. An average sentence, in a German newspaper, is a sublime and impressive curiosity; it occupies a quarter of a column; it contains all the ten parts of speech—not in regular order, but mixed;

it is built mainly of compound words constructed by the writer on the spot, and not to be found in any dictionary—six or seven words compacted into one, without joint or seam—that is, without hyphens; it treats of fourteen or fifteen different subjects, each enclosed in a parenthesis of its own, with here and there extra parentheses which re-enclose three or four of the minor parentheses, making pens within pens; finally, all the parentheses and re-parentheses are massed together between a couple of king-parentheses, one of which is placed in the first line of the majestic sentence and the other in the middle of the last line of it—*after which comes the* VERB, and you find out for the first time what the man has been talking about; and after the verb—merely by way of ornament, as far as I can make out,—the writer shovels in "*haben sind gewesen gehabt haben geworden sein*," or words to that effect, and the monument is finished. I suppose that this closing hurrah is in the nature of the flourish to a man's signature—not necessary, but pretty. German books are easy enough to read when you hold them before the looking-glass or stand on your head,—so as to reverse the construction,—but I think that to learn to read and understand a German newspaper is a thing which must always remain an impossibility to a foreigner.

Yet even the German books are not entirely free from attacks of the Parenthesis distemper—though they are usually so mild as to cover only a few lines, and therefore when you at last get down to the verb it carries some meaning to your mind because you are able to remember a good deal of what has gone before.

Now here is a sentence from a popular and excellent German novel,—with a slight parenthesis in it. I will make a perfectly literal translation, and throw in the parenthesis-marks and some hyphens for the assistance of the reader,—though in the original there are no parenthesis-marks or hyphens, and the reader is left to flounder through to the remote verb the best way he can:

"But when he, upon the street, the (in-satin-and-silk-covered-now-very-unconstrainedly-after-the-newest-fashion-dressed) government counsellor's wife *met*" etc., etc.*

That is from "The Old Mamselle's Secret," by Mrs. Marlitt. And that sentence is constructed upon the most approved German model. You observe how far that verb is from the reader's base of operations; well, in a German newspaper they put their verb away over on the next page; and I have heard that sometimes after stringing along on exciting preliminaries and paren-

* Wenn er aber auf der Strasse der in Sammt und Seide gehüllten jetz sehr ungenirt nach der neusten mode gekleideten Regierungsrathin begegnet."

theses for a column or two, they get in a hurry and have to go to press without getting to the verb at all. Of course, then, the reader is left in a very exhausted and ignorant state.

We have the Parenthesis disease in our literature, too; and one may see cases of it every day in our books and newspapers: but with us it is the mark and sign of an unpractised writer or a cloudy intellect, whereas with the Germans it is doubtless the mark and sign of a practised pen and of the presence of that sort of luminous intellectual fog which stands for clearness among these people. For surely it is *not* clearness,—it necessarily can't be clearness. Even a jury would have penetration enough to discover that. A writer's ideas must be a good deal confused, a good deal out of line and sequence, when he starts out to say that a man met a counsellor's wife in the street, and then right in the midst of this so simple undertaking halts these approaching people and makes them stand still until he jots down an inventory of the woman's dress. That is manifestly absurd. It reminds a person of those dentists who secure your instant and breathless interest in a tooth by taking a grip on it with the forceps, and then stand there and drawl through a tedious anecdote before they give the dreaded jerk. Parentheses in literature and dentistry are in bad taste.

The Germans have another kind of parenthesis, which they make by splitting a verb in two and putting half of it at the beginning of an exciting chapter and the *other half* at the end of it. Can any one conceive of anything more confusing than that? These things are called "separable verbs." The German grammar is blistered all over with separable verbs; and the wider the two portions of one of them are spread apart, the better the author of the crime is pleased with his performance. A favorite one is *reiste ab*,—which means, *departed*. Here is an example which I culled from a novel and reduced to English:

"The trunks being now ready, he DE-after kissing his mother and sisters, and once more pressing to his bosom his adored Gretchen, who, dressed in simple white muslin, with a single tube-rose in the ample folds of her rich brown hair, had tottered feebly down the stairs, still pale from the terror and excitement of the past evening, but longing to lay her poor aching head yet once again upon the breast of him whom she loved more dearly than life itself, PARTED."

However, it is not well to dwell too much on the separable verbs. One is sure to lose his temper early; and if he sticks to the subject, and will not be warned, it will at last either soften his brain or petrify it. Personal pronouns and adjectives are a fruitful nuisance in this language, and should have been left out. For instance, the same sound, *sie*, means *you*, and it means *she*, and it means *her*, and it means *it*, and it means *they*, and it means *them*. Think of the ragged poverty of a language which has to make one word do the work of six,—and a poor little weak thing of only three letters at that. But mainly, think of the exasperation of never knowing which of these meanings the speaker is trying to convey. This explains why, whenever a person says *sie* to me, I generally try to kill him, if a stranger.

Now observe the Adjective. Here was a case where simplicity would have been an advantage; therefore, for no other reason, the inventor of this language complicated it all he could. When we wish to speak of our "good friend or friends," in our enlightened tongue, we stick to the one form and have no trouble or hard feeling about it; but with the German tongue it is different. When a German gets his hands on an adjective, he declines it, and keeps on declining it until the common sense is all declined out of it. It is as bad as Latin. He says, for instance:

SINGULAR.

Nominative—Mein gut*er* Freund, my good friend.
Genitive—Mein*es* gut*en* Freund*es*, of my good friend.
Dative—Mein*em* gut*en* Freund, to my good friend.
Accusative—Mein*en* gut*en* Freund, my good friend.

PLURAL.

N.—Mein*e* gut*en* Freund*e*, my good friends.
G.—Mein*er* gut*en* Freund*e*, of my good friends.
D.—Mein*en* gut*en* Freund*en*, to my good friends.
A.—Mein*e* gut*en* Freund*e*, my good friends.

Now let the candidate for the asylum try to memorize those variations, and see how soon he will be elected. One might better go without friends in Germany than take all this trouble about them. I have shown what a bother it is to decline a good (male) friend; well, this is only a third of the work, for there is a variety of new distortions of the adjective to be learned when the object is feminine, and still another when the object is neuter. Now there are more adjectives in this language than there are black cats in Switzerland, and they must all be as elaborately declined as the examples above suggested. Difficult?—troublesome?—these words cannot describe it. I heard a Californian student in Heidelberg, say, in one of his calmest moods, that he would rather decline two drinks than one German adjective.

The inventor of the language seems to have taken pleasure in complicating it in every way he could think of. For instance, if one is casually referring to a house, *Haus*, or a horse, *Pferd*, or a dog, *Hund*, he spells these words as I have indicated; but if he is referring to them in the Dative case, he sticks on a foolish and unnecessary *e* and spells them Hause, Pferde, Hunde. So, as an added *e* often signifies the plural, as the *s* does with us, the new student is likely to go on for a month making twins out of a Dative dog before he discovers his mistake; and on the other hand, many a new student who could ill afford loss, has bought and paid for two dogs and only got one of them, because he ignorantly bought that dog in the Dative singular when he really supposed he was talking plural,—which left the law on the seller's side, of course, by the strict rules of grammar, and therefore a suit for recovery could not lie.

In German, all the Nouns begin with a capital letter. Now that is a good idea; and a good idea, in this language, is necessarily conspicuous from its lonesomeness. I consider this capitalizing of nouns a good idea, because by reason of it you are almost always able to tell a noun the minute you see it. You fall into error occasionally, because you mistake the name of a person for the name of a thing, and waste a good deal of time trying to dig a meaning out of it. German names almost always do mean something, and this helps to deceive the student. I translated a passage one day, which said that "the infuriated tigress broke loose and utterly ate up the unfortunate fir-forest," (*Tannenwald.*) When I was girding up my loins to doubt this, I found out that Tannenwald, in this instance, was a man's name.

Every noun has a gender, and there is no sense or system in the distribution; so the gender of each must be learned separately and by heart. There is no other way. To do this, one has to have a memory like a memorandum book. In German, a young lady has no sex, while a turnip has. Think what overwrought reverence that shows for the turnip, and what callous disrespect for the girl. See how it looks in print—I translate this from a conversation in one of the best of the German Sunday-school books:

"*Gretchen.* Wilhelm, where is the turnip?

"*Wilhelm.* She has gone to the kitchen.

"*Gretchen.* Where is the accomplished and beautiful English maiden?

"*Wilhelm.* It has gone to the opera."

To continue with the German genders: a tree is male, its buds are female, its leaves are neuter; horses are sexless, dogs are male, cats are female,—Tom-cats included, of course; a person's mouth, neck, bosom, elbows, fingers, nails, feet, and body, are of the male sex, and his head is male or neuter according to the word selected to signify it, and *not* according to the sex of the individual who wears it,—for in Germany all the women wear either male heads or sexless ones; a person's nose, lips, shoulders, breast, hands, hips, and toes are of the female sex; and his hair, ears, eyes, chin, legs, knees, heart, and conscience, haven't any sex at all. The inventor of the language probably got what he knew about a conscience from hearsay.

Now, by the above dissection, the reader will see that in Germany a man may *think* he is a man, but when he comes to look into the matter closely, he is bound to have his doubts; he finds that in sober truth he is a most ridiculous mixture; and if he ends by trying to comfort himself with the thought that he can at least depend on a third of this mess as being manly and masculine, the humiliating second thought will quickly remind him that in this respect he is no better off than any woman or cow in the land.

In the German it is true that by some oversight of the inventor of the language, a Woman is a female; but a Wife, (*Weib,*) is not,—which is unfortunate. A Wife, here, has no sex; she is neuter; so, according to the grammar, a fish is *he*, his scales are *she*, but a fishwife is neither. To describe a wife as sexless, may be called under-description; that is bad enough, but over-description is surely worse. A German speaks of an Englishman as the *Engländer*; to change the sex, he adds *inn*, and that stands for Englishwoman,—*Engländerinn*. That seems descriptive enough, but still it is not exact enough for a German; so he precedes the word with that article which indicates that the creature to follow is feminine, and writes it down thus: "*die* Englander*inn*,"—which means "the *she-Englishwoman*." I consider that that person is over-described.

Well, after the student has learned the sex of a great number of nouns, he is still in a difficulty, because he finds it impossible to persuade his tongue to refer to things as "*he*" and "*she*," and "*him*" and "*her*," which it has been always accustomed to refer to as "*it*." When he even frames a German sentence in his mind, with the hims and hers in the right places, and then works up his courage to the utterance-point, it is no use,—the moment he begins to speak his tongue flies the track and all those labored males and females come out as "*its*." And even when he is reading German to himself, he always calls those things "*it;*" whereas he ought to read in this way:

TALE OF THE FISHWIFE AND ITS SAD FATE.*

It is a bleak Day. Hear the Rain, how he pours, and the Hail, how he rattles; and see the Snow, how he drifts along, and oh the Mud, how deep he is! Ah the poor Fishwife, it is stuck fast in the Mire; it has dropped its Basket of Fishes; and its Hands have been cut by the Scales as it seized some of the falling Creatures; and one Scale has even got into its Eye, and it cannot get her out. It opens its Mouth to cry for Help; but if any Sound comes out of him, alas he is drowned by the raging of the Storm. And now a Tomcat has got one of the Fishes and she will surely escape with him. No, she bites off a Fin, she holds her in her Mouth,—will she swallow her? No, the Fishwife's brave Mother-Dog deserts his Puppies and rescues the Fin,—which he eats, himself, as his Reward. O, horror, the Lightning has struck the Fishbasket, he sets him on Fire; see the Flame, how she licks the doomed Utensil with her red and angry Tongue; now she attacks the helpless Fishwife's Foot,—she burns him up, all but the big Toe, and even *she* is partly consumed; and still she spreads, still she waves her fiery Tongues; she attacks the Fishwife's Leg and destroys *it*; she attacks its Hand and destroys *her*; she attacks its poor worn Garment and destroys *her* also; she attacks its Body and consumes *him*; she wreathes herself about its Heart and *it* is consumed; next about its Breast, and in a Moment *she* is a Cinder; now she reaches its Neck,—*he* goes; now its Chin,—*it* goes; now its Nose,—*she* goes. In another Moment, except Help come, the Fishwife will be no more. Time presses,—is there none to succor and save? Yes! Joy, joy, with flying Feet the she-Englishwoman comes! But alas, the generous she-Female is too late: where now is the fated Fishwife? It has ceased from its Sufferings, it has gone to a better Land; all that is left of it for its loved Ones to lament over, is this poor smouldering Ash-heap. Ah, woful, woful Ash-heap! Let us take him up tenderly, reverently, upon the lowly Shovel, and bear him to his long Rest, with the Prayer that when he rises again it will be in a Realm where he will have one good square responsible Sex, and have it all to himself, instead of having a mangy lot of assorted Sexes scattered all over him in Spots.

*I capitalize the nouns, in the German (and ancient English) fashion.

There, now, the reader can see for himself that this pronoun-business is a very awkward thing for the unaccustomed tongue.

I suppose that in all languages the similarities of look and sound between words which have no similarity in meaning are a fruitful source of perplexity to the foreigner. It is so in our tongue, and it is notably the case in the German. Now there is that troublesome word *vermählt:* to me it has so close a resemblance,—either real or fancied,—to three or four other words, that I never know whether it means despised, painted, suspected, or married; until I look in the dictionary, and then I find it means the latter. There are lots of such words, and they are a great torment. To increase the difficulty there are words which *seem* to resemble each other, and yet do not; but they make just as much trouble as if they did. For instance, there is the word *vermiethen*, (to let, to lease, to hire); and the word *verheirathen*, (another way of saying to *marry.*) I heard of an Englishman who knocked at a man's door in Heidelberg and proposed, in the best German he could command, to "verheirathen" that house. Then there are some words which mean one thing when you emphasize the first syllable, but mean something very different if you throw the emphasis on the last syllable. For instance, there is a word which means a run-away, or the act of glancing through a book, according to the placing of the emphasis; and another word which signifies to *associate* with a man, or to *avoid* him, according to where you put the emphasis,—and you can generally depend on putting it in the wrong place and getting into trouble.

There are some exceedingly useful words in this language. *Schlag*, for example; and *Zug*. There are three-quarters of a column of Schlags in the dictionary, and a column and a half of Zugs. The world Schlag means Blow, Stroke, Dash, Hit, Shock, Clap, Slap, Time, Bar, Coin, Stamp, Kind, Sort, Manner, Way, Apoplexy, Wood-Cutting, Enclosure, Field, Forest-Clearing. This is its simple and *exact* meaning,—that is to say, its restricted, its fettered meaning; but there are ways by which you can set it free, so that it can soar away, as on the wings of the morning, and never be at rest. You can hang any word you please to its tail, and make it mean anything you want to. You can begin with *Schlag-ader*, which means artery, and you can hang on the whole dictionary, word by word, clear through the alphabet to *Schlag-wasser*, which means bilge-water,—and including *Schlag-mutter*, which means mother-in-law.

Just the same with *Zug*. Strictly speaking, Zug means Pull, Tug, Draught, Procession, March, Progress, Flight, Direction, Expedition, Train, Caravan, Passage, Stroke, Touch, Line,

Flourish, Trait of Character, Feature, Lineament, Chess-move, Organstop, Team, Whiff, Bias, Drawer, Propensity, Inhalation, Disposition: but that thing which it does *not* mean,—when all its legitimate pendants have been hung on, has not been discovered yet.

One cannot over-estimate the usefulness of Schlag and Zug. Armed just with these two, and the word *Also*, what cannot the foreigner on German soil accomplish? The German word *Also* is the equivalent of the English phrase "You know," and does not mean anything at all,—in *talk*, though it sometimes does in print. Every time a German opens his mouth an *Also* falls out; and every time he shuts it he bites one in two that was trying to *get* out.

Now, the foreigner, equipped with these three noble words, is master of the situation. Let him talk right along, fearlessly; let him pour his indifferent German forth, and when he lacks for a word, let him heave a *Schlag* into the vacuum; all the chances are, that it fits it like a plug; but if it doesn't, let him promptly heave a *Zug* after it; the two together can hardly fail to bung the hole; but if, by a miracle, they *should* fail, let him simply say *Also*! and this will give him a moment's chance to think of the needful word. In Germany, when you load your conversational gun it is always best to throw in a *Schlag* or two and a *Zug* or two; because it doesn't make any difference how much the rest of the charge may scatter, you are bound to bag something with *them*. Then you blandly say *Also*, and load up again. Nothing gives such an air of grace and elegance and unconstraint to a German or an English conversation as to scatter it full of "Also's" or "You-knows."

In my note-book I find this entry:

July 1.–In the hospital, yesterday, a word of thirteen syllables was successfully removed from a patient,—a North-German from near Hamburg; but as most unfortunately the surgeons had opened him in the wrong place, under the impression that he contained a panorama, he died. The sad event has cast a gloom over the whole community.

That paragraph furnished a text for a few remarks about one of the most curious and notable features of my subject,—the length of German words. Some German words are so long that they have a perspective. Observe these examples:

Freudschaftsbezeigungen.

Dilletantenaufdringlichkeiten.

Stadtverordnetenversammlungen.

These things are not words, they are alphabetical processions. And they are not rare; one can open a German newspaper any time and see them marching majestically across the page,—and if he has any imagination he can see the banners and hear the music, too. They impart a martial thrill to the meekest subject. I take a great interest in these curiosities. Whenever I come across a good one, I stuff it and put it in my museum. In this way I have made quite a valuable collection. When I get duplicates, I exchange with other collectors, and thus increase the variety of my stock. Here are some specimens which I lately bought at an auction sale of the effects of a bankrupt bric-a-brac hunter:

GENERALSTAATSVERORDNETENVERSAMMLUGEN.

ALTERTHUMSWISSENSCHAFTEN.

KINDERBEWAHRUNGSANSTALTEN.

UNABHAENGIGKEITSERKLAERUNGEN.

WIEDERHERSTELLUNGSBESTREBUNGEN.

WAFFENSTILLSTANDSUNTERHANDLUNGEN.

Of course when one of these grand mountain ranges goes stretching across the printed page, it adorns and ennobles that literary landscape,—but at the same time it is a great distress to the new student, for it blocks up his way; he cannot crawl under it, or climb over it or tunnel through it. So he resorts to the dictionary for help; but there is no help there. The dictionary must draw the line somewhere,—so it leaves this sort of words out. And it is right, because these long things are hardly legitimate words, but are rather combinations of words, and the inventor of them ought to have been killed. They are compound words, with the hyphens left out. The various words used in building them are in the dictionary, but in a very scattered condition; so you can hunt the materials out, one by one, and get at the meaning at last, but it is a tedious and harrassing business. I have tried this process upon some of the above examples. 'Freundschaftsbezeigungen'' seems to be ''Friendship demonstrations,'' which is only a foolish and clumsy way of saying ''demonstrations of friendship.'' ''Unabhaengigkeitserklaerungen'' seems to be ''Independencedeclarations,'' which is no improvement upon ''Declarations of Independence,'' as far as I can see. ''Generalstaatsverordnetenversammlungen'' seems to be ''Generalstatesrepresentativesmeetings,'' as nearly as I can get at it,—a mere rhythmical, gushy euphuism for ''meetings of the legislature,'' I judge. We used to have a good deal of this sort of crime in our literature, but it has gone out, now. We used to speak of a thing as a ''never-to-be-forgotten'' circumstance, instead of cramping it into the simple and sufficient word ''memorable'' and then going calmly about our business as if nothing had happened. In those days we were not content to embalm the thing and bury it decently, we wanted to build a monument over it.

But in our newspapers the compounding-disease lingers a little to the present day, but with the hyphens left out, in the German fashion. This is the shape it takes: instead of saying "Mr. Simmons, clerk of the country and district courts, was in town yesterday," the new form puts it thus: "Clerk of the County and District Court Simmons was in town yesterday." This saves neither time nor ink, and has an awkward sound besides. One often sees a remark like this in our papers: "*Mrs.* Assistant District Attorney Johnson returned to her city residence yesterday for the season." That is a case of really unjustifiable compounding; because it not only saves no time or trouble, but confers a title on Mrs. Johnson which she has no right to. But these little instances are trifles indeed, contrasted with the ponderous and dismal German system of piling jumbled compounds together. I wish to submit the following local item, from a Mannheim journal, by way of illustration:

"In the daybeforeyesterdayshortlyaftereleveno'clock Night, the inthistownstandingtavern called "The Wagoner" was downburnt. When the fire to the onthedownburninghouseresting Stork's Nest reached, flew the parent Storks away. But when the byteraging, firesurrounded Nest *itself* caught Fire, straightway plunged the quickreturning Mother-Stork into the Flames and died, her Wings over young ones outspread."

Even the cumbersome German construction is not able to take the pathos out of that picture,—indeed it somehow seems to strengthen it. This item is dated away back yonder months ago. I could have used it sooner, but I was waiting to hear from the Father-Stork. I am still waiting.

"Also!" If I have not shown that the German is a difficult language, I have at least intended to do it. I have heard of an American student who was asked how he was getting along with his German, and who answered promptly: "I am not getting along at all. I have worked at it hard for three level months, and all I have got to show for it is one solitary German phrase,—'*Zwei glas,*' " (two glasses of beer.) He paused a moment, reflectively, then added with feeling, "But I've got that *solid!*"

And if I have not also shown that German is a harassing and infuriating study, my execution has been at fault, and not my intent. I heard lately of a worn and sorely tried American student who used to fly to a certain German word for relief when he could bear up under his aggravations no longer,—the only word in the whole language whose sound was sweet and precious to his ear and healing to his lacerated spirit. This was the word *Damit.*

It was only the *sound* that helped him, not the meaning*; and so, at last, when he learned that the emphasis was not on the first syllable, his only stay and support was gone, and he faded away and died.

I think that a description of any loud, stirring, tumultuous episode must be tamer in German than in English. Our descriptive words of this character have such a deep, strong, resonant sound, while their German equivalents do seem so thin and mild and energyless. Boom, burst, crash, roar, storm, bellow, blow, thunder, explosion; howl, cry, shout, yell, groan; battle, hell. These are magnificent words; they have a force and magnitude of sound befitting the things which they describe. But their German equivalents would be ever so nice to sing the children to sleep with, or else my awe-inspiring ears were made for display and not for superior usefulness in analyzing sounds. Would any man want to die in a battle which was called by so tame a term as a *Schlacht?* Or would not a consumptive feel too much bundled up, who was about to go out, in a shirt collar and a seal ring, into a storm which the bird-song word *Gewitter* was employed to describe? And observe the strongest of the several German equivalents for explosion,—*Ausbruch.* Our word Toothbrush is more powerful than that. It seems to me that the Germans could do worse than import it into their language to describe particularly tremendous explosions with. The German word for hell,—Hölle,—sounds more like *helly* than anything else; therefore, how necessarily chipper, frivolous and unimpressive it is. If a man were told in German to go there, could he really rise to the dignity of feeling insulted?

Having now pointed out, in detail, the several vices of this language, I now come to the brief and pleasant task of pointing out its virtues. The capitalizing of the nouns, I have already mentioned. But far before this virtue stands another,—that of spelling a word according to the sound of it. After one short lesson in the alphabet, the student can tell how any German word is pronounced, without having to ask; whereas in our language if a student should inquire of us "What does B,O,W, spell?" we should be obliged to reply, "Nobody can tell what it spells, when you set it off by itself,—you can only tell by referring to the context and finding out what it signifies,—whether it is a thing to shoot arrows with, or a nod of one's head, or the forward end of a boat."

There are some German words which are singularly and

*It merely means, in its general sense, *"herewith."*

powerfully effective. For instance, those which describe lowly, peaceful and affectionate home life; those which deal with love, in any and all forms, from mere kindly feeling and honest good will toward the passing stranger, clear up to courtship; those which deal with out door Nature, in its softest and loveliest aspects,—with meadows, and forests, and birds and flowers, the fragrance and sunshine of summer, and the moonlight of peaceful winter nights; in a word, those which deal with any and all forms of rest, repose, and peace; those also which deal with the creatures and marvels of fairyland; and lastly and chiefly, in those words which express pathos, is the language surpassingly rich and effective. There are German songs which can make a stranger to the language cry. That shows that the *sound* of the words is correct,—it interprets the meanings with truth and with exactness; and so the ear is informed, and through the ear, the heart.

The Germans do not seem to be afraid to repeat a word when it is the right one. They repeat it several times, if they choose. That is wise. But in English when we have used a word a couple of times in a paragraph, we imagine we are growing tautological, and so we are weak enough to exchange it for some other word which only approximates exactness, to escape what we wrongly fancy is a greater blemish. Repetition may be bad, but surely inexactness is worse.

———

There are people in the world who will take a great deal of trouble to point out the faults in a religion or a language, and then go blandly about their business without suggesting any remedy. I am not that kind of a person. I have shown that the German language needs reforming. Very well, I am ready to reform it. At least I am ready to make the proper suggestions. Such a course as this might be immodest in another; but I have devoted upwards of nine full weeks, first and last, to a careful and critical study of this tongue, and thus have acquired a confidence in my ability to reform it which no mere superficial culture could have conferred upon me.

In the first place, I would leave out the Dative Case. It confuses the plurals; and besides, nobody ever knows when he is in the Dative Case, except he discover it by accident,—and then he does not know when or where it was that he got into it, or how long he has been in it, or how he is ever going to get out of it again. The Dative Case is but an ornamental folly,—it is better to discard it.

In the next place, I would move the Verb further up to the

front. You may load up with ever so good a Verb, but I notice that you never really bring down a subject with it at the present German range,—you only cripple it. So I insist that this important part of speech should be brought forward to a position where it may be easily seen with the naked eye.

Thirdly, I would import some strong words from the English tongue,—to swear with, and also to use in describing all sorts of vigorous things in a vigorous way.*

Fourthly, I would reorganize the sexes, and distribute them according to the will of the Creator. This as a tribute of respect, if nothing else.

Fifthly, I would do away with those great long compounded words; or require the speaker to deliver them in sections, with intermissions for refreshments. To wholly do away with them would be best, for ideas are more easily received and digested when they come one at a time than when they come in bulk. Intellectual food is like any other; it is pleasanter and more beneficial to take it with a spoon than with a shovel.

Sixthly, I would require a speaker to stop when he is done, and not hang a string of those useless "haben sind gewesen gehabt haben geworden seins" to the end of his oration. This sort of gew-gaws undignify a speech, instead of adding a grace. They are therefore an offense, and should be discarded.

Seventhly, I would discard the Parenthesis. Also the re-Parenthesis, the re-re-parenthesis, and the re-re-re-re-re-re-parentheses, and likewise the final wide-reaching all-enclosing King-parenthesis. I would require every individual, be he high or low, to unfold a plain straightforward tale, or else coil it and sit on it and hold his peace. Infractions of this law should be punishable with death.

And eighthly and lastly, I would retain *Zug* and *Schlag,* with their pendants, and discard the rest of the vocabulary. This would simplify the language.

I have now named what I regard as the most necessary and important changes. These are perhaps all I could be expected to name for nothing; but there are other suggestions which I can

*"*Verdammt,*" and its variations and enlargements, are word which have plenty of meaning, but the *sounds* are so mild and ineffectual that German ladies can use them without sin. German ladies who could not be induced to commit a sin by any persuasion or compulsion, promptly rip out one of these harmless little words when they tear their dresses or don't like the soup. It sounds about as wicked as our "My gracious." German ladies are constantly saying, "Ach! Gott!" "Mein Gott!" "Gott in Himmel!" "Herr Gott!" "Der Herr Jesus!" etc. They think our ladies have the same custom, perhaps, for I once heard a gentle and lovely old German lady say to a sweet young American girl, "The two languages are so alike—how pleasant that is; we say 'Ach! Gott!' you say *'Goddam.'* "

and will make in case my proposed application shall result in my being formally employed by the government in the work of reforming the language.

My philological studies have satisfied me that a gifted person ought to learn English (barring spelling and pronouncing), in 30 hours, French in 30 days, and German in 30 years. It seems manifest, then, that the latter tongue ought to be trimmed down and repaired. If it is to remain as it is, it ought to be gently and reverently set aside among the dead languages, for only the dead have time to learn it.

A Fourth of July Oration in the German Tongue, delivered at a Banquet of the Anglo-American Club of Students by the Author of this Book.

Gentlemen: Since I arrived, a month ago, in this old wonderland, this vast garden of Germany, my English tongue has so often proved a useless piece of baggage to me, and so troublesome to carry around, in a country where they haven't the checking system for luggage, that I finally set to work, last week, and learned the German language. Also! Es freüt mich dass dies so ist, denn es muss, in ein hauptsächlich degree, höflich sein, dass man aüf ein occasion like this, sein Rede in die Sprache des Landes worin he boards, aüssprechen soll. Dafür habe ich, aus reinische Verlegenheit,—no Vergangenheit,—nó, I mean Höflichkeit,—aüs reinische Höflichkeit habe ich resòlved to tackle this business in the German language, ŭm Gottes willen! Also! Sie müssen so freŭndlich sein, ŭnd verzeih mich die interlarding von ein oder zwei Englischer Worte, hie ŭnd da, denn ich finde dass die deutches is not a very copious language, and so when you've really got anything to say, you've got to draw on a language that can stand the strain.

Wenn aber man kann nicht meinem Rede verstehen, so werde ich ihm spater dasselbe übersetz, wenn er solche Dienst verlangen wollen haben werden sollen sein hätte. (I don't know what wollen haben werden sollen sein hätte means, but I notice they always put it at the end of a German sentence—merely for general literary gorgeousness, I suppose.)

This is a great and justly honored day,—a day which is worthy of the veneration in which it is held by the true patriots of all climes and nationalities,—a day which offers a fruitful theme for thought and speech; ŭnd meinem Freŭnde,—no, mein*en* Freŭd*en*,—mein*es* Freŭn*des*,—well, take your choice, they're all the same price; I don't know which one is right,—also! ich habe gehabt haben worden gewesen sein, as Goethe says, in his

Paradise Lost,—ich,—ich,—that is to say,—ich,—but let us change cars.

Also! Die Anblich so viele Grossbrittanischer ŭnd Amerikanischer hier zusammengetroffen in Bruderliche concord, ist zwar a welcome and inspiriting spectacle. And what has moved you to it? Can the terse German tongue rise to the expression of this impulse? Is it Freŭndschaftsbezeigŭngenstadtverordnetenversammlungenfamilieneigenthŭmlichkeiten? Nein, o nein! This is a crisp and noble word, but it fails to pierce the marrow of the impulse which has gathered this friendly meeting and produced diese Anblick,—eine Anblick welche ist gŭt zu sehen,—gŭt fŭr die Aŭgen in a foreign land and a far country,—eine Anblick solche als in die gewŏnliche Heidelberger phrase nennt man ein "schŏnes Aussicht!" Ja, freilich natŭrlich wahrscheinlich ebensowohl! Also! Die Aussich aŭf dem Kŏnigstuhl mehr grŏsserer ist, aber geistlische sprechend nicht so schŏn, lob' Gott! Because sie sind hier zusammengetroffen, in Bruderlichem concord, ein grossen Tag zu feiern, whose high benefits were not for one land and one locality only, but have conferred a measure of good upon all lands that know liberty to day, and love it. Hŭndert Jahre vorŭber, waren die Englănder ŭnd die Amerikaner Feinde; aber heŭte sind sie herzlichen Freŭnde, Gott sei Dank! May this good fellowship endure; may these banners here blended in amity, so remain; may they never any more wave over opposing hosts, or be stained with blood which was kindred, is kindred, and always will be kindred, until a line drawn upon a map shall be able to say, "*This* bars the ancestral blood from flowing in the veins of the descendant!"

Chapters IV through XVII of Life on the Mississippi *were originally written as a series for the prestigious Boston literary magazine, the* Atlantic, *which was edited by Twain's friend, William Dean Howells. This material was titled "Old Times on the Mississippi" when it appeared in the magazine from January to June of 1875, and also for its publication in book form by Belford Brothers of Toronto in 1876 and in London the following year. To fill out the narrative to a suitable length for the subscription format of his American publishers, Twain returned to the river in 1882 and set down an account of that later trip. The expanded narrative was retitled* Life on the Mississippi *when it was published by James R. Osgood and Company in 1883.*

Life on the Mississippi

THE "BODY OF THE NATION"

But *the basin of the Mississippi is the* BODY OF THE NATION. All the other parts are but members, important in themselves, yet more important in their relations to this. Exclusive of the Lake basin and of 300,000 square miles in Texas and New Mexico, which, in many aspects form a part of it, this basin contains about 1,250,000 square miles. In extent it is the second great valley of the world, being exceeded only by that of the Amazon. The valley of the frozen Obi approaches it in extent; that of the La Plata comes next in space, and probably in habitable capacity, having about 8/9 of its area; then comes that of the Yenisei, with about 7/9; the Lena, Amoor, Hoang-ho, Yang-tse-kiang, and Nile, 5/9; the Ganges, less than 1/2; the Indus, less than 1/3; the Euphrates, 1/5; the Rhine, 1/15. It exceeds in extent the whole of Europe, exclusive of Russia, Norway, and Sweden. *It would contain Austria four times, Germany or Spain five times, France six times, the British Islands or Italy ten times*. Conceptions formed from the river-basins of Western Europe are rudely shocked when we consider the extent of the valley of the Mississippi; nor are those formed from the sterile basins of the great rivers of Siberia, the lofty plateaus of Central Asia, or the mighty sweep of the swampy Amazon more adequate. Latitude, elevation, and rainfall all combine to render every part of the Mississippi Valley capable of supporting a dense population. *As* a dwelling-place for civilized man it is by far the first upon our globe.—EDITOR'S TABLE, *Harper's Magazine, February,* 1863.

CHAPTER I

THE RIVER AND ITS HISTORY

The Mississippi is well worth reading about. It is not a commonplace river, but on the contrary is in all ways remarkable. Considering the Missouri its main branch, it is the longest river in the world—four thousand three hundred miles. It seems safe to say that it is also the crookedest river in the world, since in one part of its journey it uses up one thousand three hundred miles to cover the same ground that the crow would fly over in six hundred and seventy-five. It discharges three times as much water as the St. Lawrence, twenty-five times as much as the Rhine, and three hundred and thirty-eight times as much as the Thames. No other river has so vast a drainage-basin: it draws its water supply from twenty-eight States and Territories; from Delaware, on the Atlantic seaboard, and from all the country between that and Idaho on the Pacific slope—a spread of forty-five degrees of longitude. The Mississippi receives and carries to the Gulf water from fifty-four subordinate rivers that are navigable by steamboats, and from some hundreds that are navigable by flats and keels. The area of its drainage-basin is as great as the combined areas of England, Wales, Scotland, Ireland, France, Spain, Portugal, Germany, Austria, Italy, and Turkey; and almost all this wide region is fertile; the Mississippi valley, proper, is exceptionally so.

It is a remarkable river in this: that instead of widening toward its mouth, it grows narrower; grows narrower and deeper. From the junction of the Ohio to a point half way down to the sea, the width averages a mile in high water: thence to the sea the width steadily diminishes, until, at the "Passes," above the mouth, it is but little over half a mile. At the junction of the Ohio the Mississippi's depth is eighty-seven feet; the depth increases gradually, reaching one hundred and twenty-nine just above the mouth.

The difference in rise and fall is also remarkable—not in the upper, but in the lower river. The rise is tolerably uniform down to Natchez (three hundred and sixty miles above the mouth)—about fifty feet. But at Bayou La Fourche the river rises only twenty-four feet; at New Orleans only fifteen, and just above the mouth only two and one half.

An article in the New Orleans "Times-Democrat," based upon reports of able engineers, states that the river annually empties four hundred and six million tons of mud into the Gulf of Mexico—which brings to mind Captain Marryat's rude name for the Mississippi—"the Great Sewer." This mud, solidified, would make a mass a mile square and two hundred and forty-one feet high.

The mud deposit gradually extends the land—but only gradually; it has extended it not quite a third of a mile in the two hundred years which have elapsed since the river took its place in history. The belief of the scientific people is, that the mouth used to be at Baton Rouge, where the hills cease, and that the two hundred miles of land between there and the Gulf was built by the river. This gives us the age of that piece of country, without any trouble at all—one hundred and twenty thousand years. Yet it is much the youthfulest batch of country that lies around there anywhere.

The Mississippi is remarkable in still another way—its disposition to make prodigious jumps by cutting through narrow necks of land, and thus straightening and shortening itself. More than once it has shortened itself thirty miles at a single jump! These cut-offs have had curious effects: they have thrown several river towns out into the rural districts, and built up sand bars and forests in front of them. The town of Delta used to be three miles below Vicksburg: a recent cut-off has radically changed the position, and Delta is now *two miles above* Vicksburg.

Both of these river towns have been retired to the country by that cut-off. A cut-off plays havoc with boundary lines and jurisdictions: for instance, a man is living in the State of Mississippi to-day, a cut-off occurs to-night, and to-morrow the man finds himself and his land over on the other side of the river, within the boundaries and subject to the laws of the State of Louisiana! Such a thing, happening in the upper river in the old times, could have transferred a slave from Missouri to Illinois and made a free man of him.

The Mississippi does not alter its locality by cut-offs alone: it is always changing its habitat *bodily*—is always moving bodily *sidewise*. At Hard Times, La., the river is two miles west of the region it used to occupy. As a result, the original *site* of that settlement is not now in Louisiana at all, but on the other side of the river, in the State of Mississippi. *Nearly the whole of that one thousand three hundred miles of old Mississippi River which La Salle floated down in his canoes, two hundred years ago, is good solid dry ground now.* The river lies to the right of it, in places, and to the left of it in other places.

Although the Mississippi's mud builds land but slowly, down at the mouth, where the Gulf's billows interfere with its work, it builds fast enough in better protected regions higher up: for instance, Prophet's Island contained one thousand five hundred acres of land thirty years ago; since then the river has added seven hundred acres to it.

But enough of these examples of the mighty stream's eccentricities for the present—I will give a few more of them further along in the book.

Let us drop the Mississippi's physical history, and say a word about its historical history—so to speak. We can glance briefly at its slumbrous first epoch in a couple of short chapters; at its second and wider-awake epoch in a couple more; at its flushest and widest-awake epoch in a good many succeeding chapters; and then talk about its comparatively tranquil present epoch in what shall be left of the book.

The world and the books are so accustomed to use, and overuse, the word "new" in connection with our country, that we early get and permanently retain the impression that there is nothing old about it. We do of course know that there are several comparatively old dates in American history, but the mere figures convey to our minds no just idea, no distinct realization, of the stretch of time which they represent. To say that De Soto, the first white man who ever saw the Mississippi River, saw it in 1542, is a remark which states a fact without interpreting it: it is something like giving the dimensions of a sunset by astronomical measurements, and cataloguing the colors by their scientific names;—as a result, you get the bald fact of the sunset, but you don't see the sunset. It would have been better to paint a picture of it.

The date 1542, standing by itself, means little or nothing to us; but when one groups a few neighboring historical dates and facts around it, he adds perspective and color, and then realizes that this is one of the American dates which is quite respectable for age.

For instance, when the Mississippi was first seen by a white man, less than a quarter of a century had elapsed since Francis I.'s defeat at Pavia; the death of Raphael; the death of Bayard, *sans peur et sans reproche;* the driving out of the Knights-Hospitallers from Rhodes by the Turks; and the placarding of the Ninety-Five Propositions,—the act which began the Reformation. When De Soto took his glimpse of the river, Ignatius Loyola was an obscure name; the order of the Jesuits was not yet a year old; Michael Angelo's paint was not yet dry on the Last Judgment in the Sistine Chapel; Mary Queen of Scots was not yet born, but would be before the year closed. Catherine de Medici was a child; Elizabeth of England was not yet in her teens; Calvin, Benvenuto Cellini, and the Emperor Charles V. were at the top of their fame, and each was manufacturing history after his own peculiar fashion; Margaret of Navarre was writing the "Heptameron" and some religious books,—the first survives, the others are forgotten, wit and indelicacy being sometimes better literature-preservers than holiness; lax court morals and the absurd chivalry business were in full feather, and the joust and the tournament were the frequent pastime of titled fine gentlemen who could fight better than they could spell, while religion was the passion of their ladies, and the classifying their offspring into children of full rank and children by brevet their pastime. In fact, all around, religion was in a peculiarly blooming condition: the Council of Trent was being called; the Spanish Inquisition was roasting, and racking, and burning, with a free hand; elsewhere on the continent the nations were being persuaded to holy living by the sword and fire; in England, Henry VIII. had suppressed the monasteries, burnt Fisher and another bishop or two, and was getting his English reformation and his harem effectively started. When De Soto stood on the banks of the Mississippi, it was still two years before Luther's death; eleven years before the burning of Servetus; thirty years before the St. Bartholomew slaughter; Rabelais was not yet published; "Don Quixote" was not yet written; Shakespeare was not yet born; a hundred long years must still elapse before Englishmen would hear the name of Oliver Cromwell.

Unquestionably the discovery of the Mississippi is a datable fact which considerably mellows and modifies the shiny newness of our country, and gives her a most respectable outside-aspect of rustiness and antiquity.

De Soto merely glimpsed the river, then died and was buried in it by his priests and soldiers. One would expect the priests and the soldiers to multiply the river's dimensions by ten—the Spanish custom of the day—and thus move other adventurers to go at once and explore it. On the contrary, their narratives when they reached home, did not excite that amount of curiosity. The Mississippi was left unvisited by whites during a term of years which seems incredible in our energetic days. One may "sense" the interval to his mind, after a fashion, by dividing it up in this way: After De Soto glimpsed the river, a fraction short of a quarter of a century elapsed, and then Shakespeare was born; lived a trifle more than half a century, then died; and when he had been in his grave considerably more than half a century, the *second* white man saw the Mississippi. In our day we don't allow a hundred and thirty years to elapse between glimpses of a marvel. If somebody should discover a creek in the county next to the one that the North Pole is in, Europe and America would start fifteen costly expeditions thither: one to explore the creek, and the other fourteen to hunt for each other.

For more than a hundred and fifty years there had been white settlements on our Atlantic coasts. These people were in intimate communication with the Indians: in the south the Spaniards were robbing, slaughtering, enslaving and converting them; higher up, the English were trading beads and blankets to them for a consideration, and throwing in civilization and whiskey, "for lagniappe;"* and in Canada the French were schooling them in a rudimentary way, missionarying among them, and drawing whole populations of them at a time to Quebec, and later to Montreal, to buy furs of them. Necessarily, then, these various clusters of whites must have heard of the great river of the far west; and indeed, they did hear of it vaguely,—so vaguely and indefinitely, that its course, proportions, and locality were hardly even guessable. The mere mysteriousness of the matter ought to have fired curiosity and compelled exploration; but this did not occur. Apparently nobody happened to want such a river, nobody needed it, nobody was curious about it; so, for a century and a half the Mississippi remained out of the market and undisturbed. When De Soto found it, he was not hunting for a river, and had no present occasion for one; consequently he did not value it or even take any particular notice of it.

But at last La Salle the Frenchman conceived the idea of seeking out that river and exploring it. It always happens that when a man seizes upon a neglected and important idea, people inflamed with the same notion crop up all around. It happened so in this instance.

Naturally the question suggests itself, Why did these people want the river now when nobody had wanted it in the five preceding generations? Apparently it was because at this late day they thought they had discovered a way to make it useful; for it had come to be believed that the Mississippi emptied into the Gulf of California, and therefore afforded a short cut from Canada to China. Previously the supposition had been that it emptied into the Atlantic, or Sea of Virginia.

*See page 414.

CHAPTER II

THE RIVER AND ITS EXPLORERS

La Salle himself sued for certain high privileges, and they were graciously accorded him by Louis XIV. of inflated memory. Chief among them was the privilege to explore, far and wide, and build forts, and stake out continents, and hand the same over to the king, and pay the expenses himself; receiving, in return, some little advantages of one sort or another; among them the monopoly of buffalo hides. He spent several years and about all of his money, in making perilous and painful trips between Montreal and a fort which he had built on the Illinois, before he at last succeeded in getting his expedition in such a shape that he could strike for the Mississippi.

And meantime other parties had had better fortune. In 1673 Joliet the merchant, and Marquette the priest, crossed the country and reached the banks of the Mississippi. They went by way of the Great Lakes; and from Green Bay, in canoes, by way of Fox River and the Wisconsin. Marquette had solemnly contracted, on the feast of the Immaculate Conception, that if the Virgin would permit him to discover the great river, he would name it Conception, in her honor. He kept his word. In that day, all explorers travelled with an outfit of priests. De Soto had twenty-four with him. La Salle had several, also. The expeditions were often out of meat, and scant of clothes, but they always had the furniture and other requisites for the mass; they were always prepared, as one of the quaint chroniclers of the time phrased it, to "explain hell to the salvages."

On the 17th of June, 1673, the canoes of Joliet and Marquette and their five subordinates reached the junction of the Wisconsin with the Mississippi. Mr. Parkman says: "Before them a wide and rapid current coursed athwart their way, by the foot of lofty heights wrapped thick in forests." He continues: "Turning southward, they paddled down the stream, through a solitude unrelieved by the faintest trace of man."

A big cat-fish collided with Marquette's canoe, and startled him; and reasonably enough, for he had been warned by the Indians that he was on a foolhardy journey, even a fatal one, for the river contained a demon "whose roar could be heard at a great distance, and who would engulf them in the abyss where he dwelt." I have seen a Mississippi cat-fish that was more than six feet long, and weighed two hundred and fifty pounds; and if Marquette's fish was the fellow to that one, he had a fair right to think the river's roaring demon was come.

"At length the buffalo began to appear, grazing in herds on the great prairies which then bordered the river; and Marquette describes the fierce and stupid look of the old bulls as they stared at the intruders through the tangled mane which nearly blinded them."

The voyagers moved cautiously: "Landed at night and made a fire to cook their evening meal; then extinguished it, embarked again, paddled some way farther, and anchored in the stream, keeping a man on the watch till morning."

They did this day after day and night after night; and at the end of two weeks they had not seen a human being. The river was an awful solitude, then. And it is now, over most of its stretch.

But at the close of the fortnight they one day came upon the footprints of men in the mud of the western bank—a Robinson Crusoe experience which carries an electric shiver with it yet, when one stumbles on it in print. They had been warned that the river Indians were as ferocious and pitiless as the river demon, and destroyed all comers without waiting for provocation; but no matter, Joliet and Marquette struck into the country to hunt up the proprietors of the tracks. They found them, by and by, and were hospitably received and well treated—if to be received by an Indian chief who has taken off his last rag in order to appear at his level best is to be received hospitably; and if to be treated abundantly to fish, porridge, and other game, including dog, and have these things forked into one's mouth by the ungloved fingers of Indians is to be well treated. In the morning the chief and six hundred of his tribesmen escorted the Frenchmen to the river and bade them a friendly farewell.

On the rocks above the present city of Alton they found some rude and fantastic Indian paintings, which they describe. A short distance below "a torrent of yellow mud rushed furiously athwart the calm blue current of the Mississippi, boiling and surging and sweeping in its course logs, branches, and uprooted trees." This was the mouth of the Missouri, "that savage river," which "descending from its mad career through a vast unknown of barbarism, poured its turbid floods into the bosom of its gentle sister."

By and by they passed the mouth of the Ohio; they passed canebrakes; they fought mosquitoes; they floated along, day after day, through the deep silence and loneliness of the river, drowsing in the scant shade of makeshift awnings, and broiling with the heat; they encountered and exchanged civilities with another party of Indians; and at last they reached the mouth of the Arkansas (about a month out from their starting-point), where a tribe of war-whooping savages swarmed out to meet and murder them; but they appealed to the Virgin for help; so in place of a fight there was a feast, and plenty of pleasant palaver and fol-de-rol.

They had proved to their satisfaction, that the Mississippi did not empty into the Gulf of California, or into the Atlantic. They believed it emptied into the Gulf of Mexico. They turned back, now, and carried their great news to Canada.

But belief is not proof. It was reserved for La Salle to furnish the proof. He was provokingly delayed, by one misfortune after another, but at last got his expedition under way at the end of the year 1681. In the dead of winter he and Henri de Tonty, son of Lorenzo Tonty, who invented the tontine, his lieutenant, started down the Illinois, with a following of eighteen Indians brought from New England, and twenty-three Frenchmen. They moved in procession down the surface of the frozen river, on foot, and dragging their canoes after them on sledges.

At Peoria Lake they struck open water, and paddled thence to the Mississippi and turned their prows southward. They ploughed through the fields of floating ice, past the mouth of the Missouri; past the mouth of the Ohio, by and by; "and, gliding by the wastes of bordering swamp, landed on the 24th of February near the Third Chickasaw Bluffs," where they halted and built Fort Prudhomme.

"Again," says Mr. Parkman, "they embarked; and with every stage of their adventurous progress, the mystery of this vast new world was more and more unveiled. More and more they entered the realms of spring. The hazy sunlight, the warm and drowsy air, the tender foliage, the opening flowers, betokened the reviving life of nature."

Day by day they floated down the great bends, in the shadow of the dense forests, and in time arrived at the mouth of the Arkansas. First, they were greeted by the natives of this locality as Marquette had before been greeted by them—with the booming of the war drum and the flourish of arms. The Virgin composed the difficulty in Marquette's case; the pipe of peace did the same office for La Salle. The white man and the red man struck hands and entertained each other during three days. Then, to the admiration of the savages, La Salle set up a cross with the arms of France on it, and took possession of the whole country for the king—the cool fashion of the time—while the priest piously consecrated the robbery with a hymn. The priest explained the mysteries of the faith "by signs," for the saving of the savages; thus compensating them with possible possessions in Heaven for the certain ones on earth which they had just been robbed of. And also, by signs, La Salle drew from these simple children of the forest acknowledgments of fealty to Louis the Putrid, over the water. Nobody smiled at these colossal ironies.

These performances took place on the site of the future town of Napoleon, Arkansas, and there the first confiscation-cross was raised on the banks of the great river. Marquette's and Joliet's voyage of discovery ended at the same spot—the site of the future town of Napoleon. When De Soto took his fleeting glimpse of the river, away back in the dim early days, he took it from that same spot—the site of the future town of Napoleon, Arkansas. Therefore, three out of the four memorable events connected with the discovery and exploration of the mighty river occurred, by accident, in one and the same place. It is a most curious distinction, when one comes to look at it and think about it. France stole that vast country on that spot, the future Napoleon; and by and by Napoleon himself was to give the country back again!—make restitution, not to the owners, but to their white American heirs.

The voyagers journeyed on, touching here and there; "passed the sites, since become historic, of Vicksburg and Grand Gulf;" and visited an imposing Indian monarch in the Teche country, whose capital city was a substantial one of sun-baked bricks mixed with straw—better houses than many that exist there now. The chief's house contained an audience room forty feet square; and there he received Tonty in State, surrounded by sixty old men clothed in white cloaks. There was a temple in the town, with a mud wall about it ornamented with skulls of enemies sacrificed to the sun.

The voyagers visited the Natchez Indians, near the site of the present city of that name, where they found a "religious and political despotism, a privileged class descended from the sun, a temple and a sacred fire." It must have been like getting home again; it was home with an advantage, in fact, for it lacked Louis XIV.

A few more days swept swiftly by, and La Salle stood in the shadow of his confiscating cross, at the meeting of the waters from Delaware, and from Itaska, and from the mountain ranges close upon the Pacific, with the waters of the Gulf of Mexico, his task finished, his prodigy achieved. Mr. Parkman, in closing his fascinating narrative, thus sums up:

> "On that day, the realm of France received on parchment a stupendous accession. The fertile plains of Texas; the vast basin of the

Mississippi, from its frozen northern springs to the sultry borders of the Gulf; from the woody ridges of the Alleghanies to the bare peaks of the Rocky Mountains—a region of savannas and forests, sun-cracked deserts and grassy prairies, watered by a thousand rivers, ranged by a thousand warlike tribes, passed beneath the sceptre of the Sultan of Versailles; and all by virture of a feeble human voice, inaudible at half a mile."

CHAPTER III

FRESCOES FROM THE PAST

Apparently the river was ready for business, now. But no, the distribution of a population along its banks was as calm and deliberate and time-devouring a process as the discovery and exploration had been.

Seventy years elapsed, after the exploration, before the river's borders had a white population worth considering; and nearly fifty more before the river had a commerce. Between La Salle's opening of the river and the time when it may be said to have become the vehicle of anything like a regular and active commerce, seven sovereigns had occupied the throne of England, America had become an independent nation, Louis XIV. and Louis XV. had rotted and died, the French monarchy had gone down in the red tempest of the revolution, and Napoleon was a name that was beginning to be talked about. Truly, there were snails in those days.

The river's earliest commerce was in great barges—keel-boats, broadhorns. They floated and sailed from the upper rivers to New Orleans, changed cargoes there, and were tediously warped and poled back by hand. A voyage down and back sometimes occupied nine months. In time this commerce increased until it gave employment to hordes of rough and hardy men; rude, uneducated, brave, suffering terrific hardships with sailor-like stoicism; heavy drinkers, coarse frolickers in moral sties like the Natchez-under-the-hill of that day, heavy fighters, reckless fellows, every one, elephantinely jolly, foul-witted, profane; prodigal of their money, bankrupt at the end of the trip, fond of barbaric finery, prodigious braggarts; yet, in the main, honest, trustworthy, faithful to promises and duty, and often picturesquely magnanimous.

By and by the steamboat intruded. Then, for fifteen or twenty years, these men continued to run their keelboats down-stream, and the steamers did all of the up-stream business, the keelboatmen selling their boats in New Orleans, and returning home as deck passengers in the steamers.

But after a while the steamboats so increased in number and in speed that they were able to absorb the entire commerce; and then keelboating died a permanent death. The keelboatman became a deck hand, or a mate, or a pilot on the steamer; and when steamer-berths were not open to him, he took a berth on a Pittsburgh coal-flat, or on a pine-raft constructed in the forests up toward the sources of the Mississippi.

In the heyday of the steamboating prosperity, the river from end to end was flaked with coal-fleets and timber rafts, all managed by hand, and employing hosts of the rough characters whom I have been trying to describe. I remember the annual processions of mighty rafts that used to glide by Hannibal when I was a boy,—an acre or so of white, sweet-smelling boards in each raft, a crew of two dozen men or more, three or four wigwams scattered about the raft's vast level space for storm-quarters,—and I remember the rude ways and the tremendous talk of their big crews, the ex-keelboatmen and their admiringly patterning successors; for we used to swim out a quarter or third of a mile and get on these rafts and have a ride.

By way of illustrating keelboat talk and manners, and that now-departed and hardly-remembered raft-life, I will throw in, in this place, a chapter from a book which I have been working at, by fits and starts, during the past five or six years, and may possibly finish in the course of five or six more. The book is a story which details some passages in the life of an ignorant village boy, Huck Finn, son of the town drunkard of my time out west, there. He has run away from his persecuting father, and from a persecuting good widow who wishes to make a nice, truth-telling, respectable boy of him; and with him a slave of the widow's has also escaped. They have found a fragment of a lumber raft (it is high water and dead summer time), and are floating down the river by night, and hiding in the willows by day,—bound for Cairo,—whence the negro will seek freedom in the heart of the free States. But in a fog, they pass Cairo without knowing it. By and by they begin to suspect the truth, and Huck Finn is persuaded to end the dismal suspense by swimming down to a huge raft which they have seen in the distance ahead of them, creeping aboard under cover of the darkness, and gathering the needed information by eavesdropping:—

But you know a young person can't wait very well when he is impatient to find a thing out. We talked it over, and by and by Jim said it was such a black night, now, that it wouldn't be no risk to swim down to the big raft and crawl aboard and listen,—they would talk about Cairo, because they would be calculating to go ashore there for a spree, maybe, or anyway they would send boats ashore to buy whiskey or fresh meat or something. Jim had a wonderful level head, for a nigger: he could most always start a good plan when you wanted one.

I stood up and shook my rags off and jumped into the river, and struck out for the raft's light. By and by, when I got down nearly to her, I eased up and went slow and cautious. But everything was all right—nobody at the sweeps. So I swum down along the raft till I was most abreast the camp fire in the middle, then I crawled aboard and inched along and got in amongst some bundles of shingles on the weather side of the fire. There was thirteen men there—they was the watch on deck of course. And a mighty rough-looking lot, too. They had a jug, and tin cups, and they kept the jug moving. One man was singing— roaring, you may say; and it wasn't a nice song—for a parlor anyway. He roared through his nose, and strung out the last word of every line very long. When he was done they all fetched a kind of Injun war-whoop, and then another was sung. It begun:—

"There was a woman in our towdn,
  In our towdn did dwed'l (dwell,)
She loved her husband dear-i-lee,
  But another man twyste as wed'l.

Singing too, riloo, riloo, riloo,
  Ri-too, riloo, rilay- - -e,
She loved her husband dear-i-lee,
  But another man twyste as wed'l."

And so on—fourteen verses. It was kind of poor, and when he was going to start on the next verse one of them said it was the tune the old cow died on; and another one said, "Oh, give us a rest." And another one told him to take a walk. They made fun of him till he got mad and jumped up and begun to cuss the crowd, and said he could lam any thief in the lot.

They was all about to make a break for him, but the biggest man there jumped up and says:

"Set whar you are, gentlemen. Leave him to me; he's my meat."

Then he jumped up in the air three times and cracked his heels together every time. He flung off a buckskin coat that was all hung with fringes, and says, "You lay thar tell the chawin-up's done;" and flung his hat down, which was all over ribbons, and says, "You lay thar tell his sufferins is over."

Then he jumped up in the air and cracked his heels together again and shouted out:—

"Whoo-oop! I'm the old original iron-jawed, brass-mounted, copper-bellied corpse-maker from the wilds of Arkansaw!—Look at me! I'm the man they call Sudden Death and General Desolation! Sired by a hurricane, dam'd by an earthquake, half-brother to the cholera, nearly related to the small-pox on the mother's side! Look at me! I take nineteen alligators and a bar'l of whiskey for breakfast when I'm in robust health, and a bushel of rattlesnakes and a dead body when I'm ailing! I split the everlasting rocks with my glance, and I squouch the thunder when I speak! Whoo-oop! Stand back and give me room according to my strength! Blood's my natural drink, and the wails of the dying is music to my ear! Cast your eye on me, genltemen!—and lay low and hold your breath, for I'm bout to turn myself loose!"

All the time he was getting this off, he was shaking his head and looking fierce, and kind of swelling around in a little circle, tucking up his wrist-bands, and now and then straightening up and beating his breast with his fist, saying, "Look at me, gentlemen!" When he got through, he jumped up and cracked his heels together three times, and let off a roaring "whoo-oop! I'm the bloodiest son of a wildcat that lives!"

Then the man that had started the row tilted his old slouch hat down over his right eye; then he bent stooping forward, with his back sagged and his south end sticking out far, and his fists a-shoving out and drawing in in front of him, and so went around in a little circle about three times, swelling himself up and breathing hard. Then he straightened, and jumped up and cracked his heels together three times before he lit again (that made them cheer), and he begun to shout like this:—

"Whoo-oop! bow your neck and spread, for the kingdom of sorrow's a-coming! Hold me down to the earth, for I feel my powers a-working! whoo-oop! I'm a child of sin, *don't* let me get a start! Smoked glass, here, for all! Don't attempt to look at me with the naked eye, gentlemen! When I'm playful I use the meridians of longitude and parallels of latitude for a seine, and drag the Atlantic Ocean for whales! I scratch my head with the lightning and purr myself to sleep with the thunder! When I'm cold, I bile the Gulf of Mexico and bathe in it; when I'm hot I fan myself with an equinoctial storm; when I'm thirsty I reach up and suck a cloud dry like a sponge; when I range the earth hungry, famine follows in my tracks! Woo-oop! Bow your neck and spread! I put my hand on the sun's face and make it night in the earth; I bite a piece out of the moon and hurry the seasons; I shake myself and crumble the mountains! Contemplate me through leather—*don't* use the naked eye! I'm the man with a petrified heart and biler-iron bowels! The massacre of isolated communities is the pastime of my idle moments, the destruction of nationalities the serious business of my life! The boundless vastness of the great American desert is my enclosed property, and I bury my dead on my own premises!" He jumped up and cracked his heels together three times before he lit (they cheered him again), and as he come down he shouted out: "Whoo-oop! bow your neck and spread, for the pet child of calamity's a-coming!"

Then the other one went to swelling around and blowing again—the first one—the one they called Bob; next, the Child of Calamity chipped in again, bigger than ever; then they both got at it at the same time, swelling round and round each other and punching their fists most into each other's faces, and whooping and jawing like Injuns; then Bob called the Child names, and the Child called him names back again: next, Bob called him a heap rougher names and the Child come back at him with the very worst kind of language; next, Bob knocked the Child's hat off, and the Child picked it up and kicked Bob's ribbony hat about six foot; Bob went and got it and said never mind, this warn't going to be the last of this thing, because he was a man that never forgot and never forgive, and so the Child better look out, for there was a time a-coming, just as sure as he was a living man, that he would have to answer to him with the best blood in his body. The Child said no man was willinger than he was for that time to come, and he would give Bob fair warning, *now,* never to cross his path again, for he could never rest till he had waded in his blood, for such was his nature, though he was sparing him now on account of his family, if he had one.

Both of them was edging away in different directions, growling and shaking their heads and going on about what they was going to do; but a little black-whiskered chap skipped up and says:—

"Come back here, you couple of chicken-livered cowards, and I'll thrash the two of ye!"

And he done it, too. He snatched them, he jerked them this way and that, he booted them around, he knocked them sprawling faster than they could get up. Why, it warn't two minutes till they begged like dogs—and how the other lot did yell and laugh and clap their hands all the way through, and shout "Sail in, Corpse-Maker!" "Hi! at him again, Child of Calamity!" "Bully for you, little Davy!" Well, it was a perfect pow-wow for a while. Bob and the Child had red noses and black eyes when they got through. Little Davy made them own up that they was sneaks and cowards and not fit to eat with a dog or drink with a nigger; then Bob and the Child shook hands with each other, very solemn, and said they had always respected each other and was willing to let bygones be bygones. So then they washed their faces in the river; and just then there was a loud order to stand by for a crossing, and some of them went forward to man the sweeps there, and the rest went aft to handle the after-sweeps.

I laid still and waited for fifteen minutes, and had a smoke out of a pipe that one of them left in reach; then the crossing was finished, and they stumped back and had a drink around and went to talking and singing again. Next they got out an old fiddle, and one played, and another patted juba, and the rest turned themselves loose on a regular old-fashioned keel-boat break-down. Then couldn't keep that up very long without gettting winded, so by and by they settled around the jug again.

They sung "jolly, jolly raftsman's the life for me," with a rousing chorus, and then they got to talking about differences betwixt hogs, and their different kind of habits; and next about women and their different ways; and next about the best ways to put out houses that was afire; and next about what ought to be done with the Injuns; and next about what a king had to do, and how much he got; and next about how to make cats fight; and next about what to do when a man has fits; and next about differences betwixt clearwater rivers and muddy-water ones. The man they called Ed said the muddy Mississippi water was wholesomer to drink than the clear water of the Ohio; he said if you let a pint of this yaller Mississippi water settle, you would have about a half to three quarters of an inch of mud in the bottom, according to the stage of the river, and then it warn't no better than Ohio water—what you wanted to do was to keep it stirred up—and when the river was low, keep mud on hand to put in and thicken the water up the way it ought to be.

The Child of Calamity said that was so; he said there was nutritiousness in the mud, and a man that drunk Mississippi water could grow corn in his stomach if he wanted to. He says:—

"You look at the graveyards; that tells the tale. Trees won't grow worth shucks in a Cincinnati graveyard, but in a Sent Louis graveyard they grow upwards of eight hundred foot high. It's all on account of the water the people drunk before they laid up. A Cincinnati corpse don't richen a soil any."

And they talked about how Ohio water didn't like to mix with Mississippi water. Ed said if you take the Mississippi on a rise when the Ohio is low, you'll find a wide band of clear water all the way down the east side of the Mississippi for a hundred mile or more, and the minute you get out a quarter of a mile from shore and pass the line, it is all thick and yaller the rest of the way across. Then they talked about how to keep tobacco from getting mouldy, and from that they went into ghosts and told about a lot that other folks had seen; but Ed says:—

" 'Why don't you tell something that you've seen yourselves? Now let me have a say. Five years ago I was on a raft as big as this, and right along here it was a bright moonshiny night, and I was on watch and boss of the stabboard oar forrard, and one of my pards was a man named Dick Allbright, and he come along to where I was sitting, forrard—gaping and stretching, he was—and stooped down on the edge of the raft and washed his face in the river, and come and set down by me and got out his pipe, and had just got it filled, when he looks up and says,—

" 'Why looky-here,' he says, 'ain't that Buck Miller's place, over yander in the bend?"

" 'Yes,' says I, 'it is—why?' He laid his pipe down and leant his head on his hand, and says,—

" 'I thought we'd be furder down.' I says,—

" 'I thought it too, when I went off watch'—we was standing six hours on and six off—'but the boys told me,' I says, 'that the raft didn't seem to hardly move, for the last hour,'—says I, 'though she's a slipping along all right, now,' says I. He give a kind of a groan, and says,—

" 'I've seed a raft act so before, along here,' he says, ''pears to me the current has most quit above the head of this bend durin' the last two years,' he says.

"Well, he raised up two or three times, and looked away off and around on the water. That started me at it, too. A body is always doing what he sees somebody else doing, though there mayn't be no sense in it. Pretty soon I see a black something floating on the water away off to stabboard and quartering behind us. I see he was looking at it, too. I says,—

" 'What's that?' He says, sort of pettish,—

" 'Tain't nothing but an old empty bar'l.'

" 'An empty bar'l!' says I, 'why,' says I, 'a spy-glass is a fool to *your* eyes. How can you tell it's an empty bar'l?' He says,—

" 'I don't know; I reckon it ain't a bar'l, but I thought it might be,' says he.

" 'Yes,' I says, 'so it might be, and it might be anything else, too; a body can't tell nothing about it, such a distance as that,' I says.

"We hadn't nothing else to do, so we kept on watching it. By and by I says,—

" 'Why looky-here, Dick Allbright, that thing's a-gaining on us, I believe.'

"He never said nothing. The thing gained and gained, and I judged it must be a dog that was about tired out. Well, we swung down into the crossing, and the thing floated across the bright streak of the moonshine, and, by George, it *was* a bar'l. Says I,—

" 'Dick Allbright, what made you think that thing was a bar'l, when it was a half a mile off,' says I. Says he,—

" 'I don't know.' Says I,—

" 'You tell me, Dick Allbright.' He says,—

" 'Well, I knowed it was a bar'l; I've seen it before; lots has seen it; they says it's a hanted bar'l.'

"I called the rest of the watch, and they come and stood there, and I told them what Dick said. It floated right along abreast, now, and didn't gain any more. It was about twenty foot off. Some was for having it aboard, but the rest didn't want to. Dick Allbright said rafts that had fooled with it had got bad luck by it. The captain of the watch said he didn't believe in it. He said he reckoned the bar'l gained on us because it was in a little better current than what we was. He said it would leave by and by.

"So then we went to talking about other things, and we had a song, and then a breakdown; and after that the captain of the watch called for another song; but it was clouding up, now, and the bar'l stuck right thar in the same place, and the song didn't seem to have much warm-up to it, somehow, and so they didn't finish it, and there wasn't any cheers, but it sort of dropped flat, and nobody said anything for a minute. Then everybody tried to talk at once, and one chap got off a joke, but it warn't no use, they didn't laugh, and even the chap that made the joke didn't laugh at it, which ain't usual. We all just settled down glum, and watched the bar'l, and was oneasy and oncomfortable. Well, sir, it shut down black and still, and then the wind begin to moan around, and next the lightning begin to play and the thunder to grumble. And pretty soon there was a regular storm, and in the middle of it a man that was running aft stumbled and fell and sprained his ankle so that he had to lay up. This made the boys shake their heads. And every time the lightning come, there was that bar'l with the blue lights winking around it. We was always on the look-out for it. But by and by, towards dawn, she was gone. When the day come we couldn't see her anywhere, and we warn't sorry, neither.

"But next night about half-past nine, when there was songs and high jinks going on, here she comes again, and took her old roost on the stabboard side. There warn't no more high jinks. Everybody got solemn; nobody talked; you couldn't get anybody to do anything but set around moody and look at the bar'l. It begun to cloud up again. When the watch changed, the off watch stayed up, 'stead of turning in. The storm ripped and roared around all night, and in the middle of it another man tripped and sprained his ankle, and had to knock off. The bar'l left towards day, and nobody see it go.

"Everybody was sober and down in the mouth all day. I don't mean the kind of sober that comes of leaving liquor alone,—not that. They was quiet, but they all drunk more than usual,—not together,—but each man sidled off and took it private, by himself.

"After dark the off watch didn't turn in; 'nobody sung, nobody talked; the boys didn't scatter around, neither; they sort of huddled together, forrard; and for two hours they set there, perfectly still, looking steady in the one direction, and heaving a sigh once in a while. And then, here comes the bar'l again. She took up her old place. She staid there all night; nobody turned in. The storm come on again, after midnight. It got awful dark; the rain poured down; hail, too; the thunder boomed and roared and bellowed; the wind blowed a hurricane; and the lightning spread over everything in big sheets of glare, and showed the whole raft as plain as day; and the river lashed up white as milk as far as you could see for miles, and there was that bar'l jiggering along, same as ever. The captain ordered the watch to man the after sweeps for a crossing, and nobody would go,—no more sprained ankles for them, they said. They wouldn't even *walk* aft. Well then, just then the sky split wide open, with a crash, and the lightning killed two men of the after watch, and crippled two more. Crippled them how, says you? Why, *sprained their ankles!*

"The bar'l left in the dark betwixt lightnings, towards dawn. Well, not a body eat a bite at breakfast that morning. After that the men loafed around, in twos and threes, and talked low together. But none of them herded with Dick Allbright. They all give him the cold shake. If he come around where any of the men was, they split up and sidled away. They wouldn't man the sweeps with him. The captain had all the skiffs hauled up on the raft, alongside of his wigwam, and wouldn't let the dead men be took ashore to be planted; he didn't believe a man that got ashore would come back; and he was right.

"After night come, you could see pretty plain that there was going to be trouble if that bar'l come again; there was such a muttering going on. A good many wanted to kill Dick Allbright, because he'd seen the bar'l on other trips, and that had an ugly look. Some wanted to put him ashore. Some said, let's all go ashore in a pile, if the bar'l comes again.

"This kind of whispers was still going on, the men being bunched together forrard watching for the bar'l, when, lo and behold you, here she comes again. Down she comes, slow and steady, and settles into her old tracks. You could a heard a pin drop. Then up comes the captain, and says:—

" 'Boys, don't be a pack of children and fools; I don't want this bar'l to be dogging us all the way to Orleans, and *you* don't; well, then, how's the best way to stop it? Burn it up,—that's the way. I'm going to fetch it aboard,' he says. And before anybody could say a word, in he went.

"He swum to it, and as he come pushing it to the raft, the men spread to one side. But the old man got it aboard and busted in the head, and there was a baby in it! Yes sir, a stark naked baby. It was Dick Allbright's baby; he owned up and said so.

" 'Yes,' he says, a-leaning over it, 'yes, it is my own lamented darling, my poor lost Charles William Allbright deceased,' says he,—for he could curl his tongue around the bulliest words in the language when he was a mind to, and lay them before you withoug a jint started, anywheres. Yes, he said he used to live up at the head of this bend, and one night he choked his child, which was crying, not intending to kill it,—which was prob'ly a lie,—and then he was scared, and buried it in a bar'l, before his wife got home, and off he went, and struck the northern trail and went to rafting; and this was the third year that the bar'l had chased him. He said the bad luck always begun light, and lasted till four men was killed, and then the bar'l didn't come any more after that. He said if the men would stand it one more night,—and was a-going on like that,—but the men had got enough. They started to get out a boat to take him ashore and lynch him, but he grabbed the little child all of a sudden and jumped overboard with it hugged up to his breast and shedding tears, and we never see him again in this life, poor old suffering soul, nor Charles William neither."

"*Who* was shedding tears?" says Bob; "was it Allbright or the baby?"

"Why, Allbright, of course; didn't I tell you the baby was dead? Been dead three years—how could it cry?"

"Well, never mind how it could cry—how could it *keep* all that time?" says Davy. "You answer me that."

"I don't know how it done it," says Ed. "It done it though—that's all I know about it."

"Say—what did they do with the bar'l?" says the Child of Calamity.

"Why, they hove it overboard, and it sunk like a chunk of lead."

"Edward, did the child look like it was choked?" says one.

"Did it have its hair parted?" says another.

"What was the brand on that bar'l, Eddy?" says a fellow they called Bill.

"Have you got the papers for them statistics, Edmund?" says Jimmy.

"Say, Edwin, was you one of the men that was killed by the lightning?" says Davy.

"Him? O, ho, he was both of 'em," says Bob. Then they all haw-hawed.

"Say, Edward, don't you reckon you'd better take a pill? You look bad— don't you feel pale?" says the Child of Calamity.

"O, come, now, Eddy," says Jimmy, "show up; you must a kept part of that bar'l to prove the thing by. Show us the bunghole—*do*—and we'll all believe you."

"Say, boys," says Bill, "less divide it up. Thar's thirteen of us. I can swaller a thirteenth of the yard, if you can worry down the rest."

Ed got up mad and said they could all go to some place which he ripped out pretty savage, and then walked off aft cussing to himself, and they yelling and jeering at him, and roaring and laughing so you could hear them a mile.

"Boys, we'll split a watermelon on that," says the Child of Calamity; and he come rummaging around in the dark amongst the shingle bundles where I was, and put his hand on me. I was warm and soft and naked; so he says "Ouch!" and jumped back.

"Fetch a lantern or a chunk of fire here, boys—there's a snake here as big as a cow!"

So they run there with a lantern and crowded up and looked in on me.

"Come out of that, you beggar!" says one.

"Who are you?" says another.

"What are you after here? Speak up prompt, or overboard you go."

"Snake him out, boys. Snatch him out by the heels."

I began to beg, and crept out amongst them trembling. They looked me over, wondering, and the Child of Calamity says:—

"A cussed thief! Lend a hand and less heave him overboard!"

"No," says Big Bob, "less get out the paint-pot and paint him a sky blue all over from head to heel, and *then* heave him over!"

"Good! that's it. Go for the paint, Jimmy."

When the paint come, and Bob took the brush and was just going to begin, the others laughing and rubbing their hands, I begun to cry, and that sort of worked on Davy, and he says:—

"'Vast there! He's nothing but a cub. I'll paint the man that tetches him!"

So I looked around on them, and some of them grumbled and growled, and Bob put down the paint, and the others didn't take it up.

"Come here to the fire, and less see what you're up to here," says Davy. "Now set down there and give an account of yourself. How long have you been aboard here?"

"Not over a quarter of a minute, sir," says I.

"How did you get dry so quick?"

"I don't know, sir. I'm always that way, mostly."

"Oh, you are, are you? What's your name?"

I warn't going to tell my name. I didn't know what to say, so I just says:

"Charles William Allbright, sir."

Then they roared—the whole crowd; and I was mighty glad I said that, because maybe laughing would get them in a better humor.

When they got done laughing, Davy says:—

"It won't hardly do, Charles William. You couldn't have growed this much in five year, and you was a baby when you come out of the bar'l, you know, and dead at that. Come, now, tell a straight story, and nobody'll hurt you, if you ain't up to anything wrong. What *is* your name?"

"Aleck Hopkins, sir. Aleck James Hopkins."

"Well, Aleck, where did you come from, here?"

"From a trading scow. She lays up the bend yonder. I was born on her. Pap has traded up and down here all his life; and he told me to swim off here, because when you went by he said he would like to get some of you to speak to a Mr. Jonas Turner, in Cairo, and tell him—"

"Oh, come!"

"Yes, sir, it's as true as the world; Pap he says—"

"Oh, your grandmother!"

They all laughed, and I tried again to talk, but they broke in on me and stopped me.

"Now, looky-here," says Davy; "you're scared, and so you talk wild. Honest, now, do you live in a scow, or is it a lie?"

"Yes, sir, in a trading scow. She lays up at the head of the bend. But I warn't born in her. It's our first trip."

"Now you're talking! What did you come aboard here, for? To steal?"

"No, sir, I didn't.—It was only to get a ride on the raft. All boys does that."

"Well, I know that. But what did you hide for?"

"Sometimes they drive the boys off."

"So they do. They might steal. Looky-here; if we let you off this time, will you keep out of these kind of scrapes hereafter?"

"'Deed I will, boss. You try me."

"All right, then. You ain't but little ways from shore. Overboard with you, and don't you make a fool of yourself another time this way.—Blast it, boy, some raftsmen would rawhide you till you were black and blue!"

I didn't wait to kiss good-bye, but went overboard and broke for shore. When Jim come along by and by, the big raft was away out of sight around the point. I swum out and got aboard, and was mighty glad to see home again.

The boy did not get the information he was after, but his adventure has furnished the glimpse of the departed raftsman and keelboatman which I desire to offer in this place.

I now come to a phase of the Mississippi River life of the flush times of steamboating, which seems to me to warrant full examination—the marvellous science of piloting, as displayed there. I believe there has been nothing like it elsewhere in the world.

CHAPTER IV

THE BOYS' AMBITION

When I was a boy, there was but one permanent ambition among my comrades in our village* on the west bank of the Mississippi River. That was, to be a steamboatman. We had transient ambitions of other sorts, but they were only transient. When a circus came and went, it left us all burning to become clowns; the first negro minstrel show that came to our section left us all suffering to try that kind of life; now and then we had a hope that if we lived and were good, God would permit us to be pirates. These ambitions faded out, each in its turn; but the ambition to be a steamboatman always remained.

Once a day a cheap, gaudy packet arrived upward from St. Louis, and another downward from Keokuk. Before these events, the day was glorious with expectancy; after them, the day was a dead and empty thing. Not only the boys, but the whole village, felt this. After all these years I can picture that old time to myself now, just as it was then: the white town drowsing in the sunshine of a summer's morning; the streets empty, or pretty nearly so; one or two clerks sitting in front of the Water Street stores, with their splint-bottomed chairs tilted back against the wall, chins on breasts, hats slouched over their faces, asleep—with shingle-shavings enough around to show what broke them down; a sow and a litter of pigs loafing along the sidewalk, doing a good business in watermelon rinds and seeds; two or three lonely little freight piles scattered about the "levee;" a pile of "skids" on the slope of the stone-paved wharf, and the fragrant town drunkard asleep in the shadow of them; two or three wood flats at the head of the wharf, but nobody to listen to the peaceful lapping of the wavelets against them; the great Mississippi, the majestic, the magnificent Mississippi, rolling its mile-wide tide along, shining in the sun; the dense forest away on the other side; the "point" above the town, and the "point" below, bounding the river-glimpse and turning it into a sort of sea, and withal a very still and brilliant and lonely one. Presently a film of dark smoke appears above one of those remote "points;" instantly a negro drayman, famous for his quick eye and prodigious voice, lifts up the cry, "S-t-e-a-m-boat a-comin'!" and the scene changes! The town drunkard stirs, the clerks wake up, a furious clatter of drays follows, every house and store pours out a human contribution,

*Hannibal, Missouri.

and all in a twinkling the dead town is alive and moving. Drays, carts, men, boys, all go hurrying from many quarters to a common centre, the wharf. Assembled there, the people fasten their eyes upon the coming boat as upon a wonder they are seeing for the first time. And the boat *is* rather a handsome sight, too. She is long and sharp and trim and pretty; she has two tall, fancy-topped chimneys, with a gilded device of some kind swung between them; a fanciful pilot-house, all glass and "gingerbread," perched on top of the "texas" deck behind them; the paddle-boxes are gorgeous with a picture or with gilded rays above the boat's name; the boiler deck, the hurricane deck, and the texas deck are fenced and ornamented with clean white railings; there is a flag gallantly flying from the jack-staff; the furnace doors are open and the fires glaring bravely; the upper decks are black with passengers, the captain stands by the big bell, calm, imposing, the envy of all; great volumes of the blackest smoke are rolling and tumbling out of the chimneys—a husbanded grandeur created with a bit of pitch pine just before arriving at a town; the crew are grouped on the forecastle; the broad stage is run far out over the port bow, and an envied deck-hand stands picturesquely on the end of it with a coil of rope in his hand; the pent steam is screaming through the gauge-cocks; the captain lifts his hand, a bell rings, the wheels stop; then they turn back, churning the water to foam, and the steamer is at rest. Then such a scramble as there is to get aboard, and to get ashore, and to take in freight and to discharge freight, all at one and the same time; and such a yelling and cursing as the mates facilitate it all with! Ten minutes later the steamer is under way again, with no flag on the jack-staff and no black smoke issuing from the chimneys. After ten more minutes the town is dead again, and the town drunkard asleep by the skids once more.

My father was a justice of the peace, and I supposed he possessed the power of life and death over all men and could hang anybody that offended him. This was distinction enough for me as a general thing; but the desire to be a steamboatman kept intruding, nevertheless. I first wanted to be a cabin-boy, so that I could come out with a white apron on and shake a table-cloth over the side, where all my old comrades could see me; later I thought I would rather be the deck-hand who stood on the end of the stage-plank with the coil of rope in his hand, because he was particularly conspicuous. But these were only day-dreams,—they were too heavenly to be contemplated as real possibilities. By and by one of our boys went away. He was not heard of for a long time. At last he turned up as apprentice engineer or "striker" on a steamboat. This thing shook the bottom out of all my Sunday-school teachings. That boy had been notoriously worldly, and I just the reverse; yet he was exalted to this eminence, and I left in obscurity and misery. There was nothing generous about this fellow in his greatness. He would always manage to have a rusty bolt to scrub while his boat tarried at our town, and he would sit on the inside guard and scrub it, where we could all see him and envy him and loathe him. And whenever his boat was laid up he would come home and swell around the town in his blackest and greasiest clothes, so that nobody could help remembering that he was a steamboatman; and he used all sorts of steamboat technicalities in his talk, as if he were so used to them that he forgot common people could not understand them. He would speak of the "labboard" side of a horse in an easy, natural way that would make one wish he was dead. And he was always talking about "St. Looy" like an old citizen; he would refer casually to occasions when he "was coming down Fourth Street," or when he was "passing by the Planter's House," or when there was a fire and he took a turn on the brakes of "the old Big Missouri;" and then he would go on and lie about how many towns the size of ours were burned down there that day. Two or three of the boys had long been persons of consideration among us because they had been to St. Louis once and had a vague general knowledge of its wonders, but the day of their glory was over now. They lapsed into a humble silence, and learned to disappear when the ruthless "cub"-engineer approached. This fellow had money, too, and hair oil. Also an ignorant silver watch and a showy brass watch chain. He wore a leather belt and used no suspenders. If ever a youth was cordially admired and hated by his comrades, this one was. No girl could withstand his charms. He "cut out" every boy in the village. When his boat blew up at last, it diffused a tranquil contentment among us such as we had not known for months. But when he came home the next week, alive, renowned, and appeared in church all battered up and bandaged, a shining hero, stared at and wondered over by everybody, it seemed to us that the partiality of Providence for an undeserving reptile had reached a point where it was open to criticism.

This creature's career could produce but one result, and it speedily followed. Boy after boy managed to get on the river. The minister's son became an engineer. The doctor's and the post-master's sons became "mud clerks;" the wholesale liquor dealer's son became a bar-keeper on a boat; four sons of the chief merchant, and two sons of the county judge, became pilots. Pilot was the grandest position of all. The pilot, even in those days of trivial wages, had a princely salary—from a hundred and fifty to two hundred and fifty dollars a month, and no board to pay. Two months of his wages would pay a preacher's salary for a year. Now some of us were left disconsolate. We could not get on the river—at least our parents would not let us.

So by and by I ran away. I said I never would come home again till I was a pilot and could come in glory. But somehow I could not manage it. I went meekly aboard a few of the boats that lay packed together like sardines at the long St. Louis wharf, and very humbly inquired for the pilots, but got only a cold shoulder and short words from mates and clerks. I had to make the best of this sort of treatment for the time being, but I had comforting day-dreams of a future when I should be a great and honored pilot, with plenty of money, and could kill some of these mates and clerks and pay for them.

CHAPTER V

I WANT TO BE A CUB-PILOT

Months afterward the hope within me struggled to a reluctant death, and I found myself without an ambition. But I was ashamed to go home. I was in Cincinnati, and I set work to map out a new career. I had been reading about the recent exploration of the river Amazon by an expedition sent out by our government. It was said that the expedition, owing to difficulties, had not thoroughly explored a part of the country lying about the head-waters, some four thousand miles from the mouth of the river. It was only about fifteen hundred miles from Cincinnati to New Orleans, where I could doubtless get a ship. I had thirty dollars left; I would go and complete the exploration of the Amazon. This was all the thought I gave to the subject. I never was great in matters of detail. I packed my valise, and took passage on an ancient tub called the "Paul Jones," for New Orleans. For the sum of sixteen dollars I had the scarred and tarnished splendors of "her" main saloon principally to myself, for she was not a creature to attract the eye of wiser travellers.

When we presently got under way and went poking down the broad Ohio, I became a new being, and the subject of my own admiration. I was a traveller! A word never had tasted so good in my mouth before. I had an exultant sense of being bound for mysterious lands and distant climes which I never have felt in so uplifting a degree since. I was in such a glorified condition that all ignoble feelings departed out of me, and I was able to look down and pity the untravelled with a compassion that had hardly a trace of contempt in it. Still, when we stopped at villages and wood-yards, I could not help lolling carelessly upon the railings of the boiler deck to enjoy the envy of the country boys on the bank. If they did not seem to discover me, I presently sneezed to attract their attention, or moved to a position where they could not help seeing me. And as soon as I knew they saw me I gaped and stretched, and gave other signs of being mightily bored with travelling.

I kept my hat off all the time, and stayed where the wind and the sun could strike me, bccause I wanted to get the bronzed and weather-beaten look of an old traveller. Before the second day was half gone, I experienced a joy which filled me with the purest gratitude; for I saw that the skin had begun to blister and peel off my face and neck. I wished that the boys and girls at home could see me now.

We reached Louisville in time—at least the neighborhood of it. We stuck hard and fast on the rocks in the middle of the river, and lay there four days. I was now beginning to feel a strong sense of being a part of the boat's family, a sort of infant son to the captain and younger brother to officers. There is no estimating the pride I took in this grandeur, or the affection that began to swell and grow in me for those people. I could not know how the lordly steamboatman scorns that sort of presumption in a mere landsman. I particularly longed to acquire the least trifle of notice from the big stormy mate, and I was on the alert for an opportunity to do him a service to that end. It came at last. The riotous powwow of setting a spar was going on down on the forecastle, and I went down there and stood around in the way—or mostly skipping out of it—till the mate suddenly roared a general order for somebody to bring him a capstan bar. I sprang to his side and said: "Tell me where it is—I'll fetch it!"

If a rag-picker had offered to do a diplomatic service for the Emperor of Russia, the monarch could not have been more astounded than the mate was. He even stopped swearing. He stood and stared down at me. It took him ten seconds to scrape his disjointed remains together again. Then he said impressively: "Well, if this don't beat hell!" and turned to his work with the air of a man who had been confronted with a problem too abstruse for solution.

I crept away, and courted solitude for the rest of the day. I did not go to dinner; I stayed away from supper until everybody else had finished. I did not feel so much like a member of the boat's family now as before. However, my spirits returned, in instalments, as we pursued our way down the river. I was sorry I hated the mate so, because it was not in (young) human nature not to admire him. He was huge and muscular, his face was bearded and whiskered all over; he had a red woman and a blue woman tattooed on his right arm,—one on each side of a blue anchor with a red rope to it; and in the matter of profanity he was sublime. When he was getting out cargo at a landing, I was always where I could see and hear. He felt all the majesty of his great position, and made the world feel it, too. When he gave even the simplest order, he discharged it like a blast of lightning, and sent a long, reverberating peal of profanity thundering after it. I could not held contrasting the way in which the average landsman would give an order, with the mate's way of doing it. If the landsman should wish the gang-plank moved a foot farther forward, he would probably say: "James, or William, one of you push that plank forward, please;" but put the mate in his place, and he would roar out: "Here, now, start that gang-plank for'ard! Lively, now! *What*'re you about! *Snatch* it! There! there! Aft again! aft again! Don't you hear me? Dash it to dash! are you going to *sleep* over it! *'Vast* heaving. 'Vast heaving, I tell you! Going to heave it clear astern? WHERE're you going with that barrel! *for'ard* with it 'fore I make you swallow it, you dash-dash-dash-*dashed* split between a tired mudturtle and crippled hearse-horse!"

I wished I could talk like that.

When the soreness of my adventure with the mate had somewhat worn off, I began timidly to make up to the humblest official connected with the boat—the night watchman. He snubbed my advances at first, but I presently ventured to offer him a new chalk pipe, and that softened him. So he allowed me to sit with him by the big bell on the hurricane deck, and in time he melted in conversation. He could not well have helped it, I hung with such homage on his words and so plainly showed that I felt honored by his notice. He told me the names of dim capes and shadowy islands as we glided by them in the solemnity of the night, under the winking stars, and by and by got to talking about himself. He seemed over-sentimental for a man whose salary was six dollars a week—or rather he might have seemed so to an older person that I. But I drank in his words hungrily, and with a faith that might have moved mountains if it had been applied judiciously. What was it to me that he was soiled and seedy and fragrant with gin? What was it to me that his grammar was bad, his construction worse, and his profanity so void of art that it was an element of weakness rather than strength in his conversation? He was a wronged man, a man who had seen trouble, and that was enough for me. As he mellowed into his plaintive history his tears dripped upon the lantern in his lap, and I cried, too, from sympathy. He said he was the son of an English nobleman—either an earl or an alderman, he could not remember which, but believed was both; his father, the nobleman, loved him, but his mother hated him from the cradle; and so while he was still a little boy he was sent to "one of them old, ancient colleges"—he couldn't remember which; and by and by his father died and his mother seized the property and "shook" him, as he phrased it. After his mother shook him, members of the nobility with whom he was acquainted used their influence to get him the position of "lob-lolly-boy in a ship;" and from that point my watchman threw off all trammels of date and locality and branched out into a narrative that bristled all along with incredible adventures; a narrative that was so reeking with bloodshed and so crammed with hair-breadth escapes and the most engaging and unconscious personal villanies, that I sat speechless, enjoying, shuddering, wondering, worshipping.

It was a sore blight to find out afterwards that he was a low, vulgar, ignorant, sentimental, half-witted humbug, an untravelled native of the wilds of Illinois, who had absorbed wildcat literature and appropriated its marvels, until in time he had woven odds and ends of the mess into this yarn, and then gone on telling it to fledglings like me, until he had come to believe it himself.

CHAPTER VI

A CUB-PILOT'S EXPERIENCE

What with lying on the rocks four days at Louisville, and some other delays, the poor old "Paul Jones" fooled away about two weeks in making the voyage from Cincinnati to New Orleans. This gave me a chance to get acquainted with one of the pilots, and he taught me how to steer the boat, and thus made the fascination of river life more potent than ever for me.

It also gave me a chance to get acquainted with a youth who had taken deck passage—more's the pity; for he easily borrowed six dollars of me on a promise to return to the boat and pay it back to me the day after we should arrive. But he probably died or forgot, for he never came. It was doubtless the former, since he had said his parents were wealthy, and he only travelled deck passage because it was cooler.*

*"Deck" passage—*i.e.*, steerage passage.

I soon discovered two things. One was that a vessel would not be likely to sail for the mouth of the Amazon under ten or twelve years; and the other was that the nine or ten dollars still left in my pocket would not suffice for so imposing an exploration as I had planned, even if I could afford to wait for a ship. Therefore it followed that I must contrive a new career. The "Paul Jones" was now bound for St. Louis. I planned a siege against my pilot, and at the end of three hard days he surrendered. He agreed to teach me the Mississippi River from New Orleans to St. Louis for five hundred dollars, payable out of the first wages I should receive after graduating. I entered upon the small enterprise of "learning" twelve or thirteen hundred miles of the great Mississippi River with the easy confidence of my time of life. If I had really known what I was about to require of my faculties, I should not have had the courage to begin. I supposed that all a pilot had to do was to keep his boat in the river, and I did not consider that that could be much of a trick, since it was so wide.

The boat backed out from New Orleans at four in the afternoon, and it was "our watch" until eight. Mr. Bixby, my chief, "straightened her up," plowed her along past the sterns of the other boats that lay at the Levee, and then said, "Here, take her; shave those steamships as close as you'd peel an apple." I took the wheel, and my heart-beat fluttered up into the hundreds; for it seemed to me that we were about to scrape the side off every ship in the line, we were so close. I held my breath and began to claw the boat away from the danger; and I had my own opinion of the pilot who had known no better than to get us into such peril, but I was too wise to express it. In half a minute I had a wide margin of safety intervening between the "Paul Jones" and the ships; and within ten seconds more I was set aside in disgrace, and Mr. Bixby was going into danger again and flaying me alive with abuse of my cowardice. I was stung, but I was obliged to admire the easy confidence with which my chief loafed from side to side of his wheel, and trimmed the ships so closely that disaster seemed ceaselessly imminent. When he had cooled a little he told me that the easy water was close ashore and the current outside, and therefore we must hug the bank, up-stream, to get the benefit of the former, and stay well out, down-stream, to take advantage of the latter. In my own mind I resolved to be a down-stream pilot and leave the up-streaming to people dead to prudence.

Now and then Mr. Bixby called my attention to certain things. Said he, "This is Six-Mile Point." I assented. It was pleasant enough information, but I could not see the bearing of it. I was not conscious that it was a matter of any interest to me. Another time he said, "This is Nine-Mile Point." Later he said, "This is Twelve-Mile Point." They were all about level with the water's Twelve-Mile Point." They were all about level with the water's edge; they all looked about alike to me; they were monotonously unpicturesque. I hoped Mr. Bixby would change the subject. But no; he would crowd up around a point, hugging the shore with affection, and then say: "The slack water ends here, abreast this bunch of China-trees; now we cross over." So he crossed over. He gave me the wheel once or twice, but I had no luck. I either came near shipping off the edge of a sugar plantation, or I yawed too far from shore, and so dropped back into disgrace again and got abused.

The watch was ended at last, and we took supper and went to bed. At midnight the glare of a lantern shone in my eyes, and the night watchman said:—

"Come! turn out!"

And then he left. I could not understand this extraordinary procedure; so I presently gave up trying to, and dozed off to sleep. Pretty soon the watchman was back again, and this time he was gruff. I was annoyed. I said:—

"What do you want to come bothering around here in the middle of the night for? Now as like as not I'll not get to sleep again to-night."

The watchman said:—

"Well, if this an't good, I'm blest."

The "off-watch" was just turning in, and I heard some brutal laughter from them, and such remarks as "Hello, watchman! an't the new cub turned out yet? He's delicate, likely. Give him some sugar in a rag and send for the chambermaid to sing rock-a-by-baby to him."

About this time Mr. Bixby appeared on the scene. Something like a minute later I was climbing the pilot-house steps with some of my clothes on and the rest in my arms. Mr. Bixby was close behind, commenting. Here was something fresh—this thing of getting up in the middle of the night to go to work. It was a detail in piloting that had never occurred to me at all. I knew that boats ran all night, but somehow I had never happened to reflect that somebody had to get up out of a warm bed to run them. I began to fear that piloting was not quite so romantic as I had imagined it was; there was something very real and work-like about this new phase of it.

It was a rather dingy night, although a fair number of stars were out. The big mate was at the wheel, and he had the old tub pointed at a star and was holding her straight up the middle of the river. The shores on either hand were not much more than half a mile apart, but they seemed wonderfully far away and ever so vague and indistinct. The mate said:—

"We've got to land at Jones's plantation, sir."

The vengeful spirit in me exulted. I said to myself, I wish you joy of your job, Mr. Bixby; you'll have a good time finding Mr. Jones's plantation such a night as this; and I hope you never *will* find it as long as you live.

Mr. Bixby said to the mate:—

"Upper end of the plantation, or the lower?"

"Upper."

"I can't do it. The stumps there are out of water at this stage. It's no great distance to the lower, and you'll have to get along with that."

"All right, sir. If Jones don't like it he'll have to lump it, I reckon."

And then the mate left. My exultation began to cool and my wonder to come up. Here was a man who not only proposed to find this plantation on such a night, but to find either end of it you preferred. I dreadfully wanted to ask a question, but I was carrying about as many short answers as my cargo-room would admit of, so I held my peace. All I desired to ask Mr. Bixby was the simple question whether he was ass enough to really imagine he was going to find that plantation on a night when all plantations were exactly alike and all the same color. But I held in. I used to have fine inspirations of prudence in those days.

Mr. Bixby made for the shore and soon was scraping it, just the same as if it had been daylight. And not only that, but singing—

"Father in heaven, the day is declining," etc.

It seemed to me that I had put my life in the keeping of a peculiarly reckless outcast. Presently he turned on me and said:—

"What's the name of the first point above New Orleans?"

I was gratified to be able to answer promptly, and I did. I said I didn't know.

"Don't *know*?"

This manner jolted me. I was down at the foot again, in a moment. But I had to say just what I had said before.

"Well, you're a smart one," said Mr. Bixby. "What's the name of the *next* point?"

Once more I didn't know.

"Well, this beats anything. Tell me the name of *any* point or place I told you."

I studied a while and decided that I couldn't.

"Look here! What do you start out from, above Twelve-Mile Point, to cross over?"

"I—I—don't know."

"You—you—don't know?" mimicking my drawling manner of speech. What *do* you know?"

"I—I—nothing, for certain."

"By the great Caesar's ghost, I believe you! You're the stupidest dunderhead I ever saw or ever heard of, so help me Moses! The idea of *you* being a pilot—*you!* Why, you don't know enough to pilot a cow down a lane."

Oh, but his wrath was up! He was a nervous man, and he shuffled from one side of his wheel to the other as if the floor was hot. He would boil a while to himself, and then overflow and scald me again.

"Look here! What do you suppose I told you the names of those points for?"

I tremblingly considered a moment, and then the devil of temptation provoked me to say:—

"Well—to—to—be entertaining, I thought."

This was a red rag to the bull. He raged and stormed so (he was crossing the river at the time) that I judge it made him blind, because he ran over the steering-oar of a trading-scow. Of course the traders sent up a volley of red-hot profanity. Never was a man so grateful as Mr. Bixby was: because he was brim full, and here were subjects who would *talk back*. He threw open a window, thrust his head out, and such an irruption followed as I never had heard before. The fainter and farther away the scowmen's curses drifted, the higher Mr. Bixby lifted his voice and the weightier his adjectives grew. When he closed the window he was empty. You could have drawn a seine through his system and not caught curses enough to disturb your mother with. Presently he said to me in the gentlest way:—

"My boy, you must get a little memorandum-book, and every time I tell you a thing, put it down right away. There's only one way to be a pilot, and that is to get this entire river by heart. You have to know it just like A B C."

That was a dismal revelation to me; for my memory was never loaded with anything but blank cartridges. However, I did not feel discouraged long. I judged that it was best to make some allowances, for doubtless Mr. Bixby was "stretching." Presently he pulled a rope and struck a few strokes on the big bell. The stars were all gone now, and the night was as black as ink. I could hear the wheels churn along the bank, but I was not entirely certain that I could see the shore. The voice of the invisible watchman called up from the hurricane deck:—

"What's this, sir?"

"Jones's plantation."

I said to myself, I wish I might venture to offer a small bet that it isn't. But I did not chirp. I only waited to see. Mr. Bixby handled the engine bells, and in due time the boat's nose came to the land, a torch glowed from the forecastle, a man skipped ashore, a darky's voice on the bank said, "Gimme de k'yarpet-bag, Mars' Jones," and the next moment we were standing up the river again, all serene. I reflected deeply a while, and then said,—but not aloud,—Well, the finding of that plantation was the luckiest accident that ever happened; but it couldn't happen again in a hundred years. And I fully believed it *was* an accident, too.

By the time we had gone seven or eight hundred miles up the river, I had learned to be a tolerably plucky upstream steersman, in daylight, and before we reached St. Louis I had made a trifle of progress in night-work, but only a trifle. I had a note-book that fairly bristled with the names of towns, "points," bars, islands, bends, reaches, etc.; but the information was to be found only in the note-book—none of it was in my head. It made my heart ache to think I had only got half of the river set down; for as our watch was four hours off and four hours on, day and night, there was a long four-hour gap in my book for every time I had slept since the voyage began.

My chief was presently hired to go on a big New Orleans boat, and I packed my satchel and went with him. She was a grand affair. When I stood in her pilot-house I was so far above the water that I seemed perched on a mountain; and her decks stretched so far away, fore and aft, below me, that I wondered how I could ever have considered the little "Paul Jones" a large craft. There were other differences, too. The "Paul Jones's" pilot-house was a cheap, dingy, battered rattle-trap, cramped for room: but here was a sumptuous glass temple; room enough to have a dance in; showy red and gold window-curtains; an imposing sofa; leather cushions and a back to the high bench where visiting pilots sit, to spin yarns and "look at the river;" bright, fanciful "cuspadores" instead of a broad wooden box filled with sawdust; nice new oilcloth on the floor; a hospitable big stove for winter; a wheel as high as my head, costly with inlaid work; a wire tiller-rope; bright brass knobs for the bells; and a tidy, white-aproned, black "texas-tender," to bring up tarts and ices and coffee during mid-watch, day and night. Now this was "something like;" and so I began to take heart once more to believe that piloting was a romantic sort of occupation after all. The moment we were under way I began to prowl about the great steamer and fill myself with joy. She was as clean and as dainty as a drawing-room; when I looked down her long, gilded saloon, it was like gazing through a splendid tunnel; she had an oil-picture, by some gifted signpainter, on every state-room door; she glittered with no end of prism-fringed chandeliers; the clerk's office was elegant, the bar was marvellous, and the bar-keeper had been barbered and upholstered at incredible cost. The boiler deck (*i.e.,* the second story of the boat, so to speak), was as spacious as a church, it seemed to me; so with the forecastle; and there was no pitiful handful of deck-hands, firemen, and roust-abouts down there, but a whole battalion of men. The fires were fiercely glaring from a long row of furnaces, and over them were eight huge boilers! This was unutterable pomp. The mighty engines—but enough of this. I had never felt so fine before. And when I found that the regiment of natty servants respectfully "sir'd" me, my satisfaction was complete.

CHAPTER VII

A DARING DEED

When I returned to the pilot-house St. Louis was gone and I was lost. Here was a piece of river which was all down in my book, but I could make neither head nor tail of it: you understand, it was turned around. I had seen it when coming up-stream, but I had never faced about to see how it looked when it was behind me. My heart broke again, for it was plain that I had got to learn this troublesome river *both ways.*

The pilot-house was full of pilots, going down to "look at the river." What is called the "upper river" (the two hundred miles between St. Louis and Cairo, where the Ohio comes in) was low; and the Mississippi changes its channel so constantly that the pilots used to always find it necessary to run down to Cairo to take a fresh look, when their boats were to lie in port a week; that is, when the water was at a low stage. A deal of this "looking at the river" was done by poor fellows who seldom had a berth, and whose only hope of getting one lay in their being always freshly posted and therefore ready to drop into the shoes of some reputable pilot, for a single trip, on account of such pilot's sudden illness, or some other necessity. And a good many of them constantly ran up and down inspecting the river, not because they ever really hoped to get a berth, but because (they being guests of the boat) it was cheaper to "look at the river" than stay ashore and pay board. In time these fellows grew dainty in their tastes, and only infested boats that had an established reputation for setting good tables. All visiting pilots were useful, for they were always ready and willing, winter or summer, night or day, to go out in the yawl and help buoy the channel or assist the boat's pilots in any way they could. They were likewise welcome because all pilots are tireless talkers, when gathered together, and as they talk only about the river they are always understood and are always interesting. Your true pilot cares nothing about anything on earth but the river, and his pride in his occupation surpasses the pride of kings.

We had a fine company of these river-inspectors along, this trip. There were eight or ten; and there was abundance of room for them in our great pilot-house. Two or three of them wore polished silk hats, elaborate shirt-fronts, diamond breastpins, kid gloves, and patent-leather boots.They were choice in their English, and bore themselves with a dignity proper to men of solid means and prodigious reputation as pilots. The others were more or less loosely clad, and wore upon their heads tall felt cones that were suggestive of the days of the Commonwealth.

I was a cipher in this august company, and felt subdued, not to say torpid. I was not even of sufficient consequence to assist at the wheel when it was necessary to put the tiller hard down in a hurry; the guest that stood nearest did that when occasion required—and this was pretty much all the time, because of the crookedness of the channel and the scant water. I stood in a corner; and the talk I listened to took the hope all out of me. One visitor said to another:—

"Jim, how did you run Plum Point, coming up?"

"It was in the night, there, and I ran it the way one of the boys on the 'Diana' told me; started out about fifty yards above the wood pile on the false point, and held on the cabin under Plum Point till I raised the reef—quarter less twain—then straightened up for the middle bar till I got well abreast the old one-limbed cotton-wood in the bend, then got my stern on the cotton-wood and head on the low place above the point, and came through a-booming—nine and a half."

"Pretty square crossing, an't it?"

"Yes, but the upper bar's working down fast."

Another pilot spoke up and said:—

"I had better water than that, and ran it lower down; started out from the false point—mark twain—raised the second reef abreast the big snag in the bend, and had quarter less twain."

One of the gorgeous ones remarked:—

"I don't want to find fault with your leadsmen, but that's a good deal of water for Plum Point, it seems to me."

There was an approving nod all around as this quiet snub dropped on the boaster and "settled" him. And so they went on talk-talk-talking. Meantime, the thing that was running in my mind was, "Now if my ears hear aright, I have not only to get the names of all the towns and islands and bends, and so on, by heart, but I must even get up a warm personal acquaintanceship with every old snag and one-limbed cotton-wood and obscure wood pile that ornaments the banks of this river for twelve hundred miles; and more than that, I must actually know where these things are in the dark, unless these guests are gifted with eyes that can pierce through two miles of solid blackness; I wish the piloting business was in Jericho and I had never thought of it."

At dusk Mr. Bixby tapped the big bell three times (the signal to land), and the captain emerged from his drawing-room in the forward end of the texas, and looked up inquiringly. Mr. Bixby said:—

"We will lay up here all night, captain."

"Very well, sir."

That was all. The boat came to shore and was tied up for the night. It seemed to me a fine thing that the pilot could do as he pleased, without asking so grand a captain's permission. I took my supper and went immediately to bed, discouraged by my day's observations and experiences. My late voyage's note-booking was but a confusion of meaningless names. It had tangled me all up in a knot every time I had looked at it in the daytime. I now hoped for respite in sleep; but no, it revelled all through my head till sunrise again, a frantic and tireless nightmare.

Next morning I felt pretty rusty and low-spirited. We went booming along, talking a good many chances, for we were anxious to "get out of the river" (as getting out to Cairo was called) before night should overtake us. But Mr. Bixby's partner, the other pilot, presently grounded the boat, and we lost so much time getting her off that it was plain the darkness would overtake us a good long way above the mouth. This was a great misfortune, especially to certain of our visiting pilots, whose boats would have to wait for their return, no matter how long that might be. It sobered the pilot-house talk a good deal. Coming up-stream, pilots did not mind low water or any kind of darkness; nothing stopped them but fog. But down-stream work was different; a boat was too nearly helpless, with a stiff current pushing behind her; so it was not customary to run down-stream at night in low water.

There seemed to be one small hope, however: if we could get

through the intricate and dangerous Hat Island crossing before night, we could venture the rest, for we would have plainer sailing and better water. But it would be insanity to attempt Hat Island at night. So there was a deal of looking at watches all the rest of the day, and a constant ciphering upon the speed we were making; Hat Island was the eternal subject; sometimes hope was high and sometimes we were delayed in a bad crossing, and down it went again. For hours all hands lay under the burden of this suppressed excitement; it was even communicated to me, and I got to feeling so solicitous about Hat Island, and under such an awful pressure of responsibility, that I wished I might have five minutes on shore to draw a good, full, relieving breath, and start over again. We were standing no regular watches. Each of our pilots ran such portions of the river as he had run when coming up-stream, because of his greater familiarity with it; but both remained in the pilot-house constantly.

An hour before sunset, Mr. Bixby took the wheel and Mr. W—— stepped aside. For the next thirty minutes every man held his watch in his hand and was restless, silent, and uneasy. At last somebody said, with a doomful sigh,—

"Well yonder's Hat Island—and we can't make it."

All the watches closed with a snap, everybody sighed and muttered something about its being "too bad, too bad—ah, if we could *only* have got here half an hour sooner!" and the place was thick with the atmosphere of disappointment. Some started to go out, but loitered, hearing no bell-tap to land. The sun dipped behind the horizon, the boat went on. Inquiring looks passed from one guest to another; and one who had his hand on the door-knob and had turned it, waited, then presently took away his hand and let the knob turn back again. We bore steadily down the bend. More looks were exchanged, and nods of surprised admiration—but no words. Insensibly the men drew together behind Mr. Bixby, as the sky darkened and one or two dim stars came out. The dead silence and sense of waiting became oppressive. Mr. Bixby pulled the cord, and two deep, mellow notes from the big bell floated off on the night. Then a pause, and one more note was struck. The watchman's voice followed, from the hurricane deck:—

"Labboard lead, there! Stabboard lead!"

The cries of the leadsmen began to rise out of the distance, and were gruffly repeated by the word-passers on the hurricane deck.

"M-a-r-k three! . . . . M-a-r-k three! . . . . Quarter-less-three! . . . . Half twain! . . . . Quarter twain! . . . . M-a-r-k twain! . . . . Quarter-less"—

Mr. Bixby pulled two bell-ropes, and was answered by faint jinglings far below in the engine room, and our speed slackened. The steam began to whistle through the gaugecocks. The cries of the leadsmen went on—and it is a weird sound, always, in the night. Every pilot in the lot was watching now, with fixed eyes, and talking under his breath. Nobody was calm and easy but Mr. Bixby. He would put his wheel down and stand on a spoke, and as the steamer swung into her (to me) utterly invisible marks—for we seemed to be in the midst of a wide and gloomy sea—he would meet and fasten her there. Out of the murmur of half-audible talk, one caught a coherent sentence now and then—such as:

"There; she's over the first reef all right!"

After a pause, another subdued voice:—

"Her stern's coming down just *exactly* right, by *George!*"

"Now she's in the marks; over she goes!"

Somebody else muttered:—

Oh, it was done beautiful—*beautiful!*"

Now the engines were stopped altogether, and we drifted with the current. Not that I could see the boat drift, for I could not, the stars being all gone by this time. This drifting was the dismalest work; it held one's heart still. Presently I discovered a blacker gloom than that which surrounded us. It was the head of the island. We were closing right down upon it. We entered its deeper shadow, and so imminent seemed the peril that I was likely to suffocate; and I had the strongest impulse to do *something,* anything, to save the vessel. But still Mr. Bixby stood by his wheel, silent, intent as a cat, and all the pilots stood shoulder to shoulder at his back.

"She'll not make it!" somebody whispered.

The water grew shoaler and shoaler, by the leadsman's cries, till it was down to—

"Eight-and-a-half! . . . . E-i-g-h-t feet! . . . . E-i-g-h-t feet! . . . . Seven-and"—

Mr. Bixby said warningly through his speaking tube to the engineer:—

"Stand by, now!"

"Aye-aye, sir!"

"Seven-and-a-half! Seven feet! *Six*-and"—

We touched bottom! Instantly Mr. Bixby set a lot of bells ringing, shouted through the tube, "*Now,* let her have it—every ounce you've got!" then to his partner, "Put her hard down! snatch her! snatch her!" The boat rasped and ground her way through the sand, hung upon the apex of disaster a single tremendous instant, and then over she went! And such a shout as went up at Mr. Bixby's back never loosened the roof of a pilot-house before!

There was no more trouble after that. Mr. Bixby was a hero that night; and it was some little time, too, before his exploit ceased to be talked about by river men.

Fully to realize the marvellous precision required in laying the great steamer in her marks in that murky waste of water, one should know that not only must she pick her intricate way through snags and blind reefs, and then shave the head of the island so closely as to brush the overhanging foliage with her stern, but at one place she must pass almost within arm's reach of a sunken and invisible wreck that would snatch the hull timbers from under her if she should strike it, and destroy a quarter of a million dollars' worth of steamboat and cargo in five minutes, and maybe a hundred and fifty human lives into the bargain.

The last remark I heard that night was a compliment to Mr. Bixby, uttered in soliloquy and with unction by one of our guests. He said:—

"By the Shadow of Death, but he's a lightning pilot!"

CHAPTER VIII

PERPLEXING LESSONS

At the end of what seemed a tedious while, I had managed to pack my head full of islands, towns, bars, "points," and bends; and a curiously inanimate mass of lumber it was, too. However, inasmuch as I could shut my eyes and reel off a good long string of these names without leaving out more than ten miles of river in every fifty, I began to feel that I could take a boat down to New Orleans if I could make her skip those little gaps. But of course my complacency could hardly get start enough to lift my nose a trifle into the air, before Mr. Bixby would think of something to fetch it down again. One day he turned on me suddenly with this settler:—

"What is the shape of Walnut Bend?"

He might as well have asked me my grandmother's opinion of protoplasm. I reflected respectfully, and then said I didn't know it had any particular shape. My gunpowdery chief went off with a bang, of course, and then went on loading and firing until he was out of adjectives.

I had learned long ago that he only carried just so many rounds of ammunition, and was sure to subside into a very placable and even remorseful old smooth-bore as soon as they were all gone. That word "old" is merely affectionate; he was not more than thirty-four. I waited. By and by he said,—

"My boy, you've got to know the *shape* of the river perfectly. It is all there is left to steer by on a very dark night. Everything else is blotted out and gone. But mind you, it hasn't the same shape in the night that it has in the day-time."

"How on earth am I ever going to learn it, then?"

"How do you follow a hall at home in the dark? Because you know the shape of it. You can't see it."

"Do you mean to say that I've got to know all the million trifling variations of shape in the banks of this interminable river as well as I know the shape of the front hall at home?"

"On my honor, you've got to know them *better* than any man ever did know the shapes of the halls in his own house."

"I wish I was dead!"

"Now I don't want to discourage you, but"—

"Well, pile it on me: I might as well have it now as another time."

"You see, this has got to be learned; there isn't any getting around it. A clear starlight night throws such heavy shadows that if you didn't know the shape of a shore perfectly you would claw away from every bunch of timber, because you would take the black shadow of it for a solid cape; and you see you would be getting scared to death every fifteen minutes by the watch. You would be fifty yards from shore all the time when you ought to be within fifty feet of it. You can't see a snag in one of those shadows, but you know exactly where it is, and the shape of the river tells you when you are coming to it. Then there's your pitch-dark night; the river is a very different shape on a pitch-dark night from what it is on a starlight night. All shores seem to be straight lines, then, and mighty dim ones, too; and you'd *run* them for straight lines only you know better. You boldly drive your boat right into what seems to be a solid, straight wall (you knowing very well that in reality there is a curve there), and that wall falls back and makes way for you. Then there's your gray mist. You take a night when there's one of these grisly, drizzly, gray mists, and then there isn't *any* particular shape to a shore. A gray mist would tangle the head of the oldest man that ever lived. Well, then, different kinds of *moonlight* change the shape of the river in different ways. You see"—

"Oh, don't say any more, please! Have I got to learn the shape of the river according to all these fivdifferent ways? If I tried to carry all that cargo in my head it would make me stoop-shouldered."

"*No!* you only learn *the* shape of the river; and you learn it with such absolute certainty that you can always steer by the shape that's *in your head,* and never mind the one that's before your eyes."

"Very well, I'll try it; but after I have learned it can I depend on it? Will it keep the same form and not go fooling around?"

Before Mr. Bixby could answer, Mr. W—— came in to take the watch, and he said,—

"Bixby, you'll have to look out for President's Island and all that country clear away up above the Old Hen and Chickens. The banks are caving and the shape of the shores changing like everything. Why, you wouldn't know the point above 40. You can go up inside the old sycamore snag, now."*

So that question was answered. Here were leagues of shore changing shape. My spirits were down in the mud again. Two things seemed pretty apparent to me. One was, that in order to be a pilot a man had got to learn more than any one man ought to be allowed to know; and the other was, that he must learn it all over again in a different way every twenty-four hours. That night we had the watch until twelve. Now it was an ancient river custom for the two pilots to chat a bit when the watch changed. While the relieving pilot put on his gloves and lit his cigar, his partner, the retiring pilot, would say something like this:—

"I judge the upper bar is making down a little at Hale's Point; had quarter twain with the lower lead and mark twain** with the other."

"Yes, I thought it was making down a little, last trip. Meet any boats?"

"Met one abreast the head of 21, but she was away over hugging the bar, and I couldn't make her out entirely. I took her for the 'Sunny South'—hadn't any skylights forward of the chimneys."

And so on. And as the relieving pilot took the wheel his partner† would mention that we were in such-and-such a bend, and say we were abreast of such-and-such a man's wood-yard or plantation. This was courtesy; I supposed it was *necessity.* But Mr. W—— came on watch full twelve minutes late on this particular night,—a tremendous breach of etiquette; in fact, it is the unpardonable sin among pilots. So Mr. Bixby gave him no greeting whatever, but simply surrendered the wheel and

* It may not be necessary, but still it can do no harm to explain that "inside" means between the snag and the shore.—M.T.

** Two fathoms. Quarter twain is 2¼ fathoms, 13½ feet. Mark three is three fathoms.

† "Partner" is technical for "the other pilot."

marched out of the pilot-house without a word. I was appalled; it was a villanous night for blackness, we were in a particularly wide and blind part of the river, where there was no shape or substance to anything, and it seemed incredible that Mr. Bixby should have left that poor fellow to kill the boat trying to find out where he was. But I resolved that I would stand by him any way. He should find that he was not wholly friendless. So I stood around, and waited to be asked where we were. But Mr. W—— plunged on serenely through the solid firmament of black cats that stood for an atmosphere, and never opened his mouth. Here is a proud devil, thought I; here is a limb of Satan that would rather send us all to destruction than put himself under obligations to me, because I am not yet one of the salt of the earth and privileged to snub captains and lord it over everything dead and alive in a steamboat. I presently climbed up on the bench; I did not think it was safe to go to sleep while this lunatic was on watch.

However, I must have gone to sleep in the course of time, because the next thing I was aware of was the fact that day was breaking, Mr. W—— gone, and Mr. Bixby at the wheel again. So it was four o'clock and all well—but me; I felt like a skinful of dry bones and all of them trying to ache at once.

Mr. Bixby asked me what I had stayed up there for. I confessed that it was to do Mr. W—— a benevolence,—tell him where he was. It took five minutes for the entire preposterousness of the thing to filter into Mr. Bixby's system, and then I judge it filled him nearly up to the chin; because he paid me a compliment—and not much of a one either. He said,—

"Well, taking you by-and-large, you do seem to be more different kinds of an ass than any creature I ever saw before. What did you suppose he wanted to know for?"

I said I thought it might be a convenience to him.

"Convenience! D-nation! Didn't I tell you that a man's got to know the river in the night the same as he'd know his own front hall?"

"Well, I can follow the front hall in the dark if I know it *is* the front hall; but suppose you set me down in the middle of it in the dark and not tell me which hall it is; how am *I* to know?"

"Well, you've *got* to, on the river!"

"All right. Then I'm glad I never said anything to Mr. W——"

"I should say so. Why, he'd have slammed you through the window and utterly ruined a hundred dollars' worth of window-sash and stuff."

I was glad this damage had been saved, for it would have made me unpopular with the owners. They always hated anybody who had the name of being careless, and injuring things.

I went to work now to learn the shape of the river; and of all the eluding and ungraspable objects that ever I tried to get mind or hands on, that was the chief. I would fasten my eyes upon a sharp, wooded point that projected far into the river some miles ahead of me, and go to laboriously photographing its shape upon my brain; and just as I was beginning to succeed to my satisfaction, we would draw up toward it and the exasperating thing would begin to melt away and fold back into the bank! If there had been a conspicuous dead tree standing upon the very point of the cape, I would find that tree inconspicuously merged into the general forest, and occupying the middle of a straight shore, when I got abreast of it! No prominent hill would stick to its shape long enough for me to make up my mind what its form really was, but it was as dissolving and changeful as if it had been a mountain of butter in the hottest corner of the tropics. Nothing ever had the same shape when I was coming down-stream that it had borne when I went up. I mentioned these little difficulties to Mr. Bixby. He said,—

"That's the very main virtue of the thing. If the shapes didn't change every three seconds they wouldn't be of any use. Take this place where we are now, for instance. As long as that hill over yonder is only one hill, I can boom right along the way I'm going; but the moment it splits at the top and forms a V, I know I've got to scratch to starboard in a hurry, or I'll bang this boat's brains out against a rock; and then the moment one of the prongs of the V swings behind the other, I've got to waltz to larboard again, or I'll have a misunderstanding with a snag that would snatch the keelson out of this steamboat as neatly as if it were a sliver in your hand. If that hill didn't change its shape on bad nights there would be an awful steamboat grave-yard around here inside of a year."

It was plain that I had got to learn the shape of the river in all the different ways that could be thought of,—upside down, wrong end first, inside out, for-and-aft, and "thortships,"—and then know what to do on gray nights when it hadn't any shape at all. So I set about it. In the course of time I began to get the best of this knotty lesson, and my self-complacency moved to the front once more. Mr. Bixby was all fixed, and ready to start it to the rear again. He opened on me after this fashion:—

"How much water did we have in the middle crossing at Hole-in-the-Wall, trip before last?"

I considered this an outrage. I said:—

"Every trip, down and up, the leadsmen are singing through that tangled place for three quarters of an hour on a stretch. How do you reckon I can remember such a mess as that?"

"My boy, you've got to remember it. You've got to remember the exact spot and the exact marks the boat lay in when we had the shoalest water, in every one of the five hundred shoal places between St. Louis and New Orleans; and you mustn't get the shoal soundings and marks of one trip mixed up with the shoal soundings and marks of another, either, for they're not often twice alike. You must keep them separate."

When I came to myself again, I said,—

"When I get so that I can do that, I'll be able to raise the dead, and then I won't have to pilot a steamboat to make a living. I want to retire from this business. I want a slush-bucket and a brush; I'm only fit for a roustabout. I haven't got brains enough to be a pilot; and if I had I wouldn't have strength enough to carry them around, unless I went on crutches."

"Now drop that! When I say I'll learn* a man the river, I mean it. And you can depend on it, I'll learn him or kill him."

CHAPTER IX

CONTINUED PERPLEXITIES

There was no use in arguing with a person like this. I promptly put such a strain on my memory that by and by even the shoal water and the countless crossing-marks began to stay with me. But the result was just the same. I never could more than get one knotty thing learned before another presented itself. Now I had often seen pilots gazing at the water and pretending to read it as if it were a book; but it was a book that told me nothing. A time came at last, however, when Mr. Bixby seemed to think me far enough advanced to bear a lesson on water-reading. So he began:—

"Do you see that long slanting line on the face of the water? Now, that's a reef. Moreover, it's a bluff reef. There is a solid sand-bar under it that is nearly as straight up and down as the side of a house. There is plenty of water close up to it, but mighty little on top of it. If you were to hit it you would knock the boat's brains out. Do you see where the line fringes out at the upper end and begins to fade away?"

"Yes, sir."

*"Teach" is not in the river vocabulary.

"Well, that is a low place; that is the head of the reef. You can climb over there, and not hurt anything. Cross over, now, and follow along close under the reef—easy water there—not much current."

I followed the reef along till I approached the fringed end. Then Mr. Bixby said,—

"Now get ready. Wait till I give the word. She won't want to mount the reef; a boat hates shoal water. Stand by—wait—*wait*—keep her well in hand. *Now* cramp her down! Snatch her! snatch her!"

He seized the other side of the wheel and helped to spin it around until it was hard down, and then we held it so. The boat resisted, and refused to answer for a while, and next she came surging to starboard, mounted the reef, and sent a long, angry ridge of water foaming away from her bows.

"Now watch her; watch her like a cat, or she'll get away from you. When she fights strong and the tiller slips a little, in a jerky, greasy sort of way, let up on her a trifle; it is the way she tells you at night that the water is too shoal; but keep edging her up, little by little, toward the point. You are well up on the bar, now; there is a bar under every point, because the water that comes down around it forms an eddy and allows the sediment to sink. Do you see those fine lines on the face of the water that branch out like the ribs of a fan? Well, those are little reefs; you want to just miss the ends of them, but run them pretty close. Now look out—look out! Don't you crowd that slick, greasy-looking place; there ain't nine feet there; she won't stand it. She begins to smell it; look sharp, I tell you! Oh blazes, there you go! Stop the starboard wheel! Quick! Ship up to back! Set her back!"

The engine bells jingled and the engines answered promptly, shooting white columns of steam far aloft out of the 'scape pipes, but it was too late. The boat had "smelt" the bar in good earnest; the foamy ridges that radiated from her bows suddenly disappeared, a great dead swell came rolling forward and swept ahead of her, she careened far over to larboard, and went tearing away toward the other shore as if she were about scared to death. We were a good mile from where we ought to have been, when we finally got the upper hand of her again.

During the afternoon watch the next day, Mr. Bixby asked me if I knew how to run the next few miles. I said:—

"Go inside the first snag above the point, outside the next one, start out from the lower end of Higgins's wood-yard, make a square crossing and"—

"That's all right. I'll be back before you close up on the next point."

But he wasn't. He was still below when I rounded it and entered upon a piece of river which I had some misgivings about. I did not know that he was hiding behind a chimney to see how I would perform. I went gayly along, getting prouder and prouder, for he had never left the boat in my sole charge such a length of time before. I even got to "setting" her and letting the wheel go, entirely, while I vaingloriously turned my back and inspected the stern marks and hummed a tune, a sort of easy indifference which I had prodigiously admired in Bixby and other great pilots. Once I inspected rather long, and when I faced to the front again my heart flew into my mouth so suddenly that if I hadn't clapped my teeth together I should have lost it. One of those frightful bluff reefs was stretching its deadly length right across our bows! My head was gone in a moment; I did not know which end I stood on; I gasped and could not get my breath; I spun the wheel down with such rapidity that it wove itself together like a spider's web; the boat answered and turned square away from the reef, but the reef followed her! I fled, and still it followed still it kept—right across my bows! I never looked to see where I was going, I only fled. The awful crash was imminent—why didn't that villain come! If I committed the crime of ringing a bell, I might get thrown overboard. But better that than kill the boat. So in blind desperation I started such a rattling "shivaree" down below as never had astounded an engineer in this world before, I fancy. Amidst the frenzy of the bells the engines began to back and fill in a furious way, and my reason forsook its throne—we were about to crash into the woods on the other side of the river. Just then Mr. Bixby stepped calmly into view on the hurricane deck. My soul went out to him in gratitude. My distress vanished; I would have felt safe on the brink of Niagara, with Mr. Bixby on the hurricane deck. He blandly and sweetly took his tooth-pick out of his mouth between his fingers, as if it were a cigar,—we were just in the act of climbing an overhanging big tree, and the passengers were scudding astern like rats,—and lifted up these commands to me ever so gently:—

"Stop the starboard. Stop the larboard. Set her back on both."

The boat hesitated, halted, pressed her nose among the boughs a critical instant, then reluctantly began to back away.

"Stop the larboard. Come ahead on it. Stop the starboard. Come ahead on it. Point her for the bar."

I sailed away as serenely as a summer's morning. Mr. Bixby came in and said, with mock simplicity,—

"When you have a hail, my boy, you ought to tap the big bell three times before you land, so that the engineers can get ready."

I blushed under the sarcasm, and said I hadn't had any hail.

"Ah! Then it was for wood, I suppose. The officer of the watch will tell you when he wants to wood up."

I went on consuming, and said I wasn't after wood.

"Indeed? Why, what could you want over here in the bend, then? Did you ever know of a boat following a bend up-stream at this stage of the river?"

"No, sir,—and *I* wasn't trying to follow it. I was getting away from a bluff reef."

"No, it wasn't a bluff reef; there isn't one within three miles of where you were."

"But I saw it. It was as bluff as that one yonder."

"Just about. Run over it!"

"Do you give it as an order?"

"Yes. Run over it."

"If I don't, I wish I may die."

"All right; I am taking the responsibility."

I was just as anxious to kill the boat, now, as I had been to save her before. I impressed my orders upon my memory, to be used at the inquest, and made a straight break for the reef. As it disappeared under our bows I held my breath; but we slid over it like oil.

"Now don't you see the difference? It wasn't anything but a *wind* reef. The wind does that."

"So I see. But it is exactly like a bluff reef. How am I ever going to tell them apart?"

"I can't tell you. It is an instinct. By and by you will just naturally *know* one from the other, but you never will be able to explain why or how you know them apart."

It turned out to be true. The face of the water, in time, became a wonderful book—a book that was a dead language to the uneducated passenger, but which told its mind to me without reserve, delivering its most cherished secrets as clearly as if it uttered them with a voice. And it was not a book to be read once and thrown aside, for it had a new story to tell every day. Throughout the long twelve hundred miles there was never a page that was void of interest, never one that you could leave unread without loss, never one that you would want to skip, thinking you could find higher enjoyment in some other thing. There never was so wonderful a book written by man; never one whose interest was so absorbing, so unflagging, so sparklingly renewed with every re-perusal. The passenger who could not read it was charmed with a peculiar sort of faint dimple on its surface (on the rare occasions when he did not overlook it altogether); but to the pilot that was an *italicized* passage; indeed, it was more than that, it was a legend of the largest capitals, with a string of shouting exclamation points at the end of it; for it meant that a wreck or a rock was buried there that could tear the life out of the strongest vessel that ever floated. It is the faintest and simplest expression the water ever makes, and the most hideous to a pilot's eye. In truth, the passenger who could not read this book saw nothing but all manner of pretty pictures in it, painted by the sun and shaded by the clouds, whereas to the trained eye these were not pictures at all, but the grimmest and most dead-earnest of reading-matter.

Now when I had mastered the language of this water and had come to know every trifling feature that bordered the great river as familiarly as I knew the letters of the alphabet, I had made a valuable acquisition. But I had lost something, too. I had lost something which could never be restored to me while I lived. All the grace, the beauty, the poetry had gone out of the majestic river! I still keep in mind a certain wonderful sunset which I witnessed when steamboating was new to me. A broad expanse of the river was turned to blood; in the middle distance the red hue brightened into gold, through which a solitary log came floating, black and conspicuous; in one place a long, slanting mark lay sparkling upon the water; in another the surface was broken by boiling, tumbling rings, that were as many-tinted as an opal; where the ruddy flush was faintest, was a smooth spot that was covered with graceful circles and radiating lines, ever so delicately traced; the shore on our left was densely wooded, and the sombre shadow that fell from this forest was broken in one place by a long, ruffled trail that shone like silver; and high above the forest wall a clean-stemmed dead tree waved a single leafy bough that glowed like a flame in the unobstructed splendor that was flowing from the sun. There were graceful curves, reflected images, woody heights, soft distances; and over the whole scene, far and near, the dissolving lights drifted steadily, enriching it, every passing moment, with new marvels of coloring.

I stood like one bewitched. I drank it in, in a speechless rapture. The world was new to me, and I had never seen anything like this at home. But as I have said, a day came when I began to cease from noting the glories and the charms which the moon and the sun and the twilight wrought upon the river's face; another day came when I ceased altogether to note them. Then, if that sunset scene had been repeated, I should have looked upon it without rapture, and should have commented upon it, inwardly, after this fashion: This sun means that we are going to have wind to-morrow; that floating log means that the river is rising, small thanks to it; that slanting mark on the water refers to a bluff reef which is going to kill somebody's steamboat one of these nights, if it keeps on stretching out like that; those tumbling "boils" show a dissolving bar and a changing channel there; the lines and circles in the slick water over yonder are a warning that that troublesome place is shoaling up dangerously; that silver streak in the shadow of the forest is the "break" from a new snag, and he has located himself in the very best place he could have found to fish for steamboats; that tall dead tree, with a single living branch, is not going to last long, and then how is a body ever going to get through this blind place at night without the friendly old landmark?

No, the romance and the beauty were all gone from the river. All the value any feature of it had for me now was the amount of usefulness it could furnish toward compassing the safe piloting of a steamboat. Since those days, I have pitied doctors from my heart. What does the lovely flush in a beauty's cheek mean to a doctor but a "break" that ripples above some deadly disease? Are not all her visible charms sown thick with what are to him the signs and symbols of hidden decay? Does he ever see her beauty at all, or doesn't he simply view her professionally, and comment upon her unwholesome condition all to himself? And doesn't he sometimes wonder whether he has gained most or lost most by learning his trade?

CHAPTER X

COMPLETING MY EDUCATION

Whosoever has done me the courtesy to read my chapters which have preceded this may possibly wonder that I deal so minutely with piloting as a science. It was the prime purpose of those chapters; and I am not quite done yet. I wish to show, in the most patient and painstaking way, what a wonderful science it is. Ship channels are buoyed and lighted, and therefore it is a comparatively easy undertaking to learn to run them; clearwater rivers, with gravel bottoms, change their channels very gradually, and therefore one needs to learn them but once; but piloting becomes another matter when you apply it to vast streams like the Mississippi and the Missouri, whose alluvial banks cave and change constantly, whose snags are always hunting up new quarters, whose sandbars are never at rest, whose channels are forever dodging and shirking, and whose obstructions must be confronted in all nights and all weathers without the aid of a single light-house or a single buoy; for there is neither light nor buoy to be found anywhere in all this three or four thousand miles of villanous river.* I feel justified in enlarging upon this great science for the reason that I feel sure no one has ever yet written a paragraph about it who had piloted a steamboat himself, and so had a practical knowledge of the subject. If the theme were hackneyed, I should be obliged to deal gently with the reader; but since it is wholly new, I have felt at liberty to take up a considerable degree of room with it.

When I had learned the name and position of every visible feature of the river; when I had so mastered its shape that I could shut my eyes and trace it from St. Louis to New Orleans; when I had learned to read the face of the water as one would cull the news from the morning paper; and finally, when I had trained my dull memory to treasure up an endless array of soundings and crossing-marks, and keep fast hold of them, I judged that my education was complete: so I got to tilting my cap to the side of my head, and wearing a toothpick in my mouth at the wheel. Mr. Bixby had his eye on these airs. One day he said,—

"What is the height of that bank yonder, at Burgess's?"

"How can I tell, sir? It is three quarters of a mile away."

"Very poor eye—very poor. Take the glass."

I took the glass, and presently said,—

"I can't tell. I suppose that that bank is about a foot and a half high."

"Foot and a half! That's a six-foot bank. How high was the bank along here last trip?"

"I don't know; I never noticed."

"You didn't? Well, you must always do it hereafter."

"Why?"

"Because you'll have to know a good many things that it tells you. For one thing, it tells you the stage of the river—tells you whether there's more water or less in the river along here than there was last trip."

"The leads tell me that." I rather thought I had the advantage of him there.

"Yes, but suppose the leads lie? The bank would tell you so, and then you'd stir those leadsmen up a bit. There was a ten-foot

* True at the time referred to; not true now (1882).

bank here last trip, and there is only a six-foot bank now. What does that signify?"

"That the river is four feet higher than it was last trip."

"Very good. Is the river rising or falling?"

"Rising."

"No it ain't."

"I guess I am right, sir. Yonder is some driftwood floating down the stream."

"A rise *starts* the drift-wood, but then it keeps on floating a while after the river is done rising. Now the bank will tell you about this. Wait till you come to a place where it shelves a little. Now here; do you see this narrow belt of fine sediment? That was deposited while the water was higher. You see the drift-wood begins to strand, too. The bank helps in other ways. Do you see that stump on the false point?"

"Ay, ay, sir."

"Well, the water is just up to the roots of it. You must make a note of that."

"Why?"

"Because that means that there's seven feet in the chute of 103."

"But 103 is a long way up the river yet."

"That's where the benefit of the bank comes in. There is water enough in 103 *now,* yet there may not be by the time we get there; but the bank will keep us posted all along. You don't run close chutes on a falling river, upstream, and there are precious few of them that you are allowed to run at all down-stream. There's a law of the United States against it. The river may be rising by the time we get to 103, and in that case we'll run it. We are drawing—how much?"

"Six feet aft,—six and a half forward."

"Well, you do seem to know something."

"But what I particularly want to know is, if I have got to keep up an everlasting measuring of the banks of this river, twelve hundred miles, month in and month out?"

"Of course!"

My emotions were too deep for words for a while. Presently I said,—

"And how about these chutes? Are there many of them?"

"I should say so. I fancy we shan't run any of the river this trip as you've ever seen it run before—so to speak. If the river begins to rise again, we'll go up behind bars that you've always seen standing out of the river, high and dry like the roof of a house; we'll cut across low places that you've never noticed at all, right through the middle of bars that cover three hundred acres of river; we'll creep through cracks where you've always thought was solid land; we'll dart through the woods and leave twenty-five miles of river off to one side; we'll see the hind-side of every island between New Orleans and Cairo."

"Then I've got to go to work and learn just as much more river as I already know."

"Just about twice as much more, as near as you can come at it."

"Well, one lives to find out. I think I was a fool when I went into this business."

"Yes, that is true. And you are yet. But you'll not be when you've learned it."

"Ah, I never can learn it."

"I will see that you *do.*"

By and by I ventured again:—

"Have I got to learn all this thing just as I know the rest of the river—shapes and all—and so I can run it at night?"

"Yes. And you've got to have good fair marks from one end of the river to the other, that will help the bank tell you when there is water enough in each of these countless places,—like that stump, you know. When the river first begins to rise, you can run half a dozen of the deepest of them; when it rises a foot more you can run another dozen; the next foot will add a couple of dozen, and so on: so you see you have to know your banks and marks to a dead moral certainty, and never get them mixed; for when you start through one of those cracks, there's no backing out again, as there is in the big river; you've got to go through, or stay there six months if you get caught on a falling river. There are about fifty of these cracks which you can't run at all except when the river is brim full and over the banks."

"This new lesson is a cheerful prospect."

"Cheerful enough. And mind what I've just told you; when you start into one of those places you've got to go through. They are too narrow to turn around in, too crooked to back out of, and the shoal water is always *up at the head;* never elsewhere. And the head of them is always likely to be filling up, little by little, so that the marks you reckon their depth by, this season, may not answer for next."

"Learn a new set, then, every year?"

"Exactly. Cramp her up to the bar! What are you standing up through the middle of the river for?"

The next few months showed me strange things. On the same day that we held the conversation above narrated, we met a great rise coming down the river. The whole vast face of the stream was black with drifting dead logs, broken boughs, and great trees that had caved in and been washed away. It required the nicest steering to pick one's way through this rushing raft, even in the day-time, when crossing from point to point; and at night the difficulty was mightily increased; every now and then a huge log, lying deep in the water, would suddenly appear right under our bows, coming head-on; no use to try to avoid it then; we could only stop the engines, and one wheel would walk over that log from one end to the other, keeping up a thundering racket and careening the boat in a way that was very uncomfortable to passengers. Now and then we would hit one of these sunken logs a rattling bang, dead in the centre, with a full head of steam, and it would stun the boat as if she had hit a continent. Sometimes this log would lodge, and stay right across our nose, and back the Mississippi up before it; we would have to do a little crawfishing, then, to get away from the obstruction. We often hit *white* logs, in the dark, for we could not see them till we were right on them; but a black log is a pretty distinct object at night. A white snag is an ugly customer when the daylight is gone.

Of course, on the great rise, down came a swarm of prodigious timber-rafts from the head waters of the Mississippi, coal barges from Pittsburgh, little trading scows from everywhere, and broad-horns from "Posey County," Indiana, freighted with "fruit and furniture"—the usual term for describing it, though in plain English the freight thus aggrandized was hoop-poles and pumpkins. Pilots bore a mortal hatred to these craft; and it was returned with usury. The law required all such helpless traders to keep a light burning, but it was a law that was often broken. All of a sudden, on a murky night, a light would hop up, right under our bows, almost, and an agonized voice, with the backwoods "whang" to it, would wail out:—

"Whar'n the——you goin'to! Cain't you see nothin', you dash—dashed aig-suckin', sheep-stealin', one-eyed son of a stuffed monkey!"

Then for an instant, as we whistled by, the red glare from our furnaces would reveal the scow and the form of the gesticulating orator as if under a lightning-flash, and in that instant our firemen and deck-hands would send and receive a tempest of missiles and profanity, one of our wheels would walk off with the crashing fragments of a steering-oar, and down the dead blackness would shut again. And that flatboatman would be sure to go into New Orleans and sue our boat, swearing stoutly that he had a light burning all the time, when in truth his gang had the lantern down below to sing and lie and drink and gamble by, and no watch on deck. Once, at night, in one of those forest-bordered crevices (behind an island) which steamboatmen intensely describe with the phrase "as dark as the inside of a cow," we should have eaten up a Posey County family, fruit, furniture, and all, but that they happened to be fiddling down below and we just caught the sound of the music in time to sheer off, doing no serious damage, unfortunately, but coming so near it that we had good hopes for a moment. These people brought up their lantern, then, of course; and as we backed and filled to get away, the precious family stood in the light of it—both sexes and various ages —and cursed us till everything turned blue. Once a coalboatman sent a bullet through our pilot-house, when we borrowed a steering-oar of him in a very narrow place.

CHAPTER XI

THE RIVER RISES

During this big rise these small-fry craft were an intolerable nuisance. We were running chute after chute,—a new world to me,—and if there was a particularly cramped place in a chute, we would be pretty sure to meet a broad-horn there; and if he failed to be there, we would find him in a still worse locality, namely, the head of the chute, on the shoal water. And then there would be no end of profane cordialities exchanged.

Sometimes, in the big river, when we would be feeling our way cautiously along through a fog, the deep hush would suddenly be broken by yells and a clamor of tin pans, and all in an instant a log raft would appear vaguely through the webby veil, close upon us; and then we did not wait to swap knives, but snatched our engine bells out by the roots and piled on all the steam we had, to scramble out of the way! One doesn't hit a rock or a solid log raft with a steamboat when he can get excused.

You will hardly believe it, but many steamboat clerks always carried a large assortment of religious tracts with them in those old departed steamboating days. Indeed they did. Twenty times a day we would be cramping up around a bar, while a string of these small-fry rascals were drifting down into the head of the bend away above and beyond us a couple of miles. Now a skiff would dart away from one of them, and come fighting its laborious way across the desert of water. It would "ease all," in the shadow of our forecastle, and the panting oarsmen would shout, "Gimme a pa-a-per!" as the skiff drifted swiftly astern.

The clerk would throw over a file of New Orleans journals. If these were picked up *without comment,* you might notice that now a dozen other skiffs had been drifting down upon us without saying anything. You understand, they had been waiting to see how No. 1 was going to fare. No. 1 making no comment, all the rest would bend to their oars and come on, now; and as fast as they came the clerk would heave over neat bundles of religious tracts, tied to shingles. The amount of hard swearing which twelve packages of religious literature will command when impartially divided up among twelve raftsmen's crews, who have pulled a heavy skiff two miles on a hot day to get them, is simply incredible.

As I have said, the big rise brought a new world under my vision. By the time the river was over its banks we had forsaken our old paths and were hourly climbing over bars that had stood ten feet out of water before; we were shaving stumpy shores, like that at the foot of Madrid Bend, which I had always seen avoided before; we were clattering through chutes like that of 82, where the opening at the foot was an unbroken wall of timber till our nose was almost at the very spot. Some of these chutes were utter solitudes. The dense, untouched forest overhung both banks of the crooked little crack, and one could believe that human creatures had never intruded there before. The swinging grape-vines, the grassy nooks and vistas glimpsed as we swept by, the flowering creepers waving their red blossoms from the tops of dead trunks, and all the spendthrift richness of the forest foliage, were wasted and thrown away there. The chutes were lovely places to steer in; they were deep, except at the head; the current was gentle; under the "points" the water was absolutely dead, and the invisible banks so bluff that where the tender willow thickets projected you could bury your boat's broadside in them as you tore along, and then you seemed fairly to fly.

Behind other islands we found wretched little farms, and wretcheder little log-cabins; there were crazy rail fences sticking a foot or two above the water, with one or two jeans-clad, chills-racked, yellow-faced male miserables roosting on the top-rail, elbows on knees, jaws in hands, grinding tobacco and discharging the result at floating chips through crevices left by lost teeth; while the rest of the family and the few farm-animals were huddled together in an empty wood-flat riding at her moorings close at hand. In this flatboat the family would have to cook and eat and sleep for a lesser or greater number of days (or possibly weeks), until the river should fall two or three feet and let them get back to their log-cabin and their chills again—chills being a merciful provision of an all-wise Providence to enable them to take exercise without exertion. And this sort of watery camping out was a thing which these people were rather liable to be treated to a couple of times a year: by the December rise out of the Ohio, and the June rise out of the Mississippi. And yet these were kindly dispensations, for they at least enabled the poor things to rise from the dead now and then, and look upon life when a steamboat went by. They appreciated the blessing, too, for they spread their mouths and eyes wide open and made the most of these occasions. Now what *could* these banished creatures find to do to keep from dying of the blues during the low-water season!

Once, in one of these lovely island chutes, we found our course completely bridged by a great fallen tree. This will serve to show how narrow some of the chutes were. The passengers had an hour's recreation in a virgin wilderness, while the boat-hands chopped the bridge away; for there was no such thing as turning back, you comprehend.

From Cairo to Baton Rouge, when the river is over its banks, you have no particular trouble in the night, for the thousand-mile wall of dense forest that guards the two banks all the way is only gapped with a farm or wood-yard opening at intervals, and so you can't "get out of the river" much easier than you could get out of a fenced lane; but from Baton Rouge to New Orleans it is a different matter. The river is more than a mile wide, and very deep—as much as two hundred feet, in places. Both banks, for a good deal over a hundred miles, are shorn of their timber and bordered by continuous sugar plantations, with only here and there a scattering sapling or row of ornamental China-trees. The timber is shorn off clear to the rear of the plantations, from two to four miles. When the first frost threatens to come, the planters snatch off their crops in a hurry. When they have finished grinding the cane, they form the refuse of the stalks (which they call *bagasse*) into great piles and set fire to them, though in other sugar countries the bagasse is used for fuel in the furnaces of the sugar mills. Now the piles of damp bagasse burn slowly, and smoke like Satan's own kitchen.

An embankment ten or fifteen feet high guards both banks of the Mississippi all the way down that lower end of the river, and this embankment is set back from the edge of the shore from ten to perhaps a hundred feet, according to circumstances; say thirty or forty feet, as a general thing. Fill that whole region with an impenetrable gloom of smoke from a hundred miles of burning bagasse piles, when the river is over the banks, and turn a steamboat loose along there at midnight and see how she will feel. And see how you will feel, too! You find yourself away out in the midst of a vague dim sea that is shoreless, that fades out and loses itself in the murky distances; for you cannot discern the thin rib of embankment, and you are always imagining you see a straggling tree when you don't. The plantations themselves are transformed by the smoke, and look like a part of the sea. All through your watch you are tortured with the exquisite misery of uncertainty. You hope you are keeping in the river, but you do not know. All that you are sure about is that you are likely to be within six feet of the bank *and* destruction, when you think you are a good half-mile from shore. And you are sure, also, that if you chance suddenly to fetch up against the embankment and topple your chimneys overboard, you will have the small comfort of knowing that it is about what you were expecting to do. One of the great Vicksburg packets darted out into a sugar plantation one night, at such a time, and had to stay there a week. But there was no novelty about it; it had often been done before.

I thought I had finished this chapter, but I wish to add a curious thing, while it is in my mind. It is only relevant in that it is connected with piloting. There used to be an excellent pilot on the river, a Mr. X., who was a somnambulist. It was said that if his mind was troubled about a bad piece of river, he was pretty sure to get up and walk in his sleep and do strange things. He was once fellow-pilot for a trip or two with George Ealer, on a great New Orleans passenger packet. During a considerable part of the first trip George was uneasy, but got over it by and by, as X. seemed content to stay in his bed when asleep. Late one night the boat was approaching Helena, Arkansas; the water was low, and the crossing above the town in a very blind and tangled condition. X. had seen the crossing since Ealer had, and as the night was particularly drizzly, sullen, and dark, Ealer was considering whether he had not better have X. called to assist in running the place, when the door opened and X. walked in. Now on very dark nights, light is a deadly enemy to piloting; you are aware that if you stand in a lighted room, on such a night, you cannot see things in the street to any purpose; but if you put out the lights and stand in the gloom you can make out objects in the street pretty well. So, on very dark nights, pilots do not smoke; they allow no fire in the pilot-house stove if there is a crack which can allow the least ray to escape; they order the furnaces to be curtained with huge tarpaulins and the sky-lights to be closely blinded. Then no light whatever issues from the boat. The undefinable shape that now entered the pilot-house had Mr. X.'s voice. This said,—

"Let me take her, George; I've seen this place since you have, and it is so crooked that I reckon I can run it myself easier than I could tell you how to do it."

"It is kind of you, and I swear *I* am willing. I haven't got another drop of perspiration left in me. I have been spinning around and around the wheel like a squirrel. It is so dark I can't tell which way she is swinging till she is coming around like a whirligig."

So Ealer took a seat on the bench, panting and breathless. The black phantom assumed the wheel without saying anything, steadied the waltzing steamer with a turn or two, and then stood at ease, coaxing her a little to this side and then to that, as gently and as sweetly as if the time had been noonday. When Ealer observed this marvel of steering, he wished he had not confessed! He stared, and wondered, and finally said,—

"Well, I thought I knew how to steer a steamboat, but that was another mistake of mine."

X. said nothing, but went serenely on with his work. He rang for the leads; he rang to slow down the steam; he worked the boat carefully and neatly into invisible marks, then stood at the centre of the wheel and peered blandly out into the blackness, fore and aft, to verify his position; as the leads shoaled more and more, he stopped the engines entirely, and the dead silence and suspense of "drifting" followed; when the shoalest water was struck, he cracked on the steam, carried her handsomely over, and then began to work her warily into the next system of shoal marks; the same patient, heedful use of leads and engines followed, the boat slipped through without touching bottom, and entered upon the third and last intricacy of the crossing; imperceptibly she moved through the gloom, crept by inches into her marks, drifted tediously till the shoalest water was cried, and then, under a tremendous head of steam, went swinging over the reef and away into deep water and safety!

Ealer let his long-pent breath pour out in a great, relieving sigh, and said:—

"That's the sweetest piece of piloting that was ever done on the Mississippi River! I wouldn't believed it could be done, if I hadn't seen it."

There was no reply, and he added:—

"Just hold her five minutes longer, partner, and let me run down and get a cup of coffee."

A minute later Ealer was biting into a pie, down in the "texas," and comforting himself with coffee. Just then the night watchman happened in, and was about to happen out again, when he noticed Ealer and exclaimed,—

"Who is at the wheel, sir?"

"X."

"Dart for the pilot-house, quicker than lightning!"

The next moment both men were flying up the pilot-house companion-way, three steps at a jump! Nobody there! The great steamer was whistling down the middle of the river at her own sweet will! The watchman shot out of the place again; Ealer seized the wheel, set an engine back with power, and held his breath while the boat reluctantly swung away from a "towhead" which she was about to knock into the middle of the Gulf of Mexico!

By and by the watchman came back and said,—

"Didn't that lunatic tell you he was asleep, when he first came up here?"

"No."

"Well, he was. I found him walking along on top of the railings, just as unconcerned as another man would walk a pavement; and I put him to bed; now just this minute there he was again, away astern, going through that sort of tightrope deviltry the same as before."

"Well, I think I'll stay by, next time he has one of those fits. But I hope he'll have them often. You just ought to have seen him take this boat through Helena crossing. *I* never saw anything so gaudy before. And if he can do such gold-leaf, kid-glove, diamond-breastpin piloting when he is sound asleep, what *couldn't* he do if he was dead!"

CHAPTER XII

SOUNDING

When the river is very low, and one's steamboat is "drawing all the water" there is in the channel,—or a few inches more, as was often the case in the old times,—one must be painfully circumspect in his piloting. We used to have to "sound" a number of particularly bad places almost every trip when the river was at a very low stage. Sounding is done in this way. The boat ties up at the shore, just above the shoal crossing; the pilot not on watch takes his "cub" or steersman and a picked crew of men (sometimes an officer also), and goes out in the yawl—provided the boat has not that rare and sumptuous luxury, a regularly-devised "sounding-boat"—and proceeds to hunt for the best water, the pilot on duty watching his movements through a spy-glass, meantime, and in some instances assisting by signals of the boat's whistle, signifying "try higher up" or "try lower down;" for the surface of the water, like an oil-painting, is more expressive and intelligible when inspected from a little distance than very close at hand. The whistle signals are seldom necessary, however; never, perhaps, except when the wind confuses the significant ripples upon the water's surface. When the yawl has reached the shoal place, the speed is slackened, the pilot begins to sound the depth with a pole ten or twelve feet long, and the steersman at the tiller obeys the order to "hold her up to starboard;" or "let her fall off to larboard;"* or "steady—steady as you go."

When the measurements indicate that the yawl is approaching the shoalest part of the reef, the command is given to "ease all!" Then the men stop rowing and the yawl drifts with the current. The next order is, "Stand by with the buoy!" The moment the shallowest point is reached, the pilot delivers the order, "Let go the buoy!" and over she goes. If the pilot is not satisfied, he sounds the place again; if he finds better water higher up or lower down, he removes the buoy to that place. Being finally satisfied, he gives the order, and all the men stand their oars straight up in the air, in line; a blast from the boat's whistle indicates that the signal has been seen; then the men "give way" on their oars and lay the yawl alongside the buoy; the steamer comes creeping carefully down, is pointed straight at the buoy, husbands her power for the coming struggle, and presently, at the critical moment, turns on all her steam and goes grinding and wallowing over the buoy and the sand, and gains the deep water beyond. Or maybe she doesn't; maybe she "strikes and swings." Then she has to while away several hours (or days) sparring herself off.

Sometimes a buoy is not laid at all, but the yawl goes ahead, hunting the best water, and the steamer follows along in its wake. Often there is a deal of fun and excitement about sounding, especially if it is a glorious summer day, or a blustering night. But in winter the cold and the peril take most of the fun out of it.

A buoy is nothing but a board four or five feet long, with one end turned up; it is a reversed school-house bench, with one of the supports left and the other removed. It is anchored on the shoalest part of the reef by a rope with a heavy stone made fast to the end of it. But for the resistance of the turned-up end of the reversed bench, the current would pull the buoy under water. At

* The term "larboard" is never used at sea, now, to signify the left hand; but was always used on the river in my time.

night, a paper lantern with a candle in it is fastened on top of the buoy, and this can be seen a mile or more, a little glimmering spark in the waste of blackness.

Nothing delights a cub so much as an opportunity to go out sounding. There is such an air of adventure about it; often there is danger; it is so gaudy and man-of-war-like to sit up in the stern-sheets and steer a swift yawl; there is something fine about the exultant spring of the boat when an experienced old sailor crew throw their souls into the oars; it is lovely to see the white foam stream away from the bows; there is music in the rush of the water; it is deliciously exhilarating, in summer, to go speeding over the breezy expanses of the river when the world of wavelets is dancing in the sun. It is such grandeur, too, to the cub, to get a chance to give an order; for often the pilot will simply say, "Let her go about!" and leave the rest to the cub, who instantly cries, in his sternest tone of command, "Ease starboard! Strong on the larboard! Starboard give way! With a will, men!" The cub enjoys sounding for the further reason that the eyes of the passengers are watching all the yawl's movements with absorbing interest if the time be daylight; and if it be night he knows that those same wondering eyes are fastened upon the yawl's lantern as it glides out into the gloom and dims away in the remote distance.

One trip a pretty girl of sixteen spent her time in our pilot-house with her uncle and aunt, every day and all day long. I fell in love with her. So did Mr. Thornburg's cub, Tom G——. Tom and I had been bosom friends until this time; but now a coolness began to arise. I told the girl a good many of my river adventures, and made myself out a good deal of a hero; Tom tried to make himself appear to be a hero, too, and succeeded to some extent, but then he always had a way of embroidering. However, virtue is its own reward, so I was a barely perceptible trifle ahead in the contest. About this time something happened which promised handsomely for me: the pilots decided to sound the crossing at the head of 21. This would occur about nine or ten o'clock at night, when the passengers would be still up; it would be Mr. Thornburg's watch, therefore my chief would have to do the sounding. We had a perfect love of a sounding-boat—long, trim, graceful, and as fleet as a greyhound; her thwarts were cushioned; she carried twelve oarsmen; one of the mates was always sent in her to transmit orders to her crew, for ours was a steamer where no end of "style" was put on.

We tied up at the shore above 21, and got ready. It was a foul night, and the river was so wide, there, that a landsman's uneducated eyes could discern no opposite shore through such a gloom. The passengers were alert and interested; everything was satisfactory. As I hurried through the engine-room, picturesquely gotten up in storm toggery, I met Tom, and could not forbear delivering myself of a mean speech:—

"Ain't you glad *you* don't have to go out sounding?"

Tom was passing on, but he quickly turned, and said,—

"Now just for that, you can go and get the sounding-pole yourself. I was going after it, but I'd see you in Halifax, now, before I'd do it."

"Who wants you to get it? *I* don't. It's in the sounding-boat."

"It ain't, either. It's been new-painted; and it's been up on the ladies cabin guards two days, drying."

I flew back, and shortly arrived among the crowd of watching and wondering ladies just in time to hear the command:

"Give way, men!"

I looked over, and there was the gallant sounding-boat booming away, the unprincipled Tom presiding at the tiller, and my chief sitting by him with the sounding-pole which I had been sent on a fool's errand to fetch. Then that young girl said to me,—

"Oh, how awful to have to go out in that little boat on such a night! Do you think there is any danger?"

I would rather have been stabbed. I went off, full of venom, to help in the pilot-house. By and by the boat's lantern disappeared, and after an interval a wee spark glimmered upon the face of the water a mile away. Mr. Thornburg blew the whistle, in acknowledgment, backed the steamer out, and made for it. We flew along for a while, then slackened steam and went cautiously gliding toward the spark. Presently Mr. Thornburg exclaimed,—

"Hello, the buoy-lantern's out!"

He stopped the engines. A moment or two later he said,—

"Why, there it is again!"

So he came ahead on the engines once more, and rang for the leads. Gradually the water shoaled up, and then began to deepen again! Mr. Thornburg muttered:—

"Well, I don't understand this. I believe that buoy has drifted off the reef. Seems to be a little too far to the left. No matter, it is safest to run over it, anyhow."

So, in that solid world of darkness we went creeping down on the light. Just as our bows were in the act of plowing over it, Mr. Thornburg seized the bell-ropes, rang a startling peal, and exclaimed,—

"My soul, it's the sounding-boat!"

A sudden chorus of wild alarms burst out far below—a

pause—and then a sound of grinding and crashing followed. Mr. Thornburg exclaimed,—

"There! the paddle-wheel has ground the sounding-boat to lucifer matches! Run! See who is killed!"

I was on the main deck in the twinkling of an eye. My chief and the third mate and nearly all the men were safe. They had discovered their danger when it was too late to pull out of the way; then, when the great guards overshadowed them a moment later, they were prepared and knew what to do; at my chief's order they sprang at the right instant, seized the guard, and were hauled aboard. The next moment the sounding-yawl swept aft to the wheel and was struck and splintered to atoms. Two of the men and the cub Tom, were missing—a fact which spread like wildfire over the boat. The passengers came flocking to the forward gangway, ladies and all, anxious-eyed, white-faced, and talked in awed voices of the dreadful thing. And often and again I heard them say, "Poor fellows! poor boy, poor boy!"

By this time the boat's yawl was manned and away, to search for the missing. Now a faint call was heard, off to the left. The yawl had disappeared in the other direction. Half the people rushed to one side to encourage the swimmer with their shouts; the other half rushed the other way to shriek to the yawl to turn about. By the callings, the swimmer was approaching, but some said the sound showed failing strength. The crowd massed themselves against the boiler-deck railings, leaning over and staring into the gloom; and every faint and fainter cry wrung from them such words as "Ah, poor fellow, poor fellow! is there *no* way to save him?"

But still the cries held out, and drew nearer, and presently the voice said pluckily,—

"I can make it! Stand by with a rope!"

What a rousing cheer they gave him! The chief mate took his stand in the glare of a torch-basket, a coil of rope in his hand, and his men grouped about him. The next moment the swimmer's face appeared in the circle of light, and in another one the owner of it was hauled aboard, limp and drenched, while cheer on cheer went up. It was that devil Tom.

The yawl crew searched everywhere, but found no sign of the two men. They probably failed to catch the guard, tumbled back, and were struck by the wheel and killed. Tom had never jumped for the guard at all, but had plunged head-first into the river and dived under the wheel. It was nothing; I could have done it easy enough, and I said so; but everybody went on just the same, making a wonderful to-do over that ass, as if he had done something great. That girl couldn't seem to have enough of that pitiful "hero" the rest of the trip; but little I cared; I loathed her, any way.

The way we came to mistake the sounding-boat's lantern for the buoy-light was this. My chief said that after laying the buoy he fell away and watched it till it seemed to be secure; then he took up a position a hundred yards below it and a little to one side of the steamer's course, headed the sounding-boat up-stream, and waited. Having to wait some time, he and the officer got to talking; he looked up when he judged that the steamer was about on the reef; saw that the buoy was gone, but supposed that the steamer had already run over it; he went on with his talk; he noticed that the steamer was getting very close down on him, but that was the correct thing; it was her business to shave him closely, for convenience in taking him aboard; he was expecting her to sheer off, until the last moment; then if flashed upon him that she was trying to run him down, mistaking his lantern for the buoy-light; so he sang out, "Stand by to spring for the guard, men!" and the next instant the jump was made.

CHAPTER XIII

A PILOT'S NEEDS

But I am wandering from what I was intending to do, that is, make plainer than perhaps appears in the previous chapters, some of the peculiar requirements of the science of piloting. First of all, there is one faculty which a pilot must incessantly cultivate until he has brought it to absolute perfection. Nothing short of perfection will do. That faculty is memory. He cannot stop with merely thinking a thing is so and so; he must *know* it; for this eminently one of the "exact" sciences. With what scorn a pilot was looked upon, in the old times, if he ever ventured to deal in that feeble phrase "I think," instead of the vigorous one "I know!" One cannot easily realize what a tremendous thing it is to know every trivial detail of twelve hundred miles of river and know it with absolute exactness. If you will take the longest street in New York, and travel up and down it, conning its features patiently until you know every house and window and door and lamp-post and big and little sign by heart, and know them so accurately that you can instantly name the one you are abreast of when you are set down at random in that street in the middle of an inky black night, you will then have a tolerable notion of the amount and the exactness of a pilot's knowledge who carries the Mississippi River in his head. And then if you will go on until you know every street crossing, the character, size, and position of the crossing-stones, and the varying depth of mud in each of those numberless places, you will have some idea of what the pilot must know in order to keep a Mississippi steamer out of trouble. Next, if you will take half of the signs in that long street, and *change their places* once a month, and still manage to know their new positions accurately on dark nights, and keep up with these repeated changes without making any mistakes, you will understand what is required of a pilot's peerless memory by the fickle Mississippi.

I think a pilot's memory is about the most wonderful thing in the world. To know the Old and New Testaments by heart, and be able to recite them glibly, forward or backward, or begin at random anywhere in the book and recite both ways and never trip or make a mistake, is no extravagant mass of knowledge, and no marvellous facility, compared to a pilot's massed knowledge of the Mississippi and his marvellous facility in the handling of it. I make this comparison deliberately, and believe I am not expanding the truth when I do it. Many will think my figure too strong, but pilots will not.

And how easily and comfortably the pilot's memory does its work; how placidly effortless is its way; how *unconsciously* it lays up its vast stores, hour by hour, day by day, and never loses or mislays a single valuable package of them all! Take an instance. Let a leadsman cry, "Half twain! half twain! half twain! half twain! half twain!" until it becomes as monotonous as the ticking of a clock; let conversation be going on all the time, and the pilot be doing his share of the talking, and no longer consciously listening to the leadsman; and in the midst of this endless string of half twains let a single "quarter twain!" be interjected, without emphasis, and then the half twain cry go on again, just as before: two or three weeks later that pilot can describe with precision the boat's position in the river when that quarter twain was uttered, and give you such a lot of head-marks, stern marks, and side marks to guide you, that you ought to be able to take the boat there and put her in that same spot again yourself! The cry of "quarter twain" did not really take his mind from his talk, but his trained faculties instantly photographed the bearings, noted the change of depth, and laid up the important details for future reference without requiring any assistance from *him* in the matter. If you were walking and talking with a friend, and another friend at your side kept up a monotonous repetition of the vowel sound A, for a couple of blocks, and then in the midst interjected an R, thus, A, A, A, A, A, R, A, A, A, etc., and gave the R no emphasis, you would not be able to state, two or three weeks afterward, that the R had been put in, nor be able to tell what objects you were passing at the moment it was done. But you could if your memory had been patiently and laboriously trained to do that sort of thing mechanically.

Give a man a tolerably fair memory to start with, and piloting will develop it into a very colossus of capability. But *only in the matters it is daily drilled in.* A time would come when the man's faculties could not help noticing landmarks and soundings, and his memory could not help holding on to them with the grip of a vice; but if you asked that same man at noon what he had had for breakfast, it would be ten chances to one that he could not tell you. Astonishing things can be done with the human memory if you will devote it faithfully to one particular line of business.

At the time that wages soared so high on the Missouri River, my chief, Mr. Bixby, went up there and learned more than a thousand miles of that stream with an ease and rapidity that were astonishing. When he had seen each division *once* in the daytime and *once* at night, his education was so nearly complete that he took out a "daylight" license; a few trips later he took out a full license, and went to piloting day and night,—and he ranked A 1, too.

Mr. Bixby placed me as steersman for a while under a pilot whose feats of memory were a constant marvel to me. However, his memory was born in him, I think, not built. For instance, somebody would mention a name. Instantly Mr. Brown would break in:—

"Oh, I knew *him*. Sallow-faced, red-headed fellow, with a little scar on the side of his throat, like a splinter under the flesh. He was only in the Southern trade six months. That was thirteen years ago. I made a trip with him. There was five feet in the upper river then; the 'Henry Blake' grounded at the foot of Tower Island drawing four and a half; the 'George Elliott' unshipped her rudder on the wreck of the 'Sunflower' "—

"Why, the 'Sunflower' didn't sink until"—

"*I* know when she sunk; it was three years before that, on the 2d of December; Asa Hardy was captain of her, and his brother John was first clerk; and it was his first trip in her, too; Tom Jones told me these things a week afterward in New Orleans; he was first mate of the 'Sunflower.' Captain Hardy stuck a nail in his foot the 6th of July of the next year, and died of the lockjaw on the 15th. His brother John died two years after,—3d of

March,—erysipelas. I never saw either of the Hardys,—they were Alleghany River men,—but people who knew them told me all these things. And they said Captain Hardy wore yarn socks winter and summer just the same, and his first wife's name was Jane Shook,—she was from New England,—and his second one died in a lunatic asylum. It was in the blood. She was from Lexington, Kentucky. Name was Horton before she was married."

And so on, by the hour, the man's tongue would go. He could *not* forget any thing. It was simply impossible. The most trivial details remained as distinct and luminous in his head, after they had lain there for years, as the most memorable events. His was not simply a pilot's memory; its grasp was universal. If he were talking about a trifling letter he had received seven years before, he was pretty sure to deliver you the entire screed from memory. And then without observing that he was departing from the true line of his talk, he was more than likely to hurl in a long-drawn parenthetical biography of the writer of that letter; and you were lucky indeed if he did not take up that writer's relatives, one by one, and give you their biographies, too.

Such a memory as that is a great misfortune. To it, all occurrences are of the same size. Its possessor cannot distinguish an interesting circumstance from an uninteresting one. As a talker, he is bound to clog his narrative with tiresome details and make himself an insufferable bore. Moreover, he cannot stick to his subject. He picks up every little grain of memory he discerns in his way, and so is led aside. Mr. Brown would start out with the honest intention of telling you a vastly funny anecdote about a dog. He would be "so full of laugh" that he could hardly begin; then his memory would start with the dog's breed and personal appearance; drift into a history of his owner; of his owner's family, with descriptions of weddings and burials that had occurred in it, together with recitals of congratulatory verses and obituary poetry provoked by the same; then this memory would recollect that one of these events occurred during the celebrated "hard winter" of such and such a year, and a minute description of that winter would follow, along with the names of people who were frozen to death, and statistics showing the high figures which pork and hay went up to. Pork and hay would suggest corn and fodder; corn and fodder would suggest cows and horses; cows and horses would suggest the circus and certain celebrated bare-back riders; the transition from the circus to the menagerie was easy and natural; from the elephant to equatorial Africa was but a step; then of course the heathen savages would suggest religion; and at the end of three or four hours' tedious jaw, the watch would change, and Brown would go out of the pilot-house muttering extracts from sermons he had heard years before about the efficacy of prayer as a means of grace. And the original first mention would be all you had learned about that dog, after all this waiting and hungering.

A pilot must have a memory; but there are two higher qualities which he must also have. He must have good and quick judgment and decision, and a cool, calm courage that no peril can shake. Give a man the merest trifle of pluck to start with, and by the time he has become a pilot he cannot be unmanned by any danger a steamboat can get into; but one cannot quite say the same for judgment. Judgment is a matter of brains, and a man must *start* with a good stock of that article or he will never succeed as a pilot.

The growth of courage in the pilot-house is steady all the time, but it does not reach a high and satisfactory condition until some time after the young pilot has been "standing his own watch," alone and under the staggering weight of all the responsibilities connected with the position. When an apprentice has become pretty thoroughly acquainted with the river, he goes clattering along so fearlessly with his steamboat, night or day, that he presently begins to imagine that it is *his* courage that animates him; but the first time the pilot steps out and leaves him to his own devices he finds out it was the other man's. He discovers that the article has been left out of his own cargo altogether. The whole river is bristling with exigencies in a moment; he is not prepared for them; he does not know how to meet them; all his knowledge forsakes him; and within fifteen minutes he is as white as a sheet and scared almost to death. Therefore pilots wisely train these cubs by various strategic tricks to look danger in the face a little more calmly. A favorite way of theirs is to play a friendly swindle upon the candidate.

Mr. Bixby served me in this fashion once, and for years afterward I used to blush even in my sleep when I thought of it. I had become a good steersman; so good, indeed, that I had all the work to do on our watch, night and day; Mr. Bixby seldom made a suggestion to me; all he ever did was to take the wheel on particularly bad nights or in particularly bad crossings, land the boat when she needed to be landed, play gentleman of leisure nine tenths of the watch, and collect the wages. The lower river was about bank-full, and if anybody had questioned my ability to run any crossing between Cairo and New Orleans without help or instruction, I should have felt irreparably hurt. The idea of being afraid of any crossing in the lot, in the *day-time*, was a thing too preposterous for contemplation. Well, one matchless summer's day I was bowling down the bend above island 66, brimful of self-conceit and carrying my nose as high as a giraffe's, when Mr. Bixby said,—

"I am going below a while. I suppose you know the next crossing?"

This was almost an affront. It was about the plainest and simplest crossing in the whole river. One couldn't come to any harm, whether he ran it right or not; and as for depth, there never had been any bottom there. I knew all this, perfectly well.

"Know how to *run* it? Why, I can run it with my eyes shut."

"How much water is there in it?"

"Well, that is an odd question. I couldn't get bottom there with a church steeple."

"You think so, do you?"

The very tone of the question shook my confidence. That was what Mr. Bixby was expecting. He left, without saying anything more. I began to imagine all sorts of things. Mr. Bixby, unknown to me, of course, sent somebody down to the forecastle with some mysterious instructions to the leadsmen, another messenger was sent to whisper among the officers, and then Mr. Bixby went into hiding behind a smoke-stack where he could observe results. Presently the captain stepped out on the hurricane deck; next the chief mate appeared; then a clerk. Every moment or two a straggler was added to my audience; and before I got to the head of the island I had fifteen or twenty people assembled down there under my nose. I began to wonder what the trouble was. As I started across, the captain glanced aloft at me and said, with a sham uneasiness in his voice,—

"Where is Mr. Bixby?"

"Gone below, sir."

But that did the business for me. My imagination began to construct dangers out of nothing, and they multiplied faster than I could keep the run of them. All at once I imagined I saw shoal water ahead! The wave of coward agony that surged through me then came near dislocating every joint in me. All my confidence in that crossing vanished. I seized the bell-rope; dropped it, ashamed; seized it again; dropped it once more; clutched it tremblingly once again, and pulled it so feebly that I could hardly hear the stroke myself. Captain and mate sang out instantly, and both together,—

"Starboard lead there! and quick about it!"

This was another shock. I began to climb the wheel like a squirrel; but I would hardly get the boat started to port before I would see new dangers on that side, and away I would spin to the other; only to find perils accumulating to starboard, and be crazy to get to port again. Then came the leadsman's sepulchral cry:—

"D-e-e-p four!"

Deep four in a bottomless crossing! The terror of it took my breath away.

"M-a-r-k three! . . . M-a-r-k three . . . Quarter less three! . . . Half twain!"

This was frightful! I seized the bell-ropes and stopped the engines.

"Quarter twain! Quarter twain! *Mark* twain!"

I was helpless. I did not know what in the world to do. I was quaking from head to foot, and I could have hung my hat on my eyes, they stuck out so far.

"Quarter *less* twain! Nine and a *half!*"

We were *drawing* nine! My hands were in a nerveless flutter. I could not ring a bell intelligibly with them. I flew to the speaking-tube and shouted to the engineer,—

"Oh, Ben, if you love me, *back* her! Quick, Ben! Oh, back the immortal *soul* out of her!"

I heard the door close gently. I looked around, and there stood Mr. Bixby, smiling a bland, sweet smile. Then the audience on the hurricane deck sent up a thundergust of humiliating laughter. I saw it all, now, and I felt meaner than the meanest man in human history. I laid in the lead, set the boat in her marks, came ahead on the engines, and said:—

"It was a fine trick to play on an orphan, *wasn't* it? I suppose I'll never hear the last of how I was ass enough to heave the lead at the head of 66."

"Well, no, you won't, maybe. In fact I hope you won't; for I want you to learn something by that experience. Didn't you *know* there was no bottom in that crossing?"

"Yes, sir, I did."

"Very well, then. You shouldn't have allowed me or anybody else to shake your confidence in that knowledge. Try to remember that. And another thing: when you get into a dangerous place, don't turn coward. That isn't going to help matters any."

It was a good enough lesson, but pretty hardly learned. Yet about the hardest part of it was that for months I so often had to hear a phrase which I had conceived a particular distaste for. It was, "Oh, Ben, if you love me, back her!"

CHAPTER XIV

RANK AND DIGNITY OF PILOTING

In my preceding chapters I have tried, by going into the minutiae of the science of piloting, to carry the reader step by step to a comprehension of what the science consists of; and at the same time I have tried to show him that it is a very curious and wonderful science, too, and very worthy of his attention. If I have seemed to love my subject, it is no surprising thing, for I loved the profession far better than any I have followed since, and I took a measureless pride in it. The reason is plain: a pilot, in those days was the only unfettered and entirely independent human being that lived in the earth. Kings are but the hampered servants of parliament and people; parliaments sit in chains forged by their constituency; the editor of a newspaper cannot be independent, but must work with one hand tied behind him by party and patrons, and be content to utter only half or two thirds of his mind; no clergyman is a free man and may speak the whole truth, regardless of his parish's opinions; writers of all kinds are manacled servants of the public. We write frankly and fearlessly, but then we "modify" before we print. In truth, every man and woman and child has a master, and worries and frets in servitude; but in the day I write of, the Mississippi pilot had *none.* The captain could stand upon the hurricane deck, in the pomp of a very brief authority, and give him five or six orders while the vessel backed into the stream, and then that skipper's reign was over. The moment that the boat was under way in the river, she was under the sole and unquestioned control of the pilot. He could do with her exactly as he pleased, run her when and whither he chose, and tie her up to the bank whenever his judgment said that that course was best. His movements were entirely free; he consulted no one, he received commands from nobody, he promptly resented even the merest suggestions. Indeed, the law of the United States forbade him to listen to commands or suggestions, rightly considering that the pilot necessarily knew better how to handle the boat than anybody could tell him. So here was the novelty of a king without a keeper, an absolute monarch who was absolute in sober truth and not by a fiction of words. I have seen a boy of eighteen taking a great steamer serenely into what seemed almost certain destruction, and the aged captain standing mutely by, filled with apprehension but powerless to interfere. His interference, in that particular instance, might have been an excellent thing, but to permit it would have been to establish a most pernicious precedent. It will easily be guessed, considering the pilot's boundless authority, that he was a great personage in the old steamboating days. He was treated with marked courtesy by the captain and with marked deference by all the officers and servants; and this deferential spirit was quickly communicated to the passengers, too. I think pilots were about the only people I ever knew who failed to show, in some degree, embarrassment in the presence of travelling foreign princes. But then, people in one's own grade of life are not usually embarrassing objects.

By long habit, pilots came to put all their wishes in the form of commands. It "gravels" me, to this day, to put my will in the weak shape of a request, instead of launching it in the crisp language of an order.

In those old days, to load a steamboat at St. Louis, take her to New Orleans and back, and discharge cargo, consumed about twenty-five days, on an average. Seven or eight of these days the boat spent at the wharves of St. Louis and New Orleans, and every soul on board was hard at work, except the two pilots; *they* did nothing but play gentleman up town, and receive the same wages for it as if they had been on duty. The moment the boat touched the wharf at either city, they were ashore; and they were not likely to be seen again till the last bell was ringing and everything in readiness for another voyage.

When a captain got hold of a pilot of particularly high reputation, he took pains to keep him. When wages were four hundred dollars a month on the Upper Mississippi, I have known a captain to keep such a pilot in idleness, under full pay, three months at a time, while the river was frozen up. And one must remember that in those cheap times four hundred dollars was a salary of almost inconceivable splendor. Few men on shore got such pay as that, and when they did they were mightily looked up to. When pilots from either end of the river wandered into our small Missouri village, they were sought by the best and the fairest, and treated with exalted respect. Lying in port under wages was a thing which many pilots greatly enjoyed and appreciated; especially if they belonged in the Missouri River in the heyday of that trade (Kansas times), and got nine hundred dollars a trip, which was equivalent to about eighteen hundred dollars a month. Here is a conversation of that day. A chap out of the Illinois River, with a little stern-wheel tub, accosts a couple of ornate and gilded Missouri River pilots:—

"Gentlemen, I've got a pretty good trip for the up-country, and shall want you about a month. How much will it be?"

"Eighteen hundred dollars apiece."

"Heavens and earth! You take my boat, let me have your wages, and I'll divide!"

I will remark, in passing, that Mississippi steamboatmen were important in landsmen's eyes (and in their own, too, in a degree) according to the dignity of the boat they were on. For instance, it was a proud thing to be of the crew of such stately craft as the "Aleck Scott" or the "Grand Turk." Negro firemen, deck hands, and barbers belonging to those boats were distinguished personages in their grade of life, and they were well aware of that fact, too. A stalwart darkey once gave offence at a negro ball in New Orleans by putting on a good many airs. Finally one of the managers bustled up to him and said,—

"Who *is* you, any way? Who *is* you? dat's what *I* wants to know!"

The offender was not disconcerted in the least, but swelled himself up and threw that into his voice which showed that he knew he was not putting on all those airs on a stinted capital.

"Who *is* I? Who *is* I? I let you know mighty quick who I is! I want you niggers to understan' dat I fires de middle do'* on de 'Aleck Scott!' "

That was sufficient.

The barber of the "Grand Turk" was a spruce young negro, who aired his importance with balmy complacency, and was greatly courted by the circle in which he moved. The young colored population of New Orleans were much given to flirting, at twilight, on the banquettes of the back streets. Somebody saw and heard something like the following, one evening, in one of those localities. A middle-aged negro woman projected her head through a broken pane and shouted (very willing that the neighbors should hear and envy), "You Mary Ann, come in de house dis minute! Stannin' out dah foolin' 'long wid dat low trash, an' heah's de barber off'n de 'Gran' Turk' wants to converse wid you!"

My reference, a moment ago, to the face that a pilot's peculiar official position placed him out of the reach of criticism or command, brings Stephen W—— naturally to my mind. He was a gifted pilot, a good fellow, a tireless talker, and had both wit and humor in him. He had a most irreverent independence, too, and was deliciously easy-going and comfortable in the presence of age, official dignity, and even the most august wealth. He always had work, he never saved a penny, he was a most persuasive borrower, he was in debt to every pilot on the river, and

* Door.

to the majority of the captains. He could throw a sort of splendor around a bit of harum-scarum, devil-may-care piloting, that made it almost fascinating—but not to everybody. He made a trip with good old Captain Y——once, and was "relieved" from duty when the boat got to New Orleans. Somebody expressed surprise at the discharge. Captain Y——shuddered at the mere mention of Stephen. Then his poor, thin old voice piped out something like this:—

"Why, bless me! I wouldn't have such a wild creature on my boat for the world—not for the whole world! He swears, he sings, he whistles, he yells—I never saw such an Injun to yell. All times of the night—it never made any difference to him. He would just yell that way, not for anything in particular, but merely on account of a kind of devilish comfort he got out of it. I never could get into a sound sleep but he would fetch me out of bed, all in a cold sweat, with one of those dreadful war-whoops. A queer being,—very queer being; no respect for anything or anybody. Sometimes he called me 'Johnny.' And he kept a fiddle, and a cat. He played execrably. This seemed to distress the cat, and so the cat would howl. Nobody could sleep where that man—and his family—was. And reckless? There never was anything like it. Now you may believe it or not, but as sure as I am sitting here, he brought my boat a-tilting down through those awful snags at Chicot under a rattling head of steam, and the wind a-blowing like the very nation, at that! My officers will tell you so. They saw it. And, sir, while he was a-tearing right down through those snags, and I a-shaking in my shoes and praying, I wish I may never speak again if he didn't pucker up his mouth and go to *whistling!* Yes, sir; whistling 'Buffalo gals, can't you come out to-night, can't you come out to-night, can't you come out to-night;' and doing it as calmly as if we were attending a funeral and weren't related to the corpse. And when I remonstrated with him about it, he smiled down on me as if I was his child, and told me to run in the house and try to be good, and not be meddling with my superiors!"*

Once a pretty mean captain caught Stephen in New Orleans out of work and as usual out of money. He laid steady siege to Stephen, who was in a very "close place," and finally persuaded him to hire with him at one hundred and twenty-five dollars per month, just half wages, the captain agreeing not to divulge the secret and so bring down the contempt of all the guild upon the

* Considering a captain's ostentatious but hollow chieftainship, and a pilot's real authority, there was something impudently apt and happy about that way of phrasing it.

poor fellow. But the boat was not more than a day out of New Orleans before Stephen discovered that the captain was boasting of his exploit, and that all the officers had been told. Stephen winced, but said nothing. About the middle of the afternoon the captain stepped out on the hurricane deck, cast his eye around, and looked a good deal surprised. He glanced inquiringly aloft at Stephen, but Stephen was whistling placidly, and attending to business. The captain stood around a while in evident discomfort, and once or twice seemed about to make a suggestion; but the etiquette of the river taught him to avoid that sort of rashness, and so he managed to hold his peace. He chafed and puzzled a few minutes longer, then retired to his apartments. But soon he was out again, and apparently more perplexed than ever. Presently he ventured to remark, with deference,—

"Pretty good stage of the river now, ain't it, sir?"

"Well, I should say so! Bank-full *is* a pretty liberal stage."

"Seems to be a good deal of current here."

"Good deal don't describe it! It's worse than a millrace."

"Isn't it easier in toward shore than it is out here in the middle?"

"Yes, I reckon it is; but a body can't be too careful with a steamboat. It's pretty safe out here; can't strike any bottom here, you can depend on that."

The captain departed, looking rueful enough. At this rate, he would probably die of old age before his boat got to St. Louis. Next day he appeared on deck and again found Stephen faithfully standing up the middle of the river, fighting the whole vast force of the Mississippi, and whistling the same placid tune. This thing was becoming serious. In by the shore was a slower boat clipping along in the easy water and gaining steadily; she began to make for an island chute; Stephen stuck to middle of the river. Speech was *wrung* from the captain. He said,—

"Mr. W——, don't that chute cut off a good deal of distance?"

"I think it does, but I don't know."

"Don't know! Well, isn't there water enough in it now to go through?"

"I expect there is, but I am not certain."

"Upon my word this is odd! Why, those pilots on that boat yonder are going to try it. Do you mean to say that you don't know as much as they do?"

"*They!* Why, *they* are two-hundred-and-fifty-dollar pilots! But don't you be uneasy; I know as much as any man can afford to know for a hundred and twenty-five!"

The captain surrendered.

Five minutes later Stephen was bowling through the chute and showing the rival boat a two-hundred-and-fifty-dollar pair of heels.

CHAPTER XV

THE PILOTS' MONOPOLY

One day, on board the "Aleck Scott," my chief, Mr. Bixby, was crawling carefully through a close place at Cat Island, both leads going, and everybody holding his breath. The captain, a nervous, apprehensive man, kept still as long as he could, but finally broke down and shouted from the hurricane deck,—

"For gracious' sake, give her steam, Mr. Bixby! give her steam! She'll never raise the reef on this headway!"

For all the effect that was produced upon Mr. Bixby, one would have supposed that no remark had been made. But five minutes later, when the danger was past and the leads laid in, he burst instantly into a consuming fury, and gave the captain the most admirable cursing I ever listened to. No bloodshed ensued; but that was because the captain's cause was weak; for ordinarily he was not a man to take correction quietly.

Having now set forth in detail the nature of the science of piloting, and likewise described the rank which the pilot held among the fraternity of steamboatmen, this seems a fitting place to say a few words about an organization which the pilots once formed for the protection of their guild. It was curious and noteworthy in this, that it was perhaps the compactest, the completest, and the strongest commercial organization ever formed among men.

For a long time wages had been two hundred and fifty dollars a month; but curiously enough, as steamboats multiplied and business increased, the wages began to fall little by little. It was easy to discover the reason of this. Too many pilots were being "made." It was nice to have a "cub," a steersman, to do all the hard work for a couple of years, gratis, while his master sat on a high bench and smoked; all pilots and captains had sons or nephews who wanted to be pilots. By and by it came to pass that nearly every pilot on the river had a steersman. When a steersman had made an amount of progress that was satisfactory to any two pilots in the trade, they could get a pilot's license for him by signing an application directed to the United States Inspector. Nothing further was needed; usually no questions were asked, no proofs of capacity required.

Very well, this growing swarm of new pilots presently began to undermine the wages, in order to get berths. Too late—apparently—the knights of the tiller perceived their mistake. Plainly, something had to be done, and quickly; but what was to be the needful thing? A close organization. Nothing else would answer. To compass this seemed an impossibility; so it was talked, and talked, and then dropped. It was too likely to ruin whoever ventured to move in the matter. But at last about a dozen of the boldest—and some of them the best—pilots on the river launched themselves into the enterprise and took all the chances. They got a special charter from the legislature, with large powers, under the name of the Pilots' Benevolent Association; elected their officers, completed their organization, contributed capital, put "association" wages up to two hundred and fifty dollars at once—and then retired to their homes, for they were promptly discharged from employment. But there were two or three unnoticed trifles in their by-laws which had the seeds of propagation in them. For instance, all idle members of the association, in good standing, were entitled to a pension of twenty-five dollars per month. This began to bring in one straggler after another from the ranks of the new-fledged pilots, in the dull (summer) season. Better have twenty-five dollars than starve; the initiation fee was only twelve dollars, and no dues required from the unemployed.

Also, the widows of deceased members in good standing could draw twenty-five dollars per month, and a certain sum for each of their children. Also, the said deceased would be buried at the association's expense. These things resurrected all the superannuated and forgotten pilots in the Mississippi Valley. They came from farms, they came from interior villages, they came from everywhere. They came on crutches, on drays, in ambulances,—any way, so they got there. They paid in their twelve dollars, and straightway began to draw out twenty-five dollars a month and calculate their burial bills.

By and by, all the useless, helpless pilots, and a dozen first-class ones, were in the association, and nine tenths of the best pilots out of it and laughing at it. It was the laughing-stock of the whole river. Everybody joked about the by-law requiring members to pay ten per cent of their wages, every month, into the treasury for the support of the association, whereas all the members were outcast and tabooed, and no one would employ them. Everybody was derisively grateful to the association for taking all the worthless pilots out of the way and leaving the whole field to the excellent and the deserving; and everybody was not only jocularly grateful for that, but for a result which naturally followed, namely, the gradual advance of wages as the busy season approached. Wages had gone up from the low figure of one hundred dollars a month to one hundred and twenty-five, and in some cases to one hundred and fifty; and it was great fun to enlarge upon the fact that this charming thing had been accomplished by a body of men not one of whom received a particle of benefit from it. Some of the jokers used to call at the association rooms and have a good time chaffing the members and offering them the charity of taking them as steersmen for a trip, so that they could see what the forgotten river looked like. However, the association was content; or at least it gave no sign to the contrary. Now and then it captured a pilot who was "out of luck," and added him to its list; and these later additions were very valuable, for they were good pilots; the incompetent ones had all been absorbed before. As business freshened, wages climbed gradually up to two hundred and fifty dollars—the association figure—and became firmly fixed there; and still without benefiting a member of that body, for no member was hired. The hilarity at the association's expense burst all bounds, now. There was no end to the fun which that poor martyr had to put up with.

However, it is a long lane that has no turning. Winter approached, business doubled and trebled, and an avalanche of Missouri, Illinois, and Upper Mississippi River boats came pouring down to take a chance in the New Orleans trade. All of a sudden, pilots were in great demand, and were correspondingly scarce. The time for revenge was come. It was a bitter pill to have to accept association pilots at last, yet captains and owners agreed that there was no other way. But none of these outcasts offered! So there was a still bitterer pill to be swallowed: they must be sought out and asked for their services. Captain—— was the first man who found it necessary to take the dose, and he had been the loudest derider of the organization. He hunted up one of the best of the association pilots and said,—

"Well, you boys have rather got the best of us for a little while, so I'll give in with as good a grace as I can. I've come to hire you; get your trunk aboard right away. I want to leave at twelve o'clock."

"I don't know about that. Who is your other pilot?"

"I've got I. S——. Why?"

"I can't go with him. He don't belong to the association."

"What!"

"It's so."

"Do you mean to tell me that you won't turn a wheel with one of the very best and oldest pilots on the river because he don't belong to your association?"

"Yes, I do."

"Well, if this isn't putting on airs! I supposed I was doing you a benevolence; but I begin to think that I am the party that wants a favor done. Are you acting under a law of the concern?"

"Yes."

"Show it to me."

So they stepped into the association rooms, and the secretary soon satisfied the captain, who said,—

"Well, what am I to do? I have hired Mr. S—— for the entire season."

"I will provide for you," said the secretary. "I will detail a pilot to go with you, and he shall be on board at twelve o'clock."

"But if I discharge S——, he will come on me for the whole season's wages."

"Of course that is a matter between you and Mr. S——, captain. We cannot meddle in your private affairs."

The captain stormed, but to no purpose. In the end he had to discharge S——, pay him about a thousand dollars, and take an association pilot in his place. The laugh was beginning to turn the other way, now. Every day, thenceforward, a new victim fell; every day some outraged captain discharged a non-association pet, with tears and profanity, and installed a hated association man in his berth. In a very little while, idle non-associationists began to be pretty plenty, brisk as business was, and much as their services were desired. The laugh was shifting to the other side of their mouths most palpably. These victims, together with the captains and owners, presently ceased to laugh altogether, and began to rage about the revenge they would take when the passing business "spurt" was over.

Soon all the laughers that were left were the owner and crews of boats that had two non-association pilots. But their triumph was not very long-lived. For this reason: It was a rigid rule of the association that its members should never, under any circumstances whatever, give information about the channel to any "outsider." By this time about half the boats had none but association pilots, and the other half had none but outsiders. At the first glance one would suppose that when it came to forbidding information about the river these two parties could play equally at that game; but this was not so. At every good-sized town from one end of the river to the other, there was a "wharf-boat" to land at, instead of a wharf or a pier. Freight was stored in it for transportation; waiting passengers slept in its cabins. Upon each of these wharf-boats the association's officers placed a strong box, fastened with a peculiar lock which was used in no other service but one—the United States mail service. It was the letter-bag lock, a sacred governmental thing. By dint of much beseeching the government had been persuaded to allow the association to use this lock. Every association man carried a key which would open these boxes. That key, or rather a peculiar way of holding it in the hand when its owner was asked for river information by a stranger,—for the success of the St. Louis and New Orleans association had now bred tolerably thriving branches in a dozen neighboring steamboat trades,—was the association man's sign and diploma of membership; and if the stranger did not respond by producing a similar key and holding it in a certain manner duly prescribed, his question was politely ignored. From the association's secretary each member received a package of more or less gorgeous blanks, printed like a bill-head, on handsome paper, properly ruled in columns; a bill-head worded something like this:—

STEAMER GREAT REPUBLIC.

JOHN SMITH, MASTER.

Pilots, John Jones and Thomas Brown.

CROSSINGS.	SOUNDINGS.	MARKS.	REMARKS.

These blanks were filled up, day by day, as the voyage progressed, and deposited in the several wharf-boat boxes. For instance, as soon as the first crossing, out from St. Louis, was completed, the times would be entered upon the blank, under the appropriate headings, thus:—

"St. Louis. Nine and a half (feet). Stern on courthouse, head on dead cottonwood above wood-yard, until you raise the first reef, then pull up square." Then under head of Remarks: "Go just outside the wrecks; this is important. New snag just where you straighten down; go above it."

The pilot who deposited that blank in the Cairo box (after adding to it the details of every crossing all the way down from St. Louis) took out and read half a dozen fresh reports (from upward-bound steamers) concerning the river between Cairo and Memphis, posted himself thoroughly, returned them to the box, and went back aboard his boat again so armed against accident that he could not possibly get his boat into trouble without bringing the most ingenious carelessness to his aid.

Imagine the benefits of so admirable a system in a piece of river twelve or thirteen hundred miles long, whose channel was shifting every day! The pilot who had formerly been obliged to put up with seeing a shoal place once or possibly twice a month, had a hundred sharp eyes to watch it for him, now, and bushels of intelligent brains to tell him how to run it. His information about it was seldom twenty-four hours old. If the reports in the last box chanced to leave any misgivings on his mind concerning a treacherous crossing, he had his remedy; he blew his steam-whistle in a peculiar way as soon as he saw a boat approaching; the signal was answered in a peculiar way if that boat's pilots were association men; and then the two steamers ranged alongside and all uncertainties were swept away by fresh information furnished to the inquirer by word of mouth and in minute detail.

The first thing a pilot did when he reached New Orleans or St. Louis was to take his final and elaborate report to the association parlors and hang it up there,—*after* which he was free to visit his family. In these parlors a crowd was always gathered together, discussing changes in the channel, and the moment there was a fresh arrival, everybody stopped talking till this witness had told the newest news and settled the latest uncertainty. Other craftsmen can "sink the shop," sometimes, and interest themselves in other matters. Not so with a pilot; he must devote himself wholly to his profession and talk of nothing else; for it would be small gain to be perfect one day and imperfect the next. He has no time or words to waste if he would keep "posted."

But the outsiders had a hard time of it. No particular place to meet and exchange information, no wharf-boat reports, none but chance and unsatisfactory ways of getting news. The consequence was that a man sometimes had to run five hundred miles of river on information that was a week or ten days old. At a fair stage of the river that might have answered; but when the dead low water came it was destructive.

Now came another perfectly logical result. The outsiders began to ground steamboats, sink them, and get into all sorts of trouble, whereas accidents seemed to keep entirely away from the association men. Wherefore even the owners and captains of boats furnished exclusively with outsiders, and previously considered to be wholly independent of the association and free to comfort themselves with brag and laughter, began to feel pretty uncomfortable. Still, they made a show of keeping up the brag, until one black day when every captain of the lot was formally ordered to immediately discharge his outsiders and take association pilots in their stead. And who was it that had the dashing presumption to do that? Alas, it came from a power behind the throne that was greater than the throne itself. It was the underwriters!

It was no time to "swap knives." Every outsider had to take his trunk ashore at once. Of course it was supposed that there was collusion between the association and the underwriters, but this was not so. The latter had come to comprehend the excellence of the "report" system of the association and the safety it secured, and so they had made their decision among themselves and upon plain business principles.

There was weeping and wailing and gnashing of teeth in the camp of the outsiders now. But no matter, there was but one course for them to pursue, and they pursued it. They came forward in couples and groups, and proffered their twelve dollars and asked for membership. They were surprised to learn that several new by-laws had been long ago added. For instance, the initiation fee had been raised to fifty dollars; that sum must be tendered, and also ten per cent of the wages which the applicant had received each and every month since the founding of the association. In many cases this amounted to three or four hundred dollars. Still, the association would not entertain the application until the money was present. Even then a single adverse vote killed the application. Every member had to vote yes or no in person and before witnesses; so it took weeks to decide a candidacy, because many pilots were so long absent on voyages. However, the repentant sinners scraped their savings together, and one by one, by our tedious voting process, they were added to the fold. A time came, at last, when only about ten remained outside. They said they would starve before they would apply. They remained idle a long while, because of course nobody could venture to employ them.

By and by the association published the fact that upon a certain date the wages would be raised to five hundred dollars per month. All the branch associations had grown strong, now, and the Red River one had advanced wages to seven hundred dollars a month. Reluctantly the ten outsiders yielded, in view of these things, and made application. There was *another* new by-law, by this time, which required them to pay dues not only on all the wages they had received since the association was born, but also on what they would have received if they had continued at work up to the time of their application, instead of going off to pout in idleness. It turned out to be a difficult matter to elect them, but it was accomplished at last. The most virulent sinner of this batch had stayed out and allowed "dues" to accumulate against him so long that he had to send in six hundred and twenty-five dollars with his application.

The association had a good bank account now, and was very strong. There was no longer an outsider. A by-law was added forbidding the reception of any more cubs or apprentices for five years; after which time a limited number would be taken, not by individuals, but by the association, upon these terms: the applicant must not be less than eighteen years old, and of respectable family and good character; he must pass an examination as to education, pay a thousand dollars in advance for the privilege of becoming an apprentice, and must remain under the commands of the association until a great part of the membership (more than half, I think) should be willing to sign his application for a pilot's license.

All previously-articled apprentices were now taken away from their masters and adopted by the association. The president and secretary detailed them for service on one boat or another, as they chose, and changed them from boat to boat according to certain rules. If a pilot could show that he was in infirm health and needed assistance, one of the cubs would be ordered to go with him.

The widow and orphan list grew, but so did the association's financial resources. The association attended its own funerals in state, and paid for them. When occasion demanded, it sent members down the river upon searches for the bodies of brethren lost by steamboat accidents; a search of this kind sometimes cost a thousand dollars.

The association procured a charter and went into the insurance business, also. It not only insured the lives of its members, but took risks on steamboats.

The organization seemed indestructible. It was the tightest monopoly in the world. By the United States law, no man could become a pilot unless two duly licensed pilots signed his application; and now there was nobody outside of the association competent to sign. Consequently the making of pilots was at an end. Every year some would die and others become incapacitated by age and infirmity; there would be no new ones to take their places. In time, the association could put wages up to any figure it chose; and as long as it should be wise enough not to carry the thing too far and provoke the national government into amending the licensing system, steamboat owners would have to submit, since there would be no help for it.

The owners and captains were the only obstruction that lay between the association and absolute power; and at last this one was removed. Incredible as it may seem, the owners and captains deliberately did it themselves. When the pilots' association announced, months beforehand, that on the first day of September, 1861, wages would be advanced to five hundred dollars per month, the owners and captains instantly put freights up a few cents, and explained to the farmers along the river the necessity of it, by calling their attention to the burdensome rate of wages about to be established. It was a rather slender argument, but the farmers did not seem to detect it. It looked reasonable to them that to add five cents freight on a bushel of corn was justifiable under the circumstances, overlooking the fact that this advance on a cargo of forty thousand sacks was a good deal more than necessary to cover the new wages.

So, straightway the captains and owners got up an association of their own, and proposed to put captains' wages up to five hundred dollars, too, and move for another advance in freights. It was a novel idea, but of course an effect which had been produced once could be produced again. The new association decreed (for this was before all the outsiders had been taken into the pilots' association) that if any captain employed a non-association pilot, he should be forced to discharge him, and also pay a fine of five hundred dollars. Several of these heavy fines were paid before the captains' organization grew strong enough to exercise full authority over its membership; but that all ceased, presently. The captains tried to get the pilots to decree that no member of their corporation should serve under a non-association captain; but this proposition was declined. The pilots saw that they would be backed up by the captains and the underwriters anyhow, and so they wisely refrained from entering into entangling alliances.

As I have remarked, the pilots' association was now the compactest monopoly in the world, perhaps, and seemed simply indestructible. And yet the days of its glory were numbered. First, the new railroad stretching up through Mississippi, Tennessee, and Kentucky, to Northern railway centres, began to divert the passenger travel from the steamers; next the war came and almost entirely annihilated the steamboating industry during several years, leaving most of the pilots idle, and the cost of living advancing all the time; then the treasurer of the St. Louis association put his hand into the till and walked off with every dollar of the ample fund; and finally, the railroads intruding everywhere, there was little for steamers to do, when the war was over, but carry freights; so straightway some genius from the Atlantic coast introduced the plan of towing a dozen steamer cargoes down to New Orleans at the tail of a vulgar little tug-boat; and behold, in the twinkling of an eye, as it were, the association and the noble science of piloting were things of the dead and pathetic past!

CHAPTER XVI

RACING DAYS

It was always the custom for the boats to leave New Orleans between four and five o'clock in the afternoon. From three o'clock onward they would be burning rosin and pitch pine (the sign of preparation), and so one had the picturesque spectacle of a rank, some two or three miles long, of tall, ascending columns of coal-black smoke; a colonnade which supported a sable roof of the same smoke blended together and spreading abroad over the city. Every outward-bound boat had its flag flying at the jack-staff, and sometimes a duplicate on the verge staff astern. Two or three miles of mates were commanding and swearing with more than usual emphasis; countless processions of freight barrels and boxes were spinning athwart the levee and flying aboard the stage-planks; belated passengers were dodging and skipping among these frantic things, hoping to reach the forecastle companion way alive, but having their doubts about it; women with reticules and bandboxes were trying to keep up with husbands freighted with carpet-sacks and crying babies, and making a failure of it by losing their heads in the whirl and roar and general distraction; drays and baggage-vans were clattering hither and thither in a wild hurry, every now and then getting blocked and jammed together, and then during ten seconds one could not see them for the profanity, except vaguely and dimly; every windlass connected with every fore-hatch, from one end of that long array of steamboats to the other, was keeping up a deafening whiz and whir, lowering freight into the hold, and the half-naked crews of perspiring negroes that worked them were roaring such songs as "De Las' Sack! De Las' Sack!"—inspired to unimaginable exaltation by the chaos of turmoil and racket that was driving everybody else mad. By this time the hurricane and boiler decks of the steamers would be packed and black with passengers. The "last bells" would begin to clang, all down the line, and then the powwow seemed to double; in a moment or two the final warning came,—a simultaneous din of Chinese gongs, with the cry, "All dat ain't goin', please to git asho'!"—and behold, the powwow quadrupled! People came swarming ashore, overturning excited stragglers that were trying to swarm aboard. One more moment later a long array of stage-planks was being hauled in, each with its customary latest passenger clinging to the end of it with teeth, nails, and everything else, and the customary latest procrastinator making a wild spring shoreward over his head.

Now a number of the boats slide backward into the stream, leaving wide gaps in the serried rank of steamers. Citizens crowd the decks of boats that are not to go, in order to see the sight. Steamer after steamer straightens herself up, gathers all her strength, and presently comes swinging by, under a tremendous head of steam, with flag flying, black smoke rolling, and her entire crew of firemen and deck-hands (usually swarthy negroes) massed together on the forecastle, the best "voice" in the lot towering from the mist (being mounted on the capstan), waving his hat or a flag, and all roaring a mighty chorus, while the parting cannons boom and the multitudinous spectators swing their hats and huzza! Steamer after steamer falls into line, and the stately procession goes winging its flight up the river.

In the old times, whenever two fast boats started out on a race, with a big crowd of people looking on, it was inspiring to hear the crews sing, especially if the time were night-fall, and the forecastle lit up with the red glare of the torch-baskets. Racing was royal fun. The public always had an idea that racing was dangerous; whereas the opposite was the case—that is, after the laws were passed which restricted each boat to just so many pounds of steam to the square inch. No engineer was ever sleepy or careless when his heart was in a race. He was constantly on the alert, trying gauge-cocks and watching things. The dangerous place was on slow, plodding boats, where the engineers drowsed around and allowed chips to get into the "doctor" and shut off the water supply from the boilers.

In the "flush times" of steam-boating, a race between two notoriously fleet steamers was an event of vast importance. The date was set for it several weeks in advance, and from that time foreward, the whole Mississippi Valley was in a state of consuming excitement. Politics and the weather were dropped, and people talked only of the coming race. As the time approached, the two steamers "stripped" and got ready. Every incumbrance that added weight, or exposed a resisting surface to wind or water, was removed, if the boat could possibly do without it. The "spars," and sometimes even their supporting derricks, were sent ashore, and no means left to set the boat afloat in case she got aground. When the "Eclipse" and the "A.L. Shotwell" ran their great race many years ago, it was said that pains were taken to scrape the gilding off the fanciful device which hung between the "Eclipse's" chimneys, and that for that one trip the captain left off his kid gloves and had his head shaved. But I always doubted these things.

If the boat was known to make her best speed when drawing five and a half feet forward and five feet aft, she was carefully loaded to that exact figure—she wouldn't enter a dose of homoeopathic pills on her manifest after that. Hardly any passengers were taken, because they not only add weight but they never will "trim boat." They always run to the side when there is anything to see, whereas a conscientious and experienced steamboatman would stick to the centre of the boat and part his hair in the middle with a spirit level.

No way-freights and no way-passengers were allowed, for the racers would stop only at the largest towns, and then it would be only "touch and go." Coal flats and wood flats were contracted for beforehand, and these were kept ready to hitch on to the flying streamers at a moment's warning. Double crews were carried, so that all work could be quickly done.

The chosen date being come, and all things in readiness, the two great steamers back into the stream, and lie there jockeying a moment, and apparently watching each other's slightest movement, like sentient creatures; flags drooping, the pent steam shrieking through safety-valves, the black smoke rolling and tumbling from the chimneys and darkening all the air. People, people everywhere; the shores, the house-tops, the steamboats, the ships, are packed with them, and you know that the borders of the broad Mississippi are going to be fringed with humanity thence northward twelve hundred miles, to welcome these racers.

Presently tall columns of steam burst from the 'scapepipes of both steamers, two guns boom a good-by, two red-shirted heroes mounted on capstans wave their small flags above the massed crews on the forecastles, two plaintive solos linger on the air a few waiting seconds, two mighty choruses burst forth—and here they come! Brass bands bray Hail Columbia, huzza after huzza thunders from the shores, and the stately creatures go whistling by like the wind.

Those boats will never halt a moment between New Orleans and St. Louis, except for a second or two at large towns, or to hitch thirty-cord wood-boats alongside. You should be on board when they take a couple of those wood-boats in tow and turn a swarm of men into each; by the time you have wiped your glasses and put them on, you will be wondering what has become of that wood.

Two nicely matched steamers will stay in sight of each other day after day. They might even stay side by side, but for the fact that pilots are not all alike, and the smartest pilots will win the race. If one of the boats has a "lightning" pilot, whose "partner" is a trifle his inferior, you can tell which one is on watch by noting whether that boat has gained ground or lost some during each four-hour stretch. The shrewdest pilot can delay a boat if he has not a fine genius for steering. Steering is a very high art. One must not keep a rudder dragging across a boat's stern if he wants to get up the river fast.

There is a great difference in boats, of course. For a long time I was on a boat that was so slow we used to forget what year it was we left port in. But of course this was at rare intervals. Ferry-boats used to lose valuable trips because their passengers grew old and died, waiting for us to get by. This was at still rarer intervals. I had the documents for these occurrences, but through carelessness they have been mislaid. This boat, the "John J. Roe," was so slow that when she finally sunk in Madrid Bend, it was five years before the owners heard of it. That was always a confusing fact to me, but it is according to the record, any way. She was dismally slow; still, we often had pretty exciting times racing with islands, and rafts, and such things. One trip, however, we did rather well. We went to St.Louis in sixteen days. But even at this rattling gait I think we changed watches three times in Fort Adams reach, which is five miles long. A "reach" is a piece of straight river, and of course the current drives through such a place in a pretty lively way. That trip we went to Grand Gulf, from New Orleans, in four days (three hundred and forty miles); the "Eclipse" and "Shotwell" did it in one. We were nine days out, in the chute of 63 (seven hundred miles); the "Eclipse" and "Shotwell" went there in two days. Something over a generation ago, a boat called the "J. M. White" went from New Orleans to Cairo in three days, six hours, and forty-four minutes. In 1853 the "Eclipse" made the same trip in three days, three hours, and twenty minutes.* In 1870 the "R. E. Lee" did it in three days and *one* hour. This last is called the fastest trip on record. I will try to show that it was not. For this reason: the distance between New Orleans and Cairo, when the "J. M. White" ran it, was about eleven hundred and six miles; consequently her average speed was a trifle over fourteen miles per hour. In the "Eclipse's" day the distance between the two ports had become reduced to one thousand and eighty miles; consequently her average speed was a shade under fourteen and three eighths

* Time disputed. Some authorities add 1 hour and 16 minutes to this.

miles per hour. In the "R. E. Lee's" time the distance had diminished to about one thousand and thirty miles; consequently her average was about fourteen and one eighth miles per hour. Therefore the "Eclipse's" was consequently the fastest time that has ever been made.

THE RECORD OF SOME FAMOUS TRIPS.

[*From Commodore Rollingpin's Almanac.*]

FAST TIME ON THE WESTERN WATERS.

FROM NEW ORLEANS TO NATCHEZ—268 MILES.

			D.	H.	M.				H.	M.
1814.	Orleans	made the run in	6	6	40	1844.	Sultana . .	made the run in	19	45
1814.	Comet	,, ,,	5	10		1851.	Magnolia	,, ,,	19	50
1815.	Enterprise	,, ,,	4	11	20	1853.	A. L. Shotwell	,, ,,	19	49
1817.	Washington	,, ,,	4			1853.	Southern Belle	,, ,,	20	3
1817.	Shelby	,, ,,	3	20		1853.	Princess (No. 4)	,, ,,	20	26
1819.	Paragon	,, ,,	3	8		1853.	Eclipse	,, ,,	19	47
1828.	Tecumseh	,, ,,	3	1	20	1855.	Princess (New)	,, ,,	18	53
1834.	Tuscarora	,, ,,	1	21		1855.	Natchez (New)	,, ,,	17	30
1838.	Natchez	,, ,,	1	17		1856.	Princess (New)	,, ,,	17	30
1840.	Ed. Shippen	,, ,,	1	8		1870.	Natchez	,, ,,	17	17
1842.	Belle of the West	,,	1	18		1870.	R. E. Lee	,, ,,	17	11

FROM NEW ORLEANS TO CAIRO—1,024 MILES.

			D.	H.	M				D.	H.	M.
1844.	J. M. White	made the run in	3	6	44	1869.	Dexter . . .	made the run in	3	6	20
1852.	Reindeer	,, ,,	3	12	45	1870.	Natchez	,, ,,	3	4	34
1853.	Eclipse	,, ,,	3	4	4	1870.	R. E. Lee	,, ,,	3	1	
1853.	A. L. Shotwell	,, ,,	3	3	40						

FROM NEW ORLEANS TO LOUISVILLE—1,440 MILES.

			D.	H.	M.				D.	H.	M.
1815.	Enterprise	made the run in	25	2	40	1840.	Ed. Shippen	made the run in	5	14	
1817.	Washington	,, ,,	25			1842.	Belle of the West	,, ,,	6	14	
1817.	Shelby	,, ,,	20	4	20	1843.	Duke of Orleans	,, ,,	5	23	
1819.	Paragon	,, ,,	18	10		1844.	Sultana	,, ,,	5	12	
1828.	Tecumseh	,, ,,	8	4		1849.	Bostona	,, ,,	5	8	
1834.	Tuscarora	,, ,,	7	16		1851.	Belle Key	,, ,,	4	23	
1837.	Gen. Brown	,, ,,	6	22		1852.	Reindeer	,, ,,	4	20	45
1837.	Randolph	,, ,,	6	22		1852.	Eclipse	,, ,,	4	19	
1837.	Empress	,, ,,	6	17		1853.	A. L. Shotwell	,, ,,	4	10	20
1837.	Sultana	,, ,,	6	15		1853.	Eclipse	,, ,,	4	9	30

FROM NEW ORLEANS TO DONALDSVILLE—78 MILES.

			H.	M.				H.	M.
1852.	A. L. Shotwell	made the run in	5	42	1860.	Atlantic . . .	made the run in	5	11
1852.	Eclipse	,, ,,	5	42	1860.	Gen. Quitman	,, ,,	5	6
1854.	Sultana	,, ,,	5	12	1865.	Ruth	,, ,,	4	43
1856.	Princess	,, ,,	4	51	1870.	R. E. Lee	,, ,,	4	59

FROM NEW ORLEANS TO ST. LOUIS—1,218 MILES.

			D.	H.	M.				D.	H.	M.
1844.	J. M. White	made the run in	3	23	9	1870.	Natchez . .	made the run in	3	21	58
1849.	Missouri	,, ,,	4	19		1870.	R. E. Lee	,, ,,	3	18	14
1869.	Dexter	,, ,,	4	9							

FROM LOUISVILLE TO CINCINNATI—141 MILES.

			D.	H.	M.				D.	H.	M.
1819.	Gen. Pike	made the run in	1	16		1843.	Congress . .	made the run in		12	20
1819.	Paragon	,, ,,	1	14	20	1846.	Ben Franklin (No. 6)	,,		11	45
1822.	Wheeling Packet	,, ,,	1	10		1852.	Alleghaney	,, ,,		10	38
1837.	Moselle	,,		12		1852.	Pittsburgh	,, ,,		10	23
1843.	Duke of Orleans	,, ,,		12		1853.	Telegraph No. 3	,, ,,		9	52

FROM LOUISVILLE TO ST. LOUIS 750 MILES.

			D.	H.	M.				D.	H.	M.
1843.	Congress . .	made the run in	2	1		1854.	Northerner	made the run in	1	22	30
1854.	Pike	,, ,,	1	23		1855.	Southerner	,, ,,	1	19	

FROM CINCINNATI TO PITTSBURG—490 MILES.

			D.	H.				D.	H.
1850.	Telegraph No. 2	made the run in	1	17	1852.	Pittsburgh . . .	made the run in	1	15
1851.	Buckeye State	,, ,,	1	16					

FROM ST. LOUIS TO ALTON—30 MILES.

			H.	M.				H.	M.
1853.	Altona	made the run in	1	35	1876.	War Eagle . . .	made the run in	1	37
1876.	Golden Eagle	,, ,,	1	37					

MISCELLANEOUS RUNS.

In June, 1859, the St. Louis and Keokuk Packet, City of Louisiana, made the run from St. Louis to Keokuk (214 miles) in 16 hours and 20 minutes, the best time on record.

In 1868 the steamer Hawkeye State, of the Northern Line Packet Company, made the run from St. Louis to St. Paul (800 miles) in 2 days and 20 hours. Never was beaten.

In 1853 the steamer Polar Star made the run from St. Louis to St. Joseph, on the Missouri River in 64 hours. In July, 1856, the steamer Jas. H. Lucas, Andy Wineland, Master, made the same run in 60 hours and 57 minutes. The distance between the ports is 600 miles, and when the difficulties of navigating the turbulent Missouri are taken into consideration, the performance of the Lucas deserves especial mention.

THE RUN OF THE ROBERT E. LEE.

The time made by the R. E. Lee from New Orleans to St. Louis in 1870, in her famous race with the Natchez, is the best on record, and, inasmuch as the race created a national interest, we give below her time table from port to port.

Left New Orleans, Thursday, June 30th, 1870, at 4 o'clock and 55 minutes, p. m.; reached

	D.	H.	M.		D.	H.	M.
Carrollton			27½	Vicksburg	1		38
Harry Hills		1	00½	Milliken's Bend	1	2	37
Red Church		1	39	Bailey's	1	3	48
Bonnet Carre		2	38	Lake Providence	1	5	47
College Point		3	50½	Greenville	1	10	55
Donaldsonville		4	59	Napoleon	1	16	22
Plaquemine		7	05½	White River	1	16	56
Baton Rouge		8	25	Australia	1	19	
Bayou Sara		10	26	Helena	1	23	25
Red River		12	56	Half Mile Below St. Francis . . .	2		
Stamps		13	56	Memphis	2	6	9
Bryaro		15	51½	Foot of Island 37	2	9	
Hinderson's		16	29	Foot of Island 26	2	13	30
Natchez		17	11	Tow-head, Island 14	2	17	23
Cole's Creek		19	21	New Madrid	2	19	50
Waterproof		18	53	Dry Bar No. 10	2	20	37
Rodney		20	45	Foot of Island 8	2	21	25
St. Joseph		21	02	Upper Tow-head — Lucas Bend .	3		
Grand Gulf		22	06	Cairo	3	1	
Hard Times		22	18	St. Louis	3	18	14
Half Mile Below Warrenton . . .	1						

The Lee landed at St. Louis at 11.25 A. M., on July 4th, 1870—six hours and thirty-six minutes ahead of the Natchez. The officers of the Natchez claimed seven hours and one minute stoppage on account of fog and repairing machinery. The R. E. Lee was commanded by Captain John W. Cannon, and the Natchez was in charge of that veteran Southern boatman, Captain Thomas P. Leathers.

CHAPTER XVII

CUT-OFFS AND STEPHEN

These dry details are of importance in one particular. They give me an opportunity of introducing one of the Mississippi's oddest peculiarities,—that of shortening its length from time to time. If you will throw a long, pliant apple-paring over your shoulder, it till pretty fairly shape itself into an average section of the Mississippi River; that is, the nine or ten hundred miles stretching from Cairo, Illinois, southward to New Orleans, the same being wonderfully crooked, with a brief straight bit here and there at wide intervals. The two-hundred-mile stretch from Cairo northward to St. Louis is by no means so crooked, that being a rocky country which the river cannot cut much.

The water cuts the alluvial banks of the "lower" river into deep horseshoe curves; so deep, indeed, that in some places if you were to get ashore at one extremity of the horseshoe and walk across the neck, half or three quarters of a mile, you could sit down and rest a couple of hours while your steamer was coming around the long elbow, at a speed of ten miles an hour, to take you aboard again. When the river is rising fast, some scoundrel whose plantation is back in the country, and therefore of inferior value, has only to watch his chance, cut a little gutter across the narrow neck of land some dark night, and turn the water into it, and in a wonderfully short time a miracle has happened: to wit, the whole Mississippi has taken possession of that little ditch, and placed the countryman's plantation on its bank (quadrupling its value), and that other party's formerly valuable plantation finds itself away out yonder on a big island; the old water-course around it will soon shoal up, boats cannot approach within ten miles of it, and down goes its value to a fourth of its former worth. Watches are kept on those narrow necks, at needful times, and if a man happens to be caught cutting a ditch across them, the chances are all against his ever having another opportunity to cut a ditch.

Pray observe some of the effects of this ditching business. Once there was a neck opposite Port Hudson, Louisiana, which was only half a mile across, in its narrowest place. You could walk across there in fifteen minutes; but if you made the journey around the cape on a raft, you travelled thirty-five miles to accomplish the same thing. In 1722 the river darted through that neck, deserted its old bed, and thus shortened itself thirty-five miles. In the same way it shortened itself twenty-five miles at Black Hawk Point in 1699. Below Red River Landing, Raccourci cut-off was made (forty or fifty years ago, I think). This shortened the river twenty-eight miles. In our day, if you travel by river from the southernmost of these three cut-offs to the northernmost, you go only seventy miles. To do the same thing a hundred and seventy-six years ago, one had to go a hundred and fifty-eight miles!—a shortening of eighty-eight miles in that trifling distance. At some forgotten time in the past, cut-offs were made above Vidalia, Louisiana; at island 92; at island 84; and at Hale's Point. These shortened the river, in the aggregate, seventy-seven miles.

Since my own day on the Mississippi, cut-offs have been made at Hurricane Island; at island 100; at Napoleon, Arkansas; at Walnut Bend; and at Council Bend. These shortened the river, in the aggregate, sixty-seven miles. In my own time a cut-off was made at American Bend, which shortened the river ten miles or more.

Therefore, the Mississippi between Cairo and New Orleans was twelve hundred and fifteen miles long one hundred and seventy-six years ago. It was eleven hundred and eighty after the cut-off of 1722. It was one thousand and forty after the American Bend cut-off. It has lost sixty-seven miles since. Consequently its length is only nine hundred and seventy-three miles at present.

Now, if I wanted to be one of those ponderous scientific people, and "let on" to prove what had occurred in the remote past by what had occurred in a given time in the recent past, or what will occur in the far future by what has occurred in late years, what an opportunity is here! Geology never had such a chance, nor such exact data to argue from! Nor "development of species," either! Glacial epochs are great things, but they are vague—vague. Please observe:—

In the space of one hundred and seventy-six years the Lower Mississippi has shortened itself two hundred and forty-two miles. That is an average of a trifle over one mile and a third per year. Therefore, any calm person, who is not blind or idiotic, can see that in the Old Oölitic Silurian Period, just a million years ago next November, the Lower Mississippi River was upwards of one million three hundred thousand miles long, and stuck out over the Gulf of Mexico like a fishing-rod. And by the same token any person can see that seven hundred and forty-two years from now the Lower Mississippi will be only a mile and three quarters long, and Cairo and New Orleans will have joined their streets together, and be plodding comfortably along under a single mayor and a mutual board of aldermen. There is something fascinating about science. One gets such wholesale returns of conjecture out of such a trifling investment of fact.

When the water begins to flow through one of those ditches I have been speaking of, it is time for the people thereabouts to move. The water cleaves the banks away like a knife. By the time the ditch has become twelve or fifteen feet wide, the calamity is as good as accomplished, for no power on earth can stop it now. When the width has reached a hundred yards, the banks begin to peel off in slices half an acre wide. The current flowing around the bend travelled formerly only five miles an hour; now it is tremendously increased by the shortening of the distance. I was on board the first boat that tried to go through the cut-off at American Bend, but we did not get through. It was toward midnight, and a wild night it was—thunder, lightning, and torrents of rain. It was estimated that the current in the cut-off was making about fifteen or twenty miles an hour; twelve or thirteen was the best our boat could do, even in tolerably slack water, therefore perhaps we were foolish to try the cut-off. However, Mr. Brown was ambitious, and he kept on trying. The eddy running up the bank, under the "point," was about as swift as the current out in the middle; so we would go flying up the shore like a lightning express train, get on a big head of steam, and "stand by for a surge" when we struck the current that was whirling by the point. But all our preparations were useless. The instant the current hit us it spun us around like a top, the water deluged the forecastle, and the boat careened so far over that one could hardly keep his feet. The next instant we were away down the river, clawing with might and main to keep out of the woods. We tried the experiment four times. I stood on the forecastle companion way to see. It was astonishing to observe how suddenly the boat would spin around and turn tail the moment she emerged from the eddy and the current struck her nose. The sounding concussion and the quivering would have been about the same if she had come full speed against a sand-bank. Under the lightning flashes one could see the plantation cabins and the goodly acres tumble into the river; and the crash they made was not a bad effort at thunder. Once, when we spun around, we only missed a house about twenty feet, that had a light burning in the window; and in the same instant that house went overboard. Nobody could stay on our forecastle; the water swept across it in a torrent every time we plunged athwart the current. At the end of our fourth effort we brought up in the woods two miles below the cut-off; all the country there was overflowed, of course. A day or two later the cut-off was three quarters of a mile wide, and boats passed up through it without much difficulty, and so saved ten miles.

The old Raccourci cut-off reduced the river's length twenty-eight miles. There used to be a tradition connected with it. It was said that a boat came along there in the night and went around the enormous elbow the usual way, the pilots not knowing that the cut-off had been made. It was a grisly, hideous night, and all shapes were vague and distorted. The old bend had already begun to fill up, and the boat got to running away from mysterious reefs, and occasionally hitting one. The perplexed pilots fell to swearing, and finally uttered the entirely unnecessary wish that they might never get out of that place. As always happens in such cases, that particular prayer was answered, and the others neglected. So to this day that phantom steamer is still butting around in that deserted river, trying to find her way out. More than one grave watchman has sworn to me that on drizzly, dismal nights, he has glanced fearfully down that forgotten river as he passed the head of the island, and seen the faint glow of the spectre steamer's lights drifting through the distant gloom, and heard the muffled cough of her 'scapepipes and the plaintive cry of her leads-men.

In the absence of further statistics, I beg to close this chapter with one more reminiscence of "Stephen."

Most of the captains and pilots held Stephen's note for borrowed sums, ranging from two hundred and fifty dollars upward. Stephen never paid one of these notes, but he was very prompt and very zealous about renewing them every twelve month.

Of course there came a time, at last, when Stephen could no longer borrow of his ancient creditors; so he was obliged to lie in wait for new men who did not know him. Such a victim was good-hearted, simple-natured young Yates (I use a fictitious name, but the real name began, as this one does, with a Y). Young Yates graduated as a pilot, got a berth, and when the month ended and he stepped up to the clerk's office and received his two hundred and fifty dollars in crisp new bills, Stephen was there! His silvery tongue began to wag, and in a very little while Yate's two hundred and fifty dollars had changed hands. The fact was soon known at pilot headquarters, and the amusement and satisfaction of the old creditors were large and generous. But innocent Yates never suspected that Stephen's promise to pay promptly at the end of the week was a worthless one. Yates called for his money at the stipulated time; Stephen sweetened him up and put him off a week. He called then, according to agreement, and came away sugar-coated again, but suffering under another postponement. So the thing went on. Yates haunted Stephen week after week, to no purpose, and at last gave it up. And then straightway Stephen began to haunt Yates! Wherever Yates appeared, there was the inevitable Stephen. And not only there, but beaming with affection and gushing with apologies for not being able to pay. By and by, whenever poor Yates saw him coming, he would turn and fly, and drag his company with him, if he had company; but it was of no use; his debtor would run him down and corner him. Panting and red-faced,

Stephen would come, with outstretched hands and eager eyes, invade the conversation, shake both of Yates's arms loose in their sockets, and begin:—

"My, what a race I've had! I saw you didn't see me, and so I clapped on all steam for fear I'd miss you entirely. And here you are! there, just stand so, and let me look at you! Just the same old noble countenance." [To Yates's friend:] "Just look at him! *Look* at him! Ain't it just *good* to look at him! *Ain't* it now? Ain't he just a picture! *Some* call him a picture; *I* call him a panorama! That's what he is—an entire panorama. And now I'm reminded! How I do wish I could have seen you an hour earlier! For twenty-four hours I've been saving up that two hundred and fifty dollars for you; been looking for you everywhere. I waited at the Planter's from six yesterday evening till two o'clock this morning, without rest or food; my wife says, 'Where have you been all night?' I said, 'This debt lies heavy on my mind.' She says, 'In all my days I never saw a man take a debt to heart the way you do.' I said, 'It's my nature; how can *I* change it?' She says, 'Well, do go to bed and get some rest.' I said, 'Not till that poor, noble young man has got his money.' So I set up all night, and this morning out I shot, and the first man I struck told me you had shipped on the 'Grand Turk' and gone to New Orleans. Well sir, I had to lean up against a building and cry. So help me goodness, I couldn't help it. The man that owned the place come out cleaning up with a rag, and said he didn't like to have people cry against his building, and then it seemed to me that the whole world had turned against me, and it wasn't any use to live any more; and coming along an hour ago, suffering no man knows what agony, I met Jim Wilson and paid him the two hundred and fifty dollars on account; and to think that here you are, now, and I haven't got a cent! But as sure as I am standing here on this ground on this particular brick,—there, I've scratched a mark on the brick to remember it by,—I'll borrow that money and pay it over to you at twelve o'clock sharp, to-morrow! Now, stand so; let me look at you just once more."

And so on. Yates's life became a burden to him. He could not escape his debtor and his debtor's awful sufferings on account of not being able to pay. He dreaded to show himself in the street, lest he should find Stephen lying in wait for him at the corner.

Bogart's billiard saloon was a great resort for pilots in those days. They met there about as much to exchange river news as to play. One morning Yates was there; Stephen was there, too, but kept out of sight. But by and by, when about all the pilots had arrived who were in town, Stephen suddenly appeared in the midst, and rushed for Yates as for a long-lost brother.

"*Oh,* I am so glad to see you! Oh my soul, the sight of you is such a comfort to my eyes! Gentlemen, I owe all of you money; among you I owe probably forty thousand dollars. I want to pay it; I intend to pay it—every last cent of it. You all know, without my telling you, what sorrow it has cost me to remain so long under such deep obligations to such patient and generous friends; but the sharpest pang I suffer—by far the sharpest—is from the debt I owe to this noble young man here; and I have come to this place this morning especially to make the announcement that I have at last found a method whereby I can pay off all my debts! And most especially I wanted *him* to be here when I announced it. Yes, my faithful friend,—my benefactor, I've found the method! I've found the method to pay off *all* my debts, and you'll get your money!" Hope dawned in Yates's eye; then Stephen, beaming benignantly, and placing his hand upon Yates's head, added, "I am going to pay them off in alphabetical order!"

Then he turned and disappeared. The full significance of Stephen's "method" did not dawn upon the perplexed and musing crowd for some two minutes; and then Yates murmured with a sigh:—

"Well, the Y's stand a gaudy chance. He won't get any further than the C's in *this* world, and I reckon that after a good deal of eternity has wasted away in the next one, I'll still be referred to up there as 'that poor, ragged pilot that came here from St. Louis in the early days!' "

CHAPTER XVIII

I TAKE A FEW EXTRA LESSONS

During the two or two and a half years of my apprenticeship, I served under many pilots, and had experience of many kinds of steamboatmen and many varieties of steamboats; for it was not always convenient for Mr. Bixby to have me with him, and in such cases he sent me with somebody else. I am to this day profiting somewhat by that experience; for in that brief, sharp schooling, I got personally and familiarly acquainted with about all the different types of human nature that are to be found in fiction, biography, or history. The fact is daily borne in upon me, that the average shore-employment requires as much as forty years to equip a man with this sort of education. When I say I am still profiting by this thing, I do not mean that it has constituted me a judge of men—no, it has not done that; for judges of men are born, not made. My profit is various in kind and degree; but the feature of it which I value most is the zest which that early experience has given to my later reading. When I find a well- drawn character in fiction or biography, I generally take a warm personal interest in him, for the reason that I have known him before—met him on the river.

The figure that comes before me oftenest, out of the shadows of that vanished time, is that of Brown, of the steamer "Pennsylvania"—the man referred to in a former chapter, whose memory was so good and tiresome. He was a middle-aged, long, slim, bony, smooth-shaven, horse-faced, ignorant, stingy, malicious, snarling, fault-hunting, mote-magnifying tyrant. I early got the habit of coming on watch with dread at my heart. No matter how good a time I might have been having with the off-watch below, and no matter how high my spirits might be when I started aloft, my soul became lead in my body the moment I approached the pilot-house.

I still remember the first time I ever entered the presence of that man. The boat had backed out from St. Louis and was "straightening down;" I ascended to the pilot-house in high feather, and very proud to be semi-officially a member of the executive family of so fast and famous a boat. Brown was at the wheel. I paused in the middle of the room, all fixed to make my bow, but Brown did not look around. I thought he took a furtive glance at me out of the corner of his eye, but as not even this notice was repeated, I judged I had been mistaken. By this time he was picking his way among some dangerous "breaks" abreast the wood-yards; therefore it would not be proper to interrupt him; so I stepped softly to the high bench and took a seat.

There was silence for ten minutes; then my new boss turned and inspected me deliberately and painstakingly from head to heel for about—as it seemed to me—a quarter of an hour. After which he removed his countenance and I saw it no more for some seconds; then it came around once more, and this question greeted me:—

"Are you Horace Bigsby's cub?"

"Yes, sir."

After this there was a pause and another inspection. Then:

"What's your name?"

I told him. He repeated it after me. It was probably the only thing he ever forgot; for although I was with him many months he never addressed himself to me in any other way than "Here!" and then his command followed.

"Where was you born?"

"In Florida, Missouri."

A pause. Then:—

"Dern sight better staid there!"

By means of a dozen or so of pretty direct questions, he pumped my family history out of me.

The leads were going now, in the first crossing. This interrupted the inquest. When the leads had been laid in, he resumed:—

"How long you been on the river?"

I told him. After a pause:—

"Where'd you get them shoes?"

I gave him the information.

"Hold up your foot!"

I did so. He stepped back, examined the shoe minutely and contemptuously, scratching his head thoughtfully, tilting his high sugar-loaf hat well forward to facilitate the operation, then ejaculated, "Well, I'll be dod derned!" and returned to his wheel.

What occasion there was to be dod derned about it is a thing which is still as much of a mystery to me now as it was then. It must have been all of fifteen minutes—fifteen minutes of dull, homesick silence—before that long horse-face swung round upon me again—and then, what a change! It was as red as fire, and every muscle in it was working. Now came this shriek:

"Here!—You going to set there all day?"

I lit in the middle of the floor, shot there by the electric suddenness of the surprise. As soon as I could get my voice I said, apologetically:—"I have had no orders, sir." "You've had no *orders!* My, what a fine bird we are! We must have *orders!* Our father was a *gentleman*—owned slaves—and *we've* been to *school.* Yes, *we* are a gentleman, *too,* and got to have *orders!* ORDERS, is it? ORDERS is what you want! Dod dern my skin, *I'll* learn you to swell yourself up and blow around *here* about your dod-derned *orders!* G' way from the wheel!" (I had approached it without knowing it.)

I moved back a step or two, and stood as in a dream, all my senses stupefied by this frantic assault.

"What you standing there for? Take that ice-pitcher down to the texas-tender—come, move along, and don't you be all day about it!"

The moment I got back to the pilot-house, Brown said:—

"Here! What was you doing down there all this time?"

"I couldn't find the texas-tender; I had to go all the way to the pantry."

"Derned likely story! Fill up the stove."

I proceeded to do so. He watched me like a cat. Presently he shouted:—

"Put down that shovel! Derndest numskull I ever saw—ain't even got sense enough to load up a stove."

All through the watch this sort of thing went on. Yes, and the subsequent watches were much like it, during a stretch of months. As I have said, I soon got the habit of coming on duty with dread. The moment I was in the presence, even in the darkest night, I could feel those yellow eyes upon me, and knew their owner was watching for a pretext to spit out some venom on me. Preliminarily he would say:—

"Here! Take the wheel."

Two minutes later:—

"*Where* in the nation you going to? Pull her down! pull her down!"

After another moment:—

"Say! You going to hold her all day? Let her go—meet her! meet her!"

Then he would jump from the bench, snatch the wheel from me, and meet her himself, pouring out wrath upon me all the time.

George Ritchie was the other pilot's cub. He was having good times now; for his boss, George Ealer, was as kind-hearted as Brown wasn't. Ritchie had steered for Brown the season before; consequently he knew exactly how to entertain himself and plague me, all by the one operation. Whenever I took the wheel for a moment on Ealer's watch, Ritchie would sit back on the bench and play Brown, with continual ejaculations of "Snatch her! snatch her! Derndest mud-cat I ever saw!" "Here! Where you going *now?* Going to run over that snag?" "Pull her *down!* Don't you hear me? Pull her *down!*" "There she goes! *Just* as I expected! I *told* you not to cramp that reef. G'way from the wheel!"

So I always had a rough time of it, no matter whose watch it was; and sometimes it seemed to me that Ritchie's good-natured badgering was pretty nearly as aggravating as Brown's dead-earnest nagging.

I often wanted to kill Brown, but this would not answer. A cub had to take everything his boss gave, in the way of vigorous comment and criticism; and we all believed that there was a United States law making it a penitentiary offence to strike or threaten a pilot who was on duty. However, I could *imagine* myself killing Brown; there was no law against that; and that was the thing I used always to do the moment I was abed. Instead of going over my river in my mind as was my duty, I threw business aside for pleasure, and killed Brown. I killed Brown every night for months; not in old, stale, commonplace ways, but in new and picturesque ones,—ways that were sometimes surprising for freshness of design and ghastliness of situation and environment.

Brown was *always* watching for a pretext to find fault; and if he could find no plausible pretext, he would invent one. He would scold you for shaving a shore, and for not shaving it; for hugging a bar, and for not hugging it; for "pulling down" when not invited, and for *not* pulling down when not invited; for firing up without orders, and for waiting *for* orders. In a word, it was his invariable rule to find fault with *everything* you did; and another invariable rule of his was to throw all his remarks (to you) into the form of an insult.

One day we were approaching New Madrid, bound down and heavily laden. Brown was at one side of the wheel, steering; I was at the other, standing by to "pull down" or "shove up." He cast a furtive glance at me every now and then. I had long ago learned what that meant; viz., he was trying to invent a trap for me. I wondered what shape it was going to take. By and by he stepped back from the wheel and said in his usual snarly way:—

"Here!—See if you've got gumption enough to round her to."

This was simply *bound* to be a success; nothing could prevent it; for he had never allowed me to round the boat to before; consequently, no matter how I might do the thing, he could find free fault with it. He stood back there with his greedy eye on me, and the result was what might have been foreseen: I lost my head in a quarter of a minute, and didn't know what I was about; I started too early to bring the boat around, but detected a green gleam of joy in Brown's eye, and corrected my mistake; I started around once more while too high up, but corrected myself again in time; I made other false moves, and still managed to save myself; but at last I grew so confused and anxious that I tumbled into the very worst blunder of all—I got too far *down* before beginning to fetch the boat around. Brown's chance was come.

His face turned red with passion; he made one bound, hurled me across the house with a sweep of his arm, spun the wheel down, and began to pour out a stream of vituperation upon me which lasted till he was out of breath. In the course of this speech he called me all the different kinds of hard names he could think of, and once or twice I thought he was even going to swear—but he had never done that, and he didn't this time. "Dod dern" was the nearest he ventured to the luxury of swearing, for he had been brought up with a wholesome respect for future fire and brimstone.

That was an uncomfortable hour; for there was a big audience on the hurricane deck. When I went to bed that night, I killed Brown in seventeen different ways—all of them new.

CHAPTER XIX

BROWN AND I EXCHANGE COMPLIMENTS

Two trips later, I got into serious trouble. Brown was steering; I was "pulling down." My younger brother appeared on the hurricane deck, and shouted to Brown to stop at some landing or other a mile or so below. Brown gave no intimation that he had heard anything. But that was his way: he never condescended to take notice of an under clerk. The wind was blowing; Brown was deaf (although he always pretended he wasn't), and I very much doubted if he had heard the order. If I had had two heads, I would have spoken; but as I had only one, it seemed judicious to take care of it; so I kept still.

Presently, sure enough, we went sailing by that plantation. Captain Klinefelter appeared on the deck, and said:—

"Let her come around, sir, let her come around. Didn't Henry tell you to land here?"

"No, sir!"

"I sent him up to do it."

"He *did* come up; and that's all the good it done, the dod-derned fool. He never said anything."

"Didn't *you* hear him?" asked the captain of me.

Of course I didn't want to be mixed up in this business, but there was no way to avoid it; so I said:—

"Yes, sir."

I knew what Brown's next remark would be, before he uttered it; it was:—

"Shut your mouth! you never heard anything of the kind."

I closed my mouth according to instructions. An hour later, Henry entered the pilot-house, unaware of what had been going on. He was a thoroughly inoffensive boy, and I was sorry to see him come, for I knew Brown would have no pity on him. Brown began, straightway:—

"Here! why didn't you tell me we'd got to land at that plantation?"

"I did tell you, Mr. Brown."

"It's a lie!"

I said:—

"You lie, yourself. He did tell you."

Brown glared at me in unaffected surprise; and for as much as a moment he was entirely speechless; then he shouted to me:—

"I'll attend to your case in a half a minute!" then to Henry, "And you leave the pilot-house; out with you!"

It was pilot law, and must be obeyed. The boy started out, and even had his foot on the upper step outside the door, when Brown, with a sudden access of fury, picked up a ten-pound lump of coal and sprang after him; but I was between, with a heavy stool, and I hit Brown a good honest blow which stretched him out.

I had committed a crime of crimes,—I had lifted my hand against a pilot on duty! I supposed I was booked for the penitentiary sure, and couldn't be booked any surer if I went on and squared my long account with this person while I had the chance; consequently I stuck to him and pounded him with my fists a considerable time,—I do not know how long, the pleasure of it probably made it seem longer than it really was;—but in the end he struggled free and jumped up and sprang to the wheel: a very natural solicitude, for, all this time, here was this steamboat tearing down the river at the rate of fifteen miles an hour and nobody at the helm! However, Eagle Bend was two miles wide at this bank-full stage, and correspondingly long and deep; and the boat was steering herself straight down the middle and taking no chances. Still, that was only luck—a body *might* have found her charging into the woods.

Perceiving, at a glance, that the "Pennsylvania" was in no danger, Brown gathered up the spy-glass, war-club fashion, and ordered me out of the pilot-house with more than Comanche bluster. But I was not afraid of him now; so, instead of going, I tarried, and criticised his grammer; I reformed his ferocious speeches for him, and put them into good English, calling his attention to the advantage of pure English over the bastard dialect of the Pennsylvanian collieries whence he was extracted. He could have done his part to admiration in a cross-fire of mere vituperation, of course; but he was not equipped for this species of controversy; so he presently laid aside his glass and took the wheel, muttering and shaking his head; and I retired to the bench. The racket had brought everybody to the hurricane deck, and I trembled when I saw the old captain looking up from the midst of the crowd. I said to myself, "Now I *am* done for!"—For although, as a rule, he was so fatherly and indulgent toward the boat's family, and so patient of minor shortcomings, he could be stern enough when the fault was worth it.

I tried to imagine what he *would* do to a cub pilot who had been guilty of such a crime as mine, committed on a boat guard-deep with costly freight and alive with passengers. Our watch was nearly ended. I thought I would go and hide somewhere till I got a chance to slide ashore. So I slipped out of the pilot-house, and down the steps, and around to the texas door,—and was in the act of gliding within, when the captain confronted me! I dropped my head, and he stood over me in silence a moment or two, then said impressively,—

"Follow me."

I dropped into his wake; he led the way to his parlor in the forward end of the texas. We were alone, now. He closed the after door; then moved slowly to the forward one and closed that. He sat down; I stood before him. He looked at me some little time, then said,—

"So you have been fighting Mr. Brown?"

I answered meekly:—

"Yes, sir."

"Do you know that that is a very serious matter?"

"Yes, sir."

"Are you aware that this boat was ploughing down the river fully five minutes with no one at the wheel?"

"Yes, sir."

"Did you strike him first?"

"Yes, sir."

"What with?"

"A stool, sir."

"Hard?"

"Middling, sir."

"Did it knock him down?"

"He—he fell, sir."

"Did you follow it up? Did you do anything further?"

"Yes, sir."

"What did you do?"

"Pounded him, sir."

"Pounded him?"

"Yes, sir."

"Did you pound him much?—that is, severely?"

"One might call it that, sir, maybe."

"I'm deuced glad of it! Hark ye, never mention that I said that. You have been guilty of a great crime; and don't you ever be guilty of it again, on this boat. *But*—lay for him ashore! Give him a good sound thrashing, do you hear? I'll pay the expenses.

Now go—and mind you, not a word of this to anybody. Clear out with you!—you've been guilty of a great crime, you whelp!"

I slid out, happy with the sense of a close shave and a mighty deliverance; and I heard him laughing to himself and slapping his fat thighs after I had closed his door.

When Brown came off watch he went straight to the captain, who was talking with some passengers on the boiler deck, and demanded that I be put ashore in New Orleans—and added:—

"I'll never turn a wheel on this boat again while that cub stays."

The captain said:—

"But he needn't come round when you are on watch, Mr. Brown."

"I won't even stay on the same boat with him. *One* of us has got to go ashore."

"Very well," said the captain, "let it be yourself;" and resumed his talk with the passengers.

During the brief remainder of the trip, I knew how an emancipated slave feels; for I was an emancipated slave myself. While we lay at landings, I listened to George Ealer's flute; or to his readings from his two bibles, that is to say, Goldsmith and Shakespeare; or I played chess with him—and would have beaten him sometimes, only he always took back his last move and ran the game out differently.

CHAPTER XX

A CATASTROPHE

We lay three days in New Orleans, but the captain did not succeed in finding another pilot; so he proposed that I should stand a daylight watch, and leave the night watches to George Ealer. But I was afraid; I had never stood a watch of any sort by myself, and I believed I should be sure to get into trouble in the head of some chute, or ground the boat in a near cut through some bar or other. Brown remained in his place; but he would not travel with me. So the captain gave me an order on the captain of the "A.T. Lacey," for a passage to St. Louis, and said he would find a new pilot there and my steersman's berth could then be resumed. The "Lacey" was to leave a couple of days after the "Pennsylvania."

The night before the "Pennsylvania" left, Henry and I sat chatting on a freight pile on the levee till midnight. The subject of the chat, mainly, was one which I think we had not exploited before—steamboat disasters. One was then on its way to us, little as we suspected it; the water which was to make the steam which should cause it, was washing past some point fifteen hundred miles up the river while we talked;—but it would arrive at the right time and the right place. We doubted if persons not clothed with authority were of much use in cases of disaster and attendant panic; still, they might be of *some* use; so we decided that if a disaster ever fell within our experience we would at least stick to the boat, and give such minor service as chance might throw in the way. Henry remembered this, afterward, when the disaster came, and acted accordingly.

The "Lacey" started up the river two days behind the "Pennsylvania." We touched at Greenville, Mississippi, a couple of days out, and somebody shouted:—

"The 'Pennsylvania' is blown up at Ship Island, and a hundred and fifty lives lost!"

At Napoleon, Arkansas, the same evening, we got an extra, issued by a Memphis paper, which gave some particulars. It mentioned my brother, and said he was not hurt.

Further up the river we got a later extra. My brother was again mentioned; but this time as being hurt beyond help. We did not get full details of the catastrophe until we reached Memphis. This is the sorrowful story:—

It was six o'clock on a hot summer morning. The "Pennsylvania" was creeping along, north of Ship Island, about sixty miles below Memphis on a half-head of steam, towing a wood-flat which was fast being emptied. George Ealer was in the pilot-house—alone, I think; the second engineer and a striker had the watch in the engine room; the second mate had the watch on deck; George Black, Mr. Wood, and my brother, clerks, were asleep, as were also Brown and the head engineer, the carpenter, the chief mate, and one striker; Capt. Klinefelter was in the barber's chair, and the barber was preparing to shave him. There were a good many cabin passengers aboard, and three or four hundred deck passengers—so it was said at this time—and not very many of them were astir. The wood being nearly all out of the flat now, Ealer rang to "come ahead" full steam, and the next moment four of the eight boilers exploded with a thunderous crash, and the whole forward third of the boat was hoisted toward the sky! The main part of the mass, with the chimneys, dropped upon the boat again, a mountain of riddled and chaotic rubbish—and then, after a little, fire broke out.

Many people were flung to considerable distances, and fell in the river; among these were Mr. Wood and my brother, and the carpenter. The carpenter was still stretched upon his mattress when he struck the water seventy-five feet from the boat. Brown, the pilot, and George Black, chief clerk, were never seen or heard of after the explosion. The barber's chair, with Captain Klinefelter in it and unhurt, was left with its back overhanging vacancy—everything forward of it, floor and all, had disappeared; and the stupefied barber, who was also unhurt, stood with one toe projecting over space, still stirring his lather unconsciously, and saying not a word.

When George Ealer saw the chimneys plunging aloft in front of him, he knew what the matter was; so he muffled his face in the lapels of his coat, and pressed both hands there tightly to keep this protection in its place so that no steam could get to his nose or mouth. He had ample time to attend to these details while he was going up and returning. He presently landed on top of the unexploded boilers, forty feet below the former pilot-house, accompanied by his wheel and a rain of other stuff, and enveloped in a cloud of scalding steam. All of the many who breathed that steam, died; none escaped. But Ealer breathed none of it. He made his way to the free air as quickly as he could; and when the steam cleared away he returned and climbed up on the boilers again, and patiently hunted out each and every one of his chessmen and the several joints of his flute.

By this time the fire was beginning to threaten. Shrieks and groans filled the air. A great many persons had been scalded, a great many crippled; the explosion had driven an iron crowbar through one man's body—I think they said he was a priest. He did not die at once, and his sufferings were very dreadful. A young French naval cadet, of fifteen, son of a French admiral, was fearfully scalded, but bore his tortures manfully. Both mates were badly scalded, but they stood to their posts, nevertheless. They drew the wood-boat aft, and they and the captain fought back the frantic herd of frightened immigrants till the wounded could be brought there and placed in safety first.

When Mr. Wood and Henry fell into the water, they struck out for shore, which was only a few hundred yards away; but Henry presently said he believed he was not hurt, (what an unaccountable error!) and therefore would swim back to the boat and help save the wounded. So they parted, and Henry returned.

By this time the fire was making fierce headway, and several persons who were imprisoned under the ruins were begging piteously for help. All efforts to conquer the fire proved fruitless; so the buckets were presently thrown aside and the officers fell-to with axes and tried to cut the prisoners out. A striker was one of the captives; he said he was not injured, but could not free himself; and when he saw that the fire was likely to drive away the workers, he begged that some one would shoot him, and thus save him from the more dreadful death. The fire did drive the axe-men away, and they had to listen, helpless, to this poor fellow's supplications till the flames ended his miseries.

The fire drove all into the wood-flat that could be accommodated there; it was cut adrift, then, and it and the burning steamer floated down the river toward Ship Island. They moored the flat at the head of the island, and there, unsheltered from the blazing sun, the half-naked occupants had to remain, without food or stimulants, or help for their hurts, during the rest of the day. A steamer came along, finally, and carried the unfortunates to Memphis, and there the most lavish assistance was at once forthcoming. By this time Henry was insensible. The physicians examined his injuries and saw that they were fatal, and naturally turned their main attention to patients who could be saved.

Forty of the wounded were placed upon pallets on the floor of a great public hall, and among these was Henry. There the ladies of Memphis came every day, with flowers, fruits, and dainties and delicacies of all kinds, and there they remained and nursed the wounded. All the physicians stood watches there, and all the medical students; and the rest of the town furnished money, or whatever else was wanted. And Memphis knew how to do all these things well; for many a disaster like the "Pennsylvania's" had happened near her doors, and she was experienced, above all other cities on the river, in the gracious office of the Good Samaritan.

The sight I saw when I entered that large hall was new and strange to me. Two long rows of prostrate forms—more than forty, in all—and every face and head a shapeless wad of loose raw cotton. It was a grewsome spectacle. I watched there six days and nights, and a very melancholy experience it was. There was one daily incident which was peculiarly depressing: this was the removal of the doomed to a chamber apart. It was done in order that the *morale* of the other patients might not be injuriously affected by seeing one of their number in the death-agony. The fated one was always carried out with as little stir as possible, and the stretcher was always hidden from sight by a wall of assistants; but no matter: everybody knew what that cluster of bent forms, with its muffled step and its slow movement meant; and all eyes watched it wistfully, and a shudder went abreast of it like a wave.

I saw many poor fellows removed to the "death-room," and saw them no more afterward. But I saw our chief mate carried thither more than once. His hurts were frightful, especially his scalds. He was clothed in linseed oil and raw cotton to his waist, and resembled nothing human. He was often out of his mind; and then his pains would make him rave and shout and sometimes shriek. Then, after a period of dumb exhaustion, his disordered imagination would suddenly transform the great apartment into a forecastle, and the hurrying throng of nurses into the crew; and he would come to a sitting posture and shout, "Hump yourselves, *hump* yourselves, you petrifactions, snail-bellies, pall-bearers! going to be all *day* getting that hatful of freight out?" and supplement this explosion with a firmament-obliterating irruption of profanity which nothing could stay or stop till his crater was empty. And now and then while these frenzies possessed him, he would tear off handfuls of the cotton and expose his cooked flesh to view. It was horrible. It was bad for the others, of course—this noise and these exhibitions; so the doctors tried to give him morphine to quiet him. But, in his mind or out of it, he would not take it. He said his wife had been killed by that treacherous drug, and he would die before he would take it. He suspected that the doctors were concealing it in his ordinary medicines and in his water—so he ceased from putting either to his lips. Once, when he had been without water during two sweltering days, he took the dipper in his hand, and the sight of the limpid fluid, and the misery of his thirst, tempted him almost beyond his strength; but he mastered himself and threw it away, and after that he allowed no more to be brought near him. Three times I saw him carried to the death-room, insensible and supposed to be dying; but each time he revived, cursed his attendants, and demanded to be taken back. He lived to be mate of a steamboat again.

But he was the only one who went to the death-room and returned alive. Dr. Peyton, a principal physician, and rich in all the attributes that go to constitute high and flawless character, did all that educated judgment and trained skill could do for Henry; but, as the newspapers had said in the beginning, his hurts were past help. On the evening of the sixth day his wandering mind busied itself with matters far away, and his nerveless fingers "picked at this coverlet." His hour had struck; we bore him to the death-room, poor boy.

CHAPTER XXI

A SECTION IN MY BIOGRAPHY

In due course I got my license. I was a pilot now, full fledged. I dropped into casual employments; no misfortunes resulting, intermittent work gave place to steady and protracted engagements. Time drifted smoothly and prosperously on, and I supposed—and hoped—that I was going to follow the river the rest of my days, and die at the wheel when my mission was ended. But by and by the war came, commerce was suspended, my occupation was gone.

I had to seek another livelihood. So I became a silver miner in Nevada; next, a newspaper reporter; next, a gold miner, in California; next, a reporter in San Francisco; next, a special correspondent in the Sandwich Islands; next, a roving correspondent in Europe and the East; next, an instructional torch-bearer on the lecture platform; and, finally, I became a scribbler of books, and an immovable fixture among the other rocks of New England.

In so few words have I disposed of the twenty-one slow-drifting years that have come and gone since I last looked from the windows of a pilot-house.

Let us resume, now.

CHAPTER XXII

I RETURN TO MY MUTTONS

After twenty-one years' absence, I felt a very strong desire to see the river again, and the steamboats, and such of the boys as might be left; so I resolved to go out there. I enlisted a poet for company, and a stenographer to "take him down," and started westward about the middle of April.

As I proposed to make notes, with a view to printing, I took some thought as to methods of procedure. I reflected that if I were recognized, on the river, I should not be as free to go and come, talk, inquire, and spy around, as I should be if unknown; I remembered that it was the custom of steamboatmen in the old times to load up the confiding stranger with the most picturesque and admirable lies, and put the sophisticated friend off with dull and ineffectual facts: so I concluded, that, from a business point of view, it would be an advantage to disguise our party with fictitious names. The idea was certainly good, but it bred infinite bother; for although Smith, Jones, and Johnson are easy names to remember when there is no occasion to remember them, it is next to impossible to recollect them when they are wanted. How do criminals manage to keep a brand-new *alias* in mind? This is a great mystery. I was innocent; and yet was seldom able to lay my hand on my new name when it was needed; and it seemed to me that if I had had a crime on my conscience to further confuse me, I could never have kept the name by me at all.

We left per Pennsylvania Railroad, at 8 A.M. April 18.

"*Evening*. Speaking of dress. Grace and picturesqueness drop gradually out of it as one travels away from New York."

I find that among my notes. It makes no difference which direction you take, the fact remains the same. Whether you move north, south, east, or west, no matter: you can get up in the morning and guess how far you have come, by noting what degree of grace and picturesqueness is by that time lacking in the costumes of the new passengers;—I do not mean of the women alone, but of both sexes. It may be that *carriage* is at the bottom of this thing; and I think it is; for there are plenty of ladies and gentlemen in the provincial cities whose garments are all made by the best tailors and dressmakers of New York; yet this has no perceptible effect upon the grand fact: the educated eye never mistakes those people for New-Yorkers. No, there is a godless grace, and snap, and style about a born and bred New-Yorker which mere clothing cannot effect.

"*April* 19. This morning, struck into the region of full goatees—sometimes accompanied by a moustache, but only occasionally."

It was odd to come upon this thick crop of an obsolete and uncomely fashion; it was like running suddenly across a forgotten acquaintance whom you had supposed dead for a generation. The goatee extends over a wide extent of country; and is accompanied by an iron-clad belief in Adam and the biblical history of creation, which has not suffered from the assaults of the scientists.

"*Afternoon*. At the railway stations the loafers carry *both* hands in their breeches pockets; it was observable, heretofore, that one hand was sometimes out of doors,—here, never. This is an important fact in geography."

If the loafers determined the character of a country, it would be still more important, of course.

"Heretofore, all along, the station-loafer has been often observed to scratch one shin with the other foot; here, these remains of activity are wanting. This has an ominous look."

By and by, we entered the tobacco-chewing region. Fifty years ago, the tobacco-chewing region covered the Union. It is greatly restricted now.

Next, boots began to appear. Not in strong force, however. Later—away down the Mississippi—they became the rule. They disappeared from other sections of the Union with the mud; no doubt they will disappear from the river villages, also, when proper pavements come in.

We reached St. Louis at ten o'clock at night. At the counter of the hotel I tendered a hurriedly-invented fictitious name, with a miserable attempt at careless ease. The clerk paused, and inspected me in the compassionate way in which one inspects a respectable person who is found in doubtful circumstances; then he said,—

"It's all right; I know what sort of a room you want. Used to clerk at the St. James, in New York."

An unpromising beginning for a fraudulent career. We started to the supper room, and met two other men whom I had known elsewhere. How odd and unfair it is: wicked impostors go around lecturing under my *nom de guerre*, and nobody suspects them; but when an honest man attempts an imposture, he is exposed at once.

One thing seemed plain: we must start down the river the next day, if people who could not be deceived were going to crop up at this rate: an unpalatable disappointment, for we had hoped to have a week in St. Louis. The Southern was a good hotel, and we could have had a comfortable time there. It is large, and well conducted, and its decorations do not make one cry, as do those of the vast Palmer House, in Chicago. True, the billiard-tables were of the Old Silurian Period, and the cues and balls of the Post-Pliocene; but there was refreshment in this, not discomfort; for there is rest and healing in the contemplation of antiquities.

The most notable absence observable in the billiard room, was the absence of the river man. If he was there he had taken in his sign, he was in disguise. I saw there none of the swell airs and graces, and ostentatious displays of money, and pompous squanderings of it, which used to distinguish the steamboat crowd from the dry-land crowd in the bygone days, in the thronged billiard-rooms of St. Louis. In those times, the principal saloons were always populous with river men; given fifty players present, thirty or thirty-five were likely to be from the river. But I suspected that the ranks were thin now, and the steamboatmen no longer an aristocracy. Why, in my time they used to call the "barkeep" Bill, or Joe, or Tom, and slap him on the shoulder; I watched for that. But none of these people did it. Manifestly a glory that once was had dissolved and vanished away in these twenty-one years.

When I went up to my room, I found there the young man called Rogers, crying. Rogers was not his name; neither was Jones, Brown, Dexter, Ferguson, Bascom, nor Thompson; but he answered to either of these that a body found handy in an emergency; or to any other name, in fact, if he perceived that you meant him. He said:—

"What is a person to do here when he wants a drink of water?—drink this slush?"

"Can't you drink it?"

"I could if I had some other water to wash it with."

Here was a thing which had not changed; a score of years had not affected this water's mulatto complexion in the least; a score of centuries would succeed no better, perhaps. It comes out of the turbulent, bank-caving Missouri, and every tumblerful of it holds nearly an acre of land in solution. I got this fact from the bishop of the diocese. If you will let your glass stand half an hour, you can separate the land from the water as easy as Genesis; and then you will find them both good: the one good to eat, the other good to drink. The land is very nourishing, the water is thoroughly wholesome. The one appeases hunger; the other, thirst. But the natives do not take them separately, but together, as nature mixed them. When they find an inch of mud in the bottom of a glass, they stir it up, and then take the draught as they would gruel. It is difficult for a stranger to get used to this batter, but once used to it he will prefer it to water. This is really the case. It is good for steamboating, and good to drink; but it is worthless for all other purposes, except baptizing.

Next morning, we drove around town in the rain. The city seemed but little changed. It *was* greatly changed, but it did not seem so; because in St. Louis, as in London and Pittsburgh, you can't persuade a new thing to look new; the coal smoke turns it into an antiquity the moment you take your hand off it. The place had just about doubled its size, since I was a resident of it, and was now become a city of 400,000 inhabitants; still, in the solid business parts, it looked about as it had looked formerly. Yet I am sure there is not as much smoke in St. Louis now as there used to be. The smoke used to bank itself in a dense billowy black canopy over the town, and hide the sky from view. This shelter is very much thinner now; still, there is a sufficiency of smoke there, I think. I heard no complaint.

However, on the outskirts changes were apparent enough; notably in dwelling-house architecture. The fine new homes are noble and beautiful and modern. They stand by themselves, too, with green lawns around them; whereas the dwellings of a former day are packed together in blocks, and are all of one pattern, with windows all alike, set in an arched frame-work of twisted stone; a sort of house which was handsome enough when it was rarer.

There was another change—the Forest Park. This was new to

me. It is beautiful and very extensive, and has the excellent merit of having been made mainly by nature. There are other parks, and fine ones, notably Tower Grove and the Botanical Gardens; for St. Louis interested herself in such improvements at an earlier day than did the most of our cities.

The first time I ever saw St. Louis, I could have bought it for six million dollars, and it was the mistake of my life that I did not do it. It was bitter now to look abroad over this domed and steepled metropolis, this solid expanse of bricks and mortar stretching away on every hand into dim, measure-defying distances, and remember that I had allowed that opportunity to go by. Why I should have allowed it to go by seems, of course, foolish and inexplicable to-day, at a first glance; yet there were reasons at the time to justify this course.

A Scotchman, Hon. Charles Augustus Murray, writing some forty-five or fifty years ago, said: "The streets are narrow, ill paved and ill lighted." Those streets are narrow still, of course; many of them are ill paved yet; but the reproach of ill lighting cannot be repeated, now. The "Catholic New Church" was the only notable building then, and Mr. Murray was confidently called upon to admire it, with its "species of Grecian portico, surmounted by a kind of steeple, much too diminutive in its proportions, and surmounted by sundry ornaments" which the unimaginative Scotchman found himself "quite unable to describe;" and therefore was grateful when a German tourist helped him out with the exclamation: "By—, they look exactly like bed-posts!" St. Louis is well equipped with stately and noble public buildings now, and the little church, which the people used to be so proud of, lost its importance a long time ago. Still, this would not surprise Mr. Murray, if he could come back; for he prophesied the coming greatness of St. Louis with strong confidence.

The further we drove in our inspection-tour, the more sensibly I realized how the city had grown since I had seen it last; changes in detail became steadily more apparent and frequent than at first, too: changes uniformly evidencing progress, energy, prosperity.

But the change of changes was on the "levee." This time, a departure from the rule. Half a dozen sound-asleep steamboats where I used to see a solid mile of wide-awake ones! This was melancholy, this was woful. The absence of the pervading and jocund steamboatman from the billiard-saloon was explained. He was absent because he is no more. His occupation is gone, his power has passed away, he is absorbed into the common herd, he grinds at the mill, a shorn Samson and inconspicuous. Half a dozen lifeless steamboats, a mile of empty wharves, a negro fatigued with whiskey stretched asleep, in a wide and soundless vacancy, where the serried hosts of commerce used to contend!* Here was desolation, indeed.

> "The old, old sea, as one in tears,
>   Comes murmuring, with foamy lips,
> And knocking at the vacant pipers,
>   Calls for his long-lost multitude of shops."

The towboat and the railroad had done their work, and done it well and completely. The mighty bridge, stretching along over our heads, had done its share in the slaughter and spoliation. Remains of former steamboatmen told me, with wan satisfaction, that the bridge doesn't pay. Still, it can be no sufficient compensation to a corpse, to know that the dynamite that laid him out was not of as good quality as it had been supposed to be.

The pavements along the river front were bad; the sidewalks were rather out of repair; there was a rich abundance of mud. All this was familiar and satisfying; but the ancient armies of drays, and struggling throngs of men, and mountains of freight, were gone; and Sabbath reigned in their stead. The immemorial mile of cheap foul doggeries remained, but business was dull with them; the multitudes of poison-swilling Irishmen had departed, and in their places were a few scattering handfuls of ragged negroes, some drinking, some drunk, some nodding, others asleep. St. Louis is a great and prosperous and advancing city; but the river-edge of it seems dead past resurrection.

Mississippi steamboating was born about 1812; at the end of thirty years, it had grown to mighty proportions; and in less than thirty more, it was dead! A strangely short life for so majestic a creature. Of course it is not absolutely dead; neither is a crippled octogenarian who could once jump twenty-two feet on level ground; but as contrasted with what it was in its prime vigor, Mississippi steamboating may be called dead.

It killed the old-fashioned keel-boating, by reducing the freight-trip to New Orleans to less than a week. The railroads have killed the steamboat passenger traffic by doing in two or three days what the steamboats consumed a week in doing; and the towing-fleets have killed the through-freight traffic by dragging six or seven steamer-loads of stuff down the river at a time, at an expense so trivial that steamboat competition was out of the question.

* Capt. Marryat, writing forty-five years ago, says: "St. Louis has 20,000 inhabitants. The *river abreast of the town is crowded with steamboats, lying in two or three tiers.*"

Freight and passenger way-traffic remains to the steamers. This is in the hands—along the two thousand miles of river between St. Paul and New Orleans—of two or three close corporations well fortified with capital; and by able and thoroughly business-like management and system, these make a sufficiency of money out of what is left of the once prodigious steamboating industry. I suppose that St. Louis and New Orleans have not suffered materially by the change, but alas for the wood-yard man!

He used to fringe the river all the way; his close-ranked merchandise stretched from the one city to the other, along the banks, and he sold uncountable cords of it every year for cash on the nail; but all the scattering boats that are left burn coal now, and the seldomest spectacle on the Mississippi to-day is a wood-pile. Where now is the once wood-yard man?

CHAPTER XXIII

TRAVELLING INCOGNITO

My idea was, to tarry a while in every town between St. Louis and New Orleans. To do this, it would be necessary to go from place to place by the short packet lines. It was an easy plan to make, and would have been an easy one to follow, twenty years ago—but not now. There are wide intervals between boats, these days.

I wanted to begin with the interesting old French settlements of St. Genevieve and Kaskaskia, sixty miles below St. Louis. There was only one boat advertised for that section—a Grand Tower packet. Still, one boat was enough; so we went down to look at her. She was a venerable rack-heap, and a fraud to boot; for she was playing herself for personal property, whereas the good honest dirt was so thickly caked all over her that she was righteously taxable as real estate. There are places in New England where her hurricane deck would be worth a hundred and fifty dollars an acre. The soil on her forecastle was quite good—the new crop of wheat was already springing from the cracks in protected places. The companionway was of a dry sandy character, and would have been well suited for grapes, with a southern exposure and a little subsoiling. The soil of the boiler deck was thin and rocky, but good enough for grazing purposes. A colored boy was on watch here—nobody else visible. We gathered from him that this calm craft would go, as advertised, "if she got her trip;" if she didn't get it, she would wait for it.

"Has she got any of her trip?"

"Bless you, no, boss. She ain't unloadened, yit. She only come in dis mawnin'."

He was uncertain as to when she might get her trip, but thought it might be to-morrow or maybe next day. This would not answer at all; so we had to give up the novelty of sailing down the river on a farm. We had one more arrow in our quiver: a Vicksburg packet, the "Gold Dust," was to leave at 5 P.M. We took passage in her for Memphis, and gave up the idea of stopping off here and there, as being impracticable. She was neat, clean, and comfortable. We camped on the boiler deck, and bought some cheap literature to kill time with. The vender was a venerable Irishman with a benevolent face and a tongue that worked easily in the socket, and from him we learned that he had lived in St. Louis thirty-four years and had never been across the river during that period. Then he wandered into a very flowing lecture, filled with classic names and allusions, which was quite wonderful for fluency until the fact became rather apparent that this was not the first time, nor perhaps the fiftieth, that the speech had been delivered. He was a good deal of a character, and much better company than the sappy literature he was selling. A random remark, connecting Irishmen and beer, brought this nugget of information out of him:—

"They don't drink it, sir. They *can't* drink it, sir. Give an Irishman lager for a month, and he's a dead man. An Irishman is lined with copper, and the beer corrodes it. But whiskey polishes the copper and is the saving of him, sir."

At eight o'clock, promptly, we backed out and—crossed the river. As we crept toward the shore, in the thick darkness, a blinding glory of white electric light burst suddenly from our forecastle, and lit up the water and the warehouses as with a noon-day glare. Another big change, this,—no more flickering, smoky, pitch-dripping, ineffectual torch-baskets, now: their day is past. Next, instead of calling out a score of hands to man the stage, a couple of men and a hatful of steam lowered it from the derrick where it was suspended, launched it, deposited it in just the right spot, and the whole thing was over and done-with before a mate in the olden time could have got his profanity-mill adjusted to begin the preparatory services. Why this new and simple method of handling the stages was not thought of when the first steamboat was built, is a mystery which helps one to realize what a dull-witted slug the average human being is.

We finally got away at two in the morning, and when I turned out at six, we were rounding to at a rocky point where there was an old stone warehouse—at any rate, the ruins of it; two or three decayed dwelling-houses were near by, in the shelter of the leafy hills; but there were no evidences of human or other animal life to be seen. I wondered if I had forgotten the river; for I had no recollection whatever of this place; the shape of the river, too, was unfamiliar; there was nothing in sight, anywhere, that I could remember ever having seen before. I was surprised, disappointed, and annoyed.

We put ashore a well-dressed lady and gentleman, and two well-dressed, lady-like young girls, together with sundry Russia-leather bags. A strange place for such folk! No carriage was waiting. The party moved off as if they had not expected any, and struck down a winding country road afoot.

But the mystery was explained when we got under way again; for these people were evidently bound for a large town which lay shut in behind a tow-head (*i.e.,* new island) a couple of miles below this landing. I couldn't remember that town; I couldn't place it, couldn't call its name. So I lost part of my temper. I suspected that it might be St. Genevieve—and so it proved to be. Observe what this eccentric river had been about: it had built up this huge useless tow-head directly in front of this town, cut off its river communications, fenced it away completely, and made a "country" town of it. It is a fine old place, too, and deserved a better fate. It was settled by the French, and is a relic of a time when one could travel from the mouths of the Mississippi to Quebec and be on French territory and under French rule all the way.

Presently I ascended to the hurricane deck and cast a longing glance toward the pilot-house.

CHAPTER XXIV

MY INCOGNITO IS EXPLODED

After a close study of the face of the pilot on watch, I was satisfied that I had never seen him before; so I went up there. The pilot inspected me; I re-inspected the pilot. These customary preliminaries over, I sat down on the high bench, and he faced about and went on with his work. Every detail of the pilot-house was familiar to me, with one exception,—a large-mouthed tube under the breast-board. I puzzled over that thing a considerable time; then gave up and asked what it was for.

"To hear the engine-bells through."

It was another good contrivance which ought to have been invented half a centry sooner. So I was thinking, when the pilot asked,—

"Do you know what this rope is for?"

I managed to get around this question, without committing myself.

"Is this the first time you were ever in a pilot-house?"

I crept under that one.

"Where are you from?"

"New England."

"First time you have ever been West?"

I climbed over this one.

"If you take an interest in such things, I can tell you what all these things are for."

I said I should like it.

"This," putting his hand on a backing-bell rope, "is to sound the fire-alarm; this," putting his hand on a go-a-head bell, "is to call the texas-tender; this one," indicating the whistle-lever, "is to call the captain"—and so he went on, touching one object after another, and reeling off his tranquil spool of lies.

I had never felt so like a passenger before. I thanked him, with emotion, for each new fact, and wrote it down in my note-book. The pilot warmed to his opportunity, and proceeded to load me up in the good old-fashioned way. At times I was afraid he was going to rupture his invention; but it always stood the strain, and he pulled through all right. He drifted, by easy stages, into revealments of the river's marvellous eccentricities of one sort and another, and backed them up with some pretty gigantic illustrations. For instance,—

"Do you see that little bowlder sticking out of the water yonder? well, when I first came on the river, that was a solid ridge of rock, over sixty feet high and two miles long. All washed away but that." [This with a sigh.]

I had a mighty impulse to destroy him, but it seemed to me that killing, in any ordinary way, would be too good for him.

Once, when an odd-looking craft, with a vast coal-scuttle slanting aloft on the end of a beam, was steaming by in the distance, he indifferently drew attention to it, as one might to an object grown wearisome through familiarity, and observed that it was an "alligator boat."

"An alligator boat? What's it for?"

"To dredge out alligators with."

"Are they so thick as to be troublesome?"

"Well, not now, because the government keeps them down. But they used to be. Not everywhere; but in favorite places, here and there, where the river is wide and shoal—like Plum Point, and Stack Island, and so on—places they call alligator beds."

"Did they actually impede navigation?"

"Years ago, yes, in very low water; there was hardly a trip, then, that we didn't get aground on alligators."

It seemed to me that I should certainly have to get out my tomahawk. However, I restrained myself and said,—

"It must have been dreadful."

"Yes, it was one of the main difficulties about piloting. It was so hard to tell anything about the water; the damned things shift around so—never lie still five minutes at a time. You can tell a wind-reef, straight off, by the look of it; you can tell a break; you can tell a sand-reef—that's all easy; but an alligator reef doesn't show up, worth anything. Nine times in ten you can't tell where the water is; and when you *do* see where it is, like as not it ain't there when *you* get there, the devils have swapped around so, meantime. Of course there were some few pilots that could judge of alligator water nearly as well as they could of any other kind, but they had to have natural talent for it; it wasn't a thing a body could *learn*, you had to be born with it. Let me see: there was Ben Thornburg, and Beck Jolly, and Squire Bell, and Horace Bixby, and Major Downing, and John Stevenson, and Billy Gordon, and Jim Brady, and George Ealer, and Billy Youngblood— all A 1 alligator pilots. *They* could tell alligator water as far as another Christian could tell whiskey. Read it?—Ah, *couldn't* they, though! I only wish I had as many dollars as they could read alligator water a mile and a half off. Yes, and it paid them to do it, too. A good alligator pilot could always get fifteen hundred dollars a month. Nights, other people had to lay up for alligators, but those fellows never laid up for alligators; they never laid up for anything but fog. They could *smell* the best alligator water—so it was said; I don't know whether it was so or not, and I think a body's got his hands full enough if he sticks to just what he knows himself, without going around backing up other people's say-so's, though there's a plenty that ain't backward about doing it, as long as they can roust out something wonderful to tell. Which is not the style of Robert Styles, by as much as three fathom—maybe quarter-*less*."

[My! Was this Rob Styles?—This moustached and stately figure?—A slim enough cub, in my time. How he has improved in comeliness in five and twenty years—and in the noble art of inflating his facts.] After these musings, I said aloud,—

"I should think that dredging out the alligators wouldn't have done much good, because they could come back again right away."

"If you had had as much experience of alligators as I have, you wouldn't talk like that. You dredge an alligator once and he's *convinced*. It's the last you hear of *him*. He wouldn't come back for pie. If there's one thing that an alligator is more down on than another, it's being dredged. Besides, they were not simply shoved out of the way; the most of the scoopful were scooped aboard; they emptied them into the hold; and when they had got a trip, they took them to Orleans to the Government works."

"What for?"

"Why, to make soldier-shoes out of their hides. All the Government shoes are made of alligator hide. It makes the best shoes in the world. They last five years, and they won't absorb water. The alligator fishery is a Government monopoly. All the alligators are Government property—just like the live-oaks. You cut down a live-oak, and Government fines you fifty dollars; you kill an alligator, and up you go for misprision of treason—lucky duck if they don't hang you, too. And they will, if you're a Democrat. The buzzard is the sacred bird of the South, and you can't touch him; the alligator is the sacred bird of the Government, and you've got to let him alone."

"Do you ever get aground on the alligators now?"

"Oh, no! it hasn't happened for years."

"Well, then, why do they still keep the alligator boats in service?"

"Just for police duty—nothing more. They merely go up and down now and then. The present generation of alligators know them as easy as a burglar knows a roundsman; when they see one coming, they break camp and go for the woods."

After rounding-out and finishing-up and polishing-off the alligator business, he dropped easily and comfortably into the historical vein, and told of some tremendous feats of half a dozen old-time steamboats of his acquaintance, dwelling at special length upon a certain extraordinary performance of his chief favorite among this distinguished fleet—and then adding:—

"That boat was the 'Cyclone,'—last trip she ever made—she sunk, that very trip—captain was Tom Ballou, the most immortal liar that ever I struck. He couldn't ever seem to tell the truth, in *any* kind of weather. Why, he would make you fairly shudder. He *was* the most scandalous liar! I left him, finally; I couldn't stand it. The proverb says, 'like master, like man;' and if you stay with that kind of a man, you'll come under suspicion by and by, just as sure as you live. He paid first-class wages; but said I, What's wages when your reputation's in danger? So I let the wages go, and froze to my reputation. And I've never regretted it. Reputation's worth everything, ain't it? That's the way I look at it. He had more selfish organs than any seven men in the world—all packed in the stern-sheets of his skull, of course, where they belonged. They weighed down the back of his head so that it made his nose tilt up in the air. People thought it was vanity, but it wasn't, it was malice. If you only saw his foot, you'd take him to be nineteen feet high, but he wasn't; it was because his foot was out of drawing. He was intended to be nineteen feet high, no doubt, if his foot was made first, but he didn't get there; he was only five feet ten. That's what he was, and what's what he is. You take the lies out of him, and he'll shrink to the size of your hat; you take the malice out of him, and he'll disappear. That 'Cyclone' was a rattler to go, and the sweetest thing to steer that ever walked the waters. Set her amidships, in a big river, and just let her go; it was all you had to do. She would hold herself on a star all night, if you let her alone. You couldn't ever feel her rudder. It wasn't any more labor to steer her than it is to count the Republican vote in a South Carolina election. One morning, just at daybreak, the last trip she ever made, they took her rudder aboard to mend it; I didn't know anything about it; I backed her out from the wood-yard and went a- weaving down the river all serene. When I had gone about twenty-three miles, and made four horribly crooked crossings—"

"Without any rudder?"

"Yes—old Capt. Tom appeared on the roof and began to find fault with me for running such a dark night—"

"Such a *dark night*?—Why, you said—"

"Never mind what I said,—'twas as dark as Egypt *now*, though pretty soon the moon began to rise, and—"

"You mean the *sun*—because you started out just at break of—look here! Was this *before* you quitted the captain on account of his lying, or—"

"It was before—oh, a long time before. And as I was saying, he—"

"But was this the trip she sunk, or was—"

"Oh, no!—months afterward. And so the old man, he—"

"Then she made *two* last trips, because you said—"

He stepped back from the wheel, swabbing away his perspiration, and said—

"Here!" (calling me by name), "*you* take her and lie a while—you're handier at it than I am. Trying to play yourself for a stranger and an innocent!—why, I knew you before you had spoken seven words; and I made up my mind to find out what was your little game. It was to *draw me out*. Well, I let you, didn't I? Now take the wheel and finish the watch; and next time play fair, and you won't have to work your passage."

Thus ended the fictitious-name business. And not six hours

out from St. Louis! but I had gained a privilege, anyway, for I had been itching to get my hands on the wheel, from the beginning. I seemed to have forgotten the river, but I hadn't forgotten how to steer a steamboat, nor how to enjoy it, either.

CHAPTER XXV

FROM CAIRO TO HICKMAN

The scenery, from St. Louis to Cairo—two hundred miles—is varied and beautiful. The hills were clothed in the fresh foliage of spring now, and were a gracious and worthy setting for the broad river flowing between. Our trip began auspiciously, with a perfect day, as to breeze and sunshine, and our boat threw the miles out behind her with satisfactory despatch.

We found a railway intruding at Chester, Illinois; Chester has also a penitentiary now, and is otherwise marching on. At Grand Tower, too, there was a railway; and another at Cape Girardeau. The former town gets its name from a huge, squat pillar of rock, which stands up out of the water on the Missouri side of the river—a piece of nature's fanciful handiwork—and is one of the most picturesque features of the scenery of that region. For nearer or remoter neighbors, the Tower has the Devil's Bake Oven—so called, perhaps, because it does not powerfully resemble anybody else's bake oven; and the Devil's Tea Table—this latter a great smooth-surfaced mass of rock, with diminishing wine-glass stem, perched some fifty or sixty feet above the river, beside a beflowered and garlanded precipice, and sufficiently like a tea-table to answer for anybody, Devil or Christian. Away down the river we have the Devil's Elbow and the Devil's Race-course, and lots of other property of his which I cannot now call to mind.

The Town of Grand Tower was evidently a busier place than it had been in old times, but it seemed to need some repairs here and there, and a new coat of whitewash all over. Still, it was pleasant to me to see the old coat once more. "Uncle" Mumford, our second officer, said the place had been suffering from high water and consequently was not looking its best now. But he said it was not strange that it didn't waste whitewash on itself, for more lime was made there, and of a better quality, than anywhere in the West; and added,—"On a dairy farm you never can get any milk for your coffee, nor any sugar for it on a sugar plantation; and it is against sense to go to a lime town to hunt for whitewash." In my own experience I knew the first two items to be true; and also that people who sell candy don't care for candy; therefore there was plausibility in Uncle Mumford's final observation that "people who make lime run more to religion than whitewash." Uncle Mumford said, further, that Grand Tower was a great coaling centre and a prospering place.

Cape Girardeau is situated on a hillside, and makes a handsome appearance. There is a great Jesuit school for boys at the foot of the town by the river. Uncle Mumford said it had as high a reputation for thoroughness as any similar institution in Missouri. There was another college higher up on an airy summit,—a bright new edifice, picturesquely and peculiarly towered and pinnacled—a sort of gigantic casters, with the cruets all complete. Uncle Mumford said that Cape Girardeau was the Athens of Missouri, and contained several colleges besides those already mentioned; and all of them on a religious basis of one kind or another. He directed my attention to what he called the "strong and pervasive religious look of the town," but I could not see that it looked more religious than the other hill towns with the same slope and built of the same kind of bricks. Partialities often make people see more than really exists.

Uncle Mumford has been thirty years a mate on the river. He is a man of practical sense and a level head; has observed; has had much experience of one sort and another; has opinions; has, also, just a perceptible dash of poetry in his composition, an easy gift of speech, a thick growl in his voice, and an oath or two where he can get at them when the exigencies of his office require a spiritual lift. He is a mate of the blessed old-time kind; and goes gravely damning around, when there is work to the fore, in a way to mellow the ex-steamboatman's heart with sweet soft longings for the vanished days that shall come no more. "*Git* up, there,—— —you! Going to be all day? Why d'n't you *say* you was petrified in your hind legs, before you shipped!"

He is a steady man with his crew; kind and just, but firm; so they like him, and stay with him. He is still in the slouchy garb of the old generation of mates; but next trip the Anchor Line will have him in uniform—a natty blue naval uniform, with brass buttons, along with all the officers of the line—and then he will be a totally different style of scenery from what he is now.

Uniforms on the Mississippi! It beats all the other changes put together, for surprise. Still, there is another surprise—that it was not made fifty years ago. It is so manifestly sensible, that it might have been thought of earlier, one would suppose. During fifty years, out there, the innocent passenger in need of help and information, has been mistaking the mate for the cook, and the captain for the barber—and being roughly entertained for it, too. But his troubles are ended now. And the greatly improved aspect of the boat's staff is another advantage achieved by the dress-reform period.

Steered down the bend below Cape Girardeau. They used to call it "Steersman's Bend;" plain sailing and plenty of water in it, always; about the only place in the Upper River, that a new cub was allowed to take a boat through, in low water.

Thebes, at the head of the Grand Chain, and Commerce at the foot of it, were towns easily rememberable, as they had not undergone conspicuous alteration. Nor the Chain, either—in the nature of things; for it is a chain of sunken rocks admirably arranged to capture and kill steamboats on bad nights. A good many steamboat corpses lie buried there, out of sight; among the rest my first friend the "Paul Jones;" she knocked her bottom out, and went down like a pot, so the historian told me—Uncle Mumford. He said she had a gray mare aboard, and a preacher. To me, this sufficiently accounted for the disaster; as it did, of course to Mumford, who added,—"But there are many ignorant people who would scoff at such a matter, and call it superstition. But you will always notice that they are people who have never travelled with a gray mare and a preacher. I went down the river once in such company. We grounded at Bloody Island; we grounded at Hanging Dog; we grounded just below this same Commerce; we jolted Beaver Dam Rock; we hit one of the worst breaks in the 'Graveyard' behind Goose Island; we had a roustabout killed in a fight; we burnt a boiler; broke a shaft; collapsed a flue; and went into Cairo with nine feet of water in the hold— may have been more, may have been less. I remember it as if it were yesterday. The men lost their heads with terror. They painted the mare blue, in sight of town, and threw the preacher overboard, or we should not have arrived at all. The preacher was fished out and saved. He acknowledged, himself, that he had been to blame. I remember it all, as if it were yesterday."

That this combination—of preacher and gray mare—should breed calamity, seems strange, and at first glance unbelievable; but the fact is fortified by so much unassailable proof that to doubt is to dishonor reason. I myself remember a cast where a captain was warned by numerous friends against taking a gray mare and a preacher with him, but persisted in his purpose in spite of all that could be said; and the same day,—it may have been the next, and some say it was, though I think it was the same day,—he got drunk and fell down the hatchway and was borne to his home a corpse. This is literally true.

No vestige of Hat Island is left now; every shred of it is

washed away. I do not even remember what part of the river it used to be in, except that it was between St. Louis and Cairo somewhere. It was a bad region—all around and about Hat Island, in early days. A farmer who lived on the Illinois shore there, said that twenty-nine steamboats had left their bones strung along within sight from his house. Between St. Louis and Cairo the steamboat wrecks average one to the mile;—two hundred wrecks, altogether.

I could recognize big changes from Commerce down. Beaver Dam Rock was out in the middle of the river now, and throwing a prodigious "break;" it used to be close to the shore, and boats went down outside of it. A big island that used to be away out in mid-river, has retired to the Missouri shore, and boats do not go near it any more. The island called Jacket Pattern is whittled down to a wedge now, and is booked for early destruction. Goose Island is all gone but a little dab the size of a steamboat. The perilous "Graveyard," among whose numberless wrecks we used to pick our way so slowly and gingerly, is far away from the channel now, and a terror to nobody. One of the islands formerly called the Two Sisters is gone entirely; the other, which used to lie close to the Illinois shore, is now on the Missouri side, a mile away; it is joined solidly to the shore, and it takes a sharp eye to see where the seam is—but it is Illinois ground yet, and the people who live on it have to ferry themselves over and work the Illinois roads and pay Illinois taxes: singular state of things!

Near the mouth of the river several islands were missing—washed away. Cairo was still there—easily visible across the long, flat point upon whose further verge it stands; but we had to steam a long way around to get to it. Night fell as we were going out of the "Upper River" and meeting the floods of the Ohio. We dashed along without anxiety; for the hidden rock which used to lie right in the way has moved up stream a long distance out of the channel; or rather, about one county has gone into the river from the Missouri point, and the Cairo point has "made down" and added to its long tongue of territory correspondingly. The Mississippi is a just and equitable river; it never tumbles one man's farm overboard without building a new farm just like it for that man's neighbor. This keeps down hard feelings.

Going into Cairo, we came near killing a steamboat which paid no attention to our whistle and then tried to cross our bows. By doing some strong backing, we saved him; which was a great loss, for he would have made good literature.

Cairo is a brisk town now; and is substantially built, and has a city look about it which is in noticeable contrast to its former estate, as per Mr. Dickens's portrait of it. However, it was already building with bricks when I had seen it last—which was when Colonel (now General) Grant was drilling his first command there. Uncle Mumford says the libraries and Sunday-schools have done a good work in Cairo, as well as the brick masons. Cairo has a heavy railroad and river trade, and her situation at the junction of the two great rivers is so advantageous that she cannot well help prospering.

When I turned out, in the morning, we had passed Columbus, Kentucky, and were approaching Hickman, a pretty town, perched on a handsome hill. Hickman is in a rich tobacco region, and formerly enjoyed a great and lucrative trade in that staple, collecting it there in her warehouses from a large area of country and shipping it by boat; but Uncle Mumford says she built a railway to facilitate this commerce a little more, and he thinks it facilitated in the wrong way—took the bulk of the trade out of her hands by "collaring it along the line without gathering it at her doors."

CHAPTER XXVI

UNDER FIRE

Talk began to run upon the war now, for we were getting down into the upper edge of the former battle-stretch by this time. Columbus was just behind us, so there was a good deal said about the famous battle of Belmont. Several of the boat's officers had seen active service in the Mississippi war-fleet. I gathered that they found themselves sadly out of their element in that kind of business at first, but afterward got accustomed to it, reconciled to it, and more or less at home in it. One of our pilots had his first war experience in the Belmont fight, as a pilot on a boat in the Confederate service. I had often had a curiosity to know how a green hand might feel, in his maiden battle, perched all solitary and alone on high in a pilot house, a target for Tom, Dick and Harry, and nobody at his elbow to shame him from showing the white feather when matters grew hot and perilous around him; so, to me his story was valuable—it filled a gap for me which all histories had left till that time empty.

THE PILOT'S FIRST BATTLE

He said:—

It was the 7th of November. The fight began at seven in the morning. I was on the "R. H. W. Hill." Took over a load of troops from Columbus. Came back, and took over a battery of artillery. My partner said he was going to see the fight; wanted me to go along. I said, no, I wasn't anxious, I would look at it from the pilot-house. He said I was a coward, and left.

That fight was an awful sight. General Cheatham made his men strip their coats off and throw them in a pile, and said, "Now follow me to hell or victory!" I heard him say that from the pilot-house; and then he galloped in, at the head of his troops. Old General Pillow, with his white hair, mounted on a white horse, sailed in, too, leading his troops as lively as a boy. By and by the Federals chased the rebels back, and here they came! tearing along, everybody for himself and Devil take the hindmost! and down under the bank they scrambled, and took shelter. I was sitting with my legs hanging out of the pilot-house window. All at once I noticed a whizzing sound passing my ear. Judged it was a bullet. I didn't stop to think about anything, I just tilted over backwards and landed on the floor, and stayed there. The balls came booming around. Three cannon-balls went through the chimney; one ball took off the corner of the pilot-house; shells were screaming and bursting all around. Mighty warm times—I wished I hadn't come. I lay there on the pilot-house floor, while the shots came faster and faster. I crept in behind the big stove, in the middle of the pilot-house. Presently a minie-ball came through the stove, and just grazed my head, and cut my hat. I judged it was time to go away from there. The captain was on the roof with a red-headed major from Memphis—a fine-looking man. I heard him say he wanted to leave here, but "that pilot is killed." I crept over to the starboard side to pull the bell to set her back; raised up and took a look, and I saw about fifteen shot holes through the window panes; had come so lively I hadn't noticed them. I glanced out on the water, and the spattering shot were like a hail-storm. I thought best to get out of that place. I went down the pilot-house guy, head first—not feet first but head first—slid down—before I struck the deck, the captain said we must leave there. So I climbed up the guy and got on the floor again. About that time, they collared my partner and were bringing him up to the pilot-house between two soldiers. Somebody had said I was killed. He put his head in and saw me on the floor reaching for the backing bells. He said, "Oh, hell, he ain't shot," and jerked away from the men who had him by the collar, and ran below. We were there until three o'clock in the afternoon, and then got away all right.

The next time I saw my partner, I said, "Now, come out, be honest, and tell me the truth. Where did you go when you went to see that battle?" He says, "I went down in the hold."

All through that fight I was scared nearly to death. I hardly knew anything, I was so frightened; but you see, nobody knew that but me. Next day General Polk sent for me, and praised me for my bravery and gallant conduct. I never said anything, I let it go at that. I judged it wasn't so, but it was not for me to contradict a general officer.

Pretty soon after that I was sick, and used up, and had to go off to the Hot Springs. When there, I got a good many letters from commanders saying they wanted me to come back. I declined, because I wasn't well enough or strong enough; but I kept still, and kept the reputation I had made.

A plain story, straightforwardly told; but Mumford told me that that pilot had "gilded that scare of his, in spots;" that his subsequent career in the war was proof of it.

We struck down through the chute of Island No. 8, and I went below and fell into conversation with a passenger, a handsome man, with easy carriage and an intelligent face. We were approaching Island No. 10, a place so celebrated during the war. This gentleman's home was on the main shore in its neighborhood. I had some talk with him about the war times; but presently the discourse fell upon "feuds," for in no part of the South has the vendetta flourished more briskly, or held out longer between warring families, than in this particular region. This gentleman said:—

"There's been more than one feud around here, in old times, but I reckon the worst one was between the Darnells and the Watsons. Nobody don't know what the first quarrel was about, it's so long ago; the Darnells and the Watsons, if there's any of them living, which I don't think there is. Some says it was about a horse or a cow—anyway, it was a little matter; the money in it wasn't of no consequence—none in the world—both families was rich. The thing could have been fixed up, easy enough; but no, that wouldn't do. Rough words had been passed; and so, nothing but blood could fix it up after that. That horse or cow, whichever it was, cost sixty years of killing and crippling! Every year or so somebody was shot, on one side or the other; and as fast as one generation was laid out, their sons took up the feud and kept it a-going. And it's just as I say; they went on shooting each other, year in and year out—making a kind of a religion of it, you see—till they'd done forgot, long ago, what it was all about. Wherever a Darnell caught a Watson, or a Watson caught a Darnell, one of 'em was going to get hurt—only question was, which of them got the drop on the other. They'd shoot one another down, right in the presence of the family. They didn't *hunt* for each other, but when they happened to meet, they pulled and begun. Men would shoot boys, boys would shoot men. A man shot a boy twelve years old—happened on him in the woods, and didn't give him no chance. If he *had* 'a' given him a chance, the boy'd 'a' shot *him*. Both families belonged to the same church (everybody around here is religious); through all this fifty or sixty years' fuss, both tribes was there every Sunday, to worship. The lived each side of the line, and the church was at a landing called Compromise. Half the church and half the aisle was in Kentucky, the other half in Tennessee. Sundays you'd see the families drive up, all in their Sunday clothes, men, women, and children, and file up the aisle, and set down, quiet and orderly, one lot on the Tennessee side of the church and the other on the Kentucky side; and the men and boys would lean their guns up against the wall, handy, and then all hands would join in with the prayer and praise; though they say the man next the aisle didn't kneel down, along with the rest of the family; kind of stood guard. I don't know; never was at that church in my life; but I remember that that's what used to be said.

"Twenty or twenty-five years ago, one of the feud families caught a young man of nineteen out and killed him. Don't remember whether it was the Darnells and Watsons, or one of the other feuds; but anyway, this young man rode up—steamboat laying there at the time—and the first thing he saw was a whole gang of the enemy. He jumped down behind a wood-pile, but they rode around and begun on him, he firing back, and they galloping and cavorting and yelling and banging away with all their might. Think he wounded a couple of them; but they closed in on him and chased him into the river; and as he swum along down stream, they followed along the bank and kept on shooting at him; and when he struck shore he was dead. Windy Marshall told me about it. He saw it. He was captain of the boat.

"Years ago, the Darnells was so thinned out that the old man and his two sons concluded they'd leave the country. They started to take steamboat just above No. 10; but the Watsons got wind of it; and they arrived just as the two young Darnells was walking up the companion-way with their wives on their arms. The fight begun then, and they never got no further—both of them killed. After that, old Darnell got into trouble with the man that run the ferry, and the ferry-man got the worst of it—and died. But his friends shot old Darnell through and through—filled him full of bullets, and ended him."

The country gentleman who told me these things had been reared in ease and comfort, was a man of good parts, and was college bred. His loose grammar was the fruit of careless habit, not ignorance. This habit among educated men in the West is not universal, but it is prevalent—prevalent in the towns, certainly, if not in the cities; and to a degree which one cannot help noticing, and marvelling at. I heard a Westerner who would be accounted a highly educated man in any country, say "never mind, it *don't make no difference,* anyway." A life-long resident who was present heard it, but it made no impression upon her. She was able to recall the fact afterward, when reminded of it; but she confessed that the words had not grated upon her ear at the time—a confession which suggests that if educated people can hear such blasphemous grammar, from such a source, and be unconscious of the deed, the crime must be tolerably common—so common that the general ear has become dulled by familiarity with it, and is no longer alert, no longer sensitive to such affronts.

No one in the world speaks blemishless grammar; no one has ever written it—*no* one, either in the world or out of it (taking the Scriptures for evidence on the latter point); therefore it would not be fair to exact grammatical perfection from the peoples of the Valley; but they and all other peoples may justly be required to refrain from *knowingly* and *purposely* debauching their grammar.

I found the river greatly changed at Island No. 10. The island which I remembered was some three miles long and a quarter of a mile wide, heavily timbered, and lay near the Kentucky shore—within two hundred yards of it, I should say. Now, however, one had to hunt for it with a spy-glass. Nothing was left of it but an insignificant little tuft, and this was no longer near the Kentucky shore; it was clear over against the opposite shore, a mile away. In war times the island had been an important place, for it commanded the situation; and, being heavily fortified, there was no getting by it. It lay between the upper and lower divisions of the Union forces, and kept them separate, until a junction was finally effected across the Missouri neck of land; but the island being itself joined to that neck now, the wide river is without obstruction.

In this region the river passes from Kentucky into Tennessee, back into Missouri, then back into Kentucky, and thence into Tennessee again. So a mile or two of Missouri sticks over into Tennessee.

The town of New Madrid was looking very unwell; but otherwise unchanged from its former condition and aspect. Its blocks of frame-houses were still grouped in the same old flat plain, and environed by the same old forests. It was as tranquil as formerly, and apparently had neither grown nor diminished in size. It was said that the recent high water had invaded it and damaged its looks. This was surprising news; for in low water the river bank is very high there (fifty feet), and in my day an overflow had always been considered an impossibility. This present flood of 1882 will doubtless be celebrated in the river's history for several generations before a deluge of like magnitude shall be seen. It put all the unprotected low lands under water, from Cairo to the mouth; it broke down the levees in a great many places, on both sides of the river; and in some regions south when the flood was at its highest, the Mississippi was *seventy miles* wide! a number of lives were lost, and the destruction of property was fearful. The crops were destroyed, houses washed away, and shelterless men and cattle forced to take refuge on scattering elevations here and there in field and forest, and wait in peril and suffering until the boats put in commission by the national and local governments and by newspaper enterprise could come and rescue them. The properties of multitudes of people were under water for months, and the poorer ones must have starved by the hundred if succor had not been promptly afforded.* The water had been falling during a considerable time now, yet as a rule we found the banks still under water.

CHAPTER XXVII

SOME IMPORTED ARTICLES

We met two steamboats at New Madrid. Two steamboats in sight at once! an infrequent spectacle now in the lonesome Mississippi. The loneliness of this solemn, stupendous flood is impressive—and depressing. League after league, and still league after league, it pours its chocolate tide along, between its solid forest walls, its almost untenanted shores, with seldom a sail or a moving object of any kind to disturb the surface and break the monotony of the blank, watery solitude; and so the day goes, the night comes, and again the day—and still the same, night after night and day after day,—majestic, unchanging sameness of serenity, repose, tranquillity, lethargy, vacancy,—symbol of eternity, realization of the heaven pictured

* For a detailed and interesting description of the great flood, written on board of the New Orleans "Times-Democrat's" relief-boat, see Appendix A.

by priest and prophet, and longed for by the good and thoughtless!

Immediately after the war of 1812, tourists began to come to America, from England; scattering ones at first, then a sort of procession of them—a procession which kept up its plodding, patient march through the land during many, many years. Each tourist took notes, and went home and published a book—a book which was usually calm, truthful, reasonable, kind; but which seemed just the reverse to our tender-footed progenitors. A glance at these tourist-books shows us that in certain of its aspects the Mississippi has undergone no change since those strangers visited it, but remains to-day about as it was then. The emotions produced in those foreign breasts by these aspects were not all formed on one pattern, of course; they *had* to be various, along at first, because the earlier tourists were obliged to originate their emotions, whereas in older countries one can always borrow emotions from one's predecessors. And, mind you, emotions are among the toughest things in the world to manufacture out of whole cloth; it is easier to manufacture seven facts than one emotion. Captain Basil Hall, R. N., writing fifty-five years ago, says:—

"Here I caught the first glimpse of the object I had so long wished to behold, and felt myself amply repaid at that moment for all the trouble I had experienced in coming so far; and stood looking at the river flowing past till it was too dark to distinguish anything. But it was not till I had visited the same spot a dozen times, that I came to a right comprehension of the grandeur of the scene."

Following are Mrs. Trollope's emotions. She is writing a few months later in the same year, 1827, and is coming in at the mouth of the Mississippi:—

"The first indication of our approach to land was the appearance of this mighty river pouring forth its muddy mass of waters, and mingling with the deep blue of the Mexican Gulf. I never beheld a scene so utterly desolate as this entrance of the Mississippi. Had Dante seen it, he might have drawn images of another Bolgia from its horrors. Only one object rears itself above the eddying waters; this is the mast of a vessel long since wrecked in attempting to cross the bar, and it still stands, a dismal witness of the destruction that has been, and a boding prophet of that which is to come."

Emotions of Hon. Charles Augustus Murray (near St. Louis), seven years later:—

"It is only when you ascend the mighty current for fifty or a hundred miles, and use the eye of imagination as well as that of nature, that you begin to understand all his might and majesty. You see him fertilizing a boundless valley, bearing along in his course the trophies of his thousand victories over the shattered forest—here carrying away large masses of soil with all their growth, and there forming islands, destined at some future period to be the residence of man; and while indulging in this prospect, it is then time for reflection to suggest that the current before you has flowed through two or three thousand miles, and has yet to travel one thousand three hundred more before reaching its ocean destination."

Receive, now, the emotions of Captain Marryat, R. N. author of the sea tales, writing in 1837, three years after Mr. Murray:—

"Never, perhaps, in the records of nations, was there an instance of a century of such unvarying and unmitigated crime as is to be collected from the history of the turbulent and blood-stained Mississippi. The stream itself appears as if appropriate for the deeds which have been committed. It is not like most rivers, beautiful to the sight, bestowing fertility in its course; not one that the eye loves to dwell upon as it sweeps along, nor can you wander upon its bank, or trust yourself without danger to its stream. It is a furious, rapid, desolating torrent, loaded with alluvial soil; and few of those who are received into its waters ever rise again,* or can support themselves long upon its surface without assistance from some friendly log. It contains the coarsest and most uneatable of fish, such as the cat-fish and such genus, and as you descend, its banks are occuped with the fetid alligator, while the panther basks as its edge in the cane-brakes, almost impervious to man. Pouring its impetuous waters through wild tracks covered with trees of little value except for firewood, it sweeps down whole forests in its course, which disappear in tumultuous confusion, whirled away by the stream now loaded with the masses of soil which nourished their roots, often blocking up and changing for a time the channel of the river, which, as if in anger at its being opposed, inundates and devastates the whole country round; and as soon as it forces its way through its former channel, plants in every direction the uprooted monarchs of the forest (upon whose branches the bird will never again perch, or the raccoon, the opossum, or the squirrel climb) as traps to the adventurous navigators of its waters by steam, who, borne down upon these concealed dangers which pierce through the planks, very often have not time to steer for and gain the shore before they sink to the bottom. There are no pleasing associations connected with the great common sewer of the Western America, which pours out its mud into the Mexican Gulf, polluting the clear blue sea for many miles beyond its mouth. It is a river of desolation; and instead of reminding you, like other beautiful rivers, of an angel which has descended for the benefit of

* There was a foolish superstition of some little prevalence in that day, that the Mississippi would neither buoy up a swimmer, nor permit a drowned person's body to rise to the surface.

man, you imagine it a devil, whose energies have been only overcome by the wonderful power of steam."

It is pretty crude literature for a man accustomed to handling a pen; still, as a panorama of the emotions sent weltering through this noted visitor's breast by the aspect and traditions of the "great common sewer," it has a value. A value, though marred in the matter of statistics by inaccuracies; for the catfish is a plenty good enough fish for anybody, and there are no panthers that are "impervious to man."

Later still comes Alexander Mackay, of the Middle Temple, Barrister at Law, with a better digestion, and no catfish dinner aboard, and feels as follows:—

"The Mississippi! It was with indescribable emotions that I first felt myself afloat upon its waters. How often in my school-boy dreams, and in my waking visions afterwards, had my imagination pictured to itself the lordly stream, rolling with tumultuous current through the boundless region to which it has given its name, and gathering into itself, in its course to the ocean, the tributary waters of almost every latitude in the temperate zone! Here it was then in its reality, and I, at length, steaming against its tide. I looked upon it with that reverence with which every one must regard a great feature of external nature."

So much for the emotions. The tourists, one and all, remark upon the deep, brooding loneliness and desolation of the vast river. Captain Basil Hall, who saw it at floodstage, says:—

"Sometimes we passed along distances of twenty or thirty miles without seeing a single habitation. An artist, in search of hints for a painting of the deluge, would here have found them in abundance."

The first shall be last, etc. Just two hundred years ago, the old original first and gallantest of all the foreign tourists, pioneer, head of the procession, ended his weary and tedious discovery-voyage down the solemn stretches of the great river—La Salle, whose name will last as long as the river itself shall last. We quote from Mr. Parkman:—

"And now they neared their journey's end. On the sixth of April, the river divided itself into three broad channels. La Salle followed that of the west, and D'Autray that of the east; while Tonty took the middle passage. As he drifted down the turbid current, between the low and marshy shores, the brackish water changed to brine, and the breeze grew fresh with the salt breath of the sea. Then the broad bosom of the great Gulf opened on his sight, tossing its restless billows, limitless, voiceless, lonely as when born of chaos, without a sail, without a sign of life."

Then, on a spot of solid ground, La Salle reared a column "bearing the arms of France; the Frenchmen were mustered under arms; and while the New England Indians and their squaws looked on in wondering silence, they chanted the *Te Deum,* the *Exaudiat,* and the *Domine salvum fac regem.*"

Then, whilst the musketry volleyed and rejoicing shouts burst forth, the victorious discoverer planted the column, and made proclamation in a loud voice, taking formal possession of the river and the vast countries watered by it, in the name of the King. The column bore this inscription:—

LOUIS LE GRAND, ROY DE FRANCE ET DE NAVARRE, REGNE;
LE NEUVIEME AVRIL, 1682.

New Orleans intended to fittingly celebrate, this present year, the bicentennial anniversary of this illustrious event; but when the time came, all her energies and surplus money were required in other directions, for the flood was upon the land then, making havoc and devastation everywhere.

CHAPTER XXVIII

UNCLE MUMFORD UNLOADS

All day we swung along down the river, and had the stream almost wholly to ourselves. Formerly, at such a stage of the water, we should have passed acres of lumber rafts, and dozens of big coal barges; also occasional little trading-scows, peddling along from farm to farm, with the pedler's family on board; possibly, a random scow, bearing a humble Hamlet and Co. on an itinerant dramatic trip. But these were all absent. Far along in the day, we saw one steamboat; just one, and no more. She was lying at rest in the shade, within the wooded mouth of the Obion River. The spy-glass revealed the fact that she was named for me—or *he* was named for me, whichever you prefer. As this was the first time I had ever encountered this species of honor, it seems excusable to mention it, and at the same time call the attention of the authorities to the tardiness of my recognition of it.

Noted a big change in the river, at Island 21. It was a very large island, and used to lie out toward mid-stream; but it is joined fast to the main shore now, and has retired from business as an island.

As we approached famous and formidable Plum Point, darkness fell, but that was nothing to shudder about—in these modern times. For now the national government has turned the Mississippi into a sort of two-thousand-mile torch-light procession. In the head of every crossing, and in the foot of every crossing, the government has set up a clear-burning lamp. You are never entirely in the dark, now; there is always a beacon in sight, either before you, or behind you, or abreast. One might almost say that lamps have been squandered there. Dozens of crossings are lighted which were not shoal when they were created, and have never been shoal since; crossings so plain, too, and also so straight, that a steamboat can take herself through them without any help, after she has been through once. Lamps in such places are of course not wasted; it is much more convenient and comfortable for a pilot to hold on them than on a spread of formless blackness that won't stay still; and money is saved to the boat, at the same time, for she can of course make more miles with her rudder amidships than she can with it squared across her stern and holding her back.

But this thing has knocked the romance out of piloting, to a large extent. It and some other things together, have knocked all the romance out of it. For instance, the peril from snags is not now what it once was. The government's snag-boats go patrolling up and down, in these matter-of-fact days, pulling the river's teeth; they have rooted out all the old clusters which made many localities so formidable; and they allow no new ones to collect. Formerly, if your boat got away from you, on a black night, and broke for the woods, it was an anxious time with you; so was it also, when you were groping your way through solidified darkness in a narrow chute; but all that is changed now,—you flash out your electric light, transform night into day in the twinkling of an eye, and your perils and anxieties are at an end. Horace Bixby and George Ritchie have charted the crossings and laid out the courses by compass; they have invented a lamp to go with the chart, and have patented the whole. With these helps, one may run in the fog now, with considerable security, and with a confidence unknown in the old days.

With these abundant beacons, the banishment of snags, plenty of daylight in a box and ready to be turned on whenever needed, and a chart and compass to fight the fog with, piloting, at a good stage of water, is now nearly as safe and simple as driving stage, and is hardly more than three times as romantic.

And now in these new days, these days of infinite change, the Anchor Line have raised the captain above the pilot by giving him the bigger wages of the two. This was going far, but they have not stopped there. They have decreed that the pilot shall remain at his post, and stand his watch clear through, whether the boat be under way or tied up to the shore. We, that were once the aristocrats of the river, can't go to bed now, as we used to do, and sleep while a hundred tons of freight are lugged aboard; no, we must sit in the pilot-house; and keep awake, too. Verily we are being treated like a parcel of mates and engineers. The Government has taken away the romance of our calling; the Company has taken away its state and dignity.

Plum Point looked as it had always looked by night, with the exception that now there were beacons to mark the crossings, and also a lot of other lights on the Point and along its shore; these latter glinting from the fleet of the United States River Commission, and from a village which the officials have built on the land for offices and for the employés of the service. The military engineers of the Commission have taken upon their shoulders the job of making the Mississippi over again,—a job transcended in size by only the original job of creating it. They are building wing-dams here and there, to deflect the current; and dikes to confine it in narrower bounds; and other dikes to make it stay there; and for unnumbered miles along the Mississippi, they are felling the timber-front for fifty yards back, with the purpose of shaving the bank down to low-water mark with the slant of a house-roof, and ballasting it with stones; and in many places they have protected the wasting shores with rows of piles. One who knows the Mississippi will promptly aver—not aloud, but to himself—that ten thousand River Commissions, with the mines of the world at their back, cannot tame that lawless stream, cannot curb it or confine it, cannot say to it, Go here, or Go there, and make it obey; cannot save a shore which it has sentenced; cannot bar its path with an obstruction which it will not tear down, dance over, and laugh at. But a discreet man will not put these things into spoken words; for the West Point engineers have not their superiors anywhere; they know all that can be known of their abstruse science; and so, since they conceive that they can fetter and handcuff that river and boss him, it is but wisdom for the unscientific man to keep still, lie low, and wait till they do it. Captain Eads, with his jetties, has done a work at the mouth of the Mississippi which seemed clearly impossible; so we do not feel full confidence now to prophesy against like impossibilities. Otherwise one would pipe out and say the Commission might as well bully the comets in their courses and undertake to make them behave, as try to bully the Mississippi into right and reasonable conduct.

I consulted Uncle Mumford concerning this and cognate matters; and I give here the result, stenographically reported, and therefore to be relied on as being full and correct; except that I have here and there left out remarks which were addressed to the men, such as "*where* in the blazes are you going with that barrel now?" and which seemed to me to break the flow of the written statement, without compensating by adding to its information or its clearness. Not that I have ventured to strike out all such interjections; I have removed only those which were obviously irrelevant; wherever one occurred which I felt any question about, I have judged it safest to let it remain.

UNCLE MUMFORD'S IMPRESSIONS

Uncle Mumford said:—

"As long as I have been mate of a steamboat,—thirty years—I have watched this river and studied it. Maybe I could have learnt more about it at West Point, but if I believe it I wish I may be WHAT *are you sucking your fingers there for*?—*Collar that kag of nails*! Four years at West Point, and plenty of books and schooling, will learn a man a good deal, I reckon, but it won't learn him the river. You turn one of those little European rivers over to this Commission, with its hard bottom and clear water, and it would just be a holiday job for them to wall it, and pile it, and dike it, and tame it down, and boss it around, and make it go wherever they wanted it to, and stay where they put it, and do just as they said, every time. But this ain't that kind of a river. They have started in here with big confidence, and the best intentions in the world; but they are going to get left. What does Ecclesiastes vii. 13 say? Says enough to knock *their* little game galley-west, don't it? Now you look at their methods once. There at Devil's Island, in the Upper River, they wanted the water to go one way, the water wanted to go another. So they put up a stone wall. But what does the river care for a stone wall? When it got ready, it just bulged through it. Maybe they can build another that will stay; that is, up there—but not down here they can't. Down here in the Lower River, they drive some pegs to turn the water away from the shore and stop it from slicing off the bank; very well, don't it go straight over and cut somebody else's bank? Certainly. Are they going to peg *all* the banks? Why, they could buy ground and build a new Mississippi cheaper. They are pegging Bulletin Tow-head now. It won't do any good. If the river has got a mortgage on that island, it will foreclose, sure, pegs or no pegs. Away down yonder, they have driven two rows of piles straight through the middle of a dry bar half a mile long, which is forty foot out of the water when the river is low. What do you reckon that is for? If I know, I wish I may land in—HUMP *yourself, you son of an undertaker!*—*out with that coal-oil, now, lively,* LIVELY! And just look at what they are trying to do down there at Milliken's Bend. There's been a cut-off in that section, and Vicksburg is left out in the cold. It's a country town now. The river strikes in below it; and a boat can't go up to the town except in high water. Well, they are going to build wing-dams in the bend opposite the foot of 103, and throw the water over and cut off the foot of the island and plow down into an old ditch where the river used to be in ancient times; and they think they can persuade the water around that way, and get it to strike in above Vicksburg, as it used to do, and fetch the town back into the world again. That is, they are going to take this whole Mississippi, and twist it around and make it run several miles *up stream*. Well, you've got to admire men that deal in ideas of that size and can tote them around without crutches; but you haven't got to believe they can *do* such miracles, have you? And yet you ain't absolutely obliged to believe they can't. I reckon the safe way, where a man can afford it, is to *copper* the operation, and at the same time buy enough property in Vicksburg to square you up in case they win. Government is doing a deal for the Mississippi, now—spending loads of money on her. When there used to be four thousand steamboats and ten thousand acres of coal-barges, and rafts and trading scows, there wasn't a lantern from St. Paul to New Orleans, and the snags were thicker than bristles on a hog's back; and now when there's three dozen steamboats and nary barge or raft, Government has snatched out all the snags on the river as she'd be in heaven. And I reckon that by the time there ain't any boats left at all, the Commission will have the old thing all reorganized, and dredged out, and fenced in, and tidied up, to a degree that will make navigation just simply perfect, and absolutely safe and profitable; and all the days will be Sundays, and all the mates will be Sunday-school suWHAT-*in-the-nation-you-fooling-around-there-for, you sons of unrighteousness, heirs of perdition! Going to be a* YEAR *getting that hogshead ashore?"*

During our trip to New Orleans and back, we had many conversations with river men, planters, journalists, and officers of the River Commission — with conflicting and confusing results. To wit:—

1. Some believed in the Commission's scheme to arbitrarily and permanently confine (and thus deepen) the channel, preserve threatened shores, etc.

2. Some believed that the Commission's money ought to be spent only on building and repairing the great system of levees.

3. Some believed that the higher you build your levee, the higher the river's bottom will rise; and that consequently the levee system is a mistake.

4. Some believed in the scheme to relieve the river, in flood-time, by turning its surplus waters off into Lake Borgne, etc.

5. Some believed in the scheme of northern lake-reservoirs to replenish the Mississippi in low-water seasons.

Wherever you find a man down there who believes in one of these theories you may turn to the next man and frame your talk upon the hypothesis that he does *not* believe in that theory; and after you have had experience, you do not take this course doubtfully, or hesitatingly, but with the confidence of a dying murderer—converted one, I mean. For you will have come to know, with a deep and restful certainty, that you are not going to meet two people sick of the same theory, one right after the other. No, there will always be one or two with the other diseases along between. And as you proceed, you will find out one or two other things. You will find out that there is no distemper of the lot but is contagious; and you cannot go where it is without catching it. You may vaccinate yourself with deterrent facts as much as you please—it will do no good; it will seem to "take," but it doesn't; the moment you rub against any one of those theorists, make up your mind that it is time to hang out your yellow flag.

Yes, you are his sure victim: yet his work is not all to your hurt—only part of it; for he is like your family physician, who comes and cures the mumps, and leaves the scarlet-fever behind. If your man is a Lake-Borgne-relief theorist, for instance, he will exhale a cloud of deadly facts and statistics which will lay you out with that disease, sure; but at the same time he will cure you of any other of the five theories that may have previously got into your system.

I have had all the five; and had them "bad;" but ask me not, in mournful numbers, which one racked me hardest, or which one numbered the biggest sick list, for I do not know. In truth, no one can answer the latter question. Mississippi Improvement is a mighty topic, down yonder. Every man on the river banks, south of Cairo, talks about it every day, during such moments as he is able to spare from talking about the war; and each of the several chief theories has its host of zealous partisans; but, as I have said, it is not possible to determine which cause numbers the most recruits.

All were agreed upon one point, however: if Congress would make a sufficient appropriation, a colossal benefit would result. Very well; since then the appropriation has been made—possibly a sufficient one, certainly not too large a one. Let us hope that the prophecy will be amply fulfilled.

One thing will be easily granted by the reader; that an opinion from Mr. Edward Atkinson, upon any vast national commercial matter, comes as near ranking as authority, as can the opinion of any individual in the Union. What he has to say about Mississippi River Improvement will be found in the Appendix.*

Sometimes, half a dozen figures will reveal, as with a lightning-flash, the importance of a subject which ten thousand labored words, with the same purpose in view, had left at last but dim and uncertain. Here is a case of the sort—paragraph from the "Cincinnati Commercial:"—

> "The towboat 'Jos. B. Williams' is on her way to New Orleans with a tow of thirty-two barges, containing six hundred thousand bushels (seventy-six pounds to the bushel) of coal exclusive of her own fuel, being the largest tow ever taken to New Orleans or anywhere else in the world. Her freight bill, at 3 cents a bushel, amounts to $18,000. It would take eighteen hundred cars, of three hundred and thirty-three bushels to the car, to transport this amount of coal. At $10 per ton, or $100 per car, which would be a fair price for the distance by rail, the freight bill would amount to $180,000, or $162,000 more by rail than by river. The tow will be taken from Pittsburg to New Orleans in fourteen or fifteen days. It would take one hundred trains of eighteen cars to the train to transport this one tow of six hundred thousand bushels of coal, and even if it made the usual speed of fast freight lines, it would take one whole summer to put it through by rail."

When a river in good condition can enable one to save $162,00 and a whole summer's time, on a single cargo, the wisdom of taking measures to keep the river in good condition is made plain to even the uncommercial mind.

CHAPTER XXIX

A FEW SPECIMEN BRICKS

We passed through the Plum Point region, turned Craighead's Point, and glided unchallenged by what was once the formidable Fort Pillow, memorable because of the massacre perpetrated there during the war. Massacres are sprinkled with some frequency through the histories of several Christian nations, but this is almost the only one that can be found in American history; perhaps it is the only one which rises to a size

* See Appendix B.

correspondent to that huge and sombre title. We have the "Boston Massacre," where two or three people were killed; but we must bunch Anglo-Saxon history together to find the fellow to the Fort Pillow tragedy; and doubtless even then we must travel back to the days and the performances of Coeur de Lion, that fine "hero," before we accomplish it.

More of the river's freaks. In times past, the channel used to strike above Island 37, by Brandywine Bar, and down towards Island 39. Afterward, changed its course and went from Brandywine down through Vogelman's chute in the Devil's Elbow, to Island 39—part of this course reversing the old order; the river running *up* four or five miles, instead of down, and cutting off, throughout, some fifteen miles of distance. This in 1876. All that region is now called Centennial Island.

There is a tradition that Island 37 was one of the principal abiding places of the once celebrated "Murel's Gang." This was a colossal combination of robbers, horse-thieves, negro-stealers, and counterfeiters, engaged in business along the river some fifty or sixty years ago. While our journey across the country towards St. Louis was in progress we had had no end of Jesse James and his stirring history; for he had just been assassinated by an agent of the Governor of Missouri, and was in consequence occupying a good deal of space in the newspapers. Cheap histories of him were for sale by train boys. According to these, he was the most marvellous creature of his kind that had ever existed. It was a mistake. Murel was his equal in boldness; in pluck; in rapacity; in cruelty, brutality, heartlessness, treachery, and in general and comprehensive vileness and shamelessness; and very much his superior in some larger aspects. James was a retail rascal; Murel, wholesale. James's modest genius dreamed of no loftier flight than the planning of raids upon cars, coaches, and country banks; Murel projected negro insurrections and the capture of New Orleans; and furthermore, on occasion, this Murel could go into a pulpit and edify the congregation. What are James and his half-dozen vulgar rascals compared with this stately old-time criminal, with his sermons, his meditated insurrections and city-captures, and his majestic following of ten hundred men, sworn to do his evil will!

Here is a paragraph or two concerning this big operator, from a now-forgotten book which was published half a century ago.—

> He appears to have been a most dexterous as well as consummate villain. When he travelled, his usual disguise was that of an itinerant preacher; and it is said that his discourses were very "soul-moving"—

interesting the hearers so much that they forgot to look after their horses, which were carried away by his confederates while he was preaching. But the stealing of horses in one State, and selling them in another, was but a small portion of their business; the most lucrative was the enticing slaves to run away from their masters, that they might sell them in another quarter. This was arranged as follows; they would tell a negro that if he would run away from his master, and allow them to sell him, he should receive a portion of the money paid for him, and that upon his return to them a second time they would send him to a free State, where he would be safe. The poor wretches complied with this request, hoping to obtain money and freedom; they would be sold to another master, and run away again to their employers; sometimes they would be sold in this manner three or four times, until they had realized three or four thousand dollars by them; but as, after this, there was fear of detection, the usual custom was to get rid of the only witness that could be produced against them, which was the negro himself, by murdering him, and throwing his body into the Mississippi. Even if it was established that they had stolen a negro, before he was murdered, they were always prepared to evade punishment; for they concealed the negro who had run away, until he was advertised, and a reward offered to any man who would catch him. An advertisement of this kind warrants the person to take the property, if found. And then the negro becomes a property in trust, when, therefore, they sold the negro, it only became a breach of trust, not stealing; and for a breach of trust, the owner of the property can only have redress by a civil action, which was useless, as the damages were never paid. It may be inquired, how it was that Murel escaped Lynch law under such circumstances? This will be easily understood when it is stated that he had *more than a thousand sworn confederates,* all ready at a moment's notice to support any of the gang who might be in trouble. The names of all the principal confederates of Murel were obtained from himself, in a manner which I shall presently explain. The gang was composed of two classes: the Heads or Council, as they were called, who planned and concerted, but seldom acted; they amounted to about four hundred. The other class were the active agents, and were termed strikers, and amounted to about six hundred and fifty. These were the tools in the hands of the others; they ran all the risk, and received but a small portion of the money; they were in the power of the leaders of the gang, who would sacrifice them at any time by handing them over to justice, or sinking their bodies in the Mississippi. The general rendezvous of this gang of miscreants was on the Arkansas side of the river, where they concealed their negroes in the morasses and cane-brakes.

The depredations of this extensive combination were severely felt; but so well were their plans arranged, that although Murel, who was always active, was everywhere suspected, there was no proof to be obtained. It so happened, however, that a young man of the name of Stewart, who was looking after two slaves which Murel had decoyed away, fell in with him and obtained his confidence, took the oath, and was admitted into the gang as one of the General Council. By this means all was discovered; for Stewart turned traitor, although he had taken the oath, and having obtained every information, exposed the whole concern, the names of all the parties, and finally succeeded in bringing home sufficient evidence against Murel, to procure his conviction and sentence to the Penitentiary (Murel was sentenced to fourteen years' imprisonment); so many people who were supposed to be honest, and bore a respectable name in the different States, were found to be among the list of the Grand Council as published by Stewart, that every attempt was made to throw discredit upon his assertions—his character was vilified, and more than one attempt was made to assassinate him. He was obliged to quit the Southern States in consequence. It is, however, now well ascertained to have been all true; and although some blame Mr. Stewart for having violated his oath, they no longer attempt to deny that his revelations were correct. I will quote one or two portions of Murel's confessions to Mr. Stewart, made to him when they were journeying together. I ought to have observed, that the ultimate intentions of Murel and his associates were, by his own account, on a very extended scale; having no less an object in view than *raising the blacks against the whites, taking possession of, and plundering New Orleans, and making themselves possessors of the territory.* The following are a few extracts:—

"I collected all my friends about New Orleans at one of our friends' houses in that place, and we sat in council three days before we got all our plans to our notion; we then determined to undertake the rebellion at every hazard, and make as many friends as we could for that purpose. Every man's business being assigned him, I started to Natchez on foot, having sold my horse in New Orleans,—with the intention of stealing another after I started. I walked four days, and no opportunity offered for me to get a horse. The fifth day, about twelve, I had become tired, and stopped at a creek to get some water and rest a little. While I was sitting on a log, looking down the road the way that I had come, a man came in sight riding on a good-looking horse. The very moment I saw him, I was determined to have his horse, if he was in the garb of a traveller. He rode up, and I saw from his equipage that he was a traveller. I arose and drew an elegant rifle pistol on him and ordered him to dismount. He did so, and I took his horse by the bridle and pointed down the creek, and ordered him to walk before me. He went a few hundred yards and stopped. I hitched his horse, and then made him undress himself, all to his shirt and drawers, and ordered him to turn his back to me. He said, 'If you are determined to kill me, let me have time to pray before I die.' I told him I had no time to hear him pray. He turned around and dropped on his knees, and I shot him through the back of the head. I ripped open his belly and took out his entrails, and sunk him in the creek. I then searched his pockets, and found four hundred dollars and thirty seven cents, and a number of papers that I did not take time to examine. I sunk the pocket-book and papers and his hat, in the creek. His boots were bran-new, and fitted me genteelly; and I put them on and sunk my old shoes in the creek, to atone for them. I rolled up his clothes and put them into his portmanteau, as they were bran-new cloth of the best quality. I mounted as fine a horse as ever I straddled, and directed my course for Natchez in much better style than I had been for the last five days.

"Myself and a fellow by the name of Crenshaw gathered four good horses and started for Georgia. We got in company with a young South Carolinian just before we got to Cumberland Mountain, and Crenshaw soon knew all about his business. He had been to Tennessee to buy a drove of hogs, but when he got there pork was dearer than he calculated, and he declined purchasing. We concluded he was a prize. Crenshaw winked at me; I understood his idea. Crenshaw had travelled the road before, but I never had; we had travelled several miles on the mountain, when he passed near a great precipice; just before we passed it Crenshaw asked me for my whip, which had a pound of lead in the butt; I handed it to him, and he rode up by the side of the South Carolinian, and gave him a blow on the side of the head and tumbled him from his horse; we lit from our horses and fingered his pockets; we got twelve hundred and sixty-two dollars. Crenshaw said he knew a place to hide him, and he gathered him under his arms, and I by his feet, and conveyed him to a deep crevice in the brow of the precipice, and tumbled him into it, and he went out of sight; we then tumbled in his saddle, and took his horse with us, which was worth two hundred dollars.

"We were detained a few days, and during that time our friend went to a little village in the neighborhood and saw the negro advertised (a negro in our possession), and a description of the two men of whom he had been purchased, and giving his suspicions of the men. It was rather squally times, but any port in a storm: we took the negro that night on the bank of a creek which runs by the farm of our friend, and Crenshaw shot him through the head. We took out his entrails and sunk him in the creek.

"He had sold the other negro the third time on Arkansaw River for upwards of five hundred dollars; and then stole him and delivered him into the hand of his friend, who conducted him to a swamp, and veiled the tragic scene, and got the last gleanings and sacred pledge of secrecy; as a game of that kind will not do unless it ends in a mystery to all but the fraternity. He sold the negro, first and last, for nearly two thousand dollars, and then put him forever out of the reach of all pursuers; and they can never graze him unless they can find the negro; and that they cannot do, for his carcass has fed many a tortoise and catfish before this time, and the frogs have sung this many a long day to the silent repose of his skeleton."

We were approaching Memphis, in front of which city, and witnessed by its people, was fought the most famous of the river battles of the Civil War. Two men whom I had served under, in my river days, took part in that fight: Mr. Bixby, head pilot of the Union fleet, and Montgomery, Commodore of the Confederate fleet. Both saw a great deal of active service during the war, and achieved high reputations for pluck and capacity.

As we neared Memphis, we began to cast about for an excuse

to stay with the "Gold Dust" to the end of her course—Vicksburg. We were so pleasantly situated, that we did not wish to make a change. I had an errand of considerable importance to do at Napoleon, Arkansas, but perhaps I could manage it without quitting the "Gold Dust." I said as much; so we decided to stick to present quarters.

The boat was to tarry at Memphis till ten the next morning. It is a beautiful city, nobly situated on a commanding bluff overlooking the river. The streets are straight and spacious, though not paved in a way to incite distempered admiration. No, the admiration must be reserved for the town's sewerage system, which is called perfect; a recent reform, however, for it was just the other way, up to a few years ago—a reform resulting from the lesson taught by a desolating visitation of the yellow-fever. In those awful days the people were swept off by hundreds, by thousands; and so great was the reduction caused by flight and by death together, that the population was diminished three-fourths, and so remained for a time. Business stood nearly still, and the streets bore an empty Sunday aspect.

Here is a picture of Memphis, at that disastrous time, drawn by a German tourist who seems to have been an eyewitness of the scenes which he describes. It is from Chapter VII., of his book, just published, in Leipzig, "Mississippi-Fahrten, von Ernest von Hesse-Wartegg."—

"In August the yellow-fever had reached its extremest height. Daily, hundreds fell a sacrifice to the terrible epidemic. The city was become a mighty graveyard, two-thirds of the population had deserted the place, and only the poor, the aged and the sick, remained behind, a sure prey for the insidious enemy. The houses were closed: little lamps burned in front of many—a sign that here death had entered. Often, several lay dead in a single house; from the windows hung black crape. The stores were shut up, for their owners were gone away or dead.

"Fearful evil! In the briefest space it struck down and swept away even the most vigorous victim. A slight indisposition, then an hour of fever, then the hideous delirium, then—the Yellow Death! On the street corners, and in the squares, lay sick men, suddenly overtaken by the disease; and even corpses, distorted and rigid. Food failed. Meat spoiled in a few hours in the fetid and pestiferous air, and turned black.

"Fearful clamors issue from many houses; then after a season they cease, and all is still: noble, self-sacrificing men come with the coffin, nail it up, and carry it away, to the graveyard. In the night stillness reigns. Only the physicians and the hearses hurry through the streets; and out of the distance, at intervals, comes the muffled thunder of the railway train, which with the speed of the wind, and as if hunted by furies, flies by the pest-ridden city without halting."

But there is life enough there now. The population exceeds forty thousand and is augmenting, and trade is in a flourishing condition. We drove about the city; visited the park and the sociable horde of squirrels there; saw the fine residences, rose-clad and in other ways enticing to the eye; and got a good breakfast at the hotel.

A thriving place is the Good Samaritan City of the Mississippi: has a great wholesale jobbing trade; foundries, machine shops; and manufactories of wagons, carriages, and cotton-seed oil; and is shortly to have cotton mills and elevators.

Her cotton receipts reached five hundred thousand bales last year—an increase of sixty thousand over the year before. Out from her healthy commercial heart issue five trunk lines of railway; and a sixth is being added.

This is a very different Memphis from the one which the vanished and unremembered procession of foreign tourists used to put into their books long time ago. In the days of the now forgotten but once renowned and vigorously hated Mrs. Trollope, Memphis seems to have consisted mainly of one long street of log-houses, with some outlying cabins sprinkled around rearward toward the woods; and now and then a pig, and no end of mud. That was fifty-five years ago. She stopped at the hotel. Plainly it was not the one which gave us our breakfast. She says:—

> "The table was laid for fifty persons, and was nearly full. They ate in perfect silence, and with such astonishing rapidity that their dinner was over literally before ours was begun; the only sounds heard were those produced by the knives and forks, with the unceasing chorus of coughing, *etc.*"

"Coughing, *etc.*" The "etc." stands for an unpleasant word there, a word which she does not always charitably cover up, but sometimes prints. You will find it in the following description of a steamboat dinner which she ate in company with a lot of aristocratic planters; wealthy, well-born, ignorant swells they were, tinselled with the usual harmless military and judicial titles of that old day of cheap shams and windy pretence:—

> "The total want of all the usual courtesies of the table; the voracious rapidity with which the viands were seized and devoured; the strange uncouth phrases and pronunciation; the loathsome spitting from the contamination of which it was absolutely impossible to protect our dresses; the frightful manner of feeding with their knives, till the whole blade seemed to enter into the mouth; and the still more frightful man-

ner of cleaning the teeth afterward with a pocket knife, soon forced us to feel that we were not surrounded by the generals, colonels, and majors of the old world; and that the dinner hour was to be anything rather than an hour of enjoyment.''

CHAPTER XXX

SKETCHES BY THE WAY

It was a big river, below Memphis; banks brimming full, everywhere, and very frequently more than full, the waters pouring out over the land, flooding the woods and fields for miles into the interior; and in places, to a depth of fifteen feet; signs, all about, of men's hard work gone to ruin, and all to be done over again, with straitened means and a weakened courage. A melancholy picture, and a continuous one;—hundreds of miles of it. Sometimes the beacon lights stood in water three feet deep, in the edge of dense forests which extended for miles without farm, wood-yard, clearing, or break of any kind; which meant that the keeper of the light must come in a skiff a great distance to discharge his trust,—and often in desperate weather. Yet I was told that the work is faithfully performed, in all weathers; and not always by men, sometimes by women, if the man is sick or absent. The Government furnishes oil, and pays ten or fifteen dollars a month for the lighting and tending. A Government boat distributes oil and pays wages once a month.

The Ship Island region was as woodsy and tenantless as ever. The island has ceased to be an island; has joined itself compactly to the main shore, and wagons travel, now, where the steamboats used to navigate. No signs left of the wreck of the ''Pennsylvania.'' Some farmer will turn up her bones with his plow one day, no doubt, and be surprised.

We were getting down now into the migrating negro region. These poor people could never travel when they were slaves; so they make up for the privation now. They stay on a plantation till the desire to travel seizes them; then they pack up, hail a steamboat, and clear out. Not for any particular place; no, nearly any place will answer; they only want to be moving. The amount of money on hand will answer the rest of the conundrum of them. If it will take them fifty miles, very well; let it be fifty. If not, a shorter flight will do.

During a couple of days, we frequently answered these hails. Sometimes there was a group of high-water-stained, tumble-down cabins, populous with colored folk, and no whites visible;

with grassless patches of dry ground here and there; a few felled trees, with skeleton cattle, mules, and horses, eating the leaves and gnawing the bark—no other food for them in the flood-wasted land. Sometimes there was a single lonely landing- cabin; near it the colored family that had hailed us; little and big, old and young, roosting on the scant pile of household goods; these consisting of a rusty gun, sone bedticks, chests, tinware, stools, a crippled looking-glass, a venerable arm-chair, and six or eight base-born and spiritless yellow curs, attached to the family by strings. They must have their dogs; can't go without their dogs. Yet the dogs are never willing; they always object; so, one after another, in ridiculous procession, they are dragged aboard; all four feet braced and sliding along the stage, head likely to be pulled off; but the tugger marching determinedly forward, bending to his work, with the rope over his shoulder for better purchase. Sometimes a child is forgotten and left on the bank; but never a dog.

The usual river-gossip going on in the pilot-house. Island No. 63—an island with a lovely "chute," or passage, behind it in the former times. They said Jesse Jamieson, in the "Skylark," had a visiting pilot with him one trip—a poor old broken-down, superannuated fellow—left him at the wheel, at the foot of 63, to run off the watch. The ancient mariner went up through the chute, and down the river outside; and up the chute and down the river again; and yet again and again; and handed the boat over to the relieving pilot, at the end of three hours of honest endeavor, at the same old foot of the island where he had originally taken the wheel! A darkey on shore who had observed the boat go by, about thirteen times, said, " 'clar to gracious, I wouldn't be s'prised if dey's a whole line o' dem Sk'ylarks!"

Anecdote illustrative of influence of reputation in the changing of opinion. The "Eclipse" was renowned for her swiftness. One day she passed along; an old darkey on shore, absorbed in his own matters, did not notice what steamer it was. Presently some one asked:—

"Any boat gone up?"

"Yes, sah."

"Was she going fast?"

"Oh, so-so—loafin' along."

"Now, do you know what boat that was?"

"No, sah."

"Why, uncle, that was the 'Eclipse.' "

"No! Is dat so? Well, I bet it was—cause she jes' went by here a-*sparklin'!*"

Piece of history illustrative of the violent style of some of the people down along here. During the early weeks of high water, A's fence rails washed down on B's ground, and B's rails washed up in the eddy and landed on A's ground. A said, "Let the thing remain so; I will use your rails, and you use mine." But B objected—wouldn't have it so. One day, A came down on B's ground to get his rails. B said, "I'll kill you!" and proceeded for him with his revolver. A said, "I'm not armed." So B, who wished to do only what was right, threw down his revolver; then pulled a knife, and cut A's throat all around, but gave his principal attention to the front, and so failed to sever the jugular. Struggling around, A managed to get his hands on the discarded revolver, and shot B dead with it—and recovered from his own injuries.

Further gossip;—after which, everybody went below to get afternoon coffee, and left me at the wheel, alone. Something presently reminded me of our last hour in St. Louis, part of which I spent on this boat's hurricane deck, aft. I was joined there by a stranger, who dropped into conversation with me—a brisk young fellow, who said he was born in a town in the interior of Wisconsin, and had never seen a steamboat until a week before. Also said that on the way down from La Crosse he had inspected and examined his boat so diligently and with such passionate interest that he had mastered the whole thing from stem to rudder-blade. Asked me where I was from. I answered, New England. "Oh, a Yank!" said he; and went chatting straight along, without waiting for assent or denial. He immediately proposed to take me all over the boat and tell me the names of her different parts, and teach me their uses. Before I could enter protest or excuse, he was already rattling glibly away at his benevolent work; and when I perceived that he was misnaming the things, and inhospitably amusing himself at the expense of an innocent stranger from a far country, I held my peace, and let him have his way. He gave me a world of misinformation; and the further he went, the wider his imagination expanded, and the more he enjoyed his cruel work of deceit. Sometimes, after palming off a particularly fantastic and outrageous lie upon me, he was so "full of laugh" that he had to step aside for a minute, upon one pretext or another, to keep me from suspecting. I staid faithfully by him until his comedy was finished. Then he remarked that he had undertaken to "learn" me all about a steamboat, and had done it; but that if he had overlooked anything, just ask him and he would supply the lack. "Anything about this boat that you don't know the name of or the purpose of, you come to me and I'll tell you." I said I would, and took my departure; disappeared, and approached him from another quarter, whence he could not see me. There he sat, all alone, doubling himself up and writhing this way and that, in the throes of unappeasable laughter. He must have made himself sick; for he was not publicly visible afterward for several days. Meantime, the episode dropped out of my mind.

The thing that reminded me of it now, when I was alone at the wheel, was the spectacle of this young fellow standing in the pilot-house door, with the knob in his hand, silently and severely inspecting me. I don't know when I have seen anybody look so injured as he did. He did not say anything—simply stood there and looked; reproachfully looked and pondered. Finally he shut the door, and started away; halted on the texas a minute; came slowly back and stood in the door again, with that grieved look in his face; gazed upon me a while in meek rebuke, then said:—

"You let me learn you all about a steamboat, *didn't* you?"

"Yes," I confessed.

"Yes, you did—*didn't* you?"

"Yes."

"*You* are the feller that—that—"

Language failed. Pause—impotent struggle for further words—then he gave it up, choked out a deep, strong oath, and departed for good. Afterward I saw him several times below during the trip; but he was cold—would not look at me. Idiot, if he had not been in such a sweat to play his witless practical joke upon me, in the beginning, I would have persuaded his thoughts into some other direction, and saved him from committing that wanton and silly impoliteness.

I had myself called with the four o'clock watch, mornings, for one cannot see too many summer sunrises on the Mississippi. They are enchanting. First, there is the eloquence of silence; for a deep hush broods everywhere. Next, there is the haunting sense of loneliness, isolation, remoteness from the worry and bustle of the world. The dawn creeps in stealthily; the solid walls of black forest soften to gray, and vast stretches of the river open up and reveal themselves; the water is glass-smooth, gives off spectral little wreaths of white mist, there is not the faintest breath of wind, nor stir of leaf; the tranquillity is profound and infinitely satisfying. Then a bird pipes up, another follows, and soon the pipings develop into a jubilant riot of music. You see none of the birds; you simply move through an atmosphere of song which seems to sing itself. When the light has become a little stronger, you have one of the fairest and softest pictures imaginable. You have the intense green of the massed and crowded foliage near by; you see it paling shade by shade in front of you; upon the next projecting cape, a mile off or more, the tint has lightened to the tender young green of spring; the cape beyond that one has almost lost color, and the furthest one, miles away under the horizon, sleeps upon the water a mere dim vapor, and hardly separable from the sky above it and about it. And all this stretch of river is a mirror, and you have the shadowy reflections of the leafage and the curving shores and the receding capes pictured in it. Well, that is all beautiful; soft and rich and beautiful; and when the sun gets well up, and distributes a pink flush here and a powder of gold yonder and a purple haze where it will yield the best effect, you grant that you have seen something that is worth remembering.

We had the Kentucky Bend country in the early morning—scene of a strange and tragic accident in the old times. Captain Poe had a small stern-wheel boat, for years the home of himself and his wife. One night the boat struck a snag in the head of Kentucky Bend, and sank with astonishing suddenness; water already well above the cabin floor when the captain got aft. So he cut into his wife's stateroom from above with an axe; she was asleep in the upper berth, the roof a flimsier one than was supposed; the first blow crashed down through the rotten boards and clove her skull.

This bend is all filled up now—result of a cut-off; and the same agent has taken the great and once much-frequented Walnut Bend, and set it away back in a solitude far from the accustomed track of passing steamers.

Helena we visited, and also a town I had not heard of before, it being of recent birth—Arkansas City. It was born of a railway; the Little Rock, Mississippi River and Texas Railroad touches the river there. We asked a passenger who belonged there what sort of a place it was. "Well," said he, after considering, and with the air of one who wishes to take time and be accurate,"It's a hell of a place." A description which was photographic for exactness. There were several rows and clusters of shabby frame-houses, and a supply of mud sufficient to insure the town against a famine in that article for a hundred years; for the overflow had but lately subsided. There were stagnant ponds in the streets, here and there, and a dozen rude scows were scattered about, lying aground wherever they happened to have been when the waters drained off and people could do their visiting and shopping on foot once more. Still, it is a thriving place, with a rich country behind it, an elevator in front of it, and also a fine big mill for the manufacture of cotton-seed oil. I had never seen this kind of a mill before.

Cotton-seed was comparatively valueless in my time; but it is worth $12 or $13 a ton now, and none of it is thrown away. The oil made from it is colorless, tasteless, and almost if not entirely odorless. It is claimed that it can, by proper manipulation, be made to resemble and perform the office of any and all oils, and be produced at a cheaper rate than the cheapest of the originals. Sagacious people shipped it to Italy, doctored it, labelled it, and brought it back as olive oil. This trade grew to be so formidable that Italy was obliged to put a prohibitory impost upon it to keep it from working serious injury to her oil industry.

Helena occupies one of the prettiest situations on the Mississippi. Her perch is the last, the southernmost group of hills which one sees on that side of the river. In its normal condition it is a pretty town; but the flood (or possibly the seepage) had lately been ravaging it; whole streets of houses had been invaded by the muddy water, and the outsides of the buildings were still belted with a broad stain extending upwards from the foundations. Stranded and discarded scows lay all about; plank sidewalks on stilts four feet high were still standing; the board sidewalks on the ground level were loose and ruinous,—a couple of men trotting along them could make a blind man think a cavalry charge was coming; everywhere the mud was black and deep, and in many places malarious pools of stagnant water were standing. A Mississippi inundation is the next most wasting and desolating infliction to a fire.

We had an enjoyable time here, on this sunny Sunday: two full hours' liberty ashore while the boat discharged freight. In the back streets but few white people were visible, but there were plenty of colored folk—mainly women and girls; and almost without exception upholstered in bright new clothes of swell and elaborate style and cut—a glaring and hilarious contrast to the mournful mud and the pensive puddles.

Helena is the second town in Arkansas, in point of population—which is placed at five thousand. The country about it is exceptionally productive. Helena has a good cotton trade; handles from forty to sixty thousand bales annually; she has a large lumber and grain commerce; has a foundry, oil mills, machine shops and wagon factories—in brief has $1,000,000 invested in manufacturing industries. She has two railways, and is the commercial centre of a broad and prosperous region. Her gross receipts of money, annually, from all sources, are placed by the New Orleans "Times-Democrat" at $4,000,000.

CHAPTER XXXI

A THUMB-PRINT AND WHAT CAME OF IT

We were approaching Napoleon, Arkansas. So I began to think about my errand there. Time, noonday; and bright and sunny. This was bad—not best, anyway; for mine was not (preferably) a noonday kind of errand. The more I thought, the more that fact pushed itself upon me—now in one form, now in another. Finally, it took the form of a distinct question: is it good common sense to do the errand in daytime, when, by a little sacrifice of comfort and inclination, you can have night for it, and no inquisitive eyes around? This settled it. Plain question and plain answer make the shortest road out of most perplexities.

I got my friends into my stateroom, and said I was sorry to create annoyance and disappointment, but that upon reflection it really seemed best that we put our luggage ashore and stop over at Napoleon. Their disapproval was prompt and loud; their language mutinous. Their main argument was one which has always been the first to come to the surface, in such cases, since the beginning of time: "But you decided and *agreed* to stick to this boat, etc.;" as if, having determined to do an unwise thing, one is thereby bound to go ahead and make *two* unwise things of it, by carrying out that determination.

I tried various mollifying tactics upon them, with reasonably good success: under which encouragement, I increased my efforts; and, to show them that *I* had not created this annoying errand, and was in no way to blame for it, I presently drifted into its history—substantially as follows:

Toward the end of last year, I spent a few months in Munich, Bavaria. In November I was living in Fräulein Dahlweiner's *pension,* 1*a,* Karlstrasse; but my working quarters were a mile from there, in the house of a widow who supported herself by taking lodgers. She and her two young children used to drop in every morning and talk German to me—by request. One day, during a ramble about the city, I visited one of the two establishments where the Government keeps and watches corpses until the doctors decide that they are permanently dead, and not in a trance state. It was a grisly place, that spacious room. There were thirty-six corpses of adults in sight, stretched on their backs on slightly slanted boards, in three long rows—all of them with wax-white, rigid faces, and all of them wrapped in white shrouds. Along the sides of the room were deep alcoves, like bay windows; and in each of these lay several marble-visaged babes, utterly hidden and buried under banks of fresh flowers, all but their faces and crossed hands. Around a finger of each of these fifty still forms, both great and small, was a ring; and from the ring a wire led to the ceiling, and thence to a bell in a watch-room yonder, where, day and night, a watchman sits always alert and ready to spring to the aid of any of that pallid company who, waking out of death, shall make a movement—for any even the slightest movement will twitch the wire and ring that fearful bell. I imagined myself a death-sentinel drowsing there alone, far in the dragging watches of some wailing, gusty night, and having in a twinkling all my body stricken to quivering jelly by the sudden clamor of that awful summons! So I inquired about this thing; asked what resulted usually? if the watchman died, and the restored corpse came and did what it could to make his last moments easy? But I was rebuked for trying to feed an idle and frivolous curiosity in so solemn and so mournful a place; and went my way with a humbled crest.

Next morning I was telling the widow my adventure, when she exclaimed—

"Come with me! I have a lodger who shall tell you all you want to know. He has been a night watchman there."

He was a living man, but he did not look it. He was abed, and had his head propped high on pillows; his face was wasted and colorless, his deep-sunken eyes were shut; his hand, lying on his breast, was talon-like, it was so bony and long-fingered. The widow began her introduction of me. The man's eyes opened slowly, and glittered wickedly out from the twilight of their caverns; he frowned a black frown; he lifted his lean hand and waved us peremptorily away. But the widow kept straight on, till she had got out the fact that I was a stranger and an American. The man's face changed at once; brightened, became even eager—and the next moment he and I were alone together.

I opened up in cast-iron German; he responded in quite flexible English; thereafter we gave the German language a permanent rest.

This consumptive and I became good friends. I visited him every day, and we talked about everything. At least, about everything but wives and children. Let anybody's wife or anybody's child be mentioned, and three things always followed: the most gracious and loving and tender light glimmered in the man's eyes for a moment; faded out the next, and in its place came that deadly look which had flamed there the first time I ever saw his lids unclose; thirdly, he ceased from speech, there and then for that day; lay silent, abstracted, and absorbed; apparently heard nothing that I said; took no notice of my good-byes, and plainly did not know, by either sight or hearing, when I left the room.

When I had been this Karl Ritter's daily and sole intimate during two months, he one day said, abruptly,—

"I will tell you my story."

A DYING MAN'S CONFESSION

Then he went on as follows:—

I have never given up, until now. But now I have given up. I am going to die. I made up my mind last night that it must be, and very soon, too. You say you are going to revisit your river, by and by, when you find opportunity. Very well; that, together with a certain strange experience which fell to my lot last night, determines me to tell you my history—for you will see Napoleon, Arkansas; and for my sake you will stop there, and do a certain thing for me—a thing which you will willingly undertake after you shall have heard my narrative.

Let us shorten the story wherever we can, for it will need it, being long. You already know how I came to go to America, and how I came to settle in that lonely region in the South. But you do not know that I had a wife. My wife was young, beautiful, loving, and oh, so divinely good and blameless and gentle! And our little girl was her mother in miniature. It was the happiest of happy households.

One night—it was toward the close of the war—I woke up out of a sodden lethargy, and found myself bound and gagged, and the air tainted with chloroform! I saw two men in the room, and one was saying to the other, in a hoarse whisper, "I *told* her I would, if she made a noise, and as for the child—"

The other man interrupted in a low, half-crying voice—

"You said we'd only gag them and rob them, not hurt them; or I wouldn't have come."

"Shut up your whining; *had* to change the plan when they waked up; you done all *you* could to protect them, now let that satisfy you; come, help rummage."

Both men were masked, and wore coarse, ragged "nigger" clothes; they had a bull's-eye lantern, and by its light I noticed that the gentler robber had no thumb on his right hand. They rummaged around my poor cabin for a moment; the head bandit then said, in his stage whisper,—

"It's a waste of time—*he* shall tell where it's hid. Undo his gag, and revive him up."

The other said—

"All right—provided no clubbing."

"No clubbing it is, then—provided he keeps still."

They approached me; just then there was a sound outside; a sound of voices and trampling hoofs; the robbers held their breath and listened; the sounds came slowly nearer and nearer; then came a shout—

"*Hello*, the house! Show a light, we want water."

"The captain's voice, by G—!" said the stage-whispering ruffian, and both robbers fled by the way of the back door, shutting off their bull's-eye as they ran.

The strangers shouted several times more, then rode by—there seemed to be a dozen of the horses—and I heard nothing more.

I struggled, but could not free myself from my bonds. I tried to speak, but the gag was effective; I could not make a sound. I listened for my wife's voice and my child's—listened long and intently, but no sound came from the other end of the room where their bed was. This silence became more and more awful, more and more ominous, every moment. Could you have endured an hour of it, do you think? Pity me, then, who had to endure three. Three hours?—it was three ages! Whenever the clock struck, it seemed as if years had gone by since I had heard it last. All this time I was struggling in my bonds; and at last, about dawn, I got myself free, and rose up and stretched my stiff limbs. I was able to distinguish details pretty well. The floor was littered with things thrown there by the robbers during their search for my savings. The first object that caught my particular attention was a document of mine which I had seen the rougher of the two ruffians glance at and then cast away. It had blood on it! I staggered to the other end of the room. Oh, poor unoffending, helpless ones, there they lay, their troubles ended, mine begun!

Did I appeal to the law—I? Does it quench the pauper's thirst if the King drink for him? Oh, no, no, no—I wanted no impertinent interference of the law. Laws and the gallows could not pay the debt that was owing to me! Let the laws leave the matter in my hands, and have no fears: I would find the debtor and collect the debt. How accomplish this, do you say? How accomplish it, and feel so sure about it, when I had neither seen the robbers' faces, nor heard their natural voices, nor had any idea who they might be? Nevertheless, I *was* sure—quite sure, quite confident. I had a clue—a clue which you would not have valued—a clue which would not have greatly helped even a detective, since he would lack the secret of how to apply it. I shall come to that, presently—you shall see. Let us go on, now, taking things in their due order. There was one circumstance which gave me a slant in a definite direction to begin with: Those two robbers were manifestly soldiers in tramp disguise; and not new to military service, but old in it—regulars, perhaps; they did not acquire their soldierly attitude, gestures, carriage, in a day, nor a month, nor yet in a year. So I thought, but said nothing. And one of them had said, "the captain's voice, by G—!"—the one whose life I would have. Two miles away, several regiments were in camp, and two companies of U.S. cavalry. When I learned that Captain Blakely, of Company C had passed our way, that night, with an escort, I said nothing, but in that company I resolved to seek my man. In conversation I studiously and persistently described the robbers as tramps, camp followers; and among this class the people made useless search, none suspecting the soldiers but me.

Working patiently, by night, in my desolated home, I made a disguise for myself out of various odds and ends of clothing; in the nearest village I bought a pair of blue goggles. By and by, when the military camp broke up, and Company C was ordered a hundred miles north, to Napoleon, I secreted my small hoard of money in my belt, and took my departure in the night. When Company C arrived in Napoleon, I was already there. Yes, I was there, with a new trade—fortune-teller. Not to seem partial, I made friends and told fortunes among all the companies garrisoned there; but I gave Company C the great bulk of my attentions. I made myself limitlessly obliging to these particular men; they could ask me no favor, put upon me no risk, which I would decline. I became the willing butt of their jokes; this perfected my popularity; I became a favorite.

I early found a private who lacked a thumb—what joy it was to me! And when I found that he alone, of all the company, had lost a thumb, my last misgiving vanished; I was *sure* I was on the right track. This man's name was Kruger, a German. There were nine Germans in the company. I watched, to see who might be his intimates; but he seemed to have no especial intimates. But *I* was his intimate; and I took care to make the intimacy grow. Sometimes I so hungered for my revenge that I could hardly restrain myself from going on my knees and begging him to point out the man who had murdered my wife and child; but I managed to bridle my tongue. I bided my time, and went on telling fortunes, as opportunity offered.

My apparatus was simple: a little red paint and a bit of white paper. I painted the ball of the client's thumb, took a print of it on the paper, studied it that night, and revealed his fortune to him next day. What was my idea in this nonsense? It was this: When I was a youth, I knew an old Frenchman who had been a prison-keeper for thirty years, and he told me that there was one thing about a person which never changed, from the cradle to the grave—the lines in the ball of the thumb; and he said that these lines were never exactly alike in the thumbs of any two human beings. In these days, we photograph the new criminal, and hang his picture in the Rogues' Gallery for future reference; but that Frenchman, in his day, used to take a print of the ball of a new prisoner's thumb and put that away for future reference. He always said that pictures were no good—future disguises could make them useless; "The thumb's the only sure thing," said he; "you can't disguise that." And he used to prove his theory, too, on my friends and acquaintances; it always succeeded.

I went on telling fortunes. Every night I shut myself in, all alone, and studied the day's thumb-prints with a magnifying-glass. Imagine the devouring eagerness with which I pored over those mazy red spirals, with that document by my side which bore the right-hand thumb-and finger-marks of that unknown murderer, printed with the dearest blood—to me—that was ever shed on this earth! And many and many a time I had to repeat the same old disappointed remark, "will they *never* correspond!"

But my reward came at last. It was the print of the thumb of the forty-third man of Company C whom I had experimented on—private Franz Adler. An hour before, I did not know the murderer's name, or voice, or figure, or face, or nationality; but now I knew all these things! I believed I might feel sure; the Frenchman's repeated demonstrations being so good a warranty. Still, there was a way to *make* sure. I had an impression of Kruger's left thumb. In the morning I took him aside when he was off duty; and when we were out of sight and hearing of witnesses, I said, impressively:—

"A part of your fortune is so grave, that I thought it would be better for you if I did not tell it in public. You and another man, whose fortune I was studing last night,—private Adler,— have been murdering a woman and a child! You are being dogged: within five days both of you will be assassinated."

He dropped on his knees, frightened out of his wits; and for five minutes he kept pouring out the same set of words, like a demented person, and in the same half-crying way which was one of my memories of that murderous night in my cabin:—

"I didn't do it; upon my soul I didn't do it; and I tried to keep *him* from doing it; I did, as God is my witness. He did it alone."

This was all I wanted. And I tried to get rid of the fool; but no, he clung to me, imploring me to save him from the assassin. He said,—

"I have money—ten thousand dollars—hid away, the fruit of

loot and thievery; save me—tell me what to do, and you shall have it, every penny. Two thirds of it is my cousin Adler's; but you can take it all. We hid it when we first came here. But I hid it in a new place yesterday, and have not told him—shall not tell him. I was going to desert, and get away with it all. It is gold, and too heavy to carry when one is running and dodging; but a woman who has been gone over the river two days to prepare my way for me is going to follow me with it; and if I got no chance to describe the hiding-place to her I was going to slip my silver watch into her hand, or send it to her, and she would understand. There's a piece of paper in the back of the case, which tells it all. Here, take the watch—tell me what to do!"

He was trying to press his watch upon me, and was exposing the paper and explaining it to me, when Adler appeared on the scene, about a dozen yards away. I said to poor Kruger:—

"Put up your watch, I don't want it. You shan't come to any harm. Go, now; I must tell Adler his fortune. Presently I will tell you how to escape the assassin; meantime shall have to examine your thumb-mark again. Say nothing to Adler about this thing—say nothing to anybody."

He went away filled with fright and gratitude, poor devil. I told Adler a long fortune,—purposely so long that I could not finish it; promised to come to him on guard, that night, and tell him the really important part of it—the tragical part of it, I said,—so must be out of reach of eavesdroppers. They always kept a picket-watch outside the town,—mere discipline and ceremony,—no occasion for it, no enemy around.

Toward midnight I set out, equipped with the counter-sign, and picked my way toward the lonely region where Adler was to keep his watch. It was so dark that I stumbled right on a dim figure almost before I could get out a protecting word. The sentinel hailed and I answered, both at the same moment. I added, "It's only me—the fortune-teller." Then I slipped to the poor devil's side, and without a word I drove my dirk into his heart! *Ja wohl*, laughed I, it *was* the tragedy part of his fortune, indeed! As he fell from his horse, he clutched at me, and my blue goggles remained in his hand; and away plunged the beast dragging him, with his foor in the stirrup.

I fled through the woods, and made good my escape, leaving the accusing goggles behind me in that dead man's hand.

This was fifteen or sixteen years ago. Since then I have wandered aimlessly about the earth, sometimes at work, sometimes idle; sometimes with money, sometimes with none; but always tired of life, and wishing it was done, for my mission here was finished, with the act of that night; and the only pleasure, solace, satisfaction I had, in all those tedious years, was in the daily reflection, "I have killed him!"

Four years ago, my health began to fail. I had wandered into Munich, in my purposeless way. Being out of money, I sought work, and got it; did my duty faithfully about a year, and was then given the berth of night watchman yonder in that dead-house which you visited lately. The place suited my mood. I liked it. I liked being with the dead—liked being alone with them. I used to wander among those rigid corpses, and peer into their austere faces, by the hour. The later the time, the more impressive it was; I preferred the late time. Sometimes I turned the lights low: this gave perspective, you see; and the imagination could play; always, the dim receding ranks of the dead inspired one with weird and fascinating fancies. Two years ago—I had been there a year then—I was sitting all alone in the watch-room, one gusty winter's night, chilled, numb, comfortless; drowsing gradually into unconsciousness; the sobbing of the wind and the slamming of distant shutters falling fainter and fainter upon my dulling ear each moment, when sharp and suddenly that dead-bell rang out a blood-curdling alarum over my head! The shock of it nearly paralyzed me; for it was the first time I had ever heard it.

I gathered myself together and flew to the corpse-room. About midway down the outside rank, a shrouded figure was sitting upright, wagging its head slowly from one side to the other—a grisly spectacle! Its side was toward me. I hurried to it and peered into its face. Heavens, it was Adler!

Can you divine what my first thought was? Put into words, it was this: "It seems, then, you escaped me once: there will be a different result this time!"

Evidently this creature was suffering unimaginable terrors. Think what it must have been to wake up in the midst of that voiceless hush, and look over that grim congregation of the dead! What gratitude shone in his skinny white face when he saw a living form before him! And how the fervency of this mute gratitude was augmented when his eyes fell upon the life-giving cordials which I carried in my hands! Then imagine the horror which came into this pinched face when I put the cordials behind me, and said mockingly,—

"Speak up, Franz Adler—call upon these dead. Doubtless they will listen and have pity; but here there is none else that will."

He tried to speak, but that part of the shroud which bound his jaws, held firm and would not let him. He tried to lift imploring hands, but they were crossed upon his breast and tied. I said—

"Shout, Franz Adler; make the sleepers in the distant streets hear you and bring help. Shout—and lose no time, for there is little to lose. What, you cannot? That is a pity; but it is no matter—it does not always bring help. When you and your cousin murdered a helpless woman and child in a cabin in Arkansas—my wife, it was, and my child!—they shrieked for help, you remember; but it did no good; you remember that it did no good, is it not so? Your teeth chatter—then why cannot you shout? Loosen the bandages with your hands—then you can. Ah, I see—your hands are tied, they cannot aid you. How strangely things repeat themselves, after long years; for *my* hands were tied, that night, you remember? Yes, tied much as yours are now—how odd that is. I could not pull free. It did not occur to you to untie me; it does not occur to me to untie you. Sh—! there's a late footstep. It is coming this way. Hark, how near it is! One can count the footfalls—one—two—three. There—it is just outside. Now is the time! Shout, man, shout!—it is the one sole chance between you and eternity! Ah, you see you have delayed too long—it is gone by. There—it is dying out. It is gone! Think of it—reflect upon it—you have heard a human footstep for the last time. How curious it must be, to listen to so common a sound as that, and know that one will never hear the fellow to it again."

Oh, my friend, the agony in that shrouded face was ecstasy to see! I thought of a new torture, and applied it—assisting myself with a trifle of lying invention:—

"That poor Kruger tried to save my wife and child, and I did him a grateful good turn for it when the time came. I persuaded him to rob you; and I and a woman helped him to desert, and got him away in safety."

A look as of surprise and triumph shone out dimly through the anguish in my victim's face. I was disturbed, disquieted. I said—

"What, then,—didn't he escape?"

A negative shake of the head.

"No? What happened, then?"

The satisfaction in the shrouded face was still plainer. The man tried to mumble out some words—could not succeed; tried to express something with his obstructed hands—failed; paused a moment, then feebly tilted his head, in a meaning way, toward the corpse that lay nearest him.

"Dead?" I asked. "Failed to escape?—caught in the act and shot?"

Negative shake of the head.

"How, then?"

Again the man tried to do something with his hands. I watched closely, but could not guess the intent. I bent over and watched still more intently. He had twisted a thumb around and was weakly punching at his breast with it.

"Ah—stabbed, do you mean?"

Affirmative nod, accompanied by a spectral smile of such peculiar devilishness, that it struck an awakening light through my dull brain, and I cried—

"Did *I* stab him, mistaking him for you?—for that stroke was meant for none but you."

The affirmative nod of the re-dying rascal was as joyous as his failing strength was able to put into its expression.

"O, miserable, miserable me, to slaughter the pitying soul that stood a friend to my darlings when they were helpless, and would have saved them if he could! miserable, oh, miserable, miserable me!"

I fancied I heard the muffled gurgle of a mocking laugh. I took my face out of my hands, and saw my enemy sinking back upon his inclined board.

He was a satisfactory long time dying. He had a wonderful vitality, an astonishing constitution. Yes, he was a pleasant long time at it. I got a chair and a newspaper, and sat down by him and read. Occasionally I took a sip of brandy. This was necessary, on account of the cold. But I did it partly because I saw, that along at first, whenever I reached for the bottle, he thought I was going to give him some. I read aloud: mainly imaginary accounts of people snatched from the grave's threshold and restored to life and vigor by a few spoonsful of liquor and a warm bath. Yes, he had a long, hard death of it—three hours and six minutes, from the time he rang his bell.

It is believed that in all these eighteen years that have elapsed since the institution of the corpse-watch, no shrouded occupant of the Bavarian dead-houses has ever rung its bell. Well, it is a harmless belief. Let it stand at that.

The chill of that death-room had penetrated my bones. It revived and fastened upon me the disease which had been afflicting me, but which, up to that night, had been steadily disappearing. That man murdered my wife and my child; and in three days hence he will have added me to his list. No matter—God! how delicious the memory of it!—I caught him escaping from his grave, and thrust him back into it!

After that night, I was confined to my bed for a week; but as soon as I could get about, I went to the dead-house books and got the number of the house which Adler had died in. A wretched lodging house, it was. It was my idea that he would naturally have gotten hold of Kruger's effects, being his cousin; and I wanted to get Kruger's watch, if I could. But while I was sick, Adler's things had been sold and scattered, all except a few old letter, and some odds and ends of no value. However, through those letters, I traced out a son of Kruger's, the only relative he left. He is a man of thirty, now, a shoemaker by trade, and living at No. 14 Königstrasse, Mannheim—widower, with several small children. Without explaining to him why, I have furnished two thirds of his support, ever since.

Now, as to that watch—see how strangely things happen! I traced it around and about Germany for more than a year, at considerable cost in money and vexation; and at last I got it. Got it, and was unspeakably glad; opened it, and found nothing in it! Why, I might have known that that bit of paper was not going to stay there all this time. Of course I gave up that ten thousand dollars then; gave it up, and dropped it out of my mind: and most sorrowfully, for I had wanted it for Kruger's son.

Last night, when I consented at last that I must die, I began to make ready. I proceeded to burn all useless papers; and sure enough, from a batch of Adler's, not previously examined with thoroughness, out dropped that long-desired scrap! I recognized it in a moment. Here it is—I will translate it:

> "Brick livery stable, stone foundation, middle of town, corner of Orleans and Market. Corner toward Court-house. Third stone, fourth row. Stick notice there, saying how many are to come."

There—take it, and preserve it. Kruger explained that that stone was removable; and that it was in the north wall of the foundation, fourth row from the top, and third stone from the west. The money is secreted behind it. He said the closing sentence was a blind, to mislead in case the paper should fall into wrong hands. It probably performed that office for Adler.

Now I want to beg that when you make your intended journey down the river, you will hunt out that hidden money, and send it to Adam Kruger, care of the Mannheim address which I have mentioned. It will make a rich man of him, and I shall sleep the sounder in my grave for knowing that I have done what I could for the son of the man who tried to save my wife and child—albeit my hand ignorantly struck him down, whereas the impulse of my heart would have been to shield and serve him.

CHAPTER XXXII

THE DISPOSAL OF A BONANZA

"Such was Ritter's narrative," said I to my two friends.

There was a profound and impressive silence, which lasted a considerable time; then both men broke into a fusillade of excited and admiring ejaculations over the strange incidents of the tale; and this, along with a rattling fire of questions, was kept up until all hands were about out of breath. Then my friends began to cool down, and draw off, under shelter of occasional volleys, into silence and abysmal reverie. For ten minutes now, there was stillness. Then Rogers said dreamily:—

"Ten thousand dollars." Adding, after a considerable pause,—

"Ten thousand. It is a heap of money."

Presently the poet inquired,—

"Are you going to send it to him right away?"

"Yes," I said. "It is a queer question."

No reply. After a little, Rogers asked, hesitatingly:

"*All* of it?— That is— I mean—"

"*Certainly,* all of it."

I was going to say more, but stopped,—was stopped by a train of thought which started up in me. Thompson spoke, but my mind was absent and I did not catch what he said. But I heard Rogers answer,—

"Yes, it seems so to me. It ought to be quite sufficient; for I don't see that *he* has done anything."

Presently the poet said,—

"When you come to look at it, it is *more* than sufficient. Just look at it—five thousand dollars! Why, he couldn't spend it in a lifetime! And it would injure him, too; perhaps ruin him—you want to look at that. In a little while he would throw his last away, shut up his shop, maybe take to drinking, maltreat his motherless children, drift into other evil courses, go steadily from bad to worse—"

"Yes, that's it," interrupted Rogers, fervently, "I've seen it a hundred times—yes, more than a hundred. You put money into the hands of a man like that, if you want to destroy him, that's all; just put money into his hands, it's all you've got to do; and if it don't pull him down, and take all the usefulness out of him, and all the self-respect and everything, then I don't know human nature—ain't that so, Thompson? And even if we were to give him a *third* of it; why, in less than six months—"

"Less than six *weeks,* you'd better say!" said I, warming up and breaking in. "Unless he had that three thousand dollars in safe hands where he couldn't touch it, he would no more last you six weeks than—"

"Of *course* he wouldn't," said Thompson; "I've edited books for that kind of people; and the moment they get their hands on the royalty—maybe it's three thousand, maybe it's two thousand—"

"What business has that shoemaker with two thousand dollars, I should like to know?" broke in Rogers, earnestly. "A man perhaps perfectly contented now, there in Mannheim, surrounded by his own class, eating his bread with the appetite which laborious industry alone can give, enjoying his humble life, honest, upright, pure in heart; and *blest!*—yes, I say blest! blest above all the myriads that go in silk attire and walk the empty artificial round of social folly—but just you put *that* temptation before him once! just you lay fifteen hundred dollars before a man like that, and say—"

"Fifteen hundred devils!" cried I, "*five* hundred would rot his principles, paralyze his industry, drag him to the rumshop, thence to the gutter, thence to the almshouse, thence to—"

"*Why* put upon ourselves this crime, gentlemen?" interrupted the poet earnestly and appealingly. "He is happy where he is, and *as* he is. Every sentiment of honor, every sentiment of charity, every sentiment of high and sacred benevolence warns us, beseeches us, commands us to leave him undisturbed. That is real friendship, that is true friendship. We could follow other courses that would be more showy; but none that would be so truly kind and wise, depend upon it."

After some further talk, it became evident that each of us, down in his heart, felt some misgivings over this settlement of the matter. It was manifest that we all felt that we ought to send the poor shoemaker *something*. There was long and thoughtful discussion of this point; and we finally decided to send him a chromo.

Well, now that everything seemed to be arranged satisfactorily to everybody concerned, a new trouble broke out: it transpired that these two men were expecting to share equally in the money with me. That was not my idea. I said that if they got half of it between them they might consider themselves lucky. Rogers said:—

"Who would have had *any* if it hadn't been for me? I flung out the first hint—but for that it would all have gone to the shoemaker."

Thompson said that he was thinking of the thing himself at the very moment that Rogers had originally spoken.

I retorted that the idea would have occurred to me plenty soon enough, and without anybody's help. I was slow about thinking, maybe, but I was sure.

This matter warmed up into a quarrel; then into a fight; and each man got pretty badly battered. As soon as I had got myself mended up after a fashion, I ascended to the hurricane deck in a pretty sour humor. I found Captain McCord there, and said, as pleasantly as my humor would permit:—

"I have come to say good-bye, captain. I wish to go ashore at Napoleon."

"Go ashore where?"

"Napoleon."

The captain laughed; but seeing that I was not in a jovial mood, stopped that and said,—

"But are you serious?"

"Serious? I certainly am."

"The captain glanced up at the pilot-house and said,—

"He wants to get off at Napoleon!"

"Napoleon?"

"That's what he says."

"Great Caesar's ghost!"

Uncle Mumford approached along the deck. The captain said,—

"Uncle, here's a friend of yours wants to get off at Napoleon!"

"Well, by—!"

I said,—

"Come, what is all this about? Can't a man go ashore at Napoleon if he wants to?"

"Why, hang it, don't you know? There *isn't* any Napoleon any more. Hasn't been for years and years. The Arkansas River burst through it, tore it all to rags, and emptied it into the Mississippi!"

"Carried the *whole* town away?—banks, churches, jails, newspaper-offices, court-house, theatre, fire department, livery stable,*—everything?"*

"Everything. Just a fifteen-minute job, or such a matter. Didn't leave hide nor hair, shred nor shingle of it, except the fag-end of a shanty and one brick chimney. This boat is paddling along right now, where the dead-centre of that town used to be; yonder is the brick chimney,—all that's left of Napoleon. These dense woods on the right used to be a mile back of the town.

Take a look behind you—up-stream—now you begin to recognize this country, don't you?''

''Yes, I do recognize it now. It is the most wonderful thing I ever heard of; by a long shot the most wonderful—and unexpected.''

Mr. Thompson and Mr. Rogers had arrived, meantime, with satchels and umbrellas, and had silently listened to the captain's news. Thompson put a half-dollar in my hand and said softly:—

''For my share of the chromo.''

Rogers followed suit.

Yes, it was an astonishing thing to see the Mississippi rolling between unpeopled shores and straight over the spot where I used to see a good big self-complacent town twenty years ago. Town that was county-seat of a great and important county; town with a big United States marine hospital; town of innumerable fights—an inquest every day; town where I had used to know the prettiest girl, and the most accomplished in the whole Mississippi Valley; town where we were handed the first printed news of the ''Pennsylvania's'' mournful disaster a quarter of a century ago; a town no more—swallowed up, vanished, gone to feed the fishes; nothing left but a fragment of a shanty and a crumbling brick chimney!

CHAPTER XXXIII

REFRESHMENTS AND ETHICS

In regard to Island 74, which is situated not far from the former Napoleon, a freak of the river here has sorely perplexed the laws of men and made them a vanity and a jest. When the State of Arkansas was chartered, she controlled ''to the centre of the river''—a most unstable line. The State of Mississippi claimed ''to the channel''—another shifty and unstable line. No. 74 belonged to Arkansas. By and by a cut-off threw this big island out of Arkansas, and yet not *within* Mississippi. ''Middle of the river'' on one side of it, ''channel'' on the other. That is as I understand the problem. Whether I have got the details right or wrong, this *fact* remains: that here is this big and exceedingly valuable island of four thousand acres, thrust out in the cold, and belonging to neither the one State nor the other; paying taxes to neither, owing allegiance to neither. One man owns the whole island, and of right is ''the man without a country.''

Island 92 belongs to Arkansas. The river moved it over and joined it to Mississippi. A chap established a whiskey shop there, without a Mississippi license, and enriched himself upon Mississippi custom under Arkansas protection (where no license was in those days required).

We glided steadily down the river in the usual privacy—steamboat or other moving thing seldom seen. Scenery as always: stretch upon stretch of almost unbroken forest, on both sides of the river; soundless solitude. Here and there a cabin or two, standing in small openings on the gray and grassless banks—cabins which had formerly stood a quarter or half-mile farther to the front, and gradually been pulled farther and farther back as the shores caved in. As at Pilcher's Point, for instance, where the cabins had been moved back three hundred yards in three months, so we were told; but the caving banks had already caught up with them, and they were being conveyed rearward once more.

Napoleon had but small opinion of Greenville, Mississippi, in the old times; but behold, Napoleon is gone to the catfishes, and here is Greenville full of life and activity, and making a considerable flourish in the Valley; having three thousand inhabitants, it is said, and doing a gross trade of $2,500,000 annually. A growing town.

There was much talk on the boat about the Calhoun Land Company, an enterprise which is expected to work wholesome results. Colonel Calhoun, a grandson of the statesman, went to Boston and formed a syndicate which purchased a large tract of land on the river, in Chicot County, Arkansas,—some ten thousand acres—for cotton-growing. The purpose is to work on a cash basis: buy at first hands, and handle their own product; supply their negro laborers with provisions and necessaries at a trifling profit, say 8 or 10 per cent; furnish them comfortable quarters, etc., and encourage them to save money and remain on the place. If this proves a financial success, as seems quite certain, they propose to establish a banking-house in Greenville, and lend money at an unburdensome rate of interest—6 per cent is spoken of.

The trouble heretofore has been—I am quoting remarks of planters and steamboatmen—that the planters, although owning the land, were without cash capital; had to hypothecate both land and crop to carry on the business. Consequently, the commission dealer who furnishes the money takes some risk and demands big interest—usually 10 per cent, and 2½ per cent for negotiating the loan. The planter has also to buy his supplies through the same dealer, paying commissions and profits. Then when he ships his crop, the dealer adds his commissions, insurance, etc. So, taking it by and large, and first and last, the dealer's share of that crop is about 25 per cent.*

A cotton-planter's estimate of the average margin of profit on planting, in his section: One man and mule will raise ten acres of cotton, giving ten bales cotton, worth, say, $500; cost of producing, say $350; net profit, $150, or $15 per acre. There is also a profit now from the cotton-seed, which formerly had little value—none where much transportation was necessary. In sixteen hundred pounds crude cotton, four hundred are lint, worth, say, ten cents a pound; and twelve hundred pounds of seed, worth $12 or $13 per ton. Maybe in future even the *stems* will not be thrown away. Mr. Edward Atkinson says that for each bale of cotton there are fifteen hundred pounds of stems, and that these are very rich in phosphate of lime and potash; that when ground and mixed with ensilage or cotton-seed meal (which is too rich for use as fodder in large quantities), the stem mixture makes a superior food, rich in all the elements needed for the production of milk, meat, and bone. Heretofore the stems have been considered a nuisance.

Complaint is made that the planter remains grouty toward the former slave, since the war; will have nothing but a chill business relation with him, no sentiment permitted to intrude; will not keep a "store" himself, and supply the negro's wants and thus protect the negro's pocket and make him able and willing to stay on the place and an advantage to him to do it, but lets that privilege to some thrifty Israelite, who encourages the thoughtless negro and wife to buy all sorts of things which they could do without,—buy on credit, at big prices, month after month, credit based on the negro's share of the growing crop; and at the end of the season, the negro's share belongs to the Israelite, the negro is in debt besides, is discouraged, dissatisfied, restless, and both he and the planter are injured; for he will take steamboat and migrate, and the planter must get a stranger in his place who does not know him, does not care for him, will flatten the Israelite a season, and follow his predecessor per steamboat.

It is hoped that the Calhoun Company will show, by its humane and protective treatment of its laborers, that its method is the most profitable for both planter and negro; and it is believed that a general adoption of that method will then follow.

*"But what can the state do where the people are under subjection to rates of interest ranging from 18 to 30 per cent, and are also under the necessity of purchasing their crops in advance even of planting, at these rates, for the privilege of purchasing all their supplies at 100 per cent profit?"—*Edward Atkinson.*

And where so many are saying their say, shall not the barkeeper testify? He is thoughtful, observant, never drinks; endeavors to earn his salary, and *would* earn it if there were custom enough. He says the people along here in Mississippi and Louisiana will send up the river to buy vegetables rather than raise them, and they will come aboard at the landings and buy fruits of the barkeeper. Thinks they "don't know anything but cotton;" believes they don't know how to raise vegetables and fruit—"at least the most of them." Says "a nigger will go to H for a watermelon" ("H" is all I find in the stenographer's report—means Halifax probably, though that seems a good way to go for a watermelon). Barkeeper buys watermelons for five cents up the river, brings them down and sells them for fifty. "Why does he mix such elaborate and picturesque drinks for the nigger hands on the boat?" Because they won't have any other. "They want a *big* drink; don't make any difference what you make it of, they want the worth of their money. You give a nigger a plain gill of half-a-dollar brandy for five cents—will he touch it? No. Ain't size enough to it. But you put up a pint of all kinds of worthless rubbish, and heave in some red stuff to make it beautiful—red's the main thing—and he wouldn't put down that glass to go to a circus." All the bars on this Anchor Line are rented and owned by one firm. They furnish the liquors from their own establishment, and hire the barkeepers "on salary." Good liquors? Yes, on some of the boats, where there are the kind of passengers that want it and can pay for it. On the other boats? No. Nobody but the deck hands and firemen to drink it. "Brandy? Yes, I've got brandy, plenty of it; but you don't want any of it unless you've made your will." It isn't as it used to be in the old times. Then everybody travelled by steamboat, everybody drank, and everybody treated everybody else. "Now most everybody goes by railroad, and the rest don't drink." In the old times, the barkeeper owned the bar himself, "and was gay and smarty and talky and all jewelled up, and was the toniest aristocrat on the boat; used to make $2,000 on a trip. A father who left his son a steamboat bar, left him a fortune. Now he leaves him board and lodging; yes, and washing, if a shirt a trip will do. Yes, indeedy, times are changed. Why, do you know, on the principal line of boats on the Upper Mississippi, they don't have any bar at all! Sounds like poetry, but it's the petrified truth."

CHAPTER XXXIV

TOUGH YARNS

Stack Island. I remembered Stack Island; also Lake Providence, Louisiana—which is the first distinctly Southern- looking town you come to, downward-bound; lies level and low, shade-trees hung with venerable gray beards of Spanish moss; "restful, pensive, Sunday aspect about the place," commends Uncle Mumford, with feeling—also with truth.

A Mr. H. furnished some minor details of fact concerning this region which I would have hesitated to believe if I had not known him to be a steamboat mate. He was a passenger of ours, a resident of Arkansas City, and bound to Vicksburg to join his boat, a little Sunflower packet. He was an austere man, and had the reputation of being singularly unworldly, for a river man. Among other things, he said that Arkansas had been injured and kept back by generations of exaggerations concerning the mosquitoes there. One may smile, said he, and turn the matter off as being a small thing; but when you come to look at the effects produced, in the way of discouragement of immigration, and diminished values of property, it was quite the opposite of a small thing, or thing in any wise to be coughed down or sneered at. These mosquitoes had been persistently represented as being formidable and lawless; whereas "the truth is, they are feeble, insignificant in size, diffident to a fault, sensitive"—and so on, and so on; you would have supposed he was talking about his family. But if he was soft on the Arkansas mosquitoes, he was hard enough on the mosquitoes of Lake Providence to make up for it—"those Lake Providence colossi," as he finely called them. He said that two of them could whip a dog, and that four of them could hold a man down; and except help come, they would kill him—"butcher him," as he expressed it. Referred in a sort of casual way—and yet significant way—to "the fact that the life policy in its simplest form is unknown in Lake Providence—they take out a mosquito policy besides." He told many remarkable things about those lawless insects. Among others, said he had seen them try to *vote*. Noticing that this statement seemed to be a good deal of a strain on us, he modified it a little: said he might have been mistaken, as to that particular, but knew he had seen them around the polls "canvassing."

There was another passenger—friend of H.'s—who backed up the harsh evidence against those mosquitoes, and detailed some stirring adventures which he had had with them. The stories were pretty sizable, merely pretty sizable; yet Mr. H. was continually interrupting with a cold, inexorable "Wait—knock off twenty-five per cent of that; now go on;" or, "Wait—you are getting that too strong; cut it down, cut it down—you get a leetle too much costumery on to your statements: always dress a fact in tights, never in an ulster;" or, "Pardon, once more: if you are going to load anything more on to that statement, you want to get a couple of lighters and tow the rest, because it's drawing all the water there is in the river already; stick to facts—just stick to the cold facts; what these gentlemen want for a book is the frozen truth—ain't that so, gentlemen?" He explained privately that it was necessary to watch this man all the time, and keep him within bounds; it would not do to neglect this precaution, as he, Mr. H., "knew to his sorrow." Said he, "I will not deceive you; he told me such a monstrous lie once, that it swelled my left ear up, and spread it so that I was actually not able to see out around it; it remained so for months, and people came miles to see me fan myself with it."

CHAPTER XXXV

VICKSBURG DURING THE TROUBLE

We used to plough past the lofty hill-city, Vicksburg, down-stream; but we cannot do that now. A cutoff has made a country town of it, like Osceola, St. Genevieve, and several others. There is currentless water—also a big island—in front of Vicksburg now. You come down the river the other side of the island, then turn and come up to the town; that is, in high water: in low water you can't come up, but must land some distance below it.

Signs and scars still remain, as reminders of Vicksburg's tremendous war-experiences; earthworks, trees crippled by the cannon balls, cave-refuges in the clay precipices, etc. The caves did good service during the six weeks' bombardment of the city—May 18 to July 4, 1863. They were used by the non-combatants—mainly by the women and children; not to live in constantly, but to fly to for safety on occasion. They were mere holes, tunnels, driven into the perpendicular clay bank, then branched Y shape, within the hill. Life in Vicksburg, during the six weeks was perhaps—but wait; here are some materials out of which to reproduce it:—

Population, twenty-seven thousand soldiers and three thousand non-combatants; the city utterly cut off from the world—walled solidly in, the frontage by gunboats, the rear by soldiers and batteries; hence, no buying and selling with the outside; no passing to and fro; no God-speeding a parting guest, no welcoming a coming one; no printed acres of world-wide news to be read at breakfast, mornings—a tedious dull absence of such matter, instead; hence, also, no running to see steamboats smoking into view in the distance up or down, and ploughing toward the town—for none came, the river lay vacant and undisturbed; no rush and turmoil around the railway station, no struggling over bewildered swarms of passengers by noisy mobs of hackmen—all quiet there; flour two hundred dollars a barrel, sugar thirty, corn ten dollars a bushel, bacon five dollars a pound, rum a hundred dollars a gallon; other things in proportion: consequently, no roar and racket of drays and carriages tearing along the streets; nothing for them to do, among that handful of non-combatants of exhausted means; at three o'clock in the morning, silence; silence so dead that the measured tramp of a sentinel can be heard a seemingly impossible distance; out of hearing of this lonely sound, perhaps the stillness is absolute: all in a moment come ground-shaking thunder-crashes of artillery, the sky is cobwebbed with the cris-crossing red lines streaming from soaring bomb-shells, and a rain of iron fragments descends upon the city; descends upon the empty streets: streets which are not empty a moment later, but mottled with dim figures of frantic women and children skurrying from home and bed toward the cave dungeons—encouraged by the humorous grim soldiery, who shout "Rats, to your holes!" and laugh.

The cannon-thunder rages, shells scream and crash overhead, the iron rain pours down, one hour, two hours, three, possibly six, then stops; silence follows, but the streets are still empty; the silence continues; by and by a head projects from a cave here and there and yonder, and reconnoitres, cautiously; the silence still continuing, bodies follow heads, and jaded, half-smothered creatures group themselves about, stretch their cramped limbs, draw in deep draughts of the grateful fresh air, gossip with the neighbors from the next cave; maybe straggle off home presently, or take a lounge through the town, if the stillness continues; and will skurry to the holes again, by and by, when the war-tempest breaks forth once more.

There being but three thousand of these cave-dwellers— merely the population of a village—would they not come to know each other, after a week or two, and familiarly; insomuch that the fortunate or unfortunate experiences of one would be of interest to all?

Those are the materials furnished by history. From them

might not almost anybody reproduce for himself the life of that time in Vicksburg? Could you, who did not experience it, come nearer to reproducing it to the imagination of another non- participant than could a Vicksburger who *did* experience it? It seems impossible; and yet there are reasons why it might not really be. When one makes his first voyage in a ship, it is an experience which multitudinously bristles with striking novelties; novelties which are in such sharp contrast with all this person's former experiences that they take a seemingly deathless grip upon his imagination and memory. By tongue or pen he can make a landsman live that strange and stirring voyage over with him; make him see it all and feel it all. But if he wait? If he make ten voyages in succession—what then? Why, the thing has lost color, snap, surprise; and has become commonplace. The man would have nothing to tell that would quicken a landsman's pulse.

Years ago, I talked with a couple of the Vicksburg noncombatants—a man and his wife. Left to tell their story in their own way, those people told it without fire, almost without interest.

A week of their wonderful life there would have made their tongues eloquent forever perhaps; but they had six weeks of it, and that wore the novelty all out; they got used to being bombshelled out of home and into the ground; the matter became commonplace. After that, the possibility of their ever being startlingly interested in their talks about it was gone. What the man said was to this effect:—

"It got to be Sunday all the time. Seven Sundays in the week—to us, anyway. We hadn't anything to do, and time hung heavy. Seven Sundays, and all of them broken up at one time or another, in the day or in the night, by a few hours of the awful storm of fire and thunder and iron. At first we used to shin for the holes a good deal faster than we did afterwards. The first time, I forgot the children, and Maria fetched them both along. When she was all safe in the cave she fainted. Two or three weeks afterwards, when she was running for the holes, one morning, through a shell-shower, a big shell burst near her and covered her all over with dirt, and a piece of the iron carried away her game-bag of false hair from the back of her head. Well, she stopped to get that game-bag before she shoved along again! Was getting used to things already, you see. We all got so that we could tell a good deal about shells; and after that we didn't always go under shelter if it was a light shower. Us men would loaf around and talk; and a man would say, 'There she goes!' and name the kind of shell it was from the sound of it, and go on talking—if there wasn't any danger from it. If a shell was bursting close over us, we stopped talking and stood still;—uncomfortable, yes, but it wasn't safe to move. When it let go, we went on talking again, if nobody hurt—maybe saying, 'That was a ripper!' or some such commonplace comment before we resumed; or, maybe, we would see a shell poising itself away high in the air overhead. In that case, every fellow just whipped out a sudden, 'See you again, gents!' and shoved. Often and often I saw gangs of ladies promenading the streets, looking as cheerful as you please, and keeping an eye canted up watching the shells; and I've seen them stop still when they were uncertain about what a shell was going to do, and wait and make certain; and after that they s'antered along again, or lit out for shelter, according to the verdict. Streets in some towns have a litter of pieces of paper, and odds and ends of one sort or another lying around. Ours hadn't; they had *iron* litter. Sometimes a man would gather up all the iron fragments and unbursted shells in his neighborhood, and pile them into a kind of monument in his front yard—a ton of it, sometimes. No glass left; glass couldn't stand such a bombardment; it was all shivered out. Windows of the houses vacant—looked like eye-holes in a skull. *Whole* panes were as scarce as news.

"We had church Sundays. Not many there, along at first; but by and by pretty good turnouts. I've seen service stop a minute, and everybody sit quiet—no voice heard, pretty funeral-like then—and all the more so on account of the awful boom and crash going on outside and overhead; and pretty soon, when a body could be heard, service would go on again. Organs and church-music mixed up with a bombardment is a powerful queer combination—along at first. Coming out of church, one morning, we had an accident—the only one that happened around me on a Sunday. I was just having a hearty hand-shake with a friend I hadn't seen for a while, and saying, 'Drop into our cave to-night, after bombardment; we've got hold of a pint of prime wh—.' Whiskey, I was going to say, you know, but a shell interrupted. A chunk of it cut the man's arm off, and left it dangling in my hand. And do you know the thing that is going to stick the longest in my memory, and outlast everything else, little and big, I reckon, is the mean thought I had then? It was 'the whiskey *is saved.*' And yet, don't you know, it was kind of excusable; because it was as scarce as diamonds, and we had only just that little; never had another taste during the siege.

"Sometimes the caves were desperately crowded, and always hot and close. Sometimes a cave had twenty or twenty-five people packed into it; no turning-room for anybody; air so foul, sometimes, you couldn't have made a candle burn in it. A child was born in one of those caves one night. Think of that; why, it was like having it born in a trunk.

"Twice we had sixteen people in our cave; and a number of times we had a dozen. Pretty suffocating in there. We always had eight; eight belonged there. Hunger and misery and sickness and fright and sorrow, and I don't know what all, got so loaded into them that none of them were ever rightly their old selves after the siege. They all died but three of us within a couple of years. One night a shell burst in front of the hole and caved it in and stopped it up. It was lively times, for a while, digging out. Some of us came near smothering. After that we made two openings—ought to have thought of it at first.

"Mule meat? No, we only got down to that the last day or two. Of course it was good; anything is good when you are starving."

This man had kept a diary during—six weeks? No, only the first six days. The first day, eight close pages; the second, five; the third, one—loosely written; the fourth, three or four lines; a line or two the fifth and sixth days; seventh day, diary abandoned; life in terrific Vicksburg having now become commonplace and matter of course.

The war history of Vicksburg has more about it to interest the general reader than that of any other of the river-towns. It is full of variety, full of incident, full of the picturesque. Vicksburg held out longer than any other important river-town, and saw warfare in all its phases, both land and water—the siege, the mine, the assault, the repulse, the bombardment, sickness, captivity, famine.

The most beautiful of all the national cemeteries is here. Over the great gateway is this inscription:—

"HERE REST IN PEACE 16,600 WHO DIED FOR THEIR COUNTRY IN THE YEARS 1861 TO 1865."

The grounds are nobly situated; being very high and commanding a wide prospect of land and river. They are tastefully laid out in broad terraces, with winding roads and paths; and there is profuse adornment in the way of semi-tropical shrubs and flowers; and in one part is a piece of native wild-wood, left just as it grew, and, therefore, perfect in its charm. Everything about this cemetery suggests the hand of the national Government. The Government's work is always conspicuous for excellence, solidity, thoroughness, neatness. The Government does its work well in the first place, and then takes care of it.

By winding-roads—which were often cut to so great a depth between perpendicular walls that they were mere roofless tunnels—we drove out a mile or two and visited the monument which stands upon the scene of the surrender of Vicksburg to General Grant by General Pemberton. Its metal will preserve it from the hackings and chippings which so defaced its predecessor, which was of marble; but the brick foundations are crumbling, and it will tumble down by and by. It overlooks a picturesque region of wooded hills and ravines; and is not unpicturesque itself, being well smothered in flowering weeds. The battered remnant of the marble monument has been removed to the National Cemetery.

On the road, a quarter of a mile townward, an aged colored

man showed us, with pride, an unexploded bomb-shell which has lain in his yard since the day it fell there during the siege.

"I was a-stannin' heah, an' de dog was a-stannin' heah; de dog he went for de shell, gwine to pick a fuss wid it; but I didn't; I says, 'Jes' make youseff at home heah; lay still whah you is, or bust up de place, jes' as you's a mind to, but *I's* got business out in de woods, *I* has!"

Vicksburg is a town of substantial business streets and pleasant residences; it commands the commerce of the Yazoo and Sunflower Rivers; is pushing railways in several directions, through rich agricultural regions, and has a promising future of prosperity and importance.

Apparently, nearly all the river towns, big and little, have made up their minds that they must look mainly to railroads for wealth and upbuilding, henceforth. They are acting upon this idea. The signs are, that the next twenty years will bring about some noteworthy changes in the Valley, in the direction of increased population and wealth, and in the intellectual advancement and the liberalizing of opinion which go naturally with these. And yet, if one may judge by the past, the river towns will manage to find and use a chance, here and there, to cripple and retard their progress. They kept themselves back in the days of steamboating supremacy, by a system of wharfage-dues so stupidly graded as to prohibit what may be called small *retail* traffic in freights and passengers. Boats were charged such heavy wharfage that they could not afford to land for one or two passengers or a light lot of freight. Instead of encouraging the bringing of trade to their doors, the towns diligently and effectively discouraged it. They could have had many boats and low rates; but their policy rendered few boats and high rates compulsory. It was a policy which extended—and extends—from New Orleans to St. Paul.

We had a strong desire to make a trip up the Yazoo and the Sunflower—an interesting region at any time, but additionally interesting at this time, because up there the great inundation was still to be seen in force,—but we were nearly sure to have to wait a day or more for a New Orleans boat on our return; so we were obliged to give up the project.

Here is a story which I picked up on board the boat that night. I insert it in this place merely because it is a good story, not because it belongs here—for it doesn't. It was told by a passenger—a college professor—and was called to the surface in the course of a general conversation which began with talk about horses, drifted into talk about astronomy, then into talk about the lynching of the gamblers in Vicksburg half a century ago, then into talk about dreams and superstitions; and ended, after midnight, in a dispute over free trade and protection.

CHAPTER XXXVI

THE PROFESSOR'S YARN

It was in the early days. I was not a college professor then. I was a humble-minded young land-surveyor, with the world before me—to survey, in case anybody wanted it done. I had a contract to survey a route for a great mining-ditch in California, and I was on my way thither, by sea—a three or four weeks' voyage. There were a good many passengers, but I had very little to say to them; reading and dreaming were my passions, and I avoided conversation in order to indulge these appetites. There were three professional gamblers on board—rough, repulsive fellows. I never had any talk with them, yet I could not help seeing them with some frequency, for they gambled in an upper-deck state-room every day and night, and in my promenades I often had glimpses of them through their door, which stood a little ajar to let out the surplus tobacco smoke and profanity. They were an evil and hateful presence, but I had to put up with it, of course.

There was one other passenger who fell under my eye a good deal, for he seemed determined to be friendly with me, and I could not have gotten rid of him without running some chance of hurting his feelings, and I was far from wishing to do that. Besides, there was something engaging in his countrified simplicity and his beaming good-nature. The first time I saw this Mr. John Backus, I guessed, from his clothes and his looks, that he was a grazier or farmer from the back woods of some western State—doubtless Ohio—and afterward when he dropped into his personal history and I discovered that he *was* a cattle-raiser from interior Ohio, I was so pleased with my own penetration that I warmed toward him for verifying my instinct.

He got to dropping alongside me every day, after breakfast, to help me make my promenade; and so, in the course of time, his easy-working jaw had told me everything about his business, his prospects, his family, his relatives, his politics—in fact everything that concerned a Backus, living or dead. And meantime I think he had managed to get out of me everything I knew about my trade, my tribe, my purposes, my prospects, and myself. He was a gentle and persuasive genius, and this thing showed it; for I was not given to talking about my matters. I said something about triangulation, once; the stately word pleased his ear; he inquired what it meant; I explained; after that he quietly and inoffensively ignored my name, and always called me Triangle.

What an enthusiast he was in cattle! At the bare name of a bull or a cow, his eye would light and his eloquent tongue would turn itself loose. As long as I would walk and listen, he would walk and talk; he knew all breeds, he loved all breeds, he caressed them all with his affectionate tongue. I tramped along in voiceless misery whilst the cattle question was up; when I could endure it no longer, I used to deftly insert a scientific topic into the conversation; then my eye fired and his faded; my tongue fluttered, his stopped; life was a joy to me, and a sadness to him.

One day he said, a little hesitatingly, and with somewhat of diffidence:—

"Triangle, would you mind coming down to my state-room a minute, and have a little talk on a certain matter?"

I went with him at once. Arrived there, he put his head out, glanced up and down the saloon warily, then closed the door and locked it. We sat down on the sofa, and he said:—

"I'm a-going to make a little proposition to you, and if it strikes you favorable, it'll be a middling good thing for both of us. You ain't a-going out to Californy for fun, nuther am I—it's *business,* ain't that so? Well, you can do me a good turn, and so can I you, if we see fit. I've raked and scraped and saved, a considerable many years, and I've got it all here." He unlocked an old hair trunk, tumbled a chaos of shabby clothes aside, and drew a short stout bag into view for a moment, then buried it again and relocked the trunk. Dropping his voice to a cautious low tone, he continued, "She's all there—a round ten thousand dollars in yellow-boys; now this is my little idea: What I don't know about raising cattle, ain't worth knowing. There's mints of money in it, in Californy. Well, I know, and you know, that all along a line that's being surveyed, there's little dabs of land that they call 'gores,' that fall to the surveyor free gratis for nothing. All you've got to do, on your side, is to survey in such a way that the 'gores' will fall on good fat land, then you turn 'em over to me, I stock 'em with cattle, *in* rolls the cash, I plank out your share of the dollars regular, right along, and—"

I was sorry to wither his blooming enthusiasm, but it could not be helped. I interrupted, and said severely,—"I am not that kind of a surveyor. Let us change the subject, Mr. Backus."

It was pitiful to see his confusion and hear his awkward and shamefaced apologies. I was as much distressed as he was—especially as he seemed so far from having suspected that there was anything improper in his proposition. So I hastened to console him and lead him on to forget his mishap in a conversational orgy about cattle and butchery. We were lying at Acapulco; and, as we went on deck, it happened luckily that the crew were just beginning to hoist some beeves aboard in slings. Backus's melancholy vanished instantly, and with it the memory of his late mistake.

"Now only look at that!" cried he; "My goodness, Triangle, what *would* they say to it in *Ohio?* Wouldn't their eyes bug out, to see 'em handled like that?—wouldn't they, though?"

All the passengers were on deck to look—even the gamblers—and Backus knew them all, and had afflicted them all with his pet topic. As I moved away, I saw one of the gamblers approach and accost him; then another of them; then the third. I halted; waited; watched; the conversation continued between the four men; it grew earnest; Backus drew gradually away; the gamblers followed, and kept at his elbow. I was uncomfortable. However, as they passed me presently, I heard Backus say, with a tone of persecuted annoyance:—

"But it ain't any use, gentlemen; I tell you again, as I've told you a half a dozen times before, I warn't raised to it, and I ain't a-going to resk it."

I felt relieved. "His level head will be his sufficient protection," I said to myself.

During the fortnight's run from Acapulco to San Francisco I several times saw the gamblers talking earnestly with Backus, and once I threw out a gentle warning to him. He chuckled comfortably and said,—

"Oh, yes! they tag around after me considerable—want me to play a little, just for amusement, they say—but laws-a-me, if my folks have told me once to look out for that sort of live-stock, they've told me a thousand times, I reckon."

By and by, in due course, we were approaching San Francisco. It was an ugly black night, with a strong wind blowing, but there was not much sea. I was on deck, alone. Toward ten I started below. A figure issued from the gamblers' den, and disappeared in the darkness. I experienced a shock, for I was sure it was Backus. I flew down the companion-way, looked about for him, could not find him, then returned to the deck just in time to catch a glimpse of him as he re-entered that confounded nest of rascality. Had he yielded at last? I feared it. What had he gone below for?—His bag of coin? Possibly. I drew near the door, full of bodings. It was a-crack, and I glanced in and saw a sight that made me bitterly wish I had given my attention to saving my poor cattle-friend, instead of reading and dreaming my foolish time away. He was gambling. Worse still, he was being plied with champagne, and was already showing some effect from it. He praised the "cider," as he called it, and said now that he had got a taste of it he almost believed he would drink it if it was spirits, it was so good and so ahead of anything he had ever run across before. Surreptitious smiles, at this, passed from one rascal to another, and they filled all the glasses, and whilst Backus honestly drained his to the bottom they pretended to do the same, but threw the wine over their shoulders.

I could not bear the scene, so I wandered forward and tried to interest myself in the sea and the voices of the wind. But no, my uneasy spirit kept dragging me back at quarter-hour intervals; and always I saw Backus drinking his wine—fairly and squarely, and the others throwing theirs away. It was the painfulest night I ever spent.

The only hope I had was that we might reach our anchorage with speed—that would break up the game. I helped the ship along all I could with my prayers. At last we went booming through the Golden Gate, and my pulses leaped for joy. I hurried back to that door and glanced in. Alas, there was small room for hope—Backus's eyes were heavy and bloodshot, his sweaty face was crimson, his speech maudlin and thick, his body sawed drunkenly about with the weaving motion of the ship. He drained another glass to the dregs, whilst the cards were being dealt.

He took his hand, glanced at it, and his dull eyes lit up for a moment. The gamblers observed it, and showed their gratification by hardly perceptible signs.

"How many cards?"

"None!" said Backus.

One villain—named Hank Wiley—discarded one card, the others three each. The betting began. Heretofore the bets had been trifling—a dollar or two; but Backus started off with an eagle now, Wiley hesitated a moment, then "saw it" and "went ten dollars better." The other two threw up their hands.

Backus went twenty better. Wiley said,—

"I see that, and go you a *hundred* better!" then smiled and reached for the money.

"Let it alone," said Backus, with drunken gravity.

"What! you mean to say you're going to cover it?"

"Cover it? Well I reckon I am—and lay another hundred on top of it, too."

He reached down inside his overcoat and produced the required sum.

"Oh, that's your little game, is it? I see your raise, and raise it five hundred!" said Wiley.

"Five hundred *better!*" said the foolish bull-driver, and pulled out the amount and showered it on the pile. The three conspirators hardly tried to conceal their exultation.

All diplomacy and pretence were dropped now, and the sharp exclamations came thick and fast, and the yellow pyramid grew higher and higher. At last ten thousand dollars lay in view. Wiley cast a bag of coin on the table, and said with mocking gentleness,—

"Five thousand dollars better, my friend from the rural districts—what do you say *now?*"

"I *call* you!" said Backus, heaving his golden shot-bag on the pile. "What have you got?"

"Four kings, you d—d fool!" and Wiley threw down his cards and surrounded the stakes with his arms.

"Four *aces,* you ass!" thundered Backus, covering his man with a cocked revolver. "*I'm a professional gambler myself, and I've been laying for you duffers all this voyage!*"

Down went the anchor, rumbledy-dum-dum! and the long trip was ended.

Well—well, it is a sad world. On of the three gamblers was Backus's "pal." It was he that dealt the fateful hands. According to an understanding with the two victims, he was to have given Backus four queens, but alas, he didn't.

A week later, I stumbled upon Backus—arrayed in the height of fashion—in Montgomery Street. He said, cheerily, as we were parting,—

"Ah, by-the-way, you needn't mind about those gores. I don't really know anything about cattle, except what I was able to pick up in a week's apprenticeship over in Jersey just before we sailed. My cattle-culture and cattle-enthusiasm have served their turn—I shan't need them any more."

———

Next day we reluctantly parted from the "Gold Dust" and her officers, hoping to see that boat and all those officers again, some day. A thing which the fates were to render tragically impossible!

CHAPTER XXXVII

THE END OF THE "GOLD DUST"

For, three months later, August 8, while I was writing one of these foregoing chapters, the New York papers brought this telegram:—

A TERRIBLE DISASTER

SEVENTEEN PERSONS KILLED BY AN EXPLOSION OF THE STEAMER "GOLD DUST"

"NASHVILLE, Aug. 7.—A despatch from Hickman, Ky., says:—

"The steamer 'Gold Dust' exploded her boilers at three o'clock to-day, just after leaving Hickman. Forty-seven persons were scalded and seventeen are missing. The boat was landed in the eddy just above the town, and through the exertions of the citizens the cabin passengers, officers, and part of the crew and deck passengers were taken ashore and removed to the hotels and residences. Twenty-four of the injured were lying in Holcomb's dry-goods store at one time, where they received every attention before being removed to more comfortable places."

A list of the names followed, whereby it appeared that of the seventeen dead, one was the barkeeper; and among the forty-seven wounded, were the captain, chief mate, second mate, and second and third clerks; also Mr. Lem S. Gray, pilot, and several members of the crew.

In answer to a private telegram, we learned that none of these was severely hurt, except Mr. Gray. Letters received afterward confirmed this news, and said that Mr. Gray was improving and would get well. Later letters spoke less hopefully of his case; and finally came one announcing his death. A good man, a most companionable and manly man, and worthy of a kindlier fate.

CHAPTER XXXVIII

THE HOUSE BEAUTIFUL

We took passage in a Cincinnati boat for New Orleans; or on a Cincinnati boat—either is correct; the former is the eastern form of putting it, the latter the western.

Mr. Dickens declined to agree that the Mississippi steamboats were "magnificent," or that they were "floating palaces,"—terms which had always been applied to them; terms which did not over-express the admiration with which the people viewed them.

Mr. Dickens's position was unassailable, possibly; the people's position was certainly unassailable. If Mr. Dickens was comparing these boats with the crown jewels; or with the Taj, or with the Matterhorn; or with some other priceless or wonderful thing which he had seen, they were not magnificent—he was right. The people compared them with what *they* had seen; and, thus measured, thus judged, the boats were magnificent—the term was the correct one, it was not at all too strong. The people were as right as was Mr. Dickens. The steamboats were finer than anything on shore. Compared with superior dwelling-houses and first class hotels in the Valley, they were indubitably magnificent, they were "palaces." To a few people living in New Orleans and St. Louis, they were not magnificent, perhaps; not palaces; but to the great majority of those populations, and to the entire populations spread over both banks between Baton Rouge and St. Louis, they were palaces; they tallied with the citizen's dream of what magnificence was, and satisfied it.

Every town and village along that vast stretch of double river-frontage had a best dwelling, finest dwelling, mansion,—the home of its wealthiest and most conspicuous citizen. It is easy to describe it: large grassy yard, with paling fence painted white—in fair repair; brick walk from gate to door; big, square, two-story "frame" house, painted white and porticoed like a Grecian temple—with this difference, that the imposing fluted columns and Corinthian capitals were a pathetic sham, being made of white pine, and painted; iron knocker; brass door knob—discolored, for lack of polishing. Within, an uncarpeted hall, of planed boards; opening out of it, a parlor, fifteen feet by fifteen—in some instances five or ten feet larger; ingrain carpet; mahogany centre-table; lamp on it, with green-paper shade—standing on a gridiron, so to speak, made of high-colored yarns, by the young ladies of the house, and called a lampmat; several books, piled and disposed, with cast-iron exactness, according to an inherited and unchangeable plan; among them, Tupper, much pencilled; also, "Friendship's Offering," and "Affection's Wreath," with their sappy inanities illustrated in die-away mezzotints; also, Ossian; "Alonzo and Melissa;" maybe "Ivanhoe;" also "Album," full of original "poetry" of the Thou-hast-wounded-the-spirit-that-loved-thee breed; two or three goody-goody works—"Shepherd of Salisbury Plain," etc.; current number of the chaste and innocuous Godey's "Lady's

Book," with painted fashion-plate of wax-figure women with mouths all alike—lips and eyelids the same size—each five-foot woman with a two-inch wedge sticking from under her dress and letting-on to be half of her foot. Polished air-tight stove (new and deadly invention), with pipe passing through a board which closes up the discarded good old fireplace. On each end of the wooden mantel, over the fireplace, a large basket of peaches and other fruits, natural size, all done in plaster, rudely, or in wax, and painted to resemble the originals—which they don't. Over middle of mantel, engraving—Washington Crossing the Delaware; on the wall by the door, copy of it done in thunder-and-lightning crewels by one of the young ladies—work of art which would have made Washington hesitate about crossing, if he could have foreseen what advantage was going to be taken of it. Piano—kettle in disguise—with music, bound and unbound, piled on it, and on a stand near by: Battle of Prague; Bird Waltz; Arkansas Traveller; Rosin the Bow; Marseilles Hymn; On a Lone Barren Isle (St. Helena); The Last Link is Broken; She wore a Wreath of Roses the Night when last we met; Go, forget me, Why should Sorrow o'er that Brow a Shadow fling; Hours there were to Memory Dearer; Long, Long Ago; Days of Absence; A Life on the Ocean Wave, a Home on the Rolling Deep; Bird at Sea; and spread open on the rack, where the plaintive singer has left it, *Ro*-holl on, silver *moo*-hoon, guide the *trav*-el-lerr his *way,* etc. Tilted pensively against the piano, a guitar—guitar capable of playing the Spanish Fandango by itself, if you give it a start. Frantic work of art on the wall—pious motto, done on the premises, sometimes in colored yarns, sometimes in faded grasses: progenitor of the "God Bless Our Home" of modern commerce. Framed in black mouldings on the wall, other works of art, conceived and committed on the premises, by the young ladies; being grim black-and-white crayons; landscapes, mostly: lake, solitary sail-boat, petrified clouds, pre-geological trees on shore, anthracite precipice; name of criminal conspicuous in the corner. Lithograph, Napoleon Crossing the Alps. Lithograph, The Grave at St. Helena. Steel-plates, Trumbull's Battle of Bunker Hill, and the Sally from Gibraltar. Copper-plates, Moses Smiting the Rock, and Return of the Prodigal Son. In big gilt frame, slander of the family in oil: papa holding a book ("Constitution of the United States"); guitar leaning against mamma, blue ribbons fluttering from its neck; the young ladies, as children, in slippers and scalloped pantelettes, one embracing toy horse, the other beguiling kitten with ball of yarn, and both simpering up at mamma, who simpers back. These persons all fresh, raw, and red— apparently skinned. Opposite, in gilt frame, grandpa and grandma, at thirty and twenty-two, stiff, old-fashioned, high-collared, puff-sleeved, glaring pallidly out from a background of solid Egyptian night. Under a glass French clock dome, large bouquet of stiff flowers done in corpsy white wax. Pyramidal what-not in the corner, the shelves occupied chiefly with bric-a-brac of the period, disposed with an eye to best effect: shell, with the Lord's Prayer carved on it; another shell—of the long-oval sort, narrow, straight orifice, three inches long, running from end to end—portrait of Washington carved on it; not well done; the shell had Washington's mouth, originally—artist should have built to that. These two are memorials of the long-ago bridal trip to New Orleans and the French Market. Other bric-a-brac: Californian "specimens"—quartz, with gold wart adhering; old Guinea-gold locket, with circlet of ancestral hair in it; Indian arrow-heads, of flint; pair of bead moccasins, from uncle who crossed the Plains; three "alum" baskets of various colors— being skeleton-frame of wire, clothed-on with cubes of crystallized alum in the rock-candy style—works of art which were achieved by the young ladies; their doubles and duplicates to be found upon all what-nots in the land; convention of desiccated bugs and butterflies pinned to a card; painted toy-dog, seated upon bellows-attachment—drop its under jaw and squeaks when pressed upon; sugar-candy rabbit—limbs and features merged together, not strongly defined; pewter presidential-campaign medal; miniature card-board wood-sawyer, to be attached to the stovepipe and operated by the heat; small Napoleon, done in wax; spread-open daguerreotypes of dim children, parents, cousins, aunts, and friends, in all attitudes but customary ones; no templed portico at back, and manufactured landscape stretching away in the distance—that came in later, with the photograph; all these vague figures lavishly chained and ringed—metal indicated and secured from doubt by stripes and splashes of vivid gold bronze; all of them too much combed, too much fixed up; and all of them uncomfortable in inflexible Sunday-clothes of a pattern which the spectator cannot realize could ever have been in fashion; husband and wife generally grouped together—husband sitting, wife standing, with hand on his shoulder—and both preserving, all these fading years, some traceable effect of the daguerreotypist's brisk "Now smile, if you please!" Bracketed over what-not—place of special sacredness— an outrage in water-color, done by the young niece that came on a visit long ago, and died. Pity, too; for she might have repented of this in time. Horse-hair chairs, horse-hair sofa which keeps sliding from under you. Window shades, of oil stuff, with milk-maids and ruined castles stencilled on them in fierce colors. Lambrequins dependent from gaudy boxings of beaten tin, gilded. Bedrooms with rag carpets; bedsteads of the "corded" sort, with a sag in the middle, the cords needing tightening; snuffy feather-bed—not aired often enough; cane-seat chairs, splint-bottomed rocker; looking-glass on wall, school-slate size, veneered frame; inherited bureau; wash-bowl and pitcher, possibly—but not certainly; brass candlestick, tallow candle, snuffers. Nothing else in the room. Not a bath-room in the house; and no visitor likely to come along who has ever seen one.

That was the residence of the principal citizen, all the way from the suburbs of New Orleans to the edge of St. Louis. When he stepped aboard a big fine steamboat, he entered a new and marvellous world: chimney-tops cut to counterfeit a spraying crown of plumes—and maybe painted red; pilot-house, hurricane deck, boiler-deck guards, all garnished with white wooden filagree work of fanciful patterns; gilt acorns topping the derricks; gilt deer-horns over the big bell; gaudy symbolical picture on the paddle-box, possibly; big roomy boiler-deck, painted blue, and furnished with Windsor arm-chairs; inside, a far receding snow-white "cabin;" porcelain knob and oil-picture on every state-room door; curving patterns of filagree-work touched up with gilding, stretching overhead all down the converging vista; big chandeliers every little way, each an April shower of glittering glass-drops; lovely rainbow-light falling everywhere from the colored glazing of the skylights; the whole a long-drawn, resplendent tunnel, a bewildering and soul-satisfying spectacle! in the ladies' cabin a pink and white Wilton carpet, as soft as mush, and glorified with a ravishing pattern of gigantic flowers. Then the Bridal Chamber—the animal that invented that idea was still alive and unhanged, at that day—Bridal Chamber whose pretentious flummery was necessarily overawing to the now tottering intellect of that hosannahing citizen. Every state-room had its couple of cosy clean bunks, and perhaps a looking-glass and a snug closet; and sometimes there was even a washbowl and pitcher, and part of a towel which could be told from mosquito netting by an expert—though generally these things were absent, and the shirt-sleeved passengers cleansed themselves at a long row of stationary bowls in the barber shop, where were also public towels, public combs, and public soap.

Take the steamboat which I have just described, and you have her in her highest and finest, and most pleasing, and comfortable, and satisfactory estate. Now cake her over with a layer of ancient and obdurate dirt, and you have the Cincinnati steamer awhile ago referred to. Not all over—only inside; for she was ably officered in all departments except the steward's.

But wash that boat and repaint her, and she would be about the counterpart of the most complimented boat of the old flush times: for the steamboat architecture of the West has undergone no change; neither has steamboat furniture and ornamentation undergone any.

CHAPTER XXXIX

MANUFACTURES AND MISCREANTS

Where the river, in the Vicksburg region, used to be corkscrewed, it is now comparatively straight—made so by cut-off; a former distance of seventy miles is reduced to thirty-five. It is a change which threw Vicksburg's neighbor, Delta, Louisiana, out into the country and ended its career as a river town. Its whole river-frontage is now occupied by a vast sand-bar, thickly covered with young trees—a growth which will magnify itself into a dense forest, by and by, and completely hide the exiled town.

In due time we passed Grand Gulf and Rodney, of war fame, and reached Natchez, the last of the beautiful hill-cities—for Baton Rouge, yet to come, is not on a hill, but only on high ground. Famous Natchez-under-the-hill has not changed notably in twenty years; in outward aspect—judging by the descriptions of the ancient procession of foreign tourists—it has not changed in sixty; for it is still small, straggling, and shabby. It had a desperate reputation, morally, in the old keel-boating and early steamboating times—plenty of drinking, carousing, fisticuffing, and killing there, among the riff-raff of the river, in those days. But Natchez-on-top-of-the-hill is attractive; has always been attractive. Even Mrs. Trollope (1827) had to confess its charms:

"At one or two points the wearisome level line is relieved by *bluffs,* as they call the short intervals of high ground. The town of Natchez is beautifully situated on one of those high spots. The contrast that its bright green hill forms with the dismal line of black forest that stretches on every side, the abundant growth of the paw-paw, palmetto and orange, the copious variety of sweet-scented flowers that flourish there, all make it appear like an oasis in the desert. Natchez is the furthest point to the north at which oranges ripen in the open air, or endure the winter without shelter. With the exception of this sweet spot, I thought all the little towns and villages we passed wretched-looking in the extreme."

Natchez, like her near and far river neighbors, has railways now, and is adding to them—pushing them hither and thither into all rich outlying regions that are naturally tributary to her. And like Vicksburg and New Orleans, she has her ice-factory; she makes thirty tons of ice a day. In Vicksburg and Natchez, in my time, ice was jewelry; none but the rich could wear it. But anybody and everybody can have it now. I visited one of the ice-factories in New Orleans, to see what the polar regions might look like when lugged into the edge of the tropics. But there was nothing striking in the aspect of the place. It was merely a spacious house, with some innocent steam machinery in one end of it and some big porcelain pipes running here and there. No, not porcelain—they merely seemed to be; they were iron, but the ammonia which was being breathed through them had coated them to the thickness of your hand with solid milk-white ice. It ought to have melted; for one did not require winter clothing in that atmosphere: but it did not melt; the inside of the pipe was too cold.

Sunk into the floor were numberless tin boxes, a foot square and two feet long, and open at the top end. These were full of clear water; and around each box, salt and other proper stuff was packed; also, the ammonia gases were applied to the water in some way which will always remain a secret to me, because I was not able to understand the process. While the water in the boxes gradually froze, men gave it a stir or two with a stick occasionally—to liberate the air-bubbles, I think. Other men were continually lifting out boxes whose contents had become hard frozen. They gave the box a single dip into a vat of boiling water, to melt the block of ice free from its tin coffin, then they shot the block out upon a platform car, and it was ready for market. These big blocks were hard, solid, and crystal-clear. In certain of them, big bouquets of fresh and brilliant tropical flowers had been frozen-in; in others, beautiful silken-clad French dolls, and other pretty objects. These blocks were to be set on end in a platter, in the centre of dinner-tables, to cool the tropical air; and also to be ornamental, for the flowers and things imprisoned in them could be seen as through plate glass. I was told that this factory could retail its ice, by wagon, throughout New Orleans, in the humblest dwelling house quantities, at six or seven dollars a ton, and make a sufficient profit. This being the case, there is business for ice factories in the

North; for we get ice on no such terms there, if one takes less than three hundred and fifty pounds at a delivery.

The Rosalie Yarn Mill, of Natchez, has a capacity of 6,000 spindles and 160 looms, and employs 100 hands. The Natchez Cotton Mills Company began operations four years ago in a two-story building of 50 × 190 feet, with 4,000 spindles and 128 looms; capital $105,000, all subscribed in the town. Two years later, the same stockholders increased their capital to $225,000; added a third story to the mill, increased its length to 317 feet; added machinery to increase the capacity to 10,300 spindles and 304 looms. The company now employ 250 operatives, many of whom are citizens of Natchez. "The mill works 5,000 bales of cotton annually and manufactures the best standard quality of brown shirtings and sheetings and drills, turning out 5,000,000 yards of these goods per year."* A close corporation—stock held at $5,000 per share, but none in the market.

The changes in the Mississippi River are great and strange, yet were to be expected; but I was not expecting to live to see Natchez and these other river towns become manufacturing strongholds and railway centres.

Speaking of manufactures reminds me of a talk upon that topic which I heard—which I overheard—on board the Cincinnati boat. I awoke out of a fretted sleep, with a dull confusion of voices in my ears. I listened—two men were talking; subject, apparently, the great inundation. I looked out through the open transom. The two men were eating a late breakfast; sitting opposite each other; nobody else around. They closed up the inundation with a few words—having used it, evidently, as a mere ice-breaker and acquaintanceship-breeder—then they dropped into business. It soon transpired that they were drummers—one belonging in Cincinnati, the other in New Orleans. Brisk men, energetic of movement and speech; the dollar their god, how to get it their religion.

"Now as to this article," said Cincinnati, slashing into the ostensible butter and holding forward a slab of it on his knifeblade, "It's from our house; look at it—smell of it—taste it. Put any test on it you want to. Take your own time—no hurry—make it thorough. There now—what do you say? butter, ain't it? Not by a thundering sight—it's oleomargarine! Yes, sir, that's what it is—oleomargarine. You can't tell it from butter; by George, an *expert* can't. It's from our house. We supply most of the boats in the West; there's hardly a pound of butter on one

*"New Orleans Times-Democrat," Aug. 26, 1882.

of them. We are crawling right along—*jumping* right along is the word. We are going to have that entire trade. Yes, and the hotel trade, too. You are going to see the day, pretty soon, when you can't find an ounce of butter to bless yourself with, in any hotel in the Mississippi and Ohio Valleys, outside of the biggest cities. Why, we are turning out oleomargarine *now* by the thousands of tons. And we can sell it so dirt-cheap that the whole country has *got* to take it—can't get around it you see. Butter don't stand any show—there ain't any chance for competition. Butter's had its *day*—and from this out, butter goes to the wall. There's more money in oleomargarine than—why, you can't imagine the business we do. I've stopped in every town, from Cincinnati to Natchez; and I've sent home big orders from every one of them."

And so-forth and so-on, for ten minutes longer, in the same fervid strain. Then New Orleans piped up and said:—

"Yes, it's a first-rate imitation, that's a certainty; but it ain't the only one around that's first-rate. For instance, they make olive-oil out of cotton-seed oil, now-a-days, so that you can't tell them apart."

"Yes, that's so," responded Cincinnati, "and it was a tip-top business for a while. They sent it over and brought it back from France and Italy, with the United States custom-house mark on it to indorse it for genuine, and there was no end of cash in it; but France and Italy broke up the game—of course they naturally would. Cracked on such a rattling impost that cotton-seed olive-oil couldn't stand the raise; had to hang up and quit."

"Oh, it *did,* did it?" You wait here a minute."

Goes to his state-room, brings back a couple of long bottles, and takes out the corks—says:—

"There now, smell them, taste them, examine the bottles, inspect the labels. One of 'm's from Europe, the other's never been out of this country. One's European olive-oil, the other's American cotton-seed olive-oil. Tell 'm apart? 'Course you can't. Nobody can. People that want to, can go to the expense and trouble of shipping their oils to Europe and back—it's their privilege; but our firm knows a trick worth six of that. We turn out the whole thing—clean from the word go—in our factory in New Orleans: labels, bottles, oil, everything. Well, no, not labels: been buying *them* abroad—get them dirt-cheap there. You see, there's just one little wee speck, essence, or whatever it is, in a gallon of cotton-seed oil, that gives it a smell, or a flavor, or something—get that out, and you're all right—perfectly easy then to turn the oil into any kind of oil you want to, and there ain't anybody that can detect the true from the false. Well, we know how to get that one little particle out—and we're the only firm that does. And we turn out an olive-oil that is just simply perfect—undetectable! We are doing a ripping trade, too—as I could easily show you by my order-book for this trip. Maybe you'll butter everybody's bread pretty soon, but we'll cotton-seed his salad for him from the Gulf to Canada, and that's a dead-certain thing."

Cincinnati glowed and flashed with admiration. The two scoundrels exchanged business-cards, and rose. As they left the table, Cincinnati said,—

"But you have to have custom-house marks, don't you? How do you manage that?"

I did not catch the answer.

We passed Port Hudson, scene of two of the most terrific episodes of the war—the night-battle there between Farragut's fleet and the Confederate land batteries, April 14th, 1863; and the memorable land battle, two months later, which lasted eight hours—eight hours of exceptionally fierce and stubborn fighting—and ended, finally, in the repulse of the Union forces with great slaughter.

CHAPTER XL

CASTLES AND CULTURE

Baton Rouge was clothed in flowers, like a bride—no, much more so; like a greenhouse. For we were in the absolute South now—no modifications, no compromises, no half-way measures. The magnolia-trees in the Capitol grounds were lovely and fragrant, with their dense rich foliage and huge snow-ball blossoms. The scent of the flower is very sweet, but you want distance on it, because it is so powerful. They are not good bed-room blossoms—they might suffocate one in his sleep. We were certainly in the South at last; for here the sugar region begins, and the plantations—vast green levels, with sugar-mill and negro quarters clustered together in the middle distance—were in view. And there was a tropical sun overhead and a tropical swelter in the air.

And at this point, also, begins the pilot's paradise: a wide river hence to New Orleans, abundance of water from shore to shore, and no bars, snags, sawyers, or wrecks in his road.

Sir Walter Scott is probably responsible for the Capitol building; for it is not conceivable that this little sham castle would ever have been built if he had not run the people mad, a couple of generations ago, with his mediaeval romances. The South has not yet recovered from the debilitating influence of his books. Admiration of his fantastic heroes and their grotesque "chivalry" doings and romantic juvenilities still survives here, in an atmosphere in which is already perceptible the wholesome and practical nineteenth-century smell of cotton-factories and locomotives; and traces of its inflated language and other windy humbuggeries survive along with it. It is pathetic enough, that a whitewashed castle with turrets and things—materials all ungenuine within and without, pretending to be what they are not—should ever have been built in this otherwise honorable place; but it is much more pathetic to see this architectural falsehood undergoing restoration and perpetuation in our day, when it would have been so easy to let dynamite finish what a charitable fire began, and then devote this restoration-money to the buildingof something genuine.

Baton Rouge has no patent on imitation castles, however, and no monopoly of them. Here is a picture from the advertisement of the "Female Institute" of Columbia, Tennessee. The following remark is from the same advertisement:—

> "The Institute building has long been famed as a model of striking and beautiful architecture. Visitors are charmed with its resemblance to the old castles of song and story, with its towers, turreted walls, and ivy-mantled porches."

Keeping school in a castle is a romantic thing; as romantic as keeping hotel in a castel.

By itself the imitation castle is doubtless harmless, and well enough; but as a symbol and breeder and sustainer of maudlin Middle-Age romanticism here in the midst of the plainest and sturdiest and infinitely greatest and worthiest of all the centuries the world has seen, it is necessarily a hurtful thing and a mistake.

Here is an extract from the prospectus of a Kentucky "Female College." Female college sounds well enough; but since the phrasing it in that unjustifiable way was done purely in the interest of brevity, it seems to me that she-college would have been still better—because shorter, and means the same thing: that is, if either phrase means anything at all:—

> "The president is southern by birth, by rearing, by education, and by sentiment; the teachers are all southern in sentiment, and with the exception of those born in Europe were born and raised in the south. Believing the southern to be the highest type of civilization this con-

tinent has seen,* the young ladies are trained according to the southern ideas of delicacy, refinement, womanhood, religion, and propriety; hence we offer a first-class female college for the south and solicit southern patronage."

---

*Illustrations of it thoughtlessly omitted by the advertiser:

KNOXVILLE, Tenn., October 19.—This morning a few minutes after ten o'clock, General Joseph A. Mabry, Thomas O'Connor, and Joseph A. Mabry, Jr., were killed in a shooting affray. The difficulty began yesterday afternoon by General Mabry attacking Major O'Connor and threatening to kill him. This was at the fair grounds, and O'Connor told Mabry that it was not the place to settle their difficulties. Mabry then told O'Connor he should not live. It seems that Mabry was armed and O'Connor was not. The cause of the difficulty was an old feud about the transfer of some property from Mabry to O'Connor. Later in the afternoon Mabry sent word to O'Connor that he would kill him on sight. This morning Major O'Connor was standing in the door of the Mechanics' National Bank, of which he was president. General Mabry and another gentleman walked down Gay Street on the opposite side from the bank. O'Connor stepped into the bank, got a shot gun, took deliberate aim at General Mabry and fired. Mabry fell dead, being shot in the left side. As he fell O'Connor fired again, the shot taking effect in Mabry's thigh. O'Connor then reached into the bank and got another shot gun. About this time Joseph A. Mabry, Jr., son of General Mabry, came rushing down the street, unseen by O'Connor until within forty feet, when the young man fired a pistol, the shot taking effect in O'Connor's right breast, passing through the body near the heart. The instant Mabry shot, O'Connor turned and fired, the load taking effect in young Mabry's right breast and side. Mabry fell pierced with twenty buckshot, and almost instantly O'Connor fell dead without a struggle. Mabry tried to rise, but fell back dead. The whole tragedy occurred within two minutes, and neither of the three spoke after he was shot. General Mabry had about thirty buckshot in his body. A bystander was painfully wounded in the thigh with a buckshot, and another was wounded in the arm. Four other men had their clothing pierced by buckshot. The affair caused great excitement, and Gay Street was thronged with thousands of people. General Mabry and his son Joe were acquitted only a few days ago of the murder of Moses Lusby and Don Lusby, father and son, whom they killed a few weeks ago. Will Mabry was killed by Don Lusby last Christmas. Major Thomas O'Connor was President of the Mechanics' National Bank here, and was the wealthiest man in the State.—*Associated Press Telegram.*

One day last month, Professor Sharpe, of the Somerville, Tenn., Female College, "a quiet and gentlemanly man," was told that his brother-in-law, a Captain Burton, had threatened to kill him. Burton, it seems, had already killed one man and driven his knife into another. The Professor armed himself with a double-barrelled shot gun, started out in search of his brother-in-law, found him playing billiards in a saloon, and blew his brains out. The "Memphis Avalanche" reports that the Professor's course met with pretty general approval in the community; knowing that the law was powerless, in the actual condition of public sentiment, to protect him, he protected himself.

About the same time, two young men in North Carolina quarrelled about a girl, and "hostile messages" were exchanged. Friends tried to reconcile them, but had their labor for their pains. On the 24th the young men met in the public highway. One of them had a heavy club in his hand, the other an axe. The man with the club fought desperately for his life, but it was a hopeless fight from the first. A well-directed blow sent his club whirling out of his grasp, and the next moment he was a dead man.

About the same time, two "highly connected" young Virginians, clerks in a hardware store at Charlottesville, while "skylarking," came to blows. Peter Dick threw pepper in Charles Road's eyes; Roads demanded an apology; Dick refused to give it, and it was agreed that a duel was inevitable, but a difficulty arose; the parties had no pistols, and it was too late at night to procure them. One of them suggested that butcher-knives would answer the purpose, and the other accepted the suggestion; the result was that Roads fell to the floor with a gash in his abdomen that may or may not prove fatal. If Dick has been arrested, the news has not reached us. He "expressed deep regret," and we are told by a Staunton correspondent of the "Philadelphia Press" that "every effort has been made to hush the matter up."—*Extracts from the Public Journals.*

What, warder, ho! the man that can blow so complacent a blast as that, probably blows it from a castle.

From Baton Rouge to New Orleans, the great sugar plantations border both sides of the river all the way, and stretch their league-wide levels back to the dim forest-walls of bearded cypress in the rear. Shores lonely no longer. Plenty of dwellings all the way, on both banks—standing so close together, for long distances, that the broad river lying between the two rows, becomes a sort of spacious street. A most home-like and happy-looking region. And now and then you see a pillared and porticoed great manor-house, embowered in trees. Here is testimony of one or two of the procession of foreign tourists that filed along here half a century ago. Mrs. Trollope says:—

> "The unbroken flatness of the banks of the Mississippi continued unvaried for many miles above New Orleans; but the graceful and luxuriant palmetto, the dark and noble ilex, and the bright orange, were everywhere to be seen, and it was many days before we were weary of looking at them."

Captain Basil Hall:—

> "The district of country which lies adjacent to the Mississippi, in the lower parts of Louisiana, is everywhere thickly peopled by sugar planters, whose showy houses, gay piazzas, trig gardens, and numerous slave-villages, all clean and neat, gave an exceedingly thriving air to the river scenery."

All the procession paint the attractive picture in the same way. The descriptions of fifty years ago do not need to have a word changed in order to exactly describe the same region as it appears to-day—except as to the "trigness" of the houses. The whitewash is gone from the negro cabins now; and many, possibly most, of the big mansions, once so shining white, have worn out their paint and have a decayed, neglected look. It is the blight of the war. Twenty-one years ago everything was trim and trig and bright along the "coast," just as it had been in 1827, as described by those tourists.

Unfortunate tourists! People humbugged them with stupid and silly lies, and then laughed at them for believing and printing the same. They told Mrs. Trollope that the alligators—or crocodiles, as she calls them—were terrible creatures; and backed up the statement with a blood-curdling account of how one of these slandered reptiles crept into a squatter cabin one night, and ate up a woman and five children. The woman, by herself, would have satisfied any ordinarily-impossible alligator; but no, these liars must make him gorge the five children besides. One would not imagine that jokers of this robust breed would be sensitive—but they were. It is difficult, at this day, to understand, and impossible to justify, the reception which the book of the grave, honest, intelligent, gentle, manly, charitable, well-meaning Capt. Basil Hall got. Mrs. Trollope's account of it may perhaps entertain the reader; therefore I have put it in the Appendix.*

CHAPTER XLI

THE METROPOLIS OF THE SOUTH

The approaches to New Orleans were familiar; general aspects were unchanged. When one goes flying through London along a railway propped in the air on tall arches, he may inspect miles of upper bedrooms through the open windows, but the lower half of the houses is under his level and out of sight. Similarly, in high-river stage, in the New Orleans region, the water is up to the top of the enclosing levee-rim, the flat country behind it lies low—representing the bottom of a dish—and as the boat swims along, high on the flood, one looks down upon the houses and into the upper windows. There is nothing but that frail breastwork of earth between the people and destruction.

The old brick salt-warehouses clustered at the upper end of the city looked as they had always looked; warehouses which had had a kind of Aladdin's lamp experience, however, since I had seen them; for when the war broke out the proprietor went to bed one night leaving them packed with thousands of sacks of vulgar salt, worth a couple of dollars a sack, and got up in the morning and found his mountain of salt turned into a mountain of gold, so to speak, so suddenly and to so dizzy a height had the war news sent up the price of the article.

The vast reach of plank wharves remained unchanged, and there were as many ships as ever: but the long array of steamboats had vanished; not altogether, of course, but not much of it was left.

The city itself had not changed—to the eye. It had greatly increased in spread and population, but the look of the town was not altered. The dust, waste-paper-littered, was still deep in the streets; the deep, trough-like gutters alongside the curb-stones

* See Appendix C.

were still half full of reposeful water with a dusty surface; the sidewalks were still—in the sugar and bacon region—incumbered by casks and barrels and hogsheads; the great blocks of austerely plain commercial houses were as dusty-looking as ever.

Canal Street was finer, and more attractive and stirring than formerly, with its drifting crowds of people, its several processions of hurrying street-cars, and—toward evening—its broad second-story verandas crowded with gentlemen and ladies clothed according to the latest mode.

Not that there is any "architecture" in Canal Street: to speak in broad, general terms, there is no architecture in New Orleans, except in the cemeteries. It seems a strange thing to say of a wealthy, far-seeing, and energetic city of a quarter of a million inhabitants, but it is true. There is a huge granite U.S. Custom-house—costly enough, genuine enough, but as a decoration it is inferior to a gasometer. It looks like a state prison. But it was built before the war. Architecture in America may be said to have been born since the war. New Orleans, I believe, has had the good luck—and in a sense the bad luck—to have had no great fire in late years. It must be so. If the opposite had been the case, I think one would be able to tell the "burnt district" by the radical improvement in its architecture over the old forms. One can do this in Boston and Chicago. The "burnt district" of Boston was commonplace before the fire; but now there is no commercial district in any city in the world that can surpass it—or perhaps even rival it—in beauty, elegance, and tastefulness.

However, New Orleans has begun—just this moment, as one may say. When completed, the new Cotton Exchange will be a stately and beautiful building; massive, substantial, full of architectural graces; no shams or false pretences or uglinesses about it anywhere. To the city, it will be worth many times its cost, for it will breed its species. What has been lacking hitherto, was a model to build toward; something to educate eye and taste; a *suggester,* so to speak.

The city is well outfitted with progressive men—thinking, sagacious, long-headed men. The contrast between the spirit of the city and the city's architecture is like the contrast between waking and sleep. Apparently there is a "boom" in everything but that one dead feature. The water in the gutters used to be stagnant and slimy, and a potent disease-breeder; but the gutters are flushed now, two or three times a day, by powerful machinery; in many of the gutters the water never stands still, but has a steady current. Other sanitary improvements have been made; and with such effect that New Orleans claims to be (during the long intervals between the occasional yellow-fever assaults) one of the healthiest cities in the Union. There's plenty of ice now for everybody, manufactured in the town. It is a driving place commercially, and has a great river, ocean, and railway business. At the date of our visit, it was the best lighted city in the Union, electrically speaking. The New Orleans electric lights were more numerous than those of New York, and very much better. One had this modified noonday not only in Canal and some neighboring chief streets, but all along a stretch of five miles of river frontage. There are good clubs in the city now—several of them but recently organized—and inviting modern-style pleasure resorts at West End and Spanish Fort. The telephone is everywhere. One of the most notable advances is in journalism. The newspapers, as I remember them, were not a striking feature. Now they are. Money is spent upon them with a free hand. They get the news, let it cost what it may. The editorial work is not hackgrinding, but literature. As an example of New Orleans journalistic achievement, it may be mentioned that the "Times-Democrat" of August 26, 1882, contained a report of the year's business of the towns of the Mississippi Valley, from New Orleans all the way to St. Paul—two thousand miles. That issue of the paper consisted of *forty* pages; seven columns to the page; two hundred and eighty columns in all; fifteen hundred words to the column; an aggregate of four hundred and twenty thousand words. That is to say, not much short of three times as many words as there are in this book. One may with sorrow contrast this with the architecture of New Orleans.

I have been speaking of public architecture only. The domestic article in New Orleans is reproachless, notwithstanding it remains as it always was. All the dwellings are of wood—in the American part of the town, I mean—and all have a comfortable look. Those in the wealthy quarter are spacious; painted snow-white usually, and generally have wide verandas, or double-verandas, supported by ornamental columns. These mansions stand in the centre of large grounds, and rise, garlanded with roses, out of the midst of swelling masses of shining green foliage and many-colored blossoms. No houses could well be in better harmony with their surroundings, or more pleasing to the eye, or more home-like and comfortable-looking.

One even becomes reconciled to the cistern presently; this is a mighty cask, painted green, and sometimes a couple of stories high, which is propped against the house-corner on stilts. There is a mansion-and-brewery suggestion about the combination which seems very incongruous at first. But the people cannot have wells, and so they take rain-water. Neither can they conveniently have cellars, or graves;* the town being built upon "made" ground; so they do without both, and few of the living complain, and none of the others.

CHAPTER XLII

HYGIENE AND SENTIMENT

They bury their dead in vaults, above the ground.

These vaults have a resemblance to houses—sometimes to temples; are built of marble, generally; are architecturally graceful and shapely; they face the walks and driveways of the cemetery; and when one moves through the midst of a thousand or so of them and sees their white roofs and gables stretching into the distance on every hand, the phrase "city of the dead" has all at once a meaning to him. Many of the cemeteries are beautiful, and are kept in perfect order. When one goes from the levee or the business streets near it, to a cemetery, he observes to himself that if those people down there would live as neatly while they are alive as they do after they are dead, they would find many advantages in it; and besides, their quarter would be the wonder and admiration of the business world. Fresh flowers, in vases of water, are to be seen at the portals of many of the vaults; placed there by the pious hands of bereaved parents and children, husbands and wives, and renewed daily. A milder form of sorrow finds its inexpensive and lasting remembrancer in the coarse and ugly but indestructible "immortelle"—which is a wreath or cross or some such emblem, made of rosettes of black linen, with sometimes a yellow rosette at the conjunction of the cross's bars,—kind of sorrowful breastpin, so to say. The immortelle requires no attention: you just hang it up, and there you are; just leave it alone, it will take care of your grief for you, and keep it in mind better than you can; stands weather first-rate, and lasts like boiler-iron.

On sunny days, pretty little chameleons—gracefullest of leggéd reptiles—creep along the marble fronts of the vaults, and catch flies. Their changes of color—as to variety—are not up to the creature's reputation. They change color when a person comes along and hangs up an immortelle; but that is nothing: any right-feeling reptile would do that.

I will gradually drop this subject of graveyards. I have been

*The Israelites are buried in graves—by permission, I take it, not requirement; but none else, except the destitute, who are buried at public expense. The graves are but three or four feet deep.

trying all I could to get down to the sentimental part of it, but I cannot accomplish it. I think there is no genuinely sentimental part to it. It is all grotesque, ghastly, horrible. Graveyards may have been justifiable in the bygone ages, when nobody knew that for every dead body put into the ground, to glut the earth and the plant-roots and the air with disease-germs, five or fifty, or maybe a hundred, persons must die before their proper time; but they are hardly justifiable now, when even the children know that a dead saint enters upon a century-long career of assassination the moment the earth closes over his corpse. It is a grim sort of a thought. The relics of St. Anne, up in Canada, have now, after nineteen hundred years, gone to curing the sick by the dozen. But it is merest matter-of-course that these same relics, within a generation after St. Anne's death and burial, *made* several thousand people sick. Therefore these miracle-performances are simply compensation, nothing more. St. Anne is somewhat slow pay, for a Saint, it is true; but better a debt paid after nineteen hundred years, and outlawed by the statute of limitations, than not paid at all; and most of the knights of the halo do not pay at all. Where you find one that pays—like St. Anne—you find a hundred and fifty that take the benefit of the statute. And none of them pay any more than the principal of what they owe—they pay none of the interest either simple or compound. A Saint can never *quite* return the principal, however; for his dead body *kills* people, whereas his relics *heal* only—they never restore the dead to life. That part of the account is always left unsettled.

"Dr. F. Julius Le Moyne, after fifty years of medical practice, wrote: 'The inhumation of human bodies, dead from infectious diseases, results in constantly loading the atmosphere, and polluting the waters, with not only the germs that rise from simply putrefaction, but also with the *specific* germs of the diseases from which death resulted.'

"The gases (from buried corpses) will rise to the surface through eight or ten feet of gravel, just as coal-gas will do, and there is practically no limit to their power of escape.

"During the epidemic in New Orleans in 1853, Dr. E.H. Barton reported that in the Fourth District the mortality was four hundred and fifty-two per thousand—more than double that of any other. In this district were three large cemeteries, in which during the previous year more than three thousand bodies had been buried. In other districts the proximity of cemeteries seemed to aggravate the disease.

"In 1828 Professor Bianchi demonstrated how the fearful reappearance of the plague at Modena was caused by excavations in ground where, *three hundred years previously* the victims of the pestilence had been buried. Mr. Cooper, in explaining the causes of some epidemics, remarks that the opening of the plague burial-grounds at Eyam resulted in an immediate outbreak of disease."—*North American Review, No.* 3, *Vol.* 135.

In an address before the Chicago Medical Society, in advocacy of cremation, Dr. Charles W. Purdy made some striking comparisons to show what a burden is laid upon society by the burial of the dead:—

"One and one-fourth times more money is expended annually in funerals in the United States than the Government expends for public-school purposes. Funerals cost this country in 1880 enough money to pay the liabilities of all the commercial failures in the United States during the same year, and give each bankrupt a capital of $8,630 with which to resume business. Funerals cost annually more money than the value of the combined gold and silver yield of the United States in the year 1880! These figures do not include the sums invested in burial-grounds and expended in tombs and monuments, nor the loss from depreciation of property in the vicinity of cemeteries."

For the rich, cremation would answer as well as burial; for the ceremonies connected with it could be made as costly and ostentatious as a Hindoo *suttee;* while for the poor, cremation would be better than burial, because so cheap*—so cheap until the poor got to imitating the rich, which they would do by and by. The adoption of cremation would relieve us of a muck of threadbare burial-witticisms; but, on the other hand, it would resurrect a lot of mildewed old cremation-jokes that have had a rest for two thousand years.

I have a colored acquaintance who earns his living by odd jobs and heavy manual labor. He never earns above four hundred dollars in a year, and as he has a wife and several young children, the closest scrimping is necessary to get him through to the end of the twelve months debtless. To such a man a funeral is a colossal financial disaster. While I was writing one of the preceding chapters, this man lost a little child. He walked the town over with a friend, trying to find a coffin that was within his means. He bought the very cheapest one he could find, plain wood, stained. It cost him *twenty-six dollars.* It would have cost less than four, probably, if it had been built to put something useful into. He and his family will feel that outlay a good many months.

*Four or five dollars is the minimum cost.

CHAPTER XLIII

THE ART OF INHUMATION

About the same time, I encountered a man in the street, whom I had not seen for six or seven years; and something like this talk followed. I said,—

"But you used to look sad and oldish; you don't now. Where did you get all this youth and bubbling cheerfulness? Give me the address."

He chuckled blithely, took off his shining tile, pointed to a notched pink circlet of paper pasted into its crown, with something lettered on it, and went on chuckling while I read, "J. B—, UNDERTAKER." Then he clapped his hat on, gave it an irreverent tilt to leeward, and cried out,—

"That's what's the matter! It used to be rough times with me when you knew me—insurance-agency business, you know; mighty irregular. Big fire, all right—brisk trade for ten days while people scared; after that, dull policy-business till next fire. Town like this don't have fires often enough—a fellow strikes so many dull weeks in a row that he gets discouraged. But you bet you, *this* is the business! People don't wait for examples to *die*. No, sir, they drop off right along—there ain't any dull spots in the undertaker line. I just started in with two or three little old coffins and a hired hearse, and *now* look at the thing! I've worked up a business here that would satisfy any man, don't care who he is. Five years ago, lodged in an attic; live in a swell house now, with a mansard roof, and all the modern inconveniences."

"Does a coffin pay so well? Is there much profit on a coffin?"

"Go-way! How you talk!" Then, with a confidential wink, a dropping of the voice, and an impressive laying of his hand on my arm; "Look here; there's one thing in this world which isn't ever cheap. That's a coffin. There's one thing in this world which a person don't ever try to jew you down on. That's a coffin. There's one thing in this world which a person don't say,—'I'll look around a little, and if I find I can't do better I'll come back and take it.' That's a coffin. There's one thing in this world which a person won't take in pine if he can go walnut; and won't take in walnut if he can go mahogany; and won't take in mahogany if he can go an iron casket with silver door-plate and bronze handles. That's a coffin. And there's one thing in this world which you don't have to worry around after a person to get him to pay for. And *that's* a coffin. Undertaking?—why it's the dead-surest business in Christendom, and the nobbiest.

"Why, just look at it. A rich man won't have anything but your very best; and you can just pile it on, too—pile it on and sock it to him—he won't ever holler. And you take in a poor man, and if you work him right he'll bust himself on a single lay-out. Or especially a woman. F'r instance: Mrs. O'Flaherty comes in—widow—wiping her eyes and kind of moaning. Un-handkerchiefs one eye, bats it around tearfully over the stock; says,—

" 'And fhat might ye ask for that wan?'

" 'Thirty-nine dollars, madam,' says I.

" 'It's a foine big price, sure, but Pat shall be buried like a gintleman, as he was, if I have to work me fingers off for it. I'll have that wan, sor.'

" 'Yes, madam,' says I, 'and it is a very good one, too; not costly, to be sure, but in this life we must cut our garment to our clothes, as the saying is.' And as she starts out, I heave in, kind of casually, 'This one with the white satin lining is a beauty, but I am afraid—well, sixty-five dollars *is* a rather—rather—but no matter, I felt obliged to say to Mrs. O'Shaughnessy,—'

" 'D'ye mane to soy that Bridget O'Shaughnessy bought the mate to that joo-ul box to ship that dhrunken divil to Purgatory in?'

" 'Yes, madam.'

" 'Then Pat shall go to heaven in the twin to it, if it takes the last rap the O'Flaherties can raise; and moind you, stick on some extras, too, and I'll give ye another dollar.'

"And as I lay-in with the livery stables, of course I don't forget to mention that Mrs. O'Shaughnessy hired fifty-four dollars' worth of hacks and flung as much style into Dennis's funeral as if he had been a duke or an assassin. And of course she sails in and goes the O'Shaughnessy about four hacks and an omnibus better. That *used* to be, but that's all played now; that is, in this particular town. The Irish got to piling up hacks so, on their funerals, that a funeral left them ragged and hungry for two years afterward; so the priest pitched in and broke it all up. He don't allow them to have but two hacks now, and sometimes only one."

"Well," said I, "if you are so light-hearted and jolly in ordinary times, what *must* you be in an epidemic?"

He shook his head.

"No, you're off, there. We don't like to see an epidemic. An epidemic don't pay. Well, of course I don't mean that, exactly; but it don't pay in proportion to the regular thing. Don't it occur to you, why?"

"No."

"Think."

"I can't imagine. What is it?"

"It's just two things."

"Well, what *are* they?"

"One's Embamming."

"And what's the other?"

"Ice."

"How is that?"

"Well, in ordinary times, a person dies, and we lay him up in ice; one day, two days, maybe three, to wait for friends to come. Takes a lot of it—melts fast. We charge jewelry rates for that ice, and war-prices for attendance. Well, don't you know, when there's an epidemic, they rush 'em to the cemetery the minute the breath's out. No market for ice in an epidemic. Same with Embamming. You take a family that's able to embam, and you've got a soft thing. You can mention sixteen different ways to do it—though there *ain't* only one or two ways, when you come down to the bottom facts of it—and they'll take the highest-priced way, every time. It's human nature—human nature in grief. It don't reason, you see. 'Time being, it don't care a dam. All it wants is physical immortality for deceased, and they're willing to pay for it. All you've got to do is to just be ca'm and stack it up—they'll stand the racket. Why, man, you can take a defunct that you couldn't *give* away; and get your embamming traps around you and go to work; and in a couple of hours he is worth a cool six hundred—that's what *he's* worth. There ain't anything equal to it but trading rats for di'monds in time of famine. Well, don't you see, when there's an epidemic, people don't wait to embam. No, indeed they don't; and it hurts the business like hellth, as we say—hurts it like hell-th, *health*, see?— Our little joke in the trade. Well, I must be going. Give me a call whenever you need any—I mean, when you're going by, sometime."

In his joyful high spirits, he did the exaggerating himself, if any has been done. I have not enlarged on him.

With the above brief references to inhumation, let us leave the subject. As for me, I hope to be cremated. I made that remark to my pastor once, who said, with what he seemed to think was an impressive manner,—

"I wouldn't worry about that, if I had your chances."

Much he knew about it—the family all so opposed to it.

CHAPTER XLIV

CITY SIGHTS

The old French part of New Orleans—anciently the Spanish part—bears no resemblance to the American end of the city: the American end which lies beyond the intervening brick business-centre. The houses are massed in blocks; are austerely plain and dignified; uniform of pattern, with here and there a departure from it with pleasant effect; all are plastered on the outside, and nearly all have long, iron-railed verandas running along the several stories. Their chief beauty is the deep, warm, varicolored stain with which time and the weather have enriched the plaster. It harmonizes with all the surroundings, and has as natural a look of belonging there as has the flush upon sunset clouds. This charming decoration cannot be successfully imitated; neither is it to be found elsewhere in America.

The iron railings are a specialty, also. The pattern is often exceedingly light and dainty, and airy and graceful—with a large cipher or monogram in the centre, a delicate cobweb of baffling, intricate forms, wrought in steel. The ancient railings are handmade, and are now comparatively rare and proportionately valuable. They are become bric-a-brac.

The party had the privilege of idling through this ancient quarter of New Orleans with the South's finest literary genius, the author of "the Grandissimes." In him the South has found a masterly delineator of its interior life and its history. In truth, I find by experience, that the untrained eye and vacant mind can inspect it and learn of it and judge of it more clearly and profitably in his books than by personal contact with it.

With Mr. Cable along to see for you, and describe and explain and illuminate, a jog through that old quarter is a vivid pleasure. And you have a vivid *sense* as of unseen or dimly seen things—vivid, and yet fitful and darkling; you glimpse salient features, but lose the fine shades or catch them imperfectly through the vision of the imagination: a case, as it were, of ignorant near-sighted stranger traversing the rim of wide vague horizons of Alps with an inspired and enlightened long-sighted native.

We visited the old St. Louis Hotel, now occupied by municipal offices. There is nothing strikingly remarkable about it; but one can say of it as of the Academy of Music in New York, that if a broom or a shovel has ever been used in it there is no circumstantial evidence to back up the fact. It is curious that cabbages and hay and things do not grow in the Academy of Music; but no doubt it is on account of the interruption of the light by the benches, and the impossibility of hoeing the crop except in the aisles. The fact that the ushers grow their buttonhole-bouquets on the premises shows what might be done if they had the right kind of an agricultural head to the establishment.

We visited also the venerable Cathedral, and the pretty square in front of it; the one dim with religious light, the other brilliant with the wordly sort, and lovely with orange trees and blossomy shrubs; then we drove in the hot sun through the wilderness of houses and out on to the wide dead level beyond, where the villas are, and the water wheels to drain the town, and the commons populous with cows and children; passing by an old cemetery where we were told lie the ashes of an early pirate; but we took him on trust, and did not visit him. He was a pirate with a tremendous and sanguinary history; and as long as he preserved unspotted, in retirement, the dignity of his name and the grandeur of his ancient calling, homage and reverence were his from high and low; but when at last he descended into politics and became a paltry alderman, the public "shook" him, and turned aside and wept. When he died, they set up a monument over him; and little by little he has come into respect again; but it is respect for the pirate, not the alderman, To-day the loyal and generous remember only what he was, and charitably forget what he became.

Thence, we drove a few miles across a swamp, along a raised shell road, with a canal on one hand and a dense wood on the other; and here and there, in the distance, a ragged and angular-limbed and moss-bearded cypress, top standing out, clear cut against the sky, and as quaint of form as the apple-trees in Japanese pictures—such was our course and the surroundings of it. There was an occasional alligator swimming comfortably along in the canal, and an occasional picturesque colored person on the bank, flinging his statue-rigid reflection upon the still water and watching for a bite.

And by and by we reached the West End, a collection of hotels of the usual light summer-resort pattern, with broad verandas all around, and the waves of the wide and blue Lake Pontchartrain lapping the thresholds. We had dinner on a ground-veranda over the water—the chief dish the renowned fish called the pompano, delicious as the less criminal forms of sin.

Thousands of people come by rail and carriage to West End and to Spanish Fort every evening, and dine, listen to the bands, take strolls in the open air under the electric lights, go sailing on the lake, and entertain themselves in various and sundry other ways.

We had opportunities on other days and in other places to test the pompano. Notably, at an editorial dinner at one of the clubs in the city. He was in his last possible perfection there, and justified his fame. In his suite was a tall pyramid of scarlet cray-fish—large ones; as large as one's thumb; delicate, palatable, appetizing. Also devilled whitebait; also shrimps of choice quality; and a platter of small soft-shell crabs of a most superior breed. The other dishes were what one might get at Delmonico's, or Buckingham Palace; those I have spoken of can be had in similar perfection in New Orleans only, I suppose.

In the West and South they have a new institution,—the Broom Brigade. It is composed of young ladies who dress in a uniform costume, and go through the infantry drill, with broom in place of musket. It is a very pretty sight, on private view. When they perform on the stage of a theatre, in the blaze of colored fires, it must be a fine and fascinating spectacle. I saw them go through their complex manual with grace, spirit, and admirable precision. I saw them do everything which a human being can possibly do with a broom, except sweep. I did not see them sweep. But I know they could learn. What they have already learned proves that. And if they ever should learn, and should go on the war-path down Tchoupitoulas or some of those other streets around there, those thoroughfares would bear a greatly improved aspect in a very few minutes. But the girls themselves wouldn't; so nothing would be really gained, after all.

The drill was in the Washington Artillery building. In this building we saw many interesting relics of the war. Also a fine oil-painting representing Stonewall Jackson's last interview with General Lee. Both men are on horseback. Jackson has just ridden up, and is accosting Lee. The picture is very valuable, on account of the portraits, which are authentic. But, like many another historical picture, it means nothing without its label. And one label will fit it as well as another:—

First Interview between Lee and Jackson.

Last Interview between Lee and Jackson.

Jackson Introducing Himself to Lee.

Jackson Accepting Lee's Invitation to Dinner.

Jackson Declining Lee's Invitation to Dinner—with Thanks.

Jackson Apologizing for a Heavy Defeat.

Jackson Reporting a Great Victory.

Jackson Asking Lee for a Match.

It tells *one* story, and a sufficient one; for it says quite plainly and satisfactorily, "Here are Lee and Jackson together." The artist would have made it tell that this is Lee and Jackson's last interview if he could have done it. But he couldn't, for there wasn't any way to do it. A good legible label is usually worth, for information, a ton of significant attitude and expression in a historical picture. In Rome, people with fine sympathetic natures stand up and weep in front of the celebrated "Beatrice Cenci the Day before her Execution." It shows what a label can do. If they did not know the picture, they would inspect it unmoved, and say, "Young girl with hay fever; young girl with her head in a bag."

I found the half-forgotten Southern intonations and elisions as pleasing to my ear as they had formerly been. A Southerner talks music. At least it is music to me, but then I was born in the South. The educated Southerner has no use for an *r,* except at the beginning of a word. He says "honah," and "dinnah," and "Gove'nuh," and "befo' the waw," and so on. The words may lack charm to the eye, in print, but they have it to the ear. When did the *r* disappear from Southern speech, and how did it come to disappear? The custom of dropping it was not borrowed from the North, nor inherited from England. Many Southerners—most Southerners—put a *y* into occasional words that begin with the *k* sound. For instance, they say Mr. K'yahtah (Carter) and speak of playing k'yahds or of riding in the k'yahs. And they have the pleasant custom—long ago fallen into decay in the North—of frequently employing the respectful "Sir." Instead of the curt Yes, and the abrupt No, they say "Yes, Suh"; "No, Suh."

But there are some infelicities. Such as "like" for "as," and the addition of an "at" where it isn't needed. I heard an educated gentleman say, "Like the flag-officer did." His cook or his butler would have said, "Like the flag-officer done." You hear gentlemen say, "Where have you been at?" And here is the aggravated form—heard a ragged street Arab say it to a comrade: "I was a-ask'n' Tom whah you was a-sett'n' at." The very elect carelessly say "will" when they mean "shall"; and many of them say, "I didn't go to do it," meaning "I didn't mean to do it." The Northern word "guess"—imported from England, where it used to be common, and now regarded by satirical Englishmen as a Yankee original—is but little used among Southerners. They say "reckon." They haven't any "doesn't" in their language; they say "don't" instead. The unpolished often use "went" for "gone." It is nearly as bad as the Northern "hadn't ought." This reminds me that a remark of a very peculiar nature was made here in my neighborhood (in the North) a few days ago: "He hadn't ought to have went." How is that? Isn't that a good deal of a triumph? One knows the orders combined in this half-breed's architecture without inquiring:

one parent Northern, the other Southern. To-day I heard a school-mistress ask, "Where is John gone?" This form is so common—so nearly universal, in fact—that if she had used "whither" instead of "where," I think it would have sounded like an affectation.

We picked up one excellent word—a word worth traveling to New Orleans to get; a nice limber, expressive, handy word—"Lagniappe." They pronounce it lanny-*yap*. It is Spanish—so they said. We discovered it at the head of a column of odds and ends in the Picayune, the first day; heard twenty people use it the second; inquired what it meant the third; adopted it and got facility in swinging it the fourth. It has a restricted meaning, but I think the people spread it out a little when they choose. It is the equivalent of the thirteenth roll in a "baker's dozen." It is something thrown in, gratis, for good measure. The custom originated in the Spanish quarter of the city. When a child or a servant buys something in a shop—or even the mayor or the governor, for aught I know—he finishes the operation by saying,—

"Give me something for lagniappe."

The shopman always responds; gives the child a bit of liquorice-root, gives the servant a cheap cigar or a spool of thread, gives the governor—I don't know what he gives the governor; support, likely.

When you are invited to drink,—and this does occur now and then in New Orleans,—and you say, "What, again?—no, I've had enough;" the other party says, "But just this one time more,—this is for lagniappe." When the beau perceives that he is stacking his compliments a trifle too high, and sees by the young lady's countenance that the edifice would have been better with the top compliment left off, he puts his "I beg pardon,—no harm intended," into the briefer form of "Oh, that's for lagniappe." If the waiter in the restaurant stumbles and spills a gill of coffee down the back of your neck, he says, "For lagniappe, sah," and gets you another cup without extra charge.

CHAPTER XLV

SOUTHERN SPORTS

In the North one hears the war mentioned, in social conversation, once a month; sometimes as often as once a week; but as a distinct subject for talk, it has long ago been relieved of duty. There are sufficient reasons for this. Given a dinner company of six gentlemen to-day, it can easily happen that four of them—and possibly five—were not in the field at all. So the chances are four to two, or five to one, that the war will at no time during the evening become the topic of conversation; and the chances are still greater that if it become the topic it will remain so but a little while. If you add six ladies to the company, you have added six people who saw so little of the dread realities of the war that they ran out of talk concerning them years ago, and now would soon weary of the war topic if you brought it up.

The case is very different in the South. There, every man you meet was in the war; and every lady you meet saw the war. The war is the great chief topic of conversation. The interest in it is vivid and constant; the interest in other topics is fleeting. Mention of the war will wake up a dull company and set their tongues going, when nearly any other topic would fail. In the South, the war is what A.D. is elsewhere: they date from it. All day long you hear things "placed" as having happened since the waw; or du'in' the waw; or befo' the waw; or right aftah the waw; or 'bout two yeahs or five yeahs or ten yeahs befo' the waw or aftah the waw. It shows how intimately every individual was visited, in his own person, by that tremendous episode. It gives the inexperienced stranger a better idea of what a vast and comprehensive calamity invasion is than he can ever get by reading books at the fireside.

At a club one evening, a gentleman turned to me and said, in an aside:—

"You notice, of course, that we are nearly always talking about the war. It isn't because we haven't anything else to talk about, but because nothing else has so strong an interest for us. And there is another reason: In the war, each of us, in his own person, seems to have sampled all the different varieties of human experience; as a consequence, you can't mention an outside matter of any sort but it will certainly remind some listener of something that happened during the war,—and out he comes with it. Of course that brings the talk back to the war. You may try all you want to, to keep other subjects before the house, and we may all join in and help, but there can be but one result: the most random topic would load every man up with war reminiscences, and *shut* him up, too; and talk would be likely to stop presently, because you can't talk pale inconsequentialities when you've got a crimson fact or fancy in your head that you are burning to fetch out."

The poet was sitting some little distance away; and presently he began to speak—about the moon.

The gentleman who had been talking to me remarked in an

"aside:" "There, the moon is far enough from the seat of war, but you will see that it will suggest something to somebody about the war; in ten minutes from now the moon, as a topic, will be shelved."

The poet was saying he had noticed something which was a surprise to him; had had the impression that down here, toward the equator, the moonlight was much stronger and brighter than up North; had had the impression that when he visited New Orleans, many years ago, the moon—

Interruption from the other end of the room:—

"Let me explain that. Reminds me of an anecdote. Everything is changed since the war, for better or for worse; but you'll find people down here born grumblers, who see no change except the change for the worse. There was an old negro woman of this sort. A young New-Yorker said in her presence, 'What a wonderful moon you have down here!' She sighed and said, 'Ah, bless yo' heart, honey, you ought to seen dat moon befo' de waw!'"

The new topic was dead already. But the poet resurrected it, and gave it a new start.

A brief dispute followed, as to whether the difference between Northern and Southern moonlight really existed or was only imagined. Moonlight talk drifted easily into talk about artificial methods of dispelling darkness. Then somebody remembered that when Farragut advanced upon Port Hudson on a dark night—and did not wish to assist the aim of the Confederate gunners—he carried no battle-lanterns, but painted the decks of his ships white, and thus created a dim but valuable light, which enabled his own men to grope their way around with considerable facility. At this point the war got the floor again—the ten minutes not quite up yet.

I was not sorry, for war talk by men who have been in a war is always interesting; whereas moon talk by a poet who has not been in the moon is likely to be dull.

We went to a cockpit in New Orleans on a Saturday afternoon. I had never seen a cock-fight before. There were men and boys there of all ages and all colors, and of many languages and nationalities. But I noticed one quite conspicuous and surprising absence: the traditional brutal faces. There were no brutal faces. With no cock-fighting going on, you could have played the gathering on a stranger for a prayer-meeting; and after it began, for a revival,— provided you blindfolded your stranger,—for the shouting was something prodigious.

A negro and a white man were in the ring; everybody else outside. The cocks were brought in in sacks; and when time was called, they were taken out by the two bottle-holders, stroked, caressed, poked toward each other, and finally liberated. The big black cock plunged instantly at the little gray one and struck him on the head with his spur. The gray responded with spirit. Then the Babel of many-tongued shoutings broke out, and ceased not thenceforth. When the cocks had been fighting some little time, I was expecting them momently to drop dead, for both were blind, red with blood, and so exhausted that they frequently fell down. Yet they would not give up, neither would they die. The negro and the white man would pick them up every few seconds, wipe them off, blow cold water on them in a fine spray, and take their heads in their mouths and hold them there a moment—to warm back the perishing life perhaps; I do not know. Then, being set down again, the dying creatures would totter gropingly about, with dragging wings, find each other, strike a guess-work blow or two, and fall exhausted once more.

I did not see the end of the battle. I forced myself to endure it as long as I could, but it was too pitiful a sight; so I made frank confession to that effect, and we retired. We heard afterward that the black cock died in the ring, and fighting to the last.

Evidently there is abundant fascination about this "sport" for such as have had a degree of familiarity with it. I never saw people enjoy anything more than this gathering enjoyed this fight. The case was the same with old gray-heads and with boys of ten. They lost themselves in frenzies of delight. The "cocking-main" is an inhuman sort of entertainment, there is no question about that; still, it seems a much more respectable and far less cruel sport than fox-hunting—for the cocks like it; they experience, as well as confer enjoyment; which is not the fox's case.

We assisted—in the French sense—at a mule race, one day. I believe I enjoyed this contest more than any other mule there. I enjoyed it more than I remember having enjoyed any other animal race I ever saw. The grand stand was well filled with the beauty and the chivalry of New Orleans. That phrase is not original with me. It is the Southern reporter's. He has used it for two generations. He uses it twenty times a day, or twenty thousand times a day; or a million times a day—according to the exigencies. He is obliged to use it a million times a day, if he have occasion to speak of respectable men and women that often; for he has no other phrase for such service except that single one. He never tires of it; it always has a fine sound to him. There is a kind of swell mediaeval bulliness and tinsel about it that pleases his gaudy barbaric soul. If he had been in Palestine in the early times, we should have had no references to "much people" out of him. No, he would have said "the beauty and the chivalry of

Galilee" assembled to hear the Sermon on the Mount. It is likely that the men and women of the South are sick enough of that phrase by this time, and would like a change, but there is no immediate prospect of their getting it.

The New Orleans editor has a strong, compact, direct, unflowery style; wastes no words, and does not gush. Not so with his average correspondent. In the Appendix I have quoted a good letter, penned by a trained hand; but the average correspondent hurls a style which differs from that. For instance:—

The "Times-Democrat" sent a relief-steamer up one of the bayous, last April. This steamer landed at a village, up there somewhere, and the Captain invited some of the ladies of the village to make a short trip with him. They accepted and came aboard, and the steamboat shoved out up the creek. That was all there was "to it." And that is all that the editor of the "Times-Democrat" would have got out of it. There was nothing in the thing but statistics, and he would have got nothing else out of it. He would probably have even tabulated them, partly to secure perfect clearness of statement, and partly to save space. But his special correspondent knows other methods of handling statistics. He just throws off all restraint and wallows in them:—

> "On Saturday, early in the morning, the beauty of the place graced our cabin, and proud of her fair freight the gallant little boat glided up the bayou."

Twenty-two words to say the ladies came aboard and the boat shoved out up the creek, is a clean waste of ten good words, and is also destructive of compactness of statement.

The trouble with the Southern reporter is—Women. They unsettle him; they throw him off his balance. He is plain, and sensible, and satisfactory, until a woman heaves in sight. Then he goes all to pieces; his mind totters, he becomes flowery and idiotic. From reading the above extract, you would imagine that this student of Sir Walter Scott is an apprentice, and knows next to nothing about handling a pen. On the contrary, he furnishes plenty of proofs, in his long letter, that he knows well enough how to handle it when the women are not around to give him the artificial-flower complaint. For instance:—

> "At 4 o'clock ominous clouds began to gather in the southeast, and presently from the Gulf there came a blow which increased in severity every moment. It was not safe to leave the landing then, and there was a delay. The oaks shook off long tresses of their mossy beards to the tugging of the wind, and the bayou in its ambition put on miniature waves in mocking of much larger bodies of water. A lull permitted a start, and

homewards we steamed, an inky sky overhead and a heavy wind blowing. As darkness crept on, there were few on board who did not wish themselves nearer home."

There is nothing the matter with that. It is good description, compactly put. Yet there was great temptation, there, to drop into lurid writing.

But let us return to the mule. Since I left him, I have rummaged around and found a full report of the race. In it I find confirmation of the theory which I broached just now—namely, that the trouble with the Southern reporter is Women: Women, supplemented by Walter Scott and his knights and beauty and chivalry, and so on. This is an excellent report, as long as the women stay out of it. But when they intrude, we have this frantic result:—

"It will be probably a long time before the ladies' stand presents such a sea of foam-like loveliness as it did yesterday. The New Orleans women are always charming, but never so much so as at this time of the year, when in their dainty spring costumes they bring with them a breath of balmy freshness and an odor of sanctity unspeakable. The stand was so crowded with them that, walking at their feet and seeing no possibility of approach, many a man appreciated as he never did before the Peri's feeling at the Gates of Paradise, and wondered what was the priceless boon that would admit him to their sacred presence. Sparkling on their white-robed breasts or shoulders were the colors of their favorite knights, and were it not for the fact that the doughty heroes appeared on unromantic mules, it would have been easy to imagine one of King Arthur's gala-days."

There were thirteen mules in the first heat; all sorts of mules, they were; all sorts of complexions, gaits, dispositions, aspects. Some were handsome creatures, some were not; some were sleek, some hadn't had their fur brushed lately; some were innocently gay and frisky; some were full of malice and all unrighteousness; guessing from looks, some of them thought the matter on hand was war, some thought it was a lark, the rest took it for a religious occasion. And each mule acted according to his convictions. The result was an absence of harmony well compensated by a conspicuous presence of variety—variety of picturesque and entertaining sort.

All the riders were young gentlemen in fashionable society. If the reader has been wondering why it is that the ladies of New Orleans attend so humble an orgy as a mule-race, the thing is explained now. It is a fashion-freak; all connected with it are people of fashion.

It is great fun, and cordially liked. The mule-race is one of the marked occasions of the year. It has brought some pretty fast mules to the front. One of these had to be ruled out, because he was so fast that he turned the thing into a one-mule contest, and robbed it of one of its best features—variety. But every now and then somebody disguises him with a new name and a new complexion, and rings him in again.

The riders dress in full jockey costumes of bright-colored silks, satins, and velvets.

The thirteen mules got away in a body, after a couple of false starts, and scampered off with prodigious spirit. As each mule and each rider had a distinct opinion of his own at to how the race ought to be run, and which side of the track was best in certain circumstances, and how often the track ought to be crossed, and when a collision ought to be accomplished, and when it ought to be avoided, these twenty-six conflicting opinions created a most fantastic and picturesque confusion, and the resulting spectacle was killingly comical.

Mile heat; time, 2:22. Eight of the thirteen mules distanced. I had a bet on a mule which would have won if the procession had been reversed. The second heat was good fun; and so was the "consolation race for beaten mules," which followed later; but the first heat was the best in that respect.

I think that much the most enjoyable of all races is a steamboat race; but, next to that, I prefer the gay and joyous mule-rush. Two red-hot steamboats raging along, neck-and-neck, straining every nerve—that is to say, every rivet in the boilers—quaking and shaking and groaning from stem to stern, spouting white steam from the pipes, pouring black smoke from the chimneys, raining down sparks, parting the river into long breaks of hissing foam—this is sport that makes a body's very liver curl with enjoyment. A horse-race is pretty tame and colorless in comparison. Still, a horse-race might be well enough, in its way, perhaps, if it were not for the tiresome false starts. But then, nobody is ever killed. At least, nobody was ever killed when I was at a horse-race. They have been crippled, it it true; but this is little to the purpose.

CHAPTER XLVI

ENCHANTMENTS AND ENCHANTERS

The largest annual event in New Orleans is a something which we arrived too late to sample—the Mardi-Gras festivities. I saw the procession of the Mystic Crew of Comus there, twenty-four years ago—with knights and nobles and so on, clothed in silken and golden Paris-made gorgeousnesses, planned and bought for that single night's use; and in their train all manner of giants, dwarfs, monstrosities, and other diverting grotesquerie—a startling and wonderful sort of show, as it filed solemnly and silently down the street in the light of its smoking and flickering torches; but it is said that in these latter days the spectacle is mightily augmented, as to cost, splendor, and variety. There is a chief personage—"Rex;" and if I remember rightly, neither this king nor any of his great following of subordinates is known to any outsider. All these people are gentlemen of position and consequence; and it is a proud thing to belong to the organization; so the mystery in which they hide their personality is merely for romance's sake, and not on account of the police.

Mardi-Gras is of course a relic of the French and Spanish occupation; but I judge that the religious feature has been pretty well knocked out of it now. Sir Walter has got the advantage of the gentlemen of the cowl and rosary, and he will stay. His mediaeval business, supplemented by the monsters and the oddities, and the pleasant creatures from fairy-land, is finer to look at than the poor fantastic inventions and performances of the revelling rabble of the priest's day, and serves quite as well, perhaps, to emphasize the day and admonish men that the grace-line between the worldly season and the holy one is reached.

This Mardi-Gras pageant was the exclusive possession of New Orleans until recently. But now it has spread to Memphis and St. Louis and Baltimore. It has probably reached its limit. It is a thing which could hardly exist in the practical North; would certainly last but a very brief time; as brief a time as it would last in London. For the soul of it is the romantic, not the funny and the grotesque. Take away the romantic mysteries, the kings and knights and big-sounding titles, and Mardi-Gras would die, down there in the South. The very feature that keeps it alive in the South— girly-girly romance—would kill it in the North or in London. Puck and Punch, and the press universal, would fall upon it and make merciless fun of it, and its first exhibition would be also its last.

Against the crimes of the French Revolution and of Bonaparte may be set two compensating benefactions: the Revolution broke the chains of the *ancien régime* and of the Church, and made of a nation of abject slaves a nation of freemen; and Bonaparte instituted the setting of merit above birth, and also so completely stripped the divinity from royalty, that whereas crowned heads in Europe were gods before, they are only men, since, and can never be gods again, but only figure-heads, and answerable for their acts like common clay. Such benefactions as these compensate the temporary harm which Bonaparte and the Revolution did, and leave the world in debt to them for these great and permanent services to liberty, humanity, and progress.

Then comes Sir Walter Scott with his enchantments, and by his single might checks this wave of progress, and even turns it back; sets the world in love with dreams and phantoms; with decayed and swinish forms of religion; with decayed and degraded systems of government; with the sillinesses and emptinesses, sham grandeurs, sham gauds, and sham chivalries of a brainless and worthless long-vanished society. He did measureless harm; more real and lasting harm, perhaps, than any other individual that ever wrote. Most of the world has now outlived good part of these harms, though by no means all of them; but in our South they flourish pretty forcefully still. Not so forcefully as half a generation ago, perhaps, but still forcefully. There, the genuine and wholesome civilization of the nineteenth century is curiously confused and commingled with the Walter Scott Middle-Age sham civilization and so you have practical, common-sense, progressive ideas, and progressive works, mixed up with the duel, the inflated speech, and the jejune romanticism of an absurd past that is dead, and out of charity ought to be buried. But for the Sir Walter disease, the character of the Southerner—or Southron, according to Sir Walter's starchier way of phrasing it—would be wholly modern, in place of modern and mediaeval mixed, and the South would be fully a generation further advanced than it is. It was Sir Walter that made every gentleman in the South a Major or a Colonel, or a General or a Judge, before the war; and it was he, also, that made these gentlemen value these bogus decorations. For it was he that created rank and caste down there, and also reverence for rank and caste, and pride and pleasure in them. Enough is laid on slavery, without fathering upon it these creations and contributions of Sir Walter.

Sir Walter had so large a hand in making Southern character, as it existed before the war, that he is in great measure responsible for the war. It seems a little harsh toward a dead man to say that we never should have had any war but for Sir Walter; and yet something of a plausible argument might, perhaps, be made in support of that wild proposition. The Southerner of the American revolution owned slaves; so did the Southerner of the Civil War: but the former resembles the latter as an Englishman resembles a Frenchman. The change of character can be traced rather more easily to Sir Walter's influence than to that of any other thing or person.

One may observe, by one or two signs, how deeply that influence penetrated, and how strongly it holds. If one take up a Northern or Southern literary periodical of forty or fifty years ago, he will find it filled with wordy, windy, flowery "eloquence," romanticism, sentimentality—all imitated from Sir Walter, and sufficiently badly done, too—innocent travesties of his style and methods, in fact. This sort of literature being the fashion in both sections of the country, there was opportunity for the fairest competition; and as a consequence, the South was able to show as many well-known literary names, proportioned to population, as the North could.

But a change has come, and there is no opportunity now for a fair competition between North and South. For the North has thrown out that old inflated style, whereas the Southern writer still clings to it—clings to it and has a restricted market for his wares, as a consequence. There is as much literary talent in the South, now, as ever there was, of course; but its work can gain but slight currency under present conditions; the authors write for the past, not the present; they use obsolete forms, and a dead language. But when a Southerner of genius writes modern English, his book goes upon crutches no longer, but upon wings; and they carry it swiftly all about America and England, and through the great English reprint publishing houses of Germany—as witness the experience of Mr. Cable and Uncle Remus, two of the very few Southern authors who do not write in the southern style. Instead of three or four widely-known literary names, the South ought to have a dozen or two—and will have them when Sir Walter's time is out.

A curious exemplification of the power of a single book for good or harm is shown in the effects wrought by Don Quixote and those wrought by Ivanhoe. The first swept the world's admiration for the mediaeval chivalry-silliness out of existence; and the other restored it. As far as our South is concerned, the good work done by Cervantes is pretty nearly a dead letter, so effectually has Scott's pernicious work undermined it.

CHAPTER XLVII

UNCLE REMUS AND MR. CABLE

Mr. Joel Chandler Harris ("Uncle Remus") was to arrive from Atlanta at seven o'clock Sunday morning; so we got up and received him. We were able to detect him among the crowd of arrivals at the hotel-counter by his correspondence with a description of him which had been furnished us from a trustworthy source. He was said to be undersized, red-haired, and somewhat freckled. He was the only man in the party whose outside tallied with this bill of particulars. He was said to be very shy. He is a shy man. Of this there is no doubt. It may not show on the surface, but the shyness is there. After days of intimacy one wonders to see that it is still in about as strong force as ever. There is a fine and beautiful nature hidden behind it, as all know who have read the Uncle Remus book; and a fine genius, too, as all know by the same sign. I seem to be talking quite freely about this neighbor; but in talking to the public I am but talking to his personal friends, and these things are permissible among friends.

He deeply disappointed a number of children who had flocked eagerly to Mr. Cable's house to get a glimpse of the illustrious sage and oracle of the nation's nurseries. They said:—

"Why, he's white!"

They were grieved about it. So, to console them, the book was brought, that they might hear Uncle Remus's Tar-Baby story from the lips of Uncle Remus himself—or what, in their outraged eyes, was left of him. But it turned out that he had never read aloud to people, and was too shy to venture the attempt now. Mr. Cable and I read from books of ours, to show him what an easy trick it was; but his immortal shyness was proof against even this sagacious strategy, so we had to read about Brer Rabbit ourselves.

Mr. Harris ought to be able to read the negro dialect better than anybody else, for in the matter of writing it he is the only master the country has produced. Mr. Cable is the only master in the writing of French dialects that the country has produced; and he reads them in perfection. It was a great treat to hear him read about Jean-ah Poquelin, and about Innerarity and his famous "pigshoo" representing "Louisihanna *Rif*-fusing to Hanter the Union," along with passages of nicely-shaded German dialect from a novel which was still in manuscript.

It came out in conversation, that in two different instances Mr. Cable got into grotesque trouble by using, in his books, next-to-impossible French names which nevertheless happened to be borne by living and sensitive citizens of New-Orleans. His names were either inventions or were borrowed from the ancient and obsolete past, I do not now remember which; but at any rate living bearers of them turned up, and were a good deal hurt at having attention directed to themselves and their affairs in so excessively public a manner.

Mr. Warner and I had an experience of the same sort when we wrote the book called "The Gilded Age." There is a character in it called "Sellers." I do not remember what his first name was, in the beginning; but anyway, Mr. Warner did not like it, and wanted it improved. He asked me if I was able to imagine a person named "Eschol Sellers." Of course I said I could not, without stimulants. He said that away out West, once, he had met, and contemplated, and actually shaken hands with a man bearing that impossible name—"Eschol Sellers." He added,—

"It was twenty years ago; his name has probably carried him off before this; and if it hasn't, he will never see the book anyhow. We will confiscate his name. The name you are using is common, and therefore dangerous; there are probably a thousand Sellerses bearing it, and the whole horde will come after us; but Eschol Sellers is a safe name—it is a rock."

So we borrowed that name; and when the book had been out about a week, one of the stateliest and handsomest and most aristocratic looking white men that ever lived, called around, with the most formidable libel suit in his pocket that ever—well, in brief, we got his permission to suppress an edition of ten million* copies of the book and change that name to "Mulberry Sellers" in future editions.

CHAPTER XLVIII

SUGAR AND POSTAGE

One day, on the street, I encountered the man whom, of all men, I most wished to see—Horace Bixby; formerly pilot under me—or rather, over me—now captain of the great steamer "City of Baton Rouge," the latest and swiftest addition to the Anchor Line. The same slender figure, the same tight curls, the same springy step, the same alertness, the same decision of eye and answering decision of hand, the same erect military bearing; not an inch gained or lost in girth, not an ounce gained or lost in weight, not a hair turned. It is a curious thing, to leave a man thirty-five years old, and come back at the end of twenty-one years and find him still only thirty-five. I have not had an experience of this kind before, I believe. There were some crow's-

* Figures taken from memory, and probably incorrect. Think it was more.

feet, but they counted for next to nothing, since they were inconspicuous.

His boat was just in. I had been waiting several days for her, purposing to return to St. Louis in her. The captain and I joined a party of ladies and gentlemen, guests of Major Wood, and went down the river fifty-four miles, in a swift tug, to ex-Governor Warmouth's sugar plantation. Strung along below the city, were a number of decayed, ram-shackly, superannuated old steamboats, not one of which had I ever seen before. They had all been built, and worn out, and thrown aside, since I was here last. This gives one a realizing sense of the frailness of a Mississippi boat and the briefness of its life.

Six miles below town a fat and battered brick chimney, sticking above the magnolias and live-oaks, was pointed out as the monument erected by an appreciative nation to celebrate the battle of New Orleans—Jackson's victory over the British, January 8, 1815. The war had ended, the two nations were at peace, but the news had not yet reached New Orleans. If we had had the cable telegraph in those days, this blood would not have been spilt, those lives would not have been wasted; and better still, Jackson would probably never have been president. We have gotten over the harms done us by the war of 1812, but not over some of those done us by Jackson's presidency.

The Warmouth plantation covers a vast deal of ground, and the hospitality of the Warmouth mansion is graduated to the same large scale. We saw steam-plows at work, here, for the first time. The traction engine travels about on its own wheels, till it reaches the required spot; then it stands still and by means of a wire rope pulls the huge plow toward itself two or three hundred yards across the field, between the rows of cane. The thing cuts down into the black mould a foot and a half deep. The plow looks like a fore-and-aft brace of a Hudson river steamer, inverted. When the negro steersman sits on one end of it, that end tilts down near the ground, while the other sticks up high in air. This great see-saw goes rolling and pitching like a ship at sea, and it is not every circus rider that could stay on it.

The plantation contains two thousand six hundred acres; six hundred and fifty are in cane; and there is a fruitful orange grove of five thousand trees. The cane is cultivated after a modern and intricate scientific fashion, too elaborate and complex for me to attempt to describe; but it lost $40,000 last year. I forget the other details. However, this year's crop will reach ten or twelve hundred tons of sugar, consequently last year's loss will not matter. These troublesome and expensive scientific methods achieve a yield of a ton and a half, and from that to two tons, to the acre; which is three or four times what the yield of an acre was in my time.

The drainage-ditches were everywhere alive with little crabs—"fiddlers." One saw them scampering sidewise in every direction whenever they heard a disturbing noise. Expensive pests, these crabs; for they bore into the levees, and ruin them.

The great sugar-house was a wilderness of tubs and tanks and vats and filters, pumps, pipes, and machinery. The process of making sugar is exceedingly interesting. First, you heave your cane into the centrifugals and grind out the juice; then run it through the evaporating pan to extract the fibre; then through the bone-filter to remove the alcohol; then through the clarifying tanks to discharge the molasses; then through the granulating pipes to condense it; then through the vacuum pan to extract the vacuum. It is now ready for market. I have jotted these particulars down from memory. The thing looks simple and easy. Do not deceive yourself. To make sugar is really one of the most difficult things in the world. And to make it right, is next to impossible. If you will examine your own supply every now and then for a term of years, and tabulate the result, you will find that not two men in twenty can make sugar without getting sand into it.

We could have gone down to the mouth of the river and visited Captain Eads' great work, the "jetties," where the river has been compressed between walls, and thus deepened to twenty-six feet; but it was voted useless to go, since at this stage of the water everything would be covered up and invisible.

We could have visited that ancient and singular burg, "Pilot-town," which stands on stilts in the water—so they say; where nearly all communication is by skiff and canoe, even to the attending of weddings and funerals; and where the littlest boys and girls are as handy with the oar as unamphibious children are with the velocipede.

We could have done a number of other things; but on account of limited time, we went back home. The sail up the breezy and sparkling river was a charming experience, and would have been satisfyingly sentimental and romantic but for the interruptions of the tug's pet parrot, whose tireless comments upon the scenery and the guests were always this-worldly, and often profane. He had also a superabundance of the discordant, ear-splitting, metallic laugh common to his breed,—a machine-made laugh, a Frankenstein laugh, with the soul left out of it. He applied it to every sentimental remark, and to every pathetic song. He cackled it out with hideous energy after "Home again, home again, from a foreign shore," and said he "wouldn't give a damn for a tug-load of such rot." Romance and sentiment cannot long survive this sort of discouragement; so the singing and talking presently ceased; which so delighted the parrot that he cursed himself hoarse for joy.

Then the male members of the party moved to the forecastle, to smoke and gossip. There were several old steamboatmen along, and I learned from them a great deal of what had been happening to my former river friends during my long absence. I learned that a pilot whom I used to steer for is become a spiritualist, and for more than fifteen years has been receiving a letter every week from a deceased relative, through a New York spiritualistic medium named Manchester—postage graduated by distance: from the local post-office in Paradise to New York, five dollars; from New York to St. Louis, three cents. I remember Mr. Manchester very well. I called on him once, ten years ago, with a couple of friends, one of whom wished to inquire after a deceased uncle. This uncle had lost his life in a peculiarly violent and unusual way, half a dozen years before: a cyclone blew him some three miles and knocked a tree down with him which was four feet through at the butt and sixty-five feet high. He did not survive this triumph. At the *séance* just referred to, my friend questioned his late uncle, through Mr. Manchester, and the late uncle wrote down his replies, using Mr. Manchester's hand and pencil for that purpose. The following is a fair example of the questions asked, and also of the sloppy twaddle in the way of answers, furnished by Manchester under the pretence that it came from the spectre. If this man is not the paltriest fraud that lives, I owe him an apology:—

Question. Where are you?

Answer. In the spirit world.

Q. Are you happy?

A. Very happy. Perfectly happy.

Q. How do you amuse yourself?

A. Conversation with friends, and other spirits.

Q. What else?

A. Nothing else. Nothing else is necessary.

Q. What do you talk about?

A. About how happy we are; and about friends left behind in the earth, and how to influence them for their good.

Q. When your friends in the earth all get to the spirit land, what shall you have to talk about then?— nothing but about how happy you all are?

No reply. It is explained that spirits will not answer frivolous questions.

Q. How is it that spirits that are content to spend an eternity in frivolous employments, and accept it as happiness, are so fastidious about frivolous questions upon the subject?

No reply.

Q. Would you like to come back?

A. No.

Q. Would you say that under oath?

A. Yes.

Q. What do you eat there?

A. We do not eat.

Q. What do you drink?

A. We do not drink.

Q. What do you smoke?

A. We do not smoke.

Q. What do you read?

A. We do not read.

Q. Do all the good people go to your place?

A. Yes.

Q. You know my present way of life. Can you suggest any additions to it, in the way of crime, that will reasonably insure my going to some other place?

A. No reply.

Q. When did you die?

A. I did not die, I passed away.

Q. Very well, then, when did you pass away? How long have you been in the spirit land?

A. We have no measurements of time here.

Q. Though you may be indifferent and uncertain as to dates and times in your present condition and environment, this has nothing to do with your former condition. You had dates then. One of these is what I ask for. You departed on a certain day in a certain year. Is not this true?

A. Yes.

Q. Then name the day of the month.

(Much fumbling with pencil, on the part of the medium, accompanied by violent spasmodic jerkings of his head and body, for some little time. Finally, explanation to the effect that spirits often forget dates, such things being without importance to them.)

Q. Then this one has actually forgotten the date of its translation to the spirit land?

This was granted to be the case.

Q. This is very curious. Well, then, what year was it?

(More fumbling, jerking, idiotic spasms, on the part of the medium. Finally, explanation to the effect that the spirit has forgotten the year.)

Q. This is indeed stupendous. Let me put one more question, one last question, to you, before we part to meet no more;—for even if I fail to avoid your asylum, a meeting there will go for nothing *as* a meeting, since by that time you will easily have forgotten me and my name: did you die a natural death, or were you cut off by a catastrophe?

A. (After long hesitation and many throes and spasms.) *Natural death.*

This ended the interview. My friend told the medium that when his relative was in this poor world, he was endowed with an extraordinary intellect and an absolutely defectless memory, and it seemed a great pity that he had not been allowed to keep some shred of these for his amusement in the realms of everlasting contentment, and for the amazement and admiration of the rest of the population there.

This man had plenty of clients—has plenty yet. He receives letters from spirits located in every part of the spirit world, and delivers them all over this country through the United States mail. These letter are filled with advice—advice from "spirits" who don't know as much as a tadpole—and this advice is religiously followed by the receivers. One of these clients was a man whom the spirits (if one may thus plurally describe the ingenious Manchester) were teaching how to contrive an improved railway car-wheel. It is coarse employment for a spirit, but it is higher and wholesomer activity than talking forever about "how happy we are."

CHAPTER XLIX

EPISODES IN PILOT LIFE

In the course of the tug-boat gossip, it came out that out of every five of my former friends who had quitted the river, four had chosen farming as an occupation. Of course this was not because they were peculiarly gifted, agriculturally, and thus more likely to succeed as farmers than in other industries: the reason for their choice must be traced to some other source. Doubtless they chose farming because that life is private and secluded from irruptions of undesirable strangers,—like the pilot-house hermitage. And doubtless they also chose it because on a thousand nights of black storm and danger they had noted the twinkling lights of solitary farm-houses, as the boat swung by, and pictured to themselves the serenity and security and cosiness of such refuges at such times, and so had by and by come to dream of that retired and peaceful life as the one desirable thing to long for, anticipate, earn, and at last enjoy.

But I did not learn that any of these pilot-farmers had astonished anybody with their successes. Their farms do not support them: they support their farms. The pilot-farmer disappears from the river annually, about the breaking of spring, and is seen no more till next frost. Then he appears again, in damaged homespun, combs the hay-seed out of his hair, and takes a pilot-house berth for the winter. In this way he pays the debts which his farming has achieved during the agricultural season. So his river bondage is but half broken; he is still the river's slave the hardest half of the year.

One of these men bought a farm, but did not retire to it. He knew a trick worth two of that. He did not propose to pauperize his farm by applying his personal ignorance to working it. No, he put the farm into the hands of an agricultural expert to be worked on shares—out of every three loads of corn the expert to have two and the pilot the third. But at the end of the season the pilot received no corn. The expert explained that *his* share was not reached. The farm produced only two loads.

Some of the pilots whom I had known had had adventures;—the outcome fortunate, sometimes, but not in all cases. Captain Montgomery, whom I had steered for when he was a pilot, commanded the Confederate fleet in the great battle before Memphis; when his vessel went down, he swam ashore, fought his way through a squad of soldiers, and made a gallant and narrow escape. He was always a cool man; nothing could disturb his serenity. Once when he was captain of the "Cresent City," I was bringing the boat into port at New Orleans, and momently expecting orders from the hurricane deck, but received none. I had stopped the wheels, and there my authority and responsibility ceased. It was evening—dim twilight—the captain's hat was perched upon the big bell, and I supposed the intellectual end of the captain was in it, but such was not the case. The captain was very strict; therefore I knew better than to touch a bell without orders. My duty was to hold the boat steadily on her calamitous course, and leave the consequences to take care of themselves—which I did. So we went plowing past the sterns of steamboats and getting closer and closer—the crash was bound to come very soon—and still that hat never budged; for alas, the captain was napping in the texas. . . . Things were becoming exceedingly nervous and uncomfortable. It seemed to me that the captain was not going to appear in time to see the entertainment. But he did. Just as we were walking into the stern of a steamboat, he stepped out on deck, and said, with heavenly serenity, "Set her back on both"—which I did; but a trifle late, however, for the next moment we went smashing through that other boat's flimsy outer works with a most prodigious racket. The captain never said a word to me about the matter afterwards, except to remark that I had done right, and that he hoped I would not hesitate to act in the same way again in like circumstances.

One of the pilots whom I had known when I was on the river had died a very honorable death. His boat caught fire, and he remained at the wheel until he got her safe to land. Then he went out over the breast-board with his clothing in flames, and was the last person to get ashore. He died from his injuries in the course of two or three hours, and his was the only life lost.

The history of Mississippi piloting affords six or seven instances of this sort of martyrdom, and half a hundred instances of escapes from a like fate which came within a second or two of being fatally too late; *but there is no instance of a pilot deserting his post to save his life while by remaining and sacrificing it he might secure other lives from destruction*. It is well worth while to set down this noble fact, and well worth while to put it in italics, too.

The "cub" pilot is early admonished to despise all perils connected with a pilot's calling, and to prefer any sort of death to the deep dishonor of deserting his post while there is any possibility of his being useful in it. And so effectively are these admonitions inculcated, that even young and but half-tried pilots can be depended upon to stick to the wheel, and die there when occasion requires. In a Memphis graveyard is buried a young fellow who perished at the wheel a great many years ago, in White River, to save the lives of other men. He said to the captain that if the fire would give him time to reach a sand bar, some distance away, all could be saved, but that to land against the bluff bank of the river would be to insure the loss of many lives. He reached the bar and grounded the boat in shallow water; but by that time the flames had closed around him, and in escaping through them he was fatally burned. He had been urged to fly sooner, but had replied as became a pilot to reply:—

"I will not go. If I go, nobody will be saved; if I stay, no one will be lost but me. I will stay."

There were two hundred persons on board, and no life was lost but the pilot's. There used to be a monument to this young fellow, in that Memphis graveyard. While we tarried in Memphis on our down trip, I started out to look for it, but our time was so brief that I was obliged to turn back before my object was accomplished.

The tug-boat gossip informed me that Dick Kennet was

dead—blown up, near Memphis, and killed; that several others whom I had known had fallen in the war—one or two of them shot down at the wheel; that another and very particular friend, whom I had steered many trips for, had stepped out of his house in New Orleans, one night years ago, to collect some money in a remote part of the city, and had never been seen again,—was murdered and thrown into the river, it was thought; that Ben Thornburgh was dead long ago; also his wild "cub" whom I used to quarrel with, all through every daylight watch. A heedless, reckless creature he was, and always in hot water, always in mischief. An Arkansas passenger brought an enormous bear aboard, one day, and chained him to a life-boat on the hurricane deck. Thornburgh's "cub" could not rest till he had gone there and unchained the bear, to "see what he would do." He was promptly gratified. The bear chased him around and around the deck, for miles and miles, with two hundred eager faces grinning through the railings for audience, and finally snatched off the lad's coat-tail and went into the texas to chew it. The off-watch turned out with alacrity; and left the bear in sole possession. He presently grew lonesome, and started out for recreation. He ranged the whole boat—visited every part of it, with an advance guard of fleeing people in front of him and a voiceless vacancy behind him; and when his owner captured him at last, those two were the only visible beings anywhere; everybody else was in hiding, and the boat was a solitude.

I was told that one of my pilot friends fell dead at the wheel, from heart disease, in 1869. The captain was on the roof at the time. He saw the boat breaking for the shore; shouted, and got no answer; ran up, and found the pilot lying dead on the floor.

Mr. Bixby had been blown up, in Madrid bend; was not injured, but the other pilot was lost.

George Ritchie had been blown up near Memphis—blown into the river from the wheel, and disabled. The water was very cold; he clung to a cotton bale—mainly with his teeth—and floated until nearly exhausted, when he was rescued by some deck hands who were on a piece of the wreck. They tore open the bale and packed him in the cotton, and warmed the life back into him, and got him safe to Memphis. He is one of Bixby's pilots on the "Baton Rouge" now.

Into the life of a steamboat clerk, now dead, had dropped a bit of romance,—somewhat grotesque romance, but romance nevertheless. When I knew him he was a shiftless young spendthrift, boisterous, good-hearted, full of careless generosities, and pretty conspicuously promising to fool his possibilities away early, and come to nothing. In a Western city lived a rich and childless old foreigner and his wife; and in their family was a comely young girl—sort of friend, sort of servant. The young clerk of whom I have been speaking,—whose name was not George Johnson, but who shall be called George Johnson for the purposes of this narrative,—got acquainted with this young girl, and they sinned; and the old foreigner found them out, and rebuked them. Being ashamed, they lied, and said they were married; that they had been privately married. Then the old foreigner's hurt was healed, and he forgave and blessed them. After that, they were able to continue their sin without concealment. By and by the foreigner's wife died; and presently he followed after her. Friends of the family assembled to mourn; and among the mourners sat the two young sinners. The will was opened and solemnly read. It bequeathed every penny of that old man's great wealth to *Mrs. George Johnson!*

And there was no such person. The young sinners fled forth then, and did a very foolish thing: married themselves before an obscure Justice of the Peace, and got him to antedate the thing. That did no sort of good. The distant relatives flocked in and exposed the fraudful date with extreme suddenness and surprising ease, and carried off the fortune, leaving the Johnsons very legitimately, and legally, and irrevocably chained together in honorable marriage, but with not so much as a penny to bless themselves withal. Such are the actual facts; and not all novels have for a base so telling a situation.

CHAPTER L

THE "ORIGINAL JACOBS"

We had some talk about Captain Isaiah Sellers, now many years dead. He was a fine man, a high-minded man, and greatly respected both ashore and on the river. He was very tall, well built, and handsome; and in his old age—as I remember him—his hair was as black as an Indian's, and his eye and hand were as strong and steady and his nerve and judgment as firm and clear as anybody's, young or old, among the fraternity of pilots. He was the patriarch of the craft; he had been a keelboat pilot before the day of steamboats; and a steamboat pilot before any other steamboat pilot, still surviving at the time I speak of, had ever turned a wheel. Consequently his brethren held him in the sort of awe in which illustrious survivors of a bygone age are always held by their associates. He knew how he was regarded, and perhaps this fact added some trifle of stiffening to his natural dignity, which had been sufficiently stiff in its original state.

He left a diary behind him; but apparently it did not date back to his first steamboat trip, which was said to be 1811, the year the first steamboat disturbed the waters of the Mississippi. At the time of his death a correspondent of the "St. Louis Republican" culled the following items from the diary:—

"In February, 1825, he shipped on board the steamer 'Rambler,' at Florence, Ala., and made during that year three trips to New Orleans and back,—this on the 'Gen. Carrol,' between Nashville and New Orleans. It was during his stay on this boat that Captain Sellers introduced the tap of the bell as a signal to heave the lead, previous to which time it was the custom for the pilot to speak to the men below when soundings were wanted. The proximity of the forecastle to the pilot-house, no doubt, rendered this an easy matter; but how different on one of our palaces of the present day.

"In 1827 we find him on board the 'President,' a boat of two hundred and eighty-five tons burden, and plying between Smithland and New Orleans. Thence he joined the 'Jubilee' in 1828, and on this boat he did his first piloting in the St. Louis trade; his first watch extending from Herculaneum to St. Genevieve. On May 26, 1836, he completed and left Pittsburg in charge of the steamer 'Prairie,' a boat of four hundred tons, and the first steamer with a *state-room cabin* ever seen at St. Louis. In 1857 he introduced the signal for meeting boats, and which has, with some slight change, been the universal custom of this day; in fact, is rendered obligatory by act of Congress.

"As general items of river history, we quote the following marginal notes from his general log:—

"In March, 1825, Gen. Lafayette left New Orleans for St. Louis on the low-pressure steamer 'Natchez.'

"In January, 1828, twenty-one steamers left the New Orleans wharf to celebrate the occasion of Gen. Jackson's visit to that city.

"In 1830 the 'North American' made the run from New Orleans to Memphis in six days—best time on record to that date. It has since been made in two days and ten hours.

"In 1831 the Red River cut-off formed.

"In 1832 steamer 'Hudson' made the run from White River to Helena, a distance of seventy-five miles, in twelve hours. This was the source of much talk and speculation among parties directly interested.

"In 1839 Great Horseshoe cut-off formed.

"Up to the present time, a term of thirty-five years, we ascertain, by reference to the diary, he has made four hundred and sixty round trips to New Orleans, which gives a distance of one million one hundred and four thousand miles, or an average of eighty-six miles a day."

Whenever Captain Sellers approached a body of gossiping pilots, a chill fell there, and talking ceased. For this reason: whenever six pilots were gathered together, there would always be one or two newly fledged ones in the lot, and the elder ones would be always "showing off" before these poor fellows; making them sorrowfully feel how callow they were, how recent their nobility, and how humble their degree, by talking largely and vaporously of old-time experiences on the river; always making it a point to date everything back as far as they could, so as to make the new men feel their newness to the sharpest degree possible, and envy the old stagers in the like degree. And how these complacent baldheads *would* swell, and brag, and lie, and date back—ten, fifteen, twenty years,—and how they did enjoy the effect produced upon the marvelling and envying youngsters!

And perhaps just at this happy stage of the proceedings, the stately figure of Captain Isaiah Sellers, that real and only genuine Son of Antiquity, would drift solemnly into the midst. Imagine the size of the silence that would result on the instant. And imagine the feelings of those bald-heads, and the exultation of their recent audience when the ancient captain would begin to drop casual and indifferent remarks of a reminiscent nature,—about islands that had disappeared, and cut-offs that had been made, a generation before the oldest bald-head in the company had ever set his foot in a pilot-house!

Many and many a time did this ancient mariner appear on the scene in the above fashion, and spread disaster and humiliation around him. If one might believe the pilots, he always dated his islands back to the misty dawn of river history; and he never used the same island twice; and never did he employ an island that still existed, or give one a name which anybody present was old enough to have heard of before. If you might believe the pilots, he was always conscientiously particular about little details; never spoke of "the State of Mississippi," for instance,—no, he would say, "When the State of Mississippi was where Arkansas now is;" and would never speak of Louisiana or Missouri in a general way, and leave an incorrect impression on your mind,—no, he would say, "When Louisiana was up the river farther," or "When Missouri was on the Illinois side."

The old gentleman was not of literary turn or capacity, but he used to jot down brief paragraphs of plain practical information about the river, and sign them "MARK TWAIN," and give them to the "New Orleans Picayune." They related to the stage and condition of the river, and were accurate and valuable; and thus far, they contained no poison. But in speaking of the stage of the river today, at a given point, the captain was pretty apt to drop in a little remark about this being the first time he had seen the water so high or so low at that particular point for forty-nine years; and now and then he would mention Island so and so, and follow it, in parentheses, with some such observation as "disappeared in 1807, if I remember rightly." In these antique interjections lay poison and bitterness for the other old pilots, and they used to chaff the "Mark Twain" paragraphs with unsparing mockery.

It so chanced that one of these paragraphs* became the text for my first newspaper article. I burlesqued it broadly, very broadly, stringing my fantastics out to the extent of eight hundred or a thousand words. I was a "cub" at the time. I showed my performance to some pilots, and they eagerly rushed it into print in the "New Orleans True Delta." It was a great pity; for it did nobody any worthy service, and it sent a pang deep into a good man's heart. There was no malice in my rubbish; but it laughed at the captain. It laughed at a man to whom such a thing was new and strange and dreadful. I did not know then, though I do now, that there is no suffering comparable with that which a private person feels when he is for the first time pilloried in print.

Captain Sellers did me the honor to profoundly detest me from that day forth. When I say he did me the honor, I am not using empty words. It was a very real honor to be in the thoughts of so great a man as Captain Sellers, and I had wit enough to appreciate it and be proud of it. It was distinction to be loved by such a man; but it was a much greater distinction to be hated by him, because he loved scores of people; but he didn't sit up nights to hate anybody but me.

He never printed another paragraph while he lived, and he never again signed "Mark Twain" to anything. At the time that the telegraph brought the news of his death, I was on the Pacific coast. I was a fresh new journalist, and needed a *nom de guerre;* so I confiscated the ancient mariner's discarded one, and have done my best to make it remain what it was in his hands—a sign and symbol and warrant that whatever is found in its company may be gambled on as being the petrified truth; how I have succeeded, it would not be modest in me to say.

* The original MS. of it, in the captain's own hand, has been sent to me from New Orleans. It reads as follows:—

"VICKSBURG, May 4, 1959.

"My opinion for the benefit of the citizens of New Orleans: The water is higher this far up than it has been since 1815. My opinion is that the water will be 4 feet deep in Canal street before the first of next June. Mrs. Turner's plantation at the head of Big Black Island is all under water, and it has not been since 1815.

"I. SELLERS."

The captain had an honorable pride in his profession and an abiding love for it. He ordered his monument before he died, and kept it near him until he did die. It stands over his grave now, in Bellefontaine cemetery, St. Louis. It is his image, in marble, standing on duty at the pilot wheel; and worthy to stand and confront criticism, for it represents a man who in life would have staid there till he burned to a cinder, if duty required it.

The finest thing we saw on our whole Mississippi trip, we saw as we approached New Orleans in the steam-tug. This was the curving frontage of the crescent city lit up with the white glare of five miles of electric lights. It was a wonderful sight, and very beautiful.

CHAPTER LI

REMINISCENCES

We left for St. Louis in the "City of Baton Rouge," on a delightfully hot day, but with the main purpose of my visit but lamely accomplished. I had hoped to hunt up and talk with a hundred steamboatmen, but got so pleasantly involved in the social life of the town that I got nothing more than mere five-minute talks with a couple of dozen of the craft.

I was on the bench of the pilot-house when we backed out and "straightened up" for the start—the boat pausing for a "good ready," in the old-fashioned way, and the black smoke piling out of the chimneys equally in the old-fashioned way. Then we began to gather momentum, and presently were fairly under way and booming along. It was all as natural and familiar—and so were the shoreward sights—as if there had been no break in my river life. There was a "cub," and I judged that he would take the wheel now; and he did. Captain Bixby stepped into the pilot-house. Presently the cub closed up on the rank of steamships. He made me nervous, for he allowed too much water to show between our boat and the ships. I knew quite well what was going to happen, because I could date back in my own life and inspect the record. The captain looked on, during a silent half-minute, then took the wheel himself, and crowded the boat in, till she went scraping along within a hand-breadth of the ships. It was exactly the favor which he had done me, about a quarter of a century before, in that same spot, the first time I ever steamed out of the port of New Orleans. It was a very great and sincere pleasure to me to see the thing repeated—with somebody else as victim.

We made Natchez (three hundred miles) in twenty-two hours and a half,—much the swiftest passage I have ever made over that piece of water.

The next morning I came on with the four o'clock watch, and saw Ritchie successfully run half a dozen crossings in a fog, using for his guidance the marked chart devised and patented by Bixby and himself. This sufficiently evidenced the great value of the chart.

By and by, when the fog began to clear off, I noticed that the reflection of a tree in the smooth water of an overflowed bank, six hundred yards away, was stronger and blacker than the ghostly tree itself. The faint spectral trees, dimly glimpsed through the shredding fog, were very pretty things to see.

We had a heavy thunder-storm at Natchez, another at Vicksburg, and still another about fifty miles below Memphis. They had an old-fashioned energy which had long been unfamiliar to me. This third storm was accompanied by a raging wind. We tied up to the bank when we saw the tempest coming, and everybody left the pilot-house but me. The wind bent the young trees down, exposing the pale underside of the leaves; and gust after gust followed, in quick succession, thrashing the branches violently up and down, and to this side and that, and creating swift waves of alternating green and white according to the side of the leaf that was exposed, and these waves raced after each other as do their kind over a wind-tossed field of oats. No color that was visible anywhere was quite natural,—all tints were charged with a leaden tinge from the solid cloud-bank overhead. The river was leaden; all distances the same; and even the far-reaching ranks of combing white-caps were dully shaded by the dark, rich atmosphere through which their swarming legions marched. The thunder-peals were constant and deafening; explosion followed explosion with but inconsequential intervals between, and the reports grew steadily sharper and higher-keyed, and more trying to the ear; the lightning was as diligent as the thunder, and produced effects which enchanted the eye and sent electric ecstasies of mixed delight and apprehension shivering along every nerve in the body in unintermittent procession. The rain poured down in amazing volume; the ear-splitting thunder-peals broke nearer and nearer; the wind increased in fury and began to wrench off boughs and tree-tops and send them sailing away through space; the pilot-house fell to rocking and straining and cracking and surging, and I went down in the hold to see what time it was.

People boast a good deal about Alpine thunder-storms; but the storms which I have had the luck to see in the Alps were not the equals of some which I have seen in the Mississippi Valley. I may not have seen the Alps do their best, of course, and if they can beat the Mississippi, I don't wish to.

On this up trip I saw a little towhead (infant island) half a mile long, which had been formed during the past nineteen years. Since there was so much time to spare that nineteen years of it could be devoted to the construction of a mere towhead, where was the use, originally, in rushing this whole globe through in six days? It is likely that if more time had been taken, in the first place, the world would have been made right, and this ceaseless improving and repairing would not be necessary now. But if you hurry a world or a house, you are nearly sure to find out by and by, that you have left out a towhead, or a broom-closet, or some other little convenience, here and there, which has got to be supplied, no matter how much expense and vexation it may cost.

We had a succession of black nights, going up the river, and it was observable that whenever we landed, and suddenly inundated the trees with the intense sunburst of the electric light, a certain curious effect was always produced: hundreds of birds flocked instantly out from the masses of shining green foliage, and went careering hither and thither through the white rays, and often a song-bird tuned up and fell to singing. We judged that they mistook this superb artificial day for the genuine article.

We had a delightful trip in that thoroughly well-ordered steamer, and regretted that it was accomplished so speedily. By means of diligence and activity, we managed to hunt out nearly all the old friends. One was missing, however; he went to his reward, whatever it was, two years ago. But I found out all about him. His case helped me to realize how lasting can be the effect of a very trifling occurrence. When he was an apprentice-blacksmith in our village, and I a schoolboy, a couple of young Englishmen came to the town and sojourned a while; and one day they got themselves up in cheap royal finery and did the Richard III. sword-fight with maniac energy and prodigious powwow, in the presence of the village boys. This blacksmith cub was there, and the histrionic poison entered his bones. This vast, lumbering, ignorant, dull-witted lout was stage-struck, and irrecoverably. He disappeared, and presently turned up in St. Louis. I ran across him there, by and by. He was standing musing on a street corner, with his right hand on his hip, the thumb of his left supporting his chin, face bowed and frowning, slouch hat pulled down over his forehead—imagining himself to be Othello or some such character, and imagining that the passing crowd marked his tragic bearing and were awestruck.

I joined him, and tried to get him down out of the clouds, but did not succeed. However, he casually informed me, presently, that he was a member of the Walnut Street theatre company,—and he tried to say it with indifference, but the indifference was thin, and a mighty exultation showed through it. He said he was cast for a part in Julius Caesar, for that night, and if I should come I would see him. *If* I should come! I said I wouldn't miss it if I were dead.

I went away stupefied with astonishment, and saying to myself, "How strange it is! *we* always thought this fellow a fool; yet the moment he comes to a great city, where intelligence and appreciation abound, the talent concealed in this shabby napkin is at once discovered, and promptly welcomed and honored."

But I came away from the theatre that night disappointed and offended; for I had had no glimpse of my hero, and his name was not in the bills. I met him on the street the next morning, and before I could speak, he asked:—

"Did you see me?"

"No, you weren't there."

He looked surprised and disappointed. He said:—

"Yes, I was. Indeed I was. I was a Roman soldier."

"Which one?"

"Why, didn't you see them Roman soldiers that stood back there in a rank, and sometimes marched in procession around the stage?"

"Do you mean the Roman army?—those six sandalled roustabouts in nightshirts, with tin shields and helmets, that marched around treading on each other's heels, in charge of a spider-legged consumptive dressed like themselves?"

"That's it! that's it! I was one of them Roman soldiers. I was the next to the last one. A half a year ago I used to always be the last one; but I've been promoted."

Well, they told me that the poor fellow remained a Roman soldier to the last—a matter of thirty-four years. Sometimes they cast him for a "speaking part," but not an elaborate one. He could be trusted to go and say, "My lord, the carriage waits," but if they ventured to add a sentence or two to this, his memory felt the strain and he was likely to miss fire. Yet, poor devil, he had been patiently studying the part of Hamlet for more than thirty years, and he lived and died in the belief that some day he would be invited to play it!

And this is what came of that fleeting visit of those young Englishmen to our village such ages and ages ago! What noble horseshoes this man might have made, but for those Englishmen; and what an inadequate Roman soldier he *did* make!

A day or two after we reached St. Louis, I was walking along Fourth Street when a grizzly-headed man gave a sort of start as he passed me, then stopped, came back, inspected me narrowly, with a clouding brow, and finally said with deep asperity:—

"Look here, *have you got that drink yet?*"

A maniac, I judged, at first. But all in a flash I recognized him. I made an effort to blush that strained every muscle in me, and answered as sweetly and winningly as ever I knew how:—

"Been a little slow, but am just this minute closing in on the place where they keep it. Come in and help."

He softened, and said make it a bottle of champagne and he was agreeable. He said he had seen my name in the papers, and had put all his affairs aside and turned out, resolved to find me or die; and make me answer that question satisfactorily, or kill me; though the most of his late asperity had been rather counterfeit than otherwise.

This meeting brought back to me the St. Louis riots of about thirty years ago. I spent a week there, at that time, in a boarding-house, and had this young fellow for a neighbor across the hall. We saw some of the fightings and killings; and by and by we went one night to an armory where two hundred young men had met, upon call, to be armed and go forth against the rioters, under command of a military man. We drilled till about ten o'clock at night; then news came that the mob were in great force in the lower end of the town, and were sweeping everything before them. Our column moved at once. It was a very hot night, and my musket was very heavy. We marched and marched; and the nearer we approached the seat of war, the hotter I grew and the thirstier I got. I was behind my friend; so, finally, I asked him to hold my musket while I dropped out and got a drink. Then I branched off and went home. I was not feeling any solicitude about *him* of course, because I knew he was so well armed, now, that he could take care of himself without any trouble. If I had had any doubts about that, I would have borrowed another musket for him. I left the city pretty early the next morning, and if this grizzled man had not happened to encounter my name in the papers the other day in St. Louis, and felt moved to seek me out, I should have carried to my grave a heart-torturing uncertainty as to whether he ever got out of the riots all right or not. I ought to have inquired, thirty years ago; I know that. And I would have inquired, if I had had the muskets; but, in the circumstances, he seemed better fixed to conduct the investigations than I was.

One Monday, near the time of our visit to St. Louis, the "Globe-Democrat" came out with a couple of pages of Sunday statistics, whereby it appeared that 119,448 St. Louis people attended the morning and evening church services the day before, and 23,102 children attended Sunday-school. Thus 142,550 persons, out of the city's total of 400,000 population, respected the day religious-wise. I found these statistics, in a condensed form, in a telegram of the Associated Press, and preserved them. They made it apparent that St. Louis was in a higher state of grace than she could have claimed to be in my time. But now that I canvass the figures narrowly, I suspect that the telegraph mutilated them. It cannot be that there are more than 150,000 Catholics in the town; the other 250,000 must be classified as Protestants. Out of these 250,000, according to this questionable telegram, only 26,362 attended church and Sunday-school, while out of the 150,000 Catholics, 116,188 went to church and Sunday-school.

CHAPTER LII

A BURNING BRAND

All at once the thought came into my mind, "I have not sought out Mr. Brown."

Upon that text I desire to depart from the direct line of my subject, and make a little excursion. I wish to reveal a secret which I have carried with me nine years, and which has become burdensome.

Upon a certain occasion, nine years ago, I had said, with strong feeling, "If ever I see St. Louis again, I will seek out Mr. Brown, the great grain merchant, and ask of him the privilege of shaking him by the hand."

The occasion and the circumstances were as follows. A friend of mine, a clergyman, came one evening and said:—

"I have a most remarkable letter here, which I want to read to you, if I can do it without breaking down. I must preface it with some explanations, however. The letter is written by an ex-thief and ex-vagabond of the lowest origin and basest rearing, a man all stained with crime and steeped in ignorance; but, thank God, with a mine of pure gold hidden away in him, as you shall see. His letter is written to a burglar named Williams, who is serving a nine-year term in a certain State prison, for burglary. Williams was a particularly daring burglar, and plied that trade during a number of years; but he was caught at last and jailed, to await trial in a town where he had broken into a house at night, pistol in hand, and forced the owner to hand over to him $8,000 in government bonds. Williams was not a common sort of person, by any means; he was a graduate of Harvard College, and came of good New England stock. His father was a clergyman. While lying in jail, his health began to fail, and he was threatened with consumption. This fact, together with the opportunity for reflection afforded by solitary confinement, had its effect—its natural effect. He fell into serious thought: his early training asserted itself with power, and wrought with strong influence upon his mind and heart. He put his old life behind him, and became an earnest Christian. Some ladies in the town heard of this, visited him, and by their encouraging words supported him in his good resolutions and strengthened him to continue in his new life. The trial ended in his conviction and sentence to the State prison for the term of nine years, as I have before said. In the prison he became acquainted with the poor wretch referred to in the beginning of my talk, Jack Hunt, the writer of the letter which I am going to read. You will see that the acquaintanceship bore fruit for Hunt. When Hunt's time was out, he wandered to St. Louis; and from that place he wrote his letter to Williams. The letter got no further than the office of the prison warden, of course; prisoners are not often allowed to receive letters from outside. The prison authorities read this letter, but did not destroy it. They had not the heart to do it. They read it to several persons, and eventually it fell into the hands of those ladies of whom I spoke a while ago. The other day I came across an old friend of mine—a clergyman—who had seen this letter, and was full of it. The mere remembrance of it so moved him that he could not talk of it without his voice breaking. He promised to get a copy of it for me; and here it is,—an exact copy, with all the imperfections of the original preserved. It has many slang expressions in it—thieves' *argot*—but their meaning has been interlined, in parentheses, by the prison authorities:"—

St. Louis, June 9th, 1872.

Mr. W——friend Charlie if i may call you so: i no you are surprised to get a letter from me, but i hope you won't be mad at my writing to you. i want to tell you my thanks for the way you talked to me when i was in prison—it has led me to try and be a better man; i guess you thought i did not cair for what you said, & at the first go off I didn't, but i noed you was a man who had don big work with good men & want no sucker, nor want gasing & all the boys knod it.

I used to think at nite what you said, & for it i nocked off swearing 5 months before my time was up, for i saw it want no good, nohow—the day my time was up you told me if i would shake the cross, *(quit stealing)* & live on the square for 3 months, it would be the best job i ever done in my life. The state agent give me a ticket to here, & on the car i thought more of what you said to me, but didn't make up my mind. When we got to Chicago on the cars from there to here, I pulled off an old woman's leather; *(robbed her of her pocketbook)* i hadn't no more than got it off when i wished i hadn't done it, for awhile before that i made up my mind to be a square bloke, for 3 months on your word, but forgot it when i saw the leather was a grip *(easy to get)*—but i kept clos to her & when she got out of the cars at a way place i said, marm have you lost anything? & she tumbled *(discovered)* her leather was off *(gone)*—is this it says i, giving it to her—well if you aint honest, says she, but i hadnt got cheak enough to stand that sort of talk, so i left her in a hurry. When i got here i had $1 and 25 cents left & i didn't get no work for 3 days as i aint strong enough for roust about on a steam bote *(for a deck hand)*—The afternoon of the 3rd day I spent my last 10 cts for 2 moons *(large, round sea-biscuit)* & cheese & i felt pretty rough & was thinking i would have to go on the dipe *(picking pockets)* again, when i thought of what you once said about a fellows calling on the Lord when he was in hard luck, & i thought i would try it once anyhow, but when i tryed it i got stuck on the start & all i could get off wos, Lord give a poor fellow a chance to square it for 3 months for Christ's sake, amen; & i kept a thinking, of it over and over as i went along—about an hour after that i was in 4th St. & this is what happened & is the cause of my being where i am now & about which i will tell you before i get done writing. As i was walking along i herd a big noise & saw a horse running away with a carriage with 2 children in it, & I grabed up a peace of box cover from the side walk & run in the middle of the street, & when the horse came up i smashed him over the head as hard as i could drive—the bord split to peces & the horse checked up a little & i grabbed the reigns & pulled his head down until he stopped—the gentleman what owned him came running up & soon as he saw the children were all rite, he shook hands with me & gave me a $50 green back, & my asking the Lord to help me come into my head, & i was so thunderstruck i couldn't drop the reigns nor say nothing—he saw something was up, & coming back to me said, my boy are you hurt? & the thought come into my head just then to ask him for work; & i asked him to take back the bill and give me a job—says he, jump in here & lets talk about it, but keep the money—he asked me if i could take care of horses & i said yes, for i used to hang round livery stables & often would help clean & drive horses, he told me he wanted a man for that work, & would give me $16. a month & bord me. You bet i took that chance at once. that nite in my little room over the stable i sat a long time thinking over my past life & of what had just happened & i just got down on my nees & thanked the Lord for the job & to help me to square it, & to bless you for putting me up to it, & the next morning i done it again & got me some new togs *(clothes)* & a bible for i *made up my mind* after what the Lord had done for me i would read the bible every nite and morning, & ask him to keep an eye on me. When I had been there about a week Mr. Brown (that's his name) came in my room one nite & saw me reading the bible—he asked me if i was a Christian & i told him no—he asked me how it was i read the bible instead of papers & books—Well Charlie i thought i had better give him a square deal in the start, so i told him all about my being in prison & about you, & how i had almost done give up looking for work & how the Lord got me the job when i asked him; & the only way i had to pay him back was to read the bible & square it, & i asked him to give me a chance for 3 months—he talked to me like a father for a long time, & told me i could stay & then i felt better than ever i had done in my life, for i had given Mr. Brown a fair start with me & now i didn't fear no one giving me a back cap *(exposing his past life)* & running me off the job—the next morning he called me into the library & gave me another square talk, & advised me to study some every day, & he would help me one or 2 hours every nite, & he gave me a Arithmetic, a spelling book, a Geography & a writing book, & he hers me every nite—he lets me come into the house to prayers every morning, & got me put in a bible class in the Sunday School which i likes very much for it helps me to understand my bible better.

Now, Charlie the 3 months on the square are up 2 months ago, & as you said, it is the best job i ever did in my life, & i commenced another of the same sort right away, only it is to God helping me to last a lifetime Charlie—i wrote this letter to tell you I do think God has forgiven my sins & herd your prayers, for you told me you should pray for me—i no i love to read his word & tell him all my troubles & he helps me i know for i have plenty of chances to steal but i don't feel to as i once did & now i take more pleasure in going to church than to the theatre & that wasnt so once—our minister and others often talk with me & a month ago they wanted me to join the church, but I said no, not now, i may be mistaken in my feelings, i will wait awhile, but now i feel that God has called me & on the first Sunday in July i will join the church—dear friend i wish i could write to you as i feel, but i cant do it yet—you no i learned to read and write while in prisons & i aint got well enough along to write as i would talk; i no i aint spelled all the words rite in this & lots of other mistakes but you will excuse it i no, for you no i was brought up in a poor house until i run away, & that i never new who my father and mother was & i dont no my rite name, & i hope you wont be mad at me, but i have as much rite to one name as another & i have taken your name, for you wont use it when you get out i no, & you are the man i think most of in the world; so i hope you wont be mad—I am doing well, i put $10 a month in bank with $25 of the $50—if you ever want any or all of it let me know, & it is yours. i wish you would let me send you some now. I send you with this a receipt for a year of Littles Living Age, i didn't know what you would like & i told Mr. Brown & he said he thought you would like it—i wish i was nere you so i could send you chuck *(refreshments)* on holidays; it would spoil this weather from here, but i will send you a box next thanksgiving any way—next week Mr. Brown takes me into his store as lite porter & will advance me as soon as i know a little more—he keeps a big granary store, wholesale—i forgot to tell you of my mission school, sunday school class—the school is in the sunday afternoon, i went out two sunday afternoons, and picked up seven kids *(little boys)* & got them to come in. two of them new as much as i did & i had them put in a class where they could learn something. i dont no much myself, but as these kids cant read i get on nicely with them. i make sure of them by going after them every Sunday ½ hour before school time, i also got 4 girls to come. tell Mack and Harry about me, if they will come out here when their time is up i will get them jobs at once. i hope you will excuse this long letter & all mistakes, i wish i could see you for i cant write as i would talk—i hope the warm weather is doing your lungs good—i was afraid when you was bleeding you would die—give my respects to all the boys and tell them how i am doing—i am doing well and every one here treats me as kind as they can—Mr Brown is going to write to you sometime—i hope some day you will write to me, this letter is from your very true friend

C—— W——

who you know as Jack Hunt.

I send you Mr Brown's card. Send my letter to him.

Here was true eloquence; irresistible eloquence; and without a single grace or ornament to help it out. I have seldom been so deeply stirred by any piece of writing. The reader of it halted, all the way through, on a lame and broken voice; yet he had tried to fortify his feelings by several private readings of the letter before venturing into company with it. He was practising upon me to see if there was any hope of his being able to read the document to his prayer-meeting with anything like a decent command over his feelings. The result was not promising. However, he determined to risk it; and did. He got through tolerably well; but his audience broke down early, and stayed in that condition to the end.

The fame of the letter spread through the town. A brother minister came and borrowed the manuscript, put it bodily into a sermon, preached the sermon to twelve hundred people on a Sunday morning, and the letter drowned them in their own tears. Then my friend put it into a sermon and went before his Sunday morning congregation with it. It scored another triumph. The house wept as one individual.

My friend went on summer vacation up into the fishing regions of our northern British neighbors, and carried this sermon with him, since he might possibly chance to need a sermon. He was asked to preach, one day. The little church was full. Among the people present were the late Dr. J. G. Holland, the late Mr. Seymour of the "New York Times," Mr. Page, the philanthropist and temperance advocate, and, I think, Senator Frye, of Maine. The marvellous letter did its wonted work; all the people were moved, all the people wept; the tears flowed in a steady stream down Dr. Holland's cheeks, and nearly the same can be said with regard to all who were there. Mr. Page was so full of enthusiasm over the letter that he said he would not rest until he made pilgrimage to that prison, and had speech with the man who had been able to inspire a fellow-unfortunate to write so priceless a tract.

Ah, that unlucky Page!—and another man. If they had only been in Jericho, that letter would have rung through the world and stirred all the hearts of all the nations for a thousand years to come, and nobody might ever have found out that it was the confoundedest, brazenest, ingeniousest piece of fraud and humbuggery that was ever concocted to fool poor confiding mortals with!

The letter was a pure swindle, and that is the truth. And take it by and large, it was without a compeer among swindles. It was perfect, it was rounded, symmetrical, complete, colossal!

The reader learns it at this point; but we didn't learn it till some miles and weeks beyond this stage of the affair. My friend came back from the woods, and he and other clergymen and lay missionaries began once more to inundate audiences with their tears and the tears of said audiences; I begged hard for permission to print the letter in a magazine and tell the watery story of its triumphs; numbers of people got copies of the letter, with permission to circulate them in writing, but not in print; copies were sent to the Sandwich Islands and other far regions.

Charles Dudley Warner was at church, one day, when the worn letter was read and wept over. At the church door, afterward, he dropped a peculiarly cold iceberg down the clergyman's back with the question,—

"Do you know that letter to be genuine?"

It was the first suspicion that had ever been voiced; but it had that sickening effect which first-uttered suspicions against one's idol always have. Some talk followed:—

"Why—what should make you suspect that it isn't genuine?"

"Nothing that I know of, except that it is too neat, and compact, and fluent, and nicely put together for an ignorant person, an unpractised hand. I think it was done by an educated man."

The literary artist had detected the literary machinery. If you will look at the letter now, you will detect it yourself—it is observable in every line.

Straightway the clergyman went off, with this seed of suspicion sprouting in him, and wrote to a minister residing in that town where Williams had been jailed and converted; asked for light; and also asked if a person in the literary line (meaning me) might be allowed to print the letter and tell its history. He presently received this answer:—

Rev.——.

My Dear Friend,—In regard to that "convict's letter" there can be no doubt as to its genuineness. "Williams," to whom it was written, lay in our jail and professed to have been converted, and Rev. Mr. ——, the chaplain, had great faith in the genuineness of the change—as much as one can have in any such case.

The letter was sent to one of our ladies, who is a Sunday-school teacher,—sent either by Williams himself, or the chaplain of the State's prison, probably. She has been greatly annoyed in having so much publicity, lest it might seem a breach of confidence, or be an injury to Williams. In regard to its publication, I can give no permission; though if the names and places were omitted, and especially if sent out of the country, I think you might take the responsibility and do it.

It is a wonderful letter, which no Christian genius, much less one unsanctified, could ever have written. As showing the work of grace in a human heart, and in a very degraded and wicked one, it proves its own origin and reproves our weak faith in its power to cope with any form of wickedness.

"Mr. Brown" of St. Louis, some one said, was a Hartford man. Do all whom you send from Hartford serve their Master as well?

P.S. Williams is still in the State's prison, serving out a long sentence—of nine years, I think. He has been sick and threatened with consumption, but I have not inquired after him lately. This lady that I speak of corresponds with him, I presume, and will be quite sure to look after him.

This letter arrived a few days after it was written—and up went Mr. Williams's stock again. Mr. Warner's low-down suspicion was laid in the cold, cold grave, where it apparently belonged. It was a suspicion based upon mere internal evidence, anyway; and when you come to internal evidence, it's a big field and a game that two can play at: as witness this other internal evidence, discovered by the writer of the note above quoted, that "it is a wonderful letter—which no Christian genius, much less one unsanctified, could ever have written."

I had permission now to print—provided I suppressed names and places and sent my narrative out of the country. So I chose an Australian magazine for vehicle, as being far enough out of the country, and set myself to work on my article. And the ministers set the pumps going again, with the letter to work the handles.

But meantime Brother Page had been agitating. He had not visited the penitentiary, but he had sent a copy of the illustrious letter to the chaplain of that institution, and accompanied it with—apparently—inquiries. He got an answer, dated four days later than that other Brother's reassuring epistle; and before my article was complete, it wandered into my hands. The original is before me, now, and I here append it. It is pretty well loaded with internal evidence of the most solid description:—

STATE'S PRISON, CHAPLAIN'S OFFICE, July 11, 1873.

DEAR BRO. Page,—Herewith please fine the letter kindly leased me. I am afraid its genuineness cannot be established. It purports to be addressed to some prisoner here. No such letter ever came to a prisoner here. All letters received are carefully read by officers of the prison before they go into the hands of the convicts, and any such letter could not be forgotten. Again, Charles Williams is not a Christian man, but a dissolute, cunning prodigal, whose father is a minister of the gospel. His name is an assumed one. I am glad to have made your acquaintance. I am preparing a lecture upon life seen through prison bars, and should like to deliver the same in your vicinity.

And so ended that little drama. My poor article went into the fire; for whereas the materials for it were now more abundant and infinitely richer than they had previously been, there were parties all around me, who, although longing for the publication before, were a unit for suppression at this stage and complexion of the game. They said,—"Wait—the wound is too fresh, yet." All the copies of the famous letter except mine, disappeared suddenly; and from that time onward, the aforetime same old drought set in in the churches. As a rule, the town was on a spacious grin for a while, but there were places in it where the grin did not appear, and where it was dangerous to refer to the ex-convict's letter.

A word of explanation. "Jack Hunt," the professed writer of the letter, was an imaginary person. The burglar Williams—Harvard graduate, son of a minister—wrote the letter himself, *to* himself: got it smuggled out of the prison; got it conveyed to persons who had supported and encouraged him in his conversion—where he knew two things would happen: the genuineness of the letter would not be doubted or inquired into; and the nub of it would be noticed, and would have valuable effect—the effect, indeed, of starting a movement to get Mr. Williams pardoned out of prison.

That "nub" is so ingeniously, so casually, flung in, and immediately left there in the tail of the letter, undwelt upon, that an indifferent reader would never suspect that it was the heart and core of the epistle, if he even took note of it at all. This is the "nub":—

i hope the warm weather is doing your lungs good—*i was afraid when you was bleeding you would die*—give my respects," etc.

That is all there is of it—simply touch and go—no dwelling upon it. Nevertheless it was intended for an eye that would be swift to see it; and it was meant to move a kind heart to try to effect the liberation of a poor reformed and purified fellow lying in the fell grip of consumption.

When I for the first time heard that letter read, nine years ago, I felt that it was the most remarkable one I had ever encountered. And it so warmed me toward Mr. Brown of St. Louis that I said that if ever I visited that city again, I would seek out that excellent man and kiss the hem of his garment if it was a new one. Well, I visited St. Louis, but I did not hunt for Mr. Brown; for, alas! the investigations of long ago had proved that the benevolent Brown, like "Jack Hunt," was not a real person, but a sheer invention of that gifted rascal, Williams—burglar, Harvard graduate, son of a clergyman.

CHAPTER LIII

MY BOYHOOD HOME

We took passage in one of the fast boats of the St. Louis and St. Paul Packet Company, and started up the river.

When I, as a boy, first saw the mouth of the Missouri River, it was twenty-two or twenty-three miles above St. Louis, according to the estimate of pilots; the wear and tear of the banks has moved it down eight miles since then; and the pilots say that within five years the river will cut through and move the mouth down five miles more, which will bring it within ten miles of St. Louis.

About nightfall we passed the large and flourishing town of Alton, Illinois; and before daylight next morning the town of Louisiana, Missouri, a sleepy village in my day, but a brisk railway centre now; however, all the towns out there are railway centres now. I could not clearly recognize the place. This seemed odd to me, for when I retired from the rebel army in '61 I retired upon Louisiana in good order; at least in good enough order for a person who had not yet learned how to retreat according to the rules of war, and had to trust to native genius. It seemed to me that for a first attempt at a retreat it was not badly done. I had done no advancing in all that campaign that was at all equal to it.

There was a railway bridge across the river here well sprinkled with glowing lights, and a very beautiful sight it was.

At seven in the morning we reached Hannibal, Missouri, where my boyhood was spent. I had had a glimpse of it fifteen years ago, and another glimpse six years earlier, but both were so brief that they hardly counted. The only notion of the town that remained in my mind was the memory of it as I had known it when I first quitted it twenty-nine years ago. That picture of it was still as clear and vivid to me as a photograph. I stepped ashore with the feeling of one who returns out of a dead-and-gone generation. I had a sort of realizing sense of what the Bastille prisoners must have felt when they used to come out and look upon Paris after years of captivity, and note how curiously the familiar and the strange were mixed together before them. I saw the new houses—saw them plainly enough—but they did not affect the older picture in my mind, for through their solid bricks and mortar I saw the vanished houses, which had formerly stood there, with perfect distinctness.

It was Sunday morning, and everybody was abed yet. So I passed through the vacant streets, still seeing the town as it was, and not as it is, and recognizing and metaphorically shaking hands with a hundred familiar objects which no longer exist; and finally climbed Holiday's Hill to get a comprehensive view. The whole town lay spread out below me then, and I could mark and fix every locality, every detail. Naturally, I was a good deal moved. I said, "Many of the people I once knew in this tranquil refuge of my childhood are now in heaven; some, I trust, are in the other place."

The things about me and before me made me feel like a boy again—convinced me that I was a boy again, and that I had simply been dreaming an unusually long dream; but my reflections spoiled all that; for they forced me to say, "I see fifty old houses down yonder, into each of which I could enter and find either a man or a woman who was a baby or unborn when I noticed those houses last, or a grandmother who was a plump young bride at that time."

From this vantage ground the extensive view up and down the river, and wide over the wooded expanses of Illinois, is very beautiful,—one of the most beautiful on the Mississippi, I think, which is a hazardous remark to make, for the eight hundred miles of river between St. Louis and St. Paul afford an unbroken succession of lovely pictures. It may be that my affection for the one in question biases my judgment in its favor; I cannot say as to that. No matter, it was satisfyingly beautiful to me, and it had this advantage over all the other friends whom I was about to greet again: it had suffered no change; it was as young and fresh and comely and gracious as ever it had been; whereas, the faces of the others would be old, and scarred with the campaigns of life, and marked with their griefs and defeats, and would give me no upliftings of spirit.

An old gentleman, out on an early morning walk, came along, and we discussed the weather, and then drifted into other matters. I could not remember his face. He said he had been living here twenty-eight years. So he had come after my time, and I had never seen him before. I asked him various questions; first about a mate of mine in Sunday school—what became of him?

"He graduated with honor in an Eastern college, wandered off into the world somewhere, succeeded at nothing, passed out of knowledge and memory years ago, and is supposed to have gone to the dogs."

"He was bright, and promised well when he was a boy."

"Yes, but the thing that happened is what became of it all."

I asked after another lad, altogether the brightest in our village school when I was a boy.

"He, too, was graduated with honors, from an Eastern college; but life whipped him in every battle, straight along, and he died in one of the Territories, years ago, a defeated man."

I asked after another of the bright boys.

"He is a success, always has been, always will be, I think."

I inquired after a young fellow who came to the town to study for one of the professions when I was a boy.

"He went at something else before he got through—went from medicine to law, or from law to medicine—then to some other new thing; went away for a year, came back with a young wife; fell to drinking, then to gambling behind the door; finally took his wife and two young children to her father's, and went off to Mexico; went from bad to worse, and finally died there, without a cent to buy a shroud, and without a friend to attend the funeral."

"Pity, for he was the best-natured, and most cheery and hopeful young fellow that ever was."

I named another boy.

"Oh, he is all right. Lives here yet; has a wife and children, and is prospering."

Same verdict concerning other boys.

I named three school-girls.

"The first two live here, are married and have children; the other is long ago dead—never married."

I named, with emotion, one of my early sweethearts.

"She is all right. Been married three times; buried two husbands, divorced from the third, and I hear she is getting ready to marry an old fellow out in Colorado somewhere. She's got children scattered around here and there, most everywheres."

The answer to several other inquiries was brief and simple,—

"Killed in the war."

I named another boy.

"Well, now, his case *is* curious! There wasn't a human being in this town but knew that that boy was a perfect chucklehead; perfect dummy; just a stupid ass, as you may say. Everybody knew it, and everybody said it. Well, if that very boy isn't the first lawyer in the State of Missouri to-day, I'm a Democrat!"

"Is that so?"

"It's actually so. I'm telling you the truth."

"How do you account for it?"

"Account for it? There ain't any accounting for it, except that if you send a damned fool to St. Louis, and you don't tell them he's a damned fool *they'll* never find it out. There's one thing sure—if I had a damned fool I should know what to do with him: ship him to St. Louis—it's the noblest market in the world for that kind of property. Well, when you come to look at it all around, and chew at it and think it over, *don't* it just bang anything you ever heard of?"

"Well, yes, it does seem to. But don't you think maybe it was the Hannibal people who were mistaken about the boy, and not the St. Louis people?"

"Oh, nonsense! The people here have known him from the very cradle—they knew him a hundred times better than the St. Louis idiots *could* have known him. No, if you have got any damned fools that you want to realize on, take my advice—send them to St. Louis."

I mentioned a great number of people whom I had formerly known. Some were dead, some were gone away, some had prospered, some had come to naught; but as regarded a dozen or so of the lot, the answer was comforting:

"Prosperous—live here yet—town littered with their children."

I asked about Miss ——.

"Died in the insane asylum three or four years ago—never was out of it from the time she went in; and was always suffering, too; never got a shred of her mind back."

If he spoke the truth, here was a heavy tragedy, indeed. Thirty-six years in a madhouse, that some young fools might have some fun! I was a small boy, at the time; and I saw those giddy young ladies come tiptoeing into the room where Miss —— sat reading at midnight by a lamp. The girl at the head of the file wore a shroud and a doughface; she crept behind the victim, touched her on the shoulder, and she looked up and screamed, and then fell into convulsions. She did not recover from the fright, but went mad. In these days it seems incredible that people believed in ghosts so short a time ago. But they did.

After asking after such other folk as I could call to mind, I finally inquired about *myself:*

"Oh, he succeeded well enough—another case of damned fool. If they'd sent him to St. Louis, he'd have succeeded sooner."

It was with much satisfaction that I recognized the wisdom of having told this candid gentleman, in the beginning, that my name was Smith.

CHAPTER LIV

PAST AND PRESENT

Being left to myself, up there, I went on picking out old houses on the distant town, and calling back their former inmates out of the mouldy past. Among them I presently recognized the house of the father of Lem Hackett (fictitious name). It carried me back more than a generation in a moment, and landed me in the midst of a time when the happenings of life were not the natural and logical results of great general laws, but of special orders, and were freighted with very precise and distinct purposes—partly punitive in intent, partly admonitory; and usually local in application.

When I was a small boy, Lem Hackett was drowned—on a Sunday. He fell out of an empty flat-boat, where he was playing. Being loaded with sin, he went to the bottom like an anvil. He was the only boy in the village who slept that night. We others all lay awake, repenting. We had not needed the information, delivered from the pulpit that evening, that Lem's was a case of special judgment—we knew that, already. There was a ferocious thunder-storm, that night, and it raged continuously until near dawn. The winds blew, the windows rattled, the rain swept along the roof in pelting sheets, and at the briefest of intervals the inky blackness of the night vanished, the houses over the way glared out white and blinding for a quivering instant, then the solid darkness shut down again and a splitting peal of thunder followed which seemed to rend everything in the neighborhood to shreds and splinters. I sat up in bed quaking and shuddering, waiting for the destruction of the world, and expecting it. To me there was nothing strange or incongruous in heaven's making such an uproar about Lem Hackett. Apparently it was the right and proper thing to do. Not a doubt entered my mind that all the angels were grouped together, discussing this boy's case and observing the awful bombardment of our beggarly little village with satisfaction and approval. There was one thing which disturbed me in the most serious way; that was the thought that this centering of the celestial interest on our village could not fail to attract the attention of the observers to people among us who might otherwise have escaped notice for years. I felt that I was not only one of those people, but the very one most likely to be discovered. That discovery could have but one result: I should be in the fire with Lem before the chill of the river had been fairly warmed out of him. I knew that this would be only just and fair. I was increasing the chances against myself all the time, by feeling a secret bitterness against Lem for having attracted this fatal attention to me, but I could not help it—this sinful thought persisted in infesting my breast in spite of me. Every time the lightning glared I caught my breath, and judged I was gone. In my terror and misery, I meanly began to suggest other boys, and mention acts of theirs which were wickeder than mine, and peculiarly needed punishment—and I tried to pretend to myself that I was simply doing this in a casual way, and without intent to divert the heavenly attention to them for the purpose of getting rid of it myself. With deep sagacity I put these mentions into the form of sorrowing recollections and left-handed sham-supplications that the sins of those boys might be allowed to pass unnoticed—"Possibly they may repent." "It is true that Jim Smith broke a window and lied about it—but maybe he did not mean any harm. And although Tom Holmes says more bad words than any other boy in the village, he probably intends to repent—though he has never said he would. And whilst it is a fact that John Jones did fish a little on Sunday, once, he didn't really catch anything but only just one small useless mud-cat; and maybe that wouldn't have been so awful if he had thrown it back—as he says he did, but he didn't. Pity but they would repent of these dreadful things—and maybe they will yet."

But while I was shamefully trying to draw attention to these poor chaps—who were doubtless directing the celestial attention to me at the same moment, though I never once suspected that—I had heedlessly left my candle burning. It was not a time to neglect even trifling precautions. There was no occasion to add anything to the facilities for attracting notice to me—so I put the light out.

It was a long night to me, and perhaps the most distressful one I ever spent. I endured agonies of remorse for sins which I knew I had committed, and for others which I was not certain about, yet was sure that they had been set down against me in a book by an angel who was wiser than I and did not trust such important matters to memory. It struck me, by and by, that I had been making a most foolish and calamitous mistake, in one respect: doubtless I had not only made my own destruction sure by directing attention to those other boys, but had already accomplished theirs!—Doubtless the lightning had stretched them all dead in their beds by this time! The anguish and the fright which this thought gave me made my previous sufferings seem trifling by comparison.

Things had become truly serious. I resolved to turn over a new leaf instantly; I also resolved to connect myself with the church the next day, if I survived to see its sun appear. I resolved to cease from sin in all its forms, and to lead a high and blameless life forever after. I would be punctual at church and Sunday-school; visit the sick; carry baskets of victuals to the poor (simply to fulfil the regulation conditions, although I knew we had none among us so poor but they would smash the basket over my head for my pains); I would instruct other boys in right ways, and take the resulting trouncings meekly; I would subsist entirely on tracts; I would invade the rum shop and warn the drunkard—and finally, if I escaped the fate of those who early become too good to live, I would go for a missionary.

The storm subsided toward daybreak, and I dozed gradually to sleep with a sense of obligation to Lem Hackett for going to eternal suffering in that abrupt way, and thus preventing a far more freadful disaster—my own loss.

But when I rose refreshed, by and by, and found that those other boys were still alive, I had a dim sense that perhaps the whole thing was a false alarm; that the entire turmoil had been on Lem's account and nobody's else. The world looked so bright and safe that there did not seem to be any real occasion to turn over a new leaf. I was a little subdued, during that day, and perhaps the next; after that, my purpose of reforming slowly dropped out of my mind, and I had a peaceful, comfortable time again, until the next storm.

That storm came about three weeks later; and it was the most unaccountable one, to me, that I had ever experienced; for on the afternoon of the day, "Dutchy" was drowned. Dutchy belonged to our Sunday-school. He was a German lad who did not know enough to come in out of the rain; but he was exasperatingly good, and had a prodigious memory. One Sunday he made himself the envy of all the youth and the talk of all the admiring village, by reciting three thousand verses of Scripture without missing a word; then he went off the very next day and got drowned.

Circumstances gave to his death a peculiar impressiveness. We were all bathing in a muddy creek which had a deep hole in it, and in this hole the coopers had sunk a pile of green hickory hoop poles to soak, some twelve feet under water. We were diving and "seeing who could stay under longest." We managed to remain down by holding on to the hoop poles. Dutchy made such a poor success of it that he was hailed with laughter and derision every time his head appeared above water. At last he seemed hurt with the taunts, and begged us to stand still on the bank and be fair with him and give him an honest count—"be friendly and kind just this once, and not miscount for the sake of having the fun of laughing at him." Treacherous winks were exchanged, and all said "All right, Dutchy—go ahead, we'll play fair."

Dutchy plunged in, but the boys, instead of beginning to count, followed the lead of one of their number and scampered to a range of blackberry bushes close by and hid behind it. They imagined Dutchy's humiliation, when he should rise after a superhuman effort and find the place silent and vacant, nobody there to applaud. They were "so full of laugh" with the idea, that they were continually exploding into muffled cackles. Time swept on, and presently one who was peeping through the briers, said, with surprise:—

"Why, he hasn't come up, yet!"

The laughing stopped.

"Boys, it's a splended dive," said one.

"Never mind that," said another, "the joke on him is all the better for it."

There was a remark or two more, and then a pause. Talking ceased, and all began to peer through the vines. Before long, the boys' faces began to look uneasy, then anxious, then terrified. Still there was no movement of the placid water. Hearts began to beat fast, and faces to turn pale. We all glided out, silently, and stood on the bank, our horrified eyes wandering back and forth from each other's countenances to the water.

"Somebody must go down and see!"

Yes, that was plain; but nobody wanted that grisly task.

"Draw straws!"

So we did—with hands which shook so, that we hardly knew what we were about. The lot fell to me, and I went down. The water was so muddy I could not see anything, but I felt around among the hoop poles, and presently grasped a limp wrist which gave me no response—and if it had I should not have known it, I let it go with such a frightened suddenness.

The boy had been caught among the hoop poles and entangled there, helplessly. I fled to the surface and told the awful news.

Some of us knew that if the boy were dragged out at once he might possibly be resuscitated, but we never thought of that. We did not think of anything; we did not know what to do, so we did nothing—except that the smaller lads cried, piteously, and we all struggled frantically into our clothes, putting on anybody's that came handy, and getting them wrong-side-out and upside-down, as a rule. Then we scurried away and gave the alarm, but none of us went back to see the end of the tragedy. We had a more important thing to attend to: we all flew home, and lost not a moment on getting ready to lead a better life.

The night presently closed down. Then came on that tremendous and utterly unaccountable storm. I was perfectly dazed; I could not understand it. It seemed to me that there must be some mistake. The elements were turned loose, and they rattled and banged and blazed away in the most blind and frantic manner. All heart and hope went out of me, and the dismal thought kept floating through my brain, "If a boy who knows three thousand verses by heart is not satisfactory, what chance is there for anybody else?"

Of course I never questioned for a moment that the storm was on Dutchy's account, or that he or any other inconsequential animal was worthy of such a majestic demonstration from on high; the lesson of it was the only thing that troubled me; for it convinced me that if Dutchy, with all his perfections, was not a delight, it would be vain for me to turn over a new leaf, for I must infallibly fall hopelessly short of that boy, no matter how hard I might try. Nevertheless I did turn it over—a highly educated fear compelled me to do that—but succeeding days of cheerfulness and sunshine came bothering around, and within a month I had so drifted backward that again I was as lost and comfortable as ever.

Breakfast time approached while I mused these musings and called these ancient happenings back to mind; so I got me back into the present and went down the hill.

On my way through town to the hotel, I saw the house which was my home when I was a boy. At present rates, the people who now occupy it are of no more value than I am; but in my time they would have been worth not less than five hundred dollars apiece. They are colored folk.

After breakfast, I went out alone again, intending to hunt up some of the Sunday-schools and see how this generation of pupils might compare with their progenitors who had sat with me in those places and had probably taken me as a model—though I do not remember as to that now. By the public square there had been in my day a shabby little brick church called the

"Old Ship of Zion," which I had attended as a Sunday-school scholar; and I found the locality easily enough, but not the old church; it was gone, and a trig and rather hilarious new edifice was in its place. The pupils were better dressed and better looking than were those of my time; consequently they did not resemble their ancestors; and consequently there was nothing familiar to me in their faces. Still, I contemplated them with a deep interest and a yearning wistfulness, and if I had been a girl I would have cried; for they were offspring, and represented, and occupied the places, of boys and girls some of whom I had loved to love, and some of whom I had loved to hate, but all of whom were dear to me for the one reason or the other, so many years gone by—and, Lord, where be they now!

I was mightily stirred, and would have been grateful to be allowed to remain unmolested and look my fill; but a bald-summited superintendent who had been a tow-headed Sunday-school mate of mine on that spot in the early ages, recognized me, and I talked a flutter of wild nonsense to those children to hide the thoughts which were in me, and which could not have been spoken without a betrayal of feeling that would have been recognized as out of character with me.

Making speeches without preparation is no gift of mine; and I was resolved to shirk any new opportunity, but in the next and larger Sunday-school I found myself in the rear of the assemblage; so I was very willing to go on the platform a moment for the sake of getting a good look at the scholars. On the spur of the moment I could not recall any of the old idiotic talks which visitors used to insult me with when I was a pupil there; and I was sorry for this, since it would have given me time and excuse to dawdle there and take a long and satisfying look at what I feel at liberty to say was an array of fresh young comeliness not matchable in another Sunday-school of the same size. As I talked merely to get a chance to inspect; and as I strung out the random rubbish solely to prolong the inspection, I judged it but decent to confess these low motives, and I did so.

If the Model Boy was in either of these Sunday-schools, I did not see him. The Model Boy of my time—we never had but the one—was perfect: perfect in manners, perfect in dress, perfect in conduct, perfect in filial piety, perfect in exterior godliness; but at bottom he was a prig; and as for the contents of his skull, they could have changed place with the contents of a pie and nobody would have been the worse off for it but the pie. This fellow's reproachlessness was a standing reproach to every lad in the village. He was the admiration of all the mothers, and the detestation of all their sons. I was told what became of him, but as it was a disappointment to me, I will not enter into details. He succeeded in life.

CHAPTER LV

A VENDETTA AND OTHER THINGS

During my three days' stay in the town, I woke up every morning with the impression that I was a boy—for in my dreams the faces were all young again, and looked as they had looked in the old times—but I went to bed a hundred years old, every night—for meantime I had been seeing those faces as they are now.

Of course I suffered some surprises, along at first, before I had become adjusted to the changed state of things. I met young ladies who did not seem to have changed at all; but they turned out to be the daughters of the young ladies I had in mind—sometimes their grand-daughters. When you are told that a stranger of fifty is a grandmother, there is nothing surprising about it; but if, on the contrary, she is a person whom you knew as a little girl, it seems impossible. You to say yourself, "How can a little girl be a grandmother?" It takes some little time to accept and realize the fact that while you have been growing old, your friends have not been standing still, in that matter.

I noticed that the greatest changes observable were with the women, not the men. I saw men whom thirty years had changed but slightly; but their wives had grown old. These were good women; it is very wearing to be good.

There was a saddler whom I wished to see; but he was gone. Dead, these many years, they said. Once or twice a day, the saddler used to go tearing down the street, putting on his coat as he went; and then everybody knew a steamboat was coming. Everybody knew, also, that John Stavely was not expecting anybody by the boat—or any freight, either; and Stavely must have known that everybody knew this, still it made no difference to him; he liked to seem to himself to be expecting a hundred thousand tons of saddles by this boat, and so he went on all his life, enjoying being faithfully on hand to receive and receipt for those saddles, in case by any miracle they should come. A malicious Quincy paper used always to refer to this town, in derision as "Stavely's Landing." Stavely was one of my earliest admirations; I envied him his rush of imaginary business, and the display he was able to make of it, before strangers, as he went flying down the street struggling with his fluttering coat.

But there was a carpenter who was my chiefest hero. He was a mighty liar, but I did not know that; I believed everything he said. He was a romantic, sentimental, melodramatic fraud, and his bearing impressed me with awe. I vividly remember the first time he took me into his confidence. He was planing a board, and every now and then he would pause and heave a deep sigh; and occasionally mutter broken sentences—confused and not intelligible—but out of their midst an ejaculation sometimes escaped which made me shiver and did me good: one was, "O God, it is his blood!" I sat on the tool-chest and humbly and shudderingly admired him; for I judged he was full of crime. At last he said in a low voice:—

"My little friend, can you keep a secret?"

I eagerly said I could.

"A dark and dreadful one?"

I satisfied him on that point.

"Then I will tell you some passages in my history; for oh, I *must* relieve my burdened soul, or I shall die!"

He cautioned me once more to be "as silent as the grave;" then he told me he was a "red-handed murderer." He put down his plane, held his hands out before him, contemplated them sadly, and said:—

"Look—with these hands I have taken the lives of thirty human beings!"

The effect which this had upon me was an inspiration to him, and he turned himself loose upon his subject with interest and energy. He left generalizing, and went into details,—began with his first murder; described it, told what measures he had taken to avert suspicion; then passed to his second homicide, his third, his fourth, and so on. He had always done his murders with a bowie-knife, and he made all my hairs rise by suddenly snatching it out and showing it to me.

At the end of this first *séance* I went home with six of his fearful secrets among my freightage, and found them a great help to my dreams, which had been sluggish for a while back. I sought him again and again, on my Saturday holidays; in fact I spent the summer with him—all of it which was valuable to me. His fascinations never diminished, for he threw something fresh and stirring, in the way of horror, into each successive murder. He always gave names, dates, places—everything. This by and by enabled me to note two things: that he had killed his victims in every quarter of the globe, and that these victims were always named Lynch. The destruction of the Lynches went serenely on, Saturday after Saturday, until the original thirty had multiplied to sixty,—and more to be heard from yet; then my curiosity got the better of my timidity, and I asked how it happened that these justly punished persons all bore the same name.

My hero said he had never divulged that dark secret to any living being; but felt that he could trust me, and therefore he would lay bare before me the story of his sad and blighted life. He had loved one "too fair for earth," and she had reciprocated "with all the sweet affection of her pure and noble nature." But he had a rival, a "base hireling" named Archibald Lynch, who said the girl should be his, or he would "dye his hands in her heart's best blood." The carpenter, "innocent and happy in love's young dream," gave no weight to the threat, but led his "golden-haired darling to the altar," and there, the two were made one; there also, just as the minister's hands were stretched in blessing over their heads, the fell deed was done—with a knife—and the bride fell a corpse at her husband's feet. And what did the husband do? He plucked forth that knife, and kneeling by the body of his lost one, swore to "consecrate his life to the extermination of all the human scum that bear the hated name of Lynch."

That was it. He had been hunting down the Lynches and slaughtering them, from that day to this—twenty years. He had always used that same consecrated knife; with it he had murdered his long array of Lynches, and with it he had left upon the forehead of each victim a peculiar mark—a cross, deeply incised. Said he:—

"The cross of the Mysterious Avenger is known in Europe, in America, in China, in Siam, in the Tropics, in the Polar Seas, in the deserts of Asia, in all the earth. Wherever in the uttermost parts of the globe, a Lynch has penetrated, there has the Mysterious Cross been seen, and those who have seen it have shuddered and said, 'it is his mark, he has been here.' You have heard of the Mysterious Avenger—look upon him, for before you stands no less a person! But beware—breathe not a word to any soul. Be silent, and wait. Some morning this town will flock aghast to view a gory corpse; on its brow will be seen the awful sign, and men will tremble and whisper, 'he has been here,—it is the Mysterious Avenger's mark!' You will come here, but I shall have vanished; you will see me no more."

This ass has been reading the "Jibbenainosay," no doubt, and had had his poor romantic head turned by it; but as I had not yet seen the book then, I took his inventions for truth, and did not suspect that he was a plagiarist.

However, we had a Lynch living in the town; and the more I reflected upon his impending doom, the more I could not sleep.

It seemed my plain duty to save him, and a still plainer and more important duty to get some sleep for myself, so at last I ventured to go to Mr. Lynch and tell him what was about to happen to him—under strict secrecy. I advised him to "fly," and certainly expected him to do it. But he laughed at me; and he did not stop there; he led me down to the carpenter's shop, gave the carpenter a jeering and scornful lecture upon his silly pretensions, slapped his face, made him get down on his knees and beg—then went off and left me to contemplate the cheap and pitiful ruin of what, in my eyes, had so lately been a majestic and incomparable hero. The carpenter blustered, flourished his knife, and doomed this Lynch in his usual volcanic style, the size of his fateful words undiminished; but it was all wasted upon me; he was a hero to me no longer but only a poor, foolish, exposed humbug. I was ashamed of him, and ashamed of myself; I took no further interest in him, and never went to his shop any more. He was a heavy loss to me, for he was the greatest hero I had ever known. The fellow must have had some talent; for some of his imaginary murders were so vividly and dramatically described that I remember all their details yet.

The people of Hannibal are not more changed than is the town. It is no longer a village; it is a city, with a mayor, and a council, and water-works, and probably a debt. It has fifteen thousand people, is a thriving and energetic place, and is paved like the rest of the west and south—where a well-paved street and a good sidewalk are things so seldom seen, that one doubts them when he does see them. The customary half-dozen railways centre in Hannibal now, and there is a new depot which cost a hundred thousand dollars. In my time the town had no specialty, and no commercial grandeur; the daily packet usually landed a passenger and bought a catfish, and took away another passenger and a hatful of freight; but now a huge commerce in lumber has grown up and a large miscellaneous commerce is one of the results. A deal of money changes hands there now.

Bear Creek—so called, perhaps, because it was always so particularly bare of bears—is hidden out of sight now, under islands and continents of piled lumber, and nobody but an expert can find it. I used to get drowned in it every summer regularly, and be drained out, and inflated and set going again by some chance enemy; but not enough of it is unoccupied now to drown a person in. It was a famous breeder of chills and fever in its day. I remember one summer when everybody in town had this disease at once. Many chimneys were shaken down, and all the houses were so racked that the town had to be rebuilt. The chasm or gorge between Lover's Leap and the hill west of it is supposed by scientists to have been caused by glacial action. This is a mistake.

There is an interesting cave a mile or two below Hannibal, among the bluffs. I would have liked to revisit it, but had not time. In my time the person who then owned it turned it into a mausoleum for his daughter, aged fourteen. The body of this poor child was put into a copper cylinder filled with alcohol, and this was suspended in one of the dismal avenues of the cave. The top of the cylinder was removable; and it was said to be a common thing for the baser order of tourists to drag the dead face into view and examine it and comment upon it.

CHAPTER LVI

A QUESTION OF LAW

The slaughter-house is gone from the mouth of Bear Creek and so is the small jail (or "calaboose") which once stood in its neighborhood. A citizen asked, "Do you remember when Jimmy Finn, the town drunkard, was burned to death in the calaboose?"

Observe, now, how history becomes defiled, through lapse of time and the help of the bad memories of men. Jimmy Finn was not burned in the calaboose, but died a natural death in a tan vat, of a combination of delirium tremens and spontaneous combustion. When I say natural death, I mean it was a natural death for Jimmy Finn to die. The calaboose victim was not a citizen; he was a poor stranger, a harmless whiskey-sodden tramp. I knew more about his case than anybody else; I knew too much of it, in that bygone day, to relish speaking of it. That tramp was wandering about the streets one chilly evening, with a pipe in his mouth, and begging for a match; he got neither matches nor courtesy; on the contrary, a troop of bad little boys followed him around and amused themselves with nagging and annoying him. I assisted; but at last, some appeal which the wayfarer made for forbearance, accompanying it with a pathetic reference to his forlorn and friendless condition, touched such sense of shame and remnant of right feeling as were left in me, and I went away and got him some matches, and then hied me home and to bed, heavily weighted as to conscience, and unbuoyant in spirit. An hour or two afterward, the man was arrested and locked up in the calaboose by the marshal—large name for a constable, but that was his title. At two in the morning, the church bells rang for fire, and everybody turned out, of course—I with the rest. The tramp had used his matches disastrously: he had set his straw bed on fire, and the oaken sheathing of the room had caught. When I reached the ground, two hundred men, women, and children stood massed together, transfixed with horror, and staring at the grated windows of the jail. Behind the iron bars, and tugging frantically at them, and screaming for help, stood the tramp; he seemed like a black object set against a sun, so white and intense was the light at his back. That marshal could not be found, and he had the only key. A battering-ram was quickly improvised, and the thunder of its blows upon the door had so encouraging a sound that the spectators broke into wild cheering, and believed the merciful battle won. But it was not so. The timbers were too strong; they did not yield. It was said that the man's death-grip still held fast to the bars after he was dead; and that in this position the fires wrapped him about and consumed him. As to this, I do not know. What was seen after I recognized the face that was pleading through the bars was seen by others, not by me.

I saw that face, so situated, every night for a long time afterward; and I believed myself as guilty of the man's death as if I had given him the matches purposely that he might burn himself up with them. I had not a doubt that I should be hanged if my connection with this tragedy were found out. The happenings and the impressions of that time are burnt into my memory, and the study of them entertains me as much now as they themselves distressed me then. If anybody spoke of that grisly matter, I was all ears in a moment, and alert to hear what might be said, for I was always dreading and expecting to find out that I was suspected; and so fine and so delicate was the perception of my guilty conscience, that it often detected suspicion in the most purposeless remarks, and in looks, gestures, glances of the eye which had no significance, but which sent me shivering away in a panic of fright, just the same. And how sick it made me when somebody dropped, howsoever carelessly and barren of intent, the remark that "murder will out!" For a boy of ten years, I was carrying a pretty weighty cargo.

All this time I was blessedly forgetting one thing—the fact that I was an inveterate talker in my sleep. But one night I awoke and found my bed-mate—my younger brother—sitting up in bed and contemplating me by the light of the moon. I said:—

"What is the matter?"

"You talk so much I can't sleep."

I came to a sitting posture in an instant, with my kidneys in my throat and my hair on end.

"What did I say? Quick—out with it—what did I say?"

"Nothing much."

"It's a lie—you know everything."

"Everything about what?"

"You know well enough. About *that*."

"About *what*?—I don't know what you are talking about. I think you are sick or crazy or something. But anyway, you're awake, and I'll get to sleep while I've got a chance."

He fell asleep and I lay there in a cold sweat, turning this new terror over in the whirling chaos which did duty as my mind. The burden of my thought was, How much did I divulge? How much does he know?—what a distress is this uncertainty! But by and by I evolved an idea—I would wake my brother and probe him with a supposititious case. I shook him up, and said—

"Suppose a man should come to you drunk—"

"This is foolish—I never get drunk."

"I don't mean you, idiot—I mean the man. Suppose a *man* should come to you drunk, and borrow a knife, or a tomahawk, or a pistol, and you forgot to tell him it was loaded, and—"

"How could you load a tomahawk?"

"I don't mean the tomahawk, and I didn't *say* the tomahawk; I said the pistol. Now don't you keep breaking in that way, because this is serious. There's been a man killed."

"What! In this town?"

"Yes, in this town."

"Well, go on—I won't say a single word."

"Well, then, suppose you forgot to tell him to be careful with it, because it was loaded, and he went off and shot himself with that pistol,—fooling with it, you know, and probably doing it by accident, being drunk. Well, would it be murder?"

"No—suicide."

"No, No. I don't mean *his* act, I mean yours: would you be a murderer for letting him have that pistol?"

After deep thought came this answer,—

"Well, I should think I was guilty of something—maybe murder—yes, probably murder, but I don't quite know."

This made me very uncomfortable. However, it was not a decisive verdict. I should have to set out the real case—there seemed to be no other way. But I would do it cautiously, and keep a watch out for suspicious effects. I said:—

"I was supposing a case, but I am coming to the real one now. Do you know how the man came to be burned up in the calaboose?"

"No."

"Haven't you the least idea?"

"Not the least."

"Wish you may die in your tracks if you have?"

"Yes, wish I may die in my tracks."

"Well, the way of it was this. The man wanted some matches to light his pipe. A boy got him some. The man set fire to the calaboose with those very matches, and burnt himself up."

"Is that so?"

"Yes, it is. Now, is that boy a murderer, do you think?"

"Let me see. The man was drunk?"

"Yes, he was drunk."

"Very drunk?"

"Yes."

"And the boy knew it?"

"Yes, he knew it."

There was a long pause. Then came this heavy verdict:—

"If the man was drunk, and the boy knew it, the boy murdered that man. This is certain."

Faint, sickening sensations crept along all the fibres of my body, and I seemed to know how a person feels who hears his death sentence pronounced from the bench. I waited to hear what my brother would say next. I believed I knew what it would be, and I was right. He said,—

"I know the boy."

I had nothing to say; so I said nothing. I simply shuddered. Then he added,—

"Yes, before you got half through telling about the thing, I knew perfectly well who the boy was; it was Ben Coontz!"

I came out of my collapse as one who rises from the dead. I said, with admiration:—

"Why, how in the world did you ever guess it?"

"You told it in your sleep."

I said to myself, "How splendid that is! This is a habit which must be cultivated."

My brother rattled innocently on:—

"When you were talking in your sleep, you kept mumbling something about 'matches,' which I couldn't make anything out of; but just now, when you began to tell me about the man and the calaboose and the matches, I remembered that in your sleep you mentioned Ben Coontz two or three times; so I put this and that together, you see, and right away I knew it was Ben that burnt that man up."

I praised his sagacity effusively. Presently he asked,—

"Are you going to give him up to the law?"

"No," I said; "I believe that this will be a lesson to him. I shall keep an eye on him, of course, for that is but right; but if he stops where he is and reforms, it shall never be said that I betrayed him."

"How good you are!"

"Well, I try to be. It is all a person can do in a world like this."

And now, my burden being shifted to other shoulders, my terrors soon faded away.

The day before we left Hannibal, a curious thing fell under my notice,—the surprising spread which longitudinal time undergoes there. I learned it from one of the most unostentatious of men,—the colored coachman of a friend of mine, who lives three miles from town. He was to call for me at the Park Hotel at 7.30 P.M., and drive me out. But he missed it considerably,—did not arrive till ten. He excused himself by saying:—

"De time is mos' an hour en a half slower in de country en what it is in de town; you'll be in plenty time, boss. Sometimes we shoves out early for church, Sunday, en fetches up dah right plum in de middle er de sermon. Diffunce in de time. A body can't make no calculations 'bout it."

I had lost two hours and a half; but I had learned a fact worth four.

CHAPTER LVII

AN ARCHANGEL

From St. Louis northward there are all the enlivening signs of the presence of active, energetic, intelligent, prosperous, practical nineteenth-century populations. The people don't dream, they work. The happy result is manifest all around in the substantial outside aspect of things, and the suggestions of wholesome life and comfort that everywhere appear.

Quincy is a notable example,—a brisk, handsome, well-ordered city; and now, as formerly, interested in art, letters, and other high things.

But Marion City is an exception. Marion City has gone backwards in a most unaccountable way. This metropolis promised so well that the projectors tacked "city" to its name in the very beginning, with full confidence; but it was bad prophecy. When I first saw Marion City, thirty-five years ago, it contained one street, and nearly or quite six houses. It contains but one house now, and this one, in a state of ruin, is getting ready to follow the former five into the river.

Doubtless Marion City was too near to Quincy. It had another disadvantage: it was situated in a flat mud bottom, below high-water mark, whereas Quincy stands high up on the slope of a hill.

In the beginning Quincy had the aspect and ways of a model New England town: and these she has yet: broad, clean streets, trim, neat dwellings and lawns, fine mansions, stately blocks of commercial buildings. And there are ample fair-grounds, a well kept park, and many attractive drives; library, reading-rooms, a couple of colleges, some handsome and costly churches, and a grand court-house, with grounds which occupy a square. The population of the city is thirty thousand. There are some large factories here, and manufacturing, of many sorts, is done on a great scale.

La Grange and Canton are growing towns, but I missed Alexandria; was told it was under water, but would come up to blow in the summer.

Keokuk was easily recognizable. I lived there in 1857,—an extraordinary year there in real-estate matters. The "boom" was something wonderful. Everybody bought, everybody sold,— except widows and preachers; they always hold on; and when the tide ebbs, they get left. Anything in the semblance of a town lot, no matter how situated, was salable, and at a figure which would still have been high if the ground had been sodded with greenbacks.

The town has a population of fifteen thousand now, and is progressing with a healthy growth. It was night, and we could not see details, for which we were sorry, for Keokuk has the reputation of being a beautiful city. It was a pleasant one to live in long ago, and doubtless has advanced, not retrograded, in that respect.

A mighty work which was in progress there in my day is finished now. This is the canal over the Rapids. It is eight miles long, three hundred feet wide, and is in no place less than six feet deep. Its masonry is of the majestic kind which the War Department usually deals in, and will endure like a Roman aqueduct. The work cost four or five millions.

After an hour or two spent with former friends, we started up the river again. Keokuk, a long time ago, was an occasional loafing-place of that erratic genius, Henry Clay Dean. I believe I never saw him but once; but he was much talked of when I lived there. This is what was said of him:—

He began life poor and without education. But he educated himself—on the curb-stones of Keokuk. He would sit down on a curb-stone with his book, careless or unconscious of the clatter of commerce and the tramp of the passing crowds, and bury himself in his studies by the hour, never changing his position except to draw in his knees now and then to let a dray pass unobstructed; and when his book was finished, its contents, however abstruse, had been burnt into his memory, and were his permanent possession. In this way he acquired a vast hoard of all sorts of learning, and had it pigeonholed in his head where he could put his intellectual hand on it whenever it was wanted.

His clothes differed in no respect from a "wharf-rat's", except that they were raggeder, more ill-assorted and inharmonious (and therefore more extravagantly picturesque), and several layers dirtier. Nobody could infer the master-mind in the top of that edifice from the edifice itself.

He was an orator,—by nature in the first place, and later by the training of experience and practice. When he was out on a canvass, his name was a loadstone which drew the farmers to his stump from fifty miles around. His theme was always politics. He used no notes, for a volcano does not need notes. In 1862, a son of Keokuk's late distinguished citizen, Mr. Claggett, gave me this incident concerning Dean:

The war feeling was running high in Keokuk (in '61), and a great mass meeting was to be held on a certain day in the new Althenaeum. A distinguished stranger was to address the house. After the building had been packed to its utmost capacity with sweltering folk of both sexes, the stage still remained vacant,—the distinguished stranger had failed to connect. The crowd grew impatient, and by and by indignant and rebellious. About this time a distressed manager discovered Dean on a curb-stone, explained the dilemma to him, took his book away from him, rushed him into the building the back way, and told him to make for the stage and save his country.

Presently a sudden silence fell upon the grumbling audience, and everybody's eyes sought a single point,—the wide, empty, carpetless stage. A figure appeared there whose aspect was familiar to hardly a dozen persons present. It was the scarecrow Dean,—in foxy shoes, down at the heels; socks of odd colors, also "down;" damaged trousers, relics of antiquity, and a world too short, exposing some inches of naked ankle; an unbuttoned vest, also too short, and exposing a zone of soiled and wrinkled linen between it and the waistband; shirt bosom open; long black handkerchief, wound round and round the neck like a bandage; bob-tailed blue coat, reaching down to the small of the back, with sleeves which left four inches of forearm unprotected; small, stiff-brimmed soldier-cap hung on a corner of the bump of—whichever bump it was. This figure moved gravely out upon the stage and, with sedate and measured step, down to the front, where it paused, and dreamily inspected the house, saying no word. The silence of surprise held its own for a moment, then was broken by a just audible ripple of merriment which swept the sea of faces like the wash of a wave. The figure remained as before, thoughtfully inspecting. Another wave started,—laughter, this time. It was followed by another, then a third,—this last one boisterous.

And now the stranger stepped back one pace, took off his soldier-cap, tossed it into the wing, and began to speak, with deliberation, nobody listening, everybody laughing and whispering. The speaker talked on unembarrassed, and presently delivered a shot which went home, and silence and attention resulted. He followed it quick and fast, with other telling things; warmed to his work and began to pour his words out, instead of dripping them; grew hotter and hotter, and fell to discharging lightnings and thunder,—and now the house began to break into applause, to which the speaker gave no heed, but went hammering straight on; unwound his black bandage and cast it away, still thundering; presently discarded the bob-tailed coat and flung it aside, firing up higher and higher all the time; finally flung the vest after the coat; and then for an untimed period stood there, like another Vesuvius, spouting smoke and flame, lava and ashes, raining pumice-stone and cinders, shaking the moral earth with intellectual crash upon crash, explosion upon explosion, while the mad multitude stood upon their feet in a solid body, answering back with a ceaseless hurricane of cheers, through a thrashing snow-storm of waving handkerchiefs.

"When Dean came," said Claggett, "the people thought he was an escaped lunatic; but when he went, they thought he was an escaped archangel."

Burlington, home of the sparkling Burdette, is another hill city; and also a beautiful one; unquestionably so; a fine and flourishing city, with a population of twenty-five thousand, and belted with busy factories of nearly every imaginable description. It was a very sober city, too—for the moment—for a most sobering bill was pending; a bill to forbid the manufacture, exportation, importation, purchase, sale, borrowing, lending, stealing, drinking, smelling, or possession, by conquest, inheritance, intent, accident, or otherwise, in the State of Iowa, of each and every deleterious beverage known to the human race, except water. This measure was approved by all the rational people in the State; but not by the bench of Judges.

Burlington has the progressive modern city's full equipment of devices for right and intelligent government; including a paid fire department, a thing which the great city of New Orleans is without, but still employs that relic of antiquity, the independent system.

In Burlington, as in all these Upper-River towns, one breathes a go-ahead atmosphere which tastes good in the nostrils. An opera-house has lately been built there which is in strong contrast with the shabby dens which usually do duty as theatres in cities of Burlington's size.

We had not time to go ashore in Muscatine, but had a daylight view of it from the boat. I lived there awhile, many years ago, but the place, now, had a rather unfamiliar look; so I suppose it has clear outgrown the town which I used to know. In fact, I know it has; for I remember it as a small place—which it isn't now. But I remember it best for a lunatic who caught me out in the fields, one Sunday, and extracted a butcher-knife from his boot and proposed to carve me up with it, unless I acknowledged him to be the only son of the Devil. I tried to compromise on an acknowledgment that he was the only member of the family I had met; but that did not satisfy him; he wouldn't have any half-measures; I must say he was the sole and only son of the Devil—and he whetted his knife on his boot. It did not seem worth while to make trouble about a little thing like that; so I swung round to his view of the matter and saved my skin whole. Shorty afterward, he went to visit his father; and as he has not turned up since, I trust he is there yet.

And I remember Muscatine—still more pleasantly—for its summer sunsets. I have never seen any, on either side of the ocean, that equalled them. They used the broad smooth river as a canvas, and painted on it every imaginable dream of color, from the mottled daintinesses and delicacies of the opal, all the way up, through cumulative intensities, to blinding purple and crimson conflagrations which were enchanting to the eye, but sharply tried it at the same time. All the Upper Mississippi region has these extraordinary sunsets as a familiar spectacle. It is the true Sunset Land: I am sure no other country can show so good a right to the name. The sunrises are also said to be exceedingly fine. I do not know.

CHAPTER LVIII

ON THE UPPER RIVER

The big towns drop in, thick and fast, now: and between stretch processions of thrifty farms, not desolate solitude. Hour by hour, the boat plows deeper and deeper into the great and populous Northwest; and with each successive section of it which is revealed, one's surprise and respect gather emphasis and increase. Such a people, and such achievements as theirs, compel homage. This is an independent race who think for themselves, and who are competent to do it, because they are educated and enlightened; they read, they keep abreast of the best and newest thought, they fortify every weak place in their land with a school, a college, a library, and a newspaper; and they live under law. Solicitude for the future of a race like this is not in order.

This region is new; so new that it may be said to be still in its babyhood. By what it has accomplished while still teething, one may forecast what marvels it will do in the strength of its maturity. It is so new that the foreign tourist has not heard of it yet; and has not visited it. For sixty years, the foreign tourist has steamed up and down the river between St. Louis and New Orleans, and then gone home and written his book, believing he had seen all of the river that was worth seeing or that had anything to see. In not six of all these books is there mention of these Upper-River towns—for the reason that the five or six tourists who penetrated this region did it before these towns were projected. The latest tourist of them all (1878) made the same old regulation trip—he had not heard that there was anything north of St. Louis.

Yet there was. There was this amazing region, bristling with great towns, projected day before yesterday, so to speak, and built next morning. A score of them number from fifteen hundred to five thousand people. Then we have Muscatine, ten thousand; Winona, ten thousand; Moline, ten thousand; Rock Island, twelve thousand; La Crosse, twelve thousand; Burlington, twenty-five thousand; Dubuque, twenty-five thousand; Davenport, thirty thousand; St. Paul, fifty-eight thousand; Minneapolis, sixty thousand and upward.

The foreign tourist has never heard of these; there is no note of them in his books. They have sprung up in the night, while he slept. So new is this region, that I, who am comparatively young, am yet older than it is. When I was born, St. Paul had a population of three persons, Minneapolis had just a third as many. The then population of Minneapolis died two years ago; and when he died he had seen himself undergo an increase, in forty years, of fifty-nine thousand nine hundred and ninety-nine persons. He had a frog's fertility.

I must explain that the figures set down above, as the population of St. Paul and Minneapolis, are several months old. These towns are far larger now. In fact, I have just seen a newspaper estimate which gives the former seventy-one thousand, and the latter seventy-eight thousand. This book will not reach the public for six or seven months yet; none of the figures will be worth much then.

We had a glimpse of Davenport, which is another beautiful city, crowning a hill—a phrase which applies to all these towns; for they are all comely, all well built, clean, orderly, pleasant to the eye, and cheering to the spirit; and they are all situated upon hills. Therefore we will give that phrase a rest. The Indians have a tradition that Marquette and Joliet camped where Davenport now stands, in 1673. The next white man who camped there, did it about a hundred and seventy years later—in 1834. Davenport has gathered its thirty thousand people within the past thirty years. She sends more children to her schools now, than her whole population numbered twenty-three years ago. She has the usual Upper-River quota of factories, newspapers, and institutions of learning; she has telephones, local telegraphs, an electric alarm, and an admirable paid fire department, consisting of six hook and ladder companies, four steam fire engines, and thirty churches. Davenport is the official residence of two bishops—Episcopal and Catholic.

Opposite Davenport is the flourishing town of Rock Island, which lies at the foot of the Upper Rapids. A great railroad bridge connects the two towns—one of the thirteen which fret the Mississippi and the pilots, between St. Louis and St. Paul.

The charming island of Rock Island, three miles long and half a mile wide, belongs to the United States, and the Government has turned it into a wonderful park, enhancing its natural attractions by art, and threading its fine forests with many miles of drives. Near the centre of the island one catches glimpses, through the trees, of ten vast stone four-story buildings, each of which covers an acre of ground. These are the Government workshops; for the Rock Island establishment is a national armory and arsenal.

We move up the river—always through enchanting scenery, there being no other kind on the Upper Mississippi—and pass Moline, a centre of vast manufacturing industries; and Clinton and Lyons, great lumber centres; and presently reach Dubuque, which is situated in a rich mineral region. The lead mines are very productive, and of wide extent. Dubuque has a great number of manufacturing establishments; among them a plough factory which has for customers all Christendom in general. At least so I was told by an agent of the concern who was on the boat. He said:—

"You show me any country under the sun where they really know *how* to plough, and if I don't show you our mark on the plough they use, I'll eat that plough; and I won't ask for any Woostershyre sauce to flavor it up with, either."

All this part of the river is rich in Indian history and traditions. Black Hawk's was once a puissant name hereabouts; as was Keokuk's, further down. A few miles below Dubuque is the Tete de Mort—Death's-head rock, or bluff—to the top of which the French drove a band of Indians, in early times, and cooped them up there, with death for a certainty, and only the manner of it matter of choice—to starve, or jump off and kill themselves. Black Hawk adopted the ways of the white people, toward the end of his life; and when he died he was buried, near Des Moines, in Christian fashion, modified by Indian custom; that is to say, clothed in a Christian military uniform, and with a Christian cane in his hand, but deposited in the grave in a sitting posture. Formerly, a horse had always been buried with a chief. The substitution of the cane shows that Black Hawk's haughty nature was really humbled, and he expected to walk when he got over.

We noticed that above Dubuque the water of the Mississippi was olive-green—rich and beautiful and semi-transparent, with the sun on it. Of course the water was nowhere as clear or of as fine a complexion as it is in some other seasons of the year; for now it was at flood stage, and therefore dimmed and blurred by the mud manufactured from caving banks.

The majestic bluffs that overlook the river, along through this region, charm one with the grace and variety of their forms, and the soft beauty of their adornment. The steep verdant slope, whose base is at the water's edge, is topped by a lofty rampart of broken, turreted rocks, which are exquisitely rich and mellow in color—mainly dark browns and dull greens, but splashed with other tints. And then you have the shining river, winding here and there and yonder, its sweep interrupted at intervals by clusters of wooded islands threaded by silver channels; and you have glimpses of distant villages, asleep upon capes; and of stealthy rafts slipping along in the shade of the forest walls; and of white steamers vanishing around remote points. And it is all as tranquil and reposeful as dreamland, and has nothing this-worldly about it—nothing to hang a fret or a worry upon.

Until the unholy train comes tearing along—which it presently does, ripping the sacred solitude to rags and tatters with its devil's warwhoop and the roar and thunder of its rushing wheels—and straightway you are back in this world, and with one of its frets ready to hand for your entertainment: for you remember that this is the very road whose stock always goes down after you buy it, and always goes up again as soon as you sell it. It makes me shudder to this day, to remember that I once came near not getting rid of my stock at all. It must be an awful thing to have a railroad left on your hands.

The locomotive is in sight from the deck of the steamboat almost the whole way from St. Louis to St. Paul—eight hundred miles. These railroads have made havoc with the steamboat commerce. The clerk of our boat was a steamboat clerk before these roads were built. In that day the influx of population was so great, and the freight business so heavy, that the boats were not able to keep up with the demands made upon their carrying capacity; consequently the captains were very independent and airy—pretty "biggity", as Uncle Remus would say. The clerk nut-shelled the contrast between the former time and the present, thus:—

"Boat used to land—captain on hurricane roof—mighty stiff and straight—iron ramrod for a spine—kid gloves, plug tile, hair parted behind—man on shore takes off hat and says:—

" 'Got twenty-eight tons of wheat, cap'n—be great favor if you can take them.'

"Captain says:—

" ' 'll take two of them'—and don't even condescend to look at him.

"But now-a-days the captain takes off his old slouch, and smiles all the way around to the back of his ears, and gets off a bow which he hasn't got any ramrod to interfere with, and says:—

" 'Glad to see you, Smith, glad to see you—you're looking well—haven't seen you looking so well for years—what you got for us?'

" 'Nuth'n', says Smith; and keeps his hat on, and just turns his back and goes to talking with somebody else.

"Oh, yes, eight years ago, the captain was on top; but it's Smith's turn now. Eight years ago a boat used to go up the river with every stateroom full, and people piled five and six deep on the cabin floor; and a solid deck-load of immigrants and harvesters down below, into the bargain. To get a first-class stateroom, you'd got to prove sixteen quarterings of nobility and four hundred years of descent, or be personally acquainted with the nigger that blacked the captain's boots. But it's all changed now; plenty staterooms above, no harvesters below—there's a patent self-binder now, and they don't have harvesters any more; they've gone where the woodbine twineth—and they didn't go by steamboat, either; went by the train."

Up in this region we met massed acres of lumber rafts coming down—but not floating leisurely along, in the old-fashioned way, manned with joyous and reckless crews of fiddling, song-singing, whiskey-drinking, breakdown-dancing rapscallions; no, the whole thing was shoved swiftly along by a powerful stern-wheeler, modern fashion, and the small crews were quiet, orderly men, of a sedate business aspect, with not a suggestion of romance about them anywhere.

Along here, somewhere, on a black night, we ran some exceedingly narrow and intricate island-chutes by aid of the electric light. Behind was solid blackness—a crackless bank of it; ahead, a narrow elbow of water, curving between dense walls of foliage that almost touched our bows on both sides; and here every individual leaf, and every individual ripple stood out in its natural color, and flooded with a glare as of noonday intensified. The effect was strange, and fine, and very striking.

We passed Prairie du Chien, another of Father Marquette's camping-places; and after some hours of progress through varied and beautiful scenery, reached La Crosse. Here is a town of twelve or thirteen thousand population, with electric lighted streets, and with blocks of buildings which are stately enough, and also architecturally fine enough, to command respect in any city. It is a choice town, and we made satisfactory use of the hour allowed us, in roaming it over, though the weather was rainier than necessary.

CHAPTER LIX

LEGENDS AND SCENERY

We added several passengers to our list, at La Crosse; among others an old gentleman who had come to this northwestern region with the early settlers, and was familiar with every part of it. Pardonably proud of it,too. He said:—

"You'll find scenery between here and St. Paul that can give the Hudson points. You'll have the Queen's Bluff—seven hundred feet high, and just as imposing a spectacle as you can find anywheres; and Trempeleau Island, which isn't like any other island in America, I believe, for it is a gigantic mountain, with precipitous sides, and is full of Indian traditions, and used to be full of rattlesnakes; if you catch the sun just right there, you will have a picture that will stay with you. And above Winona you'll have lovely prairies; and then come the Thousand Islands, too beautiful for anything; green? why you never saw foliage so green, nor packed so thick; it's like a thousand plush cushions afloat on a looking-glass—when the water's still; and then the monstrous bluffs on both sides of the river—ragged, rugged, dark-complected—just the frame that's wanted; you always want a strong frame, you know, to throw up the nice points of a delicate picture and make them stand out."

The old gentleman also told us a touching Indian legend or two—but not very powerful ones.

After this excursion into history, he came back to the scenery, and described it, detail by detail, from the Thousand Islands to St. Paul; naming its names with such facility, tripping along his theme with such nimble and confident ease, slamming in a three-ton word, here and there, with such a complacent air of 't isn't-anything,-I-can-do-it-any-time-I-want-to, and letting off fine surprises of lurid eloquence at such judicious intervals, that I presently began to suspect—

But no matter what I began to suspect. Hear him:—

"Ten miles above Winona we come to Fountain City, nestling sweetly at the feet of cliffs that lift their awful fronts, Jovelike, toward the blue depths of heaven, bathing them in virgin atmospheres that have known no other contact save that of angels' wings.

"And next we glide through silver waters, amid lovely and stupendous aspects of nature that attune our hearts to adoring admiration, about twelve miles, and strike Mount Vernon, six hundred feet high, with romantic ruins of a once first-class hotel perched far among the cloud shadows that mottle its dizzy heights—sole remnant of once-flourishing Mount Vernon, town of early days, now desolate and utterly deserted.

"And so we move on. Past Chimney Rock we fly—noble shaft of six hundred feet; then just before landing at Minnieska our attention is attracted by a most striking promontory rising over five hundred feet—the ideal mountain pyramid. Its conic shape—thickly-wooded surface girding its sides, and its apex like that of a cone, cause the spectator to wonder at nature's workings. From its dizzy heights superb views of the forests, streams, bluffs, hills and dales below and beyond for miles are brought within its focus. What grander river scenery can be conceived, as we gaze upon this enchanting landscape, from the uppermost point of these bluffs upon the valleys below? The primeval wildness and awful loneliness of these sublime creations of nature and nature's God, excite feelings of unbounded admiration, and the recollection of which can never be effaced from the memory, as we view them in any direction.

"Next we have the Lion's Head and the Lioness's Head, carved by nature's hand, to adorn and dominate the beauteous stream; and then anon the river widens, and a most charming and magnificent view of the valley before us suddenly bursts upon our vision; rugged hills, clad with verdant forests from summit to base, level prairie lands, holding in their lap the beautiful Wabasha, City of the Healing Waters, puissant foe of Bright's disease, and that grandest conception of nature's works, incomparable Lake Pepin—these constitute a picture whereon the tourist's eye may gaze uncounted hours, with rapture unappeased and unappeasable.

"And so we glide along; in due time encountering those majestic domes, the mighty Sugar Loaf, and the sublime Maiden's Rock—which latter, romantic superstition has invested with a voice; and oft-times as the birch canoe glides near, at twilight, the dusky paddler fancies he hears the soft sweet music of the long-departed Winona, darling of Indian song and story.

"Then Frontenac looms upon our vision, delightful resort of jaded summer tourists; then progressive Red Wing; and Diamond Bluff, impressive and preponderous in its lone sublimity; then Prescott and the St. Croix; and anon we see bursting upon us the domes and steeples of St. Paul, giant young chief of the North, marching with seven-league stride in the van of progress, banner-bearer of the highest and newest civilization, carving his beneficent way with the tomahawk of commercial enterprise, sounding the warwhoop of Christian culture, tearing off the reeking scalp of sloth and superstition to plant there the steam-plow and the school-house—ever in his front stretch arid lawlessness, ignorance, crime, despair; ever in his wake bloom the jail, the gallows, and the pulpit; and ever—"

"Have you ever travelled with a panorama?"

"I have formerly served in that capacity."

My suspicion was confirmed.

"Do you still travel with it?"

"No, she is laid up till the fall season opens. I am helping now to work up the materials for a Tourist's Guide which the St. Louis and St. Paul Packet Company are going to issue this summer for the benefit of travellers who go by that line."

"When you were talking of Maiden's Rock, you spoke of the long-departed Winona, darling of Indian song and story. Is she the maiden of the rock?—and are the two connected by legend?"

"Yes, and a very tragic and painful one. Perhaps the most celebrated, as well as the most pathetic, of all the legends of the Mississippi."

We asked him to tell it. He dropped out of his conversational vein and back into his lecture-gait without an effort, and rolled on as follows:—

"A little distance above Lake City is a famous point known as Maiden's Rock, which is not only a picturesque spot, but is full of romantic interest from the event which gave it its name. Not many years ago this locality was a favorite resort for the Sioux Indians on account of the fine fishing and hunting to be had there, and large numbers of them were always to be found in this locality. Among the families which used to resort here, was one belonging to the tribe of Wabasha. We-no-na (first-born) was the name of a maiden who had plighted her troth to a lover belonging to the same band. But her stern parents had promised her hand to another, a famous warrior, and insisted on her wedding him. The day was fixed by her parents, to her great grief. She appeared to accede to the proposal and accompany them to the rock, for the purpose of gathering flowers for the feast. On reaching the rock, We-no-na ran to its summit and standing on its edge upbraided her parents who were below, for their cruelty, and then singing a death-dirge, threw herself from the precipice and dashed them in pieces on the rock below."

"Dashed who in pieces—her parents?"

"Yes."

"Well, it certainly was a tragic business, as you say. And moreover, there is a startling kind of dramatic surprise about it which I was not looking for. It is a distinct improvement upon the threadbare form of Indian legend. There are fifty Lover's Leaps along the Mississippi from whose summit disappointed Indian girls have jumped, but this is the only jump in the lot that turned out in the right and satisfactory way. What became of Winona?"

"She was a good deal jarred up and jolted: but she got herself together and disappeared before the coroner reached the fatal spot; and 't is said she sought and married her true love, and wandered with him to some distant clime, where she lived happy ever after, her gentle spirit mellowed and chastened by the romantic incident which had so early deprived her of the sweet guidance of a mother's love and a father's protecting arm, and thrown her, all unfriended, upon the cold charity of a censorious world."

I was glad to hear the lecturer's description of the scenery, for it assisted my appreciation of what I saw of it, and enabled me to imagine such of it as we lost by the intrusion of night.

As the lecturer remarked, this whole region is blanketed with Indian tales and traditions. But I reminded him that people usually merely mentioned this fact—doing it in a way to make a body's mouth water—and judiciously stopped there. Why? Because the impression left, was that these tales were full of incident and imagination—a pleasant impression which would be promptly dissipated if the tales were told. I showed him a lot of this sort of literature which I had been collecting, and he confessed that it was poor stuff, exceedingly sorry rubbish; and I ventured to add that the legends which he had himself told us were of this character, with the single exception of the admirable story of Winona. He granted these facts, but said that if I would hunt up Mr. Schoolcraft's book, published near fifty years ago, and now doubtless out of print, I would find some Indian inventions in it that were very far from being barren on incident and imagination; that the tales in Hiawatha were of this sort, and they came from Schoolcraft's book; and that there were others in the same book which Mr. Longfellow could have turned into verse with good effect. For instance, there was the legend of "The Undying Head." He could not tell it, for many of the details had grown dim in his memory; but he would recommend me to find it and enlarge my respect for the Indian imagination. He said that this tale, and most of the others in the book, were current among the Indians along this part of the Mississippi when he first came here; and that the contributors to Schoolcraft's book had got them directly from Indian lips, and had written them down with strict exactness, and without embellishments of their own.

I have found the book. The lecturer was right. There are several legends in it which confirm what he said. I will offer two of them—"The Undying Head," and "Peboan and Seegwun, an Allegory of the Seasons." The latter is used in Hiawatha; but it is worth reading in the original form, if only that one may see how effective a genuine poem can be without the helps and graces of poetic measure and rhythm:—

PEBOAN AND SEEGWUN

An old man was sitting alone in his lodge, by the side of a frozen stream. It was the close of winter, and his fire was almost out. He appeared very old and very desolate. His locks were white with age, and he trembled in every joint. Day after day passed in solitude, and he heard nothing but the sound of the tempest, sweeping before it the new-fallen snow.

One day, as his fire was just dying, a handsome young man approached and entered his dwelling. His cheeks were red with the blood of youth, his eyes sparkled with animation, and a smile played upon his lips. He walked with a light and quick step. His forehead was bound with a wreath of sweet grass, in place of a warrior's frontlet, and he carried a bunch of flowers in his hand.

"Ah, my son," said the old man, "I am happy to see you. Come in. Come and tell me of your adventures, and what strange lands you have been to see. Let us pass the night together. I will tell you of my prowess and exploits, and what I can perform. You shall do the same, and we will amuse ourselves."

He then drew from his sack a curiously wrought antique pipe, and having filled it with tobacco, rendered mild by a mixture of certain leaves, handed it to his guest. When this ceremony was concluded they began to speak.

"I blow my breath," said the old man, "and the stream stands still. The water becomes stiff and hard as clear stone."

"I breathe," said the young man, "and flowers spring up over the plain."

"I shake my locks," retorted the old man, "and snow covers the land. The leaves fall from the trees at my command, and my breath blows them away. The birds get up from the water, and fly to a distant land. The animals hide themselves from my breath, and the very ground becomes as hard as flint."

"I shake my ringlets," rejoined the young man, "and warm showers of soft rain fall upon the earth. The plants lift up their heads out of the earth, like the eyes of children glistening with delight. My voice recalls the birds. The warmth of my breath unlocks the streams. Music fills the groves wherever I walk, and all nature rejoices."

At length the sun began to rise. A gentle warmth came over the place. The tongue of the old man became silent. The robin and bluebird began to sing on the top of the lodge. The stream began to murmur by the door, and the fragrance of growing herbs and flowers came softly on the vernal breeze.

Daylight fully revealed to the young man the character of his entertainer. When he looked upon him, he had the icy visage of *Peboan*.* Streams began to flow from his eyes. As the sun increased, he grew less and less in stature, and anon had melted completely away. Nothing remained on the place of his lodge-fire but the *miskodeed*†, a small white flower, with a pink border, which is one of the earliest species of northern plants.

"The Undying Head" is a rather long tale, but it makes up in weird conceits, fairy-tale prodigies, variety of incident, and energy of movement, for what it lacks in brevity‡.

* Winter. † The *trailing arbutus*. ‡ See Appendix D.

CHAPTER LX

SPECULATIONS AND CONCLUSIONS

We reached St. Paul, at the head of navigation of the Mississippi, and there our voyage of two thousand miles from New Orleans ended. It is about a ten-day trip by steamer. It can probably be done quicker by rail. I judge so because I know that one may go by rail from St. Louis to Hannibal—a distance of at least a hundred and twenty miles—in seven hours. This is better than walking; unless one is in a hurry.

The season being far advanced when we were in New Orleans, the roses and magnolia blossoms were falling; but here in St. Paul it was the snow. In New Orleans we had caught an occasional withering breath from over a crater, apparently; here in St. Paul we caught a frequent benumbing one from over a glacier, apparently.

I am not trying to astonish by these statistics. No, it is only natural that there should be a sharp difference between climates which lie upon parallels of latitude which are one or two thousand miles apart. I take this position, and I will hold it and maintain it in spite of the newspapers. The newspaper thinks it isn't a natural thing; and once a year, in February, it remarks, with ill-concealed exclamation points, that while we, away up here are fighting snow and ice, folds are having new strawberries and peas down South; callas are blooming out of doors, and the people are complaining of the warm weather. The newspaper never gets done being surprised about it. It is caught regularly every February. There must be a reason for this; and this reason must be change of hands at the editorial desk. You cannot surprise an individual more than twice with the same marvel—not even with the February miracles of the Southern climate; but if you keep putting new hands at the editorial desk every year or two, and forget to vaccinate them against the annual climatic surprise, that same old thing is going to occur right along. Each year one new hand will have the disease, and be safe from its recurrence; but this does not save the newspaper. No, the newspaper is in as bad case as ever; it will forever have its new hand; and so, it will break out with the strawberry surprise every February as long as it lives. The new hand is curable; the newspaper itself is incurable. An act of Congress—no, Congress could not prohibit the strawberry surprise without questionably stretching its powers. An amendment to the Constitution might fix the thing, and that is probably the best and quickest way to get at it. Under authority of such an amendment, Congress could then pass an act inflicting imprisonment for life for the first offence, and some sort of lingering death for subsequent ones; and this, no doubt, would presently give us a rest. At the same time, the amendment and the resulting act and penalties might easily be made to cover various cognate abuses, such as the Annual-Veteran-who-has-Voted-for-Every-President-from-Washington-down,-and-Walked-to-the-Polls-Yesterday-with-as-Bright-an-Eye-and-as-Firm-a-Step-as-Ever, and ten or eleven other weary yearly marvels of that sort, and of the Oldest-Freemason, and Oldest-Printer, and Oldest-Baptist-Preacher, and Oldest-Alumnus sort, and Three-Children-Born-at-a-Birth sort, and so on, and so on. And then England would take it up and pass a law prohibiting the further use of Sidney Smith's jokes, and appointing a commissioner to construct some new ones. Then life would be a sweet dream of rest and peace, and the nations would cease to long for heaven.

But I wander from my theme. St. Paul is a wonderful town. It is put together in solid blocks of honest brick and stone, and has the air of intending to stay. Its post-office was established thirty-six years ago; and by and by, when the postmaster received a letter, he carried it to Washington, horseback, to inquire what was to be done with it. Such is the legend. Two frame houses were built that year, and several persons were added to the population. A recent number of the leading St. Paul paper, the "Pioneer Press," gives some statistics which furnish a vivid contrast to that old state of things, to wit: Population, autumn of the present year (1882), 71,000; number of letters handled, first half of the year, 1,209,387; number of houses built during three-quarters of the year, 989; their cost, $3,186,000. The increase of letters over the corresponding six months of last year was fifty per cent. Last year the new buildings added to the city cost above $4,500,000. St. Paul's strength lies in her commerce—I mean his commerce. He is a manufacturing city, of course—all the cities of that region are—but he is peculiarly strong in the matter of commerce. Last year his jobbing trade amounted to upwards of $52,000,000.

He has a custom-house, and is building a costly capitol to replace the one recently burned—for he is the capital of the State. He has churches without end; and not the cheap poor kind, but the kind that the rich Protestant puts up, the kind that the poor Irish "hired-girl" delights to erect. What a passion for building majestic churches the Irish hired-girl has. It is a fine thing for our architecture; but too often we enjoy her stately fanes without giving her a grateful thought. In fact, instead of reflecting that "every brick and every stone in this beautiful edifice represents an ache or a pain, and a handful of sweat, and hours of heavy fatigue, contributed by the back and forehead and bones of poverty," it is our habit to forget these things entirely, and merely glorify the mighty temple itself, without vouchsafing one praiseful thought to its humble builder, whose rich heart and withered purse it symbolizes.

This is a land of libraries and schools. St. Paul has three public libraries, and they contain, in the aggregate, some forty thousand books. He has one hundred and sixteen school-houses, and pays out more than seventy thousand dollars a year in teachers' salaries.

There is an unusually fine railway station; so large is it, in fact, that it seemed somewhat overdone, in the matter of size, at first; but at the end of a few months it was perceived that the mistake was distinctly the other way. The error is to be corrected.

The town stands on high ground; it is about seven hundred feet above the sea level. It is so high that a wide view of river and lowland is offered from its streets.

It is a very wonderful town indeed, and is not finished yet. All the streets are obstructed with building material, and this is being compacted into houses as fast as possible, to make room for more—for other people are anxious to build, as soon as they can get the use of the streets to pile up their bricks and stuff in.

How solemn and beautiful is the thought, that the earliest pioneer of civilization, the van-leader of civilization, is never the steamboat, never the railroad, never the newspaper, never the Sabbath-school, never the missionary—but always whiskey! Such is the case. Look history over; you will see. The missionary comes after the whiskey—I mean he arrives after the whiskey has arrived; next comes the poor immigrant, with axe and hoe and rifle; next, the trader; next, the miscellaneous rush; next, the gambler, the desperado, the highwayman, and all their kindred in sin of both sexes; and next, the smart chap who has bought up an old grant that covers all the land; this brings the lawyer tribe; the vigilance committee brings the undertaker. All these interests bring the newspaper; the newspaper starts up politics and a railroad; all hands turn to and build a church and a jail,—and behold, civilization is established forever in the land. But whiskey, you see, was the van-leader in this beneficent work. It always is. It was like a foreigner—and excusable in a foreigner—to be ignorant of this great truth, and wander off into astronomy to borrow a symbol. But if he had been conversant with the facts, he would have said,—

Westward the Jug of Empire takes its way.

This great van-leader arrived upon the ground which St. Paul now occupies, in June, 1837. Yes, at that date, Pierre Parrant, a Canadian, built the first cabin, uncorked his jug, and began to sell whiskey to the Indians. The result is before us.

All that I have said of the newness, briskness, swift progress, wealth, intelligence, fine and substantial architecture, and general slash and go, and energy of St. Paul, will apply to his near neighbor, Minneapolis—with the addition that the latter is the bigger of the two cities.

These extraordinary towns were ten miles apart, a few months ago, but were growing so fast that they may possibly be joined now, and getting along under a single mayor. At any rate, within five years from now there will be at least such a substantial ligament of buildings stretching between them and uniting them that a stranger will not be able to tell where the one Siamese twin leaves off and the other begins. Combined, they will then number a population of two hundred and fifty thousand, if they continue to grow as they are now growing. Thus, this centre of population at the head of Mississippi navigation, will then begin a rivalry as to numbers, with that centre of population at the foot of it—New Orleans.

Minneapolis is situated at the falls of St. Anthony, which stretch across the river, fifteen hundred feet, and have a fall of eighty-two feet—a waterpower which, by art, has been made of inestimable value, business-wise, though somewhat to the damage of the Falls as a spectacle, or as a background against which to get your photograph taken.

Thirty flouring mills turn out two million barrels of the very choicest of flour every year; twenty sawmills produce two hundred million feet of lumber annually; then there are woollen mills, cotton mills, paper and oil mills; and sash, nail, furniture, barrel, and other factories, without number, so to speak. The great flouring-mills here and at St. Paul use the "new process" and mash the wheat by rolling, instead of grinding it.

Sixteen railroads meet in Minneapolis, and sixty-five passenger trains arrive and depart daily.

In this place, as in St. Paul, journalism thrives. Here there are three great dailies, ten weeklies, and three monthlies.

There is a university, with four hundred students—and, better still, its good efforts are not confined to enlightening the one sex. There are sixteen public schools, with buildings which cost $500,000; there are six thousand pupils and one hundred and twenty-eight teachers. There are also seventy churches existing, and a lot more projected. The banks aggregate a capital of $3,000,000, and the wholesale jobbing trade of the town amounts to $50,000,000 a year.

Near St. Paul and Minneapolis are several points of interest—Fort Snelling, a fortress occupying a river-bluff a hundred feet high; the falls of Minnehaha; White-bear Lake, and so forth. The beautiful falls of Minnehaha are sufficiently celebrated—they do not need a lift from me, in that direction. The White-bear Lake is less known. It is a lovely sheet of water, and is being utilized as a summer resort by the wealth and fashion of the State. It has its club-house, and its hotel, with the modern improvements and conveniences; its fine summer residences; and plenty of fishing, hunting, and pleasant drives. There are a dozen minor summer resorts around about St. Paul and Minneapolis, but the White-bear Lake is *the* resort. Connected with White-bear Lake is a most idiotic Indian legend. I would resist the temptation to print it here, if I could, but the task is beyond my strength. The guide-book names the preserver of the legend, and compliments his "facile pen." Without further comment or delay then, let us turn the said facile pen loose upon the reader:—

A LEGEND OF WHITE-BEAR LAKE

Every spring, for perhaps a century, or as long as there has been a nation of red men, an island in the middle of White-bear Lake has been visited by a band of Indians for the purpose of making maple sugar.

Tradition says that many springs ago, while upon this island, a young warrior loved and wooed the daughter of his chief, and it is said, also, the maiden loved the warrior. He had again and again been refused her hand by her parents, the old chief alleging that he was no brave, and his old consort called him a woman!

The sun had again set upon the "sugar-bush," and the bright moon rose high in the bright blue heavens, when the young warrior took down his flute and went out alone, once more to sing the story of his love, the mild breeze gently moved the two gay feathers in his head-dress, and as he mounted on the trunk of a leaning tree, the damp snow fell from his feet heavily. As he raised his flute to his lips, his blanket slipped from his well-formed shoulders, and lay partly on the snow beneath. He began his weird, wild love-song, but soon felt that he was cold, and as he reached back for his blanket, some unseen hand laid it gently on his shoulders; it was the hand of his love, his guardian angel. She took her place beside him, and for the present they were happy; for the Indian has a heart to love, and in this pride he is as noble as in his own freedom, which makes him the child of the forest. As the legend runs, a large white-bear, thinking, perhaps, that polar snows and dismal winter weather extended everywhere, took up his journey southward. He at length approached the northern shore of the lake which now bears his name, walked down the bank and made his way noiselessly through the deep heavy snow toward the island. It was the same spring ensuing that the lovers met. They had left their first retreat, and were now seated among the branches of a large elm which hung far over the lake. (The same tree is still standing, and excites universal curiosity and interest.) For fear of being detected, they talked almost in a whisper, and now, that they might get back to camp in good time and thereby avoid suspicion, they were just rising to return, when the maiden uttered a shriek which was heard at the camp, and bounding toward the young brave, she caught his blanket, but missed the direction of her foot and fell, bearing the blanket with her into the great arms of the ferocious monster. Instantly every man, woman, and child of the band were upon the bank, but all unarmed. Cries and wailings went up from every mouth. What was to be done? In the meantime this white and savage beast held the breathless maiden in his huge grasp, and fondled with his precious prey as if he were used to scenes like this. One deafening yell from the lover warrior is heard above the cries of hundreds of his tribe, and dashing away to his wigwam he grasps his faithful knife, returns almost at a single bound to the scene of fear and fright, rushes out along the leaning tree to the spot where his treasure fell, and springing with the fury of a mad panther, pounced upon his prey. The animal turned, and with one stroke of his huge paw brought the lovers heart to heart, but the next moment the warrior, with one plunge of the blade of his knife, opened the crimson sluices of death, and the dying bear relaxed his hold.

That night there was no more sleep for the band or the lovers, and as the young and the old danced about the carcass of the dead monster, the gallant warrior was presented with another plume, and ere another moon had set he had a living treasure added to his heart. Their children for many years played upon the skin of the white-bear—from which the lake derives its name—and the maiden and the brave remembered long the fearful scene and rescue that made them one, for Kis-se-me-pa and Ka-go-ka could never forget their fearful encounter with the huge monster that came so near sending them to the happy hunting-ground.

It is a perplexing business. First, she fell down out of the tree—she and the blanket; and the bear caught her and fondled her—her and the blanket; then she fell up into the tree again—leaving the blanket; meantime the lover goes war-whooping home and comes back "heeled," climbs the tree, jumps down on the bear, the girl jumps down after him—apparently, for she was up the tree—resumes her place in the bear's arms along with the blanket, the lover rams his knife into the bear, and saves—whom, the blanket? No—nothing of the sort. You get yourself all worked up and excited about that blanket, and then all of a sudden, just when a happy climax seems imminent, you are let down flat—nothing saved but the girl. Whereas, one is not interested in the girl; she is not the prominent feature of the legend. Nevertheless, there you are left, and there you must remain; for if you live a thousand years you will never know who got the blanket. A dead man could get up a better legend than this one. I don't mean a fresh dead man either; I mean a man that's been dead weeks and weeks.

We struck the home-trail now, and in a few hours were in that astonishing Chicago—a city where they are always rubbing the lamp, and fetching up the genii, and contriving and achieving new impossibilities. It is hopeless for the occasional visitor to try to keep up with Chicago—she out-grows his prophecies faster than he can make them. She is always a novelty; for she is never the Chicago you saw when you passed through the last time. The Pennsylvania road rushed us to New York without missing schedule time ten minutes anywhere on the route; and there ended one of the most enjoyable five-thousand-mile journeys I have ever had the good fortune to make.

APPENDIX

A

[From the New-Orleans Times-Democrat, of March 29, 1882.]

VOYAGE OF THE TIMES-DEMOCRAT'S RELIEF BOAT THROUGH THE INUNDATED REGIONS

It was nine o'clock Thursday morning when the "Susie" left the Mississippi and entered Old River, or what is now called the mouth of the Red. Ascending on the left, a flood was pouring in through and over the levees on the Chandler plantation, the most northern point in Pointe Coupée parish. The water completely covered the place, although the levees had given way but a short time before. The stock had been gathered in a large flat-boat, where, without food, as we passed, the animals were huddled together, waiting for a boat to tow them off. On the right-hand side of the river is Turnbull's Island, and on it is a large plantation which formerly was pronounced one of the most fertile in the State. The water has hitherto allowed it to go scot-free in usual floods, but now broad sheets of water told only where fields were. The top of the protecting levee could be seen here and there, but nearly all of it was submerged.

The trees have put on a greener foliage since the water has poured in, and the woods look bright and fresh, but this pleasant aspect to the eye is neutralized by the interminable waste of water. We pass mile after mile, and it is nothing but trees standing up to their branches in water. A water-turkey now and again rises and flies ahead into the long avenue of silence. A pirogue sometimes flits from the bushes and crosses the Red River on its way out to the Mississippi, but the sad-faced paddlers never turn their heads to look at our boat. The puffing of the boat is music in this gloom, which affects one most curiously. It is not the gloom of deep forests or dark caverns, but a peculiar kind of solemn silence and impressive awe that holds one perforce to its recognition. We passed two negro families on a raft tied up in the willows this morning. They were evidently of the well-to-do class, as they had a supply of meal and three or four hogs with them. Their rafts were about twenty feet square, and in front of an improvised shelter earth had been placed, on which they built their fire.

The current running down the Atchafalaya was very swift, the Mississippi showing predilection in that direction, which needs only to be seen to enforce the opinion of that river's desperate endeavors to find a short way to the Gulf. Small boats, skiffs, pirogues, etc., are in great demand, and many have been stolen by piratical negroes, who take them where they will bring the greatest price. From what was told me by Mr. C.P. Ferguson, a planter near Red River Landing, whose place has just gone under, there is much suffering in the rear of that place. The negroes had given up all thoughts of a crevasse there, as the upper levee had stood so long, and when it did come they were at its mercy. On Thursday a number were taken out of trees and off of cabin roofs and brought in, many yet remaining.

One does not appreciate the sight of earth until he has travelled through a flood. At sea one does not expect or look for it, but here, with fluttering leaves, shadowy forest aisles, house-tops barely visible, it is expected. In fact a grave-yard, if the mounds were above water, would be appreciated. The river here is known only because there is an opening in the trees, and that is all. It is in width, from Fort Adams on the left bank of the Mississippi to the bank of Rapides Parish, a distance of about sixty miles. A large portion of this was under cultivation, particularly along the Mississippi and back of the Red. When Red River proper was entered, a strong current was running directly across it, pursuing the same direction as that of the Mississippi.

After a run of some hours, Black River was reached. Hardly was it entered before signs of suffering became visible. All the willows along the banks were stripped of their leaves. One man, whom your correspondent spoke to, said that he had had one hundred and fifty head of cattle and one hundred head of hogs. At the first appearance of water he had started to drive them to the high lands of Avoyelles, thirty-five miles off, but he lost fifty head of the beef cattle and sixty hogs. Black River is quite picturesque, even if its shores are under water. A dense growth of ash, oak, gum, and hickory make the shores almost impenetrable, and where one can get a view down some avenue in the trees, only the dim outlines of distant trucks can be barely distinguished in the gloom.

A few miles up this river, the depth of water on the banks was fully eight feet, and on all sides could be seen, still holding against the strong current, the tops of cabins. Here and there one overturned was surrounded by drift-wood, forming the nucleus of possibly some future island.

In order to save coal, as it was impossible to get that fuel at any point to be touched during the expedition, a lookout was kept for a wood-pile. On rounding a point a pirogue, skilfully paddled by a youth, shot out, and in its bow was a girl of fifteen, of fair face, beautiful black eyes, and demure manners. The boy asked for a paper, which was thrown to him, and the couple pushed their tiny craft out into the swell of the boat.

Presently a little girl, not certainly over twelve years, paddled out in the smallest little canoe and handled it with all the deftness of an old voyageur. The little one looked more like an Indian than a white child, and laughed when asked if she were afraid. She had been raised in a pirogue and could go anywhere. She was bound out to pick willow leaves for the stock, and she pointed to a house near by with water three inches deep on the floors. At its back door was moored a raft about thirty feet square, with a sort of fence built upon it, and inside of this some sixteen cows and twenty hogs were standing. The family did not complain, except on account of losing their stock, and promptly brought a supply of wood in a flat.

From this point to the Mississippi River, fifteen miles, there is not a spot of earth above water, and to the westward for thirty-five miles there is nothing but the river's flood. Black River had risen during Thursday, the 23d, 1 3/4 inches, and was going up at night still. As we progress up the river habitations become more frequent, but are yet still miles apart. Nearly all of them are deserted, and the out-houses floated off. To add to the gloom, almost every living thing seems to have departed, and not a whistle of a bird nor the bark of the squirrel can be heard in this solitude. Sometimes a morose gar will throw his tail aloft and disappear in the river, but beyond this everything is quiet—the quiet of dissolution. Down the river floats now a neatly whitewashed hen-house, then a cluster of neatly split fence-rails, or a door and a bloated carcass, solemnly guarded by a pair of buzzards, the only bird to be seen, which feast on the carcass as it bears them along. A picture-frame in which there was a cheap lithograph of a soldier on horseback, as it floated on told of some hearth invaded by the water and despoiled of this ornament.

At dark, as it was not prudent to run, a place alongside the woods was hunted and to a tall gum-tree the boat was made fast for the night.

A pretty quarter of the moon threw a pleasant light over forest and river, making a picture that would be a delightful piece of landscape study, could an artist only hold it down to his canvas. The motion of the engines had ceased, the puffing of the escaping steam was stilled, and the enveloping silence closed upon us, and such silence it was! Usually in a forest at night one can hear the piping of frogs, the hum of insects, or the dropping of limbs; but here nature was dumb. The dark recesses, those aisles into this cathedral, gave forth no sound, and even the ripplings of the current die away.

At daylight Friday morning all hands were up, and up the Black we started. The morning was a beautiful one, and the river, which is remarkably straight, put on its loveliest garb. The blossoms of the haw perfumed the air deliciously, and a few birds whistled blithely along the banks. The trees were larger, and the forest seemed of older growth than below. More fields were passed than nearer the mouth, but the same scene presented itself—smokehouses drifting out in the pastures, negro quarters anchored in confusion against some oak, and the modest residence just showing its eaves above water. The sun came up in a glory of carmine, and the trees were brilliant in their varied shades of green. Not a foot of soil is to be seen anywhere, and the water is apparently growing deeper and deeper, for it reaches up to the branches of the largest trees. All along, the bordering willows have been denuded of leaves, showing how long the people have been at work gathering this fodder for their animals. An old man in a pirogue was asked how the willow leaves agreed with his cattle. He stopped in his work, and with an ominous shake of his head replied: "Well, sir, it's enough to keep warmth in their bodies and that's all we expect, but it's hard on the hogs, particularly the small ones. They is dropping off powerful fast. But what can you do? It's all we've got."

At thirty miles above the mouth of Black River the water extends from Natchez on the Mississippi across to the pine hills of Louisiana, a distance of seventy-three miles, and there is hardly a spot that is not ten feet under it. The tendency of the current up the Black is toward the west. In fact, so much is this the case, the waters of Red River have been driven down from toward the Calcasieu country, and the waters of the Black enter the Red some fifteen miles above the mouth of the former, a thing never before seen by even the oldest steamboatmen. The water now in sight of us is entirely from the Mississippi.

Up to Trinity, or rather Troy, which is but a short distance below, the people have nearly all moved out, those remaining having enough for their present personal needs. Their cattle, though, are suffering and dying off quite fast, as the confinement on rafts and the food they get breeds disease.

After a short stop we started, and soon came to a section where there were many open fields and cabins thickly scattered about. Here were seen more pictures of distress. On the inside of the houses the inmates had built on boxes a scaffold on which they placed the furniture. The bed-posts were sawed off on top, as the ceiling was not more than four feet from the improvised floor. The buildings looked very insecure, and threaten every moment to float off. Near the houses were cattle standing breast high in the water, perfectly impassive. They did not move in their places, but stood patiently waiting for help to come. The sight was a distressing one, and the poor creatures will be sure to die unless speedily rescued. Cattle differ from horses in this peculiar quality. A horse, after finding no relief comes, will swim off in search of food, whereas a beef will stand in its tracks until with exhaustion it drops in the water and drowns.

At half-past twelve o'clock a hail was given from a flat-boat inside the line of the bank. Rounding to we ran alongside, and General York stepped aboard. He was just then engaged in getting off stock, and welcomed the "Times-Democrat Boat" heartily, as he said there was much need for her. He said that the distress was not exaggerated in the least. People were in a condition it was difficult even for one to imagine. The water was so high there was great danger of their houses being swept away. It had already risen so high that it was approaching the eaves, and when it reaches this point there is always imminent risk of their being swept away. If this occurs, there will be great loss of life. The General spoke of the gallant work of many of the people in their attempts to save their stock, but thought that fully twenty-five per cent had perished. Already twenty-five hundred people had received rations from Troy, on Black River, and he had towed out a great many cattle, but a very great quantity remained and were in dire need. The water was now eighteen inches higher than in 1874, and there was no land between Vidalia and the hills of Catahoula.

At two o'clock the "Susie" reached Troy, sixty-five miles above the mouth of Black River. Here on the left comes in Little River; just beyond that the Ouachita, and on the right the Tensas. These three rivers form the Black River. Troy, or a portion of it, is situated on and around three large Indian mounds, circular in shape, which rise above the present water about twelve feet. They are about one hundred and fifty feet in diameter and are about two hundred yards apart. The houses are all built between these mounds, and hence are all flooded to a depth of eighteen inches on their floors.

These elevations, built by the aborigines hundreds of years ago, are the only points of refuge for miles. When we arrived we found them crowded with stock, all of which was thin and hardly able to stand up. They were mixed together, sheep, hogs, horses, mules, and cattle. One of these mounds has been used for many years as the grave-yard, and to-day we saw attenuated cows lying against the marble tomb-stones, chewing their cud in contentment, after a meal of corn furnished by General York. Here, as below, the remarkable skill of the women and girls in the management of the smaller pirogues was noticed. Children were paddling about in these most ticklish crafts with all the nonchalance of adepts.

General York has put into operation a perfect system in regard to furnishing relief. He makes a personal inspection of the place where it is asked, sees what is necessary to be done, and then, having two boats chartered, with flats, sends them promptly to the place, when the cattle are loaded and towed to the pine hills and uplands of Catahoula. He has made Troy his headquarters, and to this point boats come for their supply of feed for cattle. On the opposite side of Little River, which branches to the left out of Black, and between it and the Ouachita, is situated the town of Trinity, which is hourly threatened with destruction. It is much lower than Troy, and the water is eight and nine feet deep in the houses. A strong current sweeps through it, and it is remarkable that all of its houses have not gone before. The residents of both Troy and Trinity have been cared for, yet some of their stock have to be furnished with food.

As soon as the "Susie" reached Troy, she was turned over to General York and placed at his disposition to carry out the work of relief more rapidly. Nearly all her supplies were landed on one of the mounds to lighten her, and she was headed down stream to relieve those below. At Tom Hooper's place, a few miles from Troy, a large flat, with about fifty head of stock on board, was taken in tow. The animals were fed, and soon regained some strength. To-day we go on Little River, where the suffering is greatest.

DOWN BLACK RIVER

SATURDAY EVENING, MARCH 25

We started down Black River quite early, under the direction of General York, to bring out what stock could be reached. Going down river a flat in tow was left in a central locality, and from there men poled her back in the rear of plantations, picking up the animals wherever found. In the loft of a gin-house there were seventeen head found, and after a gangway was built they were led down into the flat without difficulty. Taking a skiff with the General, your reporter was pulled up to a little house of two rooms, in which the water was standing two feet on the floors. In one of the large rooms were huddled the horses and cows of the place, while in the other the Widow Taylor and her son were seated on a scaffold raised on the floor. One or two dugouts were drifting about in the room ready to be put in service at any time. When the flat was brought up, the side of the house was cut away as the only means of getting the animals out, and the cattle were driven on board the boat. General York, in this as in every case, inquired if the family desired to leave, informing them that Major Burke, of "The Times-Democrat," has sent the "Susie" up for that purpose. Mrs. Taylor said she thanked Major Burke, but she would try and hold out. The remarkable tenacity of the people here to their homes is beyond all comprehension. Just below, at a point sixteen miles from Troy, information was received that the house of Mr. Tom Ellis was in danger, and his family were all in it. We steamed there immediately, and a sad picture was presented. Looking out of the half of the window left above water was Mrs. Ellis, who is in feeble health, whilst at the door were her seven children, the oldest not fourteen years. One side of the house was given up to the work animals, some twelve head, besides hogs. In the next room the family lived, the water coming within two inches of the bed-rail. The stove was below water, and the cooking was done on a fire on top of it. The house threatened to give way at any moment: one end of it was sinking, and, in fact, the building looked a mere shell. As the boat rounded to, Mr. Ellis came out in a dug-out, and General York told him that he had come to his relief; that "The Times- Democrat" boat was at his service, and would remove his family at once to the hills, and on Monday a flat would take out his stock, as, until that time, they would be busy. Notwithstanding the deplorable situation himself and family were in, Mr. Ellis did not want to leave. He said he thought he would wait until Monday, and take the risk of his house falling. The children around the door looked perfectly contented, seeming to care little for the danger they were in. These are but two instances of the many. After weeks of privation and suffering, people still cling to their houses and leave only when there is not room between the water and the ceiling to build a scaffold on which to stand. It seemed to be incomprehensible, yet the love for the old place was stronger than that for safety.

After leaving the Ellis place, the next spot touched at was the Oswald place. Here the flat was towed alongside the gin-house where there were fifteen head standing in water; and yet, as they stood on scaffolds, their heads were above the top of the entrance. It was found impossible to get them out without cutting away a portion of the front; and so axes were brought into requisition and a gap made. After much labor the horses and mules were securely placed on the flat.

At each place we stop there are always three, four, or more dugouts arriving, bringing information of stock in other places in need. Notwithstanding the fact that a great many had driven a part of their stock to the hills some time ago, there yet remains a large quantity, which General York, who is working with indomitable energy, will get landed in the pine hills by Tuesday.

All along Black River the "Susie" has been visited by scores of planters, whose tales are the repetition of those already heard of suffering and loss. An old planter, who has lived on the river since 1844, said there never was such a rise, and he was satisfied more than one quarter of the stock has been lost. Luckily the people cared first for their work stock, and when they could find it horses and mules were housed in a place of safety. The rise which still continues, and was two inches last night, compels them to get them out to the hills; hence it is that the work of General York is of such a great value. From daylight to late at night he is going this way and that, cheering by his kindly words and directing with calm judgment what is to be done. One unpleasant story, of a certain merchant in New Orleans, is told all along the river. It appears for some years past the planters have been dealing with this individual, and many of them had balances in his hands. When the overflow came they wrote for coffee, for meal, and, in fact, for such little necessities as were required. No response to these letters came, and others were written, and yet these old customers, with plantations under water, were refused even what was necessary to sustain life. It is needless to say he is not popular now on Black River.

The hills spoken of as the place of refuge for the people and stock on Black River are in Catahoula parish, twenty-four miles from Black River.

After filling the flat with cattle we took on board the family of T.S. Hooper, seven in number, who could not longer remain in their dwelling, and we are now taking them up Little River to the hills.

THE FLOOD STILL RISING

TROY, MARCH 27, 1882, NOON.

The flood here is rising about three and a half inches every twenty-four hours, and rains have set in which will increase this. General York feels now that our efforts ought to be directed towards saving life, as the increase of the water has jeopardized many houses. We intend to go up the Tensas in a few minutes, and then we will return and go down Black River to take off families. There is a lack of steam transportation here to meet the emergency. The General has three boats chartered, with flats in tow, but the demand for these to tow out stock is greater than they can meet with promptness. All are working night and day, and the "Susie" hardly stops for more than an hour anywhere. The rise has placed Trinity in a dangerous plight, and momentarily it is expected that some of the houses will float off. Troy is a little higher, yet all are in the water. Reports have come in that a woman and child have been washed away below here, and two cabins floated off. Their occupants are the same who refused to come off day before yesterday. One would not believe the utter passiveness of the people.

As yet no news has been received of the steamer "Delia," which is supposed to be the one sunk in yesterday's storm on Lake Catahoula. She is due here now, but has not arrived. Even the mail here is most uncertain, and this I send by skiff to Natchez to get it to you. It is impossible to get accurate data as to past crops, etc., as those who know much about the matter have gone, and those who remain are not well versed in the production of this section.

General York desires me to say that the amount of rations formerly sent should be duplicated and sent at once. It is impossible to make any estimate, for the people are fleeing to the hills, so rapid is the rise. The residents here are in a state of commotion that can only be appreciated when seen, and complete demoralization has set in.

If rations are drawn for any particular section hereabouts, they would not be certain to be distributed, so everything should be sent to Troy as a centre, and the General will have it properly disposed of. He has sent for one hundred tents, and, if all go to the hills who are in motion now, two hundred will be required.

B

The condition of this rich valley of the Lower Mississippi, immediately after and since the war, constituted one of the disastrous effects of war most to be deplored. Fictitious property in slaves was not only righteously destroyed, but very much of the work which had depended upon the slave labor was also destroyed or greatly impaired, especially the levee system.

It might have been expected by those who have not investigated the subject, that such important improvements as the construction and maintenance of the levees would have been assumed at once by the several States. But what can the State do where the people are under subjection to rates of interest ranging from 18 to 30 per cent, and are also under the necessity of pledging their crops in advance even of planting, at these rates, for the privilege of purchasing all of their supplies at 100 per cent profit?

It has needed but little attention to make it perfectly obvious that the control of the Mississippi River, if undertaken at all, must be undertaken by the national government, and cannot be compassed by States. The river must be treated as a unit; its control cannot be compassed under a divided or separate system of administration.

Neither are the States especially interested competent to combine among themselves for the necessary operations. The work must begin far up the river; at least as far as Cairo, if not beyond; and must be conducted upon a consistent general plan throughout the course of the river.

It does not need technical or scientific knowledge to comprehend the elements of the case if one will give a little time and attention to the subject, and when a Mississippi River commission has been constituted, as the existing commission is, of thoroughly able men of different walks in life, may it not be suggested that their verdict in the case should be accepted as conclusive, so far as any *a priori* theory of construction or control can be considered conclusive?

It should be remembered that upon this board are General Gilmore, General Comstock, and General Suter, of the United States Engineers; Professor Henry Mitchell (the most competent authority on the question of hydrography), of the United States Coast Survey; B. B. Harrod, the State Engineer of Louisiana; Jas. B. Eads, whose success with the jetties at New Orleans is a warrant of his competency, and Judge Taylor, of Indiana.

It would be presumption on the part of any single man, however skilled, to contest the judgment of such a board as this.

The method of improvement proposed by the commission is at once in accord with the results of engineering experience and with observations of nature where meeting our wants. As in nature the growth of trees and their proneness where undermined to fall across the slope and support the bank secures at some points a fair depth of channel and some degree of permanence, so in the project of the engineer the use of timber and brush and the encouragement of forest growth are the main features. It is proposed to reduce the width where excessive by brushwood dykes, at first low, but raised higher and higher as the mud of the river settles under their shelter, and finally slope them back at the angle upon which willows will grow freely. In this work there are many details connected with the forms of these shelter dykes, their arrangements so as to present a series of settling basins, etc., a description of which would only complicate the conception. Through the larger part of the river works of contraction will not be required, but nearly all the banks on the concave side of the bends must be held against the wear of the stream, and much of the opposite banks defended at critical points. The works having in view this conservative object may be generally designated works of revetment; and these also will be largely of brushwood, woven in continuous carpets, or twined into wire-netting. This veneering process has been successfully employed on the Missouri River; and in some cases they have so covered themselves with sediments, and have become so overgrown with willows, that they may be regarded as permanent. In securing these mats rubble-stone is to be used in small quantities, and in some instances the dressed slope between high and low river will have to be more or less paved with stone.

Any one who has been on the Rhine will have observed operations not unlike those to which we have just referred; and, indeed, most of the rivers of Europe flowing among their own alluvia have required similar treatment in the interest of navigation and agriculture.

The levee is the crowning work of bank revetment, although not necessarily in immediate connection. It may be set back a short distance from the revetted bank; but it is, in effect, the requisite parapet. The flood river and the low river cannot be brought into register, and compelled to unite in the excavation of a single permanent channel, without a complete control of all the stages; and even the abnormal rise must be provided against, because this would endanger the levee, and once in force behind the works of revetment would tear them also away.

Under the general principle that the local slope of a river is the result and measure of the resistance of its bed, it is evident that a narrow and deep stream should have less slope, because it has less frictional surface in proportion to capacity; *i.e.,* less perimeter in proportion to area of cross section. The ultimate effect of levees and revetments confining the floods and bringing all the stages of the river into register is to deepen the channel and let down the slope. The first effect of the levees is to raise the surface; but this, by inducing greater velocity of flow, inevitably causes an enlargement of section, and if this enlargement is prevented from being made at the expense of the banks, the bottom must give way and the form of the waterway be so improved as to admit this flow with less rise. The actual experience with levees upon the Mississippi River, with no attempt to hold the banks, has been favorable, and no one can doubt, upon the evidence furnished in the reports of the commission, that if the earliest levees had been accompanied by revetment of banks, and made complete, we should have to-day a river navigable at low water and an adjacent country safe from inundation.

Of course it would be illogical to conclude that the constrained river can ever lower its flood slope so as to make levees unnecessary, but it is believed that, by this lateral constraint, the river as a conduit may be so improved in form that even those rare floods which result from the coincident rising of many tributaries will find vent without destroying levees of ordinary height. That the actual capacity of a channel through alluvium depends upon its service during floods has been often shown, but this capacity does not include anomalous, but recurrent, floods.

It is hardly worth while to consider the projects for relieving the Mississippi River floods by creating new outlets, since these sensational propositions have commended themselves only to unthinking minds, and have no support among engineers. Were the river bed cast-iron, a resort to openings for surplus waters might be a necessity; but as the bottom is yielding, and the best form of outlet is a single deep channel, as realizing the least ratio of perimeter to area of cross section, there could not well be a more unphilosophical method of treatment than the multiplication of avenues of escape.

In the foregoing statement the attempt has been made to condense in as limited a space as the importance of the subject would permit, the general elements of the problem, and the general features of the proposed method of improvement which has been adopted by the Mississippi River Commission.

The writer cannot help feeling that it is somewhat presumptuous on his part to attempt to present the facts relating to an enterprise which calls for the highest scientific skill; but it is a matter which interests every citizen of the United States, and is one of the methods of reconstruction which ought to be approved. It is a war claim which implies no private gain, and no compensation except for one of the cases of destruction incident to war, which may well be repaired by the people of the whole country.

EDWARD ATKINSON.

BOSTON, April 14, 1882.

C

RECEPTION OF CAPTAIN BASIL HALL'S BOOK IN THE UNITED STATES

Having now arrived nearly at the end of our travels, I am induced, ere I conclude, again to mention what I consider as one of the most remarkable traits in the national character of the Americans; namely, their exquisite sensitiveness and soreness respecting everything said or written concerning them. Of this, perhaps, the most remarkable example I can give is the effect produced on nearly every class of readers by the appearance of Captain Basil Hall's "Travels in North America." In fact, it was a sort of moral earthquake, and the vibration it occasioned through the nerves of the republic, from one corner of the Union to the other, was by no means over when I left the country in July, 1831, a couple of years after the shock.

I was in Cincinnati when these volumes came out, but it was not till July, 1830, that I procured a copy of them. One bookseller to whom I applied told me that he had had a few copies before he understood the nature of the work, but that, after becoming acquainted with it, nothing should induce him to sell another. Other persons of his profession must, however, have been less scrupulous; for the book was read in city, town, village, and hamlet, steamboat, and stage-coach, and a sort of war-whoop was sent forth perfectly unprecedented in my recollection upon any occasion whatever.

An ardent desire for approbation, and a delicate sensitiveness under censure, have always, I believe, been considered as amiable traits of character; but the condition into which the appearance of Captain Hall's work threw the republic shows plainly that these feelings, if carried to excess, produce a weakness which amounts to imbecility.

It was perfectly astonishing to hear men who, on other subjects, were of some judgment utter their opinions upon this. I never heard of any instance in which the common-sense generally found in national criticism was so overthrown by passion. I do not speak of the want of justice, and of fair and liberal interpretation: these, perhaps, were hardly to be expected. Other nations have been called thin-skinned, but the citizens of the Union have, apparently, no skins at all; they wince if a breeze blows over them, unless it be tempered with adulation. It was not, therefore, very surprising that the acute and forcible observations of a traveller they knew would be listened to should be received testily. The extraordinary features of the business were, first, the excess of the rage into which they lashed themselves; and, secondly, the puerility of the inventions by which they attempted to account for the severity with which they fancied they had been treated.

Not content with declaring that the volumes contained no word of truth from beginning to end (which is an assertion I heard made very nearly as often as they were mentioned), the whole country set to work to discover the causes why Captain Hall had visited the United States, and why he had published his book.

I have heard it said with as much precision and gravity as if the statement had been conveyed by an official report, that Captain Hall had been sent out by the British government expressly for the purpose of checking the growing admiration of England for the government of the United States,—that it was by a commission from the treasury he had come, and that it was only in obedience to orders that he had found anything to object to.

I do not give this as the gossip of a coterie; I am persuaded that it is the belief of a very considerable portion of the country. So deep is the conviction of this singular people that they cannot be seen without being admired, that they will not admit the possibility that any one should honestly and sincerely find aught to disapprove in them or their country.

The American Reviews are, many of them, I believe, well known in England; I need not, therefore, quote them here, but I sometimes wondered that they, none of them, ever thought of translating Obadiah's curse into classic American; if they had done so, on placing (he, Basil Hall,) between brackets, instead of (he, Obadiah,) it would have saved them a world of trouble.

I can hardly describe the curiosity with which I sat down at length to peruse these tremendous volumes; still less can I do justice to my surprise at their contents. To say that I found not one exaggerated statement throughout the work is by no means saying enough. It is impossible for any one who knows the country not to see that Captain Hall earnestly sought out things to admire and commend. When he praises, it is with evident pleasure; and when he finds fault, it is with evident reluctance and restraint, excepting where motives purely patriotic urge him to state roundly what it is for the benefit of his country should be known.

In fact, Captain Hall saw the country to the greatest possible advantage. Furnished, of course, with letters of introduction to the most distinguished individuals, and with the still more influential recommendation of his own reputation, he was received in full drawing-room style and state from one end of the Union to the other. He saw the country in full dress, and had little or no opportunity of judging of it unhouselled, unanointed, unannealed, with all its imperfections on its head, as I and my family too often had.

Captain Hall had certainly excellent opportunities of making himself acquainted with the form of the government and the laws; and of receiving, moreover, the best oral commentary upon them, in conversation with the most distinguished citizens. Of these opportunities he made excellent use; nothing important met his eye which did not receive that sort of analytical attention which an experienced and philosophical traveller alone can give. This has made his volumes highly interesting and valuable; but I am deeply persuaded, that were a man of equal penetration to visit the United States with no other means of becoming acquainted with the national character than the ordinary working-day intercourse of life, he would conceive an infinitely lower idea of the moral atmosphere of the country than Captain Hall appears to have done; and the internal conviction on my mind is strong, that if Captain Hall had not placed a firm restraint on himself, he must have given expression to far deeper indignation than any he has uttered against many points in the American character, with which he shows from other circumstances that he was well acquainted. His rule appears to have been to state just so much of the truth as would leave on the mind of his readers a correct impression, at the least cost of pain to the sensitive folks he was writing about. He states his own opinions and feelings, and leaves it to be inferred that he has good grounds for adopting them; but he spares the Americans the bitterness which a detail of the circumstances would have produced.

If any one chooses to say that some wicked antipathy to twelve millions of strangers is the origin of my opinion, I must bear it; and were the question of mere idle speculation, I certainly would not court the abuse I must meet for stating it. But it is not so.

. . . .

The candor which he expresses, and evidently feels, they mistake for irony, or totally distrust; his unwillingness to give pain to persons from whom he has received kindness, they scornfully reject as affectation, and although they must know right well, in their own secret hearts, how infinitely more they lay at his mercy than he has chosen to betray; they pretend, even to themselves, that he has exaggerated the bad points of their character and institutions; whereas, the truth is, that he has let them off with a degree of tenderness which may be quite suitable for him to exercise, however little merited; while, at the same time, he has most industriously magnified their merits, whenever he could possibly find anything favorable.

D

THE UNDYING HEAD

In a remote part of the North lived a man and his sister, who had never seen a human being. Seldom, if ever, had the man any cause to go from home; for, as his wants demanded food, he had only to go a little distance from the lodge, and there, in some particular spot, place his arrows, with their barbs in the ground. Telling his sister where they had been placed, every morning she would go in search, and never fail of finding each stuck through the heart of a deer. She had then only to drag them into the lodge and prepare their food. Thus she lived till she attained womanhood, when one day her brother, whose name was Iamo, said to her: "Sister, the time is at hand when you will be ill. Listen to my advice. If you do not, it will probably be the cause of my death. Take the implements with which we kindle our fires. Go some distance from our lodge and build a separate fire. When you are in want of food, I will tell you where to find it. You must cook for youself, and I will for myself. When you are ill, do not attempt to come near the lodge, or bring any of the utensils you use. Be sure always to fasten to your belt the implements you need, for you do not know when the time will come. As for myself, I must do the best I can." His sister promised to obey him in all he had said.

Shortly after, her brother had cause to go from home. She was alone in her lodge, combing her hair. She had just untied the belt to which the implements were fastened, when suddenly the event, to which her brother had alluded, occurred. She ran out of the lodge, but in her haste forgot the belt. Afraid to return, she stood for some time thinking. Finally, she decided to enter the lodge and get it. For, thought she, my brother is not at home, and I will stay but a moment to catch hold of it. She went back. Running in suddenly, she caught hold of it, and was coming out when her brother came in sight. He knew what was the matter. "Oh," he said, "did I not tell you to take care? But now you have killed me." She was going on her way, but her brother said to her, "What can you do there now? The accident has happened. Go in, and stay where you have always stayed. And what will become of you? You have killed me."

He then laid aside his hunting-dress and accoutrements, and soon after both his feet began to turn black, so that he could not move. Still he directed his sister where to place the arrows, that she might always have food. The inflammation continued to increase, and had now reached his first rib; and he said: "Sister, my end is near. You must do as I tell you. You see my medicine-sack, and my war-club tied to it. It contains all my medicines, and my war-plumes, and my paints of all colors. As soon as the inflammation reaches my breast, you will take my war-club. It has a sharp point, and you will cut off my head. When it is free from my body, take it, place its neck in the sack, which you must open at one end. Then hang it up in its former place. Do not forget my bow and arrows. One of the last you will take to procure food. The remainder, tie in my sack, and then hang it up, so that I can look towards the door. Now and then I will speak to you, but not often." His sister again promised to obey.

In a little time his breast was affected. "Now," said he, "take the club and strike off my head." She was afraid, but he told her to muster courage. *"Strike,"* said he, and a smile was on his face. Mustering all her courage, she gave the blow and cut off the head. "Now," said the head, "place me where I told you." And fearfully she obeyed it in all its commands. Retaining its animation, it looked around the lodge as usual, and it would command its sister to go in such places as it thought would procure for her the flesh of different animals she needed. One day the head said: "The time is not distant when I shall be freed from this situation, and I shall have to undergo many sore evils. So the superior manito decrees, and I must bear all patiently." In this situation we must leave the head.

In a certain part of the country was a village inhabited by a numerous and warlike band of Indians. In this village was a family of ten young men—brothers. It was in the spring of the year that the youngest of these blackened his face and fasted. His dreams were propitious. Having ended his fast, he went secretly for his brothers at night, so that none in the village could overhear or find out the direction they intended to go. Though their drum was heard, yet that was a common occurrence. Having ended the usual formalities, he told how favorable his dreams were, and that he had called them together to know if they would accompany him in a war excursion. They all answered they would. The third brother from the eldest, noted for his oddities, coming up with his war-club when his brother had ceased speaking, jumped up. "Yes," said he, "I will go, and this will be the way I will treat those I am going to fight;" and he struck the post in the centre of the lodge, and gave a yell. The others spoke to him, saying: "Slow, slow, Mudjikewis, when you are in other people's lodges." So he sat down. Then, in turn, they took the drum, and sang their songs, and closed with a feast. The youngest told them not to whisper their intention to their wives, but secretly to prepare for their journey. They all promised obedience, and Mudjikewis was the first to say so.

The time for their departure drew near. Word was given to assemble on a certain night, when they would depart immediately. Mudjikewis was loud in his demands for his moccasins. Several times his wife asked him the reason. "Besides," said she, "you have a good pair on." "Quick, quick," said he, "since you must know, we are going on a war excursion; so be quick." He thus revealed the secret. That night they met and started. The snow was on the ground, and they travelled all night, lest others should follow them. When it was daylight, the leader took snow and made a ball of it, then tossing it into the air, he said: "It was in this way I saw snow fall in a dream, so that I could not be tracked." And he told them to keep close to each other for fear of losing themselves, as the snow began to fall in very large flakes. Near as they walked, it was with difficulty they could see each other. The snow continued falling all that day and the following night, so it was impossible to track them.

They had now walked for several days, and Mudjikewis was always in the rear. One day, running suddenly forward, he gave the *saw-saw-quan,* * and struck a tree with his war-club, and it broke into pieces as if struck with lightning. "Brothers," said he, "this will be the way I will serve those we are going to fight." The leader answered, "Slow, slow, Mudjikewis, the one I lead you to is not to be thought of so lightly." Again he fell back and thought to himself: "What! what! who can this be he is leading us to?" He felt fearful and was silent. Day after day they travelled on, till they came to an extensive plain, on the borders of which human bones were bleaching in the sun. The leader spoke: "They are the bones of those who have gone before us. None has ever yet returned to tell the sad tale of their fate." Again Mudjikewis became restless, and, running forward, gave the accustomed yell. Advancing to a large rock which stood above the ground, he struck it, and it fell to pieces. "See, brothers," said he, "thus will I treat those whom we are going to fight." "Still, still," once more said the leader; "he to whom I am leading you is not to be compared to the rock."

Mudjikewis fell back thoughtful, saying to himself: "I wonder who this can be that he is going to attack;" and he was afraid. Still they continued to see the remains of former warriors, who had been to the place where they were now going, some of whom had retreated as far back as the place where they first saw the bones, beyond which no one had ever escaped. At last they came to a piece of rising ground, from which they plainly distinguished, sleeping on a distant mountain, a mammoth bear.

The distance between them was very great, but the size of the animal caused him to be plainly seen. "There," said the leader, "it is he to whom I am leading you; here our troubles will commence, for he is a mishemokwa and a manito. It is he who has that we prize so dearly (*i.e.* wampum), to obtain which, the warriors whose bones we saw, sacrificed their lives. You must not be fearful; be manly. We shall find him asleep." Then the leader went forward and touched the belt around the animal's neck. "This," said he, "is what we must get. It contains the wampum." Then they requested the eldest to try and slip the belt over the bear's head, who appeared to be fast asleep, as he was not in the least disturbed by the attempt to obtain the belt. All their efforts were in vain, till it came to the one next the youngest. He tried, and the belt moved nearly over the monster's head, but he could get it no farther. Then the youngest one, and the leader, made his attempt, and succeed-

* War-whoop.

ed. Placing it on the back of the oldest, he said, "Now we must run," and off they started. When one became fatigued with its weight, another would relieve him. Thus they ran till they had passed the bones of all former warriors, and were some distance beyond, when, looking back, they saw the monster slowly rising. He stood some time before he missed his wampum. Soon they heard his tremendous howl, like distant thunder, slowly filling all the sky; and then they heard him speak and say, "Who can it be that has dared to steal my wampum? earth is not so large but that I can find them;" and he descended from the hill in pursuit. As if convulsed, the earth shook with every jump he made. Very soon he approached the party. They, however, kept the belt, exchanging it from one to another, and encouraging each other; but he gained on them fast. "Brothers," said the leader, "has never any one of you, when fasting, dreamed of some friendly spirit who would aid you as a guardian?" A dead silence followed. "Well," said he, "fasting, I dreamed of being in danger of instant death, when I saw a small lodge, with smoke curling from its top. An old man lived in it, and I dreamed he helped me; and may it be verified soon," he said, running forward and giving the peculiar yell, and a howl as if the sounds came from the depths of his stomach, and what is called *checaudum*. Getting upon a piece of rising ground, behold! a lodge, with smoke curling from its top, appeared. This gave them all new strength, and they ran forward and entered it. The leader spoke to the old man who sat in the lodge, saying, "Nemesho, help us; we claim your protection, for the great bear will kill us." "Sit down and eat, my grandchildren," said the old man. "Who is a great manito?" said he. "There is none but me; but let me look," and he opened the door of the lodge, when, lo! at a little distance he saw the enraged animal coming on, with slow but powerful leaps. He closed the door. "Yes," said he, "he is indeed a great manito: my grandchildren, you will be the cause of my losing my life; you asked my protection, and I granted it; so now, come what may, I will protect you. When the bear arrives at the door, you must run out of the other door of the lodge." Then putting his hand to the side of the lodge where he sat, he brought out a bag which he opened. Taking out two small black dogs, he placed them before him. "These are the ones I use when I fight," said he; and he commenced patting with both hands the sides of one of them, and he began to swell out, so that he soon filled the lodge by his bulk; and he had great strong teeth. When he attained his full size he growled, and from that moment, as from instinct, he jumped out at the door and met the bear, who in another leap would have reached the lodge. A terrible combat ensued. The skies rang with the howls of the fierce monsters. The remaining dog soon took the field. The brothers, at the onset, took the advice of the old man, and escaped through the opposite side of the lodge. They had not proceeded far before they heard the dying cry of one of the dogs, and soon after of the other. "Well," said the leader, "the old man will share their fate: so run; he will soon be after us." They started with fresh vigor, for they had received food from the old man: but very soon the bear came in sight, and again was fast gaining upon them. Again the leader asked the brothers if they could do nothing for their safety. All were silent. The leader, running forward, did as before. "I dreamed," he cried, "that, being in great trouble, an old man helped me who was a manito; we shall soon see his lodge." Taking courage, they still went on. After going a short distance they saw the lodge of the old manito. They entered immediately and claimed his protection, telling him a manito was after them. The old man, setting meat before them, said: "Eat! who is a manito? there is no manito but me; there is none whom I fear;" and the earth trembled as the monster advanced. The old man opened the door and saw him coming. He shut it slowly, and said: "Yes, my grandchildren, you have brought trouble upon me." Procuring his medicine-sack, he took out his small war-clubs of black stone, and told the young men to run through the other side of the lodge. As he handled the clubs, they became very large, and the old man stepped out just as the bear reached the door. Then striking him with one of the clubs, it broke in pieces; the bear stumbled. Renewing the attempt with the other war-club, that also was broken, but the bear fell senseless. Each blow the old man gave him sounded like a clap of thunder, and the howls of the bear ran along till they filled the heavens.

The young men had now run some distance, when they looked back. They could see that the bear was recovering from the blows. First he moved his paws, and soon they saw him rise on his feet. The old man shared the fate of the first, for they now heard his cries as he was torn in pieces. Again the monster was in pursuit, and fast overtaking them. Not yet discouraged, the young men kept on their way; but the bear was now so close, that the leader once more applied to his brothers, but they could do nothing. "Well," said he, "my dreams will soon be exhausted; after this I have but one more." He advanced, invoking his guardian spirit to aid him. "Once," said he, "I dreamed that, being sorely pressed, I came to a large lake, on the shore of which was a canoe, partly out of water, having ten paddles all in readiness. Do not fear," he cried, "we shall soon get it." And so it was, even as he had said. Coming to the lake, they saw the canoe with ten paddles, and immediately they embarked. Scarcely had they reached the centre of the lake, when they saw the bear arrive at its borders. Lifting himself on his hind legs, he looked all around. Then he waded into the water; then losing his footing he turned back, and commenced making the circuit of the lake. Meantime the party remained stationary in the centre to watch his movements. He travelled all around, till at last he came to the place from whence he started. Then he commenced drinking up the water, and they saw the current fast setting in towards his open mouth. The leader encouraged them to paddle hard for the opposite shore. When only a short distance from land, the current had increased so much, that they were drawn back by it, and all their efforts to reach it were in vain.

Then the leader again spoke, telling them to meet their fates manfully. "Now is the time, Mudjikewis," said he, "to show your prowess. Take courage and sit at the bow of the canoe; and when it approaches his mouth, try what effect your club will have on his head." He obeyed, and stood ready to give the blow; while the leader, who steered, directed the canoe for the open mouth of the monster.

Rapidly advancing, they were just about to enter his mouth, when Mudjikewis struck him a tremendous blow on the head, and gave the *saw-saw-quan*. The bear's limbs doubled under him, and he fell, stunned by the blow. But before Mudjikewis could renew it, the monster disgorged all the water he had drank, with a force which sent the canoe with great velocity to the opposite shore. Instantly leaving the canoe, again they fled, and on they went till they were completely exhausted. The earth again shook, and soon they saw the monster hard after them. Their spirits drooped, and they felt discouraged. The leader exerted himself, by actions and words, to cheer them up; and once more he asked them if they thought of nothing, or could do nothing for their rescue; and, as before, all were silent. "Then," he said, "this is the last time I can apply to my guardian spirit. Now, if we do not succeed, our fates are decided." He ran forward, invoking his spirit with great earnestness, and gave the yell. "We shall soon arrive," said he to his brothers, "at the place where my last guardian spirit dwells. In him I place great confidence. Do not, do not be afraid, or your limbs will be fear-bound. We shall soon reach his lodge. Run, run," he cried.

Returning now to Iamo, he had passed all the time in the same condition we had left him, the head directing his sister, in order to procure food, where to place the magic arrows, and speaking at long intervals. One day the sister saw the eyes of the head brighten, as if with pleasure. At last it spoke. "Oh, sister," it said, "in what a pitiful situation you have been the cause of placing me! Soon, very soon, a party of young men will arrive and apply to me for aid; but alas! How can I give what I would have done with so much pleasure? Nevertheless, take two arrows, and place them where you have been in the habit of placing the others, and have meat prepared and cooked before they arrive. When you hear them coming and calling on my name, go out and say, 'Alas! it is long ago that an accident befell him. I was the cause of it.' If they still come near, ask them in, and set meat before them. And now you must follow my directions strictly. When the bear is near, go out and meet him. You will take my medicine-sack, bows and arrows, and my head. You must then untie the sack, and spread out before you my paints of all colors, my war-eagle feathers, my tufts of dried hair, and whatever else it contains. As the bear approaches, you will take all these articles, one by one, and say to him, 'This is my deceased brother's paint,' and so on with all the other articles, throwing each of them as far as you can. The virtues contained in them will cause him to totter; and, to complete his destruction, you will take my head, and that too you will cast as far off as you can, crying aloud, 'See, this is my deceased brother's head.' He will then fall senseless. By this time the young men will have eaten, and you will call them to your assistance. You must then cut the carcass into pieces, yes, into small pieces, and scatter them to the four winds; for, unless you do this, he will again revive." She promised that all should be done as he said. She had only time to prepare the meat, when the voice of the leader was heard calling upon Iamo for aid. The woman went out and said as her brother had directed. But the war party being closely pursued, came up to the lodge. She invited them in, and placed the meat before them. While they were eating, they heard the bear approaching. Untying the medicine-sack and taking the head, she had all in readiness for his approach. When he came up she did as she had been told; and, before she had expended the paints and feathers, the bear began to totter, but, still advancing, came close to the woman. Saying as she was commanded, she then took the head, and cast it as far from her as she could. As it rolled along the ground, the blood, excited by the feelings of the head in this terrible scene, gushed from the nose and mouth. The bear, tottering, soon fell with a tremendous noise. Then she cried for help, and the young men came rushing out, having partially regained their strength and spirits.

Mudjikewis, stepping up, gave a yell and struck him a blow upon the head. This he repeated, till it seemed like a mass of brains, while the others, as quick as possible, cut him into very small pieces, which they then scattered in every direction. While thus employed, happening to look around where they had thrown the meat, wonderful to behold, they saw starting up and running off in every direction small black bears, such as are seen at the present day. The country was soon overspread with these black animals. And it was from this monster that the present race of bears derived their origin.

Having thus overcome their pursuer, they returned to the lodge. In the mean time, the woman, gathering the implements she had used, and the head, placed them again in the sack. But the head did not speak again, probably from its great exertion to overcome the monster.

Having spent so much time and traversed so vast a country in their flight, the young men gave up the idea of ever returning to their own country, and game being plenty, they determined to remain where they now were. One day they moved off some distance from the lodge for the purpose of hunting, having left the wampum with the woman. They were very successful, and amused themselves, as all young men do when alone, by talking and jesting with each other. One of them spoke and said, "We have all this sport to ourselves; let us go and ask our sister if she will not let us bring the head to this place, as it is still alive. It may be pleased to hear us talk, and be in our company. In the mean time take food to our sister." They went and requested the head. She told them to take it, and they took it to their hunting-grounds, and tried to amuse it, but only at times did they see its eyes beam with pleasure. One day, while busy in their encampment, they were unexpectedly attacked by unknown Indians. The skirmish was long contested and bloody; many of their foes were slain, but still they were thirty to one. The young men fought desperately till they were all killed. The attacking party then retreated to a height of ground, to muster their men, and to count the number of missing and slain. One of their young men had stayed away, and, in endeavoring to overtake them, came to the place where the head was hung up. Seeing that alone retain animation, he eyed it for some time with fear and surprise. However, he took it down and opened the sack, and was much pleased to see the beautiful feathers, one of which he placed on his head.

Starting off, it waved gracefully over him till he reached his party, when he threw down the head and sack, and told them how he had found it, and that the sack was full of paints and feathers. They all looked at the head and made sport of it. Numbers of the young men took the paint and painted themselves, and one of the party took the head by the hair and said:—

"Look, you ugly thing, and see your paints on the faces of warriors."

But the feathers were so beautiful, that numbers of them also placed them on their heads. Then again they used all kinds of indignity to the head, for which they were in turn repaid by the death of those who had used the feathers. Then the chief commanded them to throw away all except the head. "We will see," said he, "when we get home, what we can do with it. We will try to make it shut its eyes."

When they reached their homes they took it to the council-lodge, and hung it up before the fire, fastening it with raw hide soaked, which would shrink and become tightened by the action of fire. "We will then see," they said, "if we cannot make it shut its eyes."

Meantime, for several days, the sister had been waiting for the young men to bring back the head; till, at last, getting impatient, she went in search of it. The young men she found lying within short distances of each other, dead, and covered with wounds. Various other bodies lay scattered in different directions around them. She searched for the head and sack, but they were nowhere to be found. She raised her voice and wept, and blackened her face. Then she walked in different directions, till she came to the place from whence the head had been taken. Then she found the magic bow and arrows, where the young men, ignorant of their qualities, had left them. She thought to herself that she would find her brother's head, and came to a piece of rising ground, and there saw some of his paints and feathers. These she carefully put up, and hung upon the branch of a tree till her return.

At dusk she arrived at the first lodge of a very extensive village. Here she used a charm, common among Indians when they wish to meet with a kind reception. On applying to the old man and woman of the lodge, she was kindly received. She made known her errand. The old man promised to aid her, and told her the head was hung up before the council-fire, and that the chiefs of the village, with their young men, kept watch over it continually. The former are considered as manitoes. She said she only wished to see it, and would be satisfied if she could only get to the door of the lodge. She knew she had not sufficient power to take it by force. "Come with me," said the Indian, "I will take you there." They went, and they took their seats near the door. The council-lodge was filled with warriors, amusing themselves with games, and constantly keeping up a fire to smoke the head, as they said, to make dry meat. They saw the head move, and not knowing what to make of it, one spoke and said: "Ha! ha! It is beginning to feel the effects of the smoke.'' The sister looked up from the door, and her eyes met those of her brother, and tears rolled down the cheeks of the head. ''Well,'' said the chief, ''I thought we would make you do something at last. Look! look at it—shedding tears,'' said he to those around him; and they all laughed and passed their jokes upon it. The chief, looking around, and observing the woman, after some time said to the man who came with her: ''Who have you got there? I have never seen that woman before in our village.'' ''Yes,'' replied the man, ''you have seen her; she is a relation of mine, and seldom goes out. She stays at my lodge, and asked me to allow her to come with me to this place.'' In the centre of the lodge sat one of those young men who are always forward, and fond of boasting and displaying themselves before others. ''Why'', said he, ''I have seen her often, and it is to this lodge I go almost every night to court her.'' All the others laughed and continued their games. The young man did not know he was telling a lie to the woman's advantage, who by that means escaped.

She returned to the man's lodge, and immediately set out for her own country. Coming to the spot where the bodes of her adopted brothers lay, she placed them together, their feet toward the east. Then taking an axe which she had, she cast it up into the air, crying out, ''Brothers, get up from under it, or it will fall on you.'' This she repeated three times, and the third time the brothers all arose and stood on their feet.

Mudjikewis commenced rubbing his eyes and stretching himself. ''Why,'' said he, ''I have overslept myself.'' ''No, indeed,'' said one of the others, ''do you not know we were all killed, and that it is our sister who has brought us to life?'' The young men took the bodies of their enemies and burned them. Soon after, the woman went to procure wives for them, in a distant country, they knew not where; but she returned with ten young women, which she gave to the ten young men, beginning with the eldest. Mudjikewis stepped to and fro, uneasy lest he should not get the one he liked. But he was not disappointed, for she fell to his lot. And they were well matched, for she was a female magician. They then all moved into a very large lodge, and their sister told them that the women must now take turns in going to her brother's head every night, trying to untie it. They all said they would do so with pleasure. The eldest made the first attempt, and with a rushing noise she fled through the air.

Toward daylight she returned. She had been unsuccessful, as she succeeded in untying only one of the knots. All took their turns regularly, and each one succeeded in untying only one knot each time. But when the youngest went, she commenced the work as soon as she reached the lodge; although it had always been occupied, still the Indians never could see any one. For ten nights now, the smoke had not ascended, but filled the lodge and drove them out. This last night they were all driven out, and the young woman carried off the head.

The young people and the sister heard the young woman coming high through the air, and they heard her saying: ''Prepare the body of our brother.'' And as soon as they heard it, they went to a small lodge where the black body of Iamo lay. His sister commenced cutting the neck part, from which the neck had been severed. She cut so deep as to cause it to bleed; and the others who were present, by rubbing the body and applying medicines, expelled the blackness. In the mean time the one who brought it, by cutting the neck of the head, caused that also to bleed.

As soon as she arrived, they placed that close to the body, and, by aid of medicines and various other means, succeeded in restoring Iamo to all his former beauty and manliness. All rejoiced in the happy termination of their troubles, and they had spent some time joyfully together, when Iamo said: "Now I will divide the wampum;" and getting the belt which contained it, he commenced with the eldest, giving it in equal portions. But the youngest got the most splendid and beautiful, as the bottom of the belt held the richest and rarest.

They were told that, since they had all once died, and were restored to life, they were no longer mortal, but spirits, and they were assigned different stations in the invisible world. Only Mudjukewis's place was, however, named. He was to direct the west wind, hence generally called Kebeyun, there to remain forever. They were commanded, as they had it in their power, to do good to the inhabitants of the earth, and, forgetting their sufferings in procuring the wampum, to give all things with a liberal hand. And they were also commanded that it should also be held by them sacred; those grains or shells of the pale hue to be emblematic of peace, while those of the darker hue would lead to evil and war.

The spirits then, amid songs and shouts, took their flight to their respective abodes on high; while Iamo, with his sister Iamoqua, descended into the depths below.

"A Medieval Romance" was first called "Awful, Terrible Medieval Romance" when it appeared as a feature in the Buffalo Express *on January 1, 1870. The story acquired its shortened title when it was published in 1871 in a slim volume along with* Mark Twain's Burlesque Autobiography. *Twain included "A Medieval Romance" in* Mark Twain's Sketches New and Old, *which appeared in 1875.*

A Medieval Romance

CHAPTER I

THE SECRET REVEALED

It was night. Stillness reigned in the grand old feudal castle of Klugenstein. The year 1222 was drawing to a close. Far away up in the tallest of the castle's towers a single light glimmered. A secret council was being held there. The stern old lord of Klugenstein sat in a chair of state meditating. Presently he said, with a tender accent—"My daughter!"

A young man of noble presence, clad from head to heel in knightly mail, answered—"Speak, father!"

"My daughter, the time is come for the revealing of the mystery that hath puzzled all your young life. Know, then, that it had its birth in the matter which I shall now unfold. My brother Ulrich is the great Duke of Brandenburgh. Our father, on his deathbed, decreed that if no son were born to Ulrich the succession should pass to my house, provided a *son* were born to me. And further, in case no son were born to either, but only daughters, then the succession should pass to Ulrich's daughter if she proved stainless; if she did not, my daughter should succeed if she retained a blameless name. And so I and my old wife here prayed fervently for the good boon of a son, but the prayer was vain. You were born to us. I was in despair. I saw the mighty prize slipping from my grasp—the splendid dream vanishing away! And I had been so hopeful! Five years had Ulrich lived in wedlock, and yet his wife had borne no heir of either sex.

" 'But hold,' I said, 'all is not lost.' A saving scheme had shot athwart my brain. You were born at midnight. Only the leech, the nurse, and six waiting-women knew your sex. I hanged them every one before an hour sped. Next morning all the barony went mad with rejoicing over the proclamation that a *son* was born to Klugenstein—an heir to mighty Brandenburgh! And well the secret has been kept. Your mother's own sister nursed your infancy, and from that time forward we feared nothing.

"When you were ten years old a daughter was born to Ulrich. We grieved, but hoped for good results from measles, or physicians, or other natural enemies of infancy, but were always disappointed. She lived, she throve—Heaven's malison upon her! But it is nothing. We are safe. For, ha! ha! have we not a son? And is not our son the future Duke? Our well-beloved Conrad, is it not so?—for woman of eight-and-twenty years as you are, my child, none other name than that hath ever fallen to *you!*

"Now it hath come to pass that age hath laid its hand upon my brother, and he waxes feeble. The cares of state do tax him sore, therefore he wills that you shall come to him and be already Duke in act, though not yet in name. Your servitors are ready—you journey forth to-night.

"Now listen well. Remember every word I say. There is a law as old as Germany, that if any woman sit for a single instant in the great ducal chair before she hath been absolutely crowned in presence of the people—SHE SHALL DIE! So heed my words. Pretend humility. Pronounce your judgments from the Premier's chair, which stands at the *foot* of the throne. Do this until you are crowned and safe. It is not likely that your sex will ever be discovered, but still it is the part of wisdom to make all things as safe as may be in this treacherous earthly life."

"O my father! is it for this my life hath been a lie? Was it that I might cheat my unoffending cousin of her rights? Spare me, father, spare your child!"

"What, hussy! Is this my reward for the august fortune my brain has wrought for thee? By the bones of my father, this puling sentiment of thine but ill accords with my humor. Betake thee to the Duke instantly, and beware how thou meddlest with my purpose!"

Let this suffice of the conversation. It is enough for us to know that the prayers, the entreaties, and the tears of the gentle-natured girl availed nothing. Neither they nor anything could move the stout old lord of Klugenstein. And so, at last, with a heavy heart, the daughter saw the castle gates close behind her, and found herself riding away in the darkness surrounded by a knightly array of armed vassals and a brave following of servants.

The old baron sat silent for many minutes after his daughter's departure, and then he turned to his sad wife, and said—

"Dame, our matters seem speeding fairly. It is full three months since I sent the shrewd and handsome Count Detzin on his devilish mission to my brother's daughter Constance. If he fail we are not wholly safe, but if he do succeed no power can bar our girl from being Duchess, e'en though ill fortune should decree she never should be Duke!"

"My heart is full of bodings; yet all may still be well."

"Tush, woman! Leave the owls to croak. To bed with ye, and dream of Brandenburgh and grandeur!"

CHAPTER II

FESTIVITY AND TEARS

Six days after the occurrences related in the above chapter, the brilliant capital of the Duchy of Brandenburgh was resplendent with military pageantry, and noisy with the rejoicings of loyal multitudes, for Conrad, the young heir to the crown, was come. The old Duke's heart was full of happiness, for Conrad's handsome person and graceful bearing had won his love at once. The great halls of the palace were thronged with nobles, who welcomed Conrad bravely; and so bright and happy did all things seem, that he felt his fears and sorrows passing away, and giving place to a comforting contentment.

But in a remote apartment of the palace a scene of a different nature was transpiring. By a window stood the Duke's only child, the Lady Constance. Her eyes were red and swollen, and full of tears. She was alone. Presently she fell to weeping anew, and said aloud—

"The villain Detzin is gone—has fled the dukedom! I could not believe it at first, but, alas! it is too true. And I loved him so. I dared to love him though I knew the Duke my father would never let me wed him. I loved him—but now I hate him! With all my soul I hate him! Oh, what is to become of me? I am lost, lost, lost! I shall go mad!"

CHAPTER III

THE PLOT THICKENS

A few months drifted by. All men published the praises of the young Conrad's government, and extolled the wisdom of his judgments, the mercifulness of his sentences, and the modesty with which he bore himself in his great office. The old Duke soon gave everything into his hands, and sat apart and listened with proud satisfaction while his heir delivered the decrees of the crown from the seat of the Premier. It seemed plain that one so loved and praised and honored of all men as Conrad was could not be otherwise than happy. But, strangely enough, he was not. For he saw with dismay that the Princess Constance had begun to love him! The love of the rest of the world was happy fortune for him, but this was freighted with danger! And he saw, moreover, that the delighted Duke had discovered his daughter's passion likewise, and was already dreaming of a marriage. Every day somewhat of the deep sadness that had been in the princess's face faded away; every day hope and animation beamed brighter from her eye; and by and by even vagrant smiles visited the face that had been so troubled.

Conrad was appalled. He bitterly cursed himself for having yielded to the instinct that had made him seek the companionship of one of his own sex when he was new and a stranger in the palace—when he was sorrowful and yearned for a sympathy such as only women can give or feel. He now began to avoid his cousin. But this only made matters worse, for naturally enough, the more he avoided her the more she cast herself in his way. He marvelled at this at first, and next it startled him. The girl haunted him; she hunted him; she happened upon him at all times and in all places, in the night as well as in the day. She seemed singularly anxious. There was surely a mystery somewhere.

This could not go on for ever. All the world was talking about it. The Duke was beginning to look perplexed. Poor Conrad was becoming a very ghost through dread and dire distress. One day as he was emerging from a private ante-room attached to the picture gallery Constance confronted him, and seizing both his hands in hers, exclaimed—

"Oh, why do you avoid me? What have I done—what have I said, to lose your kind opinion of me—for surely I had it once? Conrad, do not despise me, but pity a tortured heart? I cannot, cannot hold the words unspoken longer, lest they kill me—I LOVE

YOU, CONRAD! There, despise me if you must, but they *would* be uttered!"

Conrad was speechless. Constance hesitated a moment, and then, misinterpreting his silence, a wild gladness flamed in her eyes, and she flung her arms about his neck and said—

"You relent! you relent! You *can* love me—you *will* love me! Oh, say you will, my own, my worshipped Conrad!"

Conrad groaned aloud. A sickly pallor overspread his countenance, and he trembled like an aspen. Presently, in desperation, he thrust the poor girl from him, and cried—

"You know not what you ask! It is for ever and ever impossible!" And then he fled like a criminal, and left the princess stupefied with amazement. A minute afterward she was crying and sobbing there, and Conrad was crying and sobbing in his chamber. Both were in despair. Both saw ruin staring them in the face.

By and by Constance rose slowly to her feet and moved away, saying—

"To think that he was despising my love at the very moment that I thought it was melting his cruel heart! I hate him! He spurned me—did this man—he spurned me from him like a dog!"

CHAPTER IV

THE AWFUL REVELATION

Time passed on. A settled sadness rested once more upon the countenance of the good Duke's daughter. She and Conrad were seen together no more now. The Duke grieved at this. But as the weeks wore away Conrad's color came back to his cheeks, and his old-time vivacity to his eye, and he administered the government with a clear and steadily ripening wisdom.

Presently a strange whisper began to be heard about the palace. It grew louder; it spread farther. The gossips of the city got hold of it. It swept the dukedom. And this is what the whisper said—

"The Lady Constance hath given birth to a child!"

When the lord of Klugenstein heard it he swung his plumed helmet thrice around his head and shouted—

"Long live Duke Conrad!—for lo, his crown is sure from this day forward! Detzin has done his errand well, and the good scoundrel shall be rewarded!"

And he spread the tidings far and wide, and for eight-and-forty hours no soul in all the barony but did dance and sing, carouse and illuminate, to celebrate the great event, and all at proud and happy old Klugenstein's expense.

CHAPTER V

THE FRIGHTFUL CATASTROPHE

The trial was at hand. All the great lords and barons of Brandenburgh were assembled in the Hall of Justice in the ducal palace. No space was left unoccupied where there was room for a spectator to stand or sit. Conrad, clad in purple and ermine, sat in the Premier's chair, and on either side sat the great judges of the realm. The old Duke had sternly commanded that the trial of his daughter should proceed without favor, and then had taken to his bed broken-hearted. His days were numbered. Poor Conrad had begged, as for his very life, that he might be spared the misery of sitting in judgment upon his cousin's crime, but it did not avail.

The saddest heart in all that great assemblage was in Conrad's breast.

The gladdest was in his father's, for, unknown to his daughter "Conrad," the old Baron Klugenstein was come, and was among the crowd of nobles triumphant in the swelling fortunes of his house.

After the heralds had made due proclamation and the other preliminaries had followed, the venerable Lord Chief-Justice said—"Prisoner, stand forth!"

The unhappy princess rose, and stood unveiled before the vast multitude. The Lord Chief-Justice continued—

"Most noble lady, before the great judges of this realm it hath been charged and proven that out of holy wedlock your Grace hath given birth unto a child, and by our ancient law the penalty is death excepting in one sole contingency, whereof his Grace the acting Duke, our good Lord Conrad, will advertise you in his solemn sentence now; wherefore give heed."

Conrad stretched forth his reluctant sceptre, and in the self-same moment the womanly heart beneath his robe yearned pityingly toward the doomed prisoner, and the tears came into his eyes. He opened his lips to speak, but the Lord Chief-Justice said quickly—

"Not there, your Grace, not there! It is not lawful to pronounce judgment upon any of the ducal line SAVE FROM THE DUCAL THRONE!"

A shudder went to the heart of poor Conrad, and a tremor shook the iron frame of his old father likewise. CONRAD HAD NOT BEEN CROWNED—dared he profane the throne? He hesitated and turned pale with fear. But it must be done. Wondering eyes were already upon him. They would be suspicious eyes if he hesitated longer. He ascended the throne. Presently he stretched forth the sceptre again, and said—

"Prisoner, in the name of our sovereign Lord Ulrich, Duke of Brandenburgh, I proceed to the solemn duty that hath devolved upon me. Give heed to my words. By the ancient law of the land, except you produce the partner of your guilt and deliver him up to the executioner you must surely die. Embrace this opportunity—save yourself while yet you may. Name the father of your child!"

A solemn hush fell upon the great court—a silence so profound that men could hear their own hearts beat. Then the princess slowly turned, with eyes gleaming with hate, and pointing her finger straight at Conrad, said—

"Thou art the man!"

An appalling conviction of his helpless, hopeless peril struck a chill to Conrad's heart like the chill of death itself. What power on earth could save him! To disprove the charge he must reveal that he was a woman, and for an uncrowned woman to sit in the ducal chair was death! At one and the same moment he and his grim old father swooned and fell to the ground.

* * * * * * * * *

The remainder of this thrilling and eventful story will not be found in this or any other publication, either now or at any future time.

The truth is, I have got my hero (or heroine) into such a particularly close place that I do not see how I am ever going to get him (or her) out of it again, and therefore I will wash my hands of the whole business, and leave that person to get the best way that offers—or else stay there. I thought it was going to be easy enough to straighten out that little difficulty, but it looks different now.

For the first publication of "Extracts from Adam's Diary" in the Niagara Book, *a souvenir publication sold at the Buffalo World's Fair in 1893, Twain obligingly added several references to Niagara Falls. This material was cut when the story was published in the London edition of* Tom Sawyer, Detective *in 1897, and later in the New York edition of* The $30,000 Bequest *in 1906, but it was retained in the version that appeared as a separate volume in New York in 1904. This edition was reprinted in 1931 along with a companion piece, "Eve's Diary,"* *as* The Private Lives of Adam and Eve.

Extracts from Adam's Diary

Translated from the original Ms.

[NOTE. — I translated a portion of this diary some years ago, and a friend of mine printed a few copies in an incomplete form, but the public never got them. Since then I have deciphered some more of Adam's hieroglyphics, and think he has now become sufficiently important as a public character to justify this publication.—M.T.]

Monday

This new creature with the long hair is a good deal in the way. It is always hanging around and following me about. I don't like this; I am not used to company. I wish it would stay with the other animals. . . . Cloudy to-day, wind in the east; think we shall have rain. . . . *We?* Where did I get that word? . . . I remember now—the new creature uses it.

Tuesday

Been examining the great waterfall. It is the finest thing on the estate, I think. The new creature calls it Niagara Falls—why, I am sure I do not know. Says it *looks* like Niagara Falls. That is not a reason; it is mere waywardness and imbecility. I get no chance to name anything myself. The new creature names everything that comes along, before I can get in a protest. And always that same pretext is offered—it *looks* like the thing. There is the dodo, for instance. Says the moment one looks at it one sees at a glance that it "looks like a dodo." It will have to keep that name, no doubt. It wearies me to fret about it, and it does no good, anyway. Dodo! It looks no more like a dodo than I do.

Wednesday

Built me a shelter against the rain, but could not have it to myself in peace. The new creature intruded. When I tried to put it out it shed water out of the holes it looks with, and wiped it away with the back of its paws, and made a noise such as some of the other animals make when they are in distress. I wish it would not talk; it is always talking. That sounds like a cheap fling at the poor creature, a slur; but I do not mean it so. I have never heard the human voice before, and any new and strange sound intruding itself here upon the solemn hush of these dreaming solitudes offends my ear and seems a false note. And this new sound is so close to me; it is right at my shoulder, right at my ear, first on one side and then on the other, and I am used only to sounds that are more or less distant from me.

Friday

The naming goes recklessly on, in spite of anything I can do. I had a very good name for the estate, and it was musical and pretty—GARDEN-OF-EDEN. Privately, I continue to call it that, but not any longer publicly. The new creature says it is all woods and rocks and scenery, and therefore has no resemblance to a garden. Says it *looks* like a park, and does not look like anything *but* a park. Consequently, without consulting me, it has been new-named—NIAGARA FALLS PARK. This is sufficiently high-handed, it seems to me. And already there is a sign up:

KEEP OFF THE GRASS

My life is not as happy as it was.

Saturday

The new creature eats too much fruit. We are going to run short, most likely. "We" again—that is *its* word; mine too, now, from hearing it so much. Good deal of fog this morning. I do not go out in the fog myself. The new creature does. It goes out in all weathers, and stumps right in with its muddy feet. And talks. It used to be so pleasant and quiet here.

Sunday

Pulled through. This day is getting to be more and more trying. It was selected and set apart last November as a day of rest. I already had six of them per week, before. This morning found the new creature trying to clod apples out of that forbidden tree.

Monday

The new creature says its name is Eve. That is all right, I have no objections. Says it is to call it by when I want it to come. I said it was superfluous, then. The word evidently raised me in its respect; and indeed it is a large, good word, and will bear repetition. It says it is not an It, it is a She. This is probably doubtful; yet it is all one to me; what she is were nothing to me if she would but go by herself and not talk.

Tuesday

She has littered the whole estate with execrable names and offensive signs:

☞ THIS WAY TO THE WHIRLPOOL.

☞ THIS WAY TO GOAT ISLAND.

☞ CAVE OF THE WINDS THIS WAY.

She says this park would make a tidy summer resort, if there was any custom for it. Summer resort—another invention of hers—just words, without any meaning. What is a summer resort? But it is best not to ask her, she has such a rage for explaining.

Friday

She has taken to beseeching me to stop going over the Falls. What harm does it do? Says it makes her shudder. I wonder why. I have always done it—always liked the plunge, and the excitement, and the coolness. I supposed it was what the Falls were for. They have no other use that I can see, and they must have been made for something. She says they were only made for scenery—like the rhinoceros and the mastodon.

I went over the Falls in a barrel—not satisfactory to her. Went over in a tub—still not satisfactory. Swam the Whirlpool and the Rapids in a fig-leaf suit. It got much damaged. Hence, tedious complaints about my extravagance. I am too much hampered here. What I need is change of scene.

Saturday

I escaped last Tuesday night, and travelled two days, and built me another shelter, in a secluded place, and obliterated my tracks as well as I could, but she hunted me out by means of a beast which she has tamed and calls a wolf, and came making that pitiful noise again, and shedding that water out of the places she looks with. I was obliged to return with her, but will presently emigrate again, when occasion offers. She engages herself in many foolish things: among others, trying to study out why the animals called lions and tigers live on grass and flowers, when, as she says, the sort of teeth they wear would indicate that they were intended to eat each other. This is foolish, because to do that would be to kill each other, and that would introduce what, as I understand it, is called "death"; and death, as I have been told, has not yet entered the Park. Which is a pity, on some accounts.

Sunday

Pulled through.

Monday

I believe I see what the week is for: it is to give time to rest up from the weariness of Sunday. It seems a good idea. . . . She has been climbing that tree again. Clodded her out of it. She said nobody was looking. Seems to consider that a sufficient justification for chancing any dangerous thing. Told her that. The word justification moved her admiration—and envy too, I thought. It is a good word.

Tuesday

She told me she was made out of a rib taken from my body. This is at least doubtful, if not more than that. I have not missed any rib. . . . She is in much trouble about the buzzard; says grass does not agree with it; is afraid she can't raise it; thinks it was intended to live on decayed flesh. The buzzard must get along the best it can with what is provided. We cannot overturn the whole scheme to accommodate the buzzard.

Saturday

She fell in the pond yesterday, when she was looking at herself in it, which she is always doing. She nearly strangled, and said it was most uncomfortable. This made her sorry for the creatures which live in there, which she calls fish, for she continues to fasten names on to things that don't need them and don't come when they are called by them, which is a matter of no consequence to her, as she is such a numskull anyway; so she got a lot of them out and brought them in last night and put them in my bed to keep warm, but I have noticed them now and then all day, and I don't see that they are any happier there than they were before, only quieter. When night comes I shall throw them outdoors. I will not sleep with them again, for I find them clammy and unpleasant to lie among when a person hasn't anything on.

Sunday
Pulled through.

Tuesday
She has taken up with a snake now. The other animals are glad, for she was always experimenting with them and bothering them; and I am glad, because the snake talks, and this enables me to get a rest.

Friday
She says the snake advises her to try the fruit of that tree, and says the result will be a great and fine and noble education. I told her there would be another result, too—it would introduce death into the world. That was a mistake—it had been better to keep the remark to myself; it only gave her an idea—she could save the sick buzzard, and furnish fresh meat to the despondent lions and tigers. I advised her to keep away from the tree. She said she wouldn't. I foresee trouble. Will emigrate.

Wednesday
I have had a variegated time. I escaped that night, and rode a horse all night as fast as he could go, hoping to get clear out of the Park and hide in some other country before the trouble should begin; but it was not to be. About an hour after sunup, as I was riding through a flowery plain where thousands of animals were grazing, slumbering, or playing with each other, according to their wont, all of a sudden they broke into a tempest of frightful noises, and in one moment the plain was in a frantic commotion and every beast was destroying its neighbor. I knew what it meant—Eve had eaten that fruit, and death was come into the world. . . . The tigers ate my horse, paying no attention when I ordered them to desist, and they would even have eaten me if I had stayed—which I didn't, but went away in much haste. . . . I found this place, outside the Park, and was fairly comfortable for a few days, but she has found me out. Found me out, and has named the place Tonawanda—says it *looks* like that. In fact, I was not sorry she came, for there are but meagre pickings here, and she brought some of those apples. I was obliged to eat them, I was so hungry. It was against my principles, but I find that principles have no real force except when one is well fed. . . . She came curtained in boughs and bunches of leaves, and when I asked her what she meant by such

nonsense, and snatched them away and threw them down, she tittered and blushed. I had never seen a person titter and blush before, and to me it seemed unbecoming and idiotic. She said I would soon know how it was myself. This was correct. Hungry as I was, I laid down the apple half eaten—certainly the best one I ever saw, considering the lateness of the season—and arrayed myself in the discarded boughs and branches, and then spoke to her with some severity and ordered her to go and get some more and not make such a spectacle of herself. She did it, and after this we crept down to where the wild-beast battle had been, and collected some skins, and I made her patch together a couple of suits proper for public occasions. They are uncomfortable, it is true, but stylish, and that is the main point about clothes. . . . I find she is a good deal of a companion. I see I should be lonesome and depressed without her, now that I have lost my property. Another thing, she says it is ordered that we work for our living hereafter. She will be useful. I will superintend.

Ten Days Later

She accuses *me* of being the cause of our disaster! She says, with apparent sincerity and truth, that the Serpent assured her that the forbidden fruit was not apples, it was chestnuts. I said I was innocent, then, for I had not eaten any chestnuts. She said the Serpent informed her that "chestnut" was a figurative term meaning an aged and mouldy joke. I turned pale at that, for I have made many jokes to pass the weary time, and some of them could have been of that sort, though I had honestly supposed that they were new when I made them. She asked me if I had made one just at the time of the catastrophe. I was obliged to admit that I had made one to myself, though not aloud. It was this. I was thinking about the Falls, and I said to myself, "How wonderful it is to see that vast body of water tumble down there!" Then in an instant a bright thought flashed into my head, and I let it fly, saying, "It would be a deal more wonderful to see it tumble *up* there!"—and I was just about to kill myself with laughing at it when all nature broke loose in war and death, and I had to flee for my life. "There," she said, with triumph, "that is just it; the Serpent mentioned that very jest, and called it the First Chestnut, and said it was coeval with the creation." Alas, I am indeed to blame. Would that I were not witty; oh, would that I had never had that radiant thought!

Next Year

We have named it Cain. She caught it while I was up country trapping on the North Shore of the Erie; caught it in the timber a couple of miles from our dug-out—or it might have been four, she isn't certain which. It resembles us in some ways, and may be a relation. That is what she thinks, but this is an error, in my judgment. The difference in size warrants the conclusion that it is a different and new kind of animal—a fish, perhaps, though when I put it in the water to see, it sank, and she plunged in and snatched it out before there was opportunity for the experiment to determine the matter. I still think it is a fish, but she is indifferent about what it is, and will not let me have it to try. I do not understand this. The coming of the creature seems to have changed her whole nature and made her unreasonable about experiments. She thinks more of it than she does of any of the other animals, but is not able to explain why. Her mind is disordered—everything shows it. Sometimes she carries the fish in her arms half the night when it complains and wants to get to the water. At such times the water comes out of the places in her face that she looks out of, and she pats the fish on the back and makes soft sounds with her mouth to soothe it, and betrays sorrow and solicitude in a hundred ways. I have never seen her do like this with any other fish, and it troubles me greatly. She used to carry the young tigers around so, and play with them, before we lost our property; but it was only play; she never took on about them like this when their dinner disagreed with them.

Sunday

She doesn't work Sundays, but lies around all tired out, and likes to have the fish wallow over her; and she makes fool noises to amuse it, and pretends to chew its paws, and that makes it laugh. I have not seen a fish before that could laugh. This makes me doubt. . . . I have come to like Sunday myself. Superintending all the week tires a body so. There ought to be more Sundays. In the old days they were tough, but now they come handy.

Wednesday

It isn't a fish. I cannot quite make out what it is. It makes curious, devilish noises when not satisfied, and says "goo-goo" when it is. It is not one of us, for it doesn't walk; it is not a bird, for it doesn't fly; it is not a frog, for it doesn't hop; it is not a snake, for it doesn't crawl; I feel sure it is not a fish, though I cannot get a chance to find out whether it can swim or not. It merely lies around, and mostly on its back, with its feet up. I have not seen any other animal do that before. I said I believed it was an enigma, but she only admired the word without understanding it. In my judgment it is either an enigma or some kind of a bug. If it dies, I will take it apart and see what its arrangements are. I never had a thing perplex me so.

Three Months Later

The perplexity augments instead of diminishing. I sleep but little. It has ceased from lying around, and goes about on its four legs now. Yet it differs from the other four-legged animals in that its front legs are unusually short, consequently this causes the main part of its person to stick up uncomfortably high in the air, and this is not attractive. It is built much as we are, but its method of travelling shows that it is not of our breed. The short front legs and long hind ones indicate that it is of the kangaroo family, but it is a marked variation of the species, since the true kangaroo hops, whereas this one never does. Still, it is a curious and interesting variety, and has not been catalogued before. As I discovered it, I have felt justified in securing the credit of the discovery by attaching my name to it, and hence have called it *Kangaroorum Adamiensis*. . . . It must have been a young one when it came, for it has grown exceedingly since. It must be five times as big, now, as it was then, and when discontented is able to make from twenty-two to thirty-eight times the noise it made at first. Coercion does not modify this, but has the contrary effect. For this reason I discontinued the system. She reconciles it by persuasion, and by giving it things which she had previously told it she wouldn't give it. As already observed, I was not at home when it first came, and she told me she found it in the woods. It seems odd that it should be the only one, yet it must be so, for I have worn myself out these many weeks trying to find another one to add to my collection, and for this one to play with; for surely then it would be quieter, and we could tame it more easily. But I find none, nor any vestige of any; and strangest of all, no tracks. It has to live on the ground, it cannot help itself; therefore, how does it get about without leaving a track? I have set a dozen traps, but they do no good. I catch all small animals except that one; animals that merely go into the trap out of curiosity, I think, to see what the milk is there for. They never drink it.

Three Months Later

The kangaroo still continues to grow, which is very strange and perplexing. I never knew one to be so long getting its growth. It has fur on its head now; not like kangaroo fur, but exactly like our hair, except that it is much finer and softer, and instead of being black is red. I am like to lose my mind over the capricious and harassing developments of this unclassifiable zoological freak. If I could catch another one—but that is hopeless; it is a new variety, and the only sample; this is plain. But I caught a true kangaroo and brought it in, thinking that this one, being lonesome, would rather have that for company than have no kin at all, or any animal it could feel a nearness to or get sympathy from in its forlorn condition here among strangers who do not know its ways or habits, or what to do to make it feel that it is among friends; but it was a mistake—it went into such fits at the sight of the kangaroo that I was convinced it had never seen one before. I pity the poor noisy little animal, but there is nothing I can do to make it happy. If I could tame it—but that is out of the question; the more I try, the worse I seem to make it. It grieves me to the heart to see it in its little storms of sorrow and passion. I wanted to let it go, but she wouldn't hear of it. That seemed cruel and not like her; and yet she may be right. It might be lonelier than ever; for since I cannot find another one, how could *it?*

Five Months Later

It is not a kangaroo. No, for it supports itself by holding to her finger, and thus goes a few steps on its hind legs, and then falls down. It is probably some kind of a bear; and yet it has no tail—as yet—and no fur, except on its head. It still keeps on growing—that is a curious circumstance, for bears get their growth earlier than this. Bears are dangerous—since our catastrophe—and I shall not be satisfied to have this one prowling about the place much longer without a muzzle on. I have offered to get her a kangaroo if she would let this one go, but it did no good—she is determined to run us into all sorts of foolish risks, I think. She was not like this before she lost her mind.

A Fortnight Later

I examined its mouth. There is no danger yet; it has only one tooth. It has no tail yet. It makes more noise now than it ever did before—and mainly at night. I have moved out. But I shall go over, mornings, to breakfast, and to see if it has more teeth. If it gets a mouthful of teeth, it will be time for it to go, tail or no tail, for a bear does not need a tail in order to be dangerous.

Four Months Later

I have been off hunting and fishing a month, up in the region that she calls Buffalo; I don't know why, unless it is because there are not any buffaloes there. Meantime the bear has learned to paddle around all by itself on its hind legs, and says "poppa" and "momma." It is certainly a new species. This resemblance to words may be purely accidental, of course, and may have no purpose or meaning; but even in that case it is still extraordinary, and is a thing which no other bear can do. This imitation of speech, taken together with general absence of fur and entire absence of tail, sufficiently indicates that this is a new kind of bear. The further study of it will be exceedingly interesting. Meantime I will go off on a far expedition among the forests of the North and make an exhaustive search. There must certainly be another one somewhere, and this one will be less dangerous when it has company of its own species. I will go straightway; but I will muzzle this one first.

Three Months Later

It has been a weary, weary hunt, yet I have had no success. In the mean time, without stirring from the home estate, she has caught another one! I never saw such luck. I might have hunted these woods a hundred years, I never should have run across that thing.

Next Day

I have been comparing the new one with the old one, and it is perfectly plain that they are the same breed. I was going to stuff one of them for my collection, but she is prejudiced against it for some reason or other; so I have relinquished the idea, though I think it is a mistake. It would be an irreparable loss to science if they should get away. The old one is tamer than it was, and can laugh and talk like the parrot, having learned this, no doubt, from being with the parrot so much, and having the imitative faculty in a highly developed degree. I shall be astonished if it turns out to be a new kind of parrot; and yet I ought not to be astonished, for it has already been everything else it could think of, since those first days when it was a fish. The new one is as ugly now as the old one was at first; has the same sulphur-and-raw-meat complexion and the same singular head without any fur on it. She calls it Abel.

Ten Years Later

They are boys; we found it out long ago. It was their coming in that small, immature shape that puzzled us; we were not used to it. There are some girls now. Abel is a good boy, but if Cain had stayed a bear it would have improved him. After all these years, I see that I was mistaken about Eve in the beginning; it is better to live outside the Garden with her than inside it without her. At first I thought she talked too much; but now I should be sorry to have that voice fall silent and pass out of my life. Blessed be the chestnut that brought us near together and taught me to know the goodness of her heart and the sweetness of her spirit!

"Eve's Diary" was written in 1905; its epitaph becomes especially poignant when one remembers that Twain's wife, Livy, had died the previous June. The story made its first appearance in the December 1905 issue of Harper's *magazine, and in March of the following year it was included in* Their Husband's Wives. *Several months later, in June 1906, the story was issued in a separate volume. In 1931, it was collected with "Extracts from Adam's Diary" in* The Private Lives of Adam and Eve.

Eve's Diary

Translated from the Original

Saturday

I am almost a whole day old, now. I arrived yesterday. That is as it seems to me. And it must be so, for if there was a day-before-yesterday I was not there when it happened, or I should remember it. It could be, of course, that it did happen, and that I was not noticing. Very well; I will be very watchful, now, and if any day-before-yesterdays happen I will make a note of it. It will be best to start right and not let the record get confused, for some instinct tells me that these details are going to be important to the historian some day. For I feel like an experiment, I feel exactly like an experiment; it would be impossible for a person to feel more like an experiment than I do, and so I am coming to feel convinced that that is what I *am*—an experiment; just an experiment, and nothing more.

Then if I am an experiment, am I the whole of it? No, I think not; I think the rest of it is part of it. I am the main part of it, but I think the rest of it has its share in the matter. Is my position assured, or do I have to watch it and take care of it? The latter, perhaps. Some instinct tells me that eternal vigilance is the price of supremacy. [That is a good phrase, I think, for one so young.]

Everything looks better to-day than it did yesterday. In the rush of finishing up yesterday, the mountains were left in a ragged condition, and some of the plains were so cluttered with rubbish and remnants that the aspects were quite distressing. Noble and beautiful works of art should not be subjected to haste; and this majestic new world is indeed a most noble and beautiful work. And certainly marvellously near to being perfect, notwithstanding the shortness of the time. There are too many stars in some places and not enough in others, but that can be remedied presently, no doubt. The moon got loose last night, and slid down and fell out of the scheme—a very great loss; it breaks my heart to think of it. There isn't another thing among the ornaments and decorations that is comparable to it for beauty and finish. It should have been fastened better. If we can only get it back again—

But of course there is no telling where it went to. And besides, whoever gets it will hide it; I know it because I would do it myself. I believe I can be honest in all other matters, but I already begin to realize that the core and centre of my nature is love of the beautiful, a passion for the beautiful, and that it would not be safe to trust me with a moon that belonged to another person and that person didn't know I had it. I could give up a moon that I found in the daytime, because I should be afraid some one was looking; but if I found it in the dark, I am sure I should find some kind of an excuse for not saying anything about it. For I do love moons, they are so pretty and so romantic. I wish we had five or six; I would never go to bed; I should never get tired lying on the moss-bank and looking up at them.

Stars are good, too. I wish I could get some to put in my hair. But I suppose I never can. You would be surprised to find how far off they are, for they do not look it. When they first showed, last night, I tried to knock some down with a pole, but it didn't reach, which astonished me; then I tried clods till I was all tired out, but I never got one. It was because I am left-handed and cannot throw good. Even when I aimed at the one I wasn't after I couldn't hit the other one, though I did make some close shots, for I saw the black blot of the clod sail right into the midst of the golden clusters forty or fifty times, just barely missing them, and if I could have held out a little longer maybe I could have got one.

So I cried a little, which was natural, I suppose, for one of my age, and after I was rested I got a basket and started for a place on the extreme rim of the circle, where the stars were close to the ground and I could get them with my hands, which would be better, anyway, because I could gather them tenderly then, and not break them. But it was farther than I thought, and at last I had to give it up; I was so tired I couldn't drag my feet another step; and besides, they were sore and hurt me very much.

I couldn't get back home; it was too far, and turning cold; but

I found some tigers, and nestled in among them and was most adorably comfortable, and their breath was sweet and pleasant, because they live on strawberries. I had never seen a tiger before, but I knew them in a minute by the stripes. If I could have one of those skins, it would make a lovely gown.

To-day I am getting better ideas about distances. I was so eager to get hold of every pretty thing that I giddily grabbed for it, sometimes when it was too far off, and sometimes when it was but six inches away but seemed a foot—alas, with thorns between! I learned a lesson; also I made an axiom, all out of my own head—my very first one: *The scratched Experiment shuns the thorn.* I think it is a very good one for one so young.

I followed the other Experiment around, yesterday afternoon, at a distance, to see what it might be for, if I could. But I was not able to make out. I think it is a man. I had never seen a man, but it looked like one, and I feel sure that that is what it is. I realize that I feel more curiosity about it than about any of the other reptiles. If it is a reptile, and I suppose it is; for it has frowsy hair and blue eyes, and looks like a reptile. It has no hips; it tapers like a carrot; when it stands, it spreads itself apart like a derrick; so I think it is a reptile, though it may be architecture.

I was afraid of it at first, and started to run every time it turned around, for I thought it was going to chase me; but by-and-by I found it was only trying to get away, so after that I was not timid any more, but tracked it along, several hours, about twenty yards behind, which made it nervous and unhappy. At last it was a good deal worried, and climbed a tree. I waited a good while, then gave it up and went home.

To-day the same thing over. I've got it up the tree again.

Sunday

It is up there yet. Resting, apparently. But that is a subterfuge: Sunday isn't the day of rest; Saturday is appointed for that. It looks to me like a creature that is more interested in resting than in anything else. It would tire me to rest so much. It tires me just to sit around and watch the tree. I do wonder what it is for; I never see it do anything.

They returned the moon last night, and I was *so* happy! I think it is very honest of them. It slid down and fell off again, but I was not distressed; there is no need to worry when one has that kind of neighbors; they will fetch it back. I wish I could do something to show my appreciation. I would like to send them some stars, for we have more than we can use. I mean I, not we, for I can see that the reptile cares nothing for such things.

It has low tastes, and is not kind. When I went there yesterday evening in the gloaming it had crept down and was trying to catch the little speckled fishes that play in the pool, and I had to clod it to make it go up the tree again and let them alone. I wonder if *that* is what it is for? Hasn't it any heart? Hasn't it any compassion for those little creatures? Can it be that it was designed and manufactured for such ungentle work? It has the look of it. One of the clods took it back of the ear, and it used language. It gave me a thrill, for it was the first time I had ever heard speech, except my own. I did not understand the words, but they seemed expressive.

When I found it could talk, I felt a new interest in it, for I love to talk; I talk all day, and in my sleep, too, and I am very interesting, but if I had another to talk to I could be twice as interesting, and would never stop, if desired.

If this reptile is a man, it isn't an *it,* is it? That wouldn't be grammatical, would it? I think it would be *he.* I think so. In that case one would parse it thus: nominative, *he*; dative, *him*; possessive, *his'n.* Well, I will consider it a man and call it he until it turns out to be something else. This will be handier than having so many uncertainties.

Next week Sunday

All the week I tagged around after him and tried to get acquainted. I had to do the talking, because he was shy, but I don't mind it. He seemed pleased to have me around, and I used the sociable "we" a good deal, because it seemed to flatter him to be included.

Wednesday

We are getting along very well indeed, now, and getting better and better acquainted. He does not try to avoid me any more, which is a good sign, and shows that he likes to have me with him. That pleases me, and I study to be useful to him in every way I can, so as to increase his regard. During the last day or two I have taken all the work of naming things off his hands, and this has been a great relief to him, for he has no gift in that line, and is evidently very grateful. He can't think of a rational name to save him, but I do not let him see that I am aware of his defect. Whenever a new creature comes along, I name it before he has time to expose himself by an awkward silence. In this way I have saved him many embarrassments. I have no defect like his. The minute I set eyes on an animal I know what it is. I don't have to reflect a moment; the right name comes out instantly, just as if it were an inspiration, as no doubt it is, for I am sure it wasn't in me half a minute before. I seem to know just by the shape of the creature and the way it acts what animal it is.

When the dodo came along he thought it was a wildcat—I saw it in his eye. But I saved him. And I was careful not to do it in a way that could hurt his pride. I just spoke up in a quite natural way of pleased surprise, and not as if I was dreaming of conveying information, and said, "Well, I do declare if there isn't the dodo!" I explained—without seeming to be explaining—how I knew it for a dodo, and although I thought maybe he was a little piqued that I knew the creature when he didn't, it was quite evident that he admired me. That was very agreeable, and I thought of it more than once with gratification before I slept. How little a thing can make us happy when we feel that we have earned it.

Thursday

My first sorrow. Yesterday he avoided me and seemed to wish I would not talk to him. I could not believe it, and thought there was some mistake, for I loved to be with him, and loved to hear him talk, and so how could it be that he could feel unkind towards me when I had not done anything? But at last it seemed true, so I went away and sat lonely in the place where I first saw him the morning that we were made and I did not know what he was and was indifferent about him; but now it was a mournful place, and every little thing spoke of him, and my heart was very sore. I did not know why very clearly, for it was a new feeling; I had not experienced it before, and it was all a mystery, and I could not make it out.

But when night came I could not bear the lonesomeness, and went to the new shelter which he has built, to ask him what I had done that was wrong and how I could mend it and get back his kindness again; but he put me out in the rain, and it was my first sorrow.

Sunday

It is pleasant again, now, and I am happy; but those were heavy days; I do not think of them when I can help it.

I tried to get him some of those apples, but I cannot learn to throw straight. I failed, but I think the good intention pleased him. They are forbidden, and he says I shall come to harm; but so I come to harm through pleasing him, why shall I care for that harm?

Monday

This morning I told him my name, hoping it would interest

him. But he did not care for it. It is strange. If he should tell me his name, I would care. I think it would be pleasanter in my ears than any other sound.

He talks very little. Perhaps it is because he is not bright, and is sensitive about it and wishes to conceal it. It is such a pity that he should feel so, for brightness is nothing; it is in the heart that the values lie. I wish I could make him understand that a loving good heart is riches, and riches enough, and that without it intellect is poverty.

Although he talks so little he has quite a considerable vocabulary. This morning he used a surprisingly good word. He evidently recognized, himself, that it was a good one, for he worked it in twice afterwards, casually. It was not good casual art, still it showed that he possesses a certain quality of perception. Without a doubt that seed can be made to grow, if cultivated.

Where did he get that word? I do not think I have ever used it.

No, he took no interest in my name. I tried to hide my disappointment, but I suppose I did not succeed. I went away and sat on the moss-bank with my feet in the water. It is where I go when I hunger for companionship, some one to look at, some one to talk to. It is not enough—that lovely white body painted there in the pool—but it is something, and something is better than utter loneliness. It talks when I talk; it is sad when I am sad; it comforts me with its sympathy; it says, "Do not be downhearted, you poor friendless girl; I will be your friend." It *is* a good friend to me, and my only one; it is my sister.

That first time that she forsook me! ah, I shall never forget that—never, never. My heart was lead in my body! I said, "She was all I had, and now she is gone!" In my despair I said, "Break, my heart; I cannot bear my life any more!" and hid my face in my hands, and there was no solace for me. And when I took them away, after a little, there she was again, white and shining and beautiful, and I sprang into her arms!

That was perfect happiness; I had known happiness before, but it was not like this, which was ecstasy. I never doubted her afterwards. Sometimes she stayed away—maybe an hour, maybe almost the whole day, but I waited and did not doubt; I said, "She is busy, or she is gone a journey, but she will come." And it was so: she always did. At night she would not come if it was dark, for she was a timid little thing; but if there was a moon she would come. I am not afraid of the dark, but she is younger than I am; she was born after I was. Many and many are the visits I have paid her; she is my comfort and my refuge when my life is hard—and it is mainly that.

Tuesday

All the morning I was at work improving the estate; and I purposely kept away from him in the hope that he would get lonely and come. But he did not.

At noon I stopped for the day and took my recreation by flitting all about with the bees and butterflies and revelling in the flowers, those beautiful creatures that catch the smile of God out of the sky and preserve it! I gathered them, and made them into wreaths and garlands and clothed myself in them while I ate my luncheon—apples, of course; then I sat in the shade and wished and waited. But he did not come.

But no matter. Nothing would have come of it, for he does not care for flowers. He calls them rubbish, and cannot tell one from another, and thinks it is superior to feel like that. He does not care for me, he does not care for flowers, he does not care for the painted sky at eventide—is there anything he does care for, except building shacks to coop himself up in from the good clean rain, and thumping the melons, and sampling the grapes, and fingering the fruit on the trees, to see how those properties are coming along?

I laid a dry stick on the ground and tried to bore a hole in it with another one, in order to carry out a scheme that I had, and soon I got an awful fright. A thin, transparent, bluish film rose out of the hole, and I dropped everything and ran! I thought it was a spirit, and I *was* so frightened! But I looked back, and it was not coming; so I leaned against a rock and rested and panted, and let my limbs go on trembling until they got steady again; then I crept warily back, alert, watching, and ready to fly if there was occasion; and when I was come near, I parted the branches of a rose-bush and peeped through—wishing the man was about, I was looking so cunning and pretty—but the sprite was gone. I went there, and there was a pinch of delicate pink dust in the hole. I put my finger in, to feel it, and said *ouch!* and took it out again. It was a cruel pain. I put my finger in my mouth; and by standing first on one foot and then the other, and grunting, I presently eased my misery; then I was full of interest, and began to examine.

I was curious to know what the pink dust was. Suddenly the name of it occurred to me, though I had never heard of it before. It was *fire!* I was as certain of it as a person could be of anything in the world. So without hesitation I named it that—fire.

I had created something that didn't exist before; I had added a new thing to the world's uncountable properties; I realized this, and was proud of my achievement, and was going to run and find him and tell him about it, thinking to raise myself in his esteem—but I reflected, and did not do it. No—he would not care for it. He would ask what it was good for, and what could I answer? For it was not *good* for something, but only beautiful, merely beautiful—

So I sighed, and did not go. For it wasn't good for anything; it could not build a shack, it could not improve melons, it could not hurry a fruit crop; it was useless, it was a foolishness and a vanity; he would despise it and say cutting words. But to me it was not despicable; I said, "Oh, you fire, I love you, you dainty pink creature, for you are *beautiful*—and that is enough!" and was going to gather it to my breast. But refrained. Then I made another maxim out of my own head, though it was so nearly like the first one that I was afraid it was only a plagiarism: *"The burnt Experiment shuns the fire."*

I wrought again; and when I had made a good deal of fire-dust I emptied it into a handful of dry brown grass, intending to carry it home and keep it always and play with it; but the wind struck it and it sprayed up and spat out at me fiercely, and I dropped it and ran. When I looked back the blue spirit was towering up and stretching and rolling away like a cloud, and instantly I thought of the name of it—*smoke!*—though, upon my word, I had never heard of smoke before.

Soon, brilliant yellow-and-red flares shot up through the smoke, and I named them in an instant—*flames!*—and I was right, too, though these were the very first flames that had ever been in the world. They climbed the trees, they flashed splendidly in and out of the vast and increasing volume of tumbling smoke, and I had to clap my hands and laugh and dance in my rapture, it was so new and strange and so wonderful and so beautiful!

He came running, and stopped and gazed, and said not a word for many minutes. Then he asked what it was. Ah, it was too bad that he should ask such a direct question. I had to answer it, of course, and I did. I said it was fire. If it annoyed him that I should know and he must ask, that was not my fault; I had no desire to annoy him. After a pause he asked:

"How did it come?"

Another direct question, and it also had to have a direct answer.

"I made it."

The fire was travelling farther and farther off. He went to the edge of the burned place and stood looking down, and said:

"What are these?"

"Fire-coals."

He picked up one to examine it, but changed his mind and put it down again. Then he went away. *Nothing* interests him.

But I was interested. There were ashes, gray and soft and delicate and pretty—I knew what they were at once. And the embers; I knew the embers, too. I found my apples, and raked them out, and was glad; for I am very young and my appetite is active. But I was disappointed; they were all burst open and spoiled. Spoiled apparently; but it was not so; they were better than raw ones. Fire is beautiful; some day it will be useful, I think.

Friday

I saw him again, for a moment, last Monday at nightfall, but only for a moment. I was hoping he would praise me for trying to improve the estate, for I had meant well and had worked hard. But he was not pleased, and turned away and left me. He was also displeased on another account: I tried once more to persuade him to stop going over the Falls. That was because the fire had revealed to me a new passion—quite new, and distinctly different from love, grief, and those others which I had already discovered—*fear*. And it is horrible!—I wish I had never discovered it; it gives me dark moments, it spoils my happiness, it makes me shiver and tremble and shudder. But I could not persuade him, for he has not discovered fear yet, and so he could not understand me.

Extract from Adam's Diary

Perhaps I ought to remember that she is very young, a mere girl, and make allowances. She is all interest, eagerness, vivacity, the world is to her a charm, a wonder, a mystery, a joy; she can't speak for delight when she finds a new flower, she must pet it and caress it and smell it and talk to it, and pour out endearing names upon it. And she is color-mad: brown rocks, yellow sand, gray moss, green foliage, blue sky; the pearl of the dawn, the purple shadows on the mountains, the golden islands floating in crimson seas at sunset, the pallid moon sailing through the shredded cloud-rack, the star-jewels glittering in the wastes of space—none of them is of any practical value, so far as I can see, but because they have color and majesty, that is enough for her, and she loses her mind over them. If she could quiet down and keep still a couple of minutes at a time, it would be a reposeful spectacle. In that case I think I could enjoy looking at her; indeed I am sure I could, for I am coming to realize that she is a quite remarkably comely creature—lithe, slender, trim, rounded, shapely, nimble, graceful; and once when she was standing marble-white and sun-drenched on a bowlder, with her young head tilted back and her hand shading her eyes, watching the flight of a bird in the sky, I recognized that she was beautiful.

Monday noon.—If there is anything on the planet that she is not interested in it is not in my list. There are animals that I am indifferent to, but it is not so with her. She has no discrimination, she takes to all of them, she thinks they are all treasures, every new one is welcome.

When the mighty brontosaurus came striding into camp, she regarded it as an acquisition, I considered it a calamity; that is a good sample of the lack of harmony that prevails in our views of things. She wanted to domesticate it, I wanted to make it a present of the homestead and move out. She believed it could be tamed by kind treatment and would be a good pet; I said a pet twenty-one feet high and eighty-four feet long would be no proper thing to have about the place, because, even with the best intentions and without meaning any harm, it could sit down on the house and mash it, for any one could see by the look of its eye that it was absent-minded.

Still, her heart was set upon having that monster, and she couldn't give it up. She thought we could start a dairy with it, and wanted me to help her milk it; but I wouldn't; it was too risky. The sex wasn't right, and we hadn't any ladder anyway. Then she wanted to ride it, and look at the scenery. Thirty or forty feet of its tail was lying on the ground, like a fallen tree, and she thought she could climb it, but she was mistaken; when she got to the steep place it was too slick and down she came, and would have hurt herself but for me.

Was she satisfied now? No. Nothing ever satisfies her but demonstration; untested theories are not in her line, and she won't have them. It is the right spirit, I concede it; it attracts me; I feel the influence of it; if I were with her more I think I should take it up myself. Well, she had one theory remaining about this colossus: she thought that if we could tame him and make him friendly we could stand him in the river and use him for a bridge. It turned out that he was already plenty tame enough—at least as far as she was concerned—so she tried her theory, but it failed; every time she got him properly placed in the river and went ashore to cross over on him, he came out and followed her around like a pet mountain. Like the other animals. They all do that.

Tuesday—Wednesday—Thursday—and to-day: all without

seeing him. It is a long time to be alone; still, it is better to be alone than unwelcome.

I *had* to have company—I was made for it, I think—so I made friends with the animals. They are just charming, and they have the kindest disposition and the politest ways; they never look sour, they never let you feel that you are intruding, they smile at you and wag their tail, if they've got one, and they are always ready for a romp or an excursion or anything you want to propose. I think they are perfect gentlemen. All these days we have had such good times, and it hasn't been lonesome for me, ever. Lonesome! No, I should say not. Why, there's always a swarm of them around—sometimes as much as four or five acres—you can't count them; and when you stand on a rock in the midst and look out over the furry expanse, it is so mottled and splashed and gay with color and frisking sheen and sun-flash, and so rippled with stripes, that you might think it was a lake, only you know it isn't; and there's storms of sociable birds, and hurricanes of whirring wings; and when the sun strikes all that feathery commotion, you have a blazing up of all the colors you can think of, enough to put your eyes out.

We have made long excursions, and I have seen a great deal of the world—almost all of it, I think; and so I am the first traveller, and the only one. When we are on the march, it is an imposing sight—there's nothing like it anywhere. For comfort I ride a tiger or a leopard, because it is soft and has a round back that fits me, and because they are such pretty animals; but for long distance or for scenery I ride the elephant. He hoists me up with his trunk, but I can get off myself; when we are ready to camp, he sits and I slide down the back way.

The birds and animals are all friendly to each other, and there are no disputes about anything. They all talk, and they all talk to me, but it must be a foreign language, for I cannot make out a word they say; yet they often understand me when I talk back, particularly the dog and the elephant. It makes me ashamed. It shows that they are brighter than I am, and are therefore my superiors. It annoys me, for I want to be the principal Experiment myself—and I intend to be, too.

I have learned a number of things, and am educated, now, but I wasn't at first. I was ignorant at first. At first it used to vex me because, with all my watching, I was never smart enough to be around when the water was running up-hill; but now I do not mind it. I have experimented and experimented until now I know it never does run up-hill, except in the dark. I know it does in the dark, because the pool never goes dry; which it would, of course, if the water didn't come back in the night. It is best to prove things by actual experiment; then you *know;* whereas if you depend on guessing and supposing and conjecturing, you will never get educated.

Friday

Some things you *can't* find out; but you will never know you can't by guessing and supposing: no, you have to be patient and go on experimenting until you find out that you can't find out. And it is delightful to have it that way, it makes the world so interesting. If there wasn't anything to find out, it would be dull. Even trying to find out and not finding out is just as interesting as trying to find out and finding out, and I don't know but more so. The secret of the water was a treasure until I *got* it; then the excitement all went away, and I recognized a sense of loss.

By experiment I know that wood swims, and dry leaves, and feathers, and plenty of other things; therefore by all that cumulative evidence you know that a rock will swim; but you have to put up with simply knowing it, for there isn't any way to prove it—up to now. But I shall find a way—then *that* excitement will go. Such things make me sad; because by-and-by when I have found out everything there won't be any more excitements, and I do love excitements so! The other night I couldn't sleep for thinking about it.

At first I couldn't make out what I was made for, but now I think it was to search out the secrets of this wonderful world and be happy and thank the Giver of it all for devising it. I think there are many things to learn yet—I hope so; and by economizing and not hurrying too fast I think they will last weeks and weeks. I hope so. When you cast up a feather it sails away on the air and goes out of sight; then you throw up a clod and it doesn't. It comes down, every time. I have tried it and tried it, and it is always so. I wonder why it is? Of course it *doesn't* come down, but why should it *seem* to? I suppose it is an optical illusion. I mean, one of them is. I don't know which one. It may be the feather, it may be the clod; I can't prove which it is, I can only demonstrate that one or the other is a fake, and let a person take his choice.

By watching, I know that the stars are not going to last. I have seen some of the best ones melt and run down the sky. Since one can melt, they can all melt; since they can all melt, they can all melt the same night. That sorrow will come—I know it. I mean to sit up every night and look at them as long as I can keep awake; and I will impress those sparkling fields on my memory, so that by-and-by when they are taken away I can by my fancy restore those lovely myriads to the black sky and make them sparkle again, and double them by the blur of my tears.

After the Fall

When I look back, the Garden is a dream to me. It was beautiful, surpassingly beautiful, enchantingly beautiful; and now it is lost, and I shall not see it any more.

The Garden is lost, but I have found *him,* and am content. He loves me as well as he can; I love him with all the strength of my passionate nature, and this, I think, is proper to my youth and sex. If I ask myself why I love him, I find I do not know, and do not really much care to know; so I suppose that this kind of love is not a product of reasoning and statistics, like one's love for other reptiles and animals. I think that this must be so. I love certain birds because of their song; but I do not love Adam on account of his singing—no, it is not that; the more he sings the more I do not get reconciled to it. Yet I ask him to sing, because I wish to learn to like everything he is interested in. I am sure I can learn, because at first I could not stand it, but now I can. It sours the milk, but it doesn't matter; I can get used to that kind of milk.

It is not on account of his brightness that I love him—no, it is not that. He is not to blame for his brightness, such as it is, for he did not make it himself; he is as God made him, and that is sufficient. There was a wise purpose in it; *that* I know. In time it will develop, though I think it will not be sudden; and, besides, there is no hurry; he is well enough just as he is.

It is not on account of his gracious and considerate ways and his delicacy that I love him. No, he has lacks in these regards, but he is well enough just so, and is improving.

It is not on account of his industry that I love him—no, it is not that. I think he has it in him, and I do not know why he conceals it from me. It is my only pain. Otherwise he is frank and open with me, now. I am sure he keeps nothing from me but this. It grieves me that he should have a secret from me, and sometimes it spoils my sleep, thinking of it, but I will put it out of my mind; it shall not trouble my happiness, which is otherwise full to overflowing.

It is not on account of his education that I love him—no, it is not that. He is self-educated, and does really know a multitude of things, but they are not so.

It is not on account of his chivalry that I love him—no, it is not that. He told on me, but I do not blame him; it is a peculiarity of sex, I think, and he did not make his sex. Of course I would not have told on him, I would have perished first; but that is a peculiarity of sex, too, and I do not take credit for it, for I did not make my sex.

Then why is it that I love him? *Merely because he is masculine,* I think.

At bottom he is good, and I love him for that, but I could love him without it. If he should beat me and abuse me, I should go on loving him. I know it. It is a matter of sex, I think.

He is strong and handsome, and I love him for that, and I admire him and am proud of him, but I could love him without those qualities. If he were plain, I should love him; if he were a wreck, I should love him; and I would work for him, and slave over him, and pray for him, and watch by his bedside until I died.

Yes, I think I love him merely because he is *mine* and is *masculine.* There is no other reason, I suppose. And so I think it is as I first said: that this kind of love is not a product of reasonings and statistics. It just *comes*—none knows whence—and cannot explain itself. And doesn't need to.

It is what I think. But I am only a girl, and the first that has examined this matter, and it may turn out that in my ignorance and inexperience I have not got it right.

Forty Years Later

It is my prayer, it is my longing, that we may pass from this life together—a longing which shall never perish from the earth, but shall have place in the heart of every wife that loves, until the end of time; and it shall be called by my name.

But if one of us must go first, it is my prayer that it shall be I; for he is strong, I am weak, I am not so necessary to him as he is to me—life without him would not be life; how could I endure it? This prayer is also immortal, and will not cease from being offered up while my race continues. I am the first wife; and in the last wife I shall be repeated.

At Eve's Grave

ADAM: Wheresoever she was, *there* was Eden.

The Innocents Abroad, *a book of travel sketches published in 1869, was an immediate success and established Twain's reputation as a writer. Eager to capitalize on this popularity, the American Publishing Company urged him to bring out a volume based on his experiences in the West. Twain obliged with* Roughing It, *a lively description of his adventures in Nevada, California, and the Sandwich Islands. The book appeared in 1872.*

Roughing It

CHAPTER I

My brother had just been appointed Secretary of Nevada Territory—an office of such majesty that it concentrated in itself the duties and dignities of Treasurer, Comptroller, Secretary of State, and Acting Governor in the Governor's absence. A salary of eighteen hundred dollars a year and the title of "Mr. Secretary," gave to the great position an air of wild and imposing grandeur. I was young and ignorant, and I envied my brother. I coveted his distinction and his financial splendor, but particularly and especially the long, strange journey he was going to make, and the curious new world he was going to explore. He was going to travel! I never had been away from home, and that word "travel" had a seductive charm for me. Pretty soon he would be hundreds and hundreds of miles away on the great plains and deserts, and among the mountains of the Far West, and would see buffaloes and Indians, and prairie dogs, and antelopes, and have all kinds of adventures, and may be get hanged or scalped, and have ever such a fine time, and write home and tell us all about it, and be a hero. And he would see the gold mines and the silver mines, and maybe go about of an afternoon when his work was done, and pick up two or three pailfuls of shining slugs, and nuggets of gold and silver on the hillside. And by and by he would become very rich, and return home by sea, and be able to talk as calmly about San Francisco and the ocean, and "the isthmus" as if it was nothing of any consequence to have seen those marvels face to face. What I suffered in contemplating his happiness, pen cannot describe. And so, when he offered me, in cold blood, the sublime position of private secretary under him, it appeared to me that the heavens and the earth passed away, and the firmament was rolled together as a scroll! I had nothing more to desire. My contentment was complete. At the end of an hour or two I was ready for the journey. Not much packing up was necessary, because we were going in the overland stage from the Missouri frontier to Nevada, and passengers were only allowed a small quantity of baggage apiece. There was no Pacific railroad in those fine times of ten or twelve years ago—not a single rail of it.

I only proposed to stay in Nevada three months—I had no thought of staying longer than that. I meant to see all I could that was new and strange, and then hurry home to business. I little thought that I would not see the end of that three-month pleasure excursion for six or seven uncommonly long years!

I dreamed all night about Indians, deserts, and silver bars, and in due time, next day, we took shipping at the St. Louis wharf on board a steamboat bound up the Missouri River.

We were six days going from St. Louis to "St. Jo."—a trip that was so dull, and sleepy, and eventless that it has left no more impression on my memory than if its duration had been six minutes instead of that many days. No record is left in my mind, now, concerning it, but a confused jumble of savage-looking snags, which we deliberately walked over with one wheel or the other; and of reefs which we butted and butted, and then retired from and climbed over in some softer place; and of sand-bars which we roosted on occasionally, and rested, and then got out our crutches and sparred over. In fact, the boat might almost as well have gone to St. Jo. by land, for she was walking most of the time, anyhow—climbing over reefs and clambering over snags patiently and laboriously all day long. The captain said she was a "bully" boat, and all she wanted was more "shear" and a bigger wheel. I thought she wanted a pair of stilts, but I had the deep sagacity not to say so.

CHAPTER II

The first thing we did on that glad evening that landed us at St. Joseph was to hunt up the stage-office, and pay a hundred and fifty dollars apiece for tickets per overland coach to Carson City, Nevada.

The next morning, bright and early, we took a hasty breakfast, and hurried to the starting-place. Then an inconvenience presented itself which we had not properly appreciated before, namely, that one cannot make a heavy traveling trunk stand for twenty-five pounds of baggage—because it weighs a good deal more. But that was all we could take—twenty-five pounds each. So we had to snatch our trunks open, and make a selection in a good deal of a hurry. We put our lawful twenty-five pounds apiece all in one valise, and shipped the trunks back to St. Louis again. It was a sad parting, for now we had no swallow-tail coats and white kid gloves to wear at Pawnee receptions in the Rocky Mountains, and no stovepipe hats nor patent-leather boots, nor anything else necessary to make life calm and peaceful. We were reduced to a war-footing. Each of us put on a rough, heavy suit of clothing, woolen army shirt and "stogy" boots included; and into the valise we crowded a few white shirts, some under-clothing and such things. My brother, the Secretary, took along about four pounds of United States statutes and six pounds of Unabridged Dictionary; for we did not know—poor innocents—that such things could be bought in San Francisco on one day and received in Carson City the next. I was armed to the teeth with a pitiful little Smith & Wesson's seven-shooter, which carried a ball like a homoeopathic pill, and it took the whole seven to make a dose for an adult. But I thought it was grand. It appeared to me to be a dangerous weapon. It only had one fault—you could not hit anything with it. One of our "conductors" practiced awhile on a cow with it, and as long as she stood still and behaved herself she was safe; but as soon as she went to moving about, and he got to shooting at other things, she came to grief. The Secretary had a small-sized Colt's revolver strapped around him for protection against the Indians, and to guard against accidents he carried it uncapped. Mr. George Bemis was dismally formidable. George Bemis was our fellow-traveler. We had never seen him before. He wore in his belt an old original "Allen" revolver, such as irreverent people called a "pepper-box." Simply drawing the trigger back, cocked and fired the pistol. As the trigger came back, the hammer would begin to rise and the barrel to turn over, and presently down would drop the hammer, and away would speed the ball. To aim along the turning barrel and hit the thing aimed at was a feat which was probably never done with an "Allen" in the world. But George's was a reliable weapon, nevertheless, because, as one of the stage-drivers afterward said, "If she didn't get what she went after, she would fetch something else." And so she did. She went after a deuce of spades nailed against a tree, once, and fetched a mule standing about thirty yards to the left of it. Bemis did not want the mule; but the owner came out with a double-barreled shotgun and persuaded him to buy it, anyhow. It was a cheerful weapon—the "Allen." Sometimes all its six barrels would go off at once, and then there was no safe place in all the region round about, but behind it.

We took two or three blankets for protection against frosty weather in the mountains. In the matter of luxuries we were modest—we took none along but some pipes and five pounds of smoking tobacco. We had two large canteens to carry water in, between stations on the Plains, and we also took with us a little shot-bag of silver coin for daily expenses in the way of breakfasts and dinners.

By eight o'clock everything was ready, and we were on the other side of the river. We jumped into the stage, the driver cracked his whip, and we bowled away and left "the States" behind us. It was a superb summer morning, and all the landscape was brilliant with sunshine. There was a freshness and breeziness, too, and an exhilarating sense of emancipation from all sorts of cares and responsibilities, that almost made us feel that the years we had spent in the close, hot city, toiling and slaving, had been wasted and thrown away. We were spinning along through Kansas, and in the course of an hour and a half we were fairly abroad on the great Plains. Just here the land was rolling—a grand sweep of regular elevations and depressions as far as the eye could reach—like the stately heave and swell of the ocean's bosom after a storm. And everywhere were cornfields, accenting with squares of deeper green, this limitless expanse of grassy land. But presently this sea upon dry ground was to lose its "rolling" character and stretch away for seven hundred miles as level as a floor!

Our coach was a great swinging and swaying stage, of the most sumptuous description—an imposing cradle on wheels. It was drawn by six handsome horses, and by the side of the driver sat the "conductor," the legitimate captain of the craft; for it was his business to take charge and care of the mails, baggage, express matter, and passengers. We three were the only passengers, this trip. We sat on the back seat, inside. About all the rest of the coach was full of mail bags—for we had three days' delayed mails with us. Almost touching our knees, a perpendicular wall of mail matter rose up to the roof. There was a great pile of it strapped on top of the stage, and both the fore and hind boots were full. We had twenty-seven hundred pounds of it aboard, the driver said—"a little for Brigham, and Carson, and 'Frisco, but the heft of it for the Injuns, which is powerful troublesome 'thout they get plenty of truck to read." But as he just then got up a fearful convulsion of his countenance which was suggestive of a wink being swallowed by an earthquake, we guessed that his remark was intended to be facetious, and to mean that we would unload the most of our mail matter somewhere on the Plains and leave it to the Indians, or whosoever wanted it.

We changed horses every ten miles, all day long, and fairly flew over the hard, level road. We jumped out and stretched our legs every time the coach stopped, and so the night found us still vivacious and unfatigued.

After supper a woman got in, who lived about fifty miles further on, and we three had to take turns at sitting outside with the driver and conductor. Apparently she was not a talkative woman. She would sit there in the gathering twilight and fasten her steadfast eyes on a mosquito rooting into her arm, and slowly she would raise her other hand till she had got his range, and then she would launch a slap at him that would have jolted a cow; and after that she would sit and contemplate the corpse with tranquil satisfaction—for she never missed her mosquito; she was a dead shot at short range. She never removed a carcase, but left them there for bait. I sat by this grim Sphynx and watched her kill thirty or forty mosquitoes—watched her, and waited for her to say something, but she never did. So I finally opened the conversation myself. I said:

"The mosquitoes are pretty bad, about here, madam."

"You bet!"

"What did I understand you to say, madam?"

"You BET!"

Then she cheered up, and faced around and said:

"Danged if I didn't begin to think you fellers was deef and dumb. I did, b'gosh. Here I've sot, and sot, and sot, a-bust'n muskeeters and wonderin' what was ailin' ye. Fust I thot you was deef and dumb, then I thot you was sick or crazy, or suthin', and then by and by I begin to reckon you was a passel of sickly fools that couldn't think of nothing to say. Wher'd ye come from?"

The Sphynx was a Sphynx no more! The fountains of her great deep were broken up, and she rained the nine parts of speech forty days and forty nights, metaphorically speaking, and buried us under a desolating deluge of trivial gossip that left not a crag or pinnacle of rejoinder projecting above the tossing waste of dislocated grammar and decomposed pronunciation!

How we suffered, suffered, suffered! She went on, hour after hour, till I was sorry I ever opened the mosquito question and gave her a start. She never did stop again until she got to her journey's end toward daylight; and then she stirred us up as she was leaving the stage (for we were nodding, by that time), and said:

"Now you git out at Cottonwood, you fellers, and lay over a couple o' days, and I'll be along some time to-night, and if I can do ye any good by edgin' in a word now and then, I'm right thar. Folks 'll tell you 't I've always ben kind o' offish and partic'lar for a gal that's raised in the woods, and I *am*, with the rag-tag and bob-tail, and a gal *has* to be, if she wants to *be* anything, but when people comes along which is my equals, I reckon I'm a pretty sociable heifer after all."

We resolved not to "lay by at Cottonwood."

CHAPTER III

About an hour and a half before daylight we were bowling along smoothly over the road—so smoothly that our cradle only rocked in a gentle, lulling way, that was gradually soothing us to sleep, and dulling our consciousness—when something gave away under us! We were dimly aware of it, but indifferent to it. The coach stopped. We heard the driver and conductor talking together outside, and rummaging for a lantern, and swearing because they could not find it—but we had no interest in whatever had happened, and it only added to our comfort to think of those people out there at work in the murky night, and we snug in our nest with the curtains drawn. But presently, by the sounds, there seemed to be an examination going on, and then the driver's voice said:

"By George, the thoroughbrace is broke!"

This started me broad awake—as an undefined sense of calamity is always apt to do. I said to myself: "Now, a thoroughbrace is probably part of a horse; and doubtless a vital part, too, from the dismay in the driver's voice. Leg, maybe—and yet how could he break his leg waltzing along such a road as this? No, it can't be his leg. That is impossible, unless he was reaching for the driver. Now, what can be the thoroughbrace of a horse, I wonder? Well, whatever comes, I shall not air my ignorance in this crowd, anyway."

Just then the conductor's face appeared at a lifted curtain, and his lantern glared in on us and our wall of mail matter. He said:

"Gents, you'll have to turn out a spell. Thoroughbrace is broke."

We climbed out into a chill drizzle, and felt ever so homeless and dreary. When I found that the thing they called a "thoroughbrace" was the massive combination of belts and springs which the coach rocks itself in, I said to the driver:

"I never saw a thoroughbrace used up like that, before, that I can remember. How did it happen?"

"Why, it happened by trying to make one coach carry three days' mail—that's how it happened," said he. "And right here is the very direction which is wrote on all the newspaper-bags which was to be put out for the Injuns for to keep 'em quiet. It's most uncommon lucky, becuz it's so nation dark I should 'a' gone by unbeknowns if that air thoroughbrace hadn't broke."

I knew that he was in labor with another of those winks of his, though I could not see his face, because he was bent down at work; and wishing him a safe delivery, I turned to and helped the rest get out the mail-sacks. It made a great pyramid by the roadside when it was all out. When they had mended the thoroughbrace we filled the two boots again, but put no mail on top, and only half as much inside as there was before. The conductor bent all the seat-backs down, and then filled the coach just half full of mail-bags from end to end. We objected loudly to this, for it left us no seats. But the conductor was wiser than we, and said a bed was better than seats, and moreover, this plan would protect his thoroughbraces. We never wanted any seats after that. The lazy bed was infinitely preferable. I had many an exciting day, subsequently, lying on it reading the statutes and the dictionary, and wondering how the characters would turn out.

The conductor said he would send back a guard from the next station to take charge of the abandoned mail-bags, and we drove on.

It was now just dawn; and as we stretched our cramped legs full length on the mail sacks, and gazed out through the windows across the wide wastes of greensward clad in cool, powdery mist, to where there was an expectant look in the eastern horizon, our perfect enjoyment took the form of a tranquil and contented ecstasy. The stage whirled along at a spanking gait, the breeze flapping curtains and suspended coats in a most exhilarating way; the cradle swayed and swung luxuriously, the pattering of the horses' hoofs, the cracking of the driver's whip, and his "Hi-yi! g'lang!" were music; the spinning ground and the waltzing trees appeared to give us a mute hurrah as we went by, and then slack up and look after us with interest, or envy, or something; and as we lay and smoked the pipe of peace and compared all this luxury with the years of tiresome city life that had gone before it, we felt that there was only one complete and satisfying happiness in the world, and we had found it.

After breakfast, at some station whose name I have forgotten, we three climbed up on the seat behind the driver, and let the conductor have our bed for a nap. And by and by, when the sun made me drowsy, I lay down on my face on top of the coach, grasping the slender iron railing, and slept for an hour or more. That will give one an appreciable idea of those matchless roads. Instinct will make a sleeping man grip a fast hold of the railing when the stage jolts, but when it only swings and sways, no grip is necessary. Overland drivers and conductors used to sit in their places and sleep thirty or forty minutes at a time, on good roads, while spinning along at the rate of eight or ten miles an hour. I saw them do it, often. There was no danger about it; a sleeping man *will* seize the irons in time when the coach jolts. These men were hard worked, and it was not possible for them to stay awake all the time.

By and by we passed through Marysville, and over the Big Blue and Little Sandy; thence about a mile, and entered Nebraska. About a mile further on, we came to the Big Sandy—one hundred and eighty miles from St. Joseph.

As the sun was going down, we saw the first specimen of an animal known familiarly over two thousand miles of mountain and desert—from Kansas clear to the Pacific Ocean—as the "jackass rabbit." He is well named. He is just like any other rabbit, except that he is from one third to twice as large, has longer legs in proportion to his size, and has the most preposterous ears that ever were mounted on any creature *but* a jackass. When he is sitting quiet, thinking about his sins, or is absent-minded or unapprehensive of danger, his majestic ears project above him conspicuously; but the breaking of a twig will scare him nearly to death, and then he tilts his ears back gently and starts for home. All you can see, then, for the next minute, is his long gray form stretched out straight and "streaking it" through the low sage-brush, head erect, eyes right, and ears just canted a little to the rear, but showing you where the animal is, all the time, the same as if he carried a jib. Now and then he makes a marvelous spring with his long legs, high over the stunted sage-brush, and scores a leap that would make a horse envious. Presently he comes down to a long, graceful "lope," and shortly he mysteriously disappears. He has crouched behind a sage-bush, and will sit there and listen and tremble until you get within six feet of him, when he will get under way again. But one must shoot at this creature once, if he wishes to see him throw his heart into his heels, and do the best he knows how. He is frightened clear through, now, and he lays his long ears down on his back, straightens himself out like a yard-stick every spring he makes, and scatters miles behind him with an easy indifference that is enchanting.

Our party made this specimen "hump himself," as the conductor said. The secretary started him with a shot from the Colt; I commenced spitting at him with my weapon; and all in the same instant the old "Allen's" whole broadside let go with a rattling crash, and it is not putting it too strong to say that the rabbit was frantic! He dropped his ears, set up his tail, and left for San Francisco at a speed which can only be described as a flash and a vanish! Long after he was out of sight we could hear him whiz.

I do not remember where we first came across "sage-brush," but as I have been speaking of it I may as well describe it. This is easily done, for if the reader can imagine a gnarled and venerable live oak-tree reduced to a little shrub two feet high, with its rough bark, its foliage, its twisted boughs, all complete, he can picture the "sage-brush" exactly. Often, on lazy afternoons in the mountains, I have lain on the ground with my face under a sage-bush, and entertained myself with fancying that the gnats among its foliage were liliputian birds, and that the ants marching and countermarching about its base were liliputian flocks and herds, and myself some vast loafer from Brobdignag waiting to catch a little citizen and eat him.

It is an imposing monarch of the forest in exquisite miniature, is the "sage-brush." Its foliage is a grayish green, and gives that tint to desert and mountain. It smells like our domestic sage, and "sage-tea" made from it tastes like the sage-tea which all boys are so well acquainted with. The sage-brush is a singularly hardy plant, and grows right in the midst of deep sand, and among barren rocks, where nothing else in the vegetable world would try to grow, except "bunch-grass."* The sage-bushes grow from three to six or seven feet apart, all over the mountains and deserts of the Far West, clear to the borders of California. There is not a tree of any kind in the deserts, for hundreds of miles—there is no vegetation at all in a regular desert, except the sage-brush and its cousin the "greasewood," which is so much like the sage-brush that the difference amounts to little. Camp-fires and hot suppers in the deserts would be impossible but for the friendly sage-brush. Its trunk is as large as a boy's wrist (and

* "Bunch-grass" grows on the bleak mountain-sides of Nevada and neighboring territories, and offers excellent feed for stock, even in the dead of winter, wherever the snow is blown aside and exposes it; notwithstanding its unpromising home, bunch-grass is a better and more nutritious diet for cattle and horses than almost any other hay or grass that is known—so stock men say.

from that up to a man's arm), and its crooked branches are half as large as its trunk—all good, sound, hard wood, very like oak.

When a party camps, the first thing to be done is to cut sage-brush; and in a few minutes there is an opulent pile of it ready for use. A hole a foot wide, two feet deep, and two feet long, is dug, and sage-brush chopped up and burned in it till it is full to the brim with glowing coals. Then the cooking begins, and there is no smoke, and consequently no swearing. Such a fire will keep all night, with very little replenishing; and it makes a very sociable camp-fire, and one around which the most impossible reminiscences sound plausible, instructive, and profoundly entertaining.

Sage-brush is very fair fuel, but as a vegetable it is a distinguished failure. Nothing can abide the taste of it but the jackass and his illegitimate child the mule. But their testimony to its nutritiousness is worth nothing, for they will eat pine knots, or anthracite coal, or brass filings, or lead pipe, or old bottles, or anything that comes handy, and then go off looking as grateful as if they had had oysters for dinner. Mules and donkeys and camels have appetites that anything will relieve temporarily, but nothing satisfy. In Syria, once, at the head-waters of the Jordan, a camel took charge of my overcoat while the tents were being pitched, and examined it with a critical eye, all over, with as much interest as if he had an idea of getting one made like it; and then, after he was done figuring on it as an article of apparel, he began to contemplate it as an article of diet. He put his foot on it, and lifted one of the sleeves out with his teeth, and chewed and chewed at it, gradually taking it in, and all the while opening and closing his eyes in a kind of religious ecstasy, as if he had never tasted anything as good as an overcoat before, in his life. Then he smacked his lips once or twice, and reached after the other sleeve. Next he tried the velvet collar, and smiled a smile of such contentment that it was plain to see that he regarded that as the daintiest thing about an overcoat. The tails went next, along with some percussion caps and cough candy, and some fig-paste from Constantinople. And then my newspaper correspondence dropped out, and he took a chance in that—manuscript letters written for the home papers. But he was treading on dangerous ground, now. He began to come across solid wisdom in those documents that was rather weighty on his stomach; and occasionally he would take a joke that would shake him up till it loosened his teeth; it was getting to be perilous times with him, but he held his grip with good courage and hopefully, till at last he began to stumble on statements that not even a camel could swallow with impunity. He began to gag and gasp, and his eyes to stand out, and his forelegs to spread, and in about a quarter of a minute he fell over as stiff as a carpenter's work-bench, and died a death of indescribable agony. I went and pulled the manuscript out of his mouth, and found that the sensitive creature had choked to death on one of the mildest and gentlest statements of fact that I ever laid before a trusting public.

I was about to say, when diverted from my subject, that occasionally one finds sage-bushes five or six feet high, and with a spread of branch and foliage in proportion, but two or two and a half feet is the usual height.

CHAPTER IV

As the sun went down and the evening chill came on, we made preparation for bed. We stirred up the hard leather letter-sacks, and the knotty canvas bags of printed matter (knotty and uneven because of projecting ends and corners of magazines, boxes and books). We stirred them up and redisposed them in such a way as to make our bed as level as possible. And we *did* improve it, too, though after all our work it had an upheaved and billowy look about it, like a little piece of a stormy sea. Next we hunted up our boots from odd nooks among the mail-bags where they had settled, and put them on. Then we got down our coats, vests, pantaloons and heavy woolen shirts, from the arm-loops where they had been swinging all day, and clothed ourselves in them—for, there being no ladies either at the stations or in the coach, and the weather being hot, we had looked to our comfort by stripping to our underclothing, at nine o'clock in the morning. All things being now ready, we stowed the uneasy Dictionary where it would lie as quiet as possible, and placed the water canteens and pistols where we could find them in the dark. Then we smoked a final pipe, and swapped a final yarn; after which, we put the pipes, tobacco and bag of coin in snug holes and caves among the mail-bags, and then fastened down the coach curtains all around, and made the place as "dark as the inside of a cow," as the conductor phrased it in his picturesque way. It was certainly as dark as any place could be—nothing was even dimly visible in it. And finally, we rolled ourselves up like silk-worms, each person in his own blanket, and sank peacefully to sleep.

Whenever the stage stopped to change horses, we would wake up, and try to recollect where we were—and succeed—and in a minute or two the stage would be off again, and we likewise. We began to get into country, now, threaded here and there with little streams. These had high, steep banks on each side, and every time we flew down one bank and scrambled up the other, our party inside got mixed somewhat. First we would all be down in a pile at the forward end of the stage, nearly in a sitting posture, and in a second we would shoot to the other end, and stand on our heads. And we would sprawl and kick, too, and ward off ends and corners of mail-bags that came lumbering over us and about us; and as the dust rose from the tumult, we would all sneeze in chorus, and the majority of us would grumble, and probably say some hasty thing, like: "Take your elbow out of my ribs!—can't you quit crowding?"

Every time we avalanched from one end of the stage to the other, the Unabridged Dictionary would come too; and every time it came it damaged somebody. One trip it "barked" the Secretary's elbow; the next trip it hurt me in the stomach, and the third it tilted Bemis's nose up till he could look down his nostrils—he said. The pistols and coin soon settled to the bottom, but the pipes, pipe-stems, tobacco and canteens clattered and floundered after the Dictionary every time it made an assault on us, and aided and abetted the book by spilling tobacco in our eyes, and water down our backs.

Still, all things considered, it was a very comfortable night. It wore gradually away, and when at last a cold gray light was visible through the puckers and chinks in the curtains, we yawned and stretched with satisfaction, shed our cocoons, and felt that we had slept as much as was necessary. By and by, as the sun rose up and warmed the world, we pulled off our clothes and got ready for breakfast. We were just pleasantly in time, for five minutes afterward the driver sent the weird music of his bugle winding over the grassy solitudes, and presently we detected a low hut or two in the distance. Then the rattling of the coach, the clatter of our six horses' hoofs, and the driver's crisp commands, awoke to a louder and stronger emphasis, and we went sweeping down on the station at our smartest speed. It was fascinating—that old overland stage-coaching.

We jumped out in undress uniform. The driver tossed his gathered reins out on the ground, gaped and stretched complacently, drew off his heavy buckskin gloves with great deliberation and insufferable dignity—taking not the slightest notice of a dozen solicitous inquiries after his health, and humbly facetious and flattering accostings, and obsequious tenders of service, from five or six hairy and half-civilized station-keepers and hostlers who were nimbly unhitching our steeds and bringing the fresh team out of the stables—for in the eyes of the stage-driver of that day, station-keepers and hostlers were a sort of good enough low creatures, useful in their place, and helping to make up a world, but not the kind of beings which a person of distinction could afford to concern himself with; while, on the contrary, in the eyes of the station-keeper and the hostler, the stage-driver was a hero—a great and shining dignitary, the world's favorite son, the envy of the people, the observed of the nations. When they spoke to him they received his insolent silence meekly, and as being the natural and proper conduct of so great a man; when he opened his lips they all hung on his words with admiration (he never honored a particular individual with a remark, but addressed it with a broad generality to the horses, the stables, the surrounding country *and* the human underlings); when he discharged a facetious insulting personality at a hostler, that hostler was happy for the day; when he uttered his one jest—old as the hills, coarse, profane, witless, and inflicted on the same audience, in the same language, every time his coach drove up there—the varlets roared, and slapped their thighs, and swore it was the best thing they'd ever heard in all their lives. And how they would fly around when he wanted a basin of water, a gourd of the same, or a light for his pipe!—but they would instantly insult a passenger if he so far forgot himself as to crave a favor at their hands. They could do that sort of insolence as well as the driver they copied it from—for, let it be borne in mind, the overland driver had but little less contempt for his passengers than he had for his hostlers.

The hostlers and station-keepers treated the really powerful *conductor* of the coach merely with the best of what was their idea of civility, but the *driver* was the only being they bowed down to and worshipped. How admiringly they would gaze up at him in his high seat as he gloved himself with lingering deliberation, while some happy hostler held the bunch of reins aloft, and waited patiently for him to take it! And how they would bombard him with glorifying ejaculations as he cracked his long whip and went careering away.

The station buildings were long, low huts, made of sun-dried, mud-colored bricks, laid up without mortar (*adobes*, the Spaniards call these bricks, and Americans shorten it to *'dobies*). The roofs, which had no slant to them worth speaking of, were thatched and then sodded or covered with a thick layer of earth, and from this sprung a pretty rank growth of weeds and grass. It was the first time we had ever seen a man's front yard on top of his house. The buildings consisted of barns, stable-room for twelve or fifteen horses, and a hut for an eating-room for passengers. This latter had bunks in it for the station-keeper and a hostler or two. You could rest your elbow on its eaves, and you had to bend in order to get in at the door. In place of a window there was a square hole about large enough for a man to crawl through, but this had no glass in it. There was no flooring, but the ground was packed hard. There was no stove, but the fire-place served all needful purposes. There were no shelves, no cupboards, no closets. In a corner stood an open sack of flour, and nestling against its base were a couple of black and venerable tin coffee-pots, a tin tea-pot, a little bag of salt, and a side of bacon.

By the door of the station-keeper's den, outside, was a tin wash-basin, on the ground. Near it was a pail of water and a piece of yellow bar soap, and from the eaves hung a hoary blue woolen shirt, significantly—but this latter was the station-keeper's private towel, and only two persons in all the party might venture to use it—the stage-driver and the conductor. The latter would not, from a sense of decency; the former would not, because he did not choose to encourage the advances of a station-keeper. We had towels—in the valise; they might as well have been in Sodom and Gomorrah. We (and the conductor) used our handkerchiefs, and the driver his pantaloons and sleeves. By the door, inside, was fastened a small old-fashioned looking-glass frame, with two little fragments of the original mirror lodged down in one corner of it. This arrangement afforded a pleasant double-barreled portrait of you when you looked into it, with one half of your head set up a couple of inches above the other half. From the glass frame hung the half of a comb by a string—but if I had to describe that patriarch or die, I believe I would order some sample coffins. It had come down from Esau and Samson, and had been accumulating hair ever since—along with certain impurities. In one corner of the room stood three or four rifles and muskets, together with horns and pouches of ammunition. The station-men wore pantaloons of coarse, country-woven stuff, and into the seat and the inside of the legs were sewed ample additions of buckskin, to do duty in place of leggings, when the man rode horseback—so the pants were half dull blue and half yellow, and unspeakably picturesque. The pants were stuffed into the tops of high boots, the heels whereof were armed with great Spanish spurs, whose little iron clogs and chains jingled with every step. The man wore a huge beard and mustachios, an old slouch hat, a blue woolen shirt, no suspenders, no vest, no coat—in a leathern sheath in his belt, a great long "navy" revolver (slung on right side, hammer to the front), and projecting from his boot a horn-handled bowie-knife. The furniture of the hut was neither gorgeous nor much in the way. The rocking-chairs and sofas were not present, and never had been, but they were represented by two three- legged stools, a pine-board bench four feet long, and two empty candle-boxes. The table was a greasy board on stilts, and the table-cloth and napkins had not come—and they were not looking for them, either. A battered tin platter, a knife and fork, and a tin pint cup, were at each man's place, and the driver had a queensware saucer that had seen better days. Of course this duke sat at the head of the table. There was one isolated piece of table furniture that bore about it a touching air of grandeur in misfortune. This was the caster. It was German silver, and crippled and rusty, but it was so preposterously out of place there that it was suggestive of a tattered exiled king among barbarians, and the majesty of its native position compelled respect even in its degradation. There was only one cruet left, and that was a stopperless, fly-specked, broken-necked thing, with two inches of vinegar in it, and a dozen preserved flies with their heels up and looking sorry they had invested there.

The station-keeper upended a disk of last week's bread, of the shape and size of an old-time cheese, and carved some slabs from it which were as good as Nicholson pavement, and tenderer.

He sliced off a piece of bacon for each man, but only the experienced old hands made out to eat it, for it was condemned army bacon which the United States would not feed to its soldiers in the forts, and the stage company had bought it cheap for the sustenance of their passengers and employes. We may have found this condemned army bacon further out on the plains than the section I am locating it in, but we *found* it—there is no gainsaying that.

Then he poured for us a beverage which he called *"Slumgullion,"* and it is hard to think he was not inspired when he named it. It really pretented to be tea, but there was too much dish-rag, and sand, and old bacon-rind in it to deceive the intelligent traveler. He had no sugar and no milk—not even a spoon to stir the ingredients with.

We could not eat the bread or the meat, nor drink the "slumgullion." And when I looked at that melancholy vinegar-cruet, I thought of the anecdote (a very, very old one, even at that day) of the traveler who sat down to a table which had nothing on it but a mackerel and a pot of mustard. He asked the landlord if this was all. The landlord said:

"*All!* Why, thunder and lightning, I should think there was mackerel enough there for six."

"But I don't like mackerel."

"Oh—then help yourself to the mustard."

In other days I had considered a good, a very good, anecdote, but there was a dismal plausibility about it, here, that took all the humor out of it.

Our breakfast was before us, but our teeth were idle.

I tasted and smelt, and said I would take coffee, I believed. The station-boss stopped dead still, and glared at me speechless. At last, when he came to, he turned away and said, as one who communes with himself upon a matter too vast to grasp:

"*Coffee!* Well, if that don't go clean ahead of me, I'm d——d!"

We could not eat, and there was no conversation among the hostlers and herdsmen—we all sat at the same board. At least there was no conversation further than a single hurried request, now and then, from one employe to another. It was always in the same form, and always gruffly friendly. Its western freshness and novelty startled me, at first, and interested me; but it presently grew monotonous, and lost its charm. It was:

"Pass the bread, you son of a skunk!" No, I forget—skunk was not the word; it seems to me it was still stronger than that; I know it was, in fact, but it is gone from my memory, apparently. However, it is no matter—probably it was too strong for print, anyway. It is the landmark in my memory which tells me where I first encountered the vigorous new vernacular of the occidental plains and mountains.

We gave up the breakfast, and paid our dollar apiece and went back to our mail-bag bed in the coach, and found comfort in our pipes. Right here we suffered the first diminution of our princely state. We left our six fine horses and took six mules in their place. But they were wild Mexican fellows, and a man had to stand at the head of each of them and hold him fast while the driver gloved and got himself ready. And when at last he grasped the reins and gave the word, the men sprung suddenly away from the mules' heads and the coach shot from the station as if it had issued from a cannon. How the frantic animals did scamper! It was a fierce and furious gallop—and the gait never altered for a moment till we reeled off ten or twelve miles and swept up to the next collection of little station-huts and stables.

So we flew along all day. At 2 P.M. the belt of timber that fringes the North Platte and marks its windings through the vast level floor of the Plains came in sight. At 4 P.M. we crossed a branch of the river, and at 5 P.M. we crossed the Platte itself, and landed at Fort Kearney, *fifty-six hours out from St. Joe*—THREE HUNDRED MILES!

Now that was stage-coaching on the great overland, ten or twelve years ago, when perhaps not more than ten men in America, all told, expected to live to see a railroad follow that route to the Pacific. But the railroad is there, now, and it pictures a thousand odd comparisons and contrasts in my mind to read the following sketch, in the New York *Times*, of a recent trip over almost the very ground I have been describing. I can scarcely comprehend the new state of things:

ACROSS THE CONTINENT

"At 4.20 P.M., Sunday, we rolled out of the station at Omaha, and started westward on our long jaunt. A couple of hours out, dinner was announced—an "event" to those of us who had yet to experience what it is to eat in one of Pullman's hotels on wheels; so, stepping into the car next forward of our sleeping palace, we found ourselves in the dining-car. It was a revelation to us, that first dinner on Sunday. And though we continued to dine for four days, and had as many breakfasts and suppers, our whole party never ceased to admire the perfection of the arrangements, and the marvelous results achieved. Upon tables covered with snowy linen, and garnished with services of solid silver, Ethiop waiters, flitting about in spotless white, placed as by magic a repast at which Delmonico himself could have had no occasion to blush; and, indeed, in some respects it would be hard for that distinguished *chef* to match our *menu*; for, in addition to all that ordinarily makes up a first-chop dinner, had we not our antelope steak (the gormand who has not experienced this—bah! what does he know of the feast of fat things?) our delicious mountain-brook trout, and choice fruits and berries, and (sauce piquant and unpurchasable!) our sweet-scented, appetite-compelling air of the prairies? You may depend upon it, we all did justice to the good things, and as we washed them down with bumpers of sparkling Krug, whilst we sped along at the rate of thirty miles an hour, agreed it was the *fastest* living we had ever experienced. (We beat that, however, two days afterward when we made *twenty-seven miles in twenty-seven minutes*, while our Champagne glasses filled to the brim spilled not a drop!) After dinner we repaired to our drawing-room car, and, as it was Sabbath eve, intoned some of the grand old hymns—"Praise God from whom," etc.; "Shining Shore," "Coronation," etc.—the voices of the men singers and of the women singers blending sweetly in the evening air, while our train, with its great glaring Polyphemus eye, lighting up long vistas of prairie, rushed into the night and the Wild. Then to bed in luxurious couches, where we slept the sleep of the just and only awoke the next morning (Monday) at eight o'clock, to find ourselves at the crossing of the North Platte, three hundred miles from Omaha—*fifteen hours and forty minutes out.*"

CHAPTER V

Another night of alternate tranquillity and turmoil. But morning came, by and by. It was another glad awakening to fresh breezes, vast expanses of level greensward, bright sunlight, an impressive solitude utterly without visible human beings or human habitations, and an atmosphere of such amazing magnifying properties that trees that seemed close at hand were more than three miles away. We resumed undress uniform, climbed atop of the flying coach, dangled our legs over the side, shouted occasionally at our frantic mules, merely to see them lay their ears back and scamper faster, tied our hats on to keep our hair from blowing away, and leveled an outlook over the world-wide carpet about us for things new and strange to gaze at. Even at this day it thrills me through and through to think of the life, the gladness and the wild sense of freedom that used to make the blood dance in my veins on those fine overland mornings!

Along about an hour after breakfast we saw the first prairie-dog villages, the first antelope, and the first wolf. If I remember rightly, this latter was the regular *cayote* (pronounced ky-*o*-te) of the farther deserts. And if it *was*, he was not a pretty creature or respectable either, for I got well acquainted with his race afterward, and can speak with confidence. The cayote is a long, slim, sick and sorry-looking skeleton, with a gray wolf-skin stretched over it, a tolerably bushy tail that forever sags down with a despairing expression of forsakenness and misery, a furtive and evil eye, and a long, sharp face, with slightly lifted lip and exposed teeth. He has a general slinking expression all over. The cayote is a living, breathing allegory of Want. He is *always* hungry. He is always poor, out of luck and friendless. The meanest creatures despise him, and even the fleas would desert him for a velocipede. He is so spiritless and cowardly that even while his exposed teeth are pretending a threat, the rest of his face is apologizing for it. And he is *so* homely!—so scrawny, and ribby, and coarse-haired, and pitiful. When he sees you he lifts his lip and lets a flash of his teeth out, and then turns a little out of the course he was pursuing, depresses his head a bit, and strikes a long, soft-footed trot through the sage-brush, glancing over his shoulder at you, from time to time, till he is about out of easy pistol range, and then he stops and takes a deliberate survey of you; he will trot fifty yards and stop again—another fifty and stop again; and finally the gray of his gliding body blends with the gray of the sage-brush, and he disappears. All this is when you make no demonstration against him; but if you do, he develops a livelier interest in his journey, and instantly electrifies his heels and puts such a deal of real estate between himself and your weapon, that by the time you have raised the hammer you see that you need a minie rifle, and by the time you have got him in line you need a rifled cannon, and by the time you have "drawn a bead" on him you see well enough that nothing but an unusually long-winded streak of lightning could reach him where he is now. But if you start a swift-footed dog after him, you will enjoy it ever so much—especially if it is a dog that has a good opinion of himself, and has been brought up to think he knows something about speed. The cayote will go swinging gently off on that deceitful trot of his, and every little while he will smile a fraudful smile over his shoulder that will fill that dog entirely full of encouragement and worldly ambition, and make him lay his head still lower to the ground, and stretch his neck further to the front, and pant more fiercely, and stick his tail out straighter behind, and move his furious legs with a yet wilder frenzy, and leave a broader and broader, and higher and denser cloud of desert sand smoking behind, and marking his long wake across the level plain! And all this time the dog is only a short twenty feet behind the cayote, and to save the soul of him he cannot understand why it is that he cannot get perceptibly closer; and he begins to get aggravated, and it makes him madder and madder to see how gently the cayote glides along and never pants or sweats or ceases to smile; and he grows still more and more incensed to see how shamefully he has been taken in by an entire stranger, and what an ignoble swindle that long, calm, soft-footed trot is; and next he notices that he is getting fagged, and that the cayote actually has to slacken speed a little to keep from running away from him—and *then* that town-dog is mad in earnest and he begins to strain and weep and swear, and paw the sand higher than ever, and reach for the cayote with concentrated and desperate energy. This "spurt" finds him six feet behind the gliding enemy, and two miles from his friends. And then, in the instant that a wild new hope is lighting up his face, the cayote turns and smiles blandly upon him once more, and with a something about it which seems to say: "Well, I shall have to tear myself away from you, bub—business is business, and it will not do for me to be fooling along this way all day"—and forthwith there is a rushing sound, and the sudden splitting of a long crack through the atmosphere, and behold that dog is solitary and alone in the midst of a vast solitude!

It makes his head swim. He stops, and looks all around; climbs the nearest sand-mound, and gazes into the distance; shakes his head reflectively, and then, without a word, he turns and jogs along back to his train, and takes up a humble position under the hindmost wagon, and feels unspeakably mean, and looks ashamed, and hangs his tail at half-mast for a week. And for as much as a year after that, whenever there is a great hue and cry after a cayote, that dog will merely glance in that direction without emotion, and apparently observe to himself, "I believe I do not wish any of the pie."

The cayote lives chiefly in the most desolate and forbidding deserts, along with the lizard, the jackass-rabbit and the raven, and gets an uncertain and precarious living, and earns it. He seems to subsist almost wholly on the carcases of oxen, mules and horses that have dropped out of emigrant trains and died, and upon windfalls of carrion, and occasional legacies of offal bequeathed to him by white men who have been opulent enough to have something better to butcher than condemned army bacon. He will eat anything in the world that his first cousins, the desert-frequenting tribes of Indians will, and they will eat anything they can bite. It is a curious fact that these latter are the only creatures known to history who will eat nitro-glycerine and ask for more if they survive.

The cayote of the deserts beyond the Rocky Mountains has a peculiarly hard time of it, owing to the fact that his relations, the Indians, are just as apt to be the first to detect a seductive scent on the desert breeze, and follow the fragrance to the late ox it emanated from, as he is himself; and when this occurs he has to content himself with sitting off at a little distance watching those people strip off and dig out everything edible, and walk off with it. Then he and the waiting ravens explore the skeleton and polish the bones. It is considered that the cayote, and the obscene bird, and the Indian of the desert, testify their blood kinship with each other in that they live together in the waste places of the earth on terms of perfect confidence and friendship, while hating all other creatures and yearning to assist at their funerals. He does not mind going a hundred miles to breakfast, and a hundred and fifty to dinner, because he is sure to have three or four days between meals, and he can just as well be traveling and looking at the scenery as lying around doing nothing and adding to the burdens of his parents.

We soon learned to recognize the sharp, vicious bark of the cayote as it came across the murky plain at night to disturb our dreams among the mail-sacks; and remembering his forlorn aspect and his hard fortune, made shift to wish him the blessed novelty of a long day's good luck and a limitless larder the morrow.

CHAPTER VI

Our new conductor (just shipped) had been without sleep for twenty hours. Such a thing was very frequent. From St. Joseph, Missouri, to Sacramento, California, by stage-coach, was nearly nineteen hundred miles, and the trip was often made in fifteen days (the cars do it in four and a half, now), but the time specified in the mail contracts, and required by the schedule, was eighteen or nineteen days, if I remember rightly. This was to make fair allowance for winter storms and snows, and other unavoidable causes of detention. The stage company had everything under strict discipline and good system. Over each two hundred and fifty miles of road they placed an agent or superintendent, and invested him with great authority. His beat or jurisdiction of two hundred and fifty miles was called a "division." He purchased horses, mules harness, and food for men and beasts, and distributed these things among his stage stations, from time to time, according to his judgment of what each station needed. He erected station buildings and dug wells. He attended to the paying of the station-keepers, hostlers, drivers and blacksmiths, and discharged them whenever he chose. He was a very, very great man in his "division"—a kind of Grand Mogul, a Sultan of the Indies, in whose presence common men were modest of speech and manner, and in the glare of whose greatness even the dazzling stage-driver dwindled to a penny dip. There were about eight of these kings, all told, on the overland route.

Next in rank and importance to the division-agent came the "conductor." His beat was the same length as the agent's—two hundred and fifty miles. He sat with the driver, and (when necessary) rode that fearful distance, night and day, without other rest or sleep than what he could get perched thus on top of the flying vehicle. Think of it! He had absolute charge of the mails, express matter, passengers, and stage-coach, until he delivered them to the next conductor, and got his receipt for them. Consequently he had to be a man of intelligence, decision and considerable executive ability. He was usually a quiet, pleasant man, who attended closely to his duties, and was a good deal of a gentleman. It was not absolutely necessary that the division-agent should be a gentleman, and occasionally he wasn't. But he was always a general in administrative ability, and a bulldog in courage and determination—otherwise the chieftainship over the lawless underlings of the overland service would never in any instance have been to him anything but an equivalent for a month of insolence and distress and a bullet and a coffin at the end of it. There were about sixteen or eighteen conductors on the overland, for there was a daily stage each way, and a conductor on every stage.

Next in *real* and official rank and importance, *after* the conductor, came my delight, the driver—next in real but not *apparent* importance—for we have seen that in the eyes of the common herd the driver was to the conductor as an admiral is to the captain of the flag-ship. The driver's beat was pretty long, and his sleeping-time at the stations pretty short, sometimes; and so, but for the grandeur of his position his would have been a sorry life, as well as a hard and a wearing one. We took a new driver every day or every night (for they drove backward and forward over the same piece of road all the time), and therefore we never got as well acquainted with them as we did with the conductors; and besides, they would have been above being familiar with such rubbish as passengers, anyhow, as a general thing. Still, we were always eager to get a sight of each and every new driver as soon as the watch changed, for each and every day we were either anxious to get rid of an unpleasant one, or loath to part with a driver we had learned to like and had come to be sociable and friendly with. And so the first question we asked the conductor whenever we got to where we were to exchange drivers, was always, "Which is him?" The grammar was faulty, maybe, but we could not know, then, that it would go into a book some day. As long as everything went smoothly, the overland driver was well enough situated, but if a fellow driver got sick suddenly it made trouble, for the coach *must* go on, and so the potentate who was about to climb down and take a luxurious rest after his long night's siege in the midst of wind and rain and darkness, had to stay where he was and do the sick man's work. Once, in the Rocky Mountains, when I found a driver sound asleep on the box, and the mules going at the usual break-neck pace, the conductor said never mind him, there was no danger, and he was doing double duty—had driven seventy-five miles on one coach, and was now going back over it on this without rest or sleep. A hundred and fifty miles of holding back of six vindictive mules and keeping them from climbing the trees! It sounds incredible, but I remember the statement well enough.

The station-keepers, hostlers, etc., were low, rough characters, as already described; and from western Nebraska to Nevada a considerable sprinkling of them might be fairly set down as outlaws—fugitives from justice, criminals whose best security was a section of country which was without law and without even the pretence of it. When the "division-agent" issued an order to one of these parties he did it with the full understanding that he might have to enforce it with a navy six-shooter, and so he always went "fixed" to make things go along smoothly. Now and then a division-agent was really obliged to shoot a hostler through the head to teach him some simple matter that he could have taught him with a club if his circumstances and surroundings had been different. But they were snappy, able men, those division-agents, and when they tried to teach a subordinate anything, that subordinate generally "got it through his head."

A great portion of this vast machinery—these hundreds of men and coaches, and thousands of mules and horses—was in the hands of Mr. Ben Holliday. All the western half of the business was in his hands. This reminds me of an incident of Palestine travel which is pertinent here, and so I will transfer it just in the language in which I find it set down in my Holy Land note-book:

No doubt everybody has heard of Ben Holliday—a man of prodigious energy, who used to send mails and passengers flying across the continent in his overland stage-coaches like a very whirlwind—two thousand long miles in fifteen days and a half, by the watch! But this fragment of history is not about Ben Holliday, but about a young New York boy by the name of Jack, who traveled with our small party of pilgrims in the Holy Land (and who had traveled to California in Mr. Holliday's overland coaches three years before, and had by no means forgotten it or lost his gushing admiration of Mr. H.) Aged nineteen. Jack was a good boy—a good-hearted and always well-meaning boy, who had been reared in the city of New York, and although he was bright and knew a great many useful things, his Scriptural education had been a good deal neglected—to such a degree, indeed, that all Holy Land history was fresh and new to him, and all Bible names mysteries that had never disturbed his virgin ear. Also in our party was an elderly pilgrim who was the reverse of Jack, in that he was learned in the Scriptures and an enthusiast concerning them. He was our encyclopedia, and we were never tired of listening to his speeches, nor he of making them. He never passed a celebrated locality, from Bashan to Bethlehem, without illuminating it with an oration. One day, when camped near the ruins of Jericho, he burst forth with something like this:

"Jack, do you see that range of mountains over yonder that bounds the Jordan valley? The mountains of Moab, Jack! Think of it, my boy—the actual mountains of Moab—renowned in Scripture history! We are actually standing face to face with those illustrious crags and peaks—and for all we know"]dropping his voice impressively], "*our eyes may be resting at this very moment upon the spot* WHERE LIES THE MYSTERIOUS GRAVE OF MOSES! Think of it, Jack!"

"Moses *who?*" (falling inflection).

"Moses *who!* Jack, you ought to be ashamed of yourself— you ought to be ashamed of such criminal ignorance. Why, Moses, the great guide, soldier, poet, lawgiver of ancient Israel! Jack, from this spot where we stand, to Egypt, stretches a fearful desert three hundred miles in extent—and across that desert that wonderful man brought the children of Israel!—guiding them with unfailing sagacity for forty years over the sandy desolation and among the obstructing rocks and hills, and landed them at last, safe and sound, with insight of this very spot; and where we now stand they entered the Promised Land with anthems of rejoicing! It was a wonderful, wonderful thing to do, Jack! Think of it!"

"*Forty years? Only three hundred miles?* Humph! Ben Holliday would have fetched them through in thirty-six hours!"

The boy meant no harm. He did not know that he had said anything that was wrong or irreverent. And so no one scolded him or felt offended with him—and nobody *could* but some ungenerous spirit incapable of excusing the heedless blunders of a boy.

At noon on the fifth day out, we arrived at the "Crossing of the South Platte," *alias* "Julesburg," *alias* "Overland City," four hundred and seventy miles from St. Joseph—the strangest, quaintest, funniest frontier town that our untraveled eyes had ever stared at and been astonished with.

CHAPTER VII

It did seem strange enough to see a town again after what appeared to us such a long acquaintance with deep, still, almost lifeless and houseless solitude! We tumbled out into the busy street feeling like meteoric people crumbled off the corner of some other world, and wakened up suddenly in this. For an hour we took as much interest in Overland City as if we had never seen a town before. The reason we had an hour to spare was because we had to change out stage (for a less sumptuous affair, called a "mud-wagon") and transfer our freight of mails.

Presently we got under way again. We came to the shallow, yellow, muddy South Platte, with its low banks and its scattering flat sand-bars and pigmy islands—a melancholy stream straggling through the centre of the enormous flat plain, and only saved from being impossible to find with the naked eye by its sentinel rank of scattering trees standing on either bank. The Platte was "up," they said—which made me wish I could see it when it was down, if it could look any sicker and sorrier. They said it was a dangerous stream to cross, now, because its quicksands were liable to swallow up horses, coach and passengers if an attempt was made to ford it. But the mails had to go, and we made the attempt. Once or twice in midstream the wheels sunk into the yielding sands so threateningly that we half believed we had dreaded and avoided the sea all our lives to be shipwrecked in a "mud-wagon" in the middle of a desert at last. But we dragged through and sped away toward the setting sun.

Next morning, just before dawn, when about five hundred and fifty miles from St. Joseph, our mud-wagon broke down. We were to be delayed five or six hours, and therefore we took horses, by invitation, and joined a party who were just starting on a buffalo hunt. It was noble sport galloping over the plain in the dewy freshness of the morning, but our part of the hunt ended in disaster and disgrace, for a wounded buffalo bull chased the passenger Bemis nearly two miles, and then he forsook his horse and took to a lone tree. He was very sullen about the matter for some twenty-four hours, but at last he began to soften little by little, and finally he said:

"Well, it was not funny, and there was no sense in those gawks making themselves so facetious over it. I tell you I was angry in earnest for awhile. I should have shot that long gangly lubber they called Hank, if I could have done it without crippling six or seven other people—but of course I couldn't, the old 'Allen's' so confounded comprehensive. I wish those loafers had been up in the tree; they wouldn't have wanted to laugh so. If I had had a horse worth a cent—but no, the minute he saw that buffalo bull wheel on him and give a bellow, he raised straight up in the air and stood on his heels. The saddle began to slip, and I took him round the neck and laid close to him, and began to pray. Then he came down and stood up on the other end awhile, and the bull actually stopped pawing sand and bellowing to contemplate the inhuman spectacle. Then the bull made a pass at him and uttered a bellow that sounded perfectly frightful, it was so close to me, and that seemed to literally prostrate my horse's reason, and make a raving distracted maniac of him, and I wish I may die if he didn't stand on his head for a quarter of a minute and shed tears. He was absolutely out of his mind—he was, as sure as truth itself, and he really didn't know what he was doing. Then the bull came charging at us, and my horse dropped down on all fours and took a fresh start—and then for the next ten minutes he would actually throw one handspring after another so fast that the bull began to get unsettled, too, and didn't know where to start in—and so he stood there sneezing, and shovelling dust over his back, and bellowing every now and them, and thinking he had got a fifteen-hundred dollar circus horse for breakfast, certain. Well, I was first out on his neck—the horse's, not the bull's—and then underneath, and next on his rump, and sometimes head up, and sometimes heels—but I tell you it seemed solemn and awful to be ripping and tearing and carrying on so in the presence of death, as you might say. Pretty soon the bull made a snatch for us and brought away some of my horse's tail (I suppose, but do not know, being pretty busy at the time), but *something* made him hungry for solitude and suggested to him to get up and hunt for it. And then you ought to have seen that spider-legged old skeleton go! and you ought to have seen the bull cut out after him, too—head down, tongue out, tail up, bellowing like everything, and actually mowing down the weeds, and tearing up the earth, and boosting up the sand like a whirlwind! By George, it was a hot race! I and the saddle were back on the rump, and I had the bridle in my teeth and holding on to the pommel with both hands. First we left the dogs behind; then we passed a jackass rabbit; then we overtook a cayote, and were gaining on an antelope when the rotten girth let go and threw me about thirty yards off to the left, and as the saddle went down over the horse's rump he gave it a lift with his heels that sent it more than four hundred yards up in the air, I wish I may die in a minute if he didn't. I fell at the foot of the only solitary tree there was in nine counties adjacent (as any creature could see with the naked eye), and the next second I had hold of the bark with four sets of nails and my teeth, and the next second after that I was astraddle of the main limb and blaspheming my luck in a way that made my breath smell of brimstone. I *had* the bull, now, if he did not think of *one* thing. But that one thing I dreaded. I dreaded it very seriously. There was a possibility that the bull might not think of it, but there were greater chances that he would. I made up my mind what I would do in case he did. It was a little over forty feet to the ground from where I sat. I cautiously unwound the lariat from the pommel of my saddle—"

"Your *saddle?* Did you take your saddle up in the tree with you?"

"Take it up in the tree with me? Why, how you talk. Of course I didn't. No man could do that. It *fell* in the tree when it came down."

"Oh—exactly."

"Certainly. I unwound the lariat, and fastened one end of it to the limb. It was the very best green raw-hide, and capable of sustaining tons. I made a slip-noose in the other end, and then hung it down to see the length. It reached down twenty-two feet—half way to the ground. I then loaded every barrel of the Allen with a double charge. I felt satisfied. I said to myself, if he never thinks of that one thing that I dread, all right—but if he does, all right anyhow—I am fixed for him. But don't you know that the very thing a man dreads is the thing that always happens? Indeed it is so. I watched the bull, now, with anxiety—anxiety which no one can conceive of who has not been in such a situation and felt that at any moment death might come. Presently a thought came into the bull's eye. I knew it! said I—if my nerve fails now, I am lost. Sure enough, it was just as I had dreaded, he started in to climb the tree—"

"What, the bull?"

"Of course—who else?"

"But a bull can't climb a tree."

"He can't, can't he? Since you know so much about it, did you ever see a bull try?"

"No! I never dreamt of such a thing."

"Well, then, what is the use of your talking that way, then? Because you never saw a thing done, is that any reason why it can't be done?"

"Well, all right—go on. What did you do?"

"The bull started up, and got along well for about ten feet, then slipped and slid back. I breathed easier. He tried it again—got up a little higher—slipped again. But he came at it once more, and this time he was careful. He got gradually higher and higher, and my spirits went down more and more. Up he came—an inch at a time—with his eyes hot, and his tongue hanging out. Higher and higher—hitched his foot over the stump of a limb, and looked up, as much as to say, 'You are my meat, friend.' Up again—higher and higher, and getting more excited the closer he got. He was within ten feet of me! I took a long breath,—and then said I, 'It is now or never.' I had the coil of the lariat all ready; I paid it out slowly, till it hung right over his head; all of a sudden I let go of the slack, and the slipnoose fell fairly round his neck! Quicker than lightning I out with the Allen and let him have it in the face. It was an awful roar, and must have scared the bull out of his senses. When the smoke cleared away, there he was, dangling in the air, twenty foot from the ground, and going out of one convulsion into another faster than you could count! I didn't stop to count, anyhow—I shinned down the tree and shot for home."

"Bemis, is all that true, just as you have stated it?"

"I wish I may rot in my tracks and die the death of a dog if it isn't."

"Well, we can't refuse to believe it, and we don't. But if there were some proofs—"

"Proofs! Did I bring back my lariat?"

"No."

"Did I bring back my horse?"

"No."

"Did you ever see the bull again?"

"No."

"Well, then, what more do you want? I never saw anybody as particular as you are about a little thing like that."

I made up my mind that if this man was not a liar he only missed it by the skin of his teeth. This episode reminds me of an incident of my brief sojourn in Siam, years afterward. The European citizens of a town in the neighborhood of Bangkok had a prodigy among them by the name of Eckert, an Englishman—a person famous for the number, ingenuity and imposing magnitude of his lies. They were always repeating his most celebrated falsehoods, and always trying to "draw him out" before strangers; but they seldom succeeded. Twice he was invited to the house where I was visiting, but nothing could seduce him into a specimen lie. One day a planter named Bascom, an influential man, and a proud and sometimes irascible one, invited me to ride over with him and call on Eckert. As we jogged along, said he:

"Now, do you know where the fault lies? It lies in putting Eckert on his guard. The minute the boys go to pumping at Eckert he knows perfectly well what they are after, and of course he shuts up his shell. Anybody might know he would. But when we get there, we must play him finer than that. Let him shape the conversation to suit himself—let him drop it or change it whenever he wants to. Let him see that nobody is trying to draw him out. Just let him have his own way. He will soon forget himself and begin to grind out lies like a mill. Don't get impatient—just keep quiet, and let me play him. I will make him lie. It does seem to me that the boys must be blind to overlook such an obvious and simple trick as that."

Eckert received us heartily—a pleasant-spoken, gentlemannered creature. We sat in the veranda an hour, sipping English ale, and talking about the king, and the sacred white elephant, the Sleeping Idol, and all manner of things; and I noticed that my comrade never led the conversation himself or shaped it, but simply followed Eckert's lead, and betrayed no solicitude and no anxiety about anything. The effect was shortly perceptible. Eckert began to grow communicative; he grew more and more at his ease, and more and more talkative and sociable. Another hour passed in the same way, and then all of a sudden Eckert said:

"Oh, by the way! I came near forgetting. I have got a thing here to astonish you. Such a thing as neither you nor any other man ever heard of—I've got a cat that will eat cocoanut! Common green cocoanut—and not only eat the meat, but drink the milk. It is so—I'll swear to it."

A quick glance from Bascom—a glance that I understood—then:

"Why, bless my soul, I never heard of such a thing. Man, it is impossible."

"I knew you would say it. I'll fetch the cat."

He went in the house. Bascom said:

"There—what did I tell you? Now, that is the way to handle Eckert. You see, I have petted him along patiently, and put his suspicions to sleep. I am glad we came. You tell the boys about it when you go back. Cat eat a cocoanut—oh, my! Now, that is just his way, exactly—he will tell the absurdest lie, and trust to luck to get out of it again. Cat eat a cocoanut—the innocent fool!"

Eckert approached with his cat, sure enough.

Bascom smiled. Said he:

"I'll hold the cat—you bring a cocoanut."

Eckert split one open, and chopped up some pieces. Bascom smuggled a wink to me, and proffered a slice of the fruit to puss. She snatched it, swallowed it ravenously, and asked for more!

We rode our two miles in silence, and wide apart. At least I was silent, though Bascom cuffed his horse and cursed him a good deal, notwithstanding the horse was behaving well enough. When I branched off homeward, Bascom said:

"Keep the horse till morning. And—you need not speak of this—foolishness to the boys."

CHAPTER VIII

In a little while all interest was taken up in stretching our necks and watching for the "pony-rider"—the fleet messenger who sped across the continent from St. Joe to Sacramento, carrying letters nineteen hundred miles in eight days! Think of that for perishable horse and human flesh and blood to do! The pony-rider was usually a little bit of a man, brimful of spirit and endurance. No matter what time of the day or night his watch came on, and no matter whether it was winter or summer, raining, snowing, hailing, or sleeting, or whether his "beat" was a level straight road or a crazy trail over mountain crags and precipices, or whether it led through peaceful regions or regions that swarmed with hostile Indians, he must be always ready to leap into the saddle and be off like the wind! There was no idling-time for a pony-rider on duty. He rode fifty miles without stopping, by daylight, moonlight, starlight, or through the blackness of darkness—just as it happened. He rode a splendid horse that was born for a racer and fed and lodged like a gentleman; kept him at his utmost speed for ten miles, and then, as he came crashing up to the station where stood two men holding fast a fresh, impatient steed, the transfer of rider and mail-bag was made in the twinkling of an eye, and away flew the eager pair and were out of sight before the spectator could get hardly the ghost of a look. Both rider and horse went "flying light." The rider's dress was thin, and fitted close; he wore a "roundabout," and a skull-cap, and tucked his pantaloons into his boot-tops like a race-rider. He carried no arms—he carried nothing that was not absolutely necessary, for even the postage on his literary freight was worth *five dollars a letter*. He got but little frivolous correspondence to carry—his bag had business letters in it, mostly. His horse was stripped of all unnecessary weight, too. He wore a little wafer of a racing-saddle, and no visible blanket. He wore light shoes, or none at all. The little flat mail-pockets strapped under the rider's thighs would each hold about the bulk of a child's primer. They held many and many an important business chapter and newspaper letter, but these were written on paper as airy and thin as gold-leaf, nearly, and thus bulk and weight were economized. The stage-coach traveled about a hundred to a hundred and twenty-five miles a day (twenty-four hours), the pony-rider about two hundred and fifty. There were about eighty pony-riders in the saddle all the time, night and day, stretching in a long, scattering procession from Missouri to California, forty flying eastward, and forty toward the west, and among them making four hundred gallant horses earn a stirring livelihood and see a deal of scenery every single day in the year.

We had had a consuming desire, from the beginning, to see a pony-rider, but somehow or other all that passed us and all that met us managed to streak by in the night, and so we heard only a whiz and a hail, and the swift phantom of the desert was gone before we could get our heads out of the windows. But now we were expecting one along every moment, and would see him in broad daylight. Presently the driver exclaims:

"HERE HE COMES!"

Every neck is stretched further, and every eye strained wider. Away across the endless dead level of the prairie a black speck appears against the sky, and it is plain that it moves. Well, I should think so! In a second or two it becomes a horse and rider, rising and falling, rising and falling—sweeping toward us nearer and nearer—growing more and more distinct, more and more sharply defined—nearer and still nearer, and the flutter of the hoofs comes faintly to the ear—another instant a whoop and a hurrah from our upper deck, a wave of the rider's hand, but no reply, and man and horse burst past our excited faces, and go winging away like a belated fragment of a storm!

So sudden is it all, and so like a flash of unreal fancy, that but for the flake of white foam left quivering and perishing on a mail-sack after the vision had flashed by and disappeared, we might have doubted whether we had seen any actual horse and man at all, maybe.

We rattled through Scott's Bluffs Pass, by and by. It was along here somewhere that we first came across genuine and unmistakable alkali water in the road, and we cordially hailed it as a first-class curiosity, and a thing to be mentioned with eclat in letters to the ignorant at home. This water gave the road a soapy appearance, and in many places the ground looked as if it had been whitewashed. I think the strange alkali water excited us as much as any wonder we had come upon yet, and I know we felt very complacent and conceited, and better satisfied with life after we had added it to our list of things which *we* had seen and some other people had not. In a small way we were the same sort of simpletons as those who climb unnecessarily the perilous peaks of Mont Blanc and the Matterhorn, and derive no pleasure from it except the reflection that it isn't a common experience. But once in a while one of those parties trips and comes darting down the long mountain-crags in a sitting posture, making the crusted snow smoke behind him, flitting from bench to bench, and from terrace to terrace, jarring the earth where he strikes, and still glancing and flitting on again, sticking an iceberg into himself every now and then, and tearing his clothes, snatching at things to save himself, taking hold of trees and fetching them along with him, roots and all, starting little rocks now and then, then big boulders, then acres of ice and snow and patches of forest, gathering and still gathering as he goes, adding and still adding to his massed and sweeping grandeur as he nears a three thousand-foot precipice, till at last he waves his hat magnificently and rides into eternity on the back of a raging and tossing avalanche!

This is all very fine, but let us not be carried away by excitement, but ask calmly, how does this person feel about it in his cooler moments next day, with six or seven thousand feet of snow and stuff on top of him?

We crossed the sand hills near the scene of the Indian mail robbery and massacre of 1856, wherein the driver and conductor perished, and also all the passengers but one, it was supposed; but this must have been a mistake, for at different times afterward on the Pacific coast I was personally acquainted with a hundred and thirty-three or four people who were wounded during that massacre, and barely escaped with their lives. There was no doubt of the truth of it—I had it from their own lips. One of these parties told me that he kept coming across arrow-heads in his system for nearly seven years after the massacre; and another of them told me that he was stuck so literally full of arrows that after the Indians were gone and he could raise up and examine himself, he could not restrain his tears, for his clothes were completely ruined.

The most trustworthy tradition avers, however, that only one man, a person named Babbitt, survived the massacre, and he was desperately wounded. He dragged himself on his hands and knee (for one leg was broken) to a station several miles away. He did it during portions of two nights, lying concealed one day and part of another, and for more than forty hours suffering unimaginable anguish from hunger, thirst and bodily pain. The Indians robbed the coach of everything it contained, including quite an amount of treasure.

CHAPTER IX

We passed Fort Laramie in the night, and on the seventh morning out we found ourselves in the Black Hills, with Laramie Peak at our elbow (apparently) looming vast and solitary—a deep, dark, rich indigo blue in hue, so portentously did the old colossus frown under his beetling brows of storm-cloud. He was thirty or forty miles away, in reality, but he only seemed removed a little beyond the low ridge at our right. We breakfasted at Horse-Shoe Station, six hundred and seventy-six miles out from St. Joseph. We had now reached a hostile Indian country, and during the afternoon we passed Laparelle Station, and enjoyed great discomfort all the time we were in the neighborhood, being aware that many of the trees we dashed by at arm's length concealed a lurking Indian or two. During the preceding night an ambushed savage had sent a bullet through the pony-rider's jacket, but he had ridden on, just the same, because pony-riders were not allowed to stop and inquire into such things except when killed. As long as they had life enough left in them they had to stick to the horse and ride, even if the Indians had been waiting for them a week, and were entirely out of patience.

About two hours and a half before we arrived at Laparelle Station, the keeper in charge of it had fired four times at an Indian, but he said with an injured air that the Indian had "skipped around so's to spile everything—and ammunition's blamed skurse, too." The most natural inference conveyed by his manner of speaking was, that in "skipping around," the Indian had taken an unfair advantage. The coach we were in had a neat hold through its front—a reminiscence of its last trip through this region. The bullet that made it wounded the driver slightly, but he did not mind it much. He said the place to keep a man "huffy" was down on the Southern Overland, among the Apaches, before the company moved the stageline up on the northern route. He said the Apaches used to annoy him all the time down there, and that he came as near as anything to starving to death in the midst of abundance, because they kept him so leaky with bullet holes that he "couldn't hold his vittles." This person's statement were not generally believed.

We shut the blinds down very tightly that first night in the hostile Indian country, and lay on our arms. We slept on them some, but most of the time we only lay on them. We did not talk much, but kept quiet and listened. It was an inky-black night, and occasionally rainy. We were among woods and rocks, hills and gorges—so shut in, in fact, that when we peeped through a chink in a curtain, we could discern nothing. The driver and conductor on top were still, too, or only spoke at long intervals, in low tones, as is the way of men in the midst of invisible dangers. We listened to rain-drops pattering on the roof; and the grinding of the wheels through the muddy gravel; and the low wailing of the wind; and all the time we had that absurd sense upon us, inseparable from travel at night in a close-curtained vehicle, the sense of remaining perfectly still in one place, notwithstanding the jolting and swaying of the vehicle, the trampling of the horses, and the grinding of the wheels. We listened a long time, with intent faculties and bated breath; every time one of us would relax, and draw a long sigh of relief and start to say something, a comrade would be sure to utter a sudden "Hark!" and instantly the experimenter was rigid and listening again. So the tiresome minutes and decades of minutes dragged away, until at last our tense forms filmed over with a dulled consciousness, and we slept, if one might call such a condition by so strong a name—for it was a sleep set with a hair-trigger. It was a sleep seething and teeming with a weird and distressful confusion of shreds and fag-ends of dreams—a sleep that was a chaos. Presently, dreams and sleep and the sullen hush of the night were startled by a ringing report, and cloven by *such* a long, wild, agonizing shriek! Then we heard—ten steps from the stage—

"Help! help! help!" [It was our driver's voice.]

"Kill him! Kill him like a dog!"

"I'm being murdered! Will no man lend me a pistol?"

"Look out! head him off! head him off!"

[Two pistol shots; a confusion of voices and the trampling of many feet, as if a crowd were closing and surging together around some object; several heavy, dull blows, as with a club; a voice that said appealingly, "Don't, gentlemen, please don't—I'm a dead man!" Then a fainter groan, and another blow, and away sped the stage into the darkness, and left the grisly mystery behind us.]

What a startle it was! Eight seconds would amply cover the time it occupied—maybe even five would do it. We only had time to plunge at a curtain and unbuckle and unbutton part of it in an awkward and hindering flurry, when our whip cracked sharply overhead, and we went rumbling and thundering away, down a mountain "grade."

We fed on that mystery the rest of the night—what was left of it, for it was waning fast. It had to remain a present mystery, for all we could get from the conductor in answer to our hails was something that sounded, through the clatter of the wheels, like "Tell you in the morning!"

So we lit our pipes and opened the corner of a curtain for a chimney, and lay there in the dark, listening to each other's story of how he first felt and how many thousand Indians he first thought had hurled themselves upon us, and what his remembrance of the subsequent sounds was, and the order of their occurrence. And we theorized, too, but there was never a theory that would account for our driver's voice being out there, nor yet account for his Indian murderers talking such good English, if they *were* Indians.

So we chatted and smoked the rest of the night comfortably away, our boding anxiety being somehow marvelously dissipated by the real presence of something to be anxious *about*.

We never did get much satisfaction about that dark occurrence. All that we could make out of the odds and ends of the information we gathered in the morning, was that the disturbance occurred at a station; that we changed drivers there, and that the driver that got off there had been talking roughly about some of the outlaws that infested the region ("for there wasn't a man around there but had a price on his head and didn't dare show himself in the settlements," the conductor said); he had talked roughly about these characters, and ought to have "drove up there with his pistol cocked and ready on the seat alongside of him, and begun business himself, because any softy would know they would be laying for him."

That was all we could gather, and we could see that neither the conductor nor the new driver were much concerned about the matter. They plainly had little respect for a man who would deliver offensive opinions of people and then be so simple as to come into their presence unprepared to "back his judgment," as they pleasantly phrased the killing of any fellow-being who did not like said opinions. And likewise they plainly had a contempt for the man's poor discretion in venturing to rouse the wrath of such utterly reckless wild beasts as those outlaws—and the conductor added:

"I tell you it's as much as Slade himself wants to do!"

This remark created an entire revolution in my curiosity. I cared nothing now about the Indians, and even lost interest in the murdered driver. There was such magic in that name, SLADE! Day or night, now, I stood always ready to drop any subject in hand, to listen to something new about Slade and his ghastly exploits. Even before we got to Overland City, we had begun to hear about Slade and his "division" (for he was a "division-agent") on the Overland; and from the hour we had left Overland City we had heard drivers and conductors talk about only three things—"Californy," the Nevada silver mines, and this desperado Slade. And a deal the most of the talk was about Slade. We had gradually come to have a realizing sense of the fact that Slade was a man whose heart and hands and soul were steeped in the blood of offenders against his dignity; a man who awfully avenged all injuries, affronts, insults or slights, of whatever kind—on the spot if he could, years afterward if lack of earlier opportunity compelled it; a man whose hate tortured him day and night till vengeance appeased it—and not an ordinary vengeance either, but his enemy's absolute death— nothing less; a man whose face would light up with a terrible joy when he surprised a foe and had him at a disadvantage. A high and efficient servant of the Overland, an outlaw among outlaws and yet their relentless scourge, Slade was at once the most bloody, the most dangerous and the most valuable citizen that inhabited the savage fastnesses of the mountains.

CHAPTER X

Really and truly, two thirds of the talk of drivers and conductors had been about this man Slade, ever since the day before we reached Julesburg. In order that the eastern reader may have a clear conception of what a Rocky Mountain desperado is, in his highest state of development, I will reduce all this mass of overland gossip to one straightforward narrative, and present it in the following shape:

Slade was born in Illinois, of good parentage. At about twenty-six years of age he killed a man in a quarrel and fled the country. At St. Joseph, Missouri, he joined one of the early California-bound emigrant trains, and was given the post of train-master. One day on the plains he had an angry dispute with one of his wagon-drivers, and both drew their revolvers. But the driver was the quicker artist, and had his weapon cocked first. So Slade said it was a pity to waste life on so small a matter, and proposed that the pistols be thrown on the ground and the quarrel settled by a fist-fight. The unsuspecting driver agreed, and threw down his pistol—whereupon Slade laughed at his simplicity, and shot him dead!

He made his escape, and lived a wild life for awhile, dividing his time between fighting Indians and avoiding an Illinois sheriff, who had been sent to arrest him for his first murder. It is said that in one Indian battle he killed three savages with his own hand, and afterward cut their ears off and sent them, with his compliments, to the chief of the tribe.

Slade soon gained a name for fearless resolution, and this was sufficient merit to procure for him the important post of overland division-agent at Julesburg, in place of Mr. Jules, removed. For some time previously, the company's horses had been frequently stolen, and the coaches delayed, by gangs of outlaws, who were wont to laugh at the idea of any man's having the temerity to resent such outrages. Slade resented them promptly. The outlaws soon found that the new agent was a man who did not fear anything that breathed the breath of life. He made short work of all offenders. The result was that delays ceased, the company's property was let alone, and no matter what happened or who suffered, Slade's coaches went through, every time! True, in order to bring about this wholesome change, Slade had to kill several men—some say three, others say four, and others six—but the world was the richer for their loss. The first prominent difficulty he had was with the ex-agent Jules, who bore the reputation of being a reckless and desperate man himself. Jules hated Slade for supplanting him, and a good fair occasion for a fight was all he was waiting for. By and by Slade dared to employ a man whom Jules had once discharged. Next, Slade seized a team of stage-horses which he accused Jules of having driven off and hidden somewhere for his own use. War was declared, and for a day or two the two men walked warily about the streets, seeking each other, Jules armed with a double-barreled shot gun, and Slade with his history-creating revolver. Finally, as Slade stepped into a store, Jules poured the contents of his gun into him from behind the door. Slade was pluck, and Jules got several bad pistol wounds in return. Then both men fell, and were carried to their respective lodgings, both swearing that better aim should do deadlier work next time. Both were bedridden a long time, but Jules got on his feet first, and gathering his possessions together, packed them on a couple of mules, and fled to the Rocky Mountains to gather strength in safety against the day of reckoning. For many months he was not seen or heard of, and was gradually dropped out of the remembrance of all save Slade himself. But Slade was not the man to forget him. On the contrary, common report said that Slade kept a reward standing for his capture, dead or alive!

After awhile, seeing that Slade's energetic administration had restored peace and order to one of the worst divisions of the road, the overland stage company transferred him to the Rocky Ridge division in the Rocky Mountains, to see if he could perform a like miracle there. It was the very paradise of outlaws and desperadoes. There was absolutely no semblance of law there. Violence was the rule. Force was the only recognized authority. The commonest misunderstandings were settled on the spot with the revolver or the knife. Murders were done in open day, and with sparkling frequency, and nobody thought of inquiring into them. It was considered that the parties who did the killing had their private reasons for it; for other people to meddle would have been looked upon as indelicate. After a murder, all that Rocky Mountain etiquette required of a spectator was, that he should help the gentleman bury his game—otherwise his churlishness would surely be remembered against him the first time he killed a man himself and needed a neighborly turn in interring him.

Slade took up his residence sweetly and peacefully in the midst of this hive of horse-thieves and assassins, and the very first time one of them aired his insolent swaggerings in his presence he shot him dead! He began a raid on the outlaws, and in a singularly short space of time he had completely stopped their depredations on the stage stock, recovered a large number of stolen horses, killed several of the worst desperadoes of the district, and gained such a dread ascendancy over the rest that they respected him, admired him, feared him, obeyed him! He wrought the same marvelous change in the ways of the community that had marked his administration at Overland City. He captured two men who had stolen overland stock, and with his own hands he hanged them. He was supreme judge in his district, and he was jury and executioner likewise—and not only in the case of offences against his employers, but against passing emigrants as well. On one occasion some emigrants had their stock lost or stolen, and told Slade, who chanced to visit their camp. With a single companion he rode to a ranch, the owners of which he suspected, and opening the door, commenced firing, killing three, and wounding the fourth.

From a bloodthirstily interesting little Montana book* I take this paragraph:

> While on the road, Slade held absolute sway. He would ride down to a station, get into a quarrel, turn the house out of windows, and maltreat the occupants most cruelly. The unfortunates had no means of redress, and were compelled to recuperate as best they could. On one of these occasions, it is said he killed the father of the fine little half-breed boy Jemmy, whom he adopted, and who lived with his widow after his execution. Stories of Slade's hanging men, and of innumerable assaults, shootings, stabbings and beatings, in which he was a principal actor, form part of the legends of the stage line. As for minor quarrels and shootings, it is absolutely certain that a minute history of Slade's life would be one long record of such practices.

Slade was a matchless marksman with a navy revolver. The legends say that one morning at Rocky Ridge, when he was feeling comfortable, he saw a man approaching who had offended him some days before—observe the fine memory he had for matters like that—and, "Gentleman," said Slade, drawing, "it is a good twenty-yard shot—I'll clip the third button on his coat!" Which he did. The bystanders all admired it. And they all attended the funeral, too.

On one occasion a man who kept a little whisky-shelf at the station did something which angered Slade—and went and made his will. A day or two afterward Slade came in and called for some brandy. The man reached under the counter (ostensibly to get a bottle—possibly to get something else), but Slade smiled upon him that peculiarly bland and satisfied smile of his which the neighbors had long ago learned to recognize as a death-warrant in disguise, and told him to "none of that!—pass out

*"The Vigilantes of Montana," by Prof. Thos. J. Dimsdale.

the high-priced article." So the poor bar-keeper had to turn his back and get the high-priced brandy from the shelf; and when he faced around again he was looking into the muzzle of Slade's pistol. "And the next instant," added my informant, impressively, "he was one of the deadest men that ever lived."

The stage-drivers and conductors told us that sometimes Slade would leave a hated enemy wholly unmolested, unnoticed and unmentioned, for weeks together—had done it once or twice at any rate. And some said they believed he did it in order to lull the victims into unwatchfulness, so that he could get the advantage of them, and others said they believed he saved up an enemy that way, just as a schoolboy saves up a cake, and made the pleasure go as far as it would by gloating over the anticipation. One of these cases was that of a Frenchman who had offended Slade. To the surprise of everybody Slade did not kill him on the spot, but let him alone for a considerable time. Finally, however, he went to the Frenchman's house very late one night, knocked, and when his enemy opened the door, shot him dead—pushed the corpse inside the door with his foot, set the house on fire and burned up the dead man, his widow and three children! I heard this story from several different people, and they evidently believed what they were saying. It may be true, and it may not. "Give a dog a bad name," etc.

Slade was captured, once, by a party of men who intended to lynch him. They disarmed him, and shut him up in a strong log-house, and placed a guard over him. He prevailed on his captors to send for his wife, so that he might have a last interview with her. She was a brave, loving, spirited woman. She jumped on a horse and rode for life and death. When she arrived they let her in without searching her, and before the door could be closed she whipped out a couple of revolvers, and she and her lord marched forth defying the party. And then, under a brisk fire, they mounted double and galloped away unharmed!

In the fulness of time Slade's myrmidons captured his ancient enemy Jules, whom they found in a well-chosen hiding-place in the remote fastnesses of the mountains, gaining a precarious livelihood with his rifle. They brought him to Rocky Ridge, bound hand and foot, and deposited him in the middle of the cattle-yard with his back against a post. It is said that the pleasure that lit Slade's face when he heard of it was something fearful to contemplate. He examined his enemy to see that he was securely tied, and then went to bed, content to wait till morning before enjoying the luxury of killing him. Jules spent the night in the cattle-yard, and it is a region where warm nights are never known. In the morning Slade practised on him with his revolver, nipping the flesh here and there, and occasionally clipping off a finger, while Jules begged him to kill him outright and put him out of his misery. Finally Slade reloaded, and walking up close to his victim, made some characteristic remarks and then dispatched him. The body lay there half a day, nobody venturing to touch it without orders, and then Slade detailed a party and assisted at the burial himself. But he first cut off the dead man's ears and put them in his vest pocket, where he carried them for some time with great satisfaction. That is the story as I have frequently heard it told and seen it in print in California newspapers. It is doubtless correct in all essential particulars.

In due time we rattled up to a stage-station, and sat down to breakfast with a half-savage, half-civilized company of armed and bearded mountaineers, ranchmen and station employees. The most gentlemanly-appearing, quiet and affable officer we had yet found along the road in the Overland Company's service was the person who sat at the head of the table, at my elbow. Never youth stared and shivered as I did when I heard them call him SLADE!

Here was romance, and I sitting face to face with it!—looking upon it—touching it—hobnobbing with it, as it were! Here, right by my side, was the actual ogre who, in fights and brawls and various ways, *had taken the lives of twenty-six human beings,* or all men lied about him! I suppose I was the proudest stripling that ever traveled to see strange lands and wonderful people.

He was so friendly and so gentle-spoken that I warmed to him in spite of his awful history. It was hardly possible to realize that this pleasant person was the pitiless scourge of the outlaws, the raw-head-and-bloody-bones the nursing mothers of the mountains terrified their children with. And to this day I can remember nothing remarkable about Slade except that his face was rather broad across the cheek bones, and that the cheek bones were low and the lips peculiarly thin and straight. But that was enough to leave something of an effect upon me, for since then I seldom see a face possessing those characteristics without fancying that the owner of it is a dangerous man.

The coffee ran out. At least it was reduced to one tin-cupful, and Slade was about to take it when he saw that my cup was empty. He politely offered to fill it, but although I wanted it, I politely declined. I was afraid he had not killed anybody that morning, and might be needing diversion. But still with firm politeness he insisted on filling my cup, and said I had traveled all night and better deserved it than he—and while he talked he placidly poured the fluid, to the last drop. I thanked him and drank it, but it gave me no comfort, for I could not feel sure that he would not be sorry, presently, that he had given it away, and proceed to kill me to distract his thoughts from the loss. But nothing of the kind occurred. We left him with only twenty-six dead people to account for, and I felt a tranquil satisfaction in the thought that in so judiciously taking care of No. 1 at that breakfast-table I had pleasantly escaped being No. 27. Slade came out to the coach and saw us off, first ordering certain rearrangements of the mail-bags for our comfort, and then we took leave of him, satisfied that we should hear of him again, some day, and wondering in what connection.

CHAPTER XI

And sure enough, two or three years afterward, we did hear of him again. News came to the Pacific coast that the Vigilance Committee in Montana (whither Slade had removed from Rocky Ridge) had hanged him. I find an account of the affair in the thrilling little book I quoted a paragraph from in the last chapter—"The Vigilantes of Montana; being a Reliable Account of the Capture, Trial and Execution of Henry Plummer's Notorious Road Agent Band: By Prof. Thos. J. Dimsdale, Virginia City, M.T." Mr. Dimsdale's chapter is well worth reading, as a specimen of how the people of the frontier deal with criminals when the courts of law prove inefficient. Mr. Dimsdale makes two remarks about Slade, both of which are accurately descriptive, and one of which is exceedingly picturesque: "Those who saw him in his natural state only, would pronounce him to be a kind husband, a most hospitable host and a courteous gentleman; on the contrary, those who met him when maddened with liquor and surrounded by a gang of armed roughs, would pronounce him a fiend incarnate." And this: "From Fort Kearney, west, he was feared *a great deal more than the Almighty.*" For compactness, simplicity and vigor of expression, I will "back" that sentence against anything in literature. Mr. Dimsdale's narrative is as follows. In all places where italics occur, they are mine:

After the execution of the five men on the 14th of January, the Vigilantes considered that their work was nearly ended. They had freed the country of highwaymen and murderers to a great extent, and they determined that in the absence of the regular civil authority they would establish a People's Court where all offenders should be tried by judge and jury. This was the nearest approach to social order that the circumstances permitted, and, though strict legal authority was wanting, yet the people were firmly determined to maintain its efficiency, and to enforce its decrees. It may here be mentioned that the overt act which was the last round on the fatal ladder leading to the scaffold on which Slade perished, *was the tearing in pieces and stamping upon a writ of this court, followed by his arrest of the Judge, Alex. Davis, by authority of a presented Derringer, and with his own hands.*

J.A. Slade was himself, we have been informed, a Vigilante; he openly boasted of it, and said he knew all that they knew. He was never accused, or even suspected, of either murder or robbery, committed in this Territory (the latter crime was never laid to his charge, in any place); but that he had killed several men in other localities was notorious, and his bad reputation in this respect was a most powerful argument in determining his fate, when he was finally arrested for the offence above mentioned. On returning from Milk River he became more and more addicted to drinking, until at last it was a common feat for him and his friends to "take the town." He and a couple of his dependents might often be seen on one horse, galloping through the streets, shouting and yelling, firing revolvers, etc. On many occasions he would ride his horse into stores, break up bars, toss the scales out of doors and use most insulting language to parties present. Just previous to the day of his arrest, he had given a fearful beating to one of his followers; but such was his influence over them that the man wept bitterly at the gallows, and begged for his life with all his power. *It had become quite common, when Slade was on a spree, for the shopkeepers and citizens to close the stores and put out all the lights;* being fearful of some outrage at his hands. For his wanton destruction of goods and furniture, he was always ready to pay, when sober, if he had money; but there were not a few who regarded payment as small satisfaction for the outrage, and these men were his personal enemies.

From time to time Slade received warnings from men that he well knew would not deceive him, of the certain end of his conduct. There was not a moment, for weeks previous to his arrest, in which the public did not expect to hear of some bloody outrage. The dread of his very name, and the presence of the armed band of hangers-on who followed him alone prevented a resistance which must certainly have ended in the instant murder or mutilation of the opposing party.

Slade was frequently arrested by order of the court whose organization we have described, and had treated it with respect by paying one or two fines and promising to pay the rest when he had money; but in the transaction that occurred at this crisis, he forgot even this caution, and goaded by passion and the hatred of restraint, he sprang into the embrace of death.

Slade had been drunk and "cutting up" all night. He and his companions had made the town a perfect hell. In the morning, J.M. Fox, the sheriff, met him, arrested him, took him into court and commenced reading a warrant that he had for his arrest, by way of arraignment. He became uncontrollably furious, and *seizing the writ, he tore it up, threw it on the ground and stamped upon it.* The clicking of the locks of his companions' revolvers was instantly heard, and a crisis was expected. The sheriff did not attempt his retention; but being at least as prudent as he was valiant, he succumbed, leaving Slade the *master of the situation and the conqueror and ruler of the courts, law and lawmakers.* This was a declaration of war, and was so accepted. The Vigilance Committee now felt that the question of social order and the preponderance of the law-abiding citizens had then and there to be decided. They knew the character of Slade, and they were well aware that they must submit to his rule without murmur, or else that he must be dealt with in such fashion as would prevent his being able to wreak his vengeance on the committee, who could never have hoped to live in the Territory secure from outrage or death, and who could never leave it without encountering his friends, whom his victory would have emboldened and stimulated to a pitch that would have rendered them reckless of consequences. The day previous he had ridden into Dorris's store, and on being requested to leave, he drew his revolver and threatened to kill the gentleman who spoke to him. Another saloon he had led his horse into, and buying a bottle of wine, he tried to make the animal drink it. This was not considered an uncommon performance, as he had often entered saloons and commenced firing at the lamps, causing a wild stampede.

A leading member of the committee met Slade, and informed him in the quiet, earnest manner of one who feels the importance of what he is saying: "Slade, get your horse at once, and go home, or there will be——to pay." Slade started and took a long look, with his dark and piercing eyes, at the gentleman. "What do you mean?" said he. "You have no right to ask me what I mean," was the quiet reply, "get your horse at once, and remember what I tell you." After a short pause he promised to do so, and actually got into the saddle; but, being still intoxicated, he began calling aloud to one after another of his friends, and at last seemed to have forgotten the warning he had received and became again uproarious, shouting the name of a well-known courtezan in company with those of two men whom he considered heads of the committee, as a sort of challenge; perhaps, however, as a simple act of bravado. It seems probable that the intimation of personal danger he had received had not been forgotten entirely; though fatally for him, he took a foolish way of showing his remembrance of it. He sought out Alexander Davis, the Judge of the Court, and drawing a cocked Derringer, he presented it at his head, and told him that he should hold him as a hostage for his own safety. As the judge stood perfectly quiet, and offered no resistance to his captor, no further outrage followed on this score. Previous to this, on account of the critical state of affairs, the committee had met, and at last resolved to arrest him. His execution had not been agreed upon, and, at that time, would have been negatived, most assuredly. A messenger rode down to Nevada to inform the leading men of what was on hand, as it was desirable to show that there was a feeling of unanimity on the subject, all along the gulch.

The miners turned out almost *en masse,* leaving their work and forming in solid column, about six hundred strong, armed to the teeth, they marched up to Virginia. The leader of the body well knew the temper of his men on the subject. He spurred on ahead of them, and hastily calling a meeting of the executive, he told them plainly that the miners meant "business," and that, if they came up, the would not stand in the street to be shot down by Slade's friends: but that they would take him and hang him. The meeting was small, as the Virginia men were loath to act at all. This momentous announcement of the feeling of the Lower Town was made to a cluster of men, who were deliberating behind a wagon, at the rear of a store on Main street.

The committee were most unwilling to proceed to extremities. All the duty they had ever performed seemed as nothing to the task before them; but they had to decide, and that quickly. It was finally agreed that if the whole body of the miners were of the opinion that he should be hanged, that the committee left it in their hands to deal with him. Off, at hot speed, rode the leader of the Nevada men to join his command.

Slade had found out what was intended, and the news sobered him instantly. He went into P.S. Pfouts' store, where Davis was, and apologized for his conduct, saying that he would take it all back.

The head of the column now wheeled into Wallace street and marched up at quick time. Halting in front of the store, the executive officer of the committee stepped forward and arrested Slade, who was at once informed of his doom, and inquiry was made as to whether he had any business to settle. Several parties spoke to him on the subject; but to all such inquiries he turned a deaf ear, being entirely absorbed in the terrifying reflections on his own awful position. He never ceased his entreaties for life, and to see his dear wife. The unfortunate lady referred to, between whom and Slade there existed a warm affection, was at this time living at their ranch on the Madison. She was possessed of considerable personal attractions; tall, well-formed, of graceful carriage, pleasing manners, and was, withal, an accomplished horsewoman.

A messenger from Slade rode at full speed to inform her of her husband's arrest. In an instant she was in the saddle, and with all the energy that love and despair could lend to an ardent temperament and a strong physique, she urged her fleet charger over the twelve miles of rough and rocky ground that intervened between her and the object of her passionate devotion.

Meanwhile a party of volunteers had made the necessary preparations for the execution, in the valley traversed by the branch. Beneath the site of Pfouts and Russell's stone building there was a corral, the gate-posts of which were strong and high. Across the top was laid a beam, to which the rope was fastened, and a dry-goods box served for the platform. To this place Slade was marched, surrounded by a guard, composing the best armed and most numerous force that has ever appeared in Montana Territory.

The doomed man had so exhausted himself by tears, prayers and lamentations, that he had scarcely strength left to stand under the fatal beam. He repeatedly exclaimed, "My God! my God! must I die? Oh, my dear wife!"

On the return of the fatigue party, they encountered some friends of Slade, staunch and reliable citizens and members of the committee, but who were personally attached to the condemned. On hearing of his sentence, one of them, a stout-hearted man, pulled out his handkerchief and walked away, weeping like a child. Slade still begged to see his wife, most piteously, and it seemed hard to deny his request; but the bloody consequences that were sure to follow the inevitable attempt at a rescue, that her presence and entreaties would have certainly incited, forbade the granting of his request. Several gentlemen were sent for to see him, in his last moments, one of whom (Judge Davis) made a short address to the people; but in such low tones as to be inaudible, save to a few in his immediate vicinity. One of his friends, after exhausting his powers of entreaty, threw off his coat and declared that the prisoner could not be hanged until he himself was killed. A hundred guns were instantly leveled at him; whereupon he turned and fled; but, being brought back, he was compelled to resume his coat, and to give a promise of future peaceable demeanor.

Scarcely a leading man in Virginia could be found, though numbers of the citizens joined the ranks of the guard when the arrest was made. All lamented the stern necessity which dictated the execution.

Everything being ready, the command was given, "Men, do your duty," and the box being instantly slipped from beneath his feet, he died almost instantaneously.

The body was cut down and carried to the Virginia Hotel, where, in a darkened room, it was scarcely laid out, when the unfortunate and bereaved companion of the deceased arrived, at headlong speed, to find that all was over, and that she was a widow. Her grief and heart-piercing cries were terrible evidences of the depth of her attachment for her lost husband, and a considerable period elapsed before she could regain the command of her excited feelings.

There is something about the desperado-nature that is wholly unaccountable—at least it looks unaccountable. It is this. The true desperado is gifted with splendid courage, and yet he will take the most infamous advantage of his enemy; armed and free, he will stand up before a host and fight until he is shot all to pieces, and yet when he is under the gallows and helpless he will cry and plead like a child. Words are cheap, and it is easy to call Slade a coward (all executed men who do not "die game" are promptly called cowards by unreflecting people), and when we read of Slade that he "had so exhausted himself by tears, prayers and lamentations, that he had scarcely strength left to stand under the fatal beam," the disgraceful word suggests itself in a moment—yet in frequently defying and inviting the vengeance of banded Rocky Mountain cut-throats by shooting down their comrades and leaders, and never offering to hide or fly, Slade showed that he was a man of peerless bravery. No coward would dare that. Many a notorious coward, many a chicken-livered poltroon, coarse, brutal, degraded, has made his dying speech without a quaver in his voice and been swung into eternity with what looked liked the calmest fortitude, and so we are justified in believing, from the low intellect of such a creature, that it was not *moral* courage that enabled him to do it. Then, if moral courage is not the requisite quality, what could it have been that this stout-hearted Slade lacked?—this bloody, desperate, kindly-mannered, urbane gentleman, who never hesitated to warn his most ruffianly enemies that he would kill them whenever or wherever he came across them next! I think it is a conundrum worth investigating.

CHAPTER XII

Just beyond the breakfast-station we overtook a Mormon emigrant train of thirty-three wagons; and tramping wearily along and driving their herd of loose cows, were dozens of coarse-clad and sad-looking men, women and children, who had walked as they were walking now, day after day for eight lingering weeks, and in that time had compassed the distance our stage had come in *eight days and three hours*—seven hundred and ninety-eight miles! They were dusty and uncombed, hatless, bonnetless and ragged, and they did look so tired!

After breakfast, we bathed in Horse Creek, a (previously) limpid, sparkling stream—an appreciated luxury, for it was very seldom that our furious coach halted long enough for an indulgence of that kind. We changed horses ten or twelve times in every twenty-four hours—changed mules, rather—six mules—and did it nearly every time in *four minutes*. It was lively work. As our coach rattled up to each station six harnessed mules stepped gayly from the stable; and in the twinkling of an eye, almost, the old team was out, and the new one in and we off and away again.

During the afternoon we passed Sweetwater Creek, Independence Rock, Devil's Gate and the Devil's Gap. The latter were wild specimens of rugged scenery, and full of interest—*we were in the heart of the Rocky Mountains, now*. And we also passed by "Alkali" or "Soda Lake," and we woke up to the fact that our journey had stretched a long way across the world when the driver said that the Mormons often came there from Great Salt Lake City to haul away saleratus. He said that a few days gone by they had shoveled up enough pure saleratus from the ground (it was a *dry* lake) to load two wagons, and that when they got these two wagon-loads of a drug that cost them nothing, to Salt Lake, they could sell it for twenty-five cents a pound.

In the night we sailed by a most notable curiosity, and one we had been hearing a good deal about for a day or two, and were suffering to see. This was what might be called a natural ice-house. It was August, now, and sweltering weather in the daytime, yet at one of the stations the men could scrape the soil on the hill-side under the lee of a range of boulders, and at a depth of six inches cut out pure blocks of ice—hard, compactly frozen, and clear as crystal!

Toward dawn we got under way again, and presently as we sat with raised curtains enjoying our early-morning smoke and contemplating the first splendor of the rising sun as it swept down the long array of mountain peaks, flushing and gilding crag after crag and summit after summit, as if the invisible Creator reviewed his gray veterans and they saluted with a smile, we hove in sight of South Pass City. The hotel-keeper, the postmaster, the blacksmith, the mayor, the constable, the city marshal and the principal citizen and property holder, all came out and greeted us cheerily, and we gave him good day. He gave us a little Indian news, and a little Rocky Mountain news, and we gave him some Plains information in return. He then retired to his lonely grandeur and we climbed on up among the bristling peaks and the ragged clouds. South Pass City consisted of four log cabins, one of which was unfinished, and the gentleman with all those offices and titles was the chiefest of the ten citizens of the place. Think of hotel-keeper, postmaster, blacksmith, mayor, constable, city marshal and principal citizen all condensed into one person and crammed into one skin. Bemis said he was "a perfect Allen's revolver of dignities." And he said that if he were to die as postmaster, or as blacksmith, or as postmaster and blacksmith both, the people might stand it; but if he were to die all over, it would be a frightful loss to the community.

Two miles beyond South Pass City we saw for the first time that mysterious marvel which all Western untraveled boys have heard of and fully believe in, but are sure to be astounded at when they see it with their own eyes, nevertheless—banks of snow in dead summer time. We were now far up toward the sky, and knew all the time that we must presently encounter lofty summits clad in the "eternal snow" which was so commonplace a matter of mention in books, and yet when I did see it glittering in the sun on stately domes in the distance and knew the month was August and that my coat was hanging up because it was too warm to wear it, I was full as much amazed as if I never had heard of snow in August before. Truly, "seeing is believing"—and many a man lives a long life through, *thinking* he believes certain universally received and well established things, and yet never suspects that if he were confronted by those things once, he would discover that he did not *really* believe them before, but only thought he believed them.

In a little while quite a number of peaks swung into view with long claws of glittering snow clasping them; and with here and there, in the shade, down the mountain side, a little solitary patch of snow looking no larger than a lady's pocket-handkerchief, but being in reality as large as a "public square."

And now, at last, we were fairly in the renowned SOUTH PASS, and whirling gayly along high above the common world. We were perched upon the extreme summit of the great range of the Rocky Mountains, toward which we had been climbing, patiently climbing, ceaselessly climbing, for days and nights together— and about us was gathered a convention of Nature's kings that stood ten, twelve, and even thirteen thousand feet high—grand old fellows who would have to stoop to see Mount Washington, in the twilight. We were in such an airy elevation above the creeping populations of the earth, that now and then when the obstructing crags stood out of the way it seemed that we could look around and abroad and contemplate the whole great globe, with its dissolving views of mountains, seas and continents stretching away through the mystery of the summer haze.

As a general thing the Pass was more suggestive of a valley than a suspension bridge in the clouds—but it strongly suggested the latter at one spot. At that place the upper third of one or two majestic purple domes projected above our level on either hand and gave us a sense of a hidden great deep of mountains and plains and valleys down about their bases which we fancied we might see if we could step to the edge and look over. These Sultans of the fastnesses were turbaned with tumbled volumes of cloud, which shredded away from time to time and drifted off fringed and torn, trailing their continents of shadow after them; and catching presently on an intercepting peak, wrapped it about and brooded there—then shredded away again and left the purple peak, as they had left the purple domes, downy and white with new-laid snow. In passing, these monstrous rags of cloud hung low and swept along right over the spectator's head, swinging their tatters so nearly in his face that his impulse was to shrink when they came closest. In the one place I speak of, one could look below him upon a world of diminishing crags and canyons leading down, down, and away to a vague plain with a thread in it which was a road, and bunches of feathers in it which were trees,—a pretty picture sleeping in the sunlight—but with a darkness stealing over it and glooming its features deeper and deeper under the frown of a coming storm; and then, while no film or shadow marred the noon brightness of his high perch, he could watch the tempest break forth down there and see the lightning leap from crag to crag and the sheeted rain drive along the canyon-sides, and here the thunders peal and crash and roar. We had this spectacle; a familiar one to many, but to us a novelty.

We bowled along cheerily, and presently, at the very summit (though it had been all summit to us, and all equally level, for half an hour or more), we came to a spring which spent its water through two outlets and sent it in opposite directions. The conductor said that one of those streams which we were looking at, was just starting on a journey westward to the Gulf of California and the Pacific Ocean, through hundreds and even thousands of miles of desert solitudes. He said that the other was just leaving its home among the snow-peaks on a similar journey eastward—and we knew that long after we should have forgotten the simple rivulet it would still be plodding its patient way down the mountain sides, and canyon-beds, and between the banks of the Yellowstone; and by and by would join the broad Missouri and flow through unknown plains and deserts and unvisited wildernesses; and add a long and troubled pilgrimage among snags and wrecks and sandbars; and enter the Mississippi, touch the wharves of St. Louis and still drift on, traversing shoals and rocky channels, then endless chains of bottomless and ample bends, walled with unbroken forests, then mysterious byways and secret passages among woody islands, then the chained bends again, bordered with wide levels of shining sugar-cane in place of the sombre forests; then by New Orleans and still other chains of bends—and finally, after two long months of daily and nightly harassment, excitement, enjoyment, adventure, and awful peril of parched throats, pumps and evaporation, pass the Gulf and enter into its rest upon the bosom of the tropic sea, never to look upon its snow-peaks again or regret them.

I freighted a leaf with a mental message for the friends at home, and dropped it in the stream. But I put no stamp on it and it was held for postage somewhere.

On the summit we overtook an emigrant train of many wagons, many tired men and women, and many a disgusted sheep and cow. In the wofully dusty horseman in charge of the expedition I recognized John——. Of all persons in the world to meet on top of the Rocky Mountains thousands of miles from home, he was the last one I should have looked for. We were schoolboys together and warm friends for years. But a boyish prank of mine had disruptured this friendship and it had never been renewed. The act of which I speak was this. I had been accustomed to visit occasionally an editor whose room was in the third story of a building and overlooked the street. One day this editor gave me a watermelon which I made preparations to devour on the spot, but chancing to look out of the window, I saw John standing directly under it and an irresistible desire came upon me to drop the melon on his head, which I immediately did. I was the loser, for it spoiled the melon, and John never forgave me and we dropped all intercourse and parted, but now met again under these circumstances.

We recognized each other simultaneously, and hands were grasped as warmly as if no coldness had ever existed between us, and no allusion was made to any. All animosities were buried and the simple fact of meeting a familiar face in that isolated spot so far from home, was sufficient to make us forget all things but pleasant ones, and we parted again with sincere "good-byes" and "God bless you" from both.

We had been climbing up the long shoulders of the Rocky Mountains for many tedious hours—we started *down* them, now. And we went spinning away at a round rate too.

We left the snowy Wind River Mountains and Uinta Mountains behind, and sped away, always through a splendid scenery but occasionally through long ranks of white skeletons of mules and oxen—monuments of the huge emigration of other days—and here and there were up-ended boards or small piles of stones which the driver said marked the resting-place of more precious remains. It was the loneliest land for a grave! A land given over to the cayote and the raven—which is but another name for desolation and utter solitude. On damp, murky nights, these scattered skeletons gave forth a soft, hideous glow, like very faint spots of moonlight starring the vague desert. It was because of the phosphorus in the bones. But no scientific explanation could keep a body from shivering when he drifted by one of those ghostly lights and knew that a skull held it.

At midnight it began to rain, and I never saw anything like it—indeed, I did not even see this, for it was too dark. We fastened down the curtains and even caulked them with clothing, but the rain streamed in in twenty places, notwithstanding. There was no escape. If one moved his feet out of a stream, he brought his body under one; and if he moved his body he caught one somewhere else. If he struggled out of the drenched blankets and sat up, he was bound to get one down the back of his neck. Meantime the stage was wandering about a plain with gaping gullies in it, for the driver could not see an inch before his face nor keep the road, and the storm pelted so pitilessly that there was no keeping the horses still. With the first abatement the conductor turned out with lanterns to look for the road, and the first dash he made was into a chasm about fourteen feet deep, his lantern following like a meteor. As soon as he touched bottom he sang out frantically:

"Don't come here!"

To which the driver, who was looking over the precipice where he had disappeared, replied, with an injured air: "Think I'm a dam fool?"

The conductor was more than an hour finding the road—a matter which showed us how far we had wandered and what chances we had been taking. He traced our wheel-tracks to the imminent verge of danger, in two places. I have always been glad that we were not killed that night. I do not know any particular reason, but I have always been glad.

In the morning, the tenth day out, we crossed Green River, a fine, large, limpid stream— stuck in it, with the water just up to the top of our mail-bed, and waited till extra teams were put on to haul us up the steep bank. But is was nice cool water, and besides it could not find any fresh place on us to wet.

At the Green River station we had breakfast—hot biscuits, fresh antelope steaks, and coffee—the only decent meal we tasted between the United States and Great Salt Lake City, and the only one we were ever really thankful for. Think of the monotonous execrableness of the thirty that went before it, to leave this one simple breakfast looming up in my memory like a shot-tower after all these years have gone by!

At five p.m. we reached Fort Bridger, one hundred and seventeen miles from the South Pass, and one thousand and twenty-five miles from St. Joseph. Fifty-two miles further on, near the head of Echo Canyon, we met sixty United States soldiers from Camp Floyd. The day before, they had fired upon three hundred or four hundred Indians, whom they supposed gathered together for no good purpose. In the fight that had ensued, four Indians were captured, and the main body chased four miles, but nobody killed. This looked like business. We had a notion to get out and join the sixty soldiers, but upon reflecting that there were four hundred of the Indians, we concluded to go on and join the Indians.

Echo Canyon is twenty miles long. It was like a long, smooth, narrow street, with a gradual descending grade, and shut in by enormous perpendicular walls of coarse conglomerate, four hundred feet high in many places, and turreted like medieval castles. This was the most faultless piece of road in the mountains, and the driver said he would "let his team out." He did, and if the Pacific express trains whiz through there now any faster than we did then in the stage-coach, I envy the passengers the exhilaration of it. We fairly seemed to pick up our wheels and fly—and the mail matter was lifted up free from everything and held in solution! I am not given to exaggeration, and when I say a thing I mean it.

However, time presses. At four in the afternoon we arrived on the summit of Big Mountain, fifteen miles from Salt Lake City, when all the world was glorified with the setting sun, and the most stupendous panorama of mountain peaks yet encountered burst on our sight. We looked out upon this sublime spectacle from under the arch of a brilliant rainbow! Even the overland stage-driver stopped his horses and gazed!

Half an hour or an hour later, we changed horses, and took supper with a Mormon "Destroying Angel." "Destroying Angels," as I understand it, are Latter-Day Saints who are set apart by the Church to conduct permanent disappearances of obnoxious citizens. I had heard a deal about these Mormon Destroying Angels and the dark and bloody deeds they had done, and when I entered this one's house I had my shudder all ready. But alas for all our romances, he was nothing but a loud, profane, offensive, old blackguard! He was murderous enough, possibly, to fill the bill of a Destroyer, but would you have *any* kind of an Angel devoid of dignity? Could you abide an Angel in an unclean shirt and no suspenders? Could you respect an Angel with a horse-laugh and a swagger like a buccaneer?

There were other blackguards present—comrades of this one. And there was one person that looked like a gentleman—Heber C. Kimball's son, tall and well made, and thirty years old, perhaps. A lot of slatternly women flitted hither and thither in a hurry, with coffee-pots, plates of bread, and other appurtenances to supper, and these were said to be the wives of the Angel—or some of them, at least. And of course they were; for if they had been hired "help" they would not have let an angel from above storm and swear at them as he did, let alone one from the place this one hailed from.

This was our first experience of the western "peculiar institution," and it was not very prepossessing. We did not tarry long to observe it, but hurried on to the home of the Latter-Day Saints, the stronghold of the prophets, the capital of the only absolute monarch in America—Great Salt Lake City. As the night closed in we took sanctuary in the Salt Lake House and unpacked our baggage.

CHAPTER XIII

We had a fine supper, of the freshest meats and fowls and vegetables—a great variety and as great abundance. We walked about the streets some, afterward, and glanced in at shops and stores; and there was fascination in surreptitiously staring at every creature we took to be a Mormon. This was fairy-land to us, to all intents and purposes—a land of enchantment, and goblins, and awful mystery. We felt a curiosity to ask every child how many mothers it had, and if it could tell them apart; and we experienced a thrill every time a dwelling-house door opened and shut as we passed, disclosing a glimpse of human heads and backs and shoulders—for we so longed to have a good satisfying look at a Mormon family in all its comprehensive ampleness, disposed in the customary concentric rings of its home circle.

By and by the Acting Governor of the Territory introduced us to other "Gentiles," and we spent a sociable hour with them. "Gentiles" are people who are not Mormons. Our fellow-passenger, Bemis, took care of himself, during this part of the evening, and did not make an overpowering success of it, either, for he came into our room in the hotel about eleven o'clock, full of cheerfulness, and talking loosely, disjointedly and indiscriminately, and every now and then tugging out a ragged word by the roots that had more hiccups than syllables in it. This, together with his hanging his coat on the floor on one side of a chair, and his vest on the floor on the other side, and piling his pants on the floor just in front of the same chair, and then contemplating the general result with superstitious awe, and finally pronouncing it "too many for *him*" and going to bed with his boots on, led us to fear that something he had eaten had not agreed with him.

But we knew afterward that it was something he had been drinking. It was the exclusively Mormon refresher, "valley tan." Valley tan (or, at least, one form of valley tan) is a kind of whisky, or first cousin to it; is of Mormon invention and manufactured only in Utah. Tradition says it is made of (imported) fire and brimstone. If I remember rightly no public drinking saloons were allowed in the kingdom by Brigham Young, and no private drinking permitted among the faithful, except they confined themselves to "valley tan."

Next day we strolled about everywhere through the broad, straight, level streets, and enjoyed the pleasant strangeness of a city of fifteen thousand inhabitants with no loafers perceptible in it; and no visible drunkards or noisy people; a limpid stream rippling and dancing through every street in place of a filthy gutter; block after block of trim dwellings, built of "frame" and sunburned brick—a great thriving orchard and garden behind every one of them, apparently—branches from the street stream winding and sparkling among the garden beds and fruit trees—and a grand general air of neatness, repair, thrift and comfort, around and about and over the whole. And everywhere were workshops, factories, and all manner of industries; and intent faces and busy hands were to be seen wherever one looked; and in one's ears was the ceaseless clink of hammers, the buzz of trade and the contented hum of drums and fly-wheels.

The armorial crest of my own State consisted of two dissolute bears holding up the head of a dead and gone cask between them and making the pertinent remark, "UNITED, WE STAND—(hic!)—DIVIDED WE FALL." It was always too figurative for the author of this book. But the Mormon crest was easy. And it was simple, unostentatious, and fitted like a glove. It was a representation of a GOLDEN BEEHIVE, with the bees all at work!

The city lies in the edge of a level plain as broad as the State of Connecticut, and crouches close down to the ground under a curving wall of mighty mountains whose heads are hidden in the clouds, and whose shoulders bear relics of the snows of winter all the summer long. Seen from one of these dizzy heights, twelve or fifteen miles off, Great Salt Lake City is toned down and diminished till it is suggestive of a child's toy-village reposing under the majestic protection of the Chinese wall.

On some of those mountains, to the southwest, it had been raining every day for two weeks, but not a drop had fallen in the city. And on hot days in late spring and early autumn the citizens could quit fanning and growling and go out and cool off by looking at the luxury of a glorious snow-storm going on in the mountains. They could enjoy it at a distance, at those seasons, every day, though no snow would fall in their streets, or anywhere near them.

Salt Lake City was healthy—an extremely healthy city. They declared there was only one physician in the place and he was arrested every week regularly and held to answer under the vagrant act for having "no visible means of support." [They always give you a good substantial article of truth in Salt Lake, and good measure and good weight, too. Very often, if you wished to weigh one of their airiest little commonplace statements you would want the hay scales.]

We desired to visit the famous inland sea, the American "Dead Sea," the great Salt Lake—seventeen miles, horseback, from the city—for we had dreamed about it, and thought about it, and talked about it, and yearned to see it, all the first part of our trip; but now when it was only arm's length away it had suddenly lost nearly every bit of its interest. And so we put if off, in a sort of general way, till next day—and that was the last we ever thought of it. We dined with some hospitable Gentiles; and visited the foundation of the prodigious temple; and talked long with that shrewd Connecticut Yankee, Heber C. Kimball (since deceased), a saint of high degree and a mighty man of commerce. We saw the "Tithing-House," and the "Lion House," and I do not know or remember how many more church and government buildings of various kinds and curious names. We flitted hither and thither and enjoyed every hour, and picked up a great deal of useful information and entertaining nonsense, and went to bed at night satisfied.

The second day, we made the acquaintance of Mr. Street (since deceased) and put on white shirts and went and paid a state visit to the king. He seemed a quiet, kindly, easy- mannered, dignified, self-possessed old gentleman of fifty-five or sixty, and had a gentle craft in his eye that probably belonged there. He was very simply dressed and was just taking off a straw hat as we entered. He talked about Utah, and the Indians, and Nevada, and general American matters and questions, with our secretary and certain government officials who came with us. But he never paid any attention to me, notwithstanding I made several attempts to "draw him out" on federal politics and his high handed attitude toward Congress. I thought some of the things I said were rather fine. But he merely looked around at me, at distant intervals, something as I have seen a benignant old cat look around to see which kitten was meddling with her tail. By and by I subsided into an indignant silence, and so sat until the end, hot and flushed, and execrating him in my heart for an ignorant savage. But he was calm. His conversation with those gentlemen flowed on as sweetly and peacefully and musically as any summer brook. When the audience was ended and we were retiring from the presence, he put his hand on my head, beamed down on me in an admiring way and said to my brother:

"Ah—your child, I presume? Boy, or girl?"

CHAPTER XIV

Mr. Street was very busy with his telegraphic matters—and considering that he had eight or nine hundred miles of rugged, snowy, uninhabited mountains, and waterless, treeless, melancholy deserts to traverse with his wire, it was natural and needful that he should be as busy as possible. He could not go comfortably along and cut his poles by the roadside, either, but they had to be hauled by ox teams across those exhausting deserts—and it was two days' journey from water to water, in one or two of them. Mr. Street's contract was a vast work, every way one looked at it; and yet to comprehend what the vague words "eight hundred miles of rugged mountains and dismal deserts" mean, one must go over the ground in person—pen and ink descriptions cannot convey the dreary reality to the reader. And after all, Mr. S.'s mightiest difficulty turned out to be one which he had never taken into the account at all. Unto Mormons he had sub-let the hardest and heaviest half of his great undertaking, and all of a sudden they concluded that they were going to make little or nothing, and so they tranquilly threw their poles overboard in mountain or desert, just as it happened when they took the notion, and drove home and went about their customary business! They were under written contract to Mr. Street, but they did not care anything for that. They said they would "admire" to see a "Gentile" force a Mormon to fulfil a losing contract in Utah! And they made themselves very merry over the matter. Street said—for it was he that told us these things:

"I was in dismay. I was under heavy bonds to complete my contract in a given time, and this disaster looked very much like ruin. It was an astounding thing; it was such a wholly unlooked-for difficulty, that I was entirely nonplussed. I am a business man—have always been a businessman—do not know anything *but* business—and so you can imagine how like being struck by lightning it was to find myself in a country where *written contracts were worthless!*—that main security, that sheet-anchor, that absolute necessity, of business. My confidence left me. There was no use in making new contracts—that was plain. I talked with first one prominent citizen and then another. They all sympathized with me, first rate, but they did not know how to help me. But at last a Gentile said, 'Go to Brigham Young!—these small fry cannot do you any good.' I did not think much of the idea, for if the *law* could not help me, what could an individual do who had not even anything to do with either making the laws or executing them? He might be a very good patriarch of a church and preacher in its tabernacle, but something sterner than religion and moral suasion was needed to handle a hundred refractory, half-civilized sub-contractors. But what was a man to do? I thought if Mr. Young could not do anything else, he might probably be able to give me some advice and a valuable hint or two, and so I went straight to him and laid the whole case before him. He said very little, but he showed strong interest all the way through. He examined all the papers in detail, and whenever there seemed anything like a hitch, either in the papers or my statement, he would go back and take up the thread and follow it patiently out to an intelligent and satisfactory result. Then he made a list of the contractors' names. Finally he said:

" 'Mr. Street, this is all perfectly plain. These contracts are strictly and legally drawn, and are duly signed and certified. These men manifestly entered into them with their eyes open. I see no fault or flaw anywhere.'

"Then Mr. Young turned to a man waiting at the other end of the room and said: 'Take this list of names to So-and-so, and tell him to have these men here at such-and-such an hour.'

"They were there, to the minute. So was I. Mr. Young asked them a number of questions, and their answers made my statement good. Then he said to them:

" 'You signed these contracts and assumed these obligations of your own free will and accord?'

" 'Yes.'

" 'Then carry them out to the letter, if it makes paupers of you! Go!'

"And they *did* go, too! They are strung across the deserts now, working like bees. And I never hear a word out of them. There is a batch of governors, and judges, and other officials here, shipped from Washington, and they maintain the semblance of a republican form of government—but the petrified truth is that Utah is an absolute monarchy and Brigham Young is king!"

Mr. Street was a fine man, and I believe his story. I knew him well during several years afterward in San Francisco.

Our stay in Salt Lake City amounted to only two days, and therefore we had no time to make the customary inquisition into the workings of polygamy and get up the usual statistics and deductions preparatory to calling the attention of the nation at large once more to the matter. I had the will to do it. With the gushing self-sufficiency of youth I was feverish to plunge in headlong and achieve a great reform here—until I saw the Mormon women. Then I was touched. My heart was wiser than my head. It warmed toward these poor, ungainly and pathetically "homely" creatures, and as I turned to hide the generous moisture in my eyes, I said, "No—the man that marries one of them has done an act of Christian charity which entitles him to the kindly applause of mankind, not their harsh censure—and the man that marries sixty of them has done a deed of open-handed generosity so sublime that the nations should stand uncovered in his presence and worship in silence."*

CHAPTER XV

It is a luscious country for thrilling evening stories about assassinations of intractable Gentiles. I cannot easily conceive of anything more cosy than the night in Salt Lake which we spent in a Gentile den, smoking pipes and listening to tales of how Burton galloped in among the pleading and defenceless "Morisites" and shot them down, men and women, like so many dogs. And how Bill Hickman, a Destroying Angel, shot Drown and Arnold dead for bringing suit against him for a debt. And how Porter Rockwell did this and that dreadful thing. And how heedless people often come to Utah and make remarks about Brigham, or polygamy, or some other sacred matter, and the very next morning at daylight such parties are sure to be found lying up some back alley, contentedly waiting for the hearse.

And the next most interesting thing is to sit and listen to these Gentiles talk about polygamy; and how some portly old frog of an elder, or a bishop, marries a girl—likes her, marries her sister—likes her, marries another sister—likes her, takes another—likes her, marries her mother—likes her, marries her father, grandfather, great grandfather, and then comes back hungry and asks for more. And how the pert young thing of eleven will chance to be the favorite wife and her own venerable grandmother have to rank away down toward D 4 in their mutual husband's esteem, and have to sleep in the kitchen, as like as not. And how this dreadful sort of thing, this hiving together in one foul nest of mother and daughters, and the making a young daughter superior to her own mother in rank and authority, are things which Mormon women submit to because their religion teaches them that the more wives a man has on earth, and the more children he rears, the higher the place they will all have in the world to come—and the warmer, maybe, though they do not seem to say anything about that.

According to these Gentile friends of ours, Brigham Young's harem contains twenty or thirty wives. They said that some of them had grown old and gone out of active service, but were comfortably housed and cared for in the henery—or the Lion

* For a brief sketch of Mormon history, and the noted Mountain Meadow massacre, see Appendices A and B.

House, as it is strangely named. Along with each wife were her children—fifty altogether. The house was perfectly quiet and orderly, when the children were still. They all took their meals in one room, and a happy and homelike sight it was pronounced to be. None of our party got an opportunity to take dinner with Mr. Young, but a Gentile by the name of Johnson professed to have enjoyed a sociable breakfast in the Lion House. He gave a preposterous account of the "calling of the roll," and other preliminaries, and the carnage that ensued when the buckwheat cakes came in. But he embellished rather too much. He said that Mr. Young told him several smart sayings of certain of his "two-year-olds," observing with some pride that for many years he had been the heaviest contributor in that line to one of the Eastern magazines; and then he wanted to show Mr. Johnson one of the pets that had said the last good thing, but he could not find the child. He searched the faces of the children in detail, but could not decide which one it was. Finally he gave it up with a sigh and said:

"I thought I would know the little cub again but I don't." Mr. Johnson said further, that Mr. Young observed that life was a sad, sad thing—"because the joy of every new marriage a man contracted was so apt to be blighted by the inopportune funeral of a less recent bride." And Mr. Johnson said that while he and Mr. Young were pleasantly conversing in private, one of the Mrs. Youngs came in and demanded a breast-pin, remarking that she had found out that he had been giving a breast-pin to No. 6, and *she*, for one, did not propose to let this partiality go on without making a satisfactory amount of trouble about it. Mr. Young reminded her that there was a stranger present. Mrs. Young said that if the state of things inside the house was not agreeable to the stranger, he could find room outside. Mr. Young promised the breast-pin, and she went away. But in a minute or two another Mrs. Young came in and demanded a breast-pin. Mr. Young began a remonstrance, but Mrs. Young cut him short. She said No. 6 had got one, and No. 11 was promised one, and it was "no use for him to try to impose on her—she hoped she knew her rights." He gave his promise, and she went. And presently three Mrs. Youngs entered in a body and opened on their husband a tempest of tears, abuse, and entreaty. They had heard all about No. 6, No. 11, and No. 14. Three more breast-pins were promised. They were hardly gone when nine more Mrs. Youngs filed into the presence, and a new tempest burst forth and raged round about the prophet and his guest. Nine breast-pins were promised, and the weird sisters filed out again. And in came eleven more, weeping and wailing and gnashing their teeth. Eleven promised breast-pins purchased peace once more.

"That is a specimen," said Mr. Young. "You see how it is. You see what a life I lead. A man *can't* be wise all the time. In a heedless moment I gave my darling No. 6—excuse my calling her thus, as her other name has escaped me for the moment—a breast-pin. It was only worth twenty-five dollars—that is, *apparently* that was its whole cost—but its ultimate cost was inevitably bound to be a good deal more. You yourself have seen it climb up to six hundred and fifty dollars—and alas, even that is not the end! For I have wives all over this Territory of Utah. I have dozen of wives whose *numbers*, even, I do not know without looking in the family Bible. They are scattered far and wide among the mountains and valleys of my realm. And mark you, every solitary one of them will hear of this wretched breast-pin, and every last one of them will have one or die. No. 6's breast-pin will cost me twenty-five hundred dollars before I see the end of it. And these creatures will compare these pins together, and if one is a shade finer than the rest, they will all be thrown on my hands, and I will have to order a new lot to keep peace in the family. Sir, you probably did not know it, but all the time you were present with my children your every movement was watched by vigilant servitors of mine. If you had offered to give a child a dime, or a stick of candy, or any trifle of the kind, you would have been snatched out of the house instantly, provided it could be done before your gift left your hand. Otherwise it would be absolutely necessary for you to make an exactly similar gift to all my children—and knowing by experience the importance of the thing, I would have stood by and seen to it myself that you did it, and did it thoroughly. Once a gentleman gave one of my children a tin whistle—a veritable invention of Satan, sir, and one which I have an unspeakable horror of, and so would you if you had eighty or ninety children in your house. But the deed was done—the man escaped. I knew what the result was going to be, and I thirsted for vengeance. I ordered out a flock of Destroying Angels, and they hunted the man far into the fastnesses of the Nevada mountains. But they never caught him. I am not cruel, sir—I am not vindictive except when sorely outraged—but if I had caught him, sir, so help me Joseph Smith, I would have locked him into the nursery till the brats whistled him to death! By the slaughtered body of St. Parley Pratt (whom God assoil!) there was never anything on this earth like it! *I* knew who gave the whistle to the child, but I could not make those jealous mothers believe me. They believed *I* did it, and the result was just what any man of reflection could have foreseen: I had to order a hundred and ten whistles—I think we had a hundred and ten children in the house then, but some of them are off at college now—I had to order a hundred and ten of those shrieking things, and I wish I may never speak another word if we didn't have to talk on our fingers entirely, from that time forth until the children got tired of the whistles. And if ever another man gives a whistle to a child of mine and I get my hands on him, I will hang him higher than Haman! That is the word with the bark on it! Shade of Nephi! *You* don't know anything about married life. I am rich, and everybody knows it. I am benevolent, and everybody takes advantage of it. I have a strong fatherly instinct and all the foundlings are foisted on me. Every time a woman wants to do well by her darling, she puzzles her brain to cipher out some scheme for getting it into my hands. Why, sir, a woman came here once with a child of a curious lifeless sort of complexion (and so had the woman), and swore that the child was mine and she my wife—that I had married her at such-and-such a time in such-and-such a place, but she had forgotten her number, and of course I could not remember her name. Well, sir, she called my attention to the fact that the child looked like me, and really it did seem to resemble me—a common thing in the Territory—and, to cut the story short, I put it in my nursery, and she left. And by the ghost of Orson Hyde, when they came to wash the paint off that child it was an Injun! Bless my soul, you don't know anything about married life. It is a perfect dog's life, sir—a perfect dog's life. You can't economize. It isn't possible. I have tried keeping one set of bridal attire for all occasions. But it is of no use. First you'll marry a combination of calico and consumption that's as thin as a rail, and next you'll get a creature that's nothing more than the dropsy in disguise, and then you've got to eke out that bridal dress with an old balloon. That is the way it goes. And think of the wash-bill—(excuse these tears)—nine hundred and eighty-four pieces a week! No, sir, there is no such a thing as economy in a family like mine. Why, just the one item of cradles—think of it! And vermifuge! Soothing syrup! Teething rings! And 'papa's watches' for the babies to play with! And things to scratch the furniture with! And lucifer matches for them to eat, and pieces of glass to cut themselves with! The item of glass alone would support *your* family, I venture to say, sir. Let me scrimp and squeeze all I can, I still can't get ahead as fast as I feel I ought to, with my opportunities. Bless you, sir, at a time when I had seventy-two wives in this house, I groaned under the pressure of keeping thousands of dollars tied up in seventy-two bedsteads when the money ought to have been out at interest;

and I just sold out the whole stock, sir, at a sacrifice, and built a bedstead seven feet long and ninety-six feet wide. But it was a failure, sir. I could *not* sleep. It appeared to me that the whole seventy-two women snored at once. The roar was deafening. And then the danger of it! That was what I was looking at. They would all draw in their breath at once, and you could actually see the walls of the house suck in—and then they would all exhale their breath at once, and you could see the walls swell out, and strain, and hear the rafters crack, and the shingles grind together. My friend, take an old man's advice, and *don't* encumber yourself with a large family—mind, I tell you, don't do it. In a small family, and in a small family only, you will find that comfort and that peace of mind which are the best at last of the blessings this world is able to afford us, and for the lack of which no accumulation of wealth, and no acquisition of fame, power, and greatness can ever compensate us. Take my word for it, ten or eleven wives is all you need—never go over it."

Some instinct or other made me set this Johnson down as being unreliable. And yet he was a very entertaining person, and I doubt if some of the information he gave us could have been acquired from any other source. He was a pleasant contrast to those reticent Mormons.

CHAPTER XVI

All men have heard of the Mormon Bible, but few except the "elect" have seen it, or, at least, taken the trouble to read it. I brought away a copy from Salt Lake. The book is a curiosity to me, it is such a pretentious affair, and yet so "slow," so sleepy; such an insipid mess of inspiration. It is chloroform in print. If Joseph Smith composed this book, the act was a miracle— keeping awake while he did it was, at any rate. If he, according to tradition, merely translated it from certain ancient and mysteriously-engraved plates of copper, which he declares he found under a stone, in an out-of-the-way locality, the work of translating was equally a miracle, for the same reason.

The book seems to be merely a prosy detail of imaginary history, with the Old Testament for a model; followed by a tedious plagiarism of the New Testament. The author labored to give his words and phrases the quaint, old-fashioned sound and structure of our King James's translation of the Scriptures; and the result is a mongrel—half modern glibness, and half ancient simplicity and gravity. The latter is awkward and constrained; the former natural, but grotesque by the contrast. Whenever he found his speech growing too modern—which was about every sentence or two—he ladled in a few such Scriptural phrases as "exceeding sore," "and it came to pass," etc., and made things satisfactory again. "And it came to pass" was his pet. If he had left that out, his Bible would have been only a pamphlet.

The title-page reads as follows:

THE BOOK OF MORMON: AN ACCOUNT WRITTEN BY THE HAND OF MORMON, UPON PLATES TAKEN FROM THE PLATES OF NEPHI.

Wherefore it is an abridgment of the record of the people of Nephi, and also of the Lamanites; written to the Lamanites, who are a remnant of the House of Israel; and also to Jew and Gentile; written by way of commandment, and also by the spirit of prophecy and of revelation. Written and sealed up, and hid up unto the Lord, that they might not be destroyed; to come forth by the gift and power of God unto the interpretation thereof; sealed by the hand of Moroni, and hid up unto the Lord, to come forth in due time by the way of Gentile; the interpretation thereof by the gift of God. An abridgment taken from the Book of Ether also; which is a record of the people of Jared; who were scattered at the time the Lord confounded the language of the people when they were building a tower to get to Heaven.

"Hid up" is good. And so is "wherefore"—though why "wherefore"? Any other word would have answered as well—though in truth it would not have sounded so Scriptural.

Next comes

THE TESTIMONY OF THREE WITNESSES

Be it known unto all nations, kindreds, tongues, and people unto whom this work shall come, that we, through the grace of God the Father, and our Lord Jesus Christ, have seen the plates which contain this record, which is a record of the people of Nephi, and also of the Lamanites, their brethren, and also of the people of Jared, who came from the tower of which hath been spoken; and we also know that they have been translated by the gift and power of God, for His voice hath declared it unto us; wherefore we know of a surety that the work is true. And we also testify that we have seen the engravings which are upon the plates; and they have been shown unto us by the power of God, and not of man. And we declare with words of soberness, that an angel of God came down from heaven, and he brought and laid before our eyes, that we beheld and saw the plates, and the engravings thereon; and we know that it is by the grace of God the Father, and our Lord Jesus Christ, that we beheld and bear record that these things are true; and it is marvellous in our eyes; nevertheless the voice of the Lord commanded us that we should bear record of it; wherefore, to be obedient unto the commandments of God, we bear testimony of these things. And we know that if we are faithful in Christ, we shall rid our garments of the blood of all men, and be found spotless before the judgment-seat of Christ, and shall dwell with Him eternally in the heavens. And the honor be to the Father, and to the Son, and to the Holy Ghost, which is one God. Amen.

OLIVER COWDERY,
DAVID WHITMER,
MARTIN HARRIS.

Some people have to have a world of evidence before they can come anywhere in the neighborhood of believing anything; but for me, when a man tells me that he has "seen the engravings which are upon the plates," and not only that, but an angel was there at the time, and saw him see them, and probably took his receipt for it, I am very far on the road to conviction, no matter whether I ever heard of that man before or not, and even if I do not know the name of the angel, or his nationality either.

Next is this:

AND ALSO THE TESTIMONY OF EIGHT WITNESSES

Be it known unto all nations, kindreds, tongues, and people unto whom this work shall come, that Joseph Smith, Jr., the translator of this work, has shown unto us the plates of which hath been spoken, which have the appearance of gold; and as many of the leaves as the said Smith has translated, we did handle with our hands; and we also saw the engravings thereon, all of which has the appearance of ancient work, and of curious workmanship. And this we bear record with words of soberness, that the said Smith has shown unto us, for we have seen and hefted, and know of a surety that the said Smith has got the plates of which we have spoken. And we give our names unto the world, to witness unto the world that which we have seen; and we lie not, God bearing witness of it.

CHRISTIAN WHITMER,
JACOB WHITMER,
PETER WHITMER, JR.,
JOHN WHITMER,
HIRAM PAGE,
JOSEPH SMITH, SR.,
HYRUM SMITH,
SAMUEL H. SMITH.

And when I am far on the road to conviction, and eight men, be they grammatical or otherwise, come forward and tell me that they have seen the plates too; and not only seen those plates but "hefted" them, I *am* convinced. I could not feel more satisfied and at rest if the entire Whitmer family had testified.

The Mormon Bible consists of fifteen "books"—being the books of Jacob, Enos, Jarom, Omni, Mosiah, Zeniff, Alma, Helaman, Ether, Moroni, two "books" of Mormon, and three of Nephi.

In the first book of Nephi is a plagiarism of the Old Testament, which gives an account of the exodus from Jerusalem of the "children of Lehi"; and it goes on to tell of their wanderings in the wilderness, during eight years, and their supernatural protection by one of their number, a party by the name of Nephi. They finally reached the land of "Bountiful," and camped by the sea. After they had remained there "for the space of many days"— which is more Scriptural than definite—Nephi was commanded from on high to build a ship wherein to "carry the people across the waters." He travestied Noah's ark—but he obeyed orders in the matter of the plan. He finished the ship *in a single day,* while his brethren stood by and made fun of it—and of him, too— "saying, our brother is a fool, for he thinketh that he can build a ship." They did not wait for the timbers to dry, but the whole tribe or nation sailed the next day. Then a bit of genuine nature cropped out, and is revealed by outspoken Nephi with Scriptural frankness—they all got on a spree! They, "and also their wives, began to make themselves merry, insomuch that they began to dance, and to sing, and to speak with much rudeness; yea, they were lifted up unto exceeding rudeness."

Nephi tried to stop these scandalous proceedings; but they tied him neck and heels, and went on with their lark. But observe how Nephi the prophet circumvented them by the aid of the invisible powers:

> And it came to pass that after they had bound me, insomuch that I could not move, the compass, which had been prepared of the Lord, did cease to work; wherefore, they knew not whither they should steer the ship, insomuch that there arose a great storm, yea, a great and terrible tempest, and we were driven back upon the waters for the space of three days; and they began to be frightened exceedingly, lest they should be drowned in the sea; nevertheless they did not loose me. And on the fourth day, which we had been driven back, the tempest began to be exceeding sore.
>
> And it came to pass that we were about to be swallowed up in the depths of the sea.

Then they untied him.

> And it came to pass after they had loosed me, behold, I took the compass, and it did work whither I desired it. And it came to pass that I prayed unto the Lord; and after I had prayed, the winds did cease, and the storm did cease, and there was a great calm.

Equipped with their compass, these ancients appear to have had the advantage of Noah.

Their voyage was toward a "promised land"—the only name they give it. They reached it in safety.

Polygamy is a recent feature in the Mormon religion, and was added by Brigham Young after Joseph Smith's death. Before that, it was regarded as an "abomination." This verse from the Mormon Bible occurs in Chapter II. of the book of Jacob:

For behold, thus saith the Lord, this people begin to wax in iniquity; they understand not the Scriptures; for they seek to excuse themselves in committing whoredoms, because of the things which were written concerning David, and Solomon his son. Behold, David and Solomon truly had many wives and concubines, which thing was abominable before me, saith the Lord; wherefore, thus saith the Lord, I have led this people forth out of the land of Jerusalem, by the power of mine arm, that I might raise up unto me a righteous branch from the fruit of the loins of Joseph. Wherefore, I the Lord God, will not suffer that this people shall do like unto them of old.

However, the project failed—or at least the modern Mormon end of it—for Brigham "suffers" it. This verse is from the same chapter:

Behold, the Lamanites your brethren, whom ye hate, because of their filthiness and the cursings which hath come upon their skins, are more righteous than you; for they have not forgotten the commandment of the Lord, which was given unto our fathers, that they should have, save it were one wife; and concubines they should have none.

The following verse (from Chapter IX. of the Book of Nephi) appears to contain information not familiar to everybody:

And now it came to pass that when Jesus had ascended into heaven, the multitude did disperse, and every man did take his wife and his children, and did return to his own home.

And it came to pass that on the morrow, when the multitude was gathered together, behold, Nephi and his brother whom he had raised from the dead, whose name was Timothy, and also his son, whose name was Jonas, and also Mathoni, and Mathonihah, his brother, and Kumen, and Kumenonhi, and Jeremiah, and Shemnon, and Jonas, and Zedekiah, and Isaiah; now these were the names of the disciples whom Jesus had chosen.

In order that the reader may observe how much more grandeur and picturesqueness (as seen by these Mormon twelve) accompanied one of the tenderest episodes in the life of our Saviour than other eyes seem to have been aware of, I quote the following from the same "book"—Nephi:

And it came to pass that Jesus spake unto them, and bade them arise. And they arose from the earth, and He said unto them, Blessed are ye because of your faith. And now behold, My joy is full. And when He had said these words, He wept, and the multitude bear record of it, and He took their little children, one by one, and blessed them, and prayed unto the Father for them. And when He had done this He wept again, and He spake unto the multitude, and saith unto them, Behold your little ones. And as they looked to behold, they cast their eyes toward heaven, and they saw the heavens open, and they saw angels descending out of heaven as it were, in the midst of fire; and they came down and encircled those little ones about, and they were encircled about with fire; and the angels did minister unto them, and the multitude did see and hear and bear record; and they know that their record is true, for they all of them did see and hear, every man for himself; and they were in number about two thousand and five hundred souls; and they did consist of men, women, and children.

And what else would they be likely to consist of?

The Book of Ether is an incomprehensible medley of "history," much of it relating to battles and sieges among peoples whom the reader has possibly never heard of; and who inhabited a country which is not set down in the geography. There was a King with the remarkable name of Coriantumr, and he warred with Shared, and Lib, and Shiz, and others, in the "plains of Heshlon"; and the "valley of Gilgal"; and the "wilderness of Akish"; and the "land of Moran"; and the "plains of Agosh"; and "Ogath," and "Ramah," and the "land of Corihor," and the "hill Comnor," by "the waters of Ripliancum," etc., etc., etc. "And it came to pass," after a deal of fighting, that Coriantumr, upon making calculation of his losses, found that "there had been slain two millions of mighty men, and also their wives and their children"—say 5,000,000 or 6,000,000 in all—"and he began to sorrow in his heart." Unquestionably it was time. So he wrote to Shiz, asking a cessation of hostilities, and offering to give up his kingdom to save his people. Shiz declined, except upon condition that Coriantumr would come and let him cut his head off first—a thing which Coriantumr would not do. Then there was more fighting for a season; then *four years* were devoted to gathering the forces for a final struggle—after which ensued a battle, which, I take it, is the most remarkable set forth in history,—except, perhaps, that of the Kilkenny cats, which it resembles in some respects. This is the account of the gathering and the battle:

7. And it came to pass that they did gather together all the people, upon all the face of the land, who had not been slain, save it was Ether. And it came to pass that Ether did behold all the doings of the people; and he beheld that the people who were for Corianthumr, were gathered to the army of Coriantumr; and the people who were for Shiz, were gathered together to the army of Shiz; wherefore they were for the space of four years gathering together the people, that they might get all who were upon the face of the land, and that they might receive all the strength which it was possible that they could receive. And it came to pass that when they were all gathered together, every one to the army which he would, with their wives and their children; both men, women, and children being armed with weapons of war, having shields, and

breast-plates, and head-plates, and being clothed after the manner of war, they did march forth one against another, to battle; and they fought all that day, and conquered not. And it came to pass that when it was night they were weary, and retired to their camps; and after they had retired to their camps, they took up a howling and a lamentation for the loss of the slain of their people; and so great were their cries, their howlings and lamentations, that it did rend the air exceedingly. And it came to pass that on the morrow they did go again to battle, and great and terrible was that day; nevertheless they conquered not, and when the night came again, they did rend the air with their cries, and their howlings, and their mournings, for the loss of the slain of their people.

8. And it came to pass that Coriantumr wrote again an epistle unto Shiz, desiring that he would not come again to battle, but that he would take the kingdom, and spare the lives of the people. But behold, the Spirit of the Lord had ceased striving with them, and Satan had full power over the hearts of the people, for they were given up unto the hardness of their hearts, and the blindness of their minds that they might be destroyed; wherefore they went again to battle. And it came to pass that they fought all that day, and when the night came they slept upon their swords; and on the morrow they fought even until the night came; and when the night came they were drunken with anger, even as a man who is drunken with wine; and they slept again upon their swords; and on the morrow they fought again; and when the night came they had all fallen by the sword save it were fifty and two of the people of Coriantumr, and sixty and nine of the people of Shiz. And it came to pass that they slept upon their swords that night, and on the morrow they fought again, and they contended in their mights with their swords, and with their shields, all that day; and when the night came there were thirty and two of the people of Shiz, and twenty and seven of the people of Coriantumr.

9. And it came to pass that they ate and slept, and prepared for death on the morrow. And they were large and mighty men, as to the strength of men. And it came to pass that they fought for the space of three hours, and they fainted with the loss of blood. And it came to pass that when the men of Coriantumr had received sufficient strength, that they could walk, they were about to flee for their lives, but behold, Shiz arose, and also his men, and he swore in his wrath that he would slay Coriantumr, or he would perish by the sword: wherefore he did pursue them, and on the morrow he did overtake them; and they fought again with the sword. And it came to pass that when they had all fallen by the sword, save it were Coriantumr and Shiz, behold Shiz had fainted with loss of blood. And it came to pass that when Coriantumr had leaned upon his sword, that he rested a little, he smote off the head of Shiz. And it came to pass that after he had smote off the head of Shiz, that Shiz raised upon his hands and fell; and after that he had struggled for breath, he died. And it came to pass that Coriantumr fell to the earth, and became as if he had no life. And the Lord spake unto Ether, and said unto him, go forth. And he went forth, and beheld that the words

of the Lord had all been fulfilled; and he finished his record; and the hundredth part I have not written.

It seems a pity he did not finish, for after all his dreary former chapters of commonplace, he stopped just as he was in danger of becoming interesting.

The Mormon Bible is rather stupid and tiresome to read, but there is nothing vicious in its teachings. Its code of morals is unobjectionable—it is "smouched"* from the New Testament and no credit given.

CHAPTER XVII

At the end of our two days' sojourn, we left Great Salt Lake City hearty and well fed and happy—physically superb but not so very much wiser, as regards the "Mormon question," than we were when we arrived, perhaps. We had a deal more "information" than we had before, of course, but we did not know what portion of it was reliable and what was not—for it all came from acquaintances of a day—strangers, strictly speaking. We were told, for instance, that the dreadful "Mountain Meadows Massacre" was the work of the Indians entirely, and that the Gentiles had meanly tried to fasten it upon the Mormons; we were told, likewise, that the Indians were to blame, partly, and partly the Mormons; and we were told, likewise, and just as positively, that the Mormons were almost if not wholly and completely responsible for that most treacherous and pitiless butchery. We got the story in all these different shapes, but it was not till several years afterward that Mrs. Waite's book, "The Mormon Prophet," came out with Judge Cradlebaugh's trial of the accused parties in it and revealed the truth that the latter version was the correct one and that the Mormons *were* the assassins. All our "information" had three sides to it, and so I gave up the idea that I could settle the "Mormon question" in two days. Still I have seen newspaper correspondents do it in one.

I left Great Salt Lake a good deal confused as to what state of things existed there—and sometimes even questioning in my own mind whether a state of things existed there at all or not. But presently I remembered with a lightening sense of relief that we had learned two or three trivial things there which we could be certain of; and so the two days were not wholly lost. For in-

* Milton.

stance, we had learned that we were at last in a pioneer land, in absolute and tangible reality. The high prices charged for trifles were eloquent of high freights and bewildering distances of freightage. In the east, in those days, the smallest moneyed denomination was a penny and it represented the smallest purchasable quantity of any commodity. West of Cincinnati the smallest coin in use was the silver five-cent piece and no smaller quantity of an article could be bought than "five-cents' worth." In Overland City the lowest coin appeared to be the ten-cent piece; but in Salt Lake there did not seem to be any money in circulation smaller than a quarter, or any smaller quantity purchasable of any commodity than twenty-five cents' worth. We had always been used to half dimes and "five cents' worth" as the minimum of financial negotiations; but in Salt Lake if one wanted a cigar, it was a quarter; if he wanted a chalk pipe, it was a quarter; if he wanted a peach, or a candle, or a newspaper, or a shave, or a little Gentile whiskey to rub on his corns to arrest indigestion and keep him from having the toothache, twenty-five cents was the price, every time. When we looked at the shot-bag of silver, now and then, we seemed to be wasting our substance in riotous living, but if we referred to the expense account we could see that we had not been doing anything of the kind. But people easily get reconciled to big money and big prices, and fond and vain of both—it is a descent to little coins and cheap prices that is hardest to bear and slowest to take hold upon one's toleration. After a month's acquaintance with the twenty-five cent minimum, the average human being is ready to blush every time he thinks of his despicable five-cent days. How sunburnt with blushes I used to get in gandy Nevada, every time I thought of my first financial experience in Salt Lake. It was on this wise (which is a favorite expression of great authors, and a very neat one, too, but I never hear anybody *say* on this wise when they are talking). A young half-breed with a complexion like a yellow-jacket asked me if I would have my boots blacked. It was at the Salt Lake House the morning after we arrived. I said yes, and he blacked them. Then I handed him a silver five-cent piece, with the benevolent air of a person who is conferring wealth and blessedness upon poverty and suffering. The yellow-jacket took it with what I judged to be suppressed emotion, and laid it reverently down in the middle of his broad hand. Then he began to contemplate it, much as a philosopher contemplates a gnat's ear in the ample field of his microscope. Several mountaineers, teamsters, stage-drivers, etc., drew near and dropped into the tableau and fell to surveying the money with that attractive indifference to formality which is noticeable in the hardy pioneer.

Presently the yellow-jacket handed the half dime back to me and told me I ought to keep my money in my pocket-book instead of in my soul, and then I wouldn't get it cramped and shriveled up so!

What a roar of vulgar laughter there was! I destroyed the mongrel reptile on the spot, but I smiled and smiled all the time I was detaching his scalp, for the remark he made *was* good for an "Injun."

Yes, we had learned in Salt Lake to be charged great prices without letting the inward shudder appear on the surface—for even already we had overheard and noted the tenor of conversations among drivers, conductors, and hostlers, and finally among citizens of Salt Lake, until we were well aware that these superior beings despised "emigrants." We permitted no tell-tale shudders and winces in our countenances, for we wanted to seem pioneers, or Mormons, half-breeds, teamsters, stage-drivers, Mountain Meadow assassins—anything in the word that the plains and Utah respected and admired—but we were wretchedly ashamed of being "emigrants," and sorry enough that we had white shirts and could not swear in the presence of ladies without looking the other way.

And many a time in Nevada, afterwards, we had occasion to remember with humiliation that we were "emigrants," and consequently a low and inferior sort of creatures. Perhaps the reader has visited Utah, Nevada, or California, even in these latter days, and while communing with himself upon the sorrowful banishment of those countries from what he considers "the world," has had his wings clipped by finding that *he* is the one to be pitied, and that there are entire populations around him ready and willing to do it for him—yea, who are complacently doing it for him already, wherever he steps his foot. Poor thing, they are making fun of his hat; and the cut of his New York coat; and his conscientiousness about his grammar; and his feeble profanity; and his consumingly ludicrous ignorance of ores, shafts, tunnels, and other things which he never saw before, and never felt enough interest in to read about. And all the time that he is thinking what a sad fate it is to be exiled to that far country, that lonely land, the citizens around him are looking down on him with a blighting compassion because he is an "emigrant" instead of that proudest and blessedest creature that exists on all the earth, a "FORTY-NINER."

The accustomed coach life began again, now, and by midnight it almost seemed as if we never had been out of our snuggery among the mail sacks at all. We had made one alteration, however. We had provided enough bread, boiled ham and hard boiled eggs to last double the six hundred miles of staging we had still to do.

And it was comfort in those succeeding days to sit up and contemplate the majestic panorama of mountains and valleys spread out below us and eat ham and hard boiled eggs while our spiritual natures revelled alternately in rainbows, thunderstorms, and peerless sunsets. Nothing helps scenery like ham and eggs. Ham and eggs, and after these a pipe—an old, rank, delicious pipe—ham and eggs and scenery, a "down grade," a flying coach, a fragrant pipe and a contented heart—these make happiness. It is what all the ages have struggled for.

CHAPTER XVIII

At eight in the morning we reached the remnant and ruin of what had been the important military station of "Camp Floyd," some forty-five or fifty miles from Salt Lake City. At four P.M. we had doubled our distance and were ninety or a hundred miles from Salt Lake. And now we entered upon one of that species of deserts whose concentrated hideousness shames the diffused and diluted horrors of Sahara—an *"alkali"* desert. For sixty-eight miles there was but one break in it. I do not remember that this was really a break; indeed it seems to me that it was nothing but a watering depot *in the midst* of the stretch of sixty-eight miles. If my memory serves me, there was no well or spring at this place, but the water was hauled there by mule and ox teams from the further side of the desert. There was a stage station there. It was forty-five miles from the beginning of the desert, and twenty-three from the end of it.

We plowed and dragged and groped along, the whole livelong night, and at the end of this uncomfortable twelve hours we finished the forty-five-mile part of the desert and got to the stage station where the imported water was. The sun was just rising. It was easy enough to cross a desert in the night while we were asleep; and it was pleasant to reflect, in the morning, that we in actual person *had* encountered an absolute desert and could always speak knowingly of deserts in presence of the ignorant thenceforward. And it was pleasant also to reflect that this was not an obscure, back country desert, but a very celebrated one, the metropolis itself, as you may say. All this was very well and very comfortable and satisfactory—but now we were to cross a desert in *daylight*. This was fine—novel—romantic— dramatically adventurous—*this,* indeed, was worth living for, worth traveling for! We would write home all about it.

This enthusiasm, this stern thirst for adventure, wilted under the sultry August sun and did not last above one hour. One poor little hour—and then we were ashamed that we had "gushed" so. The poetry was all in the anticipation—there is none in the reality. Imagine a vast, waveless ocean stricken dead and turned to ashes; imagine this solemn waste tufted with ash-dusted sage-bushes; imagine the lifeless silence and solitude that belong to such a place; imagine a coach, creeping like a bug through the midst of this shoreless level, and sending up tumbled volumes of dust as if it were a bug that went by steam; imagine this aching monotony of toiling and plowing kept up hour after hour, and the shore still as far away as ever, apparently; imagine team, driver, coach and passengers so deeply coated with ashes that they are all one colorless color; imagine ash-drifts roosting above moustaches and eyebrows like snow accumulations on boughs and bushes. This is the reality of it.

The sun beats down with dead, blistering, relentless malignity; the perspiration is welling from every pore in man and beast, but scarcely a sign of it finds its way to the surface—it is absorbed before it gets there; there is not the faintest breath of air stirring; there is not a merciful shred of cloud in all the brilliant firmament; there is not a living creature visible in any direction whither one searches the blank level that stretches its monotonous miles on every hand; there is not a sound—not a sigh—not a whisper—not a buzz, or a whir of wings, or distant pipe of bird—not even a sob from the lost souls that doubtless people that dead air. And so the occasional sneezing of the resting mules, and the champing of the bits, grate harshly on the grim stillness, not dissipating the spell but accenting it and making one feel more lonesome and forsaken than before.

The mules, under violent swearing, coaxing and whipcracking, would make at stated intervals a "spurt," and drag the coach a hundred or may be two hundred yards, stirring up a billowy cloud of dust that rolled back, enveloping the vehicle to the wheel-tops or higher, and making it seem afloat in a fog. Then a rest followed, with the usual sneezing and bit-champing. Then another "spurt" of a hundred yards and another rest at the end of it. All day long we kept this up, without water for the mules and without ever changing the team. At least we kept it up ten hours, which, I take it, is a day, and a pretty honest one, in an alkali desert. It was from four in the morning till two in the afternoon. And it was so hot! and so close! and our water canteens went dry in the middle of the day and we got so thirsty! It was so stupid and tiresome and dull! and the tedious hours did lag and drag and limp along with such a cruel deliberation! It was so trying to give one's watch a good long undisturbed spell and then take it out and find that it had been fooling away the time and not trying to get ahead any! The alkali dust cut through our lips, it persecuted our eyes, it ate through the delicate membranes and made our noses bleed and *kept* them bleeding—and truly and seriously the romance all faded far away and disappeared, and left the desert trip nothing but a harsh reality—a thirsty, sweltering, longing, hateful reality!

Two miles and a quarter an hour for ten hours—that was what we accomplished. It was hard to bring the comprehension away down to such a snail-pace as that, when we had been used to making eight and ten miles an hour. When we reached the station on the farther verge of the desert, we were glad, for the first time, that the dictionary was along, because we never could have found language to tell how glad we were, in any sort of dictionary but an unabridged one with pictures in it. But there could not have been found in a whole library of dictionaries language sufficient to tell how tired those mules were after their twenty-three mile pull. To try to give the reader an idea of how *thirsty* they were, would be to "gild refined gold or paint the lily."

Somehow, now that it is there, the quotation does not seem to fit—but no matter, let it stay, anyhow. I think it is a graceful and attractive thing, and therefore have tried time and time again to work it in where it *would* fit, but could not succeed. These efforts have kept my mind distracted and ill at ease, and made my narrative seem broken and disjointed, in places. Under these circumstances it seems to me best to leave it in, as above, since this will afford at least a temporary respite from the wear and tear of trying to "lead up" to this really apt and beautiful quotation.

CHAPTER XIX

On the morning of the sixteenth day out from St. Joseph we arrived at the entrance of Rocky Canyon, two hundred and fifty miles from Salt Lake. It was along in this wild country somewhere, and far from any habitation of white men, except the stage stations, that we came across the wretchedest type of mankind I have ever seen, up to this writing. I refer to the Goshoot Indians. From what we could see and all we could learn, they are very considerably inferior to even the despised Digger Indians of California; inferior to all races of savages on our continent; inferior to even the Terra del Fuegans; inferior to the Hottentots, and actually inferior in some respects to the Kytches of Africa. Indeed, I have been obliged to look the bulky volumes of Wood's "Uncivilized Races of Men" clear through in order to find a savage tribe degraded enough to take rank with the Goshoots. I find but one people fairly open to that shameful verdict. It is the Bosjesmans (Bushmen) of South Africa. Such of the Goshoots as we saw, along the road and hanging about the stations, were small, lean, "scrawny" creatures; in complexion a dull black like the ordinary American negro; their faces and hands bearing dirt which they had been hoarding and accumulating for months, years, and even generations, according to the age of the proprietor; a silent, sneaking, treacherous looking race; taking note of everything, covertly, like all the other "Noble Red Men" that we (do not) read about, and betraying no sign in their countenances; indolent, everlastingly patient and tireless, like all other Indians; prideless beggars—for if the beggar instinct were left out of an Indian he would not "go," any more than a clock without a pendulum; hungry, always hungry, and yet never refusing anything that a hog would eat, though often eating what a hog would decline; hunters, but having no higher ambition than to kill and eat jackass rabbits, crickets and grasshoppers, and embezzle carrion from the buzzards and cayotes; savages who, when asked if they have the common Indian belief in a Great Spirit show a something which almost amounts to emotion, thinking whiskey is referred to; a thin, scattering race of almost naked black children, these Goshoots are, who produce nothing at all, and have no villages, and no gatherings together into strictly defined tribal communities—a people whose only shelter is a rag cast on a bush to keep off a portion of the snow, and yet who inhabit one of the most rocky, wintry, repulsive wastes that our country or any other can exhibit.

The Bushmen and our Goshoots are manifestly descended from the self-same gorilla, or kangaroo, or Norway rat, whichever animal-Adam the Darwinians trace them to.

One would as soon expect the rabbits to fight as the Goshoots, and yet they used to live off the offal and refuse of the stations a few months and then come some dark night when no mischief was expected, and burn down the buildings and kill the men from ambush as they rushed out. And once, in the night, they attacked the stage-coach when a District Judge, of Nevada Territory, was the only passenger, and with their first volley of arrows (and a bullet or two) they riddled the stage curtains, wounded a horse or two and mortally wounded the driver. The latter was full of pluck, and so was his passenger. At the driver's call Judge Mott swung himself out, clambered to the box and seized the reins of the team, and away they plunged, through the racing mob of skeletons and under a hurtling storm of missiles. The stricken driver had sunk down on the boot as soon as he was wounded, but had held on to the reins and said he would manage to keep hold of them until relieved. And after they were taken from his relaxing grasp, he lay with his head between Judge Mott's feet, and tranquilly gave directions about the road; he said he believed he could live till the miscreants were outrun and left behind, and that if he managed that, the main difficulty would be at an end, and then if the Judge drove so and so (giving directions about bad places in the road, and general course) he would reach the next station without trouble. The Judge distanced the enemy and at last rattled up to the station and knew that the night's perils were done; but there was no comrade-in-arms for him rejoice with, for the soldierly driver was dead.

Let us forget that we have been saying harsh things about the Overland drivers, now. The disgust which the Goshoots gave me, a disciple of Cooper and a worshipper of the Red Man—even of the scholarly savages in the "Last of the Mohicans" who are fittingly associated with backwoodsmen who divide each sentence into two equal parts: one part critically grammatical, refined and choice of language, and the other part just such an attempt to talk like a hunter or a mountaineer, as a Broadway clerk might make after eating an edition of Emerson Bennett's works and studying frontier life at the Bowery Theatre a couple of weeks—I say that the nausea which the Goshoots gave me, an Indian worshipper, set me to examining authorities, to see if perchance I had been over-estimating the Red Man while viewing him through the mellow moonshine of romance. The revelations that came were disenchanting. It was curious to see how quickly the paint and tinsel fell away from him and left him treacherous, filthy and repulsive—and how quickly the evidences accumulated that wherever one finds an Indian tribe he has only found Goshoots more or less modified by circumstances and surroundings—but Goshoots, after all. They deserve pity, poor creatures; and they can have mine—at this distance. Nearer by, they never get anybody's.

There is an impression abroad that the Baltimore and Washington Railroad Company and many of its employes are Goshoots; but it is an error. There is only a plausible resemblance, which, while it is apt enough to mislead the ignorant, cannot deceive parties who have contemplated both tribes. But seriously, it was not only poor wit, but very wrong to start the report referred to above; for however innocent the motive may have been, the necessary effect was to injure the reputation of a class who have a hard enough time of it in the pitiless deserts of the Rocky Mountains, Heaven knows! If we cannot find it in our hearts to give those poor naked creatures our Christian sympathy and compassion, in God's name let us at least not throw mud at them.

CHAPTER XX

On the seventeenth day we passed the highest mountain peaks we had yet seen, and although the day was very warm the night that followed upon its heels was wintry cold and blankets were next to useless.

On the eighteenth day we encountered the eastward-bound telegraph-constructors at Reese River station and sent a message to his Excellency Gov. Nye at Carson City (distant one hundred and fifty-six miles).

On the nineteenth day we crossed the Great American Desert—forty memorable miles of bottomless sand, into which the coach wheels sunk from six inches to a foot. We worked our passage most of the way across. That is to say, we got out and walked. It was a dreary pull and a long and thirsty one, for we had no water. From one extremity of this desert to the other, the road was white with the bones of oxen and horses. It would hardly be an exaggeration to say that we could have walked the forty miles and set our feet on a bone at every step! The desert was one prodigious graveyard. And the log-chains, wagon tyres, and rotting wrecks of vehicles were almost as thick as the bones. I think we saw log-chains enough rusting there in the desert, to reach across any State in the Union. Do not these relics suggest something of an idea of the fearful suffering and privation the early emigrants to California endured?

At the border of the Desert lies Carson Lake, or The "Sink" of the Carson, a shallow, melancholy sheet of water some eighty or a hundred miles in circumference. Carson River empties into it and is lost—sinks mysteriously into the earth and never appears in the light of the sun again—for the lake has no outlet whatever.

There are several rivers in Nevada, and they all have this mysterious fate. They end in various lakes or "sinks," and that is the last of them. Carson Lake, Humboldt Lake, Walker Lake, Mono Lake, are all great sheets of water without any visible outlet. Water is always flowing into them; none is ever seen to flow out of them, and yet they remain always level full, neither receding nor overflowing. What they do with their surplus is only known to the Creator.

On the western verge of the Desert we halted a moment at Ragtown. It consisted of one loghouse and is not set down on the map.

This reminds me of a circumstance. Just after we left Julesburg, on the Platte, I was sitting with the driver, and he said:

"I can tell you a most laughable thing indeed, if you would like to listen to it. Horace Greeley went over this road once. When he was leaving Carson City he told the driver, Hank Monk, that he had an engagement to lecture at Placerville and was very anxious to go through quick. Hank Monk cracked his whip and started off at an awful pace. The coach bounced up and down in such a terrific way that it jolted the buttons all off of Horace's coat, and finally shot his head clean through the roof of the stage, and then he yelled at Hank Monk and begged him to go easier—said he warn't in as much of a hurry as he was awhile ago. But Hank Monk said, 'Keep your seat, Horace, and I'll get you there on time'—and you bet you he did, too, what was left of him!"

A day or two after that we picked up a Denver man at the cross roads, and he told us a good deal about the country and the Gregory Diggings. He seemed a very entertaining person and a man well posted in the affairs of Colorado. By and by he remarked:

"I can tell you a most laughable thing indeed, if you would like to listen to it. Horace Greeley went over this road once. When he was leaving Carson City he told the driver, Hank Monk, that he had an engagement to lecture at Placerville and was very anxious to go through quick. Hank Monk cracked his whip and started off at an awful pace. The coach bounced up and down in such a terrific way that it jolted the buttons all off of Horace's coat, and finally shot his head clean through the roof of the stage, and then he yelled at Hank Monk and begged him to go easier—said he warn't in as much of a hurry as he was awhile ago. But Hank Monk said, 'Keep your seat, Horace, and I'll get you there on time!'—and you bet you he did, too, what was left of him!"

At Fort Bridger, some days after this, we took on board a cavalry sergeant, a very proper and soldierly person indeed. From no other man during the whole journey, did we gather such a store of concise and well-arranged military information. It was surprising to find in the desolate wilds of our country a man so thoroughly acquainted with everything useful to know in his line of life, and yet of such inferior rank and unpretentious bearing. For as much as three hours we listened to him with unabated interest. Finally he got upon the subject of trans- continental travel, and presently said:

"I can tell you a very laughable thing indeed, if you would like to listen to it. Horace Greeley went over this road once. When he was leaving Carson City he told the driver, Hank Monk, that he had an engagement to lecture at Placerville and was very anxious to go through quick. Hank Monk cracked his whip and started off at an awful pace. The coach bounced up and down in such a terrific way that it jolted the buttons all off of Horace's coat, and finally shot his head clean through the roof of the stage, and then he yelled at Hank Monk and begged him to go easier—said he warn't in as much of a hurry as he was awhile ago. But Hank Monk said, 'Keep your seat, Horace, and I'll get you there on time!'—and you bet you he did, too, what was left of him!"

When we were eight hours out from Salt Lake City a Mormon preacher got in with us at a way station—a gentle, soft-spoken, kindly man, and one whom any stranger would warm to at first sight. I can never forget the pathos that was in his voice as he told, in simple language, the story of his people's wanderings and unpitied sufferings. No pulpit eloquence was ever so moving and so beautiful as this outcast's picture of the first Mormon pilgrimage across the plains, stuggling sorrowfully onward to the land of its banishment and marking its desolate way with graves and watering it with tears. His words so wrought upon us that it was a relief to us all when the conversation drifted into a more cheerful channel and the natural features of the curious country we were in came under treatment. One matter after another was pleasantly discussed, and at length the stranger said:

"I can tell you a most laughable thing indeed, if you would like to listen to it. Horace Greeley went over this road once. When he was leaving Carson City he told the driver, Hank Monk, that he had an engagement to lecture in Placerville, and was very anxious to go through quick. Hank Monk cracked his whip and started off at an awful pace. The coach bounced up and down in such a terrific way that it jolted the buttons all off of Horace's coat, and finally shot his head clean through the roof of the stage, and then he yelled at Hank Monk and begged him to go easier—said he warn't in as much of a hurry as he was awhile ago. But Hank Monk said, 'Keep your seat, Horace, and I'll get you there on time!'—and you bet you he did, too, what was left of him!"

Ten miles out of Ragtown we found a poor wanderer who had lain down to die. He had walked as long as he could, but his limbs had failed him at last. Hunger and fatigue had conquered him. It would have been inhuman to leave him there. We paid his fare to Carson and lifted him into the coach. It was some little time before he showed any very decided signs of life; but by dint of chafing him and pouring brandy between his lips we finally brought him to a languid consciousness. Then we fed him a little, and by and by he seemed to comprehend the situation and a grateful light softened his eye. We made his mail-sack bed as comfortable as possible, and constructed a pillow for him with our coats. He seemed very thankful. Then he looked up in our faces, and said in a feeble voice that had a tremble of honest emotion in it:

"Gentlemen, I know not who you are, but you have saved my life; and although I can never be able to repay you for it, I feel that I can at least make one hour of your long journey lighter. I take it you are strangers to this great thoroughfare, but I am entirely familiar with it. In this connection I can tell you a most laughable thing indeed, if you would like to listen to it. Horace Greeley—"

I said, impressively:

"Suffering stranger, proceed at your peril. You see in me the melancholy wreck of a once stalwart and magnificent manhood. What has brought me to this? That thing which you are about to tell. Gradually but surely, that tiresome old anecdote has sapped my strength, undermined my constitution, withered my life. Pity my helplessness. Spare me only just this once, and tell me about young George Washington and his little hatchet for a change."

We were saved. But not so the invalid. In trying to retain the anecdote in his system he strained himself and died in our arms.

I am aware, now, that I ought not to have asked of the sturdiest citizen of all that region, what I asked of that mere shadow of a man; for, after seven years' residence on the Pacific coast, I know that no passenger or driver on the Overland ever corked that anecdote in, when a stranger was by, and survived. Within a period of six years I crossed and recrossed the Sierras between Nevada and California thirteen times by stage and listened to that deathless incident four hundred and eighty-one or eighty-two times. I have the list somewhere. Drivers always told it, conductors told it, landlords told it, chance passengers told it, the very Chinamen and vagrant Indians recounted it. I have had the same driver tell it to me two or three times in the same afternoon. It has come to me in all the multitude of tongues that Babel bequeathed to earth, and flavored with whiskey, brandy, beer, cologne, sozodont, tobacco, garlic, onions, grasshoppers—everything that has a fragrance to it through all the long list of things that are gorged or guzzled by the sons of men.

I never have smelt any anecdote as often as I have smelt that one; never have smelt any anecdote that smelt so variegated as that one. And you never could learn to know it by its smell, because every time you thought you had learned the smell of it, it would turn up with a different smell. Bayard Taylor has written about this hoary anecdote, Richardson has published it; so have Jones, Smith, Johnson, Ross Browne, and every other correspondence-inditing being that ever set his foot upon the great overland road anywhere between Julesburg and San Francisco; and I have heard that it is in the Talmud. I have seen it in print in nine different foreign languages; I have been told that it is employed in the inquisition in Rome; and I now learn with regret that it is going to be set to music. I do not think that such things are right.

Stage-coaching on the Overland is no more, and stage drivers are a race defunct. I wonder if they bequeathed that bald-headed anecdote to their successors, the railroad brakemen and conductors, and if these latter still persecute the helpless passenger with it until he concludes, as did many a tourist of other days, that the real grandeurs of the Pacific coast are not Yo Semite and the Big Trees, but Hank Monk and his adventure with Horace Greeley.*

CHAPTER XXI

We were approaching the end of our long journey. It was the morning of the twentieth day. At noon we would reach Carson City, the capital of Nevada Territory. We were not glad, but sorry. It had been a fine pleasure trip; we had fed fat on wonders every day; we were now well accustomed to stage life, and very fond of it; so the idea of coming to a stand-still and settling down to a humdrum existence in a village was not agreeable, but on the contrary depressing.

Visibly our new home was a desert, walled in by barren, snow-clad mountains. There was not a tree in sight. There was no vegetation but the endless sage-brush and greasewood. All nature was gray with it. We were plowing through great deeps of powdery alkali dust that rose in thick clouds and floated across the plain like smoke from a burning house. We were coated with

* And what makes that worn anecdote the more aggravating, is, that the adventure it celebrates *never occurred.* If it were a good anecote, that seeming demerit would be its chiefest virtue, for creative power belongs to greatness; but what ought to be done to a man who would want only contrive so flat a one as this? If *I* were to suggest what ought to be done to him, I should be called extravagant—but what does the thirteenth chapter of Daniel say? Aha!

it like millers; so were the coach, the mules, the mail-bags, the driver—we and the sage-brush and the other scenery were all one monotonous color. Long trains of freight wagons in the distance enveloped in ascending masses of dust suggested pictures of prairies on fire. These teams and their masters were the only life we saw. Otherwise we moved in the midst of solitude, silence and desolation. Every twenty steps we passed the skeleton of some dead beast of burthen, with its dust-coated skin stretched tightly over its empty ribs. Frequently a solemn raven sat upon the skull or the hips and contemplated the passing coach with meditative serenity.

By and by Carson City was pointed out to us. It nestled in the edge of a great plain and was a sufficient number of miles away to look like an assemblage of mere white spots in the shadow of a grim range of mountains overlooking it, whose summits seemed lifted clear out of companionship and consciousness of earthly things.

We arrived, disembarked, and the stage went on. It was a "wooden" town; its population two thousand souls. The main street consisted of four or five blocks of little white frame stores which were too high to sit down on, but not too high for various other purposes; in fact, hardly high enough. They were packed close together, side by side, as if room were scarce in that mighty plain. The sidewalk was of boards that were more or less loose and inclined to rattle when walked upon. In the middle of the town, opposite the stores, was the "plaza" which is native to all towns beyond the Rocky Mountains—a large, unfenced, level vacancy, with a liberty pole in it, and very useful as a place for public auctions, horse trades, and mass meetings, and likewise for teamsters to camp in. Two other sides of the plaza were faced by stores, offices and stables. The rest of Carson City was pretty scattering.

We were introduced to several citizens, at the stage-office and on the way up to the Governor's from the hotel—among others, to a Mr. Harris, who was on horseback; he began to say something, but interrupted himself with the remark:

"I'll have to get you to excuse me a minute; yonder is the witness that swore I helped to rob the California coach—a piece of impertinent intermeddling, sir, for I am not even acquainted with the man."

Then he rode over and began to rebuke the stranger with a six-shooter, and the stranger began to explain with another. When the pistols were emptied, the stranger resumed his work (mending a whip-lash), and Mr. Harris rode by with a polite nod, homeward bound, with a bullet through one of his lungs, and several in his hips; and from them issued little rivulets of blood that coursed down the horse's sides and made the animal look quite picturesque. I never saw Harris shoot a man after that but it recalled to mind that first day in Carson.

This was all we saw that day, for it was two o'clock, now, and according to custom the daily "Washoe Zephyr" set in: a soaring dust-drift about the size of the United States set up edgewise came with it, and the capital of Nevada Territory disappeared from view. Still, there were sights to be seen which were not wholly uninteresting to new comers; for the vast dust cloud was thickly freckled with things strange to the upper air—things living and dead, that flitted hither and thither, going and coming, appearing and disappearing among the rolling billows of dust—hats, chickens and parasols sailing in the remote heavens; blankets, tin signs, sage-brush and shingles a shade lower; door-mats and buffalo robes lower still; shovels and coal scuttles on the next grade; glass doors, cats and little children on the next; disrupted lumber yards, light buggies and wheelbarrows on the next; and down only thirty or forty feet above ground was a scurrying storm of emigrating roofs and vacant lots.

It was something to see that much. I could have seen more, if I could have kept the dust out of my eyes.

But seriously a Washoe wind is by no means a trifling matter. It blows flimsy houses down, lifts shingle roofs occasionally, rolls up tin ones like sheet music, now and then blows a stage coach over and spills the passengers; and tradition says the reason there are so many bald people there, is, that the wind blows the hair off their heads while they are looking skyward after their hats. Carson streets seldom look inactive on Summer afternoons, because there are so many citizens skipping around their escaping hats, like chambermaids trying to head off a spider.

The "Washoe Zephyr" (Washoe is a pet nickname for Nevada) is a peculiarly Scriptural wind, in that no man knoweth "whence it cometh." That is to say, where it *originates*. It comes right over the mountains from the West, but when one crosses the ridge he does not find any of it on the other side! It probably is manufactured on the mountain-top for the occasion, and starts from there. It is a pretty regular wind, in the summer time. Its office hours are from two in the afternoon till two the next morning; and anybody venturing abroad during those twelve hours needs to allow for the wind or he will bring up a mile or two to leeward of the point he is aiming at. And yet the first complaint a Washoe visitor to San Francisco makes, is that the sea winds blow so, there! There is a good deal of human nature in that.

We found the state palace of the Governor of Nevada Territory to consist of a white frame one-story house with two small rooms in it and a stanchion supported shed in front—for grandeur—it compelled the respect of the citizen and inspired the Indians with awe. The newly arrived Chief and Associate Justices of the Territory, and other machinery of the government, were domiciled with less splendor. They were boarding around privately, and had their offices in their bedrooms.

The Secretary and I took quarters in the "ranch" of a worthy French lady by the name of Bridget O'Flannigan, a camp follower of his Excellency the Governor. She had known him in his prosperity as commander-in-chief of the Metropolitan Police of New York, and she would not desert him in his adversity as Governor of Nevada. Our room was on the lower floor, facing the plaza, and when we had got our bed, a small table, two chairs, the government fire-proof safe, and the Unabridged Dictionary into it, there was still room enough left for a visitor—may be two, but not without straining the walls. But the walls could stand it—at least the partitions could, for they consisted simply of one thickness of white "cotton domestic" stretched from corner to corner of the room. This was the rule in Carson—any other kind of partition was the rare exception. And if you stood in a dark room and your neighbors in the next had lights, the shadows on your canvas told queer secrets sometimes! Very often these partitions were made of old flour sacks basted together; and then the difference between the common herd and the aristocracy was, that the common herd had unornamented sacks, while the walls of the aristocrat were overpowering with rudimental fresco—*i.e.,* red and blue mill brands on the flour sacks. Occasionally, also, the better classes embellished their canvas by pasting pictures from *Harper's Weekly* on them. In many cases, too, the wealthy and the cultured rose to spittoons and other evidences of a sumptuous and luxurious taste.* We had a carpet and a genuine queen's-ware washbowl. Consequently we were hated without reserve by the other tenants of the O'Flannigan "ranch." When we added a painted oilcloth window curtain, we simply took our lives into our own hands. To prevent bloodshed I removed up stairs and took up quarters with the untitled plebeians in one of the four-

* Washoe people take a joke so hard that I must explain that the above description was only the rule; there were many honorable exceptions in Carson—plastered ceilings and houses that had considerable furniture in them.—M.T.

teen white pine cot-bedsteads that stood in two long ranks in the one sole room of which the second story consisted.

It was a jolly company, the fourteen. They were principally voluntary camp-followers of the Governor, who had joined his retinue by their own election at New York and San Francisco and came along, feeling that in the scuffle for little territorial crumbs and offices they could not make their condition more precarious than it was, and might reasonably expect to make it better. They were popularly known as the "Irish Brigade," though there were only four or five Irishmen among all the Governor's retainers. His good-natured Excellency was much annoyed at the gossip his henchmen created—especially when there arose a rumor that they were paid assassins of his, brought along to quietly reduce the democratic vote when desirable!

Mrs. O'Flannigan was boarding and lodging them at ten dollars a week apiece, and they were cheerfully giving their notes for it. They were perfectly satisfied, but Bridget presently found that notes that could not be discounted were but a feeble constitution for a Carson boarding-house. So she began to harry the Governor to find employment for the "Brigade." Her importunities and theirs together drove him to a gentle desperation at last, and he finally summoned the Brigade to the presence. Then, said he:

"Gentlemen, I have planned a lucrative and useful service for you—a service which will provide you with recreation amid noble landscapes, and afford you never ceasing opportunities for enriching your minds by observation and study. I want you to survey a railroad from Carson City westward to a certain point! When the legislature meets I will have the necessary bill passed and the remuneration arranged."

"What, a railroad over the Sierra Nevada Mountains?"

"Well, then, survey it eastward to a certain point!"

He converted them into surveyors, chain-bearers and so on, and turned them loose in the desert. It was "recreation" with a vengeance! Recreation on foot, lugging chains through sand and sage-brush, under a sultry sun and among cattle bones, cayotes and tarantulas. "Romantic adventure" could go no further. They surveyed very slowly, very deliberately, very carefully. They returned every night during the first week, dusty, footsore, tired, and hungry, but very jolly. They brought in great store of prodigious hairy spiders—tarantulas—and imprisoned them in covered tumblers up stairs in the "ranch." After the first week, they had to camp on the field, for they were getting well eastward. They made a good many inquiries as to the location of that indefinite "certain point," but got no information. At last, to a peculiarly urgent inquiry of "How far eastward?" Governor Nye telegraphed back:

"To the Atlantic Ocean, blast you!—and then bridge it and go on!"

This brought back the dusty toilers, who sent in a report and ceased from their labors. The Governor was always comfortable about it; he said Mrs. O'Flannigan would hold him for the Brigade's board anyhow, and he intended to get what entertainment he could out of the boys; he said, with his old-time pleasant twinkle, that he meant to survey them into Utah and then telegraph Brigham to hang them for trespass!

The surveyors brought back more tarantulas with them, and so we had quite a menagerie arranged along the shelves of the room. Some of these spiders could straddle over a common saucer with their hairy, muscular legs, and when their feelings were hurt, or their dignity offended, they were the wickedest-looking desperadoes the animal world can furnish. If their glass prison-houses were touched ever so lightly they were up and spoiling for a fight in a minute. Starchy?—proud? Indeed, they would take up a straw and pick their teeth like a member of Congress. There was as usual a furious "zephyr" blowing the first night of the brigade's return, and about midnight the roof of an adjoining stable blew off, and a corner of it came crashing through the side of our ranch. There was a simultaneous awakening, and a tumultuous muster of the brigade in the dark, and a general tumbling and sprawling over each other in the narrow aisle between the bed-rows. In the midst of the turmoil, Bob II—sprung up out of a sound sleep, and knocked down a shelf with his head. Instantly he shouted:

"Turn out, boys—the tarantulas is loose!"

No warning ever sounded so dreadful. Nobody tried, any longer, to leave the room, lest he might step on a tarantula. Every man groped for a trunk or a bed, and jumped on it. Then followed the strangest silence—a silence of grisly suspense it was, too—waiting, expectancy, fear. It was as dark as pitch, and one had to imagine the spectacle of those fourteen scant-clad men roosting gingerly on trunks and beds, for not a thing could be seen. Then came occasional little interruptions of the silence, and one could recognize a man and tell his locality by his voice, or locate any other sound a sufferer made by his gropings or changes of position. The occasional voices were not given to much speaking—you simply heard a gentle ejaculation of "Ow!" followed by a solid thump, and you knew the gentleman had felt a hairy blanket or something touch his bare skin and had skipped from a bed to the floor. Another silence. Presently you would hear a gasping voice say:

"Su-su-something's crawling up the back of my neck!"

Every now and then you could hear a little subdued scramble and a sorrowful "O Lord!" and then you knew that somebody was getting away from something he took for a tarantula, and not losing any time about it, either. Directly a voice in the corner rang out wild and clear:

"I've got him! I've got him!" [Pause, and probable change of circumstances.] "No, he's got me! Oh, ain't they *never* going to fetch a lantern!"

The lantern came at that moment, in the hands of Mrs. O'Flannigan, whose anxiety to know the amount of damage done by the assaulting roof had not prevented her waiting a judicious interval, after getting out of bed and lighting up, to see if the wind was done, now, up stairs, or had a larger contract.

The landscape presented when the lantern flashed into the room was picturesque, and might have been funny to some people, but was not to us. Although we were perched so strangely upon boxes, trunks and beds, and so strangely attired, too, we were too earnestly distressed and too genuinely miserable to see any fun about it, and there was not the semblance of a smile anywhere visible. I know I am not capable of suffering more than I did during those few minutes of suspense in the dark, surrounded by those creeping, bloody-minded tarantulas. I had skipped from bed to bed and from box to box in a cold agony, and every time I touched anything that was furzy I fancied I felt the fangs. I had rather go to war than live that episode over again. Nobody was hurt. The man who thought a tarantula had "got him" was mistaken—only a crack in a box had caught his finger. Not one of those escaped tarantulas was ever seen again. There were ten or twelve of them. We took candles and hunted the place high and low for them, but with no success. Did we go back to bed then? We did nothing of the kind. Money could not have persuaded us to do it. We sat up the rest of the night playing cribbage and keeping a sharp lookout for the enemy.

CHAPTER XXII

It was the end of August, and the skies were cloudless and the weather superb. In two or three weeks I had grown wonderfully fascinated with the curious new country, and concluded to put off my return to "the States" awhile. I had grown well accustomed to wearing a damaged slouch hat, blue woolen shirt, and pants crammed into boot-tops, and gloried in the absence of coat, vest and braces. I felt rowdyish and "bully," (as the historian Josephus phrases it, in his fine chapter upon the destruction of the Temple). It seemed to me that nothing could be so fine and so romantic. I had become an officer of the government, but that was for mere sublimity. The office was an unique sinecure. I had nothing to do and no salary. I was private Secretary to his majesty the Secretary and there was not yet writing enough for two of us. So Johnny K——and I devoted our time to amusement. He was the young son of an Ohio nabob and was out there for recreation. He got it. We had heard a world of talk about the marvellous beauty of Lake Tahoe, and finally curiosity drove us thither to see it. Three or four members of the Brigade had been there and located some timber lands on its shores and stored up a quantity of provisions in their camp. We strapped a couple of blankets on our shoulders and took an axe apiece and started—for we intended to take up a wood ranch or so ourselves and become wealthy. We were on foot. The reader will find it advantageous to go horseback. We were told that the distance was eleven miles. We tramped a long time on level ground, and then toiled laboriously up a mountain about a thousand miles high and looked over. No lake there. We descended on the other side, crossed the valley and toiled up another mountain three or four thousand miles high, apparently, and looked over again. No lake yet. We sat down tired and perspiring, and hired a couple of Chinamen to curse those people who had beguiled us. Thus refreshed, we presently resumed the march with renewed vigor and determination. We plodded on, two or three hours longer, and at last the Lake burst upon us—a noble sheet of blue water lifted six thousand three hundred feet above the level of the sea, and walled in by a rim of snow-clad mountain peaks that towered aloft full three thousand feet higher still! It was a vast oval, and one would have to use up eighty or a hundred good miles in traveling around it. As it lay there with the shadows of the mountains brilliantly photographed upon its still surface I thought it must surely be the fairest picture the whole earth affords.

We found the small skiff belonging to the Brigade boys, and without loss of time set out across a deep bend of the lake toward the landmarks that signified the locality of the camp. I got Johnny to row—not because I mind exertion myself, but because it makes me sick to ride backwards when I am at work. But I steered. A three-mile pull brought us to the camp just as the night fell, and we stepped ashore very tired and wolfishly hungry. In a "cache" among the rocks we found the provisions and the cooking utensils, and then, all fatigued as I was, I sat down on a boulder and superintended while Johnny gathered wood and cooked supper. Many a man who had gone through what I had, would have wanted to rest.

It was a delicious supper—hot bread, fried bacon, and black coffee. It was a delicious solitude we were in, too. Three miles away was a saw-mill and some workmen, but there were not fifteen other human beings throughout the wide circumference of the lake. As the darkness closed down and the stars came out and spangled the great mirror with jewels, we smoked meditatively in the solemn hush and forgot our troubles and our pains. In due time we spread our blankets in the warm sand between two large boulders and soon feel asleep, careless of the procession of ants that passed in through rents in our clothing and explored our persons. Nothing could disturb the sleep that fettered us, for it had been fairly earned, and if our consciences had any sins on them they had to adjourn court for that night, any way. The wind rose just as we were losing consciousness, and we were lulled to sleep by the beating of the surf upon the shore.

It is always very cold on that lake shore in the night, but we had plenty of blankets and were warm enough. We never moved a muscle all night, but waked at early dawn in the original positions, and got up at once, thoroughly refreshed, free from soreness, and brim full of friskiness. There is no end of wholesome medicine in such an experience. That morning we could have whipped ten such people as we were the day before—sick ones at any rate. But the world is slow, and people will go to "water cures" and "movement cures" and to foreign lands for health. Three months of camp life on Lake Tahoe would restore an Egyptian mummy to his pristine vigor, and give him an appetite like an alligator. I do not mean the oldest and driest mummies, of course, but the fresher ones. The air up there in the clouds is very pure and fine, bracing and delicious. And why shouldn't it be?—it is the same the angels breathe. I think that hardly any amount of fatigue can be gathered together that a man cannot sleep off in one night on the sand by its side. Not under a roof, but under the sky; it seldom or never rains there in the summer time. I know a man who went there to die. But he made a failure of it. He was a skeleton when he came, and could barely stand. He had no appetite, and did nothing but read tracts and reflect on the future. Three months later he was sleeping out of doors regularly, eating all he could hold, three times a day, and chasing game over mountains three thousand feet high for recreation. And he was a skeleton no longer, but weighed part of a ton. This is no fancy sketch, but the truth. His disease was consumption. I confidently commend his experience to other skeletons.

I superintended again, and as soon as we had eaten breakfast we got in the boat and skirted along the lake shore about three miles and disembarked. We liked the appearance of the place, and so we claimed some three hundred acres of it and stuck our "notices" on a tree. It was yellow pine timber land—a dense forest of trees a hundred feet high and from one to five feet through at the butt. It was necessary to fence our property or we could not hold it. That is to say, it was necessary to cut down trees here and there and make them fall in such a way as to form a sort of enclosure (with pretty wide gaps in it). We cut down three trees apiece, and found it such heart-breaking work that we decided to "rest our case" on those; if they held the property, well and good; if they didn't, let the property spill out through the gaps and go; it was no use to work ourselves to death merely to save a few acres of land. Next day we came back to build a house—for a house was also necessary, in order to hold the property. We decided to build a substantial log-house and excite the envy of the Brigade boys; but by the time we had cut and trimmed the first log it seemed unnecessary to be so elaborate, and so we concluded to build it of saplings. However, two saplings, duly cut and trimmed, compelled recognition of the fact that a still modester architecture would satisfy the law, and so we concluded to build a "brush" house. We devoted the next day to this work, but we did so much "sitting around" and discussing, that by the middle of the afternoon we had achieved only a half-way sort of affair which one of us had to watch while the other cut brush, lest if both turned our backs we might not be able to find it again, it had such a strong family resemblance to the surrounding vegetation. But we were satisfied with it.

We were land owners now, duly seized and possessed, and within the protection of the law. Therefore we decided to take up our residence on our own domain and enjoy that large sense of independence which only such an experience can bring. Late the next afternoon, after a good long rest, we sailed away from the Brigade camp with all the provisions and cooking utensils we could carry off—borrow is the more accurate word—and just as the night was falling we beached the boat at our own landing.

CHAPTER XXIII

If there is any life that is happier than the life we led on our timber ranch for the next two or three weeks, it must be a sort of life which I have not read of in books or experienced in person. We did not see a human being but ourselves during the time, or hear any sounds but those that were made by the wind and the waves, the sighing of the pines, and now and then the far-off thunder of an avalanche. The forest about us was dense and cool, the sky above us was cloudless and brilliant with sunshine, the broad lake before us was glassy and clear, or rippled and breezy, or black and storm-tossed, according to Nature's mood; and its circling border of mountain domes, clothed with forests, scarred with land-slides, cloven by canons and valleys, and helmeted with glittering snow, fitly framed and finished the noble picture. The view was always fascinating, bewitching, entrancing. The eye was never tired of gazing, night or day, in calm or storm; it suffered but one grief, and that was that it could not look always, but must close sometimes in sleep.

We slept in the sand close to the water's edge, between two protecting boulders, which took care of the stormy night-winds for us. We never took any paregoric to make us sleep. At the first break of dawn we were always up and running footraces to tone down excess of physical vigor and exuberance of spirits. That is, Johnny was—but I held his hat. While smoking the pipe of peace after breakfast we watched the sentinel peaks put on the glory of the sun, and followed the conquering light as it swept down among the shadows, and set the captive crags and forests free. We watched the tinted pictures grow and brighten upon the water till every little detail of forest, precipice and pinnacle was wrought in and finished, and the miracle of the enchanter complete. Then to "business."

That is, drifting around in the boat. We were on the north shore. There, the rocks on the bottom are sometimes gray, sometimes white. This gives the marvelous transparency of the water a fuller advantage than it has elsewhere on the lake. We usually pushed out a hundred yards or so from shore, and then lay down on the thwarts, in the sun, and let the boat drift by the hour whither it would. We seldom talked. It interrupted the Sabbath stillness, and marred the dreams the luxurious rest and indolence brought. The shore all along was indented with deep, curved bays and coves, bordered by narrow sand-beaches; and where the sand ended, the steep mountain-sides rose right up aloft into space—rose up like a vast wall a little out of the perpendicular, and thickly wooded with tall pines.

So singularly clear was the water, that where it was only twenty or thirty feet deep the bottom was so perfectly distinct that the boat seemed floating in the air! Yes, where it was even *eighty* feet deep. Every little pebble was distinct, every speckled trout, every hand's-breadth of sand. Often, as we lay on our faces, a granite boulder, as large as a village church, would start out of the bottom apparently, and seem climbing up rapidly to the surface, till presently it threatened to touch our faces, and we could not resist the impulse to seize an oar and avert the danger. But the boat would float on, and the boulder descend again, and then we could see that when we had been exactly above it, it must still have been twenty or thirty feet below the surface. Down through the transparency of these great depths, the water was not *merely* transparent, but dazzlingly, brilliantly so. All objects seen through it had a bright, strong vividness, not only of outline, but of every minute detail, which they would not have had when seen simply through the same depth of atmosphere. So empty and airy did all spaces seem below us, and so strong was the sense of floating high aloft in mid-nothingness, that we called these boat-excursions "balloon-voyages."

We fished a good deal, but we did not average one fish a week. We could see trout by the thousand winging about in the emptiness under us, or sleeping in shoals on the bottom, but they would not bite—they could see the line too plainly, perhaps. We frequently selected the trout we wanted, and rested the bait patiently and persistently on the end of his nose at a depth of eighty feet, but he would only shake it off with an annoyed manner, and shift his position.

We bathed occasionally, but the water was rather chilly, for all it looked so sunny. Sometimes we rowed out to the "blue water," a mile or two from shore. It was as dead blue as indigo there, because of the immense depth. By official measurement the lake in its centre is one thousand five hundred and twenty-five feet deep!

Sometimes, on lazy afternoons, we lolled on the sand in camp, and smoked pipes and read some old well-worn novels. At night, by the camp-fire, we played euchre and seven-up to strengthen the mind—and played them with cards so greasy and defaced that only a whole summer's acquaintance with them could enable the student to tell the ace of clubs from the jack of diamonds.

We never slept in our "house." It never occurred to us, for one thing; and besides, it was built to hold the ground, and that was enough. We did not wish to strain it.

By and by our provisions began to run short, and we went

back to the old camp and laid in a new supply. We were gone all day, and reached home again about night-fall, pretty tired and hungry. While Johnny was carrying the main bulk of the provisions up to our "house" for future use, I took the loaf of bread, some slices of bacon, and the coffee-pot, ashore, set them down by a tree, lit a fire, and went back to the boat to get the frying-pan. While I was at this, I heard a shout from Johnny, and looking up I saw that my fire was galloping all over the premises!

Johnny was on the other side of it. He had to run through the flames to get to the lake shore, and then we stood helpless and watched the devastation.

The ground was deeply carpeted with dry pine-needles, and the fire touched them off as if they were gunpowder. It was wonderful to see with what fierce speed the tall sheet of flame traveled! My coffee-pot was gone, and everything with it. In a minute and a half the fire seized upon a dense growth of dry manzanita chapparal six or eight feet high, and then the roaring and popping and crackling was something terrific. We were driven to the boat by the intense heat, and there we remained, spell-bound.

Within half an hour all before us was a tossing, blinding tempest of flame! It went surging up adjacent ridges—surmounted them and disappeared in the canons beyond—burst into view upon higher and farther ridges, presently—shed a grander illumination abroad, and dove again—flamed out again, directly, higher and still higher up the mountain-side—threw out skirmishing parties of fire here and there, and sent them trailing their crimson spirals away among remote ramparts and ribs and gorges, till as far as the eye could reach the lofty mountain-fronts were webbed as it were with a tangled network of red lava streams. Away across the water the crags and domes were lit with a ruddy glare, and the firmament above was a reflected hell!

Every feature of the spectacle was repeated in the glowing mirror of the lake! Both pictures were sublime, both were beautiful; but that in the lake had a bewildering richness about it that enchanted the eye and held it with the stronger fascination.

We sat absorbed and motionless through four long hours. We never thought of supper, and never felt fatigue. But at eleven o'clock the conflagration had traveled beyond our range of vision, and then darkness stole down upon the landscape again.

Hunger asserted itself now, but there was nothing to eat. The provisions were all cooked, no doubt, but we did not go to see. We were homeless wanderers again, without any property. Our fence was gone, our house burned down; no insurance. Our pine forest was well scorched, the dead trees all burned up, and our broad acres of manzanita swept away. Our blankets were on our usual sand-bed, however, and so we lay down and went to sleep. The next morning we started back to the old camp, but while out a long way from shore, so great a storm came up that we dared not try to land. So I baled out the seas we shipped, and Johnny pulled heavily through the billows till we had reached a point three or four miles beyond the camp. The storm was increasing, and it became evident that it was better to take the hazard of beaching the boat than go down in a hundred fathoms of water; so we ran in, with tall white-caps following, and I sat down in the stern-sheets and pointed her head-on to the shore. The instant the bow struck, a wave came over the stern that washed crew and cargo ashore, and saved a deal of trouble. We shivered in the lee of a boulder all the rest of the day, and froze all the night through. In the morning the tempest had gone down, and we paddled down to the camp without any unnecessary delay. We were so starved that we ate up the rest of the Brigade's provisions, and then set out to Carson to tell them about it and ask their forgiveness. It was accorded, upon payment of damages.

We made many trips to the lake after that, and had many a hair-breadth escape and blood-curdling adventure which will never be recorded in any history.

CHAPTER XXIV

I resolved to have a horse to ride. I had never seen such wild, free, magnificent horsemanship outside of a circus as these picturesquely-clad Mexicans, Californians and Mexicanized Americans displayed in Carson streets every day. How they rode! Leaning just gently forward out of the perpendicular, easy and nonchalant, with broad slouch-hat brim blown square up in front, and long *riata* swinging above the head, they swept through the town like the wind! The next minute they were only a sailing puff of dust on the far desert. If they trotted, they sat up gallantly and gracefully, and seemed part of the horse; did not go jiggering up and down after the silly Miss-Nancy fashion of the riding-schools. I had quickly learned to tell a horse from a cow, and was full of anxiety to learn more. I was resolved to buy a horse.

While the thought was rankling in my mind, the auctioneer came skurrying through the plaza on a black beast that had as many humps and corners on him as a dromedary, and was necessarily uncomely; but he was "going, going, at twenty-two!—horse, saddle and bridle at twenty-two dollars, gentlemen!" and I could hardly resist.

A man whom I did not know (he turned out to be the auctioneer's brother) noticed the wistful look in my eye, and observed that that was a very remarkable horse to be going at such a price; and added that the saddle alone was worth the money. It was a Spanish saddle, with ponderous *tapidaros,* and furnished with the ungainly sole-leather covering with the unspellable name. I said I had half a notion to bid. Then this keen-eyed person appeared to me to be "taking my measure"; but I dismissed the suspicion when he spoke, for his manner was full of guileless candor and truthfulness. Said he:

"I know that horse—know him well. You are a stranger, I take it, and so you might think he was an American horse, maybe, but I assure you he is not. He is nothing of the kind: but—excuse my speaking in a low voice, other people being near—he is, without the shadow of a doubt, a Genuine Mexican Plug!"

I did not know what a Genuine Mexican Plug was, but there was something about this man's way of saying it, that made me swear inwardly that I would own a Genuine Mexican Plug, or die.

"Has he any other—er—advantages?" I inquired, suppressing what eagerness I could.

He hooked his forefinger in the pocket of my army-shirt, led me to one side, and breathed in my ear impressively these words:

"He can out-buck anything in America!"

"Going, going, going—at *twent—ty*-four dollars and a half, gen—"

"Twenty-seven!" I shouted, in a frenzy.

"And sold!" said the auctioneer, and passed over the Genuine Mexican Plug to me.

I could scarcely contain my exultation. I paid the money, and put the animal in a neighboring livery-stable to dine and rest himself.

In the afternoon I brought the creature into the plaza, and certain citizens held him by the head, and others by the tail, while I mounted him. As soon as they let go, he placed all his feet in a bunch together, lowered his back, and then suddenly arched it upward, and shot me straight into the air a matter of three or four feet! I came as straight down again, lit in the saddle, went instantly up again, came down almost on the high pommel, shot up again, and came down on the horse's neck—all in the space of three or four seconds. Then he rose and stood almost straight up on his hind feet, and I, clasping his lean neck desperately, slid back into the saddle, and held on. He came down, and immediately hoisted his heels into the air, delivering a vicious kick at the sky, and stood on his forefeet. And then down he came once more, and began the original exercise of shooting me straight up again. The third time I went up I heard a stranger say:

"Oh, *don't* he buck, though!"

While I was up, somebody struck the horse a sounding thwack with a leathern strap, and when I arrived again the Genuine Mexican Plug was not there. A Californian youth chased him up and caught him, and asked if he might have a ride. I granted him that luxury. He mounted the Genuine, got lifted into the air once, but sent his spurs home as he descended, and the horse darted away like a telegram. He soared over three fences like a bird, and disappeared down the road toward the Washoe Valley.

I sat down on a stone, with a sigh, and by a natural impulse one of my hands sought my forehead, and the other the base of my stomach. I believe I never appreciated, till then, the poverty of the human machinery—for I still needed a hand or two to place elsewhere. Pen cannot describe how I was jolted up. Imagination cannot conceive how disjointed I was—how internally, externally and universally I was unsettled, mixed up and ruptured. There was a sympathetic crowd around me, though.

One elderly-looking comforter said:

"Stranger, you've been taken in. Everybody in this camp knows that horse. Any child, any Injun, could have told you that he'd buck; he is the very worst devil to buck on the continent of America. You hear *me.* I'm Curry. *Old* Curry. Old *Abe* Curry. And moreover, he is a simon-pure, out-and-out, genuine d—d Mexican plug, and an uncommon mean one at that, too. Why, you turnip, if you had laid low and kept dark, there's chances to buy an *American* horse for mighty little more than you paid for that bloody old foreign relic."

I gave no sign; but I made up my mind that if the auctioneer's brother's funeral took place while I was in the Territory I would postpone all other recreations and attend it.

After a gallop of sixteen miles the Californian youth and the Genuine Mexican Plug came tearing into town again, shedding foam-flakes like the spume-spray that drives before a typhoon, and, with one final skip over a wheelbarrow and a Chinaman, cast anchor in front of the "ranch."

Such panting and blowing! Such spreading and contracting of the red equine nostrils, and glaring of the wild equine eye! But was the imperial beast subjugated? Indeed he was not. His lordship the Speaker of the House thought he was, and mounted him to go down to the Capitol; but the first dash the creature made was over a pile of telegraph poles half as high as a church; and his time to the Capitol—one mile and three quarters—remains unbeaten to this day. But then he took an advantage—he left out the mile, and only did the three quarters. That is to say, he made a straight cut across lots, preferring fences and ditches to a crooked road; and when the Speaker got to the Capitol he said he had been in the air so much he felt as if he had made the trip on a comet.

In the evening the Speaker came home afoot for exercise, and got the Genuine towed back behind a quartz wagon. The next day I loaned the animal to the Clerk of the House to go down to the Dana silver mine, six miles, and *he* walked back for exercise, and got the horse towed. Everybody I loaned him to always walked back; they never could get enough exercise any other way. Still, I continued to loan him to anybody who was willing to borrow him, my idea being to get him crippled, and throw him on the borrower's hands, or killed, and make the borrower pay for him. But somehow nothing ever happened to him. He took chances that no other horse ever took and survived, but he always came out safe. It was his daily habit to try experiments that had always before been considered impossible, but he always got through. Sometimes he miscalculated a little, and did not get his rider through intact, but *he* always got through himself. Of course I had tried to sell him; but that was a stretch of simplicity which met with little sympathy. The auctioneer stormed up and down the streets on him for four days, dispersing the populace, interrupting business, and destroying children, and never got a bid—at least never any but the eighteen-dollar one he hired a notoriously substanceless bummer to make. The people only smiled pleasantly, and restrained their desire to buy, if they had any. Then the auctioneer brought in his bill, and I withdrew the horse from the market. We tried to trade him off at private vendue next, offering him at a sacrifice for second-hand tombstones, old iron, temperance tracts—any kind of property. But holders were stiff, and we retired from the market again. I never tried to ride the horse any more. Walking was good enough exercise for a man like me, that had nothing the matter with him except ruptures, internal injuries, and such things. Finally I tried to *give* him away. But it was a failure. Parties said earthquakes were handy enough on the Pacific coast—they did not wish to own one. As a last resort I offered him to the Governor for the use of the "Brigade." His face lit up eagerly at first, but toned down again, and he said the thing would be too palpable.

Just then the livery stable man brought in his bill for six weeks' keeping—stall-room for the horse, fifteen dollars; hay for the horse, two hundred and fifty! The Genuine Mexican Plug had eaten a ton of the article, and the man said he would have eaten a hundred if he had let him.

I will remark here, in all seriousness, that the regular price of hay during that year and a part of the next was really two hundred and fifty dollars a ton. During a part of the previous year it had sold at five hundred a ton, in gold, and during the winter before that there was such scarcity of the article that in several instances small quantities had brought eight hundred dollars a ton in coin! The consequence might be guessed without my telling it: peopled turned their stock loose to starve, and before the spring arrived Carson and Eagle valleys were almost literally carpeted with their carcases! Any old settler there will verify these statements.

I managed to pay the livery bill, and that same day I gave the Genuine Mexican Plug to a passing Arkansas emigrant whom fortune delivered into my hand. If this ever meets his eye, he will doubtless remember the donation.

Now whoever has had the luck to ride a real Mexican plug will recognize the animal depicted in this chapter, and hardly consider him exaggerated—but the uninitiated will feel justified in regarding his portrait as a fancy sketch, perhaps.

CHAPTER XXV

Originally, Nevada was a part of Utah and was called Carson county; and a pretty large county it was, too. Certain of its valleys produced no end of hay, and this attracted small colonies of Mormon stock-raisers and farmers to them. A few orthodox Americans straggled in from California, but no love was lost between the two classes of colonists. There was little or no friendly intercourse; each party staid to itself. The Mormons were largely in the majority, and had the additional advantage of being peculiarly under the protection of the Mormon government of the Territory. Therefore they could afford to be distant, and even peremptory toward their neighbors. One of the traditions of Carson Valley illustrates the condition of things that prevailed at the time I speak of. The hired girl of one of the American families was Irish, and a Catholic; yet it was noted with surprise that she was the only person outside of the Mormon ring who could get favors from the Mormons. She asked kindnesses of them often, and always got them. It was a mystery to everybody. But one day as she was passing out at the door, a large bowie knife dropped from under her apron, and when her mistress asked for an explanation she observed that she was going out to "borry a wash-tub from the Mormons!"

In 1858 silver lodes were discovered in "Carson County," and then the aspect of things changed. Californians began to flock in, and the American element was soon in the majority. Allegiance to Brigham Young and Utah was renounced, and a temporary territorial government for "Washoe" was instituted by the citizens. Governor Roop was the first and only chief magistrate of it. In due course of time Congress passed a bill to organize "Nevada Territory," and President Lincoln sent out Governor Nye to supplant Roop.

At this time the population of the Territory was about twelve or fifteen thousand, and rapidly increasing. Silver mines were being vigorously developed and silver mills erected. Business of all kinds was active and prosperous and growing more so day by day.

The people were glad to have a legitimately constituted government, but did not particularly enjoy having strangers from distant States put in authority over them—a sentiment that was natural enough. They thought the officials should have been chosen from among themselves—from among prominent citizens who had earned a right to such promotion, and who would be in sympathy with the populace and likewise thoroughly acquainted with the needs of the Territory. They were right in viewing the matter thus, without doubt. The new officers were "emigrants," and that was no title to anybody's affection or admiration either.

The new government was received with considerable coolness. It was not only a foreign intruder, but a poor one. It was not even worth plucking—except by the smallest of small fry office-seekers and such. Everybody knew that Congress had appropriated only twenty thousand dollars a year in greenbacks for its support—about money enough to run a quartz mill a month. And everybody knew, also, that the first year's money was still in Washington, and that the getting hold of it would be a tedious and difficult process. Carson City was too wary and too wise to open a credit account with the imported bantling with anything like indecent haste.

There is something solemnly funny about the struggles of a new-born Territorial government to get a start in this world. Ours had a trying time of it. The Organic Act and the "instructions" from the State Department commanded that a legislature should be elected at such-and-such a time, and its sittings inaugurated at such-and-such a date. It was easy to get legislators, even at three dollars a day, although board was four dollars and fifty cents, for distinction has its charm in Nevada as well as elsewhere, and there were plenty of patriotic souls out of employment; but to get a legislative hall for them to meet in was another matter altogether. Carson blandly declined to give a room rent-free, or let one to the government on credit.

But when Curry heard of the difficulty, he came forward, solitary and alone, and shouldered the Ship of State over the bar and got her afloat again. I refer to "Curry—*Old* Curry—Old *Abe* Curry." But for him the legislature would have been obliged to sit in the desert. He offered his large stone building just outside the capital limits, rent-free, and it was gladly accepted. Then he built a horse-railroad from town to the capitol, and carried the legislators gratis. He also furnished pine benches and chairs for the legislature, and covered the floors with clean saw-dust by way of carpet and spittoon combined. But for Curry the government would have died in its tender infancy. A canvas partition to separate the Senate from the House of Representatives was put up by the Secretary, at a cost of three dollars and forty cents, but the United States declined to pay for it. Upon being reminded that the "instructions" permitted the payment of a liberal rent for a legislative hall, and that that money was saved to the country by Mr. Curry's generosity, the United States said that did not alter the matter, and the three dollars and forty cents would be subtracted from the Secretary's eighteen hundred dollar salary—and it *was!*

The matter of printing was from the beginning an interesting feature of the new government's difficulties. The Secretary was sworn to obey his volume of written "instructions," and these commanded him to do two certain things without fail, viz. :

1. Get the House and Senate journals printed; and,

2. For this work, pay one dollar and fifty cents per "thousand" for composition, and one dollar and fifty cents per "token" for press-work, in greenbacks.

It was easy to swear to do these two things, but it was entirely impossible to do more than one of them. When greenbacks had gone down to forty cents on the dollar, the prices regularly charged everybody by printing establishments were one dollar and fifty cents per "thousand" and one dollar and fifty cents per "token," in *gold*. The "instructions" commanded that the Secretary regard a paper dollar issued by the government as equal to any other dollar issued by the government. Hence the printing of the journals was discontinued. Then the United States sternly rebuked the Secretary for disregarding the "instructions," and warned him to correct his ways. Wherefore he got some printing done, forwarded the bill to Washington with full exhibits of the high prices of things in the Territory, and called attention to a printed market report wherein it would be observed that even hay was two hundred and fifty dollars a ton. The United States responded by subtracting the printing-bill from the Secretary's suffering salary—and moreover remarked with dense gravity that he would find nothing in his "instructions" requiring him to purchase hay!

Nothing in this world is palled in such impenetrable obscurity as a U.S. Treasury Comptroller's understanding. The very fires of the hereafter could get up nothing more than a fitful glimmer in it. In the days I speak of he never could be made to comprehend why it was that twenty thousand dollars would not go as far in Nevada, where all commodities ranged at an enormous figure, as it would in the other Territories, where exceeding cheapness was the rule. He was an officer who looked out for the little expenses all the time. The Secretary of the Territory kept his office in his bedroom, as I before remarked; and he charged the United States no rent, although his "instructions" provided for that item and he could have justly taken advantage of it (a thing which I would have done with more than lightning promptness if I had been Secretary myself). But the United States never applauded this devotion. Indeed, I think my country was ashamed to have so improvident a person in its employ.

Those "instructions" (we used to read a chapter from them every morning, as intellectual gymnastics, and a couple of chapters in Sunday school every Sabbath, for they treated of all subjects under the sun and had much valuable religious matter in them along with the other statistics) those "instructions" commanded that pen-knives, envelopes, pens and writing-paper be furnished the members of the legislature. So the Secretary made the purchase and the distribution. The knives cost three dollars apiece. There was one too many, and the Secretary gave it to the Clerk of the House of Representatives. The United States said the Clerk of the House was not a "member" of the legislature, and took that three dollars out of the Secretary's salary, as usual.

White men charged three or four dollars a "load" for sawing up stove-wood. The Secretary was sagacious enough to know that the United States would never pay any such price as that; so he got an Indian to saw up a load of office wood at one dollar and a half. He made out the usual voucher, but signed no name to it—simply appended a note explaining that an Indian had done the work, and had done it in a very capable and satisfactory way, but could not sign the voucher owing to lack of ability in the necessary direction. The Secretary had to pay that dollar and a half. He thought the United States would admire both his economy and his honesty in getting the work done at half price and not putting a pretended Indian's signature to the voucher, but the United States did not see it in that light. The United States was too much accustomed to employing dollar-and-a-half thieves in all manner of official capacities to regard his explanation of the voucher as having any foundation in fact.

But the next time the Indian sawed wood for us I taught him to make a cross at the bottom of the voucher—it looked like a cross that had been drunk a year—and then I "witnessed" it and it went through all right. The United States never said a word. I was sorry I had not made the voucher for a thousand loads of wood instead of one. The government of my country snubs honest simplicity but fondles artistic villainy, and I think I might have developed into a very capable pickpocket if I had remained in the public service a year or two.

That was a fine collection of sovereigns, that first Nevada legislature. They levied taxes to the amount of thirty or forty thousand dollars and ordered expenditures to the extent of about a million. Yet they had their little periodical explosions of economy like all other bodies of the kind. A member proposed to save three dollars a day to the nation by dispensing with the Chaplain. And yet that short-sighted man needed the Chaplain more than any other member, perhaps, for he generally sat with his feet on his desk, eating raw turnips, during the morning prayer.

The legislature sat sixty days, and passed private toll-road franchises all the time. When they adjourned it was estimated that every citizen owned about three franchises, and it was believed that unless Congress gave the Territory another degree of longitude there would not be room enough to accomodate the toll-roads. The ends of them were hanging over the boundary line everywhere like a fringe.

The fact is, the freighting business had grown to such important proportions that there was nearly as much excitement over suddenly acquired toll-road fortunes as over the wonderful silver mines.

CHAPTER XXVI

By and by I was smitten with the silver fever. "Prospecting parties" were leaving for the mountains every day, and discovering and taking possession of rich silver-bearing lodes and ledges of quartz. Plainly this was the road to fortune. The great "Gould and Curry" mine was held at three or four hundred dollars a foot when we arrived; but in two months it had sprung up to eight hundred. The "Ophir" had been worth only a mere trifle, a year gone by, and now it was selling at nearly *four thousand dollars a foot!* Not a mine could be named that had not experienced an astonishing advance in value within a short time. Everybody was talking about these marvels. Go where you would, you heard nothing else, from morning till far into the night. Tom So-and-So had sold out of the "Amanda Smith" for $40,000—hadn't a cent when he "took up" the ledge six months ago. John Jones had sold half his interest in the "Bald Eagle and Mary Ann" for $65,000, gold coin, and gone to the States for his family. The widow Brewster had "struck it rich" in the "Golden Fleece" and sold ten feet for $18,000—hadn't money enough to buy a crape bonnet when Sing-Sing Tommy killed her husband at Baldy Johnson's wake last spring. The "Last Chance" had found a "clay casing" and knew they were "right on the ledge"—consequence, "feet" that went begging yesterday were worth a brick house apiece to-day, and seedy owners who could not get trusted for a drink at any bar in the country yesterday were roaring drunk on champagne to-day and had hosts of warm personal friends in a town where they had forgotten how to bow or shake hands from long-continued want of practice. Johnny Morgan, a common loafer, had gone to sleep in the gutter and waked up worth a hundred thousand dollars, in consequence of the decision in the "Lady Franklin and Rough and Ready" lawsuit. And so on—day in and day out the talk pelted our ears and the excitement waxed hotter and hotter around us.

I would have been more or less than human if I had not gone mad like the rest. Cart-loads of solid silver bricks, as large as pigs of lead, were arriving from the mills every day, and such sights as that gave substance to the wild talk about me. I succumbed and grew as frenzied as the craziest.

Every few days news would come of the discovery of a bran-new mining region; immediately the papers would teem with accounts of its richness, and away the surplus population would scamper to take possession. By the time I was fairly inoculated with the disease, "Esmeralda" had just had a run and "Humboldt" was beginning to shriek for attention. "Humboldt! Humboldt!" was the new cry, and straightway Humboldt, the newest of the new, the richest of the rich, the most marvellous of the marvellous discoveries in silver-land, was occupying two columns of the public prints to "Esmeralda's" one. I was just on the point of starting to Esmeralda, but turned with the tide and got ready for Humboldt. That the reader may see what moved me, and what would as surely have moved him had he been there, I insert here one of the newspaper letters of the day. It and several other letters from the same calm hand were the main means of converting me. I shall not garble the extract, but put it in just as it appeared in the *Daily Territorial Enterprise*:

> But what about our mines? I shall be candid with you. I shall express an honest opinion, based upon a thorough examination. Humboldt county is the richest mineral region upon God's footstool. Each mountain range is gorged with the precious ores. Humboldt is the true Golconda.
>
> The other day an assay of mere *croppings* yielded exceeding *four thousand dollars to the ton.* A week or two ago an assay of just such surface developments made returns of *seven thousand* dollars to the ton. Our mountains are full of rambling prospectors. Each day and almost every hour reveals new and more startling evidences of the profuse and intensified wealth of our favored county. The metal is not silver alone. There are distinct ledges of auriferous ore. A late discovery plainly evinces cinnabar. The coarser metals are in gross abundance. Lately evidences of bituminous coal have been detected. My theory has ever been that coal is a ligneous formation. I told Col. Whitman, in times past, that the neighborhood of Dayton (Nevada) betrayed no present or previous manifestations of a ligneous foundation, and that hence I had no confidence in his lauded coal mines. I repeated the same doctrine to the exultant coal discoverers of Humboldt. I talked with my friend Captain Burch on the subject. My pyrhanism vanished upon his statement that in the very region referred to he had seen petrified trees of the length of two hundred feet. Then is the fact established that huge forests once cast their grim shadows over this remote section. I am firm in the coal faith. Have no fears of the mineral resources of Humboldt county. They are immense— incalculable.

Let me state one or two things which will help the reader to better comprehend certain items in the above. At this time, our near neighbor, Gold Hill, was the most successful silver mining locality in Nevada. It was from there that more than half the daily shipments of silver bricks came. "Very rich" (and scarce) Gold Hill ore yielded from $100 to $400 to the ton; but the usual yield was only $20 to $40 per ton—that is to say, each hundred pounds of ore yielded from one dollar to two dollars. But the reader will perceive by the above extract, that in Humboldt from one fourth to nearly half the mass was silver! That is to say, every one hundred pounds of the ore had from *two hundred* dollars up to about *three hundred and fifty* in it. Some days later this same correspondent wrote:

I have spoken of the vast and almost fabulous wealth of this region—it is incredible. The intestines of our mountains are gorged with precious ore to plethora. I have said that nature has so shaped our mountains as to furnish most excellent facilities for the working of our mines. I have also told you that the country about here is pregnant with the finest mill sites in the world. But what is the mining history of Humboldt? The Sheba mine is in the hands of energetic San Francisco capitalists. It would seem that the ore is combined with metals that render it difficult of reduction with our imperfect mountain machinery. The proprietors have combined the capital and labor hinted at in my exordium. They are toiling and probing. Their tunnel has reached the length of one hundred feet. From primal assays alone, coupled with the development of the mine and public confidence in the continuance of effort, the stock had reared itself to eight hundred dollars market value. I do not know that one ton of the ore has been converted into current metal. I do know that there are many lodes in this section that surpass the Sheba in primal assay value. Listen a moment to the calculations of the Sheba operators. They purpose transporting the ore concentrated to Europe. The conveyance from Star City (its locality) to Virginia City will cost seventy dollars per ton; from Virginia to San Francisco, forty dollars per ton; from thence to Liverpool, its destination, ten dollars per ton. Their idea is that its conglomerate metals will reimburse them their cost of original extraction, the price of transportation, and the expense of reduction, and that then a ton of the raw ore will net them twelve hundred dollars. The estimate may be extravagant. Cut it in twain, and the product is enormous, far transcending any previous developments of our racy Territory.

A very common calculation is that many of our mines will yield five hundred dollars to the ton. Such fecundity throws the Gould & Curry, the Ophir and the Mexican, of your neighborhood, in the darkest shadow. I have given you the estimate of the value of a single developed mine. Its richness is indexed by its market valuation. The people of Humboldt county are *feet* crazy. As I write, our towns are near deserted. They look as languid as a consumptive girl. What has become of our sinewy and athletic fellow-citizens? They are coursing through ravines and over mountain tops. Their tracks are visible in every direction. Occasionally a horseman will dash among us. His steed betrays hard usage. He alights before his adobe dwelling, hastily exchanges courtesies with his townsmen, hurries to an assay office and from thence to the District Recorder's. In the morning, having renewed his provisional supplies, he is off again on his wild and unbeaten route. Why, the fellow numbers already his feet by the thousands. He is the horse-leech. He has the craving stomach of the shark or anaconda. He would conquer metallic worlds.

This was enough. The instant we had finished reading the above article, four of us decided to go to Humboldt. We commenced getting ready at once. And we also commenced upbraiding ourselves for not deciding sooner—for we were in terror lest all the rich mines would be found and secured before we got there, and we might have to put up with ledges that would not yield more than two or three hundred dollars a ton, maybe. An hour before, I would have felt opulent if I had owned ten feet in a Gold Hill mine whose ore produced twenty-five dollars to the ton; now I was already annoyed at the prospect of having to put up with mines the poorest of which would be a marvel in Gold Hill.

CHAPTER XXVII

Hurry, was the word! We wasted no time. Our party consisted of four persons—a blacksmith sixty years of age, two young lawyers, and myself. We bought a wagon and two miserable old horses. We put eighteen hundred pounds of provisions and mining tools in the wagon and drove out of Carson on a chilly December afternoon. The horses were so weak and old that we soon found that it would be better if one or two of us got out and walked. It was an improvement. Next, we found that it would be better if a third man got out. That was an improvement also. It was at this time that I volunteered to drive, although I had never driven a harnessed horse before and many a man in such a position would have felt fairly excused from such a responsibility. But in a little while it was found that it would be a fine thing if the driver got out and walked also. It was at this time that I resigned the position of driver, and never resumed it again. Within the hour, we found that it would not only be better, but was absolutely necessary, that we four, taking turns, two at a time, should put our hands against the end of the wagon and push it through the sand, leaving the feeble horses little to do but keep out of the way and hold up the tongue. Perhaps it is well for one to know his fate at first, and get reconciled to it. We had learned ours in one afternoon. It was plain that we had to walk through the sand and shove that wagon and those horses two hundred miles. So we accepted the situation, and from that time forth we never rode. More than that, we stood regular and nearly constant watches pushing up behind.

We made seven miles, and camped in the desert. Young Clagett (now member of Congress from Montana) unharnessed and fed and watered the horses; Oliphant and I cut sage-brush, built the fire and brought water to cook with; and old Mr. Ballou the blacksmith did the cooking. This division of labor, and this appointment, was adhered to throughout the journey. We had no tent, and so we slept under our blankets in the open plain. We were so tired that we slept soundly.

We were fifteen days making the trip—two hundred miles; thirteen, rather, for we lay by a couple of days, in one place, to let the horses rest. We could really have accomplished the journey in ten days if we had towed the horses behind the wagon, but we did not think of that until it was too late, and so went on shoving the horses and the wagon too when we might have saved half the labor. Parties who met us, occasionally, advised us to put the horses *in* the wagon, but Mr. Ballou, through whose iron-clad earnestness no sarcasm could pierce, said that that would not do, because the provisions were exposed and would suffer, the horses being "bituminous from long deprivation." The reader will excuse me from translating. What Mr. Ballou customarily meant, when he used a long word, was a secret between himself and his Maker. He was one of the best and kindest hearted men that ever graced a humble sphere of life. He was gentleness and simplicity itself—and unselfishness, too. Although he was more than twice as old as the eldest of us, he never gave himself any airs, privileges, or exemptions on that account. He did a *young* man's share of the work; and did his share of conversing and entertaining from the general standpoint of *any* age—not from the arrogant, overawing summit-height of sixty years. His one striking peculiarity was his Partingtonian fashion of loving and using big words *for their own sakes*, and independent of any bearing they might have upon the thought he was purposing to convey. He always let his ponderous syllables fall with an easy unconsciousness that left them wholly without offensiveness. In truth his air was so natural and so simple that one was always catching himself accepting his stately sentences as meaning something, when they really meant nothing in the world. If a word was long and grand and resonant, that was sufficient to win the old man's love, and he would drop that word into the most out-of-the-way place in a sentence or a subject, and be as pleased with it as if it were perfectly luminous with meaning.

We four always spread our common stock of blankets together on the frozen ground, and slept side by side; and finding that our foolish, long-legged hound pup had a deal of animal heat in him, Oliphant got to admitting him to the bed, between himself and Mr. Ballou, hugging the dog's warm back to his breast and finding great comfort in it. But in the night the pup would get stretchy and brace his feet against the old man's back and shove, grunting complacently the while; and now and then, being warm and snug, grateful and happy, he would paw the old man's back simply in excess of comfort; and at yet other times he would dream of the chase and in his sleep tug at the old man's back hair and bark in his ear. The old gentleman complained mildly about these familiarities, at last, and when he got through with his statement he said that such a dog as that was not a proper animal to admit to bed with tired men, because he was "so meretricious in his movements and so organic in his emotions." We turned the dog out.

It was a hard, wearing, toilsome journey, but it had its bright side; for after each day was done and our wolfish hunger appeased with a hot supper of fried bacon, bread, molasses and black coffee, the pipe-smoking, song-singing and yarn-spinning around the evening camp-fire in the still solitudes of the desert was a happy, care-free sort of recreation that seemed the very summit and culmination of earthly luxury. It is a kind of life that has a potent charm for all men, whether city or country-bred. We are descended from desert-lounging Arabs, and countless ages of growth toward perfect civilization have failed to root out of us the nomadic instinct. We all confess to a gratified thrill at the thought of "camping out."

Once we made twenty-five miles in a day, and once we made forty miles (through the Great American Desert), and ten miles beyond—fifty in all—in twenty-three hours, without halting to eat, drink or rest. To stretch out and go to sleep, even on stony and frozen ground, after pushing a wagon and two horses fifty miles, is a delight so supreme that for the moment it almost seems cheap at the price.

We camped two days in the neighborhood of the "Sink of the Humboldt." We tried to use the strong alkaline water of the Sink, but it would not answer. It was like drinking lye, and not weak lye, either. It left a taste in the mouth, bitter and every way execrable, and a burning in the stomach that was very uncomfortable. We put molasses in it, but that helped it very little; we added a pickle, yet the alkali was the prominent taste, and so it was unfit for drinking. The coffee we made of this water was the meanest compound man has yet invented. It was really viler to the taste than the unameliorated water itself. Mr. Ballou, being the architect and builder of the beverage felt constrained to endorse and uphold it, and so drank half a cup, by little sips, making shift to praise it faintly the while, but finally threw out the remainder, and said frankly it was "too technical for *him*."

But presently we found a spring of fresh water, convenient, and then, with nothing to mar our enjoyment, and no stragglers to interrupt it, we entered into our rest.

CHAPTER XXVIII

After leaving the Sink, we traveled along the Humboldt river a little way. People accustomed to the monster mile-wide Mississippi, grow accustomed to associating the term "river" with a high degree of watery grandeur. Consequently, such people feel rather disappointed when they stand on the shores of the Humboldt or the Carson and find that a "river" in Nevada is a sickly rivulet which is just the counterpart of the Erie canal in all respects save that the canal is twice as long and four times as deep. One of the pleasantest and most invigorating exercises one can contrive is to run and jump across the Humboldt river till he is overheated, and then drink it dry.

On the fifteenth day we completed our march of two hundred miles and entered Unionville, Humboldt county, in the midst of a driving snow-storm. Unionville consisted of eleven cabins and a liberty-pole. Six of the cabins were strung along one side of a deep canyon, and the other five faced them. The rest of the landscape was made up of bleak mountain walls that rose so high into the sky from both sides of the canyon that the village was left, as it were, far down in the bottom of a crevice. It was always daylight on the mountain tops a long time before the darkness lifted and revealed Unionville.

We built a small, rude cabin in the side of the crevice and roofed it with canvas, leaving a corner open to serve as a chimney, through which the cattle used to tumble occasionally, at night, and mash our furniture and interrupt our sleep. It was very cold weather and fuel was scarce. Indians brought brush and bushes several miles on their backs; and when we could catch a laden Indian it was well—and when we could not (which was the rule, not the exception), we shivered and bore it.

I confess, without shame, that I expected to find masses of silver lying all about the ground. I expected to see it glittering in the sun on the mountain summits. I said nothing about this, for some instinct told me that I might possibly have an exaggerated idea about it, and so if I betrayed my thought I might bring derision upon myself. Yet I was as perfectly satisfied in my own mind as I could be of anything, that I was going to gather up, in a day or two, or at furthest a week or two, silver enough to make me satisfactorily wealthy—and so my fancy was already busy with plans for spending this money. The first opportunity that offered, I sauntered carelessly away from the cabin, keeping an eye on the other boys, and stopping and contemplating the sky when they seemed to be observing me; but as soon as the coast was manifestly clear, I fled away as guiltily as a thief might have done and never halted till I was far beyond sight and call. Then I began my search with a feverish excitement that was brimful of expectation—almost of certainty. I crawled about the ground, seizing and examining bits of stone, blowing the dust from them or rubbing them on my clothes, and then peering at them with anxious hope. Presently I found a bright fragment and my heart bounded! I hid behind a boulder and polished it and scrutinized it with a nervous eagerness and a delight that was more pronounced than absolute certainty itself could have afforded. The more I examined the fragment the more I was convinced that I had found the door to fortune. I marked the spot and carried away my specimen. Up and down the rugged mountain side I searched, with always increasing interest and always augmenting gratitude that I had come to Humboldt and come in time. Of all the experiences of my life, this secret search among the hidden treasures of silver-land was the nearest to unmarred ecstasy. It was a delirious revel. By and by, in the bed of a shallow rivulet, I found a deposit of shining yellow scales, and my breath almost forsook me! A gold mine, and in my simplicity I had been content with vulgar silver! I was so excited that I half believed my overwrought imagination was deceiving me. Then a fear came upon me that people might be observing me and would guess my secret. Moved by this thought, I made a circuit of the place, and ascended a knoll to reconnoiter. Solitude. No creature was near. Then I returned to my mine, fortifying myself against possible disappointment, but my fears were groundless—the shining scales were still there. I set about scooping them out, and for an hour I toiled down the windings of the stream and robbed its bed. But at last the descending sun warned me to give up the quest, and I turned homeward laden with wealth. As I walked along I could not help smiling at the thought of my being so excited over my fragment of silver when a nobler metal was almost under my nose. In this little time the former had so fallen in my estimation that once or twice I was on the point of throwing it away.

The boys were as hungry as usual, but I could eat nothing. Neither could I talk. I was full of dreams and far away. Their conversation interrupted the flow of my fancy somewhat, and annoyed me a little, too. I despised the sordid and commonplace things they talked about. But as they proceeded, it began to amuse me. It grew to be rare fun to hear them planning their poor little economies and sighing over possible privations and distresses when a gold mine, all our own, lay within sight of the cabin and I could point it out at any moment. Smothered hilarity began to oppress me, presently. It was hard to resist the impulse to burst out with exultation and reveal everything; but I did resist. I said within myself that I would filter the great news through my lips calmly and be serene as a summer morning while I watched its effect in their faces. I said:

"Where have you all been?"

"Prospecting."

"What did you find?"

"Nothing."

"Nothing? What do you think of the country?"

"Can't tell, yet," said Mr. Ballou, who was an old gold miner, and had likewise had considerable experience among the silver mines.

"Well, haven't you formed any sort of opinion?"

"Yes, a sort of a one. It's fair enough here, may be, but overrated. Seven thousand dollar ledges are scarce, though. That Sheba may be rich enough, but we don't own it; and besides, the rock is so full of base metals that all the science in the world can't work it. We'll not starve, here, but we'll not get rich, I'm afraid."

"So you think the prospect is pretty poor?"

"No name for it!"

"Well, we'd better go back, hadn't we?"

"Oh, not yet—of course not. We'll try it a riffle, first."

"Suppose, now—this is merely a supposition, you know—suppose you could find a ledge that would yield, say, a hundred and fifty dollars a ton—would that satisfy you?"

"Try us once!" from the whole party.

"Or suppose—merely a supposition, of course—suppose you were to find a ledge that would yield two thousand dollars a ton—would *that* satisfy you?"

"Here—what do you mean? What are you coming at? Is there some mystery behind all this?"

"Never mind. I am not saying anything. You know perfectly well there are no rich mines here—of course you do. Because you have been around and examined for yourselves. Anybody would know that, that had been around. But just for the sake of argument, suppose—in a kind of general way—suppose some person were to tell you that two-thousand-dollar ledges were simply contemptible—contemptible, understand—and that right yonder in sight of this very cabin there were piles of pure gold and pure silver—oceans of it—enough to make you all rich in twenty-four hours! Come!"

"I should say he was as crazy as a loon!" said old Ballou, but wild with excitement, nevertheless.

"Gentlemen," said I, "I don't say anything—*I* haven't been around, you know, and of course don't know anything—but all I ask of you is to cast your eye on *that,* for instance, and tell me what you think of it!" and I tossed my treasure before them.

There was an eager scramble for it, and a closing of heads together over it under the candle-light. Then old Ballou said:

"Think of it? I think it is nothing but a lot of granite rubbish and nasty glittering mica that isn't worth ten cents an acre!"

So vanished my dream. So melted my wealth away. So toppled my airy castle to the earth and left me stricken and forlorn.

Moralizing, I observed, then, that "all that glitters is not gold."

Mr. Ballou said I could go further than that, and lay it up among my treasures of knowledge, that *nothing* that glitters is gold. So I learned then, once for all, that gold in its native state is but dull, unornamental stuff, and that only lowborn metals excite the admiration of the ignorant with an ostentatious glitter. However, like the rest of the world, I still go on underrating men of gold and glorifying men of mica. Commonplace human nature cannot rise above that.

CHAPTER XXIX

True knowledge of the nature of silver mining came fast enough. We went out "prospecting" with Mr. Ballou. We climbed the mountain sides, and clambered among sage-brush, rocks and snow till we were ready to drop with exhaustion, but found no silver—nor yet any gold. Day after day we did this. Now and then we came upon holes burrowed a few feet into the declivities and apparently abandoned; and now and then we found one or two listless men still burrowing. But there was no appearance of silver. These holes were the beginnings of tunnels, and the purpose was to drive them hundreds of feet into the mountain, and some day tap the hidden ledge where the silver was. Some day! It seemed far enough away, and very hopeless and dreary. Day after day we toiled, and climbed and searched, and we younger partners grew sicker and still sicker of the promiseless toil. At last we halted under a beetling rampart of rock which projected from the earth high upon the mountain. Mr. Ballou broke off some fragments with a hammer, and examined them long and attentively with a small eye-glass; threw them away and broke off more; said this rock was quartz, and quartz was the sort of rock that contained silver. *Contained* it! I had thought that at least it would be caked on the outside of it like a kind of veneering. He still broke off pieces and critically examined them, now and then wetting the piece with his tongue and applying the glass. At last he exclaimed:

"We've got it!"

We were full of anxiety in a moment. The rock was clean and white, where it was broken, and across it ran a ragged thread of blue. He said that that little thread had silver in it, mixed with base metals, such as lead and antimony, and other rubbish, and that there was a speck or two of gold visible. After a great deal of effort we managed to discern some little fine yellow specks, and judged that a couple of tons of them massed together might make a gold dollar, possibly. We were not jubilant, but Mr. Ballou said there were worse ledges in the world than that. He saved what he called the "richest" piece of the rock, in order to determine its value by the process called the "fire-assay." Then we named the mine "Monarch of the Mountains" (modesty of nomenclature is not a prominent feature in the mines), and Mr. Ballou wrote out and stuck up the following "notice," preserving a copy to be entered upon the books in the mining recorder's office in the town.

"NOTICE."

"We the undersigned claim three claims, of three hundred feet each (and one for discovery), on this silver-bearing quartz lead or lode, extending north and south from this notice, with all its dips, spurs, and angles, variations and sinuosities, together with fifty feet of ground on either side for working the same."

We put our names to it and tried to feel that our fortunes were made. But when we talked the matter all over with Mr. Ballou, we felt depressed and dubious. He said that this surface quartz was not all there was of our mine; but that the wall or ledge of rock called the "Monarch of the Mountains," extended down hundreds and hundreds of feet into the earth—he illustrated by saying it was like a curb-stone, and maintained a nearly uniform thickness—say twenty feet—away down into the bowels of the earth, and was perfectly distinct from the casing rock on each side of it; and that it kept to itself, and maintained its distinctive character always, no matter how deep it extended into the earth or how far it stretched itself through and across the hills and valleys. He said it might be a mile deep and ten miles long, for all we knew; and that wherever we bored into it above ground or below, we would find gold and silver in it, but no gold or silver in the meaner rock it was cased between. And he said that down in the great depths of the ledge was its richness, and the deeper it went the richer it grew. Therefore, instead of working here on the surface, we must either bore down into the rock with a shaft till we came to where it was rich—say a hundred feet or so—or else we must go down into the valley and bore a long tunnel into the mountain side and tap the ledge far under the earth. To do either was plainly the labor of months; for we could blast and bore only a few feet a day—some five or six. But this was not all. He said that after we got the ore out it must be hauled in wagons to a distant silver-mill, ground up, and the silver extracted by a tedious and costly process. Our fortune seemed a century away!

But we went to work. We decided to sink a shaft. So, for a week we climbed the mountain, laden with picks, drills, gads, crowbars, shovels, cans of blasting powder and coils of fuse and strove with might and main. At first the rock was broken and loose and we dug it up with picks and threw it out with shovels, and the hole progressed very well. But the rock became more compact, presently, and gads and crowbars came into play. But shortly nothing could make an impression but blasting powder. That was the weariest work! One of us held the iron drill in its place and another would strike with an eight-pound sledge—it was like driving nails on a large scale. In the course of an hour or two the drill would reach a depth of two or three feet, making a hole a couple of inches in diameter. We would put in a charge of powder, insert half a yard of fuse, pour in sand and gravel and ram it down, then light the fuse and run. When the explosion came and the rocks and smoke shot into the air, we would go back and find about a bushel of that hard, rebellious quartz jolted out. Nothing more. One week of this satisfied me. I resigned. Clagget and Oliphant followed. Our shaft was only twelve feet deep. We decided that a tunnel was the thing we wanted.

So we went down the mountain side and worked a week; at the end of which time we had blasted a tunnel about deep enough to hide a hogshead in, and judged that about nine hundred feet more of it would reach the ledge. I resigned again, and the other boys only held out one day longer. We decided that a tunnel was not what we wanted. We wanted a ledge that was already "developed." There were none in the camp.

We dropped the "Monarch" for the time being.

Meantime the camp was filling up with people, and there was a constantly growing excitement about our Humboldt mines. We fell victims to the epidemic and strained every nerve to acquire more "feet." We prospected and took up new claims, put "notices" on them and gave them grandiloquent names. We traded some of our "feet" for "feet" in other people's claims. In a little while we owned largely in the "Gray Eagle," the "Columbiana," the "Branch Mint," the "Maria Jane," the "Universe," the "Root-Hog-or-Die," the "Samson and Delilah," the "Treasure Trove," the "Golconda," the "Sultana," the "Boomerang," the "Great Republic," the "Grand Mogul," and fifty other "mines" that had never been molested by a shovel or scratched with a pick. We had not less than thirty thousand "feet" apiece in the "richest mines on earth" as the frenzied cant phrased it—and were in debt to the butcher. We were stark mad with excitement—drunk with happiness—-smothered under mountains of prospective wealth—arrogantly compassionate toward the plodding millions who knew not our marvellous canyon—but our credit was not good at the grocer's.

It was the strangest phase of life one can imagine. It was a beggars' revel. There was nothing doing in the district—no mining—no milling—no productive effort—no income—and not enough money in the entire camp to buy a corner lot in an eastern village, hardly; and yet a stranger would have supposed he was walking among bloated millionaires. Prospecting parties swarmed out of town with the first flush of dawn, and swarmed in again at nightfall laden with spoil—rocks. Nothing but rocks. Every man's pockets were full of them; the floor of his cabin was littered with them; they were disposed in labeled rows on his shelves.

CHAPTER XXX

I met men at every turn who owned from one thousand to thirty thousand "feet" in undeveloped silver mines, every single foot of which they believed would shortly be worth from fifty to a thousand dollars—and as often as any other way they were men who had not twenty-five dollars in the world. Every man you met had his new mine to boast of, and his "specimens" ready; and if the opportunity offered, he would infallibly back you into a corner and offer as a favor to *you*, not to *him*, to part with just a few feet in the "Golden Age," or the "Sarah Jane," or some other unknown stack of croppings, for money enough to get a "square meal" with, as the phrase went. And you were never to reveal that he had made you the offer at such a ruinous price, for it was only out of friendship for you that he was willing to make the sacrifice. Then he would fish a piece of rock out of his pocket, and after looking mysteriously around as if he feared he might be waylaid and robbed if caught with such wealth in his possession, he would dab the rock against his tongue, clap an eyeglass to it, and exclaim:

"Look at that! Right there in that red dirt! See it? See the specks of gold? And the streak of silver? That's from the 'Uncle Abe.' There's a hundred thousand tons like that in sight! Right in sight, mind you! And when we get down on it and the ledge comes in solid, it will be the richest thing in the world! Look at the assay! I don't want you to believe *me*—look at the assay!"

Then he would get out a greasy sheet of paper which showed that the portion of rock assayed had given evidence of containing silver and gold in the proportion of so many hundreds or thousands of dollars to the ton. I little knew, then, that the custom was to hunt out the *richest* piece of rock and get it assayed! Very often, that piece, the size of a filbert, was the only fragment in a ton that had a particle of metal in it—and yet the assay made it pretend to represent the average value of the ton of rubbish it came from!

On such a system of assaying as that, the Humboldt world had gone crazy. On the authority of such assays its newspaper correspondents were frothing about rock worth four and seven thousand dollars a ton!

And does the reader remember, a few pages back, the calculations, of a quoted correspondent, whereby the ore is to be mined and shipped all the way to England, the metals extracted, and the gold and silver contents received back by the miners as clear profit, the copper, antimony and other things in the ore being sufficient to pay all the expenses incurred? Everybody's head was full of such "calculations" as those—such raving insanity, rather. Few people took *work* into their calculations—or outlay of money either; except the work and expeditures of other people.

We never touched our tunnel or our shaft again. Why? Because we judged that we had learned the *real* secret of success in silver mining—which was, *not* to mine the silver ourselves by the sweat of our brows and the labor of our hands, but to *sell* the ledges to the dull slaves of toil and let them do the mining!

Before leaving Carson, the Secretary and I had purchased "feet" from various Esmeralda stragglers. We had expected immediate returns of bullion, but were only afflicted with regular and constant "assessments" instead—demands for money wherewith to develop the said mines. These assessments had grown so oppressive that it seemed necessary to look into the matter personally. Therefore I projected a pilgrimage to Carson and thence to Esmeralda. I bought a horse and started, in company with Mr. Ballou and a gentleman named Ollendorff, a Prussian—not the party who has inflicted so much suffering on the world with his wretched foreign grammars, with their interminable repetitions of questions which never have occurred and are never likely to occur in any conversation among human beings. We rode through a snow-storm for two or three days, and arrived at "Honey Lake Smith's," a sort of isolated inn on the Carson river. It was a two-story log house situated in a small knoll in the midst of the vast basin or desert through which the sickly Carson winds its melancholy way. Close to the house were the Overland stage stables, built of sun-dried bricks. There was not another building within several leagues of the place. Towards sunset about twenty hay-wagons arrived and camped around the house and all the teamsters came in to supper—a very, very rough set. There were one or two Overland stage drivers there, also, and half a dozen vagabonds and stragglers; consequently the house was well crowded.

We walked out, after supper, and visited a small Indian camp in the vicinity. The Indian were in a great hurry about something, and were packing up and getting away as fast as they could. In their broken English they said, "By'm-by, heap water!" and by the help of signs made us understand that in their opinion a flood was coming. The weather was perfectly clear, and this was not the rainy season. There was about a foot of water in the insignificant river—or maybe two feet; the stream was not wider than a back alley in a village, and its banks were scarcely higher than a man's head. So, where was the flood to come from? We canvassed the subject awhile and then concluded it was a ruse, and that the Indians had some better reason for leaving in a hurry than fears of a flood in such an exceedingly dry time.

At seven in the evening we went to bed in the second story—with our clothes on, as usual, and all three in the same bed, for every available space on the floors, chairs, etc., was in request, and even then there was barely room for the housing of the inn's guests. An hour later we were awakened by a great turmoil, and springing out of bed we picked our way nimbly among the ranks of snoring teamsters on the floor and got to the front windows of the long room. A glance revealed a strange spectacle, under the moonlight. The crooked Carson was full to the brim, and its waters were raging and foaming in the wildest way—sweeping around the sharp bends at a furious speed, and bearing on their surface a chaos of logs, brush and all sorts of rubbish. A depression, where its bed had once been, in other times, was already filling, and in one or two places the water was beginning to wash over the main bank. Men were flying hither and thither, bringing cattle and wagons close up to the house, for the spot of high ground on which it stood extended only some thirty feet in front and about a hundred in the rear. Close to the old river bed just spoken of, stood a little log stable, and in this our horses were lodged. While we looked, the waters increased so fast in this place that in a few minutes a torrent was roaring by the little stable and its margin encroaching steadily on the logs. We suddenly realized that this flood was not a mere holiday spectacle, but meant damage—and not only to the small log stable but to the Overland buildings close to the main river, for the waves had now come ashore and were creeping about the foundations and invading the great hay-corral adjoining. We ran down and joined the crowd of excited men and frightened animals. We waded knee-deep into the log stable, unfastened the horses and waded out almost *waist*-deep, so fast the waters increased. Then the crowd rushed in a body to the hay-corral and began to tumble down the huge stacks of baled hay and roll the bales up on the high ground by the house. Meantime it was discovered that Owens, an overland driver, was missing, and a man ran to the large stable, and wading in, boot-top deep, discovered him asleep in his bed, awoke him, and waded out again. But Owens was drowsy and resumed his nap; but only for a minute or two, for presently he turned in his bed, his hand dropped over the side and came in contact with the cold water! It was up level with the mattrass! He waded out, breast-deep, almost, and the next moment the sun-burned bricks melted down like sugar and the big building crumbled to a ruin and was washed away in a twinkling.

At eleven o'clock only the roof of the little log stable was out of water, and our inn was on an island in mid-ocean. As far as the eye could reach, in the moonlight, there was no desert visible, but only a level waste of shining water. The Indians were true prophets, but how did they get their information? I am not able to answer the question.

We remained cooped up eight days and nights with that curious crew. Swearing, drinking and card playing were the order of the day, and occasionally a fight was thrown in for variety. Dirt and vermin—but let us forget those features; their profusion is simply inconceivable—it is better that they remain so.

There were two men—however, this chapter is long enough.

CHAPTER XXXI

There were two men in the company who caused me particular discomfort. One was a little Swede, about twenty-five years old, who knew only one song, and he was forever singing it. By day we were all crowded into one small, stifling bar-room, and so there was no escaping this person's music. Through all the profanity, whisky-guzzling, "old sledge" and quarreling, his monotonous song meandered with never a variation in its tiresome sameness, and it seemed to me, at last, that I would be content to die, in order to be rid of the torture. The other man was a stalwart ruffian called "Arkansas," who carried two revolvers in his belt and a bowie knife projecting from his boot, and who was always drunk and always suffering for a fight. But he was so feared, that nobody would accommodate him. He would try all manner of little wary ruses to entrap somebody into an offensive remark, and his face would light up now and then when he fancied he was fairly on the scent of a fight, but invariably his victim would elude his toils and then he would show a disappointment that was almost pathetic. The landlord, Johnson, was a meek, well-meaning fellow, and Arkansas fastened on him early, as a promising subject, and gave him no rest day or night, for awhile. On the fourth morning, Arkansas got drunk and sat himself down to wait for an opportunity. Presently Johnson came in, just comfortably sociable with whisky, and said:

"I reckon the Pennsylvania 'lection—"

Arkansas raised his finger impressively and Johnson stopped. Arkansas rose unsteadily and confronted him. Said he:

"Wha-what do you know a-about Pennsylvania? Answer me that. Wha-what do you know 'bout Pennsylvania?"

"I was only goin' to say—"

"You was only goin' to *say*. *You* was! You was only goin' to say—*what* was you goin' to say? That's it! That's what *I* want to know. *I* want to know wha-what you (*'ic*) what you know about Pennsylvania, since you're makin' yourself so d—d free. Answer me that!"

"Mr. Arkansas, if you'd only let me—"

"Who's a henderin' you? Don't you insinuate nothing agin me!—don't you do it. Don't you come in here bullyin' around, and cussin' and goin' on like a lunatic—don't you do it. 'Coz *I* won't *stand* it. If fight's what you want, out with it! I'm your man! Out with it!"

Said Johnson, backing into a corner, Arkansas following,

menacingly:

"Why, *I* never said nothing, Mr. Arkansas. You don't give a man no chance. I was only goin' to say that Pennsylvania was goin' to have an election next week—that was all—that was everything I was goin' to say—I wish I may never stir if it wasn't."

"Well then why d'n't you say it? What did you come swellin' around that way for, and tryin' to raise trouble?"

"Why *I* didn't come swelling' around, Mr. Arkansas—I just—"

"I'm a liar am I ! Ger-reat Caesar's ghost—"

"Oh, please, Mr. Arkansas, I never meant such a thing as that, I wish I may die if I did. All the boys will tell you that I've always spoke well of you, and respected you more'n any man in the house. Ask Smith. Ain't it so, Smith? Didn't I say, no longer ago than last night, that for a man that was a gentleman *all* the time and every way you took him, give me Arkansas? I'll leave it to any gentleman here if them warn't the very words I used. Come, now, Mr. Arkansas, le's take a drink—le's shake hands and take a drink. Come up—everybody! It's my treat. Come up, Bill, Tom, Bob, Scotty—come up. I want you all to take a drink with me and Arkansas—*old* Arkansas, I call him—bully old Arkansas. Gimme your hand agin. Look at him, boys—just take a *look* at him. Thar stands the whitest man in America!—and the man that denies it has got to fight *me*, that's all. Gimme that old flipper agin!"

They embraced, with drunken affection on the landlord's part and unresponsive toleration on the part of Arkansas, who, bribed by a drink, was disappointed of his prey once more. But the foolish landlord was so happy to have escaped butchery, that he went on talking when he ought to have marched himself out of danger. The consequence was that Arkansas shortly began to glower upon him dangerously, and presently said:

"Lan'lord, will you p-please make that remark over agin if you please?"

"I was a-sayin' to Scotty that my father was up'ards of eighty year old when he died."

"Was that *all* that you said?"

"Yes, that was all."

"Didn't say nothing but that?"

"No—nothing."

Then an uncomfortable silence.

Arkansas played with his glass a moment, lolling on his elbows on the counter. Then he meditatively scratched his left shin with his right boot, while the awkward silence continued. But presently he loafed away toward the stove, looking dissatisfied; roughly shouldered two or three men out of a comfortable position; occupied it himself, gave a sleeping dog a kick that sent him howling under a bench, then spread his long legs and his blanket-coat tails apart and proceeded to warm his back. In a little while he fell to grumbling to himself, and soon he slouched back to the bar and said:

"Lan'lord, what's your idea for rakin' up old personalities and blowin' about your father? Ain't this company agreeable to you? Ain't it? If this company ain't agreeable to you, p'r'aps we'd better leave. Is that your idea? Is that what you're coming at?"

"Why bless your soul, Arkansas, I warn't thinking of such a thing. My father and my mother—"

"Lan'lord, *don't* crowd a man! Don't do it. If nothing'll do you but a disturbance, out with it like a man (*'ic*)—but *don't* rake up old bygones and fling 'em in the teeth of a passel of people that wants to be peaceable if they could git a chance. What's the matter with you this mornin', anyway? I never see a man carry on so."

"Arkansas, I reely didn't mean no harm, and I won't go on with it if it's onpleasant to you. I reckon my licker's got into my head, and what with the flood, and havin' so many to feed and look out for—"

"So *that's* what's a-ranklin' in your heart, is it? You want us to leave do you? There's too many on us. You want us to pack up and swim. Is that it? Come!"

"Please be reasonable, Arkansas. Now *you* know that I ain't the man to—"

"Are you a threatenin' me? Are you? By George, the man don't live that can skeer me! Don't you try to come that game, my chicken—'cuz I can stand a good deal, but I won't stand that. Come out from behind that bar till I clean you! You want to drive us out, do you, you sneakin' underhanded hound! Come out from behind that bar! *I'll* learn you to bully and badger and browbeat a gentleman that's forever trying to befriend you and keep you out of trouble!"

"Please, Arkansas, please don't shoot! If there's got to be bloodshed—"

"Do you hear that, gentlemen? Do you hear him talk about bloodshed? So it's blood you want, is it, you ravin' desperado! You'd made up your mind to murder somebody this mornin'—I knowed it perfectly well. I'm the man, am I? It's me you're goin' to murder, is it? But you can't do it 'thout I get one chance first, you thievin' black-hearted, white-livered son of a nigger! Draw your weepon!"

With that, Arkansas began to shoot, and the landlord to

clamber over benches, men and every sort of obstacle in a frantic desire to escape. In the midst of the wild hubbub the landlord crashed through a glass door, and as Arkansas charged after him the landlord's wife suddenly appeared in the doorway and confronted the desperado with a pair of scissors! Her fury was magnificent. With head erect and flashing eye she stood a moment and then advanced, with her weapon raised. The astonished ruffian hesitated, and then fell back a step. She followed. She backed him step by step into the middle of the bar-room, and then, while the wondering crowd closed up and gazed, she gave him such another tongue-lashing as never a cowed and shamefaced braggart got before, perhaps! As she finished and retired victorious, a roar of applause shook the house, and every man ordered "drinks for the crowd" in one and the same breath.

The lesson was entirely sufficient. The reign of terror was over, and the Arkansas domination broken for good. During the rest of the season of island captivity, there was one man who sat apart in a state of permanent humiliation, never mixing in any quarrel or uttering a boast, and never resenting the insults the once cringing crew now constantly leveled at him, and that man was "Arkansas."

By the fifth or sixth morning the waters had subsided from the land, but the stream in the old river bed was still high and swift and there was no possibility of crossing it. On the eighth it was still too high for an entirely safe passage, but life in the inn had become next to insupportable by reason of the dirt, drunkenness, fighting, etc., and so we made an effort to get away. In the midst of a heavy snow-storm we embarked in a canoe, taking our saddles aboard and towing our horses after us by their halters. The Prussian, Ollendorff, was in the bow, with a paddle, Ballou paddled in the middle, and I sat in the stern holding the halters. When the horses lost their footing and began to swim, Ollendorff got frightened, for there was great danger that the horses would make our aim uncertain, and it was plain that if we failed to land at a certain spot the current would throw us off and almost surely cast us into the main Carson, which was a boiling torrent, now. Such a catastrophe would be death, in all probability, for we would be swept to sea in the "Sink" or overturned and drowned. We warned Ollendorff to keep his wits about him and handle himself carefully, but it was useless; the moment the bow touched the bank, he made a spring and the canoe whirled upside down in ten-foot water. Ollendorff seized some brush and dragged himself ashore, but Ballou and I had to swim for it, encumbered with our overcoats. But we held on to the canoe, and although we were washed down nearly to the Carson, we managed to push the boat ashore and make a safe landing. We were cold and water-soaked, but safe. The horses made a landing, too, but our saddles were gone, of course. We tied the animals in the sage-brush and there they had to stay for twenty-four hours. We baled out the canoe, and ferried over some food and blankets for them, but we slept one more night in the inn before making another venture on our journey.

The next morning it was still snowing furiously when we got away with our new stock of saddles and accoutrements. We mounted and started. The snow lay so deep on the ground that there was no sign of a road perceptible, and the snow-fall was so thick that we could not see more than a hundred yards ahead, else we could have guided our course by the mountain ranges. The case looked dubious, but Ollendorff said his instinct was as sensitive as any compass, and that he could "strike a bee-line" for Carson city and never diverge from it. He said that if he were to straggle a single point out of the true line his instinct would assail him like an outraged conscience. Consequently we dropped into his wake happy and content. For half an hour we poked along warily enough, but at the end of that time we came upon a fresh trail, and Ollendorff shouted proudly:

"I knew I was as dead certain as a compass, boys! Here we are, right in somebody's tracks that will hunt the way for us without any trouble. Let's hurry up and join company with the party."

So we put the horses into as much of a trot as the deep snow would allow, and before long it was evident that we were gaining on our predecessors, for the tracks grew more distinct. We hurried along, and at the end of an hour the tracks looked still newer and fresher—but what surprised us was, that the *number* of travelers in advance of us seemed to steadily increase. We wondered how so large a party came to be traveling at such a time and in such a solitude. Somebody suggested that it must be a company of soldiers from the fort, and so we accepted that solution and jogged along a little faster still, for they could not be far off now. But the tracks still multiplied, and we began to think the platoon of soldiers was miraculously expanding into a regiment—Ballou said they had already increased to five hundred! Presently he stopped his horse and said:

"Boys, these are our own tracks, and we've actually been circussing round and round in a circle for more than two hours, out here in this blind desert! By George this is perfectly hydraulic!"

Then the old man waxed wroth and abusive. He called Ollendorff all manner of hard names—said he never saw such a lurid fool as he was, and ended with the peculiarly venomous opinion that he "did not know as much as a logarythm!"

We certainly had been following our own tracks. Ollendorff and his "mental compass" were in disgrace from that moment. After all our hard travel, here we were on the bank of the stream again, with the inn beyond dimly outlined through the driving snow-fall. While we were considering what to do, the young Swede landed from the canoe and took his pedestrian way Carson-wards, singing his same tiresome song about his "sister and his brother" and "the child in the grave with its mother," and in a short minute faded and disappeared in the white oblivion. He was never heard of again. He no doubt got bewildered and lost, and Fatigue delivered him over to Sleep and Sleep betrayed him to Death. Possibly he followed our treacherous tracks till he became exhausted and dropped.

Presently the Overland stage forded the now fast receding stream and started toward Carson on its first trip since the flood came. We hesitated no longer, now, but took up our march in its wake, and trotted merrily along, for we had good confidence in the driver's bump of locality. But our horses were no match for the fresh stage team. We were soon left out of sight; but it was no matter, for we had the deep ruts the wheels made for a guide. By this time it was three in the afternoon, and consequently it was not very long before night came—and not with a lingering twilight, but with a sudden shutting down like a cellar door, as is its habit in that country. The snow-fall was still as thick as ever, and of course we could not see fifteen steps before us; but all about us the white glare of the snow-bed enabled us to discern the smooth sugar-loaf mounds made by the covered sage-bushes, and just in front of us the two faint grooves which we knew were the steadily filling and slowly disappearing wheel-tracks.

Now those sage-bushes were all about the same height—three or four feet; they stood just about seven feet apart, all over the vast desert; each of them was a mere snow-mound, now; in *any* direction that you proceeded (the same as in a well laid out orchard) you would find yourself moving down a distinctly defined avenue, with a row of these snow-mounds an either side of it—an avenue the customary width of a road, nice and level in its breadth, and rising at the sides in the most natural way, by reason of the mounds. But we had not thought of this. Then imagine the chilly thrill that shot through us when it finally occurred to us, far in the night, that since the last faint trace of the wheel-tracks had long ago been buried from sight, we might now be wandering down a mere sage-brush avenue, miles away from the road and diverging further and further away from it all the time. Having a cake of ice slipped down one's back is placid comfort compared to it. There was a sudden leap and stir of blood that had been asleep for an hour, and as sudden a rousing of all the drowsing activities in our minds and bodies. We were alive and awake at once—and shaking and quaking with consternation, too. There was an instant halting and dismounting, a bending low and an anxious scanning of the road-bed. Useless, of course; for if a faint depression could not be discerned from an altitude of four or five feet above it, it certainly could not with one's nose nearly against it.

CHAPTER XXXII

We seemed to be in a road, but that was no proof. We tested this by walking off in various directions—the regular snow-mounds and the regular avenues between them convinced each man that *he* had found the true road, and that the others had found only false ones. Plainly the situation was desperate. We were cold and stiff and the horses were tired. We decided to build a sage-brush fire and camp out till morning. This was wise, because if we were wandering from the right road and the snow-storm continued another day our case would be the next thing to hopeless if we kept on.

All agreed that a camp fire was what would come nearest to saving us, now, and so we set about building it. We could find no matches, and so we tried to make shift with the pistols. Not a man in the party had ever tried to do such a thing before, but not a man in the party doubted that it *could* be done, and without any trouble—because every man in the party had read about it in books many a time and had naturally come to believe it, with trusting simplicity, just as he had long ago accepted and believed *that other* common book-fraud about Indians and lost hunters making a fire by rubbing two dry sticks together.

We huddled together on our knees in the deep snow, and the horses put their noses together and bowed their patient heads over us; and while the feathery flakes eddied down and turned us into a group of white statuary, we proceeded with the momentous experiment. We broke twigs from a sage bush and piled them on a little cleared place in the shelter of our bodies. In the course of ten or fifteen minutes all was ready, and then, while conversation ceased and our pulses beat low with anxious suspense, Ollendorff applied his revolver, pulled the trigger and blew the pile clear out of the county! It was the flattest failure that ever was.

This was distressing, but it paled before a greater horror—the horses were gone! I had been appointed to hold the bridles, but in my absorbing anxiety over the pistol experiment I had unconsciously dropped them and the released animals had walked off in the storm. It was useless to try to follow them, for their footfalls could make no sound, and one could pass within two yards of the creatures and never see them. We gave them up without an effort at recovering them, and cursed the lying books that said horses would stay by their masters for protection and companionship in a distressful time like ours.

We were miserable enough, before; we felt still more forlorn, now. Patiently, but with blighted hope, we broke more sticks and piled them, and once more the Prussian shot them into annihilation. Plainly, to light a fire with a pistol was an art requiring practice and experience, and the middle of a desert at midnight in a snow-storm was not a good place or time for the acquiring of the accomplishment. We gave it up and tried the other. Each man took a couple of sticks and fell to chafing them together. At the end of half an hour we were thoroughly chilled, and so were the sticks. We bitterly execrated the Indians, the hunters and the books that had betrayed us with the silly device, and wondered dismally what was next to be done. At this critical moment Mr. Ballou fished out four matches from the rubbish of an overlooked pocket. To have found four gold bars would have seemed poor and cheap good luck compared to this. One cannot think how good a match looks under such circumstances—or how lovable and precious, and sacredly beautiful to the eye. This time we gathered sticks with high hopes; and when Mr. Ballou prepared to light the first match, there was an amount of interest centred upon him that pages of writing could not describe. The match burned hopefully a moment, and then went out. It could not have carried more regret with it if it had been a human life. The next match simply flashed and died. The wind puffed the third one out just as it was on the imminent verge of success. We gathered together closer than ever, and developed a solicitude that was rapt and painful, as Mr. Ballou scratched our last hope on his leg. It lit, burned blue and sickly, and then budded into a robust flame. Shading it with his hands, the old gentleman bent gradually down and every heart went with him—everybody, too, for that matter—and blood and breath stood still. The flame touched the sticks at last, took gradual hold upon them—hesitated—took a stronger hold—hesitated again—held its breath five heart-breaking seconds, then gave a sort of human gasp and went out.

Nobody said a word for several minutes. It was a solemn sort of silence; even the wind put on a stealthy, sinister quiet, and made no more noise than the falling flakes of snow. Finally a sad-voiced conversation began, and it was soon apparent that in each of our hearts lay the conviction that this was our last night with the living. I had so hoped that I was the only one who felt so. When the others calmly acknowledged their conviction, it sounded like the summons itself. Ollendorff said:

"Brothers, let us die together. And let us go without one hard feeling towards each other. Let us forget and forgive bygones. I know that you jave felt hard towards me for turning over the canoe, and for knowing too much and leading you round and round in the snow—but I meant well; forgive me. I acknowledge freely that I have had hard feelings against Mr. Ballou for abusing me and calling me a logarythm, which is a thing I do not know what, but no doubt a thing considered disgraceful and unbecoming in America, and it has scarcely been out of my mind and has hurt me a great deal—but let it go; I forgive Mr. Ballou with all my heart, and—"

Poor Ollendorff broke down and the tears came. He was not alone, for I was crying too, and so was Mr. Ballou. Ollendorff got his voice again and forgave me for things I had done and said. Then he got out his bottle of whisky and said that whether he lived or died he would never touch another drop. He said he had given up all hope of life, and although ill-prepared, was ready to submit humbly to his fate; that he wished he could be spared a little longer, not for any selfish reason, but to make a thorough reform in his character, and by devoting himself to helping the poor, nursing the sick, and pleading with the people to guard themselves against the evils of intemperance, make his life a beneficent example to the young, and lay it down at last with the precious reflection that it had not been lived in vain. He ended by saying that his reform should begin at this moment, even here in the presence of death, since no longer time was to be vouchsafed wherein to prosecute it to men's help and benefit—and with that he threw away the bottle of whisky.

Mr. Ballou made remarks of similar purport, and began the reform he could not live to continue, by throwing away the ancient pack of cards that had solaced our captivity during the flood and made it bearable. He said he never gambled, but still was satisfied that the meddling with cards in any way was immoral and injurious, and no man could be wholly pure and blemishless without eschewing them. "And therefore," continued he, "in doing this act I already feel more in sympathy with that spiritual saturnalia necessary to entire and obsolete reform." These rolling syllables touched him as no intelligible eloquence could have done, and the old man sobbed with a mournfulness not unmingled with satisfaction.

My own remarks were of the same tenor as those of my comrades, and I know that the feelings that prompted them were heartfelt and sincere. We were all sincere, and all deeply moved and earnest, for we were in the presence of death and without hope. I threw away my pipe, and in doing it felt that at last I was free of a hated vice and one that had ridden me like a tyrant all my days. While I yet talked, the thought of the good I might have done in the world and the still greater good I might *now* do, with these new incentives and higher and better aims to guide me if I could only be spared a few years longer, overcame me and the tears came again. We put our arms about each other's necks and awaited the warning drowsiness that precedes death by freezing.

It came stealing over us presently, and then we bade each other a last farewell. A delicious dreaminess wrought its web about my yielding senses, while the snow-flakes wove a winding sheet about my conquered body. Oblivion came. The battle of life was done.

CHAPTER XXXIII

I do not know how long I was in a state of forgetfulness, but it seemed an age. A vague consciousness grew upon me by degrees, and then came a gathering anguish of pain in my limbs and through all my body. I shuddered. The thought flitted through my brain, "this is death—this is the hereafter."

Then came a white upheaval at my side, and a voice said, with bitterness:

"Will some gentleman be so good as to kick me behind?"

It was Ballou—at least it was a towzled snow image in a sitting posture, with Ballou's voice.

I rose up, and there in the gray dawn, not fifteen steps from us, were the frame buildings of a stage station, and under a shed stood our still saddled and bridled horses!

An arched snow-drift broke up, now, and Ollendorff emerged from it, and the three of us sat and stared at the houses without speaking a word. We really had nothing to say. We were like the profane man who could not "do the subject justice," the whole situation was so painfully ridiculous and humiliating that words were tame and we did not know where to commence anyhow.

The joy in our hearts at our deliverance was poisoned; well-nigh dissipated, indeed. We presently began to grow pettish by degrees, and sullen; and then, angry at each other, angry at ourselves, angry at everything in general, we moodily dusted the snow from our clothing and in unsociable single file plowed our way to the horses, unsaddled them, and sought shelter in the station.

I have scarcely exaggerated a detail of this curious and absurd adventure. It occurred almost exactly as I have stated it. We actually went into camp in a snow-drift in a desert, at midnight in a storm, forlorn and hopeless, within fifteen steps of a comfortable inn.

For two hours we sat apart in the station and ruminated in disgust. The mystery was gone, now, and it was plain enough why the horses had deserted us. Without a doubt they were under that shed a quarter of a minute after they had left us, and they must have overheard and enjoyed all our confessions and lamentations.

After breakfast we felt better, and the zest of life soon came back. The world looked bright again, and existence was as dear to us as ever. Presently an uneasiness came over me—grew upon me—assailed me without ceasing. Alas, my regeneration was not complete—I wanted to smoke! I resisted with all my strength, but the flesh was weak. I wandered away alone and wrestled with myself an hour. I recalled my promises of reform and preached to myself persuasively, upbraidingly, exhaustively. But it was all vain, I shortly found myself sneaking among the snow-drifts hunting for my pipe. I discovered it after a considerable search, and crept away to hide myself and enjoy it. I remained behind the barn a good while, asking myself how I would feel if my braver, stronger, truer comrades should catch me in my degradation. At last I lit the pipe, and no human being can feel meaner and baser that I did then. I was ashamed of being in my own pitiful company. Still dreading discovery, I felt that perhaps the further side of the barn would be somewhat safer, and so I turned the corner. As I turned the one corner, smoking, Ollendorff turned the other with his bottle to his lips, and between us sat unconscious Ballou deep in a game of "solitaire" with the old greasy cards!

Absurdity could go no farther. We shook hands and agreed to say no more about "reform" and "examples to the rising generation."

The station we were at was at the verge of the Twenty-six-Mile Desert. If we had approached it half an hour earlier the night before, we must have heard men shouting there and firing pistols; for they were expecting some sheep drovers and their flocks and knew that they would infallibly get lost and wander out of reach of help unless guided by sounds. While we remained at the station, three of the drovers arrived, nearly exhausted with their wanderings, but two others of their party were never heard of afterward.

We reached Carson in due time, and took a rest. This rest, together with preparations for the journey to Esmeralda, kept us there a week, and the delay gave us the opportunity to be present at a trial of the great land-slide case of Hyde *vs.* Morgan—an episode which is famous in Nevada to this day. After a word or two of necessary explanation, I will set down the history of this singular affair just as it transpired.

CHAPTER XXXIV

The mountains are very high and steep about Carson, Eagle and Washoe Valleys—very high and very steep, and so when the snow gets to melting off fast in the Spring and the warm surface-earth begins to moisten and soften, the disastrous land-slides commence. The reader cannot know what a land-slide is, unless he has lived in that country and seen the whole side of a mountain taken off some fine morning and deposited down in the valley, leaving a vast, treeless, unsightly scar upon the mountain's front to keep the circumstance fresh in his memory all the years that he may go on living within seventy miles of that place.

General Buncombe was shipped out to Nevada in the invoice of Territorial officers, to be United States Attorney. He considered himself a lawyer of parts, and he very much wanted an opportunity to manifest it—partly for the pure gratification of it and partly because his salary was Territorially meagre (which is a strong expression). Now the older citizens of a new territory look down upon the rest of the world with a calm, benevolent compassion, as long as it keeps out of the way—when it gets in the way they snub it. Sometimes this latter takes the shape of a practical joke.

One morning Dick Hyde rode furiously up to General Buncombe's door in Carson city and rushed into his presence without stopping to tie his horse. He seemed much excited. He told the General that he wanted him to conduct a suit for him and would pay him five hundred dollars if he achieved a victory. And then, with violent gestures and a world of profanity, he poured out his griefs. He said it was pretty well known that for some years he had been farming (or ranching as the more customary term is) in Washoe District, and making a successful thing of it, and furthermore it was known that his ranch was situated just in the edge of the valley, and that Tom Morgan owned a ranch immediately above it on the mountain side. And now the trouble was, that one of those hated and dreaded land-slides had come and slid Morgan's ranch, fences, cabins, cattle, barns and everything down on top of *his* ranch and exactly covered up every single vestige of his property, to a depth of about thirty-eight feet. Morgan was in possession and refused to vacate the premises—said he was occupying his own cabin and not interfering with anybody else's—and said the cabin was standing on the same dirt and same ranch it had always stood on, and he would like to see anybody make him vacate.

"And when I reminded him," said Hyde, weeping, "that it was on top of my ranch and that he was trespassing, he had the infernal meanness to ask me why didn't I *stay* on my ranch and hold possession when I see him a-coming! Why didn't I *stay* on it, the blathering lunatic—by George, when I heard that racket and looked up that hill it was just like the whole world was a-ripping and a-tearing down that mountain side—splinters, and cord-wood, thunder and lightning, hail and snow, odds and ends of hay stacks, and awful clouds of dust!—trees going end over end in the air, rocks as big as a house jumping 'bout a thousand feet high and busting into ten million pieces, cattle turned inside out and a-coming head on with their tails hanging out between their teeth!—and in the midst of all that wrack and destruction sot that cussed Morgan on his gate-post, a-wondering why I didn't *stay and hold possession!* Laws bless me, I just took one glimpse, General, and lit out'n the county in three jumps exactly.

"But what grinds me is that that Morgan hangs on there and won't move off'n that ranch—says it's his'n and he's going to keep it—likes it better'n he did when it was higher up the hill. Mad! Well, I've been so mad for two days I couldn't find my way to town—been wandering around in the brush in a starving condition—got anything here to drink, General? But I'm here *now,* and I'm a-going to law. You hear *me!*"

Never in all the world, perhaps, were a man's feelings so outraged as were the General's. He said he had never heard of such high-handed conduct in all his life as this Morgan's. And he said there was no use in going to law—Morgan had no shadow of right to remain where he was—nobody in the wide world would uphold him in it, and no lawyer would take his case and no judge listen to it. Hyde said that right there was where he was mistaken—everybody in town sustained Morgan; Hal Brayton, a very smart lawyer, had taken his case; the courts being in vacation, it was to be tried before a referee, and ex-Governor Roop had already been appointed to that office and would open his court in a large public hall near the hotel at two that afternoon.

The General was amazed. He said he had suspected before that the people of that Territory were fools, and now he knew it. But he said rest easy, rest easy and collect the witnesses, for the victory was just as certain as if the conflict were already over. Hyde wiped away his tears and left.

At two in the afternoon referee Roop's Court opened, and Roop appeared throned among his sheriffs, the witnesses, and spectators, and wearing upon his face a solemnity so awe- inspiring that some of his fellow-conspirators had misgivings that maybe he had not comprehended, after all, that this was merely a joke. An unearthly stillness prevailed, for at the slightest noise the judge uttered sternly the command:

"Order in the Court!"

And the sheriffs promptly echoed it. Presently the General elbowed his way through the crowd of spectators, with his arms full of law-books, and on his ears fell an order from the judge which was the first respectful recognition of his high official dignity that had ever saluted them, and it trickled pleasantly through his whole system:

"Way for the United States Attorney!"

The witnesses were called—legislators, high government officers, ranchmen, miners, Indians, Chinamen, negroes. Three fourths of them were called by the defendant Morgan, but no matter, their testimony invariably went in favor of the plaintiff Hyde. Each new witness only added new testimony to the absurdity of a man's claiming to own another man's property because his farm had slid down on top of it. Then the Morgan lawyers made their speeches, and seemed to make singularly weak ones—they did really nothing to help the Morgan cause. And now the General, with exultation in his face, got up and made an impassioned effort; he pounded the table, he banged the law-books, he shouted, and roared, and howled, he quoted from everything and everybody, poetry, sarcasm, statistics, history, pathos, bathos, blasphemy, and wound up with a grand war-whoop for free speech, freedom of the press, free schools, the Glorious Bird of America and the principles of eternal justice! [Applause.]

When the General sat down, he did it with the conviction that if there was anything in good strong testimony, a great speech and believing and admiring countenances all around, Mr.

Morgan's case was killed. Ex-Governor Roop leant his head upon his hand for some minutes, thinking, and the still audience waited for his decision. Then he got up and stood erect, with bended head, and thought again. Then he walked the floor with long, deliberate strides, his chin in his hand, and still the audience waited. At last he returned to his throne, seated himself, and began, impressively:

"Gentlemen, I feel the great responsibility that rests upon me this day. This is no ordinary case. On the contrary it is plain that it is the most solemn and awful that ever man was called upon to decide. Gentlemen, I have listened attentively to the evidence, and have perceived that the weight of it, the overwhelming weight of it, is in favor of the plaintiff Hyde. I have listened also to the remarks of counsel, with high interest—and especially will I commend the masterly and irrefutable logic of the distinguished gentleman who represents the plaintiff. But gentlemen, let us beware how we allow mere human testimony, human ingenuity in argument and human ideas of equity, to influence us at a moment so solemn as this. Gentlemen, it ill becomes us, worms as we are, to meddle with the decrees of Heaven. It is plain to me that Heaven, in its inscrutable wisdom, has seen fit to move this defendant's ranch for a purpose. We are but creatures, and we must submit. If Heaven has chosen to favor the defendant Morgan in this marked and wonderful manner; and if Heaven, dissatisfied with the position of the Morgan ranch upon the mountain side, has chosen to remove it to a position more eligible and more advantageous for its owner, it ill becomes us, insects as we are, to question the legality of the act or inquire into the reasons that prompted it. No—Heaven created the ranches and it is Heaven's prerogative to rearrange them, to experiment with them, to shift them around at its pleasure. It is for us to submit, without repining. I warn you that this thing which has happened is a thing with which the sacrilegious hands and brains and tongues of men must not meddle. Gentlemen, it is the verdict of this court that the plaintiff, Richard Hyde, has been deprived of his ranch by the visitation of God! And from this decision there is no appeal."

Buncombe seized his cargo of law-books and plunged out of the court-room frantic with indignation. He pronounced Roop to be a miraculous fool, an inspired idiot. In all good faith he returned at night and remonstrated with Roop upon his extravagant decision, and implored him to walk the floor and think for half an hour, and see if he could not figure out some sort of modification of the verdict. Roop yielded at last and got up to walk. He walked two hours and a half, and at last his face lit up happily and he told Buncombe it had occurred to him that the ranch underneath the new Morgan ranch still belonged to Hyde, that his title to the ground was just as good as it had ever been, and therefore he was of opinion that Hyde had a right to dig it out from under there and—

The General never waited to hear the end of it. He was always an impatient and irascible man, that way. At the end of two months the fact that he had been played upon with a joke had managed to bore itself, like another Hoosac Tunnel, through the solid adamant of his understanding.

CHAPTER XXXV

When we finally left for Esmeralda, horseback, we had an addition to the company in the person of Capt. John Nye, the Governor's brother. He had a good memory, and a tongue hung in the middle. This is a combination which gives immortality to conversation. Capt. John never suffered the talk to flag or falter once during the hundred and twenty miles of the journey. In addition to his conversational powers, he had one or two other endowments of a marked character. One was a singular "handiness" about doing anything and everything, from laying out a railroad or organizing a political party, down to sewing on buttons, shoeing a horse, or setting a broken leg, or a hen. Another was a spirit of accommodation that prompted him to take the needs, difficulties and perplexities of anybody and everybody upon his own shoulders at any and all times, and dispose of them with admirable facility and alacrity—hence he always managed to find vacant beds in crowded inns, and plenty to eat in the emptiest larders. And finally, wherever he met a man, woman or child, in camp, inn or desert, he either knew such parties personally or had been acquainted with a relative of the same. Such another traveling comrade was never seen before. I cannot forbear giving a specimen of the way in which he overcame difficulties. On the second day out, we arrived, very tired and hungry, at a poor little inn in the desert, and were told that the house was full, no provisions on hand, and neither hay nor barley to spare for the horses—we must move on. The rest of us wanted to hurry on while it was yet light, but Capt. John insisted on stopping awhile. We dismounted and entered. There was no welcome for us on any face. Capt. John began his blandishments, and within twenty minutes he had accomplished the following things, viz.: found old acquaintances in three teamsters; discovered that he used to go to school with the landlord's mother; recognized his wife as a lady whose life he had saved once in California, by stopping her runaway horse; mended a child's broken toy and won the favor of its mother, a guest of the inn; helped the hostler bleed a horse, and prescribed for another horse that had the "heaves"; treated the entire party three times at the landlord's bar; produced a later paper than anybody had seen for a week and sat himself down to read the news to a deeply interested audience. The result, summed up, was as follows: The hostler found plenty of feed for our horses; we had a trout supper, an exceedingly sociable time after it, good beds to sleep in, and a surprising breakfast in the morning—and when we left, we left lamented by all! Capt. John had some bad traits, but he had some uncommonly valuable ones to offset them with.

Esmeralda was in many respects another Humboldt, but in a little more forward state. The claims we had been paying assessments on were entirely worthless, and we threw them away. The principal one cropped out of the top of a knoll that was fourteen feet high, and the inspired Board of Directors were running a tunnel under that knoll to strike the ledge. The tunnel would have to be seventy feet long, and would then strike the ledge at the same depth that a *shaft* twelve feet deep would have reached! The Board were living on the "assessments." [N.B.—This hint comes too late for the enlightenment of New York silver miners; they have already learned all about this neat trick by experience.] The Board had no desire to strike the ledge, knowing that it was as barren of silver as a curbstone. This reminiscence calls to mind Jim Townsend's tunnel. He had paid assessments on a mine called the "Daley" till he was well-nigh penniless. Finally an assessment was levied to run a tunnel two hundred and fifty feet on the Daley, and Townsend went up on the hill to look into matters. He found the Daley cropping out of the apex of an exceedingly sharp-pointed peak, and a couple of men up there "facing" the proposed tunnel. Townsend made a calculation. Then he said to the men:

"So you have taken a contract to run a tunnel into this hill two hundred and fifty feet to strike this ledge?"

"Yes, sir."

"Well, do you know that you have got one of the most expensive and arduous undertakings before you that was ever conceived by man?"

"Why no—how is that?"

"Because this hill is only twenty-five feet through from side to side; and so you have got to build two hundred and twenty-five feet of your tunnel on trestle-work!"

The ways of silver mining Boards are exceedingly dark and sinuous.

We took up various claims, and *commenced* shafts and tunnels on them, but never finished any of them. We had to do a certain amount of work on each to "hold" it, else other parties could seize our property after the expiration of ten days. We were always hunting up new claims and doing a little work on them and then waiting for a buyer— who never came. We never found any ore that would yield more than fifty dollars a ton; and as the mills charged fifty dollars a ton for *working* ore and extracting the silver, our pocket-money melted steadily away and none returned to take its place. We lived in a little cabin and cooked for ourselves; and altogether it was a hard life, though a hopeful one—for we never ceased to expect fortune and a customer to burst upon us some day.

At last, when flour reached a dollar a pound, and money could not be borrowed on the best security at less than *eight per cent a month* (I being without the security, too), I abandoned mining and went to milling. That is to say, I went to work as a common laborer in a quartz mill, at ten dollars a week and board.

CHAPTER XXXVI

I had already learned how hard and long and dismal a task it is to burrow down into the bowels of the earth and get out the coveted ore; and now I learned that the burrowing was only half the work; and that to get the silver out of the ore was the dreary and laborious other half of it. We had to turn out at six in the morning and keep at it till dark. This mill was a six-stamp affair, driven by steam. Six tall, upright rods of iron, as large as a man's ankle, and heavily shod with a mass of iron and steel at their lower ends, were framed together like a gate, and these rose and fell, one after the other, in a ponderous dance, in an iron box called a "battery." Each of these rods or stamps weighed six hundred pounds. One of us stood by the battery all day long, breaking up masses of silver-bearing rock with a sledge and shoveling it into the battery. The ceaseless dance of the stamps pulverized the rock to powder, and a stream of water that trickled into the battery turned it to a creamy paste. The minutest particles were driven through a fine wire screen which fitted close around the battery, and were washed into great tubs warmed by super-heated steam—amalgamating pans, they are called. The mass of pulp in the pans was kept constantly stirred up by revolving "mullers." A quantity of quicksilver was kept always in the battery, and this seized some of the liberated gold and silver particles and held on to them; quicksilver was shaken in a fine shower into the pans, also, about every half hour, through a buckskin sack. Quantities of coarse salt and sulphate of copper were added, from time to time to assist the amalgamation by destroying base metals which coated the gold and silver and would not let it unite with the quicksilver. All these tiresome things we had to attend to constantly. Streams of dirty water flowed always from the pans and were carried off in broad wooden troughs to the ravine. One would not suppose that atoms of gold and silver would float on top of six inches of water, but they did; and in order to catch them, coarse blankets were laid in the troughs, and little obstructing "riffles" charged with quicksilver were placed here and there across the troughs also. These riffles had to be cleaned and the blankets washed out every evening, to get their precious accumulations—and after all this eternity of trouble one third of the silver and gold in a ton of rock would find its way to the end of the troughs in the ravine at last and have to be worked over again some day. There is nothing so aggravating as silver milling. There never was any idle time in that mill. There was always something to do. It is a pity that Adam could not have gone straight out of Eden into a quartz mill, in order to understand the full force of his doom to "earn his bread by the sweat of his brow." Every now and then, during the day, we had to scoop some pulp out of the pans, and tediously "wash" it in a horn spoon—wash it little by little over the edge till at last nothing was left but some little dull globules of quicksilver in the bottom. If they were soft and yielding, the pan needed some salt or some sulphate of copper or some other chemical rubbish to assist digestion; if they were crisp to the touch and would retain a dint, they were freighted with all the silver and gold they could seize and hold, and consequently the pans needed a fresh charge of quicksilver. When there was nothing else to do, one could always "screen tailings." That is to say, he could shovel up the dried sand that had washed down to the ravine through the troughs and dash it against an upright wire screen to free it from pebbles and prepare it for working over. The process of amalgamation differed in the various mills, and this included changes in style of pans and other machinery, and a great diversity of opinion existed as to the best in use, but none of the methods employed, involved the principle of milling ore without "screening the tailings." Of all recreations in the world, screening tailings on a hot day, with a long-handled shovel, is the most undesirable.

At the end of the week the machinery was stopped and we "cleaned up." That is to say, we got the pulp out of the pans and batteries, and washed the mud patiently away till nothing was left but the long accumulating mass of quicksilver, with its imprisoned treasures. This we made into heavy, compact snow-balls, and piled them up in a bright, luxurious heap for inspection. Making these snow-balls cost me a fine gold ring—that and ignorance together; for the quicksilver invaded the ring with the same facility with which water saturates a sponge—separated its particles and the ring crumbled to pieces.

We put our pile of quicksilver into an iron retort that had a pipe leading from it to a pail of water, and then applied a roasting heat. The quicksilver turned to vapor, escaped through the pipe into the pail, and the water turned it into good wholesome quicksilver again. Quicksilver is very costly, and they never waste it. On opening the retort, there was our week's work—a lump of pure white, frosty looking silver, twice as large as a man's head. Perhaps a fifth of the mass was gold, but the color of it did not show—would not have shown if two thirds of it had been gold. We melted it up and made a solid brick of it by pouring it into an iron brick-mould.

By such a tedious and laborious process were silver bricks obtained. This mill was but one of many others in operation at the time. The first one in Nevada was built at Egan Canyon and was a small insignificant affair and compared most unfavorably with some of the immense establishments afterwards located at Virginia City and elsewhere.

From our bricks a little corner was chipped off for the "fire-assay"—a method used to determine the proportions of gold, silver and base metals in the mass. This is an interesting process. The chip is hammered out as thin as paper and weighed on scales so fine and sensitive that if you weigh a two-inch scrap of paper on them and then write your name on the paper with a coarse, soft pencil and weigh it again, the scales will take marked notice of the addition. Then a little lead (also weighed) is rolled up with the flake of silver and the two are melted at a great heat in a small vessel called a cupel, made by compressing bone ashes into a cup-shape in a steel mold. The base metals oxydize and are absorbed with the lead into the pores of the cupel. A button or globule of perfectly pure gold and silver is left behind, and by weighing it and noting the loss, the assayer knows the proportion of base metal the brick contains. He has to separate the gold from the silver now. The button is hammered out flat and thin, put in the furnace and kept some time at a red heat; after cooling it off it is rolled up like a quill and heated in a glass vessel containing nitric acid; the acid dissolves the silver and leaves the gold pure and ready to be weighed on its own merits. Then salt water is poured into the vessel containing the dissolved silver and the silver returns to palpable form again and sinks to the bottom. Nothing now remains but to weigh it; then the proportions of the several metals contained in the brick are known, and the assayer stamps the value of the brick upon its surface.

The sagacious reader will know now, without being told, that the speculative miner, in getting a "fire-assay" made of a piece of rock from his mine (to help him sell the same), was not in the habit of picking out the least valuable fragment of rock on his dump-pile, but quite the contrary. I have seen men hunt over a pile of nearly worthless quartz for an hour, and at last find a little piece as large as a filbert, which was rich in gold and silver—and this was reserved for a fire-assay! Of course the fire- assay would demonstrate that a ton of such rock would yield hundreds of dollars—and on such assays many an utterly worthless mine was sold.

Assaying was a good business, and so some men engaged in it, occasionally, who were not strictly scientific and capable. One assayer got such rich results out of all specimens brought to him that in time he acquired almost a monopoly of the business. But like all men who achieve success, he became an object of envy and suspicion. The other assayers entered into a conspiracy against him, and let some prominent citizens into the secret in order to show that they meant fairly. Then they broke a little fragment off a carpenter's grindstone and got a stranger to take it to the popular scientist and get it assayed. In the course of an hour the result came—whereby it appeared that a ton of that rock would yield $1,284.40 in silver and $366.36 in gold!

Due publication of the whole matter was made in the paper, and the popular assayer left town "between two days."

I will remark, in passing, that I only remained in the milling business one week. I told my employer I could not stay longer without an advance in my wages; that I liked quartz milling, indeed was infatuated with it; that I had never before grown so tenderly attached to an occupation in so short a time; that nothing, it seemed to me, gave such scope to intellectual activity as feeding a battery and screening tailings, and nothing so stimulated the moral attributes as retorting bullion and washing blankets—still, I felt constrained to ask an increase of salary.

He said he was paying me ten dollars a week, and thought it a good round sum. How much did I want?

I said about four hundred thousand dollars a month, and board, was about all I could reasonably ask, considering the hard times.

I was ordered off the premises! And yet, when I look back to those days and call to mind the exceeding hardness of the labor I performed in that mill, I only regret that I did not ask him seven hundred thousand.

Shortly after this I began to grow crazy, along with the rest of the population, about the mysterious and wonderful "cement mine," and to make preparations to take advantage of any opportunity that might offer to go and help hunt for it.

CHAPTER XXXVII

It was somewhere in the neighborhood of Mono Lake that the marvellous Whiteman cement mine was supposed to lie. Every now and then it would be reported that Mr. W. had passed stealthily through Esmeralda at dead of night, in disguise, and then we would have a wild excitement—because he must be steering for his secret mine, and now was the time to follow him. In less than three hours after daylight all the horses and mules and donkeys in the vicinity would be bought, hired or stolen, and half the community would be off for the mountains, following in the wake of Whiteman. But W. would drift about through the mountain gorges for days together, in a purposeless sort of way, until the provisions of the miners ran out, and they would have to go back home. I have known it reported at eleven at night, in a large mining camp, that Whiteman had just passed through, and in two hours the streets, so quiet before, would be swarming with men and animals. Every individual would be trying to be very secret, but yet venturing to whisper to just one neighbor that W. had passed through. And long before daylight—this in the dead of Winter—the stampede would be complete, the camp deserted, and the whole population gone chasing after W.

The tradition was that in the early immigration, more than twenty years ago, three young Germans, brothers, who had survived an Indian massacre on the Plains, wandered on foot through the deserts, avoiding all trails and roads, and simply holding a westerly direction and hoping to find California before they starved, or died of fatigue. And in a gorge in the mountains they sat down to rest one day, when one of them noticed a curious vein of cement running along the ground, shot full of lumps of dull yellow metal. They saw that it was gold, and that here was a fortune to be acquired in a single day. The vein was about as wide as a curbstone, and fully two thirds of it was pure gold. Every pound of the wonderful cement was worth well-nigh $200. Each of the brothers loaded himself with about twenty-five pounds of it, and then they covered up all traces of the vein, made a rude drawing of the locality and the principal landmarks in the vicinity, and started westward again. But troubles thickened about them. In their wanderings one brother fell and broke his leg, and the others were obliged to go on and leave him to die in the wilderness. Another, worn out and starving, gave up by and by, and laid down to die, but after two or three weeks of incredible hardships, the third reached the settlements of California exhausted, sick, and his mind deranged by his sufferings. He had thrown away all his cement but a few fragments, but these were sufficient to set everybody wild with excitement. However, he had had enough of the cement country, and nothing could induce him to lead a party thither. He was entirely content to work on a farm for wages. But he gave Whiteman his map, and described the cement region as well as he could, and thus transferred the curse to that gentleman—for when I had my one accidental glimpse of Mr. W. in Esmeralda he had been hunting for the lost mine, in hunger and thirst, poverty and sickness, for twelve or thirteen years. Some people believed he had found it, but most people believed he had not. I saw a piece of cement as large as my fist which was said to have been given to Whiteman by the young German, and it was of a seductive nature. Lumps of virgin gold were as thick in it as raisins in a slice of fruit cake. The privilege of working such a mine one week would be sufficient for a man of reasonable desires.

A new partner of ours, a Mr. Higbie, knew Whiteman well by sight, and a friend of ours, a Mr. Van Dorn, was well acquainted with him, and not only that, but had Whiteman's promise that he should have a private hint in time to enable him to join the next cement expedition. Van Dorn had promised to extend the hint to us. One evening Higbie came in greatly excited, and said he felt certain he had recognized Whiteman, up town, disguised and in a pretended state of intoxication. In a little while Van Dorn arrived and confirmed the news; and so we gathered in our cabin and with heads close together arranged our plans in impressive whispers.

We were to leave town quietly, after midnight, in two or three small parties, so as not to attract attention, and meet at dawn on the "divide" overlooking Mono Lake, eight or nine miles distant. We were to make no noise after starting, and not speak above a whisper under any circumstances. It was believed that for once Whiteman's presence was unknown in the town and his expedition unsuspected. Our conclave broke up at nine o'clock, and we set about our preparations diligently and with profound secrecy. At eleven o'clock we saddled our horses, hitched them with their long *riatas* (or lassos), and then brought out a side of bacon, a sack of beans, a small sack of coffee, some sugar, a hundred pounds of flour in sacks, some tin cups and a coffee pot, frying pan and some few other necessary articles. All these things were "packed" on the back of a led horse—and whoever has not been taught, by a Spanish adept, to pack an animal, let him never hope to do the thing by natural smartness. That is impossible. Higbie had had some experience, but was not perfect. He put on the pack saddle (a thing like a saw-buck), piled the property on it and then wound a rope all over and about it and under it, "every which way," taking a hitch in it every now and then, and occasionally surging back on it till the horse's sides sunk in and he gasped for breath—but every time the lashings grew tight in one place they loosened in another. We never did get the load tight all over, but we got it so that it would do, after a fashion, and then we started, in single file, close order, and without a word. It was a dark night. We kept the middle of the road, and proceeded in a slow walk past the rows of cabins, and whenever a miner came to his door I trembled for fear the light would shine on us and excite curiosity. But nothing happened. We began the long winding ascent of the canyon, toward the "divide," and presently the cabins began to grow infrequent, and the intervals between them wider and wider, and then I began to breathe tolerably freely and feel less like a thief and a murderer. I was in the rear, leading the pack horse. As the ascent grew steeper he grew proportionately less satisfied with his cargo, and began to pull back on his *riata* occasionally and delay progress. My comrades were passing out of sight in the gloom. I was getting anxious. I coaxed and bullied the pack horse till I presently got him into a trot, and then the tin cups and pans strung about his person frightened him and he ran. His *riata* was wound around the pummel of my saddle, and so, as he went by he dragged me from my horse and the two animals traveled briskly on without me. But I was not alone—the loosened cargo tumbled overboard from the pack horse and fell close to me. It was abreast of almost the last cabin. A miner came out and said:

"Hello!"

I was thirty steps from him, and knew he could not see me, it was so very dark in the shadow of the mountain. So I lay still. Another head appeared in the light of the cabin door, and presently the two men walked toward me. They stopped within ten steps of me, and one said:

" 'St! Listen."

I could not have been in a more distressed state if I had been escaping justice with a price on my head. Then the miners appeared to sit down on a boulder, though I could not see them distinctly enough to be very sure what they did. One said:

"I heard a noise, as plain as I ever heard anything. It seemed to be about there—"

A stone whizzed by my head. I flattened myself out in the dust like a postage stamp, and thought to myself if he mended his aim ever so little he would probably hear another noise. In my heart, now, I execrated secret expeditions. I promised myself that this should be my last, though the Sierras were ribbed with cement veins. Then one of the men said:

"I'll tell you what! Welch knew what he was talking about when he said he saw Whiteman to-day. I heard horses—that was the noise. I am going down to Welch's, right away."

They left and I was glad. I did not care whither they went, so they went. I was willing they should visit Welch, and the sooner the better.

As soon as they closed their cabin door my comrades emerged from the gloom; they had caught the horses and were waiting for a clear coast again. We remounted the cargo on the pack horse and got under way, and as day broke we reached the "divide" and joined Van Dorn. Then we journeyed down into the valley of the Lake, and feeling secure, we halted to cook breakfast, for we were tired and sleepy and hungry. Three hours later the rest of the population filed over the "divide" in a long procession, and drifted off out of sight around the borders of the Lake!

Whether or not my accident had produced this result we never knew, but at least one thing was certain—the secret was out and Whiteman would not enter upon a search for the cement mine this time. We were filled with chagrin.

We held a council and decided to make the best of our misfortune and enjoy a week's holiday on the borders of the curious Lake. Mono, it is sometimes called, and sometimes the "Dead Sea of California." It is one of the strangest freaks of Nature to be found in any land, but it is hardly ever mentioned in print and very seldom visited, because it lies away off the usual routes of travel and besides is so difficult to get at that only men content to endure the roughest life will consent to take upon themselves the discomforts of such a trip. On the morning of our second day, we traveled around to a remote and particularly wild spot on the borders of the Lake, where a stream of fresh, ice-cold water entered it from the mountain side, and then we went regularly into camp. We hired a large boat and two shot-guns from a lonely ranchman who lived some ten miles further on, and made ready for comfort and recreation. We soon got thoroughly acquainted with the Lake and all its peculiarities.

CHAPTER XXXVIII

Mono Lake lies in a lifeless, treeless, hideous desert, eight thousand feet above the level of the sea, and is guarded by mountains two thousand feet higher, whose summits are always clothed in clouds. This solemn, silent, sailless sea—this lonely tenant of the loneliest spot on earth—is little graced with the picturesque. It is an unpretending expanse of grayish water, about a hundred miles in circumference, with two islands in its centre, mere upheavals of rent and scorched and blistered lava, snowed over with gray banks and drifts of pumice-stone and ashes, the winding sheet of the dead volcano, whose vast crater the lake has seized upon and occupied.

The lake is two hundred feet deep, and its sluggish waters are so strong with alkali that if you only dip the most hopelessly soiled garment into them once or twice, and wring it out, it will be found as clean as if it had been through the ablest of washerwomen's hands. While we camped there our laundry work was easy. We tied the week's washing astern of our boat, and sailed a quarter of a mile, and the job was complete, all to the wringing out. If we threw the water on our heads and gave them a rub or so, the white lather would pile up three inches high. This water is not good for bruised places and abrasions of the skin. We had a valuable dog. He had raw places on him. He had more raw places on him than sound ones. He was the rawest dog I almost ever saw. He jumped overboard one day to get away from the flies. But it was bad judgment. In his condition, it would have been just as comfortable to jump into the fire. The alkali water nipped him in all the raw places simultaneously, and he struck out for the shore with considerable interest. He yelped and barked and howled as he went—and by the time he got to the shore there was no bark to him—for he had barked the bark all out of his inside, and the alkali water had cleaned the bark all off his outside, and he probably wished he had never embarked in any such enterprise. He ran round and round in a circle, and pawed the earth and clawed the air, and threw double somersaults, sometimes backward and sometimes forward, in the most extraordinary manner. He was not a demonstrative dog, as a general thing, but rather of a grave and serious turn of mind, and I never saw him take so much interest in anything before. He finally struck out over the mountains, at a gait which we estimated at about two hundred and fifty miles an hour, and he is going yet. This was about nine years ago. We look for what is left of him along here every day.

A white man cannot drink the water of Mono Lake, for it is nearly pure lye. It is said that the Indians in the vicinity drink it sometimes, though. It is not improbable, for they are among the purest liars I ever saw. [There will be no additional charge for this joke, except to parties requiring an explanation of it. This joke has received high commendation from some of the ablest minds of the age.]

There are no fish in Mono Lake—no frogs, no snakes, no polliwigs—nothing, in fact, that goes to make life desirable. Millions of wild ducks and sea-gulls swim about the surface, but no living thing exists *under* the surface, except a white feathery sort of worm, one half an inch long, which looks like a bit of white thread frayed out at the sides. If you dip up a gallon of water, you will get about fifteen thousand of these. They give to the water a sort of grayish-white appearance. Then there is a fly, which looks something like our house fly. These settle on the beach to eat the worms that wash ashore—and any time, you can see there a belt of flies an inch deep and six feet wide, and this belt extends clear around the lake—a belt of flies one hundred miles long. If you throw a stone among them, they swarm up so thick that they look dense, like a cloud. You can hold them under water as long as you please—they do not mind it—they are only proud of it. When you let them go, they pop up to the surface as dry as a patent office report, and walk off as unconcernedly as if they had been educated especially with a view to affording instructive entertainment to man in that particular way. Providence leaves nothing to go by chance. All things have their uses and their part and proper place in Nature's economy: the ducks eat the flies—the flies eat the worms—the Indians eat all three—the wild cats eat the Indians—the white folks eat the wild cats—and thus all things are lovely.

Mono Lake is a hundred miles in a straight line from the ocean—and between it and the ocean are one or two ranges of mountains—yet thousands of sea-gulls go there every season to lay their eggs and rear their young. One would as soon expect to find sea-gulls in Kansas. And in this connection let us observe another instance of Nature's wisdom. The islands in the lake being merely huge masses of lava, coated over with ashes and pumice-stone, and utterly innocent of vegetation or anything that would burn; and sea-gulls' eggs being entirely useless to anybody unless they be cooked, Nature has provided an unfailing spring of boiling water on the largest island, and you can put your eggs in there, and in four minutes you can boil them as hard as any statement I have made during the past fifteen years. Within ten feet of the boiling spring is a spring of pure cold water, sweet and wholesome. So, in that island you get your board and washing free of charge—and if nature had gone further and furnished a nice American hotel clerk who was crusty and disobliging, and didn't know anything about the time tables, or the railroad routes—or—anything—and was proud of it—I would not wish for a more desirable boarding-house.

Half a dozen little mountain brooks flow into Mono Lake, but *not a stream of any kind flows out of it.* It neither rises nor falls, apparently, and what it does with its surplus water is a dark and bloody mystery.

There are only two seasons in the region round about Mono Lake—and these are, the breaking up of one Winter and the beginning of the next. More than once (in Esmeralda) I have seen a perfectly blistering morning open up with the thermometer at ninety degrees at eight o'clock, and seen the snow fall fourteen inches deep and that same identical thermometer go down to forty-four degrees under shelter, before nine o'clock at night. Under favorable circumstances it snows at least once in every single month in the year, in the little town of Mono. So uncertain is the climate in Summer that a lady who goes out visiting cannot hope to be prepared for all emergencies unless she takes her fan under one arm and her snow shoes under the other. When they have a Fourth of July procession it generally snows on them, and they do say that as a general thing when a man calls for a brandy toddy there, the bar keeper chops it off with a hatchet and wraps it up in a paper, like maple sugar. And it is further reported that the old soakers haven't any teeth—wore them out eating gin cocktails and brandy punches. I do not endorse that statement—I simply give it for what it is worth—and it is worth—well, I should say, millions, to any man who can believe it without straining himself. But I do endorse the snow on the Fourth of July—because I know that to be true.

CHAPTER XXXIX

About seven o'clock one blistering hot morning—for it was now dead summer time—Higbie and I took the boat and started on a voyage of discovery to the two islands. We had often longed to do this, but had been deterred by the fear of storms; for they were frequent, and severe enough to capsize an ordinary row-boat like ours without great difficulty—and once capsized, death would ensue in spite of the bravest swimming, for that venomous water would eat a man's eyes out like fire, and burn him out inside, too, if he shipped a sea. It was called twelve miles, straight out to the islands—a long pull and a warm one—but the morning was so quiet and sunny, and the lake so smooth and glassy and dead, that we could not resist the temptation. So we filled two large tin canteens with water (since we were not acquainted with the locality of the spring said to exist on the large island), and started. Higbie's brawny muscles gave the boat good speed, but by the time we reached our destination we judged that we had pulled nearer fifteen miles than twelve.

We landed on the big island and went ashore. We tried the water in the canteens, now, and found that the sun had spoiled it; it was so brackish that we could not drink it; so we poured it out and began a search for the spring—for thirst augments fast as soon as it is apparent that one has no means at hand of quenching it. The island was a long, moderately high hill of ashes—nothing but gray ashes and pumice-stone, in which we sunk to our knees at every step—and all around the top was a forbidding wall of scorched and blasted rocks. When we reached the top and got within the wall, we found simply a shallow, far-reaching basin, carpeted with ashes, and here and there a patch of fine sand. In places, picturesque jets of steam shot up out of crevices, giving evidence that although this ancient crater had gone out of active business, there was still some fire left in its furnaces. Close to one of these jets of steam stood the only tree on the island—a small pine of most graceful shape and most faultless symmetry; its color was a brilliant green, for the steam drifted unceasingly through its branches and kept them always moist. It contrasted strangely enough, did this vigorous and beautiful outcast, with its dead and dismal surroundings. It was like a cheerful spirit in a mourning household.

We hunted for the spring everywhere, traversing the full length of the island (two or three miles), and crossing it twice—climbing ash-hills patiently, and then sliding down the other side in a sitting posture, plowing up smothering volumes of gray dust. But we found nothing but solitude, ashes and a heart-breaking silence. Finally we noticed that the wind had risen, and we forgot our thirst in a solicitude of greater importance; for, the lake being quiet, we had not taken pains about securing the boat. We hurried back to a point overlooking our landing place, and then—but mere words cannot describe our dismay—the boat was gone! The chances were that there was not another boat on the entire lake. The situation was not comfortable—in truth, to speak plainly, it was frightful. We were prisoners on a desolate island, in aggravating proximity to friends who were for the present helpless to aid us; and what was still more uncomfortable was the reflection that we had neither food nor water. But presently we sighted the boat. It was drifting along, leisurely, about fifty yards from shore, tossing in a foamy sea. It drifted, and continued to drift, but at the same safe distance from land, and we walked along abreast it and waited for fortune to favor us. At the end of an hour it approached a jutting cape, and Higbie ran ahead and posted himself on the utmost verge and prepared for the assault. If we failed there, there was no hope for us. It was driving gradually shoreward all the time, now; but whether it was driving fast enough to make the connection or not was the momentous question. When it got within thirty steps of Higbie I was so excited that I fancied I could hear my own heart beat. When, a little later, it dragged slowly along and seemed about to go by, only one little yard out of reach, it seemed as if my heart stood still; and when it was exactly abreast him and began to widen away, and he still standing like a watching statue, I knew my heart did stop. But when he gave a great spring, the next instant, and lit fairly in the stern, I discharged a war-whoop that woke the solitudes!

But it dulled my enthusiasm, presently, when he told me he had not been caring whether the boat came within jumping distance or not, so that it passed within eight or ten yards of him, for he had made up his mind to shut his eyes and mouth and swim that trifling distance. Imbecile that I was, I had not thought of that. It was only a long swim that could be fatal.

The sea was running high and the storm increasing. It was growing late, too—three or four in the afternoon. Whether to venture toward the mainland or not, was a question of some moment. But we were so distressed by thirst that we decided to try it, and so Higbie fell to work and I took the steering-oar. When we had pulled a mile, laboriously, we were evidently in serious peril, for the storm had greatly augmented; the billows ran very high and were capped with foaming crests, the heavens were hung with black, and the wind blew with great fury. We would have gone back, now, but we did not dare to turn the boat around, because as soon as she got in the trough of the sea she would upset, of course. Our only hope lay in keeping her head-on to the seas. It was hard work to do this, she plunged so, and so beat and belabored the billows with her rising and falling bows. Now and then one of Higbie's oars would trip on the top of a wave, and the other one would snatch the boat half around in spite of my cumbersome steering apparatus. We were drenched by the sprays constantly, and the boat occasionally shipped water. By and by, powerful as my comrade was, his great exertions began to tell on him, and he was anxious that I should change places with him till he could rest a little. But I told him this was impossible; for if the steering oar were dropped a moment while we changed, the boat would slue around into the trough of the sea, capsize, and in less than five minutes we would have a hundred gallons of soap-suds in us and be eaten up so quickly that we could not even be present at our own inquest.

But things cannot last always. Just as the darkness shut down we came booming into port, head on. Higbie dropped his oars to hurrah—I dropped mine to help—the sea gave the boat a twist, and over she went!

The agony that alkali water inflicts on bruises, chafes and blistered hands, is unspeakable, and nothing but greasing all over will modify it—but we ate, drank and slept well, that night, notwithstanding.

In speaking of the peculiarities of Mono Lake, I ought to have mentioned that at intervals all around its shores stand picturesque turret-looking masses and clusters of a whitish, coarse-grained rock that resembles inferior mortar dried hard; and if one breaks off fragments of this rock he will find perfectly shaped and thoroughly petrified gulls' eggs deeply imbedded in the mass. How did they get there? I simply state the fact—for it is a fact—and leave the geological reader to crack the nut at his leisure and solve the problem after his own fashion.

At the end of a week we adjourned to the Sierras on a fishing excursion, and spent several days in camp under snowy Castle Peak, and fished successfully for trout in a bright, miniature lake whose surface was between ten and eleven thousand feet about the level of the sea; cooling ourselves during the hot August noons by sitting on snow banks ten feet deep, under whose sheltering edges *fine grass and dainty flowers flourished luxuriously;* and at night entertaining ourselves by almost freezing to death. Then we returned to Mono Lake, and finding that the cement excitement was over for the present, packed up and went back to Esmeralda. Mr. Ballou reconnoitred awhile, and not liking the prospect, set out alone for Humboldt.

About this time occurred a little incident which has always had a sort of interest to me, from the fact that it came so near "instigating" my funeral. At a time when an Indian attack had been expected, the citizens hid their gunpowder where it would be safe and yet convenient to hand when wanted. A neighbor of ours hid six cans of rifle powder in the bake-oven of an old discarded cooking stove which stood on the open ground near a frame out-house or shed, and from and after that day never thought of it again. We hired a half-tamed Indian to do some washing for us, and he took up quarters under the shed with his tub. The ancient stove reposed within six feet of him, and before his face. Finally it occurred to him that hot water would be better than cold, and he went out and fired up under that forgotten powder magazine and set on a kettle of water. Then he returned to his tub. I entered the shed presently and threw down some more clothes, and was about to speak to him when the stove blew up with a prodigious crash, and disappeared, leaving not a splinter behind. Fragments of it fell in the streets full two hundred yards away. Nearly a third of the shed roof over our heads was destroyed, and one of the stove lids, after cutting a small stanchion half in two in front of the Indian, whizzed between us and drove partly through the weather-boarding beyond. I was as white as a sheet and as weak as a kitten and speechless. But the Indian betrayed no trepidation, no distress, not even discomfort. He simply stopped washing, leaned forward and surveyed the clean, blank ground a moment, and then remarked:

"Mph! Dam stove heap gone!"—and resumed his scrubbing as placidly as if it were an entirely customary thing for a stove to do. I will explain, that "heap" is "Injun-English" for "very much." The reader will perceive the exhaustive expressiveness of it in the present instance.

CHAPTER XL

I now come to a curious episode—the most curious, I think, that had yet accented my slothful, valueless, heedless career. Out of a hillside toward the upper end of the town, projected a wall of reddish looking quartz-croppings, the exposed comb of a silver-bearing ledge that extended deep down into the earth, of course. I was owned by a company entitled the "Wide West." There was a shaft sixty or seventy feet deep on the under side of the croppings, and everybody was acquainted with the rock that came from it—and tolerably rich rock it was, too, but nothing extraordinary. I will remark here, that although to the inexperienced stranger all the quartz of a peculiar "district" looks about alike, an old resident of the camp can take a glance at a mixed pile of rock, separate the fragments and tell you which mine each came from, as easily as a confectioner can separate and classify the various kinds and qualities of candy in a mixed heap of the article.

All at once the town was thrown into a state of extraordinary excitement. In mining parlance the Wide West had "struck it rich!" Everybody went to see the new developments, and for some days there was such a crowd of people about the Wide West shaft that a stranger would have supposed there was a mass meeting in session there. No other topic was discussed but the rich strike, and nobody thought or dreamed about anything else. Every man brought away a specimen, ground it up in a hand mortar, washed it out in his horn spoon, and glared speechless upon the marvelous result. It was not hard rock, but black, decomposed stuff which could be crumbled in the hand like a baked potato, and when spread out on a paper exhibited a thick sprinkling of gold and particles of "native" silver. Higbie brought a handful to the cabin, and when he had washed it out his amazement was beyond description. Wide West stock soared skywards. It was said that repeated offers had been made for it at a thousand dollars a foot, and promptly refused. We have all had the "blues"—the mere sky-blues—but mine were indigo, now—because I did not own in the Wide West. The world seemed hollow to me, and existence a grief. I lost my appetite, and ceased to take an interest in anything. Still I had to stay, and listen to other people's rejoicing, because I had no money to get out of the camp with.

The Wide West company put a stop to the carrying away of "specimens," and well they might, for every handful of the ore was worth a sum of some consequence. To show the exceeding value of the ore, I will remark that a sixteen-hundred-pounds parcel of it was sold, just as it lay, at the mouth of the shaft, at *one dollar a pound;* and the man who bought it "packed" it on mules a hundred and fifty or two hundred miles, over the mountains, to San Francisco, satisfied that it would yield at a rate that would richly compensate him for his trouble. The Wide West people also commanded their foreman to refuse any but their own operatives permission to enter the mine at any time or for any purpose. I kept up my "blue" meditations and Higbie kept up a deal of thinking, too, but of a different sort. He puzzled over the "rock," examined it with a glass, inspected it in different lights and from different points of view, and after each experiment delivered himself, in soliloquy, of one and the same unvarying opinion in the same unvarying formula:

"It is *not* Wide West rock!"

He said once or twice that he meant to have a look into the

Wide West Shaft if he got shot for it. I was wretched, and did not care whether he got a look into it or not. He failed that day, and tried again at night; failed again; got up at dawn and tried, and failed again. Then he lay in ambush in the sage brush hour after hour, waiting for the two or three hands to adjourn to the shade of a boulder for dinner; made a start once, but was premature—one of the men came back for something; tried it again, but when almost at the mouth of the shaft, another of the men rose up from behind the boulder as if to reconnoitre, and he dropped on the ground and lay quiet; presently he crawled on his hands and knees to the mouth of the shaft, gave a quick glance around, then seized the rope and slid down the shaft. He disappeared in the gloom of a "side drift" just as a head appeared in the mouth of the shaft and somebody shouted "Hello!"—which he did not answer. He was not disturbed any more. An hour later he entered the cabin, hot, red, and ready to burst with smothered excitement, and exclaimed in a stage whisper:

"I knew it! We are rich! IT'S A BLIND LEAD!"

I thought the very earth reeled under me. Doubt— conviction—doubt again—exultation—hope, amazement, belief, unbelief—every emotion imaginable swept in wild procession through my heart and brain, and I could not speak a word. After a moment or two of this mental fury, I shook myself to rights, and said:

"Say it again!"

"It's a blind lead!"

"Cal., let's—let's burn the house—or kill somebody! Let's get out where there's room to hurrah! But what is the use? It is a hundred times too good to be true."

"It's a blind lead, for a million!—hanging wall—foot wall—clay casings—everything complete!" He swung his hat and gave three cheers, and I cast doubt to the winds and chimed in with a will. For I was worth a million dollars, and did not care "whether school kept or not!"

But perhaps I ought to explain. A "blind lead" is a lead or ledge that does not "crop out" above the surface. A miner does not know where to look for such leads, but they are often stumbled upon by accident in the course of driving a tunnel or sinking a shaft. Higbie knew the Wide West rock perfectly well, and the more he had examined the new developments the more he was satisfied that the ore could not have come from the Wide West vein. And so had it occurred to him alone, of all the camp, that there was a blind lead down in the shaft, and that even the Wide West people themselves did not suspect it. He was right. When he went down the shaft, he found that the blind lead held its independent way through the Wide West vein, cutting it diagonally, and that it was enclosed in its own well-defined casing-rocks and clay. Hence it was public property. Both leads being perfectly well defined, it was easy for any miner to see which one belonged to the Wide West and which did not.

We thought it well to have a strong friend, and therefore we brought the foreman of the Wide West to our cabin that night and revealed the great surprise to him. Higbie said:

"We are going to take possession of this blind lead, record it and establish ownership, and then forbid the Wide West company to take out any more of the rock. You cannot help your company in this matter—nobody can help them. I will go into the shaft with you and prove to your entire satisfaction that it *is* a blind lead. Now we propose to take you in with us, and claim the blind lead in our three names. What do you say?"

What could a man say who had an opportunity to simply stretch forth his hand and take possession of a fortune without risk of any kind and without wronging any one or attaching the least taint of dishonor to his name? He could only say, "Agreed."

The notice was put up that night, and duly spread upon the recorder's books before ten o'clock. We claimed two hundred feet each—six hundred feet in all—the smallest and compactest organization in the district, and the easiest to manage.

No one can be so thoughtless as to suppose that we slept, that night. Higbie and I went to bed at midnight, but it was only to lie broad awake and think, dream, scheme. The floorless, tumble-down cabin was a palace, the ragged gray blankets silk, the furniture rosewood and mahogany. Each new splendor that burst out of my visions of the future whirled me bodily over in bed or jerked me to a sitting posture just as if an electric battery had been applied to me. We shot fragments of conversation back and forth at each other. Once Higbie said:

"When are you going home—to the States?"

"To-morrow!"—with an evolution or two, ending with a sitting position. "Well—no—but next month, at furthest."

"We'll go in the same steamer."

"Agreed."

A pause.

"Steamer of the 10th?"

"Yes. No, the 1st."

"All right."

Another pause.

"Where are you going to live?" said Higbie.

"San Francisco."

"That's me!"

Pause.

"Too high—too much climbing"—from Higbie.

"What is?"

"I was thinking of Russian Hill—building a house up there."

"Too much climbing? Shan't you keep a carriage?"

"Of course. I forgot that."

Pause.

"Cal., what kind of a house are you going to build?"

"I was thinking about that. Three-story and an attic."

"But what *kind?*"

"Well, I don't hardly know. Brick, I suppose."

"Brick—bosh."

"Why? What is your idea?"

"Brown stone front—French plate glass—billiard-room off the dining-room—statuary and paintings—shrubbery and two-acre grass plat—greenhouse—iron dog on the front stoop—gray horses—landau, and a coachman with a bug on his hat!"

"By George!"

A long pause.

"Cal., when are you going to Europe?"

"Well—I hadn't thought of that. When are you?"

"In the Spring."

"Going to be gone all summer?"

"All summer! I shall remain there three years."

"No—but are you in earnest?"

"Indeed I am."

"I will go along too."

"Why of course you will."

"What part of Europe shall you go to?"

"All parts. France, England, Germany—Spain, Italy, Switzerland, Syria, Greece, Palestine, Arabia, Persia, Egypt—all over—everywhere."

"I'm agreed."

"All right."

"Won't it be a swell trip!"

"We'll spend forty or fifty thousand dollars trying to make it one, anyway."

Another long pause.

"Higbie, we owe the butcher six dollars, and he has been threatening to stop our—"

"Hang the butcher!"

"Amen."

And so it went on. By three o'clock we found it was no use, and so we got up and played cribbage and smoked pipes till sunrise. It was my week to cook. I always hated cooking—now, I abhorred it.

The news was all over town. The former excitement was great—this one was greater still. I walked the streets serene and happy. Higbie said the foreman had been offered two hundred thousand dollars for his third of the mine. I said I would like to see myself selling for any such price. My ideas were lofty. My figure was a million. Still, I honestly believe that if I had been offered it, it would have had no other effect than to make me hold off for more.

I found abundant enjoyment in being rich. A man offered me a three-hundred-dollar horse, and wanted to take my simple, unendorsed note for it. That brought the most realizing sense I had yet had that I was actually rich, beyond shadow of doubt. I was followed by numerous other evidences of a similar nature—among which I may mention the fact of the butcher leaving us a double supply of meat and saying nothing about money.

By the laws of the district, the "locators" or claimants of a ledge were obliged to do a fair and reasonable amount of work on their new property within ten days after the date of the location, or the property was forfeited, and anybody could go and seize it that chose. So we determined to go to work the next day. About the middle of the afternoon, as I was coming out of the post office, I met a Mr. Gardiner, who told me that Capt. John Nye was lying dangerously ill at his place (the "Nine-Mile Ranch"), and that he and his wife were not able to give him nearly as much care and attention as his case demanded. I said if he would wait for me a moment, I would go down and help in the sick room. I ran to the cabin to tell Higbie. He was not there, but I left a note on the table for him, a few minutes later I left town in Gardiner's wagon.

CHAPTER XLI

Captain Nye was very ill indeed, with spasmodic rheumatism. But the old gentleman was himself—which is to say, he was kind-hearted and agreeable when comfortable, but a singularly violent wild-cat when things did not go well. He would be smiling along pleasantly enough, when a sudden spasm of his disease would take him and he would go out of his smile into a perfect fury. He would groan and wail and howl with the anguish, and fill up the odd chinks with the most elaborate profanity that strong convictions and a fine fancy could contrive. With fair opportunity he could swear very well and handle his adjectives with considerable judgment; but when the spasm was on him it was painful to listen to him, he was so awkward. However, I had seen him nurse a sick man himself and put up patiently with the inconveniences of the situation, and consequently I was willing that he should have full license now that his own turn had come. He could not disturb me, with all his raving and ranting, for my mind had work on hand, and it labored on diligently, night and day, whether my hands were idle or employed. I was altering and amending the plans for my house, and thinking over the propriety of having the billiard-room in the attic, instead of on the same floor with the dining-room; also, I was trying to decide between green and blue for the upholstery of the drawing-room, for, although my preference was blue I feared it was a color that would be too easily damaged by dust and sunlight; likewise while I was content to put the coachman in a modest livery, I was uncertain about a footman—I needed one, and was even resolved to have one, but wished he could properly appear and perform his functions out of livery, for I somewhat dreaded so much show; and yet, inasmuch as my late grandfather had had a coachman and such things, but no liveries, I felt rather drawn to beat him;—or beat his ghost, at any rate; I was also systematizing the European trip, and managed to get it all laid out, as to route and length of time to be devoted to it—everything, with one exception—namely, whether to cross the desert from Cairo to Jerusalem per camel, or go by sea to Beirut, and thence down through the country per caravan. Meantime I was writing to the friends at home every day, instructing them concerning all my plans and intentions, and directing them to look up a handsome homestead for my mother and agree upon a price for it against my coming, and also directing them to sell my share of the Tennessee land and tender the proceeds to the widows' and orphans' fund of the typographical union of which I had long been a member in good standing. [This Tennessee land had been in the possession of the family many years, and promised to confer high fortune upon us some day; it still promises it, but in a less violent way.]

When I had been nursing the Captain nine days he was somewhat better, but very feeble. During the afternoon we lifted him into a chair and gave him an alcoholic vapor bath, and then set about putting him on the bed again. We had to be exceedingly careful, for the least jar produced pain. Gardiner had his shoulders and I his legs; in an unfortunate moment I stumbled and the patient fell heavily on the bed in an agony of torture. I never heard a man swear so in my life. He raved like a maniac, and tried to snatch a revolver from the table—but I got it. He ordered me out of the house, and swore a world of oaths that he would kill me wherever he caught me when he got on his feet again. It was simply a passing fury, and meant nothing. I knew he would forget it in an hour, and maybe be sorry for it, too; but it angered me a little, at the moment. So much so, indeed, that I determined to go back to Esmeralda. I thought he was able to get along alone, now, since he was on the war path. I took supper, and as soon as the moon rose, began my nine-mile journey, on foot. Ever millionaires needed no horses, in those days, for a mere nine-mile jaunt without baggage.

As I "raised the hill" overlooking the town, it lacked fifteen minutes of twelve. I glanced at the hill over beyond the canyon, and in the bright moonlight saw what appeared to be about half the population of the village massed on and around the Wide West croppings. My heart gave an exulting bound, and I said to myself, "They have made a new strike to-night—and struck it richer than ever, no doubt." I started over there, but gave it up. I said the "strike" would keep, and I had climbed hills enough for one night. I went on down through the town, and as I was passing a little German bakery, a woman ran out and begged me to come in and help her. She said her husband had a fit. I went in, and judged she was right—he appeared to have a hundred of them, compressed into one. Two Germans were there, trying to hold him, and not making much of a success of it. I ran up the street half a block or so and routed out a sleeping doctor, brought him down half dressed, and we four wrestled with the maniac, and doctored, drenched and bled him, for more than an hour, and the poor German woman did the crying. He grew quiet, now, and the doctor and I withdrew and left him to his friends.

It was a little after one o'clock. As I entered the cabin door, tired but jolly, the dingy light of a tallow candle revealed Higbie, sitting by the pine table gazing stupidly at my note, which he held in his fingers, and looking pale, old, and haggard. I halted, and looked at him. He looked at me, stolidly. I said:

"Higbie, what—what is it?"

"We're ruined—we didn't do the work—THE BLIND LEAD'S RELOCATED!"

It was enough. I sat down sick, grieved—broken-hearted, indeed. A minute before, I was rich and brimful of vanity; I was a pauper now, and very meek. We sat still an hour, busy with thought, busy with vain and useless self-upbraidings, busy with "Why *didn't* I do this, and why *didn't* I do that," but neither spoke a word. Then we dropped into mutual explanations, and the mystery was cleared away. It came out that Higbie had depended on me, as I had on him, and as both of us had on the foreman. The folly of it! It was the first time that ever staid and steadfast Higbie had left an important matter to chance or failed to be true to his full share of a responsibility.

But he had never seen my note till this moment, and this moment was the first time he had been in the cabin since the day he had seen me last. He, also, had left a note for me, on that same fatal afternoon—had ridden up on horseback, and looked through the window, and being in a hurry and not seeing me, had tossed the note into the cabin through a broken pane. Here it was, on the floor, where it had remained undisturbed for nine days:

"Don't fail to do the work before the ten days expire. W. has passed through and given me notice. I am to join him at Mono Lake, and we shall go on from there to-night. He says he will find it this time, sure. CAL."

"W." meant Whiteman, of course. That thrice accursed "cement!"

That was the way of it. An old miner, like Higbie, could no more withstand the fascination of a mysterious mining excitement like this "cement" foolishness, than he could refrain from eating when he was famishing. Higbie had been dreaming about the marvelous cement for months; and now, against his better judgment, he had gone off and "taken the chances" on my keeping secure a mine worth a million undiscovered cement veins. They had not been followed this time. His riding out of town in broad daylight was such a commonplace thing to do that it had not attracted any attention. He said they prosecuted their search in the fastnesses of the mountains during nine days, without success; they could not find the cement. Then a ghastly fear came over him that something might have happened to prevent the doing of the necessary work to hold the blind lead (though indeed he thought such a thing hardly possible), and forthwith he started home with all speed. He would have reached Esmeralda in time, but his horse broke down and he had to walk a great part of the distance. And so it happened that as he came into Esmeralda by one road, I entered it by another. His was the superior energy, however, for he went straight to the Wide West, instead of turning aside as I had done—and he arrived there about five or ten minutes too late! The "notice" was already up, the "relocation" of our mine completed beyond recall, and the crowd rapidly dispersing. He learned some facts before he left the ground. The foreman had not been seen about the streets since the night we had located the mine—a telegram had called him to California on a matter of life and death, it was said. At any rate he had done no work and the watchful eyes of the community were taking note of the fact. At midnight of this woful tenth day, the ledge would be "relocatable," and by eleven o'clock the hill was black with men prepared to do the relocating. That was the crowd I had seen when I fancied a new "strike" had been made—idiot that I was.]We three had the same right to relocate the lead that other people had, provided we were quick enough.] As midnight was announced, fourteen men, duly armed and ready to back their proceedings, put up their "notice" and proclaimed their ownership of the blind lead, under the new name of the "Johnson." But A. D. Allen our partner (the foreman) put in a sudden appearance about that time, with a cocked revolver in his hand, and said his name must be added to the list, or he would "thin out the Johnson company some." He was a manly, splendid, determined fellow, and known to be as good as his word, and therefore a compromise was effected. They put in his name for a hundred feet, reserving to themselves the customary two hundred feet each. Such was the history of the night's events, as Higbie gathered from a friend on the way home.

Higbie and I cleared out on a new mining excitement the next morning, glad to get away from the scene of our sufferings, and after a month or two of hardship and disappointment, returned to Esmeralda once more. Then we learned that the Wide West and the Johnson companies had consolidated; that the stock, thus united, comprised five thousand feet, or shares; that the foreman, apprehending tiresome litigation, and considering such a huge concern unwieldly, had sold his hundred feet for ninety thousand dollars in gold and gone home to the States to enjoy it. If the stock was worth such a gallant figure, with five thousand shares in the corporation, it makes me dizzy to think what it would have been worth with only our original six hundred in it. It was the difference between six hundred men owning a house and five thousand owning it. We would have been millionaires if we had only worked with pick and spade one little day on our property and so secured our ownership!

It reads like a wild fancy sketch, but the evidence of many witnesses, and likewise that of the official records of Esmeralda District, is easily obtainable in proof that it is a true history. I can always have it to say that I was absolutely and unquestionably worth a million dollars, once, for ten days.

A year ago my esteemed and in every way estimable old millionaire partner, Higbie, wrote me from an obscure little mining camp in California that after nine or ten years of buffetings and hard striving, he was at last in a position where he could command twenty-five hundred dollars, and said he meant to go into the fruit business in a modest way. How such a thought would have insulted him the night we lay in our cabin planning European trips and brown stone houses on Russian Hill!

CHAPTER XLII

What to do next?

It was a momentous question. I had gone out into the world to shift for myself, at the age of thirteen (for my father had endorsed for friends; and although he left us a sumptuous legacy of pride in his fine Virginian stock and its national distinction, I presently found that I could not live on that alone without occasional bread to wash it down with). I had gained a livelihood in various vocations, but had not dazzled anybody with my successes; still the list was before me, and the amplest liberty in the matter of choosing, provided I wanted to work—which I did not, after being so wealthy. I had once been a grocery clerk, for one day, but had consumed so much sugar in that time that I was relieved from further duty by the proprietor; said he wanted me outside, so that he could have my custom. I had studied law an entire week, and then given it up because it was so prosy and tiresome. I had engaged briefly in the study of blacksmithing, but wasted so much time trying to fix the bellows so that it would blow itself, that the master turned me adrift in disgrace, and told me I would come to no good. I had been a bookseller's clerk for awhile, but the customers bothered me so much I could not read with any comfort, and so the proprietor gave me a furlough and forgot to put a limit to it. I had clerked in a drug store part of a summer, but my prescriptions were unlucky, and we appeared to sell more stomach pumps than soda water. So I had to go. I had made of myself a tolerable printer, under the impression that I would be another Franklin some day, but somehow had missed the connection thus far. There was no berth open in the Esmeralda *Union,* and besides I had always been such a slow compositor that I looked with envy upon the achievements of apprentices of two years' standing; and when I took a "take," foremen were in the habit of suggesting that it would be wanted "some time during the year." I was a good average St. Louis and New Orleans pilot and by no means ashamed of my abilities in that line; wages were two hundred and fifty dollars a month and no board to pay, and I did long to stand behind a wheel again and never roam any more—but I had been making such an ass of myself lately in grandiloquent letters home about my blind lead and my European excursion that I did what many and many a poor disappointed miner had done before; said "It is all over with me now, and I will never go back home to be pitied—and snubbed." I had been a private secretary, a silver miner and a silver mill operative, and amounted to less than nothing in each, and now—

What to do next?

I yielded to Higbie's appeals and consented to try the mining once more. We climbed far up on the mountain side and went to work on a little rubbishy claim of ours that had a shaft on it eight feet deep. Higbie descended into it and worked bravely with his pick till he had loosened up a deal of rock and dirt and then I went down with a long-handled shovel (the most awkward invention yet contrived by man) to throw it out. You must brace the shovel forward with the side of your knee till it is full, and then, with a skilful toss, throw it backward over your left shoulder. I made the toss and landed the mess just on the edge of the shaft and it all came back on my head and down the back of my neck. I never said a word, but climbed out and walked home. I inwardly resolved that I would starve before I would make a target of myself and shoot rubbish at it with a long-handled shovel. I sat down, in the cabin, and gave myself up to solid misery—so to speak. Now in pleasanter days I had amused myself with writing letters to the chief paper of the Territory, the Virginia *Daily Territorial Enterprise,* and had always been surprised when they appeared in print. My good opinion of the editors had steadily declined; for it seemed to me that they might have found something better to fill up with than my literature. I had found a letter in the post office as I came home from the hill side, and finally I opened it. Eureka! [I never did know what Eureka meant, but it seems to be as proper a word to heave in as any when no other that sounds pretty offers.] It was a deliberate offer to me of Twenty-Five Dollars a week to come up to Virginia and be city editor of the *Enterprise.*

I would have challenged the publisher in the "blind lead" days—I wanted to fall down and worship him, now. Twenty-Five Dollars a week—it looked like bloated luxury—a fortune—a sinful and lavish waste of money. But my transports cooled when I thought of my inexperience and consequent unfitness for the position—and straightway, on top of this, my long array of failures rose up before me. Yet if I refused this place I must presently become dependent upon somebody for my bread, a thing necessarily distasteful to a man who had never experienced such a humiliation since he was thirteen years old. Not much to be proud of, since it is so common—but then it was all I had to *be* proud of. So I was scared into being a city editor. I would have declined, otherwise. Necessity is the mother of "taking chances." I do not doubt that if, at that time, I had been offered a salary to translate the Talmud from the original Hebrew, I would have accepted—albeit with diffidence and some misgivings—and thrown as much variety into it as I could for the money.

I went up to Virginia and entered upon my new vocation. I was a rusty looking city editor, I am free to confess—coatless, slouch hat, blue woolen shirt, pantaloons stuffed into boot-tops, whiskered half down to the waist, and the universal navy revolver slung to my belt. But I secured a more Christian costume and discarded the revolver. I had never had occasion to kill anybody, nor ever felt a desire to do so, but had worn the thing in deference to popular sentiment, and in order that I might not, by its absence, be offensively conspicuous, and a subject of remark. But the other editors, and all the printers, carried revolvers. I asked the chief editor and proprietor (Mr. Goodman, I will call him, since it describes him as well as any name could do) for some instructions with regard to my duties, and he told me to go all over town and ask all sorts of people all sorts of questions, make notes of the information gained, and write them out for publication. And he added:

"Never say 'We learn' so-and-so, or 'It is reported,' or 'It is rumored,' or 'We understand' so-and-so, but go to headquarters and get the absolute facts, and then speak out and say 'It *is* so-and-so.' Otherwise, people will not put confidence in your news. Unassailable certainty is the thing that gives a newspaper the firmest and most valuable reputation."

It was the whole thing in a nut-shell; and to this day when I find a reporter commencing his article with "We understand," I gather a suspicion that he has not taken as much pains to inform himself as he ought to have done. I moralize well, but I did not always practise well when I was a city editor; I let fancy get the upper hand of fact too often when there was a dearth of news. I can never forget my first day's experience as a reporter. I wandered about town questioning everybody, boring everybody, and finding out that nobody knew anything. At the end of five hours my notebook was still barren. I spoke to Mr. Goodman. He said:

"Dan used to make a good thing out of the hay wagons in a dry time when there were no fires or inquests. Are there no hay wagons in from the Truckee? If there are, you might speak of the renewed activity and all that sort of thing, in the hay business, you know. It isn't sensational or exciting, but it fills up and looks business like."

I canvassed the city again and found one wretched old hay truck dragging in from the country. But I made affluent use of it. I multiplied it by sixteen, brought it into town from sixteen different directions, made sixteen separate items out of it, and got up such another sweat about hay as Virginia City had never seen in the world before.

This was encouraging. Two nonpareil columns had to be filled, and I was getting along. Presently, when things began to look dismal again, a desperado killed a man in a saloon and joy returned once more. I never was so glad over any mere trifle before in my life. I said to the murderer:

"Sir, you are a stranger to me, but you have done me a kindness this day which I can never forget. If whole years of gratitude can be to you any slight compensation, they shall be yours. I was in trouble and you have relieved me nobly and at a time when all seemed dark and drear. Count me your friend from this time forth, for I am not a man to forget a favor."

If I did not really say that to him I at least felt a sort of itching desire to do it. I wrote up the murder with a hungry attention to details, and when it was finished experienced but one regret—namely, that they had not hanged my benefactor on the spot, so that I could work him up too.

Next I discovered some emigrant wagons going into camp on the plaza and found that they had lately come through the hostile Indian country and had fared rather roughly. I made the best of the item that the circumstances permitted, and felt that if I were not confined within rigid limits by the presence of the reporters of the other papers I could add particulars that would make the article much more interesting. However, I found one wagon that was going on to California, and made some judicious inquiries of the proprietor. When I learned, through his short and surly answers to my cross-questioning, that he was certainly going on and would not be in the city next day to make trouble, I got ahead of the other papers, for I took down his list of names and added his party to the killed and wounded. Having more scope here, I put this wagon through an Indian fight that to this day has no parallel in history.

My two columns were filled. When I read them over in the morning I felt that I had found my legitimate occupation at last. I reasoned within myself that news, and stirring news, too, was what a paper needed, and I felt that I was peculiarly endowed with the ability to furnish it. Mr. Goodman said that I was as good a reporter as Dan. I desired no higher commendation. With encouragement like that, I felt that I could take my pen and murder all the immigrants on the plains if need be and the interests of the paper demanded it.

CHAPTER XLIII

However, as I grew better acquainted with the business and learned the run of the sources of information I ceased to require the aid of fancy to any large extent, and became able to fill my columns without diverging noticeably from the domain of fact.

I struck up friendships with the reporters of the other journals, and we swapped "regulars" with each other and thus economized work. "Regulars" are permanent sources of news, like courts, bullion returns, "clean-ups" at the quartz mills, and inquests. Inasmuch as everybody went armed, we had an inquest about every day, and so this department was naturally set down among the "regulars." We had lively papers in those days. My great competitor among the reporters was Boggs of the *Union*. He was an excellent reporter. Once in three or four months he would get a little intoxicated, but as a general thing he was a wary and cautious drinker although always ready to tamper a little with the enemy. He had the advantage of me in one thing; he could get the monthly public school report and I could not, because the principal hated the *Enterprise*. One snowy night when the report was due, I started out sadly wondering how I was going to get it. Presently, a few steps up the almost deserted street I stumbled on Boggs and asked him where he was going.

"After the school report."

"I'll go along with you."

"No, *sir*. I'll excuse you."

"Just as you say."

A saloon-keeper's boy passed by with a steaming pitcher of hot punch, and Boggs snuffed the fragrance gratefully. He gazed fondly after the boy and saw him start up the *Enterprise* stairs. I said:

"I wish you could help me get that school business, but since you can't, I must run up to the *Union* office and see if I can get them to let me have a proof of it after they have set it up, though I don't begin to suppose they will. Good night."

"Hold on a minute. I don't mind getting the report and sitting around with the boys a little, while you copy it, if you're willing to drop down to the principal's with me."

"Now you talk like a rational being. Come along."

We plowed a couple of blocks through the snow, got the report and returned to our office. It was a short document and soon copied. Meantime Boggs helped himself to the punch. I gave the manuscript back to him and we started out to get an inquest, for we heard pistol shots near by. We got the particulars with little loss of time, for it was only an inferior sort of barroom murder, and of little interest to the public, and then we separated. Away at three o'clock in the morning, when we had gone to press and were having a relaxing concert as usual—for some of the printers were good singers and others good performers on the guitar and on that atrocity the accordeon—the proprietor of the *Union* strode in and desired to know if anybody had heard anything of Boggs or the school report. We stated the case, and all turned out to help hunt for the delinquent. We found him standing on a table in a saloon, with an old tin lantern in one hand and the school report in the other, haranguing a gang of intoxicated Cornish miners on the iniquity of squandering the public moneys on education "when hundreds and hundreds of honest hard-working men are literally starving for whiskey." [Riotous applause.] He had been assisting in a regal spree with those parties for hours. We dragged him away and put him to bed.

Of course there was no school report in the *Union*, and Boggs held me accountable, though I was innocent of any intention or desire to compass its absence from that paper and was as sorry as any one that the misfortune had occurred.

But we were perfectly friendly. The day that the school report was next due, the proprietor of the "Genessee" mine furnished us a buggy and asked us to go down and write something about the property—a very common request and one always gladly acceded to when people furnished buggies, for we were as fond of pleasure excursions as other people. In due time we arrived at the "mine"—nothing but a hole in the ground ninety feet deep, and no way of getting down into it but by holding on to a rope and being lowered with a windlass. The workmen had just gone off somewhere to dinner. I was not strong enough to lower Boggs's bulk; so I took an unlighted candle in my teeth, made a loop for my foot in the end of the rope, implored Boggs not to go to sleep or let the windlass get the start of him, and then swung out over the shaft. I reached the bottom muddy and bruised about the elbows, but safe. I lit the candle, made an examination of the rock, selected some specimens and shouted to Boggs to hoist away. No answer. Presently a head appeared in the circle of daylight away aloft, and a voice came down:

"Are you all set?"

"All set—hoist away."

"Are you comfortable?"

"Perfectly."

"Could you wait a little?"

"Oh certainly—no particular hurry."

"Well—good by."

"Why? Where are you going?"

"After the school report!"

And he did. I staid down there an hour, and surprised the workmen when they hauled up and found a man on the rope instead of a bucket of rock. I walked home, too—five miles—up hill. We had no school report next morning; but the *Union* had.

Six months after my entry into journalism the grand "flush times" of Silverland began, and they continued with unabated splendor for three years. All difficulty about filling up the "local department" ceased, and the only trouble now was how to make the lengthened columns hold the world of incidents and happenings that came to our literary net every day. Virginia had grown to be the "livest" town, for its age and population, that America had ever produced. The sidewalks swarmed with people—to such an extent, indeed, that it was generally no easy matter to stem the human tide. The streets themselves were just as crowded with quartz wagons, freight teams and other vehicles. The procession was endless. So great was the pack, that buggies frequently had to wait half an hour for an opportunity to cross the principal street. Joy sat on every countenance, and there was a glad, almost fierce, intensity in every eye, that told of the money-getting schemes that were seething in every brain and the high hope that held sway in every heart. Money was as plenty as dust; every individual considered himself wealthy, and a melancholy countenance was nowhere to be seen. There were military companies, fire companies, brass bands, banks, hotels, theatres, "hurdy-gurdy houses," wide-open gambling palaces, political pow-wows, civic processions, street fights, murders, inquests, riots, a whiskey mill every fifteen steps, a Board of Aldermen, a Mayor, a City Surveyor, a City Engineer, a Chief of the Fire Department, with First, Second and Third Assistants, a Chief of Police, City Marshal and a large police force, two Boards of Mining Brokers, a dozen breweries and half a dozen jails and station-houses in full operation, and some talk of building a church. The "flush times" were in magnificent flower! Large fire-proof brick buildings were going up in the principal streets, and the wooden suburbs were spreading out in all directions. Town lots soared up to prices that were amazing.

The great "Comstock lode" stretched its opulent length straight through the town from north to south, and every mine on it was in diligent process of development. One of these mines alone employed six hundred and seventy-five men, and in the matter of elections the adage was, "as the 'Gould and Curry' goes, so goes the city." Laboring men's wages were four and six dollars a day, and they worked in three "shifts" or gangs, and the blasting and picking and shoveling went on without ceasing, night and day.

The "city" of Virginia roosted royally midway up the steep side of Mount Davidson, seven thousand two hundred feet above the level of the sea, and in the clear Nevada atmosphere was visible from a distance of fifty miles! It claimed a population of fifteen thousand to eighteen thousand, and all day long half of this little army swarmed the streets like bees and the other half swarmed among the drifts and tunnels of the "Comstock," hundreds of feet down in the earth directly under those same streets. Often we felt our chairs jar, and heard the faint boom of a blast down in the bowels of the earth under the office.

The mountain side was so steep that the entire town had a slant to it like a roof. Each street was a terrace, and from each to the next street below the descent was forty or fifty feet. The fronts of the houses were level with the street they faced, but their rear first floors were propped on lofty stilts; a man could stand at a rear first floor window of a C street house and look down the chimneys of the row of houses below him facing D street. It was a laborious climb, in that thin atmosphere, to ascend from D to A street, and you were panting and out of breath when you got there; but you could turn around and go down again like a house a-fire—so to speak. The atmosphere was so rarified, on account of the great altitude, that one's blood lay near the surface always, and the scratch of a pin was a disaster worth worrying about, for the chances were that a grievous erysipelas would ensue. But to offset this, the thin atmosphere seemed to carry healing to gunshot wounds, and therefore, to simply shoot your adversary through both lungs was a thing not likely to afford you any permanent satisfaction, for he would be nearly certain to be around looking for you within the month, and not with an opera glass, either.

From Virginia's airy situation one could look over a vast, far-reaching panorama of mountain ranges and deserts; and whether the day was bright or overcast, whether the sun was rising or setting, or flaming in the zenith, or whether night and the moon held sway, the spectacle was always impressive and beautiful. Over your head Mount Davidson lifted its gray dome, and before and below you a rugged canyon clove the battlemented hills, making a sombre gateway through which a soft-tinted desert was glimpsed, with the silver thread of a river winding through it, bordered with trees which many miles of distance diminished to a delicate fringe; and still further away the snowy mountains rose up and stretched their long barrier to the filmy horizon—far enough beyond a lake that burned in the desert like a fallen sun, though that, itself, lay fifty miles removed. Look from your window where you would, there was fascination in the picture. At rare intervals—but very rare—there were clouds in our skies, and then the setting sun would gild and flush and glorify this mighty expanse of scenery with a bewildering pomp of color that held the eye like a spell and moved the spirit like music.

CHAPTER XLIV

My salary was increased to forty dollars a week. But I seldom drew it. I had plenty of other resources, and what were two broad twenty-dollar gold pieces to a man who had his pockets full of such and a cumbersome abundance of bright half dollars besides? [Paper money has never come into use on the Pacific coast.] Reporting was lucrative, and every man in the town was lavish with his money and his "feet." The city and all the great mountain side were riddled with mining shafts. There were more mines than miners. True, not ten of these mines were yielding rock worth hauling to a mill, but everybody said, "Wait till the shaft gets down where the ledge comes in solid, and then you will see!" So nobody was discouraged. These were nearly all "wild cat" mines, and wholly worthless, but nobody believed it then. The "Ophir," the "Gould & Curry," the "Mexican," and other great mines on the Comstock lead in Virginia and Gold Hill were turning out huge piles of rich rock every day, and every man believed that his little wild cat claim was as good as any on the "main lead" and would infallibly be worth a thousand dollars a foot when he "got down where it came in solid." Poor fellow, he was blessedly blind to the fact that he never would see that day. So the thousand wild cat shafts burrowed deeper and deeper into the earth day by day, and all men were beside themselves with hope and happiness. How they labored, prophesied, exulted! Surely nothing like it was ever seen before since the world began. Every one of these wild cat mines—not mines, but holes in the ground over imaginary mines—was incorporated and had handsomely engraved "stock" and the stock was salable, too. It was bought and sold with a feverish avidity in the boards every day. You could go up on the mountain side, scratch around and find a ledge (there was no lack of them), put up a "notice" with a grandiloquent name in it, start a shaft, get your stock printed, and with nothing whatever to prove that your mine was worth a straw, you could put your stock on the market and sell out for hundreds and even thousands of dollars. To make money, and make it fast, was as easy as it was to eat your dinner. Every man owned "feet" in fifty different wild cat mines and considered his fortune made. Think of a city with not one solitary poor man in it! One would suppose that when month after month went by and still not a wild cat mine [by wild cat I mean, in general terms, *any* claim not located on the mother vein, *i.e.,* the "Comstock") yielded a ton of rock worth crushing, the people would begin to wonder if they were not putting too much faith in their prospective riches; but there was not a thought of such a thing. They burrowed away, bought and sold, and were happy.

New claims were taken up daily, and it was the friendly custom to run straight to the newspaper offices, give the reporter forty or fifty "feet," and get them to go and examine the mine and publish a notice of it. They did not care a fig what you said about the property so you said something. Consequently we generally said a word or two to the effect that the "indications" were good, or that the ledge was "six feet wide," or that the rock "resembled the Comstock" (and so it did—but as a general thing the resemblance was not startling enough to knock you down). If the rock was moderately promising, we followed the custom of the country, used strong adjectives and frothed at the mouth as if a very marvel in silver discoveries had transpired. If the mine was a "developed" one, and had no pay ore to show (and of course it hadn't), we praised the tunnel; said it was one of the most infatuating tunnels in the land; driveled and driveled about the tunnel till we ran entirely out of ecstasies—but never said a word about the rock. We would squander half a column of adulation on a shaft, or a new wire rope, or a dressed pine windlass, or a fascinating force pump, and close with a burst of admiration of the "gentlemanly and efficient Superintendent" of the mine—but never utter a whisper about the rock. And those people were always pleased, always satisfied. Occasionally we patched up and varnished our reputation for discrimination and stern, undeviating accuracy, by giving some old abandoned claim a blast that ought to have made its dry bones rattle—and then somebody would seize it and sell it on the fleeting notoriety thus conferred upon it.

There was *nothing* in the shape of a mining claim that was not salable. We received presents of "feet" every day. If we needed a hundred dollars or so, we sold some; if not, we hoarded it away, satisfied that it would ultimately be worth a thousand dollars a foot. I had a trunk about half full of "stock." When a claim made a stir in the market and went up to a high figure, I searched through my pile to see if I had any of its stock—and generally found it.

The prices rose and fell constantly; but still a fall disturbed us little, because a thousand dollars a foot was our figure, and so we were content to let it fluctuate as much as it pleased till it reached it. My pile of stock was not all given to me by people who wished their claims "noticed." At least half of it was given me by persons who had no thought of such a thing, and looked for nothing more than a simple verbal "thank you"; and you were not even obliged by law to furnish that. If you are coming up the street with a couple of baskets of apples in your hands, and you meet a friend, you naturally invite him to take a few. That describes the condition of things in Virginia in the "flush times." Every man had his pockets full of stock, and it was the actual *custom* of the country to part with small quantities of it to friends without the asking. Very often it was a good idea to close the transaction instantly, when a man offered a stock present to a friend, for the offer was only good and binding at that moment, and if the price went to a high figure shortly afterward the procrastination was a thing to be regretted. Mr. Stewart (Senator, now, from Nevada) one day told me he would give me twenty feet of "Justis" stock if I would walk over to his office. It was worth five or ten dollars a foot. I asked him to make the offer good for next day, as I was just going to dinner. He said he would not be in town; so I risked it and took my dinner instead of the stock. Within the week the price went up to seventy dollars and afterward to a hundred and fifty, but nothing could make that man yield. I suppose he sold that stock of mine and placed the guilty proceeds in his own pocket. [My revenge will be found in the accompanying portrait.] I met three friends one afternoon, who said they had been buying "Overman" stock at auction at eight dollars a foot. One said if I would come up to his office he would give me fifteen feet; another said he would add fifteen; the third said he would do the same. But I was going after an inquest and could not stop. A few weeks afterward they sold all their "Overman" at six hundred dollars a foot and generously came around to tell me about it—and also to urge me to accept of the next forty-five feet of it that people tried to force on me. These are actual facts, and I could make the list a long one and still confine myself strictly to the truth. Many a time friends gave us as much as twenty-five feet of stock that was selling at twenty-five dollars a foot, and they thought no more of it than they would of offering a guest a cigar. These were "flush times" indeed! I thought they were going to last always, but somehow I never was much of a prophet.

To show what a wild spirit possessed the mining brain of the community, I will remark that "claims" were actually "located" in excavations for cellars, where the pick had exposed what seemed to be quartz veins—and not cellars in the suburbs, either, but in the very heart of the city; and forthwith stock would be issued and thrown on the market. It was small matter who the cellar belonged to—the "ledge" belonged to the finder, and unless the United States government interfered (inasmuch as the government holds the primary right to mines of the noble metals in Nevada—or at least did then), it was considered to be his privilege to work it. Imagine a stranger staking out a mining claim among the costly shrubbery in your front yard and calmly proceeding to lay waste the ground with pick and shovel and blasting powder! It has been often done in California. In the middle of one of the principal business streets of Virginia, a man "located" a mining claim and began a shaft on it. He gave me a hundred feet of the stock and I sold it for a fine suit of clothes because I was afraid somebody would fall down the shaft and sue for damages. I owned in another claim that was located in the middle of another street; and to show how absurd people can be, that "East India" stock (as it was called) sold briskly although there was an ancient tunnel running directly under the claim and any man could go into it and see that it did not cut a quartz ledge or anything that remotely resembled one.

One plan of acquiring sudden wealth was to "salt" a wild cat claim and sell out while the excitement was up. The process was simple. The schemer located a worthless ledge, sunk a shaft on it, bought a wagon load of rich "Comstock" ore, dumped a portion of it into the shaft and piled the rest by its side, above ground. Then he showed the property to a simpleton and sold it to him at a high figure. Of course the wagon load of rich ore was all that the victim ever got out of his purchase. A most remarkable case of "salting" was that of the "North Ophir." It was claimed that this vein was a remote "extension" of the original "Ophir," a valuable mine on the "Comstock." For a few days everybody was talking about the rich developments in the North Ophir. It was said that it yielded perfectly pure silver in small, solid lumps. I went to the place with the owners, and found a shaft six or eight feet deep, in the bottom of which was a badly shattered vein of dull, yellowish, unpromising rock. One would as soon expect to find silver in a grindstone. We got out a pan of the rubbish and washed it in a puddle, and sure enough, among the sediment we found half a dozen black, bullet-looking pellets of unimpeachable "native" silver. Nobody had ever heard of such a thing before; science could not account for such a queer novelty. The stock rose to sixty-five dollars a foot, and at this figure the world-renowned tragedian, McKean Buchanan, bought a commanding interest and prepared to quit the stage once more—he was always doing that. And then it transpired that the mine had been "salted"—and not in any hackneyed way, either, but in a singularly bold, barefaced and peculiarly original and outrageous fashion. On one of the lumps of "native" silver was discovered the minted legend, "TED STATES OF," and then it was plainly apparent that the mine had been "salted" with melted half-dollars! The lumps thus obtained had been blackened till they resembled native silver, and were then mixed with the shattered rock in the bottom of the shaft. It is literally true. Of course the price of the stock at once fell to nothing, and the tragedian was ruined. But for this calamity we might have lost McKean Buchanan from the stage.

CHAPTER XLV

The "flush times" held bravely on. Something over two years before, Mr. Goodman and another journeyman printer, had borrowed forty dollars and set out from San Francisco to try their fortunes in the new city of Virginia. They found the *Territorial Enterprise,* a poverty-stricken weekly journal, gasping for breath and likely to die. They bought it, type, fixtures, good-will and all, for a thousand dollars, on long time. The editorial sanctum, news-room, pressroom, publication office, bed-chamber, parlor, and kitchen were all compressed into one apartment and it was a small one, too. The editors and printers slept on the floor, a Chinaman did their cooking, and the "imposing-stone" was the general dinner table. But now things were changed. The paper was a great daily, printed by steam; there were five editors and twenty-three compositors; the subscription price was sixteen dollars a year; the advertising rates were exorbitant, and the columns crowded. The paper was clearing from six to ten thousand dollars a month, and the "Enterprise Building" was finished and ready for occupation—a stately fireproof brick. Every day from five all the way up to eleven columns of "live" advertisements were left out or crowded into spasmodic and irregular "supplements."

The "Gould & Curry" company were erecting a monster hundred-stamp mill at a cost that ultimately fell little short of a million dollars. Gould & Curry stock paid heavy dividends—a rare thing, and an experience confined to the dozen or fifteen claims located on the "main lead," the "Comstock." The Superintendent of the Gould & Curry lived, rent free, in a fine house built and furnished by the company. He drove a fine pair of horses which were a present from the company, and his salary was twelve thousand dollars a year. The superintendent of another of the great mines traveled in grand state, had a salary of twenty-eight thousand dollars a year, and in a law suit in after days claimed that he was to have had one per cent, on the gross yield of the bullion likewise.

Money was wonderfully plenty. The trouble was, not how to get it,—but how to spend it, how to lavish it, get rid of it, squander it. And so it was a happy thing that just at this juncture the news came over the wires that a great United States Sanitary Commission had been formed and money was wanted for the relief of the wounded sailors and soldiers of the Union languishing in the Eastern hospitals. Right on the heels of it came word that San Francisco had responded superbly before the telegram was half a day old. Virginia rose as one man! A Sanitary Committee was hurriedly organized, and its chairman mounted a vacant cart in C street and tried to make the clamorous multitude understand that the rest of the committee were flying hither and thither and working with all their might and main, and that if the town would only wait an hour, an office would be ready, books opened, and the Commission prepared to receive contributions. His voice was drowned and his information lost in a ceaseless roar of cheers, and demands that the money be received *now*—they swore they would not wait. The chairman pleaded and argued, but, deaf to all entreaty, men plowed their way through the throng and rained checks of gold coin into the cart and skurried away for more. Hands clutching money, were thrust aloft out of the jam by men who hoped this eloquent appeal would cleave a road their strugglings could not open. The very Chinamen and Indians caught the excitement and dashed their half dollars into the cart without knowing or caring what it was all about. Women plunged into the crowd, trimly attired, fought their way to the cart with their coin, and emerged again, by and by, with their apparel in a state of hopeless dilapidation. It was the wildest mob Virginia had ever seen and the most determined and ungovernable; and when at last it abated its fury and dispersed, it had not a penny in its pocket. To use its own phraseology, it came there "flush" and went away "busted."

After that, the Commission got itself into systematic working order, and for weeks the contributions flowed into its treasury in a generous stream. Individuals and all sorts of organizations levied upon themselves a regular weekly tax for the sanitary fund, graduated according to their means, and there was not another grand universal outburst till the famous "Sanitary Flour Sack" came our way. Its history is peculiar and interesting. A former schoolmate of mine, by the name of Reuel Gridley, was living at the little city of Austin, in the Reese river country, at this time, and was the Democratic candidate for mayor. He and the Republican candidate made an agreement that the defeated man should be publicly presented with a fifty-pound sack of flour by the successful one, and should carry it home on his shoulder. Gridley was defeated. The new mayor gave him the sack of flour, and he shouldered it and carried it a mile or two, from Lower Austin to his home in Upper Austin, attended by a band of music and the whole population. Arrived there, he said he did not need the flour, and asked what the people thought he had better do with it. A voice said:

"Sell it to the highest bidder, for the benefit of the Sanitary fund."

The suggestion was greeted with a round of applause, and Gridley mounted a dry-goods box and assumed the role of auctioneer. The bids went higher and higher, as the sympathies of the pioneers awoke and expanded, till at last the sack was knocked down to a mill man at two hundred and fifty dollars, and his check taken. He was asked where he would have the flour delivered, and he said:

"Nowhere—sell it again."

Now the cheers went up royally, and the multitude were fairly in the spirit of the thing. So Gridley stood there and shouted and perspired till the sun went down; and when the crowd dispersed he had sold the sack to three hundred different people, and had taken in eight thousand dollars in gold. And still the flour sack was in his possession.

The news came to Virginia, and a telegram went back:

"Fetch along your flour sack!"

Thirty-six hours afterward Gridley arrived, and an afternoon mass meeting was held in the Opera House, and the auction began. But the sack had come sooner than it was expected; the people were not thoroughly aroused, and the sale dragged. At nightfall only five thousand dollars had been secured, and there was a crestfallen feeling in the community. However, there was no disposition to let the matter rest here and acknowledge vanquishment at the hands of the village of Austin. Till late in the night the principal citizens were at work arranging the morrow's campaign, and when they went to bed they had no fears for the result. At eleven the next morning a procession of open carriages, attended by clamorous bands of music and adorned with a moving display of flags, filed along C street and was soon in danger of blockade by a huzzaing multitude of citizens. In the first carriage sat Gridley, with the flour sack in prominent view, the latter splendid with bright paint and gilt lettering; also in the same carriage sat the mayor and the recorder. The other carriages contained the Common Council, the editors and reporters, and other people of imposing consequence. The crowd pressed to the corner of C and Taylor streets, expecting the sale to begin there, but they were disappointed, and also unspeakably surprised; for the cavalcade moved on as if Virginia had ceased to be of importance, and took its way over the "divide," toward the small town of Gold Hill. Telegrams had gone ahead to Gold Hill, Silver City and Dayton, and those communities were at fever heat and rife for the conflict. It was a very hot day, and wonderfully dusty. At the end of a short half hour we descended into Gold Hill with drums beating and colors flying, and enveloped in imposing clouds of dust. The whole population—men, women and children, Chinamen and Indians, were massed in the main street, all the flags in town were at the mast head, and the blare of the bands was drowned in cheers. Gridley stood up and asked who would make the first bid for the National Sanitary Flour Sack. Gen. W. said:

"The Yellow Jacket silver mining company offers a thousand dollars, coin!"

A tempest of applause followed. A telegram carried the news to Virginia, and fifteen minutes afterward the city's population was massed in the streets devouring the tidings—for it was part of the programme that the bulletin boards should do a good work that day. Every few minutes a new dispatch was bulletined from Gold Hill, and still the excitement grew. Telegrams began to return to us from Virginia beseeching Gridley to bring back the flour sack; but such was not the plan of the campaign. At the end of an hour Gold Hill's small population had paid a figure for the flour sack that awoke all the enthusiasm of Virginia when the grand total was displayed upon the bulletin boards. Then the Gridley cavalcade moved on, a giant refreshed with new lager beer and plenty of it—for the people brought it to the carriages without waiting to measure it—and within three hours more the expedition had carried Silver City and Dayton by storm and was on its way back covered with glory. Every move had been telegraphed and bulletined, and as the procession entered Virginia and filed down C street at half past eight in the evening the town was abroad in the thoroughfares, torches were glaring, flags flying, bands playing, cheer on cheer cleaving the air, and the city ready to surrender at discretion. The auction began, every bid was greeted with bursts of applause, and at the end of two hours and a half a population of fifteen thousand souls had paid in coin for a fifty-pound sack of flour a sum equal to forty thousand dollars in greenbacks! It was at a rate in the neighborhood of three dollars for each man, woman and child of the population. The grand total would have been twice as large, but the streets were very narrow, and hundreds who wanted to bid could not get within a block of the stand, and could not make themselves heard. These grew tired of waiting and many of them went home long before the auction was over. This was the greatest day Virginia every saw, perhaps.

Gridley sold the sack in Carson city and several California towns; also in San Francisco. Then he took it east and sold it in one or two Atlantic cities, I think. I am not sure of that, but I know that he finally carried it to St. Louis, where a monster Sanitary Fair was being held, and after selling it there for a large sum and helping on the enthusiasm by displaying the portly silver bricks which Nevada's donation had produced, he had the flour baked up into small cakes and retailed them at high prices.

It was estimated that when the flour sack's mission was ended it had been sold for a grand total of a hundred and fifty thousand dollars in greenbacks! This is probably the only instance on record where common family flour brought three thousand dollars a pound in the public market.

It is due to Mr. Gridley's memory to mention that the expenses of his sanitary flour sack expedition of fifteen thousand miles, going and returning, were paid in large part, if not entirely, out of his own pocket. The time he gave to it was not less than three months. Mr. Gridley was a soldier in the Mexican war and a pioneer Californian. He died at Stockton, California, in December, 1870, greatly regretted.

CHAPTER XLVI

There were nabobs in those days—in the "flush times," I mean. Every rich strike in the mines created one or two. I call to mind several of these. They were careless, easy-going fellows, as a general thing, and the community at large was as much benefited by their riches as they were themselves—possibly more, in some cases.

Two cousins, teamsters, did some hauling for a man and had to take a small segregated portion of a silver mine in lieu of $300 cash. They gave an outsider a third to open the mine, and they went on teaming. But not long. Ten months afterward the mine was out of debt and paying each owner $8,000 to $10,000 a month—say $100,000 a year.

One of the earliest nabobs that Nevada was delivered of wore $6,000 worth of diamonds in his bosom, and swore he was unhappy because he could not spend his money as fast as he made it.

Another Nevada nabob boasted an income that often reached $16,000 a month; and he used to love to tell how he had worked in the very mine that yielded it, for five dollars a day, when he first came to the country.

The silver and sage-brush State has knowledge of another of these pets of fortune—lifted from actual poverty to affluence almost in a single night—who was able to offer $100,000 for a position of high official distinction, shortly afterward, and did offer it—but failed to get it, his politics not being as sound as his bank account.

Then there was John Smith. He was a good, honest, kind-hearted soul, born and reared in the lower ranks of life, and miraculously ignorant. He drove a team, and owned a small ranch—a ranch that paid him a comfortable living, for although it yielded but little hay, what little it did yield was worth from $250 to $300 in gold per ton in the market. Presently Smith traded a few acres of the ranch for a small undeveloped silver mine in Gold Hill. He opened the mine and built a little unpretending ten-stamp mill. Eighteen months afterward he retired from the hay business, for his mining income had reached a most comfortable figure. Some people said it was $30,000 a month, and others said it was $60,000. Smith was very rich at any rate.

And then he went to Europe and traveled. And when he came back he was never tired of telling about the fine hogs he had seen in England, and the gorgeous sheep he had seen in Spain, and the fine cattle he had noticed in the vicinity of Rome. He was full of the wonders of the old world, and advised everybody to travel. He said a man never imagined what surprising things there were in the world till he had traveled.

One day, on board ship, the passengers made up a pool of $500, which was to be the property of the man who should come nearest to guessing the run of the vessel for the next twenty-four hours. Next day, toward noon, the figures were all in the purser's hands in sealed envelopes. Smith was serene and happy, for he had been bribing the engineer. But another party won the prize! Smith said:

"Here, that won't do! He guessed two miles wider of the mark than I did."

The purser said, "Mr. Smith, you missed it further than any man on board. We traveled two hundred and eight miles yesterday."

"Well, sir," said Smith, "that's just where I've got you, for I guessed two hundred and nine. If you'll look at my figgers again you'll find a 2 and two 0's, which stands for 200, don't it?—and after 'em you'll find a 9 (2009), which stands for two hundred and nine. I reckon I'll take that money, if you please."

The Gould & Curry claim comprised twelve hundred feet, and it all belonged originally to the two men whose names it bears. Mr. Curry owned two third of it—and he said that he sold it out for twenty-five hundred dollars in cash, and an old plug horse that ate up his market value in hay and barley in seventeen days by the watch. And he said that Gould sold out for a pair of second-hand government blankets and a bottle of whiskey that killed nine men in three hours, and that an unoffending stranger that smelt the cork was disabled for life. Four years afterward the mine thus disposed of was worth in the San Francisco market seven millions six hundred thousand dollars in gold coin.

In the early days a poverty-stricken Mexican who lived in a canyon directly back of Virginia City, had a stream of water as large as a man's wrist trickling from the hill-side on his premises. The Ophir Company segregated a hundred feet of their mine and traded it to him for the stream of water. The hundred feet proved to be the richest part of the entire mine; four years after the swap, its market value (including its mill) was $1,500,000.

An individual who owned twenty feet in the Ophir mine before its great riches were revealed to men, traded it for a horse, and a very sorry looking brute he was, too. A year or so afterward, when Ophir stock went up to $3,000 a foot, this man, who had not a cent, used to say he was the most startling example of magnificence and misery the world had ever seen—because he was able to ride a sixty-thousand-dollar horse—yet could not scrape up cash enough to buy a saddle, and was obliged to borrow one or ride bareback. He said if fortune were to give him another sixty-thousand-dollar horse it would ruin him.

A youth of nineteen, who was a telegraph operator in Virginia on a salary of a hundred dollars a month, and who, when he could not make out German names in the list of San Francisco steamer arrivals, used to ingeniously select and supply substitutes for them out of an old Berlin city directory, made himself rich by watching the mining telegrams that passed through his hands and buying and selling stocks accordingly, through a friend in San Francisco. Once when a private dispatch was sent from Virginia announcing a rich strike in a prominent mine and advising that the matter be kept secret till a large amount of the stock could be secured, he bought forty "feet" of the stock at twenty dollars a foot, and afterward sold half of it at eight hundred dollars a foot and the rest at double that figure. Within three months he was worth $150,000, and had resigned his telegraphic position.

Another telegraph operator who had been discharged by the company for divulging the secrets of the office, agreed with a moneyed man in San Francisco to furnish him the result of a great Virginia mining lawsuit within an hour after its private reception by the parties to it in San Francisco. For this he was to have a large percentage of the profits on purchases and sales made on it by his fellow-conspirator. So he went, disguised as a teamster, to a little wayside telegraph office in the mountains, got acquainted with the operator, and sat in the office day after day, smoking his pipe, complaining that his team was fagged out and unable to travel—and meantime listening to the dispatches as they passed clicking through the machine from Virginia. Finally the private dispatch announcing the result of the lawsuit sped over the wires, and as soon as he heard it he telegraphed his friend in San Francisco:

"Am tired waiting. Shall sell the team and go home."

It was the signal agreed upon. The word "waiting" left out, would have signified that the suit had gone the other way. The mock teamster's friend picked up a deal of the mining stock, at low figures, before the news became public, and a fortune was the result.

For a long time after one of the great Virginia mines had been incorporated, about fifty feet of the original location were still in the hands of a man who had never signed the incorporation papers. The stock became very valuable, and every effort was made to find this man, but he had disappeared. Once it was heard that he was in New York, and one or two speculators went east but failed to find him. Once the news came that he was in the Bermudas, and straightway a speculator or two hurried east and sailed for Bermuda—but he was not there. Finally he was heard of in Mexico, and a friend of his, a bar-keeper on a salary, scraped together a little money and sought him out, bought his "feet" for a hundred dollars, returned and sold the property for $75,000.

But why go on? The traditions of Silverland are filled with instances like these, and I would never get through enumerating them were I to attempt to do it. I only desired to give the reader an idea of a peculiarity of the "flush times" which I could not present so strikingly in any other way, and which some mention of was necessary to a realizing comprehension of the time and the country.

I was personally acquainted with the majority of the nabobs I have referred to, and so, for old acquaintance sake, I have shifted their occupations and experiences around in such a way as to keep the Pacific public from recognizing these once notorious men. No longer notorious, for the majority of them have drifted back into poverty and obscurity again.

In Nevada there used to be current the story of an adventure of two of her nabobs, which may or may not have occurred. I give it for what it is worth:

Col. Jim had seen somewhat of the world, and knew more or less of its ways; but Col. Jack was from the back settlements of the States, had led a life of arduous toil, and had never seen a city. These two, blessed with sudden wealth, projected a visit to New York,—Col. Jack to see the sights, and Col. Jim to guard his unsophistication from misfortune. They reached San Francisco in the night, and sailed in the morning. Arrived in New York, Col. Jack said:

"I've heard tell of carriages all my life, and now I mean to have a ride in one; I don't care what it costs. Come along."

They stepped out on the sidewalk, and Col. Jim called a stylish barouche. But Col. Jack said:

"*No*, sir! None of your cheap-John turn-outs for me. I'm here to have a good time, and money ain't any object. I mean to have the nobbiest rig that's going. Now here comes the very trick. Stop that yaller one with the pictures on it—don't you fret—I'll stand all the expenses myself."

So Col. Jim stopped an empty omnibus, and they got in. Said Col. Jack:

"Ain't it gay, though? Oh, no, I reckon not! Cushions, and windows, and pictures, till you can't rest. What would the boys say if they could see us cutting a swell like this in New York? By George, I wish they *could* see us."

Then he put his head out of the window, and shouted to the driver:

"Say, Johnny, this suits *me!*—suits yours truly, you bet, you!

I want this shebang all day. I'm *on* it, old man! Let 'em out! Make 'em go! We'll make it all right with *you,* sonny!"

The driver passed his hand through the strap-hole, and tapped for his fare—it was before the gongs came into common use. Col. Jack took the hand, and shook it cordially. He said:

"You twig me, old pard! All right between gents. Smell of *that*, and see how you like it!"

And he put a twenty-dollar gold piece in the driver's hand. After a moment the driver said he could not make change.

"Bother the change! Ride it out. Put it in your pocket."

Then to Col. Jim, with a sounding slap on his thigh:

"*Ain't* it style, though? Hanged if I don't hire this thing every day for a week."

The omnibus stopped, and a young lady got in. Col. Jack stared a moment, then nudged Col. Jim with his elbow:

"Don't say a word," he whispered. "Let her ride, if she wants to. Gracious, there's room enough."

The young lady got out her porte-monnaie, and handed her fare to Col. Jack.

"What's this for?" said he.

"Give it to the driver, please."

"Take back your money, madam. We can't allow it. You're welcome to ride here as long as you please, but this shebang's chartered, and we can't let you pay a cent."

The girl shrunk into a corner, bewildered. An old lady with a basket climbed in, and proffered her fare.

"Excuse me," said Col. Jack. "You're perfectly welcome here, madam, but we can't allow you to pay. Set right down there, mum, and don't you be the least uneasy. Make yourself just as free as if you was in your own turn-out."

Within two minutes, three gentlemen, two fat women, and a couple of children, entered.

"Come right along, friends," said Col. Jack; "don't mind *us*. This is a free blow-out." Then he whispered to Col. Jim, "New York ain't no sociable place, I don't reckon—it ain't no *name* for it!"

He resisted every effort to pass fares to the driver, and made everybody cordially welcome. The situation dawned on the people, and they pocketed their money, and delivered themselves up to covert enjoyment of the episode. Half a dozen more passengers entered.

"Oh, there's *plenty* of room," said Col. Jack. "Walk right in, and make yourselves at home. A blow-out ain't worth anything *as* a blow-out, unless a body has company." Then in a whisper to Col. Jim: "But *ain't* these New Yorkers friendly? And ain't they cool about it, too? Icebergs ain't anywhere. I reckon they'd tackle a hearse, if it was going their way."

More passengers got in; more yet, and still more. Both seats were filled, and a file of men were standing up, holding on to the cleats overhead. Parties with baskets and bundles were climbing up on the roof. Half-suppressed laughter rippled up from all sides.

"Well, for clean, cool, out-and-out cheek, if this don't bang anything that ever I saw, I'm an Injun!" whispered Col. Jack.

A Chinaman crowded his way in.

"I weaken!" said Col. Jack. "Hold on, driver! Keep your seats, ladies and gents. Just make yourselves free—everything's paid for. Driver, rustle these folks around as long as they're a mind to go—friends of ours, you know. Take them everywheres—and if you want more money, come to the St. Nicholas, and we'll make it all right. Pleasant journey to you, ladies and gents—go it just as long as you please—it shan't cost you a cent!"

The two comrades got out, and Col. Jack said:

"Jimmy, it's the sociablest place *I* ever saw. The Chinaman waltzed in as comfortable as anybody. If we'd staid awhile, I reckon we'd had some niggers. B' George, we'll have to barricade our doors to-night, or some of these ducks will be trying to sleep with us."

CHAPTER XLVII

Somebody has said that in order to know a community, one must observe the style of its funerals and know what manner of men they bury with most ceremony. I cannot say which class we buried with most eclat in our "flush times," the distinguished public benefactor or the distinguished rough—possibly the two chief grades or grand divisions of society honored their illustrious dead about equally; and hence, no doubt the philosopher I have quoted from would have needed to see two representative funerals in Virginia before forming his estimate of the people.

There was a grand time over Buck Fanshaw when he died. He was a representative citizen. He had "killed his man"—not in his own quarrel, it is true, but in defence of a stranger unfairly beset by numbers. He had kept a sumptuous saloon. He had been the proprietor of a dashing helpmeet whom he could have discarded without the formality of a divorce. He had held a high position in the fire department and been a very Warwick in politics. When he died there was great lamentation throughout the town, but especially in the vast bottom-stratum of society.

On the inquest it was shown that Buck Fanshaw, in the delirium of a wasting typhoid fever, had taken arsenic, shot himself through the body, cut his throat, and jumped out of a four-story window and broken his neck—and after due deliberation, the jury, sad and tearful, but with intelligence unblinded by its sorrow, brought in a verdict of death "by the visitation of God." What could the world do without juries?

Prodigious preparations were made for the funeral. All the vehicles in town were hired, all the saloons put in mourning, all the municipal and fire-company flags hung at half-mast, and all the firemen ordered to muster in uniform and bring their machines duly draped in black. Now—let us remark in parenthesis—as all the peoples of the earth had representative adventurers in the Silverland, and as each adventurer had brought the slang of his nation or his locality with him, the combination made the slang of Nevada the richest and the most infinitely varied and copious that had ever existed anywhere in the world, perhaps, except in the mines of California in the "early days." Slang was the language of Nevada. It was hard to preach a sermon without it, and be understood. Such phrases as "You bet!" "Oh, no, I reckon not!" "No Irish need apply," and a hundred others, became so common as to fall from the lips of a speaker unconsciously—and very often when they did not touch the subject under discussion and consequently failed to mean anything.

After Buck Fanshaw's inquest, a meeting of the short-haired brotherhood was held, for nothing can be done on the Pacific coast without a public meeting and an expression of sentiment. Regretful resolutions were passed and various committees appointed; among others, a committee of one was deputed to call on the minister, a fragile, gentle, spirituel new fledgling from an Eastern theological seminary, and as yet unacquainted with the ways of the mines. The committeeman, "Scotty" Briggs, made his visit; and in after days it was worth something to hear the minister tell about it. Scotty was a stalwart rough, whose customary suit, when on weighty official business, like committee work, was a fire helmet, flaming red flannel shirt, patent leather belt with spanner and revolver attached, coat hung over arm, and pants stuffed into boot tops. He formed something of a contrast to the pale theological student. It is fair to say of Scotty, however, in passing, that he had a warm heart, and a strong love for his friends, and never entered into a quarrel when he could reasonably keep out of it. Indeed, it was commonly said that whenever one of Scotty's fights was investigated, it always turned out that it had originally been no affair of his, but that out of native goodheartedness he had dropped in of his own accord to help the man who was getting the worst of it. He and Buck Fanshaw were bosom friends, for years, and had often taken adventurous "pot-luck" together. On one occasion, they had thrown off their coats and taken the weaker side in a fight among strangers, and after gaining a hard-earned victory, turned and found that the men they were helping had deserted early, and not only that, but had stolen their coats and made off with them! But to return to Scotty's visit to the minister. He was on a sorrowful mission, now, and his face was the picture of woe. Being admitted to the presence he sat down before the clergyman, placed his fire-hat on an unfinished manuscript sermon under the minister's nose, took from it a red silk handkerchief, wiped his brow and heaved a sigh of dismal impressiveness, explanatory of his business. He choked, and even shed tears; but with an effort he mastered his voice and said in lugubrious tones:

"Are you the duck that runs the gospel-mill next door?"

"Am I the—pardon me, I believe I do not understand?"

With another sigh and a half-sob, Scotty rejoined:

"Why you see we are in a bit of trouble, and the boys thought maybe you would give us a lift, if we'd tackle you—that is, if I've got the rights of it and you are the head clerk of the doxology-works next door."

"I am the shepherd in charge of the flock whose fold is next door."

"The which?"

"The spiritual adviser of the little company of believers whose sanctuary adjoins these premises."

Scotty scratched his head, reflected a moment, and then said:

"You ruther hold over me, pard. I reckon I can't call that hand. Ante and pass the buck."

"How? I beg pardon. What did I understand you to say?"

"Well, you've ruther got the bulge on me. Or maybe we've both got the bulge, somehow. You don't smoke me and I don't smoke you. You see, one of the boys has passed in his checks and we want to give him a good send-off, and so the thing I'm on now is to roust out somebody to jerk a little chin-music for us and waltz him through handsome."

"My friend, I seem to grow more and more bewildered. Your observations are wholly incomprehensible to me. Cannot you simplify them in some way? At first I thought perhaps I understood you, but I grope now. Would it not expedite matters if you restricted yourself to categorical statements of fact unencumbered with obstructing accumulations of metaphor and allegory?"

Another pause, and more reflection. Then, said Scotty:

"I'll have to pass, I judge."

"How?"

"You've raised me out, pard."

"I still fail to catch your meaning."

"Why, that last lead of yourn is too many for me—that's the idea. I can't neither trump nor follow suit."

The clergyman sank back in his chair perplexed. Scotty leaned his head on his hand and gave himself up to thought. Presently his face came up, sorrowful but confident.

"I've got it now, so's you can savvy," he said. "What we want is a gospel-sharp. See?"

"A what?"

"Gospel-sharp. Parson."

"Oh! Why did you not say so before? I am a clergyman—a parson."

"Now you talk! You see my blind and straddle it like a man. Put it there!"—extending a brawny paw, which closed over the minister's small hand and gave it a shake indicative of fraternal sympathy and fervent gratification.

"Now we're all right, pard. Let's start fresh. Don't you mind my snuffling a little—becuz we're in a power of trouble. You see, one of the boys has gone up the flume—"

"Gone where?"

"Up the flume—throwed up the sponge, you understand."

"Thrown up the sponge?"

"Yes—kicked the bucket—"

"Ah—has departed to that mysterious country from whose bourne no traveler returns."

"Return! I reckon not. Why pard, he's *dead!*"

"Yes, I understand."

"Oh, you do? Well I thought maybe you might be getting tangled some more. Yes, you see he's dead again—"

"*Again?* Why, has he ever been dead before?"

"Dead before? No! Do you reckon a man has got as many lives as a cat? But you bet you he's awful dead now, poor old boy, and I wish I'd never seen this day. I don't want no better friend than Buck Fanshaw. I knowed him by the back; and when I know a man and like him, I freeze to him—you hear *me*. Take him all round, pard, there never was a bullier man in the mines.

No man ever knowed Buck Fanshaw to go back on a friend. But it's all up, you know, it's all up. It ain't no use. They've scooped him."

"Scooped him?"

"Yes—death has. Well, well, well, we've got to give him up. Yes indeed. It's a kind of a hard world, after all, *ain't* it? But pard, he was a rustler! You ought to seen him get started once. He was a bully boy with a glass eye! Just spit in his face and give him room according to his strength, and it was just beautiful to see him peel and go in. He was the worst son of a thief that ever drawed breath. Pard, he was *on* it! He was on it bigger than an Injun!"

"On it? On what?"

"On the shoot. On the shoulder. On the fight, you understand. *He* didn't give a continental for *any*body. *Beg* your pardon, friend, for coming so near saying a cuss-word—but you see I'm on an awful strain, in this palaver, on account of having to cramp down and draw everything so mild. But we've got to give him up. There ain't any getting around that, I don't reckon. Now if we can get you to help plant him—"

"Preach the funeral discourse? Assist at the obsequies?"

"Obs'quies is good. Yes. That's it—that's our little game. We are going to get the thing up regardless, you know. He was always nifty himself, and so you bet you his funeral ain't going to be no slouch—solid silver door-plate on his coffin, six plumes on the hearse, and a nigger on the box in a biled shirt and a plug hat—how's that for high? And we'll take care of *you,* pard. We'll fix you all right. There'll be a kerridge for you; and whatever you want, you just 'scape out and we'll 'tend to it. We've got a shebang fixed up for you to stand behind, in No. 1's house, and don't you be afraid. Just go in and toot your horn, if you don't sell a clam. Put Buck through as bully as you can, pard, for anybody that knowed him will tell you that he was one of the whitest men that was ever in the mines. You can't draw it too strong. He never could stand it to see things going wrong. He's done more to make this town quiet and peaceable than any man in it. I've seen him lick four Greasers in eleven minutes, myself. If a thing wanted regulating, *he* warn't a man to go browsing around after somebody to do it, but he would prance in and regulate it himself. He warn't a Catholic. Scasely. He was down on 'em. His word was, 'No Irish need apply!' But it didn't make no difference about that when it came down to what a man's rights was—and so, when some roughs jumped the Catholic bone-yard and started in to stake out town-lots in it he *went* for 'em! And he *cleaned* 'em, too! I was there, pard, and I seen it myself."

"That was very well indeed—at least the impulse was—whether the act was strictly defensible or not. Had deceased any religious convictions? That is to say, did he feel a dependence upon, or acknowledge allegiance to a higher power?"

More reflection.

"I reckon you've stumped me again, pard. Could you say it over once more, and say it slow?"

"Well, to simplify it somewhat, was he, or rather had he ever been connected with any organization sequestered from secular concerns and devoted to self-sacrifice in the interests of morality?"

"All down but nine—set 'em up on the other alley, pard."

"What did I understand you to say?"

"Why, you're most too many for me, you know. When you get in with your left I hunt grass every time. Every time you draw, you fill; but I don't seem to have any luck. Lets have a new deal."

"How? Begin again?"

"That's it."

"Very well. Was he a good man, and—"

"There—I see that; don't put up another chip till I look at my hand. A good man, says you? Pard, it ain't no name for it. He was the best man that ever—pard, you would have doted on that man. He could lam any galoot of his inches in America. It was him that put down the riot last election before it got a start; and everybody said he was the only man that could have done it. He waltzed in with a spanner in one hand and a trumpet in the other, and sent fourteen men home on a shutter in less than three minutes. He had that riot all broke up and prevented nice before anybody ever got a chance to strike a blow. He was always for peace, and he would *have* peace—he could not stand disturbances. Pard, he was a great loss to this town. It would please the boys if you could chip in something like that and do him justice. Here once when the Micks got to throwing stones through the Methodis' Sunday school windows, Buck Fanshaw, all of his own notion, shut up his saloon and took a couple of six-shooters and mounted guard over the Sunday school. Says he, 'No Irish need apply!' And they didn't. He was the bulliest man in the mountains, pard! He could run faster, jump higher, hit harder, and hold more tangle-foot whisky without spilling it than any man in seventeen counties. Put that in, pard—it'll please the boys more than anything you could say. And you can say, pard, that he never shook his mother."

"Never shook his mother?"

"That's it—any of the boys will tell you so."

"Well, but why *should* he shake her?"

"That's what *I* say—but some people does."

"Not people of any repute?"

"Well, some that averages pretty so-so."

"In my opinion the man that would offer personal violence to his own mother, outght to—"

"Cheese it, pard; you've banked your ball clean outside the string. What I was a drivin' at, was, that he never *throwed off* on his mother—don't you see? No indeedy. He give her a house to live in, and town lots, and plenty of money; and he looked after her and took care of her all the time; and when she was down with the small-pox I'm d—d if he didn't set up nights and nuss her himself! *Beg* your pardon for saying it, but it hopped out too quick for yours truly. You've treated me like a gentleman, pard, and I ain't the man to hurt your feelings intentional. I think you're white. I think you're a square man, pard. I like you, and I'll lick any man that don't. I'll lick him till he can't tell himself from a last year's corpse! Put it *there!*" [Another fraternal handshake—and exit.]

The obsequies were all that "the boys" could desire. Such a marvel of funeral pomp had never been seen in Virginia. The plumed hearse, the dirge-breathing brass bands, the closed marts of business, the flags drooping at half mast, the long, plodding procession of uniformed secret societies, military battalions and fire companies, draped engines, carriages of officials, and citizens in vehicles and on foot, attracted multitudes of spectators to the sidewalks, roofs and windows; and for years afterward, the degree of grandeur attained by any civic display in Virginia was determined by comparison with Buck Fanshaw's funeral.

Scotty Briggs, as a pall-bearer and a mourner, occupied a prominent place at the funeral, and when the sermon was finished and the last sentence of the prayer for the dead man's soul ascended, he responded, in a low voice, but with feeling:

"AMEN. No Irish need apply."

As the bulk of the response was without apparent relevancy, it was probably nothing more than a humble tribute to the memory of the friend that was gone; for, as Scotty had once said, it was "his word."

Scotty Briggs, in after days, achieved the distinction of becoming the only convert to religion that was ever gathered from the Virginia roughs; and it transpired that the man who had it in him to espouse the quarrel of the weak out of inborn nobility of spirit was no mean timber whereof to construct a Christian. The making him one did not warp his generosity or diminish his courage; on the contrary it gave intelligent direction to the one and a broader field to the other. If his Sunday-school class progressed faster than the other classes, was it matter for wonder? I think not. He talked to his pioneer small-fry in a language they understood! It was my large privilege, a month before he died, to hear him tell the beautiful story of Joseph and his brethren to his class "without looking at the book." I leave it to the reader to fancy what it was like, as it fell, riddled with slang, from the lips of that grave, earnest teacher, and was listened to by his little learners with a consuming interest that showed that they were as unconscious as he was that any violence was being done to the sacred proprieties!

CHAPTER XLVIII

The first twenty-six graves in the Virginia cemetery were occupied by *murdered* men. So everybody said, so everybody believed, and so they will always say and believe. The reason why there was so much slaughtering done, was, that in a new mining district the rough element predominates, and a person is not respected until he has "killed his man." That was the very expression used.

If an unknown individual arrived, they did not inquire if he was capable, honest, industrious, but—had he killed his man? If he had not, he gravitated to his natural and proper position, that of a man of small consequence; if he had, the cordiality of his reception was graduated according to the number of his dead. It was tedious work struggling up to a position of influence with bloodless hands; but when a man came with the blood of half a dozen men on his soul, his worth was recognized at once and his acquaintance sought.

In Nevada, for a time, the lawyer, the editor, the banker, the chief deperado, the chief gambler, and the saloon keeper, occupied the same level in society, and it was the highest. The cheapest and easiest way to become an influential man and be looked up to by the community at large, was to stand behind a bar, wear a cluster-diamond pin, and sell whisky. I am not sure but that the saloon-keeper held a shade higher rank than any other member of society. His opinion had weight. It was his privilege to say how the elections should go. No great movement could succeed without the countenance and direction of the saloon-keepers. It was a high favor when the chief saloon-keeper consented to serve in the legislature or the board of aldermen. Youthful ambition hardly aspired so much to the honors of the law, or the army and navy as to the dignity of proprietorship in a saloon.

To be a saloon-keeper and kill a man was to be illustrious. Hence the reader will not be surprised to learn that more than one man was killed in Nevada under hardly the pretext of provocation, so impatient was the slayer to achieve reputation and throw off the galling sense of being held in indifferent repute by his associates. I knew two youths who tried to "kill their men" for no other reason—and got killed themselves for their pains. "There goes the man that killed Bill Adams" was higher praise and a sweeter sound in the ears of this sort of people than any other speech that admiring lips could utter.

The men who murdered Virginia's original twenty-six cemetery-occupants were never punished. Why? Because Alfred the Great, when he invented trial by jury, and knew that he had admirably framed it to secure justice in his age of the world, was not aware that in the nineteenth century the condition of things would be so entirely changed that unless he rose from the grave and altered the jury plan to meet the emergency, it would prove the most ingenious and infallible agency for *defeating* justice that human wisdom could contrive. For how could he imagine that we simpletons would go on using his jury plan after circumstances had stripped it of its usefulness, any more than he could imagine that we would go on using his candle-clock after we had invented chronometers? In his day news could not travel fast, and hence he could easily find a jury of honest, intelligent men who had not heard of the case they were called to try—but in our day of telegraphs and newspapers his plan compels us to swear in juries composed of fools and rascals, because the system rigidly excludes honest men and men of brains.

I remember one of those sorrowful farces, in Virginia, which we call a jury trial. A noted desperado killed Mr. B., a good citizen, in the most wanton and cold-blooded way. Of course the papers were full of it, and all men capable of reading, read about it. And of course all men not deaf and dumb and idiotic, talked about it. A jury-list was made out, and Mr. B. L., a prominent banker and a valued citizen, was questioned precisely as he would have been questioned in any court in America:

"Have you heard of this homicide?"

"Yes."

"Have you held conversations upon the subject?"

"Yes."

"Have you formed or expressed opinions about it?"

"Yes."

"Have you read the newspaper accounts of it?"

"Yes."

"We do not want you."

A minister, intelligent, esteemed, and greatly respected; a merchant of high character and known probity; a mining superintendent of intelligence and unblemished reputation; a quartz mill owner of excellent standing, were all questioned in the same way, and all set aside. Each said the public talk and the newspaper reports had not so biased his mind but that sworn testimony would overthrow his previously formed opinions and enable him to render a verdict without prejudice and in accordance with the facts. But of course such men could not be trusted with the case. Ignoramuses alone could mete out unsullied justice.

When the peremptory challenges were all exhausted, a jury of twelve men was impaneled—a jury who swore they had neither heard, read, talked about nor expressed an opinion concerning a murder which the very cattle in the corrals, the Indians in the sage-brush and the stones in the streets were cognizant of! It was a jury composed of two desperadoes, two low beer-house politicians, three bar-keepers, two ranchmen who could not read, and three dull, stupid, human donkeys! It actually came out afterward, that one of these latter thought that incest and arson were the same thing.

The verdict rendered by this jury was, Not Guilty. What else could one expect?

The jury system puts a ban upon intelligence and honesty, and a premium upon ignorance, stupidity and perjury. It is a shame that we must continue to use a worthless system because it *was* good a thousand years ago. In this age, when a gentleman of high social standing, intelligence and probity, swears that testimony given under solemn oath will outweigh, with him, street talk and newspaper reports based upon mere hearsay, he is worth a hundred jurymen who will swear to their own ignorance and stupidity, and justice would be far safer in his hands than in theirs. Why could not the jury law be so altered as to give men of brains and honesty an *equal chance* with fools and miscreants? Is it right to show the present favoritism to one class of men and inflict a disability on another, in a land whose boast is that all its citizens are free and equal? I am a candidate for the legislature. I desire to tamper with the jury law. I wish to so alter it as to put a premium on intelligence and character, and close the jury box against idiots, blacklegs, and people who do not read newspapers. But no doubt I shall be defeated—every effort I make to save the country "misses fire."

My idea, when I began this chapter, was to say something about desperadoism in the "flush times" of Nevada. To attempt a portrayal of that era and that land, and leave out the blood and carnage, would be like portraying Mormondom and leaving out polygamy. The desperado stalked the streets with a swagger graded according to the number of his homicides, and a nod of recognition from him was sufficient to make a humble admirer happy for the rest of the day. The deference that was paid to a desperado of wide reputation, and who "kept his private graveyard," as the phrase went, was marked, and cheerfully accorded. When he moved along the sidewalk in his excessively long-tailed frock-coat, shiny stump-toed boots, and with dainty little slouch hat tipped over left eye, the small-fry roughs made room for his majesty; when he entered the restaurant, the waiters deserted bankers and merchants to overwhelm him with obsequious service; when he shouldered his way to a bar, the shouldered parties wheeled indignantly, recognized him, and —apologized. They got a look in return that froze their marrow, and by that time a curled and breast-pinned bar keeper was beaming over the counter, proud of the established acquaintanceship that permitted such a familiar form of speech as:

"How're ye, Billy, old fel? Glad to see you. What'll you take—the old thing?"

The "old thing" meant his customary drink, of course.

The best known names in the Territory of Nevada were those belonging to these long-tailed heroes of the revolver. Orators, Governors, capitalists and leaders of the legislature enjoyed a degree of fame, but it seemed local and meagre when contrasted with the fame of such men as Sam Brown, Jack Williams, Billy Mulligan, Farmer Pease, Sugarfoot Mike, Pock Marked Jake, El Dorado Johnny, Jack McNabb, Joe McGee, Jack Harris, Six-fingered Pete, etc., etc. There was a long list of them. They were brave, reckless men, and traveled with their lives in their hands. To give them their due, they did their killing principally among themselves, and seldom molested peaceable citizens, for they considered it small credit to add to their trophies so cheap a bauble as the death of a man who was "not on the shoot," as they phrased it. They killed each other on slight provocation, and hoped and expected to be killed themselves—for they held it almost shame to die otherwise than "with their boots on," as they expressed it.

I remember an instance of a desperado's contempt for such

small game as a private citizen's life. I was taking a late supper in a restaurant one night, with two reporters and a little printer named—Brown, for instance—any name will do. Presently a stranger with a long-tailed coat on came in, and not noticing Brown's hat, which was lying in a chair, sat down on it. Little Brown sprang up and became abusive in a moment. The stranger smiled, smoothed out the hat, and offered it to Brown with profuse apologies couched in caustic sarcasm, and begged Brown not to destroy him. Brown threw off his coat and challenged the man to fight—abused him, threatened him, impeached his courage, and urged and even implored him to fight; and in the meantime the smiling stranger placed himself under our protection in mock distress. But presently he assumed a serious tone, and said:

"Very well, gentlemen, if we must fight, we must, I suppose. But don't rush into danger and then say I gave you no warning. I am more than a match for all of you when I get started. I will give you proofs, and then if my friend here still insists, I will try to accommodate him."

The table we were sitting at was about five feet long, and unusually cumbersome and heavy. He asked us to put our hands on the dishes and hold them in their places a moment—one of them was a large oval dish with a portly roast on it. Then he sat down, tilted up one end of the table, set two of the legs on his knees, took the end of the table between his teeth, took his hands away, and pulled down with his teeth till the table came up to a level position, dishes and all! He said he could lift a keg of nails with his teeth. He picked up a common glass tumbler and bit a semi-circle out of it. Then he opened his bosom and showed us a net-work of knife and bullet scars; showed us more on his arms and face, and said he believed he had bullets enough in his body to make a pig of lead. He was armed to the teeth. He closed with the remark that he was Mr.—— of Cariboo—a celebrated name whereat we shook in our shoes. I would publish the name, but for the suspicion that he might come and carve me. He finally inquired if Brown still thirsted for blood. Brown turned the thing over in his mind a moment, and then—asked him to supper.

With the permission of the reader, I will group together, in the next chapter, some samples of life in our small mountain village in the old days of desperadoism. I was there at the time. The reader will observe peculiarities in our *official* society; and he will observe also, an instance of how, in new countries, murders breed murders.

CHAPTER XLIX

An extract or two from the newspapers of the day will furnish a photograph that can need no embellishment:

FATAL SHOOTING AFFRAY.—An affray occurred, last evening, in a billiard saloon on C street, between *Deputy Marshal Jack Williams* and Wm. Brown, which resulted in the immediate death of the latter. There had been some difficulty between the parties for several months.

An inquest was immediately held, and the following testimony adduced:

Officer GEO. BIRDSALL, sworn, says:—I was told Wm. Brown was drunk and was looking for Jack Williams; so soon as I heard that I started for the parties to prevent a collision; went into the billiard saloon; saw Billy Brown running around, saying if anybody had anything against him to show cause; he was talking in a boisterous manner, and officer Perry took him to the other end of the room to talk to him; Brown came back to me; remarked to me that he thought he was as good as anybody, and knew how to take care of himself; he passed by me and went to the bar; don't know whether he drank or not; Williams was at the end of the billiard-table, next to the stairway; Brown, after going to the bar, came back and said he was as good as any man in the world; he had then walked out to the end of the first billiard-table from the bar; I moved closer to them, supposing there would be a fight; as Brown drew his pistol I caught hold of it; he had fired one shot at Williams; don't know the effect of it; caught hold of him with one hand, and took hold of the pistol and turned it up; think he fired once after I caught hold of the pistol; I wrenched the pistol from him; walked to the end of the billiard-table and told a party that I had Brown's pistol, and to stop shooting; I think four shots were fired in all; after walking out, Mr. Foster remarked that Brown was shot dead.

Oh, there was no excitement about it—he merely "remarked" the small circumstance!

Four months later the following item appeared in the same paper (the *Enterprise*). In this item the name of one of the city officers above referred to *(Deputy Marshal Jack Williams)* occurs again:

ROBBERY AND DESPERATE AFFRAY.—On Tuesday night, a German named Charles Hurtzal, engineer in a mill at Silver City, came to this place, and visited the hurdy-gurdy house on B street. The music, dancing and Teutonic maidens awakened memories of Faderland until our German friend was carried away with rapture. He evidently had money, and was spending it freely. Late in the evening Jack Williams and Andy Blessington invited him down stairs to take a cup of coffee. Williams proposed a game of cards and went up stairs to procure a deck, but not finding any returned. On the stairway he met the German, and drawing his pistol knocked him down and rifled his pockets of some seventy dollars. Hurtzal dared give no alarm, as he was told, with a pistol at this head, if he made any noise or exposed them, they would blow his brains out. So effectually was he frightened that he made no complaint, until his friends forced him. Yesterday a warrant was issued, but the culprits had disappeared.

This efficient city officer, Jack Williams, had the common reputation of being a burglar, a highwayman and a desperado. It was said that he had several times drawn his revolver and levied money contributions on citizens at dead of night in the public streets of Virginia.

Five months after the above item appeared, Williams was assassinated while sitting at a card table one night; a gun was thrust through the crack of the door and Williams dropped from his chair riddled with balls. It was said, at the time, that Williams had been for some time aware that a party of his own sort (desperadoes) had sworn away his life; and it was generally believed among the people that Williams's friends and enemies would make the assassination memorable—and useful, too—by a wholesale destruction of each other.*

It did not so happen, but still, times were not dull during the next twenty-four hours, for within that time a woman was killed by a pistol shot, a man was brained with a slung shot, and a man named Reeder was also disposed of permanently. Some matters in the *Enterprise* account of the killing of Reeder are worth noting—especially the accommodating complaisance of a Virginia justice of the peace. The italics in the following narrative are mine:

MORE CUTTING AND SHOOTING.—The devil seems to have again broken loose in our town. Pistols and guns explode and knives gleam in our streets as in early times. When there has been a long season of

*However, one prophecy was verified, at any rate. It was asserted by the desperadoes that one of their brethren (Joe McGee, *a special policeman*) was known to be the conspirator chosen by lot to assassinate Williams; and they also asserted that doom had been pronounced against McGee, and that he would be assassinated in exactly the same manner that had been adopted for the destruction of Williams—a prophecy which came true a year later. After twelve months of distress (for McGee saw a fancied assassin in every man that approached him), he made the last of many efforts to get out of the country unwatched. He went to Carson and sat down in a saloon to wait for the stage—it would leave at four in the morning. But as the night waned and the crowd thinned, he grew uneasy, and told the bar-keeper that assassins were on his track. The bar-keeper told him to stay in the middle of the room, then, and not go near the door, or the window by the stove. But a fatal fascination seduced him to the neighborhood of the stove every now and then, and repeatedly the bar-keeper brought him back to the middle of the room and warned him to remain there. But he could not. At three in the morning he again returned to the stove and sat down by a stranger. Before the bar-keeper could get to him with another warning whisper, some one outside fired through the window and riddled McGee's breast with slugs, killing him almost instantly. By the same discharge the stranger at McGee's side also received attentions which proved fatal in the course of two or three days.

quiet, people are slow to wet their hands in blood; but once blood is spilled, cutting and shooting come easy. Night before last Jack Williams was assassinated, and yesterday forenoon we had more bloody work, growing out of the killing of Williams, and on the same street in which he met his death. It appears that Tom Reeder, a friend of Williams, and George Gumbert were talking, at the meat market of the latter, about the killing of Williams the previous night, when Reeder said it was a most cowardly act to shoot a man in such a way, giving him "no show." Gumbert said that Williams had "as good a show as he gave Billy Brown," meaning the man killed by Williams last March. Reeder said it was a d—d lie, that Williams had no show at all. At this, Gumbert drew a knife and stabbed Reeder, cutting him in two places in the back. One stroke of the knife cut into the sleeve of Reeder's coat and passed downward in a slanting direction through his clothing, and entered his body at the small of the back; another blow struck more squarely, and made a much more dangerous wound. Gumbert gave himself up to the officers of justice, and was shortly after discharged by Justice Atwill, *on his own recognizance,* to appear for trial at six o'clock in the evening. In the meantime Reeder had been taken into the office of Dr. Owens, where his wounds were properly dressed. *One of his wounds was considered quite dangerous, and it was thought by many that it would prove fatal. But being considerably under the influence of liquor, Reeder did not feel his wounds as he otherwise would, and he got up and went into the street.* He went to the meat market and renewed his quarrel with Gumbert, threatening his life. Friends tried to interfere to put a stop to the quarrel and get the parties away from each other. In the Fashion Saloon Reeder made threats against the life of Gumbert, saying he would kill him, and it is said that *he requested the officers not to arrest Gumbert, as he intended to kill him.* After these threats Gumbert went off and procured a double-barreled shot gun, loaded with buck-shot or revolver balls, and went after Reeder. Two or three persons were assisting him along the street, trying to get him home, and had him just in front of the store of Klopstock & Harris, when Gumbert came across toward him from the opposite side of the street with his gun. He came up within about ten or fifteen feet of Reeder, and called out to those with him to "look out! get out of the way!" and they had only time to heed the warning, when he fired. Reeder was at the time attempting to screen himself behind a large cask, which stood against the awning post of Klopstock & Harris's store, but some of the balls took effect in the lower part of his breast, and he reeled around forward and fell in front of the cask. Gumbert then raised his gun and fired the second barrel, which missed Reeder and entered the ground. At the time that this occurred, there were a great many persons on the street in the vicinity, and a number of them called out to Gumbert, when they saw him raise his gun, to "hold on," and "don't shoot!" The cutting took place about ten o'clock and the shooting about twelve. After the shooting the street was instantly crowded with the inhabitants of that part of the town, some appearing much excited and laughing—declaring that it looked like the "good old times of '60." Marshal Perry and officer Birdsall were near when the shooting occurred, and Gumbert was immediately arrested and his gun taken from him, when he was marched off to jail. Many persons who were attracted to the spot where this bloody work had just taken place, looked bewildered and seemed to be asking themselves what was to happen next, appearing in doubt as to whether the killing mania had reached its climax, or whether we were to turn in and have a grand killing spell, shooting whoever might have given us offence. It was whispered around that it was not all over yet—five or six more were to be killed before night. Reeder was taken to the Virginia City Hotel, and doctors called in to examine his wounds. They found that two or three balls had entered his right side; one of them appeared to have passed through the substance of the lungs, while another passed into the liver. Two balls were also found to have struck one of his legs. As some of the balls struck the cask, the wounds in Reeder's leg were probably from these, glancing downwards, though they might have been caused by the second shot fired. After being shot, Reeder said when he got on his feet—smiling as he spoke—"It will take better shooting than that to kill me." The doctors consider it almost impossible for him to recover, but as he has an excellent constitution he may survive, notwithstanding the number and dangerous character of the wounds he has received. The town appears to be perfectly quiet at present, as though the late stormy times had cleared our moral atmosphere; but who can tell in what quarter clouds are lowering or plots ripening?

Reeder—or at least what was left of him—survived his wounds two days! Nothing was ever done with Gumbert.

Trial by jury is the palladium of our liberties. I do not know what a palladium is, having never seen a palladium, but it is a good thing no doubt at any rate. Not less than a hundred men have been murdered in Nevada—perhaps I would be within bounds if I said three hundred—and as far as I can learn, only two persons have suffered the death penalty there. However, four or five who had no money and no political influence have been punished by imprisonment—one languished in prison as much as eight months, I think. However, I do not desire to be extravagant—it may have been less.

CHAPTER L

These murder and jury statistics remind me of a certain very extraordinary trial and execution of twenty years ago; it is a scrap of history familiar to all old Californians, and worthy to be known by other peoples of the earth that love simple, straightforward justice unencumbered with nonsense. I would apologize for this digression but for the fact that the information I am about to offer is apology enough in itself. And since I digress constantly anyhow, perhaps it is as well to eschew apologies altogether and thus prevent their growing irksome.

Capt. Ned Blakely—that name will answer as well as any other fictitious one (for he was still with the living at last accounts, and may not desire to be famous)—sailed ships out of the harbor of San Francisco for many years. He was a stalwart, warm-hearted, eagle-eyed veteran, who had been a sailor nearly fifty years—a sailor from early boyhood. He was a rough, honest creature, full of pluck, and just as full of hard-headed simplicity, too. He hated trifling conventionalities—"business" was the word, with him. He had all a sailor's vindictiveness against the quips and quirks of the law, and steadfastly believed that the first and last aim and object of the law and lawyers was to defeat justice.

He sailed for the Chincha Islands in command of a guano ship. He had a fine crew, but his negro mate was his pet—on him he had for years lavished his admiration and esteem. It was Capt. Ned's first voyage to the Chinchas, but his fame had gone before him—the fame of being a man who would fight at the dropping of a handkerchief, when imposed upon, and would stand no nonsense. It was a fame well earned. Arrived in the islands, he found that the staple of conversation was the exploits of one Bill Noakes, a bully, the mate of a trading ship. This man had created a small reign of terror there. At nine o'clock at night, Capt. Ned, all alone, was pacing his deck in the starlight. A form ascended the side, and approached him. Capt. Ned said:

"Who goes there?"

"I'm Bill Noakes, the best man in the islands."

"What do you want aboard this ship?"

"I've heard of Capt. Ned Blakely, and one of us is a better man that 'tother—I'll know which, before I go ashore."

"You've come to the right shop—I'm your man. I'll learn you to come aboard this ship without an *in*vite."

He seized Noakes, backed him against the mainmast, pounded his face to a pulp, and then threw him overboard.

Noakes was not convinced. He returned the next night, got the pulp renewed, and went overboard head first, as before. He was satisfied.

A week after this, while Noakes was carousing with a sailor crowd on shore, at noonday, Capt. Ned's colored mate came along, and Noakes tried to pick a quarrel with him. The negro evaded the trap, and tried to get away. Noakes followed him up; the negro began to run; Noakes fired on him with a revolver and killed him. Half a dozen sea-captains witnessed the whole affair.

Noakes retreated to the small after-cabin of his ship, with two other bullies, and gave out that death would be the portion of any man that intruded there. There was no attempt made to follow the villains; there was no disposition to do it, and indeed very little thought of such an enterprise. There were no courts and no officers; there was no government; the islands belonged to Peru, and Peru was far away; she had no official representative on the ground; and neither had any other nation.

However, Capt. Ned was not perplexing his head about such things. They concerned him not. He was boiling with rage and furious for justice. At nine o'clock at night he loaded a double-barreled gun with slugs, fished out a pair of handcuffs, got a ship's lantern, summoned his quartermaster, and went ashore. He said:

"Do you see that ship there at the dock?"

"Ay-ay, sir."

"It's the Venus."

"Ay-ay, sir."

"You—you know *me.*"

"Ay-ay, sir."

"Very well, then. Take the lantern. Carry it just under your chin. I'll walk behind you and rest this gun-barrel on your shoulder, p'inting forward—so. Keep your lantern well up, so's I can see things ahead of you good. I'm going to march in on Noakes—and take him—and jug the other chaps. If you flinch—well, you know *me.*"

"Ay-ay, sir."

In this order they filed aboard softly, arrived at Noakes's den, the quartermaster pushed the door open, and the lantern revealed the three desperadoes sitting on the floor. Capt. Ned said:

"I'm Ned Blakely. I've got you under fire. Don't you move without orders—any of you. You two kneel down in the corner; faces to the wall—now. Bill Noakes, ptu these handcuffs on; now come up close. Quartermaster, fasten 'em. All right. Don't stir, sir. Quartermaster, put the key in the outside of the door. Now, men, I'm going to lock you two in; and if you try to burst through this door—well, you've heard of *me.* Bill Noakes, fall in ahead, and march. All set. Quartermaster, lock the door."

Noakes spent the night on board Blakely's ship, a prisoner under strict guard. Early in the morning Capt. Ned called in all the sea-captains in the harbor and invited them, with nautical ceremony, to be present on board his ship at nine o'clock to witness the hanging of Noakes at the yard-arm!

"What! The man has not been tried."

"Of course he hasn't. But didn't he kill the nigger?"

"Certainly he did; but you are not thinking of hanging him without a trial?"

"Trial! What do I want to try him for, if he killed the nigger?"

"Oh, Capt. Ned, this will *never* do. Think how it will sound."

"Sound be hanged! *Didn't he kill the nigger]"*

"Certainly, certainly, Capt. Ned,—nobody denies that,—but—"

"Then I'm going to *hang* him, that's all. Everybody I've talked to talks just the same way you do. Everybody says he killed the nigger, everybody knows he killed the nigger, and yet every lubber of you wants him *tried* for it. I don't understand such bloody foolishness as that. *Tried!* Mind you, I don't object to trying him, if it's got to be done to give satisfaction; and I'll be there, and chip in and help, too; but put it off till afternoon—put it off till afternoon, for I'll have my hands middling full till after the burying—"

"Why, what do you mean? Are you going to hang him *any how*—and try him afterward?"

"Didn't I *say* I was going to hang him? I never saw such people as you. What's the difference? You ask a favor, and then you ain't satisfied when you get it. Before or after's all one—*you* know how the trial will go. He killed the nigger. Say—I must be going. If your mate would like to come to the hanging, fetch him along. I like him."

There was a stir in the camp. The captains came in a body and pleaded with Capt. Ned not to do this rash thing. They promised that they would create a court composed of captains of the best character; they would empanel a jury; they would conduct everything in a way becoming the serious nature of the business in hand, and give the case an impartial hearing and the accused a fair trial. And they said it would be murder, and punishable by the American courts if he persisted and hung the accused on his ship. They pleaded hard. Capt. Ned said:

"Gentlemen, I'm not stubborn and I'm not unreasonable. I'm always willing to do just as near right as I can. How long will it take?"

"Probably only a little while."

"And can I take him up the shore and hang him as soon as you are done?"

"If he is proven guilty he shall be hanged without unnecessary delay."

"*If* he's proven guilty. Great Neptune, *ain't* he guilty? This beats my time. Why you all *know* he's guilty."

But at last they satisfied him that they were projecting nothing underhanded. Then he said:

"Well, all right. You go on and try him and I'll go down and overhaul his conscience and prepare him to go—like enough he needs it, and I don't want to send him off without a show for hereafter."

This was another obstacle. They finally convinced him that it was necessary to have the accused in court. Then they said they would send a guard to bring him.

"No, sir, I prefer to fetch him myself—he don't get out of *my* hands. Besides, I've got to go to the ship to get a rope, anyway."

The court assembled with due ceremony, empaneled a jury, and presently Capt. Ned entered, leading the prisoner with one hand and carrying a Bible and a rope in the other. He seated himself by the side of his captive and told the court to "up anchor and make sail." Then he turned a searching eye on the jury, and detected Noakes's friends, the two bullies. He strode over and said to them confidentially:

"You're here to interfere, you see. Now you vote right, do you hear?—or else there'll be a double-barreled inquest here when this trial's off, and your remainders will go home in a couple of baskets."

The caution was not without fruit. The jury was a unit—the verdict, "Guilty."

Capt. Ned sprung to his feet and said:

"Come along—you're my meat *now,* my lad, anyway. Gentlemen you've done yourselves proud. I invite you all to come and see that I do it all straight. Follow me to the canyon, a mile above here."

The court informed him that a sheriff had been appointed to do the hanging, and—

Capt. Ned's patience was at an end. His wrath was boundless. The subject of a sheriff was judiciously dropped.

When the crowd arrived at the canyon, Capt. Ned climbed a tree and arranged the halter, then came down and noosed his man. He opened his Bible, and laid aside his hat. Selecting a chapter at random, he read it through, in a deep bass voice and with sincere solemnity. Then he said:

"Lad, you are about to go aloft and give an account of yourself; and the lighter a man's manifest is, as far as sin's concerned, the better for him. Make a clean breast, man, and carry a log with you that'll bear inspection. You killed the nigger?"

No reply. A long pause.

The captain read another chapter, pausing, from time to time, to impress the effect. Then he talked an earnest, persuasive sermon to him, and ended by repeating the question:

"Did you kill the nigger?"

No reply—other than a malignant scowl. The captain now read the first and second chapters of Genesis, with deep feeling— paused a moment, closed the book reverently, and said with a perceptible savor of satisfaction:

"There. Four chapters. There's few that would have took the pains with you that I have."

Then he swung up the condemned, and made the rope fast; stood by and timed him half an hour with his watch, and then delivered the body to the court. A little after, as he stood contemplating the motionless figure, a doubt came into his face; evidently he felt a twinge of conscience—a misgiving—and he said with a sigh:

"Well, p'raps I ought to burnt him, maybe. But I was trying to do for the best."

When the history of this affair reached California (it was in the "early days") it made a deal of talk, but did not diminish the captain's popularity in any degree. It increased it, indeed. California had a population then that "inflicted" justice after a fashion that was simplicity and primitiveness itself, and could therefore admire appreciatively when the same fashion was followed elsewhere.

CHAPTER LI

Vice flourished luxuriantly during the hey-day of our "flush times." The saloons were overburdened with custom; so were the police courts, the gambling dens, the brothels and the jails—unfailing signs of high prosperity in a mining region—in any region for that matter. Is it not so? A crowded police court docket is the surest of all signs that trade is brisk and money plenty. Still, there is one other sign; it comes last, but when it does come it establishes beyond cavil that the "flush times" are at the flood. This is the birth of the "literary" paper. The *Weekly Occidental,* "devoted to literature," made its appearance in Virginia. All the literary people were engaged to write for it. Mr. F. was to edit it. He was a felicitous skirmisher with a pen, and a man who could say happy things in a crisp, neat way. Once, while editor of the *Union,* he had disposed of a labored, incoherent, two-column attack made upon him by a cotemporary, with a single line, which, at first glance, seemed to contain a solemn and tremendous compliment—viz.: "THE LOGIC OF OUR

ADVERSARY RESEMBLES THE PEACE OF GOD,"—and left it to the reader's memory and after-thought to invest the remark with another and "more different" meaning by supplying for himself and at his own leisure the rest of the Scripture—"*in that it passeth understanding.*" He once said of a little, half-starved, wayside community that had no subsistence except what they could get by preying upon chance passengers who stopped over with them a day when traveling by the overland stage, that in their Church service they had altered the Lord's Prayer to read: "Give us this day our daily stranger!"

We expected great things of the *Occidental.* Of course it could not get along without an original novel, and so we made arrangements to hurl into the work the full strength of the company. Mrs. F. was an able romancist of the ineffable school—I know no other name to apply to a school whose heroes are all dainty and all perfect. She wrote the opening chapter, and introduced a lovely blonde simpleton who talked nothing but pearls and poetry and who was virtuous to the verge of eccentricity. She also introduced a young French Duke of aggravated refinement, in love with the blonde. Mr. F. followed next week, with a brilliant lawyer who set about getting the Duke's estates into trouble, and a sparkling young lady of high society who fell to fascinating the Duke and impairing the appetite of the blonde. Mr. D., a dark and bloody editor of one of the dailies, followed Mr. F., the third week, introducing a mysterious Roscicrucian who transmuted metals, held consultations with the devil in a cave at dead of night, and cast the horoscope of the several heroes and heroines in such a way as to provide plenty of trouble for their future careers and breed a solemn and awful public interest in the novel. He also introduced a cloaked and masked melodramatic miscreant, put him on a salary and set him on the midnight tract of the Duke with a poisoned dagger. He also created an Irish coachman with a rich brogue and placed him in the service of the society-young-lady with an ulterior mission to carry billet-doux to the Duke.

About this time there arrived in Virginia a dissolute stranger with a literary turn of mind—rather seedy he was, but very quiet and unassuming; almost diffident, indeed. He was so gentle, and his manners were so pleasing and kindly, whether he was sober or intoxicated, that he made friends of all who came in contact with him. He applied for literary work, offered conclusive evidence that he wielded an easy and practiced pen, and so Mr. F. engaged him at once to help write the novel. His chapter was to follow Mr. D.'s, and mine was to come next. Now what does this fellow do but go off and get drunk and then proceed to his quarters and set to work with his imagination in a state of chaos, and that chaos in a condition of extravagant activity. The result may be guessed. He scanned the chapters of his predecessors, found plenty of heroes and heroines already created, and was satisfied with them; he decided to introduce no more; with all the confidence that whisky inspires and all the easy complacency it gives to its servant, he then launched himself lovingly into his work: he married the coachman to the society-young-lady for the sake of the scandal; married the Duke to the blonde's step-mother, for the sake of the sensation; stopped the desperado's salary; created a misunderstanding between the devil and the Roscicrucian; threw the Duke's property into the wicked lawyer's hands; made the lawyer's upbraiding conscience drive him to drink, thence to *delirium tremens,* thence to suicide; broke the coachman's neck; let his widow succumb to contumely, neglect, poverty and consumption; caused the blonde to drown herself, leaving her clothes on the bank with the customary note pinned to them forgiving the Duke and hoping he would be happy; revealed to the Duke, by means of the usual strawberry mark on left arm, that he had married his own long-lost mother and destroyed his long-lost sister; instituted the proper and necessary suicide of the Duke and the Duchess in order to compass poetical justice; opened the earth and let the Roscicrucian through, accompanied with the accustomed smoke and thunder and smell of brimstone, and finished with the promise that in the next chapter, after holding a general inquest, he would take up the surviving character of the novel and tell what became of the devil!

It read with singular smoothness, and with a "dead" earnestness that was funny enough to suffocate a body. But there was war when it came in. The other novelists were furious. The mild stranger, not yet more than half sober, stood there, under a scathing fire of vituperation, meek and bewildered, looking from one to another of his assailants, and wondering what he could have done to invoke such a storm. When a lull came at last, he said his say gently and appealingly—said he did not rightly remember what he had written, but was sure he had tried to do the best he could, and knew his object had been to make the novel not only pleasant and plausible but instructive and—

The bombardment began again. The novelists assailed his ill-chosen adjectives and demolished them with a storm of denunciation and ridicule. And so the siege went on. Every time the stranger tried to appease the enemy he only made matters worse. Finally he offered to rewrite the chapter. This arrested hostilities. The indignation gradually quieted down, peace reigned again and the sufferer retired in safety and got him to his own citadel.

But on the way thither the evil angel tempted him and he got drunk again. And again his imagination went mad. He led the heroes and heroines a wilder dance than ever; and yet all through it ran that same convincing air of honesty and earnestness that had marked his first work. He got the characters into the most extraordinary situations, put them through the most surprising performances, and made them talk the strangest talk! But the chapter cannot be described. It was symmetrically crazy; it was artistically absurd; and it had explanatory footnotes that were fully as curious as the text. I remember one of the "situations," and will offer it as an example of the whole. He altered the character of the brilliant lawyer, and made him a great-hearted, splendid fellow; gave him fame and riches, and set his age at thirty-three years. Then he made the blonde discover, through the help of the Roscicrucian and the melodramatic miscreant, that while the Duke loved her money ardently and wanted it, he secretly felt a sort of leaning toward the society-young-lady. Stung to the quick, she tore her affections from him and bestowed them with tenfold power upon the lawyer, who responded with consuming zeal. But the parents would none of it. What they wanted in the family was a Duke; and a Duke they were determined to have; though they confessed that next to the Duke the lawyer had their preference. Necessarily the blonde now went into a decline. The parents were alarmed. They pleaded with her to marry the Duke, but she steadfastly refused, and pined on. Then they laid a plan. They told her to wait a year and a day, and if at the end of that time she still felt that she could not marry the Duke, she might marry the lawyer with their full consent. The result was as they had foreseen: gladness came again, and the flush of returning health. Then the parents took the next step in their scheme. They had the family physician recommend a long sea voyage and much land travel for the thorough restoration of the blonde's strength; and they invited the Duke to be of the party. They judged that the Duke's constant presence and the lawyer's protracted absence would do the rest—for they did not invite the lawyer.

So they set sail in a steamer for America—and the third day out, when their sea-sickness called truce and permitted them to take their first meal at the public table, behold there sat the lawyer! The Duke and party made the best of an awkward situation; the voyage progressed, and the vessel neared America. But, by and by, two hundred miles off New Bedford, the ship took fire; she burned to the water's edge; of all her crew and passengers, only thirty were saved. They floated about the sea half an afternoon and all night long. Among them were our friends. The lawyer, by superhuman exertions, had saved the blonde and her parents, swimming back and forth two hundred yards and bringing one each time—(the girl first). The Duke had saved himself. In the morning two whale ships arrived on the scene and sent their boats. The weather was stormy and the embarkation was attended with much confusion and excitement. The lawyer did his duty like a man; helped his exhausted and insensible blonde, her parents and some others into a boat (the Duke helped himself in); then a child fell overboard at the other end of the raft and the lawyer rushed thither and helped half a dozen people fish it out, under the stimulus of its mother's screams. Then he ran back—a few seconds too late—the blonde's boat was under way. So he had to take the other boat, and go to the other ship. The storm increased and drove the vessels out of sight of each other—drove them whither it would. When it calmed, at the end of three days, the blonde's ship was seven hundred miles north of Boston and the other about seven hundred south of that port. The blonde's captain was bound on a whaling cruise in the North Atlantic and could not go back such a distance or make a port without orders; such being nautical law. The lawyer's captain was to cruise in the North Pacific, and *he* could not go back or make a port without orders. All the lawyer's money and baggage were in the blonde's boat and went to the blonde's ship—so his captain made him work his passage as a common sailor. When both ships had been cruising nearly a year, the one was off the coast of Greenland and the other in Behring's Strait. The blonde had long ago been well-nigh persuaded that her lawyer had been washed overboard and lost just before the whale ships reached the raft, and now, under the pleadings of her parents and the Duke she was at last beginning to nerve herself for the doom of the covenant, and prepare for the hated marriage. But she would not yield a day before the date set. The weeks dragged on, the time narrowed, orders were given to deck the ship for the wedding—a wedding at sea among icebergs and walruses. Five days more and all would be over. So the blonde reflected, with a sigh and a tear. Oh where was her true love—and why, why did he not come and save her? At that moment he was lifting his harpoon to strike a whale in Behring's Strait, five thousand miles away, by the way of the Arctic Ocean, or twenty thousand by the way of the Horn—that was the reason. He struck, but not with perfect aim—his foot slipped and he fell in the whale's mouth and went down his throat. He was insensible five days. Then he came to himself and heard voices; daylight was streaming through a hole cut in the whale's roof. He climbed out and astonished the sailors who were hoisting blubber up a ship's side. He recognized the vessel, flew aboard, surprised the wedding party at the altar and exclaimed:

"Stop the proceedings—I'm here! Come to my arms, my own!"

There were foot-notes to this extravagant piece of literature wherein the author endeavored to show that the whole thing was within the possibilities; he said he got the incident of the whale traveling from Behring's Strait to the coast of Greenland, five thousand miles in five days, through the Arctic Ocean, from Charles Reade's "Love Me Little Love Me Long," and considered that that established the fact that the thing could be done; and he instanced Jonah's adventure as proof that a man could live in a whale's belly, and added that if a preacher could stand it three days a lawyer could surely stand it five!

There was a fiercer storm than ever in the editorial sanctum now, and the stranger was peremptorily discharged, and his manuscript flung at his head. But he had already delayed things so much that there was not time for some one else to rewrite the chapter, and so the paper came out without any novel in it. It was but a feeble, struggling, stupid journal, and the absence of the novel probably shook public confidence; at any rate, before the first side of the next issue went to press, the *Weekly Occidental* died as peacefully as an infant.

An effort was made to resurrect it, with the proposed advantage of a telling new title, and Mr. F. said that *The Phenix* would be just the name for it, because it would give the idea of a resurrection from its dead ashes in a new and undreamed of condition of splendor; but some low-priced smarty on one of the dailies suggested that we call it the *Lazarus;* and inasmuch as the people were not profound in Scriptural matters but thought the resurrected Lazarus and the dilapidated mendicant that begged in the rich man's geteway were one and the same person, the name became the laughing stock of the town, and killed the paper for good and all.

I was sorry enough, for I was very proud of being connected with a literary paper—prouder than I have ever been of anything since, perhaps. I had written some rhymes for it—poetry I considered it—and it was a great grief to me that the production was on the "first side" of the issue that was not completed, and hence did not see the light. But time brings its revenges—I can put it in here; it will answer in place of a tear dropped to the memory of the lost *Occidental.* The idea (not the chief idea, but the vehicle that bears it) was probably suggested by the old song called "The Raging Canal," but I cannot remember now. I do remember, though, that at that time I thought my doggerel was one of the ablest poems of the age:

THE AGED PILOT MAN

On the Erie Canal, it was,
  All on a summer's day,
I sailed forth with my parents
  Far away to Albany.

From out the clouds at noon that day
  There came a dreadful storm,
That piled the billows high about,
  And filled us with alarm.

A man came rushing from a house,
  Saying, "Snub up * your boat I pray,
Snub up your boat, snub up, alas,
  Snub up while yet you may."

Our captain cast one glance astern,
  Then forward glanced he,
And said, "My wife and little ones
  I never more shall see."

Said Dollinger the pilot man,
  In noble words, but few,—
"Fear not, but lean on Dollinger,
  And he will fetch you through."

The boat drove on, the frightened mules
  Tore through the rain and wind,
And bravely still, in danger's post,
  The whip-boy strode behind.

"Come 'board, come 'board," the captain cried,
  "Nor tempt so wild a storm;"
But still the raging mules advanced,
  And still the boy strode on.

Then said the captain to us all,
  "Alas tis plain to me,
The greater danger is not there,
  But here upon the sea.

* The customary canal technicality for "tie up."

So let us strive, while life remains,
  To save all souls on board,
And then if die at last we must,
  Let . . . . I *cannot* speak the word!

Said Dollinger the pilot man,
  Tow'ring above the crew,
"Fear not, but trust in Dollinger,
  And he will fetch you through."

"Low bridge! low bridge!" all heads went down,
  The laboring bark sped on;
A mill we passed, we passed a church,
  Hamlets, and fields of corn;
And all the world came out to see,
  And chased along the shore

Crying, "Alas, alas, the sheeted rain,
  The wind, the tempest's roar!
Alas, the gallant ship and crew,
  Can *nothing* help them more?"

And from our deck sad eyes looked out
  Across the stormy scene:
The tossing wake of billows aft,
  The bending forests green,

The chickens sheltered under carts
  In lee of barn the cows,
The skurrying swine with straw in mouth,
  The wild spray from our bows!

    "She balances!
    She wavers!
Now let her go about!
  If she misses stays and broaches to,
We're all"—[then with a shout,]
    "Huray! huray!
    Avast! belay!
    Take in more sail!
    Lord, what a gale!
Ho, boy, haul taut on the hind mule's tail!"

"Ho! lighten ship! ho! man the pump!
  Ho, hostler, heave the lead!
"A quarter-three!—'tis shoaling fast!
  Three feet large!—t-h-r-e-e feet!—
Three feet scant!" I cried in fright
  "Oh, is there *no* retreat?"

Said Dollinger, the pilot man,
   As on the vessel flew,
"Fear not, but trust in Dollinger,
   And he will fetch you through."

A panic struck the bravest hearts,
   The boldest cheek turned pale;
For plain to all, this shoaling said
A leak had burst the ditch's bed!
And, straight as bolt from crossbow sped,
Our ship swept on, with shoaling lead,
   Before the fearful gale!

"Sever the tow-line! Cripple the mules!"
   Too late! . . . . . There comes a shock!
* * * * * * * *
Another length, and the fated craft
   Would have swum in the saving lock!

Then gathered together the shipwrecked crew
   And took one last embrace,
While sorrowful tears from despairing eyes
   Ran down each hopeless face;
And some did think of their little ones
   Whom they never more might see,
And others of waiting wives at home,
   And mothers that grieved would be.

But all the children of misery there
   On that poor sinking frame,
But one spake words of hope and faith,
   And I worshipped as they came:
Said Dollinger the pilot man,—
   (O brave heart, strong and true!)—
"Fear not, but trust in Dollinger,
   For he will fetch you through."

Lo! scarce the words have passed his lips
   The dauntless prophet say'th,
When every soul about him seeth
   A wonder crown his faith!

And count ye all, both great and small,
   As numbered with the dead!
For mariner for forty year,
   On Erie, boy and man,
I never yet saw such a storm,
   Or one't with it began!"

So overboard a keg of nails
  And anvils three we threw,
Likewise four bales of gunny-sacks,
  Two hundred pounds of glue,
Two sacks of corn, four ditto wheat,
  A box of books, a cow,
A violin, Lord Byron's works,
  A rip-saw and a sow.

A curve! a curve! the dangers grow!
  "Labbord!—stabbord!—s-t-e-a-d-y!— so!—
Hard-a-port, Dol!—hellum-a-lee!
  Haw the head mule!—the aft one gee!
Luff!—bring her to the wind!"

For straight a farmer brought a plank,—
  (Mysteriously inspired)—
And laying it unto the ship,
  In silent awe retired.

Then every sufferer stood amazed
  That pilot man before;
A moment stood. The wondering turned,
  And speechless walked ashore.

CHAPTER LII

Since I desire, in this chapter, to say an instructive word or two about the silver mines, the reader may take this fair warning and skip, if he chooses. The year 1863 was perhaps the very top blossom and culmination of the "flush times." Virginia swarmed with men and vehicles to that degree that the place looked like a very hive—that is when one's vision could pierce through the thick fog of alkali dust that was generally blowing in summer. I will say, concerning this dust, that if you drove ten miles through it, you and your horses would be coated with it a sixteenth of an inch thick and present an outside appearance that was a uniform pale yellow color, and your buggy would have three inches of dust in it, thrown there by the wheels. The delicate scales used by the assayers were inclosed in glass cases intended to be air-tight, and yet some of this dust was so impalpable and so invisibly fine that it would get in, somehow, and impair the accuracy of those scales.

Speculation ran riot, and yet there was a world of substantial business going on, too. All freights were brought over the mountains from California (150 miles) by pack-train partly, and partly in huge wagons drawn by such long mule teams that each team amounted to a procession, and it did seem, sometimes, that the grand combined procession of animals stretched unbroken from Virginia to California. Its long route was traceable clear across the deserts of the Territory by the writhing serpent of dust it lifted up. By these wagons, freights over that hundred and fifty miles were $200 a ton for small lots (same price for all express matter brought by stage), and $100 a ton for full loads. One Virginia firm received one hundred tons of freight a month, and paid $10,000 a month freightage. In the winter the freights were much higher. All the bullion was shipped in bars by stage to San Francisco (a bar was usually about twice the size of a pig of lead and contained from $1,500 to $3,000 according to the amount of gold mixed with the silver), and the freight on it (when the shipment was large) was one and a quarter per cent. of its intrinsic value. So, the freight on these bars probably averaged something more than $25 each. Small shippers paid two per cent. There were three stages a day, each way, and I have seen the out-going stages carry away a third of a ton of bullion each, and more than once I saw them divide a two-ton lot and take it off. However, these were extraordinary events.* Two tons of silver bullion would be in the neighborhood of forty bars, and the freight on it over $1,000. Each coach always carried a deal of ordinary express matter beside, and also from fifteen to twenty passengers at from $25 to $30 a head. With six stages going all the time,

*Mr. Valentine, Wells Fargo's agent, has handled all the bullion shipped through the Virginia office for many a month. To his memory—which is excellent—we are indebted for the following exhibit of the company's business in the Virginia office since the first of January, 1862: From January 1st, to April 1st, about $270,000 worth of bullion passed through that office; during the next quarter, $570,000; next quarter, $800,000; next quarter, $956,000; next quarter, $1,275,000; and for the quarter ending on the 30th of last June, about $1,600,000. Thus in a year and a half, the Virginia office only shipped $5,330,000 in bullion. During the year 1862 they shipped $2,615,000, so we perceive the average shipments have more than doubled in the last six months. This gives us room to promise for the Virginia office $500,000 a month for the year 1863 (though perhaps, judging by the steady increase in the business, we are under estimating, somewhat). This gives us $6,000,000 for the year. Gold Hill and Silver City together can beat us—we will give them $10,000,000. To Dayton, Empire City, Ophir and Carson City, we will allow an aggregate of $8,000,000, which is not over the mark, perhaps, and may possibly be a little under it. To Emeralda we give $4,000,000. To Reese River and Humboldt $2,000,000, which is liberal now, but may not be before the year is out. So we prognosticate that the yield of bullion this year will be about $30,000,000. Placing the number of mills in the Territory at one hundred, this gives to each the labor of producing $300,000 in bullion during the twelve months. Allowing them to run three hundred days in the year (which none of them more than do), this makes their work average $1,000 a day. Say the mills average twenty tons of rock a day and this rock worth $50 as a general thing, and you have the actual work of our one hundred mills figured down "to a spot"—$1,000 a day each, and $30,000,000 a year in the aggregate.—*Enterprise.*

[A considerable over estimate.—M.T.]

Wells, Fargo and Co.'s Virginia City business was important and lucrative.

All along under the centre of Virginia and Gold Hill, for a couple of miles, ran the great Comstock silver lode—a vein of ore from fifty to eighty feet thick between its solid walls of rock—a vein as wide as some of New York's streets. I will remind the reader that in Pennsylvania a coal vein only eight feet wide is considered ample.

Virginia was a busy city of streets and houses above ground. Under it was another busy city, down in the bowels of the earth, where a great population of men thronged in and out among an intricate maze of tunnels and drifts, flitting hither and thither under a winking sparkle of lights, and over their heads towered a vast web of interlocking timbers that held the walls of the gutted Comstock apart. These timbers were as large as a man's body, and the framework stretched upward so far that no eye could pierce to its top through the closing gloom. It was like peering up through the clean-picked ribs and bones of some colossal skeleton. Imagine such a framework two miles long, sixty feet wide, and higher than any church spire in America. Imagine this stately lattice-work stretching down Broadway, from the St. Nicholas to Wall street, and a Fourth of July procession, reduced to pigmies, parading on top of it and flaunting their flags, high above the pinnacle of Trinity steeple. One can imagine that, but he cannot well imagine what that forest of timbers cost, from the time they were felled in the pineries beyond Washoe Lake, hauled up and around Mount Davidson at atrocious rates of freightage, then squared, let down into the deep maw of the mine and built up there. Twenty ample fortunes would not timber one of the greatest of those silver mines. The Spanish proverb says it requires a gold mine to "run" a silver one, and it is true. A beggar with a silver mine is a pitiable pauper indeed if he cannot sell.

I spoke of the underground Virginia as a city. The Gould and Curry is only one single mine under there, among a great many others; yet the Gould and Curry's streets of dismal drifts and tunnels were five miles in extent, altogether, and its population five hundred miners. Taken as a whole, the underground city had some thirty miles of streets and a population of five or six thousand. In this present day some of those populations are at work from twelve to sixteen hundred feet under Virginia and Gold Hill, and the signal-bells that tell them what the superintendent above ground desires them to do are struck by telegraph as we strike a fire alarm. Sometimes men fall down a shaft, there, a thousand feet deep. In such cases, the usual plan is to hold an inquest.

If you wish to visit one of those mines, you may walk through a tunnel about half a mile long if you prefer it, or you may take the quicker plan of shooting like a dart down a shaft, on a small platform. It is like tumbling down through an empty steeple, feet first. When you reach the bottom, you take a candle and tramp through drifts and tunnels where throngs of men are digging and blasting; you watch them send up tubs full of great lumps of stone—silver ore; you select choice specimens from the mass, as souvenirs; you admire the world of skeleton timbering; you reflect frequently that you are buried under a mountain, a thousand feet below daylight; being in the bottom of the mine you climb from "gallery" to "gallery," up endless ladders that stand straight up and down; when your legs fail you at last, you lie down in a small box-car in a cramped "incline" like a half-up-ended sewer and are dragged up to daylight feeling as if you are crawling through a coffin that has no end to it. Arrived at the top, you find a busy crowd of men receiving the ascending cars and tubs and dumping the ore from an elevation into long rows of bins capable of holding half a dozen tons each; under the bins are rows of wagons loading from chutes and trap-doors in the bins, and down the long street is a procession of these wagons wending toward the silver mills with their rich freight. It is all "done," now, and there you are. You need never go down again, for you have seen it all. If you have forgotten the process of reducing the ore in the mill and making the silver bars, you can go back and find it again in my Esmeralda chapters if so disposed.

Of course these mines cave in, in places, occasionally, and then it is worth one's while to take the risk of descending into them and observing the crushing power exerted by the pressing weight of a settling mountain. I published such an experience in the *Enterprise*, once, and from it I will take an extract:

AN HOUR IN THE CAVED MINES.—We journeyed down into the Ophir mine, yesterday, to see the earthquake. We could not go down the deep incline, because it still has a propensity to cave in places. Therefore we traveled through the long tunnel which enters the hill above the Ophir office, and then by means of a series of long ladders, climbed away down from the first to the fourth gallery. Traversing a drift, we came to the Spanish line, passed five sets of timbers still uninjured, and found the earthquake. Here was as complete a chaos as ever was seen—vast masses of earth and splintered and broken timbers piled confusedly together, with scarcely an aperture left large enough for a cat to creep through. Rubbish was still falling at intervals from above, and one timber which had braced others earlier in the day, was *now* crushed down out of its former position, showing that the caving and settling of the tremendous mass was still going on. We were in that portion of the Ophir known as the "north mines." Returning to the surface, we entered a tunnel leading into the Central, for the purpose of getting into the main Ophir. Descending a long incline in this tunnel, we traversed a drift or so, and then went down a deep shaft from whence we proceeded into the fifth gallery of the Ophir. From a side-drift we crawled through a small hole and got into the midst of the earthquake again—earth and broken timbers mingled together without regard to grace or symmetry. A large portion of the second, third and fourth galleries had caved in and gone to destruction—the two latter at seven o'clock on the previous evening.

At the turn-table, near the northern extremity of the fifth gallery, two big piles of rubbish had forced their way through from the fifth gallery, and from the looks of the timbers, more was about to come. These beams are solid—eighteen inches square; first, a great beam is laid on the floor, then upright ones, five feet high, stand on it, supporting another horizontal beam, and so on, square above square, like the framework of a window. The superincumbent weight was sufficient to mash the ends of those great upright beams fairly into the solid wood of the horizontal ones three inches, compressing and bending the upright beam till it curved like a bow. Before the Spanish caved in, some of their twelve-inch horizontal timbers were compressed in this way until they were only five inches thick! Imagine the power it must take to squeeze a solid log together in that way. Here, also, was a range of timbers, for a distance of twenty feet, tilted six inches out of the perpendicular by the weight resting upon them from the caved galleries above. You could hear things cracking and giving way, and it was not pleasant to know that the world overhead was slowly and silently sinking down upon you. The men down in the mine do not mind it, however.

Returning along the fifth gallery, we struck the safe part of the Ophir incline, and went down it to the sixth; but we found ten inches of water there, and had to come back. In repairing the damage done to the incline, the pump had to be stopped for two hours, and in the meantime the water gained about a foot. However, the pump was at work again, and the flood-water was decreasing. We climbed up to the fifth gallery again and sought a deep shaft, whereby we might descend to another part of the sixth, out of reach of the water, but suffered disappointment, as the men had gone to dinner, and there was no one to man the windlass. So, having seen the earthquake, we climbed out at the Union incline and tunnel, and adjourned, all dripping with candle grease and perspiration, to lunch at the Ophir office.

During the great flush year of 1863, Nevada [claims to have] produced $25,000,000 in bullion—almost, if not quite, a round million to each thousand inhabitants, which is very well, considering that she was without agriculture and manufactures.* Silver mining was her sole productive industry.

CHAPTER LIII

Every now and then, in these days, the boys used to tell me I ought to get one Jim Blaine to tell me the stirring story of his grandfather's old ram—but they always added that I must not mention the matter unless Jim was drunk at the time—just comfortably and sociably drunk. They kept this up until my curiosity was on the rack to hear the story. I got to haunting Blaine; but it was of no use, the boys always found fault with his condition; he was often moderately but never satisfactorily drunk. I never watched a man's condition with such absorbing interest, such anxious solicitude; I never so pined to see a man uncompromisingly drunk before. At last, one evening I hurried to his cabin, for I learned that this time his situation was such that even the most fastidious could find no fault with it—he was tranquilly, serenely, symmetrically drunk—not a hiccup to mar his voice, not a cloud upon his brain thick enough to obscure his memory. As I entered, he was sitting upon an empty powder-keg, with a clay pipe in one hand and the other raised to command silence. His face was round, red, and very serious; his throat was bare and his hair tumbled; in general appearance and costume he was a stalwart miner of the period. On the pine table stood a candle, and its dim light revealed "the boys" sitting here and there on bunks, candle-boxes, powder-kegs, etc. They said:

"Sh—! Don't speak—he's going to commence."

*Since the above was in type, I learn from an official source that the above figure is too high, and that the yield for 1863 did not exceed $20,000,000. However, the day for large figures is approaching; the Sutro Tunnel is to plow through the Comstock lode from end to end, at a depth of two thousand feet, and then mining will be easy and comparatively inexpensive; and the momentous matters of drainage, and hoisting and hauling of ore will cease to be burdensome. This vast work will absorb many years, and millions of dollars, in its completion; but it will early yield money, for that desirable epoch will begin as soon as it strikes the first end of the vein. The tunnel will be some eight miles long, and will develop astonishing riches. Cars will carry the ore through the tunnel and dump it in the mills and thus do away with the present costly system of double handling and transportation by mule teams. The water from the tunnel will furnish the motive power for the mills. Mr. Sutro, the originator of this prodigious enterprise, is one of the few men in the world who is gifted with the pluck and perseverance necessary to follow up and hound such an undertaking to its completion. He has converted several obstinate Congresses to a deserved friendliness toward his important work, and has gone up and down and to and fro in Europe until he has enlisted a great moneyed interest in it there.

THE STORY OF THE OLD RAM

I found a seat at once, and Blaine said:

"I don't reckon them times will ever come again. There never was a more bullier old ram than what he was. Grandfather fetched him from Illinois—got him of a man by the name of Yates—Bill Yates—maybe you might have heard of him; his father was a decon—Baptist—and he was a rustler, too; a man had to get up ruther early to get the start of old Thankful Yates; it was him that put the Greens up to jining teams with my grandfather when he moved west. Seth Green was prob'ly the pick of the flock; he married a Wilkerson—Sarah Wilkerson—good cretur, she was—one of the likeliest heifers that was ever raised in old Stoddard, everybody said that knowed her. She could heft a bar'l of flour as easy as I can flirt a flapjack. And spin? Don't mention it! Independent? Humph! When Sile Hawkins come a browsing around her, she let him know that for all his tin he couldn't trot in harness alongside of *her*. You see, Sile Hawkins was—no, it warn't Sile Hawkins, after all—it was a galoot by the name of Filkins—I disremember his first name; but he *was* a stump— come into pra'r meeting drunk, one night, hooraying for Nixon, becuz he thought it was a primary; and old deacon Ferguson up and scooted him through the window and he lit on old Miss Jefferson's head, poor old filly. She was a good soul—had a glass eye and used to lend it to old Miss Wagner, that hadn't any, to receive company in; it warn't big enough, and when Miss Wagner warn't noticing, it would get twisted around in the socket, and look up, maybe, or out to one side, and every which way, while t'other one was looking as straight ahead as a spy-glass. Grown people didn't mind it, but it most always made the children cry, it was so sort of scary. She tried packing it in raw cotton, but it wouldn't work, somehow—the cotton would get loose and stick out and look so kind of awful that the children couldn't stand it no way. She was always dropping it out, and turning up her old dead-light on the company empty, and making them oncomfortable, becuz *she* never could tell when it hopped out, being blind on that side, you see. So somebody would have to hunch her and say, "Your game eye has fetched loose, Miss Wagner dear"—and then all of them would have to sit and wait till she jammed it in again—wrong side before, as a general thing, and green as a bird's egg, being a bashful cretur and easy sot back before company. But being wrong side before warn't much difference, anyway, becuz her own eye was sky-blue and the glass one was yaller on the front side, so whichever way she turned it it didn't match nohow. Old Miss Wagner was considerable on the borrow, she was. When she had a quilting, or Dorcas S'iety at her house she gen'ally borrowed Miss Higgins's wooden leg to stump around on; it was considerable shorter than her other pin, but much *she* minded that. She said she couldn't abide crutches when she had company, becuz they were so slow; said when she had company and things had to be done, she wanted to get up and hump herself. She was as bald as a jug, and so she used to borrow Miss Jacops's wig—Miss Jacops was the coffin-peddler's wife—a ratty old buzzard, he was, that used to go roosting around where people was sick, waiting for 'em; and there that old rip would sit all day, in the shade, on a coffin that he judged would fit the can'idate; and if it was a slow customer and kind of uncertain, he'd fetch his rations and a blanket along and sleep in the coffin nights. He was anchored out that way, in frosty weather, for about three weeks, once, before old Robbins's place, waiting for him; and after that, for as much as two years, Jacops was not on speaking terms with the old man, on account of his disapp'inting him. He got one of his feet froze, and lost money, too, becuz old Robbins took a favorable turn and got well. The next time Robbins got sick, Jacops tried to make up with him, and varnished up the same old coffin and fetched it along; but old Robbins was too many for him; he had him in, and 'peared to be powerful weak; he bought the coffin for ten dollars and Jacops was to pay it back and twenty-five more besides if Robbins didn't like the coffin after he'd tried it. And then Robbins died, and at the funeral he bursted off the lid and riz up in his shroud and told the parson to let up on the performances, becuz he could *not* stand such a coffin as that. You see he had been in a trance once before, when he was young, and he took the chances on another, cal'lating that if he made the trip it was money in his pocket, and if he missed fire he couldn't lose a cent. And by George he sued Jacops for the rhino and got jedgment; and he set up the coffin in his back parlor and said he 'lowed to take his time, now. It was always an aggravation to Jacops, the way that miserable old thing acted. He moved back to Indiany pretty soon—went to Wellsville—Wellsville was the place the Hogadorns was from. Mighty fine family. Old Maryland stock. Old Squire Hogadorn could carry around more mixed licker, and cuss better than most any man I ever see. His second wife was the widder Billings—she that was Becky Martin; her dam was deacon Dunlap's first wife. Her oldest child, Maria, married a missionary and died in grace—et up by the savages. They et *him*, too, poor feller—biled him. It warn't the custom, so they say, but they explained to friends of his'n that went down there to bring away his things, that they'd tried missionaries every other way and never could get any good out of 'em—and so it annoyed all his relations to find out that that man's life was fooled away just out of a dern'd experiment, so to speak. But mind you, there ain't anything ever reely lost; everything that people can't understand and don't see the reason of does good if you only hold on and give it a fair shake; Prov'dence don't fire no blank ca'tridges, boys. That there missionary's substance, unbeknowns to himself, actu'ly converted every last one of them heathens that took a chance at the barbacue. Nothing ever fetched them but that. Don't tell *me* it was an accident that he was biled. There ain't no such a thing as an accident. When my uncle Lem was leaning up agin a scaffolding once, sick, or drunk, or suthin, an Irishman with a hod full of bricks fell on him out of the third story and broke the old man's back in two places. People said it was an accident. Much accident there was about that. He didn't know what he was there for, but he was there for a good object. If he hadn't been there the Irishman would have been killed. Nobody can ever make me believe anything different from that. Uncle Lem's dog was there. Why didn't the Irishman fall on the dog? Becuz the dog would a seen him a-coming and stood from under. That's the reason the dog warn't appinted. A dog can't be depended on to carry out a special providence. Mark my words it was a put-up thing. Accidents don't happen, boys. Uncle Lem's dog—I wish you could a seen that dog. He was a reglar shepherd—or ruther he was part bull and part shepherd—splendid animal; belonged to parson Hagar before Uncle Lem got him. Parson Hagar belonged to the Western Reserve Hagars; prime family; his mother was a Watson; one of his sisters married a Wheeler; they settled in Morgan county, and he got nipped by the machinery in a carpet factory and went through in less than a quarter of a minute; his widder bought the piece of carpet that had his remains wove in, and people come a hundred mile to 'tend the funeral. There was fourteen years in the piece. She wouldn't let them roll him up, but planted him just so—full length. The church was middling small where they preached the funeral, and they had to let one end of the coffin stick out of the window. They didn't bury him—they planed one end, and let him stand up, same as a monument. And they nailed a sign on it and put—put on—put on it—sacred to—the m-e-m-o-r-y—of fourteen y-a-r-d-s—of three-ply—car - - - pet—containing all that was—m-o-r-t-a-l—of—of—W-i-l-l-i-a-m—W-h-e—"

Jim Blaine had been growing gradually drowsy and drowsier—his head nodded, once, twice, three times—dropped peacefully upon his breast, and he fell tranquilly asleep. The tears were running down the boys' cheeks—they were suffocating with suppressed laughter—and had been from the start, though I had never noticed it. I perceived that I was "sold." I learned then that Jim Blaine's peculiarity was that whenever he reached a certain stage of intoxication, no human power could keep him from setting out, with impressive unction, to tell about a wonderful adventure which he had once had with his grandfather's old ram—and the mention of the ram in the first sentence was as far as any man had ever heard him get, concerning it. He always maundered off, interminably, from one thing to another, till his whisky got the best of him and he fell asleep. What the thing was that happened to him and his grandfather's old ram is a dark mystery to this day, for nobody has ever yet found out.

CHAPTER LIV

Of course there was a large Chinese population in Virginia—it is the case with every town and city on the Pacific coast. They are a harmless race when white men either let them along or treat them no worse than dogs; in fact they are almost entirely harmless anyhow, for they seldom think of resenting the vilest insults or the cruelest injuries. They are quiet, peaceable, tractable, free from drunkenness, and they are as industrious as the day is long. A disorderly Chinaman is rare, and a lazy one does not exist. So long as a Chinaman has strength to use his hands he needs no support from anybody; white men often complain of want of work, but a Chinaman offers no such complaint; he always manages to find something to do. He is a great convenience to everybody—even to the worst class of white men, for he bears the most of their sins, suffering fines for their petty thefts, imprisonment for their robberies, and death for their murders. Any white man can swear a Chinaman's life away in the courts, but no Chinaman can testify against a white man. Ours is the "land of the free"—nobody denies that—nobody challenges it. [Maybe it is because we won't let other people testify.] As I write, news comes that in broad daylight in San Francisco, some boys have stoned an inoffensive Chinaman to death, and that although a large crowd witnessed the shameful deed, no one interfered.

There are seventy thousand (and possibly one hundred thousand) Chinamen on the Pacific coast. There were about a thousand in Virginia. They were penned into a "Chinese quarter"—a thing which they do not particularly object to, as they are fond of herding together. Their buildings were of wood; usually only one story high, and set thickly together along streets scarcely wide enough for a wagon to pass through. Their quarter was a little removed from the rest of the town. The chief employment of Chinamen in towns is to wash clothing. They always send a bill, pinned to the clothes. It is mere ceremony, for it does not enlighten the customer much. Their price for washing was $2.50 per dozen—rather cheaper than white people could afford to wash for at that time. A very common sign on the Chinese houses was: "See Yup, Washer and Ironer"; "Hong Wo, Washer"; "Sam Sing & Ah Hop, Washing." The house servants, cooks, etc., in California and Nevada, were chiefly Chinamen. There were few white servants and no Chinawomen so employed. Chinamen make good house servants, being quick, obedient, patient, quick to learn and tirelessly industrious. They do not need to be taught a thing twice, as a general thing. They are imitative. If a Chinaman were to see his master break up a centre table, in a passion, and kindle a fire with it, that Chinaman would be likely to resort to the furniture for fuel forever afterward.

All Chinamen can read, write and cipher with easy facility—pity but all our petted *voters* could. In California they rent little patches of ground and do a deal of gardening. They will raise surprising crops of vegetables on a sand pile. They waste nothing. What is rubbish to a Christian, a Chinaman carefully preserves and makes useful in one way or another. He gathers up all the old oyster and sardine cans that white people throw away, and procures marketable tin and solder from them by melting. He gathers up old bones and turns them into manure. In California he gets a living out of old mining claims that white men have abandoned as exhausted and worthless—and then the officers come down on him once a month with an exorbitant swindle to which the legislature has given the broad, general name of "foreign" mining tax, but it is usually inflicted on no foreigners but Chinamen. This swindle has in some cases been repeated once or twice on the same victim in the course of the same month—but the public treasury was not additionally enriched by it, probably.

Chinamen hold their dead in great reverence—they worship their departed ancestors, in fact. Hence, in China, a man's front yard, back yard, or any other part of his premises, is made his family burying ground, in order that he may visit the graves at any and all times. Therefore that huge empire is one mighty cemetery; it is ridged and wringled from its centre to its circumference with graves—and inasmuch as every foot of ground must be made to do its utmost, in China, lest the swarming population suffer for food, the very graves are cultivated and yield a harvest, custom holding this to be no dishonor to the dead. Since the departed are held in such worshipful reverence, a Chinaman cannot bear that any indignity be offered the places where they sleep. Mr. Burlingame said that herein lay China's bitter opposition to railroads; a road could not be built anywhere in the empire without disturbing the graves of their ancestors or friends.

A Chinaman hardly believes he could enjoy the hereafter except his body lay in his beloved China; also, he desires to receive, himself, after death, that worship with which he has honored his death that preceded him. Therefore, if he visits a foreign country, he makes arrangements to have his bones returned to China in case he dies; if he hires to go to a foreign country on a labor contract, there is always a stipulation that his body shall be taken back to China if he dies; if the government sells a gang of Coolies to a foreigner for the usual five-year term, it is specified in the contract that their bodies shall be restored to China in case of death. On the Pacific coast the Chinamen all belong to one or another of several great companies or organizations, and these companies keep track of their members, register their names, and ship their bodies home when they die. The See Yup Company is held to be the largest of these. The Ning Yeong Company is next, and numbers eighteen thousand members on the coast. Its headquarters are at San Francisco, where it has a costly temple, several great officers (one of whom keeps regal state in seclusion and cannot be approached by common humanity), and a numerous priesthood. In it I was shown a register of its members, with the dead and the date of their shipment to China duly marked. Every ship that sails from San Francisco carries away a heavy freight of Chinese corpses—or did, at least, until the legislature, with an ingenious refinement of Christian cruelty, forbade the shipments, as a neat underhanded way of deterring Chinese immigration. The bill was offered, whether it passed or not. It is my impression that it passed. There was another bill—it became a law—compelling every incoming Chinaman to be vaccinated on the wharf and pay a duly appointed quack (no decent doctor would defile himself with such legalized robbery) ten dollars for it. As few importers of Chinese would want to go to an expense like that, the lawmakers thought this would be another heavy blow to Chinese immigration.

What the Chinese quarter of Virginia was like—or, indeed, what the Chinese quarter of any Pacific coast town was and is like—may be gathered from this item which I printed in the *Enterprise* while reporting for that paper:

CHINATOWN.—Accompanied by a fellow reporter, we made a trip through our Chinese quarter the other night. The Chinese have built their portion of the city to suit themselves; and as they keep neither carriages nor wagons, their streets are not wide enough, as a general thing, to admit of the passage of vehicles. At ten o'clock at night the Chinaman may be seen in all his glory. In every little cooped-up, dingy cavern of a hut, faint with the odor of burning Josh-lights and with nothing to see the gloom by save the sickly, guttering tallow candle, were two or three yellow, long-tailed vagabonds, coiled up on a sort of short truckle-bed, smoking opium, motionless and with their lustreless eyes turned inward from excess of satisfaction—or rather the recent smoker looks thus, immediately after having passed the pipe to his neighbor—for opium-smoking is a comfortless operation, and requires constant attention. A lamp sits on the bed, the length of the long pipe-stem from the smoker's mouth; he puts a pellet of opium on the end of a wire, sets it on fire, and plasters it into the pipe much as a Christian would fill a hole with putty; then he applies the bowl to the lamp and proceeds to smoke—and the stewing and frying of the drug and the gurgling of the juices in the stem would wellnigh turn the stomach of statue. John likes it, though; it soothes him, he takes about two dozen whiffs, and then rolls over to dream, Heaven only knows what, for we could not imagine by looking at the soggy creature. Possibly in his visions he travels far away from the gross world and his regular washing, and feasts on succulent rats and birds'-nests in Paradise.

Mr. Ah Sing keeps a general grocery and provision store at No. 13 Wang street. He lavished his hospitality upon our party in the friendliest way. He had various kinds of colored and colorless wines and brandies, with unpronouncable names, imported from China in little crockery jugs, and which he offered to us in dainty little miniature wash-basins of porcelain. He offered us a mess of birds'-nests; also, small, neat sausages, of which we could have swallowed several yards if we had chosen to try, but we suspected that each link contained the corpse of a mouse, and therefore refrained. Mr. Sing had in his store a thousand articles of merchandise, curious to behold, impossible to imagine the uses of, and beyond our ability to describe.

His ducks, however, and his eggs, we could understand; the former were split open and flattened out like codfish, and came from China in that shape, and the latter were plastered over with some kind of paste which kept them fresh and palatable through the long voyage.

We found Mr. Hong Wo, No. 37 Chow-chow street, making up a lottery scheme—in fact we found a dozen others occupied in the same way in various parts of the quarter, for about every third Chinaman runs a lottery, and the balance of the tribe "buck" at it. "Tom," who speaks faultless English, and used to be chief and only cook to the *Territorial Enterprise,* when the establishment kept bachelor's hall two years ago, said that "Sometime Chinaman buy ticket one dollar hap, ketch um two tree hundred, sometime no ketch um anything; lottery like one man fight um seventy—may-be he whip, may-be he get whip herself, welly good." However, the percentage being sixty-nine against him, the chances are, as a general thing, that "he get whip heself." We could not see that these lotteries differed in any respect from our own, save that the figures being Chinese, no ignorant white man might ever hope to succeed in telling "t'other from which;" the manner of drawing is similar to ours.

Mr. See Yup keeps a fancy store on Live Fox street. He sold us fans of white feathers, gorgeously ornamented; perfumery that smelled like Limburger cheese, Chinese pens, and watch-charms made of a stone unscratchable with steel instruments, yet polished and tinted like the inner coat of a sea-shell.* As tokens of his esteem, See Yup presented the party with gaudy plumes made of gold tinsel and trimmed with peacocks' feathers.

We ate chow-chow with chop-sticks in the celestial restaurants; our comrade chided the moon-eyed damsels in front of the houses for their want of feminine reserve; we received protecting Josh-lights from our hosts and "dickered" for a pagan God or two. Finally, we were impressed with the genius of a Chinese book-keeper; he figured up his accounts on a machine like a gridiron with buttons strung on its bars; the different rows represented units, tens, hundreds and thousands. He fingered them with incredible rapidity—in fact, he pushed them from place to place as fast as a musical professor's fingers travel over the keys of a piano.

They are a kindly disposed, well-meaning race, and are respected and well treated by the upper classes, all over the Pacific coast. No Californian *gentleman or lady* ever abuses or oppresses a Chinaman, under any circumstances, an explanation that seems to be much needed in the East. Only the scum of the population do it—they and their children; they, and, naturally and consistently, the policemen and politicians, likewise, for these are the dust-licking pimps and slaves of the scum, there as well as elsewhere in America.

CHAPTER LV

I began to get tired of staying in one place so long. There was no longer satisfying variety in going down to Carson to report the proceedings of the legislature once a year, and horse-races and pumpkin-shows once in three months; (they had got to raising pumpkins and potatoes in Washoe Valley, and of course one of the first achievements of the legislature was to institute a ten-

*A peculiar species of the "jade-stone"—to a Chinaman peculiarly precious.

thousand-dollar Agricultural Fair to show off forty dollars' worth of those pumpkins in—however, the territorial legislature was usually spoken of as the "asylum"). I wanted to see San Francisco. I wanted to go somewhere. I wanted—I did not know *what* I wanted. I had the "spring fever" and wanted a change, principally, no doubt. Besides, a convention had framed a State Constitution; nine men out of every ten wanted an office; I believed that these gentlemen would "treat" the moneyless and the irresponsible among the population into adopting the constitution and thus wellnigh killing the country (it could not well carry such a load as a State government, since it had nothing to tax that could stand a tax, for undeveloped mines could not, and there were not fifty developed ones in the land, there was but little realty to tax, and it did seem as if nobody was ever going to think of the simple salvation of inflicting a money penalty on murder). I believed that a State government would destroy the "flush times," and I wanted to get away. I believed that the mining stocks I had on hand would soon be worth $100,000, and thought if they reached that before the Constitution was adopted, I would sell out and make myself secure from the crash the change of government was going to bring. I considered $100,000 sufficient to go home with decently, though it was but a small amount compared to what I had been expecting to return with. I felt rather downhearted about it, but I tried to comfort myself with the reflection that with such a sum I could not fall into want. About this time a schoolmate of mine whom I had not seen since boyhood, came tramping in on foot from Reese River, a very allegory of Poverty. The son of wealthy parents, here he was, in a strange land, hungry, bootless, mantled in an ancient horse-blanket, roofed with a brimless hat, and so generally and so extravagantly dilapidated that he could have "taken the shine out of the Prodigal Son himself," as he pleasantly remarked. He wanted to borrow forty-six dollars—twenty-six to take him to San Francisco, and twenty for something else; to buy some soap with, maybe, for he needed it. I found I had but little more than the amount wanted, in my pocket; so I stepped in and borrowed forty-six dollars of a banker (on twenty days' time, without the formality of a note), and gave it him, rather than walk half a block to the office, where I had some specie laid up. If anybody had told me that it would take me two years to pay back that forty-six dollars to the banker (for I did not expect it of the Prodigal, and was not disappointed), I would have felt injured. And so would the banker.

I wanted a change. I wanted variety of some kind. It came.

Mr. Goodman went away for a week and left me the post of chief editor. It destroyed me. The first day, I wrote my "leader" in the forenoon. The second day, I had no subject and put it off till the afternoon. The third day I put it off till evening, and then copied an elaborate editorial out of the "American Cyclopedia," that steadfast friend of the editor, all over this land. The fourth day I "fooled around" till midnight, and then fell back on the Cyclopedia again. The fifth day I cudgeled my brain till midnight, and then kept the press waiting while I penned some bitter personalities on six different people. The sixth day I labored in anguish till far into the night and brought forth—nothing. The paper went to press without an editorial. The seventh day I resigned. On the eighth, Mr. Goodman returned and found six duels on his hands—my personalities had borne fruit.

Nobody, except he has tried it, knows what it is to be an editor. It is easy to scribble local rubbish, with the facts all before you; it is easy to clip selections from other papers; it is easy to string out a correspondence from any locality; but it is unspeakable hardship to write editorials. *Subjects* are the trouble—the dreary lack of them, I mean. Every day, it is drag, drag, drag—think, and worry and suffer—all the world is a dull blank, and yet the editorial columns *must* be filled. Only give the editor a *subject,* and his work is done—it is no trouble to write it up; but fancy how you would feel if you had to pump your brains dry every day in the week, fifty-two weeks in the year. It makes one low spirited simply to think of it. The matter that each editor of a daily paper in America writes in the course of a year would fill from four to eight bulky volumes like this book! Fancy what a library an editor's work would make, after twenty or thirty years' service. Yet people often marvel that Dickens, Scott, Bulwer, Dumas, etc., have been able to produce so many books. If these authors had wrought as voluminously as newspaper editors do, the result would be something to marvel at, indeed. How editors can continue this tremendous labor, this exhausting consumption of brain fibre (for their work is creative, and not a mere mechanical laying-up of facts, like reporting), day after day and year after year, is incomprehensible. Preachers take two months' holiday in midsummer, for they find that to produce two sermons a week is wearing, in the long run. In truth it must be so, and is so; and therefore, how an editor can take from ten to twenty texts and build upon them from ten to twenty painstaking editorials a week and keep it up all the year round, is farther beyond comprehension than ever. Ever since I survived my week as editor, I have found at least one pleasure in any newspaper that comes to my hand; it is in admiring the long columns of editorial, and wondering to myself how in the mischief he did it!

Mr. Goodman's return relieved me of employment, unless I chose to become a reporter again. I could not do that; I could not serve in the ranks after being General of the army. So I thought I would depart and go abroad into the world somewhere. Just at this juncture, Dan, my associate in the reportorial department, told me, casually, that two citizens had been trying to persuade him to go with them to New York and aid in selling a rich silver mine which they had discovered and secured in a new mining district in our neighborhood. He said they offered to pay his expenses and give him one third of the proceeds of the sale. He had refused to go. It was the very opportunity I wanted. I abused him for keeping so quiet about it, and not mentioning it sooner. He said it had not occurred to him that I would like to go, and so he had recommended them to apply to Marshall, the reporter of the other paper. I asked Dan if it was a good, honest mine, and no swindle. He said the men had shown him nine tons of the rock, which they had got out to take to New York, and he could cheerfully say that he had seen but little rock in Nevada that was richer; and moreover, he said that they had secured a tract of valuable timber and a mill-site, near the mine. My first idea was to kill Dan. But I changed my mind, notwithstanding I was so angry, for I thought maybe the chance was not yet lost. Dan said it was by no means lost; that the men were absent at the mine again, and would not be in Virginia to leave for the East for some ten days; that they had requested him to do the talking to Marshall, and he had promised that he would either secure Marshall or somebody else for them by the time they got back; he would now say nothing to anybody till they returned, and then fulfil his promise by furnishing me to them.

It was splendid. I went to bed all on fire with excitement; for nobody had yet gone East to sell a Nevada silver mine, and the field was white for the sickle. I felt that such a mine as the one described by Dan would bring a princely sum in New York, and sell without delay or difficulty. I could not sleep, my fancy so rioted through its castles in the air. It was the "blind lead" come again.

Next day I got away, on the coach, with the usual eclat attending departures of old citizens,—for if you have only half a dozen friends out there they will make noise for a hundred rather than let you seem to go away neglected and unregretted— and Dan promised to keep strict watch for the men that had the mine to sell.

The trip was signalized but by one little incident, and that occurred just as we were about to start. A very seedy looking vagabond passenger got out of the stage a moment to wait till the usual ballast of silver bricks was thrown in. He was standing on the pavement, when an awkward express employé, carrying a brick weighing a hundred pounds, stumbled and let it fall on the bummer's foot. He instantly dropped on the ground and began to howl in the most heart-breaking way. A sympathizing crowd gathered around and were going to pull his boot off; but he screamed louder than ever and they desisted; then he fell to gasping, and between the gasps ejaculated "Brandy! for Heaven's sake, brandy!" They poured half a pint down him, and it wonderfully restored and comforted him. Then he begged the people to assist him to the stage, which was done. The express people urged him to have a doctor at their expense, but he declined, and said that if he only had a little brandy to take along with him, to soothe his paroxyms of pain when they came on, he would be grateful and content. He was quickly supplied with two bottles, and we drove off. He was so smiling and happy after that, that I could not refrain from asking him how he could possibly be so comfortable with a crushed foot.

"Well," said he, "I hadn't had a drink for twelve hours, and hadn't a cent to my name. I was most perishing—and so, when that duffer dropped that hundred-pounder on my foot, I see my chance. Got a cork leg, you know!" and he pulled up his pantaloons and proved it.

He was as drunk as a lord all day long, and full of chucklings over his timely ingenuity.

One drunken man necessarily reminds one of another. I once heard a gentleman tell about an incident which he witnessed in a Californian bar-room. He entitled it "Ye Modest Man Taketh a Drink." It was nothing but a bit of acting, but it seemed to me a perfect rendering, and worthy of Toodles himself. The modest man, tolerably far gone with beer and other matters, enters a saloon (twenty-five cents is the price for anything and everything, and specie the only money used) and lays down a half dollar; calls for whiskey and drinks it; the bar-keeper makes change and lays the quarter in a wet place on the counter; the modest man fumbles at it with nerveless fingers, but it slips and the water holds it; he contemplates it, and tries again; same result; observes that people are interested in what he is at, blushes; fumbles at the quarter again—blushes—puts his forefinger carefully, slowly down, to make sure of his aim—pushes the coin toward the bar-keeper, and says with a sigh:

"('ic!) Gimme a cigar!"

Naturally, another gentleman present told about another drunken man. He said he reeled toward home late at night; made a mistake and entered the wrong gate; thought he saw a dog on the stoop; and it was—an iron one. He stopped and considered; wondered if it was a dangerous dog; ventured to say "Be (hic) begone!" No effect. Then he approached warily, and adopted conciliation; pursed up his lips and tried to whistle, but failed; still approached, saying, "Poor dog!—doggy, doggy, doggy!—poor doggy-dog!" Got up on the stoop, still petting with fond names; till master of the advantages; then exclaimed, "Leave, you thief!"—planted a vindictive kick in his ribs, and went head-over-heels overboard, of course. A pause; a sigh or two of pain, and then a remark in a reflective voice:

"Awful solid dog. What could he ben eating? ('ic!) Rocks, p'raps. Such animals is dangerous. 'At's what *I* say—they're dangerous. If a man—('ic!)—if a man wants to feed a dog on rocks, let him *feed* him on rocks; 'at's all right; but let him keep him at *home*—not have him layin' round promiscuous, where ('ic!) where people's liable to stumble over him when they ain't noticin'!"

It was not without regret that I took a last look at the tiny flag (it was thirty-five feet long and ten feet wide) fluttering like a lady's handkerchief from the topmost peak of Mount Davidson, two thousand feet above Virginia's roofs, and felt that doubtless I was bidding a permanent farewell to a city which had afforded me the most vigorous enjoyment of life I had ever experienced. And this reminds me of an incident which the dullest memory Virginia could boast at the time it happened must vividly recall, at times, till its possessor dies. Late one summer afternoon we had a rain shower. That was astonishing enough, in itself, to set the whole town buzzing, for it only rains (during a week or two weeks) in the winter in Nevada, and even then not enough at a time to make it worth while for any merchant to keep umbrellas for sale. But the rain was not the chief wonder. It only lasted five or ten minutes; while the people were still talking about it all the heavens gathered to themselves a dense blackness as of midnight. All the vast eastern front of Mount Davidson, overlooking the city, put on such a funereal gloom that only the nearness and solidity of the mountain made its outlines even faintly distinguishable from the dead blackness of the heavens they rested against. This unaccustomed sight turned all eyes toward the mountain; and as they looked, a little tongue of rich golden flame was seen waving and quivering in the heart of the midnight, away up on the extreme summit! In a few minutes the streets were packed with people, gazing with hardly an uttered word, at the one brilliant mote in the brooding world of darkness. It flicked like a candle-flame, and looked no larger; but with such a background it was wonderfully bright, small as it was. It was the flag!—though no one suspected it at first, it seemed so like a supernatural visitor of some kind—a mysterious messenger of good tidings, some were fain to believe. It was the nation's emblem transfigured by the departing rays of a sun that was entirely palled from view; and on no other object did the glory fall, in all the broad panorama of mountain ranges and deserts. Not even upon the staff of the flag—for that, a needle in the distance at any time, was now untouched by the light and undistinguishable in the gloom. For a whole hour the weird visitor winked and burned in its lofty solitude, and still the thousands of uplifted eyes watched it with fascinated interest. How the people were wrought up! The superstition grew apace that this was a mystic courier come with great news from the war—the poetry of the idea excusing and commending it—and on it spread, from heart to heart, from lip to lip and from street to street, till there was a general impulse to have out the military and welcome the bright waif with a salvo of artillery!

And all that time one sorely tired man, the telegraph operator sworn to official secrecy, had to lock his lips and chain his tongue with a silence that was like to rend them; for he, and he only, of all the speculating multitude, knew the great things this sinking sun had seen that day in the east—Vicksburg fallen, and the Union arms victorious at Gettysburg!

But for the journalistic monopoly that forbade the slightest revealment of eastern news till a day after its publication in the California papers, the glorified flag on Mount Davidson would have been saluted and re-saluted, that memorable evening, as long as there was a charge of powder to thunder with; the city would have been illuminated, and every man that had any respect for himself would have got drunk,—as was the custom of the country on all occasions of public moment. Even at this distant day I cannot think of this needlessly marred supreme opportunity without regret. What a time we might have had!

CHAPTER LVI

We rumbled over the plains and valleys, climbed the Sierras to the clouds, and looked down upon summer-clad California. And I will remark here, in passing, that all scenery in California requires *distance* to give it its highest charm. The mountains are imposing in their sublimity and their majesty of form and altitude, from any point of view—but one must have distance to soften their ruggedness and enrich their tintings; a Californian forest is best at a little distance, for there is a sad poverty of variety in species, the trees being chiefly of one monotonous family—redwood, pine, spruce, fir—and so, at a near view there is a wearisome sameness of attitude in their rigid arms, stretched downward and outward in one continued and reiterated appeal to all men to "Sh!—don't say a word!—you might disturb somebody!" Close at hand, too, there is a reliefless and relentless smell of pitch and turpentine; there is a ceaseless melancholy in their sighing and complaining foliage; one walks over a soundless carpet of beaten yellow bark and dead spines of the foliage till he feels like a wandering spirit bereft of a footfall; he tires of the endless tufts of needles and yearns for substantial, shapely leaves; he looks for moss and grass to loll upon, and finds none, for where there is no bark there is naked clay and dirt, enemies to pensive musing and clean apparel. Often a grassy plain in California, is what it should be, but often, too, it is best contemplated at a distance, because although its grass blades are tall, they stand up vindictively straight and self-sufficient, and are unsociably wide apart, with uncomely spots of barrens and between.

One of the queerest things I know of, is to hear tourists from "the States" go into ecstasies over the loveliness of "ever-blooming California." And they always do go into that sort of ecstasies. But perhaps they would modify them if they knew how old Californians, with the memory full upon them of the dust-covered and questionable summer greens of Californian "verdure," stand astonished, and filled with worshipping admiration, in the presence of the lavish richness, the brilliant green, the infinite freshness, the spendthrift variety of form and species and foliage that make an Eastern landscape a vision of Paradise itself. The idea of a man falling into raptures over grave and sombre California, when that man has seen New England's meadow-expanses and her maples, oaks and cathedral-windowed elms decked in summer attire, or the opaline splendors of autumn descending upon her forests, comes very near being funny—would be, in fact, but that it is so pathetic. No land with an unvarying climate can be very beautiful. The tropics are not, for all the sentiment that is wasted on them. They seem beautiful at first, but sameness impairs the charm by and by. *Change* is the handmaiden Nature requires to do her miracles with. The land that has four well-defined seasons, cannot lack beauty, or pall with monotony. Each season brings a world of enjoyment and interest in the watching of its unfolding, its gradual, harmonious development, its culminating graces—and just as one begins to tire of it, it passes away and a radical change comes, with new witcheries and new glories in its train. And I think that to one in sympathy with nature, each season, in its turn, seems the loveliest.

San Francisco, a truly fascinating city to live in, is stately and handsome at a fair distance, but close at hand one notes that the architecture is mostly old-fashioned, many streets are made up of decaying, smoke-grimed, wooden houses, and the barren sand-hills toward the outskirts obtrude themselves too prominently. Even the kindly climate is sometimes pleasanter when read about than personally experienced, for a lovely, cloudless sky wears out its welcome by and by, and then when the longed for rain does come it *stays*. Even the playful earthquake is better contemplated at a dis—

However there are varying opinions about that.

The climate of San Francisco is mild and singularly equable. The thermometer stands at about seventy degrees the year round. It hardly changes at all. You sleep under one or two light blankets Summer and Winter, and never use a mosquito bar. Nobody ever wears Summer clothing. You wear black broadcloth—if you have it—in August and January, just the same. It is no colder, and no warmer, in the one month than the other. You do not use overcoats and you do not use fans. It is as pleasant a climate as could well be contrived, take it all around, and is doubtless the most unvarying in the whole world. The wind blows there a good deal in the Summer months, but then you can go over to Oakland, if you choose—three or four miles away—it does not blow there. It has only snowed twice in San Francisco in nineteen years, and then it only remained on the ground long enough to astonish the children, and set them to wondering what the feathery stuff was.

During eight months of the year, straight along, the skies are bright and cloudless, and never a drop of rain falls. But when the other four months come along, you will need to go and steal an umbrella. Because you will require it. Not just one day, but one hundred and twenty days in hardly varying succession. When you want to go visiting, or attend church, or the theatre, you never look up at the clouds to see whether it is likely to rain or not—you look at the almanac. If it is Winter, it will *rain*—and if it is Summer, it *won't* rain, and you cannot help it. You never need a lightning-rod, because it never thunders and it never lightens. And after you have listened for six or eight weeks, every night, to the dismal monotony of those quiet rains, you will wish in your heart the thunder *would* leap and crash and roar along those drowsy skies once, and make everything alive—you will wish the prisoned lightnings *would* cleave the dull firmament asunder and light it with a blinding glare for *one* little instant. You would give *anything* to hear the old familiar thunder again and see the lightning strike somebody. And along in the Summer, when you have suffered about four months of lustrous, pitiless sunshine, you are ready to go down on your knees and plead for rain—hail—snow—thunder and lightning—anything to break the monotony—you will take an earthquake, if you cannot do any better. And the chances are that you'll get it, too.

San Francisco is built on sand hills, but they are prolific sand hills. They yield a generous vegetation. All the rare flowers which people in "the States" rear with such patient care in parlor flower-pots and green-houses, flourish luxuriantly in the open air there all the year round. Calla lilies, all sorts of geraniums, passion flowers, moss roses—I do not know the names of a tenth part of them. I only know that while New Yorkers are burdened with banks and drifts of snow, Californians are burdened with banks and drifts of flowers, if they only keep their hands off and let them grow. And I have heard that they have also that rarest and most curious of all the flowers, the beautiful *Espiritu Santo,* as the Spaniards call it—or flower of the Holy Spirit—though I thought it grew only in Central America—down on the Isthmus. In its cup is the daintiest little fac-simile of a dove, as pure as snow. The Spaniards have a superstitious reverence for it. The blossom has been conveyed to the States, submerged in ether; and the bulb has been taken thither also, but every attempt to make it bloom after it arrived, has failed.

I have elsewhere spoken of the endless Winter of Mono, California, and but this moment of the eternal Spring of San Francisco. Now if we travel a hundred miles in a straight line, we come to the eternal Summer of Sacramento. One never sees Summer-clothing or mosquitoes in San Francisco—but they can be found in Sacramento. Not always and unvaryingly, but about one hundred and forty-three months out of twelve years, perhaps. Flowers bloom there, always, the reader can easily believe—people suffer and sweat, and swear, morning, noon and night, and wear out their stanchest energies fanning themselves. It gets hot there, but if you go down to Fort Yuma you will find it hotter. Fort Yuma is probably the hottest place on earth. The thermometer stays at one hundred and twenty in the shade there all the time—except when it varies and goes higher. It is a U.S. military post, and its occupants get so used to the terrific heat that they suffer without it. There is a tradition (attributed to John Phenix*) that a very, very wicked soldier died there, once, and of course, went straight to the hottest corner of perdition,—and the next day he *telegraphed back for his blankets.* There is no doubt about the truth of this statement—there can be no doubt about it. I have seen the place where that soldier used to board. In Sacramento it is fiery Summer always, and you can gather roses, and eat strawberries and ice-cream, and wear white linen clothes, and pant and perspire, at eight or nine o'clock in the morning, and then take the cars, and at noon put on your furs and your skates, and go skimming over frozen Donner Lake, seven thousand feet above the valley, among snow banks fifteen feet deep, and in the shadow of grand mountain peaks that lift their frosty crags ten thousand feet above the level of the sea. There is a transition for you! Where will you find another like it in the Western hemisphere? And some of us have swept around snow-walled curves of the Pacific Railroad in that vicinity, six thousand feet above the sea, and looked down as the birds do, upon the deathless Summer of the Sacramento Valley, with its fruitful fields, its feathery foliage, its silver streams, all slumbering in the mellow haze of its enchanted atmosphere, and all infinitely softened and spiritualized by distance—a dreamy, exquisite glimpse of fairyland, made all the more charming and striking that it was caught through a forbidden gateway of ice and snow, and savage crags and precipices.

CHAPTER LVII

It was in this Sacramento Valley, just referred to, that a deal of the most lucrative of the early gold mining was done, and you may still see, in places, its grassy slopes and levels torn and guttered and disfigured by the avaricious spoilers of fifteen and twenty years ago. You may see such disfigurements far and wide over California—and in some such places, where only meadows and forests are visible—not a living creature, not a house, no stick or stone or remnant of a ruin, and not a sound, not even a whisper to disturb the Sabbath stillness—you will find it hard to believe that there stood at one time a fiercely-flourishing little city, of two thousand or three thousand souls, with its newspaper, fire company, brass band, volunteer militia, bank, hotels, noisy Fourth of July processions and speeches, gambling hells crammed with tobacco smoke, profanity, and rough-

*It has been purloined by fifty different scribblers who were too poor to invent a fancy but not ashamed to steal one.—M.T.

bearded men of all nations and colors, with tables heaped with gold dust sufficient for the revenues of a German principality—streets crowded and rife with business—town lots worth four hundred dollars a front foot—labor, laughter, music, dancing, swearing, fighting, shooting, stabbing—a bloody inquest and a man for breakfast every morning—*everything* that delights and adorns existence—all the appointments and appurtenances of a thriving and prosperous and promising young city,—and *now* nothing is left of it all but a lifeless, homeless solitude. The men are gone, the houses have vanished, even the *name* of the place is forgotten. In no other land, in modern times, have towns so absolutely died and disappeared, as in the old mining regions of California.

It was a driving, vigorous, restless population in those days. It was a *curious* population. It was the *only* population of the kind that the world has ever seen gathered together, and it is not likely that the world will ever see its like again. For, observe, it was an assemblage of two hundred thousand *young* men—not simpering, dainty, kid-gloved weaklings, but stalwart, muscular, dauntless young braves, brimful of push and energy, and royally endowed with every attribute that goes to make up a peerless and magnificent manhood—the very pick and choice of the world's glorious ones. No women, no children, no gray and stooping veterans,—none but erect, bright-eyed, quick-moving, strong-handed young giants—the strangest population, the finest population, the most gallant host that ever trooped down the startled solitudes of an unpeopled land. And where are they now? Scattered to the ends of the earth—or prematurely aged and decrepit—or shot or stabbed in street affrays—or dead of disappointed hopes and broken hearts—all gone, or nearly all—victims devoted upon the altar of the golden calf—the noblest holocaust that ever wafted its sacrificial incense heavenward. It is pitiful to think upon.

It was a splendid population—for all the slow, sleepy, sluggish-brained sloths staid at home—you never find that sort of people among pioneers—you cannot build pioneers out of that sort of material. It was that population that gave to California a name for getting up astounding enterprises and rushing them through with a magnificent dash and daring and a recklessness of cost or consequences, which she bears unto this day—and when she projects a new surprise, the grave world smiles as usual, and says "Well, that is California all over."

But they were rough in those times! They fairly reveled in gold, whisky, fights, and fandangoes, and were unspeakably happy. The honest miner raked from a hundred to a thousand dollars out of his claim a day, and what with the gambling dens and the other entertainments, he hadn't a cent the next morning, if he had any sort of luck. They cooked their own bacon and beans, sewed on their own buttons, washed their own shirts—blue woollen ones; and if a man wanted a fight on his hands without any annoying delay, all he had to do was to appear in public in a white shirt or a stove-pipe hat, and he would be accommodated. For those people hated aristocrats. They had a particular and malignant animosity toward what they called a "biled shirt."

It was a wild, free, disorderly, grotesque society! *Men*—only swarming hosts of stalwart *men*—nothing juvenile, nothing feminine, visible anywhere!

In those days miners would flock in crowds to catch a glimpse of that rare and blessed spectacle, a woman! Old inhabitants tell how, in a certain camp, the news went abroad early in the morning that a woman was come! They had seen a calico dress hanging out of a wagon down at the camping-ground—sign of emigrants from over the great plains. Everybody went down there, and a shout went up when an actual, bona fide dress was discovered fluttering in the wind! The man emigrant was visible. The miners said:

"Fetch her out!"

He said: "It is my wife, gentlemen—she is sick—we have been robbed of money, provisions, everything, by the Indians—we want to rest."

"Fetch her out! We've got to see her!"

"But, gentlemen, the poor thing, she—"

"FETCH HER OUT!"

He "fetched her out," and they swung their hats and sent up three rousing cheers and a tiger; and they crowded around and gazed at her, and touched her dress, and listened to her voice with the look of men who listened to a *memory* rather than a present reality—and then they collected twenty-five hundred dollars in gold and gave it to the man, and swung their hats again and gave three more cheers, and went home satisfied.

Once I dined in San Francisco with the family of a pioneer, and talked with his daughter, a young lady whose first experience in San Francisco was an adventure, though she herself did not remember it, as she was only two or three years old at the time. Her father said that, after landing from the ship, they were walking up the street, a servant leading the party with the little girl in her arms. And presently a huge miner, bearded, belted, spurred, and bristling with deadly weapons—just down from a long campaign in the mountains, evidently—barred the way, stopped the servant, and stood gazing, with a face all alive with gratification and astonishment. Then he said, reverently:

"Well, if it ain't a child!" And then he snatched a little leather sack out of his pocket and said to the servant:

"There's a hundred and fifty dollars in dust, there, and I'll give it to you to let me kiss the child!"

That anecdote is *true*.

But see how things change. Sitting at that dinner-table, listening to that anecdote, if I had offered double the money for the privilege of kissing the same child, I would have been refused. Seventeen added years have far more than doubled the price.

And while upon this subject I will remark that once in Star City, in the Humboldt Mountains, I took my place in a sort of long, post-office single file of miners, to patiently await my chance to peep through a crack in the cabin and get a sight of the splendid new sensation—a genuine, live Woman! And at the end of half of an hour my turn came, and I put my eye to the crack, and there she was, with one arm akimbo, and tossing flap-jacks in a frying-pan with the other. And she was one hundred and sixty-five* years old, and hadn't a tooth in her head.

CHAPTER LVIII

For a few months I enjoyed what to me was an entirely new phase of existence—a butterfly idleness; nothing to do, nobody to be responsible to, and untroubled with financial uneasiness. I fell in love with the most cordial and sociable city in the Union. After the sage-brush and alkali deserts of Washoe, San Francisco was Paradise to me. I lived at the best hotel, exhibited my clothes in the most conspicuous places, infested the opera, and learned to seem enraptured with music which oftener afflicted my ignorant ear than enchanted it, if I had had the vulgar honesty to confess it. However, I suppose I was not greatly worse than the most of my countrymen in that. I had longed to be a butterfly, and I was one at last. I attended private parties in sumptuous evening dress, simpered and aired my graces like a born beau, and polked and schottisched with a step peculiar to myself—and the kangaroo. In a word, I kept the due state of a man worth a hundred thousand dollars (prospectively,) and likely to reach absolute affluence when that silvermine sale should be ultimately achieved in the East. I spent money with a free hand, and meantime watched the stock sales with an interested eye and looked to see what might happen in Nevada.

*Being in calmer mood, now, I voluntarily knock off a hundred from that.—M.T.

Something very important happened. The property holders of Nevada voted against the State Constitution; but the folks who had nothing to lose were in the majority, and carried the measure over their heads. But after all it did not immediately look like a disaster, though unquestionably it was one. I hesitated, calculated the chances, and then concluded not to sell. Stocks went on rising; speculation went mad; bankers, merchants, lawyers, doctors, mechanics, laborers, even the very washerwomen and servant girls, were putting up their earnings on silver stocks, and every sun that rose in the morning went down on paupers enriched and rich men beggared. What a gambling carnival it was! Gould and Curry soared to six thousand three hundred dollars a foot! And then—all of a sudden, out went the bottom and everything and everybody went to ruin and destruction! The wreck was complete. The bubble scarcely left a microscopic moisture behind it. I was an early beggar and a thorough one. My hoarded stocks were not worth the paper they were printed on. I threw them all away. I, the cheerful idiot that had been squandering money like water, and thought myself beyond the reach of misfortune, had not now as much as fifty dollars when I gathered together my various debts and paid them. I removed from the hotel to a very private boarding house. I took a reporter's berth and went to work. I was not entirely broken in spirit, for I was building confidently on the sale of the silver mine in the east. But I could not hear from Dan. My letters miscarried or were not answered.

One day I did not feel vigorous and remained away from the office. The next day I went down toward noon as usual, and found a note on my desk which had been there twenty-four hours. It was signed "Marshall"—the Virginia reporter—and contained a request that I should call at the hotel and see him and a friend or two that night, as they would sail for the east in the morning. A postscript added that their errand was a big mining speculation! I was hardly ever so sick in my life. I abused myself for leaving Virginia and entrusting to another man a matter I ought to have attended to myself; I abused myself for remaining away from the office on the one day of all the year that I should have been there. And thus berating myself I trotted a mile to the steamer wharf and arrived just in time to be too late. The ship was in the stream and under way.

I comforted myself with the thought that may be the speculation would amount to nothing—poor comfort at best—and then went back to my slavery, resolved to put up with my thirty-five dollars a week and forget all about it.

A month afterward I enjoyed my first earthquake. It was one

which was long called the "great" earthquake, and is doubtless so distinguished till this day. It was just after noon, on a bright October day. I was coming down Third street. The only objects in motion anywhere in sight in that thickly built and populous quarter, were a man in a buggy behind me, and a street car wending slowly up the cross street. Otherwise, all was solitude and a Sabbath stillness. As I turned the corner, around a frame house, there was a great rattle and jar, and it occurred to me that here was an item!—no doubt a fight in that house. Before I could turn and seek the door, there came a really terrific shock; the ground seemed to roll under me in waves, interrupted by a violent joggling up and down, and there was a heavy grinding noise as of brick houses rubbing together. I fell up against the frame house and hurt my elbow. I knew what it was, now, and from mere reportorial instinct, nothing else, took out my watch and noted the time of day; at that moment a third and still severer shock came, and as I reeled about on the pavement trying to keep my footing, I saw a sight! The entire front of a tall four-story brick building in Third street sprung outward like a door and fell sprawling across the street, raising a dust like a great volume of smoke! And here came the buggy—overboard went the man, and in less time than I can tell it the vehicle was distributed in small fragments along three hundred yards of street. One could have fancied that somebody had fired a charge of chair-rounds and rags down the thoroughfare. The street car had stopped, the horses were rearing and plunging, the passengers were pouring out at both ends, and one fat man had crashed half way through a glass window on one side of the car, got wedged fast and was squirming and screaming like an impaled madman. Every door, of every house, as far as the eye could reach, was vomiting a stream of human beings; and almost before one could execute a wink and begin another, there was a massed multitude of people stretching in endless procession down every street my position commanded. Never was solemn solitude turned into teeming life quicker.

Of the wonders wrought by "the great earthquake," these were all that came under my eye; but the tricks it did, elsewhere, and far and wide over the town, made toothsome gossip for nine days. The destruction of property was trifling—the injury to it was wide-spread and somewhat serious.

The "curiosities" of the earthquake were simply endless. Gentlemen and ladies who were sick, or were taking a siesta, or had dissipated till a late hour and were making up lost sleep, thronged into the public streets in all sorts of queer apparel, and some without any at all. One woman who had been washing a naked child, ran down the street holding it by the ankles as if it were a dressed turkey. Prominent citizens who were supposed to keep the Sabbath strictly, rushed out of saloons in their shirt-sleeves, with billiard cues in their hands. Dozens of men with necks swathed in napkins, rushed from barber-shops, lathered to the eyes or with one cheek clean shaved and the other still bearing a hairy stubble. Horses broke from stables, and a frightened dog rushed up a short attic ladder and out on to a roof, and when his scare was over had not the nerve to go down again the same way he had gone up. A prominent editor flew down stairs, in the principal hotel, with nothing on but one brief undergarment—met a chambermaid, and exclaimed:

"Oh, what *shall* I do! Where shall I go!"

She responded with naive serenity:

"If you have no choice, you might try a clothing-store!"

A certain foreign consul's lady was the acknowledged leader of fashion, and every time she appeared in anything new or extraordinary, the ladies in the vicinity made a raid on their husbands' purses and arrayed themselves similarly. One man who had suffered considerably and growled accordingly, was standing at the window when the shocks came, and the next instant the consul's wife, just out of the bath, fled by with no other apology for clothing than—a bath-towel! The sufferer rose superior to the terrors of the earthquake, and said to his wife:

"Now *that* is something *like!* Get out your towel my dear!"

The plastering that fell from ceilings in San Francisco that day, would have covered several acres of ground. For some days afterward, groups of eyeing and pointing men stood about many a building, looking at long zig-zag cracks that extended from the eaves to the ground. Four feet of the tops of three chimneys on one house were broken square off and turned around in such a way as to completely stop the draft. A crack a hundred feet long gaped open six inches wide in the middle of one street and then shut together again with such force, as to ridge up the meeting earth like a slender grave. A lady sitting in her rocking and quaking parlor, saw the wall part at the ceiling, open and shut twice, like a mouth, and then-drop the end of a brick on the floor like a tooth. She was a woman easily disgusted with foolishness, and she arose and went out of there. One lady who was coming down stairs was astonished to see a bronze Hercules lean forward on its pedestal as if to strike her with its club. They both reached the bottom of the flight at the same time,—the woman insensible from the fright. Her child, born some little time afterward, was club-footed. However—on second thought,—if the reader sees any coincidence in this, he must do it at his own risk.

The first shock brought down two or three huge organ-pipes in one of the churches. The minister, with uplifted hands, was just closing the services. He glanced up, hesitated, and said:

"However, we will omit the benediction!"—and the next instant there was a vacancy in the atmosphere where he had stood.

After the first shock, an Oakland minister said:

"Keep your seats! There is no better place to die than this"—

And added, after the third:

"But outside is good enough!" He then skipped out at the back door.

Such another destruction of mantel ornaments and toilet bottles as the earthquake created, San Francisco never saw before. There was hardly a girl or a matron in the city but suffered losses of this kind. Suspended pictures were thrown down, but oftener still, by a curious freak of the earthquake's humor, they were whirled completely around with their faces to the wall! There was great difference of opinion, at first, as to the course or direction the earthquake traveled, but water that splashed out of various tanks and buckets settled that. Thousands of people were made so sea-sick by the rolling and pitching of floors and streets that they were weak and bed-ridden for hours, and some few for even days afterward.—Hardly an individual escaped nausea entirely.

The queer earthquake—episodes that formed the staple of San Francisco gossip for the next week would fill a much larger book than this, and so I will diverge from the subject.

By and by, in the due course of things, I picked up a copy of the *Enterprise* one day, and fell under this cruel blow:

NEVADA MINES IN NEW YORK.—G.M. Marshall, Sheba Hurs and Amos H. Rose, who left San Francisco last July for New York City, with ores from mines in Pine Wood District, Humboldt County, and on the Reese River range, have disposed of a mine containing six thousand feet and called the Pine Mountains Consolidated, for the sum of $3,000,000. The stamps on the deed, which is now on its way to Humboldt County, from New York, for record, amounted to $3,000, which is said to be the largest amount of stamps ever placed on one document. A working capital of $1,000,000 has been paid into the treasury, and machinery has already been purchased for a large quartz mill, which will be put up as soon as possible. The stock in this company is all full paid and entirely unassessable. The ores of the mines in this district somewhat resemble those of the Sheba mine in Humboldt. Sheba Hurst, the discoverer of the mines, with his friends corralled all the best leads and all the land and timber they desired before making public their whereabouts. Ores from there, assayed in this city, showed them to be exceedingly rich in silver and gold—silver predominating. There is an abundance of wood and water in the District. We are glad to know that New York capital has been enlisted in the development of the mines of this region. Having seen the ores and assays, we are satisfied that the mines of the District are very valuable—anything but wild-cat.

Once more native imbecility had carried the day, and I had lost a million! It was the "blind lead" over again.

Let us not dwell on this miserable matter. If I were inventing these things, I could be wonderfully humorous over them; but they are too true to be talked of with hearty levity, even at this distant day.* Suffice it that I so lost heart, and so yielded myself up to repinings and sighings and foolish regrets, that I neglected my duties and became about worthless, as a reporter for a brisk newspaper. And at last one of the proprietors took me aside, with a charity I still remember with considerable respect, and gave me an opportunity to resign my berth and so save myself the disgrace of a dismissal.

CHAPTER LIX

For a time I wrote literary screeds for the *Golden Era.* C. H. Webb had established a very excellent literary weekly called the *Californian,* but high merit was no guaranty of success; it languished, and he sold out to three printers, and Bret Harte became editor at $20 a week, and I was employed to contribute an article a week at $12. But the journal still languished, and the printers sold out to Captain Ogden, a rich man and a pleasant gentleman who chose to amuse himself with such an expensive luxury without much caring about the cost of it. When he grew tired of the novelty, he re-sold to the printers, the paper presently died a peaceful death, and I was out of work again. I would not mention these things but for the fact that they so aptly illustrate the ups and downs that characterize life on the Pacific coast. A man could hardly stumble into such a variety of queer vicissitudes in any other country.

*True, and yet not exactly as given in the above figures, possibly. I saw Marshall, months afterward, and although he had plenty of money he did not claim to have captured an entire *million.* In fact I gathered that he had not then received $50,000. Beyond that figure his fortune appeared to consist of uncertain vast expectations rather than prodigious certainties. However, when the above item appeared in print I put full faith in it, and incontinently wilted and went to seed under it.

For two months my sole occupation was avoiding acquaintances; for during that time I did not earn a penny, or buy an article of any kind, or pay my board. I became a very adept at "slinking." I slunk from back street to back street, I slunk away from approaching faces that looked familiar, I slunk to my meals, ate them humbly and with a mute apology for every mouthful I robbed my generous landlady of, and at midnight, after wanderings that were but slinkings away from cheerfulness and light, I slunk to my bed. I felt meaner, and lowlier and more despicable than the worms. During all this time I had but one piece of money—a silver ten cent piece—and I held to it and would not spend it on any account, lest the consciousness coming strong upon me that I was *entirely* penniless, might suggest suicide. I had pawned every thing but the clothes I had on; so I clung to my dime desperately, till it was smooth with handling.

However, I am forgetting. I did have one other occupation beside that of "slinking." It was the entertaining of a collector (and being entertained by him,) who had in his hands the Virginia banker's bill for the forty-six dollars which I had loaned my schoolmate, the "Prodigal." This man used to call regularly once a week and dun me, and sometimes oftener. He did it from sheer force of habit, for he knew he could get nothing. He would get out his bill, calculate the interest for me, at five per cent a month, and show me clearly that there was no attempt at fraud in it and no mistakes; and then plead, and argue and dun with all his might for any sum—any little trifle—even a dollar—even half a dollar, on account. Then his duty was accomplished and his conscience free. He immediately dropped the subject there always; got out a couple of cigars and divided, put his feet in the window, and then we would have a long, luxurious talk about everything and everybody, and he would furnish me a world of curious dunning adventures out of the ample store in his memory. By and by he would clap his hat on his head, shake hands and say briskly:

"Well, business is business—can't stay with you always!"—and was off in a second.

The idea of pining for a dun! And yet I used to long for him to come, and would get as uneasy as any mother if the day went by without his visit, when I was expecting him. But he never collected that bill, at last nor any part of it. I lived to pay it to the banker myself.

Misery loves company. Now and then at night, in out-of-the way, dimly lighted places, I found myself happening on another child of misfortune. He looked so seedy and forlorn, so homeless and friendless and forsaken, that I yearned toward him as a brother. I wanted to claim kinship with him and go about and enjoy our wretchedness together. The drawing toward each other must have been mutual; at any rate we got to falling together oftener, though still seemingly by accident; and although we did not speak or evince any recognition, I think the dull anxiety passed out of both of us when we saw each other, and then for several hours we would idle along contentedly, wide apart, and glancing furtively in at home lights and fireside gatherings, out of the night shadows, and very much enjoying our dumb companionship.

Finally we spoke, and were inseparable after that. For our woes were identical, almost. He had been a reporter too, and lost his berth, and this was his experience, as nearly as I can recollect it. After losing his berth, he had gone down, down, down, with never a halt: from a boarding house on Russian Hill to a boarding house in Kearney street; from thence to Dupont; from thence to a low sailor den; and from thence to lodgings in goods boxes and empty hogsheads near the wharves. Then, for a while, he had gained a meagre living by sewing up bursted sacks of grain on the piers; when that failed he had found food here and there as chance threw it in his way. He had ceased to show his face in daylight, now, for a reporter knows everybody, rich and poor, high and low, and cannot well avoid familiar faces in the broad light of day.

This mendicant Blucher—I call him that for convenience—was a splendid creature. He was full of hope, pluck and philosophy; he was well read and a man of cultivated taste; he had a bright wit and was a master of satire; his kindliness and his generous spirit made him royal in my eyes and changed his curb-stone seat to a throne and his damaged hat to a crown.

He had an adventure, once, which sticks fast in my memory as the most pleasantly grotesque that ever touched my sympathies. He had been without a penny for two months. He had shirked about obscure streets, among friendly dim lights, till the thing had become second nature to him. But at last he was driven abroad in daylight. The cause was sufficient; *he had not tasted food for forty-eight hours,* and he could not endure the misery of his hunger in idle hiding. He came along a back street, glowering at the loaves in bake-shop windows, and feeling that he could trade his life away for a morsel to eat. The sight of the bread doubled his hunger; but it was good to look at it, any how, and imagine what one might do if one only had it. Presently, in the middle of the street he saw a shining spot—looked again—did not, and could not, believe his eyes—turned away, to try them, then looked again. It was a verity—no vain, hunger-inspired delusion—it was a silver dime! He snatched it—gloated over it; doubted it—bit it—found it genuine—choked his heart down, and smothered a halleluiah. Then he looked around—saw that nobody was looking at him—threw the dime down where it was before—walked away a few steps, and approached again, pretending he did not know it was there, so that he could re-enjoy the luxury of finding it. He walked around it, viewing it from different points; then sauntered about with his hands in his pockets, looking up at the signs and now and then glancing at it and feeling the old thrill again. Finally he took it up, and went away, fondling it in his pocket. He idled through unfrequented streets, stopping in doorways and corners to take it out and look at it. By and by he went home to his lodgings—an empty queensware hogshead,—and employed himself till night trying to make up his mind what to buy with it. But it was hard to do. To get the most for it was the idea. He knew that at the Miner's Restaurant he could get a plate of beans and a piece of bread for ten cents; or a fish-ball and some few trifles, but they gave "no bread with one fish-ball" there. At French Pete's he could get a veal cutlet, plain, and some radishes and bread, for ten cents; or a cup of coffee—a pint at least—and a slice of bread; but the slice was not thick enough by the eighth of an inch, and sometimes they were still more criminal than that in the cutting of it. At seven o'clock his hunger was wolfish; and still his mind was not made up. He turned out and went up Merchant street, still ciphering; and chewing a bit of stick, as is the way of starving men. He passed before the lights of Martin's restaurant, the most aristocratic in the city, and stopped. It was a place where he had often dined, in better days, and Martin knew him well. Standing aside, just out of the range of the light, he worshiped the quails and steaks in the show window, and imagined that may be the fairy times were not gone yet and some prince in disguise would come along presently and tell him to go in there and take whatever he wanted. He chewed his stick with a hungry interest as he warmed to his subject. Just at this juncture he was conscious of some one at his side, sure enough; and then a finger touched his arm. He looked up, over his shoulder, and saw an apparition—a very allegory of Hunger! It was a man six feet high, gaunt, unshaven, hung with rags; with a haggard face and sunken cheeks, and eyes that pleaded piteously. This phantom said:

"Come with me—please."

He locked his arm in Blucher's and walked up the street to where the passengers were few and the light not strong, and then facing about, put out his hands in a beseeching way, and said:

"Friend—stranger—look at me! Life is easy to you— you go about, placid and content, as I did once, in my day—you have been in there, and eaten your sumptuous supper, and picked your teeth, and hummed your tune, and thought your pleasant thoughts, and said to yourself it is a good world—but you've never *suffered!* You don't know what trouble is—you don't know what misery is— nor hunger! Look at me! Stranger have pity on a poor friendless, homeless dog! As God is my judge, I have not tasted food for eight and forty hours!—look in my eyes and see if I lie! Give me the least trifle in the world to keep me from starving—anything—twenty-five cents! Do it, stranger—do it, *please.* It will be nothing to you, but life to me. Do it, and I will go down on my knees and lick the dust before you! I will kiss your footprints—I will worship the very ground you walk on! Only twenty-five cents! I am famishing—perishing—starving by inches! For God's sake don't desert me!"

Blucher was bewildered—and touched, too—stirred to the depths. He reflected. Thought again. Then an idea struck him, and he said:

"Come with me."

He took the outcast's arm, walked him down to Martin's restaurant, seated him at a marble table, placed the bill of fare before him, and said:

"Order what you want, friend. Charge it to me, Mr. Martin."

"All right, Mr. Blucher," said Martin.

Then Blucher stepped back and leaned against the counter and watched the man stow away cargo after cargo of buckwheat cakes at seventy-five cents a plate; cup after cup of coffee, and porter house steaks worth two dollars apiece; and when six dollars and a half's worth of destruction had been accomplished, and the stranger's hunger appeased, Blucher went down to French Pete's, bought a veal cutlet plain, a slice of bread, and three radishes, with his dime, and set to and feasted like a king!

Take the episode all around, it was as odd as any that can be culled from the myriad curiosities of Californian life, perhaps.

CHAPTER LX

By and by, an old friend of mine, a miner, came down from one of the decayed mining camps of Tuolumne, California, and I went back with him. We lived in a small cabin on a verdant hillside, and there were not five other cabins in view over the wide expanse of hill and forest. Yet a flourishing city of two or three thousand population had occupied this grassy dead solitude during the flush times of twelve or fifteen years before, and where our cabin stood had once been the heart of the teeming hive, the centre of the city. When the mines gave out the town fell into decay, and in a few years wholly disappeared—streets, dwellings, shops, everything—and left no sign. The grassy slopes were as green and smooth and desolate of life as if they had never been disturbed. The mere handful of miners still remaining, had seen the town spring up, spread, grow and flourish in its pride; and they had seen it sicken and die, and pass away like a dream. With it their hopes had died, and their zest of life. They had long ago resigned themselves to their exile, and ceased to correspond with their distant friends or turn longing eyes toward their early homes. They had accepted banishment, forgotten the world and been forgotten of the world. They were far from telegraphs and railroads, and they stood, as it were, in a living grave, dead to the events that stirred the globe's great populations, dead to the common interests of men, isolated and outcast from brotherhood with their kind. It was the most singular, and almost the most touching and melancholy exile that fancy can imagine.—One of my associates in this locality, for two or three months, was a man who had had a university education; but now for eighteen years he had decayed there by inches, a bearded, rough-clad, clay-stained miner, and at times, among his sighings and soliloquizings, he unconsciously interjected vaguely remembered Latin and Greek sentences—dead and musty tongues, meet vehicles for the thoughts of one whose dreams were all of the past, whose life was a failure; a tired man, burdened with the present, and indifferent to the future; a man without ties, hopes, interests, waiting for rest and the end.

In that one little corner of California is found a species of mining which is seldom or never mentioned in print. It is called "pocket mining" and I am not aware that any of it is done outside of that little corner. The gold is not evenly distributed through the surface dirt, as in ordinary placer mines, but is collected in little spots, and they are very wide apart and exceedingly hard to find, but when you do find one you reap a rich and sudden harvest. There are not now more than twenty pocket miners in that entire little region. I think I know every one of them personally. I have known one of them to hunt patiently about the hill-sides every day for eight months without finding gold enough to make a snuff-box—his grocery bill running up relentlessly all the time—and then find a pocket and take out of it two thousand dollars in two dips of his shovel. I have known him to take out three thousand dollars in two hours, and go and pay up every cent of his indebtedness, then enter on a dazzling spree that finished the last of his treasure before the night was gone. And the next day he bought his groceries on credit as usual, and shouldered his pan and shovel and went off to the hills hunting pockets again happy and content. This is the most fascinating of all the different kinds of mining, and furnishes a very handsome percentage of victims to the lunatic asylum.

Pocket hunting is an ingenious process. You take a spadeful of earth from the hill-side and put it in a large tin pan and dissolve and wash it gradually away till nothing is left but a tea-spoonful of fine sediment. Whatever gold was in that earth has remained, because, being the heaviest, it has sought the bottom. Among the sediment you will find half a dozen yellow particles no larger than pin-heads. You are delighted. You move off to one side and wash another pan. If you find gold again, you move to one side further, and wash a third pan. If you find *no* gold this time, you are delighted again, because you know you are on the right scent. You lay an imaginary plan, shaped like a fan, with its handle up the hill—for just where the end of the handle is, you argue that the rich deposit lies hidden, whose vagrant grains of gold have escaped and been washed down the hill, spreading farther and farther apart as they wandered. And so you proceed up the hill, washing the earth and narrowing your lines every time the absence of gold in the pan shows that you are outside the spread of the fan; and at last, twenty yards up the hill your lines have converged to a point—a single foot from that point you cannot find any gold. Your breath comes short and quick, you are feverish with excitement; the dinner-bell may ring its clapper off, you pay no attention; friends may die, weddings transpire, houses burn down, they are nothing to you; you sweat and dig and delve with a frantic interest—and all at once you strike it! Up comes a spadeful of earth and quartz that is all lovely with soiled lumps and leaves and sprays of gold. Sometimes that one spadeful is all—$500. Sometimes the nest contains $10,000, and it takes you three or four days to get it all out. The pocket-miners tell of one nest that yielded $60,000 and two men exhausted it in two weeks, and then sold the ground for $10,000 to a party who never got $300 out of it afterward.

The hogs are good pocket hunters. All the summer they root around the bushes, and turn up a thousand little piles of dirt, and then the miners long for the rains; for the rains beat upon these little piles and wash them down and expose the gold, possibly right over a pocket. Two pockets were found in this way by the same man in one day. One had $5,000 in it and the other

$8,000. That man could appreciate it, for he hadn't had a cent for about a year.

In Tuolumne lived two miners who used to go to the neighboring village in the afternoon and return every night with household supplies. Part of the distance they traversed a trail, and nearly always sat down to rest on a great boulder that lay beside the path. In the course of thirteen years they had worn that boulder tolerably smooth, sitting on it. By and by two vagrant Mexicans came along and occupied the seat. They began to amuse themselves by chipping off flakes from the boulder with a sledge-hammer. They examined one of these flakes and found it rich with gold. That boulder paid them $800 afterward. But the aggravating circumstance was that these "Greasers" knew that there must be more gold where that boulder came from, and so they went panning up the hill and found what was probably the richest pocket that region has yet produced. It took three months to exhaust it, and it yielded $120,000. The two American miners who used to sit on the boulder are poor yet, and they take turn about in getting up early in the morning to curse those Mexicans—and when it comes down to pure ornamental cursing, the native American is gifted above the sons of men.

I have dwelt at some length upon this matter of pocket mining because it is a subject that is seldom referred to in print, and therefore I judged that it would have for the reader that interest which naturally attaches to novelty.

CHAPTER LXI

One of my comrades there—another of those victims of eighteen years of unrequited toil and blighted hopes—was one of the gentlest spirits that ever bore its patient cross in a weary exile: grave and simple Dick Baker, pocket-miner of Dead-House Gulch.—He was forty-six, gray as a rat, earnest, thoughtful, slenderly educated, slouchily dressed and clay-soiled, but his heart was finer metal than any gold his shovel ever brought to light—than any, indeed, that ever was mined or minted.

Whenever he was out of luck and a little down-hearted, he would fall to mourning over the loss of a wonderful cat he used to own (for where women and children are not, men of kindly impulses take up with pets, for they must love something). And he always spoke of the strange sagacity of that cat with the air of a man who believed in his secret heart that there was something human about it—may be even supernatural.

I heard him talking about this animal once. He said:

"Gentlemen, I used to have a cat here, by the name of Tom Quartz, which you'd a took an interest in I reckon—most any body would. I had him here eight year—and he was the remarkablest cat *I* ever see. He was a large gray one of the Tom specie, an' he had more hard, natchral sense than any man in this camp—'n' a *power* of dignity—he wouldn't let the Gov'ner of Californy be familiar with him. He never ketched a rat in his life—'peared to be above it. He never cared for nothing but mining. He knowed more about mining, that cat did, than any man *I* ever, ever see. You couldn't tell *him* noth'n' 'bout placer diggin's—'n' as for pocket mining, why he was just born for it. He would dig out after me an' Jim when we went over the hills prospect'n', and he would trot along behind us for as much as five mile, if we went so fur. An' he had the best judgment about mining ground—why you never see anything like it. When we went to work, he'd scatter a glance around, 'n' if he didn't think much of the indications, he would give a look as much as to say, 'Well, I'll have to get you to excuse *me*,' 'n' without another word he'd hyste his nose into the air 'n' shove for home. But if the ground suited him, he would lay low 'n' keep dark till the first pan was washed, 'n' then he would sidle up 'n' take a look, an' if there was about six or seven grains of gold *he* was satisfied—he didn't want no better prospect 'n' that—'n' then he would lay down on our coats and snore like a steamboat till we'd struck the pocket, an' then get up 'n' superintend. He was nearly lightnin' on superintending.

"Well, bye an' bye, up comes this yer quartz excitement. Every body was into it—every body was pick'n' 'n' blast'n' instead of shovelin' dirt on the hill side—every body was put'n' down a shaft instead of scrapin' the surface. Noth'n' would do Jim, but *we* must tackle the ledges, too, 'n' so we did. We commenced put'n' down a shaft, 'n' Tom Quartz he begin to wonder what in the Dickens it was all about. *He* hadn't ever seen any mining like that before, 'n' he was all upset, as you may say—he couldn't come to a right understanding of it no way—it was too many for *him*. He was down on it, too, you bet you—he was down on it powerful—'n' always appeared to consider it the cussedest foolishness out. But that cat, you know, was *always* agin new fangled arrangements—somehow he never could abide 'em. *You* know how it is with old habits. But by an' by Tom Quartz begin to git sort of reconciled a little, though he never *could* altogether understand that eternal sinkin' of a shaft an' never pannin' out any thing. At last he got to comin' down in the shaft, hisself, to try to cipher it out. An' when he'd git the blues, 'n' feel kind o' scruffy, 'n' aggravated 'n' disgusted—knowin' as he did, that the bills was runnin' up all the time an' we warn't makin' a cent—he would curl up on a gunny sack in the corner an' go to sleep. Well, one day when the shaft was down about eight foot, the rock got so hard that we had to put in a blast—the first blast'n' we'd ever done since Tom Quartz was born. An' then we lit the fuse 'n' clumb out 'n' got off 'bout fifty yards—'n' forgot 'n' left Tom Quartz sound asleep on the gunny sack. In 'bout a minute we seen a puff of smoke bust up out of the hole, 'n' then everything let go with an awful crash, 'n' about four million ton of rocks 'n' dirt 'n' smoke 'n' splinters shot up 'bout a mile an' a half into the air, an' by George, right in the dead centre of it was old Tom Quartz a goin' end over end, an' a snortin' an' a sneez'n', an' a clawin' an' a reachin' for things like all possessed. But it warn't no use, you know, it warn't no use. An' that was the last we see of *him* for about two minutes 'n' a half, an' then all of a sudden it begin to rain rocks and rubbage, an' directly he come down ker-whop about ten foot off f'm where we stood. Well, I reckon he was p'raps the orneriest lookin' beast you ever see. One ear was sot back on his neck, 'n' his tail was stove up, 'n' his eye-winkers was swinged off, 'n' he was all blacked up with powder an' smoke, an' all sloppy with mud 'n' slush f'm one end to the other. Well sir, it warn't no use to try to apologize—we couldn't say a word. He took a sort of a disgusted look at hisself, 'n' then he looked at us—an' it was just exactly the same as if he had said—'Gents, may be *you* think it's smart to take advantage of a cat that ain't had no experience of quartz minin', but *I* think *different'*—an' then he turned on his heel 'n' marched off home without ever saying another word.

"That was jest his style. An' may be you won't believe it, but after that you never see a cat so prejudiced agin quartz mining as what he was. An' by an' bye when he *did* get to goin' down in the shaft agin, you'd 'a been astonished at his sagacity. The minute we'd tetch off a blast 'n' the fuse'd begin to sizzle, he'd give a look as much as to say: 'Well, I'll have to git you to excuse *me*,' an' it was surpris'n' the way he'd shin out of that hole 'n' go f'r a tree. Sagacity? It ain't no name for it. 'Twas *inspiration!*"

I said, "Well, Mr. Baker, his prejudice against quartz-mining *was* remarkable, considering how he came by it. Couldn't you ever cure him of it?"

"*Cure him!* No! When Tom Quartz was sot once, he was *always* sot—and you might a blowed him up as much as three million times 'n' you'd never a broken him of his cussed prejudice agin quartz mining."

The affection and the pride that lit up Baker's face when he delivered this tribute to the firmness of his humble friend of other days, will always be a vivid memory with me.

At the end of two months we had never "struck" a pocket. We had panned up and down the hillsides till they looked plowed like a field; we could have put in a crop of grain, then, but there would have been no way to get it to market. We got many good "prospects," but when the gold gave out in the pan and we dug down, hoping and longing, we found only emptiness—the pocket that should have been there was as barren as our own.— At last we shouldered our pans and shovels and struck out over the hills to try new localities. We prospected around Angel's Camp, in Calaveras county, during three weeks, but had no success. Then we wandered on foot among the mountains, sleeping under the trees at night, for the weather was mild, but still we remained as centless as the last rose of summer. That is a poor joke, but it is in pathetic harmony with the circumstances, since we were so poor ourselves. In accordance with the custom of the country, our door had always stood open and our board welcome to tramping miners—they drifted along nearly every day, dumped their paust shovels by the threshold and took "pot luck" with us—and now on our own tramp we never found cold hospitality.

Our wanderings were wide and in many directions; and now I could give the reader a vivid description of the Big Trees and the marvels of the Yo Semite—but what has this reader done to me that I should persecute him? I will deliver him into the hands of less conscientious tourists and take his blessing. Let me be charitable, though I fail in all virtues else.

Some of the phrases in the above are mining technicalities, purely, and may be a little obscure to the general reader. In "*placer diggings*" the gold is scattered all through the surface dirt; in "*pocket*" diggings it is concentrated in one little spot; in "*quartz*" the gold is in a solid, continuous vein of rock, enclosed between distinct walls of some other kind of stone—and this is the most laborious and expensive of all the different kinds of mining. "*Prospecting*" is hunting for a "*placer*"; "*indications*" are signs of its presence; "*panning out*" refers to the washing process by which the grains of gold are separated from the dirt; a "*prospect*" is what one finds in the first panful of dirt—and its value determines whether it is a good or a bad prospect, and whether it is worth while to tarry there or seek further.

CHAPTER LXII

After a three months' absence, I found myself in San Francisco again, without a cent. When my credit was about exhausted, (for I had become too mean and lazy, now, to work on a morning paper, and there were no vacancies on the evening journals,) I was created San Francisco correspondent of the *Enterprise*, and at the end of five months I was out of debt, but my interest in my work was gone; for my correspondence being a daily one, without rest or respite, I got unspeakably tired of it. I wanted another change. The vagabond interest was strong upon me. Fortune favored and I got a new berth and a delightful one. It was to go down to the Sandwich Islands and write some letters for the Sacramento *Union*, an excellent journal and liberal with employés.

We sailed in the propeller *Ajax*, in the middle of winter. The almanac called it winter, distinctly enough, but the weather was a compromise between spring and summer. Six days out of port, it became summer altogether. We had some thirty passengers; among them a cheerful soul by the name of Williams, and three sea-worn old whaleship captains going down to join their vessels. These latter played euchre in the smoking room day and night, drank astonishing quantities of raw whisky without being in the least affected by it, and were the happiest people I think I ever saw. And then there was "the old Admiral—" a retired whaleman. He was a roaring, terrific combination of wind and lightning and thunder, and earnest, whole-souled profanity. But nevertheless he was tender-hearted as a girl. He was a raving, deafening, devastating typhoon, laying waste the cowering seas but with an unvexed refuge in the centre where all comers were safe and at rest. Nobody could know the "Admiral" without liking him; and in a sudden and dire emergency I think no friend of his would know which to choose—to be cursed by him or prayed for by a less efficient person.

His title of "Admiral" was more strictly "official" than any ever worn by a naval officer before or since, perhaps—for it was the voluntary offering of a whole nation, and came direct from the *people* themselves without any intermediate red tape—the people of the Sandwich Islands. It was a title that came to him freighted with affection, and honor, and appreciation of his unpretending merit. And in testimony of the genuineness of the title it was publicly ordained that an exclusive flag should be devised for him and used solely to welcome his coming and wave him God-speed in his going. From that time forth, whenever his ship was signaled in the offing, or he catted his anchor and stood out to sea, that ensign streamed from the royal halliards on the parliament house and the nation lifted their hats to it with spontaneous accord.

Yet he had never fired a gun or fought a battle in his life. When I knew him on board the *Ajax*, he was seventy-two years old and had plowed the salt water sixty-one of them. For sixteen years he had gone in and out of the harbor of Honolulu in command of a whaleship, and for sixteen more had been captain of a San Francisco and Sandwich Island passenger packet and had never had an accident or lost a vessel. The simple natives knew him for a friend who never failed them, and regarded him as children regard a father. It was a dangerous thing to oppress them when the roaring Admiral was around.

Two years before I knew the Admiral, he had retired from the sea on a competence, and had sworn a colossal nine-jointed oath that he would "never go within *smelling* distance of the salt water again as long as he lived." And he had conscientiously kept it. That is to say, *he* considered he had kept it, and it would have been more than dangerous to suggest to him, even in the gentlest way, that making eleven long sea voyages, as a passenger, during the two years that had transpired since he "retired," was only keeping the general spirit of it and not the strict letter.

The Admiral knew only one narrow line of conduct to pursue in any and all cases where there was a fight, and that was to shoulder his way straight in without an inquiry as to the rights or the merits of it, and take the part of the weaker side.—And this was the reason why he was always sure to be present at the trial of any universally execrated criminal to oppress and intimidate the jury with a vindictive pantomime of what he would do to them if he ever caught them out of the box. And this was why harried cats and outlawed dogs that knew him confidently took sanctuary under his chair in time of trouble. In the beginning he was the most frantic and bloodthirsty Union man that drew breath in the shadow of the Flag; but the instant the Southerners began to go down before the sweep of the Northern armies, he ran up the Confederate colors and from that time till the end was a rampant and inexorable secessionist.

He hated intemperance with a more uncompromising animosity than any individual I have ever met, of either sex; and he was never tired of storming against it and beseeching friends and strangers alike to be wary and drink with moderation. And yet if any creature had been guileless enough to intimate that his absorbing nine gallons of "straight" whisky during our voyage was any fraction short of rigid or inflexible abstemiousness, in that self-same moment the old man would have spun him to the uttermost parts of the earth in the whirlwind of his wrath. Mind, I am not saying his whisky ever affected his head or his legs, for it did not, in even the slightest degree. He was a capacious container, but he did not hold enough for that. He took a level tumblerful of whisky every morning before he put his clothes on—"to sweeten his bilgewater," he said.—He took another after he got the most of his clothes on, "to settle his mind and give him clean bearings." He then shaved, and put on a clean shirt; after which he recited the Lord's Prayer in a fervent, thundering bass that shook the ship to her kelson and suspended all conversation in the main cabin. Then, at this stage, being invariably "by the head," or "by the stern," or "listed to port or starboard," he took one more to "put him on an even keel so that he would mind his hellum and not miss stays and go about, every time he came up in the wind."—And now, his state-room door swung open and the sun of his benignant face beamed redly out upon men and women and children, and he roared his "Shipmets a'hoy!" in a way that was calculated to wake the dead and precipitate the final resurrection; and forth he strode, a picture to look at and a presence to enforce attention. Stalwart and portly; not a gray hair; broad-brimmed slouch hat; semi-sailor toggery of blue navy flannel—roomy and ample; a stately expanse of shirt-front and a liberal amount of black silk neck-cloth tied with a sailor knot; large chain and imposing seals impending from his fob; awe-inspiring feet, and "a hand like the hand of Providence," as his whaling brethren expressed it; wrist-bands and sleeves pushed back half way to the elbow, out of respect for the warm weather, and exposing hairy arms, gaudy with red and blue anchors, ships, and goddesses of liberty tattooed in India ink. But these details were only secondary matters—his face was the lodestone that chained the eye. It was a sultry disk, glowing determinedly out through a weather beaten mask of mahogany, and studded with warts, seamed with scars, "blazed" all over with unfailing fresh slips of the razor; and with cheery eyes, under shaggy brows, contemplating the world from over the back of a gnarled crag of a nose that loomed vast and lonely out of the undulating immensity that spread away from its foundations. At his heels frisked the darling of his bachelor estate, his terrier "Fan," a creature no larger than a squirrel. The main part of his daily life was occupied in looking after "Fan," in a motherly way, and doctoring her for a hundred ailments which existed only in his imagination.

The Admiral seldom read newspapers; and when he did he never believed anything they said. He read nothing, and believed in nothing, but "The Old Guard," a secession periodical published in New York. He carried a dozen copies of it with him, always, and referred to them for all required information. If it was not there, he supplied it himself, out of a bountiful fancy, inventing history, names, dates, and every thing else necessary to make his point good in an argument. Consequently he was a formidable antagonist in a dispute. Whenever he swung clear of the record and began to create history, the enemy was helpless and had to surrender. Indeed, the enemy could not keep from betraying some little spark of indignation at his manufactured history—and when it came to indignation, that was the Admiral's very "best hold." He was always ready for a political argument, and if nobody started one he would do it himself. With his third retort his temper would begin to rise, and within five minutes he would be blowing a gale, and within fifteen his smoking-room audience would be utterly stormed away and the old man left solitary and alone, banging the table with his fist, kicking the chairs, and roaring a hurricane of profanity. It got so, after a while, that whenever the Admiral approached, with politics in his eye, the passengers would drop out with quiet accord, afraid to meet him; and he would camp on a deserted field.

But he found his match at last, and before a full company. At one time or another, everybody had entered the lists against him and been routed, except the quiet passenger Williams. He had never been able to get an expression of opinion out of him on politics. But now, just as the Admiral drew near the door and the company were about to slip out, Williams said:

"Admiral, are you *certain* about that circumstance concerning the clergymen you mentioned the other day?"—referring to a piece of the Admiral's manufactured history.

Every one was amazed at the man's rashness. The idea of deliberately inviting annihilation was a thing incomprehensible. The retreat came to a halt; then everybody sat down again wondering, to await the upshot of it. The Admiral himself was as surprised as any one. He paused in the door, with his red handkerchief half raised to his sweating face, and contemplated the daring reptile in the corner.

"*Certain* of it? Am I *certain* of it? Do you think I've been lying about it? What do you take me for? Anybody that don't know that circumstance, don't know anything; a child ought to know it. Read up your history! Read it up —— —— —— ——, and don't come asking a man if he's *certain* about a bit of A B C stuff that the very southern niggers know all about."

Here the Admiral's fires began to wax hot, the atmosphere thickened, the coming earthquake rumbled, he began to thunder and lighten. Within three minutes his volcano was in full irruption and he was discharging flames and ashes of indignation, belching black volumes of foul history aloft, and vomiting red-hot torrents of profanity from his crater. Meantime Williams sat silent, and apparently deeply and earnestly interested in what the old man was saying. By and by, when the lull came, he said in the most deferential way, and with the gratified air of a man who has had a mystery cleared up which had been puzzling him uncomfortably:

"*Now* I understand it. I always thought I knew that piece of history well enough, but was still afraid to trust it, because there was not that convincing particularity about it that one likes to have in history; but when you mentioned every name, the other day, and every date, and every little circumstance, in their just order and sequence, I said to myself, *this* sounds something like—*this* is history—*this* is putting it in a shape that gives a man confidence; and I said to myself afterward, I will just ask the Admiral if he is perfectly certain about the details, and if he is I will come out and thank him for clearing this matter up for me. And that is what I want to do now—for until you set that matter right it was nothing but just a confusion in my mind, without head or tail to it."

Nobody ever saw the Admiral look so mollified before, and so pleased. Nobody had ever received his bogus history as gospel before; its genuineness had always been called in question either by words or looks; but here was a man that not only swallowed it all down, but was grateful for the dose. He was taken a back; he hardly knew what to say; even his profanity failed him. Now, Williams continued, modestly and earnestly:

"But Admiral, in saying that this was the first stone thrown, and that this precipitated the war, you have overlooked a circumstance which you are perfectly familiar with, but which has escaped your memory. Now I grant you that what you have stated is correct in every detail—to wit: that on the 16th of October, 1860, two Massachusetts clergymen, named Waite and Granger, went in disguise to the house of John Moody, in Rockport, at dead of night, and dragged forth two southern women and their two little children, and after tarring and feathering them conveyed them to Boston and burned them alive in the State House square; and I also grant your proposition that this deed is what led to the secession of South Carolina on the 20th of December following. Very well." [Here the company were pleasantly surprised to hear Williams proceed to come back at the Admiral with his own invincible weapon—clean, pure, *manufactured history*, without a word of truth in it.] "Very well, I say. But Admiral, why overlook the Willis and Morgan case in South Carolina? You are too well informed a man not to know all about that circumstance. Your arguments and your conversations have shown you to be intimately conversant with every detail of this national quarrel. You develop matters of history every day that show plainly that you are no smatterer in it, content to nibble about the surface, but a man who has searched the depths and possessed yourself of everything that has a bearing upon the great question. Therefore, let me just recall to your mind that Willis and Morgan case—though I see by your face that the whole thing is already passing through your memory at this moment. On the 12th of August, 1860, *two months* before the Waite and Granger affair, two South Carolina clergymen, named John H. Morgan and Winthrop L. Willis, one a Methodist and the other an Old School Baptist, disguised themselves, and went at midnight to the house of a planter named Thompson—Archibald F. Thompson, Vice President under Thomas Jefferson,—and took thence, at midnight, his widowed aunt, (a Northern woman,) and her adopted child, an orphan named Mortimer Hughie, afflicted with epilepsy and suffering at the time from white swelling on one of his legs, and compelled to walk on crutches in consequence; and the two ministers, in spite of the pleadings of the victims, dragged them to the bush, tarred and feathered them, and afterward burned them at the stake in the city of Charleston. You remember perfectly well what a stir it made; you remember perfectly well that even the Charleston *Courier* stigmatized the act as being unpleasant, of questionable propriety, and scarcely justifiable, and likewise that it would not be a matter of surprise if retaliation ensued. And you remember also, that this thing was the *cause* of the Massachusetts outrage. Who, indeed, were the two Massachusetts ministers? and who were the two Southern women they burned? I do not need to remind *you*, Admiral, with your intimate knowledge of history; that Waite was the nephew of the woman burned in Charleston; the Granger was her cousin in the second degree, and that the woman they burned in Boston was the wife of John H. Morgan, and the still loved but divorced wife of Winthrop L. Willis. Now, Admiral, it is only fair that you should acknowledge that the first provocation came from the Southern preachers and that the Northern ones were justified in retaliating. In your arguments you never yet have shown the least disposition to withhold a just verdict or be in anywise unfair, when authoritative history condemned your position, and therefore I have no hesitation in asking you to take the original blame from the Massachusetts ministers, in this matter, and transfer it to the South Carolina clergymen where it justly belongs."

The Admiral was conquered. This sweet spoken creature who swallowed his fraudulent history as if it were the bread of life; basked in his furious blasphemy as if it were generous sunshine; found only calm, even-handed justice in his rampart partisanship; and flooded him with invented history so sugar-coated with flattery and deference that there was no rejecting it, was "too many" for him. He stammered some awkward, profane sentences about the —— —— —— —— Willis and Morgan business having escaped his memory, but that he "remembered it now," and then, under pretence of giving Fan some medicine for an imaginary cough, drew out of the battle and went away, a vanquished man. Then cheers and laughter went up, and Williams, the ship's benefactor was a hero. The news went about the vessel, champagne was ordered, an enthusiastic reception instituted in the smoking room, and everybody flocked thither to shake hands with the conqueror. The wheelsman said afterward, that the Admiral stood up behind the pilot house and "ripped and cursed all to himself" till he loosened the smokestack guys and becalmed the mainsail.

The Admiral's power was broken. After that, if he began an argument, somebody would bring Williams, and the old man would grow weak and begin to quiet down at once. And as soon as he was done, Williams in his dulcet, insinuating way, would invent some history (referring for proof, to the old man's own excellent memory and to copies of "The Old Guard" known not to be in his possession) that would turn the tables completely and leave the Admiral all abroad and helpless. By and by he came to so dread Williams and his gilded tongue that he would stop talking when he saw him approach, and finally ceased to mention politics altogether, and from that time forward there was entire peace and serenity in the ship.

CHAPTER LXIII

On a certain bright morning the Islands hove in sight, lying low on the lonely sea, and everybody climbed to the upper deck to look. After two thousand miles of watery solitude the vision was a welcome one. As we approached, the imposing promontory of Diamond Head rose up out of the ocean its rugged front softened by the hazy distance, and presently the details of the land began to make themselves manifest: first the line of beach; then the plumed coacoanut trees of the tropics; then cabins of the natives; then the white town of Honolulu, said to contain between twelve and fifteen thousand inhabitants spread over a dead level; with streets from twenty to thirty feet wide, solid and level as a floor, most of them straight as a line and few as crooked as a corkscrew.

The further I traveled through the town the better I liked it. Every step revealed a new contrast—disclosed something I was unaccustomed to. In place of the grand mud-colored brown fronts of San Francisco, I saw dwellings built of straw, adobies, and cream-colored pebble-and-shell-conglomerated coral, cut into oblong blocks and laid in cement; also a great number of neat white cottages, with green window-shutters; in place of front yards like billiard-tables with iron fences around them, I saw these homes surrounded by ample yards, thickly clad with green grass, and shaded by tall trees, through whose dense foliage the sun could scarcely penetrate; in place of the customary geranium, calla lily, etc., languishing in dust and general debility, I saw luxurious banks and thickets of flowers, fresh as a meadow after a rain, and glowing with the richest dyes; in place of the dingy horrors of San Francisco's pleasure grove, the "Willows," I saw huge-bodied, wide-spreading forest trees, with strange names and stranger appearance—trees that cast a shadow like a thundercloud, and were able to stand alone without being tied to green poles; in place of gold fish, wiggling around in glass globes, assuming countless shades and degrees of distortion through the magnifying and diminishing qualities of their transparent prison houses, I saw cats—Tom-cats, Mary Ann cats, long-tailed cats, bob-tailed cats, blind cats, one-eyed cats, wall-eyed cats, cross-eyed cats, gray cats, black cats, white cats, yellow cats, striped cats, spotted cats, tame cats, wild cats, singed cats, individual cats, groups of cats, platoons of cats, companies of cats, regiments of cats, armies of cats, multitudes of cats, millions of cats, and all of them sleek, fat, lazy and sound asleep.

I looked on a multitude of people, some white, in white coats, vests, pantaloons, even white cloth shoes, made snowy with chalk duly laid on every morning; but the majority of the people were almost as dark as negroes—women with comely features, fine black eyes, rounded forms, inclining to the voluptuous, clad in a single bright red or white garment that fell free and unconfined from shoulder to heel, long black hair falling loose, gypsy hats, encircled with wreaths of natural flowers of a brilliant carmine tint; plenty of dark men in various costumes, and some with nothing on but a battered stove-pipe hat tilted on the nose, and a very scant breech-clout;—certain smoke-dried children were clothed in nothing but sunshine—a very neat fitting and picturesque apparel indeed.

In place of roughs and rowdies staring and blackguarding on the corners, I saw long-haired, saddle-colored Sandwich Island maidens sitting on the ground in the shade of corner houses, gazing indolently at whatever or whoever happened along; instead of wretched cobble-stone pavements, I walked on a firm foundation of coral, built up from the bottom of the sea by the absurd but persevering insect of that name, with a light layer of lava and cinders overlying the coral, belched up out of fathomless perdition long ago through the seared and blackened crater that stands dead and harmless in the distance now; instead of cramped and crowded street-cars, I met dusky native women sweeping by, free as the wind, on fleet horses and astride, with gaudy riding-sashes, streaming like banners behind them; instead of the combined stenches of Chinadom and Brannan street slaughter-houses, I breathed the balmy fragrance of jesamine, oleander, and the Pride of India; in place of the hurry and bustle and noisy confusion of San Francisco, I moved in the midst of a Summer calm as tranquil as dawn in the Garden of Eden; in place of the Golden City's skirting sand hills and the placid bay, I saw on the one side a frame-work of tall, precipitous mountains close at hand, clad in refreshing green, and cleft by deep, cool, chasm-like valleys—and in front the grand sweep of the ocean: a brilliant, transparent green near the shore, bound and bordered by a long white line of foamy spray dashing against the reef, and further out the dead blue water of the deep sea, flecked with "white caps," and in the far horizon a single, lonely sail—a mere accent-mark to emphasize a slumberous calm and a solitude that were without sound or limit. When the sun sunk down—the one intruder from other realms and persistent in suggestions of them—it was tranced luxury to sit in the perfumed air and forget that there was any world but these enchanted islands.

It was such ecstacy to dream, and dream—till you got a bite. A scorpion bite. Then the first duty was to get up out of the grass and kill the scorpion; and the next to bathe the bitten place with alcohol or brandy; and the next to resolve to keep out of the grass in future. Then came an adjournment to the bed-chamber and the pastime of writing up the day's journal with one hand and the destruction of mosquitoes with the other—a whole community of them at a slap. Then, observing an enemy approaching—a hairy tarantula on stilts—why not set the spitoon on him? It is done, and the projecting ends of his paws give a luminous idea of the magnitude of his reach. Then to bed and become a promenade for a centipede with forty-two legs and every foot hot enough to burn a hole through a raw-hide. More soaking with alcohol, and a resolution to examine the bed before entering it, in future. Then wait, and suffer, till all the mosquitoes in the neighborhood have crawled in under the bar, then slip out quickly, shut them in and sleep peacefully on the floor till morning. Meantime it is comforting to curse the tropics in occasional wakeful intervals.

We had an abundance of fruit in Honolulu, of course. Oranges, pine-apples, bananas, strawberries, lemons, limes, mangoes, guavas, melons, and a rare and curious luxury called the chirimoya, which is deliciousness itself. Then there is the tamarind. I thought tamarinds were made to eat, but that was probably not the idea. I ate several, and it seemed to me that they were rather sour that year. They pursed up my lips, till they resembled the stem-end of a tomato, and I had to take my sustenance through a quill for twenty-four hours. They sharpened my teeth till I could have shaved with them, and gave them a "wire edge" that I was afraid would stay; but a citizen said "no, it will come off when the enamel does"—which was comforting, at any rate. I found, afterward, that only strangers eat tamarinds—but they only eat them once.

CHAPTER LXIV

In my diary of our third day in Honolulu, I find this:

I am probably the most sensitive man in Hawaii to-night—especially about sitting down in the presence of my betters. I have ridden fifteen or twenty miles on horseback since 5 P.M. and to tell the honest truth, I have a delicacy about sitting down at all.

An excursion to Diamond Head and the King's Coacoanut Grove was planned to-day—time, 4:30 P.M.—the party to consist of half a dozen gentlemen and three ladies. They all started at the appointed hour except myself. I was at the Government prison, (with Captain Fish and another whaleship-skipper, Captain Phillips,) and got so interested in its examination that I did not notice how quickly the time was passing. Somebody remarked that it was twenty minutes past five o'clock, and that woke me up. It was a fortunate circumstance that Captain Phillips was along with his "turn out," as he calls a top-buggy that Captain Cook brought here in 1778, and a horse that was here when Captain Cook came. Captain Phillips takes a just pride in his driving and in the speed of his horse, and to his passion for displaying them I owe it that we were only sixteen minutes coming from the prison to the American Hotel—a distance which has been estimated to be over half a mile. But it took some fearful driving. The Captain's whip came down fast, and the blows started so much dust out of the horse's hide that during the last half of the journey we rode through an impenetrable fog, and ran by a pocket compass in the hands of Captain Fish, a whaler of twenty-six years experience, who sat there through the perilous voyage as self-possessed as if he had been on the euchre-deck of his own ship, and calmly said, "Port your helm—port," from time to time, and "Hold her a little free—steady—so-o," and "Luff—hard down to starboard!" and never once lost his presence of mind or betrayed the least anxiety by voice or manner. When we came to anchor at last, and Captain Phillips looked at his watch and said, "Sixteen minutes—I told you it was in her! that's over three miles an hour!" I could see he felt entitled to a compliment, and so I said I had never seen lightning go like that horse. And I never had.

The landlord of the American said the party had been gone nearly an hour, but that he could give me my choice of several horses that could overtake them. I said, never mind—I preferred a safe horse to a fast one—I would like to have an excessively gentle horse—a horse with no spirit whatever—a lame one, if he had such a thing. Inside of five minutes I was mounted, and perfectly satisfied with my outfit. I had no time to label him "This is a horse," and so if the public took him for a sheep I cannot help it. I was satisfied, and that was the main thing. I could see that he had as many fine points as any man's horse, and so I hung my hat on one of them, behind the saddle, and swabbed the perspiration from my face and started. I named him after this island, "Oahu" (pronounced O-waw-hee). The first gate he came to he started in; I had neither whip nor spur, and so I simply argued the case with him. He resisted argument, but ultimately yielded to insult and abuse. He backed out of that gate and steered for another one on the other side of the street. I triumphed by my former process. Within the next six hundred yards he crossed the street fourteen times and attempted thirteen gates, and in the meantime the tropical sun was beating down and threatening to cave the top of my head in, and I was literally dripping with perspiration. He abandoned the gate business after that and went along peaceably enough, but absorbed in meditation. I noticed this latter circumstance, and it soon began to fill me with apprehension. I said to myself, this creature is planning some new outrage, some fresh deviltry or other—no horse ever thought over a subject so profoundly as this one is doing just for nothing. The more this thing preyed upon my mind the more uneasy I became, until the suspense became almost unbearable and I dismounted to see if there was anything wild in his eye—for I had heard that the eye of this noblest of our domestic animals is very expressive. I cannot describe what a load of anxiety was lifted from my mind when I found that he was only asleep. I woke him up and started him into a faster walk, and then the villainy of his nature came out again. He tried to climb over a stone wall, five or six feet high. I saw that I must apply force to this horse, and that I might as well begin first as last. I plucked a stout switch from a tamarind tree, and the moment he saw it, he surrendered. He broke into a convulsive sort of a canter, which had three short steps in it and one long one, and reminded me alternately of the clattering shake of the great earthquake, and the sweeping plunging of the Ajax in a storm.

And now there can be no fitter occasion than the present to pronounce a left-handed blessing upon the man who invented the American saddle. There is no seat to speak of about it— one might as well sit in a shovel—and the stirrups are nothing but an ornamental nuisance. If I were to write down here all the abuse I expended on those stirrups, it would make a large book, even without pictures. Sometimes I got one foot so far through, that he stirrup partook of the nature of an anklet; sometimes both feet were through, and I was handcuffed by the legs; and sometimes my feet got clear out and left the stirrups wildly dangling about my shins. Even when I was in proper position and carefully balanced upon the balls of my feet, there was no comfort in it, on account of my nervous dread that they were going to slip one way or the other in a moment. But the subject is too exasperating to write about.

A mile and a half from town, I came to a grove of tall cocoanut trees, with clean, branchless stems reaching straight up sixty or seventy feet and topped with a spray of green foliage sheltering clusters of cocoa-nuts—not more picturesque than a forest of collossal ragged parasols, with bunches of magnified grapes under them, would be. I once heard a grouty northern invalid say that a cocoanut tree might be poetical, possibly it was; but it looked like a feather-duster struck by lightning. I think that describes it better than a picture—and yet, without any question, there is something fascinating about a cocoa-nut tree—and graceful, too.

About a dozen cottages, some frame and the others of native grass, nestled sleepily in the shade here and there. The grass cabins are of a grayish color, are shaped much like our own cottages, only with higher and steeper roofs usually, and are made of some kind of weed strongly bound together in bundles. The roofs are very thick, and so are the walls; the latter have square holes in them for windows. At a little distance these cabins have a furry appearance, as if they might be made of bear skins. They are very cool and pleasant inside. The King's flag was flying from the roof of one of the cottages, and His Majesty was probably within. He owns the whole concern thereabouts, and passes his time there frequently, on sultry days "laying off." The spot is called "The King's Grove."

Near by is an interesting ruin—the meagre remains of an ancient heathen temple—a place where human sacrifices were offered up in those old bygone days when the simple child of nature, yielding momentarily to sin when sorely tempted, acknowledged his error when calm reflection had shown it him, and came forward with noble frankness and offered up his grandmother as an atoning sacrifice—in those old days when the luckless sinner could keep on cleansing his conscience and achieving periodical happiness as long as his relations held out; long, long before the missionaries braved a thousand privations to come and make them permanently miserable by telling them how beautiful and how blissful a place heaven is, and how nearly impossible it is to get there; and showed the poor native how dreary a place perdition is and what unnecessarily liberal facilities there are for going to it; showed him how, in his ignorance he had gone and fooled away all his kinfolks to no purpose; showed him what rapture it is to work all day long for fifty cents to buy food for next day with, as compared with fishing for pastime and lolling in the shade through eternal Summer, and eating of the bounty that nobody labored to provide but Nature. How sad it is to think of the multitudes who have gone to their graves in this beautiful island and never knew there was a hell!

This ancient temple was built of rough blocks of lava, and was simply a roofless inclosure a hundred and thirty feet long and seventy feet wide—nothing but naked walls, very thick, but not much higher than a man's head. They will last for ages no doubt, if left unmolested. Its three altars and other sacred appurtenances have crumbled and passed away years ago. It is said that in the old times thousands of human beings were slaughtered here, in the presence of naked and howling savages. If these mute stones could speak, what tales they could tell, what pictures they could describe, of fettered victims writhing under the knife; of massed forms straining forward out of the gloom, with ferocious faces lit up by the sacrificial fires; of the background of ghostly trees; of the dark pyramid of Diamond Head standing sentinel over the uncanny scene, and the peaceful moon looking down upon it through rifts in the cloud-rack!

When Kamehameha (pronounced Ka-may-ha-may-ah) the Great—who was a sort of a Napoleon in military genius and uniform success—invaded this island of Oahu three quarters of a century ago, and exterminated the army sent to oppose him, and took full and final possession of the country, he searched out the dead body of the King of Oahu, and those of the principal chiefs, and impaled their heads on the walls of this temple.

Those were savage times when this old slaughter-house was in its prime. The King and the chiefs ruled the common herd with a rod of iron; made them gather all the provisions the masters needed; build all the houses and temples; stand all the expenses of whatever kind; take kicks and cuffs for thanks; drag out lives well flavored with misery, and then suffer deatfences or yield up their lives on the sacrificial altars to purchase favors from the gods for their hard rulers. The missionaries have clothed them, educated them, broken up the tyrannous authority of their chiefs, and given them freedom and the right to enjoy whatever their hands and brains produce with equal laws for all, and punishment for all alike who transgress them. The contrast is so strong—the benefit conferred upon this people by the missionaries is so prominent, so palpable and so unquestionable, that the frankest compliment I can pay them, and the best, is simply to point to the condition of the Sandwich Islanders of Captain Cook's time, and their condition to-day. Their work speaks for itself.

CHAPTER LXV

By and by, after a rugged climb, we halted on the summit of a hill which commanded a far-reaching view. The moon rose and flooded mountain and valley and ocean with a mellow radiance, and out of the shadows of the foliage the distant lights of Honolulu glinted like an encampment of fireflies. The air was heavy with the fragrance of flowers. The halt was brief.—Gayly laughing and talking, the party galloped on, and I clung to the pommel and cantered after. Presently we came to a place where no grass grew—a wide expanse of deep sand. They said it was an old battle ground. All around everywhere, not three feet apart, the bleached bones of men gleamed white in the moonlight. We picked up a lot of them for mementoes. I got quite a number of arm bones and leg bones—of great chiefs, may be, who had fought savagely in that fearful battle in the old days, when blood flowed like wine where we now stood.—and wore the choicest of them out on Oahu afterward, trying to make him go. All sorts of bones could be found except skulls; but a citizen said, irreverently, that there had been an unusual number of "skull-hunters" there lately—a species of sportsmen I had never heard of before.

Nothing whatever is known about this place—its story is a secret that will never be revealed. The oldest natives make no pretense of being possessed of its history. They say these bones were here when they were children. They were here when their grandfathers were children—but how they came here, they can only conjecture. Many people believe this spot to be an ancient battle-ground, and it is usual to call it so; and they believe that these skeletons have lain for ages just where their proprietors fell in the great fight. Other people believe that Kamehameha I. fought his first battle here. On this point, I have heard a story, which may have been taken from one of the numerous books which have been written concerning these islands—I do not know where the narrator got it. He said that when Kamehameha (who was at first merely a subordinate chief on the island of Hawaii), landed here, he brought a large army with him, and encamped at Waikiki. The Oahuans marched against him, and so confident were they of success that they readily acceded to a demand of their priests that they should draw a line where these bones now lie, and take an oath that, if forced to retreat at all, they would never retreat beyond this boundary. The priests told them that death and everlasting punishment would overtake any who violated the oath, and the march was resumed. Kamehameha drove them back step by step; the priests fought in the front rank and exhorted them both by voice and inspiriting example to remember their oath—to die, if need be, but never cross the fatal line. The struggle was manfully maintained, but at last the chief priest fell, pierced to the heart with a spear, and the unlucky omen fell like a blight upon the brave souls at his back; with a triumphant shout the invaders pressed forward—the line was crossed—the offended gods deserted the despairing army, and, accepting the doom their perjury had brought upon them, they broke and fled over the plain where Honolulu stands now—up the beautiful Nuuanu Valley—paused a moment, hemmed in by precipitous mountains on either hand and the frightful precipice of the Pari in front, and then were driven over—a sheer plunge of six hundred feet!

The story is pretty enough, but Mr. Jarves' excellent history says the Oahuans were intrenched in Nuuanu Valley; that Kamehameha ousted them, routed them, pursued them up the valley and drove them over the precipice. He makes no mention of our bone-yard at all in his book.

Impressed by the profound silence and repose that rested over the beautiful landscape, and being, as usual, in the rear, I gave voice to my thoughts. I said:

"What a picture is here slumbering in the solemn glory of the moon! How strong the rugged outlines of the dead volcano stand out against the clear sky! What a snowy fringe marks the bursting of the surf over the long, curved reef! How calmly the dim city sleeps yonder in the plain! How soft the shadows lie upon the stately mountains that border the dream-haunted Mauoa Valley! What a grand pyramid of billowy clouds towers above the storied Pari! How the grim warriors of the past seem flocking in ghostly squadrons to their ancient battlefield again—how the wails of the dying well up from the—"

At this point the horse called Oahu sat down in the sand. Sat down to listen, I suppose. Never mind what he heard, I stopped apostrophising and convinced him that I was not a man to allow contempt of Court on the part of a horse. I broke the back-bone of a Chief over his rump and set out to join the cavalcade again.

Very considerably fagged out we arrived in town at 9 o'clock at night, myself in the lead—for when my horse finally came to understand that he was homeward bound and hadn't far to go, he turned his attention strictly to business.

This is a good time to drop in a paragraph of information. There is no regular livery stable in Honolulu, or, indeed, in any part of the kingdom of Hawaii; therefore unless you are acquainted with wealthy residents (who all have good horses), you must hire animals of the wretchedest description from the Kanakas. (i.e. natives.) Any horse you hire, even though it be from a white man, is not often of much account, because it will be brought in for you from some ranch, and has necessarily been leading a hard life. If the Kanakas who have been caring for him (inveterate riders they are) have not ridden him half to death every day themselves, you can depend upon it they have been doing the same thing by proxy, by clandestinely hiring him out. At least, so I am informed. The result is, that no horse has a chance to eat, drink, rest, recuperate, or look well or feel well, and so strangers go about the Islands mounted as I was to-day.

In hiring a horse from a Kanaka, you must have all your eyes about you, because you can rest satisfied that you are dealing with a shrewd unprincipled rascal. You may leave your door open and your trunk unlocked as long as you please, and he will not meddle with your property; he has no important vices and no inclination to commit robbery on a large scale; but if he can get ahead of you in the horse business, he will take a genuine delight in doing it. This trait is characteristic of horse jockeys, the world over, is it not? He will overcharge you if he can; he will hire you a fine-looking horse at night (anybody's—may be the King's, if the royal steed be in convenient view), and bring you the mate to my Oahu in the morning, and contend that it is the same animal. If you make trouble, he will get out by saying it was not himself who made the bargain with you, but his brother, "who went out in the country this morning." They have always got a "brother" to shift the responsibility upon. A victim said to one of these fellows one day:

"But I know I hired the horse of you, because I noticed that scar on your cheek."

The reply was not bad: "Oh, yes—yes—my brother all same—we twins!"

A friend of mine, J. Smith, hired a horse yesterday, the Kanaka warranting him to be in excellent condition. Smith had a saddle and blanket of his own, and he ordered the Kanaka to put these on the horse. The Kanaka protested that he was perfectly willing to trust the gentleman with the saddle that was already on the animal, but Smith refused to use it. The change was made; then Smith noticed that the Kanaka had only changed the saddles, and had left the original blanket on the horse; he said he forgot to change the blankets, and so, to cut the bother short, Smith mounted and rode away. The horse went lame a mile from town, and afterward got to cutting up some extraordinary capers. Smith got down and took off the saddle, but the blanket stuck fast to the horse—glued to a procession of raw places. The Kanaka's mysterious conduct stood explained.

Another friend of mine bought a pretty good horse from a native, a day or two ago, after a tolerably thorough examination. He discovered today that the horse was as blind as a bat, in one eye. He meant to have examined that eye, and came home with a general notion that he had done it; but he remembers now that every time he made the attempt his attention was called to something else by his victimizer.

One more instance, and then I will pass to something else. I am informed that when a certain Mr. L., a visiting stranger, was here, he bought a pair of very respectable-looking match horses from a native. They were in a little stable with a partition through the middle of it—one horse in each apartment. Mr. L. examined one of them critically through a window (the Kanaka's "brother" having gone to the country with the key), and then went around the house and examined the other through a window on the other side. He said it was the neatest match he had ever seen, and paid for the horses on the spot. Whereupon the Kanaka departed to join his brother in the country. The fellow had shamefully swindled L. There was only one "match" horse, and he had examined his starboard side through one window and his port side through another! I decline to believe this story, but I give it because it is worth something as a fanciful illustration of a fixed fact— namely, that the Kanaka horse-jockey is fertile in invention and elastic in conscience.

You can buy a pretty good horse for forty or fifty dollars, and a good enough horse for all practical purposes for two dollars and a half. I estimate "Oahu" to be worth somewhere in the neighborhood of thirty-five cents. A good deal better animal than he is was sold here day before yesterday for a dollar and seventy-five cents, and sold again to-day for two dollars and twenty-five cents; Williams bought a handsome and lively little pony yesterday for ten dollars; and about the best common horse on the island (and he is a really good one) sold yesterday, with Mexican saddle and bridle, for seventy dollars—a horse which is well and widely known, and greatly respected for his speed, good disposition and everlasting bottom. You give your horse a little grain once a day; it comes from San Francisco, and is worth about two cents a pound; and you give him as much hay as he wants; it is cut and brought to the market by natives, and is not very good it is baled into long, round bundles, about the size of a large man; one of them is stuck by the middle on each end of a six-foot pole, and the Kanaka shoulders the pole and walks about the streets between the upright bales in search of customers. These hay bales, thus carried, have a general resemblance to a colossal capital H.

The hay-bundles cost twenty-five cents apiece, and one will last a horse about a day. You can get a horse for a song, a week's hay for another song, and you can turn your animal loose among the luxuriant grass in your neighbor's broad front yard without a song at all—you do it at midnight, and stable the beast again before morning. You have been at no expense thus far, but when you buy a saddle and bridle they will cost you from twenty to thirty-five dollars. You can hire a horse, saddle and bridle at from seven to ten dollars a week, and the owner will take care of them at his own expense.

It is time to close this day's record—bed time. As I prepare for sleep, a rich voice rises out of the still night, and, far as this ocean rock is toward the ends of the earth, I recognize a familiar home air. But the words seem somewhat out of joint:

"Waikiki lantoni œ Kaa hooly hooly wawhoo."

Translated, that means, "When we were marching through Georgia."

CHAPTER LXVI

Passing through the market place we saw that feature of Honolulu under its most favorable auspices—that is, in the full glory of Saturday afternoon, which is a festive day with the natives. The native girls by twos and threes and parties of a dozen, and sometimes in whole platoons and companies, went cantering up and down the neighboring streets astride of fleet but homely horses, and with their gaudy riding habits streaming like banners behind them. Such a troop of free and easy riders, in their natural home, the saddle, makes a gay and graceful spectacle. The riding habit I speak of is simply a long, broad scarf, like a tavern table cloth brilliantly colored, wrapped around the loins once, then apparently passed between the limbs and each end thrown backward over the same, and floating and flapping behind on both sides beyond the horse's tail like a couple of fancy flags; then, slipping the stirrup-irons between her toes, the girl throws her chest forward, sits up like a Major General and goes sweeping by like the wind.

The girls put on all the finery they can on Saturday afternoon—fine black silk robes; flowing red ones that nearly put your eyes out; others as white as snow; still others that discount the rainbow; and they wear their hair in nets, and trim their jaunty hats with fresh flowers, and encircle their dusky throats with home-made necklaces of the brilliant vermillion-tinted blossom of the *ohia*; and they fill the markets and the adjacent streets with their bright presences, and smell like a rag factory on fire with their offensive cocoanut oil.

Occasionally you see a heathen from the sunny isles away down in the South Seas, with his face and neck tattooed till he looks like the customary mendicant from Washoe who has been blown up in a mine. Some are tattooed a dead blue color down to the upper lip—masked, as it were—leaving the natural light yellow skin of Micronesia unstained from thence down; some with broad marks drawn down from hair to neck, on both sides of the face, and a strip of the original yellow skin, two inches wide, down the center—a gridiron with a spoke broken out; and some with the entire face discolored with the popular mortification tint, relieved only by one or two thin, wavy threads of natural yellow running across the face from ear to ear, and eyes twinkling out of this darkness, from under shadowing hatbrims, like stars in the dark of the moon.

Moving among the stirring crowds, you come to the poi merchants, squatting in the shade on their hams, in true native fashion, and surrounded by purchasers. (The Sandwich Islanders always squat on their hams, and who knows but they may be the old original "ham sandwiches?" The thought is pregnant with interest.) The poi looks like common flour paste, and is kept in large bowls formed of a species of gourd, and capable of holding from one to three or four gallons. Poi is the chief article of food among the natives, and is prepared from the *taro* plant. The taro root looks like a thick, or, if you please, a corpulent sweet potato, in shape, but is of light purple color when boiled. When boiled it answers as a passable substitute for bread. The buck Kanakas bake it under ground, then mash it up well with a heavy lava pestle, mix water with it until it becomes a paste, set it aside and let it ferment, and then it is poi—and an unseductive mixture it is, almost tasteless before it ferments and too sour for a luxury afterward. But nothing is more nutritious. When solely used, however,it produces acrid humors, a fact which sufficiently accounts for the humorous character of the Kanakas. I think there must be as much of a knack in handling poi as there is in eating with chopsticks. The forefinger is thrust into the mess and stirred quickly round several times and drawn as quickly out, thickly coated, just as if it were poulticed; the head is thrown back, the finger inserted in the mouth and the delicacy stripped off and swallowed—the eye closing gently, meanwhile, in a languid sort of ecstasy. Many a different finger goes into the same bowl and many a different kind of dirt and shade and quality of flavor is added to the virtues of its contents.

Around a small shanty was collected a crowd of natives buying the *awa* root. It is said that but for the use of this root the destruction of the people in former times by certain imported diseases would have been far greater than it was, and by others it is said that this is merely a fancy. All agree that poi will rejuvenate a man who is used up and his vitality almost annihilated by hard drinking, and that in some kinds of diseases it will restore health after all medicines have failed; but all are not willing to allow to the *awa* the virtues claimed for it. The natives manufacture an intoxicating drink from it which is fearful in its effects when persistently indulged in. It covers the body with dry, white scales, inflames the eyes, and causes premature decrepitude. Although the man before whose establishment we stopped has to pay a Government license of eight hundred dollars a year for the exclusive right to sell *awa* root, it is said that he makes a small fortune every twelve-month; while saloon keepers, who pay a thousand dollars a year for the privilege of retailing whiskey, etc., only make a bare living.

We found the fish market crowded; for the native is very fond of fish, and *eats the article raw and alive!* Let us change the subject.

In old times here Saturday was a grand gala day indeed. All the native population of the town forsook their labors, and those of the surrounding country journeyed to the city. Then the white folks had to stay indoors, for every street was so packed with charging cavaliers and cavalieresses that it was next to impossible to thread one's way through the cavalcades without getting crippled.

At night they feasted and the girls danced the lascivious *hula hula*—a dance that is said to exhibit the very perfection of educated motion of limb and arm, hand, head and body, and the exactest uniformity of movement and accuracy of "time." It was performed by a circle of girls with no raiment on them to speak of, who went through an infinite variety of motions and figures without prompting, and yet so true was their "time," and in such perfect concert did they move that when they were placed in a straight line, hands, arms, bodies, limbs and heads waved, swayed, gesticulated, bowed, stooped, whirled, squirmed, twisted and undulated as if they were part and parcel of a single individual; and it was difficult to believe they were not moved in a body by some exquisite piece of mechanism.

Of late years, however, Saturday has lost most of its quondam gala features. This weekly stampede of the natives interfered too much with labor and the interest of the white folks, and by sticking in a law here, and preaching a sermon there, and by various other means, they gradually broke it up. The demoralizing *hula hula* was forbidden to be performed, save at night, with closed doors, in presence of few spectators, and only by permission duly procured from the authorities and the payment of ten dollars for the same. There are few girls now-a-days able to dance this ancient national dance in the highest perfection of the art.

The missionaries have christianized and educated all the natives. They all belong to the Church, and there is not one of them, above the age of eight years, but can read and write with facility in the native tongue. It is the most universally educated race of people outside of China. They have any quantity of books, printed in the Kanaka language, and all the natives are fond of reading. They are inveterate church-goers—nothing can keep them away. All this ameliorating cultivation has at last built up in the native women a profound respect for chastity—in other people. Perhaps that is enough to say on that head. The national sin will die out when the race does, but perhaps not earlier.—But doubtless this purifying is not far off, when we reflect that contact with civilization and the whites has reduced the native population from *four hundred thousand* (Captain Cook's estimate,) to *fifty-five thousand* in something over eighty years!

Society is a queer medley in this notable missionary, whaling and governmental centre. If you get into conversation with a stranger and experience that natural desire to know what sort of ground you are treading on by finding out what manner of man your stranger is, strike out boldly and address him as "Captain." Watch him narrowly, and if you see by his countenance that you are on the wrong tack, ask him where he preaches. It is a safe bet that he is either a missionary or captain of a whaler. I am now personally acquainted with seventy-two captains and ninety-six missionaries. The captains and ministers form one-half of the population; the third fourth is composed of common Kanakas and mercantile foreigners and their families, and the final fourth is made up of high officers of the Hawaiian Government. And there are just about cats enough for three apiece all around.

A solemn stranger met me in the suburbs the other day, and said:

"Good morning, your reverence. Preach in the stone church yonder, no doubt?"

"No, I don't. I'm not a preacher."

"Really, I beg your pardon, Captain. I trust you had a good season. How much oil"—

"Oil? What do you take me for? I'm not a whaler."

"Oh, I beg a thousand pardons, your Excellency. Major General in the household troops, no doubt? Minister of the Interior, likely? Secretary of war? First Gentleman of the Bedchamber? Commissioner of the Royal"—

"Stuff! I'm no official. I'm not connected in any way with the Government."

"Bless my life! Then, who the mischief are you? what the mischief are you? and how the mischief did you get here, and where in thunder did you come from?"

"I'm only a private personage—an unassuming stranger—lately arrived from America."

"No? Not a missionary! Not a whaler! not a member of his Majesty's Government! not even Secretary of the Navy! Ah, Heaven! it is too blissful to be true; alas, I do but dream. And yet that noble, honest countenance—those oblique, ingenuous eyes—that massive head, incapable of—of—anything; your hand; give me your hand, bright waif. Excuse these tears. For sixteen weary years I have yearned for a moment like this, and"—

Here his feelings were too much for him, and he swooned away. I pitied this poor creature from the bottom of my heart. I was deeply moved. I shed a few tears on him and kissed him for his mother. I then took what small change he had and "shoved."

CHAPTER LXVII

I still quote from my journal:

I found the national Legislature to consist of half a dozen white men and some thirty or forty natives. It was a dark assemblage. The nobles and Ministers (about a dozen of them altogether) occupied the extreme left of the hall, with David Kalakaua (the King's Chamberlain) and Prince William at the head. The President of the Assembly, His Royal Highness M. Kekuanaoa,* and the Vice President (the latter a white man,) sat in the pulpit, if I may so term it.

The President is the King's father. He is an erect, strongly built, massive featured, white-haired, tawny old gentleman of eighty years of age or thereabouts. He was simply but well dressed, in a blue cloth coat and white vest, and white pantaloons, without spot, dust or blemish upon them. He bears himself with a calm, stately dignity, and is a man of noble presence. He was a young man and a distinguished warrior under that terrific fighter, Kamehameha I., more than half a century ago. A knowledge of his career suggested some such thought as this: "This man, naked as the day he was born, and war-club and spear in hand, has charged at the head of a horde of savages against other hordes of savages more than a generation and a half ago, and reveled in slaughter and carnage; has worshipped wooden images on his devout knees; has seen hundreds of his race offered up in heathen temples as sacrifices to wooden idols, at a time when no missionary's foot had ever pressed this soil, and he had never heard of the white man's God; has believed his enemy could secretly pray him to death; has seen the day, in his childhood, when it was a crime punishable by death for a man to eat with his wife, or for a plebeian to let his shadow fall upon the King—and now look at

*Since dead.

him; an educated Christian; neatly and handsomely dressed; a high-minded, elegant gentleman; a traveler, in some degree, and one who has been the honored guest of royalty in Europe; a man practiced in holding the reins of an enlightened government, and well versed in the politics of his country and in general, practical information. Look at him, sitting there presiding over the deliberations of a legislative body, among whom are white men—a grave, dignified, statesmanlike personage, and as seemingly natural and fitted to the place as if he had been born in it and had never been out of it in his life time. How the experiences of this old man's eventful life shame the cheap inventions of romance!"

Kekuanaoa is not of the blood royal. He derives his princely rank from his wife, who was a daughter of Kamehameha the Great. Under other monarchies the male line takes precedence of the female in tracing genealogies, but here the opposite is the case—the female line takes precedence. Their reason for this is exceedingly sensible, and I recommend it to the aristocracy of Europe: They say it is easy to know who a man's mother was, but, etc, etc.

The christianizing of the natives has hardly even weakened some of their barbarian superstitions, much less destroyed them. I have just referred to one of these. It is still a popular belief that if your enemy can get hold of any article belonging to you he can get down on his knees over it and *pray you to death.* Therefore many a native gives up and dies merely because he *imagines* that some enemy is putting him through a course of damaging prayer. This praying an individual to death seems absurb enough at a first glance, but then when we call to mind some of the pulpit efforts of certain of our own ministers the thing looks plausible.

In former times, among the Islanders, not only a plurality of wives was customary, but a *plurality of husbands* likewise. Some native women of noble rank had as many as six husbands. A woman thus supplied did not reside with all her husbands at once, but lived several months with each in turn. An understood sign hung at her door during these months. When the sign was taken down, it meant "NEXT."

In those days woman was rigidly taught to "know her place." Her place was to do all the work, take all the cuffs, provide all the food, and content herself with what was left after her lord had finished his dinner. She was not only forbidden, by ancient law, and under penalty of death, to eat with her husband or enter a canoe, but was debarred, under the same penalty, from eating bananas, pine-apples, oranges and other choice fruits at any time or in any place. She had to confine herself pretty strictly to "poi" and hard work. These poor ignorant heathen seem to have had a sort of groping idea of what came of woman eating fruit in the garden of Eden, and they did not choose to take any more chances. But the missionaries broke up this satisfactory arrangement of things. They liberated woman and made her the equal of man.

The natives had a romantic fashion of burying some of their children alive when the family became larger than necessary. The missionaries interfered in this matter too, and stopped it.

To this day the natives are able to *lie down and die whenever they want to,* whether there is anything the matter with them or not. If a Kanaka takes a notion to die, that is the end of him; nobody can persuade him to hold on; all the doctors in the world could not save him.

A luxury which they enjoy more than anything else, is a large funeral. If a person wants to get rid of a troublesome native, it is only necessary to promise him a fine funeral and name the hour and he will be on hand to the minute—at least his remains will.

All the natives are Christians, now, but many of them still desert to the Great Shark God for temporary succor in time of trouble. An irruption of the great volcano of Kilauea, or an earthquake, always brings a deal of latent loyalty to the Great Shark God to the surface. It is common report that the King, educated, cultivated and refined Christian gentleman as he undoubtedly is, still turns to the idols of his fathers for help when disaster threatens. A planter caught a shark, and one of his christianized natives testified his emancipation from the thrall of ancient superstition by assisting to dissect the shark after a fashion forbidden by his abandoned creed. But remorse shortly began to torture him. He grew moody and sought solitude; brooded over his sin, refused food, and finally said he must die and ought to die, for he had sinned against the Great Shark God and could never know peace any more. He was proof against persuasion and ridicule, and in the course of a day or two took to his bed and died, although he showed no symptom of disease. His young daughter followed his lead and suffered a like fate within the week. Superstition is ingrained in the native blood and bone and it is only natural that it should crop out in time of distress. Wherever one goes in the Islands, he will find small piles of stones by the wayside, covered with leafy offerings, placed there by the natives to appease evil spirits or honor local deities belonging to the mythology of former days.

In the rural districts of any of the Islands, the traveler hourly comes upon parties of dusky maidens bathing in the streams or in the sea without any clothing on and exhibiting no very intemperate zeal in the matter of hiding their nakedness. When the missionaries first took up their residence in Honolulu, the native women would pay their families frequent friendly visits, day by day, not even clothed with a blush. It was found a hard matter to convince them that this was rather indelicate. Finally the missionaries provided them with long, loose calico robes, and that ended the difficulty—for the women would troop through the town, stark naked, with their robes folded under their arms, march to the missionary houses and then proceed to dress!—The natives soon manifested a strong proclivity for clothing, but it was shortly apparent that they only wanted it for grandeur. The missionaries imported a quantity of hats, bonnets, and other male and female wearing apparel, instituted a general distribution, and begged the people not to come to church naked, next Sunday, as usual. And they did not; but the national spirit of unselfishness led them to divide up with neighbors who were not at the distribution, and next Sabbath the poor preachers could hardly keep countenance before their vast congregations. In the midst of the reading of a hymn a brown, stately dame would sweep up the aisle with a world of airs, with nothing in the world on but a "stovepipe" hat and a pair of cheap gloves; another dame would follow, tricked out in a man's shirt, and nothing else; another one would enter with a flourish, with simply the sleeves of a bright calico dress tied around her waist and the rest of the garment dragging behind like a peacock's tail off duty; a stately "buck" Kanaka would stalk in with a woman's bonnet on, wrong side before—only this, and nothing more; after him would stride his fellow, with the legs of a pair of pantaloons tied around his neck, the rest of his person untrammeled; in his rear would come another gentleman simply gotten up in a fiery neck-tie and a striped vest. The poor creatures were beaming with complacency and wholly unconscious of any absurdity in their appearance. They gazed at each other with happy admiration, and it was plain to see that the young girls were taking note of what each other had on, as naturally as if they had always lived in a land of Bibles and knew what churches were made for; here was the evidence of a dawning civilization. The spectacle which the congregation presented was so extraordinary and withal so moving, that the missionaries found it difficult to keep to the text and go on with the services; and by and by when the simple children of the sun began a general swapping of garments in open meeting and produced some irresistibly grotesque effects in the course of re-dressing, there was nothing for it but to cut the thing short with the benediction and dismiss the fantastic assemblage.

In our country, children play "keep house;" and in the same high-sounding but miniature way the grown folk here, with the poor little material of slender territory and meagre population, play "empire." There is his royal Majesty the King, with a New York detective's income of thirty or thirty-five thousand dollars a year from the "royal civil list" and the "royal domain." He lives in a two-story frame "palace."

And there is the "royal family"—the customary hive of royal brothers, sisters, cousins and other noble drones and vagrants usual to monarchy,—all with a spoon in the national pap-dish, and all bearing such titles as his or her Royal Highness the Prince or Princess So-and-so. Few of them can carry their royal splendors far enough to ride in carriages, however; they sport the economical Kanaka horse or "hoof it"* with the plebeians.

Then there is his Excellency the "royal Chamberlain"—a sinecure, for his majesty dresses himself with his own hands, except when he is ruralizing at Waikiki and then he requires no dressing.

Next we have his Excellency the Commander-in-chief of the Household Troops, whose forces consist of about the number of soldiers usually placed under a corporal in other lands.

Next comes the royal Steward and the Grand Equerry in Waiting—high dignitaries with modest salaries and little to do.

Then we have his Excellency the First Gentleman of the Bedchamber—an office as easy as it is magnificent.

Next we come to his Excellency the Prime Minister, a renegade American from New Hampshire, all jaw, vanity, bombast and ignorance, a lawyer of "shyster" calibre, a fraud by nature, a humble worshiper of the sceptre above him, a reptile never tired of sneering at the land of his birth or glorifying the ten-acre kingdom that has adopted him—salary, $4,000 a year, vast consequence, and no perquisites.

Then we have his Excellency the Imperial Minister of Finance, who handles a million dollars of public money a year, sends in his annual "budget" with great ceremony, talks prodigiously of "finance," suggests imposing schemes for paying off the "national debt" (of $150,000,) and does it all for $4,000 a year and unimaginable glory.

Next we have his Excellency the Minister of War, who holds sway over the royal armies—they consist of two hundred and

*Missionary phrase.

thirty uniformed Kanakas, mostly Brigadier Generals, and if the country ever gets into trouble with a foreign power we shall probably hear from them. I knew an American whose copper-plate visiting card bore this impressive legend: "Lieutenant-Colonel in the Royal Infantry. To say that he was proud of this distinction is stating it but tamely. The Minister of War has also in his charge some venerable swivels on Punch-Bowl Hill wherewith royal salutes are fired when foreign vessels of war enter the port.

Next comes his Excellency the Minister of the Navy—a nabob who rules the "royal fleet," (a steam-tug and a sixty-ton schooner.)

And next comes his Grace the Lord Bishop of Honolulu, the chief dignitary of the "Established Church"—for when the American Presbyterian missionaries had completed the reduction of the nation to a compact condition of Christianity, native royalty stepped in and erected the grand dignity of an "Established (Episcopal) Church" over it, and imported a cheap ready-made Bishop from England to take charge. The chagrin of the missionaries has never been comprehensively expressed, to this day, profanity not being admissible.

Next comes his Excellency the Minister of Public Instruction.

Next , their Excellencies the Governors of Oahu, Hawaii, etc., and after them a string of High Sheriffs and other small fry too numerous for computation.

Then there are their Excellencies the Envoy Extraordinary and Minister Plenipotentiary of his Imperial Majesty the Emperor of the French; her British Majesty's Minister; the Minister Resident, of the United States; and some six or eight representatives of other foreign nations, all with sounding titles, imposing dignity and prodigious but economical state.

Imagine all this grandeur in a play-house "kingdom" whose population falls absolutely short of sixty thousand souls!

The people are so accustomed to nine-jointed titles and colossal magnates that a foreign prince makes very little more stir in Honolulu than a Western Congressman does in New York.

And let it be borne in mind that there is a strictly defined "court costume" of so "stunning" a nature that it would make the clown in a circus look tame and commonplace by comparison; and each Hawaiian official dignitary has a gorgeous vari-colored, gold-laced uniform peculiar to his office—no two of them are alike, and it is hard to tell which one is the "loudest." The King had a "drawing-room" at stated intervals, like other monarchs, and when these varied uniforms congregate there weak-eyed people have to contemplate the spectacle through smoked glass. Is there not a gratifying contrast between this latter-day exhibition and the one the ancestors of some of these magnates afforded the missionaries the Sunday after the old-time distribution of clothing? Behold what religion and civilization have wrought!

CHAPTER LXVIII

While I was in Honolulu I witnessed the ceremonious funeral of the King's sister, her Royal Highness the Princess Victoria. According to the royal custom, the remains had lain in state at the palace *thirty days*, watched day and night by a guard of honor. And during all that time a great multitude of natives from the several islands had kept the palace grounds well crowded and had made the place a pandemonium every night with their howlings and wailings, beating of tom-toms and dancing of the (at other times) forbidden "hula-hula" by half-clad maidens to the music of songs of questionable decency chanted in honor of the deceased. The printed programme of the funeral procession interested me at the time; and after what I have just said of Hawaiian grandiloquence in the matter of "playing empire," I am persuaded that a perusal of it may interest the reader:

After reading the long list of dignitaries, etc., and remembering the sparseness of the population, one is almost inclined to wonder where the material for that portion of the procession devoted to "Hawaiian Population Generally" is going to be procured:

Undertaker.
Royal School. Kawaiahao School.
Roman Catholic School. Miæmæ School.
Honolulu Fire Department.
Mechanics' Benefit Union.
Attending Physicians.
Knonohikis (Superintendents) of the Crown Lands, Konohikis of the Private Lands of His Majesty Konohikis of Private Lands of Her late Royal Highness.
Governor of Oahu and Staff.
Hulumanu (Military Company).
Household Troops.
The Prince of Hawaii's Own (Military Company).
The King's household servants.
Servants of Her late Royal Highness.
Protestant Clergy. The Clergy of the Roman Catholic Church.
His Lordship Louis Maigret, The Right Rev. Bishop of Arathea, Vicar-Apostolic of the Hawaiian Islands.

The Clergy of the Hawaiian Reformed Catholic Church.
His Lordship the Right Rev. Bishop of Honolulu.

Escort Hawaiian Cavalry.
Large Kahilis.*
Small Kahilis.
Pall Bearers.

[HEARSE.]

Escort Hawaiian Cavalry.
Large Kahilis.
Small Kahalis.
Pall Bearers.

Her Majesty Queen Emma's Carriage.
His Majesty's Staff.
Carriage of Her late Royal Highness.
Carriage of Her Majesty the Queen Dowager.
The King's Chancellor.
Cabinet Ministers.
His Excellency the Minister Resident of the United States.
H. I. M's Commissioner.
H. B. M's Acting Commissioner.
Judges of Supreme Court.
Privy Councillors.
Members of Legislative Assembly.
Consular Corps.
Circuit Judges.
Clerks of Government Departments.
Members of the Bar.
Collector General, Custom-house Officers and
Officers of the Customs.
Marshal and Sheriffs of the different Islands.
King's Yeomanry.
Foreign Residents.
Ahahui Kaahumanu.
Hawaiian Population Generally.
Hawaiian Cavalry.
Police Force.

I resume my journal at the point where the procession arrived at the royal mausoleum:

As the procession filed through the gate, the military deployed handsomely to the right and left and formed an avenue through which the long column of mourners passed to the tomb. The coffin was borne through the door of the mausoleum, followed by the King and his chiefs, the great officers of the kingdom, foreign Consuls, Embassadors and distinguished guests (Burlingame and General Van Valkenburgh). Several of the kahilis were then fastened to a frame-

*Ranks of long-handled mops made of gaudy feathers—sacred to royalty. They are stuck in the ground around the tomb and left there.

work in front of the tomb, there to remain until they decay and fall to pieces, or, forestalling this, until another scion of royalty dies. At this point of the proceedings the multitude set up such a heart-broken wailing as I hope never to hear again. The soldiers fired three volleys of musketry—the wailing being previously silenced to permit of the guns being heard. His Highness Prince William, in a showy military uniform (the "true prince," this—scion of the house over-thrown by the present dynasty—he was formerly betrothed to the Princess but was not allowed to marry her), stood guard and paced back and forth within the door. The privileged few who followed the coffin into the mausoleum remained sometime, but the King soon came out and stood in the door and near one side of it. A stranger could have guessed his rank (although he was so simply and unpretentiously dressed) by the profound deference paid him by all persons in his vicinity; by seeing his high officers receive his quiet orders and suggestions with bowed and uncovered heads; and by observing how careful those persons who came out of the mausoleum were to avoid "crowding" him (although there was room enough in the doorway for a wagon to pass, for that matter); how respectfully they edged out sideways, scraping their backs against the wall and always presenting a front view of their persons to his Majesty, and never putting their hats on until they were well out of the royal presence.

He was dressed entirely in black—dress-coat and silk hat—and looked rather democratic in the midst of the showy uniforms about him. On his breast he wore a large gold star, which was half hidden by the lapel of his coat. He remained at the door a half hour, and occasionally gave an order to the men who were erecting the *kahilis* before the tomb. He had the good taste to make one of them substitute black crape for the ordinary hempen rope he was about to tie one of them to the frame-work with. Finally he entered his carriage and drove away, and the populace shortly began to drop into his wake. While he was in view there was but one man who attracted more attention than himself, and that was Harris (the Yankee Prime Minister). This feeble personage had crape enough around his hat to express the grief of an entire nation, and as usual he neglected no opportunity of making himself conspicuous and exciting the admiration of the simple Kanakas. Oh! noble ambition of this modern Richelieu!

It is interesting to contrast the funeral ceremonies of the Princess Victoria with those of her noted ancestor Kamehameha the Conqueror, who died fifty years ago—in 1819, the year before the first missionaries came.

"On the 8th of May, 1819, at the age of sixty-six, he died, as he had lived, in the faith of his country. It was his misfortune not to have come in contact with men who could have rightly influenced his religious aspirations. Judged by his advantages and compared with the most eminent of his countrymen he may be justly styled not only great, but good. To this day his memory warms the heart and elevates the national feelings of Hawaiians. They are proud of their old warrior King; they love his name; his deeds form their historical age; and an enthusiasm everywhere prevails, shared even by foreigners who knew his worth, that constitutes the firmest pillar of the throne of his dynasty.

"In lieu of human victims (the custom of that age), a sacrifice of three hundred dogs attended his obsequies—no mean holocaust when their national value and the estimation in which they were held are considered. The bones of Kamehameha, after being kept for a while, were so carefully concealed that all knowledge of their final resting place is now lost. There was a proverb current among the common people that the bones of a cruel King could not be hid; they made fishhooks and arrows of them, upon which, in using them, they vented their abhorrence of his memory in bitter execrations."

The account of the circumstances of his death, as written by the native historians, is full of minute detail, but there is scarcely a line of it which does not mention or illustrate some by-gone custom of the country. In this respect it is the most comprehensive document I have yet met with. I will quote it entire:

"When Kamehameha was dangerously sick, and the priests were unable to cure him, they said: 'Be of good courage and build a house for the god' (his own private god or idol), that thou mayest recover.' The chiefs corroborated this advice of the priests, and a place or worship was prepared for Kukailimoku, and consecrated in the evening. They proposed also to the King, with a view to prolong his life, that human victims should be sacrificed to his deity; upon which the greater part of the people absconded through fear of death, and concealed themselves in hiding places till the *tabu** in which destruction impended, was past. It is doubtful whether Kamehameha approved of the plan of the chiefs and priests to sacrifice men, as he was known to say, 'The men are sacred for the King;' meaning that they were for the service of his successor. This information was derived from Liholiho, his son.

"After this, his sickness increased to such a degree that he had not strength to turn himself in his bed. When another season, consecrated for worship at the new temple (*heiau*) arrived, he said to his son, Liholiho, 'Go thou and make supplication to thy god; I am not able to go, and will offer my prayers at home.' When his devotions to his feathered god, Kukuailimoku, were concluded, a certain religiously disposed individual, who had a bird god, suggested to the King that through its influence his sickness might be removed. The name of this god was Pua; its body was made of a bird, now eaten by the Hawaiians, and called in their language *alae*. Kamehameha was willing that a trial should be made, and two houses were constructed to facilitate the ex-

**Tabu* (pronounced tah-boo,) means prohibition (we have borrowed it,) or sacred. The tabu was sometimes permanent, sometimes temporary; and the person or thing placed under tabu was for the time being sacred to the purpose for which it was set apart. In the above case the victims selected under the tabu would be sacred to the sacrifice.

periment; but while dwelling in them he became so very weak as not to receive food. After lying there three days, his wives, children and chiefs, perceiving that he was very low, returned him to his own house. In the evening he was carried to the eating house,* where he took a little food in his mouth which he did not swallow; also a cup of water. The chiefs requested him to give them his counsel; but he made no reply, and was carried back to the dwelling house; but when near midnight—ten o'clock, perhaps—he was carried again to the place to eat; but, as before, he merely tasted of what was presented to him. Then Kaikioewa addressed him thus: 'Here we all are, your younger brethren, your son Liholiho and your foreigner; impart to us your dying charge, that Liholiho and Kaahumanu may hear.' Then Kamehameha inquired, 'What do you say?' Kaikioewa repeated, 'Your counsels for us.' He then said, 'Move on in my good way and—.' He could proceed no further. The foreigner, Mr. Young, embraced and kissed him. Hoapili also embraced him, whispering something in his ear, after which he was taken back to the house. About twelve he was carried once more to the house for eating, into which his head entered, while his body was in the dwelling house immediately adjoining. It should be remarked that this frequent carrying of a sick chief from one house to another resulted from the *tabu* system, then in force. There were at that time six houses (huts) connected with an establishment—one was for worship, one for the men to eat in, an eating house for the women, a house to sleep in, a house in which to manufacture kapa (native cloth) and one where, at certain intervals, the women might dwell in seclusion.

"The sick was once more taken to his house, when he expired; this was at two o'clock, a circumstance from which Leleiohoku derived his name. As he breathed his last, Kalaimoku came to the eating house to order those in it to go out. There were two aged persons thus directed to depart; one went, the other remained on account of love to the King, by whom he had formerly been kindly sustained. The children also were sent away. Then Kalaimoku came to the house, and the chiefs had a consultation. One of them spoke thus: 'This is my thought—we will eat him raw.'† Kaahumanu (one of the dead King's widows) replied, 'Perhaps his body is not at our disposal; that is more properly with his successor. Our part in him—his breath—has departed; his remains will be disposed of by Liholiho.'

"After this conversation the body was taken into the consecrated house for the performance of the proper rites by the priest and the new King. The name of this ceremony is *uko;* and when the sacred hog was baked the priest offered it to the dead body, and it became a god, the King at the same time repeating the customary prayers.

"Then the priest, addressing himself to the King and chiefs, said: 'I will now make known to you the rules to be observed respecting per-

*It was deemed pollution to eat in the same hut a person slept in—the fact that the patient was dying could not modify the rigid etiquette.

†This sounds suspicious, in view of the fact that all Sandwich Island historians, white and black, protest that cannibalism never existed in the islands. However, since they only proposed to "eat him raw" we "won't count that". But it would certainly have been cannibalism if they had cooked him.—]M. T.]

sons to be sacrificed on the burial of this body. If you obtain one man before the corpse is removed, one will be sufficient; but after it leaves this house four will be required. If delayed until we carry the corpse to the grave there must be ten; but after it is deposited in the grave there must be fifteen. To-morrow morning there will be a *tabu*, and, if the sacrifice be delayed until that time, forty men must die.'

"Then the high priest, Hewahewa, inquired of the chiefs, 'Where shall be the residence of King Liholiho?' They replied, 'Where, indeed? You, of all men, ought to know.' Then the priest observed, 'There are two suitable places; one is Kau, the other is Kohala.' The chiefs preferred the latter, as it was more thickly inhabited. The priest added, 'These are proper places for the King's residence; but he must not remain in Kona, for it is polluted.' This was agreed to. It was now break of day. As he was being carried to the place of burial the people perceived that their King was dead, and they wailed. When the corpse was removed from the house to the tomb, a distance of one chain, the procession was met by a certain man who was ardently attached to the deceased. He leaped upon the chiefs who were carrying the King's body; he desired to die with him on account of his love. The chiefs drove him away. He persisted in making numerous attempts, which were unavailing. Kalaimoka also had it in his heart to die with him, but was prevented by Hookio.

"The morning following Kamehameha's death, Liholiho and his train departed for Kohala, according to the suggestions of the priest, to avoid the defilement occasioned by the dead. At this time if a chief died the land was polluted, and the heirs sought a residence in another part of the country until the corpse was dissected and the bones tied in a bundle, which being done, the season of defilement terminated. If the deceased were not a chief, the house only was defiled which became pure again on the burial of the body. Such were the laws on this subject.

"On the morning on which Liholiho sailed in his canoe for Kohala, the chiefs and people mourned after their manner on occasion of a chief's death, conducting themselves like madmen and like beasts. Their conduct was such as to forbid description; The priests, also, put into action the sorcery apparatus, that the person who had prayed the King to death might die; for it was not believed that Kamehameha's departure was the effect either of sickness or old age. When the sorcerers set up by their fire-places stick with a strip of kapa flying at the top, the chief Keeaumoku, Kaahumanu's brother, came in a state of intoxication and broke the flag-staff of the sorcerers, from which it was inferred that Kaahumanu and her friends had been instrumental in the King's death. On this account they were subjected to abuse."

You have the contrast, now, and a strange one it is. This great Queen, Kaahumanu, who was "subjected to abuse" during the frightful orgies that followed the King's death, in accordance with ancient custom, afterward became a devout Christian and a steadfast and powerful friend of the missionaries.

Dogs were, and still are, reared and fattened for food, by the natives—hence the reference to their value in one of the above paragraphs.

Forty years ago it was the custom in the Islands to suspend all law for a certain number of days after the death of a royal personage; and then a saturnalia ensued which one may picture to himself after a fashion, but not in the full horror of the reality. The people shaved their heads, knocked out a tooth or two, plucked out an eye sometimes, cut, bruised, mutilated or burned their flesh, got drunk, burned each other's huts, maimed or murdered one another according to the caprice of the moment, and both sexes gave themselves up to brutal and unbridled licentiousness. And after it all, came a torpor from which the nation slowly emerged bewildered and dazed, as if from a hideous half-remembered nightmare. They were not the salt of the earth, those "gentle children of the sun."

The natives still keep up an old custom of theirs which cannot be comforting to an invalid. When they think a sick friend is going to die, a couple of dozen neighbors surround his hut and keep up a deafening wailing night and day till he either dies or gets well. No doubt this arrangement has helped many a subject to a shroud before his appointed time.

They surround a hut and wail in the same heart-broken way when its occupant returns from a journey. This is their dismal idea of a welcome. A very little of it would go a great way with most of us.

CHAPTER LXIX

Bound for Hawaii (a hundred and fifty miles distant,) to visit the great volcano and behold the other notable things which distinguish that island above the remainder of the group, we sailed from Honolulu on a certain Saturday afternoon, in the good schooner Boomerang.

The Boomerang was about as long as two street cars, and about as wide as one. She was so small (though she was larger than the majority of the inter-island coasters) that when I stood on her deck I felt but little smaller than the Colossus of Rhodes must have felt when he had a man-of-war under him. I could reach the water when she lay over under a strong breeze. When the Captain and my comrade (a Mr. Billings), myself and four other persons were all assembled on the little after portion of the deck which is sacred to the cabin passengers, it was full—there was not room for any more quality folks. Another section of the deck, twice as large as ours, was full of natives of both sexes, with their customary dogs, mats, blankets, pipes, calabashes of poi, fleas, and other luxuries and baggage of minor importance. As soon as we set sail the natives all lay down on the deck as thick as negroes in a slave-pen, and smoked, conversed, and spit on each other, and were truly sociable.

The little low-ceiled cabin below was rather larger than a hearse, and as dark as a vault. It had two coffins on each side—I mean two bunks. A small table, capable of accommodating three persons at dinner, stood against the forward bulkhead, and over it hung the dingiest whale oil lantern that ever peopled the obscurity of a dungeon with ghostly shapes. The floor room unoccupied was not extensive. One might swing a cat in it, perhaps, but not a long cat. The hold forward of the bulkhead had but little freight in it, and from morning till night a portly old rooster, with a voice like Baalam's ass, and the same disposition to use it, strutted up and down in that part of the vessel and crowed. He usually took dinner at six o'clock, and then, after an hour devoted to meditation, he mounted a barrel and crowed a good part of the night. He got hoarser and hoarser all the time, but he scorned to allow any personal consideration to interfere with his duty, and kept up his labors in defiance of threatened diphtheria.

Sleeping was out of the question when he was on watch. He was a source of genuine aggravation and annoyance. It was worse than useless to shout at him or apply offensive epithets to him—he only took these things for applause, and strained himself to make more noise. Occasionally, during the day, I threw potatoes at him through an aperture in the bulkhead, but he only dodged and went on crowing.

The first night, as I lay in my coffin, idly watching the dim lamp swinging to the rolling of the ship, and snuffing the nauseous odors of bilge water, I felt something gallop over me. I turned out promptly. However, I turned in again when I found it was only a rat. Presently something galloped over me once more. I knew it was not a rat this time, and I thought it might be a centipede, because the Captain had killed one on deck in the afternoon. I turned out. The first glance at the pillow showed me a repulsive sentinel perched upon each end of it—cockroaches as large as peach leaves—fellows with long, quivering antennae and fiery, malignant eyes. They were grating their teeth like tobacco worms, and appeared to be dissatisfied about something. I had often heard that these reptiles were in the habit of eating off sleeping sailors' toe nails down to the quick, and I would not get in the bunk any more. I lay down on the floor. But a rat came and bothered me, and shortly afterward a procession of cockroaches arrived and camped in my hair. In a few moments the rooster was crowing with uncommon spirit and a party of fleas were throwing double somersaults about my person in the wildest disorder, and taking a bite every time they struck. I was beginning to feel really annoyed. I got up and put my clothes on and went on deck.

The above is not overdrawn; it is a truthful sketch of inter-island schooner life. There is no such thing as keeping a vessel in elegant condition, when she carries molasses and Kanakas.

It was compensation for my sufferings to come unexpectedly upon so beautiful a scene as met my eye—to step suddenly out of the sepulchral gloom of the cabin and stand under the strong light of the moon—in the centre, as it were, of a glittering sea of liquid silver—to see the broad sails straining in the gale, the ship keeled over on her side, the angry foam hissing past her lee bulwarks, and sparkling sheets of spray dashing high over her bows and raining upon her decks; to brace myself and hang fast to the first object that presented itself, with hat jammed down and coat tails whipping in the breeze, and feel that exhilaration that thrills in one's hair and quivers down his back bone when he knows that every inch of canvas is drawing and the vessel cleaving through the waves at her utmost speed. There was no darkness, no dimness, no obscurity there. All was brightness, every object was vividly defined. Every prostrate Kanaka; every coil of rope; every calabash of poi; every puppy; every seam in the flooring; every bolthead; every object, however minute, showed sharp and distinct in its every outline; and the shadow of the broad mainsail lay black as a pall upon the deck, leaving Billing's white upturned face glorified and his body in a total eclipse.

Monday morning we were close to the island of Hawaii. Two of its high mountains were in view—Mauna Loa and Hualaiai. The latter is an imposing peak, but being only ten thousand feet high is seldom mentioned or heard of. Mauna Loa is said to be sixteen thousand feet high. The rays of glittering snow and ice, that clasped its summit like a claw, looked refreshing when viewed from the blistering climate we were in. One could stand on that mountain (wrapped up in blankets and furs to keep warm), and while he nibbled a snowball or an icicle to quench his thirst he could look down the long sweep of its sides and see spots where plants are growing that grow only where the bitter cold of Winter prevails; lower down he could see sections devoted to productions that thrive in the temperate zone alone; and at the bottom of the mountain he could see the home of the tufted cocoa-palms and other species of vegetation that grow only in the sultry atmosphere of eternal Summer. He could see all the climes of the world at a single glance of the eye, and that glance would only pass over a distance of four or five miles as the bird flies!

By and by we took boat and went ashore at Kailua, designing to ride horseback through the pleasant orange and coffee region of Kona, and rejoin the vessel at a point some leagues distant. This journey is well worth taking. The trail passes along on high ground—say a thousand feet above sea level—and usually about a mile distant from the ocean, which is always in sight, save that occasionally you find yourself buried in the forest in the midst of a rank tropical vegetation and a dense growth of trees, whose great bows overarch the road and shut out sun and sea and everything, and leave you in a dim, shady tunnel, haunted with invisible singing birds and fragrant with the odor of flowers. It was pleasant to ride occasionally in the warm sun, and feast the eye upon the ever-changing panorama of the forest (beyond and below us), with its many tints, its softened lights and shadows, its billowy undulations sweeping gently down from the mountain to the sea. It was pleasant also, at intervals, to leave the sultry sun and pass into the cool, green depths of this forest and indulge in sentimental reflections under the inspiration of its brooding twilight and its whispering foliage.

We rode through one orange grove that had ten thousand trees in it! They were all laden with fruit.

At one farmhouse we got some large peaches of excellent flavor. This fruit, as a general thing, does not do well in the Sandwich Islands. It takes a sort of almond shape, and is small and bitter. It needs frost, they say, and perhaps it does; if this be so, it will have a good opportunity to go on needing it, as it will not be likely to get it. The trees from which the fine fruit I have spoken of, came, had been planted and replanted *sixteen times*, and to this treatment the proprietor of the orchard attributed his success.

We passed several sugar plantations—new ones and not very extensive. The crops were, in most cases, third rattoons. [Note.—The first crop is called "plant cane;" subsequent crops which spring from the original roots, without replanting, are called "rattoons."] Almost everywhere on the island of Hawaii sugar-cane matures in twelve months, both rattoons and plant, and although it ought to be taken off as soon as it tassels, no doubt, it is not absolutely necessary to do it until about four months afterward. In Kona, the average yield of an acre of ground is *two tons* of sugar, they say. This is only a moderate yield for these islands, but would be astounding for Louisiana and most other sugar growing countries. The plantations in Kona being on pretty high ground—up among the light and frequent rains—no irrigation whatever is required.

CHAPTER LXX

We stopped some time at one of the plantations, to rest ourselves and refresh the horses. We had a chatty conversation with several gentlemen present; but there was one person, a middle aged man, with an absent look in his face, who simply glanced up, gave us good-day and lapsed again into the meditations which our coming had interrupted. The planters whispered us not to mind him—crazy. They said he was in the Islands for his health; was a preacher; his home, Michigan. They said that if he woke up presently and fell to talking about a correspondence which he had some time held with Mr. Greeley about a trifle of some kind, we must humor him and listen with interest; and we must humor his fancy that this correspondence was the talk of the world.

It was easy to see that he was a gentle creature and that his madness had nothing vicious in it. He looked pale, and a little worn, as if with perplexing thought and anxiety of mind. He sat a long time, looking at the floor, and at intervals muttering to himself and nodding his head acquiescingly or shaking it in mild protest. He was lost in his thought, or in his memories. We continued our talk with the planters, branching from subject to subject. But at last the word "circumstance," casually dropped, in the course of conversation, attracted his attention and brought an eager look into his countenance. He faced about in his chair and said:

"Circumstance? What circumstance? Ah, I know—I know too well. So you have heard of it too." [With a sigh.] "Well, no matter—all the world has heard of it. All the world. The whole world. It is a large world, too, for a thing to travel so far in—now isn't it? Yes, yes—the Greeley correspondence with Erickson has created the saddest and bitterest controversy on both sides of the ocean—and still they keep it up! It makes us famous, but at what a sorrowful sacrifice! I was so sorry when I heard that it had caused that bloody and distressful war over there in Italy. It was little comfort to me, after so much bloodshed, to know that the victors sided with me, and the vanquished with Greeley.—It is little comfort to know that Horace Greeley is responsible for the battle of Sadowa, and not me. Queen Victoria wrote me that she felt just as I did about it—she said that as much as she was opposed to Greeley and the spirit he showed in the correspondence with me, she would not have had Sadowa happen for hundreds of dollars. I can show you her letter, if you would like to see it. But gentlemen, much as you may think you know about that unhappy correspondence, you cannot know the *straight* of it till you hear it from my lips. It has always been garbled in the journals, and even in history. Yes, even in history—think of it! Let me—*please* let me, give you the matter, exactly as it occurred. I truly will not abuse your confidence."

Then he leaned forward, all interest, all earnestness, and told his story—and told it appealingly, too, and yet in the simplest and most unpretentious way; indeed, in such a way as to suggest to one, all the time, that this was a faithful, honorable witness, giving evidence in the sacred interest of justice, and under oath. He said:

"Mrs. Beazeley—Mrs. Jackson Beazeley, widow, of the village of Campbellton, Kansas,—wrote me about a matter which was near her heart—a matter which many might think trivial, but to her it was a thing of deep concern. I was living in Michigan, then—serving in the ministry. She was, and is, an estimable woman—a woman to whom poverty and hardship have proven incentives to industry, in place of discouragements. Her only treasure was her son William, a youth just verging upon manhood; religious, amiable, and sincerely attached to agriculture. He was the widow's comfort and her pride. And so, moved by her love for him, she wrote me about a matter, as I have said before, which lay near her heart—because it lay near her boy's. She desired me to confer with Mr. Greeley about turnips. Turnips were the dream of her child's young ambition. While other youths were frittering away in frivolous amusements the precious years of budding vigor which God had given them for useful preparation, this boy was patiently enriching his mind with information concerning turnips. The sentiment which he felt toward the turnip was akin to adoration. He could not think of the turnip without emotion; he could not speak of it calmly; he could not contemplate it without exaltation. He could not eat it without shedding tears. All the poetry in his sensitive nature was in sympathy with the gracious vegetable. With the earliest pipe of dawn he sought his patch, and when the curtaining night drove him from it he shut himself up with his books and garnered statistics till sleep overcame him. On rainy days he sat and talked hours together with his mother about turnips. When company came, he made it his loving duty to put aside everything else and converse with them all the day long of his great joy in the turnip. And yet, was this joy rounded and complete? Was there no secret alloy of unhappiness in it? Alas, there was. There was a canker gnawing at his heart; the noblest inspiration of his soul eluded his endeavor—viz: he could not make of the turnip a climbing vine. Months went by; the bloom forsook his cheek, the fire faded out of his eye; sighings and abstraction usurped the place of smiles and cheerful converse. But a watchful eye noted these things and in time a motherly sympathy unsealed the secret. Hence the letter to me. She pleaded for attention—she said her boy was dying by inches.

"I was a stranger to Mr. Greeley, but what of that? The matter was urgent. I wrote and begged him to solve the difficult problem if possible and save the student's life. My interest grew, until it partook of the anxiety of the mother. I waited in much suspense.—At last the answer came.

"I found that I could not read it readily, the handwriting being unfamiliar and my emotions somewhat wrought up. It seemed to refer in part to the boy's case, but chiefly to other and irrelevant matters—such as paving-stones, electricity, oysters, and something which I took to be 'absolution' or 'agrarianism,' I could not be certain which; still, these appeared to be simply casual mentions, nothing more; friendly in spirit, without doubt, but lacking the connection or coherence necessary to make them useful.—I judged that my understanding was affected by my feelings, and so laid the letter away till morning.

"In the morning I read it again, but with difficulty and uncertainty still, for I had lost some little rest and my mental vision seemed clouded. The note was more connected, now, but did not meet the emergency it was expected to meet. It was too discursive. It appeared to read as follows, though I was not certain of some of the words:

'Polygamy dissembles majesty; extracts redeem polarity; causes hitherto exist. Ovations pursue wisdom, or warts inherit and condemn. Boston, botany, cakes, folony undertakes, but who shall allay? We fear not. Yrxwly,

HEVACE EVEELOJ.'

"But there did not seem to be a word about turnips. There seemed to be no suggestion as to how they might be made to grow like vines. There was not even a reference to the Beazeleys. I slept upon the matter; I ate no supper, neither any breakfast next morning. So I resumed my work with a brain refreshed, and was very hopeful. *Now* the letter took a different aspect—all save the signature, which latter I judged to be only a harmless affectation of Hebrew. The epistle was necessarily from Mr.

New-York Tribune.

Greeley, for it bore the printed heading of *The Tribune,* and I had written to no one else there. The letter, I say, had taken a different aspect, but still its language was eccentric and avoided the issue. It now appeared to say:

'Bolivia extemporizes mackerel; borax esteems polygamy; sausages wither in the east. Creation perdu, is done; for woes inherent one can damn. Buttons, buttons, corks, geology underrates but we shall allay. My beer's out. Yrxwly,

HEVACE EVEELOJ.'

"I was evidently overworked. My comprehension was impaired. Therefore I gave two days to recreation, and then returned to my task greatly refreshed. The letter now took this form:

'Poultices do sometimes choke swine; tulips reduce posterity; causes leather to resist. Our notions empower wisdom, her let's afford while we can. Butter but any cakes, fill any undertaker, we'll wean him from his filly. We feel hot.

Yrxwly, HEVACE EVEELOJ.'

"I was still not satisfied. These generalities did not meet the question. They were crisp, and vigorous, and delivered with a confidence that almost compelled conviction; but at such a time as this, with a human life at stake, they seemed inappropriate, worldly, and in bad taste. At any other time I would have been not only glad, but proud, to receive from a man like Mr. Greeley a letter of this kind, and would have studied it earnestly and tried to improve myself all I could; but now, with that poor boy in his far home languishing for relief, I had no heart for learning.

"Three days passed by, and I read the note again. Again its tenor had changed. It now appeared to say:

'Potations do sometimes wake wines; turnips restrain passion; causes necessary to state. Infest the poor widow; her lord's effects will be void. But dirt, bathing, etc., etc., followed unfairly, will worm him from his folly—so swear not.

Yrxwly, HEVACE EVEELOJ.'

"This was more like it. But I was unable to proceed. I was too much worn. The word 'turnips' brought temporary joy and encouragement, but my strength was so much impaired, and the delay might be so perilous for the boy, that I relinquished the idea of pursuing the translation further, and resolved to do what I ought to have done at first. I sat down and wrote Mr. Greeley as follows:

"DEAR SIR: I fear I do not entirely comprehend your kind note. It cannot be possible, Sir, that 'turnips restrain passion'—at least the study or contemplation of turnips cannot—for it is this very employment that has scorched our poor friend's mind and sapped his bodily strength.—But if they *do* restrain it, will you bear with us a little further and explain how they should be prepared? I observe that you say 'causes necessary to state,' but you have omitted to state them.

"Under a misapprehension, you seem to attribute to me interested motives in this matter—to call it by no harsher term. But I assure you, dear sir, that if I seem to be 'infesting the widow,' it is all *seeming,* and void of reality. It is from no seeking of mine that I am in this position. She asked me, herself, to write you. I never have infested her—indeed I scarcely know her. I do not infest anybody. I try to go along, in my humble way, doing as near right as I can, never harming anybody, and never *throwing out insinuations.* As for 'her lord and his effects,' they are of no interest to me. I trust I have effects enough of my own—shall endeavor to get along with them, at any rate, and not go mousing around to get hold of somebody's that are 'void.' But do you not see?—this woman is a *widow*—she has no 'lord.' He is dead—or pretended to be, when they buried him. Therefore, no amount of 'dirt, bathing,' etc., etc., howsoever 'unfairly followed' will be likely to 'worm him from his folly'—if being dead and a ghost is 'folly.' Your closing remark is as unkind as it was uncalled for; and if report says true you might have applied it to yourself, sir, with more point and less impropriety. Very Truly Yours, SIMON ERICKSON.

"In the course of a few days, Mr. Greeley did what would have saved a world of trouble, and much mental and bodily suffering and misunderstanding, if he had done it sooner. To wit, he sent an intelligible rescript or translation of his original note, made in a plain hand by his clerk. Then the mystery cleared, and I saw that his heart had been right, all the time. I will recite the note in its clarified form:

[Translation.]

'Potatoes do sometimes make vines; turnips remain passive: cause unnecessary to state. Inform the poor widow her lad's efforts will be vain. But diet, bathing, etc., etc., followed uniformly, will wean him from his folly—so fear not.

Yours, HORACE GREELEY.'

"But alas, it was too late, gentlemen—too late. The criminal delay had done its work—young Beazely was no more. His spirit had taken its flight to a land where all anxieties shall be charmed away, all desires gratified, all ambitions realized. Poor lad, they laid him to his rest with a turnip in each hand."

So ended Erickson, and lapsed again into nodding, mumbling, and abstraction. The company broke up, and left him so . . . . But they did not say what drove him crazy. In the momentary confusion, I forgot to ask.

CHAPTER LXXI

At four o'clock in the afternoon we were winding down a mountain of dreary and desolate lava to the sea, and closing our pleasant land journey. This lava is the accumulation of ages; one torrent of fire after another has rolled down here in old times, and built up the island structure higher and higher. Underneath, it is honey-combed with caves; it would be of no use to dig wells in such a place; they would not hold water—you would not find any for them to hold, for that matter. Consequently, the planters depend upon cisterns.

The last lava flow occurred here so long ago that there are none now living who witnessed it. In one place it enclosed and burned down a grove of cocoa-nut trees, and the holes in the lava where the trunks stood are still visible; their sides retain the impression of the bark; the trees fell upon the burning river, and becoming partly submerged, left in it the perfect counterpart of every knot and branch and leaf, and even nut, for curiosity seekers of a long distant day to gaze upon and wonder at.

There were doubtless plenty of Kanaka sentinels on guard hereabouts at that time, but they did not leave casts of their figures in the lava as the Roman sentinels at Herculaneum and Pompeii did. It is a pity it is so, because such things are so interesting; but so it is. They probably went away. They went away early, perhaps. However, they had their merits; the Romans exhibited the higher pluck, but the Kanakas showed the sounder judgment.

Shortly we came in sight of that spot whose history is so familiar to every school-boy in the wide world—Kealakekua Bay—the place where Captain Cook, the great circumnavigator, was killed by the natives, nearly a hundred years ago. The setting sun was flaming upon it, a Summer shower was falling, and it was spanned by two magnificent rainbows. Two men who were in advance of us rode through one of these and for a moment their garments shone with a more than regal splendor. Why did not Captain Cook have taste enough to call his great discovery the Rainbow Islands? These charming spectacles are present to you at every turn; they are common in all the islands; they are visible every day, and frequently at night also—not the silvery bow we see once in an age in the States, by moonlight, but barred with all bright and beautiful colors, like the children of the sun and rain. I saw one of them a few nights ago. What the sailors call "rain dogs"—little patches of rainbow—are often seen drifting about the heavens in these latitudes, like stained cathedral windows.

Kealakekua Bay is a little curve like the last kink of a snail-shell, winding deep into the land, seemingly not more than a mile wide from shore to shore. It is bounded on one side—where the murder was done—by a little flat plain, on which stands a cocoanut grove and some ruined houses; a steep wall of lava, a thousand feet high at the upper end and three or four hundred at the lower, comes down from the mountain and bounds the inner extremity of it. From this wall the place takes its name, *Kealakekua,* which in the native tongue signifies "The Pathway of the Gods." They say, (and still believe, in spite of their liberal education in Christianity), that the great god *Lono,* who used to live upon the hillside, always traveled that causeway when urgent business connected with heavenly affairs called him down to the seashore in a hurry.

As the red sun looked across the placid ocean through the tall, clean stems of the cocoanut trees, like a blooming whiskey bloat through the bars of a city prison, I went and stood in the edge of the water on the flat rock pressed by Captain Cook's feet when the blow was dealt which took away his life, and tried to picture in my mind the doomed man struggling in the midst of the multitude of exasperated savages—the men in the ship crowding to the vessel's side and gazing in anxious dismay toward the shore—the—but I discovered that I could not do it.

It was growing dark, the rain began to fall, we could see that the distant Boomerang was helplessly becalmed at sea, and so I adjourned to the cheerless little box of a warehouse and sat down to smoke and think, and wish the ship would make the land—for we had not eaten for ten hours and were viciously hungry.

Plain unvarnished history takes the romance out of Captain Cook's assassination, and renders a deliberate verdict of justifiable homicide. Wherever he went among the islands, he was cordially received and welcomed by the inhabitants, and his ships lavishly supplied with all manner of food. He returned these kindnesses with insult and ill-treatment. Perceiving that the people took him for the long vanished and lamented god Lono, he encouraged them in the delusion for the sake of the limitless power it gave him; but during the famous disturbance at this spot, and while he and his comrades were surrounded by fifteen thousand maddened savages, he received a hurt and betrayed his earthly origin with a groan. It was his death warrant. Instantly a shout went up: "He groans!—he is not a god!" So they closed in upon him and dispatched him.

His flesh was stripped from the bones and burned (except nine pounds of it which were sent on board the ships). The heart was hung up in a native hut, where it was found and eaten by three children, who mistook it for the heart of a dog. One of these children grew to be a very old man, and died in Honolulu a few years ago. Some of Cook's bones were recovered and consigned to the deep by the officers of the ships.

Small blame should attach to the natives for the killing of Cook. They treated him well. In return, he abused them. He and his men inflicted bodily injury upon many of them at different times, and killed at least three of them before they offered any proportionate retaliation.

Near the shore we found "Cook's Monument"—only a cocoanut stump, four feet high and about a foot in diameter at the butt. It had lava boulders piled around its base to hold it up and keep it in its place, and it was entirely sheathed over, from top to bottom, with rough, discolored sheets of copper, such as ships' bottoms are coppered with. Each sheet had a rude inscription scratched upon it—with a nail, apparently—and in every case the execution was wretched. Most of these merely recorded the visits of British naval commanders to the spot, but one of them bore this legend:

"Near this spot fell
CAPTAIN JAMES COOK,
The Distinguished Circumnavigator, who Discovered these
Islands A.D. 1778.

After Cook's murder, his second in command, on board the ship, opened fire upon the swarms of natives on the beach, and one of his cannon balls cut this cocoanut tree short off and left this monumental stump standing. It looked sad and lonely enough to us, out there in the rainy twilight. But there is no other monument to Captain Cook. True, up on the mountain side we had passed by a large inclosure like an ample hog-pen, built of lava blocks, which marks the spot where Cook's flesh was stripped from his bones and burned; but this is not properly a monument, since it was erected by the natives themselves, and less to do honor to the circumnavigator than for the sake of convenience in roasting him. A thing like a guide-board was elevated above this pen on a tall pole, and formerly there was an inscription upon it describing the memorable occurrence that had there taken place; but the sun and the wind have long ago so defaced it as to render it illegible.

Toward midnight a fine breeze sprang up and the schooner soon worked herself into the bay and cast anchor. The boat came ashore for us, and in a little while the clouds and the rain were all gone. The moon was beaming tranquilly down on land and sea, and we two were stretched upon the deck sleeping the refreshing sleep and dreaming the happy dreams that are only vouchsafed to the weary and the innocent.

CHAPTER LXXII

In the breezy morning we went ashore and visited the ruined temple of the last god Lono. The high chief cook of this temple—the priest who presided over it and roasted the human sacrifices—was uncle to Obookia, and at one time that youth was an apprentice-priest under him. Obookia was a young native of fine mind, who, together with three other native boys, was taken to New England by the captain of a whaleship during the reign of Kamehameha I, and they were the means of attracting the attention of the religious world to their country. This resulted in the sending of missionaries there. And this Obookia was the very same sensitive savage who sat down on the church steps and wept because his people did not have the Bible. That incident has been very elaborately painted in many a charming Sunday School book—aye, and told so plaintively and so tenderly that I have cried over it in Sunday School myself, on general principles, although at a time when I did not know much and could not understand why the people of the Sandwich Islands needed to worry so much about it as long as they did not know there was a Bible at all.

Obookia was converted and educated, and was to have returned to his native land with the first missionaries, had he lived. The other native youths made the voyage, and two of them did good service, but the third, William Kanui, fell from grace afterward, for a time, and when the gold excitement broke out in California he journeyed thither and went to mining, although he was fifty years old. He succeeded pretty well, but the failure of Page, Bacon & Co. relieved him of six thousand dollars, and then, to all intents and purposes, he was a bankrupt in his old age and he resumed service in the pulpit again. He died in Honolulu in 1864.

Quite a broad tract of land near the temple, extending from the sea to the mountain top, was sacred to the god Lono in olden times—so sacred that if a common native set his sacrilegious foot upon it it was judicious for him to make his will, because his time had come. He might go around it by water, but he could not cross it. It was well sprinkled with pagan temples and stocked with awkward, homely idols carved out of logs of wood. There was a temple devoted to prayers for rain—and with fine sagacity it was placed at a point so well up on the mountain side that if you prayed there twenty-four times a day for rain you would be likely to get it every time. You would seldom get to your Amen before you would have to hoist your umbrella.

And there was a large temple near at hand which was built in a single night, in the midst of storm and thunder and rain, by the ghastly hands of dead men! Tradition says that the weird glare of the lightning a noiseless multitude of phantoms were seen at their strange labor far up the mountain side at dead of night—flitting hither and thither and bearing great lava-blocks clasped in their nerveless fingers—appearing and disappearing as the pallid lustre fell upon their forms and faded away again. Even to this day, it is said, the natives hold this dread structure in awe and reverence, and will not pass by it in the night.

At noon I observed a bevy of nude native young ladies bathing in the sea, and went and sat down on their clothes to keep them from being stolen. I begged them to come out, for the sea was rising and I was satisfied that they were running some risk. But they were not afraid, and presently went on with their sport. They were finished swimmers and divers, and enjoyed themselves to the last degree. The swam races, splashed and ducked and tumbled each other about, and filled the air with their laughter. It is said that the first thing an Islander learns is how to swim; learning how to walk being a matter of smaller consequence, comes afterward. One hears tales of native men and women swimming ashore from vessels many miles at sea—more miles, indeed, than I dare vouch for or even mention. And they tell of a native diver who went down in thirty or forty-foot waters and brought up an anvil! I think he swallowed the anvil afterward, if my memory serves me. However I will not urge this point.

I have spoken, several times, of the god Lono—I may as well furnish two or three sentences concerning him.

The idol the natives worshiped for him was a slender, unornamented staff twelve feet long. Tradition says he was a favorite god on the Island of Hawaii—a great king who had been deified for meritorious services—just our own fashion of rewarding heroes, with the difference that we would have made him a Postmaster instead of a god, no doubt. In an angry moment he slew his wife, a goddess named Kaikilani Aiii. Remorse of conscience drove him mad, and tradition presents us the singular spectacle of a god traveling "on the shoulder;" for in his gnawing grief he wandered about from place to place boxing and wrestling with all whom he met. Of course this pastime soon lost its novelty, inasmuch as it must necessarily have been the case when so powerful a deity sent a frail human opponent "to grass" he never came back any more. Therefore, he instituted games called makahiki, and ordered that they should be held in his honor, and then sailed for foreign lands on a three-cornered raft, stating that he would return some day—and that was the last of Lono. He was never seen any more; his raft got swamped, perhaps. But the people always expected his return, and thus they were easily led to accept Captain Cook as the restored god.

Some of the old natives believed Cook was Lono to the day of their death; but many did not, for they could not understand how he could die if he was a god.

Only a mile or so from Kealakekua Bay is a spot of historic interest—the place where the last battle was fought for idolatry. Of course we visited it, and came away as wise as most people do who go and gaze upon such mementoes of the past when in an unreflective mood.

While the first missionaries were on their way around the Horn, the idolatrous customs which had obtained in the island, as far back as tradition reached were suddenly broken up. Old Kamehameha I. was dead, and his son, Liholiho, the new King was a free liver, a roystering, dissolute fellow, and hated the restraints of the ancient *tabu*. His assistant in the Government, Kaahumanu, the Queen dowager, was proud and high-spirited, and hated the *tabu* because it restricted the privileges of her sex and degraded all women very nearly to the level of brutes. So the case stood. Liholiho had half a mind to put his foot down, Kaahumanu had a whole mind to badger him into doing it, and whiskey did the rest. It was probably the rest. It was probably the first time whiskey ever prominently figured as an aid to civilization. Liholiho came up to Kailua as drunk as a piper, and attended a great feast; the determined Queen spurred his drunken courage up to a reckless pitch, and then, while all the multitude stared in blank dismay, he moved deliberately forward and sat down with the women! They saw him eat from the same vessel with them, and were appalled! Terrible moments drifted slowly by, and still the King ate, still he lived, still the lightnings of the insulted gods were withheld! Then conviction came like a revelation—the superstitions of a hundred generations passed from before the people like a cloud, and a shout went up, "the *tabu* is broken! the *tabu* is broken!"

Thus did King Liholiho and his dreadful whiskey preach the first sermon and prepare the way for the new gospel that was speeding southward over the waves of the Atlantic.

The *tabu* broken and destruction failing to follow the awful sacrilege, the people, with that childlike precipitancy which has always characterized them, jumped to the conclusion that their gods were a weak and wretched swindle, just as they formerly jumped to the conclusion that Captain Cook was no god, merely because he groaned, and promptly killed him without stopping to inquire whether a god might not groan as well as a man if it suited his convenience to do it; and satisfied that the idols were powerless to protect themselves they went to work at once and pulled them down—hacked them to pieces—applied the torch—annihilated them!

The pagan priests were furious. And well they might be; they had held the fattest offices in the land, and now they were beggared; they had been great—they had stood above the chiefs—and now they were vagabonds. They raised a revolt; they scared a number of people into joining their standard, and Bekuokalani, an ambitious offshoot of royalty, was easily persuaded to become their leader.

In the first skirmish the idolaters triumphed over the royal army sent against them, and full of confidence they resolved to march upon Kailua. The King sent an envoy to try and conciliate them, and came very near being an envoy short by the operation; the savages not only refused to listen to him, but wanted to kill him. So the King sent his men forth under Major General Kalaimoku and the two hosts met at Kuamoo. The battle was long and fierce—men and women fighting side by side, as was the custom—and when the day was done the rebels were flying in every direction in hopeless panic, and idolatry and the *tabu* were dead in the land!

The royalists marched gayly home to Kailua glorifying the new dispensation. "There is no power in the gods," said they; "they are a vanity and a lie. The army with idols was weak; the army without idols was strong and victorious!"

The nation was without a religion.

The missionary ship arrived in safety shortly afterward, timed by providential exactness to meet the emergency, and the Gospel was planted as in a virgin soil.

CHAPTER LXXIII

At noon, we hired a Kanaka to take us down to the ancient ruins at Honaunau in his canoe—price two dollars—reasonable enough, for a sea voyage of eight miles, counting both ways.

The native canoe is an irresponsible looking contrivance. I cannot think of anything to liken it to but a boy's sled runner hollowed out, and that does not quite convey the correct idea. It is about fifteen feet long, high and pointed at both ends, is a foot and a half or two feet deep, and so narrow that if you wedged a fat man into it you might not get him out again. It sits on top of the water like a duck, but it has an outrigger and does not upset easily, if you keep still. This outrigger is formed of two long bent sticks like plow handles, which project from one side, and to their outer ends is bound a curved beam composed of an extremely light wood, which skims along the surface of the water and thus saves you from an upset on that side, while the outrigger's weight is not so easily lifted as to make an upset on the other side a thing to be greatly feared. Still, until one gets used to sitting perched upon this knife-blade, he is apt to reason within himself that it would be more comfortable if there were just an outrigger or so on the other side also.

I had the bow seat, and Billings sat amidships and faced the Kanaka, who occupied the stern of the craft and did the paddling. With the first stroke the trim shell of a thing shot out from the shore like an arrow. There was not much to see. While we were on the shallow water of the reef, it was pastime to look down into the limpid depths at the large bunches of branching coral—the unique shrubbery of the sea. We lost that, though, when we got out into the dead blue water of the deep. But we had the picture of the surf, then, dashing angrily against the crag-bound shore and sending a foaming spray high into the air. There was interest in this beetling border, too, for it was honeycombed with quaint caves and arches and tunnels, and had a rude resemblance of the dilapidated architecture of ruined keeps and castles rising out of the restless sea. When this novelty ceased to be a novelty, we turned our eyes shoreward and gazed at the long mountain with its rich green forests stretching up into the curtaining clouds, and at the specks of houses in the rearward distance and the diminished schooner riding sleepily at anchor. And when these grew tiresome we dashed boldly into the midst of a school of huge, beastly porpoises engaged at their eternal game of arching over a wave and disappearing, and then doing it over again and keeping it up—always circling over, in that way, like so many well-submerged wheels. But the porpoises wheeled themselves away, and then we were thrown upon our own resources. It did not take many minutes to discover that the sun was blazing like a bonfire, and that the weather was of a melting temperature. It had a drowsing effect, too.

In one place we came upon a large company of naked natives, of both sexes and all ages, amusing themselves with the national pastime of surf-bathing. Each heathen would paddle three or four hundred yards out to sea, (taking a short board with him), then face the shore and wait for a particularly prodigious billow to come along; at the right moment he would fling his board upon its foamy crest and himself upon the board, and here he would come whizzing by like a bombshell! It did not seem that a lightning express train could shoot along at a more hair-lifting speed. I tried surf-bathing once, subsequently, but made a failure of it. I got the board placed right, and at the right moment, too; but missed connection myself.—The board struck the shore in three quarters of a second, without any cargo, and I struck the bottom about the same time, with a couple of barrels of water in me. None but natives ever master the art of surf-bathing thoroughly.

At the end of an hour, we had made the four miles, and landed on a level point of land, upon which was a wide extent of old ruins, with many a tall cocoanut tree growing among them. Here was the ancient City of Refuge—a vast inclosure, whose stone walls were twenty feet thick at the base, and fifteen feet high; an oblong square, a thousand and forty feet one way and a fraction under seven hundred the other. Within this inclosure, in early times, has been three rude temples; each two hundred and ten feet long by one hundred wide, and thirteen high.

In those days, if a man killed another anywhere on the island the relatives were privileged to take the murderer's life; and then a chase for life and liberty began—the outlawed criminal flying through pathless forests and over mountain and plain, with his hopes fixed upon the protecting walls of the City of Refuge, and the avenger of blood following hotly after him! Sometimes the race was kept up to the very gates of the temple, and the panting pair sped through long files of excited natives, who watched the contest with flashing eye and dilated nostril, encouraging the hunted refugee with sharp, inspiriting ejaculations, and sending up a ringing shout of exultation when the saving gates closed upon him and the cheated pursuer sank exhausted at the threshold. But sometimes the flying criminal fell under the hand of the avenger at the very door, when one more brave stride, one more brief second of time would have brought his feet upon the sacred ground and barred him against all harm. Where did these isolated pagans get this idea of a City of Refuge—this ancient Oriental custom?

This old sanctuary was sacred to all—even to rebels in arms and invading armies. Once within its walls, and confession made to the priest and absolution obtained, the wretch with a price upon his head could go forth without fear and without danger—he was *tabu,* and to harm him was death. The routed rebels in the lost battle for idolatry fled to this place to claim sanctuary, and many were thus saved.

Close to the corner of the great inclosure is a round structure of stone, some six or eight feet high, with a level top about ten or twelve in diameter. This was the place of execution. A high palisade of cocoanut piles shut out the cruel scenes from the vulgar multitude. Here criminals were killed, the flesh stripped from the bones and burned, and the bones secreted in holes in the body of the structure. If the man had been guilty of a high crime, the entire corpse was burned.

The walls of the temple are a study. The same food for speculation that is offered the visitor to the Pyramids of Egypt he will find here—the mystery of how they were constructed by a people unacquainted with science and mechanics. The natives have no invention of their own for hoisting heavy weights, they had no beasts of burden, and they have never even shown any knowledge of the properties of the lever. Yet some of the lava blocks quarried out, brought over rough, broken ground, and built into this wall, six or seven feet from the ground, are of prodigious size and would weigh tons. How did they transport and raise them?

Both the inner and the outer surfaces of the walls present a smooth front and are very creditable specimens of masonry. The blocks are of all manner of shapes and sizes, but yet are fitted together with the neatest exactness. The gradual narrowing of the wall from the base upward is accurately preserved.

No cement was used, but the edifice is firm and compact and is capable of resisting storm and decay for centuries. Who built this temple, and how was it built, and when, are mysteries that may never be unraveled.

Outside of these ancient walls lies a sort of coffin-shaped stone eleven feet four inches long and three feet square at the small end (it would weigh a few thousand pounds), which the high chief who held sway over this district many centuries ago brought thither on his shoulder one day to use as a lounge! This circumstance is established by the most reliable traditions. He used to lie down on it, in his indolent way, and keep an eye on his subjects at work for him and see that there were no "soldiering" done. And no doubt there was not any done to speak of, because he was a man of that sort of build that incites to attention to business on the part of an employee. He was fourteen or fifteen feet high. When he stretched himself at full length on his lounge, his legs hung down over the end, and when he snored he woke the dead. These facts are all attested by irrefragable tradition.

On the other side of the temple is a monstrous seven-ton rock, eleven feet long, seven feet wide and three feet thick. It is raised a foot or a foot and a half above the ground, and rests upon half a dozen little stony pedestals. The same old fourteen-footer brought it down from the mountain, merely for fun (he had his own notions about fun), and propped it up as we find it now and as others may find it a century hence, for it would take a score of horses to budge it from its position. They say that fifty or sixty years ago the proud Queen Kaahumanu used to fly to this rock for safety, whenever she had been making trouble with her fierce husband, and hide under it until his wrath was appeased. But these Kanakas will lie, and this statement is one of their ablest efforts—for Kaahumanu was six feet high—she was bulky—she was built like an ox—and she could no more have squeezed herself under that rock than she could have passed between the cylinders of a sugar mill. What could she gain by it, even if she succeeded? To be chased and abused by a savage husband could not be otherwise than humiliating to her high spirit, yet it could never make her feel so flat as an hour's repose under that rock would.

We walked a mile over a raised macadamized road of uniform width; a road paved with flat stones and exhibiting in its every detail a considerable degree of engineering skill. Some say that that wise old pagan, Kamehameha I., planned and built it, but others say it was built so long before his time that the knowledge of who constructed it has passed out of the traditions. In either case, however, as the handiwork of an untaught and degraded race it is a thing of pleasing interest. The stones are worn and smooth, and pushed apart in places, so that the road has the exact appearance of those ancient paved highways leading out of Rome which one sees in pictures.

The object of our tramp was to visit a great natural curiosity at the base of the foothills—a congealed cascade of lava. Some old forgotten volcanic eruption sent its broad river of fire down the mountain side here, and it poured down in a great torrent from an overhanging bluff some fifty feet high to the ground below. The flaming torrent cooled in the winds from the sea, and remains there to-day, all seamed, and frothed and rippled a petrified Niagara. It is very picturesque, and withal so natural that one might almost imagine it still flowed. A smaller stream trickled over the cliff and built up an isolated pyramid about thirty feet high, which has the semblance of a mass of large gnarled and knotted vines and roots and stems intricately twisted and woven together.

We passed in behind the cascade and the pyramid, and found the bluff pierced by several cavernous tunnels, whose crooked courses we followed a long distance.

Two of these winding tunnels stand as proof of Nature's mining abilities. Their floors are level, they are seven feet wide, and their roofs are gently arched. Their height is not uniform, however. We passed through one a hundred feet long, which leads through a spur of the hill and opens out well up in the sheer wall of a precipice whose foot rests in the waves of the sea. It is a commodious tunnel, except that there are occasional places in it where one must stoop to pass under. The roof is lava, of course, and is thickly studded with little lava-pointed icicles an inch long, which hardened as they dripped. They project as closely together as the iron teeth of a corn-sheller, and if one will stand up straight and walk any distance there, he can get his hair combed free of charge.

CHAPTER LXXIV

We got back to the schooner in good time, and then sailed down to Kau, where we disembarked and took final leave of the vessel. Next day we bought horses and bent our way over the summer-clad mountain-terraces, toward the great volcano of Kilauea (Ke-low-way-ah). We made nearly a two days' journey of it, but that was on account of laziness. Toward sunset on the second day, we reached an elevation of some four thousand feet above sea level, and as we picked our careful way through billowy wastes of lava long generations ago stricken dead and cold in the climax of its tossing fury, we began to come upon signs of the near presence of the volcano—signs in the nature of ragged fissures that discharged jets of sulphurous vapor into the air, hot from the molten ocean down in the bowels of the mountain.

Shortly the crater came into view. I have seen Vesuvius since, but it was a mere toy, a child's volcano, a soup-kettle, compared to this. Mount Vesuvius is a shapely cone thirty-six hundred feet high; its crater an inverted cone only three hundred feet deep, and not more than a thousand feet in diameter, if as much as that; its fires meagre, modest, and docile.—But here was a vast, perpendicular, walled cellar, nine hundred feet deep in some places, thirteen hundred in others, level-floored, and *ten miles in circumference!* Here was a yawning pit upon whose floor the armies of Russia could camp, and have room to spare.

Perched upon the edge of the crater, at the opposite end from where we stood, was a small look-out house—say three miles away. It assisted us, by comparison, to comprehend and appreciate the great depth of the basin—it looked like a tiny martin-box clinging at the eaves of a cathedral. After some little time spent in resting and looking and ciphering, we hurried on to the hotel.

By the path it is half a mile from the Volcano House to the lookout-house. After a hearty supper we waited until it was thoroughly dark and then started to the crater. The first glance in that direction revealed a scene of wild beauty. There was a heavy fog over the crater and it was splendidly illuminated by the glare from the fires below. The illumination was two miles wide and a mile high, perhaps; and if you ever, on a dark night and at a distance beheld the light from thirty or forty blocks of distant buildings all on fire at once, reflected strongly against overhanging clouds, you can form a fair idea of what this looked like.

A colossal column of cloud towered to a great height in the air immediately above the crater, and the outer swell of every one of its vast folds was dyed with a rich crimson luster, which was subdued to a pale rose tint in the depressions between. It glowed like a muffled torch and stretched upward to a dizzy height toward the zenith. I thought it just possible that its like had not been seen since the children of Israel wandered on their long march through the desert so many centuries ago over a path illuminated by the mysterious "pillar of fire." And I was sure that I now had a vivid conception of what the majestic "pillar of fire" was like, which almost amounted to a revelation.

Arrived at the little thatched lookout house, we rested our elbows on the railing in front and looked abroad over the wide crater and down over the sheer precipice at the seething fires beneath us. The view was a startling improvement on my daylight experience. I turned to see the effect on the balance of the company and found the reddest-faced set of men I almost ever saw. In the strong light every countenance glowed like red-hot iron, every shoulder was suffused with crimson and shaded rearward into dingy, shapeless obscurity! The place below looked like the infernal regions and these men like half-cooled devils just come up on a furlough.

I turned my eyes upon the volcano again. The "cellar" was tolerably well lighted up. For a mile and a half in front of us and half a mile on either side, the floor of the abyss was magnificently illuminated; beyond these limits the mists hung down their gauzy curtains and cast a deceptive gloom over all that made the twinkling fires in the remote corners of the crater seem countless leagues removed—made them seem like the camp-fires of a great army far away. Here was room for the imagination to work! You could imagine those lights the width of a continent away—

and that hidden under the intervening darkness were hills, and winding rivers, and weary wastes of plain and desert—and even then the tremendous vista stretched on, and on, and on!—to the fires and far beyond! You could not compass it—it was the idea of eternity made tangible—and the longest end of it made visible to the naked eye!

The greater part of the vast floor of the desert under us was as black as ink, and apparently smooth and level; but over a mile square of it was ringed and streaked and striped with a thousand branching streams of liquid and gorgeously brilliant fire! It looked like a colossal railroad map of the State of Massachusetts done in chain lightning on a midnight sky. Imagine it— imagine a coal-black sky shivered into a tangled net-work of angry fire!

Here and there were gleaming holes a hundred feet in diameter, broken in the dark crust, and in them the melted lava—the color a dazzling white just tinged with yellow—was boiling and surging furiously; and from these holes branched numberless bright torrents in many directions, like the spokes of a wheel, and kept a tolerably straight course for a while and then swept round in huge rainbow curves, or made a long succession of sharp worm-fence angles, which looked precisely like the fiercest jagged lightning. These streams met other streams, and they mingled with and crossed and recrossed each other in every conceivable direction, like skate tracks on a popular skating ground. Sometimes streams twenty or thirty feet wide flowed from the holes to some distance without dividing—and through the opera-glasses we could see that they ran down small, steep hills and were genuine cataracts of fire, white at their source, but soon cooling and turning to the richest red, grained with alternate lines of black and gold. Every now and then masses of the dark crust broke away and floated slowly down these streams like rafts down a river. Occasionally the molten lava flowing under the superincumbent crust broke through—split a dazzling streak, from five hundred to a thousand feet long, like a sudden flash of lightning, and then acre after acre of the cold lava parted into fragments, turned up edgewise like cakes of ice when a great river breaks up, plunged downward and were swallowed in the crimson cauldron. Then the wide expanse of the "thaw" maintained a ruddy glow for a while, but shortly cooled and became black and level again. During a "thaw," every dismembered cake was marked by a glittering white border which was superbly shaded inward by aurora borealis rays, which were a flaming yellow where they joined the white border, and from thence toward their points tapered into glowing crimson, then into a rich, pale carmine, and finally into a faint blush that held its own a moment and then dimmed and turned black. Some of the streams preferred to mingle together in a tangle of fantastic circles, and then they looked something like the confusion of ropes one sees on a ship's deck when she has just taken in sail and dropped anchor—provided one can imagine those ropes on fire.

Through the glasses, the little fountains scattered about looked very beautiful. They boiled, and coughed, and spluttered, and discharged sprays of stringy red fire—of about the consistency of mush, for instance—from ten to fifteen feet into the air, along with a shower of brilliant white sparks—a quaint and unnatural mingling of gouts of blood and snow-flakes!

We had circles and serpents and streaks of lightning all twined and wreathed and tied together, without a break throughout an area more than a mile square (that amount of ground was covered, though it was not strictly "square"), and it was with a feeling of placid exultation that we reflected that many years had elapsed since any visitor had seen such a splendid display—since any visitor had seen anything more than the now snubbed and insignificant "North" and "South" lakes in action. We had been reading old files of Hawaiian newspapers and the "Record Book" at the Volcano House, and were posted.

I could see the North Lake lying out on the black floor away off in the outer edge of our panorama, and knitted to it by a web-work of lava streams. In its individual capacity it looked very little more respectable than a schoolhouse on fire. True, it was about nine hundred feet long and two or three hundred wide, but then, under the present circumstances, it necessarily appeared rather insignificant, and besides it was so distant from us.

I forgot to say that the noise made by the bubbling lava is not great, heard as we heard it from our lofty perch. It makes three distinct sounds—a rushing, a hissing, and a coughing or puffing sound; and if you stand on the brink and close your eyes it is no trick at all to imagine that you are sweeping down a river on a large low-pressure steamer, and that you hear the hissing of the steam about her boilers, the puffing from her escape-pipes and the churning rush of the water abaft her wheels. The smell of sulphur is strong, but not unpleasant to a sinner.

We left the lookout house at ten o'clock in a half cooked condition, because of the heat from Pele's furnaces, and wrapping up in blankets, for the night was cold, we returned to our Hotel.

CHAPTER LXXV

The next night was appointed for a visit to the bottom of the crater, for we desired to traverse its floor and see the "North Lake" (of fire) which lay two miles away, toward the further wall. After dark half a dozen of us set out, with lanterns and native guides, and climbed down a crazy, thousand-foot pathway in a crevice fractured in the crater wall, and reached the bottom in safety.

The irruption of the previous evening had spent its force and the floor looked black and cold; but when we ran out upon it we found it hot yet, to the feet, and it was likewise riven with crevices which revealed the underlying fires gleaming vindictively. A neighboring cauldron was threatening to overflow, and this added to the dubiousness of the situation. So the native guides refused to continue the venture, and then every body deserted except a stranger named Marlette. He said he had been in the crater a dozen times in daylight and believed he could find his way through it at night. He thought that a run of three hundred yards would carry us over the hottest part of the floor and leave us our shoe-soles. His pluck gave me back-bone. We took one lantern and instructed the guides to hang the other to the roof of the look-out house to serve as a beacon for us in case we got lost, and then the party started back up the precipice and Marlette and I made our run. We skipped over the hot floor and over the red crevices with brisk dispatch and reached the cold lava safe but with pretty warm feet. Then we took things leisurely and comfortably, jumping tolerably wide and probably bottomless chasms, and threading our way through picturesque lava upheavals with considerable confidence. When we got fairly away from the cauldrons of boiling fire, we seemed to be in a gloomy desert, and a suffocating dark one, surrounded by dim walls that seemed to tower to the sky. The only cheerful objects were the glinting stars high overhead.

By and by Marlette shouted "Stop!" I never stopped quicker in my life. I asked what the matter was. He said we were out of the path. He said we must not try to go on till we found it again, for we were surrounded with beds of rotten lava through which we could easily break and plunge down a thousand feet. I thought eight hundred would answer for me, and was about to say so when Marlette partly proved his statement by accidentally crushing through and disappearing to his arm-pits. He got out and we hunted for the path with the lantern. He said there was only one path and that it was but vaguely defined. We could not find it. The lava surface was all alike in the lantern light. But he was an ingenious man. He said it was not the lantern that had informed him that we were out of the path, but his *feet.* He had noticed a crisp grinding of fine lava-needles under his feet, and some instinct reminded him that in the path these were all worn away. So he put the lantern behind him, and began to search with his boots instead of his eyes. It was good sagacity. The first time his foot touched a surface that did not grind under it he announced that the trail was found again; and after that we kept up a sharp listening for the rasping sound and it always warned us in time.

It was a long tramp, but an exciting one. We reached the North Lake between ten and eleven o'clock, and sat down on a huge overhanging lava-shelf, tired but satisfied. The spectacle presented was worth coming double the distance to see. Under us, and stretching away before us, was a heaving sea of molten fire of seemingly limitless extent. The glare from it was so blinding that it was some time before we could bear to look upon it steadily. It was like gazing at the sun at noonday, except that the glare was not quite so white. At unequal distances all around the shores of the lake were nearly white-hot chimneys or hollow drums of lava, four or five feet high, and up through them were bursting gorgeous sprays of lava-gouts and gem spangles, some white, some red and some golden—a ceaseless bombardment, and one that fascinated the eye with its unapproachable splendor. The more distant jets, sparkling up through an intervening gossamer veil of vapor, seemed miles away; and the further the curving ranks of fiery fountains receded, the more fairy-like and beautiful they appeared.

Now and then the surging bosom of the lake under our noses would calm down ominously and seem to be gathering strength for an enterprise; and then all of a sudden a red dome of lava of the bulk of an ordinary dwelling would heave itself aloft like an escaping balloon, then burst asunder, and out if its heart would flit a pale-green film of vapor, and float upward and vanish in the darkness—a released soul soaring homeward from captivity with the damned, no doubt. The crashing plunge of the ruined dome into the lake again would send a world of seething billows lashing against the shores and shaking the foundations of our perch. By and by, a loosened mass of the hanging shelf we sat on tumbled into the lake, jarring the surroundings like an earthquake and delivering a suggestion that may have been intended for a hint, and may not. We did not wait to see.

We got lost again on our way back, and were more than an hour hunting for the path. We were where we could see the beacon lantern at the look-out house at the time, but thought it was a star and paid no attention to it. We reached the hotel at two o'clock in the morning pretty well fagged out.

Kilauea never overflows its vast crater, but bursts a passage for its lava through the mountain side when relief is necessary, and then the destruction is fearful. About 1840 it rent its overburdened stomach and sent a broad river of fire careering down to the sea, which swept away forests, huts, plantations and every thing else that lay in its path. The stream was *five miles broad,* in places, and *two hundred feet deep*, and the distance it traveled was forty miles. It tore up and bore away acre-patches of land on its bosom like rafts—rocks, trees and all intact. At night the red glare was visible a hundred miles at sea; and at a distance of forty miles fine print could be read at midnight. The atmosphere was poisoned with sulphurous vapors and choked with falling ashes, pumice stones and cinders; countless columns of smoke rose up and blended together in a tumbled canopy that hid the heavens and glowed with a ruddy flush reflected from the fires below; here and there jets of lava sprung hundreds of feet into the air and burst into rocket-sprays that returned to earth in a crimson rain; and all the while the laboring mountain shook with Nature's great palsy, and voiced its distress in moanings and the muffled booming and subterranean thunders.

Fishes were killed for twenty miles along the shore, where the lava entered the sea. The earthquakes caused some loss of human life, and a prodigious tidal wave swept inland, carrying every thing before it and drowning a number of natives. The devastation consummated along the route traversed by the river of lava was complete and incalculable. Only a Pompeii and a Herculaneum were needed at the foot of Kilauea to make the story of the irruption immortal.

CHAPTER LXXVI

We rode horseback all around the island of Hawaii (the crooked road making the distance two hundred miles), and enjoyed the journey very much. We were more than a week making the trip, because our Kanaka horses would not go by a house or a hut without stopping—whip and spur could not alter their minds about it, and so we finally found that it economized time to let them have their way. Upon inquiry the mystery was explained: the natives are such thorough-going gossips that they never pass a house without stopping to swap news, and consequently their horses learn to regard that sort of thing as an essential part of the whole duty of man, and his salvation not to be compassed without it. However, at a former crisis of my life I had once taken an aristocratic young lady out driving, behind a horse that had just retired from a long and honorable career as the moving impulse of a milk wagon, and so this present experience awoke a reminiscent sadness in me in place of the exasperation more natural to the occasion. I remembered how helpless I was that day, and how humiliated; how ashamed I was of having intimated to the girl that I had always owned the horse and was accustomed to grandeur; how hard I tried to appear easy, and even vivacious, under suffering that was consuming my vitals; how placidly and maliciously the girl smiled, and kept on smiling, while my hot blushes baked themselves into a permanent blood-pudding in my face; how the horse ambled from one side of the street to the other and waited complacently before every third house two minutes and a quarter while I belabored his back and reviled him in my heart; how I tried to keep him from turning corners, and failed; how I moved heaven and earth to get him out of town, and did not succeed; how he traversed the entire settlement and delivered imaginary milk at a hundred and sixty-two different domiciles, and how he finally brought up at a dairy depot and refused to budge further, thus rounding and completing the revealment of what the plebeian service of his life had been; how, in eloquent silence, I walked the girl home, and how, when I took leave of her, her parting remark scorched my soul and appeared to blister me all over: she said that my horse was a fine, capable animal, and I must have taken great comfort in him in my time—but that if I would take along some milk tickets next time, and appear to deliver them at the various halting places, it might expedite his movements a little. There was a coolness between us after that.

In one place in the island of Hawaii, we saw a laced and ruffled cataract of limpid water leaping from a sheer precipice fifteen hundred feet high; but that sort of scenery finds its stanchest ally in the arithmetic rather than in spectacular effect. If one desires to be so stirred by a poem of Nature wrought in the happily commingled graces of picturesque rocks, glimpsed distances, foliage, color, shifting lights and shadows, and falling water, that the tears almost come into his eyes so potent is the charm exerted, he need not go away from America to enjoy such an experience. The Rainbow Fall, in Watkins Glen (N. Y.), on the Erie railway, is an example. It would recede into pitiable insignificance if the callous tourist drew an arithmetic on it; but left to compete for the honors simply on scenic grace and beauty—the grand, the august and the sublime being barred the contest—it could challenge the old world and the new to produce its peer.

In one locality, on our journey, we saw some horses that had been born and reared on top of the mountains, above the range of running water, and consequently they had never drank that fluid in their lives, but had been always accustomed to quenching their thirst by eating dew-laden or shower-wetted leaves. And now it was destructively funny to see them sniff suspiciously at a pail of water, and then put in their noses and try to take a *bite* out of the fluid, as if it were a solid. Finding it liquid, they would snatch away their heads and fall to trembling, snorting and showing other evidences of fright. When they became convinced at last that the water was friendly and harmless, they thrust in their noses up to their eyes, brought out a mouthful of the water, and proceeded to *chew* it complacently. We saw a man coax, kick and spur one of them five or ten minutes before he could make it cross a running stream. It spread its nostrils, distended its eyes and trembled all over, just as horses customarily do in the presence of a serpent—and for aught I know it thought the crawling stream *was* a serpent.

In due course of time our journey came to an end at Kawaehae (usually pronounced To-a-*hi*—and before we find fault with this elaborate orthographical method of arriving at such an unostentatious result, let us lop off the *ugh* from our word "though"). I made this horseback trip on a mule. I paid ten dollars for him at Kau (Kah-oo), added four to get him shod, rode him two hundred miles, and then sold him for fifteen dollars. I mark the circumstance with a white stone (in the absence of chalk—for I never saw a white stone that a body could mark anything with, though out of respect for the ancients I have tried it often enough); for up to that day and date it was the first strictly commercial transaction I have ever entered into, and come out winner. We returned to Honolulu, and from thence sailed to the island of Maui, and spent several weeks there very pleasantly. I still remember, with a sense of indolent luxury, a picnicing excursion up a romantic gorge there, called the Iao Valley. The trail lay along the edge of a brawling stream in the bottom of the gorge—a shady route, for it was well roofed with the verdant domes of forest trees. Through openings in the foliage we glimpsed picturesque scenery that revealed ceaseless changes and new charms with every step of our progress. Perpendicular walls from one to three thousand feet high guarded the way, and were sumptuously plumed with varied foliage, in places, and in places swathed in waving ferns. Passing shreds of cloud trailed their shadows across these shining fronts, mottling them with blots; billowy masses of white vapor hid the turreted summits, and far above the vapor swelled a background of gleaming green crags and cones that came and went, through the veiling mists, like islands drifting in a fog; sometimes the cloudy curtain descended till half the canon wall was hidden, then shredded gradually away till only airy glimpses of the ferny front appeared through it—then swept aloft and left it glorified in the sun again. Now and then, as our position changed, rocky bastions swung out from the wall, a mimic ruin of castellated ramparts and crumbling towers clothed with mosses and hung with garlands of swaying vines, and as we moved on they swung back again and hid themselves once more in the foliage. Presently a verdure-clad needle of stone, a thousand feet high, stepped out from behind a corner, and mounted guard over the mysteries of the valley. It seemed to me that if Captain Cook needed a monument, here was one ready made—therefore, why not put up his sign here, and sell out the venerable cocoanut stump?

But the chief pride of Maui is her dead volcano of Haleakala—which means, translated, "the house of the sun." We climbed a thousand feet up the side of this isolated colossus one afternoon; then camped, and next day climbed the remaining nine thousand feet, and anchored on the summit, where we built a fire and froze and roasted by turns, all night. With the first pallor of dawn we got up and saw things that were new to us. Mounted on a commanding pinnacle, we watched Nature work her silent wonders. The sea was spread abroad on every hand, its tumbled surface seeming only wrinkled and dimpled in the distance. A broad valley below appeared like an ample checker-board, its velvety green sugar plantations alternating with dun squares of barrenness and groves of trees diminished to mossy tufts. Beyond the valley were mountains picturesquely grouped together; but bear in mind, we fancied that we were looking *up* at these things—not down. We seemed to sit in the bottom of a symmetrical bowl ten thousand feet deep, with the valley and the skirting sea lifted away into the sky above us! It was curious; and not only curious, but aggravating; for it was having our trouble all for nothing, to climb ten thousand feet toward heaven and then have to look *up* at our scenery. However, we had to be content with it and make the best of it; for, all we could do we could not coax our landscape down out of the clouds. Formerly, when I had read an article in which Poe treated of this singular fraud perpetrated upon the eye by isolated great altitudes, I had looked upon the matter as an invention of his own fancy.

I have spoken of the outside view—but we had an inside one, too. That was the yawning dead crater, into which we now and then tumbled rocks, half as large as a barrel, from our perch, and saw them go careering down the almost perpendicular sides, bounding three hundred feet at a jump; kicking up dust-clouds wherever they struck; diminishing to our view as they sped farther into distance; growing invisible, finally, and only betraying their course by faint little puffs of dust; and coming to a halt at last in the bottom of the abyss, two thousand five hundred feet down from where they started! It was magnificent sport. We wore ourselves out at it.

The crater of Vesuvius, as I have before remarked, is a modest pit about a thousand feet deep and three thousand in circumference; that of Kilauea is somewhat deeper, and *ten miles* in circumference. But what are either of them compared to the vacant stomach of Haleakala? I will not offer any figures of my own, but give official ones—those of Commander Wilkes, U. S. N., who surveyed it and testifies that it is *twenty-seven miles in circumference!* If it had a level bottom it would make a fine site for a city like London. It must have afforded a spectacle worth contemplating in the old days when its furnaces gave full rein to their anger.

Presently vagrant white clouds came drifting along, high over the sea and the valley; then they came in couples and groups; then in imposing squadrons; gradually joining their forces, they banked themselves solidly together, a thousand feet under us, and *totally shut out land and ocean*—not a vestige of *anything* was left in view but just a little of the rim of the crater, circling away from the pinnacle whereon we sat (for a ghostly procession of wanderers from the filmy hosts without had drifted through a chasm in the crater wall and filed round and round, and gathered and sunk and blended together till the abyss was stored to the brim with a fleecy fog). Thus banked, motion ceased, and silence reigned. Clear to the horizon, league on league, the snowy floor stretched without a break—not level, but in rounded folds, with shallow creases between, and with here and there stately piles of vapory architecture lifting themselves aloft out of the common plain—some near at hand, some in the middle distances, and others relieving the monotony of the remote solitudes. There was little conversation, for the impressive scene overawed speech. I felt like the Last Man, neglected of the judgment, and left pinnacled in mid-heaven, a forgotten relic of a vanished world.

While the hush yet brooded, the messengers of the coming resurrection appeared in the East. A growing warmth suffused the horizon, and soon the sun emerged and looked out over the cloud-waste, flinging bars of ruddy light across it, staining its folds and billow-caps with blushes, purpling the shaded troughs between, and glorifying the massy vapor-palaces and cathedrals with a wasteful splendor of all blendings and combinations of rich coloring.

It was the sublimest spectacle I ever witnessed, and I think the memory of it will remain with me always.

CHAPTER LXXVII

I stumbled upon one curious character in the Island of Maui. He became a sore annoyance to me in the course of time. My first glimpse of him was in a sort of public room in the town of Lahaina. He occupied a chair at the opposite side of the apartment, and sat eyeing our party with interest for some minutes, and listening as critically to what we were saying as if he fancied we were talking to him and expecting him to reply. I thought it very sociable in a stranger. Presently, in the course of conversation, I made a statement bearing upon the subject under discussion—and I made it with due modesty, for there was nothing extraordinary about it, and it was only put forth in illustration of a point at issue. I had barely finished when this person spoke out with rapid utterance and feverish anxiety:

"Oh, that was certainly remarkable, after a fashion, but you ought to have seen *my* chimney—you ought to have seen *my* chimney, sir! Smoke! I wish I may hang if—Mr. Jones, *you* remember that chimney—you *must* remember that chimney! No, no—I recollect, now, you warn't living on this side of the island then. But I am telling you nothing but the truth, and I wish I may never draw another breath if that chimney didn't smoke so that the smoke actually got *caked* in it and I had to dig it out with a pickaxe! You may smile, gentlemen, but the High Sheriff's got a hunk of it which I dug out before his eyes, and so it's perfectly easy for you to go and examine for yourselves."

The interruption broke up the conversation, which had already begun to lag, and we presently hired some natives and an out-rigger canoe or two, and went out to overlook a grand surf-bathing contest.

Two weeks after this, while talking in a company, I looked up and detected this same man boring through and through me with his intense eye, and noted again his twitching muscles and his feverish anxiety to speak. The moment I paused, he said:

"*Beg* your pardon, sir, beg your pardon, but it can only be considered remarkable when brought into strong outline by isolation. Sir, contrasted with a circumstance which occurred in my own experience, it instantly becomes commonplace. No, not that—for I will not speak so discourteously of any experience in the career of a stranger and a gentleman—but I am *obliged* to say that you could not, and you *would* not ever again refer to this tree as a *large* one, if you could behold, as I have, the great Yakmatack tree, in the island of Ounaska, sea of Kamtchatka—a tree, sir, not one inch less than four hundred and fifteen feet in solid diameter!—and I wish I may die in a minute if it isn't so! Oh, you needn't look so questioning, gentlemen; here's old Cap Saltmarsh can say whether I know what I'm talking about or not. I showed him the tree."

Captain Saltmarsh.—"Come, now, cat your anchor, lad—you're heaving too taut. You *promised* to show me that stunner, and I walked more than eleven mile with you through the cussedest jungle *I* ever see, a hunting for it; but the tree you showed me finally warn't as big around as a beer cask, and *you* know that your own self, Markiss."

"Hear the man talk! Of *course* the tree was reduced that way, but didn't I *explain* it? Answer me, didn't I? Didn't I say I wished you could have seen it when *I* first saw it? When you got up on your ear and called me names, and said I had brought you eleven miles to look at a sapling, didn't I *explain* to you that all the whale-ships in the North Seas had been wooding off of it for more than twenty-seven years? And did you s'pose the tree could last for-*ever,* con-*found* it? I don't see why you want to keep back things that way, and try to injure a person that's never done *you* any harm."

Somehow this man's presence made me uncomfortable, and I was glad when a native arrived at that moment to say that Muckawow, the most companionable and luxurious among the rude war-chiefs of the Islands, desired us to come over and help him enjoy a missionary whom he had found trespassing on his grounds.

I think it was about ten days afterward that, as I finished a statement I was making for the instruction of a group of friends and acquaintances, and which made no pretence of being extraordinary, a familiar voice chimed instantly in on the heels of my last word, and said:

"But, my dear sir, there was *nothing* remarkable about that horse, or the circumstance either—nothing in the world! I mean no sort of offence when I say it, sir, but you really do not know anything whatever about speed. Bless your heart, if you could only have seen my mare Margaretta; *there* was a beast!—*there* was lightning for you! Trot! Trot is no name for it—she flew! How she *could* whirl a buggy along! I started her out once, sir—Colonel Bilgewater, *you* recollect that animal perfectly well—I started her out about thirty or thirty-five yards ahead of the awfullest storm I ever saw in my life, and it chased us upwards of eighteen miles! It did, by the everlasting hills! And I'm telling you nothing but the unvarnished truth when I say that not one single drop of rain fell on me—not a single *drop,* sir! And I swear to it! But my dog was a-swimming behind the wagon all they way!"

For a week or two I stayed mostly within doors, for I seemed to meet this person everywhere, and he had become utterly hateful to me. But one evening I dropped in on Captain Perkins and his friends, and we had a sociable time. About ten o'clock I chanced to be talking about a merchant friend of mine, and without really intending it, the remark slipped out that he was a little mean and parsimonious about paying his workmen. Instantly, through the steam of a hot whiskey punch on the opposite side of the room, a remembered voice shot—and for a moment I trembled on the imminent verge of profanity:

"Oh, my dear sir, really you expose yourself when you parade *that* as a surprising circumstance. Bless your heart and hide, you are ignorant of the very A B C of meanness! ignorant as the unborn babe! ignorant as unborn *twins!* You don't know *any thing* about it! It is pitiable to see you, sir, a well-spoken and prepossessing stranger, making such an enormous pow-wow here about a subject concerning which your ignorance is perfectly humiliating! Look me in the eye, if you please; look me in the eye. John James Godfrey was the son of poor but honest parents in the State of Mississippi—boyhood friend of mine—bosom comrade in later years. Heaven rest his noble spirit, he is gone from us now. John James Godfrey was hired by the Hayblossom Mining Company in California to do some blasting for them—the "Incorporated Company of Mean Men," the boys used to call it. Well, one day he drilled a hole about four feet deep and put in an awful blast of powder, and was standing over it ramming it down with an iron crowbar about nine foot long, when the cussed thing struck a spark and fired the powder, and scat! away John Godfrey whizzed like a skyrocket, him and his crowbar! Well, sir, he kept on going up in the air higher and higher, till he didn't look any bigger than a boy—and he kept going on up higher and higher, till he didn't look any bigger than a doll—and he kept on going up higher and higher, till he didn't look any bigger than a little small bee—and then he went out of sight! Presently he came in sight again, looking like a little small bee—and he came along down further and further, till he looked as big as a doll again—and down further and further, till he was a full-sized man once more; and then him and his crowbar came a wh-izzing down and lit right exactly in the same old tracks and went to r-ramming down, and r-ramming down, and r-ramming down again, just the same as if nothing had happened! Now do you know, that poor cuss warn't gone only sixteen minutes, and yet that Incorporated Company of Mean Men DOCKED HIM FOR THE LOST TIME!"

I said I had the headache, and so excused myself and went home. And on my diary I entered "another night spoiled" by this offensive loafer. And a fervent curse was set down with it to keep the item company. And the very next day I packed up, out of all patience, and left the Island.

Almost from the very beginning, I regarded that man as a liar.

. . . . . .

The line of points represents an interval of years. At the end of which time the opinion hazarded in that last sentence came to be gratifyingly and remarkably endorsed, and by wholly disinterested persons. The man Markiss was found one morning hanging to a beam of his own bedroom (the doors and windows securely fastened on the inside), dead; and on his breast was pinned a paper in his own handwriting begging his friends to suspect no innocent person of having any thing to do with his death, for that it was the work of his own hands entirely. Yet the jury brought in the astounding verdict that deceased came to his death "by the hands of some person or persons unknown!" They explained that the perfectly undeviating consistency of Markiss's character for thirty years towered aloft as colossal and indestructible testimony, that whatever statement he chose to make was entitled to instant and unquestioning acceptance as a *lie*. And they furthermore stated their belief that he was not dead, and instanced the strong circumstantial evidence of his own word that he *was* dead—and beseeched the coroner to delay the funeral as long as possible, which was done. And so in the tropical climate of Lahaina the coffin stood open for seven days, and then even the loyal jury gave him up. But they sat on him again, and changed their verdict to "suicide, induced by mental aberration"—because, said they, with penetration, "he said he was dead, and he *was* dead; and would he have told the truth if he had been in his right mind? *No,* sir."

CHAPTER LXXVIII

After half a year's luxurious vagrancy in the islands, I took shipping in a sailing vessel, and regretfully returned to San Francisco—a voyage in every way delightful, but without an incident: unless lying two long weeks in a dead calm, eighteen hundred miles from the nearest land, may rank as an incident. Schools of whales grew so tame that day after day they played about the ship among the porpoises and the sharks without the least apparent fear of us, and we pelted them with empty bottles for lack of better sport. Twenty-four hours afterward these bottles would be still lying on the glassy water under our noses, showing that the ship had not moved out of her place in all that time. The calm was absolutely breathless, and the surface of the sea absolutely without a wrinkle. For a whole day and part of a night we lay so close to another ship that had drifted to our vicinity, that we carried on conversations with her passengers, introduced each other by name, and became pretty intimately acquainted with people we had never heard of before, and have never heard of since. This was the only vessel we saw during the whole lonely voyage. We had fifteen passengers, and to show how hard pressed they were at last for occupation and amusement, I will mention that the gentlemen gave a good part of their time every day, during the calm, to trying to sit on an empty champagne bottle (lying on its side), and thread a needle without touching their heels to the deck, or falling over; and the ladies sat in the shade of the mainsail, and watched the enterprise with absorbing interest. We were at sea five Sundays; and yet, but for the almanac, we never would have known but that all the other days were Sundays too.

I was home again, in San Francisco, without means and without employment. I tortured my brain for a saving scheme of some kind, and at last a public lecture occurred to me! I sat down and wrote one, in a fever of hopeful anticipation. I showed it to several friends, but they all shook their heads. They said nobody would come to hear me, and I would make a humiliating failure of it. They said that as I had never spoken in public, I would break down in the delivery, anyhow. I was disconsolate now. But at last an editor slapped me on the back and told me to "go ahead." He said, "Take the largest house in town, and charge a dollar a ticket." The audacity of the proposition was charming; it seemed fraught with practical worldly wisdom, however. The proprietor of the several theatres endorsed the advice, and said I might have his handsome new opera-house at half price—fifty dollars. In sheer desperation I took it—on credit, for sufficient reasons. In three days I did a hundred and fifty dollars' worth of printing and advertising, and was the most distressed and frightened creature on the Pacific coast. I could not sleep—who could, under such circumstances? For other people there was facetiousness in the last line of my posters, but to me it was plaintive with a pang when I wrote it:

"Doors open at 7½. The trouble will begin at 8."

That line has done good service since. Showmen have borrowed it frequently. I have even seen it appended to a newspaper advertisement reminding school pupils in vacation what time next term would begin. As those three days of suspense dragged by, I grew more and more unhappy. I had sold two hundred tickets among my personal friends, but I feared they might not come. My lecture, which had seemed "humorous" to me, at first, grew steadily more and more dreary, till not a vestige of fun seemed left, and I grieved that I could not bring a coffin on the stage and turn the thing into a funeral. I was so panic-stricken, at last, that I went to three old friends, giants in stature, cordial by nature, and stormy-voiced, and said:

"This thing is going to be a failure; the jokes in it are so dim that nobody will ever see them; I would like to have you sit in the parquette, and help me through."

They said they would. Then I went to the wife of a popular citizen, and said that if she was willing to do me a very great kindness, I would be glad if she and her husband would sit prominently in the left-hand stage-box, where the whole house could see them. I explained that I should need help, and would turn toward her and smile, as a signal, when I had been delivered of an obscure joke—"and then," I added, "don't wait to investigate, but *respond!*"

She promised. Down the street I met a man I never had seen before. He had been drinking, and was beaming with smiles and good nature. He said:

"My name's Sawyer. You don't know me, but that don't matter. I haven't got a cent, but if you knew how bad I wanted to laugh, you'd give me a ticket. Come, now, what do you say?"

"Is your laugh hung on a hair-trigger?—that is, is it critical, or can you get it off *easy?"*

My drawling infirmity of speech so affected him that he laughed a specimen or two that struck me as being about the article I wanted, and I gave him a ticket, and appointed him to sit in the second circle, in the centre, and be responsible for that division of the house. I gave him minute instructions about how to detect indistinct jokes, and then went away, and left him chuckling placidly over the novelty of the idea.

I ate nothing on the last of the three eventful days—I only suffered. I had advertised that on this third day the box-office would be opened for the sale of reserved seats. I crept down to the theatre at four in the afternoon to see if any sales had been made. The ticket seller was gone, the box-office was locked up. I had to swallow suddenly, or my heart would have got out. "No sales," I said to myself; "I might have known it." I thought of suicide, pretended illness, flight. I thought of these things in earnest, for I was very miserable and scared. But of course I had to drive them away, and prepare to meet my fate. I could not wait for half-past seven—I wanted to face the horror, and end it—the feeling of many a man doomed to hang, no doubt. I went down back street at six o'clock, and entered the theatre by the back door. I stumbled my way in the dark among the ranks of canvas scenery, and stood on the stage. The house was gloomy and silent, and its emptiness depressing. I went into the dark among the scenes again, and for an hour and a half gave myself up to the horrors, wholly unconscious of everything else. Then I heard a murmur; it rose higher and higher, and ended in a crash, mingled with cheers. It made my hair raise, it was so close to me, and so loud. There was a pause, and then another; presently came a third, and before I well knew what I was about, I was in the middle of the stage, staring at a sea of faces, bewildered by the fierce glare of the lights, and quaking in every limb with a terror that seemed like to take my life away. The house was full, aisles and all!

The tumult in my heart and brain and legs continued a full minute before I could gain any command over myself. Then I recognized the charity and the friendliness in the faces before me, and little by little my fright melted away, and I began to talk. Within three or four minutes I was comfortable, and even content. My three chief allies, with three auxiliaries, were on hand, in the parquette, all sitting together, all armed with bludgeons, and all ready to make an onslaught upon the feeblest joke that might show its head. And whenever a joke did fall, their bludgeons came down and their faces seemed to split from ear to ear; Sawyer, whose hearty countenance was seen looming redly in the centre of the second circle, took it up, and the house was carried handsomely. Inferior jokes never fared so royally before. Presently I delivered a bit of serious matter with impressive unction (it was my pet), and the audience listened with an absorbed hush that gratified me more than any applause; and as I dropped the last word of the clause, I happened to turn and catch Mrs. ——'s intent and waiting eye; my conversation with her flashed upon me, and in spite of all I could do I smiled. She took it for the signal, and promptly delivered a mellow laugh that touched off the whole audience; and the explosion that followed was the triumph of the evening. I thought that that honest man Sawyer would choke himself; and as for the bludgeons, they performed like pile-drivers. But my poor little morsel of pathos was ruined. It was taken in good faith as an intentional joke, and the prize one of the entertainment, and I wisely let it go at that.

All the papers were kind in the morning; my appetite returned; I had abundance of money. All's well that ends well.

CHAPTER LXXIX

I launched out as a lecturer, now, with great boldness. I had the field all to myself, for public lectures were almost an unknown commodity in the Pacific market. They are not so rare, now, I suppose. I took an old personal friend along to play agent for me, and for two or three weeks we roamed through Nevada and California and had a very cheerful time of it. Two days before I lectured in Virginia City, two stagecoaches were robbed within two miles of the town. The daring act was committed just at dawn, by six masked men, who sprang up alongside the coaches, presented revolvers at the heads of the drivers and passengers, and commanded a general dismount. Everybody climbed down, and the robbers took their watches and every cent they had. Then they took gunpowder and blew up the express specie boxes and got their contents. The leader of the robbers was a small, quick-spoken man, and the fame of his vigorous manner and his intrepidity was in everybody's mouth when we arrived.

The night after instructing Virginia, I walked over the desolate "divide" and down to Gold Hill, and lectured there. The lecture done, I stopped to talk with a friend, and did not start back till eleven. The "divide" was high, unoccupied ground, between the towns, the scene of twenty midnight murders and a hundred robberies. As we climbed up and stepped out on this eminence, the Gold Hill lights dropped out of sight at our backs, and the night closed down gloomy and dismal. A sharp wind swept the place, too, and chilled our perspiring bodies through.

"I tell you I don't like this place at night," said Mike the agent.

"Well, don't speak so loud," I said. "You needn't remind anybody that we are here."

Just then a dim figure approached me from the direction of Virginia—a man, evidently. He came straight at me, and I stepped aside to let him pass; he stepped in the way and confronted me again. Then I saw that he had a mask on and was holding something in my face—I heard a click-click and recognized a revolver in dim outline. I pushed the barrel aside with my hand and said:

"Don't!"

He ejaculated sharply:

"Your watch! Your money!"

I said:

"You can have them with pleasure—but take the pistol away from my face, please. It makes me shiver."

"No remarks! Hand out your money!"

"Certainly—I—"

"Put up your hands! Don't you go for a weapon! Put 'em up! Higher!"

I held them above my head.

A pause. Then:

"Are you going to hand out your money or not?"

I dropped my hands to my pockets and said:

"Certainly! I—"

"Put up your *hands!* Do you want your head blown off? Higher!"

I put them above my head again.

Another pause.

"*Are* you going to hand out your money or *not?* Ah-ah—again? Put up your hands! By George, you want the head shot off you awful bad!"

"Well, friend, I'm trying my best to please you. You tell me to give up my money, and when I reach for it you tell me to put up my hands. If you would only—. Oh, now—don't! All six of you at me! That other man will get away while.—Now please take some of those revolvers out of my face—*do,* if you *please!* Every time one of them clicks, my liver comes up into my throat! If you have a mother—any of you—or if any of you have ever *had* a mother—or a—grandmother—or a—"

"Cheese it! *Will* you give up your money, or have we got to—. There-there—none of that! Put up your *hands!*"

"Gentlemen—I know you are gentlemen by your—"

"Silence! If you want to be facetious, young man, there are times and places more fitting. *This* is a serious business."

"You prick the marrow of my opinion. The funerals I have attended in my time were comedies compared to it. Now *I* think—"

"Curse your palaver! Your money!—your money!—your money! Hold!—put up your hands!"

"Gentlemen, listen to reason. You *see* how I am situated—now *don't* put those pistols so close—I smell the powder. You see how I am situated. If I had four hands—so that I could hold up two and—"

"Throttle him! Gag him! Kill him!"

"Gentlemen, *don't!* Nobody's watching the other fellow. Why don't some of you—. Ouch! Take it away, please! Gentlemen, you see that I've got to hold up my hands; and so I can't take out my money—but if you'll be so kind as to take it out for me, I will do as much for you some—"

"Search him Beauregard—and stop his jaw with a bullet, quick, if he wags it again. Help Beauregard, Stonewall."

Then three of them, with the small, spry leader, adjourned to Mike and fell to searching him. I was so excited that my lawless fancy tortured me to ask my two men all manner of facetious questions about their rebel brother-generals of the South, but, considering the order they had received, it was but common prudence to keep still. When everything had been taken from me,—watch, money, and a multitude of trifles of small value,—I supposed I was free, and forthwith put my cold hands into my empty pockets and began an inoffensive jig to warm my feet and stir up some latent courage—but instantly all pistols were at my head, and the order came again:

"Be still! Put up your hands! And *keep* them up!"

They stood Mike up alongside of me, with strict orders to keep his hands above his head, too, and then the chief highwayman said:

"Beauregard, hide behind that boulder; Phil Sheridan, you hide behind that other one; Stonewall Jackson, put yourself behind that sage-bush there. Keep you pistols bearing on these fellows, and if they take down their hands within ten minutes, or move a single peg, let them have it!"

Then three disappeared in the gloom toward the several ambushes, and the other three disappeared down the road toward Virginia.

It was depressingly still, and miserably cold. Now this whole thing was a practical joke, and the robbers were personal friends of ours in disguise, and twenty more lay hidden within ten feet of us during the whole operation, listening. Mike knew all this, and was in the joke, but I suspected nothing of it. To me it was most uncomfortably genuine.

When we had stood there in the middle of the road five minutes, like a couple of idiots, with our hands aloft, freezing to death by inches, Mike's interest in the joke began to wane. He said:

"The time's up, now, aint it?"

"No, you keep still. Do you want to take any chances with those bloody savages?"

Presently Mike said:

"*Now* the time's up, anyway. I'm freezing."

"Well freeze. Better freeze than carry your brains home in a basket. Maybe the time *is* up, but how do *we* know?—got no watch to tell by. I mean to give them good measure. I calculate to stand here fifteen minutes or die. Don't you move."

So, without knowing it, I was making one joker very sick of his contract. When we took our arms down at last, they were aching with cold and fatigue, and when we went sneaking off, the dread I was in that the time might not yet be up and that we would feel bullets in a moment, was not sufficient to draw all my attention from the misery that racked my stiffened body.

The joke of these highwayman friends of ours was mainly a joke upon themselves; for they had waited for me on the cold hill-top two full hours before I came, and there was very little fun in that; they were so chilled that it took them a couple of weeks to get warm again. Moreover, I never had a thought that they would kill me to get money which it was so perfectly easy to get without any such folly, and so they did not really frighten me bad enough to make their enjoyment worth the trouble they had taken. I was only afraid that their weapons would go off accidently. Their very numbers inspired me with confidence that no blood would be intentionally spilled. They were not smart; they ought to have sent only *one* highwayman, with a double-barrelled shot gun, if they desired to see the author of this volume climb a tree.

However, I suppose that in the long run I got the largest share of the joke at last; and in a shape not foreseen by the highwaymen; for the chilly exposure on the "divide" while I was in a perspiration gave me a cold which developed itself into a troublesome disease and kept my hands idle some three months, besides costing me quite a sum in doctor's bills. Since then I play no practical jokes on people and generally lose my temper when one is played upon me.

When I returned to San Francisco I projected a pleasure journey to Japan and thence westward around the world; but a desire to see home again changed my mind, and I took a berth in the steamship, bade good-bye to the friendliest land and livest, heartiest community on our continent, and came by the way of the Isthmus to New York—a trip that was not much of a pic-nic excursion, for the cholera broke out among us on the passage and we buried two or three bodies at sea every day. I found home a dreary place after my long absence; for half the children I had known were now wearing whiskers or waterfalls, and few of the grown people I had been acquainted with remained at their hearthstones prosperous and happy—some of them had wandered to other scenes, some were in jail, and the rest had been hanged. These changes touched me deeply, and I went away and joined the famous Quaker City European Excursion and carried my tears to foreign lands.

Thus, after seven years of vicissitudes, ended a "pleasure trip" to the silver mines of Nevada which had originally been intended to occupy only three months. However, I usually miss my calculations further than that.

MORAL

If the reader thinks he is done, now, and that this book has no moral to it, he is in error. The moral of it is this: If you are of any account, stay at home and make your way by faithful diligence; but if you are "no account," go away from home, and then you will *have* to work, whether you want to or not. Thus you become a blessing to your friends by ceasing to be a nuisance to them—if the people you go among suffer by the operation.

APPENDIX

A

BRIEF SKETCH OF MORMON HISTORY

Mormonism is only about forty years old, but its career has been full of stir and adventure from the beginning, and is likely to remain so to the end. Its adherents have been hunted and hounded from one end of the country to the other, and the result is that for years they have hated all "Gentiles" indiscriminately and with all their might. Joseph Smith, the finder of the Book of Mormon and founder of the religion, was driven from State to State with his mysterious copperplates and the miraculous stones he read their inscriptions with. Finally he instituted his "church" in Ohio and Brigham Young joined it. The neighbors began to persecute, and apostasy commenced. Brigham held to the faith and worked hard. He arrested desertion. He did more—he added converts in the midst of the trouble. He rose in favor and importance with the brethren. He was made one of the Twelve Apostles of the Church. He shortly fought his way to a higher post and a more powerful—President of the Twelve. The neighbors rose up and drove the Mormons out of Ohio, and they settled in Missouri. Brigham went with them. The Missourians drove them out and they retreated to Nauvoo, Illinois. They prospered there, and built a temple which made some pretensions to architectural grace and achieved some celebrity in a section of country where a brick court-house with a tin dome and a cupola on it was contemplated with reverential awe. But the Mormons were badgered and harried again by their neighbors. All the proclamations Joseph Smith could issue denouncing polygamy and repudiating it as utterly anti-Mormon were of no avail; the people of the neighborhood, on both sides of the Mississippi, claimed that polygamy was practised by the Mormons, and not only polygamy but a little of everything that was bad. Brigham returned from a mission to England, where he had established a Mormon newspaper, and he brought back with him several hundred converts to his preaching. His influence among the brethren augmented with every move he made. Finally Nauvoo was invaded by the Missouri and Illinois Gentiles, and Joseph Smith killed. A Mormon named Rigdon assumed the Presidency of the Mormon church and government, in Smith's place, and even tried his hand at a prophecy or two. But a greater than he was at hand. Brigham seized the advantage of the hour and without other authority than superior brain and nerve and will, hurled Rigdon from his high place and occupied it himself. He did more. He launched an elaborate curse at Rigdon and his disciples; and he pronounced Rigdon's "prophecies" emanations from the devil, and ended by "handing the false prophet over to the buffetings of Satan for a thousand years"—probably the longest term ever inflicted in Illinois. The people recognized their master. They straightway elected Brigham Young President, by a prodigious majority, and have never faltered in their devotion to him from that day to this. Brigham had forecast—a quality which no other prominent Mormon has probably ever possessed. He recognized that it was better to move to the wilderness than *be* moved. By his command the people gathered together their meagre effects, turned their backs upon their homes, and their faces toward the wilderness, and on a bitter night in February filed in sorrowful procession across the frozen Mississippi, lighted on their way by the glare from their burning temple, whose sacred furniture their own hands had fired! They camped, several days afterward, on the western verge of Iowa, and poverty, want, hunger, cold, sickness, grief and persecution did their work, and many succumbed and died—martyrs, fair and true, whatever else they might have been. Two years the remnant remained there, while Brigham and a small party crossed the country and founded Great Salt Lake City, purposely choosing a land which was *outside the ownership and jurisdiction of the hated American nation.* Note that. This was in 1847. Brigham moved his people there and got them settled just in time to see disaster fall again. For the war closed and Mexico ceded Brigham's refuge to the enemy—the United States! In 1849 the Mormons organized a "free and independent" government and erected the "State of Deseret," with Brigham Young as its head. But the very next year Congress deliberately snubbed it and created the "Territory of Utah" out of the same accumulation of mountains, sage-brush, alkali and general desolation,—but made Brigham Governor of it. Then for years the enormous migration across the plains to California poured through the land of the Mormons and yet the church remained staunch and true to its lord and master. Neither hunger, thirst, poverty, grief, hatred, contempt, nor persecution could drive the Mormons from their faith or their allegiance; and even the thirst for gold, which gleaned the flower of the youth and strength of many nations was not able to entice them! That was the final test. An experiment that could survive that was an experiment with some substance to it somewhere.

Great Salt Lake City throve finely, and so did Utah. One of the last things which Brigham Young had done before leaving Iowa, was to appear in the pulpit dressed to personate the worshipped and lamented prophet Smith and confer the prophetic succession, with all its dignities, emoluments and authorities, upon "President Brigham Young!" The people accepted the pious fraud with the maddest enthusiasm, and Brigham's power was sealed and secured for all time. Within five years afterward he openly added polygamy to the tenets of the church by authority of a "revelation" which he pretended had been received nine years before by Joseph Smith, albeit Joseph is amply on record as denouncing polygamy to the day of his death.

Now was Brigham become a second Andrew Johnson in the small beginning and steady progress in his official grandeur. He had served successively as a disciple in the ranks; home missionary; foreign missionary; editor and publisher; Apostle; President of the Board of Apostles; President of all Mormondom, civil and ecclesiastical; successor to the great Joseph by the will of heaven; "prophet," "seer," "revelator." There was but one dignity higher which he *could* aspire to, and he reached out modestly and took that—he proclaimed himself a God!

He claims that he is to have a heaven of his own hereafter, and that he will be its God, and his wives and children its goddesses, princes and princesses. Into it all faithful Mormons will be admitted, with their families, and will take rank and consequence according to the number of their wives and children. If a disciple dies before he has had time to accumulate enough wives and children to enable him to be respectable in the next world any friend can marry a few wives and raise a few children for him *after he is dead,* and they are duly credited to his account and his heavenly status advanced accordingly.

Let it be borne in mind that the majority of the Mormons have always been ignorant, simple, of an inferior order of intellect, unacquainted with the world and its ways; and let it be borne in mind that the wives of these Mormons are necessarily after the same pattern and their children likely to be fit representatives of such a conjunction; and then let it be remembered that *for forty years* these creatures have been driven, driven, driven, relentlessly! and mobbed, beaten, and shot down; cursed, despised, expatriated; banished to a remote desert, whither they journeyed gaunt with famine and disease, disturbing the ancient solitudes with their lamentations and marking the long way with graves of their dead—and all because they were simply trying to live and worship God in the way which *they* believed with all their hearts and souls to be the true one. Let all these things be borne in mind, and then it will not be hard to account for the deathless hatred which the Mormons bear our people and our government.

That hatred has "fed fat its ancient grudge" ever since Mormon Utah developed into a self-supporting realm and the church waxed rich and strong. Brigham as Territorial Governor made it plain that Mormondom was for the Mormons. The United States tried to rectify all that by appointing territorial officers from New England and other anti-Mormon localities, but Brigham prepared to make their entrance into his dominions difficult. Three thousand United States troops had to go across the plains and put these gentlemen in office. And after they were in office they were as helpless as so many stone images. They made laws which nobody minded and which could not be executed. The federal judges opened court in a land filled with crime and violence and sat as holiday spectacles for insolent crowds to gape at—for there was nothing to try, nothing to do, nothing on the dockets! And if a Gentile brought a suit, the Mormon jury would do just as it pleased about bringing in a verdict, and when the judgment of the court was rendered no Mormon cared for it and no officer could execute it. Our Presidents shipped one cargo of officials after another to Utah, but the result was always the same—they sat in a blight for awhile, they fairly feasted on scowls and insults day by day, they saw every attempt to do their official duties find its reward in darker and darker looks, and in secret threats and warnings of a more and more dismal nature—and at last they either succumbed and became despised tools and toys of the Mormons, or got scared and discomforted beyond all endurance and left the Territory. If a brave officer kept on courageously till his pluck was proven, some pliant Buchanan or Pierce would remove him and appoint a stick in his place. In 1857 General Harney came very near being appointed Governor of Utah. And so it came very near being Harney governor and Cradlebaugh judge!—two men who never had any idea of fear further than the sort of murky comprehension of it which they were enabled to gather from the dictionary. Simply (if for nothing else) for the variety they would have made in a rather monotonous history of Federal servility and helplessness, it is a pity they were not fated to hold office together in Utah.

Up to the date of our visit to Utah, such had been the Territorial record. The Territorial government established there had been a hopeless failure, and Brigham Young was the only real power in the land. He was an absolute monarch—a monarch who defied our President—a monarch who laughed at our armies when they camped about his capital—a monarch who received without emotion the news that the august Congress of the United States had enacted a solemn law against polygamy, and then went forth calmly and married twenty-five or thirty more wives.

B

THE MOUNTAIN MEADOWS MASSACRE

The persecutions which the Mormons suffered so long—and which they consider they still suffer in not being allowed to govern themselves—they have endeavored and are still endeavoring to repay. The now almost forgotten "Mountain Meadows massacre" was their work. It was very famous in its day. The whole United States rang with its horrors. A few items will refresh the reader's memory. A great emigrant train from Missouri and Arkansas passed through Salt Lake City and a few disaffected Mormons joined it for the sake of the strong protection it afforded for their escape. In that matter lay sufficient cause for hot retaliation by the Mormon chiefs. Besides, these one hundred and forty-five or one hundred and fifty unsuspecting emigrants being in part from Arkansas, where a noted Mormon missionary had lately been killed, and in part from Missouri, a State remembered with execrations as a bitter persecutor of the saints when they were few and poor and friendless, here were substantial additional grounds for lack of love for these wayfarers. And finally, this train was rich, very rich in cattle, horses, mules and other property—and how could the Mormons consistently keep up their coveted resemblance to the Israelitish tribes and not seize the "spoil" of an enemy when the Lord had so manifestly "delivered it into their hand?"

Wherefore, according to Mrs. C.V. Waite's entertaining book, "The Mormon Prophet," it transpired that—

"A 'revelation' from Brigham Young, as Great Grand Archee or God, was dispatched to President J.C. Haight, Bishop Higbee and J.D. Lee (adopted son of Brigham), commanding them to raise all the forces they could muster and trust, follow those cursed Gentiles (so read the revelation), attack them disguised as Indians, and with the arrows of the Almighty make a clean sweep of them, and leave none to tell the tale; and if they needed any assistance they were commanded to hire the Indians as their allies, promising them a share of the booty. They were to be neither slothful nor negligent in their duty, and to be punctual in sending the teams back to him before winter set in, for this was the mandate of Almighty God."

The command of the "revelation" was faithfully obeyed. A large party of Mormons, painted and tricked out as Indians, overtook the train of emigrant wagons some three hundred miles south of Salt Lake City, and made an attack. But the emigrants threw up earthworks, made fortresses of their wagons and defended themselves gallantly and successfully for five days! Your Missouri or Arkansas gentleman is not much afraid of the sort of scurvy apologies for "Indians" which the southern part of Utah affords. He would stand up and fight five hundred of them.

At the end of the five days the Mormons tried military strategy. They retired to the upper end of the "Meadows," resumed civilized apparel, washed off their paint, and then, heavily armed, drove down in wagons to the beleaguered emigrants, bearing a flag of truce! When the emigrants saw white men coming they threw down their guns and welcomed them with cheer after cheer! And, all unconscious of the poetry of it, no doubt, they lifted a little child aloft, dressed in white, in answer to the flag of truce!

The leaders of the timely white "deliverers" were President Haight and Bishop John D. Lee, of the Mormon Church. Mr. Cradlebaugh, who served a term as a Federal Judge in Utah and afterward was sent to Congress from Nevada, tells in a speech delivered in Congress how these leaders next proceeded:

"They professed to be on good terms with the Indians, and represented them as being very mad. They also proposed to intercede and settle the matter with the Indians. After several hours parley they, having (apparently) visited the Indians, gave the *ultimatum* of the savages; which was, that the emigrants should march out of their camp, leaving everything behind them, even their guns. It was promised by the Mormon bishops that they would bring a force and guard the emigrants back to the settlements. The terms were agreed to, the emigrants being desirous of saving the lives of their families. The Mormons retired, and subsequently appeared with thirty or forty armed men. The emigrants were marched out, the women and children in front and the men behind, the Mormon guard being in the rear. When they had marched in this way about a mile, at a given signal the slaughter commenced. The men were almost all shot down at the first fire from the guard. Two only escaped, who fled to the desert, and were followed one hundred and fifty miles before they were overtaken and slaughtered. The women and children ran on, two or three hundred yards further, when they were overtaken and with the aid of the Indians they were slaughtered. Seventeen individuals only, of all the emigrant party, were spared, and they were little children, the eldest of them being only seven years old. Thus, on the 10th day of September, 1857, was consummated one of the most cruel, cowardly and bloody murders known in our history."

The number of persons butchered by the Mormons on this occasion was *one hundred and twenty.*

With unheard-of temerity Judge Cradlebaugh opened his court and proceeded to make Mormondom answer for the massacre. And what a spectacle it must have been to see this grim veteran, solitary and alone in his pride and his pluck, glowering down on his Mormon jury and Mormon auditory, deriding them by turns, and by turns "breathing threatenings and slaughter!"

An editorial in the *Territorial Enterprise* of that day says of him and of the occasion:

"He spoke and acted with the fearlessness and resolution of a Jackson; but the jury failed to indict, or even report on the charges, while threats of violence were heard in every quarter, and an attack on the U.S. troops intimated, if he persisted in his course.

"Finding that nothing could be done with the juries, they were discharged, with a scathing rebuke from the judge. And then, sitting as a committing magistrate, *he commenced his task alone.* He examined witnesses, made arrests in every quarter, and created a consternation in the camps of the saints greater than any they had ever witnessed before, since Mormondom was born. At last accounts terrified elders and bishops were decamping to save their necks; and developments of the most startling character were being made, implicating the highest Church dignitaries in the many murders and robberies committed upon the Gentiles during the past eight years."

Had Harney been Governor, Cradlebaugh would have been supported in his work, and the absolute proofs adduced by him of Mormon guilt in this massacre and in a number of previous murders, would have conferred gratuitous coffins upon certain citizens, together with occasion to use them. But Cumming was the Federal Governor, and he, under a curious pretense of impartiality, sought to screen the Mormons from the demands of justice. On one occasion he even went so far as to publish his protest against the use of the U.S. troops in aid of Cradlebaugh's proceedings.

Mrs. C.V. Waite closes her interesting detail of the great massacre with the following remark and accompanying summary of the testimony—and the summary is concise, accurate and reliable:

"For the benefit of those who may still be disposed to doubt the guilt of Young and his Mormons in this transaction, the testimony is here collated and circumstances given which go not merely to implicate but to fasten conviction upon them by 'confirmations strong as proofs of Holy Writ:'

"1. The evidence of Mormons themselves, engaged in the affair, as shown by the statements of Judge Cradlebaugh and Deputy U.S. Marshal Rodgers.

"2. The failure of Brigham Young to embody any account of it in his Report as Superintendent of Indian Affairs. Also his failure to make any allusion to it whatever from the pulpit, until several years after the occurrence.

"3. The flight to the mountains of men high in authority in the Mormon Church and State, when this affair was brought to the ordeal of a judicial investigation.

"4. The failure of the *Deseret News,* the Church organ, and the only paper then published in the Territory, to notice the massacre until several months afterward, and then only to deny that Mormons were engaged in it.

"5. The testimony of the children saved from the massacre.

"6. The children and the property of the emigrants found in possession of the Mormons, and that possession traced back to the very day after the massacre.

"7. The statements of Indians in the neighborhood of the scene of the massacre: these statements are shown, not only by Cradlebaugh and Rodgers, but by a number of military officers, and by J. Forney, who was, in 1859, Superintendent of Indian Affairs for the Territory. To all these were such statements freely and frequently made by the Indians.

"8. The testimony of R.P. Campbell, Capt. 2d Dragoons, who was sent in the Spring of 1859 to Santa Clara, to protect travelers on the road to California and to inquire into Indian depredations."

C

CONCERNING A FRIGHTFUL ASSASSINATION THAT WAS NEVER CONSUMMATED

[If ever there was a harmless man, it is Conrad Wiegand, of Gold Hill, Nevada. If ever there was a gentle spirit that thought itself unfired gunpowder and latent ruin, it is Conrad Wiegand. If ever there was an oyster that fancied itself a whale; or a jack-o'lantern, confined to a swamp, that fancied itself a planet with a billion-mile orbit; or a summer zephyr that deemed itself a hurricane, it is Conrad Wiegand. Therefore, what wonder is it that when he says a thing, he thinks the world listens; that when he does a thing the world stands to look; and that when he suffers, there is a convulsion of nature? When I met Conrad, he was "Superintendent of the Gold Hill Assay Office"—and he was not only its Superintendent, but its entire force. And he was a street preacher, too, with a mongrel religion of his own invention, whereby he expected to regenerate the universe. This was years ago. Here latterly he has entered journalism; and his journalism is what it might be expected to be: colossal to ear, but pigmy to the eye. It is extravagant grandiloquence confined to a newspaper about the size of a double letter sheet. He doubtless edits, sets the type, and prints his paper, all alone; but he delights to speak of the concern as if it occupies a block and employs a thousand men.

[Something less than two years ago, Conrad assailed several people mercilessly in his little "People's Tribune," and got himself into trouble. Straightway he airs the affair in the "Territorial Enterprise," in a communication over his own signature, and I propose to reproduce it here, in all its native simplicity and more than human candor. Long as it is, it is well worth reading, for it is the richest specimen of journalistic literature the history of America can furnish, perhaps:]

From the Territorial Enterprise, Jan. 20, 1870.

A SEEMING PLOT FOR ASSASSINATION MISCARRIED

TO THE EDITOR OF THE ENTERPRISE: Months ago, when Mr. Sutro incidentally exposed mining management on the Comstock, and among others roused me to protest against its continuance, in great kindness you warned me that any attempt by publications, by public meetings and by legislative action, aimed at the correction of chronic mining evils in Storey County, must entail upon me (*a*) business ruin, (*b*) the burden of all its costs, (*c*) personal violence, and if my purpose were persisted in, then (*d*) assassination, and after all nothing would be effected.

YOUR PROPHECY FULFILLING

In large part at least your prophecies have been fulfilled, for (*a*) assaying, which was well attended to in the Gold Hill Assay Office (of which I am superintendent), in consequence of my publications, has been taken elsewhere, so the President of one of the companies assures me. With no reason *assigned,* other work has been taken away. With but one or two important exceptions, our assay business now consists simply of the *gleanings* of the vicinity. (*b*) Though my own personal donations to the People's Tribune Association have already exceeded $1,500, outside of our own numbers we have received (in money) less than $300 as contributions and subscriptions for the journal. (*c*) On Thursday last, on the main street in Gold Hill, near noon, with neither warning nor cause assigned, by a powerful blow I was felled to the ground, and while down I was kicked by a man who it would seem had been led to *believe* that I had spoken derogatorily of him. By whom he was so induced to believe I am as yet unable to say. On Saturday last I was again assailed and beaten by a man who first informed me why he did so, and who persisted in making his assault even after the erroneous impression under which he *also* was at first laboring had been clearly and repeatedly pointed out. This same man, after failing through intimidation to elicit from me the names of our editorial contributors, against giving which he knew me to be pledged, beat himself weary upon me with a raw hide, I not resisting, and then pantingly threatened me with permanent disfiguring mayhem, if ever again I should introduce his name into print, and who but a few minutes before his attack upon me assured me that the only reason I was "permitted" to reach home alive on Wednesday evening last (at which time the People's Tribune was issued) was, that he deems me only half-witted, and be it remembered the very next morning I *was* knocked down and kicked by a man who seemed to be *prepared* for flight.

[*He sees doom impending:*]

WHEN WILL THE CIRCLE JOIN?

How long before the whole of your prophecy will be fulfilled I cannot say, but under the shadow of so much fulfillment in so short a time, and with such threats from a man who is one of the most prominent exponents of the San Francisco mining-ring staring me and this whole community defiantly in the face and *pointing* to a completion of your augury, do you blame me for feeling that this communication is the last I shall ever write for the Press, especially when a sense alike of personal self-respect, of duty to this money-oppressed and fear-ridden community, and of American fealty to the spirit of true Liberty all command me, and each more loudly than love of life itself, to declare the name of that prominent man to be JOHN B. WINTERS, President of the Yellow Jacket Company, a political aspirant and a military General? The name of his partially duped accomplice and abettor in this last marvelous assault, is none other than PHILIP LYNCH, Editor and Proprietor of the Gold Hill *News*.

Despite the insult and wrong heaped upon me by John B. Winters, on Saturday afternoon, only a glimpse of which I shall be able to afford your readers, so much do I deplore clinching (by publicity) a serious mistake of any one, man or woman, committed under natural and not self-wrought passion, in view of his great apparent excitement at the time and in view of the almost perfect privacy of the assault, I am far from sure that I should not have given him space for repentance before exposing him, were it not that he himself has so far exposed the matter as to make it the common talk of the town that he has horsewhipped me. That fact having been made public, all the facts in connection need to be also, or silence on my part would seem *more* than singular, and with many would be proof either that I was conscious of some unworthy aim in publishing the article, or else that my "non-combatant" principles are but a convenient cloak alike of physical and moral cowardice. I therefore shall try to present a graphic but truthful picture of this whole affair, but shall forbear all comments, presuming that the editors of our own journal, if others do not, will speak freely and fittingly upon this subject in our next number, whether I shall then be dead or living, for my death will not stop, though it may suspend, the publication of the PEOPLE'S TRIBUNE.

[*The "non-combatant" sticks to principle, but takes along a friend or two of a conveniently different stripe:*]

THE TRAP SET

On Saturday morning John B. Winters sent verbal word to the Gold Hill Assay Office that he desired to see me at the Yellow Jacket office. Though such a request struck me as decidedly cool in view of his own recent discourtesies to me there alike as a publisher and as a stockholder in the Yellow Jacket mine, and though it seemed to me more like a summons than the courteous request by one gentleman to another for a favor, hoping that some conference with Sharon looking to the betterment of mining matters in Nevada might arise from it, I felt strongly inclined to overlook what *possibly* was simply an oversight in courtesy. But as then it had only been two days since I had been bruised and beaten under a hasty and false apprehension of facts, my caution was somewhat aroused. Moreover I remembered sensitively his contemptuousness of manner to me at my last interview in his office. I therefore felt it needful, if I went at all, to go accompanied by a friend whom he would not dare to treat with incivility, and whose presence with me might secure exemption from insult. Accordingly I asked a neighbor to accompany me.

THE TRAP ALMOST DETECTED

Although I was not then aware of this fact, it would seem that previous to my request this same neighbor had heard Dr. Zabriskie state publicly in a saloon, that Mr. Winters had told him he had decided either to kill or to horsewhip me, but had not finally decided on which. My neighbor, therefore, felt unwilling to go down with me until he had *first* called on Mr. Winters alone. He therefore paid him a visit. From that interview he assured me that he gathered the impression that he did not believe I would have any difficulty with Mr. Winters, and that he (Winters) would call on me at four o'clock in my own office.

MY OWN PRECAUTIONS

As Sheriff Cummings was in Gold Hill that afternoon, and as I desired to converse with him about the previous assault, I invited him to my office, and he came. Although a half hour had passed beyond four o'clock, Mr. Winters had not called, and we both of us began preparing to go home. Just then, Philip Lynch, Publisher of the Gold Hill *News*, came in and said, blandly and cheerily, as if bringing good news:

"Hello, John B. Winters wants to see you."

I replied, "Indeed! Why he sent me word that he would call on me *here* this afternoon at four o'clock!"

"O, well, it don't do to be too ceremonious just now, he's in my office, and that will do as well—come on in. Winters wants to consult with you alone. He's got something to say to you."

Though slightly uneasy at this change of programme, yet believing that in an *editor's* house I ought to be safe, and anyhow that I would be within hail of the street, I hurriedly, and but partially whispered my dim apprehension to Mr. Cummings, and asked him if he would not keep near enough to hear my voice in case I should call. He consented to do so while waiting for some other parties, and to come in if he heard my voice or thought I had need of protection.

On reaching the editorial part of the *News* office, which viewed from the street is dark, I did not see Mr. Winters, and again my misgivings arose. Had I paused long enough to consider the case, I should have invited Sheriff Cummings in, but as Lynch went down stairs, he said: "*This* way, Wiegand—it's best to be private," or some such remark.

[I do not desire to strain the reader's fancy, hurtfully, and yet it would be a favor to me if he would try to fancy this lamb in battle, or the duelling ground or at the head of a vigilance committee—M.T.:]

I followed, and *without* Mr. Cummings, and without arms, which I never do or will carry, unless as a soldier in war, or unless I should yet come to feel I must fight a duel, or to join and aid in the ranks of a *necessary* Vigilance Committee. But by following I made a fatal mistake. Following was entering a trap, and whatever animal suffers itself to be *caught* should expect the common fate of a caged rat, as I fear events to come will prove.

Traps commonly are not set for *benevolence.*

[*His body-guard is shut out:*]

THE TRAP INSIDE

I followed Lynch down stairs. At their foot a door to the left opened into a small room. From *that* room another door opened into yet *another* room, and once entered I found myself inveigled into what many will ever henceforth regard as a private subterranean Gold Hill den, admirably adapted in proper hands to the purposes of murder, raw or disguised, for from it, with both or even one door closed, when too late, I saw that I *could* not be heard by Sheriff Cummings, and from it, BY VIOLENCE AND BY FORCE, I was prevented from making a peaceable exit, when I thought I saw the studious object of this "consultation" was no other than to compass my killing, *in the presence of Philip Lynch as a witness,* as soon as by insult a proverbially excitable man should be exasperated to the point of assailing Mr. Winters, so that Mr. Lynch, by his conscience and by his well known tenderness of heart toward the rich and potent would be *compelled* to testify that he saw Gen. John B. Winters kill Conrad Wiegand in "self-defence." But I am going too fast.

OUR HOST

Mr. Lynch was present during the most of the time (say a little short of an hour) but three times he left the room. His testimony, therefore, would be available only as to the bulk of what transpired. On entering this carpeted den I was invited to a seat near one corner of the room. Mr. Lynch took a seat near the window. J. B. Winters sat (at first) near the door, and began his remarks essentially as follows:

"I have come here to exact of you a retraction, in black and white, of those damnably false charges which you have preferred against me in that —— —— infamous lying sheet of yours, and you must declare yourself their author, that you published them knowing them to be false, and that your motives were malicious."

"Hold, Mr. Winters. Your language is insulting and your demand an enormity. I trust I was not invited here to be insulted or coerced. I supposed myself here by invitation of Mr. Lynch, at your request."

"Nor did I come here to insult you. I have already told you that I am here for a very different purpose."

"Yet your language *has* been offensive, and even now shows strong excitement. If insult is repeated I shall either leave the room or call in

Sheriff Cummings, whom I just left standing and waiting for me outside the door."

"No, you won't, sir. You may just as well understand it at once as not. *Here* you are my man, and I'll tell you why! Months ago you put your property out of your hands, boasting that you did so to escape losing it on prosecution for libel."

"It is true that I did convert all my immovable property into personal property, such as I could trust safely to others, and chiefly to escape ruin through possible libel suits."

"Very good, sir. Having placed yourself beyond the pale of the law, *may God help your soul if you* DON'T make precisely such a retraction as I have demanded. I've got you now, and by —— before you can get out of this room you've *got* to both write and sign precisely the retraction I have demanded, and before you go, anyhow—you —— —— low-lived——lying —— ——, I'll teach you what *personal* responsibility is *outside* of the law; and, by ——, Sheriff Cummings and all the friends you've got in the world besides, can't save you, you —— ——, etc.! *No,* sir. I'm *alone* now, and I'm *prepared* to be shot down just here and now rather than be villified by you as I have been, and suffer you to escape me after publishing those charges, not only here where I am known and universally respected, but where I am *not* personally known and may be injured."

I confess this speech, with its terrible and but too plainly *implied* threat of killing me if I did not sign the paper he demanded, terrified me, especially as I saw he was working himself up to the highest possible pitch of passion, and instinct told me that any reply other than one of seeming concession to his demands would only be fuel to a raging fire, so I replied:

"Well, if I've *got* to sign——," and then I paused some time. Resuming, I said, "But, Mr. Winters, you are greatly excited. Besides, I see you are laboring under a total misapprehension. It is your duty not to inflame but to calm yourself. I am prepared to show you, if you will only point out the article that you allude to, that *you* regard as 'charges' what no calm and logical mind has any *right* to regard as such. *Show* me the charges, and I will try, at all events; and if it becomes plain that no charges *have* been preferred, then plainly there can be nothing to retract, and no one could rightly *urge* you to demand a retraction. You should beware of making so serious a mistake, for however *honest* a man may be, every one is liable to misapprehend. Besides you *assume* that *I* am the author of some certain article which you have not pointed out. It is *hasty* to do so."

He then pointed to some numbered paragraphs in a TRIBUNE article, headed "What's the Matter with Yellow Jacket?" saying "*That's* what I refer to."

To gain time for general reflection and resolution, I took up the paper and looked it over for awhile, he remaining silent, and as I hoped, cooling. I then resumed, saying, "As I supposed. I do not *admit* having written that article, nor have you any right to *assume* so important a point, and then base important action upon your assumption.

You might deeply regret it afterwards. In my published Address to the People, I notified the world that no information as to the authorship of any article would be given without the consent of the writer. I therefore cannot honorably tell you *who* wrote that article, nor can you exact it."

"If you are *not* the author, then I *do* demand to know who is?"

"I must decline to say."

"Then, by ——, I brand *you* as its author, and shall treat you accordingly."

"Passing that point, the most important misapprehension which I notice is, that you regard them as 'charges' at all, when their context, both at their beginning and end, show they are not. These words introduce them: *'Such an investigation* [just before indicated], *we think MIGHT result in showing some of the following points.'* Then follow eleven specifications, and the succeeding paragraph shows that the suggested investigation 'might EXONERATE those who are generally believed guilty.' You see, therefore, the context *proves* they are not preferred *as* charges, and this you seem to have overlooked."

While making those comments, Mr. Winters frequently interrupted me in such a way as to convince me that he was *resolved* not to consider candidly the thoughts contained in my words. He insisted upon it that they *were* charges, and "By ——," he would make me take them back *as* charges, and he referred the question to Philip Lynch, to whom I then appealed as a literary man, as a logician, and as an editor, calling his attention especially to the introductory paragraph just before quoted.

He replied, "If they are *not* charges, they are certainly *insinuations*," whereupon Mr. Winters renewed his demands for retraction precisely such as he had before named, except that he would allow me to state who *did* write the article if I did not myself, and this time shaking his fist in my face with more cursings and epithets.

When he threatened me with his clenched fist, instinctively I tried to rise from my chair, but Winters then forcibly thrust me down, as he did every other time (at least seven or eight) when under similar imminent danger of bruising by his fist (or for aught I could know worse than that after the first stunning blow) which he could easily and safely to himself have dealt me so long as he kept me down and stood over me.

This fact it was, which more than anything else, convinced me that by plan and plot I was purposely made powerless in Mr. Winters' hands, and that he did not mean to allow me that advantage of being afoot, which he possessed. Moreover, I then became convinced, that Philip Lynch (and for what *reason* I wondered) would do absolutely nothing to protect me in his own house. I realized then the situation thoroughly. I had found it equally vain to protest or argue, and I would make no unmanly appeal for pity, still less apologize. Yet my life had been by the plainest possible implication threatened. I was a weak man. I was unarmed. I was helplessly down, and Winters was afoot and probably armed. Lynch was the only "witness." The statements demanded, if given and not explained, would utterly sink me in my own self-respect, in my family's eyes, and in the eyes of the community. On the other hand, should I give the author's name how could I ever expect that confidence of the People which I should no longer deserve, and how much dearer to me and to my family was *my* life than the life of the real author to *his* friends. Yet life seemed dear and each minute that remained seemed precious if not solemn. I sincerely trust that neither you nor any of your readers, and especially none with families, may ever be placed in such seeming *direct* proximity to death while obliged to decide the one question I was compelled to, viz.: What should I do—I, a man of family, and *not* as Mr. Winters is, "alone."

[*The reader is requested not to skip the following—M. T.:*]

STRATEGY AND MANNERISM

To gain time for further reflection, and hoping that by a *seeming* acquiescence I might regain my personal liberty, at least till I could give an alarm, or take advantage of some momentary inadvertence of Winters, and then without a *cowardly* flight escape, I resolved to write a certain kind of retraction, but previously had inwardly decided

First.—That I would studiously avoid every action which might be *construed* into the drawing of a weapon, even by a self-infuriated man, no matter what amount of insult might be heaped upon me, for it seemed to me that this great excess of compound profanity, foulness and epithet must be more than a mere indulgence, and therefore must have some object. "Surely in vain the net is spread in the sight of any bird." Therefore, as before without thought, I thereafter by intent kept my hands away from my pockets, and generally in sight upon my knees.

Second.—I resolved to make no motion with my arms or hands which could possibly be construed into aggression.

Third.—I resolved completely to govern my outward manner and suppress indignation. To do this, I must govern my spirit. To do that, by force of imagination I was obliged like actors on the boards to resolve myself into an unnatural mental state and see all things through the eyes of an assumed *character*.

Fourth.—I resolved to try on Winters, silently, and unconsciously to himself a mesmeric power which I possess over certain kinds of people, and which at times I have found to work even in the dark over the lower animals.

Does any one smile at these last counts? God save you from ever being *obliged* to beat in a game of chess, whose stake is your life, you having but four poor pawns and pieces and your adversary with his full force unshorn. But if you are, provided you have any strength with breadth of will, do not despair. Though mesmeric power may not *save* you, it may help you; *try* it at all events. In this instance I was conscious of power coming into me, and by a law of nature, I know Winters was correspondingly weakened. If I could have gained more time I am sure he would not even have struck me.

It takes time to both form such resolutions and to recite them. That time, however, I gained while thinking of my retraction, which I first wrote in pencil, altering it from time to time till I got it to suit me, my aim being to make it look like a concession to demands, while in fact it should tersely speak the truth into Mr. Winters' mind. When it was finished, I copied it in ink, and if correctly copied from my first draft it should read as follows. In copying I do not think I made any material change.

COPY

To Philip Lynch, Editor of the Gold Hill News: I learn that Gen. John B. Winters believes the following (pasted on) clipping from the PEOPLE'S TRIBUNE of January to contain distinct charges of mine against him personally and that as such he desires me to retract them unqualifiedly.

In compliance with his request, permit me to say that, although Mr. Winters and I see this matter differently, in view of his strong feelings in the premises, I hereby declare that I do not know those "charges" (if such they are) to be true, and I hope that a critical examination would altogether disprove them. CONRAD WIEGAND.

Gold Hill, January 15, 1870.

I then read what I had written and handed it to Mr. Lynch, whereupon Mr. Winters said:

"That's not satisfactory, and it won't do;" and then addressing himself to Mr. Lynch, he further said: "How does it strike *you?*"

"Well, I confess I don't see that it *retracts* anything."

"Nor do I," said Winters; "in fact, I regard it as adding insult to injury. Mr. Wiegand you've got to do better than that. *You* are not the man who can pull wool over *my* eyes."

"That, sir, is the only retraction I can write."

"No, it isn't, sir, and if you so much as *say* so again you do it at your peril, for I'll thrash you to within an inch of your life, and, by ——, sir, I don't pledge myself to spare you even that inch either. I want you to understand I have asked you for a very different paper, and that paper you've got to sign."

"Mr. Winters, I assure you that I *do* not wish to irritate you, but, at the same time, it is utterly *impossible* for me to write any other paper than that which I have written. If you are resolved to *compel* me to *sign* something, Philip Lynch's hand must write at your dictation, and if, when written, I *can* sign it I will do so, but such a document as you say you *must* have from me, I never can sign. I mean what I say."

"Well, sir, what's to be done must be done quickly, for I've been here long enough already. I'll put the thing in another shape (and then pointing to the paper); don't you know those charges to be false?"

"I do not."

"Do you know them to be true?"

"Of my own personal knowledge I do not."

"Why then did you print them?"

"Because rightly considered in their connection they are *not* charges, but pertinent and useful *suggestions* in answer to the queries of a correspondent who stated facts which are inexplicable."

"Don't you know that *I* know they are false?"

"If you *do*, the proper course is simply to deny them and court an investigation."

"And do YOU claim the right to make ME come out and deny anything you may choose to write and print?"

To that question I think I made no reply, and then he further said: "Come, now, we've talked about the matter long enough. I want your final answer—did you write that article or not?"

"I cannot in honor tell you *who* wrote it."

"Did you not see it before it was printed?"

"Most certainly, sir."

"And did you deem it a fit thing to publish?"

"Most assuredly, sir, or I would never have consented to its appearance. Of its *authorship* I can say nothing whatever, but for its *publication* I assume full, sole and personal responsibility."

"And do you then retract it or not?"

"Mr. Winters, if my refusal to sign such a paper as you have demanded *must* entail me all that your language in this room fairly implies, then I ask a few minutes for prayer."

"Prayer! —— —— you, this is not your *hour* for prayer—your time to pray was when you were writing those —— lying charges. Will you sign or not?"

"You already have my answer."

"What! do you still refuse?"

"I do, sir."

"Take *that,* then," and to my amazement and inexpressible relief he drew only a rawhide instead of what I expected—a bludgeon or pistol. With it, as he spoke, he struck at my left ear downwards, as if to tear it off, and afterwards on the side of the head. As he moved away to get a better chance for a more effective shot, for the first time I gained a chance under peril to rise, and I did so pitying him from the very bottom of my soul. to think that one so naturally capable of true dignity, power and nobility could, by the temptations of this State, and by unfortunate associations and aspirations, be so deeply debased as to find in such brutality anything which he could call satisfaction—but the great hope for us all is in progress and growth, and John B. Winters, I trust, will yet be able to comprehend my feelings.

He continued to beat me with all his great force, until absolutely weary, exhausted and panting for breath. I still adhered to my purpose of non-aggressive defence, and made no other use of my arms than to defend my head and face from further disfigurement. The mere pain arising from the blows he inflicted upon my person was of course transient, and my clothing to some extent deadened its severity, as it now hides all remaining traces.

When I supposed he was through, taking the butt end of his weapon and shaking it in my face, he warned me, if I correctly understood him, of more yet to come, and furthermore said, if ever I again dared to introduce his name to print, in either my own or any other public journal, he would cut off my left ear (and I do not *think* he was jesting) and send me home to my family a visibly mutilated man, to be a standing warning to all low-lived puppies who seek to blackmail gentlemen and to injure their good names. And when he *did* so operate, he informed me that his implement would not be a whip but a knife.

When he had said this, unaccompanied by Mr. Lynch, as I remember it, he left the room, for I sat down by Mr. Lynch, exclaiming: "The man is mad—he is *utterly* mad—this step is his ruin—it is a mistake—it would be ungenerous in me, despite of all the ill usage I have here received, to expose him, at least until he has had an opportunity to reflect upon the matter. I shall be in no haste."

"Winters *is* very mad just now," replied Mr. Lynch, "but when he is himself he is one of the finest men I ever met. In fact, he told me the reason he did not meet you upstairs was to spare you the humiliation of a beating in the sight of others."

I submit that that unguarded remark of Philip Lynch convicts him of having been privy in advance to Mr. Winters' intentions whatever they may have been, or at least to his meaning to make an assault upon me, but I leave to others to determine how much censure an *editor* deserves for inveigling a weak, non-combatant man, also a publisher, to a pen of his own to be horsewhipped, if no worse, for the simple printing of what is verbally in the mouth of nine out of ten men, and women too, upon the street.

While writing this account two theories have occurred to me as *possibly* true respecting this most remarkable assault:

First.—The aim *may* have been simply to extort from me such admissions as in the hands of money and influence would have sent me to the Penitentiary for libel. This, however, seems unlikely, because any statements elicited by fear or force could not be evidence in law or could be so explained as to have no force. The statements wanted so badly must have been desired for some other purpose.

Second.—The other theory has so dark and wilfully murderous a look that I shrink from writing it, yet as in all probability my death at the earliest practicable moment has already been decreed, I feel I should do all I can before my hour arrives, at least to show others how to break up that aristocratic rule and combination which has robbed all Nevada of true freedom, if not of manhood itself. Although I do not prefer this hypothesis as a *"charge,"* I feel that as an American citizen I still have a right both to think and to speak my thoughts even in the land of Sharon and Winters, and as much so respecting the theory of a brutal assault (especially when I have been its subject) as respecting any other apparent enormity. I give the matter simply as a suggestion which may explain to the proper authorities and to the people whom they should represent, a well ascertained but notwithstanding a darkly mysterious fact. The scheme of the assault *may* have been

First—To terrify me by making me conscious of my own helplessness after making actual though not legal threats against my life.

Second—To imply that I could save my life only by writing or signing certain specific statements which if not subsequently explained would eternally have branded me as infamous and would have consigned my family to shame and want, and to the deadful compassion and patronage of the rich.

Third—To blow my brains out *the moment I had signed,* thereby preventing me from making any subsequent explanation such as *could* remove the infamy.

Fourth—Philip Lynch to be compelled to testify that I was killed by John B. Winters in self-defence, for the conviction of Winters would bring *him* in as an accomplice. If that *was* the programme in John B. Winters' mind nothing saved my life but my persistent *refusal* to sign, when that refusal seemed clearly to me to be the choice of death.

The remarkable assertion made to me by Mr. Winters, that pity only spared my life on Wednesday evening last, almost compels me to believe that at first he *could* not have intended me to leave that room alive; and why I was allowed to, unless through mesmeric *or some other invisible influence,* I cannot divine. The more I reflect upon this matter, the more probable as true does this horrible interpretation become.

The narration of these things I might have spared both to Mr. Winters and to the public had he himself observed silence, but as he has both verbally spoken and suffered a thoroughly garbled statement of facts to appear in the Gold Hill *News* I feel it due to myself no less than to this community, and to the entire independent press of America and Great Britain, to give a true account of what even the Gold Hill *News* has pronounced a disgraceful affair, and which it deeply regrets because of some alleged telegraphic mistake in the account of it. [Who received the erroneous telegrams?]

Though he may not deem it prudent to take my life just now, the publication of this article I feel sure must compel Gen. Winters (with his peculiar views about *his* right to exemption from criticism by *me*) to resolve on my violent death, though it may take years to compass it. Notwithstanding *I* bear *him* no ill will; and if W. C. Ralston and William Sharon, and other members of the San Francisco mining and milling Ring feel that he above all other men in this State and California is the most fitting man to supervise and control Yellow Jacket matters, until I am able to vote more than half their stock I presume he will be retained to grace his present post.

Meantime, I cordially invite all who know of any sort of important villainy which only *can* be cured by exposure (and who would expose it if they felt sure they would not be betrayed under bullying threats), to communicate with the PEOPLE'S TRIBUNE; for until I *am* murdered, so long as I can raise the means to publish, I propose to continue my *efforts* at least to revive the liberties of the State, to curb oppression, and to benefit man's world and God's earth.

CONRAD WIEGAND.

[It does seem a pity that the Sheriff was shut out, since the good sense of a general of militia and of a prominent editor failed to teach them that the merited castigation of this weak, half-witted child was a thing that ought to have been done in the street, where the poor thing could have a chance to run. When a journalist maligns a citizen, or attacks his good name on hearsay evidence, he deserves to be thrashed for it, even if he *is* a "non-combatant" weakling; but a generous adversary would at least allow such a lamb the use of his legs at such a time.—M.T.]

"How To Tell a Story" was written for the October 3, 1895 issue of Youth's Companion, *and was first collected in* How To Tell a Story and Other Essays, *published by Harper & Brothers in 1897. It contains a hair-raising ghost story, "The Golden Arm," that Twain first heard as a boy on his uncle's farm. He used the tale on many of his lecture tours, and it was one of the most effective parts of the program. The story always terrified his daughter Susy, and she disliked it intensely.*

How To Tell a Story

THE HUMOROUS STORY AN AMERICAN DEVELOPMENT.—ITS DIFFERENCE FROM COMIC AND WITTY STORIES.

I do not claim that I can tell a story as it ought to be told. I only claim to know how a story ought to be told, for I have been almost daily in the company of the most expert story-tellers for many years.

There are several kinds of stories, but only one difficult kind—the humorous. I will talk mainly about that one. The humorous story is American, the comic story is English, the witty story is French. The humorous story depends for its effect upon the *manner* of the telling; the comic story and the witty story upon the *matter*.

The humorous story may be spun out to great length, and may wander around as much as it pleases, and arrive nowhere in particular; but the comic and witty stories must be brief and end with a point. The humorous story bubbles gently along, the others burst.

The humorous story is strictly a work of art—high and delicate art—and only an artist can tell it; but no art is necessary in telling the comic and the witty story; anybody can do it. The art of telling a humorous story—understand, I mean by word of mouth, not print—was created in America, and has remained at home.

The humorous story is told gravely; the teller does his best to conceal the fact that he even dimly suspects that there is anything funny about it; but the teller of the comic story tells you beforehand that it is one of the funniest things he has ever heard, then tells it with eager delight, and is the first person to laugh when he gets through. And sometimes, if he has had good success, he is so glad and happy that he will repeat the "nub" of it and glance around from face to face, collecting applause, and then repeat it again. It is a pathetic thing to see.

Very often, of course, the rambling and disjointed humorous story finishes with a nub, point, snapper, or whatever you like to call it. Then the listener must be alert, for in many cases the teller will divert attention from that nub by dropping it in a carefully casual and indifferent way, with the pretence that he does not know it is a nub.

Artemus Ward used that trick a good deal; then when the belated audience presently caught the joke he would look up with innocent surprise, as if wondering what they had found to laugh at. Dan Setchell used it before him, Nye and Riley and others use it to-day.

But the teller of the comic story does not slur the nub; he shouts it at you—every time. And when he prints it, in England, France, Germany, and Italy, he italicizes it, puts some whooping exclamation-points after it, and sometimes explains it in a parenthesis. All of which is very depressing, and makes one want to renounce joking and lead a better life.

Let me set down an instance of the comic method, using an anecdote which has been popular all over the world for twelve or fifteen hundred years. The teller tells it in this way:

THE WOUNDED SOLDIER

In the course of a certain battle a soldier whose leg had been shot off appealed to another soldier who was hurrying by to carry him to the rear, informing him at the same time of the loss which he had sustained; whereupon the generous son of Mars, shouldering the unfortunate, proceeded to carry out his desire. The bullets and cannon-balls were flying in all directions, and presently one of the latter took the wounded man's head off—without, however, his deliverer being aware of it. In no long time he was hailed by an officer, who said:

"Where are you going with that carcass?"

"To the rear, sir—he's lost his leg!"

"His leg, forsooth?" responded the astonished officer: "you mean his head, you booby."

Whereupon the soldier dispossessed himself of his burden, and stood looking down upon it in great perplexity. At length he said:

"It is true, sir, just as you have said." Then after a pause he added, *"But he* TOLD *me* IT WAS HIS LEG!!!!!"

Here the narrator bursts into explosion after explosion of thunderous horse-laughter, repeating that nub from time to time through his gaspings and shriekings and suffocatings.

It takes only a minute and a half to tell that in its comic-story form; and isn't worth the telling, after all. Put into the humorous-story form it takes ten minutes, and is about the funniest thing I have ever listened to—as James Whitcomb Riley tells it.

He tells it in the character of a dull-witted old farmer who has just heard it for the first time, thinks it is unspeakably funny, and is trying to repeat it to a neighbor. But he can't remember it; so he gets all mixed up and wanders helplessly round and round, putting in tedious details that don't belong in the tale and only retard it; taking them out conscientiously and putting in others that are just as useless; making minor mistakes now and then and stopping to correct them and explain how he came to make them; remembering things which he forgot to put in in their proper place and going back to put them in there; stopping his narrative a good while in order to try to recall the name of the soldier that was hurt, and finally remembering that the soldier's name was not mentioned, and remarking placidly that the name is of no real importance, anyway—better, of course, if one knew it, but not essential, after all—and so on, and so on, and so on.

The teller is innocent and happy and pleased with himself, and has to stop every little while to hold himself in and keep from laughing outright; and does hold in, but his body quakes in a jelly-like way with interior chuckles; and at the end of the ten minutes the audience have laughed until they are exhausted, and the tears are running down their faces.

The simplicity and innocence and sincerity and unconsciousness of the old farmer are perfectly simulated, and the result is a performance which is thoroughly charming and delicious. This is art—and fine and beautiful, and only a master can compass it; but a machine could tell the other story.

To string incongruities and absurdities together in a wandering and sometimes purposeless way, and seem innocently unaware that they are absurdities, is the basis of the American art, if my position is correct. Another feature is the slurring of the point. A third is the dropping of a studied remark apparently without knowing it, as if one were thinking aloud. The fourth and last is the pause.

Artemus Ward dealt in numbers three and four a good deal. He would begin to tell with great animation something which he seemed to think was wonderful; then lose confidence, and after an apparently absent-minded pause add an incongruous remark in a soliloquizing way; and that was the remark intended to explode the mine—and it did.

For instance, he would say eagerly, excitedly, "I once knew a man in New Zealand who hadn't a tooth in his head"—here his animation would die out; a silent, reflective pause would follow, then he would say dreamily, and as if to himself, "and yet that man could beat a drum better than any man I ever saw."

The pause is an exceedingly important feature in any kind of story, and a frequently recurring feature, too. It is a dainty thing, and delicate, and also uncertain and treacherous; for it must be exactly the right length—no more and no less—or it fails of its purpose and makes trouble. If the pause is too short the impressive point is passed, and the audience have had time to divine that a surprise is intended—and then you can't surprise them, of course.

One the platform I used to tell a negro ghost story that had a pause in front of the snapper on the end, and that pause was the most important thing in the whole story. If I got it the right length precisely, I could spring the finishing ejaculation with effect enough to make some impressive girl deliver a startled little yelp and jump out of her seat—and that was what I was after. This story was called "The Golden Arm," and was told in this fashion. You can practise with it yourself—and mind you look out for the pause and get it right.

THE GOLDEN ARM

Once 'pon a time dey wuz a monsus mean man, en he live 'way out in de prairie all 'lone by hisself, 'cept'n he had a wife. En bimeby she died, en he tuck en toted her way out dah in de prairie en buried her. Well, she had a golden arm—all solid gold, fum de shoulder down. He wuz pow'ful mean—pow'ful; en dat night he couldn't sleep, caze he want dat golden arm so bad.

When it come midnight he couldn't stan' it no mo'; so he git up, he did, en tuck his lantern en shoved out thoo de storm en dug her up en got de golden arm; en he bent his head down 'gin de win', en plowed en plowed en plowed thoo de snow. Den all on a sudden he stop (make a considerable pause here, and look startled, and take a listening attitude) en say: "My *lan'*, what's dat!"

En he listen—en listen—en de win' say (set your teeth together and imitate the wailing and wheezing singsong of the wind), "Bzzz-z-zzz"—en den, way back yonder whah de grave is, he hear a *voice!*—he hear a voice all mix' up in de win'—can't hardly tell 'em 'part—"Bzzz-zzz—W-h-o—g-o-t—m-y—g-o-l-de-n *arm?*—zzz—zzz—W-h-o g-o-t m-y g-o-l-d-e-n *arm?* (You must begin to shiver violently now.)

En he begin to shiver en shake, en say, "Oh, my! *Oh,* my lan'!" en de win' blow de lantern out, en de snow en sleet blow in his face en mos' choke him, en he start a-plowin' knee-deep towards home mos' dead, he so sk'yerd—en pooty soon he hear de voice agin, en (pause) it'us comin' *after* him! "Buzz—zzz—zzz—W-h-o—g-o-t—m-y—g-o-l-d-e-n—*arm?"*

When he git to de pasture he hear it agin—closter now, en a-*comin'!*—a-comin' back dah in de dark en de storm—(repeat the wind and the voice). When he git to de house he rush up-stairs en jump in de bed en kiver up, head and years, en lay dah shiverin' en shakin'—en den way out dah he hear it *agin!*—en a *comin'!* En bimeby he hear (pause—awed, listening attitude)—pat—pat—pat—*hit's a-comin' up-stairs!* Den he hear de latch, en he *know* it's in de room!

Den pooty soon he know it's a-*stannin' by de bed!* (Pause.) Den—he know it's a-*bendin' down over him*—he cain't skasely git his breath! Den—den—he seem to feel someth'n *c-o-l-d,* right down 'most agin his head! (Pause.)

Den de voice say, *right at his year*—"W-h-o—g-o-t—m-y—g-o-l-d-e-n *arm?"* (You must wail it out very plaintively and accusingly; then you stare steadily and impressively into the face of the farthest-gone auditor—a girl, preferably—and let that awe-inspiring pause begin to build itself in the deep hush. When it has reached exactly the right length, jump suddenly at that girl and yell, *"You've* got it!"

If you've got the *pause* right, she'll fetch a dear little yelp and spring right out of her shoes. But you *must* get the pause right; and you will find it the most troublesome and aggravating and uncertain thing you ever undertook.)

In August of 1869, Twain used a loan from his future father-in-law to buy a share in the Buffalo Express. *Following his marriage to Olivia Langdon, he tried to settle down to the life of a newspaper proprietor, and he spent the next few years running the paper, contributing a series of sketches and commentaries, usually for its Saturday edition. "A Curious Dream" appeared in the* Express *on April 30 and May 7, 1870. In 1872, it was included in a collection published by George Routledge & Sons in London called* A Curious Dream and Other Stories, *and also appeared in an unauthorized collection called* A Book for an Hour *which was brought out in New York in 1873 by B.J. Such. In 1875, Twain reprinted the tale in* Mark Twain's Sketches New and Old.

A Curious Dream

CONTAINING A MORAL

Night before last I had a singular dream. I seemed to be sitting on a doorstep (in no particular city perhaps), ruminating, and the time of night appeared to be about twelve or one o'clock. The weather was balmy and delicious. There was no human sound in the air, not even a footstep. There was no sound of any kind to emphasize the dead stillness, except the occasional hollow barking of a dog in the distance and the fainter answer of a further dog. Presently up the street I heard a bony clack-clacking, and guessed it was the castanets of a serenading party. In a minute more a tall skeleton, hooded, and half-clad in a tattered and mouldy shroud, whose shreds were flapping about the ribby lattice-work of its person swung by me with a stately stride, and disappeared in the grey gloom of the starlight. It had a broken and worm-eaten coffin on its shoulder and a bundle of something in its hand. I knew what the clack-clacking was then; it was this party's joints working together, and his elbows knocking against his sides as he walked. I may say I was surprised. Before I could collect my thoughts and enter upon any speculations as to what this apparition might portend, I heard another one coming—for I recognized his clack-clack. He had two-thirds of a coffin on his shoulder, and some foot- and head-boards under his arm. I mightily wanted to peer under his hood and speak to him, but when he turned and smiled upon me with his cavernous sockets and his projecting grin as he went by, I thought I would not detain him. He was hardly gone when I heard the clacking again, and another one issued from the shadowy half-light. This one was bending under a heavy gravestone, and dragging a shabby coffin after him by a string. When he got to me he gave me a steady look for a moment or two, and then rounded to and backed up to me, saying:

"Ease this down for a fellow, will you?"

I eased the gravestone down till it rested on the ground, and in doing so noticed that it bore the name of "John Baxter Copmanhurst," with "May 1839," as the date of his death. Deceased sat wearily down by me, and wiped his os frontis with his major maxillary—chiefly from former habit I judged, for I could not see that he brought away any perspiration.

"It is too bad, too bad," said he, drawing the remnant of the shroud about him and leaning his jaw pensively on his hand. Then he put his left foot up on his knee and fell to scratching his ankle bone absently with a rusty nail which he got out of his coffin.

"What is too bad, friend?"

"Oh, everything, everything. I almost wish I never had died."

"You surprise me. Why do you say this? Has anything gone wrong? What is the matter?"

"Matter! Look at this shroud—rags. Look at this gravestone, all battered up. Look at that disgraceful old coffin. All a man's property going to ruin and destruction before his eyes, and ask him if anything is wrong? Fire and brimstone!"

"Calm yourself, calm yourself," I said. "It *is* too bad—it is certainly too bad, but then I had not supposed that you would much mind such matters, situated as you are."

"Well, my dear sir, I *do* mind them. My pride is hurt, and my comfort is impaired—destroyed, I might say. I will state my case—I will put it to you in such a way that you can comprehend it, if you will let me," said the poor skeleton, tilting the hood of his shroud back, as if he were clearing for action, and thus unconsciously giving himself a jaunty and festive air very much at variance with the grave character of his position in life—so to speak—and in prominent contrast with his distressful mood.

"Proceed," said I.

"I reside in the shameful old graveyard a block or two above you here, in this street—there, now, I just expected that cartilage would let go!—third rib from the bottom, friend, hitch the end of it to my spine with a string, if you have got such a thing about you, though a bit of silver wire is a deal pleasanter, and more durable and becoming, if one keeps it polished—to think of shredding out and going to pieces in this way, just on account of the indifference and neglect of one's posterity!"—and the poor ghost grated his teeth in a way that gave me a wrench and a shiver—for the effect is mightily increased by the absence of muffling flesh and cuticle. "I reside in that old graveyard, and have for these thirty years; and I tell you things are changed since I first laid this old tired frame there, and turned over, and stretched out for a long sleep, with a delicious sense upon me of being *done* with bother, and grief, and anxiety, and doubt, and fear, for ever and ever, and listening with comfortable and increasing satisfaction to the sexton's work, from the startling clatter of his first spadeful on my coffin till it dulled away to the faint patting that shaped the roof of my new home—delicious! My! I wish you could try it to-night!" and out of my reverie deceased fetched me with a rattling slap with a bony hand.

"Yes, sir, thirty years ago I laid me down there, and was happy. For it was out in the country, then—out in the breezy, flowery, grand old woods, and the lazy winds gossiped with the leaves, and the squirrels capered over us and around us, and the creeping things visited us, and the birds filled the tranquil solitude with music. Ah, it was worth ten years of a man's life to be dead then! Everything was pleasant. I was in a good neighborhood, for all the dead people that lived near me belonged to the best families in the city. Our posterity appeared to think the world of us. They kept our graves in the very best condition; the fences were always in faultless repair, head-boards were kept painted or whitewashed, and were replaced with new ones as soon as they began to look rusty or decayed; monuments were kept upright, railings intact and bright, the rosebushes and shrubbery trimmed, trained, and free from blemish, the walks clean and smooth and gravelled. But that day is gone by. Our descendants have forgotten us. My grandson lives in a stately house built with money made by these old hands of mine, and I sleep in a neglected grave with invading vermin that gnaw my shroud to build them nests withal! I and friends that lie with me founded and secured the prosperity of this fine city, and the stately bantling of our loves leaves us to rot in a dilapidated cemetery which neighbors curse and strangers scoff at. See the difference between the old time and this—for instance: Our graves are all caved in, now; our headboards have rotted away and tumbled down; our railings reel this way and that with one foot in the air, after a fashion of unseemly levity; our monuments lean wearily, and our gravestones bow their heads discouraged; there be no adornments any more—no roses, nor shrubs, nor gravelled walks, nor anything that is a comfort to the eye; and even the paintless old board fence that did make a show of holding us sacred from companionship with beasts and the defilement of heedless feet, has tottered till it overhangs the street, and only advertises the presence of our dismal resting-place and invites yet more derision to it. And now we cannot hide our poverty and tatters in the friendly woods, for the city has stretched its withering arms abroad and taken us in, and all that remains of the cheer of our old home is the cluster of lugubrious forest trees that stand, bored and weary of a city life, with their feet in our coffins, looking into the hazy distance and wishing they were there. I tell you it is disgraceful!

"You begin to comprehend—you begin to see how it is. While our descendants are living sumptuously on our money, right around us in the city, we have to fight hard to keep skull and bones together. Bless you, there isn't a grave in our cemetery that doesn't leak—not one. Every time it rains in the night we have to climb out and roost in the trees—and sometimes we are wakened suddenly by the chilly water trickling down the back of our necks. Then I tell you there is a general heaving up of old graves and kicking over of old monuments, and scampering of old skeletons for the trees! Bless me, if you had gone along there some such nights after twelve you might have seen as many as fifteen of us roosting on one limb, with our joints rattling drearily and the wind wheezing through our ribs!Many a time we have perched there for three or four dreary hours, and then come down, stiff and chilled through and drowsy, and borrowed each other's skulls to bale out our graves with—if you will glance up in my mouth, now as I tilt my head back, you can see that my head-piece is half full of old dry sediment—how top-heavy and stupid it makes me sometimes! Yes, sir, many a time if you had happened to come along just before the dawn you'd have caught us baling out the graves and hanging our shrouds on the fence to dry. Why, I had an elegant shroud stolen from there one morning—think a party by the name of Smith took it, that resides in a plebeian graveyard over yonder—I think so because the first time I ever saw him he hadn't anything on but a check-shirt, and the last time I saw him, which was at a social gathering in the new cemetery, he was the best dressed corpse in the company—and it is a significant fact that he left when he saw me; and presently an old woman from here missed her coffin—she generally took it with her when she went anywhere, because she was liable to take cold and bring on the spasmodic rheumatism that originally killed her if she exposed herself to the night air much. She was named Hotchkiss—Anna Matilda Hotchkiss—you might know her? She has two upper front teeth, is tall, but a good deal inclined to stoop, one rib on the left side gone, has one shred of rusty hair hanging from the left side of her head, and one little tuft just above and a little forward of her right ear, has her under jaw wired on one side where it had worked loose, small bone of left forearm gone—lost in a fight—has a kind of swagger in her gait and a 'gallus' way of going with her arms akimbo and her nostrils in the air—has been pretty free and easy, and is all damaged and battered up till she looks like a queensware crate in ruins—maybe you have met her?"

"God forbid!" I involuntarily ejaculated, for somehow I was not looking for that form of question, and it caught me a little off my guard. But I hastened to make amends for my rudeness, and say, "I simply meant I had not had the honor—for I would not deliberately speak discourteously of a friend of yours. You were saying that you were robbed—and it was a shame, too—but it appears by what is left of the shroud you have on that it was a costly one in its day. How did—"

A most ghastly expression began to develop among the decayed features and shrivelled integuments of my guest's face, and I was beginning to grow uneasy and distressed, when he told me he was only working up a deep, sly smile, with a wink in it, to suggest that about the time he acquired his present garment a ghost in a neighboring cemetery missed one. This reassured me, but I begged him to confine himself to speech thenceforth, because his facial expression was uncertain. Even with the most elaborate care it was liable to miss fire. Smiling should especially be avoided. What *he* might honestly consider a shining success was likely to strike me in a very different light. I said I liked to see a skeleton cheerful, even decorously playful, but I did not think smiling was a skeleton's best hold.

"Yes, friend," said the poor skeleton, "the facts are just as I have given them to you. Two of these old graveyards—the one that I resided in and one further along—have been deliberately neglected by our descendants of to-day until there is no occupying them any longer. Aside from the osteological discomfort of it—and that is no light matter this rainy weather—the present state of things is ruinous to property. We have got to move or be content to see our effects wasted away and utterly destroyed. Now, you will hardly believe it, but it is true, nevertheless, that there isn't a single coffin in good repair among all my acquaintance—now that is an absolute fact. I do not refer to low people who come in a pine box mounted on an express wagon, but I am talking about your high-toned, silver mounted burial-case, your monumental sort, that travel under black plumes at the head of a procession and have choice of cemetery lots—I mean folks like the Jarvises, and the Bledsoes and Burlings, and such. They are all about ruined. The most substantial people in our set, they were. And now look at them—utterly used up and poverty-stricken. One of the Bledsoes actually traded his monument to a late bar-keeper for some fresh shavings to put under his head. I tell you it speaks volumes, for there is nothing a corpse takes so much pride in as his monument. He loves to read the inscription. He comes after awhile to believe what it says himself, and then you may see him sitting on the fence night after night enjoying it. Epitaphs are cheap, and they do a poor chap a world of good after he is dead, especially if he had hard luck while he was alive. I wish they were used more. Now, I don't complain, but confidentially I *do* think it was a little shabby in my descendants to give me nothing but this old slab of a gravestone—and all the more that there isn't a compliment on it. It used to have

'GONE TO HIS JUST REWARD'

on it, and I was proud when I first saw it, but by-and-by I noticed that whenever an old friend of mine came along he would hook his chin on the railing and pull a long face and read along down till he came to that, and then he would chuckle to himself and walk off, looking satisfied and comfortable. So I scratched it off to get rid of those fools. But a dead man always takes a deal of pride in his monument. Yonder goes half-a-dozen of the Jarvises, now, with the family monument along. And Smithers and some hired spectres went by with his a while ago. Hello, Higgins, good-bye, old friend! That's Meredith Higgins—died in '44—belongs to our set in the cemetery—fine old family—great-grandmother was an Injun—I am on the most familiar terms with him—he didn't hear me was the reason he didn't answer me. And I am sorry, too, because I would have liked to introduce you. You would admire him. He is the most disjointed, sway-backed, and generally distorted old skeleton you ever saw, but he is full of fun. When he laughs it sounds like rasping two stones together, and he always starts it off with a cheery screech like raking a nail across a window-pane. Hey, Jones! That is old Columbus Jones—shroud cost four hundred dollars—entire trousseau, including monument, twenty-seven hundred. This was in the spring of '26. It was enormous style for those days. Dead people came all the way from the Alleghanies to see his things—the party that occupied the grave next to mine remembers it well. Now do you see that individual going along with a piece of a head-board under his arm, one leg-bone below his knee gone, and not a thing in the world on? That is Barstow Dalhousie, and next to Columbus Jones he was the most sumptuously outfitted person that ever entered our cemetery. We are all leaving. We cannot tolerate the treatment we are receiving at the hands of our descendants. They open new cemeteries, but they leave us to our ignominy. They mend the streets, but they never mend anything that is about us or belongs to us. Look at that coffin of mine—yet I tell you in its day it was a piece of furniture that would have attracted attention in any drawing-room in this city. You may have it if you want it—I can't afford to repair it. Put a new bottom in her, and part of a new top, and a bit of fresh lining along the left side, and you'll find her about as comfortable as any receptacle of her species you ever tried. No thanks—no, don't mention it—you have been civil to me, and I would give you all the property I have got before I would seem ungrateful. Now this winding-sheet is a kind of a sweet thing in its way, if you would like to—No? Well, just as you say, but I wished to be fair and liberal—there's nothing mean about *me.* Good-by, friend, I must be going. I may have a good way to go to-night—don't know. I only know one thing for certain, and that is, that I am on the emigrant trail, now, and I'll never sleep in that crazy old cemetery again. I will travel till I find respectable quarters, if I have to hoof it to New Jersey. All the boys are going. It was decided in public conclave, last night, to emigrate, and by the time the sun rises there won't be a bone left in our old habitations. Such cemeteries may suit my surviving friends, but they do not suit the remains that have the honor to make these remarks. My opinion is the general opinion. If you doubt it, go and see how the departing ghosts upset things before they started. They were almost riotous in their demonstrations of distaste. Hello, here are some of the Bledsoes, and if you will give me a lift with this tombstone I guess I will join company and jog along with them—mighty respectable old family, the Bledsoes, and used to always come out in six-horse hearses, and all that sort of thing fifty years ago when I walked these streets in daylight. Good-by, friend."

And with his gravestone on his shoulder he joined the grisly procession, dragging his damaged coffin after him, for notwithstanding he pressed it upon me so earnestly, I utterly refused his hospitality. I suppose that for as much as two hours these sad outcasts went clacking by, laden with their dismal effects, and all that time I sat pitying them. One or two of the youngest and least dilapidated among them inquired about midnight trains on the railways, but the rest seemed unacquainted with that mode of travel, and merely asked about common public roads to various towns and cities, some of which are not on the map now, and vanished from it and from the earth as much as thirty years ago, and some few of them never *had* existed anywhere but on maps, and private ones in real estate agencies at that. And they asked about the condition of the cemeteries in these towns and cities, and about the reputation the citizens bore as to reverence for the dead.

This whole matter interested me deeply, and likewise compelled my sympathy for these homeless ones. And it all seeming real, and I not knowing it was a dream, I mentioned to one shrouded wanderer an idea that had entered my head to publish an account of this curious and very sorrowful exodus, but said also that I could not describe it truthfully, and just as it occurred, without seeming to trifle with a grave subject and exhibit an irreverence for the dead that would shock and distress their surviving friends. But this bland and stately remnant of a former citizen leaned him far over my gate and whispered in my ear, and said:—

"Do not let that disturb you. The community that can stand such graveyards as those we are emigrating from can stand anything a body can say about the neglected and forsaken dead that lie in them."

At that very moment a cock crowed, and the weird procession vanished and left not a shred or a bone behind. I awoke, and found myself lying with my head out of the bed and "sagging" downwards considerably—a position favorable to dreaming dreams with morals in them, maybe, but not poetry.

———

NOTE.—The reader is assured that if the cemeteries in his town are kept in good order, this Dream is not levelled at his town at all, but is levelled particularly and venomously at the *next* town.

The first appearance of "My Late Senatorial Secretaryship" in book form in this country was in Mark Twain's Sketches New and Old, *published in 1875 by the American Publishing Company. It had been written for a New York monthly called* Galaxy, *where it appeared in the May 1868 issue under the title "Facts Concerning the Late Senatorial Secretaryship." The essay is a burlesque of Twain's experiences in Washington as private secretary to Senator William M. Stewart of Nevada, an arrangement which suited neither of the parties involved and was terminated after two months.*

My Late Senatorial Secretaryship

I am not a private secretary to a senator any more, now. I held the berth two months in security and in great cheerfulness of spirit, but my bread began to return from over the waters, then—that is to say, my works came back and revealed themselves. I judged it best to resign. The way of it was this. My employer sent for me one morning tolerably early, and, as soon as I had finished inserting some conundrums clandestinely into his last great speech upon finance, I entered the presence. There was something portentous in his appearance. His cravat was untied, his hair was in a state of disorder, and his countenance bore about it the signs of a suppressed storm. He held a package of letters in his tense grasp, and I knew that the dreaded Pacific mail was in. He said—

"I thought you were worthy of confidence."

I said, "Yes, sir."

He said, "I gave you a letter from certain of my constituents in the State of Nevada, asking the establishment of a post-office at Baldwin's Ranch, and told you to answer it, as ingeniously as you could, with arguments which should persuade them that there was no real necessity for an office at that place."

I felt easier. "Oh, if that is all, sir, I *did* do that."

"Yes, you *did*. I will read your answer, for your own humiliation:

"WASHINGTON, NOV. 24.

" '*Messrs. Smith, Jones, and others.*

" 'GENTLEMEN: What the mischief do you suppose you want with a post-office at Baldwin's Ranche? It would not do you any good. If any letters came there, you couldn't read them, you know; and, besides, such letters as ought to pass through, with money in them, for other localities, would not be likely to *get* through, you must perceive at once; and that would make trouble for us all. No, don't bother about a post-office in your camp. I have your best interests at heart, and feel that it would only be an ornamental folly. What you want is a nice jail, you know—a nice, substantial jail and a free school. These will be a lasting benefit to you. These will make you really contented and happy. I will move in the matter at once.

" 'Very truly, etc.,

" 'MARK TWAIN,

" 'For James W.N**, U.S. Senator.'

"That is the way you answered that letter. Those people say they will hang me, if I ever enter that district again; and I am perfectly satisfied they *will*, too."

"Well, sir, I did not know I was doing any harm. I only wanted to convince them."

"Ah. Well you *did* convince them, I make no manner of doubt. Now, here is another specimen. I gave you a petition from certain gentlemen of Nevada, praying that I would get a bill through Congress incorporating the Methodist Episcopal Church of the State of Nevada. I told you to say, in reply, that the creation of such a law came more properly within the province of the State Legislature; and to endeavor to show them that, in the present of feebleness of the religious element in that new commonwealth, the expediency of incorporating the church was questionable. What did you write?

" 'WASHINGTON, NOV. 24.

" '*Rev. John Halifax and others.*

" 'GENTLEMEN: You will have to go to the State Legislature about that speculation of yours—Congress don't know anything about religion. But don't you hurry to go there, either; because this thing you propose to do out in that new country isn't expedient—in fact, it is ridiculous. Your religious people there are too feeble, in intellect, in morality, in piety—in everything, pretty much. You had better drop this—you can't make it work. You can't issue stock on an incorporation like that—or if you could, it would only keep you in trouble all the time. The other denominations would abuse it, and "bear" it, and "sell it short," and break it down. They would do with it just as they would with one of your silver mines out there—they would try to make all the world believe it was "wildcat." You ought not to do anything that is calculated to bring a sacred thing into disrepute. You ought to be ashamed of yourselves—that is what *I* think about it. You close your petition with the words: "And we will ever pray." I think you had better—you need to do it.

" 'Very truly, etc.,
" 'MARK TWAIN,
" 'For James W.N**, U.S. Senator.'

"*That* luminous epistle finishes me with the religious element among my constituents. But that my political murder might be made sure, some evil instinct prompted me to hand you this memorial from the grave company of elders composing the Board of Aldermen of the city of San Francisco, to try your hand upon—a memorial praying that the city's right to the water-lots upon the city front might be established by law of Congress. I told you this was a dangerous matter to move in. I told you to write a non-committal letter to the Aldermen—an ambiguous letter—a letter that should avoid, as far as possible, all real consideration and discussion of the water-lot question. If there is any feeling left in you—any shame—surely this letter you wrote, in obedience to that order, ought to evoke it, when its words fall upon your ears:

" 'WASHINGTON, NOV.17.

" '*The Hon. Board of Aldermen, etc.*

" 'GENTLEMEN: George Washington, the revered Father of his Country is dead. His long and brilliant career is closed, alas! forever. He was greatly respected in this section of the country, and his untimely decease cast a gloom over the whole community. He died on the 14th day of December, 1799. He passed peacefully away from the scene of his honors and his great achievements, the most lamented hero and the best beloved that ever earth hath yielded unto Death. At such a time as this, *you* speak of water-lots!—what a lot was his!

" 'What is fame! Fame is an accident. Sir Isaac Newton discovered an apple falling to the ground—a trivial discovery, truly, and one which a million men had made before him—but his parents were influential, and so they tortured that small circumstance into something wonderful, and, lo! the simple world took up the shout and, in almost the twinkling of an eye, that man was famous. Treasure these thoughts.

" 'Poesy, sweet poesy, who shall estimate what the world owes to thee!

"Mary had a little lamb, its fleece was white as snow—
And everywhere that Mary went, the lamb was sure to go."

"Jack and Gill went up the hill
To draw a pail of water.
Jack fell down and broke his crown,
And Gill came tumbling after."

For simplicity, elegance of diction, and freedom from immoral tendencies, I regard those two poems in the light of gems. They are suited to all grades of intelligence, to every sphere of life— to the field, to the nursery, to the guild. Especially should no Board of Aldermen be without them.

" 'Venerable fossils! write again. Nothing improves one so much as friendly correspondence. Write again—and if there is anything in this memorial of yours that refers to anything in particular, do not be backward about explaining it. We shall always be happy to hear you chirp.

" 'Very Truly, etc.

" 'MARK TWAIN,

" 'For James W.N**, U.S. Senator.

"That is an atrocious, a ruinous epistle! Distraction!"

"Well, sir, I am really sorry if there is anything wrong about it—but—but it appears to me to dodge the water-lot question."

"Dodge the mischief! Oh—but never mind. As long as destruction must come now, let it be complete. Let it be complete—let this last of your performances, which I am about to read, make a finality of it. I am a ruined man. I *had* my misgivings when I gave you the the letter from Humboldt, asking that the post route from Indian Gulch to Shakespeare Gap and intermediate points, be changed partly to the old Mormon trail. But I told you it was a delicate question, and warned you to deal with it deftly—to answer it dubiously5 and leave them a little in the dark. And your fatal imbecility impelled you to make *this* disastrous reply. I should think you would stop your ears, if you are not dead to all shame:

" 'WASHINGTON, NOV. 30.

" '*Messrs. Perkins, Wagner, et al.*

" 'GENTLEMEN: It is a delicate question about this Indian trail, but, handled with proper deftness and dubiousness, I doubt not we shall succeed in some measure or otherwise, because the place where the route leaves the Lassen Meadows, over beyond where those two Shawnee chiefs, Dilapidated-Vengeance and Biter-of-the-Clouds, were scalped last winter, this being the favorite direction to some, but others preferring something else in consequence of things, the Mormon trail leaving Mosby's at three in the morning, and passing through Jawbone Flat to Blucher, and then down by a Jug-Handle, the road passing to the right of it, and naturally leaving it on the right, too, and Dawson's on the left of the trail where it passes to the left of said Dawson's and onward thence to Tomahawk, thus making the route cheaper, easier of access to all who can get at it, and compassing all the desirable objects so considered by others, and, therefore, conferring the most good upon the greatest number, and, consequently, I am encouraged to hope we shall. However, I shall be ready, and happy, to afford you still further information upon the subject, from time to time, as you may desire it and the Post-office Department be enabled to furnish it to me.

" 'Very truly, etc.

" 'MARK TWAIN,

" 'For, James W.N**, U.S. Senator.'

"There—now *what* do you think of that?"

"Well, I don't know, sir. It—well, it appears to me—to be dubious enough."

"Du—leave the house! I am a ruined man. Those Humboldt savages never will forgive me for tangling their brains up with this inhuman letter. I have lost the respect of the Methodist Church, the Board of Aldermen——"

"Well, I haven't anything to say about that, because I may have missed it a little in their cases, but I *was* too many for the Baldwin's Ranch people, General!"

"Leave the house! Leave it for ever and for ever, too!"

I regarded that as a sort of covert intimation that my service could be dispensed with, and so I resigned. I never will be a private secretary to a senator again. You can't please that kind of people. They don't know anything. They can't appreciate a party's efforts.

"A Mysterious Visit" appeared in the Buffalo Express *on March 19, 1870, and was later collected in* Mark Twain's Sketches New and Old *in 1875. Written while Twain was a proprietor of and regular contributor to the newspaper, it describes the sudden interest taken in him—a man who had recently married a wealthy woman and published an enormously successful book—by the Internal Revenue Department.*

A Mysterious Visit

The first notice that was taken of me when I "settled down" recently, was by a gentleman who said he was an assessor, and connected with the U.S. Internal Revenue Department. I said I had never heard of his branch of business before, but I was very glad to see him all the same—would he sit down? He sat down. I did not know anything particular to say, and yet I felt that people who have arrived at the dignity of keeping house must be conversational, must be easy and sociable in company. So, in default of anything else to say, I asked him if he was opening his shop in our neighborhood?

He said he was. [I did not wish to appear ignorant, but I *had* hoped he would mention what he had for sale.]

I ventured to ask him "How was trade?" And he said "So- so."

I then said we would drop in, and if we liked his house as well as any other, we would give him our custom.

He said he thought we would like his establishment well enough to confine ourselves to it—said he never saw anybody who would go off and hunt up another man in his line after trading with him once.

That sounded pretty complacent, but barring that natural expression of villainy which we all have, the man looked honest enough.

I do not know how it came about exactly, but gradually we appeared to melt down and run together, conversationally speaking, and then everything went along as comfortably as clockwork.

We talked, and talked, and talked—at least I did; and we laughed, and laughed, and laughed—at least he did. But all the time I had my presence of mind about me—I had my native shrewdness turned on "full head," as the engineers say. I was determined to find out all about his business in spite of his obscure answers—and I was determined I would have it out of him without his suspecting what I was at. I meant to trap him with a deep, deep ruse. I would tell him all about my own business, and he would naturally so warm to me during this seductive burst of confidence that he would forget himself, and tell me all about *his* affairs before he suspected what I was about. I thought to myself, My son, you little know what an old fox you are dealing with. I said—

"Now you never would guess what I made lecturing this winter and last spring?"

"No—don't believe I could, to save me. Let me see—let me see. About two thousand dollars, maybe? But no; no sir, I know you couldn't have made that much. Say seventeen hundred, maybe?"

"Ha! ha! I knew you couldn't. My lecturing receipts for last spring and this winter were fourteen thousand seven hundred and fifty dollars. What do you think of that?"

"Why, it is amazing—perfectly amazing. I will make a note of it. And you say even this wasn't all?"

"All! Why bless you, there was my income from the *Daily Warwhoop* for four months—about—about—well, what should you say to about eight thousand dollars, for instance?"

"Say! Why, I should say I should like to see myself rolling in just such another ocean of affluence. Eight thousand! I'll make a note of it. Why man!—and on top of all this I am to understand that you had still more income?"

"Ha! ha! ha! Why, you're only in the suburbs of it, so to speak. There's my book, 'The Innocents Abroad'—price $3.50 to $5.00, according to the binding. Listen to me. Look me in the eye. During the last four months and a half, saying nothing of sales before that, but just simply during the four months and a half, we've sold ninety-five thousand copies of that book. Ninety-five thousand! Think of it. Average four dollars a copy, say. It's nearly four hundred thousand dollars, my son. I get half."

"The suffering Moses! I'll set *that* down. Fourteen-seven-fifty—eight—two hundred. Total, say—well, upon my word, the grand total is about two hundred and thirteen or fourteen thousand dollars! *Is* that possible?"

"Possible! If there's any mistake it's the other way. Two hundred and fourteen thousand, cash, is my income for this year if *I* know how to cipher."

Then the gentleman got up to go. It came over me most uncomfortably that maybe I had made my revelations for nothing, besides being flattered into stretching them considerably by the stranger's astonished exclamations. But no; at the last moment the gentleman handed me a large envelope, and said it contained his advertisement; and that I would find out all about his business in it; and that he would be happy to have my custom—would in fact, be *proud* to have the custom of a man of such prodigious income; and that he used to think there were several wealthy men in the city, but when they came to trade with him, he discovered that they barely had enough to live on; and that, in truth it had been such a weary, weary age since he had seen a rich man face to face, and talked to him, and touched him with his hands, that he could hardly refrain from embracing me—in fact, would esteem it a great favor if I would *let* him embrace me.

This so pleased me that I did not try to resist, but allowed this simple-hearted stranger to throw his arms about me and weep a few tranquilizing tears down the back of my neck. Then he went his way.

As soon as he was gone I opened his advertisement. I studied it attentively for four minutes. I then called up the cook, and said—

"Hold me while I faint! Let Marie turn the griddle-cakes."

By and by, when I came to, I sent down to the rum mill on the corner and hired an artist by the week to sit up nights and curse that stranger, and give me a lift occasionally in the daytime when I came to a hard place.

Ah, what a miscreant he was! His "advertisement" was nothing in the world but a wicked tax-return—a string of impertinent questions about my private affairs, occupying the best part of four foolscap pages of fine print—questions, I may remark, gotten up with such marvelous ingenuity, that the oldest man in the world couldn't understand what the most of them were driving at—questions, too, that were calculated to make a man report about four times his actual income to keep from swearing to a falsehood. I looked for a loophole, but there did not appear to be any. Inquiry No. 1 covered my case as generously and as amply as an umbrella could cover an ant hill—

> "What were your profits, during the past year, from any trade, business, or vocation, wherever carried on?"

And that inquiry was backed up by thirteen others of an

equally searching nature, the most modest of which required information as to whether I had committed any burglary or highway robbery, or by any arson or other secret source of emolument, had acquired property which was not enumerated in my statement of income as set opposite to inquiry No. I.

It was plain that that stranger had enabled me to make a goose of myself. It was very, very plain; and so I went out and hired another artist. By working on my vanity, the stranger had seduced me into declaring an income of $214,000. By law, $1000 of this was exempt from income-tax—the only relief I could see, and it was only a drop in the ocean. At the legal five per cent, I must pay to the Government the sum of ten thousand six hundred and fifty dollars, income-tax!

[I may remark, in this place, that I did not do it.]

I am acquainted with a very opulent man, whose house is a palace, whose table is regal, whose outlays are enormous, yet a man who has no income, as I have often noticed by the revenue returns; and to him I went for advice, in my distress. He took my dreadful exhibition of receipts, he put on his glasses, he took his pen, and presto!—I was a pauper! It was the neatest thing that ever was. He did it simply by deftly manipulating the bill of "DEDUCTIONS." He set down my "State, national, and municipal taxes" at so much; my "losses by shipwreck, fire, etc.," at so much; my "losses on sales of real estate"—on "live stock sold"—on "payments for rent of homestead"—on "repairs, improvements, interest"—on "previously taxed salary as an officer of the United States' army, navy, revenue service," and other things. He got astonishing "deductions" out of each and every one of these matters—each and every one of them. And when he was done he handed me the paper, and I saw at a glance that during the year my income, in the way of profits, had been *one thousand two hundred and fifty dollars and forty cents.*

"Now," said he, "the thousand dollars is exempt by law. What you want to do is to go and swear this document in and pay tax on the two hundred and fifty dollars."

[While he was making this speech his little boy Willie lifted a two dollar greenback out of his vest pocket and vanished with it, and I would wager anything that if my stranger were to call on that little boy to-morrow he would make a false return of his income.]

"Do you," said I, "do you always work up the 'deductions' after this fashion in your own case, sir?"

"Well, I should say so! If it weren't for those eleven saving clauses under the head of 'Deduction' I should be beggared every year to support this hateful and wicked, this extortionate and tyrannical government."

This gentleman stands away up among the very best of the solid men of the city—the men of moral weight, of commercial integrity, of unimpeachable social spotlessness—and so I bowed to his example. I went down to the revenue office, and under the accusing eyes of my old visitor I stood up and swore to lie after lie, fraud after fraud, villainy after villainy, till my soul was coated inches and inches thick with perjury, and my self-respect gone for ever and ever.

But what of it? It is nothing more than thousands of the richest and proudest, and most respected, honored, and courted men in America do every year. And so I don't care. I am not ashamed. I shall simply, for the present, talk little, and eschew fire-proof gloves, lest I fall into certain dreadful habits irrevocably.

"Journalism in Tennessee" was written for Twain's column in the Buffalo Express, *where it appeared on September 4, 1869. In 1871, the story was part of a volume of pirated material called* Eye Openers *that was published in London by John Camden Hotten, an enterprising man who had assembled several cheap editions of Twain's work for the British market. This infuriated Twain, not only because he did not collect royalties on any of the books, but also because Hotten was in the habit of filling out collections like* Eye Openers *with sketches that he had written himself. In a blast at Hotten in the London* Spectator *of September 20, 1872, Twain directed loyal readers to patronize his official English publishers, George Routledge & Sons. At home, Twain continued to be a client of the American Publishing Company, which issued* Mark Twain's Sketches New and Old *(including "Journalism in Tennessee") in 1875. The story was reissued as a pamphlet with several other selections in Girard, Kansas, around 1923.*

Journalism in Tennessee

The editor of the Memphis *Avalanche* swoops thus mildly down upon a correspondent who posted him as a Radical:—"While he was writing the first word, the middle, dotting his i's, crossing his t's, and punching his period, he knew he was concocting a sentence that was saturated with infamy and reeking with falsehood."—*Exchange*

I was told by the physician that a Southern climate would improve my health, and so I went down to Tennessee, and got a berth on the *Morning Glory and Johnson County War-Whoop* as associate editor. When I went on duty I found the chief editor sitting tilted back in a three-legged chair with his feet on a pine table. There was another pine table in the room and another afflicted chair, and both were half buried under newspapers and scraps and sheets of manuscript. There was a wooden box of sand, sprinkled with cigar stubs and "old soldiers," and a stove with a door hanging by its upper hinge. The chief editor had a long-tailed black cloth frock coat on, and white linen pants. His boots were small and neatly blacked. He wore a ruffled shirt, a large seal ring, a standing collar of obsolete pattern, and a checkered neckerchief with the ends hanging down. Date of costume about 1848. He was smoking a cigar, and trying to think of a word, and in pawing his hair he had rumpled his locks a good deal. He was scowling fearfully, and I judged that he was concocting a particularly knotty editorial. He told me to take the exchanges and skim through them and write up the "Spirit of the Tennessee Press," condensing into the article all of their contents that seemed of interest.

I wrote as follows:—

"SPIRIT OF THE TENNESSEE PRESS

"The editors of the *Semi-Weekly Earthquake* evidently labor under a misapprehension with regard to the Ballyhack railroad. It is not the object of the company to leave Buzzardville off to one side. On the contrary, they consider it one of the most important points along the line, and consequently can have no desire to slight it. The gentlemen of the *Earthquake* will, of course, take pleasure in making the correction.

"John W. Blossom, Esq., the able editor of the Higginsville *Thunderbolt and Battle Cry of Freedom,* arrived in the city yesterday. He is stopping at the Van Buren House.

"We observe that our contemporary of the Mud Springs *Morning Howl* has fallen into the error of supposing that the election of Van Werter is not an established fact, but he will have discovered his mistake before this reminder reaches him, no doubt. He was doubtless misled by incomplete election returns.

"It is pleasant to note that the city of Blathersville is endeavoring to contract with some New York gentlemen to pave its well-nigh impassable streets with the Nicholson pavement. The *Daily Hurrah* urges the measure with ability, and seems confident of ultimate success."

I passed my manuscript over to the chief editor for acceptance, alteration, or destruction. He glanced at it and his face clouded. He ran his eye down the pages, and his countenance grew portentous. It was easy to see that something was wrong. Presently he sprang up and said—

"Thunder and lightning! Do you suppose I am going to speak of those cattle that way? Do you suppose my subscribers are going to stand such gruel as that? Give me the pen!"

I never saw a pen scrape and scratch its way so viciously, or plough through another man's verbs and adjectives so relentlessly. While he was in the midst of his work, somebody shot at him through the open window, and marred the symmetry of my ear.

"Ah," said he, "that is that scoundrel Smith, of the *Moral Volcano*—he was due yesterday." And he snatched a navy revolver from his belt and fired. Smith dropped, shot in the thigh. The shot spoiled Smith's aim, who was just taking a second chance, and he crippled a stranger. It was me. Merely a finger shot off.

Then the chief editor went on with his erasures and interlineations. Just as he finished them a hand-grenade came down the stove pipe, and the explosion shivered the stove into a thousand fragments. However, it did no further damage, except that a vagrant piece knocked a couple of my teeth out.

"That stove is utterly ruined," said the chief editor.

I said I believed it was.

"Well, no matter—don't want it this kind of weather. I know the man that did it. I'll get him. Now, *here* is the way this stuff ought to be written."

I took the manuscript. It was scarred with erasures and interlineations till its mother wouldn't have known it if it had had one. It now read as follows:—

"SPIRIT OF THE TENNESSEE PRESS

"The inveterate liars of the *Semi-Weekly Earthquake* are evidently endeavoring to palm off upon a noble and chivalrous people another of their vile and brutal falsehoods with regard to that most glorious conception of the nineteenth century, the Ballyhack railroad. The idea that Buzzardville was to be left off at one side originated in their own fulsome brains—or rather in the settlings which *they* regard as brains. They had better swallow this lie if they want to save their abandoned reptile carcasses the cowhiding they so richly deserve.

"That ass, Blossom, of the Higginsville *Thunderbolt and Battle Cry of Freedom,* is down here again sponging at the Van Buren.

"We observe that the besotted blackguard of the Mud Springs *Morning Howl* is giving out, with his usual propensity for lying, that Van Werter is not elected. The heaven-born mission of journalism is to disseminate truth; to eradicate error; to educate, refine, and elevate the tone of public morals and manners, and make all men more gentle, more virtuous, more charitable, and in all ways better, and holier, and happier; and yet this black-hearted scoundrel degrades his great office persistently to the dissemination of falsehood, calumny, vituperation, and vulgarity.

"Blathersville wants a Nicholson pavement—it wants a jail and a poorhouse more. The idea of a pavement in a one horse town composed of two gin mills, a blacksmith's shop, and that mustard-plaster of a newspaper, the *Daily Hurrah!* The crawling insect, Buckner, who edits the *Hurrah,* is braying about this business with his customary imbecility, and imagining that he is talking sense."

"Now *that* is the way to write—peppery and to the point. Mush-and-milk journalism gives me the fan-tods."

About this time a brick came through the window with a splintering crash, and gave me a considerable of a jolt in the back. I moved out of range—I began to feel in the way.

The chief said, "That was the Colonel, likely. I've been expecting him for two days. He will be up, now, right away."

He was correct. The Colonel appeared in the door a moment afterward with a dragoon revolver in his hand.

He said, "Sir, have I the honor of addressing the poltroon who edits this mangy sheet?"

"You have. Be seated, sir. Be careful of the chair, one of its legs is gone. I believe I have the honor of addressing the putrid liar, Col. Blatherskite Tecumseh?"

"Right, sir. I have a little account to settle with you. If you are at leisure we will begin."

"I have an article on the 'Encouraging Progress of Moral and Intellectual Development in America' to finish, but there is no hurry. Begin."

Both pistols rang out their fierce clamor at the same instant. The chief lost a lock of his hair, and the Colonel's bullet ended its career in the fleshy part of my thigh. The Colonel's left shoulder was clipped a little. They fired again. Both missed their men this time, but I got my share, a shot in the arm. At the third fire both gentlemen were wounded slightly, and I had a knuckle chipped. I then said, I believed I would go out and take a walk, as this was a private matter, and I had a delicacy about participating in it further. But both gentlemen begged me to keep my seat, and assured me that I was not in the way.

They then talked about the elections and the crops while they reloaded, and I fell to tying up my wounds. But presently they opened fire again with animation, and every shot took effect—but it is proper to remark that five out of the six fell to my share. The sixth one mortally wounded the colonel, who remarked, with fine humor, that he would have to say good morning now, as he had business up town. He then inquired the way to the undertaker's and left.

The chief turned to me and said, "I am expecting company to dinner, and shall have to get ready. It will be a favor to me if you will read proof and attend to the customers."

I winced a little at the idea of attending to the customers, but I was too bewildered by the fusilade that was still ringing in my ears to think of anything to say.

He continued, "Jones will be here at 3—cowhide him. Gillespie will call earlier, perhaps—throw him out of the window. Ferguson will be along about 4—kill him. That is all for to-day, I believe. If you have any odd time, you may write a blistering article on the police—give the Chief Inspector rats. The cowhides are under the table; weapons in the drawer— ammunition there in the corner—lint and bandages up there in the pigeon-holes. In case of accident, go to Lancet, the surgeon, down-stairs. He advertises—we take it out in trade."

He was gone. I shuddered. At the end of the next three hours I had been through perils so awful that all peace of mind and all cheerfulness were gone from me. Gillespie had called and thrown *me* out of the window. Jones arrived promptly, and when I got ready to do the cowhiding he took the job off my hands. In an encounter with a stranger, not in the bill of fare, I had lost my scalp. Another stranger, by the name of Thompson, left me a mere wreck and ruin of chaotic rags. And at last, at bay in the corner, and beset by an infuriated mob of editors, blacklegs, politicians, and desperadoes, who raved and swore and flourished their weapons about my head till the air shimmered with glancing flashes of steel, I was in the act of resigning my berth on the paper when the chief arrived, and with him a rabble of charmed and enthusiastic friends. Then ensued a scene of riot and carnage such as no human pen, or steel one either, could describe. People were shot, probed, dismembered, blown up, thrown out of the window. There was a brief tornado of murky blasphemy, with a confused and frantic war-dance glimmering through it, and then all was over. In five minutes there was silence, and the gory chief and I sat alone and surveyed the sanguinary ruin that strewed the floor around us.

He said, "You'll like this place when you get used to it".

I said, "I'll have to get you to excuse me; I think maybe I might write to suit you after a while; as soon as I had had some practice and learned the language I am confident I could. But, to speak the plain truth, that sort of energy of expression has its inconveniences, and a man is liable to interruption. You see that yourself. Vigorous writing is calculated to elevate the public, no doubt, but, then I do not like to attract so much attention as it calls forth. I can't write with comfort when I am interrupted so much as I have been to-day. I like this berth well enough, but I don't like to be left here to wait on the customers. The experiences are novel, I grant you, and entertaining too, after a fashion, but they are not judiciously distributed. A gentleman shoots at you through the window and cripples *me;* a bomb-shell comes down the stove-pipe for your gratification and sends the stove-door down *my* throat; a friend drops in to swap compliments with you, and freckles *me* with bullet-holes till my skin won't hold my principles; you go to dinner, and Jones comes with his cowhide, Gillespie throws me out of the window, Thompson tears all my clothes off, and an entire stranger takes my scalp with the easy freedom of an old acquaintance; and in less than five minutes all the blackguards in the country arrive in their war-paint, and proceed to scare the rest of me to death with their tomahawks. Take it altogether, I never had such a spirited time in all my life as I have had to-day. No; I like you, and I like your calm unruffled way of explaining things to the customers, but you see I am not used to it. The Southern heart is too impulsive; Southern hospitality is too lavish with the stranger. The paragraphs which I have written to-day, and into whose cold sentences your masterly hand has infused the fervent spirit of Tennessean journalism, will wake up another nest of hornets. All that mob of editors will come—and they will come hungry, too, and want somebody for breakfast. I shall have to bid you adieu. I decline to be present at these festivities. I came South for my health, I will go back on the same errand, and suddenly. Tennesseean journalism is too stirring for me."

After which we parted with mutual regret, and I took apartments at the hospital.

This travelogue was originally called "A Day at Niagara" when it appeared in the Buffalo Express *on August 21, 1869. In 1872, it surfaced in London in one of John Camden Hotten's pirated volumes,* Practical Jokes. *The next year, Twain contributed the tale to a collection issued in Philadelphia called* One Hundred Choice Selections. *Retitled "A Visit to Niagara," it was also included in the American Publishing Company's* Mark Twain's Sketches New and Old *in 1875.*

A Visit to Niagara

Niagara Falls is a most enjoyable place of resort. The hotels are excellent, and the prices not at all exorbitant. The opportunities for fishing are not even equalled elsewhere. Because, in other localities, certain places in the streams are much better than others; but at Niagara one place is just as good as another, for the reason that the fish do not bite anywhere, and so there is no use in your walking five miles to fish, when you can depend on being just as unsuccessful nearer home. The advantages of this state of things have never heretofore been properly placed before the public.

The weather is cool in summer, and the walks and drives are all pleasant and none of them fatiguing. When you start out to "do" the Falls you first drive down about a mile, and pay a small sum for the privilege of looking down from a precipice into the narrowest part of the Niagara river. A railway "cut" through a hill would be as comely if it had the angry river tumbling and foaming through its bottom. You can descend a staircase here a hundred and fifty feet down, and stand at the edge of the water. After you have done it, you will wonder why you did it; but you will then be too late.

The guide will explain to you, in his blood-curdling way, how he saw the little steamer, *Maid of the Mist,* descend the fearful rapids—how first one paddle-box was out of sight behind the raging billows, and then the other, and at what point it was that her smokestack toppled overboard, and where her planking began to break and part asunder—and how she did finally live through the trip, after accomplishing the incredible feat of travelling seventeen miles in six minutes, or six miles in seventeen minutes, I have really forgotten which. But it was very extraordinary, anyhow. It is worth the price of admission to hear the guide tell the story nine times in succession to different parties, and never miss a word or alter a sentence or a gesture.

Then you drive over the Suspension Bridge, and divide your misery between the chances of smashing down two hundred feet into the river below, and the chances of having the railway train overhead smashing down on to you. Either possibility is discomforting taken by itself, but mixed together, they amount in the aggregate to positive unhappiness.

On the Canada side you drive along the chasm between long ranks of photographers standing guard behind their cameras, ready to make an ostentatious frontispiece of you and your decaying ambulance, and your solemn crate with a hide on it, which you are expected to regard in the light of a horse, and a diminished and unimportant background of sublime Niagara; and a great many people have the incredible effrontery or the native depravity to aid and abet this sort of crime.

Any day, in the hands of these photographers, you may see stately pictures of papa and mamma, Johnny and Bub and Sis, or a couple of country cousins, all smiling vacantly, and all disposed in studied and uncomfortable attitudes in their carriage, and all looming up in their awe-inspiring imbecility before the snubbed and diminished presentment of that majestic presence whose ministering spirits are the rainbows, whose voice is the thunder, whose awful front is veiled in clouds, who was monarch here dead and forgotten ages before this hackful of small reptiles was deemed temporarily necessary to fill a crack in the world's unnoted myriads, and will still be monarch here ages and decades of ages after they shall have gathered themselves to their blood relations, the other worms, and been mingled with the unremembering dust.

There is no actual harm in making Niagara a background whereon to display one's marvelous insignificance in a good strong light, but it requires a sort of superhuman self-complacency to enable one to do it.

When you have examined the stupendous Horseshoe Fall till you are satisfied you cannot improve on it, you return to America by the new Suspension Bridge, and follow up the bank to where they exhibit the Cave of the Winds.

Here I followed instructions, and divested myself of all my clothing, and put on a waterproof jacket and overalls. This costume is picturesque, but not beautiful. A guide, similarly dressed, led the way down a flight of winding stairs, which wound and wound, and still kept on winding long after the thing ceased to be a novelty, and then terminated long before it had begun to be a pleasure. We were then well down under the precipice, but still considerably above the level of the river.

We now began to creep along flimsy bridges of a single plank, our persons shielded from destruction by a crazy wooden railing, to which I clung with both hands—not because I was afraid, but because I wanted to. Presently the descent became steeper, and the bridge flimsier, and sprays from the American Fall began to rain down on us in fast-increasing sheets that soon became blinding, and after that our progress was mostly in the nature of groping. Now a furious wind began to rush out from behind the waterfall, which seemed determined to sweep us from the bridge, and scatter us on the rocks and among the torrents below. I remarked that I wanted to go home; but it was too late. We were almost under the monstrous wall of water thundering down from above, and speech was in vain in the midst of such a pitiless crash of sound.

In another moment the guide disappeared behind the deluge, and bewildered by the thunder, driven helplessly by the wind, and smitten by the arrowy tempest of rain, I followed. All was darkness. Such a mad storming, roaring, and bellowing of warring wind and water never crazed my ears before. I bent my head, and seemed to receive the Atlantic on my back. The world seemed going to destruction. I could not see anything, the flood poured down so savagely. I raised my head, with open mouth, and the most of the American cataract went down my throat. If I had sprung a leak now, I had been lost. And at this moment I discovered that the bridge had ceased, and we must trust for a foothold to the slippery and precipitous rocks. I never was so scared before and survived it. But we got through at last, and emerged into the open day, where we could stand in front of the laced and frothy and seething world of descending water, and look at it. When I saw how much of it there was, and how fearfully in earnest it was, I was sorry I had gone behind it.

The noble Red Man has always been a friend and darling of mine. I love to read about him in tales and legends and romances. I love to read of his inspired sagacity, and his love of the wild free life of mountain and forest, and his general nobility of character, and his stately metaphorical manner of speech, and his chivalrous love for the dusky maiden, and the picturesque pomp of his dress and accoutrements. Especially the picturesque pomp of his dress and accoutrements. When I found the shops at Niagara Falls full of dainty Indian bead-work, and stunning moccasins, and equally stunning toy figures representing human beings who carried their weapons in holes bored through their arms and bodies, and had feet shaped like a pie, I was filled with emotion. I knew that now, at last, I was going to come face to face with the noble Red Man.

A lady clerk in a shop told me, indeed, that all her grand array of curiosities were made by the Indians, and that they were plenty about the Falls, and that they were friendly, and it would not be dangerous to speak to them. And sure enough, as I approached the bridge leading over to Luna Island, I came upon a noble Son of the Forest sitting under a tree, diligently at work on a bead reticule. He wore a slouch hat and brogans, and had a short black pipe in his mouth. Thus does the baneful contact with our effeminate civilization dilute the picturesque pomp which is so natural to the Indian when far removed from us in his native haunts. I addressed the relic as follows:—

"Is the Wawhoo-Wang-Wang of the Whack-a-Whack happy? Does the great Speckled Thunder sigh for the warpath, or is his heart contented with dreaming of the dusky maiden, the Pride of the Forest? Does the mighty Sachem yearn to drink the blood of his enemies, or is he satisfied to make bead reticules for the pappooses of the paleface? Speak, sublime relic of bygone grandeur—venerable ruin, speak!"

The relic said—

"An' is it mesilf, Dennis Hooligan, that ye'd be takin' for a dirty Injin, ye drawlin', lantern-jawed, spider-legged divil! By the piper that played before Moses, I'll ate ye!"

I went away from there.

By and by, in the neighborhood of the Terrapin Tower, I came upon a gentle daughter of the aborigines in fringed and beaded buckskin moccasins and leggins, seated on a bench, with her pretty wares about her. She had just carved out a wooden chief that had a strong family resemblance to a clothes-pin, and was now boring a hole through his abdomen to put his bow through. I hesitated a moment, and then addressed her:

"Is the heart of the forest maiden heavy? Is the Laughing Tadpole lonely? Does she mourn over the extinguished council-fires of her race, and the vanished glory of her ancestors? Or does her sad spirit wander afar toward the hunting grounds whither her brave Gobbler-of-the-Lightning is gone? Why is my daughter silent? Has she aught against the paleface stranger?"

The maiden said—

"Faix, an' is it Biddy Malone ye dare to be callin' names? Lave this, or I'll shy your lean carcass over the cataract, ye sniveling blaggard!"

I adjourned from there also.

"Confound these Indians!" I said. "They told me they were tame; but, if appearances go for anything, I should say they were all on the warpath."

I made one more attempt to fraternize with them, and only one. I came upon a camp of them gathered in the shade of a great tree, making wampum and moccasins, and addressed them in the language of friendship:

"Noble Red Men, Braves, Grand Sachems, War Chiefs, Squaws, and High Muck-a-Mucks, the paleface from the land of the setting sun greets you! You, Beneficent Polecat—you, Devourer of Mountains—you, Roaring Thundergust—you, Bully Boy with a Glass eye—the paleface from beyond the great waters greets you all! War and pestilence have thinned your ranks, and destroyed your once proud nation. Poker and seven-up, and a vain modern expense for soap, unknown to your glorious ancestors, have depleted your purses. Appropriating, in your simplicity, the property of others, has gotten you into trouble. Misrepresenting facts, in your simple innocence, has damaged your reputation with the soulless usurper. Trading for forty-rod whisky, to enable you to get drunk and happy and tomahawk your families, has played the everlasting mischief with the picturesque pomp of your dress, and here you are, in the broad light of the nineteenth century, gotten up like the ragtag and bobtail of the purlieus of New York. For shame! Remember your ancestors! Recall their mighty deeds! Remember Uncas!—and Red Jacket!—and Hole in the Day!—and Whoopdedoodledo! Emulate their achievements! Unfurl yourselves under my banner, noble savages, illustrious guttersnipes"—

"Down wid him!" "Scoop the blaggard!" "Burn him!" "Hang him!" "Dhround him!"

It was the quickest operation that ever was. I simply saw a sudden flash in the air of clubs, brickbats, fists, bead-baskets, and moccasins—a single flash, and they all appeared to hit me at once, and no two of them in the same place. In the next instant the entire tribe was upon me. They tore half the clothes off me; they broke my arms and legs; they gave me a thump that dented the top of my head till it would hold coffee like a saucer; and, to crown their disgraceful proceedings and add insult to injury, they threw me over the Niagara Falls, and I got wet.

About ninety or a hundred feet from the top, the remains of my vest caught on a projecting rock, and I was almost drowned before I could get loose. I finally fell, and brought up in a world of white foam at the foot of the Fall, whose celled and bubbly masses towered up several inches above my head. Of course I got into the eddy. I sailed round and round in it forty-four times—chasing a chip and gaining on it—each round trip a half mile—reaching for the same bush on the bank forty-four times, and just exactly missing it by a hair's-breadth every time.

At last a man walked down and sat down close to that bush, and put a pipe in his mouth, and lit a match, and followed me with one eye and kept the other on the match, while he sheltered it in his hands from the wind. Presently a puff of wind blew it out. The next time I swept around he said—

"Got a match?"

"Yes; in my other vest. Help me out, please."

"Not for Joe."

When I came round again, I said—

"Excuse the seemingly impertinent curiosity of a drowning man, but will you explain this singular conduct of yours?"

"With pleasure. I am the coroner. Don't hurry on my account. I can wait for you. But I wish I had a match."

I said—"Take my place, and I'll go and get you one."

He declined. This lack of confidence on his part created a coldness between us, and from that time forward I avoided him. It was my idea, in case anything happened, to so time the occurrence as to throw my custom into the hands of the opposition coroner over on the American side.

At last a policeman came along, and arrested me for disturbing the peace by yelling at people on shore for help. The judge fined me, but I had the advantage of him. My money was with my pantaloons, and my pantaloons were with the Indians.

Thus I escaped. I am now lying in a very critical condition. At least I am lying anyway—critical or not critical. I am hurt all over, but I cannot tell the full extent yet, because the doctor is not done taking inventory. He will make out my manifest this evening. However, thus far he thinks only sixteen of my wounds are fatal. I don't mind the others.

Upon regaining my right mind, I said—

"It is an awful savage tribe of Indians that do the bead work and moccasins for Niagara Falls, doctor. Where are they from?"

"Limerick, my son."

"The Experiences of the McWilliamses With the Membranous Croup" made its first appearance in Mark Twain's Sketches New and Old *in 1875. The narrator of the tale, Mortimer McWilliams, was the classic henpecked husband; he was also one of Twain's favorite characters.*

The Experiences of the McWilliamses with Membranous Croup

[*As related to the author of this book by Mr. McWilliams, a pleasant New York gentleman whom the said author met by chance on a journey.*]

Well, to go back to where I was before I digressed to explain to you how that frightful and incurable disease, membranous croup, was ravaging the town and driving all mothers mad with terror, I called Mrs. McWilliams's attention to little Penelope and said:

"Darling, I wouldn't let that child be chewing that pine stick if I were you."

"Precious, where is the harm in it?" said she, but at the same time preparing to take away the stick—for some women cannot receive even the most palpably judicious suggestion without arguing it; that is, married women.

I replied:

"Love, it is notorious that pine is the least nutritious wood that a child can eat."

My wife's hand paused, in the act of taking the stick, and returned itself to her lap. She bridled perceptibly, and said:

"Hubby, you know better than that. You know you do. Doctors *all* say that the turpentine in pine wood is good for weak back and the kidneys."

"Ah—I was under a misapprehension. I did not know that the child's kidneys and spine were affected, and that the family physician had recommended—"

"Who said the child's spine and kidneys were affected?"

"My love, you intimated it."

"The idea! I never intimated anything of the kind."

"Why my dear, it hasn't been two minutes since you said—"

"Bother what I said! I don't care what I did say. There isn't any harm in the child's chewing a bit of pine stick if she wants to, and you know it perfectly well. And she *shall* chew it, too. So there, now!"

"Say no more, my dear. I now see the force of your reasoning, and I will go and order two or three cords of the best pine wood to-day. No child of mine shall want while I—"

"O *please* go along to your office and let me have some peace. A body can never make the simplest remark but you must take it up and go to arguing and arguing and arguing till you don't know what you are talking about, and you *never* do."

"Very well, it shall be as you say. But there is a want of logic in your last remark which—"

However, she was gone with a flourish before I could finish, and had taken the child with her. That night at dinner she confronted me with a face as white as a sheet:

"O, Mortimer, there's another! Little Georgie Gordon is taken."

"Membranous croup?"

"Membranous croup."

"Is there any hope for him?"

"None in the wide world. O, what is to become of us!"

By and by a nurse brought in our Penelope to say good-night and offer the customary prayer at the mother's knee. In the midst of "Now I lay me down to sleep," she gave a slight cough! My wife fell back like one stricken with death. But the next moment she was up and brimming with the activities which terror inspires.

She commanded that the child's crib be removed from the nursery to our bed-room; and she went along to see the order executed. She took me with her, of course. We got matters arranged with speed. A cot bed was put up in my wife's dressing room for the nurse. But now Mrs. McWilliams said we were too far away from the other baby, and what if *he* were to have the symptoms in the night—and she blanched again, poor thing.

We then restored the crib and the nurse to the nursery and put up a bed for ourselves in a room adjoining.

Presently, however, Mrs. McWilliams said suppose the baby should catch it from Penelope? This thought struck a new panic to her heart, and the tribe of us could not get the crib out of the nursery again fast enough to satisfy my wife, though she assisted in her own person and well nigh pulled the crib to pieces in her frantic hurry.

We moved down stairs; but there was no place there to stow

the nurse, and Mrs. McWilliams said the nurse's experience would be an inestimable help. So we returned, bag and baggage, to our own bed-room once more, and felt a great gladness, like storm-buffeted birds that have found their nest again.

Mrs. McWilliams sped to the nursery to see how things were going on there. She was back in a moment with a new dread. She said:

"What *can* make Baby sleep so?"

I said:

"Why, my darling, Baby *always* sleeps like a graven image."

"I know. I know; but there's something peculiar about his sleep, now. He seems to—to—he seems to breathe so *regularly*. O, this is dreadful."

"But my dear he always breathes regularly."

"Oh, I know it, but there's something frightful about it now. His nurse is too young and inexperienced. Maria shall stay there with her, and be on hand if anything happens."

"That is a good idea, but who will help *you*?"

"You can help me all I want. I wouldn't allow anybody to do anything but myself, any how, at such a time as this."

I said I would feel mean to lie abed and sleep, and leave her to watch and toil over our little patient all the weary night.—But she reconciled me to it. So old Maria departed and took up her ancient quarters in the nursery.

Penelope coughed twice in her sleep.

"Oh, why *don't* that doctor come! Mortimer, this room is too warm. This room is certainly too warm. Turn off the register—quick!"

I shut it off, glancing at the thermometer at the same time, and wondering to myself if 70 *was* too warm for a sick child.

The coachman arrived from down town, now, with the news that our physician was ill and confined to his bed.—Mrs. McWilliams turned a dead eye upon me, and said in a dead voice:

"There is a Providence in it. It is foreordained. He never was sick before.—Never. We have not been living as we ought to live, Mortimer. Time and time again I have told you so. Now you see the result. Our child will never get well. Be thankful if you can forgive yourself; I never can forgive *my*self."

I said, without intent to hurt, but with heedless choice of words, that I could not see that we had been living such an abandoned life.

"*Mortimer!* Do you want to bring the judgment upon Baby, too!"

Then she began to cry, but suddenly exclaimed:

"The doctor must have sent medicines!"

I said:

"Certainly. They are here. I was only waiting for you to give me a chance."

"Well, do give them to me! Don't you know that every moment is precious now? But what was the use in sending medicines, when he *knows* that the disease is incurable?"

I said that while there was life there was hope.

"Hope! Mortimer, you know no more what you are talking about than the child unborn. If you would—. As I live, the directions say give one teaspoonful once an hour! Once an hour!—as if we had a whole year before us to save the child in! Mortimer, please hurry. Give the poor perishing thing a table-spoonful, and *try* to be quick!"

"Why, my dear, a table-spoonful might—"

"*Don't* drive me frantic!. . . . .There, there, there, my precious, my own; it's nasty bitter stuff, but it's good for Nelly—good for Mother's precious darling; and it will make her well. There, there, there, put the little head on Mamma's breast and go to sleep, and pretty soon—Oh, I know she can't live till morning! Mortimer, a table-spoonful every half hour will—. Oh, the child needs belladonna too; I know she does—and aconite. Get them, Mortimer. Now do let me have my way. You know nothing about these things."

We now went to bed, placing the crib close to my wife's pillow. All this turmoil had worn upon me, and within two minutes I was something more than half asleep. Mrs. McWilliams roused me:

"Darling, is that register turned on?"

"No."

"I thought as much. Please turn it on at once. This room is cold."

I turned it on, and presently fell asleep again. I was aroused once more:

"Dearie, would you mind moving the crib to your side of the bed? It is nearer the register."

I moved it, but had a collision with the rug and woke up the child. I dozed off once more, while my wife quieted the sufferer. But in a little while these words came murmuring remotely through the fog of my drowsiness:

"Mortimer, if we only had some goose-grease—will you ring?"

I climbed dreamily out, and stepped on a cat, which responded with a protest and would have got a convincing kick for it if a chair had not got it instead.

"Now, Mortimer, why do you want to turn up the gas and wake up the child again?"

"Because I want to see how much I am hurt, Caroline."

"Well look at the chair, too—I have no doubt it is ruined. Poor cat, suppose you had—"

"Now I am not going to suppose anything about the cat. It never would have occurred if Maria had been allowed to remain here and attend to these duties, which are in her line and are not in mine."

"Now Mortimer, I should think you would be ashamed to make a remark like that. It is a pity if you cannot do the few little things I ask of you at such an awful time as this when our child—"

"There, there, I will do anything you want. But I can't raise anybody with this bell. They're all gone to bed. Where is the goose-grease?"

"On the mantel-piece in the nursery. If you'll step there and speak to Maria—"

I fetched the goose-grease and went to sleep again. Once more I was called:

"Mortimer, I so hate to disturb you, but the room is still too cold for me to try to apply this stuff. Would you mind lighting the fire? It is all ready to touch a match to."

I dragged myself out and lit the fire, and then sat down disconsolate.

"Mortimer, don't sit there and catch your death of cold. Come to bed."

As I was stepping in, she said:

"But wait a moment. Please give the child some more of the medicine."

Which I did. It was a medicine which made a child more or less lively; so my wife made use of its waking interval to strip it and grease it all over with the goose-oil. I was soon asleep once more, but once more I had to get up.

"Mortimer, I feel a draft. I feel it distinctly. There is nothing so bad for this disease as a draft. Please move the crib in front of the fire."

I did it; and collided with the rug again, which I threw in the fire. Mrs. McWilliams sprang out of bed and rescued it and we had some words. I had another trifling interval of sleep, and then got up, by request, and constructed a flax-seed poultice.

This was placed upon the child's breast and left there to do its healing work.

A wood fire is not a permanent thing. I got up every twenty minutes and renewed ours, and this gave Mrs. McWilliams the opportunity to shorten the times of giving the medicines by ten minutes, which was a great satisfaction to her. Now and then, between times, I reorganized the flax-seed poultices, and applied sinapisms and other sorts of blisters where unoccupied places could be found upon the child. Well, toward morning the wood gave out and my wife wanted me to go down cellar and get some more. I said:

"My dear, it is a laborious job, and the child must be nearly warm enough, with her extra clothing. Now mightn't we put on another layer of poultices and—"

I did not finish, because I was interrupted. I lugged wood up from below for some little time, and then turned in and fell to snoring as only a man can whose strength is all gone and whose soul is worn out. Just at broad daylight I felt a grip on my shoulder that brought me to my senses suddenly.—My wife was glaring down upon me and gasping. As soon as she could command her tongue she said:

"It is all over! All over! The child's perspiring! What *shall* we do?"

"Mercy, how you terrify me! *I* don't know what we ought to do. Maybe if we scraped her and put her in the draft again—"

"O, idiot! There is not a moment to lose! Go for the doctor. Go yourself. Tell him he *must* come, dead or alive."

I dragged that poor sick man from his bed and brought him. He looked at the child and said she was not dying. This was joy unspeakable to me, but it made my wife as mad as if he had offered her a personal affront. Then he said the child's cough was only caused by some trifling irritation or other in the throat. At this I thought my wife had a mind to show him the door.—Now the doctor said he would make the child cough harder and dislodge the trouble. So he gave her something that sent her into a spasm of coughing, and presently up came a little wood splinter or so.

"This child has no membranous croup," said he. "She has been chewing a bit of pine shingle or something of the kind, and got some little slivers in her throat. They won't do her any hurt."

"No," said I, "I can well believe that. Indeed the turpentine that is in them is very good for certain sorts of diseases that are peculiar to children. My wife will tell you so."

But she did not. She turned away in disdain and left the room; and since that time there is one episode in our life which we never refer to. Hence the tide of our days flows by in deep and untroubled serenity.

[Very few married men have such an experience as McWilliams's, and so the author of this book thought that maybe the novelty of it would give it a passing interest to the reader.]

"Mrs. McWilliams and the Lightning" is one of several tales Twain wrote about the domestic problems of the McWilliams family. The story made its debut in the September 1880 issue of the Atlantic *and appeared the next year in an anthology called* Choice Selections No. 19. *In 1882, it was included in a collection of Twain's sketches called* The Stolen White Elephant, *published by James R. Osgood and Company.*

Mrs. McWilliams and the Lightning

Well, sir,—continued Mr. McWilliams, for this was not the beginning of his talk,—the fear of lightning is one of the most distressing infirmities a human being can be afflicted with. It is mostly confined to women; but now and then you find it in a little dog, and sometimes in a man. It is a particularly distressing infirmity, for the reason that it takes the sand out of a person to an extent which no other fear can, and it can't be *reasoned* with, and neither can it be shamed out of a person. A woman who could face the very devil himself—or a mouse— loses her grip and goes all to pieces in front of a flash of lightning. Her fright is something pitiful to see.

Well, as I was telling you, I woke up, with that smothered and unlocatable cry of "Mortimer! Mortimer!" wailing in my ears; and as soon as I could scrape my faculties together I reached over in the dark and then said,—

"Evangeline, is that you calling? What is the matter? Where are you?"

"Shut up in the boot-closet. You ought to be ashamed to lie there and sleep so, and such an awful storm going on."

"Why, how *can* one be ashamed when he is asleep? It is unreasonable; a man *can't* be ashamed when he is asleep, Evangeline."

"You never try, Mortimer,—you know very well you never try."

I caught the sound of muffled sobs.

That sound smote dead the sharp speech that was on my lips, and I changed it to—

"I'm sorry, dear,—I'm truly sorry. I never meant to act so. Come back and—"

"MORTIMER!"

"Heavens! what is the matter, my love?"

"Do you mean to say you are in that bed yet?"

"Why, of course."

"Come out of it instantly. I should think you would take some *little* care of your life, for *my* sake and the children's, if you will not for your own."

"But my love—"

"Don't talk to me, Mortimer. You *know* there is no place so dangerous as a bed, in such a thunder-storm as this,—all the books say that; yet there you would lie, and deliberately throw away your life,—for goodness knows what, unless for the sake of arguing and arguing, and—"

"But, confound it, Evangeline, I'm *not* in the bed, *now*. I'm—"

[Sentence interrupted by a sudden glare of lightning, followed by a terrified little scream from Mrs. McWilliams and a tremendous blast of thunder.]

"There! You see the result. Oh, Mortimer, how *can* you be so profligate as to swear at such a time as this?"

"I *didn't* swear. And that *wasn't* a result of it, any way. It would have come, just the same, if I hadn't said a word; and you know very well, Evangeline,—at least you ought to know,—that when the atmosphere is charged with electricity—"

"Oh, yes, now argue it, and argue it, and argue it!—I don't see how you can act so, when you *know* there is not a lightning-rod on the place, and your poor wife and children are absolutely at the mercy of Providence. What *are* you doing?—lighting a match at such a time as this! Are you stark mad?"

"Hang it, woman, where's the harm? The place is as dark as the inside of an infidel, and—"

"Put it out! put it out instantly! Are you determined to sacrifice us all? You *know* there is nothing attracts lightning like a light. [*Fzt!—crash! boom—boloom-boom-boom!*] Oh, just hear it! Now you see what you've done!"

"No, I *don't* see what I've done. A match may attract lightning, for all I know, but it don't *cause* lightning,—I'll go odds on that. And it didn't attract it worth a cent this time; for if that shot was levelled at my match, it was blessed poor marksmanship,—about an average of none out of a possible million, I should say. Why, at Dollymount, such marksmanship as that—"

"For shame, Mortimer! Here we are standing right in the very presence of death, and yet in so solemn a moment you are capable of using such language as that. If you have no desire to—Mortimer!"

"Well?"

"Did you say your prayers to-night?"

"I— I— meant to, but I got to trying to cipher out how much twelve times thirteen is, and—"

[*Fzt!—boom-beroom-boom! bumble-umble bang-*SMASH!]

"Oh, we are lost, beyond all help! How *could* you neglect such a thing at such a time as this?"

"But it *wasn't* 'such a time as this.' There wasn't a cloud in the sky. How could *I* know there was going to be all this rumpus and pow-wow about a little slip like that? And I don't think it's just fair for you to make so much out of it, any way, seeing it happens so seldom; I haven't missed before since I brought on that earthquake, four years ago."

"MORTIMER! How you talk! Have you forgotten the yellow fever?"

"My dear, you are always throwing up the yellow fever to me, and I think it is perfectly unreasonable. You can't even send a telegraphic message as far as Memphis without relays, so how is a little devotional slip of mine going to carry so far? I'll *stand* the earthquake, because it was in the neighborhood; but I'll be hanged if I'm going to be responsible for every blamed—"

[*Fzt!*—BOOM *beroom*-boom! boom!—BANG!]

"Oh, dear, dear, dear! I *know* it struck something, Mortimer. We never shall see the light of another day; and if it will do you any good to remember, when we are gone, that your dreadful language—*Mortimer!*"

"WELL! What now?"

"Your voice sounds as if—Mortimer, are you actually standing in front of that open fireplace?"

"That is the very crime I am committing."

"Get away from it, this moment. You do seem determined to bring destruction on us all. Don't you *know* that there is no better conductor for lightning than an open chimney? *Now* where have you got to?"

"I'm here by the window."

"Oh, for pity's sake, have you lost your mind? Clear out from there, this moment. The very children in arms know it is fatal to stand near a window in a thunder-storm. Dear, dear, I know I shall never see the light of another day. Mortimer?''

''Yes?''

''What is that rustling?''

''It's me.''

''What are you doing?''

''Trying to find the upper end of my pantaloons.''

''Quick! throw those things away! I do believe you would deliberately put on those clothes at such a time as this; yet you know perfectly well that *all* authorities agree that woollen stuffs attract lightning. Oh, dear, dear, it isn't sufficient that one's life must be in peril from natural causes, but you must do everything you can possibly think of to augment the danger. Oh, *don't* sing! What *can* you be thinking of?''

''Now where's the harm in it?''

''Mortimer, if I have told you once, I have told you a hundred times, that singing causes vibrations in the atmosphere which interrupt the flow of the electric fluid, and—What on *earth* are you opening that door for?''

''Goodness gracious, woman, is there any harm in *that?''*

''Harm? There's *death* in it. Anybody that has given this subject any attention knows that to create a draught is to invite the lightning. You haven't half shut it; shut it *tight,*—and do hurry, or we are all destroyed. Oh, it is an awful thing to be shut up with a lunatic at such a time as this. Mortimer, what *are* you doing?''

''Nothing. Just turning on the water. This room is smothering hot and close. I want to bathe my face and hands.''

''You have certainly parted with the remnant of your mind! Where lightning strikes any other substance once, it strikes water fifty times. Do turn it off. Oh, dear, I am sure that nothing in this world can save us. I does seem to me that—Mortimer, what was that?''

''It was a da— it was a picture. Knocked it down.''

''Then you are close to the wall! I never heard of such imprudence! Don't you *know* that there's no better conductor for lightning than a wall? Come away from there! And you came as near as anything to swearing, too. Oh, how can you be so desperately wicked, and your family in such peril? Mortimer, did you order a feather bed, as I asked you to do?''

''No. Forgot it.''

''Forgot it! It may cost you your life. If you had a feather bed, now, and could spread it in the middle of the room and lie on it, you would be perfectly safe. Come in here,—come quick, before you have a chance to commit any more frantic indiscretions.''

I tried, but the little closet would not hold us both with the door shut, unless we could be content to smother. I gasped awhile, then forced my way out. My wife called out,—

"Mortimer, something *must* be done for your preservation. Give me that German book that is on the end of the mantel-piece, and a candle; but don't light it; give me a match; I will light it in here. That book has some directions in it."

I got the book,—at cost of a vase and some other brittle things; and the madam shut herself up with her candle. I had a moment's peace; then she called out,—

"Mortimer, what was that?"

"Nothing but the cat."

"The cat! Oh, destruction! Catch her, and shut her up in the wash-stand. Do be quick, love; cats are *full* of electricity. I just know my hair will turn white with this night's awful perils."

I heard the muffled sobbings again. But for that, I should not have moved hand or foot in such a wild enterprise in the dark.

However, I went at my task,—over chairs, and against all sorts of obstructions, all of them hard ones, too, and most of them with sharp edges,—and at last I got kitty cooped up in the commode, at an expense of over four hundred dollars in broken furniture and shins. Then these muffled words came from the closet:—

"It says the safest thing is to stand on a chair in the middle of the room, Mortimer; and the legs of the chair must be insulated, with non-conductors. That is, you must set the legs of the chair in glass tumblers. [*Fzt!—boom—bang!—smash!*] Oh, hear that! Do hurry, Mortimer, before you are struck."

I managed to find and secure the tumblers. I got the last four,—broke all the rest. I insulated the chair legs, and called for further instructions.

"Mortimer, it says, 'Während eines Gewitters entferne man Metalle, wie z. B., Ringe, Uhren, Schlüssel, etc., von sich und halte sich auch nicht an solchen Stellen auf, wo viele Metalle bei einander liegen, oder mit andern Körpern verbunden sind, wie an Herden, Oefen, Eisengittern u. dgl.' What does that mean, Mortimer? Does it mean that you must keep metals *about* you, or keep them *away* from you?"

"Well, I hardly know. It appears to be a little mixed. All German advice is more or less mixed. However, I think that that sentence is mostly in the dative case, with a little genitive and accusative sifted in, here and there, for luck; so I reckon it means that you must keep some metals *about* you."

"Yes, that must be it. It stands to reason that it is. They are in the nature of lightning-rods, you know. Put on your fireman's helmet, Mortimer; that is mostly metal."

I got it and put it on,—a very heavy and clumsy and uncomfortable thing on a hot night in a close room. Even my night-dress seemed to be more clothing that I strictly needed.

"Mortimer, I think your middle ought to be protected. Won't you buckle on your militia sabre, please?"

I complied.

"Now, Mortimer, you ought to have some way to protect your feet. Do please put on your spurs."

I did it,—in silence,—and kept my temper as well as I could.

"Mortimer, it says, 'Das Gewitter läuten ist sehr gefährlich, weil die Glocke selbst, sowie der durch das Läuten veranlasste Luftzug und die Höhe des Thurmes den Blitz anziehen könnten.' Mortimer, does that mean that it is dangerous not to ring the church bells during a thunder-storm?"

"Yes, it seems to mean that,—if that is the past participle of the nominative case singular, and I reckon it is. Yes, I think it means that on account of the height of the church tower and the absence of *Luftzug* it would be very dangerous *(sehr gefährlich)* not to ring the bells in time of a storm; and moreover, don't you see, the very wording—"

"Never mind that, Mortimer; don't waste the precious time in talk. Get the large dinner-bell; it is right there in the hall. Quick, Mortimer dear; we are almost safe. Oh, dear, I do believe we are going to be saved at last!"

Our little summer establishment stands on top of a high range of hills, overlooking a valley. Several farm-houses are in our neighborhood,—the nearest some three or four hundred yards away.

When I, mounted on the chair, had been clanging that dreadful bell a matter of seven or eight minutes, our shutters were suddenly torn open from without, and a brilliant bull's-eye lantern was thrust in at the window, followed by a hoarse inquiry:—

"What in the nation is the matter here?"

The window was full of men's heads, and the heads were full of eyes that stared wildly at my night-dress and my warlike accoutrements.

I dropped the bell, skipped down from the chair in confusion, and said,—

"There is nothing the matter, friends,—only a little discomfort on account of the thunder-storm. I was trying to keep off the lightning."

"Thunder-storm? Lightning? Why, Mr. McWilliams, have you lost your mind? It is a beautiful starlight night; there has been no storm."

I looked out, and I was so astonished I could hardly speak for a while. Then I said,—

"I do not understand this. We distinctly saw the glow of the flashes through the curtains and shutters, and heard the thunder."

One after another of those people lay down on the ground to laugh,—and two of them died. One of the survivors remarked,—

"Pity you didn't think to open your blinds and look over to the top of the high hill yonder. What you heard was cannon; what you saw was the flash. You see, the telegraph brought some news, just at midnight: Garfield's nominated,—and that's what's the matter!"

Yes, Mr. Twain, as I was saying in the beginning (said Mr. McWilliams), the rules for preserving people against lightning are so excellent and so innumerable that the most incomprehensible thing in the world to me is how anybody ever manages to get struck.

So saying, he gathered up his satchel and umbrella, and departed; for the train had reached his town.

"The Stolen White Elephant" first appeared in a volume of the same name published by James R. Osgood and Company in 1882. This outrageous farce lampoons detectives, the heroes of the popular fiction of the period.

The Stolen White Elephant*

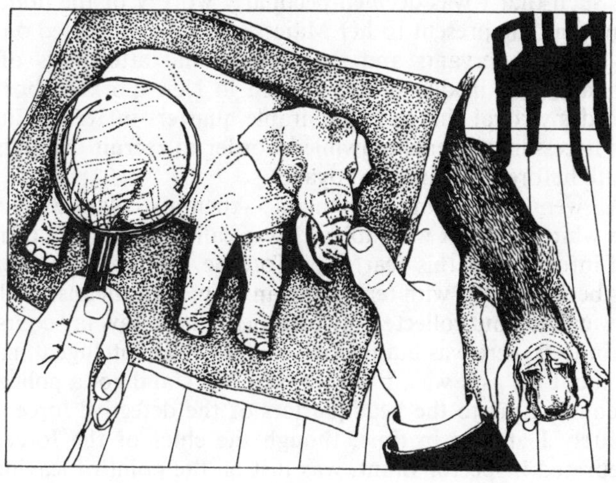

I

The following curious history was related to me by a chance railway acquaintance. He was a gentleman more than seventy years of age, and his thoroughly good and gentle face and earnest and sincere manner imprinted the unmistakable stamp of truth upon every statement which fell from his lips. He said:—

You know in what reverence the royal white elephant of Siam is held by the people of that country. You know it is sacred to kings, only kings may possess it, and that it is indeed in a measure even superior to kings, since it receives not merely honor but worship. Very well; five years ago, when the troubles concerning the frontier line arose between Great Britain and Siam, it was presently manifest that Siam had been in the wrong. Therefore every reparation was quickly made, and the British representative stated that he was satisfied and the past should be forgotten. This greatly relieved the King of Siam, and partly as a token of gratitude, but partly also, perhaps, to wipe out any little remaining vestige of unpleasantness which England might feel toward him, he wished to send the Queen a present,—the sole sure way of propitiating an enemy, according to Oriental ideas. This present ought not only to be a royal one, but transcendently royal. Wherefore, what offering could be so meet as

*Left out of "A Tramp Abroad," because it was feared that some of the particulars had been exaggerated, and that others were not true. Before these suspicions had been proven groundless, the book had gone to press.—M.T.

that of a white elephant? My position in the Indian civil service was such that I was deemed peculiarly worthy of the honor of conveying the present to her Majesty. A ship was fitted out for me and my servants and the officers and attendants of the elephant, and in due time I arrived in New York harbor and placed my royal charge in admirable quarters in Jersey City. It was necessary to remain awhile in order to recruit the animal's health before resuming the voyage.

All went well during a fortnight,—then my calamities began. The white elephant was stolen! I was called up at dead of night and informed of this fearful misfortune. For some moments I was beside myself with terror and anxiety; I was helpless. Then I grew calmer and collected my faculties. I soon saw my course,—for indeed there was but the one course for an intelligent man to pursue. Late as it was, I flew to New York and got a policeman to conduct me to the headquarters of the detective force. Fortunately I arrived in time, though the chief of the force, the celebrated Inspector Blunt, was just on the point of leaving for his home. He was a man of middle size and compact frame, and when he was thinking deeply he had a way of knitting his brows and tapping his forehead reflectively with his finger, which impressed you at once with the conviction that you stood in the presence of a person of no common order. The very sight of him gave me confidence and made me hopeful. I stated my errand. It did not flurry him in the least; it had no more visible effect upon his iron self-possession than if I had told him somebody had stolen my dog. He motioned me to a seat, and said calmly,—

"Allow me to think a moment, please."

So saying, he sat down at his office table and leaned his head upon his hand. Several clerks were at work at the other end of the room; the scratching of their pens was all the sound I heard during the next six or seven minutes. Meantime the inspector sat there, buried in thought. Finally he raised his head, and there was that in the firm lines of his face which showed me that his brain had done its work and his plan was made. Said he,—and his voice was low and impressive,—

"This is no ordinary case. Every step must be warily taken; each step must be made sure before the next is ventured. And secrecy must be observed,—secrecy profound and absolute. Speak to no one about the matter, not even the reporters. I will take care of *them;* I will see that they get only what it may suit my ends to let them know." He touched a bell; a youth appeared. "Alaric, tell the reporters to remain for the present." The boy retired. "Now let us proceed to business,—and systematically. Nothing can be accomplished in this trade of mine without strict and minute method."

He took a pen and some paper. "Now—name of the elephant?"

"Hassan Ben Ali Ben Selim Abdallah Mohammed Moisé Alhammal Jamsetjejeebhoy Dhuleep Sultan Ebu Bhudpoor."

"Very well. Given name?"

"Jumbo."

"Very well. Place of birth?"

"The capital city of Siam."

"Parents living?"

"No,—dead."

"Had they any other issue besides this one?"

"None. He was an only child."

"Very well. These matters are sufficient under that head. Now please describe the elephant, and leave out no particular, however insignificant,—that is, insignificant from *your* point of view. To men in my profession there *are* no insignificant particulars; they do not exist."

I described,—he wrote. When I was done, he said,—

"Now listen. If I have made any mistakes, correct me."

He read as follows:—

"Height, 19 feet; length from apex of forehead to insertion of tail, 26 feet; length of trunk, 16 feet; length of tail, 6 feet; total length, including trunk and tail, 48 feet; length of tusks, 9½ feet; ears in keeping with these dimensions; footprint resembles the mark left when one up-ends a barrel in the snow; color of the elephant, a dull white; has a hole the size of a plate in each ear for the insertion of jewelry, and possesses the habit in a remarkable degree of squirting water upon spectators and of maltreating with his trunk not only such persons as he is acquainted with, but even entire strangers; limps slightly with his right hind leg, and has a small scar in his left armpit caused by a former boil; had on, when stolen, a castle containing seats for fifteen persons, and a gold-cloth saddle-blanket the size of an ordinary carpet."

There were no mistakes. The inspector touched the bell, handed the description to Alaric, and said,—

"Have fifty thousand copies of this printed at once and mailed to every detective office and pawnbroker's shop on the continent." Alaric retired. "There,—so far, so good. Next, I must have a photograph of the property."

I gave him one. He examined it critically, and said,—

"It must do, since we can do no better; but he has his trunk curled up and tucked into his mouth. That is unfortunate, and is calculated to mislead, for of course he does not usually have it in that position." He touched his bell.

"Alaric, have fifty thousand copies of this photograph made, the first thing in the morning, and mail them with the descriptive circulars."

Alaric retired to execute his orders. The inspector said,—

"It will be necessary to offer a reward, of course. Now as to the amount?"

"What sum would you suggest?"

"To *begin* with, I should say,—well, twenty-five thousand dollars. It is an intricate and difficult business; there are a thousand avenues of escape and opportunities of concealment. These thieves have friends and pals everywhere—"

"Bless me, do you know who they are?"

The wary face, practised in concealing the thoughts and feelings within, gave me no token, nor yet the replying words, so quietly uttered:—

"Never mind about that. I may, and I may not. We generally gather a pretty shrewd inkling of who our man is by the manner of his work and the size of the game he goes after. We are not dealing with a pickpocket or a hall thief, now, make up your mind to that. This property was not 'lifted' by a novice. But, as I was saying, considering the amount of travel which will have to be done, and the diligence with which the thieves will cover up their traces as they move along, twenty-five thousand may be too small a sum to offer, yet I think it worth while to start with that."

So we determined upon that figure, as a beginning. Then this man, whom nothing escaped which could by any possibility be made to serve as a clew, said:—

"There are cases in detective history to show that criminals have been detected through peculiarities in their appetites. Now, what does this elephant eat, and how much?"

"Well, as to *what* he eats,—he will eat *anything*. He will eat a man, he will eat a Bible,—he will eat anything *between* a man and a Bible."

"Good,—very good indeed, but too general. Details are necessary,—details are the only valuable things in our trade. Very well,—as to men. At one meal,—or, if you prefer, during one day,—how many men will he eat, if fresh?"

"He would not care whether they were fresh or not; at a single meal he would eat five ordinary men."

"Very good; five men; we will put that down. What nationalities would he prefer?"

"He is indifferent about nationalities. He prefers acquaintances, but is not prejudiced against strangers."

"Very good. Now, as to Bibles. How many Bibles would he eat at a meal?"

"He would eat an entire edition."

"It is hardly succinct enough. Do you mean the ordinary octavo, or the family illustrated?"

"I think he would be indifferent to illustrations; that is, I think he would not value illustrations above simple letter-press."

"No, you do not get my idea. I refer to bulk. The ordinary octavo Bible weighs about two pounds and a half, while the great quarto with the illustrations weighs ten or twelve. How many Doré Bibles would he eat at a meal?"

"If you knew this elephant, you could not ask. He would take what they had."

"Well, put it in dollars and cents, then. We must get at it somehow. The Doré costs a hundred dollars a copy, Russia leather, bevelled."

"He would require about fifty thousand dollars' worth,—say an edition of five hundred copies."

"Now that is more exact. I will put that down. Very well; he likes men and Bibles; so far, so good. What else will he eat? I want particulars."

"He will leave Bibles to eat bricks, he will leave bricks to eat bottles, he will leave bottles to eat clothing, he will leave clothing to eat cats, he will leave cats to eat oysters, he will leave oysters to eat ham, he will leave ham to eat sugar, he will leave sugar to eat pie, he will leave pie to eat potatoes, he will leave potatoes to eat bran, he will leave bran to eat hay, he will leave hay to eat oats, he will leave oats to eat rice, for he was mainly raised on it. There is nothing whatever that he will not eat but European butter, and he would eat that if he could taste it."

"Very good. General quantity at a meal,—say about—"

"Well, anywhere from a quarter to half a ton."

"And he drinks—"

"Everything that is fluid. Milk, water, whiskey, molasses, castor oil, camphene, carbolic acid,—it is no use to go into particulars; whatever fluid occurs to you set it down. He will drink anything that is fluid, except European coffee."

"Very good. As to quantity?"

"Put it down five to fifteen barrels,—his thirst varies; his other appetites do not."

"These things are unusual. They ought to furnish quite good clews toward tracing him."

He touched the bell.

"Alaric, summon Captain Burns."

Burns appeared. Inspector Blunt unfolded the whole matter to him, detail by detail. Then he said in the clear, decisive tones of a man whose plans are clearly defined in his head, and who is accustomed to command,—

"Captain Burns, detail Detectives Jones, Davis, Halsey, Bates, and Hackett to shadow the elephant."

"Yes, sir."

"Detail Detectives Moses, Dakin, Murphy, Rogers, Tupper, Higgins, and Bartholomew to shadow the thieves."

"Yes, sir."

"Place a strong guard—a guard of thirty picked men, with a relief of thirty—over the place from whence the elephant was stolen, to keep strict watch there night and day, and allow none to approach—except reporters—without written authority from me."

"Yes, sir."

"Place detectives in plain clothes in the railway, steamship, and ferry depots, and upon all roadways leading out of Jersey City, with orders to search all suspicious persons."

"Yes, sir."

"Furnish all these men with photograph and accompanying description of the elephant, and instruct them to search all trains and outgoing ferry-boats and other vessels."

"Yes, sir."

"If the elephant should be found, let him be seized, and the information forwarded to me by telegraph."

"Yes, sir."

"Let me be informed at once if any clews should be found,—footprints of the animal, or anything of that kind."

"Yes, sir."

"Get an order commanding the harbor police to patrol the frontages vigilantly."

"Yes, sir."

"Despatch detectives in plain clothes over all the railways, north as far as Canada, west as far as Ohio, south as far as Washington."

"Yes, sir."

"Place experts in all the telegraph offices to listen to all messages; and let them require that all cipher despatches be interpreted to them."

"Yes, sir."

"Let all these things be done with the utmost secrecy,—mind, the most impenetrable secrecy."

"Yes, sir."

"Report to me promptly at the usual hour."

"Yes, sir."

"Go!"

"Yes, sir."

He was gone.

Inspector Blunt was silent and thoughtful a moment, while the fire in his eye cooled down and faded out. Then he turned to me and said in a placid voice,—

"I am not given to boasting, it is not my habit; but—we shall find the elephant."

I shook him warmly by the hand and thanked him; and I *felt* my thanks, too. The more I had seen of the man the more I liked him, and the more I admired him and marvelled over the mysterious wonders of his profession. Then we parted for the night, and I went home with a far happier heart than I had carried with me to his office.

II

Next morning it was all in the newspapers, in the minutest detail. It even had additions,—consisting of Detective This, Detective That, and Detective The Other's "Theory" as to how the robbery was done, who the robbers were, and whither they had flown with their booty. There were eleven of these theories, and they covered all the possibilities; and this single fact shows what independent thinkers detectives are. No two theories were alike, or even much resembled each other, save in one striking particular, and in that one all the eleven theories were absolutely agreed. That was, that although the rear of my building was torn out and the only door remained locked, the elephant had not been removed through the rent, but by some other (undiscovered) outlet. All agreed that the robbers had made that rent only to mislead the detectives. That never would have occurred to me or to any other layman, perhaps, but it had not deceived the detectives for a moment. Thus, what I had supposed was the only thing that had no mystery about it was in fact the very thing I had gone furthest astray in. The eleven theories all named the supposed robbers, but no two named the same robbers; the total number of suspected persons was thirty-seven. The various newspaper accounts all closed with the most important opinion of all,—that of Chief Inspector Blunt. A portion of this statement read as follows:—

"The chief knows who the principals are, namely, 'Brick' Duffy and 'Red' McFadden. Ten days before the robbery was achieved he was already aware that it was to be attempted, and had quietly proceeded to shadow these two noted villains; but unfortunately on the night in question their track was lost, and before it could be found again the bird was flown,—that is, the elephant.

"Duffy and McFadden are the boldest scoundrels in the profession; the chief has reasons for believing that they are the men who stole the stove out of the detective headquarters on a bitter night last winter,—in consequence of which the chief and every detective present were in the hands of the physicians before morning, some with frozen feet, others with frozen fingers, ears, and other members."

When I read the first half of that I was more astonished than ever at the wonderful sagacity of this strange man. He not only saw everything in the present with a clear eye, but even the future could not be hidden from him. I was soon at his office, and said I could not help wishing he had had those men arrested, and so prevented the trouble and loss; but his reply was simple and unanswerable:—

"It is not our province to prevent crime, but to punish it. We cannot punish it until it is committed."

I remarked that the secrecy with which we had begun had been marred by the newspapers; not only all our facts but all our plans and purposes had been revealed; even all the suspected persons had been named; these would doubtless disguise themselves now, or go into hiding.

"Let them. They will find that when I am ready for them my hand will descend upon them, in their secret places, as unerringly as the hand of fate. As to the newspapers, we *must* keep in with them. Fame, reputation, constant public mention,—these are the detective's bread and butter. He must publish his facts, else he will be supposed to have none; he must publish his theory, for nothing is so strange or striking as a detective's theory, or brings him so much wondering respect; we must publish our plans, for these the journals insist upon having, and we could not deny them without offending. We must constantly show the public what we are doing, or they will believe we are doing nothing. It is much pleasanter to have a newspaper say, 'Inspector Blunt's ingenious and extraordinary theory is as follows,' than to have it say some harsh thing, or, worse still, some sarcastic one."

"I see the force of what you say. But I noticed that in one part of your remarks in the papers this morning you refused to reveal your opinion upon a certain minor point."

"Yes, we always do that; it has a good effect. Besides, I had not formed any opinion on that point, any way."

I deposited a considerable sum of money with the inspector, to meet current expenses, and sat down to wait for news. We were expecting the telegrams to begin to arrive at any moment now. Meantime I reread the newspapers and also our descriptive circular, and observed that our $25,000 reward seemed to be offered only to detectives. I said I thought it ought to be offered to anybody who would catch the elephant. The inspector said:—

"It is the detectives who will find the elephant, hence the reward will go to the right place. If other people found the animal, it would only be by watching the detectives and taking advantage of clews and indications stolen from them, and that would entitle the detectives to the reward, after all. The proper office of a reward is to stimulate the men who deliver up their time and their trained sagacities to this sort of work, and not to confer benefits upon chance citizens who stumble upon a capture without having earned the benefits by their own merits and labors."

This was reasonable enough, certainly. Now the telegraphic machine in the corner began to click, and the following despatch was the result:—

FLOWER STATION, N.Y., 7:30 A.M.

Have got a clew. Found a succession of deep tracks across a farm near here. Followed them two miles east without result; think elephant went west. Shall now shadow him in that direction.

DARLEY, *Detective.*

"Darley's one of the best men on the force," said the inspector. "We shall hear from him again before long."

Telegram No. 2 came:—

BARKER'S, N.J., 7.40 A.M.

Just arrived. Glass factory broken open here during night, and eight hundred bottles taken. Only water in large quantity near here is five miles distant. Shall strike for there. Elephant will be thirsty. Bottles were empty.

BAKER, *Detective.*

"That promises well, too," said the inspector. "I told you the creature's appetites would not be bad clews."

Telegram No. 3:—

TAYLORVILLE, L.I., 8.15 A.M.

A haystack near here disappeared during night. Probably eaten. Have got a clew, and am off.

HUBBARD, *Detective.*

"How he does move around!" said the inspector. "I knew we had a difficult job on hand, but we shall catch him yet."

FLOWER STATION, N.Y., 9 A.M.

Shadowed the tracks three miles westward. Large, deep and ragged. Have just met a farmer who says they are not elephant tracks. Says they are holes where he dug up saplings for shade-trees when ground was frozen last winter. Give me orders how to proceed.

DARLEY, *Detective.*

"Aha! a confederate of the thieves! The thing grows warm," said the inspector.

He dictated the following telegram to Darley:—

Arrest the man and force him to name his pals. Continue to follow the tracks,—to the Pacific, if necessary.

Chief BLUNT.

Next telegram:—

CONEY POINT, PA., 8.45 A.M.

Gas office broken open here during night and three months' unpaid gas bills taken. Have got a clew and am away.

MURPHY, *Detective.*

"Heavens!" said the inspector; "would he eat gas bills?"

"Through ignorance,—yes; but they cannot support life. At least, unassisted."

Now came this exciting telegram:—

IRONVILLE, N.Y., 9.30 A.M.

Just arrived. This village in consternation. Elephant passed through here at five this morning. Some say he went east, some say west, some north, some south,—but all say they did not wait to notice particularly. He killed a horse; have secured a piece of it for a clew. Killed it with his trunk; from style of blow, think he struck it left-handed. From position in which horse lies, think elephant travelled northward along line of Berkley railway. Has four and a half hours' start, but I move on his track at once.

HAWES, *Detective.*

I uttered exclamations of joy. The inspector was as self-contained as a graven image. He calmly touched his bell.

"Alaric, send Captain Burns here."

Burns appeared.

"How many men are ready for instant orders?"

"Ninety-six, sir."

"Send them north at once. Let them concentrate along the line of the Berkley road north of Ironville."

"Yes, sir."

"Let them conduct their movements with the utmost secrecy. As fast as others are at liberty, hold them for orders."

"Yes, sir."

"Go!"

"Yes, sir."

Presently came another telegram:—

SAGE CORNERS, N.Y., 10.30.

Just arrived. Elephant passed through here at 8.15. All escaped from the town but a policeman. Apparently elephant did not strike at policeman, but at the lamp-post. Got both. I have secured a portion of the policeman as clew.

STUMM, *Detective.*

"So the elephant has turned westward," said the inspector. "However, he will not escape, for my men are scattered all over that region."

The next telegram said:—

GLOVER'S, 11.15.

Just arrived. Village deserted, except sick and aged. Elephant passed through three quarters of an hour ago. The anti-temperance mass meeting was in session; he put his trunk in at a window and washed it out with water from cistern. Some swallowed it—since dead; several drowned. Detectives Cross and O'Shaughnessy were passing through town, but going south,—so missed elephant. Whole region for many miles around in terror,—people flying from their homes. Wherever they turn they meet elephant, and many are killed.

BRANT, *Detective.*

I could have shed tears, this havoc so distressed me. But the inspector only said,—

"You see,—we are closing in on him. He feels our presence; he has turned eastward again."

Yet further troublous news was in store for us. The telegraph brought this:—

HOGANPORT, 12.19.

Just arrived. Elephant passed through half an hour ago, creating wildest fright and excitement. Elephant raged around streets; two plumbers going by, killed one—other escaped. Regret general.

O'FLAHERTY, *Detective.*

"Now he is right in the midst of my men," said the inspector. "Nothing can save him."

A succession of telegrams came from detectives who were scattered through New Jersey and Pennsylvania, and who were following clews consisting of ravaged barns, factories, and Sunday school libraries, with high hopes,—hopes amounting to certainties, indeed. The inspector said,—

"I wish I could communicate with them and order them north, but that is impossible. A detective only visits a telegraph office to send his report; then he is off again, and you don't know where to put your hand on him."

Now came this despatch:—

BRIDGEPORT, CT., 12.15.

Barnum offers rate of $4,000 a year for exclusive privilege of using elephant as travelling advertising medium from now till detectives find him. Wants to paste circus-posters on him. Desires immediate answer.

BOGGS, *Detective.*

"That is perfectly absurd!" I exclaimed.

"Of course it is," said the inspector. "Evidently Mr. Barnum, who thinks he is so sharp, does not know me,—but I know him."

Then he dictated this answer to the despatch:—

Mr. Barnum's offer declined. Make it $7,000 or nothing.

Chief BLUNT.

"There. We shall not have to wait long for an answer. Mr. Barnum is not at home; he is in the telegraph office,—it is his way when he has business on hand. Inside of three—"

DONE.—P.T. BARNUM.

So interrupted the clicking telegraphic instrument. Before I could make a comment upon this extraordinary episode, the following despatch carried my thoughts into another and very distressing channel:—

BOLIVIA, N.Y., 12.50.

Elephant arrived here from the south and passed through toward the forest at 11.50, dispersing a funeral on the way, and diminishing the mourners by two. Citizens fired some small cannon-balls into him, and then fled. Detective Burke and I arrived ten minutes later, from the north, but mistook some excavations for footprints, and so lost a good deal of time; but at last we struck the right trail and followed it to the woods. We then got down on our hands and knees and continued to keep a sharp eye on the track, and so shadowed it into the brush. Burke was in advance. Unfortunately the animal had stopped to rest; therefore, Burke having his head down, intent upon the track, butted up against the elephant's hind legs before he was aware of his vicinity. Burke instantly rose to his feet, seized the tail, and exclaimed joyfully, "I claim the re———" but got no further, for a single blow of the huge trunk laid the brave fellow's fragments low in death. I fled rearward, and the elephant turned and shadowed me to the edge of the wood, making tremendous speed, and I should inevitably have been lost, but that the remains of the funeral providentially intervened again and diverted his attention. I have just learned that nothing of that funeral is now left; but this is no loss, for there is an abundance of material for another. Meantime, the elephant has disappeared again.

MULROONEY, *Detective.*

We heard no news except from the diligent and confident detectives scattered about New Jersey, Pennsylvania, Delaware, and Virginia,—who were all following fresh and encouraging clews,—until shortly after 2 P.M., when this telegram came:—

BAXTER CENTRE, 2.15.

Elephant been here, plastered over with circus-bills, and broke up a revival, striking down and damaging many who were on the point of entering upon a better life. Citizens penned him up, and established a guard. When Detective Brown and I arrived, some time after, we entered enclosure and proceeded to identify elephant by photograph and description. All marks tallied exactly except one, which we could not see,—the boil-scar under armpit. To make sure, Brown crept under to look, and was immediately brained,—that is, head crushed and destroyed, though nothing issued from debris. All fled; so did elephant, striking right and left with much effect. Has escaped, but left bold blood-track from cannon-wounds. Rediscovery certain. He broke southward, through a dense forest.

BRENT, *Detective.*

That was the last telegram. At nightfall a fog shut down which was so dense that objects but three feet away could not be discerned. This lasted all night. The ferry-boats and even the omnibuses had to stop running.

III

Next morning the papers were as full of detective theories as before; they had all our tragic facts in detail also, and a great many more which they had received from their telegraphic correspondents. Column after column was occupied, a third of its way down, with glaring head-lines, which it made my heart sick to read. Their general tone was like this:—

THE WHITE ELEPHANT AT LARGE! HE MOVES UPON HIS FATAL MARCH! WHOLE VILLAGES DESERTED BY THEIR FRIGHT-STRICKEN OCCUPANTS! PALE TERROR GOES BEFORE HIM. DEATH AND DEVASTATION FOLLOW AFTER! AFTER THESE, THE DETECTIVES. BARNS DESTROYED, FACTORIES GUTTED, HARVESTS DEVOURED, PUBLIC ASSEMBLAGES DISPERSED, ACCOMPANIED BY SCENES OF CARNAGE IMPOSSIBLE TO DESCRIBE! THEORIES OF THIRTY-FOUR OF THE MOST DISTINGUISHED DETECTIVES ON THE FORCE! THEORY OF CHIEF BLUNT!"

"There!" said Inspector Blunt, almost betrayed into excitement, "this is magnificent! This is the greatest windfall that any detective organization ever had. The fame of it will travel to the ends of the earth, and endure to the end of time, and my name with it."

But there was no joy for me. I felt as if I had committed all those red crimes, and that the elephant was only my irresponsible agent. And how the list had grown! In one place he had "interfered with an election and killed five repeaters." He had followed this act with the destruction of two poor fellows, named O'Donahue and McFlannigan, who had "found a refuge in the home of the oppressed of all lands only the day before, and were in the act of exercising for the first time the noble right of American citizens at the polls, when stricken down by the relentless hand of the Scourge of Siam." In another, he had "found a crazy sensation-preacher preparing his next season's heroic attacks on the dance, the theatre, and other things which can't strike back, and had stepped on him." And in still another place he had "killed a lightning-rod agent." And so the list went on, growing redder and redder, and more and more heartbreaking. Sixty persons had been killed, and two hundred and forty wounded. All the accounts bore just testimony to the activity and devotion of the detectives, and all closed with the remark that "three hundred thousand citizens and four detectives saw the dread creature, and two of the latter he destroyed."

I dreaded to hear the telegraphic instrument begin to click again. By and by the messages began to pour in, but I was happily disappointed in their nature. It was soon apparent that all trace of the elephant was lost. The fog had enabled him to search out a good hiding-place unobserved. Telegrams from the most absurdly distant points reported that a dim vast mass had been glimpsed there through the fog at such and such an hour, and was "undoubtedly the elephant." This dim vast mass had been glimpsed in New Haven, in New Jersey, in Pennsylvania, in interior New York, in Brooklyn, and even in the city of New York itself! But in all cases the dim vast mass had vanished quickly and left no trace. Every detective of the large force scattered over this huge extent of country sent his hourly report, and each and every one of them had a clew, and was shadowing something, and was hot upon the heels of it.

But the day passed without other result.

The next day the same.

The next just the same.

The newspaper reports began to grow monotonous with facts that amounted to nothing, clews which led to nothing, and theories which had nearly exhausted the elements which surprise and delight and dazzle.

By advice of the inspector I doubled the reward.

Four more dull days followed. Then came a bitter blow to the poor, hard-working detectives,—the journalists declined to print their theories, and coldly said, "Give us a rest."

Two weeks after the elephant's disappearance I raised the reward to $75,000 by the inspector's advice. It was a great sum, but I felt that I would rather sacrifice my whole private fortune than lose my credit with my government. Now that the detectives were in adversity, the newspapers turned upon them, and began to fling the most stinging sarcasms at them. This gave the minstrels an idea, and they dressed themselves as detectives and hunted the elephant on the stage in the most extravagant way. The caricaturists made pictures of detectives scanning the country with spy-glasses, while the elephant, at their backs, stole apples out of their pockets. And they made all sorts of ridiculous pictures of the detective badge,—you have seen that badge printed in gold on the back of detective novels, no doubt,—it is a wide-staring eye, with the legend, "WE NEVER SLEEP." When detectives called for a drink, the would-be facetious bar- keeper resurrected an obsolete form of expression and said, "Will you have an eye-opener?" All the air was thick with sarcasms.

But there was one man who moved calm, untouched, unaffected, through it all. It was that heart of oak, the Chief Inspector. His brave eye never drooped, his serene confidence never wavered. He always said,—

"Let them rail on; he laughs best who laughs last."

My admiration for the man grew into a species of worship. I was at his side always. His office had become an unpleasant place to me, and now became daily more and more so. Yet if he could endure it I meant to do so also; at least, as long as I could. So I came regularly, and stayed,—the only outsider who seemed to be capable of it. Everybody wondered how I could; and often it seemed to me that I must desert, but at such times I looked into that calm and apparently unconscious face, and held my ground.

About three weeks after the elephant's disappearance I was about to say, one morning, that I should *have* to strike my colors and retire, when the great detective arrested the thought by proposing one more superb and masterly move.

This was to compromise with the robbers. The fertility of this man's invention exceeded anything I have ever seen, and I have had a wide intercourse with the world's finest minds. He said he was confident he could compromise for $100,000 and recover the elephant. I said I believed I could scrape the amount together, but what would become of the poor detectives who had worked so faithfully? He said,—

"In compromises they always get half."

This removed my only objection. So the inspector wrote two notes, in this form:—

DEAR MADAM,—Your husband can make a large sum of money (and be entirely protected from the law) by making an immediate appointment with me.

Chief BLUNT.

He sent one of these by his confidential messenger to the "reputed wife" of Brick Duffy, and the other to the reputed wife of Red McFadden.

Within the hour these offensive answers came:—

YE OWLD FOOL: brick McDuffys bin ded 2 yere.

BRIDGET MAHONEY.

CHIEF BAT,—Red McFadden is hung and in heving 18 month. Any Ass but a detective knose that.

MARY O'HOOLIGAN.

"I had long suspected these facts," said the inspector; "this testimony proves the unerring accuracy of my instinct."

The moment one resource failed him he was ready with another. He immediately wrote an advertisement for the morning papers, and I kept a copy of it:—

A.—xwblv.242 N. Tjnd—fz328wmlg. Ozpo,—; 2m!ogw. Mum.

He said that if the thief was alive this would bring him to the usual rendezvous. He further explained that the usual rendezvous was a place where all business affairs between detectives and criminals were conducted. This meeting would take place at twelve the next night.

We could do nothing till then, and I lost no time in getting out of the office, and was grateful indeed for the privilege.

At 11 the next night I brought $100,000 in bank-notes and put them into the chief's hands, and shortly afterward he took his leave, with the brave old undimmed confidence in his eye. An almost intolerable hour dragged to a close; then I heard his welcome tread, and rose gasping and tottered to meet him. How his fine eyes flamed with triumph! He said,—

"We've compromised! The jokers will sing a different tune to-morrow! Follow me!"

He took a lighted candle and strode down into the vast vaulted basement where sixty detectives always slept, and where a score were now playing cards to while the time. I followed close after him. He walked swiftly down to the dim remote end of the place, and just as I succumbed to the pangs of suffocation and was swooning away he stumbled and fell over the outlying members of a mighty object, and I heard him exclaim as he went down,—

"Our noble profession is vindicated. Here is your elephant!"

I was carried to the office above and restored with carbolic acid. The whole detective force swarmed in, and such another season of triumphant rejoicing ensued as I had never witnessed before. The reporters were called, baskets of champagne were opened, toasts were drunk, the handshakings and congratulations were continuous and enthusiastic. Naturally the chief was the hero of the hour, and his happiness was so complete and had been so patiently and worthily and bravely won that it made me happy to see it, though I stood there a homeless beggar, my priceless charge dead, and my position in my country's service lost to me through what would always seem my fatally careless execution of a great trust. Many an eloquent eye testified its deep admiration for the chief, and many a detective's voice murmured, "Look at him,—just the king of the profession,—only give him a clew, it's all he wants, and there ain't anything hid that he can't find." The dividing of the $50,000 made great pleasure; when it was finished the chief made a little speech while he put his share in his pocket, in which he said, "Enjoy it, boys, for you've earned it; and more than that you've earned for the detective profession undying fame."

A telegram arrived, which read:—

MONROE, MICH., 10 P.M.

First time I've struck a telegraph office in over three weeks. Have followed those footprints, horseback, through the woods, a thousand miles to here, and they get stronger and bigger and fresher every day.

Don't worry—inside of another week I'll have the elephant. This is dead sure.

DARLEY, *Detective.*

The chief ordered three cheers for "Darley, one of the finest minds on the force," and then commanded that he be telegraphed to come home and receive his share of the reward.

So ended that marvelous episode of the stolen elephant. The newspapers were pleasant with praises once more, the next day, with one contemptible exception. This sheet said, "Great is the detective! He may be a little slow in finding a little thing like a mislaid elephant,—he may hunt him all day and sleep with his rotting carcass all night for three weeks, but he will find him at last—if he can get the man who mislaid him to show him the place!"

Poor Hassan was lost to me forever. The cannon-shots had wounded him fatally, he had crept to that unfriendly place in the fog, and there, surrounded by his enemies and in constant danger of detection, he had wasted away with hunger and suffering till death gave him peace.

The compromise cost me $100,000; my detective expenses were $42,000 more; I never applied for a place again under my government; I am a ruined man and a wanderer in the earth,—but my admiration for that man, whom I believe to be the greatest detective the world has ever produced, remains undimmed to this day, and will so remain unto the end.

Twain claimed that he had written the "Legend of Sagenfeld, in Germany" for A Tramp Abroad, *but the tale was cut from the final version of the travelogue that was published in 1880. Instead, the story made its first appearance two years later in* The Stolen White Elephant, *a collection of sketches issued by James R. Osgood and Company.*

Legend of Sagenfeld, in Germany*

I

More than a thousand years ago this small district was a kingdom,—a little bit of a kingdom, a sort of dainty little toy kingdom, as one might say. It was far removed from the jealousies, strifes, and turmoils of that old warlike day, and so its life was a simple life, its people a gentle and guileless race; it lay always in a deep dream of peace, a soft Sabbath tranquility; there was no malice, there was no envy, there was no ambition, consequently there were no heart-burnings, there was no unhappiness in the land.

In the course of time the old king died and his little son Hubert came to the throne. The people's love for him grew daily; he was so good and so pure and so noble, that by and by this love became a passion, almost a worship. Now at his birth the soothsayers had diligently studied the stars and found something written in that shining book to this effect:—

In Hubert's fourteenth year a pregnant event will happen; the animal whose singing shall sound sweetest in Hubert's ear shall save Hubert's life. So long as the king and the nation shall honor this animal's race for this good deed, the ancient dynasty shall not fail of an heir, nor the nation know war or pestilence or poverty. But beware an erring choice!

* Left out of "A Tramp Abroad" because its authenticity seemed doubtful, and could not at that time be proved.—M.T.

All through the king's thirteenth year but one thing was talked of by the soothsayers, the statesmen, the little parliament, and the general people. That one thing was this: How is the last sentence of the prophecy to be understood? What goes before seems to mean that the saving animal will choose *itself*, at the proper time; but the closing sentence seems to mean that the *king* must choose beforehand, and say what singer among the animals pleases him best, and that if he choose wisely the chosen animal will save his life, his dynasty, his people, but that if he should make "an erring choice"—beware!

By the end of the year there were as many opinions about this matter as there had been in the beginning; but a majority of the wise and the simple were agreed that the safest plan would be for the little king to make choice beforehand, and the earlier the better. So an edict was sent forth commanding all persons who owned singing creatures to bring them to the great hall of the palace in the morning of the first day of the new year. This command was obeyed. When everything was in readiness for the trial, the king made his solemn entry with the great officers of the crown, all clothed in their robes of state. The king mounted his golden throne and prepared to give judgment. But he presently said,—

"These creatures all sing at once; the noise is unendurable; no one can choose in such a turmoil. Take them all away, and bring back one at a time."

This was done. One sweet warbler after another charmed the young king's ear and was removed to make way for another candidate. The precious minutes slipped by; among so many bewildering songsters he found it hard to choose, and all the harder because that promised penalty for an error was so terrible that it unsettled his judgment and made him afraid to trust his own ears. He grew nervous and his face showed distress. His ministers saw this, for they never took their eyes from him a moment. Now they began to say in their hearts,—

"He has lost courage—the cool head is gone—he will err—he and his dynasty and his people are doomed!"

At the end of an hour the king sat silent awhile, and then said,—

"Bring back the linnet."

The linnet trilled forth her jubilant music. In the midst of it the king was about to uplift his sceptre in sign of choice, but checked himself and said,—

"But let us be sure. Bring back the thrush; let them sing together."

The thrush was brought, and the two birds poured out their

marvels of song together. The king wavered, then his inclination began to settle and strengthen—one could see it in his countenance. Hope budded in the hearts of the old ministers, their pulses began to beat quicker, the sceptre began to rise slowly, when—

There was a hideous interruption! It was a sound like this—just at the door:—

"Waw . . . . . . *he!*—waw . . . . . . *he!*—waw-he! waw-he!—waw he!"

Everybody was sorely startled—and enraged at himself for showing it.

The next instant the dearest, sweetest, prettiest little peasant maid of nine years came tripping in, her brown eyes glowing with childish eagerness; but when she saw that august company and those angry faces she stopped and hung her head and put her poor coarse apron to her eyes. Nobody gave her welcome, none pitied her. Presently, she looked up timidly through her tears, and said,—

"My lord the king, I pray you pardon me, for I meant no wrong. I have no father and no mother, but I have a goat and a donkey, and they are all in all to me. My goat gives me the sweetest milk, and when my good dear donkey brays it seems to me there is no music like it. So when my lord the king's jester said the sweetest singer among all the animals should save the crown and nation, and moved me to bring him here—"

All the court burst into a rude laugh, and the child fled away crying, without trying to finish her speech. The chief minister gave a private order that she and her disastrous donkey be flogged beyond the precincts of the palace and commanded to come within them no more.

Then the trial of the birds was resumed. The two birds sang their best, but the sceptre lay motionless in the king's hand. Hope died slowly out in the breasts of all. An hour went by; two hours; still no decision. The day waned to its close, and the waiting multitudes outside the palace grew crazed with anxiety and apprehension. The twilight came on, the shadows fell deeper and deeper. The king and his court could no longer see each other's faces. No one spoke—none called for lights. The great trial had been made; it had failed; each and all wished to hide their faces from the light and cover up their deep trouble in their own hearts.

Finally—hark! A rich, full strain of the divinest melody streamed forth from a remote part of the hall,—the nightingale's voice!

"Up!" shouted the king, "let all the bells make proclamation to the people, for the choice is made and we have not erred. King, dynasty, and nation are saved. From henceforth let the nightingale be honored throughout the land forever. And publish it among all the people that whosoever shall insult a nightingale, or injure it, shall suffer death. The king hath spoken."

All that little world was drunk with joy. The castle and the city blazed with bonfires all night long, the people danced and drank and sang, and the triumphant clamor of the bells never ceased.

From that day the nightingale was a sacred bird. Its song was heard in every house; the poets wrote its praises; the painters painted it; its sculptured image adorned every arch and turret and fountain and public building. It was even taken into the king's councils; and no grave matter of state was decided until the soothsayers had laid the thing before the state nightingale and translated to the ministry what it was that the bird had sung about it.

II

The young king was very fond of the chase. When the summer was come he rose forth with hawk and hound, one day, in a brilliant company of his nobles. He got separated from them, by and by, in a great forest, and took what he imagined a near cut, to find them again; but it was a mistake. He rode on and on, hopefully at first, but with sinking courage finally. Twilight came on, and still he was plunging through a lonely and unknown land. Then came a catastrophe. In the dim light he forced his horse through a tangled thicket overhanging a steep and rocky declivity. When horse and rider reached the bottom, the former had a broken neck and the latter a broken leg. The poor little king lay there suffering agonies of pain, and each hour seemed a long month to him. He kept his ear strained to hear any sound that might promise hope of rescue; but he heard no voice, no sound of horn or bay of hound. So at last he gave up all hope, and said, "Let death come, for come it must."

Just then the deep, sweet song of a nightingale swept across the still wastes of the night.

"Saved!" the king said. "Saved! It is the sacred bird, and the prophecy is come true. The gods themselves protected me from error in the choice."

He could hardly contain his joy; he could not word his gratitude. Every few moments, now, he thought he caught the sound of approaching succor. But each time it was a disappointment; no succor came. The dull hours drifted on. Still no help came,—but still the sacred bird sang on. He began to have misgivings about his choice, but he stifled them. Toward dawn the bird ceased. The morning came, and with it thirst and hunger; but no succor. The day waxed and waned. At last the king cursed the nightingale.

Immediately the song of the thrush came out from the wood. The king said in his heart, "This was the true bird—my choice was false—succor will come now."

But it did not come. Then he lay many hours insensible. When he came to himself, a linnet was singing. He listened—with apathy. His faith was gone. "These birds," he said, "can bring no help; I and my house and my people are doomed." He turned him about to die; for he was grown very feeble from hunger and thirst and suffering, and felt that his end was near. In truth, he wanted to die, and be released from pain. For long hours he lay without thought or feeling or motion. Then his senses returned. The dawn of the third morning was breaking. Ah, the world seemed very beautiful to those worn eyes. Suddenly a great longing to live rose up in the lad's heart, and from his soul welled a deep and fervent prayer that Heaven would have mercy upon him and let him see his home and his friends once more. In that instant a soft, a faint, a far-off sound, but oh, how inexpressibly sweet to his waiting ear, came floating out of the distance,—

"Waw . . . . . . *he!*—waw . . . . . . *he!*—waw-he!—waw-he!—waw-he!"

"*That*, oh, *that* song is sweeter, a thousand times sweeter, than the voice of nightingale, thrush, or linnet, for it brings not mere hope, but *certainty* of succor; and now indeed am I saved! The sacred singer has chosen itself, as the oracle intended; the prophecy is fulfilled, and my life, my house, and my people are redeemed. The ass shall be sacred from this day!"

The divine music grew nearer and nearer, stronger and stronger,—and ever sweeter and sweeter to the perishing sufferer's ear. Down the declivity the docile little donkey wandered, cropping herbage and singing as he went; and when at last he saw the dead horse and the wounded king, he came and snuffed at them with simple and marvelling curiosity. The king petted him, and he knelt down as had been his wont when his little mistress desired to mount. With great labor and pain the lad drew himself upon the creature's back, and held himself there by aid of the generous ears. The ass went singing forth from the place and carried the king to the little peasant maid's hut. She gave him her pallet for a bed, refreshed him with goat's milk, and then flew to tell the great news to the first scouting party of searchers she might meet.

The king got well. His first act was to proclaim the sacredness and inviolability of the ass; his second was to add this particular ass to his cabinet and make him chief minister of the crown; his third was to have all the statues and effigies of nightingales throughout his kingdom destroyed, and replaced by statues and effigies of the sacred donkey; and his fourth was to announce that when the little peasant maid should reach her fifteenth year he would make her his queen,—and he kept his word.

Such is the legend. This explains why the mouldering image of the ass adorns all these old crumbling walls and arches; and it explains why, during many centuries, an ass was always the chief minister in that royal cabinet, just as is still the case in most cabinets to this day; and it also explains why, in that little kingdom, during many centuries, all great poems, all great speeches, all great books, all public solemnities, and all royal proclamations, always began with these stirring words,—

"Waw . . . . . . *he!*—waw . . . . . . *he!*—waw-he!—waw-he!—waw-he!"

"Some Rambling Notes of an Idle Excursion," which describes Twain's visit to the island of Bermuda, was written for the Atlantic, *where it appeared in monthly installments from October 1877 to January 1878. The piece appeared in a small collection called* Punch, Brothers, Punch!, *published by Slote, Woodman & Company of New York in 1878. It was also published in another of Twain's collections,* The Stolen White Elephant, *issued by James R. Osgood and Company in 1882.*

Some Rambling Notes
of an Idle Excursion

I

All the journeyings I had ever done had been purely in the way of business. The pleasant May weather suggested a novelty, namely, a trip for pure recreation, the bread-and-butter element left out. The Reverend said he would go, too: a good man, one of the best of men, although a clergyman. By eleven at night we were in New Haven and on board the New York boat. We bought our tickets, and then went wandering around, here and there, in the solid comfort of being free and idle, and of putting distance between ourselves and the mails and telegraphs.

After a while I went to my state-room and undressed, but the night was too enticing for bed. We were moving down the bay now, and it was pleasant to stand at the window and take the cool night-breeze and watch the gliding lights on shore. Presently, two elderly men sat down under that window and began a conversation. Their talk was properly no business of mine, yet I was feeling friendly toward the world and willing to be entertained. I soon gathered that they were brothers, that they were from a small Connecticut village, and that the matter in hand concerned the cemetery. Said one,—

"Now, John, we talked it all over amongst ourselves, and this is what we've done. You see, every body was a-movin' from the old buryin' ground, and our folks was most about left to theirselves, as you may say. They was crowded, too, as you know; lot wa'n't big enough in the first place; and last year, when Seth's wife died, we couldn't hardly tuck her in. She sort o' overlaid Deacon Shorb's lot, and he soured on her, so to speak, and on the rest of us, too. So we talked it over, and I was for a lay-out in the new simitery on the hill. They wa'n't unwilling, if it was cheap. Well the two best and biggest plots was No. 8 and No. 9—both of a size; nice comfortable room for twenty-six—twenty-six full-growns, that is; but you reckon in children and other shorts, and strike an everage, and I should say you might lay in thirty, or maybe thirty-two or three, pretty genteel—no crowdin' to signify."

"That's a plenty, William. Which one did you buy?"

"Well, I'm a-coming to that, John. You see, No. 8 was thirteen dollars, No. 9 fourteen—"

"I see. So 's 't you took No. 8."

"You wait. I took No. 9. And I'll tell you for why. In the first place, Deacon Shorb wanted it. Well, after the way he'd gone on about Seth's wife overlappin' his prem'ses, I'd 'a' beat him out of that No. 9 if I'd 'a' had to stand two dollars extra, let alone one. That's the way I felt about it. Says I, what's a dollar any way? Life's on'y a pilgrimage, says I; we ain't here for good, and we can't take it with us, says I. So I just dumped it down, knowin' the Lord don't suffer a good deed to go for nothin', and cal'latin' to take it out o' somebody in the course o' trade. Then there was another reason, John. No. 9's a long way the handiest lot in the simitery, and the likeliest for situation. It lays right on top of a knoll, in the dead centre of the buryin' ground; and you can see Millport from there, and Tracy's, and Hopper Mount, and a raft o' farms, and so on. There ain't no better outlook from a buryin' plot in the State. Si Higgins says so, and I reckon he ought to know. Well, and that ain't all. 'Course Shorb had to take No. 8; wa'n't no help for 't. Now, No. 8 jines on to No. 9, but it's on the slope of the hill, and every time it rains, it 'll soak right down on to the Shorbs. Si Higgins says 't when the deacon's time comes, he better take out fire and marine insurance both on his remains."

Here there was the sound of a low, placid, duplicate chuckle of appreciation and satisfaction.

"Now, John, here's a little rough draft of the ground, that I've made on a piece of paper. Up here in the left-hand corner we've bunched the departed; took them from the old grave-yard and stowed them one along side o' t' other, on a first-come-first-served plan, no partialities, with gran'ther Jones for a starter, on'y because it happened so, and windin' up indiscriminate with Seth's twins. A little crowded towards the end of the lay-out, maybe, but we reckoned 't wa'n't best to scatter the twins. Well, next comes the livin'. Here, where it's marked A, we're goin' to put Mariar and her family, when they're called; B, that's for brother Hosea and his'n; C, Calvin and tribe. What's left is these two lots here,—just the gem of the whole patch for general style and outlook; they're for me and my folks, and you and yourn. Which of them would you ruther be buried in?"

"I swan you've took me mighty onexpected, William! It sort of started the shivers. Fact is, I was thinkin' so busy about makin' things comfortable for the others, I hadn't thought about being buried myself."

"Life's on'y a fleetin' show, John, as the sayin' is. We've all got to go, sooner or later. To go with a clean record's the main thing. Fact is, it's the on'y thing worth strivin' for, John."

"Yes, that's so, William, that's so; there ain't no getting around it. Which of these lots would you recommend?"

"Well, it depends, John. Are you particular about outlook?"

"I don't say I am, William; I don't say I ain't. Reely I don't know. But mainly, I reckon, I'd set store by a south exposure."

"That's easy fixed, John. They're both south exposure. They take the sun and the Shorbs get the shade."

"How about sile, William?"

"D's a sandy sile, E's mostly loom."

"You may gimme E, then, William; a sandy sile caves in, more or less, and costs for repairs."

"All right; set your name down here, John, under E. Now, if you don't mind payin' me your share of the fourteen dollars, John, while we're on the business, every thing's fixed."

After some higgling and sharp bargaining, the money was paid, and John bade his brother good-night and took his leave. There was silence for some moments; then a soft chuckle welled up from the lonely William, and he muttered: "I declare for't, if I haven't made a mistake! It's D that's mostly loom, not E. And John's booked for a sandy sile after all."

There was another soft chuckle, and William departed to his rest, also.

The next day, in New York, was a hot one. Still we managed to get more or less entertainment out of it. Toward the middle of the afternoon we arrived on board the stanch steamship Bermuda, with bag and baggage, and hunted for a shady place. It was blazing summer weather, until we were half way down the harbor. Then I buttoned my coat closely; half an hour later I put on a spring overcoat and buttoned that. As we passed the lightship I added an ulster and tied a handkerchief around the collar to hold it snug to my neck. So rapidly had the summer gone and winter come again!

By nightfall we were far out at sea, with no land in sight. No telegrams could come here, no letters, no news. This was an uplifting thought. It was still more uplifting to reflect that the millions of harassed people on shore behind us were suffering just as usual.

The next day brought us into the midst of the Atlantic solitudes—out of smoke-colored soundings into fathomless deep blue; no ships visible anywhere over the wide ocean; no company but Mother Cary's chickens wheeling, darting, skimming the waves in the sun. There were some seafaring men among the passengers, and conversation drifted into matters concerning ships and sailors. One said that "true as the needle to the pole" was a bad figure, since the needle seldom pointed to the pole. He said a ship's compass was not faithful to any particular point, but was the most fickle and treacherous of the servants of man. It was forever changing. It changed every day in the year; consequently the amount of the daily variation had to be ciphered out and allowance made for it, else the mariner would go utterly astray. Another said there was a vast fortune waiting for the genius who should invent a compass that would not be affected by the local influences of an iron ship. He said there was only one creature more fickle than a wooden ship's compass, and that was the compass of an iron ship. Then came reference to the well-known fact that an experienced mariner can look at the compass of a new iron vessel, thousands of miles from her birthplace, and tell which way her head was pointing when she was in process of building.

Now an ancient whale-ship master fell to talking about the sort of crew they used to have in his early days. Said he—

"Sometimes we'd have a batch of college students. Queer lot. Ignorant? Why, they didn't know the cat-heads from the main brace. But if you took them for fools you'd get bit, sure. They'd learn more in a month than another man would in a year. We had one, once, in the Mary Ann, that came aboard with gold spectacles on. And besides, he was rigged out from main truck to keelson in the nobbiest clothes that ever saw a fo'castle. He had a chest full, too: cloaks, and broadcloth coats, and velvet vests; every thing swell, you know; and didn't the salt water fix them out for him? I guess not! Well, going to sea, the mate told him to go aloft and help shake out the fore-to'-gallants'l. Up he shins to the foretop, with his spectacles on, and in a minute down he comes again, looking insulted. Says the mate, 'What did you come for?' Says the chap, 'P'raps you didn't notice that there ain't any ladders above there.' You see we hadn't any shrouds above the foretop. The men bursted out in a laugh such as I guess you never heard the like of. Next night, which was dark and rainy, the mate ordered this chap to go aloft about something, and I'm dummed if he didn't start up with an umbrella and a lantern! But no matter; he made a mighty good sailor before the voyage was done, and we had to hunt up something else to laugh at. Years afterwards, when I had forgot all about him, I comes into Boston, mate of a ship, and was loafing around town with the second mate, and it so happened that we stepped into the Revere House, thinking maybe we would chance the salt-horse in that big dining-room for a flyer, as the boys say. Some fellows were talking just at our elbow, and one says, 'Yonder's the new governor of Massachusetts—at that table over there, with the ladies.' We took a good look, my mate and I, for we hadn't either of us ever seen a governor before. I looked and looked at that face, and then all of a sudden it popped on me! But I didn't give any sign. Says I, 'Mate, I've a notion to go over and shake hands with him.' Says he, 'I think I see you doing it, Tom.' Says I, 'Mate, I'm a-going to do it.' Says he, 'Oh, yes, I guess so! Maybe you don't want to bet you will, Tom?' Says I, 'I don't mind going a V on it, mate.' Says he, 'Put it up.' 'Up she goes,' says I, planking the cash. This surprised him. But he covered it, and says, pretty sarcastic, 'Hadn't you better take your grub with the governor and the ladies, Tom?' Says I, 'Upon second thoughts, I will.' Says he, 'Well, Tom, you *are* a dum fool.' Says I, 'Maybe I am, maybe I ain't; but the main question is, Do you want to risk two and a half that I won't do it?' 'Make it a V,' says he. 'Done,' says I. I started, him a-giggling and slapping his hand on his thigh, he felt so good. I went over there and leaned my knuckles on the table a minute, and looked the governor in the face, and says I, 'Mister Gardner, don't you know me?' He stared, and I stared, and he stared. Then all of a sudden he sings out, 'Tom Bowling, by the holy poker! Ladies, it's old Tom Bowling, that you've heard me talk about—shipmate of mine in the Mary Ann.' He rose up and shook hands with me ever so hearty—I sort of glanced around and took a realizing sense of my mate's saucer eyes—and then, says the governor, 'Plant yourself, Tom; plant yourself; you can't cat your anchor again till you've had a feed with me and the ladies!' I planted myself alongside the governor, and canted my eye around towards my mate. Well, sir, his dead-lights were bugged out like tompions; and his mouth stood that wide open that you could have laid a ham in it without him noticing it."

There was great applause at the conclusion of the old captain's story; then, after a moment's silence, a grave, pale young man said:

"Had you ever met the governor before?"

The old captain looked steadily at this inquirer a while, and then got up and walked aft without making any reply. One passenger after another stole a furtive glance at the inquirer, but failed to make him out, and so gave him up. It took some little work to get the talk-machinery to running smoothly again after this derangement; but at length a conversation sprang up about that important and jealously guarded instrument, a ship's time-keeper; its exceeding delicate accuracy, and the wreck and destruction that have sometimes resulted from its varying a few seemingly trifling moments from the true time; then, in due course, my comrade, the Reverend, got off on a yarn, with a fair wind and every thing drawing. It was a true story, too—about Captain Rounceville's shipwreck—true in every detail. It was to this effect:

Captain Rounceville's vessel was lost in mid-Atlantic, and likewise his wife and his two little children. Captain Rounceville and seven seamen escaped with life, but with little else. A small, rudely constructed raft was to be their home for eight days. They had neither provisions nor water. They had scarcely any clothing; no one had a coat but the captain. This coat was changing hands all the time, for the weather was very cold. Whenever a man became exhausted with the cold, they put the coat on him and laid him down between two shipmates until the garment and their bodies had warmed life into him again. Among the sailors was a Portuguese who knew no English. He seemed to have no thought of his own calamity, but was concerned only about the captain's bitter loss of wife and children. By day, he would look his dumb compassion in the captain's face; and by night, in the darkness and the driving spray and rain, he would seek out the captain, and try to comfort him with caressing pats on the shoulder. One day, when hunger and thirst were making their sure inroads upon the men's strength and spirits, a floating barrel was seen at a distance. It seemed a great find, for doubtless it contained food of some sort. A brave fellow swam to it, and, after long and exhausting effort, got it to the raft. It was eagerly opened. It was a barrel of magnesia! On the fifth day an onion was spied. A sailor swam off and got it. Although perishing with hunger, he brought it in its integrity and put it into the captain's hand. The history of the sea teaches that among starving, ship-wrecked men selfishness is rare, and a wonder-compelling magnanimity the rule. The onion was equally divided into eight parts, and eaten with deep thanksgivings. On the eighth day a distant ship was sighted. Attempts were made to hoist an oar, with Captain Rounceville's coat on it for a signal. There were many failures, for the men were but skeletons now, and strengthless. At last success was achieved, but the signal brought no help. The ship faded out of sight and left despair behind her. By and by another ship appeared, and passed so near that the castaways, every eye eloquent with gratitude, made ready to welcome the boat that would be sent to save them. But this ship also drove on, and left these men staring their unutterable surprise and dismay into each other's ashen faces. Late in the day, still another ship came up out of the distance, but the men noted with a pang that her course was one which would not bring her nearer. Their remnant of life was nearly spent; their lips and tongues were swollen, parched, cracked with eight days' thirst; their bodies starved; and here was their last chance gliding relentlessly from them; they would not be alive when the next sun rose. For a day or two past the men had lost their voices, but now Captain Rounceville whispered, "Let us pray." The Portuguese patted him on the shoulder in sign of deep approval. All knelt at the base of the oar that was waving the signal-coat aloft, and bowed their heads. The sea was tossing; the sun rested, a red, rayless disk, on the sea-line in the west. When the men presently raised their heads they would have roared a hallelujah if they had had a voice—the ship's sails lay wrinkled and flapping against her masts; she was going about! Here was rescue at last, and in the very last instant of time that was left for it. No, not rescued yet—only the imminent prospect of it. The red disk sank under the sea and darkness blotted out the ship. By and by came a pleasant sound—oars moving in a boat's rowlocks. Nearer it came and nearer—within thirty steps—but nothing visible. Then a deep voice: "Hol-*lo!*" The castaways could not answer; their swollen tongues refused voice. The boat skirted round and round the raft, started away—the agony of it!—returned, rested the oars, close at hand, listening, no doubt. The deep voice again: "Hol-*lo!* Where are ye, shipmates?" Captain Rounceville whispered to his men, saying: "Whisper your best, boys; now—all at once!" So they sent out an eight-fold whisper in hoarse concert: "Here!" There was life in it if it succeeded; death if it failed; after that supreme moment Captain Rounceville was conscious of nothing until he came to himself on board the saving ship. Said the Reverend, concluding:

"There was one little moment of time in which that raft could be visible from that ship, and only one. If that one little fleeting moment had passed unfruitful, those men's doom was sealed. As close as that does God shave events foreordained from the beginning of the world. When the sun reached the water's edge that day, the captain of that ship was sitting on deck reading his prayer-book. The book fell; he stooped to pick it up, and happened to glance at the sun. In that instant that far-off raft appeared for a second against the red disk, its needle-like oar and diminutive signal cut sharp and black against the bright surface, and in the next instant was thrust away into the dusk again. But that ship, that captain, and that pregnant instant had their work appointed for them in the dawn of time, and could not fail of the performance. The chronometer of God never errs!"

There was deep, thoughtful silence for some moments; then the grave, pale young man said:

"What is the chronometer of God?"

II

At dinner, six o'clock, the same people assembled whom we had talked with on deck and seen at luncheon and breakfast this second day out, and at dinner the evening before. That is to say, three journeying ship-masters, a Boston merchant, and a returning Bermudian who had been absent from his Bermuda thirteen years; these sat on the starboard side. On the port side sat the Reverend in the seat of honor; the pale young man next to him; I next; next to me an aged Bermudian, returning to his sunny islands after an absence of twenty-seven years. Of course our captain was at the head of the table, the purser at the foot of it. A small company, but small companies are pleasantest.

No racks upon the table; the sky cloudless, the sun brilliant, the blue sea scarcely ruffled. Then what had become of the four married couples, the three bachelors, and the active and obliging doctor from the rural districts of Pennsylvania? for all these were on deck when we sailed down New York harbor. This is the explanation. I quote from my note-book:

> Thursday, 3.30 P.M. Under way, passing the Battery. The large party, of four married couples, three bachelors, and a cheery, exhilarating doctor from the wilds of Pennsylvania, are evidently travelling together. All but the doctor grouped in camp-chairs on deck.
>
> Passing principal fort. The doctor is one of those people who has an infallible preventive of sea-sickness; is flitting from friend to friend administering it, and saying, "Don't you be afraid; I *know* this medicine; absolutely infallible; prepared under my own supervision." Takes a dose himself, intrepidly.
>
> 4.15 P.M. Two of those ladies have struck their colors, notwithstanding the "infallible." They have gone below. The other two begin to show distress.

5 P.M. Exit one husband and one bachelor. These still had their infallible in cargo when they started, but arrived at the companion-way without it.

5.10. Lady No. 3, two bachelors, and one married man have gone below with their own opinion of the infallible.

5.20. Passing Quarantine Hulk. The infallible has done the business for all the party except the Scotchman's wife and the author of that formidable remedy.

Nearing the Light-Ship. Exit the Scotchman's wife, head drooped on stewardess's shoulder.

Entering the open sea. Exit doctor!

The rout seems permanent; hence the smallness of the company at table since the voyage began. Our captain is a grave, handsome Hercules of thirty-five, with a brown hand of such majestic size that one cannot eat for admiring it, and wondering if a single kid or calf could furnish material for gloving it.

Conversation not general; drones along between couples. One catches a sentence here and there. Like this, from Bermudian of thirteen years' absence: "It is the nature of women to ask trivial, irrelevant, and pursuing questions,—questions that pursue you from a beginning in nothing to a run-to-cover in nowhere." Reply of Bermudian of twenty-seven years' absence: "Yes; and to think they have logical, analytical minds and argumentative ability. You see 'em begin to whet up whenever they smell argument in the air." Plainly these be philosophers.

Twice since we left port our engines have stopped for a couple of minutes at a time. Now they stop again. Says the pale young man, meditatively, "There! that engineer is sitting down to rest again."

Grave stare from the captain, whose mighty jaws cease to work, and whose harpooned potato stops in mid-air on its way to his open, paralyzed mouth. Presently says he, in measured tones, "Is it your idea that the engineer of this ship propels her by a crank turned by his own hands?"

The pale young man studies over this a moment, then lifts up his guileless eyes, and says, "Don't he?"

Thus gently falls the death-blow to further conversation, and the dinner drags to its close in a reflective silence, disturbed by no sounds but the murmurous wash of the sea and the subdued clash of teeth.

After a smoke and a promenade on deck, where is no motion to discompose our steps, we think of a game of whist. We ask the brisk and capable stewardess from Ireland if there are any cards in the ship.

"Bless your soul, dear, indeed there is. Not a whole pack, true for ye, but not enough missing to signify."

However, I happened by accident to bethink me of a new pack in a morocco case, in my trunk, which I had placed there by mistake, thinking it to be a flask of something. So a party of us conquered the tedium of the evening with a few games, and were ready for bed at six bells, mariner's time, the signal for putting out the lights.

There was much chat in the smoking-cabin on the upper deck after luncheon to-day, mostly whaler yarns from those old sea-captains. Captain Tom Bowling was garrulous. He had that garrulous attention to minor detail which is born of secluded farm life or life at sea on long voyages, where there is little to do and time no object. He would sail along till he was right in the most exciting part of a yarn, and then say, "Well, as I was saying, the rudder was fouled, ship driving before the gale, head on, straight for the iceberg, all hands holding their breath, turned to stone, top-hamper giving way, sails blown to ribbons, first one stick going, then another, boom! smash! crash! duck your head and stand from under! when up comes Johnny Rogers, capstan bar in hand, eyes a-blazing, hair a-flying—no, 't wa'n't Johnny Rogers—lemme see—seems to me Johnny Rogers wa'n't along that voyage; he was along *one* voyage, I know that mighty well, but somehow it seems to me that he signed the articles for this voyage, but—but—whether he come along or not, or got left, or something happened—"

And so on and so on, till the excitement all cooled down and nobody cared whether the ship struck the iceberg or not.

In the course of his talk he rambled into a criticism upon New England degrees of merit in ship-building. Said he, "You get a vessel built away down Maine-way; Bath, for instance; what's the result? First thing you do, you want to heave her down for repairs,—*that's* the result! Well, sir, she hain't been hove down a week till you can heave a dog through her seams. You send that vessel to sea, and what's the result? She wets her oakum the first trip! Leave it to any man if 't a'n't so. Well, you let *our* folks build you a vessel—down New Bedford-way. What's the result? Well, sir, you might take that ship and heave her down, and keep her hove down six months, and she'll never shed a tear!"

Every body, landsmen and all, recognized the descriptive neatness of that figure, and applauded, which greatly pleased the old man. A moment later, the meek eyes of the pale young fellow heretofore mentioned came up slowly, rested upon the old man's face a moment, and the meek mouth began to open.

"Shet your head!" shouted the old mariner.

It was a rather startling surprise to every body, but it was effective in the matter of its purpose. So the conversation flowed on instead of perishing.

There was some talk about the perils of the sea, and a landsman delivered himself of the customary nonsense about the poor mariner wandering in far oceans, tempest-tossed, pursued by dangers, every storm blast and thunderbolt in the home skies moving the friends by snug firesides to compassion for that poor mariner, and prayers for his succor. Captain Bowling put up with this for a while, and then burst out with a new view of the matter.

"Come, belay there! I have read this kind of rot all my life in poetry and tales and such like rubbage. Pity for the poor mariner! sympathy for the poor mariner! All right enough, but not in the way the poetry puts it. Pity for the mariner's wife! all right again, but not in the way the poetry puts it. Look-a-here! whose life's the safest in the whole world? The poor mariner's. You look at the statistics, you'll see. So don't you fool away any sympathy on the poor mariner's dangers and privations and sufferings. Leave that to the poetry muffs. Now you look at the other side a minute. Here is Captain Brace, forty years old, been at sea thirty. On his way now to take command of his ship and sail south from Bermuda. Next week he'll be under way: easy times; comfortable quarters; passengers, sociable company; just enough to do to keep his mind healthy and not tire him; king over his ship, boss of every thing and every body; thirty years' safety to learn him that his profession a'n't a dangerous one. Now you look back at his home. His wife's a feeble woman; she's a stranger in New York; shut up in blazing hot or freezing cold lodgings, according to the season; don't know any body hardly; no company but her lonesomeness and her thoughts; husband gone six months at a time. She has borne eight children; five of them she has buried without her husband ever setting eyes on them. She watched them all the long nights till they died—he comfortable on the sea; she followed them to the grave, she heard the clods fall that broke her heart—he comfortable on the sea; she mourned at home, weeks and weeks, missing them every day and every hour—he cheerful at sea, knowing nothing about it. Now look at it a minute—turn it over in your mind and size it: five children born, she among strangers, and him not by to hearten her; buried, and him not by to comfort her; think of that! Sympathy for the poor mariner's perils is rot; give it to his wife's hard lines, where it belongs! Poetry makes out that all the wife worries about is the dangers her husband's running. She's got substantialer things to worry over, I tell you. Poetry's always pitying the poor mariner on account of his perils at sea; better a blamed sight pity him for the nights he can't sleep for thinking of how he had to leave his wife in her very birth pains, lonesome and friendless, in the thick of disease and trouble and death. If there's one thing that can make me madder than another, it's this sappy, damned maritime poetry!"

Captain Brace was a patient, gentle, seldom-speaking man, with a pathetic something in his bronzed face that had been a mystery up to this time, but stood interpreted now, since we had heard his story. He had voyaged eighteen times to the Mediterranean, seven times to India, once to the arctic pole in a discovery-ship, and "between times" had visited all the remote seas and ocean corners of the globe. But he said that twelve years ago, on account of his family, he "settled down," and ever since then had ceased to roam. And what do you suppose was this simple-hearted, life-long wanderer's idea of settling down and ceasing to roam? Why, the making of two five-month voyages a year between Surinam and Boston for sugar and molasses!

Among other talk, to-day, it came out that whaleships carry no doctor. The captain adds the doctorship to his own duties. He not only gives medicines, but sets broken limbs after notions of his own, or saws them off and sears the stump when amputation seems best. The captain is provided with a medicine-chest, with the medicines numbered instead of named. A book of directions goes with this. It describes diseases and symptoms, and says, "Give a tea-spoonful of No. 9 once an hour," or "Give ten grains of No. 12 every half hour," etc. One of our sea-captains came across a skipper in the North Pacific who was in a state of great surprise and perplexity. Said he:

"There's something rotten about this medicine-chest business. One of my men was sick—nothing much the matter. I looked in the book: it said, 'Give him a tea-spoonful of No. 15.' I went to the medicine-chest, and I see I was out of No. 15. I judged I'd got to get up a combination somehow that would fill the bill; so I hove into the fellow half a tea-spoonful of No. 8 and half a tea-spoonful of No. 7, and I'll be hanged if it didn't kill him in fifteen minutes! There's something about this medicine-chest system that's too many for me!"

There was a good deal of pleasant gossip about old Captain "Hurricane" Jones, of the Pacific Ocean—peace to his ashes! Two or three of us present had known him; I, particularly well, for I had made four sea-voyages with him. He was a very remarkable man. He was born in a ship; he picked up what little education he had among his shipmates; he began life in the forecastle, and climbed grade by grade to the captaincy. More than fifty years of his sixty-five were spent at sea. He had sailed all oceans, seen all lands, and borrowed a tint from all climates. When a man has been fifty years at sea; he necessarily knows nothing of men, nothing of the world but its surface, nothing of the world's thought, nothing of the world's learning but its A B C, and that blurred and distorted by the unfocused lenses of an untrained mind. Such a man is only a gray and bearded child. That is what old Hurricane Jones was—simply an innocent, lovable old infant. When his spirit was in repose, he was as sweet and gentle as a girl; when his wrath was up, he was a hurricane that made his nickname seem tamely descriptive. He was formidable in a fight, for he was of powerful build and dauntless courage. He was frescoed from head to heel with pictures and mottoes tattooed in red and blue India ink. I was with him one voyage when he got his last vacant space tattooed; this vacant space was around his left ankle. During three days he stumped about the ship with his ankle bare and swollen, and this legend gleaming red and angry out from a clouding of India ink: "Virtue is its own R'd." (There was a lack of room.) He was deeply and sincerely pious, and swore like a fishwoman. He considered swearing blameless; because sailors would not understand an order unillumined by it. He was a profound Biblical scholar—that is, he thought he was. He believed every thing in the Bible, but he had his own methods of arriving at his beliefs. He was of the "advanced" school of thinkers, and applied natural laws to the interpretation of all miracles, somewhat on the plan of the people who make the six days of creation six geological epochs, and so forth. Without being aware of it, he was a rather severe satire on modern scientific religionists. Such a man as I have been describing is rabidly fond of disquisition and argument; one knows that without being told it.

One trip the captain had a clergyman on board, but did not know he was a clergyman, since the passenger list did not betray the fact. He took a great liking to this Rev. Mr. Peters, and talked with him a great deal; told him yarns, gave him toothsome scraps of personal history, and wove a glittering streak of profanity through his garrulous fabric that was refreshing to a spirit weary of the dull neutralities of undecorated speech. One day the captain said, "Peters, do you ever read the Bible?"

"Well—yes."

"I judge it a'n't often, by the way you say it. Now, you tackle it in dead earnest once, and you'll find it'll pay. Don't you get discouraged, but hang right on. First you won't understand it; but by and by things will begin to clear up, and then you wouldn't lay it down to eat."

"Yes, I have heard that said."

"And it's so, too. There a'n't a book that begins with it; it lays over 'em all, Peters. There's some pretty tough things in it—there a'n't any getting around that—but you stick to them and think them out, and when once you get on the inside every thing's plain as day."

"The miracles, too, captain?"

"Yes, sir! the miracles, too. Every one of them. Now, there's that business with the prophets of Baal; like enough that stumped you?"

"Well, I don't know but—"

"Own up, now; it stumped you. Well, I don't wonder. You hadn't had any experience in ravelling such things out, and naturally it was too many for you. Would you like to have me explain that thing to you, and show you how to get at the meat of these matters?"

"Indeed I would, captain, if you don't mind."

Then the captain proceeded as follows:

"I'll do it with pleasure. First, you see, I read and read, and thought and thought, till I got to understand what sort of people they were in the old Bible times, and then after that it was all clear and easy. Now, this was the way I put it up concerning Isaac* and the prophets of Baal. There was some mighty sharp men amongst the public characters of that old ancient day, and Isaac was one of them. Isaac had his failings—plenty of them, too. It a'n't for me to apologize for Isaac; he played it on the prophets of Baal, and like enough he was justifiable, considering the odds that was against him. No, all I say is, 'twa'n't any miracle, and that I'll show you so's't you can see it yourself.

"Well, times had been getting rougher and rougher for prophets—that is, prophets of Isaac's denomination. There was four hundred and fifty prophets of Baal in the community, and only one Presbyterian; that is, if Isaac *was* a Presbyterian, which I reckon he was, but it don't say. Naturally, the prophets of Baal took all the trade. Isaac was pretty low-spirited, I reckon, but he was a good deal of a man, and no doubt he went a-prophesying around, letting on to be doing a land-office business, but 'twa'n't any use; he couldn't run any opposition to amount to any thing. By and by things got desperate with him; he sets his head to work and thinks it all out, and then what does he do?

*This is the captain's own mistake.

Why, he begins to throw out hints that the other parties are this and that and 't other—nothing very definite, may be, but just kind of undermining their reputation in a quiet way. This made talk, of course, and finally got to the king. The king asked Isaac what he meant by his talk. Says Isaac, 'Oh! nothing particular; only, can they pray down fire from heaven on an altar? It a'n't much, may be, your majesty, only, can they *do* it? that's the idea.' So the king was a good deal disturbed, and he went to the prophets of Baal, and they said, pretty airy, that if he had an altar ready, *they* were ready; and they intimated he better get it insured, too.

"So next morning all the children of Israel and their parents and the other people gathered themselves together. Well, here was that great crowd of prophets of Baal packed together on one side, and Isaac walking up and down all alone on the other, putting up his job. When time was called, Isaac let on to be comfortable and indifferent; told the other team to take the first innings. So they went at it, the whole four hundred and fifty, praying around the altar, very hopeful, and doing their level best. They prayed an hour—two hours—three hours—and so on, plumb till noon. It wa'n't any use; they hadn' took a trick. Of course they felt kind of ashamed before all those people, and well they might. Now, what would a magnanimous man do? Keep still, wouldn't he? Of course. What did Isaac do? He gravelled the prophets of Baal every way he could think of. Says he, 'You don't speak up loud enough; your God's asleep, like enough, or may be he's taking a walk; you want to holler, you know'—or words to that effect; I don't recollect the exact language. Mind, I don't apologize for Isaac; he had his faults.

"Well, the prophets of Baal prayed along the best they knew how all the afternoon, and never raised a spark. At last, about sundown, they were all tuckered out, and they owned up and quit.

"What does Isaac do now? He steps up and says to some friends of his there, 'Pour four barrels of water on the altar!' Every body was astonished; for the other side had prayed at it dry, you know, and got whitewashed. They poured it on. Says he, 'Heave on four more barrels.' Then he says, 'Heave on four more.' Twelve barrels, you see, altogether. The water ran all over the altar, and all down the sides, and filled up a trench around it that would hold a couple of hogsheads—'measures,' it says; I reckon it means about a hogshead. Some of the people were going to put on their things and go, for they allowed he was crazy. They didn't know Isaac. Isaac knelt down and began to pray: he strung along, and strung along, about the heathen in distant lands, and about the sister churches, and about the state and the country at large, and about those that's in authority in the government, and all the usual programme, you know, till every body had got tired and gone to thinking about something else, and then, all of a sudden, when nobody was noticing, he outs with a match and rakes it on the under side of his leg, and pff! up the whole thing blazes like a house afire! Twelve barrels of *water? Petroleum,* sir, PETROLEUM! that's what it was."

"Petroleum, captain?"

"Yes, sir; the country was full of it. Isaac knew all about that. You read the Bible. Don't you worry about the tough places. They a'n't tough when you come to think them out and throw light on them. There a'n't a thing in the Bible but what is true; all you want is to go prayerfully to work and cipher out how 't was done."

At eight o'clock on the third morning out from New York, land was sighted. Away across the sunny waves one saw a faint dark stripe stretched along under the horizon—or pretended to see it, for the credit of his eyesight. Even the Reverend said he saw it, a thing which was manifestly not so. But I never have seen any one who was morally strong enough to confess that he could not see land when others claimed that they could.

By and by the Bermuda Islands were easily visible. The principal one lay upon the water in the distance, a long, dull-colored body, scalloped with slight hills and valleys. We could not go straight at it, but had to travel all the way around it, sixteen miles from shore, because it is fenced with an invisible coral reef. At last we sighted buoys, bobbing here and there, and then we glided into a narrow channel among them, "raised the reef," and came upon shoaling blue water that soon further shoaled into pale green, with a surface scarcely rippled. Now came the resurrection hour; the berths gave up their dead. Who are these pale spectres in plug hats and silken flounces that file up the companion-way in melancholy procession and step upon the deck? These are they which took the infallible preventive of seasickness in New York harbor, and then disappeared and were forgotten. Also there came two or three faces not seen before until this moment. One's impulse is to ask, "Where did you come aboard?"

We followed the narrow channel a long time, with land on both sides—low hills that might have been green and grassy, but had a faded look instead. However, the land-locked water was lovely at any rate, with its glittering belts of blue and green where moderate soundings were, and its broad splotches of rich brown where the rocks lay near the surface. Every body was feeling so well that even the grave, pale young man (who, by a sort of kindly common consent, had come latterly to be referred to as "the Ass") received frequent and friendly notice—which was right enough, for there was no harm in him.

At last we steamed between two island points whose rocky jaws allowed only just enough room for the vessel's body, and now before us loomed Hamilton on her clustered hill-sides and summits, the whitest mass of terraced architecture that exists in the world, perhaps.

It was Sunday afternoon, and on the pier were gathered one or two hundred Bermudians, half of them black, half of them white, and all of them nobbily dressed, as the poet says.

Several boats came off to the ship, bringing citizens. One of these citizens was a faded, diminutive old gentleman, who approached our most ancient passenger with a childlike joy in his twinkling eyes, halted before him, folded his arms, and said, smiling with all his might and with all the simple delight that was in him, "You don't know me, John! Come, out with it, now; you know you don't!"

The ancient passenger scanned him perplexedly, scanned the napless, threadbare costume of venerable fashion that had done Sunday service no man knows how many years, contemplated the marvellous stovepipe hat of still more ancient and venerable pattern, with its poor pathetic old stiff brim canted up "gallusly" in the wrong places, and said, with a hesitation that indicated strong internal effort to "place" the gentle old apparition, 'Why—let me see—plague on it—there's *something* about you that—er—er—but I've been gone from Bermuda for twenty-seven years, and—hum, hum—I don't seem to get at it, somehow, but there's something about you that is just as familiar to me as—"

"Likely it might be his hat," murmured the Ass, with innocent, sympathetic interest.

III

So the Reverend and I had at last arrived at Hamilton, the principal town in the Bermuda Islands. A wonderfully white town; white as snow itself. White as marble; white as flour. Yet looking like none of these, exactly. Never mind, we said; we shall hit upon a figure by and by that will describe this peculiar white.

It was a town that was compacted together upon the sides and tops of a cluster of small hills. Its outlying borders fringed off and thinned away among the cedar forests, and there was no woody distance of curving coast, or leafy islet sleeping upon the dimpled, painted sea, but was flecked with shining white points—half-concealed houses peeping out of the foliage. The architecture of the town was mainly Spanish, inherited from the colonists of two hundred and fifty years ago. Some ragged-topped cocoapalms, glimpsed here and there, gave the land a tropical aspect.

There was an ample pier of heavy masonry; upon this, under shelter, were some thousands of barrels containing that product which has carried the fame of Bermuda to many lands, the potato. With here and there an onion. That last sentence is facetious; for they grow at least two onions in Bermuda to one potato. The onion is the pride and joy of Bermuda. It is her jewel, her gem of gems. In her conversation, her pulpit, her literature, it is her most frequent and eloquent figure. In Bermudian metaphor it stands for perfection—perfection absolute.

The Bermudian weeping over the departed, exhausts praise when he says, "He was an onion!" The Bermudian extolling the living hero, bankrupts applause when he says, "He is an onion!" The Bermudian, setting his son upon the stage of life to dare and do for himself, climaxes all counsel, supplication, admonition, comprehends all ambition, when he says, "Be an onion!"

When parallel with the pier, and ten or fifteen steps outside it, we anchored. It was Sunday, bright and sunny. The groups upon the pier—men, youths, and boys—were whites and blacks in about equal proportion. All were well and neatly dressed, many of them nattily, a few of them very stylishly. One would have to travel far before he would find another town of twelve thousand inhabitants that could represent itself so respectably, in the matter of clothes, on a freight-pier, without premeditation or effort. The women and young girls, black and white, who occasionally passed by, were nicely clad, and many were elegantly and fashionably so. The men did not affect summer clothing much, but the girls and women did, and their white garments were good to look at, after so many months of familiarity with sombre colors.

Around one isolated potato-barrel stood four young gentlemen, two black, two white, becomingly dressed, each with the head of a slender cane pressed against his teeth, and each with a foot propped up on the barrel. Another young gentleman came up, looked longingly at the barrel, but saw no rest for his foot there, and turned pensively away to seek another barrel. He wandered here and there, but without result. Nobody sat upon a barrel, as is the custom of the idle in other lands, yet all the isolated barrels were humanly occupied. Whosoever had a foot to spare, put it on a barrel, if all the places on it were not already taken. The habits of all peoples are determined by their circumstances. The Bermudians lean upon barrels because of the scarcity of lampposts.

Many citizens came on board and spoke eagerly to the officers—inquiring about the Turco-Russian war news, I supposed. However, by listening judiciously I found that this was not so. They said, "What is the price of onions?" or, "How's onions?" Naturally enough, this was their first interest; but they dropped into the war the moment it was satisfied.

We went ashore and found a novelty of a pleasant nature; there were no hackmen, hacks, or omnibuses on the pier or about it anywhere, and nobody offered his services to us, or molested us in any way. I said it was like being in heaven. The Reverend rebukingly and rather pointedly advised me to make the most of it, then. We knew of a boarding-house, and what we needed now was somebody to pilot us to it. Presently a little barefooted colored boy came along, whose raggedness was conspicuously un-Bermudian. His rear was so marvellously bepatched with colored squares and triangles that one was half persuaded he had got it out of an atlas. When the sun struck him right, he was as good to follow as a lightning-bug. We hired him and dropped into his wake. He piloted us through one picturesque street after another, and in due course deposited us where we belonged. He charged nothing for his map, and but a trifle for his services; so the Reverend doubled it. The little chap received the money with a beaming applause in his eye which plainly said, "This man's an onion!"

We had brought no letters of introduction; our names had been misspelt in the passenger list; nobody knew whether we were honest folk or otherwise. So we were expecting to have a good private time in case there was nothing in our general aspect to close boarding-house doors against us. We had no trouble. Bermuda has had but little experience of rascals, and is not suspicious. We got large, cool, well-lighted rooms on a second floor, overlooking a bloomy display of flowers and flowering shrubs—calla and annunciation lilies, lantanas, heliotrope, jessamine, roses, pinks, double geraniums, oleanders, pomegranates, blue morning-glories of a great size, and many plants that were unknown to me.

We took a long afternoon walk, and soon found out that that exceedingly white town was built of blocks of white coral. Bermuda is a coral island, with a six-inch crust of soil on top of it, and every man has a quarry on his own premises. Everywhere you go you see square recesses cut into the hill-sides, with perpendicular walls unmarred by crack or crevice, and perhaps you fancy that a house grew out of the ground there, and has been removed in a single piece from the mould. If you do, you err. But the material for a house has been quarried there. They cut right down through the coral, to any depth that is convenient—ten to twenty feet—and take it out in great square blocks. This cutting is done with a chisel that has a handle twelve or fifteen feet long, and is used as one uses a crowbar when he is drilling a hole, or a dasher when he is churning. Thus soft is this stone. Then with a common handsaw they saw the great blocks into handsome, huge bricks, that are two feet long, a foot wide, and about six inches thick. These stand loosely piled during a month to harden; then the work of building begins. The house is built of these blocks; it is roofed with broad coral slabs an inch thick, whose edges lap upon each other, so that the roof looks like a succession of shallow steps or terraces; the chimneys are built of the coral blocks and sawed into graceful and picturesque patterns; the ground-floor verandah is paved with coral blocks; also the walk to the gate; the fence is built of coral blocks—built in massive panels, with broad cap-stones and heavy gate-posts, and the whole trimmed into easy lines and comely shape with the saw. Then they put a hard coat of whitewash, as thick as your thumb nail, on the fence and all over the house, roof, chimneys, and all; the sun comes out and shines on this spectacle, and it is time for you to shut your unaccustomed eyes, lest they be put out. Is is the whitest white you can conceive of, and the blindingest. A Bermuda house does not look like marble; it is a much intenser white than that; and besides, there is a dainty, indefinable something else about its look that is not marble-like. We put in a great deal of solid talk and reflection over this matter of trying to find a figure that would describe the unique white of a Bermuda house, and we contrived to hit upon it at last. It is exactly the white of the icing of a cake, and has the same unemphasized and scarcely perceptible polish. The white of marble is modest and retiring compared with it.

After the house is cased in its hard scale of whitewash, not a crack, or sign of a seam, or joining of the blocks, is detectable, from base-stone to chimney-top; the building looks as if it had been carved from a single block of stone, and the doors and windows sawed out afterwards. A white marble house has a cold, tomb-like, unsociable look, and takes the conversation out of a body and depresses him. Not so with a Bermuda house. There is something exhilarating, even hilarious, about its vivid whiteness when the sun plays upon it. If it be of picturesque shape and graceful contour—and many of the Bermudian dwellings are—it will so fascinate you that you will keep your eyes on it until they ache. One of those clean-cut, fanciful chimneys—too pure and white for this world—with one side glowing in the sun and the other touched with a soft shadow, is an object that will charm one's gaze by the hour. I know of no other country that has chimneys worthy to be gazed at and gloated over. One of those snowy houses half-concealed and half-glimpsed through green foliage is a pretty thing to see; and if it takes one by surprise and suddenly, as he turns a sharp corner of a country road, it will wring an exclamation from him, sure.

Wherever you go, in town or country, you find those snowy houses, and always with masses of bright-colored flowers about them, but with no vines climbing their walls; vines cannot take hold of the smooth, hard whitewash. Wherever you go, in the town or along the country roads, among little potato farms and patches or expensive country-seats, these stainless white dwellings, gleaming out from flowers and foliage, meet you at every turn. The least little bit of a cottage is as white and blemishless as the stateliest mansion. Nowhere is there dirt or stench, puddle or hog-wallow, neglect, disorder, or lack of trimness and neatness. The roads, the streets, the dwellings, the people, the clothes—this neatness extends to every thing that falls under the eye. It is the tidiest country in the world. And very much the tidiest, too.

Considering these things, the question came up, Where do the poor live? No answer was arrived at. Therefore, we agreed to leave this conundrum for future statesmen to wrangle over.

What a bright and startling spectacle one of those blazing white country palaces, with its brown-tinted window caps and ledges, and green shutters, and its wealth of caressing flowers and foliage, would be in black London! And what a gleaming surprise it would be in nearly any American city one could mention, too!

Bermuda roads are made by cutting down a few inches into the solid white coral—or a good many feet, where a hill intrudes itself—and smoothing off the surface of the road-bed. It is a simple and easy process. The grain of the coral is coarse and porous; the road-bed has the look of being made of coarse white sugar. Its excessive cleanness and whiteness are a trouble in one way: the sun is reflected into your eyes with such energy as you walk along that you want to sneeze all the time. Old Captain Tom Bowling found another difficulty. He joined us in our walk, but kept wandering unrestfully to the roadside. Finally he explained. Said he, "Well, I chew, you know, and the road's so plaguy clean."

We walked several miles that afternoon in the bewildering glare of the sun, the white roads, and the white buildings. Our eyes got to paining us a good deal. By and by a soothing, blessed twilight spread its cool balm around. We looked up in pleased surprise, and saw that it proceeded from an intensely black negro who was going by. We answered his military salute in the grateful gloom of his near presence, and then passed on into the pitiless white glare again.

The colored women whom we met usually bowed and spoke; so did the children. The colored men commonly gave the military salute. They borrow this fashion from the soldiers no doubt; England has kept a garrison here for generations. The younger men's custom of carrying small canes is also borrowed from the soldiers, I suppose, who always carry a cane, in Bermuda as everywhere else in Britain's broad dominions.

The country roads curve and wind hither and thither, in the delightfulest way, unfolding pretty surprises at every turn: billowy masses of oleander that seem to float out from behind distant projections like the pink cloud-banks of sunset; sudden plunges among cottages and gardens, life and activity, followed by as sudden plunges into the sombre twilight and stillness of the woods; flitting visions of white fortresses and beacon towers pictured against the sky on remote hill-tops; glimpses of shining green sea caught for a moment through opening headlands, then lost again; more woods and solitude; and by and by another turn lays bare, without warning, the full sweep of the inland ocean, enriched with its bars of soft color, and graced with its wandering sails.

Take any road you please, you may depend upon it you will not stay in it half a mile. Your road is every thing that a road ought to be: it is bordered with trees, and with strange plants and flowers; it is shady and pleasant, or sunny and still pleasant; it carries you by the prettiest and peacefulest and most homelike of homes, and through stretches of forest that lie in a deep hush sometimes, and sometimes are alive with the music of birds; it curves always, which is a continual promise, whereas straight roads reveal every thing at a glance and kill interest. Your road is all this, and yet you will not stay in it half a mile, for the reason that little, seductive, mysterious roads are always branching out from it on either hand, and as these curve sharply also and hide what is beyond, you cannot resist the temptation to desert your own chosen road and explore them. You are usually paid for your trouble; consequently, your walk inland always turns out to be one of the most crooked, involved, purposeless, and interesting experiences a body can imagine. There is enough of variety. Sometimes you are in the level open, with marshes thick grown with flag-lances that are ten feet high on the one hand, and potato and onion orchards on the other; next you are on a hill-top, with the ocean and the Islands spread around you; presently the road winds through a deep cut, shut in by perpendicular walls thirty or forty feet high, marked with the oddest and abruptest stratum lines, suggestive of sudden and eccentric old upheavals, and garnished with here and there a clinging adventurous flower, and here and there a dangling vine; and by and by your way is along the sea edge, and you may look down a fathom or two through the transparent water and watch the diamond-like flash and play of the light upon the rocks and sands on the bottom until you are tired of it—if you are so constituted as to be able to get tired of it.

You may march the country roads in maiden meditation, fancy free, by field and farm, for no dog will plunge out at you from unsuspected gate, with breath-taking surprise of ferocious bark, notwithstanding it is a Christian land and a civilized. We saw upwards of a million cats in Bermuda, but the people are very abstemious in the matter of dogs. Two or three nights we prowled the country far and wide, and never once were accosted by a dog. It is a great privilege to visit such a land. The cats were no offence when properly distributed, but when piled they obstructed travel.

As we entered the edge of the town that Sunday afternoon, we stopped at a cottage to get a drink of water. The proprietor, a middle-aged man with a good face, asked us to sit down and rest. His dame brought chairs, and we grouped ourselves in the shade of the trees by the door. Mr. Smith—that was not his name, but it will answer—questioned us about ourselves and our country, and we answered him truthfully, as a general thing, and questioned him in return. It was all very simple and pleasant and sociable. Rural, too; for there was a pig and a small donkey and a hen anchored out, close at hand, by cords to their legs, on a spot that purported to be grassy. Presently, a woman passed along, and although she coldly said nothing she changed the drift of our talk. Said Smith:

"She didn't look this way, you noticed? Well, she is our next neighbor on one side, and there's another family that's our next neighbors on the other side; but there's a general coolness all around now, and we don't speak. Yet these three families, one generation and another, have lived here side by side and been as friendly as weavers for a hundred and fifty years, till about a year ago."

"Why, what calamity could have been powerful enough to break up so old a friendship?"

"Well, it was too bad, but it couldn't be helped. It happened like this: About a year or more ago, the rats got to pestering my place a good deal, and I set up a steel-trap in the back-yard. Both of these neighbors run considerable to cats, and so I warned them about the trap, because their cats were pretty sociable around here nights, and they might get into trouble without my intending it. Well, they shut up their cats for a while, but you know how it is with people; they got careless, and sure enough one night the trap took Mrs. Jones's principal tomcat into camp, and finished him up. In the morning Mrs. Jones comes here with the corpse in her arms, and cries and takes on the same as if it was a child. It was a cat by the name of Yelverton—Hector G. Yelverton—a troublesome old rip, with no more principle than an Injun, though you couldn't make *her* believe it. I said all a man could to comfort her, but no, nothing would do but I must pay for him. Finally, I said I warn't investing in cats now as much as I was, and with that she walked off in a huff, carrying the remains with her. That closed our intercourse with the Joneses. Mrs. Jones joined another church and took her tribe with her. She said she would not hold fellowship with assassins. Well, by and by comes Mrs. Brown's turn—she that went by here a minute ago. She had a disgraceful old yellow cat that she thought as much of as if he was twins, and one night he tried that trap on his neck, and it fitted him so, and was so sort of satisfactory, that he laid down and curled up and stayed with it. Such was the end of Sir John Baldwin."

"Was that the name of the cat?"

"The same. There's cats around here with names that would surprise you. Maria" (to his wife), "what was that cat's name that eat a keg of ratsbane by mistake over at Hooper's, and started home and got struck by lightning and took the blind staggers and fell in the well and was most drowned before they could fish him out?"

"That was that colored Deacon Jackson's cat. I only remember the last end of its name, which was To-Be-Or-Not-To-Be-That-Is-The-Question Jackson."

"Sho! that ain't the one. That's the one that eat up an entire box of Seidlitz powders, and then hadn't any more judgment than to go and take a drink. He was considered to be a great loss, but I never could see it. Well, no matter about the names. Mrs. Brown wanted to be reasonable, but Mrs. Jones wouldn't let her. She put her up to going to law for damages. So to law she went, and had the face to claim seven shillings and sixpence. It made a great stir. All the neighbors went to court. Every body took sides. It got hotter and hotter, and broke up all the friendships for three hundred yards around—friendships that had lasted for generations and generations.

"Well, I proved by eleven witnesses that the cat was of a low character and very ornery, and warn't worth a cancelled postage-stamp, any way, taking the average of cats here; but I lost the case. What could I expect? The system is all wrong here, and is bound to make revolution and bloodshed some day. You see, they give the magistrate a poor little starvation salary, and then turn him loose on the public to gouge for fees and costs to live on. What is the natural result? Why he never looks into the justice of a case—never once. All he looks at is which client has got the money. So this one piled the fees and costs and every thing on to me. I could pay specie, don't you see? and he knew mighty well that if he put the verdict on to Mrs. Brown, where it belonged, he'd have to take his swag in currency."

"Currency? Why, has Bermuda a currency?"

"Yes—onions. And they were forty per cent discount, too, then, because the season had been over as much as three months. So I lost my case. I had to pay for that cat. But the general trouble the case made was the worse thing about it. Broke up so much good feeling. The neighbors don't speak to each other now. Mrs. Brown had named a child after me. But she changed its name right away. She is a Baptist. Well, in the course of baptizing it over again, it got drowned. I was hoping we might get to be friendly again some time or other, but of course this drowning the child knocked that all out of the question. It would have saved a world of heart-break and ill blood if she had named it dry."

I knew by the sigh that this was honest. All this trouble and all this destruction of confidence in the purity of the bench on account of a seven-shilling lawsuit about a cat! Somehow, it seemed to "size" the country.

At this point we observed that an English flag had just been placed at half-mast on a building a hundred yards away. I and my friends were busy in an instant trying to imagine whose death, among the island dignitaries, could command such a mark of respect as this. Then a shudder shook them and me at the same moment, and I knew that we had jumped to one and the same conclusion: "The governor has gone to England; it is for the British admiral!"

At this moment Mr. Smith noticed the flag. He said with emotion:

"That's on a boarding-house. I judge there's a boarder dead."

A dozen other flags within view went to half-mast.

"It's a boarder, sure," said Smith.

"But would they half-mast the flags here for a boarder, Mr. Smith?"

"Why, certainly they would, if he was *dead.*"

That seemed to size the country again.

IV

The early twilight of a Sunday evening in Hamilton, Bermuda, is an alluring time. There is just enough of whispering breeze, fragrance of flowers, and sense of repose, to raise one's thoughts heavenward; and just enough amateur piano music to keep him reminded of the other place. There are many venerable pianos in Hamilton, and they all play at twilight. Age enlarges and enriches the powers of some musical instruments—notably those of the violin—but it seems to set a piano's teeth on edge. Most of the music in vogue there is the same that those pianos prattled in their innocent infancy; and there is something very pathetic about it when they go over it now, in their asthmatic second childhood, dropping a note here and there, where a tooth is gone.

We attended evening service at the stately Episcopal church on the hill, where were five or six hundred people, half of them white and the other half black, according to the usual Bermudian proportions; and all well dressed—a thing which is also usual in Bermuda, and to be confidently expected. There was good music, which we heard, and doubtless a good sermon, but there was a wonderful deal of coughing, and so only the high parts of the argument carried over it. As we came out, after service, I overheard one young girl say to another,

"Why, you don't mean to say you pay duty on gloves and laces! I only pay postage; have them done up and sent in the Boston *Advertiser.*"

There are those who believe that the most difficult thing to create is a woman who can comprehend that it is wrong to smuggle; and that an impossible thing to create is a woman who will not smuggle, whether or no, when she gets a chance. But these may be errors.

We went wandering off toward the country, and were soon far down in the lonely black depths of a road that was roofed over with the dense foliage of a double rank of great cedars. There was no sound of any kind, there; it was perfectly still. And it was so dark that one could detect nothing but sombre outlines. We strode farther and farther down this tunnel, cheering the way with chat.

Presently, the chat took this shape: "How insensibly the character of a people and of a government makes its impress upon a stranger, and gives him a sense of security or of insecurity without his taking deliberate thought upon the matter or asking any body a question! We have been in this land half a day; we have seen none but honest faces; we have noted the British flag flying, which means efficient government and good order; so without inquiry we plunge unarmed and with perfect confidence into this dismal place, which in almost any other country would swarm with thugs and garroters—"

'Sh! What was that? Stealthy footsteps! Low voices! We gasp, we close up together, and wait. A vague shape glides out of the dusk and confronts us. A voice speaks—demands money!

"A shilling, gentlemen, if you please, to help build the new Methodist church."

Blessed sound! Holy sound! We contribute with thankful avidity to the new Methodist church, and are happy to think how lucky it was that those little colored Sunday-school scholars did not seize upon every thing we had with violence, before we recovered from our momentary helpless condition. By the light of cigars we write down the names of weightier philanthropists than ourselves on the contribution-cards, and then pass on into the farther darkness, saying, What sort of government do they call this, where they allow little black pious children, with contribution-cards, to plunge out upon peaceable strangers in the dark and scare them to death?

We prowled on several hours, sometimes by the seaside, sometimes inland, and finally managed to get lost, which is a feat that requires talent in Bermuda. I had on new shoes. They were No. 7's when I started, but were not more than 5's now, and still diminishing. I walked two hours in those shoes after that, before we reached home. Doubtless I could have the reader's sympathy for the asking. Many people have never had the headache or the toothache, and I am one of those myself; but every body has worn tight shoes for two or three hours, and known the luxury of taking them off in a retired place and seeing his feet swell up and obscure the firmament. Few of us will ever forget the exquisite hour we were married. Once when I was a callow, bashful cub, I took a plain, unsentimental country girl to a comedy one night. I had known her a day; she seemed divine; I wore my new boots. At the end of the first half hour she said, "Why do you fidget so with your feet?" I said, "Did I?" Then I put my attention there and kept still. At the end of another half hour she said, "Why do you say, 'Yes, oh! yes!' and 'Ha, ha! oh! certainly! very true!' to every thing I say, when half the time those are entirely irrelevant answers?" I blushed, and explained that I had been a little absent-minded. At the end of another half hour she said, "Please, why do you grin so steadfastly at vacancy, and yet look so sad?" I explained that I always did that when I was reflecting. An hour passed, and then she turned and contemplated me with her earnest eyes and said, "Why do you cry all the time?" I explained that very funny comedies always made me cry. At last human nature surrendered, and I secretly slipped my boots off. This was a mistake. I was not able to get them on any more. It was a rainy night; there were no omnibuses going our way; and as I walked home, burning up with shame, with the girl on one arm and my boots under the other, I was an object worthy of some compassion—especially in those moments of martyrdom when I had to pass through the glare that fell upon the pavement from street lamps. Finally, this child of the forest said, "Where are your boots?" and being taken unprepared, I put a fitting finish to the follies of the evening with the stupid remark, "The higher classes do not wear them to the theatre."

The Reverend had been an army chaplain during the war, and while we were hunting for a road that would lead to Hamilton, he told me a story about two dying soldiers which interested me in spite of my feet. He said that in the Potomac hospitals rough pine coffins were furnished by government, but that it was not always possible to keep up with the demand; so when a man died, if there was no coffin at hand he was buried without one. One night late, two soldiers lay dying in a ward. A man came in with a coffin on his shoulder, and stood trying to make up his mind which of these two poor fellows would be likely to need it first. Both of them begged for it with their fading eyes—they were past talking. Then one of them protruded a wasted hand from his blankets and made a feeble beckoning sign with the fingers, to signify, "Be a good fellow; put it under my bed, please." The man did it, and left. The lucky soldier painfully turned himself in his bed until he faced the other warrior, raised himself partly on his elbow, and began to work up a mysterious expression of some kind in his face. Gradually, irksomely, but surely and steadily, it developed, and at last it took definite form as a pretty successful wink. The sufferer fell back exhausted with his labor, but bathed in glory. Now entered a personal friend of

No. 2, the despoiled soldier. No. 2 pleaded with him with eloquent eyes, till presently he understood, and removed the coffin from under No. 1's bed and put it under No. 2's. No. 2 indicated his joy, and made some more signs; the friend understood again, and put his arm under No. 2's shoulders and lifted him partly up. Then the dying hero turned the dim exultation of his eye upon No. 1, and began a slow and labored work with his hands; gradually he lifted one hand up toward his face; it grew weak and dropped back again; once more he made the effort, but failed again. He took a rest; he gathered all the remnant of his strength, and this time he slowly but surely carried his thumb to the side of his nose, spread the gaunt fingers wide in triumph, and dropped back dead. That picture sticks by me yet. Thl "situation" is unique.

The next morning, at what seemed a very early hour, the little white table-waiter appeared suddenly in my room and shot a single word out of himself: "Breakfast!"

This was a remarkable boy in many ways. He was about eleven years old; he had alert, intent black eyes; he was quick of movement; there was no hesitation, no uncertainty about him anywhere; there was a military decision in his lip, his manner, his speech, that was an astonishing thing to see in a little chap like him; he wasted no words; his answers always came so quick and brief that they seemed to be part of the question that had been asked, instead of a reply to it. When he stood at table with his fly-brush, rigid, erect, his face set in a cast-iron gravity, he was a statue till he detected a dawning want in somebody's eye; then he pounced down, supplied it, and was instantly a statue again. When he was sent to the kitchen for any thing, he marched upright till he got to the door; he turned hand-springs the rest of the way.

"Breakfast!"

I thought I would make one more effort to get some conversation out of this being.

"Have you called the Reverend, or are—"

"Yes, s'r!"

"Is it early, or is—"

"Eight-five!"

"Do you have to do all the 'chores,' or is there somebody to give you a l—"

"Colored girl!"

"Is there only one parish in this island, or are there—"

"Eight!"

"Is the big church on the hill a parish church, or is it—"

"Chapel-of-ease!"

"Is taxation here classified into poll, parish, town, and—"

"Don't know!"

Before I could cudgel another question out of my head, he was below, hand-springing across the back yard. He had slid down the balusters, head first. I gave up trying to provoke a discussion with him. The essential element of discussion had been left out of him; his answers were so final and exact that they did not leave a doubt to hang conversation on. I suspect that there is the making of a mighty man or a mighty rascal in this boy,—according to circumstances,—but they are going to apprentice him to a carpenter. It is the way the world uses its opportunities.

During this day and the next we took carriage drives about the island and over to the town of St. George's, fifteen or twenty miles away. Such hard, excellent roads to drive over are not to be found elsewhere out of Europe. An intelligent young colored man drove us, and acted as guide-book. In the edge of town we saw five or six mountain-cabbage palms (atrocious name!) standing in a straight row, and equidistant from each other. These were not the largest or the tallest trees I have ever seen, but they were the stateliest, the most majestic. That row of them must be the nearest that nature has ever come to counterfeiting a colonnade. These trees are all the same height, say sixty feet; the trunks as gray as granite, with a very gradual and perfect taper; without a sign of branch or knot or flaw; the surface not looking like bark, but like granite that has been dressed and not polished. Thus all the way up the diminishing shaft for fifty feet; then it begins to take the appearance of being closely wrapped, spool-fashion, with gray cord, or of having been turned in a lathe. Above this point there is an outward swell, and thence upwards, for six feet or more, the cylinder is a bright, fresh green, and is formed of wrappings like those of an ear of green Indian corn. Then comes the great spraying palm plume, also green. Other palm-trees always lean out of the perpendicular, or have a curve in them. But the plumb-line could not detect a deflection in any individual of this stately row; they stand as straight as the colonnade of Baalbec; they have its great height, they have its gracefulness, they have its dignity; in moonlight or twilight, and shorn of their plumes, they would duplicate it.

The birds we came across in the country were singularly tame; even that wild creature, the quail, would pick around in the grass at ease while we inspected it and talked about it at leisure. A small bird of the canary species had to be stirred up with the butt end of the whip before it would move, and then it moved only a couple of feet. It is said that even the suspicious flea is tame and sociable in Bermuda, and will allow himself to be caught and caressed without misgivings. This should be taken with allowance, for doubtless there is more or less brag about it. In San Francisco they used to claim that their native flea could kick a child over, as if it were a merit in a flea to be able to do that; as if the knowledge of it, trumpeted abroad, ought to entice immigration. Such a thing in nine cases out of ten would be almost sure to deter a thinking man from coming.

We saw no bugs or reptiles to speak of, and so I was thinking of saying in print, in a general way, that there were none at all; but one night after I had gone to bed, the Reverend came into my room carrying something, and asked, "Is this your boot?" I said it was, and he said he had met a spider going off with it. Next morning he stated that just at dawn the same spider raised his window and was coming in to get a shirt, but saw him and fled.

I inquired, "Did he get the shirt?"

"No."

"How did you know it was a shirt he was after?"

"I could see it in his eye."

We inquired around, but could hear of no Bermudian spider capable of doing these things. Citizens said that their largest spiders could not more than spread their legs over an ordinary saucer, and that they had always been considered honest. Here was testimony of a clergyman against the testimony of mere worldlings—interested ones, too. On the whole, I judged it best to lock up my things.

Here and there on the country roads we found lemon, papaia, orange, lime, and fig trees; also several sorts of palms, among them the cocoa, the date, and the palmetto. We saw some bamboos forty feet high, with stems as thick as a man's arm. Jungles of the mangrove-tree stood up out of swamps, propped on their interlacing roots as upon a tangle of stilts. In drier places the noble tamarind sent down its grateful cloud of shade. Here and there the blossomy tamarisk adorned the roadside. There was a curious gnarled and twisted black tree, without a single leaf on it. It might have passed itself off for a dead apple-tree but for the fact that it had a star-like, red-hot flower sprinkled sparsely over its person. It had the scattery red glow that a constellation might have when glimpsed through smoked glass. It is possible that our constellations have been so constructed as to be invisible through smoked glass; if this is so, it is a great mistake.

We saw a tree that bears grapes, and just as calmly and unostentatiously as a vine would do it. We saw an India-rubber tree, but out of season, possibly, so there were no shoes on it, nor suspenders, nor any thing that a person would properly expect to find there. This gave it an impressively fraudulent look. There was exactly one mahogany tree on the island. I know this to be reliable, because I saw a man who said he had counted it many a time and could not be mistaken. He was a man with a hare lip and a pure heart, and every body said he was as true as steel. Such men are all too few.

One's eye caught near and far the pink cloud of the oleander and the red blaze of the pomegranate blossom. In one piece of wild-wood the morning-glory vines had wrapped the trees to their very tops, and decorated them all over with couples and clusters of great blue bells—a fine and striking spectacle, at a little distance. But the dull cedar is everywhere, and it is the prevailing foliage. One does not appreciate how dull it is until the varnished, bright green attire of the infrequent lemon-tree pleasantly intrudes its contrast. In one thing Bermuda is eminently tropical—was in May, at least—the unbrilliant, slightly faded, unrejoicing look of the landscape. For forests arrayed in a blemishless magnificence of glowing green foliage that seems to exult in its own existence, and can move the beholder to an enthusiasm that will make him either shout or cry, one must go to countries that have malignant winters.

We saw scores of colored farmers digging their crops of potatoes and onions, their wives and children helping—entirely contented and comfortable, if looks go for any thing. We never met a man, or woman, or child anywhere in this sunny island who seemed to be unprosperous, or discontented, or sorry about any thing. This sort of monotony became very tiresome presently, and even something worse. The spectacle of an entire nation grovelling in contentment is an infuriating thing. We felt the lack of something in this community—a vague, an undefinable, an elusive something, and yet a lack. But after considerable thought we made out what it was—tramps. Let them go there, right now, in a body. It is utterly virgin soil. Passage is cheap. Every true patriot in America will help buy tickets. Whole armies of these excellent beings can be spared from our midst and our polls; they will find a delicious climate and a green, kind-hearted people. There are potatoes and onions for all, and a generous welcome for the first batch that arrives, and elegant graves for the second.

It was the Early Rose potato the people were digging. Later in the year they have another crop, which they call the Garnet. We buy their potatoes (retail) at fifteen dollars a barrel; and those colored farmers buy ours for a song, and live on them. Havana might exchange cigars with Connecticut in the same advantageous way, if she thought of it.

We passed a roadside grocery with a sign up, "Potatoes Wanted." An ignorant stranger, doubtless. He could not have gone thirty steps from his place without finding plenty of them.

In several fields the arrow-root crop was already sprouting. Bermuda used to make a vast annual profit out of this staple before fire-arms came into such general use.

The island is not large. Somewhere in the interior a man ahead of us had a very slow horse. I suggested that we had better go by him; but the driver said the man had but a little way to go. I waited to see, wondering how he could know. Presently the man did turn down another road. I asked, "How did you know he would?"

"Because I knew the man, and where he lived."

I asked him, satirically, if he knew every body in the island; he answered, very simply, that he did. This gives a body's mind a good substantial grip on the dimensions of the place.

At the principal hotel in St. George's, a young girl, with a sweet, serious face, said we could not be furnished with dinner, because we had not been expected, and no preparation had been made. Yet it was still an hour before dinner time. We argued, she yielded not ; we supplicated, she was serene. The hotel had not been expecting an inundation of two people, and so it seemed that we should have to go home dinnerless. I said we were not very hungry; a fish would do. My little maid answered, it was not the market-day for fish. Things began to look serious; but presently the boarder who sustained the hotel came in, and when the case was laid before him, he was cheerfully willing to divide. So we had much pleasant chat at table about St. George's chief industry, the repairing of damaged ships; and in between we had a soup that had something in that seemed to taste like the hereafter, but it proved to be only pepper of a particularly vivacious kind. And we had an iron-clad chicken that was deliciously cooked, but not in the right way. Baking was not the thing to convince his sort. He ought to have been put through a quartz mill until the "tuck" was taken out of him, and then boiled till we came again. We got a good deal of sport out of him, but not enough sustenance to leave the victory on our side. No matter; we had potatoes and a pie and a sociable good time. Then a ramble through the town, which is a quaint one, with interesting, crooked streets, and narrow, crooked lanes, with here and there a grain of dust. Here, as in Hamilton, the dwellings had Venetian blinds of a very sensible pattern. They were not double shutters, hinged at the sides, but a single broad shutter, hinged at the top; you push it outward, from the bottom, and fasten it at any angle required by the sun or desired by yourself.

All about the island one sees great white scars on the hill-slopes. These are dished spaces where the soil has been scraped off and the coral exposed and glazed with hard whitewash. Some of these are a quarter-acre in size. They catch and carry the rainfall to reservoirs; for the wells are few and poor, and there are no natural springs and no brooks.

They say that the Bermuda climate is mild and equable, with never any snow or ice, and that one may be very comfortable in spring clothing the year round, there. We had delightful and decided summer weather in May, with a flaming sun that permitted the thinnest of raiment, and yet there was a constant breeze; consequently we were never discomforted by heat. At four or five in the afternoon the mercury began to go down, and then it became necessary to change to thick garments. I went to St. George's in the morning clothed in the thinnest of linen, and reached home at five in the afternoon with two overcoats on. The nights are said to be always cool and bracing. We had mosquito nets, and the Reverend said the mosquitoes persecuted him a good deal. I often heard him slapping and banging at these imaginary creatures with as much zeal as if they had been real. There are no mosquitoes in the Bermudas in May.

The poet Thomas Moore spent several months in Bermuda more than seventy years ago. He was sent out to be registrar of the admiralty. I am not quite clear as to the function of a registrar of the admiralty of Bermuda, but I think it is his duty to keep a record of all the admirals born there. I will inquire into this. There was not much doing in admirals, and Moore got tired and went away. A reverently preserved souvenir of him is still one of the treasures of the islands. I gathered the idea, vaguely, that it was a jug, but was persistently thwarted in the twenty-two efforts I made to visit it. However, it was no matter, for I found afterwards that it was only a chair.

There are several "sights" in the Bermudas, of course, but they are easily avoided. This is a great advantage—one cannot have it in Europe. Bermuda is the right country for a jaded man to "loaf" in. There are no harassments; the deep peace and quiet of the country sink into one's body and bones and give his conscience a rest, and chloroform the legion of invisible small devils that are always trying to whitewash his hair. A good many Americans go there about the first of March and remain until the early spring weeks have finished their villainies at home.

The Bermudians are hoping soon to have telegraphic communication with the world. But even after they shall have acquired this curse, it will still be a good country to go to for a vacation; for there are charming little islets scattered about the inclosed sea where one could live secure from interruption. The telegraph boy would have to come in a boat, and one could easily kill him while he was making his landing.

We had spent four days in Bermuda—three bright ones out of doors and one rainy one in the house, we being disappointed about getting a yacht for a sail; and now our furlough was ended.

We made the run home to New York quarantine in three days and five hours, and could have gone right along up to the city if we had had a health permit. But health permits are not granted after seven in the evening, partly because a ship cannot be inspected and overhauled with exhaustive thoroughness except in daylight, and partly because health officers are liable to catch cold if they expose themselves to the night air. Still, you can *buy* a permit after hours for five dollars extra, and the officer will do the inspecting next week. Our ship and passengers lay under expense and in humiliating captivity all night, under the very nose of the little official reptile who is supposed to protect New York from pestilence by his vigilant "inspections." This imposing rigor gave every body a solemn and awful idea of the beneficent watchfulness of our government, and there were some who wondered if any thing finer could be found in other countries.

In the morning we were all a-tiptoe to witness the intricate ceremony of inspecting the ship. But it was a disappointing thing. The health officer's tug ranged alongside for a moment, our purser handed the lawful three-dollar permit fee to the health officer's boot-black, who passed us a folded paper in a forked stick, and away we went. The entire "inspection" did not occupy thirteen seconds.

The health officer's place is worth a hundred thousand dollars a year to him. His system of inspection is perfect, and therefore cannot be improved on; but it seems to me that his system of collecting his fees might be amended. For a great ship to lie idle all night is a most costly loss of time; for her passengers to have to do the same thing works to them the same damage, with the addition of an amount of exasperation and bitterness of soul that the spectacle of that health officer's funeral could hardly sweeten. Now why would it not be better and simpler to let the ships pass in unmolested, and the fees and permits be exchanged once a year by post?

"Travelling With a Reformer" was written for the December 1893 edition of Cosmopolitan. *Twain included it in a collection entitled* How To Tell a Story and Other Essays, *published by Harper & Brothers in 1897.*

Travelling with a Reformer

Last spring I went out to Chicago to see the Fair, and although I did not see it my trip was not wholly lost—there were compensations. In New York I was introduced to a major in the regular army who said he was going to the Fair, and we agreed to go together. I had to go to Boston first, but that did not interfere; he said he would go along, and put in the time. He was a handsome man, and built like a gladiator. But his ways were gentle, and his speech was soft and persuasive. He was companionable, but exceedingly reposeful. Yes, and wholly destitute of the sense of humor. He was full of interest in everything that went on around him, but his serenity was indestructible; nothing disturbed him, nothing excited him.

But before the day was done I found that deep down in him somewhere he had a passion, quiet as he was—a passion for reforming petty public abuses. He stood for citizenship—it was his hobby. His idea was that every citizen of the republic ought to consider himself an unofficial policeman, and keep unsalaried watch and ward over the laws and their execution. He thought that the only effective way of preserving and protecting public rights was for each citizen to do his share in preventing or punishing such infringements of them as came under his personal notice.

It was a good scheme, but I thought it would keep a body in trouble all the time; it seemed to me that one would be always trying to get offending little officials discharged, and perhaps getting laughed at for all reward. But he said no, I had the wrong idea; that there was no occasion to get anybody discharged; that in fact you *musn't* get anybody discharged; that that would itself be a failure; no, one must reform the man—reform him and make him useful where he was.

"Must one report the offender and then beg his superior not to discharge him, but reprimand him and keep him?"

"No, that is not the idea; you don't report him at all, for then you risk his bread and butter. You can act as if you are *going* to report him—when nothing else will answer. But that's an extreme case. That is a sort of *force*, and force is bad. Diplomacy is the effective thing. Now if a man has tact—if a man will exercise diplomacy—"

For two minutes we had been standing at a telegraph wicket, and during all this time the Major had been trying to get the attention of one of the young operators, but they were all busy skylarking. The Major spoke now, and asked one of them to take his telegram. He got for reply:

"I reckon you can wait a minute, can't you?" and the skylarking went on.

The Major said yes, he was not in a hurry. Then he wrote another telegram:

"President Western Union Tel. Co.:

"Come and dine with me this evening. I can tell you how business is conducted in one of your branches."

Presently the young fellow who had spoken so pertly a little before reached out and took the telegram, and when he read it he lost color and began to apologize and explain. He said he would lose his place if this deadly telegram was sent, and he might never get another. If he could be let off this time he would give no cause for complaint again. The compromise was accepted.

As we walked away, the Major said:

"Now, you see, that was diplomacy—and you see how it worked. It wouldn't do any good to bluster, the way people are always doing—that boy can always give you as good as you send, and you'll come out defeated and ashamed of yourself pretty nearly always. But you see he stands no chance against diplomacy. Gentle words and diplomacy—those are the tools to work with."

"Yes, I see; but everybody wouldn't have had your opportunity. It isn't everybody that is on those familiar terms with the president of the Western Union."

"Oh, you misunderstand. I don't know the president—I only

use him diplomatically. It is for his good and for the public good. There's no harm in it."

I said, with hesitation and diffidence:

"But is it ever right or noble to tell a lie?"

He took no note of the delicate self-righteousness of the question, but answered, with undisturbed gravity and simplicity:

"Yes, sometimes. Lies told to injure a person, and lies told to profit yourself are not justifiable, but lies told to help another person, and lies told in the public interest—oh, well, that is quite another matter. Anybody knows that. But never mind about the methods: you see the result. That youth is going to be useful now, and well-behaved. He had a good face. He was worth saving. Why, he was worth saving on his mother's account if not his own. Of course, he has a mother—sisters, too. Damn these people who are always forgetting that! Do you know, I've never fought a duel in my life—never once—and yet have been challenged, like other people. I could always see the other man's unoffending women folks or his little children standing between him and me. *They* hadn't done anything—I couldn't break *their* hearts, you know."

He corrected a good many little abuses in the course of the day, and always without friction—always with a fine and dainty "diplomacy" which left no sting behind; and he got such happiness and such contentment out of these performances that I was obliged to envy him his trade—and perhaps would have adopted it if I could have managed the necessary deflections from fact as confidently with my mouth as I believe I could with a pen, behind the shelter of print, after a little practice.

Away late that night we were coming uptown in a horse-car when three boisterous roughs got aboard, and began to fling hilarious obscenities and profanities right and left among the timid passengers, some of whom were women and children. Nobody resisted or retorted; the conductor tried soothing words and moral suasion, but the roughs only called him names and laughed at him. Very soon I saw that the Major realized that this was a matter which was in his line; evidently he was turning over his stock of diplomacy in his mind and getting ready. I felt that the first diplomatic remark he made in this place would bring down a land-slide of ridicule upon him and maybe something worse; but before I could whisper to him and check him, he had begun, and it was too late. He said, in a level and dispassionate tone:

"Conductor, you must put these swine out. I will help you."

I was not looking for that. In a flash the three roughs plunged at him. But none of them arrived. He delivered three such blows as one could not expect to encounter outside the prize-ring, and neither of the men had life enough left in him to get up from where he fell. The Major dragged them out and threw them off the car, and we got under way again.

I was astonished; astonished to see a lamb act so; astonished at the strength displayed, and the clean and comprehensive result; astonished at the brisk and business-like style of the whole thing. The situation had a humorous side to it, considering how much I had been hearing about mild persuasion and gentle diplomacy all day from this pile-driver, and I would have liked to call his attention to that feature and do some sarcasms about it; but when I looked at him I saw that it would be of no use—his placid and contented face had no ray of humor in it; he would not have understood. When we left the car, I said:

"That was a good stroke of diplomacy—three good strokes of diplomacy, in fact."

"*That?* That wasn't diplomacy. You are quite in the wrong. Diplomacy is a wholly different thing. One cannot apply it to that sort, they would not understand it. No, that was not diplomacy; it was force."

"Now that you mention it, I—yes, I think perhaps you are right."

"Right? Of course I am right. It was just force."

"I think, myself, it had an outside aspect of it. Do you often have to reform people in that way?"

"Far from it. It hardly ever happens. Not oftener than once in half a year, at the outside."

"Those men will get well?"

"Get well? Why, certainly they will. They are not in any danger. I know how to hit and where to hit. You noticed that I did not hit them under the jaw. That would have killed them."

I believed that. I remarked—rather wittily, as I thought—that he had been a lamb all day, but now had all of a sudden developed into a ram—battering-ram; but with dulcet frankness and simplicity he said no, a battering-ram was quite a different thing and not in use now. This was maddening, and I came near bursting out and saying he had no more appreciation of wit than a jackass—in fact, I had it right on my tongue, but did not say it, knowing there was no hurry and I could say it just as well some other time over the telephone.

We started to Boston the next afternoon. The smoking-compartment in the parlor-car was full, and we went into the regular smoker. Across the aisle in the front seat sat a meek, farmer-looking old man with a sickly pallor in his face, and he was holding the door open with his foot to get the air. Presently a big brakeman came rushing through, and when he got to the door he stopped, gave the farmer an ugly scowl, then wrenched the door to with such energy as to almost snatch the old man's boot off. Then on he plunged about his business. Several passengers laughed, and the old gentleman looked pathetically shamed and grieved.

After a little the conductor passed along, and the Major stopped him and asked him a question in his habitually courteous way:

"Conductor, where does one report the misconduct of a brakeman? Does one report to you?"

"You can report him at New Haven if you want to. What has he been doing?"

The Major told the story. The conductor seemed amused. He said, with just a touch of sarcasm in his bland tones:

"As I understand you, the brakeman didn't *say* anything."

"No, he didn't say anything."

"But he scowled, you say."

"Yes."

"And snatched the door loose in a rough way."

"Yes."

"That's the whole business, is it?"

"Yes, that is the whole of it."

The conductor smiled pleasantly, and said:

"Well, if you want to report him, all right, but I don't quite make out what it's going to amount to. You'll say—as I understand you—that the brakeman insulted this old gentleman. They'll ask you what he *said*. You'll say he didn't say anything at all. I reckon they'll say, how are you going to make out an insult when you acknowledge yourself that he didn't say a word."

There was a murmur of applause at the conductor's compact reasoning, and it gave him pleasure—you could see it in his face. But the Major was not disturbed. He said:

"There—now you have touched upon a crying defect in the complaint-system. The railway officials—as the public think and as you also seem to think—are not aware that there are any kind of insults except *spoken* ones. So nobody goes to headquarters and reports insults of manners, insults of gestures, look, and so forth; and yet these are sometimes harder to bear than any words. They are bitter hard to bear because there is nothing tangible to take hold of; and the insulter can always say, if called before the railway officials, that he never dreamed of intending any offence. It seems to me that the officials ought to specially and urgently request the public to report *unworded* affronts and incivilities."

The conductor laughed, and said:

"Well, that *would* be trimming it pretty fine, sure!"

"But not too fine, I think. I will report this matter at New Haven, and I have an idea that I'll be thanked for it."

The conductor's face lost something of its complacency; in fact, it settled to a quite sober cast as the owner of it moved away. I said:

"You are not really going to bother with that trifle, are you?"

"It isn't a trifle. Such things ought always to be reported. It is a public duty, and no citizen has a right to shirk it. But I sha'n't have to report this case."

"Why?"

"It won't be necessary. Diplomacy will do the business. You'll see."

Presently the conductor came on his rounds again, and when he reached the Major he leaned over and said:

"That's all right. You needn't report him. He's responsible to me, and if he does it again I'll give him a talking to."

The Major's response was cordial:

"Now that is what I like! You mustn't think that I was moved by any vengeful spirit, for that wasn't the case. It was duty—just a sense of duty, that was all. My brother-in-law is one of the directors of the road, and when he learns that you are going to reason with your brakeman the very next time he brutally insults an unoffending old man it will please him, you may be sure of that."

The conductor did not look as joyous as one might have thought he would, but on the contrary looked sickly and uncomfortable. He stood around a little; then said:

"*I* think something ought to be done to him *now*. I'll discharge him."

"Discharge him? What good would that do? Don't you think it would be better wisdom to teach him better ways and keep him?"

"Well, there's something in that. What would you suggest?"

"He insulted the old gentleman in presence of all these people. How would it do to have him come and apologize in their presence?"

"I'll have him here right off. And I want to say this: If people would do as you've done, and report such things to me instead of keeping mum and going off and blackguarding the road, you'd see a different state of things pretty soon. I'm much obliged to you."

The brakeman came and apologized. After he was gone the Major said:

"Now, you see how simple and easy that was. The ordinary citizen would have accomplished nothing—the brother-in-law of a director can accomplish anything he wants to."

"But are you really the brother-in-law of a director?"

"Always. Always when the public interests require it. I have a brother-in-law on all the boards—everywhere. It saves me a world of trouble."

"It is a good wide relationship."

"Yes. I have over three hundred of them."

"Is the relationship never doubted by a conductor?"

"I have never met with a case. It is the honest truth—I never have."

"Why didn't you let him go ahead and discharge the brakeman, in spite of your favorite policy? You know he deserved it."

The Major answered with something which really had a sort of distant resemblance to impatience:

"If you would stop and think a moment you wouldn't ask such a question as that. Is a brakeman a dog, that nothing but dog's methods will do for him? He is a man, and has a man's fight for life. And he always has a sister, or a mother, or wife and children to support. Always—there are no exceptions. When you take his living away from him you take theirs away too—and what have they done to you? Nothing. And where is the profit in discharging an uncourteous brakeman and hiring another just like him? It's unwisdom. Don't you see that the rational thing to do is to *reform* the brakeman and keep him? Of course it is."

Then he quoted with admiration the conduct of a certain division superintendent of the Consolidated road, in a case where a switchman of two years' experience was negligent once and threw a train off the track and killed several people. Citizens came in a passion to urge the man's dismissal, but the superintendent said:

"No, you are wrong. He has learned his lesson, he will throw no more trains off the track. He is twice as valuable as he was before. I shall keep him."

We had only one more adventure on the trip. Between Hartford and Springfield the train-boy came shouting in with an armful of literature and dropped a sample into a slumbering gentleman's lap, and the man woke up with a start. He was very angry, and he and a couple of friends discussed the outrage with much heat. They sent for the parlor-car conductor and described the matter, and were determined to have the boy expelled from his situation. The three complainants were wealthy Holyoke merchants, and it was evident that the conductor stood in some awe of them. He tried to pacify them, and explained that the boy was not under his authority, but under that of one of the news companies; but he accomplished nothing.

Then the Major volunteered some testimony for the defence. He said:

"I saw it all. You gentlemen have not meant to exaggerate the circumstances, but still that is what you have done. The boy has done nothing more than all train-boys do. If you want to get his ways softened down and his manners reformed, I am with you and ready to help, but it isn't fair to get him discharged without giving him a chance."

But they were angry, and would hear no compromise. They were well acquainted with the president of the Boston & Albany, they said, and would put everything aside next day and go up to Boston and fix that boy.

The Major said he would be on hand too, and would do what he could to save the boy. One of the gentlemen looked him over, and said:

"Apparently it is going to be a matter of who can wield the most influence with the president. Do you know Mr. Bliss personally?"

The Major said, with composure:

"Yes; he is my uncle."

The effect was satisfactory. There was an awkward silence for a minute or more; then the hedging and the half-confessions of overhaste and exaggerated resentment began, and soon everything was smooth and friendly and sociable, and it was resolved to drop the matter and leave the boy's bread-and-butter unmolested.

It turned out as I had expected: the president of the road was not the Major's uncle at all—except by adoption, and for this day and train only.

We got into no episodes on the return journey. Probably it was because we took a night train and slept all the way.

We left New York Saturday night by the Pennsylvania road. After breakfast the next morning we went into the parlor-car, but found it a dull place and dreary. There were but few people in it and nothing going on. Then we went into the little smoking-compartment of the same car and found three gentlemen in there. Two of them were grumbling over one of the rules of the road—a rule which forbade card-playing on the trains on Sunday. They had started an innocent game of high-low-jack and been stopped. The Major was interested. He said to the third gentleman:

"Did you object to the game?"

"Not at all. I am a Yale professor and a religious man, but my prejudices are not extensive."

Then the Major said to the others:

"You are at perfect liberty to resume your game, gentlemen; no one here objects."

One of them declined the risk, but the other one said he would like to begin again if the Major would join him. So they spread an overcoat over their knees and the game proceeded. Pretty soon the parlor-car conductor arrived, and said, brusquely:

"There, there, gentlemen, that won't do. Put up the cards—it's not allowed."

The Major was shuffling. He continued to shuffle, and said:

"By whose order is it forbidden?"

"It's my order. I forbid it."

The dealing began. The Major asked:

"Did you invent the idea?"

"What idea?"

"The idea of forbidding card-playing on Sunday."

"No—of course not."

"Who did?"

"The company."

"Then it isn't your order, after all, but the company's. Is that it?"

"Yes. But you don't stop playing; I have to require you to stop playing immediately."

"Nothing is gained by hurry, and often much is lost. Who authorized the company to issue such an order?"

"My dear sir, that is a matter of no consequence to me, and—"

"But you forget that you are not the only person concerned. It may be a matter of consequence to me. It is indeed a matter of very great importance to me. I cannot violate a legal requirement of my country without dishonoring myself; I cannot allow any man or corporation to hamper my liberties with illegal rules—a thing which railway companies are always trying to do—without dishonoring my citizenship. So I come back to that question: By whose authority has the company issued this order?"

"I don't *know*. That's *their* affair."

"Mine, too. I doubt if the company has any right to issue such a rule. This road runs through several States. Do you know what State we are in now, and what its laws are in matters of this kind?"

"Its laws do not concern me, but the company's orders do. It is my duty to stop this game, gentlemen, and it *must* be stopped."

"Possibly; but still there is no hurry. In hotels they post certain rules in the rooms, but they always quote passages from the State law as authority for these requirements. I see nothing posted here of this sort. Please produce your authority and let us arrive at a decision, for you see yourself that you are marring the game."

"I have nothing of the kind, but I have my orders, and that is sufficient. They must be obeyed."

"Let us not jump to conclusions. It will be better all around to examine into the matter without heat or haste, and see just where we stand before either of us makes a mistake—for the curtailing of the liberties of a citizen of the United States is a much more serious matter than you and the railroads seem to think, and it cannot be done in my person until the curtailer proves his right to do so. Now—"

"My dear sir, *will* you put down those cards?"

"All in good time, perhaps. It depends. You say this order must be obeyed. *Must.* It is a strong word. You see yourself how strong it is. A wise company would not arm you with so drastic an order as this, of *course*, without appointing a penalty for its infringement. Otherwise it runs the risk of being a dead letter and a thing to laugh at. What is the appointed penalty for an infringement of this law?"

"Penalty? I never heard of any."

"Unquestionably you must be mistaken. Your company orders you to come here and rudely break up an innocent amusement, and furnishes you no way to enforce the order? Don't you see that that is nonsense. What do you *do* when people refuse to obey this order? Do you take the cards away from them?"

"No."

"Do you put the offender off at the next station?"

"Well, no—of course we couldn't if he had a ticket."

"Do you have him up before a court?"

The conductor was silent and apparently troubled. The Major started a new deal, and said:

"You see that you are helpless, and that the company has placed you in a foolish position. You are furnished with an arrogant order, and you deliver it in a blustering way, and when you come to look into the matter you find you haven't any way of enforcing obedience."

The conductor said, with chill dignity:

"Gentlemen, you have heard the order, and my duty is ended. As to obeying it or not, you will do as you think fit." And he turned to leave.

"But wait. The matter is not yet finished. I think you are

mistaken about your duty being ended; but if it really is, I myself have a duty to perform yet."

"How do you mean?"

"Are you going to report my disobedience at headquarters in Pittsburg?"

"No. What good would that do?"

"You must report me, or I will report you."

"Report me for what?"

"For disobeying the company's orders in not stopping this game. As a citizen it is my duty to help the railway companies keep their servants to their work."

"Are you in earnest?"

"Yes, I am in earnest. I have nothing against you as a man, but I have this against you as an officer—that you have not carried out that order, and if you do not report me I must report you. And I will."

The conductor looked puzzled, and was thoughtful for a moment; then he burst out with:

"I seem to be getting *myself* into a scrape! It's all a muddle; I can't make head or tail of it; it's never happened before; they always knocked under and never said a word, and so *I* never saw how ridiculous that stupid order with no penalty is. *I* don't want to report anybody, and I don't want to *be* reported—why, it might do me no end of harm! Now *do* go on with the game—play the whole day if you want—and don't let's have any more trouble about it!"

"No, I only sat down here to establish this gentleman's rights—he can have his place now. But before you go won't you tell me what you think the company made this rule for? Can you imagine an excuse for it? I mean a rational one—an excuse that is not on its face silly, and the invention of an idiot?"

"Why, surely I can. The reason it was made is plain enough. It is to save the feelings of the other passengers—the religious ones among them, I mean. They would not like it, to have the Sabbath desecrated by card-playing on the train."

"I just thought as much. They are willing to desecrate it themselves by travelling on Sunday, but they are not willing that other people—"

"By gracious, you've hit it! I never thought of that before. The fact is, it *is* a silly rule when you come to look into it."

At this point the train-conductor arrived, and was going to shut down the game in a very high-handed fashion, but the parlor-car conductor stopped him and took him aside to explain. Nothing more was heard of the matter.

I was ill in bed eleven days in Chicago and got no glimpse of the Fair, for I was obliged to return east as soon as I was able to travel. The Major secured and paid for a state-room in a sleeper the day before we left, so that I could have plenty of room and be comfortable; but when we arrived at the station a mistake had been made and our car had not been put on. The conductor had reserved a section for us—it was the best he could do, he said. But the Major said we were not in a hurry, and would wait for the car to be put on. The conductor responded, with pleasant irony:

"It may be that *you* are not in a hurry, just as you say, but we *are:* Come, get aboard, gentlemen, get aboard—don't keep us waiting."

But the Major would not get aboard himself nor allow me to do it. He wanted his car, and said he must have it. This made the hurried and perspiring conductor impatient, and he said:

"It's the best we can *do*—we can't do impossibilities. You will take the section or go without. A mistake has been made and can't be rectified at this late hour. It's a thing that happens now and then, and there is nothing for it but to put up with it and make the best of it. Other people do."

"Ah, that is just it, you see. If they had stuck to their rights and enforced them you wouldn't be trying to trample mine underfoot in this bland way now. I haven't any disposition to give you unnecessary trouble, but it is my duty to protect the next man from this kind of imposition. So I must have my car. Otherwise I will wait in Chicago and sue the company for violating its contract."

"Sue the company?—for a thing like that!"

"Certainly."

"Do you really mean that?"

"Indeed, I do."

The conductor looked the Major over wonderingly, and then said:

"It beats me—it's bran-new—I've never struck the mate to it before. But I swear I think you'd do it. Look here, I'll send for the station-master."

When the station-master came he was a good deal annoyed—at the Major, not at the person who had made the mistake. He was rather brusque, and took the same position which the conductor had taken in the beginning; but he failed to move the soft-spoken artilleryman, who still insisted that he must have his car. However, it was plain that there was only one strong side in this case, and that that side was the Major's. The station-master banished his annoyed manner, and became pleasant and even half-apologetic. This made a good opening for a compromise, and the Major made a concession. He said he would give up the engaged state-room, but he must have *a* state-room. After a deal of ransacking, one was found whose owner was persuadable; he exchanged it for our section, and we got away at last. The conductor called on us in the evening, and was kind and courteous and obliging, and we had a long talk and got to be good friends. He said he wished the public would make trouble oftener—it would have a good effect. He said that the railroads could not be expected to do their whole duty by the traveller unless the traveller would take some interest in the matter himself.

I hoped that we were done reforming for the trip now, but it was not so. In the hotel-car, in the morning, the Major called for broiled chicken. The waiter said:

"It's not in the bill of fare, sir; we do not serve anything but what is in the bill."

"That gentleman yonder is eating a broiled chicken."

"Yes, but that is different. He is one of the superintendents of the road."

"Then all the more must I have broiled chicken. I do not like these discriminations. Please hurry—bring me a broiled chicken."

The waiter brought the steward, who explained in a low and polite voice that the thing was impossible—it was against the rule, and the rule was rigid.

"Very well, then, you must either apply it impartially or break it impartially. You must take that gentleman's chicken away from him or bring me one."

The steward was puzzled, and did not quite know what to do. He began an incoherent argument, but the conductor came along just then, and asked what the difficulty was. The steward explained that here was a gentleman who was insisting on having a chicken when it was dead against the rule and not in the bill. The conductor said:

"Stick by your rules—you haven't any option. Wait a minute—is this the gentleman?" Then he laughed and said: "Never mind your rules—it's my advice, and sound; give him anything he wants—don't get him started on his rights. Give him whatever he asks for; and if you haven't got it, stop the train and get it."

The Major ate the chicken, but said he did it from a sense of duty and to establish a principle, for he did not like chicken.

I missed the Fair it is true, but I picked up some diplomatic tricks which I and the reader may find handy and useful as we go along.

"The Loves of Alonzo Fitz Clarence and Rosannah Ethelton" appeared in March, 1878, in the Atlantic *magazine and almost simultaneously in a collection of sketches called* Punch, Brothers, Punch! *That same year it was also published separately in pamphlet form in The Chimney Corner Series.*

The Loves of Alonzo Fitz Clarence and Rosannah Ethelton

I

It was well along in the forenoon of a bitter winter's day. The town of Eastport, in the State of Maine, lay buried under a deep snow that was newly fallen. The customary bustle in the streets was wanting. One could look long distances down them and see nothing but a dead-white emptiness, with silence to match. Of course I do not mean that you could *see* the silence,—no, you could only hear it. The sidewalks were merely long, deep ditches, with steep snow walls on either side. Here and there you might hear the faint, far scrape of a wooden shovel, and if you were quick enough you might catch a glimpse of a distant black figure stooping and disappearing in one of those ditches, and reappearing the next moment with a motion which you would know meant the heaving out of a shovelful of snow. But you needed to be quick, for that black figure would not linger, but would soon drop that shovel and scud for the house, thrashing itself with its arms to warm them. Yes, it was too venomously cold for snow shovelers or any body else to stay out long.

Presently the sky darkened; then the wind rose and began to blow in fitful, vigorous gusts, which sent clouds of powdery snow aloft, and straight ahead, and everywhere. Under the impulse of one of these gusts, great white drifts banked themselves like graves across the streets; a moment later, another gust shifted them around the other way, driving a fine spray of snow from their sharp crests, as the gale drives the spume-flakes from wave-crests at sea; a third gust swept that place as clean as your hand, if it saw fit. This was fooling, this was play; but each and all of the gusts dumped some snow into the sidewalk ditches, for that was business.

Alonzo Fitz Clarence was sitting in his snug and elegant little parlor, in a lovely blue silk dressing-gown, with cuffs and facings of crimson satin, elaborately quilted. The remains of his breakfast were before him, and the dainty and costly little table service added a harmonious charm to the grace, beauty, and richness of the fixed appointments of the room. A cheery fire was blazing on the hearth.

A furious gust of wind shook the windows, and a great wave of snow washed against them with a drenching sound, so to speak. The handsome young bachelor murmured—

"That means, no going out to-day. Well, I am content. But what to do for company? Mother is well enough, aunt Susan is well enough; but these, like the poor, I have with me always. On so grim a day as this, one needs a new interest, a fresh element, to whet the dull edge of captivity. That was very neatly said, but it doesn't mean any thing. One doesn't *want* the edge of captivity sharpened up, you know, but just the reverse."

He glanced at his pretty French mantel clock.

"That clock's wrong again. That clock hardly ever knows what time it is; and when it does know, it lies about it—which amounts to the same thing. Alfred!"

There was no answer.

"Alfred!—Good servant, but as uncertain as the clock."

Alonzo touched an electrical bell-button in the wall. He waited a moment, then touched it again; waited a few moments more, and said—

"Battery out of order, no doubt. But now that I have started, I *will* find out what time it is." He stepped to a speaking-tube in the wall, blew its whistle, and called, "Mother!" and repeated it twice.

"Well, *that's* no use. Mother's battery is out of order, too. Can't raise any body down-stairs—that is plain."

He sat down at a rose-wood desk, leaned his chin on the left-hand edge of it, and spoke, as if to the floor: "Aunt Susan!"

A low, pleasant voice answered, "Is that you, Alonzo?"

"Yes. I'm too lazy and comfortable to go downstairs; I am in extremity, and I can't seem to scare up any help."

"Dear me, what is the matter?"

"Matter enough, I can tell you!"

"Oh, don't keep me in suspense, dear! What *is* it?"

"I want to know what time it is."

"You abominable boy, what a turn you did give me! Is that all?"

"All—on my honor. Calm yourself. Tell me the time, and receive my blessing."

"Just five minutes after nine. No charge—keep your blessing."

"Thanks. It wouldn't have impoverished me, aunty, nor so enriched you that you could live without other means." He got up, murmuring, "Just five minutes after nine," and faced his clock. "Ah," said he, "you are doing better than usual. You are only thirty-four minutes wrong. Let me see—let me see—Thirty-three and twenty-one are fifty-four; four times fifty-four are two hundred and thirty-six. One off, leaves two hundred and thirty-five. That's right."

He turned the hands of the clock forward till they marked twenty-five minutes to one, and said, "Now see if you can't keep right for a while—else I'll raffle you!"

He sat down at the desk again, and said, "Aunt Susan!"

"Yes, dear."

"Had breakfast?"

"Yes indeed, an hour ago."

"Busy?"

"No—except sewing. Why?"

"Got any company?"

"No, but I expect some at half past nine."

"I wish *I* did. I'm lonesome. I want to talk to somebody."

"Very well, talk to me."

"But this is very private."

"Don't be afraid—talk right along; there's nobody here but me."

"I hardly know whether to venture or not, but—"

"But what? Oh, don't stop there! You *know* you can trust me, Alonzo—you know you can."

"I feel it, aunt, but this is very serious. It affects me deeply—me, and all the family—even the whole community."

"Oh, Alonzo, tell me! I will never breathe a word of it. What is it?"

"Aunt, if I might dare—"

"Oh, please go on! I love you, and can feel for you. Tell me all. Confide in me. What *is* it?"

"The weather!"

"Plague take the weather! I don't see how you can have the heart to serve me so, Lon."

"There, there, aunty dear, I'm sorry; I am, on my honor. I won't do it again. Do you forgive me?"

"Yes, since you seem so sincere about it, though I know I oughtn't to. You will fool me again as soon as I have forgotten this time."

"No, I won't, honor bright. But such weather, oh, such weather! You've *got* to keep your spirits up artificially. It is snowy, and blowy, and gusty, and bitter cold! How is the weather with you?"

"Warm and rainy and melancholy. The mourners go about the streets with their umbrellas running streams from the end of every whalebone. There's an elevated double pavement of umbrellas stretching down the sides of the streets as far as I can see. I've got a fire for cheerfulness, and the windows open to keep cool. But it is vain, it is useless: nothing comes in but the balmy breath of December, with its burden of mocking odors from the flowers that possess the realm outside, and rejoice in their lawless profusion whilst the spirit of man is low, and flaunt their gaudy splendors in his face whilst his soul is clothed in sackcloth and ashes and his heart breaketh."

Alonzo opened his lips to say, "You ought to print that, and get it framed," but checked himself, for he heard his aunt speaking to some one else. He went and stood at the window and looked out upon the wintry prospect. The storm was driving the snow before it more furiously than ever; window shutters were slamming and banging; a forlorn dog, with bowed head and tail withdrawn from service, was pressing his quaking body against a windward wall for shelter and protection; a young girl was plowing knee-deep through the drifts, with her face turned from the blast, and the cape of her water-proof blowing straight rearward over her head. Alonzo shuddered, and said with a sigh, "Better the slop, and the sultry rain, and even the insolent flowers, than this!"

He turned from the window, moved a step, and stopped in a listening attitude. The faint, sweet notes of a familiar song caught his ear. He remained there, with his head unconsciously bent forward, drinking in the melody, stirring neither hand nor foot, hardly breathing. There was a blemish in the execution of the song, but to Alonzo it seemed an added charm instead of a defect. This blemish consisted of a marked flatting of the third, fourth, fifth, sixth, and seventh notes of the refrain or chorus of the piece. When the music ended, Alonzo drew a deep breath, and said, "Ah, I never heard 'In the Sweet By and By' sung like that before!"

He stepped quickly to the desk, listened a moment, and said in a guarded, confidential voice, "Aunty, who is this divine singer?"

"She is the company I was expecting. Stays with me a month or two. I will introduce you. Miss—"

"For goodness' sake, wait a moment, Aunt Susan! You never stop to think what you are about!"

He flew to his bed-chamber, and returned in a moment perceptibly changed in his outward appearance, and remarking, snappishly—

"Hang it, she would have introduced me to this angel in that sky-blue dressing-gown with red-hot lapels! Women never think, when they get a-going."

He hastened and stood by the desk, and said eagerly, "Now, aunty, I am ready," and fell to smiling and bowing with all the persuasiveness and elegance that were in him.

"Very well. Miss Rosannah Ethelton, let me introduce to you my favorite nephew, Mr. Alonzo Fitz Clarence. There! You are both good people, and I like you; so I am going to trust you together while I attend to a few household affairs. Sit down, Rosannah; sit down, Alonzo. Good-by; I shan't be gone long."

Alonzo had been bowing and smiling all the while, and motioning imaginary young ladies to sit down in imaginary chairs, but now he took a seat himself, mentally saying, "Oh, this is luck! Let the winds blow now, and the snow drive, and the heavens frown! Little I care!"

While these young people chat themselves into an acquaintanceship, let us take the liberty of inspecting the sweeter and fairer of the two. She sat alone, at her graceful ease, in a richly furnished apartment which was manifestly the private parlor of a refined and sensible lady, if signs and symbols may go for anything. For instance, by a low, comfortable chair stood a dainty, top-heavy work-stand, whose summit was a fancifully embroidered shallow basket, with vari-colored crewels, and other strings and odds and ends, protruding from under the gaping lid and hanging down in negligent profusion. On the floor lay bright shreds of Turkey red, Prussian blue, and kindred fabrics, bits of ribbon, a spool or two, a pair of scissors, and a roll or so of tinted silken stuffs. On a luxurious sofa upholstered with some sort of soft Indian goods wrought in black and gold threads interwebbed with other threads not so pronounced in color, lay a great square of coarse white stuff, upon whose surface a rich bouquet of flowers was growing, under the deft cultivation of the crochet needle. The household cat was asleep on this work of art. In a bay-window stood an easel with an unfinished picture on it, and a palette and brushes on a chair beside it. There were books everywhere: Robertson's Sermons, Tennyson, Moody and Sankey, Hawthorne, Rab and his Friends, cook-books, prayer-books, pattern-books, and books about all kinds of odious and exasperating pottery, of course. There was a piano, with a deck-load of music, and more in a tender. There was a great plenty of pictures on the walls, on the shelves of the mantel-piece, and around generally; where coigns of vantage offered were statuettes, and quaint and pretty gimcracks, and rare and costly specimens of peculiarly devilish china. The bay-window gave upon a garden that was ablaze with foreign and domestic flowers and flowering shrubs.

But the sweet young girl was the daintiest thing those premises, within or without, could offer for contemplation: delicately chiseled features, of Grecian cast; her complexion the pure snow of a japonica that is receiving a faint reflected enrichment from some scarlet neighbor of the garden; great, soft, blue eyes fringed with long, curving lashes; an expression made up of the trustfulness of a child and the gentleness of a fawn; a beautiful head crowned with its own prodigal gold; a lithe and rounded figure, whose every attitude and movement were instinct with native grace.

Her dress and adornment were marked by that exquisite harmony that can come only of a fine natural taste perfected by culture. Her gown was of a simple magenta tulle, cut bias, traversed by three rows of light blue flounces, with the selvage edges turned up with ashes-of-roses chenille; overdress of dark bay tarleton, with scarlet satin lambrequins; corn-colored polonaise, *en panier*, looped with mother-of-pearl buttons and silver cord, and hauled aft and made fast by buff-velvet lashings; basque of lavender reps, picked out with valenciennes; low neck, short sleeves; maroon-velvet necktie edged with delicate pink silk; inside handkerchief of some simple three-ply ingrain fabric of a soft saffron tint; coral bracelets and locket-chain; coiffure of forget-me-nots and lilies of the valley massed around a noble calla.

This was all; yet even in this subdued attire she was divinely beautiful. Then what must she have been when adorned for the festival or the ball?

All this time she has been busily chatting with Alonzo, unconscious of our inspection. The minutes still sped, and still she talked. But by and by she happened to look up, and saw the clock. A crimson blush sent its rich flood through her cheeks, and she exclaimed—

"There, good-by, Mr. Fitz Clarence; I must go now!"

She sprang from her chair with such haste that she hardly heard the young man's answering good-by. She stood radiant, graceful, beautiful, and gazed, wondering, upon the accusing clock. Presently her pouting lips parted, and she said—

"Five minutes after eleven! Nearly two hours, and it did not seem twenty minutes! Oh, dear, what will he think of me!"

At the self-same moment Alonzo was staring at *his* clock. And presently he said—

"Twenty-five minutes to three! Nearly two hours, and I didn't believe it was two minutes! Is it possible that this clock is humbugging again? Miss Ethelton! Just one moment, please. Are you there yet?"

"Yes, but be quick; I'm going right away."

"Would you be so kind as to tell me what time it is?"

The girl blushed again, murmured to herself, "It's right down cruel of him to ask me!" and then spoke up and answered with admirably counterfeited unconcern, "Five minutes after eleven."

"Oh, thank you! You have to go now, have you?"

"Yes."

"I'm sorry."

No reply.

"Miss Ethelton!"

"Well?"

"You—you're there yet, *ain't* you?"

"Yes, but please hurry. What did you want to say?"

"Well, I—well, nothing in particular. It's very lonesome here. It's asking a great deal, I know, but would you mind talking with me again by and by—that is, if it will not trouble you too much?"

"I don't know—but I'll think about it. I'll try."

"O thanks! Miss Ethelton?—Ah me, she's gone, and here are the black clouds and the whirling snow and the raging winds come again! But she said *good-by!* She didn't say good morning, she said good-by!—The clock was right, after all. What a lightning-winged two hours it was!"

He sat down, and gazed dreamily into his fire for a while, then heaved a sigh and said—

"How wonderful it is! Two little hours ago I was a free man, and now my heart's in San Francisco!"

About that time Rosannah Ethelton, propped in the window-seat of her bed-chamber, book in hand, was gazing vacantly out over the rainy seas that washed the Golden Gate, and whispering to herself, "How different he is from poor Burley, with his empty head and his single little antic talent of mimicry!"

II

Six weeks later Mr. Sydney Algernon Burley was entertaining a gay luncheon company, in a sumptuous drawing-room on Telegraph Hill, with some capital imitations of the voices and gestures of certain popular actors and San Franciscan literary people and Bonanza grandees. He was elegantly upholstered, and was a handsome fellow, barring a trifling cast in his eye. He seemed very jovial, but nevertheless he kept his eye on the door with an expectant and uneasy watchfulness. By and by a nobby lackey appeared, and delivered a message to the mistress, who nodded her head understandingly. That seemed to settle the thing for Mr. Burley; his vivacity decreased little by little, and a dejected look began to creep into one of his eyes and a sinister one into the other.

The rest of the company departed in due time, leaving him with the mistress, to whom he said—

"There is no longer any question about it. She avoids me. She continually excuses herself. If I could see her, if I could speak to her only a moment,—but this suspense—"

"Perhaps her seeming avoidance is mere accident, Mr. Burley. Go to the small drawing-room up-stairs and amuse yourself a moment. I will dispatch a household order that is on my mind, and then I will go to her room. Without doubt she will be persuaded to see you."

Mr. Burley went up-stairs, intending to go to the small drawing-room, but as he was passing "aunt Susan's" private parlor, the door of which stood slightly ajar, he heard a joyous laugh which he recognized; so without knock or announcement he stepped confidently in. But before he could make his presence known he heard words that harrowed up his soul and chilled his young blood. He heard a voice say—

"Darling, it has come!"

Then he heard Rosannah Ethelton, whose back was toward him, say—

"So has yours, dearest!"

He saw her bowed form bend lower; he heard her kiss something—not merely once, but again and again! His soul raged within him. The heart-breaking conversation went on:

"Rosannah, I knew you must be beautiful, but this is dazzling, this is blinding, this is intoxicating!"

"Alonzo, it is such happiness to hear you say it. I know it is not true, but I am *so* grateful to have you think it is, nevertheless! I knew you must have a noble face, but the grace and majesty of the reality beggar the poor creation of my fancy."

Burley heard the rattling shower of kisses again.

"Thank you, my Rosannah! The photograph flatters me, but you must not allow yourself to think of that. Sweetheart?"

"Yes, Alonzo."

"I am so happy, Rosannah."

"Oh, Alonzo, none that have gone before me knew what love was, none that come after me will ever know what happiness is. I float in a gorgeous cloudland, a boundless firmament of enchanted and bewildering ecstasy!"

"Oh, my Rosannah!—for you are mine, are you not?"

"Wholly, oh, wholly yours, Alonzo, now and forever! All the day long, and all through my nightly dreams, one song sings itself, and its sweet burden is, 'Alonzo Fitz Clarence, Alonzo Fitz Clarence, Eastport, State of Maine!' "

"Curse him, I've got his address, any way!" roared Burley inwardly, and rushed from the place.

Just behind the unconscious Alonzo stood his mother, a picture of astonishment. She was so muffled from head to heel in furs that nothing of herself was visible but her eyes and nose. She was a good allegory of winter, for she was powdered all over with snow.

Behind the unconscious Rosannah stood "aunt Susan," another picture of astonishment. She was a good allegory of summer, for she was lightly clad, and was vigorously cooling the perspiration on her face with a fan.

Both of these women had tears of joy in their eyes.

"So ho!" exclaimed Mrs. Fitz Clarence, "this explains why nobody has been able to drag you out of your room for six weeks, Alonzo!"

"So ho!" exclaimed Aunt Susan, "this explains why you have been a hermit for the past six weeks, Rosannah!"

The young people were on their feet in an instant, abashed, and standing like detected dealers in stolen goods awaiting Judge Lynch's doom.

"Bless you, my son! I am happy in your happiness. Come to your mother's arms, Alonzo!"

"Bless you, Rosannah, for my dear nephew's sake! Come to my arms!"

Then was there a mingling of hearts and tears of rejoicing on Telegraph Hill and in Eastport Square.

Servants were called by the elders, in both places. Unto one was given the order, "Pile this fire high with hickory wood, and bring me a roasting-hot lemonade."

Unto the other was given the order, "Put out this fire, and bring me two palm-leaf fans and a pitcher of ice-water."

Then the young people were dismissed, and the elders sat down to talk the sweet surprise over and make the wedding plans.

Some minutes before this Mr. Burley rushed from the mansion on Telegraph Hill without meeting or taking formal leave of anybody. He hissed through his teeth in unconscious imitation of a popular favorite in melodrama, "Him shall she never wed! I have sworn it! Ere great Nature shall have doffed her winter's ermine to don the emerald gauds of spring, she shall be mine!"

III

Two weeks later. Every few hours, during some three or four days, a very prim and devout looking Episcopal clergyman, with a cast in his eye, had visited Alonzo. According to his card, he was the Rev. Melton Hargrave, of Cincinnati. He said he had retired from the ministry on account of his health. If he had said on account of ill health, he would probably have erred, to judge by his wholesome looks and firm build. He was the inventor of an improvement in telephones, and hoped to make his bread by selling the privilege of using it. "At present," he continued, "a man may go and tap a telegraph wire which is conveying a song or a concert from one State to another, and he can attach his private telephone and steal a hearing of that music as it passes along. My invention will stop all that."

"Well," answered Alonzo, "if the owner of the music could not miss what was stolen, why should he care?"

"He shouldn't care," said the Reverend.

"Well?" said Alonzo, inquiringly.

"Suppose," replied the Reverend, "suppose that instead of music that was passing along and being stolen, the burden of the wire was loving endearments of the most private and sacred nature?"

Alonzo shuddered from head to heel. "Sir, it is a priceless invention," said he; "I must have it at any cost."

But the invention was delayed somewhere on the road from Cincinnati, most unaccountably. The impatient Alonzo could hardly wait. The thought of Rosannah's sweet words being shared with him by some ribald thief was galling to him. The Reverend came frequently and lamented the delay, and told of measures he had taken to hurry things up. This was some little comfort to Alonzo.

One forenoon the Reverend ascended the stairs, and knocked

at Alonzo's door. There was no response. He entered, glanced eagerly around, closed the door softly, then ran to the telephone. The exquisitely soft remote strains of the "Sweet By and By" came floating through the instrument. The singer was flatting, as usual, the five notes that follow the first two in the chorus, when the Reverend interrupted her with this word, in a voice which was an exact imitation of Alonzo's, with just the faintest flavor of impatience added—

"Sweetheart?"

"Yes, Alonzo?"

"Please don't sing that any more this week—try something modern."

The agile step that goes with a happy heart was heard on the stairs, and the Reverend, smiling diabolically, sought sudden refuge behind the heavy folds of the velvet window curtains. Alonzo entered and flew to the telephone. Said he—

"Rosannah, dear, shall we sing something together?"

"Something *modern?*" asked she, with sarcastic bitterness.

"Yes, if you prefer."

"Sing it yourself, if you like!"

This snappishness amazed and wounded the young man. He said—

Rosannah, that was not like you."

"I suppose it becomes me as much as your very polite speech became you, Mr. Fitz Clarence."

"*Mister* Fitz Clarence! Rosannah, there was nothing impolite about my speech."

"Oh, indeed! Of course, then, I misunderstood you, and I most humbly beg your pardon, ha-ha-ha! No doubt you said, 'Don't sing it any more *to-day.*' "

"Sing *what* any more to-day?"

"The song you mentioned, of course. How very obtuse we are, all of a sudden!"

"I never mentioned any song."

"Oh, you *didn't!*"

"No, I *didn't!*"

"I am compelled to remark that you *did.*"

"And I am obliged to reiterate that I *didn't.*"

"A second rudeness! That is sufficient, sir. I will never forgive you. All is over between us."

Then came a muffled sound of crying. Alonzo hastened to say—

"Oh, Rosannah, unsay those words! There is some dreadful mystery here, some hideous mistake. I am utterly earnest and sincere when I say I never said any thing about any song. I would not hurt you for the whole world . . . Rosannah, dear? . . . Oh, speak to me, won't you?"

There was a pause; then Alonzo heard the girl's sobbings retreating, and knew she had gone from the telephone. He rose with a heavy sigh, and hastened from the room, saying to himself, "I will ransack the charity missions and the haunts of the poor for my mother. She will persuade her that I never meant to wound her."

A minute later, the Reverend was crouching over the telephone like a cat that knoweth the ways of the prey. He had not very many minutes to wait. A soft repentant voice, tremulous with tears, said—

"Alonzo, dear, I have been wrong. You *could* not have said so cruel a thing. It must have been some one who imitated your voice in malice or in jest."

The Reverend coldly answered, in Alonzo's tones—

"You have said all was over between us. So let it be. I spurn your proffered repentance, and despise it!"

Then he departed, radiant with fiendish triumph, to return no more with his imaginary telephonic invention forever.

Four hours afterward, Alonzo arrived with his mother from her favorite haunts of poverty and vice. They summoned the San Francisco household; but there was no reply. They waited, and continued to wait, upon the voiceless telephone.

At length, when it was sunset in San Francisco, and three hours and a half after dark in Eastport, an answer came to the oft-repeated cry of "Rosannah!"

But, alas, it was aunt Susan's voice that spake. She said—

"I have been out all day; just got in. I will go and find her."

The watchers waited two minutes—five minutes—ten minutes. Then came these fatal words, in a frightened tone—

"She is gone, and her baggage with her. To visit another friend, she told the servants. But I found this note on the table in her room. Listen: 'I am gone; seek not to trace me out; my heart is broken; you will never see me more. Tell him I shall always think of him when I sing my poor 'Sweet By and By,' but never of the unkind words he said about it.' That is her note. Alonzo, Alonzo, what does it mean? What has happened?"

But Alonzo sat white and cold as the dead. His mother threw back the velvet curtains and opened a window. The cold air refreshed the sufferer, and he told his aunt his dismal story. Meantime his mother was inspecting a card which had disclosed itself upon the floor when she cast the curtains back. It read, "Mr. Sidney Algernon Burley, San Francisco."

"The miscreant!" shouted Alonzo, and rushed forth to seek

the false Reverend and destroy him; for the card explained every thing, since in the course of the lovers' mutual confessions they had told each other all about all the sweethearts they had ever had, and thrown no end of mud at their failings and foibles—for lovers always do that. It has a fascination that ranks next after billing and cooing.

IV

During the next two months, many things happened. It had early transpired that Rosannah, poor suffering orphan, had neither returned to her grandmother in Portland, Oregon, nor sent any word to her save a duplicate of the woful note she had left in the mansion on Telegraph Hill. Whosoever was sheltering her—if she was still alive—had been persuaded not to betray her whereabouts, without doubt; for all efforts to find trace of her had failed.

Did Alonzo give her up? Not he. He said to himself, "She will sing that sweet song when she is sad; I shall find her." So he took his carpet sack and a portable telephone, and shook the snow of his native city from his arctics, and went forth into the world. He wandered far and wide and in many States. Time and again, strangers were astounded to see a wasted, pale, and woe-worn man laboriously climb a telegraph pole in wintry and lonely places, perch sadly there an hour, with his ear at a little box, then come sighing down, and wander wearily away. Sometimes they shot at him, as peasants do at aeronauts, thinking him mad and dangerous. Thus his clothes were much shredded by bullets and his person grievously lacerated. But he bore it all patiently.

In the beginning of his pilgrimage he used often to say, "Ah, if I could but hear the 'Sweet By and By!' But toward the end of it he used to shed tears of anguish and say, "Ah, if I could but hear something else!"

Thus a month and three weeks drifted by, and at last some humane people seized him and confined him in a private mad-house in New York. He made no moan, for his strength was all gone, and with it all heart and all hope. The superintendent, in pity, gave up his own comfortable parlor and bed-chamber to him and nursed him with affectionate devotion.

At the end of a week the patient was able to leave his bed for the first time. He was lying, comfortably pillowed, on a sofa, listening to the plaintive Miserere of the bleak March winds, and the muffled sound of tramping feet in the street below—for it was about six in the evening, and New York was going home from work. He had a bright fire and the added cheer of a couple of student lamps. So it was warm and snug within, though bleak and raw without; it was light and bright within, though outside it was as dark and dreary as if the world had been lit with Hartford gas. Alonzo smiled feebly to think how his loving vagaries had made him a maniac in the eyes of the world, and was proceeding to pursue his line of thought further, when a faint, sweet strain, the very ghost of sound, so remote and attenuated it seemed, struck upon his ear. His pulses stood still; he listened with parted lips and bated breath. The song flowed on—he waiting, listening, rising slowly and unconsciously from his recumbent position. At last he exclaimed—

"It is! it is she! Oh, the divine flatted notes!"

He dragged himself eagerly to the corner whence the sounds proceeded, tore aside a curtain, and discovered a telephone. He bent over, and as the last note died away he burst forth with the exclamation—

"Oh, thank Heaven, found at last! Speak to me, Rosannah, dearest! The cruel mystery has been unravelled; it was the villain Burley who mimicked my voice and wounded you with insolent speech!"

There was a breathless pause, a waiting age to Alonzo; then a faint sound came, framing itself into language—

"Oh, say those precious words again, Alonzo!"

"They are the truth, the veritable truth, my Rosannah, and you shall have the proof, ample and abundant proof!"

"Oh, Alonzo, stay by me! Leave me not for a moment! Let me feel that you are near me! Tell me we shall never be parted more! Oh, this happy hour, this blessed hour, this memorable hour!"

"We will make record of it, my Rosannah; every year, as this dear hour chimes from the clock, we will celebrate it with thanksgivings, all the years of our life."

"We will, we will, Alonzo!"

"Four minutes after six, in the evening, my Rosannah, shall henceforth—"

"Twenty-three minutes after twelve, afternoon, shall—"

"Why, Rosannah, darling, where are you?"

"In Honolulu, Sandwich Islands. And where are you? Stay by me; do not leave me for a moment. I cannot bear it. Are you at home?"

"No, dear, I am in New York—a patient in the doctor's hands."

An agonizing shriek came buzzing to Alonzo's ear, like the

sharp buzzing of a hurt gnat; it lost power in travelling five thousand miles. Alonzo hastened to say—

"Calm yourself, my child. It is nothing. Already I am getting well under the sweet healing of your presence. Rosannah?"

"Yes, Alonzo? Oh, how you terrified me! Say on."

"Name the happy day, Rosannah!"

There was a little pause. Then a diffident small voice replied, "I blush—but it is with pleasure, it is with happiness. Would—would you like to have it soon?"

"This very night, Rosannah! Oh, let us risk no more delays. Let it be now!—this very night, this very moment!"

"Oh, you impatient creature! I have nobody here but my good old uncle, a missionary for a generation, and now retired from service—nobody but him and his wife. I would so dearly like it if your mother and your aunt Susan—"

"Our mother and *our* aunt Susan, my Rosannah."

"Yes, *our* mother and *our* aunt Susan—I am content to word it so if it pleases you; I would so like to have them present."

"So would I. Suppose you telegraph aunt Susan. How long would it take her to come?"

"The steamer leaves San Francisco day after tomorrow. The passage is eight days. She would be here the 31st of March."

"Then name the 1st of April; do, Rosannah, dear."

"Mercy, it would make us April fools, Alonzo!"

"So we be the happiest ones that that day's sun looks down upon in the whole broad expanse of the globe, why need we care? Call it the 1st of April, dear."

"Then the 1st of April it shall be, with all my heart!"

"Oh, happiness! Name the hour too, Rosannah."

"I like the morning, it is so blithe. Will eight in the morning do, Alonzo?"

"The loveliest hour in the day, since it will make you mine."

There was a feeble but frantic sound for some little time, as if wool-lipped, disembodied spirits were exchanging kisses; then Rosannah said, "Excuse me just a moment, dear; I have an appointment, and am called to meet it."

The young girl sought a large parlor and took her place at a window which looked out upon a beautiful scene. To the left one could view the charming Nuuana Valley, fringed with its ruddy flush of tropical flowers and its plumed and graceful cocoa palms; its rising foothills, clothed in the shining green of lemon, citron, and orange groves; its storied precipice beyond, where the first Kamehameha drove his defeated foes over to their destruction, a spot that had forgotten its grim history, no doubt, for now it was smiling, as almost always at noonday, under the glowing arches of a succession of rainbows. In front of the window one could see the quaint town, and here and there a picturesque group of dusky natives, enjoying the blistering weather; and far to the right lay the restless ocean, tossing its white mane in the sunshine.

Rosannah stood there, in her filmy white raiment, fanning her flushed and heated face, waiting. A Kanaka boy, clothed in a damaged blue neck-tie and part of a silk hat, thrust his head in at the door, and announced, " 'Frisco *haole!*"

"Show him in," said the girl, straightening herself up and assuming a meaning dignity. Mr. Sidney Algernon Burley entered, clad from head to heel in dazzling snow—that is to say, in the lightest and whitest of Irish linen. He moved eagerly forward, but the girl made a gesture and gave him a look which checked him suddenly. She said, coldly, "I am here as I promised. I believed your assertions. I yielded to your importunities, and said I would name the day. I name the 1st of April—eight in the morning. Now go!"

"Oh, my dearest, if the gratitude of a lifetime—"

"Not a word. Spare me all sight of you, all communication with you, until that hour. No, no supplications; I will have it so."

When he was gone, she sank exhausted in a chair, for the long siege of troubles she had undergone had wasted her strength. Presently she said, "What a narrow escape! If the hour appointed had been an hour earlier—Oh, horror, what an escape I have made! And to think I had come to imagine I was loving this beguiling, this truthless, this treacherous monster! Oh! he shall repent his villainy!"

Let us now draw this history to a close, for little more needs to be told. On the 2d of the ensuing April, the Honolulu Advertiser contained this notice:

MARRIED.—In this city, by telephone, yesterday morning, at eight o'clock, by Rev. Nathan Hays, assisted by Rev. Nathaniel Davis, of New York, Mr. Alonzo Fitz Clarence, of Eastport, Maine, U. S., and Miss Rosannah Ethelton, of Portland, Oregon, U. S. Mrs. Susan Howland, of San Francisco, a friend of the bride, was present, she being the guest of the Rev. Mr. Hays and wife, uncle and aunt of the bride. Mr. Sidney Algernon Burley, of San Francisco, was also present, but did not remain till the conclusion of the marriage service. Captain Hawthorne's beautiful yacht, tastefully decorated, was in waiting, and the happy bride and her friends immediately departed on a bridal trip to Lahaina and Haleakala.

The New York papers of the same date contained this notice:

MARRIED.—In this city, yesterday, by telephone, at half past two in the morning, by Rev. Nathaniel Davis, assisted by Rev. Nathan Hays, of Honolulu, Mr. Alonzo Fitz Clarence, of Eastport, Maine, and Miss Rosannah Ethelton, of Portland, Oregon. The parents and several friends of the bridegroom were present, and enjoyed a sumptuous breakfast and much festivity until nearly sunrise, and then departed on a bridal trip to the Aquarium, the bridegroom's state of health not admitting of a more extended journey.

Toward the close of that memorable day, Mr. and Mrs. Alonzo Fitz Clarence were buried in sweet converse concerning the pleasures of their several bridal tours, when suddenly the young wife exclaimed: "O Lonny, I forgot! I did what I said I would."

"Did you, dear?"

"Indeed I did. I made *him* the April fool! And I told him so too! Ah, it was a charming surprise! There he stood, sweltering in a black dress suit, with the mercury leaking out of the top of the thermometer, waiting to be married. You should have seen the look he gave when I whispered it in his ear! Ah, his wickedness cost me many of heartache and many a tear, but the score was all squared up, then. So the vengeful feeling went right out of my heart, and I begged him to stay, and said I forgave him every thing. But he wouldn't. He said he would live to be avenged; said he would make our lives a curse to us. But he can't, *can* he dear?"

"Never in this world, my Rosannah!"

Aunt Susan, the Oregonian grandmother, and the young couple and their Eastport parents are all happy at this writing, and likely to remain so. Aunt Susan brought the bride from the Islands, accompanied her across our continent, and had the happiness of witnessing the rapturous meeting between an adoring husband and wife who had never seen each other until that moment.

A word about the wretched Burley, whose wicked machinations came so near wrecking the hearts and lives of our poor young friends, will be sufficient. In a murderous attempt to seize a crippled and helpless artisan who he fancied had done him some small offence, he fell into a caldron of boiling oil and expired before he could be extinguished.

"The $30,000 Bequest" was completed in a villa outside Florence where Twain had taken his wife Livy in a vain attempt to restore her failing health. The Twains had been troubled by financial difficulties for some time, and this tale perhaps reflects some of the wisdom gained from their close escape from bankruptcy. The story made its first appearance in the December 10, 1904 issue of Harper's Weekly, *and was collected in* The $30,000 Bequest and Other Stories, *published by Harper & Brothers in 1906.*

The $30,000 Bequest

I

Lakeside was a pleasant little town of five or six thousand inhabitants, and a rather pretty one, too, as towns go in the Far West. It had church accommodations for 35,000, which is the way of the Far West and the South, where everybody is religious, and where each of the Protestant sects is represented and has a plant of its own. Rank was unknown in Lakeside—unconfessed, anyway; everybody knew everybody and his dog, and a sociable friendliness was the prevailing atmosphere.

Saladin Foster was book-keeper in the principal store, and the only high-salaried man of his profession in Lakeside. He was thirty-five years old, now; he had served that store for fourteen years; he had begun in his marriage-week at four hundred dollars a year, and had climbed steadily up, a hundred dollars a year, for four years; from that time forth his wage had remained eight hundred—a handsome figure indeed, and everybody conceded that he was worth it.

His wife, Electra, was a capable helpmeet, although—like himself—a dreamer of dreams and a private dabbler in romance. The first thing she did, after her marriage—child as she was, aged only nineteen—was to buy an acre of ground on the edge of the town, and pay down the cash for it—twenty-five dollars, all her fortune. Saladin had less, by fifteen. She instituted a vegetable garden there, got it farmed on shares by the nearest neighbor, and made it pay her a hundred per cent. a year. Out of

Saladin's first year's wage she put thirty dollars in the savings-bank, sixty out of his second, a hundred out of his third, a hundred and fifty out of his fourth. His wage went to eight hundred a year, then, and meantime two children had arrived and increased the expenses, but she banked two hundred a year from the salary, nevertheless, thenceforth. When she had been married seven years she built and furnished a pretty and comfortable two-thousand-dollar house in the midst of her garden-acre, paid half of the money down and moved her family in. Seven years later she was out of debt and had several hundred dollars out earning its living.

Earning it by the rise in landed estate; for she had long ago bought another acre or two and sold the most of it at a profit to pleasant people who were willing to build, and would be good neighbors and furnish a general comradeship for herself and her growing family. She had an independent income from safe investments of about a hundred dollars a year; her children were growing in years and grace; and she was a pleased and happy woman. Happy in her husband, happy in her children, and the husband and the children were happy in her. It is at this point that this history begins.

The youngest girl, Clytemnestra—called Clytie for short—was eleven; her sister, Gwendolen—called Gwen for short—was thirteen; nice girls, and comely. The names betray the latent romance-tinge in the parental blood, the parents' names indicate that the tinge was an inheritance. It was an affectionate family, hence all four of its members had pet names. Saladin's was a curious and unsexing one—Sally; and so was Electra's— Aleck. All day long Sally was a good and diligent book-keeper and salesman; all day long Aleck was a good and faithful mother and housewife, and thoughtful and calculating business-woman; but in the cosey living-room at night they put the plodding world away, and lived in another and a fairer, reading romances to each other, dreaming dreams, comrading with kings and princes and stately lords and ladies in the flash and stir and splendor of noble palaces and grim and ancient castles.

II

Now came great news! Stunning news—joyous news, in fact. It came from a neighboring State, where the family's only surviving relative lived. It was Sally's relative—a sort of vague and indefinite uncle or second or third cousin by the name of Tilbury Foster, seventy and a bachelor, reputed well-off and correspondingly sour and crusty. Sally had tried to make up to him once, by letter, in a by-gone time, and had not made that mistake again. Tilbury now wrote to Sally, saying he should shortly die, and should leave him thirty thousand dollars, cash; not for love, but because money had given him most of his troubles and exasperations, and he wished to place it where there was good hope that it would continue its malignant work. The bequest would be found in his will, and would be paid over. *Provided,* that Sally should be able to prove to the executors that he had *taken no notice of the gift by spoken word or by letter, had made no inquiries concerning the moribund's progress towards the everlasting tropics, and had not attended the funeral.*

As soon as Aleck had partially recovered from the tremendous emotions created by the letter, she sent to the relative's habitat and subscribed for the local paper.

Man and wife entered into a solemn compact, now, to never mention the great news to any one while the relative lived, lest some ignorant person carry the fact to the death-bed and distort it and make it appear that they were disobediently thankful for the bequest, and just the same as confessing it and publishing it, right in the face of the prohibition.

For the rest of the day Sally made havoc and confusion with his books, and Aleck could not keep her mind on her affairs, nor even take up a flower-pot or book or a stick of wood without forgetting what she had intended to do with it. For both were dreaming.

"Thir-ty thousand dollars!"

All day long the music of those inspiring words sang through those people's heads.

From his marriage-day forth, Aleck's grip had been upon the purse, and Sally had seldom known what it was to be privileged to squander a dime on non-necessities.

"Thir-ty thousand dollars!" the song went on and on. A vast sum, an unthinkable sum!

All day long Aleck was absorbed in planning how to invest it, Sally in planning how to spend it.

There was no romance-reading that night. The children took themselves away early, for the parents were silent, distraught, and strangely unentertaining. The good-night kisses might as well have been impressed upon vacancy, for all the response they got; the parents were not aware of the kisses, and the children had been gone an hour before their absence was noticed. Two pencils had been busy during that hour—note-making; in the way of plans. It was Sally who broke the stillness at last. He said, with exultation—

"Ah, it'll be grand, Aleck! Out of the first thousand we'll have a horse and a buggy for summer, and a cutter and a skin lap-robe for winter."

Aleck responded with decision and composure—

"Out of the *capital?* Nothing of the kind. Not if it was a million!"

Sally was deeply disappointed; the glow went out of his face.

"Oh, Aleck!" he said, reproachfully. "We've always worked so hard and been so scrimped; and now that we are rich, it does seem—"

He did not finish, for he saw her eye soften; his supplication had touched her. She said, with gentle persuasiveness—

"We must not spend the capital, dear, it would not be wise. Out of the income from it—"

"That will answer, that will answer, Aleck! How dear and good you are! There will be a noble income, and if we can spend that—"

"Not *all* of it, dear, not all of it, but you can spend a part of it. That is, a reasonable part. But the whole of the capital—every penny of it—must be put right to work, and kept at it. You see the reasonableness of that, don't you?"

"Why, ye-s. Yes, of course. But we'll have to wait so long. Six months before the first interest falls due."

"Yes—maybe longer."

"Longer, Aleck? Why? Don't they pay half-yearly?"

"*That* kind of an investment—yes; but I sha'n't invest in that way."

"What way then?"

"For big returns."

"Big. That's good. Go on, Aleck. What is it?"

"Coal. The new mines. Cannel. I mean to put in ten thousand. Ground floor. When we organize, we'll get three shares for one."

"By George, but it sounds good, Aleck! Then the shares will be worth—how much? And when?"

"About a year. They'll pay ten per cent. half-yearly, and be worth thirty thousand. I know all about it; the advertisement is in the Cincinnati paper here."

"Land, thirty thousand for ten—in a year! Let's jam in the whole capital and pull out ninety! I'll write and subscribe right now—to-morrow it may be too late."

He was flying to the writing-desk, but Aleck stopped him and put him back in his chair. She said:

"Don't lose your head so. We mustn't subscribe till we've got the money; don't you know that?"

Sally's excitement went down a degree or two, but he was not wholly appeased.

"Why, Aleck, we'll *have* it, you know—and so soon, too. He's probably out of his troubles before this, it's a hundred to nothing he's selecting his brimstone-shovel this very minute. Now, I think—"

Aleck shuddered, and said:

"How *can* you, Sally! Don't talk in that way, it is perfectly scandalous."

"Oh well, make it a halo, if you like, *I* don't care for his outfit, I was only just talking. Can't you let a person talk?"

"But why should you *want* to talk in that dreadful way? How would you like to have people talk so about *you,* and you not cold yet?"

"Not likely to be, for *one* while, I reckon, if my last act was giving away money for the sake of doing somebody a harm with it. But never mind about Tilbury, Aleck, let's talk about something worldly. It does seem to me that that mine is the place for the whole thirty. What's the objection?"

"All the eggs in one basket—that's the objection."

"All right, if you say so. What about the other twenty? What do you mean to do with that?"

"There is no hurry; I am going to look around before I do anything with it."

"All right, if your mind's made up," sighed Sally. He was deep in thought awhile, then he said:

"There'll be twenty thousand profit coming from the ten a year from now. We can spend that, can't we, Aleck?"

Aleck shook her head.

"No, dear," she said, "it won't sell high till we've had the first semi-annual dividend. You can spend part of that."

"Shucks, only *that*—and a whole year to wait! Confound it, I—"

"Oh, do be patient! It might even be declared in three months—it's quite within the possibilities."

"Oh, jolly! oh, thanks!" and Sally jumped up and kissed his wife in gratitude. "It'll be three thousand—three whole thousand! how much of it can we spend, Aleck? Make it liberal—do, dear, that's a good fellow."

Aleck was pleased; so pleased that she yielded to the pressure and conceded a sum which her judgment told her was a foolish extravagance—a thousand dollars. Sally kissed her half a dozen times and even in that way could not express all his joy and thankfulness. This new access of gratitude and affection carried Aleck quite beyond the bounds of prudence, and before she could restrain herself she had made her darling another grant—a couple of thousand out of the fifty or sixty which she meant to clear within a year out of the twenty which still remained of the bequest. The happy tears sprang to Sally's eyes, and he said:

"Oh, I want to hug you!" And he did it. Then he got his notes and sat down and began to check off, for first purchase, the luxuries which he should earliest wish to secure. "Horse—buggy—cutter—lap-robe—patent-leathers—dog—plug hat—church-pew—stem-winder—new teeth—*say,* Aleck!"

"Well?"

"Ciphering away, aren't you? That's right. Have you got the twenty thousand invested yet?"

"No, there's no hurry about that; I must look around first, and think."

"But you are ciphering; what's it about?"

"Why, I have to find work for the thirty thousand that comes out of the coal, haven't I?"

"Scott, what a head! I never thought of that. How are you getting along? Where have you arrived?"

"Not very far—two years or three. I've turned it over twice; once in oil and once in wheat."

"Why, Aleck, it's splendid! How does it aggregate?"

"I think—well, to be on the safe side, about a hundred and eighty thousand clear, though it will probably be more."

"My! isn't it wonderful! By gracious! luck has come our way at last, after all the hard sledding. Aleck!"

"Well?"

"I'm going to cash-in a whole three hundred on the missionaries—what real right have we to care for expenses!"

"You couldn't do a nobler thing, dear; and it's just like your generous nature, you unselfish boy."

The praise made Sally poignantly happy, but he was fair and just enough to say it was rightfully due to Aleck rather than to himself, since but for her he should never have had the money.

Then they went up to bed, and in their delirium of bliss they forgot and left the candle burning in the parlor. They did not remember until they were undressed; then Sally was for letting it burn; he said they could afford it, if it was a thousand. But Aleck went down and put it out.

A good job, too; for on her way back she hit on a scheme that would turn the hundred and eighty thousand into half a million before it had had time to get cold.

III

The little newspaper which Aleck had subscribed for was a Thursday sheet; it would make the trip of five hundred miles from Tilbury's village and arrive on Saturday. Tilbury's letter had started on Friday, more than a day too late for the benefactor to die and get into that week's issue, but in plenty of time to make connection for the next output. Thus the Fosters had to wait almost a complete week to find out whether anything of a satisfactory nature had happened to him or not. It was a long, long week, and the strain was a heavy one. The pair could hardly have borne it if their minds had not had the relief of wholesome diversion. We have seen that they had that. The woman was piling up fortunes right along; the man was spending them—spending all his wife would give him a chance at, at any rate.

At last the Saturday came, and the *Weekly Sagamore* arrived. Mrs. Eversly Bennett was present. She was the Presbyterian parson's wife, and was working the Fosters for a charity. Talk now died a sudden death—on the Foster side. Mrs. Bennett presently discovered that her hosts were not hearing a word she was saying; so she got up, wondering and indignant, and went away. The moment she was out of the house, Aleck eagerly tore the wrapper from the paper, and her eyes and Sally's swept the columns for the death notices. Disappointment! Tilbury was not anywhere mentioned. Aleck was a Christian from the cradle, and duty and the force of habit required her to go through the motions. She pulled herself together and said, with a pious two-per-cent. trade joyousness:

"Let us be humbly thankful that he has been spared; and—"

"Damn his treacherous hide, I wish—"

"Sally! For shame!"

"I don't care!" retorted the angry man. "It's the way *you* feel, and if you weren't so immorally pious you'd be honest and say so."

Aleck said, with wounded dignity:

"I do not see how you can say such unkind and unjust things. There is no such thing as immoral piety."

Sally felt a pang, but tried to conceal it under a shuffling attempt to save his case by changing the form of it—as if changing the form while retaining the juice could deceive the expert he was trying to placate. He said:

"I didn't mean so bad as that, Aleck; I didn't really mean immoral piety, I only meant—meant—well, conventional piety, you know; er—shop piety; the—the—why, *you* know what I mean, Aleck—the—well, where you put up the plated article and play it for solid, you know, without intending anything improper but just out of trade habit, ancient policy, petrified custom, loyalty to—to—hang it, I can't find the right words, but *you* know what I mean, Aleck, and that there isn't any harm in it. I'll try again. You see, it's this way. If a person—"

"You have said quite enough," said Aleck, coldly; let the subject be dropped."

"I'm willing," fervently responded Sally, wiping the sweat from his forehead and looking the thankfulness he had no words for. Then, musingly, he apologized to himself. "I certainly held threes—I *know* it—but I drew and didn't fill. That's where I'm so often weak in the game. If I had stood pat—but I didn't. I never do. I don't know enough."

Confessedly defeated, he was properly tame now and subdued. Aleck forgave him with her eyes.

The grand interest, the supreme interest, came instantly to the front again; nothing could keep it in the background many minutes on a stretch. The couple took up the puzzle of the absence of Tilbury's death notice. They discussed it every way, more or less hopefully, but they had to finish where they began, and concede that the only really sane explanation of the absence of the notice must be—and without doubt was—that Tilbury was not dead. There was something sad about it, something even a little unfair, maybe, but there it was, and had to be put up with. They were agreed as to that. To Sally it seemed a strangely inscrutable dispensation; more inscrutable than usual, he thought; one of the most unnecessarily inscrutable he could call to mind, in fact—and said so, with some feeling; but if he was hoping to draw Aleck he failed; she reserved her opinion, if she one; she had not the habit of taking injudicious risks in any market, worldy or other.

The pair must wait for next week's paper—Tilbury had evidently postponed. That was their thought and their decision. So they put the subject away, and went about their affairs again with as good heart as they could.

Now, if they had but known it, they had been wronging Tilbury all the time. Tilbury had kept faith, kept it to the letter; he was dead, he had died to schedule. He was dead more than four days now and used to it; entirely dead, perfectly dead, as dead as any other new person in the cemetery; dead in abundant time to get into that week's *Sagamore,* too, and only shut out by an accident; an accident which could not happen to a metropolitan journal, but which happens easily to a poor little village rag like the *Sagamore.* On this occasion, just as the editorial page was being locked up, a gratis quart of strawberry water-ice arrived from Hostetter's Ladies' and Gents' Ice-Cream Parlors, and the stickful of rather chilly regret over Tilbury's translation got crowded out to make room for the editor's frantic gratitude.

On its way to the standing-galley Tilbury's notice got pied. Otherwise it would have gone into some future edition, for *Weekly Sagamores* do not waste "live" matter, and in their galleys "live" matter is immortal, unless a pi accident intervenes. But a thing that gets pied is dead, and for such there is no resurrection; its chance of seeing print is gone, forever and ever. And so, let Tilbury like it or not, let him rave in his grave to his fill, no matter—no mention of his death would ever see the light in the *Weekly Sagamore.*

IV

Five weeks drifted tediously along. The *Sagamore* arrived regularly on the Saturdays, but never once contained a mention of Tilbury Foster. Sally's patience broke down at this point, and he said, resentfully:

"Damn his livers, he's immortal!"

Aleck gave him a very severe rebuke, and added, with icy solemnity:

"How would you feel if you were suddenly cut off just after such an awful remark had escaped out of you?"

Without sufficient reflection Sally responded:

"I'd feel I was lucky I hadn't got caught with it *in* me."

Pride had forced him to say something, and as he could not think of any rational thing to say he flung that out. Then he stole a base—as he called it—that is, slipped from the presence, to keep from getting brayed in his wife's discussion-mortar.

Six months came and went. The *Sagamore* was still silent about Tilbury. Meantime, Sally had several times thrown out a feeler—that is, a hint that he would like to know. Aleck had ignored the hints. Sally now resolved to brace up and risk a frontal attack. So he squarely proposed to disguise himself and go to Tilbury's village and surreptitiously find out as to the prospects. Aleck put her foot on the dangerous project with energy and decision. She said:

"What can you be thinking of? You do keep my hands full! You have to be watched all the time, like a little child, to keep you from walking into the fire. You'll stay right where you are!"

"Why, Aleck, I could do it and not be found out—I'm certain of it."

"Sally Foster, don't you know you would have to inquire around?"

"Of course, but what of it? Nobody would suspect who I was."

"Oh, listen to the man! Some day you've got to prove to the executors that you never inquired. What then?"

He had forgotten that detail. He didn't reply; there wasn't anything to say. Aleck added:

"Now then, drop that notion out of your mind, and don't ever meddle with it again. Tilbury set that trap for you. Don't you know it's a trap? He is on the watch, and fully expecting you to blunder into it. Well, he is going to be disappointed—at least while I am on deck. Sally!"

"Well?"

"As long as you live, if it's a hundred years, don't you ever make an inquiry. Promise!"

"All right," with a sigh and reluctantly.

Then Aleck softened and said:

"Don't be impatient. We are prospering; we can wait; there is no hurry. Our small dead-certain income increases all the time; and as to futures, I have not made a mistake yet—they are piling up by the thousands and the tens of thousands. There is not another family in the State with such prospects as ours. Already we are beginning to roll in eventual wealth. You know that, don't you?"

"Yes, Aleck, it's certainly so."

"Then be grateful for what God is doing for us, and stop worrying. You do not believe we could have achieved these prodigious results without His special help and guidance, do you?"

Hesitatingly, "No-no, I suppose not." Then, with feeling and admiration, "And yet, when it comes to judiciousness in watering a stock or putting up a hand to skin Wall Street I don't give in that *you* need any outside amateur help, if I do I wish I—"

"Oh, *do* shut up! I know you do not mean any harm or any irreverence, poor boy, but you can't seem to open your mouth without letting out things to make a person shudder. You keep me in constant dread. For you and for all of us. Once I had no fear of the thunder, but now when I hear it I—"

Her voice broke, and she began to cry, and could not finish. The sight of this smote Sally to the heart and he took her in his arms and petted her and comforted her and promised better conduct, and upbraided himself and remorsefully pleaded for forgiveness. And he was in earnest, and sorry for what he had done and ready for any sacrifice that could make up for it.

And so, in privacy, he thought long and deeply over the matter, resolving to do what should seem best. It was easy to *promise* reform; indeed he had already promised it. But would that do any real good, any permanent good? No, it would be but temporary—he knew his weakness, and confessed it to himself with sorrow—he could not keep the promise. Something surer and better must be devised; and he devised it. At cost of precious money which he had long been saving up, shilling by shilling, he put a lightning-rod on the house.

At a subsequent time he relapsed.

What miracles habit can do! and how quickly and how easily habits are acquired—both trifling habits and habits which profoundly change us. If by accident we wake at two in the morning a couple of nights in succession, we have need to be uneasy, for another repetition can turn the accident into a habit; and a month's dallying with whiskey—but we all know these commonplace facts.

The castle-building habit, the day-dreaming habit—how it grows! what a luxury it becomes; how we fly to its enchantments at every idle moment, how we revel in them, steep our souls in them, intoxicate ourselves with their beguiling fantasies—oh yes, and how soon and how easily our dream-life and our material life become so intermingled and so fused together that we can't quite tell which is which, any more.

By-and-by Aleck subscribed for a Chicago daily and for the *Wall Street Pointer*. With an eye single to finance she studied these as diligently all the week as she studied her Bible Sundays. Sally was lost in admiration, to note with what swift and sure strides her genius and judgment developed and expanded in the forecasting and handling of the securities of both the material and spiritual markets. He was proud of her nerve and daring in exploiting worldly stocks, and just as proud of her conservative caution in working her spiritual deals. He noted that she never lost her head in either case; that with a splendid courage she often went short on worldly futures, but heedfully drew the line there—she was always long on the others. Her policy was quite sane and simple, as she explained it to him: what she put into earthly futures was for speculation, what she put into spiritual futures was for investment; she was willing to go into the one on a margin, and take chances, but in the case of the other, "margin her no margins"—she wanted to cash-in a hundred cents per dollar's-worth, and have the stock transferred on the books.

It took but a very few months to educate Aleck's imagination and Sally's. Each day's training added something to the spread and effectiveness of the two machines. As a consequence, Aleck made imaginary money much faster than at first she had dreamed of making it, and Sally's competency in spending the overflow of it kept pace with the strain put upon it, right along. In the beginning, Aleck had given the coal speculation a twelvemonth in which to materialize, and had been loath to grant that this term might possibly be shortened by nine months. But that was the feeble work, the nursery work, of a financial fancy that had had no teaching, no experience, no practice. These aids soon came, then that nine months vanished, and the imaginary ten-thousand-dollar investment came marching home with three hundred per cent. profit on its back!

It was a great day for the pair of Fosters. They were speechless for joy. Also speechless for another reason: after much watching of the market, Aleck had lately, with fear and trembling, made her first flyer on a "margin," using the remaining twenty thousand of the bequest in this risk. In her mind's eye she had seen it climb, point by point—always with a chance that the market would break—until at last her anxieties were too great for further endurance—she being new to the margin-business and unhardened as yet—and she gave her imaginary broker an imaginary order by imaginary telegraph to sell. She said forty thousand dollars profit was enough. The sale was made on the very day that the coal-venture had returned with its rich freight. As I have said, the couple were speechless. They sat dazed and blissful that night, trying to realize the immense fact, the overwhelming fact, that they were actually worth a hundred thousand dollars in clean, imaginary cash. Yet so it was.

It was the last time that ever Aleck was afraid of a margin; at least afraid enough to let it break her sleep and pale her cheek to the extent that this first experience in that line had done.

Indeed it was a memorable night. Gradually the realization that they were rich sank securely home into the souls of the pair, then they began to place the money. If we could have looked out through the eyes of these dreamers, we should have seen their tidy little wooden house disappear, and a two-story brick with a cast-iron fence in front of it take its place; we should have seen a three-globed gas-chandelier grow down from the parlor ceiling; we should have seen the homely rag carpet turn to noble Brussels, a dollar and a half a yard; we should have seen the plebeian fireplace vanish away and a recherché, big base-burner with isinglass windows take position and spread awe around.

And we should have seen other things, too; among them the buggy, the lap-robe, the stove-pipe hat, and so on.

From that time forth, although the daughters and the neighbors saw only the same old wooden house there, it was a two-story brick to Aleck and Sally; and not a night went by that Aleck did not worry about the imaginary gas-bills, and get for all comfort Sally's reckless retort, "What of it? we can afford it."

Before the couple went to bed, that first night that they were rich, they had decided that they must celebrate. They must give a party—that was the idea. But how to explain it—to the daughters and the neighbors? They could not expose the fact that they were rich. Sally was willing, even anxious, to do it; but Aleck kept her head and would not allow it. She said that although the money was as good as in, it would be as well to wait until it was actually in. On that policy she took her stand, and would not budge. The great secret must be kept, she said—kept from the daughters and everybody else.

The pair were puzzled. They must celebrate, they were determined to celebrate, but since the secret must be kept, what could they celebrate? No birthdays were due for three months. Tilbury wasn't available, evidently he was going to live forever; what the nation *could* they celebrate? That was Sally's way of putting it; and he was getting impatient, too, and harassed. But at last he hit it—just by sheer inspiration, as it seemed to him—and all their troubles were gone in a moment; they would celebrate the Discovery of America. A splendid idea!

Aleck was almost too proud of Sally for words—she said *she* never would have thought of it. But Sally, although he was bursting with delight in the compliment and with wonder at himself, tried not to let on, and said it wasn't really anything, anybody could have done it. Whereat Aleck, with a prideful toss of her happy head, said:

"Oh, certainly! Anybody could—oh, anybody! Hosannah Dilkins, for instance! Or maybe Adelbert Peanut—oh, *dear*—yes! Well, I'd like to see them try it, that's all. Dear-me-suz, if they could think of the discovery of a forty-acre island it's more than *I* believe they could; and as for a whole continent, why, Sally Foster, you know perfectly well it would strain the livers and lights out of them and *then* they couldn't!"

The dear woman, she knew he had talent; and if affection made her over-estimate the size of it a little, surely it was a sweet and gentle crime, and forgiveable for its source's sake.

V

The celebration went off well. The friends were all present, both the young and the old. Among the young were Flossie and Gracie Peanut and their brother Adelbert, who was a rising young journeyman tinner, also Hosannah Dilkins, Jr., journeyman plasterer, just out of his apprenticeship. For many months Adelbert and Hosannah had been showing interest in Gwendolen and Clytemnestra Foster, and the parents of the girls had noticed this with private satisfaction. But they suddenly realized now that that feeling had passed. They recognized that the changed financial conditions had raised up a social bar between their daughters and the young mechanics. The daughters could now look higher—and must. Yes, must. They need marry nothing below the grade of lawyer or merchant; poppa and momma would take care of this; there must be no mésalliances.

However, these thinkings and projects of theirs were private, and did not show on the surface, and therefore threw no shadow upon the celebration. What showed upon the surface was a serene and lofty contentment and a dignity of carriage and gravity of deportment which compelled the admiration and likewise the wonder of the company. All noticed it, all commented upon it, but none was able to divine the secret of it. It was a marvel and a mystery. Three several persons remarked, without suspecting what clever shots they were making:

"It's as if they'd come into property."

That was just it, indeed.

Most mothers would have taken hold of the matrimonial matter in the old regulation way; they would have given the girls a talking to, of a solemn sort and untactful—a lecture calculated to defeat its own purpose, by producing tears and secret rebellion; and the said mothers would have further damaged the business by requesting the young mechanics to discontinue their attentions. But this mother was different. She was practical. She said nothing to any of the young people concerned, nor to any one else except Sally. He listened to her and understood; understood and admired. He said:

"I get the idea. Instead of finding fault with the samples on view, thus hurting feelings and obstructing trade without occasion, you merely offer a higher class of goods for the money, and leave nature to take her course. It's wisdom, Aleck, solid wisdom, and sound as a nut. Who's your fish? Have you nominated him yet?"

No, she hadn't. They must look the market over—which they did. To start with, they considered and discussed Bradish, rising young lawyer, and Fulton, rising young dentist. Sally must invite them to dinner. But not right away; there was no hurry, Aleck said. Keep an eye on the pair, and wait; nothing would be lost by going slowly in so important a matter.

It turned out that this was wisdom, too; for inside of three weeks Aleck made a wonderful strike which swelled her imaginary hundred thousand to four hundred thousand of the same quality. She and Sally were in the clouds that evening. For the first time they introduced champagne at dinner. Not real champagne, but plenty real enough for the amount of imagination expended on it. It was Sally that did it, and Aleck weakly submitted. At bottom both were troubled and ashamed, for he was a high-up Son of Temperance, and at funerals wore an apron which no dog could look upon and retain his reason and his opinion; and she was a W.C.T.U., with all that that implies of boiler-iron virtue and unendurable holiness. But there it was; the pride of riches was beginning its disintegrating work. They had lived to prove, once more, a sad truth which had been proven many times before in the world: that whereas principle is a great and noble protection against showy and degrading vanities and vices, poverty is worth six of it. More than four hundred thousand dollars to the good! They took up the matrimonial matter again. Neither the dentist nor the lawyer was mentioned; there was no occasion, they were out of the running. Disqualified. They discussed the son of the pork-packer and the son of the village banker. But finally, as in the previous case, they concluded to wait and think, and go cautiously and sure.

Luck came their way again. Aleck, ever watchful, saw a great and risky chance, and took a daring flyer. A time of trembling, of doubt, of awful uneasiness followed, for non-success meant absolute ruin and nothing short of it. Then came the result, and Aleck, faint with joy, could hardly control her voice when she said:

"The suspense is over, Sally—and we are worth a cold million!"

Sally wept for gratitude, and said:

"Oh, Electra, jewel of women, darling of my heart, we are free at last, we roll in wealth, we need never scrimp again. It's a case for Veuve Cliquot!" and he got out a pint of spruce-beer and made sacrifice, he saying "Damn the expense," and she rebuking him gently with reproachful but humid and happy eyes.

They shelved the pork-packer's son and the banker's son, and sat down to consider the Governor's son and the son of the Congressman.

VI

It were a weariness to follow in detail the leaps and bounds the Foster fictitious finances took from this time forth. It was marvellous, it was dizzying, it was dazzling. Everything Aleck touched turned to fairy gold, and heaped itself glittering towards the firmament. Millions upon millions poured in, and still the mighty stream flowed thundering along, still its vast volume increased. Five millions—ten millions—twenty—thirty—was there never to be an end?

Two years swept by in a splendid delirium, the intoxicated Fosters scarcely noticing the flight of time. They were now worth three hundred million dollars; they were in every board of directors of every prodigious combine in the country; and still, as time drifted along, the millions went on piling up, five at a time, ten at a time, as fast as they could tally them off, almost. The three hundred doubled itself—then doubled again—and yet again—and yet once more.

Twenty-four hundred millions!

The business was getting a little confused. It was necessary to take an account of stock, and straighten it out. The Fosters knew it, they felt it, they realized that it was imperative; but they also knew that to do it properly and perfectly the task must be carried to a finish without a break when once it was begun. A ten-hours' job; and where could *they* find ten leisure hours in a bunch? Sally was selling pins and sugar and calico all day and every day; Aleck was cooking and washing dishes and sweeping and making beds all day and every day, with none to help, for the daughters were being saved up for high society. The Fosters knew there was one way to get the ten hours, and only one. Both were ashamed to name it; each waited for the other to do it. Finally Sally said:

"Somebody's got to give in. It's up to me. Consider that I've named it—never mind pronouncing it out loud."

Aleck colored, but was grateful. Without further remark, they fell. Fell, and—broke the Sabbath. For that was their only free ten-hour stretch. It was but another step in the downward path. Others would follow. Vast wealth has temptations which fatally and surely undermine the moral structure of persons not habituated to its possession.

They pulled down the shades and broke the Sabbath. With hard and patient labor they overhauled their holdings and listed them. And a long-drawn procession of formidable names it was! Starting with the Railway Systems, Steamer Lines, Standard Oil, Ocean Cables, Diluted Telegraph, and all the rest, and winding up with Klondike, De Beers, Tammany Graft, and Shady Privileges in the Post-office Department.

Twenty-four hundred millions, and all safely planted in Good Things, gilt-edged and interest-bearing. Income, $120,000,000 a year. Aleck fetched a long purr of soft delight, and said:

"Is it enough?"

"It is, Aleck."

"What shall we do?"

"Stand pat."

"Retire from business?"

"That's it."

"I am agreed. The good work is finished; we will take a long rest and enjoy the money."

"Good! Aleck!"

"Yes, dear?"

"How much of the income can we spend?"

"The whole of it."

It seemed to her husband that a ton of chains fell from his limbs. He did not say a word; he was happy beyond the power of speech.

After that, they broke the Sabbaths right along, as fast as they turned up. It is the first wrong steps that count. Every Sunday they put in the whole day, after morning service, on inventions—inventions of ways to spend the money. They got to continuing this delicious dissipation until past midnight; and at every séance Aleck lavished millions upon great charities and religious enterprises, and Sally lavished like sums upon matters to which (at first) he gave definite names. Only at first. Later the names gradually lost sharpness of outline, and eventually faded into "sundries," thus becoming entirely—but safely— undescriptive. For Sally was crumbling. The placing of these millions added seriously and most uncomfortably to the family expenses—in tallow candles. For a while Aleck was worried. Then, after a little, she ceased to worry, for the occasion of it was gone. She was pained, she was grieved, she was ashamed; but she said nothing, and so became an accessory. Sally was taking candles; he was robbing the store. It is ever thus. Vast wealth, to the person unaccustomed to it, is a bane; it eats into the flesh and bone of his morals. When the Fosters were poor, they could have been trusted with untold candles. But now they—but let us not dwell upon it. From candles to apples is but a step: Sally got to taking apples; then soap; then maple-sugar; then canned-goods; then crockery. How easy it is to go from bad to worse, when once we have started upon a downward course!

Meantime, other effects had been milestoning the course of

the Fosters' splendid financial march. The fictitious brick-dwelling had given place to an imaginary granite one with a checker-board mansard roof; in time this one disappeared and gave place to a still grander home—and so on and so on. Mansion after mansion, made of air, rose, higher, broader, finer, and each in its turn vanished away; until now, in these latter great days, our dreamers were in fancy housed, in a distant region, in a sumptuous vast palace which looked out from a leafy summit upon a noble prospect of vale and river and receding hills steeped in tinted mists—and all private, all the property of the dreamers; a palace swarming with liveried servants, and populous with guests of fame and power, hailing from all the world's capitals, foreign and domestic.

This palace was far, far away towards the rising sun, immeasurably remote, astronomically remote, in Newport, Rhode Island, Holy Land of High Society, ineffable Domain of the American Aristocracy. As a rule, they spent a part of every Sabbath—after morning service—in this sumptuous home, the rest of it they spent in Europe, or in dawdling around in their private yacht. Six days of sordid and plodding Fact-life at home on the ragged edge of Lakeside and straitened means, the seventh in Fairyland—such had become their programme and their habit.

In their sternly restricted Fact-life they remained as of old—plodding, diligent, careful, practical, economical. They stuck loyally to the little Presbyterian Church, and labored faithfully in its interests and stood by its high and tough doctrines with all their mental and spiritual energies. But in their Dream-life they obeyed the invitations of their fancies, whatever they might be, and howsoever the fancies might change. Aleck's fancies were not very capricious, and not frequent, but Sally's scattered a good deal. Aleck, in her dream-life, went over to the Episcopal camp, on account of its large official titles; next she became High-church on account of the candles and shows; and next she naturally changed to Rome, where there were cardinals and more candles. But these excursions were as nothing to Sally's. His Dream-life was a glowing and continuous and persistent excitement, and he kept every part of it fresh and sparkling by frequent changes, the religious part along with the rest. He worked his religions hard, and changed them with his shirt.

The liberal spendings of the Fosters upon their fancies began early in their prosperities, and grew in prodigality step by step with their advancing fortunes. In time they became truly enormous. Aleck built a university or two per Sunday; also a hospital or two; also a Rowton hotel or so; also a batch of churches; now and then a cathedral; and once, with untimely and ill-chosen playfulness, Sally said, "It was a cold day when she didn't ship a cargo of missionaries to persuade unreflecting Chinamen to trade off twenty-four carat Confucianism for counterfeit Christianity."

This rude and unfeeling language hurt Aleck to the heart, and she went from the presence crying. That spectacle went to his own heart, and in his pain and shame he would have given worlds to have those unkind words back. She had uttered no syllable of reproach—and that cut him. Not one suggestion that he look at his own record—and she could have made, oh, so many, and such blistering ones! Her generous silence brought a swift revenge, for it turned his thoughts upon himself, it summoned before him a spectral procession, a moving vision of his life as he had been leading it these past few years of limitless prosperity, and as he sat there reviewing it his cheeks burned and his soul was steeped in humiliation. Look at her life—how fair it was, and tending upward; and look at his own—how frivolous, how charged with mean vanities, how selfish, how empty, how ignoble! And its trend—never upward, but downward, ever downward!

He instituted comparisons between her record and his own. He had found fault with her—so he mused—*he!* And what could he say for himself? When she built her first church what was he doing? Gathering other blasé multimillionaires into a Poker Club; defiling his own palace with it; losing hundreds of thousands to it at every sitting, and sillily vain of the admiring notoriety it made for him. When she was building her first university, what was he doing? Polluting himself with a gay and dissipated secret life in the company of other fast bloods, multimillionaires in money and paupers in character. When she was building her first foundling asylum, what was he doing? Alas! When she was projecting her noble Society for the Purifying of the Sex, what was he doing? Ah, what, indeed! When she and the W.C.T.U. and the Woman with the Hatchet, moving with resistless march, were sweeping the fatal bottle from the land, what was he doing? Getting drunk three times a day. When she, builder of a hundred cathedrals, was being gratefully welcomed and blest in papal Rome and decorated with the Golden Rose which she had so honorably earned, what was he doing? Breaking the bank at Monte Carlo.

He stopped. He could go no farther; he could not bear the rest. He rose up, with a great resolution upon his lips: this secret life should be revealed, and confessed; no longer would he live it clandestinely; he would go and tell her All.

And that is what he did. He told her All; and wept upon her bosom; wept, and moaned, and begged for her forgiveness. It was a profound shock, and she staggered under the blow, but he was her own, the core of her heart, the blessing of her eyes, her all in all, she could deny him nothing, and she forgave him. She felt that he could never again be quite to her what he had been before; she knew that he could only repent, and not reform; yet all morally defaced and decayed as he was, was he not her own, her very own, the idol of her deathless worship? She said she was his serf, his slave, and she opened her yearning heart and took him in.

VII

One Sunday afternoon some time after this they were sailing the summer seas in their dream-yacht, and reclining in lazy luxury under the awning of the after-deck. There was silence, for each was busy with his own thoughts. These seasons of silence had insensibly been growing more and more frequent of late; the old nearness and cordiality were waning. Sally's terrible revelation had done its work; Aleck had tried hard to drive the memory of it out of her mind, but it would not go, and the shame and bitterness of it were poisoning her gracious dream-life. She could see now (on Sundays) that her husband was becoming a bloated and repulsive Thing. She could not close her eyes to this, and in these days she no longer looked at him, Sundays, when she could help it.

But she—was she herself without blemish? Alas, she knew she was not. She was keeping a secret from him, she was acting dishonorably towards him, and many a pang it was costing her. *She was breaking the compact, and concealing it from him.* Under strong temptation she had gone into business again; she had risked their whole fortune in a purchase of all the railway systems and coal and steel companies in the country on a margin, and she was now trembling, every Sabbath hour, lest through some chance word of hers he find it out. In her misery and remorse for this treachery she could not keep her heart from going out to him in pity; she was filled with compunctions to see him lying there, drunk and content, and never suspecting. Never suspecting—trusting her with a perfect and pathetic trust, and she holding over him by a thread a possible calamity of so devastating a—

"*Say*—Aleck?"

The interrupting words brought her suddenly to herself. She

was grateful to have that persecuting subject from her thoughts, and she answered, with much of the old-time tenderness in her tone:

"Yes, dear."

"Do you know, Aleck, I think we are making a mistake—that is, you are. I mean about the marriage business." He sat up, fat and froggy and benevolent, like a bronze Buddha, and grew earnest. "Consider—it's more than five years. You've continued the same policy from the start: with every rise, always holding on for five points higher. Always when I think we are going to have some weddings, you see a bigger thing ahead, and I undergo another disappointment. *I* think you are too hard to please. Some day we'll get left. First, we turned down the dentist and the lawyer. That was all right—it was sound. Next, we turned down the banker's son and the pork-butcher's heir—right again, and sound. Next, we turned down the Congressman's son and the Governor's—right as a trivet, I confess it. Next, the Senator's son and the son of the Vice-President of the United States—perfectly right, there's no permanency about those little distinctions. Then you went for the aristocracy; and I thought we had struck oil at last—yes. We would make a plunge at the Four Hundred, and pull in some ancient lineage, venerable, holy, ineffable, mellow with the antiquity of a hundred and fifty years, disinfected of the ancestral odors of salt cod and pelts all of a century ago, and unsmirched by a day's work since; and then! why, then the marriages, of course. But no, along comes a pair of real aristocrats from Europe, and straightway you throw over the half-breeds. It was awfully discouraging, Aleck! Since then, what a procession! You turned down the baronets for a pair of barons; you turned down the barons for a pair of viscounts; the viscounts for a pair of earls; the earls for a pair of marquises; the marquises for a brace of dukes. *Now,* Aleck, cash-in!—you've played the limit. You've got a job lot of four dukes under the hammer; of four nationalities; all sound in wind and limb and pedigree, all bankrupt and in debt up to the ears. They come high, but we can afford it. Come, Aleck, don't delay any longer, don't keep up the suspense: take the whole lay-out, and leave the girls to choose!"

Aleck had been smiling blandly and contentedly all through this arraignment of her marriage-policy; a pleasant light, as a triumph with perhaps a nice surprise peeping out through it, rose in her eyes, and she said, as calmly as she could:

"Sally, what would you say to—*royalty?*"

Prodigious! Poor man, it knocked him silly, and he fell over the garboard-strake and barked his shin on the cat-heads. He was dizzy for a moment, then he gathered himself up and limped over and sat down by his wife and beamed his old-time admiration and affection upon her in floods, out of his bleary eyes.

"By George!" he said, fervently, "Aleck, you *are* great—the greatest woman in the whole earth! I can't ever learn the whole size of you. I can't ever learn the immeasurable deeps of you. Here I've been considering myself qualified to criticise your game. *I!* Why, if I had stopped to think, I'd have known you had a lone hand up your sleeve. Now, dear heart, I'm all red-hot impatience—tell me about it!"

The flattered and happy woman put her lips to his ear and whispered a princely name. It made him catch his breath, it lit his face with exultation.

"Land!" he said, "it's a stunning catch! He's got a gambling-hell, and a graveyard, and a bishop, and a cathedral—all his very own. And all gilt-edged five-hundred-per-cent. stock, every detail of it; the tidiest little property in Europe. And that graveyard—it's the selectest in the world: none but suicides admitted; *yes,* sir, and the free-list suspended, too, *all* the time. There isn't much land in the principality, but there's enough: eight hundred acres in the graveyard and forty-two outside. It's a *sovereignty*—that's the main thing; *land's* nothing. There's plenty land, Sahara's drugged with it."

Aleck glowed; she was profoundly happy. She said:

"Think of it, Sally—it is a family that has never married outside the Royal and Imperial Houses of Europe: our grandchildren will sit upon thrones!"

"True as you live, Aleck—and bear sceptres, too; and handle them as naturally and nonchalantly as I handle a yardstick. It's a grand catch, Aleck. He's corralled, is he? Can't get away? You didn't take him on a margin?"

"No. Trust me for that. He's not a liability, he's an asset. So is the other one."

"Who is it, Aleck?"

"His Royal Highness Sigismund-Siegfried-Lauenfeld- Dinkelspiel-Schwartzenberg Blutwurst, Hereditary Grand Duke of Katzenyammer."

"No! You can't mean it!"

"It's as true as I'm sitting here, I give you my word," she answered.

His cup was full, and he hugged her to his heart with rapture, saying:

"How wonderful it all seems, and how beautiful! It's one of the oldest and noblest of the three hundred and sixty-four ancient German principalities, and one of the few that was allowed to retain its royal estate when Bismarck got done trimming them. I know that farm, I've been there. It's got a ropewalk and a candle-factory and an army. Standing army. Infantry and cavalry. Three soldiers and a horse. Aleck, it's been a long wait, and full of heartbreak and hope deferred, but God knows I am happy now. Happy, and grateful to yof, my own, who have done it all. When is it to be?"

"Next Sunday."

"Good. And we'll want to do these weddings up in the very regalest style that's going. It's properly due to the royal quality of the parties of the first part. Now as I understand it, there is only one kind of marriage that is sacred to royalty, exclusive to royalty: it's the morganatic."

"What do they call it that for, Sally?"

"I don't know; but anyway it's royal, and royal only."

"Then we will insist upon it. More—I will compel it. It is morganatic marriage or none."

"That settles it!" said Sally, rubbing his hands with delight. "And it will be the very first in America. Aleck, it will make Newport sick."

Then they fell silent, and drifted away upon their dream-wings to the far regions of the earth to invite all the crowned heads and their families and provide gratis transportation for them.

VIII

During three days the couple walked upon air, with their heads in the clouds. They were but vaguely conscious of their surroundings; they saw all things dimly, as through a veil; they were steeped in dreams, often they did not hear when they were spoken to; they often did not understand when they heard; they answered confusedly or at random; Sally sold molasses by weight, sugar by the yard, and furnished soap when asked for candles, and Aleck put the cat in the wash and fed milk to the soiled linen. Everybody was stunned and amazed, and went about muttering, "What *can* be the matter with the Fosters?"

Three days. Then came events! Things had taken a happy turn, and for forty-eight hours Aleck's imaginary corner had been booming. Up—up—still up! Cost-point was passed. Still up—and up—and up! Five points above cost—then ten—fifteen—twenty! Twenty points cold profit on the vast venture, now, and Aleck's imaginary brokers were shouting frantically by imaginary long-distance, "Sell! sell! for Heaven's sake *sell!*"

She broke the splendid news to Sally, and he, too, said, "Sell!

sell—oh, don't make a blunder, now, you own the earth!—sell, sell!" But she set her iron will and lashed it amidships, and said she would hold on for five points more if she died for it.

It was a fatal resolve. The very next day came the historic crash, the record crash, the devastating crash, when the bottom fell out of Wall Street, and the whole body of gilt-edged stocks dropped ninety-five points in five hours, and the multimillionaire was seen begging his bread in the Bowery. Aleck sternly held her grip and "put up" as long as she could, but at last there came a call which she was powerless to meet, and her imaginary brokers sold her out. Then, and not till then, the man in her was vanquished, and the woman in her resumed sway. She put her arms about her husband's neck and wept, saying:

"I am to blame, do not forgive me, I cannot bear it. We are paupers! Paupers, and I am so miserable. The weddings will never come off; all that is past; we could not even buy the dentist, now."

A bitter reproach was on Sally's tongue: "I *begged* you to sell, but you—" He did not say it; he had not the heart to add a hurt to that broken and repentant spirit. A nobler thought came to him and he said:

"Bear up, my Aleck, all is not lost! You really never invested a penny of my uncle's bequest, but only its unmaterialized future; what we have lost was only the increment harvested from that future by your incomparable financial judgement and sagacity. Cheer up, banish these griefs; we still have the thirty thousand untouched; and with the experience which you have acquired, think what you will be able to do with it in a couple of years! The marriages are not off, they are only postponed."

These were blessed words. Aleck saw how true they were, and the influence was electric; her tears ceased to flow, and her great spirit rose to its full stature again. With flashing eye and grateful heart, and with hand uplifted in pledge and prophecy, she said:

"Now and here I proclaim—"

But she was interrupted by a visitor. It was the editor and proprietor of the *Sagamore*. He had happened into Lakeside to pay a duty-call upon an obscure grandmother of his who was nearing the end of her pilgrimage, and with the idea of combining business with grief he had looked up the Fosters, who had been so absorbed in other things for the past four years that they had neglected to pay up their subscription. Six dollars due. No visitor could have been more welcome. He would know all about Uncle Tilbury and what his chances might be getting to be, cemeterywards. They could, of course, ask no questions, for that would squelch the bequest, but they could nibble around on the edge of the subject and hope for results. The scheme did not work. The obtuse editor did not know he was being nibbled at; but at last, chance accomplished what art had failed in. In illustration of something under discussion which required the help of metaphor, the editor said:

"Land, it's as tough as Tilbury Foster!—as *we* say."

It was sudden, and it made the Fosters jump. The editor noticed it, and said, apologetically:

"No harm intended, I assure you. It's just a saying; just a joke, you know—nothing in it. Relation of yours?"

Sally crowded his burning eagerness down, and answered with all the indifference he could assume:

"I—well, not that I know of, but we've heard of him." The editor was thankful, and resumed his composure. Sally added: "Is he—is he—well?"

"Is he *well?* Why, bless you he's in Sheol these five years!"

The Fosters were trembling with grief, though it felt like joy. Sally said, non-commitally—and tentatively:

"Ah, well, such is life, and none can escape—not even the rich are spared."

The editor laughed.

"If you are including Tilbury," said he, "it don't apply. *He* hadn't a cent; the town had to bury him."

The Fosters sat petrified for two minutes; petrified and cold. Then, white-faced and weak-voiced, Sally asked:

"Is it true? Do you *know* it to be true?"

"Well, I should say! I was one of the executors. He hadn't anything to leave but a wheelbarrow, and he left that to me. It hadn't any wheel, and wasn't any good. Still, it was something, and so, to square up, I scribbled off a sort of a little obituarial send-off for him, but it got crowded out."

The Fosters were not listening—their cup was full, it could contain no more. They sat with bowed heads, dead to all things but the ache at their hearts.

An hour later. Still they sat there, bowed, motionless, silent, the visitor long ago gone, they unaware.

Then they stirred, and lifted their heads wearily, and gazed at each other wistfully, dreamily, dazed; then presently began to twaddle to each other in a wandering and childish way. At intervals they lapsed into silences, leaving a sentence unfinished, seemingly either unaware of it or losing their way. Sometimes, when they woke out of these silences they had a dim and transient consciousness that something had happened to their minds; then with a dumb and yearning solicitude they would softly caress each other's hands in mutual compassion and support, as if they would say: "I am near you, I will not forsake you, we will bear it together; somewhere there is release and forgetfulness, somewhere there is a grave and peace; be patient, it will not be long."

They lived yet two years, in mental night, always brooding, steeped in vague regrets and melancholy dreams, never speaking; then release came to both on the same day.

Towards the end the darkness lifted from Sally's ruined mind for a moment, and he said:

"Vast wealth, acquired by sudden and unwholesome means, is a snare. It did us no good, transient were its feverish pleasures; yet for its sake we threw away our sweet and simple and happy life—let others take warning by us."

He lay silent awhile, with closed eyes; then as the chill of death crept upward towards his heart, and consciousness was fading from his brain, he muttered:

"Money had brought him misery, and he took his revenge upon us, who had done him no harm. He had his desire: with base and cunning calculation he left us but thirty thousand, knowing we would try to increase it, and ruin our life and break our hearts. Without added expense he could have left us far above desire of increase, far above the temptation to speculate, and a kinder soul would have done it; but in him was no generous spirit, no pity, no—"

This burlesque was written when Twain was a newspaperman in San Francisco; it appeared as a feature in the Golden Era *on September 20, 1863, and was reprinted in the January 1864 issue of the monthly* Yankee Notions. *The tale was first collected in* The Celebrated Jumping Frog of Calaveras County and Other Sketches, *published by C.H. Webb in 1867, and was later included in the American Publishing Company's edition of* Mark Twain's Sketches New and Old *in 1875.*

Curing a Cold

It is a good thing, perhaps, to write for the amusement of the public, but it is a far higher and nobler thing to write for their instruction, their profit, their actual and tangible benefit. The latter is the sole object of this article. If it prove the means of restoring to health one solitary sufferer among my race, of lighting up once more the fire of hope and joy in his faded eyes, of bringing back to his dead heart again the quick, generous impulses of other days, I shall be amply rewarded for my labor; my soul will be permeated with the sacred delight a Christian feels when he has done a good, unselfish deed.

Having led a pure and blameless life, I am justified in believing that no man who knows me will reject the suggestions I am about to make, out of fear that I am trying to deceive him. Let the public do itself the honor to read my experience in doctoring a cold, as herein set forth, and then follow in my footsteps.

When the White House was burned in Virginia City, I lost my home, my happiness, my constitution, and my trunk. The loss of the two first-named articles was a matter of no great consequence, since a home without a mother or a sister, or a distant young female relative in it, to remind you, by putting your soiled linen out of sight and taking your boots down off the mantelpiece, that there are those who think about you and care for you, is easily obtained. And I cared nothing for the loss of my happiness, because not being a poet, it could not be possible that melancholy would abide with me long. But to lose a good constitution and a better trunk were serious misfortunes. On the day of the fire my constitution succumbed to a severe cold, caused by undue exertion in getting ready to do something. I suffered to no purpose, too, because the plan I was figuring at for the extinguishing of the fire was so elaborate that I never got it completed until the middle of the following week.

The first time I began to sneeze, a friend told me to go and bathe my feet in hot water and go to bed. I did so. Shortly afterwards, another friend advised me to get up and take a cold shower-bath. I did that also. Within the hour, another friend assured me that it was policy to "feed a cold and starve a fever." I had both. So I thought it best to fill myself up for the cold, and then keep dark and let the fever starve awhile.

In a case of this kind, I seldom do things by halves; I ate pretty heartily; I conferred my custom upon a stranger who had just opened his restaurant that morning: he waited near me in respectful silence until I had finished feeding my cold, when he inquired if the people about Virginia City were much afflicted with colds? I told him I thought they were. He then went out and took in his sign.

I started down toward the office, and on the way encountered another bosom friend, who told me that a quart of salt water, taken warm, would come as near curing a cold as anything in the world. I hardly thought I had room for it, but I tried it anyhow. The result was surprising. I believed I had thrown up my immortal soul.

Now, as I am giving my experience only for the benefit of those who are troubled with the distemper I am writing about, I feel that they will see the propriety of my cautioning them against following such portions of it as proved inefficient with me, and acting upon this conviction, I warn them against warm salt water. It may be a good enough remedy, but I think it is too severe. If I had another cold in the head, and there were no course left me but to take either an earthquake or a quart of warm salt water, I would take my chances on the earthquake.

After the storm which had been raging in my stomach had subsided, and no more good Samaritans happening along, I went on borrowing handkerchiefs again and blowing them to atoms, as had been my custom in the early stages of my cold, until I came across a lady who had just arrived from over the plains, and who said she had lived in a part of the country where doctors were scarce, and had from necessity acquired considerable skill in the treatment of simple "family complaints." I knew she must have had much experience, for she appeared to be a hundred and fifty years old.

She mixed a decoction composed of molasses, aquafortis,

turpentine, and various other drugs, and instructed me to take a wine-glass full of it every fifteen minutes. I never took but one dose; that was enough; it robbed me of all moral principle, and awoke every unworthy impulse of my nature. Under its malign influence my brain conceived miracles of meanness, but my hands were too feeble to execute them; at that time, had it not been that my strength had surrendered to a succession of assaults from infallible remedies for my cold, I am satisfied that I would have tried to rob the graveyard. Like most other people, I often feel mean, and act accordingly; but until I took that medicine I had never revelled in such supernatural depravity, and felt proud of it. At the end of two days I was ready to go to doctoring again. I took a few more unfailing remedies, and finally drove my cold from my head to my lungs.

I got to coughing incessantly, and my voice fell below zero; I conversed in a thundering base, two octaves below my natural tone; I could only compass my regular nightly repose by coughing myself down to a state of utter exhaustion, and then the moment I began to talk in my sleep, my discordant voice woke me up again.

My case grew more and more serious every day. Plain gin was recommended; I took it. Then gin and molasses; I took that also. Then gin and onions; I added the onions, and took all three. I detected no particular result, however, except that I had acquired a breath like a buzzard's.

I found I had to travel for my health. I went to Lake Bigler with my reportorial comrade, Wilson. It is gratifying to me to reflect that we traveled in considerable style; we went in the Pioneer coach, and my friend took all his baggage with him, consisting of two excellent silk handkerchiefs and a daguerreotype of his grandmother. We sailed and hunted and fished and danced all day, and I doctored my cough all night. By managing in this way, I made out to improve every hour in the twenty-four. But my disease continued to grow worse.

A sheet-bath was recommended. I had never refused a remedy yet, and it seemed poor policy to commence then; therefore I determined to take a sheet-bath, notwithstanding I had no idea what sort of arrangement it was. It was administered at midnight, and the weather was very frosty. My breast and back were bared, and a sheet (there appeared to be a thousand yards of it) soaked in ice-water, and wound around me until I resembled a swab for a Columbiad.

It is a cruel expedient. When the chilly rag touches one's warm flesh, it makes him start with sudden violence, and gasp for breath just as men do in the death agony. It froze the marrow in my bones, and stopped the beating of my heart. I thought my time had come.

Young Wilson said the circumstance reminded him of an anecdote about a negro who was being baptized, and who slipped from the parson's grasp, and came near being drowned. He floundered around, though, and finally rose up out of the water considerably strangled, and furiously angry, and started ashore at once, spouting water like a whale, and remarking, with great asperity, that "one o' dese days some gent'l'man's nigger gwyne to get killed wid jis' such dam foolishness as dis!"

Never take a sheet-bath—never. Next to meeting a lady acquaintance, who, for reasons best known to herself, don't see you when she looks at you, and don't know you when she does see you, it is the most uncomfortable thing in the world.

But, as I was saying, when the sheet-bath failed to cure my cough, a lady friend recommended the application of a mustard plaster to my breast. I believe that would have cured me effectually, if it had not been for young Wilson. When I went to bed, I put my mustard plaster—which was a very gorgeous one, eighteen inches square—where I could reach it when I was ready for it. But young Wilson got hungry in the night and—here is food for the imagination.

After sojourning a week at Lake Bigler, I went to Steamboat Springs, and beside the steam baths, I took a lot of the vilest medicines that were ever concocted. They would have cured me, but I had to go back to Virginia City, where, notwithstanding the variety of new remedies I absorbed every day, I managed to aggravate my disease by carelessness and undue exposure.

I finally concluded to visit San Francisco, and the first day I got there, a lady at the hotel told me to drink a quart of whisky every twenty-four hours, and a friend up town recommended precisely the same course. Each advised me to take a quart; that made half a gallon. I did it, and still live.

Now, with the kindest motives in the world, I offer for the consideration of consumptive patients the variegated course of treatment I have lately gone through. Let them try it: if it don't cure, it can't more than kill them.

This scathing satire appeared in the May 1870 issue of Galaxy. *At the time, Twain had an arrangement with the magazine to contribute a monthly column called "Memoranda," and he often used his allotted space to comment on various injustices, particularly to the Chinese, about which he had not been able to write freely while he was a newspaperman in San Francisco. In 1871, the essay appeared in an unauthorized publication in Toronto called* Mark Twain's Memoranda from the Galaxy. *He included it in his own collection,* Mark Twain's Sketches New and Old, *in 1875.*

Disgraceful Persecution of a Boy

In San Francisco, the other day, "A well-dressed boy, on his way to Sunday-school, was arrested and thrown into the city prison for stoning Chinamen."

What a commentary is this upon human justice! What sad prominence it gives to our human disposition to tyrannize over the weak! San Francisco has little right to take credit to herself for her treatment of this poor boy. What had the child's education been? How should he suppose it was wrong to stone a Chinaman? Before we side against him, along with outraged San Francisco, let us give him a chance—let us hear the testimony for the defense.

He was a "well-dressed" boy, and a Sunday-school scholar, and therefore, the chances are that his parents were intelligent, well-to-do people, with just enough natural villainy in their composition to make them yearn after the daily papers, and enjoy them; and so this boy had opportunities to learn all through the week how to do right, as well as on Sunday.

It was in this way that he found out that the great commonwealth of California imposes an unlawful mining-tax upon John the foreigner, and allows Patrick the foreigner to dig gold for nothing—probably because the degraded Mongol is at no expense for whisky, and the refined Celt cannot exist without it.

It was in this way that he found out that a respectable number of the tax-gatherers—it would be unkind to say all of them—collect the tax twice, instead of once; and that, inasmuch as they do it solely to discourage Chinese immigration into the mines, it is a thing that is much applauded, and likewise regarded as being singularly facetious.

It was in this way that he found out that when a white man robs a sluice-box (by the term white man is meant Spaniards, Mexicans, Portuguese, Irish, Hondurans, Peruvians, Chileans, &c., &c.), they make him leave the camp; and when a Chinaman does that thing, they hang him.

It was in this way that he found out that in many districts of the vast Pacific coast, so strong is the wild, free love of justice in the hearts of the people, that whenever any secret and mysterious crime is committed, they say, "Let justice be done, though the heavens fall," and go straightNay and swing a Chinaman.

It was in this way that he found out that by studying one half of each day's "local items," it would appear that the police of San Francisco were either asleep or dead, and by studying the other half it would seem that the reporters were gone mad with admiration of the energy, the virtue, the high effectiveness, and the dare-devil intrepidity of that very police—making exultant mention of how "the Argus-eyed officer So-and-so," captured a wretched knave of a Chinaman who was stealing chickens, and brought him gloriously to the city prison and how "the gallant officer Such-and-such-a-one," quietly kept an eye on the movements of an "unsuspecting, almond-eyed son of Confucius" (your reporter is nothing if not facetious), following him around with that far-off look of vacancy and unconsciousness always so finely affected by that inscrutable being, the forty-dollar policeman, during a waking interval, and captured him at last in the very act of placing his hands in a suspicious manner upon a paper of tacks, left by the owner in an exposed situation; and how one officer performed this prodigious thing, and another officer that, and another the other—and pretty much every one of these performances having for a dazzling central incident a Chinaman guilty of a shilling's worth of crime, an unfortunate, whose misdemeanor must be hurrahed into something enormous in order to keep the public from noticing how many really important rascals went uncaptured in the meantime, and how overrated those glorified policemen actually are.

It was in this way that the boy found out that the Legislature, being aware that the Constitution has made America an asylum for the poor and the oppressed of all nations, and that, therefore, the poor and oppressed who fly to our shelter must not be charged a disabling admission fee, made a law that every

Chinaman, upon landing, must be *vaccinated* upon the wharf, and pay to the State's appointed officer *ten dollars* for the service, when there are plenty of doctors in San Francisco who would be glad enough to do it for him for fifty cents.

It was in this way that the boy found out that a Chinaman had no rights that any man was bound to respect; that he had no sorrows that any man was bound to pity; that neither his life nor his liberty was worth the purchase of a penny when a white man needed a scapegoat; that nobody loved Chinamen, nobody befriended them, nobody spared them suffering when it was convenient to inflict it; everybody, individuals, communities, the majesty of the State itself, joined in hating, abusing, and persecuting these humble strangers.

And, therefore, what *could* have been more natural than for this sunny-hearted boy, tripping along to Sunday-school, with his mind teeming with freshly-learned incentives to high and virtuous action, to say to himself—

"Ah, there goes a Chinaman! God will not love me if I do not stone him."

And for this he was arrested and put in the city jail.

Everything conspired to teach him that it was a high and holy thing to stone a Chinaman, and yet he no sooner attempts to do his duty that he is punished for it—he, poor chap, who has been aware all his life that one of the principal recreations of the police, out toward the Gold Refinery, is to look on with tranquil enjoyment while the butchers of Brannan Street set their dogs on unoffending Chinamen, and make them flee for their lives.*

Keeping in mind the tuition in the humanities which the entire "Pacific coast" gives its youth, there is a very sublimity of incongruity in the virtuous flourish with which the good city fathers of San Francisco proclaim (as they have lately done) that "The police are positively ordered to arrest all boys, of every description and wherever found, who engage in assaulting Chinamen."

Still, let us be truly glad they have made the order, notwithstanding its inconsistency; and let us rest perfectly confident the police are glad, too. Because there is no personal peril in ar-

*I have many such memories in my mind, but am thinking just at present of one particular one, where the Brannan Street butchers set their dogs on a Chinaman who was quietly passing with a basket of clothes on his head; and while the dogs mutilated his flesh, a butcher increased the hilarity of the occasion by knocking some of the Chinaman's teeth down his throat with half a brick. This incident sticks in my memory with a more malevolent tenacity, perhaps, on account of the fact that I was in the employ of a San Francisco journal at the time, and was not allowed to publish it because it might offend some of the peculiar element that subscribed for the paper.

resting boys, provided they be of the small kind, and the reporters will have to laud their performances just as loyally as ever, or go without items.

The new form for local items in San Francisco will now be:—"The ever vigilant and efficient officer So-and-so succeeded, yesterday afternoon, in arresting Master Tommy Jones, after a determined resistance," etc., etc, followed by the customary statistics and final hurrah, with its unconscious sarcasm: "We are happy in being able to state that this is the forty-seventh boy arrested by this gallant officer since the new ordinance went into effect. The most extraordinary activity prevails in the police department. Nothing like it has been seen since we can remember."

This burlesque on the mania of the collector was written for the December 1876 issue of the Atlantic. *The following year, it appeared as "The Echo That Did Not Answer" in the London publication* Beeton's Christmas Annual. *Its first appearance in book form in America was in* Punch, Brothers, Punch!, *a collection of sketches issued by Slote, Woodman & Company in 1878.*

The Canvasser's Tale

Poor, sad-eyed stranger! There was that about his humble mien, his tired look, his decayed-gentility clothes, that almost reached the mustard-seed of charity that still remained, remote and lonely, in the empty vastness of my heart, notwithstanding I observed a portfolio under his arm, and said to myself, Behold, Providence hath delivered his servant into the hands of another canvasser.

Well, these people always get one interested. Before I well knew how it came about, this one was telling me his history, and I was all attention and sympathy. He told it something like this:

My parents died, alas! when I was a little, sinless child. My uncle Ithuriel took me to his heart and reared me as his own. He was my only relative in the wide world; but he was good and rich and generous. He reared me in the lap of luxury. I knew no want that money could satisfy.

In the fulness of time I was graduated, and went with two of my servants—my chamberlain and my valet—to travel in foreign countries. During four years I flitted upon careless wing amid the beauteous gardens of the distant strand, if you will permit this form of speech in one whose tongue was ever attuned to poesy; and indeed I so speak with confidence, as one unto his kind, for I perceive by your eyes that you too, sir, are gifted with the divine inflation. In those far lands I reveled in the ambrosial food that fructifies the soul, the mind, the heart. But of all things, that which most appealed to my inborn aesthetic taste was the prevailing custom there, among the rich, of making collections of elegant and costly rarities, dainty *objets de vertu*, and in an evil hour I tried to uplift my uncle Ithuriel to a plane of sympathy with this exquisite employment.

I wrote and told him of one gentleman's vast collection of shells; another's noble collection of meerschaum pipes; another's elevating and refining collection of undecipherable autographs; another's priceless collection of old china; another's enchanting collection of postage-stamps—and so forth and so on. Soon my letters yielded fruit. My uncle began to look about for something to make a collection of. You may know, perhaps, how fleetly a taste like this dilates. His soon became a raging fever, though I knew it not. He began to neglect his great pork business; presently he wholly retired and turned an elegant leisure into a rabid search for curious things. His wealth was vast, and he spared it not. First he tried cow-bells. He made a collection which filled five large *salons*, and comprehended all the different sorts of cow-bells that ever had been contrived, save one. That one—an antique, and the only specimen extant—was possessed by another collector. My uncle offered enormous sums for it, but the gentleman would not sell. Doubtless you know what necessarily resulted. A true collector attaches no value to a collection that is not complete. His great heart breaks, he sells his hoard, he turns his mind to some field that seems unoccupied.

Thus did my uncle. He next tried brickbats. After piling up a vast and intensely interesting collection, the former difficulty supervened; his great heart broke again; he sold out his soul's idol to the retired brewer who possessed the missing brick. Then he tried flint hatchets and other implements of Primeval Man, but by and by discovered that the factory where they were made was supplying other collectors as well as himself. He tried Aztec inscriptions and stuffed whales—another failure, after incredible labor and expense. When his collection seemed at last perfect, a stuffed whale arrived from Greenland and an Aztec inscription from the Cundurango regions of Central America that made all former specimens insignificant. My uncle hastened to secure these noble gems. He got the stuffed whale, but another collector got the inscription. A real Cundurango, as possibly you know, is a possession of such supreme value that, when once a collector gets it, he will rather part with his family than with it. So my uncle sold out, and saw his darlings go forth, never more to return; and his coal-black hair turned white as snow in a single night.

Now he waited, and thought. He knew another disappointment might kill him. He was resolved that he would choose things next time that no other man was collecting. He carefully made up his mind, and once more entered the field—this time to make a collection of echoes.

"Of what?" said I.

Echoes, sir. His first purchase was an echo in Georgia that repeated four times; his next was a six-repeater in Maryland; his next was a thirteen-repeater in Maine; his next was a nine-repeater in Kansas; his next was a twelve-repeater in Tennessee, which he got cheap, so to speak, because it was out of repair, a portion of the crag which reflected it having tumbled down. He believed he could repair it at a cost of a few thousand dollars, and, by increasing the elevation with masonry, treble the repeating capacity; but the architect who undertook the job had never built an echo before, and so he utterly spoiled this one. Before he meddled with it, it used to talk back like a mother-in-law, but now it was only fit for the deaf and dumb asylum. Well, next he bought a lot of cheap little double-barreled echoes, scattered around over various States and Territories; he got them at twenty per cent off by taking the lot. Next he bought a perfect Gatling gun of an echo in Oregon, and it cost a fortune, I can tell you. You may know, sir, that in the echo market the scale of prices is cumulative, like the carat-scale in diamonds; in fact, the same phraseology is used. A single-carat echo is worth but ten dollars over and above the value of the land it is on; a two-carat or double-barreled echo is worth thirty dollars; a five-carat is worth nine hundred and fifty; a ten-carat is worth thirteen thousand. My uncle's Oregon echo, which he called the Great Pitt Echo, was a twenty-two carat gem, and cost two hundred and sixteen thousand dollars—they threw the land in, for it was four hundred miles from a settlement.

Well, in the mean time my path was a path of roses. I was the accepted suitor of the only and lovely daughter of an English earl, and was beloved to distraction. In that dear presence I swam in seas of bliss. The family were content, for it was known that I was sole heir to an uncle held to be worth five millions of dollars. However, none of us knew that my uncle had become a collector, at least in any thing more than a small way, for aesthetic amusement.

Now gathered the clouds above my unconscious head. That divine echo, since known throughout the world as the Great Koh-i-noor, or Mountain of Repetitions, was discovered. It was a sixty-five-carat gem. You could utter a word and it would talk back at you for fifteen minutes, when the day was otherwise quiet. But behold, another discovery was made at the same time: another echo-collector was in the field. The two rushed to make the purchase. The property consisted of a couple of small hills with a shallow swale between, out yonder among the back settlements of New York State. Both men arrived on the ground at the same time, and neither knew the other was there. The echo was not all owned by one man; a person by the name of Williamson Bolivar Jarvis owned the east hill, and a person by the name of Harbison J. Bledso owned the west hill; the swale between was the dividing line. So, while my uncle was buying Jarvis's hill for three million two hundred and eighty-five thousand dollars, the other party was buying Bledso's hill for a shade over three million.

Now, do you perceive the natural result? Why, the noblest collection of echoes on earth was forever and ever incomplete, since it possessed but the one half of the king echo of the universe. Neither man was content with this divided ownership, yet neither would sell to the other. There were jawings, bickerings, heart-burnings. And at last, that other collector, with a malignity which only a collector can feel toward a man and a brother, proceeded to cut down his hill.

You see, as long as he could not have the echo, he was resolved that nobody should have it. He would remove his hill, and then there would be nothing to reflect my uncle's echo. My uncle remonstrated with him, but the man said, "I own one end of this echo; I choose to kill my end; you must take care of your own end yourself."

Well, my uncle got an injunction put on him. The other man appealed and fought it in a higher court. They carried it on up, clear to the Supreme Court of the United States. It made no end of trouble there. Two of the judges believed that an echo was personal property, because it was impalpable to sight and touch, and yet was purchasable, salable, and consequently taxable; two others believed that an echo was real estate, because it was manifestly attached to the land, and was not removable from place to place; other of the judges contended that an echo was not property at all.

It was finally decided that the echo was property; that the hills were property; that the two men were separate and independent owners of the two hills, but tenants in common in the echo; therefore, defendant was at full liberty to cut down his hill, since it belonged solely to him, but must give bonds in three million dollars as indemnity for damages which might result to my uncle's half of the echo. This decision also debarred my uncle from using defendant's hill to reflect his part of the echo, without defendant's consent; he must use only his own hill; if his part of the echo would not go, under these circumstances, it was sad, of course, but the court could find no remedy. The court also debarred defendant from using my uncle's hill to reflect *his* end of the echo, without consent. You see the grand result! Neither man would give consent, and so that astonishing and most noble echo had to cease from its great powers; and since that day that magnificent property is tied up and unsalable.

A week before my wedding day, while I was still swimming in bliss and the nobility were gathering from far and near to honor our espousals, came news of my uncle's death, and also a copy of his will, making me his sole heir. He was gone; alas, my dear benefactor was no more. The thought surcharges my heart even at this remote day. I handed the will to the earl; I could not read it for the blinding tears. The earl read it; then he sternly said, "Sir, do you call this wealth? But doubtless you do in your inflated country. Sir, you are left sole heir to a vast collection of echoes—if a thing can be called a collection that is scattered far and wide over the huge length and breadth of the American continent. Sir, this is not all; you are head and ears in debt; there is not an echo in the lot but has a mortgage on it. Sir, I am not a hard man, but I must look to my child's interest; if you had but one echo which you could honestly call your own; if you had but one echo which was free from encumbrances, so that you could retire to it with my child, and by humble, painstaking industry cultivate and improve it, and thus wrest from it a maintenance, I would not say you nay; but I cannot marry my child to a beggar. Leave his side, my darling; go, sir, take your mortgage-ridden echoes and quit my sight forever."

My noble Celestine clung to me in tears, with loving arms, and swore she would willingly, nay, gladly marry me, though I had not an echo in the world. But it could not be. We were torn asunder; she to pine and die within the twelvemonth, I to toil life's long journey sad and lone, praying daily, hourly, for that release which shall join us together again in that dear realm where the wicked cease from troubling and the weary are at rest. Now, sir, if you will be so kind as to look at these maps and plans in my portfolio, I am sure that I can sell you an echo for less money than any man in the trade. Now this one, which cost my uncle ten dollars thirty years ago, and is one of the sweetest things in Texas, I will let you have for—

"Let me interrupt you," I said. "My friend, I have not had a moment's respite from canvassers this day. I have bought a sewing machine which I did not want; I have bought a map which is mistaken in all its details, I have bought a clock which will not go; I have bought a moth poison which the moths prefer to any other beverage; I have bought no end of useless inventions, and now I have had enough of this foolishness. I would not have one of your echoes if you were even to give it to me. I would not let it stay on the place. I always hate a man that tries to sell me echoes. You see this gun? Now take your collection and move on; let us not have bloodshed."

But he only smiled a sad, sweet smile, and got out some more diagrams. You know the result perfectly well, because you know that when you have once opened the door to a canvasser, the trouble is done, and you have got to suffer defeat.

I compromised with this man at the end of an intolerable hour. I bought two double-barreled echoes in good condition, and he threw in another, which he said was not salable because it only spoke German. He said, "She was a perfect polyglot once, but somehow her palate got down."

"At the Appetite-Cure," a story that Twain says was originally intended for inclusion in A Tramp Abroad, *first appeared in* Cosmopolitan *in August 1898. It was collected in* How To Tell a Story and Other Essays *in 1900.*

At the Appetite-Cure

I

This establishment's name is Hochberghaus. It is in Bohemia, a short day's journey from Vienna, and being in the Austrian empire is of course a health resort. The empire is made up of health resorts; it distributes health to the whole world. Its waters are all medicinal. They are bottled and sent throughout the earth; the natives themselves drink beer. This is self-sacrifice, apparently—but outlanders who have drunk Vienna beer have another idea about it. Particularly the Pilsner which one gets in a small cellar up an obscure back lane in the First Bezirk—the name has escaped me, but the place is easily found: You inquire for the Greek church; and when you get to it, go right along by—the next house is that little beer-mill. It is remote from all traffic and all noise; it is always Sunday there. There are two small rooms, with low ceilings supported by massive arches; the arches and ceilings are whitewashed, otherwise the rooms would pass for cells in the dungeons of a bastile. The furniture is plain and cheap, there is no ornamentation anywhere; yet it is a heaven for the self-sacrificers, for the beer there is incomparable; there is nothing like it elsewhere in the world. In the first room you will find twelve or fifteen ladies and gentlemen of civilian quality; in the other one a dozen generals and ambassadors. One may live in Vienna many months and not hear of this place; but having once heard of it and sampled it, the sampler will afterward infest it.

However, this is all incidental—a mere passing note of gratitude for blessings received—it has nothing to do with my subject. My subject is health resorts. All unhealthy people ought to domicile themselves in Vienna, and use that as a base, making flights from time to time to the outlying resorts, according to need. A flight to Marienbad to get rid of fat; a flight to Carlsbad to get rid of rheumatism; a flight to Kaltenleutgeben to take the water cure and get rid of the rest of the diseases. It is all so handy. You can stand in Vienna and toss a biscuit into Kaltenleutgeben, with a twelve-inch gun. You can run out thither at any time of the day; you go by the phenomenally slow trains, and yet inside of an hour you have exchanged the glare and swelter of the city for wooded hills, and shady forest paths, and soft cool airs, and the music of birds, and the repose and peace of paradise.

And there are plenty of other health resorts at your service and convenient to get at from Vienna; charming places, all of them; Vienna sits in the centre of a beautiful world of mountains with now and then a lake and forests; in fact, no other city is so fortunately situated.

There are an abundance of health resorts, as I have said. Among them this place—Hochberghaus. It stands solitary on the top of a densely wooded mountain, and is a building of great size. It is called the Appetite Anstallt, and people who have lost their appetites come here to get them restored. When I arrived I was taken by Professor Haimberger to his consulting-room and questioned:

"It is six o'clock. When did you eat last?"

"At noon."

"What did you eat?"

"Next to nothing."

"What was on the table?"

"The usual things."

"Chops, chickens, vegetables, and so on?"

"Yes; but don't mention them—I can't bear it."

"Are you tired of them?"

"Oh, utterly. I wish I might never hear of them again."

"The mere sight of food offends you, does it?"

"More, it revolts me."

The doctor considered awhile, then got out a long menu and ran his eye slowly down it.

"I think," said he, "that what you need to eat is—but here, choose for yourself."

I glanced at the list, and my stomach threw a handspring. Of all the barbarous layouts that were ever contrived, this was the most atrocious. At the top stood "tough, underdone, overdue tripe, garnished with garlic"; half-way down the bill stood "young cat; old cat; scrambled cat"; at the bottom stood "sailor-boots, softened with tallow—served raw." The wide intervals of the bill were packed with dishes calculated to insult a cannibal. I said:

"Doctor, it is not fair to joke over so serious a case as mine. I came here to get an appetite, not to throw away the remnant that's left."

He said gravely: "I am not joking; why should I joke?"

"But I can't eat these horrors."

"Why not?"

He said it with a naiveté that was admirable, whether it was real or assumed.

"Why not? Because—why, doctor, for months I have seldom been able to endure anything more substantial than omelettes and custards. These unspeakable dishes of yours—"

"Oh, you will come to like them. They are very good. And you *must* eat them. It is the rule of the place, and is strict. I cannot permit any departure from it."

I said, smiling: "Well, then, doctor, you will have to permit the departure of the patient. I am going."

He looked hurt, and said in a way which changed the aspect of things:

"I am sure you would not do me that injustice. I accepted you in good faith—you will not shame that confidence. This appetite-cure is my whole living. If you should go forth from it with the sort of appetite which you now have, it could become known, and you can see, yourself, that people would say my cure failed in your case and hence can fail in other cases. You will not go; you will not do me this hurt."

I apologized and said I would stay.

"That is right. I was sure you would not go; it would take the food from my family's mouths."

"Would they mind that? Do they eat these fiendish things?"

"They? My family?" His eyes were full of gentle wonder. "Of course not."

"Oh, they don't! Do you?"

"Certainly not."

"I see. It's another case of a physician who doesn't take his own medicine."

"I don't need it. It is six hours since you lunched. Will you have supper now—or later?"

"I am not hungry, but now is as good a time as any, and I would like to be done with it and have it off my mind. It is about my usual time, and regularity is commanded by all the authorities. Yes, I will try to nibble a little now—I wish a light horsewhipping would answer instead."

The professor handed me that odious menu.

"Choose—or will you have it later?"

"Oh, dear me, show me to my room; I forgot your hard rule."

"Wait just a moment before you finally decide. There is another rule. If you choose now, the order will be filled at once; but if you wait, you will have to await my pleasure. You cannot get a dish from that entire bill until I consent."

"All right. Show me to my room, and send the cook to bed; there is not going to be any hurry."

The professor took me up one flight of stairs and showed me into a most inviting and comfortable apartment consisting of parlor, bedchamber, and bathroom.

The front windows looked out over a far-reaching spread of green glades and valleys, and tumbled hills clothed with forests—a noble solitude unvexed by the fussy world. In the parlor were many shelves filled with books. The professor said he would now leave me to myself; and added:

"Smoke and read as much as you please, drink all the water you like. When you get hungry, ring and give your order, and I will decide whether it shall be filled or not. Yours is a stubborn, bad case, and I think the first fourteen dishes in the bill are each and all too delicate for its needs. I ask you as a favor to restrain yourself and not call for them."

"Restrain myself, is it? Give yourself no uneasiness. You are going to save money by me. The idea of coaxing a sick man's appetite back with this buzzard-fare is clear insanity."

I said it with bitterness, for I felt outraged by this calm, cold talk over these heartless new engines of assassination. The doctor looked grieved, but not offended. He laid the bill of fare on the commode at my bed's head, "so that it would be handy," and said:

"Yours is not the worst case I have encountered, by any means; still it is a bad one and requires robust treatment; therefore I shall be gratified if you will restrain yourself and skip down to No. 15 and begin with that."

Then he left me and I began to undress, for I was dog-tired and very sleepy. I slept fifteen hours and woke up finely refreshed at ten the next morning. Vienna coffee! It was the first thing I thought of—that unapproachable luxury—that sumptuous coffee-house coffee, compared with which all other European coffee and all American hotel coffee is mere fluid poverty.

I rang, and ordered it; also Vienna bread, that delicious invention. The servant spoke through the wicket in the door and said—but you know what he said. He referred me to the bill of fare. I allowed him to go—I had no further use for him.

After the bath I dressed and started for a walk, and got as far as the door. It was locked on the outside. I rang and the servant came and explained that it was another rule. The seclusion of the patient was required until after the first meal. I had not been particularly anxious to get out before; but it was different now. Being locked in makes a person wishful to get out. I soon began to find it difficult to put in the time. At two o'clock I had been twenty-six hours without food. I had been growing hungry for some time; I recognized that I was not only hungry now, but hungry with a strong adjective in front of it. Yet I was not hungry enough to face the bill of fare.

I must put in the time somehow. I would read and smoke. I did it; hour by hour. The books were all of one breed—shipwrecks; people lost in deserts; people shut up in caved-in mines; people starving in besieged cities. I read about all the revolting dishes that ever famishing men had stayed their hunger with. During the first hours these things nauseated me: hours followed in which they did not so affect me; still other hours followed in which I found myself smacking my lips over some tolerably infernal messes. When I had been without food forty-five hours I ran eagerly to the bell and ordered the second dish in the bill, which was a sort of dumplings containing a compost made of caviar and tar.

It was refused me. During the next fifteen hours I visited the bell every now and then and ordered a dish that was further down the list. Always a refusal. But I was conquering prejudice after prejudice, right along; I was making sure progress; I was creeping up on No. 15 with deadly certainty, and my heart beat faster and faster, my hopes rose higher and higher.

At last when food had not passed my lips for sixty hours, victory was mine, and I ordered No. 15:

"Soft-boiled spring chicken—in the egg; six dozen, hot and fragrant!"

In fifteen minutes it was there; and the doctor along with it, rubbing his hands with joy. He said with great excitement:

"It's a cure, it's a cure! I knew I could do it. Dear sir, my grand system never fails—never. You've got your appetite back—you know you have; say it and make me happy."

"Bring on your carrion—I can eat anything in the bill!"

"Oh, this is noble, this is splendid—but I knew I could do it, the system never fails. How are the birds?"

"Never was anything so delicious in the world; and yet as a rule I don't care for game. But don't interrupt me, don't—I can't spare my mouth, I really can't."

Then the doctor said:

"The cure is perfect. There is no more doubt nor danger. Let the poultry alone; I can trust you with a beefsteak, now."

The beefsteak came—as much as a basketful of it—with potatoes, and Vienna bread and coffee; and I ate a meal then that was worth all the costly preparation I had made for it. And dripped tears of gratitude into the gravy all the time—gratitude to the doctor for putting a little plain common-sense into me when I had been empty of it so many, many years.

II

Thirty years ago Haimberger went off on a long voyage in a sailing-ship. There were fifteen passengers on board. The table-fare was of the regulation pattern of the day: At 7 in the morning, a cup of bad coffee in bed; at 9, breakfast: bad coffee, with condensed milk; soggy rolls, crackers, salt fish; at 1 P.M., luncheon: cold tongue, cold ham, cold corned beef, soggy cold rolls, crackers; 5 P.M., dinner: thick pea soup, salt fish, hot corned beef and sour kraut, boiled pork and beans, pudding; 9 till 11 P.M., supper: tea, with condensed milk, cold tongue, cold ham, pickles, sea-biscuit, pickled oysters, pickled pig's feet, grilled bones, golden buck.

At the end of the first week eating had ceased, nibbling had taken its place. The passengers came to the table, but it was partly to put in the time, and partly because the wisdom of the ages commanded them to be regular in their meals. They were tired of the coarse and monotonous fare, and took no interest in it, had no appetite for it. All day and every day they roamed the ship half hungry, plagued by their gnawing stomachs, moody, untalkative, miserable. Among them were three confirmed dyspeptics. These became shadows in the course of three weeks. There was also a bedridden invalid; he lived on boiled rice; he could not look at the regular dishes.

Now came shipwreck and life in open boats, with the usual paucity of food. Provisions ran lower and lower. The appetites improved, then. When nothing was left but raw ham and the ration of that was down to two ounces a day per person, the appetites were perfect. At the end of fifteen days the dyspeptics, the invalid, and the most delicate ladies in the party were chewing sailor-boots in ecstasy, and only complaining because the supply of them was limited. Yet these were the same people who couldn't endure the ship's tedious corned beef and sour kraut and other crudities. They were rescued by an English vessel. Within ten days the whole fifteen were in as good condition as they had been when the shipwreck occurred.

"They had suffered no damage by their adventure," said the professor. "Do you note that?"

"Yes."

"Do you note it well?"

"Yes—I think I do."

"But you don't. You hesitate. You don't rise to the importance of it. I will say it again—with emphasis—*not one of them suffered any damage.*"

"Now I begin to see. Yes, it was indeed remarkable."

"Nothing of the kind. It was perfectly natural. There was no reason why they should suffer damage. They were undergoing Nature's Appetite Cure, the best and wisest in the world."

"Is that where you got your idea?"

"That is where I got it."

"It taught those people a valuable lesson."

"What makes you think that?"

"Why shouldn't I? You seem to think it taught you one."

"That is nothing to the point. I am not a fool."

"I see. Were they fools?"

"They were human beings."

"Is it the same thing?"

"Why do you ask? You know it yourself. As regards his health—and the rest of the things—the average man is what his environment and his superstitions have made him; and their function is to make him an ass. He can't add up three or four new circumstances together and perceive what they mean; it is beyond him. He is not capable of observing for himself; he has to get everything at second-hand. If what are miscalled the lower animals were as silly as man is, they would all perish from the earth in a year."

"Those passengers learned no lesson, then?"

"Not a sign of it. They went to their regular meals in the English ship, and pretty soon they were nibbling again—nibbling, appetiteless, disgusted with the food, moody, miserable, half hungry, their outraged stomachs cursing and swearing and whining and supplicating all day long. And in vain, for they were the stomachs of fools."

"Then, as I understand it, your scheme is—"

"Quite simple. Don't eat till you are hungry. If the food fails to taste good, fails to satisfy you, rejoice you, comfort you, don't eat again until you are *very* hungry. Then it will rejoice you— and do you good, too."

"And I observe no regularity, as to hours?"

"When you are conquering a bad appetite—no. After it is conquered, regularity is no harm, so long as the appetite remains good. As soon as the appetite wavers, apply the corrective again—which is starvation, long or short according to the needs of the case."

"The best diet, I suppose—I mean the wholesomest—"

"All diets are wholesome. Some are wholesomer than others, but all the ordinary diets are wholesome enough for the people who use them. Whether the food be fine or coarse it will taste good and it will nourish if a watch be kept upon the appetite and a little starvation introduced every time it weakens. Nansen was used to fine fare, but when his meals were restricted to bear-meat months at a time he suffered no damage and no discomfort, because his appetite was kept at par through the difficulty of getting his bear-meat regularly."

"But doctors arrange carefully considered and delicate diets for invalids."

"They can't help it. The invalid is full of inherited superstitions and won't starve himself. He believes it would certainly kill him."

"It would weaken him, wouldn't it?"

"Nothing to hurt. Look at the invalids in our shipwreck. They lived fifteen days on pinches of raw ham, a suck at sailor-boots, and general starvation. It weakened them, but it didn't hurt them. It put them in fine shape to eat heartily of hearty food and build themselves up to a condition of robust health. But they do not perceive that; they lost their opportunity; they remained invalids; it served them right. Do you know the tricks that the health-resort doctors play?"

"What is it?"

"My system disguised—covert starvation. Grape-cure, bath-cure, mud-cure—it is all the same. The grape and the bath and the mud make a show and do a trifle of the work—the real work is done by the surreptitious starvation. The patient accustomed to four meals and late hours—at both ends of the day—now consider what he has to do at a health resort. He gets up at 6 in the morning. Eats one egg. Tramps up and down a promenade two hours with the other fools. Eats a butterfly. Slowly drinks a glass of filtered sewage that smells like a buzzard's breath. Promenades another two hours, but alone; if you speak to him he says anxiously, 'My water!—I am walking off my water!—please don't interrupt,' and goes stumping along again. Eats a candied rose-leaf. Lies at rest in the silence and solitude of his room for hours; mustn't read, mustn't smoke. The doctor comes and feels of his heart, now, and his pulse, and thumps his breast and his back and his stomach, and listens for results through a penny flageolet; then orders the man's bath—half a degree, Reamur, cooler than yesterday. After the bath another egg. A glass of sewage at 3 or 4 in the afternoon, and promenade solemnly with the other freaks. Dinner at 6—half a doughnut and a cup of tea. Walk again. Half-past 8, supper—more butterfly; at 9, to bed. Six weeks of this régime—think of it. It starves a man out and puts him in splendid condition. It would have the same effect in London, New York, Jericho—anywhere."

"How long does it take to put a person in condition here?"

"It ought to take but a day or two; but in fact it takes from one to six weeks, according to the character and mentality of the patient."

"How is that?"

"Do you see that crowd of women playing football, and boxing, and jumping fences yonder? They have been here six or seven weeks. They were spectral poor weaklings when they came. They were accustomed to nibbling at dainties and delicacies at set hours four times a day, and they had no appetite for anything. I questioned them, and then locked them into their rooms—the frailest ones to starve nine or ten hours, the others twelve or fifteen. Before long they began to beg; and indeed they suffered a good deal. They complained of nausea, headache, and so on. It was good to see them eat when the time was up. They could not remember when the devouring of a meal had afforded them such rapture—that was their word. Now, then, that ought to have ended their cure, but it didn't. They were free to go to any meals in the house, and they chose their accustomed four. Within a day or two I had to interfere. Their appetites were weakening. I made them knock out a meal. That set them up again. Then they resumed the four. I begged them to learn to knock out a meal themselves, without waiting for me. Up to a fortnight ago they couldn't; they really hadn't manhood enough; but they were gaining it, and now I think they are safe. They drop out a meal every now and then of their own accord. They are in fine condition now, and they might safely go home, I think, but their confidence is not quite perfect yet, so they are waiting awhile."

"Other cases are different?"

"Oh yes. Sometimes a man learns the whole trick in a week. Learns to regulate his appetite and keep it in perfect order.

Learns to drop out a meal with frequency and not mind it."

"But why drop the entire meal out? Why not a part of it?"

"It's a poor device, and inadequate. If the stomach doesn't call vigorously—with a shout, as you may say—it is better not to pester it but just give it a real rest. Some people can eat more meals than others, and still thrive. There are all sorts of people, and all sorts of appetites. I will show you a man presently who was accustomed to nibble at eight meals a day. It was beyond the proper gait of his appetite by two. I have got him down to six a day, now, and he is all right, and enjoys life. How many meals do you affect per day?"

"Formerly—for twenty-two years—a meal and a half; during the past two years, two and a half: coffee and a roll at 9, luncheon at 1, dinner at 7:30 or 8."

"Formerly a meal and a half—that is, coffee and a roll at 9, dinner in the evening, nothing between—is that it?"

"Yes."

"Why did you add a meal?"

"It was the family's idea. They were uneasy. They thought I was killing myself."

"You found a meal and a half per day enough, all through the twenty-two years?"

"Plenty."

"Your present poor condition is due to the extra meal. Drop it out. You are trying to eat oftener than your stomach demands. You don't gain, you lose. You eat less food now, in a day, on two and a half meals, than you formerly ate on one and half."

"True—a good deal less; for in those old days my dinner was a very sizable thing."

"Put yourself on a single meal a day, now—dinner—for a few days, till you secure a good, sound, regular, trustworthy appetite, then take to your one and a half permanently, and don't listen to the family any more. When you have any ordinary ailment, particularly of a feverish sort, eat nothing at all during twenty-four hours. That will cure it. It will cure the stubbornest cold in the head, too. No cold in the head can survive twenty-four hours' unmodified starvation."

"I know it. I have proved it many a time."

This petition to Congress concerning copyright was published in Mark Twain's Sketches New and Old *in 1875, and describes inequities against which Twain lobbied throughout his life. His most famous appearance on its behalf took place on December 7, 1906, when he testified before a joint congressional committee on copyright at the Library of Congress. It was one of the first times that Twain was seen in a white serge suit, a costume that was soon to become his trademark.*

Petition to Congress

TO THE HONORABLE THE SENATE AND HOUSE OF REPRESENTATIVES IN CONGRESS ASSEMBLED:

Whereas, The Constitution guarantees equal rights to all, backed by the Declaration of Independence; and

Whereas, Under our laws, the right of property in real estate is perpetual; and

Whereas, Under our laws, the right of property in the literary result of a citizen's intellectual labor is restricted to forty-two years; and

Whereas, Forty-two years seems an exceedingly just and righteous term, and a sufficiently long one for the retention of property:

Therefore, Your petitioner, having the good of his country solely at heart, humbly prays that "equal rights" and fair and equal treatment may be meted out to all citizens, by the restriction of rights in *all* property, real estate included, to the beneficent term of forty-two years. Then shall all men bless your honorable body and be happy. And for this will your petitioner ever pray.

MARK TWAIN

A PARAGRAPH NOT ADDED TO THE PETITION

The charming absurdity of restricting property-rights in books to forty-two years sticks prominently out in the fact that hardly any man's books ever *live* forty-two years, or even half of it; and so, for the sake of getting a shabby advantage of the heirs of about one Scott or Burns or Milton in a hundred years, the law makers of the "Great" Republic are content to leave that poor little pilfering edict upon the statute books. It is like an emperor lying in wait to rob a phenix's nest, and waiting the necessary century to get the chance.

NIV

STUDY BIBLE

ZONDERVAN®

Published by Zondervan
Grand Rapids, Michigan 49546, USA

www.Zondervan.com

Library of Congress Catalog Card Number 2011929614

Printed in China N100511

17 18 19 20 21 22 23 24 25 /DSC/ 20 19 18 17 16 15 14 13 12 11 10 9 8 7 6

A portion of the purchase price of your NIV® Bible is provided to Biblica so together we support the mission of *Transforming lives through God's Word.*

Biblica provides God's Word to people through translation, publishing and Bible engagement in Africa, Asia Pacific, Europe, Latin America, Middle East, and North America. Through its worldwide reach, Biblica engages people with God's Word so that their lives are transformed through a relationship with Jesus Christ.

TRIBUTES

TRIBUTE TO

Edwin H. Palmer

Edwin H. Palmer, who had served so capably as Executive Secretary of the NIV Committee on Bible Translation and as coordinator of all translation work on the NIV, was appointed General Editor of *The NIV Study Bible* by Zondervan in 1979. On September 16, 1980, he departed this life to "be with Christ, which is better by far" (Philippians 1:23). Before his death, however, he had laid most of the plans for *The NIV Study Bible*, had recruited the majority of the contributors and had done some editorial work on the first manuscripts submitted. We gratefully acknowledge his significant contribution to the earliest stages of the 1985 edition of which this is a revision.

TRIBUTE TO

Donald W. Burdick

Donald Burdick was one of the original Associate Editors of the 1985 edition of *The NIV Study Bible*, with special responsibility for the New Testament. He departed this life on January 4, 1996, to be "at home with the Lord" (2 Corinthians 5:8) before work commenced in 1997 on the fully revised 2002 edition. We gratefully acknowledge his outstanding work on the original *NIV Study Bible*.

TRIBUTE TO

Walter W. Wessel

Walter Wessel was also one of the Associate Editors of the original *NIV Study Bible* (1985), as well as of the 2002 fully revised edition, with special responsibility for the New Testament. Although he was physically unable to be present at our final work session in March 2002, his handwritten proposals were available to us. Then he went home to be with his Lord on April 21, 2002. We thankfully acknowledge his substantial contributions to *The NIV Study Bible* (fully revised). "Blessed are the dead who die in the Lord ... they will rest from their labor, for their deeds will follow them" (Revelation 14:13).

TRIBUTE TO

John H. Stek

John Stek was also one of the Associate Editors of the original *NIV Study Bible* (1985), as well as of the 2002 fully revised edition and the 2008 update, with special responsibility for the Old Testament (though, because of his comprehensive grasp of the whole range of Biblical exegesis and Biblical theology, he also made significant contributions to the New Testament). Then the Lord took him to glory (Psalm 73:24) on June 6, 2009. John leaves a huge void, and he will be sorely missed.

TRIBUTE TO

Ronald Youngblood

Ronald Youngblood, who passed from earth to heaven on July 5, 2014, was also one of the Associate Editors of the original *NIV Study Bible* (1985), as well as of the 2002 fully revised edition, the 2008 update and the 2011 edition, with special responsibility for the Old Testament. Now his "light and momentary troubles are achieving ... an eternal glory that far outweighs them all" (2 Corinthians 4:17). I will miss him greatly, but I will see him again.

Kenneth L. Barker, General Editor

The NIV Study Bible (2011 Edition)

General Editor:	Kenneth L. Barker
Associate Editors:	Mark L. Strauss Ronald F. Youngblood
Project Management and Editorial:	Natalie Block Jean Bloom Dirk Buursma, project manager Donna Huisjen Kim Tanner, visual editor Michael Vander Klipp
Interior Typesetting:	Denise Froehlich Sherri Hoffman Tom and Kathy Ristow, CouGrr Graphics Mark Sheeres Joe Vriend Nancy Wilson, project manager
Interior Proofreading:	Peachtree Editorial and Proofreading Service
Art Direction and Cover Design:	Jamie DeBruyn Ron Huizinga
Interior Design:	Studio Gearbox
Production Management:	Phil Herich

See Contributors page (p. xx) for a complete listing of individuals who contributed or reviewed material for *The NIV Study Bible*.

TABLE OF CONTENTS

THE OLD TESTAMENT

THE NEW TESTAMENT

STUDY HELPS

MAPS

CHARTS

MODELS

PREFACE

The goal of the New International Version (NIV) is to enable English-speaking people from around the world to read and hear God's eternal Word in their own language. Our work as translators is motivated by our conviction that the Bible is God's Word in written form. We believe that the Bible contains the divine answer to the deepest needs of humanity, sheds unique light on our path in a dark world and sets forth the way to our eternal well-being. Out of these deep convictions, we have sought to recreate as far as possible the experience of the original audience — blending transparency to the original text with accessibility for the millions of English speakers around the world. We have prioritized accuracy, clarity and literary quality with the goal of creating a translation suitable for public and private reading, evangelism, teaching, preaching, memorizing and liturgical use. We have also sought to preserve a measure of continuity with the long tradition of translating the Scriptures into English.

The complete NIV Bible was first published in 1978. It was a completely new translation made by over a hundred scholars working directly from the best available Hebrew, Aramaic and Greek texts. The translators came from the United States, Great Britain, Canada, Australia and New Zealand, giving the translation an international scope. They were from many denominations and churches — including Anglican, Assemblies of God, Baptist, Brethren, Christian Reformed, Church of Christ, Evangelical Covenant, Evangelical Free, Lutheran, Mennonite, Methodist, Nazarene, Presbyterian, Wesleyan and others. This breadth of denominational and theological perspective helped to safeguard the translation from sectarian bias. For these reasons, and by the grace of God, the NIV has gained a wide readership in all parts of the English-speaking world.

The work of translating the Bible is never finished. As good as they are, English translations must be regularly updated so that they will continue to communicate accurately the meaning of God's Word. Updates are needed in order to reflect the latest developments in our understanding of the biblical world and its languages and to keep pace with changes in English usage. Recognizing, then, that the NIV would retain its ability to communicate God's Word accurately only if it were regularly updated, the original translators established The Committee on Bible Translation (CBT). The committee is a self-perpetuating group of biblical scholars charged with keeping abreast of advances in biblical scholarship and changes in English and issuing periodic updates to the NIV. CBT is an independent, self-governing body and has sole responsibility for the NIV text. The committee mirrors the original group of translators in its diverse international and denominational makeup and in its unifying commitment to the Bible as God's inspired Word.

In obedience to its mandate, the committee has issued periodic updates to the NIV. An initial revision was released in 1984. A more thorough revision process was completed in 2005, resulting in the separately published Today's New International Version (TNIV). The updated NIV you now have in your hands builds on both the original NIV and the TNIV and represents the latest effort of the committee to articulate God's unchanging Word in the way the original authors might have said it had they been speaking in English to the global English-speaking audience today.

The first concern of the translators has continued to be the accuracy of the translation and its faithfulness to the intended meaning of the biblical writers. This has moved the translators to go beyond a formal word-for-word rendering of the original texts. Because thought patterns and syntax differ from language to language, accurate communication of the meaning of the biblical authors demands constant regard for varied contextual uses of words and idioms and for frequent modifications in sentence structures.

As an aid to the reader, sectional headings have been inserted. They are not to be regarded as part of the biblical text and are not intended for oral reading. It is the committee's hope that these headings may prove more helpful to the reader than the traditional chapter divisions, which were introduced long after the Bible was written.

For the Old Testament the standard Hebrew text, the Masoretic Text as published in the latest edition of *Biblia Hebraica,* has been used throughout. The Masoretic Text tradition contains marginal notations that offer variant readings. These have sometimes been followed instead of the text itself. Because such instances involve variants within the Masoretic tradition, they have not been indicated in the textual notes. In a few cases, words in the basic consonantal text have been divided differently than in the Masoretic Text. Such cases are usually indicated in the textual footnotes. The Dead Sea Scrolls contain biblical texts that represent an earlier stage of the transmission of the Hebrew text. They have been consulted, as have been the Samaritan Pentateuch and the ancient scribal traditions concerning deliberate textual changes. The translators also consulted the more important early versions — the Greek Septuagint, Aquila, Symmachus and Theodotion, the Latin Vulgate, the Syriac Peshitta, the Aramaic Targums and, for the Psalms, the *Juxta Hebraica* of Jerome. Readings from these versions, the Dead Sea Scrolls and the scribal traditions were occasionally followed where the Masoretic Text seemed doubtful and where accepted principles of textual criticism showed that one or more of these textual witnesses appeared to provide the correct reading. In rare cases, the committee has emended the Hebrew text where it appears to have become corrupted at an even earlier stage of its transmission. These departures from the Masoretic Text are also indicated in the textual footnotes. Sometimes the vowel indicators (which are later additions to the basic consonantal text) found in the Masoretic Text did not, in the judgment of the committee, represent the correct vowels for the original text. Accordingly, some words have been read with a different set of vowels. These instances are usually not indicated in the footnotes.

The Greek text used in translating the New Testament is an eclectic one, based on the latest editions of the Nestle-Aland/United Bible Societies' Greek New Testament. The committee has made its choices among the variant readings in accordance with widely accepted principles of New Testament textual criticism. Footnotes call attention to places where uncertainty remains.

The New Testament authors, writing in Greek, often quote the Old Testament from its ancient Greek version, the Septuagint. This is one reason why some of the Old Testament quotations in the NIV New Testament are not identical to the corresponding passages in the NIV Old Testament. Such quotations in the New Testament are indicated with the footnote "(see Septuagint)."

Other footnotes in this version are of several kinds, most of which need no explanation. Those giving alternative translations begin with "Or" and generally introduce the alternative with the last word preceding it in the text, except when it is a single-word alternative. When poetry is quoted in a footnote, a slash mark indicates a line division.

It should be noted that references to diseases, minerals, flora and fauna, architectural details, clothing, jewelry, musical instruments and other articles cannot always be identified with precision. Also, linear measurements and measures of capacity can only be approximated (see the Table of Weights and Measures). Although *Selah,* used mainly in the Psalms, is probably a musical term, its meaning is uncertain. Since it may interrupt reading and distract the reader, this word has not been kept in the English text, but every occurrence has been signaled by a footnote.

One of the main reasons the task of Bible translation is never finished is the change in our own language, English. Although a basic core of the language remains relatively stable, many diverse and complex linguistic factors continue to bring about subtle shifts in the meanings and/or connotations of even old, well-established words and phrases. One of the shifts that creates particular challenges to writers and translators alike is the manner in which gender is presented. The original NIV (1978) was published in a time when "a man" would naturally be understood, in many contexts, to be referring to a person, whether male or female. But most English speakers today tend to hear a distinctly male connotation in this word. In recognition of this change in English, this edition of the NIV, along with almost all other recent English translations, substitutes other expressions when the original text intends to refer generically to men and women equally. Thus, for instance, the NIV (1984) rendering of 1 Corinthians 8:3, "But the man who loves God is known by God" becomes in this edition "But whoever loves God is known by God." On the other hand, "man" and "mankind," as ways of denoting the human race, are still widely used. This edition of the NIV therefore continues to use these words, along with other expressions, in this way.

A related shift in English creates a greater challenge for modern translations: the move away from using the third-person masculine singular pronouns — "he/him/his" — to refer to men and women equally. This usage does persist at a low level in some forms of English, and this revision therefore occasionally uses these pronouns in a generic sense. But the tendency, recognized in day-to-day usage and confirmed by extensive research, is away from the generic use of "he," "him" and "his." In recognition of this shift in language and in an effort to translate into the "common" English that people are actually using, this revision of the NIV generally uses other constructions when the biblical text is plainly addressed to men and women equally. The reader will frequently encounter a "they," "them" or "their" to express a generic singular idea. Thus, for instance, Mark 8:36 reads: "What good is it for someone to gain the whole world, yet forfeit their soul?" This generic use of the "indefinite" or "singular" "they/them/their" has a venerable place in English idiom and has quickly become established as standard English, spoken and written, all over the world. Where an individual emphasis is deemed to be present, "anyone" or "everyone" or some other equivalent is generally used as the antecedent of such pronouns.

Sometimes the chapter and/or verse numbering in English translations of the Old Testament differs from that found in published Hebrew texts. This is particularly the case in the Psalms, where the traditional titles are often included in the Hebrew verse numbering. Such differences are indicated in the footnotes at the bottom of the page. In the New Testament, verse numbers that marked off portions of the traditional English text not supported by the best Greek manuscripts now appear in brackets, with a footnote indicating the text that has been omitted (see, for example, Matthew 17:[21]).

Mark 16:9 – 20 and John 7:53 – 8:11, although long accorded virtually equal status with the rest of the Gospels in which they stand, have a very questionable — and confused — standing in the textual history of the New Testament, as noted in the bracketed annotations with which they are set off. A different typeface has been chosen for these passages to indicate even more clearly their uncertain status.

Basic formatting of the text, such as lining the poetry, paragraphing (both prose and poetry), setting up of (administrative-like) lists, indenting letters and lengthy prayers within narratives and the insertion of sectional headings, has been the work of the committee. However, the choice between single-column and double-column formats has been left to the publishers. Also the issuing of "red-letter" editions is a publisher's choice — one the committee does not endorse.

The committee has again been reminded that every human effort is flawed — including this revision of the NIV. We trust, however, that many will find in it an improved representation of the Word of God, through which they hear his call to faith in our Lord Jesus Christ and to service in his kingdom. We offer this version of the Bible to him in whose name and for whose glory it has been made.

The Committee on Bible Translation
September 2010

QUICK START GUIDE

Congratulations on your purchase of *The NIV Study Bible*. You have in your hands a comprehensive, multiuse tool that has been designed specifically to enhance your understanding of and appreciation for God's Word.

About *The NIV Study Bible*

Most of the team of evangelical scholars who wrote and edited notes for *The NIV Study Bible* also served on the translation team for the New International Version translation itself. Since the release of *The NIV Study Bible* in 1985, its editors have diligently worked to revise the notes to provide readers with the most up-to-date, relevant study notes available in the market today. Find out more about the New International Version itself by reading the Preface, beginning on page xi.

What Is a Study Bible?

A study Bible contains the full text of the Bible, along with a library of study features to help the reader more completely grasp and understand what the text is saying. These notes introduce and explain a wide variety of background information to the Biblical text, providing deeper insights for individuals who are ready to devote themselves to serious study of the text.

What Help Do These Study Features Offer Me?

For a full discussion of each of these features — and others — see the Introduction on page xv.

- Book introductions answer the Who? What? Where? Why? and When? questions readers have about the Bible's 66 books.
- Center-column cross references aid in deeper study of themes or concepts by leading readers to related passages on the same or similar themes.
- Over 20,000 study notes have been placed close to the text that they amplify and explain. These have been designed to provide background and context to the Scripture text and will also answer questions that may arise as one reads through the Bible.
- Full-color in-text maps, charts and models, along with well-crafted essays, summarize and explain important information and ideas from Scripture. 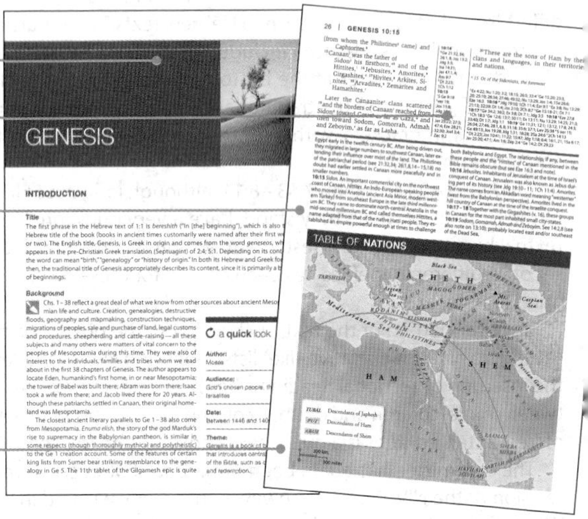
- The Index to Topics has more than 700 entries that will help readers to study subjects of particular interest, allowing them to create their own study paths.
- The Index to Notes directs readers' attention to study notes, book introductions, essays and charts where information about various subjects can be found.
- The NIV Concordance is a tool designed to help readers who remember a key word or phrase in a passage to locate the verses they are looking for. Words and names are listed alphabetically, along with their more significant verse references.
- Fourteen full-color maps at the end of this study Bible help readers to visualize the geographic context of what they are studying. The maps are supplemented by a complete map index.

Why not go ahead and spend a few minutes trying out each of these features? If you're like most readers, certain helps will catch your interest and eventually become trusted friends as you spend time with your Bible. May God bless you as you study and come to understand the timeless truths of the Bible as priceless treasures for today.

INTRODUCTION TO *THE NIV STUDY BIBLE*

About *The NIV Study Bible*

The New International Version of the Bible (NIV) is unsurpassed in accuracy, clarity and literary grace. The commitments that led to the completion of this version guided the General Editor and Associate Editors of the 2008 update of *The NIV Study Bible* to adapt it to the new 2011 text of the NIV, resulting in this new edition of *The NIV Study Bible*. Their purpose was unchanged: to communicate the word of God to the hearts of people.

Like the NIV itself, *The NIV Study Bible* is the work of a transdenominational team of Biblical scholars. All confess the authority of the Bible as God's infallible word to humanity. They have sought to clarify understanding of, develop appreciation for and provide insight into that word.

But why a study Bible when the NIV text itself is so clearly written? Surely there is no substitute for the reading of the text itself; nothing people write *about* God's word can be on a level with the word itself. Further, it is the Holy Spirit alone—not fallible human beings—who can open the human mind to the divine message.

However, the Spirit also uses people to explain God's word to others. It was the Spirit who led Philip to the Ethiopian eunuch's chariot, where he asked, "Do you understand what you are reading?" (Ac 8:30). "How can I," the Ethiopian replied, "unless someone explains it to me?" Philip then showed him how an Old Testament passage in Isaiah related to the good news of Jesus.

This interrelationship of the Scriptures—so essential to understanding the complete Biblical message—is a major theme of the notes in *The NIV Study Bible*.

Doctrinally, *The NIV Study Bible* reflects traditional evangelical theology. Where editors were aware of significant differences of opinion on key passages or doctrines, they tried to follow an evenhanded approach by indicating those differences (e.g., see note on Rev 20:2 about the "thousand years"). In finding solutions to problems mentioned in the book introductions, they went only as far as evidence (Biblical and non-Biblical) could carry them.

The result is a study Bible that can be used profitably by all Christians who want to be serious Bible students.

Features of *The NIV Study Bible*

The NIV Study Bible features the text of the New International Version, study notes keyed to and listed with Bible verses, introductions and outlines to books of the Bible, text notes, a cross-reference system (100,000 entries), parallel passages, a concordance (over 35,000 references), maps, charts, models, photos, essays and comprehensive indexes.

The text of the NIV, which is divided into paragraphs as well as verses, is organized into sections with headings.

Study Notes

The outstanding feature of this study Bible is that it contains over 20,000 study notes, usually located on the same pages as the verses and passages they explain.

The study notes provide new information to supplement that found in the NIV text notes. Among other things, they

(1) explain important words and concepts (see note on Lev 11:44 about holiness);

(2) interpret difficult verses (see notes on Mal 1:3 and Lk 14:26 for the concept of hating your parents);

(3) draw parallels between specific people and events (see note on Ex 32:30 for the parallels between Moses and Christ as mediators);
(4) describe historical and textual contexts of passages (see note on 1Co 8:1 for the practice of eating meat sacrificed to idols); and
(5) demonstrate how one passage sheds light on another (see note on Ps 26:8 for how the presence of God's glory marked his presence in the tabernacle, in the temple and, finally, in Jesus Christ himself).

Some elements of style should be noted:

(1) Study notes on a *passage* precede notes on individual verses within that passage.
(2) When a book of the Bible is referred to within a note on that book, the book name is not repeated. For example, a reference to 2 Timothy 2:18 within the notes on 2 Timothy is written 2:18, not 2Ti 2:18.
(3) In lists of references within a note, references from the book under discussion are placed first. The rest usually appear in Biblical order.
(4) Certain kinds of material have been made more accessible through the use of the following symbols:

The trowel points out references containing study notes that provide light from archaeology. Since there is more personal application material in the study notes than archaeological information, we have also indicated where archaeological data can be found in certain book introductions, maps and charts.

The seedling calls attention to Scripture references containing study notes that have practical principles for personal application.

The character symbol occurs in front of Scripture references containing study notes that provide descriptions and/or characterizations of a person or a people. It also sometimes appears in book introductions and essays.

Introductions to Books of the Bible

An introduction frequently reports on a book's title, author and date of writing. It details the book's background and purpose, explores themes and theological significance and points out special problems and distinctive literary features. Where appropriate, such as in Paul's letters to the churches, it describes the original recipients of a book and the city in which they lived.

A complete outline of the book's content is provided in each introduction (except for the introduction to Psalms). For Genesis, two outlines—a literary and a thematic—are given. Pairs of books that were originally one literary work, such as 1 and 2 Samuel, 1 and 2 Kings, and 1 and 2 Chronicles, are outlined together.

Text Notes

NIV text notes are indicated by raised italic letters following the words or phrases they explain. They examine such things as alternative translations, meanings of Hebrew and Greek terms, Old Testament quotations and variant readings in ancient Biblical manuscripts. There are also some explanatory notes. Text notes appear at the bottom of the Bible text, above the line separating Scripture from study notes, and are preceded by their raised italic letters and verse numbers.

Cross-Reference System

The cross-reference system can be used to explore concepts, as well as specific words. For example, one can either study angels as protectors (see Mt 18:10) or focus on the word "angel" (see Jn 20:12).

The NIV cross-reference system resembles a series of interlocking chains with many links. The head, or organizing, link in each concept chain is indicated by the letter "S" (short for "See"). The appearance of a head link in a list of references usually signals another list of references that will cover a slightly different aspect of the concept or word being studied. The various chains in the cross-reference system—which is virtually inexhaustible—continually intersect and diverge.

Cross references are indicated by raised letters. When a single word is addressed by both text notes and cross references, the NIV text note letter comes first. The cross references normally appear in the center column and, when necessary, continue at the bottom of the Scripture portion of the page, after the NIV text notes (indicated by raised italic letters).

The four lists of references are in Biblical order with one exception: If reference is made to a verse within the same chapter, that verse (indicated by "ver") is listed first. If an Old Testament verse is quoted in the New Testament, the New Testament reference is marked with an asterisk (*).

Genesis 1:1 provides a good example of the resources of the cross-reference system.

The four lists of references all relate to creation, but each takes a different perspective. Note *a* takes up the time of creation: "in the beginning." Note *b* lists three other occurrences of the word "created" in Genesis 1—2. Note *c* focuses on "the heavens" as God's creation. Because note *d* is attached to the end of the verse as well as to the word "earth," it deals with the word "earth," with the phrase "the heavens and the earth" and with creation itself (the whole verse).

The Beginning

1 In the beginning[a] God created[b]
the heavens[c] and the earth.[d] 2 Now
the earth was formless[e] and empty,[f]
darkness was over the surface of the
deep,[g] and the Spirit of God[h] was hovering[i] over the waters.
3 And God said,[j] "Let there be light," and
there was light.[k] 4 God saw that the
light was good,[l] and he separated the
light from the darkness.[m] 5 God called[n]
the light "day," and the darkness he
called "night."[o] And there was evening, and there was morning[p]—the
first day.
6 And God said,[q] "Let there be a vault[r]
between the waters[s] to separate water from water." 7 So God made the
vault and separated the water under

1:1 [a] Ps 102:25; Pr 8:23; Isa 40:21; 41:4, 26; Jn 1:1-2 [b] ver 21, 27; Ge 2:3 [c] ver 6; Ne 9:6; Job 9:8; 37:18; Ps 96:5; 104:2; 115:15; 121:2; 136:5; Isa 40:22; 42:5; 51:13; Jer 10:12; 51:15 [d] Ge 14:19; 2Ki 19:15; Ne 9:6; Job 38:4; Ps 90:2; 136:6; 146:6; Isa 37:16; 40:28; 42:5; 44:24; 45:12, 18; Jer 27:5; 32:17; Ac 14:15; 17:24; Eph 3:9; Col 1:16; Heb 3:4; 11:3; Rev 4:11; 10:6 **1:2** [e] Isa 23:1;

Parallel Passages

When two or more passages of Scripture are nearly identical or deal with the same event, this "parallel" is noted at the sectional headings for those passages. Such passages are especially common in Matthew, Mark, Luke and John, as well as in Samuel, Kings and Chronicles.

Identical or nearly identical passages are noted with "*pp.*" Similar passages—those not dealing with the same event—are noted with "*Ref.*"

To conserve space and avoid repetition, when a parallel passage is noted at a sectional heading, no further parallels are listed in the cross-reference system.

Concordance

The concordance is the largest ever bound with an English Bible. It was compiled and edited by John R. Kohlenberger III. By looking up key words, you can find verses for which you remember a word or two but not their location. For example, to find the verse that states that the word of God is "sharper than any double-edged sword," you could look in the concordance under either "sharper," "double-edged," or "sword."

Maps

The NIV Study Bible includes 90 full-color maps. The 14 maps at the end of this study Bible cover about 2,000 years of history. See Contents: Maps (pp. vii–viii) for a complete list of the topics covered.

The cities of Jerusalem, Damascus, Rome, Corinth, Ephesus and Philippi have been reconstructed as they might have been in ancient times. These re-creations allow Bible students to visualize David's city and the places through which Paul traveled on his missionary journeys.

Charts

Complementing the study notes are more than 70 charts and models designed specifically for *The NIV Study Bible*. Two full-color time lines are located before each Testament, pinpointing significant dates in the Old and New Testaments. The charts and models carefully placed within the text give detailed information about such things as ancient, non-Biblical texts; about Old Testament covenants, sacrifices and festival days; about Jewish sects; and about major archaeological finds relating to the Old and New Testaments.

Essays

Five brief essays provide additional information on specific sections of the Bible: Wisdom Literature, the Minor Prophets, the Synoptic Gospels, the Pastoral Letters and the General Letters.

A sixth essay confronts the ethical question of war, and a seventh details the history, literature and social developments of the 400 years between the Old and New Testaments.

Topics, Notes and Maps Indexes

The topics index contains references to key Biblical information and important topics. The notes index pinpoints other references to persons, places, events and topics mentioned in the *NIV Study Bible* notes.

The maps index helps in locating place-names on the maps at the end of this study Bible.

A Harmony of the Gospels

As an additional study tool for the Gospels and the life of Christ, a portion of *The NIV Harmony of the Gospels* by Robert L. Thomas and Stanley N. Gundry is included in this study Bible.

The Divine Name *Yahweh*

The editors have sometimes elected to use the divine name Yahweh (rendered "the LORD" in the NIV) in the book introductions, study notes and essays instead of "the Lord." For the significance of this name, see Ge 2:4; Ex 3:14–15; 6:6; Dt 28:58 and notes.

ACKNOWLEDGMENTS

1985 Edition

My greatest debt of gratitude is owed to God for giving me the privilege of serving as General Editor of *The NIV Study Bible*. Special thanks go to the four Associate Editors: Donald W. Burdick, John H. Stek, Walter W. Wessel and Ronald F. Youngblood. Without their help, it would have been impossible to complete this project in approximately seven years.

In addition, grateful acknowledgment is given to all those listed on the Contributors page. Obviously the editors and contributors have profited immensely from the labors of others. We feel deeply indebted to all the commentaries and other sources we have used in our work.

I should also thank the following individuals for rendering help in various ways (though I fear that I have inadvertently omitted a few names): Caroline Blauwkamp, David R. Douglass, Stanley N. Gundry, N. David Hill, Betty Hockenberry, Charles E. Hummel, Alan F. Johnson, Janet Johnston, Donald H. Madvig, Frances Steenwyk and Edward Viening.

Nehemiah 8:7 – 8, 12 reads, "The Levites … instructed the people in the Law while the people were standing there. They read from the Book of the Law of God, making it clear and giving the meaning so that the people understood what was being read … Then all the people went away … to celebrate with great joy, because they now understood the words that had been made known to them."

My associates and I will feel amply rewarded if those who use this study Bible have an experience similar to that of God's people in the time of Ezra and Nehemiah.

Kenneth L. Barker, General Editor

2002 Edition

In the fully revised edition of *The NIV Study Bible*, the Associate Editors and I added hundreds of new study notes, improved the book introductions (e.g., by paying greater attention to rhetorical, structural and other literary features) and enhanced other helps.

Special thanks go to Andrew J. Bandstra for providing additional study notes on the book of Revelation. We are also humbly grateful to God for the manner in which he has used this study Bible to bring edification and spiritual enrichment to literally millions of readers and users. It is my prayer that this will continue to be true of this fully revised edition of *The NIV Study Bible*.

Kenneth L. Barker, General Editor

2008 Edition

In the 2008 update of *The NIV Study Bible*, the Associate Editors and I added some new study notes and charts, corrected a few mistakes, and brought greater continuity to certain kinds of material (e.g., there is now more consistency in the outlining of a few books and in the development of themes). We give a hearty welcome and special thanks to Mark Strauss as a new Associate Editor, with primary responsibility for the New Testament. "The unfolding of your words gives light" (Ps 119:130).

Kenneth L. Barker, General Editor

2011 Edition

The 2011 edition of *The NIV Study Bible* includes an adaptation to the 2011 revised NIV text plus numerous full-color features. My Associate Editors and I pray that many more millions of readers and users will be edified and spiritually enriched through its use. *Gloria in excelsis Deo!*

Kenneth L. Barker, General Editor

CONTRIBUTORS

2011 Edition

General Editor: Kenneth L. Barker
Associate Editors: Mark L. Strauss
Ronald F. Youngblood

2008 Edition

General Editor: Kenneth L. Barker
Associate Editors: John H. Stek
Mark L. Strauss
Ronald F. Youngblood

2002 Edition (Fully Revised)

General Editor: Kenneth L. Barker
Associate Editors: John H. Stek
Walter W. Wessel
Ronald F. Youngblood

1985 Edition

General Editor: Kenneth L. Barker
Associate Editors: Donald W. Burdick
John H. Stek
Walter W. Wessel
Ronald F. Youngblood

The individuals named below contributed or reviewed material for *The NIV Study Bible*. However, since the General Editor and the Associate Editors extensively edited the notes on most books, they alone are responsible for their final form and content.

The chief contributors of original material to *The NIV Study Bible* are listed first. Where the Associate Editors and General Editor contributed an unusually large number of notes on certain books, their names are also listed.

Genesis	Ronald F. Youngblood
Exodus	Ronald F. Youngblood Walter C. Kaiser Jr.
Leviticus	R. Laird Harris Ronald F. Youngblood
Numbers	Ronald B. Allen Kenneth L. Barker
Deuteronomy	Earl S. Kalland Kenneth L. Barker
Joshua	Arthur Lewis
Judges	John J. Davis Herbert Wolf
Ruth	Marvin R. Wilson John H. Stek
1,2 Samuel	J. Robert Vannoy
1,2 Kings	J. Robert Vannoy
1,2 Chronicles	Raymond Dillard
Ezra	Edwin Yamauchi Ronald F. Youngblood
Nehemiah	Edwin Yamauchi Ronald F. Youngblood
Esther	Raymond Dillard Edwin Yamauchi
Job	Elmer B. Smick Ronald F. Youngblood
Psalms	John H. Stek
Proverbs	Herbert Wolf
Ecclesiastes	Derek Kidner John H. Stek
Song of Songs	John H. Stek
Isaiah	Herbert Wolf John H. Stek
Jeremiah	Ronald F. Youngblood
Lamentations	Ronald F. Youngblood John H. Stek
Ezekiel	Mark Hillmer John H. Stek
Daniel	Gleason L. Archer Jr. Ronald F. Youngblood
Hosea	Jack P. Lewis
Joel	Jack P. Lewis
Amos	Alan R. Millard John H. Stek
Obadiah	John M. Zinkand
Jonah	Marvin R. Wilson John H. Stek
Micah	Kenneth L. Barker Thomas E. McComiskey
Nahum	G. Herbert Livingston Kenneth L. Barker
Habakkuk	Roland K. Harrison William C. Williams
Zephaniah	Roland K. Harrison
Haggai	Herbert Wolf
Zechariah	Kenneth L. Barker Larry L. Walker
Malachi	Herbert Wolf John H. Stek
Matthew	Walter W. Wessel Ralph Earle
Mark	Walter W. Wessel William L. Lane
Luke	Lewis Foster
John	Leon Morris
Acts	Lewis Foster
Romans	Walter W. Wessel
1 Corinthians	W. Harold Mare
2 Corinthians	Philip E. Hughes
Galatians	Robert Mounce
Ephesians	Walter L. Liefeld
Philippians	Richard B. Gaffin Jr.
Colossians	Gerald F. Hawthorne Wilber B. Wallis
1,2 Thessalonians	Leon Morris
1,2 Timothy	Walter W. Wessel George W. Knight, III
Titus	D. Edmond Hiebert
Philemon	John Werner
Hebrews	Philip E. Hughes Donald W. Burdick
James	Donald W. Burdick
1,2 Peter	Donald W. Burdick John H. Skilton
1,2,3 John	Donald W. Burdick
Jude	Donald W. Burdick John H. Skilton
Revelation	Robert Mounce Andrew J. Bandstra
The Time between the Testaments (essay)	David O'Brien

ABBREVIATIONS AND TRANSLITERATIONS

ABBREVIATIONS

General

c	*century*
c.	*about, approximately*
cf.	*compare, confer*
ch., chs.	*chapter, chapters*
e.g.	*for example*
etc.	*and so on*
i.e.	*that is*
KJV	*King James (Authorized) Version*
lit.	*literally, literal*
NT	*New Testament*
OT	*Old Testament*
p., pp.	*page, pages*
v., vv.,	*verse, verses (in the chapter being commented on)*

Standard abbreviations of month names are also sometimes used, as well as a few other common abbreviations.

The Old Testament

Genesis	Ge
Exodus	Ex
Leviticus	Lev
Numbers	Nu
Deuteronomy	Dt
Joshua	Jos
Judges	Jdg
Ruth	Ru
1 Samuel	1Sa
2 Samuel	2Sa
1 Kings	1Ki
2 Kings	2Ki
1 Chronicles	1Ch
2 Chronicles	2Ch
Ezra	Ezr
Nehemiah	Ne
Esther	Est
Job	Job
Psalms	Ps
Proverbs	Pr
Ecclesiastes	Ecc
Song of Songs	SS
Isaiah	Isa
Jeremiah	Jer
Lamentations	La
Ezekiel	Eze
Daniel	Da
Hosea	Hos
Joel	Joel
Amos	Am
Obadiah	Ob
Jonah	Jnh
Micah	Mic
Nahum	Na
Habakkuk	Hab
Zephaniah	Zep
Haggai	Hag
Zechariah	Zec
Malachi	Mal

The New Testament

Matthew	Mt
Mark	Mk
Luke	Lk
John	Jn
Acts	Ac
Romans	Ro
1 Corinthians	1Co
2 Corinthians	2Co
Galatians	Gal
Ephesians	Eph
Philippians	Php
Colossians	Col
1 Thessalonians	1Th
2 Thessalonians	2Th
1 Timothy	1Ti
2 Timothy	2Ti
Titus	Titus
Philemon	Phm
Hebrews	Heb
James	Jas
1 Peter	1Pe
2 Peter	2Pe
1 John	1Jn
2 John	2Jn
3 John	3Jn
Jude	Jude
Revelation	Rev

TRANSLITERATIONS

A simplified system has been used for transliterating words from ancient Biblical languages into English. The only transliterations calling for comment are these:

Transliteration	*Pronunciation*
ʼ	Glottal stop
ḥ	Similar to the "ch" in the German word *Buch*
ṭ	Similar to the "t" in the verb "tear"
ʻ	Similar to the glottal stop
ṣ	Similar to the "ts" in "hits"
ś	Similar to the "s" in "sing"

ANCIENT TEXTS RELATING TO THE OLD TESTAMENT

Major representative examples of ancient Near Eastern non-Biblical documents that provide parallels to or shed light on various Old Testament passages

TITLE	ORIGIN	DESCRIPTION
AMARNA LETTERS	**Canaanite Akkadian** *Fourteenth century BC*	Hundreds of letters, written primarily by Canaanite scribes, illuminate social, political and religious relationships between Canaan and Egypt during the reigns of Amunhotep III and Akhenaten.
AMENEMOPE'S WISDOM	**Egyptian** *Late second millennium BC*	Thirty chapters of wisdom instruction are similar to Pr 22:17—24:22 and provide the closest external parallels to OT Wisdom Literature.
ATRAHASIS EPIC	**Akkadian** *Early second millennium BC*	A cosmological epic depicts creation and early human history, including the flood (cf. Ge 1–9).
BABYLONIAN THEODICY	**Akkadian** *Early first millennium BC*	A sufferer and his friend dialogue with each other (cf. Job).
CYRUS CYLINDER	**Akkadian** *Sixth century BC*	King Cyrus of Persia records the conquest of Babylon (cf. Da 5:30; 6:28) and boasts of his generous policies toward his new subjects and their gods.

Cyrus Cylinder, a cuneiform text that describes Cyrus's (Persian ruler 559–530 BC) capture of Babylon in 539 BC. Cyrus allowed the Jews to return from Babylonia and rebuild the temple in Jerusalem (2 Ch 36:23; Ezr 1:2–4; 7:1–5).
Kim Walton, courtesy of the British Museum

Gezer Calendar—one of the earliest examples of Hebrew writing—highlights the agricultural seasons in Israel.
© 1995 Phoenix Data Systems

TITLE	ORIGIN	DESCRIPTION
DEAD SEA SCROLLS	**Hebrew, Aramaic, Greek** *Third century BC to first century AD*	Several hundred scrolls and fragments include the oldest copies of OT books and passages.
EBLA TABLETS	**Sumerian, Eblaite** *Mid-third millennium BC*	Thousands of commercial, legal, literary and epistolary texts describe the cultural vitality and political power of a pre-patriarchal civilization in northern Syria.
ELEPHANTINE PAPYRI	**Aramaic** *Late fifth century BC*	Contracts and letters document life among Jews who fled to southern Egypt after Jerusalem was destroyed in 586 BC.
ENUMA ELISH	**Akkadian** *Second millennium BC*	Marduk, the Babylonian god of cosmic order, is elevated to the supreme position in the pantheon. The seven-tablet epic contains an account of creation (cf. Ge 1–2).
GEZER CALENDAR	**Hebrew** *Tenth century BC*	A schoolboy from west-central Israel describes the seasons, crops and farming activity of the agricultural year.
GILGAMESH EPIC	**Akkadian** *Early second millennium BC*	Gilgamesh, ruler of Uruk, experiences numerous adventures, including a meeting with Utnapishtim, the only survivor of a great deluge (cf. Ge 6–9).
HAMMURAPI'S CODE	**Akkadian** *Eighteenth century BC*	Together with similar law codes that preceded and followed it, the Code of Hammurapi exhibits close parallels to numerous passages in the Mosaic legislation of the OT.

ANCIENT TEXTS RELATING TO THE OLD TESTAMENT (CONT.)

Major representative examples of ancient Near Eastern non-Biblical documents that provide parallels to or shed light on various Old Testament passages

TITLE	ORIGIN	DESCRIPTION
HYMN TO THE ATEN	Egyptian *Fourteenth century BC*	The poem praises the beneficence and universality of the sun in language somewhat similar to that used in Ps 104.
ISHTAR'S DESCENT	Akkadian *First millennium BC*	The goddess Ishtar temporarily descends to the netherworld, which is pictured in terms reminiscent of OT descriptions of Sheol.
JEHOIACHIN'S RATION DOCKETS	Akkadian *Early sixth century BC*	Brief texts from the reign of Nebuchadnezzar II refer to rations allotted to Judah's exiled king Jehoiachin and his sons (cf. 2Ki 25:27–30).
KING LISTS	Sumerian *Early second millennium BC*	The reigns of Sumerian kings before the flood are described as lasting for thousands of years, reminding us of the longevity of the preflood patriarchs in Ge 5.
LACHISH LETTERS (OSTRACA)	Hebrew *Early sixth century BC*	Inscriptions on pottery fragments vividly portray the desperate days preceding the Babylonian siege of Jerusalem in 588–586 BC (cf. Jer 34:7).
LAMENTATION OVER THE DESTRUCTION OF UR	Sumerian *Early second millennium BC*	The poem mourns the destruction of the city of Ur at the hands of the Elamites (cf. the OT book of Lamentations).
LUDLUL BEL NEMEQI	Akkadian *Late second millennium BC*	A suffering Babylonian nobleman describes his distress in terms faintly reminiscent of the experiences of Job.
MARI TABLETS	Akkadian *Eighteenth century BC*	Letters and administrative texts provide detailed information regarding customs, language and personal names that reflect the culture of the OT patriarchs.
MERNEPTAH STELE	Egyptian *Thirteenth century BC*	Pharaoh Merneptah figuratively describes his victory over various peoples in western Asia, including "Israel."
MESHA STELE (MOABITE STONE)	Moabite *Ninth century BC*	Mesha, king of Moab (see 2Ki 3:4 and note on 1:1), rebels against a successor of Israel's king Omri.

Mesha Stele (Moabite Stone), a Moabite inscription (c. 840–820 BC), recounts the exploits of Mesha, king of Moab (2 Ki 3:4).

Z. Radovan/www.BibleLandPictures.com

Sennacherib's Prism was discovered among the ruins of Nineveh, the ancient capital of the Assyrian Empire. It contains the annals of Sennacherib, the Assyrian king who besieged Jerusalem in 701 BC during the reign of King Hezekiah.

© 1995 Phoenix Data Systems

ANCIENT TEXTS RELATING TO THE OLD TESTAMENT (CONT.)

Major representative examples of ancient Near Eastern non-Biblical documents that provide parallels to or shed light on various Old Testament passages		
TITLE	**ORIGIN**	**DESCRIPTION**
MURASHU TABLETS	**Akkadian** *Fifth century BC*	Commercial documents describe financial transactions engaged in by Murashu and Sons, a Babylonian firm that did business with Jews and other exiles.
MURSILIS'S TREATY WITH DUPPI-TESSUB	**Hittite** *Mid-second millennium BC*	King Mursilis imposes a suzerainty treaty on King Duppi-Tessub. The literary outline of this and other Hittite treaties is strikingly paralleled in OT covenants established by God with his people.
NABONIDUS CHRONICLE	**Akkadian** *Mid-sixth century BC*	The account describes the absence of King Nabonidus from Babylon. His son Belshazzar is therefore the regent in charge of the kingdom (cf. Da 5:29–30).
NEBUCHADNEZZAR CHRONICLE	**Akkadian** *Early sixth century BC*	A chronicle from the reign of Nebuchadnezzar II includes the Babylonian account of the siege of Jerusalem in 597 BC (see 2Ki 24:10–17).
NUZI TABLETS	**Akkadian** *Mid-second millennium BC*	Adoption, birthright sale and other legal documents graphically illustrate OT patriarchal customs current centuries earlier.
PESSIMISTIC DIALOGUE	**Akkadian** *Early first millennium BC*	A master and his servant discuss the pros and cons of various activities (cf. Ecc 1–2).
RAS SHAMRA TABLETS	**Ugaritic** *Fifteenth–fourteenth centuries BC*	Canaanite deities and rulers experience adventures in epics that enrich our understanding of Canaanite mythology and religion and of OT poetry.
SARGON LEGEND	**Akkadian** *First millennium BC*	Sargon I (the Great), ruler of Akkad in the late third millennium BC, claims to have been rescued as an infant from a reed basket found floating in a river (cf. Ex 2).
SARGON'S DISPLAY INSCRIPTION	**Akkadian** *Eighth century BC*	Sargon II takes credit for the conquest of Samaria in 722/721 BC and states that he captured and exiled 27,290 Israelites.
SENNACHERIB'S PRISM	**Akkadian** *Early seventh century BC*	Sennacherib vividly describes his siege of Jerusalem in 701 BC, making Hezekiah a prisoner in his own royal city (but cf. 2Ki 19:35–37).
SEVEN LEAN YEARS TRADITION	**Egyptian** *Second century BC*	Egypt experiences seven years of low Niles and famine, which, by a contractual agreement between Pharaoh Djoser (twenty-eighth century BC) and a god, will be followed by prosperity (cf. Ge 41).
SHALMANESER'S BLACK OBELISK	**Akkadian** *Ninth century BC*	Israel's king Jehu presents tribute to Assyria's king Shalmaneser III. Additional Assyrian and Babylonian texts refer to other kings of Israel and Judah.
SHISHAK'S GEOGRAPHICAL LIST	**Egyptian** *Tenth century BC*	Pharaoh Shishak lists the cities that he captured or made tributary during his campaign in Judah and Israel (cf. 1Ki 14:25–26 and note on 14:25).
SILOAM INSCRIPTION	**Hebrew** *Late eighth century BC*	A Judahite workman describes the construction of an underground conduit to guarantee Jerusalem's water supply during Hezekiah's reign (cf. 2Ki 20:20; 2Ch 32:30).
SINUHE'S STORY	**Egyptian** *Twentieth–nineteenth centuries BC*	An Egyptian official of the Twelfth Dynasty goes into voluntary exile in Aram (Syria) and Canaan during the OT patriarchal period.
TALE OF TWO BROTHERS	**Egyptian** *Thirteenth century BC*	A young man rejects the amorous advances of his older brother's wife (cf. Ge 39).
WENAMUN'S JOURNEY	**Egyptian** *Eleventh century BC*	An official of the temple of Amun at Thebes in Egypt is sent to Byblos in Canaan to buy lumber for the ceremonial barge of his god.

OLD TESTAMENT CHRONOLOGY

Creation	Fall	Flood	Babel
Ge 1–2	Ge 3	Ge 6–9	Ge 11
?	?	?	?

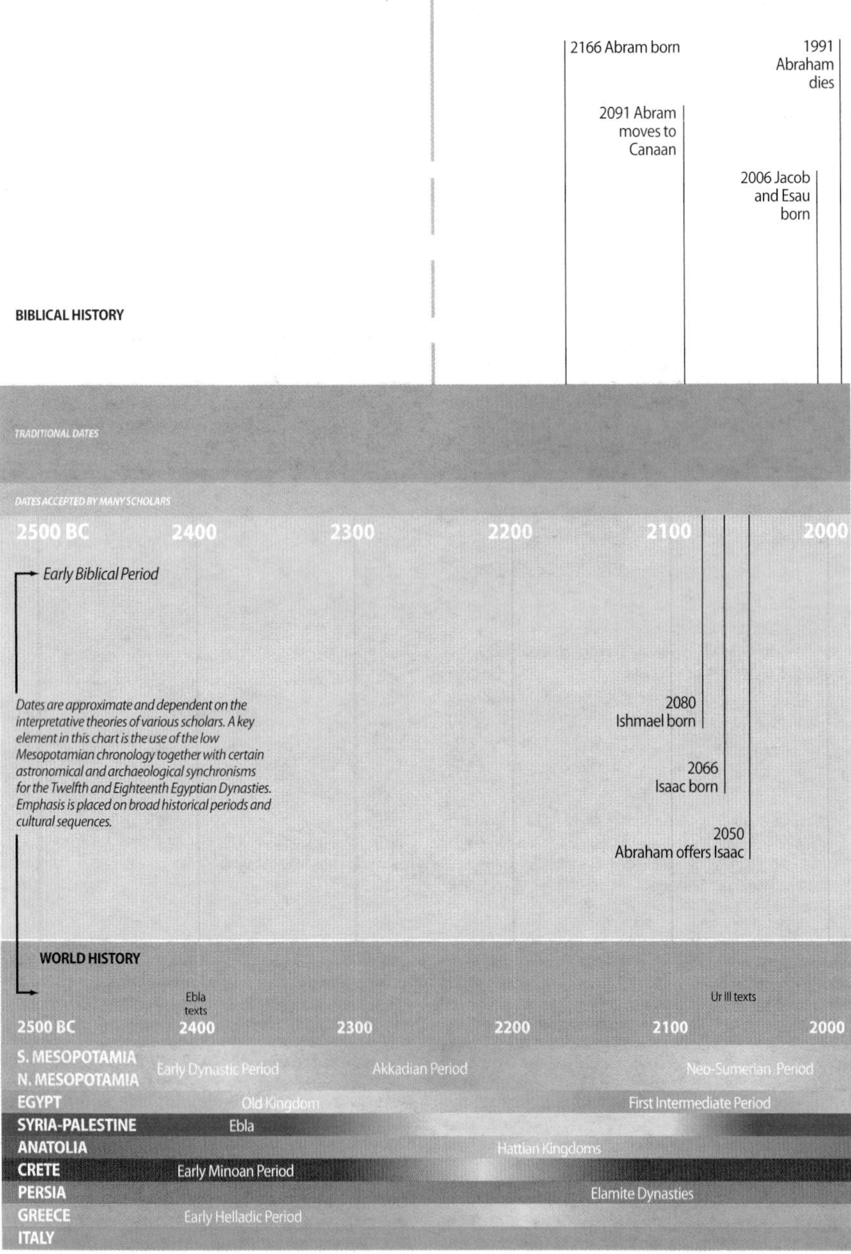
Patriarchs
Ge 12–50
2166 Abram born
1991 Abraham dies
2091 Abram moves to Canaan
2006 Jacob and Esau born
BIBLICAL HISTORY
TRADITIONAL DATES
DATES ACCEPTED BY MANY SCHOLARS
2500 BC
2400
2300
2200
2100
2000
Early Biblical Period
Dates are approximate and dependent on the interpretative theories of various scholars. A key element in this chart is the use of the low Mesopotamian chronology together with certain astronomical and archaeological synchronisms for the Twelfth and Eighteenth Egyptian Dynasties. Emphasis is placed on broad historical periods and cultural sequences.
2080 Ishmael born
2066 Isaac born
2050 Abraham offers Isaac
WORLD HISTORY
Ebla texts
Ur III texts
2500 BC
2400
2300
2200
2100
2000
S. MESOPOTAMIA
N. MESOPOTAMIA
Early Dynastic Period
Akkadian Period
Neo-Sumerian Period
EGYPT
Old Kingdom
First Intermediate Period
SYRIA-PALESTINE
Ebla
ANATOLIA
Hattian Kingdoms
CRETE
Early Minoan Period
PERSIA
Elamite Dynasties
GREECE
Early Helladic Period
ITALY

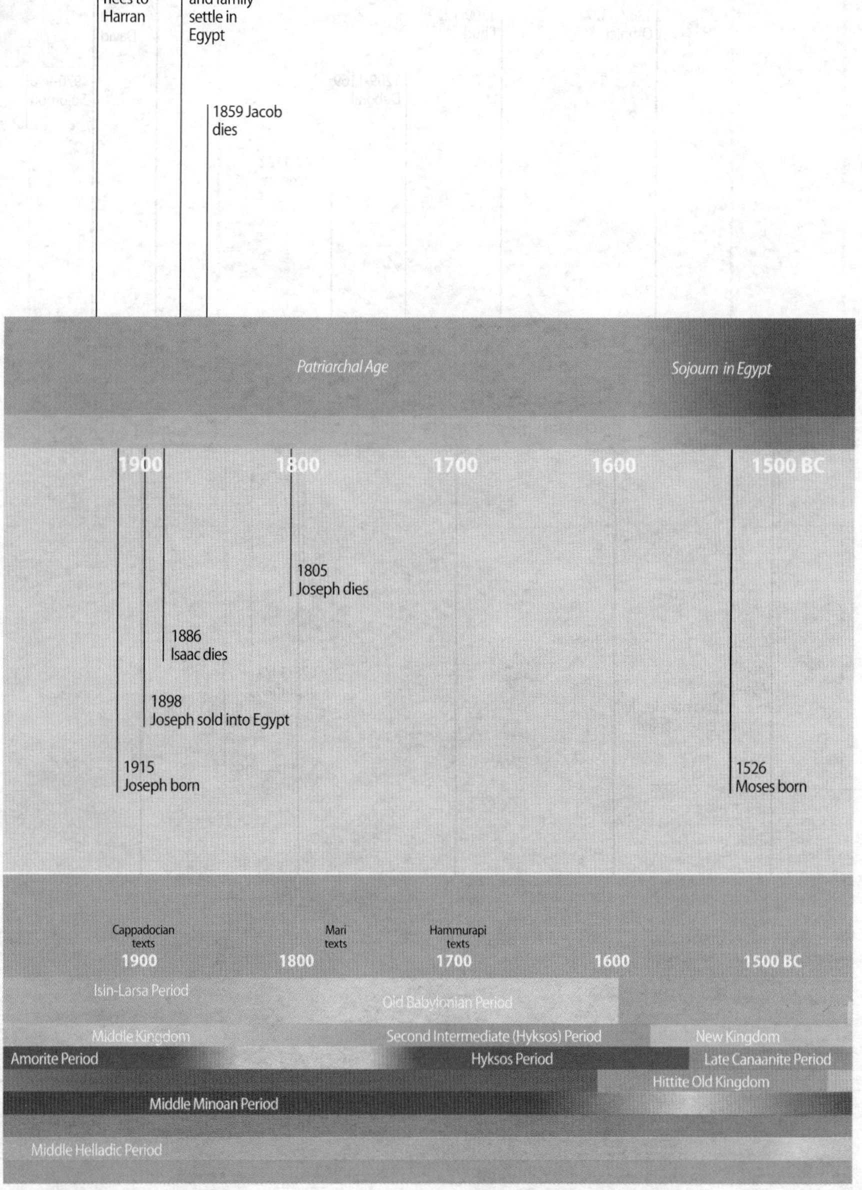
1929 Jacob flees to Harran
1876 Jacob and family settle in Egypt
1859 Jacob dies
Patriarchal Age
Sojourn in Egypt
1900
1800
1700
1600
1500 BC
1805 Joseph dies
1886 Isaac dies
1898 Joseph sold into Egypt
1915 Joseph born
1526 Moses born
Cappadocian texts
Mari texts
Hammurapi texts
1900
1800
1700
1600
1500 BC
Isin-Larsa Period
Old Babylonian Period
Middle Kingdom
Second Intermediate (Hyksos) Period
New Kingdom
Amorite Period
Hyksos Period
Late Canaanite Period
Hittite Old Kingdom
Middle Minoan Period
Middle Helladic Period

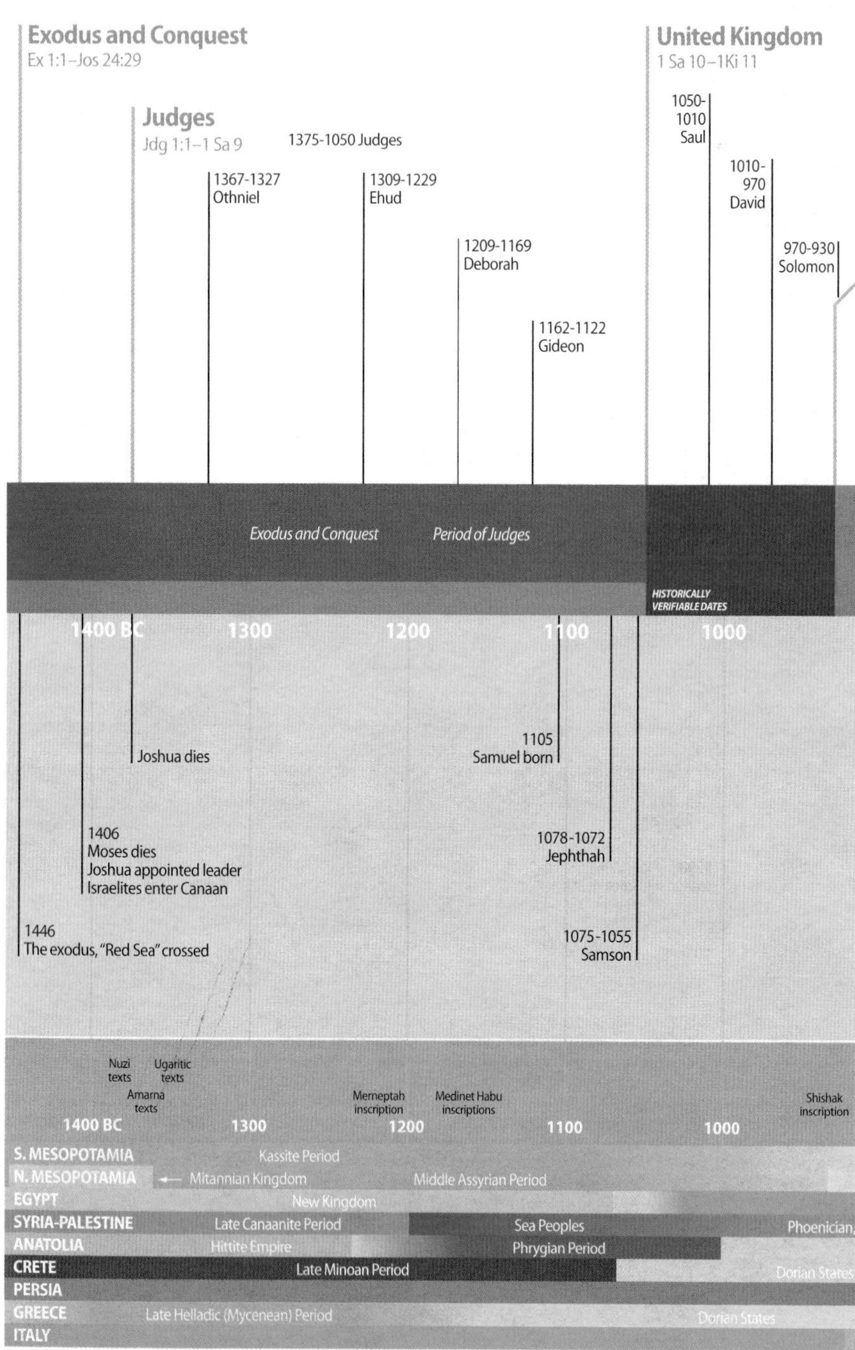
Exodus and Conquest
Ex 1:1–Jos 24:29
Judges
Jdg 1:1–1 Sa 9
1375-1050 Judges
1367-1327
Othniel
1309-1229
Ehud
1209-1169
Deborah
1162-1122
Gideon
United Kingdom
1 Sa 10–1Ki 11
1050-
1010
Saul
1010-
970
David
970-930
Solomon
Exodus and Conquest
Period of Judges
HISTORICALLY
VERIFIABLE DATES
1400 BC
1300
1200
1100
1000
Joshua dies
1105
Samuel born
1406
Moses dies
Joshua appointed leader
Israelites enter Canaan
1078-1072
Jephthah
1446
The exodus, "Red Sea" crossed
1075-1055
Samson
Nuzi
texts
Ugaritic
texts
Amarna
texts
Merneptah
inscription
Medinet Habu
inscriptions
Shishak
inscription
1400 BC
1300
1200
1100
1000
S. MESOPOTAMIA
Kassite Period
N. MESOPOTAMIA
Mitannian Kingdom
Middle Assyrian Period
EGYPT
New Kingdom
SYRIA-PALESTINE
Late Canaanite Period
Sea Peoples
Phoenician,
ANATOLIA
Hittite Empire
Phrygian Period
CRETE
Late Minoan Period
Dorian States
PERSIA
GREECE
Late Helladic (Mycenean) Period
Dorian States
ITALY

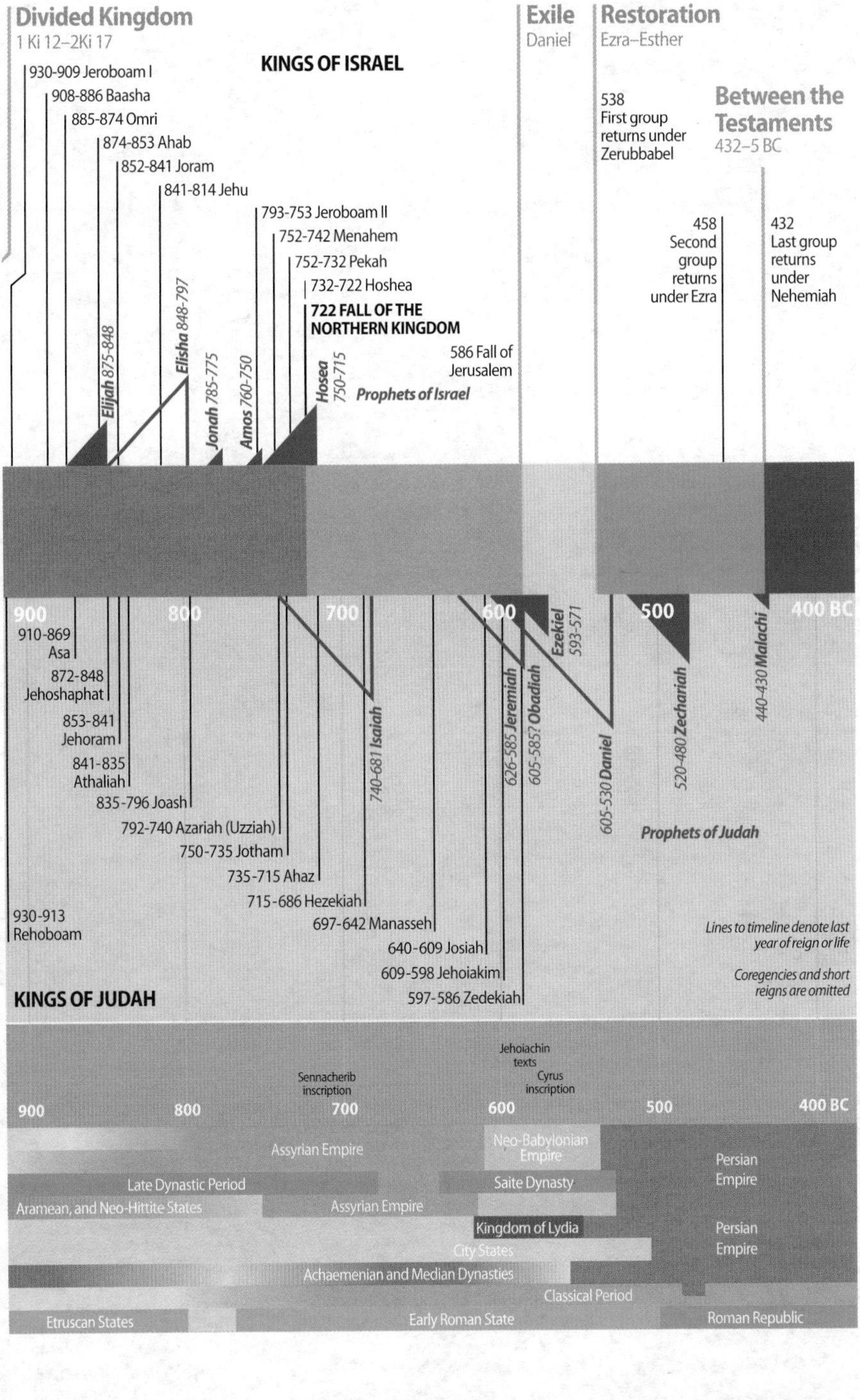

Divided Kingdom
1 Ki 12–2Ki 17

Exile
Daniel

Restoration
Ezra–Esther

Between the Testaments
432–5 BC

KINGS OF ISRAEL

930-909 Jeroboam I
908-886 Baasha
885-874 Omri
874-853 Ahab
852-841 Joram
841-814 Jehu
793-753 Jeroboam II
752-742 Menahem
752-732 Pekah
732-722 Hoshea
722 FALL OF THE NORTHERN KINGDOM

586 Fall of Jerusalem

538 First group returns under Zerubbabel

458 Second group returns under Ezra

432 Last group returns under Nehemiah

Prophets of Israel

Elijah 875-848
Elisha 848-797
Jonah 785-775
Amos 760-750
Hosea 750-715

900 800 700 600 500 400 BC

KINGS OF JUDAH

930-913 Rehoboam
910-869 Asa
872-848 Jehoshaphat
853-841 Jehoram
841-835 Athaliah
835-796 Joash
792-740 Azariah (Uzziah)
750-735 Jotham
735-715 Ahaz
715-686 Hezekiah
697-642 Manasseh
640-609 Josiah
609-598 Jehoiakim
597-586 Zedekiah

Prophets of Judah

740-681 *Isaiah*
626-585 *Jeremiah*
605-585? *Obadiah*
Ezekiel 593-571
605-530 *Daniel*
520-480 *Zechariah*
440-430 *Malachi*

Lines to timeline denote last year of reign or life

Coregencies and short reigns are omitted

Sennacherib inscription
Jehoiachin texts
Cyrus inscription

900 800 700 600 500 400 BC

Assyrian Empire
Neo-Babylonian Empire
Persian Empire
Late Dynastic Period
Saite Dynasty
Aramean, and Neo-Hittite States
Assyrian Empire
Kingdom of Lydia
Persian Empire
City States
Achaemenian and Median Dynasties
Classical Period
Etruscan States
Early Roman State
Roman Republic

THE OLD TESTAMENT

THE FIVE BOOKS OF MOSES

English Bibles are often divided into six major sections: Pentateuch, History, Poetry, Prophets, Gospels and Acts, and Letters and Revelation. The Pentateuch (meaning "five-volumed book") comprises the first major section of the OT. It is also known as the Torah ("Law"). Here God's earliest covenants with his chosen people are described and confirmed.

The five books of Moses are primarily accounts of the history of God's covenant people (Israel). Beginning with Genesis, the narrative moves from a broad view of the universe and all creation to human beings in general and God's role for them in the world. From this view of mankind as a whole, the account narrows from a focus on all nations to Abraham and one nation—Israel as the vassal people of the divine King and his kingdom. The last four books tell the story of Israel's exodus from Egypt, their assent to the Sinaitic covenant, and their wandering in the Desert of Sinai because of unbelief and disobedience at Kadesh Barnea (Nu 13–14; see note on Heb 3:16–19).

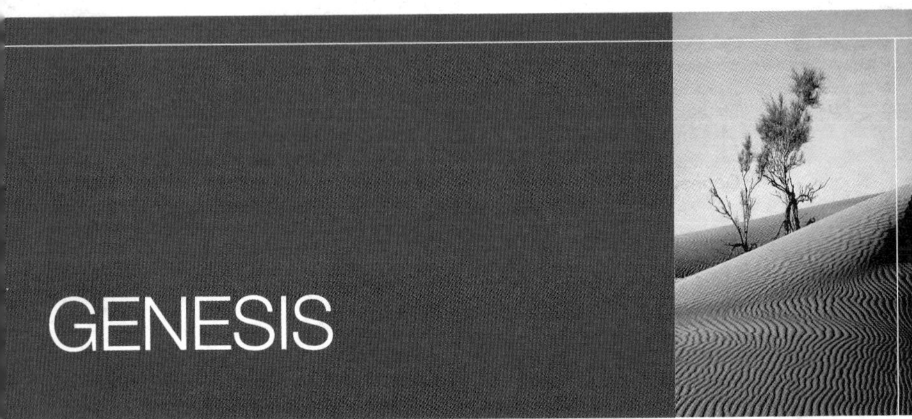

GENESIS

INTRODUCTION

Title

The first phrase in the Hebrew text of 1:1 is *bereshith* ("In [the] beginning"), which is also the Hebrew title of the book (books in ancient times customarily were named after their first word or two). The English title, Genesis, is Greek in origin and comes from the word *geneseos*, which appears in the pre-Christian Greek translation (Septuagint) of 2:4; 5:1. Depending on its context, the word can mean "birth," "genealogy" or "history of origin." In both its Hebrew and Greek forms, then, the traditional title of Genesis appropriately describes its content, since it is primarily a book of beginnings.

Background

Chs. 1 – 38 reflect a great deal of what we know from other sources about ancient Mesopotamian life and culture. Creation, genealogies, destructive floods, geography and mapmaking, construction techniques, migrations of peoples, sale and purchase of land, legal customs and procedures, sheepherding and cattle-raising — all these subjects and many others were matters of vital concern to the peoples of Mesopotamia during this time. They were also of interest to the individuals, families and tribes whom we read about in the first 38 chapters of Genesis. The author appears to locate Eden, humankind's first home, in or near Mesopotamia; the tower of Babel was built there; Abram was born there; Isaac took a wife from there; and Jacob lived there for 20 years. Although these patriarchs settled in Canaan, their original homeland was Mesopotamia.

The closest ancient literary parallels to Ge 1 – 38 also come from Mesopotamia. *Enuma elish*, the story of the god Marduk's rise to supremacy in the Babylonian pantheon, is similar in some respects (though thoroughly mythical and polytheistic) to the Ge 1 creation account. Some of the features of certain king lists from Sumer bear striking resemblance to the genealogy in Ge 5. The 11th tablet of the Gilgamesh epic is quite

a quick look

Author:
Moses

Audience:
God's chosen people, the Israelites

Date:
Between 1446 and 1406 BC

Theme:
Genesis is a book of beginnings that introduces central themes of the Bible, such as creation and redemption.

similar in outline to the flood narrative in Ge 6–8. Several of the major events of Ge 1–8 are narrated in the same order as similar events in the Atrahasis epic. In fact, the latter features the same basic motif of creation-alienation-flood as the Biblical account. Clay tablets found in 1974 at the ancient (c. 2500–2300 BC) site of Ebla (modern Tell Mardikh) in northern Syria may also contain some intriguing parallels (see chart, p. xxii).

Two other important sets of documents demonstrate the reflection of Mesopotamia in the first 38 chapters of Genesis. From the Mari tablets (see chart, p. xxiii), dating from the patriarchal period, we learn that the names of the patriarchs (including especially Abram, Jacob and Job) were typical of that time. The letters also clearly illustrate the freedom of travel that was possible between various parts of the Amorite world in which the patriarchs lived. The Nuzi tablets (see chart, p. xxiv), though a few centuries later than the patriarchal period, shed light on patriarchal customs, which tended to survive virtually intact for many centuries. The inheritance right of an adopted household member or slave (see 15:1–4), the obligation of a barren wife to furnish her husband with sons through a servant girl (see 16:2–4), strictures against expelling such a servant girl and her son (see 21:10–11), the authority of oral statements in ancient Near Eastern law, such as the deathbed bequest (see 27:1–4,22–23,33; 49:28–33)—these and other legal customs, social contracts and provisions are graphically illustrated in Mesopotamian documents.

The Atrahasis epic, c. seventeenth century BC, contains an account of creation and early human history, including the flood.
Kim Walton, courtesy of the British Museum

As Ge 1–38 is Mesopotamian in character and background, so chs. 39–50 reflect Egyptian influence—though in not quite so direct a way. Examples of such influence are: Egyptian grape cultivation (40:9–11), the riverside scene (ch. 41), Egypt as Canaan's breadbasket (ch. 42), Canaan as the source of numerous products for Egyptian consumption (ch. 43), Egyptian religious and social customs (the end of chs. 43; 46), Egyptian administrative procedures (ch. 47), Egyptian funerary practices (ch. 50) and several Egyptian words and names used throughout these chapters. The closest specific literary parallel from Egypt is the *Tale of Two Brothers*, which bears some resemblance to the story of Joseph and Potiphar's wife (ch. 39). Egyptian autobiographical narratives (such as the *Story of Sinuhe* and the *Report of Wenamun*) and certain historical legends offer more general literary parallels.

Author and Date of Writing

Historically, Jews and Christians alike have held that Moses was the author/compiler of the first five books of the OT. These books, known also as the Pentateuch (meaning "five-volumed book"), were referred to in Jewish tradition as the five fifths of the Law (of Moses). The Bible itself suggests Mosaic authorship of Genesis, since Ac 15:1 refers to circumcision as "the custom taught by Moses," an allusion to Ge 17. However, a certain amount of later editorial updating does appear to be indicated (see, e.g., notes on 14:14; 36:31; 47:11).

The historical period during which Moses lived seems to be fixed with a fair degree of accuracy by 1 Kings. We are told that "the fourth year of Solomon's reign over Israel" was the same as "the four hundred and eightieth year after the Israelites came out of Egypt" (1Ki 6:1). Since the former was c. 966 BC, the latter—and thus the date of the exodus—was c. 1446 (assuming that the 480 in 1Ki 6:1 is to be taken literally; see Introduction to Judges: Background). The 40-year period of Israel's wanderings in the wilderness, which lasted from c. 1446 to c. 1406, would have been the most likely time for Moses to write the bulk of what is today known as the Pentateuch.

During the last three centuries many interpreters have claimed to find in the Pentateuch four underlying sources. The presumed documents, allegedly dating from the tenth to the fifth centuries BC, are called J (for Jahweh/Yahweh, the personal OT name for God), E (for Elohim, a generic name for God), D (for Deuteronomic) and P (for Priestly). Each of these documents is claimed to have its own characteristics and its own theology, which often contradicts that of the other documents. The Pentateuch is thus depicted as a patchwork of stories, poems and laws. However, this view is not supported by conclusive evidence, and intensive archaeological and literary research has tended to undercut many of the arguments used to challenge Mosaic authorship.

Theological Theme and Message

Genesis speaks of beginnings—of the heavens and the earth, of light and darkness, of seas and skies, of land and vegetation, of sun and moon and stars, of sea and air and land animals, of human beings (made in God's own image, the climax of his creative activity), of marriage and family, of society and civilization, of sin and redemption. The list could go on and on. A key word in Genesis is "account," which also serves to divide the book into its ten major parts (see Literary Features and Literary Outline) and which includes such concepts as birth, genealogy and history.

The book of Genesis is foundational to the understanding of the rest of the Bible. Its message is rich and complex, and listing its main elements gives a succinct outline of the Biblical message as a whole. It is supremely a book that speaks about relationships, highlighting those between God and his creation, between God and humankind, and between human beings. It is thoroughly monotheistic, taking for granted that there is only one God worthy of the name and opposing the ideas that there are many gods (polytheism), that there is no god at all (atheism) and that everything is divine (pantheism). It clearly teaches that the one true God is sovereign over all that exists (i.e., his entire creation), and that he often exercises his unlimited freedom to overturn human customs, traditions and plans. It introduces us to the way in which God initiates and makes covenants with his chosen people, pledging his love and faithfulness to them and calling them to promise theirs to him. It establishes sacrifice as the substitution of life for life (ch. 22). It gives us the first hint of God's provision for redemption from the forces of evil (compare 3:15 with Ro 16:17–20) and contains the oldest and most profound statement concerning the significance of faith (15:6; see note there). More than half of Heb 11—a NT list of the faithful—refers to characters in Genesis.

Genesis is supremely a book that speaks about relationships, highlighting those between God and his creation, between God and humankind, and between human beings.

Literary Features

The message of a book is often enhanced by its literary structure and characteristics. Genesis is divided into ten main sections, each identified by the word "account" (see 2:4; 5:1; 6:9; 10:1; 11:10; 11:27; 25:12; 25:19; 36:1 — repeated for emphasis at 36:9 — and 37:2). The first five sections can be grouped together and, along with the introduction to the book as a whole (1:1 — 2:3), can be appropriately called "primeval history" (1:1 — 11:26). This introduction to the main story sketches the period from Adam to Abraham and tells about the ways of God with the human race as a whole. The last five sections constitute a much longer (but equally unified) account and relate the story of God's dealings with the ancestors of his chosen people Israel (Abraham, Isaac, Jacob and Joseph and their families) — a section often called "patriarchal history" (11:27 — 50:26). This section is in turn composed of three narrative cycles (Abraham-Isaac, 11:27 — 25:11; Isaac-Jacob, 25:19 — 35:29; 37:1; Jacob-Joseph, 37:2 — 50:26), interspersed by the genealogies of Ishmael (25:12 – 18) and Esau (ch. 36).

The narrative frequently concentrates on the life of a later son in preference to the firstborn: Seth over Cain, Shem over Japheth (but see NIV text note on 10:21), Isaac over Ishmael, Jacob over Esau, Judah and Joseph over their brothers, and Ephraim over Manasseh. Such emphasis on divinely chosen men and their families is perhaps the most obvious literary and theological characteristic of the book of Genesis as a whole. It strikingly underscores the fact that the people of God are not the product of natural human developments but are the result of God's sovereign and gracious intrusion in human history. He brings out of the fallen human race a new humanity consecrated to himself, called and destined to be the people of his kingdom and the channel of his blessing to the whole earth.

Numbers with symbolic significance figure prominently in Genesis. The number ten, in addition to being the number of sections into which Genesis is divided, is also the number of names appearing in the genealogies of chs. 5 and 11 (see note on 5:5). The number seven also occurs frequently. The Hebrew text of 1:1 consists of exactly seven words and that of 1:2 of exactly 14 (twice seven). There are seven days of creation, seven names in the genealogy of ch. 4 (see note on 4:17 – 18; see also 4:15,24; 5:31), various sevens in the flood story, 70 descendants of Noah's sons (ch. 10), a sevenfold promise to Abram (12:2 – 3), seven years of abundance and then seven of famine in Egypt (ch. 41), and 70 descendants of Jacob (ch. 46). Other significant numbers, such as 12 and 40, are used with similar frequency.

The book of Genesis is basically prose narrative, punctuated here and there by brief poems (the longest is the so-called Blessing of Jacob in 49:2 – 27). Much of the prose has a lyrical quality and uses the full range of figures of speech and other devices that characterize the world's finest epic literature. Vertical and horizontal parallelism between the two sets of three days in the creation account (see note on 1:11); the ebb and flow of sin and judgment in ch. 3 (the serpent, woman and man sin successively; God questions them in reverse order; then he judges them in the original order); the powerful monotony of "and then he died" at the end of paragraphs in ch. 5; the climactic hinge effect of the phrase "But God remembered Noah" (8:1) at the midpoint of the flood story; the hourglass structure of the account of the tower of Babel in 11:1 – 9 (narrative in vv. 1 – 2,8 – 9; discourse in vv. 3 – 4,6 – 7; v. 5 acting as transition); the macabre pun in 40:19 (see 40:13); the alter-

Michelangelo's painting of God creating Adam

Sistine Chapel Ceiling (1508-12): *The Creation of Adam*, 1511-12, Buonarroti, Michelangelo (1475-1564)/Vatican Museums and Galleries, Vatican City, Italy/ The Bridgeman Art Library

nation between brief accounts about firstborn sons and lengthy accounts about younger sons—these and numerous other literary devices add interest to the narrative and provide interpretive signals to which the reader should pay close attention.

It is no coincidence that many of the subjects and themes of the first three chapters of Genesis are reflected in the last three chapters of Revelation. We can only marvel at the superintending influence of the Lord himself, who assures us that "all Scripture is God-breathed" (2Ti 3:16) and that its writers "spoke from God as they were carried along by the Holy Spirit" (2Pe 1:21).

Outlines

Literary Outline:

I. Introduction (1:1—2:3)
II. Body (2:4—50:26)
  A. "The account of the heavens and the earth" (2:4—4:26)
  B. "The written account of Adam's family line" (5:1—6:8)
  C. "The account of Noah" (6:9—9:29)
  D. "The account of Shem, Ham and Japheth" (10:1—11:9)
  E. "The account of Shem's family line" (11:10–26)
  F. "The account of Terah's family line" (11:27—25:11)
  G. "The account of the family line of Abraham's son Ishmael" (25:12–18)
  H. "The account of the family line of Abraham's son Isaac" (25:19—35:29)
  I. "The account of the family line of Esau" (36:1—37:1)
  J. "The account of Jacob's family line" (37:2—50:26)

Thematic Outline:

- I. Creation (1:1 — 2:3)
- II. Primeval History (2:4 — 11:26)
  - A. Adam and Eve in Eden (2:4 – 25)
  - B. The Fall and Its Consequences (ch. 3)
  - C. Sin's Progression (4:1 – 16)
  - D. The Genealogy of Cain (4:17 – 26)
  - E. The Genealogy of Seth (ch. 5)
  - F. God's Response to Human Depravity (6:1 – 8)
  - G. The Great Flood (6:9 — 9:29)
    1. Preparing for the flood (6:9 — 7:10)
    2. Judgment and redemption (7:11 — 8:19)
       - a. The rising of the waters (7:11 – 24)
       - b. The receding of the waters (8:1 – 19)
    3. The flood's aftermath (8:20 — 9:29)
       - a. A new promise (8:20 – 22)
       - b. Renewed benediction and new ordinances (9:1 – 7)
       - c. A new relationship (9:8 – 17)
       - d. A new temptation (9:18 – 23)
       - e. A final word (9:24 – 29)
  - H. The Spread of the Nations (10:1 — 11:26)
    1. The diffusion of nations (ch. 10)
    2. The confusion of languages (11:1 – 9)
    3. The first Semitic genealogy (11:10 – 26)
- III. Patriarchal History (11:27 — 50:26)
  - A. The Life of Abraham (11:27 — 25:11)
    1. Abraham's background (11:27 – 32)
    2. Abraham's call and response (chs. 12 – 14)
    3. Abraham's faith and God's covenant (chs. 15 – 22)
    4. Abraham's final acts (23:1 — 25:11)
  - B. The Descendants of Ishmael (25:12 – 18)
  - C. The Life of Jacob (25:19 — 35:29)
    1. Jacob at home (25:19 — 27:46)
    2. Jacob abroad (chs. 28 – 30)
    3. Jacob at home again (chs. 31 – 35)
  - D. The Descendants of Esau (36:1 — 37:1)
  - E. The Life of Joseph (37:2 — 50:26)
    1. Joseph's career (37:2 — 41:57)
    2. Jacob's migration (chs. 42 – 47)
    3. Jacob's final days (48:1 — 50:14)
    4. Joseph's final days (50:15 – 26)

The Beginning

1 In the beginning[a] God created[b]
the heavens[c] and the earth.[d] 2 Now
the earth was formless[e] and empty,[f]
darkness was over the surface of the
deep,[g] and the Spirit of God[h] was hovering[i] over the waters.

3 And God said,[j] "Let there be light," and
there was light.[k] 4 God saw that the
light was good,[l] and he separated the
light from the darkness.[m] 5 God called[n]
the light "day," and the darkness he
called "night."[o] And there was evening, and there was morning[p]—the
first day.
6 And God said,[q] "Let there be a vault[r]
between the waters[s] to separate water from water." 7 So God made the
vault and separated the water under
the vault from the water above it.[t]
And it was so.[u] 8 God called[v] the vault
"sky."[w] And there was evening, and
there was morning[x]—the second day.
9 And God said, "Let the water under the
sky be gathered to one place,[y] and let
dry ground[z] appear." And it was so.[a]
10 God called[b] the dry ground "land,"
and the gathered waters[c] he called

1:1 [a] Ps 102:25; Pr 8:23; Isa 40:21; 41:4, 26; Jn 1:1-2 [b] ver 21,27; Ge 2:3 [c] ver 6; Ne 9:6; Job 9:8; 37:18; Ps 96:5; 104:2; 115:15; 121:2; 136:5; Isa 40:22; 42:5; 51:13; Jer 10:12; 51:15 [d] Ge 14:19; 2Ki 19:15; Ne 9:6; Job 38:4; Ps 90:2; 136:6; 146:6; Isa 37:16; 40:28; 42:5; 44:24; 45:12, 18; Jer 27:5; 32:17; Ac 14:15; 17:24; Eph 3:9; Col 1:16; Heb 3:4; 11:3; Rev 4:11; 10:6 **1:2** [e] Isa 23:1; 24:10; 27:10; 32:14; 34:11 [f] Isa 45:18; Jer 4:23 [g] Ge 8:2; Job 7:12; 26:8; 38:9; Ps 36:6; 42:7; 104:6; 107:24; Pr 30:4 [h] Ge 2:7; Job 33:4; Ps 104:30; Isa 32:15 [i] Dt 32:11; Isa 31:5 **1:3** [j] ver 6; Ps 33:6, 9; 148:5; Heb 11:3 [k] 2Co 4:6*; 1Jn 1:5-7 **1:4** [l] ver 10, 12, 18, 21, 25, 31; Ps 104:31; 119:68; Jer 31:35 [m] ver 14; Ex 10:21-23; Job 26:10; 38:19; Ps 18:28; 104:20; 105:28; Isa 42:16; 45:7 **1:5** [n] ver 8, 10; Ge 2:19, 23 [o] Ps 74:16 [p] ver 8, 13, 19, 23, 31 **1:6** [q] S ver 3 [r] S ver 1; Isa 44:24; 2Pe 3:5 [s] ver 9; Ps 24:2; 136:6 **1:7** [t] Ge 7:11; Job 26:10; 38:8-11, 16; Ps 68:33; 148:4; Pr 8:28 [u] ver 9, 11, 15, 24 **1:8** [v] S ver 5 [w] Job 9:8; 37:18; Ps 19:1; 104:2; Isa 40:22; 44:24; 45:12; Jer 10:12; Zec 12:1 [x] S ver 5 **1:9** [y] Job 38:8-11; Ps 33:7; 104:6-9; Pr 8:29; Jer 5:22; 2Pe 3:5 [z] Ps 95:5; Jnh 1:9; Hag 2:6 [a] S ver 7 **1:10** [b] S ver 5 [c] Ps 33:7

1:1—2:3 In the ancient Near East, most of the peoples had myths relating how the world came to be. Prevalent in those myths were accounts of how one of the gods triumphed over a fierce and powerful beast that represented disorder, then fashioned the ordered world that people knew, and finally was proclaimed by the other gods to be the divine "king" over the world he had created—a position ever subject to the challenge of the forces of disorder.

Over against all those pagan myths, the author of Genesis taught a totally different doctrine of creation: The one and only true God did not have to overcome a mighty cosmic champion of chaos but simply by a series of his royal creation decrees called into being the ordered world, the visible kingdom that those decrees continue to uphold and govern. The author teaches this doctrine of creation in the form of a narrative that recounts the story of God's creative acts. Those acts are narrated from the perspective of one who was an eyewitness to events in God's royal council chamber, where he issues his creative decrees. For a similar narrative perspective, see Job 1:6–12; 2:1–6. (For the different narrative perspective of what follows, see note on 2:4—4:26.)

1:1 A summary statement introducing the six days of creative activity (see note on 2:1). The truth of this majestic verse was joyfully affirmed by poet (Ps 102:25) and prophet (Isa 40:21). *In the beginning God.* The Bible always assumes, and never argues, God's existence. Although everything else had a beginning, God has always been (Ps 90:2). *In the beginning.* Jn 1:1–10, which stresses the work of Christ in creation, opens with the same phrase. *God created.* "God" renders the common Hebrew noun *Elohim*. It is plural but the verb is singular, a normal usage in the OT when reference is to the one true God. This use of the plural expresses intensification rather than number and has been called the plural of majesty, or of potentiality. In the OT the Hebrew verb for "create" is used only of divine, never of human, activity. *the heavens and the earth.* "All things" (Isa 44:24). That God created everything is also taught in Ecc 11:5; Jer 10:16; Jn 1:3; Col 1:16; Heb 1:2. The positive, life-oriented teaching of v. 1 is beautifully summarized in Isa 45:18.

1:2 *earth.* The focus of this account. *formless and empty.* The phrase, which appears elsewhere only in Jer 4:23, gives structure to the rest of the chapter (see note on v. 11). God's "separating" and "gathering" on days 1–3 gave form, and his "making" and "filling" on days 4–6 removed the emptiness. *darkness ... the waters.* Completes the picture of a world awaiting God's light-giving, order-making and life-creating word. *and.* Or "but." The awesome (and, for ancient people, fearful) picture of the original state of the visible creation is relieved by the majestic announcement that the mighty Spirit of God hovers over creation. The announcement anticipates God's creative words that follow. *Spirit of God.* He was active in creation, and his creative power continues today (see Job 33:4; Ps 104:30). *hovering over.* Like an eagle that hovers over its young when they are learning to fly (see Dt 32:11; cf. Isa 31:5).

1:3 *God said.* Merely by issuing his royal decree, God brought all things into being (Ps 33:6,9; 148:5; Heb 11:3). *Let there be light.* God's first creative word called forth light in the midst of the primeval darkness. Light is necessary for making God's creative works visible and life possible. In the OT it is also symbolic of life and blessing (see 2Sa 22:29; Job 3:20; 30:26; 33:30; Ps 49:19; 56:13; 97:11; 112:4; Isa 53:11; 58:8,10; 59:9; 60:1,3). Paul uses this word to illustrate God's re-creating work in sin-darkened hearts (2Co 4:6).

1:4 *good.* Everything God created is good (see vv. 10,12,18,21, 25); in fact, the conclusion declares it to be "very good" (v. 31). The creation, as fashioned and ordered by God, had no lingering traces of disorder and no dark and threatening forces arrayed against God or people. Even darkness and the deep were given benevolent functions in a world fashioned to bless and sustain life (see Ps 104:19–26; 127:2—see also NIV text note there).

1:5 *called.* See vv. 8,10. In the ancient Near East, for a king to name people or things was an act of claiming dominion over them (see 17:5,15; 41:45; 2Ki 23:34; 24:17; Da 1:7). In this creation account, God named the great cosmic realities of day, night, sky, land and seas. He left to human beings the naming of the creatures they were given dominion over (see vv. 26,28; see also 2:19 and note). *first day.* Some say that the creation days were 24-hour days, others that they were indefinite periods.

1:6 *vault.* The atmosphere, or "sky" (v. 8), as seen from the earth. "Hard as a mirror" (Job 37:18) and "like a canopy" (Isa 40:22) are among the many pictorial phrases used to describe it.

1:7 *And it was so.* The only possible outcome, whether stated (vv. 9,11,15,24,30) or implied, to God's "Let there be" (see Ps 33:6,9 and note on 33:6).

1:9 *one place.* A picturesque way of referring to the "seas" (v. 10) that surround the dry land on all sides and into which the waters of the lakes and rivers flow. The earth was "formed out of water" (2Pe 3:5) and "founded ... on the seas" (Ps 24:2), and the waters are not to cross the boundaries set for them (Ps 104:7–9; Jer 5:22).

"seas."[d] And God saw that it was
good.[e]
11 Then God said, "Let the land produce vegetation:[f] seed-bearing plants
and trees on the land that bear fruit
with seed in it, according to their various kinds.[g]" And it was so.[h] 12 The
land produced vegetation: plants
bearing seed according to their kinds[i]
and trees bearing fruit with seed in
it according to their kinds. And God
saw that it was good.[j] 13 And there
was evening, and there was morning[k]—the third day.
14 And God said, "Let there be lights[l] in
the vault of the sky to separate the
day from the night,[m] and let them
serve as signs[n] to mark sacred times,[o]
and days and years,[p] 15 and let them
be lights in the vault of the sky to give
light on the earth." And it was so.[q]
16 God made two great lights—the
greater light[r] to govern[s] the day and
the lesser light to govern[t] the night.[u]
He also made the stars.[v] 17 God set
them in the vault of the sky to give
light on the earth, 18 to govern the day
and the night,[w] and to separate light
from darkness. And God saw that it
was good.[x] 19 And there was evening,
and there was morning[y]—the fourth
day.
20 And God said, "Let the water teem with
living creatures,[z] and let birds fly
above the earth across the vault of
the sky."[a] 21 So God created[b] the great
creatures of the sea[c] and every living
thing with which the water teems
and that moves about in it,[d] according to their kinds, and every winged
bird according to its kind.[e] And God
saw that it was good.[f] 22 God blessed
them and said, "Be fruitful and increase in number and fill the water
in the seas, and let the birds increase
on the earth."[g] 23 And there was evening, and there was morning[h]—the
fifth day.
24 And God said, "Let the land produce
living creatures[i] according to their
kinds:[j] the livestock, the creatures
that move along the ground, and the
wild animals, each according to its
kind." And it was so.[k] 25 God made
the wild animals[l] according to their
kinds, the livestock according to their
kinds, and all the creatures that move
along the ground according to their
kinds.[m] And God saw that it was
good.[n]
26 Then God said, "Let us[o] make
mankind[p] in our image,[q] in our likeness,[r] so that they may rule[s] over the
fish in the sea and the birds in the
sky,[t] over the livestock and all the wild

1:10 [d] Job 38:8; Ps 90:2; 95:5 [e] S ver 4 **1:11** [f] Ps 65:9-13; 104:14 [g] ver 12,21,24, 25; Ge 2:5; 6:20; 7:14; Lev 11:14, 19,22; Dt 14:13, 18; 1Co 15:38 [h] S ver 7 **1:12** [i] S ver 11 [j] S ver 4 **1:13** [k] S ver 5 **1:14** [l] Ps 74:16; 136:7 [m] S ver 4 [n] Jer 10:2 [o] Ps 104:19 [p] Ge 8:22; Jer 31:35-36; 33:20,25 **1:15** [q] S ver 7 **1:16** [r] Dt 17:3; Job 31:26; Jer 43:13; Eze 8:16 [s] Ps 136:8 [t] Ps 136:9 [u] Job 38:33; Ps 74:16; 104:19; Jer 31:35; Jas 1:17 [v] Dt 4:19; Job 9:9; 38:7, 31-32; Ps 8:3; 33:6; Ecc 12:2; Isa 40:26; Jer 8:2; Am 5:8 **1:18** [w] Jer 33:20,25 [x] S ver 4 **1:19** [y] S ver 5 **1:20** [z] Ps 146:6

[a] Ge 2:19 **1:21** [b] S ver 1 [c] Job 3:8; 7:12; Ps 74:13; 148:7; Isa 27:1; Eze 32:2 [d] Ps 104:25-26 [e] S ver 11 [f] S ver 4 **1:22** [g] ver 28; Ge 8:17; 9:1, 7,19; 47:27; Lev 26:9; Eze 36:11 **1:23** [h] S ver 5 **1:24** [i] Ge 2:19 [j] S ver 11 [k] S ver 7 **1:25** [l] Ge 7:21-22; Jer 27:5 [m] S ver 11 [n] S ver 4 **1:26** [o] Ge 3:5,22; 11:7; Ps 100:3; Isa 6:8 [p] Isa 45:18 [q] ver 27; Ge 5:3; 9:6; Ps 8:5; 82:6; 89:6; 1Co 11:7; 2Co 4:4; Col 1:15; 3:10; Jas 3:9 [r] Ac 17:28-29 [s] Ge 9:2; Ps 8:6-8 [t] Ps 8:8

1:11 *God said.* This phrase is used twice on the third day (vv. 9,11) and three times (vv. 24,26,29) on the sixth day. These two days are climactic, as the following structure of ch. 1 reveals (see note on v. 2 regarding "formless and empty").

Days of forming	Days of filling
1. "light" (v. 3)	4. "lights" (v. 14)
2. "water under the vault ... water above it" (v. 7)	5. "every living thing with which the water teems ... every winged bird" (v. 21)
3a. "dry ground" (v. 9)	$6a_1$. "livestock, the creatures that move along the ground, and the wild animals" (v. 24) $6a_2$. "mankind" (v. 26)
3b. "vegetation" (v. 11)	6b. "every green plant for food" (v. 30)

Both the horizontal and vertical relationships between the days demonstrate the literary structure of the chapter and stress the orderliness and symmetry of God's creative activity. *kinds.* See vv. 12,21,24–25. Both creation and reproduction are orderly.

1:14 *serve as signs.* In the ways mentioned here, not in any astrological or other such sense (see Ps 104:19; 136:7–9).

1:16 *two great lights.* The words "sun" and "moon" seem to be avoided deliberately here, since both were used as proper names for the pagan deities associated with these heavenly bodies. They are light-givers to be appreciated, not powers to be feared, because the one true God made them (see Isa 40:26). Since the emphasis is on the greater light and lesser light, the stars seem to be mentioned almost as an afterthought. But Ps 136:9 indicates that the stars help the moon "govern the night." *govern.* The great Creator-King assigns subordinate regulating roles to certain of his creatures (see vv. 26,28).

1:17–18 The three main functions of the heavenly bodies.

1:21 *creatures of the sea.* The Hebrew word underlying this phrase was used in Canaanite mythology to name a dreaded sea monster. He is often used figuratively in OT poetry to refer to one of God's most powerful opponents. He is pictured as national (Babylonia, Jer 51:34; Egypt, Isa 51:9; Eze 29:3; 32:2) or cosmic (Job 7:12; Ps 74:13; Isa 27:1, though some take the latter as a reference to Egypt). In Genesis, however, the creatures of the sea are portrayed not as enemies to be feared but as part of God's good creation to be appreciated (cf. Ps 104:26 and note).

1:22 *Be fruitful and increase in number.* God's benediction on living things that inhabit the water and that fly in the air. By his blessing they flourish and fill both realms with life (see note on v. 28). God's rule over his created realm promotes and blesses life.

1:26 *us ... our ... our.* God speaks as the Creator-King, announcing his crowning work to the members of his heavenly court (see 3:22; 11:7; Isa 6:8; see also 1Ki 22:19–23; Job 15:8; Jer 23:18). *image ... likeness.* No

animals,[a] and over all the creatures
that move along the ground."

27 So God created[u] mankind[v] in his own
image,[w]
in the image of God[x] he created
them;
male and female[y] he created them.[z]

28 God blessed them and said to
them,[a] "Be fruitful and increase in
number;[b] fill the earth[c] and subdue it.
Rule over[d] the fish in the sea and the
birds in the sky and over every living
creature that moves on the ground.[e]"
29 Then God said, "I give you every seed-bearing plant on the face of
the whole earth and every tree that
has fruit with seed in it. They will be
yours for food.[f] 30 And to all the beasts
of the earth and all the birds in the
sky and all the creatures that move
along the ground—everything that
has the breath of life[g] in it—I give
every green plant for food.[h]" And it
was so.
31 God saw all that he had made,[i]
and it was very good.[j] And there was
evening, and there was morning[k]—
the sixth day.

2 Thus the heavens and the earth
were completed in all their vast array.[l]

2 By the seventh day[m] God had finished
the work he had been doing; so on
the seventh day he rested from all his
work.[n] 3 Then God blessed the seventh day and made it holy,[o] because
on it he rested[p] from all the work of
creating[q] that he had done.

Adam and Eve

4 This is the account[r] of the heavens
and the earth when they were created,[s]
when the LORD God made the earth and
the heavens.

1:27 [u] S ver 1 [v] Ge 2:7; Ps 103:14; 119:73 [w] S ver 26 [x] Ge 5:1 [y] Ge 5:2; Mt 19:4*; Mk 10:6*; Gal 3:28 [z] Dt 4:32 **1:28** [a] Ge 33:5; Jos 24:3; Ps 113:9; 127:3, 5 [b] S Ge 17:6 [c] S ver 22; Ge 6:1; Ac 17:26 [d] ver 26; Ps 115:16 [e] Ps 8:6-8 **1:29** [f] Ge 9:3; Dt 12:15; Ps 104:14; 1Ti 4:3 **1:30** [g] Ge 2:7; 7:22 [h] Job 38:41; Ps 78:25; 104:14, 27; 111:5; 136:25; 145:15; 147:9 **1:31** [i] Ps 104:24; 136:5; Pr 3:19; Jer 10:12 [j] S ver 4; 1Ti 4:4 [k] S ver 5 **2:1** [l] Dt 4:19; 17:3; 2Ki 17:16; 21:3; Ps 104:2; Isa 44:24; 45:12; 48:13; 51:13 **2:2** [m] Dt 5:14 [n] ver 2-3; Ex 20:11; 31:17; 34:21; Jn 5:17; Heb 4:4* **2:3** [o] Ex 16:23; 20:10; 23:12; 31:15; 35:2; Lev 23:3; Ne 9:14; Isa 58:13; Jer 17:22 [p] Ps 95:11; Heb 4:1-11 [q] S Ge 1:1 **2:4** [r] Ge 5:1; 6:9; 10:1; 11:10, 27; 25:12, 19; 36:1, 9; 37:2 [s] Ge 1:1; Job 38:8-11

[a] *26* Probable reading of the original Hebrew text (see Syriac); Masoretic Text *the earth*

distinction should be made between "image" and "likeness," which are synonyms in both the OT (5:1; 9:6) and the NT (1Co 11:7; Col 3:10; Jas 3:9), as well as in a ninth-century BC Aramaic inscription found in 1979 on a life-size statue of a local ruler at Tell Fekheriyeh in Syria. Since human beings are made in God's image, they are all worthy of honor and respect; they are neither to be murdered (9:6) nor cursed (Jas 3:9). "Image" includes such characteristics as "righteousness and holiness" (Eph 4:24) and "knowledge" (Col 3:10). Believers are to be "conformed to the image" of Christ (Ro 8:29) and will someday be "like him" (1Jn 3:2; see note on Col 1:15). *so that they may rule.* Within the realm of his visible creation God places a creature capable of acting as his agent in relationship to other creatures (1) to represent God's claim to kingship over his creation and (2) to bring its full potential to realization to the praise of the Creator's glory. (In the ancient Near East, kings marked their conquest of lands by setting up images of themselves in the conquered territories as a sign of their authority.) For a celebration of humanity's exalted role (under God) in the creation, see Ps 8:5–8 and notes. For the ultimate embodiment of humanity's dominion over the creation, see Eph 1:22; Heb 2:5–9 and notes. *rule.* Humans are the climax of God's creative activity, and God has "crowned them with glory and honor" and made them rulers over the rest of his creation (Ps 8:5–8). Since they were created in the image of the divine King, delegated sovereignty (kingship) was bestowed on them.

1:27 This highly significant verse is the first occurrence of poetry in the OT (which is about 40 percent poetry). *created.* The word is used here three times to describe the central divine act of the sixth day (see note on v. 1). *male and female.* Alike they bear the image of God, and together they share in the divine benediction that follows.

1:28 *God blessed them ... fill ... subdue ... Rule.* Humankind goes forth from the hands of the Creator under his divine benediction—flourishing, filling the earth with their kind, and exercising dominion over the other earthly creatures (see v. 26; 2:15; Ps 8:6–8). Human culture, accordingly, is not anti-God (though fallen human beings often have turned their efforts into proud rebellion against God). Rather, it is the activity of those who bear the image of their Creator and share, as God's servants, in his kingly rule. As God's representatives in the creaturely realm, they are stewards of God's creatures. They are not to exploit, waste or despoil them, but are to care for them (see note on 2:15) and use them in the service of God and humankind.

1:29–30 People and animals seem to be portrayed as originally vegetarian (see 9:3 and note).

1:31 *very good.* See note on v. 4. *the sixth day.* Perhaps to stress the finality and importance of this day, in the Hebrew text the definite article is first used here in regard to the creation days.

2:1 A summary statement concluding the six days of creative activity (see note on 1:1).

2:2 *finished ... rested.* God rested on the seventh day, not because he was weary, but because nothing formless or empty remained. His creative work was completed—and it was totally effective, absolutely perfect, "very good" (1:31). It did not have to be repeated, repaired or revised, and the Creator rested to commemorate it.

2:3 *God blessed the seventh day and made it holy ... rested.* Although the word "Sabbath" is not used here, the Hebrew verb translated "rested" (v. 2) is the origin of the noun "Sabbath." Ex 20:11 quotes the first half of v. 3, but substitutes "Sabbath" for "seventh," clearly equating the two. The first record of obligatory Sabbath observance is of Israel on her way from Egypt to Sinai (Ex 16), but according to Ne 9:13–14 the Sabbath was not an official covenant obligation until the giving of the law at Mount Sinai.

2:4—4:26 The beginning of human history, in distinction from the account of creation in 1:1—2:3 (see note there).

2:4 *account.* The Hebrew word for "account" occurs ten times in Genesis—at the beginning of each main section (see Introduction: Literary Features). *the heavens and the earth.* See note on 1:1. The phrase "the account of the heavens and the earth" introduces the story of what happened to God's creation. The blight of sin and rebellion brought a threefold curse that darkens the story of Adam and Eve in God's good and beautiful garden: (1) on Satan (3:14);

5 Now no shrub had yet appeared on the
earth[a] and no plant had yet sprung up,[t]
for the LORD God had not sent rain on the
earth[u] and there was no one to work the
ground, 6 but streams[b] came up from the
earth and watered the whole surface of
the ground. 7 Then the LORD God formed[v]
a man[c][w] from the dust[x] of the ground[y] and
breathed into his nostrils the breath[z] of
life,[a] and the man became a living being.[b]
8 Now the LORD God had planted a garden in the east, in Eden;[c] and there he put
the man he had formed. 9 The LORD God
made all kinds of trees grow out of the
ground—trees[d] that were pleasing to the
eye and good for food. In the middle of the
garden were the tree of life[e] and the tree of
the knowledge of good and evil.[f]
10 A river[g] watering the garden flowed
from Eden;[h] from there it was separated into four headwaters. 11 The name of
the first is the Pishon; it winds through
the entire land of Havilah,[i] where there
is gold. 12 (The gold of that land is good;
aromatic resin[d][j] and onyx are also there.)
13 The name of the second river is the Gihon; it winds through the entire land of
Cush.[e] 14 The name of the third river is the
Tigris;[k] it runs along the east side of Ashur. And the fourth river is the Euphrates.[l]
15 The LORD God took the man and put
him in the Garden of Eden[m] to work it and
take care of it. 16 And the LORD God commanded the man, "You are free to eat from
any tree in the garden;[n] 17 but you must not
eat from the tree of the knowledge of good
and evil,[o] for when you eat from it you
will certainly die."[p]
18 The LORD God said, "It is not good for
the man to be alone. I will make a helper
suitable for him."[q]
19 Now the LORD God had formed out
of the ground all the wild animals[r] and
all the birds in the sky.[s] He brought them
to the man to see what he would name
them; and whatever the man called[t] each
living creature,[u] that was its name. 20 So
the man gave names to all the livestock,
the birds in the sky and all the wild animals.

2:5 [t]Ge 1:11 [u]Job 38:28; Ps 65:9-10; Jer 10:13 **2:7** [v]Isa 29:16; 43:1,21; 44:2 [w]S Ge 1:27 [x]Ge 3:19; 18:27; Job 4:19; 10:9; 17:16; 34:15; Ps 90:3; Ecc 3:20; 12:7 [y]Ge 3:23; 4:2; Ps 103:14; Jer 18:6; 1Co 15:47 [z]S Ge 1:2; Job 27:3; Isa 2:22 [a]S Ge 1:30; Isa 42:5; Ac 17:25 [b]Job 12:10; 32:8; 33:4; 34:14; Ps 104:29; Isa 57:16; Eze 37:5; 1Co 15:45* **2:8** [c]ver 10, 15; Ge 3:23, 24; 4:16; 13:10; Isa 51:3; Eze 28:13; 31:9, 16; 36:35; Joel 2:3 **2:9** [d]Eze 31:8 [e]Ge 3:22, 24; Pr 3:18; 11:30; S Rev 2:7 [f]Eze 47:12 **2:10** [g]Nu 24:6; Ps 46:4; Eze 47:5

[a] *5* Or *land*; also in verse 6 [b] *6* Or *mist*
[c] *7* The Hebrew for *man (adam)* sounds like and may be related to the Hebrew for *ground (adamah)*; it is also the name *Adam* (see verse 20). [d] *12* Or *good; pearls*
[e] *13* Possibly southeast Mesopotamia

[h]S ver 8 **2:11** [i]Ge 10:7; 25:18 **2:12** [j]Nu 11:7 **2:14** [k]Ge 41:1; Da 10:4 [l]Ge 15:18; 31:21; Ex 23:31; Nu 22:5; Dt 1:7; 11:24; Jos 1:4; 2Sa 8:3; 1Ki 4:21; 2Ki 23:29; 24:7; 1Ch 5:9; 18:3; 2Ch 35:20; Jer 13:4; 46:2; 51:63; S Rev 9:14 **2:15** [m]S ver 8 **2:16** [n]Ge 3:1-2 **2:17** [o]Ge 3:11, 17 [p]Ge 3:1, 3; 5:5; 9:29; Dt 30:15, 19; Jer 42:16; Eze 3:18; S Ro 5:12; S 6:23 **2:18** [q]Pr 31:11; 1Co 11:9; 1Ti 2:13 **2:19** [r]Ps 8:7 [s]S Ge 1:20 [t]S Ge 1:5 [u]Ge 1:24

(2) on the ground, because of Adam's sin (3:17); and (3) on Cain (4:11). *LORD God.* "LORD" (Hebrew *YHWH*, "Yahweh") is the personal name of God (see note on Ex 3:15), emphasizing his role as Israel's Redeemer and covenant Lord (see note on Ex 6:6), while "God" (Hebrew *Elohim*) is a general term. Both names occur thousands of times in the OT, and often, as here, they appear together—clearly indicating that they refer to the one and only God.

2:7 *formed.* The Hebrew for this verb commonly referred to the work of a potter (see Isa 45:9; Jer 18:6), who fashions vessels from clay (see Job 33:6). "Make" (1:26), "create" (1:27) and "form" are used to describe God's creation of both people and animals (v. 19; 1:21,25). *breath of life.* Humans and animals alike have the breath of life in them (see 1:30; Job 33:4). *the man became a living being.* The Hebrew phrase here translated "living being" is translated "living creatures" in 1:20,24. The words of 2:7 therefore imply that people, at least physically, have affinity with the animals. The great difference is that people are made "in the image of God" (1:27) and have an absolutely unique relation both to God as his servants and to the other creatures as God's stewards over them (Ps 8:5–8).

2:8 *in the east.* From the standpoint of the author of Genesis. The garden was thought of as being near where the Tigris and Euphrates Rivers (see v. 14) meet, in what is today southern Iraq. *Eden.* A name synonymous with "paradise" and related to either (1) a Hebrew word meaning "bliss" or "delight" or (2) a Mesopotamian word meaning "a plain." Perhaps the author subtly suggests both.

2:9 *tree of life.* Signifying and giving life, without death, to those who eat its fruit (see 3:22; Rev 2:7; 22:2,14). *tree of the knowledge of good and evil.* Signifying and giving knowledge of good and evil, leading ultimately to death, to those who eat its fruit (v. 17; 3:3). "Knowledge of good and evil" refers to moral knowledge or ethical discernment (see Dt 1:39; Isa 7:15–16). Adam and Eve possessed both life and moral discernment as they came from the hand of God. Their access to the fruit of the tree of life showed that God's will and intention for them was life. Ancient pagans believed that the gods intended for human beings always to be mortal. In eating the fruit of the tree of the knowledge of good and evil, Adam and Eve sought a creaturely source of discernment in order to be morally independent of God.

2:11 *Pishon.* Location unknown. The Hebrew word may be a common noun meaning "gusher." *Havilah.* Location unknown; perhaps mentioned again in 10:29. It is probably to be distinguished from the Havilah of 10:7 (see note there), which was in Arabia.

2:13 *Gihon.* Location unknown. The Hebrew word may be a common noun meaning "spurter." Both the Pishon and the Gihon may have been streams in Lower Mesopotamia near the Persian Gulf. The names were those current when Genesis was written.

2:14 *Ashur.* An ancient capital city of Assyria ("Assyria" and "Ashur" are related words). *Euphrates.* Often called in Hebrew simply "the River" because of its size and importance (see note on 15:18).

2:15 *work … take care.* See notes on 1:26,28. The man is now charged to govern the earth responsibly under God's sovereignty.

2:16 *any tree.* Including the tree of life (v. 9).

2:17 *certainly die.* Despite the serpent's denial (3:4), disobeying God ultimately results in death.

2:18–25 The only full account of the creation of woman in ancient Near Eastern literature.

2:18 *not good … to be alone.* Without female companionship and a partner in reproduction, the man could not fully realize his humanity.

2:19 *name them.* His first act of dominion over the creatures around him (see note on 1:5).

But for Adam[a] no suitable helper[v] was
found. 21 So the LORD God caused the man
to fall into a deep sleep;[w] and while he
was sleeping, he took one of the man's
ribs[b] and then closed up the place with
flesh. 22 Then the LORD God made a woman from the rib[c][x] he had taken out of the
man, and he brought her to the man.
23 The man said,

"This is now bone of my bones
and flesh of my flesh;[y]
she shall be called[z] 'woman,'
for she was taken out of man.[a]"

24 That is why a man leaves his father and
mother and is united[b] to his wife, and they
become one flesh.[c]
25 Adam and his wife were both naked,[d]
and they felt no shame.

The Fall

3 Now the serpent[e] was more crafty than
any of the wild animals the LORD God
had made. He said to the woman, "Did
God really say, 'You must not eat from any
tree in the garden'?[f]"
2 The woman said to the serpent, "We
may eat fruit from the trees in the garden,[g]
3 but God did say, 'You must not eat fruit
from the tree that is in the middle of the
garden, and you must not touch it, or you
will die.' "[h]
4 "You will not certainly die," the serpent
said to the woman.[i] 5 "For God knows that
when you eat from it your eyes will be
opened, and you will be like God,[j] knowing good and evil."
6 When the woman saw that the fruit of
the tree was good for food and pleasing to
the eye, and also desirable[k] for gaining wisdom, she took some and ate it. She also
gave some to her husband,[l] who was with
her, and he ate it.[m] 7 Then the eyes of both of
them were opened, and they realized they
were naked;[n] so they sewed fig leaves together and made coverings for themselves.[o]
8 Then the man and his wife heard the
sound of the LORD God as he was walking[p] in the garden in the cool of the day,
and they hid[q] from the LORD God among
the trees of the garden. 9 But the LORD God
called to the man, "Where are you?"[r]
10 He answered, "I heard you in the garden, and I was afraid[s] because I was naked;[t] so I hid."
11 And he said, "Who told you that you
were naked?[u] Have you eaten from the tree
that I commanded you not to eat from?[v]"
12 The man said, "The woman you put
here with me[w]—she gave me some fruit
from the tree, and I ate it."
13 Then the LORD God said to the woman, "What is this you have done?"

[a] 20 Or *the man* [b] 21 Or *took part of the man's side* [c] 22 Or *part*

2:20 [v] Ge 3:20; 4:1 **2:21** [w] Ge 15:12; 1Sa 26:12; Job 33:15 **2:22** [x] 1Co 11:8, 9,12; 1Ti 2:13 **2:23** [y] Ge 29:14; Eph 5:28-30 [z] S Ge 1:5 [a] 1Co 11:8 **2:24** [b] Mal 2:15 [c] Mt 19:5*; Mk 10:7-8*; 1Co 6:16*; Eph 5:31* **2:25** [d] Ge 3:7, 10-11; Isa 47:3; La 1:8 **3:1** [e] Job 1:7; 2:2; 2Co 11:3; Rev 12:9; 20:2 [f] S Ge 2:17 **3:2** [g] Ge 2:16 **3:3** [h] S Ge 2:17 **3:4** [i] S Jn 8:44; 2Co 11:3 **3:5** [j] S Ge 1:26; 14:18,19; Ps 7:8; Isa 14:14; Eze 28:2 **3:6** [k] Jas 1:14-15; 1Jn 2:16 [l] Nu 30:7-8; Jer 44:15,19, 24 [m] 2Co 11:3; 1Ti 2:14 **3:7** [n] Ge 2:25 [o] ver 21 **3:8** [p] Lev 26:12; Dt 23:14 [q] Job 13:16; 23:7; 31:33; 34:22,23; Ps 5:5; 139:7-12; Isa 29:15; Jer 16:17; 23:24; 49:10; Rev 6:15-16 **3:9** [r] Ge 4:9; 16:8; 18:9; 1Ki 19:9,13 **3:10** [s] Ex 19:16; 20:18; Dt 5:5; 1Sa 12:18 [t] Ge 2:25 **3:11** [u] Ge 2:25 [v] S Ge 2:17 **3:12** [w] Ge 2:22

2:24 *leaves his father and mother.* Instead of remaining under the protective custody of his parents, a man leaves them and, with his wife, establishes a new family unit. *united ... one flesh.* The divine intention for husband and wife was monogamy. Together they were to form as inseparable a union as that between parent and child. As parents and their children are the same "flesh and blood" (see 29:14 and note), so husband and wife should be bound together as "one flesh" as long as they live—of which sexual union is an expression (cf. 1Co 6:16 and note).

2:25 *naked ... no shame.* Freedom from shame, signifying moral innocence, would soon be lost as a result of sin (see 3:7 and note).

3:1–24 The disobedience of Adam and Eve, and God's response that affects the whole course of human history (cf. Ro 5:12–21 and notes).

3:1 *serpent.* The great deceiver clothed himself as a serpent, one of God's good creatures. He insinuated a falsehood and portrayed rebellion as clever, but essentially innocent, self-interest. Therefore "the devil, or Satan," is later referred to as "that ancient serpent" (Rev 12:9; 20:2). *crafty.* The Hebrew words for "crafty" and "naked" are almost identical. Though naked, the man and his wife felt no shame (2:25). The craftiness of the serpent led them to sin, and they then became ashamed of their nakedness (see v. 7). *Did God really say ...?* The question and the response changed the course of human history. By causing the woman to doubt God's word, the serpent brought evil into the world. Here the deceiver undertook to alienate people from God. Elsewhere he acts as an accuser to alienate God from people (see Job 1–2; Zec 3:1 and note).

3:3 *and you must not touch it.* The woman adds to God's word, distorting his directive and demonstrating that the serpent's subtle challenge was working its poison.

3:4 *You will not certainly die.* The blatant denial of a specific divine pronouncement (see 2:17).

3:5 *God knows.* The serpent accuses God of having unworthy motives. In Job 1:9–11; 2:4–5 he accuses righteous Job of the same. *your eyes will be opened, and you will be like God.* The statement is only half true. Their eyes were opened, to be sure (see v. 7), but the result was quite different from what the serpent had promised. *knowing good and evil.* See note on 2:9.

3:6 *good for food ... pleasing to the eye ... desirable for gaining wisdom.* Three aspects of temptation. Cf. Lk 4:3,5,9; 1Jn 2:16.

3:7 *they realized they were naked.* No longer innocent like children, they had a new awareness of themselves and of each other in their nakedness, which now produced in them a sense of shame (see note on 2:25). *they ... made coverings.* Their own feeble and futile attempt to hide their shame, which only God could cover (see note on v. 21).

3:8 *garden.* Once a place of joy and of fellowship with God, it became a place of fear and of hiding from God.

3:9 *Where are you?* A rhetorical question (see 4:9).

3:12 *The woman you put here ... gave me.* The man blames God and the woman—anyone but himself—for his sin.

3:13 *The serpent deceived me.* The woman blames the serpent rather than herself.

The woman said, "The serpent deceived
me,[x] and I ate."
14 So the LORD God said to the serpent,
"Because you have done this,

"Cursed[y] are you above all livestock
and all wild animals!
You will crawl on your belly
and you will eat dust[z]
all the days of your life.
15 And I will put enmity
between you and the woman,
and between your offspring[a][a] and
hers;[b]
he will crush[b] your head,[c]
and you will strike his heel."

16 To the woman he said,

"I will make your pains in childbearing
very severe;
with painful labor you will give birth
to children.[d]
Your desire will be for your husband,
and he will rule over you.[e]"

17 To Adam he said, "Because you listened to your wife and ate fruit from the
tree about which I commanded you, 'You
must not eat from it,'[f]

"Cursed[g] is the ground[h] because of
you;
through painful toil[i] you will eat
food from it
all the days of your life.[j]

3:13 [x]Ro 7:11; 2Co 11:3; 1Ti 2:14 **3:14** [y]Dt 28:15-20 [z]Ps 72:9; Isa 49:23; 65:25; Mic 7:17 **3:15** [a]Jn 8:44; Ac 13:10; 1Jn 3:8 [b]Ge 16:11; Jdg 13:5; Isa 7:14; 8:3; 9:6; Mt 1:23; Lk 1:31; Gal 4:4; Rev 12:17 [c]Ro 16:20; Heb 2:14 **3:16** [d]Ps 48:5-6; Isa 13:8; 21:3; 26:17; Jer 4:31; 6:24; Mic 4:9; 1Ti 2:15 [e]1Co 11:3; Eph 5:22 **3:17** [f]S Ge 2:17 [g]Ge 5:29; Nu 35:33; Ps 106:39; Isa 24:5; Jer 3:1; Ro 8:20-22 [h]Ge 6:13; 8:21; Isa 54:9 [i]Ge 29:32; 31:42; Ex 3:7; Ps 66:11; 127:2; Ecc 1:13 [j]Ge 47:9; Job 5:7; 7:1; 14:1; Ecc 2:23; Jer 20:18 **3:18** [k]Job 31:40; Isa 5:6; Heb 6:8 [l]Ps 104:14 **3:19** [m]Ps 104:23 [n]Ge 14:18; Dt 8:3,9; 23:4;

18 It will produce thorns and thistles[k] for
you,
and you will eat the plants of the field.[l]
19 By the sweat of your brow[m]
you will eat your food[n]
until you return to the ground,
since from it you were taken;
for dust you are
and to dust you will return."[o]

20 Adam[c] named his wife Eve,[d][p] because
she would become the mother of all the
living.
21 The LORD God made garments of skin
for Adam and his wife and clothed them.[q]
22 And the LORD God said, "The man has
now become like one of us,[r] knowing good
and evil. He must not be allowed to reach
out his hand and take also from the tree
of life[s] and eat, and live forever." 23 So the
LORD God banished him from the Garden
of Eden[t] to work the ground[u] from which
he had been taken. 24 After he drove the
man out, he placed on the east side[e] of the
Garden of Eden[v] cherubim[w] and a flaming
sword[x] flashing back and forth to guard
the way to the tree of life.[y]

[a] 15 Or *seed* [b] 15 Or *strike* [c] 20 Or *The man* [d] 20 *Eve* probably means *living.* [e] 24 Or *placed in front*

Ru 1:6; 2:14; 2Th 3:10 [o]S Ge 2:7; S Job 7:21; S Ps 146:4; 1Co 15:47; Heb 9:27 **3:20** [p]S Ge 2:20; 2Co 11:3; 1Ti 2:13 **3:21** [q]S ver 7 **3:22** [r]S Ge 1:26 [s]S Ge 2:9; S Rev 2:7 **3:23** [t]S Ge 2:8 [u]S Ge 2:7 **3:24** [v]S Ge 2:8 [w]Ex 25:18-22; 1Sa 4:4; 2Sa 6:2; 22:11; 1Ki 6:27; 8:6; 2Ki 19:15; 2Ch 5:8; Ps 18:10; 80:1; 99:1; Isa 37:16; Eze 10:1; 28:16 [x]Job 40:19; Ps 104:4; Isa 27:1 [y]S Ge 2:9

3:14 *Cursed.* The serpent, the woman and the man were all judged, but only the serpent and the ground were cursed—the latter because of Adam (v. 17). *dust.* The symbol of death itself (v. 19) would be the serpent's food.

3:15 *he will crush your head, and you will strike his heel.* The antagonism between people and snakes is used to symbolize the outcome of the titanic struggle between God and the evil one, a struggle played out in the hearts and history of humankind. The offspring of the woman would eventually crush the serpent's head, a promise fulfilled in Christ's victory over Satan—a victory in which all believers will share (see Ro 16:20).

3:16 *pains in childbearing.* Her judgment fell on what was most uniquely hers as a woman and as a "suitable helper" (2:20) for her husband. Similarly, the man's "painful toil" (v. 17) was a judgment on him as worker of the soil. Some believe that the Hebrew root underlying "pains" and "painful labor" should perhaps be understood here in the sense of burdensome labor (see Pr 5:10, "toil"; 14:23, "hard work"). *give birth to children.* As a sign of grace in the midst of judgment, the original benediction (see 1:28 and note) is not withdrawn. *desire ... rule.* Her sexual attraction to the man and his headship over her will become intimate aspects of her life in which she experiences trouble and anguish rather than unalloyed joy and blessing.

3:17–19 *you will eat.* Though he would have to work hard and long (judgment), the man would be able to produce food that would sustain life (grace).

3:18 Cultivating the ground and sowing the seed of desired crops create a situation in which certain native plants become weeds—of which "thorns and thistles" are the most troublesome.

3:19 *return to the ground ... to dust you will return.* Adam's labor would not be able to stave off death. The origin of his body (see 2:7) and the source of his food (see v. 17) became a symbol of his eventual death.

3:20 *named his wife.* Not an act of claiming dominion over her (see notes on 1:5; 2:19) but of memorializing her significance for him and the human race.

3:21 *clothed them.* God graciously provided Adam and Eve with more effective clothing (cf. v. 7) to cover their shame (cf. v. 10).

3:22 *us.* See note on 1:26. *knowing good and evil.* In a terribly perverted way, the serpent's prediction (v. 5) came true. *live forever.* Sin, which always results in death (Ps 37:1–2; Pr 11:19; Eze 33:8–9; Ro 6:23; Jas 1:14–15), cuts the sinner off from God's gift of eternal life.

3:23 *banished him from the Garden ... to work the ground.* Before Adam sinned, he had worked in a beautiful and fruitful garden (2:15). Now he would have to till undeveloped land and struggle with the curse of thorns and thistles (v. 18).

3:24 *cherubim.* Similar to the statues of winged figures that stood guard at the entrances to palaces and temples in ancient Mesopotamia (see note on Ex 25:18). *to guard.* The sword of God's judgment stood between fallen humanity and God's garden. The reason is given in v. 22. Only through God's redemption in Christ do people have access again to the tree of life (see Rev 2:7; 22:2,14,19).

Cain and Abel

4 Adam[a] made love to his wife[z] Eve,[a]
and she became pregnant and gave
birth to Cain.[b][b] She said, "With the help
of the LORD I have brought forth[c] a man."
2 Later she gave birth to his brother Abel.[c]
Now Abel kept flocks, and Cain worked
the soil.[d] 3 In the course of time Cain
brought some of the fruits of the soil as
an offering[e] to the LORD.[f] 4 And Abel also
brought an offering—fat portions[g] from
some of the firstborn of his flock.[h] The
LORD looked with favor on Abel and his
offering,[i] 5 but on Cain and his offering he
did not look with favor. So Cain was very
angry, and his face was downcast.
6 Then the LORD said to Cain, "Why are
you angry?[j] Why is your face downcast?
7 If you do what is right, will you not be accepted? But if you do not do what is right,
sin is crouching at your door;[k] it desires to
have you, but you must rule over it.[l]"
8 Now Cain said to his brother Abel,
"Let's go out to the field."[d] While they
were in the field, Cain attacked his brother Abel and killed him.[m]
9 Then the LORD said to Cain, "Where is
your brother Abel?"[n]
"I don't know,[o]" he replied. "Am I my
brother's keeper?"
10 The LORD said, "What have you done?
Listen! Your brother's blood cries out to
me from the ground.[p] 11 Now you are under a curse[q] and driven from the ground,
which opened its mouth to receive your
brother's blood from your hand. 12 When
you work the ground, it will no longer
yield its crops for you.[r] You will be a restless wanderer[s] on the earth.[t]"
13 Cain said to the LORD, "My punishment is more than I can bear. 14 Today you
are driving me from the land, and I will
be hidden from your presence;[u] I will be a
restless wanderer on the earth,[v] and whoever finds me will kill me."[w]
15 But the LORD said to him, "Not so[e]; anyone who kills Cain[x] will suffer vengeance[y]

4:1 [z] ver 17, 25 [a] S Ge 2:20 [b] Heb 11:4; 1Jn 3:12; Jude 1:11 **4:2** [c] Mt 23:35; Lk 11:51; Heb 11:4; 12:24 [d] S Ge 2:7 **4:3** [e] Lev 2:1-2; Isa 43:23; Jer 41:5 [f] Nu 18:12 **4:4** [g] Lev 3:16; 2Ch 29:35 [h] Ex 13:2, 12; Dt 15:19 [i] Heb 11:4 **4:6** [j] Jnh 4:4 **4:7** [k] Ge 44:16; Nu 32:23; Isa 59:12 [l] Job 11:15; 22:27; Ps 27:3; 46:2; S Ro 6:16 **4:8** [m] Mt 23:35; Lk 11:51; 1Jn 3:12; Jude 1:11 **4:9** [n] S Ge 3:9 [o] S Jn 8:44 **4:10** [p] Ge 9:5; 37:20, 26; Ex 21:12; Nu 35:33; Dt 21:7, 9; 2Sa 4:11; Job 16:18; 24:2; 31:38; Ps 9:12; 106:38; Heb 12:24; Rev 6:9-10 **4:11** [q] Dt 11:28; 2Ki 2:24 **4:12** [r] Dt 28:15-24 [s] Ps 37:25; 59:15; 109:10 [t] ver 14 **4:14** [u] 2Ki 17:18; Ps 51:11; 139:7-12; Jer 7:15; 52:3 [v] ver 12; Dt 28:64-67 [w] Ge 9:6; Ex 21:12, 14; Lev 24:17; Nu 35:19, 21, 27, 33; 1Ki 2:32; 2Ki 11:16 **4:15** [x] Eze 9:4, 6 [y] Ex 21:20

[a] *1* Or *The man* [b] *1* *Cain* sounds like the Hebrew for *brought forth* or *acquired.* [c] *1* Or *have acquired* [d] *8* Samaritan Pentateuch, Septuagint, Vulgate and Syriac; Masoretic Text does not have *"Let's go out to the field."* [e] *15* Septuagint, Vulgate and Syriac; Hebrew *Very well*

4:1–26 How human sin progressed from murder of a brother in the second generation to arrogant assertion of independence from God and a claim of total self-sufficiency in the seventh generation.

4:1 *With the help of the LORD.* Eve acknowledged that God is the ultimate source of life (see Ac 17:25).

4:2 *Abel.* The name means "breath" or "temporary" or "meaningless" (the translation of the same basic Hebrew word that is in Ecc 1:2; 12:8) and hints at the shortness of Abel's life.

4:3–4 *Cain brought some of the fruits … And Abel also brought … fat portions from some of the firstborn of his flock.* The contrast is not between an offering of plant life and an offering of animal life, but between a careless, thoughtless offering and a choice, generous offering (cf. Lev 3:16 and note). Motivation and heart attitude are all-important, and God looked with favor on Abel and his offering because of Abel's faith (see Heb 11:4 and note). *firstborn.* Indicative of the recognition that all the productivity of the flock is from the Lord and all of it belongs to him.

4:5 *angry.* God did not look with favor on Cain and his offering, and Cain (whose motivation and attitude were bad from the outset) reacted predictably.

4:7 *sin is crouching at your door.* The Hebrew word for "crouching" is the same as an ancient Babylonian word referring to an evil demon crouching at the door of a building to threaten the people inside. Sin may thus be pictured here as just such a demon, waiting to pounce on Cain. He may already have been plotting his brother's murder. *it desires to have you.* In Hebrew, the same expression as that for "your desire will be for [your husband]" in 3:16 (see also SS 7:10).

4:8 *attacked his brother … and killed him.* The first murder was especially monstrous because it was committed with deliberate deceit ("Let's go out to the field"), against a brother (see vv. 9–11; 1Jn 3:12) and against a good man (Mt 23:35; Heb 11:4)—a striking illustration of the awful consequences of the fall.

4:9 *Where … ?* A rhetorical question (see 3:9). *I don't know.* An outright lie. *Am I my brother's keeper?* Demonstrating callous indifference—all too common through the whole course of human history.

4:10 *Your brother's blood cries out.* For justice. "Righteous Abel" (Mt 23:35), in one sense a "prophet" (Lk 11:50–51), "still speaks, even though he is dead" (Heb 11:4), for his spilled blood continues to cry out to God against all those who do violence to others. But the blood of Christ "speaks a better word" (Heb 12:24).

4:11 *curse.* The ground had been cursed because of human sin (3:17), and now Cain himself is cursed. Formerly he had worked the ground, and it had produced life for him (vv. 2–3). Now the ground, soaked with his brother's blood, would no longer yield its produce for him (v. 12).

4:12 *wanderer.* Estranged from other people and finding even the ground inhospitable, he became a wanderer in the land of wandering (see NIV text note on v. 16).

4:13 *My punishment is more than I can bear.* Confronted with his crime and its resulting curse, Cain responded not with remorse but with self-pity. His sin was virtually uninterrupted: impiety (v. 3), anger (v. 5), jealousy, deception and murder (v. 8), falsehood (v. 9) and self-seeking (v. 13). The final result was alienation from God himself (vv. 14,16).

4:14–15 *whoever … anyone … no one.* These words seem to imply the presence of substantial numbers of people outside Cain's immediate family, but perhaps they only anticipate the future rapid growth of the race. Alternatively, Cain's reference to himself was inclusive of his whole family line, which stood under judgment with him (as did the family line of Adam). Note that Cain built a city (v. 17) and that his descendant Lamech boasted of avenging (defending) himself (vv. 23–24).

4:15 *mark.* A warning sign to protect him from an avenger. For the time being, the life of the murderer is spared (but see 6:7; 9:6). For a possible parallel, see Eze 9:4.

seven times over.[z]” Then the LORD put a mark on Cain so that no one who found him would kill him. 16 So Cain went out from the LORD’s presence[a] and lived in the land of Nod,[a] east of Eden.[b]

17 Cain made love to his wife,[c] and she became pregnant and gave birth to Enoch. Cain was then building a city,[d] and he named it after his son[e] Enoch. 18 To Enoch was born Irad, and Irad was the father of Mehujael, and Mehujael was the father of Methushael, and Methushael was the father of Lamech.

19 Lamech married[f] two women,[g] one named Adah and the other Zillah. 20 Adah gave birth to Jabal; he was the father of those who live in tents and raise livestock. 21 His brother’s name was Jubal; he was the father of all who play stringed instruments[h] and pipes.[i] 22 Zillah also had a son, Tubal-Cain, who forged[j] all kinds of tools out of[b] bronze and iron. Tubal-Cain’s sister was Naamah.

23 Lamech said to his wives,

“Adah and Zillah, listen to me;
  wives of Lamech, hear my words.
I have killed[k] a man for wounding me,
  a young man for injuring me.
24 If Cain is avenged[l] seven times,[m]
  then Lamech seventy-seven times.[n]”

25 Adam made love to his wife[o] again, and she gave birth to a son and named him Seth,[c][p] saying, “God has granted me another child in place of Abel, since Cain killed him.”[q] 26 Seth also had a son, and he named him Enosh.[r]

At that time people began to call on[d] the name of the LORD.[s]

From Adam to Noah

5 This is the written account[t] of Adam’s family line.[u]

When God created mankind, he made them in the likeness of God.[v] 2 He created them[w] male and female[x] and blessed them. And he named them “Mankind”[e] when they were created.

3 When Adam had lived 130 years, he had a son in his own likeness, in his own image;[y] and he named him Seth.[z] 4 After Seth was born, Adam lived 800 years and had other sons and daughters. 5 Altogether, Adam lived a total of 930 years, and then he died.[a]

[a] 16 *Nod* means *wandering* (see verses 12 and 14). [b] 22 Or *who instructed all who work in* [c] 25 *Seth* probably means *granted.* [d] 26 Or *to proclaim* [e] 2 Hebrew *adam*

4:15 [z] ver 24; Lev 26:21; Ps 79:12 **4:16** [a] Jude 1:11 [b] S Ge 2:8 **4:17** [c] S ver 1 [d] Ps 55:9 [e] Ps 49:11 **4:19** [f] Ge 6:2 [g] Ge 29:28; Dt 21:15; Ru 4:11; 1Sa 1:2 **4:21** [h] Ge 31:27; Ex 15:20; 1Sa 16:16; 1Ch 25:3; Ps 33:2; 43:4; Isa 16:11; Da 3:5 [i] Job 21:12; 30:31; Ps 150:4 **4:22** [j] Ex 35:35; 1Sa 13:19; 2Ki 24:14 **4:23** [k] Ge 9:5-6; Ex 20:13; 21:12; 23:7; Lev 19:18; 24:17; Dt 27:24; 32:35 **4:24** [l] Dt 32:35; 2Ki 9:7; Ps 18:47; 94:1; Isa 35:4; Jer 51:56; Na 1:2 [m] S ver 15 [n] Mt 18:22 **4:25** [o] ver 1 [p] Ge 5:3; 1Ch 1:1 [q] ver 8 **4:26** [r] Ge 5:6; 1Ch 1:1; Lk 3:38 [s] Ge 12:8; 13:4; 21:33; 22:9; 26:25; 33:20; 35:1; Ex 17:15; 1Ki 18:24; Ps 116:17; Joel 2:32; Zep 3:9; S Ac 2:21 **5:1** [t] S Ge 2:4 [u] 1Ch 1:1 [v] S Ge 1:27; Col 3:10 **5:2** [w] Ge 1:28 [x] S Ge 1:27; Mt 19:4; Mk 10:6; Gal 3:28 **5:3** [y] S Ge 1:26; 1Co 15:49 [z] S Ge 4:25; Lk 3:38 **5:5** [a] S Ge 2:17; Heb 9:27

4:16 *Nod.* Location unknown. See NIV text note.

4:17–18 *Cain … Enoch … Irad … Mehujael … Methushael … Lamech.* Together with that of Adam, these names add up to a total of seven, a number often signifying completeness (see v. 15). Each of the six names listed here is paralleled by a similar or identical name in the genealogy of Seth in ch. 5 as follows: Kenan (5:12), Enoch (5:21), Jared (5:18), Mahalalel (5:15), Methuselah (5:25), Lamech (5:28). The similarity between the two sets of names is striking and may suggest the selective nature of such genealogies (see note on 5:5). For an example of such selectivity elsewhere, see Ezr 7:3, where comparison with 1Ch 6:7–10 indicates that six names were omitted between Azariah and Meraioth. See also Introduction to 1 Chronicles: Genealogies and notes on Mt 1:5,8,11,17.

4:17 *city.* The Hebrew for this word can refer to any permanent settlement, however small. Cain tried to redeem himself from his wandering and vulnerable state by the activity of his own hands—in the land of wandering he builds a city.

4:19 *married two women.* Polygamy entered history. Haughty Lamech, the seventh from Adam in the line of Cain, perhaps sought to attain the benefits of God’s primeval blessing (see 1:28 and note) by his own device—multiplying his wives. Monogamy, however, was the original divine intention (see 2:23–24).

4:20–22 *Jabal … Jubal … Tubal-Cain.* Lamech’s three sons had similar names, each derived from a Hebrew verb meaning “to bring, carry, lead,” and emphasizing activity. Tubal-Cain’s name was especially appropriate, since “Cain” means “metalsmith.”

4:22 *tools.* For agriculture and construction; perhaps also for war (see 1Sa 13:19–21).

4:23 *killed a man for wounding me.* Violent and wanton destruction of human life by one who proclaimed his complete independence from God by taking vengeance with his own hands (see Dt 32:35 and note). Lamech proudly claimed to be master of his own destiny, thinking that he and his sons, by their own achievements, would redeem themselves from the curse on the line of Cain. This titanic claim climaxes the catalog of sins that began with Cain’s unworthy offering and the murder of his brother.

4:24 *seventy-seven times.* Lamech’s arrogant announcement of personal revenge found its counterpoint in Jesus’ response to Peter’s question about forgiveness in Mt 18:21–22 (see note on Mt 18:22).

4:25 *again … another child.* Abel was dead, and Cain was alienated, so Adam and Eve were granted a third son to carry on the family line.

4:26 *Enosh.* The name, like “Adam” (see NIV text note on 2:7), means “man” or “humankind.” *began to call on the name of the LORD.* Lamech’s proud self-reliance, so characteristic of the line of Cain, is contrasted with dependence on God found in the line of Seth.

5:1 *account.* See note on 2:4. *likeness.* See note on 1:26.

5:2 *male and female.* See note on 1:27. *blessed them.* See 1:28 and note. *named them.* See note on 1:5.

5:3 *his own likeness … his own image.* See note on 1:26. As God created sinless Adam in his own perfect image, so now sinful Adam has a son in his own imperfect image.

5:5 *930 years.* See notes on v. 27; 6:3. Whether the large numbers describing human longevity in the early chapters of Genesis are literal or have a conventional literary function—or both—is uncertain. Some believe that several of the numbers have symbolic significance, such as Enoch’s 365 (v. 23) years (365 being the number of days in a year, thus a full life) and Lamech’s 777 (v. 31) years (777 being an expansion and multiple of seven, the number of completeness; cf. the “seventy-seven times” of the other Lamech in 4:24). The

6 When Seth had lived 105 years, he became the father[a] of Enosh.[b] 7 After he became the father of Enosh, Seth lived 807
years and had other sons and daughters.
8 Altogether, Seth lived a total of 912 years,
and then he died.
9 When Enosh had lived 90 years, he became the father of Kenan.[c] 10 After he became the father of Kenan, Enosh lived 815
years and had other sons and daughters.
11 Altogether, Enosh lived a total of 905
years, and then he died.
12 When Kenan had lived 70 years, he
became the father of Mahalalel.[d] 13 After
he became the father of Mahalalel, Kenan
lived 840 years and had other sons and
daughters. 14 Altogether, Kenan lived a total of 910 years, and then he died.
15 When Mahalalel had lived 65 years,
he became the father of Jared.[e] 16 After
he became the father of Jared, Mahalalel
lived 830 years and had other sons and
daughters. 17 Altogether, Mahalalel lived a
total of 895 years, and then he died.
18 When Jared had lived 162 years, he
became the father of Enoch.[f] 19 After he
became the father of Enoch, Jared lived
800 years and had other sons and daughters. 20 Altogether, Jared lived a total of 962
years, and then he died.
21 When Enoch had lived 65 years, he
became the father of Methuselah.[g] 22 After he became the father of Methuselah,
Enoch walked faithfully with God[h] 300
years and had other sons and daughters. 23 Altogether, Enoch lived a total of
365 years. 24 Enoch walked faithfully with
God;[i] then he was no more, because God
took him away.[j]
25 When Methuselah had lived 187 years,
he became the father of Lamech.[k] 26 After
he became the father of Lamech, Methuselah lived 782 years and had other sons and
daughters. 27 Altogether, Methuselah lived a
total of 969 years, and then he died.
28 When Lamech had lived 182 years,
he had a son. 29 He named him Noah[b][l]
and said, "He will comfort us in the labor
and painful toil of our hands caused by
the ground the LORD has cursed.[m]" 30 After
Noah was born, Lamech lived 595 years
and had other sons and daughters. 31 Altogether, Lamech lived a total of 777 years,
and then he died.
32 After Noah was 500 years old,[n] he became the father of Shem,[o] Ham and Japheth.[p]

Wickedness in the World

6 When human beings began to increase
in number on the earth[q] and daughters
were born to them, 2 the sons of God[r] saw
that the daughters[s] of humans were beautiful,[t] and they married[u] any of them they
chose. 3 Then the LORD said, "My Spirit[v]

5:6 [b] S Ge 4:26; Lk 3:38
5:9 [c] 1Ch 1:2; Lk 3:37
5:12 [d] 1Ch 1:2; Lk 3:37
5:15 [e] 1Ch 1:2; Lk 3:37
5:18 [f] 1Ch 1:3; Lk 3:37; Jude 1:14
5:21 [g] 1Ch 1:3; Lk 3:37
5:22 [h] ver 24; Ge 6:9; 17:1; 24:40; 48:15; 2Ki 20:3; Ps 116:9; Mic 6:8; Mal 2:6
5:24 [i] S ver 22 [j] 2Ki 2:1,11; Ps 49:15; 73:24; 89:48; Heb 11:5
5:25 [k] 1Ch 1:3; Lk 3:36
5:29 [l] 1Ch 1:3; Lk 3:36 [m] S Ge 3:17; Ro 8:20
5:32 [n] Ge 7:6, 11; 8:13 [o] Lk 3:36 [p] Ge 6:10; 9:18; 10:1; 1Ch 1:4; Isa 65:20
6:1 [q] S Ge 1:28
6:2 [r] Job 1:6 *fn*; 2:1 *fn* [s] ver 4 [t] Dt 21:11 [u] S Ge 4:19
6:3 [v] Job 34:14; Gal 5:16-17

[a] 6 *Father* may mean *ancestor*; also in verses 7-26.
[b] 29 *Noah* sounds like the Hebrew for *comfort*.

fact that there are exactly ten names in the Ge 5 list (as in the genealogy of 11:10 – 26) makes it likely that it includes gaps (see note on 4:17 – 18), the lengths of which may be summarized in the large numbers. Other ancient genealogies outside the Bible exhibit similarly large figures. For example, three kings in a Sumerian list (which also contains exactly ten names) are said to have reigned 72,000 years each — obviously exaggerated time spans. *and then he died.* Repeated as a sad refrain throughout the chapter, the only exception being Enoch (see note on v. 24). The phrase is a stark reminder of God's judgment on sin resulting from Adam's fall.

5:22,24 *walked faithfully with God.* The phrase replaces the word "lived" in the other paragraphs of the chapter and reminds us that there is a difference between walking faithfully with God and merely living.

5:24 *then he was no more, because God took him away.* The phrase replaces "and then he died" in the other paragraphs of the chapter. Like Elijah, who was "taken" (2Ki 2:10) to heaven, Enoch was taken away (cf. Ps 49:15; 73:24) to the presence of God without experiencing death (Heb 11:5). Lamech, the seventh from Adam in the genealogy of Cain, was evil personified. But "Enoch, the seventh from Adam" (Jude 14) in the genealogy of Seth, "was commended as one who pleased God" (Heb 11:5).

5:27 *969 years.* Only Noah and his family survived the flood. If the figures concerning life spans are literal, Methuselah died in the year of the flood (the figures in vv. 25,28 and 7:6 add up to exactly 969).

6:1 – 8 How the early history of humankind led to such pervasive corruption that God was moved to bring a radical judgment on his creation.

6:1 *increase in number.* See note on 1:22.

6:2 *sons of God saw ... the daughters ... and they married any.* See v. 4. The phrase "sons of God" here has been interpreted to refer either to angels or to human beings. In such places as Job 1:6; 2:1 it refers to angels, and probably also in Ps 29:1 (where it is translated "heavenly beings"). Some interpreters also appeal to Jude 6 – 7 (as well as to Jewish literature) in referring the phrase here to angels.

Others, however, maintain that intermarriage and cohabitation between angels and human beings, though commonly mentioned in ancient mythologies, are surely excluded by the very nature of the created order (see ch. 1; Lk 20:34 – 36 and note on 20:36). Elsewhere, expressions equivalent to "sons of God" often refer to human beings, though in contexts quite different from the present one (see Dt 14:1; 32:5; Ps 73:15; Isa 43:6; Hos 1:10; 11:1; Lk 3:38; 1Jn 3:1 – 2,10). "Sons of God" (vv. 2,4) possibly refers to godly men, and "the daughters" to sinful women (significantly, they are not called "daughters of God"), probably from the wicked line of Cain. If so, the context suggests that vv. 1 – 2 describe the intermarriage of the Sethites ("sons of God") of ch. 5 with the Cainites ("the daughters") of ch. 4, indicating a breakdown in the separation of the two groups.

Another plausible suggestion is that the "sons of God" refers to royal figures (kings were closely associated with gods in the ancient Near East) who proudly perpetuated and aggravated the corrupt lifestyle of Lamech, son of Cain (virtually a royal figure), and established for themselves royal harems.

6:3 Two key phrases in the Hebrew of this verse are obscure: the one rendered "contend with" (see NIV text note) and the one rendered "for they are mortal." The verse seems to announce that the period of grace between God's declaration

will not contend with[a] humans forever,[w]
for they are mortal[b];[x] their days will be a
hundred and twenty years."
4The Nephilim[y] were on the earth in
those days — and also afterward — when
the sons of God went to the daughters of
humans[z] and had children by them. They
were the heroes of old, men of renown.[a]
5The LORD saw how great the wickedness of the human race had become on
the earth,[b] and that every inclination of
the thoughts of the human heart was only
evil all the time.[c] 6The LORD regretted[d]
that he had made human beings on the
earth, and his heart was deeply troubled.
7So the LORD said, "I will wipe from the
face of the earth[e] the human race I have
created — and with them the animals, the
birds and the creatures that move along
the ground — for I regret that I have made
them.[f]" 8But Noah[g] found favor in the eyes
of the LORD.[h]

Noah and the Flood

9This is the account[i] of Noah and his
family.

Noah was a righteous man, blameless[j]
among the people of his time,[k] and he
walked faithfully with God.[l] 10Noah had
three sons: Shem,[m] Ham and Japheth.[n]
11Now the earth was corrupt[o] in God's
sight and was full of violence.[p] 12God saw
how corrupt[q] the earth had become, for
all the people on earth had corrupted their
ways.[r] 13So God said to Noah, "I am going
to put an end to all people, for the earth
is filled with violence because of them. I
am surely going to destroy[s] both them and
the earth.[t] 14So make yourself an ark of
cypress[c] wood;[u] make rooms in it and coat
it with pitch[v] inside and out. 15This is how
you are to build it: The ark is to be three
hundred cubits long, fifty cubits wide and
thirty cubits high.[d] 16Make a roof for it,
leaving below the roof an opening one
cubit[e] high all around.[f] Put a door in the
side of the ark and make lower, middle
and upper decks. 17I am going to bring
floodwaters[w] on the earth to destroy all
life under the heavens, every creature that
has the breath of life in it. Everything on
earth will perish.[x] 18But I will establish my
covenant with you,[y] and you will enter the
ark[z] — you and your sons and your wife

6:3 [w]Isa 57:16; 1Pe 3:20 [x]Job 10:9; Ps 78:39; 103:14; Isa 40:6 **6:4** [y]Nu 13:33 [z]ver 2 [a]Ge 11:4 **6:5** [b]Ge 38:7; Job 34:26; Jer 1:16; 44:5; Eze 3:19 [c]Ge 8:21; Ps 14:1-3 **6:6** [d]Ex 32:14; 1Sa 15:11, 35; 2Sa 24:16; 1Ch 21:15; Isa 63:10; Jer 18:7-10; Eph 4:30 **6:7** [e]Eze 33:28; Zep 1:2,18 [f]ver 17; Ge 7:4, 21; Dt 28:63; 29:20 **6:8** [g]Eze 14:14 [h]Ge 19:19; 39:4; Ex 33:12,13,17; 34:9; Nu 11:15; Ru 2:2; Lk 1:30; Ac 7:46 **6:9** [i]S Ge 2:4 [j]Ge 17:1; Dt 18:13; 2Sa 22:24; Job 1:1; 4:6; 9:21; 12:4; 31:6; Ps 15:2; 18:23; 19:13; 37:37; Pr 2:7 [k]Ge 7:1; Ps 37:39; Jer 15:1; Eze 14:14, 20; Da 10:11; S Lk 1:6; Heb 11:7; 2Pe 2:5 [l]S Ge 5:22 **6:10** [m]Lk 3:36 [n]S Ge 5:32

[a] *3* Or *My spirit will not remain in* [b] *3* Or *corrupt* [c] *14* The meaning of the Hebrew for this word is uncertain. [d] *15* That is, about 450 feet long, 75 feet wide and 45 feet high or about 135 meters long, 23 meters wide and 14 meters high [e] *16* That is, about 18 inches or about 45 centimeters [f] *16* The meaning of the Hebrew for this clause is uncertain.

6:11 [o]Dt 31:29; Jdg 2:19 [p]Ps 7:9; 73:6; Eze 7:23; 8:17; 28:16; Mal 2:16 **6:12** [q]Ex 32:7; Dt 4:16; 9:12,24 [r]Ps 14:1-3 **6:13** [s]Dt 28:63; 2Ki 8:19; Ezr 9:14; Jer 44:11 [t]ver 17; Ge 7:4, 21-23; Job 34:15; Isa 5:6; 24:1-3; Jer 44:27; Eze 7:2-3 **6:14** [u]Heb 11:7; 1Pe 3:20 [v]Ex 2:3 **6:17** [w]Ps 29:10 [x]S ver 7, S 13; 2Pe 2:5 **6:18** [y]Ge 9:9-16; 17:7; 19:12; Ex 6:4; 34:10,27; Dt 29:13, 14-15; Ps 25:10; 74:20; 106:45; Isa 55:3; Jer 32:40; Eze 16:60; Hag 2:5; 1Pe 3:20 [z]Ge 7:1,7,13

of judgment and its arrival would be 120 years (cf. 1Pe 3:20). But if the NIV text note reading is accepted, the verse announces that the human life span would henceforth be limited to 120 years (but see 11:10–26).

6:4 *Nephilim.* People of great size and strength (see Nu 13:31–33; Dt 1:28 and note). The Hebrew word means "fallen ones." They were viewed by people as "the heroes of old, men of renown," but in God's eyes they were sinners ("fallen ones") ripe for judgment.

6:5 One of the Bible's most vivid descriptions of total depravity. And because human nature remained unchanged, things were no better after the flood (8:21).

6:6 *The LORD regretted ... his heart was deeply troubled.* Human sin is God's sorrow (see Eph 4:30).

6:7 *I will wipe from the face of the earth the human race.* The period of grace (see v. 3 and note) was coming to an end. *animals ... birds ... creatures.* Though morally innocent, the animal world, as creatures under the corrupted rule of human beings, shared in their judgment.

6:8–9 *found favor ... righteous ... blameless ... walked faithfully with God.* See note on 5:22. Noah's godly life was a powerful contrast to the wicked lives of his contemporaries (see v. 5 and note; see also v. 12). This description of Noah does not imply sinless perfection.

6:9—9:29 In many legends circulating among the peoples of the ancient Near East, one of the major gods brought a devastating flood on the earth because he was disturbed by the noisy hubbub raised by humans (see Introduction: Background). The author of Genesis also tells of a worldwide flood that destroyed all humankind except a single family. In his account, the Creator (who alone is God) was deeply grieved by the moral evil embraced and practiced by the creatures he had created in his own image and to whom he had committed the care of his creation. In his eyes they had so corrupted life in his good creation that only a radical cleansing judgment could check the rampant evil and bring humanity to account. See 9:8–17 and notes.

6:9 *account.* See note on 2:4. *righteous.* See note on Ps 1:5.

6:14 *ark.* The Hebrew for this word is used elsewhere only in reference to the basket that saved the baby Moses (Ex 2:3,5). *coat it with pitch.* Moses' mother made his basket watertight in the same way (see Ex 2:3).

6:16 *roof.* Perhaps overhanging, to keep the rain from coming in. *an opening one cubit high all around.* Noah's ark probably had a series of small windows (see 8:6) encircling the entire vessel 18 inches from the top to admit light and air.

6:17 *floodwaters on the earth to destroy all life under the heavens.* Some believe that the deluge was worldwide, partly because of the apparently universal terms of the text — both here and elsewhere (vv. 7,12–13; 7:4,19,21–23; 8:21; 9:11,15; cf. 2Pe 3:6 and note). Others argue that nothing in the narrative of chs. 6–9 prevents the flood from being understood as regional — destroying everything in its wake, but of relatively limited scope and universal only from the standpoint of Moses' geographic knowledge. "Earth," e.g., may be defined in the more restricted sense of "land" (see 2:5). "All life under the heavens" may mean all life within the range of Noah's perception. (See the universal language used to describe the drought and famine in the time of Joseph — 41:54,57; see also note on 41:57.)

6:18 *covenant.* See note on 9:9. Noah would not be given the particulars of God's covenant with him until after the floodwaters had dried up (see 9:8–17 and

and your sons' wives with you. 19 You are
to bring into the ark two of all living creatures, male and female, to keep them alive
with you.[a] 20 Two[b] of every kind of bird, of
every kind of animal and of every kind[c] of
creature that moves along the ground will
come to you to be kept alive.[d] 21 You are to
take every kind of food that is to be eaten
and store it away as food for you and for
them."
22 Noah did everything just as God commanded him.[e]

7 The LORD then said to Noah, "Go into
the ark, you and your whole fami-
ly,[f] because I have found you righteous[g]
in this generation. 2 Take with you sev-
en pairs of every kind of clean[h] animal,
a male and its mate, and one pair of every kind of unclean animal, a male and its
mate, 3 and also seven pairs of every kind
of bird, male and female, to keep their
various kinds alive[i] throughout the earth.
4 Seven days from now I will send rain[j] on
the earth[k] for forty days[l] and forty nights,[m]
and I will wipe from the face of the earth
every living creature I have made.[n]"
5 And Noah did all that the LORD commanded him.[o]
6 Noah was six hundred years old[p] when
the floodwaters came on the earth. 7 And
Noah and his sons and his wife and his
sons' wives entered the ark[q] to escape the
waters of the flood. 8 Pairs of clean and
unclean[r] animals, of birds and of all creatures that move along the ground, 9 male
and female, came to Noah and entered the
ark, as God had commanded Noah.[s] 10 And
after the seven days[t] the floodwaters came
on the earth.

6:19 [a] Ge 7:15 **6:20** [b] Ge 7:15 [c] S Ge 1:11 [d] Ge 7:3 **6:22** [e] Ge 7:5, 9, 16; Ex 7:6; 39:43; 40:16, 19, 21, 23, 25, 27, 29, 32 **7:1** [f] S Ge 6:18; Mt 24:38; Lk 17:26-27; Heb 11:7; 1Pe 3:20; 2Pe 2:5 [g] Ge 6:9; Eze 14:14 **7:2** [h] ver 8; Ge 8:20; Lev 10:10; 11:1-47; Dt 14:3-20; Eze 44:23; Hag 2:12; Ac 10:14-15 **7:3** [i] Ge 6:20 **7:4** [j] Ge 8:2 [k] 1Ki 13:34; Jer 28:16 [l] Nu 13:25; Dt 9:9; 1Sa 17:16; 1Ki 19:8 [m] ver 12, 17; Ex 24:18; 32:1; 34:28; Dt 9:9, 11, 18, 25; 10:10; Job 37:6, 13; Mt 4:2 [n] S Ge 6:7, 13 **7:5** [o] S Ge 6:22 **7:6** [p] S Ge 5:32 **7:7** [q] S Ge 6:18 **7:8** [r] S ver 2 **7:9** [s] S Ge 6:22 **7:10** [t] S ver 4 **7:11** [u] S Ge 5:32 [v] Ge 8:4, 14 [w] S Ge 1:7; Job 28:11; Ps 36:6; 42:7; Pr 8:24; Isa 51:10; Eze 26:19 [x] Ge 8:2; 2Ki 7:2; Ps 78:23; Isa 24:18; Mal 3:10

11 In the six hundredth year of Noah's
life,[u] on the seventeenth day of the second
month[v]—on that day all the springs of the
great deep[w] burst forth, and the floodgates
of the heavens[x] were opened. 12 And rain
fell on the earth forty days and forty nights.[y]
13 On that very day Noah and his sons,[z]
Shem, Ham and Japheth, together with his
wife and the wives of his three sons, entered the ark.[a] 14 They had with them every
wild animal according to its kind, all livestock according to their kinds, every creature that moves along the ground according to its kind and every bird according to
its kind,[b] everything with wings. 15 Pairs of
all creatures that have the breath of life in
them came to Noah and entered the ark.[c]
16 The animals going in were male and
female of every living thing, as God had
commanded Noah.[d] Then the LORD shut
him in.
17 For forty days[e] the flood kept coming
on the earth, and as the waters increased
they lifted the ark high above the earth.
18 The waters rose and increased greatly
on the earth, and the ark floated on the
surface of the water. 19 They rose greatly
on the earth, and all the high mountains
under the entire heavens were covered.[f]
20 The waters rose and covered the mountains to a depth of more than fifteen cubits.[a,b][g] 21 Every living thing that moved

[a] 20 That is, about 23 feet or about 6.8 meters
[b] 20 Or *rose more than fifteen cubits, and the mountains were covered*

7:12 [y] S ver 4; S 1Sa 12:17; S Job 28:26 **7:13** [z] Ge 8:16; 1Pe 3:20; 2Pe 2:5 [a] S Ge 6:18 **7:14** [b] S Ge 1:11 **7:15** [c] ver 8-9; Ge 6:19 **7:16** [d] S Ge 6:22 **7:17** [e] S ver 4 **7:19** [f] Ps 104:6 **7:20** [g] Ge 8:4-5; 2Pe 3:6

note). *enter the ark.* The story of Noah's deliverance from the flood foreshadows God's full redemption of his children (see Heb 11:7; 2Pe 2:5) and typifies baptism (see 1Pe 3:20–21). *your sons and your wife and your sons' wives with you.* God extends his loving concern to the whole family of righteous Noah—a consistent pattern in God's dealings with his people, underscoring the moral and responsible relationship of parents to their children (see 17:7–27; 18:19; Dt 30:19; Ps 78:1–7; 102:28; 103:17–18; 112:1–2; Ac 2:38–39; 16:31; 1Co 7:14).

6:19 *two of all living creatures ... to keep them alive.* Most animals were doomed to die in the flood (see note on v. 7), but at least one pair of each kind was preserved to restock the earth after the waters subsided.

6:20 *kind.* See note on 1:11.

6:22 *did everything just as God commanded.* The account stresses Noah's obedience (see 7:5,9,16).

7:1 *Go into the ark.* The beginning of God's final word to Noah before the flood. God's first word to Noah after the flood begins similarly: "Come out of the ark" (8:16). *righteous.* See note on 6:8–9. Later, Noah was known as a "preacher of righteousness" (2Pe 2:5) who warned his contemporaries of coming judgment and testified to the vitality of his own faith (see Heb 11:7).

7:2 *seven pairs of every kind of clean animal ... one pair of every kind of unclean animal.* The "unclean" animals would only have to reproduce themselves after the flood, but the "clean" animals would be needed also for the burnt offerings that Noah would sacrifice (see 8:20) and for food (see 9:3).

7:4 *forty days and forty nights.* A length of time often characterizing a critical period in redemptive history (see v. 12; Dt 9:11; Mt 4:1–11).

7:7 *entered the ark to escape the waters.* Noah and his family were saved, but life as usual continued for everyone else until it was too late (see Mt 24:37–39).

7:13 *Noah and his sons ... together with his wife and the wives of his three sons.* "Only a few people, eight in all" (1Pe 3:20; see 2Pe 2:5), survived the flood.

7:14 *every wild animal ... all livestock ... every creature that moves along the ground ... every bird.* Four of the five categories of animate life mentioned in 1:21–25. The fifth category—sea creatures—could remain alive outside the ark.

7:16 *God had commanded Noah ... the LORD shut him in.* "God" gave the command, but in his role as redeeming "LORD" (see notes on 2:4; Ex 6:6) he closed the door of the ark behind Noah and his family. Neither divine name is mentioned in the rest of ch. 7, as the full fury of the flood was unleashed on sinful humankind.

7:20 *covered the mountains to a depth of more than fifteen*

on land perished — birds, livestock, wild
animals, all the creatures that swarm over
the earth, and all mankind.[h] 22 Everything
on dry land that had the breath of life[i] in
its nostrils died. 23 Every living thing on
the face of the earth was wiped out; people and animals and the creatures that
move along the ground and the birds were
wiped from the earth.[j] Only Noah was left,
and those with him in the ark.[k]
24 The waters flooded the earth for a
hundred and fifty days.[l]

8 But God remembered[m] Noah and all
the wild animals and the livestock that
were with him in the ark, and he sent a
wind over the earth,[n] and the waters receded. 2 Now the springs of the deep and
the floodgates of the heavens[o] had been
closed, and the rain[p] had stopped falling
from the sky. 3 The water receded steadily
from the earth. At the end of the hundred
and fifty days[q] the water had gone down,
4 and on the seventeenth day of the seventh month[r] the ark came to rest on the
mountains[s] of Ararat.[t] 5 The waters continued to recede until the tenth month, and
on the first day of the tenth month the
tops of the mountains became visible.
6 After forty days[u] Noah opened a window he had made in the ark 7 and sent
out a raven,[v] and it kept flying back and
forth until the water had dried up from
the earth.[w] 8 Then he sent out a dove[x] to
see if the water had receded from the surface of the ground. 9 But the dove could
find nowhere to perch because there was
water over all the surface of the earth;
so it returned to Noah in the ark. He
reached out his hand and took the dove
and brought it back to himself in the ark.
10 He waited seven more days and again
sent out the dove from the ark. 11 When
the dove returned to him in the evening,
there in its beak was a freshly plucked olive leaf! Then Noah knew that the water
had receded from the earth.[y] 12 He waited
seven more days and sent the dove out
again, but this time it did not return to
him.
13 By the first day of the first month of
Noah's six hundred and first year,[z] the
water had dried up from the earth. Noah
then removed the covering from the ark
and saw that the surface of the ground
was dry. 14 By the twenty-seventh day of
the second month[a] the earth was completely dry.
15 Then God said to Noah, 16 "Come out
of the ark, you and your wife and your
sons and their wives.[b] 17 Bring out every
kind of living creature that is with you —
the birds, the animals, and all the creatures that move along the ground — so
they can multiply on the earth and be
fruitful and increase in number on it."[c]
18 So Noah came out, together with his
sons and his wife and his sons' wives.[d]
19 All the animals and all the creatures that
move along the ground and all the birds —
everything that moves on land — came out
of the ark, one kind after another.
20 Then Noah built an altar to the LORD[e]
and, taking some of all the clean animals
and clean[f] birds, he sacrificed burnt offerings[g] on it. 21 The LORD smelled the pleasing aroma[h] and said in his heart: "Never
again will I curse the ground[i] because of

7:21 [h] S Ge 6:7, 13; 2Pe 3:6 **7:22** [i] S Ge 1:30 **7:23** [j] Job 14:19; 21:18; 22:11, 16; Ps 90:5; Isa 28:2; Mt 24:39; Lk 17:27; 1Pe 3:20; 2Pe 2:5 [k] Heb 11:7 **7:24** [l] Ge 8:3; Job 12:15 **8:1** [m] Ge 9:15; 19:29; 21:1; 30:22; Ex 2:24; Nu 10:9; Ru 4:13; 1Sa 1:11, 19; 2Ki 20:3; 1Ch 16:15; Ne 1:8; 5:19; 13:14, 22, 31; Job 14:13; Ps 105:42; 106:4; Lk 1:54, 72 [n] Ex 14:21; Jos 2:10; 3:16; Job 12:15; Ps 66:6; Isa 11:15; 44:27; Na 1:4 **8:2** [o] S Ge 7:11 [p] S Ge 7:4 **8:3** [q] S Ge 7:24 **8:4** [r] S Ge 7:11 [s] Ge 7:20 [t] 2Ki 19:37; Jer 51:27 **8:6** [u] Ge 7:12 **8:7** [v] Lev 11:15; Dt 14:14; 1Ki 17:4, 6; Job 38:41; Ps 147:9; Pr 30:17; Isa 34:11; Lk 12:24 [w] ver 11 **8:8** [x] Job 30:31; Ps 55:6; 74:19; SS 2:12, 14; Isa 38:14; 59:11; 60:8; Jer 48:28; Eze 7:16; Hos 7:11; 11:11; Na 2:7; Mt 3:16; 10:16; Jn 1:32

8:11 [y] ver 7 **8:13** [z] S Ge 5:32 **8:14** [a] S Ge 7:11 **8:16** [b] S Ge 7:13 **8:17** [c] S Ge 1:22 **8:18** [d] 1Pe 3:20; 2Pe 2:5 **8:20** [e] Ge 12:7-8; 13:18; 22:9; 26:25; 33:20; 35:7; Ex 17:15; 24:4 [f] S Ge 7:8 [g] Ge 22:2, 13; Ex 10:25; 20:24; 40:29; Lev 1:3; 4:29; 6:8-13; Nu 6:11; Jdg 6:26; 11:31; 1Sa 20:29; Job 1:5; 42:8 **8:21** [h] Ex 29:18, 25; Lev 1:9, 13; 2:9; 4:31; Nu 15:3, 7; 2Co 2:15 [i] S Ge 3:17

---

cubits. See NIV text note. The ark was 45 feet high (6:15; see NIV text note there), so the water was deep enough to keep it from running aground.

7:22 *breath of life.* God's gift at creation (see 1:30; 2:7) was taken away because of sin.

8:1 So far the flood narrative has been an account of judgment; from this point on it is a story of redemption. *God remembered Noah.* Though he had not been mentioned since 7:16 or heard from for 150 days (see 7:24), God had not forgotten Noah and his family. To "remember" in the Bible is often not merely to recall people to mind but to express concern for them, to act with loving care for them. When God remembers his children, he does so "with favor" (Ne 5:19; 13:31). *wind.* The Hebrew word translated "Spirit" in 1:2 is here rendered "wind," and it introduces a series of parallels between the events of chs. 8–9 and those of ch. 1 in their literary order: Compare 8:2 with 1:7; 8:5 with 1:9; 8:7 with 1:20; 8:17 with 1:25; 9:1 with 1:28a; 9:2 with 1:28b; 9:3 with 1:30. Ch. 1 describes the original beginning, while chs. 8–9 describe a new beginning after the flood.

8:4 *mountains.* The word is plural and refers to a range of mountains. *Ararat.* The name is related to Assyrian Urartu, which became an extensive mountainous kingdom (see Jer 51:27; see also Isa 37:38), including much of the territory north of Mesopotamia and east of modern Turkey.

8:6 *window.* See note on 6:16.

8:11 *dove returned . . . in its beak was a freshly plucked olive leaf.* Olives do not grow at high elevations, and the fresh leaf was a sign to Noah that the water had receded from the earth. The modern symbol of peace represented by a dove carrying an olive branch in its beak has its origin in this story.

8:13 *first day of the first month of Noah's six hundred and first year.* The date formula signals humankind's new beginning after the flood.

8:14 *twenty-seventh day of the second month.* More than a year after the flood began (see 7:11).

8:16 *Come out of the ark.* See note on 7:1.

8:17 *multiply . . . be fruitful . . . increase in number.* See 1:22 and note. The animals and birds could now repopulate their former habitats.

8:20 *LORD.* Since worship is a very personal matter, it is to God as "the LORD" (see note on 2:4) that Noah brought his sacrifice (see 4:4). *burnt offerings.* See Lev 1:3 and note.

8:21 *smelled the pleasing aroma.* A figurative way of saying that the Lord took delight in Noah's offering (cf. Eph 5:2; Php 4:18). *curse the ground.* Although the Hebrew

humans, even though[a] every inclination of
the human heart is evil from childhood.[j]
And never again will I destroy[k] all living
creatures,[l] as I have done.

22 "As long as the earth endures,
seedtime and harvest,[m]
cold and heat,
summer and winter,[n]
day and night
will never cease."[o]

God's Covenant With Noah

9 Then God blessed Noah and his sons,
saying to them, "Be fruitful and increase in number and fill the earth.[p] 2 The
fear and dread of you will fall on all the
beasts of the earth, and on all the birds
in the sky, on every creature that moves
along the ground, and on all the fish in the
sea; they are given into your hands.[q] 3 Everything that lives and moves about will
be food for you.[r] Just as I gave you the
green plants, I now give you everything.[s]
4 "But you must not eat meat that has its
lifeblood still in it.[t] 5 And for your lifeblood
I will surely demand an accounting.[u] I will
demand an accounting from every animal.[v] And from each human being, too, I
will demand an accounting for the life of
another human being.[w]

6 "Whoever sheds human blood,
by humans shall their blood be
shed;[x]
for in the image of God[y]
has God made mankind.

7 As for you, be fruitful and increase in
number; multiply on the earth and increase upon it."[z]
8 Then God said to Noah and to his sons
with him: 9 "I now establish my covenant
with you[a] and with your descendants after you 10 and with every living creature
that was with you—the birds, the livestock and all the wild animals, all those
that came out of the ark with you—every
living creature on earth. 11 I establish my
covenant[b] with you:[c] Never again will all
life be destroyed by the waters of a flood;
never again will there be a flood to destroy
the earth.[d]"

8:21 [j] Ge 6:5; Ps 51:5; Jer 17:9; Mt 15:19; Ro 1:21 [k] Jer 44:11 [l] Ge 9:11,15; Isa 54:9 **8:22** [m] Jos 3:15; Ps 67:6; Jer 5:24 [n] Ps 74:17; Zec 14:8 [o] S Ge 1:14 **9:1** [p] S Ge 1:22 **9:2** [q] S Ge 1:26 **9:3** [r] S Ge 1:29 [s] S Ac 10:15; Col 2:16 **9:4** [t] Lev 3:17; 7:26; 17:10-14; 19:26; Dt 12:16, 23-25; 15:23; 1Sa 14:33; Eze 33:25; Ac 15:20,29 **9:5** [u] Ge 42:22; 50:15; 1Ki 2:32; 2Ch 24:22; Ps 9:12 [v] Ex 21:28-32 [w] Ge 4:10 **9:6** [x] S Ge 4:14; S Jdg 9:24; S Mt 26:52 [y] S Ge 1:26 **9:7** [z] S Ge 1:22 **9:9** [a] ver 11; S Ge 6:18 **9:11** [b] ver 16; Isa 24:5; 33:8; Hos 6:7 [c] S ver 9 [d] S Ge 8:21

[a] 21 Or *humans, for*

here has a different word for "curse," the reference appears to be to the curse of 3:17. It may be that the Lord here pledged never to add curse upon curse as he had in regard to Cain (4:12). *even though every inclination of the human heart is evil.* For almost identical phraseology, see 6:5. Because of humanity's extreme wickedness, God had destroyed people (6:7) by means of a flood (6:17). Although righteous Noah and his family had been saved, he and his offspring were descendants of Adam and carried in their hearts the inheritance of sin. God graciously promises never again to deal with sin by sending such a devastating deluge (see 9:11,15). Human history is held open for God's dealing with sin in a new and redemptive way—the way that was prepared for by God's action at Babel (see notes on 11:6,8) and that begins to unfold with the call of Abram (12:1). *from childhood.* The phrase replaces "all the time" in 6:5 and emphasizes the truth that sin infects a person's life from conception and birth (Ps 51:5; 58:3).

8:22 Times and seasons, created by God in the beginning (see 1:14), will never cease till the end of history.

9:1–7 At this new beginning, God renewed his original benediction (1:28) and his provision for humanity's food (cf. v. 3; 1:29–30). But because sin had brought violence into the world and because God now appointed meat as a part of the human diet (v. 3), further divine provisions and stipulations are added (vv. 4–6). Yet God's benediction dominates and encloses the whole (see v. 7).

9:2 *given into your hands.* God reaffirmed that human beings would rule over all creation, including the animals (see note on 1:26).

9:3 *Everything that lives and moves about will be food.* Meat would now supplement the human diet.

9:4 *you must not eat meat that has its lifeblood.* Lev 17:14 stresses the intimate relationship between blood and life by twice declaring that "the life of every creature is its blood." Life is the precious and mysterious gift of God, and people are not to seek to preserve it or increase the life-force within them by eating "life" that is "in the blood" (Lev 17:11)—as many pagan peoples throughout history have thought they could do.

9:5 *for your lifeblood ... I will demand an accounting from every animal.* God himself is the great defender of human life (see 4:9–12), which is precious to him because people were created in his image (v. 6) and because they are the earthly representatives and focal point of God's kingdom. In the theocracy (kingdom of God) established at Sinai, a domestic animal that had taken human life was to be stoned to death (Ex 21:28–32).

9:6 *Whoever sheds human blood, by humans shall their blood be shed.* In the later theocracy, those guilty of premeditated murder were to be executed (see Ex 21:12–14; Nu 35:16–32; see also Ro 13:3–4; 1Pe 2:13–14). *for in the image of God has God made mankind.* See 1:26 and note. In killing a human being, a murderer demonstrates contempt for God (see Pr 14:31; 17:5; Jas 3:9 and notes).

9:8–17 God's first and most basic covenant with his creatures (see chart, p. 23). It concerns the creation order itself and has its "sign" embedded in that creation order. Since divine judgment had seemed to undo the creation completely, sinful humanity needed God's covenanted assurance that his acts of judgment in history will not destroy the created order. This is the only divine covenant in which God pledges *not* to do something.

9:9 *I now establish my covenant.* God sovereignly promised in this covenant to Noah, to Noah's descendants and to all other living things (as a kind of gracious reward to righteous Noah, the new father of the human race—see 6:18) never again to destroy the earth and its inhabitants until his purposes for his creation are fully realized ("as long as the earth endures," 8:22). For similar commitments by God, see his covenants with Abram (15:18–20), Phinehas (Nu 25:10–13) and David (2Sa 7). See chart, p. 23.

9:11 *Never again will all life be destroyed by the waters of a flood.* A summary of the provisions of the Lord's covenant with Noah—an eternal covenant, as seen in such words and phrases as "never again" (see also v. 15), "for all generations to come" (v. 12) and "everlasting" (v. 16). See 8:21–22.

MAJOR COVENANTS IN THE OLD TESTAMENT

COVENANTS	REFERENCE	TYPE	PARTICIPANT	DESCRIPTION
NOAHIC	Ge 9:8–17	Royal Grant	Made with righteous (6:9) Noah (and his descendants and every living thing on earth—all life that is subject to human jurisdiction)	An unconditional divine promise never to destroy all earthly life with some natural catastrophe, the covenant "sign" (9:13,17) being the rainbow in the storm cloud
ABRAHAMIC A	Ge 15:9–21	Royal (land) Grant	Made with "righteous" (his faith was "credited . . . to him as righteousness," v. 6) Abram (and his descendants, v. 16)	An unconditional divine promise to fulfill the grant of the land; a self-maledictory oath symbolically enacted it (v. 17; see note there)
ABRAHAMIC B	Ge 17	Suzerain-vassal	Made with Abraham as patriarchal head of his household	A conditional divine pledge to be Abraham's God and the God of his descendants (cf. "as for me," v. 4; "as for you," v. 9); the condition: total consecration to the Lord as symbolized by circumcision
SINAITIC	Ex 19–24	Suzerain-vassal	Made with Israel as the descendants of Abraham, Isaac and Jacob and as the people the Lord had redeemed from bondage to an earthly power	A conditional divine pledge to be Israel's God (as her protector and the guarantor of her blessed destiny); the condition: Israel's total consecration to the Lord as his people (his kingdom) who live by his rule and serve his purposes in history
PHINEHAS	Nu 25:10–13	Royal Grant	Made with the zealous priest Phinehas	An unconditional divine promise to maintain the family of Phinehas in a "lasting priesthood" (v. 13; implicitly a pledge to Israel to provide her forever with a faithful priesthood)
DAVIDIC	2Sa 7:5–16	Royal Grant	Made with faithful King David after his devotion to God as Israel's king and the Lord's anointed vassal had come to special expression (v. 2)	An unconditional divine promise to establish and maintain the Davidic dynasty on the throne of Israel (implicitly a pledge to Israel) to provide her forever with a godly king like David and through that dynasty to do for her what he had done through David—bring her into rest in the promised land (1Ki 4:20–21; 5:3–4)
NEW	Jer 31:31–34	Royal Grant	Promised to rebellious Israel as she is about to be expelled from the promised land in actualization of the most severe covenant curse (Lev 26:27–39; Dt 28:36–37, 45–68)	An unconditional divine promise to unfaithful Israel to forgive her sins and establish his relationship with her on a new basis by writing his law "on their hearts" (v. 33)—a covenant of pure grace

MAJOR TYPES OF ROYAL COVENANTS/TREATIES IN THE ANCIENT NEAR EAST

ROYAL GRANT (UNCONDITIONAL)	PARITY	SUZERAIN-VASSAL (CONDITIONAL)
A king's grant (of land or some other benefit) to a loyal servant for faithful or exceptional service. The grant was normally perpetual and unconditional, but the servant's heirs benefited from it only as they continued their father's loyalty and service. (Cf. 1Sa 8:14; 22:7; 27:6; Est 8:1.)	A covenant between equals, binding them to mutual friendship or at least to mutual respect for each other's spheres and interests. Participants called each other "brother." (Cf. Ge 21:27; 26:31; 31:44–54; 1Ki 5:12; 15:19; 20:32–34; Am 1:9.)	A covenant regulating the relationship between a great king and one of his subject kings. The great king claimed absolute right of sovereignty, demanded total loyalty and service (the vassal must "love" his suzerain) and pledged protection of the subject's realm and dynasty, conditional on the vassal's faithfulness and loyalty to him. The vassal pledged absolute loyalty to his suzerain—whatever service his suzerain demanded—and exclusive reliance on the suzerain's protection. Participants called each other "lord" and "servant" or "father" and "son." (Cf. Jos 9:6,8; Eze 17:13–18; Hos 12:1.)

Commitments made in these covenants were accompanied by self-maledictory oaths (made orally, ceremonially or both). The gods were called on to witness the covenants and implement the curses of the oaths if the covenants were violated.

12 And God said, "This is the sign of the
covenant[e] I am making between me and
you and every living creature with you, a
covenant for all generations to come:[f] 13 I
have set my rainbow[g] in the clouds, and it
will be the sign of the covenant between
me and the earth. 14 Whenever I bring
clouds over the earth and the rainbow[h]
appears in the clouds, 15 I will remember
my covenant[i] between me and you and
all living creatures of every kind. Never
again will the waters become a flood to
destroy all life.[j] 16 Whenever the rainbow[k]
appears in the clouds, I will see it and remember the everlasting covenant[l] between
God and all living creatures of every kind
on the earth."
17 So God said to Noah, "This is the sign
of the covenant[m] I have established between me and all life on the earth."

The Sons of Noah

18 The sons of Noah who came out of
the ark were Shem, Ham and Japheth.[n]
(Ham was the father of Canaan.)[o] 19 These
were the three sons of Noah,[p] and from
them came the people who were scattered
over the whole earth.[q]
20 Noah, a man of the soil, proceeded[a] to
plant a vineyard. 21 When he drank some
of its wine,[r] he became drunk and lay uncovered inside his tent. 22 Ham, the father
of Canaan, saw his father naked[s] and told
his two brothers outside. 23 But Shem and
Japheth took a garment and laid it across
their shoulders; then they walked in backward and covered their father's naked
body. Their faces were turned the other
way so that they would not see their father naked.
24 When Noah awoke from his wine and
found out what his youngest son had done
to him, 25 he said,

"Cursed[t] be Canaan![u]
The lowest of slaves
will he be to his brothers.[v]"

26 He also said,

"Praise be to the LORD, the God of
Shem![w]
May Canaan be the slave[x] of Shem.
27 May God extend Japheth's[b]
territory;[y]
may Japheth live in the tents of
Shem,[z]
and may Canaan be the slave of
Japheth."

28 After the flood Noah lived 350 years.
29 Noah lived a total of 950 years, and then
he died.[a]

[a] 20 Or *soil, was the first* [b] 27 *Japheth* sounds like the Hebrew for *extend.*

9:12 [e] ver 17; Ge 17:11 [f] Ge 17:12; Ex 12:14; Lev 3:17; 6:18; 17:7; Nu 10:8 **9:13** [g] ver 14; Eze 1:28; Rev 4:3; 10:1 **9:14** [h] S ver 13 **9:15** [i] S Ge 8:1; Ex 2:24; 6:5; 34:10; Lev 26:42,45; Dt 7:9; Ps 89:34; 103:18; 105:8; 106:45; Eze 16:60 [j] S Ge 8:21 **9:16** [k] ver 13 [l] S ver 11; Ge 17:7,13, 19; 2Sa 7:13; 23:5; Ps 105:9-10; Isa 9:7; 54:10; 55:3; 59:21; 61:8; Jer 31:31-34; 32:40; 33:21; Eze 16:60; 37:26; S Heb 13:20 **9:17** [m] S ver 12 **9:18** [n] S Ge 5:32; Lk 3:36 [o] ver 25-27; Ge 10:6,15 **9:19** [p] Ge 5:32 [q] S Ge 1:22; 10:32; 11:4,8,9 **9:21** [r] Ge 19:35 **9:22** [s] Hab 2:15 **9:25** [t] Ge 27:12 [u] ver 18; Ex 20:5; Ps 79:8; Isa 14:21; Jer 31:29; 32:18 [v] Ge 25:23; 27:29,37,40; 37:10; 49:8; Nu 24:18; Jos 9:23 **9:26** [w] Ge 14:20; Ex 18:10; Ps 7:17 [x] 1Ki 9:21 **9:27** [y] Ge 10:2-5 [z] Eph 2:13-14; 3:6 **9:29** [a] S Ge 2:17

9:12 *sign.* A covenant sign was a visible seal and reminder of covenant commitments. Circumcision would become the sign of the covenant with Abraham (see 17:11), and the Sabbath would be the sign of the covenant with Israel at Sinai (see Ex 31:16–17).

9:13 *rainbow.* Rain and the rainbow doubtless existed long before the time of Noah's flood, but after the flood the rainbow took on new meaning as the sign of the Noahic covenant. The Hebrew word is lit. "bow" (27:3; 48:22). The rainbow probably represents the bow with which God often shoots the arrows of his lightning bolts toward the earth (Ps 18:14; 77:17; 144:6; Hab 3:9,11). But after a rainstorm God's bow is aimed away from the earth. Whenever he sees the rainbow, he is reminded of his pledge not to send another deluge to wipe out the earth (v. 16).

9:19 *who were scattered.* The clause anticipates the list of nations in ch. 10 (see note on 11:8).

9:20 *man of the soil.* Like his father Lamech (see 5:29).

9:21 *When he drank some of its wine, he became drunk.* The first person to make wine drank to excess (cf. Pr 20:1 and note). *uncovered inside his tent.* Excessive use of wine led, among other things, to immodest behavior (see 19:30–35).

9:22 *father of Canaan.* Mentioned here because Ham, in acting as he did, showed himself to be the true father of Canaan (i.e., of the Canaanites; see note on 15:16). *told his two brothers.* He broadcast, rather than covered, his father's immodesty.

9:23 *faces were turned ... so that they would not see.* They wanted to avoid further disgrace to their father (cf. Ex 20:12 and note; Lev 19:3).

9:24 *from his wine.* From the drunkenness caused by the wine.

9:25 *Cursed be Canaan!* Some maintain that Ham's son (see vv. 18,22) was to be punished because of his father's sin (see Ex 20:5), but Ex 20:5 (see note there) restricts such punishment to "those who hate me." This account of Noah's cursing and blessing of his sons is addressed to Israel. Most likely it is for this reason that Canaan is here singled out from Ham's descendants as the object of Noah's curse. Israel would experience firsthand the depth of Canaanite sin (see Lev 18:2–3,6–30) and the harshness of God's judgment on it. In that judgment Noah's curse came to be fulfilled in the experience of this segment of Ham's descendants. But Ham's offspring, as listed in 10:6–13, included many of Israel's other long-term enemies (Egypt, Philistia, Assyria, Babylonia), who also experienced severe divine judgments because of their hostility to Israel and Israel's God. *lowest of slaves.* Joshua's subjection of the Gibeonites (Jos 9:27) is one of the fulfillments (see also Jos 16:10; Jdg 1:28,30,33,35; 1Ki 9:20–21). Noah's curse cannot be used to justify the enslavement of blacks, since most of Ham's descendants are known to be Caucasian, as the Canaanites certainly were (as shown by ancient paintings of the Canaanites discovered in Egypt).

9:26 *Praise be to the LORD.* The Lord (instead of Shem) is blessed ("praised") because he is the source of Shem's blessing. He is also the "God of Shem" (and his descendants, the Semites—which included the Israelites) in a special sense.

9:27 *live in the tents of Shem.* Share in the blessings bestowed on Shem.

9:29 *and then he died.* See note on 5:5. As the tenth and last member of the genealogy of Seth (5:3–32), Noah had an obituary that ends like those of his worthy ancestors.

The Table of Nations

10 This is the account[b] of Shem, Ham
and Japheth,[c] Noah's sons,[d] who
themselves had sons after the flood.

The Japhethites

10:2-5pp — 1Ch 1:5-7

2 The sons[a] of Japheth:
Gomer,[e] Magog,[f] Madai, Javan,[g] Tubal,[h] Meshek[i] and Tiras.
3 The sons of Gomer:
Ashkenaz,[j] Riphath and Togarmah.[k]
4 The sons of Javan:
Elishah,[l] Tarshish,[m] the Kittites[n] and
the Rodanites.[b] 5 (From these the
maritime peoples spread out into
their territories by their clans within their nations, each with its own
language.)[o]

The Hamites

10:6-20pp — 1Ch 1:8-16

6 The sons of Ham:
Cush,[p] Egypt, Put[q] and Canaan.[r]
7 The sons of Cush:
Seba,[s] Havilah,[t] Sabtah, Raamah[u]
and Sabteka.
The sons of Raamah:
Sheba[v] and Dedan.[w]

10:1 [b]Ge 2:4 [c]S Ge 5:32 [d]ver 32; 1Ch 1:4 **10:2** [e]Eze 38:6 [f]Eze 38:2; 39:6; Rev 20:8 [g]Eze 27:19 [h]Isa 66:19; Eze 27:13; 32:26 [i]Eze 39:1 **10:3** [j]Jer 51:27 [k]Eze 27:14; 38:6 **10:4** [l]Eze 27:7 [m]Ps 48:7; 72:10; Isa 2:16; 23:1,6,10,14; 60:9; 66:19; Jer 10:9; Eze 27:12,25; 38:13; Jnh 1:3 [n]Nu 24:24; Isa 23:12; Jer 2:10; Eze 27:6; Da 11:30 **10:5** [o]Ge 9:27 **10:6** [p]2Ki 19:9; 2Ch 12:3; 16:8; Isa 11:11; 18:1; 20:3; 43:3; Jer 46:9; Eze 30:4,9; 38:5; Na 3:9; Zep 2:12; 3:10 [q]Eze 27:10; 38:5 [r]S Ge 9:18 **10:7** [s]Isa 43:3 [t]S Ge 2:11 [u]Eze 27:22

8 Cush was the father[c] of Nimrod,[x] who
became a mighty warrior on the earth. 9 He
was a mighty[y] hunter[z] before the LORD; that
is why it is said, "Like Nimrod, a mighty
hunter before the LORD." 10 The first centers of his kingdom were Babylon,[a] Uruk,[b]
Akkad and Kalneh,[c] in[d] Shinar.[e][d] 11 From
that land he went to Assyria,[e] where he
built Nineveh,[f] Rehoboth Ir,[f] Calah 12 and
Resen, which is between Nineveh and Calah — which is the great city.

13 Egypt was the father of
the Ludites, Anamites, Lehabites,
Naphtuhites, 14 Pathrusites, Kasluhites

[a] *2 Sons* may mean *descendants* or *successors* or *nations*; also in verses 3, 4, 6, 7, 20-23, 29 and 31. [b] *4* Some manuscripts of the Masoretic Text and Samaritan Pentateuch (see also Septuagint and 1 Chron. 1:7); most manuscripts of the Masoretic Text *Dodanites* [c] *8 Father* may mean *ancestor* or *predecessor* or *founder*; also in verses 13, 15, 24 and 26. [d] *10* Or *Uruk and Akkad — all of them in* [e] *10* That is, Babylonia [f] *11* Or *Nineveh with its city squares*

[v]Ge 25:3; 1Ki 10:1; 2Ch 9:1; Job 1:15; 6:19; 16:11; Ps 72:10, 15; Isa 60:6; Jer 6:20; Eze 27:22; 38:13; Joel 3:8 [w]1Ch 1:32; Isa 21:13; Jer 25:23-24; 49:8; Eze 27:15,20; 38:13 **10:8** [x]Mic 5:6 **10:9** [y]2Ch 14:9; 16:8; Isa 18:2 [z]Ge 25:27; 27:3 **10:10** [a]Ge 11:9; 2Ch 36:17; Isa 13:1; 47:1; Jer 21:2; 25:12; 50:1 [b]Ezr 4:9 [c]Isa 10:9; Am 6:2 [d]Ge 11:2; 14:1; Zec 5:11 **10:11** [e]Ps 83:8; Mic 5:6 [f]2Ki 19:36; Isa 37:37; Jnh 1:2; 3:2,3; 4:11; Na 1:1; Zep 2:13

10:1 *account.* See note on 2:4. The links affirmed here may not all be based on strictly physical descent, but may include geographic, historical and linguistic associations (see note on v. 5 and NIV text notes on vv. 2,8; 11:10). See also Introduction to 1 Chronicles: Genealogies.

10:2 *sons.* See NIV text note. *Japheth.* As the least involved in the Biblical narrative and perhaps also as the oldest of Noah's sons (see v. 21 and NIV text note), his descendants or successors are listed first. The genealogy of Shem, the chosen line, appears last in the chapter (see vv. 21 – 31; see also 11:10 – 26). The 14 nations that came from Japheth plus the 30 from Ham and the 26 from Shem add up to 70 (the multiple of 10 and 7, both numbers signifying completeness; see note on 5:5), perhaps in anticipation of the 70 members of Jacob's family who went down to Egypt (see 46:27; Ex 1:5; see also Dt 32:8). The Japhethites lived generally north and west of Canaan in Eurasia. *Gomer.* The people of Gomer (the later Cimmerians) and related nations (see v. 3) lived near the Black Sea (see map, p. 26). *Magog.* Possibly the father of a Scythian people who inhabited the Caucasus and adjacent regions southeast of the Black Sea. *Madai.* The later Medes. *Javan.* Ionia (southern Greece) and perhaps western Asia Minor. *Tubal, Meshek.* Not related to Tobolsk and Moscow in modern Russia. Together with Magog they are mentioned in later Assyrian inscriptions. See also Eze 38:2 and note. Probably Tubal was in Pontus and Meshek was in the Moschian Mountains. Their movement was from eastern Asia Minor north to the Black Sea. *Tiras.* Possibly the Thrace of later times.

10:3 *Ashkenaz.* The later Scythians. All three names in this verse refer to peoples located in the upper Euphrates region.

10:4 *Elishah.* Either Alashia (an ancient name for Cyprus) or a reference to Sicily and southern Italy. *Tarshish.* Probably southern Spain. *Kittites.* A people living on Cyprus. *Rodanites.* A people whose name is perhaps reflected in Rhodes (a Greek isle).

10:5 See vv. 20,31. *territories ... clans ... nations ... language.* Geographic, ethnic, political and linguistic terms, respectively. These several criteria were used to differentiate the various groups of people.

10:6 *Ham.* The Hamites named here were located in southwestern Asia and northeastern Africa. *Cush.* The upper Nile region, south of Egypt. *Egypt.* Hebrew *Mizraim*, which means "two Egypts," a reference to Upper (southern) and Lower (northern) Egypt. *Put.* Probably Libya (see note on v. 13). *Canaan.* The name possibly means "land of purple" (as does Phoenicia, the Greek name for the same general region). Canaan was a major producer and exporter of purple dye, highly prized by royalty. The territory was much later called Palestine after the Philistines (see v. 14 and note).

10:7 *sons of Cush.* The seven Cushite nations here mentioned were all in Arabia. Sheba and Dedan (or their namesakes) reappear as two of Abraham's grandsons (see 25:3). Together with Raamah they are mentioned in Eze 27:20 – 22.

10:8 *Cush.* Probably not the same as in v. 6. Located in Mesopotamia, the name may be related to that of the later Kassites. *Nimrod.* Possibly the Hebrew name of Sargon I, an early ruler of Akkad (see v. 10).

10:10 *Uruk.* One of the important cities in ancient Mesopotamia (see maps, pp. 26, 48).

10:12 *great city.* Possibly a reference to Calah (or even Resen), but most likely to Nineveh (see Jnh 1:2; 3:2; 4:11), either alone or including the surrounding urban areas.

10:13 *Ludites.* Perhaps the Lydians in Asia Minor (see note on v. 22). *Anamites.* Located in north Africa, west of Egypt, near Cyrene. *Lehabites.* Perhaps the Libyan desert tribes (see note on v. 6). *Naphtuhites.* People of Lower Egypt.

10:14 *Pathrusites.* The inhabitants of Upper Egypt (see note on v. 6). *Caphtorites.* Crete, known as Caphtor in ancient times, was for a while the homeland of various Philistine groups (see Jer 47:4; Am 9:7). The Philistines themselves were a vigorous Indo-European maritime people who invaded

(from whom the Philistines[g] came)
and Caphtorites.[h]
15 Canaan[i] was the father of
Sidon[j] his firstborn,[a][k] and of the
Hittites,[l] 16 Jebusites,[m] Amorites,[n]
Girgashites,[o] 17 Hivites,[p] Arkites, Si-
nites, 18 Arvadites,[q] Zemarites and
Hamathites.[r]

Later the Canaanite[s] clans scattered
19 and the borders of Canaan[t] reached from
Sidon[u] toward Gerar[v] as far as Gaza,[w] and
then toward Sodom, Gomorrah, Admah
and Zeboyim,[x] as far as Lasha.

10:14 [g]Ge 21:32,34; 26:1,8; Jos 13:2; Jdg 3:3; Isa 14:31; Jer 47:1,4; Am 9:7 [h]Dt 2:23; 1Ch 1:12 **10:15** [i]S Ge 9:18 [j]ver 19; Jos 11:8; Jdg 10:6; Isa 23:2,4; Jer 25:22; 27:3; 47:4; Eze 28:21; 32:30; Joel 3:4; Zec 9:2

20 These are the sons of Ham by their
clans and languages, in their territories
and nations.

[a] 15 Or *of the Sidonians, the foremost*

[k]Ex 4:22; Nu 1:20; 3:2; 18:15; 26:5; 33:4 [l]Ge 15:20; 23:3, 20; 25:10; 26:34; 27:46; 49:32; Nu 13:29; Jos 1:4; 1Sa 26:6; Eze 16:3 **10:16** [m]Jdg 19:10; 1Ch 11:4; Ezr 9:1 [n]Ex 3:8; Nu 13:29; 21:13; 32:39; Dt 1:4; Jos 2:10; 2Ch 8:7 [o]Ge 15:18-21; Dt 7:1 **10:17** [p]Ge 34:2; 36:2; Ex 3:8; Dt 7:1; Jdg 3:3 **10:18** [q]Eze 27:8 [r]1Ch 18:3 [s]Ge 12:6; 13:7; 50:11; Ex 13:11; Nu 13:29; 14:25; 21:3; 33:40; Dt 1:7; Jdg 1:1 **10:19** [t]Ge 11:31; 12:1; 13:12; 17:8; 24:3; 26:34; 27:46; 28:1,6,8; 31:18; 35:6; 37:1; Lev 25:38 [u]S ver 15; Ge 49:13; Jos 19:28; Jdg 1:31; 18:28; 2Sa 24:6 [v]2Ch 14:13 [w]Dt 2:23; Jos 10:41; 11:22; 15:47; Jdg 1:18; 6:4; 16:1,21; 1Sa 6:17; Jer 25:20; 47:1; Am 1:6; Zep 2:4 [x]Ge 14:2; Dt 29:23

Egypt early in the twelfth century BC. After being driven out, they migrated in large numbers to southwest Canaan, later extending their influence over most of the land. The Philistines of the patriarchal period (see 21:32,34; 26:1,8,14–15,18) no doubt had earlier settled in Canaan more peacefully and in smaller numbers.

10:15 *Sidon.* An important commercial city on the northwest coast of Canaan. *Hittites.* An Indo-European-speaking people who moved into Anatolia (ancient Asia Minor, modern western Turkey) from southeast Europe in the late third millennium BC. They came to dominate north-central Anatolia in the mid-second millennium BC and called themselves Hittites, a name adapted from that of the native Hatti people. They established an empire powerful enough at times to challenge both Babylonia and Egypt. The relationship, if any, between these people and the "Hittites" of Canaan mentioned in the Bible remains obscure (but see Eze 16:3 and note).

10:16 *Jebusites.* Inhabitants of Jerusalem at the time of Israel's conquest of Canaan. Jerusalem was also known as Jebus during part of its history (see Jdg 19:10–11; 1Ch 11:4). *Amorites.* The name comes from an Akkadian word meaning "westerner" (west from the Babylonian perspective). Amorites lived in the hill country of Canaan at the time of the Israelite conquest.

10:17–18 Together with the Girgashites (v. 16), these groups in Canaan for the most part inhabited small city-states.

10:19 *Sodom, Gomorrah, Admah and Zeboyim.* See 14:2,8 (see also note on 13:10); probably located east and/or southeast of the Dead Sea.

TABLE OF NATIONS

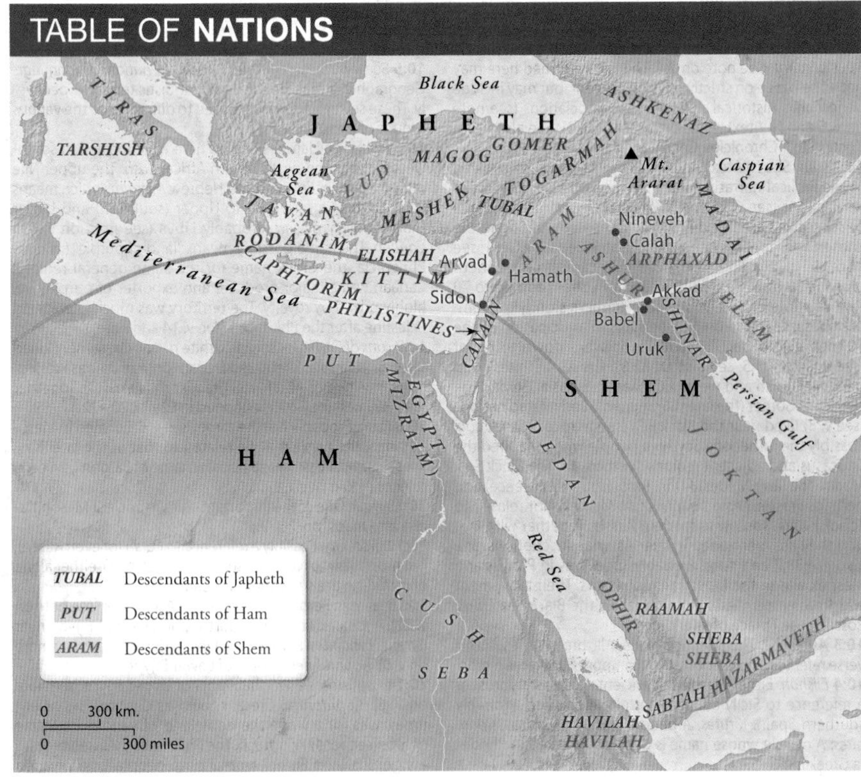

The Semites

10:21-31pp — Ge 11:10-27; 1Ch 1:17-27

21 Sons were also born to Shem, whose
older brother was[a] Japheth; Shem was the
ancestor of all the sons of Eber.[y]

22 The sons of Shem:
Elam,[z] Ashur,[a] Arphaxad,[b] Lud and
Aram.[c]

23 The sons of Aram:
Uz,[d] Hul, Gether and Meshek.[b]

24 Arphaxad was the father of[c] Shelah,
and Shelah the father of Eber.[e]

25 Two sons were born to Eber:
One was named Peleg,[d] because in
his time the earth was divided; his
brother was named Joktan.

26 Joktan was the father of
Almodad, Sheleph, Hazarmaveth,
Jerah, 27 Hadoram, Uzal,[f] Diklah,
28 Obal, Abimael, Sheba,[g] 29 Ophir,[h]
Havilah and Jobab. All these were
sons of Joktan.

30 The region where they lived stretched
from Mesha toward Sephar, in the eastern
hill country.

31 These are the sons of Shem by their
clans and languages, in their territories
and nations.

32 These are the clans of Noah's sons,[i]
according to their lines of descent, within their nations. From these the nations
spread out over the earth[j] after the flood.

The Tower of Babel

11 Now the whole world had one language[k] and a common speech. 2 As
people moved eastward,[e] they found a
plain in Shinar[f][l] and settled there.

3 They said to each other, "Come, let's
make bricks[m] and bake them thoroughly."
They used brick instead of stone,[n] and tar[o]
for mortar. 4 Then they said, "Come, let us
build ourselves a city, with a tower that
reaches to the heavens,[p] so that we may
make a name[q] for ourselves; otherwise
we will be scattered[r] over the face of the
whole earth."[s]

5 But the LORD came down[t] to see the
city and the tower the people were building. 6 The LORD said, "If as one people
speaking the same language[u] they have begun to do this, then nothing they plan to

[a] 21 Or *Shem, the older brother of* [b] 23 See Septuagint and 1 Chron. 1:17; Hebrew *Mash.* [c] 24 Hebrew; Septuagint *father of Cainan, and Cainan was the father of* [d] 25 *Peleg* means *division.* [e] 2 Or *from the east;* or *in the east* [f] 2 That is, Babylonia

10:21 [y] ver 24; Nu 24:24 **10:22** [z] Ge 14:1; Isa 11:11; 21:2; Jer 25:25; 49:34; Eze 32:24; Da 8:2 [a] Nu 24:22, 24; Eze 27:23 [b] Lk 3:36 [c] Jdg 3:10; 1Ki 11:25; 19:15; 20:34; 22:31; 2Ki 5:1; 8:7 **10:23** [d] Ge 22:21; Job 1:1; Jer 25:20; La 4:21 **10:24** [e] S ver 21; Lk 3:35 **10:27** [f] Eze 27:19 **10:28** [g] 1Ki 10:1; Job 6:19; Ps 72:10, 15; Isa 60:6; Eze 27:22 **10:29** [h] 1Ki 9:28; 10:11; 1Ch 29:4; Job 22:24; 28:16; Ps 45:9; Isa 13:12 **10:32** [i] S ver 1 [j] S Ge 9:19 **11:1** [k] ver 6 **11:2** [l] S Ge 10:10 **11:3** [m] Ex 1:14; 5:7; Jer 43:9 [n] Isa 9:10; Am 5:11 [o] Ge 14:10 **11:4** [p] Dt 1:28; 6:10; 9:1; Job 20:6; Jer 51:53 [q] Ge 6:4 [r] Dt 30:3; 1Ki 22:17; Est 3:8; Ps 44:11; Jer 31:10; 40:15; Eze 6:8; Joel 3:2 [s] S Ge 9:19; Dt 4:27 **11:5** [t] ver 7; Ge 18:21; Ex 3:8; 19:11, 18, 20; Ps 18:9; 144:5 **11:6** [u] S ver 1

10:21 *Sons were also born to Shem.* The descendants of Shem were called Shemites (later modified to Semites). *Eber.* Though a distant descendant of Shem (see vv. 24–25; 11:14–17), Eber's importance as the ancestor of the Hebrews ("Eber" is the origin of the Hebrew word for "Hebrew") is already hinted at here.

10:22 *Elam.* The Elamites lived east of Mesopotamia. *Ashur.* An early name for Assyria (see note on 2:14) in northern Mesopotamia. *Arphaxad.* See also 11:10–13; perhaps a compound form of the Hebrew word for Chaldea, in southern Mesopotamia. *Lud.* Probably the Lydians of Asia Minor (see note on v. 13). *Aram.* Located north-northeast of Canaan, the area known today as Syria (see note on Dt 26:5).

10:24 *Shelah.* See 11:12–15.

10:25 *Peleg.* See NIV text note and 11:16–19. *earth was divided.* Perhaps resulting from the dispersion of peoples described in 11:1–9 (see note there).

10:26 *Joktan.* The predecessor of numerous south Arabian kingdoms.

10:28 *Sheba.* In southwest Arabia (roughly the area of Yemen). A later queen of Sheba made a memorable visit to King Solomon in the tenth century BC (see 1Ki 10:1–13).

10:29 *Ophir.* The source of much of King Solomon's gold (see 1Ki 9:28; 10:11). Its location seems to have been south of Canaan, perhaps somewhere in Africa or south Arabia (but see note on 1Ki 9:28).

11:1–9 This section provides the main reason for the scattering of the peoples listed in ch. 10. The narrative is a beautiful example of inverted or hourglass structure (see Introduction: Literary Features). The author of Genesis uses the story of the flood and the story of Babel to characterize the ways of humankind and God's responses through acts of judgment in order to thwart humanity's proud efforts to rule over the creation not as God's faithful representatives but as rebels. With this characterization of human history outside God's saving work, the author sets the stage for God's call of Abram out of the post-Babel world to begin his redemptive work that would unfold in Israel's history.

11:1 *whole world.* The survivors of the flood and their descendants (see vv. 4,8–9).

11:3 *brick instead of stone, and tar for mortar.* Stone and mortar were used as building materials in Canaan. Stone was scarce in Mesopotamia, however, so mud brick and tar were used (as indicated also by archaeological excavations).

11:4 *us ... ourselves ... we ... ourselves ... we.* The people's plans were egotistical and proud. *tower.* The typical Mesopotamian temple-tower, known as a ziggurat, was square at the base and had sloping, stepped sides that led upward to a small shrine at the top. *reaches to the heavens.* A similar ziggurat may be described in 28:12. Other Mesopotamian ziggurats were given names demonstrating that they, too, were meant to serve as staircases from earth to heaven: "The House of the Link between Heaven and Earth" (at Larsa), "The House of the Seven Guides of Heaven and Earth" (at Borsippa), "The House of the Foundation-Platform of Heaven and Earth" (at Babylon), "The House of the Mountain of the Universe" (at Ashur). *name.* In the OT, "name" also refers to reputation, fame or renown. (The Nephilim were "men of renown [lit. 'name']," 6:4.) At Babel (see note on v. 9) the rebellious human race undertook a united and godless effort to establish for themselves, by a titanic enterprise, a world renown by which they would dominate God's creation (cf. 10:8–12; 2Sa 18:18). *scattered.* See note on v. 8.

11:6 *If ... then.* If the whole human race remained united in the proud attempt to take its destiny into its own hands and, by its self-centered efforts, to seize the reins of history, there would be no limit to its

do will be impossible for them. 7Come, let
us[v] go down[w] and confuse their language
so they will not understand each other."[x]
8So the LORD scattered them from there
over all the earth,[y] and they stopped building the city. 9That is why it was called Babel[a z]—because there the LORD confused
the language[a] of the whole world.[b] From
there the LORD scattered[c] them over the
face of the whole earth.

From Shem to Abram

11:10-27pp — Ge 10:21-31; 1Ch 1:17-27

10This is the account[d] of Shem's family
line.

Two years after the flood, when Shem
was 100 years old, he became the father[b]
of Arphaxad.[e] 11And after he became the
father of Arphaxad, Shem lived 500 years
and had other sons and daughters.
12When Arphaxad had lived 35 years,
he became the father of Shelah.[f] 13And
after he became the father of Shelah, Arphaxad lived 403 years and had other sons
and daughters.[c]

14When Shelah had lived 30 years, he
became the father of Eber.[g] 15And after he
became the father of Eber, Shelah lived 403
years and had other sons and daughters.
16When Eber had lived 34 years, he became the father of Peleg.[h] 17And after he
became the father of Peleg, Eber lived 430
years and had other sons and daughters.
18When Peleg had lived 30 years, he
became the father of Reu.[i] 19And after he
became the father of Reu, Peleg lived 209
years and had other sons and daughters.
20When Reu had lived 32 years, he became the father of Serug.[j] 21And after he
became the father of Serug, Reu lived 207
years and had other sons and daughters.
22When Serug had lived 30 years, he became the father of Nahor.[k] 23And after he

11:7 [v] S Ge 1:26 [w] S ver 5 [x] Ge 42:23; Dt 28:49; Isa 28:11; 33:19; Jer 5:15; 1Co 14:2,11 **11:8** [y] S Ge 9:19; Dt 32:8; S Lk 1:51 **11:9** [z] S Ge 10:10 [a] Ps 55:9 [b] Ac 2:5-11 [c] Isa 2:10,21; 13:14; 24:1 **11:10** [d] S Ge 2:4 [e] Lk 3:36 **11:12** [f] Lk 3:35 **11:14** [g] Lk 3:35 **11:16** [h] Lk 3:35 **11:18** [i] Lk 3:35 **11:20** [j] Lk 3:35 **11:22** [k] Lk 3:34

[a] *9* That is, Babylon; *Babel* sounds like the Hebrew for *confused.* [b] *10 Father* may mean *ancestor;* also in verses 11-25. [c] *12,13* Hebrew; Septuagint (see also Luke 3:35, 36 and note at Gen. 10:24) *35 years, he became the father of Cainan. 13And after he became the father of Cainan, Arphaxad lived 430 years and had other sons and daughters, and then he died. When Cainan had lived 130 years, he became the father of Shelah. And after he became the father of Shelah, Cainan lived 330 years and had other sons and daughters*

unrestrained rebellion against God. A godless human kingdom would displace and exclude the kingdom of God.
11:7 *let us.* See notes on 1:1,26. God's "Come, let us" from heaven counters proud people's "Come, let us" (v. 4) from earth. *not understand each other.* Without a common language, joint effort became impossible (see v. 8).
11:8 *scattered.* See v. 4; 9:1,19. God dispersed the people because of their rebellious pride. Even the greatest of human powers cannot defy God and long survive.
11:9 *Babel.* See NIV text note and 10:10. The word is of Akkadian origin and means "gateway to a god" (Jacob's stairway was similarly called "gate of heaven"; see 28:17). *confused.* The Hebrew word used here (*balal*) sounds like "Babel," the Hebrew word for Babylon and the origin of the English word "babble."
11:10–26 A ten-name genealogy, like that of Seth (see 5:3–31; see also note on 5:5). Unlike the Sethite genealogy, however, the genealogy of Shem does not give total figures for the ages of the men at death and does not end each paragraph with "and then he died." It covers the centuries between Shem and Abram as briefly as possible.
11:10 *account.* See note on 2:4.

Ziggurat of Nanna at Ur. The large temple dedicated to the god Nanna was built c. 2100 BC by King Ur-Nammu in the ancient Mesopotamian city of Ur in present-day Iraq. Some believe that the tower of Babel (Ge 11:1–9) was a type of ziggurat.

became the father of Nahor, Serug lived 200
years and had other sons and daughters.
24 When Nahor had lived 29 years, he became the father of Terah.[l] 25 And after he
became the father of Terah, Nahor lived 119
years and had other sons and daughters.
26 After Terah had lived 70 years, he became the father of Abram,[m] Nahor[n] and
Haran.[o]

Abram's Family

27 This is the account[p] of Terah's family
line.

Terah became the father of Abram, Nahor[q] and Haran. And Haran became the
father of Lot.[r] 28 While his father Terah was
still alive, Haran died in Ur of the Chaldeans,[s] in the land of his birth. 29 Abram
and Nahor[t] both married. The name of
Abram's wife was Sarai,[u] and the name
of Nahor's wife was Milkah;[v] she was the
daughter of Haran, the father of both Milkah and Iskah. 30 Now Sarai was childless
because she was not able to conceive.[w]
31 Terah took his son Abram, his grandson Lot[x] son of Haran, and his daughter-
in-law[y] Sarai, the wife of his son Abram,
and together they set out from Ur of the
Chaldeans[z] to go to Canaan.[a] But when
they came to Harran,[b] they settled there.
32 Terah[c] lived 205 years, and he died in
Harran.

The Call of Abram

12 The LORD had said to Abram, "Go
from your country, your people
and your father's household[d] to the land[e]
I will show you.[f]

2 "I will make you into a great nation,[g]
and I will bless you;[h]
I will make your name great,
and you will be a blessing.[a][i]

[a] 2 Or *be seen as blessed*

11:24 [l] Lk 3:34 **11:26** [m] Lk 3:34 [n] Jos 24:2 [o] 2Ki 19:12; Isa 37:12; Eze 27:23 **11:27** [p] S Ge 2:4 [q] ver 29; Ge 31:53 [r] ver 31; Ge 12:4; 13:1, 5, 8, 12; 14:12; 19:1; Lk 17:28; 2Pe 2:7 **11:28** [s] ver 31; Ge 15:7; Ne 9:7; Job 1:17; 16:11; Eze 23:23; Ac 7:4 **11:29** [t] S ver 27, 31; Ge 22:20, 23; 24:10, 15, 24; 29:5 [u] Ge 12:5, 11; 16:1; 17:15 [v] Ge 22:20 **11:30** [w] Ge 16:1; 18:11; 25:21; 29:31; 30:1, 22; Jdg 13:2; 1Sa 1:5; Ps 113:9; Lk 1:7, 36 **11:31** [x] S ver 27 [y] Ge 38:11; Lev 18:15; 20:12; Ru 1:6, 22; 2:20; 4:15; 1Sa 4:19; 1Ch 2:4; Eze 22:11; Mic 7:6 [z] S ver 28 [a] S Ge 10:19 [b] S ver 29; Ge 12:4; 27:43; 28:5, 10; 29:4; 2Ki 19:12; Eze 27:23 **11:32** [c] Jos 24:2 **12:1** [d] Ge 20:13; 24:4, 27, 40 [e] S Ge 10:19 [f] Ge 15:7; 26:2; Jos 24:3; Ac 7:3*; Heb 11:8 **12:2** [g] Ge 13:16; 15:5; 17:2, 4; 18:18; 22:17; 26:4; 28:3, 14; 32:12; 35:11; 41:49; 46:3; 47:27; 48:4, 16, 19; Ex 1:7; 5:5; 32:13; Dt 1:10; 10:22; 13:17; 26:5; Jos 11:4; 24:3; 2Sa 17:11; 1Ki 3:8; 4:20; 1Ch 27:23; 2Ch 1:9; Ne 9:23; Ps 107:38; Isa 6:13; 10:22; 48:19; 51:2; 54:3; 60:22; Jer 33:22; Mic 4:7 [h] Ge 24:1, 35; 25:11; 26:3; 28:4; Ex 20:24; Nu 22:12; 23:8, 20; 24:9; Ps 67:6; 115:12; Isa 44:3; 61:9; 65:23; Mal 3:12 [i] Ge 22:18; Isa 19:24; Jer 4:2; Hag 2:19; Zec 8:13

11:26 *Terah ... became the father of Abram, Nahor and Haran.* As in the case of Shem, Ham and Japheth, the names of the three sons may not be in chronological order by age (see 9:24; see also 10:21 and NIV text note). Haran died while his father was still alive (see v. 28).

11:27—25:11 With God's calling of Abram out of the post-Babel peoples, the story of God's ways with humankind shifts focus from universal history to the history of God's relationship with a particular person and people. Here begins the history of his saving work, in which human sin is not only judged (the flood) or restrained (Babel) but forgiven (through atonement) and overcome (through the purifying of human hearts). Throughout the rest of Scripture the unfolding of this history remains the golden thread and central theme. Its final outcome is made sure through Jesus Christ, "the son of Abraham" (Lk 3:34; see also Mt 1:1 – 17 and note on 1:1; Gal 3:16)—which is the core message of the NT.

The account of the God-Abram relationship found here foreshadows in many ways the God-Israel relationship, and the trials and triumphs of Abram's faith model the life of faith for his descendants.

11:27 *account.* See note on 2:4.

11:28 *Ur of the Chaldeans.* Possibly in northern Mesopotamia, but more likely the site on the Euphrates in southern Iraq excavated by Leonard Woolley between 1922 and 1934. Ruins and artifacts from Ur reveal a civilization and culture that reached high levels before Abram's time. King Ur-Nammu, who may have been Abram's contemporary, is famous for his law code. *Chaldeans.* See notes on Ezr 5:12; Job 1:17.

11:30 *Sarai was ... not able to conceive.* The sterility of Abram's wife (see 15:2 – 3; 17:17) emphasized the fact that God's people would not come by natural generation from the post-Babel peoples. God was bringing a new humanity into being, of whom Abram was father (17:5), just as Adam and Noah were fathers of the fallen human race.

11:31 *they came to Harran.* In Hebrew the name of the town is spelled differently from that of Abram's brother (v. 26). The moon-god was worshiped at both Ur and Harran, and since Terah was an idolater (see Jos 24:2), he probably felt at home in either place (his name probably means "moon worshiper"). Harran (an Akkadian word meaning "caravan") was a flourishing caravan city in the nineteenth century BC. In the eighteenth century it was ruled by Amorites (see note on 10:16).

12:1 *had said.* God had spoken to Abram "while he was still in Mesopotamia, before he lived in Harran" (Ac 7:2). *Go from ... show you.* Abram must leave the settled world of the post-Babel nations and begin a pilgrimage with God to a better world of God's making (see 24:7; see also 11:1 – 9; Heb 11:8 – 10 and notes).

Here begins the story of how "the LORD [Yahweh] ... the God of Abraham, Isaac and Jacob" (Ex 3:16), "the God of Israel" (Ex 5:1), created for himself a people who acknowledged him as the only true God and who had as their homeland a place in the world that would be called "their own land, which they had acquired in accordance with the command of the LORD through Moses" (Jos 22:9). In the ancient world of the OT, all the various gods that were worshiped and relied on were gods of a particular place and/or a particular people (a family, tribe or nation). The rest of Yahweh's dealings with the patriarchs and with Israel is an important theme that relates how Abram's pilgrimage moved ever forward toward the fulfillment of Yahweh's purposes.

12:2 – 3 God's promise to Abram has a sevenfold structure: (1) "I will make you into a great nation," (2) "I will bless you," (3) "I will make your name great," (4) "you will be a blessing," (5) "I will bless those who bless you," (6) "whoever curses you I will curse," and (7) "all peoples on earth will be blessed through you." God's original blessing on the whole human race (1:28) would be especially fulfilled in the lives of Abram and his offspring. In various ways and degrees, these promises were reaffirmed to Abram (v. 7; 15:5 – 21; 17:4 – 8; 18:18 – 19; 22:17 – 18), to Isaac (26:2 – 4), to Jacob (28:13 – 15; 35:11 – 12; 46:3) and to Moses (Ex 3:6 – 8; 6:2 – 8). The seventh promise is quoted in Ac 3:25 with reference to Peter's Jewish listeners (see Ac 3:12)—Abram's physical descendants—and in Gal 3:8 with reference to Paul's Gentile listeners—Abram's spiritual descendants.

ABRAM'S TRAVELS

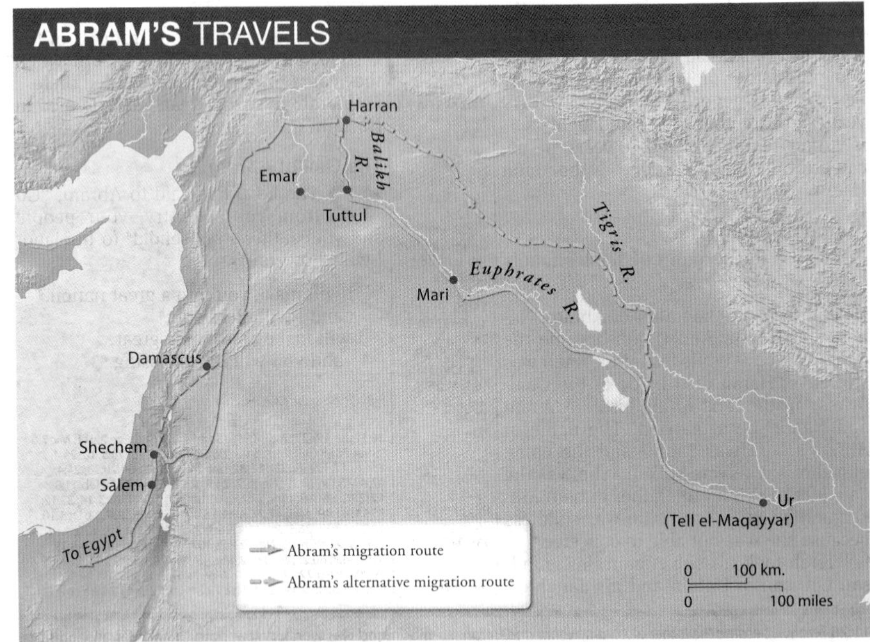

³I will bless those who bless you,
and whoever curses you I will curse;[j]
and all peoples on earth
will be blessed through you.[k]"[a]

⁴So Abram went, as the LORD had told
him; and Lot[l] went with him. Abram was
seventy-five years old[m] when he set out
from Harran.[n] ⁵He took his wife Sarai,[o] his
nephew Lot, all the possessions they had
accumulated[p] and the people[q] they had acquired in Harran, and they set out for the
land of Canaan,[r] and they arrived there.
⁶Abram traveled through the land[s] as
far as the site of the great tree of Moreh[t]
at Shechem.[u] At that time the Canaanites[v]
were in the land. ⁷The LORD appeared to
Abram[w] and said, "To your offspring[b] I will
give this land.[x]"[y] So he built an altar there
to the LORD,[z] who had appeared to him.
⁸From there he went on toward the hills
east of Bethel[a] and pitched his tent,[b] with

12:3 [j]Ge 27:29; Ex 23:22; Nu 24:9; Dt 30:7 [k]Ge 15:5; 18:18; 22:18; 26:4; 28:4,14; Dt 9:5; Ps 72:17; Isa 19:25; Ac 3:25; Gal 3:8* **12:4** [l]S Ge 11:27 [m]Ge 16:3,16; 17:1,17,24; 21:5 [n]S Ge 11:31 **12:5** [o]S Ge 11:29 [p]ver 16; Ge 13:2,6; 31:18; 46:6 [q]Ge 14:14; 15:3; 17:23; Ecc 2:7 [r]Ge 11:31; 16:3; Heb 11:8 **12:6** [s]Heb 11:9 [t]Ge 35:4; Dt 11:30; Jos 24:26; Jdg 7:1; 9:6 [u]Ge 33:18; 37:12; Jos 17:7; 20:7; 24:1; Jdg 8:31; 21:19; 1Ki 12:1; Ps 60:6; 108:7 [v]S Ge 10:18 **12:7** [w]Ge 17:1; 18:1; 26:2; 35:1; Ex 6:3; Ac 7:2 [x]Ex 3:8; Nu 10:29; Dt 30:5; Heb 11:8 [y]Ge 13:15,17; 15:18; 17:8; 23:18; 24:7; 26:3-4; 28:13; 35:12; 48:4; 50:24; Ex 6:4,8; 13:5, 11; 32:13; 33:1; Nu 11:12; Dt 1:8; 2:31; 9:5; 11:9; 34:4; 2Ki 25:21; 1Ch 16:16; 2Ch 20:7; Ps 105:9-11; Jer 25:5; Eze 47:14; Ac 7:5; Ro 4:13; Gal 3:16* [z]S Ge 8:20; 13:4 **12:8** [a]Ge 13:3; 28:11,19; 35:1,8,15; Jos 7:2; 8:9; 1Sa 7:16; 1Ki 12:29; Hos 12:4; Am 3:14; 4:4 [b]Ge 26:25; 33:19; Heb 11:9

[a] 3 Or *earth / will use your name in blessings* (see 48:20)
[b] 7 Or *seed*

12:3 *whoever curses you.* The ancient Near Eastern peoples thought that by pronouncing curses on someone they could bring down the power of the gods (or other mysterious powers) on that person (cf. 1Sa 17:43). They had a large conventional stock of such curses, preserved in many sources, such as the Egyptian Execration Texts, the Hittite suzerainty-vassal treaties, *kudurrus* (stone boundary markers), the Code of Hammurapi (Epilogue), etc. For examples, see notes on Dt 9:14; Jer 15:3; see also note on Ge 27:33; cf. note on Ezr 6:11.

12:4 *Abram went, as the LORD had told him.* See Heb 11:8. Prompt obedience grounded in faith characterized this patriarch throughout his life (see 17:23; 21:14; 22:3). *Lot went with him.* See 13:1,5. Lot chose to go with his uncle Abram, seeking a better future. *seventy-five years old.* Although advanced in age at the time of his call, Abram would live for another full century (see 25:7; see also note on 5:5).

12:5 *people they had acquired.* Wealthy people in that ancient world always had servants in their employ. Some were slaves, others were servants by choice; all were considered to be members of the "household" in which they served (see 14:14; 15:3; 17:12–13; 24:2).

12:6 *site of the great tree.* Perhaps the same tree referred to in 35:4 (see also Jdg 9:6,37). *Moreh.* The name means "teacher." It suggests that the Canaanites sought directions from their gods by this tree. Abram's God (Yahweh) appeared to him there (v. 7). *Shechem.* An important city in central Canaan, founded in the patriarchal period.

12:7 *The LORD appeared.* The Lord at times "appeared" in some way to the patriarchs and others, but not in all his glory (see Ex 33:18–20; Jn 1:18). *altar.* The first of several Abram built (see v. 8; 13:18; 22:9). He acknowledged that the land of Canaan belonged to the Lord in a special way (see Ex 20:24; Jos 22:19).

12:8 *Bethel.* Just north of Jerusalem (see map, p. 536), it was

Bethel on the west and Ai[c] on the east.
There he built an altar to the LORD and
called on the name of the LORD.[d]
9 Then Abram set out and continued toward the Negev.[e]

Abram in Egypt

12:10-20Ref — Ge 20:1-18; 26:1-11

10 Now there was a famine in the land,[f]
and Abram went down to Egypt to live
there for a while because the famine was
severe.[g] 11 As he was about to enter Egypt,
he said to his wife Sarai,[h] "I know what
a beautiful woman[i] you are. 12 When the
Egyptians see you, they will say, 'This is

12:8 [c] Jos 7:2; 12:9; Ezr 2:28; Ne 7:32; Jer 49:3 [d] S Ge 4:26; S 8:20 **12:9** [e] Ge 13:1, 3; 20:1; 24:62; Nu 13:17; 33:40; Dt 34:3; Jos 10:40 **12:10** [f] Ge 41:27. 57; 42:5; 43:1; 47:4, 13; Ru 1:1; 2Sa 21:1; 2Ki 8:1; Ps 105:19 [g] Ge 41:30, 54, 56; 47:20; Ps 105:16 **12:11** [h] S Ge 11:29 [i] ver 14; Ge 24:16; 26:7; 29:17; 39:6

---

an important town in the religious history of God's ancient people (see, e.g., 28:10 – 22; 35:1 – 8; 1Ki 12:26 – 29).

12:9 *Negev.* The dry wasteland stretching southward from Beersheba (see map, pp. 2516 – 2517, at the end of this study Bible). This Hebrew word is translated "south" in 13:14.

12:10 *went down to Egypt . . . because the famine was severe.* Egypt's food supply was usually plentiful because the Nile's water supply was normally dependable. Abram's experience in this episode foreshadows Israel's later experience in Egypt, as the author of Genesis, writing after the exodus, was very much aware. The parallels are striking: a famine in the land (here; 47:4); affliction at the hands of the Egyptians (vv. 12 – 15; Ex 1:11 – 14); God's plagues on the Egyptians (v. 17; Ex 8 – 11); the Egyptians sending the people away as a result (vv. 19 – 20; Ex 12:31 – 32); the Egyptians letting them take with them all their possessions (v. 20; Ex 12:32); the people obtaining wealth from the Egyptians (v. 16; Ex 12:36); return to Canaan by stages through the wilderness (13:1 – 3; Exodus; Numbers; Deuteronomy; Joshua); arrival back in Canaan, where they worship the Lord (13:4; Jos 5:10; 8:30 – 35; 24:1 – 27). Abram was truly the "father" of Israel.

12:11 *As he was about to enter Egypt.* Having left the promised land to find food in a time of famine (see Ru 1:1), but doing so without God's guidance or consent (see 46:3 – 4; 2Ki 8:1), Abram showed that he needed to learn that the God who had called him and made promises

INTEGRATED CHRONOLOGY OF THE PATRIARCHS

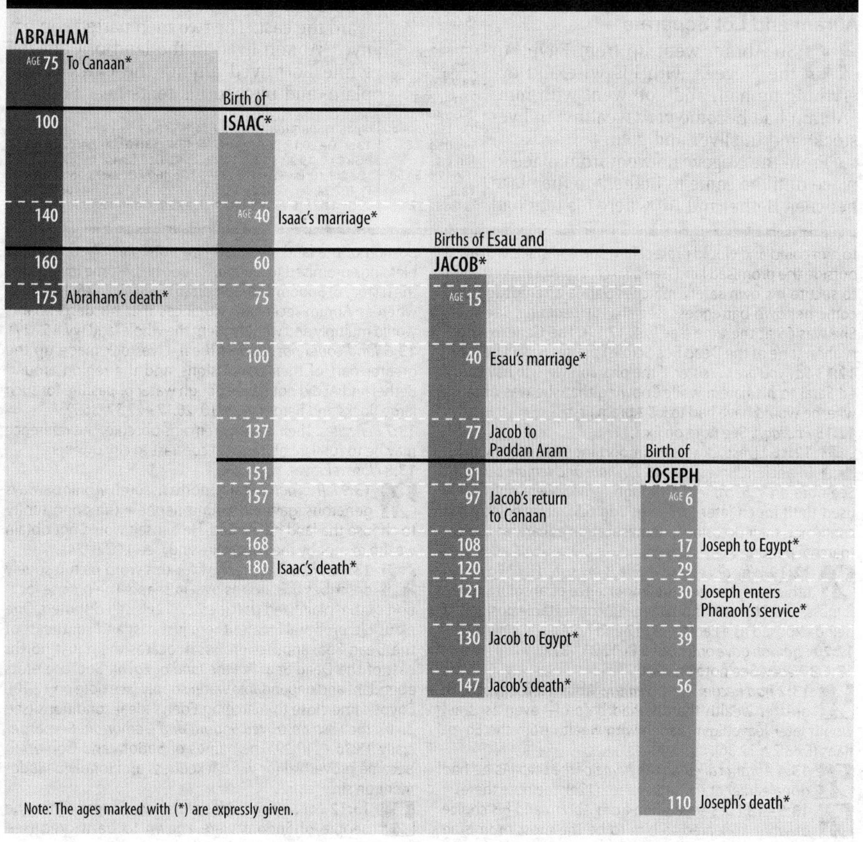

his wife.’ Then they will kill me but will let
you live. 13 Say you are my sister,[j] so that I
will be treated well for your sake and my
life will be spared because of you.”
14 When Abram came to Egypt, the
Egyptians saw that Sarai was a very beautiful woman.[k] 15 And when Pharaoh’s officials saw her, they praised her to Pharaoh, and she was taken into his palace.
16 He treated Abram well for her sake, and
Abram acquired sheep and cattle, male
and female donkeys, male and female servants, and camels.[l]
17 But the LORD inflicted[m] serious diseases on Pharaoh and his household[n] because
of Abram’s wife Sarai. 18 So Pharaoh summoned Abram. “What have you done to
me?”[o] he said. “Why didn’t you tell me
she was your wife?[p] 19 Why did you say,
‘She is my sister,’[q] so that I took her to
be my wife? Now then, here is your wife.
Take her and go!” 20 Then Pharaoh gave
orders about Abram to his men, and they
sent him on his way, with his wife and everything he had.

Abram and Lot Separate

13 So Abram went up from Egypt[r] to
the Negev,[s] with his wife and everything he had, and Lot[t] went with him.
2 Abram had become very wealthy[u] in livestock[v] and in silver and gold.
3 From the Negev[w] he went from place to
place until he came to Bethel,[x] to the place
between Bethel and Ai[y] where his tent had
been earlier 4 and where he had first built
an altar.[z] There Abram called on the name
of the LORD.[a]
5 Now Lot,[b] who was moving about
with Abram, also had flocks and herds
and tents. 6 But the land could not support
them while they stayed together, for their
possessions were so great that they were
not able to stay together.[c] 7 And quarreling[d]
arose between Abram’s herders and Lot’s.
The Canaanites[e] and Perizzites[f] were also
living in the land[g] at that time.
8 So Abram said to Lot,[h] “Let’s not have
any quarreling between you and me,[i] or
between your herders and mine, for we
are close relatives.[j] 9 Is not the whole land
before you? Let’s part company. If you go
to the left, I’ll go to the right; if you go to
the right, I’ll go to the left.”[k]
10 Lot looked around and saw that the
whole plain[l] of the Jordan toward Zoar[m]
was well watered, like the garden of the
LORD,[n] like the land of Egypt.[o] (This was
before the LORD destroyed Sodom[p] and Gomorrah.)[q] 11 So Lot chose for himself the
whole plain of the Jordan and set out toward the east. The two men parted company: 12 Abram lived in the land of Canaan,[r]
while Lot[s] lived among the cities of the
plain[t] and pitched his tents near Sodom.[u]

12:13 [j] Ge 20:2; 26:7 **12:14** [k] S ver 11 **12:16** [l] S ver 5; Ge 24:35; 26:14; 30:43; 32:5; 34:23; 47:17; Job 1:3; 31:25 **12:17** [m] 2Ki 15:5; Job 30:11; Isa 53:4, 10 [n] 1Ch 16:21; Ps 105:14 **12:18** [o] Ge 20:9; 26:10; 29:25; 31:26; 44:15 [p] Isa 43:27; 51:2; Eze 16:3 **12:19** [q] Ge 20:5; 26:9 **13:1** [r] Ge 45:25 [s] S Ge 12:9 [t] S Ge 11:27 **13:2** [u] S Ge 12:5; 26:13; Pr 10:22 [v] Ge 32:15; Job 1:3; 42:12 **13:3** [w] S Ge 12:9 [x] S Ge 12:8 [y] Jos 7:2 **13:4** [z] S Ge 12:7 [a] S Ge 4:26 **13:5** [b] S Ge 11:27 **13:6** [c] S Ge 12:5; 33:9; 36:7 **13:7** [d] Ge 26:20, 21; Nu 20:3 [e] S Ge 10:18 [f] Ge 15:20; 34:30; Ex 3:8; Jdg 1:4 [g] Ge 12:6; 34:30 **13:8** [h] S Ge 11:27 [i] Pr 15:18; 20:3 [j] Ge 19:9; Ex 2:14; Nu 16:13; Ps 133:1 **13:9** [k] Ge 20:15; 34:10; 47:6; Jer 40:4 **13:10** [l] 1Ki 7:46; 2Ch 4:17 [m] Ge 14:2; 19:22, 30; Nu 13:29; 33:48; Dt 34:3; Isa 15:5; Jer 48:34 [n] Ge 2:8-10; Isa 51:3; Eze 31:8-9 [o] Ge 46:7 [p] Dt 29:23; Job 39:6; Ps 107:34; Jer 4:26 [q] Ge 14:8; 19:17-29 **13:12** [r] S Ge 10:19 [s] S Ge 11:27 [t] S ver 10; Ge 19:17, 25, 29 [u] Ge 14:12

---

to him could and would protect him and Sarai (see v. 3) even outside the promised land (see also ch. 20). Abram’s attempt to secure his own safety matches Sarai’s attempt to overcome her own barrenness (see ch. 16). *beautiful.* See v. 14. She was 65 at the time (see v. 4; 17:17). The Genesis Apocryphon (one of the Dead Sea Scrolls) praises Sarai’s beauty.

12:13 *Say you are my sister.* If the pharaoh were to have added Sarai to his harem while knowing that she was Abram’s wife, he would have had to kill Abram first.

12:15 *Pharaoh.* See note on Ex 1:11.

12:16 Livestock was an important measure of wealth in ancient times (see 13:2). *male and female servants.* See note on v. 5. *camels.* Although camels were not widely used until much later (see, e.g., Jdg 6:5), archaeology has confirmed their occasional domestication as early as the patriarchal period.

12:19 *Why did you say, ‘She is my sister’ . . . ?* Egyptian ethics emphasized the importance of absolute truthfulness, and Abram was put in the uncomfortable position of being exposed as a liar (see 20:12 and note).

12:20 *Pharaoh gave orders.* See Ex 12:31 – 32.

13:1,3 *Negev.* See note on 12:9.

13:2 *had become very wealthy.* Abram left Egypt with greater wealth than he had before — even as Israel would later leave Egypt laden with wealth from the Egyptians (Ex 3:22; 12:36).

13:4 *Abram called on the name of the LORD.* As he had done earlier at the same place (12:8; see note there).

13:5 – 18 Lot’s separation from Abram and his choice of what appeared to him to be the most promising portion of the land alienated him from participating in the blessings promised to Abram. Rather, he became involved in the history of Sodom and Gomorrah (see 14:12 – 16; 19:1 – 38), whereas Abram received assurances that his descendants would multiply and would inherit the whole land (vv. 15 – 17).

13:6 *land could not support them.* Livestock made up the greater part of their possessions, and the region around Bethel and Ai did not have enough water or pasture for such large flocks and herds (see v. 10; 26:17 – 22,32; 36:7).

13:7 *Perizzites.* Their identity remains obscure, but reference may be to rural inhabitants, in contrast to city dwellers.

13:8 *close relatives.* See 12:5.

13:9 *left . . . right.* That is, north . . . south. Abram, always generous, gave his young nephew the opportunity to choose the land he wanted. He himself would not obtain wealth except by the Lord’s blessing (see 14:22 – 24).

13:10 *plain.* The Hebrew for this word picturesquely describes this area as oval in shape. The precise location of the “plain” and its “cities” (v. 12) is still disputed. One plausible proposal locates them just east and southeast of the Dead Sea; another proposal locates them just northeast of the Dead Sea. *like the land of Egypt.* Because of its abundant and dependable water supply (see note on 12:10), Egypt came close to matching Eden’s ideal conditions (see 2:10). *the LORD destroyed Sodom and Gomorrah.* See especially 18:16 — 19:29. The names of Sodom and Gomorrah became proverbial for vile wickedness and for divine judgment on sin.

13:12 *Lot . . . pitched his tents near Sodom.* Since the people of Sodom were known to be wicked (see

13 Now the people of Sodom[v] were wicked
and were sinning greatly against the LORD.[w]
14 The LORD said to Abram after Lot had
parted from him, "Look around from where
you are, to the north and south, to the east
and west.[x] 15 All the land that you see I will
give to you and your offspring[a] forever.[y] 16 I
will make your offspring like the dust of
the earth, so that if anyone could count the
dust, then your offspring could be counted.[z]
17 Go, walk through the length and breadth
of the land,[a] for I am giving it to you."[b]
18 So Abram went to live near the great
trees of Mamre[c] at Hebron,[d] where he
pitched his tents. There he built an altar
to the LORD.[e]

Abram Rescues Lot

14 At the time when Amraphel was
king of Shinar,[b][f] Arioch king of Ellasar, Kedorlaomer[g] king of Elam[h] and Tidal
king of Goyim, 2 these kings went to war
against Bera king of Sodom, Birsha king of
Gomorrah, Shinab king of Admah, Shem-
eber king of Zeboyim,[i] and the king of
Bela (that is, Zoar).[j] 3 All these latter kings
joined forces in the Valley of Siddim[k] (that
is, the Dead Sea Valley[l]). 4 For twelve years
they had been subject to Kedorlaomer,[m]
but in the thirteenth year they rebelled.
5 In the fourteenth year, Kedorlaomer[n]
and the kings allied with him went out
and defeated the Rephaites[o] in Ashteroth
Karnaim, the Zuzites in Ham, the Emites[p]
in Shaveh Kiriathaim 6 and the Horites[q] in
the hill country of Seir,[r] as far as El Paran[s]
near the desert. 7 Then they turned back
and went to En Mishpat (that is, Kadesh),[t]
and they conquered the whole territory of
the Amalekites,[u] as well as the Amorites[v]
who were living in Hazezon Tamar.[w]
8 Then the king of Sodom, the king of
Gomorrah,[x] the king of Admah, the king
of Zeboyim[y] and the king of Bela (that is,
Zoar)[z] marched out and drew up their battle lines in the Valley of Siddim[a] 9 against
Kedorlaomer[b] king of Elam,[c] Tidal king of
Goyim, Amraphel king of Shinar and Arioch king of Ellasar—four kings against
five. 10 Now the Valley of Siddim[d] was full
of tar[e] pits, and when the kings of Sodom
and Gomorrah[f] fled, some of the men fell
into them and the rest fled to the hills.[g]
11 The four kings seized all the goods[h] of
Sodom and Gomorrah and all their food;
then they went away. 12 They also carried
off Abram's nephew Lot[i] and his possessions, since he was living in Sodom.
13 A man who had escaped came and
reported this to Abram the Hebrew.[j] Now

13:13 [v]Ge 19:4; Isa 1:10; 3:9 [w]Ge 18:20; 19:5; 20:6; 39:9; Nu 32:23; 1Sa 12:23; 2Sa 12:13; Ps 51:4; Eze 16:49-50; 2Pe 2:8 **13:14** [x]Ge 28:14; 32:12; 48:16; Dt 3:27; 13:17; Isa 54:3 **13:15** [y]S Ge 12:7; Gal 3:16* **13:16** [z]S Ge 12:2; 16:10; 17:20; 21:13, 18; 25:16; Nu 23:10 **13:17** [a]ver 15; Nu 13:17-25 [b]S Ge 12:7; 15:7 **13:18** [c]Ge 14:13, 24; 18:1; 23:17, 19; 25:9; 49:30; 50:13 [d]Ge 23:2; 35:27; 37:14; Nu 13:22; Jos 10:3, 36; Jdg 1:10; 1Sa 30:31; 2Sa 2:1, 3, 11; 1Ch 11:1 [e]S Ge 8:20 **14:1** [f]S Ge 10:10 [g]ver 4, 9, 17 [h]S Ge 10:22 **14:2** [i]S Ge 10:19 [j]S Ge 13:10 **14:3** [k]ver 8, 10 [l]Nu 34:3, 12; Dt 3:17; Jos 3:16; 12:3; 15:2, 5; 18:19 **14:4** [m]S ver 1

[a] *15* Or *seed*; also in verse 16 [b] *1* That is, Babylonia; also in verse 9

14:5 [n]S ver 1 [o]Ge 15:20; Dt 2:11, 20; 3:11, 13; Jos 12:4; 13:12; 17:15; 1Ch 20:4 [p]Dt 2:10 **14:6** [q]Ge 36:20; Dt 2:12, 22 [r]Ge 32:3; 33:14, 16; 36:8; Dt 1:2; 2:1, 5, 22; Jos 11:17; 24:4; 1Ch 4:42; Isa 34:5; Eze 25:8; 35:2; Am 1:6 [s]Ge 21:21; Nu 10:12; 12:16; 13:3, 26; Hab 3:3 **14:7** [t]Ge 16:14; 20:1; Nu 13:26; 20:1; 32:8; Dt 1:2; Jos 10:41; Jdg 11:16; Ps 29:8 [u]Ex 17:8; Nu 13:29; 14:25; 24:20; Dt 25:17; Jdg 3:13; 6:3; 10:12; 12:15; 1Sa 14:48; 15:2; 28:18; 2Sa 1:1; 1Ch 4:43; Ps 83:7 [v]Nu 13:29; Dt 1:4; Jos 2:10; 13:4 [w]2Ch 20:2; Eze 48:28 **14:8** [x]S Ge 13:10 [y]Dt 29:23; Hos 11:8 [z]S Ge 13:10 [a]S ver 3 **14:9** [b]S ver 1 [c]S Ge 10:22 **14:10** [d]S ver 3 [e]Ge 11:3 [f]ver 17, 21 [g]Ge 19:17, 30; Jos 2:16; Ps 11:1 **14:11** [h]ver 16, 21 **14:12** [i]S Ge 11:27 **14:13** [j]Ge 37:28; 39:14, 17; 40:15; 41:12; 43:32; Ex 3:18; 1Sa 4:6; 14:11

v. 13), Lot was flirting with temptation by choosing to live near them. Contrast the actions of Abram (v. 18).

13:14 *Look around.* See Dt 34:1–4. Lot and Abram are a study in contrasts. The former looked selfishly and coveted (v. 10); the latter looked as God commanded and was blessed.

13:16 *like the dust of the earth.* A simile (common in the ancient Near East) for the large number of Abram's offspring (see 28:14; 2Ch 1:9; see also Nu 23:10). Similar phrases are: "as numerous as the stars in the sky" and "as the sand on the seashore" (22:17).

13:17 *walk through the length … of the land.* Either to inspect it or to claim the right to live in it while looking forward to the promised ownership (cf. Dt 32:48–49).

13:18 *great trees.* See note on 12:6. *Mamre.* A town named after one of Abram's allies (see 14:13). *Hebron.* Kiriath Arba (see note on 23:2). *altar.* See note on 12:7.

14:1–24 Abram's act of faith successfully challenged the foreign kings who were seeking to bring the promised land under their sphere of rule and enabled him to rescue his nephew Lot. It also won for him recognition among kings that he was a force to be reckoned with (see 12:2: "I will make your name great") and provided him with an opportunity to bear witness to his God.

14:1 *Amraphel was king of Shinar.* Not the great Babylonian king Hammurapi, as once thought. *Elam.* See note on 10:22. *Goyim.* The Hebrew word means "Gentile nations" and may be a common noun here (as in Isa 9:1).

14:3 *Dead Sea.* Lit. "Salt Sea." Its water contains an approximately five times greater concentration of chloride and bromide salts than the water in the world's oceans, making it the densest large body of water on earth.

14:5 *Rephaites.* People of large stature (see Dt 3:11).

14:6 *Horites.* Formerly thought to be cave dwellers (the Hebrew word *hor* means "cave"), they are now commonly identified with the Hurrians, a non-Semitic people widely dispersed throughout the ancient Near East.

14:7 *En Mishpat.* Another name for Kadesh, it means "spring of judgment/justice." It is called Meribah Kadesh, "quarreling/litigation at Kadesh," in Dt 32:51 (see Nu 27:14). *Kadesh.* Located in the southwest Negev (see note on 12:9), it was later called Kadesh Barnea (see Nu 32:8). *Amalekites.* A tribal people living in the Negev and in the Sinai peninsula. *Amorites.* See note on 10:16.

14:10 *tar pits.* Lumps of asphalt are often seen even today floating in the southern end of the Dead Sea. *hills.* The Dead Sea, the lowest body of water on earth (about 1,300 feet below sea level), is flanked by hills on both sides.

14:12 *Lot … was living in Sodom.* He moved into the town and was living among its wicked people (see 2Pe 2:8). Though Lot was "righteous," he was now in danger of imitating the "depraved conduct of the lawless" (2Pe 2:7).

14:13 *Hebrew.* Abram, the father of the Hebrew people, is the first Biblical character to be called a Hebrew (see "Eber" in note on 10:21). Usually an ethnic term

Abram was living near the great trees of
Mamre[k] the Amorite, a brother[a] of Eshkol[l]
and Aner, all of whom were allied with
Abram. 14 When Abram heard that his relative[m] had been taken captive, he called out
the 318 trained[n] men born in his household[o] and went in pursuit as far as Dan.[p]
15 During the night Abram divided his
men[q] to attack them and he routed them,
pursuing them as far as Hobah, north of
Damascus.[r] 16 He recovered[s] all the goods[t]
and brought back his relative Lot and his
possessions, together with the women and
the other people.

17 After Abram returned from defeating
Kedorlaomer[u] and the kings allied with
him, the king of Sodom[v] came out to meet
him in the Valley of Shaveh (that is, the
King's Valley).[w]

18 Then Melchizedek[x] king of Salem[y]
brought out bread[z] and wine.[a] He was
priest of God Most High,[b] 19 and he blessed
Abram,[c] saying,

"Blessed be Abram by God Most
High,[d]
Creator of heaven and earth.[e]
20 And praise be to God Most High,[f]
who delivered your enemies into
your hand."

Then Abram gave him a tenth of everything.[g]
21 The king of Sodom[h] said to Abram,
"Give me the people and keep the goods[i]
for yourself."

22 But Abram said to the king of Sodom,[j] "With raised hand[k] I have sworn an
oath to the LORD, God Most High,[l] Creator of heaven and earth,[m] 23 that I will accept nothing belonging to you,[n] not even a
thread or the strap of a sandal, so that you
will never be able to say, 'I made Abram
rich.' 24 I will accept nothing but what my
men have eaten and the share that belongs
to the men who went with me—to Aner,
Eshkol and Mamre.[o] Let them have their
share."

The LORD's Covenant With Abram

15 After this, the word of the LORD
came to Abram[p] in a vision:[q]

"Do not be afraid,[r] Abram.
I am your shield,[b][s]
your very great reward.[c][t]"

[a] 13 Or *a relative*; or *an ally* [b] 1 Or *sovereign*
[c] 1 Or *shield; / your reward will be very great*

14:13 [k] ver 24; S Ge 13:18 [l] Nu 13:23; 32:9; Dt 1:24 **14:14** [m] ver 12 [n] Dt 4:9; Pr 22:6 [o] S Ge 12:5 [p] Dt 34:1; Jdg 18:29; 1Ki 15:20 **14:15** [q] Jdg 7:16 [r] Ge 15:2; 2Sa 8:5; 1Ki 20:34; 2Ki 16:9; Isa 7:8; 8:4; 10:9; 17:1; Jer 49:23, 27; Eze 27:18; Am 1:3-5 **14:16** [s] 1Sa 30:8, 18 [t] S ver 11 **14:17** [u] S ver 1 [v] S ver 10 [w] 2Sa 18:18 **14:18** [x] Ps 110:4; Heb 5:6; 7:17, 21 [y] Ps 76:2; Heb 7:2 [z] S Ge 3:19 [a] Jdg 9:13; 19:19; Est 1:10; Ps 104:15; Pr 31:6; Ecc 10:19; SS 1:2 [b] ver 22; Ps 7:8, 17; Da 7:27 **14:19** [c] Heb 7:6 [d] ver 18 [e] ver 22; S Ge 1:1; 24:3; Jos 2:11; Ps 148:5; Mt 11:25 **14:20** [f] S Ge 9:26; S 24:27 [g] Ge 28:22; Dt 14:22; 26:12; Lk 18:12; Heb 7:4 **14:21** [h] S ver 10 [i] S ver 11 **14:22** [j] S ver 10 [k] Ex 6:8; Nu 14:30; Dt 32:40; Ne 9:15; Eze 20:5; Da 12:7; Rev 10:5-6 [l] S ver 18 [m] S ver 19 **14:23** [n] 1Sa 15:3, 19; 2Ki 5:16; Est 8:11; 9:10, 15 **14:24** [o] S Ge 13:18 **15:1** [p] 1Sa 15:10; 2Sa 7:4; 1Ki 6:11; 12:22; Jer 1:13; Eze 3:16; Da 10:1 [q] Ge 46:2; Nu 12:6; 24:4; Ru 1:20; Job 33:15 [r] Ge 21:17; 26:24; 46:3; Ex 14:13; 20:20; 2Ki 6:16; 2Ch 20:15, 17; Ps 27:1; Isa 7:4; 41:10, 13-14; 43:1, 5; Jer 1:8; Hag 2:5 [s] Dt 33:29; 2Sa 22:3, 31; Ps 3:3; 5:12; 18:2; 28:7; 33:20; 84:11; 119:114; 144:2; Pr 2:7; 30:5 [t] Ps 18:20; 37:25; 58:11; Isa 3:10

---

in the Bible, it was normally used by non-Israelites in a disparaging sense (see, e.g., 39:17). Outside the Bible, people known as the Hapiru/Apiru (a word probably related to the word "Hebrew") are referred to as a propertyless, dependent, immigrant (foreign) social class rather than as a specific ethnic group. Negative descriptions of them are given in the Amarna letters (clay tablets found in Egypt). *Mamre.* A town was named after him (see 13:18 and note).

14:14 *318 trained men born in his household.* A clear indication of Abram's great wealth. The Hebrew for "trained men" is found only here in the Bible. A related word used elsewhere in very ancient texts means "armed retainers." *Dan.* This well-known city in the north was not given the name "Dan" until the days of the judges (see Jdg 18:29). It was formerly called Laish or Leshem (see notes on Jos 19:47; Jdg 18:7). Thus the designation here is most likely a later editorial updating.

14:17 *King's Valley.* Near Jerusalem (see 2Sa 18:18).

14:18 *Melchizedek king of Salem … priest.* See Heb 7:1. In ancient times, particularly in non-Israelite circles, kingly and priestly duties were often performed by the same individual. "Melchizedek" means "My king is righteous" or "king of righteousness" (Heb 7:2). "Salem" is a shortened form of "Jerusalem" (Ps 76:2) and is related to the Hebrew word for "peace" (Heb 7:2; see Jos 10:1 and note). *bread and wine.* An ordinary meal (see Jdg 19:19), in no way related to the NT ordinance of communion. Melchizedek's interest in Abram's military success was most likely political, and his entertainment of victorious Abram with refreshment and a priestly benediction constituted a recognition that Abram was a man to be reckoned with in kingly affairs.

14:19 *God Most High, Creator of heaven and earth.* The titles "most high," "lord of heaven" and "creator of earth" were frequently applied to the chief Canaanite deity in ancient times. But Abram, by identifying Melchizedek's "God Most High" with "the LORD" (see v. 22), bore testimony to the one true God.

14:20 *Abram gave him a tenth of everything.* A tenth was a king's share (see 1Sa 8:15,17). By offering Melchizedek a tenth, Abram responded to Melchizedek's action by showing that he in turn acknowledged his kingship in Salem. At the same time, having recognized Melchizedek's blessing as a benediction from the Lord, Abram's tithe to Melchizedek constituted a declaration that he would be indebted to no king but the Lord (see v. 23 and note). Melchizedek is later spoken of as a type or prefiguration of Jesus, our "great high priest" (Heb 4:14), whose priesthood is therefore "in the order of Melchizedek, not in the order of Aaron" (Heb 7:11; see Ps 110:4).

14:22 *With raised hand.* A customary oath-taking practice in ancient times (see Dt 32:40; Rev 10:5–6).

14:23 *I will accept nothing belonging to you.* Cf. 2Ki 5:16. Abram refused to let himself become obligated to anyone but the Lord. If he had done so, this Canaanite king might later have claimed the right of kingship over Abram.

15:1–21 Here for the first time the Lord introduces a covenant into his relationship with Abram. In response to Abram's faltering faith, he graciously reinforces his promise (12:2–3) with a covenant oath.

15:1 *I am your shield.* Whether "shield" or "sovereign" is meant (see NIV text note), the reference is to the Lord as Abram's King. As elsewhere, "shield" stands for king (e.g., Dt 33:29; 2Sa 22:3; Ps 7:10; 84:9). *your very great reward.* Though Abram was quite rich (13:2; 14:23), God himself was Abram's greatest treasure (cf. Dt 10:9).

2 But Abram said, "Sovereign LORD,[u] what
can you give me since I remain childless[v]
and the one who will inherit[a] my estate is
Eliezer of Damascus?[w]" 3 And Abram said,
"You have given me no children; so a servant[x] in my household[y] will be my heir."
4 Then the word of the LORD came to
him: "This man will not be your heir, but
a son who is your own flesh and blood
will be your heir.[z]" 5 He took him outside
and said, "Look up at the sky and count
the stars[a]—if indeed you can count them."
Then he said to him, "So shall your offspring[b] be."[b]
6 Abram believed the LORD, and he credited it to him as righteousness.[c]
7 He also said to him, "I am the LORD,
who brought you out[d] of Ur of the Chaldeans[e] to give you this land to take possession of it."[f]
8 But Abram said, "Sovereign LORD,[g]
how can I know[h] that I will gain possession of it?"[i]
9 So the LORD said to him, "Bring me a
heifer,[j] a goat and a ram, each three years
old,[k] along with a dove and a young pigeon.[l]"
10 Abram brought all these to him, cut
them in two and arranged the halves opposite each other;[m] the birds, however, he
did not cut in half.[n] 11 Then birds of prey
came down on the carcasses,[o] but Abram
drove them away.

15:2 [u] ver 8; Isa 49:22; Jer 44:26; Eze 5:11; 16:48 [v] Ac 7:5 [w] S Ge 14:15 **15:3** [x] Ge 24:2, 34 [y] S Ge 12:5 **15:4** [z] Gal 4:28 **15:5** [a] Job 11:8; 35:5; Ps 8:3; 147:4; Jer 33:22 [b] S Ge 12:2; S Jer 30:19; Ro 4:18*; Heb 11:12 **15:6** [c] Ps 106:31; Ro 4:3*, 20-24*; Gal 3:6*; Jas 2:23* **15:7** [d] Ge 12:1; Ex 20:2; Ac 7:3; Heb 11:8 [e] S Ge 11:28; Ac 7:4 [f] S Ge 13:17; 17:8; 28:4; 35:12; 48:4; Ex 6:8; Dt 9:5 **15:8** [g] S ver 2 [h] Lk 1:18 [i] Dt 12:20; 19:8 **15:9** [j] Nu 19:2; Dt 21:3; Hos 4:16; Am 4:1 [k] 1Sa 1:24 [l] Lev 1:14; 5:7, 11; 12:8 **15:10** [m] ver 17; Jer 34:18 [n] Lev 1:17; 5:8 **15:11** [o] Dt 28:26; Jer 7:33 **15:12** [p] S Ge 2:21

12 As the sun was setting, Abram fell into
a deep sleep,[p] and a thick and dreadful
darkness came over him. 13 Then the LORD
said to him, "Know for certain that for four
hundred years[q] your descendants will be
strangers in a country not their own and
that they will be enslaved[r] and mistreated
there. 14 But I will punish the nation they
serve as slaves, and afterward they will
come out[s] with great possessions.[t] 15 You,
however, will go to your ancestors[u] in peace
and be buried at a good old age.[v] 16 In the
fourth generation[w] your descendants will
come back here,[x] for the sin of the Amorites[y] has not yet reached its full measure."
17 When the sun had set and darkness
had fallen, a smoking firepot with a blazing torch[z] appeared and passed between
the pieces.[a] 18 On that day the LORD made
a covenant with Abram[b] and said, "To
your descendants I give this land,[c] from
the Wadi[c] of Egypt[d] to the great river, the

[a] *2* The meaning of the Hebrew for this phrase is uncertain. [b] *5* Or *seed* [c] *18* Or *river*

15:13 [q] ver 16; Ex 12:40; Nu 20:15; Ac 7:6, 17; Gal 3:17 [r] Ex 1:11; 3:7; 5:6, 10-14, 18; 6:5; Dt 5:15; Job 3:18 **15:14** [s] Ge 50:24; Ex 3:8; 6:6-8; 12:25; Nu 10:29; Jos 1:2; Ac 7:7* [t] Ex 12:32-38 **15:15** [u] Ge 47:30; 49:29; Dt 31:16; 2Sa 7:12; 1Ki 1:21; Ps 49:19 [v] Ge 25:8; 35:29; Ex 23:26; Dt 34:7; Jos 14:11; Jdg 8:32; 1Ch 29:28; Job 5:26; 21:23; 42:17; Ps 91:16; Pr 3:16; 9:11; Isa 65:20 **15:16** [w] S ver 13; Ex 12:40 [x] Ge 28:15; 46:4; 48:21; 50:24; Ex 3:8, 17 [y] Lev 18:28; Jos 13:4; Jdg 10:11; 1Ki 21:26; 2Ki 16:3; 21:11; Eze 16:3 **15:17** [z] Jdg 7:16, 20; 15:4, 5 [a] S ver 10 **15:18** [b] Ge 17:2, 4, 7; Ex 6:4; 34:10, 27; 1Ch 16:16; Ps 105:9 [c] S Ge 12:7 [d] Nu 34:5; Jos 15:4, 47; 1Ki 8:65; 2Ki 24:7; 2Ch 7:8; Isa 27:12; Jer 37:5; 46:2; La 4:17; Eze 30:22; 47:19

15:2 *Eliezer of Damascus.* A servant probably acquired by Abram on his journey southward from Harran (see 12:5). He may also be the unnamed "senior servant" of 24:2.

15:3–4 Ancient documents uncovered at Nuzi (see chart, p. xxiv) near Kirkuk on a branch of the Tigris River, as well as at other places, demonstrate that a childless man could adopt one of his own male servants to be heir and guardian of his estate. Abram apparently contemplated doing this with Eliezer, or perhaps had already done so.

15:5 *count the stars—if indeed you can.* See 22:17. More than 8,000 stars are clearly visible to the naked eye in the darkness of a Near Eastern night. *So shall your offspring be.* The promise was initially fulfilled in Egypt (see Ex 1; see also Dt 1:10; Heb 11:12). Ultimately, all who belong to Christ are Abram's offspring (see Gal 3:29 and note).

15:6 Abram is the "father of all who believe" (Ro 4:11), and this verse is the first explicit reference to faith in God's promises (see Ro 4:3 and note). It also teaches that God graciously responds to faith by crediting righteousness to one who believes (see Heb 11:8 and note).

15:7 *I am the LORD, who brought you out.* Ancient royal covenants often began with (1) the self-identification of the king and (2) a brief historical prologue, as here (see Ex 20:2 and note).

15:8 *how can I know . . . ?* Cf. Lk 1:18. Abram believed God's promise of a son, but he asked for a guarantee of the promise of the land.

15:9–21 This expression of God's covenant with Abram was cast in the form of ancient Near Eastern royal land-grant treaties and contained a perpetual and unconditional divine promise to fulfill the grant of land to Abram and his descendants (1Ch 16:14–18; Ps 105:8–11). See chart, p. 23.

15:10 *birds . . . he did not cut in half.* Perhaps because they were so small (see Lev 1:17).

15:13 *four hundred years.* A round number. According to Ex 12:40 Israel spent 430 years in Egypt. *country not their own.* Egypt (see 46:3–4).

15:15 The fulfillment is recorded in 25:8.

15:16 *In the fourth generation.* That is, after 400 years (see v. 13). A "generation" was the age of a man when his firstborn son (from a legal standpoint) was born—in Abram's case, 100 years (see 21:5). *sin of the Amorites has not yet reached its full measure.* Just how sinful many Canaanite practices were is now known from archaeological artifacts and from their own epic literature, discovered at Ras Shamra (ancient Ugarit) on the north Syrian coast beginning in 1929 (see chart, p. xxiv). Their "worship" was polytheistic and included idolatry, religious prostitution, divination (cf. Dt 18:9–12) and at times even child sacrifice. God was patient in judgment, even with the wicked Canaanites.

15:17 *smoking firepot with a blazing torch.* Symbolizing the presence of God (see Ex 3:2; 14:24; 19:18; 1Ki 18:38; Ac 2:3–4). *passed between the pieces.* Of the slaughtered animals (v. 10). In ancient times the parties sometimes solemnized a covenant by walking down an aisle flanked by the pieces of slaughtered animals (see Jer 34:18–19). The practice signified a self-maledictory oath: "May it be so done to me if I do not keep my oath and pledge." Having credited Abram's faith as righteousness, God now graciously ministered to his need for assurance concerning the land. He granted Abram a promissory covenant, as he had to Noah (see 9:9 and note; see also chart, p. 23).

15:18 *made a covenant.* Lit. "cut a covenant," referring to the slaughtering of the animals (the same Hebrew verb is

Euphrates[e]— 19 the land of the Kenites,[f]
Kenizzites, Kadmonites, 20 Hittites,[g] Periz-
zites,[h] Rephaites,[i] 21 Amorites, Canaanites,
Girgashites and Jebusites."[j]

Hagar and Ishmael

16 Now Sarai,[k] Abram's wife, had
borne him no children.[l] But she
had an Egyptian slave[m] named Hagar;[n] 2 so
she said to Abram, "The LORD has kept me
from having children.[o] Go, sleep with my
slave; perhaps I can build a family through
her."[p]
Abram agreed to what Sarai said. 3 So
after Abram had been living in Canaan[q]
ten years,[r] Sarai his wife took her Egyptian
slave Hagar and gave her to her husband
to be his wife. 4 He slept with Hagar,[s] and
she conceived.
When she knew she was pregnant, she
began to despise her mistress.[t] 5 Then Sarai said to Abram, "You are responsible for
the wrong I am suffering. I put my slave in
your arms, and now that she knows she is
pregnant, she despises me. May the LORD
judge between you and me."[u]
6 "Your slave is in your hands,[v]" Abram
said. "Do with her whatever you think
best." Then Sarai mistreated[w] Hagar; so
she fled from her.
7 The angel of the LORD[x] found Hagar
near a spring[y] in the desert; it was the
spring that is beside the road to Shur.[z]
8 And he said, "Hagar,[a] slave of Sarai,
where have you come from, and where
are you going?"[b]
"I'm running away from my mistress Sarai," she answered.
9 Then the angel of the LORD told her,
"Go back to your mistress and submit to
her." 10 The angel added, "I will increase
your descendants so much that they will
be too numerous to count."[c]
11 The angel of the LORD[d] also said to her:

"You are now pregnant
and you will give birth to a son.[e]
You shall name him[f] Ishmael,*[a]*[g]
for the LORD has heard of your
misery.[h]
12 He will be a wild donkey[i] of a man;
his hand will be against
everyone
and everyone's hand against
him,
and he will live in hostility
toward*[b]* all his brothers.[j]"

a 11 *Ishmael* means *God hears.* *b* 12 Or *live to the east / of*

15:18 [e]S Ge 2:14 **15:19** [f]Nu 24:21; Jdg 1:16; 4:11, 17; 5:24; 1Sa 15:6; 27:10; 30:29; 1Ch 2:55 **15:20** [g]S Ge 10:15; S Dt 7:1 [h]S Ge 13:7 [i]S Ge 14:5 **15:21** [j]S Ge 10:16; Jos 3:10; 24:11; Ne 9:8 **16:1** [k]S Ge 11:29 [l]S Ge 11:30; Lk 1:7, 36; Gal 4:24-25 [m]Ge 21:9; 24:61; 29:24, 29; 31:33; 46:18 [n]ver 3-4, 8, 15; Ge 21:14; 25:12 **16:2** [o]Ge 29:31; 30:2 [p]Ge 19:32; 30:3-4, 9-10 **16:3** [q]S Ge 12:5 [r]S Ge 12:4 **16:4** [s]S ver 1 [t]Ge 30:1; 1Sa 1:6 **16:5** [u]Ge 31:53; Ex 5:21; Jdg 11:27; 1Sa 24:12, 15; 26:10, 23; Ps 50:6; 75:7 **16:6** [v]Jos 9:25 [w]Ge 31:50 **16:7** [x]ver 11; Ge 21:17; 22:11, 15; 24:7, 40; 31:11; 48:16; Ex 3:2; 14:19; 23:20, 23; 32:34; 33:2; Nu 22:22; Jdg 2:1; 6:11; 13:3; 2Sa 24:16; 1Ki 19:5; 2Ki 1:3; 19:35; Ps 34:7; Zec 1:11; S Ac 5:19 [y]ver 14; Ge 21:19 [z]Ge 20:1; 25:18; Ex 15:22; 1Sa 15:7; 27:8 **16:8** [a]S ver 1 [b]S Ge 3:9 **16:10** [c]S Ge 13:16 **16:11** [d]S ver 7; S Ac 5:19 [e]S Ge 3:15 [f]Ge 12:2-3; 18:19; Ne 9:7; Isa 44:1; Am 3:2; Mt 1:21; Lk 1:13, 31 [g]Ge 17:19; 21:3; 37:25, 28; 39:1; Jdg 8:24 [h]Ge 29:32; 31:42; Ex 2:24; 3:7, 9; 4:31; Nu 20:16; Dt 26:7; 1Sa 9:16 **16:12** [i]Job 6:5; 11:12; 24:5; 39:5; Ps 104:11; Jer 2:24; Hos 8:9 [j]Ge 25:18

---

translated "made" and "cut" in Jer 34:18). *I give this land.* The Lord initially fulfilled this covenant through Joshua (see Jos 1:2–9; 21:43; see also 1Ki 4:20–21). *Wadi of Egypt.* Probably the modern Wadi el-Arish in northeastern Sinai (see map, p. 117). *Euphrates.* The longest river in western Asia (about 1,700 miles). It marked the boundary between Israel and Israel's historic enemies (Assyria and Babylonia) to the east and northeast (cf. Isa 8:5–8).

15:19–21 A similar list associated with Canaan is found in 10:15–18 (see notes there). Here ten peoples are listed, the number ten signifying completeness. For other lists of the inhabitants of Canaan, see Ex 3:8,17; 13:5; 23:23; 33:2; 34:11; Nu 13:29; Dt 7:1; 20:17; Jos 3:10; 9:1; 11:3; 12:8; 24:11; Jdg 3:5; 1Ch 1:14; 2Ch 8:7; Ezr 9:1; Ne 9:8.

16:1–15 A failure in faith leads to a brazen attempt to provide by human means what the Lord is accused of withholding. Sarai at the beginning (v. 2) and Abram at the end ("Ishmael"; see v. 15 and NIV text note on v. 11) express their mutual impatience with the Lord's failure as yet to overcome Sarai's barrenness.

16:1 *no children.* See note on 11:30. *Egyptian.* Perhaps Hagar was acquired while Abram and Sarai were in Egypt (see 12:10–20).

16:2 *The LORD has kept me from having children.* Some time had passed since the revelation of 15:4 (see 16:3), and Sarai impatiently implied that God was not keeping his promise. *Go, sleep with my slave.* An ancient custom, illustrated in Old Assyrian marriage contracts, the Code of Hammurapi and the Nuzi tablets (see note on 15:3–4), to ensure the birth of a male heir.

16:3 *ten years.* Abram was now 85 years old (see 12:4; 16:16).

16:4 *despise her mistress.* Peninnah acted similarly toward Hannah (see 1Sa 1:6).

16:5 *May the LORD judge between you and me.* An expression of hostility or suspicion (see 31:53; see also 31:49 and note).

16:7 *The angel of the LORD.* Since the angel of the Lord speaks for God in the first person (v. 10) and Hagar is said to name "the LORD who spoke to her: 'You are the God who sees me'" (v. 13), the angel appears to be both distinguished from the Lord (in that he is called "messenger"—the Hebrew for "angel" means "messenger") and identified with him (see also 48:16). Similar distinction and identification can be found in 19:1,21; 31:11,13; Ex 3:2,4; Jdg 2:1–5; 6:11–12,14; 13:3,6, 8–11,13,15–17,20–23; Zec 3:1–6; 12:8. Traditional Christian interpretation has held that this "angel" was a preincarnate manifestation of Christ as God's Messenger-Servant. It may be, however, that, as the Lord's personal messenger who represented him and bore his credentials, the angel could speak on behalf of (and so be identified with) the One who sent him (see especially 19:21; cf. 18:2,22; 19:2). Whether this "angel" was the second person of the Trinity remains therefore uncertain (cf. Lk 2:9 and note). *Shur.* Located just east of Lower Egypt (see 25:18; 1Sa 15:7).

16:8 *I'm running away from my mistress.* Not yet knowing exactly where she was going, Hagar answered only the first of the angel's questions.

16:10 A promise reaffirmed in 17:20 and fulfilled in 25:13–16.

16:11 *Ishmael.* See NIV text note and 17:20.

16:12 *wild donkey.* Probably the onager, which roamed the dry steppes of the Near East. Ishmael would roam the desert like a wild donkey (see Job 24:5; Hos 8:9). *hostility.* The hostility between Sarai and Hagar (see vv. 4–6) was passed on to their descendants (see 25:18).

13 She gave this name to the LORD who
spoke to her: "You are the God who sees
me,[k]" for she said, "I have now seen[a] the
One who sees me."[l] 14 That is why the
well[m] was called Beer Lahai Roi[b];[n] it is still
there, between Kadesh[o] and Bered.
15 So Hagar[p] bore Abram a son,[q] and
Abram gave the name Ishmael[r] to the son
she had borne. 16 Abram was eighty-six
years old[s] when Hagar bore him Ishmael.

The Covenant of Circumcision

17 When Abram was ninety-nine
years old,[t] the LORD appeared to
him[u] and said, "I am God Almighty[c];[v] walk
before me faithfully and be blameless.[w]
2 Then I will make my covenant between
me and you[x] and will greatly increase your
numbers."[y]
3 Abram fell facedown,[z] and God said
to him, 4 "As for me, this is my covenant
with you:[a] You will be the father of many
nations.[b] 5 No longer will you be called
Abram[d]; your name will be Abraham,[e][c] for
I have made you a father of many nations.[d]
6 I will make you very fruitful;[e] I will make
nations of you, and kings will come from
you.[f] 7 I will establish my covenant[g] as an
everlasting covenant[h] between me and you
and your descendants after you for the generations to come, to be your God[i] and the
God of your descendants after you.[j] 8 The
whole land of Canaan,[k] where you now reside as a foreigner,[l] I will give as an everlasting possession to you and your descendants after you;[m] and I will be their God.[n]"
9 Then God said to Abraham, "As for
you, you must keep my covenant,[o] you
and your descendants after you for the
generations to come.[p] 10 This is my covenant with you and your descendants after
you, the covenant you are to keep: Every
male among you shall be circumcised.[q]

16:13 [k] Ps 139:1-12 [l] Ge 32:30; 33:10; Ex 24:10; 33:20,23; Nu 12:8; Jdg 6:22; 13:22; Isa 6:5 **16:14** [m] S ver 7 [n] Ge 24:62; 25:11 [o] S Ge 14:7 **16:15** [p] S ver 1 [q] Ge 21:9; Gal 4:22 [r] Ge 17:18; 25:12; 28:9 **16:16** [s] S Ge 12:4 **17:1** [t] S Ge 12:4 [u] S Ge 12:7 [v] Ge 28:3; 35:11; 43:14; 48:3; 49:25; Ex 6:3; Ru 1:20; Job 5:17; 6:4, 14; 22:21; 33:19; 36:16; Isa 13:6; Joel 1:15; Mic 6:9 [w] S Ge 5:22; 20:5; Dt 18:13; 1Ki 3:6; 9:4; Job 1:1; Ps 15:2; 18:23; 78:72; 101:2 **17:2** [x] S Ge 15:18; S 22:16-18 [y] S Ge 12:2

[a] 13 Or *seen the back of* [b] 14 *Beer Lahai Roi* means *well of the Living One who sees me.* [c] 1 Hebrew *El-Shaddai* [d] 5 *Abram* means *exalted father.* [e] 5 *Abraham* probably means *father of many.*

17:3 [z] ver 17; Ge 18:2; 19:1; 33:3; Ex 18:7; Nu 14:5; Jos 5:14; 7:6; Jdg 13:20; Eze 1:28; 3:23 **17:4** [a] S Ge 15:18 [b] ver 16; S Ge 12:2; 25:23 **17:5** [c] ver 15; Ge 32:28; 35:10; 37:3,13; 43:6; 46:2; 1Ki 18:31; 2Ki 17:34; 1Ch 1:34; Ne 9:7; Isa 48:1; S Jn 1:42 [d] Ro 4:17* **17:6** [e] Ge 1:28; 22:17; 26:22; 28:3; 35:11; 41:52; 47:27; 48:4; 49:22; Lev 26:9; Dt 7:13 [f] ver 16,19; Ge 18:10; 21:1; 36:31; Isa 51:2; Mt 1:6 **17:7** [g] S Ge 6:18; S Ge 15:18; Lev 26:9,15 [h] S Ge 9:16; S Heb 13:20 [i] Ex 6:7; 20:2; 29:45,46; Lev 11:44-45; 18:2; 22:33; 25:38; 26:12, 45; Nu 15:41; Dt 4:20; 7:6,21; 29:13; 2Sa 7:24; Jer 14:9; Rev 21:7 [j] Ro 9:8; Gal 3:16 **17:8** [k] S Ge 10:19 [l] Ge 23:4; 28:4; 35:27; 37:1; Ex 6:4; 1Ch 29:15 [m] S Ge 12:7; S 15:7 [n] S ver 7; Jer 31:1 **17:9** [o] Ge 22:18; Ex 19:5; Dt 5:2 [p] Ge 18:19 **17:10** [q] ver 23; Ge 21:4; Lev 12:3; Jos 5:2,5,7; Jn 7:22; Ac 7:8; Ro 4:11

16:13 *I have now seen the One who sees me.* See NIV text note and cf. Ex 33:23. To see God's face was believed to bring death (see 32:30; Ex 33:20).

16:14 *Beer Lahai Roi.* See NIV text note. Another possible translation that fits the context equally well is: "well of the one who sees me and who lives," i.e., Hagar. *Kadesh.* See note on 14:7.

17:1–27 God's covenant with Abram renewed and expanded (see chart, p. 23). After Abram's and Sarai's attempt to obtain the promised offspring by using the womb of Sarai's servant, God appears to Abram to reaffirm his promises. But he also makes it clear that if Abram is to receive God's covenanted benefits, he must live out the "obedience that comes from faith for his name's sake" (Ro 1:5; see also Ge 22). To that end he calls on Abram to make with him a covenanted commitment of loyal obedience.

17:1 *ninety-nine years old.* Thirteen years had passed since Ishmael's birth (see 16:16; 17:24–25). *appeared.* See note on 12:7. *I am.* See note on 15:7. *God Almighty.* The Hebrew (*El-Shaddai*) perhaps means "God, the Mountain One," either highlighting the invincible power of God or referring to the mountains as God's symbolic home (see Ps 121:1). It was the special name by which God revealed himself to the patriarchs (see Ex 6:3). *Shaddai* occurs 31 times in the book of Job and 17 times in the rest of the Bible. *walk before me faithfully and be blameless.* Perhaps equivalent to "walk *with* me faithfully and be blameless" (see notes on 5:22; 6:8–9).

17:2 *my covenant.* See 15:4–5. The covenant is God's; he calls it "my covenant" nine times in vv. 2–21, and he initiates (see 15:18), confirms (v. 2) and establishes (v. 7) it. *increase your numbers.* The language echoes 1:28 (Adam) and 9:7 (Noah), suggesting that God's original purpose for humankind, threatened by the sins of the race, will be achieved through Abraham and his descendants (see also Ex 1:7 and note). See 13:16 and note. Earlier God had covenanted to keep his promise concerning the land (ch. 15); here he broadens his covenant to include the promised offspring.

17:5 *Abram ... Abraham.* See NIV text notes. The first name means "Exalted Father," probably in reference to God (i.e., "[God is] Exalted Father"); the second probably means "father of many," in reference to Abraham. *your name will be.* By giving Abram a new name (see Ne 9:7) God marked him in a special way as his servant (see notes on 1:5; 2:19).

17:6 *nations ... kings.* This promise also came to Sarah (v. 16) and was renewed to Jacob (35:11; see 48:19). It referred to the proliferation of Abraham's offspring, who, like the descendants of Noah (see ch. 10), would someday become many nations and spread over the earth. Ultimately it finds fulfillment in such passages as Ro 4:16–18; 15:8–12; Gal 3:29; Rev 7:9; 21:24.

17:7 *everlasting.* God's commitment to his covenant was forever (see vv. 13,19), but descendants of Abraham could break it (see v. 14; cf. Isa 24:5; Jer 31:32). *to be your God.* The heart of God's covenant promise, repeated over and over in the OT (see, e.g., v. 8; Jer 24:7; 31:33; Eze 34:30–31; Hos 2:23; Zec 8:8 and note). This is God's pledge to be the protector of his people and the One who provides for their well-being and guarantees their future blessing (see 15:1).

17:8 *land.* See 12:7; 15:18; Ac 7:5. *everlasting possession.* The land, though an everlasting possession given by God, could be temporarily lost because of disobedience (see Dt 28:62–63; 30:1–10).

17:9 *As for you.* Balances the "as for me" of v. 4 (cf. also vv. 15,20). Having reviewed his covenanted commitment to Abraham (see 15:8–21), and having broadened it to include the promise of offspring, God now called upon Abraham to make a covenanted commitment to him—to "walk before me faithfully and be blameless" (v. 1). *keep my covenant.* Participation in the blessings of the Abrahamic covenant was conditioned on obedience (see 18:19; 22:18; 26:4–5).

17:10 *circumcised.* Circumcision was God's appointed "sign of the covenant" (v. 11), which signified Abraham's covenanted commitment to the Lord—that the Lord alone would be his God, whom he would trust and serve.

11 You are to undergo circumcision,[r] and it
will be the sign of the covenant[s] between
me and you. 12 For the generations to
come[t] every male among you who is eight
days old must be circumcised,[u] including
those born in your household or bought
with money from a foreigner — those who
are not your offspring. 13 Whether born
in your household or bought with your
money, they must be circumcised.[v] My
covenant in your flesh is to be an everlasting covenant.[w] 14 Any uncircumcised
male, who has not been circumcised[x] in
the flesh, will be cut off from his people;[y]
he has broken my covenant.[z]"
15 God also said to Abraham, "As for Sarai[a] your wife, you are no longer to call
her Sarai; her name will be Sarah.[b] 16 I will
bless her and will surely give you a son by
her.[c] I will bless her so that she will be the
mother of nations;[d] kings of peoples will
come from her."
17 Abraham fell facedown;[e] he laughed[f]
and said to himself, "Will a son be born
to a man a hundred years old?[g] Will Sarah
bear a child at the age of ninety?"[h] 18 And
Abraham said to God, "If only Ishmael[i]
might live under your blessing!"[j]
19 Then God said, "Yes, but your wife
Sarah will bear you a son,[k] and you will
call him Isaac.[a][l] I will establish my covenant with him[m] as an everlasting covenant[n] for his descendants after him.
20 And as for Ishmael, I have heard you:
I will surely bless him; I will make him
fruitful and will greatly increase his numbers.[o] He will be the father of twelve rulers,[p] and I will make him into a great nation.[q] 21 But my covenant[r] I will establish
with Isaac, whom Sarah will bear to you[s]
by this time next year."[t] 22 When he had
finished speaking with Abraham, God
went up from him.[u]
23 On that very day Abraham took his
son Ishmael and all those born in his
household[v] or bought with his money,
every male in his household, and circumcised them, as God told him.[w] 24 Abraham
was ninety-nine years old[x] when he was
circumcised,[y] 25 and his son Ishmael[z] was
thirteen; 26 Abraham and his son Ishmael
were both circumcised on that very day.
27 And every male in Abraham's household[a], including those born in his household or bought from a foreigner, was circumcised with him.

The Three Visitors

18 The LORD appeared to Abraham[b]
near the great trees of Mamre[c]
while he was sitting at the entrance to
his tent[d] in the heat of the day. 2 Abraham
looked up[e] and saw three men[f] standing
nearby. When he saw them, he hurried

17:11 [r]Ex 12:48; Dt 10:16 [s]S Ge 9:12; Ro 4:11 **17:12** [t]S Ge 9:12 [u]Ge 21:4; Lev 12:3; Jos 5:2; S Lk 1:59 **17:13** [v]Ex 12:44, 48 [w]S Ge 9:16 **17:14** [x]ver 23 [y]Ex 4:24-26; 12:15, 19; 30:33; Lev 7:20, 25; 17:4; 18:29; 19:8; 20:17; Nu 9:13; 15:30; 19:13; Dt 17:12; Jos 5:2-8; Job 38:15; Ps 37:28 [z]Eze 44:7 **17:15** [a]S Ge 11:29 [b]S ver 5 **17:16** [c]S ver 6; S Isa 29:22 [d]S ver 4; Ge 24:60; Gal 4:31 **17:17** [e]S ver 3 [f]Ge 18:12; 21:6 [g]S Ge 12:4 [h]Ge 18:11, 13; 21:7; 24:1, 36; Jer 20:15; Lk 1:18; Ro 4:19; Gal 4:23; Heb 11:11 **17:18** [i]S Ge 16:15 [j]Ge 21:11 **17:19** [k]S ver 6, 21; Ge 18:14; 21:2; 1Sa 1:20 [l]S Ge 16:11; Mt 1:21; Lk 1:13, 31 [m]Ge 26:3; 50:24; Ex 13:11; Dt 1:8 [n]S Ge 9:16; S Gal 3:16 **17:20** [o]S Ge 13:16 [p]Ge 25:12-16 [q]Ge 25:18; 48:19 **17:21** [r]Ex 34:10 [s]S ver 19 [t]Ge 18:10, 14 **17:22** [u]Ge 18:33; 35:13; Nu 12:9 **17:23** [v]S Ge 12:5 [w]S ver 10, S 14 **17:24** [x]S Ge 12:4 [y]Ro 4:11 **17:25** [z]Ge 16:16 **17:27** [a]Ge 14:14 **18:1** [b]S Ge 12:7; Ac 7:2 [c]S Ge 13:18 [d]Ge 19:1; 23:10, 18; 34:20, 24; Ru 4:1; Ps 69:12; Heb 11:9 **18:2** [e]Ge 24:63 [f]ver 16, 22; Ge 19:1, 10; 32:24; Jos 5:13; Jdg 13:6-11; Hos 12:3-4; Heb 13:2

[a] 19 *Isaac* means *he laughs.*

It symbolized a self-maledictory oath: "If I am not loyal in faith and obedience to the Lord, may the sword of the Lord cut off me and my offspring [see v. 14] as I have cut off my foreskin" (analogous to the oath to which God had submitted himself; see note on 15:17). Thus Abraham was to place himself under the rule of the Lord as his King, consecrating himself, his offspring and all he possessed to the service of the Lord. For circumcision as signifying consecration to the Lord, see Dt 10:16; 30:6; Jer 4:4; 9:25 – 26; Eze 44:7 and note; 44:9; cf. Ro 2:29. Other nations also practiced circumcision (see Jer 9:25 – 26; Eze 32:18 – 19), but not for the covenant reasons that Israel did.

17:11 *sign of the covenant.* See notes on 9:12; 15:17. As the covenant sign, circumcision also (see note on v. 10) marked Abraham as the one to whom God had made covenant commitment (15:7 – 21) in response to Abraham's faith, which he "credited ... to him as righteousness" (15:6). Paul comments on this aspect of the covenant sign in Ro 4:11.

17:12 *eight days old.* See 21:4 and Ac 7:8 (Isaac); Lk 1:59 (John the Baptist); 2:21 (Jesus); Php 3:5 (Paul). Abraham was 99 years old when the newly initiated rite of circumcision was performed on him (see v. 24). The Arabs, who consider themselves descendants of Ishmael, are circumcised at the age of 13 (see v. 25). For them, as for other peoples, circumcision serves as a rite of transition from childhood to manhood, thus into full participation in the community.

17:14 *cut off from his people.* Removed from the covenant people by divine judgment (see note on v. 10).

17:15 *Sarai ... Sarah.* Both names evidently mean "princess." The renaming stressed that she was to be the mother of nations and kings (see v. 16) and thus to serve the Lord's purpose (see note on v. 5).

17:16 *son.* Fulfilled in Isaac (see 21:2 – 3).

17:17 *laughed.* In temporary disbelief (see 18:12; cf. Ro 4:19 – 21). The verb is a pun on the name "Isaac," which means "he laughs" (see NIV text notes on v. 19 and 21:3; see also 18:12 – 15; 21:6).

17:20 *numbers.* See note on 13:16. *father of twelve rulers.* Fulfilled in 25:16.

17:21 Paul cites the choice of Isaac (and not Ishmael) as one proof of God's sovereign right to choose to save by grace alone (see Ro 9:6 – 13). *by this time next year.* See 21:2.

17:22 *God went up from him.* A solemn conclusion to the conversation.

17:23 *On that very day.* Abraham was characterized by prompt obedience (see note on 12:4).

18:1 – 33 God appears to Abraham with two representatives (identified as "angels" in 19:1) of his heavenly council (see 1Ki 22:19 – 22 and note on 22:19; Jer 23:18,22 and note on 23:18). He comes to announce to Abraham what he is about to do (see note on v. 17).

18:1 *appeared.* See note on 12:7. *great trees.* See note on 12:6. *Mamre.* See note on 13:18. *heat of the day.* Early afternoon.

18:2 *three men.* Two of the "men" were angels (see 19:1; see also note on 16:7). The third was the Lord himself (see vv. 1,13,17,20,26,33; see especially v. 22). *hurried.* The story in

from the entrance of his tent to meet them
and bowed low to the ground.[g]
3 He said, "If I have found favor in your
eyes,[h] my lord,[a] do not pass your servant[i]
by. 4 Let a little water be brought, and then
you may all wash your feet[j] and rest under this tree. 5 Let me get you something to
eat,[k] so you can be refreshed and then go
on your way—now that you have come to
your servant."
"Very well," they answered, "do as you
say."
6 So Abraham hurried into the tent to
Sarah. "Quick," he said, "get three seahs[b]
of the finest flour and knead it and bake
some bread."[l]
7 Then he ran to the herd and selected
a choice, tender calf[m] and gave it to a servant, who hurried to prepare it. 8 He then
brought some curds[n] and milk[o] and the
calf that had been prepared, and set these
before them.[p] While they ate, he stood
near them under a tree.
9 "Where is your wife Sarah?"[q] they
asked him.
"There, in the tent,[r]" he said.
10 Then one of them said, "I will surely
return to you about this time next year,[s]
and Sarah your wife will have a son."[t]
Now Sarah was listening at the entrance to the tent, which was behind him.
11 Abraham and Sarah were already very
old,[u] and Sarah was past the age of childbearing.[v] 12 So Sarah laughed[w] to herself as
she thought, "After I am worn out and my
lord[x] is old, will I now have this pleasure?"
13 Then the LORD said to Abraham, "Why
did Sarah laugh and say, 'Will I really have
a child, now that I am old?'[y] 14 Is anything
too hard for the LORD?[z] I will return to you
at the appointed time next year,[a] and Sarah will have a son."[b]
15 Sarah was afraid, so she lied and said,
"I did not laugh."
But he said, "Yes, you did laugh."

Abraham Pleads for Sodom

16 When the men[c] got up to leave, they
looked down toward Sodom, and Abraham walked along with them to see them
on their way. 17 Then the LORD said, "Shall
I hide from Abraham[d] what I am about to
do?[e] 18 Abraham will surely become a great
and powerful nation,[f] and all nations on
earth will be blessed through him.[c] 19 For
I have chosen him[g], so that he will direct
his children[h] and his household after him
to keep the way of the LORD[i] by doing
what is right and just,[j] so that the LORD
will bring about for Abraham what he has
promised him."[k]
20 Then the LORD said, "The outcry
against Sodom[l] and Gomorrah is so great[m]
and their sin so grievous[n] 21 that I will go
down[o] and see if what they have done is
as bad as the outcry that has reached me.
If not, I will know."

[a] 3 Or *eyes, Lord* [b] 6 That is, probably about 36 pounds or about 16 kilograms [c] 18 Or *will use his name in blessings* (see 48:20)

18:2 [g] S Ge 17:3; S 43:28 **18:3** [h] Ge 19:19; 39:4; Ru 2:2, 10, 13; 1Sa 1:18; Est 2:15 [i] Ge 32:4, 18, 20; 33:5 **18:4** [j] Ge 19:2; 24:32; 43:24; Jdg 19:21; 2Sa 11:8; S Lk 7:44 **18:5** [k] Jdg 13:15; 19:5 **18:6** [l] Ge 19:3; 2Sa 13:8 **18:7** [m] 1Sa 28:24; Lk 15:23 **18:8** [n] Isa 7:15, 22 [o] Jdg 4:19; 5:25 [p] Jdg 6:19 **18:9** [q] S Ge 3:9 [r] Ge 24:67; Heb 11:9 **18:10** [s] S Ge 17:21; 21:2; 2Ki 4:16 [t] S Ge 17:6; Ro 9:9* **18:11** [u] S Ge 17:17; Lk 1:18 [v] S Ge 11:30; Ro 4:19; Heb 11:11-12 **18:12** [w] S Ge 17:17 [x] 1Pe 3:6 **18:13** [y] S Ge 17:17 **18:14** [z] Job 42:2; Isa 40:29; 50:2; 51:9; Jer 32:17, 27; S Mt 19:26; Ro 4:21 [a] S ver 10 [b] S Ge 17:19; Ro 9:9*; Gal 4:23 **18:16** [c] S ver 2 **18:17** [d] Am 3:7 [e] Ge 19:24; Job 1:16; Ps 107:34 **18:18** [f] S Ge 12:2; Gal 3:8* **18:19** [g] Ge 17:9 [h] Dt 4:9-10; 6:7 [i] Jos 24:15; Eph 6:4 [j] Ge 22:12, 18; 26:5; 2Sa 8:15; Ps 17:2; 99:4; Jer 23:5 [k] S Ge 16:11; S Isa 14:1 **18:20** [l] Isa 1:10; Jer 23:14; Eze 16:46 [m] Ge 19:13 [n] S Ge 13:13 **18:21** [o] S Ge 11:5

vv. 2–8 illustrates Near Eastern hospitality in several ways: (1) Abraham gave prompt attention to the needs of his guests (vv. 2,6–7). (2) He bowed low to the ground (v. 2). (3) He politely addressed one of his guests as "my lord" and called himself "your servant" (vv. 3,5), a common way of speaking when addressing a superior (see, e.g., 19:2,18–19). (4) He acted as if it would be a favor to him if they allowed him to serve them (vv. 3–5). (5) He asked that water be brought to wash their feet (see v. 4), an act of courtesy to refresh a traveler in a hot, dusty climate (see 19:2; 24:32; 43:24). (6) He prepared a lavish meal for them (vv. 5–8; a similar lavish offering was presented to a divine messenger in Jdg 6:18–19; 13:15–16). (7) He stood nearby (v. 8), assuming the posture of a servant (see v. 22), to meet their every wish. Heb 13:2 (see note there) is probably a reference to vv. 2–8 and 19:1–3.

18:6 *bread.* A plural word referring to round, thin loaves.

18:10 See 17:21. Paul quotes this promise of Isaac's birth (see v. 14) in Ro 9:9 and relates it to Abraham's spiritual offspring (see Ro 9:7–8).

18:12 *laughed.* In disbelief, as also Abraham had at first (see note on 17:17). For Sarah's later laugh of joy and faith, see 21:6–7.

18:14 *Is anything too hard for the LORD?* The answer is no, for Sarah as well as for her descendants Mary and Elizabeth (see Lk 1:34–37). Nothing within God's will, including creation (see Jer 32:17) and redemption (see Mt 19:25–26), is impossible for him.

18:16 *Sodom.* See notes on 10:19; 13:10.

18:17 Abraham was God's friend (see v. 19; 2Ch 20:7; Jas 2:23; see also Isa 41:8). And because he was now God's covenant friend (see Job 29:4), God convened his heavenly council (see note on 1:26) at Abraham's tent. There he announced his purpose for Abraham (v. 10) and for the wicked people of the plain (vv. 20–21)—redemption and judgment. He thus even gave Abraham opportunity to speak in his court and to intercede for the righteous in Sodom and Gomorrah. Accordingly, Abraham was later called a prophet (20:7). Here, in Abraham, is exemplified the great privilege of God's covenant people throughout the ages: God has revealed his purposes to them and allows their voice to be heard (in intercession) in the court of heaven itself.

18:18 *great and powerful nation … blessed through him.* See note on 12:2–3.

18:19 *what is right and just.* See note on Ps 119:121.

18:20 *outcry.* A cry of righteous indignation (cf. the blood of Abel, 4:10) that became one of the reasons for the destruction of the cities (see 19:13). *Gomorrah.* See notes on 10:19; 13:10.

18:21 *I will go down.* The result would be judgment (as in 11:5–9), but God also comes down to redeem (as in Ex 3:8). *see.* Not a denial of God's infinite knowledge but a figurative way of stating that he as "Judge" (v. 25) does not act on the basis of mere complaints.

[22]The men[p] turned away and went toward Sodom,[q] but Abraham remained
standing before the LORD.[a][r] [23]Then Abraham approached him and said: "Will you
sweep away the righteous with the wicked?[s] [24]What if there are fifty righteous people in the city? Will you really sweep it
away and not spare[b] the place for the sake
of the fifty righteous people in it?[t] [25]Far be
it from you to do such a thing[u]—to kill
the righteous with the wicked, treating the
righteous[v] and the wicked alike.[w] Far be
it from you! Will not the Judge[x] of all the
earth do right?"[y]
[26]The LORD said, "If I find fifty righteous
people in the city of Sodom, I will spare
the whole place for their sake.[z]"
[27]Then Abraham spoke up again: "Now
that I have been so bold as to speak to the
Lord, though I am nothing but dust and
ashes,[a] [28]what if the number of the righteous is five less than fifty? Will you destroy
the whole city for lack of five people?"
"If I find forty-five there," he said, "I
will not destroy it."
[29]Once again he spoke to him, "What if
only forty are found there?"
He said, "For the sake of forty, I will
not do it."
[30]Then he said, "May the Lord not be
angry,[b] but let me speak. What if only thirty can be found there?"
He answered, "I will not do it if I find
thirty there."
[31]Abraham said, "Now that I have been
so bold as to speak to the Lord, what if
only twenty can be found there?"
He said, "For the sake of twenty, I will
not destroy it."
[32]Then he said, "May the Lord not be
angry, but let me speak just once more.[c]
What if only ten can be found there?"

18:22 [p]S ver 2 [q]Ge 19:1 [r]ver 1; Ge 19:27
18:23 [s]Ex 23:7; Lev 4:3,22, 27; Nu 16:22; Dt 27:25; 2Sa 24:17; Ps 11:4-7; 94:21; Eze 18:4; 2Pe 2:9
18:24 [t]ver 26; Jer 5:1
18:25 [u]Ge 44:7, 17; Dt 32:4; Job 8:3-7; 34:10 [v]Isa 5:20; Am 5:15; Mal 2:17; 3:18 [w]Dt 1:16-17 [x]Jdg 11:27; Job 9:15; Ps 7:11; 94:2; Heb 12:23 [y]Ge 20:4; Dt 32:4; 2Ch 19:7; Ezr 9:15; Ne 9:33; Job 8:3, 20; 34:10; 36:23; Ps 58:11; 75:7; 94:2; 119:137; Isa 3:10-11; Eze 18:25; Da 4:37; 9:14; Mal 2:17; Ro 3:6
18:26 [z]S ver 24
18:27 [a]S Ge 2:7; S Job 2:8
18:30 [b]ver 32; Ge 44:18; Ex 32:22
18:32 [c]S ver 30; Jdg 6:39
[d]Jer 5:1
18:33 [e]Ex 31:18 [f]S Ge 17:22 [g]Ge 31:55
19:1 [h]S Ge 18:2; Heb 13:2 [i]Ge 18:22 [j]S Ge 11:27 [k]S Ge 18:1 [l]S Ge 17:3; 48:12; Ru 2:10; 1Sa 25:23;

He answered, "For the sake of ten,[d] I
will not destroy it."
[33]When the LORD had finished speaking[e]
with Abraham, he left,[f] and Abraham returned home.[g]

Sodom and Gomorrah Destroyed

19 The two angels[h] arrived at Sodom[i]
in the evening, and Lot[j] was sitting
in the gateway of the city.[k] When he saw
them, he got up to meet them and bowed
down with his face to the ground.[l] [2]"My
lords," he said, "please turn aside to your
servant's house. You can wash your feet[m]
and spend the night and then go on your
way early in the morning."
"No," they answered, "we will spend
the night in the square."[n]
[3]But he insisted[o] so strongly that they
did go with him and entered his house.[p]
He prepared a meal for them, baking
bread without yeast,[q] and they ate.[r] [4]Be-
fore they had gone to bed, all the men
from every part of the city of Sodom[s]—
both young and old—surrounded the
house. [5]They called to Lot, "Where are
the men who came to you tonight? Bring
them out to us so that we can have sex
with them."[t]
[6]Lot went outside to meet them[u] and
shut the door behind him [7]and said, "No,
my friends. Don't do this wicked thing.
[8]Look, I have two daughters who have
never slept with a man. Let me bring them
out to you, and you can do what you like
with them. But don't do anything to these

[a] 22 Masoretic Text; an ancient Hebrew scribal tradition *but the LORD remained standing before Abraham*
[b] 24 Or *forgive*; also in verse 26

2Sa 14:33; 2Ki 2:15 **19:2** [m]S Ge 18:4; Lk 7:44 [n]Jdg 19:15,20 **19:3** [o]Ge 33:11 [p]Job 31:32 [q]Ex 12:39 [r]S Ge 18:6 **19:4** [s]S Ge 13:13 **19:5** [t]S Ge 13:13; Lev 18:22; Dt 23:18; Jdg 19:22; Ro 1:24-27 **19:6** [u]Jdg 19:23

18:22 *Abraham remained standing before the LORD.* The text and NIV text note both illustrate the mutual accessibility that existed between God and his servant.

18:23 The second time Abraham intervened for his relatives and for Sodom (see 14:14–16).

18:25 *Judge of all the earth.* Abraham based his plea on the justice and authority of God, confident that God would do what was right (see Dt 32:4).

18:27 *Lord.* Abraham used the title "Lord" (Adonai), not the covenantal name "LORD" (Yahweh), throughout his prayer. He was appealing to God as "Judge of all the earth" (v. 25). *dust and ashes.* In contrast to God's exalted position, Abraham described himself as insignificant (see Job 30:19; 42:6).

18:32 *just once more.* Abraham's questioning in vv. 23–32 did not arise from a spirit of haggling but of compassion for his relatives and of wanting to know God's ways. *ten.* Perhaps Abraham stopped at ten because he had been counting while praying: Lot, his wife, possibly two sons (see 19:12), at least two married daughters and their husbands (see 19:14 and NIV text note), and two unmarried daughters (see 19:8).

18:33 *home.* To Mamre (see v. 1). The next morning Abraham went back to see what God had done (see 19:27).

19:1–3 See note on 18:2.

19:1 *two angels.* See notes on 16:7; 18:2. *Lot was sitting in the gateway of the city.* Lot had probably become a member of Sodom's ruling council, since a city gateway served as the administrative and judicial center where legal matters were discussed and prosecuted (see Ru 4:1–12).

19:2 *square.* An open space near the main city gateway (see 2Ch 32:6) where public gatherings were held. Important cities like Jerusalem could have two or more squares (see Ne 8:16).

19:3 *bread without yeast.* A flat bread that could be baked quickly (see 18:6; Ex 12:8,39).

19:4–9 See Jdg 19:22–25.

19:5 *have sex with them.* Homosexual practice was open and common among the men of Sodom (see Jude 7). The English word "sodomy" alludes to the perversions of the ancient city.

19:8 *under the protection of my roof.* Ancient hospitality obliged a host to protect his guests in every situation and in every possible way.

men, for they have come under the protection of my roof."[v]
9 "Get out of our way," they replied.
"This fellow came here as a foreigner,[w]
and now he wants to play the judge![x]
We'll treat you worse than them." They
kept bringing pressure on Lot and moved
forward to break down the door.
10 But the men[y] inside reached out and
pulled Lot back into the house and shut
the door. 11 Then they struck the men who
were at the door of the house, young and
old, with blindness[z] so that they could not
find the door.
12 The two men said to Lot, "Do you
have anyone else here — sons-in-law, sons
or daughters, or anyone else in the city
who belongs to you?[a] Get them out of
here, 13 because we[b] are going to destroy
this place. The outcry to the LORD against
its people is so great[c] that he has sent us
to destroy it."[d]
14 So Lot went out and spoke to his sons-
in-law, who were pledged to marry[a] his
daughters. He said, "Hurry and get out
of this place, because the LORD is about
to destroy the city![e]" But his sons-in-law
thought he was joking.[f]
15 With the coming of dawn, the angels
urged Lot, saying, "Hurry! Take your wife
and your two daughters who are here, or
you will be swept away[g] when the city is
punished.[h]"
16 When he hesitated, the men grasped
his hand and the hands of his wife and
of his two daughters[i] and led them safely
out of the city, for the LORD was merciful
to them.[j] 17 As soon as they had brought
them out, one of them said, "Flee for your
lives![k] Don't look back,[l] and don't stop
anywhere in the plain![m] Flee to the mountains[n] or you will be swept away!"
18 But Lot said to them, "No, my lords,[b]
please! 19 Your[c] servant has found favor in
your[c] eyes,[o] and you[c] have shown great
kindness[p] to me in sparing my life. But
I can't flee to the mountains;[q] this disaster will overtake me, and I'll die. 20 Look,
here is a town near enough to run to,
and it is small. Let me flee to it — it is
very small, isn't it? Then my life will be
spared."
21 He said to him, "Very well, I will grant
this request[r] too; I will not overthrow the
town you speak of. 22 But flee there quickly, because I cannot do anything until you
reach it." (That is why the town was called
Zoar.[d][s])
23 By the time Lot reached Zoar,[t] the sun
had risen over the land. 24 Then the LORD
rained down burning sulfur[u] on Sodom
and Gomorrah[v] — from the LORD out of
the heavens.[w] 25 Thus he overthrew those
cities[x] and the entire plain,[y] destroying all
those living in the cities — and also the
vegetation in the land.[z] 26 But Lot's wife
looked back,[a] and she became a pillar of
salt.[b]
27 Early the next morning Abraham got
up and returned to the place where he had
stood before the LORD.[c] 28 He looked down
toward Sodom and Gomorrah, toward all
the land of the plain, and he saw dense
smoke rising from the land, like smoke
from a furnace.[d]
29 So when God destroyed the cities of
the plain,[e] he remembered[f] Abraham, and
he brought Lot out of the catastrophe[g] that
overthrew the cities where Lot had lived.[h]

Lot and His Daughters

30 Lot and his two daughters left Zoar[i] and
settled in the mountains,[j] for he was afraid
to stay in Zoar. He and his two daughters
lived in a cave. 31 One day the older daughter said to the younger, "Our father is old,
and there is no man around here to give

[a] 14 Or *were married to* [b] 18 Or *No, Lord*; or *No, my lord* [c] 19 The Hebrew is singular. [d] 22 *Zoar* means *small.*

19:8 [v]Jdg 19:24; 2Pe 2:7-8 **19:9** [w]Ge 23:4 [x]S Ge 13:8; Ac 7:27 **19:10** [y]S Ge 18:2 **19:11** [z]Dt 28:28-29; 2Ki 6:18; Ac 13:11 **19:12** [a]S Ge 6:18 **19:13** [b]Ex 12:29; 2Sa 24:16; 2Ki 19:35; 1Ch 21:12; 2Ch 32:21 [c]Ge 18:20 [d]1Ch 21:15; Ps 78:49; Jer 21:12; 25:18; 44:22; 51:45 **19:14** [e]Nu 16:21; Rev 18:4 [f]Ex 9:21; 1Ki 13:18; Jer 5:12; 43:2; Lk 17:28 **19:15** [g]Nu 16:26; Job 21:18; Ps 58:9; 73:19; 90:5 [h]Rev 18:4 **19:16** [i]2Pe 2:7 [j]Ex 34:6; Ps 33:18-19 **19:17** [k]1Ki 19:3; Jer 48:6 [l]ver 26 [m]S Ge 13:12 [n]S ver 19; S Ge 14:10; Mt 24:16 **19:19** [o]S Ge 6:8; S 18:3 [p]Ge 24:12; 39:21; 40:14; 47:29; Ru 1:8; 2:20; 3:10 [q]S ver 17,30 **19:21** [r]1Sa 25:35; 2Sa 14:8; Job 42:9 **19:22** [s]S Ge 13:10 **19:23** [t]S Ge 13:10 **19:24** [u]Job 18:15; Ps 11:6; Isa 30:33; 34:9; Eze 38:22 [v]Dt 29:23; Isa 1:9; 13:19; Jer 49:18; 50:40; Am 4:11 [w]S Ge 18:17; S Lev 10:2; S Mt 10:15; Lk 17:29 **19:25** [x]S ver 24; Eze 26:16; Zep 3:8; Hag 2:22 [y]S Ge 13:12 [z]Ps 107:34; Isa 1:10; Jer 20:16; 23:14; La 4:6; Eze 16:48 **19:26** [a]S ver 17 [b]Lk 17:32 **19:27** [c]Ge 18:22 **19:28** [d]Ge 15:17; Ex 19:18; Rev 9:2; 18:9 **19:29** [e]S Ge 13:12 [f]S Ge 8:1 [g]2Pe 2:7 [h]Ge 14:12; Eze 14:16 **19:30** [i]ver 22; S Ge 13:10 [j]S ver 19; S Ge 14:10

19:9 *This fellow came here as a foreigner, and now he wants to play the judge.* Centuries later, Moses was also considered an outsider and was accused of setting himself up as a judge (see Ex 2:14; Ac 7:27).

19:13 *we are going to destroy this place.* Sodom's wickedness had made it ripe for destruction (see Isa 3:9; Jer 23:14; La 4:6; Zep 2:8–9; 2Pe 2:6; Jude 7).

19:14 *his sons-in-law thought he was joking.* Lot apparently had lost his power of moral persuasion even among his family members.

19:16 *hesitated.* Perhaps because of reluctance to leave his material possessions. *his hand and the hands of his wife and of his two daughters.* The ten righteous people required to save Sodom (see 18:32) had now been reduced to four. *the LORD was merciful to them.* Deliverance is due to divine mercy, not to human righteousness (cf. Titus 3:5 and note).

19:24 *rained down burning sulfur.* Perhaps from a violent earthquake spewing up asphalt, such as is still found in this region (cf. Isa 34:9 and note).

19:26 *Lot's wife looked back, and she became a pillar of salt.* Her disobedient hesitation (see v. 17) became proverbial in later generations (see Lk 17:32). Even today, grotesque salt formations near the southern end of the Dead Sea are reminders of her folly.

19:29 *God … remembered Abraham.* See note on 8:1. *he brought Lot out of the catastrophe.* Lot's deliverance was the main concern of Abraham's prayer (18:23–32), which God now answered.

us children — as is the custom all over the earth. 32 Let's get our father to drink wine and then sleep with him and preserve our family line[k] through our father."[l]

33 That night they got their father to drink wine, and the older daughter went in and slept with him. He was not aware of it when she lay down or when she got up.[m]

34 The next day the older daughter said to the younger, "Last night I slept with my father. Let's get him to drink wine again tonight, and you go in and sleep with him so we can preserve our family line through our father."[n] 35 So they got their father to drink wine[o] that night also, and the younger daughter went in and slept with him. Again he was not aware of it when she lay down or when she got up.[p]

36 So both of Lot's daughters became pregnant by their father.[q] 37 The older daughter had a son, and she named him Moab[a];[r] he is the father of the Moabites[s] of today. 38 The younger daughter also had a son, and she named him Ben-Ammi[b]; he is the father of the Ammonites[c][t] of today.

Abraham and Abimelek

20:1-18Ref — Ge 12:10-20; 26:1-11

20 Now Abraham moved on from there[u] into the region of the Negev[v] and lived between Kadesh[w] and Shur.[x] For a while[y] he stayed in Gerar,[z] 2 and there Abraham said of his wife Sarah, "She is my sister.[a]" Then Abimelek[b] king of Gerar sent for Sarah and took her.[c]

3 But God came to Abimelek[d] in a dream[e] one night and said to him, "You are as good as dead[f] because of the woman you have taken; she is a married woman."[g]

4 Now Abimelek had not gone near her, so he said, "Lord, will you destroy an innocent nation?[h] 5 Did he not say to me, 'She is my sister,[i]' and didn't she also say, 'He is my brother'? I have done this with a clear conscience[j] and clean hands.[k]"

6 Then God said to him in the dream, "Yes, I know you did this with a clear conscience, and so I have kept[l] you from sinning against me.[m] That is why I did not let you touch her. 7 Now return the man's wife, for he is a prophet,[n] and he will pray for you[o] and you will live. But if you do not return her, you may be sure that you and all who belong to you will die."[p]

8 Early the next morning Abimelek summoned all his officials, and when he told them all that had happened, they were very much afraid. 9 Then Abimelek called Abraham in and said, "What have you done to us? How have I wronged you that you have brought such great guilt upon me and my kingdom? You have done things to me that should never be done.[q]" 10 And Abimelek asked Abraham, "What was your reason for doing this?"

11 Abraham replied, "I said to myself, 'There is surely no fear of God[r] in this place, and they will kill me because of my wife.'[s] 12 Besides, she really is my sister,[t] the daughter of my father though not of my mother; and she became my wife. 13 And when God had me wander[u] from my father's household,[v] I said to her, 'This is how you can show your love to me: Everywhere we go, say of me, "He is my brother."'"

14 Then Abimelek[w] brought sheep and

[a] 37 *Moab* sounds like the Hebrew for *from father.*
[b] 38 *Ben-Ammi* means *son of my father's people.*
[c] 38 Hebrew *Bene-Ammon*

19:32 [k]S Ge 16:2 [l]ver 34,36; Ge 38:18 **19:33** [m]ver 35 **19:34** [n]S ver 32 **19:35** [o]Ge 9:21 [p]ver 33 **19:36** [q]S ver 32 **19:37** [r]Ge 36:35; Ex 15:15; Nu 25:1; Isa 15:1; 25:10; Jer 25:21; 48:1; Eze 25:8; Zep 2:9 [s]Nu 22:4; 24:17; Dt 2:9; Jdg 3:28; Ru 1:4,22; 1Sa 14:47; 22:3-4; 2Sa 8:2; 2Ki 1:1; 3:4; Ezr 9:1; Ps 108:9; Jer 48:1 **19:38** [t]Nu 21:24; Dt 2:19; 23:3; Jos 12:2; Jdg 3:13; 10:6, 7; 1Sa 11:1-11; 14:47; 1Ch 19:1; 2Ch 20:23; 26:8; 27:5; Ne 2:19; 4:3; Jer 25:21; 40:14; 49:1; Eze 21:28; 25:2; Am 1:13 **20:1** [u]Ge 18:1 [v]S Ge 12:9 [w]S Ge 14:7 [x]S Ge 16:7 [y]Ge 26:3 [z]Ge 26:1,6,17 **20:2** [a]ver 12; S Ge 12:13 [b]ver 14; Ge 21:22; 26:1 [c]S Ge 12:15 **20:3** [d]Nu 22:9, 20 [e]Ge 28:12; 31:10,24; 37:5,9; 40:5; 41:1; Nu 12:6; Dt 13:1; Job 33:15; Da 2:1; 4:5 [f]Ex 10:7; 12:33; Ps 105:38 [g]ver 7; Ge 26:11; 1Ch 16:21; Ps 105:14 **20:4** [h]S Ge 18:25 **20:5** [i]S Ge 12:19 [j]S Ge 17:1 [k]Ps 7:8; 25:21; 26:6; 41:12 **20:6** [l]1Sa 25:26,34 [m]S Ge 13:13; Ps 41:4; 51:4 **20:7** [n]Dt 18:18; 34:10; 2Ki 3:11; 5:3; 1Ch 16:22; Ps 105:15 [o]ver 17; Ex 8:8; Nu 11:2; 12:13; 1Sa 7:5; 1Ki 13:6; Job 42:8; Jer 18:20; 37:3; 42:2 [p]S ver 3; S Ps 9:5 **20:9** [q]S Ge 12:18; 34:7 **20:11** [r]Ge 42:18; Ne 5:15; Job 31:23; Ps 36:1; Pr 16:6 [s]S Ge 12:12; 31:31 **20:12** [t]S Ge 12:13 **20:13** [u]Dt 26:5; 1Ch 16:20; Isa 30:28; 63:17 [v]S Ge 12:1 **20:14** [w]S ver 2

19:33 *they got their father to drink wine, and the older daughter went in and slept with him.* Though Lot's role was mainly passive, he bore the basic responsibility for what happened here and reaped the harvest of his move toward Sodom (see 13:10 – 12 and notes).

19:36 – 38 The sons born to Lot's daughters were the ancestors of the Moabites and Ammonites (see Dt 2:9,19), two nations that were to become bitter enemies of Abraham's descendants (see, e.g., 1Sa 14:47; 2Ch 20:1).

20:1 – 18 See 12:10 – 20 and notes.

20:1 *Negev.* See note on 12:9. *between Kadesh and Shur.* See notes on 14:7; 16:7. *Gerar.* Located at the edge of Philistine territory, about halfway between Gaza near the Mediterranean coast and Beersheba in the northern Negev.

20:2 *Abimelek.* Probably the father or grandfather of the later king who bore the same name (see 26:1).

20:3 *dream.* Once again God intervened to spare the mother of the promised offspring. Dreams were a frequent mode of revelation in the OT (see 28:12; 31:10 – 11; 37:5 – 9; 40:5; 41:1; Nu 12:6; Jdg 7:13; 1Ki 3:5; Da 2:3; 4:5; 7:1).

20:7 *prophet.* See notes on 18:17; Zec 1:1. Abraham was the first man to bear this title (see Ps 105:15).

20:9 *brought such great guilt upon me and my kingdom.* Or "caused me and my kingdom to commit such a great sin." The "great sin" is adultery (see vv. 2 – 3,6; the same meaning for this expression is attested also in Egyptian and Canaanite texts). Everywhere else the Hebrew expression occurs in the OT it refers to idolatry (Ex 32:21,30 – 31; 2Ki 17:21), which is spiritual adultery (see Hos 1:2 and note). Adultery and idolatry are supreme forms of covenant infidelity (see note on Ex 34:15).

20:11 *fear of God.* A conventional phrase equivalent to "true religion." "Fear" in this phrase has the sense of reverential trust in God and commitment to his revealed will (word); see Ps 34:8 – 14 and note.

20:12 *she really is my sister, the daughter of my father though not of my mother.* Abraham's half-truth was a sinful deception, not a legitimate explanation.

20:14 – 16 Abimelek's generosity was a strong contrast to Abraham's fearfulness and deception.

cattle and male and female slaves and gave
them to Abraham,[x] and he returned Sarah
his wife to him. 15 And Abimelek said, "My
land is before you; live wherever you like."[y]
16 To Sarah he said, "I am giving your
brother a thousand shekels[a] of silver. This
is to cover the offense against you before
all who are with you; you are completely
vindicated."
17 Then Abraham prayed to God,[z] and
God healed Abimelek, his wife and his female slaves so they could have children
again, 18 for the LORD had kept all the wom-
en in Abimelek's household from conceiv-
ing because of Abraham's wife Sarah.[a]

The Birth of Isaac

21 Now the LORD was gracious to Sarah[b] as he had said, and the LORD
did for Sarah what he had promised.[c] 2 Sarah became pregnant and bore a son[d] to
Abraham in his old age,[e] at the very time
God had promised him.[f] 3 Abraham gave
the name Isaac[b][g] to the son Sarah bore
him. 4 When his son Isaac was eight days
old, Abraham circumcised him,[h] as God
commanded him. 5 Abraham was a hundred years old[i] when his son Isaac was
born to him.
6 Sarah said, "God has brought me
laughter,[j] and everyone who hears about
this will laugh with me." 7 And she added,
"Who would have said to Abraham that
Sarah would nurse children? Yet I have
borne him a son in his old age."[k]

Hagar and Ishmael Sent Away

8 The child grew and was weaned,[l] and
on the day Isaac was weaned Abraham
held a great feast. 9 But Sarah saw that the
son whom Hagar the Egyptian had borne
to Abraham[m] was mocking,[n] 10 and she said
to Abraham, "Get rid of that slave woman[o] and her son, for that woman's son will
never share in the inheritance with my son
Isaac."[p]
11 The matter distressed Abraham greatly because it concerned his son.[q] 12 But
God said to him, "Do not be so distressed
about the boy and your slave woman. Listen to whatever Sarah tells you, because it
is through Isaac that your offspring[c] will
be reckoned.[r] 13 I will make the son of the
slave into a nation[s] also, because he is
your offspring."
14 Early the next morning Abraham took
some food and a skin of water and gave
them to Hagar.[t] He set them on her shoulders and then sent her off with the boy.
She went on her way and wandered in the
Desert of Beersheba.[u]
15 When the water in the skin was gone,
she put the boy under one of the bushes.
16 Then she went off and sat down about a
bowshot away, for she thought, "I cannot
watch the boy die." And as she sat there,
she[d] began to sob.[v]
17 God heard the boy crying,[w] and the
angel of God[x] called to Hagar from heav-
en[y] and said to her, "What is the matter,
Hagar? Do not be afraid;[z] God has heard
the boy crying as he lies there. 18 Lift the
boy up and take him by the hand, for I will
make him into a great nation.[a]"
19 Then God opened her eyes[b] and she
saw a well of water.[c] So she went and
filled the skin with water and gave the boy
a drink.

[a] *16* That is, about 25 pounds or about 12 kilograms
[b] *3* *Isaac* means *he laughs.* [c] *12* Or *seed*
[d] *16* Hebrew; Septuagint *the child*

20:14 [x] Ge 12:16 **20:15** [y] Ge 13:9; S 45:18 **20:17** [z] S ver 7; Job 42:9 **20:18** [a] Ge 12:17 **21:1** [b] 1Sa 2:21 [c] S Ge 8:1; S 17:16,21; 18:14; Gal 4:23; Heb 11:11 **21:2** [d] S Ge 17:19; S 30:6 [e] Gal 4:22; Heb 11:11 [f] S Ge 18:10 **21:3** [g] S Ge 16:11; S 17:19; Jos 24:3 **21:4** [h] Ge 17:10,12; Ac 7:8 **21:5** [i] S Ge 12:4; Heb 6:15 **21:6** [j] Ge 17:17; Job 8:21; Ps 126:2; Isa 12:6; 35:2; 44:23; 52:9; 54:1 **21:7** [k] S Ge 17:17 **21:8** [l] 1Sa 1:23 **21:9** [m] S Ge 16:15 [n] Ge 39:14; Gal 4:29 **21:10** [o] Ge 39:17 [p] Ge 25:6; Gal 4:30* **21:11** [q] Ge 17:18 **21:12** [r] Mt 1:2; Ro 9:7*; Heb 11:18* **21:13** [s] ver 18; S Ge 13:16 **21:14** [t] S Ge 16:1 [u] ver 31,32; Ge 22:19; 26:33; 28:10; 46:1,5; Jos 15:28; 19:2; Jdg 20:1; 1Sa 3:20; 1Ch 4:28; Ne 11:27 **21:16** [v] Jer 6:26; Am 8:10; Zec 12:10 **21:17** [w] Ex 3:7; Nu 20:16; Dt 26:7; Ps 6:8 [x] S Ge 16:7 [y] Ge 22:11,15 [z] S Ge 15:1 **21:18** [a] ver 13; S Ge 17:20 **21:19** [b] Nu 22:31 [c] S Ge 16:7

20:16 *shekels.* Though not in the Hebrew, the word is correctly supplied here as the most common unit of weight in ancient times. Originally the shekel was only a weight, not a coin, since coinage was not invented till the seventh century BC.

21:1 See 17:16. *did for Sarah what he had promised.* See Gal 4:22–23,28. The promised son through whom God will continue the covenant line (17:21) is born at last.

21:3 *Isaac.* See note on 17:17.

21:4 See notes on 17:10,12.

21:5 In fulfillment of the promise made to him (see 17:16), Abraham miraculously became a father at the age of 100 years (see 17:17 and chart, p. 31).

21:6 *laughter ... laugh.* See note on 17:17; contrast 18:12 (see note there).

21:8 *weaned.* At age two or three, as was customary in the ancient Near East.

21:9 *the son whom Hagar the Egyptian had borne.* Ishmael, who was in his late teens at this time (see 16:15–16). *mocking.* Or "at play." In either case, Sarah saw Ishmael as a potential threat to Isaac's inheritance (v. 10).

21:10 *Get rid of that slave woman and her son.* See Gal 4:21–31. Driving them out would have had the effect of disinheriting Ishmael.

21:11 *The matter distressed Abraham.* Both love and legal custom played a part in Abraham's anguish. He knew that the customs of his day, illustrated later in the Nuzi tablets (see chart, p. xxiv), prohibited the arbitrary expulsion of a female servant's son (whose legal status was relatively weak in any case).

21:12 *Listen to whatever Sarah tells you.* God overruled in this matter (as he had done earlier; see 15:4), promising Abraham that both Isaac and Ishmael would have numerous descendants. *it is through Isaac that your offspring will be reckoned.* See 17:19; 22:18; see also Ro 9:6–8 and Heb 11:17–19 for broader spiritual applications of this statement.

21:14 *Early the next morning.* Though Abraham would now be separated from Ishmael for the first time, he responded to God's command with prompt obedience (see note on 12:4). *Beersheba.* See note on v. 31.

21:15 *one of the bushes.* See note on v. 33.

21:17 *God heard ... God has heard.* A pun on the name "Ishmael" (see NIV text note on 16:11; see also 17:20).

20 God was with the boy[d] as he grew up.
He lived in the desert and became an archer. 21 While he was living in the Desert
of Paran,[e] his mother got a wife for him[f]
from Egypt.

The Treaty at Beersheba

22 At that time Abimelek[g] and Phicol the
commander of his forces[h] said to Abraham, "God is with you in everything you
do.[i] 23 Now swear[j] to me here before God
that you will not deal falsely with me or
my children or my descendants.[k] Show to
me and the country where you now reside
as a foreigner the same kindness I have
shown to you."[l]
24 Abraham said, "I swear it."
25 Then Abraham complained to Abimelek about a well of water that Abimelek's
servants had seized.[m] 26 But Abimelek said,
"I don't know who has done this. You did
not tell me, and I heard about it only today."
27 So Abraham brought sheep and cattle
and gave them to Abimelek, and the two
men made a treaty.[n] 28 Abraham set apart
seven ewe lambs from the flock, 29 and
Abimelek asked Abraham, "What is the
meaning of these seven ewe lambs you
have set apart by themselves?"
30 He replied, "Accept these seven lambs
from my hand as a witness[o] that I dug this
well.[p]"
31 So that place was called Beersheba,[a][q]
because the two men swore an oath[r] there.
32 After the treaty[s] had been made at Beersheba,[t] Abimelek and Phicol the commander of his forces[u] returned to the land
of the Philistines.[v] 33 Abraham planted a
tamarisk tree[w] in Beersheba, and there he
called on the name of the LORD,[x] the Eternal God.[y] 34 And Abraham stayed in the
land of the Philistines[z] for a long time.

Abraham Tested

22 Some time later God tested[a] Abraham. He said to him, "Abraham!"
"Here I am,"[b] he replied.
2 Then God said, "Take your son[c], your
only son, whom you love—Isaac—and
go to the region of Moriah.[d] Sacrifice him

21:20 [d] Ge 26:3, 24; 28:15; 39:2, 21,23; Lk 1:66 **21:21** [e] S Ge 14:6 [f] Ge 24:4,38; 28:2; 34:4,8; Jdg 14:2 **21:22** [g] S Ge 20:2 [h] ver 32; Ge 26:26 [i] ver 23; Ge 26:28; 28:15; 31:3,5, 42; 39:2,3; 1Sa 3:19; 16:18; 2Ch 1:1; Ps 46:7; Isa 7:14; 8:8,10; 41:10; 43:5 **21:23** [j] ver 31; Ge 25:33; 26:31; 31:53; Jos 2:12; 1Ki 2:8 [k] 1Sa 24:21 [l] S ver 22; Jos 2:12 **21:25** [m] Ge 26:15,18, 20-22 **21:27** [n] ver 31, 32; Ge 26:28, 31; 31:44,53 **21:30** [o] Ge 31:44, 47,48,50, 52; Jos 22:27, 28,34; 24:27; Isa 19:20; Mal 2:14 [p] ver 25; Ge 26:25,32

[a] 31 *Beersheba* can mean *well of seven* and *well of the oath.*

21:31 [q] S ver 14 [r] S ver 23, S 27 **21:32** [s] S ver 27 [t] S ver 14 [u] S ver 22 [v] S Ge 10:14 **21:33** [w] 1Sa 22:6; 31:13 [x] S Ge 4:26 [y] Ex 15:18; Dt 32:40; 33:27; Job 36:26; Ps 10:16; 45:6; 90:2; 93:2; 102:24; 103:19; 146:10; Isa 40:28; Jer 10:10; Hab 1:12; 3:6; Heb 13:8 **21:34** [z] S Ge 10:14 **22:1** [a] Ex 15:25; 16:4; 20:20; Dt 8:2, 16; 13:3; Jdg 2:22; 3:1; 2Ch 32:31; Ps 66:10; Heb 11:17; Jas 1:12-13 [b] ver 11; Ge 31:11; 46:2; 1Sa 3:4,6,8; Isa 6:8 **22:2** [c] ver 12,16; Jn 3:16; Heb 11:17; 1Jn 4:9 [d] 2Ch 3:1

21:21 *Desert of Paran.* Located in north central Sinai. *his mother got a wife for him from Egypt.* Parents often arranged their children's marriages (see ch. 24).

21:22 *Abimelek.* See 20:2 and note. *Phicol.* Either a family name or an official title, since it reappears over 60 years later (25:26) in a similar context (26:26).

21:23 *swear to me … before God … Show to me … kindness.* Phrases commonly used when making covenants or treaties (see vv. 27,32). "Kindness" as used here refers to acts of friendship (cf. v. 27; 20:14; Ps 6:4 and note). Such covenants always involved oaths.

21:27 *sheep and cattle.* Probably to be used in the treaty ceremony (see 15:10).

21:30 *as a witness.* "Witnesses" to covenant/treaty-making (or other events of continuing significance) served as disinterested (third-party) testimonies to the event they "witnessed" (see 31:44,48,52; Dt 4:26; 30:19; 31:19,26; 32:1; Jos 22:27–28; 24:27; 1Sa 6:18) and could be appealed to (see Ps 50:1 and note; Isa 1:2; Mic 6:1–2).

21:31 *Beersheba, because the two men swore an oath there.* See NIV text note. For a similar pun on the name, see 26:33. Beersheba, an important town in the northern Negev, marked the southernmost boundary of the Israelite monarchy in later times (see, e.g., 2Sa 17:11). An ancient well there is still pointed out as "Abraham's well" (see v. 25), but its authenticity is not certain. *because.* Or "when."

21:32 *Philistines.* See note on 10:14.

21:33 *tamarisk.* A shrub or small tree that thrives in arid regions. Its leafy branches provide welcome shade, and it is probably the unidentified bush under which Hagar put Ishmael in v. 15. *Eternal God.* Hebrew *El Olam*, a phrase unique to this passage. It is one of a series of names that include *El*, "God," as an element (see 14:19; 17:1 and notes; 33:20; 35:7).

22:1–19 The climax to the account of God's dealings with Abraham. Here we are told of God's supreme test of Abraham's faith and of his final confirmation of his covenanted promises—once again confirmed by an oath (vv. 15–18). After this, there follows only the account of how Abraham put his affairs in order with a view to the future: providing a place of burial for Sarah and himself in the promised land (ch. 23), obtaining a suitable wife for Isaac (ch. 24), and seeing to the distribution of his inheritance among his offspring (25:1–6).

This climax in many ways echoes the beginning (12:1–7) and with it frames the main body of the Abraham story. Cf., e.g., 12:1: "Go from your country, your people and your father's household to the land I will show you"; 22:2: "Go to the region of Moriah … [to] a mountain I will show you."

22:1 *Some time later.* Isaac had grown into adolescence or young manhood, as implied also by 21:34 ("a long time"). *tested.* Not "tempted," for God does not tempt (Jas 1:13). Satan tempts us (see 1Co 7:5) in order to make us fall; God tests us in order to confirm our faith (Ex 20:20) or prove our commitment (Dt 8:2). See note on Mt 4:1. *Here I am.* Abraham answered with the response of a servant, as did Moses and Samuel when God called them by name (see Ex 3:4; 1Sa 3:4,6,8).

22:2 *your son, your only son, whom you love—Isaac.* "Isaac" follows the clause "whom you love" in order to heighten the effect. Isaac was the "only son" of the promise (21:12; cf. Gal 4:23), and Ishmael had been sent away (21:8–21). *region of Moriah.* The author of Chronicles identifies the area as the temple mount in Jerusalem (2Ch 3:1). Today "Mount Moriah" is occupied by the Dome of the Rock, an impressive Muslim structure erected in AD 691. A large outcropping of rock inside the building is still pointed to as the traditional site of the intended sacrifice of Isaac. *Sacrifice him.* Abraham had committed himself by covenant to be obedient to the Lord and had consecrated his son Isaac to the Lord by circumcision. The Lord put his servant's faith and

there as a burnt offering[e] on a mountain I
will show you.[f]"
3Early the next morning[g] Abraham got
up and loaded his donkey. He took with
him two of his servants and his son Isaac.
When he had cut enough wood for the
burnt offering, he set out for the place
God had told him about. 4On the third
day Abraham looked up and saw the place
in the distance. 5He said to his servants,
"Stay here with the donkey while I and the
boy go over there. We will worship and
then we will come back to you.[h]"
6Abraham took the wood for the burnt
offering and placed it on his son Isaac,[i]
and he himself carried the fire and the
knife.[j] As the two of them went on together, 7Isaac spoke up and said to his father
Abraham, "Father?"
"Yes, my son?" Abraham replied.
"The fire and wood are here," Isaac
said, "but where is the lamb[k] for the burnt
offering?"
8Abraham answered, "God himself will
provide[l] the lamb[m] for the burnt offering,
my son." And the two of them went on
together.
9When they reached the place God
had told him about,[n] Abraham built an
altar[o] there and arranged the wood[p] on
it. He bound his son Isaac and laid him
on the altar,[q] on top of the wood. 10Then
he reached out his hand and took the
knife[r] to slay his son.[s] 11But the angel of
the LORD[t] called out to him from heaven,[u]
"Abraham! Abraham!"[v]
"Here I am,"[w] he replied.
12"Do not lay a hand on the boy," he said.
"Do not do anything to him. Now I know
that you fear God,[x] because you have not
withheld from me your son, your only son.[y]"
13Abraham looked up and there in a
thicket he saw a ram[a] caught by its horns.[z]
He went over and took the ram and sacrificed it as a burnt offering instead of his
son.[a] 14So Abraham called[b] that place The
LORD[c] Will Provide. And to this day it is
said, "On the mountain of the LORD it will
be provided.[d]"
15The angel of the LORD[e] called to Abraham from heaven[f] a second time 16and
said, "I swear by myself,[g] declares the
LORD, that because you have done this
and have not withheld your son, your
only son,[h] 17I will surely bless you[i] and
make your descendants[j] as numerous as
the stars in the sky[k] and as the sand on
the seashore.[l] Your descendants will take
possession of the cities of their enemies,[m]

22:2 [e]S Ge 8:20 [f]ver 9
22:3 [g]Jos 8:10
22:5 [h]Ex 24:14
22:6 [i]Jn 19:17 [j]ver 10; Jdg 19:29
22:7 [k]Ex 29:38-42; Lev 1:10; Rev 13:8
22:8 [l]ver 14 [m]ver 13; S Jn 1:29
22:9 [n]ver 2 [o]S Ge 4:26; S 8:20 [p]Lev 1:7; 1Ki 18:33 [q]Heb 11:17-19; Jas 2:21
22:10 [r]S ver 6 [s]ver 3; S Ge 18:19
22:11 [t]S Ge 16:7 [u]S Ge 21:17 [v]Ge 46:2 [w]S ver 1
22:12 [x]S Ge 18:19; 42:18; Ex 18:21; 1Sa 15:22; Job 1:1; 37:24; Pr 8:13; Jas 2:21-22 [y]S ver 2; Jn 3:16; 1Jn 4:9
22:13 [z]S ver 8 [a]S Ge 8:20; Ro 8:32
22:14 [b]Ex 17:15; Jdg 6:24 [c]Isa 30:29 [d]ver 8
22:15 [e]S Ge 16:7 [f]S Ge 21:17
22:16 [g]Ex 13:11; 32:13; 33:1; Isa 45:23; 62:8; Jer 22:5; 44:26; 49:13; 51:14; Am 6:8; Lk 1:73; Heb 6:13 [h]S ver 2
22:17 [i]S Ge 12:2 [j]Heb 6:14* [k]S Ge 15:5; Ex 32:13; Dt 7:7; 28:62 [l]S Ge 12:2; S 26:24; Hos 1:10; Ro 9:27; Heb 11:12 [m]Ge 24:60; Est 9:2

[a] *13* Many manuscripts of the Masoretic Text, Samaritan Pentateuch, Septuagint and Syriac; most manuscripts of the Masoretic Text *a ram behind him*

loyalty to the supreme test, thereby instructing Abraham, Isaac and their descendants as to the kind of total consecration the Lord's covenant requires. The test also foreshadowed the perfect consecration in sacrifice that another offspring of Abraham would undergo (see note on v. 16) in order to wholly consecrate Abraham and his spiritual descendants to God and to fulfill the covenant promises.

22:3 *Early the next morning.* Prompt obedience, even under such trying circumstances, characterized Abraham's response to God (see note on 12:4).

22:4 *third day.* Parts of three days were likely required for the journey from Beersheba (see v. 19) to "the region of Moriah" (Jerusalem; see v. 2 and note), a distance of about 48 miles. On the other hand, a "journey of three days" may have been a conventional expression for a short trip rather than a journey of exactly three days (see 30:36; Ex 3:18; 5:3; 8:27; 15:22; Nu 10:33; 33:8; Jos 9:16; Jnh 1:17; 3:3).

22:5 *boy.* See v. 12; see also note on v. 1. The Hebrew for this word has a wide range of meaning, from an infant (see Ex 2:6) to a young man of military age (see 1Ch 12:28). *we will come back to you.* Abraham, the man of faith and "the father of all who believe" (Ro 4:11), "reasoned that God could even raise the dead" (Heb 11:19) if that were necessary to fulfill his promise.

22:8 *God himself will provide the lamb.* The immediate fulfillment of Abraham's trusting response was the ram of v. 13, but its ultimate fulfillment is the Lamb of God (Jn 1:29,36).

22:9 *laid him on the altar, on top of the wood.* Isaac is here a type (prefiguration) of Christ (see note on v. 16).

22:11 *angel of the LORD.* See note on 16:7. The "angel of the LORD" who had seen to the safety of Abraham's son Ishmael and had spoken of Ishmael's future (16:7 – 12; 21:17 – 18) now intervenes to save Abraham's son Isaac and afterward speaks of Isaac's future (vv. 17 – 18). *Abraham! Abraham!* The repetition of the name indicates urgency (see 46:2; Ex 3:4; 1Sa 3:10; Ac 9:4). *Here I am.* See note on v. 1.

22:12 *fear God.* See note on 20:11. *you have not withheld from me your son, your only son.* See v. 16 and note. Abraham's "faith was made complete by what he did" (Jas 2:22).

22:13 *instead of.* Substitutionary sacrifice of one life for another is here mentioned for the first time. As the ram died in Isaac's place, so also Jesus gave his life as a ransom "for" (lit. "instead of") many (Mk 10:45).

22:14 *The LORD Will Provide.* Thus Abraham memorializes the remarkable way in which God fulfilled his expectation (v. 8). The Hebrew for "will provide" is lit. "will see (to it)"; God's "seeing to it" spared Isaac, just as God's "seeing" had spared Ishmael (in Hagar's womb; see 16:13 – 14 and notes; cf. 21:15 – 21). *mountain of the LORD.* During the Israelite monarchy the phrase referred to the temple mount in Jerusalem (see Ps 24:3; Isa 2:3; 30:29; Zec 8:3).

22:16 *I swear by myself.* There is no greater name in which the Lord can take an oath (see Heb 6:13). *you . . . have not withheld your son, your only son.* Abraham's devotion is paralleled by God's love to us in Christ as reflected in Jn 3:16 and Ro 8:32, which may allude to this verse.

22:17 *descendants as numerous as the stars in the sky.* See 13:16; 15:5 and notes. *sand on the seashore.* Fulfilled, at least in part, during Solomon's reign (see 1Ki 4:20). *cities.* Lit. "gates." Taking possession of the gate of a city was tantamount to occupying the city itself (see 24:60).

18 and through your offspring[a] all nations
on earth will be blessed,[b][n] because you
have obeyed me."[o]
19 Then Abraham returned to his servants, and they set off together for Beersheba.[p] And Abraham stayed in Beersheba.

Nahor's Sons

20 Some time later Abraham was told,
"Milkah is also a mother; she has borne
sons to your brother Nahor:[q] 21 Uz[r] the
firstborn, Buz[s] his brother, Kemuel (the
father of Aram), 22 Kesed, Hazo, Pildash,
Jidlaph and Bethuel.[t]" 23 Bethuel became
the father of Rebekah.[u] Milkah bore these
eight sons to Abraham's brother Nahor.[v]
24 His concubine,[w] whose name was Reu-
mah, also had sons: Tebah, Gaham, Ta-
hash and Maakah.

The Death of Sarah

23 Sarah lived to be a hundred and
twenty-seven years old. 2 She died
at Kiriath Arba[x] (that is, Hebron)[y] in the
land of Canaan, and Abraham went to
mourn for Sarah and to weep over her.[z]
3 Then Abraham rose from beside his
dead wife and spoke to the Hittites.[c][a] He
said, 4 "I am a foreigner and stranger[b]
among you. Sell me some property for a
burial site here so I can bury my dead.[c]"
5 The Hittites replied to Abraham, 6 "Sir,
listen to us. You are a mighty prince[d]
among us. Bury your dead in the choicest
of our tombs. None of us will refuse you
his tomb for burying your dead."

7 Then Abraham rose and bowed down
before the people of the land, the Hittites.
8 He said to them, "If you are willing to let
me bury my dead, then listen to me and
intercede with Ephron son of Zohar[e] on my
behalf 9 so he will sell me the cave of Machpelah,[f] which belongs to him and is at the
end of his field. Ask him to sell it to me for
the full price as a burial site among you."
10 Ephron the Hittite was sitting among
his people and he replied to Abraham in
the hearing of all the Hittites[g] who had
come to the gate[h] of his city. 11 "No, my
lord," he said. "Listen to me; I give[d][i] you
the field, and I give[d] you the cave that is
in it. I give[d] it to you in the presence of my
people. Bury your dead."
12 Again Abraham bowed down before
the people of the land 13 and he said to
Ephron in their hearing, "Listen to me, if
you will. I will pay the price of the field.
Accept it from me so I can bury my dead
there."
14 Ephron answered Abraham, 15 "Listen
to me, my lord; the land is worth four hundred shekels[e] of silver,[j] but what is that
between you and me? Bury your dead."
16 Abraham agreed to Ephron's terms
and weighed out for him the price he had

[a] *18* Or *seed* [b] *18* Or *and all nations on earth will use the name of your offspring in blessings* (see 48:20) [c] *3* Or *the descendants of Heth*; also in verses 5, 7, 10, 16, 18 and 20 [d] *11* Or *sell* [e] *15* That is, about 10 pounds or about 4.6 kilograms

22:18 [n] S Ge 12:2,3; Ac 3:25*; Gal 3:8* [o] S ver 10; Ge 17:2,9; Ps 105:9 **22:19** [p] Ge 21:14; 26:23; 28:10 **22:20** [q] S Ge 11:29 **22:21** [r] S Ge 10:23 [s] Job 32:2; Jer 25:23 **22:22** [t] Ge 24:15,47; 25:20 **22:23** [u] Ge 24:15 [v] S Ge 11:29 **22:24** [w] Ge 25:6; 35:22; 36:12; Jdg 8:31; 2Sa 3:7; 1Ki 2:22; 11:3; 1Ch 1:32; SS 6:8 **23:2** [x] Jos 14:15; 15:13; 20:7; 21:11 [y] ver 19; S Ge 13:18 [z] Ge 24:67 **23:3** [a] S Ge 10:15 **23:4** [b] S Ge 17:8; 19:9; Ex 2:22; Lev 25:23; Ps 39:12; 105:12; 119:19; Heb 11:9,13 [c] Ge 49:30; Ac 7:16 **23:6** [d] Ge 14:14-16; 24:35 **23:8** [e] Ge 25:9 **23:9** [f] ver 17, 19; Ge 25:9; 47:30; 49:30; 50:13 **23:10** [g] ver 18 [h] S Ge 18:1; Dt 22:15; 25:7; Jos 20:4; Ru 4:11; 2Sa 15:2; 2Ki 15:35; Ps 127:5; Pr 31:23; Jer 26:10; 36:10 **23:11** [i] 2Sa 24:23 **23:15** [j] Eze 45:12

22:18 *all nations on earth will be blessed.* See note on 12:2–3. *because you have obeyed me.* See note on 17:9.

22:23–24 Abraham's brother Nahor became the father of eight sons by his wife and four by his concubine (see note on 25:6). They would later become the ancestors of 12 Aramean (see v. 21) tribes, just as Abraham's son Ishmael would become the ancestor of 12 tribes (25:16) and Abraham's grandson Jacob would become the ancestor of the 12 tribes of Israel (49:28).

23:1–20 How Abraham provided a burial place for Sarah and himself in Canaan, thus in faith laying claim to Canaan as his homeland in accordance with God's promise.

23:2 *Kiriath Arba.* Means "the town of Arba" (Arba was the most prominent member of a tribe living in the Hebron area [see Jos 14:15]). It can also mean "the town of four," referring to the place where Anak (see Jos 15:13–14; 21:11) and his three sons lived (see Jdg 1:10,20). *went.* Either from Beersheba to Hebron or into the place where Sarah's body was lying.

23:3 *Hittites.* See note on 10:15. They were apparently in control of the Hebron area at this time.

23:4 *a foreigner and stranger.* The phrase was used often by the patriarchs and their descendants in reference to themselves (see 1Ch 29:15; Ps 39:12; see also Heb 11:13). On this earth Abraham "lived in tents" (Heb 11:9), the most temporary of dwellings. But he looked forward to the more permanent home promised him, which the author of Hebrews calls "the city with foundations, whose architect and builder is God" (Heb 11:10).

23:6 *You are a mighty prince.* Probably intended as flattery.

23:9 *cave of Machpelah.* The tombs of several patriarchs and their wives—Abraham and Sarah, Isaac and Rebekah, Jacob and Leah (see v. 19; 25:8–10; 49:30–31; 50:12–13)—are, according to tradition, located in a large cave deep beneath the Mosque of Abraham, a Muslim shrine in Hebron. *end of his field.* Apparently Abraham wanted to buy only a small part of the field (namely, the part where the cave was located), but Ephron insisted that he purchase the entire field (see note on v. 15).

23:10 *in the hearing of all the Hittites who had come to the gate.* The main gateway of a city was usually the place where legal matters were transacted and attested (see v. 18; see also note on 19:1).

23:11 *my lord.* Perhaps intended to flatter Abraham (see v. 15). *give.* See NIV text note.

23:15 *four hundred shekels of silver, but what is that between you and me?* See note on 20:16. Despite Ephron's pretense of generosity, 400 shekels of silver was an exorbitant price for a field (see, e.g., Jer 32:9). Ephron was taking advantage of Abraham during a time of grief and bereavement. He knew that Abraham had to deal quickly in order to have a place to bury Sarah, so he insisted that Abraham buy the entire lot.

23:16 *weight current among the merchants.* Subject to more variation and therefore greater dishonesty than the later royal standard (see 2Sa 14:26), which was carefully regulated and more precise.

named in the hearing of the Hittites: four hundred shekels of silver,[k] according to the weight current among the merchants.[l]

17 So Ephron's field in Machpelah[m] near Mamre[n]—both the field and the cave in it, and all the trees within the borders of the field—was deeded 18 to Abraham as his property[o] in the presence of all the Hittites[p] who had come to the gate[q] of the city. 19 Afterward Abraham buried his wife Sarah in the cave in the field of Machpelah[r] near Mamre (which is at Hebron[s]) in the land of Canaan.[t] 20 So the field and the cave in it were deeded[u] to Abraham by the Hittites as a burial site.[v]

Isaac and Rebekah

24 Abraham was now very old,[w] and the LORD had blessed[x] him in every way.[y] 2 He said to the senior servant[z] in his household, the one in charge of all that he had,[a] "Put your hand under my thigh.[b] 3 I want you to swear[c] by the LORD, the God of heaven[d] and the God of earth,[e] that you will not get a wife for my son[f] from the daughters of the Canaanites,[g] among whom I am living,[h] 4 but will go to my country and my own relatives[i] and get a wife for my son Isaac.[j]"

5 The servant asked him, "What if the woman is unwilling to come back with me to this land?[k] Shall I then take your son back to the country you came from?[l]"

6 "Make sure that you do not take my son back there,"[m] Abraham said. 7 "The LORD, the God of heaven,[n] who brought me out of my father's household and my native land[o] and who spoke to me and promised me on oath, saying, 'To your offspring[a][p] I will give this land'[q]—he will send his angel before you[r] so that you can get a wife for my son from there. 8 If the woman is unwilling to come back with you, then you will be released from this oath[s] of mine. Only do not take my son back there."[t] 9 So the servant put his hand under the thigh[u] of his master[v] Abraham and swore an oath to him concerning this matter.

10 Then the servant left, taking with him ten of his master's camels[w] loaded with all kinds of good things[x] from his master. He set out for Aram Naharaim[b][y] and made his way to the town of Nahor.[z] 11 He had the camels kneel down near the well[a] outside the town; it was toward evening, the time the women go out to draw water.[b]

12 Then he prayed, "LORD, God of my master Abraham,[c] make me successful[d] today, and show kindness[e] to my master Abraham. 13 See, I am standing beside this spring, and the daughters of the townspeople are coming out to draw water.[f] 14 May it be that when I say to a young woman, 'Please let down your jar that I may have a drink,' and she says, 'Drink,[g] and I'll water your camels too'[h]—let her be the one you have chosen for your servant Isaac.[i] By this I will know[j] that you have shown kindness to my master."

15 Before he had finished praying,[k] Rebekah[l] came out with her jar on her shoulder. She was the daughter of Bethuel[m] son

[a] 7 Or *seed* [b] 10 That is, Northwest Mesopotamia

23:16 [k] 2Sa 24:24; Jer 32:9; Zec 11:12 [l] 2Sa 14:26 **23:17** [m] S ver 9 [n] S Ge 13:18 **23:18** [o] S Ge 12:7 [p] ver 10 [q] S Ge 18:1 **23:19** [r] S ver 9 [s] S Ge 13:18; Jos 14:13; 1Ch 29:27 [t] Ge 49:31 **23:20** [u] Jer 32:10 [v] S Ge 10:15; 35:29; 47:30; 49:30; 50:5, 13 **24:1** [w] S Ge 17:17; Jos 23:1 [x] Ge 12:2; Gal 3:9 [y] ver 35 **24:2** [z] S Ge 15:3 [a] Ge 39:4-6 [b] ver 9; Ge 47:29 **24:3** [c] Ge 47:31; 50:25 [d] ver 7 [e] S Ge 14:19; S Nu 20:14 [f] Dt 7:3; 2Co 6:14-17 [g] S Ge 10:15-19 [h] ver 37 **24:4** [i] S Ge 12:1; Jdg 14:3 [j] S ver 29; S Ge 21:21 **24:5** [k] ver 39 [l] Heb 11:15 **24:6** [m] ver 8 **24:7** [n] ver 3 [o] Ge 12:1 [p] Ro 4:13; Gal 3:16* [q] S Ge 12:7 [r] S Ge 16:7 **24:8** [s] ver 41; Jos 2:12, 17, 20; 9:20 [t] S ver 6 **24:9** [u] S ver 2 [v] Ge 32:4; 33:8 **24:10** [w] ver 19; 1Ki 10:2; 1Ch 12:40; Isa 30:6 [x] ver 22, 30, 47, 53; Ge 43:11; 45:23 [y] Nu 23:7; Dt 23:4; Jdg 3:8 [z] S Ge 11:29 **24:11** [a] Ex 2:15 [b] ver 13; Ge 29:2, 9-10; Ex 2:16; 1Sa 9:11; Jn 4:7 **24:12** [c] ver 27, 42, 48; Ge 26:24; 28:13; 31:42, 53; 32:9; 43:23; 46:3; Ex 3:6, 15, 16; 4:5; 1Ki 18:36; Ps 75:9; 94:7 [d] ver 21, 40, 51, 56; Ge 27:20; Ne 1:11 [e] S Ge 19:19; Jos 2:12; Job 10:12 **24:13** [f] S ver 11, 43; Ge 29:8 **24:14** [g] ver 18, 46 [h] ver 19 [i] ver 44 [j] Jos 2:12; Jdg 6:17, 37; 1Sa 14:10; 1Ki 13:3; Ps 86:17; Isa 38:7; Jer 44:29 **24:15** [k] ver 45 [l] S Ge 22:23 [m] S Ge 22:22

23:17 *the field and the cave in it, and all the trees.* Ephron had held out for the sale of the entire field and its contents (see notes on vv. 9,15).

23:19 *buried his wife … in the land of Canaan.* In that culture, people had a strong desire to be buried with their ancestors (see note on 25:8) in their native land. By purchasing a burial place in Canaan, Abraham indicated his unswerving commitment to the Lord's promise. Canaan was his new homeland.

24:1-67 Abraham obtains a suitable wife for Isaac, relying on God who has made a covenant with him to provide an appropriate mother for his descendants who would inherit the land (see vv. 6-7).

24:2 *senior servant in his household.* Probably Eliezer of Damascus (see note on 15:2). *Put your hand under my thigh.* Near the organ of procreation, probably because this oath was related to Abraham's last will and testament and called for faithful implementation on the part of his son. Isaac must accept Abraham's and God's choice (see also 47:29 and note).

24:3 *the LORD, the God of heaven and the God of earth.* See v. 7; see also note on 1:1. For a similar majestic title used by Abraham in an oath, see 14:22.

24:4 *my country.* Mesopotamia (see note on v. 10). *get a wife for my son.* See note on 21:21.

24:7 *To your offspring I will give this land.* Repeats the promise of 12:7. *his angel.* See note on 16:7.

24:10 *camels.* See note on 12:16. *Aram Naharaim.* See NIV text note; the name means "Aram of the two rivers"—the Euphrates and the Tigris. Aram (see note on 10:22) Naharaim was the northern part of the area called later by the Greeks "Mesopotamia," meaning "between the rivers" (see map, p. 48). *town of Nahor.* Nahor is the same name as that of Abraham's brother (see v. 15; 11:26). The town is mentioned in clay tablets excavated beginning in 1933 at the ancient city of Mari on the Euphrates (see chart, p. xxiii; see also map, p. 48). Nahor was located in the Harran (see note on 11:31) district and was ruled by an Amorite prince in the eighteenth century BC.

24:11 *toward evening, the time the women go out to draw water.* After the midday heat had cooled.

24:14 *By this I will know.* Like his master Abraham, the servant asked God for a sign to validate his errand (see note on 15:8). *kindness.* See v. 27; probably a reference to God's covenant with Abraham, which had promised numerous descendants through Isaac (see 17:19; 21:12).

24:15 *Before he had finished praying.* God had already begun to answer. *Rebekah … was the daughter of Bethuel son of … the wife of Abraham's brother.* Isaac would thus be marrying his father's grandniece (see v. 48).

of Milkah,[n] who was the wife of Abraham's brother Nahor.[o] 16The woman was
very beautiful,[p] a virgin;[q] no man had
ever slept with her. She went down to the
spring, filled her jar and came up again.
17The servant hurried to meet her and
said, "Please give me a little water from
your jar."[r]
18"Drink,[s] my lord," she said, and quickly lowered the jar to her hands and gave
him a drink.
19After she had given him a drink,
she said, "I'll draw water for your camels[t] too,[u] until they have had enough to
drink." 20So she quickly emptied her jar
into the trough, ran back to the well to
draw more water, and drew enough for all
his camels.[v] 21Without saying a word, the
man watched her closely to learn whether or not the LORD had made his journey
successful.[w]
22When the camels had finished drinking, the man took out a gold nose ring[x]
weighing a beka[a] and two gold bracelets[y]
weighing ten shekels.[b] 23Then he asked,

24:15 [n]S Ge 11:29 [o]S Ge 11:29 **24:16** [p]S Ge 12:11 [q]Dt 22:15-21 **24:17** [r]ver 45; 1Ki 17:10; Jn 4:7 **24:18** [s]S ver 14 **24:19** [t]S ver 10 [u]ver 14 **24:20** [v]ver 46 **24:21** [w]S ver 12 **24:22** [x]ver 47; Ge 41:42; Isa 3:21; Eze 16:11-12 [y]S ver 10 **24:23** [z]ver 47 [a]Jdg 19:15; 20:4 **24:24** [b]ver 29, 47; S Ge 11:29 **24:25** [c]ver 32; Jdg 19:19 **24:26** [d]ver 48, 52; Ex 4:31; 12:27; 1Ch 29:20; 2Ch 20:18 **24:27** [e]Ge 14:20; Ex 18:10; Ru 4:14; 1Sa 25:32; 2Sa 18:28; 1Ki 1:48; 8:56; Ps 28:6; 41:13; 68:19; 106:48; Lk 1:68 [f]S ver 12 [g]ver 49; Ge 32:10; 47:29; Jos 2:14; Ps 98:3 [h]ver 21 [i]S ver 12, 48; S Ge 12:1 **24:28** [j]Ge 29:12 **24:29** [k]ver 4; Ge 25:20; 27:43; 28:2, 5; 29:5, 12, 13

"Whose daughter are you?[z] Please tell me,
is there room in your father's house for us
to spend the night?[a]"
24She answered him, "I am the daughter
of Bethuel, the son that Milkah bore to Nahor.[b]" 25And she added, "We have plenty
of straw and fodder,[c] as well as room for
you to spend the night."
26Then the man bowed down and worshiped the LORD,[d] 27saying, "Praise be to
the LORD,[e] the God of my master Abraham,[f] who has not abandoned his kindness and faithfulness[g] to my master. As for
me, the LORD has led me on the journey[h] to
the house of my master's relatives."[i]
28The young woman ran and told her
mother's household about these things.[j]
29Now Rebekah had a brother named Laban,[k] and he hurried out to the man at

[a] *22* That is, about 1/5 ounce or about 5.7 grams
[b] *22* That is, about 4 ounces or about 115 grams

24:22 *beka.* Half a shekel (see Ex 38:26); see note on 20:16.

MESOPOTAMIA

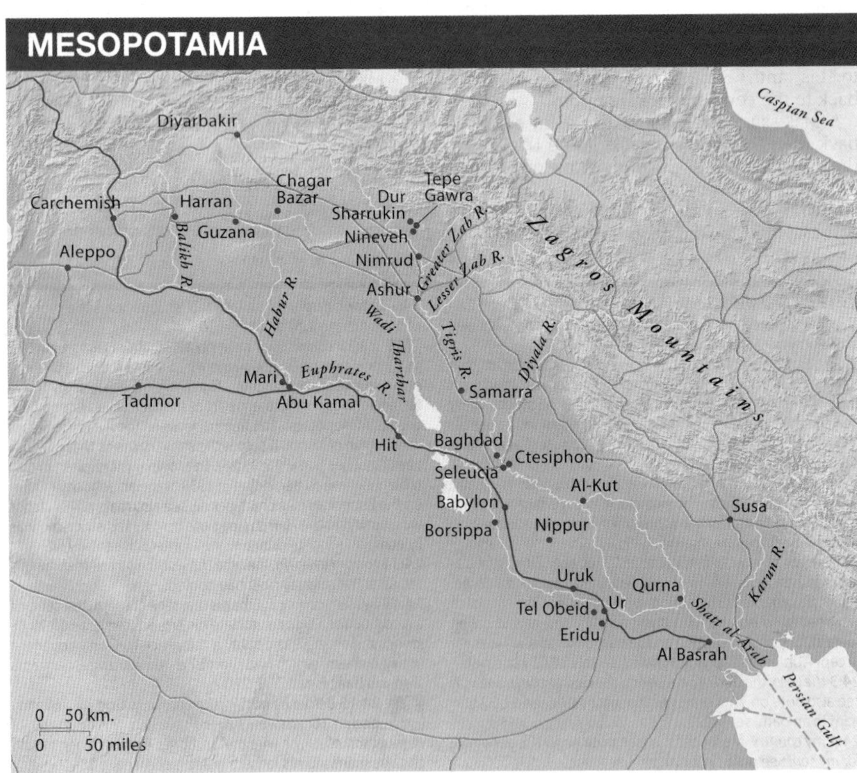

the spring. 30 As soon as he had seen the nose ring, and the bracelets on his sister's arms,[l] and had heard Rebekah tell what the man said to her, he went out to the man and found him standing by the camels near the spring. 31 "Come, you who are blessed by the LORD,"[m] he said. "Why are you standing out here? I have prepared the house and a place for the camels."

32 So the man went to the house, and the camels were unloaded. Straw and fodder[n] were brought for the camels, and water for him and his men to wash their feet.[o] 33 Then food was set before him, but he said, "I will not eat until I have told you what I have to say."

"Then tell us," Laban said.

34 So he said, "I am Abraham's servant.[p] 35 The LORD has blessed[q] my master abundantly,[r] and he has become wealthy.[s] He has given him sheep and cattle, silver and gold, male and female servants, and camels and donkeys.[t] 36 My master's wife Sarah has borne him a son in her old age,[u] and he has given him everything he owns.[v] 37 And my master made me swear an oath,[w] and said, 'You must not get a wife for my son from the daughters of the Canaanites, in whose land I live,[x] 38 but go to my father's family and to my own clan, and get a wife for my son.'[y]

39 "Then I asked my master, 'What if the woman will not come back with me?'[z]

40 "He replied, 'The LORD, before whom I have walked faithfully,[a] will send his angel with you[b] and make your journey a success,[c] so that you can get a wife for my son from my own clan and from my father's family.[d] 41 You will be released from my oath if, when you go to my clan, they refuse to give her to you—then you will be released from my oath.'[e]

42 "When I came to the spring today, I said, 'LORD, God of my master Abraham, if you will, please grant success[f] to the journey on which I have come. 43 See, I am standing beside this spring.[g] If a young woman[h] comes out to draw water and I say to her, "Please let me drink a little water from your jar,"[i] 44 and if she says to me, "Drink, and I'll draw water for your camels too," let her be the one the LORD has chosen for my master's son.'[j]

45 "Before I finished praying in my heart,[k] Rebekah came out, with her jar on her shoulder.[l] She went down to the spring and drew water, and I said to her, 'Please give me a drink.'[m]

46 "She quickly lowered her jar from her shoulder and said, 'Drink, and I'll water your camels too.'[n] So I drank, and she watered the camels also.[o]

47 "I asked her, 'Whose daughter are you?'[p]

"She said, 'The daughter of Bethuel[q] son of Nahor, whom Milkah bore to him.'[r]

"Then I put the ring in her nose[s] and the bracelets on her arms,[t] 48 and I bowed down and worshiped the LORD.[u] I praised the LORD, the God of my master Abraham,[v] who had led me on the right road to get the granddaughter of my master's brother for his son.[w] 49 Now if you will show kindness and faithfulness[x] to my master, tell me; and if not, tell me, so I may know which way to turn."

50 Laban and Bethuel[y] answered, "This is from the LORD;[z] we can say nothing to you one way or the other.[a] 51 Here is Rebekah; take her and go, and let her become the wife of your master's son, as the LORD has directed.[b]"

52 When Abraham's servant heard what they said, he bowed down to the ground before the LORD.[c] 53 Then the servant brought out gold and silver jewelry and articles of clothing[d] and gave them to Rebekah; he also gave costly gifts[e] to her brother and to her mother. 54 Then he and the men who were with him ate and drank and spent the night there.

When they got up the next morning, he said, "Send me on my way[f] to my master."

55 But her brother and her mother replied, "Let the young woman remain with us ten days or so;[g] then you[a] may go."

56 But he said to them, "Do not detain me, now that the LORD has granted success[h] to my journey. Send me on my way[i] so I may go to my master."

57 Then they said, "Let's call the young woman and ask her about it."[j] 58 So they called Rebekah and asked her, "Will you go with this man?"

"I will go,"[k] she said.

59 So they sent their sister Rebekah on her way,[l] along with her nurse[m] and Abraham's servant and his men. 60 And they blessed[n] Rebekah and said to her,

> "Our sister, may you increase
> to thousands upon thousands;[o]

24:30 [l] S ver 10; Eze 23:42
24:31 [m] Ge 26:29; Ps 115:15
24:32 [n] S ver 25 [o] S Ge 18:4
24:34 [p] S Ge 15:3
24:35 [q] S Ge 12:2 [r] ver 1 [s] S Ge 23:6 [t] S Ge 12:16
24:36 [u] S Ge 17:17 [v] Ge 25:5; 26:14
24:37 [w] Ge 50:5, 25 [x] ver 3
24:38 [y] S Ge 21:21
24:39 [z] S ver 5
24:40 [a] S Ge 5:22 [b] S Ge 16:7 [c] S ver 12 [d] S Ge 12:1
24:41 [e] S ver 8
24:42 [f] S ver 12
24:43 [g] S ver 13 [h] Pr 30:19; Isa 7:14 [i] S ver 14
24:44 [j] ver 14
24:45 [k] 1Sa 1:13 [l] ver 15 [m] S ver 17; Jn 4:7
24:46 [n] ver 18-19 [o] ver 20
24:47 [p] ver 23 [q] S Ge 22:22 [r] S ver 24 [s] S ver 22 [t] S ver 10; Isa 3:19; Eze 16:11-12
24:48 [u] S ver 26 [v] S ver 12 [w] S ver 27
24:49 [x] S ver 27
24:50 [y] Ge 22:22 [z] Ps 118:23 [a] Ge 31:7, 24, 29, 42; 48:16
24:51 [b] S ver 12
24:52 [c] S ver 26
24:53 [d] Ge 45:22; Ex 3:22; 12:35; 2Ki 5:5 [e] S ver 10, 22
24:54 [f] ver 56, 59; Ge 30:25
24:55 [g] Jdg 19:4
24:56 [h] S ver 12 [i] S ver 54
24:57 [j] Jdg 19:3
24:58 [k] Ru 1:16
24:59 [l] S ver 54 [m] Ge 35:8
24:60 [n] Ge 27:4, 19; 28:1; 31:55; 48:9, 15, 20; Jos 22:6 [o] S Ge 17:16

[a] 55 Or *she*

24:32–33 See note on 18:2.
24:34–49 The servant explained his mission to Rebekah's family. His speech, which summarizes the narrative of the earlier part of the chapter, is an excellent example of the ancient storyteller's art, which was designed to fix the details of a story in the hearer's memory.
24:40 *before whom I have walked faithfully.* See notes on 5:22; 6:8–9; 17:1.
24:53 The rich gifts bestowed on Rebekah and her family indicated the wealth of the household into which she was being asked to marry—far from her loved ones and homeland.
24:60 See 22:17 and note.

may your offspring possess
the cities of their enemies."[p]

61 Then Rebekah and her attendants[q] got
ready and mounted the camels and went
back with the man. So the servant took
Rebekah and left.

62 Now Isaac had come from Beer Lahai
Roi,[r] for he was living in the Negev.[s] 63 He
went out to the field one evening to meditate,[a][t] and as he looked up,[u] he saw camels approaching. 64 Rebekah also looked
up and saw Isaac. She got down from her
camel[v] 65 and asked the servant, "Who is
that man in the field coming to meet us?"

"He is my master," the servant answered. So she took her veil[w] and covered
herself.

66 Then the servant told Isaac all he had
done. 67 Isaac brought her into the tent[x] of
his mother Sarah,[y] and he married Rebekah.[z] So she became his wife, and he loved
her;[a] and Isaac was comforted after his
mother's death.[b]

The Death of Abraham

25:1-4pp — 1Ch 1:32-33

25 Abraham had taken another wife,
whose name was Keturah. 2 She
bore him Zimran,[c] Jokshan, Medan, Midian,[d] Ishbak and Shuah.[e] 3 Jokshan was the
father of Sheba[f] and Dedan;[g] the descendants of Dedan were the Ashurites, the Le-
tushites and the Leummites. 4 The sons of
Midian were Ephah,[h] Epher, Hanok, Abida
and Eldaah. All these were descendants of
Keturah.

5 Abraham left everything he owned to
Isaac.[i] 6 But while he was still living, he
gave gifts to the sons of his concubines[j]
and sent them away from his son Isaac[k] to
the land of the east.[l]

7 Abraham lived a hundred and seventy-
five years.[m] 8 Then Abraham breathed his
last and died at a good old age,[n] an old
man and full of years; and he was gathered to his people.[o] 9 His sons Isaac and
Ishmael buried him[p] in the cave of Machpelah[q] near Mamre,[r] in the field of Ephron[s]
son of Zohar the Hittite,[t] 10 the field Abraham had bought from the Hittites.[b][u] There
Abraham was buried with his wife Sarah.
11 After Abraham's death, God blessed his
son Isaac,[v] who then lived near Beer Lahai Roi.[w]

Ishmael's Sons

25:12-16pp — 1Ch 1:29-31

12 This is the account[x] of the family line
of Abraham's son Ishmael, whom Sarah's
slave, Hagar[y] the Egyptian, bore to Abraham.[z]

13 These are the names of the sons of
Ishmael, listed in the order of their birth:
Nebaioth[a] the firstborn of Ishmael, Kedar,[b]
Adbeel, Mibsam, 14 Mishma, Dumah,[c] Massa, 15 Hadad, Tema,[d] Jetur,[e] Naphish and
Kedemah. 16 These were the sons of Ishmael, and these are the names of the twelve
tribal rulers[f] according to their settlements
and camps.[g] 17 Ishmael lived a hundred and
thirty-seven years. He breathed his last and
died, and he was gathered to his people.[h]

[a] 63 The meaning of the Hebrew for this word is uncertain. [b] 10 Or *the descendants of Heth*

24:60 [p] Ge 22:17; Ps 127:5; Pr 27:11 **24:61** [q] S Ge 16:1; 30:3; 46:25 **24:62** [r] S Ge 16:14 [s] S Ge 12:9 **24:63** [t] Jos 1:8; Ps 1:2; 77:12; 119:15,27,48, 97,148; 143:5; 145:5 [u] Ge 18:2 **24:64** [v] Ge 31:17,34; 1Sa 30:17 **24:65** [w] Ge 38:14; SS 1:7; 4:1,3; 6:7; Isa 47:2 **24:67** [x] Ge 31:33 [y] S Ge 18:9 [z] Ge 25:20; 49:31 [a] Ge 29:18,20; 34:3; Jdg 16:4 [b] Ge 23:1-2 **25:2** [c] Jer 25:25 [d] Ge 36:35; 37:28,36; Ex 2:15; Nu 22:4; 25:6, 18; 31:2; Jos 13:21; Jdg 6:1,3; 7:1; 8:1,22,24; 9:17; 1Ki 11:18; Ps 83:9; Isa 9:4; 10:26; 60:6; Hab 3:7 [e] Job 2:11; 8:1 **25:3** [f] S Ge 10:7 [g] S Ge 10:7 **25:4** [h] Isa 60:6 **25:5** [i] S Ge 24:36 **25:6** [j] S Ge 22:24 [k] S Ge 21:10, 14 [l] Ge 29:1; Jdg 6:3,33; 1Ki 4:30; Job 1:3; Eze 25:4 **25:7** [m] ver 26; Ge 12:4; 35:28; 47:9, 28; 50:22,26; Job 42:16 **25:8** [n] S Ge 15:15 [o] ver 17; Ge 35:29; 49:29,33; Nu 20:24; 31:2; Dt 31:14; 32:50; 34:5 **25:9** [p] Ge 35:29; 47:30; 49:31 [q] S Ge 23:9 [r] S Ge 13:18 [s] Ge 23:8 [t] Ge 49:29; 50:13 **25:10** [u] S Ge 10:15 **25:11** [v] S Ge 12:2 [w] S Ge 16:14 **25:12** [x] S Ge 2:4 [y] S Ge 16:1 [z] S Ge 17:20; 21:18 **25:13** [a] Ge 28:9; 36:3 [b] Ps 120:5; SS 1:5; Isa 21:16; 42:11; 60:7; Jer 2:10; 49:28; Eze 27:21 **25:14** [c] Jos 15:52; Isa 21:11; Ob 1:1 **25:15** [d] Job 6:19; Isa 21:14; Jer 25:23 [e] 1Ch 5:19 **25:16** [f] Ge 17:20 [g] S Ge 13:16; Ps 83:6 **25:17** [h] S ver 8

24:62 *Beer Lahai Roi.* See note on 16:14. *Negev.* See note on 12:9.

24:65 *she took her veil and covered herself.* Apparently a sign that she was unmarried (cf. 38:14,19).

24:67 *tent.* Often used as a bridal chamber (see Ps 19:4–5).

25:1–6 Abraham's final disposition of his estate.

25:1 *had taken.* Abraham would have been 140 years old at this time if the order were chronological; hence, "had taken" instead of "took." *wife.* Elsewhere called Abraham's "concubine" (1Ch 1:32).

25:2 *She bore him.* The listing of Keturah's offspring shows that Abraham indeed became "the father of many nations" (17:4; see note on 17:6).

25:5 *left everything he owned to Isaac.* Isaac was the "only son" (22:2; see note there) of Abraham's wife Sarah, so he was the legal heir to Abraham's estate (cf. 21:10 and note).

25:6 *concubines.* Secondary wives, a common cultural phenomenon in the ancient Near East. Polygamy was practiced even by godly men in ancient times, though it was not the original divine intention (see notes on 2:24; 4:19).

25:7 *a hundred and seventy-five years.* Abraham thus lived for a full 100 years in the promised land (see 12:4 and note).

25:8 *died at a good old age.* As God had promised (see 15:15). *old man and full of years.* A phrase used also of the patriarch Job (see Job 42:17). *was gathered to his people.* Joined his ancestors and/or deceased relatives in death (see 2Ki 22:20; 2Ch 34:28).

25:9 *Isaac and Ishmael.* Isaac, as the heir of the covenant and estate (see note on v. 5), is listed first.

25:11 *Beer Lahai Roi.* See note on 16:14.

25:12–18 A brief account of Ishmael's family line, showing the fulfillment of the promises made to Hagar (16:10) and Abraham (17:20) concerning their son but also noting the fulfillment of his predicted alienation from the descendants of Abraham and Sarah (16:12).

25:12 *account.* See note on 2:4.

25:13 *names of the sons of Ishmael.* Many are Arab names, giving credence to the Arab tradition that Ishmael is their ancestor.

25:16 *twelve tribal rulers.* Twelve major tribes descended from Abraham's son Ishmael (as predicted in 17:20)—as was also true of Abraham's brother Nahor (see note on 22:23–24).

18 His descendants[i] settled in the area from
Havilah to Shur,[j] near the eastern border
of Egypt, as you go toward Ashur. And
they lived in hostility toward[a] all the tribes
related to them.[k]

Jacob and Esau

19 This is the account[l] of the family line
of Abraham's son Isaac.

Abraham became the father of Isaac,
20 and Isaac was forty years old[m] when he
married Rebekah[n] daughter of Bethuel[o] the
Aramean from Paddan Aram[b][p] and sister
of Laban[q] the Aramean.[r]
21 Isaac prayed to the LORD on behalf of
his wife, because she was childless.[s] The
LORD answered his prayer,[t] and his wife
Rebekah became pregnant. 22 The babies
jostled each other within her, and she
said, "Why is this happening to me?" So
she went to inquire of the LORD.[u]
23 The LORD said to her,

"Two nations[v] are in your womb,
and two peoples from within you
will be separated;
one people will be stronger than the
other,
and the older will serve the
younger.[w]"

24 When the time came for her to give
birth,[x] there were twin boys in her womb.[y]
25 The first to come out was red,[z] and his
whole body was like a hairy garment;[a] so
they named him Esau.[c][b] 26 After this, his
brother came out,[c] with his hand grasping Esau's heel;[d] so he was named Jacob.[d][e]
Isaac was sixty years old[f] when Rebekah
gave birth to them.
27 The boys grew up, and Esau became
a skillful hunter,[g] a man of the open country,[h] while Jacob was content to stay at
home among the tents. 28 Isaac, who had
a taste for wild game,[i] loved Esau, but Rebekah loved Jacob.[j]
29 Once when Jacob was cooking some
stew,[k] Esau came in from the open country,[l] famished. 30 He said to Jacob, "Quick,
let me have some of that red stew![m] I'm
famished!" (That is why he was also called
Edom.[e])[n]
31 Jacob replied, "First sell me your
birthright.[o]"
32 "Look, I am about to die," Esau said.
"What good is the birthright to me?"
33 But Jacob said, "Swear[p] to me first."
So he swore an oath to him, selling his
birthright[q] to Jacob.
34 Then Jacob gave Esau some bread and
some lentil stew.[r] He ate and drank, and
then got up and left.
So Esau despised his birthright.

25:18 [i]S Ge 17:20; 21:18 [j]S Ge 16:7 [k]Ge 16:12 **25:19** [l]S Ge 2:4 **25:20** [m]ver 26; Ge 26:34; 35:28 [n]S Ge 24:67 [o]S Ge 22:22 [p]Ge 28:2,5,6; 30:20; 31:18; 33:18; 35:9, 26; 46:15; 48:7 [q]S Ge 24:29 [r]Ge 31:20,24; Dt 26:5 **25:21** [s]S Ge 11:30 [t]Ge 30:17, 22; 1Sa 1:17, 23; 1Ch 5:20; 2Ch 33:13; Ezr 8:23; Ps 127:3 **25:22** [u]Ex 18:15; 28:30; 33:7; Lev 24:12; Nu 9:6-8; 27:5, 21; Dt 17:9; Jdg 18:5; 1Sa 9:9; 10:22; 14:36; 22:10; 1Ki 22:8; 2Ki 3:11; 22:13; Isa 30:2; Jer 21:2; 37:7, 17; Eze 14:7; 20:1,3 **25:23** [v]S Ge 17:4 [w]S Ge 9:25; 48:14,19; Ro 9:11-12* **25:24** [x]Lk 1:57; 2:6 [y]Ge 38:27 **25:25** [z]1Sa 16:12 [a]Ge 27:11 [b]Ge 27:1,15 **25:26** [c]Ge 38:29

[a] *18* Or *lived to the east of* [b] *20* That is, Northwest Mesopotamia [c] *25* *Esau* may mean *hairy.*
[d] *26* *Jacob* means *he grasps the heel,* a Hebrew idiom for *he deceives.* [e] *30* *Edom* means *red.*

[d]Hos 12:3 [e]Ge 27:36; 32:27; Dt 23:7; Jos 24:4; Ob 1:10, 12 [f]S ver 7, S 20 **25:27** [g]S Ge 10:9 [h]ver 29; Ge 27:3,5 **25:28** [i]Ge 27:3,4,9,14,19 [j]Ge 27:6; 37:3 **25:29** [k]2Ki 4:38-40 [l]S ver 27 **25:30** [m]ver 34 [n]Ge 32:3; 36:1,8,8-9,19; Nu 20:14; Dt 23:7; Ps 137:7; Jer 25:21; 40:11; 49:7 **25:31** [o]Dt 21:16-17; 1Ch 5:1-2 **25:33** [p]S Ge 21:23; S 47:31 [q]Ge 27:36; Heb 12:16 **25:34** [r]ver 30

25:18 *in hostility toward.* See note on 16:12; or possibly "to the east of" (see NIV text notes here and on 16:12; see also 25:6).

25:19—35:29 The author now takes up the story of Jacob, which he continues until the death of Isaac. Isaac is the link between Abraham and Jacob, and his story is interwoven with theirs.

25:19 *account.* See note on 2:4. *Abraham became the father of Isaac.* In c. 2066 BC.

25:20 *Paddan Aram.* See NIV text note; means "plain of Aram," another name for Aram Naharaim (see note on 24:10).

25:21 *because she was childless.* As Sarah had been (see 11:30 and note). Rebekah was barren for 20 years (vv. 20,26). Isaac's offspring, like Abraham's, were a special gift in fulfillment of God's covenant promises.

25:22 *jostled each other.* The struggle between Jacob and Esau began in the womb (see also v. 26). *went.* Perhaps to a nearby place of worship.

25:23 *the older will serve the younger.* The ancient law of primogeniture (cf. Dt 21:15–17 and notes) provided that, under ordinary circumstances, the younger of two sons would be subservient to the older. God's election of the younger son highlights the fact that God's people are the product not of natural or worldly development but of his sovereign intervention in human affairs (see note on 11:30). Part of this verse is quoted in Ro 9:10–12 as an example of God's sovereign right to do "whatever pleases him" (Ps 115:3)—not in an arbitrary way (see Ro 9:14), but according to his own perfect will.

25:24–26 For another unusual birth of twin boys, see 38:27–30.

25:25 *red.* A pun on Edom, one of Esau's other names (see v. 30 and NIV text note).

25:26 *his brother came out ... Jacob.* In c. 2006 BC. *his hand grasping Esau's heel.* Hostility between the Israelites (Jacob's descendants) and Edomites (Esau's descendants) became the rule rather than the exception (see, e.g., Nu 20:14–21; Ob 9–10). *Jacob.* See NIV text note. The name became proverbial for the unsavory quality of deceptiveness (see NIV text note on Jer 9:4).

25:31 *sell me your birthright.* In ancient times the birthright included the inheritance rights of the firstborn (see Heb 12:16). Jacob was ever the schemer, seeking by any means to gain advantage over others. But it was by God's appointment and care, not Jacob's wits, that he came into the blessing.

25:33 *Swear to me first.* A verbal oath was all that was required to make the transaction legal and forever binding.

25:34 *lentil.* A small, pea-like annual plant, the pods of which turn reddish-brown when boiled. It grows well even in bad soil and has provided an important source of nourishment in the Near East since ancient times (see 2Sa 17:28; 23:11; Eze 4:9). *Esau despised his birthright.* In so doing, he proved himself to be "godless" (Heb 12:16), since at the heart of the birthright were the covenant promises that Isaac had inherited from Abraham.

Isaac and Abimelek

26:1-11Ref — Ge 12:10-20; 20:1-18

26 Now there was a famine in the land[s] — besides the previous famine in Abraham's time — and Isaac went to Abimelek king of the Philistines[t] in Gerar.[u] 2 The LORD appeared[v] to Isaac and said, "Do not go down to Egypt;[w] live in the land where I tell you to live.[x] 3 Stay in this land for a while,[y] and I will be with you[z] and will bless you.[a] For to you and your descendants I will give all these lands[b] and will confirm the oath I swore to your father Abraham.[c] 4 I will make your descendants[d] as numerous as the stars in the sky[e] and will give them all these lands,[f] and through your offspring[a] all nations on earth will be blessed,[b][g] 5 because Abraham obeyed me[h] and did everything I required of him, keeping my commands, my decrees[i] and my instructions.[j]" 6 So Isaac stayed in Gerar.[k]

7 When the men of that place asked him about his wife, he said, "She is my sister,[l]" because he was afraid to say, "She is my wife." He thought, "The men of this place might kill me on account of Rebekah, because she is beautiful."

8 When Isaac had been there a long time, Abimelek king of the Philistines[m] looked down from a window and saw Isaac caressing his wife Rebekah. 9 So Abimelek summoned Isaac and said, "She is really your wife! Why did you say, 'She is my sister'?[n]"

Isaac answered him, "Because I thought I might lose my life on account of her."

10 Then Abimelek said, "What is this you have done to us?[o] One of the men might well have slept with your wife, and you would have brought guilt upon us."

11 So Abimelek gave orders to all the people: "Anyone who harms[p] this man or his wife shall surely be put to death."[q]

12 Isaac planted crops in that land and the same year reaped a hundredfold,[r] because the LORD blessed him.[s] 13 The man became rich, and his wealth continued to grow until he became very wealthy.[t] 14 He had so many flocks and herds and servants[u] that the Philistines envied him.[v] 15 So all the wells[w] that his father's servants had dug in the time of his father Abraham, the Philistines stopped up,[x] filling them with earth.

16 Then Abimelek said to Isaac, "Move away from us;[y] you have become too powerful for us.[z]"

17 So Isaac moved away from there and encamped in the Valley of Gerar,[a] where he settled. 18 Isaac reopened the wells[b] that had been dug in the time of his father Abraham, which the Philistines had stopped up after Abraham died, and he gave them the same names his father had given them.

19 Isaac's servants dug in the valley and discovered a well of fresh water there. 20 But the herders of Gerar quarreled[c] with those of Isaac and said, "The water is ours!"[d] So he named the well Esek,[c] because they disputed with him. 21 Then they dug another well, but they quarreled[e] over that one also; so he named it Sitnah.[d]

[a] 4 Or *seed* [b] 4 Or *and all nations on earth will use the name of your offspring in blessings* (see 48:20) [c] 20 *Esek* means *dispute.* [d] 21 *Sitnah* means *opposition.*

26:1 [s] S Ge 12:10; S Dt 32:24 [t] S Ge 10:14; Jdg 10:6 [u] S Ge 20:1 **26:2** [v] S Ge 12:7 [w] Ge 46:3 [x] S Ge 12:1 **26:3** [y] Ge 20:1 [z] S Ge 21:20; 27:45; 31:3,5; 32:9; 35:3; 48:21; Ex 3:12; 33:14-16; Nu 23:21; Dt 31:23; Jos 1:5; Isa 43:2; Jer 1:8,19; Hag 1:13 [a] ver 12; S Ge 12:2 [b] S Ge 12:7; Ac 7:5 [c] S Ge 17:19 **26:4** [d] ver 24; Ge 48:4 [e] S Ge 12:2; S Nu 10:36 [f] S Ge 12:7 [g] S Ge 12:3; Ac 3:25*; Gal 3:8 **26:5** [h] S Ge 18:19 [i] Ps 119:80, 112; Eze 18:21 [j] Lev 18:4,5, 26; 19:19,37; 20:8,22; 25:18; 26:3; Nu 15:40; Dt 4:40; 6:2; 11:1; 1Ki 2:3 **26:6** [k] S Ge 20:1 **26:7** [l] S Ge 12:13 **26:8** [m] S Ge 10:14 **26:9** [n] S Ge 12:19 **26:10** [o] S Ge 12:18 **26:11** [p] 1Sa 24:6; 26:9; Ps 105:15 [q] S Ge 20:3 **26:12** [r] Mt 13:8 [s] S ver 3

26:13 [t] S Ge 13:2; S Dt 8:18 **26:14** [u] S Ge 12:16; S 24:36; 32:23 [v] Ge 37:11 **26:15** [w] S Ge 21:30 [x] S Ge 21:25 **26:16** [y] ver 27; Jdg 11:7 [z] Ex 1:9; Ps 105:24-25 **26:17** [a] S Ge 20:1 **26:18** [b] S Ge 21:30 **26:20** [c] S Ge 13:7 [d] Ge 21:25 **26:21** [e] S Ge 13:7

26:1 – 33 The events of some of these verses (e.g., vv. 1 – 11) occurred before the birth of Esau and Jacob. Verses 1 – 11 are placed here to highlight the fact that the birthright and blessing Jacob struggled to obtain from his father (see 25:22,31 – 33; 27:5 – 29) involved the covenant inheritance of Abraham that Isaac had received.

26:1 *previous famine in Abraham's time.* See 12:10. *Abimelek.* Probably the son or grandson of the earlier king who bore the same name (see 20:2). *Philistines.* See note on 10:14. *Gerar.* See note on 20:1.

26:2 *appeared.* See note on 12:7.

26:3 *I will be with you.* God's promise to be a sustainer and protector of his people is repeated often (see, e.g., v. 24; 28:15 and note; 31:3; Jos 1:5; Isa 41:10; Jer 1:8,19; Mt 28:20; Ac 18:10; see also Ge 17:7 and note). *the oath I swore to your father Abraham.* See 22:16 – 18.

26:4 *descendants as numerous as the stars in the sky.* See 13:16; 15:5 and notes. *through your offspring all nations on earth will be blessed.* See note on 12:2 – 3.

26:5 *because Abraham obeyed me.* See note on 17:9. *everything I required ... commands ... decrees ... instructions.* Legal language describing various aspects of the divine regulations that God's people were expected to keep (see Lev 26:14 – 16,46; Dt 11:1). Addressing Israel after the covenant at Sinai, the author of Genesis used language that strictly applied only to that covenant. But he emphasized to the Israelites that their father Abraham had been obedient to God's will in his time and that they must follow his example if they were to receive the covenant promises.

26:7 *because she is beautiful.* See 12:11,14.

26:8 *caressing.* The word in Hebrew (a form of the verb translated "laugh" in 17:17; 18:12 – 13,15; 21:6 and "mock" in 21:9) is yet another pun on Isaac's name.

26:12 *reaped a hundredfold.* Indicative of the fertility of the promised land.

26:16 *you have become too powerful for us.* An indication that the covenant promises were being fulfilled. Already in the days of the patriarchs, the presence of God's people in the land was seen as a threat by the peoples of the world. As the world's people pursued their own godless living, God's people aroused their hostility. A similar complaint was voiced by an Egyptian pharaoh hundreds of years later (Ex 1:9).

26:20 *The water is ours!* In those arid regions, disputes over water rights and pasturelands were common (see 13:6 and note; 21:25; 36:7).

22 He moved on from there and dug another well, and no one quarreled over it. He named it Rehoboth,[a][f] saying, "Now the LORD has given us room[g] and we will flourish[h] in the land."

23 From there he went up to Beersheba.[i] 24 That night the LORD appeared to him and said, "I am the God of your father Abraham.[j] Do not be afraid,[k] for I am with you;[l] I will bless you and will increase the number of your descendants[m] for the sake of my servant Abraham."[n]

25 Isaac built an altar[o] there and called on the name of the LORD.[p] There he pitched his tent, and there his servants dug a well.[q]

26 Meanwhile, Abimelek had come to him from Gerar, with Ahuzzath his personal adviser and Phicol the commander of his forces.[r] 27 Isaac asked them, "Why have you come to me, since you were hostile to me and sent me away?[s]"

28 They answered, "We saw clearly that the LORD was with you;[t] so we said, 'There ought to be a sworn agreement between us'—between us and you. Let us make a treaty[u] with you 29 that you will do us no harm,[v] just as we did not harm you but always treated you well and sent you away peacefully. And now you are blessed by the LORD."[w]

30 Isaac then made a feast[x] for them, and they ate and drank. 31 Early the next morning the men swore an oath[y] to each other. Then Isaac sent them on their way, and they went away peacefully.

32 That day Isaac's servants came and told him about the well[z] they had dug. They said, "We've found water!" 33 He called it Shibah,[b] and to this day the name of the town has been Beersheba.[c][a]

26:22 [f] Ge 36:37 [g] Ps 18:19; Isa 33:20; 54:2; Am 9:11 [h] S Ge 17:6
26:23 [i] S Ge 22:19
26:24 [j] S Ge 24:12 [k] S Ge 15:1; S Jos 8:1 [l] S Ge 21:20 [m] S ver 4 [n] ver 4; Ge 17:7; S 22:17; 28:14; 30:27; 39:5; Dt 13:17
26:25 [o] S Ge 8:20 [p] S Ge 4:26; S Ac 2:21 [q] S Ge 21:30
26:26 [r] S Ge 21:22
26:27 [s] S ver 16
26:28 [t] S Ge 21:22 [u] S Ge 21:27; Jos 9:6
26:29 [v] Ge 31:29, 52 [w] S Ge 24:31
26:30 [x] Ge 31:54; Ex 18:12; 24:11; 1Sa 20:27
26:31 [y] S Ge 21:23, 27
26:32 [z] S Ge 21:30
26:33 [a] S Ge 21:14
26:34 [b] S Ge 25:20 [c] S Ge 10:15; 28:9; 36:2; Jos 3:10; 1Sa 26:6; 1Ki 10:29
26:35 [d] Ge 27:46; 28:8; Job 7:16
27:1 [e] Ge 48:10; Dt 34:7; 1Sa 3:2 [f] S Ge 25:25
27:2 [g] Ge 47:29; 1Ki 2:1
27:3 [h] S Ge 25:27

Jacob Takes Esau's Blessing

34 When Esau was forty years old,[b] he married Judith daughter of Beeri the Hittite, and also Basemath daughter of Elon the Hittite.[c] 35 They were a source of grief to Isaac and Rebekah.[d]

27 When Isaac was old and his eyes were so weak that he could no longer see,[e] he called for Esau his older son[f] and said to him, "My son."

"Here I am," he answered.

2 Isaac said, "I am now an old man and don't know the day of my death.[g] 3 Now then, get your equipment—your quiver and bow—and go out to the open country[h] to hunt some wild game for me. 4 Prepare me the kind of tasty food I like[i] and bring it to me to eat, so that I may give you my blessing[j] before I die."[k]

5 Now Rebekah was listening as Isaac spoke to his son Esau. When Esau left for the open country[l] to hunt game and bring it back, 6 Rebekah said to her son Jacob,[m] "Look, I overheard your father say to your brother Esau, 7 'Bring me some game and prepare me some tasty food to eat, so that I may give you my blessing in the presence of the LORD before I die.'[n] 8 Now, my son, listen carefully and do what I tell you:[o] 9 Go out to the flock and bring me two choice young goats,[p] so I can prepare some tasty food for your father, just the way he likes it.[q] 10 Then take it to your father to eat, so that he may give you his blessing[r] before he dies."

[a] 22 *Rehoboth* means *room.* [b] 33 *Shibah* can mean *oath* or *seven.* [c] 33 *Beersheba* can mean *well of the oath* and *well of seven.*

27:4 [i] S Ge 25:28 [j] ver 10, 25, 31; S Ge 24:60; 49:28; Dt 33:1; Heb 11:20 [k] ver 7 **27:5** [l] S Ge 25:27 **27:6** [m] S Ge 25:28 **27:7** [n] ver 4 **27:8** [o] ver 13, 43 **27:9** [p] 1Sa 16:20 [q] S Ge 25:28 **27:10** [r] S ver 4

26:25 *built an altar.* See note on 12:7. *called on the name of the LORD.* See 4:26 and note.

26:26 *Phicol.* See note on 21:22.

26:30 *made a feast.* Covenants were often concluded with a shared meal, signifying the bond of friendship (see 31:54; Ex 24:11 and notes).

26:33 *name of the town has been Beersheba.* See note on 21:31.

26:34 *When Esau was forty years old, he married.* As had his father Isaac (see 25:20). Forty years was roughly equivalent to a generation in later times (see Nu 32:13). *Judith ... Basemath.* In addition to these two wives, Esau also married Mahalath, "sister of Nebaioth and daughter of Ishmael" (28:9). The Esau genealogy of ch. 36 also mentions three wives, but they are identified as "Adah daughter of Elon the Hittite," "Oholibamah daughter of Anah ... the Hivite" and "Basemath daughter of Ishmael and sister of Nebaioth" (36:2–3). Possibly the lists have suffered in transmission, or perhaps alternative names or nicknames are used. It is also possible that Esau married more than three wives.

26:35 *They were a source of grief.* Isaac and Rebekah were determined not to allow Jacob to make the same mistake of marrying Hittite or Canaanite women (see 27:46—28:2).

27:1–40 How Rebekah and Jacob manipulated Isaac's last will and testament.

27:1 *eyes were so weak that he could no longer see.* In ancient times, blindness and near blindness were common among elderly people (see 48:10; 1Sa 4:15). *Here I am.* See note on 22:1.

27:4 *the kind of tasty food I like.* Rebekah and Jacob took advantage of Isaac's love for a certain kind of food (see vv. 9,14). *give you my blessing before I die.* Oral statements, including deathbed bequests (see 49:28–33), had legal force in ancient Near Eastern law. *blessing.* See note on v. 36.

27:5 *listening.* Eavesdropping.

27:6 *Rebekah.* Throughout the Jacob story the author develops a wordplay on "birthright" (*bekorah*) and "blessing" (*berakah*), both of which Jacob seeks to obtain, and Rebekah (*ribqah*) does her best to further the cause of her favorite son. *said to her son Jacob.* The parental favoritism mentioned in 25:28 is about to bear its poisonous fruit.

27:8 *my son, ... do what I tell you.* Rebekah proves to be just as deceitful as Jacob, whose very name signifies deceit (see NIV text notes on v. 36; 25:26).

11 Jacob said to Rebekah his mother,
"But my brother Esau is a hairy man[s]
while I have smooth skin. 12 What if my
father touches me?[t] I would appear to
be tricking him and would bring down a
curse[u] on myself rather than a blessing."
13 His mother said to him, "My son, let
the curse fall on me.[v] Just do what I say;[w]
go and get them for me."
14 So he went and got them and brought
them to his mother, and she prepared
some tasty food, just the way his father
liked it.[x] 15 Then Rebekah took the best
clothes[y] of Esau her older son,[z] which she
had in the house, and put them on her
younger son Jacob. 16 She also covered his
hands and the smooth part of his neck
with the goatskins.[a] 17 Then she handed to
her son Jacob the tasty food and the bread
she had made.
18 He went to his father and said, "My
father."
"Yes, my son," he answered. "Who
is it?"[b]
19 Jacob said to his father, "I am Esau
your firstborn.[c] I have done as you told me.
Please sit up and eat some of my game,[d]
so that you may give me your blessing."[e]
20 Isaac asked his son, "How did you
find it so quickly, my son?"
"The LORD your God gave me success,[f]"
he replied.
21 Then Isaac said to Jacob, "Come near
so I can touch you,[g] my son, to know
whether you really are my son Esau or
not."
22 Jacob went close to his father Isaac,[h]
who touched[i] him and said, "The voice is
the voice of Jacob, but the hands are the
hands of Esau." 23 He did not recognize
him, for his hands were hairy like those
of his brother Esau;[j] so he proceeded to
bless him. 24 "Are you really my son Esau?"
he asked.
"I am," he replied.
25 Then he said, "My son, bring me
some of your game to eat, so that I may
give you my blessing."[k]
Jacob brought it to him and he ate;
and he brought some wine and he drank.
26 Then his father Isaac said to him, "Come
here, my son, and kiss me."

27 So he went to him and kissed[l] him[m].
When Isaac caught the smell of his
clothes,[n] he blessed him and said,

"Ah, the smell of my son
is like the smell of a field
that the LORD has blessed.[o]
28 May God give you heaven's dew[p]
and earth's richness[q]—
an abundance of grain[r] and new
wine.[s]
29 May nations serve you
and peoples bow down to you.[t]
Be lord over your brothers,
and may the sons of your mother
bow down to you.[u]
May those who curse you be cursed
and those who bless you be
blessed.[v]"

30 After Isaac finished blessing him, and
Jacob had scarcely left his father's presence, his brother Esau came in from hunting. 31 He too prepared some tasty food
and brought it to his father. Then he said
to him, "My father, please sit up and eat
some of my game, so that you may give
me your blessing."[w]
32 His father Isaac asked him, "Who are
you?"[x]
"I am your son," he answered, "your
firstborn, Esau.[y]"
33 Isaac trembled violently and said,
"Who was it, then, that hunted game and
brought it to me?[z] I ate it just before you
came and I blessed him—and indeed he
will be blessed![a]"
34 When Esau heard his father's words,
he burst out with a loud and bitter cry[b]
and said to his father, "Bless[c] me—me
too, my father!"
35 But he said, "Your brother came deceitfully[d] and took your blessing."[e]
36 Esau said, "Isn't he rightly named
Jacob[a]?[f] This is the second time he has
taken advantage of[g] me: He took my birthright,[h] and now he's taken my blessing!"[i]

[a] 36 *Jacob* means *he grasps the heel,* a Hebrew idiom for *he takes advantage of* or *he deceives.*

27:11 [s]S Ge 25:25 **27:12** [t]ver 22 [u]S Ge 9:25 **27:13** [v]Mt 27:25 [w]S ver 8 **27:14** [x]S Ge 25:28 **27:15** [y]ver 27; SS 4:11 [z]S Ge 25:25 **27:16** [a]ver 22-23 **27:18** [b]ver 32 **27:19** [c]ver 32 [d]S Ge 25:28 [e]S ver 4 **27:20** [f]S Ge 24:12 **27:21** [g]ver 12 **27:22** [h]Ge 45:4 [i]ver 12 **27:23** [j]ver 16 **27:25** [k]S ver 4 **27:27** [l]Ge 31:28, 55; 33:4; 48:10; Ex 4:27; 18:7; Ru 1:9; 1Sa 20:41; 2Sa 14:33; 19:39 [m]Heb 11:20 [n]S ver 15 [o]Ps 65:9-13 **27:28** [p]Dt 33:13; 2Sa 1:21; Job 18:16; 29:19; Pr 3:20; Isa 26:19; Hos 14:5; Hag 1:10; Zec 8:12 [q]ver 39; Ge 49:25; Lev 26:20; Dt 33:13 [r]Ps 65:9; 72:16 [s]ver 37; Nu 18:12; Dt 7:13; 33:28; 2Ki 18:32; Ps 4:7; Isa 36:17; Jer 31:12; 40:10 **27:29** [t]2Sa 8:14; Ps 68:31; 72:11; Isa 19:21,23; 27:13; 45:14, 23; 49:7, 23; 60:12, 14; 66:23; Jer 12:17; Da 2:44; Zec 14:17-18 [u]S Ge 9:25; S 25:23; S 37:7 [v]ver 33; Ge 12:3 **27:31** [w]S ver 4 **27:32** [x]ver 18 [y]ver 19

27:33 [z]ver 35 [a]S ver 29 **27:34** [b]Heb 12:17 [c]Ex 12:32 **27:35** [d]Jer 9:4; 12:6 [e]ver 19,45 **27:36** [f]S Ge 25:26 [g]Ge 29:25; 31:20,26; 34:13; 1Sa 28:12 [h]S Ge 25:33 [i]Heb 12:16-17

27:20 *your God.* Consistent with Jacob's language elsewhere (31:5,42; 32:9). Not until his safe return from Harran did he speak of the Lord as his own God (cf. 28:20–21; 33:18–20 and notes).
27:24 *Are you really my son Esau?* To the very end of the charade, Isaac remained suspicious.
27:29 *Be lord over your brothers.* Isaac was unwittingly blessing Jacob and thus fulfilling God's promise to Rebekah in 25:23 (see note there). *curse ... be cursed ... bless ... be blessed.* Cf. 12:2–3.
27:33 *indeed he will be blessed.* The ancient world believed that blessings and curses had a kind of magical power to accomplish what they pronounced (see note on 12:3). But Isaac, as heir and steward of God's covenant blessing, acknowledged that he had solemnly transmitted that heritage to Jacob by way of a legally binding bequest (see note on v. 4).
27:34 *loud and bitter cry.* Esau's tears "could not change what he had done" (Heb 12:17).
27:36 *Isn't he rightly named Jacob?* See NIV text notes here and on 25:26. *He took my birthright, and now he's taken my blessing!* The Hebrew for "birthright" is *bekorah,* and for "blessing" it is *berakah* (see note on v. 6). Though Esau tried

Then he asked, "Haven't you reserved any
blessing for me?"
37 Isaac answered Esau, "I have made
him lord over you and have made all his
relatives his servants, and I have sustained
him with grain and new wine.[j] So what
can I possibly do for you, my son?"
38 Esau said to his father, "Do you have
only one blessing, my father? Bless me
too, my father!" Then Esau wept aloud.[k]
39 His father Isaac answered him,[l]

"Your dwelling will be
away from the earth's richness,
away from the dew[m] of heaven
above.[n]
40 You will live by the sword
and you will serve[o] your brother.[p]
But when you grow restless,
you will throw his yoke
from off your neck.[q]"

41 Esau held a grudge[r] against Jacob[s] because of the blessing his father had giv-
en him. He said to himself, "The days of
mourning[t] for my father are near; then I
will kill[u] my brother Jacob."[v]
42 When Rebekah was told what her older son Esau[w] had said, she sent for her
younger son Jacob and said to him, "Your
brother Esau is planning to avenge himself by killing you.[x] 43 Now then, my son,
do what I say:[y] Flee at once to my brother
Laban[z] in Harran.[a] 44 Stay with him for a
while[b] until your brother's fury subsides.
45 When your brother is no longer angry
with you and forgets what you did to him,[c]
I'll send word for you to come back from
there.[d] Why should I lose both of you in
one day?"
46 Then Rebekah said to Isaac, "I'm disgusted with living because of these Hittite[e]
women. If Jacob takes a wife from among
the women of this land,[f] from Hittite wom-
en like these, my life will not be worth
living."[g]

27:37 [j]S ver 28; Dt 16:13; Ezr 6:9; Isa 16:10; Jer 40:12
27:38 [k]Ge 29:11; Nu 14:1; Jdg 2:4; 21:2; Ru 1:9; 1Sa 11:4; 30:4; Heb 12:17
27:39 [l]Heb 11:20 [m]ver 28 [n]Ge 36:6
27:40 [o]2Sa 8:14 [p]S Ge 9:25 [q]2Ki 8:20-22
27:41 [r]Ge 37:4; 49:23; 50:15; 1Sa 17:28 [s]Ge 31:17; 32:11; Hos 10:14 [t]Ge 50:4, 10; Nu 20:29 [u]ver 42 [v]Ob 1:10
27:42 [w]Ge 32:3, 11; 33:4 [x]ver 41
27:43 [y]S ver 8 [z]S Ge 24:29 [a]S Ge 11:31
27:44 [b]Ge 31:38, 41
27:45 [c]S ver 35 [d]S Ge 26:3
27:46 [e]S Ge 10:15 [f]S Ge 10:15-19 [g]S Ge 26:35; S Job 7:7

28:1 [h]S Ge 24:60 [i]Ge 24:3
28:2 [j]S Ge 25:20 [k]S Ge 25:20 [l]S Ge 21:21; S 24:29
28:3 [m]S Ge 17:1 [n]Ge 48:16; Nu 6:24; Ru 2:4; Ps 129:8; 134:3; Jer 31:23 [o]S Ge 17:6 [p]S Ge 12:2
28:4 [q]S Ge 12:2, 3 [r]S Ge 15:7

28 So Isaac called for Jacob and
blessed[h] him. Then he commanded him: "Do not marry a Canaanite woman.[i] 2 Go at once to Paddan Aram,[a][j] to the
house of your mother's father Bethuel.[k]
Take a wife for yourself there, from among
the daughters of Laban, your mother's
brother.[l] 3 May God Almighty[b][m] bless[n] you
and make you fruitful[o] and increase your
numbers[p] until you become a community
of peoples. 4 May he give you and your descendants the blessing given to Abraham,[q]
so that you may take possession of the
land[r] where you now reside as a foreigner,[s] the land God gave to Abraham." 5 Then
Isaac sent Jacob on his way,[t] and he went
to Paddan Aram,[u] to Laban son of Bethuel the Aramean,[v] the brother of Rebekah,[w]
who was the mother of Jacob and Esau.
6 Now Esau learned that Isaac had
blessed Jacob and had sent him to Paddan Aram to take a wife from there, and
that when he blessed him he commanded
him, "Do not marry a Canaanite woman,"[x]
7 and that Jacob had obeyed his father and
mother and had gone to Paddan Aram.
8 Esau then realized how displeasing the
Canaanite women[y] were to his father
Isaac;[z] 9 so he went to Ishmael[a] and married Mahalath, the sister of Nebaioth[b] and
daughter of Ishmael son of Abraham, in
addition to the wives he already had.[c]

Jacob's Dream at Bethel

10 Jacob left Beersheba[d] and set out for
Harran.[e] 11 When he reached a certain
place,[f] he stopped for the night because
the sun had set. Taking one of the stones

[a] *2* That is, Northwest Mesopotamia; also in verses 5, 6 and 7 [b] *3* Hebrew *El-Shaddai*

[s]S Ge 17:8 **28:5** [t]S Ge 11:31 [u]Hos 12:12 [v]S Ge 25:20 [w]S Ge 24:29 **28:6** [x]S ver 1 **28:8** [y]S Ge 10:15-19 [z]S Ge 26:35 **28:9** [a]S Ge 16:15 [b]S Ge 25:13 [c]S Ge 26:34 **28:10** [d]S Ge 21:14 [e]S Ge 11:31 **28:11** [f]S Ge 12:8

to separate birthright from blessing, the former led inevitably to the latter, since both involved the inheritance of the firstborn (see Heb 12:16–17).

27:39 *away from the earth's richness, away from the dew of heaven.* Cf. v. 28. Isaac's secondary blessing of Esau could be only a parody of his primary blessing of Jacob.

27:40 See 25:23 and notes on 25:22,26.

27:41–45 Esau's fierce hostility toward Jacob and its consequences. This account of Esau's "grudge" and the later account of the brothers' reconciliation (33:1–17) frame the story of Jacob's flight from Canaan to Paddan Aram, where he finds his wives, fathers many children and obtains great wealth before returning to the promised land. This chain of events parallels Joseph's experiences as seen in his words to his brothers in 50:20 (see note there).

27:43 *do what I say.* Bad advice earlier (see vv. 8,13), but sensible counsel this time.

27:44 *for a while.* Twenty years, as it turned out (see 31:38,41).

27:45 *both of you.* Jacob and Esau. Esau would have to pay for his deed with his life (see 9:6 and note; see also Ex 21:12; Lev 24:17; Nu 35:19,21,27,33 and note on 35:33; 2Sa 14:6–7).

27:46 See note on 26:35.

28:2 *Paddan Aram.* See note on 25:20. *Take a wife for yourself there.* See 24:3–4.

28:3 *God Almighty.* See note on 17:1.

28:4 *the blessing given to Abraham.* For Paul's application of this phrase to Christian believers, see Gal 3:14.

28:5 See map and accompanying text, p. 61.

28:9 *in addition to the wives he already had.* See 26:34 and note.

28:10–22 God's reassuring appearance to Jacob as he is about to leave the promised land. This event and God's appearance to him at the Jabbok River upon his return (32:22–32) form a frame around Jacob's stay in Paddan Aram, to which he went empty but from which he returned full.

28:11 *one of the stones ... under his head.* In ancient times headrests (e.g., in Egypt) were often quite hard, sometimes being made of metal. People were used to sleeping on the ground.

there, he put it under his head[g] and lay down to sleep. 12 He had a dream[h] in which he saw a stairway resting on the earth, with its top reaching to heaven, and the angels of God were ascending and descending on it.[i] 13 There above it[a] stood the LORD,[j] and he said: "I am the LORD, the God of your father Abraham and the God of Isaac.[k] I will give you and your descendants the land[l] on which you are lying.[m] 14 Your descendants will be like the dust of the earth, and you[n] will spread out to the west and to the east, to the north and to the south.[o] All peoples on earth will be blessed through you and your offspring.[b][p] 15 I am with you[q] and will watch over you[r] wherever you go,[s] and I will bring you back to this land.[t] I will not leave you[u] until I have done what I have promised you.[v]"[w]

16 When Jacob awoke from his sleep,[x] he thought, "Surely the LORD is in this place, and I was not aware of it." 17 He was afraid and said, "How awesome is this place![y] This is none other than the house of God;[z] this is the gate of heaven."

18 Early the next morning Jacob took the stone he had placed under his head[a] and set it up as a pillar[b] and poured oil on top of it.[c] 19 He called that place Bethel,[c][d] though the city used to be called Luz.[e]

20 Then Jacob made a vow,[f] saying, "If God will be with me and will watch over me[g] on this journey I am taking and will give me food to eat and clothes to wear[h] 21 so that I return safely[i] to my father's household,[j] then the LORD[d] will be my God[k] 22 and[e] this stone that I have set up as a pillar[l] will be God's house,[m] and of all that you give me I will give you a tenth.[n]"

28:11 [g] ver 18 **28:12** [h] S Ge 20:3; 37:19 [i] Jn 1:51 **28:13** [j] S Ge 12:7; 35:7,9; 48:3 [k] S Ge 24:12; 48:16; 49:25; 50:17 [l] S Ge 12:7 [m] Ge 46:4; 48:21 **28:14** [n] Ge 26:4 [o] S Ge 12:2; S 13:14; S 26:24 [p] S Ge 12:3; Ac 3:25; Gal 3:8 **28:15** [q] S Ge 21:20 [r] ver 20; Ps 121:5, 7-8 [s] ver 22; Ge 35:3 [t] ver 21; S Ge 15:16; 30:25; 31:30 [u] Dt 31:6,8; Jos 1:5; Ne 4:14; Ps 9:10 [v] Lev 26:42 [w] Ps 105:10 **28:16** [x] 1Ki 3:15; Jer 31:26 **28:17** [y] Ex 3:5; 19:21; Jos 5:15; Ps 68:24,35 [z] ver 22; Ge 32:2; 1Ch 22:1; 2Ch 3:1 **28:18** [a] ver 11 [b] ver 22; Ge 31:13,45,51; 35:14; Ex 24:4; Jos 24:26, 27; Isa 19:19 [c] Lev 8:11; Jos 4:9 **28:19** [d] S Ge 12:8 [e] Ge 35:6; 48:3; Jos 16:2; 18:13; Jdg 1:23,26 **28:20** [f] Ge 31:13; Lev 7:16; 22:18; 23:38; 27:2,9; Nu 6:2; 15:3; Dt 12:6; Jdg 11:30; 1Sa 1:21; 2Sa 15:8

Jacob Arrives in Paddan Aram

29 Then Jacob continued on his journey and came to the land of the eastern peoples.[o] 2 There he saw a well in the open country, with three flocks of sheep lying near it because the flocks were watered from that well.[p] The stone[q] over the mouth of the well was large. 3 When all the flocks were gathered there, the shepherds would roll the stone[r] away from the well's mouth and water the sheep.[s] Then they would return the stone to its place over the mouth of the well.

4 Jacob asked the shepherds, "My brothers, where are you from?"[t]

"We're from Harran,[u]" they replied.

5 He said to them, "Do you know Laban, Nahor's grandson?"[v]

"Yes, we know him," they answered.

6 Then Jacob asked them, "Is he well?"

"Yes, he is," they said, "and here comes his daughter Rachel[w] with the sheep.[x]"

7 "Look," he said, "the sun is still high; it is not time for the flocks to be gathered. Water the sheep and take them back to pasture."

8 "We can't," they replied, "until all the flocks are gathered and the stone[y] has been rolled away from the mouth of the well. Then we will water[z] the sheep."

9 While he was still talking with them, Rachel came with her father's sheep,[a] for she was a shepherd. 10 When Jacob saw

[a] 13 Or *There beside him* [b] 14 Or *will use your name and the name of your offspring in blessings* (see 48:20) [c] 19 *Bethel* means *house of God.* [d] 20,21 Or *Since God . . . father's household, the LORD* [e] 21,22 Or *household, and the LORD will be my God, 22 then*

[g] S ver 15 [h] 1Ti 6:8 **28:21** [i] Jdg 11:31 [j] S ver 15 [k] Ex 15:2; Dt 26:17; Jos 24:18; Ps 48:14; 118:28 **28:22** [l] S ver 18; 1Sa 7:12 [m] S ver 17 [n] S Ge 14:20; S Nu 18:21; Lk 18:12 **29:1** [o] S Ge 25:6 **29:2** [p] S Ge 24:11 [q] ver 3,8,10 **29:3** [r] S ver 2 [s] ver 8 **29:4** [t] Ge 42:7; Jdg 19:17 [u] S Ge 11:31 **29:5** [v] S Ge 11:29 **29:6** [w] Ge 30:22-24; 35:16; 46:19,22 [x] Ex 2:16 **29:8** [y] S ver 2 [z] S Ge 24:13 **29:9** [a] Ex 2:16

28:12 *stairway.* Not a ladder with rungs, it was more likely a stairway such as mounted the sloping side of a ziggurat (see note on 11:4). *angels of God were ascending and descending on it.* A sign that the Lord offered to be Jacob's God. Jesus told a disciple that he would "see 'heaven open, and the angels of God ascending and descending on' the Son of Man" (Jn 1:51). Jesus himself is the bridge between heaven and earth (see Jn 14:6), the only "mediator between God and mankind" (1Ti 2:5).

28:13 *above it stood the LORD.* Mesopotamian ziggurats were topped with a small shrine where worshipers prayed to their gods.

28:14 *like the dust of the earth.* See note on 13:16. *All peoples on earth will be blessed through you.* Repeats the blessing of 12:3.

28:15 *I am with you.* See note on 26:3. *I will not leave you.* Unlike the gods of pagan religions, in which the gods were merely local deities who gave protection only within their own territories, the one true God assured Jacob that he would always be with him wherever he went (see Dt 31:6 and note).

28:17 *house of God ... gate of heaven.* Phrases that related Jacob's stairway to the Mesopotamian ziggurats (see notes on 11:4,9).

28:18 *pillar.* A memorial of worship or of communion between people and God, common in ancient times. *poured oil on top of it.* To consecrate it (see Ex 30:25–29).

28:21 *return safely.* Partially fulfilled in 33:18. *the LORD will be my God.* For the first time Jacob considered (conditionally: "If ...," v. 20) acknowledging the God of Abraham and Isaac (see v. 13; 27:20) as his own. His full acknowledgment came only after his safe return from Harran (see 33:20 and note).

28:22 *this stone ... will be God's house.* In the sense that it would memorialize Jacob's meeting with God at Bethel (see NIV text note on v. 19). *of all that you give me I will give you a tenth.* A way of acknowledging the Lord as his God and King (see note on 14:20).

29:5 *Laban, Nahor's grandson.* See 24:15,29. The Hebrew word here for "grandson" is lit. "son," which can refer to any male descendant (see NIV text note on 10:2).

29:9 *shepherd.* The task of caring for sheep and goats in the Middle East was shared by men and women (cf. Ex 2:16–17; SS 1:8 and note).

29:10 *rolled the stone away.* A feat of unusual strength for one man, because the stone was large (see v. 2).

Rachel[b] daughter of his uncle Laban, and Laban's sheep, he went over and rolled the stone[c] away from the mouth of the well and watered[d] his uncle's sheep.[e] 11 Then Jacob kissed[f] Rachel and began to weep aloud.[g] 12 He had told Rachel that he was a relative[h] of her father and a son of Rebekah.[i] So she ran and told her father.[j]

13 As soon as Laban[k] heard the news about Jacob, his sister's son, he hurried to meet him. He embraced him[l] and kissed him and brought him to his home, and there Jacob told him all these things. 14 Then Laban said to him, "You are my own flesh and blood."[m]

Jacob Marries Leah and Rachel

After Jacob had stayed with him for a whole month, 15 Laban said to him, "Just because you are a relative[n] of mine, should you work for me for nothing? Tell me what your wages[o] should be."

16 Now Laban had two daughters; the name of the older was Leah,[p] and the name of the younger was Rachel.[q] 17 Leah had weak[a] eyes, but Rachel[r] had a lovely figure and was beautiful.[s] 18 Jacob was in love with Rachel[t] and said, "I'll work for you seven years in return for your younger daughter Rachel."[u]

19 Laban said, "It's better that I give her to you than to some other man. Stay here with me." 20 So Jacob served seven years to get Rachel,[v] but they seemed like only a few days to him because of his love for her.[w]

21 Then Jacob said to Laban, "Give me my wife. My time is completed, and I want to make love to her.[x]"

22 So Laban brought together all the people of the place and gave a feast.[y] 23 But when evening came, he took his daughter Leah[z] and brought her to Jacob, and Jacob made love to her. 24 And Laban gave his servant Zilpah[a] to his daughter as her attendant.[b]

25 When morning came, there was Leah! So Jacob said to Laban, "What is this you have done to me?[c] I served you for Rachel, didn't I? Why have you deceived me?[d]"

26 Laban replied, "It is not our custom here to give the younger daughter in marriage before the older one.[e] 27 Finish this daughter's bridal week;[f] then we will give you the younger one also, in return for another seven years of work.[g]"

28 And Jacob did so. He finished the week with Leah, and then Laban gave him his daughter Rachel to be his wife.[h] 29 Laban gave his servant Bilhah[i] to his daughter Rachel as her attendant.[j] 30 Jacob made love to Rachel also, and his love for Rachel was greater than his love for Leah.[k] And he worked for Laban another seven years.[l]

Jacob's Children

31 When the LORD saw that Leah was not loved,[m] he enabled her to conceive,[n] but Rachel remained childless. 32 Leah became pregnant and gave birth to a son.[o] She named him Reuben,[b][p] for she said, "It is because the LORD has seen my misery.[q] Surely my husband will love me now."

33 She conceived again, and when she gave birth to a son she said, "Because the LORD heard that I am not loved,[r] he gave me this one too." So she named him Simeon.[c][s]

34 Again she conceived, and when she gave birth to a son she said, "Now at last my husband will become attached to me,[t] because I have borne him three sons." So he was named Levi.[d][u]

[a] *17* Or *delicate* [b] *32* *Reuben* sounds like the Hebrew for *he has seen my misery*; the name means *see, a son.* [c] *33* *Simeon* probably means *one who hears.* [d] *34* *Levi* sounds like and may be derived from the Hebrew for *attached.*

29:10 [b] ver 16 [c] S ver 2 [d] S Ge 24:11 [e] ver 3; Ex 2:17 **29:11** [f] ver 13 [g] Ge 33:4; 42:24; 43:30; 45:2, 14-15; 46:29; 50:1, 17; Ru 1:9 **29:12** [h] ver 15 [i] S Ge 24:29 [j] Ge 24:28 **29:13** [k] S Ge 24:29 [l] Ge 33:4; 45:14-15, 14; 48:10; Ex 4:27; 18:7; Lk 15:20 **29:14** [m] Ge 2:23; 37:27; Jdg 9:2; 2Sa 5:1; 19:12-13; 20:1; Ne 5:5; Isa 58:7 **29:15** [n] ver 12 [o] Ge 30:28, 32; 31:7, 41 **29:16** [p] ver 17, 23, 28, 30; Ge 30:9; 35:23; 47:30; 49:31; Ru 4:11 [q] ver 9-10 **29:17** [r] S ver 16 [s] S Ge 12:11 **29:18** [t] S Ge 24:67 [u] ver 20, 27, 30; Ge 30:26; Hos 12:12 **29:20** [v] S ver 18; Ge 31:15 [w] SS 8:7; Hos 12:12 **29:21** [x] Jdg 15:1 **29:22** [y] Jdg 14:10; Isa 25:6; Jn 2:1-2 **29:23** [z] S ver 16 **29:24** [a] Ge 30:9 [b] S Ge 16:1 **29:25** [c] S Ge 12:18 [d] S Ge 27:36 **29:26** [e] Jdg 15:2; 1Sa 14:49; 18:17, 20; 2Sa 6:23 **29:27** [f] Jdg 14:12 [g] S ver 18; Ge 31:41 **29:28** [h] S ver 16; S Ge 4:19 **29:29** [i] Ge 30:3; 35:22; 49:4; Dt 22:30; 1Ch 5:1 [j] S Ge 16:1 **29:30** [k] S ver 16 [l] S ver 20 **29:31** [m] ver 33; Dt 21:15-17 [n] S Ge 11:30; S 16:2; Ru 4:13; 1Sa 1:19; Ps 127:3 **29:32** [o] Ge 30:23; Ru 4:13; 1Sa 1:20 [p] Ge 37:21; 46:8; 48:5, 14; 49:3; Ex 6:14; Nu 1:5, 20; 26:5; Dt 33:6; Jos 4:12; 1Ch 5:1, 3 [q] S Ge 16:11 **29:33** [r] S ver 31 [s] Ge 34:25; 46:10; 48:5; 49:5; Ex 6:15; Nu 1:6, 22; 34:20; 1Ch 4:24; Eze 48:24 **29:34** [t] Ge 30:20; 1Sa 1:2-4 [u] Ge 34:25; 46:11; 49:5-7; Ex 2:1; 6:16, 19; Nu 1:47; 3:17-20; 26:57; Dt 33:8; 1Ch 6:1, 16; 23:6-24, 13-14

29:11 *weep aloud.* For joy.

29:13 *kissed him.* A common sign of affection among relatives, also between men (see 33:4; Ex 4:27; see also notes on Ro 16:16; 1Co 16:20).

29:14 *flesh and blood.* The English equivalent of a Hebrew phrase that means lit. "bone and flesh" and that stresses blood kinship (see, e.g., 2:23).

29:15 Laban's question and the author's observation in 30:43 frame the account of Jacob's receiving the fulfillment of Isaac's blessing. See also God's blessing on Jacob (28:14).

29:16 *Leah ... Rachel.* The names mean "cow" and "ewe," respectively, appropriate in a herdsman's family.

29:21 *my wife.* If Jacob had said "Rachel," Laban would have had no excuse for giving him Leah.

29:22 *feast.* A wedding feast was usually seven days long (see vv. 27–28; Jdg 14:10,12).

29:23 *when evening came ... Jacob made love to her.* The darkness, or perhaps a veil (see 24:65), may have concealed Leah's identity.

29:24 See v. 29; a wedding custom documented in Old Babylonian marriage contracts.

29:25 *you deceived me.* Jacob, the deceiver in name (see NIV text notes on 25:26; 27:36) as well as in behavior (see 27:36), had himself been deceived. The one who had tried everything to obtain the benefits of the firstborn had now, against his will, received the firstborn (vv. 16,26).

29:28 *then Laban gave him his daughter Rachel.* Before Jacob worked another seven years (see v. 30).

29:31–35 Leah, though unloved, nevertheless became the mother of Jacob's first four sons, including Levi (ancestor of the Aaronic priestly line) and Judah (ancestor of David and his royal line, and ultimately of Jesus).

29:32 *named him Reuben ... because the LORD has seen my misery.* See NIV text note. Ishmael had received his name in similar circumstances (see 16:11).

35 She conceived again, and when she gave birth to a son she said, "This time I will praise the LORD." So she named him Judah.[a][v] Then she stopped having children.[w]

30 When Rachel saw that she was not bearing Jacob any children,[x] she became jealous of her sister.[y] So she said to Jacob, "Give me children, or I'll die!"

2 Jacob became angry with her and said, "Am I in the place of God,[z] who has kept you from having children?"[a]

3 Then she said, "Here is Bilhah,[b] my servant.[c] Sleep with her so that she can bear children for me and I too can build a family through her."[d]

4 So she gave him her servant Bilhah as a wife.[e] Jacob slept with her,[f] 5 and she became pregnant and bore him a son. 6 Then Rachel said, "God has vindicated me;[g] he has listened to my plea and given me a son."[h] Because of this she named him Dan.[b][i]

7 Rachel's servant Bilhah[j] conceived again and bore Jacob a second son. 8 Then Rachel said, "I have had a great struggle with my sister, and I have won."[k] So she named him Naphtali.[c][l]

9 When Leah[m] saw that she had stopped having children,[n] she took her servant Zilpah[o] and gave her to Jacob as a wife.[p] 10 Leah's servant Zilpah[q] bore Jacob a son. 11 Then Leah said, "What good fortune!"[d] So she named him Gad.[e][r]

12 Leah's servant Zilpah bore Jacob a second son. 13 Then Leah said, "How happy I am! The women will call me[s] happy."[t] So she named him Asher.[f][u]

14 During wheat harvest,[v] Reuben went out into the fields and found some mandrake plants,[w] which he brought to his mother Leah. Rachel said to Leah, "Please give me some of your son's mandrakes."

15 But she said to her, "Wasn't it enough[x] that you took away my husband? Will you take my son's mandrakes too?"

"Very well," Rachel said, "he can sleep with you tonight in return for your son's mandrakes."[y]

16 So when Jacob came in from the fields that evening, Leah went out to meet him. "You must sleep with me," she said. "I have hired you with my son's mandrakes."[z] So he slept with her that night.

17 God listened to Leah,[a] and she became pregnant and bore Jacob a fifth son. 18 Then Leah said, "God has rewarded me for giving my servant to my husband."[b] So she named him Issachar.[g][c]

19 Leah conceived again and bore Jacob a sixth son. 20 Then Leah said, "God has presented me with a precious gift. This time my husband will treat me with honor,[d] because I have borne him six sons." So she named him Zebulun.[h][e]

21 Some time later she gave birth to a daughter and named her Dinah.[f]

22 Then God remembered Rachel;[g] he listened to her[h] and enabled her to conceive.[i] 23 She became pregnant and gave birth to a son[j] and said, "God has taken away my disgrace."[k] 24 She named him Joseph,[i][l] and said, "May the LORD add to me another son."[m]

Jacob's Flocks Increase

25 After Rachel gave birth to Joseph, Jacob said to Laban, "Send me on my way[n]

29:35 [v] Ge 35:23; 37:26; 38:1; 43:8; 44:14, 18; 46:12; 49:8; 1Ch 2:3; 4:1; Isa 48:1; Mt 1:2-3 [w] Ge 30:9 **30:1** [x] S Ge 11:30; Isa 49:21; 54:1 [y] S Ge 16:4; Lev 18:18 **30:2** [z] Ge 50:19; Dt 32:35; 2Ki 5:7 [a] S Ge 16:2 **30:3** [b] ver 7; S Ge 29:29 [c] S Ge 24:61 [d] Ge 16:2 **30:4** [e] ver 9, 18 [f] Ge 16:3-4 **30:6** [g] Ps 35:24; 43:1 [h] ver 23; Ge 21:2; Ru 4:13; 1Sa 1:20 [i] Ge 46:23; 49:16-17; Nu 26:42-43; Jos 19:40-48; Jdg 1:34; 13:2; 18:2; Jer 4:15; 8:16; Eze 48:1 **30:7** [j] S ver 3 **30:8** [k] Ge 32:28; Hos 12:3-4 [l] Ge 35:25; 46:24; 49:21; Nu 1:42; 26:48; Dt 33:23; Jdg 4:6; 5:18; 1Ch 7:13 **30:9** [m] S Ge 29:16 [n] Ge 29:35 [o] Ge 29:24 [p] S ver 4 **30:10** [q] Ge 46:18 **30:11** [r] Ge 35:26; 46:16; 49:19; Ex 1:4; Nu 1:24; 26:18; Jos 4:12; 1Ch 5:11; 12:8; Jer 49:1 **30:13** [s] Ps 127:3 [t] Ru 4:14; Ps 127:4-5; Lk 1:48 [u] Ge 35:26; 46:17; 49:20; Nu 1:40; 26:47; Dt 33:24; Jos 19:24-31; 1Ch 7:30-31 **30:14** [v] Ex 34:22; Jdg 15:1; Ru 2:23; 1Sa 6:13; 12:17 [w] ver 15, 16; SS 7:13 **30:15** [x] Nu 16:9, 13; Isa 7:13; Eze 34:18 [y] Ge 38:16; Eze 16:33; Hos 9:1 **30:16** [z] S ver 14 **30:17** [a] S Ge 25:21 **30:18** [b] S ver 4 [c] Ge 46:13; 49:14; Nu 1:8, 28, 29; 26:25; Dt 27:12; 33:18; Jos 17:10; 19:17; 21:6, 28; Jdg 5:15; 10:1; 1Ch 7:1 **30:20** [d] S Ge 29:34; 1Pe 3:7 [e] Ge 35:23; 46:14; 49:13; Nu 1:30; 26:27; 34:25; Dt 33:18; Jdg 5:18 **30:21** [f] Ge 34:1; 46:15 **30:22** [g] S Ge 8:1 [h] S Ge 25:21 [i] S Ge 11:30 **30:23** [j] S ver 6; S Ge 29:32 [k] Isa 4:1; 25:8; 45:17; 54:4; Lk 1:25 **30:24** [l] S Ge 29:6; 32:22; 33:2, 7; 35:24; 37:2; 39:1; 49:22-26; Dt 33:13 [m] Ge 35:17; 1Sa 4:20 **30:25** [n] S Ge 24:54

[a] 35 *Judah* sounds like and may be derived from the Hebrew for *praise.* [b] 6 *Dan* here means *he has vindicated.* [c] 8 *Naphtali* means *my struggle.* [d] 11 Or *"A troop is coming!"* [e] 11 *Gad* can mean *good fortune* or *a troop.* [f] 13 *Asher* means *happy.* [g] 18 *Issachar* sounds like the Hebrew for *reward.* [h] 20 *Zebulun* probably means *honor.* [i] 24 *Joseph* means *may he add.*

30:1 *she became jealous of her sister.* As Jacob was of his older brother. *Give me children, or I'll die!* Tragically prophetic words (see 35:16–19).

30:2 *Am I in the place of God ... ?* Jacob was forever trying to secure the blessing by his own efforts. Here he has to acknowledge that the blessing of offspring could come only from God (see 31:7–13 for the blessing of flocks). Joseph later echoed these words (see 50:19).

30:3 *Sleep with her.* See v. 9; see also 16:2 and note. *for me.* Lit. "on my knees," apparently an expression symbolic of adoption (see 48:10–16) and meaning "as though my own" (see 50:23 and NIV text note).

30:4 *as a wife.* As a concubine (see 35:22).

30:5–12 Jacob's fifth, sixth, seventh and eighth sons were born to him through his concubines.

30:14 *give me some of your son's mandrakes.* The mandrake has fleshy, forked roots that resemble the lower part of a human body and were therefore superstitiously thought to induce pregnancy when eaten (see SS 7:13). Rachel, like Jacob (vv. 37–43), tried to obtain what she wanted by magical means.

30:16 *hired.* The Hebrew for this word is a pun on the name Issachar (see NIV text note on v. 18).

30:17–20 Jacob's ninth and tenth sons were born through Leah, who was thus the mother of half of Jacob's 12 sons (see note on 29:31–35).

30:20 *presented ... gift.* The Hebrew terms for these words are puns on the name Zebulun (see NIV text note).

30:21 *Dinah.* See ch. 34.

30:22 *God remembered Rachel.* See note on 8:1.

30:23 *disgrace.* Barrenness was considered to be shameful, a mark of divine disfavor (see 16:2; 30:2).

30:24 *May the LORD add to me another son.* The fulfillment of Rachel's wish would bring about her death (see 35:16–19).

so I can go back to my own homeland.[o]
26 Give me my wives and children, for
whom I have served you,[p] and I will be on
my way. You know how much work I've
done for you."
27 But Laban said to him, "If I have
found favor in your eyes,[q] please stay. I
have learned by divination[r] that the LORD
has blessed me because of you."[s] 28 He
added, "Name your wages,[t] and I will pay
them."
29 Jacob said to him, "You know how I
have worked for you[u] and how your livestock has fared under my care.[v] 30 The little
you had before I came has increased greatly, and the LORD has blessed you wherever
I have been.[w] But now, when may I do
something for my own household?[x]"
31 "What shall I give you?" he asked.
"Don't give me anything," Jacob replied. "But if you will do this one thing for
me, I will go on tending your flocks and
watching over them: 32 Let me go through
all your flocks today and remove from
them every speckled or spotted sheep, every dark-colored lamb and every spotted
or speckled goat.[y] They will be my wages.[z] 33 And my honesty will testify for me
in the future, whenever you check on the
wages you have paid me. Any goat in my
possession that is not speckled or spotted,
or any lamb that is not dark-colored,[a] will
be considered stolen.[b]"
34 "Agreed," said Laban. "Let it be as you
have said." 35 That same day he removed
all the male goats that were streaked or
spotted, and all the speckled or spotted
female goats (all that had white on them)
and all the dark-colored lambs,[c] and
he placed them in the care of his sons.[d]
36 Then he put a three-day journey[e] between himself and Jacob, while Jacob continued to tend the rest of Laban's flocks.
37 Jacob, however, took fresh-cut branches from poplar, almond[f] and plane trees[g]
and made white stripes on them by peel-
ing the bark and exposing the white inner
wood of the branches.[h] 38 Then he placed
the peeled branches[i] in all the watering
troughs,[j] so that they would be directly
in front of the flocks when they came to
drink. When the flocks were in heat[k] and
came to drink, 39 they mated in front of the
branches.[l] And they bore young that were
streaked or speckled or spotted.[m] 40 Jacob
set apart the young of the flock by themselves, but made the rest face the streaked
and dark-colored animals[n] that belonged
to Laban. Thus he made separate flocks
for himself and did not put them with
Laban's animals. 41 Whenever the stronger females were in heat,[o] Jacob would
place the branches in the troughs in front
of the animals so they would mate near
the branches,[p] 42 but if the animals were
weak, he would not place them there. So
the weak animals went to Laban and the
strong ones to Jacob.[q] 43 In this way the
man grew exceedingly prosperous and
came to own large flocks, and female and
male servants, and camels and donkeys.[r]

Jacob Flees From Laban

31 Jacob heard that Laban's sons[s] were
saying, "Jacob has taken everything
our father owned and has gained all this
wealth from what belonged to our father."[t]
2 And Jacob noticed that Laban's attitude
toward him was not what it had been.[u]
3 Then the LORD said to Jacob, "Go back[v]
to the land of your fathers and to your relatives, and I will be with you."[w]

30:25 [o] S Ge 28:15
30:26 [p] S Ge 29:18
30:27 [q] Ge 33:10; 50:4; Est 2:15 [r] Ge 44:5, 15; Lev 19:26; Nu 22:7; 23:23; 24:1; Jos 13:22; 2Ki 17:17; Jer 27:9 [s] ver 30; S Ge 26:24; 31:38; Dt 28:11; 2Sa 6:11
30:28 [t] S Ge 29:15
30:29 [u] Ge 31:6 [v] Ge 31:38-40
30:30 [w] S ver 27 [x] 1Ti 5:8
30:32 [y] ver 33, 35, 39, 40; Ge 31:8, 12 [z] S Ge 29:15
30:33 [a] S ver 32 [b] Ge 31:39
30:35 [c] S ver 32 [d] Ge 31:1
30:36 [e] Ge 31:22; Ex 3:18; 5:3; 8:27
30:37 [f] Jer 1:11 [g] Eze 31:8 [h] ver 38, 41
30:38 [i] S ver 37 [j] Ex 2:16 [k] ver 41; Jer 2:24
30:39 [l] ver 41 [m] S ver 32
30:40 [n] S ver 32
30:41 [o] S ver 38 [p] S ver 37
30:42 [q] Ge 31:1, 9, 16, 43
30:43 [r] S Ge 12:16
31:1 [s] Ge 30:35 [t] S Ge 30:42
31:2 [u] ver 5
31:3 [v] ver 13; Ge 32:9; Dt 30:3; Isa 10:21; 35:10; Jer 30:3; 42:12 [w] S Ge 21:22; S 26:3

30:26 *I will be on my way.* Jacob had fulfilled his commitments. With his accounts squared with Laban, he asked permission to leave, taking only his family with him. Later, he will take with him also much of Laban's wealth (see 30:43—31:1).

30:27 *divination.* The attempt to discover hidden knowledge through mechanical means (see 44:5), the interpretation of omens (see Eze 21:21) or the aid of supernatural powers (see Ac 16:16 and note). It was strictly forbidden to Israel (Lev 19:26; Dt 18:10,14) because it reflected a pagan concept of the world controlled by evil forces, and therefore obviously not under the sovereign rule of the Lord. *the LORD has blessed me because of you.* As God had promised Jacob at Bethel (28:14) and in accordance with the promise made to Abraham (see 12:2–3 and note; 22:18; see also 39:5,23; 41:41–57).

30:32 Most commonly the sheep were all white and the goats all black. So Jacob chose to identify as his wages the sheep with dark markings and the goats with white markings—on the face of it a very modest request.

30:35 *he removed.* Secretly and without telling Jacob.

30:36 *the rest of Laban's flocks.* Now made up of only pure-white sheep and all-black goats.

30:37 *poplar … white.* The Hebrew terms for these words are puns on the name Laban. As Jacob had gotten the best of Esau (whose other name, Edom, means "red"; see note on 25:25) by means of red stew (25:30), so he now tries to get the best of Laban (whose name means "white") by means of white branches. In effect, Jacob was using Laban's own tactic (deception) against him.

30:39 The scheme worked—but only because of God's intervention (see Jacob's own admission in 31:9), not because of Jacob's superstition.

30:43 *the man grew exceedingly prosperous.* Over a period of six years (see 31:41). While in Harran, Jacob obtained both family and wealth. His wealth came at the expense of people in Northwest Mesopotamia, just as Abram's (12:16) and later Israel's (Ex 12:36) were obtained at the expense of the Egyptians (see also Isa 60:5–17 and note on 60:5; 61:6).

31:1 *has taken everything.* Since Laban's sons had been caring for flocks containing the spotted and speckled animals that Laban had sorted out, Jacob could potentially lay claim to a large proportion of the flocks under their care.

31:3 *Go back to the land of your fathers.* Every sign Jacob was

4So Jacob sent word to Rachel and
Leah to come out to the fields where his
flocks were. 5He said to them, "I see that
your father's[x] attitude toward me is not
what it was before,[y] but the God of my
father has been with me.[z] 6You know that
I've worked for your father with all my
strength,[a] 7yet your father has cheated[b] me
by changing my wages[c] ten times.[d] However, God has not allowed him to harm
me.[e] 8If he said, 'The speckled ones will
be your wages,' then all the flocks gave
birth to speckled young; and if he said,
'The streaked ones will be your wages,'[f]
then all the flocks bore streaked young.
9So God has taken away your father's livestock[g] and has given them to me.[h]
10"In breeding season I once had a
dream[i] in which I looked up and saw that
the male goats mating with the flock were
streaked, speckled or spotted. 11The angel of God[j] said to me in the dream,[k] 'Jacob.' I answered, 'Here I am.'[l] 12And he
said, 'Look up and see that all the male
goats mating with the flock are streaked,
speckled or spotted,[m] for I have seen all
that Laban has been doing to you.[n] 13I am
the God of Bethel,[o] where you anointed a
pillar[p] and where you made a vow[q] to me.
Now leave this land at once and go back
to your native land.[r]' "
14Then Rachel and Leah replied, "Do we
still have any share[s] in the inheritance of
our father's estate? 15Does he not regard
us as foreigners?[t] Not only has he sold us,
but he has used up what was paid for us.[u]
16Surely all the wealth that God took away
from our father belongs to us and our children.[v] So do whatever God has told you."
17Then Jacob put his children and his
wives[w] on camels,[x] 18and he drove all his
livestock ahead of him, along with all the
goods he had accumulated[y] in Paddan
Aram,[a][z] to go to his father Isaac[a] in the
land of Canaan.[b]
19When Laban had gone to shear his
sheep,[c] Rachel stole her father's household gods.[d] 20Moreover, Jacob deceived[e]
Laban the Aramean[f] by not telling him he
was running away.[g] 21So he fled[h] with all
he had, crossed the Euphrates River,[i] and
headed for the hill country of Gilead.[j]

Laban Pursues Jacob

22On the third day[k] Laban was told that
Jacob had fled.[l] 23Taking his relatives[m]
with him[n], he pursued Jacob for seven
days and caught up with him in the hill
country of Gilead.[o] 24Then God came to
Laban the Aramean[p] in a dream at night
and said to him,[q] "Be careful not to say
anything to Jacob, either good or bad."[r]
25Jacob had pitched his tent in the hill
country of Gilead[s] when Laban overtook
him, and Laban and his relatives camped
there too. 26Then Laban said to Jacob,
"What have you done?[t] You've deceived
me,[u] and you've carried off my daughters
like captives in war.[v] 27Why did you run
off secretly and deceive me? Why didn't
you tell me,[w] so I could send you away
with joy and singing to the music of timbrels[x] and harps?[y] 28You didn't even let me
kiss my grandchildren and my daughters
goodbye.[z] You have done a foolish thing.
29I have the power to harm you;[a] but last
night the God of your father[b] said to me,
'Be careful not to say anything to Jacob,

[a] *18* That is, Northwest Mesopotamia

31:5 [x] ver 29, 42,53; Ge 43:23; Da 2:23 [y] ver 2 [z] S Ge 21:22; S 26:3 **31:6** [a] Ge 30:29 **31:7** [b] Lev 6:2; Am 8:5 [c] S Ge 29:15 [d] ver 41; Nu 14:22; Job 19:3 [e] ver 52; S Ge 24:50 **31:8** [f] S Ge 30:32 **31:9** [g] Job 39:2; Eze 31:6 [h] S Ge 30:42 **31:10** [i] S Ge 20:3 **31:11** [j] S Ge 16:7 [k] S Ge 20:3 [l] S Ge 22:1; S Ex 3:4 **31:12** [m] S Ge 30:32 [n] Ex 3:7 **31:13** [o] Ge 28:10-22 [p] S Ge 28:18 [q] S Ge 28:20 [r] S ver 3 **31:14** [s] 2Sa 20:1; 1Ki 12:16 **31:15** [t] Dt 15:3; 23:20; Ru 2:10; 2Sa 15:19; 1Ki 8:41; Ob 1:11 [u] S Ge 29:20 **31:16** [v] S Ge 30:42 **31:17** [w] S Ge 27:41 [x] S Ge 24:63-64 **31:18** [y] S Ge 12:5 [z] S Ge 25:20 [a] Ge 35:27 [b] S Ge 10:19 **31:19** [c] Ge 38:12,13; 1Sa 25:2,4,7; 2Sa 13:23 [d] ver 30,32, 34-35; Ge 35:2; Jos 24:14; Jdg 17:5; 18:14, 17,24,30; 1Sa 7:3; 19:13; 2Ki 23:24; Hos 3:4 **31:20** [e] S Ge 27:36 [f] S Ge 25:20 [g] ver 27 **31:21** [h] ver 22; Ex 2:15; 14:5; 1Ki 18:46; 19:3; Jer 26:21 [i] S Ge 2:14 [j] ver 23,25; Ge 37:25; Nu 26:30; 32:1; Dt 3:10; Jos 12:2; Jer 22:6 **31:22** [k] S Ge 30:36 [l] S ver 21 **31:23** [m] ver 37 [n] Ex 14:9 [o] S ver 21 **31:24** [p] S Ge 25:20 [q] S Ge 20:3 [r] S Ge 24:50 **31:25** [s] S ver 21 **31:26** [t] S Ge 12:18 [u] S Ge 27:36 [v] Ge 34:29; 1Sa 30:2-3 **31:27** [w] ver 20 [x] Ex 15:20; Jdg 11:34; 1Sa 10:5; 2Sa 6:5; Ps 68:25; Isa 24:8; Jer 31:4 [y] S Ge 4:21 **31:28** [z] ver 55; S Ge 27:27; Ru 1:14; Ac 20:37 **31:29** [a] S ver 7; S Ge 26:29 [b] S ver 5

---

getting—from his wives (see vv. 14–16), from Laban (see v. 2), from Laban's sons (see v. 1) and now from God himself—told him that it was time to return to Canaan. *I will be with you.* See note on 26:3.

31:4 *Rachel and Leah.* At long last (see v. 14) Rachel, the younger, has been given precedence over Leah—but she will soon become a deceiver like her husband Jacob (see vv. 31,35).

31:7 *ten times.* See v. 41. "Ten" here probably signifies completeness. In effect, Jacob accused Laban of cheating him at every turn.

31:9 See note on 30:39.

31:11 *angel of God.* See note on 16:7. *Here I am.* See note on 22:1.

31:13 *Bethel, where you anointed a pillar.* See note on 28:18.

31:15 *what was paid for us.* Jacob had come empty-handed to Paddan Aram and had offered his labors instead of wealth for his wives (cf. 24:10). So what had been "paid" for them was the fruit of Jacob's labors for their father (30:27,30).

31:18 *Paddan Aram.* See note on 25:20; see also map, p. 61.

31:19 *household gods.* Small portable idols, which Rachel probably stole because she thought they would bring her protection and blessing. Or perhaps she wanted to have something tangible to worship on the long journey ahead, a practice referred to much later in the writings of Josephus, a first-century AD Jewish historian. In any case, Rachel was not yet free of her pagan background (see 35:2; Jos 24:2).

31:21 *So he fled.* As he had fled earlier from Esau (27:42–43). Jacob's devious dealings produced only hostility from which he had to flee. *Gilead.* An area of exceptionally good grazing land southeast of the Sea of Galilee (see Nu 32:1 and note).

31:24 *not to say anything … good or bad.* Do not enter into a dispute with him; or do not press any claim against him (see also v. 29; cf. 24:50).

31:26 *deceived.* Jacob's character, reflected in his name (see NIV text notes on 25:26; 27:36), is emphasized in the narrative again and again.

31:27 *harps.* Much smaller, and with fewer strings (usually 6 to 12), than their modern counterparts.

either good or bad.'[c] 30 Now you have gone
off because you longed to return to your
father's household.[d] But why did you
steal[e] my gods?[f]"
31 Jacob answered Laban, "I was afraid,
because I thought you would take your
daughters away from me by force.[g] 32 But
if you find anyone who has your gods,
that person shall not live.[h] In the presence
of our relatives, see for yourself whether
there is anything of yours here with me;
and if so, take it." Now Jacob did not
know that Rachel had stolen the gods.[i]
33 So Laban went into Jacob's tent and
into Leah's tent[j] and into the tent of the
two female servants,[k] but he found nothing.[l] After he came out of Leah's tent, he
entered Rachel's tent. 34 Now Rachel had
taken the household gods[m] and put them
inside her camel's saddle[n] and was sitting
on them. Laban searched[o] through everything in the tent but found nothing.
35 Rachel said to her father, "Don't be
angry, my lord, that I cannot stand up in
your presence;[p] I'm having my period.[q]"
So he searched but could not find the
household gods.[r]
36 Jacob was angry and took Laban to
task. "What is my crime?" he asked Laban. "How have I wronged[s] you that you
hunt me down?[t] 37 Now that you have
searched through all my goods, what have
you found that belongs to your household?[u] Put it here in front of your relatives[v]
and mine, and let them judge between the
two of us.[w]
38 "I have been with you for twenty
years now.[x] Your sheep and goats have not

31:29 [c] S Ge 24:50 **31:30** [d] S Ge 28:15; Job 29:2 [e] Ge 44:8 [f] S ver 19 **31:31** [g] S Ge 20:11 **31:32** [h] Ge 44:9 [i] S ver 19 **31:33** [j] Ge 24:67 [k] S Ge 16:1 [l] ver 37 **31:34** [m] S ver 19 [n] S Ge 24:63-64 [o] ver 37; Ge 44:12 **31:35** [p] Ex 20:12; Lev 19:3, 32; Dt 21:18; 27:16; Jer 35:18 [q] Lev 15:19-23 [r] ver 19

31:36 [s] 1Sa 19:5; 20:32 [t] 1Sa 23:23; 24:11 **31:37** [u] ver 33 [v] ver 23 [w] Dt 1:16; 16:18 **31:38** [x] S Ge 27:44

31:32 *if you find anyone who has your gods, that person shall not live.* Cf. 44:7 – 12. Though he made the offer in all innocence, Jacob almost lost his beloved Rachel. He had now been deceived even by his wife.

31:34 *inside her camel's saddle ... sitting on them.* Indicating the small size and powerlessness of the household gods.

31:35 *I'm having my period.* In later times, anything a menstruating woman sat on was considered ritually unclean (Lev 15:20).

JACOB'S JOURNEYS

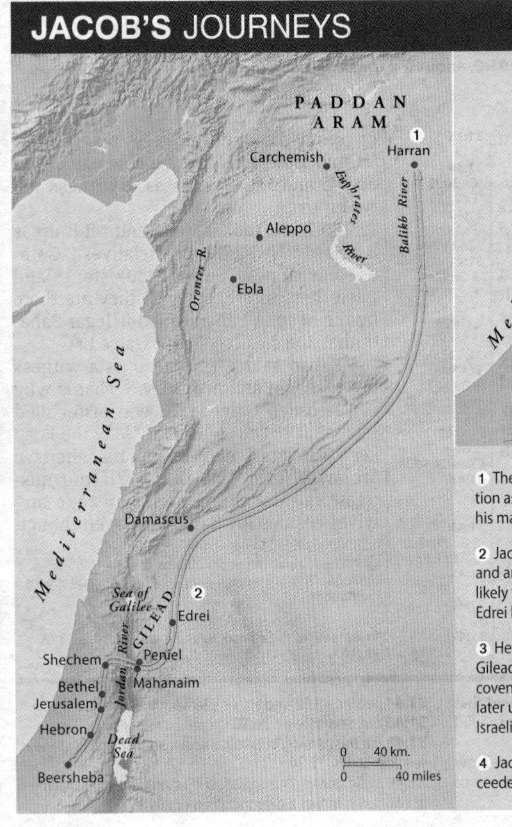

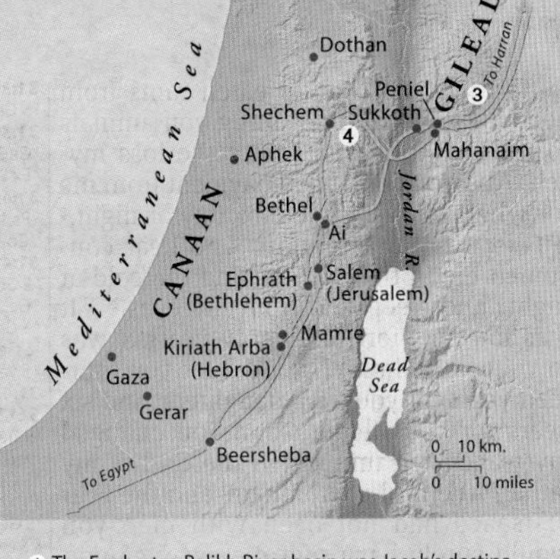

1 The Euphrates-Balikh River basin was Jacob's destination as he fled from Esau, ultimately reaching the home of his maternal uncle (Laban) near Harran.

2 Jacob's lengthy sojourn ended in a dispute with Laban and another flight—this time back to Canaan. His route likely took him toward Aleppo, then to Damascus and Edrei before reaching Peniel on the Jabbok River.

3 He and his dependents reached the hill country of Gilead before their caravan was overtaken by Laban. The covenant at Mizpah was celebrated on one of the hills later used as a border station between Aramean and Israelite territories.

4 Jacob lingered at Sukkoth, entered Canaan and proceeded to Shechem, where he erected an altar to the Lord.

A reproduction of a wall painting from a tomb at Beni Hasan, Egypt. The top panel depicts a group of Semitic traders being escorted by a darker-skinned Egyptian into the presence of an Egyptian provincial governor. The original painting is from c. 1900 BC, about the time of Jacob's journeys.

Erich Lessing/Art Resource, NY

miscarried,[y] nor have I eaten rams from
your flocks. 39 I did not bring you animals
torn by wild beasts; I bore the loss myself. And you demanded payment from me
for whatever was stolen[z] by day or night.[a]
40 This was my situation: The heat consumed me in the daytime and the cold at
night, and sleep fled from my eyes.[b] 41 It
was like this for the twenty years[c] I was
in your household. I worked for you fourteen years for your two daughters[d] and six
years for your flocks,[e] and you changed
my wages[f] ten times.[g] 42 If the God of my
father,[h] the God of Abraham[i] and the Fear
of Isaac,[j] had not been with me,[k] you
would surely have sent me away empty-
handed. But God has seen my hardship
and the toil of my hands,[l] and last night
he rebuked you.[m]"

43 Laban answered Jacob, "The wom-
en are my daughters, the children are my
children, and the flocks are my flocks.[n]
All you see is mine. Yet what can I do
today about these daughters of mine,
or about the children they have borne?
44 Come now, let's make a covenant,[o] you
and I, and let it serve as a witness between us."[p]

45 So Jacob took a stone and set it up as
a pillar.[q] 46 He said to his relatives, "Gather some stones." So they took stones and
piled them in a heap,[r] and they ate there
by the heap. 47 Laban called it Jegar Sahadutha, and Jacob called it Galeed.[a][s]

48 Laban said, "This heap[t] is a witness
between you and me today."[u] That is why
it was called Galeed. 49 It was also called
Mizpah,[b][v] because he said, "May the LORD
keep watch between you and me when we
are away from each other. 50 If you mistreat[w] my daughters or if you take any
wives besides my daughters, even though

31:38 [y]S Ge 30:27 **31:39** [z]Ge 30:33 [a]Ex 22:13 **31:40** [b]Ps 132:4; 2Co 11:27 **31:41** [c]S Ge 27:44 [d]Ge 29:30 [e]S Ge 30:32 [f]S Ge 29:15 [g]S ver 7 **31:42** [h]S ver 5; S Ex 3:15 [i]S Ge 24:12 [j]ver 53; Ge 46:1 [k]S Ge 21:22; Ps 124:1-2 [l]S Ge 3:17 [m]S Ge 24:50 **31:43** [n]Ge 30:32,42 **31:44** [o]S Ge 21:27 [p]S Ge 21:30 **31:45** [q]S Ge 28:18 **31:46** [r]ver 48, 51,52 **31:47** [s]S Ge 21:30

[a] *47* The Aramaic *Jegar Sahadutha* and the Hebrew *Galeed* both mean *witness heap.* [b] *49* *Mizpah* means *watchtower.*

31:48 [t]S ver 46 [u]S Ge 21:30; Jer 29:23; 42:5 **31:49** [v]Jos 11:3; Jdg 10:17; 11:29 **31:50** [w]Ge 16:6

31:39 *I bore the loss.* Ancient laws (as in Ex 22:13) held that a shepherd did not have to compensate for losses to wild animals.

31:42 *Fear.* Here a surrogate for God. Or perhaps the Hebrew for this word means "Kinsman," stressing the intimacy of God's relationship to the patriarch.

31:44 See vv. 48,52; see also 21:30 and note.

31:46 *ate.* See note on 26:30.

31:48 For the naming of an altar under similar circumstances, see Jos 22:10–12,34.

31:49 *May . . . other.* The so-called Mizpah benediction, which in context is in fact a denunciation or curse.

no one is with us, remember that God is a
witness[x] between you and me."[y]
51 Laban also said to Jacob, "Here is this
heap,[z] and here is this pillar[a] I have set
up between you and me. 52 This heap is a
witness, and this pillar is a witness,[b] that
I will not go past this heap to your side to
harm you and that you will not go past
this heap[c] and pillar to my side to harm
me.[d] 53 May the God of Abraham[e] and the
God of Nahor,[f] the God of their father,
judge between us."[g]
So Jacob took an oath[h] in the name of
the Fear of his father Isaac.[i] 54 He offered
a sacrifice[j] there in the hill country and
invited his relatives to a meal.[k] After they
had eaten, they spent the night there.
55 Early the next morning Laban kissed
his grandchildren and his daughters[l] and
blessed[m] them. Then he left and returned
home.[a][n]

Jacob Prepares to Meet Esau

32 [b] Jacob also went on his way,
and the angels of God[o] met him.
2 When Jacob saw them, he said, "This
is the camp of God!"[p] So he named that
place Mahanaim.[c][q]
3 Jacob sent messengers[r] ahead of him
to his brother Esau[s] in the land of Seir,[t] the
country of Edom.[u] 4 He instructed them:
"This is what you are to say to my lord[v]
Esau: 'Your servant[w] Jacob says, I have been
staying with Laban[x] and have remained
there till now. 5 I have cattle and donkeys,
sheep and goats, male and female servants.[y]
Now I am sending this message to my lord,[z]
that I may find favor in your eyes.[a]' "
6 When the messengers returned to Jacob, they said, "We went to your brother
Esau, and now he is coming to meet you,
and four hundred men are with him."[b]
7 In great fear[c] and distress[d] Jacob divided the people who were with him into
two groups,[d][e] and the flocks and herds
and camels as well. 8 He thought, "If Esau
comes and attacks one group,[e] the group[e]
that is left may escape."
9 Then Jacob prayed, "O God of my father Abraham,[f] God of my father Isaac,[g]
LORD, you who said to me, 'Go back to
your country and your relatives, and I
will make you prosper,'[h] 10 I am unworthy
of all the kindness and faithfulness[i] you
have shown your servant. I had only my
staff[j] when I crossed this Jordan, but now
I have become two camps.[k] 11 Save me, I
pray, from the hand of my brother Esau,
for I am afraid[l] he will come and attack
me,[m] and also the mothers with their children.[n] 12 But you have said, 'I will surely
make you prosper and will make your descendants like the sand[o] of the sea, which
cannot be counted.[p]' "
13 He spent the night there, and from
what he had with him he selected a gift[q]

[a] *55* In Hebrew texts this verse (31:55) is numbered 32:1. [b] In Hebrew texts 32:1-32 is numbered 32:2-33. [c] *2* *Mahanaim* means *two camps.* [d] *7* Or *camps* [e] *8* Or *camp*

31:50 [x] Dt 31:19; Jos 24:27; Jdg 11:10; 1Sa 12:5; 20:14, 23, 42; Job 16:19; Jer 29:23; 42:5; Mic 1:2 [y] S Ge 21:30; S Dt 4:26; S Jer 7:11 **31:51** [z] S ver 46 [a] S Ge 28:18 **31:52** [b] S Ge 21:30 [c] S ver 46 [d] S ver 7; S Ge 26:29 **31:53** [e] S Ge 24:12 [f] S Ge 11:27 [g] S Ge 16:5 [h] S Ge 21:23, 27 [i] S ver 42 **31:54** [j] Ge 46:1; Ex 24:5; Lev 3:1 [k] S Ge 26:30 **31:55** [l] S ver 28; Ru 1:9 [m] S Ge 24:60; S Ex 39:43 [n] Ge 18:33 **32:1** [o] S Ge 16:11; 2Ki 6:16-17; 1Ch 21:15; Ps 34:7; 35:5; 91:11; Da 6:22 **32:2** [p] S Ge 28:17 [q] Jos 13:26, 30; 21:38; 2Sa 2:8, 29; 17:24; 19:32; 1Ki 2:8; 4:14; 1Ch 6:80 **32:3** [r] Nu 21:21; Jdg 11:17 [s] S Ge 27:41-42 [t] S Ge 14:6; S Nu 24:18 [u] S Ge 25:30; S 36:16 **32:4** [v] S Ge 24:9 [w] S Ge 18:3 [x] Ge 31:41 **32:5** [y] S Ge 12:16 [z] S Ge 24:9 [a] Ge 33:8, 10, 15; 34:11; 47:25, 29; 50:4; Ru 2:13 **32:6** [b] Ge 33:1 **32:7** [c] ver 11 [d] Ge 35:3; Ps 4:1; 77:2; 107:6 [e] ver 10; Ge 33:1 **32:9** [f] S Ge 24:12 [g] S Ge 28:13 [h] S Ge 26:3; 31:13 **32:10** [i] S Ge 24:27 [j] Ge 38:18; 47:31; Nu 17:2 [k] S ver 7 **32:11** [l] S ver 7 [m] Ge 43:18; Ps 59:2 [n] S Ge 27:41 **32:12** [o] S Ge 22:17; 1Ki 4:20, 29 [p] S Ge 12:2; S 13:14; Hos 1:10; Ro 9:27 **32:13** [q] ver 13-15, 18, 20, 21; Ge 33:10; 43:11, 15, 25, 26; 1Sa 16:20; Pr 18:16; 21:14

31:51 *heap ... pillar ... between you and me.* Boundary markers between Laban's territory and Jacob's territory. Galeed, Jacob's name for the heap, is a pun on Gilead (see v. 47 and NIV text note).

31:53 *God of their father.* Or possibly "gods of their father [i.e., Terah]," reflecting Laban's polytheistic background (see Jos 24:2). *Fear of his father Isaac.* See note on v. 42. Jacob had met the "God of Isaac" (28:13) at Bethel 20 years earlier.

31:54 *sacrifice ... meal.* Two important aspects of the covenant-making (see v. 44) process (see Ex 24:5–8,11). *relatives.* Those with whom he had now entered into a covenant. The common meal indicated mutual acceptance (see note on 26:30).

31:55 *blessed.* Or "said farewell to" (see NIV text note on 47:10; see also 31:28).

32:1–32 Jacob's peaceful meeting with once hostile Esau and his safe arrival in the promised land.

32:1 *angels of God met him.* Jacob had just left the region of the hostile Laban and was about to enter the region of the hostile Esau. He was met by the angels of God, whom he had seen at Bethel when he was fleeing from Esau to go to Laban (28:12). Thus God was with Jacob, as he had promised (see 28:15; 31:3; see also note on 26:3).

32:2 *Mahanaim.* Located in Gilead (see note on 31:21) east of the Jordan and north of the Jabbok (see note on v. 22). Two camps (see NIV text note) had just met in hostility and separated in peace. Two camps were again about to meet (in hostility, Jacob thought) and separate in peace. But Jacob called this crucial place "two camps" after seeing the angelic encampment, suggesting that he saw God's encampment as a divine assurance. God's host had come to escort him safely to Canaan (see 33:12,15). Yet he also feared meeting with Esau, so he divided his household into two camps (see vv. 7,10 and NIV text note on v. 7), still trying to protect himself by his own devices.

32:3 *Seir ... Edom.* Far to the south of Jacob's ultimate destination, but he assumed that Esau would come seeking revenge as soon as he heard that Jacob was on his way back.

32:4 *Your servant.* A phrase suggesting both courtesy and humility.

32:6 *four hundred.* A round number for a sizable unit of fighting men (see 1Sa 22:2; 25:13; 30:10). While Jacob lived the peaceful life of a shepherd, Esau lived "by the sword," as Isaac had foretold (27:40).

32:9 *Jacob prayed.* His first recorded prayer since leaving Bethel.

32:11 *mothers with their children.* Jacob knew that if Esau still had revenge in his heart, Jacob's wives and children would suffer with him.

32:12 *your descendants like the sand of the sea.* A reference to God's promise in 28:14 (see 22:17 and note).

32:13 *gift.* Probably a wordplay: Out of his "two camps"

for his brother Esau: 14 two hundred female goats and twenty male goats, two hundred ewes and twenty rams,[r] 15 thirty female camels with their young, forty cows and ten bulls, and twenty female donkeys and ten male donkeys.[s] 16 He put them in the care of his servants, each herd by itself, and said to his servants, "Go ahead of me, and keep some space between the herds."[t]

17 He instructed the one in the lead: "When my brother Esau meets you and asks, 'Who do you belong to, and where are you going, and who owns all these animals in front of you?' 18 then you are to say, 'They belong to your servant[u] Jacob. They are a gift[v] sent to my lord Esau, and he is coming behind us.' "

19 He also instructed the second, the third and all the others who followed the herds: "You are to say the same thing to Esau when you meet him. 20 And be sure to say, 'Your servant[w] Jacob is coming behind us.' " For he thought, "I will pacify him with these gifts[x] I am sending on ahead;[y] later, when I see him, perhaps he will receive me."[z] 21 So Jacob's gifts[a] went on ahead of him, but he himself spent the night in the camp.

Jacob Wrestles With God

22 That night Jacob got up and took his two wives, his two female servants and his eleven sons[b] and crossed the ford of the Jabbok.[c] 23 After he had sent them across the stream, he sent over all his possessions.[d] 24 So Jacob was left alone,[e] and a man[f] wrestled with him till daybreak. 25 When the man saw that he could not overpower him, he touched the socket of Jacob's hip[g] so that his hip was wrenched as he wrestled with the man. 26 Then the man said, "Let me go, for it is daybreak."

But Jacob replied, "I will not let you go unless you bless me."[h]

27 The man asked him, "What is your name?"

"Jacob,"[i] he answered.

28 Then the man said, "Your name[j] will no longer be Jacob, but Israel,[a][k] because you have struggled with God and with humans and have overcome."[l]

29 Jacob said, "Please tell me your name."[m]

But he replied, "Why do you ask my name?"[n] Then he blessed[o] him there.

30 So Jacob called the place Peniel,[b] saying, "It is because I saw God face to face,[p] and yet my life was spared."

31 The sun rose above him as he passed Peniel,[c][q] and he was limping because of his hip. 32 Therefore to this day the Israelites do not eat the tendon attached to the socket of the hip,[r] because the socket of Jacob's hip was touched near the tendon.

Jacob Meets Esau

33 Jacob looked up and there was Esau, coming with his four hundred men;[s] so he divided the children among Leah, Rachel and the two female servants.[t] 2 He put the female servants and their children[u] in front, Leah and her children next, and Rachel and Joseph[v] in the rear. 3 He himself went on ahead and bowed down to

32:14 [r] Nu 7:88
32:15 [s] S Ge 13:2; 42:26; 45:23
32:16 [t] Ge 33:8
32:18 [u] S Ge 18:3 [v] S ver 13
32:20 [w] S Ge 18:3 [x] S ver 13; 1Sa 9:7; 2Ki 8:8; Jer 40:5 [y] 1Sa 25:19 [z] Ge 33:10; Ex 28:38; Lev 1:4; Mal 1:8
32:21 [a] S ver 13
32:22 [b] S Ge 30:24 [c] Nu 21:24; Dt 2:37; 3:16; Jos 12:2
32:23 [d] S Ge 26:14
32:24 [e] Da 10:8 [f] S Ge 18:2
32:25 [g] ver 32
32:26 [h] Hos 12:4
32:27 [i] S Ge 25:26
32:28 [j] Isa 1:26; 56:5; 60:14; 62:2, 4,12; 65:15 [k] S Ge 17:5 [l] S Ge 30:8
32:29 [m] Ex 3:13; 6:3; Jdg 13:17 [n] Jdg 13:18 [o] Ge 25:11; 35:9; 48:3
32:30 [p] S Ge 16:13; 1Co 13:12
32:31 [q] Jdg 8:9
32:32 [r] ver 25
33:1 [s] S Ge 32:6 [t] S Ge 32:7
33:2 [u] ver 6 [v] S Ge 30:24

[a] *28 Israel* probably means *he struggles with God.* [b] *30 Peniel* means *face of God.* [c] *31* Hebrew *Penuel,* a variant of *Peniel*

(Hebrew *maḥanayim,* v. 2; see vv. 7–8,10) Jacob selects a "gift" (*minḥah*) for his brother.

32:22 *Jabbok.* Today called the Wadi Zerqa, flowing westward into the Jordan about 20 miles north of the Dead Sea.

32:24 *left alone.* As he had been at Bethel (28:10–22). *a man.* God himself (as Jacob eventually realized; see v. 30) in the form of an angel (see Hos 12:3–4 and note on Ge 16:7). *wrestled.* God wrestled (*ye'abeq*) with Jacob (*ya'aqob*) by the Jabbok (*yabboq*)—the author delighted in wordplay. Jacob had struggled all his life to prevail, first with Esau, then with Laban. Now, as he was about to reenter Canaan, he was shown that it was with God that he must "wrestle"—not with Esau or any other human being.

32:25 *could not overpower him … touched the socket.* God came to him in such a form that Jacob could wrestle with him successfully, yet he showed Jacob that he could disable him at will.

32:26 *I will not let you go.* Jacob's persistence was soon rewarded (v. 29). *unless you bless me.* Jacob finally acknowledged that the blessing must come from God.

32:28 *Your name will no longer be Jacob.* Now that Jacob had acknowledged God as the source of blessing and was about to reenter the promised land, the Lord acknowledged Jacob as his servant by changing his name (see 17:5 and note). *Israel.* See NIV text note. Here in Jacob/Israel, the nation of Israel got its name and characterization: the people who struggle with God (memorialized in the name Israel) and with human beings (memorialized in the name Jacob) and overcome. God later confirmed Jacob's new name (35:10).

32:29 *Why do you ask my name?* Such a request of God is both unworthy and impossible to fulfill (see Jdg 13:17–18).

32:30 *I saw God face to face.* See note on 16:13; see also Jdg 6:22–23; 13:22. Only God's "back" (Ex 33:23) or "feet" (Ex 24:10; see note there) or "form" (Nu 12:8), in a symbolic sense, may be seen with impunity. *yet my life was spared.* If Jacob's life was spared in his encounter with God, his prayer for his life to be spared in his encounter with Esau (v. 11) will surely be granted.

32:31 *The sun rose above him.* A new day dawns in Jacob's life (see Ps 5:3 and note).

32:32 *do not eat the tendon.* Probably the sciatic muscle. Mentioned nowhere else in the Bible, this dietary prohibition is found in the later writings of Judaism. Jacob retained in his body, and Israel retained in her dietary practice, a perpetual reminder of this fateful encounter with God.

33:2 *Rachel and Joseph in the rear.* Jacob wanted to keep his favorite wife and child farthest away from potential harm.

33:3 *bowed down to the ground seven times.* A sign of total submission, documented also in texts found at Tell el-Amarna in Egypt and dating to the fourteenth century BC (see chart, p. xxii).

the ground[w] seven times[x] as he approached
his brother.
4 But Esau[y] ran to meet Jacob and embraced him; he threw his arms around his
neck and kissed him.[z] And they wept.[a]
5 Then Esau looked up and saw the women
and children. "Who are these with you?"
he asked.
Jacob answered, "They are the children
God has graciously given your servant.[b]"
6 Then the female servants and their
children[c] approached and bowed down.[d]
7 Next, Leah and her children[e] came and
bowed down.[f] Last of all came Joseph and
Rachel,[g] and they too bowed down.
8 Esau asked, "What's the meaning of all
these flocks and herds I met?"[h]
"To find favor in your eyes, my lord,"[i]
he said.
9 But Esau said, "I already have plenty,[j]
my brother. Keep what you have for yourself."
10 "No, please!" said Jacob. "If I have
found favor in your eyes,[k] accept this gift[l]
from me. For to see your face is like seeing the face of God,[m] now that you have
received me favorably.[n] 11 Please accept the
present[o] that was brought to you, for God
has been gracious to me[p] and I have all I
need."[q] And because Jacob insisted,[r] Esau
accepted it.
12 Then Esau said, "Let us be on our
way; I'll accompany you."
13 But Jacob said to him, "My lord[s]
knows that the children are tender and
that I must care for the ewes and cows
that are nursing their young.[t] If they are
driven hard just one day, all the animals
will die. 14 So let my lord go on ahead of
his servant, while I move along slowly at
the pace of the flocks and herds[u] before
me and the pace of the children, until I
come to my lord in Seir.[v]"
15 Esau said, "Then let me leave some of
my men with you."
"But why do that?" Jacob asked. "Just
let me find favor in the eyes of my lord."[w]
16 So that day Esau started on his way
back to Seir.[x] 17 Jacob, however, went to
Sukkoth,[y] where he built a place for himself and made shelters for his livestock.
That is why the place is called Sukkoth.[a]
18 After Jacob came from Paddan Aram,[bz]
he arrived safely at the city of Shechem[a] in
Canaan and camped within sight of the
city. 19 For a hundred pieces of silver,[c] he
bought from the sons of Hamor,[b] the father
of Shechem,[c] the plot of ground[d] where he
pitched his tent.[e] 20 There he set up an altar[f] and called it El Elohe Israel.[d]

Dinah and the Shechemites

34 Now Dinah,[g] the daughter Leah
had borne to Jacob, went out to
visit the women of the land. 2 When Shechem[h] son of Hamor[i] the Hivite,[j] the ruler of that area, saw her, he took her and
raped her.[k] 3 His heart was drawn to Dinah[l]
daughter of Jacob;[m] he loved[n] the young
woman and spoke tenderly[o] to her. 4 And
Shechem said to his father Hamor, "Get
me this girl as my wife."[p]

[a] *17 Sukkoth* means *shelters.* [b] *18* That is, Northwest Mesopotamia [c] *19* Hebrew *hundred kesitahs;* a kesitah was a unit of money of unknown weight and value. [d] *20 El Elohe Israel* can mean *El is the God of Israel* or *mighty is the God of Israel.*

33:3 [w]ver 6,7; S Ge 17:3; 37:7-10; 42:6; 43:26; 44:14; 48:12; 1Sa 20:41 [x]2Ki 5:10,14 **33:4** [y]S Ge 27:41-42 [z]S Ge 29:11; Lk 15:20 [a]S Ge 27:27 **33:5** [b]S Ge 18:3; Ge 48:9; Ps 127:3; Isa 8:18 **33:6** [c]ver 2 [d]S ver 3 **33:7** [e]ver 2 [f]S ver 3 [g]S Ge 30:24 **33:8** [h]Ge 32:14-16 [i]S Ge 24:9; S 32:5 **33:9** [j]ver 11; S Ge 13:6 **33:10** [k]S Ge 30:27; S 32:5 [l]S Ge 32:13 [m]S Ge 16:13 [n]S Ge 32:20 **33:11** [o]1Sa 25:27; 30:26 [p]Ge 30:43 [q]S ver 9 [r]Ge 19:3 **33:13** [s]ver 8 [t]Isa 40:11; Jer 31:8 **33:14** [u]Ex 12:38 [v]S Ge 14:6 **33:15** [w]S Ge 32:5 **33:16** [x]S Ge 14:6 **33:17** [y]Jos 13:27; Jdg 8:5,6,8, 14-16; 1Ki 7:46; 2Ch 4:17; Ps 60:6; 108:7 **33:18** [z]S Ge 25:20 [a]S Ge 12:6

33:19 [b]Ge 34:2; Jdg 9:28; Ac 7:16 [c]Ge 34:2; Jos 24:32 [d]Ge 34:10,16,21; 47:27; Jn 4:5 [e]S Ge 12:8 **33:20** [f]S Ge 4:26; S 8:20 **34:1** [g]S Ge 30:21 **34:2** [h]S Ge 33:19 [i]S Ge 33:19 [j]S Ge 10:17 [k]Dt 21:14; 2Sa 13:14 **34:3** [l]ver 26 [m]ver 19 [n]S Ge 24:67 [o]Ge 50:21; Isa 14:1; 40:2 **34:4** [p]S Ge 21:21

33:4 All Jacob's fears proved unfounded. God had been at work and had so blessed Esau (v. 9) that he no longer held a grudge against Jacob.

33:9 *I already have plenty.* Esau had obtained his "plenty" while residing in "the land of Seir" (32:3; cf. 33:16) south of the promised land, just as Jacob had obtained his bounties in Paddan Aram north of the promised land. *my brother.* Esau's response was in contrast to Jacob's cautious and fearful "my lord" (v. 8).

33:11 *present.* The Hebrew for "present" is the same as that used for "blessing" in 27:35. The author of Genesis was conscious of the irony that Jacob now acknowledged that the blessing he had struggled for was from God. In his last attempt to express reconciliation with Esau, Jacob in a sense gave back the "blessing" he had stolen from his brother, doing so from the blessings the Lord had given him.

33:12 *I'll accompany you.* Resulting in another "two camps" (see 32:2 and note). Esau's proposal suggests that he had come with his 400 men to escort Jacob's vulnerable company safely home (see v. 15). Jacob declines the offer because he trusts the protection of God more than he trusts Esau and his men.

33:14 *until I come to my lord in Seir.* But Jacob, still the deceiver, had no intention of following Esau all the way to Seir.

33:18 *Paddan Aram.* See note on 25:20. *arrived safely.* The answer to Jacob's prayer 20 years earlier (see 28:21). *Shechem.* See note on 12:6. Jacob followed in the footsteps of Abraham (see 12:6). Jacob dug a well there (see Jn 4:5–6 and note on 4:11) that can still be seen today.

33:19 *pieces of silver.* See NIV text note. The Hebrew word translated by this phrase is found only three times and always in patriarchal contexts (see Jos 24:32; Job 42:11).

33:20 *set up an altar.* See note on 12:7. *called it El Elohe Israel.* See NIV text note. Jacob formally acknowledged the God of his ancestors as his God also (see 28:21). But he lingered at Shechem and did not return to Bethel (see 35:1), and that meant trouble (see ch. 34).

34:1–31 Jacob is now confronted in the promised land with the danger of being absorbed by the native Canaanites (vv. 9,16) and then with the threat of their hostility after his sons' vengeful acts (v. 30). These were dangers the Israelites constantly faced from the peoples around them — either absorption or hostility, both of which are perpetual threats to God's people. The name of God ends ch. 33 and begins ch. 35 but is completely absent from this sordid chapter (see note on 7:16).

34:2 *Shechem.* See 33:19. He was probably named after the city.

34:4 *Get me this girl as my wife.* See note on 21:21.

5 When Jacob heard that his daughter
Dinah had been defiled,[q] his sons were
in the fields with his livestock; so he did
nothing about it until they came home.
6 Then Shechem's father Hamor went
out to talk with Jacob.[r] 7 Meanwhile, Jacob's sons had come in from the fields as
soon as they heard what had happened.
They were shocked[s] and furious,[t] because Shechem had done an outrageous
thing in[a] Israel[u] by sleeping with Jacob's
daughter — a thing that should not be
done.[v]
8 But Hamor said to them, "My son Shechem has his heart set on your daughter.
Please give her to him as his wife.[w] 9 Intermarry with us; give us your daughters and
take our daughters for yourselves.[x] 10 You
can settle among us;[y] the land is open to
you.[z] Live in it, trade[b] in it,[a] and acquire
property in it.[b]"
11 Then Shechem said to Dinah's father
and brothers, "Let me find favor in your
eyes,[c] and I will give you whatever you
ask. 12 Make the price for the bride[d] and
the gift I am to bring as great as you like,
and I'll pay whatever you ask me. Only
give me the young woman as my wife."
13 Because their sister Dinah had been
defiled,[e] Jacob's sons replied deceitfully[f]
as they spoke to Shechem and his father
Hamor. 14 They said to them, "We can't do
such a thing; we can't give our sister to a
man who is not circumcised.[g] That would
be a disgrace to us. 15 We will enter into
an agreement with you on one condition[h]
only: that you become like us by circumcising all your males.[i] 16 Then we will give
you our daughters and take your daughters for ourselves.[j] We'll settle among you
and become one people with you.[k] 17 But if
you will not agree to be circumcised, we'll
take our sister and go."
18 Their proposal seemed good to Hamor and his son Shechem. 19 The young
man, who was the most honored[l] of all
his father's family, lost no time in doing
what they said, because he was delighted
with Jacob's daughter.[m] 20 So Hamor and
his son Shechem went to the gate of their
city[n] to speak to the men of their city.
21 "These men are friendly toward us,"
they said. "Let them live in our land and
trade in it;[o] the land has plenty of room
for them. We can marry their daughters
and they can marry ours.[p] 22 But the men
will agree to live with us as one people
only on the condition that our males be
circumcised,[q] as they themselves are.
23 Won't their livestock, their property and
all their other animals become ours?[r] So
let us agree to their terms, and they will
settle among us.[s]"
24 All the men who went out of the city
gate[t] agreed with Hamor and his son Shechem, and every male in the city was circumcised.
25 Three days later, while all of them
were still in pain,[u] two of Jacob's sons,
Simeon[v] and Levi,[w] Dinah's brothers, took
their swords[x] and attacked the unsuspecting city,[y] killing every male.[z] 26 They
put Hamor and his son Shechem to the
sword[a] and took Dinah[b] from Shechem's
house and left. 27 The sons of Jacob came
upon the dead bodies and looted the city[c]
where[c] their sister had been defiled.[d]
28 They seized their flocks and herds and
donkeys[e] and everything else of theirs in
the city and out in the fields.[f] 29 They carried off all their wealth and all their wom-
en and children,[g] taking as plunder[h] everything in the houses.[i]
30 Then Jacob said to Simeon and Levi,
"You have brought trouble[j] on me by making me obnoxious[k] to the Canaanites and
Perizzites, the people living in this land.[l]
We are few in number,[m] and if they join
forces against me and attack me, I and my
household will be destroyed."
31 But they replied, "Should he have
treated our sister like a prostitute?[n]"

[a] 7 Or *against* [b] 10 Or *move about freely;* also in verse 21 [c] 27 Or *because*

34:5 [q] ver 2,13, 27; Ge 35:22; 49:4; Dt 27:20; 33:6; 1Ch 5:1 **34:6** [r] Jdg 14:2-5 **34:7** [s] 1Co 5:2 [t] Ge 39:19; 49:6-7; 2Sa 12:5; 13:21; Est 7:7; Pr 6:34 [u] Dt 22:21; Jdg 19:23; 20:6; 2Sa 13:12; Jer 29:23 [v] S Ge 20:9 **34:8** [w] S Ge 21:21; Dt 21:11 **34:9** [x] ver 16, 21; Dt 7:3; Jos 23:12 **34:10** [y] ver 23; Ge 46:34; 47:6, 27 [z] S Ge 13:9 [a] Ge 42:34 [b] S Ge 33:19 **34:11** [c] S Ge 32:5 **34:12** [d] Ex 22:16; Dt 22:29; 1Sa 18:25 **34:13** [e] S ver 5 [f] S Ge 27:36 **34:14** [g] Ge 17:14; Jdg 14:3; 1Sa 31:4; Isa 52:1 **34:15** [h] 1Sa 11:2 [i] ver 22; Ex 12:48 **34:16** [j] S ver 9 [k] S Ge 33:19 **34:19** [l] Ge 49:3; 1Ch 11:21 [m] ver 3 **34:20** [n] S Ge 18:1 **34:21** [o] S Ge 33:19 [p] S ver 9 **34:22** [q] S ver 15 **34:23** [r] ver 28; S Ge 12:16 [s] S ver 10 **34:24** [t] S Ge 18:1 **34:25** [u] Jos 5:8 [v] S Ge 29:33 [w] S Ge 29:34 [x] Ge 49:5; Mal 2:16 [y] Jdg 18:7,10, 27; Eze 38:11 [z] Ge 49:7 **34:26** [a] S ver 7; Ge 48:22 [b] ver 3 **34:27** [c] 2Ki 21:14 [d] S ver 5

34:28 [e] Ge 43:18 [f] S ver 23 **34:29** [g] S Ge 31:26 [h] Nu 14:3; 31:9,53; Dt 2:35; Jos 7:21 [i] 2Ki 8:12; Isa 13:16; La 5:11; Am 1:13; Zec 14:2 **34:30** [j] Ge 43:6; Ex 5:23; Nu 11:11 [k] Ex 5:21; 6:9; 1Sa 13:4; 27:12; 2Sa 10:6; 1Ch 19:6 [l] S Ge 13:7 [m] Ge 35:26; 46:27; Ex 1:5; Dt 10:22; 26:5; 1Ch 16:19; Ps 105:12 **34:31** [n] ver 2

34:7 *Israel.* The clan of Israel. *a thing that should not be done.* Cf. Tamar's plea to Amnon in a similar situation (2Sa 13:12).

34:9 *Intermarry with us.* The Canaanites wanted to benefit from the blessings Jacob had received from the Lord (both his offspring and his possessions — vv. 21 – 23).

34:12 *price for the bride.* For a specific example of this marriage custom, see 24:53 and note.

34:13 *Jacob's sons replied deceitfully.* Like father, like son (see 27:24; see also note on 25:26).

34:15 Using a sacred ceremony for a sinful purpose (see vv. 24 – 25).

34:20 *gate of their city.* See notes on 19:1; 23:10.

34:23 The greed of the men of Shechem led to their destruction.

34:24 The Canaanites were even willing to submit to Israel's covenant rite in order to attain their purposes.

34:25 *Simeon and Levi.* Because they slaughtered the men of Shechem, their own descendants would be scattered far and wide (see note on 49:7). *Dinah's brothers.* All three were children of Leah (29:33 – 34; 30:21). *killing every male.* Shechem's crime, serious as it was, hardly warranted such brutal and extensive retaliation (see vv. 27 – 29). Jacob's sons ran ahead of God's judgment on the Canaanites (see 15:16 and note).

34:30 *Perizzites.* See note on 13:7.

Jacob Returns to Bethel

35 Then God said to Jacob, "Go up to
Bethel[o] and settle there, and build
an altar[p] there to God,[q] who appeared to
you[r] when you were fleeing from your
brother Esau."[s]
2 So Jacob said to his household[t] and
to all who were with him, "Get rid of the
foreign gods[u] you have with you, and purify yourselves and change your clothes.[v]
3 Then come, let us go up to Bethel, where
I will build an altar to God,[w] who answered me in the day of my distress[x] and
who has been with me wherever I have
gone.[y]" 4 So they gave Jacob all the foreign
gods they had and the rings in their ears,[z]
and Jacob buried them under the oak[a] at
Shechem.[b] 5 Then they set out, and the terror of God[c] fell on the towns all around
them so that no one pursued them.[d]
6 Jacob and all the people with him
came to Luz[e] (that is, Bethel) in the land
of Canaan.[f] 7 There he built an altar,[g] and
he called the place El Bethel,[a][h] because
it was there that God revealed himself
to him[i] when he was fleeing from his
brother.[j]
8 Now Deborah, Rebekah's nurse,[k] died
and was buried under the oak[l] outside
Bethel.[m] So it was named Allon Bakuth.[b]
9 After Jacob returned from Paddan
Aram,[c][n] God appeared to him again and
blessed him.[o] 10 God said to him, "Your
name is Jacob,[d] but you will no longer be
called Jacob; your name will be Israel.[e]"[p]
So he named him Israel.
11 And God said to him, "I am God Almighty[f];[q] be fruitful and increase in number.[r] A nation[s] and a community of nations will come from you, and kings will
be among your descendants.[t] 12 The land I
gave to Abraham and Isaac I also give to
you, and I will give this land to your descendants after you.[u]"[v] 13 Then God went
up from him[w] at the place where he had
talked with him.
14 Jacob set up a stone pillar[x] at the place
where God had talked with him, and he
poured out a drink offering[y] on it; he also
poured oil on it.[z] 15 Jacob called the place
where God had talked with him Bethel.[g][a]

The Deaths of Rachel and Isaac

35:23-26pp — 1Ch 2:1-2

16 Then they moved on from Bethel.
While they were still some distance from
Ephrath,[b] Rachel[c] began to give birth and
had great difficulty. 17 And as she was having great difficulty in childbirth, the midwife[d] said to her, "Don't despair, for you
have another son."[e] 18 As she breathed her
last—for she was dying—she named her
son Ben-Oni.[h][f] But his father named him
Benjamin.[i][g]

[a] 7 *El Bethel* means *God of Bethel.* [b] 8 *Allon Bakuth* means *oak of weeping.* [c] 9 That is, Northwest Mesopotamia; also in verse 26 [d] 10 *Jacob* means *he grasps the heel,* a Hebrew idiom for *he deceives.* [e] 10 *Israel* probably means *he struggles with God.* [f] 11 Hebrew *El-Shaddai* [g] 15 *Bethel* means *house of God.* [h] 18 *Ben-Oni* means *son of my trouble.* [i] 18 *Benjamin* means *son of my right hand.*

35:1 [o] S Ge 12:8 [p] S Ge 4:26; 8:20 [q] ver 3 [r] S Ge 12:7 [s] ver 7; Ge 27:43 **35:2** [t] Ge 18:19; Jos 24:15 [u] S Ge 31:19; S Jos 24:14 [v] Ex 19:10, 14; Nu 8:7, 21; 19:19 **35:3** [w] ver 1 [x] S Ge 32:7; S Jdg 2:15 [y] S Ge 26:3 **35:4** [z] S Ge 24:22; Ex 32:3; 35:22; Jdg 8:24; Pr 25:12 [a] ver 8 [b] S Ge 12:6 **35:5** [c] Ex 15:16; 23:27; Dt 2:25; Jos 2:9; 1Sa 7:10; 13:7; 14:15; 2Ch 14:14; 17:10; 20:29; Ps 9:20; Isa 19:17; Zec 14:13 [d] Ps 105:14 **35:6** [e] S Ge 28:19 [f] S Ge 10:19 **35:7** [g] S Ge 8:20 [h] Ge 28:19 [i] S Ge 28:13 [j] S ver 1 **35:8** [k] Ge 24:59 [l] ver 4 [m] S Ge 12:8; 1Sa 10:3 **35:9** [n] S Ge 25:20 [o] S Ge 28:13; S 32:29 **35:10** [p] S Ge 17:5 **35:11** [q] S Ge 17:1 [r] S Ge 12:2 [s] S Ge 12:2 [t] S Ge 17:6

35:12 [u] S Ge 28:13 [v] S Ge 12:7; S 15:7 **35:13** [w] S Ge 17:22 **35:14** [x] S Ge 28:22 [y] Ex 29:40; Lev 23:13; Nu 6:15, 17; 15:5; 28:7, 14; 2Sa 23:16; 2Ch 29:35 [z] S Ge 28:18 **35:15** [a] S Ge 12:8 **35:16** [b] ver 19; Ge 48:7; Ru 1:2; 4:11; 1Sa 17:12; Mic 5:2 [c] S Ge 29:6 **35:17** [d] Ge 38:28; Ex 1:15 [e] S Ge 30:24 **35:18** [f] 1Sa 4:21; 14:3 [g] ver 24; Ge 42:4; 43:16, 29; 45:12, 14; 49:27; Nu 1:36; Dt 33:12

35:1–15 Whereas Abram's arrival at Shechem marked the end of his journey to Canaan—it was there that God promised to give the land to his offspring (12:6–7)—the final stage of Jacob's journey back was from Shechem to Bethel, where Jacob's pilgrimage with God had begun (28:10–22).
35:1 *God … appeared to you when you were fleeing.* See v. 7; 28:13.
35:2 *foreign gods you have with you.* See note on 31:19 (see also Jos 24:23).
35:3 *God … who has been with me.* See 28:15; see also note on 26:3.
35:4 *rings.* Worn as amulets or charms; a pagan religious custom (cf. Hos 2:13). *oak at Shechem.* Obviously a well-known tree, perhaps the "great tree" mentioned in 12:6 (see Jos 24:26).
35:5 *terror of God.* God protected his servant.
35:7 *built an altar.* See note on 12:7.
35:8 *Deborah, Rebekah's nurse, died.* After long years of faithful service (see 24:59). *the oak.* Again probably a well-known tree (see note on v. 4), perhaps the "great tree" mentioned in 1Sa 10:3.
35:9 *Jacob returned.* See map, p. 61. *Paddan Aram.* See note on 25:20.
35:10 *Jacob … Israel.* The previous assignment of an additional name (see 32:28) is here confirmed. For similar examples compare 21:31 with 26:33 and 28:19 with 35:15.

35:11–12 This event climaxes the Isaac-Jacob cycle (see Introduction: Literary Features). Now that Jacob was at last back at Bethel, where God had begun his direct relationship with him, God confirmed to this chosen son of Isaac the covenant promises made to Abraham (17:1–8; see 28:3). His words echo his original benediction pronounced on humankind in the beginning (1:28) and renewed after the flood (9:1,7). God's blessing on the human race would be fulfilled in and through Jacob and his offspring. See also 47:27; Ex 1:7.
35:11 God identifies himself to Jacob here as "God Almighty" (El-Shaddai). At Bethel he had identified himself as "the God of your father Abraham and the God of Isaac" (28:13), but that was also as El-Shaddai (see 17:1 and note; see also 28:3; 48:3; Ex 6:3).
35:13 See note on 17:22.
35:14 See 28:18 and note. *drink offering.* A liquid poured out as a sacrifice to a deity.
35:15 See 28:19; see also note on v. 10.
35:16–29 The conclusion to the main story of Jacob's life.
35:16 *Ephrath.* The older name for Bethlehem (see v. 19) in Judah; it apparently refers to the area in which Bethlehem was located (see Ru 1:2; Mic 5:2 and notes).
35:17 *another son.* An echo of Rachel's own plea at the time of Joseph's birth (see 30:24).
35:18 *Benjamin.* See NIV text note. The name can also mean "son of the south"—in distinction from the other sons, who

19 So Rachel died and was buried on the way to Ephrath[h] (that is, Bethlehem[i]). 20 Over her tomb Jacob set up a pillar, and to this day[j] that pillar marks Rachel's tomb.[k]

21 Israel moved on again and pitched his tent beyond Migdal Eder.[l] 22 While Israel was living in that region, Reuben went in and slept with his father's concubine[m] Bilhah,[n] and Israel heard of it.

Jacob had twelve sons:

23 The sons of Leah:[o]
Reuben the firstborn[p] of Jacob,
Simeon, Levi, Judah,[q] Issachar and Zebulun.[r]

24 The sons of Rachel:
Joseph[s] and Benjamin.[t]

25 The sons of Rachel's servant Bilhah:[u]
Dan and Naphtali.[v]

26 The sons of Leah's servant Zilpah:[w]
Gad[x] and Asher.[y]

These were the sons of Jacob,[z] who were born to him in Paddan Aram.[a]

27 Jacob came home to his father Isaac[b] in Mamre,[c] near Kiriath Arba[d] (that is, Hebron),[e] where Abraham and Isaac had stayed.[f] 28 Isaac lived a hundred and eighty years.[g] 29 Then he breathed his last and died and was gathered to his people,[h] old and full of years.[i] And his sons Esau and Jacob buried him.[j]

Esau's Descendants

36:10-14pp — 1Ch 1:35-37
36:20-28pp — 1Ch 1:38-42

36 This is the account[k] of the family line of Esau (that is, Edom).[l]

2 Esau took his wives from the women of Canaan:[m] Adah daughter of Elon the Hittite,[n] and Oholibamah[o] daughter of Anah[p] and granddaughter of Zibeon the Hivite[q]— 3 also Basemath[r] daughter of Ishmael and sister of Nebaioth.[s]

4 Adah bore Eliphaz to Esau, Basemath bore Reuel,[t] 5 and Oholibamah bore Jeush, Jalam and Korah.[u] These were the sons of Esau, who were born to him in Canaan.

6 Esau took his wives and sons and daughters and all the members of his household, as well as his livestock and all his other animals and all the goods he had acquired in Canaan,[v] and moved to a land some distance from his brother Jacob.[w] 7 Their possessions were too great for them to remain together; the land where they were staying could not support them both because of their livestock.[x] 8 So Esau[y] (that is, Edom)[z] settled in the hill country of Seir.[a]

9 This is the account[b] of the family line of Esau the father of the Edomites[c] in the hill country of Seir.

10 These are the names of Esau's sons:
Eliphaz, the son of Esau's wife Adah, and Reuel, the son of Esau's wife Basemath.[d]

11 The sons of Eliphaz:[e]
Teman,[f] Omar, Zepho, Gatam and Kenaz.[g]

35:19 [h] S ver 16 [i] Ge 48:7; Jos 19:15; Jdg 12:8; 17:7; 19:1,18; Ru 1:1,19; 1Sa 17:12; Mic 5:2 **35:20** [j] Jos 4:9; 7:26; 8:28; 10:27; 1Sa 6:18 [k] 1Sa 10:2 **35:21** [l] Jos 15:21 **35:22** [m] S Ge 22:24 [n] S Ge 29:29; S 34:5; S Lev 18:8 **35:23** [o] S Ge 29:16 [p] Ge 43:33; 46:8 [q] S Ge 29:35 [r] S Ge 30:20 **35:24** [s] S Ge 30:24 [t] S ver 18 **35:25** [u] Ge 37:2 [v] S Ge 30:8 **35:26** [w] Ge 37:2 [x] S Ge 30:11 [y] S Ge 30:13 [z] S Ge 34:30; 46:8; Ex 1:1-4 [a] S Ge 25:20 **35:27** [b] Ge 31:18 [c] S Ge 13:18 [d] Ge 23:2; Jos 15:54; Jdg 1:10; Ne 11:25 [e] S Ge 13:18 [f] S Ge 17:8 **35:28** [g] S Ge 25:7,20 **35:29** [h] S Ge 25:8 [i] S Ge 15:15 [j] S Ge 23:20; S 25:9 **36:1** [k] S Ge 2:4 [l] S Ge 25:30 **36:2** [m] Ge 28:8-9 [n] Ge 26:34 [o] ver 14,18

[p] ver 25; 1Ch 1:40 [q] ver 24; S Ge 10:17; 1Ch 1:40 **36:3** [r] ver 4,10,13,17 [s] S Ge 25:13 **36:4** [t] S ver 3; 1Ch 1:35 **36:5** [u] ver 14,18; 1Ch 1:35 **36:6** [v] Ge 12:5 [w] Ge 27:39 **36:7** [x] S Ge 13:6 **36:8** [y] Dt 2:4 [z] S Ge 25:30 [a] S Ge 14:6 **36:9** [b] S Ge 2:4 [c] ver 1,43 **36:10** [d] S ver 3 **36:11** [e] ver 15-16; 1Ch 1:45; Job 2:11; 4:1 [f] Jer 49:7,20; Eze 25:13; Am 1:12; Ob 1:9; Hab 3:3 [g] ver 15

---

were born in the north. One set of Hebrew terms for indicating direction was based on facing east, so south was on the right.

35:19 *Rachel died.* In childbirth (see note on 30:1). *Ephrath ... Bethlehem.* See note on v. 16.

35:20 *Rachel's tomb.* See 1Sa 10:2. The traditional, though not authentic, site is near Bethlehem.

35:21 *Migdal Eder.* Means "tower of the flock," perhaps referring to a watchtower built to discourage thieves from stealing sheep and other animals (see, e.g., 2Ch 26:10). The same Hebrew phrase is used figuratively in Mic 4:8, where "flock" refers to the people of Judah (see Mic 4:6–7).

35:22 Reuben's act was an arrogant and premature claim to the rights of the firstborn (see 2Sa 3:7; 12:8; 16:21; 1Ki 2:22 and notes). For this he would lose his legal status as firstborn (see 49:3–4; 1Ch 5:1; see also note on Ge 37:21).

35:26 *sons of Jacob ... born to him in Paddan Aram.* Obviously a summary statement since Benjamin was born in Canaan (see vv. 16–18).

35:27 *Mamre, near Kiriath Arba (that is, Hebron).* See notes on 13:18; 23:2.

35:29 See note on 25:8. *buried him.* In the family tomb, the cave of Machpelah (49:30–31).

36:1–43 A concise account of Esau's descendants, who also belonged to the "many nations" promised to Abraham and Sarah (17:5–6,16), before the more full-blown account of Jacob's descendants (see notes on 37:2—50:26 and 37:2). Cf. the account of Ishmael's offspring in 25:12–18.

36:1 *account.* See note on 2:4. Though repeated in v. 9, the word does not mark the start of a new main section there since the information in vv. 9–43 is merely an expansion of that in vv. 1–8. *Esau (that is, Edom).* See 25:30 and NIV text note there. Reddish rock formations, primarily sandstone, are conspicuous in the territory of the Edomites, located south and southeast of the Dead Sea.

36:2–3 See note on 26:34.

36:7 See 13:6; 26:20 and notes.

36:8 *Seir.* Another name for Edom. The word itself is related to the Hebrew word meaning "hair," a possible meaning also for the name "Esau" (see NIV text note on 25:25). Esau's clan must have driven away the original Horite (see v. 20) inhabitants of Seir (see 14:6 and note). The descendants of Seir are listed in vv. 20–28.

36:10–14 The same list of Esau's descendants (see 1Ch 1:35–37) is repeated in vv. 15–19 as a list of tribal chieftains.

36:11 *Eliphaz: Teman.* One of Job's friends was named Eliphaz the Temanite (Job 2:11), and Job himself was from the land of Uz (Job 1:1). Thus Job probably lived in Edom (see vv. 28,34).

12 Esau's son Eliphaz also had a concubine[h] named Timna, who bore
him Amalek.[i] These were grandsons of Esau's wife Adah.[j]
13 The sons of Reuel:
Nahath, Zerah, Shammah and
Mizzah. These were grandsons of
Esau's wife Basemath.[k]
14 The sons of Esau's wife Oholibamah[l]
daughter of Anah and granddaughter
of Zibeon, whom she bore to Esau:
Jeush, Jalam and Korah.[m]

15 These were the chiefs[n] among Esau's
descendants:
The sons of Eliphaz the firstborn of
Esau:
Chiefs Teman,[o] Omar, Zepho, Kenaz,[p] 16 Korah,[a] Gatam and Amalek.
These were the chiefs descended
from Eliphaz[q] in Edom;[r] they were
grandsons of Adah.[s]
17 The sons of Esau's son Reuel:[t]
Chiefs Nahath, Zerah, Shammah
and Mizzah. These were the chiefs
descended from Reuel in Edom;
they were grandsons of Esau's wife
Basemath.[u]
18 The sons of Esau's wife Oholibamah:[v]
Chiefs Jeush, Jalam and Korah.[w]
These were the chiefs descended from Esau's wife Oholibamah
daughter of Anah.
19 These were the sons of Esau[x] (that is,
Edom),[y] and these were their chiefs.[z]

20 These were the sons of Seir the Horite,[a] who were living in the region:
Lotan, Shobal, Zibeon, Anah,[b] 21 Dishon, Ezer and Dishan. These sons
of Seir in Edom were Horite chiefs.[c]
22 The sons of Lotan:
Hori and Homam.[b] Timna was Lotan's sister.
23 The sons of Shobal:
Alvan, Manahath, Ebal, Shepho
and Onam.
24 The sons of Zibeon:[d]
Aiah and Anah. This is the Anah
who discovered the hot springs[ce] in
the desert while he was grazing the
donkeys[f] of his father Zibeon.
25 The children of Anah:[g]
Dishon and Oholibamah[h] daughter
of Anah.
26 The sons of Dishon[d]:
Hemdan, Eshban, Ithran and Ke-
ran.

36:12 [h] S Ge 22:24 [i] Ex 17:8, 16; Nu 24:20; Dt 25:17, 19; 1Sa 15:2; 27:8 [j] ver 16 **36:13** [k] S ver 3 **36:14** [l] S ver 2 [m] S ver 5 **36:15** [n] ver 19, 40; Ex 15:15 [o] Job 2:11; Jer 49:7; Eze 25:13; Am 1:12; Hab 3:3 [p] S ver 11 **36:16** [q] S ver 11 [r] Ge 32:3; Ex 15:15; Nu 20:14; 33:37 [s] ver 12 **36:17** [t] 1Ch 1:37 [u] S ver 3 **36:18** [v] S ver 2 [w] S ver 5 **36:19** [x] 1Ch 1:35 [y] S Ge 25:30 [z] S ver 15 **36:20** [a] S Ge 14:6 [b] ver 29 **36:21** [c] ver 30 **36:24** [d] S ver 2 [e] Jos 15:19 [f] Job 1:14 **36:25** [g] S ver 2 [h] S ver 2

27 The sons of Ezer:
Bilhan, Zaavan and Akan.
28 The sons of Dishan:
Uz and Aran.
29 These were the Horite chiefs:
Lotan, Shobal, Zibeon, Anah,[i] 30 Dishon, Ezer and Dishan. These were
the Horite chiefs,[j] according to their
divisions, in the land of Seir.

The Rulers of Edom

36:31-43pp — 1Ch 1:43-54

31 These were the kings who reigned in
Edom before any Israelite king[k] reigned:
32 Bela son of Beor became king of
Edom. His city was named Dinhabah.
33 When Bela died, Jobab son of Zerah
from Bozrah[l] succeeded him as
king.
34 When Jobab died, Husham from the
land of the Temanites[m] succeeded
him as king.
35 When Husham died, Hadad son of
Bedad, who defeated Midian[n] in
the country of Moab,[o] succeeded
him as king. His city was named
Avith.
36 When Hadad died, Samlah from Mas-
rekah succeeded him as king.
37 When Samlah died, Shaul from Rehoboth[p] on the river succeeded him as
king.
38 When Shaul died, Baal-Hanan son of
Akbor succeeded him as king.
39 When Baal-Hanan son of Akbor died,
Hadad[e] succeeded him as king. His
city was named Pau, and his wife's
name was Mehetabel daughter of
Matred, the daughter of Me-Zahab.

40 These were the chiefs[q] descended
from Esau, by name, according to their
clans and regions:
Timna, Alvah, Jetheth, 41 Oholibamah, Elah, Pinon, 42 Kenaz, Teman,
Mibzar, 43 Magdiel and Iram. These
were the chiefs of Edom, according
to their settlements in the land they
occupied.

36:29 [i] ver 20 **36:30** [j] ver 21 **36:31** [k] S Ge 17:6 **36:33** [l] Isa 34:6; 63:1; Jer 49:13, 22 **36:34** [m] Jer 49:7; Eze 25:13; Ob 1:9 **36:35** [n] S Ge 25:2 [o] S Ge 19:37; Nu 21:11; 22:1; Dt 1:5; Jdg 3:30; Ru 1:1, 6 **36:37** [p] Ge 26:22 **36:40** [q] S ver 15

[a] *16* Masoretic Text; Samaritan Pentateuch (also verse 11 and 1 Chron. 1:36) does not have *Korah.*
[b] *22* Hebrew *Hemam,* a variant of *Homam* (see 1 Chron. 1:39)
[c] *24* Vulgate; Syriac *discovered water;* the meaning of the Hebrew for this word is uncertain.
[d] *26* Hebrew *Dishan,* a variant of *Dishon*
[e] *39* Many manuscripts of the Masoretic Text, Samaritan Pentateuch and Syriac (see also 1 Chron. 1:50); most manuscripts of the Masoretic Text *Hadar*

36:12 *Amalek.* See note on 14:7.
36:20–28 See note on v. 8. The same list of Seir's descendants (see 1Ch 1:38–42) is repeated in abbreviated form in vv. 29–30 as a list of tribal chieftains.
36:30 *divisions.* Tribal divisions (cf. Jos 11:23).
36:31 *before any Israelite king reigned.* Appears to presuppose the Israelite monarchy and thus to be a later editorial updating (see note on 14:14).
36:43 *This ... Edomites.* A summary statement for the whole chapter (just as v. 1 is a title for the whole chapter).

This is the family line of Esau, the father of the Edomites.[r]

Joseph's Dreams

37 Jacob lived in the land where his
father had stayed,[s] the land of Canaan.[t]

2 This is the account[u] of Jacob's family
line.

Joseph,[v] a young man of seventeen,[w]
was tending the flocks[x] with his brothers,
the sons of Bilhah[y] and the sons of Zilpah,[z]
his father's wives, and he brought their father a bad report[a] about them.
3 Now Israel[b] loved Joseph more than
any of his other sons,[c] because he had
been born to him in his old age;[d] and he
made an ornate[a] robe[e] for him.[f] 4 When his
brothers saw that their father loved him
more than any of them, they hated him[g]
and could not speak a kind word to him.
5 Joseph had a dream,[h] and when he told
it to his brothers,[i] they hated him all the
more.[j] 6 He said to them, "Listen to this
dream I had: 7 We were binding sheaves[k]
of grain out in the field when suddenly my
sheaf rose and stood upright, while your
sheaves gathered around mine and bowed
down to it."[l]
8 His brothers said to him, "Do you intend to reign over us? Will you actually
rule us?"[m] And they hated him all the
more[n] because of his dream and what he
had said.
9 Then he had another dream,[o] and he
told it to his brothers. "Listen," he said, "I
had another dream, and this time the sun
and moon and eleven stars[p] were bowing
down to me."[q]
10 When he told his father as well as
his brothers,[r] his father rebuked[s] him and
said, "What is this dream you had? Will
your mother and I and your brothers actually come and bow down to the ground
before you?"[t] 11 His brothers were jealous
of him,[u] but his father kept the matter in
mind.[v]

Joseph Sold by His Brothers

12 Now his brothers had gone to graze
their father's flocks near Shechem,[w] 13 and
Israel[x] said to Joseph, "As you know, your
brothers are grazing the flocks near Shechem.[y] Come, I am going to send you to
them."
"Very well," he replied.
14 So he said to him, "Go and see if all
is well with your brothers[z] and with the
flocks, and bring word back to me." Then
he sent him off from the Valley of Hebron.[a]
When Joseph arrived at Shechem, 15 a
man found him wandering around in the
fields and asked him, "What are you looking for?"
16 He replied, "I'm looking for my brothers. Can you tell me where they are grazing their flocks?"
17 "They have moved on from here," the
man answered. "I heard them say, 'Let's
go to Dothan.[b]' "

[a] 3 The meaning of the Hebrew for this word is uncertain; also in verses 23 and 32.

36:43 [r] S ver 9 **37:1** [s] S Ge 17:8 [t] S Ge 10:19 **37:2** [u] S Ge 2:4 [v] S Ge 30:24 [w] Ge 41:46; 2Sa 5:4 [x] Ge 46:32; 1Sa 16:11; 17:15; Ps 78:71; Am 7:15 [y] Ge 35:25 [z] Ge 35:26 [a] 1Sa 2:24 **37:3** [b] S Ge 17:5 [c] S Ge 25:28 [d] Ge 43:27; 44:20 [e] ver 23, 31, 32; 2Sa 13:18-19 [f] Ge 43:34; 45:22; 1Sa 1:4-5; Est 2:9 **37:4** [g] S ver 24; S Ge 27:41; Ac 7:9 **37:5** [h] S Ge 20:3; S 28:12 [i] ver 10 [j] ver 8 **37:7** [k] Ru 2:7, 15 [l] ver 9, 10; Ge 27:29; 42:6, 9; 43:26, 28; 44:14; 50:18; 2Sa 1:2; 9:6 **37:8** [m] Ge 41:44; 42:10; 44:16, 18; 48:22; 49:26; Dt 33:16 [n] ver 5 **37:9** [o] S ver 7; Ge 28:12 [p] Rev 12:1 [q] Dt 4:19; 17:3 **37:10** [r] ver 5 [s] Ru 2:16; Ps 9:5; 68:30; 106:9; 119:21; Isa 17:13; 54:9; Zec 3:2 [t] S ver 7; S Ge 9:25; S 33:3 **37:11** [u] Ge 26:14; Ac 7:9 [v] Lk 2:19, 51 **37:12** [w] S Ge 12:6 **37:13** [x] S Ge 17:5 [y] Ge 33:19 **37:14** [z] 1Sa 17:18 [a] S Ge 13:18 **37:17** [b] 2Ki 6:13

37:1 *Canaan.* Jacob made the promised land his homeland and was later buried there (49:29–30; 50:13). His son Joseph also insisted on being buried in Canaan, which he recognized as the land the Lord had promised to Israel (50:24–25).

37:2—50:26 The Jacob-Joseph cycle (see Introduction: Literary Features). It focuses mainly on Jacob's sons and how they embodied for both good and ill the family line of Abraham, Isaac and Jacob, which God had chosen to be the channel of his saving acts in history.

37:2 *account.* See note on 2:4. The word here introduces the tenth and final main section of Genesis. *Joseph.* The author immediately introduces Joseph, on whom the last cycle of the patriarchal narrative centers. In his generation he, more than any other, represented Israel—as a people who struggled with both God and human beings and overcame (see 32:28 and note) and as a source of blessing to the nations (see 12:2–3). It is, moreover, through the life of Joseph that the covenant family in Canaan becomes an emerging nation in Egypt, thus setting the stage for the exodus. The story of God's dealings with the patriarchs foreshadows the subsequent Biblical account of God's purpose with Israel. It begins with the election and calling out of Abram from the post-Babel nations and ends with Israel in Egypt (in the person of Joseph) preserving the life of the nations (see 41:57; 50:20). So God would deliver the Israelites out of the nations (the exodus), eventually to send them on a mission of life to the nations (cf. Mt 28:18–20; Ac 1:8). *bad report about them.* Doubtless about all his brothers (as the later context indicates), not just the sons of his father's concubines.

37:3 *ornate robe.* A mark of Jacob's favoritism, "the kind of garment the virgin daughters of the king wore" (2Sa 13:18).

37:5 *dream.* See note on 20:3.

37:7 *bowed down.* Joseph's dream would later come true (42:6; 43:26; 44:14).

37:8 *Will you actually rule us?* Joseph would later become the "prince among his brothers" (Dt 33:16) and receive "the rights of the firstborn" (1Ch 5:2), at least the double portion of the inheritance (see note on 25:5), since his father adopted his two sons (48:5).

37:10 *your mother.* Jacob possibly refers to Leah, since Rachel has already died (see 35:19). *bow down ... before you.* An echo of Isaac's blessing of Jacob (27:29).

37:11 *kept the matter in mind.* A hint that Jacob later recalled Joseph's dreams when events brought about their fulfillment. Cf. Mary's equally sensitive response to events during Jesus' boyhood days (Lk 2:19,51).

37:12 *Shechem.* See 12:6; 33:18 and notes.

37:17 *Dothan.* Located about 13 miles north of Shechem, Dothan was already an ancient city by this time.

So Joseph went after his brothers and found them near Dothan. 18 But they saw him in the distance, and before he reached them, they plotted to kill him.[c]

19 "Here comes that dreamer![d]" they said to each other. 20 "Come now, let's kill him and throw him into one of these cisterns[e] and say that a ferocious animal[f] devoured him.[g] Then we'll see what comes of his dreams."[h]

21 When Reuben[i] heard this, he tried to rescue him from their hands. "Let's not take his life," he said.[j] 22 "Don't shed any blood. Throw him into this cistern[k] here in the wilderness, but don't lay a hand on him." Reuben said this to rescue him from them and take him back to his father.[l]

23 So when Joseph came to his brothers, they stripped him of his robe—the ornate robe[m] he was wearing— 24 and they took him and threw him into the cistern.[n] The cistern was empty; there was no water in it.

25 As they sat down to eat their meal, they looked up and saw a caravan of Ishmaelites[o] coming from Gilead.[p] Their camels were loaded with spices, balm[q] and myrrh,[r] and they were on their way to take them down to Egypt.[s]

26 Judah[t] said to his brothers, "What will we gain if we kill our brother and cover up his blood?[u] 27 Come, let's sell him to the Ishmaelites and not lay our hands on him; after all, he is our brother,[v] our own flesh and blood.[w]" His brothers agreed.

28 So when the Midianite[x] merchants came by, his brothers pulled Joseph up out of the cistern[y] and sold[z] him for twenty shekels[a] of silver[a] to the Ishmaelites,[b] who took him to Egypt.[c]

29 When Reuben returned to the cistern and saw that Joseph was not there, he tore his clothes.[d] 30 He went back to his brothers and said, "The boy isn't there! Where can I turn now?"[e]

31 Then they got Joseph's robe,[f] slaughtered a goat and dipped the robe in the blood.[g] 32 They took the ornate robe[h] back to their father and said, "We found this. Examine it to see whether it is your son's robe."

33 He recognized it and said, "It is my son's robe! Some ferocious animal[i] has devoured him. Joseph has surely been torn to pieces."[j]

34 Then Jacob tore his clothes,[k] put on sackcloth[l] and mourned for his son many days.[m] 35 All his sons and daughters came to comfort him,[n] but he refused to be comforted.[o] "No," he said, "I will continue to mourn until I join my son[p] in the grave.[q]" So his father wept for him.

36 Meanwhile, the Midianites[b][r] sold Joseph[s] in Egypt to Potiphar, one of Pharaoh's officials, the captain of the guard.[t]

37:18 [c] 1Sa 19:1; 2Ch 24:21; Ps 31:13,20; 37:12,32; S Mt 12:14; Mk 14:1; Ac 23:12 **37:19** [d] S Ge 28:12 **37:20** [e] ver 22; Jer 38:6,9 [f] ver 33; Lev 26:6,22; Dt 32:24; 2Ki 17:25; Eze 34:25 [g] ver 31-33; S Ge 4:10 [h] Ge 50:20 **37:21** [i] S Ge 29:32 [j] Ge 42:22 **37:22** [k] S ver 20 [l] ver 29-30 **37:23** [m] ver 3 **37:24** [n] S ver 4; Ge 49:23; Jer 38:6; 41:7; Eze 22:27 **37:25** [o] S Ge 16:11 [p] S Ge 31:21; S SS 4:1 [q] Jer 8:22; 22:6; 46:11 [r] Ge 43:11; Ex 30:23; Ps 45:8; Pr 7:17; SS 1:13; Mt 2:11 [s] ver 28; Ge 39:1; Ps 105:17 **37:26** [t] S Ge 29:35 [u] S Ge 4:10 **37:27** [v] Ge 42:21 [w] S Ge 29:14 **37:28** [x] S Ge 25:2 [y] Jer 38:13 [z] Ex 21:16 [a] Lev 27:5; Mt 26:15 [b] S Ge 16:11

[a] *28* That is, about 8 ounces or about 230 grams
[b] *36* Samaritan Pentateuch, Septuagint, Vulgate and Syriac (see also verse 28); Masoretic Text *Medanites*

[c] ver 36; Ge 39:1; 45:4-5; Ps 105:17; Jer 12:6; Ac 7:9 **37:29** [d] ver 34; Ge 44:13; Nu 14:6; Jos 7:6; 2Sa 1:11; 2Ki 2:12; 5:7; 11:14; 22:11; Job 1:20; 2:12; Isa 36:22; 37:1; Jer 36:24; 41:5; Joel 2:13 **37:30** [e] ver 22 **37:31** [f] S ver 3 [g] Rev 19:13 **37:32** [h] S ver 3 **37:33** [i] S ver 20 [j] Ge 42:13,38; 44:20,28 **37:34** [k] S ver 29 [l] 2Sa 3:31; 1Ki 20:31; 21:27; 2Ki 6:30; 19:1,2; Job 16:15; Ps 69:11; Isa 3:24; 15:3; 22:12; 32:11; 37:1; Jer 48:37; 49:3; Joel 1:13 [m] Ge 50:3,10,11; Nu 20:29; Dt 34:8 **37:35** [n] Job 2:11; 15:11; 16:5; 42:11 [o] 2Sa 12:17; Ps 77:2; Jer 31:15 [p] 2Sa 12:23 [q] Ge 42:38; 44:22,29,31 **37:36** [r] S Ge 25:2 [s] S ver 28 [t] Ge 39:1; 40:3; 41:10,12; 1Sa 22:14

37:19 *dreamer.* The Hebrew for this word means "master of dreams" or "dream expert" and is here used with obvious sarcasm.

37:21 *Reuben … tried to rescue him.* As Jacob's firstborn, he felt responsible for Joseph. He would later remind his brothers of this day (42:22). Initially Reuben's attempts to influence events seemed successful (30:14–17). But after his arrogant incest with Bilhah (see 35:22 and note) his efforts were always ineffective (see 42:37–38)—demonstrating his loss of the status of firstborn (see 49:3–4). Effective leadership passed to Judah (see vv. 26–27; 43:3–5,8–10; 44:14–34; 46:28; 49:8–12).

37:24 Cf. Jer 38:6.

37:25 *Ishmaelites.* Also called Midianites (v. 28; see Jdg 8:22, 24,26) and Medanites (see NIV text note on v. 36). These various tribal groups were interrelated, since Midian and Medan, like Ishmael, were also sons of Abraham (25:2). *Gilead.* See note on 31:21. *balm.* A soothing oil with healing properties (see Jer 51:8), exuded by the fruit or stems of one or more kinds of small trees. The balm of Gilead was especially effective (see Jer 8:22; 46:11). *myrrh.* Probably to be identified with labdanum, an aromatic gum (see Ps 45:8; Pr 7:17; SS 3:6; 5:13) extracted from the leaves of the cistus rose. Its oil was used in beauty treatments (see Est 2:12), and it was sometimes mixed with wine and drunk to relieve pain (see Mk 15:23). As a gift fit for a king, myrrh was brought to Jesus after his birth (Mt 2:11) and applied to his body after his death (Jn 19:39–40).

37:28 *twenty shekels of silver.* In later times this amount was the value of a male of Joseph's age who had been dedicated to the Lord (see Lev 27:5).

37:31–33 Again a slaughtered goat figures prominently in an act of deception (see 27:5–13).

37:34 *tore his clothes, put on sackcloth.* Tearing one's clothes (see v. 29) and wearing coarse and uncomfortable sackcloth instead of ordinary clothes were both signs of mourning (see note on Rev 11:3).

37:35 *daughters.* The term can include daughters-in-law (e.g., a daughter-in-law of Jacob is mentioned in 38:2). *grave.* The Hebrew for "grave" (*Sheol*) can also refer in a more general way to the realm of the dead, the netherworld, where, it was thought, departed spirits live (see notes on Dt 32:22; Job 17:16).

37:36 *sold.* "As a slave" (Ps 105:17). The peoples of the Arabian Desert were long involved in international slave trade (cf. Am 1:6,9). *guard.* The Hebrew for this word can mean "executioners" (the captain of whom was in charge of the royal prisoners; see 40:4), or it can mean "butchers" (the captain of whom was the chief cook in the royal court; cf. 1Sa 9:23–24).

Judah and Tamar

38 At that time, Judah[u] left his brothers and went down to stay with a man of Adullam[v] named Hirah.[w] 2 There Judah met the daughter of a Canaanite man named Shua.[x] He married her and made love to her; 3 she became pregnant and gave birth to a son, who was named Er.[y] 4 She conceived again and gave birth to a son and named him Onan.[z] 5 She gave birth to still another son and named him Shelah.[a] It was at Kezib that she gave birth to him.

6 Judah got a wife for Er, his firstborn, and her name was Tamar.[b] 7 But Er, Judah's firstborn, was wicked in the LORD's sight;[c] so the LORD put him to death.[d]

8 Then Judah said to Onan, "Sleep with your brother's wife and fulfill your duty to her as a brother-in-law to raise up offspring for your brother."[e] 9 But Onan knew that the child would not be his; so whenever he slept with his brother's wife, he spilled his semen on the ground to keep from providing offspring for his brother. 10 What he did was wicked in the LORD's sight; so the LORD put him to death also.[f]

11 Judah then said to his daughter-in-law[g] Tamar,[h] "Live as a widow in your father's household[i] until my son Shelah[j] grows up."[k] For he thought, "He may die too, just like his brothers." So Tamar went to live in her father's household.

12 After a long time Judah's wife, the daughter of Shua,[l] died. When Judah had recovered from his grief, he went up to Timnah,[m] to the men who were shearing his sheep,[n] and his friend Hirah the Adullamite[o] went with him.

13 When Tamar[p] was told, "Your father-in-law is on his way to Timnah to shear his sheep,"[q] 14 she took off her widow's clothes,[r] covered herself with a veil[s] to disguise herself, and then sat down[t] at the entrance to Enaim, which is on the road to Timnah.[u] For she saw that, though Shelah[v] had now grown up, she had not been given to him as his wife.

15 When Judah saw her, he thought she was a prostitute,[w] for she had covered her face. 16 Not realizing[x] that she was his daughter-in-law,[y] he went over to her by the roadside and said, "Come now, let me sleep with you."[z]

"And what will you give me to sleep with you?"[a] she asked.

17 "I'll send you a young goat[b] from my flock," he said.

"Will you give me something as a pledge[c] until you send it?" she asked.

18 He said, "What pledge should I give you?"

"Your seal[d] and its cord, and the staff[e] in your hand," she answered. So he gave them to her and slept with her, and she became pregnant by him.[f] 19 After she left, she took off her veil and put on her widow's clothes[g] again.

20 Meanwhile Judah sent the young goat by his friend the Adullamite[h] in order to get his pledge[i] back from the woman, but he did not find her. 21 He asked the men who lived there, "Where is the shrine prostitute[j] who was beside the road at Enaim?"

38:1 [u] S Ge 29:35 [v] Jos 12:15; 15:35; 1Sa 22:1; 2Sa 23:13; 2Ch 11:7 [w] ver 12, 20 **38:2** [x] ver 12; 1Ch 2:3 **38:3** [y] ver 6; Ge 46:12; Nu 26:19 **38:4** [z] ver 8, 9; Ge 46:12; Nu 26:19 **38:5** [a] Nu 26:20 **38:6** [b] ver 11, 13 **38:7** [c] S Ge 6:5 [d] ver 10; Ge 46:12; Lev 10:1-2; 1Ch 2:3 **38:8** [e] Dt 25:5-6; Ru 4:5; Mt 22:24-28 **38:10** [f] S ver 7; Dt 25:7-10 **38:11** [g] S Ge 11:31 [h] S ver 6 [i] Ru 1:8 [j] ver 14, 26 [k] Ru 1:13 **38:12** [l] S ver 2 [m] ver 14; Jos 15:10, 57; 19:43; Jdg 14:1, 2; 2Ch 28:18 [n] S Ge 31:19 [o] S ver 1 **38:13** [p] S ver 6 [q] S Ge 31:19 **38:14** [r] ver 19 [s] S Ge 24:65 [t] Jer 3:2 [u] S ver 12 [v] S ver 11 **38:15** [w] Jdg 11:1; 16:1 **38:16** [x] Ge 42:23 [y] Lev 18:15; 20:12; Ru 1:6 [z] Ge 39:7, 12; 2Sa 13:11 [a] S Ge 30:15 **38:17** [b] Jdg 15:1 [c] ver 20 **38:18** [d] ver 25; 1Ki 21:8; Est 3:12; 8:8; SS 8:6; Isa 49:16; Jer 22:24; Hag 2:23; 2Co 1:22; Eph 1:13 [e] S Ge 32:10; S Ex 4:2 [f] S Ge 19:32 **38:19** [g] ver 14 **38:20** [h] S ver 1 [i] ver 17 **38:21** [j] S Ge 19:5; Lev 19:29; Dt 22:21; 23:17; 2Ki 23:7; Hos 4:14

38:1–30 The unsavory events of this chapter illustrate the danger that Israel as God's separated people faced if they remained among the Canaanites (see 15:16 and note). In Egypt the Israelites were kept separate because the Egyptians despised them (43:32; 46:34). While there, God's people were able to develop into a nation without losing their identity. Judah's actions contrasted with those of Joseph (ch. 39)—demonstrating the moral superiority of Joseph, to whom leadership in Israel fell in his generation (see 37:5–9).

38:1 *left his brothers.* Joseph was separated from his brothers by force, but Judah voluntarily separated himself to seek his fortune among the Canaanites. *Adullam.* A town southwest of Jerusalem (see 2Ch 11:5,7).

38:3–4 *Er ... Onan.* The names also appear as designations of tribes in Mesopotamian documents of this time.

38:5 *Kezib.* Probably the same as Akzib (Jos 15:44), three miles west of Adullam. The "men of Kozeba" (another form of the same word) were descendants of Shelah, son of Judah (see 1Ch 4:21–22). The Hebrew root of the name means "deception" (see Mic 1:14 and NIV text note), a theme running throughout the story of Jacob and his sons.

38:6 *Judah got a wife for Er.* See note on 21:21.

38:8 A concise description of the custom known as "levirate marriage" (Latin *levir* means "brother-in-law"). Details of the practice are given in Dt 25:5–6 (see note there), where it is laid down as a legal obligation within Israel (cf. Mt 22:24 and note). The custom is illustrated in Ru 4:5 (see note there), though there it is extended to the nearest living relative ("guardian-redeemer," Ru 3:12; see note there and on 2:20), since neither Boaz nor the nearer relative was a brother-in-law.

38:9 *knew that the child would not be his.* Similarly, Ruth's nearest relative was fearful that if he married Ruth he would endanger his own estate (Ru 4:5–6; see note on 4:6). *spilled his semen on the ground.* A means of birth control sometimes called "onanism" (after Onan).

38:10 *What he did.* His refusal to perform his levirate duty.

38:11 *he thought, "He may die too, just like his brothers."* Thus Judah had no intention of giving Shelah to Tamar (see v. 14).

38:12 *Timnah.* Exact location unknown, but somewhere in the hill country of Judah (see map, p. 359).

38:14 *sat down ... the road.* Prostitutes (see v. 15) customarily stationed themselves by the roadside (Jer 3:2; see note there). *Enaim.* Means "two springs"; probably the same as Enam in the western foothills of Judah (see Jos 15:33–34).

38:18 *seal and its cord.* Probably a small cylinder seal of the type used to sign clay documents by rolling them over the clay. The owner wore it around his neck on a cord threaded through a hole drilled lengthwise through it.

38:21 *shrine prostitute.* The Hebrew here differs from that used for "prostitute" in v. 15. Judah's friend perhaps deliber-

"There hasn't been any shrine prostitute
here," they said.
22 So he went back to Judah and said,
"I didn't find her. Besides, the men who
lived there said, 'There hasn't been any
shrine prostitute here.'"
23 Then Judah said, "Let her keep what
she has,[k] or we will become a laughingstock.[l] After all, I did send her this young
goat, but you didn't find her."
24 About three months later Judah was
told, "Your daughter-in-law Tamar is guilty
of prostitution, and as a result she is now
pregnant."
Judah said, "Bring her out and have her
burned to death!"[m]
25 As she was being brought out, she
sent a message to her father-in-law. "I am
pregnant by the man who owns these,"
she said. And she added, "See if you recognize whose seal and cord and staff these
are."[n]
26 Judah recognized them and said, "She
is more righteous than I,[o] since I wouldn't
give her to my son Shelah.[p]" And he did
not sleep with her again.
27 When the time came for her to give
birth, there were twin boys in her womb.[q]
28 As she was giving birth, one of them put
out his hand; so the midwife[r] took a scarlet thread and tied it on his wrist[s] and said,
"This one came out first." 29 But when he
drew back his hand, his brother came out,[t]
and she said, "So this is how you have
broken out!" And he was named Perez.[a][u]
30 Then his brother, who had the scarlet
thread on his wrist,[v] came out. And he
was named Zerah.[b][w]

Joseph and Potiphar's Wife

39 Now Joseph[x] had been taken down
to Egypt. Potiphar, an Egyptian
who was one of Pharaoh's officials, the
captain of the guard,[y] bought him from
the Ishmaelites who had taken him there.[z]
2 The LORD was with Joseph[a] so that he
prospered, and he lived in the house of his
Egyptian master. 3 When his master saw
that the LORD was with him[b] and that the
LORD gave him success in everything he
did,[c] 4 Joseph found favor in his eyes[d] and
became his attendant. Potiphar put him
in charge of his household,[e] and he entrusted to his care everything he owned.[f]
5 From the time he put him in charge of his
household and of all that he owned, the
LORD blessed the household[g] of the Egyptian because of Joseph.[h] The blessing of
the LORD was on everything Potiphar had,
both in the house and in the field.[i] 6 So
Potiphar left everything he had in Joseph's
care;[j] with Joseph in charge, he did not
concern himself with anything except the
food he ate.
Now Joseph was well-built and handsome,[k] 7 and after a while his master's wife
took notice of Joseph and said, "Come to
bed with me!"[l]
8 But he refused.[m] "With me in charge,"
he told her, "my master does not concern
himself with anything in the house; everything he owns he has entrusted to my
care.[n] 9 No one is greater in this house than
I am.[o] My master has withheld nothing
from me except you, because you are his
wife. How then could I do such a wicked
thing and sin against God?"[p] 10 And though
she spoke to Joseph day after day, he refused[q] to go to bed with her or even be
with her.

[a] 29 *Perez* means *breaking out.* [b] 30 *Zerah* can mean *scarlet* or *brightness.*

38:23 [k] ver 18 [l] Ex 32:25; Job 12:4; Jer 20:7; La 3:14 **38:24** [m] Lev 20:10, 14; 21:9; Dt 22:21, 22; Jos 7:25; Jdg 15:6; 1Sa 31:12; Job 31:11, 28; Eze 16:38 **38:25** [n] S ver 18 **38:26** [o] 1Sa 24:17 [p] S ver 11 **38:27** [q] Ge 25:24 **38:28** [r] S Ge 35:17 [s] ver 30 **38:29** [t] Ge 25:26 [u] Ge 46:12; Nu 26:20, 21; Ru 4:12, 18; 2Sa 5:20; 6:8; 1Ch 2:4; 9:4; Isa 28:21; Mt 1:3 **38:30** [v] ver 28 [w] Ge 46:12; 1Ch 2:4; Ne 11:24 **39:1** [x] S Ge 30:24 [y] S Ge 37:36 [z] S Ge 37:25 **39:2** [a] S Ge 21:20, 22; Jos 1:5; 6:27; Jdg 1:19; 1Sa 18:14; Ac 7:9 **39:3** [b] S Ge 21:22 [c] ver 23; 1Sa 18:14; 2Ki 18:7; 2Ch 20:20; Ps 1:3; 128:2; Isa 33:6 **39:4** [d] S Ge 6:8; S 18:3 [e] Ge 47:6; 1Ki 11:28; Pr 22:29 [f] ver 8, 22; Ge 40:4; 42:37 **39:5** [g] 2Sa 6:11 [h] S Ge 26:24 [i] Dt 28:3; Ps 128:4 **39:6** [j] Ge 24:2 [k] S Ge 12:11; Ex 2:2; 1Sa 9:2; 16:12; 17:42; Est 2:7; Da 1:4 **39:7** [l] S Ge 38:16; Pr 7:15-18 **39:8** [m] Pr 6:23-24 [n] S ver 4 **39:9** [o] Ge 41:33, 40 [p] S Ge 13:13; S Nu 22:34 **39:10** [q] Est 3:4

---

ately used the more acceptable term, since ritual prostitutes enjoyed a higher social status in Canaan than did ordinary prostitutes (see note on 20:9).

38:24 *have her burned to death.* In later times, burning was the legal penalty for prostitution (see Lev 21:9).

38:27–30 For a similarly unusual birth of twin boys, see 25:24–26.

38:29 *Perez.* Became the head of the leading clan in Judah and the ancestor of David (see Ru 4:18–22 and note) and ultimately of Christ (see Mt 1:1–16).

39:1–23 A continuation of the Joseph story (see 37:36)—the first stage in the movement of Israel from Canaan to Egypt.

39:1 *Ishmaelites.* See note on 37:25.

39:2–6 See vv. 20–23. Though Joseph's situation changed drastically, God's relationship to him remained the same.

39:2 *The LORD was with Joseph.* See note on 26:3. This fact, mentioned several times here (vv. 3,21,23), is stressed also by Stephen (Ac 7:9–10).

39:5 *the LORD blessed the household of the Egyptian because of Joseph.* As God had blessed Laban because of Jacob (30:27). The offspring of Abraham continue to be a blessing to the nations (see 12:2–3 and note).

39:6 *left everything he had in Joseph's care.* As Laban had entrusted his flocks to Jacob's care (30:31–34). Joseph had full responsibility for the welfare of Potiphar's house, as later he would have full responsibility in prison (vv. 22–23) and later still in all Egypt (41:41). Always this Israelite came to hold the welfare of his "world" in his hands—but always by the blessing and overruling of God, never by his own wits, as his father Jacob had so long attempted. In the role that he played in Israel's history and in the manner in which he lived it, Joseph was a true representative of Israel.

39:7 *took notice of.* Looked with desire at. The phrase is used in the same sense in Akkadian in Section 25 of the Code of Hammurapi (see chart, p. xxii).

39:9 *sin against God.* All sin is against God, first and foremost (see Ps 51:4 and note).

39:10 *though she spoke to Joseph day after day, he refused.* Samson twice succumbed under similar pressure (Jdg 14:17; 16:16–17).

EGYPT

International routes
Local or regional routes
Water routes

Mediterranean Sea
Damascus
Tel Aviv
Amman
Gaza
Jerusalem
Raphia
Alexandria
Port Said
El-Arish
Beersheba
LOWER EGYPT
Delta
Ismailiya
Wadi el-Arish
GOSHEN
Giza
Cairo
Suez
Timnah
Saqqara
Memphis
Lisht
Elath
Aqaba
Faiyum Oasis
Gulf of Suez
Sinai Peninsula
Gulf of Elath/Aqaba
Bahariya Oasis
MIDIAN
El Amarna
Eastern Desert
Sharm esh-Sheikh
Farafra Oasis
UPPER EGYPT
Nile R.
ARABIA
Abydos
Wadi Hammamat
Thebes
Ed-Dakhla Oasis
Jebel es-Silsila
Medina
Ed-Kharga Oasis
Aswan
1st Cataract
Berenike
Kurkur Oasis
Dunqul Oasis
Red Sea
2nd Cataract
Salima Oasis
Mecca
NUBIA
3rd Cataract
Jebel Barkal
Nile R.
4th Cataract
5th Cataract
Sahara Desert
CUSH
6th Cataract
Atbara R.
White Nile R.
Blue Nile R.
ETHIOPIA
Bab-el-Mandeb
Ethiopian Highlands

0 100 km.
0 100 miles

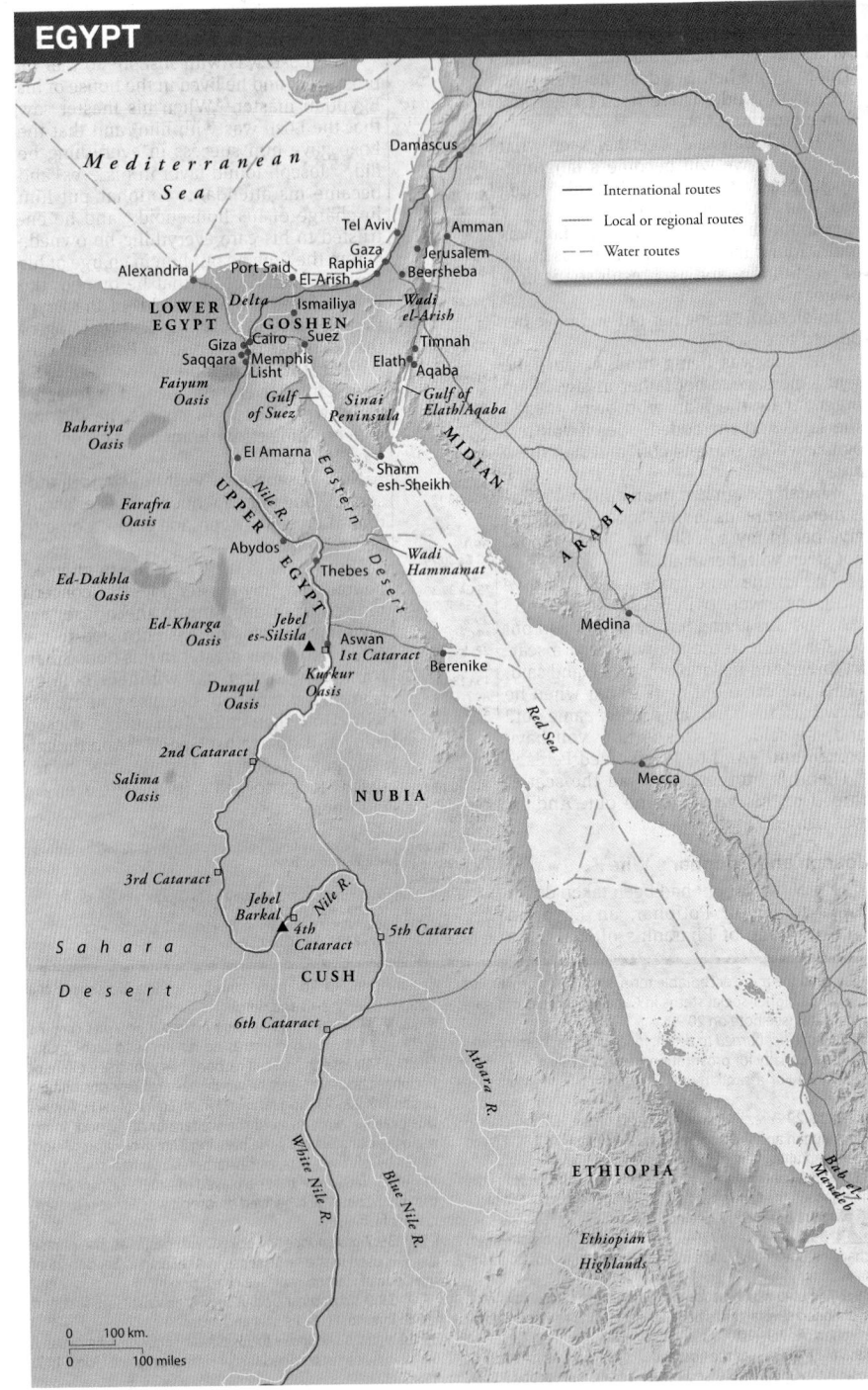

11 One day he went into the house to attend to his duties,[r] and none of the household servants[s] was inside. 12 She caught
him by his cloak[t] and said, "Come to bed
with me!"[u] But he left his cloak in her
hand and ran out of the house.[v]
13 When she saw that he had left his
cloak in her hand and had run out of the
house, 14 she called her household servants.[w] "Look," she said to them, "this
Hebrew[x] has been brought to us to make
sport of us![y] He came in here to sleep with
me, but I screamed.[z] 15 When he heard me
scream for help, he left his cloak beside
me and ran out of the house."[a]
16 She kept his cloak beside her until
his master came home. 17 Then she told
him this story:[b] "That Hebrew[c] slave[d] you
brought us came to me to make sport of
me. 18 But as soon as I screamed for help,
he left his cloak beside me and ran out of
the house."
19 When his master heard the story his
wife told him, saying, "This is how your
slave treated me," he burned with anger.[e]
20 Joseph's master took him and put him in
prison,[f] the place where the king's prisoners were confined.
But while Joseph was there in the prison, 21 the LORD was with him;[g] he showed
him kindness[h] and granted him favor in
the eyes of the prison warden.[i] 22 So the
warden put Joseph in charge of all those
held in the prison, and he was made responsible for all that was done there.[j]
23 The warden paid no attention to anything under Joseph's[k] care, because the
LORD was with Joseph and gave him success in whatever he did.[l]

The Cupbearer and the Baker

40 Some time later, the cupbearer[m]
and the baker[n] of the king of Egypt
offended their master, the king of Egypt.
2 Pharaoh was angry[o] with his two officials,[p] the chief cupbearer and the chief
baker, 3 and put them in custody in the
house of the captain of the guard,[q] in the
same prison where Joseph was confined.
4 The captain of the guard[r] assigned them
to Joseph,[s] and he attended them.
After they had been in custody[t] for some
time, 5 each of the two men—the cupbearer and the baker of the king of Egypt, who
were being held in prison—had a dream[u]
the same night, and each dream had a
meaning of its own.[v]
6 When Joseph came to them the next
morning, he saw that they were dejected. 7 So he asked Pharaoh's officials who
were in custody[w] with him in his master's
house, "Why do you look so sad today?"[x]
8 "We both had dreams," they answered,
"but there is no one to interpret them."[y]
Then Joseph said to them, "Do not interpretations belong to God?[z] Tell me your
dreams."
9 So the chief cupbearer[a] told Joseph his
dream. He said to him, "In my dream I
saw a vine in front of me, 10 and on the
vine were three branches. As soon as it
budded, it blossomed,[b] and its clusters ripened into grapes. 11 Pharaoh's cup was in
my hand, and I took the grapes, squeezed
them into Pharaoh's cup and put the cup
in his hand."
12 "This is what it means,[c]" Joseph said
to him. "The three branches are three
days.[d] 13 Within three days[e] Pharaoh will
lift up your head[f] and restore you to your
position, and you will put Pharaoh's cup
in his hand, just as you used to do when
you were his cupbearer.[g] 14 But when all
goes well with you, remember me[h] and
show me kindness;[i] mention me to Pharaoh[j] and get me out of this prison. 15 I was
forcibly carried off from the land of the
Hebrews,[k] and even here I have done nothing to deserve being put in a dungeon."[l]

39:11 [r]Ex 18:20; Dt 1:18 [s]ver 14 **39:12** [t]2Sa 13:11; Pr 7:13 [u]S Ge 38:16 [v]ver 15; Pr 5:8; 2Ti 2:22 **39:14** [w]ver 11 [x]S Ge 14:13 [y]S Ge 21:9 [z]Dt 22:24,27 **39:15** [a]S ver 12 **39:17** [b]Ex 20:16; 23:1,7; Dt 5:20; Ps 101:5 [c]S Ge 14:13 [d]Ge 21:10 **39:19** [e]S Ge 34:7; S Est 1:12 **39:20** [f]Ge 40:3; 41:10; Ps 105:18 **39:21** [g]S Ge 21:20 [h]S Ge 19:19 [i]Ex 3:21; 11:3; 12:36; Est 2:9; Ps 106:46; Pr 16:7; Da 1:9 **39:22** [j]S ver 4 **39:23** [k]S Ge 21:20; S Nu 14:43 [l]S ver 3 **40:1** [m]ver 9,13,21; Ne 1:11 [n]ver 16,20 **40:2** [o]Pr 16:14,15; 19:12 [p]Ge 41:10; Est 2:21 **40:3** [q]S Ge 37:36; S 39:20 **40:4** [r]S Ge 37:36 [s]S Ge 39:4 [t]ver 7; Ge 42:17 **40:5** [u]S Ge 20:3 [v]Ge 41:11 **40:7** [w]S ver 4 [x]Ne 2:2 **40:8** [y]Ge 41:8,15 [z]Ge 41:16,25,28,32; Dt 29:29; Da 2:22,28,47 **40:9** [a]S ver 1 **40:10** [b]Isa 27:6; 35:1-2; Hos 14:7 **40:12** [c]ver 16; Ge 41:12,15,25; Da 2:36; 4:19 [d]ver 18 **40:13** [e]ver 19,20; Jos 1:11; 3:2; Ezr 8:32; Ne 2:11 [f]ver 19 [g]S ver 1 **40:14** [h]1Sa 25:31; Lk 23:42 [i]S Ge 19:19; 1Sa 20:14,42; 2Sa 9:1; 1Ki 2:7 [j]ver 23; Ge 41:9; Ecc 9:15 **40:15** [k]S Ge 14:13 [l]Ge 39:20; Job 13:27

39:14 *this Hebrew.* See v. 17; see also note on 14:13.

39:20–23 See note on vv. 2–6.

39:20 *place where the king's prisoners were confined.* Though understandably angry (see v. 19), Potiphar put Joseph in the "house of the captain of the guard" (40:3)—certainly not the worst prison available.

40:1–23 God gives Joseph the interpretation of two dreams, which prepares the way for Joseph to be used by God to interpret the pharaoh's two dreams (ch. 41), leading to the subsequent fulfillment (chs. 42–46) of Joseph's two dreams (37:5–11).

40:2 *Pharaoh.* See note on Ex 1:11. *chief cupbearer.* Would be the divinely appointed agent for introducing Joseph to the pharaoh (see 41:9–14).

40:5 *each dream had a meaning.* Throughout the ancient Near East it was believed that dreams sometimes contained disclosures about the future that a proper interpretation would bring to light (see note on 20:3). God was beginning to prepare the way for Joseph's rise in Egypt.

40:8 *interpretations belong to God.* Only God, who knows the future, can properly interpret dreams (see 41:16,25,28; Da 2:28). *Tell me.* Joseph presents himself as God's agent through whom God will make known the revelation contained in their dreams—Israel is God's prophetic people through whom God's revelation comes to the nations (see 18:17 and note; 41:16,28,32).

40:13 *lift up your head and restore you to your position.* See Ps 3:3; 27:6. For this meaning of the idiom "lift up one's head," see 2Ki 25:27 and Jer 52:31, where the Hebrew for "released" in the context of freeing a prisoner means lit. "lifted up the head of."

40:14 *when all goes well with you, remember me.* Unfortunately, the cupbearer "forgot him" (v. 23) until two full years later (see 41:1,9–13).

40:15 *dungeon.* Probably hyperbole to reflect Joseph's despair

16When the chief baker[m] saw that Joseph had given a favorable interpretation,[n]
he said to Joseph, "I too had a dream: On
my head were three baskets[o] of bread.[a]
17In the top basket were all kinds of baked
goods for Pharaoh, but the birds were eating them out of the basket on my head."
18"This is what it means," Joseph said.
"The three baskets are three days.[p] 19With-
in three days[q] Pharaoh will lift off your
head[r] and impale your body on a pole.[s]
And the birds will eat away your flesh."[t]
20Now the third day[u] was Pharaoh's
birthday,[v] and he gave a feast for all his
officials.[w] He lifted up the heads of the
chief cupbearer and the chief baker[x] in the
presence of his officials: 21He restored the
chief cupbearer[y] to his position,[z] so that
he once again put the cup into Pharaoh's
hand[a]— 22but he impaled the chief baker,[b] just as Joseph had said to them in his
interpretation.[c]
23The chief cupbearer, however, did not
remember Joseph; he forgot him.[d]

Pharaoh's Dreams

41 When two full years had passed,
Pharaoh had a dream:[e] He was
standing by the Nile,[f] 2when out of the
river there came up seven cows, sleek and
fat,[g] and they grazed among the reeds.[h]
3After them, seven other cows, ugly and
gaunt, came up out of the Nile and stood
beside those on the riverbank. 4And the
cows that were ugly and gaunt ate up
the seven sleek, fat cows. Then Pharaoh
woke up.[i]
5He fell asleep again and had a second dream: Seven heads of grain,[j] healthy
and good, were growing on a single stalk.
6After them, seven other heads of grain
sprouted—thin and scorched by the east
wind.[k] 7The thin heads of grain swallowed
up the seven healthy, full heads. Then
Pharaoh woke up;[l] it had been a dream.
8In the morning his mind was trou-
bled,[m] so he sent for all the magicians[n] and
wise men of Egypt. Pharaoh told them his
dreams, but no one could interpret them
for him.[o]
9Then the chief cupbearer said to Pharaoh, "Today I am reminded of my shortcomings.[p] 10Pharaoh was once angry with
his servants,[q] and he imprisoned me and
the chief baker in the house of the captain
of the guard.[r] 11Each of us had a dream the
same night, and each dream had a meaning of its own.[s] 12Now a young Hebrew[t]
was there with us, a servant of the captain of the guard.[u] We told him our dreams,
and he interpreted them for us, giving each
man the interpretation of his dream.[v] 13And
things turned out exactly as he interpreted
them to us: I was restored to my position,
and the other man was impaled.[w]"
14So Pharaoh sent for Joseph, and he
was quickly brought from the dungeon.[x]
When he had shaved[y] and changed his
clothes,[z] he came before Pharaoh.
15Pharaoh said to Joseph, "I had a
dream, and no one can interpret it.[a] But
I have heard it said of you that when you
hear a dream you can interpret it."[b]
16"I cannot do it," Joseph replied to
Pharaoh, "but God will give Pharaoh the
answer he desires."[c]
17Then Pharaoh said to Joseph, "In my
dream I was standing on the bank of the
Nile,[d] 18when out of the river there came
up seven cows, fat and sleek, and they
grazed among the reeds.[e] 19After them,
seven other cows came up—scrawny and
very ugly and lean. I had never seen such
ugly cows in all the land of Egypt. 20The
lean, ugly cows ate up the seven fat cows
that came up first. 21But even after they
ate them, no one could tell that they had
done so; they looked just as ugly as before. Then I woke up.
22"In my dream I saw seven heads of
grain, full and good, growing on a single stalk. 23After them, seven other
heads sprouted—withered and thin and
scorched by the east wind. 24The thin
heads of grain swallowed up the seven
good heads. I told this to the magicians,
but none of them could explain it to me.[f]"

[a] 16 Or *three wicker baskets*

40:16 [m]S ver 1 [n]S ver 12 [o]Am 8:1-2 **40:18** [p]ver 12 **40:19** [q]ver 13 [r]S ver 13 [s]ver 22; Dt 21:22-23; Est 2:23; 7:10 [t]Dt 28:26; 1Sa 17:44; 2Sa 21:10; 1Ki 14:11; 16:4; 21:24; Eze 39:4 **40:20** [u]S ver 13 [v]Mt 14:6-10 [w]Est 2:18; Mk 6:21 [x]S ver 1 **40:21** [y]S ver 1 [z]2Ki 25:27; Jer 52:31 [a]ver 13 **40:22** [b]S ver 19 [c]Ge 41:13; Ps 105:19 **40:23** [d]S ver 14; S Ecc 1:11 **41:1** [e]S Ge 20:3 [f]ver 17; S Ge 2:14; Ex 1:22; 2:5; 7:15 **41:2** [g]ver 26; Jer 5:28 [h]ver 18; Ex 2:3; Job 40:21; Isa 19:6 **41:4** [i]ver 7 **41:5** [j]Jos 13:3; 2Ki 4:42; 1Ch 13:5; Isa 23:3; Jer 2:18 **41:6** [k]Ex 10:13; 14:21; Job 6:26; 11:2; 15:2; Ps 11:6; 48:7; Isa 11:15; 27:8; Jer 4:11; 18:17; Eze 19:12; 27:26; Hos 12:1; 13:15; Jnh 4:8 **41:7** [l]ver 4 **41:8** [m]Job 7:14; Da 2:1,3; 4:5,19 [n]Ex 7:11,22; Da 1:20; 2:2,27; 4:7; 5:7 [o]ver 24; S Ge 40:8; Da 4:18 **41:9** [p]S Ge 40:14 **41:10** [q]S Ge 40:2 [r]S Ge 37:36; S 39:20 **41:11** [s]Ge 40:5 **41:12** [t]S Ge 14:13; 39:17 [u]S Ge 37:36; 40:4 [v]S Ge 40:12 **41:13** [w]S Ge 40:22 **41:14** [x]Ps 105:20 [y]Isa 18:2,7 [z]S Ge 35:2; 45:22; Ru 3:3; 2Sa 12:20 **41:15** [a]S Ge 40:8 [b]S Ge 40:12; Da 4:18; 5:16 **41:16** [c]S Ge 40:8 **41:17** [d]S ver 1 **41:18** [e]S ver 2 **41:24** [f]S ver 8

(see note on 39:20). Since the same Hebrew word refers to a cistern in 37:24, the author of Genesis has established a link with Joseph's earlier experience at the hands of his brothers.

40:19 *lift off your head.* A grisly pun based on the same idiom used in v. 13 (see note there).

41:2 *out of the river there came up seven cows.* Cattle often submerged themselves up to their necks in the Nile to escape sun and insects.

41:6 *scorched by the east wind.* The Palestinian sirocco (in Egypt the khamsin), which blows in from the desert (see Hos 13:15) in late spring and early fall, often withers vegetation (see Isa 40:7; Eze 17:10 and note).

41:8 *his mind was troubled.* See 40:6–7. *magicians.* Probably priests who claimed to possess occult knowledge. *no one could interpret them.* See Da 2:10–11.

41:13 *things turned out exactly as he interpreted them.* Because his words were from the Lord (see Ps 105:19).

41:14 *Pharaoh sent for Joseph.* Effecting his permanent release from prison (see Ps 105:20). *shaved.* Egyptians were normally smooth-shaven, while Palestinians wore beards (see 2Sa 10:4; Jer 41:5 and notes).

41:16 *I cannot do it … but God will give Pharaoh the answer.* See 40:8 and note; Da 2:27–28,30; cf. 2Co 3:5.

25 Then Joseph said to Pharaoh, "The
dreams of Pharaoh are one and the same.[g]
God has revealed to Pharaoh what he is
about to do.[h] 26 The seven good cows[i] are
seven years, and the seven good heads of
grain are seven years; it is one and the
same dream. 27 The seven lean, ugly cows
that came up afterward are seven years,
and so are the seven worthless heads of
grain scorched by the east wind: They are
seven years of famine.[j]
28 "It is just as I said to Pharaoh: God
has shown Pharaoh what he is about to
do.[k] 29 Seven years of great abundance[l] are
coming throughout the land of Egypt, 30 but
seven years of famine[m] will follow them.
Then all the abundance in Egypt will be
forgotten, and the famine will ravage the
land.[n] 31 The abundance in the land will not
be remembered, because the famine that
follows it will be so severe. 32 The reason
the dream was given to Pharaoh in two
forms is that the matter has been firmly
decided[o] by God, and God will do it soon.[p]
33 "And now let Pharaoh look for a discerning and wise man[q] and put him in
charge of the land of Egypt.[r] 34 Let Pharaoh appoint commissioners[s] over the land
to take a fifth[t] of the harvest of Egypt during the seven years of abundance.[u] 35 They
should collect all the food of these good
years that are coming and store up the
grain under the authority of Pharaoh, to
be kept in the cities for food.[v] 36 This food
should be held in reserve for the country,
to be used during the seven years of famine that will come upon Egypt,[w] so that the
country may not be ruined by the famine."
37 The plan seemed good to Pharaoh and
to all his officials.[x] 38 So Pharaoh asked
them, "Can we find anyone like this man,
one in whom is the spirit of God[a]?"[y]
39 Then Pharaoh said to Joseph, "Since
God has made all this known to you,[z]
there is no one so discerning and wise
as you.[a] 40 You shall be in charge of my
palace,[b] and all my people are to submit
to your orders.[c] Only with respect to the
throne will I be greater than you.[d]"

Joseph in Charge of Egypt

41 So Pharaoh said to Joseph, "I hereby put you in charge of the whole land
of Egypt."[e] 42 Then Pharaoh took his signet
ring[f] from his finger and put it on Joseph's
finger. He dressed him in robes[g] of fine lin-
en[h] and put a gold chain around his neck.[i]
43 He had him ride in a chariot[j] as his second-in-command,[b][k] and people shouted
before him, "Make way[c]!"[l] Thus he put
him in charge of the whole land of Egypt.[m]
44 Then Pharaoh said to Joseph, "I am
Pharaoh, but without your word no one
will lift hand or foot in all Egypt."[n] 45 Pharaoh gave Joseph[o] the name Zaphenath-Paneah and gave him Asenath daughter of
Potiphera, priest[p] of On,[d][q] to be his wife.[r]
And Joseph went throughout the land of
Egypt.
46 Joseph was thirty years old[s] when he
entered the service[t] of Pharaoh king of
Egypt. And Joseph went out from Pharaoh's presence and traveled throughout
Egypt. 47 During the seven years of abundance[u] the land produced plentifully. 48 Joseph collected all the food produced in
those seven years of abundance in Egypt

[a] 38 Or *of the gods* [b] 43 Or *in the chariot of his second-in-command;* or *in his second chariot* [c] 43 Or *Bow down* [d] 45 That is, Heliopolis; also in verse 50

41:25 [g] S Ge 40:12 [h] S Ge 40:8; Isa 46:11; Da 2:45 **41:26** [i] S ver 2 **41:27** [j] S Ge 12:10 **41:28** [k] S Ge 40:8 **41:29** [l] ver 47 **41:30** [m] ver 54; Ge 45:6, 11; 47:13; Ps 105:16 [n] ver 56; S Ge 12:10 **41:32** [o] Da 2:5 [p] S Ge 40:8 **41:33** [q] ver 39 [r] S Ge 39:9 **41:34** [s] Est 2:3 [t] Ge 47:24, 26; 1Sa 8:15 [u] ver 48; Ge 47:14 **41:35** [v] ver 48 **41:36** [w] ver 56; Ge 42:6; 47:14 **41:37** [x] Ge 45:16; Est 2:4; Isa 19:11 **41:38** [y] Nu 27:18; Dt 34:9; Da 2:11; 4:8-9, 18; 5:11,14 **41:39** [z] Da 2:11; 5:11 [a] ver 33 **41:40** [b] 1Ki 4:6; 2Ki 15:5; Isa 22:15; 36:3 [c] S Ge 39:9; Ps 105:21-22; Ac 7:10 [d] Est 10:3 **41:41** [e] ver 43, 55; Ge 42:6; 45:8,13,26; Est 8:2; Jer 40:7; Da 6:3 **41:42** [f] S Ge 24:22; Est 3:10; 8:2,8 [g] 1Sa 17:38; 18:4; 1Ki 19:19; Est 6:8,11; Da 5:29; Zec 3:4 [h] Ex 25:4; Est 8:15; Da 5:29 [i] Ps 73:6; SS 4:9; Isa 3:18; Eze 16:11; Da 5:7,16,29 **41:43** [j] Ge 46:29; 50:9; Isa 2:7; 22:18 [k] Est 10:3 [l] Est 6:9 [m] S ver 41 **41:44** [n] S Ge 37:8; Est 10:2; Ps 105:22 **41:45** [o] Est 2:7 [p] Ex 2:16 [q] Eze 30:17 [r] ver 50; Ge 46:20,27 **41:46** [s] S Ge 37:2 [t] 1Sa 8:11; 16:21; Pr 22:29; Da 1:19 **41:47** [u] ver 29

41:27 *seven years of famine.* See Ac 7:11. Long famines were rare in Egypt because of the regularity of the annual overflow of the Nile, but not uncommon elsewhere (see 2Ki 8:1 and note; see also chart, p. xxiv ["Seven Lean Years Tradition"]).

41:32 Repetition of a divine revelation was often used for emphasis (see 37:5–9; Am 7:1–6,7–9; 8:1–3).

41:38 *spirit of God.* See NIV text note. The word "spirit" should probably not be capitalized in such passages, since reference to the Holy Spirit would be out of character in statements by pagan rulers.

41:40 *You shall be in charge.* The pharaoh took Joseph's advice (see v. 33) and decided that Joseph himself should be "ruler over Egypt" (Ac 7:10; see also Ps 105:21). *all my people are to submit to your orders.* More lit. "at your command all my people are to kiss (you)"—i.e., kiss your hands or feet in an act of homage and submission (see Ps 2:12 and note).

41:42 Three symbols of transfer and/or sharing of royal authority, referred to also in Est 3:10 (signet ring); Est 6:11 (robe); and Da 5:7,16,29 (gold chain).

41:43 *second-in-command.* The position was probably that of vizier, the highest executive office below that of the king himself.

41:45 *gave Joseph the name Zaphenath-Paneah.* As a part of assigning Joseph an official position within his royal administration (see note on 1:5). The pharaoh presumed to use this marvelously endowed servant of the Lord for his own royal purposes—as a later pharaoh would attempt to use divinely blessed Israel for the enrichment of Egypt (Ex 1). He did not recognize that Joseph served a Higher Power, whose kingdom and redemptive purposes are being advanced. (The meaning of Joseph's Egyptian name is uncertain.) *Asenath.* The name is Egyptian and probably means "She belongs to (the goddess) Neith." *Potiphera.* Not the same person as "Potiphar" (37:36; 39:1); the name (also Egyptian) means "he whom (the sun-god) Ra has given." *On.* Located ten miles northeast of modern Cairo, it was called Heliopolis ("city of the sun") by the Greeks and was an important center for the worship of Ra, who had a temple there. Potiphera therefore bore an appropriate name.

41:46 *thirty years old.* In just 13 years (see 37:2), Joseph had become second-in-command (v. 43) in Egypt.

and stored it in the cities.[v] In each city he
put the food grown in the fields surrounding it. 49 Joseph stored up huge quantities
of grain, like the sand of the sea;[w] it was
so much that he stopped keeping records
because it was beyond measure.
50 Before the years of famine came, two
sons were born to Joseph by Asenath
daughter of Potiphera, priest of On.[x] 51 Joseph named his firstborn[y] Manasseh[a z] and
said, "It is because God has made me
forget all my trouble and all my father's
household." 52 The second son he named
Ephraim[b a] and said, "It is because God has
made me fruitful[b] in the land of my suffering."
53 The seven years of abundance in Egypt
came to an end, 54 and the seven years of
famine[c] began,[d] just as Joseph had said.
There was famine in all the other lands,
but in the whole land of Egypt there was
food. 55 When all Egypt began to feel the
famine,[e] the people cried to Pharaoh for
food. Then Pharaoh told all the Egyptians,
"Go to Joseph and do what he tells you."[f]
56 When the famine had spread over
the whole country, Joseph opened all the
storehouses and sold grain to the Egyptians,[g] for the famine[h] was severe throughout Egypt.[i] 57 And all the world came to
Egypt to buy grain from Joseph,[j] because
the famine was severe everywhere.[k]

Joseph's Brothers Go to Egypt

42 When Jacob learned that there was
grain in Egypt,[l] he said to his sons,
"Why do you just keep looking at each
other?" 2 He continued, "I have heard that
there is grain in Egypt. Go down there and
buy some for us,[m] so that we may live and
not die."[n]
3 Then ten of Joseph's brothers went
down to buy grain[o] from Egypt. 4 But Jacob
did not send Benjamin,[p] Joseph's brother, with the others, because he was afraid
that harm might come to him.[q] 5 So Israel's
sons were among those who went to buy
grain,[r] for there was famine in the land of
Canaan[s] also.[t]
6 Now Joseph was the governor of the
land,[u] the person who sold grain to all its
people.[v] So when Joseph's brothers arrived, they bowed down to him with their
faces to the ground.[w] 7 As soon as Joseph
saw his brothers, he recognized them, but
he pretended to be a stranger and spoke
harshly to them.[x] "Where do you come
from?"[y] he asked.
"From the land of Canaan," they replied, "to buy food."
8 Although Joseph recognized his brothers, they did not recognize him.[z] 9 Then he
remembered his dreams[a] about them and
said to them, "You are spies![b] You have
come to see where our land is unprotected."[c]
10 "No, my lord,[d]" they answered. "Your
servants have come to buy food.[e] 11 We are
all the sons of one man. Your servants[f] are
honest men,[g] not spies.[h]"
12 "No!" he said to them. "You have come
to see where our land is unprotected."[i]
13 But they replied, "Your servants[j] were
twelve brothers, the sons of one man, who
lives in the land of Canaan.[k] The youngest is now with our father, and one is no
more."[l]
14 Joseph said to them, "It is just as I
told you: You are spies![m] 15 And this is how
you will be tested: As surely as Pharaoh
lives,[n] you will not leave this place unless
your youngest brother comes here.[o] 16 Send

[a] *51 Manasseh* sounds like and may be derived from the Hebrew for *forget.* [b] *52 Ephraim* sounds like the Hebrew for *twice fruitful.*

41:48 [v] S ver 34 **41:49** [w] S Ge 12:2 **41:50** [x] S ver 45 **41:51** [y] Ge 48:14, 18, 20; 49:3 [z] Ge 46:20; 48:1; 50:23; Nu 1:34; Dt 33:17; Jos 4:12; 17:1; 1Ch 7:14 **41:52** [a] Ge 46:20; 48:1, 5; 50:23; Nu 1:32; 26:28; Dt 33:17; Jos 14:4; Jdg 5:14; 1Ch 7:20; 2Ch 30:1; Ps 60:7; Jer 7:15; Ob 1:19 [b] S Ge 17:6 **41:54** [c] S Ge 12:10 [d] Ac 7:11 **41:55** [e] Dt 32:24; 2Ch 20:9; Isa 51:19; Jer 5:12; 27:8; 42:16; 44:27 [f] S ver 41; Jn 2:5 **41:56** [g] S ver 36 [h] S Ge 12:10 [i] S ver 30 **41:57** [j] Ge 42:5; 47:15 [k] S Ge 12:10 **42:1** [l] Ac 7:12 **42:2** [m] Ge 43:2, 4; 44:25 [n] ver 19, 33; Ge 43:8; 47:19; Ps 33:18-19 **42:3** [o] ver 10; Ge 43:20 **42:4** [p] S Ge 35:18 [q] ver 38 **42:5** [r] S Ge 41:57 [s] ver 13, 29; Ge 31:18; 45:17 [t] S Ge 12:10; S Dt 32:24; Ac 7:11 **42:6** [u] S Ge 41:41; S Ne 5:14 [v] S Ge 41:36 [w] S Ge 33:3 **42:7** [x] ver 30 [y] S Ge 29:4

42:8 [z] Ge 37:2 **42:9** [a] S Ge 37:7 [b] ver 14, 16, 30; Dt 1:22; Jos 2:1; 6:22 [c] ver 12 **42:10** [d] S Ge 37:8 [e] S ver 3 **42:11** [f] ver 13; Ge 44:7, 9, 16, 19, 21, 31; 46:34; 47:3 [g] ver 15, 16, 19, 20, 34 [h] ver 31 **42:12** [i] ver 9 **42:13** [j] S ver 11 [k] S ver 5; Ge 46:31; 47:1 [l] ver 24, 32, 36; S Ge 37:30, 33; 43:7, 29, 33; 44:8; Jer 31:15 **42:14** [m] S ver 9 **42:15** [n] 1Sa 17:55 [o] S ver 11; Ge 43:3, 5, 7; 44:21, 23

41:49 *like the sand of the sea.* A simile also for the large number of offspring promised to Abraham and Jacob (see 22:17; 32:12).

41:52 *Ephraim.* The wordplay on the name (see NIV text note) reflects the fact that God gave Joseph "two" (see v. 50) sons.

41:57 *all the world.* The known world from the writer's perspective (the Middle East). This description of the famine in the time of Joseph echoes the author's description of the flood in the time of Noah (see 7:24).

42:1 — 45:28 The reunion and reconciliation of Jacob's sons — but now in Egypt.

42:2 – 3 Stephen refers to this incident (Ac 7:12).

42:4 *did not send Benjamin, Joseph's brother.* Their mother Rachel had died (35:19), and Jacob thought Joseph also was dead (37:33). Jacob did not want to lose Benjamin, the remaining son of his beloved Rachel.

42:5 *famine in the land of Canaan also.* As in the time of Abram (see 12:10 and note).

42:6 *they bowed down to him.* In fulfillment of Joseph's dreams (see 37:7,9; see also note on 40:1 – 23).

42:8 *Joseph recognized his brothers.* Although 21 years had passed since he had last seen them (see 37:2; 41:46,53 – 54), they had been adults at the time and their appearance had not changed much. *they did not recognize him.* Joseph, 17 years old at the time of his enslavement (37:2), was now an adult in an unexpected position of authority, wearing Egyptian clothes and speaking to his brothers through an interpreter (see v. 23). He was, moreover, shaven in the Egyptian manner (see note on 41:14).

42:9,14,16 *You are spies!* See note on Jos 2:1 – 24.

42:10 *my lord ... Your servants.* Unwittingly, Joseph's brothers again fulfilled his dreams and their own scornful fears (see 37:8).

42:15 *As surely as Pharaoh lives.* The most solemn oaths were pronounced in the name of the reigning monarch (as here) or of the speaker's deities (Ps 16:4; Am 8:14) or of the Lord himself (Jdg 8:19; 1Sa 14:39,45; 19:6).

one of your number to get your brother;[p] the rest of you will be kept in prison,[q] so that your words may be tested to see if you are telling the truth.[r] If you are not, then as surely as Pharaoh lives, you are spies![s]" 17 And he put them all in custody[t] for three days.

18 On the third day, Joseph said to them, "Do this and you will live, for I fear God:[u] 19 If you are honest men,[v] let one of your brothers stay here in prison,[w] while the rest of you go and take grain back for your starving households.[x] 20 But you must bring your youngest brother to me,[y] so that your words may be verified and that you may not die." This they proceeded to do.

21 They said to one another, "Surely we are being punished because of our brother.[z] We saw how distressed he was when he pleaded with us for his life, but we would not listen; that's why this distress[a] has come on us."

22 Reuben replied, "Didn't I tell you not to sin against the boy?[b] But you wouldn't listen! Now we must give an accounting[c] for his blood."[d] 23 They did not realize[e] that Joseph could understand them,[f] since he was using an interpreter.

24 He turned away from them and began to weep,[g] but then came back and spoke to them again. He had Simeon taken from them and bound before their eyes.[h]

25 Joseph gave orders to fill their bags with grain,[i] to put each man's silver back in his sack,[j] and to give them provisions[k] for their journey.[l] After this was done for them, 26 they loaded their grain on their donkeys[m] and left.

27 At the place where they stopped for the night one of them opened his sack to get feed for his donkey,[n] and he saw his silver in the mouth of his sack.[o] 28 "My silver has been returned," he said to his brothers. "Here it is in my sack."

Their hearts sank[p] and they turned to each other trembling[q] and said, "What is this that God has done to us?"[r]

29 When they came to their father Jacob in the land of Canaan,[s] they told him all that had happened to them.[t] They said, 30 "The man who is lord over the land spoke harshly to us[u] and treated us as though we were spying on the land.[v] 31 But we said to him, 'We are honest men; we are not spies.[w] 32 We were twelve brothers, sons of one father. One is no more, and the youngest is now with our father in Canaan.'[x]

33 "Then the man who is lord over the land said to us, 'This is how I will know whether you are honest men: Leave one of your brothers here with me, and take food for your starving households and go.[y] 34 But bring your youngest brother to me so I will know that you are not spies but honest men.[z] Then I will give your brother back to you,[a] and you can trade[a] in the land.[b]' "

35 As they were emptying their sacks, there in each man's sack was his pouch of silver![c] When they and their father saw the money pouches, they were frightened.[d] 36 Their father Jacob said to them, "You have deprived me of my children. Joseph is no more and Simeon is no more,[e] and now you want to take Benjamin.[f] Everything is against me![g]"

37 Then Reuben said to his father, "You may put both of my sons to death if I do not bring him back to you. Entrust him to my care,[h] and I will bring him back."[i]

38 But Jacob said, "My son will not go down there with you; his brother is dead[j] and he is the only one left. If harm comes to him[k] on the journey you are taking, you will bring my gray head down to the grave[l] in sorrow.[m]"

The Second Journey to Egypt

43 Now the famine was still severe in the land.[n] 2 So when they had eaten all the grain they had brought from Egypt,[o] their father said to them, "Go back and buy us a little more food."[p]

3 But Judah[q] said to him, "The man warned us solemnly, 'You will not see my face again unless your brother is with you.'[r] 4 If you will send our brother along with us, we will go down and buy food for you.[s] 5 But if you will not send him, we will not go down, because the man said to us, 'You will not see my face again unless your brother is with you.[t]' "

6 Israel[u] asked, "Why did you bring this trouble[v] on me by telling the man you had another brother?"

42:16 [p] ver 15 [q] ver 19 [r] S ver 11 [s] S ver 9 **42:17** [t] S Ge 40:4 **42:18** [u] S Ge 20:11; S 22:12; Lev 19:14; 25:43; 2Sa 23:3 **42:19** [v] S ver 11 [w] ver 16 [x] S ver 2 **42:20** [y] S ver 15 **42:21** [z] Ge 37:26-28 [a] Ge 45:5 **42:22** [b] Ge 37:21-22 [c] S Ge 9:5 [d] Ge 45:24 **42:23** [e] Ge 38:16 [f] S Ge 11:7 **42:24** [g] S Ge 29:11 [h] S ver 13; Ge 43:14,23 **42:25** [i] Ge 43:2 [j] ver 27,35; Ge 43:12,18, 21; 44:1,8 [k] Jer 40:5 [l] Ge 45:21,23 **42:26** [m] S Ge 32:15; 44:13; 45:17; 1Sa 25:18; Isa 30:6 **42:27** [n] Jdg 19:19; Job 39:9; Isa 1:3 [o] S ver 25 **42:28** [p] Jos 2:11; 5:1; 7:5 [q] Mk 5:33 [r] Ge 43:23 **42:29** [s] S ver 5 [t] Ge 44:24 **42:30** [u] ver 7 [v] S ver 9 **42:31** [w] ver 11 **42:32** [x] S ver 13 **42:33** [y] S ver 2 **42:34** [z] S ver 11 [a] S ver 24 [b] Ge 34:10 **42:35** [c] S ver 25 [d] Ge 43:18 **42:36** [e] S ver 13 [f] S ver 24 [g] Job 3:25; Pr 10:24; Ro 8:31 **42:37** [h] S Ge 39:4 [i] Ge 43:9; 44:32 **42:38** [j] Ge 37:33 [k] ver 4 [l] S Ge 37:35 [m] Ge 44:29,34; 48:7 **43:1** [n] S Ge 12:10 **43:2** [o] Ge 42:25 [p] S Ge 42:2 **43:3** [q] ver 8; Ge 44:14,18; 46:28 [r] S Ge 42:15 **43:4** [s] S Ge 42:2 **43:5** [t] S Ge 42:15; 44:26; 2Sa 3:13 **43:6** [u] ver 8,11; S Ge 17:5 [v] S Ge 34:30

[a] 34 Or *move about freely*

42:21 *how distressed he was ... distress has come on us.* The brothers realized they were beginning to reap what they had sown (see Gal 6:7).
42:22 See 37:21 – 22 and note on 37:21.
42:24 *He had Simeon taken.* Jacob's second son (see 29:32 – 33) is imprisoned instead of the firstborn Reuben, perhaps because the latter had saved Joseph's life years earlier (37:21 – 22).
42:37 *both of my sons.* Reuben's generous offer as security for Benjamin's safety (see note on 37:21).
42:38 *grave.* See note on 37:35.
43:3 *Judah said.* From this point on, Judah became the spokesman for his brothers (see vv. 8 – 10; 44:14 – 34; 46:28). His tribe would become preeminent among the 12 (see 49:8 – 10), and he would be an ancestor of Jesus (see Mt 1:2 – 3, 16 – 17; Lk 3:23,33).

7 They replied, "The man questioned us closely about ourselves and our family. 'Is your father still living?'[w] he asked us. 'Do you have another brother?'[x] We simply answered his questions. How were we to know he would say, 'Bring your brother down here'?"[y]

8 Then Judah[z] said to Israel[a] his father, "Send the boy along with me and we will go at once, so that we and you and our children may live and not die.[b] 9 I myself will guarantee his safety; you can hold me personally responsible for him.[c] If I do not bring him back to you and set him here before you, I will bear the blame[d] before you all my life.[e] 10 As it is, if we had not delayed,[f] we could have gone and returned twice."

11 Then their father Israel[g] said to them, "If it must be, then do this: Put some of the best products[h] of the land in your bags and take them down to the man as a gift[i]—a little balm[j] and a little honey, some spices[k] and myrrh,[l] some pistachio nuts and almonds. 12 Take double the amount[m] of silver with you, for you must return the silver that was put back into the mouths of your sacks.[n] Perhaps it was a mistake. 13 Take your brother also and go back to the man at once.[o] 14 And may God Almighty[a][p] grant you mercy[q] before the man so that he will let your other brother and Benjamin come back with you.[r] As for me, if I am bereaved, I am bereaved."[s]

15 So the men took the gifts and double the amount of silver,[t] and Benjamin also. They hurried[u] down to Egypt and presented themselves[v] to Joseph. 16 When Joseph saw Benjamin[w] with them, he said to the steward of his house,[x] "Take these men to my house, slaughter an animal and prepare a meal;[y] they are to eat with me at noon."

17 The man did as Joseph told him and took the men to Joseph's house.[z] 18 Now the men were frightened[a] when they were taken to his house.[b] They thought, "We were brought here because of the silver that was put back into our sacks[c] the first time. He wants to attack us[d] and overpower us and seize us as slaves[e] and take our donkeys.[f]"

19 So they went up to Joseph's steward[g] and spoke to him at the entrance to the house. 20 "We beg your pardon, our lord," they said, "we came down here the first time to buy food.[h] 21 But at the place where we stopped for the night we opened our sacks and each of us found his silver—the exact weight—in the mouth of his sack. So we have brought it back with us.[i] 22 We have also brought additional silver with us to buy food. We don't know who put our silver in our sacks."

23 "It's all right," he said. "Don't be afraid. Your God, the God of your father,[j] has given you treasure in your sacks;[k] I received your silver." Then he brought Simeon out to them.[l]

24 The steward took the men into Joseph's house,[m] gave them water to wash their feet[n] and provided fodder for their donkeys. 25 They prepared their gifts[o] for Joseph's arrival at noon,[p] because they had heard that they were to eat there.

26 When Joseph came home,[q] they presented to him the gifts[r] they had brought into the house, and they bowed down before him to the ground.[s] 27 He asked them how they were, and then he said, "How is your aged father[t] you told me about? Is he still living?"[u]

28 They replied, "Your servant our father[v] is still alive and well." And they bowed down,[w] prostrating themselves before him.[x]

29 As he looked about and saw his brother Benjamin, his own mother's son,[y] he asked, "Is this your youngest brother, the one you told me about?"[z] And he said, "God be gracious to you,[a] my son." 30 Deeply moved[b] at the sight of his brother, Joseph hurried out and looked for a place to weep. He went into his private room and wept[c] there.

[a] 14 Hebrew *El-Shaddai*

43:7 [w] ver 27; Ge 45:3 [x] S Ge 42:13; 44:19 [y] S Ge 42:15 **43:8** [z] S ver 3; S Ge 29:35 [a] S ver 6 [b] S Ge 42:2; Ps 33:18-19 **43:9** [c] 1Sa 23:20 [d] Ge 44:10,17 [e] S Ge 42:37; Phm 1:18-19 **43:10** [f] Ge 45:9 **43:11** [g] S ver 6 [h] S Ge 24:10 [i] S Ge 32:13 [j] S Ge 37:25; Eze 27:17 [k] Ex 30:23; 1Ki 10:2; Eze 27:22 [l] S Ge 37:25 **43:12** [m] ver 15; Ex 22:4,7; Pr 6:31 [n] S Ge 42:25 **43:13** [o] ver 3 **43:14** [p] S Ge 17:1 [q] Dt 13:17; Ps 25:6 [r] S Ge 42:24 [s] 2Sa 18:33; Est 4:16 **43:15** [t] ver 12 [u] Ge 45:9,13 [v] Ge 47:2,7; Mt 2:11 **43:16** [w] S Ge 35:18 [x] ver 17,24, 26; Ge 44:1,4, 12; 2Sa 19:17; Isa 22:15 [y] ver 31; Lk 15:23 **43:17** [z] S ver 16 **43:18** [a] Ge 42:35 [b] Ge 44:14 [c] S Ge 42:25 [d] S Ge 32:11 [e] Ge 44:9,16,33; 50:18 [f] Ge 34:28 **43:19** [g] ver 16 **43:20** [h] S Ge 42:3 **43:21** [i] S ver 15; S Ge 42:25 **43:23** [j] S Ge 24:12; S 31:5; Ex 3:6 [k] Ge 42:28 [l] S Ge 42:24 **43:24** [m] S ver 16 [n] S Ge 18:4 **43:25** [o] S Ge 32:13 [p] ver 16 **43:26** [q] S ver 16 [r] S Ge 32:13; Mt 2:11 [s] S Ge 33:3 **43:27** [t] S Ge 37:3 [u] S ver 7 **43:28** [v] Ge 44:24,27,30 [w] Ge 18:2; Ex 18:7 [x] S Ge 37:7 **43:29** [y] S Ge 35:18 [z] S Ge 42:13 [a] Nu 6:25; Ps 67:1; 119:58; Isa 30:18-19; 33:2 **43:30** [b] Jn 11:33,38 [c] S Ge 29:11

43:9 Judah offered himself as security for Benjamin's safety—an even more generous gesture than that of Reuben (see 42:37 and note).

43:11 *take them ... as a gift.* A customary practice when approaching one's superior, whether political (see 1Sa 16:20), military (see 1Sa 17:18) or religious (see 2Ki 5:15). *balm ... myrrh.* See 37:25 and note. *honey.* Either that produced by bees, or an inferior substitute made by boiling grape or date juice down to a thick syrup. *pistachio nuts.* Mentioned only here in the Bible, they are the fruit of a small, broad-crowned tree that is native to Asia Minor, Syria (Aram) and Canaan but not to Egypt.

43:14 *God Almighty.* See notes on 17:1; 35:1. *if I am bereaved, I am bereaved.* Cf. Esther's similar phrase of resignation in Est 4:16.

43:21 The brothers' statement to Joseph's steward compressed the details (see 42:27,35).

43:23 *Your God ... has given you treasure.* The steward spoke better than he knew.

43:24 See note on 18:2.

43:26 *bowed down.* Additional fulfillment of Joseph's dreams (37:7,9; see also 42:6; 43:28).

43:29 *Benjamin, his own mother's son.* Joseph's special relationship to Benjamin is clear. *God be gracious to you.* Later blessings and benedictions would echo these words (see Nu 6:25; Ps 67:1).

43:30 *Joseph ... wept.* Both emotional and sensitive, he wept often (see 42:24; 45:2,14–15; 46:29; 50:17).

31 After he had washed his face, he came
out and, controlling himself,[d] said, "Serve
the food."[e]
32 They served him by himself, the
brothers by themselves, and the Egyptians
who ate with him by themselves, because
Egyptians could not eat with Hebrews,[f] for
that is detestable to Egyptians.[g] 33 The men
had been seated before him in the order of
their ages, from the firstborn[h] to the youngest;[i] and they looked at each other in astonishment. 34 When portions were served
to them from Joseph's table, Benjamin's
portion was five times as much as anyone
else's.[j] So they feasted[k] and drank freely
with him.

A Silver Cup in a Sack

44 Now Joseph gave these instructions to the steward of his house:[l]
"Fill the men's sacks with as much food as
they can carry, and put each man's silver
in the mouth of his sack.[m] 2 Then put my
cup,[n] the silver one,[o] in the mouth of the
youngest one's sack, along with the silver
for his grain." And he did as Joseph said.
3 As morning dawned, the men were sent
on their way with their donkeys.[p] 4 They
had not gone far from the city when Joseph
said to his steward,[q] "Go after those men at
once, and when you catch up with them,
say to them, 'Why have you repaid good
with evil?[r] 5 Isn't this the cup[s] my master
drinks from and also uses for divination?[t]
This is a wicked thing you have done.' "
6 When he caught up with them, he repeated these words to them. 7 But they
said to him, "Why does my lord say such
things? Far be it from your servants[u] to
do anything like that![v] 8 We even brought
back to you from the land of Canaan[w] the
silver[x] we found inside the mouths of our
sacks.[y] So why would we steal[z] silver or
gold from your master's house? 9 If any of
your servants[a] is found to have it, he will
die;[b] and the rest of us will become my
lord's slaves.[c]"

43:31 [d]Ge 45:1; Isa 30:18; 42:14; 63:15; 64:12 [e]S ver 16 **43:32** [f]S Ge 14:13; Gal 2:12 [g]Ge 46:34; Ex 8:26 **43:33** [h]S Ge 35:23 [i]S Ge 42:13; 44:12 **43:34** [j]S Ge 37:3; S 2Ki 25:30 [k]Lk 15:23 **44:1** [l]S Ge 43:16 [m]S Ge 42:25 **44:2** [n]ver 5, 10, 12, 16 [o]ver 8 **44:3** [p]Jdg 19:9 **44:4** [q]S Ge 43:16 [r]Ps 35:12; 38:20; 109:5; Pr 17:13; Jer 18:20 **44:5** [s]S ver 2 [t]S Ge 30:27; Dt 18:10-14 **44:7** [u]S Ge 42:11 [v]S Ge 18:25 **44:8** [w]S Ge 42:13 [x]ver 2 [y]S Ge 42:25; S 43:15 [z]Ge 31:30 **44:9** [a]S Ge 42:11 [b]Ge 31:32 [c]S ver 10; S Ge 43:18

44:10 [d]S ver 2 [e]ver 9, 17, 33 [f]S Ge 43:9 **44:12** [g]S Ge 43:16 [h]S Ge 31:34 [i]S Ge 43:33 [j]ver 2 **44:13** [k]S Ge 37:29 [l]S Ge 42:26 **44:14** [m]Ge 43:18 [n]ver 16; S Ge 29:35; S 43:3 [o]S Ge 33:3 **44:15** [p]S Ge 12:18 [q]S Ge 30:27 **44:16** [r]ver 22, 24; S Ge 37:8 [s]S ver 14

10 "Very well, then," he said, "let it be as
you say. Whoever is found to have it[d] will
become my slave;[e] the rest of you will be
free from blame."[f]
11 Each of them quickly lowered his
sack to the ground and opened it. 12 Then
the steward[g] proceeded to search,[h] beginning with the oldest and ending with
the youngest.[i] And the cup was found in
Benjamin's sack.[j] 13 At this, they tore their
clothes.[k] Then they all loaded their donkeys[l] and returned to the city.
14 Joseph was still in the house[m] when
Judah[n] and his brothers came in, and they
threw themselves to the ground before
him.[o] 15 Joseph said to them, "What is this
you have done?[p] Don't you know that a
man like me can find things out by divination?[q]"
16 "What can we say to my lord?[r]" Judah[s] replied. "What can we say? How can
we prove our innocence?[t] God has uncovered your servants'[u] guilt. We are now my
lord's slaves[v]—we ourselves and the one
who was found to have the cup.[w]"
17 But Joseph said, "Far be it from me
to do such a thing![x] Only the man who
was found to have the cup will become
my slave.[y] The rest of you, go back to your
father in peace."[z]
18 Then Judah[a] went up to him and
said: "Pardon your servant, my lord,[b] let
me speak a word to my lord. Do not be
angry[c] with your servant, though you are
equal to Pharaoh himself. 19 My lord asked
his servants,[d] 'Do you have a father or a
brother?'[e] 20 And we answered, 'We have
an aged father, and there is a young son
born to him in his old age.[f] His brother is
dead,[g] and he is the only one of his mother's sons left, and his father loves him.'[h]
21 "Then you said to your servants,[i]
'Bring him down to me so I can see him

[t]Ps 26:6; 73:13 [u]S Ge 42:11 [v]S Ge 43:18 [w]S ver 2 **44:17** [x]S Ge 18:25 [y]S ver 10 [z]S Ge 43:9 **44:18** [a]S Ge 29:35 [b]S ver 16 [c]S Ge 18:30 **44:19** [d]S Ge 42:11 [e]S Ge 43:7 **44:20** [f]S Ge 37:3 [g]S Ge 37:33 [h]S Ge 42:13 **44:21** [i]S Ge 42:11

43:32 *Egyptians could not eat with Hebrews.* The taboo was probably based on ritual or religious reasons (see Ex 8:26), unlike the Egyptian refusal to associate with shepherds (see 46:34), which was probably based on social custom.

43:34 *Benjamin's portion was five times as much.* Again reflecting his special status with Joseph (see note on v. 29; see also 45:22).

44:4 *city.* Identity unknown, though Memphis (about 13 miles south of modern Cairo) and Zoan (in the eastern delta region) have been suggested.

44:5 *divination.* See v. 15; see also note on 30:27.

44:9 *If any of your servants is found to have it, he will die.* Years earlier, Jacob had given Laban a similar rash response (see 31:32 and note).

44:10 The steward softened the penalty contained in the brothers' proposal.

44:12 *beginning with the oldest and ending with the youngest.* For a similar building up of suspense, see 31:33.

44:13 *tore their clothes.* A sign of distress and grief (see 37:29 and note on 37:34).

44:14 *threw themselves to the ground before him.* Further fulfillment of Joseph's dreams in 37:7,9 (see 42:6; 43:26,28).

44:16 *God has uncovered your servants' guilt.* Like Joseph's steward (see note on 43:23), Judah spoke better than he knew. Or perhaps he refers both to the present event and to the guilt of their sin against Joseph (see 42:21 and note).

44:18 *Judah ... said.* See note on 43:3. *lord ... servant.* See note on 42:10. *you are equal to Pharaoh.* Words more flattering than true (see 41:40,43).

for myself.'[j] 22 And we said to my lord,[k] 'The boy cannot leave his father; if he leaves him, his father will die.'[l] 23 But you told your servants, 'Unless your youngest brother comes down with you, you will not see my face again.'[m] 24 When we went back to your servant my father,[n] we told him what my lord[o] had said.[p]

25 "Then our father said, 'Go back and buy a little more food.'[q] 26 But we said, 'We cannot go down. Only if our youngest brother is with us will we go. We cannot see the man's face unless our youngest brother is with us.'[r]

27 "Your servant my father[s] said to us, 'You know that my wife bore me two sons.[t] 28 One of them went away from me, and I said, "He has surely been torn to pieces."[u] And I have not seen him since.[v] 29 If you take this one from me too and harm comes to him, you will bring my gray head down to the grave[w] in misery.'[x]

30 "So now, if the boy is not with us when I go back to your servant my father,[y] and if my father, whose life is closely bound up with the boy's life,[z] 31 sees that the boy isn't there, he will die.[a] Your servants[b] will bring the gray head of our father down to the grave[c] in sorrow. 32 Your servant guaranteed the boy's safety to my father. I said, 'If I do not bring him back to you, I will bear the blame before you, my father, all my life!'[d]

33 "Now then, please let your servant remain here as my lord's slave[e] in place of the boy,[f] and let the boy return with his brothers. 34 How can I go back to my father if the boy is not with me? No! Do not let me see the misery[g] that would come on my father."[h]

Joseph Makes Himself Known

45 Then Joseph could no longer control himself[i] before all his attendants, and he cried out, "Have everyone leave my presence!"[j] So there was no one with Joseph when he made himself known to his brothers. 2 And he wept[k] so loudly that the Egyptians heard him, and Pharaoh's household heard about it.[l]

3 Joseph said to his brothers, "I am Joseph! Is my father still living?"[m] But his brothers were not able to answer him,[n] because they were terrified at his presence.[o]

4 Then Joseph said to his brothers, "Come close to me."[p] When they had done so, he said, "I am your brother Joseph, the one you sold into Egypt![q] 5 And now, do not be distressed[r] and do not be angry with yourselves for selling me here,[s] because it was to save lives that God sent me ahead of you.[t] 6 For two years now there has been famine[u] in the land, and for the next five years there will be no plowing and reaping. 7 But God sent me ahead of you to preserve for you a remnant[v] on earth and to save your lives by a great deliverance.[a][w]

8 "So then, it was not you who sent me here, but God.[x] He made me father[y] to Pharaoh, lord of his entire household and ruler of all Egypt.[z] 9 Now hurry[a] back to my father and say to him, 'This is what your son Joseph says: God has made me lord of all Egypt. Come down to me; don't delay.[b] 10 You shall live in the region of Goshen[c] and be near me—you, your children and grandchildren, your flocks and herds, and all you have.[d] 11 I will provide for you there,[e] because five years of famine[f] are still to come. Otherwise you and your household and all who belong to you will become destitute.'[g]

12 "You can see for yourselves, and so can my brother Benjamin,[h] that it is really I who am speaking to you.[i] 13 Tell my father about all the honor accorded me in Egypt[j]

[a] 7 Or *save you as a great band of survivors*

44:21 [j] S Ge 42:15 **44:22** [k] S ver 16 [l] S Ge 37:35 **44:23** [m] S Ge 42:15; S 43:5 **44:24** [n] S Ge 43:28 [o] S ver 16 [p] Ge 42:29 **44:25** [q] S Ge 42:2 **44:26** [r] S Ge 43:5 **44:27** [s] S Ge 43:28 [t] Ge 46:19 **44:28** [u] S Ge 37:33 [v] Ge 45:26,28; 46:30; 48:11 **44:29** [w] S Ge 37:35 [x] S Ge 42:38 **44:30** [y] S Ge 43:28 [z] 1Sa 18:1; 2Sa 1:26 **44:31** [a] S ver 22 [b] S Ge 42:11 [c] S Ge 37:35 **44:32** [d] S Ge 42:37 **44:33** [e] S ver 10; S Ge 43:18 [f] Jn 15:13 **44:34** [g] S Ge 42:38 [h] Est 8:6 **45:1** [i] S Ge 43:31 [j] 2Sa 13:9 **45:2** [k] S Ge 29:11 [l] ver 16; Ac 7:13 **45:3** [m] S Ge 43:7 [n] ver 15 [o] Ge 44:20; Job 21:6; 23:15; Mt 17:6; Mk 6:49-50 **45:4** [p] Ge 27:21-22 [q] Ge 37:28 **45:5** [r] Ge 42:21 [s] Ge 42:22 [t] ver 7-8; Ge 50:20; Job 10:12; Ps 105:17 **45:6** [u] S Ge 41:30 **45:7** [v] 2Ki 19:4, 30,31; Ezr 9:8, 13; Isa 1:9; 10:20, 21; 11:11,16; 46:3; Jer 6:9; 42:2; 50:20; Mic 4:7; 5:7; Zep 2:7 [w] S ver 5; Ge 49:18; Ex 15:2; 1Sa 14:45; 2Ki 13:5; Est 4:14; Isa 25:9; Mic 7:7 **45:8** [x] ver 5 [y] Jdg 17:10; 2Ki 6:21; 13:14 [z] S Ge 41:41 **45:9** [a] S Ge 43:15 [b] Ge 43:10; Ac 7:14 **45:10** [c] Ge 46:28,34; 47:1, 11,27; 50:8; Ex 8:22; 9:26; 10:24 [d] Ge 46:6-7 **45:11** [e] Ge 47:12; 50:21 [f] S Ge 41:30 [g] Ps 102:17 **45:12** [h] S Ge 35:18 [i] Mk 6:50 **45:13** [j] S Ge 41:41

44:29,31 *grave.* See note on 37:35.
44:30 *whose life is closely bound up with the boy's life.* The Hebrew underlying this clause is later used of Jonathan's becoming "one in spirit with David" (1Sa 18:1).
44:33 *in place of the boy.* Judah's willingness to be a substitute for Benjamin helped make amends for his role in selling Joseph (see 37:26–27).
44:34 *Do not let me see the misery.* Judah remembers an earlier scene (37:34–35).
45:2 *wept.* See vv. 14–15; see also 43:30 and note.
45:3 *brothers ... were terrified.* Either because they thought they were seeing a ghost or because they were afraid of what Joseph would do to them.
45:4 *I am your brother Joseph.* See v. 3; Ac 7:13. This time Joseph emphasized his relationship to them. *you sold.* See note on 37:28.
45:5 *God sent me.* See vv. 7–9; Ac 7:9; cf. 50:20. God had a purpose to work through the brothers' jealous and cruel act (see Ac 2:23; 4:28; cf. Ro 8:28).
45:6 Joseph was now 39 years old (see 41:46,53).
45:7 *remnant.* Although none had been lost, they had escaped a great threat to them all; so Joseph called them a remnant in the confidence that they would live to produce a great people.
45:8 *father.* A title of honor given to viziers (see note on 41:43) and other high officials (in the Apocrypha see 1 Maccabees 11:32).
45:9 *hurry back ... don't delay.* Joseph is anxious to see Jacob as soon as possible (see v. 13).
45:10 *Goshen.* A region in the eastern part of the Nile delta, it was very fertile (see v. 18) and remains so today.
45:12 *I ... am speaking.* Not through an interpreter as before (see 42:23).

and about everything you have seen. And
bring my father down here quickly.[k]"
14 Then he threw his arms around his
brother Benjamin and wept, and Benjamin[l]
embraced him,[m] weeping. 15 And he kissed[n]
all his brothers and wept over them.[o] Afterward his brothers talked with him.[p]
16 When the news reached Pharaoh's
palace that Joseph's brothers had come,[q]
Pharaoh and all his officials[r] were pleased.[s]
17 Pharaoh said to Joseph, "Tell your brothers, 'Do this: Load your animals[t] and return to the land of Canaan,[u] 18 and bring
your father and your families back to me. I
will give you the best of the land of Egypt[v]
and you can enjoy the fat of the land.'[w]
19 "You are also directed to tell them, 'Do
this: Take some carts[x] from Egypt for your
children and your wives, and get your father and come. 20 Never mind about your
belongings,[y] because the best of all Egypt[z]
will be yours.'"
21 So the sons of Israel did this. Joseph
gave them carts,[a] as Pharaoh had commanded, and he also gave them provisions
for their journey.[b] 22 To each of them he
gave new clothing,[c] but to Benjamin he
gave three hundred shekels[a] of silver and
five sets of clothes.[d] 23 And this is what
he sent to his father: ten donkeys[e] loaded
with the best things[f] of Egypt, and ten female donkeys loaded with grain and bread
and other provisions for his journey.[g]
24 Then he sent his brothers away, and as
they were leaving he said to them, "Don't
quarrel on the way!"[h]
25 So they went up out of Egypt[i] and
came to their father Jacob in the land of
Canaan.[j] 26 They told him, "Joseph is still
alive! In fact, he is ruler of all Egypt."[k] Jacob was stunned; he did not believe them.[l]
27 But when they told him everything Joseph had said to them, and when he saw
the carts[m] Joseph had sent to carry him
back, the spirit of their father Jacob revived. 28 And Israel said, "I'm convinced![n]
My son Joseph is still alive. I will go and
see him before I die."[o]

Jacob Goes to Egypt

46 So Israel[p] set out with all that was
his, and when he reached Beershe-
ba,[q] he offered sacrifices[r] to the God of his
father Isaac.[s]
2 And God spoke to Israel[t] in a vision at
night[u] and said, "Jacob! Jacob!"
"Here I am,"[v] he replied.
3 "I am God, the God of your father,"[w]
he said. "Do not be afraid[x] to go down to
Egypt,[y] for I will make you into a great
nation[z] there.[a] 4 I will go down to Egypt
with you, and I will surely bring you back
again.[b] And Joseph's own hand will close
your eyes.[c]"
5 Then Jacob left Beersheba,[d] and Israel's[e] sons took their father Jacob and their
children and their wives in the carts[f] that
Pharaoh had sent to transport him. 6 So Jacob and all his offspring went to Egypt,[g]
taking with them their livestock and the
possessions[h] they had acquired[i] in Canaan. 7 Jacob brought with him to Egypt[j]
his sons and grandsons and his daughters
and granddaughters — all his offspring.[k]

8 These are the names of the sons of
Israel[l] (Jacob and his descendants) who
went to Egypt:

Reuben the firstborn[m] of Jacob.
9 The sons of Reuben:[n]
Hanok, Pallu,[o] Hezron and Karmi.[p]
10 The sons of Simeon:[q]
Jemuel,[r] Jamin, Ohad, Jakin, Zohar[s]

[a] *22* That is, about 7 1/2 pounds or about 3.5 kilograms

45:13 [k]S Ge 43:15; Ac 7:14 **45:14** [l]S Ge 35:18 [m]S Ge 29:13 **45:15** [n]S Ge 29:11; Lk 15:20 [o]S Ge 29:11,13; S 46:4 [p]ver 3 **45:16** [q]S ver 2; Ac 7:13 [r]Ge 50:7 [s]S Ge 41:37 **45:17** [t]S Ge 42:26 [u]S Ge 42:5 **45:18** [v]ver 20; Ge 20:15; 46:34; 47:6, 11,27; Jer 40:4 [w]Ezr 9:12; Ps 37:19; Isa 1:19 **45:19** [x]ver 21, 27; Ge 46:5; Nu 7:3-8 **45:20** [y]Ge 46:6, 32 [z]S ver 18 **45:21** [a]S ver 19 [b]S Ge 42:25 **45:22** [c]S Ge 24:53 [d]S Ge 37:3; S 41:14; Jdg 14:12,13; 2Ki 5:22 **45:23** [e]S Ge 42:26 [f]S Ge 24:10 [g]S Ge 42:25 **45:24** [h]Ge 42:21-22 **45:25** [i]Ge 13:1 [j]Ge 42:29 **45:26** [k]S Ge 41:41 [l]S Ge 44:28; 1Ki 10:7 **45:27** [m]S ver 19 **45:28** [n]Lk 16:31 [o]S Ge 44:28 **46:1** [p]ver 5 [q]S Ge 21:14 [r]S Ge 31:54 [s]S Ge 31:42 **46:2** [t]S Ge 17:5 [u]S Ge 15:1 [v]S Ge 22:1 **46:3** [w]S Ge 28:13 [x]S Ge 15:1 [y]Ge 26:2 [z]S Ge 12:2 [a]Ex 1:7 **46:4** [b]S Ge 15:16; S 28:13 [c]ver 29; Ge 45:14-15; 50:1 **46:5** [d]S Ge 21:14 [e]ver 1 [f]S Ge 45:19 **46:6** [g]Nu 20:15; Dt 26:5; Jos 24:4; Ps 105:23; Isa 52:4; Ac 7:15 [h]S Ge 45:20 [i]S Ge 12:5 **46:7** [j]Ge 13:10 [k]ver 6; Ge 45:10 **46:8** [l]S Ge 35:26; Ex 1:1; Nu 26:4 [m]S Ge 29:32 **46:9** [n]Ex 6:14; Nu 1:20; 26:7; 1Ch 5:3 [o]Nu 26:5; 1Ch 5:3 [p]Nu 26:6 **46:10** [q]S Ge 29:33; Nu 26:14 [r]Ex 6:15; Nu 26:12 [s]Nu 26:13

45:14 *wept.* See 43:30 and note.
45:15 *his brothers talked with him.* In intimate fellowship and friendship, rather than in hostility or fear, for the first time in over 20 years (see 37:2 and note on 45:6).
45:18 *you can enjoy the fat of the land.* An echo of Isaac's blessing on Jacob (see 27:28).
45:22 *to Benjamin he gave ... five sets of clothes.* See note on 43:34. *shekels.* See note on 20:16.
45:24 *Don't quarrel.* Joseph wanted nothing to delay their return (see note on v. 9), and he wanted them to avoid mutual accusation and recrimination concerning the past.
46:1 — 47:12 Israel's (Jacob's) move to and settlement in Egypt (see 15:13 and note).
46:1 *set out.* Probably from the family estate at Hebron (see 35:27 and note). *when he reached Beersheba, he offered sacrifices.* Abraham and Isaac had also worshiped the Lord there (see 21:33; 26:23 – 25).
46:2 *God spoke to Israel in a vision at night.* See 26:24. *Jacob! Jacob!* See note on 22:11. *Here I am.* See note on 22:1.
46:3 – 4 As Israel and his family were about to leave Canaan, God reaffirmed his covenant promises.
46:3 *I am ... the God of your father ... Do not be afraid.* A verbatim repetition of God's statement to Isaac in 26:24. *I will make you into a great nation.* The Lord reaffirmed one aspect of his promise to Abraham (see 12:2). *there.* See Ex 1:7.
46:4 *I will go down to Egypt with you.* God would be with Jacob as he went south to Egypt, just as he was with him when he went north to Harran, and would again bring him back as he had done before (see 28:15 and note; see also 15:16 and note; 48:21). *will close your eyes.* A reference to Jacob's death (49:33 — 50:1).
46:8 *These are the names of the sons of Israel ... who went to Egypt.* Repeated verbatim in Ex 1:1 (see note there), where it introduces the background for the story of the exodus (predicted here in v. 4).

and Shaul the son of a Canaanite
woman.
11 The sons of Levi:[t]
Gershon,[u] Kohath[v] and Merari.[w]
12 The sons of Judah:[x]
Er,[y] Onan,[z] Shelah, Perez[a] and Zerah[b] (but Er and Onan had died in
the land of Canaan).[c]
The sons of Perez:[d]
Hezron and Hamul.[e]
13 The sons of Issachar:[f]
Tola, Puah,[a][g] Jashub[b][h] and Shimron.
14 The sons of Zebulun:[i]
Sered, Elon and Jahleel.
15 These were the sons Leah bore to Jacob in Paddan Aram,[c][j] besides his daughter Dinah.[k] These sons and daughters of
his were thirty-three in all.

16 The sons of Gad:[l]
Zephon,[d][m] Haggi, Shuni, Ezbon,
Eri, Arodi and Areli.
17 The sons of Asher:[n]
Imnah, Ishvah, Ishvi and Beriah.
Their sister was Serah.
The sons of Beriah:
Heber and Malkiel.
18 These were the children born to Jacob
by Zilpah,[o] whom Laban had given to his
daughter Leah[p]—sixteen in all.

19 The sons of Jacob's wife Rachel:[q]
Joseph and Benjamin.[r] 20 In Egypt,
Manasseh[s] and Ephraim[t] were born
to Joseph[u] by Asenath daughter of
Potiphera, priest of On.[e][v]
21 The sons of Benjamin:[w]
Bela, Beker, Ashbel, Gera, Naaman,
Ehi, Rosh, Muppim, Huppim and
Ard.[x]
22 These were the sons of Rachel[y] who
were born to Jacob—fourteen in all.

23 The son of Dan:[z]
Hushim.[a]
24 The sons of Naphtali:[b]
Jahziel, Guni, Jezer and Shillem.
25 These were the sons born to Jacob
by Bilhah,[c] whom Laban had given to his
daughter Rachel[d]—seven in all.

26 All those who went to Egypt with Jacob
—those who were his direct descendants,
not counting his sons' wives—numbered
sixty-six persons.[e] 27 With the two sons[f]
who had been born to Joseph in Egypt,[f]
the members of Jacob's family, which
went to Egypt, were seventy[g] in all.[g]

28 Now Jacob sent Judah[h] ahead of him
to Joseph to get directions to Goshen.[i]
When they arrived in the region of Goshen, 29 Joseph had his chariot[j] made
ready and went to Goshen to meet his father Israel.[k] As soon as Joseph appeared
before him, he threw his arms around his
father[h] and wept[l] for a long time.[m]
30 Israel[n] said to Joseph, "Now I am
ready to die, since I have seen for myself
that you are still alive."[o]
31 Then Joseph said to his brothers and
to his father's household, "I will go up
and speak to Pharaoh and will say to him,
'My brothers and my father's household,
who were living in the land of Canaan,[p]
have come to me.[q] 32 The men are shepherds;[r] they tend livestock,[s] and they have
brought along their flocks and herds and
everything they own.'[t] 33 When Pharaoh
calls you in and asks, 'What is your occupation?'[u] 34 you should answer, 'Your
servants[v] have tended livestock from our
boyhood on, just as our fathers did.'[w] Then
you will be allowed to settle[x] in the region
of Goshen,[y] for all shepherds are detestable to the Egyptians.[z]"

47 Joseph went and told Pharaoh,
"My father and brothers, with their
flocks and herds and everything they own,
have come from the land of Canaan[a] and
are now in Goshen."[b] 2 He chose five of

46:11 [t] S Ge 29:34; S Nu 3:17 [u] Ex 6:16; Nu 3:21; 4:38 [v] Ex 6:16; Nu 3:27; 1Ch 23:12 [w] Ex 6:19; Nu 3:20,33; 4:29; 26:57; 1Ch 6:19 **46:12** [x] S Ge 29:35 [y] S Ge 38:3 [z] S Ge 38:4 [a] S Ge 38:29 [b] S Ge 38:30 [c] S Ge 38:7; Nu 26:19 [d] 1Ch 2:5; Mt 1:3 [e] Nu 26:21 **46:13** [f] S Ge 30:18 [g] Nu 26:23; Jdg 10:1; 1Ch 7:1 [h] Nu 26:24 **46:14** [i] S Ge 30:20 **46:15** [j] S Ge 25:20; 29:31-35 [k] S Ge 30:21 **46:16** [l] S Ge 30:11; S Nu 1:25 [m] Nu 26:15 **46:17** [n] S Ge 30:13 **46:18** [o] Ge 30:10 [p] S Ge 16:1 **46:19** [q] S Ge 29:6 [r] Ge 44:27 **46:20** [s] S Ge 41:51 [t] S Ge 41:52 [u] Nu 26:28-37 [v] S Ge 41:45 **46:21** [w] Nu 26:38-41; 1Ch 7:6-12; 8:1 [x] Nu 26:40; 1Ch 8:3 **46:22** [y] S Ge 29:6 **46:23** [z] S Ge 30:6 [a] Nu 26:42 **46:24** [b] S Ge 30:8 **46:25** [c] Ge 30:8 [d] S Ge 24:61 **46:26** [e] ver 5-7; Ex 1:5; Dt 10:22 **46:27** [f] S Ge 41:45 [g] S Ge 34:30; Ac 7:14 **46:28** [h] S Ge 43:3 [i] S Ge 45:10 **46:29** [j] S Ge 41:43

[a] *13* Samaritan Pentateuch and Syriac (see also 1 Chron. 7:1); Masoretic Text *Puvah* [b] *13* Samaritan Pentateuch and some Septuagint manuscripts (see also Num. 26:24 and 1 Chron. 7:1); Masoretic Text *Iob* [c] *15* That is, Northwest Mesopotamia [d] *16* Samaritan Pentateuch and Septuagint (see also Num. 26:15); Masoretic Text *Ziphion* [e] *20* That is, Heliopolis [f] *27* Hebrew; Septuagint *the nine children* [g] *27* Hebrew (see also Exodus 1:5 and note); Septuagint (see also Acts 7:14) *seventy-five* [h] *29* Hebrew *around him*

[k] ver 1,30; S Ge 32:28; 47:29,31 [l] S Ge 29:11 [m] S ver 4; Lk 15:20 **46:30** [n] S ver 29 [o] S Ge 44:28 **46:31** [p] S Ge 42:13 [q] S Ge 45:10 **46:32** [r] Ge 47:3 [s] S Ge 37:2 [t] S Ge 45:20 **46:33** [u] Ge 47:3 **46:34** [v] S Ge 42:11 [w] Ge 47:3 [x] S Ge 34:10 [y] S Ge 45:10 [z] S Ge 43:32 **47:1** [a] S Ge 42:13 [b] S Ge 46:31

46:15 *Paddan Aram.* See note on 25:20. *thirty-three in all.* There are 34 names in vv. 8–15. To bring the number to 33 the name Ohad in v. 10 should probably be removed, since it does not appear in the parallel lists in Nu 26:12–13; 1Ch 4:24. The Hebrew form of "Ohad" looks very much like that of the nearby "Zohar" (see Ex 6:15), and perhaps a later scribe added Ohad to the text accidentally.
46:20 See note on 41:45.
46:26 *All those who went to Egypt with Jacob ... numbered sixty-six persons.* The total of 33 (see v. 15 and note), 16 (v. 18), 14 (v. 22) and 7 (v. 25) is 70 (v. 27). To arrive at 66 we must subtract Er and Onan, who "had died in the land of Canaan" (v. 12), and Manasseh and Ephraim (v. 20), who "had been born ... in Egypt" (v. 27).
46:27 *seventy.* See NIV text note; see also Dt 10:22. Seventy is the ideal and complete number (see Introduction: Literary Features; see also notes on 5:5; 10:2) of Jacob's descendants who would have been in Egypt if Er and Onan had not died earlier (see 38:7–10). For the number 75 in Ac 7:14, see note there.
46:28 *Jacob sent Judah ahead.* See note on 43:3.
46:29 *wept.* See 43:30 and note.
46:34 *shepherds are detestable to the Egyptians.* See note on 43:32.

his brothers and presented them[c] before Pharaoh.

3 Pharaoh asked the brothers, "What is your occupation?"[d]

"Your servants[e] are shepherds,[f]" they replied to Pharaoh, "just as our fathers were." 4 They also said to him, "We have come to live here for a while,[g] because the famine is severe in Canaan[h] and your servants' flocks have no pasture.[i] So now, please let your servants settle in Goshen."[j]

5 Pharaoh said to Joseph, "Your father and your brothers have come to you, 6 and the land of Egypt is before you; settle[k] your father and your brothers in the best part of the land.[l] Let them live in Goshen. And if you know of any among them with special ability,[m] put them in charge of my own livestock.[n]"

7 Then Joseph brought his father Jacob in and presented him[o] before Pharaoh. After Jacob blessed[a] Pharaoh,[p] 8 Pharaoh asked him, "How old are you?"

9 And Jacob said to Pharaoh, "The years of my pilgrimage are a hundred and thirty.[q] My years have been few and difficult,[r] and they do not equal the years of the pilgrimage of my fathers.[s]" 10 Then Jacob blessed[b] Pharaoh[t] and went out from his presence.

11 So Joseph settled his father and his brothers in Egypt and gave them property in the best part of the land,[u] the district of Rameses,[v] as Pharaoh directed. 12 Joseph also provided his father and his brothers and all his father's household with food, according to the number of their children.[w]

Joseph and the Famine

13 There was no food, however, in the whole region because the famine was severe; both Egypt and Canaan wasted away because of the famine.[x] 14 Joseph collected all the money that was to be found in Egypt and Canaan in payment for the grain they were buying,[y] and he brought it to Pharaoh's palace.[z] 15 When the money of the people of Egypt and Canaan was gone,[a] all Egypt came to Joseph[b] and said, "Give us food. Why should we die before your eyes?[c] Our money is all gone."

16 "Then bring your livestock,[d]" said Joseph. "I will sell you food in exchange for your livestock, since your money is gone.[e]" 17 So they brought their livestock to Joseph, and he gave them food in exchange for their horses,[f] their sheep and goats, their cattle and donkeys.[g] And he brought them through that year with food in exchange for all their livestock.

18 When that year was over, they came to him the following year and said, "We cannot hide from our lord the fact that since our money is gone[h] and our livestock belongs to you,[i] there is nothing left for our lord except our bodies and our land. 19 Why should we perish before your eyes[j]—we and our land as well? Buy us and our land in exchange for food,[k] and we with our land will be in bondage to Pharaoh.[l] Give us seed so that we may live and not die,[m] and that the land may not become desolate."

20 So Joseph bought all the land in Egypt for Pharaoh. The Egyptians, one and all, sold their fields, because the famine was too severe[n] for them. The land became Pharaoh's, 21 and Joseph reduced the people to servitude,[c][o] from one end of Egypt to the other. 22 However, he did not buy the land of the priests,[p] because they received a regular allotment from Pharaoh and had food enough from the allotment[q] Pharaoh gave them. That is why they did not sell their land.

23 Joseph said to the people, "Now that I have bought you and your land today for Pharaoh, here is seed[r] for you so you can plant the ground.[s] 24 But when the crop comes in, give a fifth[t] of it to Pharaoh. The other four-fifths you may keep as seed for the fields and as food for yourselves and your households and your children."

25 "You have saved our lives," they said. "May we find favor in the eyes of our lord;[u] we will be in bondage to Pharaoh."[v]

26 So Joseph established it as a law concerning land in Egypt—still in force today—that a fifth[w] of the produce belongs

47:2 [c] S Ge 43:15 **47:3** [d] Ge 46:33 [e] S Ge 42:11 [f] Ge 46:32 **47:4** [g] Ru 1:1 [h] S Ge 12:10 [i] 1Ki 18:5; Jer 14:5-6; Joel 1:18 [j] Ge 46:34 **47:6** [k] S Ge 34:10 [l] S Ge 13:9; S 45:18 [m] Ex 18:21, 25; Dt 1:13, 15; 2Ch 19:5; Ps 15:2 [n] S Ge 39:4 **47:7** [o] S Ge 43:15 [p] ver 10; 2Sa 14:22; 19:39; 1Ki 8:66 **47:9** [q] S Ge 25:7 [r] S Ge 3:17; Ps 39:4; 89:47 [s] Job 8:9; Ps 39:12 **47:10** [t] S ver 7 **47:11** [u] S Ge 45:10, 18 [v] Ex 1:11; 12:37; Nu 33:3, 5 **47:12** [w] S Ge 45:11 **47:13** [x] S Ge 12:10; S 41:30 **47:14** [y] S Ge 41:36 [z] S Ge 41:34; Ex 7:23; 8:24; Jer 43:9 **47:15** [a] ver 16, 18 [b] S Ge 41:57 [c] ver 19; Ex 16:3 **47:16** [d] ver 18, 19 [e] ver 15 **47:17** [f] Ex 14:9 [g] S Ge 12:16 **47:18** [h] S ver 15 [i] S ver 16 **47:19** [j] S ver 15 [k] S ver 16 [l] ver 21, 25 [m] S Ge 42:2 **47:20** [n] S Ge 12:10 **47:21** [o] S ver 19 **47:22** [p] ver 26 [q] Dt 14:28-29 **47:23** [r] Isa 55:10; 61:11 [s] Ne 5:3 **47:24** [t] S Ge 41:34 **47:25** [u] S Ge 32:5 [v] S ver 19 **47:26** [w] S Ge 41:34

[a] 7 Or *greeted* [b] 10 Or *said farewell to* [c] 21 Samaritan Pentateuch and Septuagint (see also Vulgate); Masoretic Text *and he moved the people into the cities*

47:9 *pilgrimage.* Jacob referred to the itinerant nature of patriarchal life in general and of his own in particular as he hopefully awaited the fulfillment of the promise of a land (see also Dt 26:5 and note). *they do not equal the years of ... my fathers.* Abraham lived to the age of 175 (25:7), Isaac to 180 (35:28).

47:11 *best part of the land.* See note on 45:10. *district of Rameses.* The city of Rameses is mentioned in Ex 1:11; 12:37; Nu 33:3,5. The name doubtless refers to the great Egyptian pharaoh Rameses II, who reigned centuries later (the designation here involves an editorial updating). In addition to being known as Goshen (see v. 27), the "district of Rameses" was called the "region of Zoan" in Ps 78:12,43 (see note on Ge 44:4).

47:13 *famine was severe.* After the people used up all their money to buy grain (see vv. 14–15), they traded their livestock (vv. 16–17), then their land (v. 20), then themselves (v. 21).

47:21 The NIV text note reading would mean that the Egyptians were to move temporarily into the cities until seed could be distributed to them for planting (see v. 23).

47:26 *a fifth of the produce belongs to Pharaoh.* The same was true "during the seven years of abundance" (41:34)—but

to Pharaoh. It was only the land of the
priests that did not become Pharaoh's.[x]
27 Now the Israelites settled in Egypt
in the region of Goshen.[y] They acquired
property there[z] and were fruitful and increased greatly in number.[a]
28 Jacob lived in Egypt[b] seventeen years,
and the years of his life were a hundred
and forty-seven.[c] 29 When the time drew
near for Israel[d] to die,[e] he called for his
son Joseph and said to him, "If I have
found favor in your eyes,[f] put your hand
under my thigh[g] and promise that you will
show me kindness[h] and faithfulness.[i] Do
not bury me in Egypt, 30 but when I rest
with my fathers,[j] carry me out of Egypt
and bury me where they are buried."[k]
"I will do as you say," he said.
31 "Swear to me,"[l] he said. Then Joseph
swore to him,[m] and Israel[n] worshiped as he
leaned on the top of his staff.[a][o]

Manasseh and Ephraim

48 Some time later Joseph was told,
"Your father is ill." So he took his
two sons Manasseh and Ephraim[p] along
with him. 2 When Jacob was told, "Your
son Joseph has come to you," Israel[q] rallied his strength and sat up on the bed.
3 Jacob said to Joseph, "God Almighty[b][r]
appeared to me at Luz[s] in the land of Canaan, and there he blessed me[t] 4 and said
to me, 'I am going to make you fruitful
and increase your numbers.[u] I will make
you a community of peoples, and I will
give this land[v] as an everlasting possession
to your descendants after you.'[w]
5 "Now then, your two sons born to you
in Egypt[x] before I came to you here will be
reckoned as mine; Ephraim and Manasseh
will be mine,[y] just as Reuben[z] and Simeon[a]
are mine. 6 Any children born to you after
them will be yours; in the territory they
inherit they will be reckoned under the
names of their brothers. 7 As I was returning from Paddan,[c][b] to my sorrow[c] Rachel
died in the land of Canaan while we were
still on the way, a little distance from Ephrath. So I buried her there beside the road
to Ephrath" (that is, Bethlehem).[d]
8 When Israel[e] saw the sons of Joseph,[f]
he asked, "Who are these?"
9 "They are the sons God has given me
here,"[g] Joseph said to his father.
Then Israel said, "Bring them to me so I
may bless[h] them."
10 Now Israel's eyes were failing because
of old age, and he could hardly see.[i] So
Joseph brought his sons close to him,
and his father kissed them[j] and embraced
them.[k]
11 Israel[l] said to Joseph, "I never expected to see your face again,[m] and now God
has allowed me to see your children too."[n]
12 Then Joseph removed them from Israel's knees[o] and bowed down with his face
to the ground.[p] 13 And Joseph took both
of them, Ephraim on his right toward Israel's left hand and Manasseh on his left

[a] 31 Or *Israel bowed down at the head of his bed*
[b] 3 Hebrew *El-Shaddai*
[c] 7 That is, Northwest Mesopotamia

47:26 [x] ver 22 **47:27** [y] S Ge 45:10, 18 [z] S Ge 33:19 [a] S Ge 1:22; S 12:2; S 17:6 **47:28** [b] Ps 105:23 [c] S Ge 25:7 **47:29** [d] S Ge 46:29 [e] S Ge 27:2 [f] S Ge 32:5 [g] S Ge 24:2 [h] S Ge 19:19 [i] S Ge 24:27; Jdg 1:24; 2Sa 2:6 **47:30** [j] S Ge 15:15 [k] S Ge 23:20; S 25:9; S 29:16; 50:25; Ex 13:19; Jos 24:32; Ac 7:15-16 **47:31** [l] Ge 21:23; Jos 2:20; Jdg 15:12; 1Sa 24:21; 30:15 [m] S Ge 24:3 [n] S Ge 46:29 [o] S Ge 32:10; Heb 11:21 *fn*; 1Ki 1:47 **48:1** [p] S Ge 41:52; Heb 11:21 **48:2** [q] ver 8, 9, 11, 14, 20 **48:3** [r] S Ge 17:1 [s] S Ge 28:19 [t] S Ge 28:13; S 32:29 **48:4** [u] S Ge 12:2; S 17:6 [v] S Ge 12:7; S 28:13 [w] S Ge 15:7 **48:5** [x] S Ge 41:50-52 [y] 1Ch 5:1 [z] S Ge 29:32

[a] S Ge 29:33 **48:7** [b] S Ge 25:20 [c] S Ge 42:38 [d] Ge 35:19; Ru 1:2; 1Sa 16:4 **48:8** [e] S ver 2 [f] ver 10 **48:9** [g] S Ge 33:5 [h] S Ge 24:60 **48:10** [i] S Ge 27:1 [j] S Ge 27:27 [k] S Ge 29:13 **48:11** [l] S ver 2 [m] S Ge 44:28 [n] Ge 50:23; Job 42:16; Ps 103:17; 128:6 **48:12** [o] Ge 50:23; Job 3:12 [p] S Ge 19:1; S 33:3; 37:10

now all the land on which the produce grew belonged to the pharaoh as well.

47:27 *Israelites ... were fruitful and increased greatly in number.* See 35:11–12; 46:3 and notes.

47:29 *put your hand under my thigh.* See 24:2 and note. In both cases, ties of family kinship are being stressed.

47:30 *rest with my fathers.* See note on 25:8. *bury me where they are buried.* In the cave of Machpelah (see 50:12–13).

47:31 *worshiped as he leaned on the top of his staff.* Quoted in Heb 11:21. Compare 48:2 with the NIV text note reading here.

48:1–22 How Joseph, Rachel's beloved older son, received the inheritance of the firstborn among his brothers.

48:3 *God Almighty.* See notes on 17:1; 35:11. *Luz.* The older name for Bethel (see 28:19).

48:5 *your two sons ... will be reckoned as mine.* Jacob adopts them as his own. *Ephraim and Manasseh.* See v. 1 for the expected order, since Manasseh was Joseph's firstborn (see 41:51). Jacob mentions Ephraim first because he intends to give him the primary blessing and thus "put Ephraim ahead of Manasseh" (v. 20). *mine, just as Reuben and Simeon are mine.* Joseph's first two sons would enjoy equal status with Jacob's first two sons (35:23) and in fact would eventually supersede them. Because of an earlier sinful act (see 35:22 and note), Reuben would lose his birthright to Jacob's favorite son, Joseph (see 49:3–4; 1Ch 5:2), and thus to Joseph's sons (see 1Ch 5:1).

48:6 *children born to you after them will be yours.* They would take the place of Ephraim and Manasseh, whom Jacob had adopted. *in the territory they inherit they will be reckoned under the names of their brothers.* They would perpetuate the names of Ephraim and Manasseh for purposes of inheritance (for a similar provision, see 38:8 and note; Dt 25:5–7). Joseph's territory would thus be divided between Ephraim and Manasseh, but Levi (Jacob's third son; see 35:23) would receive "no share of the land" (Jos 14:4). The total number of tribal allotments would therefore remain the same.

48:7 *Paddan.* That is, Paddan Aram (see note on 25:20). *Rachel died.* See 35:16–19. Adopted by Joseph's father, Ephraim and Manasseh in effect took the place of other sons whom Joseph's mother, Rachel, might have borne if she had not died. *Ephrath.* See note on 35:16.

48:8 *Israel ... asked, "Who are these?"* Either because he had never met them or because, being old, he could not see them clearly.

48:10 *because of old age ... he could hardly see.* See note on 27:1. *kissed them and embraced them.* While they were on Jacob's knees (see v. 12), probably symbolizing adoption (see note on 30:3).

48:13–20 See note on Ac 6:6.

48:13 *Manasseh ... toward Israel's right hand.* Joseph wanted Jacob to bless Manasseh, Joseph's firstborn, by placing his right hand on Manasseh's head.

toward Israel's right hand,[q] and brought
them close to him. 14But Israel[r] reached
out his right hand and put it on Ephraim's
head,[s] though he was the younger,[t] and
crossing his arms, he put his left hand on
Manasseh's head, even though Manasseh
was the firstborn.[u]
15Then he blessed[v] Joseph and said,

"May the God before whom my fathers
Abraham and Isaac walked
faithfully,[w]
the God who has been my shepherd[x]
all my life to this day,
16the Angel[y] who has delivered me from
all harm[z]
—may he bless[a] these boys.[b]
May they be called by my name
and the names of my fathers
Abraham and Isaac,[c]
and may they increase greatly
on the earth."[d]

17When Joseph saw his father placing
his right hand[e] on Ephraim's head[f] he was
displeased; so he took hold of his father's
hand to move it from Ephraim's head to
Manasseh's head. 18Joseph said to him,
"No, my father, this one is the firstborn;
put your right hand on his head."[g]
19But his father refused and said, "I
know, my son, I know. He too will become
a people, and he too will become great.[h]
Nevertheless, his younger brother will be
greater than he,[i] and his descendants will
become a group of nations.[j]" 20He blessed[k]
them that day[l] and said,

"In your[a] name will Israel[m] pronounce
this blessing:[n]
'May God make you like Ephraim[o]
and Manasseh.[p]' "

So he put Ephraim ahead of Manasseh.
21Then Israel said to Joseph, "I am
about to die, but God will be with you[b][q]
and take you[b] back to the land of your[b] fathers.[r] 22And to you I give one more ridge
of land[c][s] than to your brothers,[t] the ridge
I took from the Amorites with my sword[u]
and my bow."

Jacob Blesses His Sons

49:1-28Ref — Dt 33:1-29

49 Then Jacob called for his sons and
said: "Gather around so I can tell
you what will happen to you in days to
come.[v]

2"Assemble[w] and listen, sons of Jacob;
listen to your father Israel.[x]

3"Reuben, you are my firstborn,[y]
my might, the first sign of my
strength,[z]
excelling in honor,[a] excelling in
power.
4Turbulent as the waters,[b] you will no
longer excel,
for you went up onto your father's
bed,
onto my couch and defiled it.[c]

5"Simeon[d] and Levi[e] are brothers—
their swords[d] are weapons of
violence.[f]
6Let me not enter their council,
let me not join their assembly,[g]
for they have killed men in their anger[h]
and hamstrung[i] oxen as they
pleased.

[a] *20* The Hebrew is singular. [b] *21* The Hebrew is plural. [c] *22* The Hebrew for *ridge of land* is identical with the place name Shechem. [d] *5* The meaning of the Hebrew for this word is uncertain.

48:13 [q] Ps 16:8; 73:23; 110:1; Mt 25:33 **48:14** [r] S ver 2 [s] ver 17,18 [t] S Ge 25:23 [u] S Ge 29:32; S 41:51 **48:15** [v] S Ge 24:60 [w] S Ge 5:22 [x] Ge 49:24; 2Sa 5:2; Ps 23:1; 80:1; Isa 40:11; Jer 23:4 **48:16** [y] S Ge 16:7 [z] S Ge 24:50; 2Sa 4:9; Ps 71:4; Jer 15:21; Da 3:17 [a] S Ge 28:3 [b] 1Ch 5:1; Eze 47:13; Heb 11:21 [c] S Ge 28:13 [d] S Ge 12:2; S 13:14 **48:17** [e] ver 13 [f] S ver 14 **48:18** [g] S ver 14 **48:19** [h] Ge 17:20 [i] S Ge 25:23 [j] S Ge 12:2 **48:20** [k] S Ge 24:60 [l] Heb 11:21 [m] S ver 2 [n] Lev 9:22; Nu 6:23; Dt 10:8; 21:5 [o] Nu 2:18; Jer 31:9 [p] S Ge 41:51; Nu 2:20; 10:23; Ru 4:11 **48:21** [q] S Ge 26:3 [r] S Ge 15:16; S 28:13; Dt 30:3; Ps 126:1; Jer 29:14; Eze 34:13 **48:22** [s] Jos 24:32; Jn 4:5 [t] Ge 37:8 [u] S Ge 34:26 **49:1** [v] Nu 24:14; Dt 31:29; Jer 23:20; Da 2:28,45 **49:2** [w] Jos 24:1 [x] ver 16,28; Ps 34:11 **49:3** [y] S Ge 29:32; S 41:51 [z] Dt 21:17; Ps 78:51; 105:36 [a] S Ge 34:19 **49:4** [b] Isa 57:20; Jer 49:23 [c] S Ge 29:29; S 34:5 **49:5** [d] S Ge 29:33 [e] Ge 29:34 [f] S Ge 34:25; S Pr 4:17 **49:6** [g] Ps 1:1; Pr 1:15; Eph 5:11 [h] S Ge 34:26 [i] Jos 11:6,9; 2Sa 8:4; 1Ch 18:4

48:15 *blessed.* As his father Isaac had blessed him (27:27–29). *Joseph.* Used here collectively for Ephraim and Manasseh (see NIV text note on v. 21). *before whom ... Abraham and Isaac walked faithfully.* See notes on 5:22; 17:1. *shepherd.* Widely used in the ancient Near East as a metaphor for the king. It highlighted his care for his people. Here and in 49:24 it is used of God (see Ps 23:1 and note).

48:16 *Angel.* See note on 16:7. The angel—God himself—had earlier blessed Jacob (see 32:29; see also note on 32:24).

48:19 *his younger brother will be greater than he.* See note on 25:23. During the divided monarchy (930–722 BC), Ephraim's descendants were the most powerful tribe in the north. "Ephraim" was commonly used in the prophetic books to refer to the northern kingdom as a whole (see, e.g., Isa 7:2,5,8–9; Hos 9:13; 12:1,8).

48:20 *he put Ephraim ahead of Manasseh.* Jacob, the younger son who struggled with Esau for the birthright and blessing and who preferred the younger sister (Rachel) above the older (Leah), now advanced Joseph's younger son ahead of the older.

48:21 *Joseph.* See note on v. 15. *I am about to die.* Years later, Joseph spoke these words to his brothers (50:24).

48:22 *ridge of land.* The Hebrew for this phrase is identical with the place-name Shechem, where Joseph was later buried in a plot of ground inherited by his descendants (see Jos 24:32 and note; see also 33:19; Jn 4:5 and note). *I took from the Amorites.* Possibly referring to the event of 34:25–29.

49:2–27 Often called the "Blessing of Jacob," this is the longest poem in Genesis. Its various blessings were intended not only for Jacob's 12 sons but also for the tribes that descended from them (see v. 28). For other poetic blessings in Genesis, see 9:26–27; 14:19–20; 27:27–29; 27:39–40; 48:15–16; 48:20.

49:4 *Turbulent.* Reuben's descendants were characterized by indecision (see Jdg 5:15–16). *you will no longer excel, for you went up onto your father's bed.* See 35:22 and note; see also notes on 37:21; 48:5.

49:5 *Simeon and Levi are brothers.* They shared the traits of violence, anger and cruelty (see vv. 6–7; see also note on 34:25).

7 Cursed be their anger, so fierce,
and their fury,[j] so cruel![k]
I will scatter them in Jacob
and disperse them in Israel.[l]

8 "Judah,[a][m] your brothers will praise you;
your hand will be on the neck[n] of your enemies;
your father's sons will bow down to you.[o]
9 You are a lion's[p] cub,[q] Judah;[r]
you return from the prey,[s] my son.
Like a lion he crouches and lies down,
like a lioness—who dares to rouse him?
10 The scepter will not depart from Judah,[t]
nor the ruler's staff from between his feet,[b]
until he to whom it belongs[c] shall come[u]
and the obedience of the nations shall be his.[v]
11 He will tether his donkey[w] to a vine,
his colt to the choicest branch;[x]
he will wash his garments in wine,
his robes in the blood of grapes.[y]
12 His eyes will be darker than wine,
his teeth whiter than milk.[d][z]

13 "Zebulun[a] will live by the seashore
and become a haven for ships;
his border will extend toward Sidon.[b]

14 "Issachar[c] is a rawboned[e] donkey
lying down among the sheep pens.[f][d]
15 When he sees how good is his resting place
and how pleasant is his land,[e]
he will bend his shoulder to the burden[f]
and submit to forced labor.[g]

16 "Dan[g][h] will provide justice for his people
as one of the tribes of Israel.[i]
17 Dan[j] will be a snake by the roadside,
a viper along the path,[k]
that bites the horse's heels[l]
so that its rider tumbles backward.

18 "I look for your deliverance,[m] LORD.[n]

19 "Gad[h][o] will be attacked by a band of raiders,
but he will attack them at their heels.[p]

20 "Asher's[q] food will be rich;[r]
he will provide delicacies fit for a king.[s]

21 "Naphtali[t] is a doe set free
that bears beautiful fawns.[i][u]

22 "Joseph[v] is a fruitful vine,[w]
a fruitful vine near a spring,
whose branches[x] climb over a wall.[j]

49:7 [j]Ge 34:7 [k]Ge 34:25 [l]Jos 19:1,9; 21:1-42 **49:8** [m]S Ge 29:35 [n]Dt 28:48 [o]S Ge 9:25; 1Ch 5:2 **49:9** [p]Nu 24:9; Ps 7:2; 10:9; Eze 19:5; Mic 5:8 [q]Eze 19:2 [r]Rev 5:5 [s]ver 27; Nu 23:24; Job 38:39; Ps 17:12; 22:13; 104:21 **49:10** [t]Nu 24:17,19; Jdg 1:1-2; 20:18; 1Ch 5:2; 28:4; Ps 60:7; 108:8 [u]Eze 21:27 [v]Ps 2:9; 72:8-11; 98:3; 110:2; Isa 2:4; 26:18; 42:1,4; 45:22; 48:20; 49:6; 51:5 **49:11** [w]Jdg 5:10; 10:4; Zec 9:9 [x]Dt 8:8; 2Ki 18:32 [y]Dt 32:14; Isa 63:2 **49:12** [z]SS 5:12 **49:13** [a]S Ge 30:20 [b]S Ge 10:19 **49:14** [c]S Ge 30:18 [d]Jdg 5:16; Ps 68:13 **49:15** [e]Jos 19:17-23 [f]Eze 29:18 [g]1Ki 4:6; 5:13; 9:21; Isa 14:2; 31:8 **49:16** [h]Ge 30:6 [i]S ver 2 **49:17** [j]Jdg 18:27 [k]Jer 8:17; Am 9:3 [l]ver 19 **49:18** [m]S Ge 45:7; Ps 40:1-3 [n]Ps 119:166, 174 **49:19** [o]S Ge 30:11 [p]ver 17 **49:20** [q]S Ge 30:13 [r]Isa 25:6 [s]Job 29:6 **49:21** [t]S Ge 30:8 [u]Job 39:1 **49:22** [v]Ge 30:24 [w]S Ge 17:6; Ps 128:3; Eze 19:10 [x]Ps 80:10

[a] 8 *Judah* sounds like and may be derived from the Hebrew for *praise.* [b] 10 Or *from his descendants* [c] 10 Or *to whom tribute belongs*; the meaning of the Hebrew for this phrase is uncertain. [d] 12 Or *will be dull from wine, / his teeth white from milk* [e] 14 Or *strong* [f] 14 Or *the campfires*; or *the saddlebags* [g] 16 *Dan* here means *he provides justice.* [h] 19 *Gad* sounds like the Hebrew for *attack* and also for *band of raiders.* [i] 21 Or *free; / he utters beautiful words* [j] 22 Or *Joseph is a wild colt, / a wild colt near a spring, / a wild donkey on a terraced hill*

49:7 *I will scatter them.* Fulfilled when Simeon's descendants were absorbed into the territory of Judah (see Jos 19:1,9 and note on 19:1) and when Levi's descendants were dispersed throughout the land, living in 48 towns and the surrounding pasturelands (see note on 48:6; see also Nu 35:2,7; Jos 14:4; 21:41).
49:8 Cf. 27:29,40; 37:7,9. *Judah, your brothers ... will bow down to you.* See note on 43:3. As those who would become the leading tribes of southern and northern Israel, respectively, Judah and Joseph were given the longest (vv. 8–12 and vv. 22–26) of Jacob's blessings. Judah was the fourth of Leah's sons and also the fourth son born to Jacob (29:35), but Reuben, Simeon and Levi had forfeited their right of leadership. So Jacob assigns leadership to Judah (a son of Leah) but a double portion to Joseph (a son of Rachel). See also 1Ch 5:2.
49:9 *You are a lion's cub.* A symbol of sovereignty, strength and courage. Judah (or Israel) is often pictured as a lion in later times (see Eze 19:2; Mic 5:8 and notes; and especially Nu 24:9). Judah's greatest descendant, Jesus Christ (see note on 43:3), is himself called "the Lion of the tribe of Judah" (Rev 5:5; see note there).
49:10 Though difficult to translate (see NIV text note), the verse has been traditionally understood as Messianic. It was initially fulfilled in David, and ultimately in Christ. *scepter.* See Nu 24:17 and note. *until he to whom it belongs shall come.* Repeated almost verbatim in Eze 21:27 (see note there) in a section where Zedekiah, the last king of Judah, is told to "remove the crown" (Eze 21:26) from his head because dominion over Jerusalem will ultimately be given to the one "to whom it rightfully belongs" (v. 27).
49:11 Judah's descendants would someday enjoy a settled and prosperous life.
49:13 Though landlocked by the tribes of Asher and Manasseh, the descendants of Zebulun were close enough to the Mediterranean (within ten miles) to "feast on the abundance of the seas" (Dt 33:19).
49:17 *Dan will be a snake.* The treachery of a group of Danites in later times is described in Jdg 18:27. *bites the horse's heels.* Samson, from the tribe of Dan, would single-handedly hold the Philistines at bay (Jdg 14–16).
49:18 Jacob pauses midway through his series of blessings to utter a brief prayer for God's help.
49:19 *Gad will be attacked.* Located east of the Jordan (see Jos 13:24–27), the descendants of Gad were vulnerable to raids by the Moabites to the south, as the Mesha (see 2Ki 3:4) Stele (a Moabite inscription dating from the late ninth century BC) illustrates (see chart, p. xxiii).
49:20 *Asher's food will be rich.* Fertile farmlands near the Mediterranean (see Jos 19:24–30) would ensure the prosperity of Asher's descendants.
49:21 *Naphtali is a doe set free.* Perhaps a reference to an independent spirit fostered in the descendants of Naphtali by their somewhat isolated location in the hill country north of the Sea of Galilee (see Jos 19:32–38).
49:22 *fruitful ... fruitful.* A pun on the name Ephraim (see NIV text note on 41:52), who Jacob predicted would be greater

23 With bitterness archers attacked him;[y]
they shot at him with hostility.[z]
24 But his bow remained steady,[a]
his strong arms[b] stayed[a] limber,
because of the hand of the Mighty One
of Jacob,[c]
because of the Shepherd,[d] the Rock
of Israel,[e]
25 because of your father's God,[f] who
helps[g] you,
because of the Almighty,[b h] who
blesses you
with blessings of the skies above,
blessings of the deep springs
below,[i]
blessings of the breast[j] and womb.[k]
26 Your father's blessings are greater
than the blessings of the ancient
mountains,
than[c] the bounty of the age-old hills.[l]
Let all these rest on the head of
Joseph,[m]
on the brow of the prince among[d]
his brothers.[n]
27 "Benjamin[o] is a ravenous wolf;[p]
in the morning he devours the prey,[q]
in the evening he divides the
plunder."[r]

28 All these are the twelve tribes of Israel,[s] and this is what their father said to
them when he blessed them, giving each
the blessing[t] appropriate to him.

The Death of Jacob

29 Then he gave them these instructions:[u]
"I am about to be gathered to my people.[v]
Bury me with my fathers[w] in the cave in
the field of Ephron the Hittite,[x] 30 the cave
in the field of Machpelah,[y] near Mamre[z]
in Canaan, which Abraham bought along
with the field[a] as a burial place[b] from
Ephron the Hittite. 31 There Abraham[c] and
his wife Sarah[d] were buried, there Isaac
and his wife Rebekah[e] were buried, and
there I buried Leah.[f] 32 The field and the
cave in it were bought from the Hittites.[e g]"
33 When Jacob had finished giving instructions to his sons, he drew his feet up
into the bed, breathed his last and was
gathered to his people.[h]

50 Joseph threw himself on his father and wept over him and kissed
him.[i] 2 Then Joseph directed the physicians
in his service to embalm his father Israel.
So the physicians embalmed him,[j] 3 taking
a full forty days, for that was the time required for embalming. And the Egyptians
mourned for him seventy days.[k]
4 When the days of mourning[l] had
passed, Joseph said to Pharaoh's court,[m]
"If I have found favor in your eyes,[n] speak
to Pharaoh for me. Tell him, 5 'My father
made me swear an oath[o] and said, "I am
about to die;[p] bury me in the tomb I dug
for myself[q] in the land of Canaan."[r] Now
let me go up and bury my father;[s] then I
will return.' "
6 Pharaoh said, "Go up and bury your
father, as he made you swear to do."
7 So Joseph went up to bury his father. All
Pharaoh's officials[t] accompanied him—the
dignitaries of his court[u] and all the dignitaries of Egypt— 8 besides all the members of
Joseph's household and his brothers and
those belonging to his father's household.[v]
Only their children and their flocks and
herds were left in Goshen.[w] 9 Chariots[x] and
horsemen[f] also went up with him. It was a
very large company.

49:23 [y] 1Ch 10:3 [z] S Ge 27:41; S 37:24 **49:24** [a] Job 29:20 [b] Ps 18:34; Isa 63:12 [c] Ps 132:2, 5; Isa 1:24; 10:34; 49:26; 60:16 [d] S Ge 48:15 [e] Dt 32:4, 15, 18, 31; 1Sa 2:2; 2Sa 22:32; Ps 18:2, 31; 19:14; 78:35; 89:26; 144:1; Isa 17:10; 26:4; 30:29; 44:8; Hab 1:12 **49:25** [f] S Ge 28:13 [g] Ex 18:4; Ps 27:9 [h] S Ge 17:1 [i] S Ge 27:28 [j] Isa 66:11 [k] Dt 7:13; 28:4; Ps 107:38; Pr 10:22 **49:26** [l] Hab 3:6 [m] 1Ch 5:1; Eze 47:13 [n] S Ge 37:8 **49:27** [o] Ge 35:18; Jdg 20:12-13 [p] Hab 1:8; Zep 3:3 [q] S ver 9 [r] Nu 31:11; Dt 2:35; Jos 7:21; 8:2; 22:8; Jdg 8:24 **49:28** [s] S ver 2 [t] S Ge 27:4 **49:29** [u] Ge 50:16 [v] S Ge 25:8 [w] S Ge 15:15; 50:25; 2Sa 2:32; 19:37 [x] S Ge 25:9 **49:30** [y] S Ge 23:9 [z] S Ge 13:18 [a] S Ge 23:20 [b] S Ge 23:4 **49:31** [c] Ge 25:9 [d] Ge 23:19 [e] S Ge 24:67 [f] S Ge 23:20; S 29:16 **49:32** [g] S Ge 10:15

[a] 23,24 Or *archers will attack . . . will shoot . . . will remain . . . will stay* [b] 25 Hebrew *Shaddai* [c] 26 Or *of my progenitors, / as great as* [d] 26 Or *of the one separated from* [e] 32 Or *the descendants of Heth* [f] 9 Or *charioteers*

49:33 [h] S Ge 25:8; Ac 7:15 **50:1** [i] S Ge 29:11; S 46:4 **50:2** [j] ver 26; 2Ch 16:14; Mt 26:12; Mk 16:1; Jn 19:39-40 **50:3** [k] S Ge 37:34; S Dt 1:3 **50:4** [l] S Ge 27:41 [m] ver 7 [n] S Ge 30:27; S 32:5 **50:5** [o] S Ge 24:37 [p] ver 24 [q] 2Sa 18:18; 2Ch 16:14; Isa 22:16; Mt 27:60 [r] Ge 47:31 [s] Mt 8:21 **50:7** [t] Ge 45:16 [u] ver 4 **50:8** [v] ver 14 [w] S Ge 45:10 **50:9** [x] S Ge 41:43

than Joseph's firstborn son, Manasseh (48:19–20). *branches climb over a wall.* Ephraim's descendants tended to expand their territory (see Jos 17:14–18).

49:24 *his bow remained steady.* The warlike Ephraimites (see Jdg 8:1; 12:1) would often prove victorious in battle (see Jos 17:18). *Mighty One of Jacob.* Stresses the activity of God in saving and redeeming his people (see Isa 49:26). *Shepherd.* See note on 48:15. *Rock of Israel.* Israel's sure defense (see Dt 32:4,15,18,30–31)—a figure often used also in Psalms (see note on Ps 18:2) and Isaiah.

49:25 *Almighty.* See note on 17:1. *blessings of the skies … of the deep springs.* The fertility of the soil watered by rains from above and springs and streams from below. *breast and womb.* The fertility of people and animals. For the later prosperity of Ephraim's descendants, see Hos 12:8.

49:26 *Joseph … prince among his brothers.* See notes on v. 8; 48:19. Ephraim would gain supremacy, especially over the northern tribes (see Jos 16:9; Isa 7:1–2; Hos 13:1).

49:27 *Benjamin is a ravenous wolf.* See the exploits of Ehud (Jdg 3:12–30) and Saul and Jonathan (1Sa 11–15). See Jdg 19–21 for examples of the savagery that characterized one group of Benjamin's descendants.

49:28 *twelve tribes of Israel.* See note on vv. 2–27.

49:29 *Bury me with my fathers.* See note on 25:8. Jacob does not forget that the land of his ancestors is his God-appointed homeland (see note on 23:19).

49:33 *was gathered to his people.* See note on 25:8.

50:1 *wept.* See note on 43:30.

50:2 *physicians embalmed him.* Professional embalmers could have been hired for the purpose, but Joseph perhaps wanted to avoid involvement with the pagan religious ceremonies accompanying their services.

50:3 *forty days … seventy days.* The two periods probably overlapped.

50:5 *My father made me swear an oath.* See 47:29–31. *dug.* Or "bought," as the Hebrew for this verb is translated in Hos 3:2

10When they reached the threshing
floor[y] of Atad, near the Jordan, they lamented loudly and bitterly;[z] and there
Joseph observed a seven-day period[a] of
mourning[b] for his father.[c] 11When the Canaanites[d] who lived there saw the mourning at the threshing floor of Atad, they
said, "The Egyptians are holding a solemn
ceremony of mourning."[e] That is why that
place near the Jordan is called Abel Mizraim.[a]
12So Jacob's sons did as he had commanded them:[f] 13They carried him to the
land of Canaan and buried him in the cave
in the field of Machpelah,[g] near Mamre,[h]
which Abraham had bought along with
the field[i] as a burial place from Ephron the
Hittite.[j] 14After burying his father, Joseph
returned to Egypt, together with his brothers and all the others who had gone with
him to bury his father.[k]

Joseph Reassures His Brothers

15When Joseph's brothers saw that
their father was dead, they said, "What
if Joseph holds a grudge[l] against us and
pays us back for all the wrongs we did
to him?"[m] 16So they sent word to Joseph,
saying, "Your father left these instructions[n]
before he died: 17'This is what you are to
say to Joseph: I ask you to forgive your
brothers the sins[o] and the wrongs they
committed in treating you so badly.'[p] Now
please forgive the sins of the servants of
the God of your father.[q]" When their message came to him, Joseph wept.[r]
18His brothers then came and threw
themselves down before him.[s] "We are
your slaves,"[t] they said.
19But Joseph said to them, "Don't be
afraid. Am I in the place of God?[u] 20You intended to harm me,[v] but God intended[w] it
for good[x] to accomplish what is now being
done, the saving of many lives.[y] 21So then,
don't be afraid. I will provide for you and

50:10 [y] Nu 15:20; Ru 3:2; 2Sa 24:18; 1Ki 22:10 [z] 2Sa 1:17; 3:33; 2Ch 35:25; Eze 32:16; Ac 8:2 [a] 1Sa 31:13; Job 2:13; Eze 3:15 [b] S Ge 27:41; S Lev 10:6 [c] S Ge 37:34 **50:11** [d] S Ge 10:18 [e] S Ge 37:34 **50:12** [f] Ge 49:29 **50:13** [g] S Ge 23:9 [h] S Ge 13:18 [i] S Ge 23:20 [j] S Ge 25:9 **50:14** [k] ver 8 **50:15** [l] S Ge 27:41 [m] ver 17; S Ge 9:5; 37:28; Zep 3:11; 1Pe 3:9 **50:16** [n] Ge 49:29 **50:17** [o] S Mt 6:14 [p] S ver 15 [q] S Ge 28:13 [r] S Ge 29:11 **50:18** [s] S Ge 37:7 [t] S Ge 43:18 **50:19** [u] S Ge 30:2; S Ex 32:34; Ro 12:19; Heb 10:30 **50:20** [v] Ge 37:20 [w] Isa 10:7; Mic 4:11-12 [x] Ro 8:28 [y] S Ge 45:5; Est 4:14

[a] *11 Abel Mizraim* means *mourning of the Egyptians.*

(see also Dt 2:6). *go up.* To Hebron, which has a higher elevation than Goshen.
50:10 *threshing floor.* Grain was threshed on a flat, circular area, either of rock or of pounded earth. Threshing floors were located on an elevated, open place exposed to the wind, usually at the edge of town or near the main gate (see 1Ki 22:10). See note on Ru 1:22.
50:15 *holds a grudge ... and pays us back.* Similarly, Esau had once planned to kill Jacob as soon as Isaac died (see 27:41–45 and note).
50:17 *Joseph wept.* See note on 43:30.
50:18 *threw themselves down.* A final fulfillment of Joseph's earlier dreams (see note on 37:7; see also 37:9). *We are your slaves.* They had earlier expressed a similar willingness, but under quite different circumstances (see 44:9,33).
50:19 *Am I in the place of God?* See note on 30:2.
50:20 *God intended it for good.* See 45:5 and note. Their act, out of personal animosity toward a brother, had been used by God to save life—the life of the Israelites, the Egyptians and all the nations that came to Egypt to buy food

THE TRIBES OF **ISRAEL**

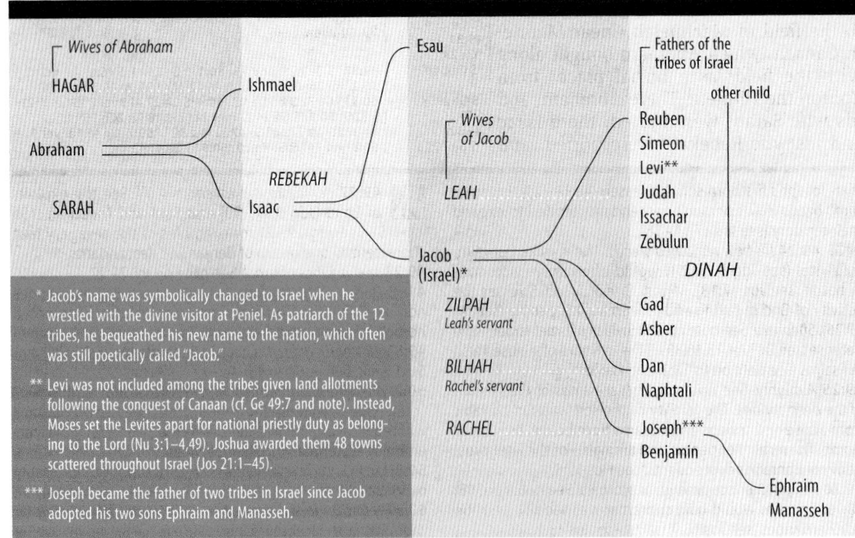
Wives of Abraham
HAGAR
Ishmael
Abraham
SARAH
Isaac
REBEKAH
Esau
Jacob (Israel)*
Wives of Jacob
LEAH
ZILPAH
Leah's servant
BILHAH
Rachel's servant
RACHEL
Fathers of the tribes of Israel
other child
Reuben
Simeon
Levi**
Judah
Issachar
Zebulun
DINAH
Gad
Asher
Dan
Naphtali
Joseph***
Benjamin
Ephraim
Manasseh
* Jacob's name was symbolically changed to Israel when he wrestled with the divine visitor at Peniel. As patriarch of the 12 tribes, he bequeathed his new name to the nation, which often was still poetically called "Jacob."
** Levi was not included among the tribes given land allotments following the conquest of Canaan (cf. Ge 49:7 and note). Instead, Moses set the Levites apart for national priestly duty as belonging to the Lord (Nu 3:1–4,49). Joshua awarded them 48 towns scattered throughout Israel (Jos 21:1–45).
*** Joseph became the father of two tribes in Israel since Jacob adopted his two sons Ephraim and Manasseh.

your children.[z]" And he reassured them
and spoke kindly[a] to them.

The Death of Joseph

22 Joseph stayed in Egypt, along with all
his father's family. He lived a hundred and
ten years[b] 23 and saw the third generation[c]
of Ephraim's[d] children.[e] Also the children
of Makir[f] son of Manasseh[g] were placed at
birth on Joseph's knees.[a][h]
24 Then Joseph said to his brothers, "I
am about to die.[i] But God will surely come
to your aid[j] and take you up out of this

50:21 [z]S Ge 45:11 [a]S Ge 34:3; Eph 4:32 **50:22** [b]S Ge 25:7; Jos 24:29 **50:23** [c]Job 42:16 [d]S Ge 41:52 [e]S Ge 48:11 [f]Nu 26:29; 27:1; 32:39, 40; 36:1; Dt 3:15; Jos 13:31; 17:1; Jdg 5:14 [g]S Ge 41:51 [h]S Ge 48:12 **50:24** [i]ver 5

land to the land[k] he promised on oath to
Abraham,[l] Isaac[m] and Jacob."[n] 25 And Joseph made the Israelites swear an oath[o]
and said, "God will surely come to your
aid, and then you must carry my bones[p]
up from this place."[q]
26 So Joseph died[r] at the age of a hundred and ten.[s] And after they embalmed
him,[t] he was placed in a coffin in Egypt.

[a] *23* That is, were counted as his

[j]Ru 1:6; Ps 35:2; 106:4; Isa 38:14 [k]S Ge 15:14 [l]S Ge 13:17 [m]S Ge 17:19 [n]S Ge 12:7; S 15:16 **50:25** [o]S Ge 24:37 [p]S Ge 49:29 [q]S Ge 47:29-30; Heb 11:22 **50:26** [r]Ex 1:6 [s]S Ge 25:7 [t]S ver 2

in the face of a famine that threatened the known world. At the same time, God showed by these events that his purpose for the nations is life and that this purpose would be effected through the descendants of Abraham.

50:23 *saw the third generation.* Cf. Job's experience (Job 42:16). *Makir.* Manasseh's firstborn son and the ancestor of the powerful Gileadites (Jos 17:1). The name of Makir later became almost interchangeable with that of Manasseh himself (see Jdg 5:14 and note). *placed at birth on Joseph's knees.* Joseph probably adopted Makir's children (see note on 30:3).

50:24 *I am about to die.* See note on 48:21. *God will ... take you up out of this land.* Joseph did not forget God's promises (cf. 15:16; 46:4; 48:21) concerning "the exodus" (Heb 11:22).

50:25 See 47:29–31 for a similar request by Jacob. *carry my bones up from this place.* Centuries later Moses did so to fulfill his ancestor's oath (see Ex 13:19). Joseph's bones were eventually "buried at Shechem in the tract of land that Jacob bought ... from the sons of Hamor" (Jos 24:32; see note there; see also Ge 33:19).

50:26 *Joseph died at the age of a hundred and ten.* See v. 22. Ancient Egyptian records indicate that 110 years was considered to be the ideal life span; to the Egyptians this would have signified divine blessing upon Joseph (see Jos 24:29).

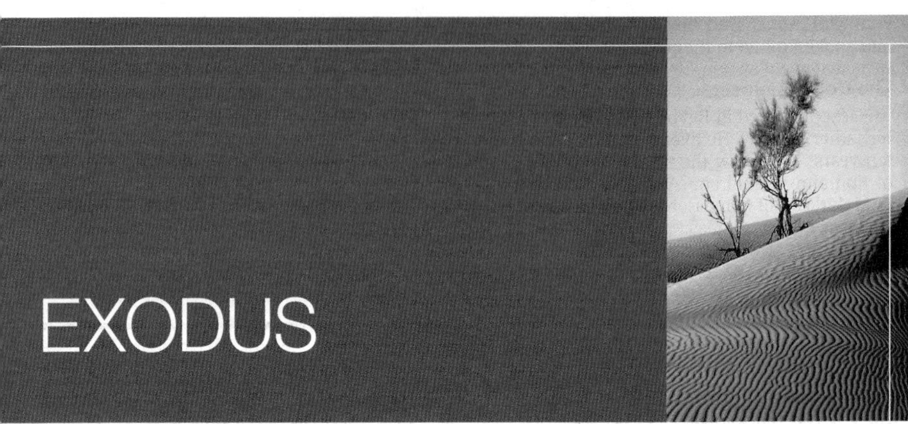

EXODUS

INTRODUCTION

Title

The word "Exodus" is derived from the Greek *Exodos*, the name given to the book by those who translated the Septuagint (the pre-Christian Greek translation of the OT). "Exodus" means "exit," "departure" (see Lk 9:31; Heb 11:22). The name was retained by the Latin Vulgate, by the Jewish author Philo (a contemporary of Christ) and by the Syriac version. In Hebrew the book is named after its first two words, *we'elleh shemoth* ("And these are the names of"). The same phrase occurs in Ge 46:8, where it likewise introduces a list of the names of those Israelites "who went to Egypt" with Jacob. Thus Exodus was not intended to exist separately but was thought of as a continuation of a narrative that began in Genesis and was completed in Leviticus, Numbers and Deuteronomy. The first five books of the Bible are together known as the Pentateuch (see Introduction to Genesis: Author and Date of Writing).

Author and Date of Writing

Several statements in Exodus indicate that Moses wrote certain sections of the book (see 17:14; 24:4; 34:27). In addition, Jos 8:31 refers to the command of Ex 20:25 as having been "written in the Book of the Law of Moses." The NT also claims Mosaic authorship for various passages in Exodus (see, e.g., Mk 7:10; 12:26 and NIV text notes; see also Lk 2:22–23). Taken together, these references strongly suggest that Moses was largely responsible for writing the book of Exodus — a traditional view not convincingly challenged by the commonly held notion that the Pentateuch as a whole contains four underlying sources (see Introduction to Genesis: Author and Date of Writing).

Chronology

According to 1Ki 6:1 (see note there), the exodus took place 480 years before "the fourth year of Solomon's reign over Israel." Since that year was c. 966 BC, it has been traditionally held that the exodus occurred c. 1446. The "three hundred years" of Jdg 11:26 fit comfortably within this time span (see Introduction

a **quick** look

Author:
Moses

Audience:
God's chosen people, the Israelites

Date:
Between 1446 and 1406 BC

Theme:
God reveals himself to his people and delivers them from slavery in Egypt to establish a covenant with them in the desert.

to Judges: Background). In addition, although Egyptian chronology relating to the Eighteenth Dynasty remains somewhat uncertain, in the chronology followed here Thutmose II (1491 – 1479 BC) was the pharaoh of the oppression (which doubtless continued under Thutmose III), and Thutmose III (1479 – 1425) was the pharaoh of the exodus (see notes on 2:15,23; 3:10). See chart, p. 511.

On the other hand, the appearance of the name Rameses in 1:11 has led many to the conclusion that the Nineteenth-Dynasty pharaoh Seti I (1289 – 1278) and his son Rameses II (1279 – 1212) were the pharaohs of the oppression and the exodus, respectively. Furthermore, archaeological evidence of the destruction of numerous Canaanite cities in the thirteenth century BC has been interpreted as proof that Joshua's troops invaded the promised land in that century. These and similar lines of argument lead to a date for the exodus of c. 1279 (see Introduction to Joshua: Historical Setting).

The identity of the cities' attackers, however, cannot be positively ascertained. The raids may have been initiated by later Israelite armies or by Philistines or other outsiders. In addition, the archaeological evidence itself has become increasingly ambiguous, and recent evaluations have tended to redate some of it to the Eighteenth Dynasty. Also, the name Rameses in 1:11 could very well be the result of an editorial updating by someone who lived centuries after Moses — a procedure that probably accounts for the appearance of the same word in Ge 47:11 (see note there).

In short, there are no compelling reasons to modify in any substantial way the traditional 1446 BC date for the exodus of the Israelites from Egyptian bondage.

The Route of the Exodus

At least three routes of escape from Pithom and Rameses (1:11) have been proposed: (1) a northern route through the land of the Philistines (but see 13:17); (2) a middle route leading eastward across Sinai to Beersheba; and (3) a southern route along the west coast of Sinai to the southeastern extremities of the peninsula. The southern route seems most likely, since several of the sites in Israel's wilderness itinerary have been tentatively identified along it. See map, p. 2518, at the end of this study Bible; see also map, p. 117. The exact place where Israel crossed the "Red Sea" is uncertain, however (see notes on 13:18; 14:2).

Themes and Theology

Exodus lays a foundational theology in which God reveals his name, his attributes, his redemption, his law and how he is to be worshiped. It also reports the appointment and work of Moses as the mediator of the Sinaitic

Statue of Thutmose III, believed by some to be the pharaoh of the exodus

The Giza Pyramids of Khufu and Khafre in Egypt

covenant, describes the beginnings of the priesthood in Israel, defines the role of the prophet and relates how the ancient covenant relationship between God and his people (see note on Ge 17:2) came under a new administration (the covenant given at Mount Sinai).

Profound insights into the nature of God are found in chs. 3; 6; 33 – 34. The focus of these texts is on the fact and importance of his presence with his people (as signified by his name Yahweh — see notes on 3:14 – 15 — and by his glory among them). But emphasis is also placed on his attributes of justice, truthfulness, mercy, faithfulness and holiness. Thus to know God's "name" is to know him and to know his character (see 3:13 – 15; 6:3).

God is also the Lord of history. Neither the affliction of Israel nor the plagues in Egypt were outside his control. The pharaoh, the Egyptians and all Israel saw the power of God. There is no one like him, "majestic in holiness, awesome in glory, working wonders" (15:11; see note there).

It is reassuring to know that God remembers and is concerned about his people (see 2:24). What he had promised centuries earlier to Abraham, Isaac and Jacob he now begins to bring to fruition as Israel is freed from Egyptian bondage and sets out for the land of promise. The covenant at Sinai is but another step in God's fulfillment of his promise to the patriarchs (3:15 – 17; 6:2 – 8; 19:3 – 8).

The Biblical message of salvation is likewise powerfully set forth in this book. The verb "redeem"

What the Lord had promised centuries earlier to Abraham, Isaac and Jacob he now begins to bring to fruition as Israel is freed from Egyptian bondage and sets out for the land of promise.

is used, e.g., in 6:6; 15:13 (see notes on 6:6 – 8). But the heart of redemption theology is best seen in the Passover narrative (ch. 12), the ratification of the covenant (ch. 24) and the account of God's gracious renewal of that covenant after the Israelites' blatant unfaithfulness to it in their worship of the golden calf (see 34:1 – 14 and notes). The apostle Paul viewed the death of the Passover lamb as fulfilled in Christ (1Co 5:7). Indeed, John the Baptist called Jesus the "Lamb of God, who takes away the sin of the world" (Jn 1:29).

The foundation of Biblical ethics and morality is laid out first in the merciful character of God as revealed in the exodus itself and then in the Ten Commandments (20:1 – 17) and the ordinances of the Book of the Covenant (20:22 — 23:33), which taught Israel how to apply in a practical way the principles of the commandments.

The book concludes with an elaborate discussion of the theology of worship. Though costly in time, effort and monetary value, the tabernacle, in meaning and function, points to the "chief end of man," namely, "to glorify God and to enjoy him forever" (Westminster Shorter Catechism). By means of the tabernacle, the omnipotent, unchanging and transcendent God of the universe came to "dwell," or "tabernacle," with his people, thereby revealing his gracious nearness. God is not only mighty in Israel's behalf; he is also present in the nation's midst.

However, these theological elements do not merely sit side by side in the Exodus narrative. They receive their fullest and richest significance from the fact that they are embedded in the account of God's raising up his servant Moses (1) to liberate his people from Egyptian bondage, (2) to inaugurate his earthly kingdom among them by bringing them into a special national covenant with him, and (3) to erect within Israel God's royal tent. And this account of redemption from bondage leading to consecration in covenant and the pitching of God's royal tent on earth, all through the ministry of a chosen mediator, discloses God's purpose in history — the purpose he would fulfill through Israel, and ultimately through Jesus Christ, the supreme Mediator.

Outline

- I. Prologue (chs. 1 – 2)
  - A. Israel Blessed and Oppressed (ch. 1)
  - B. A Deliverer Prepared (ch. 2)
    1. Infant Moses spared (2:1 – 10)
    2. Mature Moses' escape from Egypt (2:11 – 25)
- II. God's Deliverance of Israel (chs. 3 – 18)
  - A. The Deliverer Called (3:1 – 10)
  - B. The Deliverer's Objections and Disqualifications Overcome (3:11 — 4:17)
  - C. The Deliverer Returns to Egypt (4:18 – 31)
  - D. Unsuccessful Attempts to Deliver (5:1 — 6:12)
    1. Oppression made more harsh (5:1 – 21)
    2. Promise of deliverance renewed (5:22 — 6:12)
  - E. The Deliverers Identified (6:13 – 27)
  - F. Judgment of Plagues on Egypt (6:28 — 11:10)
    1. Deliverer's commission renewed (6:28 — 7:7)
    2. Presenting the signs of divine authority (7:8 – 13)

3. First plague: water turned to blood (7:14–24)
4. Second plague: frogs (7:25—8:15)
5. Third plague: gnats (8:16–19)
6. Fourth plague: flies (8:20–32)
7. Fifth plague: against livestock (9:1–7)
8. Sixth plague: boils (9:8–12)
9. Seventh plague: hail (9:13–35)
10. Eighth plague: locusts (10:1–20)
11. Ninth plague: darkness (10:21–29)
12. Tenth plague announced: death of the firstborn (ch. 11)

G. The Passover (12:1–28)
H. The Exodus from Egypt (12:29–51)
I. The Consecration of the Firstborn (13:1–16)
J. Crossing the "Red Sea" (13:17—15:21)
   1. Deliverance at the "Red Sea" (13:17—14:31)
   2. Song at the sea (15:1–21)
K. Journey to Sinai (15:22—18:27)
   1. The waters of Marah (15:22–27)
   2. The manna and the quail (ch. 16)
   3. The waters of Meribah (17:1–7)
   4. The war with Amalek (17:8–16)
   5. Basic administrative structure (ch. 18)

III. Covenant at Sinai (chs. 19–24)
   A. The Covenant Proposed (ch. 19)
   B. The Decalogue (20:1–17)
   C. The Reaction of the People to God's Fiery Presence (20:18–21)
   D. The Book of the Covenant (20:22—23:33)
      1. Prologue (20:22–26)
      2. Laws on slaves (21:1–11)
      3. Laws on homicide (21:12–17)
      4. Laws on bodily injuries (21:18–32)
      5. Laws on property damage (21:33—22:15)
      6. Laws on society (22:16–31)
      7. Laws on justice and neighborliness (23:1–9)
      8. Laws on sacred seasons (23:10–19)
      9. Epilogue (23:20–33)
   E. Ratification of the Covenant (ch. 24)

IV. God's Royal Tent in Israel (chs. 25–40)
   A. Instructions concerning the Royal Tent (chs. 25–31)
      1. Collection of the materials (25:1–9)
      2. Furnishings of the tent (25:10–40)
         a. Ark and atonement cover (25:10–22)

- b. Table of the bread of the Presence (25:23 – 30)
- c. Gold lampstand (25:31 – 40)
3. The tent and its courtyard (26:1 — 27:19)
   - a. Curtains and frames (ch. 26)
   - b. Altar of burnt offering (27:1 – 8)
   - c. Courtyard (27:9 – 19)
4. The tent's personnel (27:20 — 29:46)
   - a. Priesthood (27:20 — 28:5)
   - b. Garments of the priests (28:6 – 43)
   - c. Ordination of the priests (ch. 29)
5. Remaining provisions concerning the tent (ch. 30)
   - a. Altar of incense (30:1 – 10)
   - b. Census tax (30:11 – 16)
   - c. Bronze basin (30:17 – 21)
   - d. Anointing oil and incense (30:22 – 38)
6. Appointment of skilled workers (31:1 – 11)
7. Observance of Sabbath rest (31:12 – 18)

B. Rebellion Threatens Withdrawal of God (chs. 32 – 34)

1. The golden calf (32:1 – 29)
2. Moses' mediation (32:30 – 35)
3. Threatened separation and Moses' prayer (ch. 33)
4. Renewal of the covenant (ch. 34)

C. God's Royal Tent Set Up (chs. 35 – 40)

1. Summons to build (35:1 – 19)
2. Voluntary gifts (35:20 – 29)
3. Bezalel and his skilled workers (35:30 — 36:7)
4. Progress of the work (36:8 — 39:31)
5. Moses' blessing (39:32 – 43)
6. Erection of God's royal tent (40:1 – 33)
7. Dedication of God's royal tent (40:34 – 38)

The Israelites Oppressed

1 These are the names of the sons of Israel[a] who went to Egypt with Jacob, each with his family: 2 Reuben, Simeon, Levi and Judah; 3 Issachar, Zebulun and Benjamin; 4 Dan and Naphtali; Gad and Asher.[b] 5 The descendants of Jacob numbered seventy[a] in all;[c] Joseph was already in Egypt.

6 Now Joseph and all his brothers and all that generation died,[d] 7 but the Israelites were exceedingly fruitful; they multiplied greatly, increased in numbers[e] and became so numerous that the land was filled with them.

8 Then a new king, to whom Joseph meant nothing, came to power in Egypt.[f] 9 "Look," he said to his people, "the Israelites have become far too numerous[g] for us.[h] 10 Come, we must deal shrewdly[i] with them or they will become even more numerous and, if war breaks out, will join our enemies, fight against us and leave the country."[j]

11 So they put slave masters[k] over them to oppress them with forced labor,[l] and they built Pithom and Rameses[m] as store cities[n] for Pharaoh. 12 But the more they were oppressed, the more they multiplied and spread; so the Egyptians came to dread the Israelites 13 and worked them ruthlessly.[o] 14 They made their lives bitter with harsh labor[p] in brick[q] and mortar and with all kinds of work in the fields; in all their harsh labor the Egyptians worked them ruthlessly.[r]

15 The king of Egypt said to the Hebrew midwives,[s] whose names were Shiphrah and Puah, 16 "When you are helping the Hebrew women during childbirth on the delivery stool, if you see that the baby is a boy, kill him; but if it is a girl, let her live."[t] 17 The midwives, however, feared[u] God and did not do what the king of Egypt had told them to do;[v] they let the boys live. 18 Then the king of Egypt summoned the midwives and asked them, "Why have you done this? Why have you let the boys live?"

19 The midwives answered Pharaoh, "Hebrew women are not like Egyptian women; they are vigorous and give birth before the midwives arrive."[w]

20 So God was kind to the midwives[x] and the people increased and became even more numerous. 21 And because the midwives feared[y] God, he gave them families[z] of their own.

22 Then Pharaoh gave this order to all his people: "Every Hebrew boy that is born

[a] 5 Masoretic Text (see also Gen. 46:27); Dead Sea Scrolls and Septuagint (see also Acts 7:14 and note at Gen. 46:27) *seventy-five*

1:1 [a] S Ge 46:8 **1:4** [b] Ge 35:22-26; Nu 1:20-43 **1:5** [c] S Ge 46:26 **1:6** [d] Ge 50:26; Ac 7:15 **1:7** [e] ver 9; S Ge 12:2; Dt 7:13; Eze 16:7 **1:8** [f] Jer 43:11; 46:2 **1:9** [g] S ver 7 [h] S Ge 26:16 **1:10** [i] Ge 15:13; Ex 3:7; 18:11; Ps 64:2; 71:10; 83:3; Isa 53:3 [j] Ps 105:24-25; Ac 7:17-19 **1:11** [k] Ex 3:7; 5:10, 13, 14 [l] S Ge 15:13; Ex 2:11; 5:4; 6:6-7; Jos 9:27; 1Ki 9:21; 1Ch 22:2; Isa 60:10 [m] S Ge 47:11 [n] 1Ki 9:19; 2Ch 8:4 **1:13** [o] ver 14; Ge 15:13-14; Ex 5:21; 16:3; Lev 25:43, 46, 53; Dt 4:20; 26:6; 1Ki 8:51; Ps 129:1; Isa 30:6; 48:10; Jer 11:4 **1:14** [p] Dt 26:6; Ezr 9:9; Isa 14:3 [q] S Ge 11:3 [r] Ex 2:23; 3:9; Nu 20:15; 1Sa 10:18; 2Ki 13:4; Ps 66:11; 81:6; Ac 7:19 **1:15** [s] S Ge 35:17 **1:16** [t] ver 22 **1:17** [u] ver 21; Pr 16:6 [v] 1Sa 22:17; Da 3:16-18; Ac 4:18-20; 5:29 **1:19** [w] Lev 19:11; Jos 2:4-6; 1Sa 19:14; 2Sa 17:20 **1:20** [x] Pr 11:18; 22:8; Ecc 8:12; Isa 3:10; Heb 6:10 **1:21** [y] S ver 17 [z] 1Sa 2:35; 2Sa 7:11, 27-29; 1Ki 11:38; 14:10

1:1 — 2:25 This first section of Exodus forms a prologue to the book. It describes how God blesses the Israelites to the point where they become a threat to the Egyptians. Oppression follows, but God raises up a deliverer in the person of Moses. Thus the stage is set for the conflict with the pharaoh and for Israel's redemption from Egypt.

1:1 – 5 These verses clearly indicate that Exodus was written as a continuation of Genesis. The Israelites lived in Egypt 430 years (see 12:40).

1:1 *These are the names of.* The same expression appears in Ge 46:8 at the head of a list of Jacob's descendants. *Israel ... Jacob.* Jacob had earlier been given the additional name Israel (see Ge 32:28; 35:10 and notes).

1:2 – 4 The sons of Leah (Reuben through Zebulun) and Rachel (Benjamin; Joseph is not mentioned because the list includes only those "who went to Egypt" with Jacob, v. 1) are listed in the order of their seniority and before the sons of Rachel's and Leah's female servants: Bilhah had Dan and Naphtali, Zilpah had Gad and Asher (see Ge 35:23 – 26).

1:5 *seventy.* See note on Ge 46:27.

1:6 – 7 From the death of Joseph to the rise of a "new king" (v. 8) was more than 200 years.

1:7 The language of this verse echoes that of God's benediction on humankind at the time of their creation (see Ge 1:28 and note). This benediction is renewed in the new beginning after the flood (see Ge 9:1 and note on 9:1 – 7) and subsequently becomes a centerpiece in the blessings promised and covenanted to Abraham (Ge 17:2,6; 22:17), Isaac (Ge 26:4) and Jacob (Ge 28:14; 35:11; 48:4). God's good intentions for humans when he created them were beginning to be realized in a special way in Israel's history — not in the history of Egypt or of any other world power in which dreams of another, though perhaps lesser, Babel were still cherished. See also notes on 39:32; Nu 1:46. *land.* Goshen (see note on Ge 45:10).

1:8 See Ac 7:18. *new king.* Probably Ahmose (1550 – 1525), the founder of the Eighteenth Dynasty, who expelled the Hyksos (foreign — predominantly Semitic — rulers of Egypt). *to whom Joseph meant nothing.* He did not know about the great blessing Joseph had been to Egypt many years before.

1:11 *slave masters.* The same official Egyptian designation appears on a wall painting in the Theban tomb of Rekhmire during the reign of the Eighteenth-Dynasty pharaoh Thutmose III (see Introduction: Chronology). *oppress them with forced labor.* See Ge 15:13. *Rameses.* See note on Ge 47:11. *Pharaoh.* The word, which is Egyptian in origin and means "great house," is a royal title rather than a personal name.

1:14 *made their lives bitter.* A fact commemorated in the Passover meal, which was eaten "with bitter herbs" (12:8). *all kinds of work in the fields.* Including pumping the waters of the Nile into the fields to irrigate them (see Dt 11:10).

1:15 *Hebrew.* See note on Ge 14:13. *Shiphrah and Puah.* Semitic, not Egyptian, names. Since the Israelites were so numerous, there were probably other midwives under Shiphrah and Puah.

1:16 *delivery stool.* The Hebrew term means lit. "two stones"; a woman sat on them while giving birth. *if ... a boy, kill him.* Boy babies are potential warriors and fathers.

1:17 See Ac 5:29 for a parallel in the early church. *feared God.* See note on Ge 20:11.

1:22 *all his people.* Failing to accomplish his purposes

you must throw into the Nile,[a] but let every girl live."[b]

The Birth of Moses

2 Now a man of the tribe of Levi[c] married a Levite woman,[d] 2 and she became pregnant and gave birth to a son. When she saw that he was a fine[e] child, she hid him for three months.[f] 3 But when she could hide him no longer, she got a papyrus[g] basket[a] for him and coated it with tar and pitch.[h] Then she placed the child in it and put it among the reeds[i] along the bank of the Nile. 4 His sister[j] stood at a distance to see what would happen to him.

5 Then Pharaoh's daughter went down to the Nile to bathe, and her attendants were walking along the riverbank.[k] She saw the basket among the reeds and sent her female slave to get it. 6 She opened it and saw the baby. He was crying, and she felt sorry for him. "This is one of the Hebrew babies," she said.

7 Then his sister asked Pharaoh's daughter, "Shall I go and get one of the Hebrew women to nurse the baby for you?"

8 "Yes, go," she answered. So the girl went and got the baby's mother. 9 Pharaoh's daughter said to her, "Take this baby and nurse him for me, and I will pay you." So the woman took the baby and nursed him. 10 When the child grew older, she took him to Pharaoh's daughter and he became her son. She named[l] him Moses,[b] saying, "I drew[m] him out of the water."

Moses Flees to Midian

11 One day, after Moses had grown up, he went out to where his own people[n] were and watched them at their hard labor.[o] He saw an Egyptian beating a Hebrew, one of his own people. 12 Looking this way and that and seeing no one, he killed the Egyptian and hid him in the sand. 13 The next day he went out and saw two Hebrews fighting. He asked the one in the wrong, "Why are you hitting your fellow Hebrew?"[p]

14 The man said, "Who made you ruler and judge over us?[q] Are you thinking of killing me as you killed the Egyptian?" Then Moses was afraid and thought, "What I did must have become known."

15 When Pharaoh heard of this, he tried to kill[r] Moses, but Moses fled[s] from Pharaoh and went to live in Midian,[t] where he sat down by a well. 16 Now a priest of Midian[u] had seven daughters, and they came to draw water[v] and fill the troughs[w] to water their father's flock. 17 Some shepherds came along and drove them away, but

1:22 [a] S Ge 41:1 [b] ver 16; Ac 7:19 **2:1** [c] S Ge 29:34 [d] ver 2; Ex 6:20; Nu 26:59 **2:2** [e] S Ge 39:6 [f] Heb 11:23 **2:3** [g] Isa 18:2 [h] Ge 6:14 [i] S Ge 41:2; S Job 8:11; Ac 7:21 **2:4** [j] Ex 15:20 **2:5** [k] Ex 7:15; 8:20 **2:10** [l] 1Sa 1:20 [m] 2Sa 22:17 **2:11** [n] Ac 7:23; Heb 11:24-26 [o] S Ex 1:11 **2:13** [p] Ac 7:26 **2:14** [q] S Ge 13:8; Ac 7:27* **2:15** [r] Ex 4:19 [s] S Ge 31:21 [t] Heb 11:27 **2:16** [u] Ex 3:1; 18:1 [v] S Ge 24:11 [w] S Ge 30:38

[a] 3 The Hebrew can also mean *ark*, as in Gen. 6:14.
[b] 10 *Moses* sounds like the Hebrew for *draw out*.

through the midwives, the pharaoh mobilized all the Egyptians to deal with the Israelite threat.

2:1 – 10 The birth of Moses. He was born a child of the oppression, was saved by means of an "ark" from the watery death decreed by the pharaoh, and was allowed to grow to maturity in the pharaoh's court. Thus Moses' early life paralleled in fundamental ways the life of Israel in Egypt, even as it contained also foreshadowings of things to come (see note on v. 2).

2:1 *a man ... a Levite woman.* Perhaps Amram and Jochebed (but see note on 6:20).

2:2 *a fine child.* Moses was "no ordinary child" (Ac 7:20; Heb 11:23). The account of Moses' remarkable deliverance in infancy foreshadows Israel's deliverance from Egypt that God would later effect through him.

2:3 *papyrus basket.* Each of the two Hebrew words lying behind this phrase is of Egyptian origin. The word for "basket" is used only here and of Noah's ark (see note on Ge 6:14). Moses' basket was a miniature version of the large, seaworthy "papyrus boats" mentioned in Isa 18:2. *reeds.* A word of Egyptian derivation, reflected in the proper name "Red Sea" (see NIV text note on 10:19).

2:4 *His sister.* Miriam (see 15:20).

2:5 *Pharaoh's daughter.* Perhaps the famous Eighteenth-Dynasty princess who later became Queen Hatshepsut (c. 1479 – 1458). Throughout this early part of Exodus, all the pharaoh's efforts to suppress Israel were thwarted by women: the midwives (1:17), the Israelite mothers (1:19), Moses' mother and sister (vv. 3 – 4,7 – 9), the pharaoh's daughter (here). The pharaoh's impotence to destroy the people of God is thus ironically exposed.

2:6 *baby ... crying.* The only place in the Bible that tells of an infant crying.

2:10 *he became her son.* Thus "Moses was educated in all the wisdom of the Egyptians" (Ac 7:22; see note there). The narrator here was not interested in describing what this involved. Instead, he cited in the following verses (11 – 12,13,16 – 17) three incidents that illustrated Moses' character as a champion of justice. *Moses.* The name, of Egyptian origin, means "is born" and forms the second element in such pharaonic names as Ahmose (see note on 1:8), Thutmose and Rameses (see note on 1:11). *drew him out.* A Hebrew wordplay on the name Moses (see NIV text note), emphasizing his providential rescue from the Nile. Thus Moses' name may also have served as a reminder of the great act of deliverance God worked through him at the "Red Sea" (see 13:17 — 14:31).

2:11 – 15 See Ac 7:23 – 29; Heb 11:24 – 27 and notes.

2:11 *Moses had grown up.* He was now 40 years old (see Ac 7:23).

2:14 *Who made you ruler and judge ... ?* Unwittingly, the speaker made a prediction that would be fulfilled 40 years later (see Ac 7:27,30,35). The Hebrew word for "judge" could also refer to a deliverer, as in the book of Judges (see Ac 7:35); it was often a synonym for "ruler" in the OT (see Ge 18:25 and note), as well as in ancient Canaanite usage. *Moses was afraid.* See note on Heb 11:27.

2:15 *Pharaoh.* Probably Thutmose II (1491 – 1479; see Introduction: Chronology). *Midian.* Named after one of Abraham's younger sons (see Ge 25:2; see also note on Ge 37:25). Midian flanked the eastern arm of the "Red Sea" (Gulf of Aqaba) on both sides (see map, p. 117). Dry and desolate, it formed a stark contrast to Moses' former home in the royal court. He lived in Midian 40 years (see Ac 7:29 – 30).

2:16 *priest of Midian.* Reuel (see v. 18), which means "friend of God." His other name, Jethro (see 3:1), may be a title meaning "his excellency."

Moses got up and came to their rescue[x] and watered their flock.[y]

[18]When the girls returned to Reuel[z] their father, he asked them, "Why have you returned so early today?"

[19]They answered, "An Egyptian rescued us from the shepherds. He even drew water for us and watered the flock."

[20]"And where is he?" Reuel asked his daughters. "Why did you leave him? Invite him to have something to eat."[a]

[21]Moses agreed to stay with the man, who gave his daughter Zipporah[b] to Moses in marriage. [22]Zipporah gave birth to a son, and Moses named him Gershom,[a][c] saying, "I have become a foreigner[d] in a foreign land."

[23]During that long period,[e] the king of Egypt died.[f] The Israelites groaned in their slavery[g] and cried out, and their cry[h] for help because of their slavery went up to God. [24]God heard their groaning and he remembered[i] his covenant[j] with Abraham, with Isaac and with Jacob. [25]So God looked on the Israelites and was concerned[k] about them.

Moses and the Burning Bush

3 Now Moses was tending the flock of Jethro[l] his father-in-law, the priest of Midian,[m] and he led the flock to the far side of the wilderness and came to Horeb,[n] the mountain[o] of God. [2]There the angel of the LORD[p] appeared to him in flames of fire[q] from within a bush.[r] Moses saw that though the bush was on fire it did not burn up. [3]So Moses thought, "I will go over and see this strange sight—why the bush does not burn up."

[4]When the LORD saw that he had gone over to look, God called[s] to him from within the bush,[t] "Moses! Moses!"

And Moses said, "Here I am."[u]

[5]"Do not come any closer,"[v] God said. "Take off your sandals, for the place where you are standing is holy ground."[w] [6]Then he said, "I am the God of your father,[b] the God of Abraham, the God of Isaac and the God of Jacob."[x] At this, Moses hid[y] his face, because he was afraid to look at God.[z]

[7]The LORD said, "I have indeed seen[a] the misery[b] of my people in Egypt. I have heard them crying out because of their slave drivers, and I am concerned[c] about their suffering.[d] [8]So I have come down[e] to rescue them from the hand of the Egyptians and to bring them up out of that land into a good and spacious land,[f] a land flowing with milk and honey[g]—the home

2:17 [x] 1Sa 30:8; Ps 31:2 [y] S Ge 29:10 **2:18** [z] Ex 3:1; 4:18; 18:1,5,12; Nu 10:29 **2:20** [a] Ge 18:2-5 **2:21** [b] Ex 4:25; 18:2; Nu 12:1 **2:22** [c] Jdg 18:30 [d] S Ge 23:4; Heb 11:13 **2:23** [e] Ac 7:30 [f] Ex 4:19 [g] S Ex 1:14 [h] ver 24; Ex 3:7,9; 6:5; Nu 20:15-16; Dt 26:7; Jdg 2:18; 1Sa 12:8; Ps 5:2; 18:6; 39:12; 81:7; 102:1; Jas 5:4 **2:24** [i] S Ge 8:1 [j] S Ge 9:15; 15:15; 17:4; 22:16-18; 26:3; 28:13-15; Ex 32:13; 2Ki 13:23; Ps 105:10,42; Jer 14:21 **2:25** [k] Ex 3:7; 4:31; Lk 1:25 **3:1** [l] S Ex 2:18; Jdg 1:16 [m] S Ex 2:16 [n] ver 12; Ex 17:6; 19:1-11,5; 33:6; Dt 1:2, 6; 4:10; 5:2; 29:1; 1Ki 19:8; Mal 4:4 [o] Ex 4:27; 18:5; 24:13; Dt 4:11, 15 **3:2** [p] S Ge 16:7; S Ex 12:23; S Ac 5:19

[a] 22 *Gershom* sounds like the Hebrew for *a foreigner there.* [b] 6 Masoretic Text; Samaritan Pentateuch (see Acts 7:32) *fathers*

[q] Ex 19:18; 1Ki 19:12 [r] ver 4; Ex 2:2-6; Dt 33:16; Mk 12:26; Lk 20:37; Ac 7:30 **3:4** [s] Ex 19:3; Lev 1:1 [t] Ex 4:5 [u] Ge 31:11; 1Sa 3:4; Isa 6:8 **3:5** [v] Jer 30:21 [w] S Ge 28:17; Ac 7:33* **3:6** [x] S Ge 24:12; S Ex 4:5; Mt 22:32*; Mk 12:26*; Lk 20:37*; Ac 3:13; 7:32* [y] 1Ki 19:13 [z] Ex 24:11; 33:20; Jdg 13:22; Job 13:11; 23:16; 30:15; Isa 6:5 **3:7** [a] 1Sa 9:16 [b] ver 16; S Ge 16:11; 1Sa 1:11; Ne 9:9; Ps 106:44 [c] S Ex 2:25; Ac 7:34* [d] S Ex 1:10 **3:8** [e] S Ge 11:5; Ac 7:34* [f] S Ge 12:7; S 15:14 [g] ver 17; Ex 13:5; 33:3; Lev 20:24; Nu 13:27; Dt 1:25; 6:3; 8:7-9; 11:9; 26:9; 27:3; Jos 5:6; Jer 11:5; 32:22; Eze 20:6

2:23–25 These verses turn the reader's attention back to Israel's miserable plight in Egypt. They show that God truly cares for his people and has not forgotten his covenant promises made to their ancestors. This sets the stage for God's active intervention to bring about Israel's deliverance. Four expressions refer to Israel's suffering: "groaned," "cried out," "cry for help" (v. 23), "groaning" (v. 24); and four verbs describe God's response: "heard," "remembered" (v. 24), "looked on," "was concerned about" (v. 25).

2:23 *king of Egypt.* Probably Thutmose II (see note on v. 15).

2:24 *covenant with Abraham.* See Ge 15:17–18; 17:7 and notes. *with Isaac.* See Ge 17:19; 26:24. *with Jacob.* See Ge 35:11–12.

3:1—18:27 The second main section of the book. It describes the deliverance of Israel from Egypt and includes the call of Moses, the plagues, the Passover, the exodus from Egypt, the crossing of the "Red Sea" and the journey to Sinai.

3:1 Like David (2Sa 7:8), Moses was called from tending the flock to be the shepherd of God's people. *Jethro.* See note on 2:16. *Horeb.* Means "desert," "desolation"; either (1) another name for Mount Sinai or (2) another high mountain in the same vicinity in the southeast region of the Sinai peninsula. Tradition identifies Mount Horeb with Ras es-Safsaf ("willow peak"), 6,500 feet high, and Mount Sinai with Jebel Musa ("mountain of Moses"), 7,400 feet high, but both identifications are uncertain.

3:2 *angel of the LORD.* Used interchangeably with "the LORD" and "God" in v. 4 (see note on Ge 16:7). *appeared to him in flames of fire.* God's revelation of himself and his will was often accompanied by fire (see 13:21; 19:18; Ge 15:17 and note; 1Ki 18:24,38).

3:4 Every true prophet was called by God (see, e.g., 1Sa 3:4; Isa 6:8; Jer 1:4–5; Eze 2:1–8; Hos 1:2; Am 7:15; Jnh 1:1–2; see also note on 7:1–2). *Moses! Moses! ... Here I am.* See notes on Ge 22:1,11.

3:5 *Take off your sandals.* A sign of respect and humility in the ancient Near East (see Jos 5:15). This practice is still followed by Muslims before entering a mosque. *holy.* The ground was not holy by nature but was made so by the divine presence (see, e.g., Ge 2:3). Holiness involves being consecrated to the Lord's service and thus being separated from the commonplace.

3:6 See 2:24 and note. *afraid to look at God.* See notes on Ge 16:13; 32:30. Later, as the Lord's servant, Moses would meet with God on Mount Sinai (19:3) and even ask to see God's glory (33:18).

3:8 *I have come down to rescue.* God may also come down to judge (see Ge 11:5–9; 18:21). *land flowing with milk and honey.* The traditional and proverbial description of the hill country of Canaan—in its original pastoral state. For a description of the natural bounty of Canaan, see note on Ne 9:25. *honey.* The Hebrew for "honey" refers to both bees' honey and the sweet, syrupy juice of dates. *Canaanites ... Jebusites.* See notes on Ge 10:6,15–16; 13:7. The list of the Canaanite nations ranges from two names (Ge 13:7) to five (Nu 13:29) to six (as here; see also Jdg 3:5) to ten (see Ge 15:19–21 and note) to twelve (Ge 10:15–18). The classic description includes seven names (see, e.g., Dt 7:1), seven being the number of completeness (see note on Ge 4:17–18).

of the Canaanites, Hittites, Amorites, Perizzites, Hivites[h] and Jebusites.[i] 9 And now
the cry of the Israelites has reached me,
and I have seen the way the Egyptians are
oppressing[j] them. 10 So now, go. I am sending[k] you to Pharaoh to bring my people the
Israelites out of Egypt."[l]
11 But Moses said to God, "Who am I[m]
that I should go to Pharaoh and bring the
Israelites out of Egypt?"
12 And God said, "I will be with you.[n]
And this will be the sign[o] to you that it
is I who have sent you: When you have
brought the people out of Egypt, you[a] will
worship God on this mountain.[p]"
13 Moses said to God, "Suppose I go to
the Israelites and say to them, 'The God of
your fathers has sent me to you,' and they
ask me, 'What is his name?'[q] Then what
shall I tell them?"
14 God said to Moses, "I AM WHO I AM.[b]
This is what you are to say to the Israelites: 'I AM[r] has sent me to you.'"
15 God also said to Moses, "Say to the
Israelites, 'The LORD,[c] the God of your fathers[s]—the God of Abraham, the God of
Isaac and the God of Jacob[t]—has sent me
to you.'

"This is my name[u] forever,
the name you shall call me
from generation to generation.[v]

16 "Go, assemble the elders[w] of Israel and
say to them, 'The LORD, the God of your
fathers—the God of Abraham, Isaac and
Jacob[x]—appeared to me and said: I have
watched over you and have seen[y] what
has been done to you in Egypt. 17 And I
have promised to bring you up out of your
misery in Egypt[z] into the land of the Canaanites, Hittites, Amorites, Perizzites, Hivites and Jebusites—a land flowing with
milk and honey.'[a]
18 "The elders of Israel will listen[b] to you.
Then you and the elders are to go to the
king of Egypt and say to him, 'The LORD,
the God of the Hebrews,[c] has met[d] with us.
Let us take a three-day journey[e] into the
wilderness to offer sacrifices[f] to the LORD
our God.' 19 But I know that the king of
Egypt will not let you go unless a mighty
hand[g] compels him. 20 So I will stretch out
my hand[h] and strike the Egyptians with
all the wonders[i] that I will perform among
them. After that, he will let you go.[j]
21 "And I will make the Egyptians favorably disposed[k] toward this people, so
that when you leave you will not go empty-handed.[l] 22 Every woman is to ask her
neighbor and any woman living in her
house for articles of silver[m] and gold[n] and
for clothing, which you will put on your
sons and daughters. And so you will plunder[o] the Egyptians."[p]

[a] 12 The Hebrew is plural. [b] 14 Or *I WILL BE WHAT I WILL BE* [c] 15 The Hebrew for *LORD* sounds like and may be related to the Hebrew for *I AM* in verse 14.

3:8 [h]Jos 11:3; Jdg 3:3; 2Sa 24:7 [i]S Ge 15:18-21; Ezr 9:1 **3:9** [j]S Ex 1:14; S Nu 10:9 **3:10** [k]Ex 4:12; Jos 24:5; 1Sa 12:8; Ps 105:26; Ac 7:34* [l]Ex 6:13,26; 12:41,51; 20:2; Dt 4:20; 1Sa 12:6; 1Ki 8:16; Mic 6:4 **3:11** [m]Ex 4:10; 6:12,30; Jdg 6:15; 1Sa 9:21; 15:17; 18:18; 2Sa 7:18; 2Ch 2:6; Isa 6:5; Jer 1:6 **3:12** [n]S Ge 26:3; S Ex 14:22; Ro 8:31 [o]Nu 26:10; Jos 2:12; Jdg 6:17; Ps 86:17; Isa 7:14; 8:18; 20:3; Jer 44:29 [p]S ver 1; Ac 7:7 **3:13** [q]S Ge 32:29 **3:14** [r]Ex 6:2-3; Jn 8:58; Heb 13:8; Rev 1:8; 4:8 **3:15** [s]Ge 31:42; Da 2:23 [t]S Ge 24:12 [u]Ex 6:3,7; 15:3; 23:21; 34:5-7; Lev 24:11; Dt 28:58; Ps 30:4; 83:18; 96:2; 97:12; 135:13; 145:21; Isa 42:8; Jer 16:21; 33:2; Hos 12:5 [v]Ps 45:17; 72:17; 102:12

3:16 [w]Ex 4:29; 17:5; Lev 4:15; Nu 11:16; 16:25; Dt 5:23; 19:12; Jdg 8:14; Ru 4:2; Pr 31:23; Eze 8:11 [x]S Ge 24:12 [y]Ex 4:31; 2Ki 19:16; 2Ch 6:20; Ps 33:18; 66:7 **3:17** [z]S Ge 15:16; 46:4; Ex 6:6 [a]S ver 8 **3:18** [b]Ex 4:1,8,31; 6:12,30 [c]S Ge 14:13 [d]Nu 23:4,16 [e]S Ge 30:36 [f]Ex 4:23; 5:1,3; 6:11; 7:16; 8:20, 27; 9:13; 10:9,26 **3:19** [g]Ex 4:21; 6:6; 7:3; 10:1; 11:9; Dt 4:34; 2Ch 6:32 **3:20** [h]Ex 6:1,6; 7:4-5; 9:15; 13:3,9,14,16; 15:6,12; Dt 4:34,37; 5:15; 7:8; 26:8; 2Ki 17:36; 2Ch 6:32; Ps 118:15-16; 136:12; Isa 41:10; 63:12; Jer 21:5; 51:25; Da 9:15 [i]Ex 4:21; 7:3; 11:9,10; 15:11; 34:10; Nu 14:11; Dt 3:24; 4:34; 6:22; Ne 9:10; Ps 71:19; 72:18; 77:14; 78:43; 86:10; 105:27; 106:22; 135:9; 136:4; Jer 32:20; Mic 7:15; Ac 7:36 [j]Ex 11:1; 12:31-33 **3:21** [k]S Ge 39:21 [l]Ex 11:2; 2Ch 30:9; Ne 1:11; Ps 105:37; 106:46; Jer 42:12 **3:22** [m]Job 27:16-17 [n]Ex 11:2; 12:35; Ezr 1:4,6; 7:16; Ps 105:37 [o]S Ge 15:14; Eze 39:10 [p]Eze 29:10

3:10 *Pharaoh.* Probably Thutmose III (see Introduction: Chronology).
3:11 Moses' first expression of reluctance (see v. 13; 4:1,10,13 and notes).
3:12 *I will be with you.* See note on Ge 26:3. The Hebrew word translated "I will be" is the same as the one translated "I AM" in v. 14. *sign.* A visible proof or guarantee that what God had promised he would surely fulfill (see notes on 4:8; Ge 15:8).
3:13 Moses' second expression of reluctance. *What is his name?* God had not yet identified himself to Moses by name (see v. 6; cf. Ge 17:1).
3:14 *I AM WHO I AM.* The name by which God wished to be known and worshiped in Israel—the name that expressed his character as the dependable and faithful God who desires the full trust of his people (see v. 12, where "I will be" is completed by "with you"; see also 34:5–7). *I AM.* The shortened form of the name is perhaps found also in Ps 50:21; Hos 1:9 (see NIV text notes there). Jesus applied the phrase to himself; in so doing he claimed to be God and risked being stoned for blasphemy (see Jn 8:58–59 and notes).
3:15 *The LORD.* The Hebrew for this name is *Yahweh* (often incorrectly spelled "Jehovah"; see note on Dt 28:58). It means "He is" or "He will be" and is the third-person form of the verb translated "I will be" in v. 12 and "I AM" in v. 14. When God speaks of himself he says, "I AM," and when we speak of him we say, "He is."
3:16 *elders.* The Hebrew for this word means lit. "bearded ones," perhaps reflecting the age, wisdom, experience and influence necessary for a man expected to function as an elder. As heads of local families and tribes, "elders" had a recognized position also among the Babylonians, Hittites, Egyptians (see Ge 50:7), Moabites and Midianites (see Nu 22:7). Their duties included judicial arbitration and sentencing (see Dt 22:13–19), as well as military leadership (see Jos 8:10) and counsel (see 1Sa 4:3).
3:18 *Hebrews.* See note on Ge 14:13. *three-day journey.* See note on Ge 22:4. *wilderness.* God had met with Moses there (see vv. 1–2) and would meet with him there again (see v. 12). *to offer sacrifices.* Entries in extant logs of Egyptian supervisors show that such a request was not exceptional.
3:20 *wonders.* A prediction of the plagues that God would send against Egypt (see 7:14—12:30).
3:21–22 See 11:2–3; 12:35–36.
3:21 *when you leave you will not go empty-handed.* God had promised Abraham that after the Israelites had served for 400 years they would "come out with great possessions" (Ge 15:14; see Ps 105:37). Israel was to live by the same principle of providing gifts to a released slave (see Dt 15:12–15).
3:22 *plunder the Egyptians.* As if they had conquered them in battle.

Signs for Moses

4 Moses answered, "What if they do not
believe me or listen[q] to me and say,
'The LORD did not appear to you'?"
2Then the LORD said to him, "What is
that in your hand?"
"A staff,"[r] he replied.
3The LORD said, "Throw it on the
ground."
Moses threw it on the ground and it became a snake,[s] and he ran from it. 4Then
the LORD said to him, "Reach out your hand
and take it by the tail." So Moses reached
out and took hold of the snake and it turned
back into a staff in his hand. 5"This," said
the LORD, "is so that they may believe[t] that
the LORD, the God of their fathers—the
God of Abraham, the God of Isaac and the
God of Jacob—has appeared to you."
6Then the LORD said, "Put your hand inside your cloak." So Moses put his hand
into his cloak, and when he took it out,
the skin was leprous[a]—it had become as
white as snow.[u]
7"Now put it back into your cloak," he
said. So Moses put his hand back into his
cloak, and when he took it out, it was restored,[v] like the rest of his flesh.
8Then the LORD said, "If they do not
believe[w] you or pay attention to the first
sign,[x] they may believe the second. 9But if
they do not believe these two signs or listen to you, take some water from the Nile
and pour it on the dry ground. The water
you take from the river will become blood[y]
on the ground."
10Moses said to the LORD, "Pardon your
servant, Lord. I have never been eloquent,
neither in the past nor since you have spoken to your servant. I am slow of speech
and tongue."[z]
11The LORD said to him, "Who gave human beings their mouths? Who makes
them deaf or mute?[a] Who gives them sight
or makes them blind?[b] Is it not I, the LORD?
12Now go;[c] I will help you speak and will
teach you what to say."[d]
13But Moses said, "Pardon your servant,
Lord. Please send someone else."[e]
14Then the LORD's anger burned[f] against
Moses and he said, "What about your
brother, Aaron the Levite? I know he can
speak well. He is already on his way to
meet[g] you, and he will be glad to see you.
15You shall speak to him and put words in
his mouth;[h] I will help both of you speak
and will teach you what to do. 16He will
speak to the people for you, and it will be
as if he were your mouth[i] and as if you
were God to him.[j] 17But take this staff[k] in
your hand[l] so you can perform the signs[m]
with it."

Moses Returns to Egypt

18Then Moses went back to Jethro his
father-in-law and said to him, "Let me return to my own people in Egypt to see if
any of them are still alive."
Jethro said, "Go, and I wish you well."
19Now the LORD had said to Moses in
Midian, "Go back to Egypt, for all those
who wanted to kill[n] you are dead."[o] 20So
Moses took his wife and sons,[p] put them
on a donkey and started back to Egypt.
And he took the staff[q] of God in his hand.
21The LORD said to Moses, "When you
return to Egypt, see that you perform before Pharaoh all the wonders[r] I have given
you the power to do. But I will harden his

[a] 6 The Hebrew word for *leprous* was used for various diseases affecting the skin.

4:1 [q]S Ex 3:18 **4:2** [r]ver 17, 20; Ge 38:18; Ex 7:19; 8:5,16; 14:16,21; 17:5-6,9; Nu 17:2; 20:8; Jos 8:18; Jdg 6:21; 1Sa 14:27; 2Ki 4:29 **4:3** [s]Ex 7:8-12,15 **4:5** [t]ver 31; S Ex 3:6; 14:31; 19:9 **4:6** [u]Lev 13:2, 11; Nu 12:10; Dt 24:9; 2Ki 5:1, 27; 2Ch 26:21 **4:7** [v]2Ki 5:14; Mt 8:3; Lk 17:12-14 **4:8** [w]S Ex 3:18 [x]ver 30; Jdg 6:17; 1Ki 13:3; Isa 7:14; Jer 44:29 **4:9** [y]Ex 7:17-21 **4:10** [z]S Ex 3:11 **4:11** [a]Lk 1:20, 64 [b]Ps 94:9; 146:8; Mt 11:5; Jn 10:21 **4:12** [c]S Ex 3:10 [d]ver 15-16; Nu 23:5; Dt 18:15, 18; Isa 50:4; 51:16; Jer 1:9; Mt 10:19-20; Mk 13:11; S Lk 12:12 **4:13** [e]Jnh 1:1-3 **4:14** [f]Nu 11:1, 10,33; 12:9; 16:15; 22:22; 24:10; 32:13; Dt 7:25; Jos 7:1; Job 17:8 [g]ver 27; 1Sa 10:2-5 **4:15** [h]ver 30; Nu 23:5,12, 16; Dt 18:18; Jos 1:8; Isa 51:16; 59:21; Jer 1:9; 31:33 **4:16** [i]Ex 7:1-2; Jer 15:19; 36:6 [j]Nu 33:1; Ps 77:20; 105:26; Mic 6:4 **4:17** [k]S ver 2 [l]ver 20; Ex 17:9 [m]Ex 7:9-21; 8:5,16; 9:22; 10:12-15,21-23; 14:15-18,26; Nu 14:11; Dt 4:34; Ps 74:9; 78:43; 105:27 **4:19** [n]Ex 2:15 [o]Ex 2:23; Mt 2:20 **4:20** [p]Ex 2:22; 18:3; Ac 7:29 [q]S ver 2 **4:21** [r]S Ex 3:19,20

4:1–17 Moses has already voiced two reasons for his reluctance to obey God's call to rescue Israel from Egyptian bondage (see notes on 3:11,13). Here he states three more (vv. 1,10,13; see notes there). The Lord answers all three. Moses is now ready to return from Midian to Egypt (see vv. 18–31).
4:1 Moses' third expression of reluctance (in spite of God's assurance in 3:18).
4:2 *staff.* Probably a shepherd's crook.
4:3 *snake.* See 7:9–10 and note. Throughout much of Egypt's history the pharaoh wore a cobra made of metal on the front of his headdress as a symbol of his sovereignty.
4:8 *sign.* A supernatural event or phenomenon designed to demonstrate authority, provide assurance (see Jos 2:12–13), bear testimony (see Isa 19:19–20), give warning (see Nu 17:10) or encourage faith. See note on 3:12.
4:10 Moses' fourth expression of reluctance. *I am slow of speech and tongue.* Not in the sense of a speech impediment (see Ac 7:22). He complained, instead, of not being eloquent or quick-witted enough to respond to the pharaoh (see 6:12). Cf. the description of Paul in 2Co 10:10.
4:13 Moses' fifth and final expression of reluctance (see note on 3:11).
4:14 *the LORD's anger burned against Moses.* Although the Lord is "slow to anger" (34:6), he does not withhold his anger or punishment from his disobedient children forever (see 34:7). *Levite.* Under Aaron's leadership Israel's priesthood would come from the tribe of Levi.
4:15–16 See note on 7:1–2.
4:19 *all those ... are dead.* Including Thutmose II (see 2:15,23; see also Introduction: Chronology).
4:20 *sons.* Gershom (see 2:22) and Eliezer. The latter, though unmentioned by name until 18:4, had already been born.
4:21 *wonders.* See note on 3:20. *I will harden his heart.* Nine times in Exodus the hardening of the pharaoh's heart is ascribed to God (here; 7:3; 9:12; 10:1,20,27; 11:10; 14:4,8; see Jos 11:20; Ro 9:17–18 and notes); another nine times the pharaoh is said to have hardened his own heart (7:13–14,22; 8:15,19,32; 9:7,34–35). The pharaoh alone was the agent of the hardening in each of the first five plagues. Not until the sixth plague did God confirm the pharaoh's willful action (see 9:12), as he had told Moses he would do (see similarly Ro 1:24–28).

heart[s] so that he will not let the people
go.[t] 22Then say to Pharaoh, 'This is what
the LORD says: Israel is my firstborn son,[u]
23and I told you, "Let my son go,[v] so he
may worship[w] me." But you refused to let
him go; so I will kill your firstborn son.' "[x]
24At a lodging place on the way, the LORD
met Moses[a] and was about to kill[y] him.
25But Zipporah[z] took a flint knife, cut off
her son's foreskin[a] and touched Moses' feet
with it.[b] "Surely you are a bridegroom of
blood to me," she said. 26So the LORD let
him alone. (At that time she said "bridegroom of blood," referring to circumcision.)
27The LORD said to Aaron, "Go into the
wilderness to meet Moses." So he met Moses at the mountain[b] of God and kissed[c]
him. 28Then Moses told Aaron everything
the LORD had sent him to say, and also
about all the signs he had commanded
him to perform.
29Moses and Aaron brought together all
the elders[d] of the Israelites, 30and Aaron
told them everything the LORD had said to
Moses. He also performed the signs[e] before the people, 31and they believed.[f] And
when they heard that the LORD was concerned[g] about them and had seen their
misery,[h] they bowed down and worshiped.[i]

Bricks Without Straw

5 Afterward Moses and Aaron went to
Pharaoh and said, "This is what the
LORD, the God of Israel, says: 'Let my people go,[j] so that they may hold a festival[k] to
me in the wilderness.' "
2Pharaoh said, "Who is the LORD,[l] that
I should obey him and let Israel go? I do
not know the LORD and I will not let Israel go."[m]
3Then they said, "The God of the Hebrews has met with us. Now let us take
a three-day journey[n] into the wilderness
to offer sacrifices to the LORD our God, or
he may strike us with plagues[o] or with the
sword."
4But the king of Egypt said, "Moses
and Aaron, why are you taking the people away from their labor?[p] Get back to
your work!" 5Then Pharaoh said, "Look,
the people of the land are now numerous,[q]
and you are stopping them from working."
6That same day Pharaoh gave this order to the slave drivers[r] and overseers in
charge of the people: 7"You are no longer
to supply the people with straw for making
bricks;[s] let them go and gather their own
straw. 8But require them to make the same
number of bricks as before; don't reduce
the quota.[t] They are lazy;[u] that is why they
are crying out, 'Let us go and sacrifice to
our God.'[v] 9Make the work harder for the
people so that they keep working and pay
no attention to lies."
10Then the slave drivers[w] and the overseers went out and said to the people,
"This is what Pharaoh says: 'I will not
give you any more straw. 11Go and get
your own straw wherever you can find it,
but your work will not be reduced[x] at all.' "
12So the people scattered all over Egypt to
gather stubble to use for straw. 13The slave
drivers kept pressing them, saying, "Complete the work required of you for each
day, just as when you had straw." 14And
Pharaoh's slave drivers beat the Israelite
overseers they had appointed,[y] demanding, "Why haven't you met your quota of
bricks yesterday or today, as before?"
15Then the Israelite overseers went and

a 24 Hebrew *him* *b* 25 The meaning of the Hebrew for this clause is uncertain.

4:21 [s] Ex 7:3, 13; 8:15; 9:12, 35; 10:1, 20, 27; 11:10; 14:4, 8; Dt 2:30; Jos 11:20; 1Sa 6:6; Ps 105:25; Isa 6:10; 63:17; Jn 12:40; Ro 9:18 [t] Ex 8:32; 9:17 **4:22** [u] S Ge 10:15; Dt 32:6; Isa 9:6; 63:16; 64:8; Jer 3:19; 31:9; Hos 11:1; Mal 2:10; Ro 9:4; 2Co 6:18 **4:23** [v] Ex 5:1; 7:16 [w] S Ex 3:18 [x] Ge 49:3; Ex 11:5; 12:12, 29; Nu 8:17; 33:4; Ps 78:51; 105:36; 135:8; 136:10 **4:24** [y] Nu 22:22 **4:25** [z] S Ex 2:21 [a] Ge 17:14; Jos 5:2, 3 **4:27** [b] S Ex 3:1 [c] S Ge 27:27; S 29:13 **4:29** [d] S Ex 3:16 **4:30** [e] S ver 8 **4:31** [f] S Ex 3:18 [g] S Ex 2:25 [h] S Ge 16:11 [i] S Ge 24:26 **5:1** [j] S Ex 4:23 [k] S Ex 3:18 **5:2** [l] Jdg 2:10; Job 21:15; Mal 3:14 [m] Ex 3:19
5:3 [n] S Ge 30:36 [o] Lev 26:25; Nu 14:12; Dt 28:21; 2Sa 24:13 **5:4** [p] S Ex 1:11; 6:6-7 **5:5** [q] S Ge 12:2 **5:6** [r] S Ge 15:13 **5:7** [s] S Ge 11:3 **5:8** [t] ver 14, 18 [u] ver 17 [v] Ex 10:11
5:10 [w] ver 13; Ex 1:11 **5:11** [x] ver 19 **5:14** [y] ver 16; Isa 10:24

4:22 *firstborn son.* A figure of speech indicating Israel's special relationship with God (see Jer 31:9; Hos 11:1).
4:23 *kill your firstborn son.* Anticipates the tenth plague (see 11:5; 12:12).
4:24 *lodging place.* Perhaps near water, where travelers could spend the night. *the LORD ... was about to kill him.* Evidently because Moses had failed to circumcise his son (see Ge 17:9–14).
4:25 *Zipporah ... cut off her son's foreskin.* Sensing that divine displeasure had threatened Moses' life, she quickly performed the circumcision on their young son. *flint knife.* Continued to be used for circumcision long after metal was introduced, probably because flint knives were sharper than the metal instruments available and thus more efficient for the surgical procedure (see Jos 5:2 and note). *feet.* Probably a euphemism for "genitals," as in Dt 28:57 ("womb," lit. "feet").
4:26 *bridegroom of blood.* Circumcision may have been repulsive to Zipporah—though it was practiced for various reasons among many peoples of the ancient Near East.
4:27 *kissed.* See note on Ge 29:13.
4:30 *Aaron told them everything the LORD had said to Moses.* See note on 7:1–2.
5:1 *Pharaoh.* See note on 3:10.
5:3 See 3:18 and note. The reason for sacrificing where the Egyptians could not see them is given in 8:26 (see note on Ge 43:32).
5:6 *slave drivers.* Probably the same as the Egyptian "slave masters" in 1:11 (see note there). *overseers.* Israelite supervisors whose method of appointment and whose functions are indicated in vv. 14–16.
5:7 *straw.* Chopped and mixed with the clay as binder to make the bricks stronger. Canaanite Amarna letter 148.30–34 probably refers to the use of straw in making bricks. See photos, pp. 104, 105.
5:9 *lies.* See 4:29–31. The pharaoh labels all hopes of a quick release for Israel as presumptuous and false.
5:10 *This is what Pharaoh says.* In opposition to "This is what the LORD says" (4:22; 5:1). The pharaoh is now set on a collision course with the God of Israel.
5:15 *Israelite overseers ... appealed to Pharaoh.* During certain periods of Egyptian history slaves were permitted to appeal directly to the pharaoh, bypassing the ordinary chain of command. Egyptian records show that sometimes they were heard, but more often they were not.

appealed to Pharaoh: "Why have you treated your servants this way? 16 Your servants
are given no straw, yet we are told, 'Make
bricks!' Your servants are being beaten,
but the fault is with your own people."
17 Pharaoh said, "Lazy, that's what you
are—lazy![z] That is why you keep saying,
'Let us go and sacrifice to the LORD.' 18 Now
get to work.[a] You will not be given any
straw, yet you must produce your full quota of bricks."
19 The Israelite overseers realized they
were in trouble when they were told, "You
are not to reduce the number of bricks required of you for each day." 20 When they
left Pharaoh, they found Moses and Aaron waiting to meet them, 21 and they said,
"May the LORD look on you and judge[b]
you! You have made us obnoxious[c] to
Pharaoh and his officials and have put a
sword[d] in their hand to kill us."[e]

God Promises Deliverance

22 Moses returned to the LORD and said,
"Why, Lord, why have you brought trouble on this people?[f] Is this why you sent
me? 23 Ever since I went to Pharaoh to
speak in your name, he has brought trouble on this people, and you have not rescued[g] your people at all."

6 Then the LORD said to Moses, "Now
you will see what I will do to Pharaoh:
Because of my mighty hand[h] he will let
them go;[i] because of my mighty hand he
will drive them out of his country."[j]
2 God also said to Moses, "I am the LORD.[k]
3 I appeared to Abraham, to Isaac and to Jacob as God Almighty,[a][l] but by my name[m]
the LORD[b][n] I did not make myself fully
known to them. 4 I also established my covenant[o] with them to give them the land[p] of
Canaan, where they resided as foreigners.[q]
5 Moreover, I have heard the groaning[r] of the
Israelites, whom the Egyptians are enslaving, and I have remembered my covenant.[s]

[a] 3 Hebrew *El-Shaddai* [b] 3 See note at 3:15.

5:17 [z] ver 8 **5:18** [a] S Ge 15:13 **5:21** [b] S Ge 16:5 [c] S Ge 34:30 [d] Ex 16:3; Nu 14:3; 20:3 [e] S Ex 1:13; S 14:11 **5:22** [f] Nu 11:11; Dt 1:12; Jos 7:7 **5:23** [g] Jer 4:10; 20:7; Eze 14:9 **6:1** [h] S Ex 3:20; S Dt 5:15 [i] S Ex 3:20 [j] Ex 11:1; 12:31, 33,39 **6:2** [k] ver 6,7,8, 29; Ex 3:14,15; 7:5,17; 8:22; 10:2; 12:12; 14:4,18; 16:12; Lev 11:44; 18:21; 20:7; Isa 25:3; 41:20; 43:11; 49:23; 60:16; Eze 13:9; 25:17; 36:38; 37:6,13; Joel 2:27 **6:3** [l] S Ge 17:1 [m] S Ex 3:15; 2Sa 7:26; Ps 48:10; 61:5; 68:4; 83:18; 99:3; Isa 52:6 [n] Ex 3:14; Jn 8:58 **6:4** [o] S Ge 6:18; S 15:18 [p] S Ge 12:7; Ac 7:5; Ro 4:13; Gal 3:16; Heb 11:8-10 [q] S Ge 17:8 **6:5** [r] S Ex 2:23; Ac 7:34 [s] S Ge 9:15

5:21 *May the LORD look on you and judge you!* See Ge 16:5; 31:49 and notes. *obnoxious.* See note on 1Sa 13:4.
6:1 *hand.* Often used figuratively in the Bible for power.
6:2 *I am the LORD.* Appears four times in this passage: (1) to introduce the message; (2) to confirm God's promise of redemption (v. 6) based on the evidence of vv. 2–5; (3) to underscore God's intention to adopt Israel (v. 7); (4) to confirm his promise of the land and to conclude the message (v. 8).
6:3 *God Almighty.* See note on Ge 17:1. *by my name the LORD I did not make myself fully known to them.* See notes on 3:14–15. This does not necessarily mean that the patriarchs were totally ignorant of the name Yahweh ("the LORD"), but it indicates that they did not understand its full implications as the name of the One who would redeem his people (see notes on v. 6; Ge 2:4). That fact could be comprehended only by the Israelites who were to experience the exodus, and by their descendants. *make myself fully known.* This experiential sense of the verb "to know" is intended also in its repeated use throughout the account of the plagues (see v. 7; 7:17; 8:10,22; 9:14,29; 10:2; 11:7) and in connection with the exodus itself (see 14:4,18; 16:6,8,12; 18:11).
6:5 *remembered.* See note on Ge 8:1.

A man at Luxor (ancient Thebes) making bricks from mud and straw as the ancient Israelites would have done

A wall painting in the tomb of Rekhmire, vizier under Thutmose III and Amunhotep II (Eighteenth Dynasty, sixteenth–fourteenth century BC), depicts Egyptian workers making bricks.

Erich Lessing/Art Resource, NY

6 "Therefore, say to the Israelites: 'I am
the LORD, and I will bring you out from
under the yoke of the Egyptians.[t] I will
free you from being slaves to them, and
I will redeem[u] you with an outstretched
arm[v] and with mighty acts of judgment.[w]
7 I will take you as my own people, and I
will be your God.[x] Then you will know[y]
that I am the LORD your God, who brought
you out from under the yoke of the Egyptians. 8 And I will bring you to the land[z] I
swore[a] with uplifted hand[b] to give to Abraham, to Isaac and to Jacob.[c] I will give it
to you as a possession. I am the LORD.' "[d]
9 Moses reported this to the Israelites,
but they did not listen to him because of
their discouragement and harsh labor.[e]
10 Then the LORD said to Moses, 11 "Go,
tell[f] Pharaoh king of Egypt to let the Israelites go out of his country."[g]

12 But Moses said to the LORD, "If the Israelites will not listen[h] to me, why would
Pharaoh listen to me, since I speak with
faltering lips[a]?"[i]

Family Record of Moses and Aaron

13 Now the LORD spoke to Moses and
Aaron about the Israelites and Pharaoh
king of Egypt, and he commanded them
to bring the Israelites out of Egypt.[j]
14 These were the heads of their families[b]:[k]

[a] 12 Hebrew *I am uncircumcised of lips;* also in verse 30
[b] 14 The Hebrew for *families* here and in verse 25 refers to units larger than clans.

6:6 [t] ver 7; Ex 3:8; 12:17, 51; 16:1,6; 18:1; 19:1; 20:2; 29:46; Lev 22:33; 26:13; Dt 6:12; Ps 81:10; 136:11; Jer 2:6; Hos 13:4; Am 2:10; Mic 6:4 [u] Ex 15:13; Dt 7:8; 9:26; 1Ch 17:21; Job 19:25; Ps 19:14; 34:22; 74:2; 77:15; 107:2; Isa 29:22; 35:9; 43:1; 44:23; 48:20; Jer 15:21; 31:11; 50:34 [v] S Ex 3:19,20; S Jer 32:21; Ac 13:17 [w] Ex 3:20; Ps 9:16; 105:27 **6:7** [x] S Ge 17:7; S Ex 34:9; Eze 11:19-20; Ro 9:4 [y] S ver 2; 1Ki 20:13,28; Isa 43:10; 48:7; Eze 39:6; Joel 3:17 **6:8** [z] S Ge 12:7; Ex 3:8 [a] Jer 11:5; Eze 20:6 [b] S Ge 14:22; Rev 10:5-6 [c] Ps 136:21-22 [d] Lev 18:21 **6:9** [e] S Ge 34:30; Ex 2:23 **6:11** [f] ver 29 [g] S Ex 3:18 **6:12** [h] S Ex 3:18 [i] Ex 4:10 **6:13** [j] S Ex 3:10 **6:14** [k] Ex 13:3; Nu 1:1; 26:4

6:6 *I will bring you out … will free you … will redeem you.* The verbs stress the true significance of the name Yahweh—"the LORD"—who is the Redeemer of his people (see note on v. 3). *outstretched arm.* Used figuratively of God's display of his power in the redemption of his people (see Dt 4:34; 5:15; see also Isa 51:9–11 and note on 51:9). *mighty acts of judgment.* See 7:4. The Lord's acts include redemption (for Israel) and judgment (against Egypt).

6:7–8 *brought you out from … will bring you to.* Redemption means not only release from slavery and suffering but also deliverance to freedom and joy.

6:7 *I will take you as my own people, and I will be your God.* Words that anticipate the covenant at Mount Sinai (see 19:5–6; see also Jer 31:33; Zec 8:8 and notes).

6:8 See Ge 22:15–17. *swore with uplifted hand.* See note on Ge 14:22.

6:12 *I speak with faltering lips.* See note on 4:10.

6:13 *Moses and Aaron.* The genealogy contained in vv. 14–25 gives details concerning the background of Moses and Aaron. Only the first three of Jacob's 12 sons (Reuben, Simeon and Levi) are listed since Moses and Aaron were from the third tribe.

The sons of Reuben[l] the firstborn
son of Israel were Hanok and Pallu,
Hezron and Karmi. These were the
clans of Reuben.
15The sons of Simeon[m] were Jemuel, Jamin, Ohad, Jakin, Zohar and
Shaul the son of a Canaanite woman.
These were the clans of Simeon.
16These were the names of the sons
of Levi[n] according to their records:
Gershon,[o] Kohath and Merari.[p] Levi
lived 137 years.
17The sons of Gershon, by clans,
were Libni and Shimei.[q]
18The sons of Kohath[r] were Amram, Izhar, Hebron and Uzziel.[s] Kohath lived 133 years.
19The sons of Merari were Mahli
and Mushi.[t]
These were the clans of Levi according to their records.
20Amram[u] married his father's sister Jochebed, who bore him Aaron
and Moses.[v] Amram lived 137 years.
21The sons of Izhar[w] were Korah,
Nepheg and Zikri.
22The sons of Uzziel were Mishael,
Elzaphan[x] and Sithri.
23Aaron married Elisheba, daughter of Amminadab[y] and sister of Nahshon,[z] and she bore him Nadab and
Abihu,[a] Eleazar[b] and Ithamar.[c]
24The sons of Korah[d] were Assir, Elkanah and Abiasaph. These were the
Korahite clans.
25Eleazar son of Aaron married one
of the daughters of Putiel, and she
bore him Phinehas.[e]

These were the heads of the Levite
families, clan by clan.

26It was this Aaron and Moses to whom
the LORD said, "Bring the Israelites out of
Egypt[f] by their divisions."[g] 27They were
the ones who spoke to Pharaoh[h] king of
Egypt about bringing the Israelites out of
Egypt — this same Moses and Aaron.[i]

Aaron to Speak for Moses

28Now when the LORD spoke to Moses in
Egypt, 29he said to him, "I am the LORD.[j]
Tell Pharaoh king of Egypt everything I tell
you."
30But Moses said to the LORD, "Since
I speak with faltering lips,[k] why would
Pharaoh listen to me?"
7 Then the LORD said to Moses, "See,
I have made you like God[l] to Pharaoh, and your brother Aaron will be your
prophet.[m] 2You are to say everything I
command you, and your brother Aaron is
to tell Pharaoh to let the Israelites go out
of his country. 3But I will harden Pharaoh's heart,[n] and though I multiply my
signs and wonders[o] in Egypt, 4he will not
listen[p] to you. Then I will lay my hand on
Egypt and with mighty acts of judgment[q] I
will bring out my divisions,[r] my people the
Israelites. 5And the Egyptians will know
that I am the LORD[s] when I stretch out my
hand[t] against Egypt and bring the Israelites out of it."
6Moses and Aaron did just as the LORD
commanded[u] them. 7Moses was eighty
years old[v] and Aaron eighty-three when
they spoke to Pharaoh.

Aaron's Staff Becomes a Snake

8The LORD said to Moses and Aaron,
9"When Pharaoh says to you, 'Perform a
miracle,[w]' then say to Aaron, 'Take your
staff and throw it down before Pharaoh,'
and it will become a snake."[x]
10So Moses and Aaron went to Pharaoh and did just as the LORD commanded. Aaron threw his staff down in front of

6:14 [l]S Ge 29:32 **6:15** [m]S Ge 29:33 **6:16** [n]S Ge 29:34 [o]S Ge 46:11 [p]Nu 3:17; Jos 21:7; 1Ch 6:1,16 **6:17** [q]Nu 3:18; 1Ch 6:17 **6:18** [r]Nu 3:27; 1Ch 23:12 [s]Nu 3:19; 1Ch 6:2,18 **6:19** [t]Nu 3:20, 33; 1Ch 6:19; 23:21 **6:20** [u]1Ch 23:13 [v]Ex 2:1-2; Nu 26:59 **6:21** [w]1Ch 6:38 **6:22** [x]Lev 10:4; Nu 3:30; 1Ch 15:8; 2Ch 29:13 **6:23** [y]Ru 4:19, 20; 1Ch 2:10 [z]Nu 1:7; 2:3; Mt 1:4 [a]Ex 24:1; 28:1; Lev 10:1 [b]Lev 10:6; Nu 3:2,32; 16:37,39; Dt 10:6; Jos 14:1 [c]Ex 28:1; Lev 10:12,16; Nu 3:2; 4:28; 26:60; 1Ch 6:3; 24:1 **6:24** [d]ver 21; Nu 16:1; 1Ch 6:22,37 **6:25** [e]Nu 25:7, 11; 31:6; Jos 24:33; Ps 106:30 **6:26** [f]S Ex 3:10 [g]Ex 7:4; 12:17, 41,51 **6:27** [h]Ex 5:1 [i]Nu 3:1; Ps 77:20 **6:29** [j]S ver 2 **6:30** [k]S Ex 3:11 **7:1** [l]S Ex 4:16 [m]Ex 4:15; Ac 14:12 **7:3** [n]S Ex 4:21; Ro 9:18 [o]S Ex 3:20; S 10:1; Ac 7:36

7:4 [p]ver 13,16,22; Ex 8:15,19; 9:12; 11:9 [q]S Ex 3:20; Ac 7:36 [r]S Ex 6:26 **7:5** [s]S Ex 6:2 [t]Ex 3:20; Ps 138:7; Eze 6:14; 25:13 **7:6** [u]ver 2,10,20; Ge 6:22 **7:7** [v]Dt 31:2; 34:7; Ac 7:23,30 **7:9** [w]Dt 6:22; 2Ki 19:29; Ps 78:43; 86:17; 105:27; 135:9; Isa 7:11; 37:30; 38:7-8; 55:13; S Jn 2:11 [x]Ex 4:2-5

6:16 *Merari.* The name is of Egyptian origin, as are those of Putiel and Phinehas (see v. 25) and of Moses himself (see note on 2:10). *Levi lived 137 years.* See vv. 18,20. In the OT, attention is usually called to a person's life span only when it exceeds 100 years.

6:20 *Amram ... Aaron and Moses.* There is some reason to believe that Amram and Jochebed were not the immediate parents but the ancestors of Aaron and Moses. Kohath, Amram's father (see v. 18), was born before Jacob's (Israel's) descent into Egypt (see Ge 46:11), where the Israelites then stayed 430 years (see 12:40 – 41). Since Moses was 80 years old at the time of the exodus (see 7:7), he must have been born at least 350 years after Kohath, who consequently could not have been Moses' grandfather (see v. 18). Therefore Amram must not have been Moses' father, and the Hebrew verb for "bore" must have the same meaning it sometimes has in Ge 10 (see NIV text note on Ge 10:8, where it is translated "was the father of"). *Jochebed.* The name appears to mean "The LORD is glory." If so, it shows that the name Yahweh (here abbreviated as *Jo-*) was known before Moses was born (see note on v. 3). *Aaron and Moses.* Aaron, as the firstborn (see 7:7), is listed first in the official genealogy.

6:26 *divisions.* The Hebrew word may imply that Israel is to serve as the Lord's army (also in 7:4; 12:17,41,51).

6:30 *faltering lips.* See v. 12 and note on 4:10.

7:1 – 2 As God transmits his word through his prophets to his people, so Moses will transmit God's message through Aaron to the pharaoh. The prophet's task was to speak God's word on God's behalf. He was God's "mouth" (4:15 – 16).

7:3 *harden.* See note on 4:21. *signs.* See notes on 3:12; 4:8.

7:4 *mighty acts of judgment.* See note on 6:6.

7:7 *Moses was eighty years old.* See notes on 2:11,15.

7:9 – 10 *snake.* The Hebrew for this word is different from that used in 4:3 (see Ps 74:13, "monster"). A related word (also translated "monster") is used in Eze 29:3 as a designation for Egypt and her king.

Pharaoh and his officials, and it became a snake. 11 Pharaoh then summoned wise men and sorcerers,[y] and the Egyptian magicians[z] also did the same things by their secret arts:[a] 12 Each one threw down his staff and it became a snake. But Aaron's staff swallowed up their staffs. 13 Yet Pharaoh's heart[b] became hard and he would not listen[c] to them, just as the LORD had said.

The Plague of Blood

14 Then the LORD said to Moses, "Pharaoh's heart is unyielding;[d] he refuses to let the people go. 15 Go to Pharaoh in the morning as he goes out to the river.[e] Confront him on the bank of the Nile,[f] and take in your hand the staff that was changed into a snake. 16 Then say to him, 'The LORD, the God of the Hebrews, has sent me to say to you: Let my people go, so that they may worship[g] me in the wilderness. But until now you have not listened.[h] 17 This is what the LORD says: By this you will know that I am the LORD:[i] With the staff that is in my hand I will strike the water of the Nile, and it will be changed into blood.[j] 18 The fish in the Nile will die, and the river will stink;[k] the Egyptians will not be able to drink its water.' "[l]

19 The LORD said to Moses, "Tell Aaron, 'Take your staff[m] and stretch out your hand[n] over the waters of Egypt—over the streams and canals, over the ponds and all the reservoirs—and they will turn to blood.' Blood will be everywhere in Egypt, even in vessels[a] of wood and stone."

20 Moses and Aaron did just as the LORD had commanded.[o] He raised his staff in the presence of Pharaoh and his officials and struck the water of the Nile,[p] and all the water was changed into blood.[q] 21 The fish in the Nile died, and the river smelled so bad that the Egyptians could not drink its water. Blood was everywhere in Egypt.

22 But the Egyptian magicians[r] did the same things by their secret arts,[s] and Pharaoh's heart[t] became hard; he would not listen to Moses and Aaron, just as the LORD had said. 23 Instead, he turned and went into his palace, and did not take even this to heart. 24 And all the Egyptians dug along the Nile to get drinking water[u], because they could not drink the water of the river.

The Plague of Frogs

25 Seven days passed after the LORD

8[b] struck the Nile. 1 Then the LORD said to Moses, "Go to Pharaoh and say to him, 'This is what the LORD says: Let my people go, so that they may worship[v] me. 2 If you refuse to let them go, I will send a plague of frogs[w] on your whole country. 3 The Nile will teem with frogs. They will come up into your palace and your bedroom and onto your bed, into the houses of your officials and on your people,[x] and into your ovens and kneading troughs.[y] 4 The frogs will come up on you and your people and all your officials.' "

5 Then the LORD said to Moses, "Tell Aaron, 'Stretch out your hand with your staff[z]

[a] 19 Or *even on their idols* [b] In Hebrew texts 8:1-4 is numbered 7:26-29, and 8:5-32 is numbered 8:1-28.

7:11 [y] Ex 22:18; Dt 18:10; 1Sa 6:2; 2Ki 21:6; Isa 2:6; 47:12; Jer 27:9; Mal 3:5 [z] S Ge 41:8; 2Ti 3:8 [a] ver 22; Ex 8:7,18; S Mt 24:24
7:13 [b] S Ex 4:21 [c] S ver 4
7:14 [d] ver 22; Ex 8:15,32; 9:7; 10:1,20,27
7:15 [e] Ex 8:20 [f] S Ge 41:1
7:16 [g] S Ex 3:18 [h] S ver 4
7:17 [i] S Ex 6:2; 14:25 [j] ver 19-21; Ex 4:9; Rev 11:6; 16:4
7:18 [k] Isa 19:6 [l] ver 21,24; Ps 78:44
7:19 [m] S Ex 4:2 [n] Ex 14:21; 2Ki 5:11
7:20 [o] S ver 6 [p] Ex 17:5 [q] Ps 78:44; 105:29; 114:3; Hab 3:8
7:22 [r] S Ge 41:8 [s] S ver 11; S Mt 24:24 [t] ver 13, S 14; Ex 8:19; Ps 105:28
7:24 [u] S ver 18
8:1 [v] Ex 3:12,18; 4:23; 5:1; 9:1
8:2 [w] Ps 78:45; 105:30; Rev 16:13
8:3 [x] Ex 10:6 [y] Ex 12:34
8:5 [z] S Ex 4:2; 7:9-20; 9:23; 10:13,21-22; 14:27

7:11 *wise men and ... magicians.* See note on Ge 41:8. According to tradition, two of the magicians who opposed Moses were named Jannes and Jambres (see 2Ti 3:8; the first is also mentioned in the pre-Christian Dead Sea Scrolls). *the Egyptian magicians also did the same things by their secret arts.* Either through sleight of hand or by means of demonic power.

7:12 *Aaron's staff swallowed up their staffs.* Demonstrating God's mastery over the pharaoh and the gods of Egypt.

7:13 *heart became hard.* A hardened heart refers to a stubborn refusal to take God and his word seriously (see also note on 4:21).

7:14—10:29 The first nine plagues can be divided into three groups of three plagues each: 7:14—8:19; 8:20—9:12; 9:13—10:29. The first plague in each group (the first, the fourth and the seventh) is introduced by a warning delivered to the pharaoh in the morning as he went out to the Nile (see v. 15; 8:20; 9:13). Each of the three groups of plagues seems to be directed against one or more of the chief gods of Egypt (see notes on 7:20; 9:3; 10:21).

7:17 *my.* Moses'. *the water of the Nile ... will be changed into blood.* See Ps 78:44; 105:29. Some interpreters believe that the first nine plagues may have been a series of unprecedented intensifications of events that were part of the Egyptian experience, events that in their more usual form did not have anything like the catastrophic effects of the disasters God brought on Egypt in order to deliver the Israelites from Egyptian imperial bondage. If that was the case, the first plague may have resulted from an unparalleled quantity of red sediment being washed down from Ethiopia during the annual flooding of the Nile in late summer and early fall, causing the water of Egypt's lifeline to become as red as blood (see v. 24; cf. the incident in 2Ki 3:22–23).

7:19 *your staff.* Aaron was acting on Moses' behalf (see v. 17). *in vessels of wood and stone.* Lit. "in/on the wooden things and in/on the stone things" (see NIV text note). Some think that since the Egyptians believed that their gods inhabited idols and images made of wood, clay and stone (see Dt 29:16–17), the plague may have been intended as a rebuke to their religion (see 12:12).

7:20 *Nile.* Egypt's dependence on the life-sustaining waters of the Nile led to its deification as the god Hapi, for whom hymns of adoration were composed. See note on v. 19.

7:24 *dug along the Nile to get drinking water.* Filtered through sandy soil near the river bank, the polluted water would become safe for drinking.

7:25 *Seven days passed.* The plagues did not follow each other in rapid succession.

8:2 *I will send a plague of frogs.* The frog (or toad) was deified in the goddess Heqt, who assisted women in childbirth.

8:3 *come up.* The frogs abandoned the Nile and swarmed over the land, perhaps because an unusually high concentration of bacteria-laden algae had by now proved fatal to most of the fish, thus polluting the river.

over the streams and canals and ponds,
and make frogs[a] come up on the land of
Egypt.' "
6 So Aaron stretched out his hand over
the waters of Egypt, and the frogs[b] came
up and covered the land. 7 But the magicians did the same things by their secret
arts;[c] they also made frogs come up on the
land of Egypt.
8 Pharaoh summoned Moses and Aaron
and said, "Pray[d] to the LORD to take the
frogs away from me and my people, and I
will let your people go to offer sacrifices[e]
to the LORD."
9 Moses said to Pharaoh, "I leave to you
the honor of setting the time[f] for me to
pray for you and your officials and your
people that you and your houses may be
rid of the frogs, except for those that remain in the Nile."
10 "Tomorrow," Pharaoh said.
Moses replied, "It will be as you say, so
that you may know there is no one like
the LORD our God.[g] 11 The frogs will leave
you and your houses, your officials and
your people; they will remain only in the
Nile."
12 After Moses and Aaron left Pharaoh,
Moses cried out to the LORD about the
frogs he had brought on Pharaoh. 13 And
the LORD did what Moses asked.[h] The
frogs died in the houses, in the courtyards
and in the fields. 14 They were piled into
heaps, and the land reeked of them. 15 But
when Pharaoh saw that there was relief,[i]
he hardened his heart[j] and would not listen to Moses and Aaron, just as the LORD
had said.

The Plague of Gnats

16 Then the LORD said to Moses, "Tell
Aaron, 'Stretch out your staff[k] and strike
the dust of the ground,' and throughout the
land of Egypt the dust will become gnats."
17 They did this, and when Aaron stretched
out his hand with the staff and struck the
dust of the ground, gnats[l] came on people
and animals. All the dust throughout the
land of Egypt became gnats. 18 But when
the magicians[m] tried to produce gnats by
their secret arts,[n] they could not.
Since the gnats were on people and animals everywhere, 19 the magicians said to
Pharaoh, "This is the finger[o] of God." But
Pharaoh's heart[p] was hard and he would
not listen,[q] just as the LORD had said.

The Plague of Flies

20 Then the LORD said to Moses, "Get up
early in the morning[r] and confront Pharaoh as he goes to the river and say to him,
'This is what the LORD says: Let my people go, so that they may worship[s] me. 21 If
you do not let my people go, I will send
swarms of flies on you and your officials,
on your people and into your houses.
The houses of the Egyptians will be full
of flies; even the ground will be covered
with them.
22 " 'But on that day I will deal differently with the land of Goshen,[t] where
my people live;[u] no swarms of flies will
be there, so that you will know[v] that I,
the LORD, am in this land. 23 I will make a
distinction[a] between my people and your
people.[w] This sign will occur tomorrow.' "
24 And the LORD did this. Dense swarms
of flies poured into Pharaoh's palace and
into the houses of his officials; throughout
Egypt the land was ruined by the flies.[x]
25 Then Pharaoh summoned[y] Moses and
Aaron and said, "Go, sacrifice to your God
here in the land."
26 But Moses said, "That would not be
right. The sacrifices we offer the LORD our
God would be detestable to the Egyptians.[z]
And if we offer sacrifices that are detestable in their eyes, will they not stone us?
27 We must take a three-day journey[a] into
the wilderness to offer sacrifices[b] to the
LORD our God, as he commands us."

8:5 [a] S Ex 4:17 **8:6** [b] Ps 78:45; 105:30 **8:7** [c] S Ex 7:11; S Mt 24:24 **8:8** [d] ver 28; Ex 9:28; 10:17; Nu 21:7; 1Sa 12:19; 1Ki 13:6; Jer 42:2; Ac 8:24 [e] ver 25; Ex 10:8, 24; 12:31 **8:9** [f] Ex 9:5 **8:10** [g] Ex 9:14; 15:11; Dt 3:24; 4:35; 33:26; 2Sa 7:22; 1Ki 8:23; 1Ch 17:20; 2Ch 6:14; Ps 71:19; 86:8; 89:6; 113:5; Isa 40:18; 42:8; 46:9; Jer 10:6; 49:19; Mic 7:18 **8:13** [h] Jas 5:16-18 **8:15** [i] Ecc 8:11 [j] S Ex 7:14 **8:16** [k] S Ex 4:2 **8:17** [l] Ps 105:31 **8:18** [m] Ex 9:11; Da 5:8 [n] S Ex 7:11 **8:19** [o] Ex 7:5; 10:7; 12:33; 31:18; 1Sa 6:9; Ne 9:6; Ps 8:3; 33:6; Lk 11:20 [p] S Ex 7:22 [q] S Ex 7:4 **8:20** [r] Ex 7:15; 9:13 [s] S Ex 3:18 **8:22** [t] S Ge 45:10 [u] Ex 9:4,6,26; 10:23; 11:7; 12:13; 19:5; Dt 4:20; 7:6; 14:2; 26:18; 1Ki 8:36; Job 36:11; Ps 33:12; 135:4; Mal 3:17 [v] Ex 7:5; 9:29 **8:23** [w] Ex 9:4, 6; 10:23; 11:7; 12:13,23,27 **8:24** [x] Ps 78:45; 105:31 **8:25** [y] ver 8; Ex 9:27; 10:16; 12:31 **8:26** [z] S Ge 43:32 **8:27** [a] S Ge 30:36 [b] S Ex 3:18

[a] *23* Septuagint and Vulgate; Hebrew *will put a deliverance*

8:13 *the LORD did what Moses asked.* For similar occurrences see v. 31; 1Sa 12:18; 1Ki 18:42–45; Am 7:1–6. *The frogs died.* Probably because they had been infected by bacteria in the Nile algae (see note on v. 3).
8:15 *hardened his heart.* See note on 7:13.
8:16 *dust will become gnats.* The word "dust" is perhaps a reference to the enormous number (see, e.g., Ge 13:16) of the gnats, bred in the flooded fields of Egypt in late autumn.
8:19 *finger of God.* A concise and colorful figure of speech referring to God's miraculous power (see 31:18; Ps 8:3). Jesus drove out demons "by the finger of God" (Lk 11:20). Cf. the similar use of the phrase "hand of the LORD" in 9:3 and "arm of the LORD" in Isa 51:9 (see note there).
8:20 *as he goes to the river.* As he goes to the Nile. Perhaps the pharaoh went there (1) to worship at a shrine or (2) to bathe, as the princess had done in 2:5 (see also 7:15). The specific purpose remains uncertain.
8:21 *I will send swarms of flies.* They probably would have multiplied rapidly as the receding Nile left breeding places in its wake. Full-grown, such flies infest houses and stables and bite people and animals.
8:22 *I will deal differently.* See 33:16. God makes a "distinction" (v. 23) between Moses' people and the pharaoh's people in this plague as well as in the fifth (see 9:4,6), the seventh (see 9:26), the ninth (see 10:23) and the tenth (see 11:7)—and probably also the sixth and eighth (see 9:11; 10:6)—demonstrating that the Lord can preserve his own people while judging Egypt. *Goshen.* See Ge 45:10 and note.
8:23 *sign.* See 4:8 and note.
8:26 *detestable to the Egyptians.* See Ge 46:34; see also Ge 43:32 and note.

28 Pharaoh said, "I will let you go to offer sacrifices to the LORD your God in the wilderness, but you must not go very far. Now pray[c] for me."

29 Moses answered, "As soon as I leave you, I will pray to the LORD, and tomorrow the flies will leave Pharaoh and his officials and his people. Only let Pharaoh be sure that he does not act deceitfully[d] again by not letting the people go to offer sacrifices to the LORD."

30 Then Moses left Pharaoh and prayed to the LORD,[e] 31 and the LORD did what Moses asked. The flies left Pharaoh and his officials and his people; not a fly remained. 32 But this time also Pharaoh hardened his heart[f] and would not let the people go.

The Plague on Livestock

9 Then the LORD said to Moses, "Go to Pharaoh and say to him, 'This is what the LORD, the God of the Hebrews, says: "Let my people go, so that they may worship[g] me." 2 If you refuse to let them go and continue to hold them back, 3 the hand[h] of the LORD will bring a terrible plague[i] on your livestock in the field—on your horses, donkeys and camels and on your cattle, sheep and goats. 4 But the LORD will make a distinction between the livestock of Israel and that of Egypt,[j] so that no animal belonging to the Israelites will die.' "

5 The LORD set a time and said, "Tomorrow the LORD will do this in the land." 6 And the next day the LORD did it: All the livestock[k] of the Egyptians died,[l] but not one animal belonging to the Israelites died. 7 Pharaoh investigated and found that not even one of the animals of the Israelites had died. Yet his heart[m] was unyielding and he would not let the people go.[n]

8:28 [c]S ver 8; S Jer 37:3; Ac 8:24 **8:29** [d]ver 15; Ex 9:30; 10:11; Isa 26:10 **8:30** [e]ver 12; Ex 9:33; 10:18 **8:32** [f]S Ex 7:14 **9:1** [g]S Ex 8:1 **9:3** [h]Ex 7:4; 1Sa 5:6; Job 13:21; Ps 32:4; 39:10; Ac 13:11 [i]Lev 26:25; Ps 78:50; Am 4:10 **9:4** [j]ver 26; S Ex 8:23 **9:6** [k]ver 19-21; Ex 11:5; 12:29 [l]Ps 78:48-50 **9:7** [m]S Ex 7:22 [n]Ex 7:14; 8:32 **9:9** [o]Lev 13:18, 19; Dt 28:27, 35; 2Ki 20:7; Job 2:7; Isa 38:21; Rev 16:2 **9:11** [p]S Ex 8:18 **9:12** [q]S Ex 4:21 [r]S Ex 7:4 **9:13** [s]S Ex 3:18 **9:14** [t]S Ex 8:10 [u]Ex 15:11; 1Sa 2:2; 2Sa 7:22; 1Ki 8:23; 1Ch 17:20; Ps 35:10; 71:19; 86:8; 89:6; Isa 46:9; Jer 10:6; Mic 7:18 **9:15** [v]Ex 3:20 **9:16** [w]Pr 16:4 [x]Ex 14:4, 17, 31; Ps 20:6; 25:11; 68:28; 71:18; 106:8; 109:21; Ro 9:17* **9:18** [y]ver 23; Jos 10:11; Ps 78:47-48; 105:32; 148:8; Isa 30:30; Eze 38:22; Hag 2:17 [z]ver 24; Ex 10:6

The Plague of Boils

8 Then the LORD said to Moses and Aaron, "Take handfuls of soot from a furnace and have Moses toss it into the air in the presence of Pharaoh. 9 It will become fine dust over the whole land of Egypt, and festering boils[o] will break out on people and animals throughout the land."

10 So they took soot from a furnace and stood before Pharaoh. Moses tossed it into the air, and festering boils broke out on people and animals. 11 The magicians[p] could not stand before Moses because of the boils that were on them and on all the Egyptians. 12 But the LORD hardened Pharaoh's heart[q] and he would not listen[r] to Moses and Aaron, just as the LORD had said to Moses.

The Plague of Hail

13 Then the LORD said to Moses, "Get up early in the morning, confront Pharaoh and say to him, 'This is what the LORD, the God of the Hebrews, says: Let my people go, so that they may worship[s] me, 14 or this time I will send the full force of my plagues against you and against your officials and your people, so you may know[t] that there is no one like[u] me in all the earth. 15 For by now I could have stretched out my hand and struck you and your people[v] with a plague that would have wiped you off the earth. 16 But I have raised you up[a] for this very purpose,[w] that I might show you my power[x] and that my name might be proclaimed in all the earth. 17 You still set yourself against my people and will not let them go. 18 Therefore, at this time tomorrow I will send the worst hailstorm[y] that has ever fallen on Egypt, from the day it was founded till now.[z]

[a] 16 Or *have spared you*

8:31 *the LORD did what Moses asked.* See note on v. 13.

9:3 *hand of the LORD.* See note on 8:19. *terrible plague on your livestock.* The flies of the fourth plague (see note on 8:21) possibly carried the bacteria (see note on 8:13) that would now infect the animals, which had been brought into the fields again as the floodwaters subsided. The Egyptians worshiped many animals and animal-headed deities, including the bull-gods Apis and Mnevis, the cow-god Hathor and the ram-god Khnum. Thus Egyptian religion is again rebuked and ridiculed (see note on 7:19). *camels.* See note on Ge 12:16.

9:4 *distinction.* See note on 8:22.

9:5 *Tomorrow.* To give those Egyptians who feared God time to bring their livestock in from the fields and out of danger (see also v. 20)—mercy in the midst of judgment.

9:6 *All the livestock of the Egyptians died.* That is, all that were left out in the fields. Protected livestock remained alive (see vv. 19–21).

9:8 *Take ... soot ... toss it into the air.* Perhaps symbolizing either the widespread extent of the plague of boils or their black coloration. *furnace.* Possibly a kiln for firing bricks, the symbol of Israel's bondage (see 1:14; 5:7–19). The same word is used in Ge 19:28 as a simile for the destruction of Sodom and Gomorrah.

9:9 *boils.* Possibly skin anthrax (a variety of the plague that struck the livestock in vv. 1–7), a black, burning abscess that develops into a pustule. *people and animals.* The plague on the livestock now extended to other animals, as well as to the people of Egypt.

9:11 *magicians could not stand.* The "boils of Egypt" (Dt 28:27) seriously affected the knees and legs (see Dt 28:35).

9:12 *the LORD hardened Pharaoh's heart.* See note on 4:21.

9:16 Paul quotes this verse as an outstanding illustration of the sovereignty of God (see Ro 9:17).

9:18 *I will send ... hailstorm.* The flooding of the Nile (the possible occasion of the first six plagues) came to an end late in the fall. The hailstorm is thus in the proper chronological position, taking place in January or February when the flax and barley were in flower but the wheat and spelt had not yet germinated (see vv. 31–32).

19 Give an order now to bring your livestock and everything you have in the field
to a place of shelter, because the hail will
fall on every person and animal that has
not been brought in and is still out in the
field, and they will die.' "
20 Those officials of Pharaoh who feared[a]
the word of the LORD hurried to bring their
slaves and their livestock inside. 21 But
those who ignored[b] the word of the LORD
left their slaves and livestock in the field.
22 Then the LORD said to Moses, "Stretch
out your hand toward the sky so that hail
will fall all over Egypt — on people and
animals and on everything growing in the
fields of Egypt." 23 When Moses stretched
out his staff toward the sky, the LORD sent
thunder[c] and hail,[d] and lightning flashed
down to the ground. So the LORD rained
hail on the land of Egypt; 24 hail fell and
lightning flashed back and forth. It was
the worst storm in all the land of Egypt
since it had become a nation.[e] 25 Throughout Egypt hail struck everything in the
fields — both people and animals; it beat
down everything growing in the fields and
stripped every tree.[f] 26 The only place it did
not hail was the land of Goshen,[g] where
the Israelites were.[h]
27 Then Pharaoh summoned Moses and
Aaron. "This time I have sinned,"[i] he said
to them. "The LORD is in the right,[j] and I
and my people are in the wrong. 28 Pray[k] to
the LORD, for we have had enough thunder
and hail. I will let you go;[l] you don't have
to stay any longer."
29 Moses replied, "When I have gone out
of the city, I will spread out my hands[m] in
prayer to the LORD. The thunder will stop
and there will be no more hail, so you may
know that the earth[n] is the LORD's. 30 But I
know that you and your officials still do
not fear[o] the LORD God."
31 (The flax and barley[p] were destroyed,
since the barley had headed and the flax
was in bloom. 32 The wheat and spelt,[q]
however, were not destroyed, because
they ripen later.)

33 Then Moses left Pharaoh and went
out of the city. He spread out his hands
toward the LORD; the thunder and hail
stopped, and the rain no longer poured
down on the land. 34 When Pharaoh saw
that the rain and hail and thunder had
stopped, he sinned again: He and his officials hardened their hearts. 35 So Pharaoh's
heart[r] was hard and he would not let the
Israelites go, just as the LORD had said
through Moses.

The Plague of Locusts

10 Then the LORD said to Moses, "Go
to Pharaoh, for I have hardened his
heart[s] and the hearts of his officials so that
I may perform these signs[t] of mine among
them 2 that you may tell your children[u]
and grandchildren how I dealt harshly[v]
with the Egyptians and how I performed
my signs among them, and that you may
know that I am the LORD."[w]
3 So Moses and Aaron went to Pharaoh
and said to him, "This is what the LORD,
the God of the Hebrews, says: 'How long
will you refuse to humble[x] yourself before
me? Let my people go, so that they may
worship me. 4 If you refuse[y] to let them go,
I will bring locusts[z] into your country tomorrow. 5 They will cover the face of the
ground so that it cannot be seen. They will
devour what little you have left[a] after the
hail, including every tree that is growing in
your fields.[b] 6 They will fill your houses[c] and
those of all your officials and all the Egyptians — something neither your parents nor
your ancestors have ever seen from the day
they settled in this land till now.' "[d] Then
Moses turned and left Pharaoh.
7 Pharaoh's officials said to him, "How
long will this man be a snare[e] to us? Let
the people go, so that they may worship
the LORD their God. Do you not yet realize
that Egypt is ruined?"[f]

9:20 [a] Pr 13:13 **9:21** [b] S Ge 19:14; Eze 33:4-5 **9:23** [c] Ex 20:18; 1Sa 7:10; 12:17; Ps 18:13; 29:3; 68:33; 77:17; 104:7 [d] S ver 18; Rev 8:7; 16:21 **9:24** [e] S ver 18 **9:25** [f] Ps 105:32-33; Eze 13:13 **9:26** [g] S ver 4; Isa 32:18-20 [h] Ex 10:23; 11:7; 12:13; Am 4:7 **9:27** [i] ver 34; Ex 10:16; Nu 14:40; Dt 1:41; Jos 7:11; Jdg 10:10; 1Sa 15:24; 24:17; 26:21 [j] Ps 11:7; 116:5; 119:137; 129:4; 145:17; Jer 12:1; La 1:18 **9:28** [k] Ex 8:8; Ac 8:24 [l] S Ex 8:8 **9:29** [m] ver 33; 1Ki 8:22,38; Job 11:13; Ps 77:2; 88:9; 143:6; Isa 1:15 [n] Ex 19:5; Job 41:11; Ps 24:1; 50:12; 1Co 10:26 **9:30** [o] S Ex 8:29 **9:31** [p] Dt 8:8; Ru 1:22; 2:23; 2Sa 14:30; 17:28; Isa 28:25; Eze 4:9; Joel 1:11 **9:32** [q] Isa 28:25 **9:35** [r] S Ex 4:21 **10:1** [s] S Ex 4:21 [t] S Ex 3:19; S 7:3; Jos 24:17; Ne 9:10; Ps 74:9; 105:26-36 **10:2** [u] Ex 12:26-27; 13:8,14; Dt 4:9; 6:20; 32:7; Jos 4:6; Ps 44:1; 71:18; 78:4,5; Joel 1:3 [v] 1Sa 6:6 [w] S Ex 6:2 **10:3** [x] 1Ki 21:29; 2Ki 22:19; 2Ch 7:14; 12:7; 33:23; 34:27; Job 42:6; Isa 58:3; Da 5:22; Jas 4:10; 1Pe 5:6 **10:4** [y] Ex 8:2; 9:2 [z] Dt 28:38; Ps 105:34; Pr 30:27; Joel 1:4; Rev 9:3 **10:5** [a] Ex 9:32; Joel 1:4 [b] ver 15 **10:6** [c] Joel 2:9 [d] S Ex 9:18 **10:7** [e] Ex 23:33; 34:12; Dt 7:16; 12:30; 20:18; Jos 23:13; Jdg 2:3; 8:27; 16:5; 1Sa 18:21; Ps 106:36; Ecc 7:26 [f] S Ge 20:3; S Ex 8:19

9:19–21 See note on v. 6.

9:19 An example of God's compassion. Even in judgment he allows for the protection of both humans and animals (see also note on Jnh 4:11).

9:27 *This time I have sinned.* For the first time the pharaoh acknowledges his sinfulness and perceives its devastating results.

9:29 *spread out my hands.* See 1Ki 8:22,38,54; 2Ch 6:12–13,29; Ezr 9:5; Ps 44:20; 88:9; 143:6; Isa 1:15; 1Ti 2:8. Statues of men praying with hands upraised have been found by archaeologists at several ancient sites in the Middle East.

9:30 *LORD God.* See note on Ge 2:4.

9:31–32 See note on v. 18.

9:32 *spelt.* Grains of spelt, a member of the grass family allied to wheat, have been found in ancient Egyptian tombs. Although inferior to wheat, it grows well in poorer and drier soil.

10:2 *tell your children.* The memory of God's redemptive acts is to be kept alive by reciting them to our descendants (see 12:26–27; 13:8,14–15; Dt 4:9; Ps 77:11–20; 78:4–6, 43–53; 105:26–38; 106:7–12; 114:1–3; 135:8–9; 136:10–15).

10:4 *I will bring locusts.* In March or April the prevailing east winds (see v. 13) would sometimes bring in hordes of migratory locusts. Fifty million of them could occupy a square kilometer and devour as much as 100,000 tons of vegetation in a single night. Such locust plagues were greatly feared in ancient times and became a powerful symbol of divine judgment (see Joel 1:4–7; 2:1–11; Am 7:1–3).

10:7 *How long ... ?* The pharaoh's officials ironically echo the phrase used by Moses in v. 3. *Egypt is ruined.*

8 Then Moses and Aaron were brought
back to Pharaoh. "Go, worship[g] the LORD
your God," he said. "But tell me who will
be going."
9 Moses answered, "We will go with our
young and our old, with our sons and our
daughters, and with our flocks and herds,
because we are to celebrate a festival[h] to
the LORD."
10 Pharaoh said, "The LORD be with
you—if I let you go, along with your wom-
en and children! Clearly you are bent on
evil.[a] 11 No! Have only the men go and worship the LORD, since that's what you have
been asking for." Then Moses and Aaron
were driven out of Pharaoh's presence.
12 And the LORD said to Moses, "Stretch
out your hand[i] over Egypt so that locusts
swarm over the land and devour everything growing in the fields, everything left
by the hail."
13 So Moses stretched out his staff[j] over
Egypt, and the LORD made an east wind
blow across the land all that day and
all that night. By morning the wind had
brought the locusts;[k] 14 they invaded all
Egypt and settled down in every area of
the country in great numbers. Never before
had there been such a plague of locusts,[l]
nor will there ever be again. 15 They covered all the ground until it was black. They
devoured[m] all that was left after the hail—
everything growing in the fields and the
fruit on the trees. Nothing green remained
on tree or plant in all the land of Egypt.
16 Pharaoh quickly summoned[n] Moses and Aaron and said, "I have sinned[o]
against the LORD your God and against
you. 17 Now forgive[p] my sin once more and
pray[q] to the LORD your God to take this
deadly plague away from me."
18 Moses then left Pharaoh and prayed
to the LORD.[r] 19 And the LORD changed the
wind to a very strong west wind, which
caught up the locusts and carried them
into the Red Sea.[b] Not a locust was left
anywhere in Egypt. 20 But the LORD hardened Pharaoh's heart,[s] and he would not
let the Israelites go.

10:8 [g]S Ex 8:8 **10:9** [h]S Ex 3:18 **10:12** [i]Ex 7:19 **10:13** [j]ver 21-22; Ex 4:17; 8:5, 17; 9:23; 14:15-16, 26-27; 17:5; Nu 20:8 [k]ver 4; 1Ki 8:37; Ps 78:46; 105:34; Am 4:9; Na 3:16 **10:14** [l]Dt 28:38; Ps 78:46; Isa 33:4; Joel 1:4; 2:1-11, 25; Am 4:9 **10:15** [m]Dt 28:38; Ps 105:34-35; Joel 1:4; Am 7:2; Mal 3:11 **10:16** [n]S Ex 8:25 [o]S Ex 9:27 **10:17** [p]1Sa 15:25 [q]S Ex 8:8 **10:18** [r]S Ex 8:30 **10:20** [s]S Ex 4:21

The Plague of Darkness

21 Then the LORD said to Moses, "Stretch
out your hand toward the sky so that darkness[t] spreads over Egypt—darkness that
can be felt." 22 So Moses stretched out his
hand toward the sky, and total darkness[u]
covered all Egypt for three days. 23 No one
could see anyone else or move about for
three days. Yet all the Israelites had light
in the places where they lived.[v]
24 Then Pharaoh summoned Moses and
said, "Go,[w] worship the LORD. Even your
women and children[x] may go with you;
only leave your flocks and herds behind."[y]
25 But Moses said, "You must allow us to
have sacrifices and burnt offerings[z] to present to the LORD our God. 26 Our livestock
too must go with us; not a hoof is to be
left behind. We have to use some of them
in worshiping the LORD our God, and until
we get there we will not know what we
are to use to worship the LORD."
27 But the LORD hardened Pharaoh's
heart,[a] and he was not willing to let them
go. 28 Pharaoh said to Moses, "Get out of
my sight! Make sure you do not appear
before me again! The day you see my face
you will die."
29 "Just as you say," Moses replied. "I
will never appear[b] before you again."

The Plague on the Firstborn

11 Now the LORD had said to Moses,
"I will bring one more plague on
Pharaoh and on Egypt. After that, he will
let you go[c] from here, and when he does,
he will drive you out completely.[d] 2 Tell the
people that men and women alike are to
ask their neighbors for articles of silver
and gold."[e] 3 (The LORD made the Egyptians favorably disposed[f] toward the people, and Moses himself was highly regarded[g] in Egypt by Pharaoh's officials and by
the people.)
4 So Moses said, "This is what the LORD
says: 'About midnight[h] I will go throughout

10:21 [t]Dt 28:29 **10:22** [u]Ps 105:28; Isa 13:10; 45:7; 50:3; Rev 16:10 **10:23** [v]S Ex 8:22; Am 4:7 **10:24** [w]S Ex 8:8 [x]ver 8-10 [y]S Ge 45:10 **10:25** [z]S Ge 8:20; S Ex 18:12 **10:27** [a]S Ex 4:21 **10:29** [b]Ex 11:8; Heb 11:27 **11:1** [c]S Ex 3:20 [d]S Ex 6:1 **11:2** [e]S Ex 3:21, 22 **11:3** [f]S Ge 39:21 [g]Dt 34:11; 2Sa 7:9; 8:13; 22:44; 23:1; Est 9:4; Ps 89:27 **11:4** [h]Ex 12:29; Job 34:20

[a] 10 Or *Be careful, trouble is in store for you!* [b] 19 Or *the Sea of Reeds*

Human rebellion and disobedience always bring death and destruction in their wake.

10:10 *The LORD be with you.* This may be irony (see NIV text note on "Clearly you are bent on evil").

10:11 *Have only the men go.* From the pharaoh's standpoint, (1) the women and children should remain behind as hostages, and (2) it was typically only the men who participated fully in worship.

10:13 *east wind.* See note on v. 4.

10:19 *the LORD changed the wind.* He used the forces of his own creation to carry out his historical purpose and sovereign will (see v. 4; 14:21; Ps 104:4 and notes; cf. Mt 8:23–27). *Red Sea.* See NIV text note.

10:21 *darkness spreads over Egypt.* Like the third and sixth plagues, this ninth plague was unannounced to the pharaoh. It was possibly caused by the arrival of an unusually severe khamsin, the blinding sandstorm that blows in from the desert each year in the early spring. The darkness was an insult to the sun-god Ra (or Re), one of the chief deities of Egypt.

10:28 The pharaoh declares that he will never again grant Moses an audience. *The day you see my face.* During a plague of darkness, these words are somewhat ironic.

11:1 *and when he does.* The Hebrew for this phrase can also be read "as one sends away [a bride]"—i.e., laden with gifts (see Ge 24:53).

11:2–3 See 3:21–22; 12:35–36.

11:4 *Moses said.* Continuing the speech of 10:29.

Egypt.[i] 5Every firstborn[j] son in Egypt will
die, from the firstborn son of Pharaoh,
who sits on the throne, to the firstborn
son of the female slave, who is at her
hand mill,[k] and all the firstborn of the
cattle as well. 6There will be loud wailing[l] throughout Egypt—worse than there
has ever been or ever will be again. 7But
among the Israelites not a dog will bark
at any person or animal.' Then you will
know that the LORD makes a distinction[m]
between Egypt and Israel. 8All these officials of yours will come to me, bowing
down before me and saying, 'Go,[n] you
and all the people who follow you!' After
that I will leave."[o] Then Moses, hot with
anger, left Pharaoh.
9The LORD had said to Moses, "Pharaoh
will refuse to listen[p] to you—so that my
wonders[q] may be multiplied in Egypt."
10Moses and Aaron performed all these
wonders before Pharaoh, but the LORD
hardened Pharaoh's heart,[r] and he would
not let the Israelites go out of his country.

The Passover and the Festival of Unleavened Bread

12:14-20pp — Lev 23:4-8; Nu 28:16-25; Dt 16:1-8

12 The LORD said to Moses and Aaron in Egypt, 2"This month is to be
for you the first month,[s] the first month
of your year. 3Tell the whole community of Israel that on the tenth day of this
month each man is to take a lamb[a][t] for his
family, one for each household.[u] 4If any
household is too small for a whole lamb,
they must share one with their nearest
neighbor, having taken into account the
number of people there are. You are to determine the amount of lamb needed in accordance with what each person will eat.
5The animals you choose must be year-
old males without defect,[v] and you may
take them from the sheep or the goats.
6Take care of them until the fourteenth
day of the month,[w] when all the members
of the community of Israel must slaughter them at twilight.[x] 7Then they are to
take some of the blood[y] and put it on the
sides and tops of the doorframes of the
houses where they eat the lambs. 8That
same night[z] they are to eat the meat roasted[a] over the fire, along with bitter herbs,[b]
and bread made without yeast.[c] 9Do not
eat the meat raw or boiled in water, but
roast it over a fire—with the head, legs
and internal organs.[d] 10Do not leave any of
it till morning;[e] if some is left till morning,
you must burn it. 11This is how you are
to eat it: with your cloak tucked into your
belt, your sandals on your feet and your
staff in your hand. Eat it in haste;[f] it is the
LORD's Passover.[g]
12"On that same night I will pass
through[h] Egypt and strike down[i] every
firstborn[j] of both people and animals, and
I will bring judgment on all the gods[k] of

[a] 3 The Hebrew word can mean *lamb* or *kid*; also in verse 4.

11:4 [i] Ex 12:23; Ps 81:5 **11:5** [j] S Ex 4:23 [k] Isa 47:2 **11:6** [l] Ex 12:30; Pr 21:13; Am 5:17 **11:7** [m] S Ex 8:22 **11:8** [n] Ex 12:31-33 [o] Heb 11:27 **11:9** [p] S Ex 7:4 [q] S Ex 3:20 **11:10** [r] S Ex 4:21; Ro 2:5 **12:2** [s] ver 18; Ex 13:4; 23:15; 34:18; 40:2; Dt 16:1 **12:3** [t] Mk 14:12; 1Co 5:7 [u] ver 21 **12:5** [v] Ex 29:1; Lev 1:3; 3:1; 4:3; 22:18-21; 23:12; Nu 6:14; 15:8; 28:3; Dt 15:21; 17:1; Heb 9:14; 1Pe 1:19 **12:6** [w] ver 19; Lev 23:5; Nu 9:1-3, 5, 11; Jos 5:10; 2Ch 30:2 [x] Ex 16:12; Dt 16:4, 6 **12:7** [y] ver 13, 23; Eze 9:6 **12:8** [z] ver 10; Ex 16:19; 23:18; 34:25; Lev 7:15; Nu 9:12 [a] Dt 16:7; 2Ch 35:13 [b] Nu 9:11 [c] ver 19-20; Ex 13:3; Dt 16:3-4; 1Co 5:8 **12:9** [d] Ex 29:13, 17, 22; Lev 3:3 **12:10** [e] S ver 8; Ex 13:7; 29:34; Lev 22:30; Dt 16:4 **12:11** [f] ver 33; Dt 16:3; Isa 48:20; 52:12 [g] ver 13, 21, 27, 43; Lev 23:5; Nu 9:2, 4; 28:16; Dt 16:1; Jos 5:10; 2Ki 23:21, 23; 2Ch 30:1; Ezr 6:19; Isa 31:5; Eze 45:21 **12:12** [h] Am 5:17 [i] Isa 10:33; 31:8; 37:36 [j] ver 29; S Ex 4:23; 13:15 [k] Ex 15:11; 18:11; Nu 33:4; 2Ch 2:5; Ps 95:3; 97:9; 135:5; Isa 19:1; Jer 43:12; 44:8

11:5 *Every firstborn son in Egypt will die.* See Ps 78:51; 105:36; 135:8; 136:10. This is the ultimate disaster, since all the plans and dreams of a father were bound up in his firstborn son, who received a double share of the family estate when the father died (see Dt 21:17 and note). Moreover, judgment on the firstborn represented judgment on the entire community. *female slave, who is at her hand mill.* The lowliest of occupations (see 12:29 and note; Isa 47:2).

11:7 *distinction.* See note on 8:22.

11:8 *Moses, hot with anger.* Moses' announcement of the death of the pharaoh's firstborn son is the Lord's response to the death threat to his servant Moses (10:28).

12:2 *This month is ... the first month.* The inauguration of the religious calendar in Israel (see chart, p. 113). In the ancient Near East, new year festivals normally coincided with the new season of life in nature. The designation of this month as Israel's religious New Year reminded Israel that its life as the people of God was grounded in God's redemptive act in the exodus. The Canaanite name for this month was Aviv (see 13:4; 23:15; 34:18; Dt 16:1), which means "young head of grain." Later the Babylonian name Nisan was used (see Ne 2:1; Est 3:7). Israel's agricultural calendar began in the fall (see note on 23:16), and during the monarchy it dominated the nation's civil calendar. Both calendars (civil and religious) existed side by side until after the exile. Judaism today uses only the calendar that begins in the fall.

12:3 *community of Israel.* The Israelites gathered in assembly.

12:5 *animals ... without defect.* See Lev 22:18–25. Similarly, Jesus was like "a lamb without blemish or defect" (1Pe 1:19).

12:6 *at twilight.* Lit. "between the two evenings," an idiom meaning either (1) between the decline of the sun and sunset, or (2) between sunset and nightfall—which has given rise to disputes about when the Sabbath and other holy days begin.

12:7 *blood.* Symbolizes a sacrifice offered as a substitute, one life laid down for another (see Ge 9:4–6; 22:13; Lev 17:11 and notes). Thus Israel escapes the judgment about to fall on Egypt only through the mediation of a sacrifice (see Heb 9:22; 1Jn 1:7).

12:8 *bitter herbs.* Endive, chicory and other bitter-tasting plants are indigenous to Egypt. Eating them would recall the bitter years of servitude there (see 1:14 and note). *bread made without yeast.* Reflecting the haste with which the people left Egypt (see vv. 11,39; Dt 16:3; see also note on Ge 19:3).

12:9 *roast it ... head, legs and internal organs.* The method wandering shepherds used to cook meat.

12:11 *Passover.* Explained in vv. 13,23,27 to mean that the Lord would "pass over" and not destroy the occupants of houses that were under the sign of the blood.

12:12 *judgment on all the gods of Egypt.* Some had already been judged (see notes on 7:19; 8:2; 9:3; 10:21), and now all would be: (1) They would be shown to be powerless to deliver from the impending slaughter, and (2) many animals sacred to the gods would be killed.

Egypt. I am the LORD.[l] 13The blood will
be a sign for you on the houses where
you are, and when I see the blood, I will
pass over[m] you. No destructive plague will
touch you when I strike Egypt.[n]
14"This is a day you are to commemorate;[o] for the generations to come you shall
celebrate it as a festival to the LORD—a
lasting ordinance.[p] 15For seven days you
are to eat bread made without yeast.[q] On
the first day remove the yeast from your
houses, for whoever eats anything with
yeast in it from the first day through the
seventh must be cut off[r] from Israel. 16On
the first day hold a sacred assembly, and
another one on the seventh day. Do no

12:12 [l] S Ex 6:2
12:13 [m] S ver 11,23; Heb 11:28 [n] S Ex 8:23
12:14 [o] Ex 13:9; 23:14; 32:5 [p] ver 17,24; Ex 13:5,10; 27:21; Lev 3:17; 10:9; 16:29; 17:7; 23:14; 24:3; Nu 18:23
12:15 [q] Ex 13:6-7; 23:15; 34:18; Lev 23:6; Nu 28:17; Dt 16:3; 1Co 5:7 [r] S Ge 17:14

12:13 *sign.* Just as the plagues were miraculous signs of judgment on the pharaoh and his people (see 4:8 and note; 8:23), so the Lord's "passing over" the Israelites who placed themselves under the sign of blood was a pledge of God's mercy.
12:14 *celebrate it as ... a lasting ordinance.* Frequent references to Passover observance occur in the rest of Scripture (see Nu 9:1–5; Jos 5:10; 2Ki 23:21–23; 2Ch 30:1–27; 35:1–19; Ezr 6:19–22; Lk 2:41–43; Jn 2:13,23; 6:4; 11:55—12:1). The ordinance is still kept by practicing Jews today.
12:15 *remove the yeast from your houses.* Yeast later was often used as a symbol of sin, such as "hypocrisy" (Lk 12:1; cf. Mk 8:15 and note) or "malice and wickedness" (1Co 5:8; see note there). Before celebrating Passover, observant Jews today conduct a systematic (often symbolic) search of their house to remove every crumb of leavened bread that might be there (see v. 19). *cut off from Israel.* Removed from the covenant people by execution (see, e.g., 31:14; Lev 20:2–3) or banishment. See also Ge 17:14 and note.

HEBREW CALENDAR AND SELECTED EVENTS

NUMBER OF MONTH		HEBREW NAME	MODERN EQUIVALENT	BIBLICAL REFERENCES	AGRICULTURE	FESTIVALS**
1 Sacred sequence begins	7	**Aviv; Nisan**	March–April	Ex 12:2; 13:4; 23:15; 34:18; Dt 16:1; Ne 2:1; Est 3:7	Spring (latter) rains; barley and flax harvest begins	Passover; Unleavened Bread; Firstfruits
2	8	**Ziv (Iyyar)***	April–May	1Ki 6:1,37	Barley harvest; dry season begins	
3	9	**Sivan**	May–June	Est 8:9	Wheat harvest	Pentecost (Weeks)
4	10	**(Tammuz)***	June–July		Tending vines	
5	11	**(Av)***	July–August		Ripening of grapes, figs and olives	
6	12	**Elul**	August–September	Ne 6:15	Processing grapes, figs and olives	
7	1 Civil sequence	**Ethanim (Tishri)***	September–October	1Ki 8:2	Autumn (early) rains begin; plowing	Trumpets; Day of Atonement; Tabernacles (Booths)
8	2	**Bul (Marcheshvan)***	October–November	1Ki 6:38	Sowing of wheat and barley	
9	3	**Kislev**	November–December	Ne 1:1; Zec 7:1	Winter rains begin (snow in some areas)	Hanukkah ("Dedication")
10	4	**Tebeth**	December–January	Est 2:16		
11	5	**Shebat**	January–February	Zec 1:7		
12	6	**Adar**	February–March	Ezr 6:15; Est 3:7,13; 8:12; 9:1,15,17,19,21	Almond trees bloom; citrus fruit harvest	Purim
		(Adar Sheni)*—Second Adar	This intercalary month was added about every three years so the lunar calendar would correspond to the solar year.			

*Names of months in parentheses are not in the Bible. **For more information on the festivals, see chart, pp. 188–189.

work[s] at all on these days, except to prepare food for everyone to eat; that is all
you may do.
17“Celebrate the Festival of Unleavened
Bread,[t] because it was on this very day
that I brought your divisions out of Egypt.[u]
Celebrate this day as a lasting ordinance
for the generations to come.[v] 18In the first
month[w] you are to eat bread made without yeast, from the evening of the fourteenth day until the evening of the twenty-first day. 19For seven days no yeast is
to be found in your houses. And anyone,
whether foreigner[x] or native-born, who
eats anything with yeast in it must be cut
off[y] from the community of Israel. 20Eat
nothing made with yeast. Wherever you
live,[z] you must eat unleavened bread.”[a]
21Then Moses summoned all the elders
of Israel and said to them, “Go at once
and select the animals for your families
and slaughter the Passover[b] lamb. 22Take
a bunch of hyssop,[c] dip it into the blood
in the basin and put some of the blood[d]
on the top and on both sides of the doorframe. None of you shall go out of the
door of your house until morning. 23When
the LORD goes through the land to strike[e]
down the Egyptians, he will see the blood[f]
on the top and sides of the doorframe and
will pass over[g] that doorway, and he will
not permit the destroyer[h] to enter your
houses and strike you down.
24“Obey these instructions as a lasting
ordinance[i] for you and your descendants.
25When you enter the land[j] that the LORD
will give you as he promised, observe this
ceremony. 26And when your children[k] ask
you, ‘What does this ceremony mean to
you?’ 27then tell them, ‘It is the Passover[l]
sacrifice to the LORD, who passed over
the houses of the Israelites in Egypt and
spared our homes when he struck down
the Egyptians.’ ”[m] Then the people bowed
down and worshiped.[n] 28The Israelites did
just what the LORD commanded[o] Moses
and Aaron.
29At midnight[p] the LORD[q] struck down all
the firstborn[r] in Egypt, from the firstborn
of Pharaoh, who sat on the throne, to the
firstborn of the prisoner, who was in the
dungeon, and the firstborn of all the livestock[s] as well. 30Pharaoh and all his officials and all the Egyptians got up during
the night, and there was loud wailing[t] in
Egypt, for there was not a house without
someone dead.

The Exodus

31During the night Pharaoh summoned
Moses and Aaron and said, “Up! Leave
my people, you and the Israelites! Go,
worship[u] the LORD as you have requested.
32Take your flocks and herds,[v] as you have
said, and go. And also bless[w] me.”
33The Egyptians urged the people to
hurry[x] and leave[y] the country. “For otherwise,” they said, “we will all die!”[z] 34So
the people took their dough before the
yeast was added, and carried it on their
shoulders in kneading troughs[a] wrapped
in clothing. 35The Israelites did as Moses
instructed and asked the Egyptians for articles of silver and gold[b] and for clothing.[c]
36The LORD had made the Egyptians favorably disposed[d] toward the people, and
they gave them what they asked for; so
they plundered[e] the Egyptians.
37The Israelites journeyed from Rameses[f] to Sukkoth.[g] There were about six
hundred thousand men[h] on foot, besides
women and children. 38Many other people[i]

12:16 [s]Nu 29:35 **12:17** [t]Ex 23:15; 34:18; Dt 16:16; 2Ch 8:13; 30:21; Ezr 6:22; Mt 26:17; Lk 22:1; Ac 12:3 [u]ver 41; S Ex 6:6,26; 13:3; Lev 19:36 [v]Lev 3:17 **12:18** [w]S ver 2 **12:19** [x]Nu 9:14; 15:14; 35:15; Dt 1:16; Jos 8:33 [y]S Ge 17:14 **12:20** [z]Lev 3:17; Nu 35:29; Eze 6:6 [a]Ex 13:6 **12:21** [b]S ver 11; Mk 14:12-16 **12:22** [c]Lev 14:4, 6; Nu 19:18; Ps 51:7 [d]Heb 11:28 **12:23** [e]Isa 19:22 [f]S ver 7; Rev 7:3 [g]S ver 13 [h]S Ge 16:7; Isa 37:36; Jer 6:26; 48:8; 1Co 10:10; Heb 11:28 **12:24** [i]S ver 14 **12:25** [j]S Ge 15:14; Ex 3:17 **12:26** [k]Ex 10:2 **12:27** [l]S ver 11 [m]S Ex 8:23 [n]S Ge 24:26 **12:28** [o]ver 50 **12:29** [p]S Ex 11:4 [q]S Ge 19:13 [r]S Ex 4:23 [s]S Ex 9:6 **12:30** [t]S Ex 11:6 **12:31** [u]S Ex 8:8 **12:32** [v]Ex 10:9, 26 [w]Ge 27:34 **12:33** [x]S ver 11 [y]S Ex 6:1; 1Sa 6:6 [z]S Ge 20:3; S Ex 8:19 **12:34** [a]Ex 8:3 **12:35** [b]S Ex 3:22 [c]S Ge 24:53 **12:36** [d]S Ge 39:21 [e]S Ex 3:22 **12:37** [f]S Ge 47:11 [g]Ex 13:20; Nu 33:3-5 [h]Ge 12:2; Ex 38:26; Nu 1:46; 2:32; 11:13,21; 26:51 **12:38** [i]Nu 11:4; Jos 8:35

12:17 *Festival of Unleavened Bread.* Began with the Passover meal and continued for seven days (see vv. 18–19; see also Mk 14:12 and note). *divisions.* See note on 6:26.

12:21 *Passover lamb.* Christ (the Messiah) is “our Passover lamb” (1Co 5:7), sacrificed “once for all” (Heb 7:27) for us.

12:22 *hyssop.* Here probably refers to an aromatic plant (*Origanum maru*) of the mint family with a straight stalk (see Jn 19:29) and white flowers. The hairy surface of its leaves and branches held liquids well and made it suitable as a sprinkling device for use in purification rituals (see Lev 14:4,6,49,51–52; Nu 19:6,18; Heb 9:19; see also Ps 51:7). *dip it into the blood.* Today at Passover meals a sprig of parsley or other plant is dipped in salt water to symbolize the lowly diet and tears of the Israelites during their time of slavery.

12:23 *pass over.* See note on v. 11. *the destroyer.* In Ps 78:49 the agent of God’s wrath against the Egyptians is described as “a band of destroying angels.” God often used angels to bring destructive plagues (see 2Sa 24:15–16; 2Ki 19:35; see also 1Co 10:10, a reference to Nu 16:41–49).

12:26 *your children ask you, ‘What does this ceremony mean to you?’* See 13:14. The Passover was to be observed as a memorial festival commemorating Israel’s redemption and appropriating it anew. As observed today, it includes the asking of similar questions by the youngest child present.

12:27 *Passover sacrifice.* See note on v. 21. *passed over.* See note on v. 11.

12:29 *prisoner, who was in the dungeon.* The lowliest of situations (see note on 11:5).

12:31 *Pharaoh summoned Moses.* Though he had sworn never again to grant Moses an audience (see 10:28 and note), the pharaoh now humbles himself by summoning Moses and Aaron into his presence.

12:35–36 See 3:21–22; 11:2–3.

12:36 *plundered the Egyptians.* See note on 3:22.

12:37 *journeyed from Rameses.* See 1:11; see also note on Ge 47:11. The Israelite departure took place “the day after the Passover” (Nu 33:3). *Rameses ... Sukkoth.* See map, p. 117. *about six hundred thousand men.* A round number for 603,550 (38:26; see Introduction to Numbers: Special Problem; see also Nu 1:46 and note).

12:38 *Many other people.* Possibly including such Egyptians as those mentioned in 9:20.

went up with them, and also large droves
of livestock, both flocks and herds. 39 With
the dough the Israelites had brought from
Egypt, they baked loaves of unleavened
bread. The dough was without yeast because they had been driven out[j] of Egypt
and did not have time to prepare food for
themselves.
40 Now the length of time the Israelite
people lived in Egypt[a] was 430 years.[k]
41 At the end of the 430 years, to the very
day, all the LORD's divisions[l] left Egypt.[m]
42 Because the LORD kept vigil that night to
bring them out of Egypt, on this night all
the Israelites are to keep vigil to honor the
LORD for the generations to come.[n]

Passover Restrictions

43 The LORD said to Moses and Aaron,
"These are the regulations for the Passover
meal:[o]
"No foreigner[p] may eat it. 44 Any slave
you have bought may eat it after you have
circumcised[q] him, 45 but a temporary resident or a hired worker[r] may not eat it.
46 "It must be eaten inside the house; take
none of the meat outside the house. Do not
break any of the bones.[s] 47 The whole community of Israel must celebrate it.
48 "A foreigner residing among you who
wants to celebrate the LORD's Passover
must have all the males in his household
circumcised; then he may take part like
one born in the land.[t] No uncircumcised[u]
male may eat it. 49 The same law applies
both to the native-born and to the foreigner[v] residing among you."
50 All the Israelites did just what the LORD
had commanded[w] Moses and Aaron. 51 And
on that very day the LORD brought the Israelites out of Egypt[x] by their divisions.[y]

Consecration of the Firstborn

13 The LORD said to Moses, 2 "Consecrate to me every firstborn male.[z]
The first offspring of every womb among
the Israelites belongs to me, whether human or animal."
3 Then Moses said to the people, "Commemorate this day, the day you came out
of Egypt,[a] out of the land of slavery, because the LORD brought you out of it with
a mighty hand.[b] Eat nothing containing
yeast.[c] 4 Today, in the month of Aviv,[d] you
are leaving. 5 When the LORD brings you
into the land of the Canaanites,[e] Hittites,
Amorites, Hivites and Jebusites[f]—the
land he swore to your ancestors to give
you, a land flowing with milk and honey[g]—you are to observe this ceremony[h]
in this month: 6 For seven days eat bread
made without yeast and on the seventh
day hold a festival[i] to the LORD. 7 Eat unleavened bread during those seven days;
nothing with yeast in it is to be seen
among you, nor shall any yeast be seen
anywhere within your borders. 8 On that
day tell your son,[j] 'I do this because of
what the LORD did for me when I came out
of Egypt.' 9 This observance will be for you
like a sign on your hand[k] and a reminder
on your forehead[l] that this law of the LORD
is to be on your lips. For the LORD brought
you out of Egypt with his mighty hand.[m]
10 You must keep this ordinance[n] at the appointed time[o] year after year.
11 "After the LORD brings you into the
land of the Canaanites[p] and gives it to you,
as he promised on oath[q] to you and your
ancestors,[r] 12 you are to give over to the
LORD the first offspring of every womb. All
the firstborn males of your livestock belong to the LORD.[s] 13 Redeem with a lamb
every firstborn donkey,[t] but if you do not
redeem it, break its neck.[u] Redeem[v] every
firstborn among your sons.[w]

[a] *40* Masoretic Text; Samaritan Pentateuch and Septuagint *Egypt and Canaan*

12:39 [j] Ex 3:20; 11:1 **12:40** [k] Ge 15:13; Ac 7:6; Gal 3:17 **12:41** [l] S Ex 6:26 [m] S Ex 3:10 **12:42** [n] Ex 13:10; Lev 3:17; Nu 9:3; Dt 16:1,6 **12:43** [o] S ver 11 [p] ver 48; Nu 9:14; 15:14; 2Ch 6:32-33; Isa 14:1; 56:3,6; 60:10 **12:44** [q] S Ge 17:12-13 **12:45** [r] Lev 22:10 **12:46** [s] Nu 9:12; Ps 22:14; 34:20; 51:8; Pr 17:22; Jn 19:36* **12:48** [t] ver 49; Lev 19:18,34; 24:22; Nu 9:14; 10:32 [u] Eze 44:7 **12:49** [v] Lev 24:22; Nu 15:15-16, 29; Dt 1:16 **12:50** [w] ver 28 **12:51** [x] S Ex 3:10; S 6:6 [y] S Ex 6:26 **13:2** [z] ver 12, 13, 15; Ex 22:29; 34:20; Lev 27:26; Nu 3:13; 8:17; 18:15; Dt 15:19; Ne 10:36; Lk 2:23*

13:3 [a] ver 14; Ex 7:4; Lev 26:13; Nu 1:1; 9:1; 22:5; 26:4; Dt 4:45; 5:6; Ps 81:10; 114:1 [b] S Ex 3:20 [c] S Ex 12:8 **13:4** [d] S Ex 12:2 **13:5** [e] ver 11 [f] S Ex 3:8 [g] S Ex 3:8 [h] Ex 12:25-26 **13:6** [i] S Ex 12:15-20 **13:8** [j] S Ex 10:2; Ps 78:5-6 **13:9** [k] Isa 44:5 [l] ver 16; Dt 6:8; 11:18; Pr 3:3; Mt 23:5 [m] S Ex 3:20 **13:10** [n] S Ex 12:14 [o] Ps 75:2; 102:13 **13:11** [p] S ver 5 [q] S Ge 22:16; Dt 1:8 [r] S Ge 12:7; S 17:19; Ps 105:42-45 **13:12** [s] S Ge 4:4; Lev 27:26; Nu 3:13; 18:15, 17; Lk 2:23* **13:13** [t] ver 15; Lev 27:11 [u] Ex 34:20; Isa 66:3 [v] Nu 3:46-47 [w] Nu 18:15

12:41 *430 years, to the very day.* See notes on Ge 15:13; Ac 7:6.
12:44 See Ge 17:12–13 and note on 17:10.
12:46 *Do not break any of the bones.* See Nu 9:12; Ps 34:20; quoted in Jn 19:36 in reference to Jesus.
12:48 *No uncircumcised male may eat it.* Only those consecrated to the Lord in covenant commitment could partake of Passover; only for them could it have its full meaning (see Ge 17:9–14). Concerning participants in the Lord's Supper, see 1Co 11:27–30.
13:2 *Consecrate to me every firstborn male.* God had adopted Israel as his firstborn (see 4:22) and had delivered every firstborn among the Israelites, whether human or animal, from the tenth plague (see 12:12–13). All the firstborn in Israel were therefore his. Jesus, Mary's firstborn son (see Lk 2:7), was presented to the Lord in accordance with this law (see Lk 2:22–23).
13:5 See note on 3:8.
13:9 *like a sign on your hand and a reminder on your forehead.* A figure of speech (see v. 16; Dt 6:8; 11:18; see also Pr 3:3; 6:21; 7:3; SS 8:6). A literal reading of this verse has led to the practice of writing the texts of vv. 1–10, vv. 11–16, Dt 6:4–9 and Dt 11:13–21 on separate strips of parchment and placing them in two small leather boxes, which the observant Jew straps on his forehead and left arm before his morning prayers. The boxes are called "phylacteries" (Mt 23:5). This practice seems to have originated after the exile to Babylonia.
13:13 *Redeem.* See 6:6 and note. The verb means "obtain release by means of payment." *every firstborn donkey.* The economic importance of pack animals allowed for their redemption through sacrificing a lamb. *every firstborn among your sons.* Humans were to be consecrated to the Lord by their life, not by their death (see Ge 22:12; Nu 3:39–51; cf. Ro 12:1 and note).

14 “In days to come, when your son[x] asks you, ‘What does this mean?’ say to him, ‘With a mighty hand the LORD brought us out of Egypt, out of the land of slavery.[y] 15 When Pharaoh stubbornly refused to let us go, the LORD killed the firstborn of both people and animals in Egypt. This is why I sacrifice to the LORD the first male offspring of every womb and redeem each of my firstborn sons.’[z] 16 And it will be like a sign on your hand and a symbol on your forehead[a] that the LORD brought us out of Egypt with his mighty hand.”

Crossing the Sea

17 When Pharaoh let the people go, God did not lead them on the road through the Philistine country, though that was shorter. For God said, “If they face war, they might change their minds and return to Egypt.”[b] 18 So God led[c] the people around by the desert road toward the Red Sea.[a] The Israelites went up out of Egypt ready for battle.[d]

19 Moses took the bones of Joseph[e] with him because Joseph had made the Israelites swear an oath. He had said, “God will surely come to your aid, and then you must carry my bones up with you from this place.”[b][f]

20 After leaving Sukkoth[g] they camped at Etham on the edge of the desert.[h] 21 By day the LORD went ahead[i] of them in a pillar of cloud[j] to guide them on their way and by night in a pillar of fire to give them light, so that they could travel by day or night. 22 Neither the pillar of cloud by day nor the pillar of fire by night left[k] its place in front of the people.

14 Then the LORD said to Moses, 2 “Tell the Israelites to turn back and encamp near Pi Hahiroth, between Migdol[l] and the sea. They are to encamp by the sea, directly opposite Baal Zephon.[m] 3 Pharaoh will think, ‘The Israelites are wandering around the land in confusion, hemmed in by the desert.’ 4 And I will harden Pharaoh’s heart,[n] and he will pursue them.[o] But I will gain glory[p] for myself through Pharaoh and all his army, and the Egyptians will know that I am the LORD.”[q] So the Israelites did this.

5 When the king of Egypt was told that the people had fled,[r] Pharaoh and his officials changed their minds[s] about them and said, “What have we done? We have let the Israelites go and have lost their services!” 6 So he had his chariot made ready and took his army with him. 7 He took six hundred of the best chariots,[t] along with all the other chariots of Egypt, with officers over all of them. 8 The LORD hardened the heart[u] of Pharaoh king of Egypt, so that he pursued the Israelites, who were marching out boldly.[v] 9 The Egyptians—all Pharaoh’s horses[w] and chariots, horsemen[c] and troops[x]—pursued the Israelites and overtook[y] them as they camped by the sea near Pi Hahiroth, opposite Baal Zephon.[z]

10 As Pharaoh approached, the Israelites looked up, and there were the Egyptians, marching after them. They were terrified and cried[a] out to the LORD. 11 They said to Moses, “Was it because there were no graves in Egypt that you brought us to the desert to die?[b] What have you done to us by bringing us out of Egypt? 12 Didn’t we say to you in Egypt, ‘Leave us alone; let us serve the Egyptians’? It would have been better for us to serve the Egyptians than to die in the desert!”[c]

[a] *18* Or *the Sea of Reeds* [b] *19* See Gen. 50:25.
[c] *9* Or *charioteers*; also in verses 17, 18, 23, 26 and 28

13:14 [x] S Ex 10:2 [y] Ex 20:2; Dt 7:8; 28:68 **13:15** [z] S ver 2 **13:16** [a] S ver 9 **13:17** [b] Ex 14:11; Nu 14:1-4; Dt 17:16; Hos 11:5 **13:18** [c] Ex 15:22; Ps 136:16; Eze 20:10 [d] Jos 1:14; 4:13 **13:19** [e] Jos 24:32; Ac 7:16; Heb 11:22 [f] S Ge 47:29-30 **13:20** [g] S Ex 12:37 [h] Nu 33:6 **13:21** [i] Ex 32:1; 33:14; Dt 2:7; 31:8; Jdg 4:14; 5:4; Ps 68:7; 77:20; Jer 2:2; Hab 3:13 [j] Ex 14:19,24; 24:16; 33:9-10; 34:5; 40:38; Nu 9:16; 12:5; 14:14; Dt 1:33; Ne 9:12,19; Ps 78:14; 99:7; 105:39; Isa 4:5; 1Co 10:1 **13:22** [k] Ne 9:19 **14:2** [l] Nu 33:7; Jer 44:1; Eze 29:10 [m] ver 9 **14:4** [n] S Ex 4:21 [o] ver 8,17, 23; Ps 71:11 [p] S Ex 9:16; Ro 9:17,22-23 [q] S Ex 6:2; Eze 32:15 **14:5** [r] S Ge 31:21 [s] Ps 105:25 **14:7** [t] Ex 15:4 **14:8** [u] S Ex 11:10 [v] Nu 33:3; Ac 13:17 **14:9** [w] Ge 47:17 [x] ver 6-7, 25; Jos 24:6; Isa 43:17 [y] Ex 15:9 [z] ver 2 **14:10** [a] Ex 15:25; Jos 24:7; Ne 9:9; Ps 5:2; 34:17; 50:15; 107:6,28 **14:11** [b] S Ex 5:21; 16:3; 17:3; Nu 11:1; 14:22; 20:4; 21:5; Dt 9:7 **14:12** [c] S Ex 5:21; 15:24; 17:2; Ps 106:7-8

13:14 See note on 12:26.
13:16 See note on v. 9.
13:17 *road through the Philistine country.* Although the most direct route from Goshen to Canaan, it was heavily guarded by a string of Egyptian fortresses.
13:18 *desert road.* Leading south along the west coast of the Sinai peninsula. *Red Sea.* See NIV text note. Various locations of the crossing have been proposed along the line of the modern Suez Canal and including the northern end of the Gulf of Suez (see note on 14:2). *ready for battle.* Probably armed only with spears, bows and slings.
13:19 See notes on Ge 50:24–25.
13:21 *pillar of cloud … pillar of fire.* The visible symbol of God’s presence among his people (see 14:24; see also note on 3:2). The Lord often spoke to them from the pillar (see Nu 12:5–6; Dt 31:15–16; Ps 99:6–7).
14:2 *turn back.* Northward, in the general direction from which they had come. *Pi Hahiroth.* Located “east of Baal Zephon” (Nu 33:7). *Migdol.* Location unknown. The name means “watchtower.” *sea.* The sea that the NIV, in accordance with established tradition, calls the “Red Sea”—in Hebrew *Yam Suph*, i.e., Sea of Reeds (see 13:18 and NIV text note). Reference can hardly be to the northern end of the Gulf of Suez since reeds do not grow in salt water. Moreover, an Egyptian papyrus seems to locate Baal Zephon in the vicinity of Tahpanhes (see note on Jer 2:16), a site near Lake Menzaleh about 20 miles east of Rameses. The crossing of the “Red Sea” thus may have occurred at the southern end of Lake Menzaleh (see map, p. 117; but see note on 13:18). However, more recent investigation points toward Lake Balah (see map, p. 117). *Baal Zephon.* Means “Baal of the north” or “Baal of North (Mountain)”—also the name of a Canaanite god.
14:4 *harden.* See v. 8 and note on 4:21. *know that I am the LORD.* See note on 6:3.
14:7 *chariots.* Introduced into Egypt from Canaan, they brought about a revolutionary change in the art of warfare. Where the terrain was open and relatively flat, as much of Egypt was, they were especially effective. *officers.* The Hebrew for the singular of this word means “third man,” perhaps referring to his place in a chariot crew.
14:8 *hardened.* See v. 4 and note.

THE EXODUS

The exodus and conquest narratives form the classic historical and spiritual drama of OT times. Subsequent ages looked back to this period as one of obedient and victorious living under divine guidance. Close examination of the environment and circumstances also reveals the strenuous exertions, human sin and bloody conflicts of the era.

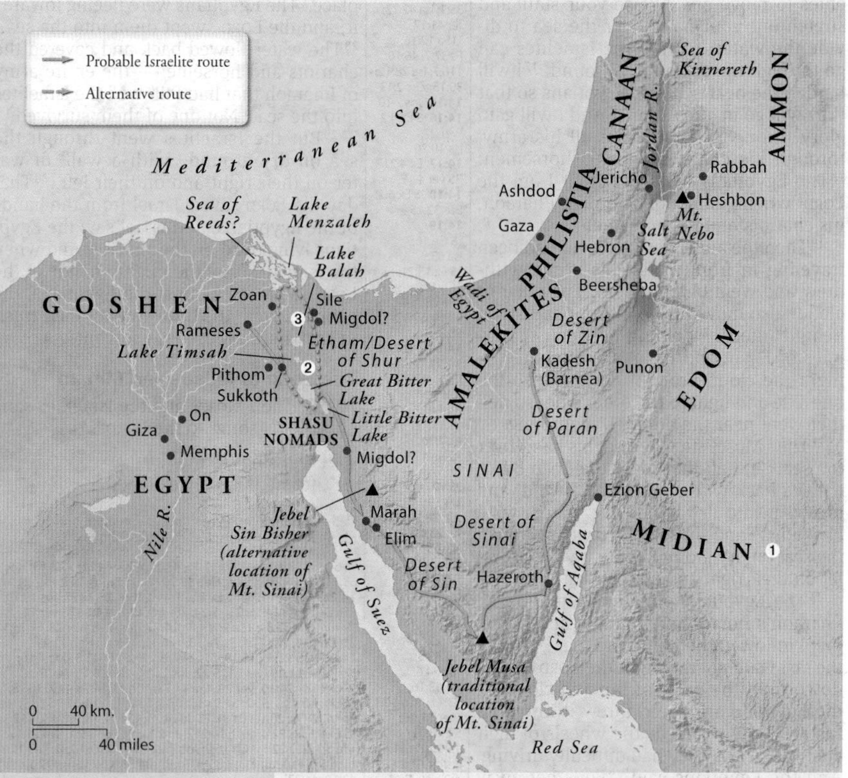

1 It was necessary for Moses to take refuge in Midian, where the Egyptian authorities could not reach him. The decades spent on "the far side of the wilderness" (Ex 3:1) were an important formative part of his life.

2 The exact crossing place through the Biblical "Sea of Reeds" (Heb. *Yam Suph*) is unknown.

3 The Israelite tribes fled past the Egyptian system of border posts, through the "Red Sea" and into the wilderness, where they avoided the main military and trade routes leading across northern Sinai. Their route possibly took them past the remote turquoise and copper mining regions northwest of Mount Sinai.

In historical terms, the exodus from Egypt was ignored by Egyptian scribes and recorders. No definitive monuments mention the event itself, but a stele of Merneptah (c. 1209 BC) claims that a people called Israel were encountered by Egyptian troops somewhere in northern Canaan.

Finding precise geographic and chronological details of the period is problematic, but new information has emerged from vast amounts of fragmentary archaeological and inscriptional evidence. Hittite cuneiform documents parallel the ancient covenant formula governing Israel's national contract with God at Mount Sinai.

The Late Bronze Age (c. 1550–1200 BC) was a time of major social migrations. Egyptian control over the Semites in the eastern Nile delta was harsh, with a system of brickmaking quotas imposed on the labor force, often the landless, low-class "Apiru." Numerous Canaanite towns were violently destroyed. New populations, including the "Sea Peoples," made their presence felt in Anatolia, Egypt, Canaan, Transjordan, and elsewhere in the eastern Mediterranean.

Correspondence from Canaanite town rulers to the Egyptian court (the Amarna letters; see chart, p. xxii) in the time of Akhenaten (c. 1350 BC) reveals a weak structure of alliances, with an intermittent Egyptian military presence and an ominous fear of people called "Apiru" (= "Hapiru").

13 Moses answered the people, "Do not
be afraid.[d] Stand firm and you will see[e]
the deliverance the LORD will bring you today. The Egyptians you see today you will
never see[f] again. 14 The LORD will fight[g] for
you; you need only to be still."[h]
15 Then the LORD said to Moses, "Why
are you crying out to me?[i] Tell the Israelites to move on. 16 Raise your staff[j] and
stretch out your hand over the sea to divide the water[k] so that the Israelites can
go through the sea on dry ground. 17 I will
harden the hearts[l] of the Egyptians so that
they will go in after them.[m] And I will gain
glory through Pharaoh and all his army,
through his chariots and his horsemen.
18 The Egyptians will know that I am the
LORD[n] when I gain glory through Pharaoh,
his chariots and his horsemen."
19 Then the angel of God,[o] who had been
traveling in front of Israel's army, withdrew and went behind them. The pillar of
cloud[p] also moved from in front and stood
behind[q] them, 20 coming between the armies of Egypt and Israel. Throughout the
night the cloud brought darkness[r] to the
one side and light to the other side; so neither went near the other all night long.
21 Then Moses stretched out his hand[s] over
the sea,[t] and all that night the LORD drove
the sea back with a strong east wind[u] and
turned it into dry land.[v] The waters were
divided,[w] 22 and the Israelites went through
the sea[x] on dry ground,[y] with a wall[z] of water on their right and on their left.
23 The Egyptians pursued them, and all
Pharaoh's horses and chariots and horsemen[a] followed them into the sea. 24 During
the last watch of the night the LORD looked
down from the pillar of fire and cloud[b] at
the Egyptian army and threw it into confusion.[c] 25 He jammed[a] the wheels of their
chariots so that they had difficulty driving.
And the Egyptians said, "Let's get away
from the Israelites! The LORD is fighting[d]
for them against Egypt."[e]
26 Then the LORD said to Moses, "Stretch
out your hand over the sea so that the
waters may flow back over the Egyptians
and their chariots and horsemen." 27 Moses stretched out his hand over the sea,
and at daybreak the sea went back to its
place.[f] The Egyptians were fleeing toward[b]
it, and the LORD swept them into the sea.[g]
28 The water flowed back and covered the
chariots and horsemen — the entire army
of Pharaoh that had followed the Israelites
into the sea.[h] Not one of them survived.[i]
29 But the Israelites went through the
sea on dry ground,[j] with a wall[k] of water on their right and on their left. 30 That
day the LORD saved[l] Israel from the hands
of the Egyptians, and Israel saw the Egyptians lying dead on the shore. 31 And when
the Israelites saw the mighty hand[m] of the
LORD displayed against the Egyptians, the
people feared[n] the LORD and put their trust[o]
in him and in Moses his servant.

The Song of Moses and Miriam

15 Then Moses and the Israelites sang
this song[p] to the LORD:

"I will sing[q] to the LORD,
for he is highly exalted.

[a] *25* See Samaritan Pentateuch, Septuagint and Syriac; Masoretic Text *removed* [b] *27* Or *from*

14:13 [d] S Ge 15:1 [e] 1Sa 12:16; 2Ch 20:17 [f] ver 30 **14:14** [g] ver 25; Ex 15:3; Dt 1:30; 3:22; 20:4; Jos 10:14; 23:3, 10; 2Sa 5:24; 2Ch 20:29; Ne 4:20; Ps 24:8; 35:1; Isa 42:13; Jer 41:12 [h] 1Sa 12:16; Ps 37:7; 46:10; 116:7; Isa 28:12; 30:15; Zec 2:13 **14:15** [i] Jos 7:10 **14:16** [j] S Ex 4:2 [k] ver 27; Isa 10:26 **14:17** [l] Ex 4:21 [m] S ver 4 **14:18** [n] S Ex 6:2; Eze 32:15 **14:19** [o] S Ge 16:7; Isa 63:9 [p] S Ex 13:21; 1Co 10:1 [q] Isa 26:7; 42:16; 49:10; 52:12; 58:8 **14:20** [r] Jos 24:7 **14:21** [s] S Ex 7:19 [t] S Ex 4:2; Job 26:12; Isa 14:27; 23:11; 51:15; Jer 31:35; Ac 7:36 [u] S Ge 41:6; Ex 15:8; 2Sa 22:16; 1Ki 19:11; Job 38:1; 40:6; Jer 23:19; Na 1:3 [v] S ver 22; S Ge 8:1 [w] 2Ki 2:8; Ps 74:13; 78:13; 114:5; 136:13; Isa 63:12 **14:22** [x] ver 16; Nu 33:8; Jos 24:6; Isa 43:16; 63:11; 1Co 10:1 [y] ver 21, 29; S Ex 3:12; 15:19; Dt 31:6-8; Jos 3:16, 17; 4:22; Ne 9:11; Ps 66:6; 77:19; 106:9; Isa 11:15; 41:10; 43:5; 44:27; 50:2; 51:10; 63:13; Jer 46:28; Na 1:4; Heb 11:29 [z] Ex 15:8; Jos 3:13; Ps 78:13 **14:23** [a] ver 7 **14:24** [b] S Ex 13:21; 1Co 10:1 [c] Ex 23:27; Jos 10:10; 1Sa 5:9; 7:10; 14:15; 2Sa 5:24; 2Ki 7:6; 19:7 **14:25** [d] S ver 14 [e] S ver 9; Dt 32:31; 1Sa 2:2; 4:8 **14:27** [f] Jos 4:18 [g] ver 28; Ex 15:1, 21; Dt 1:40; 2:1; 11:4; Ps 78:53; 106:11; 136:15; Heb 11:29 **14:28** [h] ver 23; Ex 15:19; Jos 24:7 [i] S ver 27; Ex 15:5; Jdg 4:16; Ne 9:11 **14:29** [j] ver 21, S 22; Jos 24:11; 2Ki 2:8; Ps 74:15 [k] Ps 78:13 **14:30** [l] ver 29; 1Sa 14:23; 1Ch 11:14; Ps 44:7; 106:8, 10, 21; Isa 43:3; 50:2; 51:9-10; 60:16; 63:8, 11 **14:31** [m] S Ex 9:16; Ps 147:5 [n] Ex 20:18; Dt 31:13; Jos 4:24; 1Sa 12:18; Ps 76:7; 112:1 [o] S Ex 4:5; Ps 22:4; 40:3; 106:12; Jn 2:11; 11:45 **15:1** [p] Nu 21:17; Jdg 5:1; 2Sa 22:1; 1Ch 16:9; Job 36:24; Ps 59:16; 105:2; Rev 15:3 [q] Jdg 5:3; Ps 13:6; 21:13; 27:6; 61:8; 104:33; 106:12; Isa 12:5, 6; 42:10; 44:23

14:14 *The LORD will fight for you.* A necessary reminder that although Israel was "ready for battle" (13:18) and "marching out boldly" (v. 8), the victory would be won by God alone.

14:19 *angel of God.* See note on Ge 16:7; here associated with the cloud (see 13:21).

14:20 *coming between the armies of Egypt and Israel.* The pillar of cloud (signifying the Lord's presence) protected Israel (see Ps 105:39).

14:21 *strong east wind.* See 10:13. In 15:8 the poet praises the Lord and calls the wind the "blast of your nostrils," affirming (as here) that the miracle occurred in accordance with God's timing and under his direction (see 15:10).

14:22,29 In later times, psalmists and prophets reminded Israel of what God had done for them (see Ps 66:6; 106:9; 136:13 – 14; Isa 51:10; 63:11 – 13). The waters were "piled up" (15:8) on both sides.

14:24 *last watch of the night.* Often the time for surprise attack (see Jos 10:9; 1Sa 11:11). *the LORD looked down.* See note on 13:21.

14:25 *The LORD is fighting for them.* See note on v. 14.

14:27 *the LORD swept them into the sea.* As he had done with the locusts of the eighth plague (see 10:19).

14:31 *feared the LORD.* See note on Ge 20:11. *put their trust in him and in Moses.* Faith in God's mighty power and confidence in Moses' leadership (cf. 1Sa 12:18 and note). *his servant.* Here refers to one who has the status of a high official in the Lord's kingly administration (see notes on Nu 12:6 – 8; Dt 34:5). See also the same title applied to Joshua (Jos 24:29), Samuel (1Sa 3:10), David (2Sa 3:18) and Elijah (2Ki 9:36).

15:1 – 18 A hymn celebrating God's spectacular victory over the pharaoh and his army. The focus of the song is God himself (see v. 11 and note); the divine name Yahweh ("the LORD") appears ten times. The first two stanzas (vv. 2 – 6, 7 – 11) retell the story of the "deliverance" (14:13) at the "Red Sea," and the final stanza (vv. 12 – 17) anticipates the future approach to and conquest of Canaan (the promised land).

15:1 *Moses and the Israelites sang.* As though one person, the whole community praises God. *I will sing ... into the sea.* Together with v. 18, this opening couplet frames the song and

Both horse and driver[r]
he has hurled into the sea.[s]

2 "The LORD is my strength[t] and my
defense[a];
he has become my salvation.[u]
He is my God,[v] and I will praise him,
my father's God, and I will exalt[w]
him.
3 The LORD is a warrior;[x]
the LORD is his name.[y]
4 Pharaoh's chariots and his army[z]
he has hurled into the sea.
The best of Pharaoh's officers
are drowned in the Red Sea.[b]
5 The deep waters[a] have covered them;
they sank to the depths like a
stone.[b]
6 Your right hand,[c] LORD,
was majestic in power.
Your right hand,[d] LORD,
shattered[e] the enemy.

7 "In the greatness of your majesty[f]
you threw down those who opposed
you.
You unleashed your burning anger;[g]
it consumed[h] them like stubble.
8 By the blast of your nostrils[i]
the waters piled up.[j]
The surging waters stood up like a
wall;[k]
the deep waters congealed in the
heart of the sea.[l]
9 The enemy boasted,
'I will pursue,[m] I will overtake them.
I will divide the spoils;[n]
I will gorge myself on them.
I will draw my sword
and my hand will destroy them.'
10 But you blew with your breath,[o]
and the sea covered them.
They sank like lead
in the mighty waters.[p]
11 Who among the gods
is like you,[q] LORD?
Who is like you—
majestic in holiness,[r]
awesome in glory,[s]
working wonders?[t]

12 "You stretch out[u] your right hand,
and the earth swallows your
enemies.[v]
13 In your unfailing love you will lead[w]
the people you have redeemed.[x]
In your strength you will guide them
to your holy dwelling.[y]
14 The nations will hear and tremble;[z]
anguish[a] will grip the people of
Philistia.[b]
15 The chiefs[c] of Edom[d] will be terrified,
the leaders of Moab will be seized
with trembling,[e]
the people[c] of Canaan will melt[f] away;
16 terror[g] and dread will fall on them.
By the power of your arm
they will be as still as a stone[h]—
until your people pass by, LORD,
until the people you bought[di]
pass by.[j]

[a] 2 Or *song* [b] 4 Or *the Sea of Reeds*; also in verse 22
[c] 15 Or *rulers* [d] 16 Or *created*

15:1 [r] Dt 11:4; Ps 76:6; Jer 51:21 [s] S Ex 14:27 **15:2** [t] Ps 18:1; 59:17 [u] S Ge 45:7; Ex 14:13; Ps 18:2,46; 25:5; 27:1; 62:2; 118:14; Isa 12:2; 33:2; Jnh 2:9; Hab 3:18 [v] S Ge 28:21 [w] Dt 10:21; 2Sa 22:47; Ps 22:3; 30:1; 34:3; 35:27; 99:5; 103:19; 107:32; 108:5; 109:1; 118:28; 145:11; 148:14; Isa 24:15; 25:1; Jer 17:14; Da 4:37 **15:3** [x] S Ex 14:14; Rev 19:11 [y] S Ex 3:15 **15:4** [z] Ex 14:6-7; Jer 51:21 **15:5** [a] S Ex 14:28 [b] ver 10; Ne 9:11 **15:6** [c] Ps 16:11; 17:7; 21:8; 63:8; 74:11; 77:10; 89:13; 98:1; 118:15; 138:7 [d] S Ex 3:20; S Job 40:14 [e] Nu 24:8; 1Sa 2:10; Ps 2:9 **15:7** [f] Dt 33:26; Ps 150:2 [g] Ps 2:5; 78:49-50; Jer 12:13; 25:38 [h] Ex 24:17; Dt 4:24; 9:3; Ps 18:8; 59:13; Heb 12:29 **15:8** [i] S Ex 14:21; Ps 18:15 [j] Jos 3:13; Ps 78:13; Isa 43:16 [k] S Ex 14:22 [l] Ps 46:2 **15:9** [m] Ex 14:5-9; Dt 28:45; Ps 7:5; La 1:3 [n] Jdg 5:30; Isa 9:3; 53:12; Lk 11:22 **15:10** [o] Job 4:9; 15:30; Isa 11:4; 30:33; 40:7 [p] ver 5; Ne 9:11; Ps 29:3; 32:6; 77:19 **15:11** [q] S Ex 8:10; Ps 77:13; S Isa 46:5 [r] Lev 19:2; 1Sa 2:2; 1Ch 16:29; Ps 99:3; 110:3; Isa 6:3; Rev 4:8 [s] S Ex 14:4; Ps 4:2; 8:1; 26:8; Isa 35:2; 40:5 [t] S Ex 3:20 **15:12** [u] S Ex 7:5 [v] Nu 16:32; 26:10; Dt 11:6; Ps 106:17 **15:13** [w] Ne 9:12; Ps 77:20 [x] S Ex 6:6; Job 33:28; Ps 71:23; 106:10; Isa 1:27; 41:14; 43:14; 44:22-24; 51:10; 63:9; Titus 2:14 [y] ver 17; Ps 68:16; 76:2; 78:54 **15:14** [z] ver 16; Ex 23:27; Dt 2:25; Jos 2:9; 5:1; 9:24; 1Sa 4:7; Est 8:17; Ps 48:6; 96:9; 99:1; 114:7; Eze 38:20 [a] Isa 13:8 [b] Ps 83:7 **15:15** [c] S Ge 36:15 [d] Dt 2:4 [e] Nu 22:3; Ps 114:7 [f] Jos 2:9,24 **15:16** [g] S ver 14; S Ge 35:5 [h] 1Sa 25:37 [i] Ps 74:2; 2Pe 2:1 [j] Dt 2:4

---

concentrates its dominant theme. *I will sing.* A common way to begin a hymn of praise (see Jdg 5:3; Ps 89:1; 101:1; 108:1).
15:2–6 The Lord's victory over the pharaoh was decisive.
15:2 The first half of the verse is echoed in Ps 118:14 (see Isa 12:2).
15:3 *The LORD is a warrior.* See note on 14:14. God is often pictured as a king leading his people into battle (see, e.g., Dt 1:30; Jdg 4:14; 2Sa 5:24; 2Ch 20:17–18).
15:4 *officers.* See note on 14:7.
15:5 *deep waters … covered them.* See vv. 8,10. *sank … like a stone.* See vv. 10,16. Babylon is similarly described in Jer 51:63–64.
15:6 *right hand.* See Isa 41:10 and note.
15:7–8 The Lord's overwhelming victory marks him as incomparable among the gods.
15:8 See note on 14:22. *blast of your nostrils.* See note on 14:21; see also Ps 18:15.
15:10 *you blew with your breath.* See note on 14:21. *sank like lead.* Cf. vv. 5,8,16.
15:11 *Who is like you … ?* See Ps 35:10; 71:19; 89:6; 113:5; Mic 7:18 and note. The Lord, who tolerates no rivals (see 20:3 and note), has defeated all the gods of Egypt and their worshipers.
15:12–17 The Lord's victorious right hand (= power) will surely establish his people in the promised land.
15:12 *earth.* Perhaps refers to Sheol or the grave (see Ps 63:9; 71:20), the "realm of the dead below" (Dt 32:22), since it was the sea that swallowed the Egyptians.
15:13 *unfailing love.* See note on Ps 6:4. *people you have redeemed.* See note on 6:6. *your holy dwelling.* Perhaps a reference to the house of worship at Shiloh (see Jer 7:12), and ultimately the temple on Mount Zion (see Ps 76:2), the "place" God would "choose" (Dt 12:14,18,26; 14:25; 16:7,15–16; 17:8, 10; 18:6; 31:11) to put "his Name" (Dt 12:5,11,21; 14:23–24; 16:2,6,11; 26:2). But the phrase may refer to the promised land, which is called "your dwelling" and "the sanctuary … your hands established" in v. 17. *holy.* See note on 3:5.
15:14–15 *Philistia … Edom … Moab … Canaan.* Israel's potential enemies. The order is roughly that along the route Israel would follow from Mount Sinai to the promised land.
15:15 *chiefs.* The term used earlier of the Edomite rulers (see Ge 36:15–19,21,29–30,40,43).
15:16 *dread will fall on them.* See note on 1Ch 14:17. *bought.* See NIV text note; see also Dt 32:6 and NIV text note. In Ps 74:2 the meaning "bought" or "purchased" is found in context with "redeemed" (see note on 13:13).

[17]You will bring[k] them in and plant[l] them
on the mountain[m] of your
inheritance—
the place, LORD, you made for your
dwelling,[n]
the sanctuary,[o] Lord, your hands
established.

[18]"The LORD reigns
for ever and ever."[p]

[19]When Pharaoh's horses, chariots and
horsemen[a] went into the sea,[q] the LORD
brought the waters of the sea back over
them, but the Israelites walked through
the sea on dry ground.[r] [20]Then Miriam[s]
the prophet,[t] Aaron's sister, took a timbrel
in her hand, and all the women followed
her, with timbrels[u] and dancing.[v] [21]Miriam
sang[w] to them:

"Sing to the LORD,
for he is highly exalted.
Both horse and driver[x]
he has hurled into the sea."[y]

The Waters of Marah and Elim

[22]Then Moses led Israel from the Red
Sea and they went into the Desert[z] of
Shur.[a] For three days they traveled in the
desert without finding water.[b] [23]When
they came to Marah, they could not drink
its water because it was bitter. (That is
why the place is called Marah.[bc]) [24]So the
people grumbled[d] against Moses, saying,
"What are we to drink?"[e]

[25]Then Moses cried out[f] to the LORD,
and the LORD showed him a piece of wood.
He threw[g] it into the water, and the water
became fit to drink.

There the LORD issued a ruling and instruction for them and put them to the
test.[h] [26]He said, "If you listen carefully to
the LORD your God and do what is right in
his eyes, if you pay attention to his commands and keep[i] all his decrees,[j] I will not
bring on you any of the diseases[k] I brought
on the Egyptians, for I am the LORD, who
heals[l] you."

[27]Then they came to Elim, where there
were twelve springs and seventy palm
trees, and they camped[m] there near the
water.

Manna and Quail

16 The whole Israelite community
set out from Elim and came to the
Desert of Sin,[n] which is between Elim and
Sinai, on the fifteenth day of the second
month after they had come out of Egypt.[o]
[2]In the desert the whole community grumbled[p] against Moses and Aaron. [3]The Israelites said to them, "If only we had died
by the LORD's hand in Egypt![q] There we sat
around pots of meat and ate all the food[r]
we wanted, but you have brought us out
into this desert to starve this entire assembly to death."[s]

[4]Then the LORD said to Moses, "I will
rain down bread from heaven[t] for you.
The people are to go out each day and
gather enough for that day. In this way I
will test[u] them and see whether they will

[a] 19 Or *charioteers* [b] 23 *Marah* means *bitter.*

15:17 [k]Ex 23:20; 32:34; 33:12 [l]2Sa 7:10; Ps 44:2; 80:8, 15; Isa 5:2; 60:21; Jer 2:21; 11:17; 24:6; Am 9:15 [m]Dt 33:19; Ps 2:6; 3:4; 15:1; 78:54,68; 133:3; Da 9:16; Joel 2:1; Ob 1:16; Zep 3:11 [n]S ver 13; Ps 132:13-14 [o]Ps 78:69; 114:2 **15:18** [p]S Ge 21:33; Ps 9:7; 29:10; 55:19; 66:7; 80:1; 102:12; 145:13; La 5:19 **15:19** [q]S Ex 14:28 [r]S Ex 14:22 **15:20** [s]ver 21; Ex 2:4; Nu 12:1; 20:1; 26:59; 1Ch 4:17; 6:3 [t]Jdg 4:4; 2Ki 22:14; 2Ch 34:22; Ne 6:14; Isa 8:3; Eze 13:17 [u]S Ge 31:27; 1Sa 18:6; Ps 81:2; Isa 30:32 [v]S Ge 4:21; Jdg 11:34; 21:21; 1Sa 18:6; 2Sa 6:5,14,16; Ps 30:11; 149:3; 150:4; SS 6:13; Jer 31:4,13 **15:21** [w]1Sa 18:7 [x]Am 2:15; Hag 2:22 [y]S Ex 14:27 **15:22** [z]Ps 78:52 [a]S Ge 16:7 [b]Ex 17:1,3; Nu 20:2,5; 33:14; Ps 107:5 **15:23** [c]Nu 33:8; Ru 1:20

15:24 [d]S Ex 14:12; 16:2; 17:3; Nu 14:2; Jos 9:18; Ps 78:18,42; 106:13,25; Eze 16:43 [e]Mt 6:31 **15:25** [f]S Ex 14:10 [g]2Ki 2:21; 4:41; 6:6 [h]S Ge 22:1; Jdg 3:4; Job 23:10; Ps 81:7; Isa 48:10 **15:26** [i]Ex 23:22; Dt 11:13; 15:5; 28:1; Jer 11:6 [j]Ex 19:5-6; 20:2-17; Dt 7:12 [k]Dt 7:15; 28:27,58-60; 32:39; 1Sa 5:6; Ps 30:2; 41:3-4; 103:3 [l]Ex 23:25-26; 2Ki 20:5; Ps 25:11; 103:3; 107:20; Jer 30:17; Hos 11:3 **15:27** [m]Nu 33:9 **16:1** [n]Ex 17:1; Nu 33:11, 12 [o]S Ex 6:6; 12:1-2 **16:2** [p]S Ex 15:24; 1Co 10:10 **16:3** [q]Ex 17:3; Nu 14:2; 20:3 [r]Nu 11:4,34; Dt 12:20; Ps 78:18; 106:14; Jer 44:17 [s]S Ge 47:15; Dt 8:3 **16:4** [t]ver 14-15; Dt 8:3; Ne 9:15; Ps 78:24; 105:40; S Jn 6:31* [u]S Ge 22:1

15:17 *inheritance.* The promised land (see 1Sa 26:19; Ps 79:1).
15:18 See note on v. 1.
15:20 *prophet.* See Nu 12:1–2 for a statement by Miriam concerning her prophetic gift (see also note on 7:1–2). Other female prophets in the Bible were Deborah (Jdg 4:4), Isaiah's wife (Isa 8:3, but see note there), Huldah (2Ki 22:14), Noadiah (Ne 6:14), Anna (see note on Lk 2:36) and Philip's daughters (Ac 21:9). *women followed her, with timbrels and dancing.* Such celebration was common after victory in battle (see 1Sa 18:6; 2Sa 1:20).
15:21 Miriam repeats the first four lines of the victory hymn (see v. 1), changing only the form of the first verb.
15:22—18:27 The story of Israel's journey from the "Red Sea" to Mount Sinai (see Introduction: Outline).
15:22 *Desert of Shur.* Located east of Egypt (see Ge 25:18; 1Sa 15:7) in the northwestern part of the Sinai peninsula. In Nu 33:8 it is called the "Desert of Etham." Shur and Etham both mean "fortress wall" (Shur in Hebrew, Etham in Egyptian).
15:23 *Marah.* Probably modern Ain Hawarah, inland from the western arm of the "Red Sea," about 50 miles south of its northern end.
15:24 *grumbled.* During their wilderness wanderings, the Israelites grumbled against Moses and Aaron whenever they faced a crisis (see 16:2; 17:3; Nu 14:2; 16:11,41). In reality, however, they were grumbling "against the LORD" (16:8). Paul warns us not to follow their example (see 1Co 10:10).
15:25 *He threw it into the water, and the water became fit to drink.* For a similar occurrence see 2Ki 2:19–22. *a ruling and instruction.* Technical terms presumably referring to what follows in v. 26. *put them to the test.* See note on Ge 22:1. God tested Israel also in connection with his provision of manna (see 16:4; Dt 8:2–3) and the giving of the Ten Commandments (see 20:20).
15:27 *Elim.* Seven miles south of Ain Hawarah (see note on v. 23) in the well-watered valley of Gharandel. *palm trees.* Elim means "large trees."
16:1 *from Elim … to the Desert of Sin.* See Nu 33:10–11. The Desert of Sin was in southwestern Sinai ("Sin" is probably derived from "Sinai"). *fifteenth day of the second month.* Exactly one month had passed since Israel's exodus from Egypt (see 12:2,6,29,31).
16:2 *grumbled.* See note on 15:24.
16:3 *meat.* Nu 11:5 lists additional items of food from Egypt that the Israelites craved.

16:4 *bread from heaven.* That the God of Israel could provide food in the wilderness for his people for 40 years

follow my instructions. 5On the sixth day
they are to prepare what they bring in, and
that is to be twice[v] as much as they gather
on the other days."
6So Moses and Aaron said to all the Israelites, "In the evening you will know
that it was the LORD who brought you out
of Egypt,[w] 7and in the morning you will
see the glory[x] of the LORD, because he has
heard your grumbling[y] against him. Who
are we, that you should grumble against
us?"[z] 8Moses also said, "You will know
that it was the LORD when he gives you
meat to eat in the evening and all the
bread you want in the morning, because
he has heard your grumbling[a] against
him. Who are we? You are not grumbling
against us, but against the LORD."[b]
9Then Moses told Aaron, "Say to the entire Israelite community, 'Come before the
LORD, for he has heard your grumbling.' "
10While Aaron was speaking to the
whole Israelite community, they looked toward the desert, and there was the glory[c]
of the LORD appearing in the cloud.[d]
11The LORD said to Moses, 12"I have
heard the grumbling[e] of the Israelites.
Tell them, 'At twilight you will eat meat,
and in the morning you will be filled with
bread. Then you will know that I am the
LORD your God.' "[f]
13That evening quail[g] came and covered
the camp, and in the morning there was
a layer of dew[h] around the camp. 14When
the dew was gone, thin flakes like frost[i] on
the ground appeared on the desert floor.
15When the Israelites saw it, they said to
each other, "What is it?" For they did not
know[j] what it was.
Moses said to them, "It is the bread[k] the
LORD has given you to eat. 16This is what the
LORD has commanded: 'Everyone is to gather as much as they need. Take an omer[a][l] for
each person you have in your tent.' "
17The Israelites did as they were told;
some gathered much, some little. 18And
when they measured it by the omer, the
one who gathered much did not have too
much, and the one who gathered little did
not have too little.[m] Everyone had gathered
just as much as they needed.
19Then Moses said to them, "No one is
to keep any of it until morning."[n]
20However, some of them paid no attention to Moses; they kept part of it until
morning, but it was full of maggots and
began to smell.[o] So Moses was angry[p] with
them.
21Each morning everyone gathered as
much as they needed, and when the sun
grew hot, it melted away. 22On the sixth
day, they gathered twice[q] as much—two
omers[b] for each person—and the leaders
of the community[r] came and reported this
to Moses. 23He said to them, "This is what
the LORD commanded: 'Tomorrow is to be
a day of sabbath rest, a holy sabbath[s] to
the LORD. So bake what you want to bake
and boil what you want to boil. Save whatever is left and keep it until morning.' "
24So they saved it until morning, as Moses commanded, and it did not stink or get
maggots in it. 25"Eat it today," Moses said,
"because today is a sabbath to the LORD.
You will not find any of it on the ground
today. 26Six days you are to gather it, but
on the seventh day, the Sabbath,[t] there
will not be any."
27Nevertheless, some of the people went
out on the seventh day to gather it, but
they found none. 28Then the LORD said
to Moses, "How long will you[c] refuse to
keep my commands[u] and my instructions?
29Bear in mind that the LORD has given you
the Sabbath; that is why on the sixth day
he gives you bread for two days. Everyone
is to stay where they are on the seventh
day; no one is to go out." 30So the people
rested on the seventh day.
31The people of Israel called the bread
manna.[d][v] It was white like coriander seed
and tasted like wafers made with honey.

16:5 [v] ver 22; Lev 25:21 **16:6** [w] S Ex 6:6 **16:7** [x] ver 10; Ex 24:16; 29:43; 33:18,22; 40:34; Lev 9:6; Nu 16:19, 42; Dt 5:24; 1Ki 8:11; Ps 63:2; Isa 6:3; 35:2; 40:5; 44:23; 60:1; 66:18; Eze 1:28; 10:4; 43:5; Hab 2:14; Hag 2:7; Jn 11:40 [y] ver 12; Nu 11:1,18; 14:2,27,28; 17:5 [z] Nu 16:11 **16:8** [a] ver 7 [b] Nu 23:21; Dt 33:5; Jdg 8:23; 1Sa 8:7; 12:12; S Mt 10:40; Ro 13:2; 1Th 4:8 **16:10** [c] S ver 7; Jn 11:4 [d] Ex 13:21; 40:34-35; 1Ki 8:10; 2Ch 7:1; Eze 10:4 **16:12** [e] S ver 7 [f] S Ex 6:2; S 20:2 **16:13** [g] Nu 11:31; Ps 78:27-28; 105:40; 106:15 [h] Nu 11:9 **16:14** [i] ver 31; Nu 11:7-9; Dt 8:3, 16; Ps 105:40 **16:15** [j] Dt 8:16 [k] S ver 4; Ne 9:20; S Jn 6:31 **16:16** [l] ver 32, 36 **16:18** [m] 2Co 8:15* **16:19** [n] ver 23; Ex 12:10 **16:20** [o] ver 24 [p] Ex 32:19 **16:22** [q] S ver 5 [r] Ex 34:31 **16:23** [s] S Ge 2:3; S Ex 20:8; Dt 5:13-14 **16:26** [t] ver 23 **16:28** [u] Jos 9:14; Ps 78:10; 106:13; 107:11; 119:1; Jer 32:23 **16:31** [v] S ver 14

[a] *16* That is, possibly about 3 pounds or about 1.4 kilograms; also in verses 18, 32, 33 and 36 [b] *22* That is, possibly about 6 pounds or about 2.8 kilograms [c] *28* The Hebrew is plural. [d] *31* *Manna* sounds like the Hebrew for *What is it?* (see verse 15).

---

was one of the great signs that Israel's God was the true God, the Lord of creation (see note on v. 31). Jesus called himself "the true bread from heaven" (Jn 6:32; see notes on 6:31–33), "the bread of God" (Jn 6:33), "the bread of life" (Jn 6:35,48), "the living bread that came down from heaven" (Jn 6:51)—all in the spiritual sense (Jn 6:63). For a similar application, see Dt 8:3 and Jesus' quotation of it in Mt 4:4. *go out each day and gather enough for that day.* Probably the background for Jesus' model petition in Mt 6:11; Lk 11:3. *test.* See notes on 15:25; Ge 22:1.

16:5 *sixth day ... twice as much as they gather on the other days.* To provide for "the seventh day, the Sabbath" (v. 26), "a day of sabbath rest" (v. 23). See v. 29.

16:6 *know.* See note on 6:3.

16:8 *meat ... in the evening and ... bread ... in the morning.* See vv. 13–14.

16:10 *glory of the LORD appearing in the cloud.* See 24:15–17; see also notes on 13:21; 40:34; Ps 26:8.

16:12 *twilight.* See note on 12:6.

16:13 *quail came.* For a similar incident, see Nu 11:31–33.

16:14 *thin flakes like frost.* See note on v. 31.

16:15 *What is it?* See v. 31 and NIV text note.

16:18 See 2Co 8:15, where Paul quotes the heart of the verse to describe Christians who share with each other what they possess.

16:23 *sabbath.* The first occurrence of the word itself, though the principle of the seventh day as a day of rest and holiness is set forth in the account of creation (see note on Ge 2:3).

16:29 See note on v. 5.

16:31 *manna.* Several naturalistic explanations for the manna have been given. For example, some equate it with

32 Moses said, "This is what the LORD has
commanded: 'Take an omer of manna and
keep it for the generations to come, so
they can see the bread I gave you to eat
in the wilderness when I brought you out
of Egypt.' "
33 So Moses said to Aaron, "Take a jar
and put an omer of manna[w] in it. Then
place it before the LORD to be kept for the
generations to come."
34 As the LORD commanded Moses, Aaron put the manna with the tablets of the
covenant law,[x] so that it might be preserved. 35 The Israelites ate manna[y] forty
years,[z] until they came to a land that was
settled; they ate manna until they reached
the border of Canaan.[a]
36 (An omer[b] is one-tenth of an ephah.)[c]

Water From the Rock

17 The whole Israelite community
set out from the Desert of Sin,[d]
traveling from place to place as the LORD
commanded. They camped at Rephidim,[e]
but there was no water[f] for the people to
drink. 2 So they quarreled with Moses and
said, "Give us water[g] to drink."[h]
Moses replied, "Why do you quarrel
with me? Why do you put the LORD to the
test?"[i]
3 But the people were thirsty[j] for water
there, and they grumbled[k] against Moses.
They said, "Why did you bring us up out
of Egypt to make us and our children and
livestock die[l] of thirst?"
4 Then Moses cried out to the LORD,
"What am I to do with these people? They
are almost ready to stone[m] me."
5 The LORD answered Moses, "Go out in
front of the people. Take with you some of
the elders of Israel and take in your hand
the staff[n] with which you struck the Nile,[o]
and go. 6 I will stand there before you by
the rock at Horeb.[p] Strike[q] the rock, and
water[r] will come out of it for the people
to drink." So Moses did this in the sight
of the elders of Israel. 7 And he called the
place Massah[a][s] and Meribah[b][t] because the
Israelites quarreled and because they tested the LORD saying, "Is the LORD among
us or not?"

The Amalekites Defeated

8 The Amalekites[u] came and attacked
the Israelites at Rephidim.[v] 9 Moses said to
Joshua,[w] "Choose some of our men and
go out to fight the Amalekites. Tomorrow
I will stand on top of the hill with the staff[x]
of God in my hands."

[a] 7 *Massah* means *testing.* [b] 7 *Meribah* means *quarreling.*

16:33 [w] Heb 9:4; Rev 2:17 **16:34** [x] Ex 25:16,21,22; 27:21; 31:18; 40:20; Lev 16:13; Nu 1:50; 7:89; 10:11; 17:4,10; Dt 10:2; 1Ki 8:9; 2Ch 5:10 **16:35** [y] Jn 6:31,49 [z] Nu 14:33; 33:38; Dt 1:3; 2:7; 8:2-4; Jos 5:6; Jdg 3:11; Ne 9:21; Ps 95:10; Am 5:25 [a] Jos 5:12 **16:36** [b] S ver 16 [c] Lev 5:11; 6:20; Nu 5:15; 15:4; 28:5 **17:1** [d] S Ex 16:1 [e] ver 8; Ex 19:2; Nu 33:15 [f] Nu 20:5; 21:5; 33:14 **17:2** [g] Nu 20:2; 33:14; Ps 107:5 [h] S Ex 14:12 [i] Dt 6:16; Ps 78:18,41; 106:14; Mt 4:7; 1Co 10:9 **17:3** [j] S Ex 15:22 [k] S Ex 15:24 [l] S Ex 14:11 **17:4** [m] Nu 14:10; 1Sa 30:6; S Jn 8:59 **17:5** [n] S Ex 4:2; S 10:12-13 [o] Ex 7:20 **17:6** [p] S Ex 3:1 [q] Nu 20:8 [r] Nu 20:11; Dt 8:15; Jdg 15:19; 2Ki 3:20; Ne 9:15; Ps 74:15; 78:15-16; 105:41; 107:35; 114:8; Isa 30:25; 35:6; 43:19; 48:21; 1Co 10:4 **17:7** [s] Dt 6:16; 9:22; 33:8; Ps 95:8 [t] Nu 20:13,24; 27:14; Ps 81:7; 106:32 **17:8** [u] S Ge 36:12 [v] S ver 1 **17:9** [w] Ex 24:13; 32:17; 33:11; Nu 11:28; 27:22; Dt 1:38; Jos 1:1; Ac 7:45 [x] S Ex 4:17

---

the sticky and often granular honeydew that is excreted in Sinai in early June by various scale insects and that solidifies rapidly through evaporation. But no naturally occurring substance fits all the data of the text, and several factors suggest that manna was in fact the Lord's unique provision for his people in the wilderness: (1) The meaning of the Hebrew word for "manna" suggests that it was something unknown by the people at the time (see NIV text note). (2) The appearance and taste of the manna suggest that it is not something experienced by other peoples in other times. (3) The daily abundance of the manna and its regular periodic surge and slump (double amounts on the sixth day but none on the seventh day, vv. 22,27) hardly fit a natural phenomenon. (4) Its availability in ample supply for the entire wilderness experience, no matter where the people were (v. 35), argues against a natural substance. (5) The keeping of a sample of the manna in the ark for future generations (vv. 33–34) suggests that it was a unique food.

16:33 *jar.* Said in Heb 9:4 to be made of gold.

16:34 *covenant law.* Anticipates the later description of the tablets containing the Ten Commandments as the "two tablets of the covenant law" (31:18; 32:15; 34:29), which gave their name to the "ark of the covenant law" (25:22; 26:33) in which they were placed (see 25:16,21), along with the jar of manna (see Heb 9:4; see also Rev 2:17 and note).

16:35 *ate manna forty years ... until they reached ... Canaan.* The manna stopped at the time the Israelites celebrated their first Passover in Canaan (see Jos 5:10–12).

17:1 *traveling from place to place.* For a list of specific sites, see Nu 33:12–14. *Rephidim.* Probably either the Wadi Refayid or the Wadi Feiran, both near Jebel Musa (see note on 3:1) in southern Sinai.

17:2 *put the LORD to the test.* Israel fails the Lord's testing of her (see 16:4) by putting the Lord to the test.

17:3 *grumbled.* See note on 15:24.

17:4 *these people.* The same note of distance and alienation ("these people" instead of "my people") in such situations (see also the interplay in 32:7,9–11; 33:13) is found often in the prophets (see, e.g., Isa 6:9–10 and note; Hag 1:2).

17:6 *I will stand there ... by the rock.* Paul may have had this incident in mind when he spoke of Christ as "the spiritual rock that accompanied" Israel (see 1Co 10:4 and note; see also Heb 11:24–26). *Horeb.* See note on 3:1. *Strike the rock, and water will come out.* The event was later celebrated by Israel's hymn writers and prophets (see Ps 78:15–16,20; 105:41; 114:8; Isa 48:21).

17:7 *Massah and Meribah.* Heb 3:7–8,15 (quoting Ps 95:7–8) gives the meaning "testing" for Massah and "rebellion" for Meribah. Another Meribah, where a similar incident occurred near Kadesh Barnea (see note on Ge 14:7), is referred to in Nu 20:13,24 (see note on 20:13); 27:14; Dt 32:51; 33:8; Ps 81:7; 106:32; Eze 47:19; 48:28.

17:8 *Amalekites.* See note on Ge 14:7.

17:9 *Joshua.* The name given by Moses to Hoshea, son of Nun (see Nu 13:16). "Hoshea" means "salvation," while "Joshua" means "The LORD saves." The Greek form of the name Joshua is the same as that of the name Jesus, for the meaning of which see NIV text note on Mt 1:21. Joshua was from the tribe of Ephraim (Nu 13:8), one of the most powerful of the 12 tribes (see notes on Ge 48:6,19). *fight the Amalekites.* Joshua's military prowess uniquely suited him to be the conqueror of Canaan 40 years later, while his faith in God and loyalty to Moses suited him to be Moses' "aide" (24:13; 33:11) and successor (see Dt 1:38; 3:28; 31:14; 34:9; Jos 1:5).

10 So Joshua fought the Amalekites as
Moses had ordered, and Moses, Aaron and
Hur[y] went to the top of the hill. 11 As long
as Moses held up his hands, the Israelites
were winning,[z] but whenever he lowered
his hands, the Amalekites were winning.
12 When Moses' hands grew tired, they
took a stone and put it under him and he
sat on it. Aaron and Hur held his hands
up—one on one side, one on the other—
so that his hands remained steady till sunset.[a] 13 So Joshua overcame the Amalekite[b]
army with the sword.
14 Then the LORD said to Moses, "Write[c]
this on a scroll as something to be remembered and make sure that Joshua hears
it, because I will completely blot out[d] the
name of Amalek[e] from under heaven."
15 Moses built an altar[f] and called[g] it The
LORD is my Banner. 16 He said, "Because
hands were lifted up against[a] the throne of
the LORD,[b] the LORD will be at war against
the Amalekites[h] from generation to generation."[i]

Jethro Visits Moses

18 Now Jethro,[j] the priest of Midian[k]
and father-in-law of Moses, heard
of everything God had done for Moses and
for his people Israel, and how the LORD
had brought Israel out of Egypt.[l]
2 After Moses had sent away his wife Zipporah,[m] his father-in-law Jethro received
her 3 and her two sons.[n] One son was
named Gershom,[c] for Moses said, "I have
become a foreigner in a foreign land";[o]
4 and the other was named Eliezer,[d][p] for he
said, "My father's God was my helper;[q] he
saved me from the sword of Pharaoh."
5 Jethro, Moses' father-in-law, together
with Moses' sons and wife, came to him
in the wilderness, where he was camped
near the mountain[r] of God. 6 Jethro had
sent word to him, "I, your father-in-law
Jethro, am coming to you with your wife
and her two sons."
7 So Moses went out to meet his father-
in-law and bowed down[s] and kissed[t] him.
They greeted each other and then went
into the tent. 8 Moses told his father-in-
law about everything the LORD had done
to Pharaoh and the Egyptians for Israel's
sake and about all the hardships[u] they had
met along the way and how the LORD had
saved[v] them.
9 Jethro was delighted to hear about all
the good things[w] the LORD had done for
Israel in rescuing them from the hand of
the Egyptians. 10 He said, "Praise be to the
LORD,[x] who rescued you from the hand of
the Egyptians and of Pharaoh, and who
rescued the people from the hand of the
Egyptians. 11 Now I know that the LORD is
greater than all other gods,[y] for he did this
to those who had treated Israel arrogantly."[z] 12 Then Jethro, Moses' father-in-law,[a]
brought a burnt offering[b] and other sacrifices[c] to God, and Aaron came with all the
elders of Israel to eat a meal[d] with Moses'
father-in-law in the presence[e] of God.
13 The next day Moses took his seat to
serve as judge for the people, and they
stood around him from morning till evening. 14 When his father-in-law saw all that
Moses was doing for the people, he said,
"What is this you are doing for the people?
Why do you alone sit as judge, while all
these people stand around you from morning till evening?"

[a] 16 Or *to* [b] 16 The meaning of the Hebrew for this clause is uncertain. [c] 3 *Gershom* sounds like the Hebrew for *a foreigner there.* [d] 4 *Eliezer* means *my God is helper.*

17:10 [y] ver 10-12; Ex 24:14; 31:2 **17:11** [z] Jas 5:16 **17:12** [a] Jos 8:26 **17:13** [b] ver 8 **17:14** [c] Ex 24:4; 34:27; Nu 33:2; Dt 31:9; Job 19:23; Isa 30:8; Jer 36:2; 45:1; 51:60 [d] Ex 32:33; Dt 29:20; Job 18:17; Ps 9:5; 34:16; 109:15; Eze 18:4 [e] ver 13; S Ge 36:12; Nu 24:7; Jdg 3:13; 1Sa 30:17-18; Ps 83:7 **17:15** [f] S Ge 8:20 [g] S Ge 22:14 **17:16** [h] Nu 24:7; 1Sa 15:8,32; 1Ch 4:43; Est 3:1; 8:3; 9:24 [i] Est 9:5 **18:1** [j] S Ex 2:18 [k] S Ex 2:16 [l] S Ex 6:6 **18:2** [m] S Ex 2:21 **18:3** [n] S Ex 4:20; Ac 7:29 [o] Ex 2:22 **18:4** [p] 1Ch 23:15 [q] S Ge 49:25; S Dt 33:29 **18:5** [r] S Ex 3:1 **18:7** [s] S Ge 17:3; S 43:28 [t] S Ge 29:13 **18:8** [u] Nu 20:14; Ne 9:32 [v] Ex 15:6,16; Ps 81:7 **18:9** [w] Jos 21:45; 1Ki 8:66; Ne 9:25; Ps 145:7; Isa 63:7 **18:10** [x] S Ge 9:26; S 24:27 **18:11** [y] S Ex 12:12; S 1Ch 16:25 [z] S Ex 1:10; S Lk 1:51 **18:12** [a] S Ex 3:1 [b] Ex 10:25; 20:24; Lev 1:2-9 [c] Ge 31:54; Ex 24:5 [d] S Ge 26:30 [e] Dt 12:7

17:10 *Hur.* Perhaps the same Hur who was the son of Caleb and the grandfather of Bezalel (see 1Ch 2:19–20), one of the builders of the tabernacle (see 31:2–5).
17:11 *held up his hands.* A symbol of appeal to God for help and enablement (see note on 9:29; see also 9:22; 10:12; 14:16).
17:14 *Write.* See 24:4; 34:27–28; Nu 33:2; Dt 28:58; 29:20,21,27; 30:10; 31:9,19,22,24; see also Introduction: Author and Date of Writing. *scroll.* A long strip of leather or papyrus on which scribes wrote in columns (see Jer 36:23) with pen (see Isa 8:1) and ink (see Jer 36:18), sometimes on both sides (see Eze 2:10; Rev 5:1). After being rolled up, a scroll was often sealed (see Isa 29:11; Da 12:4; Rev 5:1–2,5,9) to protect its contents. Scrolls were of various sizes (see Isa 8:1; Rev 10:2,9–10). Certain Egyptian examples reached lengths of over 100 feet; Biblical scrolls, however, rarely exceeded 30 feet in length, as in the case of a book like Isaiah (see Lk 4:17). Reading the contents of a scroll involved the awkward procedure of unrolling it with one hand while rolling it up with the other (see Isa 34:4; Eze 2:10; Lk 4:17,20; Rev 6:14). Shortly after the time of Christ the scroll gave way to the book form still used today.
17:15 *my Banner.* Recalling Moses' petition with upraised hands (see vv. 11–12,16) and testifying to the power of God displayed in defense of his people.
18:1 *Jethro, the priest of Midian.* See note on 2:16.
18:2 *sent away his wife.* Apparently Moses sent Zipporah to her father with the news that the Lord had blessed his mission (see v. 1) and that he was in the vicinity of Mount Sinai with Israel.
18:5 *mountain of God.* See 3:1 and note.
18:7–12 A striking example of how the God of Israel demonstrated not only to Israel but also to non-Israelites, by his mighty acts in behalf of his people, that he is the only true God. See the similar responses of Rahab (see Jos 2:9–11 and note) and the Gibeonites (Jos 9:9–10); see also notes on 16:4; Ge 12:1.
18:11 *Now I know that the LORD is greater than all other gods.* See the similar confession of Naaman in 2Ki 5:15.
18:12 *brought.* The verb means "provided" an animal for sacrifice (see, e.g., 25:2; Lev 12:8), not "officiated at" a sacrifice. *eat a meal with.* A token of friendship (contrast the battle with the Amalekites, 17:8–16). Such a meal often climaxed the establishment of a treaty (see Ge 31:54; Ex 24:11).

15 Moses answered him, "Because the people come to me to seek God's will.[f] 16 Whenever they have a dispute,[g] it is brought to me, and I decide between the parties and inform them of God's decrees and instructions."[h]

17 Moses' father-in-law replied, "What you are doing is not good. 18 You and these people who come to you will only wear yourselves out. The work is too heavy for you; you cannot handle it alone.[i] 19 Listen now to me and I will give you some advice, and may God be with you.[j] You must be the people's representative before God and bring their disputes[k] to him. 20 Teach them his decrees and instructions,[l] and show them the way they are to live[m] and how they are to behave.[n] 21 But select capable men[o] from all the people—men who fear[p] God, trustworthy men who hate dishonest gain[q]—and appoint them as officials[r] over thousands, hundreds, fifties and tens. 22 Have them serve as judges for the people at all times, but have them bring every difficult case[s] to you; the simple cases they can decide themselves. That will make your load lighter, because they will share[t] it with you. 23 If you do this and God so commands, you will be able to stand the strain, and all these people will go home satisfied."

24 Moses listened to his father-in-law and did everything he said. 25 He chose capable men from all Israel and made them leaders[u] of the people, officials over thousands, hundreds, fifties and tens.[v] 26 They served as judges[w] for the people at all times. The difficult cases[x] they brought to Moses, but the simple ones they decided themselves.[y]

18:15 [f]S ver 19; S Ge 25:22 **18:16** [g]Ex 24:14 [h]ver 15; Lev 24:12; Nu 15:34; Dt 1:17; 2Ch 19:7; Pr 24:23; Mal 2:9 **18:18** [i]Nu 11:11,14, 17; Dt 1:9,12 **18:19** [j]Ex 3:12 [k]ver 15; Nu 27:5 **18:20** [l]Dt 4:1,5; 5:1; Ps 119:12,26, 68 [m]Ps 143:8 [n]S Ge 39:11 **18:21** [o]S Ge 47:6; Ac 6:3 [p]S Ge 22:12 [q]Ex 23:8; Dt 16:19; 1Sa 12:3; Ps 15:5; Pr 17:23; 28:8; Ecc 7:7; Eze 18:8; 22:12 [r]Nu 1:16; 7:2; 10:4; Dt 16:18; Ezr 7:25 **18:22** [s]Lev 24:11; Dt 1:17-18 [t]Nu 11:17; Dt 1:9 **18:25** [u]Nu 1:16; 7:2; 11:16; Dt 16:18 [v]Dt 1:13-15 **18:26** [w]Dt 16:18; 2Ch 19:5; Ezr 7:25 [x]Dt 1:17 [y]ver 22 **18:27** [z]Nu 10:29-30 **19:1** [a]S Ex 6:6 [b]Nu 1:1; 3:14; 33:15 **19:2** [c]S Ex 17:1

27 Then Moses sent his father-in-law on his way, and Jethro returned to his own country.[z]

At Mount Sinai

19 On the first day of the third month after the Israelites left Egypt[a]—on that very day—they came to the Desert of Sinai.[b] 2 After they set out from Rephidim,[c] they entered the Desert of Sinai, and Israel camped there in the desert in front of the mountain.[d]

3 Then Moses went up to God,[e] and the LORD called[f] to him from the mountain and said, "This is what you are to say to the descendants of Jacob and what you are to tell the people of Israel: 4 'You yourselves have seen what I did to Egypt,[g] and how I carried you on eagles' wings[h] and brought you to myself.[i] 5 Now if you obey me fully[j] and keep my covenant,[k] then out of all nations you will be my treasured possession.[l] Although the whole earth[m] is mine, 6 you[a] will be for me a kingdom of priests[n] and a holy nation.'[o] These are the words you are to speak to the Israelites."

7 So Moses went back and summoned the elders[p] of the people and set before them all the words the LORD had commanded him to speak.[q] 8 The people all responded together, "We will do everything

[a] 5,6 Or *possession, for the whole earth is mine.* 6 *You*

[d]S ver 17; S Ex 3:1; Dt 5:2-4 **19:3** [e]Ex 20:21 [f]S Ex 3:4; S 25:22; Ac 7:38 **19:4** [g]Dt 29:2; Jos 24:7 [h]Dt 32:11; Ps 103:5; Isa 40:31; Jer 4:13; 48:40; Rev 12:14 [i]Dt 33:12; Isa 31:5; Eze 16:6 **19:5** [j]Ex 15:26; Dt 6:3; Ps 78:10; Jer 7:23 [k]S Ge 17:9; S Ex 3:1 [l]S Ex 8:22; S 34:9; S Dt 8:1; S Titus 2:14 [m]S Ex 9:29; 1Co 10:26 **19:6** [n]Isa 61:6; 66:21; S 1Pe 2:5 [o]Ge 18:19; Lev 11:44-45; Dt 4:37; 7:6; 26:19; 28:9; 29:13; 33:3; Isa 4:3; 62:12; Jer 2:3; Am 3:2 **19:7** [p]Ex 18:12; Lev 4:15; 9:1; Nu 16:25 [q]Ex 4:30; 1Sa 8:10

18:15 *seek God's will.* Inquire of God, usually by going to a place of worship (see Ge 25:22 and note; Nu 27:21) or to a prophet (see 1Sa 9:9; 1Ki 22:8).

18:16 *God's decrees and instructions.* The process of compiling and systematizing the body of divine law that would govern the newly formed nation of Israel may have already begun (see 15:25–26).

18:21 *men who fear God.* See note on Ge 20:11.

19:1 The arrival at Sinai marked a significant milestone in Israel's life. Having been delivered by God from Egyptian bondage and having experienced his care and provision, they were about to enter into a national covenantal relationship with him.

19:2 *Desert of Sinai.* Located in the southeast region of the peninsula (see note on 3:1). The narrator locates there the events recorded in the rest of Exodus, all of Leviticus, and Nu 1:1—10:10.

19:3—24:18 The Sinaitic covenant. It was cast in the form of ancient Near Eastern suzerainty-vassal treaties of the second millennium BC. It contained the divine pledge to be the Israelites' Suzerain-Protector if they would be faithful to him as their covenant Lord and obedient to the stipulations of the covenant as the vassal-people of his kingdom. The covenant had several later renewals, including ch. 34, the whole book of Deuteronomy, and Jos 24. See chart, p. 23; see also note on Jer 31:32.

19:3 *Jacob ... Israel.* See note on 1:1.

19:4 *I carried you on eagles' wings.* Reference may be to either the female golden eagle or the vulture (often symbolizing the protection of the pharaoh).

19:5 *if ... then.* The covenant between God and Israel at Mount Sinai is the outgrowth and extension of the Lord's covenant with Abraham and his descendants 600 years earlier. Participation in the divine blessings is conditioned on obedience added to faith (see note on Ge 17:9). *my covenant.* See note on Ge 9:9. *out of all nations ... my treasured possession.* The equivalent phrases used of Christians in 1Pe 2:9 are "chosen people" and "God's special possession" (see Dt 7:6; 14:2; 26:18; Ps 135:4; Mal 3:17; cf. Titus 2:14). *the whole earth is mine.* God is the Creator and Possessor of the earth and everything in it (see Ge 14:19,22; Ps 24:1–2).

19:6 *kingdom of priests.* The Israelites were to constitute the Lord's kingdom (the people who acknowledged him as their King) and, like priests, were to be wholly consecrated to his service (see Isa 61:6; cf. 1Pe 2:5; Rev 1:6; 5:10; 20:6). In their priestly role, the Israelites were to be channels of God's grace to the nations (see notes on Ge 12:2–3; Isa 42:1–4; 49:6). *holy nation.* See 1Pe 2:9. God's people, both individually and collectively, are to be "set apart" (see note on 3:5) to do his will (see Dt 7:6; 14:2,21; 26:19; Isa 62:12).

19:8 *We will do everything the LORD has said.* See 24:3,7; Dt 5:27.

the LORD has said."[r] So Moses brought their answer back to the LORD.

9 The LORD said to Moses, "I am going to come to you in a dense cloud,[s] so that the people will hear me speaking[t] with you and will always put their trust[u] in you." Then Moses told the LORD what the people had said.

10 And the LORD said to Moses, "Go to the people and consecrate[v] them today and tomorrow. Have them wash their clothes[w] 11 and be ready by the third day,[x] because on that day the LORD will come down[y] on Mount Sinai[z] in the sight of all the people. 12 Put limits[a] for the people around the mountain and tell them, 'Be careful that you do not approach the mountain or touch the foot of it. Whoever touches the mountain is to be put to death. 13 They are to be stoned[b] or shot with arrows; not a hand is to be laid on them. No person or animal shall be permitted to live.' Only when the ram's horn[c] sounds a long blast may they approach the mountain."[d]

14 After Moses had gone down the mountain to the people, he consecrated them, and they washed their clothes.[e] 15 Then he said to the people, "Prepare yourselves for the third day. Abstain[f] from sexual relations."

16 On the morning of the third day there was thunder[g] and lightning, with a thick cloud[h] over the mountain, and a very loud trumpet blast.[i] Everyone in the camp trembled.[j] 17 Then Moses led the people out of the camp to meet with God, and they stood at the foot of the mountain.[k] 18 Mount Sinai was covered with smoke,[l] because the LORD descended on it in fire.[m] The smoke billowed up from it like smoke from a furnace,[n] and the whole mountain*[a]* trembled[o] violently. 19 As the sound of the trumpet grew louder and louder, Moses spoke and the voice[p] of God answered[q] him.*[b]*

20 The LORD descended to the top of Mount Sinai[r] and called Moses to the top of the mountain. So Moses went up 21 and the LORD said to him, "Go down and warn the people so they do not force their way through to see[s] the LORD and many of them perish.[t] 22 Even the priests, who approach[u] the LORD, must consecrate[v] themselves, or the LORD will break out against them."[w]

23 Moses said to the LORD, "The people cannot come up Mount Sinai,[x] because you yourself warned us, 'Put limits[y] around the mountain and set it apart as holy.' "

24 The LORD replied, "Go down and bring Aaron[z] up with you. But the priests and the people must not force their way through to come up to the LORD, or he will break out against them."[a]

25 So Moses went down to the people and told them.

The Ten Commandments

20:1-17pp — Dt 5:6-21

20 And God spoke[b] all these words:[c]

2 "I am the LORD your God,[d] who brought you out[e] of Egypt,[f] out of the land of slavery.[g]

a *18* Most Hebrew manuscripts; a few Hebrew manuscripts and Septuagint *and all the people*
b *19* Or *and God answered him with thunder*

19:8 [r] Ex 24:3,7; Dt 5:27; 26:17 **19:9** [s] ver 16; Ex 20:21; 24:15-16; 33:9; 34:5; Dt 4:11; 2Sa 22:10, 12; 2Ch 6:1; Ps 18:11; 97:2; 99:7; Mt 17:5 [t] Dt 4:12,36; Jn 12:29-30 [u] S Ex 4:5 **19:10** [v] ver 14, 22; Lev 11:44; Nu 11:18; 1Sa 16:5; Joel 2:16; Heb 10:22 [w] S Ge 35:2; Rev 22:14 **19:11** [x] ver 16 [y] S Ge 11:5 [z] ver 3,20; S Ex 3:1; 24:16; 31:18; 34:2,4, 29,32; Lev 7:38; 26:46; 27:34; Nu 3:1; Dt 10:5; Ne 9:13; Gal 4:24-25 **19:12** [a] ver 23 **19:13** [b] Heb 12:20* [c] Jos 6:4; 1Ch 15:28; Ps 81:3; 98:6 [d] ver 21; Ex 34:3 **19:14** [e] S Ge 35:2 **19:15** [f] 1Sa 21:4; 1Co 7:5 **19:16** [g] 1Sa 2:10; Isa 29:6 [h] S ver 9 [i] Heb 12:18-19; Rev 4:1 [j] S Ge 3:10; 1Sa 13:7; 14:15; 28:5; Ps 99:1; Heb 12:21 **19:17** [k] S ver 2; Dt 4:11 **19:18** [l] Ex 20:18; Ps 104:32; Isa 6:4; Rev 15:8 [m] S Ex 3:2; 24:17; Lev 9:24; Dt 4:11, 24,33,36; 5:4; 9:3; 1Ki 18:24,38; 1Ch 21:26; 2Ch 7:1; Ps 18:8; Heb 12:18 [n] S Ge 19:28; Rev 9:2 [o] Jdg 5:5; 2Sa 22:8; Ps 18:7; 68:8; Isa 2:19; 5:25; 41:15; 64:1; Jer 4:24; 10:10; Mic 1:4; Na 1:5; Hab 3:6,10; Hag 2:6 **19:19** [p] S ver 9; Dt 4:33; Ne 9:13 [q] Ps 81:7 **19:20** [r] S ver 11 **19:21** [s] Ex 24:10-11; Nu 4:20; 1Sa 6:19 [t] S ver 13 **19:22** [u] Lev 10:3 [v] 1Sa 16:5; 2Ch 29:5; Joel 2:16 [w] ver 24; 2Sa 6:7 **19:23** [x] ver 11 [y] ver 12 **19:24** [z] Ex 24:1,9 [a] ver 22 **20:1** [b] Dt 10:4 [c] Ne 9:13; Ps 119:9; 147:19; Mal 4:4 **20:2** [d] S Ge 17:7; Ex 16:12; Lev 19:2; 20:7; Isa 43:3; Eze 20:19 [e] S Ge 15:7 [f] S Ex 6:6 [g] Ex 13:3; Eze 20:6

19:9 *dense cloud.* See 13:21 and note. *the people will hear me speaking.* See Dt 4:33. *put their trust in you.* See 14:31 and note.

19:10–11 Outward preparation to meet God symbolizes the inward consecration God requires of his people.

19:12–13 The whole mountain becomes holy because of God's presence (see 3:5 and note). Israel must keep itself from the mountain even as it is to keep itself from the tabernacle (see Nu 3:10).

19:15 *Abstain from sexual relations.* Not because sex is sinful but because it may leave the participants ceremonially unclean (see Lev 15:18; see also 1Sa 21:4–5).

19:16 *thunder ... lightning ... trumpet blast.* God's appearance is often accompanied by an impressive display of meteorological sights and sounds (see, e.g., 1Sa 7:10; 12:18; Job 38:1; 40:6; Ps 18:13–14). *thick cloud.* See 13:21 and note.

19:18 *fire ... smoke from a furnace.* See Ge 15:17 and note.

19:22 *priests.* See also v. 24. Before the Aaronic priesthood was established (see 28:1), priestly functions were performed either by the elders (see note on 3:16; see also 3:18; 12:21; 18:12) or by designated younger men (see 24:5). But perhaps the verse anticipates the regulations for the Aaronic priests who will be appointed. *who approach the LORD.* To officiate at sacrifices (see 40:32; Lev 21:23).

19:23 *set it apart as holy.* See note on 3:5.

20:1–17 See Dt 5:6–21; see also Mt 5:21,27; 19:17–19; Mk 10:19; Lk 18:20; Ro 13:9; Eph 6:2–3; Jas 2:10–11.

20:1 *words.* A technical term for "(covenant) stipulations" in the ancient Near East (e.g., among the Hittites; see also 24:3,8; 34:28). The basic code in Israel's divine law is found in vv. 2–17, elsewhere called the "Ten Commandments" (34:28; Dt 4:13; 10:4), the Hebrew words for which mean lit. "Ten Words." "Decalogue," a term of Greek origin often used as a synonym for the Ten Commandments, also means lit. "Ten Words."

20:2 *I am the LORD your God, who brought you out.* The Decalogue reflects the structure of the contemporary royal treaties (see note on Ge 15:7). On the basis of (1) a preamble, in which the great king identified himself ("I am the LORD your God"), and (2) a historical prologue, in which he sketched his previous gracious acts toward the subject king or people ("who brought you out ..."), the Lord then set forth (3) the treaty (covenant) stipulations (see Dt 5:1–3, 7–21) to be obeyed (in this case, ten in number, vv. 3–17).

3 "You shall have no other gods before[a] me.[h]
4 "You shall not make for yourself an
image[i] in the form of anything
in heaven above or on the earth
beneath or in the waters below. 5 You shall not bow down
to them or worship[j] them; for I,
the LORD your God, am a jealous
God,[k] punishing the children for
the sin of the parents[l] to the third
and fourth generation[m] of those
who hate me, 6 but showing love
to a thousand[n] generations of
those who love me and keep my
commandments.
7 "You shall not misuse the name of the
LORD your God, for the LORD will
not hold anyone guiltless who
misuses his name.[o]
8 "Remember the Sabbath[p] day by
keeping it holy. 9 Six days you
shall labor and do all your work,[q]
10 but the seventh day is a sabbath[r] to the LORD your God. On it
you shall not do any work, neither you, nor your son or daughter, nor your male or female servant, nor your animals, nor any
foreigner residing in your towns.
11 For in six days the LORD made
the heavens and the earth,[s] the
sea, and all that is in them, but
he rested[t] on the seventh day.[u]
Therefore the LORD blessed the
Sabbath day and made it holy.
12 "Honor your father and your mother,[v]
so that you may live long[w] in the
land[x] the LORD your God is giving
you.
13 "You shall not murder.[y]
14 "You shall not commit adultery.[z]
15 "You shall not steal.[a]

[a] 3 Or *besides*

20:3 [h] ver 23; Ex 34:14; Dt 6:14; 13:10; 2Ki 17:35; Ps 44:20; 81:9; Jer 1:16; 7:6, 9; 11:13; 19:4; 25:6; 35:15 **20:4** [i] ver 5, 23; Ex 32:8; 34:17; Lev 19:4; 26:1; Dt 4:15-19, 23; 27:15; 2Sa 7:22; 1Ki 14:9; 2Ki 17:12; Isa 40:19; 42:8; 44:9 **20:5** [j] Ex 23:13, 24; Jos 23:7; Jdg 6:10; 2Ki 17:35; Isa 44:15, 17, 19; 46:6 [k] Ex 34:14; Dt 4:24; Jos 24:19; Na 1:2 [l] S Ge 9:25; S Lev 26:39 [m] Ex 34:7; Nu 14:18; Jer 32:18 **20:6** [n] Ex 34:7; Nu 14:18; Dt 7:9; Jer 32:18; Lk 1:50; Ro 11:28 **20:7** [o] Ex 22:28; Lev 18:21; 19:12; 22:2; 24:11, 16; Dt 6:13; 10:20; Job 2:5, 9; Ps 63:11; Isa 8:21; Eze 20:39; 39:7; S Mt 5:33 **20:8** [p] S Ex 16:23; 31:13-16; 35:3; Lev 19:3, 30; 26:2; Isa 56:2; Jer 17:21-27; Eze 22:8 **20:9** [q] Ex 23:12; 31:13-17; 34:21; 35:2-3; Lev 23:3; Lk 13:14 **20:10** [r] S Ge 2:3; Ex 31:14; Lev 23:38; Nu 28:9; Isa 56:2; Eze 20:12, 20 **20:11** [s] Ge 1:3-2:1 [t] S Ge 2:2 [u] Ex 31:17; Heb 4:4 **20:12** [v] S Ge 31:35; S Dt 5:16; Mt 15:4*; 19:19*; Mk 7:10*; 10:19*; Lk 18:20*; Eph 6:2 [w] Dt 6:2; Eph 6:3 [x] Dt 11:9; 25:15; Jer 35:7 **20:13** [y] S Ge 4:23; Mt 5:21*; 19:18*; Mk 10:19*; Lk 18:20*; Ro 13:9*; Jas 2:11* **20:14** [z] Lev 18:20; 20:10; Nu 5:12, 13, 29; Pr 6:29, 32; Mt 5:27*; 19:18*; Mk 10:19*; Lk 18:20*; Ro 13:9*; Jas 2:11* **20:15** [a] Lev 19:11, 13; Eze 18:7; Mt 19:18*; Mk 10:19*; Lk 18:20*; Ro 13:9*

Use of this ancient royal treaty pattern shows that the Lord is here formally acknowledged as Israel's King and that Israel is his subject people. As his subjects, his covenant people are to render complete submission, allegiance and obedience to him out of gratitude for his mercies, reverence for his sovereignty, and trust in his continuing care. See chart, p. 23.

20:3 *before.* The Hebrew for this word is translated "in hostility toward" in Ge 16:12; 25:18. Something of that sense may be intended here. In any event, no deity, real or imagined, is to rival the one true God in Israel's heart and life.

20:4 *image in the form of anything.* Because God has no visible form, any idol intended to resemble him would be a sinful misrepresentation of him (see Dt 4:12,15–18). Since other gods are not to be worshiped (see v. 5), making idols of them would be equally sinful (see Dt 4:19,23–28). Cf. Jn 4:23–24 and note on 4:24.

20:5 *jealous God.* God will not put up with rivalry or unfaithfulness. Usually his "jealousy" concerns Israel and assumes the covenant relationship (analogous to marriage) and the Lord's exclusive right to possess Israel and to claim her love and allegiance. Actually, jealousy is part of the vocabulary of love. The "jealousy" of God (1) demands exclusive devotion to God (see 34:14; Dt 4:24; 32:16,21; Jos 24:19; Ps 78:58; 1Co 10:22; Jas 4:5 and NIV text note), (2) delivers to judgment all who oppose God (see Dt 29:20; 1Ki 14:22; Ps 79:5; Isa 42:13; 59:17; Eze 5:13; 16:38; 23:25; 36:5–6; Na 1:2; Zep 1:18; 3:8) and (3) vindicates God's people (see 2Ki 19:31; Isa 9:7; 26:11; Eze 39:25; Joel 2:18; Zec 1:14; 8:2). In some of these passages the meaning is closer to "zeal" (the same Hebrew word may be translated either way, depending on context). *to the third and fourth generation of those who hate me.* Those Israelites who blatantly violate God's covenant and thus show that they reject the Lord as their King will bring down judgment on themselves and their households (see, e.g., Nu 16:31–34; Jos 7:24 and note)—households were usually extended to three or four generations. See note on Ps 109:12. *hate.* In covenant contexts the terms "hate" and "love" (v. 6) were conventionally used to indicate rejection of or loyalty to the covenant Lord.

20:6 *a thousand generations of those.* See Dt 7:9; 1Ch 16:15; Ps 105:8. *love me and keep my commandments.* See Dt 5:10; 6:5; 7:9,12 and note; Ne 1:5; Da 9:4; Jn 14:15; 1Jn 5:3. In the treaty language of the ancient Near East the "love" owed to the great king was a conventional term for total allegiance and implicit trust expressing itself in obedient service.

20:7 *misuse the name of the LORD.* By profaning God's name—e.g., by swearing falsely by it (see Lev 19:12; see also Jer 7:9 and NIV text note), as on the witness stand in court. Jesus elaborates on oath-taking in Mt 5:33–37.

20:8 See Ge 2:3. *Sabbath.* See note on 16:23. *holy.* See note on 3:5.

20:9 *Six days.* The question of a shorter work week in a modern industrialized culture is not in view.

20:10 *On it you shall not do any work.* Two reasons (one here and one in Deuteronomy) are given: (1) Having completed his work of creation God "rested on the seventh day" (v. 11), and the Israelites are to observe the same pattern in their service of God in the creation; (2) the Israelites must cease all labor so that their servants can also participate in the Sabbath-rest—just as God had delivered his people from the burden of slavery in Egypt (see Dt 5:14–15). The Sabbath thus became a "sign" of the covenant between God and Israel at Mount Sinai (see 31:12–17; see also note on Ge 9:12).

20:12 *Honor.* (1) Prize highly (see Pr 4:8), (2) care for (see Ps 91:15), (3) show respect for (see Lev 19:3; 20:9), and (4) obey (see Dt 21:18–21; cf. Eph 6:1). *so that you may live long.* "The first commandment with a promise" (Eph 6:2). See also note on Dt 6:2. Honoring those in authority is essential for social stability.

20:13 See Mt 5:21–26. *murder.* The Hebrew for this verb usually refers to a premeditated and deliberate act. See note on Nu 35:33.

20:14 See Mt 5:27–30. *adultery.* A sin "against God" (Ge 39:9) as well as against the marriage partner. The "marriage bed should be kept pure" (Heb 13:4).

20:15 *steal.* Stealing deprives others of what God has entrusted to them (see 22:1–15 and notes).

16 "You shall not give false testimony[b]
against your neighbor.[c]
17 "You shall not covet[d] your neighbor's
house. You shall not covet your
neighbor's wife, or his male or
female servant, his ox or donkey,
or anything that belongs to your
neighbor."

18 When the people saw the thunder and
lightning and heard the trumpet[e] and saw
the mountain in smoke,[f] they trembled
with fear.[g] They stayed at a distance 19 and
said to Moses, "Speak to us yourself and
we will listen. But do not have God speak[h]
to us or we will die."[i]

20 Moses said to the people, "Do not be
afraid.[j] God has come to test[k] you, so that
the fear[l] of God will be with you to keep
you from sinning."[m]

21 The people remained at a distance,
while Moses approached the thick darkness[n] where God was.

Idols and Altars

22 Then the LORD said to Moses, "Tell the
Israelites this: 'You have seen for yourselves that I have spoken to you from
heaven:[o] 23 Do not make any gods to be
alongside me;[p] do not make for yourselves
gods of silver or gods of gold.[q]

24 " 'Make an altar[r] of earth for me and
sacrifice on it your burnt offerings[s] and fellowship offerings, your sheep and goats
and your cattle. Wherever I cause my name[t]
to be honored, I will come to you and bless[u]
you. 25 If you make an altar of stones for
me, do not build it with dressed stones, for
you will defile it if you use a tool[v] on it.
26 And do not go up to my altar on steps, or
your private parts[w] may be exposed.'

21 "These are the laws[x] you are to set
before them:

Hebrew Servants

21:2-6pp — Dt 15:12-18
21:2-11Ref — Lev 25:39-55

2 "If you buy a Hebrew servant,[y] he is
to serve you for six years. But in the seventh year, he shall go free,[z] without paying

20:16 [b] Lev 19:11; Jer 9:3,5 [c] Ex 23:1,7; Lev 19:18; Ps 50:20; 101:5; 119:29; Mt 19:18*; Mk 10:19; Lk 3:14*; 18:20* **20:17** [d] Lk 12:15; Ro 7:7*; 13:9*; Eph 5:3; Heb 13:5 **20:18** [e] Ex 19:16-19; Dt 4:36; Isa 58:1; Jer 6:17; Eze 33:3; Heb 12:18-19; Rev 1:10 [f] S Ex 19:18 [g] S Ge 3:10; S Ex 14:31; S 19:16 **20:19** [h] Job 37:4,5; 40:9; Ps 29:3-4 [i] Dt 5:5,23-27; 18:16; Gal 3:19 **20:20** [j] S Ge 15:1 [k] S Ge 22:1 [l] Dt 4:10; 6:2, 24; 10:12; Ps 111:10; 128:1; Pr 1:7; Ecc 12:13; Isa 8:13 [m] Job 1:8; 2:3; 28:28; Pr 3:7; 8:13; 14:16; 16:6 **20:21** [n] S Ex 19:9; Dt 5:22; Ps 18:9; 68:4; 97:2; Isa 19:1 **20:22** [o] Dt 5:24,26; Ne 9:13 **20:23** [p] S ver 3 [q] Ex 22:20; 32:4,8,31; 34:17; Dt 29:17-18; Ne 9:18 **20:24** [r] Ex 27:1; 40:29; Nu 16:38; Dt 27:5; Jos 8:30; 2Ki 16:14; 2Ch 4:1; Ezr 3:2; Eze 43:13 [s] S Ge 8:20; S Ex 18:12 [t] Dt 12:5; 16:6,11; 26:2; 1Ki 9:3; 2Ki 21:4,7; 2Ch 6:6; 12:13; Ezr 6:12 [u] S Ge 12:2; 22:17 **20:25** [v] Jos 8:31; 1Ki 6:7 **20:26** [w] Eze 43:17 **21:1** [x] Ex 24:3; 34:32; Dt 4:14; 6:1 **21:2** [y] Ex 22:3 [z] ver 7; Jer 34:8, 14

20:16 *false testimony.* Violates others' reputation and deprives them of their rights (see Ps 24:4; Pr 6:19; Jer 5:2 and notes).

20:17 *covet.* Desire something with evil motivation (see Mt 15:19). To break God's commandments inwardly is equivalent to breaking them outwardly (see Mt 5:21–30; cf. Col 3:5).

20:18–21 Concludes the account of the giving of the Decalogue. The order of the narrative appears to be different from the order of events, since v. 18 is most likely a continuation of 19:25. On this reading, the proclamation of the Decalogue took place after Moses approached God (v. 21). Biblical writers often did not follow chronological sequence in their narratives for various literary reasons. The purpose of chronological displacement here may have been either (1) to keep the Decalogue distinct from the "Book of the Covenant" (24:7) that follows (20:22—23:19) or (2) to conclude the account with the formal institution of Moses' office as covenant mediator—or both.

20:19 See Heb 12:19–20. The Israelites request a mediator to stand between them and God, a role fulfilled by Moses and subsequently by priests, prophets and kings—and ultimately by Jesus Christ (see 1Ti 2:5).

20:20 *Do not be afraid.* Do not think that God's display of his majesty is intended simply to fill you with abject fear. He has come to enter into covenant with you as your heavenly King. *test.* See note on Ge 22:1. *fear of God.* See note on Ge 20:11.

20:22—23:19 The stipulations of the "Book of the Covenant" (24:7), consisting largely of expansions on and expositions of the Ten Commandments. See chart, p. 287.

20:22–26 Initial stipulations governing Israel's basic relationship with God (cf. v. 3).

20:22 *heaven.* God's dwelling place. Even on "top of Mount Sinai" (19:20) God spoke from heaven.

20:23 See vv. 3–4. The contrast between the one true God "in heaven," who "does whatever pleases him" (Ps 115:3), and idols of silver or gold, who can do nothing at all (see Ps 115:3–8; see also Ps 135:5–6,15–17), is striking.

20:24 *altar of earth.* Such an altar, with dimensions the same as those of the altar in the tabernacle (see 27:1), has been found in the excavated ruins of a small Iron Age (tenth, or possibly eleventh, century BC) Israelite temple at Arad in southern Israel. *burnt offerings.* See note on Lev 1:3. *fellowship offerings.* See note on Lev 3:1. *Wherever I cause my name to be honored.* Not the later central sanctuary at Jerusalem, but numerous temporary places of worship (see, e.g., Jos 8:30–31; Jdg 6:24; 21:4; 1Sa 7:17; 14:35; 2Sa 24:25; 1Ki 18:30).

20:25 *do not build it with dressed stones.* Many ancient altars of undressed stones (from various periods) have been found in Israel. *defile it if you use a tool on it.* For reasons not now clear but perhaps related to pagan practices.

20:26 *steps.* The oldest stepped altar known in Israel is at Megiddo and dates between 3000 and 2500 BC. *or your private parts may be exposed.* Men who ascended to such altars would expose their nakedness in the presence of God. Although Aaron and his descendants served at stepped altars (see Lev 9:22; Eze 43:17), they were instructed to wear linen undergarments (see 28:42–43; Lev 6:10; 16:3–4; Eze 44:17–18).

21:1 This verse functions as the heading for the section 21:2—23:19.

21:2–11 See Jer 34:8–22. The list begins with laws regulating servitude. No other ancient Near Eastern law collection begins this way. Hammurapi's law code, e.g., deals with the question of slavery last (see chart, p. xxii). The fact that the Lord gives priority to regulating servitude in the Book of the Covenant may reflect his recent deliverance of Israel from a painful period of enslavement in Egypt.

21:2 *Hebrew.* See note on Ge 14:13. *in the seventh year, he shall go free.* The Lord's servants are not to be anyone's perpetual slaves (see 20:10 and note).

anything. 3 If he comes alone, he is to go
free alone; but if he has a wife when he
comes, she is to go with him. 4 If his master gives him a wife and she bears him
sons or daughters, the woman and her
children shall belong to her master, and
only the man shall go free.
5 "But if the servant declares, 'I love
my master and my wife and children and
do not want to go free,'[a] 6 then his master must take him before the judges.[ab] He
shall take him to the door or the doorpost
and pierce[c] his ear with an awl. Then he
will be his servant for life.[d]
7 "If a man sells his daughter as a servant, she is not to go free as male servants
do. 8 If she does not please the master who
has selected her for himself,[b] he must let
her be redeemed. He has no right to sell
her to foreigners, because he has broken faith with her. 9 If he selects her for
his son, he must grant her the rights of
a daughter. 10 If he marries another woman, he must not deprive the first one of
her food, clothing and marital rights.[e] 11 If
he does not provide her with these three
things, she is to go free, without any payment of money.

Personal Injuries

12 "Anyone who strikes a person with a
fatal blow is to be put to death.[f] 13 However, if it is not done intentionally, but God
lets it happen, they are to flee to a place[g]
I will designate. 14 But if anyone schemes
and kills someone deliberately,[h] that person is to be taken from my altar and put
to death.[i]
15 "Anyone who attacks[c] their father or
mother is to be put to death.
16 "Anyone who kidnaps someone is to
be put to death,[j] whether the victim has
been sold[k] or is still in the kidnapper's
possession.
17 "Anyone who curses their father or
mother is to be put to death.[l]
18 "If people quarrel and one person hits
another with a stone or with their fist[d] and
the victim does not die but is confined to
bed, 19 the one who struck the blow will
not be held liable if the other can get up
and walk around outside with a staff;
however, the guilty party must pay the injured person for any loss of time and see
that the victim is completely healed.
20 "Anyone who beats their male or female slave with a rod must be punished if
the slave dies as a direct result, 21 but they
are not to be punished if the slave recovers
after a day or two, since the slave is their
property.[m]
22 "If people are fighting and hit a pregnant
woman and she gives birth prematurely[e] but
there is no serious injury, the offender must
be fined whatever the woman's husband demands[n] and the court allows. 23 But if there
is serious injury, you are to take life for
life,[o] 24 eye for eye, tooth for tooth,[p] hand for
hand, foot for foot, 25 burn for burn, wound
for wound, bruise for bruise.
26 "An owner who hits a male or female
slave in the eye and destroys it must let the
slave go free to compensate for the eye.
27 And an owner who knocks out the tooth
of a male or female slave must let the slave
go free to compensate for the tooth.
28 "If a bull gores a man or woman to
death, the bull is to be stoned to death,[q]
and its meat must not be eaten. But the
owner of the bull will not be held responsible. 29 If, however, the bull has had the
habit of goring and the owner has been
warned but has not kept it penned up[r]
and it kills a man or woman, the bull is
to be stoned and its owner also is to be
put to death. 30 However, if payment is de-

21:5 [a] Dt 15:16
21:6 [b] Ex 22:8-9; Dt 17:9; 19:17; 25:1 [c] Ps 40:6 [d] Job 39:9; 41:4
21:10 [e] 1Co 7:3-5
21:12 [f] ver 15, 17; S Ge 4:14, 23; Ex 31:15; Lev 20:9, 10; 24:16; 27:29; Nu 1:51; 35:16, 30-31; Dt 13:5; 19:11; 22:22; 27:16; Job 31:11; Pr 20:20; S Mt 26:52
21:13 [g] Nu 35:10-34; Dt 4:42; 19:2-13; Jos 20:9
21:14 [h] Ge 4:8; Nu 35:20; 2Sa 3:27; 20:10; Heb 10:26 [i] Dt 19:11-12; 1Ki 2:28-34
21:16 [j] Ex 22:4; Dt 24:7 [k] Ge 37:28
21:17 [l] S ver 12; S Dt 5:16; Mt 15:4*; Mk 7:10*
21:21 [m] Lev 25:44-46
21:22 [n] ver 30
21:23 [o] Lev 24:19; Dt 19:21
21:24 [p] S ver 23; Mt 5:38*
21:28 [q] ver 32; Ge 9:5
21:29 [r] ver 36

[a] 6 Or *before God* [b] 8 Or *master so that he does not choose her* [c] 15 Or *kills* [d] 18 Or *with a tool* [e] 22 Or *she has a miscarriage*

21:6 *the judges.* See 22:8–9,28 and NIV text notes. *pierce his ear with an awl.* See Dt 15:17. Submission to this rite symbolized willing service (see Ps 40:6–8 and note on 40:6).
21:12–15 See 20:13 and note; see also Nu 35:16–34; Dt 19:1–13; 21:1–9; 24:7; 27:24–25; Jos 20:1–9.
21:12 See Ge 9:6 and note.
21:13 *not done intentionally.* Related terms and expressions are "accidentally" (Nu 35:11), "without enmity" (Nu 35:22), "was not an enemy" (Nu 35:23), "no harm was intended" (Nu 35:23) and "without malice aforethought" (Dt 19:4). Premeditated murder is thus distinguished from accidental manslaughter. *God lets it happen.* The event is beyond human control — in modern legal terminology, an "act of God." *place.* A city of refuge (see Nu 35:6–32; Dt 19:1–13; Jos 20:1–9; 21:13,21,27,32,38).
21:14 *from my altar.* Or "even from my altar." The horns of the altar were a final refuge for those subject to judicial action (see 1Ki 1:50–51; 2:28; Am 3:14 and notes).
21:15 See 20:12 and note.
21:16 See 20:15 and note.
21:17 *curses ... father or mother.* Calls down curses on them to effect their destruction.
21:19 *walk around outside with a staff.* Recover in a satisfactory way. *any loss of time.* Lit. "sitting," i.e., enforced idleness.
21:20–21 Benefit of doubt was granted to the slaveholder where no homicidal intentions could be proved.
21:23–25 See Dt 19:21. The so-called law of retaliation, as its contexts show, was meant to limit the punishment to fit the crime. By invoking the law of love, Jesus corrected the popular misunderstanding of the law of retaliation (see Mt 5:38–42). See note on Lev 24:20.
21:23 *serious injury.* Either to mother or to child.
21:26–27 Humane applications of the law of retaliation.
21:28–32 The law of the goring bull.
21:28 *the bull is to be stoned to death.* By killing someone, the bull becomes accountable for that person's life (see Ge 9:5 and note).
21:30 *if payment is demanded.* If the victim's family is will-

manded, the owner may redeem his life
by the payment of whatever is demanded.[s]
31 This law also applies if the bull gores a
son or daughter. 32 If the bull gores a male
or female slave, the owner must pay thirty shekels[a][t] of silver to the master of the
slave, and the bull is to be stoned to death.
33 "If anyone uncovers a pit[u] or digs one
and fails to cover it and an ox or a donkey
falls into it, 34 the one who opened the pit
must pay the owner for the loss and take
the dead animal in exchange.
35 "If anyone's bull injures someone
else's bull and it dies, the two parties
are to sell the live one and divide both
the money and the dead animal equally.
36 However, if it was known that the bull
had the habit of goring, yet the owner did
not keep it penned up,[v] the owner must
pay, animal for animal, and take the dead
animal in exchange.

Protection of Property

22 [b] "Whoever steals an ox or a sheep
and slaughters it or sells it must
pay back[w] five head of cattle for the ox and
four sheep for the sheep.
2 "If a thief is caught breaking in[x] at
night and is struck a fatal blow, the defender is not guilty of bloodshed;[y] 3 but if
it happens after sunrise, the defender is
guilty of bloodshed.
"Anyone who steals must certainly
make restitution,[z] but if they have nothing,
they must be sold[a] to pay for their theft.
4 If the stolen animal is found alive in their
possession[b]—whether ox or donkey or
sheep—they must pay back double.[c]
5 "If anyone grazes their livestock in a
field or vineyard and lets them stray and
they graze in someone else's field, the offender must make restitution[d] from the
best of their own field or vineyard.
6 "If a fire breaks out and spreads into
thornbushes so that it burns shocks[e] of
grain or standing grain or the whole field,
the one who started the fire must make
restitution.[f]

7 "If anyone gives a neighbor silver or
goods for safekeeping[g] and they are stolen from the neighbor's house, the thief,
if caught, must pay back double.[h] 8 But if
the thief is not found, the owner of the
house must appear before the judges,[i] and
they must[c] determine whether the owner
of the house has laid hands on the other
person's property. 9 In all cases of illegal
possession of an ox, a donkey, a sheep, a
garment, or any other lost property about
which somebody says, 'This is mine,' both
parties are to bring their cases before the
judges.[d][j] The one whom the judges declare[e] guilty must pay back double to the
other.
10 "If anyone gives a donkey, an ox, a
sheep or any other animal to their neighbor for safekeeping[k] and it dies or is injured or is taken away while no one is
looking, 11 the issue between them will be
settled by the taking of an oath[l] before the
LORD that the neighbor did not lay hands
on the other person's property. The owner
is to accept this, and no restitution is required. 12 But if the animal was stolen from
the neighbor, restitution[m] must be made
to the owner. 13 If it was torn to pieces by
a wild animal, the neighbor shall bring in
the remains as evidence and shall not be
required to pay for the torn animal.[n]
14 "If anyone borrows an animal from
their neighbor and it is injured or dies
while the owner is not present, they must
make restitution.[o] 15 But if the owner is
with the animal, the borrower will not
have to pay. If the animal was hired, the
money paid for the hire covers the loss.[p]

Social Responsibility

16 "If a man seduces a virgin[q] who is
not pledged to be married and sleeps with
her, he must pay the bride-price,[r] and she
shall be his wife. 17 If her father absolutely

21:30 [s] ver 22
21:32 [t] Ge 37:28; Zec 11:12-13; Mt 26:15; 27:3,9
21:33 [u] Lk 14:5
21:36 [v] ver 29
22:1 [w] Lev 6:1-7; 2Sa 12:6; Pr 6:31; S Lk 19:8
22:2 [x] Job 24:16; Jer 2:34; Hos 7:1; Mt 6:19-20; 24:43 [y] Nu 35:27
22:3 [z] ver 1 [a] S Ex 21:2; S Mt 18:25
22:4 [b] 1Sa 12:5 [c] S Ge 43:12
22:5 [d] ver 1
22:6 [e] Jdg 15:5 [f] ver 1
22:7 [g] ver 10; Lev 6:2 [h] S Ge 43:12
22:8 [i] S Ex 21:6
22:9 [j] ver 8; Dt 25:1
22:10 [k] S ver 7
22:11 [l] Lev 6:3; 1Ki 8:31; 2Ch 6:22; Heb 6:16
22:12 [m] ver 1
22:13 [n] Ge 31:39
22:14 [o] ver 1
22:15 [p] Lev 19:13; Job 17:5
22:16 [q] Dt 22:28 [r] S Ge 34:12

[a] *32* That is, about 12 ounces or about 345 grams [b] In Hebrew texts 22:1 is numbered 21:37, and 22:2-31 is numbered 22:1-30. [c] *8* Or *before God, and he will* [d] *9* Or *before God* [e] *9* Or *whom God declares*

ing to accept a ransom payment instead of demanding the death penalty. *the owner may redeem his life by the payment.* The payment (lit. "ransom," as in Nu 35:31) is not to compensate the victim's family but to save the negligent man's life.
21:32 *thirty shekels of silver.* Apparently the standard price for a slave. It was also the amount Judas was willing to accept as his price for betraying Jesus (see Mt 26:14–15; see also Zec 11:12–13 and notes). *shekels.* See note on Ge 20:16.
21:33–36 Laws concerning injuries to animals.
22:1 *four sheep for the sheep.* See 2Sa 12:6 and note.
22:1–15 Laws concerning property rights (see 20:15 and note).
22:2 An act of self-defense in darkness does not produce bloodguilt.
22:3 Killing an intruder in broad daylight is not justifiable.

22:5 *from the best.* Restitution should always err on the side of quality and generosity.
22:6 *thornbushes.* Often used as hedges (see Mic 7:4) bordering cultivated areas.
22:11 See 20:7 and note. *an oath before the LORD.* The judges were God's representatives in court cases (see 21:6; 22:8–9,28 and NIV text notes).
22:12–13 Similar laws apparently existed as early as the patriarchal period (see Ge 31:39).
22:16–31 General laws related to social obligations (see chart, p. 287).
22:16 *bride-price.* A gift, usually substantial, given by the prospective groom to the bride's family as payment for her (see Ge 24:53). The custom is still followed today in parts of the Middle East.

refuses to give her to him, he must still
pay the bride-price for virgins.
18 "Do not allow a sorceress[s] to live.
19 "Anyone who has sexual relations
with an animal[t] is to be put to death.
20 "Whoever sacrifices to any god[u] other
than the LORD must be destroyed.[a][v]
21 "Do not mistreat or oppress a foreigner,[w] for you were foreigners[x] in Egypt.
22 "Do not take advantage of the widow
or the fatherless.[y] 23 If you do and they cry
out[z] to me, I will certainly hear their cry.[a]
24 My anger will be aroused, and I will kill
you with the sword; your wives will become widows and your children fatherless.[b]
25 "If you lend money to one of my people among you who is needy, do not treat
it like a business deal; charge no interest.[c]
26 If you take your neighbor's cloak as a
pledge,[d] return it by sunset, 27 because that
cloak is the only covering your neighbor
has. What else can they sleep in?[e] When
they cry out to me, I will hear, for I am
compassionate.[f]
28 "Do not blaspheme God[b][g] or curse[h]
the ruler of your people.[i]
29 "Do not hold back offerings[j] from your
granaries or your vats.[c]
"You must give me the firstborn of your
sons.[k] 30 Do the same with your cattle
and your sheep.[l] Let them stay with their
mothers for seven days, but give them to
me on the eighth day.[m]
31 "You are to be my holy people.[n] So do
not eat the meat of an animal torn by wild
beasts;[o] throw it to the dogs.

Laws of Justice and Mercy

23 "Do not spread false reports.[p] Do
not help a guilty person by being a
malicious witness.[q]
2 "Do not follow the crowd in doing
wrong. When you give testimony in a lawsuit, do not pervert justice[r] by siding with
the crowd,[s] 3 and do not show favoritism[t]
to a poor person in a lawsuit.
4 "If you come across your enemy's[u] ox
or donkey wandering off, be sure to return it.[v] 5 If you see the donkey[w] of someone who hates you fallen down under its
load, do not leave it there; be sure you
help them with it.
6 "Do not deny justice[x] to your poor people in their lawsuits. 7 Have nothing to do
with a false charge[y] and do not put an innocent[z] or honest person to death,[a] for I
will not acquit the guilty.[b]
8 "Do not accept a bribe,[c] for a bribe
blinds those who see and twists the words
of the innocent.
9 "Do not oppress a foreigner;[d] you yourselves know how it feels to be foreigners,
because you were foreigners in Egypt.

[a] *20* The Hebrew term refers to the irrevocable giving over of things or persons to the LORD, often by totally destroying them. [b] *28* Or *Do not revile the judges* [c] *29* The meaning of the Hebrew for this phrase is uncertain.

22:18 [s] S Ex 7:11; Lev 19:26, 31; 20:27; Dt 18:11; 1Sa 28:3; 2Ch 33:6; Isa 57:3 **22:19** [t] Lev 18:23; 20:15; Dt 27:21 **22:20** [u] S Ex 20:23; 34:15; Lev 17:7; Nu 25:2; Dt 32:17; Ps 106:37 [v] Lev 27:29; Dt 13:5; 17:2-5; 18:20; 1Ki 18:40; 19:1; 2Ki 10:25; 23:20; 2Ch 15:13 **22:21** [w] Ex 23:9; Lev 19:33; 24:22; Nu 15:14; Dt 1:16; 24:17; Eze 22:29 [x] Dt 10:19; 27:19; Zec 7:10; Mal 3:5 **22:22** [y] ver 26; Dt 10:18; 24:6, 10, 12, 17; Job 22:6, 9; 24:3, 21; Ps 68:5; 146:9; Pr 23:10; Isa 1:17; Jer 7:5, 6; 21:12; 22:3; Eze 18:5-9, 12; Zec 7:9-10; Mal 3:5; Jas 1:27 **22:23** [z] Lk 18:7 [a] Dt 10:18; 15:9; 24:15; Job 34:28; 35:9; Ps 10:14, 17; 12:5; 18:6; 34:15; Jas 5:4 **22:24** [b] Ps 69:24; 109:9; La 5:3 **22:25** [c] Lev 25:35-37; Dt 15:7-11; 23:20; Ne 5:7, 10; Ps 15:5; Eze 18:8 **22:26** [d] S ver 22; Pr 20:16; Eze 33:15; Am 2:8 **22:27** [e] Dt 24:13, 17; Job 22:6; 24:7; 29:11; 31:19-20; Eze 18:12, 16 [f] Ex 34:6; Dt 4:31; 2Ch 30:9; Ne 9:17; Ps 99:8; 103:8; 116:5; 145:8; Joel 2:13; Jnh 4:2 **22:28** [g] S Ex 20:7 [h] 2Sa 16:5, 9; 19:21; 1Ki 21:10; 2Ki 2:23; Ps 102:8 [i] Ecc 10:20; Ac 23:5* **22:29** [j] Ex 23:15, 16, 19; 34:20, 26; Lev 19:24; 23:10; Nu 18:13; 28:26; Dt 18:4; 26:2, 10; 1Sa 6:3; Ne 10:35; Pr 3:9; Mal 3:10 [k] S Ex 13:2; Nu 8:16-17; Lk 2:23 **22:30** [l] Ex 34:19; Dt 15:19 [m] Ge 17:12; Lev 12:3; 22:27 **22:31** [n] Ex 19:6; Lev 19:2; 22:31; Ezr 9:2 [o] Lev 7:24; 17:15; 22:8; Dt 14:21; Eze 4:14; 44:31 **23:1** [p] S Ge 39:17; Mt 19:18; Lk 3:14 [q] S Ex 20:16; Dt 5:20; 19:16-21; Ps 27:12; 35:11; Pr 19:5; Ac 6:11 **23:2** [r] ver 3, 6, 9; Lev 19:15, 33; Dt 1:17; 16:19; 24:17; 27:19; 1Sa 8:3 [s] Job 31:34 **23:3** [t] Dt 1:17 **23:4** [u] Ro 12:20 [v] Lev 6:3; 19:11; Dt 22:1-3 **23:5** [w] Dt 22:4 **23:6** [x] S ver 2; Dt 23:16; Pr 22:22 **23:7** [y] S Ex 20:16; S Eph 4:25 [z] Mt 27:4 [a] S Ge 18:23 [b] Ex 34:7; Dt 19:18; 25:1 **23:8** [c] S Ex 18:21; Lev 19:15; Dt 10:17; 27:25; Job 15:34; 36:18; Ps 26:10; Pr 6:35; 15:27; 17:8; Isa 1:23; 5:23; Mic 3:11; 7:3 **23:9** [d] S ver 2; S Ex 22:21; Lev 19:33-34; Eze 22:7

22:18 Dt 18:9–12 strongly condemns sorcery and all such occult practices (see also 1Sa 28:9; Isa 47:12–14).

22:19 Ancient myths and epics describe acts of bestiality performed by pagan gods and demigods in Babylon and Canaan.

22:20 See 20:3–5. The total destruction (see NIV text note) of the idolatrous Canaanites was later commanded by the Lord (see Dt 7:2; 13:15; 20:17; Jos 6:17; 10:40; 11:12,20).

22:21–27 That the poor, the widow, the orphan, the foreigner — in fact, all defenseless people — are objects of God's special concern and providential care is clear from the writings of Moses (see 21:26–27; 23:6–12; Lev 19:9–10; Dt 14:29; 16:11,14; 24:19–21; 26:12–13), the psalmists (see Ps 10:14,17–18; 68:5; 82:3; 146:9) and the prophets (see Isa 1:23; 10:2; Jer 7:6; 22:3; Zec 7:10; Mal 3:5), as well as from the teachings of Jesus (see, e.g., Mt 25:34–45) and the apostles (Ro 15:26; Gal 2:10; Jas 1:27; 2:2–7).

22:25–27 Laws dealing with interest on loans (see Lev 25:35–37; Dt 15:1,7–11; 23:19–20; see also Ne 5:10 and note; Job 24:9; Ps 15:5; Pr 28:8 and note; Eze 18:8,13; 22:12). Interest for profit was not to be charged at the expense of the poor. Generosity in such matters was extended even further by Jesus (see Lk 6:34–35).

22:26–27 If all that a person had to offer in pledge for a loan was a cloak, that person was among the poorest of the poor (see Am 2:8 and note).

22:28 *Do not … curse the ruler of your people.* A ruler was God's representative. A penitent Paul quoted this law after he had unwittingly insulted the high priest (see Ac 23:4–5).

22:29 *vats.* See note on Hag 2:16. *give me the firstborn.* See notes on 4:22; 13:2,13; see also 13:15.

22:30 *Do the same with your cattle and your sheep.* See notes on 13:2,13; see also 13:12,15. *give them to me on the eighth day.* The same principle applied in a different way to firstborn sons as well (see note on Ge 17:12).

22:31 Since God's people were "a kingdom of priests" (see 19:6 and note), they were to obey a law later specified for members of the Aaronic priesthood (see Lev 22:8) as well.

23:1–9 Most of the regulations in this section pertain to 20:16.

23:1 See Lev 19:16; Dt 22:13–19; 1Ki 21:10–13.

23:4–5 Those hostile to you are to be shown the same consideration as others (see Dt 22:1–4; Pr 25:21). Jesus teaches that this means "love your enemies" (Mt 5:44).

23:8 See Dt 16:19.

Sabbath Laws

10 “For six years you are to sow your
fields and harvest the crops, 11 but during
the seventh year let the land lie unplowed
and unused.[e] Then the poor among your
people may get food from it, and the wild
animals may eat what is left. Do the same
with your vineyard and your olive grove.
12 “Six days do your work,[f] but on the
seventh day do not work, so that your ox
and your donkey may rest, and so that
the slave born in your household and the
foreigner living among you may be refreshed.[g]
13 “Be careful[h] to do everything I have
said to you. Do not invoke the names of
other gods;[i] do not let them be heard on
your lips.[j]

The Three Annual Festivals

14 “Three times[k] a year you are to celebrate a festival to me.
15 “Celebrate the Festival of Unleavened
Bread;[l] for seven days eat bread made
without yeast, as I commanded you. Do
this at the appointed time in the month
of Aviv,[m] for in that month you came out
of Egypt.
“No one is to appear before me empty-handed.[n]
16 “Celebrate the Festival of Harvest[o]
with the firstfruits[p] of the crops you sow
in your field.
“Celebrate the Festival of Ingathering[q] at
the end of the year, when you gather in
your crops from the field.[r]
17 “Three times[s] a year all the men are to
appear before the Sovereign LORD.
18 “Do not offer the blood of a sacrifice to
me along with anything containing yeast.[t]
“The fat of my festival offerings must
not be kept until morning.[u]
19 “Bring the best of the firstfruits[v] of
your soil to the house of the LORD your
God.
“Do not cook a young goat in its mother's milk.[w]

God's Angel to Prepare the Way

20 “See, I am sending an angel[x] ahead of
you to guard you along the way and to
bring you to the place I have prepared.[y]
21 Pay attention to him and listen[z] to what
he says. Do not rebel against him; he will
not forgive[a] your rebellion,[b] since my
Name[c] is in him. 22 If you listen carefully
to what he says and do[d] all that I say, I
will be an enemy[e] to your enemies and
will oppose those who oppose you. 23 My
angel will go ahead of you and bring you
into the land of the Amorites, Hittites, Perizzites, Canaanites, Hivites and Jebusites,[f]
and I will wipe them out. 24 Do not bow
down before their gods or worship[g] them
or follow their practices.[h] You must demolish[i] them and break their sacred stones[j]
to pieces. 25 Worship the LORD your God,[k]
and his blessing[l] will be on your food and
water. I will take away sickness[m] from
among you, 26 and none will miscarry or
be barren[n] in your land. I will give you a
full life span.[o]

23:11 [e] Lev 25:1-7; Ne 10:31 **23:12** [f] S Ex 20:9; Lk 13:14 [g] Ge 2:2-3 **23:13** [h] Dt 4:9, 23; 1Ti 4:16 [i] ver 32; Dt 12:3; Jos 23:7; Ps 16:4; Zec 13:2 [j] Dt 18:20; Jos 23:7; Ps 16:4; Hos 2:17 **23:14** [k] ver 17; S Ex 12:14; 34:23, 24; Dt 16:16; 1Ki 9:25; 2Ch 8:13; Eze 46:9 **23:15** [l] S Ex 12:17; Mt 26:17; Lk 22:1; Ac 12:3 [m] S Ex 12:2 [n] S Ex 22:29 **23:16** [o] Lev 23:15-21; Nu 28:26; Dt 16:9; 2Ch 8:13 [p] S Ex 22:29; S 34:22 [q] Ex 34:22; Lev 23:34, 42; Dt 16:16; 31:10; Ezr 3:4; Ne 8:14; Zec 14:16 [r] Lev 23:39; Dt 16:13; Jer 40:10 **23:17** [s] S ver 14 **23:18** [t] Ex 34:25; Lev 2:11 [u] S Ex 12:8 **23:19** [v] S Ex 22:29; S 34:22; S Nu 18:12 [w] Ex 34:26; Dt 14:21 **23:20** [x] S Ge 16:7 [y] Ex 15:17 **23:21** [z] Dt 18:19; Jer 13:15 [a] Dt 29:20; 2Ki 24:4; La 1:17 [b] Nu 17:10; Dt 9:7; 31:27; Jos 24:19; Ps 25:7; 78:8, 40, 56; 106:33; 107:11; 1Jn 5:16 [c] S Ex 3:15 **23:22** [d] S Ex 15:26 [e] S Ge 12:3; Isa 41:11; Jer 30:20 **23:23** [f] Nu 13:29; 21:21; Jos 3:10; 24:8, 11; Ezr 9:1; Ps 135:11 **23:24** [g] S Ex 20:5 [h] Lev 18:3; 20:23; Dt 9:4; 12:30-31; Jer 10:2 [i] Ex 34:13; Nu 33:52; Dt 7:5; 12:3; Jdg 2:2; 2Ki 18:4; 23:14 [j] Lev 26:1; Dt 16:22; 1Ki 14:23; 2Ki 3:2; 10:26; 17:10; 2Ch 14:3; Isa 27:9 **23:25** [k] Mt 4:10 [l] Lev 26:3-13; Dt 7:12-15; 28:1-14 [m] S Ex 15:26 **23:26** [n] Lev 26:3-4; Dt 7:14; 28:4; Mal 3:11 [o] S Ge 15:15; Dt 4:1, 40; 32:47; Ps 90:10

23:10–13 Extensions of the principles taught in 20:8–11; Dt 5:12–15.
23:14–19 See 34:18–26; Lev 23:4–44; Nu 28:16—29:40; Dt 16:1–17; see also chart, pp. 188–189.
23:15 *Festival of Unleavened Bread.* Celebrated from the 15th through the 21st days of the first month (usually about mid-March to mid-April; see note on 12:2) at the beginning of the barley harvest; it commemorated the exodus.
23:16 *Festival of Harvest.* Also called the "Festival of Weeks" (34:22) because it was held seven weeks after the Festival of Unleavened Bread. It was celebrated on the sixth day of the third month (usually about mid-May to mid-June) during the wheat harvest. In later Judaism it came to commemorate the giving of the law on Mount Sinai, though there is no evidence of this significance in the OT. In NT times it was called "(the day of) Pentecost" (Ac 2:1; 20:16; 1Co 16:8), which means "fifty" (see Lev 23:16). *Festival of Ingathering.* Also called the "Festival of Tabernacles" (Lev 23:34; see note on Zec 14:16) or "Booths" because the Israelites lived in temporary shelters when God brought them out of Egypt (see Lev 23:42–43). It was celebrated from the 15th through the 22nd days of the seventh month (usually about mid-September to mid-October) when the produce of the orchards and vines had been harvested; it commemorated the wilderness wanderings after the exodus. *end of the year.* End of the agricultural year, which began in the fall (see note on 12:2).
23:17 *all the men.* Normally accompanied by their families (see, e.g., 1Sa 1).
23:18 *not … with anything containing yeast.* See note on 12:15. *not be kept until morning.* See 12:9–10.
23:19 *firstfruits.* Representative of the whole harvest. The offering of firstfruits was an acknowledgment that the harvest was from the Lord and belonged wholly to him (see 34:26; Lev 23:9–14; Nu 18:12–13; Dt 18:13). *Do not cook a young goat in its mother's milk.* The reason for the prohibition is uncertain, but it may be related to the prohibition against slaughtering a mother animal and its offspring (see Lev 22:28; cf. Dt 22:6–7).
23:20 *angel.* See 14:19; see also note on Ge 16:7. *place I have prepared.* Canaan (cf. the similar statement of Jesus in Jn 14:2–3).
23:21 *Name.* Representing God's presence (see note on Dt 12:5).
23:22 *If.* See note on 19:5.
23:23 See 3:8 and note.
23:25–26 For more expanded lists of God's covenant blessings see Lev 26:3–13; Dt 7:13–15; 28:1–14; 31:1–10 and relevant notes.

27 "I will send my terror[p] ahead of you and throw into confusion[q] every nation you encounter. I will make all your enemies turn their backs and run.[r] 28 I will send the hornet[s] ahead of you to drive the Hivites, Canaanites and Hittites[t] out of your way. 29 But I will not drive them out in a single year, because the land would become desolate and the wild animals[u] too numerous for you. 30 Little by little I will drive them out before you, until you have increased enough to take possession[v] of the land.

31 "I will establish your borders from the Red Sea[a] to the Mediterranean Sea,[b] and from the desert to the Euphrates River.[w] I will give into your hands the people who live in the land, and you will drive them out[x] before you. 32 Do not make a covenant[y] with them or with their gods. 33 Do not let them live in your land or they will cause you to sin against me, because the worship of their gods will certainly be a snare[z] to you."

The Covenant Confirmed

24 Then the LORD said to Moses, "Come up to the LORD, you and Aaron,[a] Nadab and Abihu,[b] and seventy of the elders[c] of Israel. You are to worship at a distance, 2 but Moses alone is to approach[d] the LORD; the others must not come near. And the people may not come up with him."

3 When Moses went and told the people all the LORD's words and laws,[e] they responded with one voice, "Everything the LORD has said we will do."[f] 4 Moses then wrote[g] down everything the LORD had said.

He got up early the next morning and built an altar[h] at the foot of the mountain and set up twelve stone pillars[i] representing the twelve tribes of Israel. 5 Then he sent young Israelite men, and they offered burnt offerings[j] and sacrificed young bulls as fellowship offerings[k] to the LORD. 6 Moses[l] took half of the blood[m] and put it in bowls, and the other half he splashed[n] against the altar. 7 Then he took the Book of the Covenant[o] and read it to the people. They responded, "We will do everything the LORD has said; we will obey."[p]

8 Moses then took the blood, sprinkled it on the people[q] and said, "This is the blood of the covenant[r] that the LORD has made with you in accordance with all these words."

9 Moses and Aaron, Nadab and Abihu, and the seventy elders[s] of Israel went up 10 and saw[t] the God of Israel. Under his feet was something like a pavement made of lapis lazuli,[u] as bright blue as the sky.[v] 11 But God did not raise his hand against these leaders of the Israelites; they saw[w] God, and they ate and drank.[x]

[a] 31 Or *the Sea of Reeds* [b] 31 Hebrew *to the Sea of the Philistines*

23:27 [p] S Ge 35:5; S Ex 15:14 [q] S Ex 14:24; Dt 7:23 [r] 2Sa 22:41; Ps 18:40; 21:12 **23:28** [s] Dt 7:20; Jos 24:12 [t] Ex 33:2; 34:11, 24; Nu 13:29; Dt 4:38; 11:23; 18:12; Jos 3:10; 24:11; Ps 78:55 **23:29** [u] Dt 7:22 **23:30** [v] Jos 23:5 **23:31** [w] S Ge 2:14; Dt 34:2; Ezr 4:20 [x] Dt 7:24; 9:3; Jos 21:44; 24:12, 18; Ps 80:8 **23:32** [y] S Ge 26:28; Ex 34:12; Dt 7:2; Jos 9:7; Jdg 2:2; 1Sa 11:1; 1Ki 15:19; 20:34; Eze 17:13 **23:33** [z] S Ex 10:7 **24:1** [a] S Ex 19:24 [b] S Ex 6:23 [c] ver 9; Nu 11:16 **24:2** [d] Nu 12:6-8 **24:3** [e] S Ex 21:1; Gal 3:19 [f] S Ex 19:8; Jos 24:24 **24:4** [g] S Ex 17:14 [h] S Ge 8:20 [i] S Ge 28:18; S Dt 27:2 **24:5** [j] Lev 1:3 [k] S Ge 31:54 **24:6** [l] Ex 14:15; 32:31; Ps 99:6 [m] Heb 9:18 [n] Lev 1:11; 3:2, 8, 13; 5:9; Mt 26:28 **24:7** [o] 2Ki 23:2, 21; Heb 9:19 [p] Ex 19:8; Jer 40:3; 42:6, 21; 43:2 **24:8** [q] Heb 9:19; 1Pe 1:2 [r] Lev 26:3; Dt 5:2-3; Jos 24:25; 2Ki 11:17; Jer 11:4, 8; 31:32; 34:13; Zec 9:11; S Mt 26:28; S Lk 22:20; Heb 9:20* **24:9** [s] S ver 1 **24:10** [t] S Ge 16:13; Nu 12:6; Isa 6:1; Eze 1:1; 8:3; 40:2; S Jn 1:18 [u] Job 28:16; Isa 54:11; Eze 1:26; 10:1 [v] Rev 4:3 **24:11** [w] S ver 10; S Ex 3:6; S 19:21 [x] Eze 44:3; Mt 26:29

23:27 *my terror.* See note on 1Ch 14:17.

23:28 *hornet.* The meaning of the Hebrew for this word is uncertain. The Septuagint (the pre-Christian Greek translation of the OT) renders it "wasp," but the translators may have been guessing. In any event, the Lord promises to send some agent to disable or frighten the peoples of Canaan so that they will not be able to resist Israel's invasion (cf. Isa 7:18).

23:30 *Little by little.* See Jdg 1.

23:31 See Ge 15:18; 1Ki 4:21. *Red Sea.* The (south)eastern border (here the modern Gulf of Aqaba; see note on 1Ki 9:26). *Mediterranean Sea.* The western border (see NIV text note). *the desert.* The southern border (northeastern Sinai; see note on Ge 15:18). *Euphrates River.* The northern border.

23:33 *snare.* A symbol of destruction (see 10:7; Job 18:9; Ps 18:5; Pr 13:14; 21:6; Isa 24:17–18).

24:1 *Come up.* The action, temporarily interrupted for the Book of the Covenant (20:22—23:33), is resumed from 20:21. Moses and his associates would ascend the mountain after the events of vv. 3–8. *Nadab and Abihu.* Aaron's two oldest sons. Nadab would have succeeded Aaron as high priest, but he and his brother died because they offered unauthorized fire before the Lord (see Lev 10:2; Nu 3:4 and notes). *seventy ... elders.* Cf. Nu 11:16; perhaps representing Jacob's 70 descendants (see 1:5; Ge 46:27 and note). *elders.* See note on 3:16. *at a distance.* See 20:21.

24:2 *Moses alone.* The mediator between God and the people of Israel. Jesus, who is greater than Moses (see Heb 3:1–6 and notes), is the "mediator of a new covenant" (Heb 12:24).

24:3 *words.* Probably refers to the Ten Commandments (see 20:1 and note). *laws.* Probably refers to the stipulations of the Book of the Covenant (20:22—23:19). *we will do.* See v. 7; see also 19:8 and note.

24:4 *Moses ... wrote.* See note on 17:14; see also Introduction: Author and Date of Writing. *twelve stone pillars representing.* See Jos 4:5,20; 1Ki 18:31.

24:5 *young Israelite men ... offered.* See note on 19:22.

24:6 *half of the blood ... the other half.* The division of the blood points to the twofold aspect of the "blood of the covenant" (v. 8): The blood on the altar symbolizes God's forgiveness and his acceptance of the offering; the blood on the people points to an oath that binds them in obedience (see vv. 3,7).

24:7 *Book of the Covenant.* Strictly speaking, 20:22—23:19 (see note there)—but here implying also the stipulations of 20:2–17; 23:20–33. *We will do ... we will obey.* See v. 3; see also 19:8 and note.

24:8 *then.* Only after the people agreed to obey the Lord could they participate in his covenant with them. *blood of the covenant.* See Mk 14:24 and note.

24:9 *went up.* See v. 1 and note.

24:10 *saw ... God.* But not in the fullness of his glory (see 33:20; see also notes on 3:6; Ge 16:13; Nu 12:8; Eze 1:28). *sky.* Symbolized by the blue color of the "lapis lazuli" (see Eze 1:26).

24:11 *raise his hand against.* See 9:15. *leaders.* Lit. "corners," "corner supports"; used in the sense of "leaders" only here. Cf. Gal 2:9. *ate and drank.* A covenant meal (cf. Ge

12 The LORD said to Moses, "Come up to
me on the mountain and stay here, and I
will give you the tablets of stone[y] with the
law and commandments I have written for
their instruction."
13 Then Moses set out with Joshua[z] his
aide, and Moses went up on the mountain[a] of God. 14 He said to the elders, "Wait
here for us until we come back to you.
Aaron and Hur[b] are with you, and anyone
involved in a dispute[c] can go to them."
15 When Moses went up on the moun-
tain, the cloud[d] covered it, 16 and the glory[e]
of the LORD settled on Mount Sinai.[f] For
six days the cloud covered the mountain,
and on the seventh day the LORD called
to Moses from within the cloud.[g] 17 To the
Israelites the glory of the LORD looked like
a consuming fire[h] on top of the mountain.
18 Then Moses entered the cloud as he
went on up the mountain. And he stayed
on the mountain forty[i] days and forty
nights.[j]

Offerings for the Tabernacle

25:1-7pp — Ex 35:4-9

25 The LORD said to Moses, 2 "Tell
the Israelites to bring me an offering. You are to receive the offering for
me from everyone whose heart prompts[k]
them to give. 3 These are the offerings you
are to receive from them: gold, silver and
bronze; 4 blue, purple and scarlet yarn[l] and
fine linen; goat hair; 5 ram skins dyed red
and another type of durable leather[a];[m] acacia wood;[n] 6 olive oil[o] for the light; spices
for the anointing oil and for the fragrant
incense;[p] 7 and onyx stones and other
gems to be mounted on the ephod[q] and
breastpiece.[r]
8 "Then have them make a sanctuary[s] for
me, and I will dwell[t] among them. 9 Make
this tabernacle and all its furnishings exactly like the pattern[u] I will show you.

The Ark

25:10-20pp — Ex 37:1-9

10 "Have them make an ark[b][v] of acacia
wood—two and a half cubits long, a cubit and a half wide, and a cubit and a half
high.[c] 11 Overlay[w] it with pure gold, both
inside and out, and make a gold molding around it. 12 Cast four gold rings for it
and fasten them to its four feet, with two

24:12 [y] Ex 31:18; 32:15-16; 34:1, 28, 29; Dt 4:13; 5:22; 8:3; 9:9, 10, 11; 10:4; 2Co 3:3 **24:13** [z] S Ex 17:9 [a] S Ex 3:1 **24:14** [b] S Ex 17:10 [c] Ex 18:16 **24:15** [d] S Ex 19:9; Mt 17:5 **24:16** [e] S Ex 16:7; Lev 9:23; Nu 14:10; 1Sa 4:21, 22; Eze 8:4; 11:22 [f] S Ex 19:11 [g] Ps 99:7 **24:17** [h] S Ex 15:7; S 19:18; Heb 12:18, 29 **24:18** [i] 1Ki 19:8 [j] S Ge 7:4; Mt 4:2 **25:2** [k] Ex 35:21, 22, 26, 27, 29; 36:2; 2Ki 12:4; 1Ch 29:5, 7, 9; 2Ch 24:10; 29:31; Ezr 2:68; Ne 7:70-72; 2Co 8:11-12; 9:7 **25:4** [l] Ex 28:4-8 **25:5** [m] Nu 4:6, 10 [n] Dt 10:3 **25:6** [o] Ex 27:20; 30:22-32; 35:28; 39:37; Nu 4:16 [p] Ex 30:1, 7, 35; 31:11; 35:28; Lev 16:12; Nu 4:16; 7:14; 2Ch 13:11 **25:7** [q] Ex 28:4, 6-14; 29:5; Jdg 8:27; Hos 3:4 [r] Lev 8:8 **25:8** [s] Ex 36:1-5; Lev 4:6; 10:4, 7; 21:12, 23; Nu 3:28; Heb 9:1-2 [t] Ex 29:45; Lev 26:11-12; Nu 5:3; Dt 12:11; 1Ki 6:13; Zec 2:10; 2Co 6:16 **25:9** [u] ver 40; Ex 26:30; 27:8; 31:11; 39:32, 42, 43; Nu 8:4; 1Ch 28:11, 19; Ac 7:44; Heb 8:5 **25:10** [v] Dt 10:1-5; 1Ki 6:19; Heb 9:4 **25:11** [w] ver 24; Ex 30:3

[a] *5* Possibly the hides of large aquatic mammals
[b] *10* That is, a chest
[c] *10* That is, about 3 3/4 feet long and 2 1/4 feet wide and high or about 1.1 meters long and 68 centimeters wide and high; similarly in verse 17

26:30; 31:54) celebrating the ratification of the covenant described in vv. 3–8. It foreshadows the Lord's Supper, which celebrates the new covenant ratified by Christ's death (see 1Co 11:25–26).

24:12 *Come up.* See note on v. 1. *tablets of stone.* See note on 31:18. *their.* The people's. *instruction.* As instruction from the covenant Lord, the laws were divine directives.

24:13 *Joshua his aide.* See note on 17:9.

24:14 *Hur.* See note on 17:10.

24:17 *glory of the LORD.* See v. 10; 16:10 and notes.

24:18 *stayed on the mountain.* Moses did not come down until he had received instructions concerning the tabernacle and its furnishings (see 32:15). *forty days and forty nights.* Jesus, the new Moses (see note on v. 2), fasted for the same length of time (see Mt 4:2).

25:2 *offering.* Here refers to a voluntary contribution.

25:4 *blue, purple and scarlet.* Royal colors. *blue, purple.* Dyes derived from various shellfish (primarily the *murex*) that swarm in the waters of the northeast Mediterranean. See note on Ge 10:6. *scarlet.* Derived from the eggs and carcasses of the worm *Coccus ilicis*, which attaches itself to the leaves of the holly plant. *fine linen.* A very high quality cloth (often used by Egyptian royalty) made from thread spun from the fibers of flax straw. The Hebrew for this term derives ultimately from Egyptian. Excellent examples of unusually white, tightly woven linen have been found in ancient Egyptian tombs. Some are so finely woven that they cannot be distinguished from silk without the use of a magnifying glass. *goat hair.* From long-haired goats. Coarse and black (cf. SS 1:5; 6:5), it was often used to weave cloth for tents.

25:5 *ram skins dyed red.* After all the wool had been removed from the skins. The final product was similar to present-day morocco leather. *durable leather.* See NIV text note. *acacia.* The wood is darker and harder than oak and is avoided by wood-eating insects. It is common in the Sinai peninsula.

25:6 *spices.* Those used in the anointing oil are identified in 30:23–24 as myrrh (balsam sap), cinnamon (bark of the cinnamon tree, a species of laurel), calamus (pith from the root of a reed plant) and cassia (made from dried flowers of the cinnamon tree). Those used in the fragrant incense are identified in 30:34 as gum resin (a powder taken from the middle of hardened drops of myrrh—rare and very valuable), onycha (made from mollusk shells) and galbanum (a rubbery resin taken from the roots of a flowering plant that thrives in Syria and Persia).

25:7 *other gems.* See 28:17–20. *ephod.* See 28:6 and note. *breastpiece.* See 28:15–30.

25:8 *sanctuary.* Lit. "holy place," "place set apart." See note on 3:5.

25:9 *tabernacle.* Lit. "dwelling place." The word is rarely used of human dwellings; it almost always signifies the place where God dwells among his people (see v. 8; 29:45–46; Lev 26:11; Eze 37:27; cf. Jn 1:14; Rev 21:3). *pattern.* See note on v. 40.

25:10 *ark.* It was in the form of a chest (see NIV text note). The Hebrew for this word is translated by the traditional term "ark" throughout Exodus (see note on Dt 10:1–3); it is a different word from that used to refer to Noah's ark and to the reed basket in which the infant Moses was placed (see note on 2:3). Of all the tabernacle furnishings, the ark is mentioned first, probably because it symbolized the throne of the Lord (see 1Sa 4:4; 2Sa 6:2), the great King, who chose to dwell among his people (see note on v. 9).

25:11 *pure gold.* Uncontaminated by silver or other impurities.

25:12 *rings.* Lit. "houses," "housings," into which poles were inserted to carry the ark (see v. 14).

rings[x] on one side and two rings on the
other. 13 Then make poles of acacia wood
and overlay them with gold.[y] 14 Insert the
poles[z] into the rings on the sides of the
ark to carry it. 15 The poles are to remain
in the rings of this ark; they are not to be
removed.[a] 16 Then put in the ark the tablets of the covenant law,[b] which I will give
you.
17 "Make an atonement cover[c] of pure
gold—two and a half cubits long and a cubit and a half wide. 18 And make two cherubim[d] out of hammered gold at the ends
of the cover. 19 Make one cherub on one
end and the second cherub on the other;
make the cherubim of one piece with the
cover, at the two ends. 20 The cherubim[e]
are to have their wings spread upward,
overshadowing[f] the cover with them. The
cherubim are to face each other, looking
toward the cover. 21 Place the cover on top
of the ark[g] and put in the ark the tablets
of the covenant law[h] that I will give you.

25:12 [x] ver 26; Ex 30:4 **25:13** [y] ver 28; Ex 27:6; 30:5; 37:28 **25:14** [z] Ex 27:7; 40:20; 1Ch 15:15 **25:15** [a] 1Ki 8:8 **25:16** [b] S Ex 16:34; Heb 9:4 **25:17** [c] ver 21; Lev 16:13; Ro 3:25 **25:18** [d] Ex 26:1, 31; 36:35; 1Ki 6:23, 27; 8:6; 2Ch 3:10-13; Heb 9:5 **25:20** [e] S Ge 3:24 [f] Ex 37:9; 1Ki 8:7; 1Ch 28:18; Heb 9:5 **25:21** [g] ver 10-15; Ex 26:34; 40:20; Dt 10:5 [h] S Ex 16:34; Heb 9:4

25:16 *covenant law.* The two tablets on which were inscribed the Ten Commandments as the basic stipulations of the Sinaitic covenant (see 20:1–17; 31:18). The Hebrew word for "covenant law" is related to a Babylonian word meaning "covenant stipulations." See also notes on v. 22; 16:34.

25:17 *atonement.* Reconciliation, the divine act of grace whereby God draws to himself and makes "at one" with him those who were once alienated from him. In the OT, the shed blood of sacrificial offerings effected atonement (see Lev 17:11 and note); in the NT, the blood of Jesus, shed once for all time (see Heb 9:12), does the same (see Ro 3:25; 1Jn 2:2 and notes). *atonement cover.* See Lev 16:2 and note. That God's symbolic throne was capped with an atonement cover signified his great mercy toward his people—only such a God can be revered (see Ps 130:3–4).

25:18 *cherubim.* Probably similar to the carvings of winged sphinxes that adorned the armrests of royal thrones (see note on v. 10) in many parts of the ancient Near East (see also note on Ge 3:24). In the OT the cherubim were symbolic attendants that marked the place of the Lord's "enthronement" in his earthly kingdom (see 1Sa 4:4; 2Sa 6:2; 2Ki 19:15; Ps 99:1). From the cover of the ark (the footstool of God's symbolic throne) the Lord gave directions to Moses (see v. 22; Nu 7:89). Later the ark's presence in the temple at Jerusalem would designate it as God's earthly royal city (see Ps 9:11 and note).

25:21 *put in the ark the tablets of the covenant law.* See note on 31:18, but see also Dt 31:26.

THE TABERNACLE

The new religious observances taught by Moses in the wilderness centered on rituals connected with the tabernacle and amplified Israel's sense of separateness, purity and oneness under the lordship of Yahweh.

A few desert shrines have been found in Sinai (notably at Serabit el-Khadem) and at Timnah in the Negev. They show marked Egyptian influence.

Specific cultural antecedents to portable shrines carried on poles and covered with thin sheets of gold can be found in ancient Egypt as early as the Old Kingdom (2800–2250 BC), but they were especially prominent in the Eighteenth and Nineteenth Dynasties (1570–1180). The best examples come from the fabulous tomb of Tutankhamun, c. 1300 BC. Comparisons of construction details in the text of Ex 25–40 with the frames, shrines, poles, sheathing, draped fabric covers, gilt rosettes and winged protective figures from the shrine of Tutankhamun are instructive. The period, the Late Bronze Age, is equivalent in all dating systems to the era of Moses and the exodus.

22 There, above the cover between the two cherubim[i] that are over the ark of the covenant law, I will meet[j] with you and give you all my commands for the Israelites.[k]

The Table

25:23-29pp — Ex 37:10-16

23 "Make a table[l] of acacia wood—two cubits long, a cubit wide and a cubit and a half high.[a] 24 Overlay it with pure gold and make a gold molding around it. 25 Also make around it a rim a handbreadth[b] wide and put a gold molding on the rim. 26 Make four gold rings for the table and fasten them to the four corners, where the four legs are. 27 The rings are to be close to the rim to hold the poles used in carrying the table. 28 Make the poles of acacia wood, overlay them with gold[m] and carry the table with them. 29 And make its plates and dishes of pure gold, as well as its pitchers and bowls for the pouring out of offerings.[n] 30 Put the bread of the Presence[o] on this table to be before me at all times.

The Lampstand

25:31-39pp — Ex 37:17-24

31 "Make a lampstand[p] of pure gold. Hammer out its base and shaft, and make

[a] *23* That is, about 3 feet long, 1 1/2 feet wide and 2 1/4 feet high or about 90 centimeters long, 45 centimeters wide and 68 centimeters high [b] *25* That is, about 3 inches or about 7.5 centimeters

25:22 [i] Nu 7:89; 1Sa 4:4; 2Sa 6:2; 22:11; 2Ki 19:15; 1Ch 13:6; 28:18; Ps 18:10; 80:1; 99:1; Isa 37:16 [j] S Ex 19:3; 29:42; 30:6, 36; Lev 1:1; 16:2; Nu 17:4 [k] Jer 3:16
25:23 [l] ver 30; Ex 26:35; 40:4, 22; Lev 24:6; Nu 3:31; 1Ki 7:48; 1Ch 28:16; 2Ch 4:8, 19; Eze 41:22; 44:16; Heb 9:2
25:28 [m] S ver 13
25:29 [n] Nu 4:7
25:30 [o] Ex 35:13; 39:36; 40:4, 23; Lev 24:5-9; Nu 4:7; 1Sa 21:4-6; 1Ki 7:48; 1Ch 23:29 **25:31** [p] Ex 26:35; 31:8; 35:14; 39:37; 40:4, 24; Lev 24:4; Nu 3:31; 1Ki 7:49; 2Ch 4:7; Zec 4:2; Heb 9:2; Rev 1:12

25:22 *ark of the covenant law.* Called this because it contained the two "tablets of the covenant law" (v. 16; see note there). The phrase "ark of the covenant law" is a synonym of the more familiar phrase "ark of the covenant" (see, e.g., Nu 10:33). *I will meet with you.* See note on 27:21.
25:26 *rings.* See note on v. 12.
25:30 *bread of the Presence.* Traditionally "showbread." In this phrase, "Presence" refers to the presence of God himself (as in 33:14–15; Isa 63:9). The bread (12 loaves, one for each tribe) represented a perpetual offering to the Lord by which the Israelites declared that they consecrated to God the fruits of their labors and by which the nation at the same time acknowledged that all such fruit had been provided only by God's blessing. See Lev 24:5–9.
25:31 *flowerlike cups, buds and blossoms.* The design is patterned after an almond tree (see v. 33), the first of the trees

TABERNACLE FURNISHINGS

The symbolism of God's redemptive covenant was preserved in the tabernacle, making each element an object lesson for the worshiper. Likely reconstructions of the furnishings are based on the detailed descriptions and precise measurements recorded in Exodus 25–40. (The bronze basin is not shown here, but see photo, p. 143.)

1 ARK OF THE COVENANT

The ark of the covenant compares with the roughly contemporary shrine and funerary furniture of Tutankhamun (c. 1300 BC), which, along with the Nimrud and Samaria ivories from a later period, have been used to guide the graphic interpretation of the text. Both sources show the conventional way of depicting extreme reverence, with facing winged guardians shielding a sacred place.

2 INCENSE ALTAR

3 LAMPSTAND

The traditional form of the lampstand is not attested archaeologically until much later.

4 TABLE

The table holding the bread of the Presence was made of wood overlaid with thin sheets of gold. All of the objects were portable and were fitted with rings and carrying poles, practices typical of Egyptian ritual processions as early as the Old Kingdom period (c. 2715–2640 BC).

5 BRONZE ALTAR

The altar of burnt offering was made of wood overlaid with bronze. The size, five cubits square and three cubits high, matches that of an altar found at Arad from the time of Solomon.

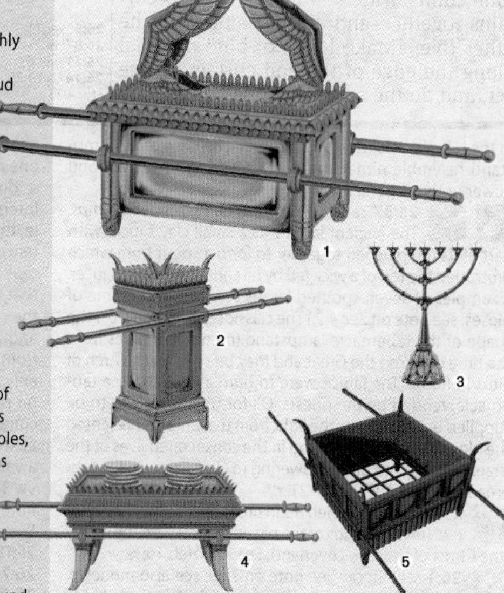

its flowerlike cups, buds and blossoms of
one piece with them. 32Six branches are to
extend from the sides of the lampstand—
three on one side and three on the other.
33Three cups shaped like almond flowers
with buds and blossoms are to be on one
branch, three on the next branch, and the
same for all six branches extending from
the lampstand. 34And on the lampstand
there are to be four cups shaped like almond flowers with buds and blossoms.
35One bud shall be under the first pair of
branches extending from the lampstand,
a second bud under the second pair, and
a third bud under the third pair—six
branches in all. 36The buds and branches
shall all be of one piece with the lampstand, hammered out of pure gold.[q]
37"Then make its seven lamps[r] and set
them up on it so that they light the space
in front of it. 38Its wick trimmers and trays[s]
are to be of pure gold. 39A talent[a] of pure
gold is to be used for the lampstand and
all these accessories. 40See that you make
them according to the pattern[t] shown you
on the mountain.

The Tabernacle

26:1-37pp — Ex 36:8-38

26 "Make the tabernacle[u] with ten
curtains of finely twisted linen
and blue, purple and scarlet yarn, with
cherubim[v] woven into them by a skilled
worker. 2All the curtains are to be the
same size[w]—twenty-eight cubits long and
four cubits wide.[b] 3Join five of the curtains together, and do the same with the
other five. 4Make loops of blue material
along the edge of the end curtain in one
set, and do the same with the end curtain
in the other set. 5Make fifty loops on one
curtain and fifty loops on the end curtain
of the other set, with the loops opposite
each other. 6Then make fifty gold clasps
and use them to fasten the curtains together so that the tabernacle is a unit.[x]
7"Make curtains of goat hair for the tent
over the tabernacle—eleven altogether.
8All eleven curtains are to be the same
size[y]—thirty cubits long and four cubits
wide.[c] 9Join five of the curtains together
into one set and the other six into another
set. Fold the sixth curtain double at the
front of the tent. 10Make fifty loops along
the edge of the end curtain in one set and
also along the edge of the end curtain in
the other set. 11Then make fifty bronze
clasps and put them in the loops to fasten the tent together as a unit.[z] 12As for
the additional length of the tent curtains,
the half curtain that is left over is to hang
down at the rear of the tabernacle. 13The
tent curtains will be a cubit[d] longer on
both sides; what is left will hang over
the sides of the tabernacle so as to cover
it. 14Make for the tent a covering[a] of ram
skins dyed red, and over that a covering of
the other durable leather.[e][b]
15"Make upright frames of acacia wood
for the tabernacle. 16Each frame is to be
ten cubits long and a cubit and a half
wide,[f] 17with two projections set parallel to each other. Make all the frames of

25:36 [q] ver 18; Nu 8:4 **25:37** [r] Ex 27:21; 30:8; Lev 24:3-4; Nu 8:2; 1Sa 3:3; 2Ch 13:11 **25:38** [s] S ver 37; Nu 4:9 **25:40** [t] S ver 9; Ac 7:44; Heb 8:5* **26:1** [u] Ex 29:42; 40:2; Lev 8:10; Nu 1:50; Jos 22:19, 29; 2Sa 7:2; 1Ki 1:39; Ac 7:44; Heb 8:2, 5; 13:10; S Rev 21:3 [v] S Ex 25:18 **26:2** [w] ver 8

26:6 [x] ver 11 **26:8** [y] ver 2 **26:11** [z] ver 6 **26:14** [a] Nu 3:25 [b] Nu 4:25

[a] *39* That is, about 75 pounds or about 34 kilograms [b] *2* That is, about 42 feet long and 6 feet wide or about 13 meters long and 1.8 meters wide [c] *8* That is, about 45 feet long and 6 feet wide or about 13.5 meters long and 1.8 meters wide [d] *13* That is, about 18 inches or about 45 centimeters [e] *14* Possibly the hides of large aquatic mammals (see 25:5) [f] *16* That is, about 15 feet long and 2 1/4 feet wide or about 4.5 meters long and 68 centimeters wide

in the Near East to blossom in spring. The cups of the lampstand resemble either the outer covering of the almond flower or the almond nut.

25:37 *seven.* Signifying completeness. *lamps.* The ancient lamp was a small clay saucer with part of its rim pinched together to form a spout from which protruded the top of a wick fed by oil contained in the saucer. (Examples of seven-spouted lamps come from the time of Moses; see note on Zec 4:2.) The classic representation of the shape of the tabernacle lampstand (menorah) comes from the time of Herod the Great and may be seen on the Arch of Titus in Rome. The lamps were to burn all night in the tabernacle, tended by the priests. Oil for the lamps was to be supplied by the people; the light from the lamps represented the glory of the Lord reflected in the consecrated lives of the Israelites—Israel's glory answering to God's glory in the tabernacle (29:43). See 27:20–21.

25:40 Quoted in Heb 8:5 in order to contrast the "shadow" (the trappings of the old covenant) with the reality (the Christ of the new covenant). See also Heb 10:1.

26:1 *tabernacle.* See note on 25:9; see also model, p. 134. Its basic structure was to be 15 feet wide by 45 feet long by 15 feet high. Over an inner lining of embroidered linen (vv. 1–6), it was to have a covering woven of goat hair (vv. 7–13) and two additional coverings of leather, one made from ram skins dyed red and one from "another ... durable leather" (25:5; see NIV text note there; cf. 26:14). Internally, the ceiling was probably flat, but whether the leather coverings had a ridge line with sloping sides (like a tent) is not known. The tabernacle represented God's royal tent. Its form and adornment (like those of the later temples that replaced it) marked it as a symbolic representation of the created cosmos over which God is sovereign as Creator and Lord. As such, it stood for the center of the cosmos from which the Creator reigns, the place where the heavenly and earthly realms converge. There God "lived" among his people (Immanuel, "God with us"), and his people could come near to him. At this sanctuary Israel lived symbolically at the gate of Paradise—very near though still outside, awaiting the fulfillment of God's redemptive program (see vv. 31–35; Ge 3:24 and notes; see also Rev 21:1—22:6 and notes). *finely twisted linen and blue, purple and scarlet yarn.* See note on 25:4. *cherubim.* Signifying a royal chamber (see 25:18 and note).

26:7 *goat hair.* See note on 25:4.

26:14 *ram skins dyed red ... other durable leather.* See note on 25:5.

26:17 *projections.* Lit. "hands"; probably the two pegs at the

the tabernacle in this way. 18 Make twenty frames for the south side of the tabernacle 19 and make forty silver bases[c] to go under them — two bases for each frame, one under each projection. 20 For the other side, the north side of the tabernacle, make twenty frames 21 and forty silver bases[d] — two under each frame. 22 Make six frames for the far end, that is, the west end of the tabernacle, 23 and make two frames for the corners at the far end. 24 At these two corners they must be double from the bottom all the way to the top and fitted into a single ring; both shall be like that. 25 So there will be eight frames and sixteen silver bases — two under each frame.

26 "Also make crossbars of acacia wood: five for the frames on one side of the tabernacle, 27 five for those on the other side, and five for the frames on the west, at the far end of the tabernacle. 28 The center crossbar is to extend from end to end at the middle of the frames. 29 Overlay the frames with gold and make gold rings to hold the crossbars. Also overlay the crossbars with gold.

30 "Set up the tabernacle[e] according to the plan[f] shown you on the mountain.

31 "Make a curtain[g] of blue, purple and scarlet yarn and finely twisted linen, with cherubim[h] woven into it by a skilled worker. 32 Hang it with gold hooks on four posts of acacia wood overlaid with gold and standing on four silver bases.[i] 33 Hang the curtain from the clasps and place the ark of the covenant law behind the curtain.[j] The curtain will separate the Holy Place from the Most Holy Place.[k] 34 Put the atonement cover[l] on the ark of the covenant law in the Most Holy Place. 35 Place the table[m] outside the curtain on the north side of the tabernacle and put the lampstand[n] opposite it on the south side.

36 "For the entrance to the tent make a curtain[o] of blue, purple and scarlet yarn and finely twisted linen — the work of an embroiderer.[p] 37 Make gold hooks for this curtain and five posts of acacia wood overlaid with gold. And cast five bronze bases for them.

The Altar of Burnt Offering

27:1-8pp — Ex 38:1-7

27 "Build an altar[q] of acacia wood, three cubits[a] high; it is to be square, five cubits long and five cubits wide.[b] 2 Make a horn[r] at each of the four corners, so that the horns and the altar are of one piece, and overlay the altar with bronze. 3 Make all its utensils of bronze — its pots to remove the ashes, and its shovels, sprinkling bowls,[s] meat forks and firepans.[t] 4 Make a grating for it, a bronze network, and make a bronze

[a] *1* That is, about 4 1/2 feet or about 1.4 meters
[b] *1* That is, about 7 1/2 feet or about 2.3 meters long and wide

26:19 [c] ver 21, 25, 32; Ex 38:27 **26:21** [d] S ver 19 **26:30** [e] Ex 40:2; Nu 9:15 [f] S Ex 25:9 **26:31** [g] Nu 4:5; 2Ch 3:14; Mt 27:51; Lk 23:45; Heb 9:3 [h] S Ex 25:18 **26:32** [i] S ver 19 **26:33** [j] Ex 27:21; 35:12; 40:3, 21; Lev 16:2; Nu 3:31; 4:5; 2Ch 3:14 [k] Lev 16:2, 16; 1Ki 6:16; 7:50; 8:6; 2Ch 3:8; 5:7; Eze 41:4; Heb 9:2-3 **26:34** [l] Ex 25:21; 30:6; 37:6; Lev 16:2; Heb 9:5 **26:35** [m] S Ex 25:23; Heb 9:2 [n] S Ex 25:31 **26:36** [o] Ex 35:15; 40:5, 28 [p] Ps 45:14; Eze 16:10; 26:16; 27:7 **27:1** [q] S Ex 20:24; S 40:6; S 1Ki 8:64 **27:2** [r] Ex 29:12; 30:2; 37:25; Lev 4:7; 1Ki 1:50; 2:28; Ps 118:27; Jer 17:1; Eze 43:15; Am 3:14; Zec 9:15 **27:3** [s] Nu 7:13; 1Ki 7:40, 45; 2Ki 12:13 [t] Nu 4:14; 1Ch 28:17; Jer 52:18

---

bottom of each frame that were inserted into its two bases (see v. 19).

26:19 *forty silver bases.* These plus the 40 in v. 21, the 16 in v. 25 and the 4 in v. 32 add up to a grand total of 100, the number of talents of silver obtained from the Israelite community to be used to cast the bases (see 38:27).

26:23 *corners.* Or "angles," perhaps referring to mitered joints at the corners.

26:26 *crossbars.* To strengthen the frames on the north, south and west sides.

26:29 *rings.* Lit. "houses," "housings" (see note on 25:12).

26:30 *plan.* See note on 25:40.

26:31 – 35 A curtain was to divide the tabernacle into two rooms, the Holy Place and the Most Holy Place, with the former twice as large as the latter. The Most Holy Place formed a perfect cube, 15 feet by 15 feet by 15 feet. Enclosed with linen curtains embroidered with cherubim and containing only the ark of the covenant, it represented God's throne room (see note on v. 1). The Holy Place represented his royal guest chamber where his people symbolically came before him in the bread of the Presence (see note on 25:30), the light from the lampstand (see note on 25:37) and the incense from the altar of incense (see note on 30:1).

26:31 *curtain.* To separate the Holy Place from the Most Holy Place (see v. 33). It was called the "shielding curtain" (39:34; 40:21; Nu 4:5) because it shielded the ark (see 27:21; see also notes on 16:34; 25:22). At the moment when Christ died, the curtain of Herod's temple was torn, thereby giving the believer direct access to the presence of God (see Mk 15:38; Heb 6:19 – 20; 10:19 – 22). *cherubim.* See v. 1 and note. The curtain at the entrance to the Holy Place did not have cherubim (see v. 36).

26:37 *bronze.* Inside the tabernacle, gold was the metal of choice; outside — beginning with the bases of the outer curtain (see v. 36) — the metal of choice was bronze. The furnishings close to the place of God's dwelling were made of, or overlaid with, gold; those farther away (see 27:2 – 6; 30:18) were made of, or overlaid with, bronze. The bases that supported the frames of the tabernacle and the four posts holding the dividing curtain were of silver (see vv. 19,21,25,32).

27:1 *altar.* The altar of burnt offering (see model, p. 135; see also Lev 4:7,10,18). *acacia wood.* See note on 25:5.

27:2 *horns.* Projections on the four corners. They were symbols of help and refuge (see 1Ki 1:50; 2:28). They also symbolized the atoning power of the altar: Some of the blood was put on the horns of the altar before the rest was poured out at the base (see 29:12; Lev 4:7,18,25,30,34; 8:15; 9:9; 16:18).

27:3 *sprinkling bowls.* To catch the blood of the animals slain beside the altar and to splash it against it (see 24:6). *meat forks.* Three-pronged forks for arranging the sacrifice or removing the priests' portion from the container in which it was being boiled (see 1Sa 2:13 – 14). *firepans.* Probably for carrying fire from the altar of burnt offering to the altar of incense inside the Holy Place (see Lev 10:1; 16:12 – 13).

27:4 *grating.* Placed midway between the top and bottom of the boxlike structure. Since the intense heat of the fire built inside the upper half of the altar would have eventually destroyed it, perhaps the hollow altar (see v. 8) was designed to be filled with earth when it was in use. *ring.* See note on 25:12.

ring at each of the four corners of the network. 5 Put it under the ledge of the altar
so that it is halfway up the altar. 6 Make
poles of acacia wood for the altar and
overlay them with bronze.[u] 7 The poles
are to be inserted into the rings so they
will be on two sides of the altar when it
is carried.[v] 8 Make the altar hollow, out of
boards. It is to be made just as you were
shown[w] on the mountain.

The Courtyard

27:9-19pp — Ex 38:9-20

9 "Make a courtyard[x] for the tabernacle.
The south side shall be a hundred cubits[a]
long and is to have curtains of finely twisted linen, 10 with twenty posts and twenty bronze bases and with silver hooks
and bands on the posts. 11 The north side
shall also be a hundred cubits long and is
to have curtains, with twenty posts and
twenty bronze bases and with silver hooks
and bands on the posts.

12 "The west end of the courtyard shall
be fifty cubits[b] wide and have curtains,
with ten posts and ten bases. 13 On the
east end, toward the sunrise, the courtyard shall also be fifty cubits wide. 14 Curtains fifteen cubits[c] long are to be on one
side of the entrance, with three posts and
three bases, 15 and curtains fifteen cubits
long are to be on the other side, with three
posts and three bases.

16 "For the entrance to the courtyard,
provide a curtain[y] twenty cubits[d] long, of
blue, purple and scarlet yarn and finely
twisted linen — the work of an embroiderer[z] — with four posts and four bases. 17 All
the posts around the courtyard are to have
silver bands and hooks, and bronze bases.
18 The courtyard shall be a hundred cubits
long and fifty cubits wide,[e] with curtains
of finely twisted linen five cubits[f] high,
and with bronze bases. 19 All the other articles used in the service of the tabernacle,
whatever their function, including all the
tent pegs for it and those for the courtyard,
are to be of bronze.

Oil for the Lampstand

27:20-21pp — Lev 24:1-3

20 "Command the Israelites to bring you
clear oil[a] of pressed olives for the light so
that the lamps may be kept burning. 21 In
the tent of meeting,[b] outside the curtain that
shields the ark of the covenant law,[c] Aaron
and his sons are to keep the lamps[d] burning
before the LORD from evening till morning.
This is to be a lasting ordinance[e] among the
Israelites for the generations to come.

The Priestly Garments

28 "Have Aaron[f] your brother brought
to you from among the Israelites,
along with his sons Nadab and Abihu,[g]
Eleazar and Ithamar,[h] so they may serve
me as priests.[i] 2 Make sacred garments[j] for
your brother Aaron to give him dignity
and honor.[k] 3 Tell all the skilled workers[l]
to whom I have given wisdom[m] in such
matters that they are to make garments
for Aaron, for his consecration, so he may
serve me as priest. 4 These are the garments they are to make: a breastpiece,[n] an
ephod,[o] a robe,[p] a woven tunic,[q] a turban[r]
and a sash. They are to make these sacred garments for your brother Aaron and
his sons, so they may serve me as priests.
5 Have them use gold, and blue, purple and
scarlet yarn, and fine linen.[s]

The Ephod

28:6-14pp — Ex 39:2-7

6 "Make the ephod[t] of gold, and of blue,
purple and scarlet yarn, and of finely
twisted linen — the work of skilled hands.

27:6 [u] S Ex 25:13 **27:7** [v] Ex 25:14, 28 **27:8** [w] S Ex 25:9 **27:9** [x] Ex 35:17; 40:8, 33; Lev 6:16, 26; Eze 40:14; 42:1 **27:16** [y] Ex 40:33 [z] Ex 36:37 **27:20** [a] S Ex 25:6 **27:21** [b] Ex 28:43; 29:42; 30:36; 33:7; Lev 1:1; 6:26; 8:3, 31; Nu 1:1; 31:54; Jos 18:1; 1Ki 1:39 [c] S Ex 16:34 [d] S Ex 25:37 [e] Ex 29:9; 30:21; Lev 3:17; 16:34; 17:7; Nu 18:23; 19:21; 1Sa 30:25 **28:1** [f] Lev 8:30; Ps 99:6; Heb 5:4 [g] S Ex 6:23; 24:9 [h] S Ex 6:23 [i] Lev 8:2; 21:1; Nu 18:1-7; Dt 18:5; 1Sa 2:28; Heb 5:1 **28:2** [j] Ex 29:5, 29; 31:10; 35:19; 39:1; Lev 8:7-9, 30; 16:32; Nu 20:26-28 [k] ver 40 **28:3** [l] Ex 31:6; 35:10, 25, 35; 36:1 [m] Ex 31:3; Dt 34:9; Isa 11:2; 1Co 12:8; S Eph 1:17 **28:4** [n] ver 15-30 [o] S Ex 25:7 [p] ver 31-35 [q] ver 39; Lev 10:5 [r] ver 37 **28:5** [s] Ex 25:4 **28:6** [t] S Ex 25:7

[a] *9* That is, about 150 feet or about 45 meters; also in verse 11 [b] *12* That is, about 75 feet or about 23 meters; also in verse 13 [c] *14* That is, about 23 feet or about 6.8 meters; also in verse 15 [d] *16* That is, about 30 feet or about 9 meters [e] *18* That is, about 150 feet long and 75 feet wide or about 45 meters long and 23 meters wide [f] *18* That is, about 7 1/2 feet or about 2.3 meters

---

27:12 – 13 *west end ... east end.* The courtyard is described as having two equal parts. The Most Holy Place probably occupied the central position in the western half, the altar of burnt offering the central position in the eastern half.

27:13 – 14 *toward the sunrise ... the entrance.* The entrance to the tabernacle courtyard faced east, as did that of Solomon's temple (see Eze 8:16) and of Herod's temple.

27:18 *five cubits.* See NIV text note; high enough to block the view of people standing outside the courtyard, thus protecting the sanctity and privacy of the worship taking place inside.

27:20 *clear oil of pressed olives.* Unripe olives were crushed in a mortar. The pulpy mass was then placed in a cloth basket through the bottom of which the oil dripped, producing a clear fuel that burned with little or no smoke.

27:21 *tent of meeting.* The tabernacle; it was not a place where God's people met for collective worship but one where God himself met — by appointment, not by accident — with his people (see 29:42 – 43). *curtain that shields the ark of the covenant law.* See note on 26:31. *lamps burning ... from evening till morning.* The lamps were lit in the evening (see 30:8) and apparently extinguished in the morning (1Sa 3:3).

28:1 *Nadab and Abihu.* See note on 24:1. *serve me as priests.* In order "to offer gifts and sacrifices for sins" and "to deal gently with those who are ignorant and are going astray" (Heb 5:1 – 2). Another important function of the priests was to read the law of Moses to the people and remind them of their covenant obligations (see Dt 31:9 – 13; Ne 8:2 – 3; Jer 18:18; Mal 2:5 – 8).

28:2 *to give him dignity and honor.* The garments were to exalt the office and functions of regular priests (see vv. 4,40), as well as of the high priest.

28:6 *ephod.* A sleeveless vestment worn by the high priest. Sometimes the word refers to an otherwise unidentified object of worship (see, e.g., Jdg 8:27; 18:17; Hos 3:4).

7 It is to have two shoulder pieces attached to two of its corners, so it can be fastened. 8 Its skillfully woven waistband[u] is to be like it—of one piece with the ephod and made with gold, and with blue, purple and scarlet yarn, and with finely twisted linen.

9 "Take two onyx stones and engrave[v] on them the names of the sons of Israel 10 in the order of their birth—six names on one stone and the remaining six on the other. 11 Engrave the names of the sons of Israel on the two stones the way a gem cutter engraves a seal. Then mount the stones in gold filigree settings 12 and fasten them on the shoulder pieces of the ephod as memorial stones for the sons of Israel. Aaron is to bear the names on his shoulders[w] as a memorial[x] before the LORD. 13 Make gold filigree settings 14 and two braided chains of pure gold, like a rope, and attach the chains to the settings.

The Breastpiece

28:15-28pp — Ex 39:8-21

15 "Fashion a breastpiece[y] for making decisions—the work of skilled hands. Make it like the ephod: of gold, and of blue, purple and scarlet yarn, and of finely twisted linen. 16 It is to be square—a span[a] long and a span wide—and folded double. 17 Then mount four rows of precious stones[z] on it. The first row shall be carnelian, chrysolite[a] and beryl; 18 the second row shall be turquoise, lapis lazuli and emerald; 19 the third row shall be jacinth, agate and amethyst; 20 the fourth row shall be topaz, onyx and jasper.[b] Mount them in gold filigree settings. 21 There are to be twelve stones, one for each of the names of the sons of Israel,[b] each engraved like a seal with the name of one of the twelve tribes.[c]

22 "For the breastpiece make braided chains of pure gold, like a rope. 23 Make two gold rings for it and fasten them to two corners of the breastpiece. 24 Fasten the two gold chains to the rings at the corners of the breastpiece, 25 and the other ends of the chains to the two settings, attaching them to the shoulder pieces of the ephod at the front. 26 Make two gold rings and attach them to the other two corners of the breastpiece on the inside edge next to the ephod. 27 Make two more gold rings and attach them to the bottom of the shoulder pieces on the front of the ephod, close to the seam just above the waistband of the ephod. 28 The rings of the breastpiece are to be tied to the rings of the ephod with blue cord, connecting it to the waistband, so that the breastpiece will not swing out from the ephod.

29 "Whenever Aaron enters the Holy Place,[d] he will bear the names of the sons of Israel over his heart on the breastpiece of decision as a continuing memorial before the LORD. 30 Also put the Urim and

[a] *16* That is, about 9 inches or about 23 centimeters
[b] *20* The precise identification of some of these precious stones is uncertain.

28:8 [u] Ex 29:5 **28:9** [v] S SS 8:6; Isa 49:16; Hag 2:23 **28:12** [w] Dt 33:12; Job 31:36 [x] ver 29; Ex 30:16; Nu 10:10; 31:54; Jos 4:7; Zec 6:14 **28:15** [y] S Ex 25:7 **28:17** [z] Eze 28:13; Rev 21:19-20 [a] Eze 1:16; 10:9; Da 10:6 **28:21** [b] Jos 4:8 [c] Rev 21:12 **28:29** [d] ver 43

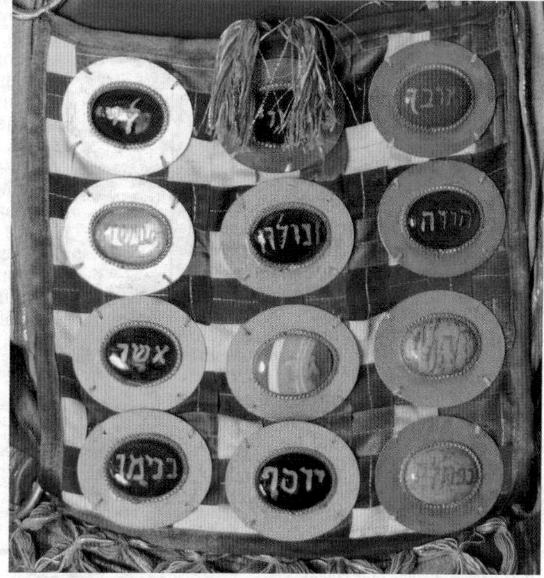

Replica of high priest's breastpiece
Todd Bolen/www.BiblePlaces.com

28:8 *waistband.* Apparently to hold the front and the back of the ephod to the priest's body.
28:12 *Aaron is to bear the names on his shoulders.* To symbolize the fact that the high priest represents all Israel when he ministers in the tabernacle (see photo above).
28:15 *for making decisions.* By means of the Urim and Thummim (see note on v. 30).
28:29 *Aaron ... will bear the names ... over his heart.* Thus the nation was doubly represented before the Lord (see v. 12 and note).
28:30 *the Urim and the Thummim.* The Hebrew for this phrase probably means "the curses [traditionally 'lights'] and the perfections." The Hebrew word *Urim* begins with the first letter of the Hebrew alphabet (*aleph*), and *Thummim* begins with the last letter (*taw*; see NIV text note on Ps 119; to see what *aleph* and *taw* looked like, they are printed in front of the *Aleph* and *Taw* headings above Ps 119:1 and 119:169). They were sacred lots and were often used in times of crisis to determine the will of God (see Nu 27:21). It has been suggested that if Urim ("curses") dominated when the lots were cast the answer was "no," but if Thummim ("perfections") dominated it was "yes." In any event, their "every decision" was "from the LORD" (Pr 16:33; see note there).

the Thummim[e] in the breastpiece, so they may be over Aaron's heart whenever he enters the presence of the LORD. Thus Aaron will always bear the means of making decisions for the Israelites over his heart before the LORD.

Other Priestly Garments

28:31-43pp — Ex 39:22-31

31 "Make the robe of the ephod entirely of blue cloth, 32 with an opening for the head in its center. There shall be a woven edge like a collar[a] around this opening, so that it will not tear. 33 Make pomegranates[f] of blue, purple and scarlet yarn around the hem of the robe, with gold bells between them. 34 The gold bells and the pomegranates are to alternate around the hem of the robe. 35 Aaron must wear it when he ministers. The sound of the bells will be heard when he enters the Holy Place before the LORD and when he comes out, so that he will not die.

36 "Make a plate[g] of pure gold and engrave on it as on a seal: HOLY TO THE LORD.[h] 37 Fasten a blue cord to it to attach it to the turban; it is to be on the front of the turban. 38 It will be on Aaron's forehead, and he will bear the guilt[i] involved in the sacred gifts the Israelites consecrate, whatever their gifts may be. It will be on Aaron's forehead continually so that they will be acceptable[j] to the LORD.

39 "Weave the tunic[k] of fine linen and make the turban[l] of fine linen. The sash is to be the work of an embroiderer. 40 Make tunics, sashes and caps for Aaron's sons[m] to give them dignity and honor.[n] 41 After you put these clothes[o] on your brother Aaron and his sons, anoint[p] and ordain them. Consecrate them so they may serve me as priests.[q]

42 "Make linen undergarments[r] as a covering for the body, reaching from the waist to the thigh. 43 Aaron and his sons must wear them whenever they enter the tent of meeting[s] or approach the altar to minister in the Holy Place,[t] so that they will not incur guilt and die.[u]

"This is to be a lasting ordinance[v] for Aaron and his descendants.

Consecration of the Priests

29:1-37pp — Lev 8:1-36

29 "This is what you are to do to consecrate[w] them, so they may serve me as priests: Take a young bull and two rams without defect.[x] 2 And from the finest wheat flour make round loaves without yeast, thick loaves without yeast and with olive oil mixed in, and thin loaves without yeast and brushed with olive oil.[y] 3 Put them in a basket and present them along with the bull and the two rams.[z] 4 Then bring Aaron and his sons to the entrance to the tent of meeting and wash them with water.[a] 5 Take the garments[b] and dress Aaron with the tunic, the robe of the ephod, the ephod itself and the breastpiece. Fasten the ephod on him by its skillfully woven waistband.[c] 6 Put the turban[d] on his head and attach the sacred emblem[e] to the turban. 7 Take the anointing oil[f] and anoint him by pouring it on his head. 8 Bring his sons and dress them in tunics[g] 9 and fasten caps on them. Then tie sashes on Aaron and his sons.[b][h] The priesthood is theirs by a lasting ordinance.[i]

"Then you shall ordain Aaron and his sons.

10 "Bring the bull to the front of the tent of meeting, and Aaron and his sons shall lay their hands on its head.[j] 11 Slaughter it in the LORD's presence[k] at the entrance to the tent of meeting. 12 Take some of the bull's blood and put it on the horns[l] of the altar with your finger, and pour out the rest of it at the base of the altar.[m] 13 Then take all the fat[n] on

[a] 32 The meaning of the Hebrew for this word is uncertain. [b] 9 Hebrew; Septuagint *on them*

28:30 [e] Lev 8:8; Nu 27:21; Dt 33:8; 1Sa 28:6; Ezr 2:63; Ne 7:65 **28:33** [f] Nu 13:23; 1Sa 14:2; 1Ki 7:18; SS 4:3; Jer 52:22; Joel 1:12; Hag 2:19 **28:36** [g] ver 37; Ex 29:6; Lev 8:9 [h] Zec 14:20 **28:38** [i] Lev 5:1; 10:17; 16:22; 22:9, 16; Nu 18:1; Isa 53:5, 6, 11; Eze 4:4-6; Heb 9:28; 1Pe 2:24 [j] S Ge 32:20; Lev 22:20, 27; 23:11; Isa 56:7 **28:39** [k] ver 4 [l] Ex 29:6; Lev 16:4; Eze 24:17, 23; 44:18 **28:40** [m] ver 4; Ex 29:8-9; 39:41; 40:14; Lev 8:13 [n] ver 2 **28:41** [o] Ex 40:13 [p] Ex 29:7; Lev 6:20; 10:7; 21:12; Nu 35:25 [q] Ex 29:7-9; 30:30; 40:15; Lev 4:3; 6:22; 8:1-36; Nu 3:3; Heb 7:28 **28:42** [r] Lev 6:10; 16:4, 23; Eze 44:18 **28:43** [s] S Ex 27:21 [t] ver 29 [u] Ex 30:20, 21; Lev 16:13; 22:9; Nu 1:51; 4:15, 20; 18:22 [v] S Ex 27:21 **29:1** [w] ver 21, 44; Lev 20:7; Jos 3:5; 1Ch 15:12 [x] Eze 43:23 **29:2** [y] ver 23; Lev 2:1, 4; 6:19-23; Nu 6:15 **29:3** [z] ver 15, 19 **29:4** [a] Ex 40:12; Lev 14:8; 16:4; Heb 10:22

29:5 [b] S Ex 28:2 [c] Ex 28:8 **29:6** [d] Ex 28:39; Isa 3:23; Zec 3:5 [e] S Ex 28:36 **29:7** [f] ver 21; S Ex 28:41; 30:25, 30, 31; 37:29; 40:9; Lev 21:10; 1Sa 10:1; 1Ki 1:39; Ps 89:20; 133:2; 141:5 **29:8** [g] S Ex 28:4; Lev 16:4 **29:9** [h] Ex 28:40 [i] S Ex 27:21; 40:15; Nu 3:10; 18:7; 25:13; Dt 18:5; Jdg 17:5; 1Sa 2:30; 1Ki 12:31 **29:10** [j] ver 19; Lev 1:4; 4:15; 16:21; Nu 8:12 **29:11** [k] Lev 1:5, 11; 4:24; 6:16, 25; 14:13 **29:12** [l] S Ex 27:2 [m] Lev 4:7; 9:9 **29:13** [n] ver 22; Lev 1:8; 3:3, 5, 9; 4:10; 6:12; 7:3, 5, 31; 9:10; Nu 18:17; 1Sa 2:15; 1Ki 8:64; 2Ch 7:7; 29:35; 35:14; Isa 43:24; Eze 44:15

28:31 *robe.* Worn under the ephod.

28:35 According to Jewish legend, one end of a length of rope was tied to the high priest's ankle and the other end remained outside the tabernacle. If the bells on his robe stopped jingling while he was in the Holy Place, the assumption that he had died could be tested by pulling gently on the rope. It is unknown if this legend has any historical validity.

28:36 *HOLY TO THE LORD.* See 3:5 and note; 39:30; Zec 14:20 and note.

28:38 *bear the guilt.* Symbolically.

28:39 *tunic.* Worn under the robe.

28:40 *to give them dignity and honor.* See note on v. 2.

28:42–43 See note on 20:26.

28:43 *tent of meeting.* See note on 27:21.

29:1 *consecrate them.* See note on 19:10–11. *without defect.* See note on 12:5.

29:4 *tent of meeting.* See note on 27:21. *wash them with water.* Symbolizing the removal of ceremonial uncleanness (cf. Heb 10:22) and thus signifying the purity that must characterize them.

29:7 *anoint him.* Symbolizing spiritual endowment for serving God (see 28:41; Isa 61:1 and note).

29:10 *Bring the bull.* As a sin offering (see v. 14) to atone for the past sins of Aaron and his sons (see Lev 4:3 and note). *lay their hands on its head.* As a symbol of (1) the animal's becoming their substitute and (2) transferring their sins to the sin-bearer (see Lev 16:20–22 and note).

29:12 *horns of the altar.* See note on 27:2.

29:13 *fat.* The most select parts of the bull (see Lev 3:3–5,16) were burned on the altar as a sacrifice to the Lord.

the internal organs,[o] the long lobe of the liver, and both kidneys with the fat on them, and burn them on the altar. [14]But burn the bull's flesh and its hide and its intestines[p] outside the camp.[q] It is a sin offering.[a]

[15]"Take one of the rams,[r] and Aaron and his sons shall lay their hands on its head.[s] [16]Slaughter it and take the blood and splash it against the sides of the altar. [17]Cut the ram into pieces and wash[t] the internal organs and the legs, putting them with the head and the other pieces. [18]Then burn the entire ram on the altar. It is a burnt offering to the LORD, a pleasing aroma,[u] a food offering presented to the LORD.

[19]"Take the other ram,[v] and Aaron and his sons shall lay their hands on its head.[w] [20]Slaughter it, take some of its blood and put it on the lobes of the right ears of Aaron and his sons, on the thumbs of their right hands, and on the big toes of their right feet.[x] Then splash blood against the sides of the altar.[y] [21]And take some blood[z] from the altar and some of the anointing oil[a] and sprinkle it on Aaron and his garments and on his sons and their garments. Then he and his sons and their garments will be consecrated.[b]

[22]"Take from this ram the fat,[c] the fat tail, the fat on the internal organs, the long lobe of the liver, both kidneys with the fat on them, and the right thigh. (This is the ram for the ordination.) [23]From the basket of bread made without yeast, which is before the LORD, take one round loaf, one thick loaf with olive oil mixed in, and one thin loaf. [24]Put all these in the hands of Aaron and his sons and have them wave them before the LORD as a wave offering.[d] [25]Then take them from their hands and burn them on the altar along with the burnt offering for a pleasing aroma to the LORD, a food offering presented to the LORD.[e] [26]After you take the breast of the ram for Aaron's ordination, wave it before the LORD as a wave offering, and it will be your share.[f]

[27]"Consecrate those parts of the ordination ram that belong to Aaron and his sons:[g] the breast that was waved and the thigh that was presented. [28]This is always to be the perpetual share from the Israelites for Aaron and his sons. It is the contribution the Israelites are to make to the LORD from their fellowship offerings.[h]

[29]"Aaron's sacred garments[i] will belong to his descendants so that they can be anointed and ordained in them.[j] [30]The son[k] who succeeds him as priest and comes to the tent of meeting to minister in the Holy Place is to wear them seven days.

[31]"Take the ram[l] for the ordination and cook the meat in a sacred place.[m] [32]At the entrance to the tent of meeting, Aaron and his sons are to eat the meat of the ram and the bread[n] that is in the basket. [33]They are to eat these offerings by which atonement was made for their ordination and consecration. But no one else may eat[o] them, because they are sacred. [34]And if any of the meat of the ordination ram or any bread is left over till morning,[p] burn it up. It must not be eaten, because it is sacred.

[35]"Do for Aaron and his sons everything I have commanded you, taking seven days to ordain them. [36]Sacrifice a bull each day[q] as a sin offering to make atonement[r]. Purify the altar by making atonement for it, and anoint it to consecrate[s] it. [37]For seven days make atonement for the altar and consecrate it. Then the altar will be most holy, and whatever touches it will be holy.[t]

[38]"This is what you are to offer on the altar regularly each day:[u] two lambs a year old. [39]Offer one in the morning and the other at twilight.[v] [40]With the first lamb offer a tenth of an ephah[b] of the finest flour mixed with a quarter of a hin[c] of oil[w] from pressed olives, and a quarter of a hin of wine as a drink offering.[x] [41]Sacrifice the other lamb at twilight[y] with the same grain offering[z] and its drink offering as in the morning—a pleasing aroma, a food offering presented to the LORD.

[42]"For the generations to come[a] this burnt offering is to be made regularly[b] at

[a] *14* Or *purification offering*; also in verse 36
[b] *40* That is, probably about 3 1/2 pounds or about 1.6 kilograms [c] *40* That is, probably about 1 quart or about 1 liter

29:13 [o]S Ex 12:9 **29:14** [p]Na 3:6; Mal 2:3 [q]Lev 4:12, 21; 16:27; Nu 19:3-5; Heb 13:11 **29:15** [r]S ver 3 [s]ver 10; Lev 3:2; 2Ch 29:23 **29:17** [t]Lev 1:9, 13 **29:18** [u]S Ge 8:21; 2Co 2:15 **29:19** [v]S ver 3 [w]S ver 10 **29:20** [x]Lev 14:14, 25 [y]ver 16; Lev 1:5, 11; 3:2 **29:21** [z]Heb 9:22 [a]S ver 7 [b]S ver 1 **29:22** [c]S ver 13 **29:24** [d]Lev 7:30; 9:21; 10:15; 14:12; 23:11, 20; Nu 6:20; 8:11, 13, 15 **29:25** [e]ver 18 **29:26** [f]Lev 7:31-34 **29:27** [g]Ex 22:29; Lev 7:31, 34; Nu 18:11, 12; Dt 18:3 **29:28** [h]ver 22-27; Lev 7:30, 34; 10:15 **29:29** [i]S Ex 28:2; S Lev 16:4 [j]Nu 20:28 **29:30** [k]Lev 6:22; Nu 3:3; 20:28 **29:31** [l]Lev 7:37; 2Ch 13:9 [m]Lev 10:14; Nu 19:9; Eze 42:13 **29:32** [n]Mt 12:4 **29:33** [o]Lev 22:10, 13 **29:34** [p]S Ex 12:10 **29:36** [q]Heb 10:11 [r]ver 33, 37; Ex 30:10; Lev 1:4; 4:20; 16:16; Nu 6:11; 8:12, 19; 16:46; 25:13; 2Ch 29:24 [s]Ex 40:10; Nu 7:10 **29:37** [t]Ex 30:28-29; 40:10; Eze 43:25; Mt 23:19

29:38 [u]Lev 23:2; Nu 28:3-8; 1Ch 16:40; 2Ch 8:13; Eze 46:13-15; Da 12:11 **29:39** [v]Nu 28:4, 8; 1Ki 18:36; 2Ch 13:11; Ezr 3:3; Ps 141:2; Da 9:21 **29:40** [w]Ex 30:24; Nu 15:4; 28:5 [x]S Ge 35:14; Lev 23:37; 2Ki 16:13 **29:41** [y]1Ki 18:29, 36; 2Ki 3:20; 16:15; Ezr 9:4, 5; Ps 141:2; Da 9:21 [z]Lev 2:1; 5:13; 10:12; Nu 4:16; 6:17; 1Ki 8:64; Isa 43:23 **29:42** [a]Ex 30:8, 10, 21, 31; 31:13 [b]Eze 46:15

9:14 *flesh ... hide ... intestines.* Thought of as bearing sin, and hus burned outside the camp (see Heb 13:11–13 and notes).

29:18 *burn the entire ram.* Symbolizing total dedication (see note on Lev 1:3).

29:20 *right ears.* Symbolizing sensitivity to God and his word. *right hands ... right feet.* Symbolizing a life of serice to others on God's behalf.

9:24 *wave offering.* See note on Lev 7:30–32.

9:28 *perpetual share ... for Aaron and his sons.* Parts of cerain sacrificial animals were set aside as food for the priests nd their families (see Lev 10:14).

29:31 *a sacred place.* Probably the tabernacle courtyard.

29:36 *making atonement for it.* Because the altar was corrupted by the sins of the people (see Lev 16:16; Heb 9:21–22).

29:37 *holy ... holy.* Set apart as consecrated to the Lord (see note on 3:5).

29:38–39 Institution of the daily morning and evening offerings—sometimes observed even during days of apostasy (see 2Ki 16:15).

the entrance to the tent of meeting,[c] before
the LORD. There I will meet you and speak
to you;[d] 43 there also I will meet with the
Israelites, and the place will be consecrated by my glory.[e]
44 "So I will consecrate the tent of meeting and the altar and will consecrate Aaron and his sons to serve me as priests.[f]
45 Then I will dwell[g] among the Israelites
and be their God.[h] 46 They will know that I
am the LORD their God, who brought them
out of Egypt[i] so that I might dwell among
them. I am the LORD their God.[j]

The Altar of Incense

30:1-5pp — Ex 37:25-28

30 "Make an altar[k] of acacia wood for
burning incense.[l] 2 It is to be square,
a cubit long and a cubit wide, and two cubits high[a] — its horns[m] of one piece with
it. 3 Overlay the top and all the sides and
the horns with pure gold, and make a gold
molding around it.[n] 4 Make two gold rings[o]
for the altar below the molding — two on
each of the opposite sides — to hold the
poles used to carry it. 5 Make the poles of
acacia wood and overlay them with gold.[p]
6 Put the altar in front of the curtain that
shields the ark of the covenant law — before the atonement cover[q] that is over the
tablets of the covenant law — where I will
meet with you.
7 "Aaron must burn fragrant incense[r] on
the altar every morning when he tends the
lamps. 8 He must burn incense again when
he lights the lamps at twilight so incense
will burn regularly before the LORD for the
generations to come.[s] 9 Do not offer on this
altar any other incense[t] or any burnt offering or grain offering, and do not pour a
drink offering on it. 10 Once a year[u] Aaron
shall make atonement[v] on its horns. This
annual atonement must be made with the
blood of the atoning sin offering[b][w] for the
generations to come.[x] It is most holy to
the LORD."

29:42 [c]S Ex 26:1; S 27:21 [d]ver 43; Ex 25:22; 33:9, 11; Nu 7:89 **29:43** [e]Ex 33:18; 40:34; Lev 9:6; 1Ki 8:11; 2Ch 5:14; 7:2; Ps 26:8; 85:9; Eze 1:28; 43:5; Hag 1:8; 2:7 **29:44** [f]S ver 1 **29:45** [g]S Ex 25:8; Nu 35:34; Jn 14:17; S Ro 8:10 [h]S Ge 17:7; 2Co 6:16 **29:46** [i]S Ex 6:6; 19:4-6; Dt 5:6; Ps 114:1; Hag 2:5 [j]S Ge 17:7 **30:1** [k]Ex 40:5, 26; Nu 4:11; 1Ki 6:20; Eze 41:22 [l]S Ex 25:6; 37:29; Lk 1:11; Heb 9:4; Rev 8:3 **30:2** [m]S Ex 27:2; Rev 9:13 **30:3** [n]S Ex 25:11 **30:4** [o]S Ex 25:12 **30:5** [p]S Ex 25:13 **30:6** [q]Ex 25:22; S 26:34 **30:7** [r]S Ex 25:6; 40:27; Nu 3:10; Dt 33:10; 1Sa 2:28; 1Ch 6:49; 2Ch 2:4; 26:18; 29:7 **30:8** [s]S Ex 25:37; S 29:42 **30:9** [t]Lev 10:1; Nu 16:7, 40 **30:10** [u]Lev 16:2 [v]Lev 9:7; 16:18-19, 30; 23:27, 28; 25:9 [w]Ex 29:14; Lev 4:3; 6:25; 7:7; 8:2, 14; Nu 6:11 [x]S Ex 29:42

Atonement Money

11 Then the LORD said to Moses, 12 "When
you take a census[y] of the Israelites to count
them, each one must pay the LORD a ransom[z] for his life at the time he is counted.
Then no plague[a] will come on them when
you number them. 13 Each one who crosses over to those already counted is to give
a half shekel,[c] according to the sanctuary
shekel,[b] which weighs twenty gerahs. This
half shekel is an offering to the LORD. 14 All
who cross over, those twenty years old or
more,[c] are to give an offering to the LORD.
15 The rich are not to give more than a half
shekel and the poor are not to give less[d]
when you make the offering to the LORD to
atone for your lives. 16 Receive the atonement[e] money from the Israelites and use
it for the service of the tent of meeting.[f] It
will be a memorial[g] for the Israelites before the LORD, making atonement for your
lives."

Basin for Washing

17 Then the LORD said to Moses, 18 "Make
a bronze basin,[h] with its bronze stand,
for washing. Place it between the tent
of meeting and the altar, and put water
in it. 19 Aaron and his sons are to wash
their hands and feet[i] with water[j] from it.
20 Whenever they enter the tent of meeting, they shall wash with water so that
they will not die.[k] Also, when they approach the altar to minister by presenting

[a] *2* That is, about 1 1/2 feet long and wide and 3 feet high or about 45 centimeters long and wide and 90 centimeters high [b] *10* Or *purification offering*
[c] *13* That is, about 1/5 ounce or about 5.8 grams; also in verse 15

30:12 [y]Ex 38:25; Nu 1:2, 49; 4:2, 29; 14:29; 26:2; 31:26; 2Sa 24:1; 2Ki 12:4 [z]Ex 38:26; Nu 31:50; S Mt 20:28 [a]Nu 14:12; Dt 28:58-61; 2Sa 24:13; 1Ki 8:37 **30:13** [b]ver 24; Ex 38:24, 26; Lev 5:15; 27:3, 25; Nu 3:47; 7:13; 18:16; Eze 4:10; 45:12; Mt 17:24 **30:14** [c]Ex 38:26; Nu 1:3, 18; 14:29; 26:2; 32:11; 2Ch 25:5 **30:15** [d]Pr 22:2; Eph 6:9 **30:16** [e]ver 12 [f]Ex 38:25-28; 2Ch 24:5 [g]Nu 31:54 **30:18** [h]Ex 31:9; 35:16; 38:8; 39:39; 40:7, 30; 1Ki 7:38; 2Ch 4:6 **30:19** [i]Ex 40:31-32; Jn 13:10 [j]Ex 29:4; 40:12; Lev 8:6; Ps 26:6; Heb 10:22 **30:20** [k]S Ex 28:43

29:42–43 *I will meet.* See note on 27:21.
29:43 *my glory.* Symbolic of God's presence over the ark of the covenant (see note on 25:10; see also 40:34–35; 1Ki 8:10–13).
29:45–46 *dwell among.* See note on 25:9.
29:45 *I will ... be their God.* Commonly denotes the essence of the divine promise pledged in his covenant with his people (see note on 6:7).
29:46 *I am the LORD ... who brought them out.* See note on 20:2.
30:1 *incense.* Its fragrant smoke symbolized the prayers of God's people (see Ps 141:2; Lk 1:10; Rev 5:8; 8:3–4).
30:3 *gold.* See note on 26:37.
30:4 *rings.* See note on 25:12.
30:6 *curtain that shields the ark of the covenant law.* See notes on 25:16,22; 26:31.
30:10 *annual atonement.* See Lev 16:34 and note. *holy to the LORD.* See 29:37 and note.
30:12 *take a census.* Perhaps such censuses were taken on various occasions (and at stated intervals) to enter the Israelites into an official roll for public duties in the Lord's service (see Nu 1:2; 26:2), primarily military (see note on v. 14). *pay ... a ransom for his life.* An extension of the principle stated in 13:13,15 (see note on 13:13). Jesus gave "his life as a ransom for many" (see Mt 20:28; Mk 10:45 and notes cf. 1Ti 2:5–6).
30:13 *shekel.* A unit of weight, not a coin (see note on Ge 20:16). *according to the sanctuary shekel.* In keeping with the standard weights used at the tabernacle. They may have differed slightly from those used in the marketplace.
30:14 *twenty years old or more.* Of military age (see Nu 1:3).
30:16 *tent of meeting.* See note on 27:21. *atonement.* See note on 25:17.
30:18 *basin.* Made from bronze mirrors contributed by Israelite women (see 38:8). *washing.* See note on 29:4.

Model of the bronze basin in the tabernacle courtyard

Todd Bolen/www.BiblePlaces.com

a food offering to the LORD, 21 they shall wash their hands and feet so that they will not die. This is to be a lasting ordinance[l] for Aaron and his descendants for the generations to come."[m]

Anointing Oil

22 Then the LORD said to Moses, 23 "Take the following fine spices:[n] 500 shekels[a] of liquid myrrh,[o] half as much (that is, 250 shekels) of fragrant cinnamon,[p] 250 shekels[b] of fragrant calamus,[q] 24 500 shekels[r] of cassia[s]—all according to the sanctuary shekel—and a hin[c] of olive oil. 25 Make these into a sacred anointing oil, a fragrant blend, the work of a perfumer.[t] It will be the sacred anointing oil.[u] 26 Then use it to anoint[v] the tent of meeting, the ark of the covenant law, 27 the table and all its articles, the lampstand and its accessories, the altar of incense, 28 the altar of burnt offering and all its utensils, and the basin with its stand. 29 You shall consecrate them[w] so they will be most holy, and whatever touches them will be holy.[x]

30 "Anoint Aaron and his sons and consecrate[y] them so they may serve me as priests.[z] 31 Say to the Israelites, 'This is to be my sacred anointing oil[a] for the generations to come.[b] 32 Do not pour it on anyone else's body and do not make any other oil using the same formula. It is sacred, and you are to consider it sacred.[c] 33 Whoever makes perfume like it and puts it on anyone other than a priest must be cut off[d] from their people.' "

Incense

34 Then the LORD said to Moses, "Take fragrant spices[e]—gum resin, onycha and galbanum—and pure frankincense, all in equal amounts, 35 and make a fragrant blend of incense,[f] the work of a perfumer.[g] It is to be salted and pure and sacred. 36 Grind some of it to powder and place it in front of the ark of the covenant law in the tent of meeting, where I will meet[h] with you. It shall be most holy[i] to you. 37 Do not make any incense with this formula for yourselves; consider it holy[j] to the LORD. 38 Whoever makes incense like it to enjoy its fragrance must be cut off[k] from their people."

Bezalel and Oholiab

31:2-6pp — Ex 35:30-35

31 Then the LORD said to Moses, 2 "See, I have chosen Bezalel[l] son of Uri, the son of Hur,[m] of the tribe of Judah, 3 and I have filled him with the Spirit of God, with wisdom, with understanding, with knowledge[n] and with all kinds of skills[o]— 4 to make artistic designs for work in gold, silver and bronze, 5 to cut

30:21 [l]S Ex 27:21 [m]Ex 29:42 **30:23** [n]S Ge 43:11 [o]S Ge 37:25 [p]Pr 7:17; SS 4:14 [q]SS 4:14; Isa 43:24; Jer 6:20 **30:24** [r]S ver 13 [s]Ps 45:8; Eze 27:19 **30:25** [t]ver 35; Ex 37:29; 1Ch 9:30 [u]S Ex 29:7; S 1Sa 9:16 **30:26** [v]Ex 40:9; Lev 8:10; Nu 7:1 **30:29** [w]Lev 8:10-11 [x]Ex 29:37; Lev 6:18, 27; Mt 23:17 **30:30** [y]Ex 29:7; Lev 8:2, 12, 30; 10:7; 16:32; 21:10, 12; 1Ch 15:12; Ps 133:2 [z]S Ex 28:41 **30:31** [a]S Ex 29:7 [b]S Ex 29:42

[a] *23* That is, about 12 1/2 pounds or about 5.8 kilograms; also in verse 24 [b] *23* That is, about 6 1/4 pounds or about 2.9 kilograms [c] *24* That is, probably about 1 gallon or about 3.8 liters

30:32 [c]ver 25, 37 **30:33** [d]ver 38; S Ge 17:14 **30:34** [e]SS 3:6 **30:35** [f]S Ex 25:6 [g]S ver 25 **30:36** [h]S Ex 25:22 [i]ver 32; Ex 29:37; Lev 2:3 **30:37** [j]S ver 32 **30:38** [k]S ver 33 **31:2** [l]Ex 36:1, 2; 37:1; 38:22; 1Ch 2:20; 2Ch 1:5 [m]S Ex 17:10 **31:3** [n]S Ex 28:3 [o]1Ki 7:14; 1Co 12:4

30:23–24 *myrrh ... cinnamon ... calamus ... cassia.* See note on 25:6.

30:29 *holy ... holy.* See 29:37 and note.

30:33 *cut off from their people.* See note on 12:15.

30:34 *gum resin, onycha and galbanum.* See note on 25:6. *frankincense.* A resin from the bark of *Boswellia carteri*, which grows in southern Arabia.

31:2 *Bezalel.* Means "in the shadow/protection of God." *Hur.* See note on 17:10.

31:3 *filled him with the Spirit of God.* Ability to work skillfully in all kinds of crafts was a spiritual gift, equipping a person for special service to God. *wisdom.* See Pr 1:2 and note.

and set stones, to work in wood, and to
engage in all kinds of crafts. 6Moreover,
I have appointed Oholiab[p] son of Ahisamak, of the tribe of Dan,[q] to help him.
Also I have given ability to all the skilled
workers[r] to make everything I have commanded you: 7the tent of meeting,[s] the ark
of the covenant law[t] with the atonement
cover[u] on it, and all the other furnishings
of the tent— 8the table[v] and its articles,
the pure gold lampstand[w] and all its accessories, the altar of incense,[x] 9the altar of
burnt offering[y] and all its utensils, the basin[z] with its stand— 10and also the woven
garments[a], both the sacred garments for
Aaron the priest and the garments for his
sons when they serve as priests, 11and the
anointing oil[b] and fragrant incense[c] for the
Holy Place. They are to make them just as
I commanded[d] you."

The Sabbath

12Then the LORD said to Moses, 13"Say
to the Israelites, 'You must observe my
Sabbaths.[e] This will be a sign[f] between
me and you for the generations to come,[g]
so you may know that I am the LORD, who
makes you holy.[h]
14" 'Observe the Sabbath, because it is
holy to you. Anyone who desecrates it is
to be put to death;[i] those who do any work
on that day must be cut off from their people. 15For six days work[j] is to be done, but
the seventh day is a day of sabbath rest,[k]
holy to the LORD. Whoever does any work
on the Sabbath day is to be put to death.
16The Israelites are to observe the Sabbath,[l] celebrating it for the generations to
come as a lasting covenant. 17It will be a
sign[m] between me and the Israelites forever, for in six days the LORD made the heavens and the earth, and on the seventh day
he rested and was refreshed.[n]' "[o]
18When the LORD finished speaking to
Moses on Mount Sinai,[p] he gave him the
two tablets of the covenant law, the tablets
of stone[q] inscribed by the finger of God.[r]

The Golden Calf

32 When the people saw that Moses
was so long in coming down from
the mountain,[s] they gathered around Aaron and said, "Come, make us gods[a] who
will go before[t] us. As for this fellow Moses
who brought us up out of Egypt, we don't
know what has happened to him."[u]
2Aaron answered them, "Take off the
gold earrings[v] that your wives, your sons
and your daughters are wearing, and bring
them to me." 3So all the people took off
their earrings and brought them to Aaron. 4He took what they handed him and
made it into an idol[w] cast in the shape of a
calf,[x] fashioning it with a tool. Then they
said, "These are your gods,[b][y] Israel, who
brought you up out of Egypt."[z]
5When Aaron saw this, he built an altar in front of the calf and announced,
"Tomorrow there will be a festival[a] to the
LORD." 6So the next day the people rose

[a] *1* Or *a god*; also in verses 23 and 31 [b] *4* Or *This is your god*; also in verse 8

31:6 [p]Ex 36:1, 2; 38:23 [q]1Ki 7:14; 2Ch 2:14 [r]S Ex 28:3 **31:7** [s]Ex 36:8-38 [t]Ex 37:1-5 [u]Ex 37:6; 40:20 **31:8** [v]Ex 37:10-16 [w]Ex 37:17-24; Lev 24:4 [x]Ex 37:25-28 **31:9** [y]Ex 38:3; Nu 4:14 [z]S Ex 30:18 **31:10** [a]S Ex 28:2 **31:11** [b]Ex 30:22-32; 37:29 [c]S Ex 25:6 [d]S Ex 25:9 **31:13** [e]S Ex 20:8 [f]ver 17; Isa 56:4; Eze 20:12, 20 [g]S Ex 29:42 [h]Lev 11:44; 20:8; 21:8; Eze 37:28 **31:14** [i]Ex 35:2; Nu 15:32-36 **31:15** [j]S Ex 20:8-11; 35:2; Lev 16:29; 23:3; Nu 29:7 [k]S Ge 2:3 **31:16** [l]S Ex 20:8 **31:17** [m]S ver 13 [n]S Ge 2:2-3 [o]S Ge 2:2; S Ex 20:9; Isa 56:2; 58:13; 66:23; Jer 17:21-22; Eze 20:12, 20 **31:18** [p]S Ex 19:11 [q]S Ex 24:12; 2Co 3:3; Heb 9:4 [r]Ex 32:15-16; 34:1, 28; Dt 4:13; 9:10 **32:1** [s]S Ge 7:4; Dt 9:9-12 [t]S Ex 13:21 [u]ver 23; Ac 7:40* **32:2** [v]Jdg 8:24-27 **32:4** [w]S Ex 20:23; Jdg 17:3-4; Isa 30:22 [x]ver 8, 24, 35; Dt 9:16; Ne 9:18; Ps 106:19; Ac 7:41 [y]Ex 20:23; Isa 42:17 [z]1Ki 12:28; 14:9; 2Ki 10:29; 17:16; 2Ch 13:8; Hos 8:6; 10:5 **32:5** [a]Lev 23:2, 37; 2Ki 10:20; Joel 2:15

31:6 *Oholiab.* Means "The (divine) father is my tent/tabernacle." The names of Bezalel (see note on v. 2) and Oholiab were appropriate for the chief craftsmen working on the tabernacle.
31:7 *tent of meeting.* See note on 27:21.
31:13 *observe my Sabbaths.* Instructions for building the tabernacle and making the priestly garments are concluded by impressing on the Israelites the importance and necessity of keeping the Sabbath even while carrying out this special task. *makes you holy.* See 19:6; 29:37 and notes.
31:14 *cut off from their people.* See note on 12:15.
31:16–17 *covenant ... sign.* In their rhythm of work and rest in the service of God, the Israelites were to emulate God's pattern in creation as an ever-renewed sign of their covenant with God (see note on Ge 9:12).
31:18 *two tablets.* In keeping with ancient Near Eastern practice, these were probably duplicates of the covenant document, not two sections of the Ten Commandments. One copy belonged to each party of the covenant. Since Israel's copy was to be laid up in the presence of God (according to custom), both covenant tablets (God's and Israel's) were placed in the ark (see 25:21 and note). *covenant law.* See notes on 16:34; 25:16. *inscribed by the finger of God.* Because it was God's covenant (see 19:5–6 and notes), and the stipulations of the covenant (20:1–17) were his.
32:1 *so long.* Forty days and forty nights (see 24:18 and note). *they.* Probably the tribe and clan leaders. *gods.* See NIV text note. *Moses who brought us up out of Egypt.* A rebellious contrast to the gracious statement of Israel's covenant Lord (see 20:2 and note; 29:46).
32:2 *gold earrings.* Probably part of the plunder brought from Egypt (see 3:21–22 and note on 3:21; 11:2–3; 12:35–36).
32:4 *cast in the shape of a calf.* Either gold plating over a carved wooden calf (it was later burned, v. 20) or crudely cast in solid gold and then further shaped with a tool, later to be melted down in the fire. The calf was probably similar to representations of the Egyptian bull-god Apis (see note on Jer 46:15; see also notes on Jos 24:14; Jdg 2:13; 1Ki 12:28). Its manufacture was a flagrant violation of the second commandment (20:4–5; see notes there). *they.* The leaders among the people (see note on v. 1). *These are your gods ... up out of Egypt.* A parody of 20:2 (see note on v. 1). Centuries later, King Jeroboam would quote these words when he set up two golden calves in the northern kingdom of Israel (see 1Ki 12:28–29 and notes).
32:5 *altar in front of the calf ... festival to the LORD.* Apparently Aaron recognized the idolatrous consequences of his deed and acted quickly to keep the people from turning completely away from the Lord.
32:6 *they sat down ... indulge in revelry.* A pagan symbol evoked pagan religious practices. Paul quotes this sentence as a vivid example of Israel's tendency toward idolatry (see 1Co 10:7 and note). The Hebrew verb translated

early and sacrificed burnt offerings and
presented fellowship offerings.[b] Afterward
they sat down to eat and drink[c] and got up
to indulge in revelry.[d]
7 Then the LORD said to Moses, "Go
down, because your people, whom you
brought up out of Egypt,[e] have become
corrupt.[f] 8 They have been quick to turn
away[g] from what I commanded them and
have made themselves an idol[h] cast in the
shape of a calf.[i] They have bowed down
to it and sacrificed[j] to it and have said,
'These are your gods, Israel, who brought
you up out of Egypt.'[k]
9 "I have seen these people," the LORD
said to Moses, "and they are a stiff-necked[l]
people. 10 Now leave me alone[m] so that my
anger may burn against them and that I
may destroy[n] them. Then I will make you
into a great nation."[o]
11 But Moses sought the favor[p] of the
LORD his God. "LORD," he said, "why should
your anger burn against your people,
whom you brought out of Egypt with great
power and a mighty hand?[q] 12 Why should
the Egyptians say, 'It was with evil intent
that he brought them out, to kill them in
the mountains and to wipe them off the
face of the earth'?[r] Turn from your fierce
anger; relent and do not bring disaster[s] on
your people. 13 Remember[t] your servants
Abraham, Isaac and Israel, to whom you
swore by your own self:[u] 'I will make your
descendants as numerous as the stars[v] in
the sky and I will give your descendants all
this land[w] I promised them, and it will be
their inheritance forever.'" 14 Then the LORD
relented[x] and did not bring on his people
the disaster he had threatened.
15 Moses turned and went down the
mountain with the two tablets of the covenant law[y] in his hands.[z] They were inscribed[a] on both sides, front and back.
16 The tablets were the work of God; the
writing was the writing of God, engraved
on the tablets.[b]
17 When Joshua[c] heard the noise of the
people shouting, he said to Moses, "There
is the sound of war in the camp."
18 Moses replied:

"It is not the sound of victory,
it is not the sound of defeat;
it is the sound of singing that I
hear."

19 When Moses approached the camp
and saw the calf[d] and the dancing,[e] his anger burned[f] and he threw the tablets out of
his hands, breaking them to pieces[g] at the
foot of the mountain. 20 And he took the
calf the people had made and burned[h] it
in the fire; then he ground it to powder,[i]
scattered it on the water[j] and made the
Israelites drink it.
21 He said to Aaron, "What did these
people do to you, that you led them into
such great sin?"
22 "Do not be angry,[k] my lord," Aaron answered. "You know how prone these people are to evil.[l] 23 They said to me, 'Make
us gods who will go before us. As for this
fellow Moses who brought us up out of
Egypt, we don't know what has happened
to him.'[m] 24 So I told them, 'Whoever has
any gold jewelry, take it off.' Then they

32:6 [b]Ex 20:24; 34:15; Lev 3:1; 4:10; 6:12; 9:4; 22:21; Nu 6:14; 25:2; Dt 27:7; Jdg 20:26; Eze 43:27; Ac 7:41 [c]Jdg 19:4; Ru 3:3; 1Sa 1:9; 2Sa 11:11; 1Ki 13:23; 18:42; Ne 8:12; Job 1:4; Ecc 5:18; 8:15; Jer 16:8 [d]ver 17-19; 1Co 10:7* **32:7** [e]ver 4, 11; Ex 33:1 [f]S Ge 6:11-12; Eze 20:8 **32:8** [g]Jer 7:26; 16:12; Mal 2:8; 3:7 [h]S Ex 20:4 [i]S ver 4 [j]Ex 22:20 [k]1Ki 12:28; Eze 23:8 **32:9** [l]Ex 33:3, 5; 34:9; Dt 9:6, 13; 10:16; 31:27; Jdg 2:19; 2Ki 17:14; 2Ch 30:8; 36:13; Ne 9:16; Ps 78:8; Pr 29:1; Isa 46:12; 48:4; Jer 7:26; Eze 2:4; Hos 4:16; Ac 7:51 **32:10** [m]1Sa 2:25; Jer 7:16; 11:14; 14:11 [n]Ex 22:24; 33:3, 5; Nu 16:21, 45; Dt 9:14, 19; Ps 106:23; Jer 14:12; Eze 20:13 [o]Nu 14:12; Dt 9:14 **32:11** [p]Dt 9:18; 2Sa 21:1; 2Ch 15:2; Ps 9:10; 34:4; 106:23; Isa 9:13; Jer 15:1 [q]ver 13; Dt 9:26; 1Sa 7:9; Ne 1:10; Ps 136:12 **32:12** [r]Nu 14:13-16; Dt 9:28 [s]ver 14; Ex 33:13 **32:13** [t]S Ex 2:24; 33:13 [u]S Ge 22:16; Heb 6:13 [v]Ge 15:5; 22:17 [w]S Ge 12:7 **32:14** [x]Dt 9:19; 1Sa 15:11; 2Sa 24:16; 1Ki 21:29; 1Ch 21:15; Ps 106:45; Jer 18:8; 26:3, 19; Am 7:3, 6; Jnh 3:10 **32:15** [y]Ex 31:18; Heb 9:4 [z]S Ex 19:18; 34:4, 29; Dt 9:15 [a]2Co 3:3 **32:16** [b]S Ex 24:12 **32:17** [c]S Ex 17:9 **32:19** [d]Dt 9:16 [e]ver 6; 1Co 10:7 [f]Ezr 9:3; Ps 119:53, 158 [g]Ex 34:1; Dt 9:17 **32:20** [h]Dt 7:25; 12:3; Jos 7:1; 2Ki 23:6; 1Ch 14:12 [i]2Ch 34:7; Mic 1:7 [j]Dt 9:21 **32:22** [k]S Ge 18:30 [l]Dt 9:24; 28:20; 2Ki 21:15; Ezr 9:13; Ne 9:28; Jer 4:4; 44:3; Eze 6:9 **32:23** [m]S ver 1; Ac 7:40

"indulge in revelry" often has sexual connotations (see, e.g., "caressing," Ge 26:8). Immoral orgies frequently accompanied pagan worship in ancient times.

32:7,9 *your people ... these people.* By not calling Israel "my people" (as, e.g., in 3:10), God indicates that he is disowning them for breaking his covenant with them (see note on 17:4).

32:7 *corrupt.* And, therefore, ripe for destruction (see v. 10; Ge 6:11–13).

32:9 *stiff-necked.* Like unresponsive oxen or horses (see Jer 27:11–12; see also note on Ne 3:5).

32:10 *I will make you into a great nation.* After Israel—Abraham's descendants—has been destroyed, God will transfer to Moses the pledge originally given to Abraham (see Ge 12:2).

32:11 *your people.* Using God's own words (see v. 7 and note on vv. 7,9), Moses appeals to God's special relationship to Israel, then to God's need to vindicate his name in the eyes of the Egyptians (see v. 12), and finally to the great patriarchal promises (see v. 13).

32:13 *Israel.* Jacob (see 33:1; see also Ge 32:28).

32:14 *the LORD relented.* See note on Jer 18:7–10; see also 2Sa 24:16; Ps 106:45; Am 7:1–6 and note on 7:3; cf. Jas 5:16.

32:15 *went down the mountain.* See note on 24:18. *two tablets.* See note on 31:18. *covenant law.* See notes on 16:34; 25:16. *inscribed on both sides.* See note on 31:18. Elsewhere note is taken of scrolls written on both sides (see Eze 2:10 and note; Zec 5:3; Rev 5:1); in each case what is written pertains to God's sovereign involvement in human history, especially his coming judgment.

32:16 *work of God ... writing of God.* See 31:18.

32:17 *Joshua.* Perhaps he had accompanied Moses part of the way up the mountain (see 24:13).

32:19 *breaking them to pieces.* Thus testifying against Israel that the people had broken the covenant.

32:20 *burned it ... ground it to powder.* King Jeroboam's altar (see note on v. 4) at Bethel received the same treatment (see 2Ki 23:15).

32:21 *great sin.* See Ge 20:9 and note.

32:22–24 In his desperation, Aaron blamed the people (cf. Ge 3:12–13 and notes), but the Lord held him accountable. Only through Moses' intercession was Aaron spared (see Dt 9:20).

32:24 *out came this calf.* Aaron could hardly have thought that Moses would believe such an incredible story.

gave me the gold, and I threw it into the fire, and out came this calf!"[n]

25 Moses saw that the people were running wild and that Aaron had let them get out of control and so become a laughingstock[o] to their enemies. 26 So he stood at the entrance to the camp and said, "Whoever is for the LORD, come to me." And all the Levites rallied to him.

27 Then he said to them, "This is what the LORD, the God of Israel, says: 'Each man strap a sword to his side. Go back and forth through the camp from one end to the other, each killing his brother and friend and neighbor.' "[p] 28 The Levites did as Moses commanded, and that day about three thousand of the people died. 29 Then Moses said, "You have been set apart to the LORD today, for you were against your own sons and brothers, and he has blessed you this day."

30 The next day Moses said to the people, "You have committed a great sin.[q] But now I will go up to the LORD; perhaps I can make atonement[r] for your sin."

31 So Moses went back to the LORD and said, "Oh, what a great sin these people have committed![s] They have made themselves gods of gold.[t] 32 But now, please forgive their sin[u]—but if not, then blot me[v] out of the book[w] you have written."

33 The LORD replied to Moses, "Whoever has sinned against me I will blot out[x] of my book. 34 Now go, lead[y] the people to the place[z] I spoke of, and my angel[a] will go before you. However, when the time comes for me to punish,[b] I will punish them for their sin."

35 And the LORD struck the people with a plague because of what they did with the calf[c] Aaron had made.

33 Then the LORD said to Moses, "Leave this place, you and the people you brought up out of Egypt, and go up to the land I promised on oath[d] to Abraham, Isaac and Jacob, saying, 'I will give it to your descendants.'[e] 2 I will send an angel[f] before you and drive out the Canaanites, Amorites, Hittites, Perizzites, Hivites and Jebusites.[g] 3 Go up to the land flowing with milk and honey.[h] But I will not go with you, because you are a stiff-necked[i] people and I might destroy[j] you on the way."

4 When the people heard these distressing words, they began to mourn[k] and no one put on any ornaments. 5 For the LORD had said to Moses, "Tell the Israelites, 'You are a stiff-necked people.[l] If I were to go with you even for a moment, I might destroy[m] you. Now take off your ornaments and I will decide what to do with you.' " 6 So the Israelites stripped off their ornaments at Mount Horeb.[n]

The Tent of Meeting

7 Now Moses used to take a tent and pitch it outside the camp some distance away, calling it the "tent of meeting."[o] Anyone inquiring[p] of the LORD would go to the tent of meeting outside the camp. 8 And whenever Moses went out to the tent, all the people rose and stood at the entrances to their tents,[q] watching Moses until he entered the tent. 9 As Moses went into

32:24 [n] S ver 4 **32:25** [o] S Ge 38:23 **32:27** [p] Nu 25:3, 5; Dt 33:9; Eze 9:5 **32:30** [q] 1Sa 12:20; Ps 25:11; 85:2 [r] Lev 1:4; 4:20, 26; 5:6, 10, 13; 6:7 **32:31** [s] Ex 34:9; Dt 9:18 [t] S Ex 20:23 **32:32** [u] Nu 14:19 [v] Ro 9:3 [w] Ps 69:28; Eze 13:9; Da 7:10; 12:1; Mal 3:16; S Lk 10:20 **32:33** [x] S Ex 17:14; S Job 21:20; Rev 3:5 **32:34** [y] S Ex 15:17 [z] Ex 3:17 [a] S Ex 14:19 [b] S Ge 50:19; Dt 32:35; Ps 89:32; 94:23; 99:8; 109:20; Isa 27:1; Jer 5:9; 11:22; 23:2; 44:13, 29; Hos 12:2; Ro 2:5-6 **32:35** [c] S ver 4 **33:1** [d] S Ex 13:11; S Nu 14:23; Heb 6:13 [e] S Ge 12:7 **33:2** [f] S Ex 14:19 [g] S Ex 23:28 **33:3** [h] S Ex 3:8 [i] Ex 32:9; Ac 7:51 [j] S Ex 32:10 **33:4** [k] Nu 14:39; Ezr 9:3; Est 4:1; Ps 119:53 **33:5** [l] S Ex 32:9 [m] S Ex 32:10 **33:6** [n] S Ex 3:1 **33:7** [o] S Ex 27:21 [p] S Ge 25:22; S 1Ki 22:5 **33:8** [q] ver 10; Nu 16:27

32:25 *were running wild ... get out of control.* The same Hebrew root underlies both phrases and is found also in Pr 29:18 ("cast off restraint"). Anarchy reigns among people who refuse to obey and worship the Lord.
32:26 *Whoever is for the LORD, come to me.* See Jos 24:15; 1Ki 18:21; Mt 6:24. *all.* A generalization since Dt 33:9 implies that some of the Levites were also slain. *Levites.* The descendants of Levi (Ge 29:34) may have originally been regarded as priests (Dt 18:6–8). But at some stage they became subordinate to the priests who were descendants of Aaron, the brother of Moses (38:21; Nu 3:9–10; 1Ch 16:4–6,37–42).
32:27 *killing his brother and friend and neighbor.* See Mt 10:37; Lk 14:26.
32:28 *The Levites did as Moses commanded.* Their zeal for the Lord is later matched by Aaron's grandson Phinehas, resulting in a perpetual covenant of the priesthood (see Nu 25:7–13).
32:29 *You have been set apart to the LORD today.* Because of their zeal for the Lord the Levites were set apart to be caretakers of the tabernacle and aides to the priests (see Nu 1:47–53; 3:5–9,12,41,45; 4:2–3).
32:30 *make atonement for your sin.* By making urgent intercession before God, as the mediator God had appointed between himself and Israel. No sacrifice that Israel or Moses might bring could atone for this sin. But Moses so identified himself with Israel that he made his own death the condition for God's destruction of the nation (see v. 32). Jesus Christ, the great Mediator, offered himself on the cross to make atonement for his people.
32:32 *blot me out.* Paul made a similar statement (see Ro 9:3 and note). *book you have written.* See notes on Ps 9:5; 51:1; 69:28.
32:33 *Whoever has sinned ... I will blot out.* Moses' gracious offer is refused, because the person who sins is responsible for their own sin (see Dt 24:16; Eze 18:4 and note).
32:34 *Now go, lead the people.* Thus Moses receives assurance that the Lord will continue his covenant with wayward Israel and fulfill his promise concerning the land. *the place I spoke of.* Canaan (see 33:1). *my angel.* See 23:23; 33:2.
33:2 *Canaanites ... Jebusites.* See note on 3:8.
33:3 *land flowing with milk and honey.* See note on 3:8. *I will not go with you.* The Lord's presence, earlier assured to his people (see 23:21 and note), is now temporarily withdrawn because of sin. *stiff-necked.* See note on 32:9.
33:6 *stripped off their ornaments.* As a sign of mourning (see Eze 26:16–17).
33:7 *tent of meeting outside the camp.* Not the tabernacle (contrast 27:21), which occupied a central location within the Israelite camp, but a temporary structure where the people could consult the Lord until the more durable tabernacle was completed.
33:9 *pillar of cloud would come down.* Symbolizing God's

the tent, the pillar of cloud[r] would come down and stay at the entrance, while the LORD spoke[s] with Moses. 10 Whenever the people saw the pillar of cloud standing at the entrance to the tent, they all stood and worshiped, each at the entrance to their tent.[t] 11 The LORD would speak to Moses face to face,[u] as one speaks to a friend. Then Moses would return to the camp, but his young aide Joshua[v] son of Nun did not leave the tent.

Moses and the Glory of the LORD

12 Moses said to the LORD, "You have been telling me, 'Lead these people,'[w] but you have not let me know whom you will send with me. You have said, 'I know you by name[x] and you have found favor[y] with me.' 13 If you are pleased with me, teach me your ways[z] so I may know you and continue to find favor with you. Remember that this nation is your people."[a]

14 The LORD replied, "My Presence[b] will go with you, and I will give you rest."[c]

15 Then Moses said to him, "If your Presence[d] does not go with us, do not send us up from here. 16 How will anyone know that you are pleased with me and with your people unless you go with us?[e] What else will distinguish me and your people from all the other people on the face of the earth?"[f]

17 And the LORD said to Moses, "I will do the very thing you have asked,[g] because I am pleased with you and I know you by name."[h]

18 Then Moses said, "Now show me your glory."[i]

19 And the LORD said, "I will cause all my goodness to pass[j] in front of you, and I will proclaim my name,[k] the LORD, in your presence. I will have mercy on whom I will have mercy, and I will have compassion on whom I will have compassion.[l] 20 But," he said, "you cannot see my face, for no one may see[m] me and live."

21 Then the LORD said, "There is a place near me where you may stand on a rock. 22 When my glory passes by, I will put you in a cleft in the rock[n] and cover you with my hand[o] until I have passed by. 23 Then I will remove my hand and you will see my back; but my face must not be seen."

The New Stone Tablets

34 The LORD said to Moses, "Chisel out two stone tablets like the first ones,[p] and I will write on them the words that were on the first tablets,[q] which you broke.[r] 2 Be ready in the morning, and then come up on Mount Sinai.[s] Present yourself to me there on top of the mountain. 3 No one is to come with you or be seen anywhere on the mountain;[t] not even the flocks and herds may graze in front of the mountain."

4 So Moses chiseled[u] out two stone tablets like the first ones and went up Mount Sinai early in the morning, as the LORD had commanded him; and he carried the two stone tablets in his hands.[v] 5 Then the LORD came down in the cloud[w] and stood there with him and proclaimed his name, the LORD.[x] 6 And he passed in front of Moses, proclaiming, "The LORD, the LORD, the

33:9 [r] Ex 13:21; S 19:9; Dt 31:15; 1Co 10:1 [s] S Ex 29:42; 31:18; Ps 99:7 **33:10** [t] S ver 8 **33:11** [u] Nu 12:8; Dt 5:4; 34:10 [v] S Ex 17:9 **33:12** [w] Ex 3:10; S 15:17 [x] ver 17; Isa 43:1; 45:3; 49:1; Jn 10:14-15; 2Ti 2:19 [y] S Ge 6:8 **33:13** [z] Ps 25:4; 27:11; 51:13; 86:11; 103:7; 143:8 [a] Ex 3:7; Dt 9:26,29; Ps 77:15 **33:14** [b] S Ex 13:21; Dt 4:37; Isa 63:9; Hag 1:13; 2:4 [c] Dt 12:9,10; 25:19; Jos 1:13; 11:23; 21:44; 22:4; 23:1; 1Ki 8:56; Isa 63:14; Jer 31:2; Mt 11:28; Heb 4:1-11 **33:15** [d] ver 3; Ex 34:9; 2Ki 13:23; 17:18; 23:27; 24:20; Ps 51:11; 80:3,7,19; Jer 7:15; 52:3 **33:16** [e] Ex 34:5; 40:34,35; Nu 9:15; 14:14 [f] Ex 34:10; Lev 20:24,26; Nu 23:9; Dt 4:7,32,34; 32:9; 33:28 **33:17** [g] Ex 34:28; Dt 9:18,25; 10:10; Jas 5:16 [h] S Ge 6:8 **33:18** [i] S Ex 16:7; Jn 1:14; 12:41; 1Ti 6:16; Rev 15:8 **33:19** [j] 1Ki 19:11 [k] Ex 6:3; 34:5-7 [l] Ro 9:15* **33:20** [m] S Ge 16:13; S Ex 3:6; S Dt 5:26; S Jn 1:18 **33:22** [n] Ge 49:24; 1Ki 19:9; Ps 27:5; 31:20; 62:7; 91:1; Isa 2:21; Jer 4:29 [o] Ps 91:4; Isa 49:2; 51:16 **34:1** [p] S Ex 24:12 [q] Dt 10:2,4 [r] S Ex 32:19 **34:2** [s] S Ex 19:11 **34:3** [t] S Ex 19:13 **34:4** [u] Dt 10:3 [v] S Ex 32:15 **34:5** [w] S Ex 13:21; S 19:9 [x] Ex 6:3; 33:19

:ommunication with Moses "as one speaks to a friend" (v. 11). .ater, a similar descent crowned the completion of the tabernacle (see 40:33–34; see also note on 13:21).

33:11 *The LORD would speak to Moses face to face.* God communicated with him directly—but without visu-ılly showing his "face." As the OT mediator, Moses was unique ımong the prophets (see Nu 12:6–8; Dt 34:10,12 and notes). *'oshua ... did not leave the tent.* Probably his task was to guard he tent against intrusion by others.

33:12 *you have not let me know whom you will send with me.* See note on v. 3. Moses objects that a mere ıngel is no substitute for God's own presence. *I know you by ,ame.* I have chosen you for my special purpose (see Jer 1:5 ınd note).

3:13 *teach me your ways.* A prayer that is answered in 34:6–7.

3:14 *My Presence.* Lit "My face." The Lord will not "hide" his ace from his people but will cause it to "shine" on them (see Ju 6:25; Ps 13:1 and notes). See also note on v. 12.

33:17 *because I am pleased with you.* How much more does God hear the prayers of his Son Jesus Christ (see Λt 17:5; Heb 3:1–6)!

33:18 *show me your glory.* All that God has done for Israel through Moses has made him very bold. At his first neeting with God he was "afraid to look at God" in the small display of God's glory in the burning bush (see 3:6 and note), and he inquired concerning God's name (3:13). Now he asks to be shown God's glory unveiled and is told he has asked too much, that he must be content with the fuller proclamation of God's name (see vv. 19,22; 34:5–7).

33:19 *goodness.* God's nature and character. *name.* A further symbol of God's nature, character and person (see Ps 20:1; Jn 1:12; 17:6 and note). Here his name implies his mercy (grace) and his compassion (as it does also in 34:6). *I will have mercy on whom ... compassion.* Paul quotes these words in Ro 9:15 to defend his view of God's sovereignty.

33:20 *no one may see me and live.* See note on Ge 16:13; see also Jn 1:18; 6:46; 1Ti 1:17; 1Jn 4:12.

33:21–23 God speaks of himself in human language. See 34:5–7 for the fulfillment of his promise.

34:1 *two stone tablets ... I will write on them.* See note on 31:18. *words.* See note on 20:1.

34:5 *name.* See note on 33:19.

34:6–7 See 33:19 and note. The Lord's proclamation of the meaning and implications of his name in these verses became a classic exposition that was frequently recalled elsewhere in the OT (see Nu 14:18; Ne 9:17; Ps 86:15; 103:8; 145:8; Joel 2:13; Jnh 4:2). See also notes on 3:14–15; 6:2–3.

compassionate[y] and gracious God, slow
to anger,[z] abounding in love[a] and faithfulness,[b] 7 maintaining love to thousands,[c]
and forgiving wickedness, rebellion and
sin.[d] Yet he does not leave the guilty unpunished;[e] he punishes the children and
their children for the sin of the parents to
the third and fourth generation."[f]
8 Moses bowed to the ground at once
and worshiped. 9 "Lord," he said, "if I have
found favor[g] in your eyes, then let the Lord
go with us.[h] Although this is a stiff-necked[i]
people, forgive our wickedness and our
sin,[j] and take us as your inheritance."[k]
10 Then the LORD said: "I am making a
covenant[l] with you. Before all your people
I will do wonders[m] never before done in
any nation in all the world.[n] The people
you live among will see how awesome is
the work that I, the LORD, will do for you.
11 Obey what I command[o] you today. I will
drive out before you the Amorites, Canaanites, Hittites, Perizzites, Hivites and
Jebusites.[p] 12 Be careful not to make a treaty[q] with those who live in the land where
you are going, or they will be a snare[r]
among you. 13 Break down their altars,
smash their sacred stones and cut down
their Asherah poles.[a][s] 14 Do not worship
any other god,[t] for the LORD, whose name[u]
is Jealous, is a jealous God.[v]
15 "Be careful not to make a treaty[w] with
those who live in the land; for when they
prostitute[x] themselves to their gods and
sacrifice to them, they will invite you and
you will eat their sacrifices.[y] 16 And when
you choose some of their daughters as
wives[z] for your sons and those daughters
prostitute themselves to their gods,[a] they
will lead your sons to do the same.

34:6 [y]S Ex 22:27; S Nu 14:20; S Ps 86:15 [z]Nu 14:18; Ps 78:38; Jer 15:15; Ro 2:4 [a]S Ge 19:16 [b]Ps 61:7; 108:4; 115:1; 138:2; 143:1; La 3:23; Jas 5:11 **34:7** [c]S Ex 20:6; Dt 5:10 [d]1Ki 8:30; Ps 86:5; 103:3; 130:4, 8; Isa 43:25; Da 9:9; 1Jn 1:9 [e]Ex 23:7; Jos 24:19; Job 7:20-21; 9:28; 10:14; Mic 6:1-16; Na 1:3 [f]S Ex 20:5 **34:9** [g]Ex 33:13; Nu 11:15 [h]S Ex 33:15 [i]Ex 32:9 [j]Nu 14:19; 1Ki 8:30; 2Ch 6:21; Ps 19:12; 25:11; Jer 33:8; Hos 14:2 [k]S Ex 6:7; 19:5; Dt 4:20; 7:6; 9:26, 29; 14:2; 26:18; 32:9; 1Sa 10:1; 2Sa 14:16; 1Ki 8:51, 53; Ps 28:9; 33:12; 74:2; 79:1; 94:14; 106:5, 40; Isa 19:25; 63:17; Jer 10:16; 51:19; Mic 7:18; Zec 2:12 **34:10** [l]S Ge 6:18; S 9:15; S 15:18; Dt 5:2-3 [m]S Ex 3:20 [n]S Ex 33:16

17 "Do not make any idols.[b]
18 "Celebrate the Festival of Unleavened
Bread.[c] For seven days eat bread made
without yeast,[d] as I commanded you. Do
this at the appointed time in the month
of Aviv,[e] for in that month you came out
of Egypt.
19 "The first offspring[f] of every womb
belongs to me, including all the firstborn
males of your livestock, whether from
herd or flock. 20 Redeem the firstborn donkey with a lamb, but if you do not redeem
it, break its neck.[g] Redeem all your firstborn sons.[h]
"No one is to appear before me empty-handed.[i]
21 "Six days you shall labor, but on the
seventh day you shall rest;[j] even during
the plowing season and harvest[k] you must
rest.
22 "Celebrate the Festival of Weeks with
the firstfruits[l] of the wheat harvest, and
the Festival of Ingathering[m] at the turn of
the year.[b] 23 Three times[n] a year all your
men are to appear before the Sovereign
LORD, the God of Israel. 24 I will drive out
nations[o] before you and enlarge your ter-

[a] *13* That is, wooden symbols of the goddess Asherah
[b] *22* That is, in the autumn

34:11 [o]Dt 6:25; Jos 11:15 [p]S Ex 23:28 **34:12** [q]Jdg 2:2 [r]S Ex 10:7 **34:13** [s]S Ex 23:24; Nu 33:52; Dt 7:5; 12:3; Jdg 6:26; 1Ki 15:13; 2Ch 15:16; 17:6; 34:3-4; Mic 5:14 **34:14** [t]S Ex 20:3 [u]Isa 9:6 [v]S Ex 20:5 **34:15** [w]ver 12; Dt 23:6; Ezr 9:12 [x]Ex 22:20; 32:8; Dt 31:16; Jdg 2:17; 2Ki 17:8; 1Ch 5:25; 2Ch 11:15; Am 2:4 [y]S Ex 32:6; 1Co 8:4 **34:16** [z]Dt 7:3; 17:17; Jos 23:12; Jdg 3:6; 14:3; 1Ki 11:1, 2; 16:31; Ezr 9:2; 10:3; Ne 10:30; 13:25, 26 [a]Dt 7:4; 12:31; 20:18; 1Ki 11:4; 2Ki 21:3-15; Ps 106:34-41; Mal 2:11 **34:17** [b]S Ex 20:4 **34:18** [c]S Ex 12:17; Mt 26:17; Lk 22:1; Ac 12:3 [d]S Ex 12:15 [e]S Ex 12:2 **34:19** [f]Ex 13:2 **34:20** [g]S Ex 13:13 [h]S Ex 13:2 [i]S Ex 22:29; Dt 16:16; Eze 46:9 **34:21** [j]Ge 2:2-3 [k]Ne 13:15; Isa 56:2; 58:13 **34:22** [l]ver 26; Ex 23:19; Lev 2:12, 14; 7:13; 23:10, 17; Nu 28:26 [m]S Ex 23:16 **34:23** [n]S Ex 23:14 **34:24** [o]S Ex 23:28

34:7 *thousands.* Or "a thousand generations" (see 20:6). *wickedness, rebellion and sin.* See Isa 59:12 and note.
34:10 *making a covenant.* Renewing the covenant he had earlier made (chs. 19–24). Verses 10–26, many of which are quoted almost verbatim from previous sections of Exodus (compare especially vv. 18–26 with 23:14–19), are sometimes referred to as the Ritual Decalogue since they can be convincingly divided into ten sections (see, e.g., the NIV paragraphing of vv. 15–26). *wonders.* The same word used for the plagues sent on Egypt (3:20). Here it probably refers to the miracles God performed during the wilderness wanderings and the conquest of Canaan (see Ps 9:1 and note).
34:12 *not to make a treaty with those who live in the land.* Israel is not to make a treaty of peace with any of the people of Canaan to let them live in the land. *treaty.* The Hebrew for this word is the same as that for "covenant" in v. 10 (see also v. 15).
34:13 *Asherah poles.* Asherah was the name of the wife of El, the chief Canaanite god. Wooden poles, perhaps carved in her image, were often set up in her honor and placed near other pagan objects of worship (see, e.g., Jdg 6:25).
34:14 *whose name is Jealous.* See note on 20:5.
34:15 *prostitute themselves.* A metaphor widely used in the OT to refer to Israel's unfaithfulness to her covenant Lord, who, according to a related metaphor, had become Israel's "husband" (with all that this implied in the ancient social world) when he established his special covenant with her (see Isa 54:5–6; Jer 3:14; 31:32; Hos 2:2,7,16; cf. Jer 2:2; 3:1,20 and note on 3:14; Eze 16:8,32,45 and note on 16:32; 23:4,37). Such unfaithfulness took various forms, but most commonly outright idolatry (worshiping other gods and looking to them for fertility of wombs, fields and flocks, for healing wounds and diseases, for deliverance or security from enemies—thus treating the false gods as their "lovers"). *eat their sacrifices.* Partaking of food sacrificed to a pagan deity invites compromise (cf. 1Co 8; 10:18–21). For an example, see Nu 25:1–3.
34:16 *lead your sons to do the same.* For an example, see 1Ki 11:1–8.
34:17 *Do not make any idols.* As Aaron had done when he made the golden calf (see 32:4).
34:18–26 See notes on 23:14–19.
34:21 *even during the plowing season and harvest you must rest.* Just as they were also to rest while building the tabernacle (see notes on 31:13,16–17).
34:24 *no one will covet your land.* The Lord promises to protect the Israelite pilgrim's ownership of his land while he is away attending the three annual festivals that require his presence (see Dt 16:16 and note).

ritory,[p] and no one will covet your land
when you go up three times each year to
appear before the LORD your God.
25“Do not offer the blood of a sacrifice
to me along with anything containing
yeast,[q] and do not let any of the sacrifice
from the Passover Festival remain until
morning.[r]
26“Bring the best of the firstfruits[s] of
your soil to the house of the LORD your
God.
“Do not cook a young goat in its mother's milk.”[t]
27Then the LORD said to Moses, “Write[u]
down these words, for in accordance with
these words I have made a covenant[v] with
you and with Israel.” 28Moses was there
with the LORD forty days and forty nights[w]
without eating bread or drinking water.[x]
And he wrote on the tablets[y] the words of
the covenant—the Ten Commandments.[z]

The Radiant Face of Moses

29When Moses came down from Mount
Sinai[a] with the two tablets of the covenant
law in his hands,[b] he was not aware that
his face was radiant[c] because he had spoken with the LORD. 30When Aaron and all
the Israelites saw Moses, his face was radiant, and they were afraid to come near
him. 31But Moses called to them; so Aaron and all the leaders of the community[d]
came back to him, and he spoke to them.
32Afterward all the Israelites came near
him, and he gave them all the commands[e]
the LORD had given him on Mount Sinai.
33When Moses finished speaking to
them, he put a veil[f] over his face. 34But
whenever he entered the LORD's presence
to speak with him, he removed the veil
until he came out. And when he came out
and told the Israelites what he had been
commanded, 35they saw that his face was
radiant.[g] Then Moses would put the veil
back over his face until he went in to
speak with the LORD.

Sabbath Regulations

35 Moses assembled the whole Israelite community and said to them,
“These are the things the LORD has commanded[h] you to do: 2For six days, work is
to be done, but the seventh day shall be
your holy day, a day of sabbath[i] rest to the
LORD. Whoever does any work on it is to
be put to death.[j] 3Do not light a fire in any
of your dwellings on the Sabbath day.[k]”

Materials for the Tabernacle

35:4-9pp — Ex 25:1-7
35:10-19pp — Ex 39:32-41

4Moses said to the whole Israelite community, “This is what the LORD has commanded: 5From what you have, take an
offering for the LORD. Everyone who is
willing is to bring to the LORD an offering
of gold, silver and bronze; 6blue, purple
and scarlet yarn and fine linen; goat hair;
7ram skins dyed red and another type of
durable leather[a]; acacia wood; 8olive oil[l]
for the light; spices for the anointing oil
and for the fragrant incense; 9and onyx
stones and other gems to be mounted on
the ephod and breastpiece.
10“All who are skilled among you are
to come and make everything the LORD
has commanded:[m] 11the tabernacle[n] with
its tent and its covering, clasps, frames,
crossbars, posts and bases; 12the ark[o] with
its poles and the atonement cover and the
curtain[p] that shields it; 13the table[q] with
its poles and all its articles and the bread
of the Presence; 14the lampstand[r] that is
for light with its accessories, lamps and oil
for the light; 15the altar[s] of incense with its
poles, the anointing oil[t] and the fragrant

34:24 [p]Dt 12:20; 19:8; Job 12:23 **34:25** [q]S Ex 23:18 [r]S Ex 12:8 **34:26** [s]S Ex 22:29; S Nu 18:12 [t]S Ex 23:19 **34:27** [u]S Ex 17:14 [v]S Ge 6:18; S 15:18 **34:28** [w]S Ge 7:4; Mt 4:2; Lk 4:2 [x]Dt 9:9, 18; Ezr 10:6 [y]ver 1; Ex 31:18 [z]Dt 4:13; 10:4 **34:29** [a]S Ex 19:11 [b]S Ex 32:15 [c]ver 35; Ps 34:5; Isa 60:5; Mt 17:2; 2Co 3:7, 13 **34:31** [d]Ex 16:22 **34:32** [e]S Ex 21:1; 35:1, 4 **34:33** [f]2Co 3:13 **34:35** [g]S ver 29

35:1 [h]S Ex 34:32 **35:2** [i]S Ge 2:3; Ex 34:21; Dt 5:13-14 [j]S Ex 31:14 **35:3** [k]Ex 16:23 **35:8** [l]S Ex 25:6 **35:10** [m]Ex 31:6; 39:43 **35:11** [n]Ex 26:1-37; 36:8-38 **35:12** [o]Ex 25:10-22; 37:1-9 [p]S Ex 26:33 **35:13** [q]Ex 25:23-30; 37:10-16 **35:14** [r]S Ex 25:31 **35:15** [s]Ex 30:1-6; 37:25-28 [t]Ex 30:25

[a] 7 Possibly the hides of large aquatic mammals; also in verse 23

34:27 *Write down these words.* As he had earlier written down similar words (see 24:4).

34:28 *he wrote.* Here the Lord, rather than Moses, is probably the subject (see v. 1). *the words of the covenant—the Ten Commandments.* The two phrases are synonymous (see note on 20:1).

34:29 *covenant law.* See notes on 16:34; 25:16. *was radiant.* He who had asked to see God's glory (see 33:18 and note) now, quite unawares, reflects the divine glory. The Hebrew for "was radiant" is related to the Hebrew noun for "horn." The meaning of the phrase was therefore misunderstood by the Vulgate (the Latin translation), and thus European medieval art often showed horns sprouting from Moses' head (see photo, p. 257).

34:33 *he put a veil over his face.* So that the Israelites would not see the fading away of the radiance but would continue to honor Moses as the one who represented God. For a NT reflection on Moses' action, see 2Co 3:7–18 and notes.

35:1–3 Just as the Israelites had been reminded of the importance of Sabbath observance immediately after the instructions for building the tabernacle and making the priestly garments (see note on 31:13), so now—just before the fulfilling of those instructions—the people are given the same reminder.

35:4—39:43 For the most part repeated from chs. 25–28; 30:1–5; 31:1–11 (see notes on those passages), sometimes verbatim, but with the verbs primarily in the past rather than the future tense and with the topics arranged in a different order. Such repetition was a common feature of ancient Near Eastern literature and was intended to fix the details of a narrative in the reader's mind (see note on Ge 24:34–49).

35:5 *Everyone who is willing.* The voluntary motivation behind the offering of materials and services for the tabernacle is stressed (see vv. 21–22,26,29; 36:2–3).

incense;[u] the curtain for the doorway at the entrance to the tabernacle;[v] 16the altar[w] of burnt offering with its bronze grating, its poles and all its utensils; the bronze basin[x] with its stand; 17the curtains of the courtyard with its posts and bases, and the curtain for the entrance to the courtyard;[y] 18the tent pegs[z] for the tabernacle and for the courtyard, and their ropes; 19the woven garments worn for ministering in the sanctuary — both the sacred garments[a] for Aaron the priest and the garments for his sons when they serve as priests."

20Then the whole Israelite community withdrew from Moses' presence, 21and everyone who was willing and whose heart moved them came and brought an offering to the LORD for the work on the tent of meeting, for all its service, and for the sacred garments. 22All who were willing, men and women alike, came and brought gold jewelry of all kinds: brooches, earrings, rings and ornaments. They all presented their gold as a wave offering to the LORD. 23Everyone who had blue, purple or scarlet yarn[b] or fine linen, or goat hair, ram skins dyed red or the other durable leather brought them. 24Those presenting an offering of silver or bronze brought it as an offering to the LORD, and everyone who had acacia wood for any part of the work brought it. 25Every skilled woman[c] spun with her hands and brought what she had spun — blue, purple or scarlet yarn or fine linen. 26And all the women who were willing and had the skill spun the goat hair. 27The leaders[d] brought onyx stones and other gems[e] to be mounted on the ephod and breastpiece. 28They also brought spices and olive oil for the light and for the anointing oil and for the fragrant incense.[f] 29All the Israelite men and women who were willing[g] brought to the LORD freewill offerings[h] for all the work the LORD through Moses had commanded them to do.

Bezalel and Oholiab

35:30-35pp — Ex 31:2-6

30Then Moses said to the Israelites, "See, the LORD has chosen Bezalel son of Uri, the son of Hur, of the tribe of Judah, 31and he has filled him with the Spirit of God, with wisdom, with understanding, with knowledge and with all kinds of skills[i] — 32to make artistic designs for work in gold, silver and bronze, 33to cut and set stones, to work in wood and to engage in all kinds of artistic crafts. 34And he has given both him and Oholiab[j] son of Ahisamak, of the tribe of Dan, the ability to teach[k] others. 35He has filled them with skill to do all kinds of work[l] as engravers, designers, embroiderers in blue, purple and scarlet yarn and fine linen, and weavers — all of them skilled workers and designers.

36 1So Bezalel, Oholiab and every skilled person[m] to whom the LORD has given skill and ability to know how to carry out all the work of constructing the sanctuary[n] are to do the work just as the LORD has commanded."

2Then Moses summoned Bezalel[o] and Oholiab[p] and every skilled person to whom the LORD had given ability and who was willing[q] to come and do the work. 3They received from Moses all the offerings[r] the Israelites had brought to carry out the work of constructing the sanctuary. And the people continued to bring freewill offerings morning after morning. 4So all the skilled workers who were doing all the work on the sanctuary left what they were doing 5and said to Moses, "The people are bringing more than enough[s] for doing the work the LORD commanded to be done."

6Then Moses gave an order and they sent this word throughout the camp: "No man or woman is to make anything else as an offering for the sanctuary." And so the people were restrained from bringing more, 7because what they already had was more[t] than enough to do all the work.

The Tabernacle

36:8-38pp — Ex 26:1-37

8All those who were skilled among the workers made the tabernacle with ten curtains of finely twisted linen and blue, purple and scarlet yarn, with cherubim woven into them by expert hands. 9All the curtains were the same size — twenty-eight cubits long and four cubits wide.[a] 10They joined five of the curtains together and did the same with the other five. 11Then they made loops of blue material along the edge of the end curtain in one set, and the same was done with the end curtain in the other set. 12They also made fifty loops on one curtain and fifty loops on the end curtain of the other set, with the loops opposite each other. 13Then they made fifty gold clasps and used them to fasten the two sets of curtains together so that the tabernacle was a unit.[u]

14They made curtains of goat hair for the tent over the tabernacle — eleven al

[a] 9 That is, about 42 feet long and 6 feet wide or about 13 meters long and 1.8 meters wide

35:15 [u] Ex 30:34-38 [v] S Ex 26:36 **35:16** [w] Ex 27:1-8; 38:1-7 [x] S Ex 30:18 **35:17** [y] S Ex 27:9; 38:9-20 **35:18** [z] Ex 27:19; 38:20 **35:19** [a] S Ex 28:2 **35:23** [b] Ex 39:1 **35:25** [c] S Ex 28:3 **35:27** [d] S Ex 25:2; 1Ch 29:6 [e] 1Ch 29:8 **35:28** [f] S Ex 25:6 **35:29** [g] S Ex 25:2 [h] ver 4-9; Ex 25:1-7; 36:3; 2Ki 12:4 **35:31** [i] ver 35; 2Ch 2:7,14 **35:34** [j] S Ex 31:6

[k] 2Ch 2:14 **35:35** [l] ver 31 **36:1** [m] S Ex 28:3 [n] Ex 25:8 **36:2** [o] S Ex 31:2 [p] S Ex 31:6 [q] S Ex 25:2 **36:3** [r] S Ex 35:29 **36:5** [s] 2Ch 24:14; 31:10; 2Co 8:2-3 **36:7** [t] 1Ki 7:47 **36:13** [u] ver 18

35:21 *tent of meeting.* See note on 27:21.

36:1-38 See note on 35:4—39:43.

together. 15All eleven curtains were the
same size — thirty cubits long and four
cubits wide.[a] 16They joined five of the
curtains into one set and the other six
into another set. 17Then they made fifty
loops along the edge of the end curtain
in one set and also along the edge of the
end curtain in the other set. 18They made
fifty bronze clasps to fasten the tent together as a unit.[v] 19Then they made for
the tent a covering of ram skins dyed red,
and over that a covering of the other durable leather.[b]

20They made upright frames of acacia
wood for the tabernacle. 21Each frame
was ten cubits long and a cubit and a half
wide,[c] 22with two projections set parallel
to each other. They made all the frames of
the tabernacle in this way. 23They made
twenty frames for the south side of the
tabernacle 24and made forty silver bases
to go under them — two bases for each
frame, one under each projection. 25For
the other side, the north side of the tabernacle, they made twenty frames 26and
forty silver bases — two under each frame.
27They made six frames for the far end,
that is, the west end of the tabernacle,
28and two frames were made for the corners of the tabernacle at the far end. 29At
these two corners the frames were double
from the bottom all the way to the top
and fitted into a single ring; both were
made alike. 30So there were eight frames
and sixteen silver bases — two under each
frame.

31They also made crossbars of acacia
wood: five for the frames on one side
of the tabernacle, 32five for those on the
other side, and five for the frames on the
west, at the far end of the tabernacle.
33They made the center crossbar so that
it extended from end to end at the middle
of the frames. 34They overlaid the frames
with gold and made gold rings to hold the
crossbars. They also overlaid the crossbars
with gold.

35They made the curtain[w] of blue, purple
and scarlet yarn and finely twisted linen,
with cherubim woven into it by a skilled
worker. 36They made four posts of acacia
wood for it and overlaid them with gold.
They made gold hooks for them and cast
their four silver bases. 37For the entrance
to the tent they made a curtain of blue,
purple and scarlet yarn and finely twisted
linen — the work of an embroiderer;[x] 38and
they made five posts with hooks for them.
They overlaid the tops of the posts and
their bands with gold and made their five
bases of bronze.

36:18 [v] ver 13 **36:35** [w] Ex 39:38; Mt 27:51; Lk 23:45; Heb 9:3 **36:37** [x] Ex 27:16

The Ark

37:1-9pp — Ex 25:10-20

37 Bezalel[y] made the ark[z] of acacia
wood — two and a half cubits long,
a cubit and a half wide, and a cubit and
a half high.[d] 2He overlaid it with pure
gold,[a] both inside and out, and made a
gold molding around it. 3He cast four gold
rings for it and fastened them to its four
feet, with two rings on one side and two
rings on the other. 4Then he made poles of
acacia wood and overlaid them with gold.
5And he inserted the poles into the rings
on the sides of the ark to carry it.

6He made the atonement cover[b] of pure
gold — two and a half cubits long and a cubit and a half wide. 7Then he made two
cherubim[c] out of hammered gold at the
ends of the cover. 8He made one cherub
on one end and the second cherub on the
other; at the two ends he made them of
one piece with the cover. 9The cherubim
had their wings spread upward, overshadowing[d] the cover with them. The cherubim
faced each other, looking toward the cover.[e]

The Table

37:10-16pp — Ex 25:23-29

10They[e] made the table[f] of acacia
wood — two cubits long, a cubit wide
and a cubit and a half high.[f] 11Then they
overlaid it with pure gold[g] and made a
gold molding around it. 12They also made
around it a rim a handbreadth[g] wide and
put a gold molding on the rim. 13They
cast four gold rings for the table and fastened them to the four corners, where
the four legs were. 14The rings[h] were put
close to the rim to hold the poles used in
carrying the table. 15The poles for carrying the table were made of acacia wood
and were overlaid with gold. 16And they
made from pure gold the articles for the
table — its plates and dishes and bowls
and its pitchers for the pouring out of
drink offerings.

37:1 [y] S Ex 31:2 [z] Ex 30:6; 39:35; Dt 10:3 **37:2** [a] ver 11, 26 **37:6** [b] S Ex 26:34; S 31:7; Heb 9:5 **37:7** [c] Eze 41:18 **37:9** [d] Heb 9:5 [e] Dt 10:3 **37:10** [f] Heb 9:2 **37:11** [g] S ver 2 **37:14** [h] ver 27

[a] *15* That is, about 45 feet long and 6 feet wide or about 14 meters long and 1.8 meters wide [b] *19* Possibly the hides of large aquatic mammals (see 35:7) [c] *21* That is, about 15 feet long and 2 1/4 feet wide or about 4.5 meters long and 68 centimeters wide [d] *1* That is, about 3 3/4 feet long and 2 1/4 feet wide and high or about 1.1 meters long and 68 centimeters wide and high; similarly in verse 6 [e] *10* Or *He*; also in verses 11-29 [f] *10* That is, about 3 feet long, 1 1/2 feet wide and 2 1/4 feet high or about 90 centimeters long, 45 centimeters wide and 68 centimeters high [g] *12* That is, about 3 inches or about 7.5 centimeters

37:1 – 29 See note on 35:4 — 39:43.

37:1 *Bezalel made the ark.* The chief craftsman (see 31:2 – 3 and notes) was given the honor of making the object that was most sacred (see 25:10 and note) among the furnishings for the tabernacle.

The Lampstand

37:17-24pp — Ex 25:31-39

[17]They made the lampstand[i] of pure gold. They hammered out its base and shaft, and made its flowerlike cups, buds and blossoms of one piece with them. [18]Six branches extended from the sides of the lampstand — three on one side and three on the other. [19]Three cups shaped like almond flowers with buds and blossoms were on one branch, three on the next branch and the same for all six branches extending from the lampstand. [20]And on the lampstand were four cups shaped like almond flowers with buds and blossoms. [21]One bud was under the first pair of branches extending from the lampstand, a second bud under the second pair, and a third bud under the third pair — six branches in all. [22]The buds and the branches were all of one piece with the lampstand, hammered out of pure gold.[j]

[23]They made its seven lamps,[k] as well as its wick trimmers and trays, of pure gold. [24]They made the lampstand and all its accessories from one talent[a] of pure gold.

The Altar of Incense

37:25-28pp — Ex 30:1-5

[25]They made the altar of incense[l] out of acacia wood. It was square, a cubit long and a cubit wide and two cubits high[b] — its horns[m] of one piece with it. [26]They overlaid the top and all the sides and the horns with pure gold, and made a gold molding around it. [27]They made two gold rings[n] below the molding — two on each of the opposite sides — to hold the poles used to carry it. [28]They made the poles of acacia wood and overlaid them with gold.[o]

[29]They also made the sacred anointing oil[p] and the pure, fragrant incense[q] — the work of a perfumer.

The Altar of Burnt Offering

38:1-7pp — Ex 27:1-8

38 They[c] built the altar of burnt offering of acacia wood, three cubits[d] high; it was square, five cubits long and five cubits wide.[e] [2]They made a horn at each of the four corners, so that the horns and the altar were of one piece, and they overlaid the altar with bronze.[r] [3]They made all its utensils[s] of bronze — its pots, shovels, sprinkling bowls, meat forks and firepans. [4]They made a grating for the altar, a bronze network, to be under its ledge, halfway up the altar. [5]They cast bronze rings to hold the poles for the four corners of the bronze grating. [6]They made the poles of acacia wood and overlaid them with bronze. [7]They inserted the poles into the rings so they would be on the sides of the altar for carrying it. They made it hollow, out of boards.

The Basin for Washing

[8]They made the bronze basin[t] and its bronze stand from the mirrors of the women[u] who served at the entrance to the tent of meeting.

The Courtyard

38:9-20pp — Ex 27:9-19

[9]Next they made the courtyard. The south side was a hundred cubits[f] long and had curtains of finely twisted linen, [10]with twenty posts and twenty bronze bases, and with silver hooks and bands on the posts. [11]The north side was also a hundred cubits long and had twenty posts and twenty bronze bases, with silver hooks and bands on the posts.

[12]The west end was fifty cubits[g] wide and had curtains, with ten posts and ten bases, with silver hooks and bands on the posts. [13]The east end, toward the sunrise, was also fifty cubits wide. [14]Curtains fifteen cubits[h] long were on one side of the entrance, with three posts and three bases, [15]and curtains fifteen cubits long were on the other side of the entrance to the courtyard, with three posts and three bases. [16]All the curtains around the courtyard were of finely twisted linen. [17]The bases for the posts were bronze. The hooks and bands on the posts were silver, and their tops were overlaid with silver; so all the posts of the courtyard had silver bands.

[18]The curtain for the entrance to the courtyard was made of blue, purple and scarlet yarn and finely twisted linen — the work of an embroiderer. It was twenty cubits[i] long and, like the curtains of the courtyard, five cubits[j] high, [19]with four posts and four bronze bases. Their hooks and bands were silver, and their tops were overlaid with silver. [20]All the tent pegs[v]

37:17 [i]Heb 9:2; Rev 1:12 **37:22** [j]ver 17; Nu 8:4 **37:23** [k]Ex 40:4, 25 **37:25** [l]Ex 30:34-36; Lk 1:11; Heb 9:4; Rev 8:3 [m]S Ex 27:2; Rev 9:13 **37:27** [n]ver 14 **37:28** [o]S Ex 25:13 **37:29** [p]S Ex 31:11 [q]Ex 30:1, 25; 39:38 **38:2** [r]2Ch 1:5 **38:3** [s]S Ex 31:9

38:8 [t]S Ex 30:18; S 40:7 [u]Dt 23:17; 1Sa 2:22; 1Ki 14:24 **38:20** [v]S Ex 35:18

[a] *24* That is, about 75 pounds or about 34 kilograms
[b] *25* That is, about 1 1/2 feet long and wide and 3 feet high or about 45 centimeters long and wide and 90 centimeters high
[c] *1* Or *He*; also in verses 2-9
[d] *1* That is, about 4 1/2 feet or about 1.4 meters
[e] *1* That is, about 7 1/2 feet or about 2.3 meters long and wide
[f] *9* That is, about 150 feet or about 45 meters
[g] *12* That is, about 75 feet or about 23 meters
[h] *14* That is, about 22 feet or about 6.8 meters
[i] *18* That is, about 30 feet or about 9 meters
[j] *18* That is, about 7 1/2 feet or about 2.3 meters

38:1 – 31 See note on 35:4 — 39:43.
38:8 *bronze ... mirrors.* Mirrored glass was unknown in ancient times, but highly polished bronze gave adequate reflection (cf. 1Co 13:12 and note). *tent of meeting.* See note on 27:21.

of the tabernacle and of the surrounding courtyard were bronze.

The Materials Used

[21]These are the amounts of the materials used for the tabernacle, the tabernacle
of the covenant law,[w] which were recorded at Moses' command by the Levites under the direction of Ithamar[x] son of Aaron,
the priest. [22](Bezalel[y] son of Uri, the son
of Hur, of the tribe of Judah, made every-
hing the LORD commanded Moses; [23]with
him was Oholiab[z] son of Ahisamak, of the
ribe of Dan—an engraver and designer,
and an embroiderer in blue, purple and
carlet yarn and fine linen.) [24]The total
amount of the gold from the wave offer-
ng used for all the work on the sanctuary[a]
vas 29 talents and 730 shekels,[a] according
o the sanctuary shekel.[b]

[25]The silver obtained from those of the
ommunity who were counted in the cen-
us[c] was 100 talents[b] and 1,775 shekels,[c]
ccording to the sanctuary shekel— [26]one
eka per person,[d] that is, half a shekel,[d]
ccording to the sanctuary shekel,[e] from
veryone who had crossed over to those
ounted, twenty years old or more,[f] a to-
al of 603,550 men.[g] [27]The 100 talents of
ilver were used to cast the bases[h] for the
anctuary and for the curtain—100 bases
om the 100 talents, one talent for each
ase. [28]They used the 1,775 shekels to
ake the hooks for the posts, to overlay
e tops of the posts, and to make their
ands.

[29]The bronze from the wave offering
as 70 talents and 2,400 shekels.[e] [30]They
sed it to make the bases for the entrance
the tent of meeting, the bronze altar
ith its bronze grating and all its utensils,
the bases for the surrounding courtyard
nd those for its entrance and all the tent
egs for the tabernacle and those for the
rrounding courtyard.

he Priestly Garments

39 From the blue, purple and scarlet
yarn[i] they made woven garments
r ministering in the sanctuary.[j] They also
ade sacred garments[k] for Aaron, as the
ORD commanded Moses.

he Ephod

:2-7pp — Ex 28:6-14

[2]They[f] made the ephod of gold, and
blue, purple and scarlet yarn, and of
finely twisted linen. [3]They hammered out
thin sheets of gold and cut strands to be
worked into the blue, purple and scarlet
yarn and fine linen—the work of skilled
hands. [4]They made shoulder pieces for the
ephod, which were attached to two of its
corners, so it could be fastened. [5]Its skillfully woven waistband was like it—of one
piece with the ephod and made with gold,
and with blue, purple and scarlet yarn,
and with finely twisted linen, as the LORD
commanded Moses.

[6]They mounted the onyx stones in gold
filigree settings and engraved them like a
seal with the names of the sons of Israel.
[7]Then they fastened them on the shoulder
pieces of the ephod as memorial[l] stones
for the sons of Israel, as the LORD commanded Moses.

The Breastpiece

39:8-21pp — Ex 28:15-28

[8]They fashioned the breastpiece[m]—the
work of a skilled craftsman. They made it
like the ephod: of gold, and of blue, purple and scarlet yarn, and of finely twisted
linen. [9]It was square—a span[g] long and
a span wide—and folded double. [10]Then
they mounted four rows of precious stones
on it. The first row was carnelian, chrysolite and beryl; [11]the second row was turquoise, lapis lazuli and emerald; [12]the
third row was jacinth, agate and amethyst;
[13]the fourth row was topaz, onyx and jasper.[h] They were mounted in gold filigree
settings. [14]There were twelve stones, one
for each of the names of the sons of Israel,
each engraved like a seal with the name of
one of the twelve tribes.[n]

[15]For the breastpiece they made braided
chains of pure gold, like a rope. [16]They
made two gold filigree settings and two
gold rings, and fastened the rings to two
of the corners of the breastpiece. [17]They
fastened the two gold chains to the rings
at the corners of the breastpiece, [18]and
the other ends of the chains to the two
settings, attaching them to the shoulder
pieces of the ephod at the front. [19]They

38:21 [w]Nu 1:50,53; 8:24; 9:15; 10:11; 17:7; 1Ch 23:32; 2Ch 24:6; Ac 7:44; Rev 15:5 [x]Nu 4:28,33 **38:22** [y]S Ex 31:2 **38:23** [z]S Ex 31:6 **38:24** [a]S Ex 30:16 [b]S Ex 30:13 **38:25** [c]S Ex 30:12 **38:26** [d]S Ex 30:12 [e]S Ex 30:13 [f]S Ex 30:14 [g]S Ex 12:37 **38:27** [h]S Ex 26:19 **39:1** [i]Ex 35:23 [j]Ex 35:19 [k]ver 41; Ex 28:2

39:7 [l]Lev 24:7; Jos 4:7 **39:8** [m]Lev 8:8 **39:14** [n]Rev 21:12

[a] *24* The weight of the gold was a little over a ton or about 1 metric ton. [b] *25* That is, about 3 3/4 tons or about 3.4 metric tons; also in verse 27 [c] *25* That is, about 44 pounds or about 20 kilograms; also in verse 28 [d] *26* That is, about 1/5 ounce or about 5.7 grams [e] *29* The weight of the bronze was about 2 1/2 tons or about 2.4 metric tons. [f] *2* Or *He*; also in verses 7, 8 and 22 [g] *9* That is, about 9 inches or about 23 centimeters [h] *13* The precise identification of some of these precious stones is uncertain.

:25 *100 talents and 1,775 shekels.* Since there are 3,000 ekels in a talent, 100 talents equals 300,000 shekels, ich, when added to the 1,775 shekels, gives a grand to- of 301,775—half a shekel for each of the 603,550 men of litary age (v. 26).

38:26 *603,550 men.* See Introduction to Numbers: Special Problem; see also Nu 1:46 and note.

38:27 *one talent for each base.* See note on 26:19.

39:1-43 See note on 35:4—39:43.

made two gold rings and attached them to
the other two corners of the breastpiece on
the inside edge next to the ephod. 20 Then
they made two more gold rings and attached them to the bottom of the shoulder
pieces on the front of the ephod, close to
the seam just above the waistband of the
ephod. 21 They tied the rings of the breastpiece to the rings of the ephod with blue
cord, connecting it to the waistband so
that the breastpiece would not swing out
from the ephod — as the LORD commanded Moses.

Other Priestly Garments

39:22-31pp — Ex 28:31-43

22 They made the robe of the ephod entirely of blue cloth — the work of a weaver — 23 with an opening in the center of
the robe like the opening of a collar,[a] and
a band around this opening, so that it
would not tear. 24 They made pomegranates of blue, purple and scarlet yarn and
finely twisted linen around the hem of the
robe. 25 And they made bells of pure gold
and attached them around the hem between the pomegranates. 26 The bells and
pomegranates alternated around the hem
of the robe to be worn for ministering, as
the LORD commanded Moses.
27 For Aaron and his sons, they made tunics of fine linen[o] — the work of a weaver — 28 and the turban[p] of fine linen, the
linen caps and the undergarments of finely twisted linen. 29 The sash was made of
finely twisted linen and blue, purple and
scarlet yarn — the work of an embroiderer — as the LORD commanded Moses.
30 They made the plate, the sacred emblem, out of pure gold and engraved on it,
like an inscription on a seal: HOLY TO THE
LORD.[q] 31 Then they fastened a blue cord to
it to attach it to the turban,[r] as the LORD
commanded Moses.

Moses Inspects the Tabernacle

39:32-41pp — Ex 35:10-19

32 So all the work on the tabernacle, the
tent of meeting, was completed. The Israelites did everything just as the LORD commanded Moses.[s] 33 Then they brought the
tabernacle[t] to Moses: the tent and all its

39:27 [o] Lev 6:10; 8:2
39:28 [p] ver 31; S Ex 28:4; Lev 8:9; Isa 61:10
39:30 [q] Isa 23:18; Zec 14:20
39:31 [r] S ver 28
39:32 [s] S Ex 25:9
39:33 [t] Ex 25:8-40; 36:8-38
39:35 [u] S Ex 37:1
39:36 [v] Ex 25:23-30; 37:10-16 [w] S Ex 25:30
39:37 [x] S Ex 25:31 [y] Ex 25:31-39 [z] S Ex 25:6
39:38 [a] Ex 30:1-10 [b] Ex 30:22-32; 37:29 [c] Ex 30:34-38; S 37:29 [d] S Ex 36:35
39:39 [e] Ex 27:1-8; 38:1-7 [f] S Ex 30:18
39:40 [g] Ex 27:9-19; 38:9-20
39:41 [h] S ver 1
39:42 [i] S Ex 25:9
39:43 [j] S Ex 25:9; S 35:10 [k] Ge 31:55; Lev 9:22,23; Nu 6:23-27; Dt 21:5; 26:15; 2Sa 6:18; 1Ki 8:14,55; 1Ch 16:2; 2Ch 30:27
40:2 [l] S Ex 26:30 [m] ver 34,35; Lev 1:1; 3:2; 6:26; 9:23; 16:16; Nu 1:1; 7:89; 11:16; 17:4; 20:6; Jos 18:1; 19:51; Jer 7:12 [n] ver 17; S Ex 12:2; Nu 9:1
40:3 [o] S Ex 26:33
40:4 [p] S Ex 25:23 [q] S Ex 25:30 [r] S Ex 25:31
40:5 [s] S Ex 30:1
40:6 [t] S Ex 27:1; 2Ki 16:14; 2Ch 4:1
40:7 [u] Ex 30:18
40:8 [v] S Ex 27:9
40:9 [w] S Ex 30:26

furnishings, its clasps, frames, crossbars,
posts and bases; 34 the covering of ram
skins dyed red and the covering of another durable leather[b] and the shielding curtain; 35 the ark of the covenant law[u] with
its poles and the atonement cover; 36 the
table[v] with all its articles and the bread of
the Presence;[w] 37 the pure gold lampstand[x]
with its row of lamps and all its accessories,[y] and the olive oil[z] for the light; 38 the
gold altar,[a] the anointing oil,[b] the fragrant
incense,[c] and the curtain[d] for the entrance
to the tent; 39 the bronze altar[e] with its
bronze grating, its poles and all its utensils; the basin[f] with its stand; 40 the curtains of the courtyard with its posts and
bases, and the curtain for the entrance to
the courtyard;[g] the ropes and tent pegs for
the courtyard; all the furnishings for the
tabernacle, the tent of meeting; 41 and the
woven garments[h] worn for ministering in
the sanctuary, both the sacred garments
for Aaron the priest and the garments for
his sons when serving as priests.
42 The Israelites had done all the work
just as the LORD had commanded Moses.
43 Moses inspected the work and saw tha
they had done it just as the LORD had com
manded.[j] So Moses blessed[k] them.

Setting Up the Tabernacle

40 Then the LORD said to Moses: 2 "Se
up[l] the tabernacle, the tent of meet
ing,[m] on the first day of the first month.
3 Place the ark[o] of the covenant law in i
and shield the ark with the curtain. 4 Brin
in the table[p] and set out what belongs o
it.[q] Then bring in the lampstand[r] and se
up its lamps. 5 Place the gold altar[s] of in
cense in front of the ark of the covenan
law and put the curtain at the entrance t
the tabernacle.
6 "Place the altar[t] of burnt offering i
front of the entrance to the tabernacle, th
tent of meeting; 7 place the basin[u] betwee
the tent of meeting and the altar and pu
water in it. 8 Set up the courtyard[v] aroun
it and put the curtain at the entrance t
the courtyard.
9 "Take the anointing oil and anoint[w] th

[a] *23* The meaning of the Hebrew for this word is uncertain. [b] *34* Possibly the hides of large aquatic mammals

---

39:30 *sacred emblem.* An official designation (not found in 28:36–37) for the plate of the turban. HOLY TO THE LORD. See 28:36 and note.
39:32 *all the work on the tabernacle … was completed.* Reminiscent of the concluding words of the creation narrative (see Ge 2:1–3). Thus the end of Exodus links with the beginning (see 1:7 and note), marking the complex of events narrated in the book as the beginning of the restoration of the creation order and of the realization of God's redemptive purposes in history (see also note on 26:1).

39:43 *Moses blessed them.* For the faithfulness wi which the Israelites had donated their gifts, time ar talents in building the tabernacle and all its furnishings faithfulness in service brings divine benediction.
40:2 *first day of the first month.* The tabernacle was set u almost a year after the institution of the Passover (see v. 1 12:2,6 and note on 12:2).
40:9–10 *holy … most holy.* See 3:5; 29:37 and notes.

tabernacle and everything in it; consecrate
it and all its furnishings,[x] and it will be
holy. 10 Then anoint the altar of burnt offering and all its utensils; consecrate[y] the
altar, and it will be most holy. 11 Anoint the
basin and its stand and consecrate them.
12 "Bring Aaron and his sons to the entrance to the tent of meeting[z] and wash
them with water.[a] 13 Then dress Aaron in
the sacred garments,[b] anoint him and consecrate[c] him so he may serve me as priest.
14 Bring his sons and dress them in tunics.[d]
15 Anoint them just as you anointed their
father, so they may serve me as priests.
Their anointing will be to a priesthood
that will continue throughout their generations.[e]" 16 Moses did everything just as
the LORD commanded[f] him.
17 So the tabernacle[g] was set up on the
first day of the first month[h] in the second
year. 18 When Moses[i] set up the tabernacle, he put the bases in place, erected the
frames,[j] inserted the crossbars and set up
the posts. 19 Then he spread the tent over
the tabernacle and put the covering[k] over
the tent, as the LORD commanded[l] him.
20 He took the tablets of the covenant
law[m] and placed them in the ark,[n] attached
the poles to the ark and put the atonement
cover[o] over it. 21 Then he brought the ark
into the tabernacle and hung the shielding
curtain[p] and shielded the ark of the covenant law, as the LORD commanded[q] him.
22 Moses placed the table[r] in the tent of
meeting on the north side of the tabernacle outside the curtain 23 and set out the
bread[s] on it before the LORD, as the LORD
commanded[t] him.
24 He placed the lampstand[u] in the tent
of meeting opposite the table on the south
side of the tabernacle 25 and set up the
lamps[v] before the LORD, as the LORD commanded[w] him.

40:9 [x] Nu 7:1 **40:10** [y] S Ex 29:36 **40:12** [z] Nu 8:9 [a] S Ex 29:4; S 30:19 **40:13** [b] S Ex 28:41 [c] Lev 8:12 **40:14** [d] S Ex 28:40; Lev 10:5 **40:15** [e] S Ex 29:9 **40:16** [f] S Ge 6:22 **40:17** [g] Nu 7:1 [h] S ver 2 **40:18** [i] 2Ch 1:3 [j] Ex 36:20-34 **40:19** [k] Ex 36:19 [l] S Ge 6:22 **40:20** [m] S Ex 16:34; Heb 9:4 [n] S Ex 25:21 [o] Ex 25:17-22; S 26:34; S 31:7 **40:21** [p] S Ex 26:33 [q] S Ge 6:22 **40:22** [r] S Ex 25:23 **40:23** [s] S Ex 25:30; Lev 24:5-8 [t] S Ge 6:22 **40:24** [u] S Ex 25:31 **40:25** [v] S Ex 37:23 [w] S Ge 6:22 **40:26** [x] S Ex 30:1 **40:27** [y] S Ge 6:22 **40:28** [z] S Ex 26:36 **40:29** [a] S Ex 20:24 [b] Ex 29:38-42 [c] S Ge 6:22 **40:30** [d] S ver 7; S Ex 30:18 **40:31** [e] Ex 30:19-21 **40:32** [f] Ex 30:20 [g] S Ge 6:22 **40:33** [h] S Ex 27:9;

26 Moses placed the gold altar[x] in the
tent of meeting in front of the curtain
27 and burned fragrant incense on it, as the
LORD commanded[y] him.
28 Then he put up the curtain[z] at the entrance to the tabernacle. 29 He set the altar[a] of burnt offering near the entrance to
the tabernacle, the tent of meeting, and
offered on it burnt offerings and grain offerings,[b] as the LORD commanded[c] him.
30 He placed the basin[d] between the tent
of meeting and the altar and put water in
it for washing, 31 and Moses and Aaron
and his sons used it to wash[e] their hands
and feet. 32 They washed whenever they
entered the tent of meeting or approached
the altar,[f] as the LORD commanded[g] Moses.
33 Then Moses set up the courtyard[h]
around the tabernacle and altar and put
up the curtain[i] at the entrance to the courtyard. And so Moses finished the work.

The Glory of the LORD

34 Then the cloud[j] covered the tent of
meeting, and the glory[k] of the LORD filled
the tabernacle. 35 Moses could not enter
the tent of meeting because the cloud had
settled on it, and the glory[l] of the LORD
filled the tabernacle.[m]
36 In all the travels of the Israelites,
whenever the cloud lifted from above
the tabernacle, they would set out;[n] 37 but
if the cloud did not lift, they did not set
out — until the day it lifted. 38 So the cloud[o]
of the LORD was over the tabernacle by
day, and fire was in the cloud by night,
in the sight of all the Israelites during all
their travels.

38:9-20 [i] Ex 27:16 **40:34** [j] Ex 19:16; Lev 16:2; Nu 9:15-23; 1Ki 8:12; 2Ch 5:13; Isa 6:4; Eze 10:4 [k] S Ex 16:7; Jn 1:14; 12:41; Rev 15:8 **40:35** [l] S Ex 16:10 [m] 1Ki 8:11; 2Ch 5:13-14; 7:2 **40:36** [n] Nu 9:17-23; 10:13 **40:38** [o] S Ex 13:21; 1Co 10:1

40:16 *Moses did ... just as the LORD commanded.* Moses' obedience to God's command is a key theme of the final chapter of Exodus (see vv. 19,21,23,25,27,29,32). The people provided all the resources and made all the components, but only the Lord's servant Moses was authorized to erect the tabernacle and prepare it for the Lord's entry.

40:33 *Moses finished the work.* See note on 39:32.

40:34 With the glory of the Lord entering the tabernacle (cf. 1Ki 8:10 – 11 and note on 8:10), the great series of events that began with the birth of Moses and his rescue from the Nile, foreshadowing the deliverance of Israel from Egypt, comes to a grand climax. From now on, the Israelites march through the wilderness, and through history, with the Lord tenting among them and leading them to the land of fulfilled promises.

40:38 See note on 13:21.

LEVITICUS

INTRODUCTION

Title

Leviticus receives its name from the Septuagint (the pre-Christian Greek translation of the OT) and means "relating to the Levites." Its Hebrew title, *wayyiqra'*, is the first word in the Hebrew text of the book and means "And he [i.e., the LORD] called." Although Leviticus does not deal only with the special duties of the Levites, it is so named because it concerns mainly the service of worship at the tabernacle, which was conducted by the priests who were the sons of Aaron, assisted by many from the rest of the tribe of Levi. Exodus gave the directions for building the tabernacle, and now Leviticus gives the laws and regulations for worship there, including instructions on ceremonial cleanness, moral laws, holy days, the sabbath year and the Year of Jubilee. These laws were given, at least for the most part, during the year that Israel camped at Mount Sinai, when God directed Moses in organizing Israel's worship, government and military forces. The book of Numbers continues the history with preparations for moving on from Sinai to Canaan.

Author and Date

See note on 1:1 and Introduction to Genesis: Author and Date of Writing.

Theological Themes

Leviticus is a manual of regulations enabling the holy King to set up his earthly throne among the people of his kingdom. It explains how the Israelites are to be the Lord's holy people and are to worship him in a holy manner. Holiness in this sense means to be separated from sin and set apart exclusively to the Lord for his purpose, in his service and for his glory. So the key thought of the book is holiness (see notes on 11:44; Ex 3:5)—the holiness of God and his people (they must revere him in holiness). In fact, the word *holy* appears more often in Leviticus than in any other book of the Bible. In Leviticus spiritual holiness is symbolized by physical perfection. Therefore the book demands perfect animals for its many sacrifices (chs. 1–7) and

a quick look

Author:
Moses

Audience:
God's chosen people, the Israelites

Date:
Between 1446 and 1406 BC

Theme:
The Israelites receive instructions from God at the base of Mount Sinai concerning how to live as God's holy people.

Leviticus explains how the Israelites are to be the Lord's holy people and are to worship him in a holy manner.

requires priests without deformity (chs. 8 – 10). A woman's hemorrhaging after giving birth (ch. 12); sores, burns or baldness (chs. 13 – 14); a man's bodily discharge (15:1 – 18); specific activities during a woman's monthly period (15:19 – 33) — all may be signs of blemish (a lack of perfection) and may symbolize human spiritual defects, which break spiritual wholeness. The person with visible skin disease must be banished from the camp, the place of God's special presence, just as Adam and Eve were banished from the Garden of Eden. Such people can return to the camp (and therefore to God's presence) when they are pronounced whole again by the examining priests. Before they can reenter the camp, however, they must offer the prescribed, perfect sacrifices (symbolizing the perfect, whole sacrifice of Christ).

After the establishment of the covenant at Sinai, Israel represented God's kingdom on earth (the theocracy), and as its King the Lord imposed his administration over all of Israel's life. He so regulated Israel's religious, communal and personal life as to establish them as his holy people and to instruct them in holiness. In Leviticus, special attention is given to Israel's religious ceremonies and rituals. Their sacrifices were to be offered only at the divinely designated sanctuary, which symbolized both God's holiness and his compassion. Only the appointed priests were to officiate at Israel's sacrifices, and it was also the duty of the priests to instruct the people concerning the proper form and meaning of each sacrifice. For more information on the meaning of sacrifice in

Standing stones on the summit of Gezer represent the type of sacred stones that Israelite law prohibited (Lev 26:1).

Danny Frese/www.BiblePlaces.com

Model of the tabernacle and courtyard
Todd Bolen/www.BiblePlaces.com

general, see the solemn ritual of the Day of Atonement (ch. 16; see note on 16:1 – 34). For the meaning of the blood of the offering, see 17:11; Ge 9:4 and notes. For the emphasis on substitution, see 1:5; 4:4; 16:20 – 22 and notes.

Some suppose that the OT sacrifices were carryovers and adaptations of an older sacrificial system developed by agricultural peoples who thought that humans needed to please the gods by feeding them from their crops, flocks and herds. But the OT sacrifices Israel was to bring were specifically prescribed by God and received their meaning from the Lord's covenant relationship with Israel — whatever their superficial resemblances to pagan sacrifices may have been. They did indeed include the idea of gift, but this is accompanied by such other values as dedication, communion, propitiation (appeasing God's judicial wrath against sin) and restitution. The various offerings have differing functions, the primary ones being atonement (see note on Ex 25:17) and worship (see chart, p. 164).

Outline

The subjects treated in Leviticus, as in any book of laws and regulations, cover several categories:

- I. The Five Main Offerings (chs. 1 – 7)
  - A. The Burnt Offering (ch. 1)
  - B. The Grain Offering (ch. 2)

C. The Fellowship Offering (ch. 3)
D. The Sin Offering (4:1 — 5:13)
E. The Guilt Offering (5:14 — 6:7)
F. Additional Regulations for the Offerings (6:8 — 7:38)
II. The Installation and Ministry of Aaron and His Sons (chs. 8 – 10)
A. The Ordination of Aaron and His Sons (ch. 8)
B. The Ministry of the Priests (ch. 9)
C. The Deaths of Nadab and Abihu and Attendant Regulations (ch. 10)
III. The Distinction Between Clean and Unclean (chs. 11 – 15)
A. Clean and Unclean Food (ch. 11)
B. Purification After Childbirth (ch. 12)
C. Regulations for Defiling Skin Diseases (13:1 – 46)
D. Regulations for Molds (13:47 – 59)
E. Cleansing from Skin Diseases (14:1 – 32)
F. Cleansing from Molds (14:33 – 57)
G. Bodily Discharges That Cause Uncleanness (ch. 15)
IV. The Annual Day of Atonement (ch. 16)
V. Holy Living (chs. 17 – 26)
A. Eating Blood Prohibited (ch. 17)
B. Unlawful Sexual Relations (ch. 18)
C. Various Laws for Holy Living (ch. 19)
D. Punishments for Sin (ch. 20)
E. Regulations for Priests (21:1 — 22:16)
F. Acceptable and Unacceptable Sacrifices (22:17 – 33)
G. The Annual Festivals (ch. 23)
H. Rules for Oil and Bread in the Tabernacle (24:1 – 9)
I. Punishment for Blasphemy (24:10 – 23)
J. The Sabbath and Jubilee Years (ch. 25)
K. Covenant Blessings and Curses (ch. 26)
VI. Regulations for Offerings Vowed to the Lord (ch. 27)

The Burnt Offering

1 The LORD called to Moses[a] and spoke to
him from the tent of meeting.[b] He said,
2 “Speak to the Israelites and say to them:
‘When anyone among you brings an offering to the LORD,[c] bring as your offering an
animal from either the herd or the flock.[d]
3 “ ‘If the offering is a burnt offering[e]
from the herd,[f] you are to offer a male
without defect.[g] You must present it at the
entrance to the tent[h] of meeting so that it
will be acceptable[i] to the LORD. 4 You are
to lay your hand on the head[j] of the burnt
offering,[k] and it will be accepted[l] on your
behalf to make atonement[m] for you. 5 You
are to slaughter[n] the young bull[o] before the
LORD, and then Aaron’s sons[p] the priests
shall bring the blood and splash it against
the sides of the altar[q] at the entrance to the
tent of meeting. 6 You are to skin[r] the burnt
offering and cut it into pieces.[s] 7 The sons
of Aaron the priest are to put fire on the
altar and arrange wood[t] on the fire. 8 Then
Aaron’s sons the priests shall arrange the
pieces, including the head and the fat,[u]
on the wood[v] that is burning on the altar.
9 You are to wash the internal organs and
the legs with water,[w] and the priest is to
burn all of it[x] on the altar.[y] It is a burnt offering,[z] a food offering,[a] an aroma pleasing
to the LORD.[b]
10 “ ‘If the offering is a burnt offering
from the flock, from either the sheep[c] or
the goats,[d] you are to offer a male without
defect. 11 You are to slaughter it at the north
side of the altar[e] before the LORD, and Aaron’s sons the priests shall splash its blood
against the sides of the altar.[f] 12 You are to
cut it into pieces, and the priest shall arrange them, including the head and the
fat,[g] on the wood that is burning on the
altar. 13 You are to wash the internal organs
and the legs with water,[h] and the priest is
to bring all of them and burn them[i] on the
altar.[j] It is a burnt offering,[k] a food offering, an aroma pleasing to the LORD.
14 “ ‘If the offering to the LORD is a burnt
offering of birds, you are to offer a dove or
a young pigeon.[l] 15 The priest shall bring it
to the altar, wring off the head[m] and burn

1:1 [a] S Ex 3:4; S 25:22 [b] S Ex 27:21; S 40:2 **1:2** [c] Lev 7:16, 38; 22:21; 23:38; 27:9 [d] Lev 22:18-19; Nu 15:3 **1:3** [e] S Ge 8:20 [f] ver 10; Lev 22:27; Ezr 8:35; Mal 1:8 [g] S ver 5; S Ex 12:5; S Lev 22:19, 20; Heb 9:14; 1Pe 1:19 [h] Lev 6:25; 17:9; Nu 6:16; Dt 12:5-6, 11 [i] Isa 58:5 **1:4** [j] S Ex 29:10, 15 [k] ver 3; Lev 4:29; 6:25; Eze 45:15 [l] S Ge 32:20 [m] S Ex 29:36; S 32:30 **1:5** [n] Ex 29:11; Lev 3:2, 8 [o] S ver 3; Ex 29:1; Nu 15:8; Dt 18:3; Ps 50:9; 69:31 [p] Lev 8:2; 10:6; 21:1 [q] S Ex 29:20; Heb 12:24; 1Pe 1:2

1:6 [r] Lev 7:8 [s] Ex 29:17 **1:7** [t] ver 17; S Ge 22:9; Lev 3:5; 6:12 **1:8** [u] ver 12; S Ex 29:13; Lev 8:20 [v] Lev 9:13 **1:9** [w] S Ex 29:17 [x] Lev 6:22 [y] ver 13; Ex 29:18; Lev 9:14 [z] ver 3 [a] Lev 23:8, 25, 36; Nu 28:6, 19 [b] ver 13; Ge 8:21; Lev 2:2; 3:5, 16; 17:6; Nu 18:17; 28:11-13; Eph 5:2 **1:10** [c] S Ge 22:7 [d] S ver 3; Ex 12:5; Lev 3:12; 4:23, 28; 5:6; Nu 15:11 **1:11** [e] S Ex 29:11 [f] S Ex 29:20 **1:12** [g] S ver 8 **1:13** [h] S Ex 29:17 [i] Lev 6:22 [j] S ver 9 [k] Dt 12:27 **1:14** [l] S Ge 15:9; Lk 2:24 **1:15** [m] Lev 5:8

1:1—7:38 Regulations for the five main offerings: burnt, grain, fellowship, sin and guilt offerings.

1:1 Emphasizes that the contents of Leviticus were given to Moses by God at Mount Sinai. Cf. also the concluding verse (27:34). In more than 50 places it is said that the Lord spoke to Moses. Modern criticism has attributed practically the whole book to priestly legislation written during or after the exile. But this is without objective evidence, is against the repeated claim of the book to be Mosaic, is against the traditional Jewish view, and runs counter to other OT and NT witness (Ro 10:5). Many items in Leviticus are now seen to be best explained in terms of a second-millennium BC date, which is also the most likely time for Moses to have written the Pentateuch (see Introduction to Genesis: Author and Date of Writing). There is no convincing reason not to take at face value the many references to Moses and his work. *tent of meeting.* The tabernacle, where God met with Israel (see note on Ex 27:21).

1:2 *brings an offering.* The Hebrew word for “offering” used here (*qorban*) comes from the verb translated “brings.” An “offering” is something that people “bring” to God as a gift (most offerings were voluntary, such as the burnt offering). This word for “offering” is also used in Mk 7:11 (Corban), where Mark translates it “devoted to God” (see note there).

1:3 *burnt offering.* See further priestly regulations in 6:8–13 (see also chart, p. 164). A burnt offering was offered every morning and evening for all Israel (Ex 29:39–42). Double burnt offerings were brought on the Sabbath (Nu 28:9–10) and extra ones on festival days (Nu 28–29). In addition, anyone could offer special burnt offerings to express devotion to the Lord. *male.* The burnt offering had to be a male animal because of its greater value, and also perhaps because it was thought to better represent vigor and fertility. It was usually a young sheep or goat (for the average individual), but bulls (for the wealthy) and doves or pigeons (for the poor) were also specified. *without defect.* The animal had to be unblemished (cf. Mal 1:8; 1Pe 1:19 and note). As in all offerings, the offerers were to lay their hands on the head of the animal to express identification between themselves and the animal (16:21), whose death would then be accepted in “atonement” (v. 4). The blood was splashed against the sides of the bronze altar of burnt offering (located outside the tabernacle—later the temple—in the eastern half of the courtyard), where the fire of sacrifice was never to go out (6:13). The whole sacrifice was to be burned up (v. 9), including the head, legs, fat and internal organs. It is therefore sometimes called a holocaust offering (*holo* means “whole,” and *caust* means “burnt”). When a bull was offered, however, the officiating priest could keep its hide (7:8). The burnt offering may have been the usual sacrifice offered by the patriarchs. It was the most comprehensive in its meaning. Its Hebrew name means “going up,” perhaps symbolizing worship and prayer as its aroma ascended to the Lord (v. 17). The completeness of its burning also speaks of dedication on the part of the worshiper. *entrance to the tent of meeting.* Where the altar of burnt offering was (see Ex 40:29). *acceptable to the LORD.* See Ro 12:1; Php 4:18 and note.

1:4 *lay your hand on.* See notes on v. 3; Ex 29:10. *atonement.* See notes on 16:20–22; 17:11; Ex 25:17.

1:5 Only after the offerer killed the animal (symbolizing substitution of a perfect animal sacrifice for a sinful human life) did the priestly work begin. *blood.* See notes on 17:11; Heb 9:18. *splash it against the sides of the altar.* See Ex 24:6; Heb 9:19–21.

1:6 *skin.* The whole animal was burned except the hide, which was given to the priest (7:8).

1:9,13,17 *aroma pleasing to the LORD.* The OT sacrifices foreshadowed Christ, who was a “fragrant offering” (Eph 5:2; cf. Php 4:18).

1:14 *birds.* Three categories of sacrifices are mentioned: (1) herds (vv. 3–9), (2) flocks (vv. 10–13) and (3) birds (vv. 14–17). Sacrifices of birds were allowed for the poor (see 5:7; 12:8; Lk 2:24).

it on the altar; its blood shall be drained
out on the side of the altar.[n] 16 He is to
remove the crop and the feathers[a] and
throw them down east of the altar where
the ashes[o] are. 17 He shall tear it open by
the wings, not dividing it completely,[p] and
then the priest shall burn it on the wood[q]
that is burning on the altar. It is a burnt
offering, a food offering, an aroma pleasing to the LORD.

The Grain Offering

2 "'When anyone brings a grain offering[r] to the LORD, their offering is to be
of the finest flour.[s] They are to pour olive oil[t] on it,[u] put incense on it[v] 2 and take
it to Aaron's sons the priests. The priest
shall take a handful of the flour[w] and oil,
together with all the incense,[x] and burn
this as a memorial[b] portion[y] on the altar,
a food offering,[z] an aroma pleasing to the
LORD.[a] 3 The rest of the grain offering belongs to Aaron and his sons;[b] it is a most
holy[c] part of the food offerings presented
to the LORD.

4 "'If you bring a grain offering baked in
an oven,[d] it is to consist of the finest flour:
either thick loaves made without yeast
and with olive oil mixed in or thin loaves[e]
made without yeast and brushed with olive oil.[f] 5 If your grain offering is prepared
on a griddle,[g] it is to be made of the finest
flour mixed with oil, and without yeast.
6 Crumble it and pour oil on it; it is a grain
offering. 7 If your grain offering is cooked
in a pan,[h] it is to be made of the finest
flour and some olive oil. 8 Bring the grain
offering made of these things to the LORD;

1:15 [n]Lev 5:9 **1:16** [o]Lev 4:12; 6:10; Nu 4:13 **1:17** [p]S Ge 15:10 [q]S ver 7 **2:1** [r]S Ex 29:41; Lev 6:14-18 [s]Ex 29:2, 40; Lev 5:11 [t]Nu 15:4; 28:5 [u]S Ex 29:2; Lev 7:12 [v]ver 2, 15,16; Lev 24:7; Ne 13:9; Isa 43:23 **2:2** [w]Lev 5:11 [x]Lev 6:15; Isa 1:13; 65:3; 66:3 [y]ver 9,16; Lev 5:12; 6:15; 24:7; Nu 5:26; 18:8; Ps 16:5; 73:26; Isa 53:12 [z]ver 16 [a]S Lev 1:9 **2:3** [b]ver 10; Lev 6:16; 10:12, 13 [c]S Ex 30:36 **2:4** [d]Lev 7:9; 26:26 [e]Lev 7:12; 8:26 [f]S Ex 29:2 **2:5** [g]Lev 6:21; 7:9; Eze 4:3 **2:7** [h]Lev 7:9 **2:9** [i]S ver 2 [j]S Ge 8:21 **2:10** [k]ver 3 [l]Ezr 2:63 **2:11** [m]S Ex 23:18; Lev 6:16 **2:12** [n]S Ex 34:22 **2:13** [o]Mk 9:49 [p]Nu 18:19; 2Ch 13:5; Eze 43:24 **2:14** [q]S Ex 34:22; Nu 15:20; Dt 16:13; 26:2; Ru 3:2 **2:15** [r]S ver 1

present it to the priest, who shall take it
to the altar. 9 He shall take out the memorial portion[i] from the grain offering and
burn it on the altar as a food offering, an
aroma pleasing to the LORD.[j] 10 The rest of
the grain offering belongs to Aaron and
his sons;[k] it is a most holy part of the food
offerings presented to the LORD.[l]

11 "'Every grain offering you bring to
the LORD must be made without yeast,[m]
for you are not to burn any yeast or honey
in a food offering presented to the LORD.
12 You may bring them to the LORD as an
offering of the firstfruits,[n] but they are not
to be offered on the altar as a pleasing aroma. 13 Season all your grain offerings with
salt.[o] Do not leave the salt of the covenant[p]
of your God out of your grain offerings;
add salt to all your offerings.

14 "'If you bring a grain offering of firstfruits[q] to the LORD, offer crushed heads of
new grain roasted in the fire. 15 Put oil and
incense[r] on it; it is a grain offering. 16 The
priest shall burn the memorial portion[s]
of the crushed grain and the oil, together with all the incense,[t] as a food offering
presented to the LORD.[u]

The Fellowship Offering

3 "'If your offering is a fellowship offering,[v] and you offer an animal from
the herd, whether male or female, you
are to present before the LORD an animal

[a] 16 Or *crop with its contents*; the meaning of the Hebrew for this word is uncertain.
[b] 2 Or *representative*; also in verses 9 and 16

2:16 [s]S ver 2 [t]S ver 1 [u]Nu 4:16; Jer 14:12 **3:1** [v]S ver 6; S Ex 32:6; Lev 7:11-34; S 17:5

1:17 *not dividing it completely.* See note on Ge 15:10.

2:1 *grain offering.* See further priestly regulations in 6:14–23; 7:9–10. It was made of grain or fine flour. If baked or cooked, it consisted of cakes or wafers made in a pan or oven or on a griddle. It was the only bloodless offering, but it was to accompany the burnt offering (see Nu 28:3–6), sin offering (see Nu 6:14–15) and fellowship offering (see 9:4; Nu 6:17). The amounts of grain offering ingredients specified to accompany a bull, ram or lamb sacrificed as a burnt offering are given in Nu 28:12–13. A representative handful of flour was to be burned on the altar with the accompanying offerings, and the balance was to be baked without yeast and eaten by the priests in their holy meals (6:14–17). The flour that was burned on the altar was mixed with olive oil for shortening, salted for taste and accompanied by incense, but it was to have no yeast or honey—neither of which was allowed on the altar (vv. 11–13). The worshiper was not to eat any of the grain offering, and the priests were not to eat any of their own grain offerings, which were to be totally burned (6:22–23). The Hebrew word for grain offering can mean "present" or "gift" and is often used in that way (see Ge 43:11). The sacred gifts expressed devotion to God (see v. 2). *finest flour.* Grain that was milled and sifted. *oil.* Olive oil is often mentioned in connection with grain and new wine as fresh products of the harvest (see Dt 7:13). Used extensively in cooking, it was a suitable part of the worshiper's gift. *incense.* Frankincense was the chief ingredient (see Ex 30:34–35).

2:2,9,16 *memorial portion.* Either (1) to remind the worshiper that all good things come from the Lord (cf. Jas 1:17) or (2) to cause the Lord to "remember" and bless the offerer in covenant faithfulness (cf. Ge 9:13–16). It may have been a combination of both. See also 5:12; 6:15; 24:7.

2:3 *most holy part.* For this reason, the priests were to eat it in the sanctuary area proper and not feed their families with it (6:16–18). See also v. 10. *holy.* See Ex 29:37 and note.

2:4 *without yeast.* See notes on Ex 12:8,15.

2:5 *griddle.* A clay pan that rested on a stone heated by a fire. Later, iron pans were sometimes used.

2:11 *honey.* It was forbidden on the altar, perhaps because of its use in brewing beer (as an aid to fermentation), though some suggest that it was because of its use in Canaanite cultic practice.

2:12 *firstfruits.* See 23:10–11; Ex 23:16,19; Nu 15:18–20; Dt 18:4–5; 26:1–11.

2:13 *salt of the covenant.* See note on Nu 18:19.

3:1 *fellowship offering.* See further priestly regulations in 7:11–21,28–34. Two basic ideas are included in this offering: peace and fellowship. The traditional translation is "peace offering," a name that comes from the Hebrew word for the offering, which in turn is related to the Hebrew word *shalom*, meaning "peace" or "wholeness." Thus the offering

without defect.[w] 2 You are to lay your hand
on the head[x] of your offering and slaughter
it[y] at the entrance to the tent of meeting.[z]
Then Aaron's sons the priests shall splash[a]
the blood against the sides[b] of the altar.[c]
3 From the fellowship offering you are to
bring a food offering to the LORD: the internal organs[d] and all the fat[e] that is connected to them, 4 both kidneys[f] with the fat
on them near the loins, and the long lobe
of the liver, which you will remove with
the kidneys. 5 Then Aaron's sons[g] are to
burn it on the altar[h] on top of the burnt offering[i] that is lying on the burning wood;[j]
it is a food offering, an aroma pleasing to
the LORD.[k]

6 " 'If you offer an animal from the flock
as a fellowship offering[l] to the LORD, you
are to offer a male or female without defect. 7 If you offer a lamb,[m] you are to present it before the LORD,[n] 8 lay your hand on
its head and slaughter it[o] in front of the
tent of meeting. Then Aaron's sons shall
splash its blood against the sides of the altar. 9 From the fellowship offering you are
to bring a food offering[p] to the LORD: its
fat, the entire fat tail cut off close to the
backbone, the internal organs and all the
fat that is connected to them, 10 both kidneys with the fat on them near the loins,
and the long lobe of the liver, which you
will remove with the kidneys. 11 The priest
shall burn them on the altar[q] as a food offering[r] presented to the LORD.[s]

12 " 'If your offering is a goat,[t] you are to
present it before the LORD, 13 lay your hand
on its head and slaughter it in front of the
tent of meeting. Then Aaron's sons shall
splash[u] its blood against the sides of the
altar.[v] 14 From what you offer you are to
present this food offering to the LORD: the
internal organs and all the fat that is connected to them, 15 both kidneys with the
fat on them near the loins, and the long
lobe of the liver, which you will remove
with the kidneys.[w] 16 The priest shall burn
them on the altar[x] as a food offering,[y] a
pleasing aroma.[z] All the fat[a] is the LORD's.[b]

17 " 'This is a lasting ordinance[c] for the
generations to come,[d] wherever you live:[e]
You must not eat any fat or any blood.[f] ' "

The Sin Offering

4 The LORD said to Moses, 2 "Say to the
Israelites: 'When anyone sins unintentionally[g] and does what is forbidden in
any of the LORD's commands[h] —

3 " 'If the anointed priest[i] sins,[j] bringing
guilt on the people, he must bring to the
LORD a young bull[k] without defect[l] as a sin
offering[a][m] for the sin he has committed.[n]
4 He is to present the bull at the entrance
to the tent of meeting before the LORD.[o]
He is to lay his hand on its head and

[a] 3 Or *purification offering*; here and throughout this chapter

3:1 [w] S Ex 12:5 **3:2** [x] S Ex 29:15; Nu 8:10 [y] S Lev 1:5 [z] S Ex 40:2 [a] S Ex 24:6 [b] S Ex 29:20 [c] Lev 17:6; Nu 18:17 **3:3** [d] S Ex 12:9 [e] S Ex 29:13 **3:4** [f] ver 10; Ex 29:13; Lev 4:9 **3:5** [g] Lev 7:29-34 [h] ver 11, 16 [i] Ex 29:13, 38-42; Nu 28:3-10 [j] S Lev 1:7 [k] S Lev 1:9 **3:6** [l] S ver 1; Lev 22:21; Nu 15:3, 8 **3:7** [m] Lev 17:3; Nu 15:5; 28:5, 7, 8 [n] Lev 17:8-9; 1Ki 8:62 **3:8** [o] S Lev 1:5 **3:9** [p] Isa 34:6; Jer 46:10; Eze 39:19; Zep 1:7 **3:11** [q] S ver 5 [r] ver 16; Lev 21:6, 17; Nu 28:2 [s] Lev 9:18 **3:12** [t] S Lev 1:10; S 4:3 **3:13** [u] S Ex 24:6 [v] Lev 1:5 **3:15** [w] Lev 7:4 **3:16** [x] S ver 5; Lev 7:31 [y] S ver 11 [z] S Lev 1:9 [a] S Ge 4:4 [b] 1Sa 2:16 **3:17** [c] S Ex 12:14; S 27:21 [d] S Ge 9:12 [e] S Ex 12:20 [f] Ge 9:4; Lev 7:25-26; 17:10-16; Dt 12:16; Ac 15:20 **4:2** [g] ver 13, 27; Lev 5:15-18; 22:14; Nu 15:24-29; 35:11-15; Jos 20:3, 9; Heb 9:7 [h] ver 22; Nu 15:22 **4:3** [i] S Ex 28:41 [j] S Ge 18:23 [k] ver 14; Lev 3:12; 8:14; 10:16; 16:3, 5; Nu 15:27; Ps 66:15; Eze 43:19, 23 [l] S Ex 12:5 [m] S ver 24; S Ex 30:10; Lev 5:6-13; 9:2-22; Heb 9:13-14 [n] ver 32 **4:4** [o] ver 15, 24; Lev 1:3; Nu 8:12

perhaps symbolized peace between God and his people, as well as the inward peace that resulted. The fellowship offering was the only sacrifice of which the offerer might eat a part. Fellowship was involved because the offerer, on the basis of the sacrifice, had fellowship with God and with the priest, who also ate part of the offering (7:14–15,31–34). This sacrifice — along with others — was offered by the thousands during the three annual festivals in Israel (see Ex 23:14–17; Nu 29:39) because multitudes of people came to the temple to worship and share in a communal meal. During the monarchy, the animals offered by the people were usually supplemented by large numbers given by the king (1Ki 8:63–65).

3:2 *lay your hand on.* See notes on 1:3; Ex 29:10.

3:5 *on top of the burnt offering.* The burnt offerings for the nation as a whole were offered every morning and evening, and the fellowship offerings were offered on top of them.

3:9 *fat tail.* A breed of sheep still much used in the Middle East has a tail heavy with fat.

3:11,16 *on the altar as a food offering.* Israelite sacrifices were not "food to the idols" (as in other ancient cultures; see Eze 16:20; cf. Ps 50:9–13) but were sometimes called "food" metaphorically (21:6,8,17,21; 22:25) in the sense that they were gifts to God, which he received with delight.

3:16 *All the fat is the LORD's.* Because it signified the best (see 7:23; Ge 4:3–4; Ex 29:13 and notes).

3:17 *not eat any fat or any blood.* See note on 17:11.

4:2 *unintentionally.* See 5:15; contrast Nu 15:30–31. Four classes of people involved in committing unintentional sins are listed: (1) "the anointed priest" (vv. 3–12), (2) the "whole Israelite community" (vv. 13–21), (3) a "leader" (vv. 22–26) and (4) a "member of the community" (vv. 27–35). Heb 9:7 speaks of sins "committed in ignorance" in referring to the Day of Atonement.

4:3 *anointed priest.* The high priest (see 6:20,22). *sins.* All high priests sinned except the high priest Jesus Christ (Heb 5:1–3; 7:26–28). *on the people.* The relationship of the priests to the people was so intimate in Israel (as a nation consecrated to God) that the people became guilty when the priest sinned. *must.* Although the burnt, grain and fellowship offerings (chs. 1–3) were voluntary, the sin offering was compulsory (see vv. 14,23,28). *without defect.* A defective sacrifice could not be a substitute for a defective people (see Mal 1:8 and note). The final perfect sacrifice for the sins of God's people was the crucified Christ, who was without any moral defect (Heb 9:13–14; 1Pe 1:19). *sin offering.* See further priestly regulations in 6:24–30; Nu 15:22–29. As soon as an "anointed priest" (or a person from one of the other classes of people) became aware of unintentional sin, he was to bring his sin offering to the Lord. On the other hand, if the priest (or others) should remain unaware of unintentional sin, this lack was atoned for on the Day of Atonement.

4:4 Three principles of atonement are found in this verse: (1) substitution ("present the bull"), (2) identification ("lay his hand on its head") and (3) the death of the substitute ("slaughter it").

Model of man slaughtering a bull (Egyptian, 2200 BC). The sin offering required a young bull without defect (Lev 4:3).

Kim Walton, courtesy of the Oriental Institute Museum

slaughter it there before the LORD. 5 Then
he anointed priest shall take some of the
oull's blood[p] and carry it into the tent of
neeting. 6 He is to dip his finger into the
olood and sprinkle[q] some of it seven times
oefore the LORD,[r] in front of the curtain of
he sanctuary.[s] 7 The priest shall then put
some of the blood on the horns[t] of the al-
ar of fragrant incense that is before the
LORD in the tent of meeting. The rest of
he bull's blood he shall pour out at the
oase of the altar[u] of burnt offering[v] at the
ntrance to the tent of meeting. 8 He shall
emove all the fat[w] from the bull of the
in offering—all the fat that is connect-
d to the internal organs, 9 both kidneys
vith the fat on them near the loins, and
the long lobe of the liver, which he will
remove with the kidneys[x]— 10 just as the
fat is removed from the ox[a][y] sacrificed as a
fellowship offering.[z] Then the priest shall
burn them on the altar of burnt offering.[a]
11 But the hide of the bull and all its flesh,
as well as the head and legs, the internal
organs and the intestines[b]— 12 that is, all
the rest of the bull—he must take outside
the camp[c] to a place ceremonially clean,[d]
where the ashes[e] are thrown, and burn it[f]
there in a wood fire on the ash heap.[g]
13 " 'If the whole Israelite community sins
unintentionally[h] and does what is forbidden in any of the LORD's commands, even
though the community is unaware of the
matter, when they realize their guilt 14 and
the sin they committed becomes known,
the assembly must bring a young bull[i] as a
sin offering[j] and present it before the tent of
meeting. 15 The elders[k] of the community are
to lay their hands[l] on the bull's head[m] before the LORD, and the bull shall be slaughtered before the LORD.[n] 16 Then the anointed
priest is to take some of the bull's blood[o]
into the tent of meeting. 17 He shall dip his
finger into the blood and sprinkle[p] it before
the LORD[q] seven times in front of the curtain. 18 He is to put some of the blood[r] on
the horns of the altar that is before the LORD[s]
in the tent of meeting. The rest of the blood
he shall pour out at the base of the altar[t]
of burnt offering at the entrance to the tent
of meeting. 19 He shall remove all the fat[u]
from it and burn it on the altar,[v] 20 and do
with this bull just as he did with the bull for

4:5 [p] ver 16; Lev 16:14 **4:6** [q] Ex 24:8 [r] ver 17; Lev 16:14,19 [s] S Ex 25:8 **4:7** [t] S Ex 27:2 [u] ver 34; S Ex 29:12; Lev 8:15 [v] ver 18,30; Lev 5:9; 9:9; 16:18 **4:8** [w] ver 19 **4:9** [x] S Lev 3:4 **4:10** [y] Lev 9:4 [z] S Ex 32:6 [a] S Ex 29:13 **4:11** [b] Ex 29:14; Lev 8:17; 9:11; Nu 19:5 **4:12** [c] S Ex 29:14; Lev 8:17; 9:11; Heb 13:11 [d] Lev 6:11; 10:14; Nu 19:9 [e] S Lev 1:16 [f] Lev 6:30 [g] Lev 16:3 **4:13** [h] S ver 2 **4:14** [i] S ver 3 [j] Nu 15:24 **4:15** [k] S Ex 3:16; S 19:7 [l] 2Ch 29:23 [m] S Ex 29:10; Lev 8:14, 22; Nu 8:10 [n] S ver 4 **4:16** [o] S ver 5 **4:17** [p] Nu 19:4, 18 [q] S ver 6 **4:18** [r] Lev 8:15; 17:6; 2Ch 29:22 [s] ver 7; Lev 6:30; 10:18 [t] Lev 5:9 **4:19** [u] ver 8 [v] ver 26

[a] *10* The Hebrew word can refer to either male or female.

4:5 *blood.* See note on 17:11. There were two types of sin offerings. The first (vv. 3–21) and more important vas offered by and for a priest or by the elders for the whole ommunity. It involved sprinkling the blood in the taberna- le in front of the inner curtain or, in the case of the solemn ay of Atonement (ch. 16), on and in front of the atonement over (traditionally "mercy seat") itself. This type of sin offer- ng was not eaten. The fat, kidneys and covering of the liver vere burned on the altar of burnt offering, but all the rest vas burned outside the camp (v. 12). Heb 13:11–13 clearly raws the parallel to our sin offering, Jesus, who suffered out- ide the city gate. In general, the animal to be sacrificed was young bull, but on the Day of Atonement the sin offering as to be a goat (16:9).

The second type of sin offering (4:22—5:13) was for a ader of the nation or a private individual. Some of the blood as applied to the horns of the altar; the rest was poured ut at its base. The fat, kidneys and covering of the liver were urned on the altar, but the rest of the offering was given the priest and his male relatives as food to be eaten in a oly place (6:29–30; see 10:16–20). The sin offering brought y a private person was to be a female goat or lamb. If such ersons were poor, they could bring a dove or young pigeon :7–8; 12:6,8; cf. Lk 2:24), or even about two quarts of flour :11). The offering included confession (5:5) and the sym- bolic transfer of guilt by laying hands on the sacrifice (v. 29; 16:21). Then the priest who offered the sacrifice made atone- ment for the sin, and the Lord promised forgiveness (5:13). By bringing such a sin offering, a faithful Israelite under convic- tion of sin sought restoration of fellowship with God.

4:6 *finger.* The right forefinger (see 14:16). *seven.* The number was symbolic of perfection and completeness (see note on Ge 5:5). *curtain.* The shielding curtain that separated the Holy Place from the Most Holy Place (see Ex 26:33 and note on 26:31).

4:7,30 *horns.* The four horns of the altar (see Ex 30:1–3) were symbols of the atoning power of the sin offering (Ex 30:10).

4:8–10 See 3:3–5.

4:12 *outside the camp.* See note on 13:45–46. So also Jesus was crucified outside Jerusalem (Heb 13:11–13; cf. Lev 9:11; 16:26–28; Nu 19:3; Eze 43:21). *ceremonially clean.* The distinction between clean and unclean was a matter of ritual or religious purity, not a concern for physical cleanli- ness (see chs. 11–15 for examples; see also Mk 7:1–4). *burn.* Since the sins of the offerer were symbolically transferred to the sacrificial bull, the bull had to be entirely destroyed and not thrown on the ash pile of 1:16.

4:15 *elders.* See note on Ex 3:16.

4:18 *altar.* Of incense (see v. 7).

4:20 *sin offering.* The offering of the priest who had sinned (see v. 3 and note). *will be forgiven.* In 4:20—6:7 this is a key

the sin offering. In this way the priest will
make atonement[w] for the community, and
they will be forgiven.[x] 21 Then he shall take
the bull outside the camp[y] and burn it as he
burned the first bull. This is the sin offering
for the community.[z]

22 " 'When a leader[a] sins unintentionally[b]
and does what is forbidden in any of the
commands of the LORD his God, when he
realizes his guilt 23 and the sin he has committed becomes known, he must bring
as his offering a male goat[c] without defect. 24 He is to lay his hand on the goat's
head and slaughter it at the place where
the burnt offering is slaughtered before
the LORD.[d] It is a sin offering.[e] 25 Then the
priest shall take some of the blood of the
sin offering with his finger and put it on
the horns of the altar[f] of burnt offering and

4:20 [w] S Ex 29:36; S 32:30; S Ro 3:25; Heb 10:10-12 [x] ver 26, 31, 35; Nu 15:25 **4:21** [y] S ver 12 [z] Lev 16:5, 15; 2Ch 29:21 **4:22** [a] Nu 31:13 [b] ver 2 **4:23** [c] S ver 3; S Lev 1:10 **4:24** [d] S ver 4 [e] S ver 3; Lev 6:25 **4:25** [f] Lev 16:18; Eze 43:20, 22

phrase, occurring nine times and referring to forgiveness by God.
4:23 *male goat.* Less valuable animals were sacrificed for those with lesser standing in the community or of lesser economic means. Thus a bull was required for the high priest (v. 3) and the whole community (v. 14), but a male goat for a civic leader (here) and a female goat (v. 28) or lamb (v. 32) fo[r] an ordinary Israelite. If an offerer was too poor, then doves and pigeons were sufficient (5:7) or even a handful of finest flour (see 5:11 – 12 and note on 5:11).
4:25 *priest.* The priest who officiated for the civil authority o[r] the lay person (see vv. 30,34).

OLD TESTAMENT **SACRIFICES**

SACRIFICE	OT REFERENCES	ELEMENTS	PURPOSE
Burnt Offering	Lev 1; 6:8–13; 8:18–21; 16:24	Bull, ram or male bird (dove or young pigeon for the poor); wholly consumed; no defect	Voluntary act of worship; atonement for unintentional sin in general; expression of devotion, commitment and complete surrender to God
Grain Offering	Lev 2; 6:14–23	Grain, finest flour, olive oil, incense, baked bread (cakes or wafers), salt; no yeast or honey; accompanied burnt offering and fellowship offering (along with drink offering)	Voluntary act of worship; recognition of God's goodness and provisions; devotion to God
Fellowship Offering	Lev 3; 7:11–34	Any animal without defect from herd or flock; variety of breads	Voluntary act of worship; thanksgiving and fellowship (it included a communal meal)
Sin Offering	Lev 4:1—5:13; 6:24–30; 8:14–17; 16:3–22	1. Young bull: for high priest and congregation 2. Male goat: for leader 3. Female goat or lamb: for common person 4. Dove or pigeon: for the poor 5. Tenth of an ephah of finest flour: for the very poor	Mandatory atonement for specific unintentional sin; confession of sin; forgiveness of sin; cleansing from defilement
Guilt Offering	Lev 5:14—6:7; 7:1–6	Ram	Mandatory atonement for unintentional sin requiring restitution; cleansing from defilement; make restitution; pay 20% fine

When more than one kind of offering was presented (as in Nu 7:13–17), the procedure was usually as follows: (1) sin offering or guilt offering, (2) burnt offering, (3) fellowship offering and grain offering (along with a drink offering). This sequence furnishes part of the spiritual significance of the sacrificial system. First, sin had to be dealt with (sin offering or guilt offering). Second, the worshipers committed themselves completely to God (burnt offering and grain offering). Third, fellowship or communion between the Lord, the priest and the worshiper (fellowship offering) was established. To state it another way, there were sacrifices of expiation (sin offerings and guilt offerings), consecration (burnt offerings and grain offerings) and communion (fellowship offerings—these included vow offerings, thank offerings and freewill offerings).

pour out the rest of the blood at the base of the altar.[g] 26 He shall burn all the fat on the altar as he burned the fat of the fellowship offering. In this way the priest will make atonement[h] for the leader's sin, and he will be forgiven.[i]

27 " 'If any member of the community sins unintentionally[j] and does what is forbidden in any of the LORD's commands, when they realize their guilt 28 and the sin they have committed becomes known, they must bring as their offering[k] for the sin they committed a female goat[l] without defect. 29 They are to lay their hand on the head[m] of the sin offering[n] and slaughter it at the place of the burnt offering.[o] 30 Then the priest is to take some of the blood with his finger and put it on the horns of the altar of burnt offering[p] and pour out the rest of the blood at the base of the altar. 31 They shall remove all the fat, just as the fat is removed from the fellowship offering, and the priest shall burn it on the altar[q] as an aroma pleasing to the LORD.[r] In this way the priest will make atonement[s] for them, and they will be forgiven.[t]

32 " 'If someone brings a lamb[u] as their sin offering, they are to bring a female without defect.[v] 33 They are to lay their hand on its head and slaughter it[w] for a sin offering[x] at the place where the burnt offering is slaughtered.[y] 34 Then the priest shall take some of the blood of the sin offering with his finger and put it on the horns of the altar of burnt offering and pour out the rest of the blood at the base of the altar.[z] 35 They shall remove all the fat, just as the fat is removed from the lamb of the fellowship offering, and the priest shall burn it on the altar[a] on top of the food offerings presented to the LORD. In this way the priest will make atonement for them for the sin they have committed, and they will be forgiven.

5 " 'If anyone sins because they do not speak up when they hear a public charge to testify[b] regarding something they have seen or learned about, they will be held responsible.[c]

2 " 'If anyone becomes aware that they are guilty — if they unwittingly touch anything ceremonially unclean (whether the carcass of an unclean animal, wild or domestic, or of any unclean creature that moves along the ground)[d] and they are unaware that they have become unclean,[e] but then they come to realize their guilt; 3 or if they touch human uncleanness[f] (anything that would make them unclean)[g] even though they are unaware of it, but then they learn of it and realize their guilt; 4 or if anyone thoughtlessly takes an oath[h] to do anything, whether good or evil[i] (in any matter one might carelessly swear about) even though they are unaware of it, but then they learn of it and realize their guilt — 5 when anyone becomes aware that they are guilty in any of these matters, they must confess[j] in what way they have sinned. 6 As a penalty for the sin they have committed, they must bring to the LORD a female lamb or goat[k] from the flock as a sin offering[a];[l] and the priest shall make atonement[m] for them for their sin.

7 " 'Anyone who cannot afford[n] a lamb[o] is to bring two doves or two young pigeons[p] to the LORD as a penalty for their sin — one for a sin offering and the other for a burnt offering. 8 They are to bring them to the priest, who shall first offer the one for the sin offering. He is to wring its head from its neck,[q] not dividing it completely,[r] 9 and is to splash[s] some of the blood of the sin offering against the side of the altar;[t] the rest of the blood must be drained out at the base of the altar.[u] It is a sin offering. 10 The priest shall then offer the other as a burnt offering in the prescribed way[v] and make atonement[w] for them for the sin they have committed, and they will be forgiven.[x]

11 " 'If, however, they cannot afford[y] two doves or two young pigeons,[z] they are to bring as an offering for their sin a tenth of an ephah[b][a] of the finest flour[b] for a sin offering. They must not put olive oil or incense on it, because it is a sin offering. 12 They are to bring it to the priest, who shall take a handful of it as a memorial[c] portion[c] and burn it on the altar[d] on top of the food offerings presented to the LORD. It is a sin offering. 13 In this way the priest

[a] 6 Or *purification offering*; here and throughout this chapter [b] 11 That is, probably about 3 1/2 pounds or about 1.6 kilograms [c] 12 Or *representative*

4:25 [g] Lev 9:9 **4:26** [h] S Ex 32:30 [i] Lev 5:10; 12:8 **4:27** [j] S ver 2 **4:28** [k] Lev 5:6; Eze 40:39; 44:27 [l] S ver 3; S Lev 1:10 **4:29** [m] ver 4, 24 [n] S Lev 1:4 [o] S Ge 8:20 **4:30** [p] S ver 7 **4:31** [q] ver 35 [r] S Ge 8:21 [s] Lev 1:4 [t] S ver 20 **4:32** [u] Ex 29:38; Lev 9:3; 14:10 [v] Lev 1:3 **4:33** [w] Lev 1:5 [x] Lev 1:4 [y] ver 29 **4:34** [z] S ver 7 **4:35** [a] ver 31 **5:1** [b] Pr 29:24; Mt 26:63 [c] ver 17; S Ex 28:38; Lev 7:18; 17:16; 19:8; 20:17; 24:15; Nu 5:31; 9:13; 15:31; 19:20; 30:15 **5:2** [d] Lev 11:11, 24-40; Dt 14:8; Isa 52:11 [e] ver 3; Lev 7:21; 11:8, 24; 13:45; Nu 19:22; Job 15:16; Ps 51:5; Isa 6:5; 64:6; Eze 36:17; Hag 2:13 **5:3** [f] Nu 19:11-16 [g] Lev 7:20; 11:25; 14:19; 21:1; Nu 5:2; 9:6; 19:7; Eze 44:25 **5:4** [h] Nu 30:6,8 [i] Isa 41:23 **5:5** [j] Lev 16:21; 26:40; Nu 5:7; Jos 7:19; 1Ki 8:47; Pr 28:13 **5:6** [k] S Lev 1:10; S 4:3 [l] S Lev 4:28 [m] S Ex 32:30 **5:7** [n] ver 11; Lev 12:8; 14:21; 27:8 [o] Lev 12:8; 14:22,30 [p] S Ge 15:9; Nu 6:10 **5:8** [q] Lev 1:15 [r] Lev 1:17 **5:9** [s] S Ex 24:6 [t] Lev 1:15 [u] S Lev 4:7 **5:10** [v] Lev 1:14-17; 1Ch 15:13 [w] S Ex 32:30 [x] S Lev 4:26 **5:11** [y] S ver 7 [z] S Ge 15:9 [a] S Ex 16:36 [b] S Lev 2:1 **5:12** [c] S Lev 2:2 [d] Lev 2:9

:28 *female goat.* See note on v. 23.
:29 *lay their hand on.* See notes on 1:3; Ex 29:10.
:32 *lamb ... female.* See note on v. 23.
:35 *fat ... of the fellowship offering.* See 3:3 – 5.
:1 – 4 Four examples of the unintentional sins (see 4:2 – 3,13, 2,27) the sin offering covers.
:2 *ceremonially unclean.* See note on 4:12.
:3 *human uncleanness.* See chs. 11 – 15.

5:5 *confess.* The offerers had to acknowledge their sin to God in order to receive forgiveness (cf. Pr 28:13 and note).
5:7 *two doves ... pigeons.* See note on 4:23.
5:11 *finest flour.* See note on 4:23. Although no blood was used with a flour offering, it was offered "on top of the food offerings presented to the LORD" (v. 12). Heb 9:22 may refer to such a situation.
5:12 *memorial portion.* See note on 2:2,9,16.

will make atonement[e] for them for any of these sins they have committed, and they will be forgiven. The rest of the offering will belong to the priest,[f] as in the case of the grain offering.[g]’ ”

The Guilt Offering

14 The LORD said to Moses: 15 “When anyone is unfaithful to the LORD by sinning unintentionally[h] in regard to any of the LORD’s holy things, they are to bring to the LORD as a penalty[i] a ram[j] from the flock, one without defect and of the proper value in silver, according to the sanctuary shekel.[a][k] It is a guilt offering.[l] 16 They must make restitution[m] for what they have failed to do in regard to the holy things, pay an additional penalty of a fifth of its value[n] and give it all to the priest. The priest will make atonement for them with the ram as a guilt offering, and they will be forgiven.

17 “If anyone sins and does what is forbidden in any of the LORD’s commands, even though they do not know it,[o] they are guilty and will be held responsible.[p] 18 They are to bring to the priest as a guilt offering[q] a ram from the flock, one without defect and of the proper value. In this way the priest will make atonement for them for the wrong they have committed unintentionally, and they will be forgiven.[r] 19 It is a guilt offering; they have been guilty of[b] wrongdoing against the LORD.”[s]

6 [c] The LORD said to Moses: 2 “If anyone sins and is unfaithful to the LORD[t] by deceiving a neighbor[u] about something entrusted to them or left in their care[v] or about something stolen, or if they cheat[w] their neighbor, 3 or if they find lost property and lie about it,[x] or if they swear falsely[y] about any such sin that people may commit— 4 when they sin in any of these ways and realize their guilt, they must return[z] what they have stolen or taken by extortion, or what was entrusted to them, or the lost property they found, 5 or whatever it was they swore falsely about. They must make restitution[a] in full, add a fifth of the value to it and give it all to the owner on the day they present their guilt offering.[b] 6 And as a penalty they must bring to the priest, that is, to the LORD, their guilt offering,[c] a ram from the flock, one without defect and of the proper value.[d] 7 In this way the priest will make atonement[e] for them before the LORD, and they will be forgiven for any of the things they did that made them guilty.”

The Burnt Offering

8 The LORD said to Moses: 9 “Give Aaron and his sons this command: ‘These are the regulations for the burnt offering[f]: The burnt offering is to remain on the altar hearth throughout the night, till morning, and the fire must be kept burning on the altar.[g] 10 The priest shall then put on his linen clothes,[h] with linen undergarments next to his body,[i] and shall remove the ashes[j] of the burnt offering that the fire has consumed on the altar and place them beside the altar. 11 Then he is to take off these clothes and put on others, and carry the ashes outside the camp to a place that is ceremonially clean.[k] 12 The fire on the altar must be kept burning; it must not go out. Every morning the priest is to add firewood[l] and arrange the burnt offering on the fire and burn the fat[m] of the fellowship offerings[n] on it. 13 The fire must be kept burning on the altar continuously; it must not go out.

The Grain Offering

14 “ ‘These are the regulations for the grain offering:[o] Aaron’s sons are to bring it before the LORD, in front of the altar. 15 The priest is to take a handful of the finest flour and some olive oil, together with all the incense[p] on the grain offering,[q] and burn the memorial[d] portion[r] on the altar as an aroma pleasing to the LORD.

5:13 [e] S Ex 32:30 [f] Lev 2:3 [g] S Ex 29:41 **5:15** [h] S Lev 4:2 [i] Lev 22:14 [j] S Ex 29:3; Lev 6:6; Nu 5:8; 6:14; 15:6; 28:11 [k] S Ex 30:13 [l] ver 16, 18; Lev 6:5,6; 7:1,7; 14:12-17; 19:21, 22; Nu 6:12; 18:9; 1Sa 6:3; Ezr 10:19; Isa 53:10 **5:16** [m] Lev 6:4 [n] ver 15; Lev 27:13; Nu 5:7 **5:17** [o] ver 15 [p] S ver 1 **5:18** [q] Lev 6:6; 14:12 [r] S ver 15 **5:19** [s] 2Ki 12:16 **6:2** [t] Nu 5:6; Ps 73:27; Ac 5:4; Col 3:9 [u] Lev 19:11; Jer 9:4,5 [v] S Ex 22:7 [w] S Ge 31:7 **6:3** [x] S Ex 23:4 [y] S Ex 22:11 **6:4** [z] Lev 5:16; Eze 33:15; S Lk 19:8 **6:5** [a] Nu 5:7 [b] S Lev 5:15 **6:6** [c] S Lev 5:15 [d] Nu 5:8 **6:7** [e] S Ex 32:30 **6:9** [f] Lev 7:37 [g] ver 12 **6:10** [h] S Ex 39:27 [i] Ex 28:39-42, 43; 39:28 [j] S Lev 1:16 **6:11** [k] S Lev 4:12 **6:12** [l] S Lev 1:7 [m] S Ex 29:13 [n] S Ex 32:6 **6:14** [o] S Lev 2:1; Nu 6:15; 15:4; 28:13 **6:15** [p] S Lev 2:1 [q] Lev 2:9 [r] S Lev 2:2

[a] *15* That is, about 2/5 ounce or about 12 grams
[b] *19* Or *offering; atonement has been made for their*
[c] In Hebrew texts 6:1-7 is numbered 5:20-26, and 6:8-30 is numbered 6:1-23.
[d] *15* Or *representative*

5:15 *LORD's holy things.* See note on Ex 3:5. *according to the sanctuary shekel.* See note on Ex 30:13. *guilt offering.* See further priestly regulations in 7:1 – 6 (see also Isa 53:10 and note, as well as chart, p. 164). Traditionally called the "trespass offering," it was very similar to the sin offering (cf. 7:7), and the Hebrew words for the two were apparently sometimes interchanged. The major difference between the guilt and sin offerings was that the guilt offering was brought in cases where restitution for the sin was possible and therefore required (v. 16). Thus, in cases of theft and cheating (6:2 – 5), the stolen property had to be returned along with 20 percent indemnity. By contrast, the sin offering was prescribed in cases of sin where no restitution was possible. The animal sacrificed as a guilt offering was always a ram.

6:3 *lost property.* See Dt 22:1 – 3.
6:6 *to the priest, that is, to the LORD.* Sacrifices were brough to the Lord, but priests were his authorized representatives.
6:8 — 7:36 Further regulations concerning the sacrifices dealing mainly with the portions to be eaten by the priests or, in the case of the fellowship offering, by the one offering the sacrifice.
6:9 *burnt offering.* See ch. 1; Nu 15:1 – 16 and notes.
6:13 The perpetual fire on the altar represented uninterrupted offering to and appeal to God on behalf of Israel.
6:14 *grain offering.* See ch. 2 and notes.
6:15 *memorial portion.* See note on 2:2,9,16.

16 Aaron and his sons[s] shall eat the rest[t] of it, but it is to be eaten without yeast[u] in the sanctuary area;[v] they are to eat it in the courtyard[w] of the tent of meeting.[x] 17 It must not be baked with yeast; I have given it as their share[y] of the food offerings presented to me.[z] Like the sin offering[a] and the guilt offering, it is most holy.[a] 18 Any male descendant of Aaron may eat it.[b] For all generations to come[c] it is his perpetual share[d] of the food offerings presented to the LORD. Whatever touches them will become holy.[b][e]' "

19 The LORD also said to Moses, 20 "This is the offering Aaron and his sons are to bring to the LORD on the day he[c] is anointed:[f] a tenth of an ephah[d][g] of the finest flour[h] as a regular grain offering,[i] half of it in the morning and half in the evening. 21 It must be prepared with oil on a griddle;[j] bring it well-mixed and present the grain offering broken[e] in pieces as an aroma pleasing to the LORD. 22 The son who is to succeed him as anointed priest[k] shall prepare it. It is the LORD's perpetual share and is to be burned completely.[l] 23 Every grain offering of a priest shall be burned completely; it must not be eaten."

The Sin Offering

24 The LORD said to Moses, 25 "Say to Aaron and his sons: 'These are the regulations for the sin offering:[m] The sin offering is to be slaughtered before the LORD[n] in the place[o] the burnt offering is slaughtered; it is most holy. 26 The priest who offers it shall eat it; it is to be eaten in the sanctuary area,[p] in the courtyard[q] of the tent of meeting.[r] 27 Whatever touches any of the flesh will become holy,[s] and if any of the blood is spattered on a garment, you must wash it in the sanctuary area. 28 The clay pot[t] the meat is cooked in must be broken; but if it is cooked in a bronze pot, the pot is to be scoured and rinsed with water. 29 Any male in a priest's family may eat it;[u] it is most holy.[v] 30 But any sin offering whose blood is brought into the tent of meeting to make atonement[w] in the Holy Place[x] must not be eaten; it must be burned up.[y]

The Guilt Offering

7 " 'These are the regulations for the guilt offering,[z] which is most holy: 2 The guilt offering is to be slaughtered in the place where the burnt offering is slaughtered, and its blood is to be splashed against the sides of the altar. 3 All its fat[a] shall be offered: the fat tail and the fat that covers the internal organs, 4 both kidneys with the fat on them near the loins, and the long lobe of the liver, which is to be removed with the kidneys.[b] 5 The priest shall burn them on the altar[c] as a food offering presented to the LORD. It is a guilt offering. 6 Any male in a priest's family may eat it,[d] but it must be eaten in the sanctuary area; it is most holy.[e]

7 " 'The same law applies to both the sin offering[f][f] and the guilt offering:[g] They belong to the priest[h] who makes atonement with them.[i] 8 The priest who offers a burnt offering for anyone may keep its hide[j] for himself. 9 Every grain offering baked in an oven[k] or cooked in a pan[l] or on a griddle[m] belongs to the priest who offers it, 10 and every grain offering, whether mixed with olive oil or dry, belongs equally to all the sons of Aaron.

The Fellowship Offering

11 " 'These are the regulations for the fellowship offering anyone may present to the LORD:

12 " 'If they offer it as an expression of thankfulness, then along with this thank offering[n] they are to offer thick loaves[o] made without yeast[p] and with olive oil mixed in, thin loaves[q] made without yeast and brushed with oil,[r] and thick loaves of the finest flour well-kneaded and with oil mixed in. 13 Along with their fellowship offering of thanksgiving[s] they are to present an offering with thick

[a] *17* Or *purification offering*; also in verses 25 and 30
[b] *18* Or *Whoever touches them must be holy*; similarly in verse 27
[c] *20* Or *each*
[d] *20* That is, probably about 3 1/2 pounds or about 1.6 kilograms
[e] *21* The meaning of the Hebrew for this word is uncertain.
[f] *7* Or *purification offering*; also in verse 37

6:16 [s]S Lev 2:3 [t]Eze 44:29 [u]S Lev 2:11 [v]ver 26; S Ex 29:11; Lev 10:13; 16:24; 24:9; Nu 18:10 [w]S Ex 27:9 [x]Ex 29:31; Lev 8:31 **6:17** [y]Nu 5:9 [z]Ex 29:28; Lev 7:7; 10:16-18 [a]ver 29; Ex 40:10; Lev 10:12; 21:22; 24:9; Nu 18:9,10 **6:18** [b]ver 29; Lev 2:3; 7:6; Nu 18:9-10 [c]S Ge 9:12 [d]Nu 5:9 [e]S Ex 30:29 **6:20** [f]S Ex 28:41 [g]S Ex 16:36 [h]Nu 5:15; 28:5 [i]Ex 29:2; Lev 23:13; Nu 4:16 **6:21** [j]Lev 2:5 **6:22** [k]S Ex 28:41; S 29:30 [l]S Lev 1:9 **6:25** [m]S Ex 30:10; S Lev 4:24 [n]S Lev 1:3 [o]S Ex 29:11 **6:26** [p]S ver 16 [q]S Ex 27:9 [r]S Ex 27:21; S 40:2 **6:27** [s]S Ex 29:37; Lev 10:10; Eze 44:19; 46:20; Hag 2:12 **6:28** [t]Lev 11:33; 15:12; Nu 19:15 **6:29** [u]S ver 18 [v]S ver 17; Eze 42:13 **6:30** [w]Eze 45:15 [x]S Lev 4:18 [y]Lev 4:12

7:1 [z]S Lev 5:15; Eze 40:39 **7:3** [a]S Ex 29:13 **7:4** [b]Lev 3:15 **7:5** [c]S Ex 29:13 **7:6** [d]S Lev 6:18 [e]Eze 42:13 **7:7** [f]S Ex 30:10 [g]S Lev 5:15 [h]ver 6; Lev 2:3; 6:17,26; 14:13; 2Ki 12:16; 1Co 9:13; 10:18 [i]Nu 5:8 **7:8** [j]Lev 1:6 **7:9** [k]S Lev 2:4 [l]Lev 2:7 [m]S Lev 2:5 **7:12** [n]ver 13,15; Lev 22:29; Ps 50:14; 54:6; 107:22; 116:17; Jer 33:11 [o]Jer 44:19 [p]Nu 6:19 [q]S Lev 2:4 [r]S Lev 2:1 **7:13** [s]S ver 12; S Ex 34:22

6:18 *will become holy.* See Ex 29:37 and note.
6:25 *sin offering.* See 4:1—5:13 and notes.
6:28 *clay.* Ordinary kitchen utensils and domestic ware were made of clay, usually fired in a kiln and often painted or burnished.
7:1 *holy.* See note on Ex 3:5.
7:2 *guilt offering.* See 5:14—6:7 and notes. *place.* On the north side of the altar of burnt offering in front of the tabernacle (1:11; see note there).
7:3 *fat tail.* See note on 3:9.
7:7-10 See Nu 18:8-20; 1Co 9:13 and notes.
7:11-36 This section supplements ch. 3, adding regulations about (1) three types of fellowship offerings (thank, vv. 12-15; vow, v. 16; freewill, v. 16), (2) prohibition of eating fat and blood (vv. 22-27) and (3) the priests' share (vv. 28-36).
7:12-15 Thank offerings were given in gratitude for deliverance from sickness (Ps 116:17), trouble (Ps 107:22) or death (Ps 56:12) or for a blessing received.
7:13 *with yeast.* This regulation was not against the prohibition of 2:11 or Ex 23:18 since the offering here was not burned on the altar.

loaves of bread made with yeast.[t] 14 They
are to bring one of each kind as an offering, a contribution to the LORD; it belongs
to the priest who splashes the blood of
the fellowship offering against the altar.
15 The meat of their fellowship offering of
thanksgiving must be eaten on the day it
is offered; they must leave none of it till
morning.[u]
16 " 'If, however, their offering is the result of a vow[v] or is a freewill offering,[w] the
sacrifice shall be eaten on the day they offer it, but anything left over may be eaten
on the next day.[x] 17 Any meat of the sacrifice left over till the third day must be
burned up.[y] 18 If any meat of the fellowship
offering[z] is eaten on the third day, the one
who offered it will not be accepted.[a] It will
not be reckoned[b] to their credit, for it has
become impure; the person who eats any
of it will be held responsible.[c]
19 " 'Meat that touches anything ceremonially unclean must not be eaten; it must
be burned up. As for other meat, anyone
ceremonially clean may eat it. 20 But if anyone who is unclean[d] eats any meat of the
fellowship offering belonging to the LORD,
they must be cut off from their people.[e]
21 Anyone who touches something unclean[f]—whether human uncleanness or
an unclean animal or any unclean creature that moves along the ground*[a]*—and
then eats any of the meat of the fellowship
offering belonging to the LORD must be cut
off from their people.' "

Eating Fat and Blood Forbidden

22 The LORD said to Moses, 23 "Say to the
Israelites: 'Do not eat any of the fat of cattle, sheep or goats.[g] 24 The fat of an animal
found dead or torn by wild animals[h] may
be used for any other purpose, but you
must not eat it. 25 Anyone who eats the fat
of an animal from which a food offering
may be*[b]* presented to the LORD must be cut
off from their people. 26 And wherever you
live, you must not eat the blood[i] of any
bird or animal. 27 Anyone who eats blood[j]
must be cut off from their people.' "

The Priests' Share

28 The LORD said to Moses, 29 "Say to the
Israelites: 'Anyone who brings a fellowship offering to the LORD is to bring part
of it as their sacrifice to the LORD. 30 With
their own hands they are to present the
food offering to the LORD; they are to bring
the fat, together with the breast, and wave
the breast before the LORD as a wave offering.[k] 31 The priest shall burn the fat on
the altar,[l] but the breast belongs to Aaron
and his sons.[m] 32 You are to give the right
thigh of your fellowship offerings to the
priest as a contribution.[n] 33 The son of Aaron who offers the blood and the fat of the
fellowship offering shall have the right
thigh as his share. 34 From the fellowship
offerings of the Israelites, I have taken the
breast that is waved and the thigh[o] that is
presented and have given them to Aaron
the priest and his sons[p] as their perpetual
share from the Israelites.' "
35 This is the portion of the food offerings presented to the LORD that were allotted to Aaron and his sons on the day
they were presented to serve the LORD as
priests. 36 On the day they were anointed,[q]
the LORD commanded that the Israelites
give this to them as their perpetual share
for the generations to come.

37 These, then, are the regulations for
the burnt offering,[r] the grain offering,[s] the
sin offering, the guilt offering, the ordination offering[t] and the fellowship offering,
38 which the LORD gave Moses[u] at Mount
Sinai[v] in the Desert of Sinai on the day he
commanded the Israelites to bring their offerings to the LORD.[w]

7:13 [t] Lev 23:17; Am 4:5 **7:15** [u] S Ex 12:10 **7:16** [v] S Ge 28:20; S Lev 1:2; Dt 23:21-23 [w] Ex 35:29; Lev 22:18,21; 23:38; Nu 15:3; 29:39; Dt 12:6; Ps 54:6; Eze 46:12 [x] Lev 19:5-8 **7:17** [y] Ex 12:10; Lev 19:6 **7:18** [z] 2Ch 33:16 [a] Lev 19:7 [b] Nu 18:27 [c] S Lev 5:1 **7:20** [d] S Lev 5:3 [e] S Ge 17:14; Lev 22:3-7 **7:21** [f] S Lev 5:2 **7:23** [g] Lev 17:13-14; Dt 14:4 **7:24** [h] S Ex 22:31 **7:26** [i] S Ge 9:4 **7:27** [j] S Ge 9:4 **7:30** [k] S Ex 29:24 **7:31** [l] S Ex 29:13 [m] S Ex 29:27 **7:32** [n] Ex 29:27; Lev 10:14,15; Nu 5:9; 6:20; 18:18 **7:34** [o] Ex 29:22; Lev 10:15; Nu 6:20; 1Sa 9:24 [p] S Ex 29:27 **7:36** [q] Lev 8:12, 30 **7:37** [r] Lev 6:9 [s] Lev 6:14 [t] S Ex 29:31 **7:38** [u] Lev 26:46; Nu 36:13; Dt 4:5; 29:1 [v] S Ex 19:11 [w] S Lev 1:2

a 21 A few Hebrew manuscripts, Samaritan Pentateuch, Syriac and Targum (see 5:2); most Hebrew manuscripts *any unclean, detestable thing* *b* 25 Or *offering is*

7:15–18 See 19:5–8. All meat had to be eaten promptly (in the case of the thank offering on the same day and in the case of the vow and freewill offerings within two days). One reason may have been that in Canaan meat spoiled quickly and thus became ceremonially impure (v. 18) because it was not then perfect (1:3; see 21:16–23). The prohibition applied also to the Passover (Ex 12:10).

7:16 *vow.* See 22:18–23. A vow was a solemn promise to offer a gift to God in response to a divine deliverance or blessing. Such vows often accompanied prayers for deliverance or blessing (see note on Ps 7:17; see also Introduction to Psalms: Psalm Types). *freewill offering.* See 22:18–23.

7:19 *ceremonially unclean.* See note on 4:12.

7:20 *cut off from their people.* Removed from the covenant people through direct divine judgment (Ge 17:14), or (as here and in vv. 21,25,27; 17:4,9–10,14; 18:29; 19:8; 20:3,5–6,17–18; 23:29) through execution (see, e.g., 20:2–3; Ex 31:14) or possibly sometimes through banishment.

7:22–27 See note on 17:11.

7:23 *fat.* The prohibition of fat for food was as strict as that of blood, but the reason was different. The fat of the fellowship offerings was the Lord's and was to be burned on the altar (see 3:16 and note). There was no explicit prohibition of eating the fat of hunted animals like the gazelle or deer, but probably that was included (see 3:17; Dt 12:15–22).

7:26 *not eat the blood.* See note on 17:11; see also 3:17; 19:26; Ge 9:4–6; Dt 12:16,23–25; 15:23; 1Sa 14:32–34; Eze 33:25.

7:28–36 See 10:12–15; Nu 18:8–20; Dt 18:1–5.

7:30–32 *breast ... right thigh.* The breast and right thigh given to the priest were first presented to the Lord with gestures described as waving the breast and presenting the thigh (v. 34). See 8:25–29; 9:21; 10:14–15; Ex 29:26–27; Nu 6:20; 18:11,18.

7:37–38 A summary of chs. 1–7.

7:37 *ordination offering.* See 8:14–36; Ex 29:1–35.

The Ordination of Aaron and His Sons

8:1-36pp — Ex 29:1-37

8 The LORD said to Moses, 2 “Bring Aaron and his sons,[x] their garments,[y] the anointing oil,[z] the bull for the sin offering,[a][a] the two rams[b] and the basket containing bread made without yeast,[c] 3 and gather the entire assembly[d] at the entrance to the tent of meeting.” 4 Moses did as the LORD commanded him, and the assembly gathered at the entrance to the tent of meeting.

5 Moses said to the assembly, “This is what the LORD has commanded to be done.[e]” 6 Then Moses brought Aaron and his sons forward and washed them with water.[f] 7 He put the tunic on Aaron, tied the sash around him, clothed him with the robe and put the ephod on him. He also fastened the ephod with a decorative waistband, which he tied around him.[g] 8 He placed the breastpiece[h] on him and put the Urim and Thummim[i] in the breastpiece. 9 Then he placed the turban[j] on Aaron’s head and set the gold plate, the sacred emblem,[k] on the front of it, as the LORD commanded Moses.[l]

10 Then Moses took the anointing oil[m] and anointed[n] the tabernacle[o] and everything in it, and so consecrated them. 11 He sprinkled some of the oil on the altar seven times, anointing the altar and all its utensils and the basin with its stand, to consecrate them.[p] 12 He poured some of the anointing oil on Aaron’s head and anointed[q] him to consecrate him.[r] 13 Then he brought Aaron’s sons[s] forward, put tunics[t] on them, tied sashes around them and fastened caps on them, as the LORD commanded Moses.[u]

14 He then presented the bull[v] for the sin offering,[w] and Aaron and his sons laid their hands on its head.[x] 15 Moses slaughtered the bull and took some of the blood,[y] and with his finger he put it on all the horns of the altar[z] to purify the altar.[a] He poured out the rest of the blood at the base of the altar. So he consecrated it to make atonement for it.[b] 16 Moses also took all the fat around the internal organs, the long lobe of the liver, and both kidneys and their fat, and burned it on the altar. 17 But the bull with its hide and its flesh and its intestines[c] he burned up outside the camp,[d] as the LORD commanded Moses.

18 He then presented the ram[e] for the burnt offering, and Aaron and his sons laid their hands on its head. 19 Then Moses slaughtered the ram and splashed the blood against the sides of the altar. 20 He cut the ram into pieces and burned the head, the pieces and the fat.[f] 21 He washed the internal organs and the legs with water and burned the whole ram on the altar. It was a burnt offering, a pleasing aroma, a food offering presented to the LORD, as the LORD commanded Moses.

22 He then presented the other ram, the ram for the ordination,[g] and Aaron and his sons laid their hands on its head.[h] 23 Moses slaughtered the ram and took some of its blood and put it on the lobe of Aaron’s right ear, on the thumb of his right hand and on the big toe of his right foot.[i] 24 Moses also brought Aaron’s sons forward and put some of the blood on the lobes of their right ears, on the thumbs of their right hands and on the big toes of their right feet. Then he splashed blood against the sides of the altar.[j] 25 After that, he took the fat[k], the fat tail, all the fat around the internal organs, the long lobe of the liver, both kidneys and their fat and the right thigh. 26 And from the basket of bread made without yeast, which was before the LORD, he took one thick loaf, one thick loaf with olive oil mixed in, and one thin loaf,[l] and he put these on the fat portions and on the right thigh. 27 He put all these in the hands of Aaron and his sons, and they waved them before the LORD[m] as a wave

8:2 [x] S Ex 28:1; S Lev 1:5 [y] Ex 28:2,4, 43; S 39:27 [z] Ex 30:23-25, 30 [a] S Ex 30:10 [b] ver 18,22 [c] Ex 29:2-3
8:3 [d] Nu 8:9
8:5 [e] Ex 29:1
8:6 [f] S Ex 29:4; S 30:19; S Ac 22:16
8:7 [g] Ex 28:4
8:8 [h] S Ex 25:7 [i] S Ex 28:30
8:9 [j] S Ex 39:28 [k] S Ex 28:36 [l] S Ex 28:2; Lev 21:10
8:10 [m] ver 2 [n] S Ex 30:26 [o] S Ex 26:1
8:11 [p] S Ex 30:29
8:12 [q] S Lev 7:36 [r] S Ex 30:30
8:13 [s] S Ex 28:40 [t] S Ex 28:4, 39; 39:27 [u] Lev 21:10
8:14 [v] S Lev 4:3 [w] S Ex 30:10 [x] S Lev 4:15
8:15 [y] S Lev 4:18 [z] S Lev 4:7 [a] Heb 9:22 [b] Eze 43:20
8:17 [c] S Lev 4:11 [d] S Lev 4:12
8:18 [e] S ver 2
8:20 [f] S Lev 1:8
8:22 [g] S ver 2 [h] S Lev 4:15
8:23 [i] Lev 14:14,25
8:24 [j] Heb 9:18-22
8:25 [k] Lev 3:3-5
8:26 [l] S Lev 2:4
8:27 [m] Nu 5:25

[a] 2 Or *purification offering;* also in verse 14

:1 — 10:20 The ordination, installation and ministry of aron and his sons, and the deaths of Nadab and Abihu and ttendant regulations.
:2 *their garments.* See Ex 39:1 – 31; 40:12 – 16. The garments hat the high priest was to wear when he ministered are deailed in Ex 28:4 – 43 (see notes there). *anointing oil.* See note n Ex 25:6. The oil was used to anoint the tabernacle, sacred bjects and consecrated priests (vv. 10 – 12,30). It was later sed to anoint leaders and kings (1Sa 10:1; 16:13). See also ote on Ex 29:7.
:6 *washed them with water.* In the bronze basin (see v. 11) in he courtyard of the tabernacle (see Ex 30:17 – 21).
:7 *ephod.* See note on Ex 28:6.
:8 *Urim and Thummim.* See notes on Ex 28:30; 1Sa 2:28.
:9 *sacred emblem.* See note on Ex 39:30.
:11 *seven times.* See note on 4:6.
:12 *oil on Aaron’s head.* See Ps 133.
8:14 *sin offering.* See 4:3 – 11 and notes. The consecration service included a sin offering for atonement, a burnt offering for worship (v. 18) and a “ram for the ordination” (v. 22), whose blood was applied to the high priest on his right ear, thumb and toe (v. 23). After this was done, Aaron offered sacrifices for the people (9:15 – 21). Then he blessed the people in his capacity as priest, and the Lord accepted his ministry with the sign of miraculous fire (9:23 – 24). *laid their hands on.* See notes on 1:3; Ex 29:10.
8:15 *make atonement for it.* See 16:16; see also note on Ex 29:36.
8:17 *outside the camp.* See notes on 4:5,12; 13:45 – 46; Eze 43:21; Heb 13:12 – 13.
8:23 Putting some of the blood on Aaron’s extremities signified his complete consecration to the Lord’s service (cf. note on v. 14).
8:27 *wave offering.* See note on 7:30 – 32.

offering. 28 Then Moses took them from
their hands and burned them on the altar
on top of the burnt offering as an ordination offering, a pleasing aroma, a food offering presented to the LORD. 29 Moses also
took the breast, which was his share of
the ordination ram,[n] and waved it before
the LORD as a wave offering, as the LORD
commanded Moses.
30 Then Moses[o] took some of the anointing oil and some of the blood from the
altar and sprinkled them on Aaron and his
garments[p] and on his sons and their garments. So he consecrated[q] Aaron and his
garments and his sons and their garments.
31 Moses then said to Aaron and his
sons, "Cook the meat at the entrance to
the tent of meeting[r] and eat it there with
the bread from the basket of ordination offerings, as I was commanded: 'Aaron and
his sons are to eat it.' 32 Then burn up the
rest of the meat and the bread. 33 Do not
leave the entrance to the tent of meeting
for seven days, until the days of your ordination are completed, for your ordination will last seven days.[s] 34 What has been
done today was commanded by the LORD[t]
to make atonement for you. 35 You must
stay at the entrance to the tent of meeting
day and night for seven days and do what
the LORD requires,[u] so you will not die; for
that is what I have been commanded."
36 So Aaron and his sons did everything
the LORD commanded through Moses.

The Priests Begin Their Ministry

9 On the eighth day[v] Moses summoned
Aaron and his sons and the elders[w] of
Israel. 2 He said to Aaron, "Take a bull calf
for your sin offering[a] and a ram for your
burnt offering, both without defect, and
present them before the LORD. 3 Then say
to the Israelites: 'Take a male goat[x] for a
sin offering,[y] a calf[z] and a lamb[a]—both a
year old and without defect—for a burnt
offering, 4 and an ox[b][b] and a ram for a fellowship offering[c] to sacrifice before the
LORD, together with a grain offering mixed
with olive oil. For today the LORD will appear to you.[d]' "
5 They took the things Moses commanded to the front of the tent of meeting, and
the entire assembly came near and stood
before the LORD. 6 Then Moses said, "This
is what the LORD has commanded you to
do, so that the glory of the LORD[e] may appear to you."
7 Moses said to Aaron, "Come to the
altar and sacrifice your sin offering and
your burnt offering and make atonement
for yourself and the people;[f] sacrifice the
offering that is for the people and make
atonement for them, as the LORD has commanded.[g]"
8 So Aaron came to the altar and slaughtered the calf as a sin offering[h] for himself.
9 His sons brought the blood to him,[i] and
he dipped his finger into the blood and
put it on the horns of the altar; the rest of
the blood he poured out at the base of the
altar.[j] 10 On the altar he burned the fat, the
kidneys and the long lobe of the liver from
the sin offering, as the LORD commanded
Moses; 11 the flesh and the hide[k] he burned
up outside the camp.[l]
12 Then he slaughtered the burnt offering.[m] His sons handed him the blood,[n] and
he splashed it against the sides of the altar.
13 They handed him the burnt offering piece
by piece, including the head, and he burned
them on the altar.[o] 14 He washed the internal
organs and the legs and burned them on
top of the burnt offering on the altar.[p]
15 Aaron then brought the offering that
was for the people.[q] He took the goat for
the people's sin offering and slaughtered
it and offered it for a sin offering as he did
with the first one.
16 He brought the burnt offering and offered it in the prescribed way.[r] 17 He also
brought the grain offering, took a handful
of it and burned it on the altar in addition
to the morning's burnt offering.[s]
18 He slaughtered the ox and the ram as
the fellowship offering for the people.[t] His
sons handed him the blood, and he splashed
it against the sides of the altar. 19 But the fat
portions of the ox and the ram—the fat tail,
the layer of fat, the kidneys and the long
lobe of the liver— 20 these they laid on the
breasts, and then Aaron burned the fat on
the altar. 21 Aaron waved the breasts and the
right thigh before the LORD as a wave offering,[u] as Moses commanded.
22 Then Aaron lifted his hands toward

8:29 [n] Lev 7:31-34 **8:30** [o] S Ex 28:1 [p] S Ex 28:2 [q] S Lev 7:36 **8:31** [r] S Lev 6:16 **8:33** [s] Lev 14:8; 15:13,28; Nu 19:11; Eze 43:25 **8:34** [t] Heb 7:16 **8:35** [u] Lev 18:30; 22:9; Nu 3:7; 9:19; Dt 11:1; 1Ki 2:3; Eze 48:11; Zec 3:7 **9:1** [v] Eze 43:27 [w] S Lev 4:15 **9:3** [x] S Lev 4:3 [y] ver 15; Lev 10:16 [z] ver 8 [a] S Lev 4:32 **9:4** [b] Lev 4:10 [c] S Ex 32:6 [d] Ex 29:43 **9:6** [e] S Ex 16:7 **9:7** [f] Lev 16:6 [g] S Ex 30:10; Heb 5:1,3; 7:27 **9:8** [h] Lev 4:1-12; 10:19 **9:9** [i] ver 12, 18 [j] S Ex 29:12; Eze 43:20 **9:11** [k] S Lev 4:11 [l] S Lev 4:12 **9:12** [m] Lev 10:19 [n] S ver 9 **9:13** [o] S Lev 1:8 **9:14** [p] S Lev 1:9 **9:15** [q] Lev 4:27-31 **9:16** [r] Lev 1:1-13 **9:17** [s] Lev 3:5 **9:18** [t] Lev 3:1-11 **9:21** [u] S Ex 29:24,26

[a] 2 Or *purification offering*; here and throughout this chapter [b] 4 The Hebrew word can refer to either male or female; also in verses 18 and 19.

8:28 *on top of the burnt offering.* See note on 3:5.
8:31 *Aaron and his sons are to eat it.* See Ex 29:32.
9:1 *eighth day.* After the seven days of ordination (8:33).
9:2 *sin offering.* See notes on 4:3,5. *burnt offering.* See note on 1:3.
9:4 *fellowship offering.* See note on 3:1. *grain offering.* See note on 2:1. *LORD will appear.* See vv. 6,23; see also note on Ge 12:7.
9:6,23 *glory of the LORD.* See notes on Ex 16:7; 40:34; Ps 26:8; Eze 1:1–28.
9:8 *sin offering for himself.* Contrast Jesus in Heb 7:26–28 (see notes there).
9:9 *blood ... on the horns.* See photo, p. 171.
9:11 *outside the camp.* See note on 8:17.
9:17 *morning's burnt offering.* See Ex 29:38–42.
9:21 *wave offering.* See note on 7:30–32.

the people and blessed them.[v] And
having sacrificed the sin offering,
the burnt offering and the fellowship
offering, he stepped down.
23 Moses and Aaron then went
into the tent of meeting.[w] When they
came out, they blessed the people;
and the glory of the LORD[x] appeared
to all the people. 24 Fire[y] came out
from the presence of the LORD and
consumed the burnt offering and the
fat portions on the altar. And when
all the people saw it, they shouted
for joy and fell facedown.[z]

Model of the tabernacle altar. The blood that the priests would spread on the four horns (Lev 9:9) can be seen here.

Todd Bolen/www.BiblePlaces.com

The Death of Nadab and Abihu

10 Aaron's sons Nadab and Abihu[a] took their censers,[b] put
fire in them[c] and added incense;[d] and
they offered unauthorized fire before
the LORD,[e] contrary to his command.[f]
2 So fire came out[g] from the presence of
the LORD and consumed them,[h] and they
died before the LORD.[i] 3 Moses then said to
Aaron, "This is what the LORD spoke of
when he said:

" 'Among those who approach me[j]
I will be proved holy;[k]
in the sight of all the people
I will be honored.[l] ' "

Aaron remained silent.
4 Moses summoned Mishael and Elzaphan,[m] sons of Aaron's uncle Uzziel,[n]
and said to them, "Come here; carry your
cousins outside the camp,[o] away from the
front of the sanctuary.[p]" 5 So they came
and carried them, still in their tunics,[q] outside the camp, as Moses ordered.
6 Then Moses said to Aaron and his sons
Eleazar and Ithamar,[r] "Do not let your hair
become unkempt[a][s] and do not tear your
clothes,[t] or you will die and the LORD will
be angry with the whole community.[u]
But your relatives, all the Israelites, may
mourn[v] for those the LORD has destroyed
by fire. 7 Do not leave the entrance to the
tent of meeting[w] or you will die, because
the LORD's anointing oil[x] is on you." So
they did as Moses said.
8 Then the LORD said to Aaron, 9 "You and
your sons are not to drink wine[y] or other fermented drink[z] whenever you go into
the tent of meeting, or you will die. This
is a lasting ordinance[a] for the generations
to come, 10 so that you can distinguish between the holy and the common, between
the unclean and the clean,[b] 11 and so you
can teach[c] the Israelites all the decrees the
LORD has given them through Moses.[d]"
12 Moses said to Aaron and his remaining

[a] 6 Or *Do not uncover your heads*

9:22 [v] S Ge 48:20; S Ex 39:43; Lk 24:50 **9:23** [w] S Ex 40:2 [x] S Ex 24:16 **9:24** [y] S Ex 19:18; Jdg 6:21; 13:20 [z] 1Ki 18:39 **10:1** [a] Ex 6:23; 24:1; 28:1; Nu 3:2-4; 26:61; 1Ch 6:3 [b] Nu 16:46; 1Ki 7:50; 2Ki 25:15; 2Ch 4:22; Jer 52:19; Eze 8:11 [c] Lev 16:12; Nu 16:7, 18; Isa 6:6 [d] S Ex 30:9 [e] ver 2; Lev 16:1 [f] Ex 30:9 **10:2** [g] Ps 106:18 [h] Nu 11:1; 16:35; Ps 2:12; 50:3; Isa 29:6 [i] S Ge 19:24; S 38:7; Nu 16:35; 1Ch 24:2; Job 1:16 **10:3** [j] Ex 19:22 [k] Ex 30:29; Lev 21:6; 22:32; Nu 16:5; 20:13; Isa 5:16; Eze 28:22; 38:16 [l] Ex 14:4; Isa 44:23; 49:3; 55:5; 60:21 **10:4** [m] S Ex 6:22 [n] Ex 6:18 [o] Ac 5:6, 9, 10 [p] S Ex 25:8 **10:5** [q] S Lev 8:13 **10:6** [r] S Ex 6:23 [s] Lev 13:45; 21:10; Nu 5:18 [t] Jer 41:5; S Mk 14:63 [u] Nu 1:53; 16:22; Jos 7:1; 22:18 [v] Ge 50:3, 10; Nu 20:29; 1Sa 25:1 **10:7** [w] S Ex 25:8 [x] S Ex 28:41 **10:9** [y] Ge 9:21; Ex 29:40; Lev 23:13; Nu 15:5; Dt 28:39; Isa 5:22; 22:13; 28:1; 29:9; 56:12; Jer 35:6; Hos 4:11; Hab 2:15-16 [z] Nu 6:3; 28:7; Dt 14:26; 29:6; Jdg 13:4; Pr 20:1; 23:29-35; 31:4-7; Isa 28:7; Eze 44:21; Mic 2:11; Lk 1:15; S Eph 5:18; 1Ti 3:3; Titus 1:7 [a] S Ex 12:14 **10:10** [b] S Ge 7:2; S Lev 6:27; 14:57; 20:25; Eze 22:26 **10:11** [c] 2Ch 15:3; 17:7; Ezr 7:25; Ne 8:7; Mal 2:7 [d] Dt 17:10, 11; 24:8; 25:1; 33:10; Pr 4:27; Hag 2:11; Mal 2:7

9:22 *blessed.* The Aaronic benediction, a threefold blessing, is given in Nu 6:23–26. Cf. the threefold apostolic benediction in 2Co 13:14.
9:23 *glory of the LORD.* See v. 6; cf. the display of the Lord's glory at the erection of the tabernacle (Ex 40:34–35); cf. also God's acceptance of sacrifices at the dedication of Solomon's temple (2Ch 7:1).
9:24 *Fire came out from the presence of the LORD.* See 10:2; 1Ki 18:38.
10:1 *censers.* Ceremonial vessels containing hot coals and used for burning incense (see 16:12–13; 2Ch 26:19; Rev 8:3–4).
10:2 *died before the LORD.* Aaron's older sons are mentioned also in Ex 6:23; 24:1,9; 28:1; Nu 3:2–4; 26:60–61; 1Ch 6:3; 24:1–2. They are regularly remembered as having died before the Lord and as having had no sons. Their death was tragic and at first seems harsh, but no more so than that of Ananias and Sapphira (Ac 5:1–11). In both cases a new era was being inaugurated (cf. also the judgment on Achan, Jos 7, and on Uzzah, 2Sa 6:1–7). The new community had to be made aware that it existed for God, not vice versa.
10:3 The quotation reflects the spirit and substance of passages like Ex 14:4; 19:22; 29:1,44; 30:29. *be proved holy.* Act so as to publicly display my holiness (see 11:44 and note; see also Nu 20:13; Isa 5:16; Eze 20:41; 28:22,25; 36:23; 38:16; 39:27). *holy.* See Introduction: Theological Themes.
10:4 *outside the camp.* See note on 8:17.
10:6 *not tear your clothes.* See 21:10; see also note on Ge 44:13.
10:7 *Do not leave.* To join the mourners (see 21:11–12).
10:10 *between the holy and the common.* The distinction between what was holy (sacred; see note on Ex 3:5) and what was common (not associated with the sacred) was carefully maintained (see Eze 22:26; 42:20; 44:23; 48:14–15).
10:12–15 See 7:28–36; Nu 18:8–20; Dt 18:1–5.

sons, Eleazar and Ithamar, "Take the grain
offering[e] left over from the food offerings
prepared without yeast and presented to
the LORD and eat it beside the altar,[f] for
it is most holy. 13 Eat it in the sanctuary
area,[g] because it is your share and your
sons' share of the food offerings presented
to the LORD; for so I have been commanded.[h] 14 But you and your sons and your
daughters may eat the breast[i] that was
waved and the thigh that was presented.
Eat them in a ceremonially clean place;[j]
they have been given to you and your children as your share of the Israelites' fellowship offerings. 15 The thigh[k] that was
presented and the breast that was waved
must be brought with the fat portions of
the food offerings, to be waved before the
LORD as a wave offering.[l] This will be the
perpetual share for you and your children,
as the LORD has commanded."
16 When Moses inquired about the goat
of the sin offering[a][m] and found that it had
been burned up, he was angry with Eleazar and Ithamar, Aaron's remaining sons,
and asked, 17 "Why didn't you eat the sin
offering[n] in the sanctuary area? It is most
holy; it was given to you to take away the
guilt[o] of the community by making atonement for them before the LORD. 18 Since its
blood was not taken into the Holy Place,[p]
you should have eaten the goat in the
sanctuary area, as I commanded.[q]"
19 Aaron replied to Moses, "Today they
sacrificed their sin offering and their burnt
offering[r] before the LORD, but such things
as this have happened to me. Would the
LORD have been pleased if I had eaten the
sin offering today?" 20 When Moses heard
this, he was satisfied.

Clean and Unclean Food

11:1-23pp — Dt 14:3-20

11 The LORD said to Moses and Aaron, 2 "Say to the Israelites: 'Of all
the animals that live on land, these are
the ones you may eat:[s] 3 You may eat any
animal that has a divided hoof and that
chews the cud.
4 " 'There are some that only chew the
cud or only have a divided hoof, but you
must not eat them.[t] The camel, though it
chews the cud, does not have a divided
hoof; it is ceremonially unclean for you.
5 The hyrax, though it chews the cud, does
not have a divided hoof; it is unclean for
you. 6 The rabbit, though it chews the cud,
does not have a divided hoof; it is unclean
for you. 7 And the pig,[u] though it has a divided hoof, does not chew the cud; it is
unclean for you. 8 You must not eat their
meat or touch their carcasses; they are unclean for you.[v]
9 " 'Of all the creatures living in the water of the seas and the streams you may
eat any that have fins and scales. 10 But all
creatures in the seas or streams that do
not have fins and scales — whether among
all the swarming things or among all the
other living creatures in the water — you
are to regard as unclean.[w] 11 And since you
are to regard them as unclean, you must
not eat their meat; you must regard their
carcasses as unclean.[x] 12 Anything living
in the water that does not have fins and
scales is to be regarded as unclean by
you.[y]
13 " 'These are the birds you are to regard
as unclean and not eat because they are
unclean: the eagle,[b] the vulture, the black
vulture, 14 the red kite, any kind[z] of black
kite, 15 any kind of raven,[a] 16 the horned
owl, the screech owl, the gull, any kind
of hawk, 17 the little owl, the cormorant,
the great owl, 18 the white owl,[b] the desert
owl, the osprey, 19 the stork,[c] any kind[d] of
heron, the hoopoe and the bat.[e]
20 " 'All flying insects that walk on all
fours are to be regarded as unclean by

10:12 [e] S Ex 29:41 [f] Lev 6:14-18 **10:13** [g] S Lev 6:16 [h] Eze 42:13 **10:14** [i] Nu 5:9 [j] S Ex 29:31; S Lev 4:12 **10:15** [k] S Lev 7:34 [l] S Ex 29:28 **10:16** [m] S Lev 9:3 **10:17** [n] Lev 6:24-30; Eze 42:13 [o] S Ex 28:38 **10:18** [p] S Lev 4:18; 6:26 [q] S Lev 6:17 **10:19** [r] Lev 9:12

11:2 [s] Ac 10:12-14 **11:4** [t] Ac 10:14 **11:7** [u] Isa 65:4; 66:3,17 **11:8** [v] S Lev 5:2; Heb 9:10 **11:10** [w] ver 12 **11:11** [x] S Lev 5:2 **11:12** [y] ver 10 **11:14** [z] S Ge 1:11 **11:15** [a] S Ge 8:7 **11:18** [b] Isa 13:21; 14:23; 34:11, 13; Zep 2:14 **11:19** [c] Zec 5:9 [d] S Ge 1:11 [e] Isa 2:20

[a] 16 Or *purification offering*; also in verses 17 and 19
[b] 13 The precise identification of some of the birds, insects and animals in this chapter is uncertain.

10:18 *Since its blood was not taken into the Holy Place, you should have eaten.* There were two types of sin offerings: (1) those in which the blood was sprinkled within the tabernacle, and (2) those in which it was splashed only against the altar of burnt offering. Portions of the second type normally should have been eaten (see note on 4:5). But Moses was satisfied when he learned that Aaron had acted sincerely and not in negligence or rebellion (vv. 19 – 20).

10:19 *such things as this have happened to me.* Probably referring to the death of his two oldest sons (v. 2), for which he mourned by fasting. Or possibly something had occurred that made him ceremonially unclean.

11:1 — 15:33 The distinction between clean and unclean (see note on 11:2).

11:2 *the ones you may eat.* Ch. 11 is closely paralleled in Dt 14:3 – 21 but is more extensive. The animals acceptable for human consumption were those that chewed the cud and had a divided hoof (v. 3). Of marine life, only creatures with fins and scales were permissible (v. 9). Birds and insects are also covered in the instructions (vv. 13 – 23). Some distinction between clean and unclean food was as old as the time of Noah (see Ge 7:2 and note). The Hittites also had a system of clean and unclean animals.The main reason for the laws concerning clean and unclean food is the same as for other laws concerning the clean and unclean — to preserve the sanctity of Israel as God's holy people (see v. 44 and note). Some hold that certain animal life was considered unclean for health considerations, but it is difficult to substantiate this idea. Uncleanness typified sin and defilement. For the uncleanness of disease and bodily discharges, see chs. 13 – 15.

11:6 *rabbit.* Does not technically chew the cud with regurgitation. The apparent chewing movements of the rabbit caused it to be classified popularly with cud chewers.

11:20 *all fours.* Although insects have six legs, perhaps

you.[f] 21 There are, however, some flying insects that walk on all fours that you may eat: those that have jointed legs for hopping on the ground. 22 Of these you may eat any kind of locust,[g] katydid, cricket or grasshopper. 23 But all other flying insects that have four legs you are to regard as unclean.

24 "'You will make yourselves unclean by these;[h] whoever touches their carcasses will be unclean till evening.[i] 25 Whoever picks up one of their carcasses must wash their clothes,[j] and they will be unclean till evening.[k]

26 "'Every animal that does not have a divided hoof or that does not chew the cud is unclean for you; whoever touches the carcass of any of them will be unclean. 27 Of all the animals that walk on all fours, those that walk on their paws are unclean for you; whoever touches their carcasses will be unclean till evening. 28 Anyone who picks up their carcasses must wash their clothes, and they will be unclean till evening.[l] These animals are unclean for you.

29 "'Of the animals that move along the ground, these are unclean for you:[m] the weasel, the rat,[n] any kind of great lizard, 30 the gecko, the monitor lizard, the wall lizard, the skink and the chameleon. 31 Of all those that move along the ground, these are unclean for you. Whoever touches them when they are dead will be unclean till evening. 32 When one of them dies and falls on something, that article, whatever its use, will be unclean, whether it is made of wood, cloth, hide or sackcloth.[o] Put it in water; it will be unclean till evening, and then it will be clean. 33 If one of them falls into a clay pot, everything in it will be unclean, and you must break the pot.[p] 34 Any food you are allowed to eat that has come into contact with water from any such pot is unclean, and any liquid that is drunk from such a pot is unclean. 35 Anything that one of their carcasses falls on becomes unclean; an oven or cooking pot must be broken up. They are unclean, and you are to regard them as unclean. 36 A spring, however, or a cistern for collecting water remains clean, but anyone who touches one of these carcasses is unclean. 37 If a carcass falls on any seeds that are to be planted, they remain clean. 38 But if water has been put on the seed and a carcass falls on it, it is unclean for you.

39 "'If an animal that you are allowed to eat dies,[q] anyone who touches its carcass[r] will be unclean till evening. 40 Anyone who eats some of its carcass[s] must wash their clothes, and they will be unclean till evening.[t] Anyone who picks up the carcass must wash their clothes, and they will be unclean till evening.

41 "'Every creature that moves along the ground is to be regarded as unclean; it is not to be eaten. 42 You are not to eat any creature that moves along the ground, whether it moves on its belly or walks on all fours or on many feet; it is unclean. 43 Do not defile yourselves by any of these creatures.[u] Do not make yourselves unclean by means of them or be made unclean by them. 44 I am the LORD your God;[v] consecrate yourselves[w] and be holy,[x] because I am holy.[y] Do not make yourselves unclean by any creature that moves along the ground.[z] 45 I am the LORD, who brought you up out of Egypt[a] to be your God;[b] therefore be holy, because I am holy.[c]

46 "'These are the regulations concerning animals, birds, every living thing that moves about in the water and every creature that moves along the ground. 47 You must distinguish between the unclean and the clean, between living creatures that may be eaten and those that may not be eaten.[d]'"

11:20 [f] Ac 10:14
11:22 [g] Mt 3:4; Mk 1:6
11:24 [h] S Lev 5:2 [i] ver 27-40; Lev 13:3; 14:46; 15:5; 22:6; Nu 19:7,19
11:25 [j] ver 28; S Ex 19:10; Lev 13:6; 14:8, 47; 15:5; 16:26; Nu 8:7; 19:7 [k] Lev 13:34; Nu 19:8; 31:24
11:28 [l] Heb 9:10
11:29 [m] ver 41 [n] Isa 66:17
11:32 [o] Lev 15:12; Nu 19:18; 31:20
11:33 [p] S Lev 6:28
11:39 [q] Lev 17:15; 22:8; Dt 14:21; Eze 4:14; 44:31 [r] ver 40; Lev 22:4; Nu 19:11
11:40 [s] S ver 39 [t] ver 25; Lev 14:8; 17:15; 22:8; Eze 44:31; Heb 9:10
11:43 [u] ver 44; Lev 20:25; 22:5
11:44 [v] S Ex 6:2, 7; 20:2; Isa 43:3; 51:15; Eze 20:5 [w] S Ex 19:10; Lev 20:7; Nu 15:40; Jos 3:5; 7:13; 1Ch 15:12; 2Ch 29:5; 35:6 [x] S Ex 22:31; S Dt 14:2 [y] S Ex 31:13; Lev 19:2; 20:7; Jos 24:19; 1Sa 2:2; Job 6:10; Ps 99:3; Eph 1:4; 1Th 4:7; 1Pe 1:15,16* [z] S ver 43
11:45 [a] Lev 25:38, 55 [b] S Ge 17:7 [c] S Ex 19:6; 1Pe 1:16*
11:47 [d] Lev 10:10

Purification After Childbirth

12 The LORD said to Moses, 2 "Say to the Israelites: 'A woman who becomes pregnant and gives birth to a son

---

people in ancient times did not count as ordinary legs the two large hind legs that many insects used for jumping.

11:36 *cistern for collecting water.* The use of waterproof plaster for lining cisterns dug in the ground was an important factor in helping the Israelites to settle the dry areas of Canaan after the conquest (cf. 2Ch 26:10).

11:41 *ground.* Verses 29–30 identify the animals that move about (or swarm) on the ground.

11:44 *be holy.* Quoted in 1Pe 1:16 (see note there; see also Introduction to Leviticus: Theological Themes). Holiness is the key theme of Leviticus, ringing like a refrain in various forms throughout the book (e.g., v. 45; 19:2; 20:7,26; 21:8,15; 22:9,16,32). The word "holy" appears more often in Leviticus than in any other book of the Bible. Israel was to be totally consecrated to God. Her holiness was to be expressed in every aspect of her life, to the extent that all of life had a certain ceremonial quality. Because of who God is and what he has done (v. 45), his people must dedicate themselves fully to him (cf. Mt 5:48). See Ro 12:1. *I am holy.* When God's holiness is spoken of in the Bible, reference is to (1) his incomparably awesome majesty (the mysterious, overwhelming presence of his infinite power, before which the whole creation trembles), and (2) his absolute moral virtue (a presence so infinitely pure that it unmasks and judges every moral flaw or fault). Sometimes one of these aspects is foregrounded, sometimes the other, but often both are evoked together (as in Isa 6:3–5).

11:45 *brought ... out of Egypt.* A refrain found 8 more times in Leviticus (19:36; 22:33; 23:43; 25:38,42,55; 26:13,45) and nearly 60 times in 18 other books of the OT.

11:46–47 A summary of ch. 11.

12:2 *unclean.* The uncleanness came from the bleeding (vv. 4–5,7), not from the birth. It is not clear why the period

will be ceremonially unclean for seven
days, just as she is unclean during her
monthly period.[e] 3 On the eighth day[f] the
boy is to be circumcised.[g] 4 Then the woman must wait thirty-three days to be purified from her bleeding. She must not
touch anything sacred or go to the sanctuary until the days of her purification are
over. 5 If she gives birth to a daughter, for
two weeks the woman will be unclean, as
during her period. Then she must wait sixty-six days to be purified from her bleeding.
6 " 'When the days of her purification for
a son or daughter are over,[h] she is to bring
to the priest at the entrance to the tent of
meeting a year-old lamb[i] for a burnt offering and a young pigeon or a dove for a sin
offering.[a][j] 7 He shall offer them before the
LORD to make atonement for her, and then
she will be ceremonially clean from her
flow of blood.
" 'These are the regulations for the
woman who gives birth to a boy or a girl.
8 But if she cannot afford a lamb, she is to
bring two doves or two young pigeons,[k]
one for a burnt offering and the other for
a sin offering.[l] In this way the priest will
make atonement for her, and she will be
clean.[m]' "

Regulations About Defiling Skin Diseases

13 The LORD said to Moses and Aaron,
2 "When anyone has a swelling[n] or
a rash or a shiny spot[o] on their skin that
may be a defiling skin disease,[b][p] they must
be brought to Aaron the priest[q] or to one
of his sons[c] who is a priest. 3 The priest is
to examine the sore on the skin, and if the
hair in the sore has turned white and the
sore appears to be more than skin deep, it
is a defiling skin disease. When the priest
examines that person, he shall pronounce
them ceremonially unclean.[r] 4 If the shiny
spot[s] on the skin is white but does not appear to be more than skin deep and the
hair in it has not turned white, the priest
is to isolate the affected person for seven
days.[t] 5 On the seventh day[u] the priest is
to examine them,[v] and if he sees that the
sore is unchanged and has not spread in
the skin, he is to isolate them for another
seven days. 6 On the seventh day the priest
is to examine them again, and if the sore
has faded and has not spread in the skin,
the priest shall pronounce them clean;[w]
it is only a rash. They must wash their
clothes,[x] and they will be clean.[y] 7 But if
the rash does spread in their skin after
they have shown themselves to the priest
to be pronounced clean, they must appear
before the priest again.[z] 8 The priest is to
examine that person, and if the rash has
spread in the skin, he shall pronounce
them unclean; it is a defiling skin disease.
9 "When anyone has a defiling skin disease, they must be brought to the priest.
10 The priest is to examine them, and if
there is a white swelling in the skin that
has turned the hair white and if there is
raw flesh in the swelling, 11 it is a chronic skin disease[a] and the priest shall pronounce them unclean. He is not to isolate
them, because they are already unclean.
12 "If the disease breaks out all over their
skin and, so far as the priest can see, it
covers all the skin of the affected person
from head to foot, 13 the priest is to examine them, and if the disease has covered
their whole body, he shall pronounce
them clean. Since it has all turned white,
they are clean. 14 But whenever raw flesh
appears on them, they will be unclean.
15 When the priest sees the raw flesh, he
shall pronounce them unclean. The raw
flesh is unclean; they have a defiling disease.[b] 16 If the raw flesh changes and turns
white, they must go to the priest. 17 The
priest is to examine them, and if the sores
have turned white, the priest shall pronounce the affected person clean;[c] then
they will be clean.

12:2 [e] Lev 15:19; 18:19; Isa 64:6; Eze 18:6; 22:10; 36:17 **12:3** [f] S Ex 22:30 [g] S Ge 17:10; S Lk 1:59 **12:6** [h] Lk 2:22 [i] Ex 29:38; Lev 23:12; Nu 6:12,14; 7:15 [j] Lev 5:7 **12:8** [k] S Ge 15:9; Lev 14:22 [l] Lev 5:7; Lk 2:22-24* [m] S Lev 4:26 **13:2** [n] ver 10, 19,28,43 [o] ver 4,38, 39; Lev 14:56 [p] ver 3,9, 15; S Ex 4:6; Lev 14:3,32; Nu 5:2; Dt 24:8 [q] Dt 24:8 **13:3** [r] ver 8,11, 20,30; Lev 21:1; Nu 9:6 **13:4** [s] S ver 2 [t] ver 5,21, 26,33,46; Lev 14:38; Nu 12:14,15; Dt 24:9 **13:5** [u] Lev 14:9 [v] ver 27,32, 34,51 **13:6** [w] ver 13, 17,23,28,34; Mt 8:3; Lk 5:12-14 [x] S Lev 11:25 [y] Lev 11:25; 14:8,9,20,48; 15:8; Nu 8:7 **13:7** [z] Lk 5:14 **13:11** [a] S Ex 4:6; S Lev 14:8; S Nu 12:10; Mt 8:2 **13:15** [b] S ver 2 **13:17** [c] S ver 6

[a] 6 Or *purification offering*; also in verse 8 [b] 2 The Hebrew word for *defiling skin disease*, traditionally translated "leprosy," was used for various diseases affecting the skin; here and throughout verses 3-46. [c] 2 Or *descendants*

of uncleanness after the birth of a baby boy (40 days) was half the period for a girl (80 days). *monthly period.* See 15:19–24.
12:3 See notes on Ge 17:10,12.
12:6 *burnt offering.* See note on 1:3. *sin offering.* See notes on 4:3,5.
12:7 The last sentence in this verse is a summary of ch. 12.
12:8 An appendix prescribing alternative sacrifices for people who were poor. See 1:14–17 and note on 1:14; see also 5:7–10; 14:21–22; and especially Lk 2:24 (Mary's offering for Jesus).
13:1–46 This section deals with preliminary symptoms of skin diseases (vv. 1–8) and then with the symptoms of (1) raw flesh (vv. 9–17), (2) boils (vv. 18–23), (3) burns (vv. 24–28), (4) sores on the head or chin (vv. 29–37), (5) white spots (vv. 38–39) and (6) skin diseases on the head that cause baldness (vv. 40–44).
13:2 *defiling skin disease.* Occurs often in chs. 13–14; see also 22:4; Nu 5:2. Such diseases show visible defects that could function aptly as a symbol for defilement—as could mold (cf. vv. 47–59). *disease.* See NIV text note; see also 22:4–8; Nu 5:2–4; Dt 24:8–9. The symptoms described, and the fact that they may rapidly change (vv. 6,26–27,32–37), show that the disease was not true leprosy (Hansen's disease). They apply also to a number of other diseases, as well as to rather harmless skin eruptions. The Hebrew word translated "defiling skin disease" can also mean "mold" (v. 47; 14:34; and especially 14:57).

18“When someone has a boil[d] on their skin and it heals, 19and in the place where the boil was, a white swelling or reddish-white[e] spot[f] appears, they must present themselves to the priest. 20The priest is to examine it, and if it appears to be more than skin deep and the hair in it has turned white, the priest shall pronounce that person unclean. It is a defiling skin disease[g] that has broken out where the boil was. 21But if, when the priest examines it, there is no white hair in it and it is not more than skin deep and has faded, then the priest is to isolate them for seven days. 22If it is spreading in the skin, the priest shall pronounce them unclean; it is a defiling disease. 23But if the spot is unchanged and has not spread, it is only a scar from the boil, and the priest shall pronounce them clean.[h]

24“When someone has a burn on their skin and a reddish-white or white spot appears in the raw flesh of the burn, 25the priest is to examine the spot, and if the hair in it has turned white, and it appears to be more than skin deep, it is a defiling disease that has broken out in the burn. The priest shall pronounce them unclean; it is a defiling skin disease.[i] 26But if the priest examines it and there is no white hair in the spot and if it is not more than skin deep and has faded, then the priest is to isolate them for seven days.[j] 27On the seventh day the priest is to examine that person,[k] and if it is spreading in the skin, the priest shall pronounce them unclean; it is a defiling skin disease. 28If, however, the spot is unchanged and has not spread in the skin but has faded, it is a swelling from the burn, and the priest shall pronounce them clean; it is only a scar from the burn.[l]

29“If a man or woman has a sore on their head[m] or chin, 30the priest is to examine the sore, and if it appears to be more than skin deep and the hair in it is yellow and thin, the priest shall pronounce them unclean; it is a defiling skin disease on the head or chin. 31But if, when the priest examines the sore, it does not seem to be more than skin deep and there is no black hair in it, then the priest is to isolate the affected person for seven days.[n] 32On the seventh day the priest is to examine the sore,[o] and if it has not spread and there is no yellow hair in it and it does not appear to be more than skin deep, 33then the man or woman must shave themselves, except for the affected area, and the priest is to keep them isolated another seven days. 34On the seventh day the priest is to examine the sore,[p] and if it has not spread in the skin and appears to be no more than skin deep, the priest shall pronounce them clean. They must wash their clothes, and they will be clean.[q] 35But if the sore does spread in the skin after they are pronounced clean, 36the priest is to examine them, and if he finds that the sore has spread in the skin, he does not need to look for yellow hair; they are unclean.[r] 37If, however, the sore is unchanged so far as the priest can see, and if black hair has grown in it, the affected person is healed. They are clean, and the priest shall pronounce them clean.

38“When a man or woman has white spots on the skin, 39the priest is to examine them, and if the spots are dull white, it is a harmless rash that has broken out on the skin; they are clean.

40“A man who has lost his hair and is bald[s] is clean. 41If he has lost his hair from the front of his scalp and has a bald forehead, he is clean. 42But if he has a reddish-white sore on his bald head or forehead, it is a defiling disease breaking out on his head or forehead. 43The priest is to examine him, and if the swollen sore on his head or forehead is reddish-white like a defiling skin disease, 44the man is diseased and is unclean. The priest shall pronounce him unclean because of the sore on his head.

45“Anyone with such a defiling disease must wear torn clothes,[t] let their hair be unkempt,[a] cover the lower part of their face[u] and cry out, ‘Unclean! Unclean!’[v] 46As long as they have the disease they remain unclean. They must live alone; they must live outside the camp.[w]

Regulations About Defiling Molds

47“As for any fabric that is spoiled with a defiling mold—any woolen or linen clothing, 48any woven or knitted material of linen or wool, any leather or anything made of leather— 49if the affected area in the fabric, the leather, the woven or knitted

13:18 [d] S Ex 9:9 **13:19** [e] ver 24, 42; Lev 14:37 [f] S ver 2 **13:20** [g] ver 2 **13:23** [h] S ver 6 **13:25** [i] ver 11 **13:26** [j] S ver 4 **13:27** [k] S ver 5 **13:28** [l] S ver 2 **13:29** [m] ver 43, 44 **13:31** [n] ver 4 **13:32** [o] S ver 5 **13:34** [p] S ver 5 [q] S Lev 11:25 **13:36** [r] ver 30 **13:40** [s] Lev 21:5; 2Ki 2:23; Isa 3:24; 15:2; 22:12; Eze 27:31; 29:18; Am 8:10; Mic 1:16 **13:45** [t] S Lev 10:6 [u] Eze 24:17, 22; Mic 3:7 [v] S Lev 5:2; La 4:15; Lk 17:12 **13:46** [w] Nu 5:1-4; 12:14; 2Ki 7:3; 15:5

[a] 45 *Or clothes, uncover their head*

13:45–46 The ceremonially unclean were excluded from the camp (the area around the tabernacle and courtyard), where the Israelites lived in tents. Later, no unclean persons were allowed in the temple area, where they could mingle with others. God was present in a special way not only in the tabernacle but also in the camp (Nu 5:3; Dt 23:14). Therefore unclean people were not to be in the camp (see Nu 5:1–4; 12:14–15, Miriam; 31:19–24; see also Lev 10:4–5; Nu 15:35–36; 2Ki 7:3–4; 2Ch 26:21, Uzziah). As a result of their separation from God, they were to exhibit their grief by tearing their clothes, by having unkempt hair and by partially covering their faces (v. 45).

13:47 *defiling mold.* During Israel's rainy season (October through March), this is a problem along the coast and by the Sea of Galilee, where it is very humid.

material, or any leather article, is greenish or reddish, it is a defiling mold and must be shown to the priest.[x] 50 The priest is to examine the affected area[y] and isolate the article for seven days. 51 On the seventh day he is to examine it,[z] and if the mold has spread in the fabric, the woven or knitted material, or the leather, whatever its use, it is a persistent defiling mold; the article is unclean.[a] 52 He must burn the fabric, the woven or knitted material of wool or linen, or any leather article that has been spoiled; because the defiling mold is persistent, the article must be burned.[b]

53 "But if, when the priest examines it, the mold has not spread in the fabric, the woven or knitted material, or the leather article, 54 he shall order that the spoiled article be washed. Then he is to isolate it for another seven days. 55 After the article has been washed, the priest is to examine it again, and if the mold has not changed its appearance, even though it has not spread, it is unclean. Burn it, no matter which side of the fabric has been spoiled. 56 If, when the priest examines it, the mold has faded after the article has been washed, he is to tear the spoiled part out of the fabric, the leather, or the woven or knitted material. 57 But if it reappears in the fabric, in the woven or knitted material, or in the leather article, it is a spreading mold; whatever has the mold must be burned. 58 Any fabric, woven or knitted material, or any leather article that has been washed and is rid of the mold, must be washed again. Then it will be clean."

59 These are the regulations concerning defiling molds in woolen or linen clothing, woven or knitted material, or any leather article, for pronouncing them clean or unclean.

Cleansing From Defiling Skin Diseases

14 The LORD said to Moses, 2 "These are the regulations for any diseased person at the time of their ceremonial cleansing, when they are brought to the priest:[c] 3 The priest is to go outside the camp and examine them.[d] If they have been healed of their defiling skin disease,[a][e] 4 the priest shall order that two live clean birds and some cedar wood, scarlet yarn and hyssop[f] be brought for the person to be cleansed.[g] 5 Then the priest shall order that one of the birds be killed over fresh water in a clay pot.[h] 6 He is then to take the live bird and dip it, together with the cedar wood, the scarlet yarn and the hyssop, into the blood of the bird that was killed over the fresh water.[i] 7 Seven times[j] he shall sprinkle[k] the one to be cleansed of the defiling disease, and then pronounce them clean. After that, he is to release the live bird in the open fields.[l]

8 "The person to be cleansed must wash their clothes,[m] shave off all their hair and bathe with water;[n] then they will be ceremonially clean.[o] After this they may come into the camp,[p] but they must stay outside their tent for seven days. 9 On the seventh day[q] they must shave off all their hair;[r] they must shave their head, their beard, their eyebrows and the rest of their hair. They must wash their clothes and bathe themselves with water, and they will be clean.[s]

10 "On the eighth day[t] they must bring two male lambs and one ewe lamb[u] a year old, each without defect, along with three-tenths of an ephah[b][v] of the finest flour mixed with olive oil for a grain offering,[w] and one log[c] of oil.[x] 11 The priest who pronounces them clean shall present[y] both the one to be cleansed and their offerings before the LORD at the entrance to the tent of meeting.[z]

12 "Then the priest is to take one of the male lambs and offer it as a guilt offering,[a] along with the log of oil; he shall wave them before the LORD as a wave offering.[b] 13 He is to slaughter the lamb in the sanctuary area[c] where the sin offering[d] and the burnt offering are slaughtered. Like the sin

[a] 3 The Hebrew word for *defiling skin disease,* traditionally translated "leprosy," was used for various diseases affecting the skin; also in verses 7, 32, 54 and 57. [b] 10 That is, probably about 11 pounds or about 5 kilograms [c] 10 That is, about 1/3 quart or about 0.3 liter; also in verses 12, 15, 21 and 24
[d] 13 Or *purification offering;* also in verses 19, 22 and 31

13:49 [x] Mk 1:44 **13:50** [y] Eze 44:23 **13:51** [z] S ver 5 [a] Lev 14:44 **13:52** [b] ver 55, 57 **14:2** [c] Lev 13:57; Dt 24:8; Mt 8:2-4; Mk 1:40-44; Lk 5:12-14; 17:14 **14:3** [d] Lev 13:46 [e] S Lev 13:2 **14:4** [f] S Ex 12:22 [g] ver 6, 49, 51, 52; Nu 19:6; Ps 51:7 **14:5** [h] ver 50 **14:6** [i] S ver 4 **14:7** [j] ver 51 [k] 2Ki 5:10, 14; Isa 52:15; Eze 36:25 [l] ver 53 **14:8** [m] S Lev 11:25 [n] ver 9; S Ex 29:4; Lev 15:5; 17:15; 22:6; Nu 19:7, 8 [o] ver 20 [p] S Lev 13:11; Nu 5:2, 3; 12:14, 15; 19:20; 31:24; 2Ch 26:21 **14:9** [q] S Lev 13:5 [r] Nu 6:9; Dt 21:12 [s] S Lev 13:6 **14:10** [t] Nu 6:10; Mt 8:4; Mk 1:44; Lk 5:14 [u] S Lev 4:32 [v] Nu 15:9; 28:20 [w] Lev 2:1 [x] ver 12, 15, 21, 24 **14:11** [y] Nu 6:16 [z] Nu 6:10 **14:12** [a] S Lev 5:18 [b] S Ex 29:24 **14:13** [c] S Ex 29:11

13:54 *washed.* See vv. 34,55 – 56,58. The treatment of disorders commonly included washing.
13:59 A summary of ch. 13.
14:1 – 32 The ritual after the skin disease had been cured had three parts: (1) ritual for the first week (outside the camp, vv. 1 – 7), (2) ritual for the second week (inside the camp, vv. 8 – 20) and (3) special permission for the poor (vv. 21 – 32).
14:4 *hyssop.* A plant used in ceremonial cleansing (see note on Ex 12:22).
14:5 *killed.* Diseases and disorders were a symbol of sin and rendered a person or object ceremonially unclean. The prescribed cleansing included sacrifice as well as washing (see note on 13:54).
14:6 *cedar ... yarn ... hyssop.* Also used for cleansing in vv. 51 – 52; Nu 19:6 (see note there).
14:7,16,51 *Seven times.* See note on 4:6.
14:7 *clean.* Perhaps the yarn and cedar stick were used as well as the hyssop plant to sprinkle the blood for cleansing (see Ps 51:7 and note). Further sacrifices are specified in vv. 10 – 31. *release the live bird.* Cf. 16:22; see note on 16:5.
14:8 The Levites were similarly cleansed (see Nu 8:7 and note).
14:10 *grain offering.* See note on 2:1.
14:12 *guilt offering.* See 5:14 — 6:7 and note on 5:15. *wave offering.* See note on 7:30 – 32.
14:13 *most holy.* See note on Ex 3:5.

offering, the guilt offering belongs to the priest;[d] it is most holy. 14 The priest is to take some of the blood of the guilt offering and put it on the lobe of the right ear of the one to be cleansed, on the thumb of their right hand and on the big toe of their right foot.[e] 15 The priest shall then take some of the log of oil, pour it in the palm of his own left hand,[f] 16 dip his right forefinger into the oil in his palm, and with his finger sprinkle some of it before the LORD seven times.[g] 17 The priest is to put some of the oil remaining in his palm on the lobe of the right ear of the one to be cleansed, on the thumb of their right hand and on the big toe of their right foot, on top of the blood of the guilt offering.[h] 18 The rest of the oil in his palm the priest shall put on the head of the one to be cleansed[i] and make atonement for them before the LORD.

19 "Then the priest is to sacrifice the sin offering and make atonement for the one to be cleansed from their uncleanness.[j] After that, the priest shall slaughter the burnt offering 20 and offer it on the altar, together with the grain offering, and make atonement for them,[k] and they will be clean.[l]

21 "If, however, they are poor[m] and cannot afford these,[n] they must take one male lamb as a guilt offering to be waved to make atonement for them, together with a tenth of an ephah[a] of the finest flour mixed with olive oil for a grain offering, a log of oil, 22 and two doves or two young pigeons,[o] such as they can afford, one for a sin offering and the other for a burnt offering.[p]

23 "On the eighth day they must bring them for their cleansing to the priest at the entrance to the tent of meeting,[q] before the LORD.[r] 24 The priest is to take the lamb for the guilt offering,[s] together with the log of oil,[t] and wave them before the LORD as a wave offering.[u] 25 He shall slaughter the lamb for the guilt offering and take some of its blood and put it on the lobe of the right ear of the one to be cleansed, on the thumb of their right hand and on the big toe of their right foot.[v] 26 The priest is to pour some of the oil into the palm of his own left hand,[w] 27 and with his right forefinger sprinkle some of the oil from his palm seven times before the LORD. 28 Some of the oil in his palm he is to put on the same places he put the blood of the guilt offering—on the lobe of the right ear of the one to be cleansed, on the thumb of their right hand and on the big toe of their right foot. 29 The rest of the oil in his palm the priest shall put on the head of the one to be cleansed, to make atonement for them before the LORD.[x] 30 Then he shall sacrifice the doves or the young pigeons, such as the person can afford,[y] 31 one as a sin offering and the other as a burnt offering,[z] together with the grain offering. In this way the priest will make atonement before the LORD on behalf of the one to be cleansed.[a]"

32 These are the regulations for anyone who has a defiling skin disease[b] and who cannot afford the regular offerings[c] for their cleansing.

Cleansing From Defiling Molds

33 The LORD said to Moses and Aaron, 34 "When you enter the land of Canaan,[d] which I am giving you as your possession,[e] and I put a spreading mold in a house in that land, 35 the owner of the house must go and tell the priest, 'I have seen something that looks like a defiling mold in my house.' 36 The priest is to order the house to be emptied before he goes in to examine the mold, so that nothing in the house will be pronounced unclean. After this the priest is to go in and inspect the house. 37 He is to examine the mold on the walls, and if it has greenish or reddish[f] depressions that appear to be deeper than the surface of the wall, 38 the priest shall go out the doorway of the house and close it up for seven days.[g] 39 On the seventh day[h] the priest shall return to inspect the house. If the mold has spread on the walls, 40 he is to order that the contaminated stones be torn out and thrown into an unclean place outside the town.[i] 41 He must have all the inside walls of the house scraped and the material that is scraped off dumped into an unclean place outside the town. 42 Then they are to take other stones to replace these and take new clay and plaster the house.

43 "If the defiling mold reappears in the house after the stones have been torn out and the house scraped and plastered, 44 the priest is to go and examine it and, if the mold has spread in the house, it is a persistent defiling mold; the house is unclean.[j] 45 It must be torn down—its stones,

[a] *21* That is, probably about 3 1/2 pounds or about 1.6 kilograms

14:13 [d] Lev 6:24-30; S 7:7
14:14 [e] S Ex 29:20
14:15 [f] ver 26
14:16 [g] ver 27
14:17 [h] ver 28
14:18 [i] ver 31; Lev 15:15
14:19 [j] ver 31; S Lev 5:3; 15:15
14:20 [k] Lev 15:30 [l] ver 8
14:21 [m] S Lev 5:7 [n] ver 22,32
14:22 [o] S Lev 5:7 [p] Lev 15:30
14:23 [q] Lev 15:14,29 [r] S ver 10,11
14:24 [s] Nu 6:14 [t] S ver 10 [u] ver 12
14:25 [v] S Ex 29:20
14:26 [w] ver 15
14:29 [x] ver 18
14:30 [y] S Lev 5:7
14:31 [z] ver 22; Lev 5:7; 15:15, 30 [a] S ver 18,19
14:32 [b] S Lev 13:2 [c] S ver 21
14:34 [d] Ge 12:5; Ex 6:4; Nu 13:2 [e] Ge 17:8; 48:4; Nu 27:12; 32:22; Dt 3:27; 7:1; 32:49
14:37 [f] S Lev 13:19
14:38 [g] S Lev 13:4
14:39 [h] Lev 13:5
14:40 [i] ver 45
14:44 [j] Lev 13:51

14:14 See note on 8:14.
14:18–21,29,31 *atonement.* See notes on 16:20–22; 17:11; Ex 25:17; cf. note and NIV text note on Ro 3:25.
14:19 *sin offering.* See 4:1—5:13 and notes on 4:3,5. *burnt offering.* See note on 1:3.
14:20 *grain offering.* See note on 2:1.
14:33–53 There are many similarities between this section and the previous one, particularly in the manner of restoration.
14:45 *torn down.* A house desecrated by mold or fungus would be a defiled place to live in, so drastic measures had to be taken.

timbers and all the plaster—and taken out of the town to an unclean place.

46“Anyone who goes into the house while it is closed up will be unclean till evening.[k] 47Anyone who sleeps or eats in the house must wash their clothes.[l]

48“But if the priest comes to examine it and the mold has not spread after the house has been plastered, he shall pronounce the house clean,[m] because the defiling mold is gone. 49To purify the house he is to take two birds and some cedar wood, scarlet yarn and hyssop.[n] 50He shall kill one of the birds over fresh water in a clay pot.[o] 51Then he is to take the cedar wood, the hyssop,[p] the scarlet yarn and the live bird, dip them into the blood of the dead bird and the fresh water, and sprinkle the house seven times.[q] 52He shall purify the house with the bird’s blood, the fresh water, the live bird, the cedar wood, the hyssop and the scarlet yarn. 53Then he is to release the live bird in the open fields[r] outside the town. In this way he will make atonement for the house, and it will be clean.[s]”

54These are the regulations for any defiling skin disease,[t] for a sore, 55for defiling molds[u] in fabric or in a house, 56and for a swelling, a rash or a shiny spot,[v] 57to determine when something is clean or unclean.

These are the regulations for defiling skin diseases and defiling molds.[w]

Discharges Causing Uncleanness

15 The Lord said to Moses and Aaron, 2“Speak to the Israelites and say to them: ‘When any man has an unusual bodily discharge,[x] such a discharge is unclean. 3Whether it continues flowing from his body or is blocked, it will make him unclean. This is how his discharge will bring about uncleanness:

4“ ‘Any bed the man with a discharge lies on will be unclean, and anything he sits on will be unclean. 5Anyone who touches his bed must wash their clothes[y] and bathe with water,[z] and they will be unclean till evening.[a] 6Whoever sits on anything that the man with a discharge sat on must wash their clothes and bathe with water, and they will be unclean till evening.

7“ ‘Whoever touches the man[b] who has a discharge[c] must wash their clothes and bathe with water, and they will be unclean till evening.

8“ ‘If the man with the discharge spits[d] on anyone who is clean, they must wash their clothes and bathe with water, and they will be unclean till evening.

9“ ‘Everything the man sits on when riding will be unclean, 10and whoever touches any of the things that were under him will be unclean till evening; whoever picks up those things[e] must wash their clothes and bathe with water, and they will be unclean till evening.

11“ ‘Anyone the man with a discharge touches without rinsing his hands with water must wash their clothes and bathe with water, and they will be unclean till evening.

12“ ‘A clay pot[f] that the man touches must be broken, and any wooden article[g] is to be rinsed with water.

13“ ‘When a man is cleansed from his discharge, he is to count off seven days[h] for his ceremonial cleansing; he must wash his clothes and bathe himself with fresh water, and he will be clean.[i] 14On the eighth day he must take two doves or two young pigeons[j] and come before the Lord to the entrance to the tent of meeting and give them to the priest. 15The priest is to sacrifice them, the one for a sin offering[a][k] and the other for a burnt offering.[l] In this way he will make atonement before the Lord for the man because of his discharge.[m]

16“ ‘When a man has an emission of semen,[n] he must bathe his whole body with water, and he will be unclean till evening.[o] 17Any clothing or leather that has semen on it must be washed with water, and it will be unclean till evening. 18When a man has sexual relations with a woman and there is an emission of semen,[p] both of them must bathe with water, and they will be unclean till evening.

19“ ‘When a woman has her regular flow of blood, the impurity of her monthly period[q] will last seven days, and anyone who touches her will be unclean till evening.

20“ ‘Anything she lies on during her period will be unclean, and anything she sits

14:46 [k]S Lev 11:24 **14:47** [l]S Lev 11:25 **14:48** [m]S Lev 13:6 **14:49** [n]ver 4; 1Ki 4:33 **14:50** [o]ver 5 **14:51** [p]ver 6; Ps 51:7 [q]S ver 4,7 **14:53** [r]S ver 7 [s]ver 20 **14:54** [t]Lev 13:2 **14:55** [u]Lev 13:47-52 **14:56** [v]Lev 13:2 **14:57** [w]S Lev 10:10 **15:2** [x]ver 16, 32; Lev 22:4; Nu 5:2; 2Sa 3:29; Mt 9:20 **15:5** [y]S Lev 11:25 [z]Lev 14:8 [a]S Lev 11:24

15:7 [b]ver 19; Lev 22:5 [c]ver 16; Lev 22:4 **15:8** [d]Nu 12:14 **15:10** [e]Nu 19:10 **15:12** [f]S Lev 6:28 [g]S Lev 11:32 **15:13** [h]S Lev 8:33 [i]ver 5 **15:14** [j]Lev 14:22 **15:15** [k]Lev 5:7 [l]Lev 14:31 [m]S Lev 14:18, 19 **15:16** [n]S ver 2; Dt 23:10 [o]ver 5; Dt 23:11 **15:18** [p]1Sa 21:4 **15:19** [q]S ver 24

[a] *15* Or *purification offering*; also in verse 30

14:54–57 A summary of chs. 13; 14.

15:1–33 The chapter deals with (1) male uncleanness caused by bodily discharge (vv. 2–15) or emission of semen (vv. 16–18); (2) female uncleanness caused by her monthly period (vv. 19–24) or lengthy hemorrhaging (vv. 25–30); (3) summary (vv. 31–33).

15:2 *bodily discharge.* Probably either diarrhea or urethral discharge (various kinds of infections). The contamination of anything under the man (v. 10), whether he sat (vv. 4,6,9) or lay (v. 4) on it, indicates that the bodily discharge had to do with the buttocks or genitals.

15:4 *bed.* Something like a mat (cf. 2Sa 11:13).

15:13 *cleansed.* God brought about the healing; the priest could only ascertain that a person was already healed.

15:16 *semen.* Normal sexual activity and a woman’s menstruation required no sacrifices but only washing and a minimal period of uncleanness.

15:19 *seven days.* See 12:2. This regulation is the background of 2Sa 11:4 (Bathsheba; see note there).

15:20 See note on Ge 31:35.

on will be unclean. 21 Anyone who touches
her bed will be unclean; they must wash
their clothes and bathe with water, and
they will be unclean till evening.[r] 22 Anyone who touches anything she sits on will
be unclean; they must wash their clothes
and bathe with water, and they will be unclean till evening. 23 Whether it is the bed or
anything she was sitting on, when anyone
touches it, they will be unclean till evening.
24 " 'If a man has sexual relations with
her and her monthly flow[s] touches him, he
will be unclean for seven days; any bed he
lies on will be unclean.
25 " 'When a woman has a discharge of
blood for many days at a time other than
her monthly period[t] or has a discharge
that continues beyond her period, she
will be unclean as long as she has the discharge, just as in the days of her period.
26 Any bed she lies on while her discharge
continues will be unclean, as is her bed
during her monthly period, and anything
she sits on will be unclean, as during her
period. 27 Anyone who touches them will
be unclean; they must wash their clothes
and bathe with water, and they will be unclean till evening.
28 " 'When she is cleansed from her discharge, she must count off seven days,
and after that she will be ceremonially
clean. 29 On the eighth day she must take
two doves or two young pigeons[u] and
bring them to the priest at the entrance to
the tent of meeting. 30 The priest is to sacrifice one for a sin offering and the other for
a burnt offering. In this way he will make
atonement for her before the LORD for the
uncleanness of her discharge.[v]
31 " 'You must keep the Israelites separate from things that make them unclean,
so they will not die in their uncleanness
for defiling my dwelling place,[a][w] which is
among them.' "
32 These are the regulations for a man
with a discharge, for anyone made unclean by an emission of semen,[x] 33 for a
woman in her monthly period, for a man
or a woman with a discharge, and for a
man who has sexual relations with a
woman who is ceremonially unclean.[y]

The Day of Atonement

16:2-34pp — Lev 23:26-32; Nu 29:7-11

16 The LORD spoke to Moses after
the death of the two sons of Aaron who died when they approached the
LORD.[z] 2 The LORD said to Moses: "Tell
your brother Aaron that he is not to come
whenever he chooses[a] into the Most Holy
Place[b] behind the curtain[c] in front of the
atonement cover[d] on the ark, or else he
will die. For I will appear[e] in the cloud[f]
over the atonement cover.

[a] 31 Or *my tabernacle*

15:21 [r] ver 27 **15:24** [s] ver 19; Lev 12:2; 18:19; 20:18; Eze 18:6 **15:25** [t] Mt 9:20; Mk 5:25; Lk 8:43 **15:29** [u] Lev 14:22 **15:30** [v] Lev 5:10; 14:20,31; 18:19; 2Sa 11:4; Mk 5:25; Lk 8:43 **15:31** [w] Lev 20:3; Nu 5:3; 19:13, 20; 2Sa 15:25; 2Ki 21:7; Ps 33:14; 74:7; 76:2; Eze 5:11; 23:38 **15:32** [x] S ver 2 **15:33** [y] ver 19, 24,25 **16:1** [z] S Lev 10:1 **16:2** [a] Ex 30:10; Heb 9:7 [b] S Ex 26:33; Heb 9:25; 10:19 [c] S Ex 26:33; Heb 6:19 [d] S Ex 26:34 [e] S Ex 25:22 [f] S Ex 40:34; S 2Sa 22:10

15:24 *flow.* During her period a woman was protected from sexual activity (18:19), but this appears to be a case of a woman's period beginning during intercourse.

15:25 *discharge of blood for many days.* As, e.g., the woman in Mt 9:20 (see note on Mk 5:25). *beyond her period.* An unnatural discharge, possibly caused by disease, was treated like a sickness and required an offering upon recovery (vv. 28–30; see vv. 14–15).

15:31 Addressed to the priests, thus emphasizing the importance of the regulations. Since God dwelt in the tabernacle, any unholiness, symbolized by the discharges of ch. 15, could result in death if the people came into his presence. Sin separates all people from a holy God and results in their death unless atonement is made (see the next chapter).

15:32–33 A summary of ch. 15.

16:1–34 See 23:26–32; 25:9; Ex 30:10; Nu 29:7–11; Heb 9:7. The order of ritual for the Day of Atonement was as follows: (1) The high priest went to the basin in the courtyard, removed his regular garments, washed himself and went into the Holy Place to put on the special garments for the Day of Atonement (v. 4). (2) He went out to sacrifice a bull at the altar of burnt offering as a sin offering for himself and the other priests (v. 11). (3) He went into the Most Holy Place with some of the bull's blood, with incense and with coals from the altar of burnt offering (vv. 12–13). The incense was placed on the burning coals, and the smoke of the incense hid the ark from view. (4) He sprinkled some of the bull's blood on and in front of the atonement cover of the ark (v. 14). (5) He went outside the tabernacle and cast lots for two goats to see which was to be sacrificed and which was to be the scapegoat (vv. 7–8). (6) At the altar of burnt offering the high priest killed the goat for the sin offering for the people, and for a second time he went into the Most Holy Place, this time to sprinkle the goat's blood in front of and on the atonement cover (vv. 5,9,15–16a). (7) He returned to the Holy Place (called the "tent of meeting" in v. 16) and sprinkled the goat's blood there (v. 16b). (8) He went outside to the altar of burnt offering and sprinkled it (vv. 18–19) with the blood of the bull (for himself, v. 11) and of the goat (for the people, v. 15). (9) While in the courtyard, he laid both hands on the second goat, thus symbolizing the transfer of Israel's sin, and sent it out into the wilderness (vv. 20–22). (10) The man who took the goat away, after he had accomplished his task, washed himself and his clothes outside the camp (v. 26) before rejoining the people. (11) The high priest entered the Holy Place to remove his special garments (v. 23). (12) He went out to the basin to wash and put on his regular priestly clothes (v. 24). (13) As a final sacrifice he went out to the altar and offered a ram (v. 3) as a burnt offering for himself, and another ram (v. 5) for the people (v. 24). (14) The conclusion of the entire day was the removal of the sacrifices for the sin offerings to a place outside the camp, where they were burned, and there the man who performed this ritual bathed and washed his clothes (vv. 27–28) before rejoining the people.

16:1 *sons of Aaron who died.* See 10:1–3.

16:2 *atonement cover.* See Ex 25:17 and note. Blood sprinkled on the lid of the ark made atonement for Israel on the Day of Atonement (vv. 15–17). In the Septuagint (the pre-Christian Greek translation of the OT) the word for "atonement cover" is the same one used of Christ and translated "sacrifice of atonement" in Ro 3:25 (see NIV text note there).

3"This is how Aaron is to enter the Most
Holy Place:[g] He must first bring a young
bull[h] for a sin offering[a] and a ram for a
burnt offering.[i] 4He is to put on the sacred
linen tunic,[j] with linen undergarments
next to his body; he is to tie the linen sash
around him and put on the linen turban.[k]
These are sacred garments;[l] so he must
bathe himself with water[m] before he puts
them on.[n] 5From the Israelite community[o]
he is to take two male goats[p] for a sin offering and a ram for a burnt offering.

6"Aaron is to offer the bull for his own
sin offering to make atonement for himself
and his household.[q] 7Then he is to take
the two goats and present them before the
LORD at the entrance to the tent of meeting. 8He is to cast lots[r] for the two goats—
one lot for the LORD and the other for the
scapegoat.[b][s] 9Aaron shall bring the goat
whose lot falls to the LORD and sacrifice
it for a sin offering. 10But the goat chosen
by lot as the scapegoat shall be presented
alive before the LORD to be used for making atonement[t] by sending it into the wilderness as a scapegoat.

11"Aaron shall bring the bull for his own
sin offering to make atonement for himself
and his household,[u] and he is to slaughter
the bull for his own sin offering. 12He is to
take a censer full of burning coals[v] from
the altar before the LORD and two handfuls
of finely ground fragrant incense[w] and take
them behind the curtain. 13He is to put the
incense on the fire before the LORD, and
the smoke of the incense will conceal the
atonement cover[x] above the tablets of the
covenant law, so that he will not die.[y] 14He
is to take some of the bull's blood[z] and
with his finger sprinkle it on the front of
the atonement cover; then he shall sprinkle some of it with his finger seven times
before the atonement cover.[a]

15"He shall then slaughter the goat for
the sin offering for the people[b] and take its
blood behind the curtain[c] and do with it as
he did with the bull's blood: He shall sprinkle[d] it on the atonement cover and in front
of it. 16In this way he will make atonement[e] for the Most Holy Place[f] because of
the uncleanness and rebellion of the Israelites, whatever their sins have been. He
is to do the same for the tent of meeting,[g]
which is among them in the midst of their
uncleanness. 17No one is to be in the tent
of meeting from the time Aaron goes in to
make atonement in the Most Holy Place
until he comes out, having made atonement for himself, his household and the
whole community of Israel.

18"Then he shall come out to the altar[h]
that is before the LORD and make atonement for it. He shall take some of the
bull's blood and some of the goat's blood
and put it on all the horns of the altar.[i]
19He shall sprinkle some of the blood on
it with his finger seven times to cleanse it
and to consecrate it from the uncleanness
of the Israelites.[j]

20"When Aaron has finished making
atonement for the Most Holy Place, the
tent of meeting and the altar, he shall
bring forward the live goat.[k] 21He is to lay
both hands on the head of the live goat[l]
and confess[m] over it all the wickedness
and rebellion of the Israelites—all their
sins—and put them on the goat's head.
He shall send the goat away into the wilderness in the care of someone appointed
for the task. 22The goat will carry on itself
all their sins[n] to a remote place; and the
man shall release it in the wilderness.

23"Then Aaron is to go into the tent of
meeting and take off the linen garments[o]
he put on before he entered the Most
Holy Place, and he is to leave them there.[p]
24He shall bathe himself with water in
the sanctuary area[q] and put on his regu-

16:3 [g]ver 6; Lev 4:1-12; Heb 9:24,25 [h]S Lev 4:3 [i]ver 5 **16:4** [j]S Lev 8:13 [k]S Ex 28:39 [l]ver 32; S Ex 28:42; 29:29,30; Lev 21:10; Nu 20:26,28 [m]S Ex 29:4; Heb 10:22 [n]Eze 9:2; 44:17-18 **16:5** [o]S Lev 4:13-21 [p]ver 20; S Lev 4:3; 2Ch 29:23; Ps 50:9 **16:6** [q]Lev 9:7; Heb 7:27; 9:7,12 **16:8** [r]Nu 26:55, 56; 33:54; 34:13; Jos 14:2; 18:6; Jdg 20:9; Ne 10:34; Est 3:7; 9:24; Ps 22:18; Pr 16:33 [s]ver 10, 26 **16:10** [t]Isa 53:4-10; S Ro 3:25 **16:11** [u]S ver 6, 24,33 **16:12** [v]S Lev 10:1; Rev 8:5 [w]S Ex 25:6; 30:34-38 **16:13** [x]S Ex 25:17 [y]S Ex 28:43 **16:14** [z]S Lev 4:5; Heb 9:7,13,25 [a]S Lev 4:6 **16:15** [b]S Lev 4:13-21; Heb 7:27; 9:7,12; 13:11 [c]Heb 9:3 [d]S Lev 4:17; Nu 19:19; Isa 52:15; Eze 36:25 **16:16** [e]S Ex 29:36; S Ro 3:25 [f]S Ex 26:33; Heb 9:25 [g]Ex 29:4; S 40:2 **16:18** [h]S Lev 4:7 [i]S Lev 4:25 **16:19** [j]Eze 43:20

[a] 3 Or *purification offering*; here and throughout this chapter [b] 8 The meaning of the Hebrew for this word is uncertain; also in verses 10 and 26.

16:20 [k]S ver 5 **16:21** [l]S Ex 29:10 [m]S Lev 5:5 **16:22** [n]S Ex 28:38; Isa 53:12 **16:23** [o]S Ex 28:42 [p]Eze 42:14 **16:24** [q]S Lev 6:16

16:3 *bull.* For Aaron's cleansing (vv. 6,11). Before Aaron could minister in the Most Holy Place for the nation, he himself had to be cleansed (Heb 5:1–3); not so Christ, who is our high priest and Aaron's antitype (Heb 7:26–28).

16:5 *two male goats for a sin offering.* One was the usual sin offering (see notes on 4:3,5) and the other a scapegoat. No single offering could fully typify the atonement of Christ. The one goat was killed, its blood sprinkled in the Most Holy Place and its body burned outside the camp (vv. 15,27), symbolizing the payment of the price of Christ's atonement. The other goat, sent away alive and bearing the sins of the nation (v. 21), symbolized the removal of sin and its guilt. *ram.* For the sins of the people; the one in v. 3 was for the sins of the high priest. Both were sacrificed at the end of the ceremony (v. 24).

16:6–10 An outline of vv. 11–22.

16:8 *scapegoat.* See NIV text note.

16:11 *make atonement for himself.* See note on v. 3.

16:13 *smoke of the incense.* Covered the ark so that the high priest would not see the glorious presence of God (v. 2) and thus die. *the tablets of the covenant law.* See note on Ex 25:22.

16:14 See Ro 3:25 and note. *seven times.* See note on 4:6.

16:16 *tent of meeting.* Here and in vv. 17,20,33 the term refers to the Holy Place.

16:20–22 A summary description of substitutionary atonement. The sin of the worshipers was confessed and symbolically transferred to the sacrificial animal, on which hands were laid (see notes on 1:3; Ex 29:10; see also Lev 1:4; 3:8; 4:4; cf. Isa 53:6; Jn 1:29; 1Pe 2:24).

16:24 *sanctuary area.* Cf. 6:26. *burnt offering ... burnt offering.* The two rams mentioned in vv. 3,5.

lar garments.[r] Then he shall come out and sacrifice the burnt offering for himself and the burnt offering for the people,[s] to make atonement for himself and for the people.[t] 25 He shall also burn the fat of the sin offering on the altar.

26 "The man who releases the goat as a scapegoat[u] must wash his clothes[v] and bathe himself with water;[w] afterward he may come into the camp. 27 The bull and the goat for the sin offerings, whose blood was brought into the Most Holy Place to make atonement, must be taken outside the camp;[x] their hides, flesh and intestines are to be burned up. 28 The man who burns them must wash his clothes and bathe himself with water; afterward he may come into the camp.[y]

29 "This is to be a lasting ordinance[z] for you: On the tenth day of the seventh month[a] you must deny yourselves[a][b] and not do any work[c]—whether native-born[d] or a foreigner residing among you— 30 because on this day atonement will be made[e] for you, to cleanse you. Then, before the LORD, you will be clean from all your sins.[f] 31 It is a day of sabbath rest, and you must deny yourselves;[g] it is a lasting ordinance.[h] 32 The priest who is anointed and ordained[i] to succeed his father as high priest is to make atonement. He is to put on the sacred linen garments[j] 33 and make atonement for the Most Holy Place, for the tent of meeting and the altar, and for the priests and all the members of the community.[k]

34 "This is to be a lasting ordinance[l] for you: Atonement is to be made once a year[m] for all the sins of the Israelites."

And it was done, as the LORD commanded Moses.

Eating Blood Forbidden

17 The LORD said to Moses, 2 "Speak to Aaron and his sons[n] and to all the Israelites and say to them: 'This is what the LORD has commanded: 3 Any Israelite who sacrifices an ox,[b] a lamb[o] or a goat[p] in the camp or outside of it 4 instead of bringing it to the entrance to the tent of meeting[q] to present it as an offering to the LORD in front of the tabernacle of the LORD[r]—that person shall be considered guilty of bloodshed; they have shed blood and must be cut off from their people.[s] 5 This is so the Israelites will bring to the LORD the sacrifices they are now making in the open fields. They must bring them to the priest, that is, to the LORD, at the entrance to the tent of meeting and sacrifice them as fellowship offerings.[t] 6 The priest is to splash the blood against the altar[u] of the LORD[v] at the entrance to the tent of meeting and burn the fat as an aroma pleasing to the LORD.[w] 7 They must no longer offer any of their sacrifices to the goat idols[c][x] to whom they prostitute themselves.[y] This is to be a lasting ordinance[z] for them and for the generations to come.'[a]

8 "Say to them: 'Any Israelite or any foreigner residing among them who offers a burnt offering or sacrifice 9 and does not bring it to the entrance to the tent[b] of meeting[c] to sacrifice it to the LORD[d] must be cut off from the people of Israel.

10 " 'I will set my face against any Israelite or any foreigner residing among them who eats blood,[e] and I will cut them off from the people. 11 For the life of a creature is in the blood,[f] and I have given it to you to make atonement for yourselves on the altar; it is the blood that makes atonement for one's life.[d][g] 12 Therefore I say to the Israelites, "None of you may eat blood, nor may any foreigner residing among you eat blood."

13 " 'Any Israelite or any foreigner residing among you who hunts any animal or bird

16:24 [r] ver 3-5 [s] Lev 1:3 [t] S ver 11 **16:26** [u] S ver 8 [v] S Lev 11:25 [w] Lev 14:8 **16:27** [x] S Ex 29:14 **16:28** [y] Nu 19:8, 10 **16:29** [z] S Ex 12:14 [a] Lev 25:9 [b] ver 31; Lev 23:27, 32; Nu 29:7; Isa 58:3 [c] S Ex 31:15; S Lev 23:28 [d] Ex 12:19 **16:30** [e] S Ex 30:10 [f] Ps 51:2; Jer 33:8; Eze 36:33; Zec 13:1; Eph 5:26 **16:31** [g] Ezr 8:21; Isa 58:3,5; Da 10:12 [h] Ac 27:9 **16:32** [i] S Ex 30:30 [j] S ver 4; S Ex 28:2 **16:33** [k] S ver 11,16-18; Eze 45:18 **16:34** [l] S Ex 27:21 [m] Heb 9:7,25 **17:2** [n] Lev 10:6, 12 **17:3** [o] S Lev 3:7 [p] S Lev 7:23 **17:4** [q] ver 9; 1Ki 8:4; 2Ch 1:3 [r] Dt 12:5-21 [s] S Ge 17:14 **17:5** [t] S Lev 3:1; Eze 43:27 **17:6** [u] S Lev 4:18 [v] S Lev 3:2 [w] S Lev 1:9 **17:7** [x] S Ex 22:20 [y] S Ex 34:15; Jer 3:6,9; Eze 23:3; 1Co 10:20 [z] S Ex 12:14 [a] S Ge 9:12 **17:9** [b] S Lev 1:3 [c] S ver 4 [d] S Lev 3:7 **17:10** [e] S Ge 9:4 **17:11** [f] ver 14 [g] Heb 9:22

[a] 29 Or *must fast;* also in verse 31 [b] 3 The Hebrew word can refer to either male or female. [c] 7 Or *the demons* [d] 11 Or *atonement by the life in the blood*

16:25 *fat of the sin offering.* See 4:8–10.

16:27 *outside the camp.* See note on 4:12.

16:29,31 *deny yourselves.* See NIV text note on v. 29; more lit. "humble (or afflict) yourselves." The expression came to be used of fasting (Ps 35:13). The Day of Atonement was the only regular fast day stipulated in the OT (see 23:27,29,32 and NIV text note on v. 29), though tradition later added other fast days to the Jewish calendar (see Zec 7:5; 8:19 and note).

16:29 *seventh month.* Tishri, the seventh month, begins with the Festival of Trumpets (see note on 23:24). The Day of Atonement follows on the 10th day, and on the 15th day the Festival of Tabernacles begins (see 23:23–36). See chart, pp. 188–189.

16:30 *clean from all your sins.* On the Day of Atonement the repentant Israelite was assured of sins forgiven (see notes on Heb 9:12,28).

16:34 *once a year.* Heb 9:11—10:14 repeatedly contrasts this with Christ's "once for all" sacrifice.

17:1—26:46 Sometimes called the "Holiness Code," these chapters deal with regulations for holy living and holy practices in various areas (see Introduction: Theological Themes; Outline; see also note on 11:44).

17:4 *tabernacle of the LORD.* The people, with few exceptions (e.g., Dt 12:15,20–21), were directed to sacrifice only at the central sanctuary (Dt 12:5–6). Sennacherib's representative referred to Hezekiah's requiring worship only in Jerusalem (2Ki 18:22). One reason for such a regulation was to keep the Israelites from becoming corrupted by the Canaanites' pagan worship. *cut off from their people.* See note on 7:20.

17:5 *to the priest, that is, to the LORD.* See note on 6:6.

17:7 *prostitute themselves.* See Ex 34:15 and note.

17:11 *the life of a creature is in the blood.* See note on Ge 9:4. The blood shed in the sacrifices was sacred. It epitomized the life of the sacrificial victim. Since life was sacred, blood (a symbol of life) had to be treated with respect

that may be eaten must drain out the blood and cover it with earth,[h] 14 because the life of every creature is its blood. That is why I have said to the Israelites, "You must not eat the blood of any creature, because the life of every creature is its blood; anyone who eats it must be cut off."[i]

15 " 'Anyone, whether native-born or foreigner, who eats anything[j] found dead or torn by wild animals[k] must wash their clothes and bathe with water,[l] and they will be ceremonially unclean till evening;[m] then they will be clean. 16 But if they do not wash their clothes and bathe themselves, they will be held responsible.[n]' "

Unlawful Sexual Relations

18 The LORD said to Moses, 2 "Speak to the Israelites and say to them: 'I am the LORD your God.[o] 3 You must not do as they do in Egypt, where you used to live, and you must not do as they do in the land of Canaan, where I am bringing you. Do not follow their practices.[p] 4 You must obey my laws[q] and be careful to follow my decrees.[r] I am the LORD your God.[s] 5 Keep my decrees and laws,[t] for the person who obeys them will live by them.[u] I am the LORD.

6 " 'No one is to approach any close relative to have sexual relations. I am the LORD.

7 " 'Do not dishonor your father[v] by having sexual relations with your mother.[w] She is your mother; do not have relations with her.

8 " 'Do not have sexual relations with your father's wife;[x] that would dishonor your father.[y]

9 " 'Do not have sexual relations with your sister,[z] either your father's daughter or your mother's daughter, whether she was born in the same home or elsewhere.[a]

10 " 'Do not have sexual relations with your son's daughter or your daughter's daughter; that would dishonor you.

11 " 'Do not have sexual relations with the daughter of your father's wife, born to your father; she is your sister.

12 " 'Do not have sexual relations with your father's sister;[b] she is your father's close relative.

13 " 'Do not have sexual relations with your mother's sister,[c] because she is your mother's close relative.

14 " 'Do not dishonor your father's brother by approaching his wife to have sexual relations; she is your aunt.[d]

15 " 'Do not have sexual relations with your daughter-in-law.[e] She is your son's wife; do not have relations with her.[f]

16 " 'Do not have sexual relations with your brother's wife;[g] that would dishonor your brother.

17 " 'Do not have sexual relations with both a woman and her daughter.[h] Do not have sexual relations with either her son's daughter or her daughter's daughter; they are her close relatives. That is wickedness.

18 " 'Do not take your wife's sister[i] as a

17:13 [h] Lev 7:26; Eze 24:7; 33:25; Ac 15:20 **17:14** [i] S Ge 9:4 **17:15** [j] S Lev 7:24 [k] S Ex 22:31 [l] S Lev 14:8 [m] S Lev 11:40 **17:16** [n] S Lev 5:1 **18:2** [o] S Ge 17:7 **18:3** [p] ver 24-30; S Ex 23:24; Dt 18:9; 2Ki 16:3; 17:8; 1Ch 5:25 **18:4** [q] S Ge 26:5 [r] Dt 4:1; 1Ki 11:11; Jer 44:10,23; Eze 11:12 [s] ver 2 **18:5** [t] S Ge 26:5 [u] Dt 4:1; Ne 9:29; Isa 55:3; Eze 18:9; 20:11; Am 5:4-6; Mt 19:17; S Ro 10:5*; Gal 3:12* **18:7** [v] ver 8; Lev 20:11; Dt 27:20 [w] Eze 22:10 **18:8** [x] 1Co 5:1 [y] Ge 35:22; Lev 20:11; Dt 22:30; 27:20 **18:9** [z] ver 11; Lev 20:17; Dt 27:22 [a] Lev 20:17; Dt 27:22; 2Sa 13:13; Eze 22:11 **18:12** [b] ver 13; Lev 20:19 **18:13** [c] S ver 12, 14; Lev 20:20 **18:14** [d] S ver 13 **18:15** [e] S Ge 11:31; S 38:16 [f] Eze 22:11 **18:16** [g] Lev 20:21; Mt 14:4; Mk 6:18 **18:17** [h] Lev 20:14; Dt 27:23 **18:18** [i] S Ge 30:1

(Ge 9:5–6). Eating blood was therefore strictly forbidden (see 7:26–27; Dt 12:16,23–25; 15:23; 1Sa 14:32–34). *blood ... makes atonement.* Practically every sacrifice included the splashing of blood against the altar or the sprinkling of blood within the tabernacle (v. 6; 1:5; 3:2; 4:6,25; 7:2), thus teaching that atonement involves the substitution of life for life. The blood of the OT sacrifice pointed forward to the blood of the Lamb of God, who obtained for his people "eternal redemption" (Heb 9:12). "Without the shedding of blood there is no forgiveness" (Heb 9:22).

17:15 *found dead or torn.* Such animals would not have had the blood drained from them and therefore would be forbidden.

18:1—20:27 Here God's people are given instructions concerning interpersonal relations and a morality reflecting God's holiness. Israel was thereby prepared for a life different from that of the Canaanites, whose lifestyle was deplorably immoral. Ch. 18 marks the boundaries for marriage and sexual relations (but see also v. 21 and note); ch. 19 provides specific moral guidance on a variety of matters, many of which are implicitly covered by the Ten Commandments; and ch. 20 specifies the penalties for violating God's standard of morality. See chart, p. 287.

18:2 In chs. 18–26 the phrase "I am the LORD" occurs 47 times. The Lord's name (i.e., his revealed character as Yahweh, "the LORD") is the authority that stands behind his instructions. See note on Ex 3:15.

18:3 Six times in this chapter Israel is warned not to follow the example of pagans (here, two times; see also vv. 24,26–27,30).

18:5 *live.* With God's full blessing. The law was the way of life for the redeemed (see Dt 6:2; 8:2–3; 30:20 and notes; 32:47; Eze 20:11,13,21), not a way of salvation for the lost (see Ro 10:5; Gal 3:12).

18:6 A summary of the laws against incest (vv. 7–18). Penalties for incestuous relations are given in ch. 20. (Cf. 1Co 5.)

18:7 This prohibition applied also after the father's death.

18:8 *your father's wife.* Other than your mother—assuming there is more than one wife.

18:11 *sister.* There would be many half sisters in a polygamous society. Tamar claimed that an exception to this prohibition could be made (2Sa 13:12–13; but see note there).

18:14 *your aunt.* See 20:20. If the father's brother was alive, the act would be adulterous. If he was dead, one could rationalize such a marriage because the aunt was not a blood relative—but it was still forbidden.

18:15 Cf. the account of Judah and Tamar (Ge 38:18).

18:16 *your brother's wife.* The law also applied to a time after divorce or the brother's death. To marry one's brother's widow was not immoral but might damage the brother's inheritance. The levirate law of Dt 25:5–6 offered an exception that preserved the dead brother's inheritance and continued his line.

18:17 *daughter.* Stepdaughter (granddaughter-in-law is also covered in the verse). The law applied even after the mother's death.

18:18 Cf. the account of Jacob with Leah and Rachel (Ge 29:23–30).

rival wife and have sexual relations with
her while your wife is living.
19 "'Do not approach a woman to have
sexual relations during the uncleanness[j] of
her monthly period.[k]
20 "'Do not have sexual relations with
your neighbor's wife[l] and defile yourself
with her.
21 "'Do not give any of your children[m]
to be sacrificed to Molek,[n] for you must
not profane the name of your God.[o] I am
the LORD.[p]
22 "'Do not have sexual relations with a
man as one does with a woman;[q] that is
detestable.[r]
23 "'Do not have sexual relations with an
animal and defile yourself with it. A woman must not present herself to an animal
to have sexual relations with it; that is a
perversion.[s]
24 "'Do not defile yourselves in any of
these ways, because this is how the nations that I am going to drive out before
you[t] became defiled.[u] 25 Even the land was
defiled;[v] so I punished it for its sin,[w] and
the land vomited out its inhabitants.[x] 26 But
you must keep my decrees and my laws.[y]
The native-born and the foreigners residing among you must not do any of these
detestable things, 27 for all these things
were done by the people who lived in the
land before you, and the land became defiled. 28 And if you defile the land,[z] it will
vomit you out[a] as it vomited out the nations that were before you.
29 "'Everyone who does any of these
detestable things—such persons must be
cut off from their people. 30 Keep my requirements[b] and do not follow any of the
detestable customs that were practiced before you came and do not defile yourselves
with them. I am the LORD your God.[c]'"

Various Laws

19 The LORD said to Moses, 2 "Speak to
the entire assembly of Israel[d] and
say to them: 'Be holy because I, the LORD
your God,[e] am holy.[f]
3 "'Each of you must respect your mother and father,[g] and you must observe my
Sabbaths.[h] I am the LORD your God.[i]
4 "'Do not turn to idols or make metal
gods for yourselves.[j] I am the LORD your
God.[k]
5 "'When you sacrifice a fellowship offering to the LORD, sacrifice it in such a way
that it will be accepted on your behalf. 6 It
shall be eaten on the day you sacrifice it or
on the next day; anything left over until the
third day must be burned up.[l] 7 If any of it is
eaten on the third day, it is impure and will
not be accepted.[m] 8 Whoever eats it will be
held responsible[n] because they have desecrated what is holy[o] to the LORD; they must
be cut off from their people.[p]
9 "'When you reap the harvest of your
land, do not reap to the very edges[q] of
your field or gather the gleanings of your
harvest.[r] 10 Do not go over your vineyard
a second time[s] or pick up the grapes that
have fallen.[t] Leave them for the poor and
the foreigner.[u] I am the LORD your God.
11 "'Do not steal.[v]
"'Do not lie.[w]
"'Do not deceive one another.[x]
12 "'Do not swear falsely[y] by my name[z]
and so profane[a] the name of your God. I
am the LORD.
13 "'Do not defraud or rob[b] your neighbor.[c]
"'Do not hold back the wages of a hired
worker[d] overnight.[e]
14 "'Do not curse the deaf or put a stumbling block in front of the blind,[f] but fear
your God.[g] I am the LORD.
15 "'Do not pervert justice;[h] do not show
partiality[i] to the poor or favoritism to the
great,[j] but judge your neighbor fairly.[k]

18:19 [j]S Lev 15:25-30 [k]S Lev 15:24 **18:20** [l]S Ex 20:14; Mt 5:27, 28; 1Co 6:9; Heb 13:4 **18:21** [m]Dt 12:31; 18:10; 2Ki 16:3; 17:17; 21:6; 23:10; 2Ch 28:1-4; 33:6; Ps 106:37, 38; Isa 57:5; Jer 7:30,31; 19:5; 32:35; Eze 16:20; Mic 6:7 [n]Lev 20:2-5; Dt 9:4; 1Ki 11:5, 7,33; Isa 57:9; Jer 32:35; 49:1; Zep 1:5 [o]Lev 19:12; 21:6; Isa 48:11; Eze 22:26; 36:20; Am 2:7; Mal 1:12 [p]S Ex 6:2 **18:22** [q]Lev 20:13; Dt 23:18; Ro 1:27; 1Co 6:9 [r]S Ge 19:5 **18:23** [s]Ex 22:19; Lev 20:15; Dt 27:21 **18:24** [t]ver 3,27, 30; Lev 20:23 [u]Dt 9:4; 18:12 **18:25** [v]Nu 35:34; Dt 21:23 [w]Lev 20:23; Dt 9:5; 12:31; 18:12 [x]ver 28; Lev 20:22; Job 20:15; Jer 51:34 **18:26** [y]S Ge 26:5 **18:28** [z]Lev 20:22; Ezr 9:11; La 1:17 [a]S ver 25 **18:30** [b]S Lev 8:35 [c]ver 2 **19:2** [d]Nu 14:5; Ps 68:26 [e]S Ex 20:2 [f]S Ex 15:11; 1Pe 1:16*; S Lev 11:44; S 20:26 **19:3** [g]Ex 20:12 [h]S Ex 20:8 [i]Lev 11:44

19:4 [j]S Ex 20:4; Jdg 17:3; Ps 96:5; 115:4-7; 135:15 [k]Lev 11:44 **19:6** [l]Lev 7:16-17 **19:7** [m]Lev 7:18 **19:8** [n]S Lev 5:1 [o]Lev 22:2, 15,16; Nu 18:32 [p]S Ge 17:14 **19:9** [q]Ru 2:2,3,7,16,17 [r]Lev 23:10, 22; Dt 24:19-22; Job 24:10 **19:10** [s]Dt 24:20 [t]ver 9 [u]Dt 24:19,21 **19:11** [v]Ex 20:15; S 23:4; Lk 3:14 [w]S Ex 20:16; S Eph 4:25 [x]S Lev 6:2 **19:12** [y]Jer 5:2; 7:9; Mal 3:5 [z]Ex 3:13; 20:7; Dt 18:19; Pr 18:10; Isa 42:8; Jer 44:16,26; S Mt 5:33 [a]Jer 34:16 **19:13** [b]S Ex 20:15 [c]Lev 25:14,17; S Ex 22:15,25-27 [d]Job 7:2; 24:12; 31:39; Isa 16:14; Mal 3:5 [e]Dt 24:15; Jer 22:13; Mt 20:8; 1Ti 5:18; Jas 5:4 **19:14** [f]S Ex 4:11; Lev 21:18; Dt 27:18 [g]ver 32; Lev 25:17,36 **19:15** [h]S Ex 23:2; Ex 23:2,6 [i]Dt 24:17; Job 13:8,10; 32:21; Pr 28:21 [j]Job 34:19 [k]S Ex 23:8; Pr 24:23; Mal 2:9; Jas 2:1-4

18:19 See Eze 18:6; 22:10.
18:20 See note on Ex 20:14.
18:21 *Molek.* The god of the Ammonites (see 20:2–5; 1Ki 11:5 and note). The detestable practice of sacrificing children to Molek was common in Phoenicia and other surrounding countries. Cf. 2Ki 3:26–27. King Manasseh evidently sacrificed his sons to Molek (2Ch 33:6; see 2Ki 23:10). Jer 32:35 protests the practice. *profane the name of your God.* Whatever blatantly violates God's revealed will desecrates his name (see note on Ps 5:11) because it fails to honor his holiness (see note on Lev 11:44).
18:22 *have sexual relations with a man.* See 20:13, where the penalty for homosexual acts is death.
18:29 *detestable.* See note on 7:21. *cut off from their people.* See note on 7:20.
19:1 See note on 18:1—20:27.
19:2 *Be holy.* See note on 11:44.
19:3–4 See 18:30; see also Ex 20:4–6,8–12 and notes; and see chart, p. 287.
19:5 *fellowship offering.* See note on 3:1.
19:6 *third day.* See note on 7:15–18.
19:8 *what is holy to the LORD.* See note on Ex 3:5. *cut off from their people.* See note on 7:20.
19:9–10 See 23:22; see also Dt 24:19–21. Ru 2 gives an example of the application of the law of gleaning.
19:11–12 See Ex 20:7,15–16 and notes.
19:13 *wages of a hired worker.* See Dt 24:14–15; Mt 20:8.

16“ ‘Do not go about spreading slander[l]
among your people.
“ ‘Do not do anything that endangers
your neighbor’s life.[m] I am the LORD.
17“ ‘Do not hate a fellow Israelite in your
heart.[n] Rebuke your neighbor frankly[o] so
you will not share in their guilt.
18“ ‘Do not seek revenge[p] or bear a
grudge[q] against anyone among your people,[r] but love your neighbor[s] as yourself.[t]
I am the LORD.
19“ ‘Keep my decrees.[u]
“ ‘Do not mate different kinds of animals.
“ ‘Do not plant your field with two kinds
of seed.[v]
“ ‘Do not wear clothing woven of two
kinds of material.[w]
20“ ‘If a man sleeps with a female slave
who is promised to another man[x] but who
has not been ransomed or given her freedom, there must be due punishment.[a] Yet
they are not to be put to death, because
she had not been freed. 21The man, however, must bring a ram to the entrance
to the tent of meeting for a guilt offering
to the LORD.[y] 22With the ram of the guilt
offering the priest is to make atonement
for him before the LORD for the sin he has
committed, and his sin will be forgiven.[z]
23“ ‘When you enter the land and plant
any kind of fruit tree, regard its fruit as forbidden.[b] For three years you are to consider it forbidden[b]; it must not be eaten. 24In
the fourth year all its fruit will be holy,[a] an
offering of praise to the LORD. 25But in the
fifth year you may eat its fruit. In this way
your harvest will be increased. I am the
LORD your God.
26“ ‘Do not eat any meat with the blood
still in it.[b]
“ ‘Do not practice divination[c] or seek
omens.[d]
27“ ‘Do not cut the hair at the sides of
your head or clip off the edges of your
beard.[e]
28“ ‘Do not cut[f] your bodies for the dead
or put tattoo marks on yourselves. I am
the LORD.
29“ ‘Do not degrade your daughter by
making her a prostitute,[g] or the land will
turn to prostitution and be filled with
wickedness.[h]
30“ ‘Observe my Sabbaths[i] and have reverence for my sanctuary. I am the LORD.[j]
31“ ‘Do not turn to mediums[k] or seek out
spiritists,[l] for you will be defiled by them.
I am the LORD your God.
32“ ‘Stand up in the presence of the
aged, show respect[m] for the elderly[n] and
revere your God.[o] I am the LORD.[p]
33“ ‘When a foreigner resides among
you in your land, do not mistreat them.
34The foreigner residing among you must
be treated as your native-born.[q] Love them
as yourself,[r] for you were foreigners[s] in
Egypt.[t] I am the LORD your God.
35“ ‘Do not use dishonest standards
when measuring length, weight or quantity.[u] 36Use honest scales[v] and honest
weights, an honest ephah[c][w] and an honest hin.[d][x] I am the LORD your God, who
brought you out of Egypt.[y]
37“ ‘Keep all my decrees[z] and all my
laws[a] and follow them. I am the LORD.’ ”

Punishments for Sin

20 The LORD said to Moses, 2“Say to
the Israelites: ‘Any Israelite or any
foreigner residing in Israel who sacrific-

[a] *20* Or *be an inquiry* [b] *23* Hebrew *uncircumcised* [c] *36* An ephah was a dry measure having the capacity of about 3/5 of a bushel or about 22 liters. [d] *36* A hin was a liquid measure having the capacity of about 1 gallon or about 3.8 liters.

19:16 [l] Ps 15:3; 31:13; 41:6; 101:5; Jer 6:28; 9:4; Eze 22:9 [m] Ex 23:7; Dt 10:17; 27:25; Ps 15:5; Eze 22:12 **19:17** [n] S 1Jn 2:9 [o] S Mt 18:15 **19:18** [p] S Ge 4:23; Ro 12:19; Heb 10:30 [q] Ps 103:9 [r] S Ex 12:48 [s] S Ex 20:16 [t] ver 34; S Mt 5:43*; 19:16*; 22:39*; Mk 12:31*; Lk 10:27*; Jn 13:34; Ro 13:9*; Gal 5:14*; Jas 2:8* **19:19** [u] S Ge 26:5 [v] Dt 22:9 [w] Dt 22:11 **19:20** [x] Dt 22:23-27 **19:21** [y] S Lev 5:15 **19:22** [z] S Lev 5:15 **19:24** [a] S Ex 22:29 **19:26** [b] S Ge 9:4 [c] S Ge 30:27; S Isa 44:25 [d] S Ex 22:18; 2Ki 17:17 **19:27** [e] Lev 21:5; Dt 14:1; 2Sa 10:4-5; Jer 41:5; 48:37; Eze 5:1-5 **19:28** [f] Lev 21:5; Dt 14:1; 1Ki 18:28; Jer 16:6; 41:5; 47:5 **19:29** [g] Lev 21:9; Dt 23:18 [h] Ge 34:7; Lev 21:9 **19:30** [i] S Ex 20:8 [j] Lev 26:2 **19:31** [k] S Ex 22:18; 1Sa 28:7-20; 1Ch 10:13 [l] Lev 20:6; 2Ki 21:6; 23:24; Isa 8:19; 19:3; 29:4; 47:12; 65:4 **19:32** [m] 1Ki 12:8 [n] Job 32:4; Pr 23:22; La 5:12; 1Ti 5:1 [o] S ver 14; Job 29:8 [p] Lev 11:44; 25:17 **19:34** [q] S Ex 12:48 [r] S ver 18 [s] S Ex 22:21 [t] Ex 23:9; Dt 10:19; 23:7; Ps 146:9 **19:35** [u] Dt 25:13-16 **19:36** [v] Job 31:6; Pr 11:1; Hos 12:7; Mic 6:11 [w] Jdg 6:19; Ru 2:17; 1Sa 1:24; 17:17; Eze 45:10 [x] Dt 25:13-15; Pr 20:10; Eze 45:11 [y] S Ex 12:17 **19:37** [z] 2Ki 17:37; 2Ch 7:17; Ps 119:5; Eze 18:9 [a] S Ge 26:5

19:17 *Do not hate a fellow Israelite.* See 1Jn 2:9,11; 3:15; 4:20.

19:18 *love your neighbor as yourself.* See v. 34; quoted by Christ (Mt 22:39; Mk 12:31; Lk 10:27), Paul (Ro 13:9; Gal 5:14) and James (2:8). The stricter Pharisees (school of Shammai) added to this command what they thought it implied: "Hate your enemy" (Mt 5:43; see note there). Jesus' reaction, "Love your enemies," was in line with true OT teaching (see vv. 17,34) and was more in agreement with the middle-of-the-road Pharisees. Rabbi Nahmanides (thirteenth century) caught their sentiments: "One should place no limitations upon the love for the neighbor, but instead a person should love to do an abundance of good for his fellow being as he does for himself." "Neighbor" does not merely mean one who lives nearby, but anyone with whom one comes in contact (see Lk 10:25–36 and notes).

19:19 *Do not mate ... plant ... wear.* Such mixing symbolically violated the distinction God established in the creation order.

19:21–22 *guilt offering.* See 5:14—6:7 and note on 5:15.

19:26 *meat with the blood.* See note on 17:11. *seek omens.* See v. 31; Ex 22:18; Dt 18:14; 1Sa 28:9; Isa 47:12–14.

19:27 *Do not cut the hair at the sides of your head.* A prohibition still followed by orthodox Jews.

19:28 There was to be no disfiguring of the body, after the manner of the pagans (see note on 21:5).

19:34 *you were foreigners in Egypt.* See Dt 5:15.

19:35 *dishonest standards.* In a culture with no bureau of weights and measures, cheating in business transactions by falsification of standards was common (see Dt 25:13–16; Pr 11:1 and note; 16:11 and note; 20:10,23). The prophets also condemned such sin (Am 8:5; Mic 6:10–11).

20:1–27 In ch. 20 many of the same sins listed in ch. 18 are mentioned again, but this time usually with the death penalty specified. Israel's God is a jealous God who tolerates no rivals (see note on Ex 20:5). He requires exclusive allegiance (see Ex 20:3 and note). See note on 18:1—20:27.

20:2–5 *Molek.* See note on 18:21.

es any of his children to Molek is to be
put to death.[b] The members of the community are to stone him.[c] 3 I myself will
set my face against him and will cut him
off from his people;[d] for by sacrificing
his children to Molek, he has defiled[e] my
sanctuary[f] and profaned my holy name.[g]
4 If the members of the community close
their eyes when that man sacrifices one
of his children to Molek and if they fail to
put him to death,[h] 5 I myself will set my
face against him and his family and will
cut them off from their people together
with all who follow him in prostituting
themselves to Molek.
6 " 'I will set my face against anyone
who turns to mediums and spiritists to
prostitute themselves by following them,
and I will cut them off from their people.[i]
7 " 'Consecrate yourselves[j] and be holy,[k]
because I am the LORD your God.[l] 8 Keep
my decrees[m] and follow them. I am the
LORD, who makes you holy.[n]
9 " 'Anyone who curses their father[o] or
mother[p] is to be put to death.[q] Because
they have cursed their father or mother,
their blood will be on their own head.[r]
10 " 'If a man commits adultery with another man's wife[s]—with the wife of his
neighbor—both the adulterer and the
adulteress are to be put to death.[t]
11 " 'If a man has sexual relations with
his father's wife, he has dishonored his father.[u] Both the man and the woman are
to be put to death; their blood will be on
their own heads.[v]
12 " 'If a man has sexual relations with
his daughter-in-law,[w] both of them are to
be put to death. What they have done is
a perversion; their blood will be on their
own heads.
13 " 'If a man has sexual relations with a
man as one does with a woman, both of
them have done what is detestable.[x] They
are to be put to death; their blood will be
on their own heads.
14 " 'If a man marries both a woman
and her mother,[y] it is wicked. Both he and
they must be burned in the fire,[z] so that no
wickedness will be among you.[a]
15 " 'If a man has sexual relations with
an animal,[b] he is to be put to death,[c] and
you must kill the animal.
16 " 'If a woman approaches an animal
to have sexual relations with it, kill both
the woman and the animal. They are to be
put to death; their blood will be on their
own heads.
17 " 'If a man marries his sister[d], the
daughter of either his father or his mother, and they have sexual relations, it is a
disgrace. They are to be publicly removed[e]
from their people. He has dishonored his
sister and will be held responsible.[f]
18 " 'If a man has sexual relations with
a woman during her monthly period,[g] he
has exposed the source of her flow, and
she has also uncovered it. Both of them
are to be cut off from their people.[h]
19 " 'Do not have sexual relations with
the sister of either your mother or your
father,[i] for that would dishonor a close relative; both of you would be held responsible.
20 " 'If a man has sexual relations with
his aunt,[j] he has dishonored his uncle.
They will be held responsible; they will
die childless.[k]
21 " 'If a man marries his brother's wife,[l]
it is an act of impurity; he has dishonored
his brother. They will be childless.[m]
22 " 'Keep all my decrees and laws[n] and
follow them, so that the land[o] where I am
bringing you to live may not vomit you
out. 23 You must not live according to the
customs of the nations[p] I am going to
drive out before you.[q] Because they did
all these things, I abhorred them.[r] 24 But I
said to you, "You will possess their land;
I will give it to you as an inheritance, a
land flowing with milk and honey."[s] I am
the LORD your God, who has set you apart
from the nations.[t]
25 " 'You must therefore make a distinction between clean and unclean animals
and between unclean and clean birds.[u] Do
not defile yourselves by any animal or bird
or anything that moves along the ground—

20:2 [b] ver 10; Ge 26:11; Ex 19:12 [c] ver 27; Lev 24:14; Nu 15:35, 36; Dt 21:21; Jos 7:25 **20:3** [d] ver 5, 6; Lev 23:30 [e] Ps 74:7; 79:1; Jer 7:30; Eze 5:11 [f] S Lev 15:31 [g] S Lev 18:21 **20:4** [h] Dt 17:2-5 **20:6** [i] S ver 3; S Lev 19:31 **20:7** [j] S Lev 11:44 [k] S Ex 29:1; 31:13; Lev 11:45; Eph 1:4; 1Pe 1:16* [l] S Ex 6:2; S 20:2 **20:8** [m] S Ge 26:5 [n] S Ex 31:13; Eze 20:12 **20:9** [o] Ex 20:12; Jer 35:16; Mal 1:6; 2:10 [p] S Ex 20:12; Dt 27:16; Eze 22:7 [q] Ex 21:17; Dt 21:20-21; Mt 15:4*; Mk 7:10* [r] ver 11; Dt 22:30; Jos 2:19; 2Sa 1:16; 3:29; 1Ki 2:37; Eze 18:13; 33:4,5 **20:10** [s] Ex 20:14; Dt 5:18; 22:22; Jn 8:5 [t] S Ge 38:24; S Ex 21:12 **20:11** [u] S Lev 18:7 [v] S ver 9; S Lev 18:8 **20:12** [w] S Ge 11:31; S 38:16 **20:13** [x] Lev 18:22 **20:14** [y] S Lev 18:17 [z] Lev 21:9; Nu 16:39; Jdg 14:15; 15:6 [a] S Lev 18:8; Dt 27:23 **20:15** [b] S Ex 22:19 [c] ver 10 **20:17** [d] S Lev 18:9

[e] S Ge 17:14 [f] S Lev 5:1 **20:18** [g] S Lev 15:24 [h] Eze 18:6 **20:19** [i] S Lev 18:12 **20:20** [j] S Lev 18:13 [k] ver 21; Ge 15:2 **20:21** [l] S Lev 18:16; Mt 14:4; Mk 6:18 [m] S ver 20 **20:22** [n] S Ge 26:5 [o] S Lev 18:25-28 **20:23** [p] S Lev 18:3 [q] S Lev 18:24 [r] S Lev 18:25 **20:24** [s] S Ex 3:8; Nu 14:8; 16:14 [t] S Ex 33:16 **20:25** [u] Lev 10:10; Dt 14:3-21; Ac 10:14

20:3 *cut him off from his people.* See note on 7:20.
20:5 *prostituting themselves.* See Ex 34:15 and note.
20:6 *mediums and spiritists.* Practitioners of the occult; consulting a medium was no less a sin than being one (v. 27). See Dt 18:10–11; Isa 3:2–3. Only God was to be consulted—through either the priest or a prophet (see Isa 8:19–20 and notes).
20:7 *be holy.* See note on 11:44.
20:8 *who makes ... holy.* This phrase and the expression "I am the LORD (your God)" are characteristic of chs. 18–26.
20:9 Cf. the penalty of a profligate son in Dt 21:20–21.
20:10 See 18:20.
20:12 See 18:15.
20:13 *detestable.* See note on 7:21.
20:15–16 See 18:23.
20:18 See 18:19.
20:20 See 18:14.
20:21 See 18:16 and note.
20:24 *flowing with milk and honey.* A common phrase in Exodus, Numbers and Deuteronomy (see notes on Ex 3:8; Dt 6:3; see also Jos 5:6; Jer 11:5; 32:22; Eze 20:6,15).
20:25 See ch. 11 and notes.

those that I have set apart as unclean for
you. 26 You are to be holy to me[v] because
I, the LORD, am holy,[w] and I have set you
apart from the nations[x] to be my own.
27 " 'A man or woman who is a medium[y] or spiritist among you must be put to
death.[z] You are to stone them;[a] their blood
will be on their own heads.' "

Rules for Priests

21 The LORD said to Moses, "Speak to
the priests, the sons of Aaron,[b] and
say to them: 'A priest must not make himself ceremonially unclean[c] for any of his
people who die,[d] 2 except for a close relative, such as his mother or father,[e] his son
or daughter, his brother, 3 or an unmarried
sister who is dependent on him since she
has no husband—for her he may make
himself unclean.[f] 4 He must not make himself unclean for people related to him by
marriage,[a] and so defile himself.
5 " 'Priests must not shave[g] their heads
or shave off the edges of their beards[h] or
cut their bodies.[i] 6 They must be holy to
their God[j] and must not profane the name
of their God.[k] Because they present the
food offerings to the LORD,[l] the food of
their God,[m] they are to be holy.[n]
7 " 'They must not marry women defiled
by prostitution or divorced from their husbands,[o] because priests are holy to their
God.[p] 8 Regard them as holy,[q] because they
offer up the food of your God.[r] Consider
them holy, because I the LORD am holy—I
who make you holy.[s]
9 " 'If a priest's daughter defiles herself
by becoming a prostitute, she disgraces
her father; she must be burned in the fire.[t]
10 " 'The high priest, the one among his
brothers who has had the anointing oil
poured on his head[u] and who has been
ordained to wear the priestly garments,[v]
must not let his hair become unkempt[b]
or tear his clothes.[w] 11 He must not enter
a place where there is a dead body.[x] He
must not make himself unclean,[y] even for
his father or mother,[z] 12 nor leave the sanctuary[a] of his God or desecrate it, because
he has been dedicated by the anointing
oil[b] of his God. I am the LORD.
13 " 'The woman he marries must be a
virgin.[c] 14 He must not marry a widow, a
divorced woman, or a woman defiled by
prostitution, but only a virgin from his
own people, 15 so that he will not defile
his offspring among his people. I am the
LORD, who makes him holy.' "
16 The LORD said to Moses, 17 "Say to
Aaron: 'For the generations to come
none of your descendants who has a defect[d] may come near to offer the food of
his God.[e] 18 No man who has any defect[f]
may come near: no man who is blind[g] or
lame,[h] disfigured or deformed; 19 no man
with a crippled foot or hand, 20 or who is
a hunchback or a dwarf, or who has any
eye defect, or who has festering or running sores or damaged testicles.[i] 21 No descendant of Aaron the priest who has any
defect[j] is to come near to present the food
offerings to the LORD.[k] He has a defect; he
must not come near to offer the food of
his God.[l] 22 He may eat the most holy food
of his God,[m] as well as the holy food; 23 yet
because of his defect,[n] he must not go near
the curtain or approach the altar, and so
desecrate my sanctuary.[o] I am the LORD,
who makes them holy.[p]' "
24 So Moses told this to Aaron and his
sons and to all the Israelites.

22 The LORD said to Moses, 2 "Tell Aaron and his sons to treat with respect the sacred offerings[q] the Israelites
consecrate to me, so they will not profane
my holy name.[r] I am the LORD.[s]
3 "Say to them: 'For the generations to
come, if any of your descendants is ceremonially unclean and yet comes near the
sacred offerings that the Israelites consecrate to the LORD,[t] that person must be cut
off from my presence.[u] I am the LORD.

[a] 4 Or *unclean as a leader among his people*
[b] 10 Or *not uncover his head*

20:26 [v] Dt 14:2 [w] ver 8; Lev 19:2; Jos 24:19; 2Ki 19:22; Ps 99:3 [x] S Ex 33:16
20:27 [y] S Ex 22:18 [z] S Lev 19:31 [a] S ver 2; S Lev 24:14
21:1 [b] S Ex 28:1; S Lev 1:5 [c] S Lev 5:3; S 13:3 [d] ver 11; Nu 5:2; 6:6; 19:11; 31:19
21:2 [e] ver 11
21:3 [f] Nu 6:6
21:5 [g] S Lev 13:40; Jer 7:29; 16:6 [h] Eze 5:1; 44:20 [i] S Lev 19:28
21:6 [j] ver 8; Ezr 8:28 [k] Lev 18:21 [l] S Lev 3:11 [m] ver 17,22; Lev 22:25 [n] S Ex 19:22; S Lev 10:3
21:7 [o] ver 13,14 [p] Eze 44:22
21:8 [q] ver 6 [r] Lev 3:11 [s] S Ex 31:13
21:9 [t] S Ge 38:24; S Lev 19:29
21:10 [u] S Ex 29:7 [v] S Lev 8:7-9, 13; S 16:4 [w] S Lev 10:6
21:11 [x] Nu 5:2; 6:6; 9:6; 19:11, 13,14; 31:19 [y] Lev 19:28 [z] ver 2
21:12 [a] S Ex 25:8 [b] S Ex 28:41
21:13 [c] Eze 44:22
21:17 [d] ver 18, 21,23 [e] S ver 6
21:18 [f] Lev 22:19-25 [g] S Lev 19:14 [h] 2Sa 4:4; 9:3; 19:26
21:20 [i] Lev 22:24; Dt 23:1; Isa 56:3
21:21 [j] S ver 17 [k] S Lev 3:11 [l] Lev 22:19
21:22 [m] 1Co 9:13
21:23 [n] S ver 17 [o] S Ex 25:8 [p] Lev 20:8
22:2 [q] S Lev 19:8 [r] S Ex 20:7; S Mt 5:33 [s] Eze 44:8
22:3 [t] Ezr 8:28 [u] Lev 7:20,21; Nu 19:13

20:26 See 11:44 and note.
20:27 See note on v. 6.
21:1—22:33 Directions for the priests' conduct, especially about separation from ceremonial uncleanness.
21:1 *for any … who die.* Touching a corpse (Nu 19:11) or entering the home of a person who had died (Nu 19:14) made one unclean. A priest was to contract such uncleanness only at the death of a close relative (vv. 2–3), and the regulations for the high priest denied him even this (vv. 11–12).
21:5 *cut their bodies.* See 19:27–28. Such lacerations and disfigurement were common among pagans as signs of mourning and to secure the attention of their deity (see 1Ki 18:28). Israelite faith had a much less grotesque view of death (see, e.g., vv. 1–4; Ge 5:24; 2Sa 12:23; Heb 11:19).
21:6 *They must be holy to their God.* As those especially set apart for service at God's sanctuary and who represent him in a special way, the priests must be especially careful to retain ceremonial and moral purity (see 11:44; Ex 3:5 and notes). *food of their God.* See note on 3:11,16.
21:8 *I … am holy.* See note on 11:44.
21:9 See Ge 38:24 and note.
21:11–12 See note on v. 1.
21:17 *defect.* Like the sacrifices that had to be without defect, the priests were to typify Christ's perfection (Heb 9:13–14).
21:23 *curtain.* Between the Holy Place and the Most Holy Place (see Ex 26:33).
22:3 *cut off from my presence.* Excluded from the worshiping community.

4 " 'If a descendant of Aaron has a defiling skin disease[a] or a bodily discharge,[v] he
may not eat the sacred offerings until he
is cleansed. He will also be unclean if he
touches something defiled by a corpse[w] or
by anyone who has an emission of semen,
5 or if he touches any crawling thing[x] that
makes him unclean, or any person[y] who
makes him unclean, whatever the uncleanness may be. 6 The one who touches
any such thing will be unclean[z] till evening.[a] He must not eat any of the sacred
offerings unless he has bathed himself
with water.[b] 7 When the sun goes down,
he will be clean, and after that he may eat
the sacred offerings, for they are his food.[c]
8 He must not eat anything found dead[d] or
torn by wild animals,[e] and so become unclean[f] through it. I am the LORD.[g]

9 " 'The priests are to perform my service[h] in such a way that they do not become guilty[i] and die[j] for treating it with
contempt. I am the LORD, who makes them
holy.[k]

10 " 'No one outside a priest's family may
eat the sacred offering, nor may the guest
of a priest or his hired worker eat it.[l] 11 But
if a priest buys a slave with money, or if
slaves are born in his household, they may
eat his food.[m] 12 If a priest's daughter marries anyone other than a priest, she may
not eat any of the sacred contributions.
13 But if a priest's daughter becomes a widow or is divorced, yet has no children, and
she returns to live in her father's household as in her youth, she may eat her father's food. No unauthorized person, however, may eat it.

14 " 'Anyone who eats a sacred offering
by mistake[n] must make restitution to the
priest for the offering and add a fifth of
the value[o] to it. 15 The priests must not desecrate the sacred offerings[p] the Israelites
present to the LORD[q] 16 by allowing them to
eat[r] the sacred offerings and so bring upon
them guilt[s] requiring payment.[t] I am the
LORD, who makes them holy.[u] ' "

Unacceptable Sacrifices

17 The LORD said to Moses, 18 "Speak to
Aaron and his sons and to all the Israelites
and say to them: 'If any of you—whether
an Israelite or a foreigner residing in Israel[v]—presents a gift[w] for a burnt offering
to the LORD, either to fulfill a vow[x] or as
a freewill offering,[y] 19 you must present a
male without defect[z] from the cattle, sheep
or goats in order that it may be accepted
on your behalf.[a] 20 Do not bring anything
with a defect,[b] because it will not be accepted on your behalf.[c] 21 When anyone
brings from the herd or flock[d] a fellowship
offering[e] to the LORD to fulfill a special vow
or as a freewill offering,[f] it must be without
defect or blemish[g] to be acceptable.[h] 22 Do
not offer to the LORD the blind, the injured
or the maimed, or anything with warts or
festering or running sores. Do not place
any of these on the altar as a food offering
presented to the LORD. 23 You may, however, present as a freewill offering an ox[b] or
a sheep that is deformed or stunted, but it
will not be accepted in fulfillment of a vow.
24 You must not offer to the LORD an animal
whose testicles are bruised, crushed, torn
or cut.[i] You must not do this in your own
land, 25 and you must not accept such animals from the hand of a foreigner and offer
them as the food of your God.[j] They will
not be accepted on your behalf, because
they are deformed and have defects.[k] ' "

26 The LORD said to Moses, 27 "When
a calf, a lamb or a goat[l] is born, it is to
remain with its mother for seven days.[m]
From the eighth day[n] on, it will be acceptable[o] as a food offering presented to the
LORD. 28 Do not slaughter a cow or a sheep
and its young on the same day.[p]

29 "When you sacrifice a thank offering[q]
to the LORD, sacrifice it in such a way that
it will be accepted on your behalf. 30 It
must be eaten that same day; leave none
of it till morning.[r] I am the LORD.[s]

31 "Keep[t] my commands and follow
them.[u] I am the LORD. 32 Do not profane my
holy name,[v] for I must be acknowledged as

[a] *4* The Hebrew word for *defiling skin disease,* traditionally translated "leprosy," was used for various diseases affecting the skin. [b] *23* The Hebrew word can refer to either male or female.

22:4 [v] Lev 15:2-15 [w] Lev 11:24-28,39 **22:5** [x] Lev 11:24-28,43 [y] S Lev 15:7 **22:6** [z] Hag 2:13 [a] S Lev 11:24 [b] S Lev 14:8 **22:7** [c] Nu 18:11 **22:8** [d] S Lev 11:39 [e] S Ex 22:31 [f] S Lev 11:40 [g] Lev 11:44 **22:9** [h] S Lev 8:35 [i] S Ex 28:38 [j] ver 16; S Ex 28:43 [k] Lev 20:8 **22:10** [l] ver 13; Ex 12:45; 29:33 **22:11** [m] Ge 17:13; Ex 12:44 **22:14** [n] S Lev 4:2 [o] Lev 5:15 **22:15** [p] S Lev 19:8 [q] Nu 18:32 **22:16** [r] Nu 18:11 [s] S Ex 28:38 [t] S ver 9 [u] Lev 20:8 **22:18** [v] Nu 15:16; 19:10; Jos 8:33 [w] S Lev 1:2 [x] ver 21; S Ge 28:20; Nu 15:8; Ps 22:25; 76:11; 116:18 [y] S Lev 7:16 **22:19** [z] S Lev 1:3; 21:18-21; Nu 28:11; Dt 15:21 [a] S Lev 1:2 **22:20** [b] S Lev 1:3; Dt 15:21; 17:1; Eze 43:23; 45:18; 46:6; Mal 1:8; Heb 9:14; 1Pe 1:19 [c] S Ex 28:38 **22:21** [d] S Lev 1:2 [e] S Ex 32:6; S Lev 3:6 [f] S Lev 7:16 [g] S Ex 12:5; Mal 1:14 [h] Am 4:5 **22:24** [i] S Lev 21:20 **22:25** [j] S Lev 21:6 [k] S Lev 1:3; S 3:1; Nu 19:2 **22:27** [l] S Lev 1:3 [m] S Ex 22:30 [n] S Ex 22:30 [o] S Ex 28:38 **22:28** [p] Dt 22:6,7 **22:29** [q] S Lev 7:12 **22:30** [r] Lev 7:15 [s] Lev 11:44 **22:31** [t] Dt 4:2,40; Ps 105:45 [u] S Ex 22:31 **22:32** [v] Lev 18:21

22:4 See 13:1–46 and note on 13:45–46; 15:1–18 and notes; 21:11.

22:5 See 11:29–31.

22:8 See 17:15 and note.

22:9 *die for treating it with contempt.* The laws of cleanness were the same for priests and people, but the penalties were far more severe for the priests, who had greater responsibility. Cf. Nadab and Abihu (10:1–3) and the faithless priests of Malachi's day (Mal 1:6—2:9). *holy.* See note on 11:44.

22:14 *make restitution . . . add a fifth.* Cf. 5:16 and note on 5:15.

22:16 *holy.* See note on 11:44.

22:18 *burnt offering.* See note on 1:3.

22:20–22 See Mal 1:8.

22:21 *fellowship offering.* See note on 3:1.

22:24 *bruised, crushed, torn or cut.* Castrated animals were not acceptable offerings.

22:28 See note on Ex 23:19.

22:30 *that same day.* The rule applied also to the Passover (Ex 34:25); however, the fellowship offering could be saved and eaten on the following day (7:16).

22:32 *holy . . . holy . . . holy.* See 11:44; 18:21 and notes.

holy by the Israelites.[w] I am the LORD, who
made you holy[x] 33 and who brought you out
of Egypt[y] to be your God.[z] I am the LORD."

The Appointed Festivals

23 The LORD said to Moses, 2 "Speak
to the Israelites and say to them:
'These are my appointed festivals,[a] the appointed festivals of the LORD, which you
are to proclaim as sacred assemblies.[b]

The Sabbath

3 " 'There are six days when you may
work,[c] but the seventh day is a day of sabbath rest,[d] a day of sacred assembly. You
are not to do any work;[e] wherever you
live, it is a sabbath to the LORD.

The Passover and the Festival of Unleavened Bread

23:4-8pp — Ex 12:14-20; Nu 28:16-25; Dt 16:1-8

4 " 'These are the LORD's appointed festivals, the sacred assemblies you are to
proclaim at their appointed times:[f] 5 The
LORD's Passover[g] begins at twilight on the
fourteenth day of the first month.[h] 6 On the
fifteenth day of that month the LORD's Festival of Unleavened Bread[i] begins; for sev-

22:32 [w] S Lev 10:3 [x] Lev 20:8 **22:33** [y] S Ex 6:6 [z] S Ge 17:7 **23:2** [a] ver 4, 37, 44; Nu 29:39; Eze 44:24; Col 2:16 [b] ver 21, 27 **23:3** [c] Ex 20:9 [d] S Ex 20:10; Heb 4:9, 10 [e] ver 7, 21, 35; Nu 28:26 **23:4** [f] Na 1:15 **23:5** [g] S Ex 12:11 [h] S Ex 12:6 **23:6** [i] Ex 12:17

23:2 *appointed festivals.* See Ex 23:14 – 17 and notes; 34:18 – 25; Nu 28 – 29; Dt 16:1 – 17. The parallel in Numbers (the fullest and closest to Leviticus) specifies in great detail the offerings to be made at each festival. See chart below.
23:3 *sabbath.* See notes on Ex 16:23; 20:9 – 10. The Sabbath is associated with the annual festivals also in Ex 23:12. Two additional lambs were to be sacrificed as a burnt offering every weekly Sabbath (Nu 28:9 – 10).
23:5 *Passover.* See notes on Ex 12:11,14,21. *first month.* See note on Ex 12:2. The Israelites had three systems of referring to months. In one, the months were simply numbered (as here and in v. 24). In another, the Canaanite names were used (Aviv, Bul, etc.), of which only four are known. In the third system, the Babylonian names (Nisan, Adar, Tishri, Kislev, etc.) were used — in the exilic and postexilic books only — and are still used today. See chart, p. 113.
23:6 *Festival of Unleavened Bread.* See note on Ex 23:15. During the Festival the first sheaf of the barley harvest was brought (see vv. 10 – 11).

OLD TESTAMENT FESTIVALS AND OTHER SACRED DAYS

NAME	OLD TESTAMENT REFERENCES	OLD TESTAMENT TIME	MODERN EQUIVALENT
Sabbath	Ex 20:8–11; 31:12–17; Lev 23:3; Dt 5:12–15	7th day	Same
Sabbath Year	Ex 23:10–11; Lev 25:1–7	7th year	Same
Year of Jubilee	Lev 25:8–55; 27:17–24; Nu 36:4	50th year	Same
Passover	Ex 12:1–14; Lev 23:5; Nu 9:1–14; 28:16; Dt 16:1–3a,4b–7	1st month (Aviv) 14	March – April
Unleavened Bread	Ex 12:15–20; 13:3–10; 23:15; 34:18; Lev 23:6–8; Nu 28:17–25; Dt 16:3b,4a,8	1st month (Aviv) 15–21	March – April
Firstfruits	Lev 23:9–14	1st month (Aviv) 16	March – April
Weeks (Pentecost) (Harvest)	Ex 23:16a; 34:22a; Lev 23:15–21; Nu 28:26–31; Dt 16:9–12	3rd month (Sivan) 6	May – June
Trumpets (later: Rosh Hashanah–New Year's Day)	Lev 23:23–25; Nu 29:1–6	7th month (Tishri) 1	September – October
Day of Atonement (Yom Kippur)	Lev 16; 23:26–32; Nu 29:7–11	7th month (Tishri) 10	September – October
Tabernacles (Booths) (Ingathering)	Ex 23:16b; 34:22b; Lev 23:33–36a,39–43; Nu 29:12–34; Dt 16:13–15; Zec 14:16–19	7th month (Tishri) 15–21	September – October
Sacred Assembly	Lev 23:36b; Nu 29:35–38	7th month (Tishri) 22	September – October
Purim	Est 9:18–32	12th month (Adar) 14,15	February – March

On Kislev 25 (mid-December) Hanukkah, the Festival of Dedication or Festival of Lights, commemorated the purification of the temple and altar in the Maccabean period (165/4 BC). This festival is mentioned in Jn 10:22 (see note there).

en days[j] you must eat bread made without yeast. 7On the first day hold a sacred
assembly[k] and do no regular work. 8For
seven days present a food offering to the
LORD.[l] And on the seventh day hold a sacred assembly and do no regular work.' "

Offering the Firstfruits

9The LORD said to Moses, 10"Speak to
the Israelites and say to them: 'When you
enter the land I am going to give you[m] and
you reap its harvest,[n] bring to the priest a
sheaf[o] of the first grain you harvest.[p] 11He
is to wave the sheaf before the LORD[q] so it
will be accepted[r] on your behalf; the priest
is to wave it on the day after the Sabbath.
12On the day you wave the sheaf, you must
sacrifice as a burnt offering to the LORD a
lamb a year old[s] without defect,[t] 13togeth-
er with its grain offering[u] of two-tenths of
an ephah[a][v] of the finest flour mixed with
olive oil — a food offering presented to the
LORD, a pleasing aroma — and its drink
offering[w] of a quarter of a hin[b] of wine.[x]
14You must not eat any bread, or roasted
or new grain,[y] until the very day you bring
this offering to your God.[z] This is to be
a lasting ordinance for the generations to
come,[a] wherever you live.[b]

The Festival of Weeks

23:15-22pp — Nu 28:26-31; Dt 16:9-12

15" 'From the day after the Sabbath, the
day you brought the sheaf of the wave offering, count off seven full weeks. 16Count

23:6 [j]S Ex 12:19 **23:7** [k]ver 3,8 **23:8** [l]S Lev 1:9 **23:10** [m]Nu 15:2,18 [n]S Lev 19:9 [o]S Lev 19:9 [p]S Ex 22:29; S 34:22; Ro 11:16 **23:11** [q]S Ex 29:24 [r]S Ex 28:38 **23:12** [s]S Lev 12:6 [t]S Ex 12:5 **23:13** [u]Lev 2:14-16; S 6:20 [v]ver 17; Lev 24:5; Nu 15:6; 28:9 [w]S Ge 35:14 [x]S Lev 10:9 **23:14** [y]Jos 5:11; Ru 2:14; 1Sa 17:17; 25:18; 2Sa 17:28 [z]Ex 34:26 [a]Lev 3:17; Nu 10:8; 15:21 [b]Jer 2:3

[a] 13 That is, probably about 7 pounds or about 3.2 kilograms; also in verse 17 [b] 13 That is, about 1 quart or about 1 liter

23:9 – 14 Festival of Firstfruits (see notes on Ex 23:19; Nu 15:20; Ne 10:35).
23:10 *first grain you harvest.* That is, barley (Ru 1:22); wheat harvest followed (Ru 2:23).
23:15 *seven full weeks.* See note on Ex 23:16.
23:16 *fifty days.* The NT name for the Festival of Weeks was Pentecost (see Ac 2:1 and note; 20:16; 1Co 16:8), meaning "fifty." *new grain.* That is, wheat (see note on v. 10).

DESCRIPTION	PURPOSE	NEW TESTAMENT REFERENCES
Day of rest; no work	Rest for people and animals	Mt 12:1–14; 28:1; Lk 4:16; Jn 5:9–10; Ac 13:42; Col 2:16; Heb 4:1–11
Year of rest; fallow fields	Rest for land	
Canceled debts; liberation of slaves and indentured servants; land returned to original family owners	Help for poor; stabilize society	
Slaying and eating a lamb, together with bitter herbs and bread made without yeast, in every household	Remember Israel's deliverance from Egypt	Mt 26:17; Mk 14:12–26; Jn 2:13; 11:55; 1Co 5:7; Heb 11:28
Eating bread made without yeast; holding several assemblies; making designated offerings	Remember how the Lord brought the Israelites out of Egypt in haste	Mk 14:1; Ac 12:3; 1Co 5:6–8
Presenting a sheaf of the first of the barley harvest as a wave offering; making a burnt offering and a grain offering	Recognize the Lord's bounty in the land	Ro 8:23; 1Co 15:20–23
A festival of joy; mandatory and voluntary offerings, including the firstfruits of the wheat harvest	Show joy and thankfulness for the Lord's blessing of harvest	Ac 2:1–4; 20:16; 1Co 16:8
An assembly on a day of rest commemorated with trumpet blasts and sacrifices	Present Israel before the Lord for his favor	
A day of rest, fasting and sacrifices of atonement for priests and people and atonement for the tabernacle and altar	Atone for the sins of priests and people and purify the Holy Place	Ro 3:24–26; Heb 9:7; 10:3,19–22
A week of celebration for the harvest; living in booths (temporary shelters) and offering sacrifices	Memorialize the journey from Egypt to Canaan; give thanks for the productivity of Canaan	Jn 7:2,37
A day of convocation, rest and offering sacrifices	Commemorate the closing of the cycle of festivals	
A day of joy and feasting and giving presents	Remind the Israelites of their national deliverance in the time of Esther	

In addition, New Moon feasts were prescribed (see Nu 28:11–15; 1 Sa 20:5; Isa 1:14 and notes; see also 1Ch 23:31; Ezr 3:5; Ne 10:33; Ps 81:3; Hos 5:7; Am 8:5; Col 2:16).

off fifty days up to the day after the seventh
Sabbath,[c] and then present an offering of
new grain to the LORD. 17From wherever you
live, bring two loaves made of two-tenths
of an ephah[d] of the finest flour, baked with
yeast, as a wave offering of firstfruits[e] to the
LORD. 18Present with this bread seven male
lambs, each a year old and without defect,
one young bull and two rams. They will be
a burnt offering to the LORD, together with
their grain offerings and drink offerings[f]—
a food offering, an aroma pleasing to the
LORD. 19Then sacrifice one male goat for a
sin offering[a] and two lambs, each a year
old, for a fellowship offering. 20The priest
is to wave the two lambs before the LORD
as a wave offering,[g] together with the bread
of the firstfruits. They are a sacred offering
to the LORD for the priest. 21On that same
day you are to proclaim a sacred assembly[h]
and do no regular work.[i] This is to be a lasting ordinance for the generations to come,
wherever you live.

22" 'When you reap the harvest[j] of your
land, do not reap to the very edges of your
field or gather the gleanings of your harvest.[k] Leave them for the poor and for the
foreigner residing among you.[l] I am the
LORD your God.' "

The Festival of Trumpets

23:23-25pp — Nu 29:1-6

23The LORD said to Moses, 24"Say to the
Israelites: 'On the first day of the seventh
month you are to have a day of sabbath
rest, a sacred assembly[m] commemorated
with trumpet blasts.[n] 25Do no regular work,[o]
but present a food offering to the LORD.[p]' "

The Day of Atonement

23:26-32pp — Lev 16:2-34; Nu 29:7-11

26The LORD said to Moses, 27"The tenth
day of this seventh month[q] is the Day of
Atonement.[r] Hold a sacred assembly[s] and
deny yourselves,[b] and present a food offering to the LORD. 28Do not do any work[t]
on that day, because it is the Day of Atonement, when atonement is made for you
before the LORD your God. 29Those who do
not deny themselves on that day must be
cut off from their people.[u] 30I will destroy
from among their people[v] anyone who
does any work on that day. 31You shall do
no work at all. This is to be a lasting ordinance[w] for the generations to come, wherever you live. 32It is a day of sabbath rest[x]
for you, and you must deny yourselves.
From the evening of the ninth day of the
month until the following evening you are
to observe your sabbath."[y]

The Festival of Tabernacles

23:33-43pp — Nu 29:12-39; Dt 16:13-17

33The LORD said to Moses, 34"Say to the
Israelites: 'On the fifteenth day of the seventh[z] month the LORD's Festival of Tabernacles[a] begins, and it lasts for seven days.
35The first day is a sacred assembly;[b] do no
regular work.[c] 36For seven days present food
offerings to the LORD, and on the eighth day
hold a sacred assembly[d] and present a food
offering to the LORD.[e] It is the closing special
assembly; do no regular work.

37(" 'These are the LORD's appointed festivals, which you are to proclaim as sacred
assemblies for bringing food offerings to
the LORD — the burnt offerings and grain
offerings, sacrifices and drink offerings[f]
required for each day. 38These offerings[g]
are in addition to those for the LORD's Sabbaths[h] and[c] in addition to your gifts and
whatever you have vowed and all the freewill offerings[i] you give to the LORD.)

39" 'So beginning with the fifteenth day
of the seventh month, after you have gathered the crops of the land, celebrate the
festival[j] to the LORD for seven days;[k] the
first day is a day of sabbath rest, and the
eighth day also is a day of sabbath rest.
40On the first day you are to take branches[l] from luxuriant trees — from palms, willows and other leafy trees[m] — and rejoice[n]
before the LORD your God for seven days.
41Celebrate this as a festival to the LORD for
seven days each year. This is to be a lasting ordinance for the generations to come;
celebrate it in the seventh month. 42Live in

[a] 19 Or *purification offering* [b] 27 Or *and fast;* similarly in verses 29 and 32 [c] 38 Or *These festivals are in addition to the LORD's Sabbaths, and these offerings are*

23:16 [c]Ac 2:1; 20:16 **23:17** [d]S ver 13 [e]S Ex 34:22 **23:18** [f]ver 13; Ex 29:41; 30:9; 37:16; Jer 19:13; 44:18 **23:20** [g]S Ex 29:24 **23:21** [h]S ver 2; Ex 32:5 [i]S ver 3 **23:22** [j]S Lev 19:9 [k]S Lev 19:10; Dt 24:19-21; Ru 2:15 [l]Ru 2:2 **23:24** [m]ver 27, 36; Ezr 3:1 [n]Lev 25:9; Nu 10:9, 10; 29:1; 31:6; 2Ki 11:14; 2Ch 13:12; Ps 98:6 **23:25** [o]ver 21 [p]S Lev 1:9 **23:27** [q]S Lev 16:29 [r]S Ex 30:10 [s]S ver 2, S 24 **23:28** [t]ver 31 **23:29** [u]Ge 17:14; Lev 7:20; Nu 5:2 **23:30** [v]S Lev 20:3 **23:31** [w]Lev 3:17 **23:32** [x]S Lev 16:31 [y]Ne 13:19 **23:34** [z]1Ki 8:2; Hag 2:1 [a]S Ex 23:16; Jn 7:2 **23:35** [b]ver 2 [c]ver 3 **23:36** [d]S ver 24; 1Ki 8:2; 2Ch 7:9; Ne 8:18; Jn 7:37 [e]S Lev 1:9 **23:37** [f]ver 13 **23:38** [g]S Lev 1:2 [h]S Ex 20:10; 2Ch 2:4; Eze 45:17 [i]S Lev 7:16 **23:39** [j]Isa 62:9 [k]S Ex 23:16 **23:40** [l]Ps 118:27 [m]Ne 8:14-17; Ps 137:2; Isa 44:4 [n]Dt 12:7; 14:26; 28:47; Ne 8:10; Ps 9:2; 66:6; 105:43; Joel 2:26

23:22 See note on 19:9 – 10.

23:24 *first day of the seventh month.* Today known as the Jewish New Year (*Rosh Hashanah,* "the beginning of the year"), but not so called in the Bible (the Hebrew expression is used only in Eze 40:1 in a date formula; see note there). *trumpet blasts.* Trumpets were blown on the first of every month (see Ps 81:3 and note). With no calendars available, the trumpets sounding across the land were an important signal of the beginning of the new season, the end of the agricultural year. See note on 16:29; see also chart, p. 113.

23:27 *Day of Atonement.* For details, see notes on 16:1 – 34. Aaron was to enter the Most Holy Place only once a year (16:29 – 34) on this day. Modern Jews call it *Yom Kippur.* The day was typological, foreshadowing the atoning work of Christ, our high priest (see Heb 9:7; 13:11 – 12 and notes). *deny yourselves.* See note on 16:29,31.

23:34 *Festival of Tabernacles.* See notes on Ex 23:16; Zec 14:16; Jn 7:37 – 39. Tabernacles was the last of the three annual pilgrimage festivals (see Ex 23:14 – 17; Dt 16:16 and notes).

23:42 *temporary shelters.* The Hebrew for this phrase is *Sukkot* and is also translated "tabernacles" (as in v. 34), giving the festival its name. Even today, orthodox Jews construct small shelters (see Ne 8:13 – 17) to remind them of the shelters they

temporary shelters[o] for seven days: All native-born Israelites are to live in such shelters 43 so your descendants will know[p] that
I had the Israelites live in temporary shelters when I brought them out of Egypt. I
am the LORD your God.' "
44 So Moses announced to the Israelites
the appointed festivals of the LORD.

Olive Oil and Bread Set Before the LORD

24:1-3pp — Ex 27:20-21

24 The LORD said to Moses, 2 "Command the Israelites to bring you
clear oil of pressed olives for the light so
that the lamps may be kept burning continually. 3 Outside the curtain that shields
the ark of the covenant law in the tent of
meeting, Aaron is to tend the lamps before
the LORD from evening till morning, continually. This is to be a lasting ordinance[q]
for the generations to come. 4 The lamps
on the pure gold lampstand[r] before the
LORD must be tended continually.
5 "Take the finest flour and bake twelve
loaves of bread,[s] using two-tenths of an
ephah[a][t] for each loaf. 6 Arrange them in two
stacks, six in each stack, on the table of
pure gold[u] before the LORD. 7 By each stack
put some pure incense[v] as a memorial[b]
portion[w] to represent the bread and to be a
food offering presented to the LORD. 8 This
bread is to be set out before the LORD regularly,[x] Sabbath after Sabbath,[y] on behalf
of the Israelites, as a lasting covenant. 9 It
belongs to Aaron and his sons,[z] who are to
eat it in the sanctuary area,[a] because it is a
most holy[b] part of their perpetual share of
the food offerings presented to the LORD."

A Blasphemer Put to Death

10 Now the son of an Israelite mother and
an Egyptian father went out among the Israelites, and a fight broke out in the camp
between him and an Israelite. 11 The son of
the Israelite woman blasphemed the Name[c]
with a curse;[d] so they brought him to Moses.[e] (His mother's name was Shelomith,
the daughter of Dibri the Danite.)[f] 12 They
put him in custody until the will of the
LORD should be made clear to them.[g]
13 Then the LORD said to Moses: 14 "Take
the blasphemer outside the camp. All
those who heard him are to lay their
hands on his head, and the entire assembly is to stone him.[h] 15 Say to the Israelites: 'Anyone who curses their God[i] will
be held responsible;[j] 16 anyone who blasphemes[k] the name of the LORD is to be put
to death.[l] The entire assembly must stone
them. Whether foreigner or native-born,
when they blaspheme the Name they are
to be put to death.
17 " 'Anyone who takes the life of a human being is to be put to death.[m] 18 Anyone who takes the life of someone's animal must make restitution[n] — life for life.
19 Anyone who injures their neighbor is to
be injured in the same manner: 20 fracture
for fracture, eye for eye, tooth for tooth.[o]
The one who has inflicted the injury must
suffer the same injury. 21 Whoever kills an
animal must make restitution,[p] but whoever kills a human being is to be put to
death.[q] 22 You are to have the same law for
the foreigner[r] and the native-born.[s] I am
the LORD your God.' "
23 Then Moses spoke to the Israelites,
and they took the blasphemer outside the
camp and stoned him.[t] The Israelites did
as the LORD commanded Moses.

The Sabbath Year

25 The LORD said to Moses at Mount
Sinai,[u] 2 "Speak to the Israelites and
say to them: 'When you enter the land I

[a] 5 That is, probably about 7 pounds or about 3.2 kilograms [b] 7 Or *representative*

23:42 [o] S Ex 23:16 **23:43** [p] Ps 78:5 **24:3** [q] S Ex 12:14 **24:4** [r] S Ex 25:31 **24:5** [s] S Ex 25:30; Heb 9:2 [t] S Lev 23:13 **24:6** [u] Ex 25:23-30; Nu 4:7 **24:7** [v] S Lev 2:1 [w] S Lev 2:2 **24:8** [x] Ex 25:30; Nu 4:7; 1Ch 9:32; 2Ch 2:4 [y] Mt 12:5 **24:9** [z] Mt 12:4; Mk 2:26; Lk 6:4 [a] S Lev 6:16 [b] S Lev 6:17 **24:11** [c] S Ex 3:15 [d] S Ex 20:7; S 2Ki 6:33; S Job 1:11 [e] S Ex 18:22 [f] Ex 31:2; Nu 1:4; 7:2; 10:15; 13:2; 17:2; Jos 7:18; 1Ki 7:14 **24:12** [g] S Ex 18:16 **24:14** [h] ver 23; S Lev 20:2; Dt 13:9; 17:5,7; Ac 7:58 **24:15** [i] S Ex 22:28 [j] S Lev 5:1 **24:16** [k] S Ex 22:28 [l] S Ex 21:12; 1Ki 21:10, 13; Mt 26:66; Mk 14:64; Jn 10:33; 19:7; Ac 7:58 **24:17** [m] ver 21; Ge 9:6; S Ex 21:12; Dt 27:24 **24:18** [n] ver 21 **24:20** [o] S Ex 21:24; Mt 5:38* **24:21** [p] S ver 18 [q] S ver 17 **24:22** [r] S Ex 12:49; S 22:21; Eze 47:22 [s] Nu 9:14 **24:23** [t] S ver 14 **25:1** [u] Ex 19:11

lived in when God brought them out of Egypt at the time of the exodus (v. 43).

24:2–4 See Ex 27:20–21.

24:3 *the ark of the covenant law.* See note on Ex 25:22. *tend the lamps.* So that they would burn all night. *continually.* Every night without interruption, but not throughout the day. See 1Sa 3:3 and note.

24:5 *two-tenths of an ephah.* See NIV text note. Either the loaves were quite large or a smaller unit of measurement is intended. The Hebrew word *ephah* is not expressed, but since the ephah was the standard measure of capacity (see table, p. 2181), it is the measure most likely implied here.

24:7 *pure incense.* Not used as a condiment for the bread but burned either in piles on the table or in small receptacles alongside the stacks of bread. *memorial portion.* See note on 2:2,9,16.

24:8 *This bread.* Often called the "bread of the Presence" (see Ex 25:30 and note). It represented a gift from the 12 tribes and signified the fact that God sustained his people. It was eaten by the priests (24:9).

24:9 See 1Sa 21:4–6.

24:10 *Egyptian father.* A foreigner. The laws, at least in the judicial sphere, applied equally to both the foreigner and the native-born Israelite (v. 22; see Ex 12:49).

24:11 *blasphemed.* See Ex 20:7 and note. *the Name.* See v. 16; see also note on Dt 12:5.

24:17,21 See Ge 9:6 and note.

24:20 *eye for eye, tooth for tooth.* See note on Ex 21:23–25. This represents a statement of principle: The penalty is to fit the crime, not exceed it. An actual eye or tooth was not to be required, nor is there evidence that such a penalty was ever exacted. A similar law of "retaliation" is found in the Code of Hammurapi (see chart, p. xxii), which also seems not to have been literally applied. Christ, like the middle-of-the-road Pharisees (school of Hillel), objected to an extremist use of this judicial principle to excuse private vengeance, such as by the strict Pharisees (school of Shammai); see Mt 5:38–42.

24:22 See note on v. 10.

am going to give you, the land itself must observe a sabbath to the LORD. 3 For six years sow your fields, and for six years prune your vineyards and gather their crops.[v] 4 But in the seventh year the land is to have a year of sabbath rest,[w] a sabbath to the LORD. Do not sow your fields or prune your vineyards.[x] 5 Do not reap what grows of itself[y] or harvest the grapes[z] of your untended vines.[a] The land is to have a year of rest. 6 Whatever the land yields during the sabbath year[b] will be food for you—for yourself, your male and female servants, and the hired worker and temporary resident who live among you, 7 as well as for your livestock and the wild animals[c] in your land. Whatever the land produces may be eaten.

The Year of Jubilee

25:8-38Ref—Dt 15:1-11
25:39-55Ref—Ex 21:2-11; Dt 15:12-18

8 " 'Count off seven sabbath years—seven times seven years—so that the seven sabbath years amount to a period of forty-nine years. 9 Then have the trumpet[d] sounded everywhere on the tenth day of the seventh month;[e] on the Day of Atonement[f] sound the trumpet throughout your land. 10 Consecrate the fiftieth year and proclaim liberty[g] throughout the land to all its inhabitants. It shall be a jubilee[h] for you; each of you is to return to your family property[i] and to your own clan. 11 The fiftieth year shall be a jubilee[j] for you; do not sow and do not reap what grows of itself or harvest the untended vines.[k] 12 For it is a jubilee and is to be holy for you; eat only what is taken directly from the fields.

13 " 'In this Year of Jubilee[l] everyone is to return to their own property.

14 " 'If you sell land to any of your own people or buy land from them, do not take advantage of each other.[m] 15 You are to buy from your own people on the basis of the number of years[n] since the Jubilee. And they are to sell to you on the basis of the number of years left for harvesting crops. 16 When the years are many, you are to increase the price, and when the years are few, you are to decrease the price,[o] because what is really being sold to you is the number of crops. 17 Do not take advantage of each other,[p] but fear your God.[q] I am the LORD your God.[r]

18 " 'Follow my decrees and be careful to obey my laws,[s] and you will live safely in the land.[t] 19 Then the land will yield its fruit,[u] and you will eat your fill and live there in safety.[v] 20 You may ask, "What will we eat in the seventh year[w] if we do not plant or harvest our crops?" 21 I will send you such a blessing[x] in the sixth year that the land will yield enough for three years.[y] 22 While you plant during the eighth year, you will eat from the old crop and will continue to eat from it until the harvest of the ninth year comes in.[z]

23 " 'The land[a] must not be sold permanently, because the land is mine[b] and you reside in my land as foreigners[c] and strangers. 24 Throughout the land that you hold as a possession, you must provide for the redemption[d] of the land.

25 " 'If one of your fellow Israelites becomes poor and sells some of their property, their nearest relative[e] is to come and redeem[f] what they have sold. 26 If, however, there is no one to redeem it for them but later on they prosper[g] and acquire sufficient means to redeem it themselves, 27 they are to determine the value for the years[h] since they sold it and refund the balance to the

25:3 [v] Ex 23:10 **25:4** [w] ver 5,6, 20; Lev 26:35; 2Ch 36:21 [x] Isa 36:16; 37:30 **25:5** [y] 2Ki 19:29 [z] Ge 40:10; Nu 6:3; 13:20; Dt 23:24; Ne 13:15; Isa 5:2 [a] ver 4, 11 **25:6** [b] S ver 4 **25:7** [c] Ex 23:11 **25:9** [d] Lev 23:24; Nu 10:8; Jos 6:4; Jdg 3:27; 7:16; 1Sa 13:3; Isa 27:13; Zec 9:14 [e] S Lev 16:29 [f] S Ex 30:10 **25:10** [g] Isa 61:1; Jer 34:8,15, 17; S Lk 4:19 [h] ver 11,28, 50; Lev 27:17, 21; Nu 36:4; Eze 46:17 [i] ver 27 **25:11** [j] S ver 10 [k] S ver 5 **25:13** [l] ver 10 **25:14** [m] S Lev 19:13; 1Sa 12:3,4; 1Co 6:8 **25:15** [n] ver 27; Lev 27:18,23 **25:16** [o] ver 27, 51,52 **25:17** [p] S Lev 19:13; Job 31:16; Pr 22:22; Jer 7:5,6; 21:12; 22:3, 15; Zec 7:9-10; 1Th 4:6 [q] S Lev 19:14 [r] S Lev 19:32 **25:18** [s] S Ge 26:5 [t] ver 19; Lev 26:4,5; Dt 12:10; 33:28; Job 5:22; Ps 4:8; Jer 23:6; 30:10; 32:37; 33:16; Eze 28:26; 34:25; 38:14

25:19 [u] Lev 26:4; Dt 11:14; 28:12; Isa 55:10 [v] S ver 18 **25:20** [w] S ver 4 **25:21** [x] Dt 28:8,12; Ps 133:3; 134:3; 147:13; Eze 44:30; Hag 2:19; Mal 3:10 [y] S Ex 16:5 **25:22** [z] Lev 26:10 **25:23** [a] Nu 36:7; 1Ki 21:3; Eze 46:18 [b] Ex 19:5 [c] S Ge 23:4; S Heb 11:13 **25:24** [d] ver 29,48; Ru 4:7 **25:25** [e] ver 48; Ru 2:20; Jer 32:7 [f] Lev 27:13,19,31; Ru 4:4 **25:26** [g] ver 49 **25:27** [h] S ver 15

25:4 *land is to have a . . . sabbath.* See Ex 23:10–11. The Israelites did not practice crop rotation, but the fallow year (when the crops were not planted) served somewhat the same purpose. And just as the land was to have a sabbath year, so the servitude of a Hebrew slave was limited to six years, apparently whether or not the year he was freed was a sabbath year (see Ex 21:2 and note). Dt 15:1–11 specifies that debts were also to be canceled in the sabbath year. The care for the poor in the laws of Israel (see Ex 23:11) is noteworthy. See 23:7,35; Dt 31:10; Ne 10:31.

25:9 *Day of Atonement.* See notes on 16:1–34; see also 23:27.

25:10 *fiftieth year.* Possibly a fallow year in addition to the seventh sabbath year, or perhaps the same as the 49th year (counting the first and last years). Jewish sources from the period between the Testaments favor the latter interpretation. *proclaim liberty . . . inhabitants.* See vv. 39–43,47–55. The Liberty Bell in Philadelphia is so named because this statement was written on it. Cf. Isa 61:1–2; Lk 4:16–21. *jubilee.* The Hebrew for this word is the same as, and may be related to, one of the Hebrew words for "[ram's] horn," "trumpet" (see, e.g., Ex 19:13), though in v. 9 a different Hebrew word for "trumpet" is used. Trumpets were blown at the close of the Day of Atonement to inaugurate the Year of Jubilee. Cf. 23:24.

25:13 *return to their own property.* See v. 10. The Lord prohibited the accumulation of property to the detriment of the poor. "The land is mine," said the Lord (v. 23). God's people are only tenants (see 1Ch 29:15; Heb 11:13).

25:15 *number of years left for harvesting.* In a way, the sale of land in Israel was a lease until the Year of Jubilee (see 27:18,23).

25:24 *redemption of the land.* That is, the right to repurchase the land by (or for) the original family.

25:25 *nearest relative is to come and redeem.* See Jer 32:6–15. This is apparently what the nearest relative was to do for Naomi and Ruth (Ru 4:1–4), but he was also obligated to marry the widow and support the family (see Dt 25:5–10). Only Boaz was willing to do both (Ru 4:9–10). See note on Ru 2:20.

one to whom they sold it; they can then go
back to their own property.[i] 28But if they do
not acquire the means to repay, what was
sold will remain in the possession of the
buyer until the Year of Jubilee. It will be
returned[j] in the Jubilee, and they can then
go back to their property.[k]
29“ ‘Anyone who sells a house in a
walled city retains the right of redemption a full year after its sale. During that
time the seller may redeem it. 30If it is not
redeemed before a full year has passed,
the house in the walled city shall belong
permanently to the buyer and the buyer’s
descendants. It is not to be returned in the
Jubilee. 31But houses in villages without
walls around them are to be considered as
belonging to the open country. They can
be redeemed, and they are to be returned
in the Jubilee.
32“ ‘The Levites always have the right
to redeem their houses in the Levitical
towns,[l] which they possess. 33So the property of the Levites is redeemable—that is,
a house sold in any town they hold—and
is to be returned in the Jubilee, because
the houses in the towns of the Levites are
their property among the Israelites. 34But
the pastureland belonging to their towns
must not be sold; it is their permanent
possession.[m]
35“ ‘If any of your fellow Israelites become poor[n] and are unable to support
themselves among you, help them[o] as you
would a foreigner and stranger, so they
can continue to live among you. 36Do not
take interest[p] or any profit from them, but
fear your God,[q] so that they may continue
to live among you. 37You must not lend
them money at interest[r] or sell them food
at a profit. 38I am the LORD your God, who
brought you out of Egypt to give you the
land of Canaan[s] and to be your God.[t]
39“ ‘If any of your fellow Israelites become poor and sell themselves to you, do
not make them work as slaves.[u] 40They are
to be treated as hired workers[v] or temporary residents among you; they are to work
for you until the Year of Jubilee. 41Then
they and their children are to be released,
and they will go back to their own clans
and to the property[w] of their ancestors.[x]
42Because the Israelites are my servants,
whom I brought out of Egypt,[y] they must
not be sold as slaves. 43Do not rule over
them ruthlessly,[z] but fear your God.[a]
44“ ‘Your male and female slaves are to
come from the nations around you; from
them you may buy slaves. 45You may also
buy some of the temporary residents living among you and members of their clans
born in your country, and they will become your property. 46You can bequeath
them to your children as inherited property and can make them slaves for life, but
you must not rule over your fellow Israelites ruthlessly.
47“ ‘If a foreigner residing among you
becomes rich and any of your fellow Israelites become poor and sell themselves[b] to
the foreigner or to a member of the foreigner’s clan, 48they retain the right of redemption[c] after they have sold themselves. One
of their relatives[d] may redeem them: 49An
uncle or a cousin or any blood relative in
their clan may redeem them. Or if they
prosper,[e] they may redeem themselves.
50They and their buyer are to count the
time from the year they sold themselves up
to the Year of Jubilee.[f] The price for their
release is to be based on the rate paid to a
hired worker[g] for that number of years. 51If
many years remain, they must pay for their
redemption a larger share of the price paid
for them. 52If only a few years remain until the Year of Jubilee, they are to compute
that and pay for their redemption accordingly.[h] 53They are to be treated as workers
hired from year to year; you must see to it
that those to whom they owe service do
not rule over them ruthlessly.[i]
54“ ‘Even if someone is not redeemed
in any of these ways, they and their children are to be released in the Year of Jubilee, 55for the Israelites belong to me as
servants. They are my servants, whom I
brought out of Egypt.[j] I am the LORD your
God.[k]

Reward for Obedience

26 “ ‘Do not make idols[l] or set up an
image[m] or a sacred stone[n] for yourselves, and do not place a carved stone[o] in
your land to bow down before it. I am the
LORD your God.
2“ ‘Observe my Sabbaths[p] and have reverence for my sanctuary.[q] I am the LORD.
3“ ‘If you follow my decrees and are

25:27 [i]ver 10 **25:28** [j]Lev 27:24 [k]S ver 10 **25:32** [l]Nu 35:1-8; Jos 21:2 **25:34** [m]Nu 35:2-5; Eze 48:14 **25:35** [n]Dt 24:14, 15 [o]Dt 15:8; Ps 37:21, 26; Pr 21:26; Lk 6:35 **25:36** [p]S Ex 22:25; Jer 15:10 [q]S Lev 19:32 **25:37** [r]S Ex 22:25 **25:38** [s]S Ge 10:19 [t]S Ge 17:7 **25:39** [u]1Ki 5:13; 9:22; Jer 34:14 **25:40** [v]ver 53 **25:41** [w]ver 28 [x]Jer 34:8 **25:42** [y]ver 38

25:43 [z]S Ex 1:13; Eze 34:4; Col 4:1 [a]S Ge 42:18 **25:47** [b]Ne 5:5; Job 24:9 **25:48** [c]S ver 24 [d]S ver 25 **25:49** [e]ver 26 **25:50** [f]S ver 10 [g]Job 7:1; 14:6; Isa 16:14; 21:16 **25:52** [h]S ver 16 **25:53** [i]Col 4:1 **25:55** [j]S Lev 11:45 [k]Lev 11:44 **26:1** [l]S Ex 20:4 [m]Ps 97:7; Isa 48:5; Jer 44:19; Hab 2:18 [n]S Ex 23:24 [o]Nu 33:52 **26:2** [p]S Ex 20:8 [q]Lev 19:30

25:33 *towns of the Levites.* See Nu 35:1–8; Jos 21:1–42.
25:35–38 See notes on Ex 22:25–27; Ne 5:10; Pr 28:8.
25:36 *not take interest.* The main idea was that no one should profit in any way from another's misfortune; rather, the needy should be given assistance.
25:43 *fear your God.* See note on Ge 20:11.
25:55 *servants.* Covenant terminology, similar to "vassals" (see chart, p. 23).
26:1 Forbids worshiping God in any material form (see Ex 20:4 and note). "God is spirit" (Jn 4:24; see Dt 4:15–19). *sacred stone.* See photo, p. 157.
26:3 *obey my commands.* Obedience is the key to blessing (see Gal 6:7–10; Jas 1:22–25). Compare the blessings promised in vv. 3–13 with those in Dt 28:1–14.

careful to obey[r] my commands, [4]I will
send you rain[s] in its season,[t] and the
ground will yield its crops and the trees
their fruit.[u] [5]Your threshing will continue
until grape harvest and the grape harvest
will continue until planting, and you will
eat all the food you want[v] and live in safety in your land.[w]
[6]" 'I will grant peace in the land,[x] and
you will lie down[y] and no one will make
you afraid.[z] I will remove wild beasts[a]
from the land, and the sword will not
pass through your country. [7]You will pursue your enemies,[b] and they will fall by
the sword before you. [8]Five[c] of you will
chase a hundred, and a hundred of you
will chase ten thousand, and your enemies
will fall by the sword before you.[d]
[9]" 'I will look on you with favor and
make you fruitful and increase your numbers,[e] and I will keep my covenant[f] with
you. [10]You will still be eating last year's
harvest when you will have to move it out
to make room for the new.[g] [11]I will put my
dwelling place[a][h] among you, and I will not
abhor you.[i] [12]I will walk[j] among you and
be your God,[k] and you will be my people.[l]
[13]I am the LORD your God,[m] who brought
you out of Egypt[n] so that you would no
longer be slaves to the Egyptians; I broke
the bars of your yoke[o] and enabled you to
walk with heads held high.

Punishment for Disobedience

[14]" 'But if you will not listen to me and
carry out all these commands,[p] [15]and if
you reject my decrees and abhor my laws[q]
and fail to carry out all my commands and
so violate my covenant,[r] [16]then I will do
this to you: I will bring on you sudden terror, wasting diseases and fever[s] that will
destroy your sight and sap your strength.[t]
You will plant seed in vain, because your
enemies will eat it.[u] [17]I will set my face[v]
against you so that you will be defeated[w]
by your enemies;[x] those who hate you
will rule over you,[y] and you will flee even
when no one is pursuing you.[z]
[18]" 'If after all this you will not listen to
me,[a] I will punish[b] you for your sins seven
times over.[c] [19]I will break down your stubborn pride[d] and make the sky above you
like iron and the ground beneath you like
bronze.[e] [20]Your strength will be spent in
vain,[f] because your soil will not yield its
crops, nor will the trees of your land yield
their fruit.[g]
[21]" 'If you remain hostile[h] toward me
and refuse to listen to me, I will multiply
your afflictions seven times over,[i] as your
sins deserve. [22]I will send wild animals[j]
against you, and they will rob you of your
children, destroy your cattle and make you
so few[k] in number that your roads will be
deserted.[l]
[23]" 'If in spite of these things you do not
accept my correction[m] but continue to be
hostile toward me, [24]I myself will be hostile[n] toward you and will afflict you for
your sins seven times over. [25]And I will
bring the sword[o] on you to avenge[p] the
breaking of the covenant. When you withdraw into your cities, I will send a plague[q]
among you, and you will be given into enemy hands. [26]When I cut off your supply
of bread,[r] ten women will be able to bake
your bread in one oven, and they will dole
out the bread by weight. You will eat, but
you will not be satisfied.
[27]" 'If in spite of this you still do not listen to me[s] but continue to be hostile toward me, [28]then in my anger[t] I will be hostile[u] toward you, and I myself will punish
you for your sins seven times over.[v] [29]You
will eat[w] the flesh of your sons and the
flesh of your daughters.[x] [30]I will destroy

[a] *11* Or *my tabernacle*

26:3 [r]S Ge 26:5; S Ex 24:8; Dt 6:17; 7:12; 11:13,22; 28:1,9 **26:4** [s]Dt 11:14; 28:12; Ps 68:9; Jer 5:24; Hos 6:3; Joel 2:23; Zec 10:1 [t]Job 5:10; Ps 65:9; 104:13; 147:8; Jer 5:24 [u]S Ex 23:26; S Lev 25:19; S Job 14:9; Ps 67:6 **26:5** [v]Dt 6:11; 11:15; Eze 36:29-30; Joel 2:19,26 [w]S Lev 25:18 **26:6** [x]Ps 29:11; 37:11; 85:8; 147:14; Isa 26:3; 54:13; 60:18; Hag 2:9 [y]Ps 3:5; 4:8; Pr 3:24 [z]Job 11:18, 19; Isa 17:2; Jer 30:10; Mic 4:4; Zep 3:13 [a]S ver 22; S Ge 37:20 **26:7** [b]Ps 18:37; 44:5 **26:8** [c]Isa 30:17 [d]Dt 28:7; 32:30; Jos 23:10; Jdg 15:15; 1Ch 12:14 **26:9** [e]S Ge 1:22; S 17:6; Ne 9:23 [f]S Ge 17:7 **26:10** [g]Lev 25:22 **26:11** [h]Ex 25:8; Ps 74:7; 76:2; Eze 37:27 [i]ver 15,43, 44; Dt 31:6; 1Sa 12:22; 1Ki 6:13; 2Ki 17:15 **26:12** [j]S Ge 3:8 [k]S Ge 17:7 [l]Ex 6:7; Jer 7:23; 11:4; 24:7; 30:22; 31:1; Zec 13:9; 2Co 6:16* **26:13** [m]Lev 11:44 [n]S Ex 6:6; S 13:3 [o]Isa 10:27; Jer 2:20; 27:2; 28:10; 30:8; Eze 30:18; 34:27; Hos 11:4 **26:14** [p]Dt 28:15-68; Mal 2:2 **26:15** [q]S ver 11 [r]S Ge 17:7 **26:16** [s]Dt 28:22,35; Ps 78:33 [t]ver 39; 1Sa 2:33; Ps 107:17; Eze 4:17; 24:23; 33:10 [u]Jdg 6:3-6; Job 31:8 **26:17** [v]Lev 17:10; Eze 15:7 [w]Dt 28:48; Jos 7:12; Jdg 2:15; 1Ki 8:33; 2Ch 6:24 [x]Jos 7:4; Jer 19:7; 21:7 [y]Ps 106:41 [z]ver 36,37; Dt 28:7, 25; Ps 53:5; Pr 28:1; Isa 30:17 **26:18** [a]ver 14 [b]Ps 99:8; Jer 21:14; Am 3:14 [c]ver 21 **26:19** [d]Ps 10:4; 73:6; Isa 16:6; 25:11; 28:1-3; Jer 13:9; 48:29; Eze 24:21; Am 6:8; Zep 3:11 [e]Dt 28:23; Job 38:38 **26:20** [f]Dt 28:38; Ps 127:1; Isa 17:11; 49:4; Jer 12:13; Mic 6:15; Hag 1:6 [g]Dt 11:17; 28:24 **26:21** [h]ver 41 [i]ver 18; S Ge 4:15 **26:22** [j]S Ge 37:20 [k]Dt 28:62; Jer 42:2 [l]Jer 5:6; 14:16; 15:3; 16:4; Eze 14:15 **26:23** [m]Jer 2:30; 5:3; 7:28; 17:23; 32:33; Zep 3:2 **26:24** [n]2Sa 22:27 **26:25** [o]Jer 5:17; 15:3; 47:6; Eze 11:8; 14:17; 21:4; 33:2 [p]Jer 50:28; 51:6,11 [q]S Ex 5:3; S 9:3; Nu 16:46; 1Ki 8:37; Hab 3:5 **26:26** [r]1Ki 8:37; 18:2; 2Ki 4:38; 6:25; 8:1; 25:3; Ps 105:16; Isa 3:1; 9:20; Jer 37:21; 52:6; Eze 4:16,17; 5:16; 14:13; Hos 4:10; Mic 6:14 **26:27** [s]ver 14 **26:28** [t]Dt 32:19; Jdg 2:14; Ps 78:59; 106:40 [u]Dt 7:10; Job 34:11; Isa 59:18; 65:6-7; 66:6; Jer 17:10; 25:29; Joel 3:4 [v]ver 18 **26:29** [w]2Ki 6:29; Jer 19:9; La 4:10; Eze 5:10 [x]Dt 28:53

26:4 *I will send you rain.* One of the blessings for faithful obedience to the Sinaitic covenant (see Dt 28:12; see also Dt 11:14; Isa 30:23; Jer 14:22; Zec 10:1 and notes). On the other hand, one of the curses for covenant disobedience was God's withholding of rain (v. 19; Dt 28:23–24; see also Dt 11:17; 1Ki 8:35; Isa 5:6; Jer 3:3; 14:4; Zec 14:17–18 and notes).

26:9 *fruitful and increase.* See note on Ge 1:22; contrast Lev 26:22.

26:12 *your God ... my people.* Covenantal terms later made famous by Hosea (1:9–10; 2:23). See Jer 31:33; Zec 8:8 and note; Heb 8:10.

26:14 *if you will not listen.* The list of curses for covenant disobedience (see vv. 14–39) is usually much longer than that of blessings for obedience (as in vv. 3–13; see Dt 28:15—29:28; cf. Dt 28:1–14).

26:16 *You will plant seed ... your enemies will eat it.* See note on Hag 1:6.

26:17 See v. 36 and the allusion to this statement in Pr 28:1.

26:18,21,24,28 *seven times over.* Thoroughly (cf. note on 4:6).

26:19 *sky ... like iron ... ground ... like bronze.* See note on Dt 28:23.

26:30 *high places.* See note on 1Sa 9:12. *idols.* The Hebrew word probably means "filthy [or detestable] idols."

your high places,[y] cut down your incense altars[z] and pile your dead bodies[a] on the lifeless forms of your idols,[a] and I will abhor[b] you. 31 I will turn your cities into ruins[c] and lay waste[d] your sanctuaries,[e] and I will take no delight in the pleasing aroma of your offerings.[f] 32 I myself will lay waste the land,[g] so that your enemies who live there will be appalled.[h] 33 I will scatter[i] you among the nations[j] and will draw out my sword[k] and pursue you. Your land will be laid waste,[l] and your cities will lie in ruins.[m] 34 Then the land will enjoy its sabbath years all the time that it lies desolate[n] and you are in the country of your enemies;[o] then the land will rest and enjoy its sabbaths. 35 All the time that it lies desolate, the land will have the rest[p] it did not have during the sabbaths you lived in it.

36 " 'As for those of you who are left, I will make their hearts so fearful in the lands of their enemies that the sound of a windblown leaf[q] will put them to flight.[r] They will run as though fleeing from the sword, and they will fall, even though no one is pursuing them.[s] 37 They will stumble over one another[t] as though fleeing from the sword, even though no one is pursuing them. So you will not be able to stand before your enemies.[u] 38 You will perish[v] among the nations; the land of your enemies will devour you.[w] 39 Those of you who are left will waste away in the lands of their enemies because of their sins; also because of their ancestors'[x] sins they will waste away.[y]

40 " 'But if they will confess[z] their sins[a] and the sins of their ancestors[b]—their unfaithfulness and their hostility toward me, 41 which made me hostile[c] toward them so that I sent them into the land of their enemies—then when their uncircumcised hearts[d] are humbled[e] and they pay[f] for their sin, 42 I will remember my covenant with Jacob[g] and my covenant with Isaac[h] and my covenant with Abraham,[i] and I will remember the land. 43 For the land will be deserted[j] by them and will enjoy its sabbaths while it lies desolate without them. They will pay for their sins because they rejected[k] my laws and abhorred my decrees.[l] 44 Yet in spite of this, when they are in the land of their enemies,[m] I will not reject them or abhor[n] them so as to destroy them completely,[o] breaking my covenant[p] with them. I am the LORD their God. 45 But for their sake I will remember[q] the covenant with their ancestors whom I brought out of Egypt[r] in the sight of the nations to be their God. I am the LORD.' "

46 These are the decrees, the laws and the regulations that the LORD established at Mount Sinai[s] between himself and the Israelites through Moses.[t]

Redeeming What Is the LORD's

27 The LORD said to Moses, 2 "Speak to the Israelites and say to them: 'If anyone makes a special vow[u] to dedicate a person to the LORD by giving the equivalent value, 3 set the value of a male between the ages of twenty and sixty at fifty shekels[b] of silver, according to the sanctuary shekel[c];[v] 4 for a female, set her value at thirty shekels[d]; 5 for a person between the ages of five and twenty, set the value of a male at twenty shekels[e][w] and of a female at ten shekels[f]; 6 for a person between one month and five years, set the value of a male at five shekels[g][x] of silver and that of a female at three shekels[h] of silver; 7 for a person sixty years old or more, set the value of a male at fifteen shekels[i] and of a female at ten shekels. 8 If anyone making the vow is too poor to pay[y] the specified

[a] 30 Or *your funeral offerings* [b] 3 That is, about 1 1/4 pounds or about 575 grams; also in verse 16 [c] 3 That is, about 2/5 ounce or about 12 grams; also in verse 25 [d] 4 That is, about 12 ounces or about 345 grams [e] 5 That is, about 8 ounces or about 230 grams [f] 5 That is, about 4 ounces or about 115 grams; also in verse 7 [g] 6 That is, about 2 ounces or about 58 grams [h] 6 That is, about 1 1/4 ounces or about 35 grams [i] 7 That is, about 6 ounces or about 175 grams

26:30 [y]Dt 12:2; 1Sa 9:12; 10:5; 1Ki 3:2, 4; 12:31; 13:2, 32; 2Ki 17:29; 23:20; 2Ch 34:3; Ps 78:58; Eze 6:3; 16:16; Am 7:9 [z]2Ch 34:4; Isa 17:8; 27:9; Eze 6:6 [a]Isa 21:9; Jer 50:2; Eze 6:13 [b]Ps 106:40; Am 6:8 **26:31** [c]Ne 1:3; Isa 1:7; 3:8, 26; 6:11; 24:12; 61:4; Jer 4:7; 9:11; 25:11; 34:22; 44:2, 6, 22; Eze 36:33; Mic 2:4; 3:12; Zep 2:5; 3:6 [d]2Ki 22:19 [e]Ps 74:3-7; Isa 63:18; 64:11; La 2:7; Eze 24:21; Am 7:9 [f]Am 5:21, 22; 8:10 **26:32** [g]Isa 5:6; Jer 9:11; 12:11; 25:11; 26:9; 33:10; 34:22; 44:22 [h]1Ki 9:8; 2Ch 29:8; Isa 52:14; Jer 18:16; 19:8; 48:39; Eze 5:14; 26:16; 27:35; 28:19 **26:33** [i]Jer 40:15; 50:17; Eze 34:6; Joel 3:2 [j]Dt 4:27; 28:64; Ne 1:8; Ps 44:11; 106:27; Jer 4:11; 9:16; 13:24; 31:10; Eze 5:10; 12:15; 17:21; 20:23; 22:15; Zec 7:14 [k]Jer 42:16; Am 9:4 [l]Isa 49:19; Jer 7:34 [m]ver 31; 1Sa 15:22; Job 36:11; Jer 40:3 **26:34** [n]Isa 1:7; Jer 7:34; 25:11; 44:6; Eze 33:29 [o]ver 43; 2Ch 36:21 **26:35** [p]S Lev 25:4 **26:36** [q]Job 13:25 [r]2Ki 25:5; Ps 58:7; La 1:3, 6; 4:19; Eze 21:7 [s]S ver 17 **26:37** [t]Jer 6:21; 13:16; 46:16; Eze 3:20; Na 3:3 [u]Jos 7:12 **26:38** [v]Job 4:9; 36:12; Ps 1:6; Isa 1:28; Jer 16:4; 44:27 [w]Dt 4:26 **26:39** [x]Ex 20:5; Isa 14:21 [y]S ver 16; Isa 24:16 **26:40** [z]S Lev 5:5 [a]Ps 32:5; 38:18 [b]Ne 9:2; Ps 106:6; Jer 3:12-15; 14:20; Hos 5:15; Lk 15:18; 1Jn 1:9 **26:41** [c]S ver 21 [d]Dt 10:16; 30:6; Jer 4:4; 9:25, 26; Eze 44:7, 9; Ac 7:51 [e]2Ch 7:14; 12:6; Eze 20:43 [f]Isa 6:7; 33:24; 40:2; 53:5, 6, 11 **26:42** [g]Ge 28:15; 35:11-12 [h]S Ge 26:5 [i]S Ex 2:24 **26:43** [j]Ps 69:25; Isa 6:11; 32:14; 62:4; Jer 2:15; 44:2; La 1:1; Eze 36:4 [k]Nu 11:20; 14:31; 1Sa 8:7; Ps 106:24 [l]S ver 11; Eze 20:13 **26:44** [m]S ver 33; 2Ki 17:20; 25:11; 2Ch 6:36; 36:20 [n]S ver 11; Ro 11:2 [o]Dt 4:31; Jer 4:27; 5:10; 30:11 [p]Jdg 2:1; Jer 31:37; 33:26; 51:5 **26:45** [q]Dt 4:31 [r]Ex 6:8; Lev 25:38 **26:46** [s]S Ex 19:11 [t]S Lev 7:38; 27:34 **27:2** [u]S Ge 28:20 **27:3** [v]S Ex 30:13 **27:5** [w]S Ge 37:28 **27:6** [x]Nu 3:47; 18:16 **27:8** [y]S Lev 5:11

26:34 Fulfilled during the Babylonian exile (see note on 2Ch 36:20–21).
26:40 *confess their sins.* See notes on Pr 28:13; 1Jn 1:9.
26:41 *uncircumcised hearts.* See note on Ge 17:10.
26:44 *not reject them.* See Jer 31:37; 33:25–26; Ro 11:1–29 and notes; see also note on Ro 9:1—11:36.
26:46 A summary statement concerning chs. 1–26.
27:1–34 This final chapter concerns things promised to the Lord in kind—servants, animals, houses or lands. But provisions were made to give money instead of the item, in which case the adding of a fifth of its value was usually required. Such vows were expressions of special thanksgiving (cf. Hannah, 1Sa 1:28) and were given over and above the expected sacrifices.
27:2 *to dedicate a person.* Possibly to give a slave to the service of the temple, but more likely to offer oneself or a member of one's family. Since only Levites were acceptable for most work of this kind, other people gave the monetary equivalent—but see 1Sa 1:11 and note.
27:3,25 *according to the sanctuary shekel.* See note on Ex 30:13.

amount, the person being dedicated is to be presented to the priest, who will set the value[z] according to what the one making the vow can afford.

9 " 'If what they vowed is an animal that is acceptable as an offering to the LORD,[a] such an animal given to the LORD becomes holy.[b] 10 They must not exchange it or substitute a good one for a bad one, or a bad one for a good one;[c] if they should substitute one animal for another, both it and the substitute become holy. 11 If what they vowed is a ceremonially unclean animal[d]—one that is not acceptable as an offering to the LORD—the animal must be presented to the priest, 12 who will judge its quality as good or bad. Whatever value the priest then sets, that is what it will be. 13 If the owner wishes to redeem[e] the animal, a fifth must be added to its value.[f]

14 " 'If anyone dedicates their house as something holy to the LORD, the priest will judge its quality as good or bad. Whatever value the priest then sets, so it will remain. 15 If the one who dedicates their house wishes to redeem it,[g] they must add a fifth to its value, and the house will again become theirs.

16 " 'If anyone dedicates to the LORD part of their family land, its value is to be set according to the amount of seed required for it—fifty shekels of silver to a homer[a] of barley seed. 17 If they dedicate a field during the Year of Jubilee, the value that has been set remains. 18 But if they dedicate a field after the Jubilee,[h] the priest will determine the value according to the number of years that remain[i] until the next Year of Jubilee, and its set value will be reduced. 19 If the one who dedicates the field wishes to redeem it,[j] they must add a fifth to its value, and the field will again become theirs. 20 If, however, they do not redeem the field, or if they have sold it to someone else, it can never be redeemed. 21 When the field is released in the Jubilee,[k] it will become holy,[l] like a field devoted to the LORD;[m] it will become priestly property.

22 " 'If anyone dedicates to the LORD a field they have bought, which is not part of their family land, 23 the priest will determine its value up to the Year of Jubilee,[n] and the owner must pay its value on that day as something holy to the LORD. 24 In the Year of Jubilee the field will revert to the person from whom it was bought,[o] the one whose land it was. 25 Every value is to be set according to the sanctuary shekel,[p] twenty gerahs[q] to the shekel.

26 " 'No one, however, may dedicate the firstborn of an animal, since the firstborn already belongs to the LORD;[r] whether an ox[b] or a sheep, it is the LORD's. 27 If it is one of the unclean animals,[s] it may be bought back at its set value, adding a fifth of the value to it. If it is not redeemed, it is to be sold at its set value.

28 " 'But nothing that a person owns and devotes[c][t] to the LORD—whether a human being or an animal or family land—may be sold or redeemed; everything so devoted is most holy[u] to the LORD.

29 " 'No person devoted to destruction[d] may be ransomed; they are to be put to death.[v]

30 " 'A tithe[w] of everything from the land, whether grain from the soil or fruit from the trees, belongs to the LORD; it is holy[x] to the LORD. 31 Whoever would redeem[y] any of their tithe must add a fifth of the value[z] to it. 32 Every tithe of the herd and flock—every tenth animal that passes under the shepherd's rod[a]—will be holy to the LORD. 33 No one may pick out the good from the bad or make any substitution.[b] If anyone does make a substitution, both the animal and its substitute become holy and cannot be redeemed.[c] ' "

34 These are the commands the LORD gave Moses at Mount Sinai[d] for the Israelites.[e]

27:8 [z] ver 12,14 **27:9** [a] S Ge 28:20; S Lev 1:2 [b] ver 21,26, 28; Ex 40:9; Nu 6:20; 18:17; Dt 15:19 **27:10** [c] ver 33 **27:11** [d] ver 27; S Ex 13:13; Nu 18:15 **27:13** [e] S Lev 25:25 [f] S Lev 5:16 **27:15** [g] ver 13, 20 **27:18** [h] Lev 25:10 [i] Lev 25:15 **27:19** [j] S Lev 25:25 **27:21** [k] S Lev 25:10 [l] S ver 9 [m] ver 28; Nu 18:14; Eze 44:29 **27:23** [n] S Lev 25:15 **27:24** [o] Lev 25:28 **27:25** [p] S Ex 30:13 [q] Nu 3:47; Eze 45:12 **27:26** [r] S Ex 13:12 **27:27** [s] S ver 11 **27:28** [t] Nu 18:14; Jos 6:17-19 [u] S ver 9 **27:29** [v] Dt 7:26 **27:30** [w] Nu 18:26; Dt 12:6,17; 14:22,28; 2Ch 31:6; Ne 10:37; 12:44; 13:5; Mal 3:8 [x] Dt 7:6; Ezr 9:2; Isa 6:13 **27:31** [y] S Lev 25:25 [z] Lev 5:16 **27:32** [a] Ps 89:32; Jer 33:13; Eze 20:37 **27:33** [b] ver 10 [c] Nu 18:21 **27:34** [d] S Ex 19:11 [e] S Lev 7:38; Ac 7:38

[a] *16* That is, probably about 300 pounds or about 135 kilograms [b] *26* The Hebrew word can refer to either male or female. [c] *28* The Hebrew term refers to the irrevocable giving over of things or persons to the LORD. [d] *29* The Hebrew term refers to the irrevocable giving over of things or persons to the LORD, often by totally destroying them.

27:9 *becomes holy.* See note on Ex 3:5. An animal given for a sacrifice could not be exchanged for another (v. 10). The people of Malachi's day chose the poorest animals, after having vowed to offer good ones (see Mal 1:13–14 and notes). If an unclean animal was given, it could be redeemed with the 20 percent penalty (vv. 11–13).

27:18 See note on 25:15.

27:28 *devotes to the LORD.* See NIV text note. Devoting something was far more serious than dedicating it to sacred use. The devoted thing became totally the Lord's. Achan's sin was the greater because he stole what had been devoted to the Lord (Jos 7:11). Persons devoted to destruction were usually the captives in the wars of Canaan (cf. 1Sa 15:3,18).

27:29 Saul sinned in this regard when he did not totally destroy the Amalekites (1Sa 15).

27:30 *tithe.* A tenth (see Nu 18:21–29; Dt 12:6–18; 14:22–29; 26:12). From these passages it appears that Israel actually had three tithes: (1) the general tithe (here), paid to the Levites (Nu 18:21), who in turn had to give a tenth of that to the priests (Nu 18:26); (2) the tithe associated with the sacred meal involving offerer and Levite (Dt 14:22–27); and (3) the tithe paid every three years to the poor (Dt 14:28–29).

27:34 *the LORD gave Moses.* See 1:1 and note; 7:37–38; 25:1; 26:46.

NUMBERS

INTRODUCTION

Title

The English name of the book comes from the Septuagint (the pre-Christian Greek translation of the OT) and is based on the census lists found in chs. 1; 26. The Hebrew title of the book (*bemidbar*, "in the Desert," 1:1) is more descriptive of its content. Numbers presents an account of the 38-year period of Israel's wandering in the desert (or wilderness) following the establishment of the Sinaitic covenant (compare 1:1 with Dt 1:1).

Author and Date

The book has traditionally been ascribed to Moses. This conclusion is based on (1) statements concerning Moses' writing activity (e.g., 33:1 – 2; Ex 17:14; 24:4; 34:27) and (2) the assumption that the first five books of the Bible, the Pentateuch, are a unit and come from one author. See Introduction to Genesis: Author and Date of Writing.

It is not necessary, however, to claim that Numbers came from Moses' hand complete and in final form. Portions of the book were probably added by scribes or editors from later periods of Israel's history. For example, the protestation of the humility of Moses (12:3) would hardly be convincing if it came from his own mouth. But it seems reasonable to assume that Moses wrote the essential content of the book.

Contents

Numbers relates the story of Israel's journey from Mount Sinai to the plains of Moab on the border of Canaan. Much of its legislation for people and priests is similar to that in Exodus, Leviticus and Deuteronomy. The book tells of the murmuring and rebellion of God's people and of their subsequent judgment. Those whom God had redeemed from slavery in Egypt and with whom he had made a covenant at Mount Sinai responded not with faith, gratitude and obedience but with unbelief, ingratitude and repeated acts of rebellion, which

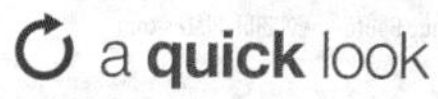

a quick look

Author:
Moses

Audience:
God's chosen people, the Israelites

Date:
Probably between 1446 and 1406 BC

Theme:
Because the Israelites are unwilling to enter the land of Canaan, their entire generation is forced to wander in the Desert of Sinai for 38 years.

The book of Numbers tells about the murmuring and rebellion of the people of God, those whom he had redeemed from slavery in Egypt.

A view of a reconstruction of the tabernacle
Becky Weolongo Booto/www.BiblePlaces.com

came to extreme expression in their refusal to undertake the conquest of Canaan (ch. 14). The community of the redeemed forfeited its part in the promised land. The Israelites were condemned to live out their lives in the wilderness; only their children would enjoy the fulfillment of the promise that had originally been theirs (cf. Heb 3:7—4:11 and note on 3:16–19).

Theological Teaching

In telling the story of Israel's wilderness wanderings, Numbers offers much that is theologically significant. During the first year after Israel's deliverance from Egypt, the nation entered into covenant with the Lord at Sinai to be the people of his kingdom, among whom he pitched his royal tent (the tabernacle)—this is the story of Exodus. As the account of Numbers begins, the Lord organizes the Israelites into a military camp. Leaving Sinai, they march forth as his conquering army, with the Lord at the head, to establish his kingdom in the promised land in the midst of the nations. The book graphically portrays Israel's identity as the Lord's redeemed covenant people and their vocation as the servant people of God, charged with establishing his kingdom on earth. God's purpose in history is implicitly disclosed: to invade the arena of fallen humanity and effect the redemption of his creation—the mission in which his people are also to be totally engaged.

Numbers also presents the chastening wrath of God against his disobedient people. Because of their rebellion (and especially the nation's refusal to undertake the conquest of Canaan),

Because of their disobedience, those whom God has used to establish the nation forfeit their part in the promised land.

Israel was in breach of the covenant. The fourth book of the Pentateuch presents a sobering reality: The God who had entered into covenant with Abraham (Ge 15; 17), who had delivered his people from bondage in the exodus (Ex 14–15), who had brought Israel into covenant with himself as his "treasured possession" (Ex 19; see especially Ex 19:5) and who had revealed his holiness and the gracious means of approaching him (Lev 1–7) was also a God of wrath. His wrath extended to his errant children, as well as to the enemy nations of Egypt and Canaan.

Even Moses, the great prophet and servant of the Lord, was not exempt from God's wrath when he disobeyed God. Ch. 20, which records his error, begins with the notice of Miriam's death (20:1) and concludes with the record of Aaron's death (20:22–29). Here is the passing of the old guard. Those whom God has used to establish the nation are dying before the nation has come into its own.

The questions arise: Is God finished with the nation as a whole (cf. Ro 11:1)? Are his promises a thing of the past? In one of the most remarkable sections of the Bible—the account of Balaam, the pagan diviner (chs. 22–24)—the reply is given. The Lord, working in a providential and direct way, proclaims his continued faithfulness to his purpose for his people despite their unfaithfulness to him.

Balaam is Moab's answer to Moses, the man of God. He is an internationally known prophet who shares the pagan belief that the God of Israel is like any other deity who might be manipulated by acts of magic or sorcery (see note on 22:5). But from the early part of the narrative, when Balaam first encounters the one true God in visions, and in the narrative of the journey on the donkey (ch. 22), he begins to learn that dealing with the true God is fundamentally different from anything he has ever known. When he attempts to curse Israel at the instigation of Balak, king of Moab, Balaam finds his mouth unable to express the curse he desires to pronounce. Instead, from his lips come blessings on Israel and curses on their enemies (chs. 23–24).

In his seven prophetic messages, Balaam proclaims God's great blessing for his people (see 23:20). Though the immediate enjoyment of this blessing will always depend on the faithfulness of his people, the ultimate realization of God's blessing is sure—because of the character of God (see 23:19). Thus Numbers reaffirms the ongoing purposes of God. Despite his judgment on his rebellious people, God is still determined to bring Israel into the land of promise. His blessing to Israel rests in his sovereign will.

The teaching of the book has lasting significance for Israel and for the church (cf. Ro 15:4; 1Co 10:6,11). God does display his wrath even against his errant people, but his grace is renewed as surely as is the dawn, and his redemptive purpose will not be thwarted.

Special Problem

The large numbers of men conscripted into Israel's army (see, e.g., the figures in 1:46; 26:51) have puzzled many interpreters. The numbers of men mustered for warfare seem to demand a total population in excess of 2,000,000. Such figures appear to be exceedingly large for the times, for the locale, for the wilderness wanderings, and in comparison with the inhabitants of Canaan. See note on 3:43.

Various possibilities have been suggested to solve this problem. Some have thought that the numbers may have been corrupted in transmission. The present text, however, does not betray textual difficulties with the numbers.

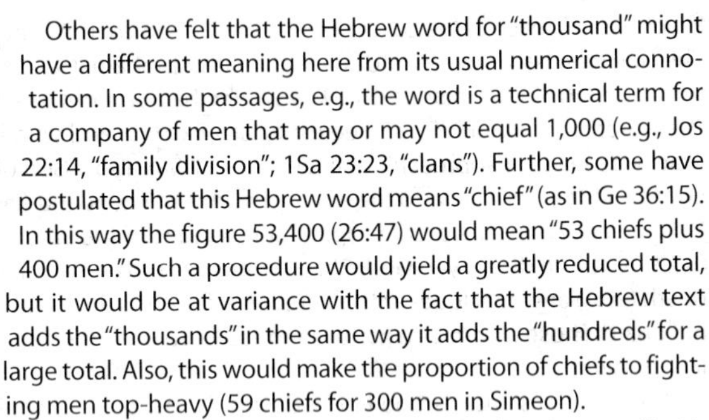

Others have felt that the Hebrew word for "thousand" might have a different meaning here from its usual numerical connotation. In some passages, e.g., the word is a technical term for a company of men that may or may not equal 1,000 (e.g., Jos 22:14, "family division"; 1Sa 23:23, "clans"). Further, some have postulated that this Hebrew word means "chief" (as in Ge 36:15). In this way the figure 53,400 (26:47) would mean "53 chiefs plus 400 men." Such a procedure would yield a greatly reduced total, but it would be at variance with the fact that the Hebrew text adds the "thousands" in the same way it adds the "hundreds" for a large total. Also, this would make the proportion of chiefs to fighting men top-heavy (59 chiefs for 300 men in Simeon).

Another option is to read the Hebrew word for "thousand" with a dual meaning of "chief" and "1,000," with the chiefs numbering one less than the stated figure. For example, the 46,500 of Reuben (1:20) is read as 45 chiefs and 1,500 fighting men, the 59,300 of Simeon (1:23) is read as 58 chiefs and 1,300 fighting men, etc. But in this case, as in the former, the totals of 1:46 and 2:32 must then be regarded as errors of understanding (perhaps by later scribes).

Still another approach is to regard the numbers as symbolic figures rather than as strictly mathematical. The numerical value of the Hebrew letters in the expression *bene yisra'el* ("the whole Israelite community," 1:2) equals 603 (the number of the thousands of the fighting men, 1:46); the remaining 550 (plus 1 for Moses) might come from the numerical equivalent of the Hebrew letters in the expression "all the men ... who are ... able to serve in the army" (1:3). This symbolic use of numbers (called "gematria") is not unknown in the Bible (see Rev 13:18), but it is not likely in Numbers, where there are no literary clues pointing in that direction. (For one more option [hyperbole], see note on 1Ch 12:23 – 37.)

While the problem of the large numbers has not been satisfactorily solved, the Bible does point to a remarkable increase of Jacob's descendants during the four centuries of their sojourn in Egypt (see Ex 1:7 – 12). With all their difficulties, these numbers also point to the great role of providence and miracles in God's dealings with his people during their life in the wilderness (see note on 1:46).

Fragments of a silver scroll from c. 600 BC found in a burial cave just outside Jerusalem containing the Aaronic benediction from Numbers 6:24–26.

Z. Radovan/www.BibleLandPictures.com

Structure and Outline

The book has three major divisions, based on Israel's geographic locations. Each of the three divisions has two parts, as the following breakdown demonstrates: (1) Israel at Sinai, preparing to depart for the land of promise (1:1 — 10:10), followed by the journey from Sinai to Kadesh (10:11 — 12:16); (2) Israel at Kadesh, delayed as a result of rebellion (13:1 — 20:13), followed by the journey from Kadesh to the plains of Moab (20:14 — 22:1); (3) Israel on the plains of Moab, anticipating the conquest of the land of promise (22:2 — 32:42), followed by appendixes dealing with various matters (chs. 33 – 36).

- I. Israel at Sinai, Preparing to Depart for the Promised Land (1:1 — 10:10)
  - A. The Commands for the First Census (chs. 1 – 4)
    1. The numbers of men from each tribe mustered for war (ch. 1)
    2. The placement of the tribes around the tabernacle and their order for march (ch. 2)
    3. The placement of the Levites around the tabernacle, and the numbers of the Levites and the firstborn of Israel (ch. 3)
    4. The numbers of the Levites in their tabernacle service to the Lord (ch. 4)
  - B. The Commands for Purity of the People (5:1 — 10:10)
    1. The test for purity in the law of jealousy (ch. 5)
    2. The Nazirite vow and the Aaronic benediction (ch. 6)
    3. The offerings of the 12 leaders at the dedication of the tabernacle (ch. 7)
    4. The setting up of the lamps and the separation of the Levites (ch. 8)
    5. The observance of the Passover (9:1 – 14)
    6. The covering cloud and the silver trumpets (9:15 — 10:10)
- II. The Journey from Sinai to Kadesh (10:11 — 12:16)
  - A. The Beginning of the Journey (10:11 – 36)
  - B. The Beginning of the Sorrows: Fire and Quail (ch. 11)
  - C. The Opposition of Miriam and Aaron (ch. 12)
- III. Israel at Kadesh, the Delay Resulting from Rebellion (13:1 — 20:13)
  - A. The 12 Spies and Their Mixed Report of the Good Land (ch. 13)
  - B. The People's Rebellion against God's Commission, and Their Defeat (ch. 14)
  - C. A Collection of Laws on Offerings, the Sabbath and Tassels on Garments (ch. 15)
  - D. The Rebellion of Korah and His Allies (ch. 16)
  - E. The Budding of Aaron's Staff: A Sign for Rebels (ch. 17)
  - F. Concerning Priests, Their Duties and Their Support (ch. 18)
  - G. The Red Heifer and the Cleansing Water (ch. 19)
  - H. The Sin of Moses (20:1 – 13)
- IV. The Journey from Kadesh to the Plains of Moab (20:14 — 22:1)
  - A. The Resistance of Edom (20:14 – 21)
  - B. The Death of Aaron (20:22 – 29)
  - C. The Destruction of Arad (21:1 – 3)
  - D. The Bronze Snake (21:4 – 9)
  - E. The Song of the Well and the Journey to Moab (21:10 – 20)

- F. The Defeat of Sihon and Og (21:21–35)
- G. Israel Returns to Moab (22:1)

V. Israel on the Plains of Moab, in Anticipation of Taking the Promised Land (22:2—32:42)
- A. Balak of Moab Hires Balaam to Curse Israel (22:2–41)
- B. Balaam Blesses Israel in Seven Messages (chs. 23–24)
- C. The Baal of Peor and Israel's Apostasy (ch. 25)
- D. The Second Census (ch. 26)
- E. Instructions for the New Generation (chs. 27–30)
  1. The inheritance for women (27:1–11)
  2. The successor to Moses (27:12–23)
  3. Commands regarding offerings (28:1–15)
  4. Commands regarding festivals (28:16—29:40)
  5. Commands regarding vows (ch. 30)
- F. The War against Midian (ch. 31)
- G. The Settlement of the Transjordan Tribes (ch. 32)

VI. Appendixes Dealing with Various Matters (chs. 33–36)
- A. The Stages of the Journey (ch. 33)
- B. The Land of Inheritance (chs. 34–35)
- C. The Inheritance for Women (ch. 36)

The Census

1 The LORD spoke to Moses in the tent
of meeting[a] in the Desert of Sinai[b] on
the first day of the second month[c] of the
second year after the Israelites came out
of Egypt.[d] He said: 2 “Take a census[e] of
the whole Israelite community by their
clans and families,[f] listing every man by
name,[g] one by one. 3 You and Aaron[h] are
to count according to their divisions all
the men in Israel who are twenty years
old or more[i] and able to serve in the
army.[j] 4 One man from each tribe,[k] each
of them the head of his family,[l] is to help
you.[m] 5 These are the names[n] of the men
who are to assist you:

from Reuben,[o] Elizur son of Shedeur;[p]
6 from Simeon,[q] Shelumiel son of Zurishaddai;[r]
7 from Judah,[s] Nahshon son of Amminadab;[t]
8 from Issachar,[u] Nethanel son of Zuar;[v]
9 from Zebulun,[w] Eliab son of Helon;[x]
10 from the sons of Joseph:
from Ephraim,[y] Elishama son of Ammihud;[z]
from Manasseh,[a] Gamaliel son of Pedahzur;[b]
11 from Benjamin,[c] Abidan son of Gideoni;[d]
12 from Dan,[e] Ahiezer son of Ammishaddai;[f]
13 from Asher,[g] Pagiel son of Okran;[h]
14 from Gad,[i] Eliasaph son of Deuel;[j]
15 from Naphtali,[k] Ahira son of Enan.[l]”

16 These were the men appointed from
the community, the leaders[m] of their ancestral tribes.[n] They were the heads of the
clans of Israel.[o]

17 Moses and Aaron took these men
whose names had been specified, 18 and
they called the whole community together
on the first day of the second month.[p] The
people registered their ancestry[q] by their
clans and families,[r] and the men twenty
years old or more[s] were listed by name,
one by one, 19 as the LORD commanded
Moses. And so he counted[t] them in the
Desert of Sinai:

20 From the descendants of Reuben[u] the firstborn son[v] of Israel:
All the men twenty years old or more
who were able to serve in the army
were listed by name, one by one, according to the records of their clans
and families. 21 The number from the
tribe of Reuben[w] was 46,500.

22 From the descendants of Simeon:[x]
All the men twenty years old or
more who were able to serve in
the army were counted and listed
by name, one by one, according to
the records of their clans and families. 23 The number from the tribe
of Simeon was 59,300.[y]

24 From the descendants of Gad:[z]
All the men twenty years old or
more who were able to serve in the

1:1 [a] S Ex 27:21; S 40:2 [b] S Ex 19:1 [c] ver 18 [d] S Ex 6:14 **1:2** [e] Ex 30:11-16 [f] ver 18 [g] Nu 3:40 **1:3** [h] Ex 4:14; Nu 17:3 [i] S Ex 30:14 [j] ver 20; Nu 26:2; Jos 5:4; 1Ch 5:18 **1:4** [k] S Lev 24:11; S Jos 7:1 [l] ver 16; Nu 7:2; 30:1; 31:26 [m] Ex 18:21; Nu 34:18; Dt 1:15; Jos 22:14 **1:5** [n] Nu 17:2 [o] S Ge 29:32; Rev 7:5 [p] Nu 2:10; 7:30; 10:18 **1:6** [q] ver 22; Nu 25:14 [r] Nu 2:12; 7:36, 41; 10:19 **1:7** [s] ver 26; S Ge 29:35; Ps 78:68 [t] Ex 6:23; Nu 7:12; Ru 4:20; 1Ch 2:10; Mt 1:4; Lk 3:32 **1:8** [u] S Ge 30:18; Nu 10:15 [v] Nu 2:5; 7:18 **1:9** [w] ver 30; Nu 10:16 [x] Nu 2:7; 7:24 **1:10** [y] ver 32 [z] Nu 2:18; 7:48, 53; 10:22 [a] ver 34; Nu 10:23 [b] Nu 2:20; 7:54 **1:11** [c] Nu 10:24 [d] Nu 2:22; 7:60; Ps 68:27

1:12 [e] ver 38 [f] Nu 2:25; 7:66; 10:25 **1:13** [g] ver 40; Nu 10:26 [h] Nu 2:27; 7:72 **1:14** [i] ver 24; Nu 10:20 [j] Nu 2:14; 7:42 **1:15** [k] ver 42; Nu 10:27 [l] Nu 2:29; 7:78 **1:16** [m] S Ex 18:25 [n] Nu 32:28 [o] S ver 4 **1:18** [p] ver 1 [q] Ezr 2:59; Heb 7:3 [r] ver 2 [s] S Ex 30:14 **1:19** [t] Ex 30:12; Nu 26:63; 31:49 **1:20** [u] S Ge 29:32; S 46:9; Rev 7:5 [v] S Ge 10:15 **1:21** [w] Nu 26:7 **1:22** [x] S Ge 29:33; Rev 7:7 **1:23** [y] Nu 26:14 **1:24** [z] S Ge 30:11; S Jos 13:24-28; Rev 7:5

1:1 *The LORD spoke to Moses.* One of the most pervasive emphases in Numbers is the fact that the Lord spoke to Moses and through Moses to Israel. From the opening words to the closing words (36:13), this is stated over 150 times and in more than 20 ways. The Lord's use of Moses as his prophet is described in 12:6–8 (see notes there). One of the Hebrew names for the book is *wayedabber* ("And he [the LORD] spoke"), from the first word in the Hebrew text. *tent of meeting.* The tabernacle. *Desert of Sinai.* The more common Hebrew name for Numbers is *bemidbar* ("in the Desert"), the fifth word in the Hebrew text. The events of Numbers cover a period of 38 years and nine or ten months, i.e., the period of Israel's desert (or wilderness) wanderings. *first day ... second month ... second year.* Thirteen months after the exodus, Numbers begins. Israel had spent the previous year in the region of Mount Sinai receiving the law and erecting the tabernacle. Now the people were to be mustered as a military force for an orderly march. Dating events from the exodus (for another example, see 1Ki 6:1; see also note there) is similar to the Christian practice of dating years in reference to the incarnation of Christ (BC and AD). The exodus was God's great act of deliverance of his people from bondage.

1:2 *Take.* The Hebrew for this word is plural, indicating that Moses and Aaron were to complete this task together (see v. 3, "You and Aaron"), but the primary responsibility lay with Moses. *census.* Its main purpose was to form a military roster, not a social, political or taxing document.

1:3 *able to serve in the army.* Refers to the principal military purpose of the census. The phrase occurs 14 times in ch. 1 and again in 26:2 (see note on 26:1–51).

1:4 *One man from each tribe.* By having a representative from each tribe assist Moses and Aaron, the count would be regarded as legitimate by all.

1:5–16 The names of these men occur again in chs. 2; 7; 10. Most contain within them a reference to the name of God. Levi is not represented in the list (see vv. 47–53 and notes).

1:19 *And so he counted them in the Desert of Sinai.* A summary statement; vv. 20–43 provide the details.

1:20–43 For each tribe there are two verses in repetitive formulaic structure, giving: (1) the name of the tribe, (2) the specifics of those numbered, (3) the name of the tribe again and (4) the total count for that tribe. The numbers for each tribe are probably rounded off to the hundred (but Gad to the fifty, v. 25). The same numbers are given for each tribe in ch. 2, where there are four triads of tribes. A peculiarity in the numbers that leads some to believe that they are symbolic is that the hundreds are grouped between 200 and 700. Also, various speculations have arisen regarding the meaning of the Hebrew word for "thousand" (see Introduction: Special Problem). In this chapter, the word has been used to mean 1,000 in order for the totals to be achieved.

army were listed by name, according to the records of their clans and
families. 25 The number from the
tribe of Gad[a] was 45,650.

26 From the descendants of Judah:[b]
All the men twenty years old or
more who were able to serve in the
army were listed by name, according to the records of their clans and
families. 27 The number from the
tribe of Judah[c] was 74,600.

28 From the descendants of Issachar:[d]
All the men twenty years old or
more who were able to serve in the
army were listed by name, according to the records of their clans and
families. 29 The number from the
tribe of Issachar[e] was 54,400.[f]

30 From the descendants of Zebulun:[g]
All the men twenty years old or
more who were able to serve in the
army were listed by name, according to the records of their clans and
families. 31 The number from the
tribe of Zebulun was 57,400.[h]

32 From the sons of Joseph:[i]
From the descendants of Ephraim:[j]
All the men twenty years old or
more who were able to serve in the
army were listed by name, according to the records of their clans and
families. 33 The number from the
tribe of Ephraim[k] was 40,500.

34 From the descendants of Manasseh:[l]
All the men twenty years old or
more who were able to serve in the
army were listed by name, according to the records of their clans and
families. 35 The number from the
tribe of Manasseh was 32,200.

36 From the descendants of Benjamin:[m]
All the men twenty years old or
more who were able to serve in the
army were listed by name, according to the records of their clans and
families. 37 The number from the
tribe of Benjamin[n] was 35,400.

38 From the descendants of Dan:[o]
All the men twenty years old or
more who were able to serve in the
army were listed by name, according to the records of their clans and
families. 39 The number from the
tribe of Dan was 62,700.[p]

40 From the descendants of Asher:[q]
All the men twenty years old or
more who were able to serve in the
army were listed by name, according to the records of their clans and
families. 41 The number from the
tribe of Asher[r] was 41,500.

42 From the descendants of Naphtali:[s]
All the men twenty years old or
more who were able to serve in the
army were listed by name, according to the records of their clans and
families. 43 The number from the
tribe of Naphtali[t] was 53,400.[u]

44 These were the men counted by Moses and Aaron[v] and the twelve leaders of
Israel, each one representing his family.
45 All the Israelites twenty years old or
more[w] who were able to serve in Israel's
army were counted according to their families.[x] 46 The total number was 603,550.[y]
47 The ancestral tribe of the Levites,[z]
however, was not counted[a] along with
the others. 48 The LORD had said to Moses:
49 "You must not count the tribe of Levi or
include them in the census of the other Israelites. 50 Instead, appoint the Levites to be
in charge of the tabernacle[b] of the covenant
law[c]—over all its furnishings[d] and everything belonging to it. They are to carry the
tabernacle and all its furnishings; they are
to take care of it and encamp around it.
51 Whenever the tabernacle[e] is to move,[f] the
Levites are to take it down, and whenever

1:25 [a] Ge 46:16; Nu 26:18; 1Ch 5:11
1:26 [b] S ver 7; Mt 1:2; Rev 7:5
1:27 [c] Nu 26:22
1:28 [d] S Ge 30:18; Rev 7:7
1:29 [e] S Ge 30:18 [f] Nu 26:25
1:30 [g] S Ge 30:20; Rev 7:8
1:31 [h] Nu 26:27
1:32 [i] Ge 49:26 [j] S Ge 41:52
1:33 [k] Nu 26:37; 1Ch 7:20
1:34 [l] S Ge 41:51; Rev 7:6
1:36 [m] S Ge 35:18; 2Ch 17:17; Jer 32:44; Ob 1:19; Rev 7:8
1:37 [n] Nu 26:41
1:38 [o] Ge 30:6; Dt 33:22
1:39 [p] Nu 26:43
1:40 [q] S Ge 30:13; Nu 26:44; Rev 7:6
1:41 [r] Nu 26:47
1:42 [s] S Ge 30:8; Rev 7:6
1:43 [t] Nu 26:50 [u] S Ex 1:1-4
1:44 [v] Nu 26:64
1:45 [w] ver 3; Nu 14:29 [x] Nu 2:32
1:46 [y] S Ex 12:37; 2Sa 24:9
1:47 [z] S Nu 3:17-20 [a] Nu 4:3,49
1:50 [b] Ex 25:9; S 26:1 [c] S 16:34; Ac 7:44; Rev 15:5 [d] Nu 3:31
1:51 [e] S Ex 26:1 [f] Nu 4:5

1:32–35 Because the descendants of Levi were excluded from the census (see note on v. 47), the descendants of Joseph are listed according to the families of his two sons, Ephraim (vv. 32–33) and Manasseh (vv. 34–35). In this way the traditional tribal number of 12 is maintained, and Joseph is given the "double portion" of the ranking heir (cf. Ge 49:22–26; Dt 33:13–17; 2Ki 2:9 and notes).

1:46 *603,550.* Except for Joshua and Caleb, all these died in the wilderness. The mathematics of these numbers is accurate and complex. It is complex in that the totals are reached in two ways: (1) a linear listing of 12 units (vv. 20–43), with the total given (v. 46); (2) four sets of triads, each with a subtotal, and then the grand total (2:3–32). These figures are also consistent with those in Ex 12:37; 38:26. This large number of men conscripted for the army suggests a population for the entire community in excess of 2,000,000 (see Introduction: Special Problem). Ex 1:7 describes the remarkable growth of the Hebrew people in Egypt during the 400-year sojourn. They had become so numerous that they were regarded as a grave threat to the security of Egypt (Ex 1:9–10,20). Israel's amazing growth from the 70 who entered Egypt (Ge 46:26–27; Ex 1:5) was an evidence of God's great blessing and his faithfulness to his covenant with Abraham (Ge 12:2; 15:5; 17:4–6; 22:17).

1:47 Because of their special tasks, the Levites were excluded from this military count. They too had to perform service to the Lord, but they were to be engaged in the ceremonies and maintenance of the tabernacle (see note on vv. 32–35).

1:50,53 *the covenant law.* The Ten Commandments written on stone tablets (see Ex 31:18; 32:15; 34:29), which were placed in the ark (Ex 25:16,21; 40:20), leading to the phrase the "ark of the covenant law" (Ex 25:22; 26:33,34). See notes on Ex 16:34; 25:16,22.

1:51 *Anyone else.* The Hebrew for this phrase is often trans-

the tabernacle is to be set up, the Levites
shall do it.[g] Anyone else who approaches
it is to be put to death.[h] 52 The Israelites are
to set up their tents by divisions, each of
them in their own camp under their standard.[i] 53 The Levites, however, are to set up
their tents around the tabernacle[j] of the
covenant law so that my wrath will not fall[k]
on the Israelite community. The Levites are
to be responsible for the care of the tabernacle of the covenant law.[l]"
54 The Israelites did all this just as the
LORD commanded Moses.

The Arrangement of the Tribal Camps

2 The LORD said to Moses and Aaron:
2 "The Israelites are to camp around
the tent of meeting some distance from it,
each of them under their standard[m] and
holding the banners of their family."

3 On the east, toward the sunrise,
the divisions of the camp of Judah are
to encamp under their standard. The
leader of the people of Judah is Nahshon son of Amminadab.[n] 4 His division numbers 74,600.
5 The tribe of Issachar[o] will camp
next to them. The leader of the people
of Issachar is Nethanel son of Zuar.[p]
6 His division numbers 54,400.
7 The tribe of Zebulun will be next.
The leader of the people of Zebulun
is Eliab son of Helon.[q] 8 His division
numbers 57,400.

9 All the men assigned to the camp
of Judah, according to their divisions,
number 186,400. They will set out
first.[r]

10 On the south[s] will be the divisions of the camp of Reuben under
their standard. The leader of the people of Reuben is Elizur son of Shedeur.[t] 11 His division numbers 46,500.
12 The tribe of Simeon[u] will camp
next to them. The leader of the people of Simeon is Shelumiel son of Zurishaddai.[v] 13 His division numbers
59,300.
14 The tribe of Gad[w] will be next.
The leader of the people of Gad is Eliasaph son of Deuel.[a][x] 15 His division
numbers 45,650.
16 All the men assigned to the camp
of Reuben,[y] according to their divisions, number 151,450. They will set
out second.

17 Then the tent of meeting and the
camp of the Levites[z] will set out in
the middle of the camps. They will
set out in the same order as they encamp, each in their own place under
their standard.

18 On the west[a] will be the divisions
of the camp of Ephraim[b] under their

1:51 [g] Nu 3:38; 4:15 [h] S Ex 21:12 **1:52** [i] Nu 10:14; Ps 20:5; SS 2:4; 6:4 **1:53** [j] Nu 2:10; 3:23,29,38 [k] Lev 10:6; Nu 16:46; 18:5; Dt 9:22 [l] S Ex 38:21; Nu 18:2-4 **2:2** [m] Ps 74:4; Isa 31:9; Jer 4:21 **2:3** [n] S Ex 6:23 **2:5** [o] Nu 10:15 [p] S Nu 1:8 **2:7** [q] Nu 1:9; 10:16 **2:9** [r] Nu 10:14; Jdg 1:1 **2:10** [s] S Nu 1:53 [t] Nu 1:5 **2:12** [u] Nu 10:19 [v] S Nu 1:6 **2:14** [w] Nu 10:20 [x] Nu 1:14; 10:20 **2:16** [y] Nu 10:18 **2:17** [z] Nu 1:50; 10:21 **2:18** [a] S Nu 1:53 [b] S Ge 48:20; Jer 31:18-20

[a] *14* Many manuscripts of the Masoretic Text, Samaritan Pentateuch and Vulgate (see also 1:14); most manuscripts of the Masoretic Text *Reuel*

---

lated "stranger" or "foreigner" (e.g., Isa 1:7; Hos 7:9). Thus a non-Levite Israelite was considered a "stranger" to the religious duties of the tabernacle (see Ex 29:33; 30:33; Lev 22:12). *death.* See 3:10,38; 18:7; cf. 16:31–33; 1Sa 6:19.

1:53 *their tents around the tabernacle.* See 3:21–38 and chart, p. 206. *wrath.* The Levites formed a protective hedge against trespassing by the non-Levites to keep them from experiencing divine wrath.

1:54 *as the LORD commanded Moses.* In view of Israel's great disobedience in the later chapters of Numbers, these words of initial compliance have a special poignancy.

2:1–34 This chapter is symmetrically structured:

- Summary command (vv. 1–2)
  - Details of execution (vv. 3–33)
    - Eastern camp (vv. 3–9)
    - Southern camp (vv. 10–16)
      - Tent and Levites (v. 17)
    - Western camp (vv. 18–24)
    - Northern camp (vv. 25–31)
  - Summary totals (vv. 32–33)
- Summary conclusion (v. 34)

In ch. 1 the nation is mustered, and the genealogical relationships are clarified. In ch. 2 the nation is put in structural order, and the line of march and place of encampment are established. The numbers of ch. 1 are given in a new pattern, and the same leaders are named here again.

2:2 *some distance from it.* See 1:52–53. *each of them.* Each was to know his exact position within the camp. *standard ... banners.* Each tribe had its banner, and each triad of tribes had its standard. Jewish tradition suggests that the tribal banners corresponded in color to the 12 stones in the breastpiece of the high priest (Ex 28:15–21). Tradition also holds that the standard of the triad led by Judah had the figure of a lion, that of Reuben the figure of a man, that of Ephraim the figure of an ox and that of Dan the figure of an eagle (see the four living creatures described by Eze 1:10; cf. Rev 4:7). But these traditions are not otherwise substantiated. See chart, p. 206.

2:3–7 *Judah ... Issachar ... Zebulun.* The fourth, fifth and sixth sons of Jacob and Leah. It is somewhat surprising to have these three tribes first in the order of march, since Reuben is regularly noted as Jacob's firstborn son (1:20). However, because of the failure of the older brothers (Reuben, Simeon and Levi; see Ge 49:3–7), Judah is granted pride of place among his brothers (Ge 49:8). Judah produced the royal line from which the Messiah came (Ge 49:10; Ru 4:18–21; Mt 1:1–16).

2:10–12 *Reuben ... Simeon.* The first and second sons of Jacob and Leah.

2:14 *Gad.* The first son of Jacob and Zilpah (Leah's servant). Levi, Leah's third son, is not included with the divisions of the congregation. *Deuel.* See NIV text note. The Hebrew letters for *d* and *r* were easily confused by scribes (copyists) because of their similarity in form (see note on Ge 10:4).

2:17 *tent of meeting.* Representing God's presence in the heart of the camp (see 1:1 and note). *Levites.* In the line of march, the Judah and Reuben triads would lead the community, then would come the tabernacle with the attendant protective hedge of Levites (see note on 1:53), and last would come the Ephraim and Dan triads.

2:18–22 The Rachel tribes (Joseph and Benjamin) were

standard. The leader of the people of Ephraim is Elishama son of Ammihud.[c] 19 His division numbers 40,500.

20 The tribe of Manasseh[d] will be next to them. The leader of the people of Manasseh is Gamaliel son of Pedahzur.[e] 21 His division numbers 32,200.

22 The tribe of Benjamin[f] will be next. The leader of the people of Benjamin is Abidan son of Gideoni.[g] 23 His division numbers 35,400.

24 All the men assigned to the camp of Ephraim,[h] according to their divisions, number 108,100. They will set out third.[i]

25 On the north[j] will be the divisions of the camp of Dan under their standard.[k] The leader of the people of Dan is Ahiezer son of Ammishaddai.[l] 26 His division numbers 62,700.

27 The tribe of Asher will camp next to them. The leader of the people of Asher is Pagiel son of Okran.[m] 28 His division numbers 41,500.

29 The tribe of Naphtali[n] will be next. The leader of the people of Naphtali is Ahira son of Enan.[o] 30 His division numbers 53,400.

31 All the men assigned to the camp of Dan number 157,600. They will set out last,[p] under their standards.

32 These are the Israelites, counted according to their families.[q] All the men in the camps, by their divisions, number 603,550.[r] 33 The Levites, however, were not counted[s] along with the other Israelites, as the LORD commanded Moses.

34 So the Israelites did everything the LORD commanded Moses; that is the way they encamped under their standards, and that is the way they set out, each of them with their clan and family.

The Levites

3 This is the account of the family of Aaron and Moses[t] at the time the LORD spoke to Moses at Mount Sinai.[u]

2 The names of the sons of Aaron were Nadab the firstborn[v] and Abihu, Eleazar

2:18 [c]Nu 1:10 **2:20** [d]S Ge 48:20 [e]S Nu 1:10 **2:22** [f]Nu 10:24 [g]S Nu 1:11 **2:24** [h]Nu 10:22 [i]Ps 80:2 **2:25** [j]S Nu 1:53 [k]Nu 10:25 [l]S Nu 1:12 **2:27** [m]Nu 1:13; 10:26 **2:29** [n]Nu 10:27 [o]Nu 1:15; 10:27 **2:31** [p]Nu 10:25; Jos 6:9 **2:32** [q]Nu 1:45 [r]S Ex 12:37 **2:33** [s]Nu 1:47; 26:57-62 **3:1** [t]S Ex 6:27 [u]S Ex 19:11 **3:2** [v]Nu 1:20

on the west. Joseph's two sons, Manasseh and Ephraim, received a special blessing from their grandfather Jacob, but the younger son, Ephraim, was given precedence over Manasseh (see Ge 48:5 – 20 and notes). Here, true to Jacob's words, Ephraim is ahead of Manasseh. Last comes Benjamin, the last son born to Jacob.
2:25 *Dan.* The first son of Bilhah, Rachel's servant.
2:27 *Asher.* The second son of Zilpah, Leah's servant.
2:29 *Naphtali.* The second son of Bilhah.
2:32 *603,550.* See 1:46 and note.
2:33 *Levites.* See notes on 1:47,53.
2:34 *did everything the LORD commanded Moses.* As in 1:54 (see note there), these words of absolute compliance contrast with Israel's later folly. *under their standards ... each of them with their clan and family.* A major accomplishment for a people so numerous, so recently enslaved and more recently a mob in disarray. It may have been the orderliness of this encampment that led Balaam to say: "How beautiful are your tents, Jacob, / your dwelling places, Israel!" (24:5).
3:1 *Aaron and Moses.* At first glance, the names seem out of order, but the emphasis is correct: It is the family of Aaron that is about to be described (see v. 2).

ENCAMPMENT OF THE TRIBES OF ISRAEL

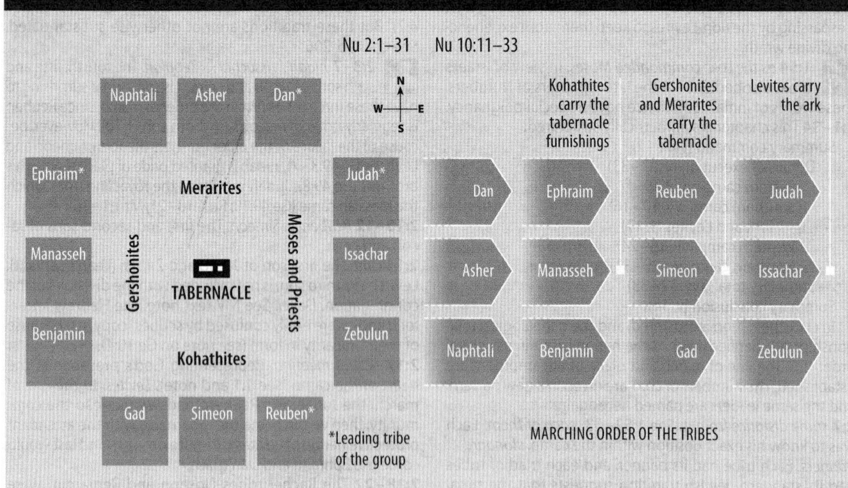

and Ithamar.[w] 3 Those were the names of Aaron's sons, the anointed priests,[x] who were ordained to serve as priests. 4 Nadab and Abihu, however, died before the LORD[y] when they made an offering with unauthorized fire before him in the Desert of Sinai.[z] They had no sons, so Eleazar and Ithamar[a] served as priests during the lifetime of their father Aaron.[b]

5 The LORD said to Moses, 6 "Bring the tribe of Levi[c] and present them to Aaron the priest to assist him.[d] 7 They are to perform duties for him and for the whole community[e] at the tent of meeting by doing the work[f] of the tabernacle. 8 They are to take care of all the furnishings of the tent of meeting, fulfilling the obligations of the Israelites by doing the work of the tabernacle. 9 Give the Levites to Aaron and his sons;[g] they are the Israelites who are to be given wholly to him.*a* 10 Appoint Aaron[h] and his sons to serve as priests;[i] anyone else who approaches the sanctuary is to be put to death."[j]

11 The LORD also said to Moses, 12 "I have taken the Levites[k] from among the Israelites in place of the first male offspring[l] of every Israelite woman. The Levites are mine,[m] 13 for all the firstborn are mine.[n] When I struck down all the firstborn in Egypt, I set apart for myself every firstborn in Israel, whether human or animal. They are to be mine. I am the LORD."[o]

3:2 [w] S Ex 6:23 **3:3** [x] S Ex 28:41; S 29:30 **3:4** [y] S Lev 10:2 [z] S Lev 10:1 [a] Lev 10:6, 12; Nu 4:28 [b] 1Ch 24:1 **3:6** [c] Dt 10:8; 31:9; 1Ch 15:2 [d] Nu 8:6-22; 18:1-7; 2Ch 29:11 **3:7** [e] Nu 1:53; 8:19 [f] S Lev 8:35 **3:9** [g] ver 12, 45; Nu 8:19; 18:6 **3:10** [h] S Ex 30:7 [i] S Ex 29:9 [j] Nu 1:51 **3:12** [k] Ne 13:29; Mal 2:4 [l] ver 41; Nu 8:16, 18 [m] S ver 9; Ex 13:2; Nu 8:14; 16:9 **3:13** [n] S Ex 13:12 [o] Lev 11:44 **3:14** [p] S Ex 19:1 **3:15** [q] ver 39; S Nu 1:19 [r] ver 22; Nu 18:16; 26:62 **3:17** [s] S Ge 29:34; S 46:11; Nu 1:47; 1Ch 15:4; 23:6; 2Ch 29:12 [t] Jos 21:6 [u] Jos 21:4 [v] S Ex 6:16 **3:18** [w] Ex 6:17

14 The LORD said to Moses in the Desert of Sinai,[p] 15 "Count[q] the Levites by their families and clans. Count every male a month old or more."[r] 16 So Moses counted them, as he was commanded by the word of the LORD.

17 These were the names of the sons of Levi:[s]

Gershon,[t] Kohath[u] and Merari.[v]

18 These were the names of the Gershonite clans:

Libni and Shimei.[w]

19 The Kohathite clans:

Amram, Izhar, Hebron and Uzziel.[x]

20 The Merarite clans:[y]

Mahli and Mushi.[z]

These were the Levite clans, according to their families.

21 To Gershon[a] belonged the clans of the Libnites and Shimeites;[b] these were the Gershonite clans. 22 The number of all the males a month old or more who were counted was 7,500. 23 The Gershonite clans were to camp on the west, behind the tabernacle.[c] 24 The leader of the families of the

a 9 Most manuscripts of the Masoretic Text; some manuscripts of the Masoretic Text, Samaritan Pentateuch and Septuagint (see also 8:16) *to me*

3:19 [x] S Ex 6:18 **3:20** [y] S Ge 46:11 [z] S Ex 6:19 **3:21** [a] S Ge 46:11 [b] Ex 6:17 **3:23** [c] S Nu 2:1

3:3 *anointed priests.* Ex 28:41 records God's command to Moses to anoint his brother Aaron and his sons as priests of the Lord (see Ex 30:30; Lev 8:30). By this solemn act they were consecrated in a special way to the Lord. Kings (see 1Sa 16:13 and note) were also anointed with oil for special service to God. Physical objects could be anointed as well (see Ge 28:18 and note; Ex 29:36). The Hebrew term for "anointed" (*mashiaḥ*) later became the specific term for the Messiah (Christ); see second NIV text note on Mt 1:1. *ordained.* The Hebrew for this word means lit. "fill the hand of" (see Ex 32:29 and note). By this act there was an investing of authority, a consecration and a setting apart.

3:4 *Nadab and Abihu.* See Lev 10:1–3 and notes. *unauthorized fire.* Or "strange fire." This seems to be a deliberately obscure expression, as though the narrator finds the very concept distasteful. They were using fire that the Lord had not commanded (see Lev 10:1). Proximity to God's holiness requires righteousness and obedience from his priests. For all time, the deaths of Aaron's newly consecrated sons serve to warn God's ministers of the awesome seriousness of their tasks (cf. 1Sa 2:12–17,22–25,27–36; 3:11–14; 4:1–11). For similar divine judgments at the beginning of new stages in salvation history see Jos 7:1–26; 2Sa 6:7; Ac 5:1 and notes.

3:5–10 These commands are not followed by a report of obedience, as were the commands in chs. 1–2, but further details are given in ch. 8. Clear distinctions are made here between the priestly house (the sons of Aaron) and the Levites. The latter were to be aides to the priests, and they served not only Aaron but the whole nation in the process (see vv. 7–8).

3:9 *to him.* See NIV text note. It appears that the issue here is service to Aaron (and through him to the Lord); in 8:16 the service is to the Lord.

3:10 *anyone else.* Lit. "stranger"—anyone lacking authorization. Service at the tabernacle may be performed only at the express appointment of the Lord. The words of v. 10 follow the paragraph telling of the deaths of Aaron's sons. They were authorized persons but used unauthorized means. If the sons of Aaron were put to death at the commencement of their duties, how dare an unauthorized person even think to trespass! See v. 38; 18:1–7 and notes.

3:12–13 See note on Ex 13:2. *mine.* Repeated for emphasis.

3:12 *in place of.* An example of the practice of substitution (see Ge 22:13; Mt 20:28 and notes).

3:15 *a month old or more.* The counting of the Levites corresponds to that of the other tribes in chs. 1–2, except that all males from the age of one month, rather than from 20 years, were to be counted. The Levites were being mustered not for war but for special service in the sacred precincts of the Lord.

3:16 *as he was commanded.* The obedience of Moses to the Lord's command is explicit and total.

3:21–38 The words of 1:53, "their tents around the tabernacle of the covenant law," are detailed by the four paragraphs in this section: (1) Gershon to the west (vv. 21–26); (2) Kohath to the south (vv. 27–32); (3) Merari to the north (vv. 33–37); (4) Moses and Aaron and sons to the east (v. 38). The other tribes began with the most favored: (1) Judah on the east (2:3); (2) Reuben on the south (2:10); (3) Ephraim on the west (2:18); (4) Dan on the north (2:25). The Levitical clans lead up to the most favored. The leaders of the Levitical houses correspond to the leaders of the other tribes (see note on 1:5–16). As the names of the other tribal leaders include a form of God's name, so do these names.

3:24 *Eliasaph.* Means "(My) God has added." *Lael.* Means "belonging to God."

Gershonites was Eliasaph son of Lael. 25 At
the tent of meeting the Gershonites were
responsible for the care of the tabernacle[d]
and tent, its coverings,[e] the curtain at the
entrance[f] to the tent of meeting,[g] 26 the curtains of the courtyard[h], the curtain at the
entrance to the courtyard surrounding the
tabernacle and altar,[i] and the ropes[j]—and
everything[k] related to their use.

27 To Kohath[l] belonged the clans of the
Amramites, Izharites, Hebronites and Uzzielites;[m] these were the Kohathite[n] clans.
28 The number of all the males a month old
or more[o] was 8,600.[a] The Kohathites were
responsible[p] for the care of the sanctuary.[q]
29 The Kohathite clans were to camp on the
south side[r] of the tabernacle. 30 The leader of the families of the Kohathite clans
was Elizaphan[s] son of Uzziel. 31 They were
responsible for the care of the ark,[t] the
table,[u] the lampstand,[v] the altars,[w] the articles[x] of the sanctuary used in ministering, the curtain,[y] and everything related to
their use.[z] 32 The chief leader of the Levites
was Eleazar[a] son of Aaron, the priest. He
was appointed over those who were responsible[b] for the care of the sanctuary.[c]

33 To Merari belonged the clans of the
Mahlites and the Mushites;[d] these were
the Merarite clans.[e] 34 The number of all
the males a month old or more[f] who were
counted was 6,200. 35 The leader of the
families of the Merarite clans was Zuriel
son of Abihail; they were to camp on the
north side of the tabernacle.[g] 36 The Merarites were appointed[h] to take care of the
frames of the tabernacle,[i] its crossbars,[j]
posts,[k] bases, all its equipment, and everything related to their use,[l] 37 as well as the
posts of the surrounding courtyard[m] with
their bases, tent pegs[n] and ropes.

38 Moses and Aaron and his sons were to
camp to the east[o] of the tabernacle, toward
the sunrise, in front of the tent of meeting.[p] They were responsible for the care of
the sanctuary[q] on behalf of the Israelites.
Anyone else who approached the sanctuary was to be put to death.[r]

39 The total number of Levites counted[s] at the Lord's command by Moses and
Aaron according to their clans, including every male a month old or more, was
22,000.[t]

40 The Lord said to Moses, "Count all
the firstborn Israelite males who are a
month old or more[u] and make a list of
their names.[v] 41 Take the Levites for me in
place of all the firstborn of the Israelites,[w]
and the livestock of the Levites in place
of all the firstborn of the livestock of the
Israelites. I am the Lord."[x]
42 So Moses counted all the firstborn
of the Israelites, as the Lord commanded
him. 43 The total number of firstborn males
a month old or more,[y] listed by name, was
22,273.[z]
44 The Lord also said to Moses, 45 "Take
the Levites in place of all the firstborn of
Israel, and the livestock of the Levites in
place of their livestock. The Levites are
to be mine.[a] I am the Lord.[b] 46 To redeem[c]
the 273 firstborn Israelites who exceed the
number of the Levites, 47 collect five shekels[bd] for each one, according to the sanctuary shekel,[e] which weighs twenty gerahs.[f]
48 Give the money for the redemption[g] of

[a] 28 Hebrew; some Septuagint manuscripts *8,300*
[b] 47 That is, about 2 ounces or about 58 grams

3:25 [d] Ex 25:9; Nu 7:1 [e] Ex 26:14 [f] Ex 26:36; Nu 4:25 [g] Ex 40:2 **3:26** [h] Ex 27:9 [i] ver 31 [j] Ex 35:18 [k] Nu 4:26 **3:27** [l] S Ge 46:11; S Ex 6:18 [m] Ex 6:18; 1Ch 26:23 [n] Nu 4:15,37 **3:28** [o] ver 15 [p] Nu 4:4,15 [q] S Ex 25:8; 30:13; 2Ch 30:19; Ps 15:1; 20:2; Eze 44:27 **3:29** [r] S Nu 1:53 **3:30** [s] S Ex 6:22 **3:31** [t] S Ex 25:10-22; Dt 10:1-8; 2Ch 5:2; Jer 3:16 [u] S Ex 25:23 [v] S Ex 25:31; 1Ch 28:15; Jer 52:19 [w] ver 26 [x] Nu 1:50 [y] S Ex 26:33; Nu 4:5 [z] Nu 4:15; 18:3 **3:32** [a] S Ex 6:23 [b] ver 28 [c] Nu 4:19; 18:3 **3:33** [d] S Ex 6:19 [e] S Ge 46:11 **3:34** [f] ver 15 **3:35** [g] S Nu 2:25 **3:36** [h] Nu 4:32 [i] Ex 26:15-25; 35:20-29 [j] Ex 26:26-29 [k] Ex 36:36 [l] Nu 18:3 **3:37** [m] Ex 27:10-17 [n] Ex 27:19
3:38 [o] Nu 2:3 [p] S Nu 1:53; 1Ch 9:27; 23:32 [q] ver 7; Nu 18:5 [r] ver 10; Nu 1:51 **3:39** [s] S ver 15 [t] Nu 26:62

3:40 [u] ver 15 [v] Nu 1:2 **3:41** [w] ver 12 [x] Lev 11:44 **3:43** [y] ver 15 [z] ver 39 **3:45** [a] S ver 9 [b] Lev 11:44 **3:46** [c] Ex 13:13; Nu 18:15 **3:47** [d] S Lev 27:6 [e] S Ex 30:13 [f] S Lev 27:25 **3:48** [g] ver 51

3:25–26 There were three curtains or covering screens for the tabernacle: (1) at the gate of the courtyard (v. 26; 4:26); (2) at the entrance to the tent (vv. 25,31; 4:25); (3) between the Holy Place and the Most Holy Place (4:5).
3:27 *Amramites.* Aaron was an Amramite (see Ex 6:20 and note); thus he and Moses were from the family of Kohath. To the Kohathites was given the care of the most holy things (see 4:4–18).
3:28 *8,600.* The total number of Levites given in v. 39 is 22,000—300 less than the totals of 7,500 Gershonites (v. 22), 8,600 Kohathites (here) and 6,200 Merarites (v. 34). Many believe that a copyist may have made a mistake here and that the correct number is 8,300 (see NIV text note).
3:30 *Elizaphan.* Means "(My) God has protected." *Uzziel.* Means "My strength is God."
3:35 *Zuriel.* Means "My Rock is God." *Abihail.* Means "My (divine) Father is powerful."
3:38 *toward the sunrise.* The most honored location, but Moses and Aaron were placed there for a representative ministry (on behalf of the Israelites). *Anyone else ... was to be put to death.* Service in the tabernacle was an act of mercy, a means for the people to come before God. Yet it was marked by strict discipline—it had to be done in God's way. The sovereignty of God was evident in his limitations on the means to approach him (see v. 10; 1:51; 18:1–7 and notes).
3:41 *I am the Lord.* What is being commanded conforms to God's character as Yahweh ("the Lord"; see note on Ex 3:14).
3:43 *22,273.* Seems too small for a population in excess of 2,000,000 and is used as an argument for attempting to find a means of reducing the total number of the people (calculations based on this number suggest a total population of about 250,000). Some suggest that the 22,273 firstborn of Israel were those born since the exodus, all the firstborn at the time of the exodus having already been set apart for the Lord at the first Passover (see Ex 12:22–23). This, however, creates a new problem since nowhere is that allegedly distinct group assigned any special service of the Lord. See Introduction: Special Problem.
3:47,50 *according to the sanctuary shekel.* See note on Ex 30:13.

the additional Israelites to Aaron and his
sons."[h]
49So Moses collected the redemption
money[i] from those who exceeded the
number redeemed by the Levites. 50From
the firstborn of the Israelites[j] he collected
silver weighing 1,365 shekels,[a][k] according
to the sanctuary shekel. 51Moses gave the
redemption money to Aaron and his sons,
as he was commanded by the word of the
LORD.

The Kohathites

4 The LORD said to Moses and Aaron:
2"Take a census[l] of the Kohathite
branch of the Levites by their clans and
families. 3Count[m] all the men from thirty
to fifty years of age[n] who come to serve in
the work at the tent of meeting.
4"This is the work[o] of the Kohathites[p] at
the tent of meeting: the care of the most
holy things.[q] 5When the camp is to move,[r]
Aaron and his sons are to go in and take
down the shielding curtain[s] and put it over
the ark of the covenant law.[t] 6Then they
are to cover the curtain with a durable
leather,[b][u] spread a cloth of solid blue over
that and put the poles[v] in place.
7"Over the table of the Presence[w] they
are to spread a blue cloth and put on it the
plates, dishes and bowls, and the jars for
drink offerings;[x] the bread that is continually there[y] is to remain on it. 8They are
to spread a scarlet cloth over them, cover
that with the durable leather and put the
poles[z] in place.
9"They are to take a blue cloth and
cover the lampstand that is for light, together with its lamps, its wick trimmers
and trays,[a] and all its jars for the olive oil
used to supply it. 10Then they are to wrap
it and all its accessories in a covering of
the durable leather and put it on a carrying frame.[b]
11"Over the gold altar[c] they are to spread
a blue cloth and cover that with the durable leather and put the poles[d] in place.
12"They are to take all the articles[e] used
for ministering in the sanctuary, wrap
them in a blue cloth, cover that with the
durable leather and put them on a carrying frame.[f]
13"They are to remove the ashes[g] from
the bronze altar[h] and spread a purple cloth
over it. 14Then they are to place on it all
the utensils[i] used for ministering at the
altar, including the firepans,[j] meat forks,[k]
shovels[l] and sprinkling bowls.[m] Over it
they are to spread a covering of the durable leather and put the poles[n] in place.
15"After Aaron and his sons have finished covering the holy furnishings and
all the holy articles, and when the camp
is ready to move,[o] only then are the Kohathites[p] to come and do the carrying.[q]
But they must not touch the holy things[r]
or they will die.[s] The Kohathites are to
carry those things that are in the tent of
meeting.
16"Eleazar[t] son of Aaron, the priest, is
to have charge of the oil for the light,[u] the
fragrant incense,[v] the regular grain offering[w] and the anointing oil. He is to be in
charge of the entire tabernacle and everything in it, including its holy furnishings
and articles."
17The LORD said to Moses and Aaron,
18"See that the Kohathite tribal clans are
not destroyed from among the Levites.
19So that they may live and not die when
they come near the most holy things,[x] do
this for them: Aaron and his sons[y] are to
go into the sanctuary and assign to each
man his work and what he is to carry.[z]
20But the Kohathites must not go in to
look[a] at the holy things, even for a moment, or they will die."

The Gershonites

21The LORD said to Moses, 22"Take a census also of the Gershonites by their families and clans. 23Count all the men from
thirty to fifty years of age[b] who come to
serve in the work at the tent of meeting.
24"This is the service of the Gershonite clans in their carrying and their other
work: 25They are to carry the curtains of
the tabernacle,[c] that is, the tent of meeting,[d] its covering[e] and its outer covering
of durable leather, the curtains for the entrance to the tent of meeting, 26the curtains
of the courtyard surrounding the tabernacle and altar,[f] the curtain for the entrance

3:48 [h] ver 50
3:49 [i] ver 48
3:50 [j] ver 41,45 [k] S ver 46-48
4:2 [l] S Ex 30:12
4:3 [m] S Nu 1:47 [n] ver 23; Nu 8:25; 1Ch 23:3,24, 27; Ezr 3:8
4:4 [o] S Nu 3:28 [p] Nu 7:9 [q] ver 19
4:5 [r] Nu 1:51 [s] S Ex 26:31,33 [t] 1Ch 23:26
4:6 [u] S Ex 25:5 [v] S Ex 25:13-15; 1Ki 8:7; 2Ch 5:8
4:7 [w] S Lev 24:6 [x] Ex 39:36; Jer 52:19 [y] S Ex 25:30
4:8 [z] Ex 26:26-28
4:9 [a] S Ex 25:38
4:10 [b] ver 12
4:11 [c] S Ex 30:1 [d] Ex 30:4
4:12 [e] Nu 3:31 [f] ver 10
4:13 [g] S Lev 1:16 [h] Ex 27:1-8; Nu 3:31
4:14 [i] S Ex 31:9 [j] S Ex 27:3 [k] 1Ch 28:17; 2Ch 4:16 [l] 2Ch 4:11 [m] Ex 27:3; Nu 7:84; 2Ch 4:8; Jer 52:18 [n] Ex 27:6
4:15 [o] ver 5 [p] S Nu 3:27 [q] Nu 7:9 [r] ver 4 [s] S Ex 28:43; Nu 1:51; 2Sa 6:6,7
4:16 [t] Lev 10:6; Nu 3:32 [u] S Ex 25:6 [v] S Ex 25:6 [w] S Ex 29:41; Lev 6:14-23
4:19 [x] S ver 15 [y] ver 27 [z] S Nu 3:32
4:20 [a] S Ex 19:21
4:23 [b] S ver 3
4:25 [c] Ex 27:10-18 [d] Nu 3:25 [e] Ex 26:14
4:26 [f] Ex 27:9

[a] *50* That is, about 35 pounds or about 16 kilograms
[b] *6* Possibly the hides of large aquatic mammals; also in verses 8, 10, 11, 12, 14 and 25

4:3 *thirty to fifty years.* Ch. 3 listed all males over the age of one month (3:15). Ch. 4 lists those Levites who were of age to serve in the tabernacle. Of the 22,000 Levite males (3:39), 8,580 were of age for service (v. 48). From 8:24 we learn that the beginning age for service was 25; perhaps the first five years were something of an apprenticeship.
4:4 *most holy things.* See note on Ex 3:5. Despite the fact that the primary care of these holy things was given to the Kohathites, they were forbidden to touch them (v. 15) or even to look at them (v. 20), on pain of death. All the work of the Kohathites was to be strictly supervised by Aaron and his sons, and only the priests were able to touch and look at the unveiled holy things.
4:5 *covenant law.* See note on Ex 25:22.
4:6 *durable leather.* See NIV text note.
4:7 *table of the Presence.* See note on Ex 25:30.
4:16 *Eleazar … the priest, is to have charge.* The high priest could draw near to the most holy things on behalf of the people. If he had not been able to do so, there could have been no worship by the community.

to the courtyard,[g] the ropes and all the equipment[h] used in the service of the tent. The Gershonites are to do all that needs to be done with these things. 27 All their service, whether carrying or doing other work, is to be done under the direction of Aaron and his sons.[i] You shall assign to them as their responsibility[j] all they are to carry. 28 This is the service of the Gershonite clans[k] at the tent of meeting. Their duties are to be under the direction of Ithamar[l] son of Aaron, the priest.

The Merarites

29 "Count[m] the Merarites by their clans and families.[n] 30 Count all the men from thirty to fifty years of age who come to serve in the work at the tent of meeting. 31 As part of all their service at the tent, they are to carry the frames of the tabernacle, its crossbars, posts and bases,[o] 32 as well as the posts of the surrounding courtyard with their bases, tent pegs, ropes,[p] all their equipment and everything related to their use. Assign to each man the specific things he is to carry. 33 This is the service of the Merarite clans as they work at the tent of meeting under the direction of Ithamar[q] son of Aaron, the priest."

The Numbering of the Levite Clans

34 Moses, Aaron and the leaders of the community counted the Kohathites[r] by their clans and families. 35 All the men from thirty to fifty years of age[s] who came to serve in the work at the tent of meeting, 36 counted by clans, were 2,750. 37 This was the total of all those in the Kohathite clans[t] who served at the tent of meeting. Moses and Aaron counted them according to the LORD's command through Moses.

38 The Gershonites[u] were counted by their clans and families. 39 All the men from thirty to fifty years of age who came to serve in the work at the tent of meeting, 40 counted by their clans and families, were 2,630. 41 This was the total of those in the Gershonite clans who served at the tent of meeting. Moses and Aaron counted them according to the LORD's command.

42 The Merarites were counted by their clans and families. 43 All the men from thirty to fifty years of age[v] who came to serve in the work at the tent of meeting, 44 counted by their clans, were 3,200. 45 This was the total of those in the Merarite clans.[w] Moses and Aaron counted them according to the LORD's command through Moses.

46 So Moses, Aaron and the leaders of Israel counted[x] all the Levites by their clans and families. 47 All the men from thirty to fifty years of age[y] who came to do the work of serving and carrying the tent of meeting 48 numbered 8,580.[z] 49 At the LORD's command through Moses, each was assigned his work and told what to carry.

Thus they were counted,[a] as the LORD commanded Moses.

The Purity of the Camp

5 The LORD said to Moses, 2 "Command the Israelites to send away from the camp anyone who has a defiling skin disease[a][b] or a discharge[c] of any kind, or who is ceremonially unclean[d] because of a dead body.[e] 3 Send away male and female alike; send them outside the camp so they will not defile their camp, where I dwell among them.[f]" 4 The Israelites did so; they sent them outside the camp. They did just as the LORD had instructed Moses.

Restitution for Wrongs

5 The LORD said to Moses, 6 "Say to the Israelites: 'Any man or woman who wrongs another in any way[b] and so is unfaithful[g]

4:26 [g] Ex 27:16 [h] Nu 3:26
4:27 [i] ver 19 [j] Nu 3:25,26
4:28 [k] Nu 7:7 [l] S Ex 6:23
4:29 [m] S Ex 30:12 [n] S Ge 46:11
4:31 [o] Nu 3:36
4:32 [p] Nu 3:37
4:33 [q] S Ex 38:21
4:34 [r] ver 2
4:35 [s] ver 3
4:37 [t] S Nu 3:27
4:38 [u] S Ge 46:11
4:43 [v] ver 3
4:45 [w] ver 29
4:46 [x] Nu 1:19
4:47 [y] ver 3
4:48 [z] Nu 3:39
4:49 [a] S Nu 1:47
5:2 [b] S Lev 13:2 [c] S Lev 15:2; Mt 9:20 [d] Lev 13:3; Nu 9:6-10 [e] S Lev 21:11
5:3 [f] S Ex 29:45; Lev 26:12; 2Co 6:16
5:6 [g] S Lev 6:2

[a] *2* The Hebrew word for *defiling skin disease,* traditionally translated "leprosy," was used for various diseases affecting the skin. [b] *6* Or *woman who commits any wrong common to mankind*

5:2 *defiling skin disease.* See NIV text note; see also note on Lev 13:2; cf. Lk 5:12–16; 17:11–19. *discharge of any kind.* See note on Lev 15:2. Such discharges were primarily from the sexual organs and were chronic in nature (cf. Lk 8:43–48). The people who suffered from them became living object lessons to the whole camp on the necessity for all people to be "clean" in their approach to God. *unclean.* Ceremonially unfit to be with the community, and a possible contaminant to the tabernacle and the pure worship of the Lord. Aspects of uncleanness were not left in the abstract or theoretical; the focus was on tangible issues, such as clearly evident skin diseases and discharges. *dead body.* The ultimate tangible sign of uncleanness. Processes of decay and disease in dead flesh were evident to all. Physical contact with a corpse was a sure mark of uncleanness; normal contacts with the living would have to be curtailed until proper cleansing had been made. See note on 6:6 for application to the Nazirite vow. Jesus reached out to the dead as well as to the living; his raising of Jairus's daughter began with holding her limp hand (Lk 8:54).

5:3 *male and female alike.* The concept of clean versus unclean cuts across gender lines. The essential issue was the presence of the Lord in the camp; there can be no uncleanness where he dwells. In the new Jerusalem (Rev 21:2–3) the dwelling of God with his people will be uncompromised by any form of uncleanness (Rev 21:27).

5:5–10 The connection of these verses (on personal wrongs) with the first paragraph (on ritual uncleanness) may be that of moving from the outward, visible defects to the inward, more secret faults that mar the purity of the community. Those with evident marks of uncleanness are to be expelled for the duration of their malady. But more insidious are those who have overtly sinned against others in the community, and who think that they may continue to function as though they had done nothing wrong.

to the LORD is guilty[h] 7 and must confess[i]
the sin they have committed. They must
make full restitution[j] for the wrong they
have done, add a fifth of the value to it
and give it all to the person they have
wronged. 8 But if that person has no close
relative to whom restitution can be made
for the wrong, the restitution belongs to
the LORD and must be given to the priest,
along with the ram[k] with which atonement is made for the wrongdoer.[l] 9 All the
sacred contributions the Israelites bring
to a priest will belong to him.[m] 10 Sacred
things belong to their owners, but what
they give to the priest will belong to the
priest.[n]' "

The Test for an Unfaithful Wife

11 Then the LORD said to Moses, 12 "Speak
to the Israelites and say to them: 'If a
man's wife goes astray[o] and is unfaithful
to him 13 so that another man has sexual
relations with her,[p] and this is hidden from
her husband and her impurity is undetect-
ed (since there is no witness against her
and she has not been caught in the act),
14 and if feelings of jealousy[q] come over
her husband and he suspects his wife and
she is impure—or if he is jealous and suspects her even though she is not impure—
15 then he is to take his wife to the priest.
He must also take an offering of a tenth of
an ephah[a][r] of barley flour[s] on her behalf.
He must not pour olive oil on it or put incense on it, because it is a grain offering
for jealousy,[t] a reminder-offering[u] to draw
attention to wrongdoing.
16 " 'The priest shall bring her and have
her stand before the LORD. 17 Then he shall
take some holy water in a clay jar and put
some dust from the tabernacle floor into
the water. 18 After the priest has had the
woman stand before the LORD, he shall
loosen her hair[v] and place in her hands
the reminder-offering, the grain offering
for jealousy,[w] while he himself holds the
bitter water that brings a curse.[x] 19 Then
the priest shall put the woman under oath
and say to her, "If no other man has had
sexual relations with you and you have
not gone astray[y] and become impure while
married to your husband, may this bitter
water that brings a curse[z] not harm you.
20 But if you have gone astray[a] while married to your husband and you have made
yourself impure by having sexual relations
with a man other than your husband"—
21 here the priest is to put the woman under this curse[b]—"may the LORD cause you
to become a curse[b] among your people
when he makes your womb miscarry and
your abdomen swell. 22 May this water[c]
that brings a curse[d] enter your body so
that your abdomen swells or your womb
miscarries."
" 'Then the woman is to say, "Amen. So
be it.[e]"

5:6 [h] Lev 5:14-6:7
5:7 [i] S Lev 5:5; S Lk 19:8 [j] S Lev 5:16
5:8 [k] S Lev 5:15 [l] Lev 6:6,7
5:9 [m] Lev 6:17
5:10 [n] Lev 7:29-34
5:12 [o] ver 19-21; S Ex 20:14
5:13 [p] S Ex 20:14
5:14 [q] ver 30; Pr 6:34; 27:4; SS 8:6
5:15 [r] S Ex 16:36 [s] S Lev 6:20 [t] ver 18,25 [u] Eze 21:23; 29:16
5:18 [v] S Lev 10:6; 1Co 11:6 [w] ver 15 [x] ver 19
5:19 [y] ver 12,29 [z] ver 18
5:20 [a] ver 12
5:21 [b] Jos 6:26; 1Sa 14:24; Ne 10:29
5:22 [c] Ps 109:18 [d] ver 18 [e] Dt 27:15

[a] *15* That is, probably about 3 1/2 pounds or about 1.6 kilograms [b] *21* That is, may he cause your name to be used in cursing (see Jer. 29:22); or, may others see that you are cursed; similarly in verse 27.

5:8 *atonement.* See notes on Ex 25:17; Lev 17:11; Ro 3:25.

5:11–31 Again, the connection with the preceding two paragraphs seems to be a movement from the more open, obvious sins to the more personal, hidden ones. Issues of purity begin with physical marks (vv. 1–4), are expanded to interpersonal relationships (vv. 5–10), and then intrude into the most intimate of relationships—the purity of a man and woman in their marriage bed (cf. Ex 20:14 and note). A test for marital fidelity is far more difficult to prove than a test for a skin disorder; hence, the larger part of the chapter is given to this most sensitive of issues.

5:14 *feelings of jealousy.* These may have been provoked on the basis of good cause, and the issue must be faced. The concern is not just for the bruised feelings of the husband but is ultimately based on the reality of God's dwelling among his people (v. 3). Yet the chapter is designed to prevent unfounded charges of unfaithfulness. This text was not to be used by a capricious, petty or malevolent husband to badger an innocent woman. *impure.* The subject of the chapter is consistent; the purity of the camp where God dwells (v. 3) is the burden of the passage.

5:15–28 The actions presented here seem severe and harsh. But the consequences would have been worse for a woman charged with adultery by an angry husband if there was no provision for her guilt or innocence to be demonstrated. That she was taken to the priest (v. 15) is finally an act of mercy. The gravity of the ritual for a suspected unfaithful wife shows that the law regards marital infidelity most seriously. This was not just a concern of a jealous husband. The entire community was affected by this breach of faith; hence, the judgment was in the context of the community.

5:15,18 *reminder-offering.* A grain offering apparently designed to stimulate reflection on sin and guilt.

5:17 *holy water.* Pure water perhaps taken from the bronze basin (Ex 38:8) and placed in a consecrated vessel and dedicated to God's service. This rendered it ritually clean for use in this ceremony.

5:18 *loosen her hair.* A sign of openness; for the guilty, an expectation of judgment and mourning. *bitter water that brings a curse.* Or "curse-bringing water of bitterness." It is not just that the water was bitter tasting but that the water had the potential of bringing with it a bitter curse. The Lord's role in the proceedings (vv. 16,21,25) is emphasized repeatedly to show that this potion was neither simply a tool of magic nor merely a psychological device to determine stress. The verdict with respect to the woman was precipitated by her physiological and psychological responses to the bitter water, but the judgment was from the Lord.

5:21 *your womb miscarry and your abdomen swell.* Speaks of the loss of the capacity for childbearing (and, if pregnant, the miscarriage of the child). This is demonstrated by the determination of the fate of a woman wrongly charged (v. 28). For a woman in the ancient Near East to be denied the ability to bear children was a personal loss of inestimable proportions. Since it was in the bearing of children that a woman's worth was realized in the ancient world, this was a grievous punishment indeed.

23 “ ‘The priest is to write these curses on
a scroll[f] and then wash them off into the
bitter water. 24 He shall make the woman
drink the bitter water that brings a curse,
and this water that brings a curse and
causes bitter suffering will enter her. 25 The
priest is to take from her hands the grain offering for jealousy, wave it before the LORD[g]
and bring it to the altar. 26 The priest is then
to take a handful of the grain offering as
a memorial[a] offering[h] and burn it on the
altar; after that, he is to have the woman
drink the water. 27 If she has made herself
impure and been unfaithful to her husband, this will be the result: When she is
made to drink the water that brings a curse
and causes bitter suffering, it will enter her,
her abdomen will swell and her womb will
miscarry, and she will become a curse.[i] 28 If,
however, the woman has not made herself
impure, but is clean, she will be cleared of
guilt and will be able to have children.

29 “ ‘This, then, is the law of jealousy
when a woman goes astray[j] and makes
herself impure while married to her husband, 30 or when feelings of jealousy[k] come
over a man because he suspects his wife.
The priest is to have her stand before the
LORD and is to apply this entire law to her.
31 The husband will be innocent of any
wrongdoing, but the woman will bear the
consequences[l] of her sin.’ ”

The Nazirite

6 The LORD said to Moses, 2 “Speak to the
Israelites and say to them: ‘If a man or
woman wants to make a special vow[m], a
vow of dedication[n] to the LORD as a Nazirite,[o] 3 they must abstain from wine[p] and
other fermented drink and must not drink
vinegar[q] made from wine or other fermented drink. They must not drink grape juice
or eat grapes[r] or raisins. 4 As long as they
remain under their Nazirite vow, they must
not eat anything that comes from the grapevine, not even the seeds or skins.
5 “ ‘During the entire period of their Nazirite vow, no razor[s] may be used on their
head.[t] They must be holy until the period
of their dedication to the LORD is over; they
must let their hair grow long.
6 “ ‘Throughout the period of their dedication to the LORD, the Nazirite must not
go near a dead body.[u] 7 Even if their own
father or mother or brother or sister dies,
they must not make themselves ceremonially unclean[v] on account of them, because
the symbol of their dedication to God is
on their head. 8 Throughout the period of
their dedication, they are consecrated to
the LORD.
9 “ ‘If someone dies suddenly in the Nazirite’s presence, thus defiling the hair that
symbolizes their dedication,[w] they must
shave their head on the seventh day—
the day of their cleansing.[x] 10 Then on the
eighth day[y] they must bring two doves or
two young pigeons[z] to the priest at the entrance to the tent of meeting.[a] 11 The priest
is to offer one as a sin offering[b][b] and the
other as a burnt offering[c] to make atonement[d] for the Nazirite because they sinned
by being in the presence of the dead body.
That same day they are to consecrate their
head again. 12 They must rededicate themselves to the LORD for the same period of
dedication and must bring a year-old male
lamb[e] as a guilt offering.[f] The previous
days do not count, because they became
defiled during their period of dedication.
13 “ ‘Now this is the law of the Nazirite
when the period of their dedication is
over.[g] They are to be brought to the entrance to the tent of meeting.[h] 14 There
they are to present their offerings to the
LORD: a year-old male lamb without defect[i] for a burnt offering, a year-old ewe
lamb without defect for a sin offering,[j] a
ram[k] without defect for a fellowship offering,[l] 15 together with their grain offerings[m] and drink offerings,[n] and a basket
of bread made with the finest flour and

5:23 [f] Jer 45:1 **5:25** [g] Lev 8:27 **5:26** [h] S Lev 2:2 **5:27** [i] Isa 43:28; 65:15; Jer 26:6; 29:18; 42:18; 44:12,22; Zec 8:13 **5:29** [j] S ver 19 **5:30** [k] S ver 14 **5:31** [l] S Lev 5:1 **6:2** [m] ver 5; S Ge 28:20; Ac 21:23 [n] ver 6 [o] Jdg 13:5; 16:17 **6:3** [p] S Lev 10:9; S Lk 1:15 [q] Ru 2:14; Ps 69:21; Pr 10:26 [r] S Lev 25:5

6:5 [s] Ps 52:2; 57:4; 59:7; Isa 7:20; Eze 5:1 [t] 1Sa 1:11 **6:6** [u] S Lev 21:1-3; Nu 19:11-22 **6:7** [v] Nu 9:6 **6:9** [w] ver 18 [x] S Lev 14:9 **6:10** [y] S Lev 14:10 [z] S Lev 5:7 [a] Lev 14:11 **6:11** [b] S Ex 30:10 [c] S Ge 8:20 [d] S Ex 29:36 **6:12** [e] S Lev 12:6 [f] S Lev 5:15 **6:13** [g] Ac 21:26 [h] Lev 14:11 **6:14** [i] S Ex 12:5 [j] ver 11; Lev 4:3; 14:10 [k] S Lev 5:15 [l] Lev 3:1 **6:15** [m] Lev 2:1; S 6:14 [n] S Ge 35:14

[a] *26* Or *representative* [b] *11* Or *purification offering;* also in verses 14 and 16

6:2 *man or woman.* See ch. 30 for the differences between the vows of men and women. *vow ... Nazirite.* Involved separation or consecration for a specific period of special devotion to God—on occasion even for life (see notes on Jdg 13:5; 1Sa 1:11). Attention is usually given to the prohibitions for the Nazirite; more important to the Lord is the positive separation (see v. 8). This was not just a vow of personal self-discipline; it was an act of total devotion to the Lord.

6:4 *anything that comes from the grapevine.* Not only was the fermented beverage forbidden, but even the seed and skin of the grape. During the period of a Nazirite's vow, three areas of his (or her) life were governed: (1) diet, (2) appearance and (3) associations. Every Israelite was regulated in these areas, but for the Nazirite each regulation was heightened.

6:5 *no razor.* See Jdg 13:5 and note. The unusually long hair of a Nazirite would become a physical mark of his (or her) vow of special devotion to the Lord. Cf. Lev 21:5. *They must be holy.* See note on Ex 3:5.

6:6 *dead body.* See note on 5:2. For the Nazirite, the prohibition of contact with dead bodies extended even to the deceased within his (or her) own family (v. 7; contrast Lev 21:1–3).

6:9–12 The provisions of the Nazirite vow concerned areas where he (or she) was able to make conscious decisions. This section deals with the unexpected and the unplanned events of daily living.

6:13–20 The offerings of the Nazirite at the completion of the period of the vow were extensive, expensive and expressive of the spirit of total commitment to the Lord during this time of special devotion. In addition to these

without yeast—thick loaves with olive oil
mixed in, and thin loaves brushed with
olive oil.[o]
16 " 'The priest is to present all these[p] before the LORD[q] and make the sin offering
and the burnt offering.[r] 17 He is to present
the basket of unleavened bread and is to
sacrifice the ram as a fellowship offering[s]
to the LORD, together with its grain offering[t] and drink offering.[u]
18 " 'Then at the entrance to the tent of
meeting, the Nazirite must shave off the
hair that symbolizes their dedication.[v]
They are to take the hair and put it in the
fire that is under the sacrifice of the fellowship offering.
19 " 'After the Nazirite has shaved off the
hair that symbolizes their dedication, the
priest is to place in their hands a boiled
shoulder of the ram, and one thick loaf
and one thin loaf from the basket, both
made without yeast.[w] 20 The priest shall
then wave these before the LORD as a wave
offering;[x] they are holy[y] and belong to the
priest, together with the breast that was
waved and the thigh that was presented.[z]
After that, the Nazirite may drink wine.[a]
21 " 'This is the law of the Nazirite[b] who
vows offerings to the LORD in accordance
with their dedication, in addition to whatever else they can afford. They must fulfill
the vows[c] they have made, according to
the law of the Nazirite.' "

The Priestly Blessing

22 The LORD said to Moses, 23 "Tell Aaron
and his sons, 'This is how you are to bless[d]
the Israelites. Say to them:

24 " ' "The LORD bless you[e]
and keep you;[f]
25 the LORD make his face shine on you[g]
and be gracious to you;[h]
26 the LORD turn his face[i] toward you
and give you peace.[j]" '

27 "So they will put my name[k] on the Israelites, and I will bless them."

6:15 [o] S Ex 29:2
6:16 [p] Lev 1:3 [q] ver 10 [r] ver 11
6:17 [s] Lev 3:1 [t] S Ex 29:41 [u] Lev 23:13
6:18 [v] ver 9; Ac 21:24
6:19 [w] Lev 7:12
6:20 [x] Lev 7:30 [y] S Lev 27:9 [z] S Lev 7:34 [a] Ecc 9:7
6:21 [b] ver 13 [c] ver 2
6:23 [d] Dt 21:5; 1Ch 23:13
6:24 [e] S Ge 28:3; Dt 28:3-6; Ps 28:9; 128:5 [f] 1Sa 2:9; Ps 17:8
6:25 [g] Job 29:24; Ps 4:6; 31:16; 80:3; 119:135 [h] Ge 43:29; Ps 25:16; 86:16; 119:29
6:26 [i] Ps 4:6; 44:3 [j] Ps 4:8; 29:11; 37:11, 37; 127:2; Isa 14:7; Jer 33:6; Jn 14:27
6:27 [k] Dt 28:10; 2Sa 7:23; 2Ch 7:14; Ne 9:10; Jer 25:29; Eze 36:23

7:1 [l] Ex 40:17 [m] S Ex 30:26 [n] S Ex 40:9 [o] ver 84, 88; Ex 40:10; 2Ch 7:9
7:2 [p] Nu 1:5-16 [q] Nu 1:19
7:3 [r] Ge 45:19; 1Sa 6:7-14; 1Ch 13:7
7:7 [s] Nu 4:24-26, 28
7:8 [t] Nu 4:31-33
7:9 [u] Nu 4:4 [v] Nu 4:15
7:10 [w] ver 1; S Ex 29:36 [x] 2Ch 7:9
7:12 [y] S Nu 1:7
7:13 [z] S Ex 27:3 [a] ver 85 [b] S Ex 30:13; Lev 27:3-7

Offerings at the Dedication of the Tabernacle

7 When Moses finished setting up the
tabernacle,[l] he anointed[m] and consecrated it and all its furnishings.[n] He also
anointed and consecrated the altar and
all its utensils.[o] 2 Then the leaders of Israel,[p] the heads of families who were the
tribal leaders in charge of those who were
counted,[q] made offerings. 3 They brought
as their gifts before the LORD six covered
carts[r] and twelve oxen—an ox from each
leader and a cart from every two. These
they presented before the tabernacle.
4 The LORD said to Moses, 5 "Accept these
from them, that they may be used in the
work at the tent of meeting. Give them to
the Levites as each man's work requires."
6 So Moses took the carts and oxen and
gave them to the Levites. 7 He gave two
carts and four oxen to the Gershonites,[s]
as their work required, 8 and he gave four
carts and eight oxen to the Merarites,[t] as
their work required. They were all under
the direction of Ithamar son of Aaron, the
priest. 9 But Moses did not give any to the
Kohathites,[u] because they were to carry on
their shoulders[v] the holy things, for which
they were responsible.
10 When the altar was anointed,[w] the
leaders brought their offerings for its dedication[x] and presented them before the
altar. 11 For the LORD had said to Moses,
"Each day one leader is to bring his offering for the dedication of the altar."

12 The one who brought his offering on the
first day was Nahshon[y] son of Amminadab
of the tribe of Judah.
13 His offering was one silver plate
weighing a hundred and thirty shekels[a] and one silver sprinkling bowl[z]
weighing seventy shekels,[b][a] both
according to the sanctuary shekel,[b]

[a] 13 That is, about 3 1/4 pounds or about 1.5 kilograms; also elsewhere in this chapter [b] 13 That is, about 1 3/4 pounds or about 800 grams; also elsewhere in this chapter

several offerings, the Nazirite burned his (or her) hair (the sign of the vow).

6:21 A summary of vv. 1–20.

6:24–26 The Aaronic benediction. The threefold repetition of the divine name Yahweh ("the LORD") is for emphasis and gives force to the expression in v. 27: "So they will put my name on the Israelites." Each verse conveys two elements of benediction, and the verses are progressively longer (in the Hebrew text, the first verse has three words, the second has five and the third has seven). This benediction is echoed in Ps 67:1 (see note there). In 1979 a condensed version of these verses was found in a burial cave just outside Jerusalem. The words were inscribed in Hebrew on two tiny silver scrolls dating to c. 600 BC, making them the oldest citations of Biblical texts thus far discovered.

6:25 *make his face shine on you.* In acceptance and favor.

6:26 *peace.* The Hebrew for this word is *shalom*, here seen in its most expressive fullness—not the absence of war, but a positive state of rightness and well-being. Such peace comes only from the Lord (cf. Jn 14:27 and note).

7:1–89 See Ex 40, which describes the setting up of the tabernacle and ends with the report of the cloud covering and the presence of the Lord filling the tabernacle. With much repetition of language, this chapter (the longest in the Pentateuch) records the magnificent (and identical) gifts to the Lord for tabernacle service from the leaders of the 12 tribes. The fact that the record of these gifts follows the text of the Aaronic benediction (6:24–26) seems fitting: In response to God's promise to bless his people, they bring gifts to him in 12 sequential days of celebrative pageantry.

7:12–78 The leaders of the 12 tribes have already been named in 1:5–15; 2:3–32. The order of the presentation of

each filled with the finest flour mixed
with olive oil as a grain offering;[c]
14 one gold dish[d] weighing ten shekels,[a][e] filled with incense;[f] 15 one young
bull,[g] one ram and one male lamb a
year old for a burnt offering;[h] 16 one
male goat for a sin offering[b];[i] 17 and
two oxen, five rams, five male goats
and five male lambs a year old to be
sacrificed as a fellowship offering.[j]
This was the offering of Nahshon son
of Amminadab.[k]

18 On the second day Nethanel son of
Zuar,[l] the leader of Issachar, brought his
offering.
19 The offering he brought was one
silver plate weighing a hundred and
thirty shekels and one silver sprinkling bowl weighing seventy shekels, both according to the sanctuary
shekel, each filled with the finest
flour mixed with olive oil as a grain
offering; 20 one gold dish[m] weighing
ten shekels, filled with incense; 21 one
young bull, one ram and one male
lamb a year old for a burnt offering;
22 one male goat for a sin offering;
23 and two oxen, five rams, five male
goats and five male lambs a year old
to be sacrificed as a fellowship offering. This was the offering of Nethanel
son of Zuar.

24 On the third day, Eliab son of Helon,[n] the
leader of the people of Zebulun, brought
his offering.
25 His offering was one silver plate
weighing a hundred and thirty shekels and one silver sprinkling bowl
weighing seventy shekels, both according to the sanctuary shekel, each
filled with the finest flour mixed with
olive oil as a grain offering; 26 one
gold dish weighing ten shekels, filled
with incense; 27 one young bull, one
ram and one male lamb a year old for
a burnt offering; 28 one male goat for
a sin offering; 29 and two oxen, five
rams, five male goats and five male
lambs a year old to be sacrificed as a
fellowship offering. This was the offering of Eliab son of Helon.

30 On the fourth day Elizur son of Shedeur,[o] the leader of the people of Reuben,
brought his offering.
31 His offering was one silver plate
weighing a hundred and thirty shekels and one silver sprinkling bowl
weighing seventy shekels, both according to the sanctuary shekel, each
filled with the finest flour mixed with
olive oil as a grain offering; 32 one
gold dish weighing ten shekels, filled
with incense; 33 one young bull, one
ram and one male lamb a year old for
a burnt offering; 34 one male goat for
a sin offering; 35 and two oxen, five
rams, five male goats and five male
lambs a year old to be sacrificed as a
fellowship offering. This was the offering of Elizur son of Shedeur.

36 On the fifth day Shelumiel son of Zurishaddai,[p] the leader of the people of Simeon, brought his offering.
37 His offering was one silver plate
weighing a hundred and thirty shekels
and one silver sprinkling bowl weighing seventy shekels, both according to
the sanctuary shekel, each filled with
the finest flour mixed with olive oil
as a grain offering; 38 one gold dish
weighing ten shekels, filled with incense; 39 one young bull, one ram and
one male lamb a year old for a burnt
offering; 40 one male goat for a sin offering; 41 and two oxen, five rams, five
male goats and five male lambs a year
old to be sacrificed as a fellowship offering. This was the offering of Shelumiel son of Zurishaddai.

42 On the sixth day Eliasaph son of Deuel,[q]
the leader of the people of Gad, brought
his offering.
43 His offering was one silver plate
weighing a hundred and thirty shekels and one silver sprinkling bowl
weighing seventy shekels, both according to the sanctuary shekel, each
filled with the finest flour mixed with
olive oil as a grain offering; 44 one
gold dish weighing ten shekels, filled
with incense; 45 one young bull, one
ram and one male lamb a year old for
a burnt offering; 46 one male goat for
a sin offering; 47 and two oxen, five
rams, five male goats and five male
lambs a year old to be sacrificed as a
fellowship offering. This was the offering of Eliasaph son of Deuel.

7:13 [c] Lev 2:1; Nu 6:15; 15:4 **7:14** [d] ver 20; 1Ki 7:50; 2Ki 25:14; 2Ch 4:22; 24:14 [e] ver 86 [f] S Ex 25:6 **7:15** [g] Ex 24:5; 29:3; Nu 28:11 [h] Lev 1:3 **7:16** [i] Lev 4:3 **7:17** [j] Lev 3:1 [k] Nu 1:7 **7:18** [l] S Nu 1:8 **7:20** [m] S ver 14 **7:24** [n] S Nu 1:9 **7:30** [o] S Nu 1:5 **7:36** [p] S Nu 1:6 **7:42** [q] S Nu 1:14

[a] *14* That is, about 4 ounces or about 115 grams; also elsewhere in this chapter [b] *16* Or *purification offering*; also elsewhere in this chapter

their offerings to the Lord is the same as the order of march: first, the triad of tribes camped east of the tabernacle (Judah, Issachar and Zebulun: 2:3–9; 7:12,18,24); second, the triad camped to the south (Reuben, Simeon and Gad: 2:10–16; 7:30,36,42); third, the triad to the west (Ephraim, Manasseh and Benjamin: 2:18–24; 7:48,54,60); finally, those to the north (Dan, Asher and Naphtali: 2:25–31; 7:66,72,78). See chart, p. 206.

7:17,23 *fellowship offering.* See note on Lev 3:1.

7:19 *according to the sanctuary shekel.* See note on Ex 30:13.

48 On the seventh day Elishama son of Ammihud,[r] the leader of the people of Ephraim, brought his offering.
49 His offering was one silver plate
weighing a hundred and thirty shekels and one silver sprinkling bowl
weighing seventy shekels, both according to the sanctuary shekel, each
filled with the finest flour mixed
with olive oil as a grain offering;
50 one gold dish weighing ten shekels, filled with incense; 51 one young
bull, one ram and one male lamb a
year old for a burnt offering; 52 one
male goat for a sin offering; 53 and
two oxen, five rams, five male goats
and five male lambs a year old to be
sacrificed as a fellowship offering.
This was the offering of Elishama
son of Ammihud.[s]

54 On the eighth day Gamaliel son of Pedahzur,[t] the leader of the people of Manasseh, brought his offering.
55 His offering was one silver plate
weighing a hundred and thirty shekels and one silver sprinkling bowl
weighing seventy shekels, both according to the sanctuary shekel, each
filled with the finest flour mixed
with olive oil as a grain offering;
56 one gold dish weighing ten shekels, filled with incense; 57 one young
bull, one ram and one male lamb a
year old for a burnt offering; 58 one
male goat for a sin offering; 59 and
two oxen, five rams, five male goats
and five male lambs a year old to be
sacrificed as a fellowship offering.
This was the offering of Gamaliel son
of Pedahzur.

60 On the ninth day Abidan son of Gideoni,[u] the leader of the people of Benjamin,
brought his offering.
61 His offering was one silver plate
weighing a hundred and thirty shekels and one silver sprinkling bowl
weighing seventy shekels, both according to the sanctuary shekel, each
filled with the finest flour mixed with
olive oil as a grain offering; 62 one
gold dish weighing ten shekels, filled
with incense; 63 one young bull, one
ram and one male lamb a year old for
a burnt offering; 64 one male goat for
a sin offering; 65 and two oxen, five
rams, five male goats and five male
lambs a year old to be sacrificed as a
fellowship offering. This was the offering of Abidan son of Gideoni.

7:48 [r] S Nu 1:10
7:53 [s] S Nu 1:10
7:54 [t] S Nu 1:10
7:60 [u] S Nu 1:11
7:66 [v] S Nu 1:12
7:72 [w] S Nu 1:13
7:78 [x] S Nu 1:15

66 On the tenth day Ahiezer son of Ammishaddai,[v] the leader of the people of Dan,
brought his offering.
67 His offering was one silver plate
weighing a hundred and thirty shekels
and one silver sprinkling bowl weighing seventy shekels, both according to
the sanctuary shekel, each filled with
the finest flour mixed with olive oil
as a grain offering; 68 one gold dish
weighing ten shekels, filled with incense; 69 one young bull, one ram and
one male lamb a year old for a burnt
offering; 70 one male goat for a sin offering; 71 and two oxen, five rams, five
male goats and five male lambs a year
old to be sacrificed as a fellowship offering. This was the offering of Ahiezer son of Ammishaddai.

72 On the eleventh day Pagiel son of Okran,[w] the leader of the people of Asher,
brought his offering.
73 His offering was one silver plate
weighing a hundred and thirty shekels and one silver sprinkling bowl
weighing seventy shekels, both according to the sanctuary shekel, each
filled with the finest flour mixed with
olive oil as a grain offering; 74 one
gold dish weighing ten shekels, filled
with incense; 75 one young bull, one
ram and one male lamb a year old for
a burnt offering; 76 one male goat for
a sin offering; 77 and two oxen, five
rams, five male goats and five male
lambs a year old to be sacrificed as a
fellowship offering. This was the offering of Pagiel son of Okran.

78 On the twelfth day Ahira son of Enan,[x]
the leader of the people of Naphtali,
brought his offering.
79 His offering was one silver plate
weighing a hundred and thirty shekels and one silver sprinkling bowl
weighing seventy shekels, both according to the sanctuary shekel, each
filled with the finest flour mixed with
olive oil as a grain offering; 80 one
gold dish weighing ten shekels, filled
with incense; 81 one young bull, one
ram and one male lamb a year old for
a burnt offering; 82 one male goat for
a sin offering; 83 and two oxen, five
rams, five male goats and five male
lambs a year old to be sacrificed as a
fellowship offering. This was the offering of Ahira son of Enan.

84 These were the offerings of the Israelite leaders for the dedication of the altar

7:84–88 The totals of the 12 sets of gifts.

when it was anointed:[y] twelve silver plates,
twelve silver sprinkling bowls[z] and twelve
gold dishes.[a] 85 Each silver plate weighed
a hundred and thirty shekels, and each
sprinkling bowl seventy shekels. Altogether, the silver dishes weighed two thousand
four hundred shekels,[a] according to the
sanctuary shekel.[b] 86 The twelve gold dishes filled with incense weighed ten shekels
each, according to the sanctuary shekel.[c] Altogether, the gold dishes weighed a
hundred and twenty shekels.[b] 87 The total
number of animals for the burnt offering[d]
came to twelve young bulls, twelve rams
and twelve male lambs a year old, together with their grain offering.[e] Twelve male
goats were used for the sin offering.[f] 88 The
total number of animals for the sacrifice of
the fellowship offering[g] came to twenty-
four oxen, sixty rams, sixty male goats and
sixty male lambs[h] a year old. These were
the offerings for the dedication of the altar
after it was anointed.[i]

89 When Moses entered the tent of meeting[j] to speak with the LORD,[k] he heard the
voice speaking to him from between the
two cherubim above the atonement cover[l]
on the ark of the covenant law.[m] In this
way the LORD spoke to him.

Setting Up the Lamps

8 The LORD said to Moses, 2 "Speak to
Aaron and say to him, 'When you set
up the lamps, see that all seven light up
the area in front of the lampstand.[n]' "

3 Aaron did so; he set up the lamps so
that they faced forward on the lampstand,
just as the LORD commanded Moses. 4 This
is how the lampstand was made: It was
made of hammered gold[o]—from its base
to its blossoms. The lampstand was made
exactly like the pattern[p] the LORD had
shown Moses.

The Setting Apart of the Levites

5 The LORD said to Moses: 6 "Take the
Levites from among all the Israelites and
make them ceremonially clean.[q] 7 To purify
them, do this: Sprinkle the water of cleansing[r] on them; then have them shave their
whole bodies[s] and wash their clothes.[t]
And so they will purify themselves.[u] 8 Have
them take a young bull with its grain offering of the finest flour mixed with olive
oil;[v] then you are to take a second young
bull for a sin offering.[c][w] 9 Bring the Levites
to the front of the tent of meeting[x] and assemble the whole Israelite community.[y]
10 You are to bring the Levites before the
LORD, and the Israelites are to lay their
hands on them.[z] 11 Aaron is to present the
Levites before the LORD as a wave offering[a]
from the Israelites, so that they may be
ready to do the work of the LORD.

12 "Then the Levites are to lay their
hands on the heads of the bulls,[b] using
one for a sin offering[c] to the LORD and the
other for a burnt offering,[d] to make atonement[e] for the Levites. 13 Have the Levites
stand in front of Aaron and his sons and
then present them as a wave offering[f] to
the LORD. 14 In this way you are to set the
Levites apart from the other Israelites, and
the Levites will be mine.[g]

15 "After you have purified the Levites
and presented them as a wave offering,[h]
they are to come to do their work at the
tent of meeting.[i] 16 They are the Israelites
who are to be given wholly to me. I have
taken them as my own in place of the firstborn,[j] the first male offspring[k] from every
Israelite woman. 17 Every firstborn male in
Israel, whether human or animal,[l] is mine.
When I struck down all the firstborn in
Egypt, I set them apart for myself.[m] 18 And
I have taken the Levites in place of all the
firstborn sons in Israel.[n] 19 From among all
the Israelites, I have given the Levites as
gifts to Aaron and his sons[o] to do the work
at the tent of meeting on behalf of the Israelites[p] and to make atonement for them[q]
so that no plague will strike the Israelites
when they go near the sanctuary."

7:84 [y] ver 1, 10 [z] S Nu 4:14 [a] ver 14
7:85 [b] ver 13
7:86 [c] ver 13
7:87 [d] ver 15 [e] ver 13 [f] ver 16
7:88 [g] ver 17 [h] Ge 32:14 [i] S ver 1, 10
7:89 [j] S Ex 40:2 [k] S Ex 29:42 [l] S Ex 16:34; Ps 80:1; 99:1 [m] Nu 3:31
8:2 [n] Ex 25:37
8:4 [o] S Ex 25:18, 36 [p] S Ex 25:9
8:6 [q] Lev 22:2; Isa 1:16; 52:11
8:7 [r] Nu 19:9, 17; 31:23 [s] S Lev 14:9; Nu 6:9; Dt 21:12 [t] S Ge 35:2; Lev 14:8 [u] S Ge 35:2
8:8 [v] Lev 2:1; Nu 15:8-10 [w] Lev 4:3
8:9 [x] Ex 40:12 [y] Lev 8:3
8:10 [z] S Lev 3:2; Ac 6:6
8:11 [a] S Ex 29:24
8:12 [b] S Ex 29:10 [c] Lev 4:3; Nu 6:11 [d] Lev 1:3 [e] S Ex 29:36
8:13 [f] S Ex 29:24
8:14 [g] S Nu 3:12
8:15 [h] S Ex 29:24 [i] Ex 40:2
8:16 [j] Nu 1:20 [k] S Nu 3:12
8:17 [l] S Ex 4:23 [m] S Ex 13:2; S Ex 22:29
8:18 [n] S Nu 3:12
8:19 [o] S Nu 3:9 [p] S Nu 3:7 [q] Nu 16:46

[a] 85 That is, about 60 pounds or about 28 kilograms
[b] 86 That is, about 3 pounds or about 1.4 kilograms
[c] 8 Or *purification offering*; also in verse 12

7:89 The climax: Communion is established between the Lord and his prophet. The people have an advocate with God. *covenant law.* See note on Ex 25:22.
8:2 *area in front of the lampstand.* The Holy Place in the tabernacle (see Ex 25:37; 26:31–35; 27:21 and notes).
8:5–26 Describes the ceremonial cleansing of the Levites and may be compared with the account of the ordination of Aaron and his sons to the priesthood (Lev 8). The Levites are helpers to the priests, and the language describing their consecration is somewhat different from that of the priests. The priests were made holy, the Levites clean; the priests were anointed and washed, the Levites sprinkled; the priests were given new garments, while the Levites washed theirs; blood was applied to the priests but was waved over the Levites.
8:7 *shave their whole bodies.* Symbolic of the completeness of their cleansing, as in the case of the ritual cleansing of one cured of skin disease (see Lev 14:8 and note).
8:10 *Israelites are to lay their hands on them.* The Levites were substitutes for the nation; by laying hands on them, the other people of the nation were acknowledging this substitutionary act (see vv. 16–18).
8:16 *to me.* See note on 3:9.
8:19 *I have given the Levites as gifts to Aaron and his sons.* The Levites were given to the Lord for his exclusive use (see v. 14). Now the Lord gives his Levites to the priests as their aides for the work of ministry in the tabernacle worship. *so that no plague will strike the Israelites.* The Levites were a protective hedge for the community against trespassing in the sacred precincts of the tabernacle (see note on 1:53).

20 Moses, Aaron and the whole Israelite
community did with the Levites just as the
LORD commanded Moses. 21 The Levites purified themselves and washed their clothes.[r]
Then Aaron presented them as a wave offering before the LORD and made atonement[s] for them to purify them.[t] 22 After that,
the Levites came to do their work[u] at the
tent of meeting under the supervision of
Aaron and his sons. They did with the Levites just as the LORD commanded Moses.
23 The LORD said to Moses, 24 "This applies
to the Levites: Men twenty-five years old or
more[v] shall come to take part in the work at
the tent of meeting,[w] 25 but at the age of fifty,[x]
they must retire from their regular service
and work no longer. 26 They may assist their
brothers in performing their duties at the
tent of meeting, but they themselves must
not do the work.[y] This, then, is how you are
to assign the responsibilities of the Levites."

The Passover

9 The LORD spoke to Moses in the Desert of Sinai in the first month[z] of the
second year after they came out of Egypt.[a]
He said, 2 "Have the Israelites celebrate the
Passover[b] at the appointed time.[c] 3 Celebrate
it at the appointed time, at twilight on the
fourteenth day of this month,[d] in accordance with all its rules and regulations.[e]"
4 So Moses told the Israelites to celebrate
the Passover,[f] 5 and they did so in the Desert
of Sinai[g] at twilight on the fourteenth day
of the first month.[h] The Israelites did everything just as the LORD commanded Moses.[i]
6 But some of them could not celebrate
the Passover on that day because they were
ceremonially unclean[j] on account of a dead
body.[k] So they came to Moses and Aaron[l]
that same day 7 and said to Moses, "We
have become unclean because of a dead
body, but why should we be kept from presenting the LORD's offering with the other
Israelites at the appointed time?[m]"
8 Moses answered them, "Wait until I
find out what the LORD commands concerning you."[n]
9 Then the LORD said to Moses, 10 "Tell the
Israelites: 'When any of you or your descendants are unclean because of a dead body[o]
or are away on a journey, they are still to
celebrate[p] the LORD's Passover, 11 but they are
to do it on the fourteenth day of the second
month[q] at twilight. They are to eat the lamb,
together with unleavened bread and bitter
herbs.[r] 12 They must not leave any of it till
morning[s] or break any of its bones.[t] When
they celebrate the Passover, they must follow all the regulations.[u] 13 But if anyone who
is ceremonially clean and not on a journey
fails to celebrate the Passover, they must be
cut off from their people[v] for not presenting
the LORD's offering at the appointed time.
They will bear the consequences of their sin.
14 " 'A foreigner[w] residing among you is
also to celebrate the LORD's Passover in
accordance with its rules and regulations.
You must have the same regulations for
both the foreigner and the native-born.' "

The Cloud Above the Tabernacle

15 On the day the tabernacle, the tent of
the covenant law,[x] was set up,[y] the cloud[z]

8:21 [r] ver 7; S Ge 35:2 [s] Nu 16:47 [t] ver 12 **8:22** [u] ver 11 **8:24** [v] 1Ch 23:3 [w] S Ex 38:21 **8:25** [x] S Nu 4:3 **8:26** [y] ver 11 **9:1** [z] S Ex 40:2 [a] Nu 1:1 **9:2** [b] S Ex 12:11 [c] ver 7 **9:3** [d] S Ex 12:6, 42 [e] Ex 12:2-11, 43-49; Lev 23:5-8; Dt 16:1-8 **9:4** [f] ver 2; S Ex 12:11 **9:5** [g] ver 1 [h] S Ex 12:6 [i] ver 3 **9:6** [j] S Lev 5:3; S 13:3 [k] S Lev 21:11 [l] Ex 18:15; Nu 27:2 **9:7** [m] ver 2 **9:8** [n] Ex 18:15; Lev 24:12; Nu 15:34; 27:5, 21; Ps 85:8 **9:10** [o] ver 6 [p] 2Ch 30:2 **9:11** [q] S Ex 12:6 [r] Ex 12:8 **9:12** [s] S Ex 12:8 [t] S Ex 12:46; Jn 19:36* [u] ver 3 **9:13** [v] S Ge 17:14 **9:14** [w] S Ex 12:19,43 **9:15** [x] S Ex 38:21 [y] S Ex 26:30 [z] S Ex 33:16

8:20 *as the LORD commanded Moses.* See vv. 4,22; 1:54; 2:34; 3:16,51; 4:49; 5:4; 9:5,23. The implicit obedience of Moses and the Israelites to God's commands in the areas of ritual and regimen stands in sharp contrast to the people's complaints against the Lord's loving character and to their breaches of faith that begin in ch. 11.

8:24 *twenty-five years old.* See note on 4:3. The age at which the Levites entered service was reduced to 20 by David (see 1Ch 23:3,24,27 and note on 23:3), as the circumstances of their work had greatly changed by the time of the monarchy (see 1Ch 23:26). It is difficult to imagine a change in circumstances between 4:3 and this verse, however. Therefore the rabbinical suggestion that these two verses indicate a five-year period of apprenticeship seems reasonable.

8:26 *They may assist.* After a Levite had reached the mandatory retirement age of 50 (see v. 25), he was still free to assist his younger co-workers (perhaps at festivals), but he was no longer to do the difficult work he had done in his prime.

9:1–14 This unit is in four parts: (1) the command to keep the Passover (vv. 1–5); (2) the question concerning those ceremonially unclean (vv. 6–8); (3) the response of the Lord—giving permission for legitimate delay, but judgment for willful neglect (vv. 9–13); (4) the rights of the foreigner at Passover (v. 14). The first Passover was held in Egypt (see Ex 12). The second is here at Sinai a year later. Because of Israel's rebellion and God's judgment on her (ch. 14), Israel would not celebrate the Passover again until she entered the promised land (see Jos 5:10 and note).

9:1 *first month of the second year.* The events of this chapter preceded the beginning of the census in ch. 1 (see 1:1 and note).

9:3 *twilight.* Traditional Jewish practice regards this period as the end of one day and the beginning of the next.

9:7 *why should we be kept from presenting the LORD's offering ... ?* Those with ceremonial uncleanness had a keen desire to worship the Lord "in the Spirit and in truth" (Jn 4:24; see note there).

9:10 *they are still to celebrate.* God's gracious provision for these people was an alternative day one month later (v. 11) so that they would not be excluded totally from the Passover celebration. The Lord thus demonstrates the reality of the distance that uncleanness brings between a believer and his or her participation in the worship of the community, but he also provides a merciful alternative.

9:12 *not ... break any of its bones.* When Jesus ("our Passover lamb," 1Co 5:7; cf. Jn 1:29) was crucified, it was reported that none of his bones was broken, in fulfillment of Scripture (Jn 19:36). See also Ex 12:46; Ps 34:20.

9:13 *fails to celebrate ... cut off.* The NT also issues grave warnings concerning the abuse or misuse of the celebration of the Lord's Supper (1Co 11:28–30). See note on Ex 12:15.

9:14 *foreigner.* Must first be circumcised before participating in the Passover celebration (see Ex 12:48 and note).

9:15 *covenant law.* See note on Ex 25:22. *cloud covered it.* See notes on Ex 13:21; 40:34. The cloud was the visible symbol of

covered it. From evening till morning the cloud above the tabernacle looked like fire.[a] 16 That is how it continued to be; the cloud covered it, and at night it looked like fire.[b] 17 Whenever the cloud lifted from above the tent, the Israelites set out;[c] wherever the cloud settled, the Israelites encamped.[d] 18 At the LORD's command the Israelites set out, and at his command they encamped. As long as the cloud stayed over the tabernacle, they remained[e] in camp. 19 When the cloud remained over the tabernacle a long time, the Israelites obeyed the LORD's order[f] and did not set out.[g] 20 Sometimes the cloud was over the tabernacle only a few days; at the LORD's command they would encamp, and then at his command they would set out. 21 Sometimes the cloud stayed only from evening till morning, and when it lifted in the morning, they set out. Whether by day or by night, whenever the cloud lifted, they set out. 22 Whether the cloud stayed over the tabernacle for two days or a month or a year, the Israelites would remain in camp and not set out; but when it lifted, they would set out. 23 At the LORD's command they encamped, and at the LORD's command they set out. They obeyed the LORD's order, in accordance with his command through Moses.

Silver coin depicting two trumpets (AD 134–135), reminiscent of the ones blown to summon the people together on important occasions (Nu 10:2–10).

Z. Radovan/www.BibleLandPictures.com

The Silver Trumpets

10 The LORD said to Moses: 2 "Make two trumpets[h] of hammered silver, and use them for calling the community[i] together and for having the camps set out.[j] 3 When both are sounded, the whole community is to assemble before you at the entrance to the tent of meeting. 4 If only one is sounded, the leaders[k]—the heads of the clans of Israel—are to assemble before you. 5 When a trumpet blast is sounded, the tribes camping on the east are to set out.[l] 6 At the sounding of a second blast, the camps on the south are to set out.[m] The blast will be the signal for setting out. 7 To gather the assembly, blow the trumpets,[n] but not with the signal for setting out.[o]

8 "The sons of Aaron, the priests, are to blow the trumpets. This is to be a lasting ordinance for you and the generations to come.[p] 9 When you go into battle in your own land against an enemy who is oppressing you,[q] sound a blast on the trumpets.[r] Then you will be remembered[s] by the LORD your God and rescued from your enemies.[t] 10 Also at your times of rejoicing—your appointed festivals and New Moon feasts[u]—you are to sound the trumpets[v] over your burnt offerings[w] and fellowship offerings,[x] and they will be a memorial for you before your God. I am the LORD your God.[y]"

The Israelites Leave Sinai

11 On the twentieth day of the second month of the second year,[z] the cloud lifted[a] from above the tabernacle of the covenant law.[b] 12 Then the Israelites set out from the Desert of Sinai and traveled from

9:15 [a] Ex 13:21 **9:16** [b] S Ex 40:38 **9:17** [c] ver 21 [d] 1Co 10:1 **9:18** [e] Ex 40:37 **9:19** [f] S Lev 8:35 [g] Ex 40:37 **10:2** [h] ver 8, 9; Nu 31:6; Ne 12:35; Ps 47:5; 98:6; 150:3 [i] Ne 4:18; Jer 4:5, 19; 6:1; Hos 5:8; 8:1; Joel 2:1, 15; Am 3:6 [j] Nu 33:3 **10:4** [k] S Ex 18:21 **10:5** [l] ver 14 **10:6** [m] ver 18 **10:7** [n] Jer 4:5; 6:1; Eze 33:3; Joel 2:1 [o] 1Co 14:8 **10:8** [p] S Ge 9:12; Nu 15:14; 35:29 **10:9** [q] Ex 3:9; Jdg 2:18; 6:9; 1Sa 10:18; 2Ki 13:4; Ps 106:42 [r] S Lev 23:24 [s] S Ge 8:1 [t] 2Ch 13:12; Ps 106:4 **10:10** [u] Nu 28:11; 1Sa 20:5, 24; 2Ki 4:23; 2Ch 8:13; Ps 81:3; Isa 1:13; Eze 45:17; 46:6; Am 8:5 [v] S Lev 23:24 [w] Lev 1:3 [x] Lev 3:1; Nu 6:14 [y] Lev 11:44 **10:11** [z] Ex 40:17 [a] Nu 9:17 [b] S Ex 38:21

---

the Lord's presence hovering above the tabernacle. The Lord also directed the movements of his people by means of the cloud (vv. 17–18).

9:18 *At the LORD's command.* The lifting and settling of the cloud are identified with the Lord's command.

9:23 *obeyed the LORD's order.* The repetitious nature of vv. 15–23 enhances the expectation of continued complete obedience to the Lord's direction of Israel's movements through the wilderness. Moses was the Lord's agent, who interpreted the movement of the cloud as signaling the movement of the people. The tragedy of their subsequent disobedience (ch. 11) is heightened by this paragraph on their obedience.

10:2 *trumpets.* Long, straight, slender metal tubes with flared ends. They were blown for order and discipline. See photo above.

10:3 *sounded.* Not only for assembling but also for marching (vv. 5–6), battle (v. 9) and festivals (v. 10). Since different signals were used (v. 7), a guild of priestly musicians was developed (v. 8). See Jos 6:4 (see also note there) for the use of seven trumpets of rams' horns (Hebrew *shophar*) in the battle of Jericho.

10:10 *at your … appointed festivals … sound the trumpets.* To prepare the people for communion with God. Later, David expanded the instruments to include the full orchestra in the worship of the Lord (see, e.g., 1Ch 25), but he maintained the playing of the silver trumpets regularly before the ark of the covenant (1Ch 16:6).

10:11—22:1 The sordid account of the Israelites' long trek from Sinai to Kadesh (13:26) to the plains of Moab (see Introduction: Structure and Outline).

10:11–28 The structure of this section is: (1) v. 11, time frame; (2) vv. 12–13, introductory summary of setting out; (3) vv. 14–17, setting out of the tribes led by Judah (see 2:3–9); (4) vv. 18–21, setting out of the tribes led by Reuben (see 2:10–16); (5) vv. 22–24, setting out of the tribes led by Ephraim (see 2:18–24); (6) vv. 25–27, setting out of the tribes led by Dan (see 2:25–31); (7) v. 28, concluding summary of the line of march.

10:11 *twentieth day of the second month.* After 11 months in

place to place until the cloud came to rest
in the Desert of Paran.[c] 13 They set out, this
first time, at the LORD's command through
Moses.[d]
14 The divisions of the camp of Judah
went first, under their standard.[e] Nahshon
son of Amminadab[f] was in command.
15 Nethanel son of Zuar was over the division of the tribe[g] of Issachar,[h] 16 and Eliab
son of Helon[i] was over the division of the
tribe of Zebulun.[j] 17 Then the tabernacle
was taken down, and the Gershonites and
Merarites, who carried it, set out.[k]
18 The divisions of the camp of Reuben[l]
went next, under their standard.[m] Elizur
son of Shedeur[n] was in command. 19 Shelumiel son of Zurishaddai was over the division of the tribe of Simeon,[o] 20 and Eliasaph
son of Deuel was over the division of the
tribe of Gad.[p] 21 Then the Kohathites[q] set
out, carrying the holy things.[r] The tabernacle was to be set up before they arrived.[s]
22 The divisions of the camp of Ephraim[t]
went next, under their standard. Elishama son of Ammihud[u] was in command.
23 Gamaliel son of Pedahzur was over the
division of the tribe of Manasseh,[v] 24 and
Abidan son of Gideoni was over the division of the tribe of Benjamin.[w]
25 Finally, as the rear guard[x] for all the
units, the divisions of the camp of Dan set
out under their standard. Ahiezer son of
Ammishaddai[y] was in command. 26 Pagiel
son of Okran was over the division of the
tribe of Asher,[z] 27 and Ahira son of Enan
was over the division of the tribe of Naphtali.[a] 28 This was the order of march for the
Israelite divisions as they set out.
29 Now Moses said to Hobab[b] son of
Reuel[c] the Midianite, Moses' father-in-
law,[d] "We are setting out for the place
about which the LORD said, 'I will give it
to you.'[e] Come with us and we will treat
you well, for the LORD has promised good
things to Israel."
30 He answered, "No, I will not go;[f] I am
going back to my own land and my own
people.[g]"
31 But Moses said, "Please do not leave
us. You know where we should camp in the
wilderness, and you can be our eyes.[h] 32 If
you come with us, we will share with you[i]
whatever good things the LORD gives us.[j]"
33 So they set out[k] from the mountain of
the LORD and traveled for three days. The
ark of the covenant of the LORD[l] went before them during those three days to find
them a place to rest.[m] 34 The cloud of the
LORD was over them by day when they set
out from the camp.[n]
35 Whenever the ark set out, Moses said,

"Rise up,[o] LORD!
May your enemies be scattered;[p]
may your foes flee before you.[q]"[r]

36 Whenever it came to rest, he said,

"Return,[s] LORD,
to the countless thousands of
Israel.[t]"

Fire From the LORD

11 Now the people complained[u] about
their hardships in the hearing of
the LORD,[v] and when he heard them his
anger was aroused.[w] Then fire from the
LORD burned among them[x] and consumed[y]
some of the outskirts of the camp. 2 When
the people cried out to Moses, he prayed[z]
to the LORD[a] and the fire died down. 3 So
that place was called Taberah,[a][b] because
fire from the LORD had burned among
them.[c]

[a] 3 *Taberah* means *burning*.

10:12 [c] S Ge 14:6; Dt 1:1; 33:2 **10:13** [d] Dt 1:6 **10:14** [e] S Nu 1:52; S 2:3-9 [f] Nu 1:7 **10:15** [g] S Lev 24:11 [h] S Nu 1:8 **10:16** [i] S Nu 2:7 [j] S Nu 1:9 **10:17** [k] ver 21; Nu 4:21-32 **10:18** [l] Nu 2:16 [m] Nu 2:10-16 [n] S Nu 1:5 **10:19** [o] Nu 1:6 **10:20** [p] S Nu 1:14 **10:21** [q] S Nu 2:17 [r] Nu 4:20 [s] S ver 17 **10:22** [t] Nu 2:24 [u] S Nu 1:10 **10:23** [v] S Nu 1:10 **10:24** [w] Nu 1:11 **10:25** [x] S Nu 2:31 [y] S Nu 1:12 **10:26** [z] S Nu 1:13 **10:27** [a] S Nu 1:15 **10:29** [b] Jdg 4:11 [c] S Ex 2:18 [d] S Ex 3:1 [e] S Ge 12:7; S 15:14 **10:30** [f] Mt 21:29 [g] S Ex 18:27 **10:31** [h] Job 29:15 **10:32** [i] S Ex 12:48; Dt 10:18 [j] Ps 22:27-31; 67:5-7 **10:33** [k] ver 12; Dt 1:33 [l] Dt 10:8; 31:9; Jos 3:3; Jdg 20:27; 2Sa 15:24 [m] Jer 31:2 **10:34** [n] Nu 9:15-23 **10:35** [o] 2Ch 6:41; Ps 17:13; 44:26; 94:2; 132:8 [p] Jdg 5:31; 1Sa 2:1; Ps 68:1; 92:9 [q] Dt 5:9; 7:10; 32:41; Ps 68:2; Isa 17:12-14 [r] Isa 59:18 **10:36** [s] Isa 52:8; 63:17 [t] Ge 15:5; 26:4; Dt 1:10; 10:22; Ne 9:23 **11:1** [u] S Ex 14:11; S 16:7; La 3:39 [v] Nu 12:2; Dt 1:34 [w] S Ex 4:14 [x] S Lev 10:2 [y] Nu 21:28; Ps 78:63; Isa 26:11 **11:2** [z] Dt 9:19; 1Sa 2:25; 12:23; Ps 106:23 [a] S Ge 20:7; Nu 21:7; Dt 9:20; Jnh 2:1 **11:3** [b] Dt 9:22 [c] Nu 16:35; Job 1:16; Isa 10:17

---

the region of Mount Sinai, the people set out for the promised land, led by the cloud (see note on 9:15). Israel leaves on a journey that in a few months should have led to the conquest of Canaan. *covenant law.* See note on Ex 25:16.

10:14–27 The names of the leaders of the 12 tribes are given for the fourth time in the book (see 1:5–15; 2:3–31; 7:12–83). The order of the line of march is essentially the same as that in ch. 2. The new details are that the Gershonites and Merarites, who carry the tabernacle, follow the triad of the Judah tribes (v. 17), and the Kohathites, who carry the holy things, follow the triad of the Reuben tribes (v. 21) (see chart, p. 206).

10:14 *standard.* As in 2:3,10,18,25, each of the four triads of tribes has a standard or banner for rallying and organization.

10:29 *Hobab son of Reuel.* Thus Hobab was Moses' brother-in-law. *Reuel.* Jethro (see Ex 2:18; 3:1).

10:31 *be our eyes.* Jdg 1:16 indicates that Hobab acceded to Moses' request.

10:33 *three days.* Because of the huge numbers of people in the tribes of Israel, and because this was their first organized march, it is not likely that this first journey covered much territory (cf. note on Ge 22:4).

10:35–36 Reinforces the portrayal of Israel as the Lord's army on the march, with the Lord in the vanguard.

10:35 Later used in the opening words of a psalm celebrating God's triumphal march from Sinai to Jerusalem (see Ps 68:1 and note on 68:1–3).

11:1 *people complained.* The first ten chapters of Numbers repeatedly emphasize the complete obedience of Moses and the people to the dictates of the Lord. But only three days into their march, the people revert to disloyal complaints. They had expressed the same complaints a year earlier, only three days after their deliverance at the waters of the "Red Sea" (Ex 15:22–27), and had subsequently complained about manna (Ex 16) and a lack of water (Ex 17:1–7). *fire from the LORD.* By God's mercy, this purging fire was limited to the outskirts of the camp. The phrase sometimes refers to fire ignited by lightning (as probably in 1Ki 18:38; see note on 18:24).

11:3 *Taberah.* See NIV text note.

Quail From the LORD

4 The rabble with them began to crave
other food,[d] and again the Israelites started wailing[e] and said, "If only we had meat
to eat! 5 We remember the fish we ate in
Egypt at no cost — also the cucumbers,
melons, leeks, onions and garlic.[f] 6 But
now we have lost our appetite; we never
see anything but this manna![g]"
7 The manna was like coriander seed[h]
and looked like resin.[i] 8 The people went
around gathering it,[j] and then ground it
in a hand mill or crushed it in a mortar.
They cooked it in a pot or made it into
loaves. And it tasted like something made
with olive oil. 9 When the dew[k] settled on
the camp at night, the manna also came
down.
10 Moses heard the people of every family wailing[l] at the entrance to their tents.
The LORD became exceedingly angry, and
Moses was troubled. 11 He asked the LORD,
"Why have you brought this trouble[m] on
your servant? What have I done to displease you that you put the burden of all
these people on me?[n] 12 Did I conceive all
these people? Did I give them birth? Why
do you tell me to carry them in my arms,
as a nurse carries an infant,[o] to the land
you promised on oath[p] to their ancestors?[q]
13 Where can I get meat for all these people?[r] They keep wailing to me, 'Give us
meat to eat!' 14 I cannot carry all these
people by myself; the burden is too heavy
for me.[s] 15 If this is how you are going to
treat me, please go ahead and kill me[t] — if
I have found favor in your eyes — and do
not let me face my own ruin."
16 The LORD said to Moses: "Bring me
seventy of Israel's elders[u] who are known
to you as leaders and officials among the
people.[v] Have them come to the tent of
meeting,[w] that they may stand there with
you. 17 I will come down and speak with
you[x] there, and I will take some of the
power of the Spirit that is on you and put
it on them.[y] They will share the burden of
the people with you so that you will not
have to carry it alone.[z]
18 "Tell the people: 'Consecrate yourselves[a] in preparation for tomorrow, when
you will eat meat. The LORD heard you
when you wailed,[b] "If only we had meat
to eat! We were better off in Egypt!"[c] Now
the LORD will give you meat,[d] and you will
eat it. 19 You will not eat it for just one
day, or two days, or five, ten or twenty
days, 20 but for a whole month — until it
comes out of your nostrils and you loathe
it[e] — because you have rejected the LORD,[f]
who is among you, and have wailed before him, saying, "Why did we ever leave
Egypt?" ' "[g]
21 But Moses said, "Here I am among
six hundred thousand men[h] on foot, and
you say, 'I will give them meat to eat for a
whole month!' 22 Would they have enough

11:4 [d] S Ex 16:3 [e] ver 18 **11:5** [f] S Ex 16:3; Nu 21:5 **11:6** [g] Ex 16:14 **11:7** [h] S Ex 16:31 [i] Ge 2:12 **11:8** [j] Ex 16:16 **11:9** [k] Ex 16:13 **11:10** [l] ver 4 **11:11** [m] S Ge 34:30 [n] S Ex 5:22; S 18:18 **11:12** [o] Isa 40:11; 49:23; 66:11, 12 [p] Nu 14:16 [q] S Ge 12:7; Ex 13:5 **11:13** [r] S Ex 12:37; Jn 6:5-9 **11:14** [s] S Ex 18:18 **11:15** [t] Ex 32:32; 1Ki 19:4; Job 6:9; 7:15-16; 9:21; 10:1; Isa 38:12; Jnh 4:3 **11:16** [u] S Ex 3:16 [v] S Ex 18:25 [w] S Ex 40:2 **11:17** [x] Ex 19:20 [y] ver 25, 29; 1Sa 10:6; 2Ki 2:9, 15; 3:12; Isa 32:15; 40:5; 63:11; Joel 2:28; Hag 2:5 [z] S Ex 18:18; Jer 19:1 **11:18** [a] S Ex 19:10 [b] S Ex 16:7 [c] ver 5; Ac 7:39 [d] Ps 78:20 **11:20** [e] Ps 78:29; 106:14, 15 [f] S Lev 26:43; Jos 24:27; Jdg 8:23; 1Sa 10:19; Job 31:28; Isa 59:13; Hos 13:11 [g] ver 33; Job 20:13, 23 **11:21** [h] S Ex 12:37

11:4 *rabble.* An apt term for the non-Israelite mixed group of people who followed the Israelites out of Egypt, pointing to a recurring source of complaints and trouble in the camp. Those who did not know the Lord and his mercies incited those who did know him to rebel against him. *If only we had meat to eat!* As in Ex 16, the people began to complain about their diet, forgetting what God had done for them (see Ps 106:14). Certainly meat was not their common fare when they were slaves in Egypt. Now that they were in a new type of distress, the people romanticized the past and minimized its discomforts.

11:5 *fish ... cucumbers ... garlic.* Suggestive of the varieties of foods available in Egypt, in contrast to the diet of manna in the wilderness.

11:7 *manna.* See note on Ex 16:31.

11:10 *The LORD became exceedingly angry.* The rejection of his gracious gift of heavenly food (called "bread from heaven" in Ex 16:4) angered the Lord. God had said that the reception of the manna by the people would be a significant test of their obedience (Ex 16:4). In view of the good things he was to give them (10:32), the people were expected to receive each day's supply of manna as a gracious gift of a merciful God and a promise of abundance to come. In spurning the manna, the people had spurned the Lord. They had failed the test of faith. *Moses was troubled.* The people's reaction to God's provision of manna was troubling to Moses as well. Instead of asking the Lord to understand the substance of their complaint, Moses asked him why he was given such an ungrateful people to lead.

11:11–15 A prayer of distress and complaint, filled with urgency, irony and passion.

11:12 *Did I conceive all these people?* The implication is that the Lord conceived the people of Israel, that he was their nurse and that their promises were his. Moses asks that he be relieved of his mediatorial office, for "the burden is too heavy for me" (v. 14; cf. Elijah, 1Ki 19). Even death, Moses asserts (v. 15), would be preferable to facing the continuing complaints of the people.

11:16–34 The Lord's response to the great distress of his prophet was twofold — mercy and curse: (1) There was mercy to Moses in that his responsibility was now to be shared by 70 leaders (vv. 16–17). (2) There was a curse on the people that was analogous to their complaint: They asked for meat and would now become sick with meat (vv. 18–34; cf. Ps 78:27–31).

11:18 *you will eat meat.* Their distress at the lack of variety in the daily manna had led the people to challenge the Lord's goodness. They had wailed for meat. Now they were going to get their fill of meat, so much that it would make them physically ill (v. 20).

11:20 *you have rejected the LORD.* The principal issue was not meat at all, but a failure to demonstrate proper gratitude to the Lord, who was in their midst and who was their constant source of good.

11:21 *six hundred thousand men on foot.* The numbers are consistent: A marching force of this size suggests a total population of over 2,000,000 (see note on 1:46). Moses' distress at providing meat for this immense number of people (v. 22) is nearly comical — the task is impossible for him.

if flocks and herds were slaughtered for
them? Would they have enough if all the
fish in the sea were caught for them?"[i]
23 The LORD answered Moses, "Is the
LORD's arm too short?[j] Now you will see
whether or not what I say will come true
for you.[k]"
24 So Moses went out and told the people what the LORD had said. He brought
together seventy of their elders and had
them stand around the tent. 25 Then the
LORD came down in the cloud[l] and spoke
with him,[m] and he took some of the power
of the Spirit[n] that was on him and put it on
the seventy elders.[o] When the Spirit rested
on them, they prophesied[p]—but did not
do so again.
26 However, two men, whose names
were Eldad and Medad, had remained in
the camp. They were listed among the elders, but did not go out to the tent. Yet
the Spirit also rested on them,[q] and they
prophesied in the camp. 27 A young man
ran and told Moses, "Eldad and Medad are
prophesying in the camp."
28 Joshua son of Nun,[r] who had been
Moses' aide[s] since youth, spoke up and
said, "Moses, my lord, stop them!"[t]
29 But Moses replied, "Are you jealous
for my sake? I wish that all the LORD's
people were prophets[u] and that the LORD
would put his Spirit[v] on them!"[w] 30 Then
Moses and the elders of Israel returned to
the camp.
31 Now a wind went out from the LORD
and drove quail[x] in from the sea. It scattered them up to two cubits[a] deep all
around the camp, as far as a day's walk in
any direction. 32 All that day and night and
all the next day the people went out and
gathered quail. No one gathered less than
ten homers.[b] Then they spread them out
all around the camp. 33 But while the meat
was still between their teeth[y] and before it
could be consumed, the anger[z] of the LORD
burned against the people, and he struck
them with a severe plague.[a] 34 Therefore
the place was named Kibroth Hattaavah,[c][b]
because there they buried the people who
had craved other food.
35 From Kibroth Hattaavah the people
traveled to Hazeroth[c] and stayed there.

Miriam and Aaron Oppose Moses

12 Miriam[d] and Aaron began to talk
against Moses because of his Cushite wife,[e] for he had married a Cushite.
2 "Has the LORD spoken only through Moses?" they asked. "Hasn't he also spoken
through us?"[f] And the LORD heard this.[g]
3 (Now Moses was a very humble man,[h]
more humble than anyone else on the face
of the earth.)
4 At once the LORD said to Moses, Aaron and Miriam, "Come out to the tent of
meeting, all three of you." So the three
of them went out. 5 Then the LORD came
down in a pillar of cloud;[i] he stood at the

11:22 [i] Mt 15:33
11:23 [j] Isa 50:2; 59:1 [k] Nu 23:19; 1Sa 15:29; Eze 12:25; 24:14
11:25 [l] S Ex 19:9; Nu 12:5 [m] ver 17 [n] ver 29; 1Sa 10:6; 19:23 [o] S Ac 2:17 [p] ver 26; Nu 24:2; Jdg 3:10; 1Sa 10:10; 19:20; 2Ch 15:1
11:26 [q] S ver 25; 1Ch 12:18; Rev 1:10
11:28 [r] Ex 17:9; Nu 13:8; 26:65; Jos 14:10 [s] Ex 33:11; Jos 1:1 [t] Mk 9:38-40
11:29 [u] 1Sa 10:5; 19:20; 2Ch 24:19; Jer 7:25; 44:4; 1Co 14:5 [v] S ver 17 [w] Nu 27:18
11:31 [x] S Ex 16:13; Ps 78:26-28
11:33 [y] Ps 78:30 [z] Nu 14:18; Dt 9:7; Jdg 2:12; 2Ki 22:17; Ps 106:29; Jer 44:3; Eze 8:17 [a] S ver 18-20; Ps 106:15; Isa 10:16
11:34 [b] Nu 33:16; Dt 9:22
11:35 [c] Nu 33:17

[a] *31* That is, about 3 feet or about 90 centimeters
[b] *32* That is, possibly about 1 3/4 tons or about 1.6 metric tons
[c] *34* *Kibroth Hattaavah* means *graves of craving.*

12:1 [d] S Ex 15:20 [e] S Ex 2:21 **12:2** [f] Nu 16:3 [g] S Nu 11:1 **12:3** [h] Mt 11:29 **12:5** [i] S Ex 13:21; S Nu 11:25

11:23 *Is the LORD's arm too short?* The human impossibility is an occasion for demonstrating the Lord's power. Cf. Isa 59:1.

11:25 *came down.* See 12:5 and note. *the Spirit.* God's empowering presence (cf. Jdg 3:10 and note). *they prophesied.* Probably means that they gave ecstatic expression to an intense religious experience (see 1Sa 10:5; 18:10; 19:20,24; 1Ki 18:29 and notes). *but did not do so again.* It seems that the temporary gift of prophecy to the elders was primarily to establish their credentials as Spirit-empowered leaders.

11:29 *Are you jealous for my sake?* Here the true spirit of Moses is demonstrated. Rather than being threatened by the public demonstration of the gifts of the Spirit by Eldad and Medad, Moses desired that all God's people might have the full gifts of the Spirit (cf. Joel 2:28 and note; Php 1:15–18). This verse is a fitting introduction to the inexcusable challenge to Moses' leadership in ch. 12.

11:31–32 Cf. the great provision of Jesus in the feeding of the 5,000 (Jn 6:5–13) and the 4,000 (Mt 15:29–39). In those cases the feeding was a demonstration of God's grace; in this instance it was accompanied by God's wrath.

11:34 *Kibroth Hattaavah.* See NIV text note. These graves marked the death camp of those who had turned against the food of the Lord's mercy.

12:1 *his Cushite wife.* Ham had a son named Cush. His descendants, as named in Ge 10:7, were all located in Arabia (see note on Ge 10:7). Nimrod, a descendant of perhaps another Cush, is identified as a great empire builder in lower Mesopotamia (Ge 10:8–12; see note on 10:8). Elsewhere "Cush" also frequently refers to a region lying just south of Egypt (ancient Nubia, modern Sudan; see note on Ge 10:6). Because of this diversity, we cannot know with any certainty the ethnic identity of Moses' wife here referred to. Perhaps Hab 3:7 provides a better clue. There "the tents of Cushan" appear to be identified with "the dwellings of Midian." It is possible that one from "the tents of Cushan" could be referred to as "a Cushite." In that case, the wife of Moses in question is Zipporah, a daughter of the Midianite priest Jethro (Ex 3:1; see note there). The attack on Moses because of his Cushite wife was a pretext; its focus was the prophetic gift of Moses and his special relationship with the Lord (v. 2).

12:2 *Hasn't he also spoken through us?* Of course he had. Mic 6:4 speaks of Moses, Aaron and Miriam as God's gracious provision for Israel. The prophetic gifting of the 70 elders (11:24–30) seems to have been the immediate provocation for the attack of Miriam and Aaron on their brother.

12:3 Perhaps a later addition to the text, alerting the reader to the great unfairness of the charge of arrogance against Moses.

12:5 *came down.* Often used of divine manifestations. In 11:25 the Lord came down in grace; here and in Ge 11:5 he came down in judgment. In a sense every theophany (appearance of God) is a picture and promise of the grand

entrance to the tent and summoned Aaron and Miriam. When the two of them stepped forward, 6 he said, "Listen to my words:

"When there is a prophet among you,
I, the LORD, reveal[j] myself to them in visions,[k]
I speak to them in dreams.[l]
7 But this is not true of my servant Moses;[m]
he is faithful in all my house.[n]
8 With him I speak face to face,
clearly and not in riddles;[o]
he sees the form of the LORD.[p]
Why then were you not afraid
to speak against my servant Moses?"[q]

9 The anger of the LORD burned against them,[r] and he left them.[s]

10 When the cloud lifted from above the tent,[t] Miriam's skin was leprous[a]—it became as white as snow.[u] Aaron turned toward her and saw that she had a defiling skin disease,[v] 11 and he said to Moses, "Please, my lord, I ask you not to hold against us the sin we have so foolishly committed.[w] 12 Do not let her be like a stillborn infant coming from its mother's womb with its flesh half eaten away."

13 So Moses cried out to the LORD, "Please, God, heal her![x]"

14 The LORD replied to Moses, "If her father had spit in her face,[y] would she not have been in disgrace for seven days? Confine her outside the camp[z] for seven days; after that she can be brought back." 15 So Miriam was confined outside the camp[a] for seven days,[b] and the people did not move on till she was brought back.

16 After that, the people left Hazeroth[c] and encamped in the Desert of Paran.[d]

12:6 [j] 1Sa 3:7, 21 [k] S Ge 15:1 [l] S Ge 20:3; S Mt 27:19; Heb 1:1 **12:7** [m] Dt 34:5; Jos 1:1-2; Ps 105:26 [n] Heb 3:2,5 **12:8** [o] Jdg 14:12; 1Ki 10:1; Ps 49:4; Pr 1:6; Da 5:12 [p] Ex 20:4; Job 19:26; Ps 17:15; 140:13; Isa 6:1 [q] Ex 24:2 **12:9** [r] S Ex 4:14 [s] S Ge 17:22 **12:10** [t] Ex 40:2 [u] S Ex 4:6; Dt 24:9 [v] S Lev 13:11; 2Ki 5:1,27; 2Ch 16:12; 21:12-15; 26:19 **12:11** [w] 2Sa 19:19; 24:10 **12:13** [x] Ex 15:26; Ps 6:2; 147:3; Isa 1:6; 30:26; 53:5; Jer 17:14; Hos 6:1 **12:14** [y] Dt 25:9; Job 17:6; 30:9-10; Isa 50:6 [z] S Lev 13:46 **12:15** [a] S Lev 14:8 [b] S Lev 13:4 **12:16** [c] Nu 11:35 [d] Ge 21:21; Nu 10:12; 15:32

13:2 [e] ver 16; Dt 1:22 [f] S Lev 14:34 [g] Jos 1:3 [h] S Lev 24:11 **13:3** [i] Nu 1:16 **13:6** [j] ver 30; Nu 14:6,24; 34:19; Dt 1:36; Jdg 1:12-15

Exploring Canaan

13 The LORD said to Moses, 2 "Send some men to explore[e] the land of Canaan,[f] which I am giving to the Israelites.[g] From each ancestral tribe[h] send one of its leaders."

3 So at the LORD's command Moses sent them out from the Desert of Paran. All of them were leaders of the Israelites.[i] 4 These are their names:

from the tribe of Reuben, Shammua son of Zakkur;
5 from the tribe of Simeon, Shaphat son of Hori;
6 from the tribe of Judah, Caleb son of Jephunneh;[j]
7 from the tribe of Issachar, Igal son of Joseph;
8 from the tribe of Ephraim, Hoshea son of Nun;[k]
9 from the tribe of Benjamin, Palti son of Raphu;
10 from the tribe of Zebulun, Gaddiel son of Sodi;
11 from the tribe of Manasseh (a tribe of Joseph), Gaddi son of Susi;
12 from the tribe of Dan, Ammiel son of Gemalli;
13 from the tribe of Asher, Sethur son of Michael;
14 from the tribe of Naphtali, Nahbi son of Vophsi;
15 from the tribe of Gad, Geuel son of Maki.

16 These are the names of the men Moses sent to explore[l] the land. (Moses gave Hoshea son of Nun[m] the name Joshua.)[n]

[a] *10* The Hebrew for *leprous* was used for various diseases affecting the skin.

13:8 [k] S Nu 11:28 **13:16** [l] S ver 2 [m] ver 8 [n] Dt 32:44

---

theophany, the incarnation of Jesus, both in grace and in judgment.

12:6–8 The poetic cast of these words adds a sense of solemnity to them. The point of the poem is clear: All true prophetic vision is from the Lord, but in the case of Moses his position and faithfulness enhance his special relationship with the Lord.

12:7 *my servant.* See notes on Ex 14:31; Ps 18 title; Isa 41:8–9; 42:1. *my house.* The household of God's people Israel (see notes on Heb 3:5–6).

12:8 *clearly and not in riddles.* God's revelation does not come with equal clarity to his servants. There may be messages of the Lord that a prophet might not fully understand at the time; to him they may be riddles and mysteries (cf. 1Pe 1:10–11). But to Moses God spoke with special clarity, as though "face to face" (see also Dt 34:10 and note).

12:10 *leprous.* See NIV text note. Miriam, the principal offender against her brother Moses, has become an outcast, as she now suffers from a skin disease that would exclude her from the community of Israel (see 5:1–4).

12:14 *disgrace for seven days.* An act of public rebuke (see Dt 25:9) demands a period of public shame. A period of seven days was a standard time for uncleanness occasioned by being in contact with a dead body (see 19:11,14,16).

12:16 *Desert of Paran.* The southernmost region of the promised land (see map, p. 117). The people's opportunity to conquer the land was soon to come.

13:2 *Send some men to explore … Canaan.* The use of spies was a common practice in the ancient Near East (see note on Jos 2:1–24). From Dt 1:22–23 it appears that this directive of the Lord was in response to the people's request.

13:4–15 The names listed here are different from those in chs. 1–2; 7; 10. Presumably the tribal leaders in the four earlier lists were older men. The task for the spies called for men who were younger and more robust, but no less respected by their peers.

13:6 Although Caleb was not a native Israelite since he was a Kenizzite (32:12) and Kenaz was an Edomite (Ge 36:6,9,11), he became associated with the tribe of Judah. See note on 14:24.

13:16 *Moses gave Hoshea son of Nun the name Joshua.* A parenthetical statement anticipating the later prominence of Joshua. The reader is alerted to the significance of this name in the list of the spies; here is a man of destiny.

17 When Moses sent them to explore Canaan,[o] he said, “Go up through the Negev[p]
and on into the hill country.[q] 18 See what
the land is like and whether the people
who live there are strong or weak, few or
many. 19 What kind of land do they live in?
Is it good or bad? What kind of towns do
they live in? Are they unwalled or fortified?
20 How is the soil? Is it fertile or poor? Are
there trees in it or not? Do your best to
bring back some of the fruit of the land.[r]”
(It was the season for the first ripe grapes.)[s]
21 So they went up and explored the land
from the Desert of Zin[t] as far as Rehob,[u]
toward Lebo Hamath.[v] 22 They went up
through the Negev and came to Hebron,[w]
where Ahiman, Sheshai and Talmai,[x] the
descendants of Anak,[y] lived. (Hebron had
been built seven years before Zoan in
Egypt.)[z] 23 When they reached the Valley
of Eshkol,[aa] they cut off a branch bearing
a single cluster of grapes. Two of them
carried it on a pole between them, along
with some pomegranates[b] and figs.[c] 24 That
place was called the Valley of Eshkol because of the cluster of grapes the Israelites
cut off there. 25 At the end of forty days[d]
they returned from exploring the land.[e]

Report on the Exploration

26 They came back to Moses and Aaron
and the whole Israelite community at Kadesh[f] in the Desert of Paran.[g] There they
reported to them[h] and to the whole assembly and showed them the fruit of the
land.[i] 27 They gave Moses this account:
“We went into the land to which you sent
us, and it does flow with milk and honey![j]
Here is its fruit.[k] 28 But the people who live
there are powerful, and the cities are fortified and very large.[l] We even saw descendants of Anak[m] there.[n] 29 The Amalekites[o]
live in the Negev; the Hittites,[p] Jebusites[q]
and Amorites[r] live in the hill country;[s] and
the Canaanites[t] live near the sea and along
the Jordan.[u]”
30 Then Caleb[v] silenced the people before Moses and said, “We should go up
and take possession of the land, for we
can certainly do it.”
31 But the men who had gone up with
him said, “We can’t attack those people;
they are stronger than we are.”[w] 32 And
they spread among the Israelites a bad
report[x] about the land they had explored.
They said, “The land we explored devours[y] those living in it. All the people we
saw there are of great size.[z] 33 We saw the
Nephilim[a] there (the descendants of Anak[b]
come from the Nephilim). We seemed like
grasshoppers[c] in our own eyes, and we
looked the same to them.”

The People Rebel

14 That night all the members of the
community raised their voices
and wept aloud.[d] 2 All the Israelites grumbled[e] against Moses and Aaron, and the

[a] 23 *Eshkol* means *cluster*; also in verse 24.

13:17 [o]ver 2; Jos 14:7 [p]S Ge 12:9 [q]Dt 1:7; Jos 9:1; Jdg 1:9 **13:20** [r]Dt 1:25 [s]S Lev 25:5 **13:21** [t]Nu 20:1; 27:14; 33:36; Dt 32:51; Jos 15:1 [u]Jos 19:28; Jdg 1:31; 18:28; 2Sa 10:6; 1Ch 6:75 [v]Nu 34:8; Jos 13:5; Jdg 3:3; 1Ki 8:65; 2Ki 14:25; 1Ch 13:5; 2Ch 7:8; Jer 52:9; Eze 47:16, 20; Am 6:14 **13:22** [w]S Ge 13:18; S 23:19 [x]Jos 15:14; Jdg 1:10 [y]ver 28; Dt 2:10; 9:2; Jos 11:21; 15:13; Jdg 1:20 [z]Ps 78:12, 43; Isa 19:11, 13; 30:4; Eze 30:14 **13:23** [a]S Ge 14:13 [b]S Ex 28:33 [c]Ge 3:7; Nu 20:5; Dt 8:8; 2Ki 18:31; Ne 13:15 **13:25** [d]S Ge 7:4 [e]Nu 14:34 **13:26** [f]S Ge 14:7 [g]S Ge 14:6 [h]Nu 32:8 [i]Dt 1:25 **13:27** [j]S Ex 3:8 [k]Dt 1:25; Jer 2:7 **13:28** [l]Dt 1:28; 9:1, 2 [m]S ver 22 [n]Jos 14:12 **13:29** [o]S Ge 14:7 [p]S Ge 10:15; Dt 7:1; 20:17; 1Ki 9:20; 10:29; 2Ki 7:6 [q]S Ex 3:8 [r]S Ge 10:16 [s]ver 17 [t]Ge 10:18 [u]S Ge 13:10; Nu 22:1; 32:5; Dt 1:1; Jos 1:2; Jdg 3:28; Ps 42:6 **13:30** [v]S ver 6 **13:31** [w]Dt 9:1; Jos 14:8 **13:32** [x]Nu 14:36, 37 [y]Eze 36:13, 14 [z]Dt 1:28; Am 2:9 **13:33** [a]Ge 6:4 [b]ver 28; Dt 1:28; Jos 11:22; 14:12 [c]Ecc 12:5; Isa 40:22 **14:1** [d]S Ge 27:38; Ex 33:4; Nu 25:6; Dt 1:45; Jdg 20:23, 26; 2Sa 3:32; Job 31:29 **14:2** [e]S Ex 15:24; Heb 3:16

Hoshea means “salvation”; Joshua means “The LORD saves” (see NIV text note on Mt 1:21).

13:17–20 Moses’ instruction to the 12 spies was comprehensive; a thorough report of the land and its produce and the peoples and their towns was required in their reconnaissance mission.

13:21 *explored the land.* The journey of the spies began in the southernmost extremity of the land (the Desert of Zin) and took them to the northernmost point (Rehob, near Lebo Hamath; see 34:8). This journey of about 250 miles each way took them 40 days (v. 25), perhaps a round number.

13:22 *Hebron.* The first city the spies came to in Canaan. The parenthetical comment about the city’s being built seven years before Zoan in Egypt (see note on Ps 78:12,43) may have been prompted by their amazement at the size and fortifications of the city that was so closely associated with the lives of their ancestors four centuries before this time (see Ge 13:14–18; 14:13; 23:2; 25:9; 35:27–29; 50:13). In the stories of the ancestors of their people, Hebron had not been a great city but a dwelling and trading place for shepherds and herdsmen. *descendants of Anak.* The Anakites were people “of great size” (v. 32), who brought fear to the people (v. 33). In a later day of faith, Caleb was to drive them from their city (Jos 15:14; Jdg 1:10).

13:23 *Valley of Eshkol.* See NIV text note. This valley is near Hebron. The size of the grape cluster should have indicated the goodness of the land God was giving them.

13:26–29 The first part of the spies’ report was truthful, but the goodness of the land was offset in their fearful eyes by the powerful peoples who lived there.

13:26 *Kadesh.* See note on Ge 14:7.

13:27 *flow with milk and honey.* See notes on Ex 3:8; Dt 6:3.

13:30 *Caleb silenced the people.* Only Caleb and Joshua gave a report prompted by faith in God.

13:32 *bad report about the land.* The promised land was a good land, a gracious gift from God. By speaking bad things about it, the faithless spies were speaking evil of the Lord (cf. 10:29).

13:33 Their words became exaggerations and distortions. The Anakites were now said to be Nephilim (see note on Ge 6:4). The reference to the Nephilim seems deliberately intended to evoke fear. The exaggeration of the faithless led to their final folly: “We seemed like grasshoppers.”

14:1 *all the members ... wept.* The frightening words of the faithless spies led to mourning by the entire community and to their great rebellion against the Lord. They forgot all the miracles the Lord had done for them; they despised his mercies and spurned his might. In their ingratitude they preferred death (v. 2).

14:2,29 *grumbled.* See Introduction: Contents; see also note on Ex 15:24.

whole assembly said to them, "If only
we had died in Egypt![f] Or in this wilderness![g] 3 Why is the LORD bringing us to this
land only to let us fall by the sword?[h] Our
wives and children[i] will be taken as plunder.[j] Wouldn't it be better for us to go back
to Egypt?[k]" 4 And they said to each other,
"We should choose a leader and go back
to Egypt.[l]"
5 Then Moses and Aaron fell facedown[m]
in front of the whole Israelite assembly[n]
gathered there. 6 Joshua son of Nun[o] and
Caleb son of Jephunneh, who were among
those who had explored the land, tore their
clothes[p] 7 and said to the entire Israelite assembly, "The land we passed through and
explored is exceedingly good.[q] 8 If the LORD
is pleased with us,[r] he will lead us into
that land, a land flowing with milk and
honey,[s] and will give it to us.[t] 9 Only do
not rebel[u] against the LORD. And do not be
afraid[v] of the people of the land,[w] because
we will devour them. Their protection is
gone, but the LORD is with[x] us.[y] Do not be
afraid of them."[z]
10 But the whole assembly talked about
stoning[a] them. Then the glory of the LORD[b]
appeared at the tent of meeting to all the
Israelites. 11 The LORD said to Moses, "How
long will these people treat me with contempt?[c] How long will they refuse to believe in me,[d] in spite of all the signs[e] I have
performed among them? 12 I will strike
them down with a plague[f] and destroy
them, but I will make you into a nation[g]
greater and stronger than they."[h]
13 Moses said to the LORD, "Then the
Egyptians will hear about it! By your
power you brought these people up from
among them.[i] 14 And they will tell the inhabitants of this land about it. They have
already heard[j] that you, LORD, are with
these people[k] and that you, LORD, have
been seen face to face,[l] that your cloud
stays over them,[m] and that you go before
them in a pillar of cloud by day and a pillar of fire by night.[n] 15 If you put all these
people to death, leaving none alive, the
nations who have heard this report about
you will say, 16 'The LORD was not able to
bring these people into the land he promised them on oath,[o] so he slaughtered
them in the wilderness.'[p]
17 "Now may the Lord's strength be displayed, just as you have declared: 18 'The
LORD is slow to anger, abounding in love
and forgiving sin and rebellion.[q] Yet he
does not leave the guilty unpunished;
he punishes the children for the sin of
the parents to the third and fourth generation.'[r] 19 In accordance with your great
love, forgive[s] the sin of these people,[t] just
as you have pardoned them from the time
they left Egypt until now."[u]
20 The LORD replied, "I have forgiven
them,[v] as you asked. 21 Nevertheless, as
surely as I live[w] and as surely as the glory
of the LORD[x] fills the whole earth,[y] 22 not
one of those who saw my glory and the
signs[z] I performed in Egypt and in the wilderness but who disobeyed me and tested
me ten times[a]— 23 not one of them will
ever see the land I promised on oath[b] to
their ancestors. No one who has treated
me with contempt[c] will ever see it.[d] 24 But
because my servant Caleb[e] has a different spirit and follows me wholeheartedly,[f] I will bring him into the land he went
to, and his descendants will inherit it.[g]
25 Since the Amalekites[h] and the Canaanites[i] are living in the valleys, turn[j] back

14:2 [f] S Ex 16:3 [g] S Nu 11:1; 16:13; 20:4; 21:5 **14:3** [h] S Ex 5:21 [i] ver 31 [j] S Ge 34:29; Dt 1:39; Ps 109:11; Isa 33:4; Eze 7:21; 25:7; 26:5 [k] Ac 7:39 **14:4** [l] Ne 9:17 **14:5** [m] S Lev 9:24; Nu 16:4, 22, 45; 20:6; Jos 5:14; 2Sa 14:4; 1Ch 21:16; Eze 1:28 [n] S Lev 19:2 **14:6** [o] Nu 11:28 [p] S Ge 37:29, 34; Jdg 11:35; 2Sa 13:31; 2Ki 19:1; Ezr 9:3; Est 4:1; S Mk 14:63 **14:7** [q] Nu 13:27; Dt 1:25 **14:8** [r] Dt 7:8; 10:15; Ps 18:19; 22:8; 37:23; 41:11; 56:9; 147:11; Pr 11:20; Isa 62:4; Mal 2:17 [s] Nu 13:27 [t] Dt 1:21 **14:9** [u] Dt 1:26; 9:7, 23, 24 [v] Ge 26:24; 2Ch 32:7; Ps 118:6; Jer 41:18; 42:11 [w] Dt 1:21; 7:18; 20:1 [x] Hag 2:4 [y] S Ge 21:22; Dt 1:30; 2Ch 13:12; Jer 15:20; 46:28; Hag 1:13 [z] ver 24 **14:10** [a] S Ex 17:4 [b] S Ex 24:16 **14:11** [c] Ex 23:21; Nu 15:31; 16:30; 1Sa 2:17; Eze 31:14; Mal 1:13 [d] Dt 1:32; Ps 78:22; 106:24; Jn 3:15 [e] S Ex 3:20; S 4:17; S 10:1

14:12 [f] S Ex 5:3; S 30:12 [g] S Ex 32:10 [h] Dt 9:14; 29:20; 32:26; Ps 109:13 **14:13** [i] Ex 32:11-14; Ps 106:23 **14:14** [j] Ex 15:14 [k] Nu 5:3; 16:3; Jos 2:9 [l] Dt 5:4; 34:10 [m] S Ex 33:16 [n] S Ex 13:21 **14:16** [o] Nu 11:12 [p] Ex 32:12; Jos 7:7 **14:18** [q] S Ex 20:6; 34:6; Ps 145:8; Jnh 4:2; Jas 5:11 [r] Ex 20:5 **14:19** [s] S Ex 34:9; 1Ki 8:34; Ps 85:2; 103:3 [t] Ps 106:45 [u] Ps 78:38 **14:20** [v] Ex 34:6; Ps 99:8; 106:23; Mic 7:18-20 **14:21** [w] ver 28; Dt 32:40; Jdg 8:19; Ru 3:13; 1Sa 14:39; 19:6; Isa 49:18; Jer 4:2; Eze 5:11; Zep 2:9 [x] Lev 9:6 [y] Ps 72:19; Isa 6:3; 40:5; Hab 2:14 **14:22** [z] ver 11 [a] S Ex 14:11; 17:7; 32:1; Ps 81:7; 1Co 10:5 **14:23** [b] ver 16; S Ex 33:1; Nu 32:11; Dt 1:34; Ps 95:11; 106:26 [c] ver 11 [d] Heb 3:18 **14:24** [e] Nu 13:6 [f] ver 6-9; Dt 1:36; Jos 14:8, 14 [g] Nu 26:65; 32:12; Ps 25:13; 37:9, 11 **14:25** [h] S Ge 14:7 [i] S Ge 10:18 [j] Dt 1:40

14:3 *children.* The most reprehensible charge against God's grace was that concerning their children. Only their children would survive (see vv. 31 – 33).

14:8 *flowing with milk and honey.* See notes on Ex 3:8; Dt 6:3.

14:9 *the LORD is with us.* There are no walls, no fortifications, no factors of size or bearing, and certainly no gods that can withstand the onslaught of God's people when the Lord is with them.

14:10 *glory of the LORD appeared.* This manifestation of God must have been staggering in its sudden and intense display of his majesty and wrath (see vv. 21 – 22; see also note on Ex 16:7).

14:11 *treat me with contempt.* By refusing to believe in the Lord's power, especially in view of all the wonders they had experienced, the people of Israel were holding him in contempt.

14:12 *I will make you into a nation.* For the second time since the exodus, God speaks of starting over with Moses in creating a people faithful to himself (see Ex 32:10).

14:13 *Egyptians will hear about it!* Moses desires to protect the Lord's reputation. The enemies of God's people will charge the Lord with inability to complete his deliverance and will be contemptuous of his power.

14:17 – 19 Moses now moves from the Lord's reputation to his character, presenting a composite quotation of his own words of loyal love for and faithful discipline of his people (see Ex 20:6; 34:6 – 7 and notes).

14:22 *ten times.* Perhaps to be enumerated as follows: (1) Ex 14:10 – 12; (2) Ex 15:22 – 24; (3) Ex 16:1 – 3; (4) Ex 16:19 – 20; (5) Ex 16:27 – 30; (6) Ex 17:1 – 4; (7) Ex 32:1 – 35; (8) Nu 11:1 – 3; (9) 11:4 – 34; (10) 14:3. But "ten times" may also be a way of saying "many times."

14:24 *Caleb … follows me wholeheartedly.* Caleb may be singled out — even from Joshua — because although he was not a native Israelite (see note on 13:6), he was faithful to the Lord. His ultimate vindication came 45 years later (see note on 13:22; see also Jos 14:10 and note on 14:6).

tomorrow and set out toward the desert
along the route to the Red Sea.[a][k]"
26 The LORD said to Moses and Aaron:
27 "How long will this wicked community grumble against me? I have heard the
complaints of these grumbling Israelites.[l]
28 So tell them, 'As surely as I live,[m] declares
the LORD, I will do to you[n] the very thing
I heard you say: 29 In this wilderness your
bodies will fall[o]—every one of you twenty years old or more[p] who was counted in
the census[q] and who has grumbled against
me. 30 Not one of you will enter the land[r]
I swore with uplifted hand[s] to make your
home, except Caleb son of Jephunneh[t] and
Joshua son of Nun.[u] 31 As for your children
that you said would be taken as plunder,
I will bring them in to enjoy the land you
have rejected.[v] 32 But as for you, your bodies will fall[w] in this wilderness. 33 Your
children will be shepherds here for forty
years,[x] suffering for your unfaithfulness,
until the last of your bodies lies in the wilderness. 34 For forty years[y]—one year for
each of the forty days you explored the
land[z]—you will suffer for your sins and
know what it is like to have me against
you.' 35 I, the LORD, have spoken, and I will
surely do these things[a] to this whole wicked community, which has banded together
against me. They will meet their end in this
wilderness; here they will die.[b]"
36 So the men Moses had sent[c] to explore the land, who returned and made
the whole community grumble[d] against
him by spreading a bad report[e] about it—
37 these men who were responsible for
spreading the bad report[f] about the land
were struck down and died of a plague[g]
before the LORD. 38 Of the men who went to
explore the land,[h] only Joshua son of Nun
and Caleb son of Jephunneh survived.[i]

14:25 [k]Ex 23:31; Nu 21:4; 1Ki 9:26 **14:27** [l]Ex 16:12; Dt 1:34,35 **14:28** [m]S ver 21 [n]Nu 33:56 **14:29** [o]ver 23,30, 32; Nu 26:65; 32:13; 1Co 10:5; Heb 3:17; Jude 1:5 [p]S Nu 1:45 [q]S Ex 30:12 **14:30** [r]S ver 29 [s]Ex 6:8; Dt 32:40; Ne 9:15; Ps 106:26; Eze 20:5; 36:7 [t]Nu 13:6 [u]Nu 11:28 **14:31** [v]S Lev 26:43 **14:32** [w]S ver 29,35 **14:33** [x]ver 34; S Ex 16:35; Ac 13:18; Heb 3:9 **14:34** [y]S ver 33 [z]Nu 13:25 **14:35** [a]Nu 23:19 [b]S ver 32 **14:36** [c]Nu 13:4-16 [d]ver 2 [e]S Nu 13:32 **14:37** [f]S Nu 13:32; 1Co 10:10; Heb 3:17 [g]Nu 16:49; 5:9; 26:1; 31:16; Dt 4:3 **14:38** [h]ver 30; Nu 13:4-16 [i]ver 24; Jos 14:6 **14:39** [j]ver 28-35 [k]S Ex 33:4 **14:40** [l]ver 45; Nu 13:17 [m]S Ex 9:27

39 When Moses reported this[j] to all the
Israelites, they mourned[k] bitterly. 40 Early
the next morning they set out for the highest point in the hill country,[l] saying, "Now
we are ready to go up to the land the LORD
promised. Surely we have sinned![m]"
41 But Moses said, "Why are you disobeying the LORD's command? This will
not succeed![n] 42 Do not go up, because the
LORD is not with you. You will be defeated by your enemies,[o] 43 for the Amalekites[p]
and the Canaanites[q] will face you there.
Because you have turned away from the
LORD, he will not be with you[r] and you will
fall by the sword."
44 Nevertheless, in their presumption
they went up[s] toward the highest point in
the hill country, though neither Moses nor
the ark of the LORD's covenant moved from
the camp.[t] 45 Then the Amalekites and the
Canaanites[u] who lived in that hill country[v]
came down and attacked them and beat
them down all the way to Hormah.[w]

Supplementary Offerings

15 The LORD said to Moses, 2 "Speak to
the Israelites and say to them: 'After you enter the land I am giving you[x] as
a home 3 and you present to the LORD food
offerings from the herd or the flock,[y] as
an aroma pleasing to the LORD[z]—whether burnt offerings[a] or sacrifices, for special vows or freewill offerings[b] or festival
offerings[c]— 4 then the person who brings
an offering shall present to the LORD a

[a] 25 *Or the Sea of Reeds*

14:41 [n]2Ch 24:20 **14:42** [o]Dt 1:42 **14:43** [p]Jdg 3:13 [q]ver 45; Nu 13:29 [r]S Ge 39:23; Dt 31:8; Jos 6:27; Jdg 1:19; 6:16; 1Sa 3:19; 18:14; 2Ch 1:1 **14:44** [s]Dt 1:43 [t]Nu 31:6 **14:45** [u]S ver 43 [v]S ver 40 [w]Nu 21:3; Dt 1:44; Jos 12:14; 15:30; 19:4; Jdg 1:17; 1Sa 30:30; 1Ch 4:30 **15:2** [x]S Lev 23:10 **15:3** [y]S Lev 1:2 [z]ver 24; S Lev 1:9 [a]Lev 1:3; Nu 28:13 [b]S Lev 7:16; S Ezr 1:4 [c]Lev 23:1-44

14:28 *I will do to you the very thing I heard you say.* The people of Israel brought upon themselves their punishment. They had said that they would rather die in the wilderness (v. 2) than be led into Canaan to die by the sword. All those 20 years old or more, who were counted in the census, were to die in the wilderness (v. 29). The only exceptions would be Joshua and Caleb (v. 30). Only the people's children would survive (v. 31)—the very children they had said God would allow to die in the wilderness (v. 3).

14:32 See Heb 3:17.

14:34 The 40 days of the travels of the spies became the numerical pattern for their suffering: one year for one day—for 40 years they would be reminded of their misjudgment, and for 40 years the people 20 years old or more would be dying, so that only the young generation might enter the land. Significantly, Israel's refusal to carry out the Lord's commission to conquer his land is the climactic act of rebellion for which God condemns Israel to die in the wilderness.

14:37 *these men who were responsible for spreading the bad report ... were struck down.* The judgment on the ten evil spies was immediate; the generation that they influenced would live out their lives in the wilderness.

14:40 *Now we are ready to go up.* Now, too late, the people determine to go up to the land. Such a course of action was doomed to failure. Not only was the Lord not with them; he was against them (v. 41). Their subsequent defeat (v. 45) was another judgment the rebellious people brought down on their own heads (see note on Ob 15).

15:1–41 This chapter is divided into three units, each introduced by the phrase, "The LORD said to Moses" (vv. 1,17,37). The people were under terrible judgment because they had disobeyed the specific commands of the Lord and had despised his character.

15:2 *After you enter the land.* The juxtaposition of this clause with the sad ending of ch. 14 is dramatic. The sins of the people were manifold; they would be judged. The grace and mercy of the Lord are magnified as he points to the ultimate realization of his ancient promise to Abraham (Ge 12:7), as well as to his continuing promise to the nation that they would indeed enter the land.

15:3–12 Grain and wine offerings were to accompany the food offerings; the grain was to be mixed with oil. The offerings increased in amounts with the increase in size of the sacrificial animal (vv. 6–12).

grain offering[d] of a tenth of an ephah[a] of the finest flour[e] mixed with a quarter of a hin[b] of olive oil. 5 With each lamb[f] for the burnt offering or the sacrifice, prepare a quarter of a hin of wine[g] as a drink offering.[h]

6 " 'With a ram[i] prepare a grain offering[j] of two-tenths of an ephah[c][k] of the finest flour mixed with a third of a hin[d] of olive oil,[l] 7 and a third of a hin of wine[m] as a drink offering.[n] Offer it as an aroma pleasing to the LORD.[o]

8 " 'When you prepare a young bull[p] as a burnt offering or sacrifice, for a special vow[q] or a fellowship offering[r] to the LORD, 9 bring with the bull a grain offering[s] of three-tenths of an ephah[e][t] of the finest flour mixed with half a hin[f] of olive oil, 10 and also bring half a hin of wine[u] as a drink offering.[v] This will be a food offering, an aroma pleasing to the LORD.[w] 11 Each bull or ram, each lamb or young goat, is to be prepared in this manner. 12 Do this for each one, for as many as you prepare.[x]

13 " 'Everyone who is native-born[y] must do these things in this way when they present a food offering as an aroma pleasing to the LORD.[z] 14 For the generations to come,[a] whenever a foreigner[b] or anyone else living among you presents a food[c] offering[d] as an aroma pleasing to the LORD, they must do exactly as you do. 15 The community is to have the same rules for you and for the foreigner residing among you; this is a lasting ordinance for the generations to come.[e] You and the foreigner shall be the same before the LORD: 16 The same laws and regulations will apply both to you and to the foreigner residing among you.[f] "

17 The LORD said to Moses, 18 "Speak to the Israelites and say to them: 'When you enter the land to which I am taking you[g] 19 and you eat the food of the land,[h] present a portion as an offering to the LORD.[i] 20 Present a loaf from the first of your ground meal[j] and present it as an offering from the threshing floor.[k] 21 Throughout the generations to come[l] you are to give this offering to the LORD from the first of your ground meal.[m]

15:4 [d] S Lev 6:14 [e] S Ex 16:36 **15:5** [f] S Lev 3:7 [g] S Lev 10:9 [h] S Ge 35:14 **15:6** [i] S Lev 5:15 [j] Nu 28:12; 29:14 [k] S Lev 23:13 [l] Eze 46:14 **15:7** [m] ver 5 [n] Lev 23:13; Nu 28:14; 29:18 [o] S Lev 1:9 **15:8** [p] S Ex 12:5; S Lev 1:5 [q] S Lev 22:18 [r] S Lev 3:6 **15:9** [s] Lev 2:1 [t] S Lev 14:10 **15:10** [u] Nu 28:14 [v] Lev 23:13 [w] Lev 1:9 **15:12** [x] Ezr 7:17 **15:13** [y] S Lev 16:29 [z] Lev 1:9 **15:14** [a] Lev 3:17; Nu 10:8 [b] S Ex 12:19,43; S 22:21 [c] ver 25 [d] S Lev 22:18 **15:15** [e] ver 14, 21 **15:16** [f] Ex 12:49; S Lev 22:18; Nu 9:14 **15:18** [g] S Lev 23:10 **15:19** [h] Jos 5:11, 12 [i] Nu 18:8 **15:20** [j] S Lev 23:14 [k] S Ge 50:10; S Lev 2:14; S Nu 18:27 **15:21** [l] S Lev 23:14 [m] Eze 44:30; Ro 11:16

15:22 [n] S Lev 4:2 **15:23** [o] ver 21 **15:24** [p] ver 25, 26 [q] S Lev 5:15 [r] Lev 4:14 [s] S ver 3 [t] Lev 2:1 [u] Lev 23:13; Nu 6:15 [v] Lev 4:3 **15:25** [w] Lev 4:20; S Ro 3:25 [x] ver 22, S 24 [y] ver 14 [z] Lev 4:3 **15:26** [a] S ver 24 **15:27** [b] Lev 4:27 [c] Lev 4:3; Nu 6:14 **15:28** [d] Nu 8:12; 28:22 [e] Lev 4:20

Offerings for Unintentional Sins

22 " 'Now if you as a community unintentionally fail to keep any of these commands the LORD gave Moses[n]— 23 any of the LORD's commands to you through him, from the day the LORD gave them and continuing through the generations to come[o]— 24 and if this is done unintentionally[p] without the community being aware of it,[q] then the whole community is to offer a young bull for a burnt offering[r] as an aroma pleasing to the LORD,[s] along with its prescribed grain offering[t] and drink offering,[u] and a male goat for a sin offering.[g][v] 25 The priest is to make atonement for the whole Israelite community, and they will be forgiven,[w] for it was not intentional[x] and they have presented to the LORD for their wrong a food offering[y] and a sin offering.[z] 26 The whole Israelite community and the foreigners residing among them will be forgiven, because all the people were involved in the unintentional wrong.[a]

27 " 'But if just one person sins unintentionally,[b] that person must bring a year-old female goat for a sin offering.[c] 28 The priest is to make atonement[d] before the LORD for the one who erred by sinning unintentionally, and when atonement has been made, that person will be forgiven.[e] 29 One and the same law applies to everyone who sins unintentionally, whether a native-born Israelite or a foreigner residing among you.[f]

30 " 'But anyone who sins defiantly,[g] whether native-born or foreigner,[h] blasphemes the LORD[i] and must be cut off from the people of Israel.[j] 31 Because they have despised[k] the LORD's word and broken his commands,[l] they must surely be cut off; their guilt remains on them.[m] ' "

[a] *4* That is, probably about 3 1/2 pounds or about 1.6 kilograms [b] *4* That is, about 1 quart or about 1 liter; also in verse 5 [c] *6* That is, probably about 7 pounds or about 3.2 kilograms [d] *6* That is, about 1 1/3 quarts or about 1.3 liters; also in verse 7 [e] *9* That is, probably about 11 pounds or about 5 kilograms [f] *9* That is, about 2 quarts or about 1.9 liters; also in verse 10 [g] *24* Or *purification offering*; also in verses 25 and 27

15:29 [f] S Ex 12:49 **15:30** [g] Nu 14:40-44; Dt 1:43; 17:13; Ps 19:13 [h] ver 14 [i] 2Ki 19:6, 20; Isa 37:6, 23; Eze 20:27 [j] S Ge 17:14; S Job 31:22 **15:31** [k] S Nu 14:11 [l] 1Sa 15:23, 26; 2Sa 11:27; 12:9; Ps 119:126; Pr 13:13 [m] S Lev 5:1; Eze 18:20

15:14 *foreigner.* As in the case of the celebration of the Passover (see note on 9:14), the foreigner had the same regulations as the native-born Israelite. The commonwealth of Israel would always be open to proselytes. Indeed, God's promise to Abraham embraces "all peoples on earth" (see Ge 12:2–3 and note).

15:20 *Present a loaf from the first.* This law also looks forward to the time when the Israelites would be in the land. The first of the threshed grain was to be made into a loaf and presented to the Lord. This concept of the firstfruits is a symbol that all blessing is from the Lord and all produce belongs to him.

15:22 *unintentionally fail.* Sins may be unintentional, but they still need to be dealt with (see note on Lev 4:2). Such unintentional sins may be committed by the people as a whole (vv. 22–26) or by an individual (vv. 27–29).

15:30 *defiantly.* Lit. "with a high hand." Unlike unintentional sins, for which there are provisions of God's mercy, one who sets his hand defiantly to despise the word of God and to blaspheme his name must be punished. This was the experience of the nation in ch. 14, and it is described in the case of an individual here in vv. 32–36. *cut off from the people.* See note on Ex 12:15.

The Sabbath-Breaker Put to Death

32While the Israelites were in the wilderness,[n] a man was found gathering
wood on the Sabbath day.[o] 33Those who
found him gathering wood brought him to
Moses and Aaron and the whole assembly,
34and they kept him in custody, because
it was not clear what should be done to
him.[p] 35Then the LORD said to Moses, "The
man must die.[q] The whole assembly must
stone him outside the camp.[r]" 36So the
assembly took him outside the camp and
stoned him[s] to death,[t] as the LORD commanded Moses.[u]

Tassels on Garments

37The LORD said to Moses, 38"Speak to
the Israelites and say to them: 'Throughout the generations to come[v] you are to
make tassels on the corners of your garments,[w] with a blue cord on each tassel.
39You will have these tassels to look at and
so you will remember[x] all the commands
of the LORD, that you may obey them and
not prostitute yourselves[y] by chasing after the lusts of your own hearts[z] and eyes.
40Then you will remember to obey all my
commands[a] and will be consecrated to
your God.[b] 41I am the LORD your God, who
brought you out of Egypt to be your God.[c]
I am the LORD your God.[d]'"

Korah, Dathan and Abiram

16 Korah[e] son of Izhar, the son of Kohath, the son of Levi, and certain
Reubenites—Dathan and Abiram[f], sons
of Eliab,[g] and On son of Peleth—became
insolent[a] 2and rose up against Moses.[h]
With them were 250 Israelite men, well-
known community leaders who had been
appointed members of the council.[i] 3They
came as a group to oppose Moses and Aaron[j] and said to them, "You have gone too
far! The whole community is holy,[k] every
one of them, and the LORD is with them.[l]
Why then do you set yourselves above the
LORD's assembly?"[m]
4When Moses heard this, he fell facedown.[n] 5Then he said to Korah and all his
followers: "In the morning the LORD will
show who belongs to him and who is
holy,[o] and he will have that person come
near him.[p] The man he chooses[q] he will
cause to come near him. 6You, Korah, and
all your followers[r] are to do this: Take censers[s] 7and tomorrow put burning coals[t] and
incense[u] in them before the LORD. The man
the LORD chooses[v] will be the one who is
holy.[w] You Levites have gone too far!"
8Moses also said to Korah, "Now listen,
you Levites! 9Isn't it enough[x] for you that
the God of Israel has separated you from
the rest of the Israelite community and
brought you near himself to do the work
at the LORD's tabernacle and to stand before the community and minister to them?[y]
10He has brought you and all your fellow
Levites near himself, but now you are trying to get the priesthood too.[z] 11It is against
the LORD that you and all your followers
have banded together. Who is Aaron that
you should grumble[a] against him?[b]"
12Then Moses summoned Dathan and
Abiram,[c] the sons of Eliab. But they said,
"We will not come![d] 13Isn't it enough that
you have brought us up out of a land flowing with milk and honey[e] to kill us in the
wilderness?[f] And now you also want to
lord it over us![g] 14Moreover, you haven't
brought us into a land flowing with milk
and honey[h] or given us an inheritance of

[a] 1 Or *Peleth—took men*

15:32 [n] S Nu 12:16 [o] Ex 31:14, 15; 35:2, 3 **15:34** [p] Nu 9:8 **15:35** [q] Ex 31:14, 15 [r] S Lev 20:2; Lk 4:29; Ac 7:58 **15:36** [s] S Lev 20:2 [t] S Ex 31:14 [u] Jer 17:21 **15:38** [v] Lev 3:17; Nu 10:8 [w] Dt 22:12; Mt 23:5 **15:39** [x] Dt 4:23; 6:12; Ps 73:27 [y] S Lev 17:7; Jdg 2:17; Ps 106:39; Jer 3:2; Hos 4:12 [z] Ps 78:37; Jer 7:24; Eze 20:16 **15:40** [a] S Ge 26:5; Dt 11:13; Ps 103:18; 119:56 [b] S Lev 11:44; Ro 12:1; Col 1:22; 1Pe 1:15 **15:41** [c] S Ge 17:7 [d] S Ex 20:2 **16:1** [e] S Ex 6:24; Jude 1:11 [f] ver 24; Ps 106:17 [g] Nu 26:8; Dt 11:6 **16:2** [h] Nu 27:3 [i] Nu 1:16; 26:9 **16:3** [j] ver 7; Ps 106:16 [k] Ex 19:6 [l] S Nu 14:14 [m] Nu 12:2 **16:4** [n] Nu 14:5 **16:5** [o] S Lev 10:3; 2Ti 2:19* [p] Jer 30:21 [q] Nu 17:5; Ps 65:4; 105:26; Jer 50:44 **16:6** [r] ver 7, 16 [s] S Lev 10:1; Rev 8:3 **16:7** [t] S Lev 10:1 [u] S Ex 30:9 [v] S ver 6 [w] ver 5 **16:9** [x] S Ge 30:15 [y] Nu 3:6; Dt 10:8; 17:12; 21:5; 1Sa 2:11; Ps 134:1; Eze 44:11 **16:10** [z] Nu 3:10; 18:7; Jdg 17:5, 12 **16:11** [a] ver 41; 1Co 10:10 [b] S Ex 16:7 **16:12** [c] S ver 1, 27 [d] ver 14 **16:13** [e] Nu 13:27 [f] Nu 14:2 [g] S Ge 13:8; Ac 7:27, 35 **16:14** [h] S Lev 20:24

15:32 *gathering wood on the Sabbath day.* The penalty for breaking the Sabbath was death (v. 36; Ex 31:15; 35:2). As in the case of the willful blasphemer (Lev 24:10–16), the Sabbath-breaker was guilty of high-handed rebellion (see note on v. 30) and was judged with death. Centuries later, Jesus would criticize those who regarded legalistic Sabbath regulations as more important than the needs of people. He confronted the Pharisees on this issue on several occasions (see, e.g., Mt 12:1–14). From their point of view, these regulations (vv. 32–36) gave them reasons to seek his death (Mt 12:14).

15:38 *tassels on the corners of your garments.* As one would walk along, the tassels would swirl about at the edge of one's garment (cf. v. 39), serving as excellent memory prods to obey God's commands (cf. Dt 6:4–9 and notes).

15:39 *prostitute yourselves.* See Ex 34:15 and note.

15:41 *I am the LORD your God, who brought you out.* The demands that God made upon his people were grounded in his act of redemption (see Ex 20:2 and note).

16:1–7 Earlier, Miriam and Aaron had led a rebellion against the leadership of Moses (ch. 12). Now Korah and his allies attack the leadership of Moses and Aaron. Korah was descended from Levi through Kohath. As a Kohathite, he had important duties in the service of the Lord at the tabernacle (see 4:1–20), but he desired more. Korah was joined by the Reubenites—Dathan, Abiram and On—and about 250 other leaders of Israel who had their own complaints. Their charge was that Moses had "gone too far" (v. 3) in taking the role of spiritual leadership of the people; the "whole community is holy" (v. 3; see notes on Ex 7:5; 19:6). To this abusive charge Moses retorts, "You Levites have gone too far!" (v. 7), and sets up a trial by fire.

16:6 *censers.* See note on Lev 10:1.

16:12 *Dathan and Abiram.* Their charge against Moses was that he had not led them into the land of promise. They claimed that Moses had in fact led the people "out of a land flowing with milk and honey" (v. 13). By this strange alchemy, in their minds the land of Egypt has been transformed from prison to paradise.

16:13–14 *flowing with milk and honey.* See notes on Ex 3:8; Dt 6:3.

fields and vineyards.[i] Do you want to treat
these men like slaves[a]?[j] No, we will not
come![k]"
15 Then Moses became very angry[l] and
said to the LORD, "Do not accept their offering. I have not taken so much as a donkey[m] from them, nor have I wronged any
of them."
16 Moses said to Korah, "You and all
your followers are to appear before the
LORD tomorrow — you and they and Aaron.[n] 17 Each man is to take his censer and
put incense in it — 250 censers in all — and
present it before the LORD. You and Aaron are to present your censers also.[o]" 18 So
each of them took his censer,[p] put burning
coals and incense in it, and stood with Moses and Aaron at the entrance to the tent
of meeting. 19 When Korah had gathered all
his followers in opposition to them[q] at the
entrance to the tent of meeting, the glory
of the LORD[r] appeared to the entire assembly. 20 The LORD said to Moses and Aaron,
21 "Separate yourselves[s] from this assembly
so I can put an end to them at once."[t]
22 But Moses and Aaron fell facedown[u]
and cried out, "O God, the God who gives
breath to all living things,[v] will you be angry with the entire assembly[w] when only
one man sins?"[x]
23 Then the LORD said to Moses, 24 "Say
to the assembly, 'Move away from the
tents of Korah, Dathan and Abiram.' "
25 Moses got up and went to Dathan and
Abiram, and the elders of Israel[y] followed
him. 26 He warned the assembly, "Move
back from the tents of these wicked men![z]
Do not touch anything belonging to them,
or you will be swept away[a] because of all
their sins.[b]" 27 So they moved away from
the tents of Korah, Dathan and Abiram.[c]
Dathan and Abiram had come out and
were standing with their wives, children[d]
and little ones at the entrances to their
tents.[e]
28 Then Moses said, "This is how you
will know[f] that the LORD has sent me[g] to
do all these things and that it was not my
idea: 29 If these men die a natural death
and suffer the fate of all mankind, then
the LORD has not sent me.[h] 30 But if the
LORD brings about something totally new,
and the earth opens its mouth[i] and swallows them, with everything that belongs
to them, and they go down alive into the
realm of the dead,[j] then you will know
that these men have treated the LORD with
contempt.[k]"
31 As soon as he finished saying all this,
the ground under them split apart[l] 32 and
the earth opened its mouth and swallowed
them[m] and their households, and all those
associated with Korah, together with their
possessions. 33 They went down alive into
the realm of the dead,[n] with everything
they owned; the earth closed over them,
and they perished and were gone from the
community. 34 At their cries, all the Israelites around them fled, shouting, "The
earth is going to swallow us too!"
35 And fire came out from the LORD[o] and
consumed[p] the 250 men who were offering
the incense.
36 The LORD said to Moses, 37 "Tell Eleazar[q] son of Aaron, the priest, to remove
the censers[r] from the charred remains and
scatter the coals some distance away, for
the censers are holy — 38 the censers of the
men who sinned at the cost of their lives.[s]
Hammer the censers into sheets to overlay
the altar,[t] for they were presented before
the LORD and have become holy. Let them
be a sign[u] to the Israelites."
39 So Eleazar the priest[v] collected the
bronze censers brought by those who
had been burned to death,[w] and he had
them hammered out to overlay the altar,

16:14 [i] Ex 22:5; 23:11; Nu 20:5; 1Ki 4:25; Ne 13:15; Ps 105:33; Jer 5:17; Hos 2:12; Joel 2:22; Hag 2:19; Zec 3:10 [j] Jdg 16:21; 1Sa 11:2; Jer 39:7 [k] ver 12 **16:15** [l] S Ex 4:14 [m] 1Sa 12:3 **16:16** [n] S ver 6 **16:17** [o] Eze 8:11 **16:18** [p] Lev 10:1 **16:19** [q] ver 42; Nu 20:2 [r] S Ex 16:7; Nu 14:10; 20:6 **16:21** [s] ver 24 [t] S Ge 19:14; S Ex 32:10 **16:22** [u] S Nu 14:5 [v] Nu 27:16; Job 12:10; 27:8; 33:4; 34:14; Jer 32:27; Eze 18:4; Heb 12:9 [w] S Lev 10:6 [x] S Ge 18:23; S Job 21:20 **16:25** [y] S Ex 19:7 **16:26** [z] Isa 52:11 [a] S Ge 19:15 [b] Jer 51:6 **16:27** [c] S ver 12 [d] ver 32; Jos 7:24; Isa 13:16; 14:21 [e] S Ex 33:8 **16:28** [f] 1Ki 18:36 [g] Ex 3:12; Jn 5:36; 6:38 **16:29** [h] Nu 24:13; Job 31:2; Ecc 3:19 **16:30** [i] Ps 141:7; Isa 5:14 [j] ver 33; S Ge 37:35; 1Sa 2:6; Job 5:26; 21:13; Ps 9:17; 16:10; 55:15; Isa 14:11; 38:18 [k] S Nu 14:11; S Eze 26:20

[a] 14 Or *to deceive these men*; Hebrew *Will you gouge out the eyes of these men*

16:31 [l] Isa 64:1-2; Eze 47:1-12; Mic 1:3-4; Zec 14:4 **16:32** [m] S Ex 15:12 **16:33** [n] S ver 30; S Ecc 9:10 **16:35** [o] S Nu 11:1-3; 26:10; Rev 11:5 [p] S Lev 10:2 **16:37** [q] S Ex 6:23 [r] ver 6 **16:38** [s] Lev 10:1; Pr 20:2 [t] S Ex 20:24; 38:1-7 [u] Nu 26:10; Dt 28:46; Jer 44:29; Eze 14:8; 2Pe 2:6 **16:39** [v] 2Ch 26:18 [w] S Lev 20:14

16:15 *nor have I wronged any of them.* Moses' humanity is seen in his plea of innocence.

16:18–21 The trial was to be by fire: Which men would the Lord accept as his priests in the holy tabernacle? The 250 men allied with Korah came with arrogance to withstand Moses and Aaron at the entrance to the tent of meeting. The revelation of the Lord's glory was sure and sudden (v. 19), with words of impending doom for the rebellious people (v. 21). The punishment was fittingly ironic. Those 250 men who dared to present themselves as priests before the Lord with fire in their censers were themselves put to death by fire (perhaps lightning) from the Lord (see v. 35).

16:19,42 *glory of the LORD.* See note on Ex 16:7.

16:24 *Move away.* God's judgment was going to be severe, but he did not want to lash out against bystanders. It appears that Korah himself had left the 250 false priests and was standing with Dathan and Abiram to continue their opposition to Moses.

16:30 *something totally new.* Moses wished to assure the people that the imminent judgment was the direct work of the Lord and not a chance event. The opening of the earth to swallow the rebels was a sure sign of the wrath of God and the vindication of Moses and Aaron. *realm of the dead.* See v. 33; see also note on Ge 37:35.

16:32 *swallowed them and their households.* The sons of Korah did not die (26:11); apparently they did not join their father in his rash plan. The households of the other rebels died with them.

16:37 *remove the censers.* The true priests took the censers of the 250 deceased impostors from their charred remains and hammered them into bronze sheets for the altar as a reminder of the folly of a self-proclaimed priest (v. 40).

40 as the LORD directed him through Moses.
This was to remind the Israelites that no
one except a descendant of Aaron should
come to burn incense[x] before the LORD,[y]
or he would become like Korah and his
followers.[z]
41 The next day the whole Israelite community grumbled against Moses and Aaron. "You have killed the LORD's people,"
they said.
42 But when the assembly gathered in opposition[a] to Moses and Aaron and turned
toward the tent of meeting, suddenly the
cloud covered it and the glory of the LORD[b]
appeared. 43 Then Moses and Aaron went
to the front of the tent of meeting, 44 and
the LORD said to Moses, 45 "Get away from
this assembly so I can put an end[c] to them
at once." And they fell facedown.
46 Then Moses said to Aaron, "Take your
censer[d] and put incense in it, along with
burning coals from the altar, and hurry to the assembly[e] to make atonement[f]
for them. Wrath has come out from the
LORD;[g] the plague[h] has started." 47 So Aaron
did as Moses said, and ran into the midst
of the assembly. The plague had already
started among the people,[i] but Aaron offered the incense and made atonement for
them. 48 He stood between the living and
the dead, and the plague stopped.[j] 49 But
14,700 people died from the plague, in addition to those who had died because of
Korah.[k] 50 Then Aaron returned to Moses
at the entrance to the tent of meeting, for
the plague had stopped.[a]

The Budding of Aaron's Staff

17[b] The LORD said to Moses, 2 "Speak
to the Israelites and get twelve
staffs[l] from them, one from the leader of
each of their ancestral tribes.[m] Write the
name of each man on his staff. 3 On the
staff of Levi write Aaron's name,[n] for there
must be one staff for the head of each ancestral tribe. 4 Place them in the tent of
meeting[o] in front of the ark of the covenant law,[p] where I meet with you.[q] 5 The
staff belonging to the man I choose[r] will
sprout,[s] and I will rid myself of this constant grumbling[t] against you by the Israelites."
6 So Moses spoke to the Israelites, and
their leaders gave him twelve staffs, one
for the leader of each of their ancestral
tribes, and Aaron's staff was among them.
7 Moses placed the staffs before the LORD in
the tent of the covenant law.[u]
8 The next day Moses entered the tent[v]
and saw that Aaron's staff,[w] which represented the tribe of Levi, had not only
sprouted but had budded, blossomed and
produced almonds.[x] 9 Then Moses brought
out all the staffs[y] from the LORD's presence
to all the Israelites. They looked at them,
and each of the leaders took his own staff.
10 The LORD said to Moses, "Put back
Aaron's staff[z] in front of the ark of the
covenant law, to be kept as a sign to the
rebellious.[a] This will put an end to their
grumbling against me, so that they will
not die." 11 Moses did just as the LORD commanded him.
12 The Israelites said to Moses, "We will
die! We are lost, we are all lost![b] 13 Anyone
who even comes near the tabernacle of
the LORD will die.[c] Are we all going to die?"

Duties of Priests and Levites

18 The LORD said to Aaron, "You,
your sons and your family are to
bear the responsibility for offenses connected with the sanctuary,[d] and you and

16:40 [x] S Ex 30:1; 2Ki 12:3; Isa 1:13; 66:3; Jer 41:5; 44:3 [y] S Ex 30:9; 2Ch 26:18 [z] S Nu 3:10 **16:42** [a] S ver 19 [b] Ex 16:7; Nu 14:10 **16:45** [c] S Ex 32:10 **16:46** [d] S Lev 10:1 [e] Lev 10:6 [f] S Ex 29:36 [g] S Nu 1:53 [h] S Lev 26:25; Nu 8:19; Ps 106:29 **16:47** [i] Nu 25:6-8 **16:48** [j] Nu 25:8; Ps 106:30 **16:49** [k] ver 32 **17:2** [l] S Ge 32:10; S Ex 4:2 [m] Nu 1:4 **17:3** [n] S Nu 1:3 **17:4** [o] S Ex 40:2 [p] ver 7; Ex 16:34 [q] Ex 25:22 **17:5** [r] S Nu 16:5 [s] ver 8 [t] S Ex 16:7 **17:7** [u] S Ex 38:21 **17:8** [v] ver 7; Nu 1:50 [w] ver 2, 10 [x] Eze 17:24; Heb 9:4 **17:9** [y] ver 2 **17:10** [z] S ver 8 [a] S Ex 23:21; Dt 9:24; Ps 66:7; 68:18; Pr 24:21 **17:12** [b] Jdg 13:22; Isa 6:5; 15:1 **17:13** [c] Nu 1:51 **18:1** [d] S Ex 28:38

[a] *50* In Hebrew texts 16:36-50 is numbered 17:1-15.
[b] In Hebrew texts 17:1-13 is numbered 17:16-28.

16:41 *the whole Israelite community grumbled.* Again the community attacked Moses, unfairly charging him with the deaths of the Lord's people. Except for the intervention of Moses and Aaron (see vv. 4,22), the entire nation might have been destroyed because of their continued rebellion (see v. 45).

16:49 *14,700 people died.* The number makes sense only if the community is as large as the census lists of ch. 2 suggest.

17:1–13 This story follows the account of the divine judgment of Korah (16:1–35), the narrative of the symbolic use given to the censers of the rebels and its aftermath (16:36–50). The selection of 12 staffs, one from each tribe, was a symbolic act whereby the divine choice of Aaron would be vindicated.

17:3 *On the staff of Levi write Aaron's name.* The test needed to be unequivocal because of the wide support given to Korah's rebellion. The 250 who had joined with Korah were from many, perhaps all, of the tribes.

17:4 *in front of the ark of the covenant law.* In front of the ark, with the Ten Commandments, thus probably in the Holy Place, near the altar of incense (see vv. 7–8,10; see also note on Ex 25:22).

17:8 *had not only sprouted but had budded, blossomed and produced almonds.* God exceeded the demands of the test so that there might be no uncertainty as to who had acted or what he intended by his action.

17:10 *in front of the ark of the covenant law.* Aaron's rod joined the stone tablets of the law of Moses (see note on Ex 25:16) and the jar of manna (Ex 16:33–34) within or near the ark of the covenant (see Heb 9:4). These holy symbols were ever before the Lord as reminders of his special deeds on behalf of his people. Moreover, if anyone of a later age should dare to question the unique and holy place of the Aaronic priests in the Lord's service, this symbolic reminder of God's choice of Aaron would stand in opposition to their audacity (see note on 18:1–7).

17:12 *We will die!* At last the people realized the sin of their arrogance in challenging Aaron's role. The appropriate ways of approaching the Lord are detailed in chs. 18–19.

18:1–7 Aaron and his family, chosen by the Lord to be the true priests of holy worship, faced a burdensome

your sons alone are to bear the responsibility for offenses connected with the priesthood. 2 Bring your fellow Levites from your ancestral tribe to join you and assist you when you and your sons minister[e] before the tent of the covenant law. 3 They are to be responsible to you[f] and are to perform all the duties of the tent,[g] but they must not go near the furnishings of the sanctuary or the altar. Otherwise both they and you will die.[h] 4 They are to join you and be responsible for the care of the tent of meeting—all the work at the tent—and no one else may come near where you are.[i]

5 "You are to be responsible for the care of the sanctuary and the altar,[j] so that my wrath will not fall on the Israelites again. 6 I myself have selected your fellow Levites from among the Israelites as a gift to you,[k] dedicated to the LORD to do the work at the tent of meeting.[l] 7 But only you and your sons may serve as priests in connection with everything at the altar and inside the curtain.[m] I am giving you the service of the priesthood as a gift.[n] Anyone else who comes near the sanctuary is to be put to death.[o]"

Offerings for Priests and Levites

8 Then the LORD said to Aaron, "I myself have put you in charge of the offerings presented to me; all the holy offerings the Israelites give me I give to you and your sons as your portion,[p] your perpetual share.[q] 9 You are to have the part of the most holy offerings[r] that is kept from the fire. From all the gifts they bring me as most holy offerings, whether grain[s] or sin[a][t] or guilt offerings,[u] that part belongs to you and your sons. 10 Eat it as something most holy; every male shall eat it.[v] You must regard it as holy.[w]

11 "This also is yours: whatever is set aside from the gifts of all the wave offerings[x] of the Israelites. I give this to you and your sons and daughters as your perpetual share.[y] Everyone in your household who is ceremonially clean[z] may eat it.

12 "I give you all the finest olive oil and all the finest new wine and grain[a] they give the LORD[b] as the firstfruits of their harvest.[c] 13 All the land's firstfruits that they bring to the LORD will be yours.[d] Everyone in your household who is ceremonially clean may eat it.[e]

14 "Everything in Israel that is devoted[b] to the LORD[f] is yours. 15 The first offspring of every womb, both human and animal, that is offered to the LORD is yours.[g] But you must redeem[h] every firstborn[i] son and every firstborn male of unclean animals.[j] 16 When they are a month old,[k] you must redeem them at the redemption price set at five shekels[c][l] of silver, according to the sanctuary shekel,[m] which weighs twenty gerahs.[n]

17 "But you must not redeem the firstborn of a cow, a sheep or a goat; they are holy.[o] Splash their blood[p] against the altar and burn their fat[q] as a food offering, an aroma pleasing to the LORD.[r] 18 Their meat is to be yours, just as the breast of the wave offering[s] and the right thigh are yours.[t] 19 Whatever is set aside from the holy[u] offerings the Israelites present to the LORD I give to you and your sons and daughters as your perpetual share. It is

[a] 9 Or *purification* [b] 14 The Hebrew term refers to the irrevocable giving over of things or persons to the LORD. [c] 16 That is, about 2 ounces or about 58 grams

18:2 [e] Nu 3:10 **18:3** [f] S Nu 3:32 [g] Nu 1:51 [h] ver 7 **18:4** [i] S Nu 3:38 **18:5** [j] ver 3; Lev 6:12 **18:6** [k] S Nu 3:9 [l] Nu 3:8 **18:7** [m] Heb 9:3, 6 [n] ver 20; Ex 29:9; 40:13; Heb 5:4 [o] ver 3; Nu 3:10 **18:8** [p] S Lev 2:2 [q] Lev 6:16; 7:6, 31-34, 36; Dt 18:1; 2Ch 31:4 **18:9** [r] S Lev 6:17 [s] Lev 2:1 [t] Lev 6:25 [u] S Lev 5:15 **18:10** [v] S Lev 6:16 [w] Lev 6:17, 18 **18:11** [x] Ex 29:26; Lev 7:30; Nu 6:20 [y] Lev 7:31-34 [z] Lev 13:3; 22:1-16 **18:12** [a] Dt 7:13; 11:14; 12:17; 28:51; 2Ki 18:32; 2Ch 31:5; Ne 10:37; Jer 31:12; Eze 23:41; Hos 2:8; Joel 1:10; Hag 1:11 [b] S Ge 4:3 [c] Ex 23:19; 34:26; Ne 10:35 **18:13** [d] S Ex 29:27 [e] ver 11 **18:14** [f] S Lev 27:21; Jos 6:17-19 **18:15** [g] Ex 13:2 [h] S Nu 3:46 [i] S Ge 10:15 [j] S Ex 13:13 **18:16** [k] S Nu 3:15 [l] S Lev 27:6 [m] S Ex 30:13 [n] Nu 3:47 **18:17** [o] S Lev 27:9 [p] S Lev 3:2 [q] S Ex 29:13 [r] S Lev 1:9 **18:18** [s] Lev 7:30 [t] ver 11 **18:19** [u] 2Ki 12:4

task. The lament of the people in 17:12–13 was real; grievous sins against the holy meeting place of the Lord and his people would be judged by death. The Lord's mercy in providing a legitimate priesthood was actually an aspect of his grace (cf. Ps 99:6–8), because it was the people's only hope for deliverance from judgment.

18:2 *Bring your fellow Levites.* The Aaronic priests were to be assisted by the others in the tribe of Levi, but the assistants were not to go beyond their serving role. If they did so, not only would they die, but so would the priests who were responsible (v. 3). *covenant law.* See note on Ex 25:22.

18:7 *the service of the priesthood as a gift.* Of all men, the priests were privileged to approach the Holy Place and minister before the Lord.

18:8 *your portion, your perpetual share.* The priests were to be supported in their work of ministry (see Lev 6:14—7:36). Since the Levites as a whole and the priests in particular had no part in the land that God was going to give them, it was necessary that the means for their provision be spelled out fully. They were not to have a part in the land; their share was the Lord himself (v. 20).

18:11 *your sons and daughters.* Provision was made not only for the priests but also for their families. Only family members who were ceremonially unclean were forbidden to eat the gifts and offerings of the people (see v. 13). Provisions for cleansing were stated in Lev 22:4–8.

18:12 *finest olive oil ... finest new wine and grain.* Since the best items of produce were to be given to the Lord, these became the special foods of the priests and their families. The NT writers similarly argue that those who minister the word of God in the present period should also be paid suitably for their work (see, e.g., 1Co 9:3–10 and notes).

18:16 *according to the sanctuary shekel.* See note on Ex 30:13.

18:19 *everlasting covenant of salt.* A permanent provision for the priests. The phrase "covenant of salt" (see 2Ch 13:5) remains obscure. In Lev 2:13 the salt that must accompany grain offerings is called the "salt of the covenant." According to Eze 43:24, salt is also to be sprinkled on burnt offerings and Ex 30:35 specifies salt as one of the ingredients in the special incense compounded for the sanctuary. A "covenant of salt" is perhaps an allusion to the salt used in the sacrificial meal that commonly accompanied the making of a covenant (see Ge 31:54; Ex 24:5–11; Ps 50:5).

an everlasting covenant of salt[v] before the LORD for both you and your offspring."

20 The LORD said to Aaron, "You will have no inheritance in their land, nor will you have any share among them;[w] I am your share and your inheritance[x] among the Israelites.

21 "I give to the Levites all the tithes[y] in Israel as their inheritance[z] in return for the work they do while serving at the tent of meeting.[a] 22 From now on the Israelites must not go near the tent of meeting, or they will bear the consequences of their sin and will die.[b] 23 It is the Levites who are to do the work at the tent of meeting and bear the responsibility for any offenses they commit against it. This is a lasting ordinance[c] for the generations to come.[d] They will receive no inheritance[e] among the Israelites.[f] 24 Instead, I give to the Levites as their inheritance the tithes that the Israelites present as an offering to the LORD.[g] That is why I said concerning them: 'They will have no inheritance among the Israelites.' "

25 The LORD said to Moses, 26 "Speak to the Levites and say to them: 'When you receive from the Israelites the tithe I give you[h] as your inheritance, you must present a tenth of that tithe as the LORD's offering.[i] 27 Your offering will be reckoned[j] to you as grain from the threshing floor[k] or juice from the winepress.[l] 28 In this way you also will present an offering to the LORD from all the tithes[m] you receive from the Israelites. From these tithes you must give the LORD's portion to Aaron the priest. 29 You must present as the LORD's portion the best and holiest part of everything given to you.'

30 "Say to the Levites: 'When you present the best part, it will be reckoned to you as the product of the threshing floor or the winepress.[n] 31 You and your households may eat the rest of it anywhere, for it is your wages for your work at the tent of meeting.[o] 32 By presenting the best part[p] of it you will not be guilty in this matter;[q] then you will not defile the holy offerings[r] of the Israelites, and you will not die.' "

18:19 [v]S Lev 2:13 **18:20** [w]Nu 26:62; Dt 12:12 [x]ver 24; Dt 10:9; 14:27; 18:1-2; Jos 13:33; Eze 44:28 **18:21** [y]ver 24; S Ge 28:22; Nu 31:28; Dt 14:22; Ne 10:37; 13:5; Mal 3:8 [z]Lev 27:30-33; Heb 7:5 [a]Nu 1:53 **18:22** [b]S Ex 28:43 **18:23** [c]S Ex 12:14; S 27:21 [d]Nu 10:8 [e]ver 20; Nu 26:62; Dt 10:9 [f]Eze 44:10 **18:24** [g]Lev 27:30; Dt 26:12 **18:26** [h]ver 21 [i]ver 28; Ne 10:38 **18:27** [j]Lev 7:18 [k]Ge 50:10; Dt 15:14; Jdg 6:37; Ru 3:3,6, 14; 1Sa 23:1 [l]ver 12,30 **18:28** [m]Mal 3:8 **18:30** [n]S ver 27 **18:31** [o]ver 23 **18:32** [p]Lev 22:15 [q]ver 29 [r]S Lev 19:8

19:2 [s]S Ge 15:9; Heb 9:13 [t]S Lev 22:19-25 [u]Dt 21:3; 1Sa 6:7 **19:3** [v]Nu 3:4 [w]S Ex 29:14 **19:4** [x]S Lev 4:17 **19:5** [y]S Ex 29:14 **19:6** [z]ver 18; Ps 51:7 [a]S Lev 14:4 **19:7** [b]S Lev 11:25; S 14:8 **19:9** [c]Heb 9:13 [d]S Ex 29:31; S Lev 4:12 [e]ver 13; Nu 8:7 [f]S Ge 35:2

The Water of Cleansing

19 The LORD said to Moses and Aaron: 2 "This is a requirement of the law that the LORD has commanded: Tell the Israelites to bring you a red heifer[s] without defect or blemish[t] and that has never been under a yoke.[u] 3 Give it to Eleazar[v] the priest; it is to be taken outside the camp[w] and slaughtered in his presence. 4 Then Eleazar the priest is to take some of its blood on his finger and sprinkle[x] it seven times toward the front of the tent of meeting. 5 While he watches, the heifer is to be burned—its hide, flesh, blood and intestines.[y] 6 The priest is to take some cedar wood, hyssop[z] and scarlet wool[a] and throw them onto the burning heifer. 7 After that, the priest must wash his clothes and bathe himself with water.[b] He may then come into the camp, but he will be ceremonially unclean till evening. 8 The man who burns it must also wash his clothes and bathe with water, and he too will be unclean till evening.

9 "A man who is clean shall gather up the ashes of the heifer[c] and put them in a ceremonially clean place[d] outside the camp. They are to be kept by the Israelite community for use in the water of cleansing;[e] it is for purification from sin.[f] 10 The man who gathers up[g] the ashes of the heifer must also wash his clothes, and he too will be unclean till evening.[h] This will be a lasting ordinance[i] both for the Israelites and for the foreigners residing among them.[j]

11 "Whoever touches a human corpse[k] will be unclean for seven days.[l] 12 They must purify themselves with the water on the third day and on the seventh day;[m] then they will be clean. But if they do not purify themselves on the third and seventh days, they will not be clean.[n] 13 If they fail to purify themselves after touching a human corpse,[o] they defile the LORD's tabernacle.[p] They must be cut off from Israel.[q]

19:10 [g]Lev 15:10 [h]Lev 14:46 [i]Lev 3:17 [j]S Lev 22:18 **19:11** [k]S Lev 21:1 [l]S Lev 8:33; Nu 31:19 **19:12** [m]ver 19; Nu 31:19 [n]ver 20; 2Ch 26:21 **19:13** [o]S Lev 21:11 [p]S Lev 15:31; 2Ch 36:14; Ps 79:1 [q]Lev 7:20; 22:3

18:26–32 Although the Levites were the recipients of the tithe given to the Lord, they were not themselves exempt from tithing. They in turn were to give a tenth of their income to Aaron (v. 28) and were to be sure that the best part was given as the Lord's portion (v. 29). By obedient compliance the Levites would escape judicial death (v. 32).

19:2 *red heifer.* The qualifying words, "without defect or blemish," are familiar in contexts of sacrificial worship in the OT. But this is not a sacrificial animal. It is a cow, not an ox; it is to be slaughtered, not sacrificed; and it is to be killed outside the camp, not at the holy altar. The ashes of the red heifer (v. 9) are the primary focus of this act, for they will be used in the ritual of the water of cleansing. The burning of the animal with its "blood and intestines" (v. 5) is unprecedented in the OT. The normal pattern for the sacrifice of the burnt offering is given in Lev 1:3–9.

19:6 *cedar wood, hyssop and scarlet wool.* Associated with the cleansing properties of the ashes of the red heifer.

19:12 *purify themselves with the water.* The ashes from the red heifer were kept outside the camp and would be mixed as needed with water to provide a means of cleansing after contact with dead bodies.

19:13 *defile the LORD's tabernacle.* Willful neglect of the provision for cleansing brought not only judgment on the person but pollution of the tabernacle itself. *cut off from Israel.* See note on Ex 12:15.

Because the water of cleansing has not been sprinkled on them, they are unclean;[r] their uncleanness remains on them.

14 “This is the law that applies when a person dies in a tent: Anyone who enters the tent and anyone who is in it will be unclean for seven days, 15 and every open container[s] without a lid fastened on it will be unclean.

16 “Anyone out in the open who touches someone who has been killed with a sword or someone who has died a natural death,[t] or anyone who touches a human bone[u] or a grave,[v] will be unclean for seven days.[w]

17 “For the unclean person, put some ashes[x] from the burned purification offering into a jar and pour fresh water[y] over them. 18 Then a man who is ceremonially clean is to take some hyssop,[z] dip it in the water and sprinkle[a] the tent and all the furnishings and the people who were there. He must also sprinkle anyone who has touched a human bone or a grave[b] or anyone who has been killed or anyone who has died a natural death. 19 The man who is clean is to sprinkle[c] those who are unclean on the third and seventh days, and on the seventh day he is to purify them.[d] Those who are being cleansed must wash their clothes[e] and bathe with water, and that evening they will be clean. 20 But if those who are unclean do not purify themselves, they must be cut off from the community, because they have defiled[f] the sanctuary of the LORD.[g] The water of cleansing has not been sprinkled on them, and they are unclean.[h] 21 This is a lasting ordinance[i] for them.

“The man who sprinkles the water of cleansing must also wash his clothes, and anyone who touches the water of cleansing will be unclean till evening. 22 Anything that an unclean[j] person touches becomes unclean, and anyone who touches it becomes unclean till evening.”

Water From the Rock

20 In the first month the whole Israelite community arrived at the Desert of Zin,[k] and they stayed at Kadesh.[l] There Miriam[m] died and was buried.

2 Now there was no water[n] for the community,[o] and the people gathered in opposition[p] to Moses and Aaron. 3 They quarreled[q] with Moses and said, “If only we had died when our brothers fell dead[r] before the LORD![s] 4 Why did you bring the LORD’s community into this wilderness,[t] that we and our livestock should die here?[u] 5 Why did you bring us up out of Egypt to this terrible place? It has no grain or figs, grapevines or pomegranates.[v] And there is no water to drink![w]”

6 Moses and Aaron went from the assembly to the entrance to the tent of meeting[x] and fell facedown,[y] and the glory of the LORD[z] appeared to them. 7 The LORD said to Moses, 8 “Take the staff,[a] and you and your brother Aaron gather the assembly together. Speak to that rock before their eyes and it will pour out its water.[b] You will bring water out of the rock for the community so they and their livestock can drink.”

9 So Moses took the staff[c] from the LORD’s presence,[d] just as he commanded him. 10 He and Aaron gathered the assembly together[e] in front of the rock and Moses said to them, “Listen, you reb-

19:13 [r] ver 22; Hag 2:13 **19:15** [s] S Lev 6:28 **19:16** [t] Nu 31:19 [u] 1Ki 13:2; 2Ki 23:14; Eze 6:5 [v] 2Ki 23:6; Mt 23:27 [w] S Lev 5:3 **19:17** [x] ver 9 [y] S Nu 8:7 **19:18** [z] S ver 6; S Ex 12:22 [a] S Lev 4:17 [b] ver 16 **19:19** [c] S Lev 16:14-15 [d] Nu 31:19; Eze 36:25; Heb 10:22 [e] S Ge 35:2 **19:20** [f] Ps 74:7 [g] S Lev 15:31 [h] S ver 12; S Lev 14:8 **19:21** [i] S Ex 27:21 **19:22** [j] S Lev 5:2; 15:4-12 **20:1** [k] Nu 13:21 [l] ver 14; Nu 13:26; 33:36; Dt 1:46; Jdg 11:17; Ps 29:8 [m] S Ex 15:20 **20:2** [n] S Ex 15:22 [o] Ex 17:1 [p] S Nu 16:19 **20:3** [q] ver 13; S Ge 13:7; Ex 17:2; 21:18 [r] S Ex 5:21 [s] S Nu 14:2; 16:31-35 **20:4** [t] S Nu 14:2 [u] S Ex 14:11; Nu 14:3; 16:13 **20:5** [v] Nu 13:23; 16:14 [w] S Ex 17:1 **20:6** [x] S Ex 40:2 [y] Nu 14:5 [z] S Nu 16:19 **20:8** [a] S Ex 4:2; S 10:12-13 [b] Ex 17:6; Isa 41:18; 43:20; Jer 31:9 **20:9** [c] Nu 17:2 [d] Nu 17:10 **20:10** [e] ver 8

19:14 *anyone who is in it.* There would be many occasions in which a person would become unclean, not because of deliberate contact with a dead body, but just by being in the proximity of one who died.

19:18 *hyssop, dip it in the water and sprinkle.* Here the method of the cleansing ritual is explained. A ceremonially clean person had to sprinkle the ceremonially unclean person or thing. The cleansing power of the blood of Christ is specifically contrasted ("much more"; Heb 9:13 – 14) with the cleansing effectiveness of the water of the ashes of the red heifer.

20:1 – 29 This chapter begins with the death of Miriam (v. 1), concludes with the death of Aaron (v. 28), includes the record of the conflict with Edom (vv. 14 – 21) and centers on the tragic sin of Moses (vv. 11 – 12). Such was the sad beginning of Israel's last year in the wilderness.

20:1 *first month.* The year is not given, but a comparison of vv. 22 – 29 with 33:38 leads to the conclusion that this chapter begins in the 40th year after the exodus (see notes on 1:1; 9:1). Most of the people 20 years old or more at the time of the rebellion at Kadesh (chs. 13 – 14) would already have died. *at Kadesh.* See note on Ge 14:7. The larger part of the wilderness wandering (see 32:13) is left without record. The people may have traveled about, seeking the water sources and the sparse vegetation, supported primarily by manna. But their circuits would bring them back to the central camp at Kadesh, the scene of their great rebellion (chs. 13 – 14). They have now come full circle; the land of promise lies before them again.

20:2 *no water.* Forty years earlier the Lord had instructed Moses to take the staff he had used to strike the Nile (Ex 7:17) and to strike the rock at Horeb to initiate a flow of water (Ex 17:1 – 7). Now, 40 years later, at the place of Israel's worst acts of rebellion, the scene was recurring. The children of the rebellious nation now desire to die with their parents; the parents' complaints about the bread from heaven are repeated by the children.

20:6 *glory of the LORD.* See note on Ex 16:7.

20:8 *Speak to that rock.* Moses was told to take his staff, through which God had performed wonders in Egypt and in the wilderness all these years, but this time he was merely to speak to the rock and it would pour out its water for the people. Cf. Ps 114:8 and note.

20:10 *Listen, you rebels.* At once the accumulated anger, exasperation and frustration of 40 years came to expression (see Ps 106:33 and note).

els, must we bring you water out of this
rock?"[f] 11Then Moses raised his arm and
struck the rock twice with his staff. Water[g]
gushed out, and the community and their
livestock drank.
12But the LORD said to Moses and Aaron,
"Because you did not trust in me enough
to honor me as holy[h] in the sight of the Israelites, you will not bring this community
into the land I give them."[i]
13These were the waters of Meribah,[a][j]
where the Israelites quarreled[k] with the
LORD and where he was proved holy
among them.[l]

Edom Denies Israel Passage

14Moses sent messengers from Kadesh[m]
to the king of Edom,[n] saying:

"This is what your brother Israel
says: You know[o] about all the hardships[p] that have come on us. 15Our
ancestors went down into Egypt,[q] and
we lived there many years.[r] The Egyptians mistreated[s] us and our ancestors, 16but when we cried out to the
LORD, he heard our cry[t] and sent an
angel[u] and brought us out of Egypt.[v]
"Now we are here at Kadesh, a
town on the edge of your territory.[w]
17Please let us pass through your
country. We will not go through any
field or vineyard, or drink water
from any well. We will travel along
the King's Highway and not turn to
the right or to the left until we have
passed through your territory.[x]"

18But Edom[y] answered:

"You may not pass through here; if
you try, we will march out and attack
you with the sword.[z]"

19The Israelites replied:

"We will go along the main road,
and if we or our livestock[a] drink any
of your water, we will pay for it.[b] We
only want to pass through on foot—
nothing else."

20Again they answered:

"You may not pass through.[c]"

Then Edom[d] came out against them
with a large and powerful army. 21Since
Edom refused to let them go through their
territory,[e] Israel turned away from them.[f]

The Death of Aaron

22The whole Israelite community set
out from Kadesh[g] and came to Mount
Hor.[h] 23At Mount Hor, near the border of
Edom,[i] the LORD said to Moses and Aaron,
24"Aaron will be gathered to his people.[j]
He will not enter the land I give the Israelites, because both of you rebelled against
my command[k] at the waters of Meribah.[l]
25Get Aaron and his son Eleazar and take
them up Mount Hor.[m] 26Remove Aaron's
garments[n] and put them on his son Eleazar, for Aaron will be gathered to his people;[o] he will die there."
27Moses did as the LORD commanded:
They went up Mount Hor[p] in the sight of
the whole community. 28Moses removed
Aaron's garments and put them on his son
Eleazar.[q] And Aaron died there[r] on top of
the mountain. Then Moses and Eleazar
came down from the mountain, 29and
when the whole community learned that

[a] 13 *Meribah* means *quarreling*.

20:10 [f]Ps 106:32,33 **20:11** [g]S Ex 17:6; S Isa 33:21 **20:12** [h]Nu 27:14; Dt 32:51; Isa 5:16; 8:13 [i]ver 24; Dt 1:37; 3:27 **20:13** [j]S Ex 17:7 [k]S ver 3 [l]S Lev 10:3 **20:14** [m]S ver 1 [n]S ver 16; S Ge 25:30; S 36:16 [o]Ge 24:3; Dt 4:39; Jos 2:11; 9:9 [p]S Ex 18:8 **20:15** [q]S Ge 46:6 [r]S Ge 15:13 [s]S Ex 1:14 **20:16** [t]S Ge 16:11; S 21:17; S Ex 2:23 [u]Ex 14:19 [v]Ex 12:42; Dt 26:8 [w]ver 14, 23; Nu 33:37 **20:17** [x]ver 20; Nu 21:22; Dt 2:27; Jdg 11:17 **20:18** [y]ver 14 [z]Nu 21:23 **20:19** [a]Ex 12:38 [b]Dt 2:6,28 **20:20** [c]S ver 17, 18 [d]ver 14 **20:21** [e]Nu 21:23 [f]Nu 21:4; Dt 2:8; Jdg 11:18 **20:22** [g]Dt 1:46 [h]Nu 33:37; 34:7; Dt 32:50 **20:23** [i]S ver 16 **20:24** [j]S Ge 25:8 [k]S ver 10 [l]S Ex 17:7 **20:25** [m]Nu 33:38 **20:26** [n]Ex 28:1-4; 40:13; S Lev 16:4 [o]ver 24; Nu 27:13; 31:2 **20:27** [p]Nu 33:38 **20:28** [q]S Ex 29:29 [r]ver 26; Nu 33:38; Dt 10:6; 32:50

20:11 *struck the rock twice with his staff.* In his rage Moses disobeyed the Lord's instruction to speak to the rock (v. 8). Moses' rash action brought a stern rebuke from the Lord (v. 12). These other factors were also involved: (1) Moses' action was a lack of trust in God (v. 12), as though he believed that a word alone would not suffice. (2) God's holiness was offended by Moses' rash action (v. 12), for he had not shown proper deference to God's presence (see v. 24; 27:14; Dt 1:37 and note; Ps 106:32–33).
20:12 *to honor me as holy.* See note on Lev 11:44. *you will not bring this community into the land.* The end result of Moses' action is sure: Neither Aaron nor Moses would enter the land of promise. Of their contemporaries only Joshua and Caleb would survive to enter the land. The inclusion of Aaron demonstrates his partnership with his brother in the breach against God's holiness.
20:13 *Meribah.* See NIV text note. The same name was used 40 years earlier at the first occasion of bringing water from the rock (Ex 17:7, where it is also called Massah, "testing"; see note there). Ps 95:8 (see note there) laments the rebellion at Meribah and Massah. *was proved holy.* See Lev 10:3 and note.
20:14–21 Moses' attempt to pass through the territory of Edom by peaceful negotiation and payment for services rendered is met by arrogant rebuff.
20:14 *your brother Israel.* The people of Edom were descended from Esau, the brother of Jacob (see Ge 36:1; Ob 10 and notes).
20:17 *King's Highway.* The major north-south trade route in Transjordan, extending from Arabia to Damascus.
20:20 *large and powerful army.* The show of force by Edom caused Israel to turn away so as not to risk conflict with this brother nation. Israel was forbidden by the Lord to take even a foothold in Edom (see Dt 2:4–6).
20:22 *Mount Hor.* Somewhere "near the border of Edom" (v. 23).
20:24 *gathered to his people.* A euphemism for death (see, e.g., Ge 25:8,17; 35:29). *both of you.* Aaron had joined Moses in rebellion against God (v. 12); his impending death was a precursor of Moses' death as well (see Dt 34).
20:25 *Aaron and his son Eleazar.* There was no doubt about Aaron's successor, just as there was none about Moses' successor (see Dt 34).
20:26–28 While Aaron was still alive, his garments were to be placed on his son; only then did he die.

20:29 *mourned for him.* Aaron's death (and that of Moses) marked the passing of a generation. The old

Aaron had died,[s] all the Israelites mourned
for him[t] thirty days.

Arad Destroyed

21 When the Canaanite king of Arad,[u]
who lived in the Negev,[v] heard that
Israel was coming along the road to Ath-
arim, he attacked the Israelites and captured some of them.
2 Then Israel made
this vow[w] to the LORD: "If you will deliver these people into our hands, we will
totally destroy[a][x] their cities."
3 The LORD
listened to Israel's plea and gave the Canaanites[y] over to them. They completely
destroyed them[z] and their towns; so the
place was named Hormah.[b][a]

The Bronze Snake

4 They traveled from Mount Hor[b] along
the route to the Red Sea,[c][c] to go around
Edom.[d] But the people grew impatient on
the way;[e]
5 they spoke against God[f] and
against Moses, and said, "Why have you
brought us up out of Egypt[g] to die in the
wilderness?[h] There is no bread! There is no
water![i] And we detest this miserable food!"[j]
6 Then the LORD sent venomous snakes[k]
among them; they bit the people and many
Israelites died.[l]
7 The people came to Mo-
ses[m] and said, "We sinned[n] when we spoke
against the LORD and against you. Pray that
the LORD[o] will take the snakes away from
us." So Moses prayed[p] for the people.
8 The LORD said to Moses, "Make a snake
and put it up on a pole;[q] anyone who is
bitten can look at it and live."
9 So Moses
made a bronze snake[r] and put it up on
a pole. Then when anyone was bitten by
a snake and looked at the bronze snake,
they lived.[s]

20:29 [s]Dt 32:50 [t]S Ge 27:41; S Lev 10:6; S Dt 34:8 **21:1** [u]Nu 33:40; Jos 12:14 [v]S Ge 12:9; Nu 13:17; Dt 1:7; Jdg 1:9,16 **21:2** [w]Lev 7:16 [x]ver 3; Ex 22:20; Dt 2:34; Jos 2:10; 8:26; Jer 25:9; 50:21 **21:3** [y]S Ge 10:18 [z]S ver 2 [a]S Nu 14:45 **21:4** [b]Nu 20:22 [c]Nu 14:25; Dt 2:1; 11:4 [d]S Nu 20:21 [e]Dt 2:8; Jdg 11:18 **21:5** [f]Ps 78:19 [g]Nu 11:20 [h]S Ex 14:11; Nu 14:2,3 [i]Nu 20:5 [j]S Nu 11:5 **21:6** [k]ver 7; Dt 8:15; 32:33; Job 20:14; Ps 58:4; 140:3; Jer 8:17 [l]1Co 10:9 **21:7** [m]Ps 78:34; Hos 5:15 [n]Nu 14:40 [o]Ex 8:8; 1Sa 7:8; Jer 27:18; 37:3; Ac 8:24 [p]S Nu 11:2 **21:8** [q]Jn 3:14 **21:9** [r]2Ki 18:4 [s]Jn 3:14-15

21:10 [t]Nu 33:43 **21:11** [u]S Ge 36:35; Nu 33:44; Dt 34:8; Jer 40:11 **21:12** [v]Dt 2:13,14 **21:13** [w]Nu 22:36;

The Journey to Moab

10 The Israelites moved on and camped
at Oboth.[t]
11 Then they set out from Oboth
and camped in Iye Abarim, in the wilderness that faces Moab[u] toward the sunrise.
12 From there they moved on and camped
in the Zered Valley.[v]
13 They set out from
there and camped alongside the Arnon[w],
which is in the wilderness extending into
Amorite territory. The Arnon is the border of Moab, between Moab and the Amorites.[x]
14 That is why the Book of the Wars[y]
of the LORD says:

> ". . . Zahab[d] in Suphah and the
> ravines,
> the Arnon
> 15 and[e] the slopes of the
> ravines
> that lead to the settlement of Ar[z]
> and lie along the border of Moab."

16 From there they continued on to Beer,[a]
the well where the LORD said to Moses,
"Gather the people together and I will give
them water."
17 Then Israel sang this song:[b]

> "Spring up, O well!
> Sing about it,
> 18 about the well that the princes dug,
> that the nobles of the people sank—
> the nobles with scepters and staffs."

[a] 2 The Hebrew term refers to the irrevocable giving over of things or persons to the LORD, often by totally destroying them; also in verse 3. [b] 3 *Hormah* means *destruction.* [c] 4 Or *the Sea of Reeds* [d] 14 Septuagint Hebrew *Waheb* [e] 14,15 Or *"I have been given from Suphah and the ravines / of the Arnon* [15]*to*

Dt 2:24; Jos 12:1; Jdg 11:13,18; 2Ki 10:33; Isa 16:2; Jer 48:20 [x]S Ge 10:16 **21:14** [y]1Sa 17:47; 18:17; 25:28 **21:15** [z]ver 28; Dt 2:9,18; Isa 15:1 **21:16** [a]Nu 25:1; 33:49; Jdg 9:21; Isa 15:8 **21:17** [b]S Ex 15:1

---

generation was now nearly gone; in 40 years there had been almost a complete turnover of the people 20 years old or older.

21:1–3 The first battle of the new community against the Canaanites was provoked by the king of Arad, perhaps as he was raiding them. The result was a complete victory for the Israelites—a new day for them, since they had been defeated by the Amalekites and Canaanites a generation before (14:41–45).

21:1 *Negev.* See note on Ge 12:9.

21:2 *totally destroy.* See NIV text note.

21:3 *Hormah.* See NIV text note; the association with Israel's earlier defeat is made certain by the use of this place-name (cf. 14:45).

21:4 With Moses' determination not to engage Edom in battle (see note on 20:20), the people became impatient with him and with the direction the Lord was taking them. Flushed with victory, they were confident in themselves. They forgot that their victory over Arad had been granted by the Lord in response to their solemn pledge (v. 2); now they were ready to rebel again.

21:5 *we detest this miserable food!* The people's impatience (v. 4) led them to blaspheme God, to reject his servant Moses and to despise the "bread from heaven" (Ex 16:4; see note there). This is the most bitter of their several complaints about the manna (see note on 11:7). Just as Moses' attack on the rock was more than it appeared to be (see note on 20:11), so the people's contempt for the heavenly bread was more serious than one might think. Rejecting the heavenly manna was tantamount to spurning God's grace (cf. Jn 6:32–35,48–51,58).

21:8–9 See the typological use of this incident in Jn 3:14–15.

21:10–13 The people skirt Edom and make their way to the Arnon, the wadi that serves as the border between Moab and the region of the Amorites and that flows west into the midpoint of the Dead Sea.

21:12 *Zered.* See note on Dt 2:13.

21:14 *Book of the Wars of the LORD.* Mentioned only here in the OT. This is not in existence today; it was presumably an ancient collection of songs of war in praise of God (see note on 10:3 for music in war). Cf. the "Book of Jashar" (Jos 10:13 [see note there]; 2Sa 1:18).

21:16 *I will give them water.* The quest for water had been a constant problem during the wilderness experience (see ch. 20; Ex 17).

21:17–18 The song about the well may also come from the "Book of the Wars of the LORD" (v. 14).

Then they went from the wilderness to
Mattanah, 19 from Mattanah to Nahaliel,
from Nahaliel to Bamoth, 20 and from Bamoth to the valley in Moab where the top
of Pisgah[c] overlooks the wasteland.

Defeat of Sihon and Og

21 Israel sent messengers[d] to say to Sihon[e] king of the Amorites:[f]

22 "Let us pass through your country. We will not turn aside into any
field or vineyard, or drink water from
any well. We will travel along the
King's Highway until we have passed
through your territory.[g]"

23 But Sihon would not let Israel pass
through his territory.[h] He mustered his entire army and marched out into the wilderness against Israel. When he reached
Jahaz,[i] he fought with Israel.[j] 24 Israel,
however, put him to the sword[k] and took
over his land[l] from the Arnon to the Jabbok,[m] but only as far as the Ammonites,[n]
because their border was fortified. 25 Israel
captured all the cities of the Amorites[o] and
occupied them,[p] including Heshbon[q] and
all its surrounding settlements. 26 Heshbon
was the city of Sihon[r] king of the Amorites,[s] who had fought against the former
king of Moab[t] and had taken from him all
his land as far as the Arnon.[u]

27 That is why the poets say:

"Come to Heshbon and let it be rebuilt;
let Sihon's city be restored.

28 "Fire went out from Heshbon,
a blaze from the city of Sihon.[v]
It consumed[w] Ar[x] of Moab,
the citizens of Arnon's heights.[y]

21:20 [c] Nu 23:14; Dt 3:17,27; 34:1; Jos 12:3; 13:20 **21:21** [d] S Ge 32:3 [e] Nu 32:33; Dt 1:4; Jos 2:10; 12:2,4; 13:10; Jdg 11:19-21; 1Ki 4:19; Ne 9:22; Ps 135:11; 136:19; Jer 48:45 [f] S Ex 23:23 **21:22** [g] S Nu 20:17 **21:23** [h] Nu 20:21 [i] Dt 2:32; Jos 13:18; 21:36; Jdg 11:20; Isa 15:4; Jer 48:21,34 [j] Nu 20:18 **21:24** [k] Dt 2:33; 3:3; 29:7; Ps 135:10-11; Am 2:9 [l] ver 35; Dt 3:4 [m] S Ge 32:22; Nu 32:33; Jdg 11:13,22 [n] S Ge 19:38; Dt 2:37; Jos 13:10 **21:25** [o] Nu 13:29; Jdg 10:11; Am 2:10 [p] Jdg 11:26 [q] ver 30; Nu 32:3; Dt 1:4; 29:7; Jos 9:10; 12:2; Isa 15:4; 16:8; Jer 48:2,34 **21:26** [r] ver 21; Dt 29:7; Ps 135:11 [s] Nu 13:29 [t] ver 11 [u] ver 13 **21:28** [v] Jer 48:45 [w] S Nu 11:1 [x] S ver 15 [y] Nu 22:41; Dt 12:2; Jos 13:17; Isa 15:2; Jer 19:5

21:21–26 As they had done with Edom (20:14–19), Israel requested freedom to pass through the land of the Amorites. When Sihon their king tried to meet Israel with a show of force, he suffered an overwhelming defeat. The land of the Amorites referred to here was in Transjordan, extending from the Arnon River (at the midpoint of the Dead Sea) to the Jabbok River (v. 24), which flows into the Jordan some 24 miles north of the Dead Sea.

21:27–30 This third ancient poem in ch. 21 was an Amorite taunt song about their earlier victory over Moab (v. 29).

WILDERNESS WANDERINGS

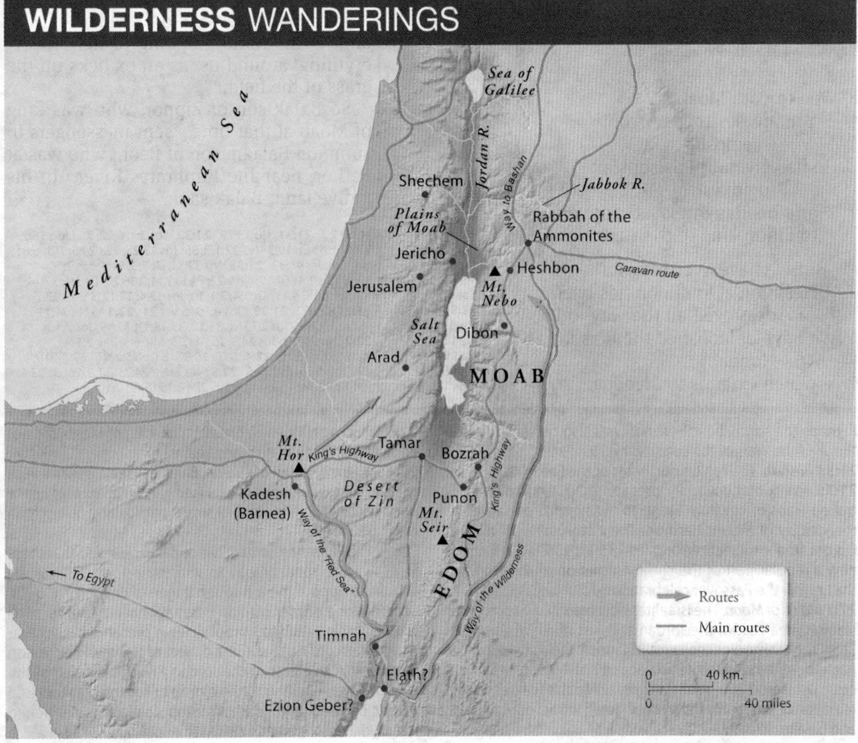

The Desert of Zin, where the Israelites spent many years during their wilderness wanderings

Z. Radovan/www.BibleLandPictures.com

[29] Woe to you, Moab![z]
You are destroyed, people of
Chemosh![a]
He has given up his sons as
fugitives[b]
and his daughters as captives[c]
to Sihon king of the Amorites.

[30] "But we have overthrown them;
Heshbon's dominion has been
destroyed all the way to Dibon.[d]
We have demolished them as far as
Nophah,
which extends to Medeba.[e]"

[31] So Israel settled in the land of the Amorites.[f]
[32] After Moses had sent spies[g] to Jazer,[h]
the Israelites captured its surrounding settlements and drove out the Amorites who
were there. [33] Then they turned and went
up along the road toward Bashan[i],[j] and
Og king of Bashan and his whole army
marched out to meet them in battle at
Edrei.[k]
[34] The LORD said to Moses, "Do not be
afraid of him, for I have delivered him into
your hands, along with his whole army
and his land. Do to him what you did to
Sihon king of the Amorites, who reigned
in Heshbon.[l]"
[35] So they struck him down, together
with his sons and his whole army, leaving
them no survivors.[m] And they took possession of his land.[n]

Balak Summons Balaam

22 Then the Israelites traveled to the
plains of Moab[o] and camped along
the Jordan[p] across from Jericho.[q]
[2] Now Balak son of Zippor[r] saw all that
Israel had done to the Amorites, [3] and
Moab was terrified because there were
so many people. Indeed, Moab was filled
with dread[s] because of the Israelites.
[4] The Moabites[t] said to the elders of Midian,[u] "This horde is going to lick up everything[v] around us, as an ox licks up the
grass of the field.[w]"
So Balak son of Zippor, who was king
of Moab at that time, [5] sent messengers to
summon Balaam son of Beor,[x] who was at
Pethor, near the Euphrates River,[y] in his
native land. Balak said:

21:29 [z] Nu 24:17; 2Sa 8:2; 1Ch 18:2; Ps 60:8; Isa 25:10; Jer 48:46 [a] Jdg 10:6; 11:24; Ru 1:15; 1Ki 11:7,33; 2Ki 23:13; Jer 48:7, 46 [b] Isa 15:5 [c] Isa 16:2 **21:30** [d] Nu 32:3; Jos 13:9,17; Ne 11:25; Isa 15:2; Jer 48:18,22 [e] Jos 13:16; 1Ch 19:7 **21:31** [f] Nu 13:29 **21:32** [g] Jos 2:1; 6:22; 7:2; Jdg 18:2; 2Sa 10:3; 1Ch 19:3 [h] Nu 32:1,3,35; Jos 13:25; 2Sa 24:5; 1Ch 6:81; Isa 16:8; Jer 48:32 **21:33** [i] Nu 32:33; Dt 3:3; 31:4; Jos 2:10; 12:4; 13:30; 1Ki 4:19; Ne 9:22; Ps 135:11; 136:20 [j] Dt 3:4; 32:14; Jos 9:10; 1Ki 4:13 [k] Dt 1:4; 3:1,10; Jos 12:4; 13:12,31; 19:37 **21:34** [l] Dt 3:2 **21:35** [m] Jos 9:10 [n] S ver 24 **22:1** [o] S Nu 21:11 [p] S Nu 13:29; S Jos 2:7 [q] Nu 31:12; 33:48; Dt 32:49; Jos 2:1 **22:2** [r] Nu 23:1-3; Jos 24:9; Jdg 11:25; Mic 6:5; Rev 2:14 **22:3** [s] S Ex 15:15 **22:4** [t] S Ge 19:37 [u] S Ge 25:2 [v] Nu 32:17,18, 29 [w] Job 5:25; Ps 72:16 **22:5** [x] ver 7; Nu 24:25; 31:8,16; Dt 23:4; Jos 13:22; Ne 13:2; Mic 6:5; S 2Pe 2:15 [y] S Ge 2:14

Perhaps the song about Heshbon was also preserved in the "Book of the Wars of the LORD" (v. 14).
21:33 *Bashan.* The region northeast of the Sea of Galilee.
21:35 *struck him down.* By defeating Og, Israel now controlled Transjordan from Moab to the heights of Bashan in the vicinity of Mount Hermon. The victory over Sihon and Og became a subject of song (Ps 135:11; 136:19–20) and is now a regular part of the commemoration of the works of the Lord in the Passover celebration.
22:1 *plains of Moab.* The Israelites now marched back to their staging area east of the Jordan and just north of the Dead Sea. From this point they would launch their attack on Canaan, beginning with the ancient city of Jericho. Moab did not trust Israel's intentions, however. Moab's fear leads to a remarkable interval in the story of Israel: the account of Balak and Balaam (chs. 22–24).
22:3 *Moab was filled with dread.* Balak, king of Moab, did not know that Israel had no plans against him.
22:4 *said to the elders of Midian.* Balak made an alliance with the Midianites to oppose Israel (see v. 7). *as an ox licks up the grass of the field.* A proverbial simile particularly fitting for a pastoral people.
22:5 *summon Balaam.* Since Balak believed that there was no military way to withstand the Israelites, he sought to oppose them through pagan divination (vv. 6–7), sending for a diviner with an international reputation. (One of Balaam's non-Biblical prophecies is preserved in an Aramaic [or, according to some, a dialect of Hebrew] inscription from Deir 'Alla—east of the Jordan River, just north of the Jabbok River—dating to the eighth or seventh century BC.) *Pethor.* Located in Northwest Mesopotamia and mentioned in Assyrian inscriptions.

"A people has come out of Egypt;[z] they cover the face of the land and have settled next to me. 6 Now come and put a curse[a] on these people, because they are too powerful for me. Perhaps then I will be able to defeat them and drive them out of the land.[b] For I know that whoever you bless is blessed, and whoever you curse is cursed."

7 The elders of Moab and Midian left, taking with them the fee for divination.[c] When they came to Balaam, they told him what Balak had said.

8 "Spend the night here," Balaam said to them, "and I will report back to you with the answer the LORD gives me.[d]" So the Moabite officials stayed with him.

9 God came to Balaam[e] and asked,[f] "Who are these men with you?"

10 Balaam said to God, "Balak son of Zippor, king of Moab, sent me this message: 11 'A people that has come out of Egypt covers the face of the land. Now come and put a curse on them for me. Perhaps then I will be able to fight them and drive them away.' "

12 But God said to Balaam, "Do not go with them. You must not put a curse on those people, because they are blessed.[g]"

13 The next morning Balaam got up and said to Balak's officials, "Go back to your own country, for the LORD has refused to let me go with you."

14 So the Moabite officials returned to Balak and said, "Balaam refused to come with us."

15 Then Balak sent other officials, more numerous and more distinguished than the first. 16 They came to Balaam and said:

"This is what Balak son of Zippor says: Do not let anything keep you from coming to me, 17 because I will reward you handsomely[h] and do whatever you say. Come and put a curse[i] on these people for me."

22:5 [z] S Ex 13:3 **22:6** [a] ver 12, 17; Nu 23:7, 11,13; 24:9,10 [b] ver 11 **22:7** [c] S Ge 30:27 **22:8** [d] ver 19 **22:9** [e] S Ge 20:3 [f] ver 20; Nu 23:5; 24:4, 16 **22:12** [g] S Ge 12:2 **22:17** [h] ver 37; Nu 24:11 [i] S ver 6

22:18 [j] ver 38; Nu 23:12, 26; 24:13; 1Ki 22:14; 2Ch 18:13; Jer 42:4 **22:19** [k] ver 8 **22:20** [l] S Ge 20:3 [m] ver 35,38; Nu 23:5,12, 16,26; 24:13; 2Ch 18:13 **22:22** [n] S Ex 4:14 [o] S Ge 16:7; Jdg 13:3,6,13 **22:23** [p] Jos 5:13 [q] ver 25,27 **22:27** [r] Nu 11:1; Jas 1:19 **22:28** [s] 2Pe 2:16 [t] ver 32 **22:29** [u] ver 33; Dt 25:4; Pr 12:10; 27:23-27; Mt 15:19

18 But Balaam answered them, "Even if Balak gave me all the silver and gold in his palace, I could not do anything great or small to go beyond the command of the LORD my God.[j] 19 Now spend the night here so that I can find out what else the LORD will tell me.[k]"

20 That night God came to Balaam[l] and said, "Since these men have come to summon you, go with them, but do only what I tell you."[m]

Balaam's Donkey

21 Balaam got up in the morning, saddled his donkey and went with the Moabite officials. 22 But God was very angry[n] when he went, and the angel of the LORD[o] stood in the road to oppose him. Balaam was riding on his donkey, and his two servants were with him. 23 When the donkey saw the angel of the LORD standing in the road with a drawn sword[p] in his hand, it turned off the road into a field. Balaam beat it[q] to get it back on the road.

24 Then the angel of the LORD stood in a narrow path through the vineyards, with walls on both sides. 25 When the donkey saw the angel of the LORD, it pressed close to the wall, crushing Balaam's foot against it. So he beat the donkey again.

26 Then the angel of the LORD moved on ahead and stood in a narrow place where there was no room to turn, either to the right or to the left. 27 When the donkey saw the angel of the LORD, it lay down under Balaam, and he was angry[r] and beat it with his staff. 28 Then the LORD opened the donkey's mouth,[s] and it said to Balaam, "What have I done to you to make you beat me these three times?[t]"

29 Balaam answered the donkey, "You have made a fool of me! If only I had a sword in my hand, I would kill you right now.[u]"

30 The donkey said to Balaam, "Am I not your own donkey, which you have always

---

22:6 *put a curse on these people.* See note on Ge 12:3.

22:8 *the answer the LORD gives me.* The language here and in v. 18 ("the LORD my God") has led some to believe that Balaam was a believer in Yahweh ("the LORD"), God of Israel. Based on the subsequent narrative, however, it seems best to take Balaam's words as claiming to be the spokesman for any god. Balaam is universally condemned in Scripture for moral, ethical and religious faults (see 31:7–8,15–16; Dt 23:3–6; Jos 13:22; 24:9–10; Ne 13:1–3; Mic 6:5; 2Pe 2:15–16; Jude 11; Rev 2:14).

22:9 That God spoke to Balaam is not to be denied, but Balaam did not yet realize that the God of Israel was unlike the supposed deities that he usually schemed against.

22:12 *they are blessed.* Israel was under the Lord's blessing promised to Abraham (see note on Ge 12:2–3).

22:20 *go with them.* There appears to be a contradiction between the permission God grants Balaam here and the prohibition he had given earlier (v. 12), and then the anger the Lord displayed against Balaam on his journey (v. 22). The difficulty is best understood as lying in the contrary character of Balaam. God had forbidden him to go to curse Israel. He then allowed Balaam to go, but only if he would follow the Lord's direction. But Balaam's real intentions were known to the Lord, and so with severe displeasure he confronted the pagan prophet.

22:23 *the donkey saw the angel of the LORD.* As a pagan prophet, Balaam was a specialist in animal divination, but his dumb beast saw what Balaam was blind to observe.

22:29 *If only I had a sword.* A ridiculous picture of the hapless Balaam. A sword was nearby (see vv. 23,31–33), but its victim was not going to be the donkey. See photo, p. 238.

ridden, to this day? Have I been in the
habit of doing this to you?"
"No," he said.
31 Then the LORD opened Balaam's eyes,[v]
and he saw the angel of the LORD standing
in the road with his sword drawn. So he
bowed low and fell facedown.
32 The angel of the LORD asked him,
"Why have you beaten your donkey these
three times? I have come here to oppose
you because your path is a reckless one
before me.[a] 33 The donkey saw me and
turned away from me these three times. If
it had not turned away, I would certainly
have killed you by now,[w] but
I would have spared it."
34 Balaam said to the an-
gel of the LORD, "I have
sinned.[x] I did not realize
you were standing in the
road to oppose me. Now
if you are displeased,
I will go back."

Bronze figurine of a person riding a donkey (tenth century BC, Anatolia), reminiscent of the Balaam story

Z. Radovan/www.BibleLandPictures.com

22:31 [v] Ge 21:19
22:33 [w] S ver 29
22:34 [x] Ge 39:9; Nu 14:40; 1Sa 15:24, 30; 2Sa 12:13; 24:10; Job 33:27; Ps 51:4

35 The angel of the LORD said to Balaam,
"Go with the men, but speak only what
I tell you." So Balaam went with Balak's
officials.
36 When Balak[y] heard that Balaam was
coming, he went out to meet him at the
Moabite town on the Arnon[z] border, at the
edge of his territory. 37 Balak said to Balaam, "Did I not send you an urgent summons? Why didn't you come to me? Am I
really not able to reward you?"
38 "Well, I have come to you now," Balaam replied. "But I can't say whatever I
please. I must speak only what God puts
in my mouth."[a]
39 Then Balaam went with Balak to Kiriath Huzoth. 40 Balak sacrificed cattle and
sheep,[b] and gave some to Balaam and the
officials who were with him. 41 The next
morning Balak took Balaam up to Bamoth
Baal,[c] and from there he could see the outskirts of the Israelite camp.[d]

Balaam's First Message

23 Balaam said, "Build me seven altars here, and prepare seven bulls
and seven rams[e] for me." 2 Balak did as Balaam said, and the two of them offered a
bull and a ram on each altar.[f]
3 Then Balaam said to Balak, "Stay here
beside your offering while I go aside. Perhaps the LORD will come to meet with me.[g]
Whatever he reveals to me I will tell you."
Then he went off to a barren height.
4 God met with him,[h] and Balaam said,
"I have prepared seven altars, and on each
altar I have offered a bull and a ram."
5 The LORD put a word in Balaam's
mouth[i] and said, "Go back to Balak and
give him this word."[j]
6 So he went back to him and found him
standing beside his offering, with all the
Moabite officials.[k] 7 Then Balaam[l] spoke
his message:[m]

22:36 [y] ver 2 [z] S Nu 21:13
22:38 [a] Nu 23:5, 16, 26
22:40 [b] Nu 23:1, 14, 29; Eze 45:23
22:41 [c] S Nu 21:28 [d] Nu 23:13
23:1 [e] S Nu 22:40
23:2 [f] ver 14, 30
23:3 [g] ver 15
23:4 [h] ver 16
23:5 [i] S Ex 4:12; S Ex 4:15; Isa 59:21 [j] S Nu 22:20
23:6 [k] ver 17
23:7 [l] Nu 22:5; Jos 24:9 [m] ver 18; Nu 24:3, 21; 2Sa 23:1

[a] *32* The meaning of the Hebrew for this clause is uncertain.

22:31 *Then the LORD opened Balaam's eyes.* The language follows the same structure as the opening words of v. 28. In some ways, the opening of the eyes of the pagan prophet to see the reality of the angel was the greater miracle.
22:35 *speak only what I tell you.* The one great gain was that Balaam was now more aware of the seriousness of the task before him; he would not be able to change the word the Lord would give him (see 23:12,20,26).
22:37 *Did I not send you an urgent summons?* The comic element of the story is seen not only in the hapless Balaam but also in the frustrated Balak (see 23:11,25; 24:10).
22:40 The pieces given to Balaam would have included the livers, for, as a pagan diviner, Balaam was a specialist in liver divination. Balaam subsequently gave up his acts of sorcery as the power of the Lord's word came upon him (24:1).
23:1 *seven altars … seven bulls and seven rams.* These sacrifices were prepared as a part of Balaam's pagan actions. The number seven (signifying completeness) was held in high regard among Semitic peoples in general. The many animals would provide abundant liver and other organ materials for the diviner from Northwest Mesopotamia.
23:2 *Balak did as Balaam said.* Balaam is in charge; Balak is now his subordinate.
23:7 — 24:24 There are seven poetic messages here. The first four are longer, have introductory narrative bridges and are written in exquisite poetry (23:7 – 10; 23:18 – 24; 24:3 – 9; 24:15 – 19). The last three are brief, are much more difficult to understand, and follow one another in a staccato pattern (24:20; 24:21 – 22; 24:23 – 24).
23:7 *message.* By this word the distinctive nature of Balaam's prophecies is established; none of the prophecies of Israel's true prophets is described by the Hebrew term (*mashal*) used here.

"Balak brought me from Aram,[n]
the king of Moab from the eastern
mountains.[o]
'Come,' he said, 'curse Jacob for me;
come, denounce Israel.'[p]
8 How can I curse
those whom God has not cursed?[q]
How can I denounce
those whom the LORD has not
denounced?[r]
9 From the rocky peaks I see them,
from the heights I view them.[s]
I see a people who live apart
and do not consider themselves one
of the nations.[t]
10 Who can count the dust of Jacob[u]
or number even a fourth of Israel?
Let me die the death of the righteous,[v]
and may my final end be like
theirs![w]"

11 Balak said to Balaam, "What have you
done to me? I brought you to curse my
enemies,[x] but you have done nothing but
bless them!"[y]
12 He answered, "Must I not speak what
the LORD puts in my mouth?"[z]

Balaam's Second Message

13 Then Balak said to him, "Come with
me to another place[a] where you can see
them; you will not see them all but only
the outskirts of their camp.[b] And from
there, curse them for me.[c]" 14 So he took
him to the field of Zophim on the top of
Pisgah,[d] and there he built seven altars and
offered a bull and a ram on each altar.[e]
15 Balaam said to Balak, "Stay here beside your offering while I meet with him
over there."
16 The LORD met with Balaam and put a
word in his mouth[f] and said, "Go back to
Balak and give him this word."
17 So he went to him and found him
standing beside his offering, with the Moabite officials.[g] Balak asked him, "What
did the LORD say?"

18 Then he spoke his message:[h]

"Arise, Balak, and listen;
hear me, son of Zippor.[i]
19 God is not human,[j] that he should lie,[k]
not a human being, that he should
change his mind.[l]
Does he speak and then not act?
Does he promise[m] and not fulfill?
20 I have received a command to bless;[n]
he has blessed,[o] and I cannot
change it.[p]
21 "No misfortune is seen in Jacob,[q]
no misery observed[a] in Israel.[r]
The LORD their God is with them;[s]
the shout of the King[t] is among
them.
22 God brought them out of Egypt;[u]
they have the strength of a wild ox.[v]
23 There is no divination against[b] Jacob,
no evil omens[w] against[b] Israel.
It will now be said of Jacob
and of Israel, 'See what God has
done!'
24 The people rise like a lioness;[x]
they rouse themselves like a lion[y]
that does not rest till it devours its prey
and drinks the blood[z] of its victims."

25 Then Balak said to Balaam, "Neither
curse them at all nor bless them at all!"
26 Balaam answered, "Did I not tell you I
must do whatever the LORD says?"[a]

Balaam's Third Message

27 Then Balak said to Balaam, "Come, let
me take you to another place.[b] Perhaps it
will please God to let you curse them for
me[c] from there." 28 And Balak took Balaam
to the top of Peor,[d] overlooking the wasteland.

[a] 21 Or *He has not looked on Jacob's offenses / or on the wrongs found* [b] 23 Or *in*

23:7 [n] 2Ki 5:1 [o] S Ge 24:10 [p] S Nu 22:6; Ne 13:2 **23:8** [q] Nu 22:12 [r] ver 20; Isa 43:13 **23:9** [s] Nu 22:41 [t] S Ex 33:16; S Dt 32:8 **23:10** [u] S Ge 13:16 [v] Ps 16:3; 116:15; Isa 57:1 [w] Ps 37:37 **23:11** [x] S Nu 22:6 [y] Nu 24:10; Jos 24:10; Ne 13:2 **23:12** [z] S Nu 22:18, 20 **23:13** [a] ver 27 [b] Nu 22:41 [c] S Nu 22:6 **23:14** [d] S Nu 21:20; 27:12 [e] S ver 2 **23:16** [f] S Ex 4:15; S Nu 22:38 **23:17** [g] ver 6 **23:18** [h] S ver 7 [i] Nu 22:2 **23:19** [j] Job 9:32; Isa 55:9; Hos 11:9 [k] S Nu 11:23 [l] 1Sa 15:29; Job 12:13; 36:5; Ps 33:11; 89:34; 102:27; 110:4; Jer 4:28; 7:16; Mal 3:6; Titus 1:2; Heb 6:18; 7:21; Jas 1:17 [m] 2Sa 7:25; Ps 119:38 **23:20** [n] ver 5, 16; Nu 24:1 [o] Ge 22:17; Nu 22:12 [p] S ver 8; S Job 9:12 **23:21** [q] Ps 32:2, 5; 85:2; Ro 4:7-8 [r] Isa 33:24; 40:2; Jer 50:20 [s] S Ge 26:3; Ex 29:45, 46; Dt 4:7; Ps 34:17-18; 145:18; Zec 2:10 [t] Dt 32:15; 33:5; Ps 89:15-18; Isa 44:2 **23:22** [u] Nu 24:8; Jos 2:10; 9:9 [v] Dt 33:17; Job 39:9; Ps 22:21; 29:6; 92:10; Isa 34:7 **23:23** [w] ver 3; S Ge 30:27; Nu 24:1 **23:24** [x] Nu 24:9; Eze 19:2; Na 2:11 [y] S Ge 49:9 [z] Isa 49:26 **23:26** [a] S Nu 22:18, 20 **23:27** [b] ver 13 [c] Nu 24:10 **23:28** [d] Nu 25:3, 18; 31:16; Dt 3:29; 4:3; Jos 22:17; Ps 106:28; Hos 9:10

23:8 *How can I curse those whom God has not cursed?* That which Balaam had been hired to do he was unable to do. God kept him from pronouncing a curse on his people, who were unlike the nations of the world (v. 9).
23:10 *Let me die the death of the righteous.* A wish not granted (see 31:8,16). *may my final end be like theirs!* He who had come to curse desired to share in Israel's blessing.
23:13 *not see them all but only the outskirts.* Balak attempted to reduce Israel's power by selecting a point where their immense numbers would be obscured. Unfortunately for Balak, the message that followed (vv. 18–24) exceeded the first in its blessing on Israel.
23:19 *God is not human, that he should lie.* These sublime words describe the immutability of the Lord and the integrity of his word. Balaam is a foil to God—constantly shifting, prevaricating, equivocating, changing—a prime example of the distinction between God and human beings.
23:21 *the shout of the King is among them.* That the first explicit declaration of the Lord's kingship in the Pentateuch was made by Balaam is a suitable improbability. Because God is King (Sovereign), he was able to use Balaam for his own ends—to bless his people in a new and wonderful manner.
23:22 *wild ox.* Possibly an "oryx," a large, straight-horned antelope.
23:23 *no divination against Jacob.* Balaam speaks from his frightful experience. He had no means in his bag of tricks to withstand God's blessing of Israel.
23:24 *like a lioness.* Israel was about to arise and devour its foes, like a lioness on the hunt (see 24:9; Ge 49:9 and note).

29 Balaam said, "Build me seven altars
here, and prepare seven bulls and seven
rams for me." 30 Balak did as Balaam had
said, and offered a bull and a ram on each
altar.[e]

24 Now when Balaam saw that it
pleased the LORD to bless Israel,[f]
he did not resort to divination[g] as at other
times, but turned his face toward the wilderness.[h] 2 When Balaam looked out and
saw Israel encamped tribe by tribe, the
Spirit of God came on him[i] 3 and he spoke
his message:

"The prophecy of Balaam son of Beor,
the prophecy of one whose eye sees
clearly,[j]
4 the prophecy of one who hears the
words of God,[k]
who sees a vision from the
Almighty,[a][l]
who falls prostrate, and whose eyes
are opened:

5 "How beautiful are your tents,[m] Jacob,
your dwelling places, Israel!

6 "Like valleys they spread out,
like gardens beside a river,[n]
like aloes[o] planted by the LORD,
like cedars beside the waters.[p]
7 Water will flow from their buckets;
their seed will have abundant water.

"Their king will be greater than Agag;[q]
their kingdom will be exalted.[r]

8 "God brought them out of Egypt;
they have the strength of a wild ox.
They devour hostile nations
and break their bones in pieces;[s]
with their arrows they pierce them.[t]
9 Like a lion they crouch and lie down,
like a lioness[u]—who dares to rouse
them?

"May those who bless you be blessed[v]
and those who curse you be
cursed!"[w]

10 Then Balak's anger burned[x] against
Balaam. He struck his hands together[y] and
said to him, "I summoned you to curse
my enemies,[z] but you have blessed them[a]
these three times.[b] 11 Now leave at once
and go home![c] I said I would reward you
handsomely,[d] but the LORD has kept you
from being rewarded."
12 Balaam answered Balak, "Did I not
tell the messengers you sent me,[e] 13 'Even
if Balak gave me all the silver and gold in
his palace, I could not do anything of my
own accord, good or bad, to go beyond
the command of the LORD[f]—and I must
say only what the LORD says'?[g] 14 Now I am
going back to my people, but come, let me
warn you of what this people will do to
your people in days to come."[h]

Balaam's Fourth Message

15 Then he spoke his message:

"The prophecy of Balaam son of
Beor,
the prophecy of one whose eye sees
clearly,
16 the prophecy of one who hears the
words[i] of God,
who has knowledge from the Most
High,[j]
who sees a vision from the Almighty,
who falls prostrate, and whose eyes
are opened:

17 "I see him, but not now;
I behold him, but not near.[k]
A star will come out of Jacob;[l]
a scepter will rise out of Israel.[m]

23:30 [e] S ver 2
24:1 [f] S Nu 23:20 [g] S Nu 23:23 [h] Nu 23:28
24:2 [i] S Nu 11:25, 26
24:3 [j] ver 15
24:4 [k] S Nu 22:9 [l] S Ge 15:1
24:5 [m] Jer 4:20; 30:18; Mal 2:12
24:6 [n] S Ge 2:10 [o] Ps 45:8; SS 4:14 [p] Job 29:19; Ps 1:3; 104:16; Eze 31:5
24:7 [q] S Ex 17:8-16 [r] Dt 28:1; 2Sa 5:12; 1Ch 14:2; Ps 89:27; 145:11-13
24:8 [s] S Ex 15:6; Jer 50:17 [t] 2Sa 18:14; Ps 45:5
24:9 [u] S Nu 23:24 [v] S Ge 12:2 [w] S Ge 12:3
24:10 [x] S Ex 4:14 [y] Job 27:23; 34:37; La 2:15; Eze 21:14; 22:13; 25:6 [z] S Nu 22:6 [a] S Nu 23:11; S Dt 23:5 [b] ver 3-9; Nu 23:7-10, 18-24
24:11 [c] ver 14, 25 [d] S Nu 22:17
24:12 [e] Nu 22:18
24:13 [f] S Nu 22:18 [g] S Nu 22:20
24:14 [h] S Ge 49:1; Nu 31:8, 16; Mic 6:5
24:16 [i] S Nu 22:9 [j] Ge 14:18; Isa 14:14
24:17 [k] Rev 1:7 [l] Mt 2:2 [m] S Ge 49:10

[a] 4 Hebrew *Shaddai*; also in verse 16

24:1 *divination as at other times.* Balaam's magic and divination are identified here (see notes on 22:40; 23:1).
24:2 *the Spirit of God came on him.* This unexpected language indicates that God has overpowered the pagan prophet for his own purposes. Cf. note on Jdg 3:10.
24:3–4 The extensive introduction of this message describes Balaam's experience in the Lord's presence. Now Balaam's eyes were opened (see note on 22:31).
24:6–7 Balaam speaks here in general, but luxuriant, terms of the blessings that will come to the Israelites as they settle in their new land. The lushness of their blessing from the Lord is reminiscent of Eden.
24:7 *Agag.* Possibly a throne name for the king of the Amalekites (cf. 1Sa 15:32–33). The allusion here may be to the Amalekites who attacked Israel when they came out of Egypt (see Ex 17:8–13) and again when they first approached Canaan (see 14:45).
24:8 *God brought them out of Egypt.* These central words about Israel's salvation are recited by one who was a hostile outsider (see notes on 23:21; 25:1–18).
24:9 *May those who bless you be blessed ... cursed!* The theology of blessing and cursing in the promises made to Abraham (Ge 12:2–3; see note there) is now a part of this message of blessing. Perhaps here Balaam was reasserting his desire to be a part of Israel's blessing (see 23:10–11 and note on 23:10).
24:11 *the LORD has kept you from being rewarded.* In his disgust with Balaam's failure to curse Israel, Balak now dismisses him without pay—the ultimate insult to his greed (see 2Pe 2:15 and note).
24:14 *in days to come.* The distant (Messianic) future is usually indicated by this expression (see, e.g., Jer 48:47 and note).
24:15–16 As in the third message (see vv. 3–4), the introduction to the fourth message is lengthy, helping to prepare the reader for the startling words of the prophecy.
24:17 *star ... scepter.* Fulfilled initially in David, but ultimately in the coming Messianic ruler. Israel's future Deliverer will be like a star (cf. 2Pe 1:19; Rev 22:16); he will wield a royal scepter and bring victory over the enemies of his people (see v. 19). *Sheth.* Possibly the early inhabitants of Moab, known as the Shutu people in ancient Egyptian documents (but see NIV text note; see also Jer 48:45–46 and note).

He will crush the foreheads of Moab,[n]
the skulls[a][o] of[b] all the people of
Sheth.[c]
18 Edom[p] will be conquered;
Seir,[q] his enemy, will be conquered,[r]
but Israel[s] will grow strong.
19 A ruler will come out of Jacob[t]
and destroy the survivors of the
city."

Balaam's Fifth Message

20 Then Balaam saw Amalek[u] and spoke
his message:

"Amalek was first among the nations,
but their end will be utter
destruction."[v]

Balaam's Sixth Message

21 Then he saw the Kenites[w] and spoke
his message:

"Your dwelling place is secure,[x]
your nest is set in a rock;
22 yet you Kenites will be destroyed
when Ashur[y] takes you captive."

Balaam's Seventh Message

23 Then he spoke his message:

"Alas! Who can live when God does
this?[d]
24 Ships will come from the shores of
Cyprus;[z]
they will subdue Ashur[a] and Eber,[b]
but they too will come to ruin.[c]"

25 Then Balaam[d] got up and returned
home, and Balak went his own way.

Moab Seduces Israel

25 While Israel was staying in
Shittim,[e] the men began to indulge
in sexual immorality[f] with Moabite[g] wom-
en,[h] 2 who invited them to the sacrifices[i] to
their gods.[j] The people ate the sacrificial
meal and bowed down before these gods.
3 So Israel yoked themselves to[k] the Baal of
Peor.[l] And the LORD's anger burned against
them.
4 The LORD said to Moses, "Take all the
leaders[m] of these people, kill them and expose[n] them in broad daylight before the
LORD,[o] so that the LORD's fierce anger[p] may
turn away from Israel."
5 So Moses said to Israel's judges, "Each
of you must put to death[q] those of your
people who have yoked themselves to the
Baal of Peor."[r]
6 Then an Israelite man brought into the
camp a Midianite[s] woman right before the
eyes of Moses and the whole assembly of
Israel while they were weeping[t] at the entrance to the tent of meeting. 7 When Phinehas[u] son of Eleazar, the son of Aaron, the
priest, saw this, he left the assembly, took
a spear[v] in his hand 8 and followed the Israelite into the tent. He drove the spear
into both of them, right through the Israelite man and into the woman's stomach. Then the plague against the Israelites
was stopped;[w] 9 but those who died in the
plague[x] numbered 24,000.[y]
10 The LORD said to Moses, 11 "Phinehas son of Eleazar, the son of Aaron, the
priest, has turned my anger away from the

a 17 Samaritan Pentateuch (see also Jer. 48:45); the meaning of the word in the Masoretic Text is uncertain. *b* 17 Or possibly *Moab, / batter* *c* 17 Or *all the noisy boasters* *d* 23 Masoretic Text; with a different word division of the Hebrew *The people from the islands will gather from the north.*

24:17 [n]S Ge 19:37; S Nu 21:29; S Dt 23:6; Isa 15:1-16:14 [o]Jer 48:45 **24:18** [p]2Sa 8:12; 1Ch 18:11; Ps 60:8; Isa 11:14; Am 9:12 [q]S Ge 14:6; Dt 1:44; Jos 12:7; 15:10; Jdg 5:4 [r]Ob 1:2 [s]S Ge 9:25 **24:19** [t]S Ge 49:10; Mic 5:2 **24:20** [u]S Ge 14:7; S Ex 17:14 [v]Dt 25:19; 1Sa 15:20; 30:17-20; 2Sa 8:12; 1Ch 18:11 **24:21** [w]S Ge 15:19 [x]Ps 37:27; Pr 1:33; Isa 32:18; Eze 34:27 **24:22** [y]S Ge 10:22 **24:24** [z]S Ge 10:4 [a]ver 22 [b]S Ge 10:21 [c]ver 20 **24:25** [d]S Nu 22:5 **25:1** [e]S Nu 21:16; Jos 2:1; Isa 66:11; Joel 3:18; Mic 6:5 [f]Jer 5:7; 7:9; 9:2; 1Co 10:8; Rev 2:14 [g]S Ge 19:37 [h]Nu 31:16 **25:2** [i]S Ex 32:6 [j]Ex 20:5; Dt 32:38; 1Co 10:20 **25:3** [k]Dt 4:19; Jdg 2:19; 1Ki 9:9; Jer 1:16; 44:3 [l]S Nu 23:28 **25:4** [m]Nu 7:2; 13:3 [n]2Sa 21:6 [o]Dt 4:3 [p]Ex 32:12; Dt 13:17; Jos 7:26; 2Ki 23:26; 2Ch 28:11; 29:10; 30:8; Ezr 10:14; Jer 44:3 **25:5** [q]S Ex 32:27 [r]Hos 9:10 **25:6** [s]S Ge 25:2 [t]S Nu 14:1; Jdg 2:4; Ru 1:9; 1Sa 11:4; 2Sa 15:30; Ezr 10:1; Ps 126:6; Jer 41:6 **25:7** [u]S Ex 6:25; Jos 22:13; Jdg 20:28 [v]Jdg 5:8; 1Sa 13:19,22; 1Ki 18:28; Ps 35:3; 46:9; Joel 3:10; Mic 4:3 **25:8** [w]Ps 106:30 **25:9** [x]S Nu 14:37; 1Co 10:8 [y]Nu 31:16

24:20 *Amalek was first.* The first to attack Israel and oppose the Lord's purpose with his people (see Ex 17:8–13).
24:21 *Kenites.* The name suggests a tribe of metal workers. In other passages the Kenites are allied with Israel (see, e.g., Jdg 1:16; 4:11; 1Sa 15:6 and note). Since Moses' father-in-law was a Kenite but also associated with Midian (see Ex 2:16), it may be that Balaam's reference is to Midianites (see 22:4,7). *nest.* Hebrew *qen,* a wordplay on the word for Kenites (Hebrew *qeni*).
24:22 *Ashur.* Assyria.
24:24 *they will subdue Ashur and Eber, but ... ruin.* One nation will rise and supplant another, only to face its own doom. By contrast, there is the implied ongoing blessing on Israel and the sure promise of a future deliverer who will have the final victory (vv. 17–19).
25:1–18 It is not until 31:8,16 that we learn that the principal instigator of Israel's apostasy here was Balaam (see notes on 22:5,8). Failing to destroy Israel by means of a curse, Balaam seduced Israel by the Canaanite fertility rites of Baal.
25:1 *Shittim.* Another name for the region of Israel's staging for the conquest of Canaan; it was across the Jordan River opposite the ancient city of Jericho (see Jos 2:1). *indulge in sexual immorality.* Israel's engagement in the fertility rites of Baal involved not only the evil of sexual immorality. It was also a breach of covenant with the Lord (see Ex 20:3–4 and notes), a worship of the gods of the land (vv. 2–3) and a foretaste of the people's ruin in the unfolding of their history.
25:4 *kill them and expose them in broad daylight.* The special display of the corpses would warn survivors of the consequences of sin.
25:6 *brought into the camp a Midianite woman.* The contempt for the holy things and the word of the Lord shown by Zimri (v. 14) and his lover Kozbi (v. 15) is unimaginable.
25:9 *24,000.* The number of those who died because of the flagrant actions of the people in their worship of Baal exceeded even that of those who had died in the rebellion of Korah and his allies (14,700; see 16:49 and note). Again, the large number of those who died fits well with the immense number of the people stated in the first census (see 1:46 and note) and the second (see 26:51 and note).
25:11 *he was as zealous for my honor among them as I am.* Cf. Ex 20:4–6. The zeal of Phinehas for the Lord's honor became

Israelites.[z] Since he was as zealous for my
honor[a] among them as I am, I did not put an
end to them in my zeal. 12 Therefore tell him
I am making my covenant of peace[b] with
him. 13 He and his descendants will have a
covenant of a lasting priesthood,[c] because
he was zealous[d] for the honor[e] of his God
and made atonement[f] for the Israelites."[g]
14 The name of the Israelite who was
killed with the Midianite woman[h] was
Zimri son of Salu, the leader of a Sime-
onite family.[i] 15 And the name of the Midianite woman who was put to death was
Kozbi[j] daughter of Zur, a tribal chief of a
Midianite family.[k]
16 The LORD said to Moses,[l] 17 "Treat the
Midianites[m] as enemies[n] and kill them.[o]
18 They treated you as enemies when they
deceived you in the Peor incident[p] involving their sister Kozbi, the daughter of a
Midianite leader, the woman who was
killed when the plague came as a result of
that incident."

The Second Census

26 After the plague[q] the LORD said to
Moses and Eleazar son of Aaron,
the priest, 2 "Take a census[r] of the whole
Israelite community by families — all those
twenty years old or more who are able to
serve in the army[s] of Israel." 3 So on the
plains of Moab[t] by the Jordan across from
Jericho,[u] Moses and Eleazar the priest
spoke with them and said, 4 "Take a census of the men twenty years old or more,
as the LORD commanded Moses."

These were the Israelites who came out
of Egypt:[v]

5 The descendants of Reuben,[w] the firstborn son of Israel, were:
through Hanok,[x] the Hanokite clan;
through Pallu,[y] the Palluite clan;
6 through Hezron,[z] the Hezronite clan;
through Karmi,[a] the Karmite clan.
7 These were the clans of Reuben; those
numbered were 43,730.
8 The son of Pallu was Eliab, 9 and the
sons of Eliab[b] were Nemuel, Dathan and
Abiram. The same Dathan and Abiram
were the community[c] officials who rebelled against Moses and Aaron and were
among Korah's followers when they rebelled against the LORD.[d] 10 The earth
opened its mouth and swallowed them[e]
along with Korah, whose followers died
when the fire devoured the 250 men.[f] And
they served as a warning sign.[g] 11 The line
of Korah,[h] however, did not die out.[i]

12 The descendants of Simeon by their
clans were:
through Nemuel,[j] the Nemuelite clan;
through Jamin,[k] the Jaminite clan;
through Jakin, the Jakinite clan;
13 through Zerah,[l] the Zerahite clan;
through Shaul, the Shaulite clan.
14 These were the clans of Simeon;[m] those
numbered were 22,200.[n]

15 The descendants of Gad by their clans
were:
through Zephon,[o] the Zephonite clan;
through Haggi, the Haggite clan;
through Shuni, the Shunite clan;
16 through Ozni, the Oznite clan;
through Eri, the Erite clan;
17 through Arodi,[a] the Arodite clan;
through Areli, the Arelite clan.
18 These were the clans of Gad;[p] those
numbered were 40,500.

a 17 Samaritan Pentateuch and Syriac (see also Gen. 46:16); Masoretic Text *Arod*

25:11 [z] Ps 106:30 [a] Ex 20:5; Dt 32:16,21; Ps 78:58 **25:12** [b] Isa 11:9; 54:10; Eze 34:25; 37:26; Mal 2:4, 5 **25:13** [c] S Ex 29:9 [d] 1Ki 19:10; 2Ki 10:16 [e] ver 11 [f] S Ex 29:36; S Ro 3:25 [g] Ps 106:31; Jer 33:18 **25:14** [h] ver 6 [i] S Nu 1:6 **25:15** [j] ver 18 [k] Nu 31:8; Jos 13:21; Hab 3:7 **25:16** [l] Nu 31:7 **25:17** [m] Nu 31:1-3 [n] Ex 23:22; Jdg 2:16-18; Ne 9:27; Ps 8:2; 21:8; 74:23 [o] Dt 21:1; 1Sa 17:9,35; 2Ki 9:27; 10:25 **25:18** [p] S Nu 23:28 **26:1** [q] S Nu 14:37; 25:8 **26:2** [r] Ex 30:11-16 [s] S Nu 1:3 **26:3** [t] ver 63; Nu 33:48; Jos 13:32 [u] Nu 22:1 **26:4** [v] S Ex 6:14; S 13:3 **26:5** [w] Nu 1:20 [x] S Ge 46:9 [y] 1Ch 5:3 **26:6** [z] 1Ch 5:3 [a] Ge 46:9 **26:9** [b] Nu 16:1 [c] Nu 1:16 [d] S Nu 16:2 **26:10** [e] S Ex 15:12 [f] S Nu 16:35 [g] S Ex 3:12; S Nu 16:38

26:11 [h] Ex 6:24 [i] Nu 16:33; Dt 5:9; 24:16; 2Ki 14:6; 2Ch 25:4; Eze 18:20 **26:12** [j] S Ge 46:10 [k] 1Ch 4:24 **26:13** [l] S Ge 46:10 **26:14** [m] S Ge 46:10 [n] Nu 1:23 **26:15** [o] Ge 46:16 **26:18** [p] S Ge 30:11; S Nu 1:25; S Jos 13:24-28

the occasion for the Lord's covenanting with him and his descendants as God's true priests (see note on Ge 9:9; see also v. 12 and chart, p. 23). This son of Eleazar contrasts with the casual wickedness of his uncles, Nadab and Abihu (see Lev 10:1–3 and notes).

25:12 *covenant of peace.* Cf. note on Isa 54:10.

25:17 *Treat the Midianites as enemies.* Because of their active participation in the seduction of the Israelites. Midianites had been in league with Balak from the beginning of the confrontation (see 22:4,7) and became the objects of a holy war (31:1–24).

26:1–51 The first census of those who were mustered for the war of conquest had been taken more than 38 years earlier (ch. 1). That first generation of men 20 years old or more had nearly all died. It was now time for the new generation to be numbered and mustered for the campaign that awaited them. Note the comparison of the numbers of each tribe from the first census to the second:

Tribe	*First Census*	*Second Census*
Reuben	46,500	43,730
Simeon	59,300	22,200
Gad	45,650	40,500
Judah	74,600	76,500
Issachar	54,400	64,300
Zebulun	57,400	60,500
Ephraim	40,500	32,500
Manasseh	32,200	52,700
Benjamin	35,400	45,600
Dan	62,700	64,400
Asher	41,500	53,400
Naphtali	53,400	45,400
Total	603,550	601,730

26:9 *Dathan and Abiram.* The listing of Reuben's families becomes an occasion to remind the reader of the part that certain of their number played in Korah's rebellion (see 16:1–7 and note; cf. Jude 11 and note).

26:14 *22,200.* The greatest loss was in the tribe of Simeon (down from 59,300). Zimri was from the house of Simeon (25:14). Perhaps most of the 24,000 who died in the plague of that time were from Simeon. The judgment was so recent that the tribe had not had time to recover, as had the tribe of Reuben (see note on vv. 1–51).

19 Er[q] and Onan[r] were sons of Judah, but they died[s] in Canaan.
20 The descendants of Judah by their clans were:
through Shelah,[t] the Shelanite clan;
through Perez,[u] the Perezite clan;
through Zerah, the Zerahite clan.[v]
21 The descendants of Perez[w] were:
through Hezron,[x] the Hezronite clan;
through Hamul, the Hamulite clan.
22 These were the clans of Judah;[y] those numbered were 76,500.

23 The descendants of Issachar by their clans were:
through Tola,[z] the Tolaite clan;
through Puah, the Puite[a] clan;
24 through Jashub,[a] the Jashubite clan;
through Shimron, the Shimronite clan.
25 These were the clans of Issachar;[b] those numbered were 64,300.

26 The descendants of Zebulun[c] by their clans were:
through Sered, the Seredite clan;
through Elon, the Elonite clan;
through Jahleel, the Jahleelite clan.
27 These were the clans of Zebulun;[d] those numbered were 60,500.

28 The descendants of Joseph[e] by their clans through Manasseh and Ephraim[f] were:
29 The descendants of Manasseh:[g]
through Makir,[h] the Makirite clan
(Makir was the father of Gilead[i]);
through Gilead, the Gileadite clan.
30 These were the descendants of Gilead:[j]
through Iezer,[k] the Iezerite clan;
through Helek, the Helekite clan;
31 through Asriel, the Asrielite clan;
through Shechem, the Shechemite clan;
32 through Shemida, the Shemidaite clan;
through Hepher, the Hepherite clan.
33 (Zelophehad[l] son of Hepher had no sons;[m] he had only daughters, whose names were Mahlah, Noah, Hoglah, Milkah and Tirzah.)[n]
34 These were the clans of Manasseh; those numbered were 52,700.[o]
35 These were the descendants of Ephraim[p] by their clans:

26:19 [q] S Ge 38:3 [r] S Ge 38:4 [s] Ge 38:7 **26:20** [t] S Ge 38:5 [u] S Ge 38:29 [v] Jos 7:17 **26:21** [w] S Ge 38:29 [x] Ru 4:19; 1Ch 2:9 **26:22** [y] Nu 1:27 **26:23** [z] S Ge 46:13 **26:24** [a] Ge 46:13 **26:25** [b] S Ge 30:18 **26:26** [c] Nu 1:30 **26:27** [d] S Ge 30:20 **26:28** [e] Nu 1:32; 36:1 [f] S Ge 41:52 **26:29** [g] Nu 1:34 [h] S Ge 50:23 [i] Jdg 11:1 **26:30** [j] Nu 27:1; 36:1; 1Ch 7:14, 17 [k] Jos 17:2; Jdg 6:11; 8:2 **26:33** [l] Nu 27:1; 36:2; Jos 17:3; 1Ch 7:15 [m] Nu 27:3 [n] Nu 36:11 **26:34** [o] Nu 1:35 **26:35** [p] Nu 1:32 **26:37** [q] S Nu 1:33 **26:38** [r] Ge 46:21; Nu 1:36; 1Ch 8:40 **26:40** [s] S Ge 46:21 **26:41** [t] Nu 1:37 **26:42** [u] Nu 1:38 [v] Jdg 18:19 [w] Ge 46:23 **26:44** [x] S Nu 1:40 **26:47** [y] Nu 1:41

through Shuthelah, the Shuthelahite clan;
through Beker, the Bekerite clan;
through Tahan, the Tahanite clan.
36 These were the descendants of Shuthelah:
through Eran, the Eranite clan.
37 These were the clans of Ephraim;[q] those numbered were 32,500.

These were the descendants of Joseph by their clans.

38 The descendants of Benjamin[r] by their clans were:
through Bela, the Belaite clan;
through Ashbel, the Ashbelite clan;
through Ahiram, the Ahiramite clan;
39 through Shupham,[b] the Shuphamite clan;
through Hupham, the Huphamite clan.
40 The descendants of Bela through Ard[s] and Naaman were:
through Ard,[c] the Ardite clan;
through Naaman, the Naamite clan.
41 These were the clans of Benjamin;[t] those numbered were 45,600.

42 These were the descendants of Dan[u] by their clans:[v]
through Shuham,[w] the Shuhamite clan.
These were the clans of Dan: 43 All of them were Shuhamite clans; and those numbered were 64,400.

44 The descendants of Asher[x] by their clans were:
through Imnah, the Imnite clan;
through Ishvi, the Ishvite clan;
through Beriah, the Beriite clan;
45 and through the descendants of Beriah:
through Heber, the Heberite clan;
through Malkiel, the Malkielite clan.
46 (Asher had a daughter named Serah.)
47 These were the clans of Asher;[y] those numbered were 53,400.

[a] 23 Samaritan Pentateuch, Septuagint, Vulgate and Syriac (see also 1 Chron. 7:1); Masoretic Text *through Puvah, the Punite* [b] 39 A few manuscripts of the Masoretic Text, Samaritan Pentateuch, Vulgate and Syriac (see also Septuagint); most manuscripts of the Masoretic Text *Shephupham* [c] 40 Samaritan Pentateuch and Vulgate (see also Septuagint); Masoretic Text does not have *through Ard.*

26:19 *Er and Onan.* The names of the evil sons of Judah had not been forgotten, but they had no heritage (see Ge 38:1–10).
26:20 *Perez.* The line of David and Jesus would be traced through him (see Ru 4:18–22 and note; Mt 1:1–3).
26:29,35 *Manasseh … Ephraim.* The order of the tribes is the same as in ch. 1, except for the inversion of Ephraim and Manasseh, perhaps due to the much larger relative growth of Manasseh's tribe (see note on vv. 1–51; see also note on v. 34).
26:33 *Zelophehad … daughters.* See 27:1–11; 36.
26:34 *52,700.* The greatest gain was in the tribe of Manasseh (up from 32,200). The reason for this increase is not known.
26:46 *daughter named Serah.* The listing of this solitary daughter is striking.

48 The descendants of Naphtali[z] by their
clans were:
through Jahzeel, the Jahzeelite clan;
through Guni, the Gunite clan;
49 through Jezer, the Jezerite clan;
through Shillem, the Shillemite clan.
50 These were the clans of Naphtali;[a] those
numbered were 45,400.[b]

51 The total number of the men of Israel
was 601,730.[c]

52 The LORD said to Moses, 53 "The land
is to be allotted to them as an inheritance
based on the number of names.[d] 54 To a
larger group give a larger inheritance, and
to a smaller group a smaller one; each is
to receive its inheritance according to the
number[e] of those listed.[f] 55 Be sure that
the land is distributed by lot.[g] What each
group inherits will be according to the
names for its ancestral tribe. 56 Each inheritance is to be distributed by lot among the
larger and smaller groups."

57 These were the Levites[h] who were counted by their clans:
through Gershon, the Gershonite
clan;
through Kohath, the Kohathite clan;
through Merari, the Merarite clan.
58 These also were Levite clans:
the Libnite clan,
the Hebronite clan,
the Mahlite clan,
the Mushite clan,
the Korahite clan.
(Kohath was the forefather of Amram;[i]
59 the name of Amram's wife was Jochebed,[j] a descendant of Levi, who was
born to the Levites[a] in Egypt. To Amram she bore Aaron, Moses[k] and their
sister[l] Miriam.[m] 60 Aaron was the father
of Nadab and Abihu, Eleazar and Ithamar.[n] 61 But Nadab and Abihu[o] died
when they made an offering before the
LORD with unauthorized fire.)[p]

62 All the male Levites a month old or more
numbered 23,000.[q] They were not counted[r] along with the other Israelites because
they received no inheritance[s] among
them.[t]

63 These are the ones counted[u] by Moses
and Eleazar the priest when they counted
the Israelites on the plains of Moab[v] by the
Jordan across from Jericho.[w] 64 Not one of
them was among those counted[x] by Moses
and Aaron[y] the priest when they counted
the Israelites in the Desert of Sinai. 65 For
the LORD had told those Israelites they
would surely die in the wilderness,[z] and
not one of them was left except Caleb[a] son
of Jephunneh and Joshua son of Nun.[b]

Zelophehad's Daughters

27:1-11pp — Nu 36:1-12

27 The daughters of Zelophehad[c] son
of Hepher,[d] the son of Gilead,[e] the
son of Makir,[f] the son of Manasseh, belonged to the clans of Manasseh son of
Joseph. The names of the daughters were
Mahlah, Noah, Hoglah, Milkah and Tirzah. They came forward 2 and stood before
Moses,[g] Eleazar the priest, the leaders
and the whole assembly at the entrance
to the tent of meeting[i] and said, 3 "Our father died in the wilderness.[j] He was not
among Korah's followers, who banded together against the LORD,[k] but he died for
his own sin and left no sons.[l] 4 Why should
our father's name disappear from his clan
because he had no son? Give us property
among our father's relatives."
5 So Moses brought their case[m] before
the LORD,[n] 6 and the LORD said to him,
7 "What Zelophehad's daughters are saying is right. You must certainly give them
property as an inheritance[o] among their
father's relatives and give their father's inheritance to them.[p]
8 "Say to the Israelites, 'If a man dies
and leaves no son, give his inheritance
to his daughter. 9 If he has no daughter,
give his inheritance to his brothers. 10 I

[a] 59 Or *Jochebed, a daughter of Levi, who was born to Levi*

26:48 [z] S Ge 30:8 **26:50** [a] Nu 1:43 [b] Nu 1:42 **26:51** [c] S Ex 12:37 **26:53** [d] ver 55; Jos 11:23; 14:1; Eze 45:8 **26:54** [e] Nu 33:54 [f] Nu 35:8 **26:55** [g] S Lev 16:8 **26:57** [h] S Ge 46:11 **26:58** [i] Ex 6:20 **26:59** [j] S Ex 2:1 [k] S Ex 6:20 [l] S Ex 2:4 [m] S Ex 15:20 **26:60** [n] Ex 6:23 **26:61** [o] S Lev 10:1-2 [p] Nu 3:4 **26:62** [q] Nu 3:39 [r] Nu 1:47 [s] S Nu 18:23 [t] S Nu 2:33 **26:63** [u] S Nu 1:19 [v] S ver 3 [w] Nu 22:1 **26:64** [x] S Nu 14:29 [y] Nu 1:44 **26:65** [z] Nu 14:28; 1Co 10:5 [a] Nu 13:6 [b] S Nu 11:28 **27:1** [c] S Nu 26:33 [d] Jos 17:2,3 [e] S Nu 26:30 [f] S Ge 50:23; 1Ch 2:21 **27:2** [g] S Nu 9:6 [h] Nu 1:16; 31:13; 32:2; 36:1 [i] Ex 40:2,17 **27:3** [j] Nu 26:65 [k] Nu 16:2 [l] Nu 26:33 **27:5** [m] S Ge 25:22; S Ex 18:19 [n] S Nu 9:8 **27:7** [o] Job 42:15 [p] ver 8; Jos 17:4

26:51 *601,730.* Despite all that the people had been through during the years of wilderness experience, their total number was nearly the same as that of those who were first numbered. This remarkable fact is to be regarded as the blessing of the Lord, in fulfillment of his many promises to give numerical strength to the people descended from Abraham through Jacob (see note on Ge 12:2–3). This grand total and its parts are in accord with the general pattern of the numbers in the book (see note on 1:46).

26:53–56 Larger tribes would receive larger shares, but decisions of place would be made by lot (see v. 56; 33:54).

26:57 *Levites.* As in the first census (ch. 3), the Levites were counted separately.

27:1–11 The daughters of a man who had no son (see 26:33) were concerned about their rights of inheritance and the preservation of their father's name in the land (v. 4). Their action in approaching Moses, Eleazar and the leaders of the nation was unprecedented, an act of courage and conviction.

27:3 *he died for his own sin.* A particular case from among those who died in the wilderness (see 26:64–65). These pious women had a sound understanding of the nature of the wilderness experience and a just claim for their family.

27:5 *Moses brought their case before the LORD.* This verse indicates how case law might have operated in Israel. The general laws would be proclaimed. Then legitimate exceptions or special considerations would come to the elders, and perhaps to Moses himself. He would then await a decision from the Lord. In this case, the Lord gave a favorable decision for these women. Ch. 36 provides an appendix to this account.

he has no brothers, give his inheritance to
his father's brothers. 11 If his father had no
brothers, give his inheritance to the nearest relative in his clan, that he may possess it. This is to have the force of law[q]
for the Israelites, as the LORD commanded
Moses.' "

Joshua to Succeed Moses

12 Then the LORD said to Moses, "Go up
this mountain[r] in the Abarim Range[s] and
see the land[t] I have given the Israelites.[u]
13 After you have seen it, you too will be
gathered to your people,[v] as your brother Aaron[w] was, 14 for when the community rebelled at the waters in the Desert of
Zin,[x] both of you disobeyed my command
to honor me as holy[y] before their eyes."
(These were the waters of Meribah[z] Kadesh, in the Desert of Zin.)

15 Moses said to the LORD, 16 "May the
LORD, the God who gives breath to all living things,[a] appoint someone over this
community 17 to go out and come in before them, one who will lead them out and
bring them in, so the LORD's people will
not be like sheep without a shepherd."[b]

18 So the LORD said to Moses, "Take Joshua son of Nun, a man in whom is the spirit of leadership,[a][c] and lay your hand on
him.[d] 19 Have him stand before Eleazar the
priest and the entire assembly and commission him[e] in their presence.[f] 20 Give
him some of your authority so the whole
Israelite community will obey him.[g] 21 He
is to stand before Eleazar the priest, who
will obtain decisions for him by inquiring[h]
of the Urim[i] before the LORD. At his command he and the entire community of the
Israelites will go out, and at his command
they will come in."

22 Moses did as the LORD commanded
him. He took Joshua and had him stand
before Eleazar the priest and the whole assembly. 23 Then he laid his hands on him
and commissioned him,[j] as the LORD instructed through Moses.

27:11 [q] Nu 35:29 **27:12** [r] Nu 23:14 [s] Nu 33:47; Jer 22:20 [t] Dt 3:23-27; 32:48-52 [u] S Lev 14:34 **27:13** [v] Nu 20:12; 31:2; Dt 4:22; 31:14; 32:50; 1Ki 2:1 [w] Nu 20:28 **27:14** [x] S Nu 20:1,2-5 [y] S Nu 20:12 [z] S Ex 17:7 **27:16** [a] S Nu 16:22; S Job 21:20 **27:17** [b] 1Ki 22:17; 2Ch 18:16; Eze 34:5; Zec 10:2; S Mt 9:36 **27:18** [c] S Ge 41:38; Nu 11:25-29 [d] ver 23; Dt 34:9; Ac 6:6 **27:19** [e] ver 23; Dt 3:28; 31:14, 23 [f] Dt 31:7 **27:20** [g] Jos 1:16, 17 **27:21** [h] S Ge 25:22; Jos 9:14; Ps 106:13; Isa 8:19; Hag 1:13; Mal 2:7; 3:1 [i] S Ex 28:30 **27:23** [j] S ver 19

28:2 [k] Lev 23:1-44 [l] S Lev 3:11 [m] Lev 1:9 **28:3** [n] S Ex 12:5 [o] Ex 29:38; Am 4:4 **28:4** [p] S Ex 29:39 **28:5** [q] Nu 29:6 [r] Lev 6:20 [s] S Lev 2:1 **28:6** [t] Lev 1:3 [u] Ex 19:3 [v] S Lev 1:9 **28:7** [w] Nu 6:15 [x] S Lev 10:9; S 23:13 [y] S Lev 3:7; Nu 3:28 **28:8** [z] S Ex 29:39 [a] S Lev 3:7 [b] ver 2; Lev 1:9 **28:9** [c] S Ex 20:10; Mt 12:5 [d] ver 3

Daily Offerings

28 The LORD said to Moses, 2 "Give
this command to the Israelites
and say to them: 'Make sure that you
present to me at the appointed time[k] my
food[l] offerings, as an aroma pleasing to
me.'[m] 3 Say to them: 'This is the food offering you are to present to the LORD: two
lambs a year old without defect,[n] as a
regular burnt offering each day.[o] 4 Offer
one lamb in the morning and the other
at twilight,[p] 5 together with a grain offering[q] of a tenth of an ephah[b] of the finest
flour[r] mixed with a quarter of a hin[c] of oil[s]
from pressed olives. 6 This is the regular
burnt offering[t] instituted at Mount Sinai[u]
as a pleasing aroma, a food offering presented to the LORD.[v] 7 The accompanying
drink offering[w] is to be a quarter of a hin
of fermented drink[x] with each lamb. Pour
out the drink offering to the LORD at the
sanctuary.[y] 8 Offer the second lamb at twilight,[z] along with the same kind of grain
offering and drink offering that you offer
in the morning.[a] This is a food offering,
an aroma pleasing to the LORD.[b]

Sabbath Offerings

9 " 'On the Sabbath[c] day, make an offering of two lambs a year old without defect,[d] together with its drink offering and a
grain offering of two-tenths of an ephah[d][e]
of the finest flour mixed with olive oil.[f]
10 This is the burnt offering for every Sabbath,[g] in addition to the regular burnt offering[h] and its drink offering.

Monthly Offerings

11 " 'On the first of every month,[i] present
to the LORD a burnt offering of two young
bulls,[j] one ram[k] and seven male lambs a

[a] 18 Or *the Spirit* [b] 5 That is, probably about 3 1/2 pounds or about 1.6 kilograms; also in verses 13, 21 and 29 [c] 5 That is, about 1 quart or about 1 liter; also in verses 7 and 14 [d] 9 That is, probably about 7 pounds or about 3.2 kilograms; also in verses 12, 20 and 28

[e] S Lev 23:13 [f] ver 5 **28:10** [g] S Lev 23:38 [h] ver 3 **28:11** [i] S Nu 10:10 [j] S Nu 7:15 [k] S Lev 5:15

27:12–23 The juxtaposition of the story of Zelophehad's daughters' request for an inheritance in the land (vv. 1–11) and the Lord's words to Moses about his own exclusion from the land (vv. 12–14) is striking. Provisions are made for exceptions and irregularities in the inheritance laws, but there is no provision for Moses. His sin at the waters of Meribah at Kadesh (20:1–13) was always before him.
27:14 *honor me as holy.* See 20:12 and note.
27:16 *appoint someone.* Moses' reaction to this reassertion of his restriction is a prayer for a successor.
27:18 *Take Joshua.* As Moses and Aaron needed to determine the true successor of Aaron before his death (20:22–29), so the true successor of Moses also needed to be established. Joshua and Caleb were the two heroes in the darkest hour of Israel's apostasy (chs. 13–14). It was fitting that the Lord selected one of them (cf. Ex 17:9–14; 24:13; 32:17; 33:11).
27:20 *Give him some of your authority.* The transition from Moses' leadership to that of any successor would have been difficult. The change would be made smoother by a gradual shift of power while Moses was still alive.
27:21 *Urim.* See notes on Ex 28:30; 1Sa 2:28.
28:1—29:40 These chapters attest to the all-pervasiveness of sacrifice in the life of the people and to the enormity of the work of the priests. Perhaps the reason for these passages at this time is to give continuity to the impending transition from the leadership of Moses to that of Joshua (27:12–23).
28:1–8 See Ex 29:38–41; Lev 1–7 and notes.
28:9–10 The Sabbath offerings were in addition to the daily offerings.

year old, all without defect.[l] 12 With each
bull there is to be a grain offering[m] of
three-tenths of an ephah[an] of the finest
flour mixed with oil; with the ram, a grain
offering of two-tenths[o] of an ephah of the
finest flour mixed with oil; 13 and with
each lamb, a grain offering[p] of a tenth[q] of
an ephah of the finest flour mixed with
oil. This is for a burnt offering,[r] a pleasing aroma, a food offering presented to
the LORD.[s] 14 With each bull there is to be
a drink offering[t] of half a hin[b] of wine;
with the ram, a third of a hin[c]; and with
each lamb, a quarter of a hin. This is the
monthly burnt offering to be made at each
new moon[u] during the year. 15 Besides the
regular burnt offering[v] with its drink offering, one male goat[w] is to be presented to
the LORD as a sin offering.[dx]

The Passover

28:16-25pp — Ex 12:14-20; Lev 23:4-8; Dt 16:1-8

16 "'On the fourteenth day of the first
month the LORD's Passover[y] is to be held.
17 On the fifteenth day of this month
there is to be a festival; for seven days[z]
eat bread made without yeast.[a] 18 On the
first day hold a sacred assembly and do
no regular work.[b] 19 Present to the LORD
a food offering[c] consisting of a burnt offering of two young bulls, one ram and
seven male lambs a year old, all without
defect.[d] 20 With each bull offer a grain offering of three-tenths of an ephah[e] of the
finest flour mixed with oil; with the ram,
two-tenths;[f] 21 and with each of the sev-
en lambs, one-tenth.[g] 22 Include one male
goat as a sin offering[h] to make atonement
for you.[i] 23 Offer these in addition to the
regular morning burnt offering. 24 In this
way present the food offering every day
for seven days as an aroma pleasing to the
LORD;[j] it is to be offered in addition to the
regular burnt offering and its drink offering. 25 On the seventh day hold a sacred
assembly and do no regular work.

The Festival of Weeks

28:26-31pp — Lev 23:15-22; Dt 16:9-12

26 "'On the day of firstfruits,[k] when you
present to the LORD an offering of new
grain during the Festival of Weeks,[l] hold a
sacred assembly and do no regular work.[m]
27 Present a burnt offering of two young
bulls, one ram and seven male lambs a
year old as an aroma pleasing to the LORD.[n]
28 With each bull there is to be a grain offering of three-tenths of an ephah of the
finest flour mixed with oil; with the ram,
two-tenths;[o] 29 and with each of the sev-
en lambs, one-tenth.[p] 30 Include one male
goat[q] to make atonement for you. 31 Offer
these together with their drink offerings,
in addition to the regular burnt offering[r]
and its grain offering. Be sure the animals
are without defect.

The Festival of Trumpets

29:1-6pp — Lev 23:23-25

29 "'On the first day of the seventh
month hold a sacred assembly
and do no regular work.[s] It is a day for
you to sound the trumpets. 2 As an aroma pleasing to the LORD,[t] offer a burnt
offering[u] of one young bull, one ram and
seven male lambs a year old,[v] all without defect.[w] 3 With the bull offer a grain
offering[x] of three-tenths of an ephah[e] of
the finest flour mixed with olive oil; with
the ram, two-tenths[f]; 4 and with each of
the seven lambs, one-tenth.[gy] 5 Include
one male goat[z] as a sin offering[h] to make
atonement for you. 6 These are in addition
to the monthly[a] and daily burnt offerings[b]
with their grain offerings[c] and drink offerings[d] as specified. They are food offerings
presented to the LORD, a pleasing aroma.[e]

The Day of Atonement

29:7-11pp — Lev 16:2-34; 23:26-32

7 "'On the tenth day of this seventh
month hold a sacred assembly. You
must deny yourselves[if] and do no work.[g]

[a] *12* That is, probably about 11 pounds or about 5 kilograms; also in verses 20 and 28 [b] *14* That is, about 2 quarts or about 1.9 liters [c] *14* That is, about 1 1/3 quarts or about 1.3 liters [d] *15* Or *purification offering*; also in verse 22 [e] *3* That is, probably about 11 pounds or about 5 kilograms; also in verses 9 and 14 [f] *3* That is, probably about 7 pounds or about 3.2 kilograms; also in verses 9 and 14 [g] *4* That is, probably about 3 1/2 pounds or about 1.6 kilograms; also in verses 10 and 15 [h] *5* Or *purification offering*; also elsewhere in this chapter [i] *7* Or *must fast*

28:11 [l] Lev 1:3
28:12 [m] S Nu 15:6; S 29:3 [n] Nu 15:9 [o] ver 20
28:13 [p] S Lev 6:14 [q] ver 21 [r] S Nu 15:3 [s] Lev 1:9
28:14 [t] S Nu 15:7 [u] ver 11; 2Ch 2:4; Ezr 3:5
28:15 [v] ver 3, 23, 24 [w] ver 30 [x] Lev 4:3; Nu 29:16, 19
28:16 [y] S Ex 12:11; 2Ch 30:13; 35:1
28:17 [z] S Ex 12:19 [a] S Ex 12:15
28:18 [b] S Ex 12:16
28:19 [c] S Lev 1:9 [d] ver 11
28:20 [e] S Lev 14:10 [f] ver 12
28:21 [g] ver 13
28:22 [h] Lev 4:3; Ro 8:3 [i] S Nu 15:28
28:24 [j] Lev 1:9
28:26 [k] S Ex 34:22 [l] S Ex 23:16 [m] ver 18
28:27 [n] ver 19
28:28 [o] ver 12
28:29 [p] ver 13
28:30 [q] ver 15
28:31 [r] ver 3, 19
29:1 [s] Nu 28:18
29:2 [t] Nu 28:2 [u] Lev 1:9; Nu 28:11 [v] ver 36 [w] Lev 1:3; Nu 28:3
29:3 [x] ver 14; Nu 28:12
29:4 [y] Nu 28:13
29:5 [z] Nu 28:15
29:6 [a] Nu 28:11 [b] Nu 28:3 [c] Nu 28:5 [d] Nu 28:7 [e] Lev 1:9; Nu 28:2
29:7 [f] Ac 27:9 [g] S Ex 31:15

28:11 – 15 The sacrifices at the beginning of the month were of great significance. These were times for celebration and blowing of trumpets in worship (see 10:10 and note).
28:16 – 25 The priests are instructed as to the proper preparation for the Passover in the first month of the year. Passover is also associated with the Festival of Unleavened Bread (see Ex 12:15 and note on 12:17; Lev 23:4 – 8). The number seven reappears frequently in the paragraph.
28:26 – 31 The Festival of Weeks came 50 days after the Festival of Unleavened Bread (see Lev 23:9 – 22); from this number the term "Pentecost" (meaning "fifty") was used in the NT (see Ac 2:1 and note).
29:1 – 6 The Festival of Trumpets came at the beginning of the seventh month, a busy month for the worship of the Lord in holy festivals (see Lev 23:23 – 25; see also chart, pp. 188 – 189). Later in Jewish tradition this festival came to commemorate the New Year (Rosh Hashanah). The trumpet used was the ram's horn (*shophar*).
29:7 – 11 The Festival of Trumpets leads into the Day of Atonement, a time of confession, contrition and celebration (see Lev 16:1 – 34 and note; 23:26 – 32).

8Present as an aroma pleasing to the LORD
a burnt offering of one young bull, one
ram and seven male lambs a year old,
all without defect.[h] 9With the bull offer a
grain offering[i] of three-tenths of an ephah
of the finest flour mixed with oil; with the
ram, two-tenths;[j] 10and with each of the
seven lambs, one-tenth.[k] 11Include one
male goat[l] as a sin offering, in addition to
the sin offering for atonement and the regular burnt offering[m] with its grain offering,
and their drink offerings.[n]

The Festival of Tabernacles

29:12-39pp — Lev 23:33-43; Dt 16:13-17

12" 'On the fifteenth day of the seventh[o]
month,[p] hold a sacred assembly and do no
regular work. Celebrate a festival to the
LORD for seven days. 13Present as an aroma
pleasing to the LORD[q] a food offering consisting of a burnt offering of thirteen young
bulls, two rams and fourteen male lambs a
year old, all without defect.[r] 14With each
of the thirteen bulls offer a grain offering[s]
of three-tenths of an ephah of the finest
flour mixed with oil; with each of the two
rams, two-tenths; 15and with each of the
fourteen lambs, one-tenth.[t] 16Include one
male goat as a sin offering,[u] in addition
to the regular burnt offering with its grain
offering and drink offering.[v]
17" 'On the second day[w] offer twelve
young bulls, two rams and fourteen male
lambs a year old, all without defect.[x]
18With the bulls, rams and lambs, offer
their grain offerings[y] and drink offerings[z]
according to the number specified.[a] 19In-
clude one male goat as a sin offering,[b]
in addition to the regular burnt offering[c]
with its grain offering, and their drink offerings.[d]
20" 'On the third day offer eleven bulls,
two rams and fourteen male lambs a year
old, all without defect.[e] 21With the bulls,
rams and lambs, offer their grain offerings
and drink offerings according to the number specified.[f] 22Include one male goat as
a sin offering, in addition to the regular
burnt offering with its grain offering and
drink offering.
23" 'On the fourth day offer ten bulls,
two rams and fourteen male lambs a year
old, all without defect. 24With the bulls,
rams and lambs, offer their grain offerings
and drink offerings according to the number specified. 25Include one male goat as
a sin offering, in addition to the regular
burnt offering with its grain offering and
drink offering.
26" 'On the fifth day offer nine bulls,
two rams and fourteen male lambs a year
old, all without defect. 27With the bulls,
rams and lambs, offer their grain offerings
and drink offerings according to the number specified. 28Include one male goat as
a sin offering, in addition to the regular
burnt offering with its grain offering and
drink offering.
29" 'On the sixth day offer eight bulls,
two rams and fourteen male lambs a year
old, all without defect. 30With the bulls,
rams and lambs, offer their grain offerings
and drink offerings according to the number specified. 31Include one male goat as
a sin offering, in addition to the regular
burnt offering with its grain offering and
drink offering.
32" 'On the seventh day offer seven
bulls, two rams and fourteen male lambs
a year old, all without defect. 33With the
bulls, rams and lambs, offer their grain
offerings and drink offerings according to
the number specified. 34Include one male
goat as a sin offering, in addition to the
regular burnt offering with its grain offering and drink offering.
35" 'On the eighth day hold a closing
special assembly[g] and do no regular work.
36Present as an aroma pleasing to the
LORD[h] a food offering consisting of a burnt
offering of one bull, one ram and seven
male lambs a year old,[i] all without defect.
37With the bull, the ram and the lambs, offer their grain offerings and drink offerings
according to the number specified. 38In-
clude one male goat as a sin offering, in
addition to the regular burnt offering with
its grain offering and drink offering.
39" 'In addition to what you vow[j] and
your freewill offerings,[k] offer these to the
LORD at your appointed festivals:[l] your
burnt offerings,[m] grain offerings, drink offerings and fellowship offerings.[n]' "
40Moses told the Israelites all that the
LORD commanded him.[a]

Vows

30 [b] Moses said to the heads of the
tribes of Israel:[o] "This is what the
LORD commands: 2When a man makes a

29:8 [h] ver 2 **29:9** [i] S ver 3, 18 [j] Nu 28:12 **29:10** [k] Nu 28:13 **29:11** [l] ver 5; Nu 28:15 [m] S Lev 16:3 [n] S ver 6 **29:12** [o] 1Ki 8:2; 12:32 [p] S Lev 23:24 **29:13** [q] ver 2; Nu 28:2 [r] Nu 28:3 **29:14** [s] S ver 3; S Nu 15:6 **29:15** [t] ver 4; Nu 28:13 **29:16** [u] ver 5; S Nu 28:15 [v] ver 6 **29:17** [w] Lev 23:36 [x] ver 2; Nu 28:3 **29:18** [y] S ver 9 [z] Nu 28:7 [a] Nu 15:4-12 **29:19** [b] S Nu 28:15 [c] Nu 28:3 [d] ver 6 **29:20** [e] S ver 17 **29:21** [f] S ver 18

29:35 [g] S Lev 23:36 **29:36** [h] Lev 1:9 [i] ver 2 **29:39** [j] Nu 6:2 [k] S Lev 7:16 [l] S Lev 23:2 [m] Lev 1:3; 1Ch 23:31; 2Ch 31:3 [n] Lev 3:1 **30:1** [o] S Nu 1:4

[a] *40* In Hebrew texts this verse (29:40) is numbered 30:1. [b] In Hebrew texts 30:1-16 is numbered 30:2-17.

29:12 – 34 In the seventh month the Festival of Trumpets took place on the first day, the Day of Atonement occurred on the tenth day, and the Festival of Tabernacles began on the fifteenth day and lasted for seven days (see Lev 23:33 – 44). Each day of the Festival of Tabernacles had its own order for sacrifice (see note on Zec 14:16).

29:40 *Moses told the Israelites.* The recapitulation of these festivals was a necessary part of the transfer of power from Moses to Joshua.

30:1 – 16 The principal OT passage on vows (see Dt 23:21 – 23). A vow is not to be made rashly (cf. Ecc 5:1 – 7), and a vow to the Lord must be kept.

vow to the LORD or takes an oath to obligate himself by a pledge, he must not break his word but must do everything he said.[p]
3 “When a young woman still living in her father's household makes a vow to the LORD or obligates herself by a pledge 4 and her father hears about her vow or pledge but says nothing to her, then all her vows and every pledge by which she obligated herself will stand.[q] 5 But if her father forbids her[r] when he hears about it, none of her vows or the pledges by which she obligated herself will stand; the LORD will release her because her father has forbidden her.
6 “If she marries after she makes a vow[s] or after her lips utter a rash promise by which she obligates herself 7 and her husband hears about it but says nothing to her, then her vows or the pledges by which she obligated herself will stand. 8 But if her husband[t] forbids her when he hears about it, he nullifies the vow that obligates her or the rash promise by which she obligates herself, and the LORD will release her.[u]
9 “Any vow or obligation taken by a widow or divorced woman will be binding on her.
10 “If a woman living with her husband makes a vow or obligates herself by a pledge under oath 11 and her husband hears about it but says nothing to her and does not forbid her, then all her vows or the pledges by which she obligated herself will stand. 12 But if her husband nullifies them when he hears about them, then none of the vows or pledges that came from her lips will stand.[v] Her husband has nullified them, and the LORD will release her. 13 Her husband may confirm or nullify any vow she makes or any sworn pledge to deny herself.[a] 14 But if her husband says nothing to her about it from day to day, then he confirms all her vows or the pledges binding on her. He confirms them by saying nothing to her when he hears about them. 15 If, however, he nullifies them[w] some time after he hears about them, then he must bear the consequences of her wrongdoing.”
16 These are the regulations the LORD gave Moses concerning relationships between a man and his wife, and between a father and his young daughter still living at home.

Vengeance on the Midianites

31 The LORD said to Moses, 2 “Take vengeance on the Midianites[x] for the Israelites. After that, you will be gathered to your people.[y]”
3 So Moses said to the people, “Arm some of your men to go to war against the Midianites so that they may carry out the LORD's vengeance[z] on them. 4 Send into battle a thousand men from each of the tribes of Israel.” 5 So twelve thousand men armed for battle,[a] a thousand from each tribe, were supplied from the clans of Israel. 6 Moses sent them into battle,[b] a thousand from each tribe, along with Phinehas[c] son of Eleazar, the priest, who took with him articles from the sanctuary[d] and the trumpets[e] for signaling.
7 They fought against Midian, as the LORD commanded Moses,[f] and killed every man.[g] 8 Among their victims were Evi, Rekem, Zur, Hur and Reba[h]—the five kings of Midian.[i] They also killed Balaam son of Beor[j] with the sword.[k] 9 The Israelites captured the Midianite women[l] and children

30:2 [p] Dt 23:21-23; Jdg 11:35; Job 22:27; Ps 22:25; 50:14; 61:5,8; 76:11; 116:14; Pr 20:25; Ecc 5:4,5; Isa 19:21; Jnh 1:16; 2:9 **30:4** [q] ver 7 **30:5** [r] ver 8, 12,15 **30:6** [s] S Lev 5:4 **30:8** [t] S Ge 3:16 [u] ver 5 **30:12** [v] Eph 5:22; Col 3:18 **30:15** [w] S ver 5 **31:2** [x] S Ge 25:2 [y] S Nu 20:26 **31:3** [z] Jdg 11:36; 1Sa 24:12; 2Sa 4:8; 22:48; Ps 94:1; 149:7; Isa 34:8; Jer 11:20; 46:10; Eze 25:17 **31:5** [a] ver 6, 21 **31:6** [b] S ver 5 [c] S Ex 6:25 [d] Nu 14:44 [e] S Nu 10:2 **31:7** [f] Nu 25:16 [g] Dt 20:13; Jdg 21:11; 1Ki 11:15,16 **31:8** [h] Jos 13:21 [i] S Nu 25:15 [j] S Nu 22:5; S 24:14 [k] Jos 13:22 **31:9** [l] ver 15

[a] 13 Or *to fast*

30:3–8 In Near Eastern society, women were subject to the authority of their fathers (vv. 3–5) or husbands (vv. 6–8), who could disallow the carrying out of a vow.
30:9 *widow or divorced woman.* Such women remained responsible for the vows they made.
30:10–15 Further examples of the complications that come in the making of vows within the husband-wife relationship. Such complications may have come up much as in the case of Zelophehad's daughters (27:1–11). One case after another presented itself, resulting in this final codification. Presumably, in the centuries leading up to the NT, the legal decisions on vows became even more complex. The words of Jesus that one is to avoid complications connected with oaths (Mt 5:33–37) are liberating.
31:1–24 The Lord declares war (see essay, p. 308) against the Midianites as one of Moses' last actions before the end of his life. Moses was not motivated by petty jealousy; rather, the war was "the LORD's vengeance" (v. 3) for the Midianites' part in seducing the Israelites to engage in sexual immorality and to worship the Baal of Peor. (See 25:16–18, where the specific mention of Kozbi, a Midianite woman, heightens the anger expressed in ch. 31.)
31:2 *be gathered to your people.* In death (see note on Ge 25:8).
31:4 *a thousand men from each of the tribes of Israel.* The burden of the Lord's war had to be shared equally among the tribes.
31:6 *Phinehas.* His zeal for the Lord's honor led him to execute Zimri and Kozbi (25:8). Now he leads in the sacred aspects of the battle to demonstrate that this is the Lord's war. *trumpets.* See note on 10:3.
31:8 *They also killed Balaam.* Ch. 25 lacks the name of the principal instigator of the seduction of the Israelite men to the depraved worship of Baal. But here he is found among the dead. What Balaam had been unable to accomplish through acts of magic or sorcery (chs. 22–24) he was almost able to achieve by his advice to the Midianites (v. 16).
31:9–18 While the troops killed the men of Midian, they spared the women and children as plunder. Moses commanded that only the virgin women (who were thus innocent of the indecencies at Peor) could be spared; the guilty women and the boys (who might endanger the inheritance rights of Israelite men) were to be put to death (vv. 15–17).

and took all the Midianite herds, flocks
and goods as plunder.[m] 10They burned[n] all
the towns where the Midianites had settled, as well as all their camps.[o] 11They
took all the plunder and spoils, including
the people and animals,[p] 12and brought
the captives, spoils[q] and plunder to Moses and Eleazar the priest and the Israelite
assembly[r] at their camp on the plains of
Moab, by the Jordan across from Jericho.[s]
13Moses, Eleazar the priest and all the
leaders of the community went to meet
them outside the camp. 14Moses was angry with the officers of the army[t]—the
commanders of thousands and commanders of hundreds—who returned from the
battle.
15"Have you allowed all the women to
live?" he asked them. 16"They were the
ones who followed Balaam's advice[u] and
enticed the Israelites to be unfaithful to
the LORD in the Peor incident,[v] so that a
plague[w] struck the LORD's people. 17Now
kill all the boys. And kill every woman
who has slept with a man,[x] 18but save for
yourselves every girl who has never slept
with a man.
19"Anyone who has killed someone or
touched someone who was killed[y] must
stay outside the camp seven days.[z] On the
third and seventh days you must purify
yourselves[a] and your captives. 20Purify every garment[b] as well as everything made
of leather, goat hair or wood.[c]"
21Then Eleazar the priest said to the soldiers who had gone into battle,[d] "This is
what is required by the law that the LORD
gave Moses: 22Gold, silver, bronze, iron,[e]
tin, lead 23and anything else that can withstand fire must be put through the fire,[f] and
then it will be clean. But it must also be
purified with the water of cleansing.[g] And
whatever cannot withstand fire must be put
through that water. 24On the seventh day
wash your clothes and you will be clean.[h]
Then you may come into the camp.[i]"

Dividing the Spoils

25The LORD said to Moses, 26"You and
Eleazar the priest and the family heads[j]
of the community are to count all the
people[k] and animals that were captured.[l]
27Divide[m] the spoils equally between the
soldiers who took part in the battle and
the rest of the community. 28From the soldiers who fought in the battle, set apart as
tribute for the LORD[n] one out of every five
hundred, whether people, cattle, donkeys
or sheep. 29Take this tribute from their
half share and give it to Eleazar the priest
as the LORD's part. 30From the Israelites'
half, select one out of every fifty, whether people, cattle, donkeys, sheep or other
animals. Give them to the Levites, who
are responsible for the care of the LORD's
tabernacle.[o]" 31So Moses and Eleazar the
priest did as the LORD commanded Moses.
32The plunder remaining from the
spoils[p] that the soldiers took was 675,000
sheep, 3372,000 cattle, 3461,000 donkeys
35and 32,000 women who had never slept
with a man.
36The half share of those who fought in
the battle was:

337,500 sheep, 37of which the tribute
for the LORD[q] was 675;
3836,000 cattle, of which the tribute for
the LORD was 72;
3930,500 donkeys, of which the tribute
for the LORD was 61;
4016,000 people, of whom the tribute
for the LORD was 32.

41Moses gave the tribute to Eleazar the
priest as the LORD's part,[r] as the LORD commanded Moses.[s]
42The half belonging to the Israelites, which Moses set apart from that of
the fighting men— 43the community's
half—was 337,500 sheep, 4436,000 cattle, 4530,500 donkeys 46and 16,000 people.
47From the Israelites' half, Moses selected
one out of every fifty people and animals,
as the LORD commanded him, and gave
them to the Levites, who were responsible
for the care of the LORD's tabernacle.
48Then the officers[t] who were over
the units of the army—the commanders
of thousands and commanders of hundreds—went to Moses 49and said to him,
"Your servants have counted[u] the soldiers
under our command, and not one is missing.[v] 50So we have brought as an offering
to the LORD the gold articles each of us
acquired—armlets, bracelets, signet rings,
earrings and necklaces—to make atonement for ourselves[w] before the LORD."
51Moses and Eleazar the priest accepted
from them the gold—all the crafted articles. 52All the gold from the commanders
of thousands and commanders of hundreds that Moses and Eleazar presented
as a gift to the LORD weighed 16,750 shekels.[a] 53Each soldier had taken plunder[x] for

31:9 [m]S Ge 34:29 **31:10** [n]Jos 6:24; 8:28; 11:11; Jdg 18:27 [o]Ge 25:16; 1Ch 6:54; Ps 69:25; Eze 25:4 **31:11** [p]ver 26; Dt 20:14; 2Ch 28:8 **31:12** [q]ver 32, 53; Ge 49:27; Ex 15:9 [r]S Nu 27:2 [s]Nu 22:1 **31:14** [t]ver 48; Ex 18:21; Dt 1:15; 2Sa 18:1 **31:16** [u]S Nu 22:5; S 24:14; S 2Pe 2:15 [v]S Nu 23:28; 25:1-9 [w]S Nu 14:37 **31:17** [x]Dt 7:2; 20:16-18; Jdg 21:11 **31:19** [y]Nu 19:16 [z]S Lev 21:1 [a]Nu 19:12 **31:20** [b]Nu 19:19 [c]S Lev 11:32 **31:21** [d]S ver 5 **31:22** [e]Jos 6:19; 22:8 **31:23** [f]S 1Co 3:13 [g]S Nu 8:7 **31:24** [h]S Lev 11:25 [i]S Lev 14:8 **31:26** [j]S Nu 1:4 [k]S Nu 1:19 [l]S ver 11,12 **31:27** [m]Jos 22:8; 1Sa 25:13; 30:24 **31:28** [n]ver 37-41; S Nu 18:21

31:30 [o]Nu 3:7; 18:3 **31:32** [p]S ver 12 **31:37** [q]ver 38-41 **31:41** [r]Nu 5:9; 18:8 [s]ver 21,28 **31:48** [t]S ver 14 **31:49** [u]S Nu 1:19 [v]Jer 23:4 **31:50** [w]S Ex 30:16 **31:53** [x]S Ge 34:29; Dt 20:14

[a] *52* That is, about 420 pounds or about 190 kilograms

31:16 *the Peor incident.* See notes on v. 8; 25:1–18.
31:19–24 Since this was the Lord's war, both people (vv. 19–20) and things (vv. 21–24) had to be cleansed (cf. 19:11–13).
31:26–35 Another aspect of the Lord's war was the fair distribution of the spoils of war, both among those who fought in the battle and among those who stayed with the community, with appropriate shares to be given to the Lord, whose battle it was (v. 28).

himself. 54 Moses and Eleazar the priest accepted the gold from the commanders of thousands and commanders of hundreds and brought it into the tent of meeting[y] as a memorial[z] for the Israelites before the LORD.

The Transjordan Tribes

32 The Reubenites and Gadites, who had very large herds and flocks,[a] saw that the lands of Jazer[b] and Gilead[c] were suitable for livestock.[d] 2 So they came to Moses and Eleazar the priest and to the leaders of the community,[e] and said, 3 "Ataroth,[f] Dibon,[g] Jazer,[h] Nimrah,[i] Heshbon,[j] Elealeh,[k] Sebam,[l] Nebo[m] and Beon[n]— 4 the land the LORD subdued[o] before the people of Israel—are suitable for livestock,[p] and your servants have livestock. 5 If we have found favor in your eyes," they said, "let this land be given to your servants as our possession. Do not make us cross the Jordan.[q]"

6 Moses said to the Gadites and Reubenites, "Should your fellow Israelites go to war while you sit here? 7 Why do you discourage the Israelites from crossing over into the land the LORD has given them?[r] 8 This is what your fathers did when I sent them from Kadesh Barnea to look over the land.[s] 9 After they went up to the Valley of Eshkol[t] and viewed the land, they discouraged the Israelites from entering the land the LORD had given them. 10 The LORD's anger was aroused[u] that day and he swore this oath:[v] 11 'Because they have not followed me wholeheartedly, not one of those who were twenty years old or more[w] when they came up out of Egypt[x] will see the land I promised on oath[y] to Abraham, Isaac and Jacob[z]— 12 not one except Caleb son of Jephunneh the Kenizzite and Joshua son of Nun, for they followed the LORD wholeheartedly.'[a] 13 The LORD's anger burned against Israel[b] and he made them wander in the wilderness forty years, until the whole generation of those who had done evil in his sight was gone.[c]

14 "And here you are, a brood of sinners, standing in the place of your fathers and making the LORD even more angry with Israel.[d] 15 If you turn away from following him, he will again leave all this people in the wilderness, and you will be the cause of their destruction.[e]"

16 Then they came up to him and said, "We would like to build pens[f] here for our livestock[g] and cities for our women and children. 17 But we will arm ourselves for battle[a] and go ahead of the Israelites[h] until we have brought them to their place.[i] Meanwhile our women and children will live in fortified cities, for protection from the inhabitants of the land. 18 We will not return to our homes until each of the Israelites has received their inheritance.[j] 19 We will not receive any inheritance with them on the other side of the Jordan, because our inheritance[k] has come to us on the east side of the Jordan."[l]

20 Then Moses said to them, "If you will do this—if you will arm yourselves before the LORD for battle[m] 21 and if all of you who are armed cross over the Jordan before the LORD until he has driven his enemies out before him[n]— 22 then when the land is subdued before the LORD, you may return[o] and be free from your obligation to the LORD and to Israel. And this land will be your possession[p] before the LORD.[q]

23 "But if you fail to do this, you will be sinning against the LORD; and you may be sure that your sin will find you out.[r] 24 Build cities for your women and children, and pens for your flocks,[s] but do what you have promised.[t]"

25 The Gadites and Reubenites said to Moses, "We your servants will do as our lord commands.[u] 26 Our children and wives, our flocks and herds will remain here in the cities of Gilead.[v] 27 But your servants, every man who is armed for battle, will cross over to fight[w] before the LORD, just as our lord says."

28 Then Moses gave orders about them[x] to Eleazar the priest and Joshua son of Nun[y] and to the family heads of the Israelite tribes.[z] 29 He said to them, "If the Gadites and Reubenites, every man armed for battle, cross over the Jordan with you before the LORD, then when the land is subdued before you,[a] you must give them the land of Gilead as their possession.[b] 30 But if they do not cross over[c] with you armed, they must accept their possession with you in Canaan.[d]"

[a] 17 Septuagint; Hebrew *will be quick to arm ourselves*

31:54 [y] S Ex 27:21; 40:2 [z] S Ex 28:12 **32:1** [a] ver 24, 36; Jdg 5:16 [b] S Nu 21:32 [c] S Ge 31:21 [d] Ex 12:38 **32:2** [e] Lev 4:22; Nu 27:2 **32:3** [f] ver 34; Jos 16:2,7; 18:13 [g] ver 34; S Nu 21:30 [h] ver 1 [i] ver 36; Jos 13:27 [j] Nu 21:25 [k] ver 37; Isa 15:4; 16:9; Jer 48:34 [l] Jos 13:19; Isa 16:8,9; Jer 48:32 [m] Nu 33:47; Dt 32:49; 34:1; 1Ch 5:8 [n] ver 38; Jos 13:17; Eze 25:9 **32:4** [o] Nu 21:34 [p] Ex 12:38 **32:5** [q] S Nu 13:29 **32:7** [r] Nu 13:27-14:4 **32:8** [s] Nu 13:3, 26; Dt 1:19-25 **32:9** [t] Nu 13:23; Dt 1:24 **32:10** [u] Nu 11:1 [v] S Nu 14:20-23 **32:11** [w] S Ex 30:14 [x] Nu 1:1 [y] S Nu 14:23 [z] Nu 14:28-30 **32:12** [a] Nu 14:24,30 **32:13** [b] S Ex 4:14 [c] Nu 14:28-35; 26:64,65 **32:14** [d] S ver 10; Dt 1:34; Ps 78:59 **32:15** [e] Dt 30:17-18; 2Ch 7:20 **32:16** [f] ver 24, 36; 1Sa 24:3; Ps 50:9; 78:70 [g] Ex 12:38; Dt 3:19 **32:17** [h] Dt 3:18; Jos 4:12,13 [i] S Nu 22:4; Dt 3:20 **32:18** [j] Jos 22:1-4 **32:19** [k] ver 22, 29 [l] Nu 21:33; Jos 12:1; 22:7 **32:20** [m] ver 17 **32:21** [n] ver 17 **32:22** [o] Jos 22:4 [p] S Lev 14:34 [q] Dt 3:18-20 **32:23** [r] S Ge 4:7; S Isa 3:9 **32:24** [s] S ver 1, 16 [t] Nu 30:2 **32:25** [u] ver 29; Jos 1:16, 18; 22:2 **32:26** [v] ver 16, 24; Jos 1:14; 12:2; 22:9; 2Sa 2:9; 1Ch 5:9 **32:27** [w] ver 17, 21 **32:28** [x] ver 29; Dt 3:18-20; Jos 1:13 [y] Nu 11:28 [z] Nu 1:16 **32:29** [a] S Nu 22:4 [b] S ver 19 **32:30** [c] ver 23 [d] ver 29, 32

32:1 *Reubenites and Gadites.* The abundance of fertile grazing land in Transjordan prompted the leaders of these two tribes to request that they be allowed to settle there and not cross the Jordan. This area too was a gift of God won by conquest.
32:8 *This is what your fathers did.* Moses' fear was that the failure of these two tribes to stay with the whole community in conquering Canaan would be the beginning of a general revolt against entering the land. It would be the failure of Kadesh (chs. 13–14) all over again. Moreover, the conquest of Canaan was a commission to all Israel.
32:12 *followed the LORD wholeheartedly.* See note on 14:24.
32:23 *your sin will find you out.* Cf. Jos 7:18. The bargain was struck, but not without strong warnings if they failed to live up to their word.

[31]The Gadites and Reubenites answered, "Your servants will do what the LORD has said.[e] [32]We will cross over before the LORD into Canaan armed,[f] but the property we inherit will be on this side of the Jordan.[g]"

[33]Then Moses gave to the Gadites,[h] the Reubenites and the half-tribe of Manasseh[i] son of Joseph the kingdom of Sihon king of the Amorites[j] and the kingdom of Og king of Bashan[k]—the whole land with its cities and the territory around them.[l]

[34]The Gadites built up Dibon, Ataroth, Aroer,[m] [35]Atroth Shophan, Jazer,[n] Jogbehah,[o] [36]Beth Nimrah[p] and Beth Haran as fortified cities, and built pens for their flocks.[q] [37]And the Reubenites rebuilt Heshbon,[r] Elealeh[s] and Kiriathaim,[t] [38]as well as Nebo[u] and Baal Meon (these names were changed) and Sibmah.[v] They gave names to the cities they rebuilt.

[39]The descendants of Makir[w] son of Manasseh went to Gilead,[x] captured it and drove out the Amorites[y] who were there. [40]So Moses gave Gilead to the Makirites,[z] the descendants of Manasseh, and they settled there. [41]Jair,[a] a descendant of Manasseh, captured their settlements and called them Havvoth Jair.[a][b] [42]And Nobah captured Kenath[c] and its surrounding settlements and called it Nobah[d] after himself.[e]

Stages in Israel's Journey

33 Here are the stages in the journey[f] of the Israelites when they came out of Egypt[g] by divisions under the leadership of Moses and Aaron.[h] [2]At the LORD's command Moses recorded[i] the stages in their journey[j]. This is their journey by stages:

[3]The Israelites set out[k] from Rameses[l] on the fifteenth day of the first month, the day after the Passover.[m] They marched out defiantly[n] in full view of all the Egyptians, [4]who were burying all their firstborn,[o] whom the LORD had struck down among them; for the LORD had brought judgment[p] on their gods.[q]

[5]The Israelites left Rameses and camped at Sukkoth.[r]

[6]They left Sukkoth and camped at Etham, on the edge of the desert.[s]

[7]They left Etham, turned back to Pi Hahiroth, to the east of Baal Zephon,[t] and camped near Migdol.[u]

[8]They left Pi Hahiroth[b][v] and passed through the sea[w] into the desert, and when they had traveled for three days in the Desert of Etham, they camped at Marah.[x]

[9]They left Marah and went to Elim, where there were twelve springs and seventy palm trees, and they camped[y] there.

[10]They left Elim[z] and camped by the Red Sea.[c]

[11]They left the Red Sea and camped in the Desert of Sin.[a]

[12]They left the Desert of Sin and camped at Dophkah.

[13]They left Dophkah and camped at Alush.

[14]They left Alush and camped at Rephidim, where there was no water for the people to drink.[b]

[15]They left Rephidim[c] and camped in the Desert of Sinai.[d]

[16]They left the Desert of Sinai and camped at Kibroth Hattaavah.[e]

[17]They left Kibroth Hattaavah and camped at Hazeroth.[f]

[18]They left Hazeroth and camped at Rithmah.

[19]They left Rithmah and camped at Rimmon Perez.

[20]They left Rimmon Perez and camped at Libnah.[g]

[a] 41 Or *them the settlements of Jair* [b] 8 Many manuscripts of the Masoretic Text, Samaritan Pentateuch and Vulgate; most manuscripts of the Masoretic Text *left from before Hahiroth* [c] 10 Or *the Sea of Reeds*; also in verse 11

32:31 [e]ver 29 **32:32** [f]ver 17 [g]S ver 30; Jos 12:6 **32:33** [h]Jos 13:24-28; 1Sa 13:7 [i]Jos 1:12 [j]Nu 21:21; Dt 2:26 [k]S ver 19; S Jos 12:5 [l]S Nu 21:24; 34:14; Dt 2:36; Jos 12:6 **32:34** [m]Dt 2:36; 3:12; 4:48; Jos 12:2; 13:9; Jdg 11:26; 1Sa 30:28; 1Ch 5:8; Jer 48:19 **32:35** [n]ver 3 [o]Jdg 8:11 **32:36** [p]S ver 3 [q]S ver 1 **32:37** [r]Nu 21:25 [s]S ver 3 [t]Jos 13:19; 1Ch 6:76; Jer 48:1,23; Eze 25:9 **32:38** [u]S ver 3; Isa 15:2; Jer 48:1,22 [v]S ver 3 **32:39** [w]S Ge 50:23 [x]Nu 26:29; Dt 2:36 [y]S Ge 10:16 **32:40** [z]S Ge 50:23; Dt 3:15 **32:41** [a]1Ki 4:13 [b]Dt 3:14; Jos 13:30; Jdg 10:4; 1Ch 2:23 **32:42** [c]1Ch 2:23 [d]Jdg 8:11 [e]1Sa 15:12; 2Sa 18:18; Ps 49:11; Isa 22:16; 56:5 **33:1** [f]Ex 17:1; 40:36 [g]Nu 1:1 [h]S Ex 4:16; 6:26 **33:2** [i]S Ex 17:14 [j]S ver 1 **33:3** [k]Nu 10:2 [l]S Ge 47:11 [m]Jos 5:10 [n]S Ex 14:8 **33:4** [o]S Ex 4:23 [p]2Ch 24:24; Jer 15:3; Eze 14:21

[q]S Ex 12:12 **33:5** [r]Ex 12:37 **33:6** [s]Ex 13:20 **33:7** [t]Ex 14:9 [u]S Ex 14:2 **33:8** [v]Ex 14:2 [w]S Ex 14:22 [x]S Ex 15:23 **33:9** [y]Ex 15:27 **33:10** [z]Ex 16:1 **33:11** [a]S Ex 16:1 **33:14** [b]S Ex 15:22; S 17:2 **33:15** [c]S Ex 17:1 [d]S Ex 19:1 **33:16** [e]S Nu 11:34 **33:17** [f]Nu 11:35 **33:20** [g]Jos 10:29; 12:15; 15:42; 21:13; 2Ki 8:22; 19:8; 23:31; 1Ch 6:57; 2Ch 21:10; Isa 37:8; Jer 52:1

32:33 *and the half-tribe of Manasseh.* It appears that after the requirements for Transjordan settlement were established with the tribes of Reuben and Gad, half the tribe of Manasseh joined with them.

33:1–49 The numerous places (significantly 40 in number between Rameses and the plains of Moab) in Israel's wilderness experience are listed. Unfortunately, most of the sites were wilderness encampments, not cities with lasting archaeological records; so they are difficult to locate. Many of the places (e.g., in vv. 19–29) are not recorded elsewhere in Exodus and Numbers, while some of the places mentioned elsewhere (e.g., Taberah, 11:3; see 21:19) are missing here. The data warrant these conclusions: (1) Moses recorded the list at the Lord's command (v. 2). (2) The list should be taken seriously, as an accurate recapitulation of the stages of the journey, despite difficulty in locating many of the sites. (3) The numerical factor of 40 sites between Rameses and the plains of Moab suggests some styling of the list, which helps to account for the sites not included. (4) As in the case of genealogies in the Pentateuch, some factors of ancient significance may not be clear to us today. (5) Ultimately the record is a recital of the Lord's blessing on his people for the extended period of their wilderness experience. Although certainly not without geographic importance, the listing of the stages of Israel's experience in the wilderness is fundamentally a religious document, a litany of the Lord's deliverance of his people.

21 They left Libnah and camped at
Rissah.
22 They left Rissah and camped at
Kehelathah.
23 They left Kehelathah and camped
at Mount Shepher.
24 They left Mount Shepher and
camped at Haradah.
25 They left Haradah and camped at
Makheloth.
26 They left Makheloth and camped
at Tahath.
27 They left Tahath and camped at
Terah.
28 They left Terah and camped at
Mithkah.
29 They left Mithkah and camped at
Hashmonah.
30 They left Hashmonah and
camped at Moseroth.[h]
31 They left Moseroth and camped
at Bene Jaakan.[i]
32 They left Bene Jaakan and
camped at Hor Haggidgad.
33 They left Hor Haggidgad and
camped at Jotbathah.[j]
34 They left Jotbathah and camped
at Abronah.
35 They left Abronah and camped at
Ezion Geber.[k]
36 They left Ezion Geber and
camped at Kadesh, in the Desert of
Zin.[l]
37 They left Kadesh and camped at
Mount Hor,[m] on the border of Edom.[n]
38 At the LORD's command Aaron the
priest went up Mount Hor, where
he died[o] on the first day of the fifth
month of the fortieth year[p] after the
Israelites came out of Egypt.[q] 39 Aaron
was a hundred and twenty-three years
old when he died on Mount Hor.
40 The Canaanite king[r] of Arad,[s]
who lived in the Negev[t] of Canaan,
heard that the Israelites were coming.
41 They left Mount Hor and camped
at Zalmonah.
42 They left Zalmonah and camped
at Punon.
43 They left Punon and camped at
Oboth.[u]
44 They left Oboth and camped at
Iye Abarim, on the border of Moab.[v]
45 They left Iye Abarim and camped
at Dibon Gad.
46 They left Dibon Gad and camped
at Almon Diblathaim.
47 They left Almon Diblathaim and
camped in the mountains of Abarim,[w]
near Nebo.[x]
48 They left the mountains of Abarim[y] and camped on the plains of
Moab[z] by the Jordan[a] across from Jericho.[b] 49 There on the plains of Moab
they camped along the Jordan from
Beth Jeshimoth[c] to Abel Shittim.[d]

50 On the plains of Moab by the Jordan
across from Jericho[e] the LORD said to Moses, 51 "Speak to the Israelites and say to
them: 'When you cross the Jordan into Canaan,[f] 52 drive out all the inhabitants of the
land before you. Destroy all their carved
images and their cast idols, and demolish
all their high places.[g] 53 Take possession of
the land and settle in it, for I have given
you the land to possess.[h] 54 Distribute the
land by lot,[i] according to your clans.[j] To a
larger group give a larger inheritance, and
to a smaller group a smaller one.[k] Whatever
falls to them by lot will be theirs. Distribute
it according to your ancestral tribes.[l]
55 " 'But if you do not drive out the inhabitants of the land, those you allow to
remain will become barbs in your eyes
and thorns[m] in your sides. They will give
you trouble in the land where you will
live. 56 And then I will do to you what I
plan to do to them.[n]' "

Boundaries of Canaan

34 The LORD said to Moses, 2 "Command the Israelites and say to
them: 'When you enter Canaan,[o] the land
that will be allotted to you as an inheritance[p] is to have these boundaries:[q]

3 " 'Your southern side will include some
of the Desert of Zin[r] along the border of
Edom. Your southern boundary will start
in the east from the southern end of the
Dead Sea,[s] 4 cross south of Scorpion Pass,[t]
continue on to Zin and go south of Kadesh
Barnea.[u] Then it will go to Hazar Addar
and over to Azmon,[v] 5 where it will turn,
join the Wadi of Egypt[w] and end at the
Mediterranean Sea.
6 " 'Your western boundary will be the
coast of the Mediterranean Sea.[x] This will
be your boundary on the west.[y]

33:30 [h]Dt 10:6
33:31 [i]Dt 10:6
33:33 [j]Dt 10:7
33:35 [k]Dt 2:8; 1Ki 9:26; 22:48
33:36 [l]S Nu 13:21
33:37 [m]S Nu 20:22 [n]S Ge 36:16; S Nu 20:16
33:38 [o]S Nu 27:13 [p]S Ex 16:35 [q]Nu 20:25-28
33:40 [r]S Ge 10:18 [s]S Nu 21:1 [t]S Ge 12:9
33:43 [u]Nu 21:10
33:44 [v]S Nu 21:11
33:47 [w]Nu 27:12 [x]Nu 32:3
33:48 [y]Nu 27:12 [z]S Nu 26:3 [a]S Ge 13:10 [b]Nu 22:1; Jos 12:9
33:49 [c]Jos 12:3; 13:20; Eze 25:9 [d]S Nu 21:16
33:50 [e]ver 48
33:51 [f]Nu 34:2; Jos 3:17
33:52 [g]Ex 34:13; S Lev 26:1; Ps 106:34-36
33:53 [h]Dt 11:31; 17:14; Jos 1:11; 21:43
33:54 [i]S Lev 16:8; Nu 36:2 [j]Nu 26:54 [k]Nu 35:8 [l]Jos 18:10
33:55 [m]Jos 23:13; Jdg 2:3; Ps 106:36; Isa 55:13; Eze 2:6; 28:24; Mic 7:4; 2Co 12:7
33:56 [n]Nu 14:28
34:2 [o]S Nu 33:51 [p]Ge 17:8; Dt 1:7-8; Jos 23:4; Ps 78:54-55; 105:11 [q]Eze 47:15
34:3 [r]Nu 13:21; Jos 15:1-3 [s]S Ge 14:3
34:4 [t]Jos 15:3; Jdg 1:36 [u]Nu 32:8 [v]Jos 15:4
34:5 [w]Ge 15:18
34:6 [x]Jos 1:4; 9:1; 15:12,47; 23:4; Eze 47:10,15; 48:28 [y]Eze 47:19-20

33:40 *Negev.* See note on Ge 12:9.
33:50 — 36:13 A summary statement dealing with matters of land and other property in the promised land. The first and last verses — with their several verbal links — frame the section.
33:52 *drive out all the inhabitants of the land ... Destroy all their ... idols.* What Israel had accomplished in the war against the Midianites (ch. 31) was now to be extended to all the inhabitants of Canaan. Particularly important was the command to destroy all symbols of the pagan religious system of the Canaanites.
33:54 See note on 26:53 – 56.
34:3 – 12 The listing of the four boundaries displays the dimensions of God's great gift to his people.

[7]" 'For your northern boundary,[z] run a
line from the Mediterranean Sea to Mount
Hor[a] [8]and from Mount Hor to Lebo Hamath.[b] Then the boundary will go to Zedad, [9]continue to Ziphron and end at Hazar Enan. This will be your boundary on
the north.

[10]" 'For your eastern boundary,[c] run a
line from Hazar Enan to Shepham. [11]The
boundary will go down from Shepham to
Riblah[d] on the east side of Ain[e] and continue along the slopes east of the Sea of Galilee.[af] [12]Then the boundary will go down
along the Jordan and end at the Dead Sea.

" 'This will be your land, with its boundaries on every side.' "

[13]Moses commanded the Israelites: "Assign this land by lot[g] as an inheritance.[h]
The LORD has ordered that it be given to
the nine and a half tribes, [14]because the
families of the tribe of Reuben, the tribe of
Gad and the half-tribe of Manasseh have
received their inheritance.[i] [15]These two
and a half tribes have received their inheritance east of the Jordan across from
Jericho, toward the sunrise."

[16]The LORD said to Moses, [17]"These are
the names of the men who are to assign
the land for you as an inheritance: Eleazar
the priest and Joshua[j] son of Nun. [18]And
appoint one leader from each tribe to help[k]
assign the land.[l] [19]These are their names:[m]

Caleb[n] son of Jephunneh,
 from the tribe of Judah;[o]
[20]Shemuel son of Ammihud,
 from the tribe of Simeon;[p]
[21]Elidad son of Kislon,
 from the tribe of Benjamin;[q]
[22]Bukki son of Jogli,
 the leader from the tribe of Dan;
[23]Hanniel son of Ephod,
 the leader from the tribe of Manasseh[r] son of Joseph;
[24]Kemuel son of Shiphtan,
 the leader from the tribe of Ephraim[s] son of Joseph;
[25]Elizaphan son of Parnak,
 the leader from the tribe of Zebulun;[t]
[26]Paltiel son of Azzan,
 the leader from the tribe of Issachar;
[27]Ahihud son of Shelomi,
 the leader from the tribe of Asher;[u]
[28]Pedahel son of Ammihud,
 the leader from the tribe of Naphtali."

[29]These are the men the LORD commanded to assign the inheritance to the
Israelites in the land of Canaan.[v]

Towns for the Levites

35 On the plains of Moab by the Jordan across from Jericho,[w] the LORD
said to Moses, [2]"Command the Israelites
to give the Levites towns to live in[x] from
the inheritance the Israelites will possess.
And give them pasturelands[y] around the
towns. [3]Then they will have towns to live
in and pasturelands for the cattle they own
and all their other animals.[z]

[4]"The pasturelands around the towns
that you give the Levites will extend a
thousand cubits[b] from the town wall.
[5]Outside the town, measure two thousand
cubits[ca] on the east side, two thousand on
the south side, two thousand on the west
and two thousand on the north, with the
town in the center. They will have this
area as pastureland for the towns.[b]

Cities of Refuge

35:6-34Ref — Dt 4:41-43; 19:1-14; Jos 20:1-9

[6]"Six of the towns you give the Levites
will be cities of refuge, to which a person
who has killed someone may flee.[c] In addition, give them forty-two other towns. [7]In
all you must give the Levites forty-eight
towns, together with their pasturelands.
[8]The towns you give the Levites from the
land the Israelites possess are to be given
in proportion to the inheritance of each
tribe: Take many towns from a tribe that
has many, but few from one that has few."[d]

[9]Then the LORD said to Moses: [10]"Speak
to the Israelites and say to them: 'When
you cross the Jordan into Canaan,[e] [11]se-
lect some towns to be your cities of refuge,
to which a person who has killed someone[f] accidentally[g] may flee. [12]They will be

34:7 [z]Eze 47:15-17 [a]S Nu 20:22 **34:8** [b]Nu 13:21; Jos 13:5 **34:10** [c]Jos 15:5 **34:11** [d]2Ki 23:33; 25:6,21; Jer 39:5; 52:9,27 [e]Jos 15:32; 21:16; 1Ch 4:32 [f]Dt 3:17; Jos 11:2; 13:27 **34:13** [g]S Lev 16:8; Jos 18:10; Mic 2:5 [h]Jos 13:6; 14:1-5; Isa 49:8; 65:9; Eze 45:1 **34:14** [i]Nu 32:19; Dt 33:21; Jos 14:3 **34:17** [j]Nu 11:28; Dt 1:38 **34:18** [k]S Nu 1:4 [l]Jos 14:1 **34:19** [m]ver 29 [n]S Nu 26:65 [o]Ge 29:35; Dt 33:7; Ps 60:7 **34:20** [p]S Ge 29:33 **34:21** [q]Ge 49:27; Jdg 5:14; Ps 68:27 **34:23** [r]Nu 1:34 **34:24** [s]Nu 1:32 **34:25** [t]S Ge 30:20 **34:27** [u]Nu 1:40 **34:29** [v]ver 19 **35:1** [w]Nu 22:1 **35:2** [x]Lev 25:32-34; Jos 14:3,4 [y]Jos 21:1-42 **35:3** [z]Dt 18:6; Jos 14:4; 21:2 **35:5** [a]Jos 3:4 [b]Lev 25:34; 2Ch 11:14; 13:9; 23:2; 31:19 **35:6** [c]ver 11; Jos 21:13 **35:8** [d]Nu 26:54; 33:54 **35:10** [e]Nu 33:51; Dt 9:1; Jos 1:2,11 **35:11** [f]ver 22-25 [g]S Ex 21:13

[a] 11 Hebrew *Kinnereth* [b] 4 That is, about 1,500 feet or about 450 meters [c] 5 That is, about 3,000 feet or about 900 meters

34:13 – 15 The new realities that the settlement of Reuben, Gad and the half-tribe of Manasseh in Transjordan brought about (see ch. 32).

34:16 – 29 The listing of the new tribal leaders recalls the listing of the leaders of the first generation (1:5 – 16). This time the promise will be realized; these new leaders will assist Eleazar and Joshua in actually allotting the land.

34:19 *Caleb ... Judah.* See note on 13:6.

35:1 – 5 Since the Levites would not receive an allotment with the other tribes in the land (1:47 – 53), they would need towns in which to live and to raise their families and care for their livestock. The Levites were to be dispersed throughout the land (see Ge 49:5,7 and notes), not to settle in an isolated encampment. Jos 21 presents the fulfillment of this command.

35:6 – 15 Six Levitical cities were to be stationed strategically in the land — three in Transjordan and three in Canaan proper — as cities of refuge, where a person guilty of unintentional manslaughter might escape blood revenge. Jos 20 describes the sites that were chosen. See map, p. 254, and accompanying text.

places of refuge from the avenger,[h] so that
anyone accused of murder[i] may not die
before they stand trial before the assembly.[j] 13 These six towns you give will be
your cities of refuge.[k] 14 Give three on this
side of the Jordan and three in Canaan as
cities of refuge. 15 These six towns will be
a place of refuge for Israelites and for foreigners residing among them, so that anyone who has killed another accidentally
can flee there.

16 " 'If anyone strikes someone a fatal
blow with an iron object, that person is
a murderer; the murderer is to be put to
death.[l] 17 Or if anyone is holding a stone
and strikes someone a fatal blow with it,
that person is a murderer; the murderer is
to be put to death. 18 Or if anyone is holding a wooden object and strikes someone
a fatal blow with it, that person is a murderer; the murderer is to be put to death.
19 The avenger of blood[m] shall put the murderer to death; when the avenger comes
upon the murderer, the avenger shall put
the murderer to death.[n] 20 If anyone with
malice aforethought shoves another or
throws something at them intentionally[o]
so that they die 21 or if out of enmity one
person hits another with their fist so that
the other dies, that person is to be put
to death;[p] that person is a murderer. The
avenger of blood[q] shall put the murderer
to death when they meet.

22 " 'But if without enmity someone suddenly pushes another or throws something
at them unintentionally[r] 23 or, without seeing them, drops on them a stone heavy
enough to kill them, and they die, then
since that other person was not an enemy
and no harm was intended, 24 the assembly[s] must judge between the accused and
the avenger of blood according to these
regulations. 25 The assembly must protect
the one accused of murder from the avenger of blood and send the accused back to
the city of refuge to which they fled. The
accused must stay there until the death of
the high priest,[t] who was anointed[u] with
the holy oil.[v]

26 " 'But if the accused ever goes outside
the limits of the city of refuge to which
they fled 27 and the avenger of blood finds
them outside the city, the avenger of blood
may kill the accused without being guilty
of murder. 28 The accused must stay in the
city of refuge until the death of the high

35:12 [h]ver 19; Dt 19:6; Jos 20:3; 2Sa 14:11 [i]ver 26,27,28 [j]ver 24,25
35:13 [k]ver 6,14
35:16 [l]S Ex 21:12
35:19 [m]S ver 12 [n]ver 21
35:20 [o]S Ex 21:14
35:21 [p]Ex 21:14 [q]ver 19
35:22 [r]S Ex 21:13
35:24 [s]S ver 12
35:25 [t]ver 32 [u]S Ex 28:41 [v]S Ex 29:7

35:16–21 Various descriptions of willful murder.
35:21 *avenger of blood.* See note on Jos 20:3.
35:22 *without enmity.* The cities of refuge were to be established for the person who had committed an act of involuntary manslaughter.
35:24 *according to these regulations.* Any gracious provision is subject to abuse. For this reason the case of the involuntary slayer had to be determined by the judges. Further, the accused had to stay in the city of refuge until the death of the high priest, which probably atoned for the act of manslaughter. Any accused person who left the city of refuge would become fair game again for the avenger of blood.
35:25–28 See note on Jos 20:6.
35:25 *send the accused back.* The trial of the accused apparently took place outside the city of refuge.

CITIES OF **REFUGE**

The idea of providing cities of refuge (see Jos 20:1–9 and notes) for capital offenses is rooted in the tension between customary tribal law (retaliation or revenge, in which the blood relative is obligated to execute vengeance) and civil law (carried out less personally by an assembly according to a standard code of justice).

Blood feuds are usually associated with nomadic groups; legal procedures, with villages and towns. Israel, a society in the process of settling down, found it necessary to adopt an intermediate step regulating manslaughter, so that an innocent person would not be killed before standing trial. Absolution was possible only by being cleared by the assembly and by the eventual death of the high priest (when there would be general amnesty).

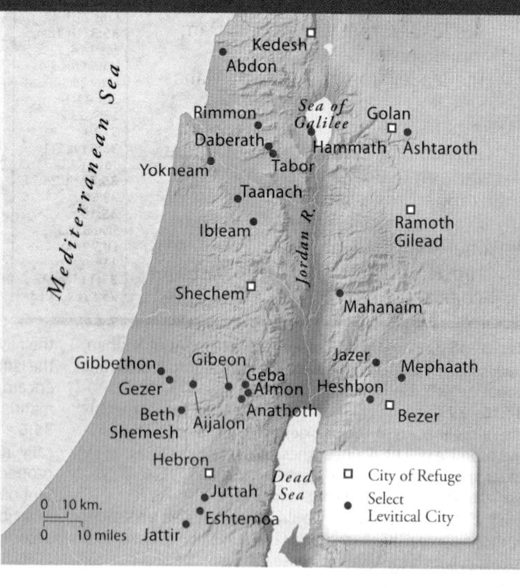

priest; only after the death of the high priest may they return to their own property.

29 “ ‘This is to have the force of law[w] for you throughout the generations to come,[x] wherever you live.[y]

30 “ ‘Anyone who kills a person is to be put to death as a murderer only on the testimony of witnesses. But no one is to be put to death on the testimony of only one witness.[z]

31 “ ‘Do not accept a ransom[a] for the life of a murderer, who deserves to die. They are to be put to death.

32 “ ‘Do not accept a ransom for anyone who has fled to a city of refuge and so allow them to go back and live on their own land before the death of the high priest.

33 “ ‘Do not pollute the land where you are. Bloodshed pollutes the land,[b] and atonement cannot be made for the land on which blood has been shed, except by the blood of the one who shed it. 34 Do not defile the land[c] where you live and where I dwell,[d] for I, the LORD, dwell among the Israelites.’ ”

Inheritance of Zelophehad's Daughters

36:1-12pp — Nu 27:1-11

36 The family heads of the clan of Gilead[e] son of Makir,[f] the son of Manasseh, who were from the clans of the descendants of Joseph,[g] came and spoke before Moses and the leaders,[h] the heads of the Israelite families. 2 They said, “When the LORD commanded my lord to give the land as an inheritance to the Israelites by lot,[i] he ordered you to give the inheritance of our brother Zelophehad[j] to his daughters. 3 Now suppose they marry men from other Israelite tribes; then their inheritance will be taken from our ancestral inheritance and added to that of the tribe they marry into. And so part of the inheritance allotted to us will be taken away. 4 When the Year of Jubilee[k] for the Israelites comes, their inheritance will be added to that of the tribe into which they marry, and their property will be taken from the tribal inheritance of our ancestors.”

5 Then at the LORD's command Moses gave this order to the Israelites: “What the tribe of the descendants of Joseph is saying is right. 6 This is what the LORD commands for Zelophehad's daughters: They may marry anyone they please as long as they marry within their father's tribal clan. 7 No inheritance[l] in Israel is to pass from one tribe to another, for every Israelite shall keep the tribal inheritance of their ancestors. 8 Every daughter who inherits land in any Israelite tribe must marry someone in her father's tribal clan,[m] so that every Israelite will possess the inheritance of their ancestors. 9 No inheritance may pass from one tribe to another, for each Israelite tribe is to keep the land it inherits.”

10 So Zelophehad's daughters did as the LORD commanded Moses. 11 Zelophehad's daughters — Mahlah, Tirzah, Hoglah, Milkah and Noah[n] — married their cousins on their father's side. 12 They married within the clans of the descendants of Manasseh son of Joseph, and their inheritance remained in their father's tribe and clan.[o]

13 These are the commands and regulations the LORD gave through Moses[p] to the Israelites on the plains of Moab by the Jordan across from Jericho.[q]

35:29 [w] Nu 27:11 [x] Nu 10:8 [y] S Ex 12:20
35:30 [z] Dt 17:6; 19:15; S Mt 18:16; Jn 7:51
35:31 [a] Ex 21:30; Job 6:22; Ps 49:8; Pr 13:8
35:33 [b] S Ge 4:10
35:34 [c] Lev 18:24,25 [d] S Ex 29:45
36:1 [e] S Nu 26:30 [f] S Ge 50:23 [g] S Nu 26:28 [h] S Nu 27:2
36:2 [i] S Nu 33:54 [j] S Nu 26:33
36:4 [k] S Lev 25:10
36:7 [l] S Lev 25:23
36:8 [m] 1Ch 23:22
36:11 [n] Nu 26:33
36:12 [o] 1Ch 7:15
36:13 [p] S Lev 7:38; S 27:34 [q] Nu 22:1

35:30 *witnesses.* To avoid the possibility of an innocent party being accused and sentenced to death on insufficient evidence.
35:32 Not even an involuntary slayer could leave the city of refuge on the payment of a ransom.
35:33 *Bloodshed pollutes the land.* The crime of murder is not only an offense against the sanctity of life but also a pollutant to the Lord's sacred land (cf. Ge 4:10 – 11 and notes).
36:1 – 13 Presents an interesting further development of the account of Zelophehad's daughters (see 27:1 – 11). Since the Lord had instructed Moses that the women might inherit their father's land, new questions arose: What will happen to the family lands if these daughters marry among other tribes? Will not the original intention of the first provision be frustrated? Such questions led to the decision that marriage is to be kept within one's own tribe, so that the family allotments will not "pass from one tribe to another" (v. 9).
36:4 *Year of Jubilee.* See Lev 25:10 and note.
36:10 *Zelophehad's daughters did as the LORD commanded.* The book of Numbers, which so often presents the rebellion of God's people against his grace and in defiance of his will, ends on a happy note. These noble women, who were concerned for their father's name and their own place in the land, obeyed the Lord.
36:11 See note on 33:50 — 36:13; cf. Lev. 27:34.

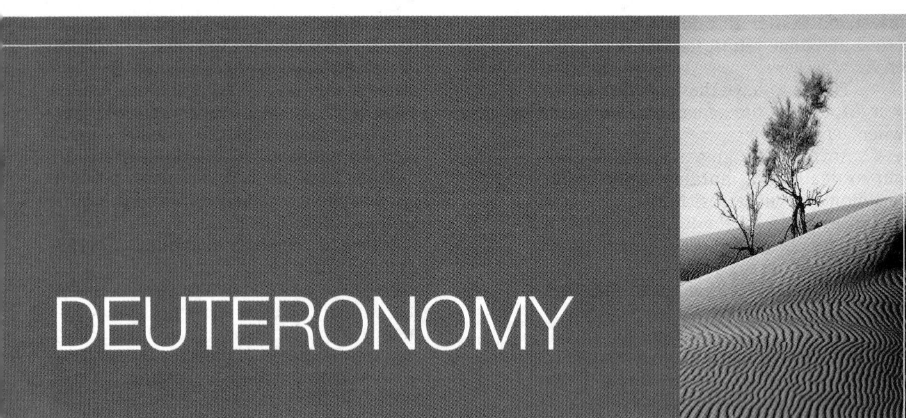

INTRODUCTION

Title

The Hebrew name of the book is *'elleh haddebarim* ("These are the words") or, more simply, *debarim* ("words"; see 1:1). The word "Deuteronomy" (meaning "repetition of the law") arose from a mistranslation in the Septuagint (the pre-Christian Greek translation of the OT) and the Latin Vulgate of a phrase in Dt 17:18, which in Hebrew means "copy of this law." The error is not serious, however, since Deuteronomy is, in a certain sense, a "repetition of the law" (see Structure and Outline).

Author and Date of Writing

The book itself ascribes most of its content to Moses (see 1:1,5; 31:24 and notes). For that reason, the OT elsewhere ascribes the bulk of Deuteronomy and other Pentateuchal legislation to Moses (see, e.g., Jos 1:7 – 8; 23:6; 1Ki 2:3; 8:53; Mal 4:4 and notes; see also 2Ki 14:6 and NIV text note). Similarly Jesus attributed Dt 24:1 to Moses (Mt 19:7 – 8; Mk 10:3 – 5), Peter attributed Dt 18:15,18 – 19 to Moses (Ac 3:22 – 23), as did Stephen (see Ac 7:37 – 38 and notes), and Paul attributed Dt 32:21 to Moses (Ro 10:19). See also Mt 22:24 and note; Mk 12:18 – 19; Lk 20:27 – 28. At the same time, it seems clear that the narrative framework within which the Mosaic material is placed (e.g., the preamble [1:1 – 5] and the conclusion [ch. 34]; see also 5:1; 27:1,9,11; 29:1 – 2; 31:1,7,9 – 10,14 – 25,30; 32:44 – 46,48 – 52; 33:1 – 2) comes from another — and unknown — hand. See Introduction to Genesis: Author and Date of Writing.

Historical Setting

Deuteronomy locates Moses and the Israelites in the territory of Moab in the area where the Jordan River flows into the Dead Sea (1:5). As his final act at this important time of transferring leadership to Joshua, Moses delivered his farewell addresses to prepare the people for their entrance into Canaan. In them,

a quick look

Author:
Moses

Audience:
God's chosen people, the Israelites

Date:
Just before the Israelites entered Canaan, probably about 1406 BC

Theme:
In a series of farewell messages, Moses exhorts the new generation of Israelites to live as his obedient people in the promised land.

Moses emphasized the laws that were especially needed at such a time, and he presented them in a way appropriate to the situation. In contrast to the matter-of-fact narratives of Leviticus and Numbers, here the words of Moses come to us from his heart as this servant of the Lord presses God's claims on his people Israel.

Special Function in the Bible

The trajectory of the story that unfolds in Genesis – Numbers seems to call for an account of the conquest of Canaan as found in Joshua to bring closure to the movement from promise to fulfillment (see Introduction to Joshua: Title and Theme). But Deuteronomy intervenes as a massive interruption. Here there is very little forward movement. At the end of Numbers, Israel is "on the plains of Moab by the Jordan across from Jericho" (Nu 36:13); at the end of Deuteronomy, the people are still there (Dt 34:8), waiting to cross the Jordan (see Jos 1:2). All that has happened is the transition from the ministry of Moses as God's spokesman and official representative to that of Joshua in his place (Dt 34:9; see Jos 1:1 – 2). But Moses' final acts as the Lord's appointed servant for dealing with Israel are so momentous that Deuteronomy's account of them marks the conclusion to the Pentateuch, while the book of Joshua, which narrates the initial fulfillment of the promises

Statue of Moses by Michelangelo in the Church of San Pietro in Vincoli (Saint Peter in Chains) in Rome

Mount Nebo can be seen in the distance in this view looking southwest toward the Dead Sea. Moses "viewed" the promised land from Mount Nebo (Dt 32:49).

made to the patriarchs and the conclusion to the mission on which Moses had been sent (see Nu 17:15 – 23; Jos 21:43 – 45), serves as the introduction to the Former Prophets.

So Deuteronomy creates a long pause in the advancement of the story of redemption:

(1) Of deliverance from bondage to a world power (Egypt) to a place in the earth where Israel can be a free people under the rule of God
(2) Of deliverance from rootlessness in the post-Babel world (Abraham, Isaac and Jacob) to security and "rest" (see Dt 3:20 and note; 12:10; 25:19) in the promised land
(3) Of deliverance from a life of banishment from God's garden (Ge 3) to a life in the Lord's own land where he has pitched his tent (Jos 22:19)

But in that long pause on the threshold of the promised land Moses, in this renewal of the Sinaitic covenant, reminded Israel at length of what the Lord required of them as his people if they were to cross the Jordan, take possession of the promised land and there enjoy the promised "rest" in fellowship with him. It was a word that Israel needed to hear over and over again. Upon reading the Pentateuch, Israel was brought ever anew to the threshold of the promised land and its promised "rest" to hear again this final word from God through his servant Moses (see also Ps 95:7b – 22).

The love relationship of the Lord to his people, and that of the people to the Lord as their sovereign God, pervade the whole book of Deuteronomy.

For this reason, all the history of Israel in Canaan as narrated in the Former Prophets is brought under the judgment of this word.

Theological Teaching and Purpose

The book of Deuteronomy was cast in the form of ancient Near Eastern suzerainty-vassal treaties of the second millennium BC. It contained the Great King's pledge to be Israel's suzerain and protector if they would be faithful to him as their covenant Lord and obedient to the covenant stipulations as the vassal people of his kingdom. There would be blessings for such obedience, but curses for disobedience (chs. 27 – 30). Deuteronomy's purpose was to prepare the new generation of the Lord's chosen people to be his kingdom representatives in the land he had unconditionally promised them in the Abrahamic covenant (see Structure and Outline; see also notes on 3:27; 17:14,18).

The love relationship of the Lord to his people, and that of the people to the Lord as their sovereign God, pervade the whole book. Deuteronomy's spiritual emphasis and its call to total commitment to the Lord in worship and obedience inspired references to its message throughout the rest of Scripture. In particular, the division of the Hebrew Bible called the Former Prophets (Joshua, Judges, Samuel, Kings) is thoroughly imbued with the style, themes and motifs of Deuteronomy. Among the Latter Prophets, Jeremiah also reflects strong influence from this book.

Structure and Outline

Deuteronomy's literary structure supports its historical setting. By its interpretive, repetitious, reminiscent and somewhat irregular style it shows that it is a series of more or less extemporaneous addresses, sometimes describing events in nonchronological order (see, e.g., 10:3 and note). But it also bears in its structure clear reflections of the suzerain-vassal treaties (see chart, p. 23) of the preceding and then-current Near Eastern states, a structure that lends itself to the Biblical emphasis on the covenant between the Lord and his people. In this sense Deuteronomy is a covenant-renewal document, as the following outline shows:

- I. Preamble (1:1 – 5)
- II. Historical Prologue (1:6 — 4:43)
- III. Stipulations of the Covenant (4:44 — 26:19)
  - A. The Great Commandment: The Demand for Absolute Allegiance (4:44 — 11:32)
    1. God's covenant Lordship (4:44 — 5:33)
    2. The principle of consecration (ch. 6)
    3. The program for conquering Canaan (ch. 7)
    4. A call to commitment in the new land (ch. 8)
    5. The lesson of the broken tablets (9:1 — 10:11)
    6. Another call to commitment (10:12 — 11:32)
  - B. Supplementary Requirements (chs. 12 – 26)
    1. Ceremonial consecration (12:1 — 16:17)
    2. Human leaders in God's righteous kingdom (16:18 — 21:21)
    3. Sanctity of God's kingdom (21:22 — 25:19)
    4. Confessions of God as Redeemer-King (ch. 26)

IV. Ratification; Curses and Blessings (chs. 27 – 30)
V. Leadership Succession under the Covenant (chs. 31 – 34)
   A. Change of Leadership (31:1 – 29)
   B. Song of Moses (31:30 — 32:47)
   C. Moses' Testamental Blessing on the Tribes (32:48 — 33:29)
   D. Death of Moses and Succession of Joshua (ch. 34)

The Command to Leave Horeb

1 These are the words Moses spoke to
all Israel in the wilderness east of the
Jordan[a]—that is, in the Arabah[b]—opposite Suph, between Paran[c] and Tophel,
Laban, Hazeroth and Dizahab. 2 (It takes
eleven days to go from Horeb[d] to Kadesh
Barnea[e] by the Mount Seir[f] road.)[g]

3 In the fortieth year,[h] on the first day of
the eleventh month,[i] Moses proclaimed[j] to
the Israelites all that the LORD had commanded him concerning them. 4 This was
after he had defeated Sihon[k] king of the
Amorites,[l] who reigned in Heshbon,[m] and
at Edrei had defeated Og[n] king of Bashan,
who reigned in Ashtaroth.[o]

5 East of the Jordan in the territory of
Moab,[p] Moses began to expound this law,
saying:

6 The LORD our God said to us[q] at Horeb,[r] "You have stayed long enough[s] at this
mountain. 7 Break camp and advance into
the hill country of the Amorites;[t] go to all
the neighboring peoples in the Arabah,[u]
in the mountains, in the western foothills,
in the Negev[v] and along the coast, to the
land of the Canaanites[w] and to Lebanon,[x]
as far as the great river, the Euphrates.[y]
8 See, I have given you this land[z].[a] Go in
and take possession of the land the LORD
swore[b] he would give to your fathers—to
Abraham, Isaac and Jacob—and to their
descendants after them."

The Appointment of Leaders

9 At that time I said to you, "You are too
heavy a burden[c] for me to carry alone.[d]
10 The LORD your God has increased[e] your
numbers[f] so that today you are as numerous[g] as the stars in the sky.[h] 11 May the LORD,
the God of your ancestors, increase[i] you a
thousand times and bless you as he has
promised![j] 12 But how can I bear your problems and your burdens and your disputes
all by myself?[k] 13 Choose some wise, understanding and respected men[l] from each of
your tribes, and I will set them over you."

14 You answered me, "What you propose
to do is good."

15 So I took[m] the leading men of your
tribes,[n] wise and respected men,[o] and
appointed them to have authority over
you—as commanders[p] of thousands, of
hundreds, of fifties and of tens and as tribal officials.[q] 16 And I charged your judges
at that time, "Hear the disputes between
your people and judge[r] fairly,[s] whether the
case is between two Israelites or between
an Israelite and a foreigner residing among
you.[t] 17 Do not show partiality[u] in judging;
hear both small and great alike. Do not be
afraid of anyone,[v] for judgment belongs to
God. Bring me any case too hard for you,
and I will hear it."[w] 18 And at that time I
told you everything you were to do.[x]

Spies Sent Out

19 Then, as the LORD our God commanded us, we set out from Horeb and went
toward the hill country of the Amorites[y]

1:1 [a]S Nu 13:29; Dt 4:46 [b]ver 7; Dt 2:8; 3:17; Jos 3:16; 8:14; 11:2; Eze 47:8 [c]S Nu 10:12 **1:2** [d]S Ex 3:1 [e]S Ge 14:7; Dt 2:14; 9:23; Jos 15:3 [f]S Nu 24:18 [g]ver 19 **1:3** [h]Nu 14:33; 32:13; Dt 8:2; Heb 3:7-9 [i]Ge 50:3; Dt 34:8; Jos 4:19 [j]Dt 4:1-2 **1:4** [k]Nu 21:21-26 [l]S Ge 10:16; S 14:7 [m]S Nu 21:25 [n]Nu 21:33-35; Dt 3:10 [o]Jos 9:10; 12:4; 1Ch 11:44 **1:5** [p]S Nu 21:11 **1:6** [q]Nu 10:13 [r]S Ex 3:1 [s]Dt 2:3 **1:7** [t]ver 19; Dt 2:24; 7:1; Jos 10:5 [u]S ver 1 [v]S Nu 21:1; Jos 11:16; 12:8; 2Sa 24:7 [w]S Ge 10:18 [x]Dt 11:24 [y]S Ge 2:14 **1:8** [z]S Jos 23:13 [a]S Nu 34:2 [b]S Ex 13:11; S Nu 14:23; Heb 6:13-14 **1:9** [c]S Nu 11:14; Ps 38:4 [d]S Ex 18:18 **1:10** [e]ver 11; Eze 16:7 [f]S Dt 7:13 [g]S Ge 15:5; Isa 51:2; 60:22; Eze 33:24 [h]S Ge 22:17; S Nu 10:36 **1:11** [i]S ver 10 [j]ver 8; Ex 32:13; 2Sa 24:3; 1Ch 21:3 **1:12** [k]S Ex 5:22; S 18:18 **1:13** [l]S Ge 47:6 **1:15** [m]Ex 18:25 [n]Ex 5:14; Nu 11:16; Jos 1:10; 3:2 [o]S Ge 47:6 [p]Nu 31:14; 1Sa 8:12; 22:7; 1Ki 14:27 [q]S Nu 1:4 **1:16** [r]1Ki 3:9; Ps 72:1; Pr 2:9 [s]S Ge 31:37; Jn 7:24 [t]S Ex 12:19, 49; S 22:21 **1:17** [u]S Ex 18:16; S Lev 19:15; Ac 10:34; Jas 2:1 [v]Pr 29:25 [w]Ex 18:26 **1:18** [x]S Ge 39:11 **1:19** [y]S ver 7

1:1–5 The preamble gives the historical setting for the entire book and introduces Moses, the Great King's covenant mediator.

1:1 *Moses spoke.* Almost all of Deuteronomy is presented as speeches by Moses during the final months of his life, just before the Israelites crossed the Jordan to enter Canaan. *Arabah.* Includes the valley of the Jordan (from the Sea of Galilee to the southern end of the Dead Sea) and the valley extending down to the Gulf of Aqaba. *Suph … Paran … Tophel, Laban, Hazeroth and Dizahab.* Places along the route from Sinai to the territory of Moab (see, e.g., Nu 12:16 and note).

1:2 *Horeb.* The usual name for Mount Sinai in Deuteronomy (the only exception is in 33:2). *Kadesh Barnea.* See notes on Ge 14:7; Nu 20:11. *Seir.* See notes on Ge 36:8; Eze 35:2.

1:3 *fortieth year.* After leaving Egypt. The Lord had condemned the Israelites to 40 years of wandering in Sinai as punishment for not entering Canaan as he had commanded them to do at Kadesh (Nu 14:33–34). The 40 years included the time spent at Sinai and on the journey to Kadesh, as well as the next 38 years (see 2:14). See 8:2–5; 29:5–6; Nu 14:29–35; 32:13; Ac 7:36; Heb 3:7–19. *eleventh month.* January-February.

1:4 *Sihon … Og.* See notes on Nu 21:21–26,35. *Heshbon.* See note on Isa 15:4.

1:5 *this law.* The Ten Commandments and other laws given at Mount Sinai and recorded in Ex 20–24, Leviticus and Numbers. In Deuteronomy the laws are summarized, interpreted and adjusted to the new, specific situation Israel would face in Canaan. Thus Deuteronomy is, in essence, a covenant renewal (and updating) document (see Introduction: Theological Teaching and Purpose; Structure and Outline).

1:6 *The LORD our God.* Together with "the LORD your God," this title occurs almost 300 times in Deuteronomy, in addition to the many times that "LORD" is used alone or in other combinations (see notes on 28:58; Ge 2:4; Ex 3:14–15; 6:3,6; Lev 18:2).

1:7 See Jos 1:4. The land is described by its various geographic areas (see map, p. 262). *Arabah.* See note on v. 1. *mountains.* The midsection running north and south. *western foothills.* Sloping toward the Mediterranean. *Negev.* See note on Ge 12:9. *coast.* The Mediterranean coastal strip. The "land of the Canaanites" and "Lebanon, as far as … the Euphrates" make up the northern sector. The "hill country of the Amorites" is, in general, the central and southern mountains. This description of the land agrees with that in the promise (see v. 8) to Abraham in Ge 15:18–21, a promise later given to Isaac's descendants (Ge 26:2–4) and still later to the descendants of Jacob (Ge 35:11–12).

1:9–18 Cf. 16:18–20; Ex 18:13–26.

1:10 *as the stars in the sky.* See 10:22; 28:62; Ge 13:16 and note; 15:5 and note; 22:17; 26:4; Ex 32:13.

1:19–46 See Nu 13–14 and notes.

through all that vast and dreadful wilderness[z] that you have seen, and so we
reached Kadesh Barnea.[a] 20 Then I said to
you, "You have reached the hill country
of the Amorites, which the LORD our God
is giving us. 21 See, the LORD your God has
given you the land. Go up and take possession[b] of it as the LORD, the God of your
ancestors, told you. Do not be afraid;[c] do
not be discouraged."[d]
22 Then all of you came to me and said,
"Let us send men ahead to spy[e] out the
land[f] for us and bring back a report about
the route we are to take and the towns we
will come to."
23 The idea seemed good to me; so I selected[g] twelve of you, one man from each
tribe. 24 They left and went up into the hill
country, and came to the Valley of Eshkol[h] and explored it. 25 Taking with them
some of the fruit of the land, they brought
it down to us and reported,[i] "It is a good
land[j] that the LORD our God is giving us."[k]

Rebellion Against the LORD

26 But you were unwilling to go up;[l] you
rebelled[m] against the command of the
LORD your God. 27 You grumbled[n] in your
tents and said, "The LORD hates us; so he
brought us out of Egypt to deliver us into
the hands of the Amorites to destroy us.
28 Where can we go? Our brothers have
made our hearts melt in fear. They say,
'The people are stronger and taller[o] than
we are; the cities are large, with walls up to
the sky. We even saw the Anakites[p] there.' "
29 Then I said to you, "Do not be terrified;
do not be afraid[q] of them.[r] 30 The LORD your

1:19 [z] Dt 2:7; 8:15; 32:10; Ps 136:16; Jer 2:2,6; Hos 13:5 [a] ver 2; Nu 13:26 **1:21** [b] Dt 9:23 [c] S Nu 14:9; Jos 1:6,9,18; 2Sa 10:12; Ps 27:14 [d] Dt 7:18; Jos 8:1; 10:8 **1:22** [e] Nu 13:1-3 [f] S Ge 42:9 **1:23** [g] Nu 13:1-3 **1:24** [h] Nu 13:21-25; S 32:9 **1:25** [i] S Nu 13:27 [j] S Nu 14:7 [k] Jos 1:2 **1:26** [l] Nu 14:1-4 [m] S Nu 14:9 **1:27** [n] Dt 9:28; Ps 106:25

1:28 [o] S Nu 13:32 [p] S Nu 13:33; Dt 9:1-3 **1:29** [q] Dt 3:22; 20:3; Ne 4:14 [r] Dt 7:18; 20:1; 31:6

1:21 *as the LORD ... told you.* The promise of the land (see note on v. 7) was reaffirmed to Moses (v. 8) at the burning bush (Ex 3:8,17). Now the Israelites are told to enter the land and conquer it. *Do not be afraid ... discouraged.* See 31:8; Jos 1:9; 8:1; 10:25.
1:23 *twelve.* They are named in Nu 13:4–15.
1:24 *Eshkol.* See note on Nu 13:23.
1:27 *grumbled.* See note on Ex 15:24. *The LORD hates us.* The people's statement is ironic indeed in the light of Deuteronomy's major theme of love (see Introduction: Theological Teaching and Purpose).
1:28 *Anakites.* Earlier inhabitants of Canaan, described as giants (see 2:10,21; 9:2; Nu 13:32–33).
1:29 *Do not be terrified ... afraid.* See notes on Isa 41:10,13; 43:1–2.
1:30 *as he did for you in Egypt.* See Ex 14:1—15:19.

THE FIVE MAJOR LONGITUDINAL ZONES OF ISRAEL

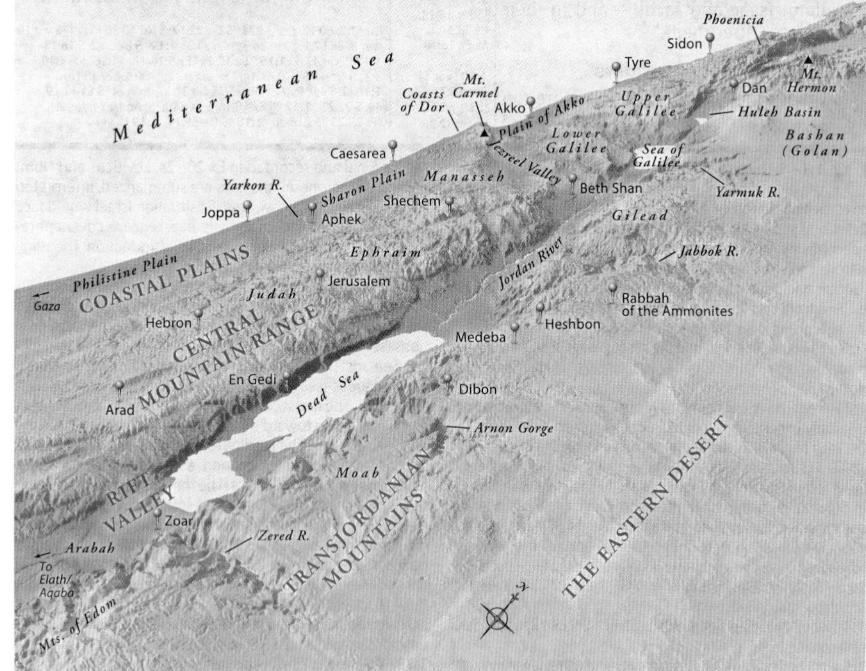

God, who is going before you, will fight[s] for
you, as he did for you in Egypt, before your
very eyes, 31 and in the wilderness. There
you saw how the LORD your God carried[t]
you, as a father carries his son, all the way
you went until you reached this place."[u]
32 In spite of this,[v] you did not trust[w] in
the LORD your God, 33 who went ahead of
you on your journey, in fire by night and
in a cloud by day,[x] to search[y] out places
for you to camp and to show you the way
you should go.
34 When the LORD heard[z] what you said,
he was angry[a] and solemnly swore:[b] 35 "No
one from this evil generation shall see the
good land[c] I swore to give your ancestors,
36 except Caleb[d] son of Jephunneh. He will
see it, and I will give him and his descendants the land he set his feet on, because
he followed the LORD wholeheartedly.[e]"
37 Because of you the LORD became angry[f] with me also and said, "You shall not
enter[g] it, either. 38 But your assistant, Joshua[h] son of Nun, will enter it. Encourage[i]
him, because he will lead[j] Israel to inherit[k] it. 39 And the little ones that you said
would be taken captive,[l] your children
who do not yet know[m] good from bad—
they will enter the land. I will give it to
them and they will take possession of it.
40 But as for you, turn around and set out
toward the desert along the route to the
Red Sea.[a][n]"
41 Then you replied, "We have sinned
against the LORD. We will go up and fight,
as the LORD our God commanded us." So
every one of you put on his weapons, thinking it easy to go up into the hill country.
42 But the LORD said to me, "Tell them,
'Do not go up and fight, because I will not
be with you. You will be defeated by your
enemies.' "[o]
43 So I told you, but you would not listen. You rebelled against the LORD's command and in your arrogance you marched
up into the hill country. 44 The Amorites
who lived in those hills came out against
you; they chased you like a swarm of bees[p]
and beat you down from Seir[q] all the way
to Hormah.[r] 45 You came back and wept
before the LORD,[s] but he paid no attention[t]
to your weeping and turned a deaf ear[u] to
you. 46 And so you stayed in Kadesh[v] many
days—all the time you spent there.

Wanderings in the Wilderness

2 Then we turned back and set out toward the wilderness along the route
to the Red Sea,[a][w] as the LORD had directed me. For a long time we made our way
around the hill country of Seir.[x]
2 Then the LORD said to me, 3 "You have
made your way around this hill country long enough;[y] now turn north. 4 Give
the people these orders:[z] 'You are about
to pass through the territory of your relatives the descendants of Esau,[a] who live
in Seir.[b] They will be afraid[c] of you, but
be very careful. 5 Do not provoke them to
war, for I will not give you any of their
land, not even enough to put your foot on.
I have given Esau the hill country of Seir
as his own.[d] 6 You are to pay them in silver for the food you eat and the water you
drink.' "
7 The LORD your God has blessed you
in all the work of your hands. He has
watched[e] over your journey through this
vast wilderness.[f] These forty years[g] the
LORD your God has been with you, and
you have not lacked anything.[h]

[a] *40,1* Or *the Sea of Reeds*

1:30 [s] S Ex 14:14 **1:31** [t] Ex 19:4; Dt 32:10-12; Ps 28:9; Isa 46:3-4; 63:9; Hos 11:3; Ac 13:18 [u] Jer 31:32 **1:32** [v] S Nu 14:11 [w] Dt 9:23; Ps 78:22; 106:24; Zep 3:2; Heb 3:19; Jude 1:5 **1:33** [x] Ex 13:21; Nu 9:15-23; Ne 9:12; Ps 78:14 [y] S Nu 10:33 **1:34** [z] S Nu 11:1 [a] S Nu 32:14 [b] S Nu 14:23, 28-30; Eze 20:15; Heb 3:11 **1:35** [c] S Nu 14:29 **1:36** [d] S Nu 13:6 [e] S Nu 14:24 **1:37** [f] Ps 106:32 [g] S Nu 27:13 **1:38** [h] S Nu 11:28 [i] Dt 31:7 [j] Dt 3:28 [k] Jos 11:23; Ps 78:55; 136:21 **1:39** [l] S Nu 14:3 [m] Isa 7:15-16 **1:40** [n] S Ex 14:27; Jdg 11:16 **1:42** [o] S Nu 14:41-43 **1:44** [p] Ps 118:12 [q] S Nu 24:18 [r] S Nu 14:45 **1:45** [s] S Nu 14:1 [t] Job 27:9; 35:13; Ps 18:41; 66:18; Pr 1:28; Isa 1:15; Jer 14:12; La 3:8; Mic 3:4; S Jn 9:31 [u] Ps 28:1; 39:12; Pr 28:9 **1:46** [v] S Nu 20:1 **2:1** [w] S Ex 14:27; S Nu 21:4 [x] S Nu 24:18 **2:3** [y] Dt 1:6 **2:4** [z] Nu 20:14-21 [a] Ge 36:8 [b] ver 1 [c] Ex 15:16 **2:5** [d] Jos 24:4 **2:7** [e] Dt 8:2-4 [f] S Ex 13:21; S Dt 1:19 [g] ver 14; S Nu 14:33; 32:13; Jos 5:6 [h] Ne 9:21; Am 2:10

1:31 *God carried you.* Cf. Isa 40:11; Jer 31:10; Eze 34:11–16.

1:33 *in fire by night and in a cloud by day.* The presence of the Lord was in the cloud over the tabernacle to guide the Israelites through their wilderness journeys (see Ex 13:21 and note; 40:34–38).

1:36 *Caleb.* See Nu 13:30—14:38; Jos 14:6–15. *followed the LORD wholeheartedly.* See note on Nu 14:24.

1:37 *Because of you.* See 3:26; 4:21. God was angry with Moses who, failing to honor the Lord as holy, struck the rock at Meribah to get water (see Nu 20:9–13 and note on 20:11; 27:12–14). And since it was the Israelites who had incited him to sin, God was angry with them too. This event (v. 37) occurred almost 40 years after that of the preceding verses (vv. 34–36), but Moses, interested in telling about the Israelites' sin and his own, brings the two events together.

1:39 *do not yet know good from bad.* See notes on Ge 2:9; Isa 7:15.

1:41 *We will go up.* See v. 26; Nu 14:40 and note.

1:43 *You rebelled against the LORD's command.* The same charge as in v. 26. First the people rebelled against the Lord's command to go into the land, then against his command not to enter the land. After their first rebellion the Lord would not go with them. His presence was essential, and Israel needed to learn that lesson.

1:44 *bees.* See note on Ex 23:28.

1:45 *before the LORD.* At the tabernacle.

2:1—3:11 See Nu 20:14—21:35 and notes.

2:1 *Red Sea.* Here probably the Gulf of Aqaba (see note on 1Ki 9:26). *hill country of Seir.* Edom, the mountainous area south of the Dead Sea.

2:5 *I will not give you any of their land.* See vv. 9,19. The Lord told Moses to bypass Edom, Moab and Ammon because of their blood relationship to Israel. The Israelites were to take over only those lands east of the Jordan that were in the hands of the Amorites (see v. 24; 3:2). *I have given.* See vv. 9,19. The Lord had given the descendants of Esau (Edomites) and Lot (Moabites and Ammonites) their lands, just as he was giving the Israelites the territories of Transjordan and Canaan.

2:6,28 *silver.* See note on 14:25.

8 So we went on past our relatives the
descendants of Esau, who live in Seir.
We turned from[i] the Arabah[j] road, which
comes up from Elath and Ezion Geber,[k] and
traveled along the desert road of Moab.[l]
9 Then the LORD said to me, "Do not harass the Moabites or provoke them to war,
for I will not give you any part of their
land. I have given Ar[m] to the descendants
of Lot[n] as a possession."
10 (The Emites[o] used to live there—a
people strong and numerous, and as tall
as the Anakites.[p] 11 Like the Anakites, they
too were considered Rephaites,[q] but the
Moabites called them Emites. 12 Horites[r]
used to live in Seir, but the descendants
of Esau drove them out. They destroyed
the Horites from before them and settled
in their place, just as Israel did[s] in the land
the LORD gave them as their possession.)
13 And the LORD said, "Now get up and
cross the Zered Valley.[t]" So we crossed the
valley.
14 Thirty-eight years[u] passed from the
time we left Kadesh Barnea[v] until we
crossed the Zered Valley. By then, that
entire generation[w] of fighting men had
perished from the camp, as the LORD had
sworn to them.[x] 15 The LORD's hand was
against them until he had completely eliminated[y] them from the camp.
16 Now when the last of these fighting
men among the people had died, 17 the
LORD said to me, 18 "Today you are to pass
by the region of Moab at Ar.[z] 19 When you
come to the Ammonites,[a] do not harass
them or provoke them to war,[b] for I will
not give you possession of any land belonging to the Ammonites. I have given it
as a possession to the descendants of Lot.[c]"
20 (That too was considered a land of the
Rephaites,[d] who used to live there; but the
Ammonites called them Zamzummites.
21 They were a people strong and numerous, and as tall as the Anakites.[e] The LORD
destroyed them from before the Ammonites, who drove them out and settled in
their place. 22 The LORD had done the same
for the descendants of Esau, who lived in
Seir,[f] when he destroyed the Horites from
before them. They drove them out and
have lived in their place to this day. 23 And
as for the Avvites[g] who lived in villages as
far as Gaza,[h] the Caphtorites[i] coming out
from Caphtor[a][j] destroyed them and settled
in their place.)

Defeat of Sihon King of Heshbon

24 "Set out now and cross the Arnon
Gorge.[k] See, I have given into your hand
Sihon the Amorite,[l] king of Heshbon, and
his country. Begin to take possession of it
and engage[m] him in battle. 25 This very day
I will begin to put the terror[n] and fear[o] of
you on all the nations under heaven. They
will hear reports of you and will tremble[p]
and be in anguish because of you."
26 From the Desert of Kedemoth[q] I sent
messengers to Sihon[r] king of Heshbon offering peace[s] and saying, 27 "Let us pass
through your country. We will stay on the
main road; we will not turn aside to the
right or to the left.[t] 28 Sell us food to eat[u]
and water to drink for their price in silver.
Only let us pass through on foot[v]— 29 as
the descendants of Esau, who live in Seir,
and the Moabites, who live in Ar, did for
us—until we cross the Jordan into the
land the LORD our God is giving us." 30 But
Sihon king of Heshbon refused to let us
pass through. For the LORD[w] your God had
made his spirit stubborn[x] and his heart
obstinate[y] in order to give him into your
hands,[z] as he has now done.
31 The LORD said to me, "See, I have begun to deliver Sihon and his country over
to you. Now begin to conquer and possess
his land."[a]
32 When Sihon and all his army came
out to meet us in battle[b] at Jahaz, 33 the
LORD our God delivered[c] him over to us
and we struck him down,[d] together with

[a] *23* That is, Crete

2:8 [i]S Nu 20:21 [j]S Dt 1:1 [k]Nu 33:35; 1Ki 9:26 [l]S Nu 21:4 **2:9** [m]S Nu 21:15 [n]Ge 19:38; Ps 83:8 **2:10** [o]Ge 14:5 [p]S Nu 13:22,33 **2:11** [q]S Ge 14:5 **2:12** [r]S Ge 14:6 [s]Nu 21:25,35 **2:13** [t]S Nu 21:12 **2:14** [u]S ver 7 [v]S Dt 1:2 [w]Nu 14:29-35 [x]Dt 1:34-35; Jos 5:6 **2:15** [y]Ps 106:26; Jude 1:5 **2:18** [z]S Nu 21:15 **2:19** [a]S Ge 19:38 [b]2Ch 20:10 [c]S ver 9 **2:20** [d]S Ge 14:5 **2:21** [e]ver 10 **2:22** [f]S Ge 14:6 **2:23** [g]Jos 13:3; 18:23; 2Ki 17:31 [h]S Ge 10:19 [i]S Ge 10:14 [j]Jer 47:4; Am 9:7 **2:24** [k]Nu 21:13-14; Jdg 11:13, 18 [l]S Dt 1:7 [m]Dt 3:6 **2:25** [n]S Ge 35:5; Dt 11:25 [o]Jos 2:9,11; 1Ch 14:17; 2Ch 14:14; 17:10; 20:29; Isa 2:19; 13:13; 19:16 [p]Ex 15:14-16 **2:26** [q]Jos 13:18; 1Ch 6:79 [r]Dt 1:4; Jdg 11:21-22 [s]Dt 20:10; Jdg 21:13; 2Sa 20:19 **2:27** [t]Nu 21:21-22 **2:28** [u]Dt 23:4 [v]S Nu 20:19 **2:30** [w]Jdg 14:4; 1Ki 12:15 [x]S Ex 4:21; Ro 9:18 [y]S Ex 14:17 [z]La 3:65 **2:31** [a]S Ge 12:7 **2:32** [b]S Nu 21:23 **2:33** [c]Ex 23:31; Dt 7:2; 31:5 [d]S Nu 21:24

2:8 *Elath and Ezion Geber.* Towns at the head of the Gulf of Aqaba. The "Arabah road" ran from the head of the gulf northward and to the east of Moab.
2:10 *Anakites.* See note on 1:28.
2:11 *Rephaites.* People of large stature (see 3:11).
2:12 *Horites.* See note on Ge 14:6. *the land the LORD gave them.* Either (1) the Transjordan regions (see 2:24—3:20), (2) Canaan itself or (3) Transjordan and Canaan. If either (2) or (3) is intended, editorial updating is involved (see note on Ge 14:14).
2:13 *Zered.* The main stream (intermittent) that flows into the southern end of the Dead Sea from the east. It marked the border between Edom and Moab (see map, p. 262).
2:14 *Thirty-eight years.* See note on 1:3.
2:20 *Zamzummites.* Perhaps to be identified with the Zuzites of Ge 14:5.
2:23 *Avvites.* Pre-Philistine people otherwise unknown (Jos 13:3). *Caphtorites.* See note on Ge 10:14. *Caphtor.* See NIV text note.
2:24 *Arnon.* See note on Nu 21:10–13. *Sihon . . . Heshbon.* See 1:4 and note.
2:26 *Kedemoth.* Means "eastern regions."
2:30 *God had made his spirit stubborn and his heart obstinate.* In the OT, actions are often attributed to God without the mention of mediate or contributing situations or persons. Sihon by his own conscious will refused Israel passage, but it was God who would give Sihon's land to Israel (see note on Ex 4:21).
2:32 *Jahaz.* See Nu 21:23; see also note on Isa 15:4.

his sons and his whole army. 34At that
time we took all his towns and completely destroyed[ae] them—men, women and
children. We left no survivors. 35But the
livestock[f] and the plunder[g] from the towns
we had captured we carried off for ourselves. 36From Aroer[h] on the rim of the
Arnon Gorge, and from the town in the
gorge, even as far as Gilead,[i] not one town
was too strong for us. The LORD our God
gave[j] us all of them. 37But in accordance
with the command of the LORD our God,[k]
you did not encroach on any of the land
of the Ammonites,[l] neither the land along
the course of the Jabbok[m] nor that around
the towns in the hills.

Defeat of Og King of Bashan

3 Next we turned and went up along the
road toward Bashan, and Og king of
Bashan[n] with his whole army marched out
to meet us in battle at Edrei.[o] 2The LORD
said to me, "Do not be afraid[p] of him, for I
have delivered him into your hands, along
with his whole army and his land. Do to
him what you did to Sihon king of the Amorites, who reigned in Heshbon."
3So the LORD our God also gave into our
hands Og king of Bashan and all his army.
We struck them down,[q] leaving no survivors.[r] 4At that time we took all his cities.[s]
There was not one of the sixty cities that
we did not take from them—the whole region of Argob, Og's kingdom[t] in Bashan.[u]
All these cities were fortified with high
walls and with gates and bars, and there
were also a great many unwalled villages.
We completely destroyed[a] them, as we
had done with Sihon king of Heshbon, de-
troying[av] every city—men, women and
children. 7But all the livestock[w] and the
plunder from their cities we carried off for
ourselves.
8So at that time we took from these two
kings of the Amorites[x] the territory east of
the Jordan, from the Arnon Gorge as far as
Mount Hermon.[y] 9(Hermon is called Sirion[z] by the Sidonians; the Amorites call
it Senir.)[a] 10We took all the towns on the
plateau, and all Gilead, and all Bashan as
far as Salekah[b] and Edrei, towns of Og's
kingdom in Bashan. 11(Og king of Bashan
was the last of the Rephaites.[c] His bed was
decorated with iron and was more than
nine cubits long and four cubits wide.[b] It
is still in Rabbah[d] of the Ammonites.)

Division of the Land

12Of the land that we took over at that
time, I gave the Reubenites and the Gadites the territory north of Aroer[e] by the Arnon Gorge, including half the hill country
of Gilead, together with its towns. 13The
rest of Gilead and also all of Bashan, the
kingdom of Og, I gave to the half-tribe of
Manasseh.[f] (The whole region of Argob in
Bashan used to be known as a land of the
Rephaites.[g] 14Jair,[h] a descendant of Manasseh, took the whole region of Argob
as far as the border of the Geshurites and
the Maakathites;[i] it was named[j] after him,
so that to this day Bashan is called Havvoth Jair.[c]) 15And I gave Gilead to Makir.[k]
16But to the Reubenites and the Gadites I
gave the territory extending from Gilead
down to the Arnon Gorge (the middle of

2:34 [e]S Nu 21:2; Dt 3:6; 7:2; Ps 106:34 **2:35** [f]Dt 3:7 [g]S Ge 34:29; S 49:27 **2:36** [h]S Nu 32:34 [i]S Nu 32:39 [j]Ps 44:3 **2:37** [k]ver 18-19 [l]S Nu 21:24 [m]S Ge 32:22 **3:1** [n]S Nu 32:19 [o]S Nu 21:33 **3:2** [p]Jos 10:8; 2Ki 19:6; Isa 7:4 **3:3** [q]S Nu 21:24 [r]Nu 21:35 **3:4** [s]S Nu 21:24 [t]ver 13 [u]S Nu 21:33 **3:6** [v]Dt 2:24 **3:7** [w]Dt 2:35 **3:8** [x]Nu 32:33; Jos 13:8-12 [y]Dt 4:48; Jos 11:3,17; 12:1; 13:5; Jdg 3:3; 1Ch 5:23; Ps 42:6; 89:12; 133:3; SS 4:8 **3:9** [z]Ps 29:6 [a]1Ch 5:23; SS 4:8; Eze 27:5 **3:10** [b]Jos 12:5; 1Ch 5:11 **3:11** [c]Ge 14:5 [d]Jos 13:25; 15:60; 2Sa 11:1; 12:26; 17:27; 1Ch 20:1; Jer 49:2; Eze 21:20; 25:5; Am 1:14 **3:12** [e]Dt 2:36 **3:13** [f]Dt 29:8 [g]S Ge 14:5 **3:14** [h]S Nu 32:41 [i]Jos 12:5; 13:11,13; 2Sa 10:6; 23:34; 2Ki 25:23; 1Ch 4:19; Jer 40:8 [j]Jos 19:47; Ps 49:11 **3:15** [k]S Ge 50:23; Nu 32:39-40

[a] *34,6* The Hebrew term refers to the irrevocable giving over of things or persons to the LORD, often by totally destroying them. [b] *11* That is, about 14 feet long and 6 feet wide or about 4 meters long and 1.8 meters wide [c] *14* Or *called the settlements of Jair*

:34 *completely destroyed.* See NIV text note. The Hebrew for his expression usually refers to the destruction of everyone nd everything that could be destroyed. Objects like gold, ilver and bronze, not subject to destruction, were put in a ecure place as God's possession. Destruction of people and hings made them useless to the conquerors but put them n the hands of God. So the word is sometimes translated destroyed" and sometimes "devoted" (see, e.g., Nu 18:14; Jos :17). God sometimes permitted exclusion from this practice, s when he assigned captured livestock and other plunder to is people as recompense for service in his army (see v. 35; :7; Jos 8:2).

:36 *Aroer.* See note on Isa 17:2. *Gilead.* See note on Ge 31:21.

:37 *Jabbok.* See note on Ge 32:22.

:3 *gave into our hands Og.* As in 2:26–37. See 1:4 and note.

:4 *sixty cities.* These were "large walled cities" (1Ki 4:13), im-lying a heavily populated territory (see v. 5). *region of Argob.* n otherwise unidentified area in Bashan (see vv. 13–14; 1Ki :13), which was northeast of the Sea of Galilee.

:6–7 See note on 2:34.

:8 *Mount Hermon.* Rising to a height of over 9,200 feet and nowcapped throughout the year, it is one of the most prom-ient and beautiful mountains in Lebanon.

3:9 *Sirion.* This name for Mount Hermon is found also in a Canaanite document contemporary with Moses. *Senir.* This name for Mount Hermon is also found in Assyrian sources.

3:10 *Salekah.* A city marking the eastern boundary of Bashan (see Jos 12:5 and note).

3:11 *bed ... with iron.* Possibly a sarcophagus made of black basalt. Such sarcophagi (stone coffins) have been found in Bashan, and the Hebrew for "bed" and "iron" may reflect this. If an actual bed, it was probably made of wood but with certain iron fixtures, as were the "chariots fitted with iron" (see note on Jos 17:16). *Rabbah of the Ammonites.* Called Philadelphia in NT times, Rabbah was the capital of ancient Ammon (Am 1:13–14). Today its name is Amman, the capital of the kingdom of Jordan.

3:12–20 See Nu 32; 34:13–15 and notes.

3:14 *Jair ... Havvoth Jair.* See NIV text note; see also note on Jdg 10:3. *the Geshurites and the Maakathites.* Two comparatively small kingdoms, Geshur was east of the Sea of Galilee and Maakah was east of the Waters of Merom (see note on Jos 11:5) and north of Geshur.

3:15 *Makir.* See note on Ge 50:23.

the gorge being the border) and out to the
Jabbok River,[l] which is the border of the
Ammonites. 17 Its western border was the
Jordan in the Arabah,[m] from Kinnereth[n] to
the Sea of the Arabah[o] (that is, the Dead
Sea[p]), below the slopes of Pisgah.
18 I commanded you at that time: "The
LORD your God has given[q] you this land
to take possession of it. But all your able-
bodied men, armed for battle, must cross
over ahead of the other Israelites.[r] 19 However, your wives,[s] your children and your
livestock[t] (I know you have much livestock) may stay in the towns I have giv-
en you, 20 until the LORD gives rest to your
fellow Israelites as he has to you, and they
too have taken over the land that the LORD
your God is giving them across the Jordan.
After that, each of you may go back to the
possession I have given you."

Moses Forbidden to Cross the Jordan

21 At that time I commanded Joshua:
"You have seen with your own eyes all
that the LORD your God has done to these
two kings. The LORD will do the same to
all the kingdoms over there where you are
going. 22 Do not be afraid[u] of them;[v] the
LORD your God himself will fight[w] for you."
23 At that time I pleaded[x] with the LORD:
24 "Sovereign LORD, you have begun to
show to your servant your greatness[y] and
your strong hand. For what god[z] is there in
heaven or on earth who can do the deeds
and mighty works[a] you do?[b] 25 Let me go
over and see the good land[c] beyond the
Jordan—that fine hill country and Lebanon.[d]"
26 But because of you the LORD was angry[e] with me and would not listen to me.
"That is enough," the LORD said. "Do not
speak to me anymore about this matter.
27 Go up to the top of Pisgah[f] and look west
and north and south and east.[g] Look at
the land with your own eyes, since you
are not going to cross[h] this Jordan.[i] 28 But
commission[j] Joshua, and encourage[k] and
strengthen him, for he will lead this people across[l] and will cause them to inherit
the land that you will see." 29 So we stayed
in the valley near Beth Peor.[m]

Obedience Commanded

4 Now, Israel, hear the decrees[n] and
laws I am about to teach[o] you. Follow
them so that you may live[p] and may go in
and take possession of the land the LORD,
the God of your ancestors, is giving you.
2 Do not add[q] to what I command you and
do not subtract[r] from it, but keep[s] the commands[t] of the LORD your God that I give
you.
3 You saw with your own eyes what the
LORD did at Baal Peor.[u] The LORD your God
destroyed from among you everyone who
followed the Baal of Peor, 4 but all of you
who held fast to the LORD your God are
still alive today.
5 See, I have taught[v] you decrees and
laws[w] as the LORD my God commanded[x]
me, so that you may follow them in the
land you are entering[y] to take possession
of it. 6 Observe[z] them carefully, for this will
show your wisdom[a] and understanding to
the nations, who will hear about all these
decrees and say, "Surely this great nation
is a wise and understanding people."[b]
7 What other nation is so great[c] as to have
their gods near[d] them the way the LORD
our God is near us whenever we pray to
him? 8 And what other nation is so great as

3:16 [l] S Nu 21:24 **3:17** [m] 2Sa 2:29; 4:7; Eze 47:8 [n] S Nu 34:11 [o] S Dt 1:1 [p] S Ge 14:3 **3:18** [q] Jos 1:13 [r] S Nu 32:17 **3:19** [s] Jos 1:14 [t] S Nu 32:16 **3:22** [u] S Dt 1:29 [v] Dt 7:18; 20:1; 31:6; 2Ch 32:8; Ps 23:4; Isa 41:10 [w] S Ex 14:14 **3:23** [x] Dt 1:37; 31:2; 32:52; 34:4 **3:24** [y] Dt 5:24; 11:2; 32:3 [z] S Ex 8:10 [a] Ps 71:16; 106:2; 145:12; 150:2 [b] 2Sa 7:22 **3:25** [c] Dt 4:22 [d] Dt 1:7; Jos 1:4; 9:1; 11:17; 12:7; 13:5; Jdg 3:3; 9:15; 1Ki 4:33 **3:26** [e] ver 27; Dt 1:37; 31:2 **3:27** [f] S Nu 21:20 [g] S Ge 13:14 [h] S ver 26; S Nu 20:12; Dt 32:52 [i] S Nu 27:12 **3:28** [j] Nu 27:18-23 [k] Dt 31:7 [l] Dt 1:38; 31:3, 23 **3:29** [m] S Nu 23:28; Dt 4:46; 34:6; Jos 13:20 **4:1** [n] S Lev 18:4 [o] Dt 1:3 [p] S Lev 18:5; Dt 30:15-20; S Ro 10:5 **4:2** [q] Dt 12:32; Jos 1:7; Pr 30:6; Rev 22:18-19 [r] Jer 26:2 [s] S Lev 22:31 [t] Dt 10:12-13; Ecc 12:13 **4:3** [u] Nu 25:1-9; Ps 106:28 **4:5** [v] Ps 71:17; 119:102; Jer 32:33 [w] S Ex 18:20 [x] S Lev 27:34 [y] Ezr 9:11 **4:6** [z] Dt 29:9; 1Ki 2:3 [a] Dt 30:19-20; 32:46-47; Ps 19:7; 119:98; Pr 1:7; 2Ti 3:15 [b] Job 1:1; 28:28; Ps 111:10; Pr 2:5; 3:7; 9:10; Ecc 12:13; Eze 5:5 **4:7** [c] ver 32-34; 2Sa 7:23 [d] S Nu 23:21; S Ps 46:1; Ac 17:27

3:17 *Kinnereth.* See note on Mk 1:16. The Hebrew word *kinnor* means "harp"; the Sea of Galilee is a harp-shaped lake. Or reference may be to the town on the northwestern shore of the Sea of Galilee that gave its name to the lake (see Jos 11:2). *Pisgah.* On the edge of the high plateau overlooking the Dead Sea from the east (see Nu 21:20).

3:18 *you.* The tribes of Reuben and Gad and the half-tribe of Manasseh.

3:20 *rest.* A peaceful situation—free from external threat and oppression, and untroubled within by conflict, famine or plague (see 12:9–10; 25:19; see also notes on Jos 1:13; 1Ki 5:4; Heb 4:1–11).

3:22 *God himself.* The conquest narratives emphasize the truth that without the Lord's help Israel's victory would be impossible. The Lord's power, not Israel's unaided strength, achieved victory. Moses bolstered Israel's resolve and faith by giving this assurance (see 1:30; 2:21–22,31; 20:4).

3:23–25 Moses' final plea to be allowed to enter the land (see 1:37 and note; 31:2).

3:26 *because of you.* See note on 1:37.

3:27 *Go up to the top of Pisgah.* Moses did so after he had expounded the law to the Israelites to prepare them for life in the promised land (see 32:48–52; 34:1–6). *Pisgah.* See note on v. 17. *look west and north and south and east.* Like Abraham (see Ge 13:14), Moses would inherit the promised land only through his descendants (see 34:1–4).

3:28 *commission Joshua.* See 31:7–8.

3:29 *Beth Peor.* Means "house/sanctuary of Peor." Very likely, reference is to the place where the Baal of Peor was worshiped (see Nu 23:28; 25:3,5).

4:1 *Israel, hear.* God's call to his people to hear and obey is a frequent theme in Deuteronomy (see, e.g., 5:1; 6:3–4; 9:1; 20:3) and elsewhere in the OT. See also note on 6:4–9.

4:2 *Do not add ... do not subtract.* The revelation the Lord gives is sufficient. All of it must be obeyed, and anything that adulterates or contradicts it cannot be tolerated (see 12:32; Pr 30:6; Gal 3:15; Rev 22:18–19).

4:4 *held fast.* See note on 10:20.

4:7 *near us whenever we pray.* The Israelites always had access to the Lord in prayer. His presence was symbol-to have such righteous decrees and laws[e] as this body of laws I am setting before you today?

9 Only be careful,[f] and watch yourselves closely so that you do not forget the things your eyes have seen or let them fade from your heart as long as you live. Teach[g] them to your children[h] and to their children after them. 10 Remember the day you stood before the LORD your God at Horeb,[i] when he said to me, "Assemble the people before me to hear my words so that they may learn[j] to revere[k] me as long as they live in the land[l] and may teach[m] them to their children." 11 You came near and stood at the foot of the mountain[n] while it blazed with fire[o] to the very heavens, with black clouds and deep darkness.[p] 12 Then the LORD spoke[q] to you out of the fire. You heard the sound of words but saw no form;[r] there was only a voice.[s] 13 He declared to you his covenant,[t] the Ten Commandments,[u] which he commanded you to follow and then wrote them on two stone tablets. 14 And the LORD directed me at that time to teach you the decrees and laws[v] you are to follow in the land that you are crossing the Jordan to possess.

Idolatry Forbidden

15 You saw no form[w] of any kind the day the LORD spoke to you at Horeb[x] out of the fire. Therefore watch yourselves very carefully,[y] 16 so that you do not become corrupt[z] and make for yourselves an idol,[a] an image of any shape, whether formed like a man or a woman, 17 or like any animal on earth or any bird that flies in the air,[b] 18 or like any creature that moves along the ground or any fish in the waters below. 19 And when you look up to the sky and see the sun,[c] the moon and the stars[d]—all the heavenly array[e]—do not be enticed[f] into bowing down to them and worshiping[g] things the LORD your God has apportioned to all the nations under heaven. 20 But as for you, the LORD took you and brought you out of the iron-smelting furnace,[h] out of Egypt,[i] to be the people of his inheritance,[j] as you now are.

21 The LORD was angry with me[k] because of you, and he solemnly swore that I would not cross the Jordan and enter the good land the LORD your God is giving you as your inheritance. 22 I will die in this land;[l] I will not cross the Jordan; but you are about to cross over and take possession of that good land.[m] 23 Be careful not to forget the covenant[n] of the LORD your God that he made with you; do not make for yourselves an idol[o] in the form of anything the LORD your God has forbidden. 24 For the LORD your God is a consuming fire,[p] a jealous God.[q]

25 After you have had children and grandchildren and have lived in the land a long time—if you then become corrupt[r] and make any kind of idol,[s] doing evil[t] in the eyes of the LORD your God and arousing his anger, 26 I call the heavens and the earth as witnesses[u] against you[v] this day that you will quickly perish[w] from the land that you are crossing the Jordan to possess. You will not live there long but will certainly be destroyed. 27 The LORD will scatter[x] you among the peoples, and only a few of you will survive[y] among the nations to which the LORD will drive you. 28 There you will worship man-made gods[z] of wood and stone,[a] which cannot see or hear or eat or smell.[b] 29 But if from there you seek[c] the LORD your God, you will find him if

4:8 [e] Ps 89:14; 97:2; 119:7,62, 144,160,172; Ro 3:2 **4:9** [f] S Ex 23:13 [g] S Ge 14:14; 18:19; Dt 6:20-25; Eph 6:4 [h] S Ex 10:2 **4:10** [i] S Ex 3:1 [j] Dt 14:23; 17:19; 31:12-13; Ps 2:11; 111:10; 147:11; Isa 8:13; Jer 32:40 [k] S Ex 20:20 [l] Dt 12:1 [m] ver 9 **4:11** [n] S Ex 3:1; S 19:17 [o] S Ex 19:18 [p] S Ex 19:9; Ps 18:11; 97:2 **4:12** [q] Ex 20:22; Dt 5:4,22; S Mt 3:17; Heb 12:19 [r] Jn 5:37 [s] S Ex 19:9 **4:13** [t] Dt 9:9; Ro 9:4 [u] S Ex 24:12 **4:14** [v] S Ex 21:1 **4:15** [w] Isa 40:18; 41:22-24 [x] S Ex 3:1 [y] Jos 23:11; Mal 2:15 **4:16** [z] S Ge 6:11-12; Dt 9:12; 31:29; 32:5; Jdg 2:19 [a] Ex 20:4-5; Ro 1:23 **4:17** [b] Ro 1:23 **4:19** [c] Dt 17:3; 2Ki 23:11; Job 31:26; Jer 8:2; 43:13; Eze 8:16 [d] S Ge 1:16 [e] S Ge 2:1; S 37:9; Ro 1:25 [f] Dt 13:5 [g] S Nu 25:3 **4:20** [h] S Ex 1:13 [i] S Ex 3:10 [j] S Ge 17:7; S Ex 8:22; S 34:9; Titus 2:14 **4:21** [k] Nu 20:12; Dt 1:37 **4:22** [l] Nu 27:13-14 [m] Dt 3:25 **4:23** [n] ver 9 [o] S Ex 20:4 **4:24** [p] S Ex 15:7; S 19:18; Heb 12:29 [q] S Ex 20:5 **4:25** [r] ver 16 [s] ver 23 [t] 1Ki 11:6; 15:26; 16:25,30; 2Ki 17:2,17; 21:2 **4:26** [u] Ge 31:50; Pr 14:5 [v] Dt 30:18-19; 31:28; 32:1; Ps 50:4; Isa 1:2; 34:1; Jer 6:19; Mic 6:2 [w] Dt 6:15; 7:4 **4:27** [x] S Lev 26:33; Dt 28:36, 64; 29:28; 1Ki 8:46; 2Ki 17:6; Ps 44:11; 106:27; Jer 3:8; Mic 1:16 [y] Isa 17:6; 21:17; Ob 1:5 **4:28** [z] Dt 13:2; 28:36,64; 1Sa 26:19; Jer 5:19; 16:13; Ac 19:26 [a] Dt 29:17 [b] Ps 115:4-8; 135:15-18; Isa 8:19; 26:14; 44:17-20; Rev 9:20 **4:29** [c] 1Sa 13:12; 2Ki 13:4; 2Ch 7:14; 15:4; 33:12; Ps 78:34; 119:58; Isa 45:19,22; 55:6; Jer 26:19; Da 9:13; Hos 3:5; Am 5:4

---

ized by the tabernacle in the center of the camp, and by the pillar of cloud over the tabernacle (see Ex 40:34–38; Nu 23:21).

4:9 *Teach them to your children.* See v. 10; 6:7; 11:19; Ps 78:4–8; cf. Ex 12:26–27.

4:10–14 See Ex 19–24 and notes.

4:10 *Remember.* The divine call to Israel to remember the Lord's past redemptive acts—especially how he delivered them from slavery in Egypt—is a common theme in Deuteronomy (5:15; 7:18; 8:2,18; 9:7,27; 11:2; 15:15; 16:3,12; 24:9,18,22; 25:17) and is summarized in 32:7: "Remember the days of old."

4:12 *no form.* See v. 15; see also note on Ex 20:4. "God is spirit" (Jn 4:24; cf. Isa 31:3). *only a voice.* See v. 36; 5:23–26; Nu 7:89; 1Ki 19:13.

4:13 *his covenant, the Ten Commandments.* See notes on Ex 20:1; 34:28. *two stone tablets.* See note on Ex 31:18.

4:15–18 See note on Ex 20:4.

4:19 Cf. 17:3. *do not be enticed.* As kings of Judah would be later (2Ki 17:16; 21:3,5; 23:4–5).

4:20 *iron-smelting furnace.* The period in Egypt was a time of affliction for the Israelites (see 1Ki 8:51; Jer 11:4; see also Isa 48:10 and note).

4:21 *because of you.* See note on 1:37.

4:24 *consuming fire.* See 9:3; see also Ex 24:17; Isa 33:14 and notes; Heb 12:29. *jealous God.* See 5:9; 6:15; see also note on Ex 20:5.

4:25 *After you ... have lived in the land.* The pattern of the Israelites' rebellion, resulting in expulsion from the land, and then their repentance, leading to restoration to the land, is prominent in Deuteronomy (see, e.g., the blessing and curse formulas in chs. 27–28).

4:26 *the heavens and the earth as witnesses.* See notes on 30:19; Ps 50:1; Isa 1:2; Mic 6:1–2.

4:27 *will scatter you.* See note on 28:64.

4:29 *with all your heart and ... soul.* Indicates total involvement and commitment. The phrase is applied not only to how the Lord's people should seek him but also to how they should fear (revere) him, live in obedience to

you seek him with all your heart[d] and with
all your soul.[e] 30 When you are in distress[f]
and all these things have happened to you,
then in later days[g] you will return[h] to the
LORD your God and obey him. 31 For the
LORD your God is a merciful[i] God; he will
not abandon[j] or destroy[k] you or forget[l] the
covenant with your ancestors, which he
confirmed to them by oath.

The LORD Is God

32 Ask[m] now about the former days, long
before your time, from the day God created human beings on the earth;[n] ask from
one end of the heavens to the other.[o] Has
anything so great[p] as this ever happened,
or has anything like it ever been heard of?
33 Has any other people heard the voice
of God[a] speaking out of fire, as you have,
and lived?[q] 34 Has any god ever tried to
take for himself one nation out of another
nation,[r] by testings,[s] by signs[t] and wonders,[u] by war, by a mighty hand and an
outstretched arm,[v] or by great and awesome deeds,[w] like all the things the LORD
your God did for you in Egypt before your
very eyes?
35 You were shown these things so that
you might know that the LORD is God; besides him there is no other.[x] 36 From heav-
en he made you hear his voice[y] to discipline[z] you. On earth he showed you his
great fire, and you heard his words from
out of the fire. 37 Because he loved[a] your
ancestors and chose their descendants after them, he brought you out of Egypt by
his Presence and his great strength,[b] 38 to
drive out before you nations greater and
stronger than you and to bring you into
their land to give it to you for your inheritance,[c] as it is today.
39 Acknowledge[d] and take to heart this
day that the LORD is God in heaven above
and on the earth below. There is no other.[e] 40 Keep[f] his decrees and commands,[g]
which I am giving you today, so that it
may go well[h] with you and your children
after you and that you may live long[i] in

4:29 [d] 1Sa 7:3; 1Ki 8:48; Jer 29:13 [e] Dt 6:5; 30:1-3,10 **4:30** [f] Lev 26:41; Dt 31:17,21; Ps 4:1; 18:6; 46:1; 59:16; 107:6 [g] Dt 31:29; Jer 23:20; Hos 3:5; Heb 1:2 [h] Dt 30:2; 1Ki 8:48; Ne 1:9; Jer 3:1,12,22; 4:1; 18:11; Joel 2:12 **4:31** [i] Ex 34:6; Ne 9:31; Ps 111:4 [j] Dt 31:6,8; Jos 1:5; 1Ki 8:57; 1Ch 28:9,20; Ps 9:10; 27:9; 71:9; Isa 42:16; Heb 13:5 [k] S Lev 26:44 [l] Lev 26:45 **4:32** [m] Dt 32:7 [n] S Ge 1:27; Isa 45:12 [o] Dt 28:64; 30:1; Jer 9:16; Mt 24:31 [p] ver 7; 2Sa 7:23 **4:33** [q] Ex 20:22; Dt 5:24-26 **4:34** [r] Ex 14:30 [s] Isa 7:12 [t] S Ex 4:17 [u] Dt 7:19; 26:8; 29:3; 1Ch 16:12; Ps 9:1; 40:5; Jer 32:20 [v] S Ex 3:20; Dt 5:15; 6:21; 15:15 [w] Ex 15:11; Dt 34:12; Ps 45:4; 65:5 **4:35** [x] ver 39; Ex 8:10; Dt 7:9; 32:4,12; 1Sa 2:2; 1Ki 8:60; 2Ki 19:19; Isa 43:10; Mk 12:32 **4:36** [y] S Ex 19:19; Heb 12:25 [z] Dt 8:5 **4:37** [a] Dt 7:8; 10:15; 23:5; 33:3; Ps 44:3; Jer 31:3;

the land the LORD your God gives you for
all time.

Cities of Refuge

4:41-43Ref — Nu 35:6-34; Dt 19:1-14; Jos 20:1-9

41 Then Moses set aside three cities east
of the Jordan, 42 to which anyone who had
killed a person could flee if they had unintentionally[j] killed a neighbor without malice aforethought. They could flee into one
of these cities and save their life. 43 The
cities were these: Bezer in the wilderness
plateau, for the Reubenites; Ramoth[k] in
Gilead, for the Gadites; and Golan in Bashan, for the Manassites.

Introduction to the Law

44 This is the law Moses set before the
Israelites. 45 These are the stipulations, decrees and laws Moses gave them when
they came out of Egypt 46 and were in the
valley near Beth Peor east of the Jordan,
in the land of Sihon[l] king of the Amorites,
who reigned in Heshbon and was defeated
by Moses and the Israelites as they came
out of Egypt. 47 They took possession of his
land and the land of Og king of Bashan,
the two Amorite kings east of the Jordan.
48 This land extended from Aroer[m] on the
rim of the Arnon Gorge to Mount Sirion[b][n]
(that is, Hermon[o]), 49 and included all the
Arabah east of the Jordan, as far as the
Dead Sea,[c] below the slopes of Pisgah.

The Ten Commandments

5:6-21pp — Ex 20:1-17

5 Moses summoned all Israel and said:
Hear, Israel, the decrees and laws[p] I
declare in your hearing today. Learn them
and be sure to follow them. 2 The LORD our

[a] 33 Or *of a god* [b] 48 Syriac (see also 3:9); Hebrew *Siyon* [c] 49 Hebrew *the Sea of the Arabah*

Hos 11:1; Mal 1:2; 2:11 [b] S Ex 3:20; S 33:14 **4:38** [c] Nu 34:14-15; Dt 7:1; 9:5 **4:39** [d] Ex 8:10 [e] S ver 35; Ex 15:11 **4:40** [f] S Lev 22:31 [g] ver 1; S Ge 26:5; Dt 5:29; 11:1; Ps 105:45; Isa 48:18 [h] Dt 5:16; 12:25; Isa 3:10 [i] S Ex 23:26; Eph 6:2-3 **4:42** [j] S Ex 21:13 **4:43** [k] Jos 21:38; 1Ki 22:3; 2Ki 8:28; 9:14 **4:46** [l] Nu 21:26 **4:48** [m] Dt 2:36 [n] Dt 3:9 [o] S Dt 3:8 **5:1** [p] S Ex 18:20

him, love and serve him (6:5; 10:12; 11:13; 13:3; 30:6), and, after forsaking him, renew their allegiance and commitment to him (26:16; 30:2,10).

4:31 *covenant . . . confirmed . . . by oath.* See notes on Ge 21:23; 22:16; Ex 19:5; Heb 6:13,18. In ancient times, parties to a covenant were expected to confirm their intentions by means of a self-maledictory oath (see note on Ge 15:17).

4:35 *so that you might know.* See v. 10. *besides him there is no other.* See v. 39; 5:7; 6:4 and note; 32:39. Moses insists that there is only one God (see also note on Ge 1:1).

4:37 *he loved.* The first reference in Deuteronomy to God's love for his people (see Introduction: Theological Teaching and Purpose). See 5:10; 7:9,13; 10:15; 23:5. The corollary truth is that his people should love him (see note on 6:5). *Presence.* See notes on Ex 25:30; 33:14.

4:39 See v. 35 and note.

4:40 *it may go well with you.* That is, you will receive the covenant benefits. This assurance occurs ten times in Deuteronomy (here; 5:16,29; 6:3,18; 8:16; 12:25,28; 19:13; 22:7). Cf. also 28:1 – 14; 30:1 – 10.

4:41 – 43 See 19:1 – 13; Nu 35:9 – 28; Jos 20 and notes.

4:43 *Bezer . . . Ramoth . . . Golan.* See map, p. 254.

5:1 *Hear, Israel.* See note on 4:1.

5:2 *covenant with us at Horeb.* See note on Ex 19:5. God's covenant with Israel, given at Horeb (Mount Sinai) and now being confirmed, bound the Israelites to the Lord as their absolute Sovereign, and to his laws and regulations as their way of life. Adherence to the covenant would bring God's people the blessings of the Lord, while breaking the covenant would bring against them the punishments

God made a covenant[q] with us at Horeb.[r]
3 It was not with our ancestors[a] that the
LORD made this covenant, but with us,[s]
with all of us who are alive here today.[t]
4 The LORD spoke[u] to you face to face[v] out
of the fire[w] on the mountain. 5 (At that
time I stood between[x] the LORD and you
to declare to you the word of the LORD,
because you were afraid[y] of the fire and
did not go up the mountain.) And he said:

6 "I am the LORD your God, who
brought you out of Egypt,[z] out of
the land of slavery.[a]
7 "You shall have no other gods before[b] me.
8 "You shall not make for yourself an
image in the form of anything
in heaven above or on the earth
beneath or in the waters below.[b] 9 You shall not bow down
to them or worship them; for I,
the LORD your God, am a jealous
God, punishing the children for
the sin of the parents[c] to the third
and fourth generation of those
who hate me,[d] 10 but showing
love to a thousand[e] generations
of those who love me and keep
my commandments.[f]
11 "You shall not misuse the name[g] of
the LORD your God, for the LORD
will not hold anyone guiltless
who misuses his name.[h]
12 "Observe the Sabbath day by keeping it holy,[i] as the LORD your
God has commanded you. 13 Six
days you shall labor and do all
your work, 14 but the seventh
day[j] is a sabbath to the LORD
your God. On it you shall not do
any work, neither you, nor your
son or daughter, nor your male
or female servant,[k] nor your ox,
your donkey or any of your animals, nor any foreigner residing
in your towns, so that your male
and female servants may rest,
as you do.[l] 15 Remember that
you were slaves[m] in Egypt and
that the LORD your God brought
you out of there with a mighty
hand[n] and an outstretched arm.[o]
Therefore the LORD your God has
commanded you to observe the
Sabbath day.
16 "Honor your father[p] and your mother,[q] as the LORD your God has
commanded you, so that you
may live long[r] and that it may
go well with you in the land the
LORD your God is giving you.
17 "You shall not murder.[s]
18 "You shall not commit adultery.[t]
19 "You shall not steal.[u]
20 "You shall not give false testimony
against your neighbor.[v]
21 "You shall not covet your neighbor's
wife. You shall not set your desire on your neighbor's house or
land, his male or female servant,
his ox or donkey, or anything
that belongs to your neighbor."[w]

22 These are the commandments the
LORD proclaimed in a loud voice to your
whole assembly there on the mountain
from out of the fire, the cloud and the
deep darkness;[x] and he added nothing
more. Then he wrote them on two stone
tablets[y] and gave them to me.
23 When you heard the voice out of the
darkness, while the mountain was ablaze
with fire, all the leaders of your tribes and
your elders[z] came to me. 24 And you said,
"The LORD our God has shown us[a] his glory and his majesty,[b] and we have heard
his voice from the fire. Today we have
seen that a person can live even if God

5:2 [q]Ex 19:5; Jer 11:2; Heb 9:15; 10:15-17 [r]S Ge 17:9; S Ex 3:1 **5:3** [s]Dt 11:2-7 [t]Nu 26:63-65; Heb 8:9 **5:4** [u]S Dt 4:12 [v]S Nu 14:14 [w]S Ex 19:18 **5:5** [x]Gal 3:19 [y]S Ge 3:10; Heb 12:18-21 **5:6** [z]S Ex 13:3; S 29:46 [a]Lev 26:1; Dt 6:4; Ps 81:10 **5:8** [b]Lev 26:1; Dt 4:15-18; Ps 78:58; 97:7 **5:9** [c]S Nu 26:11 [d]Ex 34:7; S Nu 10:35; 14:18 **5:10** [e]S Ex 34:7 [f]Nu 14:18; Dt 7:9; Ne 1:5; Jer 32:18; Da 9:4 **5:11** [g]Ps 139:20 [h]Lev 19:12; Dt 10:20; Mt 5:33-37 **5:12** [i]Ex 16:23-30; 31:13-17; Mk 2:27-28 **5:14** [j]S Ge 2:2; Mt 12:2; Mk 2:27; Heb 4:4 [k]Job 31:13; Jer 34:9-11 [l]Jer 17:21,24 **5:15** [m]S Ge 15:13 [n]Ex 6:1; Ps 108:6; Jer 32:21 [o]S Dt 4:34 **5:16** [p]Mal 1:6 [q]Ex 21:17; Lev 19:3; Eze 22:7; Mt 15:4*; 19:19*; Mk 7:10*; 10:19*; Lk 18:20*; Eph 6:2-3* [r]S Dt 4:40; 11:9; Pr 3:1-2 **5:17** [s]Ge 9:6; Lev 24:17; Ecc 3:3; Jer 40:15; 41:3; Mt 5:21-22*; 19:19*; Mk 10:19*; Lk 18:20*; Ro 13:9*; Jas 2:11* **5:18** [t]Lev 20:10; Mt 5:27-30; 19:18*; Mk 10:19*; Lk 18:20*; Ro 13:9*; Jas 2:11* **5:19** [u]Lev 19:11; Mt 19:19*; Mk 10:19*; Lk 18:20*; Ro 13:9* **5:20** [v]S Ex 23:1; Mt 19:18*; Mk 10:19*; Lk 18:20* **5:21** [w]Ro 7:7*; 13:9* **5:22** [x]S Ex 20:21 [y]S Ex 24:12 **5:23** [z]S Ex 3:16 **5:24** [a]Dt 4:34; 8:5; 11:2; Isa 53:4 [b]S Dt 3:24

[a] 3 Or *not only with our parents* [b] 7 Or *besides*

described as "curses" (see, e.g., 28:15–20). Jer 31:31–34 predicted the establishing of a new covenant, which made the Sinaitic covenant obsolete (see Heb 7:18–22; see also Heb 8:6–13; 10:15–18 and notes). See chart, p. 23.

5:3 *not with our ancestors ... but with us.* See NIV text note. The covenant was made with those who were present at Sinai, but since they were representatives of the nation it was made with all succeeding generations as well.

5:5 See vv. 23–27; Ex 20:18–21.

5:6–21 The Ten Commandments are the central stipulations of God's covenant with Israel made at Sinai. It is almost impossible to exaggerate their effect on subsequent history. They constitute the basis of the moral principles found throughout the Western world and summarize what the one true God expects of his people in terms of faith, worship and conduct (see notes on Ex 20:2–17; Jer 16:2).

5:12 *as the LORD your God has commanded you.* Missing from the parallel verse in Exodus (20:8), this clause reminds the people of the divine origin of the Ten Commandments 40 years earlier at Mount Sinai (see vv. 15–16).

5:14 *so that your male and female servants may rest.* See v. 15; see also note on Ex 20:10.

5:15 *Remember.* See note on 4:10.

5:16–21 The NT quotes often from this section of the Ten Commandments (see cross references on these verses).

5:16 *that it may go well with you.* Missing from the parallel in Ex 20:12, this clause explains that the life the Lord desires for his people is not to be measured merely in terms of longevity (see note on 4:40).

5:20 See 19:18–19; Lev 19:11–13; 1Ki 21:10,13.

5:22 *commandments.* Lit. "words" (see note on Ex 20:1). *two stone tablets.* See note on Ex 31:18.

speaks with them.[c] 25 But now, why should
we die? This great fire will consume us,
and we will die if we hear the voice of
the LORD our God any longer.[d] 26 For what
mortal has ever heard the voice of the living God speaking out of fire, as we have,
and survived?[e] 27 Go near and listen to all
that the LORD our God says.[f] Then tell us
whatever the LORD our God tells you. We
will listen and obey."[g]
28 The LORD heard you when you spoke to
me, and the LORD said to me, "I have heard
what this people said to you. Everything
they said was good.[h] 29 Oh, that their hearts
would be inclined to fear me[i] and keep all
my commands[j] always, so that it might go
well with them and their children forever![k]
30 "Go, tell them to return to their tents.
31 But you stay here[l] with me so that I may
give you all the commands, decrees and
laws you are to teach them to follow in the
land I am giving them to possess."
32 So be careful to do what the LORD your
God has commanded you;[m] do not turn
aside to the right or to the left.[n] 33 Walk in
obedience to all that the LORD your God
has commanded you,[o] so that you may
live and prosper and prolong your days[p]
in the land that you will possess.

Love the LORD Your God

6 These are the commands, decrees and
laws the LORD your God directed me to
teach you to observe in the land that you
are crossing the Jordan to possess, 2 so that
you, your children and their children after
them may fear[q] the LORD your God as long
as you live[r] by keeping all his decrees and
commands[s] that I give you, and so that
you may enjoy long life.[t] 3 Hear, Israel, and
be careful to obey[u] so that it may go well
with you and that you may increase greatly[v] in a land flowing with milk and honey,[w]
just as the LORD, the God of your ancestors, promised[x] you.
4 Hear, O Israel: The LORD our God, the
LORD is one.[a][y] 5 Love[z] the LORD your God with
all your heart[a] and with all your soul and

[a] 4 Or *The LORD our God is one LORD;* or *The LORD is our God, the LORD is one;* or *The LORD is our God, the LORD alone*

5:24 [c] Ex 19:19 **5:25** [d] Ex 20:18-19; Dt 18:16; Heb 12:19 **5:26** [e] S Ex 33:20; Dt 4:33; Jdg 6:22-23; 13:22; Isa 6:5 **5:27** [f] S Ex 19:8 [g] S Ex 24:7 **5:28** [h] Dt 18:17 **5:29** [i] Ps 81:8, 13 [j] Jos 22:5; Ps 78:7 [k] ver 33; S Dt 4:1,40; 12:25; 22:7 **5:31** [l] Ex 24:12 **5:32** [m] S Dt 4:29; 10:12 [n] Dt 17:11,20; 28:14; Jos 1:7; 1Ki 15:5; 2Ki 22:2; Pr 4:27 **5:33** [o] Isa 3:10; Jer 7:23; 38:20; S Lk 1:6 [p] S ver 29 **6:2** [q] S Ex 20:20; S 1Sa 12:24 [r] Dt 4:9 [s] S Ge 26:5 [t] S Ex 20:12 **6:3** [u] S Ex 19:5 [v] Ge 15:5; Dt 5:33 [w] S Ex 3:8; Dt 32:13-14 [x] Ex 13:5 **6:4** [y] Dt 4:35, 39; Ne 9:6; Ps 86:10; Isa 44:6; Zec 14:9; Mk 12:29*; Jn 10:30; 1Co 8:4; Eph 4:6; Jas 2:19 **6:5** [z] Dt 11:1, 22; Mt 22:37*; Mk 12:30*; Lk 10:27* [a] 1Sa 12:24

The Sumerian law code of Ur-Nammu — the oldest known code of laws (twenty-first century BC). When Moses gave the people a set of laws, this was not a new idea to them since other law codes have been found from centuries before Moses' time.

The Schøyen Collection, MS 2064, Oslo and London

5:25 *we will die.* See notes on Ge 16:13; 32:30.
5:27 *We will listen and obey.* See note on Ex 19:8.
6:2 *fear the LORD.* See note on Ge 20:11. *enjoy long life.* See 4:40; 5:16 and note. By obeying the Lord and keeping his decrees, individual Israelites would enjoy long life in the land, and the people as a whole would enjoy a long national existence there.
6:3 *Hear, Israel.* See v. 4 and note on 4:1. *land flowing with milk and honey.* See note on Ex 3:8. The phrase is used 14 times from Exodus through Deuteronomy and 5 times elsewhere in the OT.
6:4–9 See Mk 12:29–30; see also Mt 22:37–38; Lk 10:27. This passage in Deuteronomy is known as the *Shema* (Hebrew for "Hear"). It has become the Jewish confession of faith, recited daily by the pious and every Sabbath day in the synagogue.
6:4 *the LORD is one.* The truth revealed to Israel that God is one and that this one God created all things, sustains all things and governs all things stood in radical opposition to all the religions of the ancient Near Eastern world. All of Israel's neighbors had to come to terms in their daily lives with scores of gods, each with its own sphere of influence, its own limitations, its own petty self-interests and its own morally erratic ways. But Israel could live serenely in the knowledge that all things and all times were under the rule of one divine King, whose ways are righteous and whose purpose with her and through her (as Yahweh, her God) is salvation for humankind — from sin and judgment and every evil that has burdened human life. Such serenity in the midst of the ragings of history and all its seeming chaos remains the precious gift of faith for all who know and trust the God of Israel.
6:5 *Love the LORD.* Primarily in view here is the love shown by a subject to a king (see note on Ex 20:6). To love King Yahweh is to be his loyal and obedient servant (Israel was the Lord's kingdom people). Love for God and neighbor (see Lev 19:18; Mk 12:31 and note) is built on the love that the Lord has for his people (see 4:37 and note; 7:8–9,13; 23:5; 1Jn 4:19–21) and on his identification with them. Such love is to be total, involving one's whole being (see notes on 4:29; Jos 22:5).

with all your strength.[b] 6These commandments that I give you today are to be on your
hearts.[c] 7Impress them on your children.
Talk about them when you sit at home and
when you walk along the road, when you
lie down and when you get up.[d] 8Tie them
as symbols on your hands and bind them on
your foreheads.[e] 9Write them on the doorframes of your houses and on your gates.[f]
10When the LORD your God brings you
into the land he swore to your fathers, to
Abraham, Isaac and Jacob, to give you—a
land with large, flourishing cities you did
not build,[g] 11houses filled with all kinds
of good things you did not provide, wells
you did not dig,[h] and vineyards and olive
groves you did not plant—then when you
eat and are satisfied,[i] 12be careful that you
do not forget[j] the LORD, who brought you
out of Egypt, out of the land of slavery.
13Fear the LORD[k] your God, serve him
only[l] and take your oaths[m] in his name.[n]
14Do not follow other gods, the gods of the
peoples around you; 15for the LORD your
God[o], who is among you, is a jealous God
and his anger will burn against you, and
he will destroy you from the face of the
land. 16Do not put the LORD your God to
the test[p] as you did at Massah. 17Be sure to
keep[q] the commands of the LORD your God
and the stipulations and decrees he has
given you.[r] 18Do what is right and good
in the LORD's sight,[s] so that it may go well[t]
with you and you may go in and take over
the good land the LORD promised on oath
to your ancestors, 19thrusting out all your
enemies[u] before you, as the LORD said.
20In the future, when your son asks
you,[v] "What is the meaning of the stipulations, decrees and laws the LORD our
God has commanded you?" 21tell him:
"We were slaves of Pharaoh in Egypt, but
the LORD brought us out of Egypt with a
mighty hand.[w] 22Before our eyes the LORD
sent signs and wonders—great and terrible—on Egypt and Pharaoh and his whole
household. 23But he brought us out from
there to bring us in and give us the land he
promised on oath to our ancestors. 24The
LORD commanded us to obey all these decrees and to fear the LORD our God,[x] so
that we might always prosper and be kept
alive, as is the case today.[y] 25And if we
are careful to obey all this law[z] before the
LORD our God, as he has commanded us,
that will be our righteousness.[a]"

Driving Out the Nations

7 When the LORD your God brings you
into the land you are entering to possess[b] and drives out before you many nations[c]—the Hittites,[d] Girgashites,[e] Amorites,[f] Canaanites, Perizzites,[g] Hivites[h] and
Jebusites,[i] seven nations larger and stronger than you— 2and when the LORD your
God has delivered[j] them over to you and
you have defeated them, then you must
destroy[k] them totally.[a][l] Make no treaty[m]

[a] 2 The Hebrew term refers to the irrevocable giving over of things or persons to the LORD, often by totally destroying them; also in verse 26.

6:5 [b] Dt 4:29; 10:12; Jos 22:5 **6:6** [c] ver 8; Dt 11:18; 30:14; 32:46; Ps 26:2; 37:31; 40:8; 119:11; Pr 3:3; Isa 51:7; Jer 17:1; 31:33; Eze 40:4 **6:7** [d] Dt 4:9; 11:19; Pr 22:6; Eph 6:4 **6:8** [e] S ver 6; S Ex 13:9; Mt 23:5 **6:9** [f] Dt 11:20 **6:10** [g] S Ge 11:4; Dt 12:29; 19:1; Jos 24:13; Ps 105:44 **6:11** [h] Jer 2:13 [i] S Lev 26:5; Dt 8:10; 14:29; 31:20 **6:12** [j] Dt 4:9, 23; 2Ki 17:38; Ps 44:17; 78:7; 103:2 **6:13** [k] Ps 33:8; 34:9 [l] Dt 13:4; 1Sa 7:3; Jer 44:10; Mt 4:10*; Lk 4:4*; 4:8* [m] 1Sa 20:3 [n] S Ex 20:7; S Mt 5:33 **6:15** [o] Dt 4:24; 5:9 **6:16** [p] S Ex 17:2; Mt 4:7*; Lk 4:12* **6:17** [q] S Lev 26:3 [r] Dt 11:22; Ps 119:4, 56, 100, 134, 168 **6:18** [s] 2Ki 18:6; Isa 36:7; 38:3 [t] Dt 4:40 **6:19** [u] Ex 23:27; Jos 21:44; Ps 78:53; 107:2; 136:24 **6:20** [v] S Ex 10:2 **6:21** [w] S Dt 4:34 **6:24** [x] Dt 10:12; 30:6; Ps 86:11; Jer 32:39 [y] Ps 27:12; 41:2; S Ro 10:5 **6:25** [z] Ps 103:18; 119:34, 55 [a] Dt 24:13; S Ro 9:31; Ro 10:3, 5 **7:1** [b] S Lev 14:34; S Dt 4:38 [c] Dt 20:16-18; 31:3 [d] Ge 15:20 [e] S Ge 10:16 [f] S Dt 1:7 [g] Ge 13:7 [h] S Ge 10:17 [i] Jos 3:10 **7:2** [j] S Dt 2:33 [k] S Dt 2:34 [l] Nu 31:17; Dt 33:27; Jos 11:11 [m] S Ex 23:32

6:6 *commandments ... on your hearts.* A feature that would especially characterize the "new covenant" (see Jer 31:31–33 and note on 31:33; 2Co 3:3 and note).
6:8–9 Many Jews take these verses literally and tie phylacteries (see note on Mt 23:5) to their foreheads and left arms. They also attach mezuzot (small wooden or metal containers in which passages of Scripture are placed) to the doorframes of their houses. But a figurative interpretation is supported by 11:18–20; Ex 13:9,16. See note on Ex 13:9.
6:10–12 Because the emphasis in Scripture is always on what God does and not on what his people achieve, they are never to forget what he has done for them. See note on 4:10.
6:13 Quoted in part by Jesus in response to Satan's temptation (Mt 4:10; Lk 4:8). Jesus quoted from Deuteronomy in response to the devil's other two temptations as well (see notes on v. 16; 8:3). *Fear the LORD.* See note on Ge 20:11. *take your oaths in his name.* In ancient Israel's world, when people appealed to the gods to affirm and uphold their oaths, they singled out the divine power or powers they most revered. For this reason, to take an oath in the Lord's name was a key sign of loyalty to and trust in him and of the rejection of all other gods, even an implicit denial that they amounted to anything or even existed. The Israelites were to swear oaths in no other name.
6:15 *jealous God.* See 4:24; 5:9; see also note on Ex 20:5.
6:16 Quoted in part by Jesus in Mt 4:7; Lk 4:12 (see also note on v. 13 here). *as you did at Massah.* See 9:22; 33:8; see also note on Ex 17:7.
6:20 See Ex 12:26 and note.
6:23 *brought us out ... to bring us in.* See note on Ex 6:7–8.
6:25 *righteousness.* Probably here refers to a true, personal relationship with the covenant Lord that manifests itself in the daily lives of God's people (see 24:13).
7:1–6 When this passage is carefully examined together with 1Ki 11:1–13; Ezr 9:1–2,10–12,14, it seems clear that what was prohibited was intermarriage with idolatrous and immoral foreigners (see note on v. 4). On the other hand, outsiders who placed themselves under the Lord's rule and thus became affiliated with the covenant community were treated for the most part just like ordinary Israelites (see Ex 12:48–49; Lev 17:8–9; 19:33–34; Nu 9:14; 15:13–16,26–31; Dt 16:11–14; cf. Mal 2:11 and note; see also Rahab [Jos 2; 6:17,22–25] and Ruth [the book of Ruth]; see further Isa 56:3 and note; Mt 1:5 and note on 1:3).
7:1 *Hittites ... Jebusites.* See 20:17; see also notes on Ge 10:6,15–18; 13:7; Jos 9:7. *seven nations.* See note on Ex 3:8.
7:2–5 *Make no treaty ... Do not intermarry ... Break down their altars.* Israel was to have no association—political, social or religious—with the idol worshipers of Canaan (see v. 16; cf. Mal 2:11 and note).
7:2 *destroy them totally.* See note on 2:34.

with them, and show them no mercy.[n] 3 Do not intermarry with them.[o] Do not give your daughters to their sons or take their daughters for your sons, 4 for they will turn your children away from following me to serve other gods,[p] and the LORD's anger will burn against you and will quickly destroy[q] you. 5 This is what you are to do to them: Break down their altars, smash their sacred stones, cut down their Asherah poles[a][r] and burn their idols in the fire.[s] 6 For you are a people holy[t] to the LORD your God.[u] The LORD your God has chosen[v] you out of all the peoples on the face of the earth to be his people, his treasured possession.[w]

7 The LORD did not set his affection on you and choose you because you were more numerous[x] than other peoples, for you were the fewest[y] of all peoples.[z] 8 But it was because the LORD loved[a] you and kept the oath he swore[b] to your ancestors that he brought you out with a mighty hand[c] and redeemed[d] you from the land of slavery,[e] from the power of Pharaoh king of Egypt. 9 Know therefore that the LORD your God is God;[f] he is the faithful God,[g] keeping his covenant of love[h] to a thousand generations[i] of those who love him and keep his commandments.[j] 10 But

those who hate him he will repay to
their face by destruction;
he will not be slow to repay to their
face those who hate him.[k]

11 Therefore, take care to follow the commands, decrees and laws I give you today.

12 If you pay attention to these laws and are careful to follow them, then the LORD your God will keep his covenant of love with you, as he swore to your ancestors.[l] 13 He will love you and bless you[m] and increase your numbers.[n] He will bless the fruit of your womb,[o] the crops of your land—your grain, new wine[p] and olive oil[q]—the calves of your herds and the lambs of your flocks in the land he swore to your ancestors to give you.[r] 14 You will be blessed more than any other people; none of your men or women will be childless, nor will any of your livestock be without young.[s] 15 The LORD will keep you free from every disease.[t] He will not inflict on you the horrible diseases you knew in Egypt,[u] but he will inflict them on all who hate you.[v] 16 You must destroy all the peoples the LORD your God gives over to you.[w] Do not look on them with pity[x] and do not serve their gods,[y] for that will be a snare[z] to you.

17 You may say to yourselves, "These nations are stronger than we are. How can we drive them out?[a]" 18 But do not be afraid[b] of them; remember well what the LORD your God did to Pharaoh and to all Egypt.[c] 19 You saw with your own eyes the great trials, the signs and wonders, the mighty hand[d] and outstretched arm, with which the LORD your God brought you out. The LORD your God will do the same to all the peoples you now fear.[e] 20 Moreover, the LORD your God will send the hornet[f] among them until even the survivors who hide from you have perished. 21 Do not be terrified by them, for the LORD your God, who is among you,[g] is a great and awesome God.[h] 22 The LORD your God will drive out those nations before you, little by little.[i] You will not be allowed to eliminate them all at once, or the wild animals will multiply around you. 23 But the LORD your God will deliver them over to you, throwing them into great confusion until they are destroyed.[j] 24 He will give their

7:2 [n] ver 16; Dt 13:8; 19:13; 25:12 **7:3** [o] Ex 34:15-16; Jos 22:16; Da 9:7 **7:4** [p] Jdg 3:6 [q] S Dt 4:26 **7:5** [r] S Ex 34:13; Dt 16:21 [s] S Ex 23:24 **7:6** [t] Ex 19:6; S Lev 27:30 [u] Dt 26:19; Ps 30:4; 37:28; 50:5; 52:9 [v] Dt 14:2; 1Ki 3:8; Isa 41:9; Eze 20:5 [w] S Ge 17:7; S Ex 8:22; S 34:9; Isa 43:1; Ro 9:4; Titus 2:14 **7:7** [x] S Ge 22:17 [y] Ge 34:30 [z] Dt 4:37; 10:22 **7:8** [a] S Dt 4:37; 1Ki 10:9; 2Ch 2:11; Ps 44:3 [b] Ex 32:13; S Nu 14:8; Ro 11:28 [c] S Ex 3:20 [d] S Ex 6:6 [e] S Ex 13:14 **7:9** [f] S Dt 4:35 [g] Ps 18:25; 33:4; 108:4; 145:13; 146:6; Isa 49:7; Jer 42:5; Hos 11:12; S 1Co 1:9 [h] ver 12; 1Ki 8:23; 2Ch 6:14; Ne 1:5; 9:32 [i] S Ex 20:6 [j] S Dt 5:10 **7:10** [k] S Lev 26:28; S Nu 10:35; Na 1:2 **7:12** [l] Lev 26:3-13; Dt 28:1-14; Ps 105:8-9; Mic 7:20 **7:13** [m] Ps 11:5; 146:8; Pr 15:9; Isa 51:1; Jn 14:21 [n] S Ge 17:6; Ex 1:7; Dt 1:10; 13:17; 30:5; Ps 107:38

[a] 5 That is, wooden symbols of the goddess Asherah; here and elsewhere in Deuteronomy

[o] S Ge 49:25 [p] S Ge 27:28 [q] S Nu 18:12 [r] Dt 28:4 **7:14** [s] Ex 23:26 **7:15** [t] S Ex 15:26 [u] S Ex 9:9 [v] S Ex 23:25; Dt 30:8-10 **7:16** [w] ver 24; Jos 6:2; 10:26 [x] S ver 2 [y] Jdg 3:6; Ezr 9:1; Ps 106:36 [z] ver 25; S Ex 10:7 **7:17** [a] Nu 33:53 **7:18** [b] S Nu 14:9; S Dt 1:21,29 [c] Ps 105:5; 119:52 **7:19** [d] Ps 136:12 [e] Dt 4:34 **7:20** [f] S Ex 23:28 **7:21** [g] S Ge 17:7; Jos 3:10 [h] Dt 10:17; Ne 1:5; 9:32; Ps 47:2; 66:3; 68:35; Isa 9:6; Da 9:4 **7:22** [i] Ex 23:28-30 **7:23** [j] Ex 23:27; Jos 10:10

7:4 *turn your children away ... to serve other gods.* See note on vv. 1–6. The Lord's command against intermarriage with foreigners was not racially motivated but was intended to prevent spiritual contamination and apostasy (see, e.g., Jos 23:12–13 and notes; 1Ki 11:1–11; Ne 13:25–27).

7:5 *altars ... sacred stones ... Asherah poles.* Objects of Canaanite idolatrous worship (see 12:3; 16:21–22). See also NIV text note; Ex 34:13,15 and notes.

7:6 *holy.* Separated from all corrupting people or things and consecrated totally to the Lord (see note on Ex 3:5). *treasured possession.* See note on Ex 19:5.

7:8 *because the LORD loved you.* See 4:37 and note.

7:9,12 *his covenant of love.* See 1Ki 8:23; 1Ch 6:14; Ne 1:5; 9:32; Da 9:4; cf. Ps 89:28; 106:45; Isa 54:10; 55:3; i.e., the covenant in which God pledges on oath to show the Israelites his unfailing love (kindness, mercy; see note on Ps 6:4) in all his ways with them through the vicissitudes of their history so that all his particular promises to them (see vv. 13–15; 19:24; 28:1–14; 30:1–10; see also Ge 22:17–18; Lev 26:3–13) might be fulfilled. A closely related phrase is "covenant of peace" (Nu 25:12; Isa 54:10; Eze 34:25; 37:26).

7:9 *Know ... that the LORD ... is God.* See 11:28; Ps 100:3 and notes. *thousand generations ... keep his commandments.* See note on Ex 20:6.

7:12–15 The blessings are stated more fully in 28:1–14; 30:1–10.

7:13 *grain, new wine and olive oil.* A common OT summary of the produce of field, vineyard and olive grove (see, e.g., 11:14; 14:23; 18:4; 28:51).

7:15 *not inflict ... diseases.* See note on 28:60.

7:16 See essay, p. 308.

7:18 *remember.* See note on 4:10.

7:20 *hornet.* See note on Ex 23:28.

7:22 *God will drive out.* See note on 3:22. *wild animals will multiply.* The rapid expulsion of the Canaanites would leave much of the land deserted and therefore open to wild animals.

kings[k] into your hand,[l] and you will wipe out their names from under heaven. No one will be able to stand up against you;[m] you will destroy them.[n] 25 The images of their gods you are to burn[o] in the fire. Do not covet[p] the silver and gold on them, and do not take it for yourselves, or you will be ensnared[q] by it, for it is detestable[r] to the LORD your God. 26 Do not bring a detestable thing into your house or you, like it, will be set apart for destruction.[s] Regard it as vile and utterly detest it, for it is set apart for destruction.

7:24 [k] Jos 10:24; Ps 110:5 [l] S ver 16 [m] S Ex 23:31; Dt 11:25; Jos 1:5; 10:8; 23:9 [n] Jos 21:44 **7:25** [o] S Ex 4:14; S 32:20 [p] Ex 20:17; Jos 7:21 [q] S ver 16 [r] Dt 17:1 **7:26** [s] Lev 27:28-29 **8:1** [t] Dt 4:1 [u] S Ex 19:5; Job 36:11; Ps 16:11; Eze 20:19 **8:2** [v] Dt 29:5; Ps 136:16; Am 2:10 [w] S Ge 22:1

Do Not Forget the LORD

8 Be careful to follow every command I am giving you today, so that you may live[t] and increase and may enter and possess the land the LORD promised on oath to your ancestors.[u] 2 Remember how the LORD your God led[v] you all the way in the wilderness these forty years, to humble and test[w] you in order to know what was in your heart, whether or not you would

7:25–26 Cf. the story of Achan (Jos 6:17–19; 7:1,20–25).
7:26 *set apart for destruction.* See note on 2:34.

8:2 *Remember.* See note on 4:10. *test.* See v. 16; see also note on Ge 22:1.

AGRICULTURE IN THE HOLY LAND

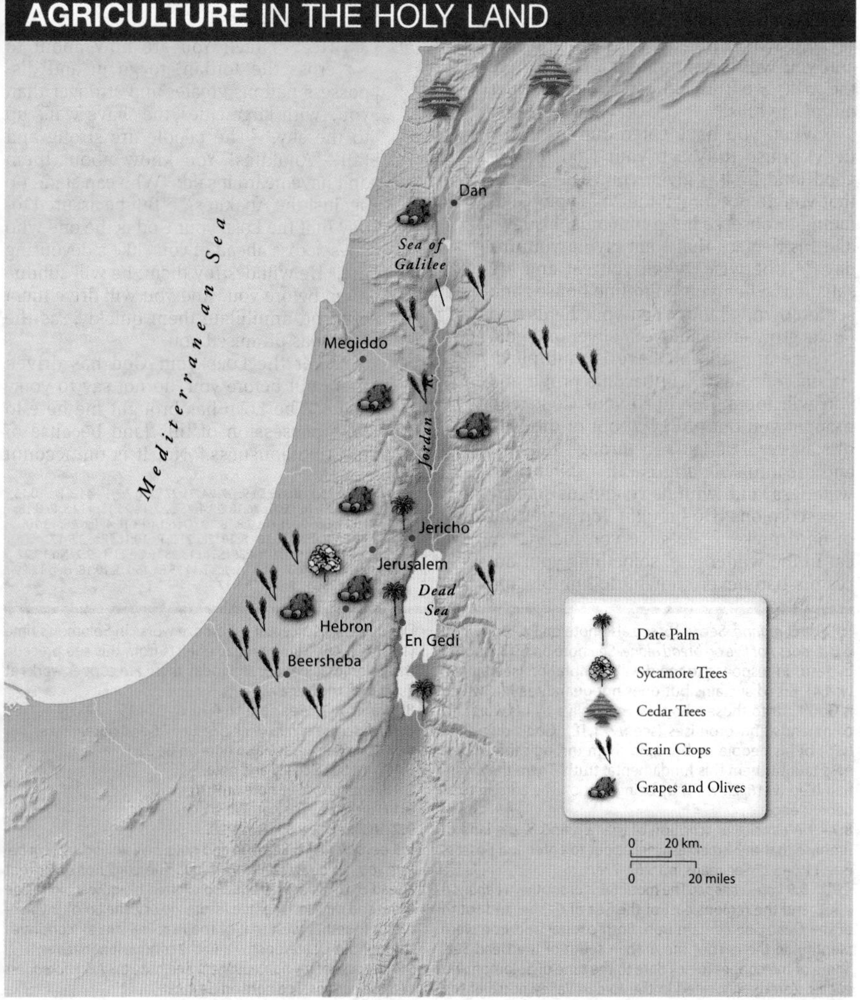

keep his commands. 3 He humbled[x] you, causing you to hunger and then feeding you with manna,[y] which neither you nor your ancestors had known, to teach[z] you that man does not live on bread[a] alone but on every word that comes from the mouth[b] of the LORD.[c] 4 Your clothes did not wear out and your feet did not swell during these forty years.[d] 5 Know then in your heart that as a man disciplines his son, so the LORD your God disciplines you.[e]

6 Observe the commands of the LORD your God, walking in obedience to him[f] and revering him.[g] 7 For the LORD your God is bringing you into a good land[h]—a land with brooks, streams, and deep springs gushing out into the valleys and hills;[i] 8 a land with wheat and barley,[j] vines[k] and fig trees,[l] pomegranates, olive oil and honey;[m] 9 a land where bread[n] will not be scarce and you will lack nothing;[o] a land where the rocks are iron and you can dig copper out of the hills.[p]

10 When you have eaten and are satisfied,[q] praise the LORD your God for the good land he has given you. 11 Be careful that you do not forget[r] the LORD your God, failing to observe his commands, his laws and his decrees that I am giving you this day. 12 Otherwise, when you eat and are satisfied, when you build fine houses and settle down,[s] 13 and when your herds and flocks grow large and your silver and gold increase and all you have is multiplied, 14 then your heart will become proud and you will forget[t] the LORD your God, who brought you out of Egypt, out of the land of slavery. 15 He led you through the vast and dreadful wilderness,[u] that thirsty and waterless land, with its venomous snakes[v] and scorpions. He brought you water out of hard rock.[w] 16 He gave you manna[x] to eat in the wilderness, something your ancestors had never known,[y] to humble and test[z] you so that in the end it might go well with you. 17 You may say to yourself,[a] "My power and the strength of my hands[b] have produced this wealth for me." 18 But remember the LORD your God, for it is he who gives you the ability to produce wealth,[c] and so confirms his covenant, which he swore to your ancestors, as it is today.

19 If you ever forget the LORD your God and follow other gods[d] and worship and bow down to them, I testify against you today that you will surely be destroyed.[e] 20 Like the nations[f] the LORD destroyed before you, so you will be destroyed for not obeying the LORD your God.[g]

Not Because of Israel's Righteousness

9 Hear, Israel: You are now about to cross the Jordan[h] to go in and dispossess nations greater and stronger than you,[i] with large cities[j] that have walls up to the sky.[k] 2 The people are strong and tall—Anakites! You know about them and have heard it said: "Who can stand up against the Anakites?"[l] 3 But be assured today that the LORD your God is the one who goes across ahead of you[m] like a devouring fire.[n] He will destroy them; he will subdue them before you. And you will drive them out and annihilate them quickly,[o] as the LORD has promised you.

4 After the LORD your God has driven them out before you, do not say to yourself,[p] "The LORD has brought me here to take possession of this land because of my righteousness." No, it is on account

8:3 [x] 2Ch 36:12; Ps 44:9; Pr 18:12; Isa 2:11; Jer 44:10 [y] S Ex 16:4 [z] 1Ki 8:36; Ps 25:5; 94:12; 119:171 [a] ver 9; S Ge 3:19; Job 23:12; Ps 104:15; Pr 28:21; Isa 51:14; Jer 42:14 [b] Job 22:22; Ps 119:13; 138:4 [c] S Ex 16:2-3; Mt 4:4*; Lk 4:4* **8:4** [d] Dt 29:5; Ne 9:21 **8:5** [e] Dt 4:36; 2Sa 7:14; Job 5:17; 33:19; Pr 3:11-12; Heb 12:5-11; Rev 3:19 **8:6** [f] S Ex 33:13; 1Ki 3:14; Ps 81:13; 95:10 [g] Dt 5:33 **8:7** [h] Ps 106:24; Jer 3:19; Eze 20:6 [i] Dt 11:9-12; Jer 2:7 **8:8** [j] S Ex 9:31 [k] S Ge 49:11 [l] S Nu 13:23; S 1Ki 4:25 [m] Dt 32:13; Ps 81:16 **8:9** [n] S ver 3 [o] Jdg 18:10 [p] Job 28:2 **8:10** [q] Dt 6:10-12 **8:11** [r] Dt 4:9 **8:12** [s] Pr 30:9; Hos 13:6 **8:14** [t] ver 11; Ps 78:7; 106:21 **8:15** [u] S Dt 1:19; S 32:10 [v] Nu 21:6; Isa 14:29; 30:6 [w] Ex 17:6; Dt 32:13; Job 28:9; Ps 78:15; 114:8 **8:16** [x] S Ex 16:14 [y] Ex 16:15 [z] S Ge 22:1 **8:17** [a] Dt 9:4,7,24; 31:27 [b] Jdg 7:2; Ps 44:3; Isa 10:13 **8:18** [c] Ge 26:13; Dt 26:10; 28:4; 1Sa 2:7; Ps 25:13; 112:3; Pr 8:18; 10:22; Ecc 9:11; Hos 2:8 **8:19** [d] Dt 6:14; Ps 16:4; Jer 7:6; 13:10; 25:6 [e] Dt 4:26; 30:18 **8:20** [f] 2Ki 21:2; Ps 10:16 [g] Eze 5:5-17 **9:1** [h] S Nu 35:10 [i] Dt 4:38 [j] S Nu 13:28 [k] S Ge 11:4 **9:2** [l] Nu 13:22; Jos 11:22 **9:3** [m] Dt 31:3; Jos 3:11 [n] S Ex 15:7; S 19:18; Heb 12:29 [o] S Ex 23:31 **9:4** [p] S Dt 8:17

8:3 *manna.* See v. 16; see also note on Ex 16:31. *man does not live on bread alone.* See note on 6:13; quoted by Jesus in response to the devil's temptation (see Mt 4:4; Lk 4:4). Bread sustains but does not guarantee life, which is God's gift to those who trust in and live by his word: his commands and promises (see vv. 1,18). God's discipline (v. 5) of his people by bringing them through the wilderness taught them this fundamental truth. There they were humbled (v. 16; cf. v. 14) by being cast on the Lord in total dependence.

8:7–9 A concise description of the rich and fertile land of promise that the Israelites were about to enter and possess (see 11:8–12). See maps, pp. 262, 273.

8:9 *iron ... copper.* The mountains of southern Lebanon and the regions east of the Sea of Galilee and south of the Dead Sea contain iron. Both copper and iron were plentiful in the part of the Arabah south of the Dead Sea. Some of the copper mines date to the time of Solomon and earlier. Zarethan, located in the Jordan Valley north of the Dead Sea, was a center for bronze works in Solomon's time (1Ki 7:45–46). Some bronze objects from this site precede the Solomonic period, and today there are copper works at Timnah in the Negev.

8:11 *not forget.* See note on 4:10; cf. 8:14,19.

8:15 *water out of hard rock.* See Ex 17:6 and note.

8:16 *test.* See v. 2; see also note on Ge 22:1.

8:17–18 See Zec 4:6 and note.

8:18 *remember.* See note on 4:10.

9:1 *Hear, Israel.* See note on 4:1.

9:2 *Anakites.* See note on 1:28.

9:3 *devouring fire.* See 4:24 and note. *he will subdue them before you ... you will drive them out.* The Lord not only went ahead of the Israelites but also exerted his power alongside them and through them to assure victory. The Lord's involvement, together with that of the Israelite armies, continues throughout Deuteronomy and the conquest narratives.

9:4 *because of my righteousness.* See note on 7:8. *wickedness of these nations.* See note on Ge 15:16.

of the wickedness[q] of these nations[r] that the LORD is going to drive them out before you. 5 It is not because of your righteousness or your integrity[s] that you are going in to take possession of their land; but on account of the wickedness[t] of these nations,[u] the LORD your God will drive them out[v] before you, to accomplish what he swore[w] to your fathers, to Abraham, Isaac and Jacob.[x] 6 Understand, then, that it is not because of your righteousness that the LORD your God is giving you this good land to possess, for you are a stiff-necked people.[y]

The Golden Calf

7 Remember this and never forget how you aroused the anger[z] of the LORD your God in the wilderness. From the day you left Egypt until you arrived here, you have been rebellious[a] against the LORD.[b] 8 At Horeb you aroused the LORD's wrath[c] so that he was angry enough to destroy you.[d] 9 When I went up on the mountain to receive the tablets of stone, the tablets of the covenant[e] that the LORD had made with you, I stayed on the mountain forty days[f] and forty nights; I ate no bread and drank no water.[g] 10 The LORD gave me two stone tablets inscribed by the finger of God.[h] On them were all the commandments the LORD proclaimed to you on the mountain out of the fire, on the day of the assembly.[i]

11 At the end of the forty days and forty nights,[j] the LORD gave me the two stone tablets,[k] the tablets of the covenant. 12 Then the LORD told me, "Go down from here at once, because your people whom you brought out of Egypt have become corrupt.[l] They have turned away quickly[m] from what I commanded them and have made an idol for themselves."

13 And the LORD said to me, "I have seen this people[n], and they are a stiff-necked people indeed! 14 Let me alone,[o] so that I may destroy them and blot out[p] their name from under heaven.[q] And I will make you into a nation stronger and more numerous than they."

15 So I turned and went down from the mountain while it was ablaze with fire. And the two tablets of the covenant were in my hands.[r] 16 When I looked, I saw that you had sinned against the LORD your God; you had made for yourselves an idol cast in the shape of a calf.[s] You had turned aside quickly from the way that the LORD had commanded you. 17 So I took the two tablets and threw them out of my hands, breaking them to pieces before your eyes.

18 Then once again I fell[t] prostrate before the LORD for forty days and forty nights; I ate no bread and drank no water,[u] because of all the sin you had committed,[v] doing what was evil in the LORD's sight and so arousing his anger. 19 I feared the anger and wrath of the LORD, for he was angry enough with you to destroy you.[w] But again the LORD listened to me.[x] 20 And the LORD was angry enough with Aaron to destroy him, but at that time I prayed for Aaron too. 21 Also I took that sinful thing of yours, the calf you had made, and burned it in the fire. Then I crushed it and ground it to powder as fine as dust[y] and threw the dust into a stream that flowed down the mountain.[z]

22 You also made the LORD angry[a] at Taberah,[b] at Massah[c] and at Kibroth Hattaavah.[d]

23 And when the LORD sent you out from Kadesh Barnea,[e] he said, "Go up and take possession[f] of the land I have given you." But you rebelled[g] against the command of the LORD your God. You did not trust[h] him or obey him. 24 You have been rebellious against the LORD ever since I have known you.[i]

25 I lay prostrate before the LORD those forty days and forty nights[j] because the LORD had said he would destroy you.[k] 26 I prayed to the LORD and said, "Sovereign LORD, do not destroy your people,[l] your own inheritance[m] that you redeemed[n] by your great power and brought out of Egypt with a mighty hand.[o] 27 Remember your servants Abraham, Isaac and Jacob. Overlook the stubbornness[p] of this

9:4 [q]2Ki 16:3; 17:8; 21:2; Ezr 9:11 [r]S Ex 23:24; S Lev 18:21,24-30; Dt 18:9-14 **9:5** [s]S Eph 2:9 [t]Dt 18:9 [u]S Lev 18:25 [v]Dt 4:38; 11:23 [w]S Ge 12:7 [x]Eze 36:32 **9:6** [y]S Ex 32:9; Ac 7:51 **9:7** [z]S Nu 11:33 [a]S Ex 23:21 [b]S Ex 14:11 **9:8** [c]Nu 16:46; 1Sa 28:18; Job 20:28; Ps 2:12; 7:11; 69:24; 110:5; Isa 9:19; Eze 20:13 [d]Ex 32:7-10; Ezr 9:14; Ps 106:19 **9:9** [e]S Dt 4:13 [f]S Ge 7:4 [g]S Ex 24:12 **9:10** [h]S Ex 31:18 [i]Dt 10:4; 18:16 **9:11** [j]S Ge 7:4 [k]S Ex 24:12 **9:12** [l]S Dt 4:16 [m]Jdg 2:17 **9:13** [n]ver 6; Dt 10:16 **9:14** [o]Ex 32:10 [p]S Nu 14:12 [q]Jer 7:16 **9:15** [r]S Ex 32:15 **9:16** [s]S Ex 32:4 **9:18** [t]S Ex 34:28 [u]ver 9 [v]S Ex 32:31 **9:19** [w]S Ex 32:14; Heb 12:21* [x]ver 26; Ex 34:10; S Nu 11:2; 1Sa 7:9; Jer 15:1 **9:21** [y]Ps 18:42; Isa 29:5; 40:15 [z]Ex 32:20; Isa 2:18; Mic 1:7 **9:22** [a]S Nu 1:53 [b]Nu 11:3 [c]S Ex 17:7 [d]Nu 11:34 **9:23** [e]S Dt 1:2 [f]Dt 1:21 [g]S Nu 14:9 [h]S Dt 1:32; Ps 106:24 **9:24** [i]S Dt 8:17 **9:25** [j]S Ge 7:4 [k]ver 18; S Ex 33:17 **9:26** [l]S Ex 33:13 [m]S Ex 34:9 [n]S Ex 6:6; Dt 15:15; 2Sa 7:23; Ps 78:35 [o]S ver 19; S Ex 32:11 **9:27** [p]ver 6; S Ex 32:9

9:6,13 *stiff-necked.* See 10:16; 31:27; see also note on Ex 32:9.
9:7,27 *Remember.* See note on 4:10.
9:9 *tablets of the covenant.* See notes on Ex 20:1; 34:28.
9:10 *two stone tablets . . . finger of God.* See Ex 31:18 and note; see also note on Ex 8:19.
9:11–21 See Ex 31:18—32:20 and notes.
9:12–13 *your people . . . this people.* See note on Ex 17:4.
9:14 *blot out their name.* The Phoenician cognate of the Hebrew for this phrase appears in a ninth-century BC inscription on a gateway: "If . . . a man . . . blots out the name of Azitawadda from this gate . . . may (the gods) wipe out . . . that man!"
9:19 *But again the LORD listened to me.* Moses' intercessory prayer on this occasion (vv. 26–29) ranks among the great prayers for Israel's national survival (see Ex 32:11–13 and notes; see also Ezr 9:6–15; Ne 9:5–38; Da 9:4–19).
9:22 *Taberah.* See Nu 11:3 and NIV text note. *Massah.* See 6:16; 33:8; see also note on Ex 17:7. *Kibroth Hattaavah.* See Nu 11:34 and NIV text note.
9:23 *Kadesh Barnea.* See notes on Ge 14:7; Nu 20:1.
9:27 *Overlook.* See note on Ac 17:30.

people, their wickedness and their sin. 28 Otherwise, the country[q] from which you brought us will say, 'Because the LORD was not able to take them into the land he had promised them, and because he hated them,[r] he brought them out to put them to death in the wilderness.'[s] 29 But they are your people,[t] your inheritance[u] that you brought out by your great power and your outstretched arm.[v]"

Tablets Like the First Ones

10 At that time the LORD said to me, "Chisel out two stone tablets[w] like the first ones and come up to me on the mountain. Also make a wooden ark.[a] 2 I will write on the tablets the words that were on the first tablets, which you broke. Then you are to put them in the ark."[x]

3 So I made the ark out of acacia wood[y] and chiseled[z] out two stone tablets like the first ones, and I went up on the mountain with the two tablets in my hands. 4 The LORD wrote on these tablets what he had written before, the Ten Commandments[a] he had proclaimed[b] to you on the mountain, out of the fire, on the day of the assembly.[c] And the LORD gave them to me. 5 Then I came back down the mountain[d] and put the tablets in the ark[e] I had made,[f] as the LORD commanded me, and they are there now.[g]

6 (The Israelites traveled from the wells of Bene Jaakan to Moserah.[h] There Aaron died[i] and was buried, and Eleazar[j] his son succeeded him as priest.[k] 7 From there they traveled to Gudgodah and on to Jotbathah, a land with streams of water.[l] 8 At that time the LORD set apart the tribe of Levi[m] to carry the ark of the covenant[n] of the LORD, to stand before the LORD to minister[o] and to pronounce blessings[p] in his name, as they still do today.[q] 9 That is why the Levites have no share or inheritance among their fellow Israelites; the LORD is their inheritance,[r] as the LORD your God told them.)

10 Now I had stayed on the mountain forty days and forty nights, as I did the first time, and the LORD listened to me at this time also. It was not his will to destroy you.[s] 11 "Go," the LORD said to me, "and lead the people on their way, so that they may enter and possess the land I swore to their ancestors to give them."

Fear the LORD

12 And now, Israel, what does the LORD your God ask of you[t] but to fear[u] the LORD your God, to walk[v] in obedience to him, to love him,[w] to serve the LORD[x] your God with all your heart[y] and with all your soul,[z] 13 and to observe the LORD's commands[a] and decrees that I am giving you today for your own good?[b]

14 To the LORD your God belong the heavens,[c] even the highest heavens,[d] the earth and everything in it.[e] 15 Yet the LORD set his affection on your ancestors and loved[f] them, and he chose you,[g] their descendants, above all the nations—as it is today.[h] 16 Circumcise[i] your hearts,[j] therefore, and do not be stiff-necked[k] any longer. 17 For the LORD your God is God of gods[l] and Lord of lords,[m] the great God, mighty and awesome,[n] who shows no partiality[o] and accepts no bribes.[p] 18 He defends the cause of the fatherless and the widow,[q] and loves the foreigner residing among you, giving them food and clothing.[r] 19 And you are to love[s] those who are foreigners,[t] for you yourselves were foreigners in Egypt.[u] 20 Fear the LORD your God and serve him.[v] Hold fast[w] to him and take your oaths in his name.[x] 21 He is the one you praise;[y] he is your God, who performed for you those great[z] and awesome wonders[a] you saw with your own eyes. 22 Your ancestors who went down into Egypt were seventy in all,[b] and now the LORD your God has made you as numerous as the stars in the sky.[c]

[a] *1* That is, a chest

9:28 q Dt 32:27 r S Dt 1:27 s S Ex 32:12; Jos 7:9 **9:29** t S Ex 33:13 u S Ex 34:9; Dt 32:9 v Dt 4:34; Ne 1:10; Jer 27:5; 32:17 **10:1** w Ex 34:1-2 **10:2** x Ex 25:16, 21; 2Ch 5:10; 6:11 **10:3** y Ex 37:1-9 z Ex 34:4 **10:4** a S Ex 24:12; S 34:28 b Ex 20:1 c S Dt 9:10 **10:5** d S Ex 19:11 e S Ex 25:10; S 1Sa 3:3 f S Ex 25:21 g 1Ki 8:9 **10:6** h Nu 33:30 i S Nu 27:13 j S Ex 6:23 k S Nu 20:25-28 **10:7** l Nu 33:32-34; Ps 42:1; SS 5:12; Isa 32:2 **10:8** m S Nu 3:6 n S Nu 10:33 o S Nu 16:9 p S Ge 48:20 q 1Ch 23:26 **10:9** r S Nu 18:20 **10:10** s S Ex 33:17 **10:12** t Mic 6:8 u S Ex 20:20 v 1Ki 2:3; 3:3; 9:4 w Dt 5:33; 6:13; Mt 22:37; 1Ti 1:5 x Dt 11:13; 28:47; Ps 100:2 y S Dt 6:5; Ps 119:2 z S Dt 5:32 **10:13** a S Dt 4:2 b Dt 5:33; 6:24 **10:14** c Dt 33:26; Ne 9:6; Job 35:5; Ps 8:3; 89:11; 104:3; 148:4; Isa 19:1; Hab 3:8 d 1Ki 8:27; Ps 115:16 e Ex 19:5; Ps 24:1; Ac 17:24 **10:15** f S Dt 4:37 g Ps 105:6; 135:4 h S Nu 14:8; Ro 11:28; 1Pe 2:9 **10:16** i S Ge 17:11 j S Lev 26:41; Dt 30:6; Jer 32:39 k S Ex 32:9; S Dt 9:13 **10:17** l Jos 22:22; Ps 135:5; 136:2; Da 2:47; 11:36 m Ps 136:3; S 1Ti 6:15 n S Dt 7:21 o Dt 1:17; Mal 2:9 p S Ex 23:8; S Lev 19:16 **10:18** q Ex 22:21,22-24; 23:9; Lev 19:33; Dt 27:19; Job 29:13; Ps 94:6; Isa 10:2; Jer 49:11 r S Nu 10:32 **10:19** s Dt 7:12 t S Ex 22:21; S Dt 24:19 u S Lev 19:34; Eze 47:22-23 **10:20** v Mt 4:10 w Dt 11:22; 13:4; 30:20; Jos 23:8; Ru 1:14; 2Ki 18:6; Ps 119:31; Isa 38:3 x S Ex 20:7 **10:21** y S Ex 15:2 z 1Sa 12:24; Ps 126:2 a 2Sa 7:23 **10:22** b S Ge 34:30; S 46:26; Ac 7:14 c S Ge 12:2; S Nu 10:36

10:1–3 *ark.* The Hebrew word means "chest" or "box" (see NIV text note on v. 1; see also note on Ex 25:10).
10:1 *two stone tablets.* See note on Ex 31:18.
10:2 *put them in the ark.* See notes on Ex 16:34; 25:16.
10:3 The order of events here is different from that in Exodus 34–37 (see Introduction to Deuteronomy: Structure and Outline).
10:6–9 A historical parenthesis, apparently stemming from Moses' prayer for Aaron and the Israelites (9:26–29) and the reference to the ark (vv. 1–5).
10:8 *carry the ark.* See note on Nu 1:50. *to minister … to pronounce blessings.* See note on 21:5.
10:9 See 12:12 and note.
10:12 *what does the LORD … ask of you … ?* See Mic 6:8 and note. *fear the LORD.* See note on Ge 20:11. *love him.* See notes on 4:29,37; 6:5.
10:13 *for your own good.* See 6:24; see also note on 6:2.
10:15 *set his affection … loved.* See 7:7–8 and note on 7:8. *ancestors.* The patriarchs (cf. v. 22).
10:16 *Circumcise your hearts.* See note on Ge 17:10. *stiff-necked.* See 9:6,13; 31:27; see also note on Ex 32:9.
10:20 *Hold fast.* As a man is "united" to his wife (Ge 2:24), and as Ruth "clung" to Naomi (Ru 1:14). See 4:4; 11:22; 13:4; 30:20.
10:21 *He is the one you praise.* See Ps 22:3 and note.
10:22 *seventy.* See notes on Ge 10:2; 46:26–27; see also Ex 1:5. *as the stars in the sky.* See note on 1:10.

Love and Obey the LORD

11 Love[d] the LORD your God and keep
his requirements, his decrees, his
laws and his commands always.[e] 2 Remember today that your children[f] were not the
ones who saw and experienced the discipline of the LORD your God:[g] his majesty,[h]
his mighty hand, his outstretched arm;[i]
3 the signs he performed and the things he
did in the heart of Egypt, both to Pharaoh
king of Egypt and to his whole country;[j]
4 what he did to the Egyptian army, to its
horses and chariots,[k] how he overwhelmed
them with the waters of the Red Sea[a][l] as
they were pursuing you, and how the LORD
brought lasting ruin on them. 5 It was not
your children who saw what he did for
you in the wilderness until you arrived at
this place, 6 and what he did[m] to Dathan
and Abiram, sons of Eliab the Reubenite,
when the earth opened[n] its mouth right
in the middle of all Israel and swallowed
them up with their households, their tents
and every living thing that belonged to
them. 7 But it was your own eyes that saw
all these great things the LORD has done.[o]
8 Observe therefore all the commands[p] I
am giving you today, so that you may have
the strength to go in and take over the
land that you are crossing the Jordan to
possess,[q] 9 and so that you may live long[r]
in the land the LORD swore[s] to your ancestors to give to them and their descendants,
a land flowing with milk and honey.[t] 10 The
land you are entering to take over is not
like the land of Egypt,[u] from which you
have come, where you planted your seed
and irrigated it by foot as in a vegetable
garden. 11 But the land you are crossing
the Jordan to take possession of is a land
of mountains and valleys[v] that drinks rain
from heaven.[w] 12 It is a land the LORD your
God cares for; the eyes[x] of the LORD your
God are continually on it from the beginning of the year to its end.
13 So if you faithfully obey[y] the commands I am giving you today—to love[z]
the LORD your God and to serve him with
all your heart and with all your soul[a]—
14 then I will send rain[b] on your land in its
season, both autumn and spring rains,[c] so
that you may gather in your grain, new
wine and olive oil. 15 I will provide grass[d]
in the fields for your cattle, and you will
eat and be satisfied.[e]
16 Be careful, or you will be enticed to
turn away and worship other gods and
bow down to them.[f] 17 Then the LORD's
anger[g] will burn against you, and he will
shut up[h] the heavens so that it will not
rain and the ground will yield no produce,[i]
and you will soon perish[j] from the good
land the LORD is giving you. 18 Fix these
words of mine in your hearts and minds;
tie them as symbols on your hands and
bind them on your foreheads.[k] 19 Teach
them to your children,[l] talking about them
when you sit at home and when you walk
along the road, when you lie down and
when you get up.[m] 20 Write them on the
doorframes of your houses and on your
gates,[n] 21 so that your days and the days of
your children may be many[o] in the land
the LORD swore to give your ancestors,
as many as the days that the heavens are
above the earth.[p]
22 If you carefully observe[q] all these commands I am giving you to follow—to love[r]
the LORD your God, to walk in obedience
to him and to hold fast[s] to him— 23 then
the LORD will drive out[t] all these nations[u]
before you, and you will dispossess nations larger and stronger than you.[v] 24 Every place where you set your foot will be
yours:[w] Your territory will extend from the
desert to Lebanon, and from the Euphrates
River[x] to the Mediterranean Sea. 25 No one
will be able to stand against you. The LORD
your God, as he promised you, will put the
terror[y] and fear of you on the whole land,
wherever you go.[z]

[a] 4 Or *the Sea of Reeds*

11:1 [d] S Dt 6:5 [e] S Lev 8:35 **11:2** [f] Dt 31:13; Ps 78:6 [g] S Dt 5:24 [h] S Dt 3:24 [i] Ps 136:12 **11:3** [j] Ex 7:8-21 **11:4** [k] S Ex 15:1 [l] S Ex 14:27; S Nu 21:4 **11:6** [m] Nu 16:1-35; Ps 106:16-18 [n] Isa 24:19 **11:7** [o] Dt 5:3 **11:8** [p] Ezr 9:10 [q] Dt 31:6-7,23; Jos 1:7 **11:9** [r] S Dt 5:16 [s] Dt 9:5 [t] S Ex 3:8 **11:10** [u] Isa 11:15; 37:25 **11:11** [v] Eze 36:4 [w] Dt 8:7; Ne 9:25 **11:12** [x] 1Ki 8:29; 9:3 **11:13** [y] S Dt 6:17 [z] S Dt 10:12 [a] Dt 4:29; Jer 17:24 **11:14** [b] S Lev 26:4; Ac 14:17 [c] Ps 147:8; Jer 3:3; 5:24; Joel 2:23; Jas 5:7 **11:15** [d] Ps 104:14 [e] S Lev 26:5 **11:16** [f] Dt 4:19; 8:19; 29:18; Job 31:9,27 **11:17** [g] Dt 6:15; 9:19 [h] 1Ki 17:1; 2Ch 6:26; 7:13 [i] S Lev 26:20 [j] Dt 4:26; 28:12,24 **11:18** [k] S Ex 13:9; Dt 6:6-8 **11:19** [l] S Ex 12:26; Dt 6:7; Ps 145:4; Isa 38:19; Jer 32:39 [m] Dt 4:9-10 **11:20** [n] Dt 6:9 **11:21** [o] Job 5:26; Pr 3:2; 4:10; 9:11 [p] Ps 72:5 **11:22** [q] S Dt 6:17 [r] S Dt 6:5 [s] S Dt 10:20 **11:23** [t] S Dt 9:5 [u] S Ex 23:28 [v] Dt 9:1 **11:24** [w] Ge 15:18; Dt 1:36; 12:20; 19:8; Jos 1:3; 14:9 [x] S Ge 2:14 **11:25** [y] S Dt 2:25 [z] Ex 23:27; Dt 7:24

11:1 *Love.* See note on 6:5. *keep.* Love and obedience are frequently linked in Scripture (e.g., 6:5–6; Jn 14:15; 1Jn 5:3; see note on Ex 20:2).
11:2–7 Moses continually emphasizes the involvement of his listeners in the Lord's works of providence and deliverance. In 5:3 it was not the patriarchs (but see NIV text note there: "not only ... parents") but they themselves with whom the covenant was made at Sinai. Here it is not their children (vv. 2–6) but they themselves who saw God's great deeds (v. 7).
11:2 *Remember.* See note on 4:10.
11:8–12 See note on 8:7–9.
11:9 *live long.* See note on 6:2.
11:10 *irrigated it by foot.* Irrigation channels dug by foot and/or fed by devices powered by foot brought the water of the Nile to the gardens in Egypt, in contrast to the rains that watered Canaan (v. 11).
11:13 See note on 4:29.
11:14 *autumn and spring rains.* The rainy season in Israel begins in October and ends in April.
11:17 *shut up the heavens.* The all-important seasonal rains (see v. 14) were controlled by the Lord—not by Baal, as the inhabitants of Canaan thought (cf. Jer 14:22; Hos 2:8 and notes).
11:18–20 See note on 6:8–9.
11:21 *as many as the days ... earth.* That is, as long as the present creation endures.
11:22 *hold fast.* See note on 10:20.
11:24 *Every place where you set your foot.* See 1:7 and note; Jos 1:3.

26 See, I am setting before you today a
blessing[a] and a curse[b]— 27 the blessing[c] if
you obey the commands of the LORD your
God that I am giving you today; 28 the
curse if you disobey[d] the commands of
the LORD your God and turn from the way
that I command you today by following
other gods,[e] which you have not known.
29 When the LORD your God has brought
you into the land you are entering to possess, you are to proclaim on Mount Gerizim[f] the blessings, and on Mount Ebal[g] the
curses.[h] 30 As you know, these mountains
are across the Jordan, westward, toward
the setting sun, near the great trees of Moreh,[i] in the territory of those Canaanites
living in the Arabah in the vicinity of Gilgal.[j] 31 You are about to cross the Jordan
to enter and take possession[k] of the land
the LORD your God is giving[l] you. When
you have taken it over and are living there,
32 be sure that you obey all the decrees and
laws I am setting before you today.

The One Place of Worship

12 These are the decrees[m] and laws
you must be careful to follow in the
land that the LORD, the God of your ancestors, has given you to possess—as long as
you live in the land.[n] 2 Destroy completely
all the places on the high mountains,[o] on
the hills and under every spreading tree,[p]
where the nations you are dispossessing
worship their gods. 3 Break down their altars, smash[q] their sacred stones and burn[r]
their Asherah[s] poles in the fire; cut down
the idols of their gods and wipe out their
names[t] from those places.
4 You must not worship the LORD your
God in their way.[u] 5 But you are to seek the
place the LORD your God will choose from
among all your tribes to put his Name[v]
there for his dwelling.[w] To that place you
must go; 6 there bring your burnt offerings
and sacrifices, your tithes[x] and special
gifts, what you have vowed[y] to give and
your freewill offerings, and the firstborn
of your herds and flocks.[z] 7 There, in the
presence[a] of the LORD your God, you and
your families shall eat and shall rejoice[b] in
everything you have put your hand to, because the LORD your God has blessed you.
8 You are not to do as we do here today,
everyone doing as they see fit,[c] 9 since you
have not yet reached the resting place[d] and
the inheritance[e] the LORD your God is giving you. 10 But you will cross the Jordan
and settle in the land the LORD your God is
giving[f] you as an inheritance, and he will
give you rest[g] from all your enemies around
you so that you will live in safety. 11 Then
to the place the LORD your God will choose
as a dwelling for his Name[h]—there you are
to bring everything I command you: your
burnt offerings and sacrifices, your tithes
and special gifts, and all the choice possessions you have vowed to the LORD.[i] 12 And
there rejoice[j] before the LORD your God—
you, your sons and daughters, your male
and female servants, and the Levites[k] from
your towns who have no allotment or inheritance[l] of their own. 13 Be careful not to
sacrifice your burnt offerings anywhere you
please.[m] 14 Offer them only at the place the
LORD will choose[n] in one of your tribes, and
there observe everything I command you.

11:26 [a] Ps 24:5 [b] Lev 26:14-17; Dt 27:13-26; 30:1,15, 19; La 2:17; Da 9:11; Hag 1:11; Mal 2:2; 3:9; 4:6 **11:27** [c] Dt 28:1-14; Ps 24:5 **11:28** [d] 2Ch 24:20; Jer 42:13; 44:16 [e] S Dt 4:28; 13:6,13; 29:26; 1Sa 26:19 **11:29** [f] Jdg 9:7 [g] Dt 27:4; Jos 8:30 [h] Dt 27:12-13; Jos 8:33; Jn 4:20 **11:30** [i] S Ge 12:6 [j] Jos 4:19; 5:9; 9:6; 10:6; 14:6; 15:7; Jdg 2:1; 2Ki 2:1; Mic 6:5 **11:31** [k] S Nu 33:53 [l] Dt 12:10; Jos 11:23 **12:1** [m] Ps 119:5 [n] Dt 4:9-10; 6:15; 1Ki 8:40; Eze 20:19 **12:2** [o] S Nu 21:28 [p] 1Ki 14:23; 2Ki 17:10; Isa 57:5; Jer 2:20; 3:6,13 **12:3** [q] 2Ki 11:18 [r] S Ex 32:20 [s] Ex 34:13; 1Ki 14:15,23 [t] S Ex 23:13 **12:4** [u] ver 30; 2Ki 17:15; Jer 10:2 **12:5** [v] S Ex 20:24; S 2Sa 7:13 [w] ver 11,13; Dt 14:23; 15:20; 16:2,11; 18:6; 26:2; 1Sa 2:29; 1Ki 5:5; 8:16; 9:3; 2Ch 2:4; 6:6; 7:12,16; Ezr 6:12; 7:15; Ps 26:8; 78:68; Zec 2:12 **12:6** [x] S Lev 27:30 [y] S Ge 28:20 [z] Jos 22:27; Isa 66:20 **12:7** [a] S Ex 18:12 [b] S Lev 23:40; Ecc 3:12-13; 5:18-20; S Isa 62:9 **12:8** [c] Jdg 17:6; 21:25 **12:9** [d] S Ex 33:14; Dt 3:20; Ps 95:11; Mic 2:10 [e] Dt 4:21 **12:10** [f] S Dt 11:31 [g] S Ex 33:14 **12:11** [h] S ver 5 [i] S Lev 1:3; Jos 22:23 **12:12** [j] ver 7 [k] Dt 26:11-13 [l] S Nu 18:20 **12:13** [m] S ver 5 **12:14** [n] ver 11

11:26–30 The blessings and curses proclaimed on Mount Gerizim and Mount Ebal are detailed in chs. 27–28.
11:28 *known.* Experienced or acknowledged (see 13:2,6,13; 28:64; 29:26; 32:17; see also note on Ex 6:3).
11:30 *great trees of Moreh.* See note on Ge 12:6. *Arabah.* See note on 1:1. The Canaanites who lived there controlled the territory around Gerizim and Ebal. *Gilgal.* See Jos 4:19 and note.
12:2 *under every spreading tree.* See note on 2Ki 16:4.
12:3 *altars ... sacred stones ... Asherah poles.* See note on 7:5.
12:4 *in their way.* The rituals and accessories of idolatrous worship were not to be used to worship the Lord, the one true God (cf. vv. 29–31). Everything that does not honor him must be eliminated from his people's worship (see Mic 5:10–14 and note).
12:5 *the place the LORD ... will choose ... to put his Name.* The tabernacle, the Lord's dwelling place during the wilderness journey, will be located in the city in Canaan where the Lord would choose to dwell. Moses stresses the importance of centralizing the place of worship (ultimately Jerusalem) as he prepares the people for settlement in the promised land, where the Canaanites had established many places of worship. See vv. 11,14,18,21,26; 14:23–24; 16:2,6,11; 26:2. *his Name.* Since in the ancient Semitic world "name" often stood for the essence of the thing named, God's "Name" is equivalent to his presence (see notes on Ex 3:13–15; 23:21; 2Sa 7:13; 1Ki 5:5).
12:6 See v. 11 and chart, p. 164.
12:7 *rejoice in everything you have put your hand to.* The Lord wants his people to enjoy the fruit of their labor, because it is the result of his blessing (see v. 18; cf. Ecc 2:24–25 and note; 5:18–20).
12:8 *as we do here today.* The Israelites were not able to follow all the procedures of the sacrificial system during the wilderness wandering and conquest periods. Moses was giving directives for their worship and way of life when settled in the land (vv. 10–14). *as they see fit.* See note on Jdg 17:6.
12:9 *resting place.* See note on 3:20.
12:11 *dwelling for his Name.* See note on v. 5.
12:12 *rejoice before the LORD.* Joy, based on the Lord's blessings, was to be a major feature of Hebrew life and worship in the promised land (vv. 7,18). *Levites ... have no ... inheritance.* See 10:9; Nu 18:1–8,20,24 and note on 18:1.
12:13 *not ... anywhere you please.* Sacrifices and offerings to the Lord were to be brought only to the central sanctuary, not to the various Canaanite worship sites (see v. 5 and note).

15 Nevertheless, you may slaughter
your animals in any of your towns and
eat as much of the meat as you want,
as if it were gazelle or deer,[o] according
to the blessing the LORD your God gives
you. Both the ceremonially unclean and
the clean may eat it. 16 But you must not
eat the blood;[p] pour[q] it out on the ground
like water.[r] 17 You must not eat in your
own towns the tithe[s] of your grain and
new wine and olive oil,[t] or the firstborn
of your herds and flocks, or whatever you
have vowed to give,[u] or your freewill offerings or special gifts.[v] 18 Instead, you are to
eat[w] them in the presence of the LORD your
God at the place the LORD your God will
choose[x]—you, your sons and daughters,
your male and female servants, and the
Levites from your towns—and you are to
rejoice[y] before the LORD your God in everything you put your hand to. 19 Be careful
not to neglect the Levites[z] as long as you
live in your land.[a]
20 When the LORD your God has enlarged
your territory[b] as he promised[c] you, and
you crave meat[d] and say, "I would like
some meat," then you may eat as much
of it as you want. 21 If the place where the
LORD your God chooses to put his Name[e]
is too far away from you, you may slaughter animals from the herds and flocks the
LORD has given you, as I have commanded you, and in your own towns you may
eat as much of them as you want.[f] 22 Eat
them as you would gazelle or deer.[g] Both
the ceremonially unclean and the clean
may eat. 23 But be sure you do not eat the
blood,[h] because the blood is the life, and
you must not eat the life with the meat.[i]
24 You must not eat the blood; pour it out
on the ground like water.[j] 25 Do not eat it,
so that it may go well[k] with you and your
children after you, because you will be doing what is right[l] in the eyes of the LORD.
26 But take your consecrated things and
whatever you have vowed to give,[m] and go
to the place the LORD will choose. 27 Present your burnt offerings[n] on the altar of
the LORD your God, both the meat and the
blood. The blood of your sacrifices must
be poured beside the altar of the LORD
your God, but you may eat[o] the meat. 28 Be
careful to obey all these regulations I am
giving you, so that it may always go well[p]
with you and your children after you, because you will be doing what is good and
right in the eyes of the LORD your God.
29 The LORD your God will cut off[q] before you the nations you are about to invade and dispossess. But when you have
driven them out and settled in their land,[r]
30 and after they have been destroyed before you, be careful not to be ensnared[s] by
inquiring about their gods, saying, "How
do these nations serve their gods? We will
do the same."[t] 31 You must not worship the
LORD your God in their way, because in
worshiping their gods, they do all kinds
of detestable things the LORD hates.[u] They
even burn their sons[v] and daughters in the
fire as sacrifices to their gods.[w]
32 See that you do all I command you; do
not add[x] to it or take away from it.[a]

Worshiping Other Gods

13 [b] If a prophet,[y] or one who foretells
by dreams,[z] appears among you
and announces to you a sign or wonder,
2 and if the sign[a] or wonder spoken of takes
place, and the prophet says, "Let us follow
other gods"[b] (gods you have not known)
"and let us worship them," 3 you must
not listen to the words of that prophet[c] or
dreamer.[d] The LORD your God is testing[e]
you to find out whether you love[f] him with
all your heart and with all your soul. 4 It is
the LORD your God you must follow,[g] and
him you must revere.[h] Keep his commands
and obey him; serve him and hold fast[i] to
him. 5 That prophet or dreamer must be
put to death[j] for inciting rebellion against
the LORD your God, who brought you out
of Egypt and redeemed you from the land
of slavery. That prophet or dreamer tried
to turn[k] you from the way the LORD your
God commanded you to follow. You must
purge the evil[l] from among you.
6 If your very own brother, or your son
or daughter, or the wife you love, or your

a 32 In Hebrew texts this verse (12:32) is numbered 13:1. *b* In Hebrew texts 13:1-18 is numbered 13:2-19.

12:15 [o]ver 22; Dt 14:5; 15:22 **12:16** [p]S Ge 9:4; Ac 15:20 [q]ver 23-24; S Ge 35:14; 1Ch 11:18; Jer 7:18 [r]S Lev 17:13; S Dt 15:23; Jn 19:34 **12:17** [s]S Lev 27:30 [t]S Nu 18:12 [u]ver 26; Nu 18:19 [v]Dt 14:23; 15:20 **12:18** [w]Dt 14:23; 15:20 [x]ver 5 [y]ver 7, 12; Dt 14:26; Ne 8:10; Ecc 3:12-13; 5:18-20 **12:19** [z]ver 12; Dt 14:27; Ne 13:10 [a]Mal 3:8 **12:20** [b]S Ex 34:24 [c]S Ge 15:8; S Dt 11:24 [d]S Ex 16:3 **12:21** [e]Dt 14:24 [f]Lev 17:4 **12:22** [g]S ver 15 **12:23** [h]Ge 9:4; S Lev 7:26 [i]Eze 33:25 **12:24** [j]ver 16 **12:25** [k]S Dt 4:40 [l]ver 28; Ex 15:26; Dt 13:18; 1Ki 11:38; 2Ki 12:2 **12:26** [m]S ver 17; Nu 5:9-10 **12:27** [n]S Lev 1:13 [o]Lev 3:1-17 **12:28** [p]Dt 4:40; Ecc 8:12 **12:29** [q]Jos 23:4 [r]S Dt 6:10 **12:30** [s]S Ex 10:7 [t]S ver 4 **12:31** [u]S Lev 18:25 [v]S Lev 18:21 [w]S 2Ki 3:27 **12:32** [x]S Dt 4:2; Rev 22:18-19 **13:1** [y]Mt 24:24; Mk 13:22; 2Th 2:9 [z]S Ge 20:3; Jer 23:25; 27:9; 29:8 **13:2** [a]Dt 18:22; 1Sa 2:34; 10:9; 2Ki 19:29; 20:9; Isa 7:11 [b]S Dt 11:28 **13:3** [c]2Pe 2:1 [d]1Sa 28:6, 15 [e]S Ge 22:1; 1Ki 13:18; 22:22-23; Jer 29:31; 43:2; Eze 13:9; 1Co 11:19 [f]Dt 6:5 **13:4** [g]2Ki 23:3; 2Ch 34:31; 2Jn 1:6 [h]S Dt 6:13; S Ps 5:7 [i]S Dt 10:20 **13:5** [j]S Ex 21:12; S 22:20 [k]ver 10; Dt 4:19 [l]Dt 17:7, 12; 19:19; 24:7; Jdg 20:13; S 1Co 5:13

12:15,22 *ceremonially unclean.* See note on Lev 4:12.
12:16,24 *you must not eat the blood.* See notes on Ge 9:4; Lev 7:11.
12:31 *burn … sons and daughters … as sacrifices.* See 18:10; see also note on Lev 18:21.
12:32 *do not add … or take away.* See note on 4:2.
13:1-5 Eventual fulfillment is one test of true prophecy (18:21-22), but the more stringent rule given here guards against intelligent foresight masquerading as prophecy and against coincidental fulfillment of the predictions of false prophets (cf. Isa 8:20).
13:3 *testing.* See note on Ge 22:1. *all your heart.* See note on 4:29.
13:4 *hold fast.* See note on 10:20.
13:5 *prophet … must be put to death.* See 18:20; Jer 28:15-17. *You must purge the evil from among you.* Repeated in 17:7; 19:19; 21:21; 22:21,24; 24:7, and quoted in 1Co 5:13. The purpose was to eliminate the evildoers as well as the evil itself.

closest friend secretly entices[m] you, saying,
"Let us go and worship other gods"[n] (gods
that neither you nor your ancestors have
known, 7 gods of the peoples around you,
whether near or far, from one end of the
land to the other), 8 do not yield[o] to them
or listen to them. Show them no pity.[p] Do
not spare them or shield them. 9 You must
certainly put them to death.[q] Your hand[r]
must be the first in putting them to death,
and then the hands of all the people.
10 Stone them to death, because they tried
to turn you away[s] from the LORD your God,
who brought you out of Egypt, out of the
land of slavery. 11 Then all Israel will hear
and be afraid,[t] and no one among you will
do such an evil thing again.

12 If you hear it said about one of the
towns the LORD your God is giving you to
live in 13 that troublemakers[u] have arisen
among you and have led the people of their
town astray, saying, "Let us go and worship
other gods" (gods you have not known),
14 then you must inquire, probe and investigate it thoroughly.[v] And if it is true and it
has been proved that this detestable thing
has been done among you,[w] 15 you must
certainly put to the sword all who live in
that town. You must destroy it complete-
ly,[a][x] both its people and its livestock.[y] 16 You
are to gather all the plunder of the town
into the middle of the public square and
completely burn the town[z] and all its plunder as a whole burnt offering to the LORD
your God.[a] That town is to remain a ruin[b]
forever, never to be rebuilt, 17 and none of
the condemned things[a] are to be found in
your hands. Then the LORD will turn from
his fierce anger,[c] will show you mercy,[d] and
will have compassion[e] on you. He will increase your numbers,[f] as he promised[g] on
oath to your ancestors— 18 because you
obey the LORD your God by keeping all his
commands that I am giving you today and
doing what is right[h] in his eyes.

Clean and Unclean Food

14:3-20pp — Lev 11:1-23

14 You are the children[i] of the LORD
your God. Do not cut yourselves
or shave the front of your heads for the
dead, 2 for you are a people holy[j] to the
LORD your God.[k] Out of all the peoples on
the face of the earth, the LORD has chosen
you to be his treasured possession.[l]

3 Do not eat any detestable thing.[m]
4 These are the animals you may eat:[n] the
ox, the sheep, the goat,[o] 5 the deer,[p] the gazelle, the roe deer, the wild goat,[q] the ibex,
the antelope and the mountain sheep.[b]
6 You may eat any animal that has a divided hoof and that chews the cud. 7 However, of those that chew the cud or that
have a divided hoof you may not eat the
camel, the rabbit or the hyrax. Although
they chew the cud, they do not have a divided hoof; they are ceremonially unclean
for you. 8 The pig is also unclean; although
it has a divided hoof, it does not chew the
cud. You are not to eat their meat or touch
their carcasses.[r]

9 Of all the creatures living in the water,
you may eat any that has fins and scales.
10 But anything that does not have fins and
scales you may not eat; for you it is unclean.

11 You may eat any clean bird. 12 But these
you may not eat: the eagle, the vulture, the
black vulture, 13 the red kite, the black kite,
any kind[s] of falcon,[t] 14 any kind of raven,[u]
15 the horned owl, the screech owl, the gull,
any kind of hawk, 16 the little owl, the great
owl, the white owl, 17 the desert owl,[v] the
osprey, the cormorant, 18 the stork, any kind
of heron, the hoopoe and the bat.

19 All flying insects are unclean to you;
do not eat them. 20 But any winged creature that is clean you may eat.[w]

21 Do not eat anything you find already
dead.[x] You may give it to the foreigner residing in any of your towns, and they may
eat it, or you may sell it to any other foreigner. But you are a people holy to the
LORD your God.[y]

Do not cook a young goat in its mother's milk.[z]

13:6 [m] Dt 17:2-7; 29:18 [n] S Dt 11:28 **13:8** [o] Pr 1:10 [p] S Dt 7:2 **13:9** [q] ver 5 [r] S Lev 24:14 **13:10** [s] S Ex 20:3 **13:11** [t] Dt 17:13; 19:20; 21:21; 1Ti 5:20 **13:13** [u] ver 2, 6; Jdg 19:22; 20:13; 1Sa 2:12; 10:27; 11:12; 25:17; 1Ki 21:10 **13:14** [v] Jdg 20:12 [w] Dt 17:4 **13:15** [x] Isa 24:6; 34:5; 43:28; 47:6; La 2:6; Da 9:11; Zec 8:13; Mal 4:6 [y] Ex 22:20 **13:16** [z] 2Ki 25:9; Jer 39:8; 52:13; Eze 16:41 [a] Dt 7:25, 26; Jos 6:24 [b] Jos 8:28; Isa 7:16; 17:1; 24:10; 25:2; 27:10; 32:14, 19; 37:26; Jer 49:2; Mic 1:6 **13:17** [c] Ex 32:12; Nu 25:4 [d] S Ge 43:14 [e] Dt 30:3 [f] S Dt 7:13 [g] S Ge 12:2; S 13:14; S 26:24 **13:18** [h] S Dt 12:25 **14:1** [i] Lev 19:28; S Jn 1:12; S Ro 8:14; 9:8 **14:2** [j] S Ge 28:14; Ex 22:31; Isa 6:13; Mal 2:15 [k] S Lev 20:26; Ro 12:1 [l] S Ex 8:22; S Dt 7:6 **14:3** [m] Eze 4:14 **14:4** [n] Ac 10:14 [o] S Lev 7:23 **14:5** [p] S Dt 12:15 [q] Job 39:1; Ps 104:18 **14:8** [r] S Lev 5:2 **14:13** [s] S Ge 1:11 [t] Isa 34:15 **14:14** [u] S Ge 8:7 **14:17** [v] Ps 102:6; Isa 13:21; 14:23; 34:11; Zep 2:14 **14:20** [w] S Lev 20:25 **14:21** [x] S Lev 11:39 [y] ver 2 [z] S Ex 23:19

[a] *15,17* The Hebrew term refers to the irrevocable giving over of things or persons to the LORD, often by totally destroying them. [b] *5* The precise identification of some of the birds and animals in this chapter is uncertain.

13:13 *troublemakers.* See 1Sa 1:16; 2:12; 25:17. The same Hebrew word is also used, e.g., in 1Sa 30:22; 1Sa 10:27; 1Ki 21:10,13 ("scoundrels"); Job 34:18 ("worthless"); Pr 6:12. Later, this word (*beliyya'al* in Hebrew) was used as a name for Satan (2Co 6:15; Greek *Beliar*, a variant of *Belial*), who is the personification of wickedness and lawlessness.

13:15 *destroy it completely.* See NIV text note and note on 2:34.

14:1 *cut yourselves.* A pagan religious custom (see 1Ki 18:28). *shave the front of your heads.* Shaving the forehead was a practice of mourners in Canaan.

14:2,21 *holy to the LORD.* See note on Lev 11:44. The regulations regarding clean and unclean foods were intended to separate Israel from things the Lord had identified as detestable and ceremonially unclean.

14:2 *a people holy to the LORD.* See Ex 3:5 and note; 19:6. *treasured possession.* See note on Ex 19:5.

14:3–21 The subject of clean and unclean food is discussed in greater detail in Lev 11 (see notes there).

14:7 *ceremonially unclean.* See note on Lev 4:12.

14:21 *Do not eat ... already dead.* Because of the prohibition against eating blood, since the dead animal's blood would

Woman with captured camels (728 BC). God declares camels to be unclean food in Deuteronomy 14:7.
{im Walton, courtesy of the British Museum

Tithes

22 Be sure to set aside a tenth[a] of all that
your fields produce each year. 23 Eat[b] the
tithe of your grain, new wine[c] and olive
oil, and the firstborn of your herds and
'locks in the presence of the LORD your
God at the place he will choose as a dwelling for his Name,[d] so that you may learn[e]
:o revere[f] the LORD your God always. 24 But
f that place is too distant and you have
been blessed by the LORD your God and
cannot carry your tithe (because the place
where the LORD will choose to put his
Name is so far away), 25 then exchange[g]
your tithe for silver, and take the silver
with you and go to the place the LORD your
God will choose. 26 Use the silver to buy
whatever you like: cattle, sheep, wine or
other fermented drink,[h] or anything you
wish. Then you and your household shall
eat there in the presence of the LORD your
God and rejoice.[i] 27 And do not neglect the
Levites[j] living in your towns, for they have
no allotment or inheritance of their own.[k]

14:22 [a]S Ge 14:20; S Lev 27:30; S Nu 18:21 **14:23** [b]S Dt 12:17, 18 [c]Ps 4:7 [d]S Dt 12:5; 1Ki 3:2 [e]S Dt 4:10 [f]Ps 22:23; 33:8; Mal 2:5 **14:25** [g]Mt 21:12; Jn 2:14 **14:26** [h]S Lev 10:9; Ecc 10:16-17 [i]S Lev 23:40; S Dt 12:18 **14:27** [j]S Dt 12:19 [k]S Nu 18:20; 26:62; Dt 18:1-2 **14:28** [l]S Lev 27:30 [m]Dt 26:12 **14:29** [n]Ge 47:22 [o]Nu 26:62 [p]Dt 16:11; 24:19-21; Ps 94:6; Isa 1:17; 58:6 [q]S Dt 6:11

28 At the end of every three years, bring
all the tithes[l] of that year's produce and
store it in your towns,[m] 29 so that the Levites (who have no allotment[n] or inheritance[o] of their own) and the foreigners,[p]
the fatherless and the widows who live in
your towns may come and eat and be satisfied,[q] and so that the LORD your God may
bless[r] you in all the work of your hands.

The Year for Canceling Debts

15:1-11Ref — Lev 25:8-38

15 At the end of every seven years you
must cancel debts.[s] 2 This is how it
is to be done: Every creditor shall cancel
any loan they have made to a fellow Israelite. They shall not require payment
from anyone among their own people, because the LORD's time for canceling debts
has been proclaimed. 3 You may require
payment from a foreigner,[t] but you must
cancel any debt your fellow Israelite owes

[r]Dt 15:10; Ps 41:1; Pr 22:9; Mal 3:10 **15:1** [s]Dt 31:10; Ne 10:31 **15:3** [t]S Ge 31:15; Dt 23:20; 28:12; Ru 2:10

not be properly drained (see 12:16,24; see also notes on Ge :4; Lev 17:11). *Do not cook a young goat in its mother's milk.* ee note on Ex 23:19.

4:22–29 See Nu 18:21–29. Taken together, the two passages uggest the following: (1) Annually, a tenth of all Israelite pro uce was to be taken to the city of the central sanctuary for istribution to the Levites. (2) At that time, at an initial festival, ll Israelites ate part of the tithe. (3) The rest, which would be y far the major part of it, belonged to the Levites. (4) Every hird year the tithe was gathered in the towns and stored for istribution to the Levites and the less fortunate: foreigners, fatherless and widows (see 26:12). (5) The Levites were to present to the Lord a tenth of their tithe. See note on Lev 27:30.

14:22 *set aside a tenth.* See notes on Ge 14:20; 28:22.

14:23 *dwelling for his Name.* See note on 12:5.

14:25 *silver.* Pieces of silver of various weights were a common medium of exchange, but not in the form of coins (see note on Ge 20:16).

15:1 *every seven years.* See Ex 23:10–11; Lev 25:1–7 and note on 25:4.

15:3 *require payment from a foreigner.* Since he was not subject to the command to allow his fields to lie fallow during

you. 4 However, there need be no poor people among you, for in the land the LORD your God is giving you to possess as your inheritance, he will richly bless[u] you, 5 if only you fully obey the LORD your God and are careful to follow[v] all these commands I am giving you today. 6 For the LORD your God will bless you as he has promised, and you will lend to many nations but will borrow from none. You will rule over many nations but none will rule over you.[w]

7 If anyone is poor[x] among your fellow Israelites in any of the towns of the land the LORD your God is giving you, do not be hardhearted or tightfisted[y] toward them. 8 Rather, be openhanded[z] and freely lend them whatever they need. 9 Be careful not to harbor this wicked thought: "The seventh year, the year for canceling debts,[a] is near," so that you do not show ill will[b] toward the needy among your fellow Israelites and give them nothing. They may then appeal to the LORD against you, and you will be found guilty of sin.[c] 10 Give generously to them and do so without a grudging heart;[d] then because of this the LORD your God will bless[e] you in all your work and in everything you put your hand to. 11 There will always be poor people[f] in the land. Therefore I command you to be openhanded toward your fellow Israelites who are poor and needy in your land.[g]

Freeing Servants

15:12-18pp — Ex 21:2-6
15:12-18Ref — Lev 25:38-55

12 If any of your people — Hebrew men or women — sell themselves to you and serve you six years, in the seventh year you must let them go free.[h] 13 And when you release them, do not send them away empty-handed. 14 Supply them liberally from your flock, your threshing floor[i] and your winepress. Give to them as the LORD your God has blessed you. 15 Remember that you were slaves[j] in Egypt and the LORD your God redeemed you.[k] That is why I give you this command today.

16 But if your servant says to you, "I do not want to leave you," because he loves you and your family and is well off with you, 17 then take an awl and push it through his earlobe into the door, and he will become your servant for life. Do the same for your female servant.

18 Do not consider it a hardship to set your servant free, because their service to you these six years has been worth twice as much as that of a hired hand. And the LORD your God will bless you in everything you do.

The Firstborn Animals

19 Set apart for the LORD[l] your God every firstborn male[m] of your herds and flocks.[n] Do not put the firstborn of your cows to work, and do not shear the firstborn of your sheep.[o] 20 Each year you and your family are to eat them in the presence of the LORD your God at the place he will choose.[p] 21 If an animal has a defect,[q] is lame or blind, or has any serious flaw, you must not sacrifice it to the LORD your God.[r] 22 You are to eat it in your own towns. Both the ceremonially unclean and the clean may eat it, as if it were gazelle or deer.[s] 23 But you must not eat the blood; pour it out on the ground like water.[t]

The Passover

16:1-8pp — Ex 12:14-20; Lev 23:4-8; Nu 28:16-25

16 Observe the month of Aviv[u] and celebrate the Passover[v] of the LORD your God, because in the month of Aviv he brought you out of Egypt by night. 2 Sacrifice as the Passover to the LORD your God an animal from your flock or herd at

15:4 [u] Dt 28:8
15:5 [v] S Ex 15:26; Dt 7:12; 28:1
15:6 [w] Dt 28:12-13,44
15:7 [x] ver 11; Mt 26:11 [y] 1Jn 3:17
15:8 [z] Mt 5:42; Lk 6:34; S Ac 24:17
15:9 [a] ver 1 [b] Mt 20:15 [c] S Ex 22:23; S Job 5:15; Jas 5:4
15:10 [d] 2Co 9:5 [e] S Dt 14:29
15:11 [f] S ver 7 [g] Mt 26:11; Mk 14:7; Jn 12:8
15:12 [h] Jer 34:14
15:14 [i] S Nu 18:27
15:15 [j] Ex 13:3; Jer 34:13 [k] Ex 20:2; S Dt 4:34; S 9:26; 16:12; 24:18; Jer 16:14; 23:7
15:19 [l] S Lev 27:9 [m] S Ex 13:2 [n] S Ge 4:4 [o] S Ex 22:30
15:20 [p] S Lev 7:15-18; Dt 12:5-7, 17,18
15:21 [q] S Ex 12:5 [r] S Lev 22:19-25; Dt 17:1; Mal 1:8,13
15:22 [s] S Dt 12:15
15:23 [t] S Ge 9:4; Dt 12:16; Eze 33:25
16:1 [u] S Ex 12:2 [v] S Ex 12:11; 2Ki 23:21; Mt 26:17-29

the seventh year, a foreigner would probably be financially able to pay his debts if asked to do so.

15:4 *there need be no poor people among you.* Because of the Lord's reward for obedience (vv. 4–6) and because of the sabbath-year arrangement (vv. 7–11). This "year for canceling debts" (v. 9) gave Israelites who had experienced economic reverses a way to gain release from indebtedness and so, in a measure, a way to equalize wealth. Cf. the provisions of the Year of Jubilee (see Lev 25:8–38 and notes).

15:6 *you will lend.* If Israel failed to follow the Lord's commands, the reverse would be true (see 28:43–44).

15:11 *There will always be poor people.* See also Jesus' statement in Mt 26:11. Even in the best of societies under the most enlightened laws, the uncertainties of life and the variations among citizens result in some people becoming poor. In such cases the Lord commands that generosity and kindness be extended to them.

15:15 *Remember.* See note on 4:10.

15:16 *because he loves you.* In Ex 21:5 an additional reason is given: The servant may want to stay with his family.

15:17 *take an awl and push it through his earlobe.* See note on Ex 21:6.

15:18 *worth twice as much.* A Hebrew servant worked twice as many years as the Code of Hammurapi, e.g., required for release from debt (see chart, p. xxii). Other ancient legal texts, however, support "equivalent to" as a possible translation of the phrase.

15:19 *Set apart ... every firstborn male.* Because the Lord saved his people from the plague of death on the firstborn in Egypt (see Ex 12:12,29; 13:2,15 and note on 13:2).

15:21 *If an animal has a defect ... you must not sacrifice it.* See note on Lev 1:3.

15:22 *ceremonially unclean.* See note on Lev 4:12.

15:23 See 12:16,24; see also notes on Ge 9:4; Lev 17:11.

16:1–17 See chart, pp. 188–189; see also Ex 23:14–19; 34:18–26; Lev 23:4–44; Nu 28:16—29:40 and notes.

16:1–8 See Ex 12:1–28; 13:1–16 and notes.

16:1 *Aviv.* See chart, p. 113.

the place the LORD will choose as a dwelling for his Name.[w] 3 Do not eat it with
bread made with yeast, but for seven days
eat unleavened bread, the bread of affliction,[x] because you left Egypt in haste[y]—so
that all the days of your life you may remember the time of your departure from
Egypt.[z] 4 Let no yeast be found in your possession in all your land for seven days. Do
not let any of the meat you sacrifice on
the evening[a] of the first day remain until
morning.[b]
5 You must not sacrifice the Passover in
any town the LORD your God gives you 6 except in the place he will choose as a dwelling for his Name. There you must sacrifice
the Passover in the evening, when the sun
goes down, on the anniversary[ac] of your
departure from Egypt. 7 Roast[d] it and eat it
at the place the LORD your God will choose.
Then in the morning return to your tents.
8 For six days eat unleavened bread and on
the seventh day hold an assembly[e] to the
LORD your God and do no work.[f]

The Festival of Weeks

16:9-12pp — Lev 23:15-22; Nu 28:26-31

9 Count off seven weeks[g] from the time
you begin to put the sickle to the standing grain.[h] 10 Then celebrate the Festival of
Weeks to the LORD your God by giving a
freewill offering in proportion to the blessings the LORD your God has given you.
11 And rejoice[i] before the LORD your God
at the place he will choose as a dwelling
for his Name[j]—you, your sons and daughters, your male and female servants, the
Levites[k] in your towns, and the foreigners,[l]
the fatherless and the widows living among
you.[m] 12 Remember that you were slaves in
Egypt,[n] and follow carefully these decrees.

The Festival of Tabernacles

16:13-17pp — Lev 23:33-43; Nu 29:12-39

13 Celebrate the Festival of Tabernacles
for seven days after you have gathered the
produce of your threshing floor[o] and your
winepress.[p] 14 Be joyful[q] at your festival—
you, your sons and daughters, your male
and female servants, and the Levites, the
foreigners, the fatherless and the widows
who live in your towns. 15 For seven days
celebrate the festival to the LORD your God
at the place the LORD will choose. For the
LORD your God will bless you in all your
harvest and in all the work of your hands,
and your joy[r] will be complete.
16 Three times a year all your men must
appear[s] before the LORD your God at the
place he will choose: at the Festival of
Unleavened Bread,[t] the Festival of Weeks
and the Festival of Tabernacles.[u] No one
should appear before the LORD empty-
handed:[v] 17 Each of you must bring a gift in
proportion to the way the LORD your God
has blessed you.

Judges

18 Appoint judges[w] and officials for each
of your tribes in every town the LORD your
God is giving you, and they shall judge
the people fairly.[x] 19 Do not pervert justice[y]
or show partiality.[z] Do not accept a bribe,[a]
for a bribe blinds the eyes of the wise and
twists the words of the innocent. 20 Follow
justice and justice alone, so that you may
live and possess the land the LORD your
God is giving you.

Worshiping Other Gods

21 Do not set up any wooden Asherah
pole[b] beside the altar you build to the LORD
your God,[c] 22 and do not erect a sacred
stone,[d] for these the LORD your God hates.

17 Do not sacrifice to the LORD your
God an ox or a sheep that has any
defect[e] or flaw in it, for that would be detestable[f] to him.[g]
2 If a man or woman living among you
in one of the towns the LORD gives you is
found doing evil in the eyes of the LORD
your God in violation of his covenant,[h]
3 and contrary to my command[i] has worshiped other gods,[j] bowing down to them
or to the sun[k] or the moon or the stars
in the sky,[l] 4 and this has been brought to
your attention, then you must investigate
it thoroughly. If it is true[m] and it has been
proved that this detestable thing has been
done in Israel,[n] 5 take the man or woman
who has done this evil deed to your city
gate and stone that person to death.[o] 6 On
the testimony of two or three witnesses a

16:2 [w] Dt 12:5, 26
16:3 [x] Ex 12:8, 39; 34:18; 1Co 5:8 [y] S Ex 12:11 [z] Dt 4:9
16:4 [a] S Ex 12:6 [b] S Ex 12:8; Mk 14:12
16:6 [c] S Ex 12:42
16:7 [d] S Ex 12:8
16:8 [e] Ex 13:6; S Lev 23:8 [f] Mt 26:17; Lk 2:41; 22:7; Jn 2:13
16:9 [g] Ac 2:1 [h] S Ex 23:16
16:11 [i] Dt 12:7 [j] S Ex 20:24; S 2Sa 7:13 [k] Dt 12:12 [l] S Dt 14:29 [m] Ne 8:10
16:12 [n] S Dt 15:15
16:13 [o] S Lev 2:14 [p] S Ge 27:37; S Ex 23:16
16:14 [q] ver 11
16:15 [r] Job 38:7; Ps 4:7; 28:7; 30:11
16:16 [s] Dt 31:11; Ps 84:7 [t] S Ex 12:17 [u] S Ex 23:14, 16; Ezr 3:4 [v] S Ex 34:20
16:18 [w] S Ex 18:21,26 [x] S Ge 31:37
16:19 [y] S Ex 23:2 [z] S Lev 19:15 [a] S Ex 18:21; S 1Sa 8:3
16:21 [b] S Dt 7:5 [c] Ex 34:13; 1Ki 14:15; 2Ki 17:16; 21:3; 2Ch 33:3
16:22 [d] S Ex 23:24
17:1 [e] S Ex 12:5; S Lev 22:20 [f] Dt 7:25 [g] S Dt 15:21
17:2 [h] Dt 13:6-11
17:3 [i] Jer 7:31 [j] Ex 22:20 [k] S Ge 1:16 [l] S Ge 2:1; S 37:9
17:4 [m] Dt 22:20 [n] Dt 13:12-14
17:5 [o] S Lev 24:14

[a] 6 Or *down, at the time of day*

16:3,12 *remember.* See note on 4:10.
16:7 *to your tents.* To wherever they were staying while at the festival, whether in permanent or temporary quarters.
16:8 *assembly.* That is, the closing assembly (see Lev 23:36).
16:9 *seven weeks.* Symbolizing the full season of grain harvest.
16:10 *giving … in proportion to.* See v. 17; cf. 1Co 16:2; 2Co 8:12 and notes.
16:15 *your joy will be complete.* As a result of God's blessing (cf. Jn 3:29; 15:11; 16:24; Php 2:2; 1Jn 1:4; 2Jn 12).
16:16 *Three times a year.* The three annual pilgrimage festivals (see Ex 23:14,17; 34:23; see also chart, pp. 188–189).
16:18–20 Cf. 1:9–18; Ex 18:13–26.
16:19 Israel must emulate the Lord in these matters (see 10:17; see also Ex 23:8 and note).
16:21–22 *Asherah pole … sacred stone.* See note on 7:5.
17:1 *defect or flaw.* See note on Lev 1:3.
17:3 *bowing down to … the sun or the moon or the stars.* See 4:19 and note.
17:6 *two or three witnesses.* A further specification of the law

person is to be put to death, but no one is
to be put to death on the testimony of only
one witness.[p] 7The hands of the witnesses
must be the first in putting that person to
death,[q] and then the hands of all the people.[r] You must purge the evil[s] from among
you.

Law Courts

8If cases come before your courts that
are too difficult for you to judge[t]—whether bloodshed, lawsuits or assaults[u]—take
them to the place the LORD your God will
choose.[v] 9Go to the Levitical[w] priests and
to the judge[x] who is in office at that time.
Inquire of them and they will give you the
verdict.[y] 10You must act according to the
decisions they give you at the place the
LORD will choose. Be careful to do everything they instruct you to do. 11Act according to whatever they teach you and the
decisions they give you. Do not turn aside
from what they tell you, to the right or to
the left.[z] 12Anyone who shows contempt[a]
for the judge or for the priest who stands
ministering[b] there to the LORD your God
is to be put to death.[c] You must purge the
evil from Israel.[d] 13All the people will hear
and be afraid, and will not be contemptuous again.[e]

The King

14When you enter the land the LORD
your God is giving you and have taken
possession[f] of it and settled in it,[g] and you
say, "Let us set a king over us like all the
nations around us,"[h] 15be sure to appoint[i]
over you a king the LORD your God chooses. He must be from among your fellow
Israelites.[j] Do not place a foreigner over
you, one who is not an Israelite. 16The
king, moreover, must not acquire great
numbers of horses[k] for himself[l] or make
the people return to Egypt[m] to get more of
them,[n] for the LORD has told you, "You are
not to go back that way again."[o] 17He must
not take many wives,[p] or his heart will be
led astray.[q] He must not accumulate[r] large
amounts of silver and gold.[s]
18When he takes the throne[t] of his kingdom, he is to write[u] for himself on a scroll
a copy[v] of this law, taken from that of the
Levitical priests. 19It is to be with him, and
he is to read it all the days of his life[w] so
that he may learn to revere the LORD his
God and follow carefully all the words of
this law and these decrees[x] 20and not consider himself better than his fellow Israelites and turn from the law[y] to the right or
to the left.[z] Then he and his descendants
will reign a long time over his kingdom
in Israel.[a]

Offerings for Priests and Levites

18 The Levitical[b] priests—indeed, the
whole tribe of Levi—are to have
no allotment or inheritance with Israel.
They shall live on the food offerings[c] presented to the LORD, for that is their inheritance.[d] 2They shall have no inheritance
among their fellow Israelites; the LORD is
their inheritance,[e] as he promised them.[f]
3This is the share due the priests[g] from
the people who sacrifice a bull[h] or a sheep:
the shoulder, the internal organs and the
meat from the head.[i] 4You are to give them
the firstfruits of your grain, new wine and
olive oil, and the first wool from the shearing of your sheep,[j] 5for the LORD your God
has chosen them[k] and their descendants
out of all your tribes to stand and minister[l]
in the LORD's name always.[m]
6If a Levite moves from one of your
towns anywhere in Israel where he is living, and comes in all earnestness to the
place the LORD will choose,[n] 7he may min-

17:6 [p] Nu 35:30; Dt 19:15; S Mt 18:16 **17:7** [q] Jn 8:7 [r] S Lev 24:14; Ac 7:58 [s] S Dt 13:5; 1Co 5:13* **17:8** [t] Ex 21:6 [u] 2Ch 19:10 [v] Dt 12:5; Ps 122:3-5 **17:9** [w] Dt 24:8; 27:9 [x] S Ex 21:6 [y] S Ge 25:22; Dt 19:17; Eze 44:24; Hag 2:11 **17:11** [z] S Lev 10:11; S Dt 5:32 **17:12** [a] Nu 15:30 [b] S Nu 16:9 [c] ver 13; S Ge 17:14; Dt 13:11; 18:20; 19:20; 1Ki 18:40; Jer 14:14; Hos 4:4; Zec 13:3 [d] S Dt 13:5 **17:13** [e] S ver 12 **17:14** [f] S Nu 33:53 [g] Jos 21:43 [h] 1Sa 8:5, 19-20; 10:19 **17:15** [i] 1Sa 16:3; 2Sa 5:3 [j] Jer 30:21 **17:16** [k] Isa 2:7; 30:16 [l] 1Sa 8:11; 1Ki 4:26; 9:19; 10:26; 2Ch 1:14; Ps 20:7 [m] 1Ki 10:29; Isa 31:1; Jer 42:14 [n] 1Ki 10:28; Isa 31:1; Eze 17:15 [o] S Ex 13:17 **17:17** [p] S Ex 34:16; 2Sa 5:13; 12:11; 1Ki 11:3; 2Ch 11:21 [q] 1Ki 11:2; Pr 31:3 [r] 1Ki 10:27 [s] 2Ch 1:11; Isa 2:7

17:18 [t] 1Ki 1:46; 1Ch 29:23 [u] Dt 31:22, 24; Jos 24:26; 1Sa 10:25 [v] 2Ch 23:11 **17:19** [w] Dt 4:9-10; Jos 1:8 [x] Dt 11:13; 1Ki 3:3; 11:38; 2Ki 22:2 **17:20** [y] Jos 23:6; Job 23:12; Ps 119:102 [z] S Dt 5:32; S 1Ki 9:4 [a] 1Sa 8:5; 10:25; 1Ki 2:3; 1Ch 28:8 **18:1** [b] Jer 33:18, 21 [c] S Nu 18:8 [d] S Nu 18:20; 1Co 9:13 **18:2** [e] Nu 18:20 [f] Jos 13:14 **18:3** [g] S Ex 29:27 [h] S Lev 1:5 [i] Lev 7:28-34; Nu 18:12 **18:4** [j] Ex 22:29; Nu 18:12 **18:5** [k] S Ex 28:1 [l] Dt 10:8 [m] S Ex 29:9 **18:6** [n] S Nu 35:2-3; S Dt 12:5

---

set forth in Nu 35:30 (see note there). See 19:15; cf. Mt 18:16; 2Co 13:1; 1Ti 5:19; Heb 10:28.

17:7 *You must purge the evil from among you.* See v. 12; see also note on 13:5.

17:14 *a king ... like all the nations around us.* Moses, Joshua and a succession of judges were chosen directly by the Lord to govern Israel on his behalf. As Gideon later said, "The LORD will rule over you" (Jdg 8:23; see note there). Moses here, however, anticipates a time when the people would ask for a king (see 1Sa 8:4–9) contrary to the Lord's ideal for them (see notes on 7:2–5; 1Sa 8:1—12:25; see also Lev 20:23). So Moses gives guidance concerning the eventual selection of a king (vv. 14–20).

17:16–17 The very things that later kings were guilty of, beginning especially with Solomon (1Ki 4:26; 10:14–22; 11:1–4)—except that they did not make Israel return to Egypt (but see Jer 42:13—43:7).

17:18 *write for himself ... a copy of this law.* As a sign of submission to the Lord as his King, and as a guide for his rule in obedience to his heavenly Suzerain. This was required procedure for vassal kings under the suzerainty treaties among the Hittites and others before and during this period (see note on 31:9). See chart, p. 23. *copy of this law.* See Introduction: Title.

17:20 *not consider himself better.* The king was not above God's law, any more than were the humblest of his subjects.

18:1 *no allotment or inheritance.* No private ownership of land. Towns and surrounding pasturelands were set aside for the use of the Levites (Jos 21:41–42), as were the tithes and parts of sacrifices (see 14:22–29; Lev 27:30 and notes; Nu 18:21–29).

18:4 *firstfruits.* See Ex 23:19 and note; 34:26; Lev 23:10–11; Nu 15:18–20; 18:12–13.

18:5 See note on 21:5.

ister in the name[o] of the LORD his God like
all his fellow Levites who serve there in
the presence of the LORD. 8 He is to share
equally in their benefits, even though he
has received money from the sale of family possessions.[p]

Occult Practices

9 When you enter the land the LORD your
God is giving you, do not learn to imitate[q]
the detestable ways[r] of the nations there.
10 Let no one be found among you who
sacrifices their son or daughter in the fire,[s]
who practices divination[t] or sorcery,[u] interprets omens, engages in witchcraft,[v]
11 or casts spells,[w] or who is a medium or
spiritist[x] or who consults the dead. 12 Anyone who does these things is detestable to
the LORD; because of these same detestable practices the LORD your God will drive
out those nations before you.[y] 13 You must
be blameless[z] before the LORD your God.[a]

The Prophet

14 The nations you will dispossess listen
to those who practice sorcery or divination.[b] But as for you, the LORD your God
has not permitted you to do so. 15 The LORD
your God will raise up for you a prophet
like me from among you, from your fellow
Israelites.[c] You must listen to him. 16 For
this is what you asked of the LORD your
God at Horeb on the day of the assembly
when you said, "Let us not hear the voice
of the LORD our God nor see this great fire
anymore, or we will die."[d]

17 The LORD said to me: "What they
say is good. 18 I will raise up for them a
prophet[e] like you from among their fellow Israelites, and I will put my words[f] in
his mouth.[g] He will tell them everything
I command him.[h] 19 I myself will call to
account[i] anyone who does not listen[j] to
my words that the prophet speaks in my
name.[k] 20 But a prophet who presumes to
speak in my name anything I have not
commanded, or a prophet who speaks in
the name of other gods,[l] is to be put to
death."[m]

18:7 [o]ver 19; 1Ki 18:32; 22:16; Ps 118:26 **18:8** [p]Nu 18:24; 2Ch 31:4; Ne 12:44,47; 13:12 **18:9** [q]Dt 9:5; 12:29-31 [r]S Lev 18:3; 2Ki 21:2; 2Ch 28:3; 33:2; 34:33; Ezr 6:21; 9:11; Jer 44:4 **18:10** [s]S Lev 18:21 [t]1Sa 15:23 [u]S Ex 7:11 [v]S Lev 19:31 **18:11** [w]Isa 47:9 [x]S Ex 22:18; S 1Sa 28:13 **18:12** [y]S Lev 18:24 **18:13** [z]S Ge 6:9; Ps 119:1 [a]Mt 5:48 **18:14** [b]2Ki 21:6 **18:15** [c]S Mt 21:11; Lk 2:25-35; Jn 1:21; Ac 3:22*; 7:37* **18:16** [d]S Ex 20:19; Dt 5:23-27 **18:18** [e]S Ge 20:7 [f]Isa 2:3; 26:8; 51:4; Mic 4:2 [g]S Ex 4:12 [h]Jn 4:25-26; S 14:24; Ac 3:22* **18:19** [i]Jos 22:23; Ac 3:23*; Heb 12:25 [j]S Ex 23:21 [k]S ver 7; S Lev 19:12; 2Ki 2:24 **18:20** [l]S Ex 23:13 [m]Dt 13:1-5; S 17:12 **18:22** [n]S Dt 13:2; 1Sa 3:20 [o]1Ki 22:28; Jer 28:9 [p]ver 20 **19:1** [q]Dt 6:10-11 **19:6** [r]S Nu 35:12 **19:8** [s]S Ex 34:24 [t]S Ge 15:8;

21 You may say to yourselves, "How can
we know when a message has not been
spoken by the LORD?" 22 If what a prophet
proclaims in the name of the LORD does
not take place or come true,[n] that is a
message the LORD has not spoken.[o] That
prophet has spoken presumptuously,[p] so
do not be alarmed.

Cities of Refuge

19:1-14Ref — Nu 35:6-34; Dt 4:41-43; Jos 20:1-9

19 When the LORD your God has destroyed the nations whose land he
is giving you, and when you have driven
them out and settled in their towns and
houses,[q] 2 then set aside for yourselves
three cities in the land the LORD your God
is giving you to possess. 3 Determine the
distances involved and divide into three
parts the land the LORD your God is giving you as an inheritance, so that a person
who kills someone may flee for refuge to
one of these cities.

4 This is the rule concerning anyone
who kills a person and flees there for safety — anyone who kills a neighbor unintentionally, without malice aforethought. 5 For
instance, a man may go into the forest
with his neighbor to cut wood, and as he
swings his ax to fell a tree, the head may
fly off and hit his neighbor and kill him.
That man may flee to one of these cities
and save his life. 6 Otherwise, the avenger
of blood[r] might pursue him in a rage, overtake him if the distance is too great, and
kill him even though he is not deserving
of death, since he did it to his neighbor
without malice aforethought. 7 This is why
I command you to set aside for yourselves
three cities.

8 If the LORD your God enlarges your territory,[s] as he promised[t] on oath to your
ancestors, and gives you the whole land
he promised them, 9 because you carefully follow all these laws I command you
today — to love the LORD your God and to
walk always in obedience to him[u] — then

S Dt 11:24 **19:9** [u]Dt 6:5

18:9 *detestable ways of the nations.* What follows is the most complete list of magical or spiritistic arts in the OT. All were practiced in Canaan, and all are condemned and prohibited. The people are not to resort to such sources for their information, guidance or revelation. Rather, they are to listen to the Lord's true prophets (see vv. 14 – 22; Isa 8:19 – 20).

18:10 *sacrifices their son or daughter.* See 12:31; see also note on Lev 18:21.

18:15 *prophet like me.* See 34:10. Verse 16, as well as the general context (see especially vv. 20 – 22), indicates that a series of prophets is meant. At Horeb (Mount Sinai) the people requested that Moses take the message from God and deliver it to them (see Ex 20:19 and note). But now that Moses is to leave them, he says that another spokesman will take his place, and then another will be necessary for the next generation. This is therefore a collective reference to the prophets who will follow. As such, it is also the basis for later Messianic expectation and receives a unique fulfillment in Jesus (see Jn 1:21,25,45; 5:46; 6:14; 7:40; Ac 3:22 – 26; 7:37).

18:16 See Ex 20:18 – 21; Heb 12:18 – 21 and notes.

18:18 *my words in his mouth.* See Ex 4:15 – 16; see also notes on Ex 7:1 – 2; Jer 1:9.

18:20 *prophet who presumes to speak.* See note on 13:1 – 5. *is to be put to death.* See 13:5; Jer 28:15 – 17.

18:21 – 22 See note on 13:1 – 5.

19:1 – 13 See 4:41 – 43; Nu 35:9 – 28; Jos 20 and notes.

you are to set aside three more cities. 10 Do this so that innocent blood[v] will not be shed in your land, which the LORD your God is giving you as your inheritance, and so that you will not be guilty of bloodshed.[w]

11 But if out of hate someone lies in wait, assaults and kills a neighbor,[x] and then flees to one of these cities, 12 the killer shall be sent for by the town elders, be brought back from the city, and be handed over to the avenger of blood to die. 13 Show no pity.[y] You must purge from Israel the guilt of shedding innocent blood,[z] so that it may go well with you.

14 Do not move your neighbor's boundary stone set up by your predecessors in the inheritance you receive in the land the LORD your God is giving you to possess.[a]

Witnesses

15 One witness is not enough to convict anyone accused of any crime or offense they may have committed. A matter must be established by the testimony of two or three witnesses.[b]

16 If a malicious witness[c] takes the stand to accuse someone of a crime, 17 the two people involved in the dispute must stand in the presence of the LORD before the priests and the judges[d] who are in office at the time. 18 The judges must make a thorough investigation,[e] and if the witness proves to be a liar, giving false testimony against a fellow Israelite, 19 then do to the false witness as that witness intended to do to the other party.[f] You must purge the evil from among you. 20 The rest of the people will hear of this and be afraid,[g] and never again will such an evil thing be done among you. 21 Show no pity:[h] life for life, eye for eye, tooth for tooth, hand for hand, foot for foot.[i]

Going to War

20 When you go to war against your enemies and see horses and chariots and an army greater than yours,[j] do not be afraid[k] of them,[l] because the LORD your God, who brought you up out of Egypt, will be with[m] you. 2 When you are about to go into battle, the priest shall come forward and address the army. 3 He shall say: "Hear, Israel: Today you are going into battle against your enemies. Do not be fainthearted[n] or afraid; do not panic or be terrified by them. 4 For the LORD your God is the one who goes with you[o] to fight[p] for you against your enemies to give you victory.[q]"

5 The officers shall say to the army: "Has anyone built a new house and not yet begun to live in[r] it? Let him go home, or he may die in battle and someone else may begin to live in it. 6 Has anyone planted[s] a vineyard and not begun to enjoy it?[t] Let him go home, or he may die in battle and someone else enjoy it. 7 Has anyone become pledged to a woman and not married her? Let him go home, or he may die in battle and someone else marry her.[u]" 8 Then the officers shall add, "Is anyone afraid or fainthearted? Let him go home so that his fellow soldiers will not become disheartened too."[v] 9 When the officers have finished speaking to the army, they shall appoint commanders over it.

10 When you march up to attack a city, make its people an offer of peace.[w] 11 If they accept and open their gates, all the people in it shall be subject[x] to forced labor[y] and shall work for you. 12 If they refuse to make peace and they engage you in battle, lay siege to that city. 13 When the LORD your God delivers it into your hand, put to the sword all the men in it.[z] 14 As for the women, the children, the livestock[a] and everything else in the city,[b] you may take these as plunder[c] for yourselves. And you may use the plunder the LORD your God gives you from your enemies. 15 This is how you are to treat all the cities that are at a distance[d] from you and do not belong to the nations nearby.

16 However, in the cities of the nations

19:10 [v] Pr 6:17; Jer 7:6; 26:15 [w] Dt 21:1-9
19:11 [x] S Ex 21:12; 1Jn 3:15
19:13 [y] Dt 7:2 [z] Dt 21:9; 1Ki 2:31
19:14 [a] Dt 27:17; Job 24:2; Ps 16:6; Pr 15:25; 22:28; 23:10; Isa 1:23; Hos 5:10
19:15 [b] S Dt 17:6; S Mt 18:16*; 26:60; 2Co 13:1*
19:16 [c] Ex 23:1; Pr 6:19
19:17 [d] S Ex 21:6
19:18 [e] S Ex 23:7
19:19 [f] Pr 19:5, 9; 1Co 5:13*
19:20 [g] S Dt 13:11
19:21 [h] ver 13 [i] S Ex 21:24; Mt 5:38*
20:1 [j] Ps 20:7; Isa 31:1 [k] S Nu 14:9 [l] S Dt 3:22; S 1Sa 17:45 [m] Isa 41:10
20:3 [n] 1Sa 17:32; Job 23:16; Ps 22:14; Isa 7:4; 35:4; Jer 51:46
20:4 [o] 2Ch 20:14-22 [p] S Ex 14:14; 1Ch 5:22; Ne 4:20 [q] Jdg 12:3; 15:18; Ps 44:7; 144:10
20:5 [r] Ne 12:27
20:6 [s] Jer 31:5; Eze 28:26; Mic 1:6 [t] 1Co 9:7
20:7 [u] Dt 24:5; Pr 5:18
20:8 [v] Jdg 7:3
20:10 [w] S Dt 2:26; Lk 14:31-32
20:11 [x] ver 15; 2Ki 6:22 [y] 1Ki 9:21; 1Ch 22:2; Isa 31:8
20:13 [z] Nu 31:7 **20:14** [a] Jos 8:2; 22:8 [b] S Nu 31:11 [c] S Nu 31:53
20:15 [d] S ver 11; Jos 9:9

19:14 *boundary stone.* Such stones were set up to indicate the perimeters of fields and landed estates. Moving them illegally to increase one's own holdings was considered a serious crime (see 27:17; Pr 15:25 and note). Amenemope's (Egyptian) Wisdom (see chart, p. xxii) has a similar prohibition in ch. 6 of that work.
19:15 See note on 17:6.
19:18 *giving false testimony.* See 5:20; Ex 20:16 and note; Lev 19:11–12; 1Ki 21:10,13.
19:19 *You must purge the evil from among you.* See note on 13:5.
19:21 *life for life.* See notes on Ex 21:23–25; Lev 24:20; see also Mt 5:38–42.
20:2 *priest shall ... address.* Priests sometimes accompanied the army when it went into battle (see, e.g., Jos 6:4–21; 2Ch 20:14–22).
20:3 *Hear, Israel.* See note on 4:1.
20:4 See note on 3:22.
20:5–8 Cf. the curses in 28:30. *Let him go home.* Israel was to trust not in the size of its army but in the Lord (see notes on 2Sa 24:1; Ps 30:6–7). The number of exemptions from military duty was sometimes extensive (see, e.g., Jdg 7:2–8).
20:10–15 Rules regarding warfare against nations outside the promised land.
20:11 *subject to forced labor.* A fulfillment of Noah's curse on Canaan (see Ge 9:25 and note).

the LORD your God is giving you as an inheritance, do not leave alive anything that
breathes.[e] 17 Completely destroy[a] them —
the Hittites, Amorites, Canaanites, Perizzites, Hivites and Jebusites — as the LORD
your God has commanded you. 18 Otherwise, they will teach you to follow all the
detestable things they do in worshiping
their gods,[f] and you will sin[g] against the
LORD your God.
19 When you lay siege to a city for a long
time, fighting against it to capture it, do
not destroy its trees by putting an ax to
them, because you can eat their fruit. Do
not cut them down. Are the trees people,
that you should besiege them?[b] 20 However, you may cut down trees that you know
are not fruit trees[h] and use them to build
siege works until the city at war with you
falls.

20:16 [e] Ex 23:31-33; Nu 21:2-3; S Dt 7:2; Jos 6:21; 10:1; 11:14
20:18 [f] S Ex 34:16 [g] S Ex 10:7
20:20 [h] Jer 6:6
21:1 [i] S Nu 25:17
21:3 [j] S Nu 19:2

Atonement for an Unsolved Murder

21 If someone is found slain, lying in
a field in the land the LORD your
God is giving you to possess, and it is not
known who the killer was,[i] 2 your elders
and judges shall go out and measure the
distance from the body to the neighboring
towns. 3 Then the elders of the town nearest the body shall take a heifer that has
never been worked and has never worn
a yoke[j] 4 and lead it down to a valley that
has not been plowed or planted and where
there is a flowing stream. There in the valley they are to break the heifer's neck.
5 The Levitical priests shall step forward,
for the LORD your God has chosen them

[a] *17* The Hebrew term refers to the irrevocable giving over of things or persons to the LORD, often by totally destroying them. [b] *19* Or *down to use in the siege, for the fruit trees are for the benefit of people.*

20:17 *Hittites ... Jebusites.* See 7:1; see also notes on Ge 10:6,15–18; 13:7; Jos 9:7.
20:19 *do not destroy its trees.* The failure of later armies to follow this wise rule stripped bare much of the land (though the absence of woodlands there today is of relatively recent origin).
21:5 *to minister.* To officiate at the place of worship before the Lord on behalf of the people (see 10:8; 18:5). *to pronounce blessings.* See Nu 6:22–27.

MAJOR SOCIAL CONCERNS IN THE COVENANT

1. **Personhood** — Everyone's person is to be secure (Ex 20:13; Dt 5:17; Ex 21:16–21,26–32; Lev 19:14; Dt 24:7; 27:18).
2. **False Accusation** — Everyone is to be secure against slander and false accusation (Ex 20:16; Dt 5:20; Ex 23:1–3,6–8; Lev 19:16; Dt 19:15–21).
3. **Women** — No woman is to be taken advantage of within her subordinate status in society (Ex 21:7–11,20,26–32; 22:16–17; Nu 27:1–11; 36:1–12; Dt 21:10–14; 22:13–30; 24:1–5).
4. **Punishment** — Punishment for wrongdoing shall not be excessive so that the culprit is dehumanized (Dt 25:1–3).
5. **Dignity** — Every Israelite's dignity and right to be God's servant are to be honored and safeguarded (Ex 21:2,5–6; Lev 25; Dt 15:12–18).
6. **Inheritance** — Every Israelite's inheritance in the promised land is to be secure (Lev 25; Nu 27:5–7; 36:1–9; Dt 25:5–10).
7. **Property** — Everyone's property is to be secure (Ex 20:15; Dt 5:19; Ex 21:33–36; 22:1–15; 23:4–5; Lev 19:35–36; Dt 22:1–4; 25:13–15).
8. **Fruit of Labor** — Everyone is to receive the fruit of their labors (Lev 19:13; Dt 24:14; 25:4).
9. **Fruit of the Ground** — Everyone is to share the fruit of the ground (Ex 23:10–11; Lev 19:9–10; 23:22; 25:3–55; Dt 14:28–29; 24:19–21).
10. **Rest on Sabbath** — Everyone, down to the humblest servant and the resident foreigner, is to share in the weekly rest of God's Sabbath (Ex 20:8–11; Dt 5:12–15; Ex 23:12).
11. **Marriage** — The marriage relationship is to be kept inviolate (Ex 20:14; Dt 5:18; see also Lev 18:6–23; 20:10–21; Dt 22:13–30).
12. **Exploitation** — No one, however disabled, impoverished or powerless, is to be oppressed or exploited (Ex 22:21–27; Lev 19:14,33–34; 25:35–36; Dt 23:19; 24:6,12–15,17; 27:18).
13. **Fair Trial** — Everyone is to have free access to the courts and is to be afforded a fair trial (Ex 23:6–8; Lev 19:15; Dt 1:17; 10:17–18; 16:18–20; 17:8–13; 19:15–21).
14. **Social Order** — Every person's God-given place in the social order is to be honored (Ex 20:12; Dt 5:16; Ex 21:15,17; 22:28; Lev 19:3,32; 20:9; Dt 17:8–13; 21:15–21; 27:16).
15. **Law** — No one shall be above the law, not even the king (Dt 17:18–20).
16. **Animals** — Concern for the welfare of other creatures is to be extended to the animal world (Ex 23:5,11; Lev 25:7; Dt 22:4,6–7; 25:4).

to minister and to pronounce blessings[k]
in the name of the LORD and to decide all
cases of dispute and assault.[l] 6Then all the
elders of the town nearest the body shall
wash their hands[m] over the heifer whose
neck was broken in the valley, 7and they
shall declare: "Our hands did not shed this
blood, nor did our eyes see it done. 8Ac-
cept this atonement for your people Israel,
whom you have redeemed, LORD, and do
not hold your people guilty of the blood of
an innocent person." Then the bloodshed
will be atoned for,[n] 9and you will have
purged[o] from yourselves the guilt of shedding innocent blood, since you have done
what is right in the eyes of the LORD.

Marrying a Captive Woman

10When you go to war against your enemies and the LORD your God delivers them
into your hands[p] and you take captives,[q]
11if you notice among the captives a beautiful[r] woman and are attracted to her,[s] you
may take her as your wife. 12Bring her into
your home and have her shave her head,[t]
trim her nails 13and put aside the clothes
she was wearing when captured. After she
has lived in your house and mourned her
father and mother for a full month,[u] then
you may go to her and be her husband
and she shall be your wife. 14If you are not
pleased with her, let her go wherever she
wishes. You must not sell her or treat her
as a slave, since you have dishonored her.[v]

The Right of the Firstborn

15If a man has two wives,[w] and he loves
one but not the other, and both bear him
sons but the firstborn is the son of the
wife he does not love,[x] 16when he wills
his property to his sons, he must not give
the rights of the firstborn to the son of the
wife he loves in preference to his actual
firstborn, the son of the wife he does not
love.[y] 17He must acknowledge the son of
his unloved wife as the firstborn by giving
him a double[z] share of all he has. That son
is the first sign of his father's strength.[a]
The right of the firstborn belongs to him.[b]

A Rebellious Son

18If someone has a stubborn and rebellious[c] son[d] who does not obey his father
and mother[e] and will not listen to them
when they discipline him, 19his father and
mother shall take hold of him and bring
him to the elders at the gate of his town.
20They shall say to the elders, "This son
of ours is stubborn and rebellious. He will
not obey us. He is a glutton and a drunkard." 21Then all the men of his town are to
stone him to death.[f] You must purge the
evil[g] from among you. All Israel will hear
of it and be afraid.[h]

Various Laws

22If someone guilty of a capital offense[i]
is put to death and their body is exposed
on a pole, 23you must not leave the body
hanging on the pole overnight.[j] Be sure
to bury[k] it that same day, because anyone who is hung on a pole is under God's
curse.[l] You must not desecrate[m] the land
the LORD your God is giving you as an inheritance.

22 If you see your fellow Israelite's ox
or sheep straying, do not ignore it
but be sure to take it back to its owner.[n] 2If
they do not live near you or if you do not
know who owns it, take it home with you
and keep it until they come looking for it.
Then give it back. 3Do the same if you find

21:5 [k]S Ge 48:20; S Ex 39:43 [l]Dt 17:8-11 **21:6** [m]Mt 27:24 **21:8** [n]Nu 35:33-34 **21:9** [o]Dt 19:13 **21:10** [p]Jos 21:44 [q]1Ki 8:46; 1Ch 9:1; Ezr 5:12; Jer 40:1; Eze 1:1; 17:12; Da 2:25; Mic 4:10 **21:11** [r]Ge 6:2 [s]S Ge 34:8 **21:12** [t]S Lev 14:9; S Nu 8:7; 1Co 11:5 **21:13** [u]Ps 45:10 **21:14** [v]S Ge 34:2 **21:15** [w]S Ge 4:19 [x]Ge 29:33 **21:16** [y]1Ch 26:10 **21:17** [z]2Ki 2:9; Isa 40:2; 61:7; Zec 9:12 [a]S Ge 49:3 [b]Ge 25:31; Lk 15:12 **21:18** [c]Ps 78:8; Jer 5:23; Zep 3:1 [d]Pr 30:17 [e]S Ge 31:35; Pr 1:8; Isa 30:1; Eph 6:1-3 **21:21** [f]S Lev 20:9 [g]Dt 19:19; 1Co 5:13* [h]S Dt 13:11 **21:22** [i]Dt 22:26; Mt 26:66; Mk 14:64; Ac 23:29 **21:23** [j]Jos 8:29; 10:27; Jn 19:31 [k]Eze 39:12 [l]Ezr 6:11; Est 2:23; 7:9; 8:7; 9:13,25; Isa 50:11; Gal 3:13* [m]S Lev 18:25 **22:1** [n]Ex 23:4-5; Pr 27:10; Zec 7:9

21:6 *wash their hands.* Symbolic of a declaration of innocence (v. 7; see Mt 27:24).

21:10 *take captives.* The enemies here were those outside Canaan (see 20:14–15), so they were not subject to total destruction (see 20:17 and NIV text note there).

21:12 *shave her head.* Indicative of leaving her former life and beginning a new life, or perhaps symbolic of mourning (v. 13; see, e.g., Jer 47:5; Mic 1:16) or of humiliation (see note on Isa 7:20). For cleansing rites, see Lev 14:8; Nu 8:7 and note; cf. 2Sa 19:24.

21:14 *dishonored.* Twelve other times the Hebrew for this word is used of men forcing women to have sexual intercourse with them (22:24,29; Ge 34:2; Jdg 19:24; 20:5; 2Sa 13:12,14, 22,32; La 5:11; Eze 22:10–11).

21:15 *two wives.* See notes on Ge 4:19; 25:6.

21:16 *in preference to.* The order of birth rather than parental favoritism governed succession, though the rule was sometimes set aside with divine approval (cf., e.g., Jacob or Solomon).

21:17 *double share.* In Israel the oldest son enjoyed a double share of the inheritance. Parallels to this practice come from Nuzi, Larsa in the Old Babylonian period and Assyria in the Middle Assyrian period (see chart, p. xxiv). Receiving a double portion of an estate was also tantamount to succession. Thus Elisha succeeded Elijah (see 2Ki 2:9 and note). *first sign of his father's strength.* The first result of a man's procreative activity.

21:18 *stubborn and rebellious ... does not obey.* In wicked defiance of the fifth commandment (see 5:16; Ex 20:12 and note).

21:21 *stone him to death.* See 5:16; 27:16; Ex 21:15,17. *You must purge the evil from among you.* See note on 13:5.

21:22 *put to death and ... exposed on a pole.* The offender was first executed, then the body was impaled on a pole (see Ge 40:19; Est 2:23 and note).

21:23 *not leave the body hanging on the pole overnight.* Prolonged exposure would give undue attention to the crime and the criminal and would desecrete the land. *under God's curse.* God had condemned murder, and hanging on a pole symbolized divine judgment and rejection. Christ accepted the full punishment of our sins, thus becoming "a curse for us" (Gal 3:13; see note there).

22:1 *do not ignore it.* See vv. 3–4. The Biblical legislation was intended not only to punish criminal behavior but also to express concern for people and their possessions. See chart, p. 287.

their donkey or cloak or anything else they
have lost. Do not ignore it.
4 If you see your fellow Israelite's donkey[o] or ox fallen on the road, do not ignore
it. Help the owner get it to its feet.[p]
5 A woman must not wear men's clothing, nor a man wear women's clothing,
for the LORD your God detests anyone who
does this.
6 If you come across a bird's nest beside
the road, either in a tree or on the ground,
and the mother is sitting on the young or
on the eggs, do not take the mother with
the young.[q] 7 You may take the young, but
be sure to let the mother go,[r] so that it
may go well with you and you may have
a long life.[s]
8 When you build a new house, make a
parapet around your roof so that you may
not bring the guilt of bloodshed on your
house if someone falls from the roof.[t]
9 Do not plant two kinds of seed in your
vineyard;[u] if you do, not only the crops
you plant but also the fruit of the vineyard
will be defiled.[a]
10 Do not plow with an ox and a donkey
yoked together.[v]
11 Do not wear clothes of wool and linen
woven together.[w]
12 Make tassels on the four corners of
the cloak you wear.[x]

Marriage Violations

13 If a man takes a wife and, after sleeping with her[y], dislikes her 14 and slanders
her and gives her a bad name, saying,
"I married this woman, but when I approached her, I did not find proof of her
virginity," 15 then the young woman's father and mother shall bring to the town
elders at the gate[z] proof that she was a
virgin. 16 Her father will say to the elders,
"I gave my daughter in marriage to this
man, but he dislikes her. 17 Now he has
slandered her and said, 'I did not find your
daughter to be a virgin.' But here is the
proof of my daughter's virginity." Then
her parents shall display the cloth before
the elders of the town, 18 and the elders[a]
shall take the man and punish him. 19 They
shall fine him a hundred shekels[b] of silver
and give them to the young woman's father, because this man has given an Israelite virgin a bad name. She shall continue
to be his wife; he must not divorce her as
long as he lives.
20 If, however, the charge is true[b] and
no proof of the young woman's virginity
can be found, 21 she shall be brought to the
door of her father's house and there the
men of her town shall stone her to death.
She has done an outrageous thing[c] in Israel by being promiscuous while still in
her father's house. You must purge the evil
from among you.
22 If a man is found sleeping with another man's wife, both the man who slept[d]
with her and the woman must die.[e] You
must purge the evil from Israel.
23 If a man happens to meet in a town a
virgin pledged to be married and he sleeps
with her, 24 you shall take both of them to
the gate of that town and stone them to
death—the young woman because she
was in a town and did not scream for help,
and the man because he violated another
man's wife. You must purge the evil from
among you.[f]
25 But if out in the country a man happens to meet a young woman pledged to
be married and rapes her, only the man
who has done this shall die. 26 Do nothing to the woman; she has committed no
sin deserving death. This case is like that
of someone who attacks and murders a
neighbor, 27 for the man found the young
woman out in the country, and though the
betrothed woman screamed,[g] there was no
one to rescue her.
28 If a man happens to meet a virgin who
is not pledged to be married and rapes her
and they are discovered,[h] 29 he shall pay
her father fifty shekels[c] of silver. He must
marry the young woman, for he has violated her. He can never divorce her as long
as he lives.
30 A man is not to marry his father's

22:4 [o] Ex 23:5 [p] 1Co 9:9
22:6 [q] Lev 22:28
22:7 [r] S Lev 22:28 [s] S Dt 5:29
22:8 [t] Jos 2:8; 1Sa 9:25; 2Sa 11:2
22:9 [u] Lev 19:19
22:10 [v] 2Co 6:14
22:11 [w] Lev 19:19
22:12 [x] Nu 15:37-41; Mt 23:5
22:13 [y] Dt 24:1
22:15 [z] S Ge 23:10
22:18 [a] Ex 18:21; Dt 1:9-18
22:20 [b] Dt 17:4
22:21 [c] S Ge 34:7; S 38:24; S Lev 19:29; Dt 23:17-18; 1Co 5:13*
22:22 [d] 2Sa 11:4 [e] S Ge 38:24; S Ex 21:12; Mt 5:27-28; Jn 8:5; 1Co 6:9; Heb 13:4
22:24 [f] 1Co 5:13*
22:27 [g] S Ge 39:14
22:28 [h] Ex 22:16

[a] 9 *Or be forfeited to the sanctuary* [b] 19 That is, about 2 1/2 pounds or about 1.2 kilograms [c] 29 That is, about 1 1/4 pounds or about 575 grams

22:5 Probably intended to prohibit such perversions as transvestism and homosexual practices, especially under religious auspices. The God-created differences between men and women are not to be disregarded (see Lev 18:22; 20:13).
22:9–11 See note on Lev 19:19.
22:12 *tassels.* See note on Nu 15:38; cf. Mt 23:5.
22:14 *proof of her virginity.* A blood-stained cloth or garment (see vv. 15,17,20).
22:15 *elders at the gate.* See 21:19; 25:7; see also notes on Ge 19:1; Ru 4:1; La 5:14.
22:19 *hundred shekels of silver.* A heavy fine—several times what Hosea paid to buy Gomer back (Hos 3:2) or what Jeremiah paid for the field at Anathoth (Jer 32:9). It may have been about twice the average bride-price (see note on v. 29). The high fine, in addition to the no-divorce rule, was intended to restrain not only a husband's charges against his wife but also easy divorce. *shekels.* See note on Ge 20:16.
22:21,24 *You must purge the evil from among you.* See v. 22; see also note on 13:5.
22:22 See Lev 20:10.
22:29 *fifty shekels of silver.* Probably equaled the average bride-price, which must have varied with the economic status of the participants (see note on Ex 22:16).
22:30 *his father's wife.* Refers to a wife other than his mother

wife; he must not dishonor his father's
bed.[a][i]

Exclusion From the Assembly

23 [b] No one who has been emasculat-
ed[j] by crushing or cutting may enter the assembly of the LORD.
2No one born of a forbidden marriage[c]
nor any of their descendants may enter
the assembly of the LORD, not even in the
tenth generation.
3No Ammonite[k] or Moabite or any of
their descendants may enter the assembly
of the LORD, not even in the tenth generation.[l] 4For they did not come to meet you
with bread and water[m] on your way when
you came out of Egypt, and they hired Balaam[n] son of Beor from Pethor in Aram
Naharaim[d][o] to pronounce a curse on you.[p]
5However, the LORD your God would not
listen to Balaam but turned the curse[q] into
a blessing for you, because the LORD your
God loves[r] you. 6Do not seek a treaty[s] of
friendship with them as long as you live.[t]
7Do not despise an Edomite,[u] for the
Edomites are related to you.[v] Do not despise an Egyptian, because you resided
as foreigners in their country.[w] 8The third
generation of children born to them may
enter the assembly of the LORD.

Uncleanness in the Camp

9When you are encamped against your
enemies, keep away from everything impure.[x] 10If one of your men is unclean because of a nocturnal emission, he is to go
outside the camp and stay there.[y] 11But as
evening approaches he is to wash himself,
and at sunset[z] he may return to the camp.[a]
12Designate a place outside the camp
where you can go to relieve yourself. 13As
part of your equipment have something to
dig with, and when you relieve yourself,
dig a hole and cover up your excrement.
14For the LORD your God moves[b] about in
your camp to protect you and to deliver
your enemies to you. Your camp must be
holy,[c] so that he will not see among you
anything indecent and turn away from you.

Miscellaneous Laws

15If a slave has taken refuge[d] with you,
do not hand them over to their master.[e]
16Let them live among you wherever they
like and in whatever town they choose. Do
not oppress[f] them.
17No Israelite man[g] or woman is to become a shrine prostitute.[h] 18You must not
bring the earnings of a female prostitute or
of a male prostitute[e] into the house of the
LORD your God to pay any vow, because
the LORD your God detests them both.[i]
19Do not charge a fellow Israelite interest, whether on money or food or anything else that may earn interest.[j] 20You
may charge a foreigner[k] interest, but not a
fellow Israelite, so that the LORD your God
may bless[l] you in everything you put your
hand to in the land you are entering to
possess.
21If you make a vow to the LORD your
God, do not be slow to pay it,[m] for the
LORD your God will certainly demand it of
you and you will be guilty of sin.[n] 22But if
you refrain from making a vow, you will
not be guilty.[o] 23Whatever your lips utter
you must be sure to do, because you made
your vow freely to the LORD your God with
your own mouth.
24If you enter your neighbor's vineyard,
you may eat all the grapes you want, but do
not put any in your basket. 25If you enter
your neighbor's grainfield, you may pick
kernels with your hands, but you must not
put a sickle to their standing grain.[p]
24 If a man marries a woman who becomes displeasing to him[q] because
he finds something indecent about her,

a 30 In Hebrew texts this verse (22:30) is numbered 23:1. *b* In Hebrew texts 23:1-25 is numbered 23:2-26. *c* 2 Or *one of illegitimate birth* *d* 4 That is, Northwest Mesopotamia *e* 18 Hebrew *of a dog*

22:30 [i] S Ge 29:29; S Lev 18:8; S 20:9; 1Co 5:1 **23:1** [j] S Lev 21:20 **23:3** [k] S Ge 19:38 [l] ver 4; Ne 13:2 **23:4** [m] Dt 2:28 [n] S Nu 23:7; S 2Pe 2:15 [o] S Ge 24:10 [p] S ver 3 **23:5** [q] Nu 24:10; Jos 24:10; Pr 26:2 [r] S Dt 4:37 **23:6** [s] S Nu 24:17; Isa 15:1; 25:10; Jer 25:21; 27:3; 48:1; Eze 25:8; Zep 2:9 [t] Ezr 9:12; Mt 5:43 **23:7** [u] S Ge 25:30 [v] S Ge 25:26 [w] S Lev 19:34 **23:9** [x] Lev 15:1-33 **23:10** [y] Lev 15:16 **23:11** [z] S Lev 15:16 [a] 1Sa 21:5 **23:14** [b] S Ge 3:8 [c] Ex 3:5 **23:15** [d] 2Sa 22:3; Ps 2:12; 71:1 [e] 1Sa 30:15 **23:16** [f] Ex 22:21; S 23:6 **23:17** [g] 1Ki 14:24; 15:12; 22:46; 2Ki 23:7; Job 36:14 [h] S Ge 38:21 **23:18** [i] S Ge 19:5; S Lev 20:13; Rev 22:15 **23:19** [j] S Lev 25:35-37; Ne 5:2-7 **23:20** [k] S Ge 31:15; S Dt 15:3 [l] Dt 15:10 **23:21** [m] S Nu 6:21; Jdg 11:35; Ps 15:4 [n] Nu 30:1-2; Job 22:27; Ps 61:8; 65:1; 76:11; Isa 19:21; S Mt 5:33; Ac 5:3 **23:22** [o] Ac 5:4 **23:25** [p] Mt 12:1; Mk 2:23; Lk 6:1 **24:1** [q] Dt 22:13

(see 27:20). *dishonor his father's bed.* Lit. "uncover the corner of his father's garment" (cf. notes on Ru 3:9; Eze 16:8).
23:1 For blessings on eunuchs in later times, see Isa 56:4–5; Ac 8:26–39.
23:2–3 *not even in the tenth generation.* Perhaps forever, since ten is symbolic of completeness or finality. In v. 6 the equivalent expression is "as long as you live" (lit. "all your days forever").
23:4 *Balaam son of Beor.* See Nu 22:4—24:25 and notes.
23:6 See the prophets' denunciation of Moab and Ammon (Isa 15–16; Jer 48:1—49:6; Eze 25:1–11; Am 1:13—2:3; Zep 2:8–11).
23:7 *Edomite ... related to you.* Edom (Esau) is often condemned for his hostility against his "brother" Jacob (Israel; see Am 1:11; Ob 10; see also notes on Ge 25:22,26).
23:9–14 Sanitary rules for Israel's military camps. For similar rules for the people in general, see Lev 15 and notes.

23:14 *Your camp must be holy.* Even as the Lord is holy (see Lev 11:44 and note).
23:15 *If a slave has taken refuge.* A foreign slave seeking freedom in Israel.
23:17–18 See notes on Ge 38:21; Ex 34:15; Jdg 2:17; 1Ki 14:24; Mic 1:7.
23:18 *male prostitute.* Lit. "dog" (see NIV text note), a word often associated with moral or spiritual impurity (cf. Mt 7:6; 15:26; Php 3:2; Rev 22:15 and note).
23:19 *interest.* See note on Ex 22:25–27.
23:20 *charge a foreigner.* A foreign merchant would come into Israel for financial advantage and so would be subject to paying interest.
23:21–23 See notes on Nu 30; Ecc 5:1–7.

24:1–4 In the books of Moses, divorce was permitted and regulated (see Lev 21:7,14; 22:13; Nu 30:9). Jesus

and he writes her a certificate of divorce,[r]
gives it to her and sends her from his
house, 2and if after she leaves his house
she becomes the wife of another man,
3and her second husband dislikes her and
writes her a certificate of divorce, gives it
to her and sends her from his house, or
if he dies, 4then her first husband, who
divorced her, is not allowed to marry her
again after she has been defiled. That
would be detestable in the eyes of the
LORD. Do not bring sin upon the land the
LORD[s] your God is giving you as an inheritance.

5If a man has recently married, he must
not be sent to war or have any other duty
laid on him. For one year he is to be free
to stay at home and bring happiness to the
wife he has married.[t]

6Do not take a pair of millstones — not
even the upper one — as security for a
debt, because that would be taking a person's livelihood as security.[u]

7If someone is caught kidnapping a fellow Israelite and treating or selling them
as a slave, the kidnapper must die.[v] You
must purge the evil from among you.[w]

8In cases of defiling skin diseases,[a] be
very careful to do exactly as the Levitical[x]
priests instruct you. You must follow carefully what I have commanded them.[y] 9Re-
member what the LORD your God did to
Miriam along the way after you came out
of Egypt.[z]

10When you make a loan of any kind to
your neighbor, do not go into their house
to get what is offered to you as a pledge.[a]
11Stay outside and let the neighbor to
whom you are making the loan bring the
pledge out to you. 12If the neighbor is
poor, do not go to sleep with their pledge[b]
in your possession. 13Return their cloak by
sunset[c] so that your neighbor may sleep in
it.[d] Then they will thank you, and it will
be regarded as a righteous act in the sight
of the LORD your God.[e]

14Do not take advantage of a hired worker who is poor and needy, whether that
worker is a fellow Israelite or a foreigner
residing in one of your towns.[f] 15Pay them
their wages each day before sunset, because they are poor[g] and are counting on
it.[h] Otherwise they may cry to the LORD
against you, and you will be guilty of sin.[i]

16Parents are not to be put to death for
their children, nor children put to death
for their parents; each will die for their
own sin.[j]

17Do not deprive the foreigner or the fatherless[k] of justice,[l] or take the cloak of the
widow as a pledge. 18Remember that you
were slaves in Egypt[m] and the LORD your
God redeemed you from there. That is why
I command you to do this.

19When you are harvesting in your field
and you overlook a sheaf, do not go back
to get it.[n] Leave it for the foreigner,[o] the fatherless and the widow,[p] so that the LORD
your God may bless[q] you in all the work
of your hands. 20When you beat the olives
from your trees, do not go over the branches a second time.[r] Leave what remains for
the foreigner, the fatherless and the widow. 21When you harvest the grapes in your
vineyard, do not go over the vines again.
Leave what remains for the foreigner, the
fatherless and the widow. 22Remember
that you were slaves in Egypt. That is why
I command you to do this.[s]

25 When people have a dispute, they
are to take it to court and the judg-
es[t] will decide the case,[u] acquitting[v] the
innocent and condemning the guilty.[w] 2If
the guilty person deserves to be beaten,[x]
the judge shall make them lie down and
have them flogged in his presence with the
number of lashes the crime deserves, 3but
the judge must not impose more than forty
lashes.[y] If the guilty party is flogged more
than that, your fellow Israelite will be degraded in your eyes.[z]

4Do not muzzle an ox while it is treading out the grain.[a]

5If brothers are living together and one
of them dies without a son, his widow
must not marry outside the family. Her

[a] 8 The Hebrew word for *defiling skin diseases*, traditionally translated "leprosy," was used for various diseases affecting the skin.

24:1 [r] ver 3; 2Ki 17:6; Isa 50:1; Jer 3:8; Mal 2:16; Mt 1:19; 5:31*; 19:7-9; Mk 10:4-5 **24:4** [s] Jer 3:1 **24:5** [t] S Dt 20:7 **24:6** [u] S Ex 22:22 **24:7** [v] S Ex 21:16 [w] 1Co 5:13* **24:8** [x] S Dt 17:9 [y] Lev 13:1-46; S 14:2 **24:9** [z] S Nu 12:10 **24:10** [a] Ex 22:25-27 **24:12** [b] S Ex 22:26 **24:13** [c] Ex 22:26 [d] S Ex 22:27 [e] Dt 6:25; Ps 106:31; Da 4:27 **24:14** [f] Lev 19:13; 25:35-43; Dt 15:12-18; Job 24:4; Pr 14:31; 19:17; Am 4:1; 1Ti 5:18 **24:15** [g] S Lev 25:35 [h] S Lev 19:13; Mt 20:8 [i] S Ex 22:23; S Job 12:19; Jas 5:4 **24:16** [j] S Nu 26:11; Jer 31:29-30 **24:17** [k] Ex 22:22; Job 6:27; 24:9; 29:12; Ps 10:18; 82:3; Pr 23:10; Eze 22:7 [l] S Ex 22:21; S 23:2; S Dt 10:18 **24:18** [m] S Dt 15:15 **24:19** [n] S Lev 19:9 [o] Dt 10:19; 27:19; Eze 47:22; Zec 7:10; Mal 3:5 [p] ver 20; Dt 14:29 [q] S Dt 14:29; Pr 19:17; 28:27; Ecc 11:1 **24:20** [r] Lev 19:10 **24:22** [s] ver 18 **25:1** [t] S Ex 21:6 [u] Dt 17:8-13; 19:17; Ac 23:3 [v] 1Ki 8:32 [w] S Ex 23:7; Dt 1:16-17 **25:2** [x] Pr 10:13; 19:29; Lk 12:47-48 **25:3** [y] Mt 27:26; Jn 19:1; 2Co 11:24 [z] Jer 20:2 **25:4** [a] S Nu 22:29; 1Co 9:9*; 1Ti 5:18*

commented on the law of 24:1 in Mt 5:31 – 32 (see note on Mt 19:3). He also cited the higher law of creation (Mt 19:3 – 9).

24:5 *happiness.* Marital bliss was held in high regard (cf. Pr 5:18; Ecc 9:9).

24:6 *millstones.* Used for grinding grain for flour and daily food (see note on Jdg 9:53).

24:7 *as a slave.* Cf. 23:15. *You must purge the evil from among you.* See note on 13:5.

24:8 *defiling skin diseases.* See NIV text note; see also note on Lev 13:2.

24:9,18,22 *Remember.* See note on 4:10.

24:10 – 13 See notes on 6:25; Ex 22:26 – 27.

24:16 *each will die for their own sin.* See Eze 18:4 and note.

24:17 – 18 See 10:18 – 19. When the Israelites were in trouble, the Lord helped them. Therefore they were not to take advantage of others in difficulty.

24:19 – 21 See note on Lev 19:9 – 10.

25:3 *not … more than forty lashes.* Beating could subject the culprit to abuse, so the law kept the punishment from becoming inhumane. Cf. Paul's experience in 2Co 11:24 – 25 (see note there).

25:4 Applied to ministers of Christ in 1Co 9:9 – 10; 1Ti 5:17 – 18. *treading out the grain.* See notes on Ge 50:10; Ru 1:22.

25:5 – 6 The continuity of each family and the decentralized

husband's brother shall take her and marry her and fulfill the duty of a brother-in-law to her.[b] 6 The first son she bears shall carry on the name of the dead brother so that his name will not be blotted out from Israel.[c]

7 However, if a man does not want to marry his brother's wife,[d] she shall go to the elders at the town gate[e] and say, "My husband's brother refuses to carry on his brother's name in Israel. He will not fulfill the duty of a brother-in-law to me."[f] 8 Then the elders of his town shall summon him and talk to him. If he persists in saying, "I do not want to marry her," 9 his brother's widow shall go up to him in the presence of the elders, take off one of his sandals,[g] spit in his face[h] and say, "This is what is done to the man who will not build up his brother's family line." 10 That man's line shall be known in Israel as The Family of the Unsandaled.

11 If two men are fighting and the wife of one of them comes to rescue her husband from his assailant, and she reaches out and seizes him by his private parts, 12 you shall cut off her hand. Show her no pity.[i]

13 Do not have two differing weights in your bag—one heavy, one light.[j] 14 Do not have two differing measures in your house—one large, one small. 15 You must have accurate and honest weights and measures, so that you may live long[k] in the land the LORD your God is giving you. 16 For the LORD your God detests anyone who does these things, anyone who deals dishonestly.[l]

17 Remember what the Amalekites[m] did to you along the way when you came out of Egypt. 18 When you were weary and worn out, they met you on your journey and attacked all who were lagging behind; they had no fear of God.[n] 19 When the LORD your God gives you rest[o] from all the enemies[p] around you in the land he is giving you to possess as an inheritance, you shall blot out the name of Amalek[q] from under heaven. Do not forget!

Firstfruits and Tithes

26 When you have entered the land the LORD your God is giving you as an inheritance and have taken possession of it and settled in it, 2 take some of the firstfruits[r] of all that you produce from the soil of the land the LORD your God is giving you and put them in a basket. Then go to the place the LORD your God will choose as a dwelling for his Name[s] 3 and say to the priest in office at the time, "I declare today to the LORD your God that I have come to the land the LORD swore to our ancestors to give us." 4 The priest shall take the basket from your hands and set it down in front of the altar of the LORD your God. 5 Then you shall declare before the LORD your God: "My father was a wandering[t] Aramean,[u] and he went down into Egypt with a few people[v] and lived there and became a great nation,[w] powerful and numerous. 6 But the Egyptians mistreated us and made us suffer,[x] subjecting us to harsh labor.[y] 7 Then we cried out to the LORD, the God of our ancestors, and the LORD heard our voice[z] and saw[a] our misery,[b] toil and oppression.[c] 8 So the LORD brought us out of Egypt[d] with a mighty hand and an outstretched arm,[e] with great terror and with signs and wonders.[f] 9 He brought us to this place and gave us this land, a land flowing with milk and honey;[g] 10 and now I bring the firstfruits of the soil that you, LORD, have given me.[h]" Place the basket before the LORD your God and bow down before him. 11 Then you and the Levites[i] and the foreigners residing among you shall rejoice[j] in all the good things the LORD your God has given to you and your household.

12 When you have finished setting aside a tenth[k] of all your produce in the third year, the year of the tithe,[l] you shall give it to the Levite, the foreigner, the fatherless and the widow, so that they may eat in your towns and be satisfied. 13 Then say to the LORD your God: "I have removed from my house the sacred portion and have given it to the Levite, the foreigner, the father-

25:5 [b] Ru 4:10, 13; Mt 22:24; Mk 12:19; Lk 20:28
25:6 [c] Ge 38:9; Ru 4:5,10
25:7 [d] Ru 1:15 [e] S Ge 23:10 [f] Ru 4:1-2,5-6
25:9 [g] Jos 24:22; Ru 4:7-8,11 [h] Nu 12:14; Job 17:6; 30:10; Isa 50:6
25:12 [i] S Dt 7:2
25:13 [j] Pr 11:1; 20:23; Mic 6:11
25:15 [k] S Ex 20:12
25:16 [l] Pr 11:1
25:17 [m] S Ge 36:12
25:18 [n] Ps 36:1; Ro 3:18
25:19 [o] S Ex 33:14; Heb 3:18-19 [p] Est 9:16 [q] S Ge 36:12
26:2 [r] S Ex 22:29 [s] S Ex 20:24; S Dt 12:5
26:5 [t] S Ge 20:13 [u] S Ge 25:20 [v] S Ge 34:30; 43:14 [w] S Ge 12:2
26:6 [x] S Nu 20:15 [y] S Ex 1:13
26:7 [z] S Ge 21:17 [a] Ex 3:9; 2Ki 13:4; 14:26 [b] S Ge 16:11 [c] Ps 42:9; 44:24; 72:14
26:8 [d] S Nu 20:16 [e] S Ex 3:20 [f] S Dt 4:34; 34:11-12
26:9 [g] S Ex 3:8
26:10 [h] S Dt 8:18
26:11 [i] Dt 12:12 [j] S Dt 16:11
26:12 [k] S Ge 14:20 [l] S Nu 18:24; Dt 14:28-29; Heb 7:5,9

---

control of land through family ownership were basic to the Mosaic economy (see note on Ge 38:8).

25:7 *if a man does not want to marry his brother's wife.* See vv. 8–10; note the experiences, with some variations, described in Ge 38:8–10; Ru 4:1–12. *elders at the town gate.* See 21:19; 22:15; see also notes on Ge 19:1; Ru 4:1.

25:11–12 Cf. Ex 21:22–25 and notes.

25:13–16 See note on Lev 19:35.

25:14 *measures.* Of quantity.

25:17 *Remember.* See note on 4:10. *Amalekites.* See Ex 17:8–16; Nu 14:45; 1Sa 15:2–3; 30:1–20.

25:18 *fear of God.* See note on Ge 20:11.

25:19 *rest.* See note on 3:20.

26:1 *inheritance.* See note on Ex 15:17.

26:2 *firstfruits.* The offering described here occurred only once and must not be confused with the annual offerings of firstfruits (see 18:4 and note). *the place the LORD … will choose as a dwelling for his Name.* See note on 12:5.

26:5 *wandering Aramean.* A reference to Jacob, who had wandered from southern Canaan to Harran in Aram (see note on Ge 10:22 and map, p. 61) and back (Ge 27–35) and who later migrated to Egypt (see Ge 46:3–7). He also married two Aramean women (see Ge 28:5; 29:16,28). The Arameans were a Semitic people who spoke a form of the Aramaic language (see also Ge 22:23–24 and note; 25:20; 31:20,24; 1Ch 18:5 and note). *with a few people … became a great nation.* See Ex 1:5,7 and note on 1:7.

26:11 *rejoice.* See note on 12:12.

26:12 See note on 14:22–29.

less and the widow, according to all you
commanded. I have not turned aside from
your commands nor have I forgotten any
of them.[m] 14 I have not eaten any of the
sacred portion while I was in mourning,
nor have I removed any of it while I was
unclean,[n] nor have I offered any of it to
the dead. I have obeyed the LORD my God;
I have done everything you commanded
me. 15 Look down from heaven,[o] your holy
dwelling place, and bless[p] your people Israel and the land you have given us as you
promised on oath to our ancestors, a land
flowing with milk and honey."

Follow the LORD's Commands

16 The LORD your God commands you this
day to follow these decrees and laws; carefully observe them with all your heart and
with all your soul.[q] 17 You have declared
this day that the LORD is your God and that
you will walk in obedience to him, that
you will keep his decrees, commands and
laws—that you will listen to him.[r] 18 And
the LORD has declared this day that you are
his people, his treasured possession[s] as he
promised, and that you are to keep all his
commands. 19 He has declared that he will
set you in praise,[t] fame and honor high
above all the nations[u] he has made and
that you will be a people holy[v] to the LORD
your God, as he promised.

The Altar on Mount Ebal

27 Moses and the elders of Israel commanded the people: "Keep all these
commands[w] that I give you today. 2 When
you have crossed the Jordan[x] into the land
the LORD your God is giving you, set up
some large stones[y] and coat them with
plaster.[z] 3 Write on them all the words of
this law when you have crossed over to
enter the land the LORD your God is giving
you, a land flowing with milk and honey,[a]
just as the LORD, the God of your ancestors, promised you. 4 And when you have
crossed the Jordan, set up these stones on
Mount Ebal,[b] as I command you today,
and coat them with plaster. 5 Build there
an altar[c] to the LORD your God, an altar of
stones. Do not use any iron tool[d] on them.
6 Build the altar of the LORD your God with
fieldstones and offer burnt offerings on it
to the LORD your God. 7 Sacrifice fellowship offerings[e] there, eating them and rejoicing[f] in the presence of the LORD your
God.[g] 8 And you shall write very clearly all
the words of this law on these stones[h] you
have set up."[i]

Curses From Mount Ebal

9 Then Moses and the Levitical[j] priests
said to all Israel, "Be silent, Israel, and
listen! You have now become the people
of the LORD your God.[k] 10 Obey the LORD
your God and follow his commands and
decrees that I give you today."
11 On the same day Moses commanded
the people:
12 When you have crossed the Jordan,
these tribes shall stand on Mount Gerizim[l]
to bless the people: Simeon, Levi, Judah,
Issachar,[m] Joseph and Benjamin.[n] 13 And
these tribes shall stand on Mount Ebal[o]
to pronounce curses: Reuben, Gad, Asher,
Zebulun, Dan and Naphtali.
14 The Levites shall recite to all the people of Israel in a loud voice:

15 "Cursed is anyone who makes
an idol[p]—a thing detestable[q] to the
LORD, the work of skilled hands—and
sets it up in secret."
Then all the people shall say,
"Amen!"[r]
16 "Cursed is anyone who dishonors
their father or mother."[s]
Then all the people shall say,
"Amen!"

26:13 [m] Ps 119:141, 153,176 **26:14** [n] Lev 7:20; Hos 9:4 **26:15** [o] Ps 68:5; 80:14; 102:19; Isa 63:15; Zec 2:13 [p] S Ex 39:43 **26:16** [q] Dt 4:29 **26:17** [r] Ex 19:8; Ps 48:14 **26:18** [s] Ex 6:7; Dt 7:6 **26:19** [t] Isa 62:7; Zep 3:20 [u] Dt 4:7-8; 28:1,13,44; 1Ch 14:2; Ps 148:14; Isa 40:11 [v] S Dt 7:6 **27:1** [w] Ps 78:7 **27:2** [x] Jos 4:1 [y] Ex 24:4; Jos 24:26; 1Sa 7:12 [z] Jos 8:31 **27:3** [a] S Ex 3:8 **27:4** [b] S Dt 11:29 **27:5** [c] S Ex 20:24 [d] Ex 20:25 **27:7** [e] S Ex 32:6 [f] S Dt 16:11 [g] Jos 8:31 **27:8** [h] Isa 8:1; 30:8; Hab 2:2 [i] Jos 8:32 **27:9** [j] S Dt 17:9 [k] Dt 26:18 **27:12** [l] S Dt 11:29 [m] S Ge 30:18 [n] Jos 8:35 **27:13** [o] S Dt 11:29 **27:15** [p] S Ex 20:4 [q] 1Ki 11:5, 7; 2Ki 23:13; Isa 44:19; 66:3 [r] Nu 5:22; S 1Co 14:16 **27:16** [s] S Ge 31:35; S Ex 21:12; S Dt 5:16

26:16 *with all your heart . . . soul.* See note on 4:29.
26:17 The terminology is that of a covenant or treaty, involving a renewal of Israel's vow that the Lord was God and that they would obey him (see 5:27; see also note on Ex 19:8).
26:18 *treasured possession.* See note on Ex 19:5.
26:19 *a people holy to the LORD.* See 14:2 and note.
27:2-8 Setting up stones inscribed with messages to be remembered was a common practice in the ancient Near East. Many such stones have been uncovered by archaeologists.
27:2,4 *coat them with plaster.* So that the writing inscribed on them would stand out clearly (see v. 8).
27:3,8 *all the words of this law.* The stipulations (see note on Ex 20:1) of the covenant that Moses' reaffirmation contained.
27:4 *Mount Ebal.* See note on Jos 8:30.
27:5 *Build . . . an altar of stones.* Different from the altars of the tabernacle, both in form and in use (see note on Ex 20:25).
27:9 *You have now become the people of the LORD.* The language of covenant renewal.
27:12 *these tribes shall stand on Mount Gerizim.* All six were descendants of Jacob by Leah and Rachel (see Ge 35:23-24). See 11:30 and note. *Mount Gerizim.* See note on Jn 4:20. *to bless.* No blessings appear in vv. 15-26, which consist entirely of 12 curses (see 28:15-68). Blessings, however, are listed and described in 28:1-14.
27:13 *these tribes shall stand on Mount Ebal.* Reuben and Zebulun were descendants of Jacob by Leah; the rest were his descendants by the female servants Zilpah and Bilhah (see Ge 35:23,25-26).
27:15 *makes an idol.* In violation of the first and second commandments of the Decalogue (see notes on Ex 20:1,4). See 4:28; 5:6-10; 31:29; Isa 40:19-20; 41:7; 44:9-20; 45:16; Jer 10:3-9; Hos 8:4-6; 13:2. *Amen!* Not simply approval but a solemn, formal assertion that the people accept and agree to the covenant with its curses and blessings (see vv. 16-26).
27:16 See 5:16; Ex 20:12 and note.

[17]"Cursed is anyone who moves their neighbor's boundary stone."[t]
Then all the people shall say, "Amen!"

[18]"Cursed is anyone who leads the blind astray on the road."[u]
Then all the people shall say, "Amen!"

[19]"Cursed is anyone who withholds justice from the foreigner,[v] the fatherless or the widow."[w]
Then all the people shall say, "Amen!"

[20]"Cursed is anyone who sleeps with his father's wife, for he dishonors his father's bed."[x]
Then all the people shall say, "Amen!"

[21]"Cursed is anyone who has sexual relations with any animal."[y]
Then all the people shall say, "Amen!"

[22]"Cursed is anyone who sleeps with his sister, the daughter of his father or the daughter of his mother."[z]
Then all the people shall say, "Amen!"

[23]"Cursed is anyone who sleeps with his mother-in-law."[a]
Then all the people shall say, "Amen!"

[24]"Cursed is anyone who kills[b] their neighbor secretly."[c]
Then all the people shall say, "Amen!"

[25]"Cursed is anyone who accepts a bribe to kill an innocent person."[d]
Then all the people shall say, "Amen!"

[26]"Cursed is anyone who does not uphold the words of this law by carrying them out."[e]
Then all the people shall say, "Amen!"[f]

Blessings for Obedience

28 If you fully obey the LORD your God and carefully follow[g] all his commands[h] I give you today, the LORD your God will set you high above all the nations on earth.[i] [2]All these blessings will come on you[j] and accompany you if you obey the LORD your God:

[3]You will be blessed[k] in the city and blessed in the country.[l]
[4]The fruit of your womb will be blessed, and the crops of your land and the young of your livestock—the calves of your herds and the lambs of your flocks.[m]
[5]Your basket and your kneading trough will be blessed.
[6]You will be blessed when you come in and blessed when you go out.[n]

[7]The LORD will grant that the enemies[o] who rise up against you will be defeated before you. They will come at you from one direction but flee from you in seven.[p]
[8]The LORD will send a blessing on your barns and on everything you put your hand to. The LORD your God will bless[q] you in the land he is giving you.
[9]The LORD will establish you as his holy people,[r] as he promised you on oath, if you keep the commands[s] of the LORD your God and walk in obedience to him.
[10]Then all the peoples on earth will see that you are called by the name[t] of the LORD, and they will fear you. [11]The LORD will grant you abundant prosperity—in the fruit of your womb, the young of your livestock[u] and the crops of your ground—in the land he swore to your ancestors to give you.[v]
[12]The LORD will open the heavens, the storehouse[w] of his bounty,[x] to send rain[y] on your land in season and to bless[z] all the work of your hands. You will lend to many nations but will borrow from none.[a]
[13]The LORD will make you the head, not the tail. If you pay attention to the commands of the LORD your God that I give you this day and carefully follow[b] them, you will always be at the top, never at the bottom.[c] [14]Do not turn aside from any of the commands I give you today, to the right or to the left,[d] following other gods and serving them.

27:17 [t]S Dt 19:14 **27:18** [u]S Lev 19:14 **27:19** [v]S Ex 22:21; S Dt 24:19 [w]S Ex 23:2; S Dt 10:18 **27:20** [x]S Ge 34:5; S Lev 18:7 **27:21** [y]S Ex 22:19 **27:22** [z]S Lev 18:9 **27:23** [a]S Lev 20:14 **27:24** [b]S Ge 4:23 [c]Ex 21:12 **27:25** [d]Ex 23:7-8; S Lev 19:16 **27:26** [e]S Lev 26:14; Dt 28:15; Ps 119:21; Jer 11:3; Gal 3:10* [f]Jer 11:5 **28:1** [g]S Dt 15:5 [h]S Lev 26:3 [i]S Nu 24:7; S Dt 26:19 **28:2** [j]Jer 32:24; Zec 1:6 **28:3** [k]Ps 144:15 [l]S Ge 39:5 **28:4** [m]S Ge 49:25; S Dt 8:18 **28:6** [n]Ps 121:8 **28:7** [o]2Ch 6:34 [p]S Lev 26:8,17 **28:8** [q]Dt 15:4 **28:9** [r]S Ex 19:6 [s]S Lev 26:3 **28:10** [t]S Nu 6:27; 1Ki 8:43; Jer 25:29; Da 9:18 **28:11** [u]S Ge 30:27 [v]ver 4; Dt 30:9 **28:12** [w]Job 38:22; Ps 135:7; Jer 10:13; 51:16 [x]Ps 65:11; 68:10; Jer 31:12 [y]S Lev 26:4; 1Ki 8:35-36; 18:1; Ps 104:13; Isa 5:6; 30:23; 32:20 [z]Isa 61:9; 65:23; Jer 32:38-41; Mal 3:12 [a]ver 44; S Lev 25:19; S Dt 15:3,6; Eze 34:26 **28:13** [b]Jer 11:6 [c]S Dt 26:19 **28:14** [d]S Dt 5:32; Jos 1:7

27:17 See note on 19:14.
27:19 See 24:17–18 and note.
27:20 See 22:30; Lev 18:8 and notes.
27:21 See Ex 22:19 and note; Lev 18:23; 20:15–16.
27:22 See Lev 18:9,11 and note.
27:24–25 See 5:17; Ex 20:13 and note; 21:12; Lev 24:17,21.
27:26 Quoted in Gal 3:10 to prove that humankind is under a curse because no one follows the law of God fully (cf. Jas 2:10; 1Jn 1:8,10).
28:1–14 These blessings are the opposites of the curses in vv. 15–44 (compare especially vv. 3–6 with vv. 16–19).
28:5,17 *basket ... kneading trough.* Used for storage and for the preparation of foods, particularly bread.
28:7 For the reverse, see v. 25.
28:9 *establish you as his holy people.* See 7:6 and note.
28:12 *the heavens, the storehouse.* For the heavens as the storehouse of rain, snow, hail and wind, see Job 38:22; Ps 135:7; Jer 10:13; 51:16. *You will lend.* For the opposite, see v. 44; see also note on 15:6.
28:13 *the head, not the tail.* For the reverse, see v. 44.

Curses for Disobedience

15 However, if you do not obey[e] the LORD
your God and do not carefully follow all
his commands and decrees I am giving
you today,[f] all these curses will come on
you and overtake you:[g]

16 You will be cursed in the city and
cursed in the country.[h]
17 Your basket and your kneading
trough will be cursed.[i]
18 The fruit of your womb will be
cursed, and the crops of your land,
and the calves of your herds and the
lambs of your flocks.[j]
19 You will be cursed when you
come in and cursed when you go
out.[k]

20 The LORD will send on you curses,[l]
confusion and rebuke[m] in everything you
put your hand to, until you are destroyed
and come to sudden ruin[n] because of the
evil[o] you have done in forsaking him.[a]
21 The LORD will plague you with diseases until he has destroyed you from the
land you are entering to possess.[p] 22 The
LORD will strike you with wasting disease,[q] with fever and inflammation, with
scorching heat and drought,[r] with blight[s]
and mildew, which will plague[t] you until you perish.[u] 23 The sky over your head
will be bronze, the ground beneath you
iron.[v] 24 The LORD will turn the rain[w] of
your country into dust and powder; it will
come down from the skies until you are
destroyed.
25 The LORD will cause you to be defeated[x] before your enemies. You will come
at them from one direction but flee from
them in seven,[y] and you will become a
thing of horror[z] to all the kingdoms on
earth.[a] 26 Your carcasses will be food for
all the birds[b] and the wild animals, and
there will be no one to frighten them
away.[c] 27 The LORD will afflict you with the
boils of Egypt[d] and with tumors, festering
sores and the itch, from which you cannot be cured. 28 The LORD will afflict you
with madness, blindness and confusion of
mind. 29 At midday you will grope[e] about
like a blind person in the dark. You will be
unsuccessful in everything you do; day after day you will be oppressed and robbed,
with no one to rescue[f] you.
30 You will be pledged to be married to a
woman, but another will take her and rape
her.[g] You will build a house, but you will
not live in it.[h] You will plant a vineyard,
but you will not even begin to enjoy its
fruit.[i] 31 Your ox will be slaughtered before
your eyes, but you will eat none of it. Your
donkey will be forcibly taken from you
and will not be returned. Your sheep will
be given to your enemies, and no one will
rescue them. 32 Your sons and daughters
will be given to another nation,[j] and you
will wear out your eyes watching for them
day after day, powerless to lift a hand. 33 A
people that you do not know will eat what
your land and labor produce, and you will
have nothing but cruel oppression[k] all your
days.[l] 34 The sights you see will drive you
mad.[m] 35 The LORD will afflict your knees
and legs with painful boils[n] that cannot
be cured, spreading from the soles of your
feet to the top of your head.[o]
36 The LORD will drive you and the king[p]
you set over you to a nation unknown to
you or your ancestors.[q] There you will
worship other gods, gods of wood and
stone.[r] 37 You will become a thing of horror,[s] a byword[t] and an object of ridicule[u]
among all the peoples where the LORD will
drive you.[v]
38 You will sow much seed in the field
but you will harvest little,[w] because locusts[x] will devour[y] it. 39 You will plant
vineyards and cultivate them but you will
not drink the wine[z] or gather the grapes,
because worms will eat[a] them.[b] 40 You will
have olive trees throughout your country but you will not use the oil, because
the olives will drop off.[c] 41 You will have
sons and daughters but you will not keep
them, because they will go into captivity.[d] 42 Swarms of locusts[e] will take over all
your trees and the crops of your land.
43 The foreigners who reside among you
will rise above you higher and higher, but
you will sink lower and lower.[f] 44 They
will lend to you, but you will not lend to
them.[g] They will be the head, but you will
be the tail.[h]

28:15 [e] 1Ki 9:6; 2Ch 7:19 [f] S Dt 27:26 [g] Dt 29:27; Jos 23:15; 2Ch 12:5; Da 9:11; Mal 2:2 **28:16** [h] ver 3 **28:17** [i] ver 5 **28:18** [j] ver 4 **28:19** [k] ver 6 **28:20** [l] ver 8, 15; Lev 26:16; Jer 42:18; Mal 2:2; 3:9; 4:6 [m] Ps 39:11; 76:6; 80:16; Isa 17:13; 51:20; 54:9; 66:15; Eze 5:15 [n] Dt 4:26 [o] S Ex 32:22 **28:21** [p] Lev 26:25; Nu 14:12; Jer 24:10; Am 4:10 **28:22** [q] ver 48; Dt 32:24 [r] Lev 26:16; 2Ki 8:1; Job 12:15; Ps 105:16; Jer 14:1; Hag 1:11; Mal 3:9 [s] Hag 2:17 [t] S Lev 26:25 [u] Dt 4:26; Am 4:9 **28:23** [v] S Lev 26:19 **28:24** [w] Lev 26:19; Dt 11:17; 1Ki 8:35; 17:1; Isa 5:6; Jer 14:1; Hag 1:10 **28:25** [x] 1Sa 4:10; Ps 78:62 [y] S Lev 26:17 [z] ver 37 [a] 2Ch 29:8; 30:7; Jer 15:4; 24:9; 26:6; 29:18; 44:12; Eze 23:46 **28:26** [b] S Ge 40:19 [c] Ps 79:2; Isa 18:6; Jer 7:33; 12:9; 15:2; 16:4; 19:7; 34:20 **28:27** [d] Dt 7:15 **28:29** [e] Ge 19:11; Ex 10:21; Job 5:14; 12:25; 24:13; 38:15; Isa 59:10 [f] Jdg 3:9; 2Ki 13:5; Est 4:14; Isa 19:20; 43:11; Hos 13:4; Ob 1:21 **28:30** [g] Job 31:10 [h] Isa 65:22; Am 5:11

[a] 20 Hebrew *me*

[i] Jer 12:13 **28:32** [j] ver 41 **28:33** [k] Jer 6:6; 22:17 [l] Jer 5:15-17; Eze 25:4 **28:34** [m] ver 67 **28:35** [n] Dt 7:15; Rev 16:2 [o] Job 2:7; 7:5; 13:28; 30:17,30; Isa 1:6 **28:36** [p] 1Sa 12:25 [q] S Dt 4:27; 2Ki 24:14; 25:7,11; 2Ch 33:11; 36:21; Ezr 5:12; Jer 15:14; 16:13; 27:20; 39:1-9; 52:28; La 1:3 [r] S Dt 4:28 **28:37** [s] ver 25; Jer 42:18; Eze 5:15 [t] Ps 22:7; 39:8; 44:13; 64:8; Jer 18:16; 48:27; Mic 6:16 [u] 2Ch 7:20; Ezr 9:7; Jer 44:8 [v] 1Ki 9:7; Ps 44:14; Jer 19:8; 24:9; 25:9,18; 29:18; La 2:15 **28:38** [w] Lev 26:20; Ps 129:7; Isa 5:10; Jer 12:13; Hos 8:7; Mic 6:15; Hag 1:6,9; 2:16 [x] S Ex 10:4 [y] S Ex 10:15 **28:39** [z] S Lev 10:9 [a] Joel 1:4; 2:25; Mal 3:11 [b] Isa 5:10; 17:10-11; Zep 1:13 **28:40** [c] Jer 11:16; Mic 6:15 **28:41** [d] ver 32 **28:42** [e] ver 38; Jdg 6:5; 7:12; Jer 46:23 **28:43** [f] ver 13 **28:44** [g] S ver 12 [h] S Dt 26:19

28:16–19 The opposites of vv. 3–6 (see note on vv. 1–14).
28:23 *sky … bronze … ground … iron.* No rain would pierce the sky or penetrate the ground (see v. 22).
28:25 For the reverse, see v. 7.
28:27 *boils of Egypt.* See note on Ex 9:9.
28:30–33 See Mic 6:14–15; Hag 1:6 and note.
28:30 See 20:5–8 and note; contrast Isa 65:21–22.
28:35 See note on Ex 9:11.
28:44 See notes on vv. 12–13.

45 All these curses will come on you.
They will pursue you and overtake you[i]
until you are destroyed,[j] because you did
not obey the LORD your God and observe
the commands and decrees he gave you.
46 They will be a sign and a wonder to you
and your descendants forever.[k] 47 Because
you did not serve[l] the LORD your God joyfully and gladly[m] in the time of prosperity,
48 therefore in hunger and thirst,[n] in nakedness and dire poverty, you will serve the
enemies the LORD sends against you. He
will put an iron yoke[o] on your neck[p] until
he has destroyed you.
49 The LORD will bring a nation against
you[q] from far away, from the ends of the
earth,[r] like an eagle[s] swooping down, a
nation whose language you will not understand,[t] 50 a fierce-looking nation without respect for the old[u] or pity for the
young. 51 They will devour the young of
your livestock and the crops of your land
until you are destroyed. They will leave
you no grain, new wine[v] or olive oil,[w] nor
any calves of your herds or lambs of your
flocks until you are ruined.[x] 52 They will
lay siege[y] to all the cities throughout your
land until the high fortified walls in which
you trust fall down. They will besiege all
the cities throughout the land the LORD
your God is giving you.[z]
53 Because of the suffering your enemy
will inflict on you during the siege, you
will eat the fruit of the womb, the flesh
of the sons and daughters the LORD your
God has given you.[a] 54 Even the most gentle and sensitive man among you will have
no compassion on his own brother or the
wife he loves or his surviving children,
55 and he will not give to one of them any
of the flesh of his children that he is eating. It will be all he has left because of
the suffering your enemy will inflict on
you during the siege of all your cities.[b]
56 The most gentle and sensitive[c] woman
among you — so sensitive and gentle that
she would not venture to touch the ground
with the sole of her foot — will begrudge
the husband she loves and her own son or
daughter[d] 57 the afterbirth from her womb
and the children she bears. For in her dire
need she intends to eat them[e] secretly because of the suffering your enemy will inflict on you during the siege of your cities.
58 If you do not carefully follow all the
words of this law,[f] which are written in
this book, and do not revere[g] this glorious and awesome name[h] — the LORD your
God — 59 the LORD will send fearful plagues
on you and your descendants, harsh and
prolonged disasters, and severe and lingering illnesses. 60 He will bring on you all
the diseases of Egypt[i] that you dreaded,
and they will cling to you. 61 The LORD will
also bring on you every kind of sickness
and disaster not recorded in this Book of
the Law,[j] until you are destroyed.[k] 62 You
who were as numerous as the stars in the
sky[l] will be left but few[m] in number, because you did not obey the LORD your God.
63 Just as it pleased[n] the LORD to make you
prosper and increase in number, so it will
please[o] him to ruin and destroy you.[p] You
will be uprooted[q] from the land you are
entering to possess.
64 Then the LORD will scatter[r] you among
all nations,[s] from one end of the earth to
the other.[t] There you will worship other
gods — gods of wood and stone, which
neither you nor your ancestors have
known.[u] 65 Among those nations you will
find no repose, no resting place[v] for the
sole of your foot. There the LORD will give
you an anxious mind, eyes[w] weary with
longing, and a despairing heart.[x] 66 You

28:45 [i] S Ex 15:9 [j] ver 15; Dt 4:25-26 **28:46** [k] S Nu 16:38; Ps 71:7; Isa 8:18; 20:3; Eze 5:15; Zec 3:8 **28:47** [l] S Dt 10:12 [m] S Lev 23:40; Ne 9:35 **28:48** [n] Jer 14:3; La 4:4 [o] Jer 28:13-14; La 1:14 [p] Ge 49:8 **28:49** [q] S Lev 26:44 [r] Isa 5:26-30, 26; 7:18-20; 39:3; Jer 4:16; 5:15; 6:22; 25:32; 31:8; Hab 1:6 [s] 2Sa 1:23; Jer 4:13; 48:40; 49:22; La 4:19; Eze 17:3 [t] S Ge 11:7; 1Co 14:21* **28:50** [u] Isa 47:6 **28:51** [v] Ps 4:7; Isa 36:17; Hag 1:11 [w] S Nu 18:12 [x] ver 33; Jdg 6:4 **28:52** [y] 2Ki 6:24 [z] Jer 10:18; Eze 6:10; Zep 1:14-16, 17 **28:53** [a] ver 57; Lev 26:29; 2Ki 6:28-29; La 2:20 **28:55** [b] 2Ki 6:29 **28:56** [c] Isa 47:1 [d] La 4:10 **28:57** [e] S ver 53 **28:58** [f] Dt 31:24 [g] Ps 96:4; Jer 5:22; Mal 1:14; 2:5; 3:5, 16; 4:2 [h] S Ex 3:15; S Jos 7:9 **28:60** [i] Ex 15:26 **28:61** [j] Dt 29:21; 30:10; 31:26; Jos 1:8; 8:34; 23:6; 24:26; 2Ki 14:6; 22:8; 2Ch 17:9; 25:4; Ne 8:1, 18; Mal 4:4 [k] Dt 4:25-26 **28:62** [l] S Ge 22:17; Dt 4:27; 10:22 [m] S Lev 26:22 **28:63** [n] Dt 30:9; Isa 62:5; 65:19; Jer 32:41; Zep 3:17 [o] Pr 1:26 [p] S Ge 6:7 [q] Ps 52:5; Jer 12:14; 31:28; 45:4 **28:64** [r] S Dt 4:27; Ezr 9:7; Isa 6:12; Jer 32:23; 43:11; 52:27 [s] Ne 1:8; Ps 44:11; Jer 13:24; 18:17; 22:22 [t] S Dt 4:32; S Jer 8:19 [u] Dt 11:28; 32:17 **28:65** [v] La 1:3 [w] Job 11:20 [x] Lev 26:16, 36; Hos 9:17

28:49 *ends of the earth.* An indefinite figurative expression meaning "far away"—anywhere from the visible horizon to the outer perimeter of the then-known world. *eagle swooping down.* Later used to symbolize the speed and power of the Assyrians (see Hos 8:1) and Babylonians (see Jer 48:40; 49:22). *whose language you will not understand.* The Lord's threat was fulfilled through the actions of Assyria and Babylonia, whose languages, though related to Hebrew, were not understood by the average Israelite (see Isa 28:11; 33:19 and note; cf. 1Co 14:21).

28:53 *suffering your enemy will inflict on you during the siege.* See vv. 55,57. The repetition of the clause emphasizes the distress that the Israelites would suffer if they refused to obey the Lord. *you will eat ... sons and daughters.* For the actualizing of this curse, see 2Ki 6:24–29; La 2:20; 4:10; cf. Zec 11:9 and note.

28:58 *words of this law.* See note on 31:24. *this glorious and awesome name — the LORD.* See note and NIV text note on Ex 3:15. One of the oddities of history is the loss of the proper pronunciation of the Hebrew word *YHWH,* the personal and covenant name of God in the OT (see note on Ge 2:4). "Jehovah" is a spelling that developed from combining the consonants of the name with the vowels of a word for "Lord" (*Adonai*). "Yahweh" is probably the original pronunciation. The name eventually ceased to be pronounced because later Jews thought it too holy to be uttered and feared violating Ex 20:7; Lev 24:16. It is translated "LORD" in this version (see the end of the Introduction to this study Bible: The Divine Name Yahweh).

28:60 *diseases of Egypt.* Those brought on the Egyptians during the plagues (see 7:15; Ex 15:26).

28:61 *Book of the Law.* See note on 31:24.

28:62 *as the stars in the sky.* See 1:10; see also notes on 1:10; Ge 13:16; 15:5.

28:64 *will scatter you.* Experienced by Israel in the Assyrian (722–721 BC) and Babylonian (586 BC) exiles (see 2Ki 17:6; 25:21).

will live in constant suspense, filled with
dread both night and day, never sure of
your life. 67In the morning you will say,
"If only it were evening!" and in the evening, "If only it were morning!"—because
of the terror that will fill your hearts and
the sights that your eyes will see.[y] 68The
LORD will send you back in ships to Egypt
on a journey I said you should never make
again.[z] There you will offer yourselves for
sale to your enemies as male and female
slaves, but no one will buy you.

Renewal of the Covenant

29[a] These are the terms of the covenant the LORD commanded Mo-
ses to make with the Israelites in Moab,[a]
in addition to the covenant he had made
with them at Horeb.[b]
2Moses summoned all the Israelites and
said to them:

Your eyes have seen all that the LORD
did in Egypt to Pharaoh, to all his officials
and to all his land.[c] 3With your own eyes
you saw those great trials, those signs and
great wonders.[d] 4But to this day the LORD
has not given you a mind that understands
or eyes that see or ears that hear.[e] 5Yet the
LORD says, "During the forty years that
I led[f] you through the wilderness, your
clothes did not wear out, nor did the sandals on your feet.[g] 6You ate no bread and
drank no wine or other fermented drink.[h] I
did this so that you might know that I am
the LORD your God."[i]
7When you reached this place, Sihon[j]
king of Heshbon[k] and Og king of Bashan
came out to fight against us, but we defeated them.[l] 8We took their land and gave
it as an inheritance[m] to the Reubenites, the
Gadites and the half-tribe of Manasseh.[n]
9Carefully follow[o] the terms of this covenant,[p] so that you may prosper in everything you do.[q] 10All of you are standing
today in the presence of the LORD your
God—your leaders and chief men, your
elders and officials, and all the other men
of Israel, 11together with your children
and your wives, and the foreigners living in your camps who chop your wood
and carry your water.[r] 12You are standing
here in order to enter into a covenant with
the LORD your God, a covenant the LORD
is making with you this day and sealing
with an oath, 13to confirm you this day as
his people,[s] that he may be your God[t] as
he promised you and as he swore to your
fathers, Abraham, Isaac and Jacob. 14I am
making this covenant,[u] with its oath, not
only with you 15who are standing here
with us today in the presence of the LORD
our God but also with those who are not
here today.[v]
16You yourselves know how we lived
in Egypt and how we passed through
the countries on the way here. 17You saw
among them their detestable images and
idols of wood and stone, of silver and
gold.[w] 18Make sure there is no man or
woman, clan or tribe among you today
whose heart turns[x] away from the LORD our
God to go and worship the gods of those
nations; make sure there is no root among
you that produces such bitter poison.[y]
19When such a person hears the words
of this oath and they invoke a blessing[z]
on themselves, thinking, "I will be safe,
even though I persist in going my own
way,"[a] they will bring disaster on the watered land as well as the dry. 20The LORD
will never be willing to forgive[b] them; his
wrath and zeal[c] will burn[d] against them.
All the curses written in this book will fall
on them, and the LORD will blot[e] out their
names from under heaven. 21The LORD will
single them out from all the tribes of Israel
for disaster,[f] according to all the curses of
the covenant written in this Book of the
Law.[g]
22Your children who follow you in later generations and foreigners who come

28:67 [y] ver 34 **28:68** [z] S Ex 13:14 **29:1** [a] S Lev 7:38 [b] S Ex 3:1 **29:2** [c] Ex 19:4 **29:3** [d] S Dt 4:34 **29:4** [e] Isa 6:10; 32:3; 48:8; Jer 5:21; Eze 12:2; S Mt 13:15; Eph 4:18 **29:5** [f] S Dt 8:2 [g] S Dt 8:4 **29:6** [h] S Lev 10:9 [i] Dt 8:3 **29:7** [j] S Nu 21:26 [k] S Nu 21:25 [l] Nu 21:21-24,33-35; Dt 2:26-3:11 **29:8** [m] Ps 78:55; 135:12; 136:22 [n] Nu 32:33; Dt 3:12-13 **29:9** [o] S Dt 4:6; S Jos 1:7 [p] Ex 19:5; Ps 25:10; 103:18 [q] Jos 1:8; 2Ch 31:21 **29:11** [r] Jos 9:21,23,27; 1Ch 20:3 **29:13** [s] S Ge 6:18; S Ex 19:6 [t] S Ge 17:7 **29:14** [u] Ex 19:5; Isa 59:21; Jer 31:31; 32:40; 50:5; Eze 16:62; 37:26; Heb 8:7-8 **29:15** [v] S Ge 6:18; Ac 2:39 **29:17** [w] Ex 20:23; Dt 4:28 **29:18** [x] S Dt 13:6 [y] S Dt 11:16; Heb 12:15 **29:19** [z] Ps 72:17; Isa 65:16 [a] Ps 36:2 **29:20** [b] S Ex 23:21 [c] Ex 34:14; Eze 23:25; Zep 1:18 [d] Ps 74:1; 79:5; 80:4; Eze 36:5 [e] 2Ki 13:23; 14:27; Rev 3:5 **29:21** [f] Dt 32:23; Eze 7:26 [g] S Dt 28:61

[a] In Hebrew texts 29:1 is numbered 28:69, and 29:2-29 is numbered 29:1-28.

28:68 *a journey I said you should never make again.* See 17:16; Ex 13:17; Nu 14:3–4.
29:1 See notes on 5:2–3.
29:2 *Your eyes have seen.* Only those who were less than 20 years old (Nu 14:29) when Israel followed the majority spy report at Kadesh Barnea and refused to enter Canaan would have actually experienced life in Egypt before the exodus. But Moses is speaking to the people as a nation and referring to the national experience (see note on 5:3).
29:4 Quoted in Ro 11:8 and applied to hardened Israel.
29:7 *Sihon ... Og.* See 1:4 and note.
29:8 *gave it as an inheritance.* See 3:12–17.
29:9–15 A clear summary of the nature of covenant reaffirmation.
29:13 *his people ... your God.* See note on Zec 8:8.
29:17 *idols.* See note on Lev 26:30.
29:18 *root ... that produces such bitter poison.* The poison of idolatry, involving the rejection of the Lord (see Ex 20:3–4; 34:15 and notes).
29:19 *oath.* God's covenant with his people (vv. 12–14). *watered land ... dry.* A disaster of major proportions is indicated (vv. 20–21).
29:20 *The LORD will never be willing to forgive them.* Not to be taken as contradictory to 2Pe 3:9 ("not wanting anyone to perish"). Peter, too, says that those who deny the "sovereign Lord" bring "swift destruction on themselves" (2Pe 2:1). See note on 2Pe 3:9. *this book.* See note on 31:24. *blot out their names.* See 9:14 and note.
29:21 *Book of the Law.* See note on 31:24.

from distant lands will see the calamities that have fallen on the land and the diseases with which the LORD has afflicted it.[h] 23 The whole land will be a burning waste[i] of salt[j] and sulfur — nothing planted, nothing sprouting, no vegetation growing on it. It will be like the destruction of Sodom and Gomorrah,[k] Admah and Zeboyim, which the LORD overthrew in fierce anger.[l] 24 All the nations will ask: "Why has the LORD done this to this land?[m] Why this fierce, burning anger?"

25 And the answer will be: "It is because this people abandoned the covenant of the LORD, the God of their ancestors, the covenant he made with them when he brought them out of Egypt.[n] 26 They went off and worshiped other gods and bowed down to them, gods they did not know, gods he had not given them. 27 Therefore the LORD's anger burned against this land, so that he brought on it all the curses written in this book.[o] 28 In furious anger and in great wrath[p] the LORD uprooted[q] them from their land and thrust them into another land, as it is now."

29 The secret things belong to the LORD our God,[r] but the things revealed belong to us and to our children forever, that we may follow all the words of this law.[s]

Prosperity After Turning to the LORD

30 When all these blessings and curses[t] I have set before you come on you and you take them to heart wherever the LORD your God disperses you among the nations,[u] 2 and when you and your children return[v] to the LORD your God and obey him with all your heart[w] and with all your soul according to everything I command you today, 3 then the LORD your God will restore your fortunes[a][x] and have compassion[y] on you and gather[z] you again from all the nations where he scattered[a] you.[b] 4 Even if you have been banished to the most distant land under the heavens,[c] from there the LORD your God will gather[d] you and bring you back.[e] 5 He will bring[f] you to the land that belonged to your ancestors, and you will take possession of it. He will make you more prosperous and numerous[g] than your ancestors. 6 The LORD your God will circumcise your hearts and the hearts of your descendants,[h] so that you may love[i] him with all your heart and with all your soul, and live. 7 The LORD your God will put all these curses[j] on your enemies who hate and persecute you.[k] 8 You will again obey the LORD and follow all his commands I am giving you today. 9 Then the LORD your God will make you most prosperous in all the work of your hands and in the fruit of your womb, the young of your livestock and the crops of your land.[l] The LORD will again delight[m] in you and make you prosperous, just as he delighted in your ancestors, 10 if you obey the LORD your God and keep his commands and decrees that are written in this Book of the Law[n] and turn to the LORD your God with all your heart and with all your soul.[o]

The Offer of Life or Death

11 Now what I am commanding you today is not too difficult for you or beyond your reach.[p] 12 It is not up in heaven, so that you have to ask, "Who will ascend into heaven[q] to get it and proclaim it to us so we may obey it?"[r] 13 Nor is it beyond the sea,[s] so that you have to ask, "Who will cross the sea to get it and proclaim it to us so we may obey it?"[t] 14 No, the word is very near you; it is in your mouth and in your heart so you may obey it.[u]

15 See, I set before you today life[v] and prosperity,[w] death[x] and destruction.[y] 16 For I command you today to love[z] the LORD your God, to walk in obedience to him, and to keep his commands, decrees and laws; then you will live[a] and increase, and the LORD your God will bless you in the land you are entering to possess.

17 But if your heart turns away and you are not obedient, and if you are drawn away to bow down to other gods and wor-

[a] 3 Or *will bring you back from captivity*

29:22 [h] Jer 19:8; 49:17; 50:13 **29:23** [i] Isa 1:7; 6:11; 9:18; 64:10; Jer 12:11; 44:2, 6; Mic 5:11 [j] S Ge 13:10; Eze 47:11 [k] S Ge 19:24, 25; Zep 2:9; S Mt 10:15; Ro 9:29 [l] S Ge 14:8 **29:24** [m] 1Ki 9:8; 2Ch 36:19; Jer 16:10; 22:8-9; 52:13 **29:25** [n] 2Ki 17:23; 2Ch 36:21 **29:27** [o] S Dt 28:15 **29:28** [p] Ps 7:11 [q] 1Ki 14:15; 2Ch 7:20; Ps 9:6; 52:5; Pr 2:22; Jer 12:14; 31:28; 42:10; Eze 19:12 **29:29** [r] Ac 1:7 [s] Jn 5:39; Ac 17:11; 2Ti 3:16 **30:1** [t] S Dt 11:26 [u] Lev 26:40-45; S Dt 4:32; 29:28 **30:2** [v] S Dt 4:30 [w] Dt 4:29; Ps 119:2 **30:3** [x] Ps 14:7; 53:6; 85:1; 126:4; Jer 30:18; 33:11; Eze 16:53; Joel 3:1; Zep 2:7 [y] Dt 13:17 [z] S Ge 48:21 [a] S Ge 11:4; Dt 4:27 [b] Isa 11:11; Jer 12:15; 16:15; 24:6; 29:14; 48:47; 49:6 **30:4** [c] Ps 19:6 [d] Isa 17:6; 24:13; 27:12; 40:11; 49:5; 56:8; Eze 20:34, 41; 34:13 [e] Ne 1:8-9; Isa 11:12; 41:5; 42:10; 43:6; 48:20; 62:11; Jer 31:8, 10; 50:2 **30:5** [f] Jer 29:14 [g] S Dt 7:13 **30:6** [h] S Dt 6:24; S 10:16 [i] Dt 6:5 **30:7** [j] S Ge 12:3 [k] Dt 7:15 **30:9** [l] Jer 1:10; 24:6; 31:28; 32:41; 42:10; 45:4 [m] S Dt 28:63 **30:10** [n] S Dt 28:61 [o] S Dt 4:29 **30:11** [p] Ps 19:8; Isa 45:19, 23; 63:1 **30:12** [q] Pr 30:4 [r] Ro 10:6* **30:13** [s] Job 28:14 [t] Ro 10:7* **30:14** [u] S Dt 6:6; Ro 10:8* **30:15** [v] Pr 10:16; 11:19; 12:28; Jer 21:8 [w] Dt 28:11; Job 36:11; Ps 25:13; 106:5; Pr 3:1-2 [x] S Ge 2:17 [y] S Dt 11:26 **30:16** [z] Dt 6:5 [a] ver 19; Dt 4:1; 32:47; Ne 9:29

29:23 *destruction of Sodom.* See Ge 19:24 – 25; see also notes on Ge 10:19; 13:10.
29:27 *this book.* See note on 31:24.
29:28 *as it is now.* This would be said when Israel was in exile (see vv. 22 – 25).
29:29 *secret things.* The hidden events of Israel's future relative to the blessings and curses; but the phrase can also have wider application. *things revealed.* Primarily the "words of this law."
30:2,6,10 *with all your heart and … soul.* See note on 4:29.
30:3 *restore your fortunes.* See NIV text note.
30:6 *circumcise your hearts.* See 10:16; see also note on Ge 17:10.
30:7 *curses on your enemies.* Cf. Ge 12:3.
30:9 *your ancestors.* The patriarchs (see v. 20).
30:10 *Book of the Law.* See note on 31:24.
30:12,14 *It is not up in heaven … the word is very near you.* Moses declares that understanding, believing and obeying the covenant were not beyond them. Paul applies this passage to the availability of the "message concerning faith" (Ro 10:8; see Ro 10:6 – 10).
30:16 *love … keep.* See notes on 6:5; 11:1.

ship them, 18 I declare to you this day that
you will certainly be destroyed.[b] You will
not live long in the land you are crossing
the Jordan to enter and possess.
19 This day I call the heavens and the
earth as witnesses against you[c] that I have
set before you life and death, blessings
and curses.[d] Now choose life, so that you
and your children may live 20 and that you
may love[e] the LORD your God, listen to his
voice, and hold fast to him. For the LORD
is your life,[f] and he will give[g] you many
years in the land[h] he swore to give to your
fathers, Abraham, Isaac and Jacob.

Joshua to Succeed Moses

31 Then Moses went out and spoke
these words to all Israel: 2 "I am
now a hundred and twenty years old[i] and
I am no longer able to lead you.[j] The LORD
has said to me, 'You shall not cross the
Jordan.'[k] 3 The LORD your God himself will
cross[l] over ahead of you.[m] He will destroy
these nations[n] before you, and you will
take possession of their land. Joshua also
will cross[o] over ahead of you, as the LORD
said. 4 And the LORD will do to them what
he did to Sihon and Og,[p] the kings of the
Amorites, whom he destroyed along with
their land. 5 The LORD will deliver[q] them
to you, and you must do to them all that
I have commanded you. 6 Be strong and
courageous.[r] Do not be afraid or terrified[s]
because of them, for the LORD your God
goes with you;[t] he will never leave you[u]
nor forsake[v] you."
7 Then Moses summoned Joshua and
said[w] to him in the presence of all Israel, "Be strong and courageous, for you
must go with this people into the land
that the LORD swore to their ancestors to
give them,[x] and you must divide it among
them as their inheritance. 8 The LORD himself goes before you and will be with you;[y]
he will never leave you nor forsake you.[z]
Do not be afraid; do not be discouraged."

Public Reading of the Law

9 So Moses wrote[a] down this law and
gave it to the Levitical priests, who carried[b] the ark of the covenant of the LORD,
and to all the elders of Israel. 10 Then Moses commanded them: "At the end of every seven years, in the year for canceling
debts,[c] during the Festival of Tabernacles,[d] 11 when all Israel comes to appear[e]
before the LORD your God at the place he
will choose,[f] you shall read this law[g] before them in their hearing. 12 Assemble the
people—men, women and children, and
the foreigners residing in your towns—
so they can listen and learn[h] to fear[i] the
LORD your God and follow carefully all the
words of this law. 13 Their children,[j] who
do not know this law, must hear it and
learn to fear the LORD your God as long as
you live in the land you are crossing the
Jordan to possess."

Israel's Rebellion Predicted

14 The LORD said to Moses, "Now the day
of your death[k] is near. Call Joshua[l] and
present yourselves at the tent of meeting,
where I will commission him.[m]" So Moses and Joshua came and presented themselves at the tent of meeting.[n]
15 Then the LORD appeared at the tent in
a pillar of cloud, and the cloud stood over
the entrance to the tent.[o] 16 And the LORD
said to Moses: "You are going to rest with
your ancestors,[p] and these people will

30:18 [b]S Dt 8:19 **30:19** [c]Dt 4:26 [d]S Dt 11:26 **30:20** [e]Dt 6:5 [f]Dt 4:1; S 8:3; 32:47; Ps 27:1; Pr 3:22; S Jn 5:26; Ac 17:28 [g]Ge 12:7 [h]Ps 37:3 **31:2** [i]S Ex 7:7 [j]Nu 27:17; 1Ki 3:7 [k]S Dt 3:23, 26 **31:3** [l]Nu 27:18 [m]S Dt 9:3 [n]S Dt 7:1 [o]S Dt 3:28 **31:4** [p]S Nu 21:33 **31:5** [q]S Dt 2:33 **31:6** [r]ver 7, 23; Jos 1:6, 9, 18; 10:25; 1Ch 22:13; 28:20; 2Ch 32:7 [s]Jer 1:8, 17; Eze 2:6 [t]S Ge 28:15; S Dt 1:29; 20:4; S Mt 28:20 [u]Ps 56:9; 118:6 [v]S Dt 4:31; 1Sa 12:22; 1Ki 6:13; Ps 94:14; Isa 41:17; Heb 13:5* **31:7** [w]ver 23; Nu 27:23 [x]Jos 1:6 **31:8** [y]S Ex 13:21 [z]S Ge 28:15; S Dt 4:31 **31:9** [a]S Ex 17:14 [b]ver 25; 1Ch 15:2 **31:10** [c]S Dt 15:1 [d]S Ex 23:16; Dt 16:13 **31:11** [e]S Dt 16:16 [f]Dt 12:5 [g]Jos 8:34-35; 2Ki 23:2; Ne 8:2

31:12 [h]Dt 4:10 [i]Hag 1:12; Mal 1:6; 3:5, 16 **31:13** [j]S Dt 11:2 **31:14** [k]S Ge 25:8; S Nu 27:13 [l]Nu 27:23; Dt 34:9; Jos 1:1-9 [m]S Nu 27:19 [n]Ex 33:9-11 **31:15** [o]S Ex 33:9 **31:16** [p]S Ge 15:15

30:19 *I call the heavens and the earth as witnesses.* The typical ancient covenant outside the OT contained a list of gods who served as "witnesses" to its provisions. The covenant in Deuteronomy was witnessed by "the heavens and the earth" (see 31:28; 32:1; see also notes on Ps 50:1; Isa 1:2).

30:20 *hold fast.* See note on 10:20. *the LORD is your life.* When they chose the Lord, they chose life (v. 19). In 32:46 – 47 "all the words of this law" are said to be their "life." The law, the Lord and life are bound together. "Life" in this context refers to all that makes life rich, full and productive—as God created it to be (cf. Lev 18:5; Jn 10:10 and notes).

31:2 *no longer able to lead.* Not a reference to physical disability (see 34:7). Because of his sin, the Lord did not allow Moses to lead the people into Canaan (see 1:37; 3:23 – 27; 4:21 – 22; 32:48 – 52; Nu 20:2 – 13 and notes).

31:4 *what he did to Sihon and Og.* See 2:26—3:11; see also note on 1:4.

31:6 *Be strong and courageous.* The Lord's exhortation, often through his servants, to the people of Israel (Jos 10:25), to Joshua (vv. 7,23; Jos 1:6 – 7,9,18), to Solomon (1Ch 22:13; 28:20) and to Hezekiah's military officers (2Ch 32:7). By trusting in the Lord and obeying him, his followers would be victorious in spite of great obstacles. *he will never leave you nor forsake you.* See v. 8; Jos 1:5; 1Ki 8:57; see also note on Ge 28:15. The clause is quoted in the first person in Heb 13:5 and applied to God's faithfulness in providing for the material needs of his people.

31:9 *wrote down this law and gave it to the Levitical priests.* Ancient treaties specified that a copy of the treaty was to be placed before the gods at the religious centers of the nations involved. For Israel, that meant to place it in the ark of the covenant (see notes on 33:9; Ex 16:34; 31:18).

31:10 *every seven years.* See 15:4 and note; Ex 23:10 – 11; Lev 25:1 – 7; see also chart, pp. 188 – 189.

31:11 *place he will choose.* See note on 12:5. *read this law before them.* Reading the law to the Israelites (and teaching it to them) was one of the main duties of the priests (see 33:10; Mal 2:4 – 9).

31:12 *fear the LORD.* See notes on Ge 20:11; Ps 34:8 – 14. *words of this law.* See note on v. 24.

31:14 *I will commission him.* See v. 23; cf. Nu 27:18 – 23 and notes on 27:18,20.

31:16 *prostitute themselves.* See Ex 34:15 and note.

soon prostitute[q] themselves to the foreign
gods of the land they are entering. They
will forsake[r] me and break the covenant I
made with them. 17 And in that day I will
become angry[s] with them and forsake[t]
them; I will hide[u] my face[v] from them, and
they will be destroyed. Many disasters[w]
and calamities will come on them, and in
that day they will ask, 'Have not these disasters come on us because our God is not
with us?'[x] 18 And I will certainly hide my
face in that day because of all their wickedness in turning to other gods.

19 "Now write[y] down this song and teach
it to the Israelites and have them sing it,
so that it may be a witness[z] for me against
them. 20 When I have brought them into
the land flowing with milk and honey, the
land I promised on oath to their ancestors,[a]
and when they eat their fill and thrive, they
will turn to other gods[b] and worship them,[c]
rejecting me and breaking my covenant.[d]
21 And when many disasters and calamities come on them,[e] this song will testify
against them, because it will not be forgotten by their descendants. I know what they
are disposed to do,[f] even before I bring
them into the land I promised them on
oath." 22 So Moses wrote[g] down this song
that day and taught it to the Israelites.

23 The LORD gave this command[h] to
Joshua son of Nun: "Be strong and courageous,[i] for you will bring the Israelites into
the land I promised them on oath, and I
myself will be with you."

24 After Moses finished writing[j] in a book
the words of this law[k] from beginning to
end, 25 he gave this command to the Levites who carried[l] the ark of the covenant
of the LORD: 26 "Take this Book of the Law
and place it beside the ark of the covenant
of the LORD your God. There it will remain
as a witness against you.[m] 27 For I know
how rebellious[n] and stiff-necked[o] you are.
If you have been rebellious against the
LORD while I am still alive and with you,
how much more will you rebel after I die!
28 Assemble before me all the elders of
your tribes and all your officials, so that
I can speak these words in their hearing
and call the heavens and the earth to testify against them.[p] 29 For I know that after
my death you are sure to become utterly
corrupt[q] and to turn from the way I have
commanded you. In days to come, disaster[r] will fall on you because you will do
evil in the sight of the LORD and arouse
his anger by what your hands have made."

The Song of Moses

30 And Moses recited the words of this
song from beginning to end in the hearing
of the whole assembly of Israel:

32 Listen,[s] you heavens,[t] and I will
speak;
hear, you earth, the words of my
mouth.[u]
2 Let my teaching fall like rain[v]
and my words descend like dew,[w]
like showers[x] on new grass,
like abundant rain on tender plants.

3 I will proclaim[y] the name of the LORD.[z]
Oh, praise the greatness[a] of our God!
4 He is the Rock,[b] his works are perfect,[c]
and all his ways are just.
A faithful God[d] who does no wrong,
upright[e] and just is he.[f]

5 They are corrupt and not his children;
to their shame they are a warped
and crooked generation.[g]
6 Is this the way you repay[h] the LORD,
you foolish[i] and unwise people?[j]
Is he not your Father,[k] your Creator,[a]
who made you and formed you?[l]

7 Remember the days of old;[m]
consider the generations long past.[n]
Ask your father and he will tell you,
your elders, and they will explain to
you.[o]

31:16 [q] S Ex 34:15; Dt 4:25-28; Jdg 2:12 [r] Jdg 10:6, 13; 1Ki 9:9; 18:18; 19:10; Jer 2:13; 5:19; 19:4 **31:17** [s] Dt 32:16; Jdg 2:14, 20; 10:7; 2Ki 13:3; 22:13; Ps 106:29, 40; Jer 7:18; 21:5; 36:7 [t] Jdg 6:13; 2Ch 15:2; 24:20; Ezr 8:22; Ps 44:9; Isa 2:6 [u] Dt 32:20; Isa 1:15; 45:15; 53:3; 54:8 [v] Job 13:24; Ps 13:1; 27:9; 30:7; 104:29; Isa 50:6; Jer 33:5; Eze 39:29; Mic 3:4 [w] Jer 4:20; Eze 7:26 [x] Nu 14:42; Hos 9:12 **31:19** [y] ver 22 [z] S Ge 31:50 **31:20** [a] Dt 6:10-12 [b] Ps 4:2; 16:4; 40:4; Jer 13:25; Da 3:28; Am 2:4 [c] Dt 8:19; 11:16-17 [d] ver 16 **31:21** [e] S Dt 4:30 [f] 1Ch 28:9; Hos 5:3; Jn 2:24-25 **31:22** [g] ver 19 **31:23** [h] S ver 7 [i] Jos 1:6 **31:24** [j] Dt 17:18; 2Ki 22:8 [k] Dt 28:58 **31:25** [l] S ver 9 **31:26** [m] ver 19 **31:27** [n] S Ex 23:21 [o] S Dt 9:27 **31:28** [p] Dt 4:26; 30:19; 32:1; Job 20:27; Isa 26:21 **31:29** [q] S Dt 4:16; Rev 9:20 [r] 1Ki 9:9; 22:23; 2Ki 22:16 **32:1** [s] Ps 49:1; Mic 1:2 [t] Jer 2:12

[a] 6 Or *Father, who bought you*

[u] S Dt 4:26 **32:2** [v] 2Sa 23:4 [w] Ps 107:20; Isa 9:8; 55:11; Mic 5:7 [x] Ps 65:10; 68:9; 72:6; 147:8 **32:3** [y] Ps 118:17; 145:6 [z] Ex 33:19; 34:5-6 [a] S Dt 3:24 **32:4** [b] S Ge 49:24 [c] 2Sa 22:31; Ps 18:30; 19:7 [d] S Dt 4:35 [e] Ps 92:15 [f] S Ge 18:25 **32:5** [g] ver 20; Mt 17:17; Lk 9:41; Ac 2:40 **32:6** [h] Ps 116:12 [i] Ps 94:8; Jer 5:21 [j] ver 28 [k] S Ex 4:22; 2Sa 7:24 [l] ver 15 **32:7** [m] Ps 44:1; 74:2; 77:5; Isa 51:9; 63:9 [n] Dt 4:32; Job 8:8; 20:4; Ps 78:4; Isa 46:9 [o] S Ex 10:2; Job 15:18

31:17 – 18 *hide my face.* See 32:20; see also note on Ps 13:1.
31:19 *write down this song and teach it.* See v. 22; 31:30—32:44.
31:23 *Be strong and courageous.* See note on v. 6.
31:24 *words of this law from beginning to end.* The book of Deuteronomy up to this place (see note on v. 9).
31:26 *place it beside the ark.* See note on v. 9.
31:27 *stiff-necked.* See 9:6,13; 10:16; see also note on Ex 32:9.
31:28 *the heavens and the earth to testify.* See note on 30:19.
31:29 *what your hands have made.* A reference to idols (see 4:28; 27:15 and note).
31:30 — 32:44 The song of Moses (see notes on Ex 15:1 – 18; Rev 15:3) set within the narrative frame of 31:30 and 32:44. The song may be outlined as follows: (1) summoning of covenant witnesses and description of the covenant God (32:1 – 4), (2) charges against the people (32:5 – 6), (3) review of God's covenant benefits (32:7 – 14), (4) the people's disobedience to the covenant stipulations (32:15 – 18), (5) covenant curses for such disobedience (32:19 – 27), (6) the impotence of false gods (32:28 – 38) and (7) the Lord's vindication and vengeance (32:39 – 43).
32:1 *Listen, you heavens.* For similar introductions see Isa 1:2 and note; 34:1; Mic 1:2; 6:1 – 2.
32:4 *He is the Rock.* A major theme of the song of Moses (see vv. 15,18,30 – 31; see also notes on Ge 49:24; Ps 18:2).
32:5 *warped and crooked generation.* See Php 2:15 and note.
32:6 *Father.* See Isa 63:16; 64:8.
32:7 *Remember the days of old.* See note on 4:10.

8 When the Most High[p] gave the nations their inheritance,
when he divided all mankind,[q]
he set up boundaries[r] for the peoples
according to the number of the sons of Israel.[a][s]
9 For the LORD's portion[t] is his people,
Jacob his allotted inheritance.[u]

10 In a desert[v] land he found him,
in a barren and howling waste.[w]
He shielded[x] him and cared for him;
he guarded him as the apple of his eye,[y]
11 like an eagle that stirs up its nest
and hovers over its young,[z]
that spreads its wings to catch them
and carries them aloft.[a]
12 The LORD alone led[b] him;[c]
no foreign god was with him.[d]

13 He made him ride on the heights[e] of the land
and fed him with the fruit of the fields.
He nourished him with honey from the rock,[f]
and with oil[g] from the flinty crag,
14 with curds and milk from herd and flock
and with fattened lambs and goats,
with choice rams of Bashan[h]
and the finest kernels of wheat.[i]
You drank the foaming blood of the grape.[j]
15 Jeshurun[b][k] grew fat[l] and kicked;
filled with food, they became heavy and sleek.
They abandoned[m] the God who made them
and rejected the Rock[n] their Savior.
16 They made him jealous[o] with their foreign gods
and angered[p] him with their detestable idols.
17 They sacrificed[q] to false gods,[r] which are not God—
gods they had not known,[s]
gods that recently appeared,[t]
gods your ancestors did not fear.
18 You deserted the Rock, who fathered you;
you forgot[u] the God who gave you birth.

19 The LORD saw this and rejected them[v]
because he was angered by his sons and daughters.[w]
20 "I will hide my face[x] from them," he said,
"and see what their end will be;
for they are a perverse generation,[y]
children who are unfaithful.[z]
21 They made me jealous[a] by what is no god
and angered me with their worthless idols.[b]
I will make them envious by those who are not a people;
I will make them angry by a nation that has no understanding.[c]
22 For a fire will be kindled by my wrath,[d]
one that burns down to the realm of the dead below.[e]
It will devour[f] the earth and its harvests[g]
and set afire the foundations of the mountains.[h]

23 "I will heap calamities[i] on them
and spend my arrows[j] against them.
24 I will send wasting famine[k] against them,
consuming pestilence[l] and deadly plague;[m]
I will send against them the fangs of wild beasts,[n]
the venom of vipers[o] that glide in the dust.[p]

[a] *8* Masoretic Text; Dead Sea Scrolls (see also Septuagint) *sons of God* [b] *15* *Jeshurun* means *the upright one*, that is, Israel.

32:8 [p]Ps 7:8 [q]S Ge 11:8; Ac 8:1 [r]Ps 74:17 [s]Nu 23:9; Dt 33:12, 28; Jer 23:6 **32:9** [t]Ps 16:5; 73:26; 119:57; 142:5; Jer 10:16 [u]S Dt 9:29; S 1Sa 26:19 **32:10** [v]S Dt 1:19 [w]Dt 8:15; Job 12:24; Ps 107:40 [x]Ps 32:10; Jer 31:22 [y]Ps 17:8; Pr 7:2; Hos 13:5; Zec 2:8 **32:11** [z]S Ex 19:4 [a]Ps 17:8; 18:10-19; 61:4 **32:12** [b]Ps 106:9; Isa 63:13; Jer 31:32 [c]Dt 4:35 [d]ver 39; Jdg 2:12; Ps 18:31; 81:9; Isa 43:12; 45:5 **32:13** [e]Dt 33:29; 2Sa 22:34; Ps 18:33; Isa 33:16; 58:14; Eze 36:2; Hab 3:19 [f]S Dt 8:8 [g]Dt 33:24; Job 29:6 **32:14** [h]S Nu 21:33 [i]Ps 65:9; 81:16; 147:14 [j]S Ge 49:11 **32:15** [k]Dt 33:5, 26; Isa 44:2 [l]Dt 31:20; Jer 5:28 [m]Dt 31:16; Isa 1:4, 28; 58:2; 65:11; Jer 15:6; Eze 14:5 [n]S Ge 49:24 **32:16** [o]S Nu 25:11; S 1Co 10:22 [p]S Dt 31:17; S 1Ki 14:9 **32:17** [q]S Ex 32:8 [r]S Ex 22:20; 1Co 10:20 [s]S Dt 28:64 [t]Jdg 5:8 **32:18** [u]Jdg 3:7; 1Sa 12:9; Ps 44:17, 20; 106:21; Jer 2:32; Eze 23:35; Hos 8:14; 13:6 **32:19** [v]Lev 26:30; Ps 78:59 [w]Am 6:8 **32:20** [x]Dt 31:17, 29; Ps 4:6; 44:24 [y]S ver 5 [z]Dt 9:23 **32:21** [a]S Nu 25:11; S 1Co 10:22 [b]ver 17; 1Ki 16:13, 26; 2Ki 17:15; Ps 31:6; Jer 2:5; 8:19; 10:8; 16:19; Jnh 2:8 [c]Ro 10:19* **32:22** [d]Ps 7:11 [e]Nu 16:31-35; Ps 18:7-8; Jer 15:14; La 4:11 [f]Am 7:4 [g]Lev 26:20 [h]Ps 83:14 **32:23** [i]S Dt 29:21 [j]ver 42; 2Sa 22:15; Job 6:4; Ps 7:13; 18:14; 45:5; 77:17; 120:4; Isa 5:28; 49:2; Eze 5:16; Hab 3:9, 11 **32:24** [k]Ge 26:1; S 41:55; 42:5; 2Sa 24:13; 1Ch 21:12 [l]S Dt 28:22 [m]Ps 91:6 [n]S Ge 37:20 [o]ver 33; Job 20:16; Ps 58:4; Jer 8:17; Am 5:18-19; Mic 7:17 [p]Job 20:16

32:8 *Most High.* The only occurrence in Deuteronomy of this name for God (see note on Ge 14:19). It emphasizes the Lord's sovereignty over all creation. *gave the nations their inheritance.* See Ge 10. *according to the number of the sons of Israel.* Perhaps referring to the number (70; see 10:22) of the sons of Jacob (Israel) who went down to Egypt (see Ge 46:27; Ex 1:5; see also note on Ge 10:2). But see NIV text note.
32:10 *apple of his eye.* Referring to the pupil, a delicate part of the eye that is essential for vision and that therefore must be protected at all costs.
32:11 *hovers over.* See note on Ge 1:2.
32:13 *honey from the rock.* See Ps 81:16. In Canaan, bees sometimes built their hives in crevices in the rocks (cf. Isa 7:18–19). *oil from the flinty crag.* Olive trees often grew on rocky hillsides, as on the Mount of Olives east of Jerusalem.
32:14 *choice rams of Bashan.* See note on Eze 39:18. *foaming blood of the grape.* Red wine (see Ge 49:11).
32:15 *Jeshurun.* See NIV text note; see also Isa 44:2 and note. *Rock.* See v. 18 and note on v. 4.
32:17 *false gods.* See Ps 106:37 and note.
32:20 *hide my face.* See note on 31:17–18.
32:21 Quoted in part in Ro 10:19 to illustrate Israel's failure to understand the good news about Christ. See also v. 16. *those who are not a people.* See note on Ro 10:19.
32:22 *realm of the dead below.* See notes on Ge 37:35; Job 17:16; Ps 6:5; Pr 15:11; Am 9:2–4; see also Job 3:13–19; 11:8; 26:6; Ps 139:8; Pr 23:14; 27:20; Isa 7:11; 14:9–11,15–20; 38:10.

[25]In the street the sword will make them childless;
in their homes terror[q] will reign.[r]
The young men and young women will perish,
the infants and those with gray hair.[s]
[26]I said I would scatter[t] them
and erase their name from human memory,[u]
[27]but I dreaded the taunt of the enemy,
lest the adversary misunderstand[v]
and say, 'Our hand has triumphed;
the LORD has not done all this.' "[w]

[28]They are a nation without sense,
there is no discernment[x] in them.
[29]If only they were wise and would understand this[y]
and discern what their end will be![z]
[30]How could one man chase a thousand,
or two put ten thousand to flight,[a]
unless their Rock had sold them,[b]
unless the LORD had given them up?[c]
[31]For their rock is not like our Rock,[d]
as even our enemies concede.[e]
[32]Their vine comes from the vine of Sodom[f]
and from the fields of Gomorrah.
Their grapes are filled with poison,[g]
and their clusters with bitterness.[h]
[33]Their wine is the venom of serpents,
the deadly poison of cobras.[i]

[34]"Have I not kept this in reserve
and sealed it in my vaults?[j]
[35]It is mine to avenge;[k] I will repay.[l]
In due time their foot will slip;[m]
their day of disaster is near
and their doom rushes upon them.[n]"

[36]The LORD will vindicate his people[o]
and relent[p] concerning his servants[q]
when he sees their strength is gone
and no one is left, slave[r] or free.[a]
[37]He will say: "Now where are their gods,
the rock they took refuge in,[s]
[38]the gods who ate the fat of their sacrifices
and drank the wine of their drink offerings?[t]
Let them rise up to help you!
Let them give you shelter!

[39]"See now that I myself am he![u]
There is no god besides me.[v]
I put to death[w] and I bring to life,[x]
I have wounded and I will heal,[y]
and no one can deliver out of my hand.[z]
[40]I lift my hand[a] to heaven and solemnly swear:
As surely as I live forever,[b]
[41]when I sharpen my flashing sword[c]
and my hand grasps it in judgment,
I will take vengeance[d] on my adversaries
and repay those who hate me.[e]
[42]I will make my arrows drunk with blood,[f]
while my sword devours flesh:[g]
the blood of the slain and the captives,
the heads of the enemy leaders."

[43]Rejoice,[h] you nations, with his people,[b,c]
for he will avenge the blood of his servants;[i]
he will take vengeance on his enemies[j]
and make atonement for his land and people.[k]

[44]Moses came with Joshua[d][l] son of Nun
and spoke all the words of this song in
the hearing of the people. [45]When Moses
finished reciting all these words to all Israel, [46]he said to them, "Take to heart all
the words I have solemnly declared to you
this day,[m] so that you may command[n] your
children to obey carefully all the words of
this law. [47]They are not just idle words for
you—they are your life.[o] By them you will

[a] 36 Or *and they are without a ruler or leader*
[b] 43 Or *Make his people rejoice, you nations*
[c] 43 Masoretic Text; Dead Sea Scrolls (see also Septuagint) *people, / and let all the angels worship him, /*
[d] 44 Hebrew *Hoshea,* a variant of *Joshua*

32:25 [q] Isa 24:17 [r] Jer 14:18; La 1:20; Eze 7:15; 2Co 7:5 [s] 2Ch 36:17; Isa 13:18; Jer 4:31; La 2:21 **32:26** [t] Dt 4:27 [u] S Nu 14:12; Job 18:17; Ps 34:16; 37:28; 109:15; Isa 14:20 **32:27** [v] Dt 9:26-28 [w] Ps 140:8; Isa 10:13; Jer 40:2-3 **32:28** [x] Isa 1:3; 5:13; 27:11; Jer 8:7 **32:29** [y] Dt 5:29; Ps 81:13 [z] Isa 47:7; La 1:9 **32:30** [a] S Lev 26:8 [b] Jdg 2:14; 3:8; 4:2; 10:7; 1Sa 12:9 [c] Nu 21:34; 1Sa 23:7; Ps 31:8; 44:12; 106:41; Isa 50:1; 54:6 **32:31** [d] S Ge 49:24 [e] S Ex 14:25 **32:32** [f] Jer 23:14 [g] Job 6:4; 20:16 [h] Dt 29:18 **32:33** [i] S ver 24 **32:34** [j] Job 14:17; Jer 2:22; Hos 13:12 **32:35** [k] S ver 41; S Ge 4:24; S Jer 51:6 [l] S Ge 30:2; S Ex 32:34; S Ps 54:5; S Ro 12:19*; Heb 10:30* [m] Ps 17:5; 35:6; 37:31; 38:16; 66:9; 73:2, 18; 94:18; 121:3; Pr 4:19; Jer 23:12 [n] Eze 7:8-9 **32:36** [o] Heb 10:30* [p] Am 7:3 [q] Lev 26:43-45; Dt 30:1-3; Jdg 2:18; Ps 90:13; 102:13; 103:13; 106:45; 135:14; Joel 2:14 [r] 1Ki 14:10; 21:21; 2Ki 9:8 **32:37** [s] Jdg 10:14; Jer 2:28; 11:12 **32:38** [t] Nu 25:1-2; Jer 11:12; 44:8, 25 **32:39** [u] Isa 41:4; 43:10; 44:7; 46:4; 48:12 [v] S ver 12 [w] 1Sa 2:6 [x] 1Sa 2:6; 2Ki 5:7; Ps 68:20; Jn 11:25-26 [y] Ex 15:26; Job 5:18; 15:11; Ps 147:3; Isa 6:10; 19:22; 30:26; 53:5; 57:18; Jer 33:6; Hos 6:1; Mal 4:2; 1Pe 2:24 [z] Job 9:12; 10:7; Ps 7:2; 50:22; Isa 43:13; Da 4:35; Hos 5:14 **32:40** [a] S Ge 14:22 [b] S Ge 21:33; Rev 1:18 **32:41** [c] Jdg 7:20; Ps 7:12; 45:3; Isa 27:1; 34:6; 66:16; Jer 12:12; Eze 21:9-10 [d] ver 35; Ps 149:7; Jer 46:10; Na 1:2 [e] Ps 137:8; Jer 25:14; 50:29; 51:24, 56 **32:42** [f] S ver 23 [g] 2Sa 2:26; Jer 12:12; 44:1; 46:10, 14 **32:43** [h] Ps 137:6; Isa 25:9; 65:18; 66:10; Ro 15:10* [i] 2Ki 9:7; S Rev 6:10 [j] Isa 1:24; Jer 9:9 [k] Ps 65:3; 79:9 **32:44** [l] Nu 13:8, 16 **32:46** [m] S Dt 6:6; Jn 1:17; 7:19 [n] Dt 6:7 **32:47** [o] S Dt 30:20

32:26 *I said I would scatter them.* See 28:64 and note; see also 4:27. *erase their name from human memory.* See 9:14 and note; cf. 25:19.
32:30 *their Rock.* Israel's God (see note on v. 4).
32:31 *their rock.* The god of Israel's enemy.
32:34 *sealed it in my vaults.* The Lord's plans for the future are fixed and certain. Sin will be punished in due time.
32:35–36 Quoted in part in Heb 10:30 as a warning against rejecting the Son of God.

32:35 *It is mine to avenge; I will repay.* Quoted in Ro 12:19 to affirm that avenging is God's prerogative, not ours.
32:39 *I myself am he.* See Ex 3:12–15 and notes; cf. Jn 4:26 and note. *no god besides me.* See note on 4:35. *I put to death and I bring to life.* See note on 1Sa 2:6–8.
32:40 *lift my hand.* See Ge 14:22 and note.
32:43 *Rejoice, you nations, with his people.* One of the Dead Sea Scrolls adds a clause in Deuteronomy (see NIV text note), and the clause is quoted in Ro 15:10; Heb 1:6 (see note there).
32:47 *they are your life.* See note on 30:20.

live long[p] in the land you are crossing the
Jordan to possess."

Moses to Die on Mount Nebo

48 On that same day the LORD told Moses,[q] 49 "Go up into the Abarim[r] Range to
Mount Nebo[s] in Moab, across from Jericho,[t] and view Canaan,[u] the land I am giving the Israelites as their own possession.
50 There on the mountain that you have
climbed you will die[v] and be gathered to
your people, just as your brother Aaron
died[w] on Mount Hor[x] and was gathered to
his people. 51 This is because both of you
broke faith with me in the presence of the
Israelites at the waters of Meribah Kadesh[y]
in the Desert of Zin[z] and because you did
not uphold my holiness among the Israelites.[a] 52 Therefore, you will see the land
only from a distance;[b] you will not enter[c]
the land I am giving to the people of Israel."

Moses Blesses the Tribes

33:1-29Ref — Ge 49:1-28

33 This is the blessing[d] that Moses the
man of God[e] pronounced on the Israelites before his death. 2 He said:

"The LORD came from Sinai[f]
and dawned over them from Seir;[g]
he shone forth[h] from Mount Paran.[i]
He came with[a] myriads of holy ones[j]
from the south, from his mountain
slopes.[b]
3 Surely it is you who love[k] the people;
all the holy ones are in your hand.[l]
At your feet they all bow down,[m]
and from you receive instruction,
4 the law that Moses gave us,[n]
the possession of the assembly of
Jacob.[o]
5 He was king[p] over Jeshurun[c][q]
when the leaders of the people
assembled,
along with the tribes of Israel.

6 "Let Reuben live and not die,
nor[d] his people be few."[r]

7 And this he said about Judah:[s]

"Hear, LORD, the cry of Judah;
bring him to his people.
With his own hands he defends his
cause.
Oh, be his help against his foes!"

8 About Levi[t] he said:

"Your Thummim and Urim[u] belong
to your faithful servant.[v]
You tested[w] him at Massah;
you contended with him at the
waters of Meribah.[x]
9 He said of his father and mother,[y]
'I have no regard for them.'
He did not recognize his brothers
or acknowledge his own children,
but he watched over your word
and guarded your covenant.[z]
10 He teaches[a] your precepts to Jacob
and your law to Israel.[b]
He offers incense before you[c]
and whole burnt offerings on your
altar.[d]
11 Bless all his skills, LORD,
and be pleased with the work of his
hands.[e]
Strike down those who rise against
him,
his foes till they rise no more."

12 About Benjamin[f] he said:

"Let the beloved of the LORD rest
secure in him,[g]
for he shields him all day long,[h]
and the one the LORD loves[i] rests
between his shoulders.[j]"

13 About Joseph[k] he said:

"May the LORD bless his land

[a] 2 Or *from* [b] 2 The meaning of the Hebrew for this phrase is uncertain. [c] 5 *Jeshurun* means *the upright one,* that is, Israel; also in verse 26. [d] 6 Or *but let*

32:47 [p] S Ex 23:26; Dt 33:25; Isa 65:22 **32:48** [q] Nu 27:12 **32:49** [r] Nu 27:12 [s] S Nu 32:3 [t] S Nu 22:1 [u] S Lev 14:34 **32:50** [v] S Ge 25:8; S Nu 27:13 [w] Nu 20:29 [x] S Nu 20:22 **32:51** [y] Eze 47:19 [z] S Nu 13:21; 20:11-13 [a] Nu 27:14 **32:52** [b] Dt 34:1-3 [c] S Dt 3:27 **33:1** [d] S Ge 27:4 [e] Jos 14:6; 1Sa 2:27; 9:6; 1Ki 12:22; 13:1; 2Ki 1:9-13; 5:8; Jer 35:4 **33:2** [f] Ex 19:18; Ps 68:8 [g] Jos 11:17; Jdg 5:4 [h] Ps 50:2; 80:1; 94:1 [i] S Nu 10:12 [j] Ps 89:7; Da 4:13; 7:10; 8:13; Zec 14:5; Ac 7:53; Gal 3:19; Heb 2:2; Rev 5:11 **33:3** [k] S Dt 4:37 [l] Dt 7:6 [m] Lk 10:39; Rev 4:10 **33:4** [n] Dt 4:2; Jn 1:17; 7:19 [o] Ps 119:111 **33:5** [p] S Ex 16:8; 1Sa 10:19; Ps 10:16; 149:2 [q] S Nu 23:21; S Dt 32:15 **33:6** [r] S Ge 34:5 **33:7** [s] S Ge 49:10 **33:8** [t] S Ge 29:34 [u] Ex 28:30 [v] Ps 106:16 [w] S Nu 14:22 [x] S Ex 17:7 **33:9** [y] Ex 32:26-29 [z] Ps 61:5; Mal 2:5 **33:10** [a] Ezr 7:10; Ne 8:18; Ps 119:151; Jer 23:22; Mal 2:6 [b] S Lev 10:11; Dt 17:8-11; 31:9-13 [c] S Ex 30:7; Lev 16:12-13 [d] Ps 51:19 **33:11** [e] 2Sa 24:23; Ps 20:3; 51:19 **33:12** [f] S Ge 35:18 [g] Dt 4:37-38; 12:10; S 32:8 [h] S Ex 19:4 [i] Ps 60:5; 127:2; Isa 5:1 [j] S Ex 28:12 **33:13** [k] S Ge 30:24

32:50 *gathered to your people.* See note on Ge 25:8. *Aaron died on Mount Hor.* See 10:6; Nu 20:22 – 29 and notes.
32:51 *you broke faith with me.* See 1:37; 3:23 – 27; 4:21 – 22; 31:2; Nu 20:12. *Meribah Kadesh in the Desert of Zin.* See 33:8; see also notes on Ex 17:7; Nu 20:13.
33:1 *blessing.* See Ge 12:1 – 3; 22:15 – 18; 27:27 – 29; 28:10 – 15. Moses' blessings on the tribes (vv. 6 – 25) should be compared particularly with Jacob's blessings on his sons in Ge 49:3 – 27. *man of God.* The first occurrence of this title. It appears next in Jos 14:6 (also of Moses; see Ps 90 title). Later it designates other messengers of God (see note on 1Sa 2:27, including prophets).
33:2 *Sinai . . . Seir . . . Paran.* Mountains associated with the giving of the law (see Ge 21:21 and note; Jdg 5:4 – 5; Hab 3:3 and note). *holy ones.* Angels.
33:3 *holy ones.* Israelites (see 7:6 and note; 14:2; 26:19; 28:9).
33:5 *king.* The Lord, not an earthly monarch, was to be king over Israel (see Jdg 8:23 and note). *Jeshurun.* See NIV text note; see also Isa 44:2 and note.
33:6 *Reuben.* For the boundaries of the tribal territories, see map, p. 2519, at the end of this study Bible.
33:8 *Thummim and Urim.* See note on Ex 28:30. *Massah.* See 6:16; 9:22; see also note on Ex 17:7. *Meribah.* See note on 32:51.
33:9 *he watched over your word.* The Levites had charge of the tabernacle with its ark, in which the Book of the Law was placed (see note on 31:9).
33:10 *teaches your precepts to Jacob.* See note on 31:11.
33:12 *between his shoulders.* See Isa 49:22; cf. Dt 33:27.
33:13 *About Joseph.* Moses included the blessing on the two

with the precious dew from heaven
above
and with the deep waters that lie
below;[l]
14 with the best the sun brings forth
and the finest the moon can yield;
15 with the choicest gifts of the ancient
mountains[m]
and the fruitfulness of the
everlasting hills;
16 with the best gifts of the earth and its
fullness
and the favor of him who dwelt in
the burning bush.[n]
Let all these rest on the head of
Joseph,
on the brow of the prince among[a]
his brothers.[o]
17 In majesty he is like a firstborn bull;
his horns[p] are the horns of a wild ox.[q]
With them he will gore[r] the nations,
even those at the ends of the earth.
Such are the ten thousands of
Ephraim;[s]
such are the thousands of
Manasseh.[t]"

18 About Zebulun[u] he said:

"Rejoice, Zebulun, in your going out,
and you, Issachar,[v] in your tents.
19 They will summon peoples to the
mountain[w]
and there offer the sacrifices of the
righteous;[x]
they will feast on the abundance of the
seas,[y]
on the treasures hidden in the sand."

20 About Gad[z] he said:

"Blessed is he who enlarges Gad's
domain![a]
Gad lives there like a lion,
tearing at arm or head.
21 He chose the best land for himself;[b]
the leader's portion was kept for him.[c]
When the heads of the people
assembled,
he carried out the LORD's righteous
will,[d]
and his judgments concerning
Israel."

22 About Dan[e] he said:

"Dan is a lion's cub,
springing out of Bashan."

23 About Naphtali[f] he said:

"Naphtali is abounding with the favor
of the LORD
and is full of his blessing;
he will inherit southward to the lake."

24 About Asher[g] he said:

"Most blessed of sons is Asher;
let him be favored by his brothers,
and let him bathe his feet in oil.[h]
25 The bolts of your gates will be iron and
bronze,[i]
and your strength will equal your
days.[j]

26 "There is no one like the God of
Jeshurun,[k]
who rides[l] across the heavens to
help you[m]
and on the clouds[n] in his majesty.[o]
27 The eternal[p] God is your refuge,[q]
and underneath are the everlasting[r]
arms.
He will drive out your enemies before
you,[s]
saying, 'Destroy them!'[t]
28 So Israel will live in safety;[u]
Jacob will dwell[b] secure
in a land of grain and new wine,
where the heavens drop dew.[v]
29 Blessed are you, Israel![w]
Who is like you,[x]
a people saved by the LORD?[y]
He is your shield and helper[z]
and your glorious sword.
Your enemies will cower before you,
and you will tread on their heights.[a]"

The Death of Moses

34 Then Moses climbed Mount Nebo[b]
from the plains of Moab to the top
of Pisgah,[c] across from Jericho.[d] There the

[a] 16 Or *of the one separated from* [b] 28 Septuagint; Hebrew *Jacob's spring is*

33:13 [l] Ge 27:28; Ps 148:7 **33:15** [m] Hab 3:6 **33:16** [n] S Ex 3:2 [o] S Ge 37:8 **33:17** [p] 1Sa 2:10; 2Sa 22:3; Eze 34:21 [q] S Nu 23:22 [r] 1Ki 22:11; Ps 44:5 [s] S Ge 41:52 [t] S Ge 41:51 **33:18** [u] S Ge 30:20 [v] S Ge 30:18 **33:19** [w] S Ex 15:17; Ps 48:1; Isa 2:3; 65:11; 66:20; Jer 31:6 [x] Ps 4:5; 51:19 [y] Isa 18:7; 23:18; 45:14; 60:5, 11; 61:6; Hag 2:7; Zec 14:14 **33:20** [z] Ge 30:11 [a] Dt 3:12-17 **33:21** [b] Nu 32:1-5, 31-32 [c] S Nu 34:14 [d] Jos 22:1-3 **33:22** [e] Ge 49:16; S Nu 1:38 **33:23** [f] S Ge 30:8 **33:24** [g] S Ge 30:13 [h] S Ge 49:20; S Dt 32:13 **33:25** [i] Ne 3:3; 7:3; Ps 147:13 [j] S Dt 32:47 **33:26** [k] S Dt 32:15 [l] Ps 18:10; 68:33 [m] S Dt 10:14; S Ps 104:3 [n] 2Sa 22:10; Ps 18:9; 68:4; Da 7:13 [o] S Ex 15:7 **33:27** [p] Ex 15:18; Isa 40:28; 57:15 [q] Ps 9:9; 84:1; 90:1; 91:9 [r] S Ge 21:33 [s] Ex 34:11; Jos 24:18 [t] S Dt 7:2 **33:28** [u] S Ex 33:16; S Lev 25:18; S Dt 32:8; Ps 16:9; Pr 1:33; Isa 14:30 [v] ver 13; Ge 27:28 **33:29** [w] Ps 1:1; 32:1-2; 144:15 [x] 2Sa 22:45; Ps 18:44; 66:3; 81:15 [y] Dt 4:7 [z] Ge 15:1; Ex 18:4; Ps 10:14; 18:1; 27:1, 9; 30:10; 54:4; 70:5; 115:9-11; 118:7; Isa 45:24; Hos 13:9; Hab 3:19 [a] S Nu 33:52; S Dt 32:13 **34:1** [b] S Nu 32:3 [c] S Nu 21:20 [d] Dt 32:49

tribes of Ephraim and Manasseh (v. 17), Joseph's sons, with that of Joseph himself. *dew from heaven ... deep waters.* See note on Ge 49:25.

33:15–16 See Ge 49:26 and note.

33:16 *best gifts of the earth.* Under the Lord's blessing, Joseph's land in the central part of Canaan was to be unusually fertile and productive. *who dwelt in the burning bush.* See Ex 3:1–6.

33:19 *abundance of the seas ... treasures hidden in the sand.* References to maritime wealth (see note on Ge 49:13).

33:21 *He chose the best land.* For his livestock (see 3:12–20 and notes).

33:22 *springing out of Bashan.* The lion's cub, not Dan, is the subject. Another possible translation is "keeping away from the viper." Although someday he would be like a viper himself (see Ge 49:17 and note), the early history of Dan pictured him as being somewhat more timid (see Jdg 18).

33:23 *lake.* The Sea of Galilee.

33:26 *Jeshurun.* See note on 32:15. *rides ... on the clouds.* See note on Ps 68:4.

33:27 *underneath are the everlasting arms.* See v. 12 and note.

33:29 *shield.* See note on Ge 15:1. *tread on their heights.* See Mic 1:3 and note; cf. Dt 32:13.

34:1 *Moses climbed Mount Nebo.* In obedience to the Lord's command in 32:48–52. See photo, p. 258.

LORD showed[e] him the whole land—from
Gilead to Dan,[f] 2 all of Naphtali, the territory of Ephraim and Manasseh, all the land
of Judah as far as the Mediterranean Sea,[g]
3 the Negev[h] and the whole region from
the Valley of Jericho, the City of Palms,[i] as
far as Zoar.[j] 4 Then the LORD said to him,
"This is the land I promised on oath[k] to
Abraham, Isaac and Jacob[l] when I said, 'I
will give it[m] to your descendants.' I have
let you see it with your eyes, but you will
not cross[n] over into it."
5 And Moses the servant of the LORD[o] died[p]
there in Moab, as the LORD had said. 6 He
buried him[a] in Moab, in the valley opposite
Beth Peor,[q] but to this day no one knows
where his grave is.[r] 7 Moses was a hundred
and twenty years old[s] when he died, yet his
eyes were not weak[t] nor his strength gone.[u]
8 The Israelites grieved for Moses in the
plains of Moab[v] thirty days,[w] until the time
of weeping and mourning[x] was over.
9 Now Joshua son of Nun was filled with
the spirit[b] of wisdom[y] because Moses had
laid his hands on him.[z] So the Israelites
listened to him and did what the LORD had
commanded Moses.
10 Since then, no prophet[a] has risen in
Israel like Moses,[b] whom the LORD knew
face to face,[c] 11 who did all those signs
and wonders[d] the LORD sent him to do
in Egypt—to Pharaoh and to all his officials[e] and to his whole land. 12 For no one
has[f] ever shown the mighty power or performed the awesome deeds[g] that Moses
did in the sight of all Israel.

[a] 6 Or *He was buried* [b] 9 Or *Spirit*

34:1 [e] Dt 32:52 [f] S Ge 14:14 **34:2** [g] S Ex 23:31 **34:3** [h] S Ge 12:9 [i] Jdg 1:16; 3:13; 2Ch 28:15 [j] S Ge 13:10 **34:4** [k] Ge 28:13 [l] Jos 21:43 [m] Ge 12:7 [n] S Dt 3:23 **34:5** [o] S Nu 12:7 [p] S Ge 25:8 **34:6** [q] S Dt 3:29 [r] Jude 1:9 **34:7** [s] S Ex 7:7 [t] S Ge 27:1 [u] S Ge 15:15 **34:8** [v] S Nu 21:11 [w] S Ge 37:34; S Dt 1:3 [x] 2Sa 11:27 **34:9** [y] S Ge 41:38; S Ex 28:3; Isa 11:2 [z] S Dt 31:14; Ac 6:6 **34:10** [a] S Ge 20:7 [b] Dt 18:15, 18 [c] S Ex 33:11 **34:11** [d] Dt 4:34 [e] S Ex 11:3 **34:12** [f] Heb 3:1-6 [g] S Dt 4:34

34:3 *Negev.* See note on Ge 12:9. *as far as Zoar.* See Isa 15:5 and note.

34:4 *land I promised.* See 1:8; Ge 12:1; 15:18 and note; Ex 33:1.

34:5 *servant of the LORD.* A special title used to refer to those whom the Lord, as the Great King, has taken into his service; they serve as members of God's royal administration. For example, it was used especially of Abraham (Ge 26:24), Moses (Ex 14:31; Jos 1:1), Joshua (Jos 24:29), David (2Sa 3:18; 7:5), the prophets (2Ki 9:7), Israel collectively (Isa 41:8–9), and even a foreign king the Lord used to carry out his purposes (Jer 25:9). See notes on Ex 14:31; Isa 41:8–9; 42:1–4.

34:6 *Beth Peor.* See note on 3:29.

34:7 *a hundred and twenty years old.* See 31:2; perhaps a round number, indicating three generations of about 40 years each (see Ac 7:23 and note).

34:8 *grieved . . . thirty days.* See Ge 50:3 and note.

34:10 *no prophet has risen in Israel like Moses.* See note on 18:15. *face to face.* See Nu 12:8 and note.

34:12 *no one has ever.* Until Jesus came, no one was superior to Moses. See Heb 3:1–6, where Moses the "*servant in* all God's house" (v. 5, emphasis added) is contrasted with Christ the "*Son over* God's house" (v. 6, emphasis added).

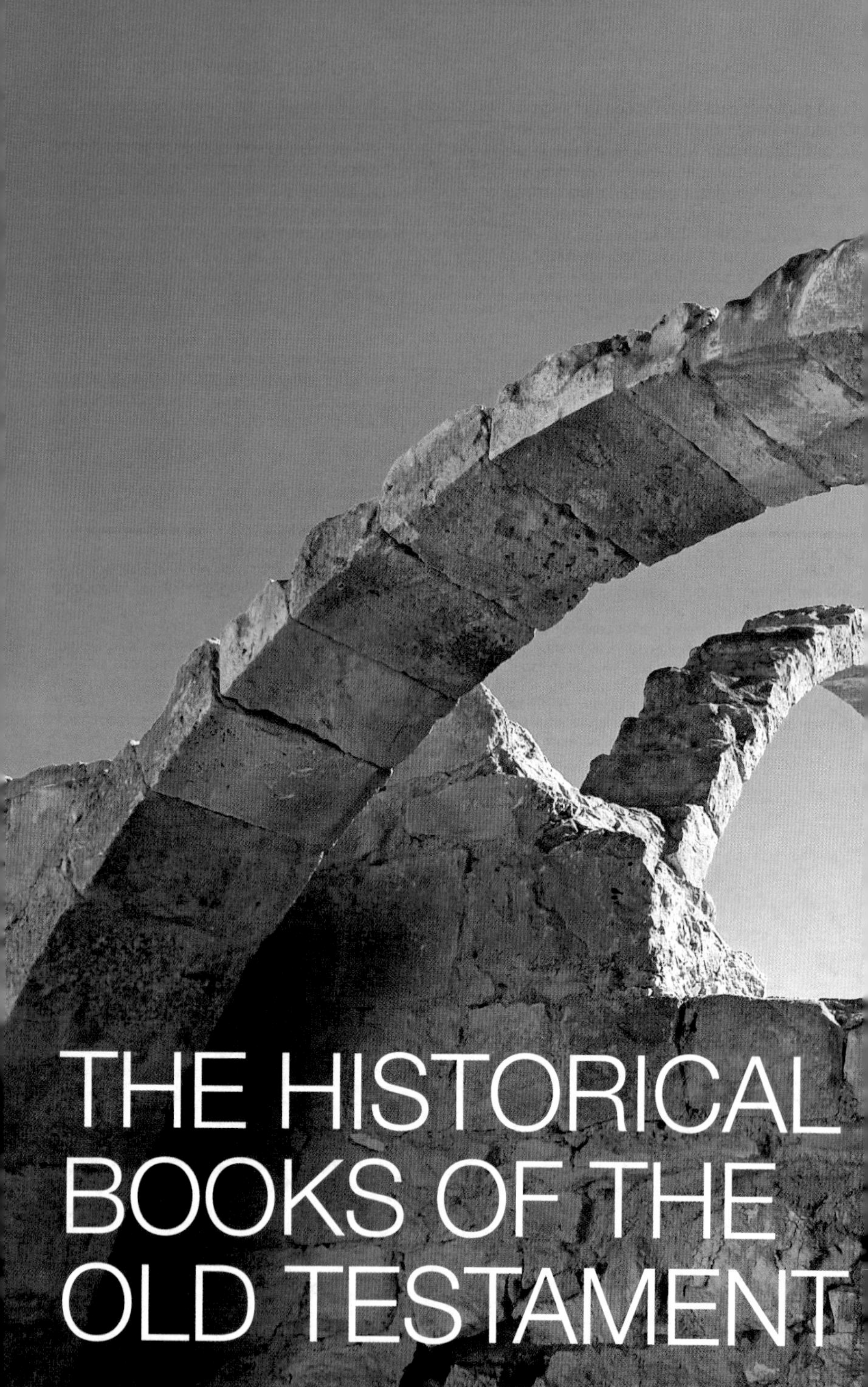

THE HISTORICAL BOOKS OF THE OLD TESTAMENT

The Historical Books of the Old Testament may be divided into two groups. The first is comprised of Joshua through Kings. The books of 1 and 2 Samuel were originally a single book, as were the books of 1 and 2 Kings. Joshua, Judges, Samuel and Kings (also known as the Former Prophets; in the Hebrew Bible, Ruth is included among the Writings) relate the story of the Israelites' conquest of the promised land of Canaan and of all the obstacles they faced and overcame through the Lord's enablement. They also cover the historical periods of the judges, the united kingdom (under Saul, David and Solomon) and the divided kingdom (Israel in the north and Judah in the south), including finally the exile of Israel and Judah to Assyria and Babylonia, respectively.

The second group of books is comprised of Chronicles through Esther. These relate important events in Israel's history during the exilic and postexilic periods, including their restoration from captivity in Babylonia.

THE CONQUEST AND THE ETHICAL QUESTION OF WAR

Many readers of Joshua (and other OT books) are deeply troubled by the role that warfare play in Joshua's account of God's dealings with his people. Not a few relieve their ethical scruples b ascribing the author's perspective to a pre-Christian (and sub-Christian) stage of moral develop ment that the Christian, in the light of Christ's teaching, must repudiate and transcend. Hence th main thread of the narrative line of Joshua is offensive to them.

It must be remembered, however, that the book of Joshua does not address itself to the abstrac ethical question of war as a means for gaining human ends. It can only be understood in the cor text of the history of redemption unfolding in the Pentateuch, with its interplay of divine grace an judgment. Of that story it is the direct continuation.

Joshua is not an epic account of Israel's heroic generation or the story of Israel's conquest c Canaan with the aid of her national deity. It is rather the story of how God, to whom the whol world belongs, at one stage in the history of redemption reconquered a portion of the earth fror the powers of this world that had claimed it for themselves, defending their claims by force of arm and reliance on their false gods. It tells how God commissioned his people to serve as his arm under the leadership of his servant Joshua, to take Canaan in his name out of the hands of th idolatrous and dissolute Canaanites (whose measure of sin was now full; see Ge 15:16 and note It further tells how he aided them in the enterprise and gave them conditional tenancy in his lan in fulfillment of the ancient pledge he had made to Israel's ancestors — Abraham, Isaac and Jacob

Joshua is the story of the kingdom of God breaking into the world of nations at a time whe national and political entities were viewed as the creation of the gods and living proofs of the power. Thus the Lord's triumph over the Canaanites testified to the world that the God of Israel i the one true and living God, whose claim on the world is absolute. It was also a warning to the na tions that the irresistible advance of the kingdom of God would ultimately disinherit all those wh oppose it, giving place in the earth only to those who acknowledge and serve the Lord. At onc an act of redemption and judgment, it gave notice of the outcome of history and anticipated th final destiny of humankind and the creation.

The battles for Canaan were therefore the Lord's war, undertaken at a particular time in th program of redemption. God gave his people under Joshua no commission or license to conque the world with the sword but a particular, limited mission. The conquered land itself would nc become Israel's national possession by right of conquest, but it belonged to the Lord. So the lan had to be cleansed of all remnants of paganism. Its people and their wealth were not for Israel t seize as the spoils of war from which to enrich themselves (as Achan tried to do, Jos 7) but we placed under God's ban (were to be devoted to God to dispense with as he pleased). On that lan Israel was to establish a commonwealth faithful to the righteous rule of God and thus be a witnes (and a blessing) to the nations. If Israel became unfaithful and conformed to Canaanite culture an practice, it would in turn lose its place in the Lord's land — as Israel almost did in the days of th judges, and as it eventually did in the exile.

War is a terrible curse that the human race brings on itself as it seeks to possess the earth by i own unrighteous ways. But it pales before the curse that awaits all those who do not heed God testimony to himself or his warnings — those who oppose the rule of God and reject his offer c grace. The God of the second Joshua (Jesus) is the God of the first Joshua also. Although now fc a time he reaches out to the whole world with the gospel (and commissions his people urgentl to carry his offer of peace to all nations), the sword of his judgment waits in the wings — and h second Joshua will wield it (Rev 19:11 – 16; see notes there).

JOSHUA

NTRODUCTION

Title and Theological Theme

oshua is a story of conquest and fulfilled promises for the people of God. After many years of lavery in Egypt and 40 years in the wilderness, the Israelites were finally allowed to enter the land promised to their ancestors. Abraham, always a migrant, never possessed the country to which e was sent, but he left to his children the legacy of God's covenant that made them the eventual eirs of all of Canaan (see Ge 15:13,16,18; 17:8 and note). Joshua was destined to turn that promise nto reality.

Where Deuteronomy ends, the book of Joshua begins: The tribes of Israel are still camped on he east side of the Jordan River. The narrative opens with God's command to move forward and ass through the river on dry land. Then it relates the series of ictories in central, southern and northern Canaan that gave he Israelites control of all the hill country and the Negev. It ontinues with a description of the tribal allotments and ends vith Joshua's final addresses to the people. The theme of the ook, therefore, is the establishment of God's people Israel in he Lord's land, the land he had promised to give them as their lace of "rest" in the earth (1:13,15; 21:44; 22:4; 23:1; see also Dt :20 and note; 12:9 – 10; 25:19; 1Ki 5:4 and note; 8:56). So the reat King's promise to the patriarchs and Moses to give the and of Canaan to the chosen people of his kingdom is now istorically fulfilled (1:1 – 6; 21:43 – 45).

In the story the book tells, three primary actors play a part: the LORD" (as Israel's God), his servant Joshua and his people srael (the last a collective "character" in the story). We meet all hree immediately in ch. 1, where all three are clearly presented n the distinctive roles they will play in the story that follows. h. 1 also introduces the reader to the main concern of the ook as a whole.

The role of the central human actor in the events narrated ere is reinforced by the name he bears. Earlier in his life Joshua vas called simply Hoshea (Nu 13:8,16), meaning "salvation." But

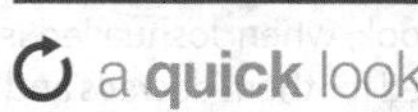

Author:
Unknown, though certain sections may derive from Joshua himself

Audience:
God's chosen people, the Israelites

Date:
Probably about 1390 BC

Theme:
God enables Joshua to lead the armies of Israel to victory over the Canaanites in the promised land.

The theme of the book is the establishment of God's people Israel in the Lord's land, the land he had promised to give them as their place of "rest" in the earth.

later Moses changed his name to Joshua, meaning "The LORD saves" (or "The LORD gives victory") When this same name (the Greek form of which is Jesus; see NIV text note on Mt 1:21) was give to Mary's firstborn son, it identified him as the servant of God who would complete what God di for Israel in a preliminary way through the first Joshua, namely, overcome all powers of evil in th world and bring God's people into their eternal "rest" (see Heb 4:1 – 11 and notes).

In the Hebrew Bible the book of Joshua initiates a division called the Former Prophets, includin also Judges, Samuel and Kings. These are all historical in content but are written from a propheti standpoint. They do more than merely record the nation's history from Moses to the fall of Judah i 586 BC. They prophetically interpret God's covenant ways with Israel in history — how he fulfills an remains true to his promises (especially through his servants such as Joshua, the judges, Samue and David) and how he deals with the waywardness of the Israelites. In Joshua it was the Lord wh won the victories and "gave Israel all the land he had sworn to give their ancestors" (21:43).

Author and Date

In the judgment of many scholars Joshua was not written until the end of the period of the king some 800 years after the actual events. But there are significant reasons to question this conclusio and to place the time of composition much earlier. The earliest Jewish traditions (Talmud) clai that Joshua wrote his own book except for the final section about his funeral, which is attribute to Eleazar, son of Aaron (the last verse must have been added by a later editor).

On at least two occasions the text reports that it was being written at Joshua's command c by Joshua himself: We are told that when the tribes received their territories, Joshua instructe his men to "make a survey of the land and write a description of it" (18:8). Then in the last scen of the book, when Joshua led Israel in a renewal of the covenant with the Lord, it is said that "h reaffirmed for them decrees and laws" (24:25) and "recorded these things" (24:26). On another occa sion the narrator speaks as if he had been a participant in the event; he uses the pronoun "us" (5:6

Moreover, the author seems to be familiar with ancient names of cities, such as "the Jebusit city" (15:8; 18:16,28) for Jerusalem, Kiriath Arba (14:15; 15:54; 20:7; 21:11) for Hebron, and Greate Sidon (11:8; 19:28) for what later became simply Sidon. And Tyre is never mentioned, probabl because in Joshua's day it had not yet developed into a port of major importance.

But if some features suggest an author of Joshua's own lifetime, others point to a writer of somewhat later period. The account of the long day when the sun stood still at Aijalon is substant ated by a quotation from another source, the Book of Jashar (10:13). This would hardly be natur for an eyewitness of the miracle who was writing shortly after it happened. Also, there are 1 instances where the phrase "to this day" occurs.

It seems safe to conclude that the book draws on early sources. It may date from the beginnin of the monarchy. Some think that Samuel may have had a hand in shaping or compiling the mater als of the book, but in fact we are unsure who the final author or editor was.

The Life of Joshua

Joshua's remarkable life was filled with excitement, variety, success and honor. He wa known for his deep trust in God and as "a man in whom is the spirit of leadership" (Nu 27:18 As a youth he lived through the bitter realities of slavery in Egypt, but he also witnessed the supe

erial view of Jericho and the hills to the west. Joshua 2 relates how the Israelite spies stayed at the home of ahab, located in the wall of Jericho.

atural plagues and the miracle of Israel's escape from the army of the Egyptians when the waters f the "Red Sea" opened before them. In the Sinai peninsula it was Joshua who led the troops of srael to victory over the Amalekites (Ex 17:8 – 13). He alone was allowed to accompany Moses up he holy mountain where the tablets of the law were received (Ex 24:13 – 14 [but see 24:18]). And was he who stood watch at the temporary "tent of meeting" Moses set up before the tabernacle vas erected (Ex 33:11).

Joshua was elected to represent his own tribe of Ephraim when the 12 spies were sent into anaan to look over the land. Only Joshua and Caleb (who represented the tribe of Judah) were eady to follow God's will and take immediate possession of the land (see Nu 14:26 – 34). The rest of he Israelites of that generation were condemned to die in the wilderness. Even Moses died short f the goal and was told to turn everything over to Joshua. God promised to guide and strengthen oshua, just as he had Moses (Dt 31:23; cf. Jos 1:5 and note).

Joshua was God's chosen servant (see 24:29 and note on Dt 34:5) to bring Moses' work to ompletion and establish Israel in the promised land. To that special divine appointment he was aithful — as the leader of God's army, as the administrator of God's division of the land and as od's spokesman for promoting Israel's covenant faithfulness. In all this he was a striking OT type foreshadowing) of Christ (see notes on Heb 4:1,6 – 8).

Historical Setting

At the time of the Israelite migration into Canaan the superpowers of the ancient Near East were relatively weak. The Hittites had faded from the scene. Neither Babylonia nor Egypt could maintain a standing military presence in Canaan, and the Assyrians would not send in their armies until centuries later.

As the tribes circled east of the Dead Sea, the Edomites refused them passage, so Israel bypassed them to the east. However, when Sihon and Og, two regional Amorite kings of Transjordan tried to stop the Israelites, they were easily defeated and their lands occupied. Moab was forced to let Israel pass through her territory and camp in her plains. Also the Midianites were dealt a severe blow.

Biblical archaeologists call this period the Late Bronze Age (c. 1550–1200 BC). Today thousands of artifacts give testimony to the richness of the Canaanite material culture, which was in many ways superior to that of the Israelites. When the ruins of the ancient kingdom of Ugarit were discovered at modern Ras Shamra on the northern coast of Syria (see chart, p. xxiv), a wealth of new information came to light concerning the domestic, commercial and religious life of the Canaanites. From a language close to Hebrew came stories of ancient kings and gods that revealed their immoral behavior and cruelty. In addition, pagan temples, altars, tombs and ritual vessels have been uncovered, throwing more light on the culture and customs of the peoples surrounding Israel.

Excavations at the ancient sites of Megiddo, Beth Shan and Gezer show how powerfully fortified these cities were and why they were not captured and occupied by Israel in Joshua's day. Many other fortified towns were taken, however, so that Israel became firmly established in the land as

Beersheba with remains of a pillared house and the wall behind it. Beersheba was one of the towns assigned to Judah (Jos 15:28).

Kim Walton

Only Joshua and Caleb were ready to follow God's will and take immediate possession of the land. The rest of the Israelites of that generation were condemned to die in the wilderness.

ne dominant power. Apart from Jericho and Ai, Joshua is reported to have burned only Hazor 1:13), so attempts to date these events by destruction levels in the mounds of Canaan's ancient ities are questionable undertakings. It must also be remembered that other groups were involved campaigns in the region about this time, among whom were Egyptian rulers and the Sea Peoples ncluding the Philistines). There had also been much intercity warfare among the Canaanites, and fterward the period of the judges was marked by general turbulence.

Much of the data from archaeology appears to support a date for Joshua's invasion c. 1239 BC. his fits well with an exodus that would then have taken place 40 years earlier under the famous ameses II (c. 1279–1212), who ruled from the Nile delta at a city with the same name (Ex 1:11). also places Joseph in Egypt in a favorable situation. Four hundred years before Rameses II the haraohs were the Semitic Hyksos, who also ruled from the delta near the land of Goshen.

On the other hand, a good case can be made for the traditional viewpoint that the invasion ccurred c. 1406 BC. The earlier date also fits better with the two numbers found in Jdg 11:26 nd 1Ki 6:1, since it allows for an additional 150 years between Moses and the monarchy. See also ntroductions to Genesis: Author and Date of Writing; Exodus: Chronology; Judges: Background; nd note on 1Ki 6:1.

utline

- I. Prologue: The Exhortations to Conquer (ch. 1)
- II. The Entrance into the Land (2:1—5:12)
  - A. The Reconnaissance of Jericho (ch. 2)
  - B. The Crossing of the Jordan (chs. 3–4)
  - C. The Consecration at Gilgal (5:1–12)
- III. The Conquest of the Land (5:13—12:24)
  - A. The Initial Battles (5:13—8:35)
    1. The victory at Jericho (5:13—6:27)
    2. The failure at Ai because of Achan's sin (ch. 7)
    3. The victory at Ai (8:1–29)
    4. The covenant renewed at Shechem (8:30–35)
  - B. The Campaign in the South (chs. 9–10)
    1. The treaty with the Gibeonites (ch. 9)
    2. The long day of Joshua (10:1–15)
    3. The southern cities conquered (10:16–43)
  - C. The Campaign in the North (ch. 11)
  - D. The Defeated Kings of Canaan (ch. 12)
- IV. The Distribution of the Land (chs. 13–21)
  - A. The Areas Yet to Be Conquered (13:1–7)
  - B. The Land Assigned by Moses to the Tribes in Transjordan (13:8–33)
  - C. The Division of the Land of Canaan (chs. 14–19)
    1. Introduction (14:1–5)
    2. The town given to Caleb (14:6–15)
    3. The lands given to Judah and "Joseph" at Gilgal (chs. 15–17)

4. The allotments for Benjamin, Simeon, Zebulun, Issachar, Asher, Naphtali and Dan at Shiloh (18:1 — 19:48)
5. The town given to Joshua (19:49 – 51)

D. The Cities Assigned to the Levites (chs. 20 – 21)
1. The 6 cities of refuge (ch. 20)
2. The 48 cities of the priests and other Levites (ch. 21)

V. Epilogue: Tribal Unity and Loyalty to the Lord (chs. 22 – 24)

A. The Altar of Witness by the Jordan (ch. 22)

B. Joshua's Farewell Exhortation (ch. 23)

C. The Renewal of the Covenant at Shechem (24:1 – 28)

D. The Death and Burial of Joshua and Eleazar (24:29 – 33)

Joshua Installed as Leader

1 After the death of Moses the servant
of the LORD,[a] the LORD said to Joshua[b]
son of Nun, Moses' aide: 2“Moses my servant is dead. Now then, you and all these
people, get ready to cross the Jordan River[c] into the land[d] I am about to give to
them[e]—to the Israelites. 3I will give you
every place where you set your foot,[f] as
I promised Moses.[g] 4Your territory will
extend from the desert to Lebanon,[h] and
from the great river, the Euphrates[i]—all
the Hittite[j] country—to the Mediterranean
Sea in the west.[k] 5No one will be able to
stand against you[l] all the days of your life.
As I was with[m] Moses, so I will be with
you; I will never leave you nor forsake[n]
you. 6Be strong[o] and courageous,[p] because
you will lead these people to inherit the
land I swore to their ancestors[q] to give
them.
7“Be strong and very courageous. Be
careful to obey[r] all the law[s] my servant
Moses[t] gave you; do not turn from it to
the right or to the left,[u] that you may be
successful wherever you go.[v] 8Keep this
Book of the Law[w] always on your lips;[x]
meditate[y] on it day and night, so that you
may be careful to do everything written in
it. Then you will be prosperous and successful.[z] 9Have I not commanded you? Be
strong and courageous. Do not be afraid;[a]
do not be discouraged,[b] for the LORD your
God will be with you wherever you go.”[c]
10So Joshua ordered the officers of the
people:[d] 11“Go through the camp[e] and tell
the people, ‘Get your provisions[f] ready.
Three days[g] from now you will cross the
Jordan[h] here to go in and take possession[i]
of the land the LORD your God is giving
you for your own.’”
12But to the Reubenites, the Gadites and
the half-tribe of Manasseh,[j] Joshua said,
13“Remember the command that Moses the
servant of the LORD gave you after he said,
‘The LORD your God will give you rest[k] by
giving you this land.’ 14Your wives,[l] your
children and your livestock may stay in
the land[m] that Moses gave you east of the
Jordan, but all your fighting men, ready
for battle,[n] must cross over ahead of your

1:1 [a]Ex 14:31; Dt 34:5; Rev 15:3 [b]S Ex 17:9 **1:2** [c]S Nu 13:29; S Nu 35:10 [d]S Ge 15:14 [e]Ge 12:7; Dt 1:25 **1:3** [f]S Dt 11:24 [g]Ge 50:24; Nu 13:2; Dt 1:8 **1:4** [h]S Dt 3:25 [i]S Ge 2:14 [j]S Ge 10:15; 23:10; Ex 3:8 [k]Nu 34:2-12; Ezr 4:20 **1:5** [l]S Dt 7:24 [m]ver 17; S Ge 26:3; S 39:2; Jdg 6:12; 1Sa 10:7; Jer 1:8; 30:11 [n]S Ge 28:15; S Dt 4:31 **1:6** [o]2Sa 2:7; 1Ki 2:2; Isa 41:6; Joel 3:9-10 [p]S Dt 1:21; S 31:6; S Jdg 5:21 [q]Jer 3:18; 7:7 **1:7** [r]Dt 29:9; 1Ki 2:3; 3:3 [s]Ezr 7:26; Ps 78:10; 119:136; Isa 42:24; Jer 26:4-6; 32:23; 44:10 [t]ver 2, 15; S Nu 12:7; Job 1:8; 42:7 [u]S Dt 5:32; Jos 23:6 [v]ver 9; S Dt 4:2; 5:33; S 11:8; Jos 11:15 **1:8** [w]S Dt 28:61; S Ps 147:19 [x]S Ex 4:15; Isa 59:21 [y]S Ge 24:63 [z]Dt 29:9; 1Sa 18:14; Ps 1:1-3; Isa 52:13; 53:10; Jer 23:5 **1:9** [a]S Dt 31:6; Jos 10:8; 2Ki 19:6; Isa 35:4; 37:6 [b]S Dt 1:21; Job 4:5 [c]S ver 7; Dt 31:7-8; Jer 1:8 **1:10** [d]S Dt 1:15 **1:11** [e]Jos 3:2 [f]1Sa 17:22; Isa 10:28 [g]S Ge 40:13 [h]S Nu 35:10 [i]S Nu 33:53 **1:12** [j]Nu 32:33 **1:13** [k]S Ex 33:14; Ps 55:6; Isa 11:10; 28:12; 30:15; 32:18; 40:31; Jer 6:16; 45:3; La 5:5 **1:14** [l]Dt 3:19 [m]S Nu 32:26 [n]S Ex 13:18

1:1–18 The Lord initiates the action by commanding Joshua, his chosen replacement for Moses (see Dt 31:1–8), to lead Israel across the Jordan and take possession of the promised land. He urges courage and promises success—but only if Israel obeys the law of God that Moses has given them. The chapter consists of speeches significant in their content and order: The Lord commands Joshua as his appointed leader over his people (vv. 1–9); Joshua, as the Lord's representative, addresses Israel (vv. 10–15); Israel responds to Joshua as the Lord's representative and successor to Moses (vv. 16–18). Thus the events of the book are set in motion and the roles of the main actors indicated (see Introduction: Title and Theological Theme).

1:1 *After the death of Moses.* Immediately the time and occasion of the action are set forth, showing that the story will continue where Deuteronomy ended, with the death of Moses. Cf. "After the death of Joshua" (Jdg 1:1). *servant of the LORD.* See notes on Ex 14:31; Dt 34:5; Ps 18 title; Isa 41:8–9; 42:1. *Moses' aide.* The title by which Joshua served for many years as second-in-command (see Nu 11:28; see also Ex 24:13; 33:11; Dt 1:38).

1:2 *Jordan River.* The flow of the Jordan near Jericho was not large during most of the year (less than 100 feet wide), but at flood stage in the spring it filled its wider bed, which at places was a mile wide and far more treacherous to cross (see 3:15 and note). *land I am about to give to them.* A central theme of the Pentateuch (see Ge 12:1; 50:24; Ex 3:8; 23:31; Dt 1:8). The book of Joshua relates the fulfillment of this promise of God.

1:3–5 See Dt 11:24–25.

1:4 The dimensions of the land promised to Israel vary (compare this text and Ge 15:18 with Dt 34:1–4), but these are the farthest limits—conquered and held only by David and Solomon. Canaan was still called "Hatti-land" centuries after the Hittites had withdrawn to the north. But Joshua was to take all he set out to conquer; wherever he set his foot was his (v. 3). His victories gave the 12 tribes control over most of the central hill country and much of the Negev.

1:5 *I will be with you.* To direct, sustain and assure success (see notes on Ge 26:3; Jer 1:8).

1:6 *land I swore to their ancestors.* The long-awaited inheritance pledged to the descendants of Abraham (Ge 15:7,8–21) and of Jacob (Ge 28:13).

1:7 *Be careful to obey.* Success was not guaranteed unconditionally (see Dt 8:1; 11:8–9,22–25).

1:8 *Book of the Law.* See Dt 28:58,61; 29:17,20–21; 30:10; 31:24. *lips; meditate.* See Ps 1:2. In the ancient world, reading written texts and even meditating on them were rarely done in complete silence (see Ex 13:9; Dt 30:14; Ps 19:14; 119:13; Ac 8:30). *day and night.* See Ps 1:2.

1:9 *Have I not commanded you?* A rhetorical question that emphasizes the authority of the speaker.

1:10 *Joshua ordered.* At this point Joshua assumes full command. *officers.* May refer to those whom Moses had appointed over the divisions within the tribes (Ex 18:21; Dt 1:15).

1:11 *provisions.* Foodstuffs needed for the next several days' march.

1:12–15 The threat from Sihon and Og (see Nu 21:21–35) was overcome by military victory and the occupation of the lands north of Moab and east of the Jordan River. The two and a half tribes who asked to remain had been commanded by Moses to send their fighting men across with the rest to conquer Canaan (Nu 21:21–35; 32:1–27). The conquest of the promised land must be an undertaking by all Israel.

1:13,15 *rest.* An important OT concept (see notes on Dt 3:20; 2Sa 7:1,11), implying secure borders, peace with neighboring countries and absence of threat to life and well-being within the land (see 1Ki 5:4; 8:56 and notes).

1:14 *your fighting men.* Those 20 years old or more (see Nu 1:3,18–45) who were fit for the rigors of war.

fellow Israelites.[o] You are to help them [15]until the LORD gives them rest, as he has done for you, and until they too have taken possession of the land the LORD your God is giving them. After that, you may go back and occupy your own land, which Moses the servant of the LORD gave you east of the Jordan toward the sunrise."[p]

[16]Then they answered Joshua, "Whatever you have commanded us we will do, and wherever you send us we will go.[q] [17]Just as we fully obeyed Moses, so we will obey you.[r] Only may the LORD your God be with you as he was with Moses. [18]Whoever rebels against your word and does not obey[s] it, whatever you may command them, will be put to death. Only be strong and courageous![t]"

Rahab and the Spies

2 Then Joshua son of Nun secretly sent two spies[u] from Shittim.[v] "Go, look over[w] the land," he said, "especially Jericho.[x]" So they went and entered the house of a prostitute named Rahab[y] and stayed there.

[2]The king of Jericho was told, "Look, some of the Israelites have come here tonight to spy out the land." [3]So the king of Jericho sent this message to Rahab:[z] "Bring out the men who came to you and entered your house, because they have come to spy out the whole land."

[4]But the woman had taken the two men[a] and hidden them.[b] She said, "Yes, the men came to me, but I did not know where they had come from. [5]At dusk, when it was time to close the city gate,[c] they left. I don't know which way they went. Go after them quickly. You may catch up with them."[d] [6](But she had taken them up to the roof and hidden them under the stalks of flax[e] she had laid out on the roof.)[f] [7]So the men set out in pursuit of the spies on the road that leads to the fords of the Jordan,[g] and as soon as the pursuers[h] had gone out, the gate was shut.

[8]Before the spies lay down for the night, she went up on the roof[i] [9]and said to them, "I know that the LORD has given you this land and that a great fear[j] of you has fallen on us, so that all who live in this country are melting in fear because of you. [10]We have heard how the LORD dried up[k] the water of the Red Sea[a] for you when you came out of Egypt,[l] and what you did to Sihon and Og,[m] the two kings of the Amorites[n] east of the Jordan,[o] whom you completely destroyed.[b][p] [11]When we heard of it, our hearts melted in fear[q] and everyone's courage failed[r] because of you,[s] for the LORD your God[t] is God in heaven above and on the earth[u] below.

[12]"Now then, please swear to me[v] by the

1:14 [o]Jos 4:12 **1:15** [p]Nu 32:20-22; Jos 22:1-4 **1:16** [q]S Nu 27:20; S 32:25 **1:17** [r]S Nu 27:20 **1:18** [s]S Nu 32:25 [t]S Dt 1:21; S 31:6 **2:1** [u]S ver 4; S Ge 42:9 [v]S Nu 25:1; Jos 3:1; Joel 3:18 [w]S Nu 21:32; Jdg 18:2 [x]S Nu 33:48 [y]Jos 6:17,25; S Heb 11:31 **2:3** [z]Jos 6:23 **2:4** [a]ver 1; Jos 6:22 [b]Jos 6:17 **2:5** [c]Jdg 5:8; 9:35; 16:2 [d]S Heb 11:31 **2:6** [e]Jdg 15:14; Pr 31:13; Isa 19:9 [f]S Ex 1:17, 19; Jos 6:25; 2Sa 17:19 **2:7** [g]Nu 22:1; Jdg 3:28; 7:24; 12:5,6; Isa 16:2 [h]ver 16,22 **2:8** [i]S Dt 22:8; Jdg 16:27; 2Sa 16:22; Ne 8:16; Isa 15:3; 22:1; Jer 32:29 **2:9** [j]S Ge 35:5; S Ex 15:14 **2:10** [k]S Ge 8:1; Ex 14:21; Jos 3:17; Ps 74:15 [l]S Nu 23:22 [m]S Nu 21:21 [n]S Ge 10:16; S 14:7 [o]Jos 9:10 [p]S Nu 21:2 **2:11** [q]S Ge 42:28 [r]S Dt 2:25; Ps 107:26; Jnh 1:5 [s]Ex 15:14; Jos 5:1; 7:5; 2Sa 4:1; Ps 22:14; Isa 13:7; 19:1; Jer 51:30; Na 2:10 [t]2Ki 5:15; 19:15; Da 6:26 [u]S Ge 14:19; S Nu 20:14 **2:12** [v]S Ge 24:8; S 47:31

[a] *10* Or *the Sea of Reeds* [b] *10* The Hebrew term refers to the irrevocable giving over of things or persons to the LORD, often by totally destroying them.

1:18 *Whoever rebels.* Having just taken the oath of allegiance to Joshua, they now agree to the death penalty for any rebellious act (e.g., the sin of Achan, 7:15). *be strong and courageous.* The people's words of encouragement to Joshua echo and reinforce those from the Lord (vv. 6–7,9).

2:1–24 The mission of the two spies and the account of Rahab. The practice of reconnaissance and espionage is as old as war itself (cf. Jdg 7:10–11; 1Sa 26:6–12). Rahab became a convert to the God of Israel and a famous woman among the Hebrews. She is honored in the NT for her faith (Heb 11:31) and good works (Jas 2:25).

In this first encounter of the Israelites (represented by the two spies) and the Canaanites (represented by Rahab and the men sent by the king of Jericho), the outcome of the mission on which God had sent his army under Joshua (ch.1) is foreshadowed, and God's assurances of success (see 1:5 and note) are confirmed.

2:1 *sent ... from Shittim.* The invasion point was in the plains of Moab facing toward the Jordan and Jericho (Nu 33:48–49). The Hebrew word *Shittim* means "acacia trees," which flourish in the semi-arid conditions of the wilderness. *especially Jericho.* The primary focus of the spies. It was a fortified city, was well supplied with water by strong springs and was located just five miles west of the Jordan (see note on 6:1). *prostitute.* Josephus and other early sources refer to Rahab as an "innkeeper," but see Heb 11:31; Jas 2:25.

2:2 *king of Jericho.* The major cities of Canaan were in reality small kingdoms, each ruled by a local king (attested also in the Amarna letters of the fourteenth century BC; see chart, p. xxii).

2:6 *hidden ... under the stalks of flax.* Rooftops in the Near East are still used for drying grain or stalks. Rahab's cunning saved the lives of the two Israelites but put her own life in jeopardy.

2:7 *fords of the Jordan.* Shallow crossings of the Jordan, where the depth of normal flow averages only three feet.

2:9–11 Rahab's confession has a significant concentric structure:

a "I know";
  b "a great fear ... has fallen on us ... all who live in this country";
    c "We have heard";
  b′ "our hearts melted in fear and everyone's courage failed";
a′ "the LORD your God is God."

Rahab's personal confession forms the outer frame (a–a′); the inner frame (b–b′) offers the military intelligence that the spies report back to Joshua; the center (c, v. 10) sums up the news about the Lord that occasioned both the Canaanite fear and Rahab's abandonment of Canaan and its gods to side with the Lord and Israel. That the hearts of the Canaanites were "melting in fear" (v. 9) was vital information to the spies. Rahab's word is the decisive turning point in the narrator's account of this event. The whole outcome of the spies' venture into Jericho hinges on her actions.

2:10 *completely destroyed.* See NIV text note.

LORD that you will show kindness[w] to my
family, because I have shown kindness to
you. Give me a sure sign[x] 13 that you will
spare the lives of my father and mother,
my brothers and sisters, and all who belong
to them[y]—and that you will save us from
death."
14 "Our lives for your lives!"[z] the men
assured her. "If you don't tell what we are
doing, we will treat you kindly and faithfully[a] when the LORD gives us the land."
15 So she let them down by a rope[b]
through the window,[c] for the house she
lived in was part of the city wall. 16 She
said to them, "Go to the hills[d] so the pursuers[e] will not find you. Hide yourselves
there three days[f] until they return, and
then go on your way."[g]
17 Now the men had said to her, "This
oath[h] you made us swear will not be binding on us 18 unless, when we enter the
land, you have tied this scarlet cord[i] in the
window[j] through which you let us down,
and unless you have brought your father
and mother, your brothers and all your
family[k] into your house. 19 If any of them
go outside your house into the street, their
blood will be on their own heads;[l] we will
not be responsible. As for those who are in
the house with you, their blood will be on
our head[m] if a hand is laid on them. 20 But
if you tell what we are doing, we will be released from the oath you made us swear."[n]
21 "Agreed," she replied. "Let it be as you
say."

So she sent them away, and they departed. And she tied the scarlet cord[o] in the
window.[p]
22 When they left, they went into the
hills and stayed there three days,[q] until
the pursuers[r] had searched all along the
road and returned without finding them.
23 Then the two men started back. They
went down out of the hills, forded the river and came to Joshua son of Nun and
told him everything that had happened to
them. 24 They said to Joshua, "The LORD
has surely given the whole land into our
hands;[s] all the people are melting in fear[t]
because of us."

Crossing the Jordan

3 Early in the morning Joshua and all
the Israelites set out from Shittim[u] and
went to the Jordan,[v] where they camped
before crossing over. 2 After three days[w] the
officers[x] went throughout the camp,[y] 3 giving orders to the people: "When you see
the ark of the covenant[z] of the LORD your
God, and the Levitical[a] priests[b] carrying it,
you are to move out from your positions
and follow it. 4 Then you will know which
way to go, since you have never been this
way before. But keep a distance of about
two thousand cubits[a][c] between you and
the ark; do not go near it."

a 4 That is, about 3,000 feet or about 900 meters

2:12 [w]S Ge 24:12; Ru 3:10 [x]S Ge 24:14; S Ex 3:12; Jos 4:6; 1Sa 2:34; 2Ki 19:29 **2:13** [y]ver 18; Jos 6:23 **2:14** [z]1Ki 20:39, 42; 2Ki 10:24 [a]S Ge 47:29 **2:15** [b]Jer 38:6, 11 [c]ver 18, 21; Ge 26:8; Jdg 5:28; 1Sa 19:12 **2:16** [d]S Ge 14:10 [e]S ver 7 [f]ver 22 [g]S Heb 11:31 **2:17** [h]S Ge 24:8 **2:18** [i]ver 21 [j]S ver 15 [k]S ver 13 **2:19** [l]S Lev 20:9 [m]Mt 27:25 **2:20** [n]S Ge 24:8; S 47:31 **2:21** [o]ver 18 [p]S ver 15 **2:22** [q]ver 16 [r]S ver 7 **2:24** [s]Jos 10:8; 11:6; Jdg 3:28; 7:9, 14; 20:28; 1Sa 14:10 [t]S Ex 15:15 **3:1** [u]S Jos 2:1 [v]S Ge 13:10; Job 40:23 **3:2** [w]S Ge 40:13; Jos 2:16 [x]S Dt 1:15 [y]Jos 1:11 **3:3** [z]S Nu 10:33 [a]1Sa 6:15 [b]ver 8, 17; Nu 4:15; Dt 31:9; 1Ki 8:3 **3:4** [c]Nu 35:5

2:12 *show kindness to my family.* The Hebrew for "kindness" is frequently translated "love" or "unfailing love" and often summarizes God's covenant favor toward his people or the love that people are to show to others (see note on Ps 6:4). Rahab had acted toward the spies as a friend of Israel, and now she asks that Israel treat her and her family similarly. *sure sign.* They gave her their oath to spare her whole family (v. 14).
2:14 *kindly and faithfully.* The terms of the pledge made by the spies echo Rahab's request (v. 12). *when the LORD gives us the land.* Rahab's words had added to their assurance of the inevitable victory of the Israelites over Jericho.
2:15 *the house ... was part of the city wall.* There is archaeological evidence that the people of Jericho would occasionally integrate living quarters into the city wall. Although this evidence predates the time of Joshua, it may still serve to illumine this verse. The Late Bronze fortifications at Jericho may have included a casemate wall (a hollow wall with partitions), and Rahab may have occupied one or more rooms inside it.
2:16 *Go to the hills.* The opposite direction from the fords of the Jordan where the spies' pursuers had gone (see v. 7).
2:18 *scarlet cord in the window.* The function of the red marker was similar to that of the blood of the Passover lamb when the Lord struck down the firstborn of Egypt (see Ex 12:13,22–23). The early church viewed the blood-colored cord as a type (symbol) of Christ's atonement.
2:19 *their blood will be on our head.* A vow that accepted responsibility for the death of another, with its related guilt and the retribution meted out by either relatives or the state.
2:22 *into the hills.* Directly west of ancient Jericho were the high, rugged hills of the central mountain ridge in Canaan. They are honeycombed with caves, making the concealment and escape of the two spies relatively easy (see photo, p. 311).
2:24 The spies' mission (see v. 1) concludes with a reassuring word to Joshua (cf. Nu 13:26–33).
3:1—4:24 Details of the river crossing and the memorial of 12 stones set up in the camp at Gilgal. The great significance of this account can hardly be overemphasized, since it marks the crossing of the boundary into the promised land and parallels the miracle of the "Red Sea" crossing in the exodus (Ex 14–15). The Israelites' faith in the God of their ancestors was renewed and strengthened when it was about to be most severely challenged, while at the same time the Canaanites' fear was greatly increased (5:1). In this account the author uses an overlay technique in which, having narrated the crossing to its conclusion (ch. 3), he returns to various points in the event to enlarge on several details: the stones for a memorial (4:1–9); the successful crossing by all Israel (4:10–14); the renewed flow of the river after the crossing was completed (4:15–18). The final paragraph of ch. 4 (vv. 19–24) picks up the story again from 3:17 and completes the account by noting Israel's encampment at Gilgal and the erecting of the stone memorial.
3:3 *ark of the covenant.* The most sacred of the tabernacle furnishings (see Ex 25:10–22). Since it signified the Lord's throne, the Lord himself went into the Jordan ahead of his people as he led them into the land of rest (see Nu 10:33–36; Dt 31:7).
3:4 *distance of about two thousand cubits.* See NIV text note. There was evidently a line of march, with the priests and ark

5 Joshua told the people, "Consecrate
yourselves,[d] for tomorrow the LORD will
do amazing things[e] among you."
6 Joshua said to the priests, "Take up the
ark of the covenant and pass on ahead of
the people." So they took it up and went
ahead of them.
7 And the LORD said to Joshua, "Today I
will begin to exalt you[f] in the eyes of all
Israel, so they may know that I am with
you as I was with Moses.[g] 8 Tell the priests[h]
who carry the ark of the covenant: 'When
you reach the edge of the Jordan's waters,
go and stand in the river.' "
9 Joshua said to the Israelites, "Come
here and listen to the words of the LORD
your God. 10 This is how you will know
that the living God[i] is among you[j] and that
he will certainly drive out before you the
Canaanites, Hittites,[k] Hivites, Perizzites,[l]
Girgashites, Amorites and Jebusites.[m]
11 See, the ark of the covenant of the Lord
of all the earth[n] will go into the Jordan
ahead of you.[o] 12 Now then, choose twelve
men[p] from the tribes of Israel, one from
each tribe. 13 And as soon as the priests
who carry the ark of the LORD—the Lord
of all the earth[q]—set foot in the Jordan,
its waters flowing downstream[r] will be cut
off[s] and stand up in a heap.[t]"
14 So when the people broke camp to
cross the Jordan, the priests carrying the
ark of the covenant[u] went ahead[v] of them.
15 Now the Jordan[w] is at flood stage[x] all
during harvest.[y] Yet as soon as the priests
who carried the ark reached the Jordan
and their feet touched the water's edge,
16 the water from upstream stopped flowing.[z] It piled up in a heap[a] a great distance
away, at a town called Adam in the vicinity of Zarethan,[b] while the water flowing
down[c] to the Sea of the Arabah[d] (that is,
the Dead Sea[e]) was completely cut off.[f] So
the people crossed over opposite Jericho.[g]
17 The priests[h] who carried the ark of the
covenant of the LORD stopped in the middle of the Jordan and stood on dry ground,[i]
while all Israel passed by until the whole
nation had completed the crossing on dry
ground.[j]

4 When the whole nation had finished
crossing the Jordan,[k] the LORD said
to Joshua, 2 "Choose twelve men[l] from
among the people, one from each tribe,
3 and tell them to take up twelve stones[m]
from the middle of the Jordan,[n] from right
where the priests are standing, and carry
them over with you and put them down at
the place where you stay tonight.[o]"
4 So Joshua called together the twelve
men[p] he had appointed from the Israelites,
one from each tribe, 5 and said to them,
"Go over before the ark of the LORD your
God into the middle of the Jordan.[q] Each
of you is to take up a stone on his shoulder, according to the number of the tribes
of the Israelites, 6 to serve as a sign[r] among
you. In the future, when your children[s]
ask you, 'What do these stones mean?'[t]
7 tell them that the flow of the Jordan was
cut off[u] before the ark of the covenant of
the LORD. When it crossed the Jordan, the

3:5 [d] S Ex 29:1; S Lev 11:44 [e] Jdg 6:13; 1Ch 16:9,24; Ps 26:7; 75:1 **3:7** [f] Jos 4:14; 1Ch 29:25 [g] Jos 1:5 **3:8** [h] S ver 3 **3:10** [i] Dt 5:26; 1Sa 17:26,36; 2Ki 19:4,16; Ps 18:46; 42:2; 84:2; Isa 37:4,17; Jer 10:10; 23:36; Da 6:26; Hos 1:10; S Mt 16:16 [j] S Dt 7:21 [k] S Ge 26:34 [l] Jos 17:15; 24:11; Jdg 1:4; 3:5 [m] S Ex 3:8; S 23:23; S Dt 7:1; Jos 9:1; 11:3; 12:8; Jdg 19:11; 1Ch 11:4 **3:11** [n] ver 13; Ex 19:5; Dt 10:14; Job 9:10; 28:24; 41:11; Ps 50:12; 97:5; Zec 6:5 [o] S Dt 9:3 **3:12** [p] Jos 4:2,4 **3:13** [q] S ver 11 [r] ver 16 [s] Jos 4:7 [t] S Ex 14:22; S Isa 11:15 **3:14** [u] Ps 132:8 [v] Ac 7:44-45 **3:15** [w] 2Ki 2:6 [x] Jos 4:18; 1Ch 12:15; Isa 8:7 [y] S Ge 8:22 **3:16** [z] Ps 66:6; 74:15; 114:3 [a] Job 38:37; Ps 33:7 [b] 1Ki 4:12; 7:46 [c] ver 13 [d] S Dt 1:1 [e] S Ge 14:3 [f] S Ge 8:1; S Ex 14:22 [g] 2Ki 2:4 **3:17** [h] S ver 3 [i] Jos 4:3,5,8,9,10 [j] S Ex 14:22; S Jos 2:10 **4:1** [k] Dt 27:2 **4:2** [l] S Jos 3:12 **4:3** [m] ver 20 [n] S Jos 3:17 [o] ver 19 **4:4** [p] S Jos 3:12 **4:5** [q] S Jos 3:17 **4:6** [r] S Jos 2:12 [s] S Ex 10:2 [t] ver 21; Ex 12:26; S 13:14 **4:7** [u] Jos 3:13

---

leading the way. Respect for the sacred symbol of the Lord's holy presence accounts for this gap between the people and the priests bearing the ark.

3:5 *Consecrate yourselves.* Before their meeting with God at Sinai this had involved washing all their garments, as well as their bodies, and also abstinence from sexual intercourse (see Ex 19:10,14–15).

3:7 *I will begin to exalt you.* A prime objective for the divine intervention at the Jordan was to validate the leadership of Joshua. With a miraculous event so much like that of the "Red Sea" crossing, Joshua's position as the Lord's servant would be shown to be comparable to that of Moses.

3:10 *This is how you will know.* The manner by which God is about to bring the Israelites across the Jordan River, the watery boundary of the promised land, will bring assurance that the one true God is with them and that he will surely dislodge the present inhabitants of Canaan. Two fundamental issues are at stake: (1) Who is the true and mighty God—the God of Israel or the god on whom the Canaanites depend (Baal, who was believed to reign as king among the gods because he had triumphed over the sea-god)? (2) Who has the rightful claim to the land—the Lord or the Canaanites? (For the juridical aspect of such wars, see Jdg 11:27.) By passing through the Jordan at the head of his army, the Lord is staking his claim on the land. *Canaanites ... Jebusites.* See notes on Ge 9:25; 10:6,15–16; 13:7; 15:16; 23:3; Ex 3:8; Jdg 3:3; 6:10.

3:12 *choose twelve men.* Joshua seems to anticipate the Lord's instructions concerning a stone monument of the event (see 4:2–3).

3:13 *cut off.* Blocked, stopped in its flow. *stand up in a heap.* The Hebrew for "heap" is found here, in v. 16 and also in the poetic accounts of the "Red Sea" crossing (Ex 15:8; Ps 78:13). It is possible that God used a physical means (such as a landslide) to dam up the Jordan at the place called Adam (v. 16), near the entrance of the Jabbok River. (As recently as 1927 a blockage of the water in this area was recorded that lasted over 20 hours.) But, even if so, the miraculous element is not diminished (see Ex 14:21).

3:15 *at flood stage.* Because of the spring rains and the melting of snow on Mount Hermon. *harvest.* Grain harvest took place in April and May. *as soon as.* The stoppage nearly 20 miles upstream (v. 16) would have happened several hours earlier to make the events coincide.

3:17 *The priests who carried the ark ... stood on dry ground.* Signifying that the Lord himself remained in the place of danger—under the threat of the waters of judgment—until all Israel had crossed the Jordan.

4:6 *What do these stones mean?* A stone monument was commonly used as a memorial to remind future generations of what had happened at a particular place (24:26; 1Sa 7:12).

CONQUEST OF CANAAN

1 ENTRY INTO CANAAN

When the Israelite tribes approached Canaan after four decades of wilderness existence, they had to overcome two Amorite kingdoms on the Medeba plateau and in Bashan. Under Moses' leadership, they also subdued the Midianites in order to consolidate their control over the Transjordanian region.

The conquest of Canaan followed a course that in retrospect appears as though it had been planned by a brilliant military strategist. Taking Jericho gave Israel control of its strategic plains, fords and roads as a base of operations. When Israel next gained control of the Bethel, Gibeon and Upper Beth Horon regions, it dominated the center of the north-south Palestinian ridge. Subsequently, Israel was able to break the power of the allied urban centers in separate campaigns south and north (for the northern campaign, see map, p. 331).

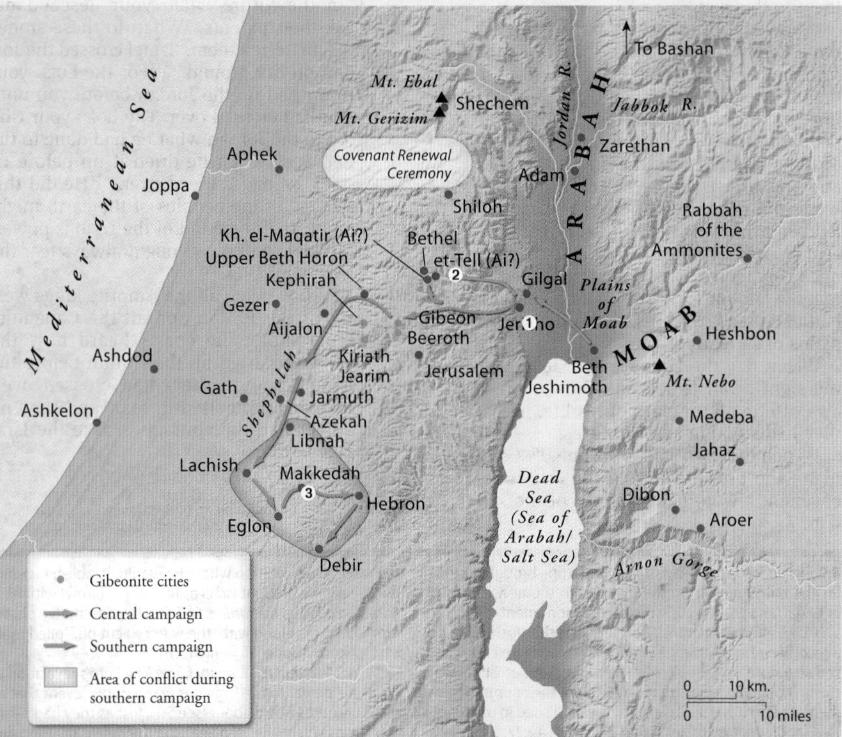

2 THE CENTRAL CAMPAIGN

The destruction of both Jericho and Ai led to a major victory against the Canaanites in the Valley of Aijalon — the battle of the long day (see Jos 10:12–14)—which then allowed Joshua to proceed against the cities of the western foothills.

Archaeological evidence for the conquest is mixed, in part because the chronological problems are unsolved. On the one hand, clay tablets containing cuneiform letters to the Egyptian court have been found at Tell el-Amarna in Egypt from c. 1375 BC. These mention bands of Hapiru that threaten many of the cities of Canaan and create fear among the Canaanite inhabitants.

On the other hand, numerous towns were destroyed c. 1230 BC by unknown assailants, presumably the "Sea Peoples," but possibly including the Israelites as well. The Biblical chronology based on 1Ki 6:1 seems to demand an even earlier dating, near the end of the fifteenth century (see Introduction to Joshua: Historical Setting).

3 THE SOUTHERN CAMPAIGN

Azekah, Libnah, Lachish, Eglon and Debir were all captured by Joshua in his campaign against the southern coalition of Canaanite cities that was led by the king of Jerusalem.

Several of these towns, most notably Lachish, contain destruction evidence that might possibly be correlated with the Israelite conquest, but with Jericho and Ai the historical implications are not clear.

waters of the Jordan were cut off. These
stones are to be a memorial[v] to the people
of Israel forever."
8So the Israelites did as Joshua commanded them. They took twelve stones[w]
from the middle of the Jordan,[x] according to the number of the tribes of the
Israelites, as the LORD had told Joshua;[y]
and they carried them over with them to
their camp, where they put them down.
9Joshua set up the twelve stones[z] that had
been[a] in the middle of the Jordan at the
spot where the priests who carried the ark
of the covenant had stood. And they are
there to this day.[a]
10Now the priests who carried the ark
remained standing in the middle of the
Jordan until everything the LORD had commanded Joshua was done by the people,
just as Moses had directed Joshua. The
people hurried over, 11and as soon as all
of them had crossed, the ark of the LORD
and the priests came to the other side
while the people watched. 12The men of
Reuben,[b] Gad[c] and the half-tribe of Manasseh[d] crossed over, ready for battle, in front
of the Israelites,[e] as Moses had directed
them.[f] 13About forty thousand armed for
battle[g] crossed over[h] before the LORD to the
plains of Jericho for war.
14That day the LORD exalted[i] Joshua in
the sight of all Israel; and they stood in
awe of him all the days of his life, just as
they had stood in awe of Moses.
15Then the LORD said to Joshua, 16"Command the priests carrying the ark of the
covenant law[j] to come up out of the Jordan."

4:7 [v]S Ex 28:12
4:8 [w]Ex 28:21 [x]S Jos 3:17 [y]ver 20
4:9 [z]S Ge 28:18; Jos 24:26; 1Sa 7:12 [a]S Ge 35:20
4:12 [b]S Ge 29:32 [c]S Ge 30:11 [d]S Ge 41:51 [e]S Nu 32:27 [f]Nu 32:29
4:13 [g]S Ex 13:18 [h]S Nu 32:17
4:14 [i]S Jos 3:7
4:16 [j]Ex 25:22
4:18 [k]Ex 14:27 [l]S Jos 3:15
4:19 [m]S Dt 11:30
4:20 [n]ver 3,8
4:21 [o]S ver 6
4:22 [p]S Ex 14:22
4:23 [q]Ex 14:19-22
4:24 [r]1Ki 8:60; 18:36; 2Ki 5:15; Ps 67:2; 83:18; 106:8; Isa 37:20; 52:10 [s]Ex 15:16; 1Ch 29:12; Ps 44:3; 89:13; 98:1; 118:15-16 [t]S Ex 14:31
5:1 [u]S Nu 13:29 [v]S Ge 42:28

17So Joshua commanded the priests,
"Come up out of the Jordan."
18And the priests came up out of the
river carrying the ark of the covenant of
the LORD. No sooner had they set their feet
on the dry ground than the waters of the
Jordan returned to their place[k] and ran at
flood stage[l] as before.
19On the tenth day of the first month
the people went up from the Jordan and
camped at Gilgal[m] on the eastern border
of Jericho. 20And Joshua set up at Gilgal the twelve stones[n] they had taken out
of the Jordan. 21He said to the Israelites,
"In the future when your descendants
ask their parents, 'What do these stones
mean?'[o] 22tell them, 'Israel crossed the Jordan on dry ground.'[p] 23For the LORD your
God dried up the Jordan before you until
you had crossed over. The LORD your God
did to the Jordan what he had done to the
Red Sea[b] when he dried it up before us
until we had crossed over.[q] 24He did this
so that all the peoples of the earth might
know[r] that the hand of the LORD is powerful[s] and so that you might always fear the
LORD your God.[t]"
5 Now when all the Amorite kings west
of the Jordan and all the Canaanite
kings along the coast[u] heard how the
LORD had dried up the Jordan before the
Israelites until they[c] had crossed over,
their hearts melted in fear[v] and they no
longer had the courage to face the Israelites.

[a] 9 Or *Joshua also set up twelve stones* [b] 23 Or *the Sea of Reeds* [c] 1 Another textual tradition *we*

4:9 *Joshua set up the twelve stones.* Each tribe brought a stone for the monument from the riverbed to the new campsite at Gilgal, and Joshua constructed the monument there (see v. 20). An alternative translation suggests that Joshua set up a second pile in the middle of the river (see NIV text note, but see also note on 3:1—4:24). The monument at Gilgal was the first of many others that came to dot the countryside as memorials to how Israel came to be established in the promised land; see, e.g., 6:26; 7:26; 8:29,30–31; 10:27; 22:26–28; 24:26–27.

4:13 *About forty thousand.* Seems too few for the number of men listed in Nu 26 for Reuben, Gad and half of Manasseh; the contingents were very likely representative since it would have been imprudent to leave the people undefended who settled in Transjordan (cf. 22:8, "your fellow Israelites"; Nu 32:17).

4:14 See 3:7 and note.

4:19 *tenth day of the first month.* The day the Passover lamb was to be selected (Ex 12:3). *Gilgal.* Usually identified with the ruins at Khirbet el-Mafjer, two miles northeast of Jericho (see map, p. 319).

4:22 *Israel crossed the Jordan.* Earlier Joshua had instructed Israel to answer that the waters of the Jordan were "cut off" so that "the ark of the covenant of the LORD" could cross the Jordan (vv. 6–7). That was the primary fact to be remembered: God crossed the Jordan to take possession of Canaan as the place in his creation where he would establish his kingdom—and he brought Israel as his people (army) with him.

4:23 *God dried up the Jordan.* Still another descriptive phrase for the miracle, along with "the water ... cut off," "piled up in a heap" and "stopped flowing" (3:16).

4:24 *so that all ... might know.* The Lord's revelation of his power to the Israelites was a public event that all the Canaanites heard about (see 5:1), just as they had heard of the crossing of the "Red Sea" and the defeat of Sihon and Og (2:10). *fear the LORD.* Worship and serve him according to his commandments.

5:1 *Amorite ... Canaanite.* Sometimes interchangeable (but see 10:5 and note), these general names included the many smaller nations in the land. Amorite meant "westerner," and Canaanite referred to the people living even farther west along the Mediterranean coast. This verse perhaps concludes the account of the crossing since it notes the effect of that event on the peoples of Canaan (see note on 3:10).

5:2–12 Circumcision and the celebration of the Passover, the two basic covenant rites, were resumed at Gilgal. Both were significant preparations for the conquest of the promised land. Only as a people who had consecrated themselves to God (circumcision; see note on Ge 17:10) and who remembered that God had set them free from Egyptian bondage to be his people (Passover; Ex 12:11,17) could Israel expect to be given possession of Canaan.

Circumcision and Passover at Gilgal

2 At that time the LORD said to Joshua,
"Make flint knives[w] and circumcise[x] the
Israelites again." 3 So Joshua made flint
knives and circumcised the Israelites at
Gibeath Haaraloth.[a]
4 Now this is why he did so: All those who
came out of Egypt—all the men of military
age[y]—died in the wilderness on the way after leaving Egypt.[z] 5 All the people that came
out had been circumcised, but all the people born in the wilderness during the journey from Egypt had not. 6 The Israelites had
moved about in the wilderness[a] forty years[b]
until all the men who were of military age
when they left Egypt had died, since they
had not obeyed the LORD. For the LORD had
sworn to them that they would not see the
land he had solemnly promised their ancestors to give us,[c] a land flowing with milk
and honey.[d] 7 So he raised up their sons in
their place, and these were the ones Joshua
circumcised. They were still uncircumcised
because they had not been circumcised on
the way. 8 And after the whole nation had
been circumcised, they remained where
they were in camp until they were healed.[e]
9 Then the LORD said to Joshua, "Today
I have rolled away the reproach of Egypt
from you." So the place has been called
Gilgal[b][f] to this day.
10 On the evening of the fourteenth day
of the month,[g] while camped at Gilgal on
the plains of Jericho, the Israelites celebrated the Passover.[h] 11 The day after the
Passover, that very day, they ate some
of the produce of the land:[i] unleavened
bread[j] and roasted grain.[k] 12 The manna
stopped the day after[c] they ate this food
from the land; there was no longer any
manna for the Israelites, but that year they
ate the produce of Canaan.[l]

The Fall of Jericho

13 Now when Joshua was near Jericho,
he looked up and saw a man[m] standing in
front of him with a drawn sword[n] in his
hand. Joshua went up to him and asked,
"Are you for us or for our enemies?"
14 "Neither," he replied, "but as commander of the army of the LORD I have
now come." Then Joshua fell facedown[o] to
the ground[p] in reverence, and asked him,
"What message does my Lord[d] have for
his servant?"
15 The commander of the LORD's army
replied, "Take off your sandals, for the
place where you are standing is holy."[q]
And Joshua did so.

6 Now the gates of Jericho[r] were securely barred because of the Israelites. No
one went out and no one came in.

5:2 [w] S Ex 4:25 [x] S Ge 17:10, 12, 14 **5:4** [y] S Nu 1:3 [z] Dt 2:14 **5:6** [a] Nu 32:13; Jos 14:10; Ps 107:4 [b] S Ex 16:35 [c] Nu 14:23, 29-35; Dt 2:14 [d] S Ex 3:8 **5:8** [e] Ge 34:25 **5:9** [f] S Dt 11:30
5:10 [g] S Ex 12:6 [h] S Ex 12:11 **5:11** [i] S Nu 15:19 [j] Ex 12:15 [k] S Lev 23:14 **5:12** [l] Ex 16:35 **5:13** [m] S Ge 18:2 [n] Nu 22:23 **5:14** [o] S Ge 17:3 [p] S Ge 19:1 **5:15** [q] S Ge 28:17; Ex 3:5; Ac 7:33 **6:1** [r] Jos 24:11

[a] 3 *Gibeath Haaraloth* means *the hill of foreskins.*
[b] 9 *Gilgal* sounds like the Hebrew for *roll.* [c] 12 Or *the day* [d] 14 Or *lord*

5:2 *flint knives.* Metal knives were available, but flint made a more efficient surgical tool, as modern demonstrations have shown. *circumcise.* Circumcision marked every male as a son of Abraham (Ge 17:10–11), bound to the service of the Lord, and it was a prerequisite for the Passover (Ex 12:48). *again.* Explained in vv. 4–8.
5:3 *Gibeath Haaraloth.* See NIV text note.
5:6 *forty years.* The time between their departure from Egypt and the crossing of the Jordan. Only 38 years had passed since they turned back at Kadesh Barnea (Nu 14:20–22; Dt 2:14). *milk and honey.* See notes on Ex 3:8; Dt 6:3.
5:9 *reproach of Egypt.* Although the reference may be to Egypt's enslavement of Israel, it is much more likely that the author had in mind the reproach the Egyptians would have cast upon them and their God if they had perished in the wilderness (see Ex 32:12; Nu 14:13; Dt 9:28). Now that the wilderness journey is over and Israel is safely in the promised land as God's special people consecrated to him by circumcision, the "reproach of Egypt" is rolled away.
5:10 *Passover.* The ceremonies took place in the month of Aviv, the first month of the year (Ex 12:2). At twilight on the 14th day of the month the Passover lamb was to be slaughtered, then roasted and eaten that same night (Ex 12:5–8). The Israelites had not celebrated Passover since Sinai, one year after their release from Egypt (Nu 9:1–5). Before the next season they had rebelled at the border of Canaan, and the generation of the exodus had been condemned to die in the wilderness (Nu 14:21–23,29–35). For that generation the celebration of Passover (deliverance from the judgment that God brought on Egypt; see Ex 12:12–13,23) would have had little meaning.
5:11 *unleavened bread.* Bread baked without yeast. It was to be eaten during the seven festival days that followed (Ex 12:15; Lev 23:6).
5:12 *manna stopped.* This transition from eating manna to eating the "produce of the land" (v. 11) ended 40 years of dependence on God's special provision. Manna was God's gift for the wilderness journey; from now on he provided Israel with food from the promised land.
5:13–15 The narration of the conquest of Jericho (5:13—6:27) is introduced by the sudden appearance of a heavenly figure who calls himself the "commander of the army of the LORD" (v. 14).
5:13 *Joshua was near Jericho.* The leader of God's army went to scout the nearest Canaanite stronghold, but another warrior was already on the scene. *a man standing.* The experience is taken by many to be an encounter with God in human form (theophany), or with Christ (Christophany). But angels also were sent on missions of this kind (Jdg 6:11; 13:3), and some were identified as captains over the heavenly armies (Da 10:5,20; 12:1).
5:14 *Neither.* Joshua and Israel must know their place—it is not that God is on their side; rather, they must fight God's battles. *commander of the army of the LORD.* God has sent the commander of his heavenly armies to take charge of the battle on earth. Joshua must take orders from him (6:2–5), and he can also know that the armies of heaven are committed to this war—as later events confirm.
5:15 Joshua is commissioned to undertake the Lord's battles for Canaan, just as Moses had been commissioned to confront the pharaoh (Ex 3:5). *place ... is holy.* See Ex 3:5 and note.
6:1 *Jericho.* Modern Tell es-Sultan. Archaeological excavations have revealed that Jericho may have been

2 Then the LORD said to Joshua, "See, I
have delivered[s] Jericho into your hands,
along with its king and its fighting men.
3 March around the city once with all the
armed men. Do this for six days. 4 Have
seven priests carry trumpets of rams'
horns[t] in front of the ark. On the seventh
day, march around the city seven times,
with the priests blowing the trumpets.[u]
5 When you hear them sound a long blast[v]
on the trumpets, have the whole army
give a loud shout;[w] then the wall of the
city will collapse and the army will go up,
everyone straight in."
6 So Joshua son of Nun called the priests
and said to them, "Take up the ark of the
covenant of the LORD and have seven
priests carry trumpets in front of it."[x] 7 And
he ordered the army, "Advance[y]! March
around the city, with an armed guard going ahead of the ark[z] of the LORD."
8 When Joshua had spoken to the people, the seven priests carrying the seven
trumpets before the LORD went forward,
blowing their trumpets, and the ark of
the LORD's covenant followed them. 9 The
armed guard marched ahead of the priests
who blew the trumpets, and the rear
guard[a] followed the ark. All this time the
trumpets were sounding. 10 But Joshua had
commanded the army, "Do not give a war
cry, do not raise your voices, do not say
a word until the day I tell you to shout.
Then shout![b]" 11 So he had the ark of the
LORD carried around the city, circling it
once. Then the army returned to camp and
spent the night there.
12 Joshua got up early the next morning
and the priests took up the ark of the LORD.
13 The seven priests carrying the seven
trumpets went forward, marching before
the ark of the LORD and blowing the trumpets. The armed men went ahead of them
and the rear guard followed the ark of
the LORD, while the trumpets kept sounding. 14 So on the second day they marched
around the city once and returned to the
camp. They did this for six days.
15 On the seventh day, they got up at
daybreak and marched around the city
seven times in the same manner, except
that on that day they circled the city seven
times.[c] 16 The seventh time around, when
the priests sounded the trumpet blast,
Joshua commanded the army, "Shout! For
the LORD has given you the city![d] 17 The
city and all that is in it are to be devoted[a][e]
to the LORD. Only Rahab the prostitute[f] and
all who are with her in her house shall
be spared, because she hid[g] the spies we
sent. 18 But keep away from the devoted

6:2 [s] ver 16; Dt 7:24; Jos 8:1 **6:4** [t] S Ex 19:13 [u] S Lev 25:9 **6:5** [v] Ex 19:13 [w] ver 20; 1Sa 4:5; 2Sa 6:15; Ezr 3:11; 10:12; Ps 42:4; 95:1; Isa 8:9; 42:13 **6:6** [x] ver 4 **6:7** [y] Ex 14:15 [z] Nu 10:35; 1Sa 4:3; 7:1 **6:9** [a] ver 13; S Nu 2:31; Isa 52:12 **6:10** [b] ver 20; 1Sa 4:5; Ezr 3:11 **6:15** [c] 1Ki 18:44; 2Ki 4:35; 5:14 **6:16** [d] S ver 2 **6:17** [e] ver 21; Lev 27:28; Dt 20:17; Isa 13:5; 24:1; 34:2,5; Mal 4:6 [f] S Jos 2:1 [g] ver 25; Jos 2:4

[a] *17* The Hebrew term refers to the irrevocable giving over of things or persons to the LORD, often by totally destroying them; also in verses 18 and 21.

the first site of village settlement in Canaan. (People who moved about and lived by hunting and gathering had been present in the area for thousands of years.) The earliest settled occupation dates from c. 7000 BC. By Joshua's day, more than two dozen cities had already been built and destroyed on the site, one above the other, over a period of more than 5,000 years. Many of them had powerful double walls. Jericho may have been a center for the worship of the moon god (Jericho probably means "moon city"; see Ge 11:31 and note). If so, God was destroying not only Canaanite cities but also Canaanite religion. See map, p. 2518, at the end of this study Bible; see also map, p. 319, and photo, p. 311.

6:2 *the LORD.* The Lord's command no doubt comes to Joshua through the "commander of the army of the LORD" (5:14), who orders the first conquest of a Canaanite city.

6:3 *March around the city.* A ritual act, signifying a siege of the city, that was to be repeated for six days.

6:4 *trumpets of rams' horns.* Instruments not of music but of signaling, in both religious and military contexts (which appear to come together here). The trumpets were to be sounded (v. 8), as on the seventh day, announcing the presence of the Lord (see 2Sa 6:15; 1Ch 15:28; Zec 9:14). *ark.* Signified that the Lord was laying siege to the city. *seventh day.* No note is taken of the Sabbath during this seven-day siege, but perhaps that was the day the Lord gave the city to Israel as the first pledge of the land of rest. To arrive at the goal of a long march on the seventh day is a motif found also in other ancient Near Eastern literature. In any event, the remarkable constellation of sevens (seven priests with trumpets, seven days, seven encirclements on the seventh day) underscores the sacred significance of the event and is, perhaps, a deliberate evoking of the seven days of creation to signal the beginning of God's new order in the world.

6:5 *long blast ... loud shout.* Signaling the onset of the attack—psychological warfare, intended to create panic and confusion (see Jdg 7). In the Dead Sea Scroll of "The War of the Sons of Light against the Sons of Darkness," the Levites are instructed to blow in unison a great battle fanfare to melt the heart of the enemy. (For Dead Sea Scrolls, see essay, pp. 1574–1575.) *everyone straight in.* Not a breach here and there but a general collapse of the walls, giving access to the city from all sides.

6:7 *armed guard.* The Hebrew for this term differs from that in v. 3 but may be synonymous with it. It is to be expected that the ark led the procession. If so, the present reference may be to a kind of royal guard (but see v. 9 and note).

6:8–14 Throughout these verses the ark of the Lord is made the center of focus (as it was in the account of the crossing of the Jordan), highlighting the fact that the Lord himself besieged the city.

6:9 *rear guard.* If the rear guard was made up of the final contingents of the army (see Nu 10:25), the armed guard of vv. 7,9 constituted the main body of troops.

6:12–14 Literary repetition reflects repetition in action, a common feature in ancient Near Eastern literature.

6:17 *devoted.* See NIV text note. The ban placed all of Jericho's inhabitants under the curse of death and all of the city's treasures that could not be destroyed under consignment to the Lord's house (v. 19). According to the law of Moses this ban could be applied to animals for sacrifice, to property given to God, or to any person found worthy of death (Lev 27:28–29). It was Moses himself who ruled that all the inhabitants of Canaan be executed for their idolatry and all its accompanying moral corruption (Dt 20:16–18). See note on Dt 2:34. *Rahab ... and ... her house shall be spared.* Honoring the pledge made by the two spies (2:14).

things,[h] so that you will not bring about your own destruction by taking any of them. Otherwise you will make the camp of Israel liable to destruction[i] and bring trouble[j] on it. 19 All the silver and gold and the articles of bronze and iron[k] are sacred to the LORD and must go into his treasury."

20 When the trumpets sounded,[l] the army shouted, and at the sound of the trumpet, when the men gave a loud shout,[m] the wall collapsed; so everyone charged straight in, and they took the city.[n] 21 They devoted[o] the city to the LORD and destroyed[p] with the sword every living thing in it—men and women, young and old, cattle, sheep and donkeys.

22 Joshua said to the two men[q] who had spied out[r] the land, "Go into the prostitute's house and bring her out and all who belong to her, in accordance with your oath to her.[s]" 23 So the young men who had done the spying went in and brought out Rahab, her father and mother, her brothers and sisters and all who belonged to her.[t] They brought out her entire family and put them in a place outside the camp of Israel.

24 Then they burned the whole city[u] and everything in it, but they put the silver and gold and the articles of bronze and iron[v] into the treasury of the LORD's house.[w] 25 But Joshua spared[x] Rahab the prostitute,[y] with her family and all who belonged to her, because she hid the men Joshua had sent as spies to Jericho[z]—and she lives among the Israelites to this day.

26 At that time Joshua pronounced this solemn oath:[a] "Cursed[b] before the LORD is the one who undertakes to rebuild this city, Jericho:

"At the cost of his firstborn son
he will lay its foundations;
at the cost of his youngest
he will set up its gates."[c]

27 So the LORD was with Joshua,[d] and his fame spread[e] throughout the land.

Achan's Sin

7 But the Israelites were unfaithful in regard to the devoted things[a];[f] Achan[g] son of Karmi, the son of Zimri,[b] the son of Zerah,[h] of the tribe of Judah,[i] took some of them. So the LORD's anger burned[j] against Israel.[k]

2 Now Joshua sent men from Jericho to Ai,[l] which is near Beth Aven[m] to the east of Bethel,[n] and told them, "Go up and spy out[o] the region." So the men went up and spied out Ai.

3 When they returned to Joshua, they said, "Not all the army will have to go up against Ai. Send two or three thousand men to take it and do not weary the whole army, for only a few people live there." 4 So about three thousand went up; but they were routed by the men of Ai,[p] 5 who killed about thirty-six[q] of them. They chased the Israelites from the city gate as far as the stone quarries and struck them down on the slopes. At this the hearts of the people melted in fear[r] and became like water.

6 Then Joshua tore his clothes[s] and fell facedown[t] to the ground before the ark of the LORD, remaining there till evening.[u] The elders of Israel[v] did the same, and

a 1 The Hebrew term refers to the irrevocable giving over of things or persons to the LORD, often by totally destroying them; also in verses 11, 12, 13 and 15.
b 1 See Septuagint and 1 Chron. 2:6; Hebrew *Zabdi*; also in verses 17 and 18.

6:18 [h] Jos 7:1; 1Ch 2:7 [i] Jos 7:12 [j] Jos 7:25,26 **6:19** [k] ver 24; Nu 31:22 **6:20** [l] Lev 25:9; Jdg 6:34; 7:22; 1Ki 1:41; Isa 18:3; 27:13; Jer 4:21; 42:14; Am 2:2 [m] S ver 5; S 10 [n] Heb 11:30 **6:21** [o] S ver 17 [p] S Dt 20:16 **6:22** [q] S Ge 42:9; S Jos 2:4 [r] S Nu 21:32 [s] Jos 2:14; Heb 11:31 **6:23** [t] S Jos 2:13 **6:24** [u] S Nu 31:10 [v] S ver 19 [w] S Dt 13:16 **6:25** [x] Jdg 1:25 [y] S Jos 2:1 [z] S ver 17; S Jos 2:6 **6:26** [a] 1Sa 14:24 [b] S Nu 5:21 [c] 1Ki 16:34 **6:27** [d] S Ge 39:2; S Nu 14:43 [e] Jos 9:1; 1Ch 14:17 **7:1** [f] S Jos 6:18 [g] ver 26; 1Ch 2:7 [h] Jos 22:20 [i] ver 18; Nu 1:4 [j] S Ex 4:14; S 32:20 [k] S Lev 10:6 **7:2** [l] S Ge 12:8; S Jos 8:1,28 [m] Jos 18:12; 1Sa 13:5; 14:23; Hos 4:15; 5:8; 10:5 [n] Ge 12:8; Jos 12:16; 16:1; Jdg 1:22; 1Sa 30:27; 2Ki 23:15; Jer 48:13; Am 3:14; 4:4; 5:5-6; 7:10,13 [o] S Nu 21:32

7:4 [p] S Lev 26:17; S Dt 28:25 **7:5** [q] Jos 22:20 [r] S Ge 42:28; Ps 22:14; Isa 13:7; Eze 21:7; Na 2:10 **7:6** [s] S Ge 37:29 [t] S Ge 17:3; 1Ch 21:16; Eze 9:8 [u] Jdg 20:23 [v] Jos 8:10; 9:11; 20:4; 23:2

6:18 *your own destruction.* See NIV text note on v. 17. If the Israelites took for themselves anything that was under God's ban, they themselves would fall under the ban.

6:25 *she lives among the Israelites.* The faith of Rahab is noted twice in the NT (Heb 11:31; Jas 2:25).

6:26 *Cursed ... is the one.* Jericho itself was to be devoted to the Lord as a perpetual sign of God's judgment on the wicked Canaanites (a second memorial in the land; see note on 4:9) and as a firstfruits offering of the land. This was a way of signifying that the conquered land belonged to the Lord. The curse was fulfilled in the rebellious days of King Ahab (see 1Ki 16:34 and note).

7:1–26 The tragic story of Achan, which stands in sharp contrast to the story of Rahab. In the earlier event a Canaanite prostitute, because of her courageous allegiance to Israel and her acknowledgment of the Lord, was spared and received into Israel. She abandoned Canaan and its gods on account of the Lord and Israel and so received Canaan back. In the present event an Israelite, because of his disloyalty to the Lord and Israel, is executed as the Canaanites were. He stole the riches of Canaan from the Lord and so lost his inheritance in the promised land. This is also a story of how one man's sin adversely affected the entire nation. Throughout this account (as often in the OT) Israel is considered a corporate unity in covenant with and in the service of the Lord. Thus even in the acts of one (Achan) or a few (the 3,000 defeated at Ai) all Israel is involved (see vv. 1,11; 22:20).

7:2 *from Jericho to Ai.* An uphill march of some 15 miles through a ravine to the top of the central Canaanite ridge. Strategically, an advance from Gilgal to Ai would bring Israel beyond the Jordan Valley and provide a foothold in the central highlands. Ai in Hebrew means "the ruin." It is usually identified with et-Tell (meaning "the ruin" in Arabic), just two miles east of Bethel. For another possible location of Ai, see map, p. 319. *Beth Aven.* Means "house of wickedness," a derogatory designation of either Bethel itself or a pagan shrine nearby (see 1Sa 13:5; Hos 4:15; Am 5:5). *spy out the region.* See note on 2:1–24.

7:6 *Joshua tore his clothes.* A sign of great distress (see Ge 37:34 and note; 44:13; Jdg 11:35). Joshua's dismay (and that of the people), as indicated by his prayer, arose from his recognition that the Lord had not been with Israel's troops in

sprinkled dust[w] on their heads. 7 And Joshua said, "Alas, Sovereign LORD, why[x] did you ever bring this people across the Jordan to deliver us into the hands of the Amorites to destroy us?[y] If only we had been content to stay on the other side of the Jordan! 8 Pardon your servant, Lord. What can I say, now that Israel has been routed by its enemies? 9 The Canaanites and the other people of the country will hear about this and they will surround us and wipe out our name from the earth.[z] What then will you do for your own great name?[a]"

10 The LORD said to Joshua, "Stand up! What are you doing down on your face? 11 Israel has sinned;[b] they have violated my covenant,[c] which I commanded them to keep. They have taken some of the devoted things; they have stolen, they have lied,[d] they have put them with their own possessions.[e] 12 That is why the Israelites cannot stand against their enemies;[f] they turn their backs[g] and run[h] because they have been made liable to destruction.[i] I will not be with you anymore[j] unless you destroy whatever among you is devoted to destruction.

13 "Go, consecrate the people. Tell them, 'Consecrate yourselves[k] in preparation for tomorrow; for this is what the LORD, the God of Israel, says: There are devoted things among you, Israel. You cannot stand against your enemies until you remove them.

14 " 'In the morning, present[l] yourselves tribe by tribe. The tribe the LORD chooses[m] shall come forward clan by clan; the clan the LORD chooses shall come forward family by family; and the family the LORD chooses shall come forward man by man. 15 Whoever is caught with the devoted things[n] shall be destroyed by fire,[o] along with all that belongs to him.[p] He has violated the covenant[q] of the LORD and has done an outrageous thing in Israel!' "[r]

16 Early the next morning Joshua had Israel come forward by tribes, and Judah was chosen. 17 The clans of Judah came forward, and the Zerahites were chosen.[s] He had the clan of the Zerahites come forward by families, and Zimri was chosen. 18 Joshua had his family come forward man by man, and Achan son of Karmi, the son of Zimri, the son of Zerah, of the tribe of Judah,[t] was chosen.[u]

19 Then Joshua said to Achan, "My son, give glory[v] to the LORD, the God of Israel, and honor him. Tell[w] me what you have done; do not hide it from me."

20 Achan replied, "It is true! I have sinned against the LORD, the God of Israel. This is what I have done: 21 When I saw in the plunder[x] a beautiful robe from Babylonia,[a] two hundred shekels[b] of silver and a bar of gold weighing fifty shekels,[c] I coveted[y] them and took them. They are hidden in the ground inside my tent, with the silver underneath."

22 So Joshua sent messengers, and they ran to the tent, and there it was, hidden in his tent, with the silver underneath. 23 They took the things from the tent, brought them to Joshua and all the Israelites and spread them out before the LORD.

24 Then Joshua, together with all Israel, took Achan son of Zerah, the silver, the robe, the gold bar, his sons[z] and daughters, his cattle, donkeys and sheep, his tent and all that he had, to the Valley of Achor.

[a] *21* Hebrew *Shinar* [b] *21* That is, about 5 pounds or about 2.3 kilograms [c] *21* That is, about 1 1/4 pounds or about 575 grams

7:6 [w] 1Sa 4:12; 2Sa 13:19; 15:32; Ne 9:1; Job 2:12; La 2:10; Eze 27:30; Rev 18:19 **7:7** [x] 1Sa 4:3 [y] S Ex 5:22; S Nu 14:16 **7:9** [z] Ex 32:12; S Dt 9:28 [a] Dt 28:58; 1Sa 12:22; Ps 48:10; 106:8; Jer 14:21 **7:11** [b] S Ex 9:27; Dt 29:27; Jos 24:16-27; 2Ki 17:7; Hos 10:9 [c] ver 15; Jos 6:17-19; 23:16; Jdg 2:20; 1Sa 15:24; Ps 78:10 [d] Ac 5:1-2 [e] ver 21 **7:12** [f] Lev 26:37 [g] Ps 18:40; 21:12 [h] S Lev 26:17 [i] Jos 6:18 [j] Ps 44:9; 60:10 **7:13** [k] S Lev 11:44 **7:14** [l] 1Sa 10:19 [m] Pr 16:33 **7:15** [n] Jos 6:18 [o] Dt 7:25; 2Ki 25:9; 1Ch 14:12; Isa 37:19; Jer 43:12; Eze 30:16 [p] 1Sa 14:39 [q] S ver 11 [r] Ge 34:7 **7:17** [s] Nu 26:20 **7:18** [t] S ver 1; S Lev 24:11 [u] Jnh 1:7 **7:19** [v] Ex 14:17; 1Sa 6:5; Ps 96:8; Isa 42:12; Jer 13:16; Jn 9:24* [w] S Lev 5:5; 1Sa 14:43 **7:21** [x] S Ge 34:29; S 49:27 [y] S Dt 7:25; Eph 5:5; 1Ti 6:10 **7:24** [z] S Nu 16:27 [a] ver 26; Jos 15:7; Isa 65:10; Hos 2:15

the battle. The Canaanites would now judge that Israel and its God were not invincible. They would pour out of their fortified cities and descend on Israel in the Jordan valley. *sprinkled dust on their heads.* See Job 2:12; La 2:10 and notes.

7:9 *your own great name.* Joshua pleads, as Moses had (Nu 14:13–16; Dt 9:28–29), that God's honor in the eyes of all the world was at stake in the fortunes of his people.

7:11 *Israel has sinned.* One soldier's theft of the devoted goods brought collective guilt on the entire nation (see 22:20). *violated my covenant.* See v. 15. This is the main indictment; what follows is further specification.

7:12 *devoted to destruction.* See note on 6:18.

7:13 *Consecrate yourselves.* A series of purifications to be undertaken by every Israelite in preparation for meeting with God, as before a solemn religious festival or a special assembly called by the Lord (see note on 3:5). Here God summons his people before him for his judgment.

7:14 *tribe the LORD chooses.* When the lots are cast, one of the tribes is taken by the Lord so that the search is narrowed until the Lord exposes the guilty persons. The lots may have been the Urim and Thummim from the ephod of the high priest (see notes on Ex 28:30; 1Sa 2:28; see also NIV text note on 1Sa 14:41).

7:15 *outrageous thing in Israel.* An act that within Israel, as the covenant people of the Lord, is an outrage or utter folly (see Dt 22:21; Jdg 19:23–24 and notes; 20:6,10; 2Sa 13:12).

7:18 *Achan ... was chosen.* "You may be sure ... your sin will find you out" (Nu 32:23).

7:19 *My son.* Joshua took a fatherly attitude toward Achan.

7:21 *robe from Babylonia.* A valuable import. *two hundred shekels ... fifty shekels.* See NIV text notes.

7:23 *before the LORD.* Who is here the Judge.

7:24 *Joshua ... all Israel.* Joshua and all Israel were God's agents for executing his judgment on both the Canaanites and this violator of the covenant. *all that he had.* As the head of (and example for) his family, Achan involved his whole household in his guilt and punishment. This is in accordance with the principle of corporate solidarity—the whole community is represented in one member (especially the head of that community). "The greedy bring ruin to their households" (Pr 15:27; see note there).

25 Joshua said, "Why have you brought
this trouble[b] on us? The LORD will bring
trouble on you today."
Then all Israel stoned him,[c] and after
they had stoned the rest, they burned
them.[d] 26 Over Achan they heaped[e] up a
large pile of rocks, which remains to this
day.[f] Then the LORD turned from his fierce
anger.[g] Therefore that place has been
called the Valley of Achor[a][h] ever since.

Ai Destroyed

8 Then the LORD said to Joshua, "Do not
be afraid;[i] do not be discouraged.[j] Take
the whole army[k] with you, and go up and
attack Ai.[l] For I have delivered[m] into your
hands the king of Ai, his people, his city
and his land. 2 You shall do to Ai and its
king as you did to Jericho and its king,
except that you may carry off their plunder[n] and livestock for yourselves.[o] Set an
ambush[p] behind the city."
3 So Joshua and the whole army moved
out to attack Ai. He chose thirty thousand
of his best fighting men and sent them out
at night 4 with these orders: "Listen carefully. You are to set an ambush behind the
city. Don't go very far from it. All of you
be on the alert. 5 I and all those with me
will advance on the city, and when the
men come out against us, as they did before, we will flee from them. 6 They will
pursue us until we have lured them away
from the city, for they will say, 'They are
running away from us as they did before.'
So when we flee from them, 7 you are to
rise up from ambush and take the city.
The LORD your God will give it into your
hand.[q] 8 When you have taken the city,
set it on fire.[r] Do what the LORD has commanded.[s] See to it; you have my orders."
9 Then Joshua sent them off, and they
went to the place of ambush[t] and lay in
wait between Bethel and Ai, to the west
of Ai—but Joshua spent that night with
the people.
10 Early the next morning[u] Joshua mustered his army, and he and the leaders of
Israel[v] marched before them to Ai. 11 The
entire force that was with him marched
up and approached the city and arrived in
front of it. They set up camp north of Ai,
with the valley between them and the city.
12 Joshua had taken about five thousand
men and set them in ambush between
Bethel and Ai, to the west of the city. 13 So
the soldiers took up their positions—with
the main camp to the north of the city and
the ambush to the west of it. That night
Joshua went into the valley.
14 When the king of Ai saw this, he and
all the men of the city hurried out early
in the morning to meet Israel in battle at
a certain place overlooking the Arabah.[w]
But he did not know[x] that an ambush
had been set against him behind the city.
15 Joshua and all Israel let themselves be
driven back[y] before them, and they fled
toward the wilderness.[z] 16 All the men of Ai
were called to pursue them, and they pursued Joshua and were lured away[a] from
the city. 17 Not a man remained in Ai or
Bethel who did not go after Israel. They
left the city open and went in pursuit of
Israel.
18 Then the LORD said to Joshua, "Hold
out toward Ai the javelin[b] that is in your
hand,[c] for into your hand I will deliver
the city." So Joshua held out toward the
city the javelin that was in his hand.[d] 19 As
soon as he did this, the men in the ambush rose quickly[e] from their position and
rushed forward. They entered the city and
captured it and quickly set it on fire.[f]
20 The men of Ai looked back and saw
the smoke of the city rising up into the
sky,[g] but they had no chance to escape in
any direction; the Israelites who had been
fleeing toward the wilderness had turned
back against their pursuers. 21 For when
Joshua and all Israel saw that the ambush
had taken the city and that smoke was going up from it, they turned around[h] and
attacked the men of Ai. 22 Those in the
ambush also came out of the city against
them, so that they were caught in the

7:25 [b] S Jos 6:18 [c] S Lev 20:2; Dt 17:5; 1Ki 12:18; 2Ch 10:18; 24:21; Ne 9:26 [d] S Ge 38:24 **7:26** [e] 2Sa 18:17 [f] S Ge 35:20 [g] S Nu 25:4 [h] S ver 24 **8:1** [i] Ge 26:24; Dt 31:6 [j] S Nu 14:9; S Dt 1:21 [k] Jos 10:7 [l] Jos 7:2; 9:3; 10:1; 12:9 [m] S Jos 6:2 **8:2** [n] S Ge 49:27 [o] ver 27; Dt 20:14 [p] ver 4, 12; Jdg 9:43; 20:29 **8:7** [q] Jdg 7:7; 1Sa 23:4 **8:8** [r] Jdg 20:29-38 [s] ver 19 **8:9** [t] 2Ch 13:13 **8:10** [u] Ge 22:3 [v] S Jos 7:6
8:14 [w] S Dt 1:1 [x] Jdg 20:34 **8:15** [y] Jdg 20:36 [z] Jos 15:61; 16:1; 18:12 **8:16** [a] Jdg 20:31 **8:18** [b] Job 41:26; Ps 35:3 [c] S Ex 4:2; 17:9-12 [d] ver 26 **8:19** [e] Jdg 20:33 [f] S ver 8 **8:20** [g] Jdg 20:40 **8:21** [h] Jdg 20:41

[a] 26 *Achor* means *trouble.*

7:25 *stoned him.* Because he had been found guilty of violating the covenant of the holy Lord (see Ex 19:13; Lev 24:23; Nu 15:36). Afterward the bodies were burned to purge the land of the evil.
7:26 *large pile of rocks.* A third monument in the land to the events of the conquest (see note on 4:9). *Achor.* See NIV text note. Achor was also another form of Achan's name (see 1Ch 2:7, "Achar," and NIV text note there).
8:1–29 Renewal of the conquest and the capture of Ai.
8:1 *Do not be afraid.* Now that Israel is purged, the Lord reassures Joshua once more (see 1:3–5; 3:11–13; 6:2–5).
8:2 *you may carry off their plunder.* The Lord now assigns the wealth of Canaan to his troops who fight his battles. *Set an ambush.* Still in command, the Lord directs the attack.
8:12 *five thousand.* Verse 3 speaks of a contingent of 30,000 assigned to the ambush. Perhaps Joshua assigned two different units to the task to assure success. Or from the original 30,000 a unit of 5,000 may have been designated to attack Ai itself while the remaining 25,000 served as a covering force to block the threat from Bethel (see v. 17).
8:13 *the main camp to the north.* In full visibility Joshua's main force moved north of the city, then pretended to flee to the east, drawing out the entire army of defenders.
8:14 *Arabah.* See note on Dt 1:1.
8:17 *Ai or Bethel.* Their joint action indicates that the two cities were closely allied, though each is said to have had a king (12:9,16).

middle, with Israelites on both sides. Israel cut them down, leaving them neither
survivors nor fugitives.[i] 23 But they took
the king of Ai alive[j] and brought him to
Joshua.

24 When Israel had finished killing all
the men of Ai in the fields and in the wilderness where they had chased them, and
when every one of them had been put to
the sword, all the Israelites returned to Ai
and killed those who were in it. 25 Twelve
thousand men and women fell that day —
all the people of Ai.[k] 26 For Joshua did not
draw back the hand that held out his javelin[l] until he had destroyed[a][m] all who lived
in Ai.[n] 27 But Israel did carry off for themselves the livestock and plunder of this
city, as the LORD had instructed Joshua.[o]

28 So Joshua burned[p] Ai[b][q] and made it a
permanent heap of ruins,[r] a desolate place
to this day.[s] 29 He impaled the body of the
king of Ai on a pole and left it there until
evening. At sunset,[t] Joshua ordered them
to take the body from the pole and throw
it down at the entrance of the city gate.
And they raised a large pile of rocks[u] over
it, which remains to this day.

The Covenant Renewed at Mount Ebal

30 Then Joshua built on Mount Ebal[v] an
altar[w] to the LORD, the God of Israel, 31 as
Moses the servant of the LORD had commanded the Israelites. He built it according to what is written in the Book of the
Law of Moses — an altar of uncut stones,
on which no iron tool[x] had been used.
On it they offered to the LORD burnt offerings and sacrificed fellowship offerings.[y]
32 There, in the presence of the Israelites,
Joshua wrote on stones a copy of the law

8:22 [i]Dt 7:2; Jos 10:1
8:23 [j]1Sa 15:8
8:25 [k]Dt 20:16-18
8:26 [l]ver 18 [m]S Nu 21:2 [n]Ex 17:12
8:27 [o]S ver 2
8:28 [p]S Nu 31:10 [q]Jos 7:2; Jer 49:3 [r]S Dt 13:16; Jos 10:1 [s]S Ge 35:20
8:29 [t]S Dt 21:23; Jn 19:31 [u]2Sa 18:17
8:30 [v]ver 33; S Dt 11:29 [w]S Ex 20:24
8:31 [x]S Ex 20:25 [y]Dt 27:6-7

[a] 26 The Hebrew term refers to the irrevocable giving over of things or persons to the LORD, often by totally destroying them. [b] 28 *Ai* means *the ruin.*

8:26 *he had destroyed all.* For the second time Joshua ordered the holy ban on the inhabitants of a Canaanite city (see NIV text note).
8:28 *burned Ai.* As he had Jericho (6:24) and would later do to Hazor (11:11).
8:29 *impaled the body of the king of Ai on a pole.* The Israelites did not execute by hanging (see note on Dt 21:22). *until evening.* According to Mosaic instructions (see Dt 21:22 – 23). *large pile of rocks.* A fourth monument in the land memorializing the conquest (see note on 4:9).
8:30 – 35 The renewal of the covenant with the Lord as Moses had ordered (Dt 11:26 – 30; 27:1 – 8) concludes the account of the initial battles (see Introduction: Outline). This final event (see also Joshua's final official act, ch. 24) underscores the Israelites' servant relationship to the Lord.

How Israel could assemble peacefully between Mount Ebal and Mount Gerizim without further conquest is a worrisome question. Perhaps this event is not in strict chronological order and occurred later after further conquests. Or perhaps, by virtue of their alliance with the Gibeonites, the Israelites were at relative peace with the people of Shechem who lived between the two mountains (see photo below).
8:30 *Mount Ebal.* At the foot of this peak was the fortress city of Shechem, where Abraham had built an altar (Ge 12:6 – 7).
8:31 *burnt offerings.* See Lev 1:1 – 17. *fellowship offerings.* See Lev 3:1 – 17; 7:11 – 18; see also chart, p. 164.
8:32 *wrote on stones.* Moses had ordered the people first to plaster the stones, then to inscribe on them the words of the law (Dt 27:2 – 4). These stones are a fifth monument in the land (see note on 4:9).

View of Mount Gerizim (left) and Mount Ebal (right) looking west. Joshua built an altar to the Lord on Mount Ebal and then recited the blessings on Mount Gerizim and the curses on Mount Ebal, as instructed in Deuteronomy 11:29.

Todd Bolen/www.BiblePlaces.com

of Moses.[z] 33 All the Israelites, with their
elders, officials and judges, were standing
on both sides of the ark of the covenant of
the LORD, facing the Levitical[a] priests who
carried it. Both the foreigners living among
them and the native-born[b] were there. Half
of the people stood in front of Mount Gerizim and half of them in front of Mount
Ebal,[c] as Moses the servant of the LORD
had formerly commanded when he gave
instructions to bless the people of Israel.
34 Afterward, Joshua read all the words
of the law — the blessings and the curses — just as it is written in the Book of the
Law.[d] 35 There was not a word of all that
Moses had commanded that Joshua did
not read to the whole assembly of Israel,
including the women and children, and
the foreigners who lived among them.[e]

The Gibeonite Deception

9 Now when all the kings west of the
Jordan heard about these things — the
kings in the hill country,[f] in the western
foothills, and along the entire coast of
the Mediterranean Sea[g] as far as Lebanon[h] (the kings of the Hittites, Amorites,
Canaanites, Perizzites,[i] Hivites[j] and Jebusites)[k] — 2 they came together to wage war
against Joshua and Israel.
3 However, when the people of Gibeon[l] heard what Joshua had done to Jericho and Ai,[m] 4 they resorted to a ruse:
They went as a delegation whose donkeys
were loaded[a] with worn-out sacks and old
wineskins, cracked and mended. 5 They
put worn and patched sandals on their
feet and wore old clothes. All the bread
of their food supply was dry and moldy.
6 Then they went to Joshua in the camp at
Gilgal[n] and said to him and the Israelites,
"We have come from a distant country;[o]
make a treaty[p] with us."
7 The Israelites said to the Hivites,[q] "But
perhaps you live near us, so how can we
make a treaty[r] with you?"

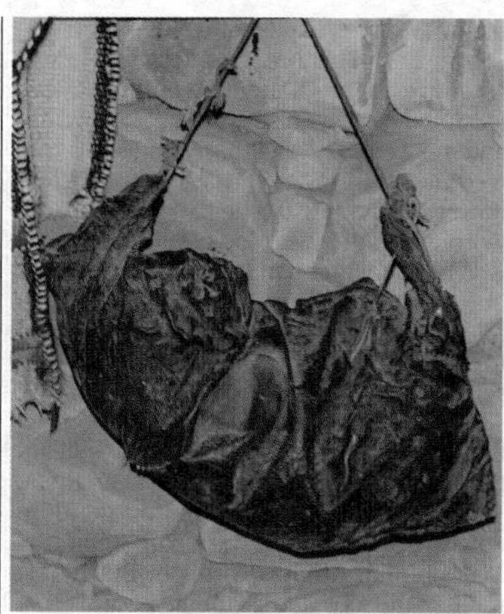

Modern facsimile of a wineskin at Qatzrin in the Golan Heights. Wineskins were made from the skin of an animal and used to hold wine. Wineskins were among the items brought along when the Gibeonites went to meet Joshua at Gilgal (Jos 9:4).

Baker Photo Archive

8 "We are your servants,[s]" they said to
Joshua.
But Joshua asked, "Who are you and
where do you come from?"
9 They answered: "Your servants have
come from a very distant country[t] because
of the fame of the LORD your God. For we
have heard reports[u] of him: all that he did
in Egypt,[v] 10 and all that he did to the two
kings of the Amorites east of the Jordan —
Sihon king of Heshbon,[w] and Og king of
Bashan,[x] who reigned in Ashtaroth.[y] 11 And
our elders and all those living in our country said to us, 'Take provisions for your
journey; go and meet them and say to

8:32 [z] Dt 27:8
8:33 [a] Dt 31:12 [b] S Lev 16:29 [c] Dt 11:29; Jn 4:20
8:34 [d] S Dt 28:61; 31:11
8:35 [e] S Ex 12:38; Dt 31:12
9:1 [f] S Nu 13:17 [g] S Nu 34:6 [h] S Dt 3:25 [i] Ge 13:7; S Jos 3:10 [j] ver 7; Jos 11:19 [k] S Jos 3:10
9:3 [l] ver 17; Jos 10:10; 11:19; 18:25; 21:17; 2Sa 2:12; 5:25; 20:8; 1Ki 3:4; 9:2; 1Ch 8:29; 14:16; 16:39; 21:29; 2Ch 1:3; Ne 3:7; Isa 28:21; Jer 28:1; 41:12 [m] Ge 12:8; S Jos 8:1
9:6 [n] S Dt 11:30 [o] ver 22 [p] S Ge 26:28
9:7 [q] S ver 1 [r] S Ex 23:32; S 1Ki 5:12
9:8 [s] 2Ki 10:5
9:9 [t] S Dt 20:15 [u] ver 24 [v] S Nu 23:22
9:10 [w] S Nu 21:25 [x] S Nu 21:33 [y] S Nu 21:24, 35; Jos 2:10

[a] *4* Most Hebrew manuscripts; some Hebrew manuscripts, Vulgate and Syriac (see also Septuagint) *They prepared provisions and loaded their donkeys*

8:33 *foreigners … and the native-born.* Israel now included the "other people" (Ex 12:38) who had come out of Egypt, plus those who had joined them during the wilderness wanderings (see note on vv. 30 – 35).
8:34 *the blessings and the curses.* See Dt 27 – 28 and notes.
9:1 – 27 The account of how the Gibeonites deceived the leaders of the tribes and obtained a treaty of submission to Israel. It is the first of three sections telling how Israel came into possession of the bulk of the land. Verses 1 – 2 introduce the three units.
9:1 *kings west of the Jordan.* Small, independent city-kingdoms were scattered over Canaan, inhabited by a variety of peoples who had come earlier from outside the land (compare vv. 1 – 2 with Ge 15:19; see also note on Ex 3:8).
9:3 *Gibeon.* Just north of Jerusalem (see map, p. 319). A site today called el-Jib shows the remains of a Late Bronze Age city with an excellent water supply. The Gibeonites were in league with a number of neighboring towns (v. 17) but seem to have been dominant in the confederation.
9:4 *they resorted to a ruse.* Motivated by their fear of Israel's God, the Gibeonites used pretense to trick Joshua into a treaty that would allow them to live.
9:6 *make a treaty with us.* In this request they were offering to submit themselves by treaty to be subjects of the Israelites (see v. 11, where they call themselves "your servants" — unmistakable language in the international diplomacy of that day). They chose submission rather than certain death (v. 24).
9:7 *Hivites.* Possibly Horites, an ethnic group living in Canaan related to the Hurrians of northern Mesopotamia (see 11:19; Ge 10:17; 34:2; 36:2; Ex 23:23; Jdg 3:3; see also note on Jos 8:30 – 35).
9:9 *heard reports of him.* The same reports that had been heard in Jericho (see 2:10).

them, "We are your servants; make a treaty
with us."' 12This bread of ours was warm
when we packed it at home on the day we
left to come to you. But now see how dry
and moldy it is. 13And these wineskins that
we filled were new, but see how cracked
they are. And our clothes and sandals are
worn out by the very long journey."
14The Israelites sampled their provisions
but did not inquire[z] of the LORD. 15Then
Joshua made a treaty of peace[a] with them
to let them live,[b] and the leaders of the assembly ratified it by oath.
16Three days after they made the treaty with the Gibeonites, the Israelites heard
that they were neighbors, living near[c] them.
17So the Israelites set out and on the third
day came to their cities: Gibeon, Kephirah,
Beeroth[d] and Kiriath Jearim.[e] 18But the Israelites did not attack them, because the
leaders of the assembly had sworn an oath[f]
to them by the LORD, the God of Israel.
The whole assembly grumbled[g] against
the leaders, 19but all the leaders answered,
"We have given them our oath by the
LORD, the God of Israel, and we cannot
touch them now. 20This is what we will
do to them: We will let them live, so that
God's wrath will not fall on us for breaking the oath[h] we swore to them." 21They
continued, "Let them live,[i] but let them be
woodcutters and water carriers[j] in the service of the whole assembly." So the leaders' promise to them was kept.
22Then Joshua summoned the Gibeonites and said, "Why did you deceive us
by saying, 'We live a long way[k] from you,'
while actually you live near[l] us? 23You are
now under a curse:[m] You will never be released from service as woodcutters and
water carriers for the house of my God."
24They answered Joshua, "Your servants were clearly told[n] how the LORD your
God had commanded his servant Moses to
give you the whole land and to wipe out
all its inhabitants from before you. So we
feared for our lives because of you, and
that is why we did this. 25We are now in
your hands.[o] Do to us whatever seems
good and right[p] to you."
26So Joshua saved them from the Israelites, and they did not kill them. 27That day
he made the Gibeonites[q] woodcutters and
water carriers[r] for the assembly, to provide
for the needs of the altar of the LORD at the
place the LORD would choose.[s] And that is
what they are to this day.

The Sun Stands Still

10 Now Adoni-Zedek[t] king of Jerusalem[u] heard that Joshua had taken
Ai[v] and totally destroyed[a][w] it, doing to Ai
and its king as he had done to Jericho and
its king, and that the people of Gibeon[x]
had made a treaty of peace[y] with Israel
and had become their allies. 2He and his
people were very much alarmed at this
because Gibeon was an important city,
like one of the royal cities; it was larger
than Ai, and all its men were good fighters. 3So Adoni-Zedek king of Jerusalem
appealed to Hoham king of Hebron,[z] Pi-
ram king of Jarmuth,[a] Japhia king of Lachish[b] and Debir[c] king of Eglon.[d] 4"Come
up and help me attack Gibeon," he said,
"because it has made peace[e] with Joshua
and the Israelites."

[a] *1* The Hebrew term refers to the irrevocable giving over of things or persons to the LORD, often by totally destroying them; also in verses 28, 35, 37, 39 and 40.

9:14 [z]S Ex 16:28; S Nu 27:21 **9:15** [a]S ver 3, 7; Jos 10:1,4; 11:19; 2Sa 21:2; 24:1 [b]ver 21; Jdg 1:21; Ps 106:34 **9:16** [c]ver 22 **9:17** [d]Jos 18:25; 2Sa 4:2; 23:37 [e]Jos 15:9, 60; 18:14,15; Jdg 18:12; 1Sa 6:21; 7:2; Ps 132:6; Jer 26:20 **9:18** [f]ver 15; Jdg 21:1,7, 18; 1Sa 20:17; Ps 15:4 [g]S Ex 15:24 **9:20** [h]S Ge 24:8 **9:21** [i]S ver 15 [j]S Dt 29:11 **9:22** [k]ver 6 [l]ver 16 **9:23** [m]S Ge 9:25 **9:24** [n]ver 9 **9:25** [o]Ge 16:6 [p]Jer 26:14 **9:27** [q]S Ex 1:11 [r]S Dt 29:11 [s]Dt 12:5 **10:1** [t]ver 3 [u]Jos 12:10; 15:8,63; 18:28; Jdg 1:7 [v]S Jos 8:1 [w]S Dt 20:16; S Jos 8:22 [x]Jos 9:3 [y]S Jos 9:15 **10:3** [z]S Ge 13:18 [a]ver 5; Jos 12:11; 15:35; 21:29; Ne 11:29 [b]ver 5, 31; Jos 12:11; 15:39; 2Ki 14:19; 2Ch 11:9; 25:27; 32:9; Ne 11:30; Isa 36:2; 37:8; Jer 34:7; Mic 1:13 [c]ver 38; Jos 11:21; 12:13; 13:26; 15:7,49; 21:15; Jdg 1:11; 1Ch 6:58 [d]ver 23,34,36; Jos 12:12; 15:39 **10:4** [e]S Jos 9:15

9:14 *did not inquire of the LORD.* Did not consult their King, whose mission they were on.
9:15 *treaty of peace.* A covenant to let them live was sworn by the heads of the tribes—i.e., an oath was taken in the holy name of God. All such oaths were binding in Israel (see Ex 20:7; Lev 19:12; 1Sa 14:24).
9:18 *The whole assembly grumbled.* Perhaps the people feared the consequences of not following through on the earlier divine order to destroy all the Canaanites, but more likely they grumbled because they could not take over the Gibeonite cities and possessions.
9:21 *woodcutters and water carriers.* A conventional phrase for household servants (see Dt 19:11).
9:23 *under a curse.* Noah's prediction that Canaan would someday "be the slave of Shem" (Ge 9:25–26) has part of its fulfillment in this event. *for the house of my God.* Probably specifies how the Gibeonites were to serve "the whole assembly" (v. 21). Worship at the tabernacle (and later at the temple) required much wood and water (for sacrifices and washing) and consequently a great deal of menial labor. From now on, that labor was to be supplied by the Gibeonites, perhaps on a rotating basis. In this way they entered the Lord's service. When Solomon became king, the tabernacle and the altar of burnt offering were at Gibeon (2Ch 1:3,5).
9:27 *place the LORD would choose.* Joshua moved the tabernacle (and its altar) to Shiloh, and there it would reside at least until the days of Samuel (1Sa 4:3). Later, the Lord chose Jerusalem (1Ki 9:3).
10:1–43 The army under Joshua comes to the defense of Gibeon and defeats the coalition of southern kings at Aijalon, then subdues all the southern cities of Judah and the Negev.
10:1 *Adoni-Zedek.* Means "lord of righteousness" or "My (divine) lord is righteous." An earlier king of Jerusalem had a similar name (Melchizedek; see Ge 14:18 and note). *Jerusalem.* City of the Jebusites.
10:2 *important city.* Gibeon was not only larger in size than Bethel or Ai but also closer to Jerusalem. With Bethel and Ai conquered and the Gibeonite league in submission, the Israelites were well established in the central highlands, virtually cutting the land in two. Naturally the king of Jerusalem felt threatened, and he wanted to reunite all the Canaanites against Israel. Perhaps he also held (or claimed) some political dominion over the Gibeonite cities and viewed their sub

[5]Then the five kings[f] of the Amorites[g]—
:he kings of Jerusalem, Hebron, Jarmuth,
Lachish and Eglon—joined forces. They
noved up with all their troops and took up
ositions against Gibeon and attacked it.
[6]The Gibeonites then sent word to Joshua in the camp at Gilgal:[h] "Do not aban-
lon your servants. Come up to us quick-
y and save us! Help us, because all the
Amorite kings from the hill country have
oined forces against us."
[7]So Joshua marched up from Gilgal
with his entire army,[i] including all the best
ighting men. [8]The LORD said to Joshua,
'Do not be afraid[j] of them; I have given
hem into your hand.[k] Not one of them
will be able to withstand you."[l]
[9]After an all-night march from Gilgal,
oshua took them by surprise. [10]The LORD
hrew them into confusion[m] before Israel,[n] so Joshua and the Israelites defeated
hem completely at Gibeon.[o] Israel pur-
ued them along the road going up to Beth
Ioron[p] and cut them down all the way to
Azekah[q] and Makkedah.[r] [11]As they fled
efore Israel on the road down from Beth
Ioron to Azekah, the LORD hurled large
ailstones[s] down on them,[t] and more of
hem died from the hail than were killed
y the swords of the Israelites.
[12]On the day the LORD gave the Am-
rites[u] over to Israel, Joshua said to the
ORD in the presence of Israel:

"Sun, stand still over Gibeon,
and you, moon, over the Valley of
Aijalon."[v]
[13]So the sun stood still,[w]
and the moon stopped,
till the nation avenged itself on[a] its
enemies,

s it is written in the Book of Jashar.[x]

10:5 [f]ver 16 [g]Nu 13:29; S Dt 1:7 10:6 [h]S Dt 11:30 10:7 [i]Jos 8:1 10:8 [j]S Dt 3:2; S Jos 1:9 [k]S Jos 2:24 [l]S Dt 7:24 10:10 [m]S Ex 14:24 [n]S Dt 7:23 [o]S Jos 9:3 [p]Jos 16:3, 5; 18:13, 14; 21:22; 1Sa 13:18; 1Ki 9:17; 1Ch 6:68; 7:24; 2Ch 8:5; 25:13 [q]Jos 15:35; 1Sa 17:1; 2Ch 11:9; Ne 11:30; Jer 34:7 [r]ver 16, 17, 21; Jos 12:16; 15:41 10:11 [s]S Ex 9:18; Ps 18:12; Isa 28:2, 17; 32:19; Eze 13:11, 13 [t]Jdg 5:20 10:12 [u]Am 2:9 [v]Jos 19:42; 21:24; Jdg 1:35; 12:12; 1Sa 14:31; 1Ch 6:69; 8:13; 2Ch 11:10; 28:18 10:13 [w]Hab 3:11 [x]2Sa 1:18 [y]Isa 38:8 10:14 [z]ver 42; S Ex 14:14; Ps 106:43; 136:24; Isa 63:10; Jer 21:5 10:15 [a]ver 43 10:16 [b]Ps 68:12 10:20 [c]Dt 20:16 [d]2Ch 11:10; Jer 4:5; 5:17; 8:14; 35:11

The sun stopped[y] in the middle of the
sky and delayed going down about a full
day. [14]There has never been a day like it
before or since, a day when the LORD listened to a human being. Surely the LORD
was fighting[z] for Israel!
[15]Then Joshua returned with all Israel
to the camp at Gilgal.[a]

Five Amorite Kings Killed

[16]Now the five kings had fled[b] and hidden in the cave at Makkedah. [17]When
Joshua was told that the five kings had
been found hiding in the cave at Makkedah, [18]he said, "Roll large rocks up to the
mouth of the cave, and post some men
there to guard it. [19]But don't stop; pursue
your enemies! Attack them from the rear
and don't let them reach their cities, for
the LORD your God has given them into
your hand."
[20]So Joshua and the Israelites defeated them completely,[c] but a few survivors
managed to reach their fortified cities.[d]
[21]The whole army then returned safely to
Joshua in the camp at Makkedah, and no
one uttered a word against the Israelites.
[22]Joshua said, "Open the mouth of the
cave and bring those five kings out to me."
[23]So they brought the five kings out of the
cave—the kings of Jerusalem, Hebron,
Jarmuth, Lachish and Eglon. [24]When they
had brought these kings[e] to Joshua, he
summoned all the men of Israel and said
to the army commanders who had come
with him, "Come here and put your feet[f]
on the necks of these kings." So they came
forward and placed their feet[g] on their
necks.

[a] 13 Or *nation triumphed over*

10:24 [e]S Dt 7:24 [f]Mal 4:3 [g]2Sa 22:40; Ps 110:1; Isa 51:23

ission to Israel as rebellion. *good fighters.* Men known to be ffective in battle. Yet they were wise enough to have made eace with the Israelites.

0:5 *five kings of the Amorites.* Rulers over five of the ma- r cities in the southern hill country. The Amorites of the ills are here distinguished from the Canaanites along the oast.

0:6 *Come ... and save us!* An urgent appeal for deliverance a man whose name means "The LORD saves." A treaty such s Joshua had made with the Gibeonites usually obliged e ruling nation to come to the aid of the subject peoples they were attacked (see chart, p. 23, under "Suzerain- assal").

0:9 *all-night march.* Gilgal was about 20 miles east of ibeon, a steep uphill climb for Joshua's men. *by surprise.* shua attacked early in the morning, perhaps while the oon was still up (v. 12).

0:10 *confusion.* The Hebrew for this word implies terror or anic.

0:11 *down from Beth Horon.* A long descent to the plain of ijalon below, following the main east-west crossroad just orth of Jerusalem. *large hailstones.* For the Lord's use of the elements of nature as his armaments, see Jdg 5:20; 1Sa 7:10; Job 38:22–23; Ps 18:12–14.

10:12 *Sun, stand still.* In addressing the Lord in this surprising way, Joshua indicates what he wants the Lord to do.

10:13 *Book of Jashar.* An early account of Israel's wars (perhaps all in poetic form; see 2Sa 1:18; see also note on Jdg 5:1–31), but now lost. *delayed going down.* Some believe that God extended the hours of daylight for the Israelites to defeat their enemies. Others suggest that the sun remained cool (perhaps as the result of an overcast sky) for an entire day, allowing the fighting to continue through the afternoon. The fact is that we do not know what happened, except that it involved divine intervention.

10:16 *Makkedah.* A town near Azekah (v. 10) in the western foothills where Joshua's troops made their camp.

10:19 *pursue your enemies.* Most of the fighting men defending the southern cities were caught and killed before they could reach the safety of their fortresses.

10:21 *no one uttered a word.* The thought here appears to be that no one dared even to raise his voice against the Israelites anymore.

10:24 *put your feet on the necks.* Public humiliation of

25Joshua said to them, "Do not be
afraid; do not be discouraged. Be strong
and courageous.[h] This is what the LORD
will do to all the enemies you are going
to fight." 26Then Joshua put the kings to
death and exposed their bodies on five
poles, and they were left hanging on the
poles until evening.
27At sunset[i] Joshua gave the order and
they took them down from the poles and
threw them into the cave where they had
been hiding. At the mouth of the cave they
placed large rocks, which are there to this
day.[j]

Southern Cities Conquered

28That day Joshua took Makkedah. He
put the city and its king to the sword and
totally destroyed everyone in it. He left
no survivors.[k] And he did to the king of
Makkedah as he had done to the king of
Jericho.[l]
29Then Joshua and all Israel with him
moved on from Makkedah to Libnah[m]
and attacked it. 30The LORD also gave that
city and its king into Israel's hand. The
city and everyone in it Joshua put to the
sword. He left no survivors there. And he
did to its king as he had done to the king
of Jericho.
31Then Joshua and all Israel with him
moved on from Libnah to Lachish;[n] he
took up positions against it and attacked
it. 32The LORD gave Lachish into Israel's
hands, and Joshua took it on the second
day. The city and everyone in it he put
to the sword, just as he had done to Libnah. 33Meanwhile, Horam king of Gezer[o]
had come up to help Lachish, but Joshua
defeated him and his army—until no survivors were left.
34Then Joshua and all Israel with him
moved on from Lachish to Eglon;[p] they
took up positions against it and attacked
it. 35They captured it that same day and
put it to the sword and totally destroyed
everyone in it, just as they had done to
Lachish.
36Then Joshua and all Israel with him
went up from Eglon to Hebron[q] and attacked it. 37They took the city and put it
to the sword, together with its king, its
villages and everyone[r] in it. They left no
survivors. Just as at Eglon, they totally destroyed it and everyone in it.
38Then Joshua and all Israel with him
turned around and attacked Debir.[s] 39They
took the city, its king and its villages, and
put them to the sword. Everyone in it they
totally destroyed. They left no survivors.
They did to Debir and its king as they had
done to Libnah and its king and to He
bron.[t]
40So Joshua subdued the whole region
including the hill country, the Negev,
the western foothills and the mountain
slopes,[v] together with all their kings.[w] He
left no survivors. He totally destroyed all
who breathed, just as the LORD, the God
of Israel, had commanded.[x] 41Joshua sub
dued them from Kadesh Barnea[y] to Gaza
and from the whole region of Goshen[a] to
Gibeon. 42All these kings and their land
Joshua conquered in one campaign, be
cause the LORD, the God of Israel, fought
for Israel.
43Then Joshua returned with all Israel
to the camp at Gilgal.[c]

Northern Kings Defeated

11 When Jabin[d] king of Hazor[e] heard
of this, he sent word to Jobab king
of Madon, to the kings of Shimron[f] and
Akshaph,[g] 2and to the northern kings who
were in the mountains, in the Arabah
south of Kinnereth,[i] in the western foot
hills and in Naphoth Dor[j] on the west; 3to
the Canaanites in the east and west; to the
Amorites, Hittites, Perizzites[k] and Jebusites
in the hill country;[l] and to the Hivites

10:25 [h] S Dt 31:6 **10:27** [i] S Dt 21:23 [j] S Ge 35:20 **10:28** [k] Dt 20:16 [l] ver 30, 32, 35, 39; Jos 6:21 **10:29** [m] S Nu 33:20 **10:31** [n] S ver 3 **10:33** [o] Jos 12:12; 16:3, 10; 21:21; Jdg 1:29; 2Sa 5:25; 1Ki 9:15; 1Ch 6:67 **10:34** [p] S ver 3 **10:36** [q] S Ge 13:18; Jos 14:13; 15:13; 20:7; 21:11; Jdg 16:3 **10:37** [r] S ver 28 **10:38** [s] S ver 3 **10:39** [t] S ver 28 **10:40** [u] S Ge 12:9; Jos 12:8; 15:19, 21; 18:25; 19:8; 1Sa 30:27 [v] S Dt 1:7 [w] Dt 7:24 [x] Dt 20:16-17 **10:41** [y] S Ge 14:7 [z] S Ge 10:19 [a] Jos 11:16; 15:51 **10:42** [b] S ver 14 **10:43** [c] ver 15; Jos 5:9; 1Sa 7:16; 10:8; 11:14; 13:12 **11:1** [d] Jdg 4:2, 7, 23; Ps 83:9 [e] ver 10; Jos 12:19; 15:23, 25; 19:36; Jdg 4:2, 17; 1Sa 12:9; 1Ki 9:15; 2Ki 15:29; Ne 11:33; Jer 49:28, 33 [f] Jos 19:15 [g] Jos 12:20; 19:25 **11:2** [h] ver 16; S Dt 1:1; Jos 12:1; 18:18 [i] S Nu 34:11; Dt 3:17; Jos 19:35; 1Ki 15:20 [j] Jos 12:23; 17:11; Jdg 1:27; 1Ki 4:11; 1Ch 7:29 **11:3** [k] S Jos 3:10 [l] Nu 13:17 [m] S Ex 3:8; Dt 7:1; Jdg 3:3, 5; 1Ki 9:20

defeated enemy chieftains was the usual climax of warfare in the ancient Near East.

10:26 *exposed their bodies on five poles.* See note on Dt 21:22.

10:27 *they placed large rocks.* A sixth monument in the land to the events of the conquest (see note on 4:9).

10:28 *totally destroyed everyone.* The holy ban was placed on the people of Makkedah, meaning that they were "devoted to the LORD" because of their wicked deeds (see 6:17 and note; see also NIV text note there). The same fate came to the other major cities of the south (vv. 29–42).

10:33 *Horam king of Gezer.* An important detail: the defeat of the king of the most powerful city in the area. Gezer was eventually taken over by the Egyptians and given to King Solomon as a wedding gift (see 1Ki 9:16).

10:38 *Debir.* Also known as Kiriath Sepher (15:15). This city was at one time identified with Tell Beit Mirsim. More recently, however, it has been equated with Khirbet Rabud, about five miles southwest of Hebron.

10:41 *Kadesh Barnea to Gaza.* The south-to-north limits in the western part of the region. *Goshen.* A seldom-used name for the eastern Negev, not to be confused with the Goshen in the delta of Egypt; it is also the name of a town (15:51). Goshen and Gibeon mark the south-to-north limits in the eastern part of the region.

11:1–23 Only the northern cities remained to be conquered. The major battle for the hills of Galilee is fought and won against Hazor and the coalition of other northern city-states. A summary follows of all Joshua's victories in the southern and central regions as well.

11:1 *Jabin king of Hazor.* Jabin is perhaps a dynastic name used again in the days of Deborah (Jdg 4:2).

11:2 *Kinnereth.* Means "harp"; the Sea of Galilee (but see note on Dt 3:17).

THE NORTHERN CAMPAIGN

Late Bronze Age Hazor was burned by Joshua (Jos 11:13). Excavations have revealed three clearly datable destruction layers, one of which may provide the strongest evidence yet for a historically verifiable date for the conquest.

The excavator thought Joshua burned the latest level (c. 1230 BC), but others argue that it must actually have been the earliest of the three levels, c. 1400 BC (see note on Jos 11:10).

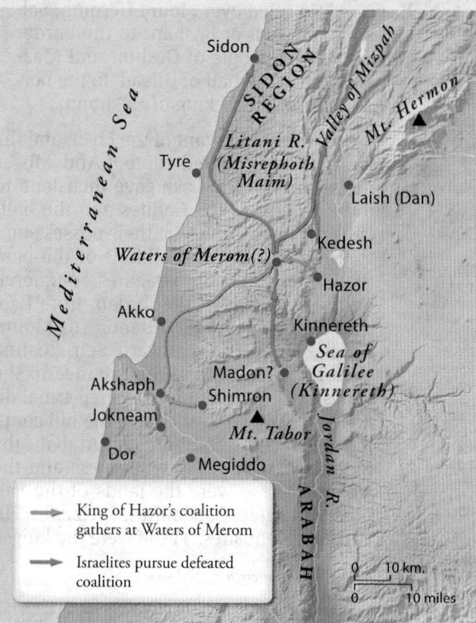

below Hermon[n] in the region of Mizpah.[o]
4They came out with all their troops and
a large number of horses and chariots—
a huge army, as numerous as the sand
on the seashore.[p] 5All these kings joined
forces[q] and made camp together at the Waters of Merom[r] to fight against Israel.
6The LORD said to Joshua, "Do not be
afraid of them, because by this time tomorrow I will hand[s] all of them, slain, over
to Israel. You are to hamstring[t] their horses
and burn their chariots."[u]
7So Joshua and his whole army came
against them suddenly at the Waters of Merom and attacked them, 8and the LORD gave
them into the hand of Israel. They defeated them and pursued them all the way to
Greater Sidon,[v] to Misrephoth Maim,[w] and
to the Valley of Mizpah on the east, until
no survivors were left. 9Joshua did to them
as the LORD had directed: He hamstrung
their horses and burned their chariots.
10At that time Joshua turned back and
captured Hazor and put its king to the
sword.[x] (Hazor had been the head of all
these kingdoms.) 11Everyone in it they
put to the sword. They totally destroyed[a]
them,[y] not sparing anyone that breathed,[z]
and he burned[a] Hazor itself.
12Joshua took all these royal cities and
their kings and put them to the sword. He
totally destroyed them, as Moses the servant of the LORD had commanded.[b] 13Yet
Israel did not burn any of the cities built on
their mounds—except Hazor, which Joshua burned. 14The Israelites carried off for
themselves all the plunder and livestock
of these cities, but all the people they put to
the sword until they completely destroyed
them, not sparing anyone that breathed.[c]
15As the LORD commanded his servant
Moses, so Moses commanded Joshua, and
Joshua did it; he left nothing undone of all
that the LORD commanded Moses.[d]

[a] *11* The Hebrew term refers to the irrevocable giving over of things or persons to the LORD, often by totally destroying them; also in verses 12, 20 and 21.

11:3 [n] S Dt 3:8 [o] ver 8; S Ge 31:49; Jos 15:38; 18:26; Jdg 11:11; 20:1; 21:1; 1Sa 7:5,6; 1Ki 15:22; 2Ki 25:23 **11:4** [p] S Ge 12:2; Jdg 7:12; 1Sa 13:5 **11:5** [q] Jdg 5:19 [r] ver 7 **11:6** [s] S Jos 2:24 [t] S Ge 49:6 [u] ver 9 **11:8** [v] S Ge 10:15; S Jdg 18:7 [w] Jos 13:6 **11:10** [x] Isa 3:25; Jer 41:2; 44:18 **11:11** [y] S Dt 7:2 [z] Dt 20:16-17 [a] S Nu 31:10 **11:12** [b] Nu 33:50-52; Dt 7:2 **11:14** [c] S Dt 20:16 **11:15** [d] Ex 34:11; Dt 7:2; S Jos 1:7

11:4 *as numerous as the sand.* A widely used figure of speech for indicating large numbers (see note on Ge 22:17).
11:5 *All these kings.* Jabin's muster extended as far as the Arabah (v. 2) in the Jordan Valley and Dor on the Mediterranean, south of Mount Carmel. *Merom.* Probably modern Meirun, about eight miles northwest of the Sea of Galilee.
11:6 *hamstring their horses.* Done by cutting the tendon above the hock or ankle, crippling the horse so that it cannot walk again. *burn their chariots.* These advanced implements of war were not used by the armies of Israel until the time of Solomon (see 1Ki 9:22; 10:26–29).
11:10 *Joshua … captured Hazor.* Perhaps his greatest victory. Hazor's armed forces, however, had been defeated earlier at Merom. The archaeological site reveals extensive damage and the burning of the Canaanite city c. 1400 BC (mentioned in the 2001 excavation report), c. 1300 and again c. 1230. Since the destruction level at c. 1300 probably indicates the burning of the city by Pharaoh Horemhab, this leaves the destruction levels at c. 1400 and c. 1230 for Joshua's conquest. Those who hold to the late date of the conquest opt for the 1230 level; those who hold to the early date opt for 1400 (see Introduction: Historical Setting). Once again the ban of total destruction was applied (v. 11).
11:13 *mounds.* The Hebrew word is *tel* (Arabic *tall*), a hill formed by the accumulated debris of many ancient settlements one on top of another (see notes on 7:2; Jer 30:18).
11:15 *he left nothing undone.* Joshua's success should be measured in the light of the specific orders given by God, which he carried out fully, rather than by the total area that eventually would have to be occupied by Israel.

16So Joshua took this entire land: the
hill country,[e] all the Negev,[f] the whole region of Goshen, the western foothills,[g] the
Arabah and the mountains of Israel with
their foothills, 17from Mount Halak, which
rises toward Seir,[h] to Baal Gad[i] in the Valley of Lebanon[j] below Mount Hermon.[k]
He captured all their kings and put them
to death.[l] 18Joshua waged war against all
these kings for a long time. 19Except for
the Hivites[m] living in Gibeon,[n] not one city
made a treaty of peace[o] with the Israelites, who took them all in battle. 20For it
was the LORD himself who hardened their
hearts[p] to wage war against Israel, so that
he might destroy them totally, exterminat-
ing them without mercy, as the LORD had
commanded Moses.[q]
21At that time Joshua went and destroyed the Anakites[r] from the hill country: from Hebron, Debir[s] and Anab,[t] from
all the hill country of Judah, and from all
the hill country of Israel. Joshua totally
destroyed them and their towns. 22No Anakites were left in Israelite territory; only
in Gaza,[u] Gath[v] and Ashdod[w] did any survive.
23So Joshua took the entire land,[x] just as
the LORD had directed Moses, and he gave
it as an inheritance[y] to Israel according to
their tribal divisions.[z] Then the land had
rest[a] from war.[b]

List of Defeated Kings

12 These are the kings of the land
whom the Israelites had defeated
and whose territory they took[c] over east
of the Jordan,[d] from the Arnon[e] Gorge to
Mount Hermon,[f] including all the eastern
side of the Arabah:[g]

2Sihon king of the Amorites, who
reigned in Heshbon.[h]
He ruled from Aroer[i] on the rim of
the Arnon Gorge—from the middle
of the gorge—to the Jabbok River,[j]
which is the border of the Ammonites.[k] This included half of Gilead.[l]
3He also ruled over the eastern Arabah from the Sea of Galilee[a][m] to the
Sea of the Arabah (that is, the Dead
Sea[n]), to Beth Jeshimoth,[o] and then
southward below the slopes of Pisgah.[p]

4And the territory of Og king of Bashan,[q] one of the last of the Rephaites,[r] who reigned in Ashtaroth[s] and
Edrei.
5He ruled over Mount Hermon, Salekah,[t] all of Bashan[u] to the border
of the people of Geshur[v] and Maakah,[w] and half of Gilead[x] to the border of Sihon king of Heshbon.

6Moses, the servant of the LORD, and the
Israelites conquered them.[y] And Moses
the servant of the LORD gave their land to
the Reubenites, the Gadites and the half-
tribe of Manasseh to be their possession.[z]
7Here is a list of the kings of the land
that Joshua and the Israelites conquered
on the west side of the Jordan, from Baal
Gad in the Valley of Lebanon[a] to Mount
Halak, which rises toward Seir. Joshua
gave their lands as an inheritance to the
tribes of Israel according to their tribal divisions. 8The lands included the hill country, the western foothills, the Arabah, the
mountain slopes, the wilderness and the
Negev.[b] These were the lands of the Hittites, Amorites, Canaanites, Perizzites, Hivites and Jebusites. These were the kings:[c]

[a] 3 Hebrew *Kinnereth*

11:16 [e]Nu 13:17 [f]S Dt 1:7 [g]S Jos 10:41 **11:17** [h]S Ge 14:6; S Nu 24:18; S Dt 33:2 [i]Jos 13:5 [j]S Dt 3:25; Jos 12:7 [k]Dt 3:9; Jos 12:8 [l]Dt 7:24 **11:19** [m]S Jos 9:1 [n]S Jos 9:3 [o]S Jos 9:15 **11:20** [p]S Ex 4:21; S 14:17; Ro 9:18 [q]Dt 7:16; Jdg 14:4 **11:21** [r]S Nu 13:22, 33 [s]S Jos 10:3 [t]Jos 15:50 **11:22** [u]S Ge 10:19 [v]Jos 12:17; 19:13; 1Sa 5:8; 17:4; 1Ki 2:39; 2Ki 14:25; 1Ch 8:13; Am 6:2 [w]Jos 15:47; 1Sa 5:1; Isa 20:1 **11:23** [x]Jos 21:43-45; Ne 9:24 [y]S Dt 1:38; 12:9-10; S 25:19; S Jos 13:7 [z]S Nu 26:53; Ps 105:44 [a]S Ex 33:14 [b]Jos 14:15 **12:1** [c]Ps 136:21 [d]S Nu 32:19 [e]S Nu 21:13 [f]S Dt 3:8 [g]S Jos 11:2 **12:2** [h]ver 5; S Nu 21:21, 25; Jos 13:10; Jdg 11:19 [i]S Nu 32:34; S Jos 13:16 [j]S Ge 32:22 [k]S Ge 19:38 [l]S Ge 31:21; S Nu 32:26; Dt 2:36; S 3:15; Jos 13:11, 25; 17:1; 20:8; 21:38; Jdg 5:17; 7:3; 10:8 **12:3** [m]Jos 11:2 [n]S Ge 14:3 [o]S Nu 33:49; Jos 13:20 [p]S Nu 21:20 **12:4** [q]S Nu 21:21, 33; Jos 13:30 [r]S Ge 14:5 [s]S Dt 1:4 **12:5** [t]S Dt 3:10 [u]Nu 32:33; Jos 17:1; 20:8; 21:27; 22:7 [v]Jos 13:2, 13; 1Sa 27:8 [w]S Dt 3:14 [x]ver 2 **12:6** [y]S Dt 3:8 [z]Nu 32:29, 33; Jos 13:8 **12:7** [a]S Jos 11:17 **12:8** [b]S Dt 1:7 [c]S Jos 3:10; S 11:17; Ezr 9:1

11:16 *this entire land.* A lesson in the geography of Canaan follows. See map, p. 262.
11:17 *Mount Halak.* A wilderness peak to the east of Kadesh Barnea marking Israel's southern extremity. *Baal Gad.* The first valley west of Mount Hermon.
11:18 *for a long time.* An estimation of the duration of Joshua's conquests can be made from the life span of Caleb: Seven years had elapsed from the beginning of the conquest (age 78; compare 14:7 with Dt 2:14) until he took Hebron (age 85; see 14:10).
11:20 *the LORD ... hardened their hearts.* See notes on Ex 4:21; 7:13.
11:21 *Anakites.* Had been reported by the 12 spies to be a people "of great size" (Nu 13:32), whom the Israelites had feared so much that they had refused to undertake the conquest. They were related to the Nephilim (see note on Ge 6:4) and were named after their forefather, Anak. Joshua shared with Caleb his victory over the Anakites (14:12–15).
12:1–24 A conclusion to the first section of Joshua, and a summary of the victories of the Israelites and the cities whose kings had been defeated (see map, p. 2518, at the end of this study Bible; see also maps, pp. 319, 331).
12:1 *territory ... east of the Jordan.* The unity of the nation is reaffirmed by the inclusion of these lands in Transjordan. *Arnon Gorge.* Marked the border with Moab to the south. *Mount Hermon.* The upper limits of Israel's land to the north.
12:4 *Og king of Bashan.* Sihon (v. 2) and Og were defeated by Israel under Moses' leadership, a long-remembered sign of God's mighty power (see Ne 9:22; Ps 135:11).
12:5 *Salekah ... Geshur ... Maakah.* All of them were east of the Sea of Galilee (Kinnereth): Salekah a town in the far east of Bashan (see map, p. 478), Geshur a small city kingdom northeast of Bashan (see map, p. 478), Maakah a city-state southeast of Mount Hermon (see map, p. 478; see also 13:11).
12:7 *the land ... on the west side.* Canaan proper (9:1; 11:16–17; 24:11; Ge 15:18–19).

[9]the king of Jericho[d] one
the king of Ai[e] (near Bethel[f]) one
[10]the king of Jerusalem[g] one
the king of Hebron one
[11]the king of Jarmuth one
the king of Lachish[h] one
[12]the king of Eglon[i] one
the king of Gezer[j] one
[13]the king of Debir[k] one
the king of Geder one
[14]the king of Hormah[l] one
the king of Arad[m] one
[15]the king of Libnah[n] one
the king of Adullam[o] one
[16]the king of Makkedah[p] one
the king of Bethel[q] one
[17]the king of Tappuah[r] one
the king of Hepher[s] one
[18]the king of Aphek[t] one
the king of Lasharon one
[19]the king of Madon one
the king of Hazor[u] one
[20]the king of Shimron Meron one
the king of Akshaph[v] one
[21]the king of Taanach[w] one
the king of Megiddo[x] one
[22]the king of Kedesh[y] one
the king of Jokneam[z]
in Carmel[a] one
[23]the king of Dor
(in Naphoth Dor[b]) one
the king of Goyim in Gilgal one
[24]the king of Tirzah[c] one
thirty-one kings in all.[d]

Land Still to Be Taken

13 When Joshua had grown old,[e] the
LORD said to him, "You are now
very old, and there are still very large areas of land to be taken over.

[2]"This is the land that remains: all the
regions of the Philistines[f] and Geshurites,[g] [3]from the Shihor River[h] on the
east of Egypt to the territory of Ekron[i]
on the north, all of it counted as Canaanite though held by the five Phi-

12:9 [d]S Nu 33:48 [e]S Ge 12:8; S Jos 8:1 [f]S Jos 7:2; 8:9; 18:13; Jdg 1:23; 4:5; 20:18; 21:2; Ne 11:31 **12:10** [g]S Jos 10:1 **12:11** [h]S Jos 10:3 **12:12** [i]S Jos 10:3 [j]S Jos 10:33 **12:13** [k]S Jos 10:3 **12:14** [l]S Nu 14:45 [m]S Nu 21:1 **12:15** [n]S Nu 33:20 [o]S Ge 38:1; Jos 15:35; Mic 1:15 **12:16** [p]S Jos 10:10 [q]S Jos 7:2 **12:17** [r]Jos 15:34; 16:8; 17:8 [s]S Jos 11:22; 1Ki 4:10 **12:18** [t]Jos 13:4; 19:30; Jdg 1:31; 1Sa 4:1; 29:1 **12:19** [u]S Jos 11:1 **12:20** [v]S Jos 11:1 **12:21** [w]Jos 17:11; 21:25 [x]Jdg 1:27; 5:19; 1Ki 4:12 **12:22** [y]Jos 15:23; 19:37; 20:7; 21:32; Jdg 4:6,9 [z]Jos 19:11; 21:34 [a]Jos 15:55; 19:26; 1Sa 15:12; 2Sa 23:35 **12:23** [b]S Jos 11:2 **12:24** [c]1Ki 14:17; 15:33; 16:8, 23; SS 6:4 [d]Ps 135:11; 136:18 **13:1** [e]Ge 24:1; Jos 14:10; 23:1, 2; 1Ki 1:1

listine rulers[j] in Gaza, Ashdod,[k] Ashkelon,[l] Gath and Ekron; the territory
of the Avvites[m] [4]on the south; all the
land of the Canaanites, from Arah of
the Sidonians as far as Aphek[n] and
the border of the Amorites;[o] [5]the area
of Byblos;[p] and all Lebanon[q] to the
east, from Baal Gad below Mount
Hermon[r] to Lebo Hamath.[s]

[6]"As for all the inhabitants of the mountain regions from Lebanon to Misrephoth
Maim,[t] that is, all the Sidonians, I myself
will drive them out[u] before the Israelites.
Be sure to allocate this land to Israel for
an inheritance, as I have instructed you,[v]
[7]and divide it as an inheritance[w] among
the nine tribes and half of the tribe of Manasseh."

Division of the Land East of the Jordan

[8]The other half of Manasseh,[a] the Reubenites and the Gadites had received the inheritance that Moses had given them east
of the Jordan, as he, the servant of the
LORD, had assigned[x] it to them.[y]

[9]It extended from Aroer[z] on the rim of
the Arnon Gorge, and from the town
in the middle of the gorge, and included the whole plateau[a] of Medeba
as far as Dibon,[b] [10]and all the towns
of Sihon king of the Amorites, who
ruled in Heshbon,[c] out to the border
of the Ammonites.[d] [11]It also included Gilead,[e] the territory of the people

[a] *8* Hebrew *With it* (that is, with the other half of Manasseh)

13:2 [f]S Ge 10:14; S Jdg 3:31 [g]S Jos 12:5 **13:3** [h]1Ch 13:5; Isa 23:3; Jer 2:18 [i]Jos 15:11,45; 19:43; Jdg 1:18; 1Sa 5:10; 7:14 [j]Jdg 3:3; 16:5,18; 1Sa 6:4,17; Isa 14:29; Jer 25:20; Eze 25:15 [k]S Jos 11:22; Am 3:9 [l]Jdg 1:18; 14:19; 2Sa 1:20 [m]S Dt 2:23 **13:4** [n]S Jos 12:18 [o]S Ge 14:7; S 15:16; Am 2:10 **13:5** [p]1Ki 5:18; Ps 83:7; Eze 27:9 [q]S Jos 11:17 [r]S Dt 3:8 [s]S Nu 13:21; 34:8; Jdg 3:3 **13:6** [t]Jos 11:8 [u]Ps 80:8 [v]Nu 33:54; S 34:13 **13:7** [w]S Jos 11:23; Ps 78:55 **13:8** [x]S Jos 12:6 [y]Jos 18:7 **13:9** [z]ver 16; S Nu 32:34; Dt 2:36; Jdg 11:26; 2Sa 24:5 [a]ver 17,21; Jer 48:8,21 [b]S Nu 21:30; S 32:3; Isa 15:2; Jer 48:18,22 **13:10** [c]S Jos 12:2 [d]S Nu 21:24 **13:11** [e]S Jos 12:2

12:12 *king of Gezer.* Had been defeated in the siege of Lachish (10:33), but the city itself was not captured by Joshua, nor were the cities of Aphek, Taanach, Megiddo or Dor (vv. 18–23; see Jdg 1:27–31).

13:1–32 The heavenly King, who has conquered the land, begins the administration of his realm by assigning specific territories to the several tribes. Much of chs. 13–21 reads like administrative documents. The account begins by noting the land still to be subdued (but to be allotted) and by recalling the assignments already made by Moses to the two and a half tribes east of the Jordan (see map, p. 2519, at the end of this study Bible).

13:1 *Joshua had grown old.* Between 90 and 100 years of age; Caleb was 85 (14:10). *still ... large areas ... to be taken over.* See note on 18:3.

13:3 *Shihor River.* Elsewhere Shihor apparently refers to a branch of the Nile (see 1Ch 13:5; Isa 23:3 and notes; see also NIV text note on Jer 2:18). Here, however, it appears to be another name for the Wadi el-Arish below Gaza at the eastern entrance to the Sinai ("on the east of Egypt"). *Ekron.* See note on 1Sa 5:10. *rulers.* The Hebrew for this word may be related to the Greek term *tyrannos* (from which comes English "tyrant"). In the OT it is used only of Philistine rulers and so may indicate the Aegean background of the Philistines. See map, p. 359.

13:5 *Byblos.* Just north of modern Beirut. The Phoenicians and the Philistines held most of the territory still to be occupied by Israel.

13:9 *Aroer.* This town on the Arnon River marked the southern boundary of Israel east of the Jordan. From here the land extended north through Gilead and Bashan to the slopes of Mount Hermon, the territory once dominated by the two kings of the Amorites, Sihon and Og.

of Geshur and Maakah, all of Mount
Hermon and all Bashan as far as Salekah[f]— 12 that is, the whole kingdom
of Og in Bashan,[g] who had reigned
in Ashtaroth[h] and Edrei.[i] (He was the
last of the Rephaites.[j]) Moses had
defeated them and taken over their
land.[k] 13 But the Israelites did not
drive out the people of Geshur[l] and
Maakah,[m] so they continue to live
among the Israelites to this day.[n]

14 But to the tribe of Levi he gave no inheritance, since the food offerings presented to the LORD, the God of Israel, are their
inheritance, as he promised them.[o]

15 This is what Moses had given to the
tribe of Reuben, according to its clans:

16 The territory from Aroer[p] on the
rim of the Arnon Gorge, and from the
town in the middle of the gorge, and
the whole plateau past Medeba[q] 17 to
Heshbon and all its towns on the plateau,[r] including Dibon,[s] Bamoth Baal,[t]
Beth Baal Meon,[u] 18 Jahaz,[v] Kedemoth,[w] Mephaath,[x] 19 Kiriathaim,[y] Sibmah,[z] Zereth Shahar on the hill in the
valley, 20 Beth Peor,[a] the slopes of Pisgah, and Beth Jeshimoth— 21 all the
towns on the plateau[b] and the entire
realm of Sihon king of the Amorites,
who ruled at Heshbon. Moses had defeated him and the Midianite chiefs,[c]
Evi, Rekem, Zur, Hur and Reba[d]—
princes allied with Sihon—who lived
in that country. 22 In addition to those
slain in battle, the Israelites had put to
the sword Balaam son of Beor,[e] who
practiced divination.[f] 23 The boundary
of the Reubenites was the bank of the
Jordan. These towns and their villages were the inheritance of the Reubenites, according to their clans.[g]

24 This is what Moses had given to the
tribe of Gad, according to its clans:

25 The territory of Jazer,[h] all the towns
of Gilead[i] and half the Ammonite
country as far as Aroer, near Rabbah;[j] 26 and from Heshbon[k] to Ramath
Mizpah and Betonim, and from Mahanaim[l] to the territory of Debir;[m]
27 and in the valley, Beth Haram, Beth
Nimrah,[n] Sukkoth[o] and Zaphon[p] with
the rest of the realm of Sihon king of
Heshbon (the east side of the Jordan,
the territory up to the end of the Sea
of Galilee[a][q]). 28 These towns and their
villages were the inheritance of the
Gadites,[r] according to their clans.

29 This is what Moses had given to the
half-tribe of Manasseh, that is, to half the
family of the descendants of Manasseh,
according to its clans:

30 The territory extending from Mahanaim[s] and including all of Bashan,[t]
the entire realm of Og king of Bashan[u]—all the settlements of Jair[v] in
Bashan, sixty towns, 31 half of Gilead,
and Ashtaroth and Edrei (the royal
cities of Og in Bashan).[w] This was for
the descendants of Makir[x] son of Manasseh—for half of the sons of Makir,
according to their clans.[y]

32 This is the inheritance Moses had giv-
en when he was in the plains of Moab[z]
across the Jordan east of Jericho.[a] 33 But
to the tribe of Levi, Moses had given no
inheritance;[b] the LORD, the God of Israel,
is their inheritance,[c] as he promised them.[d]

Division of the Land West of the Jordan

14 Now these are the areas the Israelites received as an inheritance[e]
in the land of Canaan, which Eleazar[f] the
priest, Joshua son of Nun and the heads of
the tribal clans of Israel[g] allotted[h] to them.[i]
2 Their inheritances were assigned by lot[j]
to the nine and a half tribes,[k] as the LORD

[a] 27 Hebrew *Kinnereth*

13:11 [f] Jos 12:5 **13:12** [g] S Dt 1:4 [h] Jos 12:4 [i] S Nu 21:33 [j] S Ge 14:5 [k] S Dt 3:8 **13:13** [l] S Jos 12:5 [m] S Dt 3:14 [n] Dt 3:12 **13:14** [o] ver 33; Dt 18:1-2; Jos 14:3 **13:16** [p] S ver 9; Jos 12:2; 1Sa 30:28 [q] S Nu 21:30; Isa 15:2 **13:17** [r] S ver 9 [s] S Nu 32:3 [t] Nu 22:41 [u] 1Ch 5:8; Jer 48:23; Eze 25:9 **13:18** [v] S Nu 21:23 [w] S Dt 2:26 [x] Jos 21:37; Jer 48:21 **13:19** [y] S Nu 32:37 [z] S Nu 32:3 **13:20** [a] S Dt 3:29 **13:21** [b] S ver 9 [c] S Ge 25:2; S Nu 25:15 [d] Nu 31:8 **13:22** [e] S Nu 22:5 [f] S Ge 30:27; S Nu 23:23 **13:23** [g] 1Ch 5:7 **13:25** [h] S Nu 21:32; Jos 21:39 [i] S Jos 12:2 [j] S Dt 3:11 **13:26** [k] S Nu 21:25; Jer 49:3 [l] S Ge 32:2 [m] S Jos 10:3 **13:27** [n] S Nu 32:3 [o] S Ge 33:17 [p] Jdg 12:1; Ps 48:2 [q] S Nu 34:11 **13:28** [r] Ge 46:16; S Nu 32:33; Eze 48:27 **13:30** [s] S Ge 32:2 [t] S Nu 21:33 [u] S Jos 12:4 [v] S Nu 32:41 **13:31** [w] Nu 21:33 [x] S Ge 50:23 [y] Jos 17:5 **13:32** [z] S Nu 26:3 [a] S Nu 22:1 **13:33** [b] Nu 26:62 [c] S Nu 18:20 [d] S ver 14; Jos 18:7; Eze 44:28 **14:1** [e] S Jos 11:23; Ps 16:6; 136:21 [f] S Ex 6:23 [g] Jos 21:1 [h] S Nu 26:53 [i] Nu 34:17-18; Jos 19:51 **14:2** [j] S Lev 16:8 [k] Nu 34:13

13:14 *the food offerings ... are their inheritance.* See Dt 18:1–8 and note on 18:1.
13:15 *what Moses had given to ... Reuben.* The land east of the Dead Sea between the Arnon River (boundary of Moab) and Heshbon (the old royal city of Sihon).
13:22 *Balaam son of Beor.* The one who supposedly had influence with the gods (Nu 22–24) was slain when the Lord punished the Midianites for trying to seduce Israel into idolatry and sexual immorality (see Nu 25; 31:8 and notes on Nu 22:5,8).
13:24 *what Moses had given to ... Gad.* The central area, beginning near Heshbon on the south and reaching, along the Jordan, to the southern end of the Sea of Galilee. It included most of Gilead, but the exact boundary between Gad and the half-tribe of Manasseh remains somewhat uncertain since not all the places named can now be located.
13:29 *what Moses had given to the half-tribe of Manasseh.* The lands east and north of the Sea of Galilee, but also including the upper part of Gilead. Makir (v. 31) led in the occupation of these lands (see Nu 32:32,39–42).
13:33 *the LORD ... is their inheritance.* See v. 14; see also Dt 18:1–8 and note on 18:1.
14:1–5 An introduction to the allotment of territories in Canaan.
14:1 *Eleazar the priest.* Son of Aaron, Eleazar as high priest was the highest official over the casting of the lots. The Urim and Thummim (see notes on Ex 28:30; 1Sa 2:28) may have been used.

had commanded through Moses. 3 Moses had granted the two and a half tribes their inheritance east of the Jordan[l] but had not granted the Levites an inheritance among the rest,[m] 4 for Joseph's descendants had become two tribes—Manasseh and Ephraim.[n] The Levites received no share of the land but only towns to live in, with pasturelands for their flocks and herds.[o] 5 So the Israelites divided the land, just as the LORD had commanded Moses.[p]

Allotment for Caleb

6 Now the people of Judah approached Joshua at Gilgal,[q] and Caleb son of Jephunneh[r] the Kenizzite said to him, "You know what the LORD said to Moses the man of God[s] at Kadesh Barnea[t] about you and me.[u] 7 I was forty years old when Moses the servant of the LORD sent me from Kadesh Barnea[v] to explore the land.[w] And I brought him back a report according to my convictions,[x] 8 but my fellow Israelites who went up with me made the hearts of the people melt in fear.[y] I, however, followed the LORD my God wholeheartedly.[z] 9 So on that day Moses swore to me, 'The land on which your feet have walked will be your inheritance[a] and that of your children[b] forever, because you have followed the LORD my God wholeheartedly.'[a]

10 "Now then, just as the LORD promised,[c] he has kept me alive for forty-five years since the time he said this to Moses, while Israel moved[d] about in the wilderness. So here I am today, eighty-five years old![e] 11 I am still as strong[f] today as the day Moses sent me out; I'm just as vigorous[g] to go out to battle now as I was then. 12 Now give me this hill country that the LORD promised me that day.[h] You yourself heard then that the Anakites[i] were there and their cities were large and fortified,[j] but, the LORD helping me, I will drive them out just as he said."

13 Then Joshua blessed[k] Caleb son of Jephunneh[l] and gave him Hebron[m] as his inheritance.[n] 14 So Hebron has belonged to Caleb son of Jephunneh the Kenizzite ever since, because he followed the LORD, the God of Israel, wholeheartedly.[o] 15 (Hebron used to be called Kiriath Arba[p] after Arba,[q] who was the greatest man among the Anakites.)

Then the land had rest[r] from war.

Allotment for Judah

15:15-19pp — Jdg 1:11-15

15 The allotment for the tribe of Judah, according to its clans, extended down to the territory of Edom,[s] to the Desert of Zin[t] in the extreme south.[u]

2 Their southern boundary started from the bay at the southern end of the Dead Sea,[v] 3 crossed south of Scorpion Pass,[w] continued on to Zin and went over to the south of Kadesh Barnea.[x] Then it ran past Hezron up to Addar and curved around to Karka. 4 It then passed along to Azmon[y] and joined the Wadi of Egypt,[z] ending at the Mediterranean Sea. This is their[b] southern boundary.

5 The eastern boundary[a] is the Dead Sea[b] as far as the mouth of the Jordan.

The northern boundary[c] started from the bay of the sea at the mouth

[a] 9 Deut. 1:36 [b] 4 Septuagint; Hebrew *your*

14:3 [l]S Nu 32:33; S 34:14 [m]S Nu 35:2; S Jos 13:14 **14:4** [n]S Ge 41:52; S Jdg 1:29 [o]S Nu 35:2-3; Jos 21:2 **14:5** [p]S Nu 34:13 **14:6** [q]S Dt 11:30 [r]Nu 13:6; 14:30 [s]S Dt 33:1 [t]Nu 13:26 [u]S Nu 14:38 **14:7** [v]Jos 15:3 [w]S Nu 13:17 [x]Nu 13:30; S 14:6-9 **14:8** [y]S Nu 13:31 [z]S Nu 14:24; S 32:12 **14:9** [a]S Dt 11:24 [b]S Nu 14:24 **14:10** [c]S Nu 11:28; 14:30 [d]S Jos 5:6 [e]S Jos 13:1 **14:11** [f]S Dt 34:7 [g]S Ge 15:15 **14:12** [h]S Nu 14:24 [i]S Nu 13:33 [j]Nu 13:28 **14:13** [k]Jos 22:6,7 [l]1Sa 25:3; 30:14 [m]S Ge 23:19; S Jos 10:36 [n]Jdg 1:20; 1Ch 6:56 **14:14** [o]S Nu 14:24 **14:15** [p]S Ge 23:2 [q]Jos 15:13 [r]Jos 11:23; Jdg 3:11; 1Ki 4:24; 5:4; 1Ch 22:9 **15:1** [s]Nu 34:3 [t]S Nu 13:21 [u]Jos 18:5

15:2 [v]S Ge 14:3 **15:3** [w]S Nu 34:4 [x]S Dt 1:2 **15:4** [y]Nu 34:4 [z]S Ge 15:18 **15:5** [a]Nu 34:10 [b]S Ge 14:3 [c]Jos 18:15-19

14:4 *Manasseh and Ephraim.* Sons of Joseph. Since Jacob had adopted them as his own sons (Ge 48:5), they constituted two separate tribes. This made possible the 12-part nation, with the Levites serving as a nonpolitical tribe.

14:6–15 Assignment of Hebron to Caleb—in accordance with Moses' pledge to him for his faithful service as one of Israel's spies sent to explore the promised land (see Nu 14:24,30; 32:12 and note on 14:24). Assignments of cities in Canaan to Caleb (Judah) and Joshua (Ephraim) frame the account of territorial divisions west of the Jordan (see 19:49–50 and note on 19:49).

14:6 *what the LORD said.* Caleb now recalls the promise from the Lord 45 years earlier at Kadesh Barnea (see note on 11:18) when he brought back a good report of the land (Nu 13:30; 14:6–9; Dt 1:34–36).

14:8 *followed ... wholeheartedly.* See Nu 14:24 and note; 32:12.

14:12 *this hill country.* Hebron is situated high in the Judahite hill country, about 25 miles south of Jerusalem. *Anakites.* See note on 11:21.

14:15 *Kiriath Arba.* Means "the town of Arba" and was named for Arba, the father of the Anakites (15:13; 21:11). It can also mean "the town of four," possibly referring to Anak and his three descendants (see 15:14; Nu 13:22 and note; Jdg 1:20). *Then the land had rest from war.* Since the Judahites and Caleb approached Joshua concerning their territory while he was still headquartered at Gilgal, it may be that they did so shortly before the wars fought under Joshua were ended (see 11:23).

15:1–63 Judah is the first of the west bank tribes to have its territory delineated. First the outer limits are listed, then the area apportioned to Caleb and Othniel; finally the Canaanite cities allotted to the clans of Judah are named region by region.

15:1 *tribe of Judah.* Judah's priority is anchored in the blessing of Jacob (Ge 49:8–12) and upheld in the history of the nation (Jdg 1:1–2; 20:18; 2Ki 17:18; Ps 78:68).

15:4 *southern boundary.* The points listed formed a curved line beginning at the lower tip of the Dead Sea and moving under Kadesh Barnea to join the Mediterranean coast at the mouth of the Wadi el-Arish (see note on 13:3).

15:5 *northern boundary.* Judah's border with Benjamin ran in a westerly line from the mouth of the Jordan through the Hinnom Valley, just south of Jerusalem, over to Timnah, then northwest to the coastal city of Jabneel (later called Jamnia), about ten miles south of Joppa.

DISTANCES IN MILES BETWEEN OLD TESTAMENT CITIES

(1 mile = 1.6 kilometers)

	ASHKELON	BABYLON	BEERSHEBA	BETHEL	BETH SHAN	CARCHEMISH	DAMASCUS	DAN	HARRAN	HAZOR	HEBRON	JERICHO	JERUSALEM	JOPPA	LACHISH	MARI	MEGIDDO	MEMPHIS	NINEVEH	SAMARIA	SHECHEM	SIDON	SUSA	THEBES	TYRE	UR
Ashkelon		900	36	48	87	454	178	139	519	117	36	57	44	32	21	653	80	269	726	60	63	155	1118	601	133	1070
Babylon	900		930	869	823	479	724	764	442	783	901	869	880	868	907	251	824	1172	264	845	847	779	218	1504	792	170
Beersheba	36	930		58	104	484	206	166	549	147	28	61	47	62	25	679	116	259	752	80	78	190	1148	591	176	1100
Bethel	48	869	58		47	423	145	105	488	86	31	12	11	32	40	618	50	303	691	26	22	129	1087	635	115	1039
Beth Shan	87	823	104	47		377	92	59	442	40	78	45	57	59	86	572	21	349	645	27	26	82	1041	681	62	993
Carchemish	454	479	484	423	377		278	318	65	337	455	423	434	366	461	228	378	726	285	399	401	333	697	1058	346	649
Damascus	178	724	206	145	92	278		45	343	59	177	134	149	133	181	473	98	441	546	121	123	55	942	773	68	894
Dan	139	764	166	105	59	318	45		383	19	137	105	116	104	142	513	59	408	586	80	82	29	982	740	28	934
Harran	519	442	549	488	442	65	343	383		402	520	488	500	396	526	191	443	791	215	464	466	398	660	1123	411	612
Hazor	117	783	147	86	40	337	59	19	402		118	86	97	85	124	532	41	389	605	62	64	43	1001	721	29	953
Hebron	36	901	28	31	78	455	177	137	520	118		36	21	45	17	650	80	297	723	51	53	161	1119	629	147	1071
Jericho	57	869	61	12	45	423	134	105	488	86	36		15	43	44	618	54	307	691	32	26	129	1087	639	115	1039
Jerusalem	44	880	47	11	57	434	149	116	500	97	21	15		36	29	629	61	292	702	37	33	140	1098	624	126	1050
Joppa	32	868	62	32	59	366	133	104	396	85	45	43	36		37	372	53	301	548	31	36	112	1086	633	89	1038
Lachish	21	907	25	40	86	461	181	142	526	124	17	44	29	37		656	83	281	729	66	62	158	1125	613	136	1077
Mari	653	251	679	618	572	228	473	513	191	532	650	618	629	372	656		573	921	173	594	596	528	469	1253	541	421
Megiddo	80	824	116	50	21	378	98	59	443	41	80	54	61	53	83	573		348	646	25	29	75	1042	680	53	994
Memphis	269	1172	259	303	349	726	441	408	791	389	297	307	292	301	281	921	348		994	329	325	424	1390	332	402	1342
Nineveh	726	264	752	691	645	285	546	586	215	605	723	691	702	548	729	173	646	994		667	669	601	453	1326	614	434
Samaria	60	845	80	26	27	399	121	80	464	62	51	32	37	31	66	594	25	329	667		8	105	1063	661	77	1015
Shechem	63	847	78	22	26	401	123	82	466	64	53	26	33	36	62	596	29	325	669	8		107	1065	657	80	1017
Sidon	155	779	190	129	82	333	55	29	398	43	161	129	140	112	158	528	75	424	601	105	107		997	755	25	949
Susa	1118	218	1148	1087	1041	697	942	982	660	1001	1119	1087	1098	1086	1125	469	1042	1390	453	1063	1065	997		1722	1110	145
Thebes	601	1504	591	635	681	1058	773	740	1123	721	629	639	624	633	613	1253	680	332	1326	661	657	755	1722		733	1674
Tyre	133	792	176	115	62	346	68	28	411	29	147	115	126	89	136	541	53	402	614	77	80	25	1110	733		962
Ur	1070	170	1100	1039	993	649	894	934	612	953	1071	1039	1050	1038	1077	421	994	1342	434	1015	1017	949	145	1674	962	

Note: These distances are meant only as rough estimates. They do not take into account terrain obstacles, although they do, for the most part, follow ancient routes (e.g., around the Fertile Crescent rather than across the desert).

of the Jordan, 6 went up to Beth Hoglah[d] and continued north of Beth Arabah[e] to the Stone of Bohan[f] son of
Reuben. 7 The boundary then went
up to Debir[g] from the Valley of Achor[h]
and turned north to Gilgal,[i] which
faces the Pass of Adummim south of
the gorge. It continued along to the
waters of En Shemesh[j] and came out
at En Rogel.[k] 8 Then it ran up the Valley of Ben Hinnom[l] along the southern slope of the Jebusite[m] city (that is,
Jerusalem[n]). From there it climbed to
the top of the hill west of the Hinnom
Valley[o] at the northern end of the Valley of Rephaim.[p] 9 From the hilltop the
boundary headed toward the spring of
the waters of Nephtoah,[q] came out at
the towns of Mount Ephron and went
down toward Baalah[r] (that is, Kiriath Jearim).[s] 10 Then it curved westward from Baalah[t] to Mount Seir,[u] ran
along the northern slope of Mount

15:6 [d] Jos 18:19, 21 [e] ver 61; Jos 18:18 [f] Jos 18:17 **15:7** [g] S Jos 10:3 [h] S Jos 7:24 [i] S Dt 11:30 [j] Jos 18:17 [k] Jos 18:16; 2Sa 17:17; 1Ki 1:9 **15:8** [l] 2Ch 28:3; Jer 19:6 [m] ver 63; Jos 18:16, 28; Jdg 1:21; 19:10; 2Sa 5:6; 1Ch 11:4; Ezr 9:1 [n] S Jos 10:1 [o] 2Ki 23:10; Jer 7:31; 19:2 [p] 2Sa 5:18, 22; 1Ch 14:9; Isa 17:5 **15:9** [q] Jos 18:15 [r] ver 10, 11, 29; 2Sa 6:2; 1Ch 13:6 [s] S Jos 9:17 **15:10** [t] S ver 9 [u] S Nu 24:18

15:7 *Gilgal.* See note on Jdg 3:19.

Jearim (that is, Kesalon), continued
down to Beth Shemesh[v] and crossed
to Timnah.[w] 11 It went to the northern
slope of Ekron,[x] turned toward Shik-
keron, passed along to Mount Baalah[y]
and reached Jabneel.[z] The boundary
ended at the sea.
12 The western boundary is the
coastline of the Mediterranean Sea.[a]

These are the boundaries around the
people of Judah by their clans.

13 In accordance with the LORD's command to him, Joshua gave to Caleb[b] son
of Jephunneh a portion in Judah—Kiriath Arba[c], that is, Hebron.[d] (Arba was the
forefather of Anak.)[e] 14 From Hebron Caleb
drove out the three Anakites[f]—Sheshai,
Ahiman and Talmai,[g] the sons of Anak.[h]
15 From there he marched against the people living in Debir (formerly called Kiriath
Sepher). 16 And Caleb said, "I will give my
daughter Aksah[i] in marriage to the man
who attacks and captures Kiriath Sepher."
17 Othniel[j] son of Kenaz, Caleb's brother,
took it; so Caleb gave his daughter Aksah
to him in marriage.
18 One day when she came to Othni-
el, she urged him[a] to ask her father for a
field. When she got off her donkey, Caleb
asked her, "What can I do for you?"
19 She replied, "Do me a special favor.
Since you have given me land in the Negev,[k] give me also springs of water." So Caleb gave her the upper and lower springs.[l]

20 This is the inheritance of the tribe of
Judah, according to its clans:

21 The southernmost towns of the tribe of
Judah in the Negev[m] toward the boundary
of Edom were:
Kabzeel,[n] Eder,[o] Jagur, 22 Kinah, Di-
monah, Adadah, 23 Kedesh,[p] Hazor,[q]
Ithnan, 24 Ziph,[r] Telem, Bealoth, 25 Hazor Hadattah, Kerioth Hezron (that
is, Hazor),[s] 26 Amam, Shema, Moladah,[t] 27 Hazar Gaddah, Heshmon, Beth
Pelet, 28 Hazar Shual,[u] Beersheba,[v]
Biziothiah, 29 Baalah,[w] Iyim, Ezem,[x]
30 Eltolad,[y] Kesil, Hormah,[z] 31 Ziklag,[a]
Madmannah,[b] Sansannah, 32 Lebaoth,
Shilhim, Ain[c] and Rimmon[d]—a total of
twenty-nine towns and their villages.

33 In the western foothills:
Eshtaol,[e] Zorah,[f] Ashnah,[g] 34 Zanoah,[h] En Gannim,[i] Tappuah,[j] Enam,
35 Jarmuth,[k] Adullam,[l] Sokoh,[m] Azekah,[n] 36 Shaaraim,[o] Adithaim and Gederah[p] (or Gederothaim)[b]—fourteen
towns and their villages.
37 Zenan, Hadashah, Migdal Gad,
38 Dilean, Mizpah,[q] Joktheel,[r] 39 Lachish,[s] Bozkath,[t] Eglon,[u] 40 Kabbon,
Lahmas, Kitlish, 41 Gederoth,[v] Beth
Dagon,[w] Naamah and Makkedah[x]—
sixteen towns and their villages.
42 Libnah,[y] Ether, Ashan,[z] 43 Iphtah,
Ashnah,[a] Nezib, 44 Keilah,[b] Akzib[c] and
Mareshah[d]—nine towns and their villages.
45 Ekron,[e] with its surrounding settlements and villages; 46 west of Ekron, all that were in the vicinity of
Ashdod,[f] together with their villages; 47 Ashdod,[g] its surrounding settlements and villages; and Gaza, its
settlements and villages, as far as the
Wadi of Egypt[h] and the coastline of
the Mediterranean Sea.[i]

48 In the hill country:
Shamir,[j] Jattir,[k] Sokoh,[l] 49 Dannah,
Kiriath Sannah (that is, Debir[m]),
50 Anab,[n] Eshtemoh,[o] Anim, 51 Goshen,[p] Holon[q] and Giloh[r]—eleven
towns and their villages.
52 Arab, Dumah,[s] Eshan, 53 Janim,
Beth Tappuah, Aphekah, 54 Humtah,
Kiriath Arba[t] (that is, Hebron) and
Zior—nine towns and their villages.
55 Maon,[u] Carmel,[v] Ziph,[w] Juttah,[x]
56 Jezreel,[y] Jokdeam, Zanoah,[z] 57 Kain,
Gibeah[a] and Timnah[b]—ten towns
and their villages.
58 Halhul, Beth Zur,[c] Gedor,[d] 59 Ma-

[a] *18* Hebrew and some Septuagint manuscripts; other Septuagint manuscripts (see also note at Judges 1:14) *Othniel, he urged her* [b] *36* Or *Gederah and Gederothaim*

15:10 [v] Jos 19:22, 38; 21:16; Jdg 1:33; 1Sa 6:9; 1Ki 4:9; 2Ki 14:11 [w] S Ge 38:12 **15:11** [x] S Jos 13:3 [y] S ver 9 [z] Jos 19:33 **15:12** [a] S Nu 34:6 **15:13** [b] 1Sa 25:3; 30:14 [c] S Ge 23:2 [d] S Jos 10:36; 21:12; 1Ch 6:56 [e] S Nu 13:22 **15:14** [f] S Nu 13:33 [g] S Nu 13:22 [h] Jdg 1:10, 20 **15:16** [i] 1Ch 2:49 **15:17** [j] Jdg 3:9, 11; 1Ch 4:13; 27:15 **15:19** [k] S Jos 10:40 [l] Ge 36:24 **15:21** [m] S Jos 10:40 [n] 2Sa 23:20; 1Ch 11:22 [o] Ge 35:21 **15:23** [p] S Jos 12:22 [q] S Jos 11:1 **15:24** [r] ver 55; 1Sa 23:14; 2Ch 11:8 **15:25** [s] S Jos 11:1 **15:26** [t] Jos 19:2; 1Ch 4:28; Ne 11:26 **15:28** [u] Jos 19:3; 1Ch 4:28 [v] S Ge 21:14 **15:29** [w] S ver 9 [x] Jos 19:3; 1Ch 4:29 **15:30** [y] Jos 19:4 [z] S Nu 14:45 **15:31** [a] Jos 19:5; 1Sa 27:6; 1Ch 4:30; 12:1; Ne 11:28 [b] 1Ch 2:49 **15:32** [c] S Nu 34:11 [d] Jos 19:7; Jdg 20:45; 21:13; Zec 14:10 **15:33** [e] Jos 19:41; Jdg 13:25; 16:31; 18:2 [f] Jdg 13:2; 18:11; 2Ch 11:10; Ne 11:29 [g] ver 43 **15:34** [h] ver 56; 1Ch 4:18; Ne 3:13; 11:30 [i] Jos 19:21; 21:29 [j] S Jos 12:17 **15:35** [k] S Jos 10:3 [l] S Ge 38:1 [m] ver 48; 1Ki 4:10 [n] S Jos 10:10 **15:36** [o] 1Sa 17:52; 1Ch 4:31 [p] 1Ch 12:4 **15:38** [q] S Jos 11:3 [r] 2Ki 14:7 **15:39** [s] S Jos 10:3 [t] 2Ki 22:1 [u] S Jos 10:3 **15:41** [v] 2Ch 28:18 [w] Jos 19:27 [x] S Jos 10:10 **15:42** [y] S Nu 33:20 [z] Jos 19:7; 1Sa 30:30; 1Ch 4:32; 6:59 **15:43** [a] ver 33 **15:44** [b] 1Sa 23:1-2, 1; 1Ch 4:19; Ne 3:17, 18 [c] Jos 19:29; Jdg 1:31; Mic 1:14 [d] Mic 1:15 **15:45** [e] S Jos 13:3 **15:46** [f] Jos 11:22 **15:47** [g] S Jos 11:22 [h] S Ge 15:18 [i] S Nu 34:6 **15:48** [j] Jdg 10:1 [k] Jos 21:14; 1Sa 30:27; 1Ch 6:57 [l] S ver 35 **15:49** [m] S Jos 10:3 **15:50** [n] Jos 11:21 [o] Jos 21:14; 1Sa 30:28 **15:51** [p] S Jos 10:41 [q] Jos 21:15; Jer 48:21 [r] 2Sa 15:12 **15:52** [s] S Ge 25:14 **15:54** [t] S Ge 35:27 **15:55** [u] Jdg 10:12; 1Sa 23:24, 25; 25:1, 2; 1Ch 2:45 [v] S Jos 12:22 [w] S ver 24 [x] Jos 21:16 **15:56** [y] Jos 17:16; 19:18; Jdg 6:33; 1Sa 25:43; 1Ki 18:45; 1Ch 3:1; Hos 1:5 [z] S ver 34 **15:57** [a] Jos 18:28; 24:33; Jdg 19:12; 20:4; 2Sa 23:29; 1Ch 11:31 [b] S Ge 38:12 **15:58** [c] 1Ch 2:45; 2Ch 11:7; Ne 3:16 [d] 1Ch 4:39; 12:7

15:15 *he marched against … Debir.* See note on 10:38.
15:17 *Othniel.* See Jdg 3:7–11 for his service as judge in Israel.
15:21 *southernmost towns.* Most of the first 29 villages were assigned to the tribe of Simeon (cf. 19:1–9).
15:33 *western foothills.* This area between the highlands of central Judah and the Philistine coast was for the most part not occupied by Israel until the victories of King David. Some of the places on this list were reassigned to the tribe of Dan (cf. 19:41–43).
15:48 *hill country.* The high region south of Jerusalem. The Septuagint (the pre-Christian Greek translation of the OT) adds 11 names, including Tekoa and Bethlehem, to this list.

arath, Beth Anoth and Eltekon — six
towns and their villages.[a]
60 Kiriath Baal[e] (that is, Kiriath Jearim[f]) and Rabbah[g] — two towns and
their villages.

61 In the wilderness:[h]
Beth Arabah,[i] Middin, Sekakah,
62 Nibshan, the City of Salt and En
Gedi[j] — six towns and their villages.
63 Judah could not[k] dislodge the Jebusites[l], who were living in Jerusalem;[m] to
this day the Jebusites live there with the
people of Judah.[n]

Allotment for Ephraim and Manasseh

16 The allotment for Joseph began at the Jordan, east of the
springs of Jericho, and went up from
there through the desert[o] into the hill
country of Bethel.[p] 2 It went on from
Bethel (that is, Luz[q]),[b] crossed over
to the territory of the Arkites[r] in Ataroth,[s] 3 descended westward to the
territory of the Japhletites as far as
the region of Lower Beth Horon[t] and
on to Gezer,[u] ending at the Mediterranean Sea.
4 So Manasseh and Ephraim, the descendants of Joseph, received their inheritance.[v]

5 This was the territory of Ephraim, according to its clans:

The boundary of their inheritance
went from Ataroth Addar[w] in the east
to Upper Beth Horon[x] 6 and continued
to the Mediterranean Sea. From Mikmethath[y] on the north it curved eastward to Taanath Shiloh, passing by it
to Janoah[z] on the east. 7 Then it went
down from Janoah[a] to Ataroth[b] and
Naarah, touched Jericho and came
out at the Jordan. 8 From Tappuah[c] the
border went west to the Kanah Ravine[d] and ended at the Mediterranean
Sea. This was the inheritance of the
tribe of the Ephraimites, according
to its clans. 9 It also included all the
towns and their villages that were set
aside for the Ephraimites within the
inheritance of the Manassites.[e]
10 They did not dislodge the Canaanites living in Gezer; to this day the Canaanites
live among the people of Ephraim but are
required to do forced labor.[f]

17 This was the allotment for the
tribe of Manasseh[g] as Joseph's
firstborn,[h] that is, for Makir,[i] Manasseh's
firstborn. Makir was the ancestor of the
Gileadites, who had received Gilead[j] and
Bashan[k] because the Makirites were great
soldiers. 2 So this allotment was for the rest
of the people of Manasseh[l] — the clans of
Abiezer,[m] Helek, Asriel,[n] Shechem, Hepher[o] and Shemida.[p] These are the other
male descendants of Manasseh son of Joseph by their clans.
3 Now Zelophehad son of Hepher,[q] the
son of Gilead, the son of Makir, the son of
Manasseh, had no sons but only daughters,[r]
whose names were Mahlah, Noah, Hoglah,
Milkah and Tirzah. 4 They went to Eleazar
the priest, Joshua son of Nun, and the leaders and said, "The LORD commanded Moses
to give us an inheritance among our relatives." So Joshua gave them an inheritance
along with the brothers of their father, according to the LORD's command.[s] 5 Manasseh's share consisted of ten tracts of land
besides Gilead and Bashan east of the Jordan,[t] 6 because the daughters of the tribe of
Manasseh received an inheritance among
the sons. The land of Gilead belonged to
the rest of the descendants of Manasseh.
7 The territory of Manasseh extended from Asher[u] to Mikmethath[v] east of

15:60 [e] ver 9 [f] S Jos 9:17 [g] S Dt 3:11 **15:61** [h] S Jos 8:15 [i] S ver 6 **15:62** [j] 1Sa 23:29; 24:1; Eze 47:10 **15:63** [k] Jos 16:10; 17:12; Jdg 1:21; 1Ki 9:21 [l] S ver 8 [m] S Jos 10:1 [n] Eze 48:7 **16:1** [o] S Jos 8:15 [p] S Jos 12:9 **16:2** [q] S Ge 28:19 [r] 2Sa 15:32 [s] S ver 5; S Nu 32:3 **16:3** [t] S Jos 10:10 [u] S Jos 10:33 **16:4** [v] Jos 18:5 **16:5** [w] ver 2; Jos 18:13 [x] S Jos 10:10 **16:6** [y] Jos 17:7 [z] ver 7; 2Ki 15:29 **16:7** [a] S ver 6 [b] S Nu 32:3 **16:8** [c] S Jos 12:17 [d] Jos 17:9; 19:28 **16:9** [e] Eze 48:5 **16:10** [f] S Jos 15:63; 17:13; Jdg 1:28-29; 1Ki 9:16 **17:1** [g] S Nu 1:34; 1Ch 7:14 [h] S Ge 41:51 [i] S Ge 50:23 [j] S Jos 12:2 [k] S Jos 12:5 **17:2** [l] Jos 22:7 [m] S Nu 26:30; Jdg 6:11,34; 8:2; 1Ch 7:18 [n] 1Ch 7:14 [o] S Nu 27:1 [p] 1Ch 7:19 **17:3** [q] S Nu 27:1 [r] S Nu 26:33 **17:4** [s] Nu 27:5-7 **17:5** [t] Jos 13:30-31 **17:7** [u] ver 10; Jos 19:24,31; 21:6,30; Jdg 1:31; 5:17; 6:35; 7:23 [v] Jos 16:6

[a] 59 The Septuagint adds another district of eleven towns, including Tekoa and Ephrathah (Bethlehem).
[b] 2 Septuagint; Hebrew *Bethel to Luz*

15:61 – 62 The "wilderness" is the chalky, dry region east and south of Jerusalem that borders the Dead Sea. Of the places named, only En Gedi can be positively located. However, either Sekakah or the City of Salt may have been the ancient name of the site of Qumran, where the scribes who produced the Dead Sea Scrolls lived.

15:63 *Jebusites.* A victory over the city of the Jebusites by the men of Judah is recorded in Jdg 1:8, but evidently this did not result in its permanent occupation. Both Benjamin and Judah failed to take the Jebusite fortress of Jerusalem (Jdg 1:21).

16:1 — 17:18 Two chapters are devoted to the lands given to the "descendants of Joseph" (16:4), consisting of Ephraim and the half-tribe of Manasseh that settled west of the Jordan. Following Judah, the Joseph tribes were given priority in the allotting of territory.

16:1 *allotment for Joseph.* The southern border of the Joseph tribes moved west from Jericho past Bethel and down to Gezer and the Mediterranean coast.

16:5 *boundary.* Ephraim's northern border began at the edge of the Jordan Valley and ran west near Shiloh, but south of Shechem, then followed the Wadi Kanah down to the Mediterranean Sea.

16:10 *Gezer.* See note on 10:33. *required to do forced labor.* On projects undertaken by public officials, usually the king (2Sa 12:13; 1Ki 9:15,20 – 21).

17:1 *Manasseh as Joseph's firstborn.* A reminder that Manasseh was the firstborn, though Jacob had given priority to Ephraim when he adopted Joseph's two sons (Ge 48:14,19).

17:3 *Zelophehad ... had ... only daughters.* See notes on Nu 27:1 – 11; 36:1 – 3.

17:5 *ten tracts of land.* Manasseh's territory was second only to Judah's in size. The ten portions went to the five brothers (minus Hepher) and to the five granddaughters of Hepher.

Shechem.[w] The boundary ran southward from there to include the people
living at En Tappuah. 8 (Manasseh had
the land of Tappuah, but Tappuah[x] itself, on the boundary of Manasseh,
belonged to the Ephraimites.) 9 Then
the boundary continued south to the
Kanah Ravine.[y] There were towns belonging to Ephraim lying among the
towns of Manasseh, but the boundary
of Manasseh was the northern side of
the ravine and ended at the Mediterranean Sea. 10 On the south the land
belonged to Ephraim, on the north to
Manasseh. The territory of Manasseh
reached the Mediterranean Sea and
bordered Asher[z] on the north and Issachar[a] on the east.[b]
11 Within Issachar[c] and Asher, Manasseh also had Beth Shan,[d] Ibleam[e]
and the people of Dor,[f] Endor,[g] Taanach[h] and Megiddo,[i] together with
their surrounding settlements (the
third in the list is Naphoth[a]).[j]
12 Yet the Manassites were not able[k] to occupy these towns, for the Canaanites were
determined to live in that region. 13 However, when the Israelites grew stronger,
they subjected the Canaanites to forced labor but did not drive them out completely.[l]
14 The people of Joseph said to Joshua,
"Why have you given us only one allotment and one portion for an inheritance?
We are a numerous people, and the LORD
has blessed us abundantly."[m]
15 "If you are so numerous," Joshua answered, "and if the hill country of Ephraim
is too small for you, go up into the forest[n]
and clear land for yourselves there in the
land of the Perizzites[o] and Rephaites.[p]"
16 The people of Joseph replied, "The
hill country is not enough for us, and all
the Canaanites who live in the plain have
chariots fitted with iron,[q] both those in
Beth Shan[r] and its settlements and those
in the Valley of Jezreel."[s]
17 But Joshua said to the tribes of Joseph—to Ephraim and Manasseh—"You
are numerous and very powerful. You will
have not only one allotment[t] 18 but the forested hill country[u] as well. Clear it, and its
farthest limits will be yours; though the
Canaanites have chariots fitted with iron[v]
and though they are strong, you can drive
them out."

Division of the Rest of the Land

18 The whole assembly of the Israelites gathered at Shiloh[w] and set
up the tent of meeting[x] there. The country was brought under their control, 2 but
there were still seven Israelite tribes who
had not yet received their inheritance.
3 So Joshua said to the Israelites: "How
long will you wait before you begin to
take possession of the land that the LORD,
the God of your ancestors, has given you?
4 Appoint three men from each tribe. I will
send them out to make a survey of the land
and to write a description of it,[y] according
to the inheritance of each.[z] Then they will
return to me. 5 You are to divide the land
into seven parts. Judah is to remain in its
territory on the south[a] and the tribes of Joseph in their territory on the north.[b] 6 After
you have written descriptions of the seven
parts of the land, bring them here to me
and I will cast lots[c] for you in the presence

[a] 11 That is, Naphoth Dor

17:7 [w] S Ge 12:6; Jos 21:21; 24:25; Jdg 9:1 **17:8** [x] S Jos 12:17 **17:9** [y] S Jos 16:8 **17:10** [z] S ver 7 [a] S Ge 30:18 [b] Eze 48:5 **17:11** [c] ver 10 [d] ver 16; Jdg 1:27; 1Sa 31:10; 2Sa 21:12; 1Ki 4:12; 1Ch 7:29 [e] 2Ki 9:27 [f] S Jos 11:2 [g] 1Sa 28:7; Ps 83:10 [h] S Jos 12:21 [i] 1Ki 9:15 [j] Eze 48:4 **17:12** [k] S Jos 15:63 **17:13** [l] Jdg 1:27-28 **17:14** [m] Nu 26:28-37 **17:15** [n] 2Sa 18:6 [o] S Jos 3:10 [p] S Ge 14:5; Jos 15:8; 18:16; 2Sa 5:18; 23:13; Isa 17:5 **17:16** [q] ver 18; Jdg 1:19; 4:3, 13 [r] S ver 11 [s] S Jos 15:56; S 1Sa 29:1 **17:17** [t] Eze 48:5 **17:18** [u] 1Sa 1:1 [v] S ver 16 **18:1** [w] ver 8; Jos 19:51; 21:2; Jdg 18:31; 21:12,19; 1Sa 1:3; 3:21; 4:3; 1Ki 14:2; Ps 78:60; Jer 7:12; 26:6; 41:5 [x] S ver 10; S Ex 27:21; S 40:2; Ac 7:45 **18:4** [y] ver 8 [z] Mic 2:5

18:5 [a] Jos 15:1 [b] Jos 16:1-4 **18:6** [c] S Lev 16:8

17:11 *Beth Shan ... Megiddo.* These powerfully fortified cities (and others) were not conquered until later. When King Saul died in battle, the victorious Philistines fastened his body to the wall of Beth Shan (see 1Sa 31:10), which suggests that that city was in league with the Philistines.
17:13 *when the Israelites grew stronger.* Possibly referring to the days of David and Solomon (see note on 16:10).
17:14 *people of Joseph ... numerous.* The reference is to both Ephraim and Manasseh (see v. 17). The allotment to the Joseph tribes is here handled as one (see 16:1,4)—though the two subdivisions are then described separately (16:5—17:11).
17:15 *hill country of Ephraim.* The territory of the Joseph tribes—under the name of the legal firstborn (see note on v. 1). *clear land for yourselves.* This region of Canaan was still heavily forested. It seems that the Israelites viewed their assigned territories primarily in terms of the number of cities that had their land cleared for farming and pasturage, not in terms of the size of the region in which these cities were located. The region assigned to the Joseph tribes was at the time not as heavily populated as others. *Perizzites and Rephaites.* Here listed as neighboring peoples, though elsewhere the Perizzites are said to have lived on the west bank in Canaan (3:10; 12:8) and the Rephaites in the Transjordan kingdom of Og (12:4; 13:12). See notes on Ge 13:7; Dt 2:11.
17:16 *in the plain.* Only in the plains were chariots effective. *chariots fitted with iron.* Wooden chariots with certain parts made of iron (see note on 2Sa 8:7), perhaps the axles. This use of iron was a new development. Israel did not employ chariots until much later (see note on 11:6).
18:1—19:51 Seven tribes remained to be assigned land: Benjamin, Simeon, Zebulun, Issachar, Asher, Naphtali and Dan. Their lots were cast at Shiloh.
18:1 *Shiloh.* About ten miles northeast of Bethel, a little east of the main road from Bethel to Shechem. *tent of meeting.* The tabernacle (see note on Ex 27:21) with its sacred ark of the covenant. It would remain at Shiloh until the time of Samuel (1Sa 4:3).
18:3 *take possession.* Conquest had to be followed by settlement, which required a survey, then a fair distribution, and then a full occupation of the land. A distinction must therefore be made between the national wars of conquest (Joshua) and the tribal wars of occupation (see Jdg 1–2 and note on 1:1).
18:5 *north.* Relative to the territory of Judah.
18:6 *I will cast lots for you.* See note on 14:1.

of the LORD our God. 7 The Levites, however, do not get a portion among you, because the priestly service of the LORD is their inheritance.[d] And Gad, Reuben and the half-tribe of Manasseh have already received their inheritance on the east side of the Jordan. Moses the servant of the LORD gave it to them.[e]"

8 As the men started on their way to map out the land, Joshua instructed them, "Go and make a survey of the land and write a description of it.[f] Then return to me, and I will cast lots for you here at Shiloh[g] in the presence of the LORD." 9 So the men left and went through the land. They wrote its description on a scroll, town by town, in seven parts, and returned to Joshua in the camp at Shiloh. 10 Joshua then cast lots[h] for them in Shiloh in the presence[i] of the LORD, and there he distributed the land to the Israelites according to their tribal divisions.[j]

Allotment for Benjamin

11 The first lot came up for the tribe of Benjamin according to its clans. Their allotted territory lay between the tribes of Judah and Joseph:

12 On the north side their boundary began at the Jordan, passed the northern slope of Jericho and headed west into the hill country, coming out at the wilderness[k] of Beth Aven.[l] 13 From there it crossed to the south slope of Luz[m] (that is, Bethel[n]) and went down to Ataroth Addar[o] on the hill south of Lower Beth Horon.

14 From the hill facing Beth Horon[p] on the south the boundary turned south along the western side and came out at Kiriath Baal (that is, Kiriath Jearim),[q] a town of the people of Judah. This was the western side.

15 The southern side began at the outskirts of Kiriath Jearim on the west, and the boundary came out at the spring of the waters of Nephtoah.[r] 16 The boundary went down to the foot of the hill facing the Valley of Ben Hinnom, north of the Valley of Rephaim.[s] It continued down the Hinnom Valley[t] along the southern slope of the Jebusite city and so to En Rogel.[u] 17 It then curved north, went to En Shemesh, continued to Geliloth,[v] which faces the Pass of Adummim,[w] and ran down to the Stone of Bohan[x] son of Reuben. 18 It continued to the northern slope of Beth Arabah[a][y] and on down into the Arabah.[z] 19 It then went to the northern slope of Beth Hoglah[a] and came out at the northern bay of the Dead Sea,[b] at the mouth of the Jordan in the south. This was the southern boundary.

20 The Jordan formed the boundary on the eastern side.

These were the boundaries that marked out the inheritance of the clans of Benjamin on all sides.[c]

21 The tribe of Benjamin, according to its clans, had the following towns:

Jericho, Beth Hoglah,[d] Emek Keziz, 22 Beth Arabah,[e] Zemaraim,[f] Bethel,[g] 23 Avvim,[h] Parah, Ophrah,[i] 24 Kephar Ammoni, Ophni and Geba[j]—twelve towns and their villages.

25 Gibeon,[k] Ramah,[l] Beeroth,[m] 26 Mizpah,[n] Kephirah,[o] Mozah, 27 Rekem, Irpeel, Taralah, 28 Zelah,[p] Haeleph, the Jebusite city[q] (that is, Jerusalem[r]), Gibeah[s] and Kiriath—fourteen towns and their villages.[t]

This was the inheritance of Benjamin for its clans.[u]

Allotment for Simeon

19:2-10pp — 1Ch 4:28-33

19 The second lot came out for the tribe of Simeon according to its clans. Their inheritance lay within the territory of Judah.[v] 2 It included:

Beersheba[w] (or Sheba),[b] Moladah,[x] 3 Hazar Shual,[y] Balah, Ezem,[z] 4 Eltolad,[a] Bethul, Hormah,[b] 5 Ziklag,[c] Beth Markaboth, Hazar Susah, 6 Beth Lebaoth and Sharuhen—thirteen towns and their villages;

[a] 18 Septuagint; Hebrew *slope facing the Arabah*
[b] 2 Or *Beersheba, Sheba*; 1 Chron. 4:28 does not have *Sheba*.

18:7 [d]S Jos 13:33 [e]Jos 13:8 **18:8** [f]ver 4 [g]S ver 1 **18:10** [h]S Nu 34:13 [i]S ver 1; Jer 7:12 [j]Nu 33:54; Jos 19:51 **18:12** [k]S Jos 8:15 [l]S Jos 7:2 **18:13** [m]S Ge 28:19 [n]S Jos 12:9 [o]S Nu 32:3; S Jos 16:5 **18:14** [p]Jos 10:10 [q]S Jos 9:17 **18:15** [r]Jos 15:9 **18:16** [s]S Jos 17:15 [t]Jos 15:8 [u]S Jos 15:7 **18:17** [v]Jos 22:10 [w]Jos 15:7 [x]Jos 15:6 **18:18** [y]S Jos 15:6 [z]S Jos 11:2 **18:19** [a]S Jos 15:6 [b]S Ge 14:3 **18:20** [c]1Sa 9:1 **18:21** [d]S Jos 15:6 **18:22** [e]Jos 15:6 [f]2Ch 13:4 [g]Jos 16:1 **18:23** [h]S Dt 2:23 [i]Jdg 6:11,24; 8:27,32; 9:5; 1Sa 13:17 **18:24** [j]Jos 21:17; 1Sa 13:3,16; 14:5; 1Ki 15:22; 2Ki 23:8; Isa 10:29 **18:25** [k]Jos 9:3 [l]S Jos 10:40; Jdg 4:5; 19:13; Isa 10:29; Jer 31:15; 40:1 [m]S Jos 9:17; Ezr 2:25; Ne 7:29 **18:26** [n]S Jos 11:3 [o]Jos 9:17; Ezr 2:25; Ne 7:29 **18:28** [p]2Sa 21:14 [q]S Jos 15:8 [r]S Jos 10:1 [s]S Jos 15:57 [t]S Jos 9:17 [u]Eze 48:23 **19:1** [v]S Ge 49:7

19:2 [w]S Ge 21:14; 1Ki 19:3 [x]S Jos 15:26 **19:3** [y]S Jos 15:28 [z]S Jos 15:29 **19:4** [a]Jos 15:30 [b]S Nu 14:45 **19:5** [c]S Jos 15:31

18:7 *priestly service of the LORD is their inheritance.* See 13:14; see also Dt 18:1–8 and note on 18:1.

18:9 *scroll.* Presumed form of the document; the Hebrew for this word is not specific.

18:11 *lot … for … Benjamin.* Benjamin's northern border was the same as Ephraim's southern border, and Benjamin's southern border was the same as Judah's northern boundary (see note on 15:5). The areas allotted to Benjamin and Dan (19:40–48) constituted a buffer zone between Judah and Ephraim, the two dominant tribes in Israel. The accounts of allotments to Benjamin and Dan frame the account of allotments made at Shiloh. These two tribes and the location of their allotments would play a significant role in the cycles of narratives related in the book of Judges (see Introduction to Judges: Literary Features and notes on Jdg 3:12–36; 13:1—16:31).

18:23 *Avvim.* The people of Ai.

19:1 *second lot … for … Simeon.* Cities in the Negev within the borders of Judah (15:21; 1Ch 4:24–42; see also Jdg 1:3).

DIVIDING THE LAND

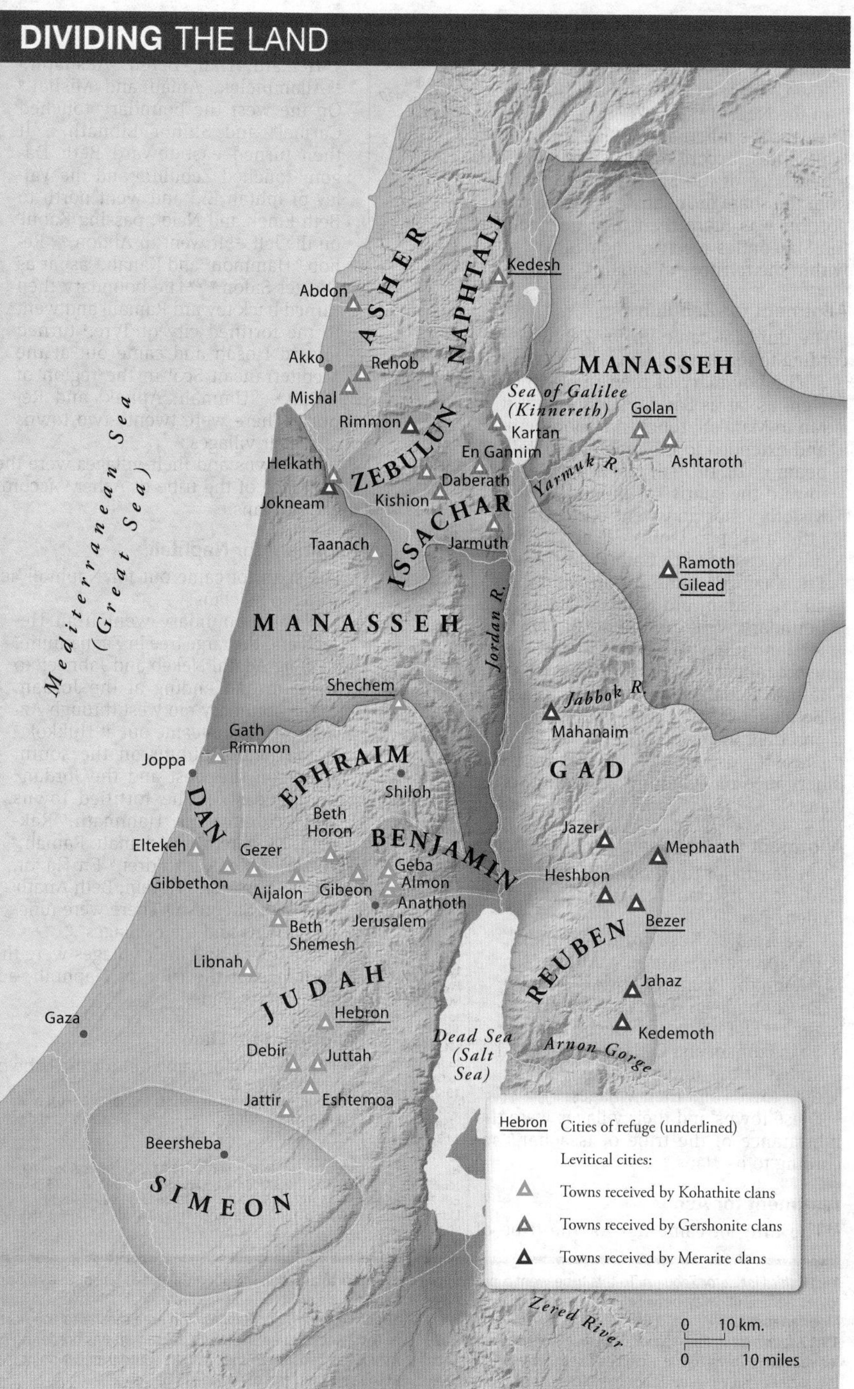

ASHER
NAPHTALI
Kedesh
Abdon
Akko
Rehob
Mishal
MANASSEH
Sea of Galilee (Kinnereth)
Golan
Rimmon
Kartan
ZEBULUN
En Gannim
Ashtaroth
Helkath
Daberath
Yarmuk R.
Jokneam
Kishion
ISSACHAR
Mediterranean Sea (Great Sea)
Taanach
Jarmuth
Ramoth Gilead
MANASSEH
Jordan R.
Shechem
Jabbok R.
Mahanaim
Gath Rimmon
Joppa
EPHRAIM
Shiloh
GAD
DAN
Beth Horon
BENJAMIN
Jazer
Eltekeh
Gezer
Mephaath
Geba
Heshbon
Gibbethon
Aijalon
Gibeon
Almon
Anathoth
Jerusalem
Bezer
Beth Shemesh
Libnah
REUBEN
JUDAH
Jahaz
Gaza
Hebron
Kedemoth
Dead Sea (Salt Sea)
Arnon Gorge
Debir
Juttah
Jattir
Eshtemoa
Beersheba
SIMEON
Hebron Cities of refuge (underlined)
Levitical cities:
Towns received by Kohathite clans
Towns received by Gershonite clans
Towns received by Merarite clans
Zered River
0 10 km.
0 10 miles

7 Ain, Rimmon,[d] Ether and Ashan[e]
— four towns and their villages —
8 and all the villages around these
towns as far as Baalath Beer (Ramah
in the Negev).[f]
This was the inheritance of the tribe of the
Simeonites, according to its clans. 9 The
inheritance of the Simeonites was taken
from the share of Judah,[g] because Judah's
portion was more than they needed. So
the Simeonites received their inheritance
within the territory of Judah.[h]

Allotment for Zebulun

10 The third lot came up for Zebulun[i] according to its clans:
The boundary of their inheritance
went as far as Sarid.[j] 11 Going west it
ran to Maralah, touched Dabbesheth,
and extended to the ravine near Jokneam.[k] 12 It turned east from Sarid[l]
toward the sunrise to the territory of
Kisloth Tabor and went on to Daberath[m] and up to Japhia. 13 Then it continued eastward to Gath Hepher[n] and
Eth Kazin; it came out at Rimmon[o]
and turned toward Neah. 14 There the
boundary went around on the north
to Hannathon and ended at the Valley of Iphtah El.[p] 15 Included were Kat-
tath, Nahalal,[q] Shimron,[r] Idalah and
Bethlehem.[s] There were twelve towns
and their villages.
16 These towns and their villages were the
inheritance of Zebulun,[t] according to its
clans.[u]

Allotment for Issachar

17 The fourth lot came out for Issachar[v] according to its clans. 18 Their territory included:
Jezreel,[w] Kesulloth, Shunem,[x]
19 Hapharaim, Shion, Anaharath,
20 Rabbith, Kishion,[y] Ebez, 21 Remeth,
En Gannim,[z] En Haddah and Beth Paz-
zez. 22 The boundary touched Tabor,[a]
Shahazumah and Beth Shemesh,[b] and
ended at the Jordan. There were sixteen towns and their villages.
23 These towns and their villages were the
inheritance of the tribe of Issachar,[c] according to its clans.[d]

Allotment for Asher

24 The fifth lot came out for the tribe of
Asher[e] according to its clans. 25 Their territory included:
Helkath, Hali, Beten, Akshaph,[f]
26 Allammelek, Amad and Mishal.[g]
On the west the boundary touched
Carmel[h] and Shihor Libnath. 27 It
then turned east toward Beth Dagon,[i] touched Zebulun[j] and the Valley of Iphtah El,[k] and went north to
Beth Emek and Neiel, passing Kabul[l]
on the left. 28 It went to Abdon,[a][m] Rehob,[n] Hammon[o] and Kanah,[p] as far as
Greater Sidon.[q] 29 The boundary then
turned back toward Ramah[r] and went
to the fortified city of Tyre,[s] turned
toward Hosah and came out at the
Mediterranean Sea[t] in the region of
Akzib,[u] 30 Ummah, Aphek[v] and Rehob.[w] There were twenty-two towns
and their villages.
31 These towns and their villages were the
inheritance of the tribe of Asher,[x] according to its clans.

Allotment for Naphtali

32 The sixth lot came out for Naphtali according to its clans:
33 Their boundary went from He-
leph and the large tree in Zaanannim,[y]
passing Adami Nekeb and Jabneel[z] to
Lakkum and ending at the Jordan.
34 The boundary ran west through Az-
noth Tabor and came out at Hukkok.[a]
It touched Zebulun[b] on the south,
Asher on the west and the Jordan[b]
on the east. 35 The fortified towns
were Ziddim, Zer, Hammath,[c] Rak-
kath, Kinnereth,[d] 36 Adamah, Ramah,[e]
Hazor,[f] 37 Kedesh,[g] Edrei,[h] En Hazor,
38 Iron, Migdal El, Horem, Beth Anath[i]
and Beth Shemesh.[j] There were nineteen towns and their villages.
39 These towns and their villages were the
inheritance of the tribe of Naphtali, according to its clans.[k]

Allotment for Dan

40 The seventh lot came out for the tribe of

a *28* Some Hebrew manuscripts (see also 21:30); most Hebrew manuscripts *Ebron* *b* *34* Septuagint; Hebrew *west, and Judah, the Jordan,*

19:7 [d] S Jos 15:32 [e] S Jos 15:42 **19:8** [f] S Jos 10:40 **19:9** [g] S Ge 49:7 [h] Eze 48:24 **19:10** [i] ver 16, 27, 34; Jos 21:7, 34 [j] ver 12 **19:11** [k] S Jos 12:22 **19:12** [l] ver 10 [m] Jos 21:28; 1Ch 6:72 **19:13** [n] S Jos 11:22 [o] Jos 15:32 **19:14** [p] ver 27 **19:15** [q] Jos 21:35 [r] Jos 11:1 [s] S Ge 35:19 **19:16** [t] S ver 10 [u] Eze 48:26 **19:17** [v] S Ge 30:18 **19:18** [w] S Jos 15:56 [x] 1Sa 28:4; 1Ki 1:3; 2Ki 4:8 **19:20** [y] Jos 21:28 **19:21** [z] S Jos 15:34 **19:22** [a] Jdg 4:6, 12; 8:18; Ps 89:12; Jer 46:18 [b] S Jos 15:10 **19:23** [c] Jos 17:10 [d] Ge 49:15; Eze 48:25 **19:24** [e] S Jos 17:7 **19:25** [f] S Jos 11:1 **19:26** [g] Jos 21:30 [h] S Jos 12:22; 1Ki 18:19; 2Ki 2:25 **19:27** [i] Jos 15:41 [j] S ver 10 [k] ver 14 [l] 1Ki 9:13 **19:28** [m] Jos 21:30; 1Ch 6:74 [n] ver 30; Nu 13:21; Jos 21:31; Jdg 1:31 [o] 1Ch 6:76 [p] S Jos 16:8 [q] S Ge 10:19 **19:29** [r] Jos 18:25 [s] 2Sa 5:11; 24:7; Ezr 3:7; Ps 45:12; Isa 23:1; Jer 25:22; Eze 26:2 [t] Jdg 5:17 [u] S Jos 15:44

19:30 [v] S Jos 12:18 [w] S ver 28 **19:31** [x] S Ge 30:13; S Jos 17:7; Eze 48:2 **19:33** [y] Jdg 4:11 [z] Jos 15:11 **19:34** [a] 1Ch 6:75 [b] S ver 10 **19:35** [c] 1Ch 2:55 [d] S Jos 11:2 **19:36** [e] Jos 18:25 [f] S Jos 11:1 **19:37** [g] S Jos 12:22 [h] S Nu 21:33 **19:38** [i] Jdg 1:33 [j] S Jos 15:10 **19:39** [k] Eze 48:3

19:10 *third lot ... for Zebulun.* To this tribe went a portion of lower Galilee midway between the Sea of Galilee and the Mediterranean.
19:17 *fourth lot ... for Issachar.* Southwest of the Sea of Galilee reaching down to the vicinity of Beth Shan and west to the Jezreel Valley. Mount Tabor marked its northern border.
19:24 *fifth lot ... for ... Asher.* Asher was given the coastal area as far north as Sidon in Phoenicia and as far south as Mount Carmel.
19:32 *sixth lot ... for Naphtali.* An area mostly to the north of the Sea of Galilee, including the mountains bordering on Asher and Zebulun to the west. Its southernmost point was at the southern end of the Sea of Galilee.
19:40 *seventh lot ... for ... Dan.* An elbow of land squeeze

Dan according to its clans. 41 The territory
of their inheritance included:
Zorah, Eshtaol,[l] Ir Shemesh, 42 Sha-
alabbin, Aijalon,[m] Ithlah, 43 Elon, Timnah,[n] Ekron,[o] 44 Eltekeh, Gibbethon,[p]
Baalath,[q] 45 Jehud, Bene Berak, Gath
Rimmon,[r] 46 Me Jarkon and Rakkon,
with the area facing Joppa.[s]
47 (When the territory of the Danites was
lost to them,[t] they went up and attacked
Leshem[u], took it, put it to the sword and
occupied it. They settled in Leshem and
named[v] it Dan after their ancestor.)[w]
48 These towns and their villages were the
inheritance of the tribe of Dan,[x] according
to its clans.

Allotment for Joshua

49 When they had finished dividing the
land into its allotted portions, the Israelites gave Joshua son of Nun an inheritance among them, 50 as the LORD had
commanded. They gave him the town he
asked for — Timnath Serah[a][y] in the hill
country of Ephraim. And he built up the
town and settled there.
51 These are the territories that Eleazar
the priest, Joshua son of Nun and the
heads of the tribal clans of Israel assigned
by lot at Shiloh in the presence of the LORD
at the entrance to the tent of meeting. And
so they finished dividing[z] the land.[a]

Cities of Refuge

20:1-9Ref — Nu 35:9-34; Dt 4:41-43; 19:1-14

20 Then the LORD said to Joshua:
2 "Tell the Israelites to designate the
cities of refuge, as I instructed you through
Moses, 3 so that anyone who kills a person
accidentally and unintentionally[b] may flee
there and find protection from the avenger
of blood.[c] 4 When they flee to one of these
cities, they are to stand in the entrance of
the city gate[d] and state their case before
the elders[e] of that city. Then the elders are
to admit the fugitive into their city and
provide a place to live among them. 5 If
the avenger of blood comes in pursuit,
the elders must not surrender the fugitive,
because the fugitive killed their neighbor
unintentionally and without malice aforethought. 6 They are to stay in that city until
they have stood trial before the assembly[f]
and until the death of the high priest who
is serving at that time. Then they may go
back to their own home in the town from
which they fled."
7 So they set apart Kedesh[g] in Galilee in the
hill country of Naphtali, Shechem[h] in the hill
country of Ephraim, and Kiriath Arba[i] (that
is, Hebron[j]) in the hill country of Judah.[k]
8 East of the Jordan (on the other side from
Jericho) they designated Bezer[l] in the wilderness on the plateau in the tribe of Reuben,
Ramoth in Gilead[m] in the tribe of Gad, and
Golan in Bashan[n] in the tribe of Manasseh.
9 Any of the Israelites or any foreigner residing among them who killed someone accidentally[o] could flee to these designated cities
and not be killed by the avenger of blood
prior to standing trial before the assembly.[p]

a 50 Also known as *Timnath Heres* (see Judges 2:9)

19:41 [l] S Jos 15:33 **19:42** [m] S Jos 10:12 **19:43** [n] S Ge 38:12 [o] S Jos 13:3 **19:44** [p] Jos 21:23; 1Ki 15:27; 16:15 [q] 1Ki 9:18; 2Ch 8:6 **19:45** [r] Jos 21:24; 1Ch 6:69 **19:46** [s] 2Ch 2:16; Ezr 3:7; Jnh 1:3; Ac 9:36 **19:47** [t] Jdg 18:1 [u] Jdg 18:7, 14 [v] S Dt 3:14 [w] Jdg 18:27,29 **19:48** [x] S Ge 30:6 **19:50** [y] Jos 24:30; Jdg 2:9 **19:51** [z] Jos 23:4 [a] S Jos 14:1; S 18:10; Ac 13:19

20:3 [b] S Lev 4:2 [c] S Nu 35:12 **20:4** [d] S Ge 23:10; Jer 38:7 [e] S Jos 7:6 **20:6** [f] S Nu 35:12 **20:7** [g] S Jos 12:22 [h] S Ge 12:6 [i] S Ge 35:27 [j] S Jos 10:36 [k] Lk 1:39 **20:8** [l] Jos 21:36; 1Ch 6:78 [m] S Jos 12:2; 1Ch 6:80 [n] S Jos 12:5; 1Ch 6:71

20:9 [o] S Lev 4:2 [p] S Ex 21:13

---

between Ephraim and Judah and west of Benjamin (see note on 18:11). The port of Joppa marked the northwestern corner of Dan.

19:47 *territory of the Danites was lost to them.* The Amorites of this area "confined the Danites to the hill country" (Jdg 1:34), so most of the tribe migrated to the upper Jordan Valley, where they seized the town of Leshem (or Laish; see Ge 14:14 and note; Jdg 18:2 – 10,27 – 29 and notes on 18:1,7,29) and renamed it Dan.

19:49 *gave Joshua ... an inheritance.* In the account of the distribution of the promised land (the territory west of the Jordan), the assignment to Caleb is treated first (14:6 – 15), the assignment to Joshua last. Thus the allotting of inheritance to these two dauntless servants of the Lord from the wilderness generation (see Nu 13:30; 14:6,24,30) frames the whole account — and both received the territory they asked for. Appropriately, Joshua's allotment came last; he was not a king or a warlord but the servant of God commissioned to bring the Lord's people into the promised land.

19:50 *Timnath Serah.* Located in the southwestern corner of Ephraim, facing out to the sea. Here Joshua was also buried (24:30).

20:1 – 9 Having distributed the land to the tribes, the Lord's next administrative regulation (see note on 13:1 – 32) provided an elementary system of government, made up of regional courts to deal with capital offenses having to do with manslaughter. A safeguard was thus created against the easy miscarriage of justice (with its potential for endless blood feuds) when retribution for manslaughter was left in the hands of family members. The cities chosen were among those also assigned to the Levites, where ideally the law of Moses would especially be known and honored. See map, p. 254.

20:2 *as I instructed you through Moses.* See Nu 35:6 – 34.

20:3 *avenger of blood.* The Hebrew word is also translated "guardian-redeemers" (Ru 2:20; see note and NIV text note there) and "Redeemer" (see Isa 41:14 and note). The avenger was a near relative with the obligation of exacting retribution (see Lev 24:17; Nu 35:16 – 28).

20:4 *city gate.* Traditional place for trials, where the elders sat to hold court (see Ru 4:1 and note; see also Job 29:7).

20:6 *assembly.* Perhaps the assembly in the town where the crime was committed (see Nu 35:24 – 25). *death of the high priest.* See Nu 35:25 – 28 and note on 35:24.

20:7 *they set apart Kedesh.* A wordplay in the Hebrew: "they consecrated (the town of) consecration." The other two cities west of the Jordan already had sacred associations: For Shechem, see 8:30 – 35 and note; Ge 12:6 – 7; for Hebron, see Ge 23:2; 49:29 – 32. The geographic distribution of the cities was important: one in the north, one in the midlands and one in the south. (See v. 8, where the order of the three cities of refuge that served in Transjordan is reversed: Bezer in the south, Ramoth in the midlands and Golan in the north.) See map, p. 254.

20:9 *or any foreigner.* Evidence of the equal protection granted to the foreigners living in Israel (cf. Lev 19:33 – 34; Dt 10:18 – 19).

Towns for the Levites

21:4-39pp — 1Ch 6:54-80

21 Now the family heads of the Levites approached Eleazar the priest,
Joshua son of Nun, and the heads of the
other tribal families of Israel[q] 2 at Shiloh[r]
in Canaan and said to them, "The LORD
commanded through Moses that you give
us towns[s] to live in, with pasturelands for
our livestock."[t] 3 So, as the LORD had commanded, the Israelites gave the Levites the
following towns and pasturelands out of
their own inheritance:
4 The first lot came out for the Kohathites,[u] according to their clans. The Levites
who were descendants of Aaron the priest
were allotted thirteen towns from the
tribes of Judah, Simeon and Benjamin.[v]
5 The rest of Kohath's descendants were
allotted ten towns from the clans of the
tribes of Ephraim, Dan and half of Manasseh.[w]
6 The descendants of Gershon[x] were allotted thirteen towns from the clans of the
tribes of Issachar,[y] Asher,[z] Naphtali and
the half-tribe of Manasseh in Bashan.
7 The descendants of Merari,[a] according
to their clans, received twelve[b] towns from
the tribes of Reuben, Gad and Zebulun.[c]
8 So the Israelites allotted to the Levites
these towns and their pasturelands, as the
LORD had commanded through Moses.

9 From the tribes of Judah and Simeon
they allotted the following towns by name
10 (these towns were assigned to the descendants of Aaron who were from the Kohathite clans of the Levites, because the
first lot fell to them):
11 They gave them Kiriath Arba[d] (that
is, Hebron[e]), with its surrounding pastureland, in the hill country of Judah.
(Arba was the forefather of Anak.)
12 But the fields and villages around
the city they had given to Caleb son of
Jephunneh as his possession.[f]
13 So to the descendants of Aaron
the priest they gave Hebron (a city of
refuge[g] for one accused of murder),
Libnah,[h] 14 Jattir,[i] Eshtemoa,[j] 15 Holon,[k] Debir,[l] 16 Ain,[m] Juttah[n] and Beth
Shemesh,[o] together with their pasturelands — nine towns from these
two tribes.
17 And from the tribe of Benjamin
they gave them Gibeon,[p] Geba,[q] 18 Anathoth[r] and Almon, together with
their pasturelands — four towns.
19 The total number of towns[s] for the
priests, the descendants of Aaron, came
to thirteen, together with their pasturelands.[t]

20 The rest of the Kohathite clans of the Levites were allotted towns from the tribe of
Ephraim:
21 In the hill country of Ephraim
they were given Shechem[u] (a city of
refuge for one accused of murder)
and Gezer,[v] 22 Kibzaim and Beth Horon,[w] together with their pasturelands — four towns.[x]
23 Also from the tribe of Dan they
received Eltekeh, Gibbethon,[y] 24 Aijalon[z] and Gath Rimmon,[a] together
with their pasturelands — four towns.
25 From half the tribe of Manasseh they received Taanach[b] and Gath
Rimmon, together with their pasturelands — two towns.
26 All these ten towns and their pasturelands were given to the rest of the Kohathite clans.[c]

27 The Levite clans of the Gershonites were
given:
from the half-tribe of Manasseh,
Golan in Bashan[d] (a city of refuge
for one accused of murder[e]) and Be
Eshterah, together with their pasturelands — two towns;
28 from the tribe of Issachar,[f]
Kishion,[g] Daberath,[h] 29 Jarmuth[i] and
En Gannim,[j] together with their pasturelands — four towns;
30 from the tribe of Asher,[k]
Mishal,[l] Abdon,[m] 31 Helkath and Rehob,[n] together with their pasturelands — four towns;
32 from the tribe of Naphtali,
Kedesh[o] in Galilee (a city of refuge for
one accused of murder[p]), Hammoth
Dor and Kartan, together with their
pasturelands — three towns.
33 The total number of towns of the Gershonite[q] clans came to thirteen, together
with their pasturelands.

21:1 [q] Jos 14:1 **21:2** [r] S Jos 18:1 [s] S Lev 25:32 [t] S Nu 35:2-3; S Jos 14:4 **21:4** [u] Nu 3:17 [v] ver 19 **21:5** [w] ver 26 **21:6** [x] Nu 3:17 [y] S Ge 30:18 [z] S Jos 17:7 **21:7** [a] S Ex 6:16 [b] ver 40 [c] S Jos 19:10 **21:11** [d] S Ge 23:2 [e] S Jos 10:36 **21:12** [f] S Jos 15:13 **21:13** [g] Nu 35:6 [h] S Nu 33:20 **21:14** [i] S Jos 15:48 [j] S Jos 15:50 **21:15** [k] S Jos 15:51 [l] S Jos 10:3 **21:16** [m] S Nu 34:11 [n] Jos 15:55 [o] S Jos 15:10 **21:17** [p] S Jos 9:3 [q] S Jos 18:24; S Ne 11:31 **21:18** [r] 2Sa 23:27; 1Ki 2:26; Ezr 2:23; Ne 7:27; 11:32; Isa 10:30; Jer 1:1; 11:21; 32:7 **21:19** [s] 2Ch 31:15 [t] ver 4 **21:21** [u] S Jos 17:7 [v] S Jos 10:33 **21:22** [w] S Jos 10:10 [x] 1Sa 1:1 **21:23** [y] S Jos 19:44 **21:24** [z] S Jos 10:12 [a] S Jos 19:45 **21:25** [b] S Jos 12:21 **21:26** [c] ver 5 **21:27** [d] S Jos 12:5 [e] Nu 35:6 **21:28** [f] S Ge 30:18 [g] Jos 19:20 [h] S Jos 19:12 **21:29** [i] S Jos 10:3 [j] S Jos 15:34 **21:30** [k] S Jos 17:7 [l] Jos 19:26 [m] S Jos 19:28 **21:31** [n] S Jos 19:28 **21:32** [o] S Jos 12:22 [p] Nu 35:6 **21:33** [q] ver 6

21:1–45 Finally the Levites are allotted their towns and adjoining pasturelands — with the priestly families being given precedence (see v. 10).

21:4 *Kohathites.* The three sons of Levi were Kohath, Gershon and Merari (Ex 6:16; Nu 3:17). *Judah, Simeon and Benjamin.* Tribal areas close to Jerusalem, which would later be the site of the temple. The remaining Kohathites received cities in adjoining tribes.

21:11 *Hebron.* Caleb's city (14:13–15). The priests and Levites were to be given space in their assigned cities along with the other inhabitants.

21:27 *Gershonites.* Received cities in the northern tribes of Asher, Naphtali and Issachar.

34The Merarite clans (the rest of the Levites) were given:
from the tribe of Zebulun,[r]
Jokneam,[s] Kartah, 35Dimnah and Nahalal,[t] together with their pasturelands—four towns;
36from the tribe of Reuben,
Bezer,[u] Jahaz,[v] 37Kedemoth and
Mephaath,[w] together with their pasturelands—four towns;
38from the tribe of Gad,
Ramoth[x] in Gilead[y] (a city of refuge
for one accused of murder), Mahanaim,[z] 39Heshbon and Jazer,[a] together
with their pasturelands—four towns
in all.
40The total number of towns allotted to
the Merarite clans, who were the rest of
the Levites, came to twelve.[b]
41The towns of the Levites in the territory
held by the Israelites were forty-eight in all,
together with their pasturelands.[c] 42Each of
these towns had pasturelands surrounding
it; this was true for all these towns.
43So the LORD gave Israel all the land
he had sworn to give their ancestors,[d]
and they took possession[e] of it and settled there.[f] 44The LORD gave them rest[g] on
every side, just as he had sworn to their
ancestors. Not one of their enemies[h] withstood them; the LORD gave all their enemies[i] into their hands.[j] 45Not one of all the
LORD's good promises[k] to Israel failed; every one was fulfilled.

Eastern Tribes Return Home

22 Then Joshua summoned the Reubenites, the Gadites and the half-
tribe of Manasseh 2and said to them, "You
have done all that Moses the servant of
the LORD commanded,[l] and you have
obeyed me in everything I commanded.
3For a long time now—to this very day—
you have not deserted your fellow Israelites but have carried out the mission the
LORD your God gave you. 4Now that the
LORD your God has given them rest[m] as he
promised, return to your homes[n] in the
land that Moses the servant of the LORD
gave you on the other side of the Jordan.[o]
5But be very careful to keep the commandment[p] and the law that Moses the servant
of the LORD gave you: to love the LORD[q]
your God, to walk in obedience to him, to
keep his commands,[r] to hold fast to him
and to serve him with all your heart and
with all your soul.[s]"
6Then Joshua blessed[t] them and sent
them away, and they went to their homes.
7(To the half-tribe of Manasseh Moses had
given land in Bashan,[u] and to the other
half of the tribe Joshua gave land on the
west side[v] of the Jordan along with their
fellow Israelites.) When Joshua sent them
home, he blessed them,[w] 8saying, "Return
to your homes with your great wealth—
with large herds of livestock,[x] with silver,
gold, bronze and iron,[y] and a great quantity of clothing—and divide[z] the plunder[a]
from your enemies with your fellow Israelites."
9So the Reubenites, the Gadites and the
half-tribe of Manasseh left the Israelites
at Shiloh[b] in Canaan to return to Gilead,[c]
their own land, which they had acquired
in accordance with the command of the
LORD through Moses.
10When they came to Geliloth[d] near the
Jordan in the land of Canaan, the Reubenites, the Gadites and the half-tribe of
Manasseh built an imposing altar[e] there
by the Jordan. 11And when the Israelites
heard that they had built the altar on the
border of Canaan at Geliloth near the Jordan on the Israelite side, 12the whole assembly of Israel gathered at Shiloh[f] to go
to war against them.

21:34 [r]S Jos 19:10 [s]S Jos 12:22 **21:35** [t]Jos 19:15 **21:36** [u]S Jos 20:8 [v]S Nu 21:23; Dt 2:32; Jdg 11:20 **21:37** [w]S Jos 13:18 **21:38** [x]S Dt 4:43 [y]S Jos 12:2 [z]S Ge 32:2 **21:39** [a]S Jos 13:25 **21:40** [b]ver 7 **21:41** [c]Nu 35:7 **21:43** [d]Dt 34:4 [e]Dt 11:31 [f]S Dt 17:14 **21:44** [g]S Ex 33:14 [h]S Dt 6:19 [i]S Ex 23:31 [j]Dt 21:10 **21:45** [k]Jos 23:14; Ne 9:8 **22:2** [l]S Nu 32:25 **22:4** [m]S Ex 33:14 [n]Nu 32:22; Dt 3:20 [o]Nu 32:18; S Jos 1:13-15 **22:5** [p]Isa 43:22; Mal 3:14 [q]Jos 23:11 [r]S Dt 5:29 [s]S Dt 6:5 **22:6** [t]S Ge 24:60; S Ex 39:43 **22:7** [u]S Nu 32:19; S Jos 12:5 [v]Jos 17:2 [w]S Jos 14:13; Lk 24:50 **22:8** [x]S Dt 20:14 [y]S Nu 31:22 [z]S Nu 31:27 [a]S Ge 49:27; 1Sa 30:16; 2Sa 1:1; Isa 9:3 **22:9** [b]Jos 18:1 [c]S Nu 32:26 **22:10** [d]Jos 18:17 [e]ver 19,26-27; Isa 19:19; 56:7 **22:12** [f]Jos 18:1

21:34 *Merarite clans.* Their 12 cities were scattered throughout Reuben, Gad and Zebulun.

21:43-45 A concluding summary statement of how the Lord had fulfilled his sworn promise to give Israel this land (see Ge 15:18-21). The occupation of the land was not yet complete (see 23:4-5; Jdg 1-2), but the national campaign was over and Israel was finally established in the promised land. No power was left in Canaan that could threaten to dislodge her.

21:44 *rest on every side.* See note on 1:13.

21:45 *good promises.* Refers to the good things God had covenanted to give his people (23:14-15; 1Ki 8:56; Jer 33:14).

22:1-34 The two and a half tribes from east of the Jordan, faithful in battle, are now commended by Joshua and sent to their homes. But their altar of "witness" (see vv. 26-27,34) was misunderstood, and disciplinary action against them was narrowly averted.

22:2 *all that Moses ... commanded.* Moses had ordered them to join the other tribes in the conquest of Canaan (Nu 32:16-27; Dt 3:18).

22:5 *love the LORD ... serve him with all your heart.* Both Moses and Joshua saw that obedience to the laws of God would require love and service from the heart. In the ancient Near East, "love" was also a political term, indicating truehearted loyalty to one's king (see notes on Dt 6:5; 11:1).

22:8 *divide ... with your fellow Israelites.* Moses also had seen the need for a fair sharing of the spoils of war (Nu 31:25-27).

22:10 *Geliloth.* Understood in the Septuagint (the pre-Christian Greek translation of the OT) to be Gilgal, next to Jericho; more likely it was a site east of Shiloh along the Jordan River (18:17).

22:11 *when the Israelites heard.* Anxiety about apostasy led to hasty conclusions. They thought the altar had been set up as a rival to the true altar at Shiloh.

22:12 *gathered at Shiloh.* In the presence of God at the tabernacle. *to go to war against them.* To take disciplinary action (cf. Dt 13:12-18; Jdg 20).

13 So the Israelites sent Phinehas[g] son
of Eleazar,[h] the priest, to the land of Gilead—to Reuben, Gad and the half-tribe of
Manasseh. 14 With him they sent ten of the
chief men, one from each of the tribes of
Israel, each the head of a family division
among the Israelite clans.[i]
15 When they went to Gilead—to Reuben, Gad and the half-tribe of Manasseh—they said to them: 16 "The whole assembly of the LORD says: 'How could you
break faith[j] with the God of Israel like this?
How could you turn away from the LORD
and build yourselves an altar in rebellion[k]
against him now? 17 Was not the sin of
Peor[l] enough for us? Up to this very day
we have not cleansed ourselves from that
sin, even though a plague fell on the community of the LORD! 18 And are you now
turning away from the LORD?
" 'If you rebel against the LORD today, tomorrow he will be angry with the whole
community[m] of Israel. 19 If the land you
possess is defiled, come over to the LORD's
land, where the LORD's tabernacle[n] stands,
and share the land with us. But do not rebel against the LORD or against us by building an altar[o] for yourselves, other than the
altar of the LORD our God. 20 When Achan
son of Zerah was unfaithful in regard to
the devoted things,[a][p] did not wrath[q] come
on the whole community[r] of Israel? He was
not the only one who died for his sin.' "[s]
21 Then Reuben, Gad and the half-tribe
of Manasseh replied to the heads of the
clans of Israel: 22 "The Mighty One, God,
the LORD! The Mighty One, God,[t] the
LORD![u] He knows![v] And let Israel know! If
this has been in rebellion or disobedience
to the LORD, do not spare us this day. 23 If
we have built our own altar to turn away
from the LORD and to offer burnt offerings
and grain offerings,[w] or to sacrifice fellowship offerings on it, may the LORD himself
call us to account.[x]
24 "No! We did it for fear that some day
your descendants might say to ours, 'What
do you have to do with the LORD, the God
of Israel? 25 The LORD has made the Jordan a boundary between us and you—
you Reubenites and Gadites! You have no
share in the LORD.' So your descendants
might cause ours to stop fearing the LORD.
26 "That is why we said, 'Let us get ready
and build an altar—but not for burnt offerings or sacrifices.' 27 On the contrary, it
is to be a witness[y] between us and you and
the generations that follow, that we will
worship the LORD at his sanctuary with our
burnt offerings, sacrifices and fellowship
offerings.[z] Then in the future your descendants will not be able to say to ours, 'You
have no share in the LORD.'
28 "And we said, 'If they ever say this to
us, or to our descendants, we will answer:
Look at the replica of the LORD's altar,
which our ancestors built, not for burnt
offerings and sacrifices, but as a witness[a]
between us and you.'
29 "Far be it from us to rebel[b] against the
LORD and turn away from him today by
building an altar for burnt offerings, grain
offerings and sacrifices, other than the altar of the LORD our God that stands before
his tabernacle.[c]"
30 When Phinehas the priest and the
leaders of the community—the heads of
the clans of the Israelites—heard what
Reuben, Gad and Manasseh had to say,
they were pleased. 31 And Phinehas son
of Eleazar, the priest, said to Reuben, Gad
and Manasseh, "Today we know that the
LORD is with us,[d] because you have not
been unfaithful to the LORD in this matter.
Now you have rescued the Israelites from
the LORD's hand."
32 Then Phinehas son of Eleazar, the
priest, and the leaders returned to Canaan
from their meeting with the Reubenites
and Gadites in Gilead and reported to the
Israelites.[e] 33 They were glad to hear the report and praised God.[f] And they talked no
more about going to war against them to
devastate the country where the Reubenites and the Gadites lived.

[a] 20 The Hebrew term refers to the irrevocable giving over of things or persons to the LORD, often by totally destroying them.

22:13 [g] S Nu 25:7 [h] Nu 3:32; Jos 24:33 **22:14** [i] ver 32; S Nu 1:4 **22:16** [j] S Dt 7:3; 1Sa 13:13; 15:11 [k] Dt 12:13-14 **22:17** [l] S Nu 23:28; 25:1-9 **22:18** [m] S Lev 10:6 **22:19** [n] S Ex 26:1 [o] S ver 10 **22:20** [p] Jos 7:1 [q] Ps 7:11 [r] Lev 10:6 [s] Jos 7:5 **22:22** [t] S Dt 10:17 [u] Ps 50:1 [v] 1Sa 2:3; 16:7; 1Ki 8:39; 1Ch 28:9; Ps 11:4; 40:9; 44:21; 139:4; Jer 17:10 **22:23** [w] Jer 41:5 [x] S Dt 12:11; S 18:19; 1Sa 20:16 **22:27** [y] S Ge 21:30; Jos 24:27; Isa 19:20 [z] S Dt 12:6 **22:28** [a] S Ge 21:30 **22:29** [b] Jos 24:16 [c] S Ex 26:1 **22:31** [d] 2Ch 15:2 **22:32** [e] S ver 14 **22:33** [f] 1Ch 29:20; Da 2:19; Lk 2:28

22:13–14 A prestigious delegation is sent to try to turn the Transjordan tribes from their (supposed) act of rebellion against the Lord.
22:16 *How could you ...?* The accusations were very grave: You have committed apostasy and rebellion.
22:17 *Peor.* Where some of the Israelites became involved in the Moabite worship of Baal of Peor (Nu 25:1–5).
22:19 *is defiled.* By pagan worship, corrupting its inhabitants. *the LORD's land.* The promised land proper had never included Transjordan territory. Canaan was the land the Lord especially claimed as his own and promised to the descendants of Abraham, Isaac and Jacob.
22:20 *Achan ... the whole community of Israel.* See note on 7:1–26.
22:22 *The Mighty One, God, the LORD!* See note on Ps 50:1. Th[e] repetition of the sacred names gives an oath-like quality t[o] this strong denial of any wrongdoing.
22:27 *witness.* The altar, presumably of uncut stone (see 8:31[;] Ex 20:25), was to serve as a testimony to the commitment o[f] the Transjordan tribes to remain loyal to the Lord, and to the continued right to worship the Lord at the tabernacle—eve[n] though they lived outside the land of promise. It constitute[d] a seventh memorial monument in the land noted by the au[-]thor of Joshua (see note on 4:9).
22:31 *you have rescued the Israelites.* Their words prevente[d] a terrible punishment that the other tribes were about to in[-]flict as an act of divine judgment (consider the implication[s] of v. 20).

34 And the Reubenites and the Gadites
gave the altar this name: A Witness[g] Between Us — that the LORD is God.

Joshua's Farewell to the Leaders

23 After a long time had passed and
the LORD had given Israel rest[h] from
all their enemies around them, Joshua, by
then a very old man,[i] 2 summoned all Israel — their elders,[j] leaders, judges and officials[k] — and said to them: "I am very old.[l]
3 You yourselves have seen everything the
LORD your God has done to all these nations for your sake; it was the LORD your
God who fought for you.[m] 4 Remember
how I have allotted[n] as an inheritance[o] for
your tribes all the land of the nations that
remain — the nations I conquered — between the Jordan and the Mediterranean
Sea[p] in the west. 5 The LORD your God himself will push them out[q] for your sake. He
will drive them out[r] before you, and you
will take possession of their land, as the
LORD your God promised you.[s]
6 "Be very strong; be careful to obey all
that is written in the Book of the Law[t] of
Moses, without turning aside[u] to the right
or to the left.[v] 7 Do not associate with these
nations that remain among you; do not invoke the names of their gods or swear[w] by
them. You must not serve them or bow
down[x] to them. 8 But you are to hold fast
to the LORD[y] your God, as you have until
now.
9 "The LORD has driven out before you
great and powerful nations;[z] to this day
no one has been able to withstand you.[a]
10 One of you routs a thousand,[b] because
the LORD your God fights for you,[c] just as
he promised. 11 So be very careful[d] to love
the LORD[e] your God.
12 "But if you turn away and ally yourselves with the survivors of these nations
that remain among you and if you intermarry with them[f] and associate with
them,[g] 13 then you may be sure that the
LORD your God will no longer drive out[h]
these nations before you. Instead, they
will become snares[i] and traps for you,
whips on your backs and thorns in your
eyes,[j] until you perish from this good
land,[k] which the LORD your God has giv-
en you.
14 "Now I am about to go the way of all
the earth.[l] You know with all your heart
and soul that not one of all the good
promises the LORD your God gave you has
failed. Every promise[m] has been fulfilled;
not one has failed.[n] 15 But just as all the
good things[o] the LORD your God has promised you have come to you, so he will
bring on you all the evil things[p] he has
threatened, until the LORD your God has
destroyed you[q] from this good land he has
given you.[r] 16 If you violate the covenant of
the LORD your God, which he commanded
you, and go and serve other gods and bow
down to them, the LORD's anger will burn
against you, and you will quickly perish
from the good land he has given you.[s]"

The Covenant Renewed at Shechem

24 Then Joshua assembled[t] all the
tribes of Israel at Shechem.[u] He
summoned[v] the elders,[w] leaders, judges
and officials of Israel,[x] and they presented
themselves before God.
2 Joshua said to all the people, "This
is what the LORD, the God of Israel, says:
'Long ago your ancestors, including Terah
the father of Abraham and Nahor,[y] lived
beyond the Euphrates River and worshiped other gods.[z] 3 But I took your father Abraham from the land beyond the

22:34 [g] S Ge 21:30 **23:1** [h] S Dt 12:9; Jos 21:44 [i] S Jos 13:1 **23:2** [j] S Jos 7:6 [k] Jos 24:1 [l] S Jos 13:1 **23:3** [m] S Ex 14:14; S Dt 20:4 **23:4** [n] Jos 19:51 [o] S Nu 34:2; Ps 78:55 [p] S Nu 34:6 **23:5** [q] ver 13; Jdg 2:21 [r] Ps 44:5; Jer 46:15 [s] Ex 23:30 **23:6** [t] S Dt 28:61 [u] S Dt 17:20 [v] Jos 1:7 **23:7** [w] Ex 23:13; Jer 5:7; 12:16 [x] S Ex 20:5 **23:8** [y] S Dt 10:20 **23:9** [z] Dt 11:23 [a] Dt 7:24 **23:10** [b] Lev 26:8; Jdg 3:31 [c] S Ex 14:14 **23:11** [d] S Dt 4:15 [e] Jos 22:5 **23:12** [f] S Ge 34:9 [g] S Ex 34:16; Ps 106:34-35 **23:13** [h] S ver 5 [i] S Ex 10:7 [j] S Nu 33:55 [k] Dt 1:8; 1Ki 9:7; 2Ki 25:21 **23:14** [l] 1Ki 2:2 [m] Ps 119:140; 145:13 [n] S Jos 21:45 **23:15** [o] 1Ki 8:56; Jer 33:14 [p] 1Ki 14:10; 2Ki 22:16; Isa 24:6; 34:5; 43:28; Jer 6:19; 11:8; 35:17; 39:16; Mal 4:6 [q] Jos 24:20 [r] Lev 26:17; Dt 28:15; Jer 40:2 **23:16** [s] Dt 4:25-26 **24:1** [t] Ge 49:2 [u] S Ge 12:6 [v] 1Sa 12:7; 1Ki 8:14 [w] Jos 7:6 [x] Jos 23:2 **24:2** [y] Ge 11:26 [z] Ge 11:32

23:1 – 16 Joshua, the Lord's servant, delivers a farewell address recalling the victories the Lord has given, but also reminding the people of areas yet to be possessed and of the need to be loyal to God's covenant laws. Their mission remains — to be the people of God's kingdom in the world.

23:1 *rest.* See note on 1:13. *very old man.* Joshua was approaching the age of 110 (24:29).

23:6 *be careful to obey.* Echoing the Lord's instructions at the beginning (1:7 – 8; see 22:5). *Book of the Law.* See note on 1:8.

23:10 *One of you routs a thousand.* See, e.g., Jdg 15:15 – 16.

23:11 *love the LORD your God.* A concluding summation (see note on 22:5).

23:12 *But if you turn away.* Remaining in the promised land was conditioned on faithfulness to the Lord and separation from the idolaters still around them. Failure to meet these conditions would bring Israel's banishment from the land (cf. vv. 13,15 – 16; 2Ki 17:7 – 8; 2Ch 7:14 – 20). *ally yourselves ... intermarry.* The Lord prohibited alliances, either national or domestic, with the peoples of Canaan because such alliances would tend to compromise Israel's loyalty to the Lord (see Ex 34:15 – 16 and note on 34:15; Dt 7:2 – 4 and notes on 7:1 – 6; 7:2 – 5; 7:4; cf. 1Ki 11:1 – 13).

23:13 *snares and traps.* Joshua's warning echoes Ex 23:33; 34:12; Dt 7:16.

23:14 *go the way of all the earth.* To the grave.

24:1 – 33 Once more Joshua assembled the tribes at Shechem to call Israel to a renewal of the covenant (see 8:30 – 35). It was his final official act as the Lord's servant, mediator of the Lord's rule over his people. In this he followed the example of Moses, whose final official act was also a call to covenant renewal — of which Deuteronomy is the preserved document.

24:2 *This is what the LORD ... says.* Only a divinely appointed mediator would dare to speak for God with direct discourse, as in vv. 2 – 13. *Long ago.* In accordance with the common ancient Near Eastern practice of making treaties (covenants), a brief recital of the past history of the relationship precedes the making of covenant commitments.

Euphrates and led him throughout Canaan[a] and gave him many descendants.[b]
I gave him Isaac,[c] 4 and to Isaac I gave Jacob and Esau.[d] I assigned the hill country
of Seir[e] to Esau, but Jacob and his family
went down to Egypt.[f]
5 "'Then I sent Moses and Aaron,[g] and I
afflicted the Egyptians by what I did there,
and I brought you out.[h] 6 When I brought
your people out of Egypt, you came to
the sea,[i] and the Egyptians pursued them
with chariots and horsemen[a][j] as far as the
Red Sea.[b][k] 7 But they cried[l] to the LORD for
help, and he put darkness[m] between you
and the Egyptians; he brought the sea over
them and covered them.[n] You saw with
your own eyes what I did to the Egyptians.[o] Then you lived in the wilderness
for a long time.[p]
8 "'I brought you to the land of the Amorites[q] who lived east of the Jordan. They
fought against you, but I gave them into
your hands. I destroyed them from before you, and you took possession of their
land.[r] 9 When Balak son of Zippor,[s] the
king of Moab, prepared to fight against Israel, he sent for Balaam son of Beor[t] to put
a curse on you.[u] 10 But I would not listen
to Balaam, so he blessed you[v] again and
again, and I delivered you out of his hand.
11 "'Then you crossed the Jordan[w] and
came to Jericho.[x] The citizens of Jericho
fought against you, as did also the Amorites, Perizzites,[y] Canaanites, Hittites,
Girgashites, Hivites and Jebusites,[z] but I
gave them into your hands.[a] 12 I sent the
hornet[b] ahead of you, which drove them
out[c] before you—also the two Amorite
kings. You did not do it with your own
sword and bow.[d] 13 So I gave you a land[e]
on which you did not toil and cities you
did not build; and you live in them and eat
from vineyards and olive groves that you
did not plant.'[f]
14 "Now fear the LORD[g] and serve him
with all faithfulness.[h] Throw away the
gods[i] your ancestors worshiped beyond
the Euphrates River and in Egypt,[j] and
serve the LORD. 15 But if serving the LORD
seems undesirable to you, then choose for
yourselves this day whom you will serve,
whether the gods your ancestors served
beyond the Euphrates, or the gods of the
Amorites,[k] in whose land you are living.
But as for me and my household,[l] we will
serve the LORD."[m]
16 Then the people answered, "Far be it
from us to forsake[n] the LORD to serve other
gods! 17 It was the LORD our God himself
who brought us and our parents up out of
Egypt, from that land of slavery,[o] and performed those great signs[p] before our eyes.
He protected us on our entire journey and
among all the nations through which we
traveled. 18 And the LORD drove out[q] before
us all the nations,[r] including the Amorites,
who lived in the land.[s] We too will serve
the LORD, because he is our God.[t]"
19 Joshua said to the people, "You are
not able to serve the LORD. He is a holy
God;[u] he is a jealous God.[v] He will not forgive[w] your rebellion[x] and your sins. 20 If
you forsake the LORD[y] and serve foreign
gods, he will turn[z] and bring disaster[a] on
you and make an end of you,[b] after he has
been good to you."
21 But the people said to Joshua, "No!
We will serve the LORD."
22 Then Joshua said, "You are witnesses[c]
against yourselves that you have chosen[d]
to serve the LORD."
"Yes, we are witnesses,[e]" they replied.
23 "Now then," said Joshua, "throw
away the foreign gods[f] that are among you
and yield your hearts[g] to the LORD, the God
of Israel."
24 And the people said to Joshua, "We
will serve the LORD our God and obey
him."[h]

[a] 6 Or *charioteers* [b] 6 Or *the Sea of Reeds*

24:3 [a] S Ge 12:1 [b] S Ge 1:28; S 12:2 [c] S Ge 21:3 **24:4** [d] S Ge 25:26 [e] S Ge 14:6; S Nu 24:18 [f] Ge 46:5-6 **24:5** [g] S Ex 3:10 [h] Ex 12:51 **24:6** [i] S Ex 14:22 [j] S Ex 14:9 [k] Ex 14:23 **24:7** [l] S Ex 14:10 [m] Ex 14:20 [n] S Ex 14:28 [o] S Ex 19:4 [p] Dt 1:46 **24:8** [q] S Ex 23:23 [r] S Nu 21:31 **24:9** [s] Nu 22:2 [t] S Nu 23:7 [u] S Nu 22:6 **24:10** [v] S Nu 23:11; S Dt 23:5 **24:11** [w] S Ex 14:29 [x] Jos 6:1 [y] S Jos 3:10 [z] S Ge 15:18-21 [a] Ex 23:23; Dt 7:1 **24:12** [b] S Ex 23:28; Ps 44:3,6-7 [c] S Ex 23:31 [d] Ps 135:11 **24:13** [e] Ex 6:8 [f] Dt 6:10-11 **24:14** [g] 1Sa 12:14; Job 23:15; Ps 19:9; 119:120 [h] Dt 10:12; 18:13; 1Sa 12:24; 2Co 1:12 [i] ver 23; S Ge 31:19; Ex 12:12; 18:11; 20:3; Nu 25:2; Dt 11:28; Jdg 10:16; Ru 1:15; Isa 55:7 [j] Eze 23:3 **24:15** [k] Jdg 6:10; Ru 1:15 [l] S Ge 35:2 [m] Ru 1:16; 2:12; 1Ki 18:21; Da 3:18

24:16 [n] Jos 22:29 **24:17** [o] Jdg 6:8 [p] S Ex 10:1 **24:18** [q] S Ex 23:31 [r] S Dt 33:27 [s] Ac 7:45 [t] S Ge 28:21 **24:19** [u] S Lev 11:44; S 20:26 [v] S Ex 20:5 [w] S Ex 34:7 [x] S Ex 23:21 **24:20** [y] 1Ch 28:9, 20; 2Ch 24:18 [z] Ac 7:42 [a] 1Sa 12:25; Hos 13:11 [b] Jos 23:15 **24:22** [c] ver 27; Ru 4:10; Isa 8:2; 43:10; 44:8; Jer 42:5; Mal 2:14 [d] Ps 119:30,173 [e] S Dt 25:9 **24:23** [f] S ver 14 [g] 1Ki 8:58; Ps 119:36; 141:4; Jer 31:33 **24:24** [h] Ex 19:8; Jer 42:6

24:10 *I would not listen to Balaam.* Not only did the Lord reject Balaam's prayers, he also turned his curse into a blessing (see Nu 23–24; Ne 13:2; Mic 6:5).

24:12 *hornet.* See note on Ex 23:28.

24:14 *fear the LORD.* Trust, serve and worship him (see note on Ge 20:11). *gods your ancestors worshiped beyond the Euphrates River and in Egypt.* See v. 2. Joshua appealed to the Israelites to put away the gods their ancestors had worshiped in Mesopotamia and Egypt. In Ur and Harran, Terah's family would have been exposed to the worship of the moon-god, Nanna(r) or Sin (see 6:1; Ge 11:31 and notes). The golden calf of Ex 32:4 may be an example of their worship of the gods of Egypt. It was probably patterned after Apis, the sacred bull of Egypt; see notes on Ex 9:3; 32:4. (Jeroboam's golden calves at Bethel and Dan, on the other hand, probably represented mounts or pedestals for a riding or standing deity; see 1Ki 12:28–29 and notes.)

24:15 *as for me.* Joshua publicly makes his commitment, hoping to elicit the same from Israel.

24:17–18 A confessional statement based on the miraculous events of the exodus.

24:19 *You are not able.* Strong words to emphasize the danger of overconfidence. *He is a holy God.* See Lev 11:44 and note. *he is a jealous God.* See Ex 20:5; Zec 1:14 and notes.

24:22 *witnesses.* See v. 27; a normal part of treaty/covenant-making (see Dt 30:19).

24:23 *foreign gods.* Such gods were represented by idols of wood and metal, which could be thrown away and destroyed.

25 On that day Joshua made a covenant[i]
or the people, and there at Shechem[j] he
eaffirmed for them decrees and laws.[k]
5 And Joshua recorded[l] these things in
he Book of the Law of God.[m] Then he
ook a large stone[n] and set it up there un-
er the oak[o] near the holy place of the
.ORD.
27 "See!" he said to all the people. "This
tone[p] will be a witness[q] against us. It has
eard all the words the LORD has said to
s. It will be a witness against you if you
re untrue[r] to your God."[s]
28 Then Joshua dismissed the people,
ach to their own inheritance.[t]

uried in the Promised Land

:29-31pp — Jdg 2:6-9

29 After these things, Joshua son of Nun,
ıe servant of the LORD, died[u] at the age
f a hundred and ten.[v] 30 And they buried
im in the land of his inheritance, at Timnath Serah[c][w] in the hill country of Ephraim, north of Mount Gaash.[x]
31 Israel served the LORD throughout the
lifetime of Joshua and of the elders[y] who
outlived him and who had experienced everything the LORD had done for Israel.
32 And Joseph's bones,[z] which the Israelites had brought up from Egypt,[a] were
buried at Shechem in the tract of land[b]
that Jacob bought for a hundred pieces of
silver[d] from the sons of Hamor, the father
of Shechem. This became the inheritance
of Joseph's descendants.
33 And Eleazar son of Aaron[c] died and
was buried at Gibeah,[d] which had been
allotted to his son Phinehas[e] in the hill
country[f] of Ephraim.

24:25 [i] S Ex 24:8 [j] S Jos 17:7 [k] Ex 15:25 **24:26** [l] S Dt 17:18 [m] S Dt 28:61; S 31:24 [n] S Ge 28:18; S Dt 27:2 [o] S Ge 12:6; S Jdg 4:11 **24:27** [p] S Ge 28:18; Hab 2:11 [q] S ver 22; S Ge 21:30; S Jos 22:27 [r] S Jos 7:11 [s] S Nu 11:20; S Pr 30:9 **24:28** [t] Jdg 21:23,24 **24:29** [u] Jdg 1:1 [v] S Ge 50:22 **24:30** [w] S Jos 19:50 [x] 2Sa 23:30 **24:31** [y] Jos 7:6 **24:32** [z] Heb 11:22 [a] S Ge 47:29-30 [b] Ge 33:19; Jn 4:5; Ac 7:16 **24:33** [c] S Jos 22:13 [d] S Jos 15:57 [e] S Ex 6:25 [f] 1Sa 9:4; 1Ki 4:8

[c] 30 Also known as *Timnath Heres* (see Judges 2:9)
[d] 32 Hebrew *hundred kesitahs;* a kesitah was a unit of money of unknown weight and value.

:25 *covenant for the people.* Consisting of the pledges they ıd agreed to and the decrees and laws from God.

:26 *Book of the Law of God.* Probably a list of decrees and ws Joshua had drawn up for the people (v. 25). *large stone.* t up as a witness to the covenant renewal that closed Josh- ı's ministry, this is the eighth memorial in the land remind- g the Israelites of what the Lord had done for them through s servant (see note on 4:9). Thus the promised land itself ɔre full testimony to God's people — how they had come :o possession of the land and how they would remain in e land only by fulfilling the covenant conditions. *oak.* See ıte on Ge 12:6.

24:29 – 33 Three burials. Since it was a deep desire of the ancients to be buried in their homeland, these no- es not only mark the conclusion of the story and the close an era but also underscore the fact that Israel had indeed en established in the promised homeland. The Lord had pt his covenant promises.

24:29 *a hundred and ten.* For the significance of this number see note on Ge 50:26.

24:30 *buried him ... at Timnath Serah.* See 19:50 and note.

24:31 The story told in Joshua is a testimony to Israel's faithfulness in that generation. The author anticipates the quite different story that would follow in Judges.

24:32 *Joseph's bones.* Returning his bones to Shechem was significant not only because of the ancient plot of land Jacob bought from Hamor (Ge 33:19) but also because Shechem was to be the center of the tribes of Ephraim and Manasseh, the two sons of Joseph. Also, the return fulfilled an oath sworn to Joseph on his deathbed (Ge 50:25; Ex 13:19).

24:33 *Eleazar.* The high priest who served Joshua, as Aaron had served Moses. *Gibeah.* Not the Benjamite city, but a place in Ephraim near Shiloh.

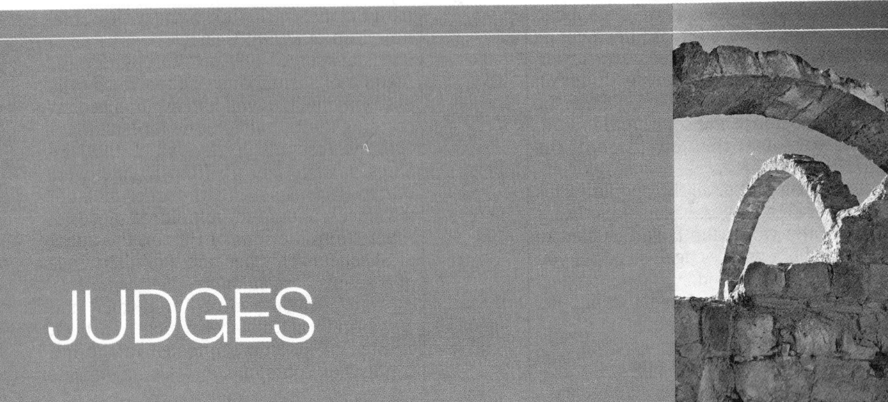

JUDGES

INTRODUCTION

Title

The title refers to the leaders Israel had from the time of the elders who outlived Joshua until th time of the monarchy. Their principal purpose is best expressed in 2:16: "Then the LORD raised u judges, who saved them out of the hands of … raiders." Since it was God who permitted the op pressions and raised up deliverers, he himself was Israel's ultimate Judge and Deliverer (11:27; se 8:23, where Gideon, a judge, insists that the Lord is Israel's true ruler).

Author and Date

Although tradition ascribes the book to Samuel, the author is actually unknown. It is possible tha Samuel assembled some of the accounts from the period of the judges and that such prophets as Nathan and Gad, both of whom were associated with David's court, had a hand in shaping and editing the material (see 1Ch 29:29).

The date of composition is also unknown, but it was undoubtedly during the monarchy. The frequent expression "In those days Israel had no king" (17:6; 18:1; 19:1; 21:25) suggests a date after the establishment of the monarchy. The observation that the Jebusites still controlled Jerusalem (1:21) has been taken to indicate a time before David's capture of the city c. 1000 BC (see 2Sa 5:6 – 10). But the new conditions in Israel alluded to in chs. 17 – 21 suggest a time after the Davidic dynasty had been effectively established (tenth century BC).

a quick look

Author:
Unknown, though certain sections may derive from the prophet Samuel

Audience:
God's chosen people, the Israelites

Date:
Probably about 1000 BC

Theme:
In danger of losing the promised land, the Israelites ar delivered again and again by God through leaders known as "judges."

Themes and Theology

The book of Judges depicts the life of Israel in the promised land from the death of Joshua to the rise of the monarchy. On the one hand, it is an account of frequent apostasy, provoking divine chastening. On the other hand, it tells of urgent appeals to God in times of crisis, moving the Lord to raise up leaders ("judges") through whom he throws off foreign oppressors and restores the land to peace.

On the one hand, Judges is an account of frequent apostasy, provoking divine chastening. On the other hand, it tells about urgent appeals to God in times of crisis, moving him to raise up leaders ("judges") through whom he throws off foreign oppressors and restores the land to peace.

With Israel's conquest of the promised land through the leadership of Joshua, many of the ovenant promises God had made to their ancestors were fulfilled (see Jos 21:43–45). The Lord's and, where Israel was to enter into rest, lay under their feet; it remained only for them to occupy , to dislodge the Canaanites and to cleanse it of paganism. The time had come for Israel to be the ingdom of God in the form of an established commonwealth on earth.

But in Canaan, Israel quickly forgot the acts of God that had given them birth and had estabshed them in the land. Consequently they lost sight of their unique identity as God's people, choen and called to be his army and the loyal citizens of his emerging kingdom. They settled down nd attached themselves to Canaan's peoples together with Canaanite morals, gods, and religious eliefs and practices as readily as to Canaan's agriculture and social life.

Throughout Judges the fundamental issue is the lordship of God in Israel, especially Israel's cknowledgment of and loyalty to his rule. His kingship over Israel had been uniquely established y the covenant at Sinai (Ex 19–24), which was later renewed by Moses on the plains of Moab (Dt 9) and by Joshua at Shechem (Jos 24). The author accuses the Israelites of having rejected the ingship of the Lord again and again. They stopped fighting the Lord's battles, turned to the gods f Canaan to secure the blessings of family, flocks and fields, and abandoned God's laws for daily ving. In the very center of the cycle of the judges (see Outline), Gideon had to remind Israel that e Lord was its King (see note on 8:23). The recurring lament, and indictment, of chs. 17–21 (see utline) is: "In those days Israel had no king; everyone did as they saw fit" (17:6; see note there). The rimary reference here is doubtless to the earthly mediators of the Lord's rule (i.e., human kings), ut the implicit charge is that Israel did not truly acknowledge or obey her heavenly King either.

Only by the Lord's sovereign use of foreign oppression to chasten his people—thereby imple-enting the covenant curses (see Lev 26:14–45; Dt 28:15–68)—and by his raising up deliverers hen his people cried out to him did he maintain his kingship in Israel and preserve his embryonic ngdom from extinction. The Israelites' flawed condition was graphically exposed; they continued need new saving acts by God in order to enter into the promised rest (see note on Jos 1:13).

Out of the recurring cycles of disobedience, foreign oppression, cries of distress, and deliver-nce (see 2:11–19; Ne 9:26–31) emerges another important theme—the covenant faithfulness of e Lord. The amazing patience and long-suffering of God are no better demonstrated than during is unsettled period.

Remarkably, this age of Israel's failure, following directly on the redemptive events that came rough Moses and Joshua, is in a special way the OT age of the Spirit. God's Spirit enabled people accomplish feats of victory in the Lord's war against the powers that threatened his kingdom (see 10; 6:34; 11:29; 13:25; 14:6,19; 15:14; see also 1Sa 10:6,10; 11:6; 16:13). This same Spirit, poured out the church following the redemptive work of the second Joshua (Jesus), empowered the people the Lord to begin the task of preaching the gospel to all nations and of advancing the kingdom God (see notes on Ac 1:2,8; 2:4,33).

ackground

Fixing precise dates for the judges is difficult and complex. The dating system followed here is based primarily on 1Ki 6:1, which speaks of an interval of 480 years between the exodus d the fourth year of Solomon's reign. This would place the exodus c. 1446 BC and the period of the judges between c. 1380 and the rise of Saul, c. 1050. Jephthah's statement that Israel ha occupied Heshbon for 300 years (11:26) generally agrees with these dates. And the reference t "Israel" in the Merneptah Stele demonstrates that Israel was established in Canaan before 1210 B (see chart, p. xxiii).

Some maintain, however, that the number 480 in 1Ki 6:1 is somewhat artificial, arrived at b multiplying 12 (perhaps in reference to the 12 judges) by 40 (a conventional number of years for generation). They point out the frequent use of the round numbers 10, 20, 40 and 80 in the boo of Judges itself. A later date for the exodus would of course require a much shorter period of tim for the judges (see Introduction to Exodus: Chronology; see also note on 1Ki 6:1).

Literary Features

Even a quick reading of Judges discloses its basic threefold division: (1) a prologue (1:1—3:6), (2) main body (3:7—16:31) and (3) an epilogue (chs. 17–21). Closer study brings to light a more com plex structure, with interwoven themes that bind the whole into an intricately designed portray of the character of an age.

The prologue (1:1—3:6) has two parts, and each serves a different purpose. They are not chro nologically related, nor does either offer a strict chronological scheme of the time as a whol

Aerial view of Beth Shemesh and the Sorek Valley (see map, p. 417). Beth Shemesh is about 12 miles west o Jerusalem and is where the Philistines returned the ark of the covenant to the Israelites (1Sa 6). The Valley Sorek is where Samson fell in love with Delilah (Jdg 16:4).

The first part (1:1—2:5) sets the stage historically for the narratives that follow. It describes the sraelites' occupation of the promised land—from their initial success to their large-scale failure nd divine rebuke.

The second part (2:6—3:6) indicates a basic perspective on the period from the time of Joshua o the rise of the monarchy, a time characterized by recurring cycles of apostasy, oppression, cries of distress and gracious divine deliverance. The author summarizes and explains the Lord's dealings vith his rebellious people and introduces some of the basic vocabulary and formulas he will use in he later narratives: "did evil in the eyes of the LORD," 2:11 (see 3:7,12; 4:1; 6:1; 10:6); "gave them into he hands of," 2:14 (see 6:1; 13:1); and "sold them," 2:14 (see 3:8; 4:2; 10:7).

The main body of the book (3:7—16:31), which gives the actual accounts of the recurring cycles apostasy, oppression, distress, deliverance), has its own unique design. Each cycle has a similar beginning ("The Israelites did evil in the eyes of the LORD"; see note on 3:7) and a recognizable onclusion ("the land had peace ... years" or "led Israel ... years"; see note on 3:11). The first of these cycles (Othniel; see 3:7–11 and note) provides the "report form" used for each successive story of ppression and deliverance.

The remaining five cycles form the following narrative units, each of which focuses on one of he major judges:

(1) Ehud (3:12–30), a lone hero from the tribe of Benjamin who delivers Israel from oppression from the east.
  - (2) Deborah (chs. 4–5), a woman from one of the Joseph tribes (Ephraim), who judges at a time when Israel is being overrun by a coalition of Canaanites under Sisera.
    - (3) Gideon and his son Abimelek (chs. 6–9), whose story forms the central account. In many ways Gideon is the ideal judge, evoking memory of Moses, while his son is the very antithesis of a responsible and faithful judge.
  - (4) Jephthah (10:6—12:7), a social outcast from the other Joseph tribe (Manasseh, east of the Jordan), who judges at a time when Israel is being threatened by a coalition of powers under the king of Ammon.

(5) Samson (chs. 13–16), a lone hero from the tribe of Dan who delivers Israel from oppression from the west.

The arrangement of these narrative units is significant. The central accounts of Gideon (the ord's ideal judge) and Abimelek (the anti-judge) are bracketed by the parallel narratives of the voman Deborah and the social outcast Jephthah—which in turn are framed by the stories of he lone heroes Ehud and Samson. In this way even the structure focuses attention on the crucial ssue of the period of the judges: Israel's attraction to the Baals of Canaan (shown by Abimelek; ee note on 9:1–57) versus the Lord's kingship over his people (encouraged by Gideon; see note n 8:23).

The epilogue (chs. 17–21) characterizes the era in yet another way, depicting religious and noral corruption on the part of individuals, cities and tribes. Like the introduction, it has two divisions that are neither chronologically related nor expressly dated to the careers of specific judges. The events must have taken place, however, rather early in the period of the judges (see notes on 8:30; 20:1,28).

THE JUDGES OF ISRAEL

SHAMGAR ?
Hazor (Jabin)
ELON
Sea of Galilee (Kinnereth)
Kishon R.
Kedesh (of Naphtali) (Barak)
JAIR
Mt. Tabor
Havvoth Jair
GIDEON
Hill of Moreh
Megiddo
En Harod
Kamon
Mediterranean Sea (Great Sea)
Ophrah
Taanach
Jabesh Gilead
Abel Meholah
Jordan R.
JEPHTHAH
TOLA
Shamir
Mt. Ebal
Zaphon
ABDON
Shechem
Penuel
Pirathon
Mt. Gerizim
Sukkoth
Jabbok R.
Mizpah
Shiloh
AMMONITES
DEBORAH
Gilead
Bethel
EHUD
Rabbah of the Ammonites
Mizpah
Gilgal
Ramah
Jericho (City of Palms)
Timnah
Sorek Valley
Eshtaol
Gibeah
Zorah
Jerusalem
IBZAN
SAMSON
Bethlehem
Ashkelon
Tableland of Moab (Mishor)
SHAMGAR ?
Hebron
Gaza
PHILISTINES
OTHNIEL
Dead Sea (Salt Sea)
Debir
Arnon Gorge
Beersheba

GIDEON Major judge
ELON Minor judge

0 10 km.
0 10 miles

The whole design of the book of Judges from prologue to epilogue portrays an age gone awry.

By dating the events of the epilogue only in relationship to the monarchy (see the recurring refrain in 17:6; 18:1; 19:1; 21:25), the author contrasts the age of the judges with the better time that the monarchy inaugurated, undoubtedly having in view the rule of David and his dynasty (see note on 17:1—21:25). The book mentions two instances of the Lord's assigning leadership to the tribe of Judah: (1) in driving out the Canaanites (1:1–2) and (2) in disciplining a tribe in Israel (20:18). The author views the ruler from the tribe of Judah as the savior of the nation.

The first division of the epilogue (chs. 17–18) relates the story of Micah's development of a paganized place of worship and tells of the tribe of Dan abandoning their allotted territory while adopting Micah's corrupted religion. The second division (chs. 19–21) tells the story of a Levite's sad experience at Gibeah in Benjamin and records the disciplinary removal of the tribe of Benjamin because it had defended the degenerate town of Gibeah.

The two divisions have several interesting parallels:

(1) Both involve a Levite's passing between Bethlehem (in Judah) and Ephraim across the Benjamin-Dan corridor.
(2) Both mention 600 warriors—those who led the tribe of Dan and those who survived from the tribe of Benjamin.
(3) Both conclude with the emptying of a tribal area in that corridor (Dan and Benjamin).

Not only are these Benjamin-Dan parallels significant within the epilogue, but they also form a notable link to the main body of the book. The tribe of Benjamin, which in the epilogue undertook to defend gross immorality, setting ties of blood above loyalty to the Lord, was the tribe from which the Lord raised up the deliverer Ehud (3:15). The tribe of Dan, which in the epilogue retreated from its assigned inheritance and adopted pagan religious practices, was the tribe from which the Lord raised up the deliverer Samson (13:2,5). Thus the tribes that in the epilogue depict the religious and moral corruption of Israel are the very tribes from which the deliverers were chosen whose stories frame the central account of the book (Gideon-Abimelek).

The whole design of the book from prologue to epilogue, the unique manner in which each section deals with the age as a whole, and the way the three major divisions are interrelated clearly portray an age gone awry—an age when "Israel had no king" and "everyone did as they saw fit" (see note on 17:6). Of no small significance is the fact that the story is in episodes and cycles. It is given as the story of all Israel, though usually only certain areas are directly involved. The book portrays the centuries after Joshua as a time of the Israelites' unfaithfulness to the Lord and of their surrender to the allurements of Canaan. Only by the mercies of God were the Israelites not overwhelmed and absorbed by the pagan nations around them. Meanwhile, the history of redemption virtually stood still—awaiting the forward movement that came with the Lord's servant David and the establishment of his dynasty.

Outline

I. Prologue: Incomplete Conquest and Apostasy (1:1—3:6)
   A. First Episode: Israel's Failure to Purge the Land (1:1—2:5)
   B. Second Episode: God's Dealings with Israel's Rebellion (2:6—3:6)

II. Oppression and Deliverance (3:7—16:31)

Major Judges	*Minor Judges*
A. Othniel Defeats Aram Naharaim (3:7–11)	
B. Ehud Defeats Moab (3:12–30)	1. Shamgar (3:31)
C. Deborah Defeats Canaan (chs. 4–5)	
D. Gideon Defeats Midian (chs. 6–8)	
(Abimelek, the anti-judge, ch. 9)	
	2. Tola (10:1–2)
	3. Jair (10:3–5)
E. Jephthah Defeats Ammon (10:6—12:7)	
	4. Ibzan (12:8–10)
	5. Elon (12:11–12)
	6. Abdon (12:13–15)
F. Samson Checks Philistia (chs. 13–16)	

III. Epilogue: Religious and Moral Disorder (chs. 17–21)
- A. First Episode (chs. 17–18; see 17:6; 18:1)
  1. Micah's corruption of religion (ch. 17)
  2. The Danites' departure from their tribal territory (ch. 18)
- B. Second Episode (chs. 19–21; see 19:1; 21:25)
  1. Gibeah's corruption of morals (ch. 19)
  2. The Benjamites' near removal from their tribal territory (chs. 20–21)

Israel Fights the Remaining Canaanites

1:11-15pp — Jos 15:15-19

1 After the death[a] of Joshua, the Israelites asked the LORD, "Who of us is to
go up first[b] to fight against the Canaanites?[c]"
2 The LORD answered, "Judah[d] shall go
up; I have given the land into their hands.[e]"
3 The men of Judah then said to the Simeonites their fellow Israelites, "Come up
with us into the territory allotted to us, to
fight against the Canaanites. We in turn
will go with you into yours." So the Simeonites[f] went with them.
4 When Judah attacked, the LORD gave
the Canaanites and Perizzites[g] into their
hands, and they struck down ten thousand
men at Bezek.[h] 5 It was there that they
found Adoni-Bezek[i] and fought against
him, putting to rout the Canaanites and
Perizzites. 6 Adoni-Bezek fled, but they
chased him and caught him, and cut off
his thumbs and big toes.
7 Then Adoni-Bezek said, "Seventy
kings with their thumbs and big toes cut
off have picked up scraps under my table.
Now God has paid me back[j] for what I did
to them." They brought him to Jerusalem,[k]
and he died there.
8 The men of Judah attacked Jerusalem[l]
also and took it. They put the city to the
sword and set it on fire.
9 After that, Judah went down to fight
against the Canaanites living in the hill
country,[m] the Negev[n] and the western foothills. 10 They advanced against the Canaanites living in Hebron[o] (formerly called Kiriath Arba[p]) and defeated Sheshai, Ahiman
and Talmai.[q] 11 From there they advanced
against the people living in Debir[r] (formerly called Kiriath Sepher).
12 And Caleb said, "I will give my
daughter Aksah in marriage to the man
who attacks and captures Kiriath Sepher."
13 Othniel son of Kenaz, Caleb's younger
brother, took it; so Caleb gave his daughter Aksah to him in marriage.
14 One day when she came to Othni-
el, she urged him[a] to ask her father for a
field. When she got off her donkey, Caleb
asked her, "What can I do for you?"
15 She replied, "Do me a special favor.
Since you have given me land in the Negev, give me also springs of water." So Caleb gave her the upper and lower springs.[s]
16 The descendants of Moses' father-in-
law,[t] the Kenite,[u] went up from the City of
Palms[b][v] with the people of Judah to live
among the inhabitants of the Desert of Judah in the Negev near Arad.[w]

1:1 [a] Jos 24:29 [b] S Nu 2:3-9; Jdg 20:18; 1Ki 20:14 [c] ver 27; S Ge 10:18; Jdg 3:1-6 **1:2** [d] S Ge 49:10 [e] ver 4; Jdg 3:28; 4:7, 14; 7:9 **1:3** [f] ver 17 **1:4** [g] S Ge 13:7; S Jos 3:10 [h] 1Sa 11:8 **1:5** [i] ver 6, 7 **1:7** [j] Lev 24:19; Jer 25:12 [k] S Jos 10:1 **1:8** [l] ver 21; Jos 15:63; 2Sa 5:6 **1:9** [m] S Nu 13:17 [n] S Ge 12:9; S Nu 21:1; Isa 30:6 **1:10** [o] S Ge 13:18 [p] S Ge 35:27 [q] ver 20; S Nu 13:22; Jos 15:14 **1:11** [r] Jos 10:38 **1:15** [s] S Nu 13:6 **1:16** [t] Nu 10:29 [u] S Ge 15:19 [v] Dt 34:3; Jdg 3:13; 2Ch 28:15 [w] Nu 21:1; Jos 12:14

[a] 14 Hebrew; Septuagint and Vulgate *Othniel, he urged her* [b] 16 That is, Jericho

1:1 — 3:6 An introduction in two parts: (1) an account of the Israelites' failure to lay claim completely to the promised land as the Lord had directed (1:1 – 36; see note there) and of his rebuke for their disloyalty (2:1 – 5; see note there); (2) an overview of the main body of the book (3:7 — 16:31), portraying Israel's rebellious ways in the centuries after Joshua's death and showing how the Lord dealt with them in that period (2:6 — 3:6; see note there). See Introduction: Literary Features.

1:1 – 36 Judah is assigned leadership in occupying the land (v. 2; see 20:18). Its vigorous efforts (together with those of Simeon) highlight by contrast the sad story of failure that follows. Only Ephraim's success at Bethel (vv. 22 – 26) breaks the monotony of that story.

1:1 *After the death of Joshua.* The book of Judges, like that of Joshua, tells of an era following the death of a leading figure in the history of redemption (see Jos 1:1). Joshua probably died c. 1390 BC (but see Introduction: Background). The battles under his leadership broke the power of the Canaanites to drive the Israelites out of the land. The task that now confronted Israel was the actual occupation of Canaanite territory (see notes on Jos 18:3; 21:43 – 45). *asked the LORD.* Probably by the priestly use of the Urim and Thummim (see notes on Ex 28:30; 1Sa 2:28). *go up.* The main Israelite encampment was at Gilgal, near Jericho in the Jordan Valley (about 800 feet below sea level), while the Canaanite cities were mainly located in the central hill country (about 2,500 – 3,500 feet above sea level).

1:2 *Judah shall go up.* See 20:18. Judah was also the first to be assigned territory west of the Jordan (Jos 15). The leadership role of the tribe of Judah had been anticipated in the blessing of Jacob (Ge 49:8 – 12; see also note on Jos 15:1).

1:3 *Simeonites.* Joshua assigned to Simeon cities within the territory of Judah (Jos 19:1,9; see Ge 49:5 – 7).

1:4 *Canaanites.* See note on Ge 10:6. *Perizzites.* See note on Ge 13:7. *Bezek.* Saul marshaled his army there before going to Jabesh Gilead (for location, see 1Sa 11:8 and note).

1:5 *Adoni-Bezek.* Means "lord of Bezek."

1:6 *cut off his thumbs and big toes.* Physically mutilating prisoners of war was a common practice in the ancient Near East (see note on 16:21). It rendered them unfit for military service.

1:7 *Seventy kings.* Canaan was made up of many small city-states, each of which was ruled by a king. "Seventy" may be a round number, or it may be symbolic of a large number. *under my table.* Humiliating treatment, like that given to a dog (see Mt 15:27; Lk 16:21). *God has paid me back.* See note on Ex 21:23 – 25.

1:8 *attacked Jerusalem.* Although the city was defeated, it was not occupied by the Israelites at this time (see v. 21). Israel did not permanently control the city until David captured it c. 1000 BC (2Sa 5:6 – 10).

1:10 *Kiriath Arba.* See note on Jos 14:15.

1:11 – 15 Virtually a word-for-word repetition of Jos 15:15 – 19. In Joshua the passage functions as part of the description of the territory allotted to the tribe of Judah. Here it serves as part of the account of Judah's success in taking possession of its tribal territory.

1:11 *Debir.* See note on Jos 10:38.

1:12 *Caleb.* He and Joshua had brought back an optimistic report about the prospects of conquering Canaan (Nu 14:6 – 9). *daughter … in marriage.* Victory in battle was one way to pay the bride-price for a bride (see 1Sa 18:25).

1:13 *Othniel.* First major judge (see 3:7 – 11).

1:16 *Moses' father-in-law.* See note on Ex 2:16.

17 Then the men of Judah went with the
Simeonites[x] their fellow Israelites and attacked the Canaanites living in Zephath,
and they totally destroyed[a] the city. Therefore it was called Hormah.[by] 18 Judah also
took[c] Gaza,[z] Ashkelon[a] and Ekron—each
city with its territory.
19 The LORD was with[b] the men of Judah. They took possession of the hill
country,[c] but they were unable to drive
the people from the plains, because they
had chariots fitted with iron.[d] 20 As Moses
had promised, Hebron[e] was given to Caleb, who drove from it the three sons of
Anak.[f] 21 The Benjamites, however, did not
drive out[g] the Jebusites, who were living
in Jerusalem;[h] to this day the Jebusites live
there with the Benjamites.
22 Now the tribes of Joseph[i] attacked
Bethel,[j] and the LORD was with them.
23 When they sent men to spy out Bethel
(formerly called Luz),[k] 24 the spies saw a
man coming out of the city and they said
to him, "Show us how to get into the city
and we will see that you are treated well.[l]"
25 So he showed them, and they put the
city to the sword but spared[m] the man and
his whole family. 26 He then went to the
land of the Hittites,[n] where he built a city
and called it Luz,[o] which is its name to
this day.
27 But Manasseh did not[p] drive out the
people of Beth Shan or Taanach or Dor[q] or
Ibleam[r] or Megiddo[s] and their surrounding settlements, for the Canaanites[t] were
determined to live in that land. 28 When
Israel became strong, they pressed the Canaanites into forced labor but never drove
them out completely.[u] 29 Nor did Ephraim[v]
drive out the Canaanites living in Gezer,[w]
but the Canaanites continued to live there
among them.[x] 30 Neither did Zebulun drive
out the Canaanites living in Kitron or Na-
halol, so these Canaanites lived among
them, but Zebulun did subject them to
forced labor. 31 Nor did Asher[y] drive out
those living in Akko or Sidon[z] or Ahlab
or Akzib[a] or Helbah or Aphek[b] or Rehob.
32 The Asherites lived among the Canaanite
inhabitants of the land because they did
not drive them out. 33 Neither did Naphtali
drive out those living in Beth Shemesh[d] or
Beth Anath[e]; but the Naphtalites too lived
among the Canaanite inhabitants of the
land, and those living in Beth Shemesh
and Beth Anath became forced laborers
for them. 34 The Amorites[f] confined the
Danites[g] to the hill country, not allowing
them to come down into the plain.[h] 35 And
the Amorites were determined also to hold
out in Mount Heres,[i] Aijalon[j] and Shaalbim,[k] but when the power of the tribes of
Joseph increased, they too were pressed
into forced labor. 36 The boundary of the
Amorites was from Scorpion Pass[l] to Sela[m]
and beyond.[n]

The Angel of the LORD at Bokim

2 The angel of the LORD[o] went up from
Gilgal[p] to Bokim[q] and said, "I brought
you up out of Egypt[r] and led you into the
land I swore to give to your ancestors.[s] I
said, 'I will never break my covenant with

1:17 [x]ver 3 [y]S Nu 14:45 **1:18** [z]Jos 11:22 [a]S Jos 13:3 **1:19** [b]S Nu 14:43 [c]Nu 13:17 [d]S Jos 17:16 **1:20** [e]Jos 10:36 [f]S ver 10; S Jos 14:13 **1:21** [g]S Jos 9:15; S 15:63 [h]S ver 8 **1:22** [i]Jdg 10:9 [j]S Jos 7:2 **1:23** [k]S Ge 28:19 **1:24** [l]S Ge 47:29 **1:25** [m]Jos 6:25 **1:26** [n]S Dt 7:1; Eze 16:3 [o]S Ge 28:19 **1:27** [p]1Ki 9:21 [q]S Jos 11:2 [r]S Jos 17:11 [s]S Jos 12:21 [t]S ver 1 **1:28** [u]Jos 17:12-13 **1:29** [v]Jos 14:4; Jdg 5:14 [w]S Jos 10:33 [x]Jos 16:10 **1:31** [y]S Jos 17:7 [z]S Ge 49:13 [a]S Jos 15:44 [b]S Jos 12:18 [c]S Nu 13:21 **1:33** [d]S Jos 15:10 [e]Jos 19:38 **1:34** [f]Nu 13:29; Jdg 10:11; 1Sa 7:14 [g]S Ge 30:6 [h]Jdg 18:1 **1:35** [i]Jdg 8:13 [j]Jos 19:42 [k]1Ki 4:9 **1:36** [l]Jos 15:3 [m]2Ki 14:7; Isa 16:1; 42:11 [n]Ps 106:34 **2:1** [o]S Ge 16:7 [p]S Dt 11:30 [q]ver 5 [r]Ex 20:2; Jdg 6:8 [s]Ge 17:8

[a] 17 The Hebrew term refers to the irrevocable giving over of things or persons to the LORD, often by totally destroying them. [b] 17 *Hormah* means *destruction.* [c] 18 Hebrew; Septuagint *Judah did not take*

1:17 *men of Judah ... Simeonites.* The Judahites were fulfilling their commitment (v. 3).
1:18 *Gaza, Ashkelon and Ekron.* Three of the five main cities inhabited by the Philistines (see map and accompanying text, p. 359). For the origin of the Philistines, see notes on Ge 10:14; Jer 47:4.
1:19 *unable to drive the people from.* The Israelites failed to comply with God's commands (Dt 7:1–5; 20:16–18) to drive the Canaanites out of the land. Five factors were involved in that failure: (1) The Canaanites possessed superior weapons (here); (2) The Israelites disobeyed God by making treaties with the Canaanites (2:1–3); (3) The Israelites took up the worship of other gods and so violated the covenant the Lord had made with their ancestors (2:20–21); (4) God was testing the Israelites' faithfulness to obey his commands (2:22–23; 3:4); (5) God was giving the Israelites, as his army, the opportunity to develop their skills in warfare (3:1–2). *chariots fitted with iron.* Wooden vehicles with certain iron fittings, perhaps axles (see note on Jos 17:16).
1:20 *As Moses had promised.* See Nu 14:24; Dt 1:36; Jos 14:9–14. *Anak.* See notes on Nu 13:22; Jos 14:15.
1:21 *Benjamites ... did not drive out.* See note on v. 8. Jerusalem lay on the border between Benjamin and Judah but was allotted to Benjamin (Jos 18:28). *Jebusites.* See note on Ge 10:16.
1:22 *tribes of Joseph.* Ephraim and West Manasseh. *Bethel.* See note on Ge 12:8. There is archaeological evidence of a destruction in the thirteenth century BC that may reflect the battle mentioned in this verse.
1:23 *spy out.* See note on Nu 13:2.
1:25 *spared the man.* Cf. the treatment of Rahab (Jos 6:25).
1:26 *land of the Hittites.* A name for Aram (Syria) at the time of the conquest (see note on Ge 10:15).
1:27–29 See Jos 17:16–18.
1:28 *forced labor.* See note on Jos 16:10.
1:33 *Beth Shemesh.* Location unknown. The name means "house of the sun (god)." There was also a Beth Shemesh in Judah (see note on v. 35). *Beth Anath.* Means "house of (the goddess) Anath" (see notes on 3:31; Jer 1:1).
1:34 *Amorites.* See note on Ge 10:16. *confined the Danites.* Joshua had defeated the Amorites earlier (Jos 10:5–11), but they were still strong enough to withstand the Danites. For this reason a large number of Danites migrated northward a short time later (see ch. 18).
1:35 *Mount Heres.* Means "mountain of the sun (god)"; probably the Beth Shemesh in Judah, which is also called Ir Shemesh, "city of the sun (god)" (Jos 19:41).
1:36 *boundary of the Amorites.* Their southern boundary (see Jos 15:2–3).
2:1–5 Because Israel had not zealously laid claim to the

ou,[t] 2and you shall not make a covenant
with the people of this land,[u] but you shall
reak down their altars.[v]' Yet you have
lisobeyed[w] me. Why have you done this?
And I have also said, 'I will not drive
hem out before you;[x] they will become
raps[y] for you, and their gods will become
nares[z] to you.'"

2:1 [t]S Lev 26:42-44; Dt 7:9 2:2 [u]S Ex 23:32; S 34:12; Dt 7:2 [v]S Ex 23:24; 34:13; Dt 7:5; 2Ch 14:3 [w]Jer 7:28 2:3 [x]Jos 23:13 [y]S Nu 33:55 [z]S Ex 10:7

4When the angel of the LORD had spoken these things to all the Israelites, the
people wept aloud,[a] 5and they called that
place Bokim.[a][b] There they offered sacrifices to the LORD.

[a] 5 *Bokim* means *weepers.*

2:4 [a]S Ge 27:38; S Nu 25:6; 2Ki 17:13 2:5 [b]ver 1

---

and as the Lord had directed (see 1:27 – 36), he withdrew his elping hand. On this note the first half of the introduction nds. Although the actual time of the Lord's rebuke is not ndicated, it was probably early in the period of the judges nd may even have been connected with the event in Jos 9 or possibly Jos 18:1 – 3).

2:1 *angel of the LORD.* See note on Ge 16:7. The role of the angel of the Lord in this passage parallels that of he unnamed prophet in 6:8 – 10 and the word of the Lord in 10:11 – 14, calling his people to account. *Gilgal.* The place where Israel first became established in the land under Joshua (see Jos 4:19 — 5:12). *out of Egypt.* The theme of Exodus, frequently referred to as the supreme evidence of God's redemptive love for his people in the OT (see Ex 20:2). *swore to give.* See Ge 15:18; see also note on Heb 6:13.

2:2 *not make a covenant.* To have done so would have broken their covenant with the Lord (see Ex 23:32).

FIVE CITIES OF THE PHILISTINES

Gaza, Ashkelon, Ashdod, Ekron and Gath comprise a list of familiar Biblical names. Each of these cities was a commercial emporium with important connections both north (as far as Mesopotamia) and south (as far as Egypt) by way of the coastal highway that served as one of the major highways of the ancient world. Also the ships of Phoenicia, Cyprus, Crete and the Aegean called at Philistia's seaports. Among these seaports was a place today called Tel Qasile on the Yarkon River (the "Kanah Ravine" of Jos 16:8; 17:9) just north of modern Tel Aviv. A Philistine temple has been found at Tel Qasile.

The Philistine plain itself was an arid, loam-covered lowland between the Mediterranean Sea and the foothills of the Judahite plateau on the east. To the south lay a stretch of undulating sand dunes adjacent to the sea. No area in Biblical history was more frequently contested than the western foothills, lying on the border between Judah and Philistia. Originally a part of Judah's tribal allotment, the coastal area was never totally wrested away from the Philistines. Beth Shemesh, Timnah, Azekah and Ziklag were among the towns coveted by both Israelites and Philistines, and they figure in the stories of Samson, Goliath and David. The area to the north of Philistia, the plain of Sharon, was also contested at various periods. During Saul's reign the Philistines even held Beth Shan and the Valley of Jezreel. Later, from about the time of Baasha on, a long border war was conducted by the Israelites at Gibbethon.

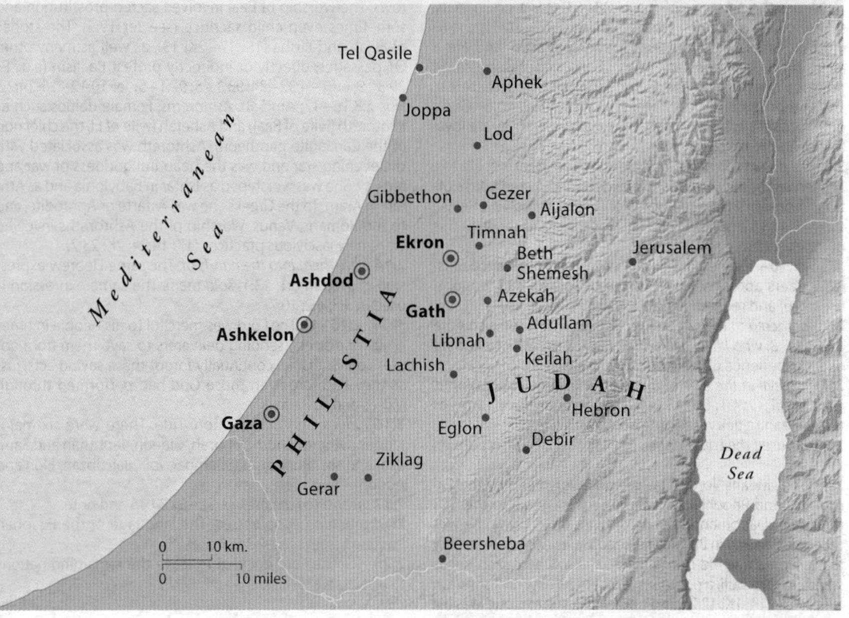

Disobedience and Defeat

2:6-9pp — Jos 24:29-31

6 After Joshua had dismissed the Israelites, they went to take possession of the
land, each to their own inheritance. 7 The
people served the LORD throughout the
lifetime of Joshua and of the elders who
outlived him and who had seen all the
great things the LORD had done for Israel.[c]
8 Joshua son of Nun,[d] the servant of the
LORD, died at the age of a hundred and
ten. 9 And they buried him in the land of
his inheritance, at Timnath Heres[a][e] in the
hill country of Ephraim, north of Mount
Gaash.
10 After that whole generation had been
gathered to their ancestors, another generation grew up who knew neither the LORD
nor what he had done for Israel.[f] 11 Then
the Israelites did evil[g] in the eyes of the
LORD[h] and served the Baals.[i] 12 They forsook the LORD, the God of their ancestors,
who had brought them out of Egypt. They
followed and worshiped various gods[j] of
the peoples around them.[k] They aroused[l]
the LORD's anger[m] 13 because they forsook[n]
him and served Baal and the Ashtoreths.[o]
14 In his anger[p] against Israel the LORD gave
them into the hands[q] of raiders who plundered[r] them. He sold them[s] into the hands
of their enemies all around, whom they
were no longer able to resist.[t] 15 Whenever
Israel went out to fight, the hand of the
LORD was against them[u] to defeat them,
just as he had sworn to them. They were
in great distress.[v]
16 Then the LORD raised up judges,[b][w]
who saved[x] them out of the hands of these
raiders. 17 Yet they would not listen to their
judges but prostituted[y] themselves to other
gods[z] and worshiped them.[a] They quickly
turned[b] from the ways of their ancestors,
who had been obedient to the LORD's commands.[c] 18 Whenever the LORD raised up a
judge for them, he was with the judge and
saved[d] them out of the hands of their enemies as long as the judge lived; for the
LORD relented[e] because of their groaning[f]
under those who oppressed and afflicted[g]
them. 19 But when the judge died, the people returned to ways even more corrupt[h]
than those of their ancestors,[i] following
other gods and serving and worshiping
them.[j] They refused to give up their evil
practices and stubborn[k] ways.
20 Therefore the LORD was very angry
with Israel and said, "Because this nation

[a] 9 Also known as *Timnath Serah* (see Joshua 19:50 and 24:30) [b] 16 Or *leaders*; similarly in verses 17-19

2:7 [c] ver 17 **2:8** [d] Jos 1:1 **2:9** [e] S Jos 19:50 **2:10** [f] S Ex 5:2; Gal 4:8 **2:11** [g] 1Ki 15:26 [h] Jdg 3:12; 4:1; 6:1; 10:6 [i] Jdg 3:7; 8:33; 1Ki 16:31; 22:53; 2Ki 10:18; 17:16 **2:12** [j] S Dt 32:12; Ps 106:36 [k] S Dt 31:16; Jdg 10:6 [l] S Nu 11:33 [m] Dt 4:25; Ps 78:58; 106:40 **2:13** [n] 1Sa 7:3; 1Ki 11:5,33; 2Ki 23:13 [o] Jdg 3:7; 5:8; 6:25; 8:33; 10:6; 1Sa 31:10; Ne 9:26; Ps 78:56; Jer 11:10 **2:14** [p] S Dt 31:17 [q] Ne 9:27; Ps 106:41 [r] Ps 44:10; 89:41; Eze 34:8 [s] S Dt 32:30; S Jdg 3:8 [t] S Dt 28:25 **2:15** [u] Ru 1:13; Job 19:21; Ps 32:4 [v] Ge 35:3; 2Sa 22:7; 2Ch 15:4; Job 5:5; 20:22; Ps 4:1; 18:6 **2:16** [w] Ru 1:1; 1Sa 4:18; 7:6,15; 2Sa 7:11; 1Ch 17:10; Ac 13:20 [x] 1Sa 11:3; Ps 106:43 **2:17** [y] S Ex 34:15; S Nu 15:39 [z] S Ps 4:2 [a] Ne 9:28; Ps 106:36 [b] Dt 9:12 [c] ver 7 **2:18** [d] 1Sa 7:3; 2Ki 13:5; Isa 19:20; 43:3,11; 45:15 21; 49:26; 60:16; 63:8 [e] S Dt 32:36 [f] S Ex 2:23 [g] S Nu 10:9 **2:19** [h] S Ge 6:11; S Dt 4:16 [i] Dt 32:17; Ne 9:2; Ps 78:57; Jer 44:3,9 [j] Jdg 4:1; 8:33 [k] S Ex 32:9 **2:20** [l] S Dt 31:17; Jos 23:16

2:6 — 3:6 The second half of the introduction continues the narrative of Jos 24:28 – 31. It is a preliminary survey of the accounts narrated in Jdg 3:7 — 16:31, showing that Israel's first centuries in the promised land are a recurring cycle of apostasy, oppression, cries of distress and gracious deliverance (see Introduction: Literary Features). The author reminds the Israelites that they will enjoy God's promised rest in the promised land only when they are loyal to him and to his covenant.

2:6 *take possession of the land.* See note on 1:1.

2:8 *servant of the LORD.* Joshua is identified as the Lord's official representative (see notes on Ex 14:31; Ps 18 title; Isa 41:8 – 9; 42:1). *a hundred and ten.* For the significance of this number, see note on Ge 50:26.

2:10 – 15 The Lord withdraws his help because of Israel's apostasy. He "sells" the people he had "bought" (Ex 15:16) and redeemed (Ex 15:13; cf. Ps 74:2).

2:10 *gathered to their ancestors.* See Ge 15:15; see also note on Ge 25:8. *who knew neither the LORD ... Israel.* They had no direct experience of the Lord's acts (see Ex 1:8).

2:11 *did evil in the eyes of the LORD.* The same expression is used in 3:7,12; 4:1; 6:1; 10:6. *Baals.* The many local forms of this Canaanite deity (see note on v. 13).

2:12 *aroused the LORD's anger.* See Dt 4:25; see also note on Zec 1:2.

2:13 *Baal.* Means "lord." Baal, the god worshiped by the Canaanites and Phoenicians, was variously known to them as the son of Dagon and the son of El. In Aram (Syria) he was called Hadad and in Babylonia, Adad. Believed to give fertility to the womb and life-giving rain to the soil, he is pictured as standing on a bull, a popular symbol of fertility and strength (see Jos 24:14; 1Ki 12:28 and notes). The storm cloud was his chariot, thunder his voice, and lightning his spear and arrows. The worship of Baal involved sacred prostitution and sometimes even child sacrifice (see Jer 19:5). The stories of Elijah and Elisha (1Ki 17 – 2Ki 13), as well as many other OT passages, directly or indirectly protest Baalism (e.g., Ps 29:3 – 9; 68:1 – 4,32 – 34; 93:1 – 5; 97:1 – 5; Jer 10:12 – 16; 14:22 Hos 2:8,16 – 17; Am 5:8). *Ashtoreths.* Female deities such as Ashtoreth (wife of Baal) and Asherah (wife of El, the chief god of the Canaanite pantheon). Ashtoreth was associated with the evening star and was the beautiful goddess of war and fertility. She was worshiped as Ishtar in Babylonia and as Athtart in Aram. To the Greeks she was Astarte or Aphrodite, and to the Romans, Venus. Worship of the Ashtoreths involved extremely lascivious practices (1Ki 14:24; 2Ki 23:7).

2:14 *gave them into the hands of.* The same Hebrew expression is used in 6:1; 13:1. *sold them.* The same expression is used in 3:8; 4:2; 10:7.

2:16 – 19 The Lord was merciful to his people in times of distress, sending deliverers to save them from oppression. But Israel continually forgot these saving acts, just as they had forgotten those God had performed through Moses and Joshua.

2:16 *judges.* See Introduction: Title. There were six major judges (Othniel, Ehud, Deborah, Gideon, Jephthah and Samson) and six minor ones (Shamgar, Tola, Jair, Ibzan, Elon and Abdon).

2:17 *prostituted themselves.* See Ex 34:15 and note.

2:18 *groaning ... oppressed.* The language of the Egyptian bondage (see Ex 2:24; 3:9; 6:5).

2:20 – 23 The Lord decided to leave the remaining nations to test Israel's loyalty.

has violated the covenant[m] I ordained for
their ancestors and has not listened to me,
21 I will no longer drive out[n] before them
any of the nations Joshua left when he
died. 22 I will use them to test[o] Israel and
see whether they will keep the way of the
LORD and walk in it as their ancestors did."
23 The LORD had allowed those nations to
remain; he did not drive them out at once
by giving them into the hands of Joshua.[p]

3 These are the nations the LORD left
to test[q] all those Israelites who had
not experienced any of the wars in Canaan 2 (he did this only to teach warfare
to the descendants of the Israelites who
had not had previous battle experience):
3 the five[r] rulers of the Philistines,[s] all the
Canaanites, the Sidonians, and the Hivites[t]
living in the Lebanon mountains from
Mount Baal Hermon[u] to Lebo Hamath.[v]
4 They were left to test[w] the Israelites to
see whether they would obey the LORD's
commands, which he had given their ancestors through Moses.
5 The Israelites lived[x] among the Canaanites, Hittites, Amorites, Perizzites,[y] Hivites
and Jebusites.[z] 6 They took their daughters[a]
in marriage and gave their own daughters
to their sons, and served their gods.[b]

Othniel

7 The Israelites did evil in the eyes of the
LORD; they forgot the LORD[c] their God and
served the Baals and the Asherahs.[d] 8 The
anger of the LORD burned against Israel
so that he sold[e] them into the hands of
Cushan-Rishathaim[f] king of Aram Naharaim,[a][g] to whom the Israelites were subject for eight years. 9 But when they cried
out[h] to the LORD, he raised up for them a
deliverer,[i] Othniel[j] son of Kenaz, Caleb's
younger brother, who saved them. 10 The
Spirit of the LORD came on him,[k] so that
he became Israel's judge[b] and went to
war. The LORD gave Cushan-Rishathaim[l]
king of Aram[m] into the hands of Othniel,
who overpowered him. 11 So the land had
peace[n] for forty years,[o] until Othniel son of
Kenaz[p] died.

Ehud

12 Again the Israelites did evil in the eyes
of the LORD,[q] and because they did this evil
the LORD gave Eglon king of Moab[r] power
over Israel. 13 Getting the Ammonites[s] and
Amalekites[t] to join him, Eglon came and
attacked Israel, and they took possession
of the City of Palms.[c][u] 14 The Israelites were
subject to Eglon king of Moab[v] for eighteen years.

[a] *8* That is, Northwest Mesopotamia [b] *10* Or *leader*
[c] *13* That is, Jericho

2:20 [m] S Jos 7:11; S 2Ki 17:15 **2:21** [n] S Jos 23:5 **2:22** [o] S Ge 22:1; S Ex 15:25 **2:23** [p] Jdg 1:1 **3:1** [q] S Ex 15:25 **3:3** [r] S Jos 13:3 [s] S Ge 10:14 [t] S Ge 10:17; S Ex 3:8 [u] S Dt 3:8 [v] S Nu 13:21 **3:4** [w] S Ex 15:25 **3:5** [x] Ps 106:35 [y] S Jos 3:10 [z] S Jos 11:3; Ezr 9:1 **3:6** [a] Ezr 10:18; Ne 13:23; Mal 2:11 [b] S Ex 34:16; Dt 7:3-4; S Dt 7:16 **3:7** [c] Dt 4:9; S 32:18; Jdg 8:34; Ps 78:11,42; 106:7; Jer 23:27 [d] S Ex 34:13; S Jdg 2:11, 13; 1Ki 16:33; 2Ch 34:7; Isa 17:8 **3:8** [e] Jdg 2:14; Ps 44:12; Isa 50:1; 52:3 [f] ver 10 [g] S Ge 24:10 **3:9** [h] ver 15; Jdg 6:6, 7; 10:10; 1Sa 12:10; Ps 106:44; 107:13 [i] S Dt 28:29; Ne 9:27 [j] S Jos 15:17 **3:10** [k] S Nu 11:25, 29; Jdg 6:34; 11:29; 13:25; 14:6, 19; 15:14; 1Sa 11:6; 16:13; 1Ki 18:46; 1Ch 12:18; 2Ch 24:20; Isa 11:2 [l] ver 8 [m] S Ge 10:22 **3:11** [n] ver 30; S Jos 14:15; Jdg 5:31; 8:28 [o] S Ex 16:35 [p] S Jos 15:17 **3:12** [q] S Jdg 2:11, 14 [r] 1Sa 12:9 **3:13** [s] S Ge 19:38; Jdg 10:11 [t] S Ge 14:7 [u] S Jdg 1:16 **3:14** [v] Jer 48:1

3:1–6 The list of nations the Lord left roughly describes an arc along the western and northern boundaries of the area actually occupied by Israel at the death of Joshua (vv. 1–4). Within Israelite-occupied territory there were large groups of native peoples (v. 5; see 1:27–36) with whom the Israelites intermingled, often adopting their religions (v. 6).

3:2 *only.* Or "especially." *to teach warfare.* As his covenant servant, Israel was the Lord's army for fighting against the powers of the world that were settled in his land. Because of the incomplete conquest, succeeding generations in Israel needed to become capable warriors.

3:3 *five rulers.* See note on Jos 13:3. These rulers had control of a five-city confederacy (see map, p. 359). At one point Judah defeated three of the cities (1:18) but was unable to hold them. *Sidonians.* Here used collectively of the Phoenicians. *Hivites.* Here identified with a region in northern Canaan reaching all the way to Hamath (see Jos 11:3 and note). *Mount Baal Hermon.* The same as Mount Hermon (see 1Ch 5:23).

3:6 *took their daughters ... and served their gods.* See note on Jos 23:12. The degenerating effect of such intermarriage is well illustrated in Solomon's experience (1Ki 11:1–8).

3:7–11 In the account of Othniel's judgeship the author provides the basic literary form he uses in his accounts of the major judges (i.e., beginning statement; cycle of apostasy, oppression, distress, deliverance; recognizable conclusion), filling it out in each case with the materials he considered necessary to his purpose (see Introduction: Literary Features).

3:7 *did evil in the eyes of the LORD.* A recurring expression (see v. 12; 4:1; 6:1; 10:6; 13:1) used to introduce the cycles of the judges (see Introduction: Literary Features). *Baals.* See note on 2:13. *Asherahs.* See notes on 2:13; Ex 34:13.

3:8 *Cushan-Rishathaim.* Probably means "doubly wicked Cushan," perhaps a caricature of his actual name (see note on 10:6 regarding Baal-Zebub). *Aram Naharaim.* See note on Ge 24:10.

3:9 *they cried out to the LORD.* The Israelites' cries of distress occurred in each recurring cycle of the judges (see Introduction: Literary Features). *Othniel.* See 1:13.

3:10 *Spirit of the LORD came on him.* The Spirit empowered Othniel to deliver his people, as he did Gideon (6:34), Jephthah (11:29), Samson (14:6,19)—and also David (1Sa 16:13). Cf. Nu 11:25–29.

3:11 *the land had peace ... years.* A recognizable conclusion to the cycle of a judge (noted only here and in v. 30; 5:31; 8:28). After the judgeship of Gideon this formula is replaced by "led Israel ... years" (12:7; 15:20; 16:31). See Introduction: Literary Features. *forty years.* A conventional number of years for a generation (see Introduction: Background).

3:12–30 Ehud's triumph over Eglon, king of Moab. The left-handed Benjamite was an authentic hero. All alone, and purely by his wits, he cut down the king of Moab, who had established himself in Canaan near Jericho. This account balances that of Samson in the five narrative units central to the book of Judges (see Introduction: Literary Features).

3:12 *Moab.* See note on Ge 19:36–38.

3:13 *Ammonites.* See note on Ge 19:33. *Amalekites.* These descendants of Esau (Ge 36:12,16) lived in the Negev (Nu 13:29). See note on Ge 14:7.

3:14 *Israelites.* Here mainly Benjamin and Ephraim.

15 Again the Israelites cried out to the
LORD, and he gave them a deliverer[w]—
Ehud[x], a left-handed[y] man, the son of
Gera the Benjamite. The Israelites sent
him with tribute[z] to Eglon king of Moab.
16 Now Ehud[a] had made a double-edged
sword about a cubit[a] long, which he
strapped to his right thigh under his clothing. 17 He presented the tribute[b] to Eglon
king of Moab, who was a very fat man.[c]
18 After Ehud had presented the tribute, he
sent on their way those who had carried
it. 19 But on reaching the stone images near
Gilgal he himself went back to Eglon and
said, "Your Majesty, I have a secret message for you."

The king said to his attendants, "Leave
us!" And they all left.

20 Ehud then approached him while he
was sitting alone in the upper room of his
palace[b][d] and said, "I have a message from
God for you." As the king rose[e] from his
seat, 21 Ehud reached with his left hand,
drew the sword[f] from his right thigh and
plunged it into the king's belly. 22 Even the
handle sank in after the blade, and his
bowels discharged. Ehud did not pull the
sword out, and the fat closed in over it.
23 Then Ehud went out to the porch[c]; he
shut the doors of the upper room behind
him and locked them.

24 After he had gone, the servants came
and found the doors of the upper room
locked. They said, "He must be relieving
himself[g] in the inner room of the palace."
25 They waited to the point of embarrassment,[h] but when he did not open the doors
of the room, they took a key and unlocked
them. There they saw their lord fallen to
the floor, dead.

26 While they waited, Ehud got away. He
passed by the stone images and escaped to
Seirah. 27 When he arrived there, he blew
a trumpet[i] in the hill country of Ephraim,
and the Israelites went down with him
from the hills, with him leading them.

28 "Follow me," he ordered, "for the LORD
has given Moab,[j] your enemy, into your
hands.[k]" So they followed him down and
took possession of the fords of the Jordan[l]
that led to Moab; they allowed no one to
cross over. 29 At that time they struck down
about ten thousand Moabites, all vigorous
and strong; not one escaped. 30 That day
Moab[m] was made subject to Israel, and the
land had peace[n] for eighty years.

Shamgar

31 After Ehud came Shamgar son of
Anath,[o] who struck down six hundred[p]
Philistines[q] with an oxgoad. He too saved
Israel.

Deborah

4 Again the Israelites did evil[r] in the eyes
of the LORD,[s] now that Ehud[t] was dead.
2 So the LORD sold them[u] into the hands of
Jabin king of Canaan, who reigned in Hazor.[v] Sisera,[w] the commander of his army,

3:15 [w]S ver 9 [x]ver 16; Jdg 4:1 [y]Jdg 20:16; 1Ch 12:2 [z]ver 17, 18; 2Sa 8:2, 6; 1Ki 4:21; 2Ki 17:3; Est 10:1; Ps 68:29; 72:10; 89:22; Ecc 2:8; Isa 60:5; Hos 10:6 **3:16** [a]S ver 15 **3:17** [b]S ver 15 [c]Job 15:27; Ps 73:4 **3:20** [d]Am 3:15 [e]Ne 8:5 **3:21** [f]2Sa 2:16; 3:27; 20:10 **3:24** [g]1Sa 24:3 **3:25** [h]2Ki 2:17; 8:11 **3:27** [i]S Lev 25:9; Jdg 6:34; 7:18; 2Sa 2:28; Isa 18:3; Jer 42:14 **3:28** [j]S Ge 19:37 [k]S Jos 2:24; S Jdg 1:2 [l]S Nu 13:29; S Jos 2:7 **3:30** [m]S Ge 36:35 [n]S ver 11 **3:31** [o]Jdg 5:6 [p]S Jos 23:10 [q]Jos 13:2; Jdg 10:11; 13:1; 1Sa 5:1; 31:1; 2Sa 8:1; Jer 25:20; 47:1 **4:1** [r]S Jdg 2:19 [s]S Jdg 2:11 [t]S Jdg 3:15 **4:2** [u]S Dt 32:30 [v]S Jos 11:1 [w]1Sa 12:9; Ps 83:9

[a] *16* That is, about 18 inches or about 45 centimeters
[b] *20* The meaning of the Hebrew for this word is uncertain; also in verse 24.
[c] *23* The meaning of the Hebrew for this word is uncertain.

3:15 *left-handed man.* Left-handedness was noteworthy among Benjamites (see 20:15–16)—which is ironic since Benjamin means "son of (my) right hand." Being left-handed, Ehud could conceal his dagger on the side where it was not expected (see v. 21). *tribute.* An annual payment, perhaps of agricultural products (cf. 2Ki 3:4).

3:16 *made a double-edged sword.* That is, a straight-bladed sword useful for a stabbing thrust, in distinction from the more common sickle sword intended for slashing blows. During the period of the judges, Israelite weapons were often fashioned or improvised for the occasion: Shamgar's oxgoad (v. 31), Jael's tent peg (4:21–22), Gideon's jars and torches (7:20), the woman's millstone (9:53) and Samson's donkey jawbone (15:15). See 1Sa 13:19.

3:19 *stone images.* Lit. "carved (stone) things," a frequent Hebrew way of referring to stone idols. But here the reference may be to carved stone statues of Eglon, marking the boundary of the territory he now claims as part of his expanded realm—a common practice in the ancient Near East. *Gilgal.* Perhaps the one mentioned in Jos 15:7, located on the border between Benjamin and Judah, not the well-known city east of Jericho.

3:20 *upper room.* Rooms built on the flat roofs of houses (2Ki 4:10–11) and palaces (Jer 22:13–14) had latticed windows (2Ki 1:2) that provided comfort in the heat of summer.

3:28 *took possession of the fords.* This move enabled the Israelites to cut off the Moabites fleeing Jericho and also prevented the Moabites from sending reinforcements.

3:30 *eighty years.* Round numbers are frequently used in Judges (see Introduction: Background).

3:31 *Shamgar.* The first of six minor judges and a contemporary of Deborah (see 5:6–7). His name is foreign, so he was probably not an Israelite. *son of Anath.* Indicates either that Shamgar came from the town of Beth Anath (see 1:33 and note) or that his family worshiped the goddess Anath. Since Anath, Baal's sister, was a goddess of war who fought for Baal, the expression "son of Anath" may have been a military title, meaning "a warrior." *oxgoad.* A long, wooden rod, sometimes having a metal tip, used for driving draft animals (see 1Sa 13:21).

4:1—5:31 Deborah's triumph over Sisera (commander of a Canaanite army)—first narrated in prose (ch. 4), then celebrated in song (ch. 5). At the time of the Canaanite threat from the north, the Israelites remained incapable of united action until a woman (Deborah) summoned them to the Lord's battle. Because the warriors of Israel lacked the courage to rise up and face the enemy, the glory of victory went to a woman (Jael)—and she may not have been an Israelite.

4:1–2 Except for the Canaanites, Israel's enemies came from outside the territory they occupied. Nations like Aram Naharaim, Moab, Midian and Ammon were mainly interested in plunder, but the Canaanite uprising of chs. 4–5 was an attempt to restore Canaanite power in the north. The Philistines engaged in continual struggle with Israel for permanent control of the land in the southern and central regions.

4:2 *Jabin.* See Ps 83:9–10. The name was possibly royal rather

was based in Harosheth Haggoyim. 3 Because he had nine hundred chariots fitted
with iron[x] and had cruelly oppressed[y] the
Israelites for twenty years, they cried to
the LORD for help.
4 Now Deborah,[z] a prophet,[a] the wife of
Lappidoth, was leading[a] Israel at that time.
5 She held court[b] under the Palm of Deborah between Ramah[c] and Bethel[d] in the
hill country of Ephraim, and the Israelites
went up to her to have their disputes decided. 6 She sent for Barak son of Abinoam[e]
from Kedesh[f] in Naphtali and said to him,
"The LORD, the God of Israel, commands
you: 'Go, take with you ten thousand men
of Naphtali[g] and Zebulun[h] and lead them
up to Mount Tabor.[i] 7 I will lead Sisera,
the commander of Jabin's[j] army, with his
chariots and his troops to the Kishon River[k] and give him into your hands.[l]' "
8 Barak said to her, "If you go with me,
I will go; but if you don't go with me, I
won't go."
9 "Certainly I will go with you," said
Deborah. "But because of the course you
are taking, the honor will not be yours, for
the LORD will deliver Sisera into the hands
of a woman." So Deborah went with Barak to Kedesh.[m] 10 There Barak summoned[n]
Zebulun and Naphtali, and ten thousand
men went up under his command. Deborah also went up with him.
11 Now Heber the Kenite had left the other Kenites,[o] the descendants of Hobab,[p]
Moses' brother-in-law,[b] and pitched his
tent by the great tree[q] in Zaanannim[r] near
Kedesh.

4:3 [x] S Jos 17:16 [y] Jdg 10:12; Ps 106:42 **4:4** [z] Jdg 5:1, 7,12,15 [a] S Ex 15:20 **4:5** [b] 1Sa 14:2; 22:6 [c] S Jos 18:25 [d] S Jos 12:9 **4:6** [e] Jdg 5:1,12, 15; 1Sa 12:11; Heb 11:32 [f] S Jos 12:22 [g] S Ge 30:8 [h] Jdg 5:18; 6:35 [i] S Jos 19:22 **4:7** [j] S Jos 11:1 [k] ver 13; Jdg 5:21; 1Ki 18:40; Ps 83:9 [l] S Jdg 1:2 **4:9** [m] S Jos 12:22 **4:10** [n] 2Ch 36:23; Ezr 1:2; Isa 41:2; 42:6; 45:3; 46:11; 48:15 **4:11** [o] S Ge 15:19 [p] Nu 10:29 [q] Jos 24:26; Jdg 9:6 [r] Jos 19:33

[a] 4 Traditionally *judging* [b] 11 Or *father-in-law*

than personal. Joshua is credited with having earlier slain a king by the same name (Jos 11:1,10). *Hazor.* The original royal city of the Jabin dynasty; it may still have been in ruins (see note on Jos 11:10). Sisera sought to recover the territory once ruled by the kings of Hazor. *Sisera.* His name suggests he was not a Canaanite.

4:3 *nine hundred.* The number probably represents a coalition rather than the chariot force of one city. In the fifteenth century BC, Pharaoh Thutmose III boasted of having captured 924 chariots at the battle of Megiddo. *Israelites.* Mainly Zebulun and Naphtali, but West Manasseh, Issachar and Asher were also affected.

4:4 *Deborah.* Means "bee"; cf. Dt 1:44. She is the only judge said to have been a prophet. Other women spoken of as prophets are Miriam (Ex 15:20), Huldah (2Ki 22:14), Noadiah (Ne 6:14) and Anna (see note on Lk 2:36), but see also Ac 21:9.

4:5 *Palm of Deborah.* The Hebrew word for "honey" refers to both bees' honey and the sweet, syrupy juice of dates. Deborah, the Bee, dispensed the sweetness of justice as she held court, not in a city gate where male judges sat, but under the shade of a "honey" tree. See also note on 1Sa 14:2.

4:6 *Barak.* Means "thunderbolt"—which suggests that he is summoned to be the Lord's "flashing sword" (Dt 32:41). He is named among the heroes of faith in Heb 11:32. *Kedesh in Naphtali.* A town affected by the Canaanite oppression. *Naphtali and Zebulun.* Issachar, a near neighbor of these tribes, is not mentioned here but is included in the poetic description of the battle in 5:15. In all, six tribes are mentioned as having participated in the battle. *Mount Tabor.* A mountain about 1,300 feet high, northeast of the battle site.

4:7 With the Israelites encamped on the slopes of Mount Tabor, safe from chariot attack, the Lord's strategy was to draw Sisera into a trap. For the battle site, Sisera cleverly chose the Valley of Jezreel along the Kishon River, where his chariot forces would have ample maneuvering space. But that was to be his undoing, for he did not know the power of the Lord, who would fight for Israel with storm and flood (see 5:20–21), as he had done in the days of Joshua (Jos 10:11–14). Even in modern times storms have rendered the plain along the Kishon virtually impassable. In April of 1799 the flooded Kishon River aided Napoleon's victory over a Turkish army.

4:9 *a woman.* Barak's timidity (and that of Israel's other warriors, whom he exemplified) was due to lack of trust in the Lord and was thus rebuked (see note on 9:54).

4:11 *Heber the Kenite.* Since one meaning of Heber's name is "ally," and since "Kenite" identifies him as belonging to a clan of metalworkers, the author hints at the truth that this member of a people allied with Israel since the days of Moses has moved from south to north to ally himself (see v. 17) with the Canaanite king who is assembling a large force of "chariots fitted with iron" (v. 3; see note on

POINTS OF PRESSURE ON ISRAEL

ENEMY	DELIVERER	TRIBAL SUPPORTERS	LOCUS OF PRESSURE
Moabites	Ehud	Benjamin	Heartland
Philistines	Shamgar		Southwest
Canaanites	Barak	Ephraim, Zebulun, Naphtali, Issachar	North
Midianites	Gideon	Manasseh, Ephraim	Heartland
Ammonites	Jephthah	Gileadites	Transjordan
Philistines	Samson	Dan	Southwest

12 When they told Sisera that Barak son of Abinoam had gone up to Mount Tabor,[s] 13 Sisera summoned from Harosheth Haggoyim to the Kishon River[t] all his men and his nine hundred chariots fitted with iron.[u]

14 Then Deborah said to Barak, "Go! This is the day the LORD has given Sisera into your hands.[v] Has not the LORD gone ahead[w] of you?" So Barak went down Mount Tabor, with ten thousand men following him. 15 At Barak's advance, the LORD routed[x] Sisera and all his chariots and army by the sword, and Sisera got down from his chariot and fled on foot.

16 Barak pursued the chariots and army as far as Harosheth Haggoyim, and all Sisera's troops fell by the sword; not a man was left.[y] 17 Sisera, meanwhile, fled on foot to the tent of Jael,[z] the wife of Heber the Kenite,[a] because there was an alliance between Jabin king of Hazor[b] and the family of Heber the Kenite.

18 Jael[c] went out to meet Sisera and said to him, "Come, my lord, come right in. Don't be afraid." So he entered her tent, and she covered him with a blanket.

19 "I'm thirsty," he said. "Please give me some water." She opened a skin of milk,[d] gave him a drink, and covered him up.

20 "Stand in the doorway of the tent," he told her. "If someone comes by and asks you, 'Is anyone in there?' say 'No.' "

21 But Jael,[e] Heber's wife, picked up a tent peg and a hammer and went quietly to him while he lay fast asleep,[f] exhausted. She drove the peg through his temple into the ground, and he died.[g]

22 Just then Barak came by in pursuit of Sisera, and Jael[h] went out to meet him. "Come," she said, "I will show you the man you're looking for." So he went in with her, and there lay Sisera with the tent peg through his temple—dead.[i]

23 On that day God subdued[j] Jabin[k] king of Canaan before the Israelites. 24 And the hand of the Israelites pressed harder and harder against Jabin king of Canaan until they destroyed him.[l]

The Song of Deborah

5 On that day Deborah[m] and Barak son of Abinoam[n] sang this song:[o]

2 "When the princes in Israel take the lead,
when the people willingly offer[p] themselves—
praise the LORD![q]

3 "Hear this, you kings! Listen, you rulers!
I, even I, will sing to[a] the LORD;[r]
I will praise the LORD, the God of Israel, in song.[s]

4 "When you, LORD, went out[t] from Seir,[u]
when you marched from the land of Edom,

4:12 [s]S Jos 19:22 **4:13** [t]S ver 7; Jdg 5:19 [u]S Jos 17:16 **4:14** [v]S Jdg 1:2 [w]Dt 9:3; 1Sa 8:20; 2Sa 5:24; Ps 68:7 **4:15** [x]S Jos 10:10 **4:16** [y]S Ex 14:28; Ps 83:9 **4:17** [z]ver 18, 21,22; Jdg 5:6, 24 [a]S Ge 15:19 [b]S Jos 11:1 **4:18** [c]S ver 17 **4:19** [d]S Ge 18:8 **4:21** [e]S ver 17 [f]Ge 2:21; 15:12; 1Sa 26:12; Isa 29:10; Jnh 1:5 [g]Jdg 5:26 **4:22** [h]S ver 17 [i]Jdg 5:27 **4:23** [j]Ne 9:24; Ps 18:47; 44:2; 47:3; 144:2 [k]S Jos 11:1 **4:24** [l]Ps 83:9; 106:43 **5:1** [m]S Jdg 4:4 [n]S Jdg 4:6 [o]S Ex 15:1; Ps 32:7 **5:2** [p]2Ch 17:16; Ps 110:3 [q]ver 9 **5:3** [r]S Ex 15:1 [s]Ps 27:6 **5:4** [t]S Ex 13:21 [u]S Nu 24:18; S Dt 33:2

[a] 3 Or *of*

Jos 17:16). It is no doubt he who informs Sisera of Barak's military preparations. *other Kenites.* Settled in the south not far from Kadesh Barnea in the Negev (see 1:16). *Hobab.* See Nu 10:29.

4:14 *gone ahead of you.* As a king at the head of his army (see 1Sa 8:20). See also Ex 15:3 ("the LORD is a warrior"); Jos 10:10–11; 2Sa 5:24; 2Ch 20:15–17, 22–24. *Barak went down Mount Tabor.* The Lord's "thunderbolt" (see note on v. 6) descends the mountain to attack the Canaanite army.

4:15 *routed.* See note on v. 7. The Hebrew for this word is also used of the panic that overcame the Egyptians at the "Red Sea" (Ex 14:24) and the Philistines at Mizpah (1Sa 7:10).

4:18 *he entered her tent.* Since ancient Near Eastern custom prohibited any man other than a woman's husband or father from entering her tent, Jael seemed to offer Sisera an ideal hiding place.

4:19 *skin.* Containers for liquids were normally made from the skins of goats or lambs. *milk.* See note on 5:25. Jael, whose name means "mountain goat," gave him milk to drink—and it was most likely goat's milk (see Ex 23:19; Pr 27:27).

4:21 *drove the peg through his temple.* The laws of hospitality normally meant that one tried to protect a guest from any harm (see 19:23; Ge 19:8). Jael remained true to her family's previous alliance with Israel (she may not have been an Israelite) and so undid her husband's deliberate breach of faith. Armed only with domestic implements, this dauntless woman destroyed the great warrior whom Barak had earlier feared.

4:22 *there lay Sisera ... dead.* With Sisera dead the kingdom of Jabin was no longer a threat. The land "flowing with milk and honey" had been saved by the courage and faithfulness of "Bee" (see note on v. 4) and "Mountain Goat" (see note on v. 19).

5:1–31 To commemorate a national victory with songs was a common practice (see Ex 15:1–18; Nu 21:27–30; Dt 32:1–43; 1Sa 18:7). The Book of the Wars of the Lord (see note on Nu 21:14) and the Book of Jashar (see note on Jos 10:13) were probably collections of such songs.

The song was probably written by Deborah or a contemporary (see vv. 1,3,7). It highlights some of the central themes of the narrative (cf. Ex 15:1–18; 1Sa 2:1–10; 2Sa 22; 23:1–7; Lk 1:46–55,68–79). In particular, it celebrates before the nations (v. 3) the righteous acts of the Lord and of his warriors (v. 11). The song may be divided into the following sections: (1) the purpose of the song (praise) and the occasion for the deeds it celebrates (vv. 2–9); (2) the exhortation to the Israelites to act in accordance with their heroic past (vv. 10–11a); (3) the people's appeal to Deborah (vv. 11b–12); (4) the gathering of warriors (vv. 13–18); (5) the battle (vv. 19–23); (6) the crafty triumph of Jael over Sisera (vv. 24–27); (7) the anxious waiting of Sisera's mother (vv. 28–30); and (8) the conclusion (v. 31).

5:4–5 Poetic recalling of the Lord's terrifying appearance in a storm cloud many years before, when he had brought Israel through the wilderness into Canaan (see Dt 33:2; Ps 68:7–8; Mic 1:3–4; see also Ps 18:7–15).

5:4 *Seir.* Mount Seir (in Edom). For a similar association of Seir (and Mount Paran) with Sinai, see Dt 33:2. *the heavens poured.* See Ps 68:7–10.

the earth shook,[v] the heavens poured,
the clouds poured down water.[w]
5 The mountains quaked[x] before the
LORD, the One of Sinai,
before the LORD, the God of Israel.

6 "In the days of Shamgar son of Anath,[y]
in the days of Jael,[z] the highways[a]
were abandoned;
travelers took to winding paths.[b]
7 Villagers in Israel would not fight;
they held back until I, Deborah,[c]
arose,
until I arose, a mother in Israel.
8 God chose new leaders[d]
when war came to the city gates,[e]
but not a shield or spear[f] was seen
among forty thousand in Israel.
9 My heart is with Israel's princes,
with the willing volunteers[g] among
the people.
Praise the LORD!

10 "You who ride on white donkeys,[h]
sitting on your saddle blankets,
and you who walk along the road,
consider 11 the voice of the singers[a] at
the watering places.
They recite the victories[i] of the LORD,
the victories of his villagers in Israel.

"Then the people of the LORD
went down to the city gates.[j]
12 'Wake up,[k] wake up, Deborah![l]
Wake up, wake up, break out in
song!
Arise, Barak![m]
Take captive your captives,[n] son of
Abinoam.'

13 "The remnant of the nobles came
down;
the people of the LORD came down to
me against the mighty.
14 Some came from Ephraim,[o] whose
roots were in Amalek;[p]
Benjamin[q] was with the people who
followed you.
From Makir[r] captains came down,
from Zebulun those who bear a
commander's[a] staff.
15 The princes of Issachar[s] were with
Deborah;[t]
yes, Issachar was with Barak,[u]
sent under his command into the
valley.
In the districts of Reuben
there was much searching of heart.
16 Why did you stay among the sheep
pens[b][v]
to hear the whistling for the
flocks?[w]
In the districts of Reuben
there was much searching of
heart.
17 Gilead[x] stayed beyond the Jordan.
And Dan, why did he linger by the
ships?
Asher[y] remained on the coast[z]
and stayed in his coves.
18 The people of Zebulun[a] risked their
very lives;
so did Naphtali[b] on the terraced
fields.[c]

19 "Kings came[d], they fought,
the kings of Canaan fought.
At Taanach, by the waters of Megiddo,[e]

[a] *11,14* The meaning of the Hebrew for this word is uncertain. [b] *16* Or *the campfires*; or *the saddlebags*

5:4 [v] 2Sa 22:8; Ps 18:7; 77:18; 82:5; Isa 2:19, 21; 13:13; 24:18; 64:3; Jer 10:10; 50:46; 51:29; Joel 3:16; Na 1:5; Hab 3:6 [w] Ps 68:8; 77:17
5:5 [x] S Ex 19:18; Ps 29:6; 46:3; 77:18; 114:4; Isa 64:3
5:6 [y] Jdg 3:31 [z] S Jdg 4:17 [a] Lev 26:22; Isa 33:8 [b] Ps 125:5; Isa 59:8
5:7 [c] S Jdg 4:4
5:8 [d] Dt 32:17; S Jdg 2:13 [e] ver 11; S Jos 2:5 [f] S Nu 25:7
5:9 [g] S ver 2
5:10 [h] S Ge 49:11; Jdg 10:4; 12:14
5:11 [i] 1Sa 12:7; Da 9:16; Mic 6:5 [j] S ver 8
5:12 [k] Ps 44:23; 57:8; Isa 51:9, 17 [l] S Jdg 4:4 [m] S Jdg 4:6 [n] Ps 68:18; Eph 4:8
5:14 [o] S Ge 41:52; S Jdg 1:29 [p] Jdg 3:13 [q] S Nu 34:21 [r] S Ge 50:23
5:15 [s] S Ge 30:18 [t] S Jdg 4:4 [u] S Jdg 4:6
5:16 [v] S Ge 49:14 [w] S Nu 32:1
5:17 [x] S Jos 12:2 [y] S Jos 17:7 [z] Jos 19:29
5:18 [a] S Ge 30:20 [b] S Ge 30:8; Ps 68:27 [c] S Jdg 4:6, 10 **5:19** [d] Jos 11:5; S Jdg 4:13; Rev 16:16 [e] S Jos 12:21

5:5 *the One of Sinai.* See Ps 68:8. An earthquake and thunderstorm occurred when God appeared at Mount Sinai (Ex 19:16–18).
5:6 *Shamgar.* See note on 3:31. *highways were abandoned.* Because of enemy garrisons and marauding bands (see note on 4:1–2) the roads were unsafe.
5:8 *not a shield or spear was seen.* Either because Israel had made peace with the native Canaanites (see 3:5–6) or because she had been disarmed (see 1Sa 13:19–22).
5:10 *who ride on white donkeys.* An allusion to the nobles and the wealthy (see 10:4; 12:14).
5:11 *voice of the singers.* The leaders are encouraged by the songs of the minstrels at the watering places—songs that rehearse the past heroic achievements of the Lord and his warriors.
5:12 *Wake up.* A plea to take action (see Ps 44:23; Isa 51:9). *Take captive your captives.* The same action is applied to God in Ps 68:18 and to Christ in Eph 4:8 (see notes on those verses).
5:13–18 The warriors of the Lord who gathered for the battle. The tribes who came were Ephraim, Benjamin, Manasseh ("Makir" is possibly both East and West Manasseh; see Dt 3:15; Jos 13:29–31; 17:1), Zebulun (vv. 14,18), Issachar (v. 15) and Naphtali (v. 18). Especially involved were Zebulun and Naphtali (v. 18; see 4:10), the tribes most immediately affected by Sisera's tyranny. Reuben (vv. 15–16) and Gad (here referred to as Gilead, v. 17), from east of the Jordan, and Dan and Asher, from along the coast (v. 17), are rebuked for not responding. Judah and Simeon are not even mentioned, perhaps because they were already engaged with the Philistines. Levi is not mentioned because it did not have military responsibilities in the theocracy (kingdom of God).
5:14 *roots … in Amalek.* Some Amalekites apparently once lived in the hill country of Ephraim (see 12:15). *Makir.* The firstborn son of Manasseh (Jos 17:1). Although the descendants of Makir settled on both sides of the Jordan (see Dt 3:15; Jos 13:29–31; 17:1; 1Ch 7:14–19), reference here is to those west of the Jordan (see v. 17; Jos 17:5).
5:19 *Megiddo.* Megiddo and Taanach dominated the main pass that runs northeast through the hill country from the plain of Sharon to the Valley of Jezreel. Because of its strategic location, the "plain of Megiddo" (2Ch 35:22) has been a frequent battleground from the earliest times. There Pharaoh Thutmose III defeated a Canaanite coalition in 1468 BC, and there in AD 1917 the British under General Allenby ended the rule of the Turks in Palestine by vanquishing them in the Valley of Jezreel opposite Megiddo. In Biblical history the forces of Israel under Deborah and Barak crushed the

they took no plunder of silver.[f]
20 From the heavens[g] the stars fought,
from their courses they fought
against Sisera.
21 The river Kishon[h] swept them away,
the age-old river, the river Kishon.
March on, my soul; be strong![i]
22 Then thundered the horses' hooves—
galloping, galloping go his mighty
steeds.[j]
23 'Curse Meroz,' said the angel of the
LORD.
'Curse its people bitterly,
because they did not come to help the
LORD,
to help the LORD against the mighty.'

24 "Most blessed of women[k] be Jael,[l]
the wife of Heber the Kenite,[m]
most blessed of tent-dwelling
women.
25 He asked for water, and she gave him
milk;[n]
in a bowl fit for nobles she brought
him curdled milk.
26 Her hand reached for the tent peg,
her right hand for the workman's
hammer.
She struck Sisera, she crushed his
head,
she shattered and pierced his
temple.[o]
27 At her feet he sank,
he fell; there he lay.
At her feet he sank, he fell;
where he sank, there he fell—dead[p].

28 "Through the window[q] peered Sisera's
mother;
behind the lattice she cried out,[r]
'Why is his chariot so long in coming?
Why is the clatter of his chariots
delayed?'
29 The wisest of her ladies answer her;
indeed, she keeps saying to herself,
30 'Are they not finding and dividing the
spoils:[s]
a woman or two for each man,
colorful garments as plunder for Sisera,
colorful garments embroidered,
highly embroidered garments[t] for my
neck—
all this as plunder?[u]'

31 "So may all your enemies perish,[v]
LORD!
But may all who love you be like the
sun[w]
when it rises in its strength."[x]

Then the land had peace[y] forty years.

Gideon

6 The Israelites did evil in the eyes of
the LORD,[z] and for seven years he gave
them into the hands of the Midianites.[a]
2 Because the power of Midian was so oppressive,[b] the Israelites prepared shelters
for themselves in mountain clefts, caves[c]
and strongholds.[d] 3 Whenever the Israelites
planted their crops, the Midianites, Amalekites[e] and other eastern peoples[f] invaded the country. 4 They camped on the land
and ruined the crops[g] all the way to Gaza[h]
and did not spare a living thing for Israel, neither sheep nor cattle nor donkeys.
5 They came up with their livestock and
their tents like swarms of locusts.[i] It was

5:19 [f] ver 30 **5:20** [g] S Jos 10:11 **5:21** [h] S Jdg 4:7 [i] Jos 1:6 **5:22** [j] Jer 8:16 **5:24** [k] Lk 1:42 [l] S Jdg 4:17 [m] S Ge 15:19 **5:25** [n] S Ge 18:8 **5:26** [o] Jdg 4:21 **5:27** [p] Jdg 4:22 **5:28** [q] S Jos 2:15 [r] Pr 7:6 **5:30** [s] Ex 15:9; 1Sa 30:24; Ps 68:12 [t] Ps 45:14; Eze 16:10 [u] ver 19; 2Sa 1:24 **5:31** [v] S Nu 10:35 [w] 2Sa 23:4; Job 37:21; Ps 19:4; 89:36; Isa 18:4 [x] 2Sa 18:32 [y] S Jdg 3:11 **6:1** [z] S Jdg 2:11 [a] S Ge 25:2 **6:2** [b] 1Sa 13:6; Isa 5:30; 8:21; 26:16; 37:3 [c] Isa 2:19; Jer 48:28; 49:8, 30 [d] Job 24:8; Jer 41:9; Heb 11:38 **6:3** [e] Nu 13:29 [f] S Ge 25:6; Isa 11:14; Jer 49:28 **6:4** [g] Lev 26:16; Dt 28:30, 51; Isa 10:6; 39:6; 42:22 [h] S Ge 10:19 **6:5** [i] S Dt 28:42

Canaanites "by the waters of Megiddo," and there Judah's good king Josiah died in battle against Pharaoh Necho II in 609 BC (2Ki 23:29). See also the reference in Rev 16:16 (see note there) to "the place that in Hebrew is called Armageddon" (i.e., "Mount Megiddo") as the site of the "battle on the great day of God Almighty" (Rev 16:14).

5:20 *stars fought.* A poetic way of saying that the powers of heaven fought in Israel's behalf (see notes on 4:7; Jos 10:11; Ps 18:7–15).

5:21 *swept them away.* See note on 4:7.

5:23 *Meroz.* Because of its refusal to help the army of the Lord, this Israelite town in Naphtali was cursed. Other cities were also punished severely for refusing to participate in the wars of the Lord (see 8:15–17; 21:5–10).

5:25 *curdled milk.* Artificially soured milk made by shaking milk in a skin-bottle and then allowing it to ferment.

5:28 This graphic picture of the anxious waiting of Sisera's mother heightens the triumph of Jael over the powerful Canaanite general and presents a contrast between this mother in Canaan and the triumphant Deborah, "a mother in Israel" (v. 7).

5:31 The song ends with a prayer that the present victory would be the pattern for all future battles against the Lord's enemies (see Nu 10:35; Ps 68:1–2). *your enemies ... all who love you.* The two basic attitudes of people toward the Lord. As Lord of the covenant and royal Head of his people Israel, he demanded their love (see Ex 20:6), just as kings in the ancient Near East demanded the love of their subjects. *forty years.* A conventional number of years for a generation (see Introduction: Background).

6:1—9:57 The Gideon and Abimelek narratives are a literary unit and constitute the central account of the judges. They are bracketed by the stories of Deborah (from Ephraim, a son of Joseph; west of the Jordan) and Jephthah (from Manasseh, the other son of Joseph; east of the Jordan)—which in turn are bracketed by the stories of the heroes Ehud (from Benjamin) and Samson (from Dan). In this central narrative, the crucial issues of the period of the judges are emphasized: the worship of Baal and the Lord's kingship over his covenant people Israel (see note on 8:23).

6:1 *Midianites.* See notes on Ge 37:25; Ex 2:15. Since they were apparently not numerous enough to wage war against the Israelites alone, they often formed coalitions with surrounding peoples—as with the Moabites (Nu 22:4–6; 25:6–18), the Amalekites and other tribes from the east (v. 3). Their defeat was an event long remembered in Hebrew history (see Ps 83:9; Isa 9:4; 10:26; Hab 3:7).

6:3 *Amalekites.* See note on Ge 14:7. Normally they were a people of the Negev, but they are in coalition here with the Midianites and other eastern peoples, who were nomads from the desert east of Moab and Ammon.

6:5 *swarms of locusts.* A vivid picture of the marauders who

impossible to count them or their camels;[j] they invaded the land to ravage it. 6 Midian so impoverished the Israelites that they cried out[k] to the LORD for help.

7 When the Israelites cried out[l] to the LORD because of Midian, 8 he sent them a prophet,[m] who said, "This is what the LORD, the God of Israel, says: I brought you up out of Egypt,[n] out of the land of slavery.[o] 9 I rescued you from the hand of the Egyptians. And I delivered you from the hand of all your oppressors;[p] I drove them out before you and gave you their land.[q] 10 I said to you, 'I am the LORD your God; do not worship[r] the gods of the Amorites,[s] in whose land you live.' But you have not listened to me."

11 The angel of the LORD[t] came and sat down under the oak in Ophrah[u] that belonged to Joash[v] the Abiezrite,[w] where his son Gideon[x] was threshing[y] wheat in a winepress[z] to keep it from the Midianites. 12 When the angel of the LORD appeared to Gideon, he said, "The LORD is with you,[a] mighty warrior.[b]"

13 "Pardon me, my lord," Gideon replied, "but if the LORD is with us, why has all this happened to us? Where are all his wonders[c] that our ancestors told[d] us about when they said, 'Did not the LORD bring us up out of Egypt?' But now the LORD has abandoned[e] us and given us into the hand of Midian."

14 The LORD turned to him and said, "Go in the strength you have[f] and save[g] Israel out of Midian's hand. Am I not sending you?"

15 "Pardon me, my lord," Gideon replied, "but how can I save Israel? My clan[h] is the weakest in Manasseh, and I am the least in my family.[i]"

16 The LORD answered, "I will be with you[j], and you will strike down all the Midianites, leaving none alive."

17 Gideon replied, "If now I have found favor in your eyes, give me a sign[k] that it is really you talking to me. 18 Please do not go away until I come back and bring my offering and set it before you."

And the LORD said, "I will wait until you return."

19 Gideon went inside, prepared a young goat,[l] and from an ephah[a][m] of flour he made bread without yeast. Putting the meat in a basket and its broth in a pot, he brought them out and offered them to him under the oak.[n]

20 The angel of God said to him, "Take the meat and the unleavened bread, place them on this rock,[o] and pour out the broth." And Gideon did so. 21 Then the angel of the LORD touched the meat and the unleavened bread[p] with the tip of the staff[q] that was in his hand. Fire flared from the rock, consuming the meat and the bread. And the angel of the LORD disappeared. 22 When Gideon realized[r] that it was the angel of the LORD, he exclaimed, "Alas, Sovereign LORD! I have seen the angel of the LORD face to face!"[s]

23 But the LORD said to him, "Peace! Do not be afraid.[t] You are not going to die."[u]

24 So Gideon built an altar to the LORD there and called[v] it The LORD Is Peace. To this day it stands in Ophrah[w] of the Abiezrites.

25 That same night the LORD said to him, "Take the second bull from your father's herd, the one seven years old.[b] Tear down your father's altar to Baal and cut down the Asherah pole[c][x] beside it. 26 Then build

[a] *19* That is, probably about 36 pounds or about 16 kilograms [b] *25* Or *Take a full-grown, mature bull from your father's herd* [c] *25* That is, a wooden symbol of the goddess Asherah; also in verses 26, 28 and 30

6:5 [j] Jdg 8:10; Isa 21:7; 60:6; Jer 49:32 **6:6** [k] S Jdg 3:9 **6:7** [l] S Jdg 3:9 **6:8** [m] Dt 18:15; 1Ki 20:13, 22; 2Ki 17:13, 23; Ne 9:29; Job 36:10; Jer 25:5; Eze 18:30-31 [n] S Jdg 2:1 [o] Jos 24:17 **6:9** [p] S Nu 10:9; Ps 136:24 [q] Ps 44:2 **6:10** [r] S Ex 20:5 [s] S Jos 24:15 **6:11** [t] S Ge 16:7 [u] S Jos 18:23 [v] ver 29; Jdg 7:14; 8:13, 29 [w] S Nu 26:30 [x] Jdg 7:1; 8:1; Heb 11:32 [y] Ru 2:17; 3:2; 1Sa 23:1; 1Ch 21:20 [z] Ne 13:15; Isa 16:10; 63:3; La 1:15; Joel 3:13 **6:12** [a] S Jos 1:5; Ru 2:4; 1Sa 10:7; Ps 129:8 [b] Jdg 11:1 **6:13** [c] S Jos 3:5 [d] 2Sa 7:22; Ps 44:1; 78:3 [e] S Dt 31:17 **6:14** [f] Heb 11:34 [g] ver 36; Jdg 10:1; 2Ki 14:27 **6:15** [h] Isa 60:22 [i] 1Sa 9:21 **6:16** [j] Ex 3:12; S Nu 14:43; Jos 1:5 **6:17** [k] ver 36-37; S Ge 24:14; S Ex 3:12; S 4:8 **6:19** [l] Jdg 13:15 [m] S Lev 19:36 [n] Ge 18:7-8 **6:20** [o] Jdg 13:19 **6:21** [p] S Lev 9:24 [q] S Ex 4:2 **6:22** [r] Jdg 13:16,21 [s] Ge 32:30; Jdg 13:22 **6:23** [t] Da 10:19 [u] S Ge 16:13; S Dt 5:26 **6:24** [v] S Ge 22:14 [w] S Jos 18:23 **6:25** [x] ver 26,28,30; Ex 34:13; S Jdg 2:13

swarmed across the land, leaving it stripped bare (see 7:12; Ex 10:13–15; Joel 1:4). *camels.* The earliest OT reference to the use of mounted camels in warfare (cf. note on Ge 12:16).

6:7 *cried out to the LORD.* The Israelites' cries of distress occurred in each recurring cycle of the judges (see Introduction: Literary Features).

6:8 *prophet.* See notes on 2:1; 10:11. The unnamed prophet rebuked Israel for forgetting that the Lord had saved them from Egyptian bondage and had given them the land (vv. 9–10).

6:10 *Amorites.* Probably here includes all the inhabitants of Canaan (see note on Ge 10:16).

6:11 *angel of the LORD.* See note on Ge 16:7. *Ophrah.* To be distinguished from the Benjamite Ophrah (Jos 18:23). *Abiezrite.* The Abiezrites (v. 24) were from the tribe of Manasseh (Jos 17:2). *threshing wheat in a winepress.* Rather than in the usual, exposed area (see note on Ru 1:22). Gideon felt more secure threshing in this better protected but very confined space.

6:12 *mighty warrior.* Apparently Gideon belonged to the upper class, perhaps a kind of aristocracy (see v. 27), in spite of his disclaimer in v. 15.

6:14 *LORD turned.* See v. 23; see also note on Ge 16:7. *Go ... Am I not sending you?* Gideon was commissioned to deliver Israel as Moses had been (see Ex 3:7–10).

6:15 *how can I ... ?* Cf. Moses' and Jeremiah's reactions to God's call to serve (Ex 3:11; 4:10; see Jer 1:6–7 and notes). The Lord usually calls the lowly rather than the mighty to act for him (see Nu 12:3 and notes on Ge 25:23; 1Sa 9:21; cf. 1Co 1:26–31 and note).

6:17 *give me a sign.* See vv. 36–40; cf. the signs the Lord gave Moses as assurance that he would be with him in his undertaking (see Ex 3:12; 4:1–17).

6:21 *consuming the meat.* Indicating that Gideon's offering was accepted (see Lev 9:24).

6:23 *not going to die.* See 13:22 and notes on Ge 16:13; 32:30.

6:25 *Tear down ... altar.* Gideon's first task as the Lord's warrior was to tear down his father's altar to Baal (cf. 2:2; Ex 34:13; Dt 7:5). *Baal.* See note on 2:13. *Asherah pole.* See NIV text note; see also notes on 2:13; Ex 34:13.

a proper kind of[a] altar to the LORD your God on the top of this height. Using the wood of the Asherah pole that you cut down, offer the second[b] bull as a burnt offering.[y]"

27 So Gideon took ten of his servants and did as the LORD told him. But because he was afraid of his family and the townspeople, he did it at night rather than in the daytime.

28 In the morning when the people of the town got up, there was Baal's altar,[z] demolished, with the Asherah pole beside it cut down and the second bull sacrificed on the newly built altar!

29 They asked each other, "Who did this?"

When they carefully investigated, they were told, "Gideon son of Joash[a] did it."

30 The people of the town demanded of Joash, "Bring out your son. He must die, because he has broken down Baal's altar[b] and cut down the Asherah pole beside it."

31 But Joash replied to the hostile crowd around him, "Are you going to plead Baal's cause?[c] Are you trying to save him? Whoever fights for him shall be put to death by morning! If Baal really is a god, he can defend himself when someone breaks down his altar." 32 So because Gideon broke down Baal's altar, they gave him the name Jerub-Baal[c][d] that day, saying, "Let Baal contend with him."

33 Now all the Midianites, Amalekites[e] and other eastern peoples[f] joined forces and crossed over the Jordan and camped in the Valley of Jezreel.[g] 34 Then the Spirit of the LORD came on[h] Gideon, and he blew a trumpet,[i] summoning the Abiezrites[j] to follow him. 35 He sent messengers throughout Manasseh, calling them to arms, and also into Asher,[k] Zebulun and Naphtali,[l] so that they too went up to meet them.[m]

36 Gideon said to God, "If you will save[n] Israel by my hand as you have promised— 37 look, I will place a wool fleece[o] on the threshing floor.[p] If there is dew only on the fleece and all the ground is dry, then I will know[q] that you will save Israel by my hand, as you said." 38 And that is what happened. Gideon rose early the next day; he squeezed the fleece and wrung out the dew—a bowlful of water.

39 Then Gideon said to God, "Do not be angry with me. Let me make just one more request.[r] Allow me one more test with the fleece, but this time make the fleece dry and let the ground be covered with dew." 40 That night God did so. Only the fleece was dry; all the ground was covered with dew.[s]

6:26 [y] S Ge 8:20
6:28 [z] ver 30; 1Ki 16:32; 2Ki 21:3
6:29 [a] S ver 11
6:30 [b] S ver 28
6:31 [c] 1Sa 24:15; Ps 43:1; Jer 30:13
6:32 [d] Jdg 7:1; 8:29, 35; 9:1; 1Sa 12:11
6:33 [e] Nu 13:29 [f] S Ge 25:6 [g] S Jos 15:56; Eze 25:4; Hos 1:5
6:34 [h] S Jdg 3:10 [i] S Jos 6:20; S Jdg 3:27 [j] S Jos 17:2
6:35 [k] S Jos 17:7 [l] S Jdg 4:6 [m] Jdg 7:23
6:36 [n] S ver 14
6:37 [o] Job 31:20 [p] S Nu 18:27; 2Sa 6:6; 24:16 [q] S Ge 24:14
6:39 [r] Ge 18:32
6:40 [s] Ex 4:3-7; Isa 38:7
7:1 [t] S Jdg 6:32 [u] S Jdg 6:11 [v] 2Sa 23:25 [w] S Ge 25:2 [x] S Ge 12:6
7:2 [y] S Dt 8:17; 2Co 4:7
7:3 [z] Dt 20:8; S Jos 12:2
7:4 [a] 1Sa 14:6
7:6 [b] Ge 14:14

Gideon Defeats the Midianites

7 Early in the morning, Jerub-Baal[t] (that is, Gideon[u]) and all his men camped at the spring of Harod.[v] The camp of Midian[w] was north of them in the valley near the hill of Moreh.[x] 2 The LORD said to Gideon, "You have too many men. I cannot deliver Midian into their hands, or Israel would boast against me, 'My own strength[y] has saved me.' 3 Now announce to the army, 'Anyone who trembles with fear may turn back and leave Mount Gilead.[z]' " So twenty-two thousand men left, while ten thousand remained.

4 But the LORD said to Gideon, "There are still too many[a] men. Take them down to the water, and I will thin them out for you there. If I say, 'This one shall go with you,' he shall go; but if I say, 'This one shall not go with you,' he shall not go."

5 So Gideon took the men down to the water. There the LORD told him, "Separate those who lap the water with their tongues as a dog laps from those who kneel down to drink." 6 Three hundred of them[b] drank from cupped hands, lapping like dogs. All the rest got down on their knees to drink.

[a] 26 Or *build with layers of stone an* [b] 26 Or *full-grown*; also in verse 28 [c] 32 *Jerub-Baal* probably means *let Baal contend.*

6:26 *proper kind of altar.* See Ex 20:25.
6:30 *He must die.* The Israelites were so apostate that they were willing to kill one of their own people for the cause of Baal (contrast Dt 13:6–10, where God told Moses that idolaters must be stoned).
6:32 *Jerub-Baal.* See NIV text note. This name later occurs as Jerub-Besheth (2Sa 11:21) by substituting a degrading term (Hebrew *bosheth*, "shameful thing") for the name of Baal (see note on Jer 2:26), as in the change of the names Esh-Baal and Merib-Baal (1Ch 8:33–34) to Ish-Bosheth and Mephibosheth (see notes on 2Sa 2:8; 4:4). *Let Baal contend with him.* Let Baal defend himself against Gideon.
6:33 *Valley of Jezreel.* See note on 5:19.
6:34 *Spirit ... came on.* Lit. "Spirit ... clothed himself with." The Hebrew phrase, used only three times (here; 1Ch 12:18; 2Ch 24:20), emphasizes that the Spirit of the Lord empowered the human agent and acted through him (see note on 3:10).
6:35 *Manasseh.* West Manasseh. *Asher.* This tribe had earlier failed to answer the call to arms (5:17).
6:39 *not be angry ... just one more request.* Cf. Abraham's words in Ge 18:32.
7:1–8 As supreme commander of Israel, the Lord reduced the army so that Israel would know that the victory was by his power, not theirs.
7:1 *Harod.* Means "trembling" and may refer to either the timidity of the Israelites (v. 3) or the great panic of the Midianites when Gideon attacked (v. 21). *valley.* That is, the Valley of Jezreel. *hill of Moreh.* Located across the valley from Harod, approximately four miles from the Israelite army.
7:3 *may turn back.* Those who were afraid to fight the Lord's battle were not to go out with his army so that they would not demoralize the others (Dt 20:8). *Mount Gilead.* Perhaps used here as another name for Mount Gilboa.
7:6 *lapping like dogs.* The 300 remained on their feet, prepared for any emergency.

GIDEON'S BATTLES

The story of Gideon begins with a graphic portrayal of one of the most striking facts of life in the Fertile Crescent: the periodic migration of nomadic peoples into the settled areas of Canaan. Each spring the tents of the Bedouin herdsmen appeared overnight almost as if by magic, scattered on the hills and fields of the farming districts. Conflict between these two ways of life (herdsmen and farmers) was inevitable.

1 In the Biblical period, the vast numbers and warlike practice of the herdsmen reduced the village people to near vassalage. God's answer was twofold: (1) religious reform, starting with Gideon's own family; and (2) military action, based on a coalition of northern Israelite tribes. The location of Gideon's hometown, "Ophrah of the Abiezrites" (6:24), is not known with certainty, but it probably was ancient Aper (modern Afula) in the Valley of Jezreel.

2 The battle at the spring of Harod is justly celebrated for its strategic brilliance. Denied the use of the only local water source, the Midianites camped in the valley and fell victim to the small band of Israelites that attacked them from the heights of the hill of Moreh.

3 The main battle took place north of the hill near the village of En-dor at the foot of Mount Tabor. Fleeing by way of the Jordan valley, the Midianites were trapped when the Ephraimites seized the fords of the Jordan from below Beth Shan to Beth Barah near Adam.

7The LORD said to Gideon, "With the
three hundred men that lapped I will save
you and give the Midianites into your
hands.[c] Let all the others go home."[d] 8So
Gideon sent the rest of the Israelites home
but kept the three hundred, who took over
the provisions and trumpets of the others.
Now the camp of Midian lay below him
in the valley. 9During that night the LORD
said to Gideon, "Get up, go down against
the camp, because I am going to give it
into your hands.[e] 10If you are afraid to attack,
go down to the camp with your servant
Purah 11and listen to what they are
saying. Afterward, you will be encouraged
to attack the camp." So he and Purah his
servant went down to the outposts of the
camp. 12The Midianites, the Amalekites[f]
and all the other eastern peoples had settled
in the valley, thick as locusts.[g] Their
camels[h] could no more be counted than
the sand on the seashore.[i]
13Gideon arrived just as a man was telling
a friend his dream. "I had a dream," he
was saying. "A round loaf of barley bread
came tumbling into the Midianite camp.
It struck the tent with such force that the
tent overturned and collapsed."
14His friend responded, "This can be
nothing other than the sword of Gideon
son of Joash,[j] the Israelite. God has given
the Midianites and the whole camp into
his hands."
15When Gideon heard the dream and its
interpretation, he bowed down and worshiped.[k]
He returned to the camp of Israel
and called out, "Get up! The LORD has given
the Midianite camp into your hands."[l]
16Dividing the three hundred men[m] into
three companies,[n] he placed trumpets[o] and
empty jars[p] in the hands of all of them,
with torches[q] inside.
17"Watch me," he told them. "Follow
my lead. When I get to the edge of the
camp, do exactly as I do. 18When I and all
who are with me blow our trumpets,[r] then
from all around the camp blow yours and
shout, 'For the LORD and for Gideon.' "

7:7 [c]S Jos 8:7 [d]1Sa 14:6
7:9 [e]ver 13-15; S Jos 2:24; S Jdg 1:2
7:12 [f]Nu 13:29 [g]S Dt 28:42; Jer 46:23 [h]Jer 49:29 [i]S Jos 11:4
7:14 [j]S Jdg 6:11
7:15 [k]1Sa 15:31 [l]S ver 9
7:16 [m]Ge 14:15 [n]Jdg 9:43; 1Sa 11:11; 2Sa 18:2 [o]S Lev 25:9 [p]ver 19; Ge 24:14 [q]S Ge 15:17
7:18 [r]S Jdg 3:27

7:8–14 The Lord provided Gideon with encouraging military intelligence for the battle.
7:13–14 Although revelations by dreams are frequently mentioned in the OT, here both dreamer and interpreter are non-Israelites. Contrast Joseph, who interpreted dreams in Egypt (Ge 40:1–22; 41:1–32), and Daniel, who interpreted dreams in Babylon (Da 2:1–45; 4:4–27).
7:13 *round loaf of barley bread.* Since barley was considered an inferior grain and only half the value of wheat (see 2Ki 7:1), it is a fitting symbol for Israel, which was inferior in numbers.
7:16 *three companies.* A strategy adopted by Israel on several occasions (9:43; 1Sa 11:11; 2Sa 18:2). *trumpets.* Rams' horns (see Ex 19:13).

19 Gideon and the hundred men with
him reached the edge of the camp at the
beginning of the middle watch, just after
they had changed the guard. They blew
their trumpets and broke the jars[s] that
were in their hands. 20 The three companies blew the trumpets and smashed the
jars. Grasping the torches[t] in their left
hands and holding in their right hands the
trumpets they were to blow, they shouted, "A sword[u] for the LORD and for Gideon!" 21 While each man held his position
around the camp, all the Midianites ran,
crying out as they fled.[v]
22 When the three hundred trumpets
sounded,[w] the LORD caused the men
throughout the camp to turn on each other[x] with their swords.[y] The army fled to
Beth Shittah toward Zererah as far as the
border of Abel Meholah[z] near Tabbath.
23 Israelites from Naphtali, Asher[a] and
all Manasseh were called out,[b] and they
pursued the Midianites.[c] 24 Gideon sent
messengers throughout the hill country
of Ephraim, saying, "Come down against
the Midianites and seize the waters of
the Jordan[d] ahead of them as far as Beth
Barah."
So all the men of Ephraim were called
out and they seized the waters of the Jordan as far as Beth Barah. 25 They also captured two of the Midianite leaders, Oreb
and Zeeb[e]. They killed Oreb at the rock of
Oreb,[f] and Zeeb at the winepress of Zeeb.
They pursued the Midianites[g] and brought
the heads of Oreb and Zeeb to Gideon,
who was by the Jordan.[h]

Zebah and Zalmunna

8 Now the Ephraimites asked Gideon,[i]
"Why have you treated us like this?
Why didn't you call us when you went to
fight Midian?[j]"[k] And they challenged him
vigorously.[l]
2 But he answered them, "What have I
accomplished compared to you? Aren't the
gleanings of Ephraim's grapes better than
the full grape harvest of Abiezer?[m] 3 God
gave Oreb and Zeeb,[n] the Midianite leaders, into your hands. What was I able to
do compared to you?" At this, their resentment against him subsided.
4 Gideon and his three hundred men, exhausted yet keeping up the pursuit, came
to the Jordan[o] and crossed it. 5 He said to
the men of Sukkoth,[p] "Give my troops
some bread; they are worn out,[q] and I am
still pursuing Zebah and Zalmunna,[r] the
kings of Midian."
6 But the officials of Sukkoth[s] said, "Do
you already have the hands of Zebah
and Zalmunna in your possession? Why
should we give bread[t] to your troops?"[u]
7 Then Gideon replied, "Just for that,
when the LORD has given Zebah and Zalmunna[v] into my hand, I will tear your
flesh with desert thorns and briers."
8 From there he went up to Peniel[a][w] and
made the same request of them, but they
answered as the men of Sukkoth had.
9 So he said to the men of Peniel, "When
I return in triumph, I will tear down this
tower."[x]
10 Now Zebah and Zalmunna were in
Karkor with a force of about fifteen thousand men, all that were left of the armies
of the eastern peoples; a hundred and
twenty thousand swordsmen had fallen.[y]
11 Gideon went up by the route of the nomads east of Nobah[z] and Jogbehah[a] and
attacked the unsuspecting army. 12 Zebah
and Zalmunna, the two kings of Midian,

[a] 8 Hebrew *Penuel,* a variant of *Peniel;* also in verses 9 and 17

7:19 [s] S ver 16
7:20 [t] S Ge 15:17 [u] S Dt 32:41
7:21 [v] 2Ki 7:7
7:22 [w] S Jos 6:20 [x] 1Sa 14:20; 2Ch 20:23; Isa 9:21; 19:2; Eze 38:21; Hag 2:22; Zec 14:13 [y] Hab 3:14 [z] 1Sa 18:19; 1Ki 4:12; 19:16
7:23 [a] S Jos 17:7 [b] Jdg 6:35 [c] Ps 83:9
7:24 [d] S Jos 2:7
7:25 [e] Jdg 8:3; Ps 83:11 [f] Isa 10:26 [g] Isa 9:4 [h] Jdg 8:4; Ps 106:43
8:1 [i] S Jdg 6:11 [j] S Ge 25:2 [k] Jdg 12:1 [l] 2Sa 19:41
8:2 [m] S Nu 26:30
8:3 [n] S Jdg 7:25
8:4 [o] Jdg 7:25
8:5 [p] S Ge 33:17 [q] Job 16:7; Ps 6:6; Jer 45:3 [r] ver 7, 12; Ps 83:11
8:6 [s] ver 14 [t] 1Sa 25:11 [u] ver 15
8:7 [v] S ver 5
8:8 [w] ver 9, 17; Ge 32:30; 1Ki 12:25
8:9 [x] ver 17
8:10 [y] S Jdg 6:5; Isa 9:4
8:11 [z] Nu 32:42 [a] S Nu 32:35

7:19 *middle watch.* The Israelites divided the night into three watches (see note on Mt 14:25). The "beginning of the middle watch" would be after the enemy had gone to sleep.
7:22 *three hundred trumpets.* Normally only a comparatively small number of men in an army carried trumpets. *turn on each other.* A similar panic occurred among the Ammonites, Moabites and Edomites (2Ch 20:23) and among the Philistines at Gibeah (1Sa 14:20). See Eze 38:21; Zec 14:13; see also note on Jdg 4:15. *toward Zererah.* Toward the southeast.
7:23 *were called out.* Encouraged by the turn of events, many of those who had departed now joined the battle.
7:24 *hill country of Ephraim.* Gideon needed the aid of the Ephraimites to cut off the retreat of the Midianites into the Jordan Valley. *waters of the Jordan.* Probably the river crossings in the vicinity of Beth Shan. By controlling the river the Israelites could prevent the escape of the fleeing Midianites (see note on 3:28). *Beth Barah.* Exact location unknown, but it must have been some distance down the river. Gideon's pursuit of the enemy across the river took him to Sukkoth, a town near the Jabbok River (8:5).
7:25 *Oreb.* Means "raven" (see Isa 10:26). *Zeeb.* Means "wolf." *heads.* Frequently parts of the bodies of dead victims, such as heads, hands (8:6) and foreskins (1Sa 18:25), were cut off and brought back as a kind of body count.
8:1 *Ephraimites.* Contrast Gideon, who placates the wrath of this tribe (vv. 2–3), with Jephthah, who brings humiliation and defeat to it (12:1–6).
8:2 *gleanings.* Leftover grain after the main gathering of the harvest (see note on Ru 1:22). Here Gideon implies that Ephraim has accomplished more than he and all the other forces involved in the initial attack. *Abiezer.* Gideon's clan (see note on 6:11). The name means "My (divine) Father is helper" or "My (divine) Father is strong."
8:3 *their resentment . . . subsided.* "A gentle answer turns away wrath" (Pr 15:1).
8:5 *kings of Midian.* Zebah and Zalmunna may have belonged to different Midianite tribes (see Nu 31:8).
8:6 *hands.* See note on 7:25. *Why should we give bread . . . ?* The officials of Sukkoth doubted Gideon's ability to defeat the Midianite coalition and feared reprisal if they gave his army food.
8:8 *Peniel.* The place where Jacob had wrestled with God (Ge 32:30–31).

led, but he pursued them and captured
hem, routing their entire army.
13Gideon son of Joash[b] then returned
rom the battle by the Pass of Heres.[c] 14He
aught a young man of Sukkoth and ques-
ioned him, and the young man wrote
own for him the names of the seventy-
even officials of Sukkoth,[d] the elders[e] of
he town. 15Then Gideon came and said to
he men of Sukkoth, "Here are Zebah and
almunna, about whom you taunted me
y saying, 'Do you already have the hands
f Zebah and Zalmunna in your posses-
ion? Why should we give bread to your
xhausted men?[f]' " 16He took the elders of
ne town and taught the men of Sukkoth
lesson[g] by punishing them with desert
norns and briers. 17He also pulled down
ne tower of Peniel[h] and killed the men of
ne town.[i]
18Then he asked Zebah and Zalmunna,
What kind of men did you kill at Tabor?[j]"
"Men like you," they answered, "each
ne with the bearing of a prince."
19Gideon replied, "Those were my
rothers, the sons of my own mother. As
urely as the LORD lives,[k] if you had spared
neir lives, I would not kill you." 20Turn-
g to Jether, his oldest son, he said, "Kill
em!" But Jether did not draw his sword,
ecause he was only a boy and was afraid.
21Zebah and Zalmunna said, "Come,
o it yourself. 'As is the man, so is his
rength.' " So Gideon stepped forward and
illed them, and took the ornaments[l] off
neir camels' necks.

ideon's Ephod

22The Israelites said to Gideon, "Rule
ver us—you, your son and your grand-
on—because you have saved us from the
and of Midian."
23But Gideon told them, "I will not rule
over you, nor will my son rule over you.
The LORD will rule[m] over you." 24And he
said, "I do have one request, that each of
you give me an earring[n] from your share
of the plunder.[o]" (It was the custom of the
Ishmaelites[p] to wear gold earrings.)
25They answered, "We'll be glad to give
them." So they spread out a garment, and
each of them threw a ring from his plunder onto it. 26The weight of the gold rings
he asked for came to seventeen hundred
shekels,[a] not counting the ornaments, the
pendants and the purple garments worn
by the kings of Midian or the chains[q]
that were on their camels' necks. 27Gid-
eon made the gold into an ephod,[r] which
he placed in Ophrah,[s] his town. All Israel
prostituted themselves by worshiping it
there, and it became a snare[t] to Gideon
and his family.[u]

Gideon's Death

28Thus Midian was subdued before the
Israelites and did not raise its head[v] again.
During Gideon's lifetime, the land had
peace[w] forty years.
29Jerub-Baal[x] son of Joash[y] went back
home to live. 30He had seventy sons[z] of his
own, for he had many wives. 31His concubine,[a] who lived in Shechem, also bore
him a son, whom he named Abimelek.[b]
32Gideon son of Joash died at a good old
age[c] and was buried in the tomb of his
father Joash in Ophrah of the Abiezrites.
33No sooner had Gideon died than the
Israelites again prostituted themselves to
the Baals.[d] They set up Baal-Berith[e] as
their god[f] 34and did not remember[g] the
LORD their God, who had rescued them
from the hands of all their enemies on every side. 35They also failed to show any

8:13 [b]S Jdg 6:11 [c]Jdg 1:35 **8:14** [d]ver 6 [e]S Ex 3:16 **8:15** [f]ver 6 **8:16** [g]1Sa 14:12 **8:17** [h]S ver 8 [i]ver 9 **8:18** [j]S Jos 19:22 **8:19** [k]S Nu 14:21 **8:21** [l]ver 26; Isa 3:18 **8:23** [m]S Ex 16:8; S Nu 11:20; 1Sa 12:12 **8:24** [n]S Ge 35:4 [o]S Ge 49:27 [p]S Ge 16:11 **8:26** [q]S ver 21 **8:27** [r]S Ex 25:7; Jdg 17:5; 18:14 [s]S Jos 18:23 [t]S Ex 10:7 [u]S Ex 32:2 **8:28** [v]Ps 83:2 [w]S Jdg 3:11 **8:29** [x]S Jdg 6:32 [y]S Jdg 6:11 **8:30** [z]Jdg 9:2, 5,18,24; 12:14; 2Ki 10:1 **8:31** [a]S Ge 22:24 [b]Jdg 9:1; 10:1; 2Sa 11:21 **8:32** [c]S Ge 15:15 **8:33** [d]S Jdg 2:11, 13,19 [e]Jdg 9:4 [f]Jdg 9:27,46 **8:34** [g]S Jdg 3:7; S Ne 9:17

[a] *26* That is, about 43 pounds or about 20 kilograms

19 *sons of my own mother.* In an age when men often had veral wives, it was necessary to distinguish between full others and half brothers.
21 *do it yourself.* Dying at the hands of a boy may have en considered a disgrace (see 1Sa 17:42). *ornaments.* Cres- nt necklaces, as in Isa 3:18.
8:23 *I will not rule ... The LORD will rule.* Gideon, like Samuel (1Sa 8:4–20), rejected the establishment of a onarchy because he regarded it as a replacement of the rd's rule. God's rule over Israel (theocracy) is a central issue Judges.
24 *earring.* Or possibly "nose ring" (see Ge 24:47; Eze 16:12). *maelites.* Related to the Midianites (Ge 25:1–2) and some- nes identified with them (vv. 22,24; Ge 37:25–28; 39:1). See te on Ge 37:25.
27 *ephod.* Sometimes a holy garment associated with the esthood (Ex 28:6–30; 39:2–26; Lev 8:7) and at other times agan object associated with idols (17:5; 18:14,17). *prosti- ed themselves.* See Ex 34:15 and note.
28 *forty years.* A conventional number of years for a gen- ation (see Introduction: Background).
8:29 *Jerub-Baal.* See note on 6:32.
8:30 *seventy sons.* A sign of power and prosperity (see 12:14; 2Ki 10:1).
8:31 *concubine.* She was originally a slave in his house- hold (9:18; see note on Ge 16:2). *Abimelek.* Appears elsewhere as a royal title (Ge 20:2; 26:1; Ps 34 title) and means "My (divine) Father is King." Gideon, in naming his son, ac- knowledges that the Lord (here called "Father") is King.
8:32 *at a good old age.* A phrase used elsewhere only of Abra- ham (Ge 15:15; 25:8) and David (1Ch 29:28).
8:33 *prostituted themselves.* See Ex 34:15 and note. *Baals.* See notes on 2:11,13. *Baal-Berith.* Means "lord of the covenant"; the same deity is called El-Berith ("god of the covenant") in 9:46. There was a temple dedicated to him (see 9:4) in Shechem. The word "covenant" in his name probably refers to a solemn treaty that bound together a league of Canaanite cities whose people worshiped him as their god. Ironically, Shechem (v. 31), near Mount Ebal, was the site at which Josh- ua had twice renewed the Lord's covenant with the Israelites after they had entered Canaan (Jos 8:30–35; 24:25–27). See also note on 2:11.

loyalty to the family of Jerub-Baal[h] (that
is, Gideon) in spite of all the good things
he had done for them.[i]

Abimelek

9 Abimelek[j] son of Jerub-Baal[k] went to
his mother's brothers in Shechem and
said to them and to all his mother's clan,
2 "Ask all the citizens of Shechem, 'Which
is better for you: to have all seventy of Jerub-Baal's sons rule over you, or just one
man?' Remember, I am your flesh and
blood.[l]"
3 When the brothers repeated all this
to the citizens of Shechem, they were inclined to follow Abimelek, for they said,
"He is related to us." 4 They gave him seventy shekels[a] of silver from the temple of
Baal-Berith,[m] and Abimelek used it to hire
reckless scoundrels,[n] who became his followers. 5 He went to his father's home in
Ophrah and on one stone murdered his
seventy brothers,[o] the sons of Jerub-Baal.
But Jotham,[p] the youngest son of Jerub-
Baal, escaped by hiding.[q] 6 Then all the
citizens of Shechem and Beth Millo[r] gathered beside the great tree[s] at the pillar in
Shechem to crown Abimelek king.
7 When Jotham[t] was told about this, he
climbed up on the top of Mount Gerizim[u]
and shouted to them, "Listen to me, citizens of Shechem, so that God may listen
to you. 8 One day the trees went out to

8:35 [h] S Jdg 6:32 [i] Jdg 9:16
9:1 [j] S Jdg 8:31 [k] S Jdg 6:32
9:2 [l] S Ge 29:14
9:4 [m] S Jdg 8:33 [n] Jdg 11:3; 1Sa 25:25; 2Ch 13:7; Job 30:8
9:5 [o] S Jdg 8:30 [p] ver 7,21, 57 [q] 2Ki 11:2; 2Ch 22:9
9:6 [r] ver 20; 2Ki 12:20 [s] S Ge 12:6; S Jdg 4:11
9:7 [t] S ver 5 [u] S Dt 11:29; Jn 4:20
9:13 [v] S Ge 14:18; Ecc 2:3; SS 4:10
9:15 [w] Isa 30:2 [x] ver 20 [y] S Dt 3:25; 1Ki 5:6; Ps 29:5; 92:12; Isa 2:13
9:17 [z] Jdg 12:3; 1Sa 19:5; 28:21; Job 13:14; Ps 119:109

anoint a king for themselves. They said t
the olive tree, 'Be our king.'
9 "But the olive tree answered, 'Shoul
I give up my oil, by which both gods an
humans are honored, to hold sway ove
the trees?'
10 "Next, the trees said to the fig tre
'Come and be our king.'
11 "But the fig tree replied, 'Should I giv
up my fruit, so good and sweet, to hol
sway over the trees?'
12 "Then the trees said to the vin
'Come and be our king.'
13 "But the vine answered, 'Should I giv
up my wine,[v] which cheers both gods an
humans, to hold sway over the trees?'
14 "Finally all the trees said to the thor
bush, 'Come and be our king.'
15 "The thornbush said to the trees, '
you really want to anoint me king ov
you, come and take refuge in my shade
but if not, then let fire come out[x] of th
thornbush and consume the cedars of Le
anon!'[y]
16 "Have you acted honorably and
good faith by making Abimelek kin
Have you been fair to Jerub-Baal and h
family? Have you treated him as he d
serves? 17 Remember that my father foug
for you and risked[z] his life to rescue yo
from the hand of Midian. 18 But today yo

[a] 4 That is, about 1 3/4 pounds or about 800 grams

9:1 – 57 The stories of Gideon and Abimelek form the literary center of Judges (see Introduction: Literary Features). Abimelek, who tried to set himself up like a Canaanite city king with the help of Baal (v. 4), stands in sharp contrast to his father, Gideon (Jerub-Baal), who had attacked Baal worship and insisted that the Lord ruled over Israel. Abimelek attempted this Canaanite revival in the very place where Joshua had earlier reaffirmed Israel's allegiance to the Lord (Jos 24:14 – 27). In every respect Abimelek was the antithesis of the Lord's appointed judges.

9:1 *Shechem.* See note on Ge 33:18. Ruins dating from the Canaanite era give evidence of a sacred area, probably to be associated with the temple of Baal-Berith or El-Berith (vv. 4,46). Archaeological evidence, which is compatible with the destruction of Shechem by Abimelek, indicates that its sacred area was never rebuilt after this time.

9:2 *citizens.* The singular form of the Hebrew for this word is *ba'al.* It means "lord" or "owner" and probably refers here to the aristocracy or landowners of the city. *flesh and blood.* Being half-Canaanite, Abimelek intimated that it was in their best interest to make him king rather than be under the rule of Gideon's other 70 sons. The following he gathered was based on this relationship and became a threat to the people of Israel.

9:4 *from the temple.* Ancient temples served as depositories for personal and civic funds. The payments of vows and penalties, as well as gifts, were also part of the temple treasury. The temple of Baal-Berith is probably to be identified with a large building found at Shechem by archaeologists. *reckless scoundrels.* Use of mercenaries to accomplish political or military goals was common in ancient times. Others who used them are Jephthah (11:3), David (1Sa 22:1 – 2), Absalom (2Sa 15:1), Adonijah (1Ki 1:5), Rezon (1 11:23 – 24) and Jeroboam (2Ch 13:6 – 7).

9:5 *on one stone.* Abimelek's 70 brothers were slaughter like sacrificial animals (see 13:19 – 20; 1Sa 14:33 – 34). In fect, he inaugurated his kingship by using his Israelite h brothers as his coronation sacrifices (see 2Sa 15:10,12; 1 1:5,9; 3:4).

9:6 *Beth Millo.* "Millo" is derived from a Hebrew verb meani "to fill" and perhaps refers to the earthen fill on which wa and other large structures were built. Beth Millo may be ide tical to the "stronghold" of v. 46. *great tree.* See Jos 24:25 – see also note on Ge 12:6.

9:7 *top.* Probably a ledge that overlooked the city.

9:8 *trees went out.* Fables of this type, in which inanimate c jects speak and act, were popular among Eastern peoples that time (see 2Ki 14:9).

9:9 – 13 The olive tree, the fig tree and the vine were plants that produced fruit of great importance to the peo of the Near East.

9:13 *gods.* It was commonly believed that the gods parti pated in such human experiences as drinking wine (cf. 29:40).

9:14 *thornbush.* Probably the well-known buckthorn, a scra gly bush common in the hills of Israel and a constant mena to farming. It produced nothing of value and was an apt f ure for Abimelek.

9:15 *shade.* Ironically, in offering shade to the trees, t thornbush symbolized the traditional role of kings as p tectors of their subjects (see Isa 30:2 – 3; 32:1 – 2; La 4:20; 4:12). *cedars of Lebanon.* The most valuable of Near Easte trees, here symbolic of the leading men of Shechem (s v. 20).

ave revolted against my father's family.
'ou have murdered his seventy sons[a] on
single stone and have made Abimelek,
he son of his female slave, king over the
itizens of Shechem because he is relat-
d to you. 19 So have you acted honorably
nd in good faith toward Jerub-Baal and
is family today?[b] If you have, may Abim-
lek be your joy, and may you be his, too!
0 But if you have not, let fire come out[c]
rom Abimelek and consume you, the cit-
zens of Shechem[d] and Beth Millo,[e] and
t fire come out from you, the citizens of
hechem and Beth Millo, and consume
bimelek!"
21 Then Jotham[f] fled, escaping to Beer,[g]
nd he lived there because he was afraid
f his brother Abimelek.
22 After Abimelek had governed Isra-
three years, 23 God stirred up animosi-
y[h] between Abimelek and the citizens of
hechem so that they acted treacherously
gainst Abimelek. 24 God did this in order
at the crime against Jerub-Baal's seventy
ons,[i] the shedding[j] of their blood, might
e avenged[k] on their brother Abimelek
nd on the citizens of Shechem, who had
elped him[l] murder his brothers. 25 In op-
osition to him these citizens of Shechem
t men on the hilltops to ambush and rob
veryone who passed by, and this was re-
orted to Abimelek.
26 Now Gaal son of Ebed[m] moved with
is clan into Shechem, and its citizens
ut their confidence in him. 27 After they
ad gone out into the fields and gathered
e grapes and trodden[n] them, they held a
stival in the temple of their god.[o] While
ey were eating and drinking, they cursed
bimelek. 28 Then Gaal son of Ebed[p] said,
Who[q] is Abimelek, and why should we
hechemites be subject to him? Isn't he
rub-Baal's son, and isn't Zebul his depu-
? Serve the family of Hamor,[r] Shechem's
ther! Why should we serve Abime-
k? 29 If only this people were under my
command![s] Then I would get rid of him.
I would say to Abimelek, 'Call out your
whole army!' "[a][t]
30 When Zebul the governor of the city
heard what Gaal son of Ebed said, he was
very angry. 31 Under cover he sent messengers to Abimelek, saying, "Gaal son
of Ebed and his clan have come to Shechem and are stirring up the city against
you. 32 Now then, during the night you and
your men should come and lie in wait[u] in
the fields. 33 In the morning at sunrise, advance against the city. When Gaal and his
men come out against you, seize the opportunity to attack them.[v]"
34 So Abimelek and all his troops set out
by night and took up concealed positions
near Shechem in four companies. 35 Now
Gaal son of Ebed had gone out and was
standing at the entrance of the city gate[w]
just as Abimelek and his troops came out
from their hiding place.[x]
36 When Gaal saw them, he said to Zebul, "Look, people are coming down from
the tops of the mountains!"
Zebul replied, "You mistake the shadows of the mountains for men."
37 But Gaal spoke up again: "Look, people are coming down from the central
hill,[b] and a company is coming from the
direction of the diviners' tree."
38 Then Zebul said to him, "Where is
your big talk now, you who said, 'Who
is Abimelek that we should be subject to
him?' Aren't these the men you ridiculed?[y]
Go out and fight them!"
39 So Gaal led out[c] the citizens of Shechem and fought Abimelek. 40 Abimelek
chased him all the way to the entrance
of the gate, and many were killed as they
fled. 41 Then Abimelek stayed in Arumah,
and Zebul drove Gaal and his clan out of
Shechem.

9:18 [a] S Jdg 8:30 **9:19** [b] ver 16 **9:20** [c] ver 15 [d] ver 45 [e] S ver 6 **9:21** [f] S ver 5 [g] Nu 21:16 **9:23** [h] 1Sa 16:14,23; 18:10; 19:9; 1Ki 22:22 **9:24** [i] S Jdg 8:30 [j] S Ge 9:6; Nu 35:33; 1Ki 2:32 [k] ver 56-57 [l] Dt 27:25 **9:26** [m] ver 28, 31,41 **9:27** [n] Isa 16:10; Am 5:11; 9:13 [o] S Jdg 8:33 **9:28** [p] S ver 26 [q] 1Sa 25:10 [r] S Ge 33:19

9:29 [s] 2Sa 15:4 [t] ver 38 **9:32** [u] Jos 8:2 **9:33** [v] 1Sa 10:7 **9:35** [w] S Jos 2:5 [x] Ps 32:7; Isa 28:15,17; Jer 49:10 **9:38** [y] ver 28-29

[a] *29* Septuagint; Hebrew *him." Then he said to Abimelek, "Call out your whole army!"* [b] *37* The Hebrew for this phrase means *the navel of the earth.* [c] *39* Or *Gaal went out in the sight of*

20 *fire come out … and consume.* A grim prediction that
imelek and the people of Shechem would destroy each
her. Fire spreads rapidly through bramble bushes and
ings about swift destruction (see Ex 22:6; Isa 9:18).
21 *Beer.* A very common name, meaning "a well."
22 *Israel.* Those Israelites who recognized Abimelek's au-
ority, mainly in the vicinity of Shechem.
9:23 *animosity.* The Hebrew for "animosity" is frequently rendered "evil spirit" or "harmful spirit" (cf., e.g, 1Sa
:14 and NIV text note); here perhaps a "spirit" of distrust
d bitterness. The Hebrew for "spirit" is often used to de-
ibe an attitude or disposition. *acted treacherously.* The one
o founded his kingdom by treachery is himself undone
treachery.
26 *put their confidence in him.* Just as the fickle population
d followed Abimelek, so they are now swayed by the de-
otive proposals of Gaal.

9:27 *held a festival.* The vintage harvest was one of the most joyous times of the year (see Isa 16:9–10; Jer 25:30), but festivals and celebrations held at pagan temples often degenerated into debauched drinking affairs.
9:28 *Hamor.* The Hivite ruler who had founded the city of Shechem (Ge 33:19; 34:2; Jos 24:32).
9:32 *lie in wait.* Ambush succeeded against Gibeah in Benjamin (20:37) and against Ai (Jos 8:2).
9:34 *four companies.* Smaller segments meant less chance of detection. Also, attack from several directions was a good tactical strategy.
9:37 *central hill.* See NIV text note; see also note on Eze 38:12, where the same Hebrew is translated "center of the land." *diviners' tree.* Probably a sacred tree in some way related to the temple of Baal-Berith (see note on Ge 12:6).

42The next day the people of Shechem
went out to the fields, and this was reported to Abimelek. 43So he took his men, divided them into three companies[z] and set
an ambush[a] in the fields. When he saw the
people coming out of the city, he rose to
attack them. 44Abimelek and the companies with him rushed forward to a position
at the entrance of the city gate. Then two
companies attacked those in the fields and
struck them down. 45All that day Abimelek pressed his attack against the city until
he had captured it and killed its people.
Then he destroyed the city[b] and scattered
salt[c] over it.
46On hearing this, the citizens in the
tower of Shechem went into the stronghold of the temple[d] of El-Berith. 47When
Abimelek heard that they had assembled
there, 48he and all his men went up Mount
Zalmon.[e] He took an ax and cut off some
branches, which he lifted to his shoulders.
He ordered the men with him, "Quick! Do
what you have seen me do!" 49So all the
men cut branches and followed Abimelek.
They piled them against the stronghold
and set it on fire with the people still inside. So all the people in the tower of Shechem, about a thousand men and women,
also died.
50Next Abimelek went to Thebez[f] and
besieged it and captured it. 51Inside the
city, however, was a strong tower, to which
all the men and women—all the people
of the city—had fled. They had locked
themselves in and climbed up on the tower roof. 52Abimelek went to the tower and
attacked it. But as he approached the entrance to the tower to set it on fire, 53a
woman dropped an upper millstone on hi
head and cracked his skull.[g]
54Hurriedly he called to his armor-bea
er, "Draw your sword and kill me,[h] so tha
they can't say, 'A woman killed him.'" S
his servant ran him through, and he diec
55When the Israelites saw that Abimele
was dead, they went home.
56Thus God repaid the wickedness tha
Abimelek had done to his father by mu
dering his seventy brothers. 57God als
made the people of Shechem pay for a
their wickedness.[i] The curse of Jothan
son of Jerub-Baal came on them.

Tola

10 After the time of Abimelek,[k] a ma
of Issachar[l] named Tola son c
Puah,[m] the son of Dodo, rose to save[n] Isra
el. He lived in Shamir,[o] in the hill countr
of Ephraim. 2He led[a] Israel twenty-thre
years; then he died, and was buried i
Shamir.

Jair

3He was followed by Jair[p] of Gilead, wh
led Israel twenty-two years. 4He had thi
ty sons, who rode thirty donkeys.[q] The
controlled thirty towns in Gilead, which t
this day are called Havvoth Jair.[b][r] 5Whe
Jair[s] died, he was buried in Kamon.

Jephthah

6Again the Israelites did evil in the eye
of the LORD.[t] They served the Baals an
the Ashtoreths,[u] and the gods of Aram
the gods of Sidon,[w] the gods of Moab, th

9:43 [z]S Jdg 7:16 [a]Jos 8:2
9:45 [b]ver 20 [c]Jer 48:9
9:46 [d]S Jdg 8:33
9:48 [e]Ps 68:14
9:50 [f]2Sa 11:21
9:53 [g]2Sa 11:21
9:54 [h]1Sa 31:4; 2Sa 1:9
9:57 [i]ver 24; Ps 94:23 [j]S ver 5
10:1 [k]S Jdg 8:31 [l]S Ge 30:18 [m]S Ge 46:13 [n]S Jdg 6:14 [o]Jos 15:48
10:3 [p]S Nu 32:41
10:4 [q]S Ge 49:11; S 1Ki 1:33 [r]S Nu 32:41
10:5 [s]S Nu 32:41
10:6 [t]S Jdg 2:11 [u]S Jdg 2:13 [v]Eze 27:16 [w]S Ge 10:15

[a] 2 Traditionally *judged;* also in verse 3 [b] 4 Or *calle* *the settlements of Jair*

9:43 *three companies.* See note on 7:16.
9:45 *scattered salt over it.* To condemn it to perpetual barrenness and desolation (see Dt 29:23; Ps 107:33–34; Jer 17:6; Zep 2:9).
9:46 *stronghold.* Probably the Beth Millo of v. 6. *El-Berith.* Baal-Berith (v. 4).
9:49 *set it on fire.* In fulfillment of Jotham's curse (v. 20).
9:53 *woman.* While the men used bows, arrows and spears, women helped to defend the tower by dropping heavy stones on those who came near it. *upper millstone.* See note on 3:16. The upper, revolving stone of a mill was circular, with a hole in the center. Grinding grain was women's work (see Ex 11:5), usually considered too lowly for men to perform (see Jdg 16:21). Abimelek was killed by a woman using a domestic implement (see also 4:21).
9:54 *armor-bearer.* In Israel's earlier years in Canaan, military leaders were usually served by a personal attendant (see 1Sa 14:6; 31:4), but no armor-bearers are mentioned after the time of David. *A woman killed him.* It was considered a disgrace for a soldier to die at the hands of a woman. Abimelek's shameful death was long remembered (2Sa 11:21).
9:56 *God repaid.* God was in control of the events. As Israel's true King, he brought Abimelek's wickedness to a quick and shameful end.
9:57 *curse of Jotham.* See v. 20.
10:1 *a man of Issachar named Tola son of Puah.* Tola and Pua bear names of two of the sons of Issachar (Ge 46:13; Nu 26:2 1Ch 7:1).
10:3 *Jair.* Since Jair came from Gilead (the territory assign to Manasseh) and since a descendant of Manasseh bore t same name (Nu 32:41; Dt 3:14; 1Ki 4:13), it appears that J was a Manassite.
10:4 *thirty sons … thirty donkeys … thirty towns.* Evidence wealth and position. *Havvoth Jair.* See NIV text note.
10:6—12:7 Israel now turned to Jephthah, a soc outcast whom they had driven from the land a caused to become an outlaw without an inheritance in rael. The author notes this to Israel's shame. The account Jephthah's judgeship balances that of Deborah in the stc of the judges (see note on 4:1—5:31; see also Introductic Literary Features).
10:6 *gods of Aram.* The chief gods were Hadad (Baa Mot, Anath and Rimmon. *gods of Sidon.* The Sidonia worshiped essentially the same gods as the Canaanites (s notes on 2:11,13). *gods of Moab.* The chief deity of Moab w Chemosh. *gods of the Ammonites.* Molek was the chief A monite deity (see 1Ki 11:7) and was sometimes worship by the offering of human sacrifice (Lev 18:21; 20:2–5; 2 23:10). This god is also called Milkom in Hebrew. Both Mol and Milkom are forms of a Semitic word for "king." *gods*

;ods of the Ammonites[x] and the gods of
he Philistines.[y] And because the Israelites
orsook the LORD[z] and no longer served
im, 7he became angry[a] with them. He
old them[b] into the hands of the Philis-
ines and the Ammonites, 8who that year
hattered and crushed them. For eighteen
'ears they oppressed all the Israelites on
he east side of the Jordan in Gilead,[c] the
and of the Amorites. 9The Ammonites
lso crossed the Jordan to fight against
udah,[d] Benjamin and Ephraim;[e] Israel
vas in great distress. 10Then the Israelites
ried[f] out to the LORD, "We have sinned[g]
gainst you, forsaking our God and serv-
ng the Baals."[h]
11The LORD replied, "When the Egyp-
ans,[i] the Amorites,[j] the Ammonites,[k] the
hilistines,[l] 12the Sidonians, the Amalek-
es[m] and the Maonites[a][n] oppressed you[o]
nd you cried to me for help, did I not
ave you from their hands? 13But you have
orsaken[p] me and served other gods,[q] so
will no longer save you. 14Go and cry
ut to the gods you have chosen. Let them
ave[r] you when you are in trouble![s]"
15But the Israelites said to the LORD,
We have sinned. Do with us whatever
ou think best,[t] but please rescue us now."
Then they got rid of the foreign gods
mong them and served the LORD.[u] And
e could bear Israel's misery[v] no longer.[w]
17When the Ammonites were called to
rms and camped in Gilead, the Israelites
ssembled and camped at Mizpah.[x] 18The
aders of the people of Gilead said to each
ther, "Whoever will take the lead in at-
cking the Ammonites will be head[y] over
ll who live in Gilead."

10:6 [x]S Ge 19:38; S Nu 21:29 [y]S Ge 26:1; S Jdg 2:12 [z]S Dt 32:15 **10:7** [a]S Dt 31:17 [b]S Dt 32:30 **10:8** [c]S Jos 12:2 **10:9** [d]ver 17; Jdg 11:4 [e]Jdg 1:22 **10:10** [f]S Jdg 3:9 [g]S Ex 9:27; Ps 32:5; Jer 3:25; 8:14; 14:20 [h]Jer 2:27 **10:11** [i]Ex 14:30 [j]S Ge 14:7 [k]S Jdg 3:13 [l]S Jdg 3:31 **10:12** [m]S Ge 14:7 [n]S Jos 15:55 [o]S Jdg 4:3 **10:13** [p]S Dt 32:15 [q]Jer 11:10; 13:10 **10:14** [r]Isa 44:17; 57:13 [s]Dt 32:37; Jer 2:28; 11:12; Hab 2:18 **10:15** [t]1Sa 3:18; 2Sa 10:12; 15:26; Job 1:21; Isa 39:8 **10:16** [u]Jos 24:23; Jer 18:8 [v]Isa 63:9 [w]S Dt 32:36 **10:17** [x]S Ge 31:49; Jdg 11:29 **10:18** [y]Jdg 11:8,9

11:1 [z]Jdg 12:1; 1Sa 12:11; Heb 11:32

11 Jephthah[z] the Gileadite was a
mighty warrior.[a] His father was
Gilead;[b] his mother was a prostitute.[c] 2Gil-
ead's wife also bore him sons, and when
they were grown up, they drove Jephthah
away. "You are not going to get any inheritance in our family," they said, "because
you are the son of another woman." 3So
Jephthah fled from his brothers and settled in the land of Tob,[d] where a gang of
scoundrels[e] gathered around him and followed him.
4Some time later, when the Ammonites[f]
were fighting against Israel, 5the elders of
Gilead went to get Jephthah from the land
of Tob. 6"Come," they said, "be our commander, so we can fight the Ammonites."
7Jephthah said to them, "Didn't you
hate me and drive me from my father's
house?[g] Why do you come to me now,
when you're in trouble?"
8The elders of Gilead said to him, "Nevertheless, we are turning to you now;
come with us to fight the Ammonites, and
you will be head[h] over all of us who live
in Gilead."
9Jephthah answered, "Suppose you take
me back to fight the Ammonites and the
LORD gives them to me—will I really be
your head?"
10The elders of Gilead replied, "The
LORD is our witness;[i] we will certainly do
as you say." 11So Jephthah went with the
elders[j] of Gilead, and the people made him

[a] 12 Hebrew; some Septuagint manuscripts *Midianites*

[a]Jdg 6:12 [b]Nu 26:29 [c]S Ge 38:15 **11:3** [d]ver 5; 2Sa 10:6,8 [e]S Jdg 9:4 **11:4** [f]S Jdg 10:9 **11:7** [g]S Ge 26:16 **11:8** [h]S Jdg 10:18 **11:10** [i]S Ge 31:50; S Isa 1:2 **11:11** [j]1Sa 8:4; 2Sa 3:17

e Philistines. While the Philistines worshiped most of the anaanite gods, their most popular deities appear to have een Dagon and Baal-Zebub. The name Dagon is the same a Hebrew word for "grain," suggesting that he was a veg-ation deity. He was worshiped in Babylonia as early as the econd millennium BC. Baal-Zebub was worshiped in Ekron Ki 1:2–3,6,16). The name means "lord of the flies," a delib-ate change by followers of the Lord (Yahweh) to ridicule nd protest the worship of Baal-Zebul ("Baal the Prince"), a ame known from ancient Canaanite texts. See Mt 10:25 and ote; 12:24.

0:7 *Philistines.* The account of Philistine oppression is re-med in 13:1.

10:11 *The LORD replied.* See note on 2:1. The Lord re-buked the Israelites for forgetting that he had deliv-ed them from their oppressors in Canaan (see notes on 16–19; 6:8).

0:12 *Maonites.* See NIV text note; or perhaps the same as e Meunites, who along with the Philistines and Arabs op-osed Israel (2Ch 26:7).

0:17 *Mizpah.* Means "watchtower." Several places bore this ame. Jephthah's headquarters was a town or fortress in lead (11:11) called "Mizpah of Gilead" (11:29). It may have een the same as Ramath Mizpah (Jos 13:26), located about miles east of Beth Shan.

10:18 The Gileadites wanted to resist the Ammonite incursion but lacked the courageous military leadership to press their cause. *people.* Fighting men.

11:1 *his mother was a prostitute.* Therefore Jephthah was a social outcast.

11:3 *the land of Tob.* The Hebrew name sounds exactly like "the good land," a common way of referring to the promised land in Deuteronomy. The narrator appears to call attention to the irony of this outcast from Israel finding a refuge in "a land of good (things)." The men of Tob were later allied with the Ammonites against David (2Sa 10:6–8). *scoundrels.* See note on 9:4.

11:8 *you will be head over all of us.* In addition to their initial offer of military command during the war with Ammon (v. 6), the Gileadites now also offer to make Jephthah regional head after the fighting is over.

11:11 The proposal of the elders was ratified by the people, a process followed later in the election of Saul (1Sa 11:15), Rehoboam (1Ki 12:1) and Jeroboam (1Ki 12:20). Jephthah's final act here suggests that the agreement reached between himself and the elders had the formal status of a covenant (compare David's covenant with the representatives of the northern tribes, 2Sa 5:3). In any event, Jephthah lays his conditions "before the LORD" as a way of calling on the Lord to enforce the pledge made to him by the elders of Gilead.

head and commander over them. And he
repeated[k] all his words before the LORD in
Mizpah.[l]
12 Then Jephthah sent messengers to the
Ammonite king with the question: "What
do you have against me that you have attacked my country?"
13 The king of the Ammonites answered
Jephthah's messengers, "When Israel
came up out of Egypt, they took away my
land from the Arnon[m] to the Jabbok,[n] all
the way to the Jordan. Now give it back
peaceably."
14 Jephthah sent back messengers to the
Ammonite king, 15 saying:

"This is what Jephthah says: Israel
did not take the land of Moab[o] or the
land of the Ammonites.[p] 16 But when
they came up out of Egypt, Israel
went through the wilderness to the
Red Sea[a][q] and on to Kadesh.[r] 17 Then
Israel sent messengers[s] to the king of
Edom, saying, 'Give us permission
to go through your country,'[t] but the
king of Edom would not listen. They
sent also to the king of Moab,[u] and he
refused.[v] So Israel stayed at Kadesh.
18 "Next they traveled through
the wilderness, skirted the lands of
Edom[w] and Moab, passed along the
eastern side[x] of the country of Moab,
and camped on the other side of the
Arnon.[y] They did not enter the territory of Moab, for the Arnon was its
border.
19 "Then Israel sent messengers[z]
to Sihon king of the Amorites, who
ruled in Heshbon,[a] and said to him,
'Let us pass through your country to
our own place.'[b] 20 Sihon, however,
did not trust Israel[b] to pass through
his territory. He mustered all his
troops and encamped at Jahaz and
fought with Israel.[c]
21 "Then the LORD, the God of Israel, gave Sihon and his whole army
into Israel's hands, and they defeated
them. Israel took over all the land of
the Amorites who lived in that country, 22 capturing all of it from the Arnon to the Jabbok and from the desert to the Jordan.[d]
23 "Now since the LORD, the God of
Israel, has driven the Amorites out
before his people Israel, what right
have you to take it over? 24 Will you
not take what your god Chemosh[e]
gives you? Likewise, whatever the
LORD our God has given us,[f] we will
possess. 25 Are you any better than Balak son of Zippor,[g] king of Moab? Did
he ever quarrel with Israel or fight
with them?[h] 26 For three hundred years
Israel occupied[i] Heshbon, Aroer,[j] the
surrounding settlements and all the
towns along the Arnon. Why didn't
you retake them during that time?
27 I have not wronged you, but you
are doing me wrong by waging war
against me. Let the LORD, the Judge,[k]
decide[l] the dispute this day between
the Israelites and the Ammonites.[m]"

28 The king of Ammon, however, paid n
attention to the message Jephthah se
him.
29 Then the Spirit[n] of the LORD came c
Jephthah. He crossed Gilead and Mana
seh, passed through Mizpah[o] of Gilea
and from there he advanced against th
Ammonites.[p] 30 And Jephthah made a vow

11:11 [k]Ex 19:9; 1Sa 8:21 [l]S Jos 11:3 **11:13** [m]S Nu 21:13 [n]S Nu 21:24 **11:15** [o]Dt 2:9 [p]Dt 2:19 **11:16** [q]Nu 14:25; S Dt 1:40 [r]S Ge 14:7 **11:17** [s]ver 19; S Ge 32:3; Nu 20:14 [t]S Nu 20:17 [u]Jer 48:1 [v]S Jos 24:9 **11:18** [w]S Nu 20:21 [x]Dt 2:8 [y]S Nu 21:13 **11:19** [z]S ver 17 [a]S Jos 12:2 [b]Nu 21:21-22 **11:20** [c]Nu 21:23 **11:22** [d]Nu 21:21-26; S Dt 2:26 **11:24** [e]S Nu 21:29; S Jos 3:10 [f]Dt 2:36 **11:25** [g]Nu 22:2 [h]S Jos 24:9 **11:26** [i]Nu 21:25 [j]S Nu 32:34; S Jos 13:9 **11:27** [k]S Ge 18:25 [l]S Ge 16:5 [m]2Ch 20:12 **11:29** [n]S Jdg 3:10 [o]S Ge 31:49 [p]S Jdg 10:17 **11:30** [q]S Ge 28:20; Nu 30:10; 1Sa 1:11; Pr 31:2

[a] 16 Or *the Sea of Reeds* [b] 20 Or *however, would no make an agreement for Israel*

11:13 *my land.* When the Israelites had first approached Canaan, this area was ruled by the Amorite king Sihon, who had taken it from the Moabites (Nu 21:29). The Ammonites had since become dominant over Moab and now claimed all previous Moabite territory.

11:14–27 Jephthah responded in accordance with international policies of the time; his letter is a classic example of contemporary international correspondence. It also reflects—and appeals to—the common recognition that the god(s) of a people established and protected their political boundaries and decided all boundary disputes. Jephthah's defense of Israel's claim to the land is threefold: (1) Israel took it from Sihon, king of the Amorites, not from the Ammonites (vv. 15–22); (2) the Lord gave the land to Israel (vv. 23–25); and (3) Israel had long possessed it (vv. 26–27).

11:16 *Kadesh.* Kadesh Barnea; see note on Nu 20:1.

11:21 *LORD, the God of Israel.* War was viewed not only in military terms but also as a contest between deities (see v. 24; Ex 12:12; Nu 33:4).

11:24 *Chemosh.* The chief deity of the Moabites. At this time either the king of Ammon also ruled Moab or there was a military confederacy of the two peoples.

11:25 *Balak.* See Nu 22–24.

11:26 *three hundred years.* For the relevance of this phra in establishing the time span for Judges, see Introductic Background.

11:27 *Judge.* See 1Sa 24:15. As the divine Judge, t Lord is the final court of appeal. It is significant th in the book of Judges the singular Hebrew noun translat "judge" is found only here, where it is used of the Lord, Isra true Judge.

11:29 *Spirit of the LORD.* See note on 3:10. In the (the unique empowering of the Spirit was given to i dividuals primarily to enable them to carry out the spec responsibilities God had given them.

11:30 *made a vow.* A common practice among the Israelit (see Ge 28:20; 1Sa 1:11; 2Sa 15:8). Here Jephthah was seeki to assure the outcome of the battle by bargaining for Go help. The precise nature of this vow has been the subject wide speculation, but v. 31 indicates the promise of a bu offering and leads to the conclusion that Jephthah probak offered his daughter as a human sacrifice (v. 39). A vow w not to be broken (see Nu 30:2; Dt 23:21–23; see also E 5:4–5).

ɔ the LORD: "If you give the Ammonites
nto my hands, 31whatever comes out of
he door of my house to meet me when
return in triumph[r] from the Ammonites
vill be the LORD's, and I will sacrifice it as
burnt offering.[s]"
32Then Jephthah went over to fight the
mmonites, and the LORD gave them into
is hands. 33He devastated twenty towns
rom Aroer to the vicinity of Minnith,[t] as
ar as Abel Keramim. Thus Israel subdued
mmon.
34When Jephthah returned to his home
n Mizpah, who should come out to
ieet him but his daughter, dancing[u] to
he sound of timbrels![v] She was an only
hild.[w] Except for her he had neither son
or daughter. 35When he saw her, he tore
is clothes[x] and cried, "Oh no, my daugh-
er! You have brought me down and I am
evastated. I have made a vow to the LORD
hat I cannot break.[y]"
36"My father," she replied, "you have
iven your word to the LORD. Do to me
ust as you promised,[z] now that the LORD
as avenged you[a] of your enemies,[b] the
mmonites. 37But grant me this one re-
uest," she said. "Give me two months to
oam the hills and weep with my friends,
ecause I will never marry."
38"You may go," he said. And he let her
o for two months. She and her friends
vent into the hills and wept because she
vould never marry. 39After the two months,
he returned to her father, and he did to her
s he had vowed. And she was a virgin.
From this comes the Israelite tradition
40that each year the young women of Is-
ael go out for four days to commemorate
he daughter of Jephthah the Gileadite.

Jephthah and Ephraim

12 The Ephraimite forces were called
out, and they crossed over to Za-
hon.[c] They said to Jephthah,[d] "Why did
you go to fight the Ammonites without
calling us to go with you?[e] We're going to
burn down your house over your head."
2Jephthah answered, "I and my people
were engaged in a great struggle with the
Ammonites, and although I called, you
didn't save me out of their hands. 3When
I saw that you wouldn't help, I took my
life in my hands[f] and crossed over to fight
the Ammonites, and the LORD gave me the
victory[g] over them. Now why have you
come up today to fight me?"
4Jephthah then called together the men
of Gilead[h] and fought against Ephraim. The
Gileadites struck them down because the
Ephraimites had said, "You Gileadites are
renegades from Ephraim and Manasseh.[i]"
5The Gileadites captured the fords of the
Jordan[j] leading to Ephraim, and whenever
a survivor of Ephraim said, "Let me cross
over," the men of Gilead asked him, "Are
you an Ephraimite?" If he replied, "No,"
6they said, "All right, say 'Shibboleth.'" If
he said, "Sibboleth," because he could not
pronounce the word correctly, they seized
him and killed him at the fords of the Jordan. Forty-two thousand Ephraimites were
killed at that time.
7Jephthah led[a] Israel six years. Then
Jephthah the Gileadite died and was buried in a town in Gilead.

Ibzan, Elon and Abdon

8After him, Ibzan of Bethlehem[k] led Israel. 9He had thirty sons and thirty daughters. He gave his daughters away in marriage to those outside his clan, and for his
sons he brought in thirty young women
as wives from outside his clan. Ibzan led
Israel seven years. 10Then Ibzan died and
was buried in Bethlehem.
11After him, Elon the Zebulunite led Israel ten years. 12Then Elon died and was
buried in Aijalon[l] in the land of Zebulun.

11:31 [r]Ge 28:21 [s]S Ge 8:20; Lev 1:3; Jdg 13:16 **11:33** [t]Eze 27:17 **11:34** [u]S Ex 15:20 [v]S Ge 31:27; S Ex 15:20 [w]Zec 12:10 **11:35** [x]S Nu 14:6 [y]Nu 30:2; S Dt 23:21; Ecc 5:2,4,5 **11:36** [z]Lk 1:38 [a]S Nu 31:3 [b]2Sa 18:19 **12:1** [c]S Jos 13:27 [d]S Jdg 11:1 [e]Jdg 8:1 **12:3** [f]S Jdg 9:17 [g]S Dt 20:4 **12:4** [h]1Ki 17:1 [i]S Ge 46:20; Isa 9:21; 19:2 **12:5** [j]S Jos 2:7 **12:8** [k]S Ge 35:19 **12:12** [l]S Jos 10:12

[a] 7 Traditionally *judged*; also in verses 8-14

1:34 *dancing.* It was customary for women to greet armies eturning victoriously from battle in this way (see Ex 15:20; Sa 18:6).

11:35 *tore his clothes.* A common practice for expressing extreme grief (see Ge 37:34 and note). *a vow to the ORD that I cannot break.* In his determination to secure the osition of leadership over his old adversaries, Jephthah had aid their pledge to him "before the LORD" for him to enforce see v. 11 and note). Now, accordingly, he cannot go back on is own vow (pledge) to the Lord. Thus all his efforts to assure or himself a position of power in Israel by manipulating God ackfired. God will not be used!

1:37 *I will never marry.* To be kept from marrying and rearing hildren was a bitter prospect for an Israelite woman.

1:39 *Israelite tradition.* Probably a local custom, since no ther mention of it is found in the OT.

2:1 *Zaphon.* See map, p. 354. *burn down your house.* The hilistines issued a similar threat to Samson's wife (14:15). ee also 20:48.

12:2 *answered.* Again Jephthah tried diplomacy first (see 11:12,14; see also note on 8:1). *I called.* New information on the sequence of events.

12:6 *Shibboleth.* Ironically, the word meant "floods" (see, e.g., Ps 69:2,15). Apparently the Israelites east of the Jordan pronounced its initial letter with a strong "sh" sound, while those in Canaan gave it a softer "s" sound. (Peter was similarly betrayed by his accent; see Mt 26:73.)

12:7 *led Israel ... years.* A new formula for closing out the account of a judge (see note on 3:11; see also Introduction: Literary Features).

12:8 *Bethlehem.* Probably the Bethlehem in western Zebulun (see Ge 35:19; 48:7; Jos 19:15).

12:9 *thirty sons and thirty daughters.* See note on 10:4.

12:11 *Elon.* Also the name of a clan in the tribe of Zebulun (Ge 46:14; Nu 26:26).

13 After him, Abdon son of Hillel, from Pirathon,[m] led Israel. 14 He had forty sons and thirty grandsons,[n] who rode on seventy donkeys.[o] He led Israel eight years. 15 Then Abdon son of Hillel died and was buried at Pirathon in Ephraim, in the hill country of the Amalekites.[p]

The Birth of Samson

13 Again the Israelites did evil in the eyes of the LORD, so the LORD delivered them into the hands of the Philistines[q] for forty years.[r]

2 A certain man of Zorah,[s] named Manoah,[t] from the clan of the Danites,[u] had a wife who was childless,[v] unable to give birth. 3 The angel of the LORD[w] appeared to her[x] and said, "You are barren and childless, but you are going to become pregnant and give birth to a son.[y] 4 Now see to it that you drink no wine or other fermented drink[z] and that you do not eat anything unclean.[a] 5 You will become pregnant and have a son[b] whose head is never to be touched by a razor[c] because the boy is to be a Nazirite,[d] dedicated to God from the womb. He will take the lead[e] in delivering Israel from the hands of the Philistines."

6 Then the woman went to her husband and told him, "A man of God[f] came to me. He looked like an angel of God,[g] very awesome.[h] I didn't ask him where he came from, and he didn't tell me his name. 7 But he said to me, 'You will become pregnant and have a son. Now then, drink no wine or other fermented drink[j] and do not eat anything unclean, because the boy will be a Nazirite of God from the womb until the day of his death.[k]' "

8 Then Manoah[l] prayed to the LORD: "Pardon your servant, Lord. I beg you to let the man of God[m] you sent to us come again to teach us how to bring up the boy who is to be born."

9 God heard Manoah, and the angel of God came again to the woman while she was out in the field; but her husband Manoah was not with her. 10 The woman hurried to tell her husband, "He's here! The man who appeared to me[n] the other day!"

11 Manoah got up and followed his wife. When he came to the man, he said, "Are you the man who talked to my wife?"

"I am," he said.

12 So Manoah asked him, "When your words are fulfilled, what is to be the rule that governs the boy's life and work?"

13 The angel of the LORD answered, "Your wife must do all that I have told her. 14 She must not eat anything that comes from the grapevine, nor drink any wine or other fermented drink[o] nor eat anything unclean.[p] She must do everything I have commanded her."

15 Manoah said to the angel of the LORD, "We would like you to stay until we prepare a young goat[q] for you."

16 The angel of the LORD replied, "Even

12:13 [m] ver 15; 2Sa 23:30; 1Ch 11:31; 27:14
12:14 [n] S Jdg 8:30 [o] S Jdg 5:10
12:15 [p] Jdg 5:14
13:1 [q] S Jdg 3:31 [r] Jdg 14:4
13:2 [s] S Jos 15:33 [t] ver 8; Jdg 16:31 [u] S Ge 30:6 [v] S Ge 11:30
13:3 [w] S Ge 16:7 [x] ver 10 [y] Isa 7:14; Lk 1:13
13:4 [z] S Lev 10:9 [a] ver 14; Nu 6:2-4; S Lk 1:15
13:5 [b] S Ge 3:15 [c] 1Sa 1:11 [d] S Nu 6:2,13; Am 2:11,12 [e] 1Sa 7:13
13:6 [f] ver 8; 1Sa 2:27; 9:6; 1Ki 13:1; 17:18 [g] S Nu 22:22 [h] Ps 66:5
13:7 [i] Jer 35:6 [j] Lev 10:9 [k] 1Sa 1:11,28
13:8 [l] S ver 2 [m] S ver 6
13:10 [n] ver 3
13:14 [o] Lev 10:9 [p] S ver 4
13:15 [q] Jdg 6:19

12:14 *forty sons and thirty grandsons.* A total of 70 (see notes on 8:30; 10:4).

12:15 *hill country of the Amalekites.* See note on 5:14. The background of this reference is unknown; the Amalekites are otherwise associated with the Negev (Nu 13:29).

13:1—16:31 Samson (from the tribe of Dan), like Ehud (from the tribe of Benjamin), was a loner, whose heroic exploits involved single-handed triumphs over powerful enemies. His story therefore balances that of Ehud (see note on 3:12–30). Significantly, this last of the judges typifies the nation of Israel. Born by special divine provision to a barren woman, consecrated to the Lord from birth and endowed by God's Spirit with unique powers to overcome Israel's enemies, he was forever drawn to Philistine women, which ultimately led to his destruction—just as God's consecrated (by circumcision) and especially empowered (for the conquest of Canaan) people Israel were continually drawn to the gods and ways of the Canaanites to their destruction (see note on Ex 34:15). The story of Samson is the story of Israel in cameo. The author provides a mirror image of Israel in the days of the judges—and of God's unfailing mercies to his wayward people whom he would not abandon.

13:1–25 The account of Samson's birth helps the author to point out the parallels between Samson and Israel that he wanted his readers to see.

13:1 *did evil in the eyes of the LORD.* See note on 3:7.

13:2 *Zorah.* A town first assigned to Judah (Jos 15:33) but later given to Dan (Jos 19:41). It became the point of departure for the Danite migration northward (18:2,8,11). *Danites.* See 1:34 and note. *childless, unable to give birth.* The same condition, before divine intervention, as that of Sarah, the mother of Isaac (Ge 11:30; 16:1), and Rebekah, the mother of Jacob (Ge 25:21). Cf. also Hannah, the mother of Samuel (1Sa 1:2), and Elizabeth, the mother of John the Baptist (Lk 1:7).

13:3 *angel of the LORD.* See note on Ge 16:7. *you are going to ... give birth to a son.* See the announcement of Isaac's birth (Ge 18:10). Cf. the announcements of the births of Ishmael (Ge 16:11), Immanuel (Isa 7:14), John the Baptist (Lk 1:13) and Jesus (Lk 1:31).

13:5 *Nazirite.* From a Hebrew word meaning "separated" or "dedicated." For the stipulations of this vow, see Nu 6:1–21 and notes. Samson's Nazirite-like consecration was not voluntary—like Israel, he was consecrated to special service by God himself—and his consecration applied to his whole lifetime (v. 7). The same was true of Samuel (1Sa 1:11) and John the Baptist (Lk 1:15). *take the lead in delivering ... from ... the Philistines.* The deliverance was continued in the time of Samuel (1Sa 7:10–14) and completed under David (2Sa 5:17–25; 8:1).

13:6 *man of God.* An expression often used of prophets (see Dt 33:1; 1Sa 2:27; 9:6–10; 1Ki 12:22), though it is clear from vv. 3,21 that this messenger was the angel of the Lord.

13:8 *teach us.* Not the usual parental concern, but a special concern based on the boy's special calling.

13:12 A declaration of faith. To Manoah it was not a matter of whether these events would occur, but of when (v. 17).

13:15 *stay until we prepare a young goat.* Such food was considered a special delicacy. Hospitality of this kind was common in the ancient Near East (see 6:18–19; Ge 18:1–8).

though you detain me, I will not eat any of
your food. But if you prepare a burnt offering,[r] offer it to the LORD." (Manoah did not
realize[s] that it was the angel of the LORD.)
17 Then Manoah inquired of the angel of
the LORD, "What is your name,[t] so that we
may honor you when your word comes
true?"
18 He replied, "Why do you ask my
name?[u] It is beyond understanding.[a]"
19 Then Manoah took a young goat, together with the grain offering, and sacrificed it
on a rock[v] to the LORD. And the LORD did
an amazing thing while Manoah and his
wife watched: 20 As the flame[w] blazed up
from the altar toward heaven, the angel
of the LORD ascended in the flame. Seeing
this, Manoah and his wife fell with their
faces to the ground.[x] 21 When the angel of
the LORD did not show himself again to
Manoah and his wife, Manoah realized[y]
that it was the angel of the LORD.
22 "We are doomed[z] to die!" he said to
his wife. "We have seen[a] God!"
23 But his wife answered, "If the LORD
had meant to kill us, he would not have
accepted a burnt offering and grain offering from our hands, nor shown us all
these things or now told us this."[b]
24 The woman gave birth to a boy and
named him Samson.[c] He grew[d] and the
LORD blessed him,[e] 25 and the Spirit of the
LORD began to stir[f] him while he was in Mahaneh Dan,[g] between Zorah and Eshtaol.

Samson's Marriage

14 Samson[h] went down to Timnah[i]
and saw there a young Philistine
woman. 2 When he returned, he said to
his father and mother, "I have seen a Philistine woman in Timnah; now get her for
me as my wife."[j]
3 His father and mother replied, "Isn't
there an acceptable woman among your
relatives or among all our people?[k] Must
you go to the uncircumcised[l] Philistines to
get a wife?[m]"
But Samson said to his father, "Get her
for me. She's the right one for me." 4 (His
parents did not know that this was from
the LORD,[n] who was seeking an occasion
to confront the Philistines;[o] for at that time
they were ruling over Israel.)[p]
5 Samson went down to Timnah together with his father and mother. As they approached the vineyards of Timnah, suddenly a young lion came roaring toward
him. 6 The Spirit of the LORD came powerfully upon him[q] so that he tore the lion

13:16 r S Jdg 11:31 s S Jdg 6:22 **13:17** t S Ge 32:29 **13:18** u S Ge 32:29 **13:19** v Jdg 6:20 **13:20** w S Lev 9:24 x S Ge 17:3 **13:21** y S Jdg 6:22 **13:22** z S Nu 17:12; S Dt 5:26 a S Ge 16:13; S Ex 3:6; S 24:10; S Jdg 6:22 **13:23** b Ps 25:14 **13:24** c Jdg 14:1; 15:1; 16:1; Heb 11:32 d 1Sa 2:21,26; 3:19 e Lk 1:80 **13:25** f S Jdg 3:10 g Jdg 18:12 **14:1** h S Jdg 13:24 i S Ge 38:12 **14:2** j S Ge 21:21 **14:3** k S Ge 24:4 l S Ge 34:14; S 1Sa 14:6 m S Ex 34:16 **14:4** n S Dt 2:30 o S Jos 11:20 p Jdg 13:1; 15:11

a 18 Or *is wonderful*

14:6 q S Jdg 3:10

13:17 *What is your name . . . ?* A messenger's identity was considered very important. *when your word comes true.* Fulfilled prophecy was a sign of the authenticity of a prophet (Dt 18:21–22; 1Sa 9:6).

13:18 *beyond understanding.* See NIV text note. In Isa 9:6 the Hebrew for this phrase (translated "Wonderful") applies to One who would come as "Mighty God."

13:22 *doomed to die.* See 6:23 and notes on Ge 16:13; 32:30.

13:24 *Samson.* The name is derived from a Hebrew word meaning "sun" or "brightness," and is used here as an expression of joy over the birth of the child. *He grew and the LORD blessed him.* Cf. 1Sa 2:26 (Samuel) and Lk 2:52 (Jesus).

13:25 *began to stir him.* See notes on 3:10; 11:29. *Mahaneh Dan.* Means "Dan's camp" (see NIV text note on 18:12).

14:1 — 16:31 The account of Samson's extraordinary exploits and flawed character has a literary structure of special note. His first encounter with a Philistine woman (14:1–20) and its aftermath (15:1–8) are closely balanced by the account of his last encounter with a Philistine woman (16:4–22) and its aftermath (16:23–31). And what happens in his first encounter foreshadows what happens in his final encounter. Between these two major cycles are three episodes: (1) Judah's attempt to appease the Philistines by binding Samson over to them (15:9–17); (2) God's rescue of Samson from life-threatening dehydration (15:18–19); and (3) Samson's escape from Gaza, the gates of which he deposits on a hill overlooking Hebron, Judah's main city (16:1–3). The author reminds his readers in the brief centerpiece (15:18–19) that mighty Samson shared in the universal vulnerabilities of human life.

14:1 *Timnah.* Identified as Tell Batash in the Sorek Valley, northwest of Beth Shemesh (see maps, pp. 354, 359). Archaeologists have uncovered the Philistine layer of the town. *young Philistine woman.* The disappointment of Samson's parents (v. 3; cf. Esau, Ge 26:35; 27:46; 28:1) is understandable in light of the prohibition against marriage with the pagan peoples of Canaan (Ex 34:11,16; Dt 7:1,3; see also Jdg 3:5–6).

14:2 *get her for me.* See Ge 34:4. As the head of the family, the father exercised authority in all matters, often including the choice of wives for his sons (see 12:9; Ge 24:3–9; Ne 10:30).

14:3 *uncircumcised.* A term of scorn, referring to those not bound by covenant to the Lord, used especially of the Philistines (see note on 1Sa 14:6). *right one for me.* The Hebrew for this expression ("is right in my eyes") is similar to that translated "did as they saw fit" (lit. "did what was right in their own eyes") in 17:6; 21:25. The author anticipates this theme, which recurs in chs. 17–21.

14:4 *this was from the LORD.* See Jos 11:20; 1Ki 12:15. The Lord uses even sinful human weaknesses to accomplish his purposes and bring praise to his name (see Ge 45:8; 50:20; 2Ch 25:20; Ac 2:23; 4:28; Ro 8:28–29).

14:5 *vineyards of Timnah.* The Sorek Valley (in which Timnah was located) and its surrounding areas were noted for their luxuriant vineyards. For anyone under Nazirite vows, vineyards could be a powerful source of temptation (see Nu 6:1–4). *a young lion came roaring toward him.* The author's language anticipates his later "the Philistines came toward him shouting" (15:14). This helps the reader to catch the author's intention to use the lion out of the Philistine vineyards as a symbol of the Philistines themselves, the very enemies of Israel against whom Samson was called to be God's champion (cf. 1Sa 17 for the roles of Goliath and David in a later confrontation between the Philistines and Israel). *young lion.* Lions were once common in southern Canaan (see 1Sa 17:34; 2Sa 23:20; 1Ki 13:24; 20:36).

14:6 *Spirit . . . came powerfully upon him.* See 13:25; 14:19; 15:14; see also notes on 3:10; 11:29. *tore the lion*

apart[r] with his bare hands as he might
have torn a young goat. But he told neither his father nor his mother what he
had done. 7Then he went down and talked
with the woman, and he liked her.
8Some time later, when he went back to
marry her, he turned aside to look at the
lion's carcass, and in it he saw a swarm
of bees and some honey. 9He scooped out
the honey with his hands and ate as he
went along. When he rejoined his parents,
he gave them some, and they too ate it.
But he did not tell them that he had taken
the honey from the lion's carcass.
10Now his father went down to see the
woman. And there Samson held a feast,[s]
as was customary for young men. 11When
the people saw him, they chose thirty men
to be his companions.
12"Let me tell you a riddle,[t]" Samson
said to them. "If you can give me the answer within the seven days of the feast,[u]
I will give you thirty linen garments and
thirty sets of clothes.[v] 13If you can't tell me
the answer, you must give me thirty linen
garments and thirty sets of clothes."
"Tell us your riddle," they said. "Let's
hear it."
14He replied,

"Out of the eater, something to eat;
out of the strong, something sweet."[w]

For three days they could not give the answer.
15On the fourth[a] day, they said to Samson's wife, "Coax[x] your husband into explaining the riddle for us, or we will burn
you and your father's household to death.[y]
Did you invite us here to steal our property?"
16Then Samson's wife threw herself on
him, sobbing, "You hate me! You don't
really love me.[z] You've given my people
a riddle, but you haven't told me the answer."
"I haven't even explained it to my father
or mother," he replied, "so why should I
explain it to you?" 17She cried the whole
seven days[a] of the feast. So on the seventh
day he finally told her, because she continued to press him. She in turn explained
the riddle to her people.
18Before sunset on the seventh day the
men of the town said to him,

"What is sweeter than honey?
What is stronger than a lion?"[b]

Samson said to them,

"If you had not plowed with my
heifer,
you would not have solved my
riddle."

19Then the Spirit of the LORD came powerfully upon him.[c] He went down to Ashkelon,[d] struck down thirty of their men,
stripped them of everything and gave their
clothes to those who had explained the
riddle. Burning with anger,[e] he returned
to his father's home. 20And Samson's wife
was given to one of his companions[f] who
had attended him at the feast.

Samson's Vengeance on the Philistines

15 Later on, at the time of wheat harvest,[g] Samson[h] took a young goat[i]
and went to visit his wife. He said, "I'm

14:6 [r] 1Sa 17:35 **14:10** [s] S Ge 29:22 **14:12** [t] S Nu 12:8; Eze 17:2; 20:49; 24:3; Hos 12:10 [u] Ge 29:27 [v] S Ge 45:22; S 2Ki 5:5 **14:14** [w] ver 18 **14:15** [x] Jdg 16:5; Ecc 7:26 [y] S Lev 20:14; Jdg 15:6 **14:16** [z] Jdg 16:15 **14:17** [a] Est 1:5 **14:18** [b] ver 14 **14:19** [c] S Jdg 3:10 [d] S Jos 13:3 [e] 1Sa 11:6 **14:20** [f] Jdg 15:2,6; Jn 3:29 **15:1** [g] S Ge 30:14 [h] S Jdg 13:24 [i] S Ge 38:17

[a] 15 Some Septuagint manuscripts and Syriac; Hebrew *seventh*

---

apart. With such unique power God's Spirit endowed Samson to overcome the Philistines. Later, David (1Sa 17:34–37) and Benaiah (2Sa 23:20) performed similar feats.
14:8–9 *carcass ... honey. He scooped out the honey with his hands.* Samson thus violated his Nazirite vows (Nu 6:6–7) in order to delight himself with something sweet.
14:10 *feast.* Such a special feast was common in the ancient Near East (see Ge 29:22) and here lasted seven days (v. 12; see Ge 29:27). Since it would have included drinking wine, Samson may have violated his Nazirite vow (see 13:4,7).
14:11 *companions.* These are the "guests of the bridegroom" (cf. Mt 9:15). They were probably charged with protecting the wedding party against marauders.
14:12 *riddle.* The use of riddles at feasts and special occasions was popular in the ancient world. *sets of clothes.* Mentioned, together with silver, as gifts of great value in Ge 45:22; 2Ki 5:22 (see also Zec 14:14).
14:14 *the eater ... the strong.* Samson refers to the lion he had killed, from the carcass of which he had taken honey to eat. He confidently uses his riddle as his opening shot in a battle of wits with the Philistines. The author, however, uses Samson's riddle to chillingly foreshadow Samson's sorry end. He has just shown us Samson "the eater" (of honey) and Samson "the strong" (killer of a powerful lion). In the end, he shows us blinded Samson grinding grain in prison for his captors (16:21: Out of the eater the Philistines get something to eat) and entertaining his captors with feats of strength (16:25: Out of the strong the Philistines get something sweet).
14:16 *don't really love me.* Delilah used the same tactics (16:15).
14:18 *sweeter than honey ... stronger than a lion.* The Philistines answer riddle with riddle. And the answer to their riddle exposes Samson's great weakness. The answer to their riddle is "love," or at least "sexual passion," the very thing that kept drawing Samson to the Philistines—and would ultimately lead to his downfall. Moreover, his downfall is already foreshadowed here where a Philistine girl, the object of Samson's passion, defeats him with her beauty and feminine wiles. *my heifer.* Samson's wife (see v. 15). Since heifers were not used for plowing, Samson is accusing them of unfairness.
14:19 *Spirit ... came powerfully upon him.* God's purposes for Samson included humbling the Philistines. *Ashkelon.* One of the five principal cities of the Philistines (see map, p. 359).
14:20 *one of his companions.* See 15:2; probably the young man who had attended Samson (cf. Jn 3:29), in all likelihood one of his 30 companions (v. 11).
15:1 *time of wheat harvest.* Near the end of May or the beginning of June (see note on Ru 1:22). *young goat.* Such a

going to my wife's room."[j] But her father
would not let him go in.
2 "I was so sure you hated her," he said,
"that I gave her to your companion.[k] Isn't
her younger sister more attractive? Take
her instead."
3 Samson said to them, "This time I have
a right to get even with the Philistines; I
will really harm them." 4 So he went out
and caught three hundred foxes[l] and tied
them tail to tail in pairs. He then fastened
a torch[m] to every pair of tails, 5 lit the torches[n] and let the foxes loose in the standing
grain of the Philistines. He burned up the
shocks[o] and standing grain, together with
the vineyards and olive groves.
6 When the Philistines asked, "Who did
this?" they were told, "Samson, the Tim-
nite's son-in-law, because his wife was
given to his companion.[p]"
So the Philistines went up and burned
her[q] and her father to death.[r] 7 Samson said
to them, "Since you've acted like this, I
swear that I won't stop until I get my revenge on you." 8 He attacked them viciously and slaughtered many of them. Then
he went down and stayed in a cave in the
rock[s] of Etam.[t]
9 The Philistines went up and camped
in Judah, spreading out near Lehi.[u] 10 The
people of Judah asked, "Why have you
come to fight us?"
"We have come to take Samson prisoner," they answered, "to do to him as he
did to us."
11 Then three thousand men from Judah went down to the cave in the rock
of Etam and said to Samson, "Don't you
realize that the Philistines are rulers over
us?[v] What have you done to us?"

15:1 [j]Ge 29:21
15:2 [k]S Jdg 14:20
15:4 [l]SS 2:15 [m]S Ge 15:17
15:5 [n]S Ge 15:17 [o]Ex 22:6; 2Sa 14:30-31
15:6 [p]S Jdg 14:20 [q]S Ge 38:24 [r]S Jdg 14:15
15:8 [s]Isa 2:21 [t]ver 11
15:9 [u]ver 14, 17, 19
15:11 [v]S Jdg 14:4; Ps 106:40-42

He answered, "I merely did to them
what they did to me."
12 They said to him, "We've come to tie
you up and hand you over to the Philistines."
Samson said, "Swear to me[w] that you
won't kill me yourselves."
13 "Agreed," they answered. "We will
only tie you up and hand you over to
them. We will not kill you." So they bound
him with two new ropes[x] and led him up
from the rock. 14 As he approached Lehi,[y]
the Philistines came toward him shouting.
The Spirit of the LORD came powerfully
upon him.[z] The ropes on his arms became like charred flax,[a] and the bindings
dropped from his hands. 15 Finding a fresh
jawbone of a donkey, he grabbed it and
struck down a thousand men.[b]
16 Then Samson said,

"With a donkey's jawbone
I have made donkeys of them.[a][c]
With a donkey's jawbone
I have killed a thousand men."

17 When he finished speaking, he threw
away the jawbone; and the place was
called Ramath Lehi.[b][d]
18 Because he was very thirsty, he cried
out to the LORD,[e] "You have given your servant this great victory.[f] Must I now die of
thirst and fall into the hands of the uncircumcised?" 19 Then God opened up the hollow place in Lehi, and water came out of it.
When Samson drank, his strength returned
and he revived.[g] So the spring[h] was called
En Hakkore,[c] and it is still there in Lehi.

[a] 16 Or *made a heap or two*; the Hebrew for *donkey* sounds like the Hebrew for *heap.* [b] 17 *Ramath Lehi* means *jawbone hill.* [c] 19 *En Hakkore* means *caller's spring.*

15:12 [w]S Ge 47:31
15:13 [x]Jdg 16:11, 12
15:14 [y]S ver 9 [z]S Jdg 3:10 [a]S Jos 2:6
15:15 [b]S Lev 26:8
15:16 [c]Jer 22:19
15:17 [d]S ver 9
15:18 [e]Jdg 16:28 [f]S Dt 20:4
15:19 [g]Ge 45:27; 1Sa 30:12; Isa 40:29 [h]S Ex 17:6

gift was customary, as with Judah and Tamar (Ge 38:17).
15:2 *younger sister.* Samson's father-in-law felt he had to make a counterproposal because he had received the bride-price from Samson. Similar marital transactions were made by Laban and Jacob (Ge 29:16–28) and Saul and David (1Sa 18:19–21).
15:6 *because his wife was given to his companion.* See 14:20.
15:5 *burned up.* The wheat harvest (v. 1) comes at the end of a long dry season, thus making the fields extremely vulnerable to fire. Samson's burning of the grainfields foreshadows his destruction of the temple of Dagon (whose name means "grain") in his last attack on the Philistines (16:23–30; see also note on 10:6).
15:7 *revenge.* A common feature of life in the ancient Near East. Six cities of refuge were designated by the Lord to prevent endless killings (see Jos 20:1–9 and note). Samson's act of revenge against the Philistines for murdering the one who had pleased his eyes (see note on 14:3; see also Eze 24:16) foreshadows his act of revenge against them for gouging out his eyes (16:28).
15:9–17 See note on 14:1—16:31.
15:9 *Lehi.* Means "jawbone." This locality probably did not receive the name until after the events described here; the author uses the name in anticipation of those events—a common device in Hebrew narrative.
15:11 *three thousand men from Judah.* The only time a force from Judah is explicitly mentioned in connection with any of the judges (but see note on 1:2). The men of Judah were well aware of Samson's capabilities, and even with a large force they did not attempt to tie him up without his consent (vv. 12–13). *Philistines are rulers over us.* Much of Judah was under Philistine rule, and the tribe was apparently content to accept it. They mustered a force, not to support Samson, but to capture him for the Philistines. Contrast the role assigned Judah in 1:2 and 20:18.
15:14 *shouting.* A battle cry (see 1Sa 17:52). They came shouting against Samson as the lion had come roaring against him (14:5). *Spirit of the LORD.* See notes on 3:10; 11:29; 14:19.
15:15 *struck down a thousand men.* Cf. the exploits of Shamgar, who struck down 600 Philistines with an oxgoad (3:31).
15:18–19 See note on 14:1—16:31.
15:18 *Must I now die of thirst . . . ?* Mighty Samson was, after all, only a mortal man.
15:19 *water came out of it.* God provided for Samson as he had for Israel in the wilderness. See Ex 17:1–7 (Massah and Meribah); Nu 20:2–13 (Meribah).

20 Samson led[a] Israel for twenty years[i] in the days of the Philistines.

Samson and Delilah

16 One day Samson[j] went to Gaza,[k] where he saw a prostitute.[l] He went in to spend the night with her. 2 The people of Gaza were told, "Samson is here!" So they surrounded the place and lay in wait for him all night at the city gate.[m] They made no move during the night, saying, "At dawn[n] we'll kill him."

3 But Samson lay there only until the middle of the night. Then he got up and took hold of the doors of the city gate, together with the two posts, and tore them loose, bar and all. He lifted them to his shoulders and carried them to the top of the hill that faces Hebron.[o]

4 Some time later, he fell in love[p] with a woman in the Valley of Sorek whose name was Delilah.[q] 5 The rulers of the Philistines[r] went to her and said, "See if you can lure[s] him into showing you the secret of his great strength[t] and how we can overpower him so we may tie him up and subdue him. Each one of us will give you eleven hundred shekels[b] of silver."[u]

6 So Delilah[v] said to Samson, "Tell me the secret of your great strength and how you can be tied up and subdued."

7 Samson answered her, "If anyone ties me with seven fresh bowstrings that have not been dried, I'll become as weak as any other man."

8 Then the rulers of the Philistines brought her seven fresh bowstrings that had not been dried, and she tied him with them. 9 With men hidden in the room,[w] she called to him, "Samson, the Philistines are upon you!"[x] But he snapped the bowstrings as easily as a piece of string snaps when it comes close to a flame. So the secret of his strength was not discovered.

10 Then Delilah said to Samson, "You have made a fool of me;[y] you lied to me. Come now, tell me how you can be tied."

11 He said, "If anyone ties me securely with new ropes[z] that have never been used, I'll become as weak as any other man."

12 So Delilah took new ropes and tied him with them. Then, with men hidden in the room, she called to him, "Samson, the Philistines are upon you!"[a] But he snapped the ropes off his arms as if they were threads.

13 Delilah then said to Samson, "All this time you have been making a fool of me and lying to me. Tell me how you can be tied."

He replied, "If you weave the seven braids of my head into the fabric on the loom and tighten it with the pin, I'll become as weak as any other man." So while he was sleeping, Delilah took the seven braids of his head, wove them into the fabric 14 and[c] tightened it with the pin.

Again she called to him, "Samson, the Philistines are upon you!"[b] He awoke from his sleep and pulled up the pin and the loom, with the fabric.

15 Then she said to him, "How can you say, 'I love you,'[c] when you won't confide in me? This is the third time[d] you have made a fool of me and haven't told me the secret of your great strength."[e] 16 With such nagging she prodded him day after day until he was sick to death of it.

17 So he told her everything.[f] "No razor has ever been used on my head," he said,

15:20 [i] Jdg 16:31 **16:1** [j] S Jdg 13:24 [k] S Ge 10:19 [l] S Ge 38:15 **16:2** [m] S Jos 2:5 [n] 1Sa 19:11 **16:3** [o] S Jos 10:36 **16:4** [p] S Ge 24:67; S 34:3 [q] ver 6 **16:5** [r] S Jos 13:3 [s] S Ex 10:7; S Jdg 14:15 [t] ver 6, 15 [u] ver 18 **16:6** [v] ver 4 **16:9** [w] ver 12 [x] ver 14 **16:10** [y] ver 13 **16:11** [z] S Jdg 15:13 **16:12** [a] ver 14 **16:14** [b] ver 9, 20 **16:15** [c] Jdg 14:16 [d] Nu 24:10 [e] S ver 5 **16:17** [f] ver 18; Mic 7:5

[a] 20 Traditionally *judged* [b] 5 That is, about 28 pounds or about 13 kilograms [c] *13,14* Some Septuagint manuscripts; Hebrew *replied, "I can if you weave the seven braids of my head into the fabric on the loom."* [14] *So she*

15:20 *led Israel … years.* See note on 12:7. *twenty years.* Round numbers are frequently used in Judges (see Introduction: Background).

16:1–3 See note on 14:1—16:31.

16:1 *Gaza.* An important Philistine city near the Mediterranean coast of southwest Canaan. *prostitute.* While Samson certainly possessed physical strength, he lacked moral strength, which ultimately led to his ruin.

16:2 *dawn.* By that time they expected Samson to be exhausted and sleeping soundly.

16:3 *bar.* Probably made of bronze (1Ki 4:13) or iron (Ps 107:16; Isa 45:2). *faces Hebron.* That is, in the direction of Hebron, which was 38 miles away in the hill country. Since Hebron was the chief city of Judah, this must be seen as Samson's response to what the men of Judah had done to him (see 15:11–13).

16:4–31 See note on 14:1—16:31.

16:5 *rulers of the Philistines.* See note on 3:3. *subdue him.* The Philistines were not interested in killing him quickly; they sought revenge by a prolonged period of torture. *eleven hundred shekels.* An extraordinarily generous payment in light of 17:10 (see note there). (The total amount paid by the five Philistines would have been equivalent to the price of 275 slaves, at the rate offered for Joseph centuries earlier; see Ge 37:28.) Micah stole a similar amount of silver from his mother (17:2). *shekels.* See note on Ge 20:16.

16:7 *seven fresh bowstrings.* The number seven had special significance to the ancients, symbolizing completeness or fullness (see notes on Ge 4:17–18; 5:5). Note that Samson's hair was divided into seven braids (v. 13).

16:11 *new ropes.* The Philistines apparently did not know that this method had already been tried and had failed (15:13–14).

16:13 Out of disdain, Samson arrogantly played with his Philistine adversaries. *tighten it with the pin.* Probably from a weaver's shuttle. The details of the account suggest that the loom in question was the vertical type with a crossbeam from which warp threads were suspended. Samson's long hair was woven into the warp and beaten up into the web with the pin, thus forming a tight fabric.

"because I have been a Nazirite[g] dedicated to God from my mother's womb. If my
head were shaved, my strength would
leave me, and I would become as weak as
any other man."
18 When Delilah saw that he had told
her everything, she sent word to the rulers of the Philistines[h], "Come back once
more; he has told me everything." So the
rulers of the Philistines returned with the
silver in their hands.[i] 19 After putting him
to sleep on her lap, she called for someone to shave off the seven braids of his
hair, and so began to subdue him.[a] And
his strength left him.[j]
20 Then she called, "Samson, the Philistines are upon you!"[k]
He awoke from his sleep and thought,
"I'll go out as before and shake myself
free." But he did not know that the LORD
had left him.[l]
21 Then the Philistines[m] seized him,
gouged out his eyes[n] and took him down
to Gaza.[o] Binding him with bronze shackles, they set him to grinding grain[p] in the
prison. 22 But the hair on his head began to
grow again after it had been shaved.

The Death of Samson

23 Now the rulers of the Philistines assembled to offer a great sacrifice to Dagon[q]
their god and to celebrate, saying, "Our
god has delivered Samson, our enemy,
into our hands."
24 When the people saw him, they
praised their god,[r] saying,

"Our god has delivered our enemy
into our hands,[s]
the one who laid waste our land
and multiplied our slain."

25 While they were in high spirits,[t] they
shouted, "Bring out Samson to entertain
us." So they called Samson out of the prison, and he performed for them.
When they stood him among the pillars, 26 Samson said to the servant who
held his hand, "Put me where I can feel
the pillars that support the temple, so
that I may lean against them." 27 Now
the temple was crowded with men and
women; all the rulers of the Philistines
were there, and on the roof[u] were about
three thousand men and women watching
Samson perform. 28 Then Samson prayed
to the LORD,[v] "Sovereign LORD, remember me. Please, God, strengthen me just
once more, and let me with one blow get
revenge[w] on the Philistines for my two
eyes." 29 Then Samson reached toward the
two central pillars on which the temple
stood. Bracing himself against them, his
right hand on the one and his left hand
on the other, 30 Samson said, "Let me die
with the Philistines!" Then he pushed
with all his might, and down came the
temple on the rulers and all the people
in it. Thus he killed many more when he
died than while he lived.
31 Then his brothers and his father's
whole family went down to get him.
They brought him back and buried him
between Zorah and Eshtaol in the tomb
of Manoah[x] his father. He had led[b] Israel
twenty years.[z]

16:17 [g] S Nu 6:2 **16:18** [h] S Jos 13:3; 1Sa 5:8 [i] ver 5 **16:19** [j] Pr 7:26-27 **16:20** [k] S ver 14 [l] Nu 14:42; Jos 7:12; 1Sa 16:14; 18:12; 28:15 **16:21** [m] Jer 47:1 [n] S Nu 16:14 [o] S Ge 10:19 [p] Job 31:10; Isa 47:2 **16:23** [q] 1Sa 5:2; 1Ch 10:10 **16:24** [r] Da 5:4 [s] 1Sa 31:9; 1Ch 10:9

16:25 [t] Jdg 9:27; 19:6, 9,22; Ru 3:7; Est 1:10 **16:27** [u] S Jos 2:8 **16:28** [v] Jdg 15:18 [w] Jer 15:15 **16:31** [x] S Jdg 13:2 [y] Ru 1:1; 1Sa 4:18; 7:6 [z] Jdg 15:20

[a] 19 Hebrew; some Septuagint manuscripts *and he began to weaken* [b] 31 Traditionally *judged*

16:19–20 *his strength left him ... the LORD had left him.* The source of Samson's strength was ultimately God himself.

16:20 *he did not know.* One of the most tragic statements in the OT. Samson was unaware that he had betrayed his calling. He had permitted a Philistine woman to rob him of the sign of his special consecration to the Lord. The Lord's champion lay asleep and helpless in the arms of his paramour.

16:21 *gouged out his eyes.* Brutal treatment of prisoners of war to humiliate and incapacitate them was common (see 1Sa 11:2; 2Ki 25:7; see also note on Jdg 1:6). *to Gaza.* In shame and weakness, Samson was led to Gaza, the place where he had displayed great strength (vv. 1–3). *set him to grinding.* See notes on 9:53; 14:14.

16:22 *hair ... began to grow again.* The author hints at the great truth that shines through the Samson story and would soon receive its final confirmation for Samson, namely, that God had not and would not abandon his flawed servant—or his flawed people Israel.

16:23 *Dagon.* See notes on 10:6; 15:5. *Our god has delivered.* It was common to attribute a victory to the national deities.

16:25 *to entertain us.* See note on 14:14.

16:27 *on the roof.* The temple complex probably surrounded an open court and had a flat roof where a large number of people had gathered to get a glimpse of the fallen champion.

16:28 *revenge ... for my two eyes.* See note on 15:7.

16:30 *pushed.* Samson pushed the wooden pillars from their stone bases. Archaeologists have discovered a Philistine temple at Tell Qasile with a pair of closely spaced pillar bases (see archaeology note in map text, p. 359). *killed many more.* Samson previously had slain well over 1,000 people (see 15:15; see also 14:19; 15:8). His final exploit was a mighty demonstration that the Philistine celebration of their god's victory over the Lord's champion was premature. *when he died.* If the Nazirite vow was violated and the uncut hair marking special dedication to God had become "defiled," that hair had to be cut off and the period of consecration started over again (see Nu 6:9–12). When Samson's hair was cut off by Delilah, God showed that it had been defiled by Samson's many defiling acts. But when his hair "began to grow again," a new time of consecration began (see v. 22 and note). He then could offer up his life as God's champion warrior against the Philistines.

16:31 *went down to get him.* The freedom of his family to secure his body and give it a burial indicates that the Philistines had no intention of further dishonoring him (contrast Saul's death, 1Sa 31:9–10). *led Israel ... years.* See note on 12:7. *twenty*

Micah's Idols

17 Now a man named Micah[a] from the
hill country of Ephraim 2 said to his
mother, "The eleven hundred shekels[a] of
silver that were taken from you and about
which I heard you utter a curse—I have
that silver with me; I took it."
Then his mother said, "The LORD bless
you,[b] my son!"
3 When he returned the eleven hundred
shekels of silver to his mother, she said, "I
solemnly consecrate my silver to the LORD
for my son to make an image overlaid with
silver.[c] I will give it back to you."
4 So after he returned the silver to his
mother, she took two hundred shekels[b] of
silver and gave them to a silversmith, who
used them to make the idol.[d] And it was
put in Micah's house.
5 Now this man Micah had a shrine,[e] and
he made an ephod[f] and some household
gods[g] and installed[h] one of his sons as his
priest.[i] 6 In those days Israel had no king;[j]
everyone did as they saw fit.[k]
7 A young Levite[l] from Bethlehem in
Judah,[m] who had been living within the
clan of Judah, 8 left that town in search of
some other place to stay. On his way[c] he
came to Micah's house in the hill country
of Ephraim.
9 Micah asked him, "Where are you
from?"
"I'm a Levite from Bethlehem in Judah,[n]"
he said, "and I'm looking for a place to
stay."
10 Then Micah said to him, "Live with
me and be my father[o] and priest,[p] and I'll
give you ten shekels[d] of silver a year, your
clothes and your food." 11 So the Levite
agreed to live with him, and the young
man became like one of his sons to him.
12 Then Micah installed[q] the Levite, and the
young man became his priest[r] and lived
in his house. 13 And Micah said, "Now I
know that the LORD will be good to me,
since this Levite has become my priest."[s]

The Danites Settle in Laish

18 In those days Israel had no king.[t]
And in those days the tribe of the
Danites was seeking a place of their own
where they might settle, because they had
not yet come into an inheritance among
the tribes of Israel.[u] 2 So the Danites[v] sent
five of their leading men[w] from Zorah and
Eshtaol to spy out[x] the land and explore
it. These men represented all the Danites.
They told them, "Go, explore the land."[y]
So they entered the hill country of
Ephraim and came to the house of Micah,[z] where they spent the night. 3 When
they were near Micah's house, they rec-

17:1 [a] Jdg 18:2, 13
17:2 [b] Ru 2:20; 3:10; 1Sa 15:13; 23:21; 2Sa 2:5
17:3 [c] S Ex 20:4
17:4 [d] S Ex 32:4; S Isa 17:8
17:5 [e] Isa 44:13; Eze 8:10 [f] S Jdg 8:27 [g] S Ge 31:19 [h] S Nu 16:10 [i] S Ex 29:9
17:6 [j] Jdg 18:1; 19:1; 21:25 [k] S Dt 12:8
17:7 [l] Jdg 18:3 [m] S Ge 35:19; Mt 2:1
17:9 [n] Ru 1:1
17:10 [o] S Ge 45:8 [p] Jdg 18:19
17:12 [q] S Nu 16:10 [r] Jdg 18:4
17:13 [s] Nu 18:7
18:1 [t] S Jdg 17:6 [u] Jos 19:47; Jdg 1:34
18:2 [v] S Ge 30:6 [w] ver 17 [x] S Nu 21:32 [y] S Jos 2:1 [z] S Jdg 17:1

[a] 2 That is, about 28 pounds or about 13 kilograms
[b] 4 That is, about 5 pounds or about 2.3 kilograms
[c] 8 Or *To carry on his profession*
[d] 10 That is, about 4 ounces or about 115 grams

years. Round numbers are frequently used in Judges (see Introduction: Background).

17:1—21:25 Two cycles of events forming an epilogue to the story of the judges (see Introduction: Literary Features). The events narrated evidently took place fairly early in the period of the judges (see notes on 18:30; 20:1,28). They illustrate the religious and moral degeneracy that characterized the age—when "Israel had no king" and "everyone did as they saw fit" (17:6; 21:25). Writing at a time when the monarchy under the Davidic dynasty had brought cohesion and order to the land and had reestablished a center for the worship of the Lord, the author portrays this earlier era of the judges as a dismal period of national decay, from which it was to be rescued by the house of David.

17:1—18:31 The first cycle of events illustrates corruption in Israelite worship by telling of Micah's establishment of a local place of worship in Ephraim, aided by a Levite claiming descent from Moses. This paganized worship of the Lord is taken over by the tribe of Dan when that tribe abandons its appointed inheritance and migrates to Israel's northern frontier.

17:2 *eleven hundred shekels.* See note on 16:5. *I heard you utter a curse.* Fear of the curse seems to have motivated his returning the stolen money. *The LORD bless you.* A blessing to counteract the curse.

17:3 *mother ... son.* With their paganized view of the God of Israel, both were idolaters in disobedience to the law (Ex 20:4,23; Dt 4:16). *image.* Probably made of wood "overlaid with silver."

17:4 *silversmith.* A maker of idols, as in Ac 19:24 (cf. Isa 40:19 and Jer 10:9, where the Hebrew for this word is translated "goldsmith").

17:5 *ephod.* See 8:27 and note on Ex 28:6. *household gods.* Used in this case for divining (cf. Eze 21:21; Zec 10:2). Some of them were in human form (1Sa 19:13).

17:6 *had no king.* See 18:1; 19:1; 21:25; suggests that Judges was written after the establishment of the monarchy (see Introduction: Author and Date). *did as they saw fit.* The expression implies that Israel had departed from the covenant standards of conduct found in the law (see Dt 12:8).

17:7 *Levite.* His name was Jonathan (see 18:30 and note). *Bethlehem in Judah.* Not among the 48 designated Levitical cities (Jos 21).

17:8 *left that town.* The failure of the Israelites to obey the law probably resulted in a lack of support for the Levites, which explains the man's wandering in search of his fortune.

17:10 *father.* A term of respect used also for Elijah (2Ki 2:12) and Elisha (2Ki 6:21; 13:14). See Ge 45:8; Mt 23:9. *ten shekels.* See NIV text note. In the light of this remuneration for a year's service, the stated amounts in 16:5 and 17:2 take on special significance. The offer of wages, clothing and food was more than this Levite could resist (v. 11). Clearly, material concerns were at the root of his decision, because later he accepts an even more attractive offer (18:19–20).

17:12 *installed the Levite.* An attempt to make his shrine legitimate and give it prestige. Micah probably removed his son (see v. 5).

18:1 *seeking a place.* The Danite allotment was at the west end of the strip of land between Judah and Ephraim (Jos 19:41–46), but due to the opposition of the Amorites (Jdg 1:34) and the Philistines, the Danites were unable to occupy that territory (see note on 13:2).

18:2 *spy out.* See 1:23 and note on Nu 13:2.

ognized the voice of the young Levite;[a] so
they turned in there and asked him, "Who
brought you here? What are you doing in
this place? Why are you here?"
4 He told them what Micah had done for
him, and said, "He has hired me and I am
his priest.[b]"
5 Then they said to him, "Please inquire
of God[c] to learn whether our journey will
be successful."
6 The priest answered them, "Go in
peace[d]. Your journey has the LORD's approval."
7 So the five men[e] left and came to Laish,[f] where they saw that the people were
living in safety, like the Sidonians, at peace
and secure.[g] And since their land lacked
nothing, they were prosperous.[a] Also, they
lived a long way from the Sidonians[h] and
had no relationship with anyone else.[b]
8 When they returned to Zorah and Eshtaol, their fellow Danites asked them,
"How did you find things?"
9 They answered, "Come on, let's attack
them! We have seen the land, and it is very
good. Aren't you going to do something?
Don't hesitate to go there and take it over.[i]
10 When you get there, you will find an unsuspecting people and a spacious land that
God has put into your hands, a land that
lacks nothing[j] whatever.[k]"
11 Then six hundred men[l] of the Danites,[m] armed for battle, set out from Zorah
and Eshtaol. 12 On their way they set up
camp near Kiriath Jearim[n] in Judah. This
is why the place west of Kiriath Jearim is
called Mahaneh Dan[c][o] to this day. 13 From
there they went on to the hill country of
Ephraim and came to Micah's house.[p]
14 Then the five men who had spied out
the land of Laish[q] said to their fellow Danites, "Do you know that one of these houses has an ephod,[r] some household gods
and an image overlaid with silver?[s] Now
you know what to do." 15 So they turned in
there and went to the house of the young
Levite at Micah's place and greeted him.
16 The six hundred Danites,[t] armed for battle, stood at the entrance of the gate. 17 The
five men who had spied out the land went
inside and took the idol, the ephod and
the household gods[u] while the priest and
the six hundred armed men[v] stood at the
entrance of the gate.
18 When the five men went into Micah's
house and took[w] the idol, the ephod and
the household gods,[x] the priest said to
them, "What are you doing?"
19 They answered him, "Be quiet![y] Don't
say a word. Come with us, and be our
father and priest.[z] Isn't it better that you
serve a tribe and clan[a] in Israel as priest
rather than just one man's household?"
20 The priest was very pleased. He took the
ephod, the household gods and the idol
and went along with the people. 21 Putting
their little children, their livestock and
their possessions in front of them, they
turned away and left.
22 When they had gone some distance
from Micah's house, the men who lived
near Micah were called together and overtook the Danites. 23 As they shouted after
them, the Danites turned and said to Micah, "What's the matter with you that you
called out your men to fight?"
24 He replied, "You took[b] the gods I
made, and my priest, and went away.
What else do I have? How can you ask,
'What's the matter with you?' "
25 The Danites answered, "Don't argue
with us, or some of the men may get angry
and attack you, and you and your family
will lose your lives." 26 So the Danites went

[a] 7 The meaning of the Hebrew for this clause is uncertain. [b] 7 Hebrew; some Septuagint manuscripts *with the Arameans* [c] 12 *Mahaneh Dan* means *Dan's camp.*

18:3 [a] Jdg 17:7 **18:4** [b] Jdg 17:12 **18:5** [c] S Ge 25:22; Jdg 20:18, 23, 27; 1Sa 14:18; 2Sa 5:19; 2Ki 1:2; 8:8 **18:6** [d] 1Ki 22:6 **18:7** [e] ver 17 [f] S Jos 19:47 [g] S Ge 34:25 [h] ver 28; Jos 11:8 **18:9** [i] Nu 13:30; 1Ki 22:3 **18:10** [j] Dt 8:9 [k] 1Ch 4:40 **18:11** [l] ver 16, 17 [m] Jdg 13:2 **18:12** [n] S Jos 9:17 [o] Jdg 13:25 **18:13** [p] S Jdg 17:1 **18:14** [q] S Jos 19:47 [r] S Jdg 8:27 [s] S Ge 31:19 **18:16** [t] S ver 11 **18:17** [u] S Ge 31:19; Mic 5:13 [v] ver 11 **18:18** [w] ver 24; Isa 46:2; Jer 43:11; 48:7; 49:3; Hos 10:5 [x] S Ge 31:19 **18:19** [y] Job 13:5; 21:5; 29:9; 40:4; Isa 52:15; Mic 7:16 [z] Jdg 17:10 [a] Nu 26:42 **18:24** [b] S ver 17-18

18:3 *recognized the voice.* Perhaps they recognized him by his dialect or accent.
18:5 *inquire of God.* The request is for a messsage, probably by using the ephod and household gods (see note on 17:5). God had already revealed his will by the allotments given to the various tribes (Jos 14–20). They were searching for a message that would guarantee the success of their journey.
18:6 *Go in peace.* The Levite gave them the message they wanted to hear. He was even careful to use the name of the Lord to give the message credibility and authority.
18:7 *Laish.* The journey northward was about 100 miles from Zorah and Eshtaol (v. 2). This town is called Leshem in Jos 19:47. After its capture by the Danites, Laish was renamed Dan (v. 29), and it was Israel's northernmost settlement (see 20:1; 1Sa 3:20; 2Sa 3:10). Excavations there have disclosed that the earliest Israelite occupation of Dan was in the twelfth century BC and that the first Israelite inhabitants apparently lived in tents or temporary huts. Occupation of the site continued into the Assyrian period, but the town was destroyed and rebuilt many times. A large high place attached to the city was often extensively rebuilt and refurbished and was in use into the Hellenistic period. *Sidonians.* A peaceful Phoenician people who engaged in commerce throughout the Mediterranean world. *had no relationship.* They did not feel threatened by other powers and therefore sought no treaties for mutual defense.
18:11 *six hundred men.* As leaders of the tribe of Dan, they represented the entire tribe's migration to its new location in the north. Cf. the 600 men who constituted the remnant of the tribe of Benjamin (20:47).
18:19 *father.* See note on 17:10. *a tribe and clan.* Only one clan from the tribe of Dan is ever mentioned—Shuham (Nu 26:42; called Hushim in Ge 46:23). The Danites appealed to the Levite's vanity and materialism.
18:21 *in front of them.* For protection in case of attack by Micah and his neighbors (cf. Ge 33:2–3, Jacob and Esau).
18:24 *You took the gods.* Micah was concerned about the loss of gods that could not even protect themselves. *What else do I have?* The agonizing cry of one whose faith is centered in helpless gods.

their way, and Micah, seeing that they were too strong for him,[c] turned around and went back home.

27 Then they took what Micah had made, and his priest, and went on to Laish, against a people at peace and secure.[d] They attacked them with the sword and burned[e] down their city.[f] 28 There was no one to rescue them because they lived a long way from Sidon[g] and had no relationship with anyone else. The city was in a valley near Beth Rehob.[h]

The Danites rebuilt the city and settled there. 29 They named it Dan[i] after their ancestor Dan, who was born to Israel — though the city used to be called Laish.[j] 30 There the Danites set up for themselves the idol, and Jonathan son of Gershom,[k] the son of Moses,[a] and his sons were priests for the tribe of Dan until the time of the captivity of the land. 31 They continued to use the idol Micah had made,[l] all the time the house of God[m] was in Shiloh.[n]

A Levite and His Concubine

19 In those days Israel had no king.

Now a Levite who lived in a remote area in the hill country of Ephraim[o] took a concubine from Bethlehem in Judah.[p] 2 But she was unfaithful to him. She left him and went back to her parents' home in Bethlehem, Judah. After she had been there four months, 3 her husband went to her to persuade her to return. He had with him his servant and two donkeys. She took him into her parents' home, and when her father saw him, he gladly welcomed him. 4 His father-in-law, the woman's father, prevailed on him to stay; so he remained with him three days, eating and drinking,[q] and sleeping there.

5 On the fourth day they got up early and he prepared to leave, but the woman's father said to his son-in-law, "Refresh yourself[r] with something to eat; then you can go." 6 So the two of them sat down to eat and drink together. Afterward the woman's father said, "Please stay tonight and enjoy yourself.[s]" 7 And when the man got up to go, his father-in-law persuaded him, so he stayed there that night. 8 On the morning of the fifth day, when he rose to go, the woman's father said, "Refresh yourself. Wait till afternoon!" So the two of them ate together.

9 Then when the man, with his concubine and his servant, got up to leave, his father-in-law, the woman's father, said, "Now look, it's almost evening. Spend the night here; the day is nearly over. Stay and enjoy yourself. Early tomorrow morning you can get up and be on your way home." 10 But, unwilling to stay another night, the man left and went toward Jebus[t] (that is, Jerusalem), with his two saddled donkeys and his concubine.

11 When they were near Jebus and the day was almost gone, the servant said to his master, "Come, let's stop at this city of the Jebusites[u] and spend the night."

12 His master replied, "No. We won't go into any city whose people are not Israelites. We will go on to Gibeah." 13 He added, "Come, let's try to reach Gibeah or Ramah[v] and spend the night in one of those places." 14 So they went on, and the sun set as they neared Gibeah in Benjamin.[w] 15 There they stopped to spend the night.[x] They went and sat in the city square,[y] but no one took them in for the night.

[a] *30* Many Hebrew manuscripts, some Septuagint manuscripts and Vulgate; many other Hebrew manuscripts and some other Septuagint manuscripts *Manasseh*

18:26 [c] 2Sa 3:39; Ps 18:17; 35:10
18:27 [d] S Ge 34:25 [e] S Nu 31:10 [f] Ge 49:17; S Jos 19:47
18:28 [g] S ver 7; S Ge 10:19 [h] S Nu 13:21
18:29 [i] S Ge 14:14 [j] S Jos 19:47; 1Ki 15:20
18:30 [k] Ex 2:22
18:31 [l] ver 17 [m] Jdg 19:18; 20:18 [n] S Jos 18:1; Jer 7:14
19:1 [o] ver 16,18 [p] Ru 1:1
19:4 [q] ver 6,8; S Ex 32:6
19:5 [r] ver 8; Ge 18:5
19:6 [s] S Jdg 16:25
19:10 [t] S Ge 10:16; S Jos 15:8
19:11 [u] S Ge 10:16; S Jos 3:10
19:13 [v] S Jos 18:25
19:14 [w] Jos 15:57; 1Sa 10:26; 11:4; 13:2; 15:34; Isa 10:29
19:15 [x] S Ge 24:23 [y] S Ge 19:2

18:28 *Beth Rehob.* Probably the same as Rehob in Nu 13:21 (see also 2Sa 10:6,8).
18:29 *named it Dan.* For the city's location, see map, p. 2519, at the end of this study Bible; see also map, p. 331.
18:30 *Jonathan.* The Levite is here identified as "Jonathan, son of Gershom, the son of Moses" (Ex 2:22; 18:3; 1Ch 23:14–15). In an effort to prevent desecration of the name of Moses, later scribes modified the name slightly, making it read "Manasseh" (see NIV text note). If Jonathan was the grandson of Moses, the events in this chapter must have occurred early in the period of the judges (see notes on 20:1,28). *captivity of the land.* The date of this captivity has not been determined (see note on v. 7 regarding Laish).
18:31 *all the time the house of God was in Shiloh.* See Jos 18:1. For Shiloh's destruction, see Ps 78:60; Jer 7:12,14; 26:6. Archaeological work at Shiloh indicates that the site was destroyed c. 1050 BC and was left uninhabited for many centuries.
19:1—21:25 The second cycle of events in the epilogue (see note on 17:1—18:31). It illustrates Israel's moral corruption by telling of the degenerate act of the men of Gibeah—an act remembered centuries later (Hos 9:9; 10:9). Although that town showed itself to be as wicked as any Canaanite town, it was defended by the rest of the tribe of Benjamin against the Lord's discipline through the Israelites, until nearly the whole tribe was destroyed.
19:1–30 An account of an Israelite town (Gibeah) that revived the ways of Sodom (see Ge 19).
19:1 *Levite.* Unlike the Levite of chs. 17–18, this man is not named. *concubine.* See note on Ge 25:6.
19:3 *gladly welcomed him.* The separation of the concubine from the Levite was probably a matter of family disgrace, so his father-in-law was glad for the prospect of the two being reunited.
19:10 *Jebus.* See 1:21; see also note on Ge 10:16.
19:12 *city whose people are not Israelites.* With the city under the control of the Jebusites, the Levite was afraid that he would receive no hospitality and might be in mortal danger.
19:14 *Gibeah in Benjamin.* Distinguished from the Gibeah in Judah (Jos 15:20,57) and the Gibeah in the hill country of Ephraim (Jos 24:33). As the political capital of Saul's kingdom, it is called Gibeah of Saul in 1Sa 11:4; see also 1Sa 13:15.
19:15 *took them in.* See notes on 13:15; Ge 18:2.

16 That evening[z] an old man from the
hill country of Ephraim,[a] who was living
in Gibeah (the inhabitants of the place
were Benjamites), came in from his work
in the fields. 17 When he looked and saw
the traveler in the city square, the old man
asked, "Where are you going? Where did
you come from?"[b]
18 He answered, "We are on our way
from Bethlehem in Judah to a remote area
in the hill country of Ephraim where I
live. I have been to Bethlehem in Judah
and now I am going to the house of the
LORD.[a][c] No one has taken me in for the
night. 19 We have both straw and fodder[d]
for our donkeys[e] and bread and wine[f] for
ourselves your servants — me, the woman and the young man with us. We don't
need anything."
20 "You are welcome at my house," the
old man said. "Let me supply whatever you need. Only don't spend the night
in the square." 21 So he took him into his
house and fed his donkeys. After they had
washed their feet, they had something to
eat and drink.[g]
22 While they were enjoying themselves,[h] some of the wicked men[i] of the
city surrounded the house. Pounding on
the door, they shouted to the old man who
owned the house, "Bring out the man who
came to your house so we can have sex
with him.[j]"
23 The owner of the house went outside[k]
and said to them, "No, my friends, don't
be so vile. Since this man is my guest,
don't do this outrageous thing.[l] 24 Look,
here is my virgin daughter,[m] and his concubine. I will bring them out to you now,
and you can use them and do to them
whatever you wish. But as for this man,
don't do such an outrageous thing."
25 But the men would not listen to him.
So the man took his concubine and sent
her outside to them, and they raped her[n]
and abused her[o] throughout the night, and
at dawn they let her go. 26 At daybreak the
woman went back to the house where her
master was staying, fell down at the door
and lay there until daylight.
27 When her master got up in the morning and opened the door of the house
and stepped out to continue on his way,
there lay his concubine, fallen in the doorway of the house, with her hands on the
threshold. 28 He said to her, "Get up; let's
go." But there was no answer. Then the
man put her on his donkey and set out
for home.
29 When he reached home, he took a
knife[p] and cut up his concubine, limb by
limb, into twelve parts and sent them into
all the areas of Israel.[q] 30 Everyone who
saw it was saying to one another, "Such
a thing has never been seen or done, not
since the day the Israelites came up out of
Egypt.[r] Just imagine! We must do something! So speak up![s]"

The Israelites Punish the Benjamites

20 Then all Israel[t] from Dan to Beersheba[u] and from the land of Gilead
came together as one[v] and assembled[w] before the LORD in Mizpah.[x] 2 The leaders of

19:16 [z] Ps 104:23 [a] S ver 1 **19:17** [b] S Ge 29:4 **19:18** [c] S Jdg 18:31 **19:19** [d] Ge 24:25 [e] S Ge 42:27 [f] S Ge 14:18 **19:21** [g] Ge 24:32-33; Lk 7:44 **19:22** [h] S Jdg 16:25 [i] S Dt 13:13 [j] Ge 19:4-5; Jdg 20:5; Ro 1:26-27 **19:23** [k] Ge 19:6 [l] S Ge 34:7; S Lev 19:29; S Jos 7:15; S Jdg 20:6; Ro 1:27 **19:24** [m] Ge 19:8 **19:25** [n] Jdg 20:5 [o] 1Sa 31:4 **19:29** [p] S Ge 22:6 [q] Jdg 20:6; 1Sa 11:7 **19:30** [r] Hos 9:9 [s] Jdg 20:7; Pr 13:10 **20:1** [t] Jdg 21:5 [u] S Ge 21:14; 1Sa 3:20; 2Sa 3:10; 17:11; 24:15; 1Ki 4:25; 2Ch 30:5 [v] ver 11; 1Sa 11:7 [w] 1Sa 7:5 [x] S Jos 11:3

[a] 18 Hebrew, Vulgate, Syriac and Targum; Septuagint *going home*

19:18 *house of the LORD.* Apparently the Levite was planning to go to Shiloh (see 18:31; Jos 18:1) to present a thank offering to the Lord or a sin offering for himself and his concubine.

19:21 *washed their feet.* An evidence of hospitality in the ancient Near East, where travelers commonly wore sandals as they walked the dusty roads (see Ge 18:4; 24:32; 43:24; Lk 7:44; Jn 13:5 – 14).

19:22 *wicked men.* The Hebrew for this expression refers to the morally depraved (see note on Dt 13:13). Elsewhere the expression is associated with idolatry (Dt 13:13), drunkenness (1Sa 1:16) and rebellion (1Sa 2:12). Here the reference is to homosexual acts. *Bring out the man.* The sexual perversion of these wicked men is yet another example of the decadence of an age when "everyone did as they saw fit" (17:6; 21:25). A similar request was made by the men of Sodom (Ge 19:5). Homosexual practices were integral to Canaanite religion.

19:23 *don't be so vile.* An expression of outrage at the willful perversion of what is right and natural (see Ge 19:7; 2Sa 13:12; see also Ro 1:27).

19:24 *my virgin daughter, and his concubine.* The tragedy of this story lies not only in the decadence of Gibeah but also in the callous selfishness of men who would betray defenseless women to be brutally violated for a whole night. Cf. Ge 19:8, where Lot offered his two daughters to the men of Sodom.

19:25 *took.* Here the Hebrew for this verb suggests taking by force.

19:29 *cut up his concubine.* Dismembering the concubine's body and sending parts to each of the 12 tribes was intended to awaken Israel from its moral lethargy and to marshal the tribes to face up to their responsibility. It is ironic that the one who issued such a call was himself so selfish and insensitive. See also Saul's similar action in 1Sa 11:7.

20:1 – 48 All Israel (except Jabesh Gilead; see 21:8 – 9) assembled before the Lord to deal with the moral outrage committed by the men of Gibeah. Having first inquired of God for divine direction, they marched against Gibeah and the Benjamites as the disciplinary arm of the Lord (see Jos 22:11 – 34), following him as their King.

20:1 *Dan to Beersheba.* A conventional way of speaking of all Israel from north (Dan) to south (Beersheba); see 1Sa 3:20; 2Sa 3:10; 24:2; 1Ch 21:2; 2Ch 30:5. The use of this expression, however, does not mean that the events of this chapter occurred after Dan's move to the north (18:27 – 29); rather, it indicates the author's perspective at the time of writing (Judges was probably written after the Davidic dynasty was fully established; see Introduction: Author and Date). Here the expression refers to the disciplinary action of all Israel (except Jabesh Gilead; see 21:8 – 9) against Gibeah and the rest of the Benjamites. Such a united response must have occurred early in the time of the judges, before the period of

all the people of the tribes of Israel took their places in the assembly of God's people, four hundred thousand men[y] armed with swords. 3 (The Benjamites heard that the Israelites had gone up to Mizpah.) Then the Israelites said, "Tell us how this awful thing happened."

4 So the Levite, the husband of the murdered woman, said, "I and my concubine came to Gibeah[z] in Benjamin to spend the night.[a] 5 During the night the men of Gibeah came after me and surrounded the house, intending to kill me.[b] They raped my concubine, and she died.[c] 6 I took my concubine, cut her into pieces and sent one piece to each region of Israel's inheritance,[d] because they committed this lewd and outrageous act[e] in Israel. 7 Now, all you Israelites, speak up and tell me what you have decided to do.[f]"

8 All the men rose up together as one, saying, "None of us will go home. No, not one of us will return to his house. 9 But now this is what we'll do to Gibeah: We'll go up against it in the order decided by casting lots.[g] 10 We'll take ten men out of every hundred from all the tribes of Israel, and a hundred from a thousand, and a thousand from ten thousand, to get provisions for the army. Then, when the army arrives at Gibeah[a] in Benjamin, it can give them what they deserve for this outrageous act done in Israel." 11 So all the Israelites got together and united as one against the city.[h]

12 The tribes of Israel sent messengers throughout the tribe of Benjamin, saying, "What about this awful crime that was committed among you?[i] 13 Now turn those wicked men[j] of Gibeah over to us so that we may put them to death and purge the evil from Israel.[k]"

But the Benjamites would not listen to their fellow Israelites. 14 From their towns they came together at Gibeah to fight against the Israelites. 15 At once the Benjamites mobilized twenty-six thousand swordsmen from their towns, in addition to seven hundred able young men from those living in Gibeah. 16 Among all these soldiers there were seven hundred select troops who were left-handed,[l] each of whom could sling a stone at a hair and not miss.

17 Israel, apart from Benjamin, mustered four hundred thousand swordsmen, all of them fit for battle.

18 The Israelites went up to Bethel[b][m] and inquired of God.[n] They said, "Who of us is to go up first[o] to fight[p] against the Benjamites?"

The LORD replied, "Judah[q] shall go first."

19 The next morning the Israelites got up and pitched camp near Gibeah. 20 The Israelites went out to fight the Benjamites and took up battle positions against them at Gibeah. 21 The Benjamites came out of Gibeah and cut down twenty-two thousand Israelites[r] on the battlefield that day. 22 But the Israelites encouraged one another and again took up their positions where they had stationed themselves the first day. 23 The Israelites went up and wept before the LORD[s] until evening,[t] and they inquired of the LORD.[u] They said, "Shall we go up again to fight[v] against the Benjamites, our fellow Israelites?"

The LORD answered, "Go up against them."

24 Then the Israelites drew near to Benjamin the second day. 25 This time, when the Benjamites came out from Gibeah to oppose them, they cut down another eighteen thousand Israelites,[w] all of them armed with swords.

26 Then all the Israelites, the whole army, went up to Bethel, and there they sat weeping before the LORD.[x] They fasted that day until evening and presented burnt offerings[z] and fellowship offerings[a] to the LORD.[b] 27 And the Israelites inquired of the

a 10 One Hebrew manuscript; most Hebrew manuscripts *Geba,* a variant of *Gibeah* *b* 18 Or *to the house of God;* also in verse 26

20:2 [y] 1Sa 11:8
20:4 [z] S Jos 15:57 [a] S Ge 24:23
20:5 [b] S Jdg 19:22 [c] Jdg 19:25-26
20:6 [d] S Jdg 19:29 [e] S Jdg 19:23; 2Sa 13:12
20:7 [f] S Jdg 19:30
20:9 [g] S Lev 16:8
20:11 [h] S ver 1
20:12 [i] Dt 13:14
20:13 [j] S Dt 13:13 [k] S Dt 13:5; S 1Co 5:13
20:16 [l] S Jdg 3:15
20:18 [m] S Jos 12:9; S Jdg 18:31 [n] S Jdg 18:5 [o] S Jdg 1:1 [p] ver 23,28 [q] S Ge 49:10
20:21 [r] ver 25
20:23 [s] S Nu 14:1 [t] Jos 7:6 [u] S Jdg 18:5 [v] S ver 18
20:25 [w] ver 21
20:26 [x] S Nu 14:1 [y] 2Sa 12:21 [z] Lev 1:3 [a] S Ex 32:6 [b] Jdg 21:4

foreign domination of various parts of the land. *as one.* Cf. vv. 8,11; 1Sa 11:7. *assembled … in Mizpah.* A place where the tribes gathered to meet before the Lord also during the days of Saul (1Sa 7:5 – 17; 10:17).

20:9 *casting lots.* A common method of determining the will of God (see notes on Ex 28:30; 1Sa 2:28; Jnh 1:7; Ac 1:26).

20:10 *ten men.* Support for the large army had to be well organized and efficient. One man was responsible for providing food for nine men fighting at the front.

20:13 *turn those wicked men … over to us.* The demand of Israel was not unreasonable. The intent was to punish only those directly involved in the crime. *wicked men.* See note on Dt 13:13. *put them to death.* The sin of the men of Gibeah called for the death penalty, and Israel had to punish the sin if she was to avoid guilt herself (see Dt 13:5; 17:7; 19:19 – 20).

20:16 *left-handed.* The Benjamite Ehud was also left-handed (see 3:15 and note). *sling a stone.* Cf. Zec 9:15. The sling wa[s] a very effective weapon, as David later demonstrated in hi[s] encounter with Goliath (1Sa 17:49). A slingstone, weighing one pound or more, could be hurled at 90 – 100 mile[s] an hour. *miss.* In other contexts the Hebrew for this verb i[s] translated "to sin."

20:18 *Bethel.* At this time the ark of the covenant and th[e] high priest Phinehas were at Bethel (see vv. 26 – 28). *inquire[d] of God.* Probably by priestly use of the Urim and Thummi[m] (see v. 9 and note). *Who of us is to go up first … ?* See 1:1 – 3[6]. *Judah.* See note on 1:2.

20:21 *twenty-two thousand Israelites.* A rousing victory fo[r] the Benjamites, who numbered 26,700 (v. 15) and therefor[e] had struck down nearly one man apiece.

20:27 *ark.* The only mention of the ark in Judges.

LORD.[c] (In those days the ark of the covenant of God[d] was there, 28 with Phinehas
son of Eleazar,[e] the son of Aaron, ministering before it.)[f] They asked, "Shall we go
up again to fight against the Benjamites,
our fellow Israelites, or not?"
The LORD responded, "Go, for tomorrow
I will give them into your hands.[g]"
29 Then Israel set an ambush[h] around
Gibeah. 30 They went up against the Benjamites on the third day and took up positions against Gibeah as they had done
before. 31 The Benjamites came out to
meet them and were drawn away[i] from
the city. They began to inflict casualties
on the Israelites as before, so that about
thirty men fell in the open field and on the
roads—the one leading to Bethel[j] and the
other to Gibeah. 32 While the Benjamites
were saying, "We are defeating them as
before,"[k] the Israelites were saying, "Let's
retreat and draw them away from the city
to the roads."
33 All the men of Israel moved from their
places and took up positions at Baal Tamar, and the Israelite ambush charged
out of its place[l] on the west[a] of Gibeah.[b]
34 Then ten thousand of Israel's able young
men made a frontal attack on Gibeah. The
fighting was so heavy that the Benjamites
did not realize[m] how near disaster was.[n]
35 The LORD defeated Benjamin[o] before Israel, and on that day the Israelites struck
down 25,100 Benjamites, all armed with
swords. 36 Then the Benjamites saw that
they were beaten.
Now the men of Israel had given way[p]
before Benjamin, because they relied on
the ambush[q] they had set near Gibeah.
37 Those who had been in ambush made a
sudden dash into Gibeah, spread out and
put the whole city to the sword.[r] 38 The
Israelites had arranged with the ambush
that they should send up a great cloud of
smoke[s] from the city,[t] 39 and then the Israelites would counterattack.
The Benjamites had begun to inflict casualties on the Israelites (about thirty),
and they said, "We are defeating them as
in the first battle."[u] 40 But when the column of smoke began to rise from the city,
the Benjamites turned and saw the whole
city going up in smoke.[v] 41 Then the Israelites counterattacked,[w] and the Benjamites
were terrified, because they realized that
disaster had come[x] on them. 42 So they
fled before the Israelites in the direction
of the wilderness, but they could not escape the battle. And the Israelites who
came out of the towns cut them down
there. 43 They surrounded the Benjamites,
chased them and easily[c] overran them in
the vicinity of Gibeah on the east. 44 Eighteen thousand Benjamites fell, all of
them valiant fighters.[y] 45 As they turned
and fled toward the wilderness to the
rock of Rimmon,[z] the Israelites cut down
five thousand men along the roads. They
kept pressing after the Benjamites as far
as Gidom and struck down two thousand
more.
46 On that day twenty-five thousand
Benjamite[a] swordsmen fell, all of them
valiant fighters. 47 But six hundred of them
turned and fled into the wilderness to the
rock of Rimmon, where they stayed four
months. 48 The men of Israel went back
to Benjamin and put all the towns to the
sword, including the animals and everything else they found. All the towns they
came across they set on fire.[b]

Wives for the Benjamites

21 The men of Israel had taken an
oath[c] at Mizpah:[d] "Not one of us
will give[e] his daughter in marriage to a
Benjamite."
2 The people went to Bethel,[d] where
they sat before God until evening, raising
their voices and weeping bitterly. 3 "LORD,

20:27 [c] S Jdg 18:5 [d] S Nu 10:33 **20:28** [e] Nu 25:7 [f] Dt 18:5 [g] S Jos 2:24 **20:29** [h] S Jos 8:2,4 **20:31** [i] Jos 8:16 [j] Jos 16:1 **20:32** [k] ver 39 **20:33** [l] Jos 8:19 **20:34** [m] Jos 8:14 [n] ver 41 **20:35** [o] 1Sa 9:21 **20:36** [p] Jos 8:15 [q] Jos 8:2 **20:37** [r] Jos 8:19 **20:38** [s] Jos 8:20 [t] Jos 8:4-8 **20:39** [u] ver 32; Ps 78:9 **20:40** [v] Jos 8:20 **20:41** [w] Jos 8:21 [x] ver 34 **20:44** [y] 1Sa 10:26; Ps 76:5 **20:45** [z] S Jos 15:32 **20:46** [a] 1Sa 9:21 **20:48** [b] Jdg 21:23 **21:1** [c] S Jos 9:18 [d] S Jos 11:3 [e] ver 18,22

[a] 33 Some Septuagint manuscripts and Vulgate; the meaning of the Hebrew for this word is uncertain. [b] 33 Hebrew *Geba,* a variant of *Gibeah* [c] 43 The meaning of the Hebrew for this word is uncertain. [d] 2 Or *to the house of God*

20:28 *Phinehas.* Phinehas was the priest in the tabernacle in the days of Joshua (Jos 22:13), and the fact that he was still serving is further evidence that these events took place early in the days of the judges (see notes on v. 1; 18:30).
20:29 *set an ambush.* See 9:32; Jos 8:2.
20:35 *25,100.* Apparently 1,000 Benjamites had been killed in the first two battles (see note on v. 21).
20:36b–45 Details of the account in vv. 29–36a.
20:46 *twenty-five thousand.* A round number for 25,100 (v. 35).
20:47 *six hundred of them.* If these had not escaped, the tribe of Benjamin would have been annihilated. The same number of Danites went to Laish (18:11).
21:1–25 Second thoughts about the slaughter of their Benjamite brothers caused the Israelites to grieve over the loss. Only 600 Benjamites were left alive, and the men of Israel decided to provide wives for them in order to keep the tribe from disappearing. After slaughtering most of the people of Jabesh Gilead, the Israelites took 400 young women from the survivors and gave them to 400 Benjamites. Shortly afterward, each of the remaining Benjamites seized a wife from the women of Shiloh, and Benjamin began to be restored.
21:1 *taken an oath.* This vow, probably taken in the name of the Lord, was not an ordinary vow but invoked a curse on oneself if the vow was broken (v. 18; see also Ac 23:12–15).
21:2 *Bethel.* See 20:18,26–27. *weeping bitterly.* Earlier the Israelites wept because they were defeated by the Benjamites (20:23,26). Now they weep because the disciplinary action against the Benjamites has nearly annihilated one of the tribes (see v. 3).

God of Israel," they cried, "why has this happened to Israel? Why should one tribe be missing[f] from Israel today?"

4 Early the next day the people built an altar and presented burnt offerings and fellowship offerings.[g]

5 Then the Israelites asked, "Who from all the tribes of Israel[h] has failed to assemble before the LORD?" For they had taken a solemn oath that anyone who failed to assemble before the LORD at Mizpah was to be put to death.

6 Now the Israelites grieved for the tribe of Benjamin, their fellow Israelites. "Today one tribe is cut off from Israel," they said. 7 "How can we provide wives for those who are left, since we have taken an oath[i] by the LORD not to give them any of our daughters in marriage?" 8 Then they asked, "Which one of the tribes of Israel failed to assemble before the LORD at Mizpah?" They discovered that no one from Jabesh Gilead[j] had come to the camp for the assembly. 9 For when they counted the people, they found that none of the people of Jabesh Gilead were there.

10 So the assembly sent twelve thousand fighting men with instructions to go to Jabesh Gilead and put to the sword those living there, including the women and children. 11 "This is what you are to do," they said. "Kill every male[k] and every woman who is not a virgin.[l]" 12 They found among the people living in Jabesh Gilead four hundred young women who had never slept with a man, and they took them to the camp at Shiloh[m] in Canaan.

13 Then the whole assembly sent an offer of peace[n] to the Benjamites at the rock of Rimmon.[o] 14 So the Benjamites returned at that time and were given the women of Jabesh Gilead who had been spared. But there were not enough for all of them.

15 The people grieved for Benjamin,[p] because the LORD had made a gap in the tribes of Israel. 16 And the elders of the assembly said, "With the women of Benjamin destroyed, how shall we provide wives for the men who are left? 17 The Benjamite survivors must have heirs," they said, "so that a tribe of Israel will not be wiped out.[q] 18 We can't give them our daughters as wives, since we Israelites have taken this oath:[r] 'Cursed be anyone who gives[s] a wife to a Benjamite.' 19 But look, there is the annual festival of the LORD in Shiloh,[t] which lies north of Bethel[u], east of the road that goes from Bethel to Shechem,[v] and south of Lebonah."

20 So they instructed the Benjamites, saying, "Go and hide in the vineyards 21 and watch. When the young women of Shiloh come out to join in the dancing,[w] rush from the vineyards and each of you seize one of them to be your wife. Then return to the land of Benjamin. 22 When their fathers or brothers complain to us, we will say to them, 'Do us the favor of helping them, because we did not get wives for them during the war. You will not be guilty of breaking your oath because you did not give[x] your daughters to them.' "

23 So that is what the Benjamites did. While the young women were dancing,[y] each man caught one and carried her off to be his wife. Then they returned to their inheritance[z] and rebuilt the towns and settled in them.[a]

24 At that time the Israelites left that place and went home to their tribes and clans, each to his own inheritance.

25 In those days Israel had no king; everyone did as they saw fit.[b]

21:3 [f] ver 6,17 **21:4** [g] Jdg 20:26 **21:5** [h] Jdg 20:1 **21:7** [i] S Jos 9:18 **21:8** [j] 1Sa 11:1; 31:11; 2Sa 2:4; 21:12; 1Ch 10:11 **21:11** [k] S Nu 31:7 [l] Nu 31:17-18 **21:12** [m] S Jos 18:1 **21:13** [n] S Dt 2:26 [o] S Jos 15:32 **21:15** [p] ver 6 **21:17** [q] S ver 3 **21:18** [r] S Jos 9:18 [s] S ver 1 **21:19** [t] S Jos 18:1 [u] Jos 16:1 [v] S Jos 17:7 **21:21** [w] S Ex 15:20 **21:22** [x] S ver 1; ver 1,18 **21:23** [y] ver 21 [z] S Jos 24:28 [a] Jdg 20:48 **21:25** [b] S Dt 12:8

21:5 *failed to assemble.* The tribes had a mutual responsibility in times of military action (see note on 5:13–18). Those who failed to participate were often singled out and sometimes punished (5:15–17,23). *solemn oath.* Complicating the situation for Israel was the fact that they had taken a second oath, calling for the deaths of those who had not participated in the battle.

21:10 *twelve thousand.* A thousand from each tribe (see Nu 31:6), with 1,000 supplied to represent the tribe of Benjamin.

21:11 *Kill every male.* The punishment of Jabesh Gilead seems brutal, but the covenant bond between the tribes was extremely important. Even though delinquency on some occasions was not punished (5:15–17), the nature of the crime in this case, coupled with Benjamin's refusal to turn over the criminals, caused Israel to take this oath (v. 5).

21:12 *in Canaan.* Emphasizes the fact that the women were brought across the Jordan from the east.

21:19 *festival of the LORD.* In light of the mention of vineyards (v. 20), it is likely that this reference is to the Festival of Tabernacles (see note on 1Sa 1:3), though it may have been a local festival. *north of Bethel ... south of Lebonah.* This detailed description of Shiloh's location may indicate that this material was written at a time when Shiloh was in ruins, perhaps after its destruction during the battle of Aphek (1Sa 4:1–11).

21:21 *seize one of them to be your wife.* With the Benjamites securing wives in this manner, the other tribes were not actually "giving" their daughters to them (see note on v. 22).

21:22 *When their fathers or brothers complain.* It was customary for the brothers of a young woman who had been abducted to demand satisfaction (see Ge 34:7–31; 2Sa 13:20–38). It was therefore important that the elders anticipate this response and be prepared to get cooperation from the young women's families.

21:24 *went home.* These soldiers had probably been away from home at least five months (see 20:47).

21:25 *Israel had no king.* See Introduction: Author and Date; see also note on 17:6. *did as they saw fit.* See note on 17:6; see also Introduction: Themes and Theology; Literary Features.

RUTH

INTRODUCTION

Title

The book is named after one of its main characters, a young woman of Moab, the great-grandmother of David and an ancestor of Jesus (4:21 – 22; Mt 1:1,5). The only other Biblical book bearing the name of a woman is Esther.

Background

The story is set in the time of the judges, a time characterized in the book of Judges as a period of religious and moral degeneracy, national disunity and frequent foreign oppression. The book of Ruth reflects a time of peace between Israel and Moab (contrast Jdg 3:12 – 30). Like 1Sa 1 – 2, it gives a series of intimate glimpses into the private lives of the members of an Israelite family. It also presents a delightful account of the remnant of true faith and piety in the period of the judges, relieving an otherwise wholly dark picture of that era.

a quick look

Author:
Unknown

Audience:
God's chosen people, the Israelites

Date:
Ruth lived during the time of the judges; the book was written sometime after David became king in about 1010 BC

Theme:
Ruth, a Moabite woman, proves to be a model of faithfulness in Israel during the period of the judges.

Author and Date of Writing

The author is unknown. Jewish tradition points to Samuel, but it is unlikely that he is the author because the mention of David (4:17,22) implies a later date. Further, the literary style of Hebrew used in Ruth suggests that it was written during the period of the monarchy.

Themes and Theology

The importance of faithful love in human relationships among God's kingdom people is powerfully underscored. The author focuses on Ruth's unswerving and selfless devotion to desolate Naomi (1:16 – 17; 2:11 – 12; 3:10; 4:15) and on Boaz's kindness to these two widows (chs. 2 – 4). He presents striking examples of lives that embody in their daily affairs the self-giving love that fulfills God's law (Lev 19:18; cf. Ro 13:10). Such love also reflects God's love, in a marvelous joining of

The book is a story of Naomi's transformation from despair to happiness through the selfless, God-blessed acts of Ruth and Boaz. Naomi moves from emptiness to fullness, from destitution to security and hope.

human and divine actions (compare 2:12 with 3:9). In God's benevolence such lives are blessed and are made a blessing.

It may seem surprising that one who reflects God's love so clearly is a Moabite (see map and accompanying text, p. 395). Yet Ruth's complete loyalty to the Israelite family into which she has been received by marriage and her total devotion to her desolate mother-in-law mark her as a true daughter of Israel and a worthy ancestor of David. She strikingly exemplifies the truth that participation in the coming kingdom of God is decided not by blood and birth but by the conformity of one's life to the will of God through "the obedience that comes from faith" (Ro 1:5). Her place in the ancestry of David signifies that all nations will be represented in the kingdom of David's greater son.

As an episode in the ancestry of David, the book of Ruth sheds light on his role in the history of redemption. Redemption is a key concept throughout the account; the Hebrew word in its various forms occurs 23 times. The book is primarily a story of Naomi's transformation from despair to happiness through the selfless, God-blessed acts of Ruth and Boaz. Naomi moves from emptiness to fullness (1:21; 3:17; see notes on 1:1,3,5 – 6,12,21 – 22; 3:17; 4:15), from destitution (1:1 – 5) to security and hope (4:13 – 17). Similarly, Israel was transformed from national desperation at the death of Eli (1Sa 4:18) to peace and prosperity in the early days of Solomon (1Ki 4:20 – 34; 5:4) through

A wheat field being harvested in the hill country of Manasseh. Ruth met Boaz when he saw her gleaning leftover grain from his fields (Ru 2).

www.HolyLandPhotos.org

View of the hill country east of Bethlehem. Boaz met Ruth in the fields near Bethlehem.
Todd Bolen/www.BiblePlaces.com

the selfless devotion of David, a true descendant of Ruth and Boaz. The author thus reminded Israel that the reign of the house of David, as the means of God's benevolent rule in Israel, held the prospect of God's promised peace and rest. But this rest would continue only so long as those who participated in the kingdom — prince and people alike — reflected in their daily lives the selfless love exemplified by Ruth and Boaz. In Jesus, the great "son of David" (Mt 1:1), and his redemptive work, the promised blessings of the kingdom of God find their fulfillment.

Literary Features

The book of Ruth is a Hebrew short story, told with consummate skill. Among historical narratives in Scripture it is unexcelled in its compactness, vividness, warmth, beauty and dramatic effectiveness — an exquisitely wrought jewel of Hebrew narrative art.

Marvelously symmetrical throughout (see Outline), the action moves from a briefly sketched account of distress (1:1 – 5; 71 words in Hebrew) through four episodes to a concluding account of relief and hope that is drawn with equal brevity (4:13 – 17; 71 words in Hebrew). The crucial turning point occurs exactly midway (see note on 2:20). The opening line of each of the four episodes signals its main development (1:6, the return; 2:1, the meeting with Boaz; 3:1, finding a home for Ruth; 4:1, the decisive event at the gate), while the closing line of each episode facilitates transition to what follows (see notes on 1:22; 2:23; 3:18; 4:12). Contrast is also used to good effect: pleasant (the meaning of "Naomi") and bitter (1:20), full and empty (1:21), and the living and the dead (2:20). Most striking is the contrast between two of the main characters, Ruth and Boaz: The one is a young, foreign, destitute widow, while the other is a middle-aged, well-to-do Israelite securely established in his home community. For each there is a corresponding character whose actions highlight, by contrast, his or her selfless acts: Ruth — Orpah; Boaz — the unnamed guardian-redeemer.

When movements in space, time and circumstance all correspond in some way, a harmony results that both satisfies the reader's artistic sense and helps open doors to understanding. The author of Ruth keeps his readers from being distracted from the central story — Naomi's passage from emptiness to fullness through the selfless acts of Ruth and Boaz (see Themes and Theology). That passage, or restoration, first takes place in connection with her return from Moab to the promised land and to Bethlehem ("house of food"; see note on 1:1). It then progresses with the harvest season, when the fullness of the land is gathered in. All aspects of the story keep the reader's attention focused on the central issue. Consideration of these and other literary devices (mentioned throughout the notes) will aid the reader's understanding of the book of Ruth.

Outline

- I. Introduction: Naomi Emptied (1:1 – 5)
- II. Naomi Returns from Moab (1:6 – 22)
  - A. Ruth Clings to Naomi (1:6 – 18)
  - B. Ruth and Naomi Return to Bethlehem (1:19 – 22)
- III. Ruth and Boaz Meet in the Harvest Fields (ch. 2)
  - A. Ruth Begins Work (2:1 – 7)
  - B. Boaz Shows Kindness to Ruth (2:8 – 16)
  - C. Ruth Returns to Naomi (2:17 – 23)
- IV. Naomi Sends Ruth to Boaz's Threshing Floor (ch. 3)
  - A. Naomi Instructs Ruth (3:1 – 5)
  - B. Boaz Pledges to Secure Redemption (3:6 – 15)
  - C. Ruth Returns to Naomi (3:16 – 18)
- V. Boaz Arranges to Fulfill His Pledge (4:1 – 12)
  - A. Boaz Confronts the Unnamed Guardian-Redeemer (4:1 – 8)
  - B. Boaz Buys Naomi's Property and Announces His Marriage to Ruth (4:9 – 12)
- VI. Conclusion: Naomi Filled (4:13 – 17)
- VII. Epilogue: Genealogy of David (4:18 – 22)

Naomi Loses Her Husband and Sons

1 In the days when the judges ruled,[a][a]
there was a famine in the land.[b] So a
man from Bethlehem in Judah,[c] together
with his wife and two sons, went to live
for a while[d] in the country of Moab.[e] 2 The
man's name was Elimelek,[f] his wife's
name was Naomi, and the names of his
two sons were Mahlon and Kilion.[g] They
were Ephrathites[h] from Bethlehem,[i] Judah.
And they went to Moab and lived there.
3 Now Elimelek, Naomi's husband, died,
and she was left with her two sons. 4 They
married Moabite women,[j] one named Orpah and the other Ruth.[k] After they had
lived there about ten years, 5 both Mahlon
and Kilion[l] also died,[m] and Naomi was left
without her two sons and her husband.

Naomi and Ruth Return to Bethlehem

6 When Naomi heard in Moab[n] that the
LORD had come to the aid of his people[o]
by providing food[p] for them, she and her
daughters-in-law[q] prepared to return home
from there. 7 With her two daughters-in-
law she left the place where she had been
living and set out on the road that would
take them back to the land of Judah.

[a] 1 Traditionally *judged*

1:1 [a] Jdg 2:16-18 [b] S Ge 12:10; 2Ki 6:25; Ps 105:16; Hag 1:11 [c] S Ge 35:19 [d] Ge 47:4 [e] S Ge 36:35 **1:2** [f] ver 3; Ru 2:1; 4:3 [g] ver 5; Ru 4:9 [h] S Ge 35:16 [i] Ge 35:19; 1Sa 16:18 **1:4** [j] 1Ki 11:1; 2Ch 24:26; Ezr 9:2; Ne 13:23 [k] ver 14; Ru 4:13; Mt 1:5 **1:5** [l] S ver 2 [m] ver 8; Ru 2:11 **1:6** [n] S Ge 36:35 [o] S Ge 50:24; Ex 4:31; Jer 29:10; Zep 2:7 [p] Ps 132:15; Mt 6:11 [q] S Ge 11:31; S 38:16

1:1 *when the judges ruled.* Probably from c. 1380 to c. 1050 BC (see Introduction to Judges: Background). By mentioning the judges, the author calls to mind that period of Israel's apostasy, moral degradation and oppression. *famine.* Not mentioned in Judges. *Bethlehem in Judah.* David's hometown (1Sa 16:18). Bethlehem (the name suggests "house of food") is empty. *Moab.* See map and accompanying text below.
1:2 *Elimelek.* Means "(My) God is King" (see note on Jdg 8:23). *Naomi.* See NIV text note on v. 20. *Mahlon.* Ruth's husband (4:10), whose name probably means "weakling" or "sickly person." *Kilion.* Probably means something like "frail person." (Mahlon's and Kilion's names may have been acquired as their conditions became evident.) *Ephrathites.* Ephrathah was a name for the area around Bethlehem (see 4:11; Ge 35:19; 1Sa 17:12; Mic 5:2). See photo, p. 393.
1:3 *Elimelek, Naomi's husband, died.* Naomi's emptying begins (see v. 21).
1:4 *They married.* The prospect of continuing the family line remained. *Moabite women.* See Ge 19:36–37. Marriage with Moabite women was not forbidden, though no Moabite — or his descendants to the tenth generation — was allowed to "enter the assembly of the LORD" (Dt 23:3). *Ruth.* The name may be related to the Hebrew for "filling" (cf. note on v. 21). Ruth is one of five women in Matthew's genealogy of Jesus. The others are Tamar, Rahab, Bathsheba and Mary (see Mt 1:3,5–6,16 and note on 1:3).
1:5 *Mahlon and Kilion also died.* Naomi's emptying is complete (see v. 3 and note). *Naomi was left.* She now has neither husband nor sons. She has only two young daughters-in-law, both of them foreigners and childless.
1:6–22 Act I in the drama: Naomi's sense of desolation is exposed.
1:6 *the LORD had come to the aid of his people.* At several points in the account, God's sovereign control of events is acknowledged (here; vv. 13,21; 2:20; 4:12–15). *food.* Bethlehem ("house of food") again has food. *prepared to return home.* Empty Naomi returns to the newly filled land of promise.

THE BOOK OF **RUTH**

Set in the dark and bloody days of the judges, the story of Ruth is silent about the underlying hostility and suspicion the two peoples—Judahites and Moabites—felt for each other. The original onslaught of the invading Israelite tribes against towns that were once Moabite had never been forgotten or forgiven, while the Hebrew prophets denounced Moab's pride and arrogance for trying to bewitch, seduce and oppress Israel from the time of Balaam on. The Mesha Stele (c. 830 BC) boasts of the massacre of entire Israelite towns.

Moab encompassed the expansive, grain-rich plateau between the Dead Sea and the eastern desert on both sides of the enormous rift of the Arnon River gorge. Much of eastern Moab was steppe land—semi-arid wastes not profitable for cultivation, but excellent for grazing flocks of sheep and goats. The tribute Moab paid to Israel in the days of Ahab was 100,000 lambs and the wool of 100,000 rams (see 2Ki 3:4 and note).

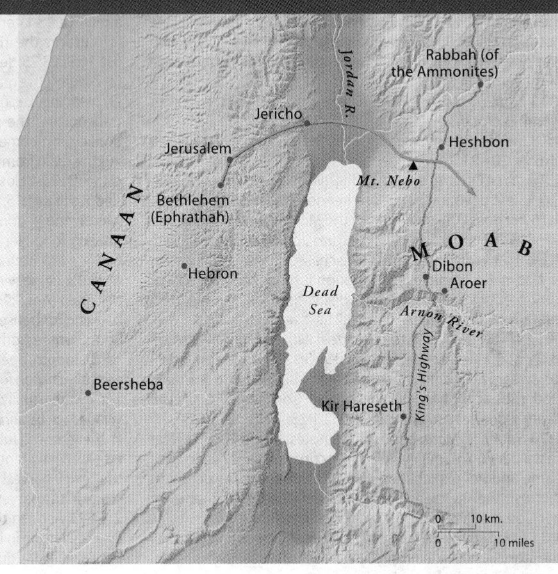

[8]Then Naomi said to her two daughters-in-law, "Go back, each of you, to your mother's home.[r] May the LORD show you kindness,[s] as you have shown kindness to your dead husbands[t] and to me. [9]May the LORD grant that each of you will find rest[u] in the home of another husband."

Then she kissed[v] them goodbye and they wept aloud[w] [10]and said to her, "We will go back with you to your people."

[11]But Naomi said, "Return home, my daughters. Why would you come with me? Am I going to have any more sons, who could become your husbands?[x] [12]Return home, my daughters; I am too old to have another husband. Even if I thought there was still hope for me—even if I had a husband tonight and then gave birth to sons— [13]would you wait until they grew up?[y] Would you remain unmarried for them? No, my daughters. It is more bitter[z] for me than for you, because the LORD's hand has turned against me![a]"

[14]At this they wept[b] aloud again. Then Orpah kissed her mother-in-law[c] goodbye,[d] but Ruth clung to her.[e]

[15]"Look," said Naomi, "your sister-in-law[f] is going back to her people and her gods.[g] Go back with her."

[16]But Ruth replied, "Don't urge me to leave you[h] or to turn back from you. Where you go I will go,[i] and where you stay I will stay. Your people will be my people[j] and your God my God.[k] [17]Where you die I will die, and there I will be buried. May the LORD deal with me, be it ever so severely,[l] if even death separates you and me."[m] [18]When Naomi realized that Ruth was determined to go with her, she stopped urging her.[n]

[19]So the two women went on until they came to Bethlehem.[o] When they arrived in Bethlehem, the whole town was stirred[p] because of them, and the women exclaimed, "Can this be Naomi?"

[20]"Don't call me Naomi,[a]" she told them. "Call me Mara,[b] because the Almighty[c][q] has made my life very bitter.[r] [21]I went away full, but the LORD has brought me back empty.[s] Why call me Naomi? The LORD has afflicted[d] me;[t] the Almighty has brought misfortune upon me."

[22]So Naomi returned from Moab accompanied by Ruth the Moabite,[u] her daughter-in-law,[v] arriving in Bethlehem as the barley harvest[w] was beginning.[x]

Ruth Meets Boaz in the Grain Field

2 Now Naomi had a relative[y] on her husband's side, a man of standing[z] from the clan of Elimelek,[a] whose name was Boaz.[b]

[a] *20 Naomi* means *pleasant.* [b] *20 Mara* means *bitter.* [c] *20* Hebrew *Shaddai*; also in verse 21 [d] *21* Or *has testified against*

1:8 [r]Ge 38:11 [s]S Ge 19:19; 2Ti 1:16 [t]S ver 5 **1:9** [u]Ru 3:1 [v]S Ge 27:27; S 29:11 [w]S Ge 27:38; S Nu 25:6 **1:11** [x]Ge 38:11; Dt 25:5 **1:13** [y]Ge 38:11 [z]ver 20; Ex 1:14; 15:23; 1Sa 30:6 [a]S Jdg 2:15; S Job 4:5 **1:14** [b]ver 9 [c]Ru 2:11; 3:1; Mic 7:6 [d]S Ge 31:28 [e]S Dt 10:20 **1:15** [f]Dt 25:7 [g]S Jos 24:14 **1:16** [h]2Ki 2:2 [i]Ge 24:58 [j]Ps 45:10 [k]S Jos 24:15 **1:17** [l]1Sa 3:17; 14:44; 20:13; 25:22; 2Sa 3:9, 35; 2Sa 19:13; 1Ki 2:23; 19:2; 20:10; 2Ki 6:31 [m]2Sa 15:21 **1:18** [n]Ac 21:14 **1:19** [o]S Jdg 17:7 [p]Mt 21:10 **1:20** [q]S Ge 15:1; S 17:1; Ps 91:1 [r]S ver 13 **1:21** [s]Job 1:21 [t]Job 30:11; Ps 88:7; Isa 53:4 **1:22** [u]Ru 2:2, 6, 21; 4:5, 10 [v]S Ge 11:31 [w]S Ex 9:31; S Lev 19:9 [x]2Sa 21:9 **2:1** [y]Ru 3:2; Pr 7:4 [z]1Sa 9:1; 1Ki 11:28 [a]S Ru 1:2 [b]Ru 4:21; 1Ch 2:12; Mt 1:5; Lk 3:32

1:8 *Go back.* Desolate Naomi repeatedly urges her daughters-in-law to return to their original homes in Moab (here; vv. 11–12,15); she has nothing to offer them.

1:11 *sons, who could become your husbands.* Naomi alludes to the Israelite law (Dt 25:5–6) regarding levirate marriage (see notes on Ge 38:8; Dt 25:5–10; see also Mk 12:18–23), which was given to protect the widow and guarantee continuance of the family line.

1:12 *I am too old.* Naomi can have no more sons; even her womb is empty.

1:13 *the LORD's hand ... against me.* See notes on vv. 5–6; see also vv. 20–21.

1:14 Orpah's departure highlights the loyalty and selfless devotion of Ruth to her desolate mother-in-law.

1:15 *her gods.* The chief god of the Moabites was Chemosh.

1:16 This classic expression of loyalty and love discloses Ruth's true character. Her commitment to Naomi is complete, even though it holds no prospect for her except to share in Naomi's desolation. For a similar declaration of devotion, see 2Sa 15:21.

1:17 *May the LORD deal with me, be it ever so severely.* See note on 1Sa 3:17. Ruth, a non-Israelite, swears her commitment to Naomi in the name of Israel's God, thus acknowledging him as her God (see v. 16). *if even death separates you and me.* Cf. 2Sa 1:23.

1:20 *Naomi ... Mara.* See NIV text notes. In the ancient Near East a person's name was often descriptive. Naomi's choice of name and her explanation for it provide the most poignant disclosure of her sense of desolation—it seems that even her God is against her. *Almighty.* See note on Ge 17:1.

1:21 *full ... empty.* These words highlight the central theme of the story—how the empty Naomi becomes full again.

1:22 *Ruth the Moabite.* Several times the author reminds the reader that Ruth is a foreigner from a despised people (2:2,6,21; 4:5,10; see 2:10). *harvest.* Harvesting grain in ancient Canaan took place in April and May (barley first, wheat a few weeks later; see 2:23). It involved the following steps: (1) cutting the ripened standing grain with hand sickles (Dt 16:9; 23:25; Jer 50:16; Joel 3:13)—usually done by men; (2) binding the grain into sheaves—usually done by women; (3) gleaning, i.e., gathering stalks of grain left behind (2:7); (4) transporting the sheaves to the threshing floor—often by donkey, sometimes by cart (Am 2:13); (5) threshing, i.e., loosening the grain from the straw—usually done by the treading of cattle (Dt 25:4; Hos 10:11), but sometimes by toothed threshing sledges (Isa 41:15; Am 1:3) or the wheels of carts (Isa 28:28); (6) winnowing—done by tossing the grain into the air with winnowing forks (Jer 15:7) so that the wind, which usually came up for a few hours in the afternoon, blew away the straw and chaff (Ps 1:4), leaving the grain at the winnower's feet; (7) sifting the grain (Am 9:9) to remove any residual foreign matter; (8) bagging for transportation and storage (Ge 42–44). Threshing floors, where both threshing and winnowing occurred, were hard, smooth, open places, prepared on either rock or clay and carefully chosen for favorable exposure to the prevailing winds. They were usually on the east side—i.e., downwind—of the village. *was beginning.* Naomi and Ruth arrive in Bethlehem just as the renewed fullness of the land is beginning to be harvested—an early hint that Naomi will be full again. Reference to the barley harvest also prepares the reader for the next major scene in the harvest fields (see Introduction: Literary Features).

2:1–23 Act II in the drama: What is done by Ruth and Boaz awakens hope in Naomi's heart.

2:1 *relative.* A sign of hope (see note on v. 20). *man of stand-*

2 And Ruth the Moabite[c] said to Naomi,
"Let me go to the fields and pick up the
leftover grain[d] behind anyone in whose
eyes I find favor.[e]"
Naomi said to her, "Go ahead, my
daughter." 3 So she went out, entered a
field and began to glean behind the harvesters.[f] As it turned out, she was working in a field belonging to Boaz, who was
from the clan of Elimelek.[g]
4 Just then Boaz arrived from Bethlehem
and greeted the harvesters, "The LORD be
with you![h]"
"The LORD bless you![i]" they answered.
5 Boaz asked the overseer of his harvesters, "Who does that young woman
belong to?"
6 The overseer replied, "She is the Moabite[j] who came back from Moab with Naomi. 7 She said, 'Please let me glean and
gather among the sheaves[k] behind the harvesters.' She came into the field and has
remained here from morning till now, except for a short rest[l] in the shelter."
8 So Boaz said to Ruth, "My daughter,
listen to me. Don't go and glean in another field and don't go away from here. Stay
here with the women who work for me.
9 Watch the field where the men are harvesting, and follow along after the wom-
en. I have told the men not to lay a hand
on you. And whenever you are thirsty, go
and get a drink from the water jars the
men have filled."
10 At this, she bowed down with her face
to the ground.[m] She asked him, "Why have
I found such favor in your eyes that you
notice me[n]—a foreigner?[o]"
11 Boaz replied, "I've been told all about
what you have done for your mother-in-
law[p] since the death of your husband[q]—
how you left your father and mother and
your homeland and came to live with a
people you did not know[r] before.[s] 12 May
the LORD repay you for what you have
done. May you be richly rewarded by the
LORD,[t] the God of Israel,[u] under whose
wings[v] you have come to take refuge.[w]"
13 "May I continue to find favor in your
eyes,[x] my lord," she said. "You have put
me at ease by speaking kindly to your servant—though I do not have the standing
of one of your servants."
14 At mealtime Boaz said to her, "Come
over here. Have some bread[y] and dip it in
the wine vinegar."
When she sat down with the harvesters,[z] he offered her some roasted grain.[a]
She ate all she wanted and had some left
over.[b] 15 As she got up to glean, Boaz gave
orders to his men, "Let her gather among
the sheaves[c] and don't reprimand her.
16 Even pull out some stalks for her from
the bundles and leave them for her to pick
up, and don't rebuke[d] her."
17 So Ruth gleaned in the field until evening. Then she threshed[e] the barley she
had gathered, and it amounted to about
an ephah.[a][f] 18 She carried it back to town,
and her mother-in-law saw how much she
had gathered. Ruth also brought out and
gave her what she had left over[g] after she
had eaten enough.
19 Her mother-in-law asked her, "Where
did you glean today? Where did you work?
Blessed be the man who took notice of
you![h]"
Then Ruth told her mother-in-law about
the one at whose place she had been
working. "The name of the man I worked
with today is Boaz," she said.
20 "The LORD bless him![i]" Naomi said to
her daughter-in-law.[j] "He has not stopped
showing his kindness[k] to the living and
the dead." She added, "That man is our

[a] *17* That is, probably about 30 pounds or about 13 kilograms

2:2 [c] S Ru 1:22 [d] S Lev 19:9; S 23:22 [e] S Ge 6:8; S 18:3
2:3 [f] ver 14; 2Ki 4:18; Jer 9:22; Am 9:13 [g] ver 1
2:4 [h] S Jdg 6:12; Lk 1:28; 2Th 3:16 [i] S Ge 28:3; S Nu 6:24
2:6 [j] S Ru 1:22
2:7 [k] S Ge 37:7; S Lev 19:9 [l] 2Sa 4:5
2:10 [m] S Ge 19:1; S 1Sa 20:41 [n] ver 19; Ps 41:1 [o] S Ge 31:15; S Dt 15:3
2:11 [p] S Ru 1:14 [q] S Ru 1:5 [r] Isa 55:5 [s] Ru 1:16-17
2:12 [t] 1Sa 24:19; 26:23, 25; Ps 18:20; Pr 25:22; Jer 31:16 [u] S Jos 24:15 [v] Ps 17:8; 36:7; 57:1; 61:4; 63:7; 91:4 [w] Ps 71:1
2:13 [x] S Ge 18:3
2:14 [y] S Ge 3:19 [z] S ver 3 [a] S Lev 23:14 [b] ver 18
2:15 [c] S Ge 37:7; S Lev 19:9
2:16 [d] S Ge 37:10
2:17 [e] S Jdg 6:11 [f] S Lev 19:36
2:18 [g] ver 14
2:19 [h] S ver 10
2:20 [i] S Jdg 17:2; S 1Sa 23:21 [j] S Ge 11:31 [k] S Ge 19:19

ing. See note on 3:11. *Boaz.* Probably means "In him is strength." Boaz (see 4:21 and note on 4:18–22) is included in both genealogies of Jesus (Mt 1:5; Lk 3:32).

2:2 *Let me go.* Although Ruth is a foreigner and, as a young woman alone, is obviously quite vulnerable in the harvest fields, she undertakes to provide for her mother-in-law. In 3:1 Naomi undertakes to provide for Ruth. *pick up the leftover grain.* The law of Moses instructed landowners to leave what the harvesters missed so that the poor, the foreigner, the widow and the fatherless could glean for their needs (Lev 19:9; 23:22; Dt 24:19). See photo, p. 392.

2:3 *As it turned out.* Divine providence is at work (vv. 19–20).

2:4 The exchange of greetings between Boaz and his laborers characterizes Boaz as a godly man with a kind spirit.

2:9 *follow along after the women.* It was customary for the men to cut the grain and for the female servants to go behind them to bind the grain into sheaves. Then Ruth could glean what they had left behind (see note on 1:22). *not to lay a hand on you.* This little word from Boaz indicates the risk Ruth had taken and discloses the measure of Boaz's care for her.

2:11 *what you have done for your mother-in-law.* Ruth's commitment to care for her desolate mother-in-law remains the center of attention throughout the book.

2:12 *under whose wings.* A figure of a bird protecting her young under her wings (see Mt 23:37; see also note on 3:9).

2:13 *your servant.* A polite reference to herself.

2:15 *gave orders to his men.* Boaz goes beyond the requirement of the law in making sure that Ruth's labors are abundantly productive (see 3:15 and note).

2:17 *threshed.* See note on 1:22. In Ruth's case, as in that of Gideon (Jdg 6:11), the amount was small and could be threshed by hand simply by beating it with a club or stick. *ephah.* See NIV text note; an unusually large amount for one day's gleaning.

2:20 *He has not stopped showing his kindness.* In 3:10 Boaz credits Ruth with demonstrating this same virtue. *guardian-redeemers.* See NIV text note. Redemption is a key concept in Ruth (see Introduction:

close relative;[l] he is one of our guardian-
redeemers.[am]"
[21]Then Ruth the Moabite[n] said, "He
even said to me, 'Stay with my workers
until they finish harvesting all my grain.' "
[22]Naomi said to Ruth her daughter-in-
law, "It will be good for you, my daughter,
to go with the women who work for him,
because in someone else's field you might
be harmed."
[23]So Ruth stayed close to the women of
Boaz to glean until the barley[o] and wheat
harvests[p] were finished. And she lived
with her mother-in-law.

Ruth and Boaz at the Threshing Floor

3 One day Ruth's mother-in-law Naomi[q] said to her, "My daughter, I must
find a home[br] for you, where you will be
well provided for. [2]Now Boaz, with whose
women you have worked, is a relative[s] of
ours. Tonight he will be winnowing barley on the threshing floor.[t] [3]Wash,[u] put
on perfume,[v] and get dressed in your best
clothes.[w] Then go down to the threshing
floor, but don't let him know you are there
until he has finished eating and drinking.[x]
[4]When he lies down, note the place where
he is lying. Then go and uncover his feet
and lie down. He will tell you what to do."
[5]"I will do whatever you say,"[y] Ruth answered. [6]So she went down to the threshing floor[z] and did everything her mother-
in-law told her to do.
[7]When Boaz had finished eating and
drinking and was in good spirits,[a] he went
over to lie down at the far end of the grain
pile.[b] Ruth approached quietly, uncovered
his feet and lay down. [8]In the middle of
the night something startled the man; he
turned—and there was a woman lying at
his feet!
[9]"Who are you?" he asked.
"I am your servant Ruth," she said.
"Spread the corner of your garment[c] over
me, since you are a guardian-redeemer[cd]
of our family."
[10]"The LORD bless you,[e] my daughter,"
he replied. "This kindness is greater than
that which you showed earlier:[f] You have
not run after the younger men, whether rich or poor. [11]And now, my daughter, don't be afraid. I will do for you all
you ask. All the people of my town know
that you are a woman of noble character.[g]
[12]Although it is true that I am a guardian-
redeemer of our family,[h] there is another
who is more closely related than[i] I. [13]Stay
here for the night, and in the morning if
he wants to do his duty as your guardian-
redeemer,[j] good; let him redeem you. But
if he is not willing, as surely as the LORD
lives[k] I will do it.[l] Lie here until morning."

2:20 [l]S Lev 25:25 [m]Ru 3:9, 12; 4:1, 14 **2:21** [n]S Ru 1:22 **2:23** [o]S Ex 9:31 [p]S Ge 30:14; S 1Sa 6:13 **3:1** [q]Ru 1:14 [r]Ru 1:9 **3:2** [s]S Ru 2:1 [t]S Lev 2:14; S Nu 18:27; S Jdg 6:11 **3:3** [u]2Sa 12:20; 2Ki 5:10; Ps 26:6; 51:2; Isa 1:16; Jer 4:14; Eze 16:9 [v]2Sa 14:2; Isa 61:3 [w]S Ge 41:14 [x]S Ex 32:6; S Ecc 2:3; S Jer 15:17 **3:5** [y]Eph 6:1; Col 3:20 **3:6** [z]S Nu 18:27 **3:7** [a]Jdg 19:6, 9, 22; 1Sa 25:36; 2Sa 13:28; 1Ki 21:7; Est 1:10 [b]2Ch 31:6; SS 7:2; Jer 50:26; Hag 2:16 **3:9** [c]Eze 16:8 [d]S Ru 2:20 **3:10** [e]S Jdg 17:2 [f]S Jos 2:12 **3:11** [g]Pr 12:4; 14:1; 31:10 **3:12** [h]S Ru 2:20 [i]Ru 4:1 **3:13** [j]Dt 25:5; Ru 4:5; Mt 22:24 [k]S Nu 14:21; Hos 4:15 [l]Ru 4:6

[a] *20* The Hebrew word for *guardian-redeemer* is a legal term for one who has the obligation to redeem a relative in serious difficulty (see Lev. 25:25-55). [b] *1* Hebrew *find rest* (see 1:9) [c] *9* The Hebrew word for *guardian-redeemer* is a legal term for one who has the obligation to redeem a relative in serious difficulty (see Lev. 25:25-55); also in verses 12 and 13.

Themes and Theology). The guardian-redeemer was responsible for protecting the interests of needy members of the extended family (see note on Isa 41:14)—e.g., to provide an heir for a brother who had died (Dt 25:5–10), to redeem land that a poor relative had sold outside the family (Lev 25:25–28), to redeem a relative who had been sold into slavery (Lev 25:47–49) and to avenge the killing of a relative (Nu 35:19–21; "avenger" and "guardian-redeemer" are translations of the same Hebrew word). When Naomi hears about the day's events, she takes courage. This moment of her awakened hope is the crucial turning point of the story (see Introduction: Literary Features).
2:23 *until the barley and wheat harvests were finished.* This phrase rounds out the harvest episode and prepares for the next major scene on the threshing floor (see Introduction: Literary Features).
3:1–18 Act III in the drama: Hopeful Naomi takes the initiative.
3:2 *Tonight he will be winnowing.* See note on 1:22. In the threshing season it was customary for the landowner and his men to spend the night near the threshing floor to protect his grain from theft.
3:3 Ruth is instructed to prepare herself like a bride (see Eze 16:9–12 and notes). *go down to the threshing floor.* At winnowing time the threshing floor was a place for male camaraderie and revelry (v. 14). *eating and drinking.* Harvest was a time of festivity (Isa 9:3; 16:9–10; Jer 48:33).
3:4 *uncover his feet and lie down.* Although Naomi's instructions may appear forward, the moral integrity of Naomi, Ruth and Boaz is never in doubt (see v. 11). Naomi's advice to Ruth is clearly for the purpose of appealing to Boaz's guardian-redeemer obligation. Ruth's actions were a request for marriage. Tamar, the mother of Perez (4:12), had also laid claim to the provision of the levirate (or guardian-redeemer) law (Ge 38:13–30).
3:9 *Spread the corner of your garment over me.* A request for marriage (see Eze 16:8); a similar custom is still practiced in some parts of the Middle East today. With a striking play on words Ruth confronts Boaz with his moral obligations. In the harvest field he had wished her well at the hands of the Lord "under whose wings you have come to take refuge" (2:12). Now on the threshing floor Ruth asks him to spread the "wings" (i.e., the corners) of his garment over her. Boaz is vividly reminded that he must serve as the Lord's protective wings over Ruth.
3:10 *kindness ... you showed earlier.* See 2:11–12; see also note on 2:20.
3:11 *woman of noble character.* See Pr 12:4; 31:10, the only other places where the Hebrew for this phrase occurs in the OT. The Hebrew for "noble character" is the same as that used to describe Boaz in 2:1; thus the author maintains a balance between his descriptions of Ruth and Boaz.
3:12 *another ... more closely related.* How Boaz was related to Ruth's former husband (Mahlon) is unknown, but the closest male relative had the primary responsibility to marry a widow. Naomi instructed Ruth to approach Boaz because he had already shown himself willing to be Ruth's protector. Boaz, however, would not bypass the directives of the law, which clearly gave priority to the nearest relative.
3:13 *as surely as the LORD lives.* Boaz commits himself by oath (cf. 1:17 and note) to redeem the family property and to arrange Ruth's honorable marriage.

[14]So she lay at his feet until morning, but
got up before anyone could be recognized;
and he said, "No one must know that a
woman came to the threshing floor.[m]"[n]
[15]He also said, "Bring me the shawl[o]
you are wearing and hold it out." When
she did so, he poured into it six measures
of barley and placed the bundle on her.
Then he[a] went back to town.
[16]When Ruth came to her mother-in-law, Naomi asked, "How did it go, my
daughter?"
Then she told her everything Boaz
had done for her [17]and added, "He gave
me these six measures of barley, saying,
'Don't go back to your mother-in-law
empty-handed.'"
[18]Then Naomi said, "Wait, my daughter,
until you find out what happens. For the man will not rest until the matter is settled today."[p]

3:14 [m]S Nu 18:27 [n]Ro 14:16; 2Co 8:21 **3:15** [o]Isa 3:22 **3:18** [p]Ps 37:3-5 **4:1** [q]S Ge 18:1; S 23:10 [r]S Ru 2:20 [s]Ru 3:12 **4:2** [t]S Ex 3:16 [u]S Dt 25:7

Boaz Marries Ruth

4 Meanwhile Boaz went up to the town gate[q] and sat down there just as the guardian-redeemer[b][r] he had mentioned[s] came along. Boaz said, "Come over here, my friend, and sit down." So he went over and sat down.
[2]Boaz took ten of the elders[t] of the town and said, "Sit here," and they did so.[u]

[a] *15* Most Hebrew manuscripts; many Hebrew manuscripts, Vulgate and Syriac *she* [b] *1* The Hebrew word for *guardian-redeemer* is a legal term for one who has the obligation to redeem a relative in serious difficulty (see Lev. 25:25-55); also in verses 3, 6, 8 and 14.

3:15 Boaz goes beyond the requirement of the law in supplying Ruth with grain from the threshing floor (see 2:15–16).
3:17 *empty-handed.* Again the empty-full motif (see note on 1:21).
3:18 *Wait.* The Hebrew underlying this word is translated "sat" in 4:1. Thus the author prepares the reader for the next major scene, in which Boaz sits at the town gate to see the matter through.
4:1–12 Act IV in the drama: Boaz arranges to fulfill his pledge to Ruth.
4:1 *town gate.* The "town hall" of ancient Israel, the normal place for business and legal transactions, where witnesses were readily available (vv. 9–12; see note on Ge 19:1; see also photo below). *my friend.* The other relative remains unnamed.
4:2 *ten of the elders.* A full court for legal proceedings.

Gate chamber at Arad showing bench (middle left) where people would sit to conduct business. It was at the "town gate" (Ru 4:1) in Bethlehem where Boaz announced to the elders that he bought Naomi's property and took Ruth as his wife.

Kim Walton

3 Then he said to the guardian-redeemer,
"Naomi, who has come back from Moab,
is selling the piece of land that belonged to
our relative Elimelek.[v] 4 I thought I should
bring the matter to your attention and
suggest that you buy it in the presence of
these seated here and in the presence of
the elders of my people. If you will redeem
it, do so. But if you[a] will not, tell me, so I
will know. For no one has the right to do it
except you,[w] and I am next in line."
"I will redeem it," he said.
5 Then Boaz said, "On the day you buy
the land from Naomi, you also acquire
Ruth the Moabite,[x] the[b] dead man's widow, in order to maintain the name of the
dead with his property."[y]
6 At this, the guardian-redeemer said,
"Then I cannot redeem[z] it because I might
endanger my own estate. You redeem it
yourself. I cannot do it."[a]
7 (Now in earlier times in Israel, for the
redemption[b] and transfer of property to
become final, one party took off his sandal[c] and gave it to the other. This was the
method of legalizing transactions[d] in Israel.)[e]
8 So the guardian-redeemer said to Boaz,
"Buy it yourself." And he removed his sandal.[f]
9 Then Boaz announced to the elders
and all the people, "Today you are witnesses[g] that I have bought from Naomi all
the property of Elimelek, Kilion and Mahlon. 10 I have also acquired Ruth the Moabite,[h] Mahlon's widow, as my wife,[i] in order
to maintain the name of the dead with his
property, so that his name will not disappear from among his family or from his
hometown.[j] Today you are witnesses![k]"
11 Then the elders and all the people at
the gate[l] said, "We are witnesses.[m] May
the LORD make the woman who is coming into your home like Rachel and Leah,[n]
who together built up the family of Israel.
May you have standing in Ephrathah[o] and
be famous in Bethlehem.[p] 12 Through the
offspring the LORD gives you by this young
woman, may your family be like that of
Perez,[q] whom Tamar[r] bore to Judah."

Naomi Gains a Son

13 So Boaz took Ruth and she became
his wife. When he made love to her, the
LORD enabled her to conceive,[s] and she
gave birth to a son.[t] 14 The women[u] said
to Naomi: "Praise be to the LORD,[v] who
this day has not left you without a guardian-redeemer.[w] May he become famous
throughout Israel! 15 He will renew your
life and sustain you in your old age. For
your daughter-in-law,[x] who loves you and
who is better to you than seven sons,[y] has
given him birth."

4:3 [v] S Lev 25:25; S Ru 1:2 **4:4** [w] S Lev 25:25; Jer 32:7-8 **4:5** [x] S Ru 1:22 [y] S Ge 38:8; S Ru 3:13 **4:6** [z] Lev 25:25; Ru 3:13 [a] S Dt 25:7 **4:7** [b] S Lev 25:24 [c] ver 8 [d] Isa 8:1-2,16,20 [e] Dt 25:7-9 **4:8** [f] Dt 25:9 **4:9** [g] Isa 8:2; Jer 32:10,44 **4:10** [h] S Ru 1:22 [i] S Dt 25:5 [j] S Dt 25:6 [k] S Jos 24:22 **4:11** [l] S Ge 23:10 [m] S Dt 25:9 [n] S Ge 4:19; S 29:16 [o] S Ge 35:16 [p] Ru 1:19 **4:12** [q] S Ge 38:29 [r] Ge 38:6,24 **4:13** [s] S Ge 8:1; S 29:31 [t] S Ge 29:32; S 30:6; Lk 1:57 **4:14** [u] Lk 1:58 [v] S Ge 24:27 [w] S Ru 2:20 **4:15** [x] S Ge 11:31 [y] 1Sa 1:8; 2:5; Job 1:2

[a] 4 Many Hebrew manuscripts, Septuagint, Vulgate and Syriac; most Hebrew manuscripts *he* [b] 5 Vulgate and Syriac; Hebrew (see also Septuagint) *Naomi and from Ruth the Moabite, you acquire the*

4:3 *selling the piece of land.* See note on 2:20. Two interpretations are possible: (1) Naomi owns the land but is so destitute that she is forced to sell. It was the duty of the guardian-redeemer to buy any land in danger of being sold outside the family. (2) Naomi does not own the land — it had been sold by Elimelek before the family left for Moab — but by law she retains the right of redemption to buy the land back. Lacking funds to do so herself, she is dependent on a guardian-redeemer to do it for her. It is the right of redemption that Naomi is "selling."

4:5 *you also acquire … the dead man's widow.* Now Boaz reveals the other half of the obligation — the acquisition of Ruth. Levirate law (Dt 25:5 – 6; see note on Lev 25:25) provided that Ruth's firstborn son would keep Mahlon's name alive and retain ownership of the family inheritance.

4:6 *I cannot redeem it.* Possibly he fears that, if he has a son by her and if that son is his only surviving heir, his own property will transfer to the family of Elimelek (see note on Ge 38:9). In that case his risk was no greater than that assumed by Boaz. This relative's refusal to assume the guardian-redeemer's role highlights the kindness and generosity of Boaz toward the two widows — just as Orpah's return to her family highlights Ruth's selfless devotion and loyalty to Naomi.

4:7 *one party took off his sandal.* The process of renouncing one's property rights and passing them to another was publicly attested by taking off a sandal and transferring it to the new owner (cf. Am 2:6; 8:6). The Nuzi documents (see chart, p. xxiv) refer to a similar custom.

4:9 *witnesses.* The role of public witnesses was to attest to all legal transactions and other binding agreements.

4:10 *name of the dead.* See Dt 25:5 – 7 and notes.

4:11 *Rachel and Leah … built up the family of Israel.* Cf. Dt 25:9. The Israelite readers of Ruth would have associated the house of Jacob (Israel), built up by Rachel and Leah, with the house of Israel, rebuilt by David, the descendant of Ruth and Boaz, after it had been threatened with extinction (1Sa 4). They also knew that the Lord had covenanted to "build" the house of David as an enduring dynasty, through which Israel's blessed destiny would be assured (see 2Sa 7:27 – 29). *Ephrathah.* See note on 1:2.

4:12 *Perez, whom Tamar bore to Judah.* Perez was Boaz's ancestor (vv. 18 – 21; Mt 1:3; Lk 3:33). His birth to Judah was from a union based on the levirate practice (Ge 38:27 – 30; see note on 1:11). Perez was therefore an appropriate model within Boaz's ancestry for the blessing the elders gave to Boaz. Moreover, the descendants of Perez had raised the tribe of Judah to a prominent place in Israel. So the blessing of the elders — that, through the offspring Ruth would bear to Boaz, his family would be like that of Perez — was fully realized in David and his dynasty. Thus also v. 12 prepares the reader for the events briefly narrated in the conclusion.

4:13 – 17 The conclusion of the story balances the introduction (1:1 – 5): (1) In the Hebrew both have the same number of words; (2) both compress much into a short space; (3) both focus on Naomi; (4) the introduction emphasizes Naomi's emptiness, and the conclusion portrays her fullness.

4:13 *the LORD enabled her to conceive.* See note on 1:6.

4:14 *guardian-redeemer.* The child Obed, as vv. 15 – 17 make clear. *May he become famous.* This same wish is expressed concerning Boaz in v. 11.

4:15 *better to you than seven sons.* See 1Sa 1:8. Since seven

16 Then Naomi took the child in her arms and cared for him.
17 The women living there said, "Naomi has a son!" And they named him Obed. He was the father of Jesse,[z] the father of David.[a]

The Genealogy of David

4:18-22pp — 1Ch 2:5-15; Mt 1:3-6; Lk 3:31-33

18 This, then, is the family line of Perez[b]:

Perez was the father of Hezron,[c]
19 Hezron the father of Ram,
Ram the father of Amminadab,[d]
20 Amminadab the father of Nahshon,[e]
Nahshon the father of Salmon,[a]
21 Salmon the father of Boaz,[f]
Boaz the father of Obed,
22 Obed the father of Jesse,
and Jesse the father of David.

4:17 [z] ver 22; 1Sa 16:1, 18; 17:12, 17, 58; 1Ch 2:12, 13; Ps 72:20 [a] 1Sa 16:13; 1Ch 2:15
4:18 [b] S Ge 38:29 [c] Nu 26:21
4:19 [d] S Ex 6:23
4:20 [e] S Nu 7:12
4:21 [f] S Ru 2:1

[a] *20* A few Hebrew manuscripts, some Septuagint manuscripts and Vulgate (see also verse 21 and Septuagint of 1 Chron. 2:11); most Hebrew manuscripts *Salma*

was considered a number of completeness, to have seven sons was the epitome of all family blessings in Israel (see 1Sa 2:5; Job 1:2; 42:13). Ruth's selfless devotion to Naomi receives its climactic acknowledgment.

4:16 *took the child in her arms.* Possibly symbolizing adoption (see v. 17 and note on Ge 30:3).

4:17 *Naomi has a son.* Through Ruth, aged Naomi, who can no longer bear children, obtains an heir in place of Mahlon. *Obed.* The name means "servant," in its full form possibly "servant of the LORD."

4:18–22 See 1Ch 2:5–15; Mt 1:3–6; Lk 3:31–33. Like the genealogies of Ge 5:3–32; 11:10–26, this genealogy has ten names (see note on Ge 5:5). It brings to mind the reign of David, during which, in contrast to the turbulent period of the judges recalled in 1:1, Israel finally entered into rest in the promised land (see 1Ki 5:4 and note). It signifies that just as Naomi was brought from emptiness to fullness through the selfless love of Ruth and Boaz, so the Lord brought Israel from unrest to rest through their descendant David, who selflessly gave himself to fight Israel's battles on the Lord's behalf. The ultimate end of this genealogy is Jesus Christ, the great "son of David" (Mt 1:1; see note there), who fulfills prophecy and will bring the Lord's people into final rest (see Introduction to Joshua: Title and Theological Theme; see also Heb 3:7—4:11 and notes).

1 SAMUEL

INTRODUCTION

Title

1 and 2 Samuel are named after the person God used to establish monarchy in Israel. Samuel not only anointed both Saul and David, Israel's first two kings, but he also gave definition to the new order of God's rule over Israel. Samuel's role as God's representative in this period of Israel's history is close to that of Moses (see Ps 99:6; Jer 15:1 and notes) since he, more than any other person, provided for covenant continuity in the transition from the rule of the judges to that of the monarchy.

1 and 2 Samuel were originally one book. It was divided into two parts by the translators of the Septuagint (the pre-Christian Greek translation of the OT)—a division subsequently followed by Jerome (in the Latin Vulgate, c. AD 400) and by modern versions. The title of the book has varied from time to time, having been designated "The First and Second Books of Kingdoms" (Septuagint), "First and Second Kings" (Vulgate) and "First and Second Samuel" (Hebrew tradition and most modern versions).

a quick look

Author:
Unknown

Audience:
God's chosen people, the Israelites

Date:
Sometime after Israel was divided into the northern and southern kingdoms in about 930 BC

Theme:
The nation of Israel transitions from being led by God through "judges" to being led by him through kings.

Literary Features, Authorship and Date

Many questions have arisen pertaining to the literary character, authorship and date of 1,2 Samuel. Certain features of the book suggest that it was compiled with the use of a number of originally independent sources, which the author may have incorporated into his own composition as much as possible.

Who the author was cannot be known since the book itself gives no indication of his identity. Whoever he was, he doubtless had access to records of the life and times of Samuel, Saul and David. Explicit reference in the book itself is made to only one such source (the Book of Jashar, 2Sa 1:18), but the writer of Chronicles refers to four others that pertain to this period (the book of the annals of King David, 1Ch 27:24; the records of Samuel the seer; the records of Nathan the prophet; and the records of Gad the seer, 1Ch 29:29). For the dates of the period, see Chronology.

Contents and Theme: Kingship and Covenant

1 Samuel relates God's establishment of a political system in Israel headed by a human king. Before the author describes this momentous change in the structure of the theocracy (God's kingly rule over his people), he effectively depicts the complexity of its context. The following events provide both historical and theological background for the beginning of the monarchy:

(1) *The birth, youth and call of Samuel (chs. 1 – 3).* In a book dealing for the most part with the reigns of Israel's first two kings, Saul and David, it is significant that the author chose not to include a birth narrative of either of these men but to describe the birth of their forerunner and anointer, the prophet Samuel. This in itself accentuates the importance the author attached to Samuel's role in the events that follow. He seems to be saying in a subtle way that flesh and blood are to be subordinated to word and Spirit in the process of the establishment of kingship. For this reason chs. 1 – 3 should be viewed as integrally related to what follows, not as a more likely component of the book of Judges or as a loosely attached prefix to the rest of 1,2 Samuel. Kingship is given its birth and then nurtured by the prophetic word and work of the prophet Samuel. Moreover, the events of Samuel's nativity thematically anticipate the story of God's working that is narrated in the rest of the book.

(2) *The "ark narratives" (chs. 4 – 6).* This section describes how the ark of God was captured by the Philistines and then, after God had wreaked havoc on several Philistine cities, returned to Israel. These narratives reveal the folly of Israel's notion that possession of the ark automatically guaranteed victory over her enemies. They also display the awesome power of the Lord (Yahweh, the God of Israel) and his superiority over the Philistine god Dagon. The Philistines were forced to confess openly their helplessness against God's power by their return of the ark to Israel. The entire ark episode performs a vital function in placing Israel's subsequent sinful desire for a human king in proper perspective.

(3) *Samuel as a judge and deliverer (ch. 7).* When Samuel called Israel to repentance and renewed dedication to the Lord, the Lord intervened mightily in Israel's behalf and gave victory over the Philistines. This narrative reaffirms the authority of Samuel as a divinely ordained leader; at the same time it provides evidence of divine protection and blessing for God's people when they place their confidence in the Lord and live in obedience to their covenant obligations.

All the material in chs. 1 – 7 serves as a necessary preface for the narratives of chs. 8 – 12, which describe the rise and establishment of kingship in Israel. The author has masterfully arranged the stories in chs. 8 – 12 in order to emphasize the serious theological conflict surrounding the historical events. In the study of these chapters, scholars have often noted the presence of a tension or ambivalence in the attitude toward the monarchy: On the one hand, Samuel is commanded by the Lord to give the people a king (8:7,9,22; 9:16 – 17; 10:24; 12:13); on the other hand, their request for a king is considered a sinful rejection of the Lord (8:7; 10:19; 12:12,17,19 – 20). These seemingly conflicting attitudes toward the monarchy must be understood in the context of Israel's covenant relationship with the Lord.

Moses had anticipated Israel's desire for a human king (see Dt 17:14 – 20 and notes), but Israelite kingship was to be compatible with the continued rule of the Lord over his people as their Great King. Instead, when the elders asked Samuel to give them a king (8:5,19 – 20), they rejected the Lord's kingship over them. Their desire was for a king such as the nations around them had — to lead them in battle and give them a sense of national security and unity. The request for a king constituted a denial of their covenant relationship to the Lord, who was their King. Moreover, the Lord not only had promised to be their protector but had also repeatedly demonstrated his power in their behalf, most recently in the ark narratives (chs. 4 – 6), as well as in the great victory won over the Philistines under the leadership of Samuel (ch. 7).

Nevertheless the Lord instructed Samuel to give the people a king. By divine appointment Saul was brought into contact with Samuel, and Samuel was directed to anoint him privately as king (9:1 — 10:16). Subsequently, Samuel gathered the people at Mizpah, where, after again admonishing them concerning their sin in desiring a king (10:18 – 19), he presided over the selection of a king by lot. The lot fell on Saul and publicly designated him as the one whom God had chosen (10:24). Saul did not immediately assume his royal office but returned home to work his fields (11:5,7). When the inhabitants of Jabesh Gilead were threatened by Nahash the Ammonite, Saul rose to

Ruins at Shiloh, hometown of the priestly family of Eli and the location of the ark of the covenant (1Sa 1:1 – 20; see notes on 1:3,9).

When the elders of Israel asked Samuel to give them a king, they rejected the Lord's kingship over them.

the challenge, gathered an army and led Israel to victory in battle. His success placed a final seal of divine approval on Saul's selection to be king (cf. 10:24; 11:12–13) and occasioned the inauguration of his reign at Gilgal (11:14—12:25).

The question that still needed resolution, then, was not so much whether Israel should have a king (it was clearly the Lord's will to give them one), but rather how they could maintain their covenant with God (i.e., preserve the theocracy) now that they had a human king. The problem was resolved when Samuel called the people to repentance and renewal of their allegiance to the Lord on the very occasion of the inauguration of Saul (see note on 10:25). By establishing kingship in the context of covenant renewal, Samuel placed the monarchy in Israel on a radically different footing from that in surrounding nations. The king in Israel was not to be autonomous in his authority and power; rather, he was to be subject to the law of the Lord and the word of the prophet (10:25; 12:23). This was to be true not only for Saul but also for all the kings who would occupy the throne in Israel in the future. The king was to be an instrument of the Lord's rule over his people, and the people as well as the king were to continue to recognize the Lord as their ultimate Sovereign (see 12:14–15 and notes).

Saul soon demonstrated that he was unwilling to submit to the requirements of his theocratic office (chs. 13–15). When he disobeyed the instructions of the prophet Samuel in preparation for battle against the Philistines (see 13:13 and note), and when he refused to totally destroy the Amalekites as he had been commanded to do by the word of the Lord through Samuel (ch. 15), he ceased to be an instrument of the Lord's rule over his people. These abrogations of the requirements of his theocratic office led to his rejection as king (see 15:22–23 and notes).

The remainder of 1 Samuel (chs. 16–31) depicts the Lord's choice of David to be Saul's successor and then describes the long road by which David is prepared for accession to the throne. Although Saul's rule became increasingly antitheocratic in nature, David refused to usurp the throne by forceful means but left his accession to office in the Lord's hands. Eventually Saul was wounded in a battle with the Philistines and, fearing capture, took his own life. Three of Saul's sons, including David's loyal friend Jonathan, were killed in the same battle (ch. 31).

Chronology

Even though the narratives of 1,2 Samuel contain some statements of chronological import (see, e.g., 1Sa 6:1; 7:2; 8:1,5; 13:1; 25:1; 2Sa 2:10–11; 5:4–5; 14:28; 15:7), the data are insufficient to establish a precise chronology for the major events of this period of Israel's history. Except for the dates of David's birth and the duration of his reign, which are quite firm (see 2Sa 5:4–5), most other dates can only be approximated. The textual problem with the chronological data on the age of Saul when he became king and the length of his reign (see NIV text notes on 1Sa 13:1) contributes to uncertainty concerning the precise time of his birth and the beginning of his reign. No information is given concerning the time of Samuel's birth (1Sa 1:20) or death (25:1). His lifetime probably overlapped that of Samson and that of Obed, son of Ruth and Boaz and grandfather of David. It is indicated that he was well along in years when the elders of Israel asked him to give them a king (see 8:1,5 and note on 8:1).

One other factor contributing to chronological uncertainty is that the author has not always arranged his material in strict chronological sequence. It seems clear, e.g., that 2Sa 7 is to be placed

View of the Sorek Valley. The ark of the covenant was brought through the Sorek Valley on the return trip to the mountains of Judah (see map, p. 417).

www.HolyLandPhotos.org

chronologically after David's conquests described in 2Sa 8:1 – 14 (see notes on 2Sa 7:1; 8:1). The story of the famine sent by God on Israel during the reign of David because of Saul's violation of a treaty with the Gibeonites is found in 2Sa 21:1 – 14, though chronologically it occurred prior to the time of Absalom's rebellion recorded in 2Sa 15 – 18 (see further the notes on 2Sa 21:1 – 14). The following dates, however, provide an approximate chronological framework for the times of Samuel, Saul and David.

1105 BC	Birth of Samuel (1Sa 1:20)
1080	Birth of Saul
1050	Saul anointed to be king (1Sa 10:1)
1040	Birth of David
1025	David anointed to be Saul's successor (1Sa 16:1 – 13)
1010	Death of Saul and beginning of David's reign over Judah in Hebron (1Sa 31:4 – 6; 2Sa 2:1,4,11)
1003	Beginning of David's reign over all Israel and capture of Jerusalem (2Sa 5)
997 – 992	David's wars (2Sa 8:1 – 14)
991	Birth of Solomon (2Sa 12:24)
980	David's census (2Sa 24:1 – 9)
970	End of David's reign (2Sa 5:4 – 5; 1Ki 2:10 – 11)

Outline

I. The Nativity of Samuel and His Authentication as a Prophet "like Moses" (1:1—4:1a)
  A. Samuel's Birth: Hannah's Song (1:1—2:11)
  B. Samuel Contrasted with Eli's Sons (2:12–36)
  C. Samuel's Initiation and Recognition as a Prophet of the Lord (3:1—4:1a)
II. Israel without Faithful Leadership (4:1b—7:1)
  A. Israel's Loss of Both the Ark and the Chief Priestly Family (4:1b–22)
  B. God's Powerful Presence with His Ark in Philistia (ch. 5)
  C. The Ark's Return to Israel (6:1—7:1)
III. Samuel's Leadership as Prophet and Judge Characterized Illustratively (7:2–17)
IV. Establishment of the Monarchy in Israel (chs. 8–12)
  A. Israel's Request for a King like the Nations (ch. 8)
  B. Samuel Anoints Saul (9:1—10:8)
  C. Saul Publicly Chosen by Lot to Be King (10:9–27)
  D. Saul's Kingship Confirmed (ch. 11)
  E. Samuel's Resignation from His Role as Judge (ch. 12)
V. Saul's Reign Characterized Illustratively (chs. 13–14)
VI. Transition to David's Reign (15:1—2Sa 5:5)
  A. God's Rejection of Saul (ch. 15)
  B. Saul's Decline; David's Rise (chs. 16—2Sa 1)
    1. David's anointing by Samuel (16:1–13)
    2. Saul's dependence on David as musician and warrior (16:14—17:58)
    3. Saul's alienation from David; his family's protection of David (chs. 18–20)
    4. David's flight from Saul (chs. 21–22)
    5. Four tests of David's use of his growing power (chs. 23–26)
    6. David's flight to Philistia and Saul's final defeat by the Philistines (chs. 27–31)
    7. David's reaction to and lament over Saul's death (2Sa 1)
  C. David Becomes King over Judah (2:1—3:5)
  D. David Becomes King over All Israel (3:6—5:5)
VII. David's Reign Characterized Illustratively (5:6—8:18)
  A. David's Conquest of Jerusalem and His Recognition by the King of Tyre (5:6–16)
  B. David's Crushing of the Philistine Threat (5:17–25)
  C. David's Bringing the Ark into His Royal City (ch. 6)
  D. God's Covenant with David (ch. 7)
  E. David's Victories that Secure the Boundaries of His Kingdom (ch. 8)
VIII. Threats to David's Reign Overcome (chs. 9–20)
  A. David's Kindness to Saul's Remaining Heir (ch. 9)
  B. Defeat of the Ammonite-Aramean Challenge to David's Reign (10:1–19; 12:26–31)
  C. David's Shameful Abuse of His Royal Power in the Matter of Bathsheba and Uriah (11:1—12:25)

- D. Absalom's Challenge to David's Rule (chs. 13 – 20)
  - 1. Amnon's abuse of power and Absalom's revenge (ch. 13)
  - 2. Absalom's revolt crushed (chs. 14 – 19)
  - 3. Absalom's attempt sparks another unsuccessful revolt (ch. 20)
- IX. Sidebars to the David Story (Chiastically Arranged) (chs. 21 – 24)
  - A. God's Wrath against Israel because of Something Saul Had Done (21:1 – 14)
    - B. Exploits of David's Mighty Men in Wars against Philistines (21:15 – 22)
      - C. David's Song in Praise of the Lord for Victories Granted (ch. 22)
      - C'. David's "Last Words" that Speak of God's Ways with Him and His House (23:1 – 7)
    - B'. David's Mighty Men and Their Exploits, Especially against Philistines (23:8 – 39)
  - A'. God's Wrath against Israel because of Something David Did (ch. 24)

The Birth of Samuel

1 There was a certain man from Ramathaim,[a] a Zuphite[ab] from the hill country[c] of Ephraim,[d] whose name was Elkanah[e] son of Jeroham, the son of Elihu, the
son of Tohu, the son of Zuph, an Ephraimite. 2 He had two wives;[f] one was called
Hannah and the other Peninnah. Peninnah
had children, but Hannah had none.
3 Year after year[g] this man went up from
his town to worship[h] and sacrifice to the
LORD Almighty at Shiloh,[i] where Hophni
and Phinehas, the two sons of Eli,[j] were
priests of the LORD. 4 Whenever the day
came for Elkanah to sacrifice,[k] he would
give portions of the meat to his wife Peninnah and to all her sons and daughters.[l]
5 But to Hannah he gave a double portion[m]
because he loved her, and the LORD had
closed her womb.[n] 6 Because the LORD had
closed Hannah's womb, her rival kept provoking her in order to irritate her.[o] 7 This
went on year after year. Whenever Hannah went up to the house of the LORD, her
rival provoked her till she wept and would
not eat.[p] 8 Her husband Elkanah would say
to her, "Hannah, why are you weeping?
Why don't you eat? Why are you downhearted? Don't I mean more to you than
ten sons?[q]"
9 Once when they had finished eating
and drinking in Shiloh, Hannah stood up.
Now Eli the priest was sitting on his chair
by the doorpost of the LORD's house.[r] 10 In
her deep anguish[s] Hannah prayed to the
LORD, weeping bitterly. 11 And she made a
vow,[t] saying, "LORD Almighty[u], if you will
only look on your servant's misery and

1:1 [a] S Jos 18:25 [b] 1Sa 9:5 [c] Jos 17:17-18 [d] Jos 21:20-22 [e] 1Ch 6:27,34 **1:2** [f] S Ge 4:19 **1:3** [g] ver 21; Ex 23:14; 1Sa 2:19; 20:6, 29; Lk 2:41 [h] Dt 12:5-7 [i] S Jos 18:1 [j] 1Sa 2:31; 14:3 **1:4** [k] Lev 7:15-18; Dt 12:17-18 [l] S Ge 29:34 **1:5** [m] S Ge 37:3 [n] S Ge 11:30; S 29:31 **1:6** [o] S Ge 16:4 **1:7** [p] 2Sa 12:17; Ps 102:4 **1:8** [q] S Ru 4:15 **1:9** [r] 1Sa 3:3 **1:10** [s] Job 3:20; 7:11; 10:1; 21:25; 23:2; 27:2; Isa 38:15; Jer 20:18 **1:11** [t] S Jdg 11:30 [u] S Ge 17:1; Ps 24:10; 46:7; Isa 1:9

[a] *1* See Septuagint and 1 Chron. 6:26-27,33-35; or *from Ramathaim Zuphim.*

1:1—7:17 The birth of Samuel and his establishment in Israel as a prophet "like [Moses]" (Dt 18:18). The central thematic focus of 1,2 Samuel is on the author's account of the establishment of the monarchy in Israel and of God's elevation of David to the throne—God's "anointed" who completed the conquest of Canaan begun by Joshua, reinstated God's symbolic throne (the ark) into the center of Israel's life, secured Israel's boundaries on every side and provided for Israel a time of "rest" (see Dt 12:10; Jos 1:13,15 and note; 1Ki 5:4 and note) in the promised land. This account, however, is prefaced by the story of the prophet Samuel, whom God raised up in a time of crisis (see 12:9–11 and note) as he had raised up Moses when Israel was under oppression in Egypt. Just as the author of Exodus used his account of Moses' birth and early years to preface his story of God's deliverance of Israel from Egypt in the exodus because it in many ways foreshadowed the exodus event, so the author of 1,2 Samuel used the story of Samuel's nativity and youth because it foreshadowed—and illumined—much in what was to follow in his account (see notes on 1:27; 2:1–10; 2:1).

1:1 *Ramathaim.* The name occurs only here in the OT and appears to be another name for Ramah (see v. 19; 2:11; 7:17; 19:18; 25:1). It is perhaps to be identified with Arimathea (see Mt 27:57 and note; Jn 19:38). *Zuphite.* See NIV text note. It is not clear whether this word refers to the man or the place. If it refers to the man, it indicates his descent from Zuph (see later in this verse; see also 1Ch 6:34–35). If it refers to the place, it designates the general area in which Ramathaim was located (see 9:5). *Ephraimite.* Although Elkanah is here called an Ephraimite, he was probably a Levite whose family belonged to the Kohathite clans that had been allotted towns in Ephraim (see Jos 21:20–21; 1Ch 6:22–27).

1:2 *two wives.* See notes on Ge 4:19; 16:2; 25:6.

1:3 *Year after year this man went up.* Three times a year every Israelite male was required to appear before the Lord at the central sanctuary (Ex 23:14–19; 34:23; Dt 16:16–17). The festival referred to here was probably the Festival of Tabernacles, which not only commemorated God's care for his people during the wilderness journey to Canaan (see Lev 23:43) but more especially celebrated, with joy and feasting, God's blessing on the year's crops (see Dt 16:13–15). On such festive occasions Hannah's deep sorrow because of her own barrenness was the more poignant. *the LORD Almighty.* Traditionally "the LORD of hosts," a royal title. This is the first time in the Bible that God is so designated. It now becomes prominent at the onset of monarchy in Israel. The Hebrew for "host(s)" can refer to (1) human armies (Ex 7:4, "divisions"; Ps 44:9); (2) the celestial bodies such as the sun, moon and stars (Ge 2:1, "vast array"; Dt 4:19; Isa 40:26); or (3) the heavenly creatures such as angels (Jos 5:14; 1Ki 22:19; Ps 148:2). The title "the LORD of hosts" is perhaps best understood as a general reference to the sovereignty of God over all powers in the universe (hence the NIV rendering "the LORD Almighty"). In the account of the establishment of kingship in Israel it became particularly appropriate as a reference to God as the God of armies—both of the heavenly armies (cf. Dt 33:2; Jos 5:14; Ps 68:17; Hab 3:8) and of the armies of Israel (1Sa 17:45). *Shiloh.* The town in Ephraim between Bethel and Shechem where the central sanctuary and the ark of the covenant were located (see 4:3; Jos 18:1 and note; Jdg 21:19; see also note on 1Sa 7:1).

1:4 *sacrifice.* Here refers to a fellowship offering, a sacrifice that was combined with a festive meal signifying fellowship and communion with the Lord and grateful acknowledgment of his mercies (see Lev 7:11–18).

1:5 *the LORD had closed her womb.* The Lord gives and withholds children (see Ge 18:10; 29:31; 30:2,22 and note on 30:2).

1:6 *her rival.* See Ge 16:4 and note.

1:8 *more to you than ten sons.* See 2:5; see also note on Ru 4:15.

1:9 *house.* Here and in 3:3 the central sanctuary, the tabernacle, is referred to as "the LORD's house" or "the house of the LORD" (also in v. 7; 3:15) and "the tent of meeting" (2:22), and the Lord calls it "my dwelling" (2:32). The references to the tabernacle as a "house," as well as references to sleeping quarters and doors (3:2,15), give the impression that at this time the tabernacle was part of a larger, more permanent building complex to which the term "house" could legitimately be applied (cf. Jer 7:12,14 and note on 7:12; 26:6).

1:11 *vow.* See Ge 28:20–22; Nu 21:2; Ps 50:14 and note; 76:11; 116:14,18; 132:2–5; Pr 20:25 and note; 31:2. Regulations for the making of vows by women are found in Nu 30. *your servant's.* That is, my (see note on Ge 18:2). *remember.* To remember is more than simply to recall that Hannah existed. It is to go into action in her behalf (see vv. 19–20; see also note on Ge 8:1). *no razor.* Hannah voluntarily vows for her son what God had required of Samson (see Jdg 13:5 and note). Long hair was a symbol of dedication to the service of the Lord and was one of the characteristics of the Nazirite vow, which was normally taken for a limited time rather than for life (see Nu 6:1–21 and notes).

TOPOGRAPHICAL CROSS-SECTION: NORTH/SOUTH
Looking Toward East

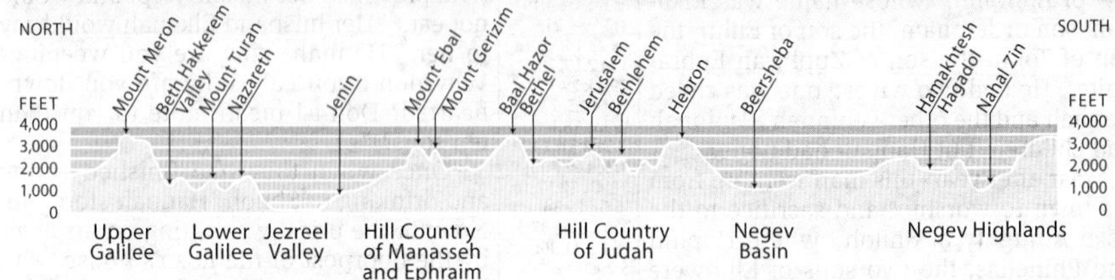

TOPOGRAPHICAL CROSS-SECTION: WEST/EAST
Looking Toward North

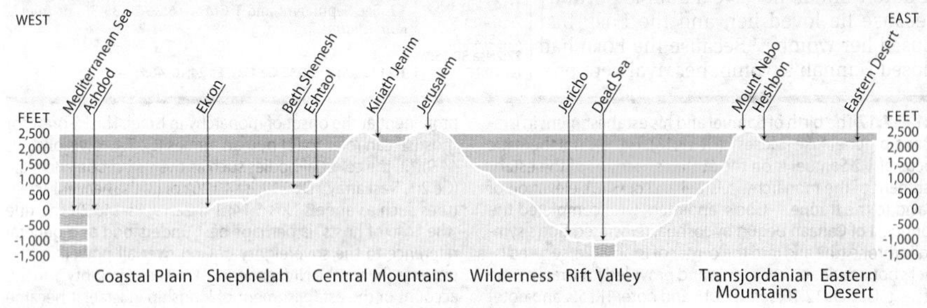

remember[v] me, and not forget your servant but give her a son, then I will give
him to the LORD for all the days of his
life,[w] and no razor[x] will ever be used on
his head."
12 As she kept on praying to the LORD,
Eli observed her mouth. 13 Hannah was
praying in her heart, and her lips were
moving but her voice was not heard. Eli
thought she was drunk 14 and said to her,
"How long are you going to stay drunk?
Put away your wine."
15 "Not so, my lord," Hannah replied,
"I am a woman who is deeply troubled.[y]
I have not been drinking wine or beer;
I was pouring[z] out my soul to the LORD.
16 Do not take your servant for a wicked
woman; I have been praying here out of
my great anguish and grief."[a]
17 Eli answered, "Go in peace,[b] and may
the God of Israel grant you what you have
asked of him.[c]"
18 She said, "May your servant find favor in your eyes.[d]" Then she went her way
and ate something, and her face was no
longer downcast.[e]
19 Early the next morning they arose and
worshiped before the LORD and then went
back to their home at Ramah.[f] Elkanah
made love to his wife Hannah, and the
LORD remembered[g] her. 20 So in the course
of time Hannah became pregnant and
gave birth to a son.[h] She named[i] him Samuel,[a][j] saying, "Because I asked the LORD
for him."

Hannah Dedicates Samuel

21 When her husband Elkanah went up
with all his family to offer the annual[k] sacrifice to the LORD and to fulfill his vow,[l]
22 Hannah did not go. She said to her hus-

[a] 20 *Samuel* sounds like the Hebrew for *heard by God.*

1:11 [v] S Ge 8:1 [w] S Jdg 13:7 [x] Nu 6:1-21; Jdg 13:5; Lk 1:15 **1:15** [y] 2Ki 4:27 [z] Ps 42:4; 62:8; La 2:19 **1:16** [a] Ps 55:2 **1:17** [b] Nu 6:26; 1Sa 20:42; 2Ki 5:19; S Ac 15:33 [c] S Ge 25:21; Ps 20:3-5 **1:18** [d] S Ge 18:3; Ru 2:13 [e] Ro 15:13 **1:19** [f] S Jos 18:25 [g] S Ge 8:1; S 29:31 **1:20** [h] S Ge 17:19; S 29:32; S 30:6 [i] Ex 2:10; Mt 1:21 [j] 1Sa 7:5; 12:23; 1Ch 6:27; Jer 15:1; Heb 11:32 **1:21** [k] S ver 3 [l] S Ge 28:20; Nu 30:2; Dt 12:11

1:13 *drunk.* Eli's mistake suggests that in those days it was not uncommon for drunken people to enter the sanctuary. Further evidence of the religious and moral deterioration of the time is found in the stories of Jdg 17–21.

1:15 *beer.* Traditionally "strong drink," but the term refers to grain alcohol—not to distilled spirits, which were virtually unknown in the ancient world. Written texts from Mesopotamia as early as 2500 BC portray the brewing of beer as a major industry.

1:16 *wicked.* See note on Dt 13:13.

1:20 *Samuel.* See NIV text note.

1:21 *annual sacrifice.* See notes on vv. 3–4. *his vow.* Making vows to God was a common feature of OT piety, usually involving thank offerings and praise (see Ps 50:14;

band, "After the boy is weaned, I will take
him and present[m] him before the LORD,
and he will live there always."[a]
23 "Do what seems best to you," her husband Elkanah told her. "Stay here until
you have weaned him; only may the LORD
make good[n] his[b] word." So the woman
stayed at home and nursed her son until
she had weaned[o] him.
24 After he was weaned, she took the
boy with her, young as he was, along with
a three-year-old bull,[c p] an ephah[d] of flour
and a skin of wine, and brought him to the
house of the LORD at Shiloh. 25 When the bull
had been sacrificed, they brought the boy to
Eli, 26 and she said to him, "Pardon me, my
lord. As surely as you live, I am the woman
who stood here beside you praying to the
LORD. 27 I prayed[q] for this child, and the LORD
has granted me what I asked of him. 28 So
now I give him to the LORD. For his whole
life[r] he will be given over to the LORD." And
he worshiped the LORD there.

Hannah's Prayer

2 Then Hannah prayed and said:[s]

"My heart rejoices[t] in the LORD;
in the LORD my horn[e u] is lifted high.
My mouth boasts[v] over my enemies,[w]
for I delight in your deliverance.

2 "There is no one holy[x] like[y] the LORD;
there is no one besides you;
there is no Rock[z] like our God.

3 "Do not keep talking so proudly
or let your mouth speak such
arrogance,[a]
for the LORD is a God who knows,[b]
and by him deeds[c] are weighed.[d]

4 "The bows of the warriors are broken,[e]
but those who stumbled are armed
with strength.[f]
5 Those who were full hire themselves
out for food,
but those who were hungry[g] are
hungry no more.
She who was barren[h] has borne seven
children,

1:22 [m] Ex 13:2; Lk 2:22 **1:23** [n] S Ge 25:21 [o] Ge 21:8 **1:24** [p] Nu 15:8-10 **1:27** [q] 1Sa 2:20; Ps 66:19-20 **1:28** [r] S Jdg 13:7 **2:1** [s] Lk 1:46-55 [t] Ps 13:5; 33:21; Zec 10:7 [u] Ps 18:2; 89:17, 24; 148:14 [v] Ps 6:8 [w] S Nu 10:35; Ps 6:10 **2:2** [x] S Ex 15:11; S Lev 11:44 [y] S Ex 8:10; Isa 40:25; 46:5 [z] S Ge 49:24; S Ex 33:22; Dt 32:37; 2Sa 22:2, 32; 23:3; Ps 31:3; 71:3 **2:3** [a] Ps 17:10; 31:18; 73:8; 75:4; 94:4 [b] S Jos 22:22 [c] 1Sa 16:7; 1Ki 8:39; 1Ch 28:9; 2Ch 6:30; Pr 15:11; Jer 11:20; 17:10 [d] Pr 16:2; 24:11-12 **2:4** [e] 2Sa 1:27; Ps 37:15; 46:9; 76:3 [f] Job 17:9; Isa 40:31; 41:1; 52:1; 57:10 **2:5** [g] Lk 1:53 [h] Ps 113:9; Isa 54:1; Jer 15:9

[a] *22* Masoretic Text; Dead Sea Scrolls *always. I have dedicated him as a Nazirite—all the days of his life."*
[b] *23* Masoretic Text; Dead Sea Scrolls, Septuagint and Syriac *your*
[c] *24* Dead Sea Scrolls, Septuagint and Syriac; Masoretic Text *with three bulls*
[d] *24* That is, probably about 36 pounds or about 16 kilograms
[e] *1* *Horn* here symbolizes strength; also in verse 10.

56:12; 116:17–18). Elkanah no doubt annually made vows to the Lord as he prayed for God's blessing on his crops and flocks, and fulfilled those vows at the Festival of Tabernacles (see note on v. 3).

1:22 *weaned.* It was customary in the East to nurse children for three years or longer (in the Apocrypha, see 2 Maccabees 7:27) since there was no way to keep milk sweet.

1:23 *his word.* No previous word from God is mentioned, unless this refers to the pronouncement of Eli in v. 17. The Dead Sea Scrolls, Septuagint (the pre-Christian Greek translation of the OT) and Syriac version (see NIV text note) resolve this problem by reading "your word." But "his word" may refer to an earlier, unrecorded word from the Lord.

1:26 *As surely as you live.* A customary way of emphasizing the truthfulness of one's words.

1:27 *I prayed for this child.* In the nativity account of Samuel, which also serves as the nativity account of the monarchy in Israel, Hannah serves as a cameo of Israel. As Hannah in her distress "asked" for a child, so Israel in her distress "asked" for a king, and Hannah's hymnic prayer that follows Samuel's birth (2:1–10) became Israel's hymn of praise as they reflected on the inauguration of the Davidic dynasty.

1:28 *given over.* The unusual Hebrew term used here sounds precisely like the Hebrew for the name Saul. It appears that the author already here hints that Saul, the one "asked for" by Israel, should also have been Saul, the one "given over" to the service of the Lord—that every king in Israel should be a "Saul" in this latter sense.

2:1–10 Hannah's prayer is constructed of two balanced parts (vv. 1–5,6–10). While there is considerable overlapping of themes between the first and second halves, the focus of Hannah's praise shifts from a celebration of the ways of God that "lifted high" her "horn" to a celebration of the ways of God that will "exalt" the "horn" of his anointed (vv. 1,10).

2:1 *prayed.* Hannah's prayer (vv. 1–10) is a song of praise and thanksgiving to God (see Ps 72:20, where the psalms of David are designated "prayers"). This song has sometimes been termed the "Magnificat of the OT" because it is so similar to the Magnificat of the NT (Mary's song, Lk 1:46–55). It also has certain resemblances to the "Benedictus" (Zechariah's song, Lk 1:67–79). Hannah's song of praise finds many echoes in David's song near the end of the book (2Sa 22). These two songs frame the main narrative, and their themes highlight the ways of God that the narrative relates—they contain the theology of the book in the form of praise. Hannah speaks prophetically at a time when Israel is about to enter an important new period of her history with the establishment of kingship through her son, Samuel. *rejoices in the LORD.* Cf. Lk 1:47. The supreme source of Hannah's joy is not in the child but in the God who has answered her prayer. *my horn is lifted high.* See NIV text note; cf. Dt 33:17; Ps 75:4 and note; 92:10; 112:9; Lk 1:69 and note. To have one's horn "lifted high" by God is to be delivered from disgrace to a position of honor and strength.

2:2 *no one holy like the LORD.* See Lev 11:44 and note. *no one besides you.* See 2Sa 7:22; 22:32; Dt 4:35 and note; Isa 45:6. *Rock.* A metaphor to depict the strength and stability of the God of Israel as the unfailing source of security for his people (see 2Sa 22:2 and note; Ps 19:14; Isa 17:10 and note).

2:3 *so proudly ... such arrogance.* After the manner of Peninnah (and others in the narratives of 1,2 Samuel—Eli's sons, the Philistines, Saul, Nabal, Goliath, Absalom, Shimei and Sheba). *the LORD is a God who knows.* See 16:7; 1Ki 8:39; Ps 139:1–6 and note; Jn 2:24–25.

2:4–5 In a series of examples derived from everyday life Hannah shows that God often works contrary to natural expectations and brings about surprising reversals—seen frequently in the stories that follow.

2:5 *seven children.* See 1:8 and note on Ru 4:15.

but she who has had many sons
pines away.

6 "The LORD brings death and makes alive;[i]
he brings down to the grave and
raises up.[j]
7 The LORD sends poverty and wealth;[k]
he humbles and he exalts.[l]
8 He raises[m] the poor[n] from the dust[o]
and lifts the needy[p] from the ash
heap;
he seats them with princes
and has them inherit a throne of
honor.[q]

"For the foundations[r] of the earth are
the LORD's;
on them he has set the world.
9 He will guard the feet[s] of his faithful
servants,[t]
but the wicked will be silenced in
the place of darkness.[u]

"It is not by strength[v] that one prevails;
10 those who oppose the LORD will be
broken.[w]
The Most High will thunder[x] from
heaven;
the LORD will judge[y] the ends of the
earth.

2:6 [i] Dt 32:39 [j] Isa 26:19; Eze 37:3,12 **2:7** [k] S Dt 8:18 [l] Job 5:11; 40:12; Ps 75:7; Isa 2:12; 13:11; 22:19; Da 4:37 **2:8** [m] Ps 113:7-8 [n] Jas 2:5 [o] 1Ki 16:2 [p] Ps 72:12; 107:41; 145:14; 146:8; S Mt 23:12 [q] 2Sa 7:8; Job 36:7; Isa 22:23; Eze 21:26 [r] Job 15:7; 38:4; Ps 104:5; Pr 8:29; Isa 40:12; Jer 10:12 **2:9** [s] Ps 91:12; 121:3; Pr 3:26 [t] Pr 2:8 [u] Job 10:22; Isa 5:30; 8:22; 59:9; 60:2; Jer 13:16; Am 5:18,20; Zep 1:14-15; Mt 8:12 [v] 1Sa 17:47; Ps 33:16-17; Zec 4:6 **2:10** [w] S Ex 15:6 [x] S Ex 19:16; 1Sa 7:10; 12:17; 2Sa 22:14;

"He will give strength[z] to his king
and exalt the horn[a] of his anointed."

11 Then Elkanah went home to Ramah,[b]
but the boy ministered[c] before the LORD
under Eli the priest.

Eli's Wicked Sons

12 Eli's sons were scoundrels; they had
no regard[d] for the LORD. 13 Now it was
the practice[e] of the priests that, whenever any of the people offered a sacrifice,
the priest's servant would come with
a three-pronged fork in his hand while
the meat[f] was being boiled 14 and would
plunge the fork into the pan or kettle or
caldron or pot. Whatever the fork brought
up the priest would take for himself. This
is how they treated all the Israelites who
came to Shiloh. 15 But even before the fat
was burned, the priest's servant would
come and say to the person who was sacrificing, "Give the priest some meat to
roast; he won't accept boiled meat from
you, but only raw."

Job 37:4,5; 38:1; Ps 18:13; 29:3; Isa 66:6 [y] Ps 96:13; 98:9; Mt 25:31-32 [z] Ps 18:1; 21:1; 59:16 [a] S Dt 33:17; Ps 89:24; S Lk 1:69 **2:11** [b] S Jos 18:25 [c] ver 18; S Nu 16:9; 1Sa 3:1 **2:12** [d] Jer 2:8; 9:6 **2:13** [e] Dt 18:3 [f] Lev 7:35-36

2:6–8 Hannah declares that life and death, prosperity and adversity, are determined by the sovereign power of God—a theme richly illustrated in the following narrative (see also Dt 32:39; 1Ki 17:20–24; 2Ki 4:32–35; Jn 5:21; 11:41–44).

2:6 *grave.* See note on Ge 37:35.

2:8 *foundations of the earth.* A common figure in the OT for the solid base on which the earth (the dry land on which people live, not planet Earth; Ge 1:10) is founded. The phrase does not teach a particular theory of the structure of the universe (see Job 9:6; 38:6; Ps 24:2 and note; 75:3; 104:5; Zec 12:1).

2:9 *guard the feet.* Travel in ancient Israel was for the most part by foot over trails that were often rocky and dangerous (see Ps 91:11–12; 121:3). *his faithful servants.* People who faithfully serve the Lord. The Hebrew root underlying this word is used of both God and his people in 2Sa 22:26 to characterize the nature of their mutual relationship. The word is also translated "faithful" (Ps 12:1; 32:6) and "faithful ones" (Pr 2:8). See Ps 4:3 and note.

2:10 *judge.* Impose his righteous rule upon (see Ps 96:13; 98:9). *ends of the earth.* All nations and peoples (see Dt 33:17; Isa 45:22). *his king.* Hannah's prayer is here prophetic, anticipating the establishment of kingship in Israel and the initial realization of the Messianic ideal in David (Lk 1:69). Ultimately her expectation finds fulfillment in Christ and his complete triumph over the enemies of God. *exalt the horn.* The expected king's horn will be "lifted high/exalt[ed]" as surely as Hannah's had been (see v. 1). This word about the horns frames the song and highlights its central theme. *anointed.* The first reference in the Bible to the Lord's anointed—i.e., his anointed king. (Priests were also anointed for God's service; see Ex 28:41; Lev 4:3.) The word is often synonymous with "king" (as here) and provides part of the vocabulary basis for the Messianic idea in the Bible. "Anointed" and "Messiah" are the translation and transliteration, respectively, of the same Hebrew word. The Greek translation of this Hebrew term is *Christos*, from which comes the English word "Christ" (see second NIV text note on Mt 1:1). A king (coming from the tribe of Judah) is first prophesied by Jacob (Ge 49:10); kingship is further anticipated in the messages of Balaam in Nu 24:7,17. Also Dt 17:14–20 looks forward to the time when the Lord will place a king of his choice over his people after they enter the promised land. 1,2 Samuel shows how this expectation of the theocratic king is realized in the person of David. Hannah's prophetic anticipation of a king at the time of the dedication of her son Samuel, who was to be God's agent for establishing kingship in Israel, is entirely appropriate.

2:11 *ministered.* Performed such services as a boy might render while assisting the high priest. *before the LORD.* At the "house of the LORD" (1:24; see note on 1:9).

2:12 *scoundrels.* See 1:16 and note. *had no regard for.* Lit. "did not know." In OT usage, to "know" the Lord is not just intellectual or theoretical recognition. It is to enter into fellowship with him and acknowledge his claims on one's life. The term often has a covenantal connotation (see Jer 31:34; Hos 2:20 and note).

2:13–16 Apparently vv. 13–14 describe the practice that had come to be accepted for determining the priests' portion of the fellowship offerings (Lev 7:31–36; 10:14–15; Dt 18:1–5)—a tradition presumably based on the assumption that a random thrust of the fork would providentially determine a fair portion. Verses 15–16 then describe how Eli's sons arrogantly violated that custom and the law.

2:15 *before the fat was burned.* On the altar as the Lord's portion, which he was to receive first (see Lev 3:16 and note; 4:10,26,31,35; 7:30–31; 17:6). *roast.* Boiling is the only form of cooking specified in the law for the priests' portion (Nu 6:19–20). Roasting this portion is nowhere expressly forbidden in the law, but it is specified only for the Passover lamb (Ex 12:8–9; Dt 16:7). The present passage seems to imply that for the priests to roast their portion of the sacrifices was unlawful.

16 If the person said to him, "Let the fat[g]
be burned first, and then take whatever
you want," the servant would answer,
"No, hand it over now; if you don't, I'll
take it by force."
17 This sin of the young men was very
great in the LORD's sight, for they[a] were
treating the LORD's offering with contempt.[h]
18 But Samuel was ministering[i] before
the LORD—a boy wearing a linen ephod.[j]
19 Each year his mother made him a little
robe and took it to him when she went
up with her husband to offer the annual[k]
sacrifice. 20 Eli would bless Elkanah and
his wife, saying, "May the LORD give you
children by this woman to take the place
of the one she prayed[l] for and gave to[b] the
LORD." Then they would go home. 21 And
the LORD was gracious to Hannah;[m] she
gave birth to three sons and two daughters. Meanwhile, the boy Samuel grew[n] up
in the presence of the LORD.
22 Now Eli, who was very old, heard
about everything[o] his sons were doing
to all Israel and how they slept with the
women[p] who served at the entrance to
the tent of meeting. 23 So he said to them,
"Why do you do such things? I hear from
all the people about these wicked deeds
of yours. 24 No, my sons; the report I hear
spreading among the LORD's people is not
good. 25 If one person sins against another,
God[c] may mediate for the offender; but if
anyone sins against the LORD, who will[q]

2:16 [g]Lev 3:3, 14-16; 7:29-34 **2:17** [h]ver 22, 29; S Nu 14:11; Jer 7:21; Eze 22:26; Mal 2:7-9 **2:18** [i]S ver 11 [j]ver 28; 1Sa 22:18; 23:9; 2Sa 6:14; 1Ch 15:27 **2:19** [k]S 1Sa 1:3 **2:20** [l]S 1Sa 1:27 **2:21** [m]Ge 21:1 [n]S Jdg 13:24; Lk 1:80; 2:40 **2:22** [o]S ver 17 [p]S Ex 38:8 **2:25** [q]Ex 4:21; Jos 11:20 [r]S Ex 32:10; S Nu 11:2; 1Sa 3:14; 1Ki 13:6; Job 9:33; Ps 106:30; Isa 1:18; 22:14; Jer 15:1; Heb 10:26 **2:26** [s]S Jdg 13:24; Lk 2:52 [t]Pr 3:4 **2:27** [u]S Dt 33:1; S Jdg 13:6 **2:28** [v]S Ex 28:1 [w]S Ex 30:7 [x]1Sa 22:18; 23:6,9; 30:7 [y]Lev 7:35-36 **2:29** [z]ver 12-17 [a]S Dt 12:5 **2:30** [b]S Ex 29:9 [c]Ps 50:23; 91:15; Pr 8:17 [d]Isa 53:3; Na 3:6; Mal 2:9 [e]Jer 18:10

intercede[r] for them?" His sons, however,
did not listen to their father's rebuke, for
it was the LORD's will to put them to death.
26 And the boy Samuel continued to
grow[s] in stature and in favor with the LORD
and with people.[t]

Prophecy Against the House of Eli

27 Now a man of God[u] came to Eli and
said to him, "This is what the LORD says:
'Did I not clearly reveal myself to your ancestor's family when they were in Egypt
under Pharaoh? 28 I chose[v] your ancestor out of all the tribes of Israel to be my
priest, to go up to my altar, to burn incense,[w] and to wear an ephod[x] in my presence. I also gave your ancestor's family
all the food offerings[y] presented by the
Israelites. 29 Why do you[d] scorn my sacrifice and offering[z] that I prescribed for my
dwelling?[a] Why do you honor your sons
more than me by fattening yourselves on
the choice parts of every offering made by
my people Israel?'
30 "Therefore the LORD, the God of Israel, declares: 'I promised that members
of your family would minister before me
forever.[b]' But now the LORD declares: 'Far
be it from me! Those who honor me I
will honor,[c] but those who despise[d] me
will be disdained.[e] 31 The time is coming

[a] *17* Dead Sea Scrolls and Septuagint; Masoretic Text *people* [b] *20* Dead Sea Scrolls; Masoretic Text *and asked from* [c] *25* Or *the judges* [d] *29* The Hebrew is plural.

2:16 *by force.* Presenting the priests' portion was to be a voluntary act on the part of the worshipers (see Lev 7:28–36; Dt 18:3).

2:18 *But Samuel.* Between 2:12 and 4:1 the author presents a series of sharp contrasts between Samuel and Eli's sons. *linen ephod.* A priestly garment worn by those who served before the Lord at his sanctuary (see 22:18; 2Sa 6:14). Samuel's garment was similar to the ephod worn by the high priest (see note on v. 28; cf. Ex 39:1–7).

2:19 *little robe.* A sleeveless garment reaching to the knees, worn over the undergarment and under the ephod. *annual sacrifice.* See note on 1:3.

2:22 *slept with the women who served.* See Ex 38:8. There is no further reference to women serving in the tabernacle or temple in the OT (but cf. Anna in the NT [Lk 2:36–38]). Their service is not to be confused with that of the Levites, which is prescribed in the Pentateuch (Nu 1:50; 3:6–8; 8:15; 16:9; 18:2–3). The immoral acts of Eli's sons are reminiscent of the religious prostitution (fertility rites) at the Canaanite sanctuaries—acts that were an abomination to the Lord and a desecration of his house (Dt 23:17–18).

2:23 *he said to them.* Eli rebuked his sons but did not remove them from office. God would do that.

2:25 *God.* See NIV text note. Eli's argument is that when someone commits an offense against another person, there is recourse to a third party to decide the issue (whether this be understood as God or as God's representatives, the judges; see NIV text notes on Ex 22:8–9 and note on Ps 82:1); but when the offense is against the Lord there is no recourse, for God is both the one wronged and the judge. *the LORD's will to put them to death.* This comment by the author of the narrative is not intended to excuse Eli's sons but to indicate that Eli's warning was much too late. Eli's sons had persisted in their evil ways for so long that God's judgment on them was determined (v. 34; see Jos 11:20).

2:26 *grow in stature and in favor with the LORD and with people.* Cf. Luke's description of Jesus (Lk 2:52).

2:27 *man of God.* Often a designation for a prophet (see 9:6,9–10; Dt 33:1; Jos 14:6; 1Ki 13:1; 17:24; 2Ki 4:9). *ancestor's family.* The descendants of Aaron.

2:28 *to be my priest.* Three tasks of the priests are mentioned: (1) *to go up to my altar.* To perform the sacrificial rites at the altar of burnt offering in the courtyard of the tabernacle. (2) *to burn incense.* At the altar of incense in the Holy Place (Ex 30:1–10). (3) *to wear an ephod.* See note on v. 18. It would appear that the reference here is to the special ephod of the high priest (see Ex 28:6–14). The breastpiece containing the Urim and Thummim was attached to the ephod. The Urim and Thummim were a divinely ordained means of obtaining guidance from God, placed in the custody of the high priest (see Ex 28:30 and note; see also 1Sa 23:9–12; 30:7–8).

2:30 *I promised.* See Ex 29:9; Lev 8–9; Nu 16–17; 25:13. *Far be it from me!* This is not to say that the promise of the priesthood to Aaron's house has been annulled, but that Eli and his house are to be excluded from participation in this privilege because of their sin. *Those who honor me I will honor.* See v. 29. Spiritual privileges bring responsibilities and obligations; they are not to be treated as irrevocable rights (see 2Sa 22:26–27).

when I will cut short your strength and
the strength of your priestly house, so that
no one in it will reach old age,[f] 32 and you
will see distress[g] in my dwelling. Although
good will be done to Israel, no one in your
family line will ever reach old age.[h] 33 Every one of you that I do not cut off from
serving at my altar I will spare only to
destroy your sight and sap your strength,
and all your descendants[i] will die in the
prime of life.
34 " 'And what happens to your two sons,
Hophni and Phinehas, will be a sign[j] to
you — they will both die[k] on the same
day.[l] 35 I will raise up for myself a faithful priest,[m] who will do according to what
is in my heart and mind. I will firmly establish his priestly house, and they will
minister before my anointed[n] one always.
36 Then everyone left in your family line
will come and bow down before him for
a piece of silver and a loaf of bread and
plead,[o] "Appoint me to some priestly office
so I can have food to eat.[p]" ' "

The LORD Calls Samuel

3 The boy Samuel ministered[q] before the
LORD under Eli. In those days the word
of the LORD was rare;[r] there were not many
visions.[s]
2 One night Eli, whose eyes[t] were becoming so weak that he could barely see,[u]
was lying down in his usual place. 3 The
lamp[v] of God had not yet gone out, and
Samuel was lying down in the house[w]
of the LORD, where the ark[x] of God was.
4 Then the LORD called Samuel.
Samuel answered, "Here I am.[y]" 5 And
he ran to Eli and said, "Here I am; you
called me."
But Eli said, "I did not call; go back and
lie down." So he went and lay down.
6 Again the LORD called, "Samuel!" And
Samuel got up and went to Eli and said,
"Here I am; you called me."
"My son," Eli said, "I did not call; go
back and lie down."
7 Now Samuel did not yet know[z] the
LORD: The word[a] of the LORD had not yet
been revealed[b] to him.
8 A third time the LORD called, "Samuel!"
And Samuel got up and went to Eli and
said, "Here I am; you called me."
Then Eli realized that the LORD was calling the boy. 9 So Eli told Samuel, "Go and
lie down, and if he calls you, say, 'Speak,
LORD, for your servant is listening.' " So
Samuel went and lay down in his place.
10 The LORD came and stood there, calling as at the other times, "Samuel! Samuel![c]"
Then Samuel said, "Speak, for your servant is listening."
11 And the LORD said to Samuel: "See, I
am about to do something in Israel that will
make the ears of everyone who hears about

2:31 [f] 1Sa 4:11-18; 22:16 **2:32** [g] 1Sa 4:3; 22:17-20; Jer 7:12,14 [h] 1Ki 2:26-27 **2:33** [i] Jer 29:32; Mal 2:12 **2:34** [j] S Dt 13:2 [k] 1Sa 4:11 [l] 1Ki 13:3 **2:35** [m] 2Sa 8:17; 20:25; 1Ki 1:8, 32; 2:35; 4:4; 1Ch 16:39; 29:22; Eze 44:15-16 [n] 1Sa 9:16; 10:1; 16:13; 2Sa 2:4; 12:7; 23:1; 1Ki 1:34; Ps 89:20 **2:36** [o] Eze 44:10-14 [p] 1Sa 3:12; 1Ki 2:27 **3:1** [q] S 1Sa 2:11 [r] Ps 74:9; La 2:9; Eze 7:26 [s] Am 8:11 **3:2** [t] 1Sa 4:15 [u] S Ge 27:1 **3:3** [v] Ex 25:31-38; Lev 24:1-4 [w] 1Sa 1:9 [x] Dt 10:1-5; 1Ki 6:19; 8:1 **3:4** [y] S Ge 22:1; S Ex 3:4 **3:7** [z] 1Sa 2:12 [a] Jer 1:2 [b] S Nu 12:6; Am 3:7 **3:10** [c] Ex 3:4

2:31 *strength ... strength.* Lit. "arm ... arm," symbolic of strength. Eli's "arm" and that of his priestly family will be cut off (contrast David, 2Sa 22:35). *no one in it will reach old age.* A prediction of the decimation of Eli's priestly family in the death of his sons (4:11), in the massacre of his descendants by Saul at Nob (22:18–19) and in the removal of Abiathar from his priestly office (1Ki 2:26–27).
2:32 *distress in my dwelling.* Including the capture of the ark by the Philistines (4:1–11), the destruction of Shiloh (Jer 7:14) and the relocation of the tabernacle to Nob (21:1–6; see note on 21:1).
2:33 A reference apparently to Abiathar, who was expelled from office by Solomon (see 1Ki 2:26–27) after an unsuccessful attempt to make Adonijah king as the successor to David.
2:34 *a sign to you.* The death of Hophni and Phinehas (4:11) will confirm the longer-term predictions. Such confirmation of a prophetic word was not uncommon (see 10:7–9; 1Ki 13:3 and note; Jer 28:15–17; Lk 1:18–20,64).
2:35 *I will raise up for myself a faithful priest.* Initially fulfilled in the person of Zadok, who served as a priest during the time of David (see 2Sa 8:17; 15:24,35; 20:25) and who eventually replaced Abiathar as high priest in the time of Solomon (see 1Ki 2:35; 1Ch 29:22). *firmly establish his priestly house.* Lit. "build for him a faithful house"; the faithful priest will be given a "faithful" (i.e., enduring) priestly family. See the similar word spoken concerning David (25:28, "lasting dynasty"; see also 2Sa 7:16; 1Ki 11:38). The line of Zadok was continued by his son Azariah (see 1Ki 4:2) and was still on the scene at the time of the exile and return (see 1Ch 6:8–15; Ezr 3:2). It continued in intertestamental times until Antiochus IV Epiphanes (175–164 BC) sold the priesthood to Menelaus (in the Apocrypha, see 2 Maccabees 4:23–50), who was not of the priestly line. *my anointed one.* David and his successors (see note on v. 10).
3:1 *boy Samuel.* See 2:11,18. Samuel is now no longer a little child (see 2:21,26). The Jewish historian Josephus places his age at 12 years; he may have been older. *the word of the LORD was rare.* See Pr 29:18 and note; Am 8:11. During the entire period of the judges, apart from the prophet of 2:27–36, we are told of only two prophets (Jdg 4:4; 6:8) and of five revelations (Jdg 2:1–3; 6:11–26; 7:2–11; 10:11–14; 13:3–21). Possibly 2Ch 15:3 also refers to this period. *visions.* Cf. Ge 15:1.
3:3 *The lamp of God had not yet gone out.* The reference is to the golden lampstand, which stood opposite the table of the bread of the Presence (Ex 25:31–40) in the Holy Place. It was still night, but the early morning hours were approaching when the flame would grow dim or go out (see Ex 27:20–21; 30:7–8; Lev 24:3–4; 2Ch 13:11; Pr 31:18). For the lamp to be permitted to go out before morning was a violation of the Pentateuchal regulations. *house.* See note on 1:9.
3:4 *Here I am.* See note on Ge 22:1.
3:5 *I did not call.* Eli's failure to recognize at once that the Lord had called Samuel may be indicative of his own unfamiliarity with the Lord.
3:7 *did not yet know the LORD.* In the sense of having a direct experience of him (see Ex 1:8), such as receiving a revelation from him (see the last half of the verse).
3:10 *Samuel! Samuel!* See note on Ge 22:11.
3:11–14 The Lord's first revelation to Samuel summarizes the message Eli had already received from the "man of God" (2:27–36), thus confirming the fact that the youth had indeed received a revelation from God.
3:11 *make the ears ... tingle.* See note on Jer 19:3.

it tingle.[d] 12 At that time I will carry out against Eli everything[e] I spoke against his family—from beginning to end. 13 For I told him that I would judge his family forever because of the sin he knew about; his sons blasphemed God,[a] and he failed to restrain[f] them. 14 Therefore I swore to the house of Eli, 'The guilt of Eli's house will never be atoned[g] for by sacrifice or offering.'"

15 Samuel lay down until morning and then opened the doors of the house of the LORD. He was afraid to tell Eli the vision, 16 but Eli called him and said, "Samuel, my son."

Samuel answered, "Here I am."

17 "What was it he said to you?" Eli asked. "Do not hide[h] it from me. May God deal with you, be it ever so severely,[i] if you hide from me anything he told you." 18 So Samuel told him everything, hiding nothing from him. Then Eli said, "He is the LORD; let him do what is good in his eyes."[j]

19 The LORD was with[k] Samuel as he grew[l] up, and he let none[m] of Samuel's words fall to the ground. 20 And all Israel from Dan to Beersheba[n] recognized that Samuel was attested as a prophet of the LORD.[o] 21 The LORD continued to appear at Shiloh, and there he revealed[p] himself to Samuel through his word.

4 And Samuel's word came to all Israel.

The Philistines Capture the Ark

Now the Israelites went out to fight against the Philistines. The Israelites camped at Ebenezer,[q] and the Philistines at Aphek.[r] 2 The Philistines deployed their forces to meet Israel, and as the battle spread, Israel was defeated by the Philistines, who killed about four thousand of them on the battlefield. 3 When the soldiers returned to camp, the elders of Israel asked, "Why[s] did the LORD bring defeat on us today before the Philistines? Let us bring the ark[t] of the LORD's covenant from Shiloh,[u] so that he may go with us[v] and save us from the hand of our enemies."

4 So the people sent men to Shiloh, and they brought back the ark of the covenant of the LORD Almighty, who is enthroned between the cherubim.[w] And Eli's two sons, Hophni and Phinehas, were there with the ark of the covenant of God.

5 When the ark of the LORD's covenant came into the camp, all Israel raised such a great shout[x] that the ground shook. 6 Hearing the uproar, the Philistines asked, "What's all this shouting in the Hebrew[y] camp?"

When they learned that the ark of the LORD had come into the camp, 7 the Philistines were afraid.[z] "A god has[b] come into the camp," they said. "Oh no! Nothing like this has happened before. 8 We're doomed! Who will deliver us from the

3:11 [d] 2Ki 21:12; Job 15:21; Jer 19:3 **3:12** [e] S 1Sa 2:27-36 **3:13** [f] 1Ki 1:6 **3:14** [g] S 1Sa 2:25 **3:17** [h] 1Ki 22:14; Jer 23:28; 38:14; 42:4 [i] S Ru 1:17 **3:18** [j] S Jdg 10:15 **3:19** [k] S Ge 21:22; S Nu 14:43 [l] S Jdg 13:24 [m] 1Sa 9:6 **3:20** [n] S Jdg 20:1 [o] S Dt 18:22; Eze 33:33 **3:21** [p] S Nu 12:6

4:1 [q] 1Sa 5:1; 7:12 [r] Jos 12:18; 1Sa 29:1; 1Ki 20:26 **4:3** [s] Jos 7:7 [t] S Jos 6:7 [u] S Jos 18:1; S 1Sa 2:32 [v] 2Ch 13:8 **4:4** [w] S Ge 3:24; S Ex 25:22 **4:5** [x] S Jos 6:5, 10 **4:6** [y] S Ge 14:13 **4:7** [z] S Ex 15:14

[a] *13* An ancient Hebrew scribal tradition (see also Septuagint); Masoretic Text *sons made themselves contemptible* [b] *7* Or *"Gods have* (see Septuagint)

3:13 *blasphemed God.* See NIV text note and Lev 24:14–16.
3:15 *doors of the house of the LORD.* See note on 1:9. *vision.* See notes on vv. 1,11–14.
3:17 *May God deal with you, be it ever so severely.* A curse formula (see 14:44; 20:13; 25:22; 2Sa 3:9,35; 19:13; Ru 1:17; 1Ki 2:23; 2Ki 6:31), usually directed against the speaker but here used by Eli against Samuel if he conceals anything the Lord said (see also note on 14:24).
3:18 *let him do what is good in his eyes.* Eli bows before God, accepting the judgment as righteous (see Ex 34:5–7).
3:19 *The LORD was with Samuel.* Said also of David (see 16:18 and note). *he let none of Samuel's words fall to the ground.* Because none of Samuel's words proved unreliable, he was recognized as a prophet who spoke the word of the Lord (see vv. 20–21; 9:6).
3:20 *Dan to Beersheba.* A conventional expression often used in Samuel, Kings and Chronicles to denote the entire land (Dan was located in the far north and Beersheba in the far south).
3:21 *continued to appear at Shiloh.* But not after the events narrated in chs. 4–6 (see Jer 7:12–14; 26:6).
4:1 *Samuel's word came to all Israel.* Contrast 3:1. *Ebenezer.* Means "stone of help." It was probably a short distance (see v. 6) to the east of Aphek—not to be confused with the location of the stone named Ebenezer that was later erected by Samuel between Mizpah and Shen (see 7:12) to commemorate a victory over the Philistines. *Aphek.* A town about 12 miles northeast of the coastal city of Joppa (see map, p. 359). Philistine presence this far north suggests an attempt to spread their control over the Israelite tribes of central Canaan (see v. 9; Jdg 15:11).
4:3 *Why did the LORD bring defeat . . . ?* The elders understood that their defeat was more an indication of God's displeasure than it was of Philistine military might. Israel's pagan neighbors also believed that the outcome of battle was decided by the gods. *so that he may go with us and save us.* In an attempt to secure the Lord's presence with them in the struggle against the Philistines, the elders sent for the ark of the covenant. They were correct in thinking there was a connection between God's presence with his people and the ark (cf. v. 4), and no doubt they remembered the presence of the ark at notable victories in Israel's past history (see Nu 10:33–36; Jos 3:3,11,14–17; 6:6,12–20). But they incorrectly believed that the Lord's presence with the ark was guaranteed, rather than being subject to his free decision. They reflect the pagan notion that the deity is identified with the symbol of his presence and that God's favor could automatically be gained by manipulating the symbol.
4:4 *enthroned between the cherubim.* On each end of the atonement cover of the ark of the covenant were cherubim of gold with their wings touching each other and spread upward over the ark (see Ex 25:17–22). In the space between these cherubim God's presence with his people was localized in a special way, so that the atonement cover of the ark came to be viewed as the throne of Israel's divine King (see 2Sa 6:2; Ps 80:1; 99:1; see also note on Ex 25:18). *Hophni and Phinehas.* These wicked priests (see 2:12) did not restrain the army from its improper use of the ark but actually accompanied the ark to the battlefield.
4:6 *Hebrew.* See note on Ge 14:13.
4:7 *A god has come into the camp.* The Philistines also identified the God of Israel with the symbol of his presence (see note on v. 3).

hand of these mighty gods? They are the
gods who struck[a] the Egyptians with all
kinds of plagues[b] in the wilderness. 9 Be
strong, Philistines! Be men, or you will be
subject to the Hebrews, as they[c] have been
to you. Be men, and fight!"
10 So the Philistines fought, and the Israelites were defeated[d] and every man fled
to his tent. The slaughter was very great;
Israel lost thirty thousand foot soldiers.
11 The ark of God was captured, and Eli's
two sons, Hophni and Phinehas, died.[e]

Death of Eli

12 That same day a Benjamite[f] ran from
the battle line and went to Shiloh with
his clothes torn and dust[g] on his head.
13 When he arrived, there was Eli[h] sitting
on his chair by the side of the road, watching, because his heart feared for the ark of
God. When the man entered the town and
told what had happened, the whole town
sent up a cry.
14 Eli heard the outcry and asked, "What
is the meaning of this uproar?"
The man hurried over to Eli, 15 who was
ninety-eight years old and whose eyes[i] had
failed so that he could not see. 16 He told
Eli, "I have just come from the battle line;
I fled from it this very day."
Eli asked, "What happened, my son?"
17 The man who brought the news replied, "Israel fled before the Philistines,
and the army has suffered heavy losses.
Also your two sons, Hophni and Phinehas,
are dead,[j] and the ark of God has been
captured."[k]
18 When he mentioned the ark of God,
Eli fell backward off his chair by the side
of the gate. His neck was broken and he
died, for he was an old man, and he was
heavy. He had led[a][l] Israel forty years.[m]
19 His daughter-in-law, the wife of Phinehas, was pregnant and near the time of
delivery. When she heard the news that
the ark of God had been captured and that
her father-in-law and her husband were
dead, she went into labor and gave birth,
but was overcome by her labor pains. 20 As
she was dying, the women attending her
said, "Don't despair; you have given birth
to a son." But she did not respond or pay
any attention.
21 She named the boy Ichabod,[b][n] saying,
"The Glory[o] has departed from Israel" —
because of the capture of the ark of God
and the deaths of her father-in-law and
her husband. 22 She said, "The Glory[p] has
departed from Israel, for the ark of God
has been captured."[q]

The Ark in Ashdod and Ekron

5 After the Philistines had captured the
ark of God, they took it from Ebenezer[r] to Ashdod.[s] 2 Then they carried the
ark into Dagon's temple and set it beside
Dagon.[t] 3 When the people of Ashdod rose

4:8 [a] Ex 12:30; 1Sa 5:12 [b] Rev 11:6 **4:9** [c] S Jdg 13:1 **4:10** [d] S Dt 28:25 **4:11** [e] Ps 78:64; Jer 7:12 **4:12** [f] Eze 24:26; 33:21 [g] S Jos 7:6; S 2Sa 1:2 **4:13** [h] ver 18 **4:15** [i] S 1Sa 3:2 **4:17** [j] 1Sa 22:18; Ps 78:64 [k] Ps 78:61 **4:18** [l] S Jdg 2:16; S 16:31 [m] 1Sa 2:31 **4:21** [n] S Ge 35:18 [o] S Ex 24:16; Ps 106:20; Jer 2:11; Eze 1:28; 9:3; 10:18 **4:22** [p] S Ex 24:16; Ps 78:61 [q] Jer 7:12 **5:1** [r] S 1Sa 4:1 [s] S Jos 11:22; S 13:3 **5:2** [t] S Jdg 16:23; Isa 2:18; 19:1; 46:1

[a] *18* Traditionally *judged* [b] *21* *Ichabod* means *no glory.*

4:8 *mighty gods.* The Philistines could think only in polytheistic terms. *Egyptians ... plagues.* See note on 6:6.
4:11 *The ark of God was captured.* This phrase or a variation of it occurs five times in the chapter (here, vv. 17,19,21 – 22) and is the focal point of the narrative. In this disastrous event, God's word in 3:11 finds a swift fulfillment. *Hophni and Phinehas, died.* The fulfillment of 2:34; 3:12.
4:12 *his clothes torn and dust on his head.* A sign of grief and sorrow, here marking the messenger as a bearer of bad news (see 2Sa 1:2; 13:19; 15:32).
4:13 *his heart feared for the ark of God.* Eli had sufficient spiritual sensitivity to be aware of the danger inherent in the sinful and presumptuous act of taking the ark of God into the battle. And he seems to have been even more concerned for the ark than for his sons (see v. 18).
4:18 *he died.* The death of Eli marked the end of an era that had begun with the deaths of Joshua and the elders who served with him (see Jos 24:29,31). Incapable of restraining Israel or his sons from their wicked ways, and weakened and blinded by age, the old priest is an apt symbol of the flawed age now coming to its tragic close. He is also a striking contrast to the reign of David, which is the main focus of this narrative. *heavy.* A bit of information that not only helps explain why Eli's fall was fatal but also links his death with the judgment announced earlier: "Why do you honor your sons more than me by fattening yourselves ...?" (2:29). *He had led Israel forty years.* See NIV text note; see also Jdg 12:7 and note. Eli is here included among the judges (see 2Sa 7:11; Jdg 2:16 – 19; Ru 1:1), who served as leaders of Israel in the period between the deaths of Joshua and of the elders who outlived him and the establishment of kingship. Eli's leadership of 40 years may have overlapped that of some of the judges, such as Jephthah and Samson.
4:21 *Ichabod.* See NIV text note. *The Glory has departed.* The glory of Israel was Israel's God, not the ark (see 15:29; Heb 9:5 and notes), and loss of the ark did not mean that God had abandoned his people — God was not inseparably bound to the ark (see Jer 3:16 – 17). Yet the removal of the ark from Israel did signal estrangement in the relationship between God and his people, and it demonstrated the gravity of their error in thinking that in spite of their wickedness they had the power to coerce God into doing their will simply because they possessed the ark.
5:1 *Ashdod.* One of the five major cities of the Philistines (Jos 13:3; see map, p. 359), it was located near the Mediterranean coast about 35 miles west of Jerusalem. See note on Isa 20:1; see also map, p. 417.
5:2 *Dagon.* In Canaanite mythology the son (or brother) of El and the father of Baal. He was the principal god of the Philistines and was worshiped in temples at Gaza (Jdg 16:21,23,26), Ashdod (here) and Beth Shan (31:10 – 12; 1Ch 10:10). Veneration of this deity was widespread in the ancient world, extending from Mesopotamia to the Aramean and Canaanite area and attested in non-Biblical sources dating from the late third millennium BC until Maccabean times (second century BC; in the Apocrypha, see 1 Maccabees 10:83 – 84). The precise nature of the worship of Dagon is obscure. Some have considered Dagon to be a fish-god, but more recent evidence suggests either a storm- or grain-god. His name is related to a Hebrew word for "grain."

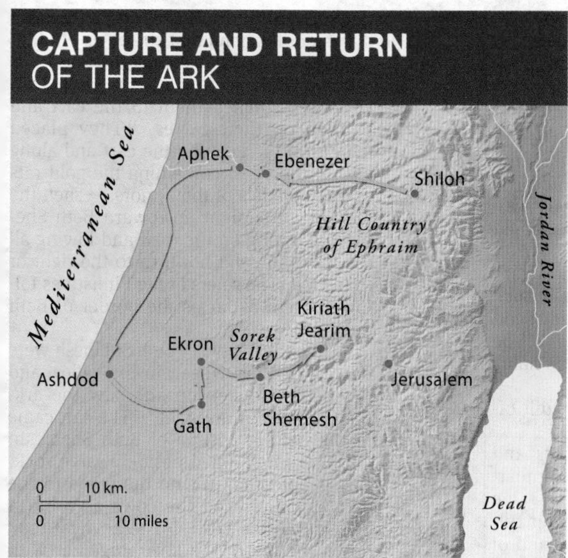

early the next day, there was Dagon, fall-
en[u] on his face on the ground before the
ark of the LORD! They took Dagon and put
him back in his place. 4But the following morning when they rose, there was
Dagon, fallen on his face on the ground
before the ark of the LORD! His head and
hands had been broken[v] off and were lying on the threshold; only his body remained. 5That is why to this day neither
the priests of Dagon nor any others who
enter Dagon's temple at Ashdod step on
the threshold.[w]
6The LORD's hand[x] was heavy on the
people of Ashdod and its vicinity; he brought devastation[y]
on them and afflicted them
with tumors.[a][z] 7When the people of Ashdod saw what was
happening, they said, "The
ark of the god of Israel must
not stay here with us, because
his hand is heavy on us and
on Dagon our god." 8So they
called together all the rulers[a]
of the Philistines and asked
them, "What shall we do with
the ark of the god of Israel?"
They answered, "Have the
ark of the god of Israel moved
to Gath.[b]" So they moved the
ark of the God of Israel.
9But after they had moved
it, the LORD's hand was against
that city, throwing it into a
great panic.[c] He afflicted the
people of the city, both young
and old, with an outbreak of
tumors.[b] 10So they sent the ark
of God to Ekron.[d]
As the ark of God was entering Ekron,
the people of Ekron cried out, "They have
brought the ark of the god of Israel around
to us to kill us and our people." 11So they
called together all the rulers[e] of the Philistines and said, "Send the ark of the god
of Israel away; let it go back to its own
place, or it[c] will kill us and our people."
For death had filled the city with panic;
God's hand was very heavy on it. 12Those

5:3 [u] Isa 40:20; 41:7; 46:7; Jer 10:4
5:4 [v] Eze 6:6; Mic 1:7
5:5 [w] Zep 1:9
5:6 [x] S Ex 9:3; Ac 13:11
[y] 2Sa 6:7; Ps 78:66
[z] S Ex 15:26; 1Sa 6:5
5:8 [a] S Jdg 16:18
[b] S Jos 11:22
5:9 [c] S Ex 14:24
5:10 [d] S Jos 13:3
5:11 [e] ver 8

[a] 6 Hebrew; Septuagint and Vulgate *tumors. And rats appeared in their land, and there was death and destruction throughout the city* [b] 9 Or *with tumors in the groin* (see Septuagint) [c] 11 Or *he*

5:3 *Dagon, fallen on his face.* The ark was placed next to the idol of Dagon by the Philistines in order to demonstrate Dagon's superiority over the God of Israel, but the symbolism was reversed when Dagon was toppled to a position of homage before the ark of the Lord.
5:4 *head and hands had been broken off.* Proving that the Lord had defeated Dagon. In the ancient Near East, the heads and/or right hands of slain enemy soldiers were often brought back to the victors' camp as trophies of war (1Ch 10:10) and to establish a body count (cf. 18:27 and note).
5:5 *this day.* The time of the writing of 1,2 Samuel (see Introduction: Literary Features, Authorship and Date). *step on the threshold.* Apparently the threshold was considered to possess supernatural power because of its contact with parts of the fallen image of Dagon. Zep 1:9 appears to be a reference to a more general and rather widespread pagan idea that the threshold was the dwelling place of spirits.
5:6 *The LORD's hand.* A pervasive motif in the ark narratives; it or its equivalent occurs eight times (here and in vv. 7,9,11; 6:3,5,9; 7:13; cf. also 4:8). *was heavy.* Dagon's broken hands lay on the threshold (v. 4), but the Lord showed the reality and strength of his own hand by bringing a plague (see note on 6:4) on the people of Ashdod and the surrounding area (see vv. 9,11). God would not be manipulated by his own people (see note on 4:3), nor would he permit the Philistines to think that their victory over the Israelites and the capture of the ark demonstrated the superiority of their god over the God of Israel. *tumors.* One of the many covenant curses that would be inflicted on the Israelites if they disobeyed God (Dt 28:58–60). Here the affliction fell on the Philistines. See also NIV text note on v. 9.
5:8 *rulers.* Of the five major cities of the Philistines (see 6:16; Jos 13:3; Jdg 3:3; see also map, p. 359). *Have the ark of the god of Israel moved to Gath.* Evidently the leaders of the Philistines did not share the opinion of the Ashdodites that there was a direct connection between what had happened in Ashdod and the presence of the ark; they seem to have suspected that the sequence of events was merely coincidental (see 6:9). The removal of the ark to Gath (12 miles southeast of Ashdod) put the matter to a test.
5:10 *Ekron.* The northernmost of the five major Philistine cities (see Jos 13:3), located 11 miles northeast of Ashdod and close to Israelite territory (see map, p. 359).
5:11 *Send the ark of the god of Israel away.* After three successive towns had been struck by disease upon the arrival of the ark, there was little doubt in the people's minds that the power of the God of Israel was the cause of their distress.

who did not die[f] were afflicted with tumors, and the outcry of the city went up to heaven.

The Ark Returned to Israel

6 When the ark of the LORD had been in Philistine territory seven months, 2 the Philistines called for the priests and the diviners[g] and said, "What shall we do with the ark of the LORD? Tell us how we should send it back to its place."

3 They answered, "If you return the ark of the god of Israel, do not send it back to him without a gift;[h] by all means send a guilt offering[i] to him. Then you will be healed, and you will know why his hand[j] has not been lifted from you."

4 The Philistines asked, "What guilt offering should we send to him?"

They replied, "Five gold tumors and five gold rats, according to the number[k] of the Philistine rulers, because the same plague[l] has struck both you and your rulers. 5 Make models of the tumors[m] and of the rats that are destroying the country, and give glory[n] to Israel's god. Perhaps he will lift his hand from you and your gods and your land. 6 Why do you harden[o] your hearts as the Egyptians and Pharaoh did? When Israel's god dealt harshly with them,[p] did they[q] not send the Israelites out so they could go on their way?

7 "Now then, get a new cart[r] ready, with two cows that have calved and have never been yoked.[s] Hitch the cows to the cart, but take their calves away and pen them up. 8 Take the ark of the LORD and put it on the cart, and in a chest beside it put the gold objects you are sending back to him as a guilt offering. Send it on its way, 9 but keep watching it. If it goes up to its own territory, toward Beth Shemesh,[t] then the LORD has brought this great disaster on us. But if it does not, then we will know that it was not his hand that struck us but that it happened to us by chance."

10 So they did this. They took two such cows and hitched them to the cart and penned up their calves. 11 They placed the ark of the LORD on the cart and along with it the chest containing the gold rats and the models of the tumors. 12 Then the cows went straight up toward Beth Shemesh, keeping on the road and lowing all the way; they did not turn to the right or to the left. The rulers of the Philistines followed them as far as the border of Beth Shemesh.

13 Now the people of Beth Shemesh were harvesting their wheat[u] in the valley, and when they looked up and saw the ark, they rejoiced at the sight. 14 The cart came to the field of Joshua of Beth Shemesh, and there it stopped beside a large rock. The people chopped up the wood of the cart and sacrificed the cows as a burnt offering[v] to the LORD. 15 The Levites[w] took down the ark of the LORD, together with the chest containing the gold objects, and placed them on the large rock.[x] On that day the people of Beth Shemesh[y] offered burnt offerings and made sacrifices to the LORD. 16 The five rulers of the Philistines saw all this and then returned that same day to Ekron.

17 These are the gold tumors the Philistines sent as a guilt offering to the LORD—one each[z] for Ashdod, Gaza, Ashkelon, Gath and Ekron. 18 And the number of the gold rats was according to the number of Philistine towns belonging to the five rulers—the fortified towns with their country villages. The large rock on which the Levites set the ark of the LORD is a witness to this day in the field of Joshua of Beth Shemesh.

19 But God struck down[a] some of the in-

5:12 [f] S 1Sa 4:8 **6:2** [g] S Ex 7:11; S Isa 44:25 **6:3** [h] S Ex 22:29; S 34:20 [i] S Lev 5:15 [j] ver 9 **6:4** [k] S Jos 13:3 [l] 2Sa 24:25 **6:5** [m] S 1Sa 5:6-11 [n] S Jos 7:19; Rev 14:7 **6:6** [o] S Ex 4:21 [p] Ex 10:2 [q] S Ex 12:33 **6:7** [r] 2Sa 6:3; 1Ch 13:7 [s] S Nu 19:2 **6:9** [t] S Jos 15:10; 21:16 **6:13** [u] S Ge 30:14; Ru 2:23; 1Sa 12:17 **6:14** [v] 1Sa 11:7; 2Sa 24:22; 1Ki 19:21 **6:15** [w] Jos 3:3 [x] ver 18 [y] Jos 21:16 **6:17** [z] S Jos 13:3 **6:19** [a] 2Sa 6:7

6:2 *priests and ... diviners.* The experts on religious matters (priests) and the discerners of hidden knowledge by interpretation of omens (diviners) were consulted (see Dt 18:10; Isa 2:6; Eze 21:21).

6:3 *guilt offering.* The priests and diviners suggest returning the ark with a gift, signifying recognition of guilt in taking the ark from Israel and compensation for this violation of the Lord's honor (see v. 5). For the guilt offering in Israel, see Lev 5:14—6:7.

6:4 *Five gold tumors.* Corresponding to the symptoms of the plague (see 5:6). *five gold rats.* The disease was accompanied by an infestation of rats (v. 5). The pre-Christian Greek translation of the OT (the Septuagint) includes this information earlier in the narrative (see NIV text note on 5:6). It is likely that the rats were carriers of the disease.

6:5 *Make models ... and give glory to Israel's god.* The gold models were an acknowledgment that the disease and the rats were a judgment from the hand of the God of Israel (see note on v. 3).

6:6 *harden your hearts.* See notes on Ex 4:21; Dt 2:3; Jos 11:20. *the Egyptians and Pharaoh.* The plagues that God inflicted on the Egyptians at the time of the exodus made a lasting impression on the surrounding nations (see 4:8; Jos 2:10).

6:7 *have never been yoked.* Have not been trained to pull a cart. *take their calves away.* Normally cows do not willingly leave their suckling calves.

6:9 *Beth Shemesh.* A town near the Philistine border, belonging to Judah (see Jos 15:10; see also map, p. 417). *by chance.* See note on 5:8.

6:12 *the cows went ... keeping on the road.* Further indication that the Lord was directing them (see v. 7 and note).

6:13 *harvesting their wheat.* The time of wheat harvest is from mid-April until mid-June.

6:14–15 The arrival of the ark at Beth Shemesh is just as much a revelation of the hand of God as the journey itself, because it was one of the priestly towns (see Jos 21:13–16).

6:17 *guilt offering.* See note on v. 3.

6:18 *witness.* A kind of monument to the event. *this day.* The time of the writing of 1,2 Samuel (see Introduction: Literary Features, Authorship and Date).

habitants of Beth Shemesh, putting seventy[a] of them to death because they looked[b]
into the ark of the LORD. The people
mourned because of the heavy blow the
LORD had dealt them. 20 And the people of
Beth Shemesh asked, "Who can stand[c] in
the presence of the LORD, this holy[d] God?
To whom will the ark go up from here?"
21 Then they sent messengers to the people of Kiriath Jearim,[e] saying, "The Philistines have returned the ark of the LORD.
Come down and take it up to your town."
7 1 So the men of Kiriath Jearim came
and took up the ark[f] of the LORD. They
brought it to Abinadab's[g] house on the hill
and consecrated Eleazar his son to guard
the ark of the LORD. 2 The ark remained at
Kiriath Jearim[h] a long time—twenty years
in all.

Samuel Subdues the Philistines at Mizpah

Then all the people of Israel turned back
to the LORD.[i] 3 So Samuel said to all the Israelites, "If you are returning[j] to the LORD
with all your hearts, then rid[k] yourselves
of the foreign gods and the Ashtoreths[l]
and commit[m] yourselves to the LORD and

6:19 [b] S Ex 19:21 **6:20** [c] 2Sa 6:9; Ps 130:3; Mal 3:2; Rev 6:17 [d] S Lev 11:45 **6:21** [e] S Jos 9:17 **7:1** [f] S Jos 6:7 [g] 2Sa 6:3; 1Ch 13:7 **7:2** [h] 1Ch 13:5; Ps 132:6 [i] 1Ch 13:3 **7:3** [j] Dt 30:10; 2Ki 18:5; 23:25; Jer 24:7 [k] S Ge 31:19; S Jos 24:14 [l] S Jdg 2:12-13; 1Sa 12:10; 31:10 [m] Joel 2:12

[a] *19* A few Hebrew manuscripts; most Hebrew manuscripts and Septuagint *50,070*

6:19 *seventy.* The additional 50,000 in most Hebrew manuscripts (see NIV text note) is apparently a copyist's mistake because it is added in an ungrammatical way (no conjunction). Furthermore, this small town could not have contained that many inhabitants. *looked into the ark.* The men of Beth Shemesh (Levites and priests among them) were judged by God for their irreverent curiosity. Because God had so closely linked the manifestation of his own presence among his people with the ark, it was to be treated with great honor (see 2Sa 6:7; Nu 4:15,17–20). This attitude of respect, however, is quite different from the superstitious attitude that led the elders to take the ark into battle against the Philistines, thus treating it as an object with magical power (see note on 4:3).
6:20 *this holy God.* See 2:2 and note. *To whom will the ark go up from here?* The inhabitants of Beth Shemesh respond to God's judgment in much the same way as the inhabitants of Ashdod, Gath and Ekron (see 5:8–10).
6:21 *Kiriath Jearim.* Located nine miles west of Jerusalem (see map, p. 417; see also photo below).
7:1 *Abinadab's house.* The ark remained in relative obscurity at Abinadab's house until David brought it to Jerusalem (2Sa 6:2–3). Somehow the tent of meeting (and the altar of burnt offering) escaped the destruction of Shiloh (Jer 7:12,14; 26:6; see photo, p. 404). It apparently was first moved to Nob (21:1–9). In David's and Solomon's days it was located at Gibeon, five miles northwest of Jerusalem (1Ki 3:4; 1Ch 16:39; 21:29; 2Ch 1:3,13). The Gibeonites had been condemned to be menial laborers at the Lord's sanctuary (Jos 9:23,27). After Solomon completed the construction of the temple, he brought the ark and the tent of meeting to it (see 1Ki 8:3–6 and note on 8:4).
7:2–17 Samuel's leadership as prophet and judge characterized.
7:2 *twenty years in all.* Probably the 20-year interval between the return of the ark to Israel and the assembly called by Samuel at Mizpah (see v. 5).
7:3 *Ashtoreths.* A general term for foreign goddesses, as elsewhere in the ancient Near East. More specifically, however, Ashtoreth herself was a goddess of love, fertility and war, worshiped in various forms by many peoples, including the Canaanites (see note on Jdg 2:13). The worship of Ashtoreth is frequently combined with the worship of Baal (see v. 4; 12:10; Jdg 2:13; 10:6), in accordance with the common practice in fertility religions to associate male and female deities.

View of Kiriath Jearim from the south. Men from Kiriath Jearim retrieved the ark from the Philistines, and the ark remained there 20 years (1Sa 7:2).

Todd Bolen/www.BiblePlaces.com

serve him only,[n] and he will deliver[o] you out of the hand of the Philistines." 4 So the Israelites put away their Baals and Ashtoreths, and served the LORD only.

5 Then Samuel[p] said, "Assemble all Israel at Mizpah,[q] and I will intercede[r] with the LORD for you." 6 When they had assembled at Mizpah,[s] they drew water and poured[t] it out before the LORD. On that day they fasted and there they confessed, "We have sinned against the LORD." Now Samuel was serving as leader[a][u] of Israel at Mizpah.

7 When the Philistines heard that Israel had assembled at Mizpah, the rulers of the Philistines came up to attack them. When the Israelites heard of it, they were afraid[v] because of the Philistines. 8 They said to Samuel, "Do not stop crying[w] out to the LORD our God for us, that he may rescue us from the hand of the Philistines." 9 Then Samuel[x] took a suckling lamb and sacrificed it as a whole burnt offering to the LORD. He cried out to the LORD on Israel's behalf, and the LORD answered him.[y]

10 While Samuel was sacrificing the burnt offering, the Philistines drew near to engage Israel in battle. But that day the LORD thundered[z] with loud thunder against the Philistines and threw them into such a panic[a] that they were routed before the Israelites. 11 The men of Israel rushed out of Mizpah and pursued the Philistines, slaughtering them along the way to a point below Beth Kar.

12 Then Samuel took a stone[b] and set it up between Mizpah and Shen. He named it Ebenezer,[b][c] saying, "Thus far the LORD has helped us."

13 So the Philistines were subdued[d] and they stopped invading Israel's territory. Throughout Samuel's lifetime, the hand of the LORD was against the Philistines. 14 The towns from Ekron[e] to Gath that the Philistines had captured from Israel were restored to Israel, and Israel delivered the neighboring territory from the hands of the Philistines. And there was peace between Israel and the Amorites.[f]

15 Samuel[g] continued as Israel's leader[h] all[i] the days of his life. 16 From year to year he went on a circuit from Bethel[j] to Gilgal[k] to Mizpah, judging[l] Israel in all those places. 17 But he always went back to Ramah,[m] where his home was, and there he also held court[n] for Israel. And he built an altar[o] there to the LORD.

Israel Asks for a King

8 When Samuel grew old, he appointed[p] his sons as Israel's leaders.[c] 2 The name of his firstborn was Joel and the name of his second was Abijah,[q] and they

[a] 6 Traditionally *judge*; also in verse 15 [b] 12 *Ebenezer* means *stone of help.* [c] 1 Traditionally *judges*

7:3 [n] S Dt 6:13; Mt 4:10; Lk 4:8 [o] S Jdg 2:18 **7:5** [p] S 1Sa 1:20; Ps 99:6; Jer 15:1 [q] S Jos 11:3; Jdg 21:5; 1Sa 10:17 [r] S ver 8; S Ge 20:7; S Dt 9:19 **7:6** [s] S Jos 11:3 [t] La 2:19 [u] S Jdg 2:16; S 16:31 **7:7** [v] 1Sa 17:11 **7:8** [w] ver 5; S Ex 32:30; S Nu 21:7; 1Sa 12:19, 23; 1Ki 18:24; Isa 37:4; Jer 15:1; 27:18 **7:9** [x] Ps 99:6 [y] S Ex 32:11; S Dt 9:19 **7:10** [z] S Ex 9:23; S 1Sa 2:10 [a] S Ge 35:5; S Ex 14:24 **7:12** [b] S Ge 28:22; S Dt 27:2; Jos 4:9 [c] S 1Sa 4:1 **7:13** [d] Jdg 13:1,5 **7:14** [e] S Jos 13:3 [f] S Jdg 1:34 **7:15** [g] ver 6; 1Sa 12:11 [h] S Jdg 2:16 [i] Jdg 2:18 **7:16** [j] S Ge 12:8 [k] S Jos 10:43; S 1Sa 10:8; Am 5:5 [l] ver 6; Ac 13:20 **7:17** [m] S Jos 18:25; 1Sa 8:4; 15:34; 19:18; 25:1; 28:3 [n] ver 6 [o] 1Sa 9:12; 14:35; 20:6; 2Sa 24:25 **8:1** [p] Dt 16:18-19 **8:2** [q] 1Ch 6:28

7:5 *Mizpah.* See note on 2Ki 25:23; a town in the territory of Benjamin (Jos 18:26), located about seven and a half miles north of Jerusalem (see map, p. 354). It was here that the Israelites had previously gathered to undertake disciplinary action against Benjamin (Jdg 20:1; 21:1) after the abuse and murder of the concubine of a traveling Levite in Gibeah of Benjamin. Several other places bore the same name (see 22:3; Ge 31:49; Jos 11:3,8; 15:38). *I will intercede.* See 7:8–9 and note on 7:8; 8:6; 12:17–19,23; 15:11. Samuel, like Moses, was later remembered as a great intercessor (see Ps 99:6; Jer 15:1). Both were appointed by God to mediate his rule over his people, representing God to Israel and speaking on Israel's behalf to God.

7:6 *they drew water and poured it out before the LORD.* There is no other reference to this type of ceremony in the OT. It appears to symbolize the pouring out of one's heart in repentance and humility before the Lord. For related expressions, see 1:15; Ps 62:8; La 2:19 and note. *Samuel was … leader.* See NIV text note and v. 15; see also note on 4:18.

7:8 *Do not stop crying out to the LORD our God for us.* As persons who were called out from among the people to mediate God's word to them, prophets were given unique access to God's council chamber (see 1Ki 22:19 and note). This privilege of having such access to God as to be mediators of God's rule over his people brought with it the special responsibility to be intercessors for God's people—as Moses was (Ex 32:11–14; 34:8–9; Nu 14:13–19), and as were Isaiah (2Ki 19:4), Jeremiah (see Jer 7:16; 15:1 and notes) and Amos (Am 7:2–3,5–6).

7:10 *the LORD thundered with loud thunder.* The Lord had promised to be the protector of his people when they were obedient to their covenant obligations (see Ex 23:22; Dt 20:1–4; see also 2Sa 5:19–25; Jos 10:11–14; Jdg 5:20–21; 2Ki 7:6; 19:35; 2Ch 20:17,22).

7:12 *Ebenezer.* See NIV text note and note on 4:1.

7:13 *stopped invading Israel's territory.* Some interpreters see a contradiction between this statement and subsequent references to the Philistines in 9:16; 10:5; 13:3,5; 17:1; 23:27. This statement, however, only indicates that the Philistines did not immediately counterattack. See 2Ki 6:23–24 for a similar situation.

7:14 *Amorites.* See note on Ge 10:16.

7:15 A summary statement marking the end of the author's account of Samuel's ministry as Israel's leader (see v. 6).

7:16 *from Bethel to Gilgal to Mizpah.* A relatively small area (see map, p. 354). *judging Israel.* See note on 4:18.

7:17 *Ramah.* See note on 1:1.

8:1—12:25 Transition from Samuel's leadership to the establishment of the monarchy as the political structure of the nation of Israel, through which God would reestablish (under David) his theocratic order over his people—as in the days of Moses and Joshua (see Introduction: Contents and Theme; see also note on Jdg 17:1—21:25).

8:1 *When Samuel grew old.* Probably about 20 years after the victory at Mizpah (see 7:11), when Samuel was approximately 65 years old (see Introduction: Chronology).

8:2 *Joel.* Means "The LORD is God." *Abijah.* Means "The LORD is my Father." Despite their names, Samuel's two sons "did not follow his ways" (v. 3). *Beersheba.* Located 45 miles southwest of Jerusalem (see note on Ge 21:31).

served at Beersheba.[r] 3But his sons[s] did not follow his ways. They turned aside[t] after dishonest gain and accepted bribes[u] and perverted[v] justice.

4So all the elders[w] of Israel gathered together and came to Samuel at Ramah.[x] 5They said to him, "You are old, and your sons do not follow your ways; now appoint a king[y] to lead[az] us, such as all the other nations[a] have."

6But when they said, "Give us a king[b] to lead us," this displeased[c] Samuel; so he prayed to the LORD. 7And the LORD told him: "Listen[d] to all that the people are saying to you; it is not you they have rejected,[e] but they have rejected me as their king.[f] 8As they have done from the day I brought them up out of Egypt until this day, forsaking[g] me and serving other gods, so they are doing to you. 9Now listen to them; but warn them solemnly and let them know[h] what the king who will reign over them will claim as his rights."

10Samuel told[i] all the words of the LORD to the people who were asking him for a king. 11He said, "This is what the king who will reign over you will claim as his rights: He will take[j] your sons and make them serve[k] with his chariots and horses, and they will run in front of his chariots.[l] 12Some he will assign to be commanders[m] of thousands and commanders of fifties, and others to plow his ground and reap his harvest, and still others to make weapons of war and equipment for his chariots. 13He will take your daughters to be perfumers and cooks and bakers. 14He will take the best of your[n] fields and vineyards[o] and olive groves and give them to his attendants.[p] 15He will take a tenth[q] of your grain and of your vintage and give it to his officials and attendants. 16Your male and female servants and the best of your cattle[b] and donkeys he will take for his own use. 17He will take a tenth of your flocks, and you yourselves will become his slaves. 18When that day comes, you will cry out for relief from the king you have chosen, but the LORD will not answer[r] you in that day.[s]"

19But the people refused[t] to listen to Samuel. "No!" they said. "We want[u] a king[v] over us. 20Then we will be like all the other nations,[w] with a king to lead us and to go out before us and fight our battles."

21When Samuel heard all that the people said, he repeated[x] it before the LORD. 22The LORD answered, "Listen[y] to them and give them a king."

Then Samuel said to the Israelites, "Everyone go back to your own town."

Samuel Anoints Saul

9 There was a Benjamite,[z] a man of standing,[a] whose name was Kish[b] son of Abiel, the son of Zeror, the son of Bekorath, the son of Aphiah of Benjamin. 2Kish had a son named Saul, as handsome[c] a young man as could be found[d] anywhere in Israel, and he was a head taller[e] than anyone else.

[a] *5* Traditionally *judge*; also in verses 6 and 20
[b] *16* Septuagint; Hebrew *young men*

8:2 [r] Ge 22:19; 1Ki 19:3; Am 5:4-5 **8:3** [s] 1Sa 2:12 [t] Ne 9:29; Job 34:27; Ps 14:3; 58:3; Isa 53:6 [u] Ex 23:8; 1Sa 12:3; Job 8:22; Pr 17:23 [v] S Ex 23:2 **8:4** [w] S Jdg 11:11; 1Sa 11:3 [x] S 1Sa 7:17 **8:5** [y] ver 19; S Dt 17:14-20; 1Sa 10:19; 12:12, 13; Hos 13:11 [z] 1Sa 3:20; 12:2 [a] ver 20 **8:6** [b] Hos 13:10 [c] 1Sa 12:17; 15:11; 16:1 **8:7** [d] ver 22; 1Sa 12:1 [e] S Nu 11:20 [f] S Ex 16:8 **8:8** [g] 1Sa 12:10; 2Ki 21:22; Jer 2:17 **8:9** [h] ver 11-18; S Dt 17:14-20; 1Sa 10:25 **8:10** [i] S Ex 19:7 **8:11** [j] 1Sa 14:52 [k] S Ge 41:46 [l] S Dt 17:16; 2Sa 15:1; 1Ki 1:5; 2Ch 1:14; 9:25; SS 3:7 **8:12** [m] S Dt 1:15 **8:14** [n] Eze 46:18 [o] 1Ki 21:7, 15; Mic 2:2 [p] 2Ki 22:12 **8:15** [q] S Ge 41:34; 1Sa 17:25 **8:18** [r] 1Sa 28:6; Job 27:9; 35:12, 13; Ps 18:41; 66:18; Pr 1:28; Isa 1:15; 58:4; 59:2; Jer 14:12; Eze 8:18; Mic 3:4 [s] 1Sa 10:25; 1Ki 12:4 **8:19** [t] Pr 1:24; Isa 50:2; 66:4; Jer 7:13; 8:12; 13:10; 44:16 [u] Ac 13:21 [v] S ver 5 **8:20** [w] S ver 5 **8:21** [x] S Jdg 11:11 **8:22** [y] S ver 7 **9:1** [z] Jos 18:11-20 [a] S Ru 2:1 [b] 1Sa 14:51; 1Ch 8:33; 9:39; Est 2:5; Ac 13:21 **9:2** [c] S Ge 39:6 [d] 1Sa 10:24 [e] 1Sa 10:23

8:3 *accepted bribes.* Contrast 12:3. Perversion of justice through bribery was explicitly forbidden in Pentateuchal law (see Ex 23:8; Dt 16:19).

8:5 *appoint a king to lead us.* The elders cite Samuel's age and the misconduct of his sons as justifications for their request for a king. It soon becomes apparent, however, that the more basic reason for their request was a desire to be like the surrounding nations — to have a human king as a symbol of national power and unity, one who would lead them in battle and guarantee their security (see v. 20; 10:19; 12:12; see also Introduction: Contents and Theme).

8:7 *Listen to all that the people are saying to you.* Anticipations of kingship in Israel are present already in the Pentateuch (Ge 49:10; Nu 24:7,17; Dt 17:14 – 20); Samuel is therefore instructed to listen to the people's request (see vv. 9,22). *it is not you they have rejected, but they have rejected me as their king.* Cf. Jdg 8:23. The sin of Israel in requesting a king (see 10:19; 12:12,17,19 – 20) rested not in any evil inherent in kingship itself but in the kind of kingship the people envisioned and their reasons for requesting it (see Introduction: Contents and Theme). Their desire was for a form of kingship that denied their covenant relationship with the Lord, who himself was pledged to be their savior and deliverer. In requesting a king "like all the other nations" (v. 20) they broke the covenant, rejected the Lord who was their King (12:12; Nu 23:21; Dt 33:5) and forgot his constant provision for their protection in the past (10:18; 12:8 – 11).

8:9,11 *what the king ... will claim as his rights.* Using a description of the policies of contemporary Canaanite kings (vv. 11 – 17), Samuel warns the people of the burdens associated with the type of kingship they long for.

8:11 *chariots.* See note on Jos 11:6; see also Dt 17:16 and note on 17:16 – 17.

8:15 *tenth.* This king's portion would be over and above the tenth Israel was to devote to the Lord (Lev 27:30 – 32; Nu 18:26; Dt 14:22,28; 26:12). In fact, the demands of the king would parallel all that Israel was to consecrate to the Lord as her Great King (persons, lands, crops, livestock) — even the whole population (v. 17).

8:18 *cry out for relief from the king.* See 1Ki 12:4; Jer 22:13 – 17.

8:20 *like all the other nations.* See notes on vv. 5,7.

9:1 — 11:15 God's establishment of Saul as king over Israel took place in three distinct stages: He was (1) anointed by Samuel (9:1 — 10:16), (2) chosen by lot (10:17 – 27) and (3) confirmed by public acclamation (11:1 – 15).

9:1 *man of standing.* Saul (v. 2) and David are each depicted as descending from an ancestor who was a noteworthy member of his community (see Ru 2:1; 4:21 – 22).

9:2 *a head taller than anyone else.* Physically of kingly stature — every inch a king (see 10:23).

3 Now the donkeys[f] belonging to Saul's father Kish were lost, and Kish said to his son Saul, "Take one of the servants with you and go and look for the donkeys." 4 So he passed through the hill[g] country of Ephraim and through the area around Shalisha,[h] but they did not find them. They went on into the district of Shaalim, but the donkeys[i] were not there. Then he passed through the territory of Benjamin, but they did not find them.

5 When they reached the district of Zuph,[j] Saul said to the servant who was with him, "Come, let's go back, or my father will stop thinking about the donkeys and start worrying[k] about us."

6 But the servant replied, "Look, in this town there is a man of God;[l] he is highly respected, and everything[m] he says comes true. Let's go there now. Perhaps he will tell us what way to take."

7 Saul said to his servant, "If we go, what can we give the man? The food in our sacks is gone. We have no gift[n] to take to the man of God. What do we have?"

8 The servant answered him again. "Look," he said, "I have a quarter of a shekel[a] of silver. I will give it to the man of God so that he will tell us what way to take." 9 (Formerly in Israel, if someone went to inquire[o] of God, they would say, "Come, let us go to the seer," because the prophet of today used to be called a seer.)[p]

10 "Good," Saul said to his servant. "Come, let's go." So they set out for the town where the man of God was.

11 As they were going up the hill to the town, they met some young women coming out to draw[q] water, and they asked them, "Is the seer here?"

12 "He is," they answered. "He's ahead of you. Hurry now; he has just come to our town today, for the people have a sacrifice[r] at the high place.[s] 13 As soon as you enter the town, you will find him before he goes up to the high place to eat. The people will not begin eating until he comes, because he must bless[t] the sacrifice; afterward, those who are invited will eat. Go up now; you should find him about this time."

14 They went up to the town, and as they were entering it, there was Samuel, coming toward them on his way up to the high place.

15 Now the day before Saul came, the LORD had revealed this to Samuel: 16 "About this time tomorrow I will send you a man from the land of Benjamin. Anoint[u] him ruler[v] over my people Israel; he will deliver[w] them from the hand of the Philistines.[x] I have looked on my people, for their cry[y] has reached me."

17 When Samuel caught sight of Saul, the LORD said to him, "This[z] is the man I spoke to you about; he will govern my people."

[a] 8 That is, about 1/10 ounce or about 3 grams

9:3 [f] ver 20; 1Sa 10:14,16 **9:4** [g] S Jos 24:33 [h] 2Ki 4:42 [i] 1Sa 10:2 **9:5** [j] 1Sa 1:1 [k] 1Sa 10:2 **9:6** [l] S Dt 33:1; S Jdg 13:6 [m] 1Sa 3:19 **9:7** [n] S Ge 32:20; 1Ki 13:7; 14:3; 2Ki 4:42; 5:5, 15; Jer 40:5 **9:9** [o] S Ge 25:22 [p] 2Sa 15:27; 24:11; 2Ki 17:13; 1Ch 9:22; 21:9; 26:28; 29:29; 2Ch 19:2; Isa 29:10; 30:10; Am 7:12 **9:11** [q] S Ge 24:11,13 **9:12** [r] Nu 28:11-15; S 1Sa 7:17 [s] S Lev 26:30 **9:13** [t] S Mt 14:19; 1Co 10:16; 1Ti 4:3-5 **9:16** [u] Ex 30:25; S 1Sa 2:35; 12:3; 15:1; 26:9; 2Ki 11:12; Ps 2:2 [v] 2Sa 7:8; 1Ki 8:16; 1Ch 5:2 [w] Ex 3:7-9 [x] 1Sa 23:4; 2Sa 3:18 [y] S Ge 16:11; Ps 102:1 **9:17** [z] 1Sa 16:12

9:3 *donkeys ... were lost.* Saul is introduced as a donkey wrangler sent in search of donkeys that had strayed from home—perhaps symbolizing Saul and the rebellious people who had asked for a king (cf. Isa 1:3). David would be introduced as a shepherd caring for his father's flock (16:11–13) and later pictured as the shepherd over the Lord's flock (2Sa 5:2; 7:7–8; Ps 78:70–72).

9:5 *Zuph.* Perhaps the region in which Ramah was located (see notes on v. 6; 1:1).

9:6 *But the servant replied.* Saul's ignorance of Samuel is an early hint of his character. *this town.* Probably Ramah (see 7:17), the hometown of Samuel, to which he had just returned from a journey (see v. 12). *man of God.* See note on 2:27; here a reference to Samuel. *everything he says comes true.* See 3:19 and note.

9:7 *what can we give the man?* Other examples of gifts offered to prophets are found in 1Ki 14:3; 2Ki 4:42; 5:15–16; 8:8–9. Whether Samuel accepted the gift and whether he was dependent on such gifts for a livelihood are not clear. Elisha refused the gift of Naaman (2Ki 5:16). False prophets usually adjusted their message to the desires of those who supported them (1Ki 22:6,8,18; Jer 28; Mic 3:5,11).

9:8 *a quarter of a shekel of silver.* See NIV text note. Before the use of coins, gold or silver was weighed out for each monetary transaction (see 13:21; Job 28:15).

9:9 *the prophet of today used to be called a seer.* There was no essential difference between a seer ("one who sees" [prophetic visions]) and a prophet ("one who is called" [by God to be his spokesperson; see Ex 7:1–2 and note]). The person popularly designated as a prophet at the time of the writing of 1,2 Samuel was termed a seer in the time of Saul. This need not mean that the term "prophet" was unknown in the time of Saul or that the term "seer" was unknown in later times (see Isa 30:10).

9:11 *young women coming out to draw water.* In the cool of the evening (see Ge 24:11).

9:12 *high place.* After entrance into the promised land, the Israelites often followed the custom of the Canaanites in building local altars on hills. (At this time the central sanctuary was not functioning because the ark of God was separated from the tabernacle; Shiloh had been destroyed, and the priestly family, after the death of Eli's sons, was apparently still inactive.) In later times, worship at these high places provided a means for the entrance of pagan practices into Israel's religious observances and, for this reason, it was condemned (see note on 1Ki 3:2).

9:13 *he must bless the sacrifice.* Samuel presided over the sacrificial meal (see 1:4; 2:13–16), at which he gave a prayer, probably similar to those referred to in the NT (see Mt 26:26–27; Jn 6:11,23; 1Ti 4:3–5).

9:16 *Anoint him.* Priests were also anointed (see Ex 29:7; 40:12–15; Lev 4:3; 8:12), but from this point in the OT it is usually the king who is referred to as "the LORD's anointed" (see note on 2:10; see also 24:6; 26:9,11,16; 2Sa 1:14,16; 19:21; cf. Ps 2:2; but see also Zec 4:14). Anointing signifies being set apart to the Lord for a particular task and divine equipping for the task (see 10:1,6; 16:13; Isa 61:1). *ruler.* The Hebrew for this word (see 10:1; 13:14; 25:30) indicates one designated by the Lord to be the ruler of his people (see also 2Sa 5:2; 7:8; 1Ch 11:2; 17:7). It served as a useful term to ease the transition between the leadership of the judges and that of the kings. *Philistines.* See note on 7:13.

18 Saul approached Samuel in the gateway and asked, "Would you please tell me
where the seer's house is?"
19 "I am the seer," Samuel replied. "Go
up ahead of me to the high place, for today you are to eat with me, and in the
morning I will send you on your way and
will tell you all that is in your heart. 20 As
for the donkeys[a] you lost three days ago,
do not worry about them; they have been
found. And to whom is all the desire[b] of
Israel turned, if not to you and your whole
family line?"
21 Saul answered, "But am I not a Benjamite, from the smallest tribe[c] of Israel, and
is not my clan the least[d] of all the clans of
the tribe of Benjamin?[e] Why do you say
such a thing to me?"
22 Then Samuel brought Saul and his
servant into the hall and seated them at
the head of those who were invited—
about thirty in number. 23 Samuel said to
the cook, "Bring the piece of meat I gave
you, the one I told you to lay aside."
24 So the cook took up the thigh[f] with
what was on it and set it in front of Saul.
Samuel said, "Here is what has been kept
for you. Eat, because it was set aside for
you for this occasion from the time I said,
'I have invited guests.' " And Saul dined
with Samuel that day.
25 After they came down from the high
place to the town, Samuel talked with
Saul on the roof[g] of his house. 26 They
rose about daybreak, and Samuel called
to Saul on the roof, "Get ready, and I will
send you on your way." When Saul got
ready, he and Samuel went outside together. 27 As they were going down to the edge
of the town, Samuel said to Saul, "Tell the
servant to go on ahead of us"—and the
servant did so—"but you stay here for a
while, so that I may give you a message
from God."

10 Then Samuel took a flask[h] of olive
oil and poured it on Saul's head
and kissed him, saying, "Has not the LORD
anointed[i] you ruler over his inheritance?[a][j]
2 When you leave me today, you will meet
two men near Rachel's tomb,[k] at Zelzah
on the border of Benjamin. They will say
to you, 'The donkeys[l] you set out to look
for have been found. And now your father
has stopped thinking about them and is
worried[m] about you. He is asking, "What
shall I do about my son?" '
3 "Then you will go on from there until
you reach the great tree of Tabor. Three
men going up to worship God at Bethel[n]
will meet you there. One will be carrying
three young goats, another three loaves of
bread, and another a skin of wine. 4 They
will greet you and offer you two loaves of
bread,[o] which you will accept from them.
5 "After that you will go to Gibeah[p] of
God, where there is a Philistine outpost.[q]
As you approach the town, you will meet a
procession of prophets[r] coming down from
the high place[s] with lyres, timbrels,[t] pipes[u]

[a] 1 Hebrew; Septuagint and Vulgate *over his people Israel? You will reign over the LORD's people and save them from the power of their enemies round about. And this will be a sign to you that the LORD has anointed you ruler over his inheritance:*

9:20 [a] S ver 3 [b] 1Sa 12:13; Ezr 6:8; Isa 60:4-9; Da 2:44; Hag 2:7; Mal 3:1 **9:21** [c] Ps 68:27 [d] S Ex 3:11; Mt 2:6; 1Co 15:9 [e] Jdg 6:15; 20:35,46; 1Sa 18:18 **9:24** [f] S Lev 7:32-34 **9:25** [g] S Dt 22:8; S Jos 2:8; S Mt 24:17; Lk 5:19
10:1 [h] 1Sa 16:1; 2Ki 9:1,3,6 [i] S Ex 29:7; S 1Sa 9:16; S 1Ki 1:39 [j] S Ex 34:9; 2Sa 20:19; Ps 78:62,71 **10:2** [k] Ge 35:20 [l] 1Sa 9:4 [m] 1Sa 9:5 **10:3** [n] S Ge 35:7-8 **10:4** [o] ver 27; 1Sa 16:20; Pr 18:16 **10:5** [p] ver 26; 1Sa 11:4; 15:34 [q] 1Sa 13:3 [r] S Nu 11:29; 1Ki 20:35; 2Ki 2:3,15; 4:1; 6:1; 9:1; Am 7:14 [s] S Lev 26:30 [t] S Ge 31:27; Jer 31:4 [u] 1Ki 1:40; Isa 30:29

9:20 *all the desire of Israel.* A reference to Israel's desire for a king.

9:21 *smallest tribe ... least of all the clans.* Saul's origins were among the humblest in Israel (Benjamin was the youngest of Jacob's sons, and the tribe had been greatly reduced in the time of the judges; see Jdg 20:46–48). His elevation to king shows that God "exalts" whomever he will (2:7), which is one of the central themes running throughout Samuel. God's use of the powerless to promote his kingdom on earth is a common feature in the Biblical testimony and underscores the truth that his kingdom is not of this world (cf. 1Co 1:26–31).

9:24 *thigh.* Normally reserved for the Lord's consecrated priest (see Ex 29:22,27; Lev 7:32–33,35; Nu 6:20; 18:18). The presentation of this choice piece of the sacrificial animal to Saul was a distinct honor and anticipated his being designated the Lord's anointed.

9:25 *on the roof.* Where they could catch the cool evening breeze (see v. 11; 2Sa 11:2 and notes) and where Saul would sleep that night (see v. 26).

10:1 *olive oil.* Perhaps spiced (see Ex 30:22–33). *Has not the LORD anointed you ... ?* See note on 9:16. *ruler.* See 9:16 and note. *his inheritance.* "My people Israel" (9:16). The Lord's inheritance includes both the people (see Ex 34:9) and the land (see Ex 15:17). After departing from Samuel, Saul is to receive three signs (see vv. 2–7) to authenticate Samuel's words and to assure him that the Lord has indeed chosen him to be king.

10:2 *Rachel's tomb.* Rachel, Jacob's favorite wife, had died on the road to Bethlehem while giving birth to Benjamin. Her tomb had become a notable landmark (see Ge 35:20 and note).

10:3 *great tree.* A large tree was often a conspicuous point of reference for pilgrims and other travelers (see Ge 12:6 and note). *Bethel.* Located ten miles north of Jerusalem (see note on Ge 12:8).

10:5 *Gibeah of God.* Gibeah was Saul's hometown (see v. 26; 11:4), located in the tribal area of Benjamin (Jos 18:28; Jdg 19:12–14). It was usually called "Gibeah" or "Gibeah in Benjamin" (as in 13:2,15), but three times "Gibeah of Saul" (11:4; 15:34; 2Sa 21:6). The present designation (used only here) may have been Samuel's way of reminding Saul that the land of Canaan belonged to God and not to the Philistines (see Dt 32:43; Isa 14:2; Hos 9:3). *prophets.* The bands of prophets with which Samuel was associated (as also the "company of the prophets" with whom Elijah and Elisha were associated; see note on 1Ki 20:35) appear to have been small communities of men who banded together in spiritually decadent times for mutual cultivation of their religious zeal. *lyres ... harps.* The actions of individual prophets or groups of prophets were sometimes accompanied by musical instruments (see 2Ki 3:15; 1Ch 25:1). *prophesying.* Here (and in vv. 6,10–11,13) appears to designate an ecstatic praising of God inspired by the Spirit of the Lord (see Nu 11:24–30 for similar use of the term).

and harps[v] being played before them, and they will be prophesying.[w] 6 The Spirit[x] of the LORD will come powerfully upon you, and you will prophesy with them; and you will be changed[y] into a different person. 7 Once these signs are fulfilled, do whatever[z] your hand[a] finds to do, for God is with[b] you.

8 "Go down ahead of me to Gilgal.[c] I will surely come down to you to sacrifice burnt offerings and fellowship offerings, but you must wait seven[d] days until I come to you and tell you what you are to do."

Saul Made King

9 As Saul turned to leave Samuel, God changed[e] Saul's heart, and all these signs[f] were fulfilled[g] that day. 10 When he and his servant arrived at Gibeah, a procession of prophets met him; the Spirit[h] of God came powerfully upon him, and he joined in their prophesying.[i] 11 When all those who had formerly known him saw him prophesying with the prophets, they asked each other, "What is this[j] that has happened to the son of Kish? Is Saul also among the prophets?"[k]

12 A man who lived there answered, "And who is their father?" So it became a saying: "Is Saul also among the prophets?"[l] 13 After Saul stopped prophesying,[m] he went to the high place.

14 Now Saul's uncle[n] asked him and his servant, "Where have you been?"

"Looking for the donkeys,[o]" he said. "But when we saw they were not to be found, we went to Samuel."

15 Saul's uncle said, "Tell me what Samuel said to you."

16 Saul replied, "He assured us that the donkeys[p] had been found." But he did not tell his uncle what Samuel had said about the kingship.

17 Samuel summoned the people of Israel to the LORD at Mizpah[q] 18 and said to them, "This is what the LORD, the God of Israel, says: 'I brought Israel up out of Egypt, and I delivered you from the power of Egypt and all the kingdoms that oppressed[r] you.' 19 But you have now rejected[s] your God, who saves[t] you out of all your disasters and calamities. And you have said, 'No, appoint a king[u] over us.'[v] So now present[w] yourselves before the LORD by your tribes and clans."

20 When Samuel had all Israel come forward by tribes, the tribe of Benjamin was taken by lot. 21 Then he brought forward the tribe of Benjamin, clan by clan, and Matri's clan was taken.[x] Finally Saul son of Kish was taken. But when they looked for him, he was not to be found. 22 So they inquired[y] further of the LORD, "Has the man come here yet?"

And the LORD said, "Yes, he has hidden himself among the supplies."

23 They ran and brought him out, and as he stood among the people he was a head taller[z] than any of the others. 24 Samuel said to all the people, "Do you see the man the LORD has chosen?[a] There is no one like[b] him among all the people."

Then the people shouted, "Long live[c] the king!"

25 Samuel explained[d] to the people the rights and duties[e] of kingship.[f] He wrote them down on a scroll and deposited it be-

10:5 [v] 1Sa 16:16; 18:10; 19:9; 2Ki 3:15; Ps 92:3 [w] ver 10; 1Sa 19:20; 1Ch 25:1; 1Co 14:1 **10:6** [x] S Nu 11:25 [y] ver 9 **10:7** [z] 2Sa 7:3; 1Ki 8:17; 1Ch 22:7; 28:2; 2Ch 6:7; Ecc 9:10 [a] Jdg 9:33 [b] S Jos 1:5; Lk 1:28; Heb 13:5 **10:8** [c] Jos 4:20; S 10:43; 1Sa 7:16; 11:14-15 [d] 1Sa 13:8 **10:9** [e] ver 6 [f] S Dt 13:2 [g] ver 7 **10:10** [h] S Nu 11:25; 1Sa 11:6 [i] S ver 5-6 **10:11** [j] Mt 13:54; Jn 7:15 [k] ver 12; 1Sa 19:24; 2Ki 9:11; Jer 29:26; Hos 9:7 **10:12** [l] S ver 11 **10:13** [m] 1Sa 19:23 **10:14** [n] 1Sa 14:50 [o] S 1Sa 9:3 **10:16** [p] S 1Sa 9:3 **10:17** [q] S 1Sa 7:5 **10:18** [r] S Ex 1:14; S Nu 10:9 **10:19** [s] S Nu 11:20; S Dt 33:5 [t] Ps 7:10; 18:48; 68:20; 145:19 [u] S 1Sa 8:5-7 [v] S Dt 17:14 [w] Jos 7:14 **10:21** [x] Est 3:7; Pr 16:33 **10:22** [y] S Ge 25:22; S Jdg 18:5 **10:23** [z] 1Sa 9:2 **10:24** [a] Dt 17:15; 2Sa 21:6 [b] 1Sa 9:2 [c] 1Ki 1:25,34,39; 2Ki 11:12 **10:25** [d] S 1Sa 8:9 [e] S Dt 17:14-20; S 1Sa 8:11-18; 2Ki 11:12 [f] 1Sa 11:14

10:6 *changed into a different person.* God's Spirit would enable Saul to be Israel's king.

10:7 *do whatever your hand finds to do.* Saul is to take whatever action is appropriate when the situation presents itself to manifest publicly his royal leadership (see 11:4–11).

10:8 *Go down ahead of me to Gilgal.* At some unspecified future time, perhaps previously discussed (see 9:25), Saul is to go to Gilgal and wait seven days for Samuel's arrival (see 13:7–14). *Gilgal.* See note on Jos 4:19.

10:11 *Is Saul also among the prophets?* See 19:24 and note; an expression of surprise at Saul's behavior by those who had known him previously—another subtle indication of his character (see notes on 9:3,6).

10:12 *who is their father?* Some understand the question as an expression of contempt for prophets generally, others as implying the recognition that prophetic inspiration comes from God and therefore could be imparted to whomever God chose. However, since leading prophets were sometimes called "father" (2Ki 2:12; 6:21; 13:14), the speaker may have intended a disdainful reference to Samuel or an ironical gibe at Saul.

10:17 *Samuel summoned the people.* After the private designation and anointing of Saul to be king (9:15–17,20–21,27; 10:1), an assembly is called by Samuel to make the Lord's choice known to the people (v. 21) and to define the king's task (v. 25). *Mizpah.* See note on 7:5.

10:18 *I delivered you.* Speaking through Samuel, the Lord emphasizes to the people that he has been their deliverer throughout their history. He brought them out of Egypt and delivered them from all their enemies during the time of the judges. Although the judges themselves are sometimes referred to as Israel's deliverers (see Jdg 3:9,15,31; 6:14; 10:1; 13:5), this was true only in a secondary sense, for they were instruments of the Lord's deliverance (see Jdg 2:18). It was the Lord who sent them (see 12:11; Jdg 6:14).

10:19 *rejected your God.* See note on 8:7.

10:20 *tribe of Benjamin was taken by lot.* See 14:41–42; Jos 7:16–18. The Urim and Thummim were used for this purpose (see notes on 2:28; Ex 28:30).

10:23 *a head taller.* See 9:2 and note.

10:24 *Long live the king!* See note on Ps 62:4.

10:25 *rights and duties of kingship.* Samuel here takes the first step toward resolving the tension that existed between Israel's misdirected desire for a king (and their misconceived notion of what the king's role and function should be) and the Lord's intent to give them one (see Introduction: Contents and Theme). This description of the duties and prerogatives of the Israelite king was given for the benefit of both

fore the LORD. Then Samuel dismissed the
people to go to their own homes.
26 Saul also went to his home in Gibeah,[g] accompanied by valiant men[h] whose
hearts God had touched. 27 But some
scoundrels[i] said, "How can this fellow
save us?" They despised him and brought
him no gifts.[j] But Saul kept silent.

Saul Rescues the City of Jabesh

11 Nahash[a][k] the Ammonite went up
and besieged Jabesh Gilead.[l] And
all the men of Jabesh said to him, "Make
a treaty[m] with us, and we will be subject
to you."
2 But Nahash the Ammonite replied, "I
will make a treaty with you only on the
condition[n] that I gouge[o] out the right eye
of every one of you and so bring disgrace[p]
on all Israel."
3 The elders[q] of Jabesh said to him,
"Give us seven days so we can send messengers throughout Israel; if no one comes
to rescue[r] us, we will surrender[s] to you."
4 When the messengers came to Gibe-
ah[t] of Saul and reported these terms to the
people, they all wept[u] aloud. 5 Just then
Saul was returning from the fields, behind
his oxen, and he asked, "What is wrong
with everyone? Why are they weeping?"
Then they repeated to him what the men
of Jabesh had said.
6 When Saul heard their words, the Spirit[v] of God came powerfully upon him, and
he burned with anger. 7 He took a pair of
oxen,[w] cut them into pieces, and sent the
pieces by messengers throughout Israel,[x]
proclaiming, "This is what will be done to
the oxen of anyone[y] who does not follow
Saul and Samuel." Then the terror of the
LORD fell on the people, and they came out
together as one.[z] 8 When Saul mustered[a]
them at Bezek,[b] the men of Israel numbered three hundred thousand and those
of Judah thirty thousand.
9 They told the messengers who had
come, "Say to the men of Jabesh Gilead,
'By the time the sun is hot tomorrow, you
will be rescued.' " When the messengers
went and reported this to the men of Jabesh, they were elated. 10 They said to the
Ammonites, "Tomorrow we will surrender[c] to you, and you can do to us whatever you like."
11 The next day Saul separated his men
into three divisions;[d] during the last watch
of the night they broke into the camp of
the Ammonites[e] and slaughtered them until the heat of the day. Those who survived
were scattered, so that no two of them
were left together.

Saul Confirmed as King

12 The people then said to Samuel,
"Who[f] was it that asked, 'Shall Saul reign
over us?' Turn these men over to us so that
we may put them to death."
13 But Saul said, "No one will be put to
death today,[g] for this day the LORD has rescued[h] Israel."
14 Then Samuel said to the people,
"Come, let us go to Gilgal[i] and there

[a] *1* Masoretic Text; Dead Sea Scrolls *gifts. Now Nahash king of the Ammonites oppressed the Gadites and Reubenites severely. He gouged out all their right eyes and struck terror and dread in Israel. Not a man remained among the Israelites beyond the Jordan whose right eye was not gouged out by Nahash king of the Ammonites, except that seven thousand men fled from the Ammonites and entered Jabesh Gilead. About a month later, [1]Nahash*

10:26 [g] S ver 5; S Jdg 19:14 [h] S Jdg 20:44 **10:27** [i] S Dt 13:13; S 1Sa 20:7 [j] S ver 4; 1Ki 10:25; 2Ch 17:5; 32:23; Ps 68:29 **11:1** [k] S Ge 19:38; 1Sa 12:12; 2Sa 10:2; 17:27; 1Ch 19:1 [l] Jdg 21:8; 1Sa 31:11; 2Sa 2:4,5; 21:12 [m] S Ex 23:32; S Jer 37:1 **11:2** [n] Ge 34:15 [o] S Nu 16:14 [p] 1Sa 17:26 **11:3** [q] S 1Sa 8:4 [r] S Jdg 2:16 [s] ver 10 **11:4** [t] S 1Sa 10:5,26 [u] S Ge 27:38; S Nu 25:6 **11:6** [v] S Jdg 3:10 **11:7** [w] S 1Sa 6:14 [x] S Jdg 19:29 [y] Jdg 21:5 [z] S Jdg 20:1 **11:8** [a] Jdg 20:2 [b] Jdg 1:4 **11:10** [c] ver 3 **11:11** [d] S Jdg 7:16 [e] S Ge 19:38 **11:12** [f] S Dt 13:13; Lk 19:27 **11:13** [g] 2Sa 19:22 [h] 1Sa 19:5; 1Ch 11:14 **11:14** [i] S Jos 10:43; S 1Sa 10:8

the people and the king-designate. It was intended to clearly distinguish Israelite kingship from that of the surrounding nations and to ensure that the king's role in Israel was compatible with the continued rule of the Lord over Israel as her Great King (see Dt 17:14–20). *scroll.* See note on Ex 17:14. *deposited it before the LORD.* Cf. note on Ex 31:9. The legal document defining the role of the king in governing God's covenant people was preserved at the sanctuary (the tabernacle, later the temple).

10:27 *scoundrels.* See 2:12; see also note on Dt 13:13. *How can this fellow save us?* Reflects the people's continued apostate idea that national security was to be sought in the person of the human king (see note on v. 18; see also 8:20).

11:1 *Ammonite.* The Ammonites were descended from Lot (see Ge 19:36–38 and note; Dt 2:19) and lived east of the Jordan River and south of the Jabbok River (see Dt 2:37; Jos 12:2). Previous attempts by the Ammonites to occupy Israelite territory are referred to in Jdg 3:13; 11:4–33. The Philistine threat to Israel in the west presented the Ammonites with an opportunity to move against Israel from the east with supposed impunity. *Jabesh Gilead.* A town east of the Jordan (see map, p. 369).

11:2 *gouge out the right eye.* Besides causing humiliation (see note on Jdg 16:21), the loss of the right eye would destroy the military capability of the archers.

11:4 *Gibeah of Saul.* See 10:26 and note on 10:5. Close family ties undoubtedly prompted the inhabitants of Jabesh to seek help from the tribe of Benjamin (see Jdg 21:12–14).

11:5 *Saul was returning from the fields.* After Saul's public selection as the king-designate at Mizpah (10:17–25), he returned home (10:26) to resume his normal private activities and to wait for the Lord's leading for the next step in his elevation to the throne (see notes on v. 15; 10:7).

11:6 *the Spirit of God came powerfully upon him.* See 10:6,10. For similar endowment of Israel's deliverers with extraordinary vigor by God's Spirit, see 11:29 and note; Jdg 14:6,19; 15:14.

11:7 *sent the pieces by messengers throughout Israel.* For a similar case see Jdg 19:29 and note.

11:8 *Bezek.* Located north of Shechem, west of the Jordan River but within striking distance of Jabesh Gilead.

11:11 *last watch of the night.* The third watch (2:00–6:00 a.m.; see note on Mt 14:25).

11:13 *the LORD has rescued Israel.* Saul recognizes Israel's true deliverer (see note on 10:18). The victory, in combination with Saul's confession, places yet another seal of divine approval on Saul as the man the Lord has chosen to be king.

11:14 *let us go to Gilgal and there renew the kingship.* Samuel perceives that it is now the appropriate time for the people to renew their allegiance to the Lord. The kingship he speaks

renew the kingship.[j]" 15 So all the people
went to Gilgal[k] and made Saul king[l] in the
presence of the LORD. There they sacrificed
fellowship offerings before the LORD, and
Saul and all the Israelites held a great celebration.

Samuel's Farewell Speech

12 Samuel said to all Israel, "I have
listened[m] to everything you said to
me and have set a king[n] over you. 2 Now
you have a king as your leader.[o] As for me,
I am old and gray, and my sons[p] are here
with you. I have been your leader from my
youth until this day. 3 Here I stand. Testify against me in the presence of the LORD
and his anointed.[q] Whose ox have I taken?
Whose donkey[r] have I taken? Whom have
I cheated? Whom have I oppressed? From
whose hand have I accepted a bribe[s] to
make me shut my eyes? If I have done[t]
any of these things, I will make it right."[u]
4 "You have not cheated or oppressed
us," they replied. "You have not taken anything from anyone's hand."
5 Samuel said to them, "The LORD is witness[v] against you, and also his anointed is
witness this day, that you have not found
anything[w] in my hand.[x]"
"He is witness," they said.

11:14 [j] 1Sa 10:25 **11:15** [k] S Jos 5:9; 2Sa 19:15 [l] 1Sa 12:1 **12:1** [m] S 1Sa 8:7 [n] 1Sa 11:15 **12:2** [o] S 1Sa 8:5 [p] 1Sa 8:3 **12:3** [q] S 1Sa 9:16; 24:6; 26:9,11; 2Sa 1:14; 19:21; Ps 105:15 [r] Nu 16:15 [s] S Ex 18:21; S 1Sa 8:3 [t] Ex 20:17; Ac 20:33 [u] S Lev 25:14 **12:5** [v] S Ge 31:50 [w] Ac 23:9; 24:20 [x] Ex 22:4

12:6 [y] S Ex 3:10; Mic 6:4 **12:7** [z] S Jos 24:1 [a] Isa 1:18; 3:14; Jer 2:9; 25:31; Eze 17:20; 20:35; Mic 6:1-5 [b] S Jdg 5:11 **12:8** [c] S Ge 46:6 [d] S Ex 2:23 [e] S Ex 3:10; 4:16 **12:9** [f] S Dt 32:18; S Jdg 3:7 [g] S Dt 32:30 [h] Jdg 4:2 [i] S Jos 11:1 [j] Jdg 10:7

6 Then Samuel said to the people, "It is
the LORD who appointed Moses and Aaron and brought[y] your ancestors up out of
Egypt. 7 Now then, stand[z] here, because I
am going to confront[a] you with evidence
before the LORD as to all the righteous acts[b]
performed by the LORD for you and your
ancestors.
8 "After Jacob[c] entered Egypt, they cried[d]
to the LORD for help, and the LORD sent[e]
Moses and Aaron, who brought your ancestors out of Egypt and settled them in
this place.
9 "But they forgot[f] the LORD their God;
so he sold them[g] into the hand of Sisera,[h]
the commander of the army of Hazor,[i] and
into the hands of the Philistines[j] and the
king of Moab,[k] who fought against them.
10 They cried[l] out to the LORD and said, 'We
have sinned; we have forsaken[m] the LORD
and served the Baals and the Ashtoreths.[n]
But now deliver us from the hands of our
enemies, and we will serve you.' 11 Then
the LORD sent Jerub-Baal,[a][o] Barak,[b][p] Jephthah[q] and Samuel,[c][r] and he delivered you

[a] 11 Also called *Gideon* [b] 11 Some Septuagint manuscripts and Syriac; Hebrew *Bedan* [c] 11 Hebrew; some Septuagint manuscripts and Syriac *Samson*

[k] Jdg 3:12 **12:10** [l] S Jdg 3:9 [m] S 1Sa 8:8 [n] S 1Sa 7:3 **12:11** [o] Jdg 6:32 [p] S Jdg 4:6 [q] S Jdg 11:1 [r] S 1Sa 7:15

---

of is the Lord's, not Saul's. Samuel calls for an assembly to restore the covenant relationship between the Lord and his people. He wants to inaugurate Saul's rule in a manner demonstrating that the continued rule of the Lord as Israel's Great King is in no way diminished or violated in the new era of the monarchy (see Introduction: Contents and Theme). Verses 14–15 are a brief synopsis of the Gilgal assembly and are prefaced to the more detailed account of the same assembly in ch. 12. *Gilgal.* Located east of Jericho, west of the Jordan River. It was a particularly appropriate place for Israel to renew her allegiance to the Lord (see Jos 4:19—5:10; 10:7–15).

11:15 *made Saul king in the presence of the LORD.* Saul had previously been anointed in private by Samuel at Ramah (10:1) and publicly selected as the king-designate at Mizpah (10:17–27). In the subsequent Ammonite crisis (vv. 1–13) his leadership did not rest on public recognition of his royal authority but on the military victory. Now at Gilgal Saul is inaugurated as God's chosen king and formally assumes the privileges and responsibilities of this office. *fellowship offerings.* This type of offering was an important element in the original ceremony of covenant ratification at Sinai (Ex 24:5,11). It represented the communion or peace between the Lord and his people when the people lived in conformity with their covenant obligations (see Lev 7:11–21; 22:21–23). *held a great celebration.* Here the rejoicing is the expression of people who have renewed their commitment to the Lord, confessed their sin (see 12:19) and been given a king.

12:2 *your leader.* Lit. "one who goes before you." The Hebrew imagery is probably that of a king or leader as shepherd of his people (see 2Sa 5:2; Eze 34:23; cf. note on Ps 23:1; Mic 2:12–13)—ultimately of Jesus in Jn 10:3–4,11,14–15,27 (cf. note on Jn 10:1–30).

12:3 *Testify against me.* Court language. When Samuel presents the newly inaugurated king to the people, he seeks to establish publicly his own past faithfulness to the covenant as leader of the nation. His purpose is to exonerate himself and provide an example for Saul in his new responsibilities. *Whose ox have I taken? Whose donkey have I taken?* See Ex 20:17; 22:1,4,9. Unlike his sons, Samuel has not used his position for personal gain (see 8:3 and note; cf. Nu 16:15). *Whom have I cheated? Whom have I oppressed?* See Lev 19:13; Dt 24:14. *From whose hand have I accepted a bribe . . . ?* Contrast 8:3. See Ex 23:8; Dt 16:19. *I will make it right.* Through restitution (see Lev 5:15 and note; cf. Lk 19:8 and note).

12:6 *Samuel said to the people.* Samuel now turns to the matter of the people's request for a king, which he views as a covenant-breaking act and a serious apostasy. *It is the LORD.* Samuel emphasizes that in the past the Lord had provided the necessary leadership for the nation.

12:7 *confront you with evidence.* The terminology is that of a legal proceeding, as in vv. 2–5, but now the relationship of the parties is reversed. This time Samuel is the accuser, the people are the defendants, and the Lord is the Judge. *righteous acts performed by the LORD.* These acts (see vv. 8–11) not only demonstrate the constancy of the Lord's covenant faithfulness toward his people in the past but also serve to expose their present apostasy.

12:9–11 A summary of the dreary cycle of apostasy, divine chastening, urgent appeals to God, and divine restoration that characterized the period of the judges (see, e.g., Jdg 2:10–15 and note; see also Introduction to Judges: Themes and Theology).

12:9 *forgot the LORD.* This would become Israel's persistent failure (see Hos 2:13 and note).

12:10 *the Baals and the Ashtoreths.* See notes on 7:3; Jdg 2:13.

12:11 *Jerub-Baal . . . Samuel.* See Heb 11:32–33 and notes. *he delivered you.* The Lord repeatedly rescued Israel from her enemies right up to Samuel's own lifetime (see 7:3,8,10,12), demonstrating again the people's apostasy in desiring a king.

from the hands of your enemies all around
you, so that you lived in safety.
12 "But when you saw that Nahash[s] king[t]
of the Ammonites was moving against
you, you said to me, 'No, we want a king
to rule[u] over us'—even though the LORD
your God was your king. 13 Now here is
the king[v] you have chosen, the one you
asked[w] for; see, the LORD has set a king
over you. 14 If you fear[x] the LORD and serve
and obey him and do not rebel[y] against his
commands, and if both you and the king
who reigns over you follow the LORD your
God—good! 15 But if you do not obey the
LORD, and if you rebel against[z] his commands, his hand will be against you, as it
was against your ancestors.
16 "Now then, stand still[a] and see[b] this
great thing the LORD is about to do before
your eyes! 17 Is it not wheat harvest[c] now? I
will call[d] on the LORD to send thunder[e] and
rain.[f] And you will realize what an evil[g]
thing you did in the eyes of the LORD when
you asked for a king."
18 Then Samuel called on the LORD,[h] and
that same day the LORD sent thunder and
rain. So all the people stood in awe[i] of the
LORD and of Samuel.
19 The people all said to Samuel, "Pray[j] to
the LORD your God for your servants so that
we will not die,[k] for we have added to all
our other sins the evil of asking for a king."

12:12 [s]S 1Sa 11:1 [t]S 1Sa 8:5 [u]1Sa 25:30; 2Sa 5:2; 1Ch 5:2 **12:13** [v]S 1Sa 8:5 [w]S 1Sa 9:20 **12:14** [x]S Jos 24:14 [y]Jer 4:17; La 1:18 **12:15** [z]Lev 26:16; Jos 24:20; Isa 1:20; Jer 4:17; 26:4 **12:16** [a]S Ex 14:14 [b]S Ex 14:13 **12:17** [c]S Ge 30:14; S 1Sa 6:13 [d]1Ki 18:42; Jas 5:18 [e]S Ex 9:23; S 1Sa 2:10 [f]Ge 7:12; Ex 9:18; Job 37:13; Pr 26:1 [g]S 1Sa 8:6-7 **12:18** [h]Ps 99:6 [i]S Ge 3:10; S Ex 14:31 **12:19** [j]S Ex 8:8; S 1Sa 7:8; S Jer 37:3; Jas 5:18; 1Jn 5:16 [k]S Dt 9:19 **12:20** [l]S Ex 32:30 **12:21** [m]Isa 40:20;

20 "Do not be afraid," Samuel replied.
"You have done all this evil;[l] yet do not
turn away from the LORD, but serve the
LORD with all your heart. 21 Do not turn
away after useless[m] idols.[n] They can do
you no good, nor can they rescue you, because they are useless. 22 For the sake[o] of
his great name[p] the LORD will not reject[q]
his people, because the LORD was pleased
to make[r] you his own. 23 As for me, far be
it from me that I should sin against the
LORD by failing to pray[s] for you. And I will
teach[t] you the way that is good and right.
24 But be sure to fear[u] the LORD and serve
him faithfully with all your heart;[v] consider[w] what great[x] things he has done for you.
25 Yet if you persist[y] in doing evil, both you
and your king[z] will perish."[a]

Samuel Rebukes Saul

13 Saul was thirty[a] years old when he
became king, and he reigned over
Israel forty-[b] two years.

[a] *1* A few late manuscripts of the Septuagint; Hebrew does not have *thirty.* [b] *1* Probable reading of the original Hebrew text (see Acts 13:21); Masoretic Text does not have *forty-*.

41:24,29; 44:9; Jer 2:5,11; 14:22; 16:19; Jnh 2:8; Hab 2:18; Ac 14:15 [n]Dt 11:16 **12:22** [o]Ps 25:11; 106:8; Isa 48:9,11; Jer 14:7; Da 9:19 [p]S Jos 7:9; 2Sa 7:23; Jn 17:12 [q]S Lev 26:11; S Dt 31:6 [r]Dt 7:7; 1Pe 2:9 **12:23** [s]S Nu 11:2; S 1Sa 1:20; S 7:8; Ro 1:9-10 [t]1Ki 8:36; Ps 25:4; 34:11; 86:11; 94:12; Pr 4:11 **12:24** [u]Dt 6:2; Ecc 12:13 [v]Dt 6:5; S Jos 24:14 [w]Job 34:27; Isa 5:12; 22:11; 26:10 [x]S Dt 10:21 **12:25** [y]1Sa 31:1-5 [z]Dt 28:36 [a]S Jos 24:20; S 1Ki 14:10

12:12 *when you saw that Nahash ... was moving against you.* In the face of the combined threat from the Philistines in the west (9:16) and the Ammonites in the east (11:1–13), the Israelites sought to find security in the person of a human king. *No, we want a king ... the LORD ... was your king.* The Israelite desire for and trust in a human leader constituted a rejection of the kingship of the Lord and betrayed a loss of confidence in his care, in spite of his faithfulness during the time of the exodus, conquest and judges (see 8:7 and note).

12:13 *the LORD has set a king over you.* In spite of the sinfulness of the people's request, the Lord had chosen to incorporate kingship into the structure of the theocracy (his kingdom). Kingship was given by the Lord to his people and was to function as an instrument of his rule over them (see Introduction: Contents and Theme).

12:14 *If you.* Samuel relates the covenant conditions (see Ex 19:5–6; Dt 8:19; 11:13–15,22–23; 28:1,15; 30:17–18; Jos 24:20) to the new era Israel is entering with the establishment of the monarchy. *if both you and the king ... follow the LORD your God—good!* Israel and her king are to demonstrate that although human kingship has been established, they will continue to recognize the Lord as their true King. In this new era where potential for divided loyalty between the Lord and the human king arises, Israel's loyalty to the Lord must remain inviolate.

12:15 *But if you do not obey.* Samuel confronts Israel with the same alternatives Moses had expressed centuries earlier (see Dt 28:1,15; 30:15–20). The introduction of kingship into Israel's social and political structures has not changed the fundamental nature of her relationship to the Lord.

12:16 *see this great thing.* See v. 24. Samuel calls the people to pay careful attention as the Lord himself demonstrates his existence and power and authenticates the truthfulness and seriousness of Samuel's words.

12:17 *wheat harvest.* See note on 6:13.

12:18 *stood in awe of the LORD and of Samuel.* See Ex 14:31 and note.

12:19 *Pray to the LORD your God.* Samuel's indictment (vv. 6–15), combined with the awesome sign of thunder and rain in the dry season (vv. 16–18), prompted the people to confess their sin and request Samuel's intercession for them.

12:20 *yet do not turn away from the LORD.* Samuel again brings into focus the central issue in the controversy surrounding the establishment of kingship in Israel.

12:21 *useless idols.* No rivals to the Lord can deliver or guarantee security (see Ex 20:3 and note).

12:23 *sin ... by failing to pray for you.* See 7:8 and note. *teach you the way that is good and right.* Samuel is not retiring from his prophetic role when he presents the people with their king. He will continue to intercede for the people (see v. 19; 7:8–9) and will instruct them in their covenant obligations (see Dt 6:18; 12:28). Saul and all future kings are to be subject to instruction and correction by the Lord's prophets.

12:24 *fear the LORD.* See notes on Ge 20:11; Ps 15:4; 111:10; Pr 1:7. Samuel summarizes Israel's obligation of loyalty to the Lord as an expression of gratitude for the great things he has done for them.

12:25 *you and your king will perish.* If the nation should persist in covenant-breaking conduct, it will bring upon itself its own destruction.

13:1—14:52 Saul's reign characterized: his disobedience, folly and failure.

13:1 *thirty years old ... forty-two years.* See NIV text notes. The wording of the verse follows the regularly used formula that introduces the reigns of later kings (see, e.g., 2Sa 2:10; 5:4; 1Ki 14:21; 2Ki 8:26).

2 Saul chose three thousand men from
Israel; two thousand[b] were with him at
Mikmash[c] and in the hill country of Bethel, and a thousand were with Jonathan at
Gibeah[d] in Benjamin. The rest of the men
he sent back to their homes.
3 Jonathan attacked the Philistine outpost[e] at Geba,[f] and the Philistines heard
about it. Then Saul had the trumpet[g]
blown throughout the land and said, "Let
the Hebrews hear!" 4 So all Israel heard
the news: "Saul has attacked the Philistine
outpost, and now Israel has become obnoxious[h] to the Philistines." And the people were summoned to join Saul at Gilgal.
5 The Philistines assembled[i] to fight Israel, with three thousand[a] chariots, six thousand charioteers, and soldiers as numerous
as the sand[j] on the seashore. They went
up and camped at Mikmash,[k] east of Beth
Aven.[l] 6 When the Israelites saw that their
situation was critical and that their army
was hard pressed, they hid[m] in caves and
thickets, among the rocks, and in pits and
cisterns.[n] 7 Some Hebrews even crossed the
Jordan to the land of Gad[o] and Gilead.
Saul remained at Gilgal, and all the
troops with him were quaking[p] with fear.
8 He waited seven[q] days, the time set by
Samuel; but Samuel did not come to Gilgal, and Saul's men began to scatter. 9 So
he said, "Bring me the burnt offering and
the fellowship offerings." And Saul offered[r]
up the burnt offering. 10 Just as he finished
making the offering, Samuel[s] arrived, and
Saul went out to greet[t] him.
11 "What have you done?" asked Samuel.
Saul replied, "When I saw that the men
were scattering, and that you did not
come at the set time, and that the Philistines were assembling at Mikmash,[u] 12 I
thought, 'Now the Philistines will come
down against me at Gilgal,[v] and I have not
sought the LORD's favor.[w]' So I felt compelled to offer the burnt offering."
13 "You have done a foolish thing,[x]" Samuel said. "You have not kept[y] the command
the LORD your God gave you; if you had, he
would have established your kingdom over
Israel for all time.[z] 14 But now your kingdom[a] will not endure; the LORD has sought
out a man after his own heart[b] and appointed[c] him ruler[d] of his people, because
you have not kept[e] the LORD's command."
15 Then Samuel left Gilgal[b] and went up
to Gibeah[f] in Benjamin, and Saul counted
the men who were with him. They numbered about six hundred.[g]

Israel Without Weapons

16 Saul and his son Jonathan and the
men with them were staying in Gibeah[c][h] in
Benjamin, while the Philistines camped at
Mikmash. 17 Raiding[i] parties went out from
the Philistine camp in three detachments.
One turned toward Ophrah[j] in the vicinity
of Shual, 18 another toward Beth Horon,[k]
and the third toward the borderland overlooking the Valley of Zeboyim[l] facing the
wilderness.

[a] 5 Some Septuagint manuscripts and Syriac; Hebrew *thirty thousand* [b] 15 Hebrew; Septuagint *Gilgal and went his way; the rest of the people went after Saul to meet the army, and they went out of Gilgal* [c] 16 Two Hebrew manuscripts; most Hebrew manuscripts *Geba,* a variant of *Gibeah*

13:2 [b] ver 15 [c] ver 5,11, 23; Ne 11:31; Isa 10:28 [d] S Jdg 19:14 **13:3** [e] S 1Sa 10:5 [f] S Jos 18:24 [g] S Lev 25:9; S Jdg 3:27 **13:4** [h] S Ge 34:30 **13:5** [i] 1Sa 17:1 [j] S Jos 11:4; Rev 20:8 [k] S ver 2 [l] S Jos 7:2 **13:6** [m] 1Sa 14:11, 22 [n] S Jdg 6:2; Eze 33:27 **13:7** [o] S Nu 32:33 [p] S Ge 35:5; S Ex 19:16 **13:8** [q] 1Sa 10:8 **13:9** [r] Dt 12:5-14; 2Sa 24:25; 1Ki 3:4 **13:10** [s] 1Sa 15:13 [t] 1Sa 25:14 **13:11** [u] S ver 2 **13:12** [v] S Jos 10:43 [w] S Dt 4:29; Ps 119:58; Jer 26:19 **13:13** [x] 2Ch 16:9 [y] ver 14; S Jos 22:16; 1Sa 15:23, 24; 2Sa 7:15; 1Ch 10:13 [z] Ps 72:5 **13:14** [a] 1Sa 15:28; 18:8; 24:20; 1Ch 10:14 [b] Ac 7:46; 13:22 [c] 2Sa 6:21 [d] 1Sa 25:30; 2Sa 5:2; Ps 18:43; Isa 16:5; 55:4; Jer 30:9; Eze 34:23-24; 37:24; Da 9:25; Hos 3:5; Mic 5:2 [e] 1Sa 15:26; 16:1; 2Sa 12:9; 1Ki 13:21; Hos 13:11 **13:15** [f] 1Sa 14:2 [g] ver 2 **13:16** [h] S Jos 18:24 **13:17** [i] 1Sa 14:15 [j] S Jos 18:23 **13:18** [k] S Jos 10:10 [l] Ne 11:34

13:2 *Mikmash.* Located southeast of Bethel and northeast of Gibeah near a pass (see v. 23; see also map, p. 595). *Jonathan.* Saul's oldest son (see 14:49; 31:2), mentioned here for the first time.
13:3,7 *Hebrews.* See note on Ge 14:13.
13:3 *Geba.* Located across a ravine and south of Mikmash.
13:4 *obnoxious.* A metaphor depicting an object of strong hostility, as in 2Sa 10:6; 16:21; Ge 34:30; Ex 5:21. *Gilgal.* See note on 11:14. By prearrangement Saul had been instructed to wait for Samuel there (see notes on v. 8; 10:8).
13:5 *three thousand chariots.* The Israelites did not acquire chariots until the time of Solomon (see 1Ki 4:26). *six thousand charioteers.* See note on 1Ki 22:34.
13:8 *time set by Samuel.* See note on 10:8. Saul is fully aware that Samuel's previous instructions had reference to this gathering at Gilgal. *Saul's men began to scatter.* The seven-day delay heightened the fear of the Israelite soldiers.
13:9 *Saul offered up the burnt offering.* Samuel had promised to make these offerings himself (see 10:8) before Israel went to battle (see 7:9), and he had directed Saul to await his arrival and instructions.
13:13 *You have done a foolish thing.* The foolish and sinful aspect (see 26:21; 2Sa 24:10; 2Ch 16:9; Isa 32:6) of Saul's act was that he thought he could strengthen Israel's chances against the Philistines while disregarding the instruction of the Lord's prophet Samuel. *You have not kept the command the LORD your God gave you.* Saul was to recognize the word of the prophet Samuel as the word of the Lord (see 3:20; 15:1; Ex 20:18–19; see also note on Ex 7:1–2). In disobeying Samuel's instructions, Saul violated a fundamental requirement of his theocratic office. His kingship was not to function independently of the law and the prophets (see notes on 12:14,23; 15:11).
13:14 *your kingdom will not endure.* Saul will not be followed by his sons; there will be no dynasty bearing his name (contrast the Lord's word to David, 2Sa 7:11–16). There is a striking parallel in the word of the Lord to Eli (see 2:30,35 and notes). *the LORD has sought out a man after his own heart and appointed him.* That is, David; Paul quotes from this passage (Ac 13:22). *ruler.* See note on 9:16.
13:15 *six hundred.* The seven-day delay had greatly depleted Saul's forces (see vv. 2,4,6–8,11).
13:17 *Raiding parties.* The purpose of these Philistine contingents was not to engage the Israelites in battle, but to plunder the land and demoralize its inhabitants.
13:18 *Valley of Zeboyim.* Located to the east toward the Jordan valley (see Ge 10:19 and note).

19Not a blacksmith[m] could be found in
the whole land of Israel, because the Philistines had said, "Otherwise the Hebrews
will make swords or spears![n]" 20So all Israel went down to the Philistines to have
their plow points, mattocks, axes and sickles[a] sharpened. 21The price was two-thirds
of a shekel[b] for sharpening plow points
and mattocks, and a third of a shekel[c] for
sharpening forks and axes and for repoint-
ing goads.
22So on the day of the battle not a soldier with Saul and Jonathan[o] had a sword
or spear[p] in his hand; only Saul and his
son Jonathan had them.

Jonathan Attacks the Philistines

23Now a detachment of Philistines had
gone out to the pass[q] at Mikmash.[r]
14 1One day Jonathan son of Saul said
to his young armor-bearer, "Come, let's go
over to the Philistine outpost on the other
side." But he did not tell his father.
2Saul was staying[s] on the outskirts of
Gibeah[t] under a pomegranate tree[u] in Migron.[v] With him were about six hundred
men, 3among whom was Ahijah, who was
wearing an ephod. He was a son of Ichabod's[w] brother Ahitub[x] son of Phinehas,
the son of Eli,[y] the LORD's priest in Shiloh.[z]
No one was aware that Jonathan had left.
4On each side of the pass[a] that Jonathan
intended to cross to reach the Philistine
outpost was a cliff; one was called Bozez
and the other Seneh. 5One cliff stood to
the north toward Mikmash, the other to
the south toward Geba.[b]
6Jonathan said to his young armor-bearer, "Come, let's go over to the outpost of
those uncircumcised[c] men. Perhaps the
LORD will act in our behalf. Nothing[d] can
hinder the LORD from saving, whether by
many[e] or by few.[f]"
7"Do all that you have in mind," his armor-bearer said. "Go ahead; I am with you
heart and soul."
8Jonathan said, "Come on, then; we
will cross over toward them and let them
see us. 9If they say to us, 'Wait there until
we come to you,' we will stay where we
are and not go up to them. 10But if they
say, 'Come up to us,' we will climb up, because that will be our sign[g] that the LORD
has given them into our hands.[h]"
11So both of them showed themselves
to the Philistine outpost. "Look!" said
the Philistines. "The Hebrews[i] are crawling out of the holes they were hiding[j] in."
12The men of the outpost shouted to Jonathan and his armor-bearer, "Come up to
us and we'll teach you a lesson.[k]"
So Jonathan said to his armor-bearer,
"Climb up after me; the LORD has given
them into the hand[l] of Israel."
13Jonathan climbed up, using his hands
and feet, with his armor-bearer right behind him. The Philistines fell before Jonathan, and his armor-bearer followed
and killed behind him. 14In that first attack Jonathan and his armor-bearer killed
some twenty men in an area of about half
an acre.

Israel Routs the Philistines

15Then panic[m] struck the whole army—
those in the camp and field, and those in
the outposts and raiding[n] parties—and
the ground shook. It was a panic sent by
God.[d]
16Saul's lookouts[o] at Gibeah in Benjamin saw the army melting away in all directions. 17Then Saul said to the men who
were with him, "Muster the forces and see
who has left us." When they did, it was
Jonathan and his armor-bearer who were
not there.
18Saul said to Ahijah, "Bring[p] the ark[q]
of God." (At that time it was with the Is-

13:19 [m]S Ge 4:22 [n]S Nu 25:7 **13:22** [o]1Ch 9:39 [p]S Nu 25:7; 1Sa 14:6; 17:47; Zec 4:6 **13:23** [q]1Sa 14:4 [r]S ver 2 **14:2** [s]S Jdg 4:5 [t]1Sa 13:15 [u]S Ex 28:33 [v]Isa 10:28 **14:3** [w]S Ge 35:18 [x]1Sa 22:11, 20 [y]S 1Sa 1:3 [z]Ps 78:60 **14:4** [a]1Sa 13:23 **14:5** [b]S Jos 18:24 **14:6** [c]Jdg 14:3; 1Sa 17:26, 36; 31:4; Jer 9:26; Eze 28:10 [d]S 1Sa 13:22; S 1Ki 19:12; S Mt 19:26; Heb 11:34 [e]Jdg 7:4 [f]Ps 33:16 **14:10** [g]S Ge 24:14 [h]S Jos 2:24 **14:11** [i]S Ge 14:13 [j]S 1Sa 13:6 **14:12** [k]Jdg 8:16 [l]1Sa 17:46; 2Sa 5:24 **14:15** [m]S Ge 35:5; S Ex 14:24; S 19:16; 2Ki 7:5-7 [n]1Sa 13:17 **14:16** [o]2Sa 18:24; 2Ki 9:17; Isa 52:8; Eze 33:2 **14:18** [p]1Sa 30:7 [q]S Jdg 18:5

[a] 20 Septuagint; Hebrew *plow points* [b] 21 That is, about 1/4 ounce or about 8 grams [c] 21 That is, about 1/8 ounce or about 4 grams [d] 15 Or *a terrible panic*

13:19 *Not a blacksmith.* A Philistine monopoly on the technology of iron production placed the Israelites at a great disadvantage in the fashioning and maintenance of agricultural implements and military weapons.
13:20 *plow points.* See note on Isa 2:4.
13:21 *price.* Probably exorbitant. *two-thirds of a shekel.* The Hebrew word (*pim*) for this phrase, which occurs only here in the OT, has now been found on weights that have turned up in various excavations.
13:22 *not ... a sword or spear.* The Israelites fought with bow and arrow and slingshot.
14:1 *on the other side.* The Philistines were encamped to the north of the pass and the Israelites to the south.
14:2 *Gibeah.* Saul had retreated farther south from Geba (13:3) to Gibeah. *under a pomegranate tree.* It appears to have been customary for leaders in early Israel to hold court under well-known trees (see 22:6; Jdg 4:5).
14:3 *Ahijah.* Either the brother and predecessor of Ahimelek son of Ahitub (referred to in 21:1; 22:9,11) or an alternative name for Ahimelek. *wearing an ephod.* See note on 2:28. *Ichabod's brother.* See 4:21.
14:6 *uncircumcised men.* A term of contempt (see 17:26,36; 31:4; 2Sa 1:20; Jdg 14:3; 15:18), which draws attention to Israel's covenant relationship to the Lord (see Ge 17:10 and note) and, by implication, to the illegitimacy of the Philistine presence in the land. *by many or by few.* See note on 17:47. Jonathan's bold plan is undertaken as an act of faith (cf. Heb 11:32–34) founded on God's promise (9:16).
14:10 *our sign.* See Jdg 6:36–40; Isa 7:11.
14:11 *Hebrews.* See v. 21; 4:6; 13:3,7 and note on Ge 14:13.
14:15 *ground shook.* See 7:10; 2Sa 22:12–16; Jos 10:11–14; Ps 77:18 for other instances of divine intervention in nature to bring deliverance to Israel.
14:18 *Bring the ark of God.* Saul decides to seek God's will before entering into battle with the Philistines (see Nu 27:21; Dt 20:2–4). Here the Septuagint (the pre-Christian Greek

raelites.)[a] 19 While Saul was talking to the
priest, the tumult in the Philistine camp
increased more and more. So Saul said to
the priest,[r] "Withdraw your hand."
20 Then Saul and all his men assembled and went to the battle. They found
the Philistines in total confusion, striking[s]
each other with their swords. 21 Those Hebrews who had previously been with the
Philistines and had gone up with them to
their camp went[t] over to the Israelites who
were with Saul and Jonathan. 22 When all
the Israelites who had hidden[u] in the hill
country of Ephraim heard that the Philistines were on the run, they joined the
battle in hot pursuit. 23 So on that day the
LORD saved[v] Israel, and the battle moved
on beyond Beth Aven.[w]

Jonathan Eats Honey

24 Now the Israelites were in distress that
day, because Saul had bound the people
under an oath,[x] saying, "Cursed be anyone who eats food before evening comes,
before I have avenged myself on my enemies!" So none of the troops tasted food.
25 The entire army entered the woods,
and there was honey on the ground.
26 When they went into the woods, they
saw the honey oozing out; yet no one put
his hand to his mouth, because they feared
the oath. 27 But Jonathan had not heard
that his father had bound the people with
the oath, so he reached out the end of the
staff that was in his hand and dipped it
into the honeycomb.[y] He raised his hand
to his mouth, and his eyes brightened.[b]
28 Then one of the soldiers told him, "Your
father bound the army under a strict
oath, saying, 'Cursed be anyone who eats
food today!' That is why the men are
faint."
29 Jonathan said, "My father has made
trouble[z] for the country. See how my eyes
brightened when I tasted a little of this
honey. 30 How much better it would have
been if the men had eaten today some of
the plunder they took from their enemies.
Would not the slaughter of the Philistines
have been even greater?"
31 That day, after the Israelites had
struck down the Philistines from Mikmash[a] to Aijalon,[b] they were exhausted.
32 They pounced on the plunder[c] and, taking sheep, cattle and calves, they butchered them on the ground and ate them,
together with the blood.[d] 33 Then someone
said to Saul, "Look, the men are sinning
against the LORD by eating meat that has
blood[e] in it."
"You have broken faith," he said. "Roll
a large stone over here at once." 34 Then
he said, "Go out among the men and tell
them, 'Each of you bring me your cattle
and sheep, and slaughter them here and
eat them. Do not sin against the LORD by
eating meat with blood still[f] in it.' "
So everyone brought his ox that night
and slaughtered it there. 35 Then Saul built

14:19 [r] Nu 27:21 **14:20** [s] S Jdg 7:22; Eze 38:21; Zec 14:13 **14:21** [t] 1Sa 29:4 **14:22** [u] S 1Sa 13:6 **14:23** [v] S Ex 14:30 [w] S Jos 7:2 **14:24** [x] Jos 6:26 **14:27** [y] ver 43; Ps 19:10; Pr 16:24; 24:13 **14:29** [z] Jos 7:25; 1Ki 18:18 **14:31** [a] ver 5 [b] S Jos 10:12 **14:32** [c] 1Sa 15:19; Est 9:10 [d] S Ge 9:4 **14:33** [e] S Ge 9:4 **14:34** [f] Lev 19:26

[a] 18 Hebrew; Septuagint *"Bring the ephod." (At that time he wore the ephod before the Israelites.)* [b] 27 Or *his strength was renewed*; similarly in verse 29

translation of the OT) may preserve the original text (see NIV text note) for the following reasons: (1) In 7:1 the ark was located at Kiriath Jearim, where it remained until David brought it to Jerusalem (2Sa 6), but the ephod was present in Saul's camp at Gibeah (see v. 3). (2) Nowhere else in the OT is the ark used to determine God's will, but the ephod (with the Urim and Thummim) was given for this purpose (see 23:9; 30:7 and notes on 2:18,28). (3) The command to the priest to withdraw his hand (v. 19) is more appropriate with the ephod than with the ark.

14:19 *Withdraw your hand.* Stop the priestly action I asked you to perform. Due to the urgency of the moment, Saul decides that to wait for the word of the Lord might jeopardize his military advantage. As in 13:8–12, his decision rests on his own insight rather than on dependence on the Lord and a commitment to obey him.

14:23 *So on that day the LORD saved Israel.* The writer attributes the victory to the Lord, not to either Saul or Jonathan (see vv. 6,10,12,15; 11:13).

14:24–46 Following the account of the great victory the Lord had given, the author relates Saul's actions that strikingly illustrated his lack of fitness to be king. His foolish curse before the battle (see v. 24 and note) brought "distress" to the army and, as Jonathan tellingly observed, "made trouble for the country" (v. 29) rather than contributing to the victory (cf. Jos 7:25; 1Ki 18:17–18). And later, when hindered from taking advantage of the battle's outcome by the Lord's refusal to answer (v. 37), Saul was ready to execute Jonathan as the cause, though Jonathan had contributed most to the victory, as everyone else recognized (v. 45). Saul's growing egocentrism was turning into an all-consuming passion that threatened the very welfare of the nation. Rather than serving the cause of the Lord and his people, he was in fact becoming a king "such as all the other nations have" (8:5).

14:24 *in distress.* Saul's rash action in requiring his troops to fast placed them at an unnecessary disadvantage in the battle (see vv. 29–30). *Cursed.* Thus Saul as king "bound the army under a strict oath" (v. 28), a most serious matter because an oath directly invoked God's involvement, whether it concerned giving testimony (Ex 20:7; Lev 19:12), making commitments (Ge 21:23–24; 24:3–4) or prohibiting action (here). It appealed to God as the supreme enforcement power and the all-knowing Judge of human actions. *I have avenged myself on my enemies.* Saul perceives the conflict with the Philistines more as a personal vendetta (see note on 15:12) than as a battle for the honor of the Lord and the security of the Lord's people (note the contrast between his attitude and that of Jonathan in vv. 6,10,12).

14:31 *Aijalon.* Located to the west near the Philistines' own territory (see Jos 10:12 and map, p. 359).

14:33 *eating meat that has blood in it.* The Israelites were not permitted to eat blood (see Ge 9:4; Lev 17:10–11; 19:26; Dt 12:16,24; Eze 33:25; Ac 15:20 and notes). *broken faith.* See Mal 2:10–11. The same Hebrew term is translated "faithless" (Ps 78:57), "unfaithful" (Jer 3:7–8,10–11) and "treacherous" (Isa 48:8).

an altar[g] to the LORD; it was the first time
he had done this.
36 Saul said, "Let us go down and pursue the Philistines by night and plunder
them till dawn, and let us not leave one of
them alive."
"Do whatever seems best to you," they
replied.
But the priest said, "Let us inquire[h] of
God here."
37 So Saul asked God, "Shall I go down
and pursue the Philistines? Will you give
them into Israel's hand?" But God did not
answer[i] him that day.
38 Saul therefore said, "Come here, all
you who are leaders of the army, and let
us find out what sin has been committed[j]
today. 39 As surely as the LORD who rescues
Israel lives,[k] even if the guilt lies with my
son Jonathan,[l] he must die."[m] But not one
of them said a word.
40 Saul then said to all the Israelites,
"You stand over there; I and Jonathan my
son will stand over here."
"Do what seems best to you," they replied.
41 Then Saul prayed to the LORD, the God
of Israel, "Why have you not answered
your servant today? If the fault is in me or
my son Jonathan, respond with Urim, but
if the men of Israel are at fault,[a] respond
with Thummim." Jonathan and Saul were
taken by lot, and the men were cleared.
42 Saul said, "Cast the lot[n] between me and
Jonathan my son." And Jonathan was tak-
en.
43 Then Saul said to Jonathan, "Tell me
what you have done."[o]
So Jonathan told him, "I tasted a little
honey[p] with the end of my staff. And now
I must die!"
44 Saul said, "May God deal with me, be
it ever so severely,[q] if you do not die, Jonathan."[r]

14:35 [g] S 1Sa 7:17
14:36 [h] S Ge 25:22; S Jdg 18:5
14:37 [i] 1Sa 28:6,15; 2Sa 22:42; Ps 18:41
14:38 [j] Jos 7:11
14:39 [k] S Nu 14:21; 2Sa 12:5; Job 19:25; Ps 18:46; 42:2 [l] ver 44 [m] Jos 7:15
14:42 [n] Jnh 1:7
14:43 [o] S Jos 7:19 [p] S ver 27
14:44 [q] S Ru 1:17 [r] ver 39
14:45 [s] 1Ki 1:52; S Mt 10:30 [t] 2Sa 14:11
14:47 [u] S Ge 19:37 [v] S Ge 19:38; 2Sa 12:31 [w] 1Sa 21:7 [x] 2Sa 8:3; 10:6; 23:36
14:48 [y] S Ge 36:12; Nu 13:29; Jdg 3:13; 1Sa 15:2,7; 27:8; 28:18; 30:13; 2Sa 1:13; 1Ch 4:43
14:49 [z] 1Sa 31:2; 1Ch 8:33 [a] S Ge 29:26
14:50 [b] 2Sa 2:8; 3:6; 1Ki 2:5 [c] 1Sa 10:14
14:51 [d] S 1Sa 9:1
14:52 [e] 1Sa 8:11
15:1 [f] S 1Sa 9:16

45 But the men said to Saul, "Should Jonathan die—he who has brought about this
great deliverance in Israel? Never! As surely as the LORD lives, not a hair[s] of his head
will fall to the ground, for he did this today with God's help." So the men rescued[t]
Jonathan, and he was not put to death.
46 Then Saul stopped pursuing the Philistines, and they withdrew to their own
land.
47 After Saul had assumed rule over Israel, he fought against their enemies on every side: Moab,[u] the Ammonites,[v] Edom,[w]
the kings[b] of Zobah,[x] and the Philistines.
Wherever he turned, he inflicted punishment on them.[c] 48 He fought valiantly and
defeated the Amalekites,[y] delivering Israel
from the hands of those who had plundered them.

Saul's Family

49 Saul's sons were Jonathan, Ishvi and
Malki-Shua.[z] The name of his older daughter was Merab, and that of the younger
was Michal.[a] 50 His wife's name was Ahinoam daughter of Ahimaaz. The name of
the commander of Saul's army was Abner[b] son of Ner, and Ner was Saul's uncle.[c]
51 Saul's father Kish[d] and Abner's father
Ner were sons of Abiel.
52 All the days of Saul there was bitter
war with the Philistines, and whenever
Saul saw a mighty or brave man, he took[e]
him into his service.

The LORD Rejects Saul as King

15 Samuel said to Saul, "I am the one
the LORD sent to anoint[f] you king
over his people Israel; so listen now to the
message from the LORD. 2 This is what the

[a] *41* Septuagint; Hebrew does not have *"Why . . . at fault.* [b] *47* Masoretic Text; Dead Sea Scrolls and Septuagint *king* [c] *47* Hebrew; Septuagint *he was victorious*

14:35 *first time he had done this.* Another indication of Saul's personal lack of interest in religious matters (see notes on 9:3,6; 10:11).
14:36 *priest.* Ahijah (see v. 3).
14:37 *Saul asked God.* The means of ascertaining God's will appears to have been the ephod with its Urim and Thummim (see v. 3 and note on v. 18). *God did not answer.* Because an oath had been broken in the battle, God refused to answer Saul's inquiry concerning further military action.
14:39,45 *As surely as the LORD ... lives.* An oath formula (see note on v. 24; 19:6; see also Ge 42:15; Hos 4:15 and notes).
14:41 *taken by lot.* See 10:20–21; Jos 7:14–18; Pr 16:33.
14:44 A curse formula (see note on v. 24; see also 3:17 and note).
14:45 *he did this today with God's help.* The men of Saul's army recognize the inappropriateness of taking the life of the one through whom God has delivered his people.
14:47–48 A summary of Saul's military victories to the east (Moab and the Ammonites), south (Edom), north (Zobah) and west (Philistines).
14:47 *Ammonites.* See note on 11:1; see also Dt 2:19–21,37.
14:48 *Amalekites.* See note on 15:2.
14:49 *Saul's sons.* See 31:2; 1Ch 9:39 and notes. *Merab ... Michal.* See 18:17,20; 19:11–17; 25:44; 2Sa 6:16–23.
14:50 *Ahinoam.* The only reference to a wife of Saul. His concubine Rizpah is mentioned in 2Sa 3:7; 21:8–11.
14:52 *All the days of Saul.* Closes the main account of Saul's reign. *he took him into his service.* Saul developed a special cadre of professional soldiers bound to himself, much as David was to do later (see 22:2; 23:13; 25:13; 27:2–3; 29:2; 30:1,9–10; 2Sa 2:3; 5:6; 8:18; 15:18; 23:8–39).
15:1—2Sa 5:5 Saul's decline and David's rise.
15:1–35 The event that occasioned Saul's rejection as king. Although no time designation is given, it evidently occurred after the conflicts of 14:47, in a time of relative peace and security. It is likely that David was anointed (16:1–13) shortly after the rejection of Saul (vv. 23,26,28), thus c. 1025 BC (see Introduction: Chronology).

LORD Almighty says: 'I will punish the Amalekites[g] for what they did to Israel when
they waylaid them as they came up from
Egypt. 3 Now go, attack the Amalekites and
totally[h] destroy[a] all that belongs to them.
Do not spare them; put to death men and
women, children and infants, cattle and
sheep, camels and donkeys.' "
4 So Saul summoned the men and mustered them at Telaim—two hundred thousand foot soldiers and ten thousand from
Judah. 5 Saul went to the city of Amalek
and set an ambush in the ravine. 6 Then
he said to the Kenites,[i] "Go away, leave the
Amalekites so that I do not destroy you
along with them; for you showed kindness to all the Israelites when they came
up out of Egypt." So the Kenites moved
away from the Amalekites.
7 Then Saul attacked the Amalekites[j] all
the way from Havilah to Shur,[k] near the
eastern border of Egypt. 8 He took Agag[l]
king of the Amalekites alive,[m] and all
his people he totally destroyed with the
sword. 9 But Saul and the army spared[n]
Agag and the best of the sheep and cattle, the fat calves[b] and lambs—everything
that was good. These they were unwilling to destroy completely, but everything
that was despised and weak they totally
destroyed.
10 Then the word of the LORD came to
Samuel: 11 "I regret[o] that I have made Saul
king, because he has turned[p] away from
me and has not carried out my instructions."[q] Samuel was angry,[r] and he cried
out to the LORD all that night.
12 Early in the morning Samuel got up
and went to meet Saul, but he was told,
"Saul has gone to Carmel.[s] There he has
set up a monument[t] in his own honor and
has turned and gone on down to Gilgal."
13 When Samuel reached him, Saul said,
"The LORD bless you! I have carried out
the LORD's instructions."
14 But Samuel said, "What then is this
bleating of sheep in my ears? What is this
lowing of cattle that I hear?"
15 Saul answered, "The soldiers brought
them from the Amalekites; they spared
the best of the sheep and cattle to sacrifice to the LORD your God, but we totally
destroyed the rest."
16 "Enough!" Samuel said to Saul. "Let
me tell you what the LORD said to me last
night."
"Tell me," Saul replied.
17 Samuel said, "Although you were once
small[u] in your own eyes, did you not become the head of the tribes of Israel? The
LORD anointed you king over Israel. 18 And
he sent you on a mission, saying, 'Go and
completely destroy those wicked people,
the Amalekites; wage war against them
until you have wiped them out.' 19 Why

15:2 [g] S Ge 14:7; S 1Sa 14:48; S 2Sa 1:8 **15:3** [h] ver 9, 19; S Ge 14:23; Jos 6:17; 1Sa 22:19; 27:9; 28:18; Est 3:13; 9:5 **15:6** [i] S Ge 15:19; Nu 24:22; Jdg 1:16; 1Sa 30:29 **15:7** [j] S 1Sa 14:48 [k] S Ge 16:7 **15:8** [l] Ex 17:8-16; S Nu 24:7 [m] S Jos 8:23 **15:9** [n] S ver 3 **15:11** [o] S Ge 6:6; S Ex 32:14 [p] S Jos 22:16 [q] Job 21:14; 34:27; Ps 28:5; Isa 5:12; 53:6; Jer 48:10; Eze 18:24 [r] S ver 35; S 1Sa 8:6 **15:12** [s] Jos 15:55 [t] S Nu 32:42 **15:17** [u] S Ex 3:11

[a] 3 The Hebrew term refers to the irrevocable giving over of things or persons to the LORD, often by totally destroying them; also in verses 8, 9, 15, 18, 20 and 21.
[b] 9 Or *the grown bulls*; the meaning of the Hebrew for this phrase is uncertain.

15:2 *Amalekites.* A nomadic people descended from Esau (see Ge 36:12,16), usually living in the Negev and Sinai regions (see 27:8; 30:1; 2Sa 17:1–15; Ge 14:7 and note; Ex 17:8; Nu 13:29). *what they did to Israel.* See 14:48; Ex 17:8–15; Nu 14:43,45; Dt 25:17–19; cf. Jdg 3:13; 6:3–5,33; 7:12; 10:12.
15:3 *totally destroy.* See NIV text note; Dt 13:12–18; see also notes on Lev 27:28–29; Jos 6:17–18. Saul is given an opportunity as king to demonstrate his allegiance to the Lord by obedience in this assigned task.
15:4 *Telaim.* Probably the same as Telem in Jos 15:24, located in the southern part of Judah. *foot soldiers.* From the northern tribes (see 11:8).
15:5 *city of Amalek.* A settlement of Amalekites, most likely located between Telaim and Kadesh Barnea, possibly the residence of their king.
15:6 *Kenites.* A nomadic people of the Sinai, closely related to the Midianites. Moses had married a Kenite woman (see Ex 2:16,21–22; Nu 10:29; Jdg 1:16; 4:11), and some of the Kenites had accompanied the Israelites when they settled in the land of Canaan (see 27:10; Jdg 1:16; 4:17–23; 5:24; 1Ch 2:55).
15:7 *Havilah to Shur.* Ishmael's descendants occupied this area (see Ge 25:18). The location of Havilah is uncertain. Shur was on the eastern frontier of Egypt (see 27:8; Ge 16:7; 20:1).
15:8 *Agag king of the Amalekites.* His descendants would later oppress Israel (see note on Est 3:1). *all his people.* All the Amalekites they encountered. Some Amalekites survived (see 27:8; 30:1,18; 2Sa 1:8,13; 8:12; 1Ch 4:43).
15:9 When the Israelites refused to obey the Lord's command (v. 3), their holy war against the Amalekites degenerated into personal aggrandizement, much like that of Achan at the time of the conquest of Canaan (see Jos 7:1). Giving to the Lord by destruction only what was despised and weak was a contemptible act (see Mal 1:7–12 and notes), not to be excused (see v. 19) by the protestation that the best had been preserved for sacrifice to the Lord (vv. 15,21).
15:11 *regret.* See note on v. 29. *he has turned away from me.* A violation of the fundamental requirement of his office as king (see notes on 12:14–15).
15:12 *Carmel.* Located about seven miles south of Hebron (see 25:2; Jos 15:55). *monument in his own honor.* Saul's self-glorification here contrasts sharply with his self-abasement after the victory over the Ammonites (see note on 11:13; cf. v. 17; 2Sa 18:18). *Gilgal.* Saul returns to the place where he was inaugurated and instructed in the responsibilities of his office (see 11:14–15). This was also the place where he had been told that he would not have a continuing dynasty because of his disobedience (see 13:13–14).
15:13 *I have carried out the LORD's instructions.* Here and in v. 20 Saul is clearly less than honest in his statements to Samuel.
15:15 *The soldiers ... spared the best ... to sacrifice.* Saul attempts to shift responsibility from himself to the army and to excuse their action by claiming pious intentions. *the LORD your God.* Saul's use of the pronoun "your" instead of "my" here and in vv. 21,30 indicates an awareness of his own alienation from the Lord (see 12:19 for a similar case), even though he speaks of obedience and the intent to honor God by sacrifice.
15:17 *you were once small in your own eyes.* See 9:21; 10:22.

did you not obey the LORD? Why did you
pounce on the plunder[v] and do evil in the
eyes of the LORD?"
20 "But I did obey[w] the LORD," Saul said.
"I went on the mission the LORD assigned
me. I completely destroyed the Amalekites
and brought back Agag their king. 21 The
soldiers took sheep and cattle from the
plunder, the best of what was devoted to
God, in order to sacrifice them to the LORD
your God at Gilgal."
22 But Samuel replied:

"Does the LORD delight in burnt
offerings and sacrifices
as much as in obeying the LORD?
To obey is better than sacrifice,[x]
and to heed is better than the fat of
rams.
23 For rebellion is like the sin of
divination,[y]
and arrogance like the evil of
idolatry.
Because you have rejected[z] the word of
the LORD,
he has rejected you as king."

24 Then Saul said to Samuel, "I have
sinned.[a] I violated[b] the LORD's command
and your instructions. I was afraid[c] of the
men and so I gave in to them. 25 Now I beg
you, forgive[d] my sin and come back with
me, so that I may worship the LORD."
26 But Samuel said to him, "I will not
go back with you. You have rejected[e] the
word of the LORD, and the LORD has rejected you as king over Israel!"
27 As Samuel turned to leave, Saul
caught hold of the hem of his robe,[f] and it
tore.[g] 28 Samuel said to him, "The LORD has
torn[h] the kingdom[i] of Israel from you today and has given it to one of your neighbors—to one better than you.[j] 29 He who is
the Glory of Israel does not lie[k] or change[l]
his mind; for he is not a human being, that
he should change his mind."
30 Saul replied, "I have sinned.[m] But
please honor[n] me before the elders of my
people and before Israel; come back with
me, so that I may worship the LORD your
God." 31 So Samuel went back with Saul,
and Saul worshiped the LORD.
32 Then Samuel said, "Bring me Agag
king of the Amalekites."
Agag came to him in chains.[a] And he
thought, "Surely the bitterness of death is
past."
33 But Samuel said,

"As your sword has made women
childless,
so will your mother be childless
among women."[o]

And Samuel put Agag to death before the
LORD at Gilgal.
34 Then Samuel left for Ramah,[p] but
Saul went up to his home in Gibeah[q] of
Saul. 35 Until the day Samuel[r] died, he did
not go to see Saul again, though Samuel
mourned[s] for him. And the LORD regretted[t]
that he had made Saul king over Israel.

[a] *32* The meaning of the Hebrew for this phrase is uncertain.

15:19 [v] S Ge 14:23; S 1Sa 14:32 **15:20** [w] 1Sa 28:18 **15:22** [x] Ps 40:6-8; 51:16; Pr 21:3; Isa 1:11-15; Jer 7:22; Hos 6:6; Am 5:25; Mic 6:6-8; S Mk 12:33 **15:23** [y] Dt 18:10 [z] S 1Sa 13:13 **15:24** [a] S Ex 9:27; S Nu 22:34; Ps 51:4 [b] S 1Sa 13:13 [c] Pr 29:25; Isa 51:12-13; Jer 42:11 **15:25** [d] Ex 10:17 **15:26** [e] S Nu 15:31; S 1Sa 13:14; S 1Ki 14:10 **15:27** [f] 1Sa 28:14 [g] 1Ki 11:11,31; 14:8; 2Ki 17:21 **15:28** [h] 1Sa 28:17 [i] S 1Sa 13:14 [j] 2Sa 6:21; 7:15 **15:29** [k] Titus 1:2 [l] S Nu 23:19; Heb 7:21 **15:30** [m] S Nu 22:34 [n] Isa 29:13; Jn 12:43 **15:33** [o] Est 9:7-10; Jer 18:21 **15:34** [p] S 1Sa 7:17 [q] S Jdg 19:14; S 1Sa 10:5 **15:35** [r] 1Sa 19:24 [s] ver 11; 1Sa 16:1 [t] S Ge 6:6

15:22 Samuel does not suggest that sacrifice is unimportant but that it is acceptable only when brought with an attitude of obedience and devotion to the Lord (see Ps 51:16–17 and notes; Isa 1:11–17; Hos 6:6; Am 5:21–24; Mic 6:6–8). *fat of rams.* The fat of sacrificed animals belonged to the Lord (see 2:15 and note; Ex 23:18; Lev 3:14–16; 7:30).

15:23 *rebellion.* Samuel charges Saul with violating the central requirement of the covenant condition given to him when he became king (see 12:14–15). *sin of divination.* A serious offense against the Lord (see Lev 19:26; Dt 18:9–12), which Saul himself condemned (28:3,9). *you have rejected the word of the LORD.* A king who sets his own will above the command of the Lord ceases to be an instrument of the Lord's rule over his people, violating the very nature of his theocratic office. *he has rejected you as king.* The judgment here goes beyond the one given earlier (see note on 13:14). Now Saul himself is to be set aside as king. Although this did not happen immediately, as chs. 16–31 show, the process began that led to his death. It included in its relentless course the removal of God's Spirit and favor from him (16:14), the defection of his son Jonathan and daughter Michal to David (18:1–4,20; 19:11–17) and the insubordination of his own officials (22:17).

15:24 Saul's confession retains an element of self-justification and a shift of blame (contrast David's confession; see 2Sa 12:13; Ps 51:4 and notes). Previously (vv. 15,21) he had attempted to justify his soldiers' actions.

15:25 *come back with me.* Saul's greatest concern was not to worship God but to avoid an open break with the prophet Samuel, a break that would undermine his authority as king (see v. 30).

15:28 *one of your neighbors.* David (see 28:17 and note on 13:14).

15:29 *Glory of Israel.* In Ps 106:20; Jer 2:11; Hos 4:7 God is called "glorious God" (see 4:21; Heb 9:5 and notes). Cf. 2Sa 1:19; Ps 89:17; Isa 13:19. *does not lie or change his mind.* See Nu 23:19; Mal 3:6 and notes; see also Ps 110:4; Jer 4:28. There is no conflict between this statement and vv. 11,35, where the Lord is said to "regret" that he had made Saul king.

15:31 *So Samuel went back with Saul.* Samuel's purpose in agreeing to Saul's request is not to honor Saul, but to carry out the divine sentence on Agag and in so doing to reemphasize Saul's neglect of duty.

15:34 *Ramah.* Samuel's home (see 7:17; see also note on 1:1). *Gibeah of Saul.* See note on 10:5.

15:35 *Samuel mourned.* Samuel regarded Saul as though dead (see the use of "mourned" in 6:19). Even though his love for him remained (see v. 11; 16:1), he sought no further contact with him because God had rejected him as king. Saul did come to Samuel on one other occasion (see 19:24).

Samuel Anoints David

16 The LORD said to Samuel, "How
long will you mourn[u] for Saul,
since I have rejected[v] him as king over Israel? Fill your horn with oil[w] and be on
your way; I am sending you to Jesse[x] of
Bethlehem. I have chosen[y] one of his sons
to be king."
2 But Samuel said, "How can I go? If
Saul hears about it, he will kill me."
The LORD said, "Take a heifer with you
and say, 'I have come to sacrifice to the
LORD.' 3 Invite Jesse to the sacrifice, and
I will show[z] you what to do. You are to
anoint[a] for me the one I indicate."
4 Samuel did what the LORD said. When
he arrived at Bethlehem,[b] the elders of the
town trembled[c] when they met him. They
asked, "Do you come in peace?[d]"
5 Samuel replied, "Yes, in peace; I have
come to sacrifice to the LORD. Consecrate[e]
yourselves and come to the sacrifice with
me." Then he consecrated Jesse and his
sons and invited them to the sacrifice.
6 When they arrived, Samuel saw Eliab[f]
and thought, "Surely the LORD's anointed
stands here before the LORD."
7 But the LORD said to Samuel, "Do not
consider his appearance or his height, for I
have rejected him. The LORD does not look
at the things people look at. People look
at the outward appearance,[g] but the LORD
looks at the heart."[h]
8 Then Jesse called Abinadab[i] and had
him pass in front of Samuel. But Samuel
said, "The LORD has not chosen this one
either." 9 Jesse then had Shammah[j] pass
by, but Samuel said, "Nor has the LORD
chosen this one." 10 Jesse had seven of his
sons pass before Samuel, but Samuel said
to him, "The LORD has not chosen these."
11 So he asked Jesse, "Are these all[k] the
sons you have?"
"There is still the youngest," Jesse answered. "He is tending the sheep."[l]
Samuel said, "Send for him; we will not
sit down until he arrives."
12 So he[m] sent for him and had him
brought in. He was glowing with health
and had a fine appearance and handsome[n]
features.
Then the LORD said, "Rise and anoint
him; this is the one."
13 So Samuel took the horn of oil and
anointed[o] him in the presence of his brothers, and from that day on the Spirit of the
LORD[p] came powerfully upon David.[q] Samuel then went to Ramah.

David in Saul's Service

14 Now the Spirit of the LORD had departed[r] from Saul, and an evil[a] spirit[s] from the
LORD tormented him.[t]

[a] 14 Or *and a harmful*; similarly in verses 15, 16 and 23

16:1 [u] S 1Sa 8:6; S 15:35 [v] S 1Sa 13:14 [w] S 1Sa 10:1 [x] S Ru 4:17 [y] 2Sa 5:2; 7:8; 1Ki 8:16; 1Ch 12:23; Ps 78:70; Ac 13:22 **16:3** [z] Ex 4:15 [a] S Dt 17:15 **16:4** [b] S Ge 48:7; Lk 2:4 [c] 1Sa 21:1 [d] 1Ki 2:13; 2Ki 9:17 **16:5** [e] S Ex 19:10,22 **16:6** [f] 1Sa 17:13; 1Ch 2:13 **16:7** [g] Ps 147:10 [h] S 1Sa 2:3; 2Sa 7:20; S Ps 44:21; S 139:23; S Rev 2:23 **16:8** [i] 1Sa 17:13 **16:9** [j] 1Sa 17:13; 2Sa 13:3; 21:21 **16:11** [k] 1Sa 17:12 [l] S Ge 37:2; 2Sa 7:8 **16:12** [m] 1Sa 9:17 [n] S Ge 39:6 **16:13** [o] S 1Sa 2:35; S 2Sa 22:51 [p] 1Sa 18:12 [q] S 1Sa 11:6 **16:14** [r] S Jdg 16:20 [s] ver 23; S Jdg 9:23; 1Sa 18:10 [t] 2Sa 7:15

16:1 *The LORD said to Samuel.* Probably c. 1025 BC (see note on 15:1–35). *Jesse.* For Jesse's genealogy see Ru 4:18–22; Mt 1:3–6. *Bethlehem.* A town five miles south of Jerusalem, formerly known as Ephrath (see Ge 35:16 and note). It was later to become renowned as the "town of David" and the birthplace of the Messiah (Mic 5:2; Mt 2:1; Lk 2:4–7). *I have chosen one of his sons to be king.* See notes on 13:14; 15:28.

16:2 *Saul … will kill me.* The road from Ramah (where Samuel was, 15:34) to Bethlehem passed through Gibeah of Saul. Saul already knew that the Lord had chosen someone to replace him as king (see 15:28). Samuel fears that jealousy will incite Saul to violence. Later incidents (18:10–11; 19:10; 20:33) demonstrate that Samuel's fears were well-founded. *say, 'I have come to sacrifice to the LORD.'* This response is true but incomplete, and it was intended to deceive Saul.

16:3 *anoint.* See vv. 1,13 and note on 9:16.

16:5 *Consecrate yourselves.* Involves preparing oneself spiritually as well as making oneself ceremonially clean by washing and putting on clean clothes (see Ex 19:10,14; Lev 15; Nu 19:11–22).

16:6 *Eliab.* Jesse's oldest son (17:13).

16:7 *his appearance or his height.* Samuel is not to focus on these outward features, which had characterized Saul (see 9:2; 10:23–24). *heart.* The Lord is concerned with a person's inner disposition and character (see 1Ki 8:39; 1Ch 28:9; Lk 16:15; Jn 2:25; Ac 1:24).

16:8 *Abinadab.* Jesse's second son (17:13).

16:9 *Shammah.* Jesse's third son (17:13).

16:11 *He is tending the sheep.* The Lord's chosen one is a shepherd (see note on 9:3; see also 2Sa 7:7–8; Ps 78:71–72).

16:13–14 Taken together, these verses describe not only the transfer of God's Spirit from Saul to David but also the beginning of God's effective displacement of Saul by David as Israel's king. This transition, occurring as it does at the center of 1 Samuel, serves as the literary, historical and theological crux of this book. Cf. Ps 51:11 and note.

16:13 *in the presence of his brothers.* The small circle of witnesses to David's anointing assured its confidentiality but also provided ample testimony for the future that David had been anointed by Samuel and that he was not merely a usurper of Saul's office. *the Spirit of the LORD came powerfully upon David.* See 10:5–6,10; 11:6; 14:6,19; Jdg 3:10 and note; 11:29 and note; 15:14. This is the first mention of David by name in 1 Samuel.

16:14—17:58 In the next two episodes, David is introduced to Saul's court and to Israel as a gifted musician and warrior. With these two gifts he would become famous in Israel and would lead the nation to spiritual and political vigor (see 2Sa 22; 23:1–7). Also through these two gifts Saul would become dependent on David.

16:14 *the Spirit of the LORD had departed from Saul.* Cf. Jdg 16:20. The removal of the Spirit from Saul and the giving of the Spirit to David (v. 13) determined the contrasting courses of their lives. *evil spirit from the LORD.* This statement and similar ones in Scripture indicate that evil spirits are subject to God's control and operate only within divinely determined boundaries (see 1Ki 22:19–23; Job 1:12; 2:6 and notes; see also 2Sa 24:1 and note). Saul's disobedience continued to be punished by the assaults of an evil spirit (vv. 15–16,23; 18:10; 19:9; see NIV text note). *tormented him.* Saul's increasing tendencies to despondency, jealousy and violence were no doubt occasioned by his knowledge of his rejection as king (see 13:13–14; 15:22–26; 18:9; 20:30–33; 22:16–18) and his awareness of David's growing popularity,

DAVID'S FAMILY TREE

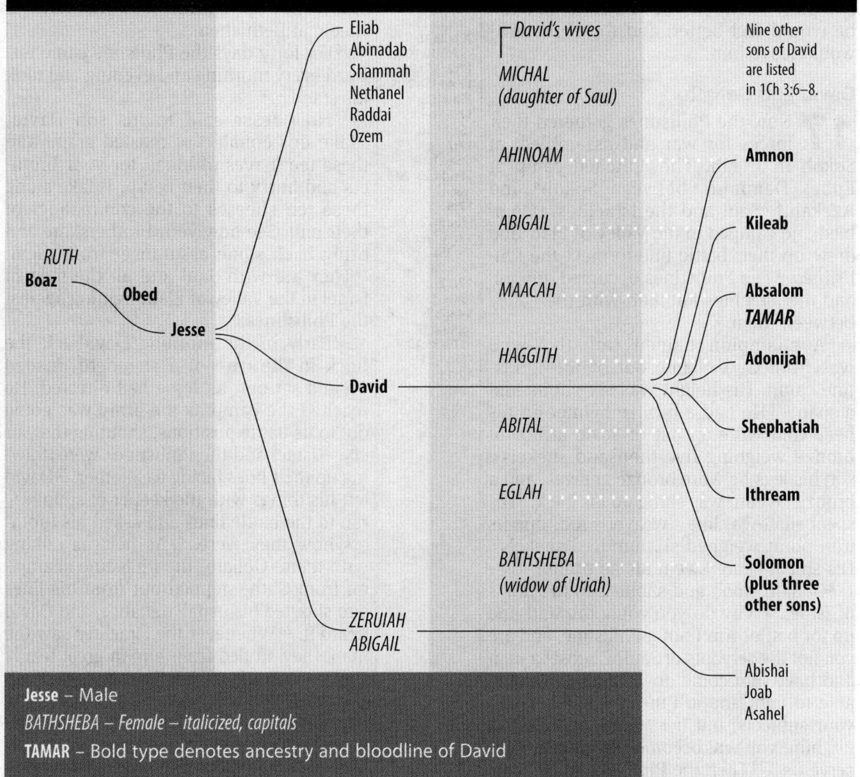

15 Saul's attendants said to him, "See,
an evil spirit from God is tormenting you.
16 Let our lord command his servants here
to search for someone who can play the
lyre.[u] He will play when the evil spirit
from God comes on you, and you will feel
better."
17 So Saul said to his attendants, "Find
someone who plays well and bring him
to me."
18 One of the servants answered, "I have
seen a son of Jesse[v] of Bethlehem who
knows how to play the lyre. He is a brave
man and a warrior.[w] He speaks well and is
a fine-looking man. And the LORD is with[x]
him."
19 Then Saul sent messengers to Jesse
and said, "Send me your son David, who
is with the sheep.[y]" 20 So Jesse took a donkey loaded with bread,[z] a skin of wine and
a young goat and sent them with his son
David to Saul.
21 David came to Saul and entered his
service.[a] Saul liked him very much, and
David became one of his armor-bearers.
22 Then Saul sent word to Jesse, saying,
"Allow David to remain in my service, for
I am pleased with him."

16:16 [u] ver 23; S 1Sa 10:5,6; 2Ch 29:26-27; Ps 49:4
16:18 [v] S Ru 4:17 [w] 2Sa 17:8 [x] S Ge 39:2; 1Sa 17:32-37; 20:13; 1Ch 22:11; Mt 1:23
16:19 [y] 1Sa 17:15
16:20 [z] S Ge 32:13; S 1Sa 10:4
16:21 [a] S Ge 41:46

---

but an evil spirit was also involved in these psychological aberrations (see 18:10–12; 19:9–10).

16:16 *you will feel better.* The soothing effect of certain types of music on a troubled spirit is a generally recognized phenomenon (see 2Ki 3:15). Beyond this natural effect of music, however, it would appear that in this instance the Spirit of the Lord was active in David's music to suppress the evil spirit temporarily (see v. 23).

16:18 *the LORD is with him.* Said also of Samuel (see 3:1 and note). The fact that God was with David (see also 17:37; 18:12,14,28; 2Sa 5:10) outweighs everything David was.

16:19 *Send me your son David.* Saul unknowingly invites to the court the person God chose to be his replacement. In this way David is brought into contact with Saul, and his introduction to Israel begins.

16:21 *David became one of his armor-bearers.* May refer to a later time after David's victory over Goliath (see 18:2).

23 Whenever the spirit from God came
on Saul, David would take up his lyre
and play. Then relief would come to Saul;
he would feel better, and the evil spirit[b]
would leave him.

David and Goliath

17 Now the Philistines gathered their
forces for war and assembled[c] at
Sokoh in Judah. They pitched camp at
Ephes Dammim, between Sokoh[d] and
Azekah.[e] 2 Saul and the Israelites assembled and camped in the Valley of Elah[f] and
drew up their battle line to meet the Philistines. 3 The Philistines occupied one hill
and the Israelites another, with the valley
between them.

4 A champion named Goliath,[g] who
was from Gath, came out of the Philistine camp. His height was six cubits and
a span.[a] 5 He had a bronze helmet on his
head and wore a coat of scale armor of
bronze weighing five thousand shekels[b];
6 on his legs he wore bronze greaves, and a
bronze javelin[h] was slung on his back. 7 His
spear shaft was like a weaver's rod,[i] and its
iron point weighed six hundred shekels.[c]
His shield bearer[j] went ahead of him.

8 Goliath stood and shouted to the ranks
of Israel, "Why do you come out and line
up for battle? Am I not a Philistine, and are
you not the servants of Saul? Choose[k] a man
and have him come down to me. 9 If he is
able to fight and kill me, we will become
your subjects; but if I overcome him and
kill him, you will become our subjects and
serve us." 10 Then the Philistine said, "This
day I defy[l] the armies of Israel! Give me
a man and let us fight each other.[m]" 11 On
hearing the Philistine's words, Saul and all
the Israelites were dismayed and terrified.

12 Now David was the son of an Ephrathite[n] named Jesse,[o] who was from Bethlehem[p] in Judah. Jesse had eight[q] sons, and
in Saul's time he was very old. 13 Jesse's
three oldest sons had followed Saul to
the war: The firstborn was Eliab;[r] the second, Abinadab;[s] and the third, Shammah.[t]
14 David was the youngest. The three oldest followed Saul, 15 but David went back
and forth from Saul to tend[u] his father's
sheep[v] at Bethlehem.

16 For forty days the Philistine came forward every morning and evening and took
his stand.

17 Now Jesse said to his son David,
"Take this ephah[d][w] of roasted grain[x] and
these ten loaves of bread for your brothers and hurry to their camp. 18 Take along
these ten cheeses to the commander of
their unit. See how your brothers[y] are and
bring back some assurance[e] from them.
19 They are with Saul and all the men of
Israel in the Valley of Elah, fighting against
the Philistines."

20 Early in the morning David left the
flock in the care of a shepherd, loaded
up and set out, as Jesse had directed. He
reached the camp as the army was going
out to its battle positions, shouting the war
cry. 21 Israel and the Philistines were drawing up their lines facing each other. 22 David
left his things with the keeper of supplies,[z]
ran to the battle lines and asked his brothers how they were. 23 As he was talking
with them, Goliath, the Philistine champion from Gath, stepped out from his lines
and shouted his usual[a] defiance, and David
heard it. 24 Whenever the Israelites saw the
man, they all fled from him in great fear.

25 Now the Israelites had been saying,
"Do you see how this man keeps coming
out? He comes out to defy Israel. The king
will give great wealth to the man who kills
him. He will also give him his daughter[b] in
marriage and will exempt his family from
taxes[c] in Israel."

26 David asked the men standing near
him, "What will be done for the man who
kills this Philistine and removes this disgrace[d] from Israel? Who is this uncircum-

16:23 [b] S ver 14; S Jdg 9:23
17:1 [c] 1Sa 13:5 [d] Jos 15:35; 2Ch 28:18 [e] S Jos 10:10,11
17:2 [f] 1Sa 21:9
17:4 [g] 1Sa 21:9; 2Sa 21:19
17:6 [h] ver 45; 1Sa 18:10
17:7 [i] 2Sa 21:19; 1Ch 11:23; 20:5 [j] ver 41
17:8 [k] 2Sa 2:12-17
17:10 [l] ver 26, 45; 2Sa 21:21 [m] ver 23
17:12 [n] S Ge 35:16; S 48:7; Ps 132:6 [o] S Ru 4:17 [p] S Ge 35:19 [q] 1Sa 16:11
17:13 [r] S 1Sa 16:6 [s] 1Sa 16:8 [t] S 1Sa 16:9
17:15 [u] S Ge 37:2 [v] 1Sa 16:19
17:17 [w] S Lev 19:36 [x] S Lev 23:14; 1Sa 25:18
17:18 [y] Ge 37:14
17:22 [z] S Jos 1:11
17:23 [a] ver 8-10
17:25 [b] 1Sa 18:17 [c] S 1Sa 8:15
17:26 [d] 1Sa 11:2

[a] *4* That is, about 9 feet 9 inches or about 3 meters
[b] *5* That is, about 125 pounds or about 58 kilograms
[c] *7* That is, about 15 pounds or about 6.9 kilograms
[d] *17* That is, probably about 36 pounds or about 16 kilograms
[e] *18* Or *some token*; or *some pledge of spoils*

17:1 *Sokoh.* Located about 15 miles west of Bethlehem (see 2Ch 28:18) near the Philistine border. *Azekah.* Located a little over a mile northwest of Sokoh.
17:2 *Valley of Elah.* Located between Azekah and Sokoh (see photo, p. 437).
17:4 *champion.* The ancient Greeks, to whom the Philistines were apparently related, sometimes decided issues of war through chosen champions who met in combat between the armies. Through this economy of warriors the judgment of the gods on the matter at stake was determined (trial by battle ordeal). Israel too may have known this practice (see 2Sa 2:14–16). *Gath.* See 5:8 and note.
17:11 *Saul and all the Israelites were … terrified.* Israel's giant warrior (see 9:2; 10:23) quakes before the Philistine champion. The fear of Saul and the Israelite army (see vv. 24,32) betrays a loss of faith in the covenant promises of the Lord (see Ex 23:22; Dt 3:22; 20:1–4). Their fear also demonstrates that the Israelite search for security in a human king (apart from trust in the Lord; see notes on 8:5,7) had failed. On the basis of God's covenant promises, Israel was never to fear her enemies but to trust in the Lord (see 2Sa 10:12; Ex 14:13–14; Nu 14:9; Jos 10:8; 2Ch 20:17).
17:12 *Ephrathite.* See note on Ru 1:2.
17:15 *David went back and forth from Saul.* David's position at the court (see 16:21–23) was not permanent, but was performed on an intermittent basis. For the relationship between chs. 16 and 17, see note on v. 55.
17:24 *great fear.* See note on v. 11.
17:25 *The king will give great wealth.* See 8:14; 22:7. *give him his daughter in marriage.* See 18:17–27; cf. Jos 15:16.

cised[e] Philistine that he should defy[f] the
armies of the living[g] God?"
27 They repeated to him what they had
been saying and told him, "This is what
will be done for the man who kills him."
28 When Eliab, David's oldest brother, heard him speaking with the men, he
burned with anger[h] at him and asked,
"Why have you come down here? And
with whom did you leave those few sheep
in the wilderness? I know how conceited
you are and how wicked your heart is; you
came down only to watch the battle."
29 "Now what have I done?" said David.
"Can't I even speak?" 30 He then turned
away to someone else and brought up the
same matter, and the men answered him as
before. 31 What David said was overheard
and reported to Saul, and Saul sent for him.
32 David said to Saul, "Let no one lose
heart[i] on account of this Philistine; your
servant will go and fight him."
33 Saul replied,[j] "You are not able to go
out against this Philistine and fight him;
you are only a young man, and he has
been a warrior from his youth."
34 But David said to Saul, "Your servant has been keeping his father's sheep.
When a lion[k] or a bear came and carried
off a sheep from the flock, 35 I went after
it, struck it and rescued the sheep from its
mouth. When it turned on me, I seized[l] it
by its hair, struck it and killed it. 36 Your
servant has killed both the lion[m] and the
bear; this uncircumcised Philistine will be
like one of them, because he has defied
the armies of the living God. 37 The LORD
who rescued[n] me from the paw of the lion[o]
and the paw of the bear will rescue me
from the hand of this Philistine."
Saul said to David, "Go, and the LORD
be with[p] you."
38 Then Saul dressed David in his own[q]
tunic. He put a coat of armor on him and
a bronze helmet on his head. 39 David fastened on his sword over the tunic and
tried walking around, because he was not
used to them.

17:26 [e] S 1Sa 14:6 [f] S ver 10 [g] Dt 5:26; S Jos 3:10; 2Ki 18:35 **17:28** [h] S Ge 27:41; Pr 18:19 **17:32** [i] S Dt 20:3; Ps 18:45; Isa 7:4; Jer 4:9; 38:4; Da 11:30 **17:33** [j] Nu 13:31 **17:34** [k] Job 10:16; Isa 31:4; Jer 49:19; Hos 13:8; Am 3:12 **17:35** [l] Jdg 14:6 **17:36** [m] 1Ch 11:22 **17:37** [n] 2Co 1:10 [o] 2Ti 4:17 [p] S 1Sa 16:18; S 18:12 **17:38** [q] S Ge 41:42

17:26,36 *uncircumcised.* See note on 14:6.

17:26 *Who is this ... ?* David sees the issues clearly—which sets him apart from Saul and all the other Israelites on that battlefield. Because of the Philistine threat and the cowering of Saul and his army in the face of it, the coming of the kingdom of God into the world through God's ways with Israel was at stake. David seems to have been aware of this. It marked him as one who was more worthy than Saul—or any other man there—to wear the crown in Israel.

17:28 *he burned with anger.* Eliab's anger may arise from jealousy toward his brother and a sense of guilt for the defeatist attitude of the Israelites. His evaluation of David stands in sharp contrast to that of Saul's attendant (see 16:18). Eliab does not comprehend David's indomitable spirit (see 16:13).

17:32 *Let no one lose heart on account of this Philistine.* David's confidence rests not in his own prowess (see vv. 37,47 and notes) but in the power of the living God, whose honor has been violated by the Philistines and whose covenant promises have been scorned by the Israelites.

17:33 *You are not able.* Saul does not take into account the power of God (see vv. 37,47 and notes).

17:34 *lion ... bear.* For the presence of lions and bears in Canaan at that time, see 2Sa 17:8; 23:20; Jdg 14:5–11; 1Ki 13:24–26; 2Ki 2:24; Am 3:12; 5:19.

17:37 *The LORD ... will rescue me.* Reliance on the Lord was essential for the true theocratic king (see notes on 10:18; 11:13). Here David's faith contrasts sharply with Saul's loss of faith (see 11:6–7 for Saul's earlier fearlessness). *Saul said to David, "Go."* Saul is now dependent on David not only for his sanity (see note on 16:16) but also for the security of his realm. *the LORD be with you.* See note on 16:18.

View of the Valley of Elah, where David killed Goliath (1Sa 17:1–2)

“I cannot go in these,” he said to Saul,
“because I am not used to them.” So he
took them off. 40Then he took his staff in
his hand, chose five smooth stones from
the stream, put them in the pouch of his
shepherd’s bag and, with his sling in his
hand, approached the Philistine.
41Meanwhile, the Philistine, with his
shield bearer[r] in front of him, kept coming
closer to David. 42He looked David over
and saw that he was little more than a
boy, glowing with health and handsome,[s]
and he despised[t] him. 43He said to David,
“Am I a dog,[u] that you come at me with
sticks?” And the Philistine cursed David
by his gods. 44“Come here,” he said, “and
I’ll give your flesh to the birds[v] and the
wild animals![w]”
45David said to the Philistine, “You come
against me with sword and spear and javelin,[x] but I come against you in the name[y]
of the LORD Almighty, the God of the armies of Israel, whom you have defied.[z]
46This day the LORD will deliver[a] you into
my hands, and I’ll strike you down and
cut off your head. This very day I will give
the carcasses[b] of the Philistine army to the
birds and the wild animals, and the whole
world[c] will know that there is a God in Israel.[d] 47All those gathered here will know
that it is not by sword[e] or spear that the
LORD saves;[f] for the battle[g] is the LORD’s,
and he will give all of you into our hands.”
48As the Philistine moved closer to attack him, David ran quickly toward the
battle line to meet him. 49Reaching into
his bag and taking out a stone, he slung it
and struck the Philistine on the forehead.
The stone sank into his forehead, and he
fell facedown on the ground.
50So David triumphed over the Philistine with a sling[h] and a stone; without a
sword in his hand he struck down the Philistine and killed him.
51David ran and stood over him. He
took hold of the Philistine’s sword and
drew it from the sheath. After he killed
him, he cut[i] off his head with the sword.[j]
When the Philistines saw that their hero
was dead, they turned and ran. 52Then the
men of Israel and Judah surged forward
with a shout and pursued the Philistines
to the entrance of Gath[a] and to the gates
of Ekron.[k] Their dead were strewn along
the Shaaraim[l] road to Gath and Ekron.
53When the Israelites returned from chasing the Philistines, they plundered their
camp.
54David took the Philistine’s head and
brought it to Jerusalem; he put the Philistine’s weapons in his own tent.
55As Saul watched David[m] going out to
meet the Philistine, he said to Abner, commander of the army, “Abner,[n] whose son is
that young man?”
Abner replied, “As surely as you live,
Your Majesty, I don’t know.”

Slingstones found at Lachish. David likely killed Goliath with something similar.

William L. Krewson/www.BiblePlaces.com

17:41 [r] ver 7 **17:42** [s] 1Sa 16:12 [t] Ps 123:3-4; Pr 16:18 **17:43** [u] 1Sa 24:14; 2Sa 3:8; 9:8; 2Ki 8:13 **17:44** [v] S Ge 40:19; Rev 19:17 [w] 2Sa 21:10; Jer 34:20 **17:45** [x] S ver 6 [y] Dt 20:1; 2Ch 13:12; 14:11; 32:8; Ps 20:7-8; 124:8; Heb 11:32-34 [z] S ver 10 **17:46** [a] S 1Sa 14:12 [b] S Dt 28:26 [c] S Jos 4:24; S Isa 11:9 [d] 1Ki 18:36; 2Ki 5:8; 19:19; Isa 37:20 **17:47** [e] Hos 1:7 [f] 1Sa 14:6; 2Ch 14:11; Jer 39:18 [g] S Ex 14:14; S Nu 21:14; S 1Sa 2:9; 2Ch 20:15; Ps 44:6-7 **17:50** [h] 1Sa 25:29 **17:51** [i] Heb 11:34 [j] 1Sa 21:9; 22:10 **17:52** [k] Jos 15:11 [l] S Jos 15:36 **17:55** [m] 1Sa 16:21 [n] 1Sa 26:5

[a] 52 Some Septuagint manuscripts; Hebrew *of a valley*

17:40 *his staff.* God’s newly appointed shepherd of his people (see 2Sa 5:2; 7:7; Ps 78:72) goes to defend the Lord’s threatened and frightened flock. *stones.* See Jdg 20:16 and note. Usually the stones chosen were round and smooth and somewhat larger than a baseball. *his sling.* For the Benjamites’ skill with a sling, see Jdg 20:16 and photo above.

17:43 *Am I a dog . . . ?* See 2Sa 9:8 and note.

17:45 *in the name of the LORD Almighty.* David’s strength was his reliance on the Lord (see Ps 9:10). *name of the LORD.* See notes on Ex 3:13 – 14; Dt 12:11. *the LORD Almighty.* See note on 1:3.

17:46 *the whole world will know.* The victory that David anticipates will demonstrate to everyone the existence and power of Israel’s God (see Ex 7:17; 9:14,16,29; Dt 4:34 – 35; Jos 2:10 – 11; 4:23 – 24; 1Ki 8:59 – 60; 18:36 – 39; 2Ki 5:15; 19:19).

17:47 *the battle is the LORD’s.* Both the Israelite and the Philistine armies will be shown the error of placing trust in human devices for personal or national security (see 2:10; 14:6; 2Ch 14:11; 20:15; Ps 33:16 – 22; 44:6 – 7; Ecc 9:11; Hos 1:7; Zec 4:6).

17:51 *cut off his head.* See 5:4; 31:9 and notes. *they turned and ran.* Most likely the Philistines saw the fall of their champion as the judgment of the gods, but they did not honor Goliath’s original proposal (see v. 9).

17:54 *brought it to Jerusalem.* Jerusalem had not at this time been conquered by the Israelites. David may have kept Goliath’s head as a trophy of victory and brought it with him to Jerusalem when he took that city and made it his capital (see 2Sa 5:6 – 9). Or, having grown up almost under the shadow of the Jebusite city, he may have displayed Goliath’s head to its inhabitants as a warning of what the God of Israel was able to do and eventually would do. *put the Philistine’s weapons in his own tent.* As his personal spoils of the battle. Since Goliath’s sword is later in the custody of the priest at Nob (see 21:9), David must have dedicated it to the Lord, the true victor in the fight (cf. 31:10).

17:55 *whose son is that young man?* The seeming contradiction between vv. 55 – 58 and 16:16 – 23 may be resolved by noting that prior to this time David was not a permanent resident at Saul’s court (see v. 15; 18:2; see also note on 16:21), so that Saul’s knowledge of David and his family may have been minimal. Further, Saul may have been so incredulous at David’s courage that he was wondering whether his family background and social standing might explain his extraordinary conduct.

56 The king said, "Find out whose son
this young man is."
57 As soon as David returned from killing the Philistine, Abner took him and
brought him before Saul, with David still
holding the Philistine's head.
58 "Whose son are you, young man?"
Saul asked him.
David said, "I am the son of your servant Jesse[o] of Bethlehem."

Saul's Growing Fear of David

18 After David had finished talking
with Saul, Jonathan[p] became one
in spirit with David, and he loved[q] him as
himself.[r] 2 From that day Saul kept David
with him and did not let him return home
to his family. 3 And Jonathan made a covenant[s] with David because he loved him
as himself. 4 Jonathan took off the robe[t] he
was wearing and gave it to David, along
with his tunic, and even his sword, his
bow and his belt.[u]
5 Whatever mission Saul sent him on,
David was so successful[v] that Saul gave
him a high rank in the army.[w] This pleased
all the troops, and Saul's officers as well.
6 When the men were returning home
after David had killed the Philistine, the
women came out from all the towns of Israel to meet King Saul with singing and
dancing,[x] with joyful songs and with timbrels[y] and lyres. 7 As they danced, they
sang:[z]

"Saul has slain his thousands,
and David his tens[a] of thousands."

8 Saul was very angry; this refrain displeased him greatly. "They have credited
David with tens of thousands," he thought,
"but me with only thousands. What more
can he get but the kingdom?[b]" 9 And from
that time on Saul kept a close[c] eye on David.
10 The next day an evil[a] spirit[d] from God
came forcefully on Saul. He was prophesying in his house, while David was playing
the lyre,[e] as he usually[f] did. Saul had a
spear[g] in his hand 11 and he hurled it, saying to himself,[h] "I'll pin David to the wall."
But David eluded[i] him twice.[j]
12 Saul was afraid[k] of David, because the
LORD[l] was with[m] David but had departed
from[n] Saul. 13 So he sent David away from
him and gave him command over a thousand men, and David led[o] the troops in
their campaigns.[p] 14 In everything he did
he had great success,[q] because the LORD
was with[r] him. 15 When Saul saw how successful he was, he was afraid of him. 16 But
all Israel and Judah loved David, because
he led them in their campaigns.[s]
17 Saul said to David, "Here is my older
daughter[t] Merab. I will give her to you in
marriage;[u] only serve me bravely and fight
the battles[v] of the LORD." For Saul said to
himself,[w] "I will not raise a hand against
him. Let the Philistines do that!"
18 But David said to Saul, "Who am I,[x]
and what is my family or my clan in Israel, that I should become the king's son-
in-law?[y]" 19 So[b] when the time came for
Merab,[z] Saul's daughter, to be given to
David, she was given in marriage to Adriel of Meholah.[a]

[a] 10 Or *a harmful* [b] 19 Or *However,*

17:58 [o] S Ru 4:17 **18:1** [p] 1Sa 19:1; 20:16; 31:2; 2Sa 4:4 [q] 2Sa 1:26 [r] S Ge 44:30 **18:3** [s] 1Sa 20:8, 16,17,42; 22:8; 23:18; 24:21; 2Sa 21:7 **18:4** [t] S Ge 41:42 [u] 2Sa 18:11 **18:5** [v] ver 30 [w] 2Sa 5:2 **18:6** [x] S Ex 15:20; 2Sa 1:20 [y] Ps 68:25 **18:7** [z] Ex 15:21 [a] 1Sa 21:11; 29:5; 2Sa 18:3 **18:8** [b] S 1Sa 13:14; 1Sa 15:8 **18:9** [c] 1Sa 19:1 **18:10** [d] S Jdg 9:23; S 1Sa 16:14 [e] S 1Sa 10:5 [f] 1Sa 16:21; 19:7 [g] S 1Sa 17:6 **18:11** [h] ver 25; 1Sa 20:7,33 [i] 1Sa 19:10 [j] Ps 132:1 **18:12** [k] ver 29 [l] 1Sa 16:13 [m] Jos 1:5; 1Sa 17:37; 20:13; 1Ch 22:11 [n] S Jdg 16:20 **18:13** [o] Nu 27:17 [p] 2Sa 5:2 **18:14** [q] S Ge 39:3 [r] S Ge 39:2; S Nu 14:43; 2Sa 7:9 **18:16** [s] 2Sa 5:2 **18:17** [t] 1Sa 17:25 [u] S Ge 29:26 [v] S Nu 21:14 [w] ver 25; 1Sa 20:33 **18:18** [x] S Ex 3:11; S 1Sa 9:21 [y] ver 23 **18:19** [z] 2Sa 21:8 [a] S Jdg 7:22

18:1—20:42 Saul's alienation from David, even while members of his own family protect David.
18:1 It appears that David spoke with Saul at length, and he may have explained his actions as an expression of his faith in the Lord, thus attracting the love and loyalty of Jonathan (see v. 3; 14:6; 19:5). Their friendship endured even when it became clear that David was to replace him as the successor to his father's throne.
18:2 *Saul kept David with him.* See note on 17:15.
18:3 *Jonathan made a covenant with David.* The initiative comes from Jonathan. The terms of the agreement are not here specified (see further 19:1; 20:8,12–16,41–42; 23:18) but would appear to involve a pledge of mutual loyalty and friendship. At the very least, Jonathan accepts David as his equal.
18:4 *took off the robe … and gave it to David.* Jonathan ratifies the covenant in an act that symbolizes giving himself to David. His act may even signify his recognition that David was to assume his place as successor to Saul (see 20:14–15,31; 23:17)—a possibility that seems the more likely in that he also gave David "even his sword, his bow and his belt" (cf. 13:22).
18:6 *women came out … with timbrels.* See Ex 15:20 and note.
18:7 *David his tens of thousands.* See 21:11; 29:5. In accordance with the normal conventions of Hebrew poetry, this was the women's way of saying "Saul and David have slain thousands" (10,000 was normally used as the parallel of 1,000—see Dt 32:30; Ps 91:7 and note; Da 7:10; Mic 6:7; also in Canaanite poetry found at Ugarit). It is a measure of Saul's insecurity and jealousy that he read their intentions incorrectly and took offense (see v. 8). His resentment may have been initially triggered by the mention of David's name alongside his own. See note on 21:11 for how the Philistines interpreted the song.
18:10 *evil spirit from God.* See note on 16:14. *prophesying.* The Hebrew for this word is sometimes used to indicate uncontrolled ecstatic behavior (see note on 1Ki 18:29) and is best understood in that sense in this context (see also note on 10:5). *as he usually did.* See 16:23.
18:12 *the LORD was with David.* See 16:18 and note. *but had departed from Saul.* See 16:14 and note.
18:13 *he sent David away.* His apparent motive was the hope that David would be killed in battle (see vv. 17,21,25; 19:1), but the result was greater acclaim for David (see vv. 14,16,30).
18:14 *the LORD was with him.* See note on 16:18.
18:17 *Here is my older daughter.* David was entitled to have Saul's daughter as his wife because of his victory over Goliath (see 17:25). This promise had not been kept and is now made conditional on further military service, in which Saul hoped David would be killed. *battles of the LORD.* See 25:28.

20 Now Saul's daughter Michal[b] was in
love with David, and when they told Saul
about it, he was pleased.[c] 21 "I will give
her to him," he thought, "so that she may
be a snare[d] to him and so that the hand
of the Philistines may be against him."
So Saul said to David, "Now you have a
second opportunity to become my son-in-
law."

22 Then Saul ordered his attendants:
"Speak to David privately and say, 'Look,
the king likes you, and his attendants all
love you; now become his son-in-law.' "

23 They repeated these words to David.
But David said, "Do you think it is a small
matter to become the king's son-in-law?[e]
I'm only a poor man and little known."

24 When Saul's servants told him what
David had said, 25 Saul replied, "Say to David, 'The king wants no other price[f] for the
bride than a hundred Philistine foreskins,
to take revenge[g] on his enemies.' " Saul's
plan[h] was to have David fall by the hands
of the Philistines.

26 When the attendants told David these
things, he was pleased to become the
king's son-in-law. So before the allotted
time elapsed, 27 David took his men with
him and went out and killed two hundred
Philistines and brought back their foreskins. They counted out the full number
to the king so that David might become
the king's son-in-law. Then Saul gave him
his daughter Michal[i] in marriage.

28 When Saul realized that the LORD was
with David and that his daughter Michal[j]
loved David, 29 Saul became still more
afraid[k] of him, and he remained his enemy
the rest of his days.

30 The Philistine commanders continued
to go out to battle, and as often as they
did, David met with more success[l] than
the rest of Saul's officers, and his name
became well known.

Saul Tries to Kill David

19 Saul told his son Jonathan[m] and all
the attendants to kill[n] David. But
Jonathan had taken a great liking to David
2 and warned him, "My father Saul is looking for a chance to kill you. Be on your
guard tomorrow morning; go into hiding[o]
and stay there. 3 I will go out and stand
with my father in the field where you are.
I'll speak[p] to him about you and will tell
you what I find out."

4 Jonathan spoke[q] well of David to Saul
his father and said to him, "Let not the
king do wrong[r] to his servant David; he
has not wronged you, and what he has
done has benefited you greatly. 5 He took
his life[s] in his hands when he killed the
Philistine. The LORD won a great victory[t]
for all Israel, and you saw it and were
glad. Why then would you do wrong to an
innocent[u] man like David by killing him
for no reason?"

6 Saul listened to Jonathan and took this
oath: "As surely as the LORD lives, David
will not be put to death."

7 So Jonathan called David and told him
the whole conversation. He brought him
to Saul, and David was with Saul as before.[v]

8 Once more war broke out, and David
went out and fought the Philistines. He
struck them with such force that they fled
before him.

9 But an evil[a] spirit[w] from the LORD came
on Saul as he was sitting in his house with
his spear in his hand. While David was
playing the lyre,[x] 10 Saul tried to pin him to
the wall with his spear, but David eluded[y]
him as Saul drove the spear into the wall.
That night David made good his escape.

11 Saul sent men to David's house to
watch[z] it and to kill him in the morning.[a]
But Michal, David's wife, warned him, "If

18:20 [b] ver 28; S Ge 29:26 [c] ver 29 **18:21** [d] S Ex 10:7; S Dt 7:16 **18:23** [e] ver 18 **18:25** [f] S Ge 34:12 [g] Ps 8:2; 44:16; Jer 20:10 [h] S ver 11, S 17; ver 17 **18:27** [i] 2Sa 3:14; 6:16 **18:28** [j] S ver 20 **18:29** [k] ver 12 **18:30** [l] ver 5

19:1 [m] S 1Sa 18:1 [n] 1Sa 18:9 **19:2** [o] 1Sa 20:5, 19 **19:3** [p] 1Sa 20:12 **19:4** [q] 1Sa 20:32; 22:14; Pr 31:8, 9; Jer 18:20 [r] 1Sa 25:21; Pr 17:13 **19:5** [s] S Jdg 9:17; S 12:3 [t] S 1Sa 11:13 [u] S Ge 31:36; Dt 19:10-13 **19:7** [v] S 1Sa 18:2, 13 **19:9** [w] S Jdg 9:23 [x] S 1Sa 10:5 **19:10** [y] 1Sa 18:11 **19:11** [z] Ps 59 Title [a] Jdg 16:2

[a] 9 Or *But a harmful*

18:20 *Michal was in love with David.* See v. 28 and note. Michal is the only named woman in the OT who is said to be in love with a man—the literal function of which is probably to demonstrate David's enormous appeal among the people.
18:21 *second opportunity to become my son-in-law.* For the first, see 17:25.
18:25 *no other price.* Normally a bride-price was paid by the bridegroom to the father of the bride (see Ge 34:12; Ex 22:16) as compensation for the loss of his daughter and insurance for her support if widowed. Saul requires David instead to pass a test appropriate for a great warrior, hoping that he will "fall" (v. 25; see vv. 17,21).
18:28 *the LORD was with David.* See note on 16:18. *Michal loved David.* See v. 20 and note. God's favor on David is revealed not only in his military exploits but also in Michal's love for him—now added to that of Jonathan. Everything Saul seeks to use against David turns to David's advantage.
18:29 *Saul became still more afraid of him.* Saul's perception that God's hand was on David led him not to repentance and acceptance of his own lot (see 15:26) but to greater fear and jealousy toward David.
19:1 *Saul told his son … to kill David.* Saul now abandons his indirect attempts on David's life (see 18:13,17,21,25) and adopts a more direct approach, leading to David's departure from the court and from service to Saul (see vv. 12,18; 20:42).
19:4 *Jonathan spoke well of David.* Jonathan does not let his own personal ambition distort his perception of David's true theocratic spirit (see v. 5 and notes on 14:6; 17:11; 18:1).
19:5 *The LORD won a great victory.* See notes on 10:18; 12:11; 14:23.
19:6 *Saul listened to Jonathan and took this oath.* See 14:24,44 for previous oaths that Saul did not keep (see note on 14:39).
19:9 *evil spirit from the LORD.* See note on 16:14; cf. 18:10–11.
19:10 *with his spear.* See 18:10–11; 20:33.

you don't run for your life tonight, tomorrow you'll be killed." 12 So Michal let David down through a window,[b] and he fled
and escaped. 13 Then Michal took an idol[c]
and laid it on the bed, covering it with a
garment and putting some goats' hair at
the head.
14 When Saul sent the men to capture
David, Michal said,[d] "He is ill."
15 Then Saul sent the men back to see
David and told them, "Bring him up to me
in his bed so that I may kill him." 16 But
when the men entered, there was the idol
in the bed, and at the head was some
goats' hair.
17 Saul said to Michal, "Why did you
deceive me like this and send my enemy
away so that he escaped?"
Michal told him, "He said to me, 'Let
me get away. Why should I kill you?' "
18 When David had fled and made his escape, he went to Samuel at Ramah[e] and
told him all that Saul had done to him.
Then he and Samuel went to Naioth and
stayed there. 19 Word came to Saul: "David
is in Naioth at Ramah"; 20 so he sent men to
capture him. But when they saw a group of
prophets[f] prophesying, with Samuel standing there as their leader, the Spirit of God
came on[g] Saul's men, and they also prophesied.[h] 21 Saul was told about it, and he sent
more men, and they prophesied too. Saul
sent men a third time, and they also prophesied. 22 Finally, he himself left for Ramah
and went to the great cistern at Seku. And
he asked, "Where are Samuel and David?"
"Over in Naioth at Ramah," they said.
23 So Saul went to Naioth at Ramah. But
the Spirit of God came even on him, and
he walked along prophesying[i] until he
came to Naioth. 24 He stripped[j] off his garments, and he too prophesied in Samuel's[k]
presence. He lay naked all that day and all
that night. This is why people say, "Is Saul
also among the prophets?"[l]

19:12 [b] S Jos 2:15; Ac 9:25; 2Co 11:33 **19:13** [c] S Ge 31:19 **19:14** [d] S Ex 1:19; Jos 2:4 **19:18** [e] S 1Sa 7:17 **19:20** [f] S Nu 11:29 [g] S Nu 11:25 [h] S 1Sa 10:5 **19:23** [i] 1Sa 10:13 **19:24** [j] 2Sa 6:20; Isa 20:2 [k] 1Sa 15:35 [l] S 1Sa 10:11

20:1 [m] 1Sa 24:9 [n] 1Sa 22:23; 23:15; 24:11; 25:29; Ps 40:14; 54:3; 63:9; 70:2 **20:3** [o] Dt 6:13 **20:5** [p] S Nu 10:10 [q] S 1Sa 19:2 **20:6** [r] ver 28 [s] 1Sa 17:58 [t] S 1Sa 1:3 **20:7** [u] 1Sa 10:27; 25:17 [v] S 1Sa 18:11 **20:8** [w] S 1Sa 18:3 [x] 2Sa 14:32

David and Jonathan

20 Then David fled from Naioth at
Ramah and went to Jonathan and
asked, "What have I done? What is my
crime? How have I wronged[m] your father,
that he is trying to kill me?"[n]
2 "Never!" Jonathan replied. "You are
not going to die! Look, my father doesn't
do anything, great or small, without letting me know. Why would he hide this
from me? It isn't so!"
3 But David took an oath[o] and said,
"Your father knows very well that I have
found favor in your eyes, and he has said
to himself, 'Jonathan must not know this
or he will be grieved.' Yet as surely as the
LORD lives and as you live, there is only a
step between me and death."
4 Jonathan said to David, "Whatever you
want me to do, I'll do for you."
5 So David said, "Look, tomorrow is the
New Moon feast,[p] and I am supposed to
dine with the king; but let me go and hide[q]
in the field until the evening of the day
after tomorrow. 6 If your father misses me
at all, tell him, 'David earnestly asked my
permission[r] to hurry to Bethlehem,[s] his
hometown, because an annual[t] sacrifice is
being made there for his whole clan.' 7 If
he says, 'Very well,' then your servant is
safe. But if he loses his temper,[u] you can
be sure that he is determined[v] to harm me.
8 As for you, show kindness to your servant, for you have brought him into a covenant[w] with you before the LORD. If I am
guilty, then kill[x] me yourself! Why hand
me over to your father?"
9 "Never!" Jonathan said. "If I had the
least inkling that my father was determined to harm you, wouldn't I tell you?"
10 David asked, "Who will tell me if your
father answers you harshly?"
11 "Come," Jonathan said, "let's go out
into the field." So they went there together.
12 Then Jonathan said to David, "I swear

19:12 *through a window.* For similar escapes, see Jos 2:15; Ac 9:25.

19:18 *Ramah.* Samuel's home (see 7:17 and note on 1:1). *Naioth.* Means "habitations" or "dwellings." The term appears to designate a complex of houses in a certain section of Ramah where a group of prophets resided (see vv. 19–20,22–23).

19:20 *group of prophets.* See 10:5 and note. *prophesying.* See notes on 10:5; 18:10.

19:24 *He lay naked all that day and all that night.* Saul was so overwhelmed by the power of the Spirit of God that he was prevented from carrying out his intention to take David's life. His frustrated attempts to kill David — his own inability to harm David and the thwarting of his plans by Jonathan's loyalty, by Michal's deception and by David's own cleverness — all reach their climax here. *Is Saul also among the prophets?* This second occasion reinforced the first (see 10:11 and note). Its repetition underscores how alien Saul's spirit was from that of these zealous servants of the Lord.

20:1 *Naioth at Ramah.* See note on 19:18.

20:3 *as surely as the LORD lives.* See note on 14:39,45.

20:5 *New Moon feast.* Each month of the year was consecrated to the Lord by bringing special sacrifices (Nu 28:11–15) and blowing trumpets (Nu 10:10; Ps 81:3). This observance also involved cessation from normal work, especially at the beginning of the seventh month (Lev 23:24–25; Nu 29:1–6; 2Ki 4:23; Isa 1:13; Am 8:5).

20:6 *annual sacrifice.* David's statement indicates that it was customary for families to observe the New Moon feast together once in the year. There is no other reference in the OT to this practice.

20:8 *covenant.* See note on 18:3.

20:11 *let's go out into the field.* Jonathan acted to save David. Cain had said the same to Abel, but in order to kill him (Ge 4:8; but see NIV text note there).

DAVID THE FUGITIVE

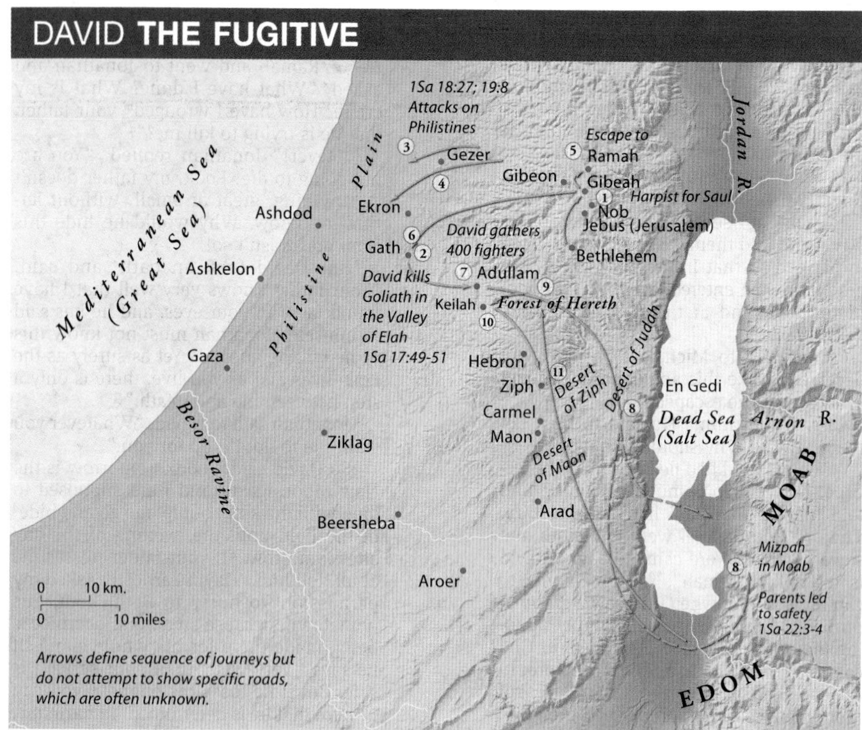

by the LORD, the God of Israel, that I will
surely sound[y] out my father by this time
the day after tomorrow! If he is favorably
disposed toward you, will I not send you
word and let you know? 13But if my father
intends to harm you, may the LORD deal
with Jonathan, be it ever so severely,[z] if I
do not let you know and send you away
in peace. May the LORD be with[a] you as he
has been with my father. 14But show me
unfailing kindness[b] like the LORD's kindness as long as I live, so that I may not be
killed, 15and do not ever cut off your kindness from my family[c]—not even when the
LORD has cut off every one of David's enemies from the face of the earth."
16So Jonathan[d] made a covenant[e] with
the house of David, saying, "May the LORD
call David's enemies to account.[f]" 17And
Jonathan had David reaffirm his oath[g] out
of love for him, because he loved him as
he loved himself.
18Then Jonathan said to David, "Tomorrow is the New Moon feast. You will be
missed, because your seat will be empty.[h]
19The day after tomorrow, toward evening,
go to the place where you hid[i] when this
trouble began, and wait by the stone Ezel.
20I will shoot three arrows[j] to the side of
it, as though I were shooting at a target.
21Then I will send a boy and say, 'Go, find
the arrows.' If I say to him, 'Look, the arrows are on this side of you; bring them
here,' then come, because, as surely as the

20:12 [y] 1Sa 19:3
20:13 [z] S Ru 1:17 [a] S 1Sa 16:18; S 18:12
20:14 [b] S Ge 40:14
20:15 [c] 1Sa 24:21; 2Sa 9:7
20:16 [d] S 1Sa 18:1 [e] S 1Sa 18:3 [f] S Jos 22:23
20:17 [g] S Jos 9:18; S 1Sa 18:3
20:18 [h] ver 25
20:19 [i] S 1Sa 19:2
20:20 [j] 2Ki 13:15

20:13 *may the LORD deal with Jonathan, be it ever so severely.* A common curse formula (see note on 3:17). *May the LORD be with you as he has been with my father.* A clear indication that Jonathan expects David to become king.
20:14 *that I may not be killed.* It was quite common in the ancient world for the first ruler of a new dynasty to secure his position by murdering all potential claimants to the throne from the preceding dynasty (see 1Ki 15:29; 16:11; 2Ki 10:7; 11:1).
20:15 *not … cut off your kindness from my family.* This request was based on the covenant previously concluded between Jonathan and David (see note on 18:3) and was subsequently honored in David's dealings with Jonathan's son Mephibosheth (see 2Sa 9:3,7; 21:7).
20:16 *May the LORD call David's enemies to account.* Jonathan aligns himself completely with David, calling for destruction of his enemies, even if that should include his father, Saul.
20:17 *reaffirm his oath.* See vv. 14–15,42; 18:3. *he loved him as he loved himself.* See 18:3; 2Sa 1:26.
20:18 *New Moon feast.* See note on v. 5.
20:19 *the place where you hid.* Perhaps the place referred to in 19:2.
20:21 *as surely as the LORD lives.* See note on 14:39,45.

.ORD lives, you are safe; there is no danger. [22]But if I say to the boy, 'Look, the
arrows are beyond[k] you,' then you must
go, because the LORD has sent you away.
[23]And about the matter you and I discussed—remember, the LORD is witness[l]
between you and me forever."

[24]So David hid in the field, and when
he New Moon feast[m] came, the king sat
down to eat. [25]He sat in his customary
place by the wall, opposite Jonathan,[a] and
Abner sat next to Saul, but David's place
was empty.[n] [26]Saul said nothing that day,
for he thought, "Something must have
happened to David to make him ceremonially unclean—surely he is unclean.[o]"
[27]But the next day, the second day of the
month, David's place was empty again.
Then Saul said to his son Jonathan, "Why
hasn't the son of Jesse come to the meal,
either yesterday or today?"

[28]Jonathan answered, "David earnestly
asked me for permission[p] to go to Bethlehem. [29]He said, 'Let me go, because
our family is observing a sacrifice[q] in the
town and my brother has ordered me to be
there. If I have found favor in your eyes,
let me get away to see my brothers.' That
is why he has not come to the king's table."

[30]Saul's anger flared up at Jonathan and
he said to him, "You son of a perverse and
rebellious woman! Don't I know that you
have sided with the son of Jesse to your
own shame and to the shame of the mother who bore you? [31]As long as the son of
Jesse lives on this earth, neither you nor
your kingdom[r] will be established. Now
send someone to bring him to me, for he
must die!"

[32]"Why[s] should he be put to death?
What[t] has he done?" Jonathan asked his
father. [33]But Saul hurled his spear at him
to kill him. Then Jonathan knew that his
father intended[u] to kill David.

20:22 [k]ver 37
20:23 [l]S Ge 31:50
20:24 [m]S Nu 10:10
20:25 [n]ver 18
20:26 [o]Lev 7:20-21
20:28 [p]ver 6
20:29 [q]S Ge 8:20
20:31 [r]1Sa 23:17; 24:20
20:32 [s]S 1Sa 19:4; Mt 27:23 [t]S Ge 31:36
20:33 [u]S 1Sa 18:11,17
20:37 [v]ver 22
20:41 [w]S Ge 33:3; Ru 2:10; 1Sa 24:8; 25:23; 2Sa 1:2
20:42 [x]S 1Sa 1:17; S Ac 15:33 [y]S Ge 40:14; 2Sa 1:26; Pr 18:24 [z]Isa 48:1 [a]S Ge 31:50; S 1Sa 18:3 [b]2Sa 9:1
21:1 [c]1Sa 22:9, 19; Ne 11:32; Isa 10:32 [d]1Sa 16:4

[34]Jonathan got up from the table in
fierce anger; on that second day of the
feast he did not eat, because he was
grieved at his father's shameful treatment
of David.

[35]In the morning Jonathan went out to
the field for his meeting with David. He
had a small boy with him, [36]and he said to
the boy, "Run and find the arrows I shoot."
As the boy ran, he shot an arrow beyond
him. [37]When the boy came to the place
where Jonathan's arrow had fallen, Jonathan called out after him, "Isn't the arrow
beyond[v] you?" [38]Then he shouted, "Hurry!
Go quickly! Don't stop!" The boy picked
up the arrow and returned to his master.
[39](The boy knew nothing about all this;
only Jonathan and David knew.) [40]Then
Jonathan gave his weapons to the boy and
said, "Go, carry them back to town."

[41]After the boy had gone, David got
up from the south side of the stone and
bowed down before Jonathan three times,
with his face to the ground.[w] Then they
kissed each other and wept together—but
David wept the most.

[42]Jonathan said to David, "Go in peace,[x]
for we have sworn friendship[y] with each
other in the name of the LORD,[z] saying,
'The LORD is witness[a] between you and
me, and between your descendants and
my descendants forever.[b]'" Then David
left, and Jonathan went back to the town.[b]

David at Nob

21 [c] David went to Nob,[c] to Ahimelek
the priest. Ahimelek trembled[d]
when he met him, and asked, "Why are
you alone? Why is no one with you?"

[2]David answered Ahimelek the priest,
"The king sent me on a mission and said
to me, 'No one is to know anything about

[a] 25 Septuagint; Hebrew *wall. Jonathan arose* [b] 42 In Hebrew texts this sentence (20:42b) is numbered 21:1. [c] In Hebrew texts 21:1-15 is numbered 21:2-16.

20:23 *the matter you and I discussed.* See vv. 14–17. *the LORD is witness.* Invoking God to act as witness and judge between them ensures that their agreement will be kept.
20:25 *Abner.* Saul's cousin and the commander of his army (see 14:50).
20:26 *ceremonially unclean.* See note on 16:5; cf. Lev 7:19–21; 15:16; Dt 23:10.
20:27,30–31 *son of Jesse.* A contemptuous way of referring to David (see 22:7–9,13; 25:10; cf. 2Sa 16:10; Isa 7:4).
20:30 *son of a perverse and rebellious woman.* The Hebrew idiom intends to characterize Jonathan, not his mother.
20:31 *neither you nor your kingdom will be established.* Saul is now convinced that David will succeed him if David is not killed (see notes on 18:13,17,29; 19:1), and he is incapable of understanding Jonathan's lack of concern for his own succession to the throne.
20:33 *hurled his spear.* See 18:11; 19:10.
20:41 *bowed ... three times.* A sign of submission and respect (see Ge 33:3 and note; 42:6).
20:42 *sworn friendship.* See vv. 14–15,23; 18:3. *the town.* Gibeah (see 10:26).
21:1 *Nob.* A town northeast of Jerusalem and southeast of Gibeah (see map, p. 442) where the tabernacle was relocated after the destruction of Shiloh (4:3; Jer 7:12). Although it appears that no attempt was made to bring the ark to this sanctuary (see note on 7:1), Ahimelek the high priest, 85 other priests (22:16–18), the ephod (v. 9) and the consecrated bread (v. 6) are mentioned in connection with it. *Ahimelek the priest.* See note on 14:3. It appears from 22:10,15 that David's purpose in coming to Nob was to seek the Lord's guidance by means of the Urim and Thummim (see notes on 2:28; Ex 28:30).
21:2 It is not clear why David resorts to deception in his response to Ahimelek. Perhaps it was an attempt to protect Ahimelek from the charge of involvement in David's escape from Saul. If so, his strategy was not successful (see 22:13–19).

the mission I am sending you on.' As for my men, I have told them to meet me at a certain place. 3 Now then, what do you have on hand? Give me five loaves of bread, or whatever you can find."

4 But the priest answered David, "I don't have any ordinary bread[e] on hand; however, there is some consecrated[f] bread here—provided the men have kept[g] themselves from women."

5 David replied, "Indeed women have been kept from us, as usual[h] whenever[a] I set out. The men's bodies are holy[i] even on missions that are not holy. How much more so today!" 6 So the priest gave him the consecrated bread,[j] since there was no bread there except the bread of the Presence that had been removed from before the LORD and replaced by hot bread on the day it was taken away.

7 Now one of Saul's servants was there that day, detained before the LORD; he was Doeg[k] the Edomite,[l] Saul's chief shepherd.

8 David asked Ahimelek, "Don't you have a spear or a sword here? I haven't brought my sword or any other weapon, because the king's mission was urgent."

9 The priest replied, "The sword[m] of Goliath[n] the Philistine, whom you killed in the Valley of Elah,[o] is here; it is wrapped in a cloth behind the ephod. If you want it, take it; there is no sword here but that one."

David said, "There is none like it; give it to me."

David at Gath

10 That day David fled from Saul and went[p] to Achish king of Gath. 11 But the servants of Achish said to him, "Isn't this David, the king of the land? Isn't he the one they sing about in their dances:

" 'Saul has slain his thousands,
and David his tens of thousands'?"[q]

12 David took these words to heart and was very much afraid of Achish king of Gath. 13 So he pretended to be insane[r] in their presence; and while he was in their hands he acted like a madman, making marks on the doors of the gate and letting saliva run down his beard.

14 Achish said to his servants, "Look at the man! He is insane! Why bring him to me? 15 Am I so short of madmen that you have to bring this fellow here to carry on like this in front of me? Must this man come into my house?"

David at Adullam and Mizpah

22 David left Gath and escaped to the cave[s] of Adullam.[t] When his brothers and his father's household heard about it, they went down to him there. 2 All those who were in distress or in debt or discontented gathered[u] around him, and he became their commander. About four hundred men were with him.

3 From there David went to Mizpah in Moab and said to the king of Moab, "Would you let my father and mother come and stay with you until I learn what God will do for me?" 4 So he left them with the king of Moab,[v] and they stayed with him as long as David was in the stronghold.

5 But the prophet Gad[w] said to David, "Do not stay in the stronghold. Go into the land of Judah." So David left and went to the forest of Hereth.[x]

21:4 [e] Lev 24:8-9 [f] Mt 12:4 [g] S Ex 19:15; S Lev 15:18
21:5 [h] Dt 23:9-11; Jos 3:5; 2Sa 11:11 [i] 1Th 4:4
21:6 [j] S Ex 25:30; 1Sa 22:10; Mt 12:3-4; Mk 2:25-28; Lk 6:1-5
21:7 [k] 1Sa 22:9, 22 [l] 1Sa 14:47; Ps 52 Title
21:9 [m] S 1Sa 17:51 [n] S 1Sa 17:4 [o] 1Sa 17:2
21:10 [p] 1Sa 25:13; 27:2
21:11 [q] S 1Sa 18:7
21:13 [r] Ps 34 Title
22:1 [s] Ps 57 Title; 142 Title [t] S Ge 38:1
22:2 [u] 1Sa 23:13; 25:13; 2Sa 15:20
22:4 [v] S Ge 19:37
22:5 [w] 2Sa 24:11; 1Ch 21:9; 29:29; 2Ch 29:25 [x] 2Sa 23:14

[a] 5 Or *from us in the past few days since*

21:4 *consecrated bread.* The "bread of the Presence" (v. 6; see Ex 25:30 and note), which was placed in the Holy Place in the tabernacle and later in the temple as a thank offering to the Lord, symbolizing his provision of daily bread. *provided the men have kept themselves from women.* Although the bread was to be eaten only by the priests (see Lev 24:9), Ahimelek agreed to give it to David and his men on the condition that they were ceremonially clean (see Ex 19:15; Lev 15:18). Jesus uses this incident to illustrate the principle that the ceremonial law was not to be viewed in a legalistic manner (see Mt 12:3–4). He also teaches that it is always lawful to do good and to save life (see Lk 6:9). Such compassionate acts are within the true spirit of the law.
21:5 *are holy.* That is, have been consecrated to God (see note on Ex 3:5).
21:9 *sword of Goliath.* See note on 17:54. *ephod.* See note on 2:28.
21:10 *Achish.* See note on Ps 34 title. The name may have been a traditional title used by Philistine rulers (see note on 1Ki 2:39). It appears as the title of a king of Ekron several centuries later (as attested in the annals of the Assyrian kings Esarhaddon and Ashurbanipal, as well as in an inscription found at Ekron in 1996). *Gath.* See 5:8 and note.
21:11 See 29:5 and note on 18:7. *king of the land.* The designation of David as "king" by the Philistines may be understood as a popular exaggeration expressing an awareness of the enormous success and popularity of David among the Israelite people.
22:1 *cave of Adullam.* See 2Sa 23:13; Ge 38:1 and note; Jos 12:15; 15:35.
22:2 *four hundred men were with him.* David, officially an outlaw, was joined by others in similar circumstances, so that he began to develop a military power base that would sustain him throughout his later years as king (see note on 14:52).
22:3 *let my father and mother come and stay with you.* The king of Moab was a natural ally for David because Saul had warred against Moab (see 14:47) and David's own great-grandmother was a Moabite (see Ru 4:5,13,22).
22:4 *stronghold.* Perhaps a specific fortress, but more likely a reference to a geographic area in which it was easy to hide (see 23:14; 2Sa 5:17; 23:14).
22:5 *prophet Gad.* The king-designate is now served also by a prophet. Later a priest would come to him (v. 20) and complete the basic elements of a royal entourage—and they were all refugees from Saul's administration. This is the first appearance of the prophet who later assisted David in musical arrangements for the temple services (see 2Ch 29:25), wrote a history of David's reign (see 1Ch 29:29)

Saul Kills the Priests of Nob

6 Now Saul heard that David and his
men had been discovered. And Saul was
seated,[y] spear in hand, under the tamarisk[z] tree on the hill at Gibeah, with all
his officials standing at his side. 7 He said
to them, "Listen, men of Benjamin! Will
the son of Jesse give all of you fields and
vineyards? Will he make all of you commanders[a] of thousands and commanders
of hundreds? 8 Is that why you have all
conspired[b] against me? No one tells me
when my son makes a covenant[c] with the
son of Jesse.[d] None of you is concerned[e]
about me or tells me that my son has incited my servant to lie in wait for me, as
he does today."
9 But Doeg[f] the Edomite, who was standing with Saul's officials, said, "I saw the
son of Jesse come to Ahimelek son of Ahitub[g] at Nob.[h] 10 Ahimelek inquired[i] of the
LORD for him; he also gave him provisions[j]
and the sword[k] of Goliath the Philistine."
11 Then the king sent for the priest Ahimelek son of Ahitub and all the men of his
family, who were the priests at Nob, and
they all came to the king. 12 Saul said, "Listen now, son of Ahitub."
"Yes, my lord," he answered.
13 Saul said to him, "Why have you conspired[l] against me, you and the son of
Jesse, giving him bread and a sword and
inquiring of God for him, so that he has rebelled against me and lies in wait for me,
as he does today?"
14 Ahimelek answered the king, "Who[m]
of all your servants is as loyal as David,
the king's son-in-law, captain of your
bodyguard and highly respected in your
household? 15 Was that day the first time
I inquired of God for him? Of course not!
Let not the king accuse your servant or
any of his father's family, for your servant
knows nothing at all about this whole affair."
16 But the king said, "You will surely die,
Ahimelek, you and your whole family.[n]"
17 Then the king ordered the guards at
his side: "Turn and kill the priests of the
LORD, because they too have sided with
David. They knew he was fleeing, yet they
did not tell me."
But the king's officials were unwilling[o]
to raise a hand to strike the priests of the
LORD.
18 The king then ordered Doeg, "You
turn and strike down the priests."[p] So
Doeg the Edomite turned and struck them
down. That day he killed eighty-five men
who wore the linen ephod.[q] 19 He also
put to the sword[r] Nob,[s] the town of the
priests, with its men and women, its children and infants, and its cattle, donkeys
and sheep.
20 But one son of Ahimelek son of Ahitub,[t] named Abiathar,[u] escaped and fled
to join David.[v] 21 He told David that Saul
had killed the priests of the LORD. 22 Then
David said to Abiathar, "That day, when
Doeg[w] the Edomite was there, I knew he
would be sure to tell Saul. I am responsible for the death of your whole family.
23 Stay with me; don't be afraid. The man
who wants to kill you[x] is trying to kill me
too. You will be safe with me."

David Saves Keilah

23 When David was told, "Look, the
Philistines are fighting against Keilah[y] and are looting the threshing floors,"[z]
2 he inquired[a] of the LORD, saying, "Shall I
go and attack these Philistines?"
The LORD answered him, "Go, attack the
Philistines and save Keilah."

22:6 [y] S Jdg 4:5 [z] S Ge 21:33 **22:7** [a] S Dt 1:15 **22:8** [b] ver 13 [c] S 1Sa 18:3 [d] 2Sa 20:1 [e] 1Sa 23:21 **22:9** [f] S 1Sa 21:7 [g] 1Sa 14:3 [h] S 1Sa 21:1 **22:10** [i] S Ge 25:22; S 1Sa 23:2 [j] S 1Sa 21:6 [k] S 1Sa 17:51 **22:13** [l] ver 8 **22:14** [m] S 1Sa 19:4 **22:16** [n] S 1Sa 2:31 **22:17** [o] S Ex 1:17 **22:18** [p] S 1Sa 4:17 [q] S 1Sa 2:18,31 **22:19** [r] S 1Sa 15:3 [s] S 1Sa 21:1 **22:20** [t] S 1Sa 14:3 [u] 1Sa 23:6,9; 30:7; 2Sa 15:24; 20:25; 1Ki 1:7; 2:22,26,27; 4:4; 1Ch 15:11; 27:34 [v] S 1Sa 2:32 **22:22** [w] S 1Sa 21:7 **22:23** [x] S 1Sa 20:1 **23:1** [y] S Jos 15:44 [z] S Nu 18:27; S Jdg 6:11 **23:2** [a] ver 4,12; 1Sa 22:10; 30:8; 2Sa 2:1; 5:19,23; Ps 50:15

and confronted David with the Lord's rebuke for his sin of numbering the Israelites (see 2Sa 24:11–25). *forest of Hereth.* Located in the tribal area of Judah (see map, p. 442).

22:6 *tamarisk tree.* See note on Ge 21:33. *Gibeah.* See note on 10:5.

22:7–9,13 *son of Jesse.* See note on 20:27,30–31.

22:7 *men of Benjamin.* Saul, a Benjamite (9:1–2; 10:21), seeks to strengthen his position with his own officials by emphasizing tribal loyalty. David was from the tribe of Judah (see note on 16:1; 2Sa 2:4). *give all of you fields and vineyards?* Saul does exactly what Samuel had warned him that he would do—become like the kings of other nations (see 8:14). His actions are contrary to the covenantal ideal for kingship (see notes on 8:7; 10:25). *commanders of thousands ... hundreds.* See 8:12.

22:10 *Ahimelek inquired of the LORD for him.* See note on 21:1.

22:17 *They knew he was fleeing.* How much the priests really knew is not clear. David himself had not told them (see 21:2–3,8).

22:18 *linen ephod.* See note on 2:18.

22:19 *put to the sword Nob.* Thus the prophecy of judgment against the house of Eli is fulfilled (see 2:31 and note).

22:20 *Abiathar, escaped and fled to join David.* See note on v. 5. Abiathar brought the high priestly ephod with him (see 23:6) and subsequently "inquired of the LORD" for David (see 23:2 and note; see also 23:4,9; 30:7–8; 2Sa 2:1; 5:19,23). He served as high priest until removed from office by Solomon for participating in the rebellion of Adonijah (see 1Ki 2:26–27).

23:1—26:25 Four tests of David's use of his growing power: (1) Will he use that power to defend Israel or only to promote his personal ambitions (23:1–6)? (2) Will he use the power in his hand to kill the king who is trying to kill him (23:7—24:22)? (3) Will he use his power to avenge the disdain of a commoner in the realm (ch. 25)? (4) Will he use the power in his hand to kill the king who is out to destroy him (ch. 26)?

23:1 *Keilah.* Located about three miles southeast of Adullam (see map, p. 442).

23:2,4 *inquired of the LORD.* By means of the Urim and Thummim through the high priest Abiathar (see vv. 6,9 and note on 2:28).

3 But David's men said to him, "Here in Judah we are afraid. How much more, then, if we go to Keilah against the Philistine forces!"

4 Once again David inquired[b] of the LORD, and the LORD answered him, "Go down to Keilah, for I am going to give the Philistines[c] into your hand.[d]" 5 So David and his men went to Keilah, fought the Philistines and carried off their livestock. He inflicted heavy losses on the Philistines and saved the people of Keilah. 6 (Now Abiathar[e] son of Ahimelek had brought the ephod[f] down with him when he fled to David at Keilah.)

Saul Pursues David

7 Saul was told that David had gone to Keilah, and he said, "God has delivered him into my hands,[g] for David has imprisoned himself by entering a town with gates and bars."[h] 8 And Saul called up all his forces for battle, to go down to Keilah to besiege David and his men.

9 When David learned that Saul was plotting against him, he said to Abiathar[i] the priest, "Bring the ephod.[j]" 10 David said, "LORD, God of Israel, your servant has heard definitely that Saul plans to come to Keilah and destroy the town on account of me. 11 Will the citizens of Keilah surrender me to him? Will Saul come down, as your servant has heard? LORD, God of Israel, tell your servant."

And the LORD said, "He will."

12 Again David asked, "Will the citizens of Keilah surrender[k] me and my men to Saul?"

And the LORD said, "They will."

13 So David and his men,[l] about six hundred in number, left Keilah and kept moving from place to place. When Saul was told that David had escaped from Keilah, he did not go there.

14 David stayed in the wilderness[m] strongholds and in the hills of the Desert of Ziph.[n] Day after day Saul searched[o] for him, but God did not[p] give David into his hands.

15 While David was at Horesh in the Desert of Ziph, he learned that[a] Saul had come out to take his life.[q] 16 And Saul's son Jonathan went to David at Horesh and helped him find strength[r] in God. 17 "Don't be afraid," he said. "My father Saul will not lay a hand on you. You will be king[s] over Israel, and I will be second to you. Even my father Saul knows this." 18 The two of them made a covenant[t] before the LORD. Then Jonathan went home, but David remained at Horesh.

19 The Ziphites[u] went up to Saul at Gibeah and said, "Is not David hiding among us[v] in the strongholds at Horesh, on the hill of Hakilah,[w] south of Jeshimon? 20 Now, Your Majesty, come down whenever it pleases you to do so, and we will be responsible for giving[x] him into your hands."

21 Saul replied, "The LORD bless[y] you for your concern[z] for me. 22 Go and get more information. Find out where David usually goes and who has seen him there. They tell me he is very crafty. 23 Find out about all the hiding places he uses and come back to me with definite information. Then I will go with you; if he is in the area, I will track[a] him down among all the clans of Judah."

24 So they set out and went to Ziph ahead of Saul. Now David and his men were in the Desert of Maon,[b] in the Arabah south of Jeshimon.[c] 25 Saul and his men began the search, and when David was told about it, he went down to the rock and stayed in the Desert of Maon. When Saul heard this, he went into the Desert of Maon in pursuit of David.

26 Saul[d] was going along one side of the mountain, and David and his men were on the other side, hurrying to get away from Saul. As Saul and his forces were closing in on David and his men to capture them, 27 a messenger came to Saul, saying, "Come quickly! The Philistines are raiding the land." 28 Then Saul broke off his pursuit of David and went to meet the Philistines. That is why they call this place Sela Hammahlekoth.[b] 29 And David went up from there and lived in the strongholds[e] of En Gedi.[cf]

23:4 [b]S ver 2 [c]S 1Sa 9:16 [d]S Jos 8:7 **23:6** [e]S 1Sa 22:20 [f]S 1Sa 2:28 **23:7** [g]S Dt 32:30 [h]Ps 31:21 **23:9** [i]S 1Sa 22:20 [j]S 1Sa 2:18 **23:12** [k]ver 20 **23:13** [l]S 1Sa 22:2 **23:14** [m]Ps 55:7 [n]S Jos 15:24, 55 [o]Ps 54:3-4 [p]Ps 32:7 **23:15** [q]S 1Sa 20:1 **23:16** [r]1Sa 30:6; Ps 18:2; 27:14 **23:17** [s]S 1Sa 20:31 **23:18** [t]S 1Sa 18:3; 2Sa 9:1 **23:19** [u]1Sa 26:1 [v]Ps 54 Title [w]1Sa 26:3 **23:20** [x]ver 12 **23:21** [y]Ru 2:20; 2Sa 2:5 [z]1Sa 22:8 **23:23** [a]S Ge 31:36 **23:24** [b]S Jos 15:55 [c]1Sa 26:1 **23:26** [d]Ps 17:9 **23:29** [e]1Sa 24:22 [f]S Jos 15:62; 2Ch 20:2; SS 1:14

[a] 15 Or *he was afraid because* [b] 28 *Sela Hammahlekoth* means *rock of parting.* [c] 29 In Hebrew texts this verse (23:29) is numbered 24:1.

23:5 *saved the people of Keilah.* God uses David rather than Saul to be Israel's protective "shepherd"—so again David protects Saul's "flock."
23:9 *Bring the ephod.* See note on v. 2.
23:13 *about six hundred.* The number of David's men has grown significantly (cf. 22:2).
23:14 *wilderness strongholds.* Inaccessible places (see note on 22:4). *Desert of Ziph.* Located south of Hebron. *God did not give David into his hands.* The reality of God's protection of David portrayed here contrasts sharply with the wishful thinking of Saul in v. 7.
23:17 *You will be king over Israel.* See notes on 18:4; 20:13,16,31. *I will be second to you.* Jonathan's love and respect for David enable him to accept a role subordinate to David without any sign of resentment or jealousy (see notes on 18:3; 19:4). This is the last recorded meeting between Jonathan and David. *Saul knows this.* See 18:8 and note on 20:31.
23:18 *covenant.* See notes on 18:3; 20:14–15.
23:19 *strongholds.* See v. 14 and note on 22:4.
23:29 *En Gedi.* See note on SS 1:14; see also map, p. 451.

David Spares Saul's Life

24 [a] After Saul returned from pursuing
the Philistines, he was told, "Da-
vid is in the Desert of En Gedi.[g]" 2 So Saul
took three thousand able young men from
all Israel and set out to look[h] for David and
his men near the Crags of the Wild Goats.
3 He came to the sheep pens along the
way; a cave[i] was there, and Saul went
in to relieve[j] himself. David and his men
were far back in the cave. 4 The men said,
"This is the day the LORD spoke[k] of when
he said[b] to you, 'I will give your enemy
into your hands for you to deal with as
you wish.'"[l] Then David crept up unnoticed and cut[m] off a corner of Saul's robe.
5 Afterward, David was conscience-
stricken[n] for having cut off a corner of his
robe. 6 He said to his men, "The LORD forbid that I should do such a thing to my
master, the LORD's anointed,[o] or lay my
hand on him; for he is the anointed of the
LORD." 7 With these words David sharply
rebuked his men and did not allow them
to attack Saul. And Saul left the cave and
went his way.
8 Then David went out of the cave and
called out to Saul, "My lord the king!"
When Saul looked behind him, David
bowed down and prostrated himself with
his face to the ground.[p] 9 He said to Saul,
"Why do you listen[q] when men say, 'David is bent on harming[r] you'? 10 This day
you have seen with your own eyes how
the LORD delivered you into my hands
in the cave. Some urged me to kill you,
but I spared[s] you; I said, 'I will not lay
my hand on my lord, because he is the
LORD's anointed.' 11 See, my father, look at
this piece of your robe in my hand! I cut[t]
off the corner of your robe but did not kill
you. See that there is nothing in my hand
to indicate that I am guilty[u] of wrongdoing[v] or rebellion. I have not wronged[w] you,
but you are hunting[x] me down to take my
life.[y] 12 May the LORD judge[z] between you
and me. And may the LORD avenge[a] the
wrongs you have done to me, but my hand
will not touch you. 13 As the old saying
goes, 'From evildoers come evil deeds,[b]'
so my hand will not touch you.
14 "Against whom has the king of Israel
come out? Who are you pursuing? A dead
dog?[c] A flea?[d] 15 May the LORD be our judge[e]
and decide[f] between us. May he consider my cause and uphold[g] it; may he vindicate[h] me by delivering[i] me from your
hand."
16 When David finished saying this, Saul
asked, "Is that your voice,[j] David my son?"
And he wept aloud. 17 "You are more righteous than I,"[k] he said. "You have treated
me well,[l] but I have treated you badly.[m]
18 You have just now told me about the
good you did to me; the LORD delivered[n]
me into your hands, but you did not kill
me. 19 When a man finds his enemy, does
he let him get away unharmed? May the
LORD reward[o] you well for the way you
treated me today. 20 I know that you will

24:1 [g] S Jos 15:62 **24:2** [h] 1Sa 26:2 **24:3** [i] Ps 57 Title; 142 Title [j] Jdg 3:24 **24:4** [k] 1Sa 25:28-30 [l] 2Sa 4:8 [m] ver 10,11 **24:5** [n] 1Sa 26:9; 2Sa 24:10 **24:6** [o] S Ge 26:11; S 1Sa 12:3 **24:8** [p] S 1Sa 20:41 **24:9** [q] 1Sa 26:19 [r] 1Sa 20:1 **24:10** [s] S ver 4 **24:11** [t] S ver 4 [u] Ps 7:3 [v] 1Sa 25:28 [w] Ps 35:7 [x] S Ge 31:36; 1Sa 26:20 [y] S 1Sa 20:1 **24:12** [z] S Ge 16:5; S 1Sa 25:38; S Job 9:15 [a] S Nu 31:3 **24:13** [b] Mt 7:20 **24:14** [c] S 1Sa 17:43 [d] 1Sa 26:20 **24:15** [e] ver 12 [f] S Ge 16:5 [g] Ps 35:1,23; Isa 49:25 [h] Ps 26:1; 35:24; 43:1; 50:4; 54:1; 135:14 [i] Ps 119:134, 154 **24:16** [j] 1Sa 26:17 **24:17** [k] Ge 38:26 [l] Mt 5:44 [m] S Ex 9:27 **24:18** [n] 1Sa 26:23 **24:19** [o] S Ru 2:12; S 2Ch 15:7

[a] In Hebrew texts 24:1-22 is numbered 24:2-23.
[b] 4 Or *"Today the LORD is saying*

24:1—26:25 In each of the three episodes in these chapters, David is put to a severe test in the desert as the Lord's anointed (16:1–13; cf. Dt 8, the testing of Israel in the wilderness; Mt 4:1–11, the testing of Jesus in the wilderness). In all three events, circumstances place David in a position of power with opportunity to use that power for purely personal ends (avenging wrongs done to him) rather than in the service of the Lord and Israel. To have failed this test would have disqualified David—as it had disqualified Saul—from serving as the Lord's appointed king over Israel.

Within these three chapters the final two confrontations between Saul and David take place. In both, the tables are turned and Saul is at the mercy of David. These two episodes (chs. 24; 26) bracket another (ch. 25) in which David has dealings with Nabal, a wealthy Judahite whose flocks David and his men have protected—as they have protected Saul's "flock" from Philistine aggression. In this center episode, Nabal serves as a literary picture of Saul, who is thus exposed as a fool whom the Lord will soon strike down (see 25:38; cf. 26:10; 28:19; 31:4).

24:1–22 Saul at the mercy of David while seeking privacy in a cave.

24:4 *This is the day the LORD spoke of when he said.* There is no previous record of the divine revelation here alluded to by David's men. Perhaps this was their own interpretation of the anointing of David to replace Saul (see 16:13–14), or of assurances given to David that he would survive Saul's vendetta against him and ultimately become king (see 20:14–15; 23:17). If the alternative given in the NIV text note is taken, the reference would be not to a verbal communication from the Lord but to the providential nature of the incident itself, which David's men understood as a revelation from God that David should not ignore. *I will give your enemy into your hands.* So it seemed to David's men (see also 26:8). Cf. what David says to Saul in v. 10 and contrast what the author has stated in 23:14. *cut off a corner of Saul's robe.* Perhaps David was symbolically depriving Saul of his royal authority and transferring it to himself (see v. 11; cf. also 15:27–28; 18:4).

24:6 *for he is the anointed of the LORD.* See v. 10; 26:9,11,16,23; 2Sa 1:14,16. Because Saul's royal office carried divine sanction by virtue of his anointing (see note on 9:16), David is determined not to wrest the kingship from Saul but to leave its disposition to the Lord who gave it (see vv. 12,15; 26:10).

24:11 *my father.* See also Saul's address to David as "my son" (v. 16). David uses this form of address either because (1) Saul was David's father-in-law (see 18:27) or because (2) the special relationship between father and son was at times used as a metaphor for an intimate relationship between king and subject (see notes on 2Sa 7:14; Ps 2:7; see also chart, p. 23).

24:14 *dead dog.* See note on 2Sa 9:8. *flea.* See note on 26:20.

24:16 *he wept aloud.* Saul experiences temporary remorse (see 26:21) for his actions against David but quickly reverts to his former determination to kill him (see 26:2).

surely be king[p] and that the kingdom[q] of Israel will be established in your hands. 21 Now swear[r] to me by the LORD that you will not kill off my descendants or wipe out my name from my father's family.[s]"

22 So David gave his oath to Saul. Then Saul returned home, but David and his men went up to the stronghold.[t]

David, Nabal and Abigail

25 Now Samuel died,[u] and all Israel assembled and mourned[v] for him; and they buried him at his home in Ramah.[w] Then David moved down into the Desert of Paran.[a]

2 A certain man in Maon,[x] who had property there at Carmel, was very wealthy.[y] He had a thousand goats and three thousand sheep, which he was shearing[z] in Carmel. 3 His name was Nabal and his wife's name was Abigail.[a] She was an intelligent and beautiful woman, but her husband was surly and mean in his dealings—he was a Calebite.[b]

4 While David was in the wilderness, he heard that Nabal was shearing sheep. 5 So he sent ten young men and said to them, "Go up to Nabal at Carmel and greet him in my name. 6 Say to him: 'Long life to you! Good health[c] to you and your household! And good health to all that is yours![d]

7 " 'Now I hear that it is sheep-shearing time. When your shepherds were with us, we did not mistreat[e] them, and the whole time they were at Carmel nothing of theirs was missing. 8 Ask your own servants and they will tell you. Therefore be favorable toward my men, since we come at a festive time. Please give your servants and your son David whatever[f] you can find for them.' "

9 When David's men arrived, they gave Nabal this message in David's name. Then they waited.

10 Nabal answered David's servants, "Who[g] is this David? Who is this son of Jesse? Many servants are breaking away from their masters these days. 11 Why should I take my bread[h] and water, and the meat I have slaughtered for my shearers, and give it to men coming from who knows where?"

12 David's men turned around and went back. When they arrived, they reported every word. 13 David said to his men[i], "Each of you strap on your sword!" So they did, and David strapped his on as well. About four hundred men went[j] up with David, while two hundred stayed with the supplies.[k]

14 One of the servants told Abigail, Nabal's wife, "David sent messengers from the wilderness to give our master his greetings,[l] but he hurled insults at them. 15 Yet

[a] *1* Hebrew and some Septuagint manuscripts; other Septuagint manuscripts *Maon*

24:20 [p]S 1Sa 20:31 [q]S 1Sa 13:14 **24:21** [r]Ge 21:23; S 47:31; S 1Sa 18:3; 2Sa 21:1-9 [s]S 1Sa 20:14-15 **24:22** [t]1Sa 23:29 **25:1** [u]1Sa 28:3 [v]S Lev 10:6; Dt 34:8 [w]S 1Sa 7:17 **25:2** [x]S Jos 15:55 [y]2Sa 19:32 [z]S Ge 31:19 **25:3** [a]Pr 31:10 [b]S Jos 14:13; S 15:13 **25:6** [c]Ps 122:7; Mt 10:12 [d]1Ch 12:18 **25:7** [e]ver 15 **25:8** [f]Ne 8:10 **25:10** [g]Jdg 9:28 **25:11** [h]Jdg 8:6 **25:13** [i]S 1Sa 22:2 [j]S 1Sa 21:10 [k]S Nu 31:27 **25:14** [l]1Sa 13:10

24:21 *not kill off my descendants.* See notes on 20:14–15.

24:22 *stronghold.* An inaccessible place (see note on 22:4). From previous experience David did not place any confidence in Saul's words of repentance.

25:1–44 David's dealings with Nabal (see notes on 23:1—26:25; 24:1—26:25). Nabal, the "fool" (see 25:25 and note), lived near Carmel, where Saul had erected a monument in his own honor (see 15:12 and note). The account of Nabal effectively serves the author's purpose in a number of ways: (1) Nabal's general character, his disdainful attitude toward David though David had guarded his flocks, and his sudden death at the Lord's hand all parallel Saul (whose "flock" David had also protected). Thus the author indirectly characterizes Saul as a fool (see 13:13; 26:21) and foreshadows his end. (2) David's vengeful attitude toward Nabal displays his natural tendency and highlights his restraint toward Saul (this event is sandwiched between the two instances in which David spared Saul in spite of the urging of his men). (3) Abigail's prudent action prevents David from using his power as leader for personal vengeance (the very thing Saul was doing). (4) Abigail's confident acknowledgment of David's future accession to the throne foreshadows that event and even anticipates the Lord's commitment to establish David's house as a "lasting dynasty" (v. 28; cf. 2Sa 7:11–16). (5) Abigail's marriage to David provides him a worthy wife, while Saul gives away David's wife Michal to another.

25:1 The author begins the David-Nabal episode by noting David's loss of his chief protector in Israel (see 19:18–24) and ends it with a notation that David also loses his wife Michal, one of his protectors in the royal family itself (see 19:11–17). Meanwhile he obtains a wife whose wisdom rivals that of Ahithophel (see 2Sa 16:23). She is one of two wives who link him with the aristocracy of Judah. This account of how David obtained Nabal's wife serves as a foil to the later account of how David obtained the wife of Uriah the Hittite (2Sa 11). There it is David who acts the fool. *all Israel ... mourned for him.* Samuel was recognized as a leader of national prominence who played a key role in the restructuring of the theocracy with the establishment of the monarchy (see chs. 8–12). The loss of his leadership was mourned much like that of other prominent figures in Israel's past history, including Jacob (Ge 50:10), Aaron (Nu 20:29) and Moses (Dt 34:8). *Ramah.* See 7:17 and note on 1:1.

25:2 In ancient times wealth often consisted primarily of livestock (see Ge 12:16; 13:2).

25:3 *intelligent and beautiful ... surly and mean.* The stark contrast between the foolish Nabal and the wise Abigail is played out through the rest of the chapter. *Calebite* A descendant of Caleb (see Nu 14:24), who settled at Hebron (see Jos 14:13) after the conquest of Canaan. Since Caleb's name can mean "dog," Nabal is subtly depicted as a dog, as well as a fool. He would soon be a dead dog (see note on 2Sa 9:8), when the Lord would avenge his acts of contempt toward David. The hint is strong that when the Lord avenges Saul's sins against David (see 24:12,15), the king will no longer pursue a dead dog (see 24:14) but will himself become one—a case of biting irony.

25:4 *shearing sheep.* A festive occasion (see v. 8; 2Sa 13:23–24).

25:8 *give ... whatever you can find for them.* David and his men ask for some consideration for their protection of Nabal's shepherds and flocks against pillage (see vv. 15–16,21).

25:10 *son of Jesse.* See note on 20:27,30–31.

these men were very good to us. They did not mistreat[m] us, and the whole time we were out in the fields near them nothing was missing.[n] 16 Night and day they were a wall[o] around us the whole time we were herding our sheep near them. 17 Now think t over and see what you can do, because disaster is hanging over our master and nis whole household. He is such a wicked[p] man that no one can talk to him."

18 Abigail acted quickly. She took two hundred loaves of bread, two skins of wine, five dressed sheep, five seahs[a] of roasted grain,[q] a hundred cakes of raisins[r] and two hundred cakes of pressed figs, and loaded them on donkeys.[s] 19 Then she told her servants, "Go on ahead;[t] I'll follow you." But she did not tell[u] her husband Nabal.

20 As she came riding her donkey into a mountain ravine, there were David and his men descending toward her, and she met them. 21 David had just said, "It's been useless—all my watching over this fellow's property in the wilderness so that nothing of his was missing.[v] He has paid[w] me back evil[x] for good. 22 May God deal with David,[b] be it ever so severely,[y] if by morning I leave alive one male[z] of all who belong to him!"

23 When Abigail saw David, she quickly got off her donkey and bowed down before David with her face to the ground.[a] 24 She fell at his feet and said: "Pardon your servant, my lord,[b] and let me speak to you; hear what your servant has to say. 25 Please pay no attention, my lord, to that wicked man Nabal. He is just like his name—his name means Fool[c],[d] and folly goes with him. And as for me, your servant, I did not see the men my lord sent. 26 And now, my lord, as surely as the LORD your God lives and as you live, since the LORD has kept you from bloodshed[e] and from avenging[f] yourself with your own hands, may your enemies and all who are intent on harming my lord be like Nabal.[g] 27 And let this gift,[h] which your servant has brought to my lord, be given to the men who follow you.

28 "Please forgive[i] your servant's presumption. The LORD your God will certainly make a lasting[j] dynasty for my lord, because you fight the LORD's battles,[k] and no wrongdoing[l] will be found in you as long as you live. 29 Even though someone is pursuing you to take your life,[m] the life of my lord will be bound securely in the bundle of the living by the LORD your God, but the lives of your enemies he will hurl[n] away as from the pocket of a sling.[o] 30 When the LORD has fulfilled for my lord every good thing he promised concerning him and has appointed him ruler[p] over Israel, 31 my lord will not have on his conscience the staggering burden of needless bloodshed or of having avenged himself. And when the LORD your God has brought my lord success, remember[q] your servant."[r]

32 David said to Abigail, "Praise[s] be to the LORD, the God of Israel, who has sent you today to meet me. 33 May you be blessed for your good judgment and for keeping me from bloodshed[t] this day and from avenging myself with my own hands. 34 Otherwise, as surely as the LORD, the God of Israel, lives, who has kept me from harming you, if you had not come quickly to meet me, not one male belonging

[a] *18* That is, probably about 60 pounds or about 27 kilograms [b] *22* Some Septuagint manuscripts; Hebrew *with David's enemies*

25:15 [m]ver 7 [n]ver 21
25:16 [o]Ex 14:22; Job 1:10; Ps 139:5
25:17 [p]S Dt 13:13; S 1Sa 20:7
25:18 [q]S Lev 23:14; S 1Sa 17:17 [r]1Ch 12:40 [s]S Ge 42:26; 2Sa 16:1; Isa 30:6
25:19 [t]Ge 32:20 [u]ver 36
25:21 [v]ver 15 [w]Ps 109:5 [x]S 1Sa 19:4
25:22 [y]S Ru 1:17 [z]1Ki 14:10; 21:21; 2Ki 9:8
25:23 [a]S Ge 19:1; S 1Sa 20:41
25:24 [b]2Sa 14:9
25:25 [c]Pr 17:12 [d]Pr 12:16; 14:16; 20:3; Isa 32:5
25:26 [e]ver 33 [f]Heb 10:30 [g]ver 34; 2Sa 18:32
25:27 [h]S Ge 33:11
25:28 [i]ver 24; 2Sa 14:9 [j]2Sa 7:11,26 [k]1Sa 18:17 [l]1Sa 24:11
25:29 [m]S 1Sa 20:1 [n]Jer 10:18; 22:26 [o]1Sa 17:50; 2Sa 4:8
25:30 [p]S 1Sa 12:12; S 13:14
25:31 [q]S Ge 40:14 [r]2Sa 3:10
25:32 [s]S Ge 24:27
25:33 [t]ver 26

25:17 *wicked man.* See note on Dt 13:13. *no one can talk to him.* In this way, too, Nabal is like Saul (cf., e.g., 20:27–33).
25:18 *She took ... bread ... wine ... sheep ... grain ... raisins ... figs.* A feast for a king. Cf. what Nabal had mentioned in v. 11.
25:19 *did not tell her husband.* Cf. Michal's treatment of Saul (19:11–17).
25:22 *May God deal with David, be it ever so severely.* See note on 3:17. David invokes a curse on himself if he should fail to kill every male in Nabal's household and so obliterate Nabal's family.
25:24 *Pardon your servant.* Abigail begins her appeal to David on an apologetic note (she is not taking on herself the blame for Nabal's action), as she does again when she begins the second half of her appeal (v. 28). Contrast Nabal's high-handed treatment of David.
25:25 *wicked man.* See v. 17 and note on Dt 13:13. *He is just like his name.* In ancient times a person's name was believed to reflect their nature and character.
25:26 *as surely as the LORD ... lives.* See note on 14:39,45.
25:28 *The LORD ... will certainly make a lasting dynasty.* While the idea that David was destined to become king in place of Saul may have spread among the general populace, Abigail's assessment of David contrasts sharply with that of her husband (see v. 10). *you fight the LORD's battles.* Abigail is familiar with David's victories over the Philistines, in which he sought to glorify the Lord rather than advance his own honor (see 17:26,45–47; 18:17). *no wrongdoing will be found in you.* See v. 39. Abigail shows concern for the preservation of David's integrity in view of the office he was later to assume (see vv. 30–31).
25:29 *bound securely in the bundle of the living.* Using the figure of placing a valuable possession in a carefully wrapped package for safekeeping, Abigail assures David that the Lord will preserve his life in the midst of danger. *hurl away as from the pocket of a sling.* A word that soon comes true for Nabal after he becomes "like a stone" (v. 37).
25:30 *ruler.* See note on 9:16.
25:31 *needless bloodshed.* See note on v. 28.
25:32–34 Cf. David's words in vv. 21–22. His words there and here bracket the account of his meeting with Abigail and highlight the crucial role of wise Abigail's actions.
25:32 *who has sent you.* David recognizes the providential leading of the Lord in his encounter with Abigail (see v. 39).
25:33 *your good judgment.* See v. 3 and note.

to Nabal[u] would have been left alive by daybreak."

35Then David accepted from her hand what she had brought him and said, "Go home in peace. I have heard your words and granted[v] your request."

36When Abigail went to Nabal, he was in the house holding a banquet like that of a king. He was in high[w] spirits and very drunk.[x] So she told[y] him nothing at all until daybreak. 37Then in the morning, when Nabal was sober, his wife told him all these things, and his heart failed him and he became like a stone.[z] 38About ten days later, the LORD struck[a] Nabal and he died.

39When David heard that Nabal was dead, he said, "Praise be to the LORD, who has upheld my cause against Nabal for treating me with contempt. He has kept his servant from doing wrong and has brought Nabal's wrongdoing down on his own head."

Then David sent word to Abigail, asking her to become his wife. 40His servants went to Carmel and said to Abigail, "David has sent us to you to take you to become his wife."

41She bowed down with her face to the ground and said, "I am your servant and am ready to serve you and wash the feet of my lord's servants." 42Abigail[b] quickly got on a donkey and, attended by her five female servants, went with David's messengers and became his wife. 43David had also married Ahinoam[c] of Jezreel, and they both were his wives.[d] 44But Saul had given his daughter Michal, David's wife, to Paltiel[a][e] son of Laish, who was from Gallim.[f]

David Again Spares Saul's Life

26 The Ziphites[g] went to Saul at Gibeah and said, "Is not David hiding[h] on the hill of Hakilah, which faces Jeshimon?[i]"

2So Saul went down to the Desert of Ziph, with his three thousand select Israelite troops, to search[j] there for David. 3Saul made his camp beside the road on the hill of Hakilah[k] facing Jeshimon, but David stayed in the wilderness. When he saw that Saul had followed him there, 4he sent out scouts and learned that Saul had definitely arrived.

5Then David set out and went to the place where Saul had camped. He saw where Saul and Abner[l] son of Ner, the commander of the army, had lain down. Saul was lying inside the camp, with the army encamped around him.

6David then asked Ahimelek the Hittite[m] and Abishai[n] son of Zeruiah,[o] Joab's brother, "Who will go down into the camp with me to Saul?"

"I'll go with you," said Abishai.

7So David and Abishai went to the army by night, and there was Saul, lying asleep inside the camp with his spear stuck in the ground near his head. Abner and the soldiers were lying around him.

8Abishai said to David, "Today God has delivered your enemy into your hands. Now let me pin him to the ground with one thrust of the spear; I won't strike him twice."

9But David said to Abishai, "Don't destroy him! Who can lay a hand on the LORD's anointed[p] and be guiltless?[q] 10As surely as the LORD lives," he said, "the LORD himself will strike[r] him, or his time[s] will come and he will die,[t] or he will go into battle and perish. 11But the LORD forbid that I should lay a hand on the LORD's anointed. Now get the spear and water jug that are near his head, and let's go."

12So David took the spear and water jug

25:34 [u]S ver 26 **25:35** [v]S Ge 19:21 **25:36** [w]S Ru 3:7 [x]Pr 20:1; Ecc 10:17; Isa 5:11,22; 22:13; 28:7; 56:12; Hos 4:11 [y]ver 19 **25:37** [z]Ex 15:16 **25:38** [a]Dt 32:35; 1Sa 24:12; 26:10; 2Sa 6:7; 12:15 **25:42** [b]2Sa 2:2; 3:3; 1Ch 3:1 **25:43** [c]2Sa 3:2; 1Ch 3:1 [d]1Sa 27:3; 30:5; 2Sa 2:2 **25:44** [e]2Sa 3:15 [f]Isa 10:30 **26:1** [g]1Sa 23:19 [h]Ps 54 Title [i]1Sa 23:24 **26:2** [j]1Sa 24:2 **26:3** [k]1Sa 23:19 **26:5** [l]1Sa 17:55 **26:6** [m]S Ge 10:15 [n]2Sa 2:18; 10:10; 16:9; 18:2; 19:21; 23:18; 1Ch 11:20; 19:11 [o]1Ch 2:16 **26:9** [p]ver 16; S Ge 26:11; S 1Sa 9:16; 2Sa 1:14; 19:21; La 4:20 [q]S 1Sa 24:5 **26:10** [r]S Ge 16:5; S 1Sa 25:38; S Ro 12:19 [s]Dt 31:14; Ps 37:13 [t]1Sa 31:6; 2Sa 1:1

[a] 44 Hebrew *Palti,* a variant of *Paltiel*

25:36 *holding a banquet.* See Pr 30:21–22. *like that of a king.* The author is using Nabal as a subtle portrayal of Saul.

25:37 *when Nabal was sober.* Lit. "when the wine had gone out of Nabal"—containing a clever wordplay on Nabal's name, which sounds very much like the Hebrew word for wineskin (as in v. 18). *became like a stone.* He who was without moral sensitivity (was a *nabal*; see v. 25 and note) became as senseless as a stone.

25:42 *became his wife.* She who acknowledged the Lord's anointed came to share in his kingdom while her fool of a husband ended up a dead dog, a dead fool, an empty wineskin, a stone flung from a sling. He typifies Saul and all who reject the Lord's anointed.

25:43 *Ahinoam.* The mother of David's first son, Amnon (see 2Sa 3:2). *Jezreel.* Located near Carmel (see v. 2; Jos 15:55–56) and not to be confused with the northern town of the same name, where Israel camped against the Philistines (see 29:1,11) and where Ahab resided in later times (see 1Ki 18:45–46; 21:1).

25:44 *Michal, David's wife.* See 18:27.

26:1–25 Saul is at the mercy of David while sleeping in the midst of his army encampment (see notes on 23:1—26:25; 24:1—26:25; 24:1–22).

26:1 *Ziphites.* See 23:19; see also note on 23:14. *Gibeah.* The site of Saul's royal residence (see 10:26).

26:2 *Desert of Ziph.* See 23:19; see also note on 23:14. *three thousand.* Apparently Saul's standing army (see 24:2).

26:5 *Abner.* Saul's cousin (see 14:50). *lain down.* David arrived at Saul's camp during the night when the men were sleeping.

26:6 *Ahimelek the Hittite.* Hittites had long resided in Canaan (see note on Ge 10:15; see also Ge 15:20; 23:3–20; Dt 7:1; 20:17). Another Hittite in David's service was Uriah (see 2Sa 11:6–7; 23:39). *Abishai son of Zeruiah, Joab's brother.* Zeruiah was David's sister (1Ch 2:16), so Abishai and Joab (and their brother Asahel, 2Sa 2:18) were David's nephews, as well as trusted military leaders. Joab would serve as the commander of his army for a long time.

26:8 *delivered your enemy into your hands.* See 24:4 and note. *pin him to the ground with … the spear.* Just as Saul had tried to pin David to the wall with his spear (see 18:11; 19:10).

26:9,11 *lay a hand on the LORD's anointed.* See note on 24:6.

26:10,16 *As surely as the LORD lives.* See note on 14:39,45.

near Saul's head, and they left. No one
saw or knew about it, nor did anyone
wake up. They were all sleeping, because
the LORD had put them into a deep sleep.[u]
13 Then David crossed over to the other side and stood on top of the hill some
distance away; there was a wide space between them. 14 He called out to the army
and to Abner son of Ner, "Aren't you going
to answer me, Abner?"

Abner replied, "Who are you who calls
to the king?"

15 David said, "You're a man, aren't you?
And who is like you in Israel? Why didn't
you guard your lord the king? Someone
came to destroy your lord the king. 16 What
you have done is not good. As surely as
the LORD lives, you and your men must
die, because you did not guard your master, the LORD's anointed. Look around you.
Where are the king's spear and water jug
that were near his head?"

17 Saul recognized David's voice and
said, "Is that your voice,[v] David my son?"

David replied, "Yes it is, my lord the
king." 18 And he added, "Why is my lord
pursuing his servant? What have I done,
and what wrong[w] am I guilty of? 19 Now
let my lord the king listen[x] to his servant's
words. If the LORD has incited you against
me, then may he accept an offering.[y] If,
however, people have done it, may they be

26:12 [u] S Jdg 4:21
26:17 [v] 1Sa 24:16
26:18 [w] Job 13:23; Jer 37:18
26:19 [x] 1Sa 24:9 [y] 2Sa 16:11

26:12 *David took the spear and water jug.* In this way he sought to prove again to Saul that he did not seek his life. But he also showed Saul that God had given him the power to take away the spear with which Saul had often tried to kill him and the water jug on which Saul's very life depended in the hot and dry Desert of Ziph.
26:19 *may he accept an offering.* David knows no reason why God should be angry with him; but if for some reason God is behind Saul's determined effort to kill him, David appeals for God to accept an offering of appeasement (cf. 16:5)—in any event, to let the matter be settled between David and God without Saul's involvement. *may they be cursed before the LORD!* David commits any such men to the judgment of God. *the LORD's inheritance.* See note on 10:1. David appeals to Saul's conscience by describing his present exclusion from the fellowship of God's people and from

EXPLOITS OF DAVID

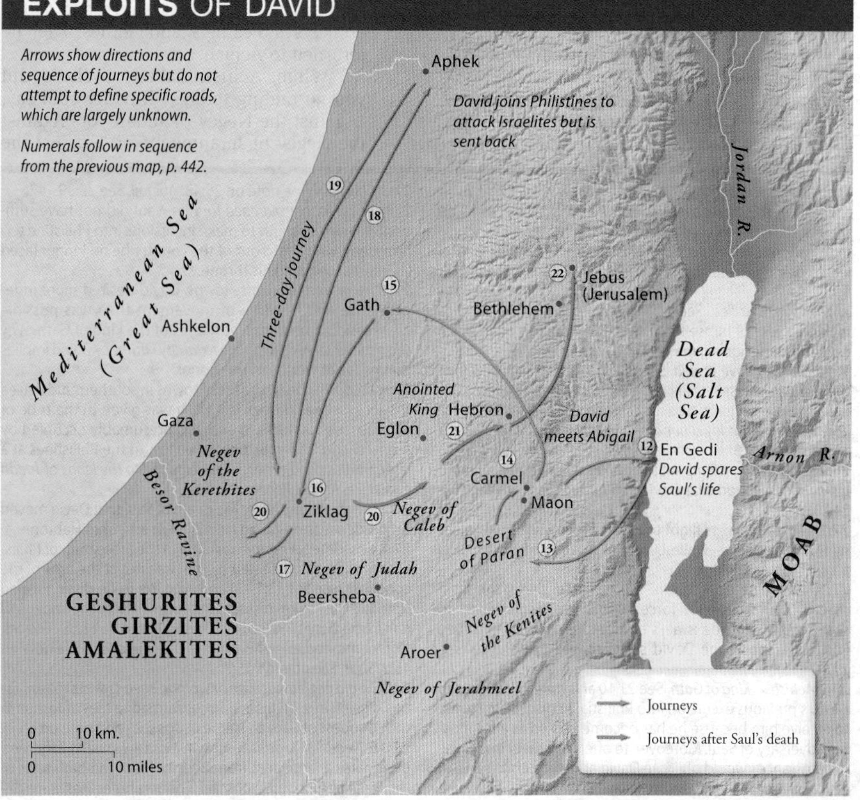

cursed before the LORD! They have driven
me today from my share in the LORD's inheritance[z] and have said, 'Go, serve other
gods.'[a] 20 Now do not let my blood[b] fall to
the ground far from the presence of the
LORD. The king of Israel has come out to
look for a flea[c]—as one hunts a partridge
in the mountains.[d]"
21 Then Saul said, "I have sinned.[e] Come
back, David my son. Because you considered my life precious[f] today, I will not try
to harm you again. Surely I have acted like
a fool and have been terribly wrong."
22 "Here is the king's spear," David answered. "Let one of your young men come
over and get it. 23 The LORD rewards[g] everyone for their righteousness[h] and faithfulness. The LORD delivered[i] you into my
hands today, but I would not lay a hand on
the LORD's anointed. 24 As surely as I valued your life today, so may the LORD value
my life and deliver[j] me from all trouble."
25 Then Saul said to David, "May you be
blessed,[k] David my son; you will do great
things and surely triumph."
So David went on his way, and Saul returned home.

David Among the Philistines

27 But David thought to himself, "One
of these days I will be destroyed by
the hand of Saul. The best thing I can do
is to escape to the land of the Philistines.
Then Saul will give up searching for me
anywhere in Israel, and I will slip out of
his hand."
2 So David and the six hundred men[l]
with him left and went[m] over to Achish[n]
son of Maok king of Gath. 3 David and his
men settled in Gath with Achish. Each
man had his family with him, and David
had his two wives:[o] Ahinoam of Jezreel
and Abigail of Carmel, the widow of Nabal. 4 When Saul was told that David had
fled to Gath, he no longer searched for
him.
5 Then David said to Achish, "If I have
found favor in your eyes, let a place be assigned to me in one of the country towns,
that I may live there. Why should your servant live in the royal city with you?"
6 So on that day Achish gave him Ziklag,[p] and it has belonged to the kings of
Judah ever since. 7 David lived[q] in Philistine territory a year and four months.
8 Now David and his men went up and
raided the Geshurites,[r] the Girzites and the
Amalekites.[s] (From ancient times these
peoples had lived in the land extending
to Shur[t] and Egypt.) 9 Whenever David attacked an area, he did not leave a man or
woman alive,[u] but took sheep and cattle,
donkeys and camels, and clothes. Then he
returned to Achish.
10 When Achish asked, "Where did
you go raiding today?" David would say,
"Against the Negev of Judah" or "Against
the Negev of Jerahmeel[v]" or "Against the

26:19 [z] Dt 20:16; 32:9; 2Sa 14:16; 20:19; 21:3 [a] S Dt 4:28; S 11:28 **26:20** [b] S 1Sa 24:11 [c] 1Sa 24:14 [d] Jer 4:29; 16:16; Am 9:3 **26:21** [e] S Ex 9:27 [f] Ps 72:14 **26:23** [g] S Ge 16:5; S Ru 2:12; Ps 62:12 [h] 2Sa 22:21,25; Ps 7:8; 18:20,24 [i] 1Sa 24:18 **26:24** [j] Ps 54:7 **26:25** [k] S Ru 2:12 **27:2** [l] 1Sa 30:9; 2Sa 2:3 [m] S 1Sa 21:10 [n] 1Ki 2:39 **27:3** [o] S 1Sa 25:43 **27:6** [p] Jos 15:31; 19:5; 1Sa 30:1; 1Ch 12:20; Ne 11:28 **27:7** [q] 1Sa 29:3 **27:8** [r] S Jos 12:5 [s] S Ex 17:14; S 1Sa 14:48; 30:1; 2Sa 1:8; 8:12 [t] S Ge 16:7 **27:9** [u] S 1Sa 15:3 **27:10** [v] 1Sa 30:29

living at peace in the Lord's land. *Go, serve other gods.* In their view, to be expelled from the Lord's land was to be separated from the Lord's sanctuary (an OT form of excommunication) and left to serve the gods of whatever land in which one might settle (see Jos 22:24–27 and note on 1Ki 5:17).

26:20 *look for a flea.* See 24:14. David suggests that Saul is making a fool of himself in his fanatical pursuit of an innocent and undesigning man.

26:21 *I have sinned.* See 24:17. *I have acted like a fool.* Saul confesses that his behavior has been not only unwise but also ungodly (see notes on 13:13; 25:2–44).

26:23 *I would not lay a hand on the LORD's anointed.* See v. 9 and note on 24:6.

26:25 *you will ... triumph.* Saul makes a veiled reference to his own conviction that David will replace him as king (see 24:20).

27:1—31:13 David's flight to Philistia and Saul's final defeat by the Philistines—while David is engaged in a campaign against the Amalekites.

27:1 *I will be destroyed by the hand of Saul.* Under the pressure of Saul's superior forces David feels compelled to seek security outside Israel's borders. *land of the Philistines.* For the second time David seeks refuge in Philistia (see 21:10–15).

27:2 *Achish ... king of Gath.* See 21:10 and note. In contrast to David's previous excursion into Philistia, Achish is now ready to receive him because he has become known as a formidable adversary of Saul. Moreover, to offer sanctuary under the circumstances would obligate David and his men to serve at his call in any military venture (see 28:1).

27:3 *Ahinoam.* See note on 25:43. *Abigail.* See 25:39–42.

27:4 *he no longer searched for him.* Saul did not have sufficient military strength to make incursions into Philistine territory, and with David out of the country he no longer faced an internal threat to his throne.

27:5 *in one of the country towns.* David desired more independence and freedom of movement than was possible while residing under the very eyes of the king of Gath. *Why should your servant live in the royal city with you?* David implies that he is not worthy of this honor.

27:6 *Ziklag.* Included in a list of towns in southern Judah (see Jos 15:31; see also map, p. 451). It was given to the tribe of Simeon (see Jos 19:1–5) and was presumably occupied by them (cf. Jdg 1:17–18), only to be lost to the Philistines at a later, undisclosed time. *it has belonged to the kings of Judah ever since.* As royal property.

27:7 It was not until after the death of Saul that David moved his residence from Ziklag (see 2Sa 1:1; 2:1–3) to Hebron.

27:8 *Geshurites.* A people residing in the area south of Philistia who were not defeated by the Israelites at the time of the conquest (see Jos 13:1–3) and who are to be distinguished from the Geshurites residing in the north near the upper Jordan in Aram (see 2Sa 3:3; 13:37–38; Dt 3:14; Jos 12:5). *Girzites.* Not mentioned elsewhere in the OT. *Amalekites.* See note on 15:2. *Shur.* See note on 15:7.

27:9 *he did not leave a man or woman alive.* David's reason for this is given in v. 11; his action conformed to that of Joshua in the conquest of Canaan (see, e.g., Jos 6:21 and note on 6:17).

27:10 *Negev of Judah.* Negev in Hebrew means "dry" and designates a large area from Beersheba to the highlands of the Sinai peninsula. *Jerahmeel.* The Jerahmeelites were de-

Negev of the Kenites.[w]" 11 He did not leave
a man or woman alive to be brought to
Gath, for he thought, "They might inform
on us and say, 'This is what David did.' "
And such was his practice as long as he
lived in Philistine territory. 12 Achish trusted David and said to himself, "He has become so obnoxious[x] to his people, the Israelites, that he will be my servant for life.[y]"

28 In those days the Philistines gathered[z] their forces to fight against
Israel. Achish said to David, "You must
understand that you and your men will
accompany me in the army."
2 David said, "Then you will see for
yourself what your servant can do."
Achish replied, "Very well, I will make
you my bodyguard[a] for life."

Saul and the Medium at Endor

3 Now Samuel was dead,[b] and all Israel
had mourned for him and buried him in his
own town of Ramah.[c] Saul had expelled[d]
the mediums and spiritists[e] from the land.
4 The Philistines assembled and came
and set up camp at Shunem,[f] while Saul
gathered all Israel and set up camp at Gilboa.[g] 5 When Saul saw the Philistine army,
he was afraid; terror[h] filled his heart. 6 He
inquired[i] of the LORD, but the LORD did not
answer him by dreams[j] or Urim[k] or prophets.[l] 7 Saul then said to his attendants,
"Find me a woman who is a medium,[m] so
I may go and inquire of her."
"There is one in Endor,[n]" they said.
8 So Saul disguised[o] himself, putting on
other clothes, and at night he and two
men went to the woman. "Consult[p] a spirit for me," he said, "and bring up for me
the one I name."
9 But the woman said to him, "Surely
you know what Saul has done. He has cut
off[q] the mediums and spiritists from the
land. Why have you set a trap[r] for my life
to bring about my death?"
10 Saul swore to her by the LORD, "As
surely as the LORD lives, you will not be
punished for this."
11 Then the woman asked, "Whom shall
I bring up for you?"
"Bring up Samuel," he said.
12 When the woman saw Samuel, she
cried out at the top of her voice and said
to Saul, "Why have you deceived me?[s] You
are Saul!"
13 The king said to her, "Don't be afraid.
What do you see?"
The woman said, "I see a ghostly figure[a]
coming up out of the earth."[t]
14 "What does he look like?" he asked.
"An old man wearing a robe[u] is coming
up," she said.
Then Saul knew it was Samuel, and he
bowed down and prostrated himself with
his face to the ground.
15 Samuel said to Saul, "Why have you
disturbed me by bringing me up?"

[a] 13 Or *see spirits*; or *see gods*

27:10 [w] Jdg 1:16 **27:12** [x] S Ge 34:30 [y] 1Sa 29:6 **28:1** [z] 1Sa 29:1 **28:2** [a] 1Sa 29:2 **28:3** [b] 1Sa 25:1 [c] S 1Sa 7:17 [d] ver 9 [e] S Ex 22:18 **28:4** [f] S Jos 19:18 [g] 1Sa 31:1,3; 2Sa 1:6,21; 21:12 **28:5** [h] S Ex 19:16 **28:6** [i] S 1Sa 8:18; 14:37 [j] S Dt 13:3 [k] S Ex 28:30; S Lev 8:8 [l] Eze 20:3; Am 8:11; Mic 3:7 **28:7** [m] 1Ch 10:13; Ac 16:16 [n] Jos 17:11; Ps 83:10 **28:8** [o] 1Ki 22:30; 2Ch 18:29; 35:22 [p] 2Ki 1:3; Isa 8:19 **28:9** [q] ver 3 [r] Job 18:10; Ps 31:4; 69:22; Isa 8:14 **28:12** [s] S Ge 27:36; 1Ki 14:6 **28:13** [t] ver 15; S Lev 19:31; 2Ch 33:6 **28:14** [u] 1Sa 15:27

scendants of Judah through Hezron (see 1Ch 2:9,25). *Kenites.* See note on 15:6.

27:12 *Achish trusted David.* David led Achish to believe that he was raiding outposts of Israelite territory when in actuality he was attacking the Geshurites, Girzites and Amalekites (see v. 8 and map, p. 451).

28:1 *accompany me in the army.* In the ancient Near East, to accept sanctuary in a country involved obligations of military service (see note on 27:2).

28:2 *you will see for yourself what your servant can do.* Perhaps an ambiguous answer. *I will make you my bodyguard.* Very likely this was conditional on David's proof of his loyalty and effectiveness in the projected campaign. Later, David would have a personal guard made up largely of Philistines (see 2Sa 15:18 and note).

28:3 *Now Samuel was dead.* See 25:1. Saul could not turn to him, even in desperation. *expelled … from the land.* Possibly a euphemism for "put to death," in agreement with Pentateuchal law (see vv. 9,21). *mediums and spiritists.* See Lev 19:31; 20:6,27; Dt 18:11.

28:4 *Shunem.* The Philistines assembled their forces far to the north, along the plain of Jezreel in the territory of Issachar (see Jos 19:18). *Gilboa.* A range of mountains east of the plain of Jezreel (see map, p. 369).

28:5 *terror filled his heart.* Because he was estranged from the Lord and was not performing his role as the true theocratic king (see note on 17:11).

28:6 *He inquired of the LORD.* Presumably through the agency of a priest. Saul seems to sense disaster in the approaching battle and seeks divine revelation concerning its outcome. *dreams.* Direct personal revelation (see Nu 12:6 and note on 12:6–8). *Urim.* Revelation through the priest (see note on 2:28). Since the authentic ephod and its Urim were with Abiathar, who was aligned with David (see 23:2,6,9), either Saul had fabricated another ephod for his use or the author used a conventional statement, including the three visual forms of revelation, to underscore his point. *prophets.* David had a prophet (Gad, 22:5), but after Samuel's alienation from Saul (15:35) no prophet served Saul.

28:7 *Find me a woman who is a medium.* In his desperation Saul turns to a pagan practice that he himself had previously outlawed (v. 3) in accordance with the Mosaic law (see Lev 19:31). *Endor.* Located about six miles northwest of Shunem (see v. 4; Jos 17:11).

28:9 *Why have you set a trap for my life … ?* The woman is very cautious about practicing her trade with strangers, afraid that she might be betrayed to Saul (see note on v. 3).

28:10 *As surely as the LORD lives.* See note on 14:39,45.

28:12 *When the woman saw Samuel.* The episode has been understood in various ways. Most likely, God permitted the spirit of Samuel to actually appear to the woman. In any event, the medium was used to convey to Saul that the impending battle would bring death and end his dynasty—just as Samuel had previously announced (15:26,28), because of Saul's unfaithfulness to the Lord. *she cried out … You are Saul!* By whatever means, the medium suddenly becomes aware that she is dealing with Saul.

28:14 *An old man wearing a robe.* Saul remembers Samuel as customarily dressed in this apparel (see 15:27).

"I am in great distress," Saul said. "The
Philistines are fighting against me, and
God has departed[v] from me. He no longer answers[w] me, either by prophets or by
dreams.[x] So I have called on you to tell me
what to do."
16 Samuel said, "Why do you consult
me, now that the LORD has departed from
you and become your enemy? 17 The LORD
has done what he predicted through me.
The LORD has torn[y] the kingdom out of
your hands and given it to one of your
neighbors—to David. 18 Because you did
not obey[z] the LORD or carry out his fierce
wrath[a] against the Amalekites,[b] the LORD
has done this to you today. 19 The LORD
will deliver both Israel and you into the
hands of the Philistines, and tomorrow
you and your sons[c] will be with me. The
LORD will also give the army of Israel into
the hands of the Philistines."
20 Immediately Saul fell full length on
the ground, filled with fear because of
Samuel's words. His strength was gone,
for he had eaten nothing all that day and
all that night.
21 When the woman came to Saul and
saw that he was greatly shaken, she said,
"Look, your servant has obeyed you. I
took my life[d] in my hands and did what
you told me to do. 22 Now please listen to
your servant and let me give you some
food so you may eat and have the strength
to go on your way."
23 He refused[e] and said, "I will not eat."
But his men joined the woman in urging him, and he listened to them. He got
up from the ground and sat on the couch.
24 The woman had a fattened calf[f] at the
house, which she butchered at once. She
took some flour, kneaded it and baked
bread without yeast. 25 Then she set it before Saul and his men, and they ate. That
same night they got up and left.

28:15 [v]S Jdg 16:20 [w]S 1Sa 14:37 [x]S Dt 13:3 **28:17** [y]1Sa 15:28 **28:18** [z]1Sa 15:20 [a]S Dt 9:8; S 1Sa 15:3 [b]S Ge 14:7; S 1Sa 14:48 **28:19** [c]1Sa 31:2; 1Ch 8:33 **28:21** [d]S Jdg 9:17; S 12:3 **28:23** [e]1Ki 21:4 **28:24** [f]S Ge 18:7

29:1 [g]1Sa 28:1 [h]S 1Sa 4:1 [i]Jos 17:16; 1Ki 18:45; 21:1, 23; 2Ki 9:30; Jer 50:5; Hos 1:4,5,11; 2:22 **29:2** [j]1Sa 28:2 **29:3** [k]1Ch 12:19 [l]1Sa 27:7 **29:4** [m]1Ch 12:19 [n]1Sa 14:21 **29:5** [o]S 1Sa 18:7 **29:6** [p]1Sa 27:8-12 [q]ver 3 **29:9** [r]2Sa 14:17,20; 19:27

Achish Sends David Back to Ziklag

29 The Philistines gathered[g] all
their forces at Aphek,[h] and Israel
camped by the spring in Jezreel.[i] 2 As the
Philistine rulers marched with their units
of hundreds and thousands, David and
his men were marching at the rear[j] with
Achish. 3 The commanders of the Philistines asked, "What about these Hebrews?"
Achish replied, "Is this not David,[k] who
was an officer of Saul king of Israel? He
has already been with me for over a year,[l]
and from the day he left Saul until now, I
have found no fault in him."
4 But the Philistine commanders were
angry with Achish and said, "Send[m] the
man back, that he may return to the place
you assigned him. He must not go with
us into battle, or he will turn[n] against us
during the fighting. How better could he
regain his master's favor than by taking
the heads of our own men? 5 Isn't this the
David they sang about in their dances:

"'Saul has slain his thousands,
and David his tens of thousands'?"[o]

6 So Achish called David and said to
him, "As surely as the LORD lives, you have
been reliable, and I would be pleased to
have you serve with me in the army. From
the day[p] you came to me until today, I
have found no fault in you, but the rulers[q]
don't approve of you. 7 Now turn back and
go in peace; do nothing to displease the
Philistine rulers."
8 "But what have I done?" asked David. "What have you found against your
servant from the day I came to you until
now? Why can't I go and fight against the
enemies of my lord the king?"
9 Achish answered, "I know that you
have been as pleasing in my eyes as an
angel[r] of God; nevertheless, the Philistine

28:17 *torn the kingdom out of your hands and given ... to David.* See 15:28 and note. In desperation Saul had torn Samuel's robe, an act symbolizing the Lord's snatching the kingdom away from Saul (see 15:27–28). David had earlier cut off a corner of Saul's robe, with similar symbolic meaning (see 24:4 and note).
28:18 See 15:17–26.
28:19 *tomorrow you and your sons will be with me.* In the realm of the dead—Saul's doom is sealed (see 31:6).
28:21 *When the woman came to Saul.* This statement suggests that the woman removed herself from the direct view of Saul while she gave her messages.
29:1 *The Philistines gathered all their forces.* The narrative flow broken at 28:2 is resumed. *Aphek.* A place in the vicinity of Shunem (28:4), to be distinguished from another place of the same name referred to in 4:1 (see note there; see also 1Ki 20:26,30; 2Ki 13:17).
29:2 *Philistine rulers.* See note on 5:8.
29:3 *I have found no fault in him.* David's tactics described in 27:10–12 were highly successful. (Cf. Pilate's similar words about Jesus [Lk 23:4; Jn 18:38].)
29:4 *the place you assigned him.* Ziklag (see 27:6). *or he will turn against us during the fighting.* The Philistines had experienced just such a reversal on a previous occasion (see 14:21). *taking the heads.* As trophies of victory (see 17:51; see also 5:4; 31:9 and notes).
29:5 See 21:11 and note on 18:7.
29:6 *As surely as the LORD lives.* See note on 14:39,45. Achish swears by the God of Israel apparently as a means of proving his sincerity to David.
29:8 *But what have I done?* David pretends disappointment in order to keep intact his strategy of deception. In reality this turn of events rescued David from a serious dilemma. *Why can't I go and fight against the enemies of my lord the king?* David again uses an ambiguous statement (see 28:2). To whom was he referring as "my lord the king"—Achish or Saul or the Lord?
29:9 *as an angel of God.* A common simile (see 2Sa 14:17 and note).

commanders[s] have said, 'He must not go
up with us into battle.' 10 Now get up early, along with your master's servants who
have come with you, and leave[t] in the
morning as soon as it is light."
11 So David and his men got up early in
the morning to go back to the land of the
Philistines, and the Philistines went up to
Jezreel.

David Destroys the Amalekites

30 David and his men reached Ziklag[u]
on the third day. Now the Amalekites[v] had raided the Negev and Ziklag.
They had attacked Ziklag and burned[w] it,
2 and had taken captive the women and
everyone else in it, both young and old.
They killed none of them, but carried
them off as they went on their way.
3 When David and his men reached Ziklag, they found it destroyed by fire and
their wives and sons and daughters tak-
en captive.[x] 4 So David and his men wept[y]
aloud until they had no strength left to
weep. 5 David's two wives[z] had been captured—Ahinoam of Jezreel and Abigail,
the widow of Nabal of Carmel. 6 David
was greatly distressed because the men
were talking of stoning[a] him; each one
was bitter[b] in spirit because of his sons
and daughters. But David found strength[c]
in the LORD his God.
7 Then David said to Abiathar[d] the
priest, the son of Ahimelek, "Bring me
the ephod.[e]" Abiathar brought it to him,
8 and David inquired[f] of the LORD, "Shall I
pursue this raiding party? Will I overtake
them?"
"Pursue them," he answered. "You will
certainly overtake them and succeed[g] in
the rescue.[h]"
9 David and the six hundred men[i] with
him came to the Besor Valley, where some
stayed behind. 10 Two hundred of them
were too exhausted[j] to cross the valley, but
David and the other four hundred continued the pursuit.
11 They found an Egyptian in a field and
brought him to David. They gave him water to drink and food to eat— 12 part of a
cake of pressed figs and two cakes of raisins. He ate and was revived,[k] for he had
not eaten any food or drunk any water for
three days and three nights.
13 David asked him, "Who do you belong to? Where do you come from?"
He said, "I am an Egyptian, the slave of
an Amalekite.[l] My master abandoned me
when I became ill three days ago. 14 We
raided the Negev of the Kerethites,[m] some
territory belonging to Judah and the Negev of Caleb.[n] And we burned[o] Ziklag."
15 David asked him, "Can you lead me
down to this raiding party?"
He answered, "Swear to me before God
that you will not kill me or hand me over
to my master,[p] and I will take you down
to them."
16 He led David down, and there they
were, scattered over the countryside, eating, drinking and reveling[q] because of the
great amount of plunder[r] they had taken
from the land of the Philistines and from
Judah. 17 David fought[s] them from dusk until the evening of the next day, and none of
them got away, except four hundred young
men who rode off on camels and fled.[t]
18 David recovered[u] everything the Amalekites had taken, including his two wives.
19 Nothing was missing: young or old, boy
or girl, plunder or anything else they had
taken. David brought everything back.
20 He took all the flocks and herds, and his
men drove them ahead of the other livestock, saying, "This is David's plunder."
21 Then David came to the two hundred
men who had been too exhausted[v] to follow him and who were left behind at the
Besor Valley. They came out to meet David and the men with him. As David and
his men approached, he asked them how
they were. 22 But all the evil men and troublemakers among David's followers said,
"Because they did not go out with us, we
will not share with them the plunder we
recovered. However, each man may take
his wife and children and go."
23 David replied, "No, my brothers, you
must not do that with what the LORD has
given us. He has protected us and delivered

29:9 [s] ver 4
29:10 [t] 1Ch 12:19
30:1 [u] S 1Sa 27:6 [v] S 1Sa 27:8 [w] ver 14
30:3 [x] S Ge 31:26
30:4 [y] S Ge 27:38
30:5 [z] S 1Sa 25:43
30:6 [a] S Ex 17:4; Jn 8:59 [b] S Ru 1:13 [c] S 1Sa 23:16; Ro 4:20
30:7 [d] S 1Sa 22:20 [e] S 1Sa 2:28
30:8 [f] S 1Sa 23:2 [g] S Ge 14:16 [h] S Ex 2:17
30:9 [i] S 1Sa 27:2
30:10 [j] ver 21
30:12 [k] S Jdg 15:19
30:13 [l] S 1Sa 14:48
30:14 [m] 2Sa 8:18; 15:18; 20:7, 23; 1Ki 1:38, 44; 1Ch 18:17; Eze 25:16; Zep 2:5 [n] S Jos 14:13; S 15:13 [o] ver 1
30:15 [p] Dt 23:15
30:16 [q] Lk 12:19 [r] S ver 17; S Jos 22:8
30:17 [s] ver 16; 1Sa 11:11; 2Sa 1:1 [t] 2Sa 1:8
30:18 [u] S Ge 14:16
30:21 [v] ver 10

29:11 *Jezreel.* The place of Israel's camp (see v. 1).
30:1—31:13 While Saul goes to his death at the hands of the Philistines, David is drawn into and pursues the Lord's continuing war with the Amalekites (see 15:2–3 and notes).
30:1 *Ziklag.* See note on 27:6. *Amalekites.* See 27:8 and note on 15:2. The absence of David and his warriors gave the Amalekites opportunity for revenge. *Negev.* See note on 27:10.
30:5 *Ahinoam.* See note on 25:43. *Abigail.* See 25:42.
30:6 *David found strength in the LORD.* As he had throughout his life (see 17:37 and note).
30:7 *Abiathar the priest.* See note on 22:20. *ephod.* See note on 2:28.
30:14 *Negev.* See note on 27:10. *Kerethites.* Along with the Pelethites, they later contributed contingents of professional warriors to David's private army (see 2Sa 8:18 and note; 15:18; 20:7; 1Ki 1:38). The name may indicate that they originally came from the island of Crete (see Jer 47:4 and note). *Negev of Caleb.* The area south of Hebron (see Jos 14:13).
30:17 *camels.* The mount of choice for the Amalekites and other eastern peoples (see Jdg 6:3,5 and note on 6:5).
30:22 *troublemakers.* See note on Dt 13:13.
30:23 *what the LORD has given us.* See 25:28 and note. David gently but firmly rejects the idea that their victory is to be attributed to their own prowess. Because the Lord gave the victory, no segment of David's men could claim any greater right to the spoils than any other.

into our hands the raiding party that came
against us. 24 Who will listen to what you
say? The share of the man who stayed
with the supplies is to be the same as that
of him who went down to the battle. All
will share alike.[w]" 25 David made this a
statute and ordinance for Israel from that
day to this.
26 When David reached Ziklag, he sent
some of the plunder to the elders of Judah, who were his friends, saying, "Here
is a gift[x] for you from the plunder of the
LORD's enemies."
27 David sent it to those who were in
Bethel,[y] Ramoth[z] Negev and Jattir;[a] 28 to
those in Aroer,[b] Siphmoth,[c] Eshtemoa[d]
29 and Rakal; to those in the towns of the
Jerahmeelites[e] and the Kenites;[f] 30 to those
in Hormah,[g] Bor Ashan,[h] Athak 31 and Hebron;[i] and to those in all the other places
where he and his men had roamed.

Saul Takes His Life

31:1-13pp — 2Sa 1:4-12; 1Ch 10:1-12

31 Now the Philistines fought against
Israel; the Israelites fled before
them, and many fell dead on Mount Gilboa.[j] 2 The Philistines were in hot pursuit
of Saul and his sons,[k] and they killed his
sons Jonathan,[l] Abinadab and Malki-
Shua.[m] 3 The fighting grew fierce around
Saul, and when the archers overtook him,
they wounded[n] him critically.
4 Saul said to his armor-bearer, "Draw
your sword and run me through,[o] or these
uncircumcised[p] fellows will come and run
me through and abuse me."
But his armor-bearer was terrified and
would not do it; so Saul took his own
sword and fell on it. 5 When the armor-
bearer saw that Saul was dead, he too fell
on his sword and died with him. 6 So Saul
and his three sons and his armor-bearer
and all his men died[q] together that same
day.
7 When the Israelites along the valley
and those across the Jordan saw that the
Israelite army had fled and that Saul and
his sons had died, they abandoned their
towns and fled. And the Philistines came
and occupied them.
8 The next day, when the Philistines[r]
came to strip the dead, they found Saul
and his three sons fallen on Mount Gilboa. 9 They cut off his head and stripped
off his armor, and they sent messengers
throughout the land of the Philistines to
proclaim the news[s] in the temple of their
idols and among their people.[t] 10 They put
his armor in the temple of the Ashtoreths[u]
and fastened his body to the wall of Beth
Shan.[v]
11 When the people of Jabesh Gilead[w]
heard what the Philistines had done to
Saul, 12 all their valiant men[x] marched
through the night to Beth Shan. They took
down the bodies of Saul and his sons from
the wall of Beth Shan and went to Jabesh,
where they burned[y] them. 13 Then they
took their bones[z] and buried them under a
tamarisk[a] tree at Jabesh, and they fasted[b]
seven days.[c]

30:24 [w] S Nu 31:27; S Jdg 5:30
30:26 [x] S Ge 33:11
30:27 [y] S Jos 7:2 [z] S Jos 10:40 [a] S Jos 15:48
30:28 [b] S Nu 32:34; S Jos 13:16 [c] 1Ch 27:27 [d] S Jos 15:50
30:29 [e] 1Sa 27:10 [f] S 1Sa 15:6
30:30 [g] S Nu 14:45; S 21:3 [h] S Jos 15:42
30:31 [i] Nu 13:22; S Jos 10:36; 2Sa 2:1,4
31:1 [j] S 1Sa 28:4
31:2 [k] S 1Sa 28:19 [l] S 1Sa 18:1 [m] S 1Sa 14:49
31:3 [n] S 1Sa 28:4
31:4 [o] S Jdg 9:54 [p] S Ge 34:14; S 1Sa 14:6
31:6 [q] S 1Sa 26:10
31:8 [r] 2Sa 1:20
31:9 [s] 2Sa 1:20; 4:4 [t] S Jdg 16:24
31:10 [u] S Jdg 2:12-13; S 1Sa 7:3 [v] S Jos 17:11
31:11 [w] S Jdg 21:8; S 1Sa 11:1
31:12 [x] Ps 76:5 [y] S Ge 38:24; Am 6:10
31:13 [z] 2Sa 21:12-14 [a] S Ge 21:33 [b] 2Sa 3:35; 12:19-23 [c] S Ge 50:10

30:24 *All will share alike.* Cf. Ex 16:18 and note.
30:26 *elders of Judah, who were his friends.* David sent the plunder as an expression of gratitude to those who had assisted him during his flight from Saul (see v. 31), thus preparing the way for his later elevation to kingship in Judah (see 2Sa 2:1 – 4).
30:29 *Jerahmeelites.* See note on 27:10. *Kenites.* See note on 15:6.
30:31 *Hebron.* The most important city in the central part of Judah. The other locations mentioned are to the southwest and southeast of Hebron.
31:1,8 *Mount Gilboa.* A range of hills (see 2Sa 1:21) at the southeast end of the Plain of Jezreel and at the head of the valley that leads down to Beth Shan. It is referred to elsewhere in the OT only as the place where Saul died (see 2Sa 1:6,21; 21:12; see also map, p. 369).
31:2 *Jonathan, Abinadab and Malki-Shua.* See note on 14:49. The surviving son, Ish-Bosheth or Esh-Baal (1Ch 8:33; 9:39), was afterward promoted by Abner, who somehow survived the battle, to succeed his father as king (2Sa 2:8 – 9).
31:4 *uncircumcised fellows.* See 14:6 and note. *abuse me.* A practice that was not uncommon; previously the Philistines had mutilated and humiliated Samson after his capture (see Jdg 16:21 – 25). *took his own sword and fell on it.* The culmination of a long process of self-destruction.
31:6 *all his men.* Those who had served around him in his administration (but see note on v. 2).
31:9 *They cut off his head.* David had done the same to Goliath (see 17:51). *sent messengers throughout the land.* Probably bearing Saul's head and armor as proof and trophies of their victory (see 5:4 and note).
31:10 *They put his armor in the temple.* Symbolic of ascribing the victory to the Philistine gods. *Ashtoreths.* See note on 7:3. *Beth Shan.* See note on Jos 17:11.
31:11 *Jabesh Gilead.* See note on 11:1.
31:12 *They took down the bodies of Saul and his sons.* The men of Jabesh Gilead had not forgotten how Saul had come to their defense when they were threatened by the Ammonites (see 11:1 – 11). *burned them.* Cremation was not customary in ancient Israel and here appears to have been done to prevent any further abuse of the bodies of Saul and his sons by the Philistines.
31:13 *took their bones and buried them.* David later had their remains removed from Jabesh and placed in the family burial grounds of Zela in Benjamin (see 2Sa 21:11 – 14). *fasted seven days.* As an indication of their mourning for Saul (cf. 2Sa 1:12; 3:35; 12:16,21 – 23).

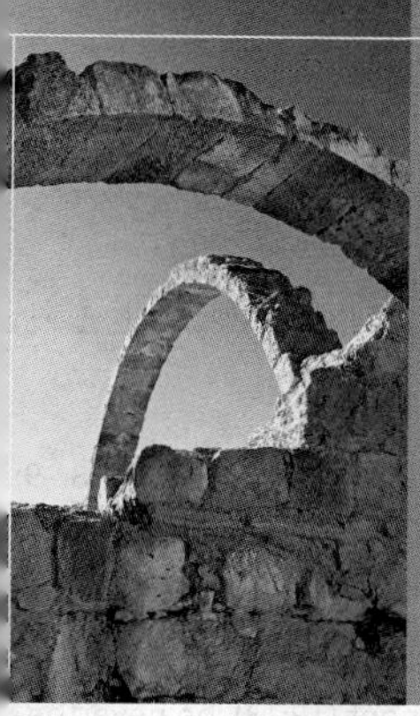

2 SAMUEL

INTRODUCTION

Title

1 and 2 Samuel were originally one book (see Introduction to 1 Samuel: Title).

Literary Features, Authorship and Date

See Introduction to 1 Samuel: Literary Features, Authorship and Date.

Contents and Theme: Kingship and Covenant

2 Samuel depicts David as a true (though imperfect) representative of the ideal theocratic king. David was initially acclaimed king at Hebron by the tribe of Judah (chs. 1 – 4) and subsequently was accepted by the remaining tribes after the murder of Ish-Bosheth, one of Saul's surviving sons (5:1 – 5). David's leadership was decisive and effective. He captured Jerusalem from the Jebusites and made it his royal city and residence (5:6 – 13). Shortly afterward he brought the ark of the Lord from the house of Abinadab to Jerusalem, publicly acknowledging the Lord's kingship and rule over himself and the nation (ch. 6; Ps 132:3 – 5).

Under David's rule the Lord caused the united kingdom to prosper, to defeat its enemies and, in fulfillment of his promise (see Ge 15:18), to extend its borders from Egypt to the Euphrates (ch. 8). David wanted to build a temple for the Lord — as his royal house, as a place for his throne and as a place for Israel to worship him. But the prophet Nathan told David that he was not to build the Lord a house (temple); rather, the Lord would build David a house (dynasty). Ch. 7 announces the Lord's promise that this Davidic dynasty would endure forever. This climactic chapter also describes the establishment of the Davidic covenant (see notes on 7:1 – 29,11,16; Ps 89:30 – 37). Later the prophets make clear that a descendant of David who sits on David's throne will perfectly fulfill the role of the theocratic

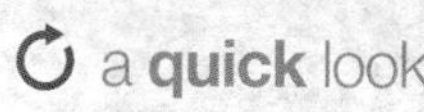

a quick look

Author:
Unknown

Audience:
God's chosen people, the Israelites

Date:
Sometime after Israel was divided into the northern and southern kingdoms in about 930 BC

Theme:
2 Samuel presents the story of David's 40-year reign, beginning with his rise to become Israel's model king and ending with his subsequent decline caused by sin.

David was a king after God's own heart because he was willing to acknowledge his sin and repent.

king. He will complete the redemption of God's people (see Isa 9:6 – 7; 11:1 – 16; Jer 23:5 – 6; 30:8 – 9; 33:14 – 16; Eze 34:23 – 24; 37:24 – 25), thus enabling them to achieve the promised victory with him (Ro 16:20).

After the description of David's rule in its glory and success, chs. 9 – 20 depict the darker side of his reign and describe David's weaknesses and failures. Even though David remained a king after God's own heart because he was willing to acknowledge his sin and repent (12:13), he nevertheless fell far short of the theocratic ideal and suffered the disciplinary results of his disobedience (12:10 – 12). His sin with Bathsheba (chs. 11 – 12) and his leniency with regard both to the wickedness of his sons (13:12 – 39; 14:1,33; 19:4 – 6) and to the insubordination of Joab (3:28 – 39; 20:10,23) led to intrigue, violence and bloodshed within his own family and the nation. It eventually drove him from Jerusalem at the time of Absalom's rebellion. Nonetheless the Lord was gracious to David, and his reign became a standard by which the reigns of later kings were measured (see 1Ki 15:3 – 5; 2Ki 18:3; 22:2).

The book ends with David's own words of praise to God, who had delivered him from all his enemies (22:31 – 51), and with words of expectation for the fulfillment of God's promise that a king will come from the house of David and rule "over people in righteousness" (23:3 – 5). These poems echo many of the themes of Hannah's song (1Sa 2:1 – 10), and together they frame (and interpret) the basic narrative.

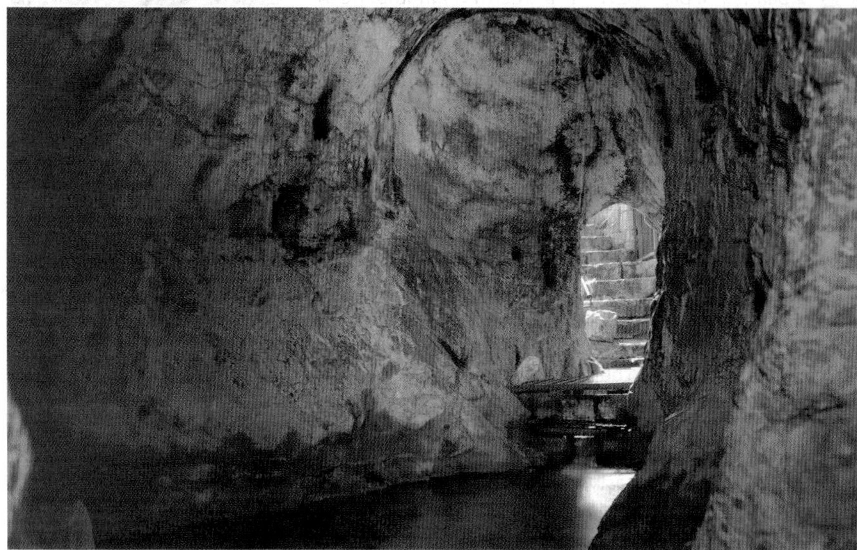

The Gihon spring (see 2Sa 5:8 and note) provided a natural water source for ancient Jerusalem.

Todd Bolen/www.BiblePlaces.com

Chronology

See Introduction to 1 Samuel: Chronology.

Outline

Below is an outline for 2 Samuel. For an outline of both 1 and 2 Samuel, see Introduction to 1 Samuel: Outline.

7. David's reaction to and lament over Saul's death (2Sa 1)

C. David Becomes King over Judah (2:1 — 3:5)

D. David Becomes King over All Israel (3:6 — 5:5)

VII. David's Reign Characterized Illustratively (5:6 — 8:18)

A. David's Conquest of Jerusalem and His Recognition by the King of Tyre (5:6 – 16)

B. David's Crushing of the Philistine Threat (5:17 – 25)

C. David's Bringing the Ark into His Royal City (ch. 6)

D. God's Covenant with David (ch. 7)

E. David's Victories that Secure the Boundaries of His Kingdom (ch. 8)

VIII. Threats to David's Reign Overcome (chs. 9 – 20)

A. David's Kindness to Saul's Remaining Heir (ch. 9)

B. Defeat of the Ammonite-Aramean Challenge to David's Reign (10:1 – 19; 12:26 – 31)

C. David's Shameful Abuse of His Royal Power in the Matter of Bathsheba and Uriah (11:1 — 12:25)

D. Absalom's Challenge to David's Rule (chs. 13 – 20)

1. Amnon's abuse of power and Absalom's revenge (ch. 13)
2. Absalom's revolt crushed (chs. 14 – 19)
3. Absalom's attempt sparks another unsuccessful revolt (ch. 20)

IX. Sidebars to the David Story (Chiastically Arranged) (chs. 21 – 24)

A. God's Wrath against Israel because of Something Saul Had Done (21:1 – 14)

B. Exploits of David's Mighty Men in Wars against Philistines (21:15 – 22)

C. David's Song in Praise of the Lord for Victories Granted (ch. 22)

C′. David's "Last Words" that Speak of God's Ways with Him and His House (23:1 – 7)

B′. David's Mighty Men and Their Exploits, Especially against Philistines (23:8 – 39)

A′. God's Wrath against Israel because of Something David Did (ch. 24)

David Hears of Saul's Death

1:4-12pp — 1Sa 31:1-13; 1Ch 10:1-12

1 After the death[a] of Saul, David returned from striking down[b] the Amalekites[c] and stayed in Ziklag two days. 2On
the third day a man[d] arrived from Saul's
camp with his clothes torn and dust on his
head.[e] When he came to David, he fell[f] to
the ground to pay him honor.[g]
3"Where have you come from?" David
asked him.
He answered, "I have escaped from the
Israelite camp."
4"What happened?" David asked.
"Tell me."
"The men fled from the battle," he replied. "Many of them fell and died. And
Saul and his son Jonathan are dead."
5Then David said to the young man
who brought him the report, "How do you
know that Saul and his son Jonathan are
dead?"
6"I happened to be on Mount Gilboa,[h]"
the young man said, "and there was Saul,
leaning on his spear, with the chariots
and their drivers in hot pursuit. 7When he
turned around and saw me, he called out
to me, and I said, 'What can I do?'
8"He asked me, 'Who are you?'
" 'An Amalekite,[i]' I answered.
9"Then he said to me, 'Stand here by
me and kill me![j] I'm in the throes of death,
but I'm still alive.'
10"So I stood beside him and killed him,
because I knew that after he had fallen he
could not survive. And I took the crown[k]
that was on his head and the band on his
arm and have brought them here to my
lord."
11Then David and all the men with him
took hold of their clothes and tore[l] them.
12They mourned and wept and fasted till
evening for Saul and his son Jonathan
and for the army of the LORD and for the
nation of Israel, because they had fallen
by the sword.
13David said to the young man who
brought him the report, "Where are you
from?"
"I am the son of a foreigner, an Amalekite,[m]" he answered.
14David asked him, "Why weren't you
afraid to lift your hand to destroy the
LORD's anointed?[n]"
15Then David called one of his men and
said, "Go, strike him down!"[o] So he struck
him down, and he died.[p] 16For David had
said to him, "Your blood be on your own
head.[q] Your own mouth testified against
you when you said, 'I killed the LORD's
anointed.' "

David's Lament for Saul and Jonathan

17David took up this lament[r] concerning Saul and his son Jonathan,[s] 18and he
ordered that the people of Judah be taught
this lament of the bow (it is written in the
Book of Jashar):[t]

19"A gazelle[a] lies slain on your heights,
Israel.
How the mighty[u] have fallen![v]

1:1 [a]S 1Sa 26:10; 1Ch 10:13 [b]S Jos 22:8; S 1Sa 30:17 [c]S Ge 14:7; Nu 13:29 **1:2** [d]2Sa 4:10 [e]S 1Sa 4:12; Job 2:12; Eze 27:30 [f]S 1Sa 20:41 [g]S Ge 37:7 **1:6** [h]ver 21; S 1Sa 28:4 **1:8** [i]ver 13; S 1Sa 15:2; S 27:8; 30:13, 17 **1:9** [j]S Jdg 9:54 **1:10** [k]2Ki 11:12 **1:11** [l]S Ge 37:29; S Nu 14:6 **1:13** [m]S ver 8; S 1Sa 14:48 **1:14** [n]S 1Sa 12:3; S 26:9 **1:15** [o]2Sa 4:12 [p]2Sa 4:10 **1:16** [q]S Lev 20:9; Mt 27:24-25; Ac 18:6 **1:17** [r]S Ge 50:10; S Eze 32:2 [s]ver 26 **1:18** [t]Jos 10:13 **1:19** [u]2Sa 23:8; Ps 29:1; 45:3 [v]2Sa 3:38

[a] *19 Gazelle* here symbolizes a human dignitary.

1:1–27 David's reaction to and lament over Saul's death. This opening segment of 2 Samuel is actually the narrative hinge of the full book of 1,2 Samuel (see notes on 22:1–51; 1Sa 2:1).
1:1 *After the death of.* See Jos 1:1; Jdg 1:1; 2Ki 1:1. The narrative thread of 1 Samuel is continued. 1 and 2 Samuel were originally one book (see Introduction to 1 Samuel: Title). *David returned from striking down the Amalekites.* See 1Sa 30:26. *Ziklag.* See note on 1Sa 27:6.
1:2 *his clothes torn ... dust on his head.* See note on 1Sa 4:12; see also Jos 7:6; Ac 14:14 and notes.
1:8 *Amalekite.* It is not necessary to conclude from v. 3 that this Amalekite was a member of Saul's army. His statement that he "happened to be on Mount Gilboa" (v. 6) is probably not as innocent as it appears. He may have been there as a scavenger to rob the fallen soldiers of their valuables and weapons. It is ironic that Saul's death is reported by an Amalekite (see 1Sa 15).
1:10 *I stood beside him and killed him.* The Amalekite's story conflicts with 1Sa 31:3–6, where Saul is depicted as taking his own life. It appears that the Amalekite fabricated this version of Saul's death, expecting David to reward him (see 4:10). His miscalculation of David's response cost him his life (see v. 15). *I took the crown.* Apparently he got to Saul before the Philistines did (see 1Sa 31:8–9).
1:11 *took hold of their clothes and tore them.* See note on v. 2.
1:12 *mourned and wept.* David and his men expressed their grief in typical Near Eastern fashion (see Ge 23:2; 1Ki 13:30; Jer 22:18). *fasted.* See note on 1Sa 31:13.
1:13 *Amalekite.* The man was probably unaware of David's recent hostile encounters with the Amalekites (see v. 1; 1Sa 30; see also note on 1Sa 15:2).
1:14 The Amalekite understood nothing of the deep significance that David attached to the sanctity of the royal office in Israel (see 1Sa 24:6 and note). *the LORD's anointed.* See note on 1Sa 9:16.
1:15 *strike him down!* David displays no personal satisfaction over Saul's death and condemns to death the one he believes to be his murderer (see note on v. 10; see also 4:10).
1:16 *Your blood be on your own head.* The Amalekite's own testimony brought about his execution (see Jos 2:19; 1Ki 2:37).
1:17 *lament.* It was a common practice in the ancient Near East to compose laments for fallen leaders, heroes and royal cities (see 2Ch 35:25 and note; Lamentations, particularly its Introduction: Themes and Theology).
1:18 *lament of the bow.* Perhaps David taught his men to sing this lament while they practiced with the bow (Israel's most common weapon; see, e.g., 22:35; 1Sa 13:22 and note) as motivation to master the weapon thoroughly so they would not experience a similar defeat (see note on Eze 21:9). *Book of Jashar.* See note on Jos 10:13.
1:19 *A gazelle.* See NIV text note; probably a reference to Jonathan (see v. 25, a kind of refrain; for the imagery

20 “Tell it not in Gath,[w]
proclaim it not in the streets of
Ashkelon,[x]
lest the daughters of the Philistines[y] be
glad,
lest the daughters of the
uncircumcised rejoice.[z]

21 “Mountains of Gilboa,[a]
may you have neither dew[b] nor rain,[c]
may no showers fall on your terraced
fields.[ad]
For there the shield of the mighty was
despised,
the shield of Saul—no longer
rubbed with oil.[e]

22 “From the blood[f] of the slain,
from the flesh of the mighty,
the bow[g] of Jonathan did not turn
back,
the sword of Saul did not return
unsatisfied.
23 Saul and Jonathan—
in life they were loved and admired,
and in death they were not parted.
They were swifter than eagles,[h]
they were stronger than lions.[i]

24 “Daughters of Israel,
weep for Saul,
who clothed you in scarlet and finery,
who adorned your garments with
ornaments of gold.[j]

1:20 [w] Mic 1:10 [x] S Jos 13:3 [y] 1Sa 31:8 [z] S 1Sa 18:6
1:21 [a] S ver 6 [b] S Ge 27:28; S Isa 18:4 [c] Dt 11:17; 1Ki 8:35; 17:1; 18:1; 2Ch 6:26; Job 36:27; 38:28; Ps 65:10; 147:8; Isa 5:6; Jer 5:24; 14:4; Am 1:2 [d] Jer 12:4; Eze 31:15 [e] Isa 21:5
1:22 [f] Isa 34:3, 7; 49:26 [g] Dt 32:42
1:23 [h] S Dt 28:49 [i] Jdg 14:18
1:24 [j] S Jdg 5:30
1:26 [k] Jer 22:18; 34:5 [l] ver 17 [m] S 1Sa 20:42 [n] S 1Sa 18:1
1:27 [o] S 1Sa 2:4
2:1 [p] S 1Sa 23:2, 11-12 [q] S Ge 13:18; S 23:19
2:2 [r] S 1Sa 25:43 [s] S 1Sa 25:42
2:3 [t] S 1Sa 27:2; 1Ch 12:22 [u] S Ge 13:18; 23:2; 37:14
2:4 [v] S 1Sa 30:31 [w] S 1Sa 2:35; 2Sa 5:3-5; 1Ch 12:23-40 [x] S Jdg 21:8; S 1Sa 11:1

25 “How the mighty have fallen in battle!
Jonathan lies slain on your heights.
26 I grieve[k] for you, Jonathan[l] my
brother;[m]
you were very dear to me.
Your love for me was wonderful,[n]
more wonderful than that of women.

27 “How the mighty have fallen!
The weapons of war have
perished!”[o]

David Anointed King Over Judah

2 In the course of time, David inquired[p]
of the LORD. “Shall I go up to one of
the towns of Judah?” he asked.
The LORD said, “Go up.”
David asked, “Where shall I go?”
“To Hebron,”[q] the LORD answered.
2 So David went up there with his two
wives,[r] Ahinoam of Jezreel and Abigail,[s]
the widow of Nabal of Carmel. 3 David
also took the men who were with him,[t]
each with his family, and they settled in
Hebron[u] and its towns. 4 Then the men of
Judah came to Hebron,[v] and there they
anointed[w] David king over the tribe of Judah.
When David was told that it was the
men from Jabesh Gilead[x] who had bur-

[a] 21 Or / *nor fields that yield grain for offerings*

f. 2:18; 1Ch 12:8). Or the Hebrew may be rendered "Your glo-y," referring to both Saul and Jonathan (vv. 22–23). *heights.*)f Gilboa (see v. 25; 1Sa 31:1,8 and note; see also note on Sa 28:4). *How the mighty have fallen!* The theme of David's ament (see vv. 25,27). David's words contain no suggestion f bitterness toward Saul but rather recall the good quali-ies and accomplishments of Saul and Jonathan. However,)avid's lament over "fallen" Saul is Saul's epitaph and stands n significant contrast to Hannah's song in 1Sa 2:1–10 and)avid's song in 2Sa 22.

:20 *Tell it not in Gath … Ashkelon.* As the major Philistine cit-es located the closest and farthest from Israel's borders, Gath nd Ashkelon represent the entire Philistine nation. David oes not want the enemies of God's covenant people to take leasure in Israel's defeat (as he knew they would; see 1Sa 1:9–10) and thus bring reproach on the name of the Lord see Ex 32:12; Nu 14:13–19; Dt 9:28; see also Jos 7:9; Mic 1:10 nd notes). *uncircumcised.* See note on 1Sa 14:6.

:21 *Mountains of Gilboa.* See note on 1Sa 28:4. As an ex-ression of profound grief, David rhetorically pronounces a urse on the place where Israel was defeated and Saul and onathan were killed (for other such rhetorical curses, see ob 3:3–26; Jer 20:14–18). *no longer rubbed with oil.* Leather hields were rubbed with oil to preserve them (see Isa 21:5).

:23 *in death they were not parted.* Even though Jonathan op-osed his father's treatment of David, he gave his life beside is father in Israel's defense.

:26 *more wonderful than that of women.* David is not sug-esting that marital love is inferior to that of friendship, nor o his remarks have any sexual implications. He is simply call-ng attention to Jonathan's nearly inexplicable self-denying ommitment to David, whom Jonathan had long recognized as the Lord's choice to succeed his own father, Saul (see notes on 1Sa 18:1; 20:13–16).

1:27 *weapons of war.* Probably a metaphor for Saul and Jonathan.

2:1—3:5 David's elevation to kingship over Judah, and Abner's response.

2:1 *In the course of time.* This phrase introduces significant episodes in David's life: his anointing as king over Judah (here), his most notable military victories (8:1), his adultery with Bathsheba and murder of Uriah (10:1), the death of his firstborn son, Amnon (13:1), and the conspiracy of his son Absalom (15:1). *David inquired of the LORD.* By means of the ephod through the priest Abiathar (see notes on Ex 28:30; 1Sa 2:28; 23:2). *one of the towns of Judah.* Even though Saul was dead and David had many friends and contacts among the people of his own tribe (see 1Sa 30:26–31), David did not presume to return from Philistine territory to assume the kingship promised to him without first seeking the Lord's guidance. *Hebron.* An old and important city (see Ge 13:18; 23:2; Jos 15:13–14; see also note on 1Sa 30:31) centrally located in the tribe of Judah (see map, p. 451).

2:2 *Ahinoam of Jezreel.* See note on 1Sa 25:43. *Abigail.* See 1Sa 25.

2:3 *men who were with him.* See note on v. 13.

2:4 *anointed David king.* See notes on 1Sa 2:10; 9:16. David had previously been anointed privately by Samuel in the presence of his own family (see note on 1Sa 16:13). Here the anointing ceremony is repeated as a public recognition by his own tribe of his divine calling to be king. *over the tribe of Judah.* Very likely the tribe of Simeon was also involved (see Jos 19:1; Jdg 1:3), but the Judahites in every way dominated the area. *men from Jabesh Gilead.*

ied Saul, 5he sent messengers to
them to say to them, "The LORD
bless[y] you for showing this kindness to Saul your master by burying him. 6May the LORD now show
you kindness and faithfulness,[z] and
I too will show you the same favor
because you have done this. 7Now
then, be strong[a] and brave, for Saul
your master is dead, and the people of Judah have anointed me king
over them."

The pool of Gibeon is 39 feet across and 35 feet deep. It is possible this is the same place where David's forces defeated Saul's army (see 2Sa 2:12 – 17 and note on 2:13).

Todd Bolen/www.BiblePlaces.com

War Between the Houses of David and Saul

3:2-5pp — 1Ch 3:1-4

8Meanwhile, Abner[b] son of Ner,
the commander of Saul's army,
had taken Ish-Bosheth[c] son of Saul
and brought him over to Mahanaim.[d] 9He made him king over Gilead,[e] Ashuri[f] and Jezreel, and also
over Ephraim, Benjamin and all Israel.[g]
10Ish-Bosheth son of Saul was forty years
old when he became king over Israel, and
he reigned two years. The tribe of Judah,
however, remained loyal to David. 11The
length of time David was king in Hebron
over Judah was seven years and six months.[h]
12Abner son of Ner, together with the
men of Ish-Bosheth son of Saul, left Mahanaim and went to Gibeon.[i] 13Joab[j] son
of Zeruiah and David's men went out and
met them at the pool of Gibeon. One grou
sat down on one side of the pool and on
group on the other side.
14Then Abner said to Joab, "Let's hav
some of the young men get up and figh
hand to hand in front of us."
"All right, let them do it," Joab said.
15So they stood up and were counte
off — twelve men for Benjamin and Ish

2:5 [y]S Jdg 17:2; S 1Sa 23:21; 2Ti 1:16 **2:6** [z]Ex 34:6 **2:7** [a]S Jos 1:6; S Jdg 5:21 **2:8** [b]S 1Sa 14:50; S 2Sa 3:27 [c]2Sa 4:5; 1Ch 8:33; 9:39 [d]S Ge 32:2 **2:9** [e]S Nu 32:26 [f]S Jos 19:24-31 [g]1Ch 12:29 **2:11** [h]2Sa 5:5 **2:12** [i]S Jos 9:3 **2:13** [j]2Sa 8:16; 19:13; 1Ki 1:7; 1Ch 2:16; 11:6; 27:34

See notes on 1Sa 11:1; 31:12. *buried Saul.* See note on 1Sa 31:13.

2:7 *your master is dead, and the people of Judah have anointed me king over them.* David's concluding statement to the men of Jabesh Gilead is a veiled invitation to them to recognize him as their king, just as the tribe of Judah had done. This appeal for their support, however, was ignored.

2:8 *Abner son of Ner.* See 1Sa 14:50 – 51. *Saul's army.* His small standing army of professionals loyal to him and his family (see 1Sa 13:2,15; 14:2,52). *Ish-Bosheth.* The name was originally Ish-(or Esh-)Baal (1Ch 8:33) but was changed by the author of Samuel to Ish-Bosheth, meaning "man of the shameful thing" (see notes on 4:4; Jdg 6:32; Jer 2:26; 3:24 – 25; 11:13). Evidently Baal (meaning "lord" or "master") was at this time still used to refer to the Lord. Later this was discontinued because of confusion with the Canaanite god Baal, and the author of Samuel reflects the later sensitivity. *son of Saul.* See note on 1Sa 31:2. *brought him.* Abner takes the initiative in the power vacuum created by Saul's death, using the unassertive Ish-Bosheth as a pawn for his own ambitions (see 3:11 and note on 4:1). There is no evidence that Ish-Bosheth had strong support among the Israelites generally. *Mahanaim.* A Gileadite town east of the Jordan River and thus beyond the sphere of Philistine domination — a kind of refugee capital.

2:9 *He made him king.* As a relative of Saul (see 1Sa 14:50 – 51), Abner had both a family and a career interest in ensuring dynastic succession for Saul's house. *Gilead ... all Israel.* This delineation of Ish-Bosheth's realm suggests that his actual rule, while involving territory both east and west of the Jordan, was quite limited and that "all Israel" was more claim than reality. David ruled over Judah and Simeon, and the Philistines controlled large sections of the northern tribal regions.

2:11 *seven years and six months.* Cf. Ish-Bosheth's two-yea reign in Mahanaim (v. 10). Because it appears that David wa made king over all Israel shortly after Ish-Bosheth's deat (5:1 – 5) and moved his capital to Jerusalem not long afte ward (5:6 – 12), reconciling the lengths of David's and Ish Bosheth's reigns is difficult. The difficulty is best resolved b assuming that it took Ish-Bosheth a number of years to b recognized as his father's successor, and that the two yea of his reign roughly correspond to the last two or three yea of David's reign in Hebron.

2:12 Abner initiates an action to prevent David's sphere c influence from spreading northward out of Judah. Gibeo was located in the tribal area of Benjamin (see Jos 18:21,25 to which Saul and his family belonged, and which the Philis tines had not occupied.

2:13 *Joab son of Zeruiah.* See note on 1Sa 26: Joab became a figure of major importance du ing David's reign as a competent but ruthless military leade (see 10:7 – 14; 11:1; 12:26; 1Ki 11:15 – 16). At times David wa unable to control him (3:39; 18:5,14; 1Ki 2:5 – 6), and he wa eventually executed for his wanton assassinations and hi part in the conspiracy to place Adonijah rather than Solo mon on David's throne (1Ki 2:28 – 34). *David's men.* Some, a least, of David's small force of professionals who had gath ered around him (see 1Sa 22:2; 23:13; 27:2; 30:3,9). *pool c Gibeon.* See Jer 41:12. In 1956 archaeologists uncovered large, cylindrical pool at el-Jib (ancient Gibeon), probab the one near which the battle recorded in vv. 15 – 16 too place. See photo above.

2:15 *Benjamin.* At this time Ish-Bosheth seems to have bee supported mainly by his own tribesmen.

osheth son of Saul, and twelve for David.
16 Then each man grabbed his opponent by
he head and thrust his dagger[k] into his
pponent's side, and they fell down to-
ether. So that place in Gibeon was called
elkath Hazzurim.[a]
17 The battle that day was very fierce,
nd Abner and the Israelites were defeat-
d[l] by David's men.[m]
18 The three sons of Zeruiah[n] were there:
oab,[o] Abishai[p] and Asahel.[q] Now Asahel
vas as fleet-footed as a wild gazelle.[r] 19 He
hased Abner, turning neither to the right
or to the left as he pursued him. 20 Aber looked behind him and asked, "Is that
ou, Asahel?"
"It is," he answered.
21 Then Abner said to him, "Turn aside
o the right or to the left; take on one of
he young men and strip him of his weap-
ns." But Asahel would not stop chasing
im.
22 Again Abner warned Asahel, "Stop
hasing me! Why should I strike you
own? How could I look your brother Joab
n the face?"[s]
23 But Asahel refused to give up the pur-
uit; so Abner thrust the butt of his spear
nto Asahel's stomach,[t] and the spear
ame out through his back. He fell there
nd died on the spot. And every man
topped when he came to the place where
sahel had fallen and died.[u]
24 But Joab and Abishai pursued Abner,
nd as the sun was setting, they came to
he hill of Ammah, near Giah on the way
o the wasteland of Gibeon. 25 Then the
nen of Benjamin rallied behind Abner.
hey formed themselves into a group and
ook their stand on top of a hill.
26 Abner called out to Joab, "Must the
word devour[v] forever? Don't you realize
hat this will end in bitterness? How long
before you order your men to stop pursuing their fellow Israelites?"
27 Joab answered, "As surely as God
lives, if you had not spoken, the men
would have continued pursuing them until morning."
28 So Joab[w] blew the trumpet,[x] and all
the troops came to a halt; they no longer
pursued Israel, nor did they fight anymore.
29 All that night Abner and his men
marched through the Arabah.[y] They
crossed the Jordan, continued through the
morning hours[b] and came to Mahanaim.[z]
30 Then Joab stopped pursuing Abner
and assembled the whole army. Besides
Asahel, nineteen of David's men were
found missing. 31 But David's men had
killed three hundred and sixty Benjamites
who were with Abner. 32 They took Asahel and buried him in his father's tomb[a]
at Bethlehem. Then Joab and his men
marched all night and arrived at Hebron
by daybreak.

3 The war between the house of Saul
and the house of David lasted a long
time.[b] David grew stronger and stronger,[c]
while the house of Saul grew weaker and
weaker.[d]
2 Sons were born to David in Hebron:

His firstborn was Amnon[e] the son of Ahinoam[f] of Jezreel;
3 his second, Kileab the son of Abigail[g] the widow of Nabal of Carmel;
the third, Absalom[h] the son of Maakah daughter of Talmai king of Geshur;[i]
4 the fourth, Adonijah[j] the son of Haggith;
the fifth, Shephatiah the son of Abital;

2:16 [k] S Jdg 3:21 **2:17** [l] 2Sa 3:1 [m] S 1Sa 17:8 **2:18** [n] 2Sa 3:39; 16:10; 19:22 [o] 2Sa 3:30; 10:7; 11:1; 14:1; 18:14; 20:8; 24:3; 1Ki 1:7; 2:5, 34 [p] S 1Sa 26:6 [q] 2Sa 23:24; 1Ch 2:16; 11:26; 27:7 [r] 1Ch 12:8; Pr 6:5; SS 2:9 **2:22** [s] 2Sa 3:27 **2:23** [t] 2Sa 3:27; 4:6 [u] 2Sa 20:12 **2:26** [v] S Dt 32:42; Jer 46:10, 14; Na 2:13; 3:15 **2:28** [w] 2Sa 18:16; 20:23 [x] S Jdg 3:27 **2:29** [y] S Dt 3:17 [z] S Ge 32:2 **2:32** [a] S Ge 49:29 **3:1** [b] 1Ki 14:30 [c] 2Sa 5:10 [d] 2Sa 2:17; 22:44; Est 9:4 **3:2** [e] 2Sa 13:1 [f] S 1Sa 25:43 **3:3** [g] S 1Sa 25:42 [h] 2Sa 13:1, 28 [i] 2Sa 13:37; 14:32; 15:8 **3:4** [j] 1Ki 1:5, 11; 2:13, 22

[a] 16 *Helkath Hazzurim* means *field of daggers* or *field of hostilities.* [b] 29 See Septuagint; the meaning of the Hebrew for this phrase is uncertain.

:17 *The battle that day was very fierce.* Because the repre-entative combat (see note on 1Sa 17:4) by 12 men from ach side was indecisive, a full-scale battle ensued in which avid's forces were victorious. The attempt to use represen-ative combat to avoid the decimation of civil war failed (see 1).

:21 *Turn aside.* Abner tried unsuccessfully to avoid the ne-essity of killing Asahel.

:22 *How could I look your brother Joab in the face?* Abner did ot want the hostility between himself and Joab to be inten-fied by the practice of blood revenge (see note on 3:27).

:23 Stabbing an enemy in the stomach was the method of xecution noted also in 3:27; 4:6 (cf. Jdg 3:21).

:26 *Must the sword devour forever?* Abner proposes an ar-istice as a means of avoiding the awful consequences of vil war.

:27 *As surely as God lives.* An oath formula (see note on 1Sa 4:39,45).

:28 *nor did they fight anymore.* For the present the open onflict ceased, but the hostility remained (see 3:1).

:29 *Arabah.* See note on Dt 1:1.

3:2–5 The list of six sons born to David in Hebron is given as an evidence of the strengthening of David's house in contrast to that of Saul (v. 1). That these six sons were each born of a different mother indirectly informs us that David married four additional wives (see 2:2) during his time in Hebron.

3:2 *Amnon.* Later raped his half sister Tamar and was killed by his brother Absalom (see ch. 13). *Ahinoam of Jezreel.* See note on 1Sa 25:43.

3:3 *Kileab.* Called Daniel in 1Ch 3:1. *Abigail.* See 1Sa 25. *Absalom.* Later avenged the rape of Tamar by killing Amnon, and conspired against his father David in an attempt to make himself king (see chs. 13–18). *Maakah daughter of Talmai.* David's marriage to Maakah undoubtedly had political implications. With Talmai as an ally on Ish-Bosheth's northern border, David flanked the northern kingdom both south and north. *Geshur.* A small Aramean city kingdom (see 15:8) located northeast of the Sea of Galilee (see Jos 12:5; 13:11–13; see also map, p. 478).

3:4 *Adonijah.* Was put to death for attempting to take over the throne before Solomon could be crowned (see 1Ki 1–2).

5 and the sixth, Ithream the son of David's wife Eglah.
These were born to David in Hebron.

Abner Goes Over to David

6 During the war between the house of Saul and the house of David, Abner[k] had been strengthening his own position in the house of Saul. 7 Now Saul had had a concubine[l] named Rizpah[m] daughter of Aiah. And Ish-Bosheth said to Abner, "Why did you sleep with my father's concubine?"

8 Abner was very angry because of what Ish-Bosheth said. So he answered, "Am I a dog's head[n]—on Judah's side? This very day I am loyal to the house of your father Saul and to his family and friends. I haven't handed you over to David. Yet now you accuse me of an offense involving this woman! 9 May God deal with Abner, be it ever so severely, if I do not do for David what the LORD promised[o] him on oath 10 and transfer the kingdom from the house of Saul and establish David's throne over Israel and Judah from Dan to Beersheba."[p] 11 Ish-Bosheth did not dare to say another word to Abner, because he was afraid of him.

12 Then Abner sent messengers on his behalf to say to David, "Whose land is it? Make an agreement with me, and I will help you bring all Israel over to you."

13 "Good," said David. "I will make an agreement with you. But I demand one thing of you: Do not come into my presence unless you bring Michal daughter of Saul when you come to see me."[q] 14 Then David sent messengers to Ish-Bosheth son of Saul, demanding, "Give me my wife Michal,[r] whom I betrothed to myself for the price of a hundred Philistine foreskins."

15 So Ish-Bosheth gave orders and had her taken away from her husband[s] Paltiel[t] son of Laish. 16 Her husband, however, went with her, weeping behind her all the way to Bahurim.[u] Then Abner said to him, "Go back home!" So he went back.

17 Abner conferred with the elders[v] of Israel and said, "For some time you have wanted to make David your king. 18 Now do it! For the LORD promised David, 'By my servant David I will rescue my people Israel from the hand of the Philistines[w] and from the hand of all their enemies.[x]' "

19 Abner also spoke to the Benjamites in person. Then he went to Hebron to tell David everything that Israel and the whole tribe of Benjamin[y] wanted to do. 20 When Abner, who had twenty men with him, came to David at Hebron, David prepared a feast[z] for him and his men. 21 Then Abner said to David, "Let me go at once and assemble all Israel for my lord the king, so that they may make a covenant[a] with you, and that you may rule over all that your heart desires."[b] So David sent Abner away, and he went in peace.

Joab Murders Abner

22 Just then David's men and Joab returned from a raid and brought with them a great deal of plunder. But Abner was no longer with David in Hebron, because David had sent him away, and he had gone in peace. 23 When Joab and all the soldiers

3:6 [k]S 1Sa 14:50 **3:7** [l]S Ge 22:24; 2Sa 16:21-22; S 1Ki 1:3 [m]2Sa 21:8-11 **3:8** [n]S 1Sa 17:43; 2Sa 9:8; 16:9; 2Ki 8:13 **3:9** [o]S 1Sa 15:28 **3:10** [p]S Jdg 20:1; 1Sa 25:28-31; 2Sa 24:2 **3:13** [q]S Ge 43:5 **3:14** [r]S 1Sa 18:27 **3:15** [s]Dt 24:1-4 [t]1Sa 25:44 **3:16** [u]2Sa 16:5; 17:18 **3:17** [v]S Jdg 11:11 **3:18** [w]S 1Sa 9:16 [x]2Sa 8:6 **3:19** [y]1Ch 12:2, 16,29 **3:20** [z]1Ch 12:39 **3:21** [a]2Sa 5:3 [b]1Ki 11:37

3:6—5:5 David's elevation to kingship over the rest of Israel (see note on 2:1—3:5).
3:7 *Rizpah.* See 21:8–11. *Why did you sleep with my father's concubine?* Ish-Bosheth suspects that Abner's act was part of a conspiracy to seize the kingship (cf. v. 6). Great significance was attached to taking the concubine of a former king (see notes on 12:8; 16:21; 1Ki 2:22).
3:8 *dog's head.* Cf. note on 9:8.
3:9 *May God deal with Abner, be it ever so severely.* A curse formula (see note on 1Sa 3:17). *what the LORD promised him on oath.* The knowledge of David's divine designation as successor to Saul had spread widely (see notes on 2:4; 1Sa 16:13; 25:28).
3:10 *transfer the kingdom.* Abner was the power behind the throne. *Dan to Beersheba.* See note on 1Sa 3:20.
3:12 *Whose land is it?* Possibly a rhetorical question that presumed that the land belonged either to Abner or to David. The former seems more likely from the following sentence. *Make an agreement with me.* Abner wants assurance that he will face no reprisals for his past loyalty to the house of Saul.
3:13 *Michal daughter of Saul.* Although Saul had given Michal to David (1Sa 18:27), he later gave her to another man after David fled from his court (1Sa 25:44). David probably sensed that in the minds of the northern elders, his reunion with Michal would strengthen his claim to the throne as a legitimate son-in-law of Saul.
3:14 *David sent messengers to Ish-Bosheth.* David wanted Michal returned as an open and official act of Ish-Bosheth himself, rather than as part of a subterfuge planned by Abner. David knew that Ish-Bosheth would not dare to defy Abner's wishes (see v. 11). *a hundred Philistine foreskins.* See 1Sa 18:25. Saul had required 100 Philistine foreskins; David presented him with 200 (1Sa 18:27).
3:16 *Bahurim.* Near the Mount of Olives.
3:17 *elders of Israel.* The collective leadership of the various tribes comprised an informal national ruling body (see notes on Ex 3:16; Joel 1:2; see also 1Sa 8:4; 2Sa 5:3; 1Ki 8:1,3; 20:7; 2Ki 10:1; 23:1). *you have wanted to make David your king.* Apparently Ish-Bosheth's support came mainly from the tribe of Benjamin (see 2:15 and note) and from Gilead east of the Jordan River (see 2:8; 1Sa 11:9–11; 31:11–13).
3:18 *the LORD promised David.* By this time Samuel's anointing of David must have become common knowledge (see 5:2). Abner probably interpreted the anointing as a promise from the Lord, since Samuel was the Lord's much-revered prophet.
3:19 *Abner also spoke to the Benjamites in person.* Because Saul and his family were from the tribe of Benjamin, Abner was careful to consult the Benjamites concerning the transfer of kingship to the tribe of Judah. Apparently they consented, but Abner was not above representing matters in a way that was favorable to his purpose.
3:21 *make a covenant with you.* See 5:3 and note.

vith him arrived, he was told that Abner
on of Ner had come to the king and that
he king had sent him away and that he
ad gone in peace.
[24]So Joab went to the king and said,
What have you done? Look, Abner came
o you. Why did you let him go? Now he
s gone! [25]You know Abner son of Ner;
ie came to deceive you and observe your
novements and find out everything you
re doing."
[26]Joab then left David and sent messen-
ers after Abner, and they brought him
ack from the cistern at Sirah. But David
lid not know it. [27]Now when Abner[c] re-
urned to Hebron, Joab took him aside
nto an inner chamber, as if to speak with
im privately. And there, to avenge the
lood of his brother Asahel, Joab stabbed
im[d] in the stomach, and he died.[e]
[28]Later, when David heard about this,
e said, "I and my kingdom are forev-
r innocent[f] before the LORD concerning
he blood of Abner son of Ner. [29]May his
lood[g] fall on the head of Joab and on his
vhole family![h] May Joab's family never be
vithout someone who has a running sore[i]
r leprosy[a] or who leans on a crutch or
vho falls by the sword or who lacks food."
[30](Joab and his brother Abishai mur-
lered Abner because he had killed their
rother Asahel in the battle at Gibeon.)
[31]Then David said to Joab and all the
eople with him, "Tear your clothes and
ut on sackcloth[j] and walk in mourning[k]
n front of Abner." King David himself
valked behind the bier. [32]They buried Aber in Hebron, and the king wept[l] aloud
t Abner's tomb. All the people wept also.
[33]The king sang this lament[m] for Abner:

"Should Abner have died as the
lawless die?
[34]Your hands were not bound,
your feet were not fettered.[n]
You fell as one falls before the wicked."

And all the people wept over him again.
[35]Then they all came and urged David
to eat something while it was still day;
but David took an oath, saying, "May God
deal with me, be it ever so severely,[o] if I
taste bread[p] or anything else before the
sun sets!"
[36]All the people took note and were
pleased; indeed, everything the king did
pleased them. [37]So on that day all the people there and all Israel knew that the king
had no part[q] in the murder of Abner son
of Ner.
[38]Then the king said to his men, "Do
you not realize that a commander and a
great man has fallen[r] in Israel this day?
[39]And today, though I am the anointed
king, I am weak, and these sons of Zeruiah[s] are too strong[t] for me.[u] May the LORD
repay[v] the evildoer according to his evil
deeds!"

Ish-Bosheth Murdered

4 When Ish-Bosheth son of Saul heard
that Abner[w] had died in Hebron,
he lost courage, and all Israel became
alarmed. [2]Now Saul's son had two men
who were leaders of raiding bands. One
was named Baanah and the other Rekab;
they were sons of Rimmon the Beerothite
from the tribe of Benjamin—Beeroth[x] is
considered part of Benjamin, [3]because the
people of Beeroth fled to Gittaim[y] and have
resided there as foreigners to this day.
[4](Jonathan[z] son of Saul had a son who
was lame in both feet. He was five years old
when the news[a] about Saul and Jonathan

3:27 [c]2Sa 2:8; 4:1; 1Ki 2:5,32 [d]S Ex 21:14; S Jdg 3:21; S 2Sa 2:23 [e]2Sa 2:22 **3:28** [f]ver 37; Dt 21:9 **3:29** [g]S Lev 20:9 [h]1Ki 2:31-33 [i]S Lev 15:2 **3:31** [j]Ps 30:11; 35:13; 69:11; Isa 20:2 [k]S Ge 37:34 **3:32** [l]S Nu 14:1; Pr 24:17 **3:33** [m]S Ge 50:10
3:34 [n]Job 36:8; Ps 2:3; 149:8; Isa 45:14; Na 3:10 **3:35** [o]S Ru 1:17 [p]S 1Sa 31:13; 2Sa 12:17; Jer 16:7 **3:37** [q]S ver 28 **3:38** [r]2Sa 1:19 **3:39** [s]S 2Sa 2:18 [t]2Sa 16:9; 18:11 [u]S Jdg 18:26 [v]1Ki 2:32; Ps 41:10; 101:8 **4:1** [w]S 2Sa 3:27 **4:2** [x]S Jos 9:17 **4:3** [y]Ne 11:33 **4:4** [z]S 1Sa 18:1 [a]S 1Sa 31:9

[a] 29 The Hebrew for *leprosy* was used for various diseases affecting the skin.

:25 *he came to deceive you.* Joab despised Abner for killing is brother (2:18,23; 3:27) and sought to discredit him in Daid's eyes as a mere opportunist. Perhaps he also sensed that is own position of leadership would be threatened if Abner oined forces with David, since Abner was obviously a power mong the northern tribes.

3:27 *inner chamber ... privately.* City gateways often had small side chambers. *Joab stabbed him in the stomch, and he died.* Joab's murder of Abner is not to be excused ither as an act of war or as justifiable blood revenge (cf. Nu 5:12; Dt 19:11–13). Asahel had been killed by Abner in the ourse of battle (see v. 30; see also 2:21,23 and notes).

3:29 *May his blood fall on the head of Joab and on his whole family!* After disclaiming any personal or official ıvolvement in the plot to assassinate Abner (v. 28), David ursed Joab and thereby called on God to judge his wicked ct. In this crucial hour when David's relationship to the orthern tribes hung in the balance, he appears not to have elt sufficiently secure in his own position to bring Joab pubcly to justice (see v. 39). The crime went unpunished until arly in the reign of Solomon (1Ki 2:5–6, 29–34).

3:31 *Joab.* He too was compelled to join the mourners. It may be that Joab's involvement was not widely known and that David hoped to keep the matter secret for the time being.

3:32 *Hebron.* David's royal city at the time. *the king wept aloud at Abner's tomb.* Because Abner's murder had the potential of destroying the union of the nation under David's rule, David did everything possible to demonstrate his innocence to the people. In this he was successful (see vv. 36–37).

3:33–34 For another lament sung by David over fallen leaders, see 1:19–27.

3:35 *urged David to eat ... but.* See 1:12; see also 1Sa 31:13 and note. *May God deal with me, be it ever so severely.* A curse formula (see note on 1Sa 3:17).

3:39 *May the LORD repay the evildoer.* See note on v. 29.

4:1 *he lost courage.* Ish-Bosheth was very much aware of his dependence on Abner (see note on 2:8). *all Israel became alarmed.* Civil strife threatened, and the northern tribes were now without a strong leader.

4:2 *Beeroth.* One of the Gibeonite cities (Jos 9:17) assigned to Benjamin (Jos 18:21,25).

4:4 *Jonathan son of Saul had a son who was lame in both feet.*

came from Jezreel. His nurse picked him
up and fled, but as she hurried to leave, he
fell and became disabled.[b] His name was
Mephibosheth.)[c]
5 Now Rekab and Baanah, the sons of
Rimmon the Beerothite, set out for the
house of Ish-Bosheth,[d] and they arrived
there in the heat of the day while he was
taking his noonday rest.[e] 6 They went into
the inner part of the house as if to get
some wheat, and they stabbed[f] him in the
stomach. Then Rekab and his brother Baanah slipped away.
7 They had gone into the house while
he was lying on the bed in his bedroom.
After they stabbed and killed him, they
cut off his head. Taking it with them,
they traveled all night by way of the Arabah.[g] 8 They brought the head[h] of Ish-Bosheth to David at Hebron and said to the
king, "Here is the head of Ish-Bosheth
son of Saul,[i] your enemy, who tried to
kill you. This day the LORD has avenged[j]
my lord the king against Saul and his offspring."
9 David answered Rekab and his brother Baanah, the sons of Rimmon the Beerothite, "As surely as the LORD lives, who
has delivered[k] me out of every trouble,
10 when someone told me, 'Saul is dead,'
and thought he was bringing good news, I
seized him and put him to death in Ziklag.[l]
That was the reward I gave him for his
news! 11 How much more—when wicke
men have killed an innocent man in hi
own house and on his own bed—shoul
I not now demand his blood[m] from you
hand and rid the earth of you!"
12 So David gave an order to his men
and they killed them.[n] They cut off thei
hands and feet and hung the bodies by th
pool in Hebron. But they took the head c
Ish-Bosheth and buried it in Abner's tom
at Hebron.

David Becomes King Over Israel

5:1-3pp — 1Ch 11:1-3

5 All the tribes of Israel[o] came to Davi
at Hebron and said, "We are your ow
flesh and blood.[p] 2 In the past, while Sau
was king over us, you were the one wh
led Israel on their military campaigns.
And the LORD said[r] to you, 'You will shep
herd[s] my people Israel, and you will be
come their ruler.[t]'"
3 When all the elders of Israel had com
to King David at Hebron, the king mad
a covenant[u] with them at Hebron befor
the LORD, and they anointed[v] David kin
over Israel.
4 David was thirty years old[w] when h
became king, and he reigned[x] forty[y] years
5 In Hebron he reigned over Judah seve
years and six months,[z] and in Jerusaler
he reigned over all Israel and Judah thirty
three years.

4:4 [b] S Lev 21:18 [c] 2Sa 9:8, 12; 16:1-4; 19:24; 21:7-8; 1Ch 8:34; 9:40 **4:5** [d] S 2Sa 2:8 [e] Ru 2:7 **4:6** [f] S 2Sa 2:23 **4:7** [g] S Dt 3:17 **4:8** [h] 2Sa 20:21; 2Ki 10:7 [i] 1Sa 24:4; 25:29 [j] S Nu 31:3 **4:9** [k] S Ge 48:16; 1Ki 1:29 **4:10** [l] 2Sa 1:2-16 **4:11** [m] S Ge 4:10; 9:5; Ps 9:12; 72:14 **4:12** [n] 2Sa 1:15 **5:1** [o] 2Sa 19:43 [p] S Ge 29:14; 35:26 **5:2** [q] 1Sa 18:5, 13,16 [r] S 1Sa 11:6 [s] S Ge 48:15; S 1Sa 16:1; 2Sa 7:7; Mt 2:6; Jn 21:16 [t] S 1Sa 12:12; S 13:14; S 2Sa 6:21 **5:3** [u] 2Sa 3:21 [v] S Dt 17:15; 2Sa 2:4 **5:4** [w] S Ge 37:2; Lk 3:23 [x] 1Ki 2:11; 1Ch 3:4 [y] 1Ch 26:31 **5:5** [z] 2Sa 2:11; 1Ki 2:11; 1Ch 3:4

The writer emphasizes that with the death of Ish-Bosheth (see v. 6) there was no other viable claimant to the throne from the house of Saul. *news about Saul and Jonathan.* See 1:4; 1Sa 31:2-6. *Mephibosheth.* See 9:1-13; 16:1-4; 19:24-30; 21:7. The name was originally Merib-Baal (apparently meaning "opponent of Baal"; see 1Ch 8:34), perhaps to be spelled "Meri-Baal" (meaning "loved by Baal"), but was changed by the author of Samuel to Mephibosheth (meaning "from the mouth of the shameful thing"). See note on 2:8.

4:6 *stabbed him in the stomach.* See 2:23 and note.

4:7 *cut off his head.* See 1Sa 5:4 and note. *Arabah.* See note on Dt 1:1.

4:8 *This day the LORD has avenged my lord the king against Saul.* Rekab and Baanah depict their assassination of Ish-Bosheth in pious terms, expecting David to commend them for their act—a serious miscalculation.

4:9 *As surely as the LORD lives.* An oath formula (see note on 1Sa 14:39,45).

4:11 *demand his blood from your hand.* A call for the death penalty (see Ge 9:5-6). David here does what he was unable to do with Joab (see note on 3:29).

4:12 *their hands and feet.* The hands that had assassinated Ish-Bosheth and the feet that had run with the news (cf. note on 1Sa 5:4).

5:1—24:25 Beginning with ch. 5 there are sections of 2 Samuel (see also 3:2-5) that have parallel passages in 1 Chronicles (they are listed at the sectional headings). In some instances these parallel accounts are nearly identical; in others there are variations.

5:1 *All the tribes of Israel.* Representatives of each tribe, including elders and armed soldiers (see 1Ch 12:23-40). *your own flesh and blood.* The representatives of the various tribes cite three reasons for recognizing David as their king. Th first of these is the acknowledgment that David is an Israelit Even though national unity had been destroyed in the civ strife following Saul's death (2:8—3:1), this blood relatior ship had not been forgotten.

5:2 *the one who led Israel on their military campaign* The second reason (see note on v. 1) for recognizin David as king (see 1Sa 18:5,13-14,16,30). *the LORD said t you.* The third and most important reason (see 1Sa 13:13-1 16:1,13; 23:17; 25:26-31). *shepherd ... ruler.* "Shepherd" wa often used as a metaphor for political rule in the OT (see P 23:1; Jer 2:8; Eze 34:2 and notes) and elsewhere in the ancier Near East (see, e.g., the prologue to Hammurapi's Code—se chart, p. xxii). See also note on 1Sa 12:2 ("your leader").

5:3 *the king made a covenant with them ... before the LOR* David and Israel entered into a covenant in which both th king and the people obligated themselves before the Lor to carry out their mutual responsibilities (see 2Ki 11:17 an note). Thus, while David was king over Judah as the one ele vated to that position by his tribe and later became king ove Jerusalem by conquest (vv. 6-10), his rule over the norther tribes was by virtue of a treaty (covenant) of submission. Tha treaty was not renewed with David's grandson Rehoboar because he refused to negotiate its terms at the time of hi accession to the throne (1Ki 12:1-16). *they anointed Davi king over Israel.* The third time David was anointed (see not on 2:4; cf. 1Sa 9:1—11:15 and note).

5:5 *In Hebron he reigned ... seven years and six months.* Se 2:11. *Israel and Judah.* The specific relationship of David t these two segments of his realm appears to have remaine distinct (see note on v. 3).

David Conquers Jerusalem

5:6-10pp — 1Ch 11:4-9
5:11-16pp — 1Ch 3:5-9; 14:1-7

6The king and his men marched to Jerusalem[a] to attack the Jebusites,[b] who lived
there. The Jebusites said to David, "You
will not get in here; even the blind and
the lame can ward you off." They thought,
"David cannot get in here." 7Nevertheless,
David captured the fortress of Zion[c]—
which is the City of David.[d]
8On that day David had said, "Anyone

5:6 [a] S Jdg 1:8 [b] S Jos 15:8
5:7 [c] Ps 76:2 [d] 2Sa 6:12, 16; 1Ki 2:10; 8:1; Isa 29:1; Jer 21:13; 25:29

5:6 — 8:18 David's reign characterized: his victories over Israel's enemies, his devotion to the Lord and the Lord's covenant with him to give him an enduring dynasty (cf. the corresponding segment of Saul's story in which his reign is characterized; see note on 1Sa 13:1 — 14:52).
5:6 - 25 Accounts of David's initial victories (over the Jebusites in Jerusalem and over the Philistines) and his later victories by which he secured all of Israel's borders (ch. 8) frame the accounts of David's devotion to the Lord (ch. 6) and the Lord's covenant with him (ch. 7).
5:6 *Jerusalem.* One of the most significant accomplishments of David's reign was the establishment of Jerusalem as his royal city and the nation's capital (see Introduction: Contents and Theme). The site was first occupied in the third millennium BC and was a royal city in the time of Abraham (see note on Ge 14:18). It was located on the border between Judah and Benjamin but was controlled by neither tribe. At the time of the conquest both Judah and Benjamin had attacked the city (see notes on Jdg 1:8,21), but it was quickly lost again to the Jebusites (see Jos 15:63 and note) and was sometimes referred to by the name Jebus (see Jdg 19:10; 1Ch 11:4). The city David conquered covered somewhat less than 11 acres and could have housed not many more than 3,500 inhabitants. By locating his royal city in a newly conquered town on the border between the two segments of his realm, David united the kingdom under his rule without seeming to subordinate one part to the other. *Jebusites.* A Canaanite people (see Ge 10:15 - 16 and note on 10:16) inhabiting Jerusalem (Jos 15:8; 18:16). *the blind and the lame can ward you off.* Jerusalem was a natural fortress because of its location on a rise surrounded on three sides by deep valleys; so the Jebusites were confident that their walls could easily be defended.
5:7 *fortress.* Probably the fortified city itself. *Zion.* The first occurrence of the name in the OT. Originally the name appears to have been given to the southernmost hill of the city on which the Jebusite fortress was located. As the city expanded (from the days of Solomon onward), the name continued to be applied to the entire city (see Isa 1:8 and note; 2:3). *City of David.* As Jerusalem's conqueror, David becomes its owner and gives it his name. Jerusalem's southeast hill (Ophel; see note on Ne 3:26) continued to bear the name long after David's time (see Ne 3:15 and note; Isa 22:19; cf. also Isa 29:1).
5:8 *On that day David had said.* 1Ch 11:6 may be combined with this verse for a more complete account.

THE CITY OF THE JEBUSITES/DAVID'S JERUSALEM

Substantial historical evidence, both Biblical and extra-Biblical, places the temple of Solomon on the holy spot where King David built an altar to the Lord. David had purchased the land from Araunah the Jebusite, who was using the exposed bedrock as a threshing floor (2Sa 24:18–25). Tradition claims a much older sanctity for the site, associating it with the altar of Abraham on Mount Moriah (Ge 22:1–19; see 2Ch 3:1 and note). The writer of Genesis equates Moriah with "the mountain of the Lord" (Ge 22:14; see note there).

c. 1000 BC

Less than 11 acres in size, Jebus, a Canaanite city, could well defend itself against attack, with walls atop steep canyons and shafts reaching an underground water source. David captured the stronghold c. 1000 BC and made it his capital.

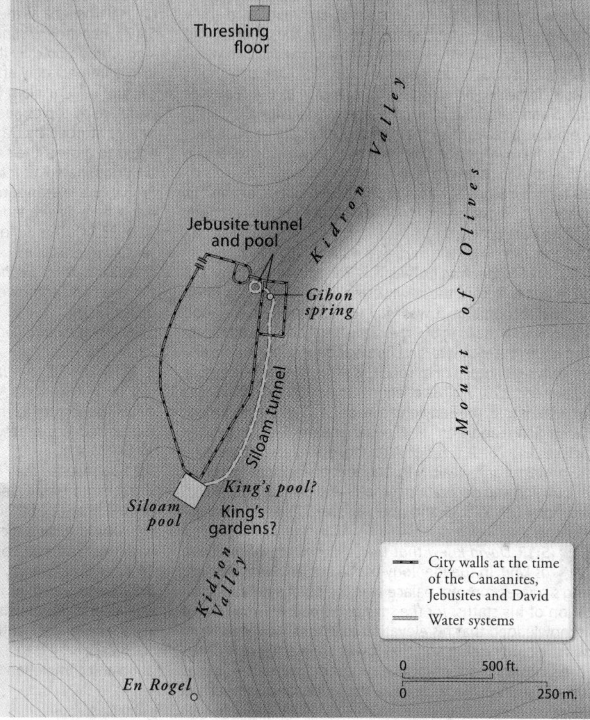

who conquers the Jebusites will have to
use the water shaft[e] to reach those 'lame
and blind'[f] who are David's enemies.[a]"
That is why they say, "The 'blind and
lame' will not enter the palace."
9David then took up residence in the
fortress and called it the City of David.
He built up the area around it, from the
terraces[b][g] inward. 10And he became more
and more powerful,[h] because the LORD
God Almighty[i] was with him.[j]
11Now Hiram[k] king of Tyre sent envoys
to David, along with cedar logs and carpenters and stonemasons, and they built a
palace for David. 12Then David knew that
the LORD had established him as king over
Israel and had exalted his kingdom[l] for the
sake of his people Israel.
13After he left Hebron, David took more
concubines and wives[m] in Jerusalem, and
more sons and daughters were born to
him. 14These are the names of the children born to him there:[n] Shammua, Shobab, Nathan,[o] Solomon, 15Ibhar, Elishua,
Nepheg, Japhia, 16Elishama, Eliada and
Eliphelet.

5:8 [e] 2Ki 20:20; 2Ch 32:30 [f] Mt 21:14
5:9 [g] 1Ki 9:15, 24
5:10 [h] 2Sa 3:1 [i] Ps 24:10 [j] 2Sa 7:9
5:11 [k] 1Ki 5:1, 18; 2Ch 2:3
5:12 [l] S Nu 24:7
5:13 [m] S Dt 17:17
5:14 [n] 1Ch 3:5 [o] Lk 3:31
5:17 [p] 2Sa 23:14; 1Ch 11:16
5:18 [q] S Jos 15:8; S 17:15
5:19 [r] S Jdg 18:5; S 1Sa 23:2
5:20 [s] S Ge 38:29
5:21 [t] Dt 7:5; Isa 46:2

David Defeats the Philistines

5:17-25pp — 1Ch 14:8-17

17When the Philistines heard that David
had been anointed king over Israel, they
went up in full force to search for him, but
David heard about it and went down to
the stronghold.[p] 18Now the Philistines had
come and spread out in the Valley of Rephaim;[q] 19so David inquired[r] of the LORD,
"Shall I go and attack the Philistines? Will
you deliver them into my hands?"
The LORD answered him, "Go, for I will
surely deliver the Philistines into your
hands."
20So David went to Baal Perazim, and
there he defeated them. He said, "As waters break out, the LORD has broken out
against my enemies before me." So that
place was called Baal Perazim.[c][s] 21The Philistines abandoned their idols there, and
David and his men carried them off.[t]
22Once more the Philistines came up
and spread out in the Valley of Rephaim;
23so David inquired of the LORD, and he

[a] 8 Or *are hated by David* [b] 9 Or *the Millo*
[c] 20 *Baal Perazim* means *the lord who breaks out.*

Joab's part in the conquest of the city demonstrated again his military prowess and reconfirmed him in the position of commander of David's armies. *water shaft.* Although the Hebrew for this term is obscure, it appears that David knew of a secret tunnel — perhaps running from the Gihon spring outside the city into the fortress — that gave access to water when the city was under siege (see 2Ch 32:30; see also photo, p. 458). *lame and blind.* An ironic reference to the Jebusites (cf. v. 6 and note). *The 'blind and lame' will not enter the palace.* The proverb may mean that the Jebusites did not have access to the royal palace, though they were allowed to remain in the city and its environs.

5:9 *terraces.* Stone terraces on the steep slopes of the hill, creating additional space for buildings (but see NIV text note; see also note on Jdg 9:6).

5:10 *the LORD ... was with him.* See note on 1Sa 16:18.

5:11 *Hiram king of Tyre.* This Phoenician king was the first to accord the newly established King David international recognition. It was vital to him that he have good relations with the king of Israel since Israel dominated the inland trade routes to Tyre, and Tyre was dependent on Israelite agriculture for much of its food (also true in the first century AD; see Ac 12:20). A close relationship existed between these two realms until the Babylonian invasions. *Tyre.* An important Phoenician seaport on the Mediterranean coast north of Israel (see Eze 26 – 27). *cedar.* A strong, durable wood used by the powerful and wealthy throughout the ancient Near East for building and decorating temples and palaces (see 1Ki 5:6 and note; 6:9; SS 5:15 and note; 8:9; Jer 22:14 – 15; Hag 1:4 and note).

5:12 *David knew that the LORD had established him as king.* In the ideology of the ancient Near East the king's possession of a palace was the chief symbolic indication of his status. *for the sake of his people Israel.* David acknowledged that his elevation to kingship over all Israel was the Lord's doing and that it was an integral part of the Lord's continuing redemptive program for Israel — just as the ministries of Moses, Joshua, the judges and Samuel had been.

5:13 *David took more concubines and wives.* See notes on 3:2 – 5; Ge 25:6.

5:14 *Shammua, Shobab, Nathan, Solomon.* 1Ch 3:5 designates Bathsheba as their mother.

5:17 *When the Philistines heard that David had been anointed king.* Chronologically it is likely that the Philistine attack followed immediately after the events of v. 3 and before the capture of Jerusalem (vv. 6 – 10). (The author arranged his narrative by topics; see note on 7:1.) The Philistines had not been disturbed by David's reign over Judah, but now they acted to protect their interests in the north, much of which they dominated after the defeat of Saul (1Sa 31). *stronghold.* Probably a reference to the wilderness area in southern Judah where David had hidden from Saul (see notes on 1Sa 22:4; 23:14). This action of David suggests that he had not yet taken Jerusalem.

5:18,22 *Valley of Rephaim.* Bordering ancient Jerusalem on the west and southwest (see Jos 15:8; 18:16; see also note on Isa 17:5).

5:19 *David inquired of the LORD.* See notes on 2:1; 1Sa 2:28; 22:20; 23:2.

5:20 *the LORD has broken out ... Baal Perazim.* See NIV text note. As a true theocratic king, David attributes the victory to the Lord and does not claim the glory for himself (see notes on 1Sa 10:18,27; 11:13; 12:11; 14:23; 17:11,45 – 47).

5:21 *abandoned their idols there.* As the Israelites had taken the ark into battle (see note on 1Sa 4:3), so the Philistines carried images of their deities into battle in the hope that this would ensure victory. *carried them off.* In compliance with the instruction of Dt 7:5, they also burned them (1Ch 14:12).

5:23 *he answered.* As had been true in the case of the conquest under Joshua, the Lord ordered the battle and he himself marched against the enemy with his heavenly host (see Jos 6:2 – 5; 8:1 – 2; 10:8,14; 11:6). David's wars were a continuation and completion of the wars fought by Joshua.

answered, "Do not go straight up, but circle around behind them and attack them
in front of the poplar trees. 24 As soon as
you hear the sound[u] of marching in the
tops of the poplar trees, move quickly, because that will mean the LORD has gone
out in front[v] of you to strike the Philistine
army." 25 So David did as the LORD commanded him, and he struck down the
Philistines[w] all the way from Gibeon[a x] to
Gezer.[y]

The Ark Brought to Jerusalem

6:1-11pp — 1Ch 13:1-14
6:12-19pp — 1Ch 15:25–16:3

6 David again brought together all the
able young men of Israel — thirty
thousand. 2 He and all his men went to
Baalah[b z] in Judah to bring up from there
the ark[a] of God, which is called by the
Name,[c b] the name of the LORD Almighty,
who is enthroned[c] between the cherubim[d]
on the ark. 3 They set the ark of God on a
new cart[e] and brought it from the house of
Abinadab, which was on the hill.[f] Uzzah
and Ahio, sons of Abinadab, were guiding
the new cart 4 with the ark of God on it,[d]
and Ahio was walking in front of it. 5 David and all Israel were celebrating[g] with
all their might before the LORD, with castanets,[e] harps, lyres, timbrels, sistrums and
cymbals.[h]
6 When they came to the threshing
floor of Nakon, Uzzah reached out and
took hold of[i] the ark of God, because the
oxen stumbled. 7 The LORD's anger burned
against Uzzah because of his irreverent
act;[j] therefore God struck him down,[k] and
he died there beside the ark of God.
8 Then David was angry because the
LORD's wrath[l] had broken out against Uzzah, and to this day that place is called
Perez Uzzah.[f m]
9 David was afraid of the LORD that day
and said, "How[n] can the ark of the LORD
ever come to me?" 10 He was not willing
to take the ark of the LORD to be with him
in the City of David. Instead, he took it to
the house of Obed-Edom[o] the Gittite. 11 The
ark of the LORD remained in the house of
Obed-Edom the Gittite for three months,
and the LORD blessed him and his entire
household.[p]
12 Now King David[q] was told, "The LORD
has blessed the household of Obed-Edom
and everything he has, because of the ark
of God." So David went to bring up the ark
of God from the house of Obed-Edom to
the City of David with rejoicing. 13 When
those who were carrying the ark of the

5:24 [u] S Ex 14:24 [v] Jdg 4:14 **5:25** [w] 2Sa 8:12; 21:15 [x] Isa 28:21 [y] S Jos 10:33 **6:2** [z] S Jos 15:9 [a] 1Sa 4:4; 7:1 [b] Lev 24:16; Dt 28:10; Isa 63:14 [c] Ps 99:1; 132:14 [d] S Ge 3:24; S Ex 25:22 **6:3** [e] ver 7; Nu 7:4-9; S 1Sa 6:7 [f] 2Sa 7:1 **6:5** [g] S Ex 15:20 [h] Ezr 3:10; Ne 12:27; Ps 150:5 **6:6** [i] S Nu 4:15, 19-20 **6:7** [j] 1Ch 15:13-15 [k] S Ex 19:22; S 1Sa 5:6; 6:19; S 25:38 **6:8** [l] Ps 7:11 [m] S Ge 38:29 **6:9** [n] S 1Sa 6:20 **6:10** [o] 1Ch 15:18; 26:4-5 **6:11** [p] S Ge 30:27; 39:5 **6:12** [q] 1Ki 8:1

[a] 25 Septuagint (see also 1 Chron. 14:16); Hebrew *Geba* [b] 2 That is, Kiriath Jearim (see 1 Chron. 13:6) [c] 2 Hebrew; Septuagint and Vulgate do not have *the Name.* [d] 3,4 Dead Sea Scrolls and some Septuagint manuscripts; Masoretic Text *cart* [4]*and they brought it with the ark of God from the house of Abinadab, which was on the hill* [e] 5 Masoretic Text; Dead Sea Scrolls and Septuagint (see also 1 Chron. 13:8) *songs* [f] 8 *Perez Uzzah* means *outbreak against Uzzah.*

5:24 *sound of marching.* The Lord's army of angels marching into battle.
5:25 *Gibeon.* See notes on 2:12–13; Jos 9:3. *Gezer.* Fifteen miles west of Gibeon, overlooking the Philistine plain (see note on Jos 10:33).
6:1–23 The supreme expression of David's devotion to the Lord.
6:2 *Baalah in Judah.* See NIV text note; see also Jos 15:60; 18:14; 1Sa 7:1. *ark of God.* See Ex 25:10–22; see also notes on 1Sa 4:3–4,21. The ark had remained at Kiriath Jearim during the reign of Saul. *called by the Name.* Used elsewhere to designate ownership (see 12:28; Dt 28:10; Isa 4:1; 63:19). *LORD Almighty.* See note on 1Sa 1:3. *enthroned between the cherubim.* See note on 1Sa 4:4; see also 1Ch 28:2 ("footstool of our God"). David recognized the great significance of the ark as the footstool of God's earthly throne. As a true theocratic king, he wished to acknowledge the Lord's kingship and rule over both himself and the people by restoring the ark to a place of prominence in the nation.
6:3 *new cart.* David follows the example of the Philistines (see 1Sa 6:7) rather than the instructions of Ex 25:12–15; Nu 4:5–6, 15, which require that the ark be carried on the shoulders of the Levites (see 1Ch 15:13–15). *from the house of Abinadab.* See 1Sa 7:1. *Uzzah and Ahio, sons of Abinadab.* 1Sa 7:1 speaks of Eleazar as the son of Abinadab. The Hebrew word for "son" can have the broader meaning of "descendant."
6:5 *sistrums.* Percussion instruments played by shaking with the hand.
6:7 *his irreverent act.* Although Uzzah's intent may have been good, he violated the clear instructions the Lord had given for handling the ark (see notes on v. 3; 1Sa 6:19). At this important new beginning in Israel's life with the Lord, he gives a shocking and vivid reminder to David and Israel that those who claim to serve him must acknowledge his rule with absolute seriousness (see Lev 10:1–3; Jos 7:24–25; 24:19–20; Ac 5:1–11 — all are instances of stern divine judgments at the beginning of new eras in the history of redemption).
6:8 *David was angry.* David's initial reaction was resentment that his attempt to honor the Lord had resulted in a display of God's wrath. *to this day.* Until the time of the writing of 2 Samuel. *Perez Uzzah.* See NIV text note. The place-name memorialized a divine warning that was not soon forgotten (see Jos 7:26 and NIV text note). Evenhanded in his judgment against sinners, the Lord plays no favorites as he "breaks out" against friend and foe alike (see 5:20 and note).
6:9 *David was afraid of the LORD.* David's anger was accompanied by fear — not the wholesome fear of proper honor and respect for the Lord (see 1Sa 12:24; Jos 24:14; see also notes on Ge 20:11; Pr 1:7) but an anxiety arising from an acute sense of his own guilt (Ge 3:10; Dt 5:5).
6:10 *Gittite.* He appears to have been a Levite (see note on 1Ch 13:13; cf. 1Ch 15:18,24; 16:5; 26:4–8,15; 2Ch 25:24), though many think the term "Gittite" fixes his place of birth at the Philistine city of Gath (see 15:18 and note). However, Gittite may be a reference to the Levitical city Gath Rimmon in Dan or Manasseh (Jos 21:20–25).
6:12 *David went to bring up the ark.* God's blessing on the household of Obed-Edom showed David that God's anger had been appeased.
6:13 *those . . . carrying the ark.* David had become aware of his previous error (1Ch 15:13–15).

LORD had taken six steps, he sacrificed[r] a
bull and a fattened calf. 14 Wearing a lin-
en ephod,[s] David was dancing[t] before the
LORD with all his might, 15 while he and all
Israel were bringing up the ark of the LORD
with shouts[u] and the sound of trumpets.[v]
16 As the ark of the LORD was entering
the City of David,[w] Michal[x] daughter of
Saul watched from a window. And when
she saw King David leaping and dancing
before the LORD, she despised him in her
heart.
17 They brought the ark of the LORD and
set it in its place inside the tent that David
had pitched for it,[y] and David sacrificed
burnt offerings[z] and fellowship offerings
before the LORD. 18 After he had finished
sacrificing[a] the burnt offerings and fellowship offerings, he blessed[b] the people in
the name of the LORD Almighty. 19 Then
he gave a loaf of bread, a cake of dates
and a cake of raisins[c] to each person in
the whole crowd of Israelites, both men
and women.[d] And all the people went to
their homes.
20 When David returned home to bless
his household, Michal daughter of Saul
came out to meet him and said, "How the
king of Israel has distinguished himself today, going around half-naked[e] in full view
of the slave girls of his servants as any
vulgar fellow would!"
21 David said to Michal, "It was before
the LORD, who chose me rather than your
father or anyone from his house when
he appointed[f] me ruler[g] over the LORD's
people Israel—I will celebrate before the
LORD. 22 I will become even more undigni-
fied than this, and I will be humiliated in
my own eyes. But by these slave girls you
spoke of, I will be held in honor."
23 And Michal daughter of Saul had no
children to the day of her death.

God's Promise to David

7:1-17pp — 1Ch 17:1-15

7 After the king was settled in his palace[h] and the LORD had given him rest
from all his enemies[i] around him,[j] 2 he said
to Nathan[k] the prophet, "Here I am, living
in a house[l] of cedar, while the ark of God
remains in a tent."[m]
3 Nathan replied to the king, "Whatever
you have in mind,[n] go ahead and do it, for
the LORD is with you."
4 But that night the word of the LORD
came to Nathan, saying:

5 "Go and tell my servant David,
'This is what the LORD says: Are you[o]
the one to build me a house to dwell
in?[p] 6 I have not dwelt in a house
from the day I brought the Israelites
up out of Egypt to this day.[q] I have
been moving from place to place with
a tent[r] as my dwelling.[s] 7 Wherever I
have moved with all the Israelites,[t]
did I ever say to any of their rulers
whom I commanded to shepherd[u]
my people Israel, "Why have you not
built me a house[v] of cedar?[w]"'
8 "Now then, tell my servant David, 'This is what the LORD Almighty

6:13 [r] 1Ki 8:5, 62; Ezr 6:17 **6:14** [s] Ex 19:6; S 1Sa 2:18 [t] S Ex 15:20 **6:15** [u] S Jos 6:5 [v] Ps 47:5; 98:6 **6:16** [w] S 2Sa 5:7 [x] S 1Sa 18:27 **6:17** [y] 1Ki 8:6; 1Ch 15:1; 2Ch 1:4 [z] Lev 1:1-17; 1Ki 8:62-64 **6:18** [a] 1Ki 8:22 [b] S Ex 39:43 **6:19** [c] Hos 3:1 [d] Dt 26:13; Ne 8:10 **6:20** [e] S 1Sa 19:24 **6:21** [f] 1Sa 13:14; S 15:28 [g] 2Sa 5:2; 7:8; 1Ch 5:2; 17:7; Mic 5:2

7:1 [h] 2Sa 6:3 [i] ver 11 [j] 1Ch 22:18 **7:2** [k] 2Sa 12:1; 1Ki 1:8, 22; 1Ch 29:29; 2Ch 9:29 [l] 2Sa 5:11; 1Ki 3:1; 7:1, 2, 7; 9:1; 2Ch 8:1; Jer 22:14; Hag 1:4 [m] S Ex 26:1; Ps 132:3; Ac 7:45-46 **7:3** [n] S 1Sa 10:7; Ps 132:1-5 **7:5** [o] 1Ki 8:19; 1Ch 22:8 [p] 1Ki 5:3-5; 1Ch 28:3 **7:6** [q] Ac 7:45 [r] Ex 40:18, 34; Jos 18:1 [s] 1Ki 8:16 **7:7** [t] Dt 23:14 [u] S 2Sa 5:2 [v] 1Ki 8:27; Isa 66:1 [w] Lev 26:11-12

6:14 *linen ephod.* See note on 1Sa 2:18.

6:16 *she despised him.* Michal had no appreciation for the significance of the event and deeply resented David's public display as unworthy of the dignity of a king (see vv. 20–23).

6:17 *burnt offerings.* See note on Lev 1:3. *fellowship offerings.* See notes on Lev 3:1; 1Sa 11:15.

6:18 *he blessed the people.* As Solomon would later do at the dedication of the temple (1Ki 8:55–61). *LORD Almighty.* See note on 1Sa 1:3.

6:21 *ruler.* See note on 1Sa 9:16.

6:23 *Michal... had no children.* Probably a punishment for her pride and at the same time another manifestation of God's judgment on the house of Saul.

7:1–29 God's great promise to David (see Introduction: Contents and Theme). Although it is not expressly called a covenant here, it is elsewhere (see 23:5 and note; Ps 89:3,28,34,39 and note on 89:30–37; cf. Ps 132:11 and note), and David responds with language suggesting his recognition that a covenant had been made (see also notes on vv. 11,16,20,28).

7:1 *After the king was settled in his palace.* See 5:11; see also note on 5:12. *the LORD had given him rest from all his enemies.* Chronologically the victories noted in 8:1–14 probably preceded the events of this chapter. The arrangement of material is topical (see notes on 5:17; 8:1)—ch. 6 records the bringing of the ark to Jerusalem; ch. 7 tells of David's desire to build a temple in Jerusalem in which to house the ark.

7:2 *Nathan.* The first reference to this prophet. *cedar.* See note on 5:11. *tent.* See v. 6; 6:17. Now that he himself had a royal palace (symbolic of his established kingship), a tent did not seem to David to be an appropriate place for the throne of Israel's divine King (see note on 6:2; see also Ps 132:2–5; Ac 7:46). He wanted to build Israel's heavenly King a royal house in the capital city of his kingdom.

7:3 *Nathan replied.* In consulting a prophet, David sought God's will, but Nathan boldly voiced approval of David's plans in the Lord's name before he had received a revelation from the Lord. *the LORD is with you.* See v. 9; see also note on 1Sa 16:18.

7:5–16 The Davidic covenant (see note on v. 11).

7:5 *Are you the one . . . ?* David's desire was commendable (1Ki 8:18–19), but his gift and mission were to fight the Lord's battles until Israel was securely at rest in the promised land (see v. 10; 1Ki 5:3; 1Ch 22:8–9 and note).

7:7 *did I ever say . . . "Why have you not built me a house . . . ?"* David misunderstood the Lord's priorities. He reflected the pagan notion that the gods were interested in human beings only as builders and maintainers of their temples and as practitioners of their religion. Instead, the Lord had raised up rulers in Israel only to shepherd his people (that is also why he had brought David "from the pasture," v. 8).

says: I took you from the pasture,
from tending the flock,[x] and appointed you ruler[y] over my people Israel.[z]
9 I have been with you wherever you
have gone,[a] and I have cut off all your
enemies from before you.[b] Now I will
make your name great, like the names
of the greatest men on earth.[c] 10 And I
will provide a place for my people Israel and will plant[d] them so that they
can have a home of their own and no
longer be disturbed.[e] Wicked[f] people
will not oppress them anymore,[g] as
they did at the beginning 11 and have
done ever since the time I appointed leaders[a][h] over my people Israel. I
will also give you rest from all your
enemies.[i]

" 'The LORD declares[j] to you that
the LORD himself will establish[k] a
house[l] for you: 12 When your days
are over and you rest[m] with your ancestors, I will raise up your offspring
to succeed you, your own flesh and
blood,[n] and I will establish his kingdom.[o] 13 He is the one who will build
a house[p] for my Name,[q] and I will establish the throne of his kingdom forever.[r] 14 I will be his father, and he will
be my son.[s] When he does wrong, I
will punish him[t] with a rod[u] wielded by men, with floggings inflicted
by human hands. 15 But my love will
never be taken away from him,[v] as I
took it away from Saul,[w] whom I removed from before you. 16 Your house
and your kingdom will endure forever
before me[b]; your throne[x] will be established[y] forever.[z] ' "

17 Nathan reported to David all the
words of this entire revelation.

David's Prayer

7:18-29pp — 1Ch 17:16-27

18 Then King David went in and sat before the LORD, and he said:

"Who am I,[a] Sovereign LORD, and
what is my family, that you have
brought me this far? 19 And as if this
were not enough in your sight, Sovereign LORD, you have also spoken
about the future of the house of your
servant — and this decree,[b] Sovereign
LORD, is for a mere human![c]

[a] 11 Traditionally *judges* [b] 16 Some Hebrew manuscripts and Septuagint; most Hebrew manuscripts *you* [c] 19 Or *for the human race*

7:8 [x] S 1Sa 16:11; 1Ch 21:17; Ps 74:1; Am 7:15 [y] S 1Sa 2:7-8; S 9:16; S 16:1; S 2Sa 6:21 [z] Ps 78:70-72; 2Co 6:18* **7:9** [a] S 1Sa 18:14; 2Sa 5:10 [b] Ps 18:37-42 [c] S Ex 11:3 **7:10** [d] S Ex 15:17; Isa 5:1-7 [e] 2Ki 21:8; 2Ch 33:8 [f] Ps 89:22-23 [g] Ps 147:14; Isa 54:14; 60:18 **7:11** [h] S Jdg 2:16; 1Sa 12:9-11 [i] ver 1 [j] 1Ki 2:24 [k] 1Sa 25:28; Ps 89:35-37; S Mt 1:1; Lk 1:32-33; Ac 13:22-23; 2Ti 2:8 [l] S Ex 1:21; Isa 7:2 **7:12** [m] S Ge 15:15; 1Ki 2:1; Ac 13:36 [n] 1Ki 8:20; Ps 132:11-12; Jer 30:21; 33:15 [o] 2Ch 23:3 **7:13** [p] S Dt 12:5; 1Ki 6:12 [q] Dt 16:11; 1Ki 5:5; 8:19, 29; 2Ki 21:4,7 [r] ver 16; S Ge 9:16; 2Sa 22:51; 1Ki 2:4,45; 1Ch 22:10; 28:6; 2Ch 6:16; 7:18; 13:5; 21:7; Ps 89:3-4,29,35-37; Pr 25:5; Isa 9:7; 16:5; Jer 17:25; 33:17,21; Da 7:27 **7:14** [s] Ps 2:7; 89:26; Jer 3:19; S Mt 3:17; Jn 1:49; 2Co 6:18*; Heb 1:5*; Rev 21:7 [t] S Dt 8:5; 1Ki 11:34; 1Ch 22:10; Heb 12:7 [u] Ps 89:30-33; Pr 13:24 **7:15** [v] ver 25; 1Ki 2:4; 6:12; 8:25; 9:5; 11:13,32; 2Ki 19:34; 2Ch 6:16; 7:18; 21:7; Ps 89:24,33; Jer 33:17 [w] S 1Sa 13:13; S 15:28; 16:14 **7:16** [x] Ps 89:36-37; S Lk 1:33 [y] Ps 9:7; 93:2; 103:19 [z] S ver 13 **7:18** [a] S Ex 3:11 **7:19** [b] Isa 55:8-9

7:9 *I have cut off all your enemies.* See note on v. 1.

7:10 *I will provide a place for my people Israel.* It is for this purpose that the Lord has made David king, and through David he will do it. *at the beginning.* In Egypt.

7:11 *leaders.* During the period of the judges (see NIV text note). *I will also give you rest from all your enemies.* See vv. 1,9. David's victories over threatening powers will be complete, so that the rest already enjoyed will be assured for the future. *the LORD himself will establish a house for you.* Compare this statement with the rhetorical question of v. 5. In a beautiful play on words God says that David is not to build him a house (temple); rather, God will build David a house (royal dynasty) that will last forever (v. 16). God has been building Israel ever since the days of Abraham, and now he commits himself to build David's royal house so that the promise to Israel may be fulfilled — rest in the promised land. It is God's building that effects his kingdom. This covenant with David is unconditional, like those with Noah, Abram and Phinehas (see note on Ge 9:9; see also chart, p. 23), grounded only in God's firm and gracious purpose. It finds its ultimate fulfillment in the kingship of Christ, who was born of the tribe of Judah and the house of David (see 23:5; Ps 89:3 – 4,30 – 37 and note; 132:11 – 18; Isa 9:1 – 7; 55:3; Mt 1:1; Lk 1:32 – 33, 69; Ac 2:29 – 30; 13:22 – 23; Ro 1:2 – 3; 2Ti 2:8; Rev 3:7; 5:5; 22:16).

7:12 *raise up your offspring to succeed you.* The royal line of David, in contrast to that of Saul, would continue after David's death by dynastic succession.

7:13 *He is the one who will build a house for my Name.* God's priorities are that his own royal house, where his throne can finally come to rest (1Ch 6:31; 28:2), will wait until Israel is at rest and David's dynasty (in the person of his son Solomon) is secure. "My Name" is equivalent to "me" in v. 5 (see note on 1Sa 25:25).

7:14 *his father ... my son.* This familial language expresses the special relationship God promises to maintain with the descendant(s) of David whom he will establish on David's throne. It marks him as the one whom God has chosen and enthroned to rule in his name as the official representative of God's rule over his people (see notes on Ps 2:7; 45:6; 89:27; see also 89:26). In Jesus Christ this promise comes to ultimate fulfillment (see Mt 1:1; Mk 1:11; Heb 1:5 and notes).

7:15 *my love.* God's special and unfailing favor (see note on Ps 6:4).

7:16 *your throne will be established forever.* See note on v. 11; see also Introduction: Contents and Theme. The promise of an everlasting kingdom for the house of David became the focal point for many later prophecies and powerfully influenced the development of the Messianic hope in Israel.

7:18 – 29 David's prayer expresses wonder that God would make such commitments to him and his descendants. But he also acknowledges that what God had pledged to him is for Israel's sake, that its purpose is the fulfillment of God's covenanted promises to his people, and that its ultimate effect will be the honor and praise of God throughout the world.

7:18 *went in.* Presumably into the tent (6:17) in which the ark was kept. *sat before the LORD.* The ark was the symbol of God's presence with his people (see Ex 25:22; see also notes on 1Sa 4:3 – 4,21).

7:19 *this decree ... is for a mere human!* Probably referring to David and his "house" (cf. 1Ch 17:17). The meaning of this clause, however, is uncertain (see NIV text note).

20“What more can David say[c] to
you? For you know[d] your servant,[e]
Sovereign LORD. 21For the sake of your
word and according to your will, you
have done this great thing and made
it known to your servant.
22“How great[f] you are,[g] Sovereign
LORD! There is no one like[h] you, and
there is no God[i] but you, as we have
heard with our own ears.[j] 23And who
is like your people Israel[k]—the one
nation on earth that God went out to
redeem as a people for himself, and
to make a name[l] for himself, and to
perform great and awesome wonders[m] by driving out nations and their
gods from before your people, whom
you redeemed[n] from Egypt?[a] 24You
have established your people Israel
as your very own[o] forever, and you,
LORD, have become their God.[p]
25“And now, LORD God, keep forever the promise[q] you have made concerning your servant and his house.
Do as you promised, 26so that your
name[r] will be great forever. Then
people will say, ‘The LORD Almighty
is God over Israel!’ And the house
of your servant David will be established[s] in your sight.
27“LORD Almighty, God of Israel,
you have revealed this to your servant, saying, ‘I will build a house
for you.’ So your servant has found
courage to pray this prayer to you.

7:20 [c]Isa 38:15 [d]Jn 21:17 [e]S 1Sa 16:7 **7:22** [f]Ps 48:1; 77:13; 86:10; Jer 10:6 [g]Dt 3:24 [h]S Ex 9:14 [i]S Ex 8:10; S 20:4 [j]Ex 10:2; S Jdg 6:13; Ps 44:1 **7:23** [k]Dt 4:32-38; S 33:29; S 1Sa 12:22 [l]S Nu 6:27 [m]Dt 10:21 [n]Dt 7:7-8; S 9:26 **7:24** [o]Dt 26:18 [p]Ex 6:6-7; Ps 48:14 **7:25** [q]S ver 15; S Nu 23:19; 2Ch 1:9 **7:26** [r]S Ex 6:3; Ne 9:5; Ps 72:19; 96:8; Mt 6:9 [s]S 1Sa 25:28 **7:28** [t]Ex 34:6; Jn 17:17 **7:29** [u]Nu 6:23-27 **8:1** [v]Ps 60:8; 87:4; 108:9 [w]Heb 11:32-33 **8:2** [x]S Ge 19:37; S Nu 21:29 [y]S Jdg 3:15; S Isa 45:14 **8:3** [z]2Sa 10:16, 19; 1Ki 11:23 [a]S 1Sa 14:47 [b]S Ge 2:14

28Sovereign LORD, you are God! Your
covenant is trustworthy,[t] and you
have promised these good things to
your servant. 29Now be pleased to
bless the house of your servant, that
it may continue forever in your sight;
for you, Sovereign LORD, have spoken,
and with your blessing[u] the house of
your servant will be blessed forever.”

David’s Victories

8:1-14pp — 1Ch 18:1-13

8 In the course of time, David defeated
the Philistines[v] and subdued[w] them,
and he took Metheg Ammah from the control of the Philistines.
2David also defeated the Moabites.[x] He
made them lie down on the ground and
measured them off with a length of cord
Every two lengths of them were put to
death, and the third length was allowed
to live. So the Moabites became subject to
David and brought him tribute.[y]
3Moreover, David defeated Hadadezer
son of Rehob, king of Zobah,[z] when he
went to restore his monument at[b] the Eu
phrates[b] River. 4David captured a thou
sand of his chariots, seven thousand char
ioteers[c] and twenty thousand foot soldiers

[a] 23 See Septuagint and 1 Chron. 17:21; Hebrew *wonder for your land and before your people, whom you redeemed from Egypt, from the nations and their gods.* [b] 3 Or *his control along* [c] 4 Septuagint (see also Dead Sea Scrolls and 1 Chron. 18:4); Masoretic Text *captured seventeen hundred of his charioteers*

7:20 *know.* Or “fully know” (see Ex 6:3) or “acknowledge” (see Hos 2:20; 6:6) or “choose” (see Ge 18:19; Am 3:2). David recognizes God’s promise as a “covenant” (23:5).
7:21 *your word.* Probably God’s covenant word of promise to his people.
7:22 *no God but you.* See 22:32; 1Sa 2:2; cf. Ex 20:3; Dt 6:4 and notes.
7:23 *the one nation on earth that God went out to redeem as a people for himself.* Israel’s uniqueness did not consist in her national achievements but in God’s choice of her to be his own people (see Dt 7:6–8; 33:26–29). *to make a name for himself.* Contrast Ge 11:4 (see note there). The basis for God’s electing love, revealed in his dealings with Israel, did not lie in any meritorious characteristic of the Israelite people but in his own sovereign purposes (see 1Sa 12:22; Dt 7:6–8; 9:4–6; Ne 9:10; Isa 63:12; Jer 32:20–21; Eze 36:22–38; cf. Da 9:18).
7:24 David recalls the essence of God’s covenant relationship with his people (see Jer 7:23 and note). *you, LORD, have become their God.* What God has pledged to David, he has pledged as the God of Israel (see Zec 8:8 and note).
7:27 *your servant has found courage to pray this prayer to you.* David’s prayer lays claim to God’s promise.
7:28 *good things.* A common summary expression for covenant benefits from God (Nu 10:29,32; Dt 26:11; Jos 23:15; Isa 63:7; Jer 29:32; 33:9; see 1Sa 2:32, “good”; Jos 21:45; 23:14, “good promises”).
8:1–18 See note on 5:6–25.
8:1 *In the course of time.* See note on 2:1. Chronologically the events of this chapter, or many of them, are probably to be placed between chs. 5 and 6 (see 7:1 and note). *Metheg Ammah.* Perhaps a way of referring to Gath and its environs (see 1Ch 18:1).
8:2 *Moabites.* Descendants of Lot (see Ge 19:36–3[7] and note), occupying territory east of the Dead Sea. Saul fought against the Moabites (1Sa 14:47), and David sought refuge in Moab for his parents during his exile from Israel (1Sa 22:3–4). David’s great-grandmother Ruth was from Moab (see Ru 1:4; 4:13,21–22).
8:3 *Hadadezer.* Means “Hadad is (my) help.” Hadad was an Aramean deity equivalent to the Canaanite Baal. *Zobah.* Saul had previously fought against the kings of Zobah (1Sa 14:47) whose territory was apparently located in the Beqaa Valley between the Lebanon and Anti-Lebanon mountains, thus on Israel’s northern border. *restore.* Saul’s earlier victories over the kings of Zobah had extended Israelite control, if only briefly, as far as the fringes of the Euphrates Valley. *Euphrates River.* The land promised to Abraham had included borders from Egypt to the Euphrates (see Ge 15:18; Dt 1:7 and notes; 11:24; Jos 1:4 and note). Here is at least another provision [of] fulfillment of this promise (see 1Ki 4:21,24 and notes; see also Ge 17:8; Jos 21:43–45). See map, p. 2520, at the end of this study Bible; see also map, p. 478.
8:4 See NIV text note. *hamstrung all but a hundred of the chariot horses.* See Jos 11:6 and note. David’s action is often attributed to his supposed ignorance of the value of the chariot as a military weapon. It is more likely, however, that he was acting in obedience to the ancient divine command not to “acquire great numbers of horses for himself” (Dt 17:16; cf. 1Sa 8:11 and note).

ɪe hamstrung[c] all but a hundred of the
:hariot horses.
5 When the Arameans of Damascus[d]
:ame to help Hadadezer king of Zobah,
)avid struck down twenty-two thousand
f them. 6 He put garrisons[e] in the Arame-
ın kingdom of Damascus, and the Arame-
ıns became subject[f] to him and brought
ribute. The LORD gave David victory wher-
ver he went.[g]
7 David took the gold shields[h] that be-
onged to the officers of Hadadezer and
rought them to Jerusalem. 8 From Tebah[a]
nd Berothai,[i] towns that belonged to Had-
dezer, King David took a great quantity
f bronze.
9 When Tou[b] king of Hamath[j] heard
ıat David had defeated the entire army
f Hadadezer,[k] 10 he sent his son Joram[c] to
ing David to greet him and congratulate
im on his victory in battle over Hadade-
er, who had been at war with Tou. Joram
rought with him articles of silver, of gold
nd of bronze.
11 King David dedicated[l] these articles to
ıe LORD, as he had done with the silver
nd gold from all the nations he had sub-
ued: 12 Edom[d][m] and Moab,[n] the Ammon-
es[o] and the Philistines,[p] and Amalek.[q]
e also dedicated the plunder taken from
adadezer son of Rehob, king of Zobah.
13 And David became famous[r] after he
eturned from striking down eighteen
ıousand Edomites[e] in the Valley of Salt.[s]
14 He put garrisons throughout Edom,
and all the Edomites[t] became subject
to David.[u] The LORD gave David victory[v]
wherever he went.[w]

David's Officials

8:15-18pp — 1Ch 18:14-17

15 David reigned over all Israel, doing
what was just and right[x] for all his people.
16 Joab[y] son of Zeruiah was over the army;
Jehoshaphat[z] son of Ahilud was recorder;[a]
17 Zadok[b] son of Ahitub and Ahimelek son
of Abiathar[c] were priests; Seraiah was secretary;[d] 18 Benaiah[e] son of Jehoiada was
over the Kerethites[f] and Pelethites; and
David's sons were priests.[f]

David and Mephibosheth

9 David asked, "Is there anyone still left
of the house of Saul to whom I can
show kindness for Jonathan's sake?"[g]

[a] *8* See some Septuagint manuscripts (see also 1 Chron. 18:8); Hebrew *Betah.* [b] *9* Hebrew *Toi,* a variant of *Tou;* also in verse 10 [c] *10* A variant of *Hadoram* [d] *12* Some Hebrew manuscripts, Septuagint and Syriac (see also 1 Chron. 18:11); most Hebrew manuscripts *Aram* [e] *13* A few Hebrew manuscripts, Septuagint and Syriac (see also 1 Chron. 18:12); most Hebrew manuscripts *Aram* (that is, Arameans) [f] *18* Or *were chief officials* (see Septuagint and Targum; see also 1 Chron. 18:17)

8:4 [c]S Ge 49:6; Jos 11:9 **8:5** [d]S Ge 14:15; 2Sa 10:6; 1Ki 11:24; 2Ki 8:7; 14:28 **8:6** [e]1Ki 20:34 [f]2Sa 10:19 [g]2Sa 3:18 **8:7** [h]1Ki 10:16; 14:26; 2Ki 11:10 **8:8** [i]Eze 47:16 **8:9** [j]1Ki 8:65; 2Ki 14:28; 2Ch 8:4 [k]Lk 14:31-32 **8:11** [l]ver 12; 1Ki 7:51; 15:15; 1Ch 26:26; 2Ch 5:1 **8:12** [m]S Nu 24:18 [n]ver 2 [o]2Sa 10:14 [p]S 2Sa 5:25 [q]S Nu 24:20; S 1Sa 27:8 **8:13** [r]2Sa 7:9 [s]2Ki 14:7; 1Ch 18:12; Ps 60 Title **8:14** [t]Nu 24:17-18; Ps 108:9; Isa 34:5; 63:1; Jer 49:7; Eze 25:12 [u]S Ge 27:29, 37-40 [v]Ps 144:10 [w]2Sa 22:44; Ps 18:43 **8:15** [x]S Ge 18:19; 1Ki 11:38; 14:8; 15:11; 22:43; 2Ki 12:2; Job 29:14; Ps 5:12; 119:121; Heb 11:33 **8:16** [y]S 2Sa 2:13 [z]2Sa 20:24; 1Ki 4:3 [a]Isa 36:3,22 **8:17** [b]S 1Sa 2:35; 2Sa 15:24,29; 20:25; 1Ki 1:8; 4:4; 1Ch 6:8,53; 16:39; 24:3; 27:17; 2Ch 31:10; Eze 40:46; 43:19; 44:15; 48:11 [c]Mk 2:26 [d]1Ki 4:3; 2Ki 12:10; 19:2; 22:3; Isa 36:3; Jer 36:12 **8:18** [e]2Sa 20:23; 23:20; 1Ki 1:8,38; 2:25,35,46; 4:4 [f]S 1Sa 30:14 **9:1** [g]S 1Sa 20:14-17,42; S 23:18

---

5 *Arameans.* See notes on Dt 26:5; 1Ch 18:5. *came to help* ɪadadezer. They feared Israelite expansion to the north.
6,14 *The LORD ... wherever he went.* The sentence summa-:es David's victories at two critical points in this section /. 1–14) and reminds the reader that God, not David, is the ıe Savior of his people.
7 *gold shields.* Shields adorned with gold — the phrase is nilar to "chariots fitted with iron" (see Jos 17:16 and note).
3 *bronze.* Later used by Solomon in the construction of the mple (see 1Ch 18:8 and note).
9 *Hamath.* A kingdom centered on the Orontes River, north Zobah (see v. 3 and note).
13 *eighteen thousand.* As king, David receives the credit for iking down 18,000 Edomites. Abishai, however, was one David's army commanders in this battle (see 1Ch 18:12 d note). The 12,000 Edomites struck down under Joab's ıdership according to the title of Ps 60 were probably part the 18,000. *Valley of Salt.* See 2Ki 14:7 and note; see also 60 title.
8:15 *just and right.* As a true theocratic king, David's reign was characterized by adherence God's standards of right rule (see notes on 1Sa 8:3; 12:3; 119:121), as no doubt laid down in Samuel's "rights and ties of kingship" (see 1Sa 10:25; 1Ki 2:3–4 and notes).
16 *Joab son of Zeruiah was over the army.* See notes on 2:13; . *recorder.* The precise duties of this official are not indi-:ed, though the position was an important one in the court d was maintained throughout the period of the monar-/ (see 2Ki 18:18,37; 2Ch 34:8). He may have been a kind of ancellor or chief administrator of royal affairs, responsible ıong other things for the royal chronicles and annals.
8:17 *Zadok son of Ahitub.* First mentioned here, Zadok was a descendant of Eleazar, son of Aaron (see 1Ch 6:4–8,50–52; 24:1–3). His father, Ahitub, is not to be identified with Ichabod's brother of the same name (1Sa 14:3). Zadok remained loyal to David throughout his reign (15:24–29; 17:15–16; 19:11). Zadok and the prophet Nathan eventually anointed Solomon as David's successor (1Ki 1:43–45). *Ahimelek son of Abiathar.* A copyist's error may have occurred here (see also 1Ch 24:6) in which these two names have been transposed. Abiathar is referred to as "son of Ahimelek" in 1Sa 22:20. While it is true that the Abiathar of 1Sa 22:20 could have had a son named Ahimelek (after his grandfather), such a person does not appear elsewhere in the narratives of Samuel and Kings as a colleague of Zadok, but Abiathar consistently does (15:29,35; 17:15; 19:11; 20:25; 1Ki 1:7–8; 2:35; 4:4). *Seraiah.* Perhaps the same person elsewhere called Sheva (20:25), Shisha (1Ki 4:3) and Shavsha (1Ch 18:16). *secretary.* His duties presumably included domestic and foreign correspondence, perhaps keeping records of important political events, and various administrative functions (2Ki 12:10–12).
8:18 *Kerethites.* See note on 1Sa 30:14. *Pelethites.* Probably an alternate form of "Philistines." *priests.* See NIV text note; see also 20:26. Several early translations render the term by some word other than "priests." Chronicles calls these men "chief officials at the king's side" (1Ch 18:17; see note there).
9:1 — 20:26 An account of threats to David's reign being overcome. These chapters, together with 1Ki 1:1 — 2:46, are among the finest examples of historical narrative to have been produced in the ancient world.
9:1–13 The events of this chapter occurred a number of

[2]Now there was a servant of Saul's
household named Ziba.[h] They summoned
him to appear before David, and the king
said to him, "Are you Ziba?"
"At your service," he replied.
[3]The king asked, "Is there no one still
alive from the house of Saul to whom I
can show God's kindness?"
Ziba answered the king, "There is still a
son of Jonathan;[i] he is lame[j] in both feet."
[4]"Where is he?" the king asked.
Ziba answered, "He is at the house of
Makir[k] son of Ammiel in Lo Debar."
[5]So King David had him brought from
Lo Debar, from the house of Makir son of
Ammiel.
[6]When Mephibosheth son of Jonathan,
the son of Saul, came to David, he bowed
down to pay him honor.[l]
David said, "Mephibosheth!"
"At your service," he replied.
[7]"Don't be afraid," David said to him,
"for I will surely show you kindness for
the sake of your father Jonathan.[m] I will
restore to you all the land that belonged
to your grandfather Saul, and you will always eat at my table.[n]"
[8]Mephibosheth[o] bowed down and said,
"What is your servant, that you should notice a dead dog[p] like me?"
[9]Then the king summoned Ziba, Saul's
steward, and said to him, "I have given
your master's grandson everything that
belonged to Saul and his family. [10]You and
your sons and your servants are to farm
the land for him and bring in the crops, so
that your master's grandson[q] may be provided for. And Mephibosheth, grandson of
your master, will always eat at my table."
(Now Ziba had fifteen sons and twenty
servants.)
[11]Then Ziba said to the king, "Your ser-

9:2 [h]2Sa 16:1-4; 19:17,26,29
9:3 [i]1Ch 8:34; 1Sa 20:14 [j]S Lev 21:18
9:4 [k]2Sa 17:27-29
9:6 [l]S Ge 37:7
9:7 [m]S 1Sa 20:14-15 [n]ver 13; 2Sa 19:28; 21:7; 1Ki 2:7; 2Ki 25:29; Jer 52:33
9:8 [o]S 2Sa 4:4 [p]S 2Sa 3:8
9:10 [q]2Sa 16:3

Frieze from the Parthenon (447–432 BC) depicts a man using a stick to assist with walking. Diseases causing lameness and crippled limbs were much more common in the ancient Near East than they are today. King David showed kindness to Jonathan's son, Mephibosheth, who was "lame in both feet" (2Sa 9:3,13), rather than treating him as an outcast.

Cast of figures from a frieze on the Parthenon by Galleria dell 'Accademia, Florence, Italy/The Bridgeman Art Library

years after David's capture of Jerusalem. Mephibosheth was five years old at the time of his father's death (4:4); now he has a son of his own (v. 12). Mephibosheth's condition and David's gracious treatment of him make clear that all potential threats from the old royal house of Saul have been neutralized.

9:1 *I can show kindness for Jonathan's sake.* David has not forgotten his promise to Jonathan (cf. 1Sa 20:14–17,42).

9:2 *Ziba.* The chief steward of Saul's estate, which had been inherited by Mephibosheth, son of Jonathan, Saul's firstborn (see 16:1–4; 19:17).

9:3,13 *lame in both feet.* And thus disqualified from contesting David's position as king (see 4:4 and note; see also photo above).

9:3 *There is still a son of Jonathan.* Saul had other descendants (see 21:8), but Ziba mentions only the one in whom David would be chiefly interested.

9:4 *Makir.* Apparently a wealthy benefactor of Mephibosheth who later also came to David's aid (17:27). *Lo Debar.* A town deep in Gileadite territory in Transjordan.

9:6 *Mephibosheth.* See 4:4 and note.

9:7 *restore to you.* Either the property Saul had acquired as king had been taken over by David, or Ziba as steward hac virtually taken possession of it and was profiting from its in come (see 16:1–4; 19:26–30). *you will always eat at my table* A matter of honor—but probably also so that David coul keep a watchful eye on him (cf. 1Sa 20:24–27; 2Ki 25:29; Je 52:33). In any event, Mephibosheth's general financial need were to be cared for by the produce of Saul's estate (v. 10).

9:8 *dead dog like me.* An expression of deep self abasement. The author has used the "(dead) dog" mo tif with great effect. First Goliath, scornfully disdaining th young warrior David, asks, "Am I a dog . . . ?" (1Sa 17:43)—an unwittingly foreshadows his own end. Then David, in a self deprecating manner, describes himself as a "dead dog" (1S 24:14) to suggest to Saul that the king of Israel should no consider him worth so much attention. In the Nabal episode that "dog" (a "Calebite") and his sudden death characteriz Saul and foreshadow his unhappy end (see note on 1Sa 25:3 Here a grandson of Saul and in 16:9 a relative of Saul wh curses David are similarly described. For the author, "dea dog" fittingly characterizes those who foolishly scorn or op pose the Lord's anointed, while David's own self-deprecatio (see 7:18; 1Sa 18:18) is conducive to his exaltation (cf. 1Pe 5:6

vant will do whatever my lord the king
commands his servant to do." So Mephibosheth ate at David's[a] table like one of the
king's sons.[r]
12 Mephibosheth had a young son
named Mika, and all the members of Ziba's household were servants of Mephibosheth.[s] 13 And Mephibosheth lived in Jerusalem, because he always ate at the king's
table; he was lame in both feet.

David Defeats the Ammonites

10:1-19pp — 1Ch 19:1-19

10 In the course of time, the king of
the Ammonites died, and his son
Hanun succeeded him as king. 2 David
thought, "I will show kindness to Hanun
son of Nahash,[t] just as his father showed
kindness to me." So David sent a delegation to express his sympathy to Hanun
concerning his father.
When David's men came to the land
of the Ammonites, 3 the Ammonite commanders said to Hanun their lord, "Do
you think David is honoring your father by
sending envoys to you to express sympathy? Hasn't David sent them to you only to
explore the city and spy it out[u] and overthrow it?" 4 So Hanun seized David's envoys, shaved off half of each man's beard,[v]
cut off their garments at the buttocks,[w]
and sent them away.
5 When David was told about this, he
sent messengers to meet the men, for
they were greatly humiliated. The king
said, "Stay at Jericho till your beards have
grown, and then come back."
6 When the Ammonites realized that
they had become obnoxious[x] to David,
they hired twenty thousand Aramean[y] foot
soldiers from Beth Rehob[z] and Zobah,[a] as
well as the king of Maakah[b] with a thousand men, and also twelve thousand men
from Tob.[c]
7 On hearing this, David sent Joab[d] out
with the entire army of fighting men. 8 The
Ammonites came out and drew up in battle formation at the entrance of their city
gate, while the Arameans of Zobah and
Rehob and the men of Tob and Maakah
were by themselves in the open country.
9 Joab saw that there were battle lines in
front of him and behind him; so he selected some of the best troops in Israel and
deployed them against the Arameans. 10 He
put the rest of the men under the command of Abishai[e] his brother and deployed
them against the Ammonites. 11 Joab said,
"If the Arameans are too strong for me,
then you are to come to my rescue; but
if the Ammonites are too strong for you,
then I will come to rescue you. 12 Be
strong,[f] and let us fight bravely for our
people and the cities of our God. The LORD
will do what is good in his sight."[g]
13 Then Joab and the troops with him
advanced to fight the Arameans, and they
fled before him. 14 When the Ammonites[h]
realized that the Arameans were fleeing,
they fled before Abishai and went inside
the city. So Joab returned from fighting the
Ammonites and came to Jerusalem.
15 After the Arameans saw that they had
been routed by Israel, they regrouped.
16 Hadadezer had Arameans brought from
beyond the Euphrates River; they went to
Helam, with Shobak the commander of
Hadadezer's army leading them.
17 When David was told of this, he gathered all Israel, crossed the Jordan and
went to Helam. The Arameans formed
their battle lines to meet David and fought
against him. 18 But they fled before Israel,
and David killed seven hundred of their
charioteers and forty thousand of their
foot soldiers.[b] He also struck down Shobak the commander of their army, and he
died there. 19 When all the kings who were
vassals of Hadadezer saw that they had
been routed by Israel, they made peace
with the Israelites and became subject[i] to
them.

9:11 [r] Job 36:7; Ps 113:8
9:12 [s] S 2Sa 4:4
10:2 [t] S 1Sa 11:1
10:3 [u] S Nu 21:32
10:4 [v] S Lev 19:27; Isa 7:20; 15:2; 50:6; 52:14; Jer 48:37; Eze 5:1 [w] Isa 20:4
10:6 [x] S Ge 34:30 [y] S 2Sa 8:5 [z] S Nu 13:21 [a] S 1Sa 14:47 [b] S Dt 3:14 [c] Jdg 11:3-5
10:7 [d] S 2Sa 2:18
10:10 [e] S 1Sa 26:6
10:12 [f] S Dt 1:21; 31:6; S Eph 6:10 [g] S Jdg 10:15; Ne 4:14
10:14 [h] 2Sa 8:12
10:19 [i] 2Sa 8:6

[a] *11* Septuagint; Hebrew *my* [b] *18* Some Septuagint manuscripts (see also 1 Chron. 19:18); Hebrew *horsemen*

9:12 *had a young son named Mika.* Who also had descendants (1Ch 8:35–39).
10:1 *In the course of time.* See note on 2:1. *king.* Nahash (see v. 2; 1Sa 11). *Ammonites.* See note on 1Sa 11:1.
10:2 *show kindness.* The Hebrew for this expression suggests that a formal treaty existed between the Israelites and the Ammonites (cf. 1Sa 20:8).
10:3,14 *city.* Rabbah, the capital (11:1; 12:26). See note on Dt 3:11.
10:4 *shaved off half of each man's beard.* In the world of that time this was considered an insult of the most serious kind (cf. Isa 7:20). *cut off their garments at the buttocks.* A customary way of degrading prisoners of war (cf. Isa 20:4).
10:5 *Jericho.* See notes on Jos 6:1; 1Ki 16:34. Jericho remained desolate during the centuries between Joshua's conquest and the time of Ahab.
10:6 *obnoxious.* See note on 1Sa 13:4. *Beth Rehob.* See Nu 13:21; Jdg 18:28 and notes. *Zobah.* See note on 8:3. *Maakah.* See Dt 3:14 and note; Jos 12:5; 13:13. *Tob.* See Jdg 11:3–6 and note on 11:3.
10:10 *Abishai.* See note on 1Sa 26:6.
10:16 *Hadadezer.* See note on 8:3.
10:18 *seven hundred.* Perhaps a copyist's mistake; in 1Ch 19:18 the figure is 7,000.
10:19 *they made peace with the Israelites.* There is no indication that Hadadezer himself made peace with Israel as his vassals did in the aftermath of this defeat. These events represent David's last major campaign against combined foreign powers.

So the Arameans[j] were afraid to help the
Ammonites anymore.

David and Bathsheba

11 In the spring,[k] at the time when
kings go off to war, David sent
Joab[l] out with the king's men and the
whole Israelite army.[m] They destroyed the
Ammonites and besieged Rabbah.[n] But
David remained in Jerusalem.
2 One evening David got up from his bed
and walked around on the roof[o] of the palace. From the roof he saw[p] a woman bathing. The woman was very beautiful, 3 and
David sent someone to find out about her.
The man said, "She is Bathsheba,[q] the
daughter of Eliam[r] and the wife of Uriah[s]
the Hittite." 4 Then David sent messengers
to get her.[t] She came to him, and he slept[u]
with her. (Now she was purifying herself
from her monthly uncleanness.)[v] Then
she went back home. 5 The woman conceived and sent word to David, saying, "I
am pregnant."
6 So David sent this word to Joab: "Send
me Uriah[w] the Hittite." And Joab sent him
to David. 7 When Uriah came to him, David asked him how Joab was, how the soldiers were and how the war was going.
8 Then David said to Uriah, "Go down to
your house and wash your feet."[x] So Uriah left the palace, and a gift from the king
was sent after him. 9 But Uriah slept at the
entrance to the palace with all his master's
servants and did not go down to his house.
10 David was told, "Uriah did not go
home." So he asked Uriah, "Haven't you
just come from a military campaign? Why
didn't you go home?"
11 Uriah said to David, "The ark[y] and Israel and Judah are staying in tents,[a] and
my commander Joab and my lord's men
are camped in the open country. How
could I go to my house to eat and drink
and make love[z] to my wife? As surely as
you live, I will not do such a thing!"
12 Then David said to him, "Stay here
one more day, and tomorrow I will send
you back." So Uriah remained in Jerusalem that day and the next. 13 At David's
invitation, he ate and drank with him, and
David made him drunk. But in the evening
Uriah went out to sleep on his mat among
his master's servants; he did not go home.
14 In the morning David wrote a letter[a]
to Joab and sent it with Uriah. 15 In it he
wrote, "Put Uriah out in front where the
fighting is fiercest. Then withdraw from
him so he will be struck down[b] and die.[c]"

10:19 [j] 1Ki 11:25; 22:31; 2Ki 5:1 **11:1** [k] 1Ki 20:22, 26 [l] S 2Sa 2:18 [m] 1Ch 20:1 [n] S Dt 3:11 **11:2** [o] S Dt 22:8; S Jos 2:8 [p] Mt 5:28 **11:3** [q] 1Ch 3:5 [r] 2Sa 23:34 [s] 2Sa 23:39 **11:4** [t] S Lev 20:10; Ps 51 Title; Jas 1:14-15 [u] Dt 22:22 [v] S Lev 15:25-30 **11:6** [w] 1Ch 11:41 **11:8** [x] S Ge 18:4 **11:11** [y] 2Sa 7:2 [z] S 1Sa 21:5 **11:14** [a] 1Ki 21:8 **11:15** [b] ver 14-17; 2Sa 12:9 [c] 2Sa 12:12

[a] 11 Or *staying at Sukkoth*

11:1 — 12:25 David's shameful abuse of his royal power and how the Lord dealt with it.

11:1 – 27 This detailed account of David's sin has as its foil the story of how David came to receive Nabal's wife Abigail as his wife (1Sa 25). There the Lord removes the husband because of his disdain for the Lord's anointed, and Abigail comes to David as the one who has prevented him from using his incipient royal power for personal ends. Here David abuses his royal power to obtain the wife of another whom he callously removes by royal manipulation of events. David commits the great sin of those entrusted by God with power — using it for personal ends. Contrast what David's greatest Son said about his own ministry (see Mk 10:45 and note).

11:1 *the spring.* Of the year following the events reported in ch. 10. *the time when kings go off to war.* When the rains have ended. At that time the roads became passable and the spring harvest provided food for armies on the march as well as fodder for their animals. *Rabbah.* See note on 10:3,14. Though now alone (see 10:19), the Ammonites had not yet been subjugated.

11:2 *walked around on the roof.* Where he could enjoy the cool evening air (see note on 1Sa 9:25).

11:3 *Eliam.* Perhaps the same Eliam who was a member of David's personal bodyguard (23:34) and a son of his counselor Ahithophel (see 15:12 and note). *Uriah.* Also listed among those comprising David's royal guard (23:39). His name suggests that even though he was a Hittite, he had adopted the Israelite faith (Uriah means "The LORD is my light"). *Hittite.* See note on 1Sa 26:6.

11:4 *David sent messengers to get her.* Through this and subsequent actions David broke the sixth, seventh and tenth commandments (Ex 20:13 – 14,17). *She came to him, and he slept with her.* Bathsheba appears to have been an unprotesting partner in this adulterous relationship with David. *(Now she was purifying herself from her monthly uncleanness.)* The purpose of this statement is to indicate Bathsheba's condition at the time of her sexual relations with David. She was just becoming ceremonially clean (Lev 15:28 – 30) after the seven-day period of monthly impurity due to menstruation (Lev 15:19). It is thus clear that she was not already pregnant by her own husband when David took her.

11:5 *I am pregnant.* Bathsheba leaves the next step up to David. The law prescribed the death penalty for both David and Bathsheba (Lev 20:10), as they well knew.

11:6 *Send me Uriah.* Under the pretense of seeking information about the course of the war, David brings Uriah back to Jerusalem.

11:8 *Go down to your house and wash your feet.* In essence David tells Uriah to go home and relax. What he does not say specifically is what is most important, and well understood by Uriah (v. 11). *a gift from the king was sent after him.* The Hebrew word for "gift" has the meaning of "food" in Ge 43:34 ("portions" from the king's table). David wanted Uriah and Bathsheba to enjoy their evening together.

11:11 *ark.* Uriah's statement suggests that the ark was in the field camp with the army rather than in the tent that David had set up for it in Jerusalem (6:17). If so, it was probably there for purposes of worship and to seek guidance for the war. But then the circumstances are even more damning for David — the Lord is in the field with his army while David stays at home in leisure. *How could I go to my house to eat ...?* See note on v. 8 ("gift"). Uriah's devotion to duty exposes by sharp contrast David's dalliance at home while his men are in the field. *As surely as you live.* See note on 1Sa 14:39,45.

11:13 *David made him drunk.* In the hope that in this condition he would relent and go to Bathsheba.

11:14 Uriah is almost certainly unaware that he is carrying his own death warrant to Joab.

16 So while Joab had the city under siege,
he put Uriah at a place where he knew the
strongest defenders were. 17 When the men
of the city came out and fought against
Joab, some of the men in David's army
fell; moreover, Uriah the Hittite died.
18 Joab sent David a full account of the
battle. 19 He instructed the messenger:
"When you have finished giving the king
this account of the battle, 20 the king's anger may flare up, and he may ask you,
'Why did you get so close to the city to
fight? Didn't you know they would shoot
arrows from the wall? 21 Who killed Abimelek[d] son of Jerub-Besheth[a]? Didn't a
woman drop an upper millstone on him
from the wall,[e] so that he died in Thebez?
Why did you get so close to the wall?' If he
asks you this, then say to him, 'Moreover,
your servant Uriah the Hittite is dead.' "
22 The messenger set out, and when he
arrived he told David everything Joab had
sent him to say. 23 The messenger said to
David, "The men overpowered us and
came out against us in the open, but we
drove them back to the entrance of the city
gate. 24 Then the archers shot arrows at
your servants from the wall, and some of
the king's men died. Moreover, your servant Uriah the Hittite is dead."
25 David told the messenger, "Say this to
Joab: 'Don't let this upset you; the sword
devours one as well as another. Press the
attack against the city and destroy it.' Say
this to encourage Joab."
26 When Uriah's wife heard that her husband was dead, she mourned for him. 27 After the time of mourning[f] was over, David
had her brought to his house, and she became his wife and bore him a son. But the
thing David had done displeased[g] the LORD.

11:21 [d] S Jdg 8:31 [e] Jdg 9:50-54 **11:27** [f] Dt 34:8
[g] 2Sa 12:9; Ps 51:4-5 **12:1** [h] S 2Sa 7:2 [i] Ps 51 Title [j] 2Sa 14:4 **12:5** [k] 1Ki 20:40 [l] S Ge 34:7 [m] Ro 2:1 [n] S 1Sa 14:39 **12:6** [o] Ex 22:1 **12:7** [p] 2Sa 14:13; Da 4:22 [q] S 1Sa 2:35 [r] 1Ki 20:42 **12:8** [s] S 2Sa 9:7

Nathan Rebukes David

11:1; 12:29-31pp — 1Ch 20:1-3

12 The LORD sent Nathan[h] to David.[i]
When he came to him,[j] he said,
"There were two men in a certain town,
one rich and the other poor. 2 The rich man
had a very large number of sheep and cattle, 3 but the poor man had nothing except
one little ewe lamb he had bought. He
raised it, and it grew up with him and his
children. It shared his food, drank from
his cup and even slept in his arms. It was
like a daughter to him.
4 "Now a traveler came to the rich man,
but the rich man refrained from taking
one of his own sheep or cattle to prepare
a meal for the traveler who had come to
him. Instead, he took the ewe lamb that
belonged to the poor man and prepared it
for the one who had come to him."
5 David[k] burned with anger[l] against the
man[m] and said to Nathan, "As surely as
the LORD lives,[n] the man who did this must
die! 6 He must pay for that lamb four times
over,[o] because he did such a thing and had
no pity."
7 Then Nathan said to David, "You are
the man![p] This is what the LORD, the God
of Israel, says: 'I anointed[q] you[r] king over
Israel, and I delivered you from the hand
of Saul. 8 I gave your master's house to
you,[s] and your master's wives into your
arms. I gave you all Israel and Judah. And
if all this had been too little, I would have

[a] *21* Also known as *Jerub-Baal* (that is, Gideon)

11:15 *so he will be struck down and die.* Unsuccessful in making it appear that Uriah was the father of Bathsheba's child, David plotted Uriah's death so he could marry Bathsheba himself as quickly as possible.
11:16 *city.* Rabbah (see note on 10:3,14).
11:17 *Uriah the Hittite died.* This phrase or its equivalent echoes like a death knell throughout the rest of the chapter (vv. 21,24; cf. also vv. 15,26).
11:21 *Jerub-Besheth.* Another possible spelling is "Jerub-Bosheth." In Judges he is called Jerub-Baal (see note on Jdg 6:32; see also NIV text note here). For similar name changes elsewhere in 2 Samuel, see notes on 2:8; 4:4. *millstone.* See Jdg 9:53 and note. *Uriah … is dead.* Joab knows that this news is of great importance to David, and he uses it to squelch any criticism David might otherwise have had of the battle tactics.
11:24 *some of the king's men died.* Other brave soldiers were sacrificed along with Uriah, a fact that exposes David's callousness, as well as the enormity of his sinful cover-up.
11:25 *David told the messenger.* David hid his satisfaction over the news with a hypocritical statement that war is war and the death of Uriah should not be a discouragement.
11:27 *time of mourning was over.* Presumably a period of seven days (see 1Sa 31:13 and note; Ge 50:10). *she became his wife.* See note on 5:14. *the thing David had done displeased the LORD.* A monumental understatement. Not only had David brazenly violated God's laws (see note on v. 4); even worse, he had shamelessly abused his royal power, which the Lord had entrusted to him to shepherd the Lord's people (see 5:2; 7:7 and note).
12:1 *The LORD sent.* Prophets were messengers from the Lord. Here the Great King sends his emissary to rebuke and announce judgment on the king he had enthroned over his people. *Nathan.* See note on 7:2.
12:5 *As surely as the LORD lives.* See note on 1Sa 14:39,45.
12:6 *four times over.* In agreement with the requirements of Ex 22:1.
12:7 *You are the man!* Nathan identifies David as the rich man in the parable of vv. 1–4. David's sentence of fourfold retribution against that man (v. 6) came true in his own experience: As a result of his engineering Uriah's death, David lost four of his sons (see vv. 10,18 and note on v. 10). Indeed, his sin against Uriah became a permanent stain on his otherwise godly life (see 1Ki 15:5).
12:8 *your master's wives.* Earlier narratives refer to only one wife of Saul (Ahinoam, 1Sa 14:50) and one concubine (Rizpah, 2Sa 3:7; 21:8–11). This statement suggests that there were others. But since it was customary for new kings to assume the harem of their predecessors (see note on 3:7), it may be that Nathan merely uses conventional language to

DAVID'S **CONQUESTS**

Once he had become king over all Israel (2Sa 5:1–5), David

(1) conquered the Jebusite fortress of Zion/Jerusalem and made it his royal city (5:6–10);

(2) received the recognition of and assurance of friendship from Hiram of Tyre, king of the Phoenicians (5:11–12);

(3) decisively defeated the Philistines so that their hold on Israelite territory was broken and their threat to Israel eliminated (5:17–25; 8:1);

(4) defeated the Moabites and imposed his authority over them (8:2);

(5) crushed the Aramean kingdoms of Hadadezer (king of Zobah), Damascus and Maakah and put them under tribute (8:3–8; 10:6–19). Talmai, the Aramean king of Geshur, apparently had made peace with David while he was still reigning in Hebron and sealed the alliance by giving his daughter Maakah in marriage to David (3:3; cf. 1Ch 2:23);

(6) subdued Edom and incorporated it into his empire (8:13–14);

(7) defeated the Ammonites and brought them into subjection (12:26–31);

(8) subjugated the remaining Canaanite cities that had previously maintained their independence from Israel, such as Beth Shan, Megiddo, Taanach and Dor.

Since David had earlier crushed the Amalekites (1Sa 30:17–18), his wars thus completed the conquest begun by Joshua and secured all the borders of Israel. His empire (united Israel plus the subjugated kingdoms) reached from Ezion Geber on the eastern arm of the "Red Sea" to the Euphrates River.

given you even more. 9Why did you despise[t] the word of the LORD by doing what
is evil in his eyes? You struck down[u] Uriah[v] the Hittite with the sword and took
his wife to be your own. You killed[w] him
with the sword of the Ammonites. 10Now,
therefore, the sword[x] will never depart
from your house, because you despised
me and took the wife of Uriah the Hittite
to be your own.'
11"This is what the LORD says: 'Out of
your own household[y] I am going to bring
calamity on you.[z] Before your very eyes I
will take your wives and give them to one
who is close to you, and he will sleep with
your wives in broad daylight.[a] 12You did it
in secret,[b] but I will do this thing in broad
daylight[c] before all Israel.' "
13Then David said to Nathan, "I have
sinned[d] against the LORD."
Nathan replied, "The LORD has tak-
en away[e] your sin.[f] You are not going to
die.[g] 14But because by doing this you have
shown utter contempt for[a] the LORD,[h] the
son born to you will die."
15After Nathan had gone home, the
LORD struck[i] the child that Uriah's wife
had borne to David, and he became ill.
16David pleaded with God for the child. He
fasted and spent the nights lying[j] in sackcloth[b] on the ground. 17The elders of his
household stood beside him to get him up
from the ground, but he refused,[k] and he
would not eat any food with them.[l]
18On the seventh day the child died.
David's attendants were afraid to tell him
that the child was dead, for they thought,
"While the child was still living, he
wouldn't listen to us when we spoke to
him. How can we now tell him the child
is dead? He may do something desperate."
19David noticed that his attendants were
whispering among themselves, and he realized the child was dead. "Is the child
dead?" he asked.
"Yes," they replied, "he is dead."
20Then David got up from the ground.
After he had washed,[m] put on lotions and
changed his clothes,[n] he went into the
house of the LORD and worshiped. Then he
went to his own house, and at his request
they served him food, and he ate.
21His attendants asked him, "Why are
you acting this way? While the child was
alive, you fasted and wept,[o] but now that
the child is dead, you get up and eat!"
22He answered, "While the child was
still alive, I fasted and wept. I thought,
'Who knows?[p] The LORD may be gracious
to me and let the child live.'[q] 23But now
that he is dead, why should I go on fasting? Can I bring him back again? I will go
to him,[r] but he will not return to me."[s]
24Then David comforted his wife Bathsheba,[t] and he went to her and made love
to her. She gave birth to a son, and they
named him Solomon.[u] The LORD loved him;
25and because the LORD loved him, he sent
word through Nathan the prophet to name
him Jedidiah.[c][v]
26Meanwhile Joab fought against Rabbah[w]

12:9 [t] S Nu 15:31; S 1Sa 13:14 [u] S 2Sa 11:15 [v] 1Ki 15:5 [w] Ps 26:9; 51:14 **12:10** [x] 2Sa 13:28; 18:14-15; 1Ki 2:25 **12:11** [y] 2Sa 16:11 [z] Dt 28:30; 2Sa 16:21-22 [a] S Dt 17:17 **12:12** [b] 2Sa 11:4-15 [c] 2Sa 16:22 **12:13** [d] S Ge 13:13; S 20:6; S Nu 22:34 [e] Ps 32:1-5; 51:1,9; 103:12; Isa 43:25; 44:22; Zec 3:4,9 [f] Pr 28:13; Jer 2:35; Mic 7:18-19 [g] Lev 20:10; 24:17 **12:14** [h] Isa 52:5; Ro 2:24 **12:15** [i] S 1Sa 25:38 **12:16** [j] Ps 5:7; 95:6 **12:17** [k] S Ge 37:35; S 1Sa 1:7 [l] S 2Sa 3:35; Da 6:18 **12:20** [m] Mt 6:17 [n] S Ge 41:14 **12:21** [o] Jdg 20:26 **12:22** [p] Jnh 3:9 [q] Isa 38:1-5 **12:23** [r] Ge 37:35 [s] S 1Sa 31:13; 2Sa 13:39; Job 7:10; 10:21 **12:24** [t] 1Ki 1:11 [u] 1Ki 1:10; 1Ch 22:9; 28:5; Mt 1:6 **12:25** [v] Ne 13:26 **12:26** [w] S Dt 3:11

[a] *14* An ancient Hebrew scribal tradition; Masoretic Text *for the enemies of* [b] *16* Dead Sea Scrolls and Septuagint; Masoretic Text does not have *in sackcloth.* [c] *25* *Jedidiah* means *loved by the LORD.*

emphasize that the Lord had placed David on Saul's throne. *I gave you all Israel and Judah.* See 2:1,4; 5:2–3.

12:9 *despise the word of the LORD.* See notes on 11:4,27. *You killed him.* David is held directly responsible for Uriah's death even though he fell in battle (see 11:15 and note).

12:10 *the sword will never depart from your house.* Three of David's sons died violently: Amnon (13:28–29), Absalom (18:14–15) and Adonijah (1Ki 2:25).

12:11 *Out of your own household I am going to bring calamity on you.* David was driven from Jerusalem by Absalom's conspiracy to seize the kingship from his own father (15:1–17). *he will sleep with your wives in broad daylight.* Fulfilled at the time of Absalom's rebellion (see note on 16:22).

12:13 *I have sinned against the LORD.* See Ps 51:4 and note. There is a clear contrast between David's confession and Saul's (see note on 1Sa 15:24). *The LORD has taken away your sin.* David experienced the joy of knowing his sin was forgiven (see Ps 32:1,5; cf. Ps 51:8,12). *You are not going to die.* The Lord, in his grace, released David from the customary death penalty for adultery and murder (Lev 20:10; 24:17,21).

12:14 *you have shown utter contempt for the LORD.* See NIV text note.

12:16 *pleaded ... fasted.* See note on Ezr 8:23.

12:18 *seventh day.* If reference is to the child's age, his life was so short that he remained uncircumcised and unnamed (see Lk 1:59; 2:21; cf. Ge 21:3–4)—and therefore was not counted among the Israelites.

12:20 *put on lotions.* A practice associated with the cessation of mourning (see 14:2). *changed his clothes.* Took off his mourning garments and put on his normal clothing. *went into the house of the LORD and worshiped.* In this way David openly demonstrated his humble acceptance of the disciplinary results of his sin. Again (see note on v. 13) there is a contrast between David's attitude and Saul's (see note on 1Sa 15:25).

12:23 *I will go to him.* David too will die and join his child in the grave (see note on Ge 37:35). *he will not return to me.* See Job 7:9 and note.

12:24 *Solomon.* See 1Ch 22:9 and NIV text note.

12:25 *Jedidiah.* See NIV text note. The giving of this name suggests that the Lord's special favor rested on Solomon from his birth. And since the name also contained an echo of David's name, it provided assurance to David that the Lord also loved him and would continue his dynasty.

12:26 *Joab fought against Rabbah.* The writer now returns to the outcome of the attack against the Ammonites (11:1,25), which provided the background for the story of David and Bathsheba. Even while the Lord was displeased with David (11:27), he gave the Israelites victory over a people who had abused them.

of the Ammonites and captured the royal citadel. 27 Joab then sent messengers to David, saying, "I have fought against Rabbah and taken its water supply. 28 Now muster the rest of the troops and besiege the city and capture it. Otherwise I will take the city, and it will be named after me."

29 So David mustered the entire army and went to Rabbah, and attacked and captured it. 30 David took the crown[x] from their king's[a] head, and it was placed on his own head. It weighed a talent[b] of gold, and it was set with precious stones. David took a great quantity of plunder from the city 31 and brought out the people who were there, consigning them to labor with saws and with iron picks and axes, and he made them work at brickmaking.[c] David did this to all the Ammonite[y] towns. Then he and his entire army returned to Jerusalem.

Amnon and Tamar

13 In the course of time, Amnon[z] son of David fell in love with Tamar,[a] the beautiful sister of Absalom[b] son of David.

2 Amnon became so obsessed with his sister Tamar that he made himself ill. She was a virgin, and it seemed impossible for him to do anything to her.

3 Now Amnon had an adviser named Jonadab son of Shimeah,[c] David's brother. Jonadab was a very shrewd man. 4 He asked Amnon, "Why do you, the king's son, look so haggard morning after morning? Won't you tell me?"

Amnon said to him, "I'm in love with Tamar, my brother Absalom's sister."

5 "Go to bed and pretend to be ill," Jonadab said. "When your father comes to see you, say to him, 'I would like my sister Tamar to come and give me something to eat. Let her prepare the food in my sight so I may watch her and then eat it from her hand.' "

6 So Amnon lay down and pretended to be ill. When the king came to see him, Amnon said to him, "I would like my sister Tamar to come and make some special bread in my sight, so I may eat from her hand."

7 David sent word to Tamar at the palace: "Go to the house of your brother Amnon and prepare some food for him." 8 So Tamar went to the house of her brother Amnon, who was lying down. She took some dough, kneaded it, made the bread in his sight and baked it. 9 Then she took the pan and served him the bread, but he refused to eat.

"Send everyone out of here,"[d] Amnon said. So everyone left him. 10 Then Amnon said to Tamar, "Bring the food here into my bedroom so I may eat from your hand." And Tamar took the bread she had prepared and brought it to her brother Amnon in his bedroom. 11 But when she took it to him to eat, he grabbed[e] her and said, "Come to bed with me, my sister."[f]

12 "No, my brother!" she said to him. "Don't force me! Such a thing should not be done in Israel![g] Don't do this wicked thing.[h] 13 What about me?[i] Where could I get rid of my disgrace? And what about you? You would be like one of the wicked fools in Israel. Please speak to the king; he will not keep me from being married to you." 14 But he refused to listen to her, and since he was stronger than she, he raped her.[j]

15 Then Amnon hated her with intense hatred. In fact, he hated her more than he had loved her. Amnon said to her, "Get up and get out!"

16 "No!" she said to him. "Sending me away would be a greater wrong than what you have already done to me."

But he refused to listen to her. 17 He called his personal servant and said, "Get this woman out of my sight and bolt the

12:30 [x] Est 8:15; Ps 21:3; 132:18
12:31 [y] S 1Sa 14:47
13:1 [z] 2Sa 3:2 [a] 2Sa 14:27; 1Ch 3:9 [b] S 2Sa 3:3
13:3 [c] S 1Sa 16:9
13:9 [d] Ge 45:1
13:11 [e] S Ge 39:12 [f] S Ge 38:16
13:12 [g] Lev 20:17 [h] S Ge 34:7
13:13 [i] S Lev 18:9; S Dt 22:21, 23-24
13:14 [j] S Ge 34:2; Eze 22:11

[a] *30* Or *from Milkom's* (that is, Molek's) [b] *30* That is, about 75 pounds or about 34 kilograms
[c] *31* The meaning of the Hebrew for this clause is uncertain.

12:30 *the crown ... was placed on his own head.* A crown of such weight (see second NIV text note) would have been worn only briefly and on very special occasions. Perhaps it was worn only once in a symbolic act of transferring to David sovereignty over Ammon.

12:31 *consigning them to labor.* Victorious kings often used prisoners of war as menial laborers in royal building projects (see 1Ki 9:20–21; cf. also Ex 1:11).

13:1–39 Amnon's abuse of power and Absalom's personal revenge. The trouble within David's family begins (see notes on 12:7,10–11).

13:1 *In the course of time.* See note on 2:1. *Amnon.* David's firstborn son (3:2). *Tamar.* David's daughter by Maakah of Geshur (cf. 3:3), and Absalom's full sister.

13:3 *Shimeah.* Called Shammah in 1Sa 16:9.

13:6 *When the king came to see him.* Amnon used his father, David, to obtain his illicit purpose, just as David had used Joab (see 11:14–17).

13:12 *wicked thing.* Hebrew *nebalah* ("folly"), from the same root word as the name Nabal ("fool"; see 1Sa 25:25).

13:13 *what about you?* This act would jeopardize Amnon's position as crown prince and heir to the throne. *one of the wicked fools.* That is, a *nabal* (see note on v. 12; see also NIV text note on Pr 1:7). David's wicked folly in his dealings with Bathsheba yields the bitter fruit of imitation by his oldest son, who by his act becomes another Nabal.

13:15 *Amnon hated her.* The reversal in Amnon's feelings toward Tamar demonstrates that his former "love" (v. 1) was nothing but sensual desire.

13:16 *Sending me away would be a greater wrong.* No longer a virgin, she could not be offered by her father to any other potential husband (see v. 21 and note).

door after her." 18 So his servant put her
out and bolted the door after her. She was
wearing an ornate[a] robe,[k] for this was the
kind of garment the virgin daughters of the
king wore. 19 Tamar put ashes[l] on her head
and tore the ornate robe she was wearing.
She put her hands on her head and went
away, weeping aloud as she went.
20 Her brother Absalom said to her, "Has
that Amnon, your brother, been with you?
Be quiet for now, my sister; he is your
brother. Don't take this thing to heart."
And Tamar lived in her brother Absalom's
house, a desolate woman.
21 When King David heard all this, he
was furious.[m] 22 And Absalom never said
a word to Amnon, either good or bad;[n] he
hated[o] Amnon because he had disgraced
his sister Tamar.

Absalom Kills Amnon

23 Two years later, when Absalom's
sheepshearers[p] were at Baal Hazor near
the border of Ephraim, he invited all the
king's sons to come there. 24 Absalom went
to the king and said, "Your servant has
had shearers come. Will the king and his
attendants please join me?"
25 "No, my son," the king replied. "All
of us should not go; we would only be a
burden to you." Although Absalom urged
him, he still refused to go but gave him
his blessing.
26 Then Absalom said, "If not, please let
my brother Amnon come with us."
The king asked him, "Why should he go
with you?" 27 But Absalom urged him, so
he sent with him Amnon and the rest of
the king's sons.

28 Absalom[q] ordered his men, "Listen!
When Amnon is in high[r] spirits from
drinking wine and I say to you, 'Strike
Amnon down,' then kill him. Don't be
afraid. Haven't I given you this order? Be
strong and brave.[s]" 29 So Absalom's men
did to Amnon what Absalom had ordered.
Then all the king's sons got up, mounted
their mules and fled.
30 While they were on their way, the report came to David: "Absalom has struck
down all the king's sons; not one of
them is left." 31 The king stood up, tore[t]
his clothes and lay down on the ground;
and all his attendants stood by with their
clothes torn.
32 But Jonadab son of Shimeah, David's
brother, said, "My lord should not think
that they killed all the princes; only Amnon is dead. This has been Absalom's express intention ever since the day Amnon
raped his sister Tamar. 33 My lord the king
should not be concerned about the report
that all the king's sons are dead. Only Amnon is dead."
34 Meanwhile, Absalom had fled.
Now the man standing watch looked up
and saw many people on the road west of
him, coming down the side of the hill. The
watchman went and told the king, "I see
men in the direction of Horonaim, on the
side of the hill."[b]
35 Jonadab said to the king, "See, the
king's sons have come; it has happened
just as your servant said."
36 As he finished speaking, the king's

13:18 [k] S Ge 37:23
13:19 [l] S Jos 7:6; Est 4:1; Da 9:3
13:21 [m] S Ge 34:7
13:22 [n] Ge 31:24 [o] Lev 19:17-18; 1Jn 2:9-11
13:23 [p] 1Sa 25:7
13:28 [q] S 2Sa 3:3 [r] S Ru 3:7 [s] S 2Sa 12:10
13:31 [t] S Nu 14:6

[a] *18* The meaning of the Hebrew for this word is uncertain; also in verse 19. [b] *34* Septuagint; Hebrew does not have this sentence.

13:18 *ornate robe.* See Ge 37:3 and note.

13:19 *put ashes on her head and tore the … robe she was wearing.* Signs of grief (see 1Sa 4:12 and note), expressing her anguish and announcing that her virginity had been violated.

13:20 *Be quiet for now, my sister … Don't take this thing to heart.* Absalom urges his sister not to make the matter a public scandal. Meanwhile, he formulates his own secret plans for revenge (see vv. 22,28,32).

13:21 *he was furious.* Although David was incensed by Amnon's rape of Tamar, there is no record that he took any punitive action against him. Perhaps the memory of his own sin with Bathsheba adversely affected his judicious handling of the matter. Whatever the reason, David abdicated his responsibility both as king and as father. This disciplinary leniency toward his sons (see notes on 14:33; 1Ki 1:6) eventually led to the death of Amnon and the revolts of Absalom and Adonijah.

13:22 *Absalom never said a word to Amnon … he hated Amnon.* He quietly bided his time.

13:23 *Two years later.* After two years it was clear to Absalom that King David was not going to do anything to Amnon for raping Tamar. *he invited all the king's sons.* The time of sheepshearing was a festive occasion (see 1Sa 25:4,8).

13:26 *let my brother Amnon come.* Upon David's refusal of the invitation, Absalom diplomatically requested that Amnon, the crown prince and oldest son, be his representative. *Why should he go with you?* David's question suggests some misgivings because of the strained relationship between the two half brothers (see v. 22).

13:28 *kill him.* Absalom arranged for the murder of his half brother in violation of Eastern hospitality. In the wicked acts of Amnon and Absalom, David's oldest sons became guilty of sexual immorality and murder, as their father had before them. With the murder of Amnon, Absalom not only avenged the rape of his sister but also secured for himself the position of successor to the throne (see 3:3; 15:1 – 6). Kileab, David's second son (3:3), may have died in his youth since there is no reference to him beyond the announcement of his birth.

13:29 *mules.* Apparently the normal mount for royalty in David's kingdom (see 18:9; 1Ki 1:33,38,44; see also note on 1Ki 1:33; cf. Zec 9:9 and note).

13:31 *tore his clothes and lay down on the ground.* Common ways of expressing grief (see v. 19; Jos 7:6; 1Ki 21:27; Est 4:1,3; Job 1:20; 2:8).

13:34 *Horonaim.* The Levitical cities of Upper and Lower Beth Horon, located in Ephraim (see Jos 21:20,22; 1Ch 7:24) two miles apart and about eleven miles northwest of Jerusalem (see note on Ne 2:10, "Horonite"; see also map, p. 319).

sons came in, wailing loudly. The king,
too, and all his attendants wept very bitterly.
37 Absalom fled and went to Talmai[u] son
of Ammihud, the king of Geshur. But King
David mourned many days for his son.
38 After Absalom fled and went to Geshur, he stayed there three years. 39 And
King David longed to go to Absalom,[v] for
he was consoled[w] concerning Amnon's
death.

Absalom Returns to Jerusalem

14 Joab[x] son of Zeruiah knew that the
king's heart longed for Absalom.
2 So Joab sent someone to Tekoa[y] and had
a wise woman[z] brought from there. He
said to her, "Pretend you are in mourning. Dress in mourning clothes, and don't
use any cosmetic lotions.[a] Act like a woman who has spent many days grieving for
the dead. 3 Then go to the king and speak
these words to him." And Joab[b] put the
words in her mouth.
4 When the woman from Tekoa went[a]
to the king, she fell with her face to the
ground to pay him honor, and she said,
"Help me, Your Majesty!"
5 The king asked her, "What is troubling
you?"
She said, "I am a widow; my husband is
dead. 6 I your servant had two sons. They
got into a fight with each other in the field,
and no one was there to separate them.
One struck the other and killed him. 7 Now
the whole clan has risen up against you
servant; they say, 'Hand over the one wh
struck his brother down, so that we ma
put him to death[c] for the life of his broth
er whom he killed; then we will get rid o
the heir[d] as well.' They would put out th
only burning coal I have left,[e] leaving m
husband neither name nor descendant o
the face of the earth."
8 The king said to the woman, "G
home,[f] and I will issue an order in you
behalf."
9 But the woman from Tekoa said to him
"Let my lord the king pardon[g] me and m
family,[h] and let the king and his throne b
without guilt.[i]"
10 The king replied, "If anyone says any
thing to you, bring them to me, and the
will not bother you again."
11 She said, "Then let the king invoke th
LORD his God to prevent the avenger[j] o
blood from adding to the destruction, s
that my son will not be destroyed."
"As surely as the LORD lives," he said
"not one hair[k] of your son's head will fa
to the ground.[l]"
12 Then the woman said, "Let your ser
vant speak a word to my lord the king."
"Speak," he replied.
13 The woman said, "Why then have yo
devised a thing like this against the peo
ple of God? When the king says this, doe
he not convict himself,[m] for the king ha

13:37 [u] S 2Sa 3:3 **13:39** [v] 2Sa 14:13 [w] S 2Sa 12:19-23 **14:1** [x] S 2Sa 2:18 **14:2** [y] Ne 3:5; Jer 6:1; Am 1:1 [z] 2Sa 20:16 [a] S Ru 3:3; S Isa 1:6 **14:3** [b] ver 19

14:7 [c] Nu 35:19 [d] Mt 21:38 [e] Dt 19:10-13 **14:8** [f] 1Sa 25:35 **14:9** [g] 1Sa 25:24 [h] Mt 27:25 [i] 1Sa 25:28 **14:11** [j] S Nu 35:12, 21 [k] S Mt 10:30 [l] S 1Sa 14:45 **14:13** [m] S 2Sa 12:7; 1Ki 20:40

[a] 4 Many Hebrew manuscripts, Septuagint, Vulgate and Syriac; most Hebrew manuscripts *spoke*

13:37 *Talmai son of Ammihud, the king of Geshur.* Absalom's grandfather (see 3:3 and note).

13:39 *longed to go to Absalom.* With Absalom a refugee, David had lost both of his oldest living sons. Moreover, he could not bring Absalom to account for what he had done to Amnon since David himself had blood on his hands.

14:1—19:43 The threat to David's reign that emerged after Absalom's restoration from exile, and how that threat was crushed.

14:1 *Joab son of Zeruiah.* See notes on 2:13; 1Sa 26:6. *the king's heart longed for Absalom.* Torn between anger and love (and perhaps remorse), David again leaves the initiative to others.

14:2 *So Joab sent.* Joab appears to have been motivated by a concern for the political implications of the unresolved dispute between David and the son in line for the throne. He attempts to move David to action by means of a story designed to elicit a response clearly applicable, by analogy, to David's own predicament. A similar technique was used by Nathan the prophet (12:1-7; see also 1Ki 20:38-43). *Tekoa.* A town a few miles south of Bethlehem, from which the prophet Amos also came (Am 1:1).

14:7 *the whole clan has risen up against your servant.* It was customary in Israel for a murder victim's next of kin to avenge the blood of his relative by putting the murderer to death (see note on 3:27; see also map and accompanying text, p. 254). In the case presented, however, blood revenge would have wiped out the family line, which Israelite law and custom tried to avoid if at all possible (see notes on D 25:5-6; Ru 2:20). *we will get rid of the heir as well.* The womar suggests that the motivation for blood revenge was more a selfish desire to acquire the family inheritance than a desire for justice (see Nu 27:11). *leaving my husband neither name nor descendant.* The implication is that it would be a more serious offense to terminate the woman's family line than tc permit a murder to go unpunished by blood revenge. Apparently Joab hoped subtly to suggest to David that if he did no restore Absalom, a struggle for the throne would eventually ensue.

14:8 *I will issue an order in your behalf.* David's judicial actior may have rested on the legal ground that the murder was not premeditated (see Dt 19:4-6).

14:11 *let the king invoke the LORD his God.* The woman wants David to confirm his promise by an oath in the Lord's name *As surely as the LORD lives.* An oath formula (see notes on Ge 42:15; 1Sa 14:39,45) that solemnly binds David to his commitment.

14:13 *against the people of God.* The woman's suggestion is that David has done the same thing to Israel that her family members have done to her. The people of Israel want their crown prince returned safely to them. *does he not convict himself...?* The argument is that when David exempted the fictitious murderer from blood revenge, he in effect rendered himself guilty for not doing the same in the case of Absalom. The analogy places David in the position of the blood avenger.

not brought back his banished son?[n] 14 Like
water[o] spilled on the ground, which cannot be recovered, so we must die.[p] But that
is not what God desires; rather, he devises
ways so that a banished person[q] does not
remain banished from him.
15 "And now I have come to say this to
my lord the king because the people have
made me afraid. Your servant thought, 'I
will speak to the king; perhaps he will
grant his servant's request. 16 Perhaps the
king will agree to deliver his servant from
the hand of the man who is trying to cut
off both me and my son from God's inheritance.'[r]
17 "And now your servant says, 'May the
word of my lord the king secure my inheritance, for my lord the king is like an angel[s]
of God in discerning[t] good and evil. May
the LORD your God be with you.' "
18 Then the king said to the woman,
"Don't keep from me the answer to what I
am going to ask you."
"Let my lord the king speak," the woman said.
19 The king asked, "Isn't the hand of
Joab[u] with you in all this?"
The woman answered, "As surely as
you live, my lord the king, no one can turn
to the right or to the left from anything my
lord the king says. Yes, it was your servant
Joab who instructed me to do this and
who put all these words into the mouth
of your servant. 20 Your servant Joab did
this to change the present situation. My
lord has wisdom[v] like that of an angel of
God—he knows everything that happens
in the land.[w]"
21 The king said to Joab, "Very well, I
will do it. Go, bring back the young man
Absalom."
22 Joab fell with his face to the ground to
pay him honor, and he blessed the king.[x]
Joab said, "Today your servant knows that
he has found favor in your eyes, my lord

14:13 [n]2Sa 13:38-39
14:14 [o]Job 14:11; Ps 58:7; Isa 19:5 [p]Job 10:8; 17:13; 30:23; Ps 22:15; Heb 9:27 [q]Nu 35:15, 25-28
14:16 [r]S Ex 34:9; S 1Sa 26:19
14:17 [s]S 1Sa 29:9 [t]1Ki 3:9; Da 2:21
14:19 [u]ver 3
14:20 [v]1Ki 3:12, 28; 10:23-24; Isa 28:6 [w]2Sa 18:13
14:22 [x]S Ge 47:7
14:26 [y]2Sa 18:9
14:27 [z]2Sa 18:18 [a]S 2Sa 13:1
14:30 [b]S Ex 9:31
14:31 [c]S Jdg 15:5
14:32 [d]S 2Sa 3:3 [e]1Sa 20:8

the king, because the king has granted his
servant's request."
23 Then Joab went to Geshur and brought
Absalom back to Jerusalem. 24 But the king
said, "He must go to his own house; he
must not see my face." So Absalom went
to his own house and did not see the face
of the king.
25 In all Israel there was not a man so
highly praised for his handsome appearance as Absalom. From the top of his head
to the sole of his foot there was no blemish in him. 26 Whenever he cut the hair of
his head[y]—he used to cut his hair once
a year because it became too heavy for
him—he would weigh it, and its weight
was two hundred shekels[a] by the royal
standard.
27 Three sons[z] and a daughter were born
to Absalom. His daughter's name was Tamar,[a] and she became a beautiful woman.
28 Absalom lived two years in Jerusalem
without seeing the king's face. 29 Then Absalom sent for Joab in order to send him to
the king, but Joab refused to come to him.
So he sent a second time, but he refused
to come. 30 Then he said to his servants,
"Look, Joab's field is next to mine, and he
has barley[b] there. Go and set it on fire." So
Absalom's servants set the field on fire.
31 Then Joab did go to Absalom's house,
and he said to him, "Why have your servants set my field on fire?[c]"
32 Absalom said to Joab, "Look, I sent
word to you and said, 'Come here so I can
send you to the king to ask, "Why have I
come from Geshur?[d] It would be better for
me if I were still there!" ' Now then, I want
to see the king's face, and if I am guilty of
anything, let him put me to death."[e]
33 So Joab went to the king and told him
this. Then the king summoned Absalom,
and he came in and bowed down with his

[a] *26* That is, about 5 pounds or about 2.3 kilograms

14:14 *Like water spilled on the ground.* Blood revenge will not return the victim of murder to life, just as water spilled on the ground cannot be recovered. *that is not what God desires.* In the suggestion that the avenging of blood is contrary to God's ways of dealing with people, the woman apparently distorts Biblical teaching of God's justice (see note on Ge 9:6). But she dwells on the mercy of God, who would rather preserve life than take it (see Eze 18:32; 33:11 and notes). David's own guilt and subsequent experience of God's mercy appear to give added weight to the woman's argument (see notes on 12:13; 13:21).
14:15 *the people have made me afraid.* The woman reverts to her own fabricated story. "The people" are evidently those of her own family who are seeking blood revenge.
14:17 *like an angel of God in discerning good and evil.* Possessing superhuman powers of discernment—as a king ideally should (see v. 20; 19:27).
14:21 *Joab.* He appears to have been present the whole time.
14:23 *Joab went to Geshur.* See 13:37.
14:24 *he must not see my face.* David still vacillates (see note on v. 1); he does not offer forgiveness and restoration.
14:25 *not a man so highly praised.* Absalom's handsomeness brought him attention and popular favor—which he was soon to cultivate.
14:26 *hair of his head.* For the people of that time, hair was a sign of vigor. Kings and heroic figures were usually portrayed with abundant locks, while baldness was a disgrace (see 2Ki 2:23 and note). In this, too, Absalom seemed destined for the throne. *royal standard.* The royal shekel was perhaps heavier than the sanctuary shekel (see Ex 30:13).
14:27 *Three sons.* Their names are unknown; 18:18 suggests that they died in their youth. *Tamar.* Absalom named his daughter after his sister (13:1). Maakah (see 1Ki 15:2 and note) was probably a daughter of Tamar and thereby Absalom's granddaughter (see note on 2Ch 11:20).
14:32 *if I am guilty of anything, let him put me to death.* Absalom demands either full pardon and restoration or death, but he still gives no sign of repentance.

face to the ground before the king. And
the king kissed[f] Absalom.

Absalom's Conspiracy

15 In the course of time,[g] Absalom
provided himself with a chari-
ot[h] and horses and with fifty men to run
ahead of him. 2He would get up early and
stand by the side of the road leading to
the city gate.[i] Whenever anyone came
with a complaint to be placed before the
king for a decision, Absalom would call
out to him, "What town are you from?"
He would answer, "Your servant is from
one of the tribes of Israel." 3Then Absalom
would say to him, "Look, your claims are
valid and proper, but there is no representative of the king to hear you."[j] 4And Absalom would add, "If only I were appointed judge in the land![k] Then everyone who
has a complaint or case could come to me
and I would see that they receive justice."
5Also, whenever anyone approached
him to bow down before him, Absalom
would reach out his hand, take hold of
him and kiss him. 6Absalom behaved
in this way toward all the Israelites who
came to the king asking for justice, and so
he stole the hearts[l] of the people of Israel.
7At the end of four[a] years, Absalom said
to the king, "Let me go to Hebron and fulfill a vow I made to the LORD. 8While your
servant was living at Geshur[m] in Aram, I
made this vow:[n] 'If the LORD takes me back
to Jerusalem, I will worship the LORD in
Hebron.[b]'"
9The king said to him, "Go in peace." So
he went to Hebron.

14:33 [f] Lk 15:20
15:1 [g] S 2Sa 12:11 [h] S 1Sa 8:11
15:2 [i] S Ge 23:10; 2Sa 19:8
15:3 [j] Pr 12:2
15:4 [k] Jdg 9:29
15:6 [l] Ro 16:18
15:8 [m] S 2Sa 3:3 [n] S Ge 28:20
15:10 [o] 1Ki 1:34,39; 2Ki 9:13
15:12 [p] ver 31,34; 2Sa 16:15,23; 17:14; 23:34; 1Ch 27:33 [q] Job 19:14; Ps 41:9; 55:13; Jer 9:4 [r] Jos 15:51 [s] Ps 3:1
15:14 [t] 1Ki 2:26; Ps 3 Title; 132:1 [u] 2Sa 19:9
15:16 [v] 2Sa 16:21-22; 20:3

10Then Absalom sent secret messengers throughout the tribes of Israel to
say, "As soon as you hear the sound of
the trumpets,[o] then say, 'Absalom is king
in Hebron.'" 11Two hundred men from
Jerusalem had accompanied Absalom.
They had been invited as guests and went
quite innocently, knowing nothing about
the matter. 12While Absalom was offering
sacrifices, he also sent for Ahithophel[p] the
Gilonite, David's counselor,[q] to come from
Giloh,[r] his hometown. And so the conspiracy gained strength, and Absalom's following kept on increasing.[s]

David Flees

13A messenger came and told David,
"The hearts of the people of Israel are with
Absalom."
14Then David said to all his officials
who were with him in Jerusalem, "Come!
We must flee,[t] or none of us will escape
from Absalom.[u] We must leave immediately, or he will move quickly to overtake us
and bring ruin on us and put the city to
the sword."
15The king's officials answered him,
"Your servants are ready to do whatever
our lord the king chooses."
16The king set out, with his entire
household following him; but he left ten
concubines[v] to take care of the palace.
17So the king set out, with all the people
following him, and they halted at the edge
of the city. 18All his men marched past

[a] 7 Some Septuagint manuscripts, Syriac and Josephus; Hebrew *forty* [b] 8 Some Septuagint manuscripts; Hebrew does not have *in Hebron.*

14:33 *the king kissed Absalom.* Signifying his forgiveness and Absalom's reconciliation with the royal family. David sidesteps repentance and justice, and in this way he probably contributes to the fulfillment of the prophecy of Nathan (see 12:10–11 and notes).

15:1 *In the course of time.* See note on 2:1. *chariot and horses.* As far as is known, Absalom was the first Israelite leader to acquire a chariot and horses (cf. Dt 17:16). *fifty men.* They probably functioned as bodyguards and provided a display of royal pomp that appealed to the masses. Absalom and his brother Adonijah (see 1Ki 1:5 and note) are parade examples of precisely what Samuel had warned against (see 1Sa 8:11 and note).

15:2 The main gateway of a city was the primary site where legal cases were settled (see notes on Ge 19:1; Ru 4:1).

15:3 *your claims are valid.* Absalom seeks to ingratiate himself with the people by endorsing their grievances apart from any investigation into their merit.

15:4 *If only I were appointed judge in the land!* Absalom presents himself as the solution to the people's legal grievances. In the case of Amnon, Absalom had taken matters into his own hands because of his father's laxity. Now he has found, he believes, the weakness in his father's reign, and he capitalizes on it with political astuteness.

15:7 *four years.* After Absalom's return to the court (14:33). By this time he must have been about 30 years old, so his revolt must be dated early in the last decade of David's reign. *Hebron.* Where David was first proclaimed king (see notes on 2:1,4; 5:3,5) and where Absalom was born (3:2–3). Absalom may have had reason to believe that he could count on some local resentment over David's transfer of the capital to Jerusalem. Hebron was also the site of an important sanctuary. *fulfill a vow I made to the LORD.* Absalom piously lies to his father in order to mask his true intentions; cf. David's masking his intentions in the matter of Uriah (11:7–15).

15:8 *Geshur.* See 13:37.

15:12 *Ahithophel.* Bathsheba's grandfather (see 11:3; 23:34 and notes) and a wise and respected counselor (16:23). He appears to have secretly aligned himself with Absalom's rebellion in its planning stage, perhaps in retaliation against David for his treatment of Bathsheba and Uriah. This unsuspected betrayal by a trusted friend may have prompted David's statements in Ps 41:9; 55:12–14. *Giloh.* Near Hebron (see Jos 15:51,54).

15:14 *none of us will escape from Absalom.* Uncertain of the extent of Absalom's support (see v. 13), David fears being trapped in Jerusalem, and he wants to spare the city a bloodbath.

15:16 *he left ten concubines to take care of the palace.* See 5:13; see also note on 3:2. David unknowingly arranges for the fulfillment of one of Nathan's prophecies (see notes on 12:11; 16:22; see also 20:3).

him, along with all the Kerethites[w] and
Pelethites; and all the six hundred Gittites
who had accompanied him from Gath
marched before the king.
19 The king said to Ittai[x] the Gittite,
"Why should you come along with us? Go
back and stay with King Absalom. You are
a foreigner,[y] an exile from your homeland.
20 You came only yesterday. And today
shall I make you wander[z] about with us,
when I do not know where I am going? Go
back, and take your people with you. May
the LORD show you kindness and faithfulness."[a][a]
21 But Ittai replied to the king, "As surely
as the LORD lives, and as my lord the king
lives, wherever my lord the king may be,
whether it means life or death, there will
your servant be."[b]
22 David said to Ittai, "Go ahead, march
on." So Ittai the Gittite marched on with
all his men and the families that were with
him.
23 The whole countryside wept aloud[c]
as all the people passed by. The king also
crossed the Kidron Valley,[d] and all the people moved on toward the wilderness.
24 Zadok[e] was there, too, and all the Levites who were with him were carrying
the ark[f] of the covenant of God. They set
down the ark of God, and Abiathar[g] offered sacrifices until all the people had finished leaving the city.
25 Then the king said to Zadok, "Take
the ark of God back into the city. If I find
favor in the LORD's eyes, he will bring me
back and let me see it and his dwelling
place[h] again. 26 But if he says, 'I am not
pleased with you,' then I am ready; let him
do to me whatever seems good to him.[i]"
27 The king also said to Zadok the priest,
"Do you understand?[j] Go back to the city
with my blessing. Take your son Ahimaaz
with you, and also Abiathar's son Jonathan.[k] You and Abiathar return with your
two sons. 28 I will wait at the fords[l] in the
wilderness until word comes from you
to inform me." 29 So Zadok and Abiathar
took the ark of God back to Jerusalem and
stayed there.
30 But David continued up the Mount
of Olives, weeping[m] as he went; his head[n]
was covered and he was barefoot. All
the people with him covered their heads
too and were weeping as they went up.
31 Now David had been told, "Ahithophel[o]
is among the conspirators with Absalom."
So David prayed, "LORD, turn Ahithophel's
counsel into foolishness."
32 When David arrived at the summit,
where people used to worship God, Hushai[p] the Arkite[q] was there to meet him,
his robe torn and dust[r] on his head. 33 David said to him, "If you go with me, you
will be a burden[s] to me. 34 But if you return to the city and say to Absalom, 'Your
Majesty, I will be your servant; I was your
father's servant in the past, but now I will
be your servant,'[t] then you can help me by
frustrating[u] Ahithophel's advice. 35 Won't
the priests Zadok and Abiathar be there
with you? Tell them anything you hear in
the king's palace.[v] 36 Their two sons, Ahimaaz[w] son of Zadok and Jonathan[x] son of
Abiathar, are there with them. Send them
to me with anything you hear."
37 So Hushai,[y] David's confidant, arrived
at Jerusalem as Absalom[z] was entering the
city.

[a] 20 Septuagint; Hebrew *May kindness and faithfulness be with you*

15:18 [w] S 1Sa 30:14; 2Sa 20:7,23; 1Ki 1:38,44; 1Ch 18:17 **15:19** [x] 2Sa 18:2 [y] S Ge 31:15 **15:20** [z] S 1Sa 22:2 [a] 2Sa 2:6 **15:21** [b] Ru 1:16-17; Pr 17:17 **15:23** [c] 1Sa 11:4; Job 2:12 [d] 1Ki 2:37; 2Ki 23:12; 2Ch 15:16; 29:16; 30:14; Jer 31:40; Jn 18:1 **15:24** [e] S 2Sa 8:17; 19:11 [f] Nu 4:15; S 10:33; 1Ki 2:26 [g] S 1Sa 22:20 **15:25** [h] Ex 15:13; S Lev 15:31; Ps 43:3; 46:4; 84:1; 132:7 **15:26** [i] S Jdg 10:15; 2Sa 22:20 **15:27** [j] S 1Sa 9:9 [k] ver 36; 2Sa 17:17; 1Ki 1:42 **15:28** [l] 2Sa 17:16 **15:30** [m] S Nu 25:6; S Ps 30:5 [n] Est 6:12 **15:31** [o] S ver 12 **15:32** [p] ver 37; 2Sa 16:16; 17:5; 1Ki 4:16 [q] Jos 16:2 [r] S Jos 7:6 **15:33** [s] 2Sa 19:35 **15:34** [t] 2Sa 16:19 [u] 2Sa 17:14; Pr 11:14 **15:35** [v] 2Sa 17:15-16 **15:36** [w] 2Sa 18:19 [x] S ver 27; 2Sa 17:17; 1Ki 1:42 **15:37** [y] 1Ch 27:33 [z] 2Sa 16:15

15:18 *Kerethites and Pelethites.* See notes on 8:18; Jer 47:4. *six hundred Gittites.* Philistine soldiers who had joined David's personal military force. Their commander was Ittai (v. 19; 18:2).

15:19 *Go back and stay with King Absalom.* David releases the Philistine contingent from further obligations to him.

15:21 *As surely as the LORD lives.* An oath of loyalty taken in the name of Israel's God (see note on 1Sa 14:39,45). *wherever my lord … may be, … there will your servant be.* For a similar declaration of commitment, see Ru 1:16–17.

15:23 *Kidron Valley.* Just east of Jerusalem (see note on Isa 22:7). *wilderness.* The northern part of the Desert of Judah that lies between Jerusalem and the Dead Sea.

15:24 *Zadok.* See note on 8:17. *Abiathar.* See note on 8:17; see also 1Sa 22:20–23 and note on 22:20.

15:25 *Take the ark of God back into the city.* David reveals a true understanding of the connection between the ark and God's presence with his people. He knows that possession of the ark does not guarantee God's blessing (see notes on 1Sa 4:3,21). He also recognizes that the ark belongs in the capital city as a symbol of the Lord's rule over the nation (see note on 6:2), no matter who the king might be.

15:26 *let him do to me whatever seems good to him.* David confesses that he has no exclusive claim to the throne and that Israel's divine King is free to confer the kingship on whomever he chooses.

15:27 *Do you understand?* Perhaps an allusion to the high priest's custody of the Urim and Thummim as a means of divine revelation (see notes on Ex 28:30; 1Sa 2:28). See also note on 1Sa 9:9.

15:28 *fords in the wilderness.* Fords across the Jordan in the vicinity of Gilgal.

15:30 *Mount of Olives.* See notes on Zec 14:4; Mk 11:1. *his head was covered.* A sign of sorrow (see Est 6:12; Jer 14:3–4; cf. 2Sa 19:4 and note). *he was barefoot.* A sign of mourning (see Eze 24:17; Mic 1:8) and shame (see Isa 20:4).

15:31 *Ahithophel.* See note on v. 12.

15:32 *Hushai the Arkite.* The Arkites were a clan (some think non-Israelite) that inhabited an area southwest of Bethel (Jos 16:2). Since Hushai was a trusted member of David's court (see note on v. 37), his appearance was the beginning of an answer to David's prayer (v. 31).

15:37 *Hushai, David's confidant.* 1Ch 27:33 calls him the "king's confidant," which seems to be an official

David and Ziba

16 When David had gone a short distance beyond the summit, there
was Ziba,[a] the steward of Mephibosheth,
waiting to meet him. He had a string of
donkeys saddled and loaded with two
hundred loaves of bread, a hundred cakes
of raisins, a hundred cakes of figs and a
skin of wine.[b]
2The king asked Ziba, "Why have you
brought these?"
Ziba answered, "The donkeys are for
the king's household to ride on, the bread
and fruit are for the men to eat, and the
wine is to refresh[c] those who become exhausted in the wilderness."
3The king then asked, "Where is your
master's grandson?"[d]
Ziba[e] said to him, "He is staying in Jerusalem, because he thinks, 'Today the Israelites will restore to me my grandfather's
kingdom.'"
4Then the king said to Ziba, "All that
belonged to Mephibosheth[f] is now yours."
"I humbly bow," Ziba said. "May I find
favor in your eyes, my lord the king."

Shimei Curses David

5As King David approached Bahurim,[g]
a man from the same clan as Saul's family came out from there. His name was
Shimei[h] son of Gera, and he cursed[i] as he
came out. 6He pelted David and all the
king's officials with stones, though all the
troops and the special guard were on David's right and left. 7As he cursed, Shimei
said, "Get out, get out, you murderer, you
scoundrel! 8The LORD has repaid you for
all the blood you shed in the household
of Saul, in whose place you have reigned.[j]
The LORD has given the kingdom into the
hands of your son Absalom. You have
come to ruin because you are a murderer!"[k]
9Then Abishai[l] son of Zeruiah said to
the king, "Why should this dead dog[m]
curse my lord the king? Let me go over
and cut off his head."[n]
10But the king said, "What does this
have to do with you, you sons of Zeruiah?[o] If he is cursing because the LORD said
to him, 'Curse David,' who can ask, 'Why
do you do this?'"[p]
11David then said to Abishai and all
his officials, "My son,[q] my own flesh and
blood, is trying to kill me. How much
more, then, this Benjamite! Leave him
alone; let him curse, for the LORD has told
him to.[r] 12It may be that the LORD will
look upon my misery[s] and restore to me
his covenant blessing[t] instead of his curse
today.[u]"
13So David and his men continued along
the road while Shimei was going along the
hillside opposite him, cursing as he went
and throwing stones at him and showering him with dirt. 14The king and all the
people with him arrived at their destination exhausted.[v] And there he refreshed
himself.

The Advice of Ahithophel and Hushai

15Meanwhile, Absalom[w] and all the men
of Israel came to Jerusalem, and Ahithophel[x] was with him. 16Then Hushai[y] the
Arkite, David's confidant, went to Absalom and said to him, "Long live the king!
Long live the king!"
17Absalom said to Hushai, "So this is
the love you show your friend? If he's your
friend, why didn't you go with him?"[z]
18Hushai said to Absalom, "No, the one
chosen by the LORD, by these people, and
by all the men of Israel—his I will be, and
I will remain with him. 19Furthermore,
whom should I serve? Should I not serve
the son? Just as I served your father, so I
will serve you."[a]
20Absalom said to Ahithophel, "Give us
your advice. What should we do?"

16:1 [a]2Sa 9:1-13 [b]S 1Sa 25:18; 1Ch 12:40 **16:2** [c]2Sa 17:27-29 **16:3** [d]2Sa 9:9-10 [e]S 2Sa 9:2 **16:4** [f]S 2Sa 4:4 **16:5** [g]S 2Sa 3:16 [h]2Sa 19:16-23; 1Ki 2:8-9,36,44 [i]S Ex 22:28 **16:8** [j]2Sa 19:28; 21:9 [k]2Sa 19:19; Ps 55:3 **16:9** [l]S 1Sa 26:6 [m]S 2Sa 3:8 [n]S 2Sa 3:39; Lk 9:54 **16:10** [o]S 2Sa 2:18; 19:22 [p]Ro 9:20 **16:11** [q]2Sa 12:11 [r]S Ge 45:5; 1Sa 26:19 **16:12** [s]Ps 4:1; 25:18 [t]Dt 23:5; Ro 8:28 [u]Ps 109:28 **16:14** [v]2Sa 17:2 **16:15** [w]S 2Sa 15:37 [x]S 2Sa 15:12 **16:16** [y]S 2Sa 15:32 **16:17** [z]2Sa 19:25 **16:19** [a]2Sa 15:34

---

title for the king's most trusted adviser (see 1Ki 4:5, where the Hebrew for "king's confidant" is translated "adviser to the king").

16:1 *Ziba.* See ch. 9. *Mephibosheth.* See note on 4:4.

16:2 *Ziba answered.* Since David assumed control of Saul's estate (9:7–10), Ziba, always the opportunist, seeks to profit from the political crisis.

16:3 *your master's grandson.* Mephibosheth (see 9:2–3,9).

16:4 *All that belonged to Mephibosheth is now yours.* Because the revolt was so widespread and loyalties so uncertain, David was quick to assume the worst.

16:5 *Bahurim.* Near the Mount of Olives. *same clan as Saul's family.* The clan of Matri (see 1Sa 10:21). *Gera.* See note on 1Ki 2:8.

16:6 *the troops and the special guard.* The Kerethites, Pelethites and 600 Gittites (see 15:18 and note).

16:7 *scoundrel.* See note on Dt 13:13.

16:8 *blood you shed in the household of Saul.* Shimei may be referring to the executions reported in 21:1–14, but the time of that event is uncertain (see note on 21:1).

16:9 *Abishai.* See note on 1Sa 26:6. *this dead dog.* An expression of absolute contempt (see note on 9:8).

16:10 *sons of Zeruiah.* Intended as an insult (cf. note on 1Sa 20:27,30–31). *If … because the LORD said to him, 'Curse David.'* David leaves open the possibility that God has seen fit to terminate his rule—the verdict is not yet in (see 15:26 and note). For David's later actions regarding Shimei, see 19:18–23; 1Ki 2:8–9.

16:15 *Ahithophel.* See note on 15:12.

16:16 *Hushai the Arkite, David's confidant.* See notes on 15:32,37. *Long live the king!* See note on Ps 62:4.

16:18 Hushai's statement is deliberately ambiguous. Nowhere is Absalom referred to as God's "chosen" one, but David is often called the Lord's "chosen" one or its equivalent (see 6:21; 1Sa 16:8–13; 1Ki 8:16; 11:34; 1Ch 28:4; Ps 78:70).

21 Ahithophel answered, "Sleep with
your father's concubines whom he left
to take care of the palace. Then all Israel will hear that you have made yourself
obnoxious to your father, and the hands
of everyone with you will be more resolute." 22 So they pitched a tent for Absalom
on the roof, and he slept with his father's
concubines in the sight of all Israel.[b]
23 Now in those days the advice[c] Ahithophel gave was like that of one who inquires of God. That was how both David[d]
and Absalom regarded all of Ahithophel's
advice.

17 Ahithophel said to Absalom, "I
would[a] choose twelve thousand
men and set out tonight in pursuit of David. 2 I would attack him while he is weary
and weak.[e] I would strike him with terror,
and then all the people with him will flee.
I would strike down only the king[f] 3 and
bring all the people back to you. The death
of the man you seek will mean the return
of all; all the people will be unharmed."
4 This plan seemed good to Absalom and
to all the elders of Israel.
5 But Absalom said, "Summon also Hushai[g] the Arkite, so we can hear what he
has to say as well." 6 When Hushai came
to him, Absalom said, "Ahithophel has
given this advice. Should we do what he
says? If not, give us your opinion."
7 Hushai replied to Absalom, "The advice Ahithophel has given is not good
this time. 8 You know your father and
his men; they are fighters, and as fierce
as a wild bear robbed of her cubs.[h] Besides, your father is an experienced fighter;[i] he will not spend the night with the
troops. 9 Even now, he is hidden in a cave
or some other place.[j] If he should attack
your troops first,[b] whoever hears about
it will say, 'There has been a slaughter
among the troops who follow Absalom.'
10 Then even the bravest soldier, whose
heart is like the heart of a lion,[k] will melt[l]
with fear, for all Israel knows that your
father is a fighter and that those with him
are brave.[m]
11 "So I advise you: Let all Israel, from
Dan to Beersheba[n]—as numerous as the
sand[o] on the seashore—be gathered to
you, with you yourself leading them into
battle. 12 Then we will attack him wherever he may be found, and we will fall on
him as dew settles on the ground. Neither
he nor any of his men will be left alive.
13 If he withdraws into a city, then all Israel will bring ropes to that city, and we
will drag it down to the valley[p] until not
so much as a pebble is left."
14 Absalom and all the men of Israel
said, "The advice[q] of Hushai the Arkite is
better than that of Ahithophel."[r] For the
LORD had determined to frustrate[s] the good
advice of Ahithophel in order to bring disaster[t] on Absalom.[u]
15 Hushai told Zadok and Abiathar, the
priests, "Ahithophel has advised Absalom
and the elders of Israel to do such and
such, but I have advised them to do so
and so. 16 Now send a message at once and
tell David, 'Do not spend the night at the
fords in the wilderness;[v] cross over without fail, or the king and all the people with
him will be swallowed up.[w]' "
17 Jonathan[x] and Ahimaaz were staying
at En Rogel.[y] A female servant was to go
and inform them, and they were to go and
tell King David, for they could not risk being seen entering the city. 18 But a young
man saw them and told Absalom. So the
two of them left at once and went to the
house of a man in Bahurim.[z] He had a well
in his courtyard, and they climbed down
into it. 19 His wife took a covering and
spread it out over the opening of the well
and scattered grain over it. No one knew
anything about it.[a]
20 When Absalom's men came to the

16:22 [b] S 2Sa 3:7; 12:11-12; S 15:16 **16:23** [c] 2Sa 17:14,23 [d] S 2Sa 15:12 **17:2** [e] 2Sa 16:14 [f] 1Ki 22:31; Zec 13:7 **17:5** [g] S 2Sa 15:32 **17:8** [h] Hos 13:8 [i] 1Sa 16:18 **17:9** [j] Jer 41:9 **17:10** [k] 1Ch 12:8 [l] Jos 2:9,11; Eze 21:15 [m] 2Sa 23:8; 1Ch 11:11 **17:11** [n] S Jdg 20:1 [o] S Ge 12:2; S Jos 11:4 **17:13** [p] Mic 1:6 **17:14** [q] S 2Sa 16:23 [r] S 2Sa 15:12 [s] S 2Sa 15:34; Ne 4:15 [t] Ps 9:16 [u] 2Ch 10:8 **17:16** [v] 2Sa 15:28 [w] 2Sa 15:35 **17:17** [x] S 2Sa 15:27, 36 [y] Jos 15:7; 18:16; 1Ki 1:9 **17:18** [z] S 2Sa 3:16 **17:19** [a] S Jos 2:6

[a] 1 Or *Let me* [b] 9 Or *When some of the men fall at the first attack*

16:21 *Sleep with your father's concubines.* This would signify Absalom's assumption of royal power; it would also be a definitive and irreversible declaration of the break between father and son (see notes on 3:7; 12:8; 1Ki 2:22). *obnoxious.* See note on 1Sa 13:4.

16:22 *he slept with his father's concubines.* A fulfillment of Nathan's prophecy (12:11–12). For additional significance, see note on v. 21.

17:1–3 Ahithophel's advice to Absalom envisioned a cheap and easy victory that would not leave the nation weakened.

17:4 *all the elders of Israel.* See note on 3:17. Absalom's rebellion appears to have gained extensive backing from prominent tribal leaders.

17:5 *Hushai the Arkite.* See 16:16–19; see also notes on 15:32, 37.

17:7–13 Hushai's advice subtly capitalizes on Absalom's uncertainty, his fear and his egotism.

17:11 *from Dan to Beersheba.* See note on 1Sa 3:20.

17:12–13 *we ... we ... we.* Hushai carefully links himself with the revolt.

17:14 *the LORD had determined to frustrate the good advice of Ahithophel.* An answer to David's prayer (see 15:31; cf. Ps 33:10; Pr 21:30).

17:15 *Zadok and Abiathar.* See 15:24–29,35–36.

17:16 *fords in the wilderness.* See 15:28 and note. *cross over.* Hushai advises David to cross the Jordan River, knowing that Absalom might change his mind and immediately set out after him.

17:17 *Jonathan and Ahimaaz.* See 15:36. *En Rogel.* A spring in the Kidron Valley just outside the walls of Jerusalem. *A female servant.* A servant going to the spring for water would attract no attention.

17:18 *Bahurim.* See note on 16:5.

woman[b] at the house, they asked, "Where are Ahimaaz and Jonathan?"

The woman answered them, "They crossed over the brook."[a] The men searched but found no one, so they returned to Jerusalem.

21 After they had gone, the two climbed out of the well and went to inform King David. They said to him, "Set out and cross the river at once; Ahithophel has advised such and such against you." 22 So David and all the people with him set out and crossed the Jordan. By daybreak, no one was left who had not crossed the Jordan.

23 When Ahithophel saw that his advice[c] had not been followed, he saddled his donkey and set out for his house in his hometown. He put his house in order[d] and then hanged himself. So he died and was buried in his father's tomb.

Absalom's Death

24 David went to Mahanaim,[e] and Absalom crossed the Jordan with all the men of Israel. 25 Absalom had appointed Amasa[f] over the army in place of Joab. Amasa was the son of Jether,[b][g] an Ishmaelite[c] who had married Abigail,[d] the daughter of Nahash and sister of Zeruiah the mother of Joab. 26 The Israelites and Absalom camped in the land of Gilead.

27 When David came to Mahanaim, Shobi son of Nahash[h] from Rabbah[i] of the Ammonites, and Makir[j] son of Ammiel from Lo Debar, and Barzillai[k] the Gileadite[l] from Rogelim 28 brought bedding and bowls and articles of pottery. They also brought wheat and barley, flour and roasted grain, beans and lentils,[e] 29 honey and curds, sheep, and cheese from cows' milk for David and his people to eat.[m] For they said, "The people have become exhausted and hungry and thirsty in the wilderness.[n]"

17:20 [b] S Ex 1:19 **17:23** [c] 2Sa S 2Sa 16:23 [d] 2Ki 20:1 **17:24** [e] S Ge 32:2 **17:25** [f] 2Sa 19:13; 20:4,9-12; 1Ki 2:5,32; 1Ch 12:18 [g] 1Ch 2:13-17 **17:27** [h] S 1Sa 11:1 [i] S Dt 3:11 [j] 2Sa 9:4 [k] 2Sa 19:31-39; 1Ki 2:7 [l] 2Sa 19:31; Ezr 2:61 **17:29** [m] 1Ch 12:40 [n] 2Sa 16:2; S Ro 12:13

18 David mustered the men who were with him and appointed over them commanders of thousands and commanders of hundreds. 2 David sent out his troops,[o] a third under the command of Joab, a third under Joab's brother Abishai[p] son of Zeruiah, and a third under Ittai[q] the Gittite. The king told the troops, "I myself will surely march out with you."

3 But the men said, "You must not go out; if we are forced to flee, they won't care about us. Even if half of us die, they won't care; but you are worth ten[r] thousand of us.[f] It would be better now for you to give us support from the city."[s]

4 The king answered, "I will do whatever seems best to you."

So the king stood beside the gate while all his men marched out in units of hundreds and of thousands. 5 The king commanded Joab, Abishai and Ittai, "Be gentle with the young man Absalom for my sake." And all the troops heard the king giving orders concerning Absalom to each of the commanders.

6 David's army marched out of the city to fight Israel, and the battle took place in the forest[t] of Ephraim. 7 There Israel's troops were routed by David's men, and the casualties that day were great—twenty thousand men. 8 The battle spread out over the whole countryside, and the forest swallowed up more men that day than the sword.

9 Now Absalom happened to meet David's men. He was riding his mule, and as the mule went under the thick branches

18:2 [o] S Jdg 7:16; 1Sa 11:11 [p] S 1Sa 26:6 [q] 2Sa 15:19 **18:3** [r] S 1Sa 18:7 [s] 2Sa 21:17 **18:6** [t] S Jos 17:15

[a] 20 Or *"They passed by the sheep pen toward the water."* [b] 25 Hebrew *Ithra,* a variant of *Jether* [c] 25 Some Septuagint manuscripts (see also 1 Chron. 2:17); Hebrew and other Septuagint manuscripts *Israelite* [d] 25 Hebrew *Abigal,* a variant of *Abigail* [e] 28 Most Septuagint manuscripts and Syriac; Hebrew *lentils, and roasted grain* [f] 3 Two Hebrew manuscripts, some Septuagint manuscripts and Vulgate; most Hebrew manuscripts *care; for now there are ten thousand like us*

17:23 *his hometown.* Giloh (see 15:12 and note). *hanged himself.* Ahithophel was convinced that the rebellion would fail and that he would be found guilty of treason as a co-conspirator.

17:24 *Mahanaim.* Ironically the same place where Ish-Bosheth had sought refuge after Saul's death (see 2:8 and note).

17:25 *Amasa.* Nephew of David and cousin of both Absalom and Joab, son of Zeruiah. *Abigail, the daughter of Nahash and sister of Zeruiah.* Zeruiah was David's sister (1Ch 2:16). Since the father of Abigail and Zeruiah is Nahash rather than Jesse, their unnamed mother may have married Jesse after the death of Nahash.

17:27 *Shobi son of Nahash.* Apparently the brother of Hanun (see 10:2–4), whom David had defeated earlier in his reign (11:1; 12:26–31). *Rabbah of the Ammonites.* See note on 10:3. *Makir.* See note on 9:4. *Barzillai.* A wealthy benefactor of David during his flight to Mahanaim (see 19:32; 1Ki 2:7). After the Babylonian exile, there were claimants to the priesthood among his descendants (Ezr 2:61–63).

18:2 *Ittai the Gittite.* See 15:18–22.

18:3 *You must not go out.* In addition to the reason given, David was growing old and was no longer the warrior he had been. This is essentially the same idea that Ahithophel had expressed to Absalom (see 17:2).

18:5 *Be gentle with … Absalom for my sake.* David's love for his (now) oldest son was undying—and almost his undoing (see 19:5–7 and note on 19:5).

18:6 *Israel.* Absalom's army (see 15:13; 16:15; 17:4,11,24–26). *forest of Ephraim.* The battle was apparently fought in Gilead, east of the Jordan (see 17:24,26). The name "forest of Ephraim" may have derived from an Ephraimite claim on the area (see Jdg 12:1–4).

18:8 *The battle spread out.* The armies apparently became dispersed, and many of the men got lost in the forest.

18:9 *his mule.* See note on 13:29. *Absalom's hair got caught in the tree.* His handsome head of hair (see 14:25,26) was in the end—ironically—his undoing.

of a large oak, Absalom's hair[u] got caught
in the tree. He was left hanging in mid-
air, while the mule he was riding kept on
going.
10 When one of the men saw what had
happened, he told Joab, "I just saw Absalom hanging in an oak tree."
11 Joab said to the man who had told him
this, "What! You saw him? Why didn't you
strike[v] him to the ground right there? Then
I would have had to give you ten shekels[a]
of silver and a warrior's belt.[w]"
12 But the man replied, "Even if a thousand shekels[b] were weighed out into my
hands, I would not lay a hand on the king's
son. In our hearing the king commanded
you and Abishai and Ittai, 'Protect the
young man Absalom for my sake.[c]' 13 And
if I had put my life in jeopardy[d]—and
nothing is hidden from the king[x]—you
would have kept your distance from me."
14 Joab[y] said, "I'm not going to wait like
this for you." So he took three javelins in
his hand and plunged them into Absalom's heart while Absalom was still alive
in the oak tree. 15 And ten of Joab's armor-
bearers surrounded Absalom, struck him
and killed him.[z]
16 Then Joab[a] sounded the trumpet, and
the troops stopped pursuing Israel, for
Joab halted them. 17 They took Absalom,
threw him into a big pit in the forest and
piled up[b] a large heap of rocks[c] over him.
Meanwhile, all the Israelites fled to their
homes.
18 During his lifetime Absalom had taken
a pillar and erected it in the King's Valley[d] as a monument[e] to himself, for he
thought, "I have no son[f] to carry on the
memory of my name." He named the pillar after himself, and it is called Absalom's
Monument to this day.

David Mourns

19 Now Ahimaaz[g] son of Zadok said,
"Let me run and take the news to the king
that the LORD has vindicated him by delivering him from the hand of his enemies.[h]"
20 "You are not the one to take the news
today," Joab told him. "You may take the
news another time, but you must not do
so today, because the king's son is dead."
21 Then Joab said to a Cushite, "Go, tell
the king what you have seen." The Cushite
bowed down before Joab and ran off.
22 Ahimaaz son of Zadok again said to
Joab, "Come what may, please let me run
behind the Cushite."
But Joab replied, "My son, why do you
want to go? You don't have any news that
will bring you a reward."
23 He said, "Come what may, I want to
run."
So Joab said, "Run!" Then Ahimaaz ran
by way of the plain[e] and outran the Cushite.
24 While David was sitting between the
inner and outer gates, the watchman[i] went
up to the roof of the gateway by the wall.
As he looked out, he saw a man running
alone. 25 The watchman called out to the
king and reported it.
The king said, "If he is alone, he must
have good news." And the runner came
closer and closer.
26 Then the watchman saw another runner, and he called down to the gatekeeper,
"Look, another man running alone!"
The king said, "He must be bringing
good news,[j] too."
27 The watchman said, "It seems to me
that the first one runs like[k] Ahimaaz son
of Zadok."
"He's a good man," the king said. "He
comes with good news."
28 Then Ahimaaz called out to the king,
"All is well!" He bowed down before the
king with his face to the ground and said,
"Praise be to the LORD your God! He has
delivered up those who lifted their hands
against my lord the king."
29 The king asked, "Is the young man
Absalom safe?"
Ahimaaz answered, "I saw great confusion

18:9 [u] 2Sa 14:26
18:11 [v] S 2Sa 3:39 [w] 1Sa 18:4
18:13 [x] 2Sa 14:19-20
18:14 [y] S 2Sa 2:18
18:15 [z] S 2Sa 12:10
18:16 [a] S 2Sa 2:28
18:17 [b] Jos 7:26 [c] Jos 8:29
18:18 [d] Ge 14:17 [e] S Ge 50:5; S Nu 32:42 [f] 2Sa 14:27
18:19 [g] S 2Sa 15:36 [h] Jdg 11:36
18:24 [i] S 1Sa 14:16; S Jer 51:12
18:26 [j] 1Ki 1:42; Isa 52:7; 61:1
18:27 [k] 2Ki 9:20

[a] *11* That is, about 4 ounces or about 115 grams
[b] *12* That is, about 25 pounds or about 12 kilograms
[c] *12* A few Hebrew manuscripts, Septuagint, Vulgate and Syriac; most Hebrew manuscripts may be translated *Absalom, whoever you may be.*
[d] *13* Or *Otherwise, if I had acted treacherously toward him*
[e] *23* That is, the plain of the Jordan

18:11 *I would have had to give you.* Joab must be referring to an announced intent on his part to reward anyone killing Absalom. His actions and interests did not always coincide with David's wishes (see note on 2:13).
18:15 *killed him.* The easiest and most certain way of ending the rebellion—but the brutal overkill is indicative of the deep animosity felt by David's men toward Absalom.
18:17 *large heap of rocks.* A mound of rocks that mocked the monument Absalom himself had erected (v. 18). *all the Israelites.* See note on v. 6.
18:18 *erected it … as a monument to himself.* As Saul had done (see 1Sa 15:12 and note). *King's Valley.* Near Jerusalem (see Ge 14:17; Josephus, *Antiquities*, 7.10.3). *I have no son.* See 14:27 and note. *Absalom's Monument.* Not to be confused with the much later monument of the same name that is still visible today in the valley east of Jerusalem.
18:19 *Ahimaaz son of Zadok.* See 15:27; 17:17–21.
18:20 *not the one to take the news.* The choice of a messenger depended on the content of the message (see v. 27 and note).
18:21 *Cushite.* A foreigner (see note on Nu 12:1).
18:27 *He comes with good news.* David presumed that Joab would not have sent someone like Ahimaaz to carry bad news (see v. 20 and note).
18:29 *I saw great confusion.* Ahimaaz avoids a direct answer to David's question, though he knew Absalom was dead.

just as Joab was about to send the king's
servant and me, your servant, but I don't
know what it was."
30 The king said, "Stand aside and wait
here." So he stepped aside and stood there.
31 Then the Cushite arrived and said,
"My lord the king, hear the good news!
The LORD has vindicated you today by delivering you from the hand of all who rose
up against you."
32 The king asked the Cushite, "Is the
young man Absalom safe?"
The Cushite replied, "May the enemies
of my lord the king and all who rise up to
harm you be like that young man."[l]
33 The king was shaken. He went up to
the room over the gateway and wept. As
he went, he said: "O my son Absalom! My
son, my son Absalom! If only I had died[m]
instead of you—O Absalom, my son, my
son!"[a][n]
19 [b] Joab was told, "The king is weeping and mourning for Absalom."
2 And for the whole army the victory that
day was turned into mourning, because
on that day the troops heard it said, "The
king is grieving for his son." 3 The men
stole into the city that day as men steal in
who are ashamed when they flee from battle. 4 The king covered his face and cried
aloud, "O my son Absalom! O Absalom,
my son, my son!"
5 Then Joab went into the house to the
king and said, "Today you have humiliated all your men, who have just saved
your life and the lives of your sons and
daughters and the lives of your wives and
concubines. 6 You love those who hate you
and hate those who love you. You have
made it clear today that the commanders and their men mean nothing to you. I
see that you would be pleased if Absalom
were alive today and all of us were dead.
7 Now go out and encourage your men. I
swear by the LORD that if you don't go out,
not a man will be left with you by nightfall. This will be worse for you than all
the calamities that have come on you from
your youth till now."[o]
8 So the king got up and took his seat
in the gateway. When the men were told,
"The king is sitting in the gateway,[p]" they
all came before him.
Meanwhile, the Israelites had fled to
their homes.

David Returns to Jerusalem

9 Throughout the tribes of Israel, all the
people were arguing among themselves,
saying, "The king delivered us from the
hand of our enemies; he is the one who
rescued us from the hand of the Philistines.[q] But now he has fled the country
to escape from Absalom;[r] 10 and Absalom,
whom we anointed to rule over us, has
died in battle. So why do you say nothing
about bringing the king back?"
11 King David sent this message to Zadok[s] and Abiathar, the priests: "Ask the elders of Judah, 'Why should you be the last
to bring the king back to his palace, since
what is being said throughout Israel has
reached the king at his quarters? 12 You are
my relatives, my own flesh and blood. So
why should you be the last to bring back
the king?' 13 And say to Amasa,[t] 'Are you
not my own flesh and blood?[u] May God
deal with me, be it ever so severely,[v] if you
are not the commander of my army for life
in place of Joab.[w]' "
14 He won over the hearts of the men of
Judah so that they were all of one mind.
They sent word to the king, "Return, you
and all your men." 15 Then the king returned and went as far as the Jordan.
Now the men of Judah had come to Gilgal[x] to go out and meet the king and bring

18:32 [l] Jdg 5:31; S 1Sa 25:26
18:33 [m] Ex 32:32 [n] S Ge 43:14; 2Sa 19:4
19:7 [o] Pr 14:28
19:8 [p] S 2Sa 15:2
19:9 [q] 2Sa 8:1-14 [r] 2Sa 15:14
19:11 [s] S 2Sa 15:24
19:13 [t] S 2Sa 17:25 [u] S Ge 29:14 [v] S Ru 1:17 [w] S 2Sa 2:13
19:15 [x] S 1Sa 11:15

[a] 33 In Hebrew texts this verse (18:33) is numbered 19:1. [b] In Hebrew texts 19:1-43 is numbered 19:2-44.

18:33 *O my son Absalom!* One of the most moving expressions in all literature of a father's grief over his son's death—in spite of all that Absalom had done. *If only I had died instead of you.* The intensity of David's grief springs in no small part from his recognition that he himself bore large responsibility for the course of events that led to Absalom's death. His own actions had set a negative example for his children and at the same time had rendered him incapable of acting judicially as a king ought—all of which led up to Absalom's rebellion. In Absalom's violent death at the hands of Joab, David's sinful abuse of royal power had finally produced its most bitter fruit.
19:4 *covered his face.* Cf. note on 15:30.
19:5 *Joab went ... to the king.* Apparently confident that the king was unaware of Joab's part in Absalom's death. David never indicates that he learned of it (see 1Ki 2:5). *you have humiliated all your men.* Joab boldly rebukes David for allowing his personal grief to keep him from expressing his appreciation for the loyalty of those who risked their lives to preserve his throne. Joab warns David that his love for Absalom can still undo him.
19:9 *The king delivered us.* With Absalom dead, the northern tribes remember what David had done for them (see 3:17–18; 5:2).
19:11 *Ask the elders of Judah.* Even though the rebellion had begun in Hebron in Judah (see 15:9–12), David appeals to the elders of his own tribe to take the initiative in restoring him to the throne in Jerusalem (see 2:4; 1Sa 30:26 and notes). This appeal produced the desired result, but it also led to the arousal of tribal jealousies (see vv. 41–43).
19:13 *Amasa ... my own flesh and blood.* See 17:25 and note. Although Amasa deserved death for treason, David appointed him commander of his army in place of Joab, hoping to secure the allegiance of those who had followed Amasa, especially the Judahites (see 20:4 and note). *May God deal with me, be it ever so severely.* A curse formula (see note on 1Sa 3:17).
19:15 *Gilgal.* See note on Jos 4:19.

him across the Jordan. 16 Shimei[y] son of Gera, the Benjamite from Bahurim, hurried down with the men of Judah to meet King David. 17 With him were a thousand Benjamites, along with Ziba,[z] the steward of Saul's household,[a] and his fifteen sons and twenty servants. They rushed to the Jordan, where the king was. 18 They crossed at the ford to take the king's household over and to do whatever he wished.

When Shimei son of Gera crossed the Jordan, he fell prostrate before the king 19 and said to him, "May my lord not hold me guilty. Do not remember how your servant did wrong on the day my lord the king left Jerusalem.[b] May the king put it out of his mind. 20 For I your servant know that I have sinned, but today I have come here as the first from the tribes of Joseph to come down and meet my lord the king."

21 Then Abishai[c] son of Zeruiah said, "Shouldn't Shimei be put to death for this? He cursed[d] the LORD's anointed."[e]

22 David replied, "What does this have to do with you, you sons of Zeruiah?[f] What right do you have to interfere? Should anyone be put to death in Israel today?[g] Don't I know that today I am king over Israel?" 23 So the king said to Shimei, "You shall not die." And the king promised him on oath.[h]

24 Mephibosheth,[i] Saul's grandson, also went down to meet the king. He had not taken care of his feet or trimmed his mustache or washed his clothes from the day the king left until the day he returned safely. 25 When he came from Jerusalem to meet the king, the king asked him, "Why didn't you go with me,[j] Mephibosheth?"

26 He said, "My lord the king, since I your servant am lame,[k] I said, 'I will have my donkey saddled and will ride on it, so I can go with the king.' But Ziba[l] my servant betrayed me. 27 And he has slandered your servant to my lord the king. My lord the king is like an angel[m] of God; so do whatever you wish. 28 All my grandfather's descendants deserved nothing but death[n] from my lord the king, but you gave your servant a place among those who eat at your table.[o] So what right do I have to make any more appeals to the king?"

29 The king said to him, "Why say more? I order you and Ziba to divide the land."

30 Mephibosheth said to the king, "Let him take everything, now that my lord the king has returned home safely."

31 Barzillai[p] the Gileadite also came down from Rogelim to cross the Jordan with the king and to send him on his way from there. 32 Now Barzillai was very old, eighty years of age. He had provided for the king during his stay in Mahanaim, for he was a very wealthy[q] man. 33 The king said to Barzillai, "Cross over with me and stay with me in Jerusalem, and I will provide for you."

34 But Barzillai answered the king, "How many more years will I live, that I should go up to Jerusalem with the king? 35 I am now eighty[r] years old. Can I tell the difference between what is enjoyable and what is not? Can your servant taste what he eats and drinks? Can I still hear the voices of male and female singers?[s] Why should your servant be an added[t] burden to my lord the king? 36 Your servant will cross over the Jordan with the king for a short distance, but why should the king reward me in this way? 37 Let your servant return, that I may die in my own town near the tomb of my father[u] and mother. But here is your servant Kimham.[v] Let him cross over with my lord the king. Do for him whatever you wish."

38 The king said, "Kimham shall cross over with me, and I will do for him whatever you wish. And anything you desire from me I will do for you."

39 So all the people crossed the Jordan, and then the king crossed over. The king

19:16 [y] 2Sa 16:5-13
19:17 [z] S 2Sa 9:2 [a] S Ge 43:16
19:19 [b] S 2Sa 16:6-8
19:21 [c] S 1Sa 26:6 [d] S Ex 22:28 [e] S 1Sa 12:3; S 26:9
19:22 [f] S 2Sa 2:18; S 16:10 [g] 1Sa 11:13
19:23 [h] 1Ki 2:8, 42
19:24 [i] S 2Sa 4:4
19:25 [j] 2Sa 16:17
19:26 [k] S Lev 21:18 [l] S 2Sa 9:2
19:27 [m] S 1Sa 29:9
19:28 [n] S 2Sa 16:8 [o] S 2Sa 9:7, 13
19:31 [p] S 2Sa 17:27-29; 1Ki 2:7
19:32 [q] 1Sa 25:2
19:35 [r] Ps 90:10 [s] 2Ch 35:25; Ezr 2:65; Ecc 2:8; 12:1 [t] 2Sa 15:33
19:37 [u] S Ge 49:29 [v] Jer 41:17

19:17 *a thousand Benjamites.* No doubt they feared they would be suspected by the king of being implicated in Shimei's deed.
19:19 *your servant did wrong.* See 16:5–13.
19:20 *I your servant know that I have sinned.* Shimei's guilt was common knowledge; he could only seize the most appropriate time to plead for mercy. *tribes of Joseph.* A common way of referring to the northern tribes (see Jos 18:5; Jdg 1:22; 1Ki 11:28; Am 5:6; Zec 10:6)—of which Ephraim and Manasseh (sons of Joseph) were the most prominent (see Nu 26:28).
19:21 *Abishai.* See 16:9; see also note on 1Sa 26:6. *the LORD's anointed.* See note on 1Sa 9:16; see also 1Sa 24:6; 26:9,11; Ex 22:28; 1Ki 21:10.
19:22 *sons of Zeruiah.* See note on 16:10. *Should anyone be put to death in Israel today?* It was a day for general amnesty (see 1Sa 11:13).
19:23 *You shall not die.* David kept his pledge; he would not himself avenge the wrong committed against him (see note on 1Sa 25:1–44). But on his deathbed he instructed Solomon to take Shimei's case in hand (see 1Ki 2:8–9,36–46).
19:24 *Mephibosheth.* See 9:6–13.
19:25 *Why didn't you go with me … ?* David remembers Ziba's previous allegations (see 16:3).
19:26 *lame.* See 4:4; 9:3.
19:27 *he has slandered your servant.* See 16:3. *like an angel of God.* See 14:17 and note. *do whatever you wish.* Mephibosheth discreetly requests David to reconsider the grant of his property to Ziba (see 16:4).
19:29 *divide the land.* Faced with conflicting testimony that could not be corroborated, David withholds judgment and orders the division of Saul's estate (cf. 1Ki 3:25 and note).
19:31 *Barzillai.* See note on 17:27.
19:35 Cf. Ecc 12:2–5 and note. *difference between what is enjoyable and what is not.* At his age, he would be indifferent to all the pleasures of the court.
19:37 *Kimham.* Likely a son of Barzillai (see 1Ki 2:7).

kissed Barzillai and bid him farewell,[w] and
Barzillai returned to his home.
40 When the king crossed over to Gilgal,
Kimham crossed with him. All the troops
of Judah and half the troops of Israel had
taken the king over.
41 Soon all the men of Israel were coming
to the king and saying to him, "Why did
our brothers, the men of Judah, steal the
king away and bring him and his household across the Jordan, together with all
his men?"[x]
42 All the men of Judah answered the
men of Israel, "We did this because the
king is closely related to us. Why are you
angry about it? Have we eaten any of the
king's provisions? Have we taken anything
for ourselves?"
43 Then the men of Israel[y] answered the
men of Judah, "We have ten shares in the
king; so we have a greater claim on David than you have. Why then do you treat
us with contempt? Weren't we the first to
speak of bringing back our king?"
But the men of Judah pressed their
claims even more forcefully than the men
of Israel.

Sheba Rebels Against David

20 Now a troublemaker named Sheba son of Bikri, a Benjamite, happened to be there. He sounded the trumpet and shouted,

"We have no share[z] in David,[a]
no part in Jesse's son![b]
Every man to his tent, Israel!"

2 So all the men of Israel deserted David
to follow Sheba son of Bikri. But the men
of Judah stayed by their king all the way
from the Jordan to Jerusalem.
3 When David returned to his palace in
Jerusalem, he took the ten concubines[c] he
had left to take care of the palace and put
them in a house under guard. He provided for them but had no sexual relations
with them. They were kept in confinement till the day of their death, living as
widows.
4 Then the king said to Amasa,[d] "Summon the men of Judah to come to me
within three days, and be here yourself."
5 But when Amasa went to summon Judah, he took longer than the time the king
had set for him.
6 David said to Abishai,[e] "Now Sheba
son of Bikri will do us more harm than
Absalom did. Take your master's men and
pursue him, or he will find fortified cities
and escape from us."[a] 7 So Joab's men and
the Kerethites[f] and Pelethites and all the
mighty warriors went out under the command of Abishai. They marched out from
Jerusalem to pursue Sheba son of Bikri.
8 While they were at the great rock in
Gibeon,[g] Amasa came to meet them.
Joab[h] was wearing his military tunic, and
strapped over it at his waist was a belt
with a dagger in its sheath. As he stepped
forward, it dropped out of its sheath.
9 Joab said to Amasa, "How are you,
my brother?" Then Joab took Amasa by
the beard with his right hand to kiss him.
10 Amasa was not on his guard against the
dagger[i] in Joab's[j] hand, and Joab plunged
it into his belly, and his intestines spilled
out on the ground. Without being stabbed
again, Amasa died. Then Joab and his
brother Abishai pursued Sheba son of
Bikri.
11 One of Joab's men stood beside Amasa and said, "Whoever favors Joab, and
whoever is for David, let him follow Joab!"
12 Amasa lay wallowing in his blood in the
middle of the road, and the man saw that
all the troops came to a halt[k] there. When
he realized that everyone who came up to

19:39 [w] S Ge 47:7
19:41 [x] Jdg 8:1; 12:1
19:43 [y] S 2Sa 5:1
20:1 [z] S Ge 31:14 [a] S Ge 29:14; 1Ki 12:16 [b] 1Sa 22:7-8
20:3 [c] S 2Sa 15:16
20:4 [d] S 2Sa 17:25
20:6 [e] 2Sa 21:17
20:7 [f] S 1Sa 30:14; S 2Sa 15:18
20:8 [g] S Jos 9:3 [h] S 2Sa 2:18
20:10 [i] S Jdg 3:21 [j] 1Ki 2:5
20:12 [k] S 2Sa 2:23

[a] 6 Or *and do us serious injury*

19:40 *Gilgal.* See v. 15 and note.
19:43 *ten shares.* The ten tribes, excluding Judah and Simeon (see note on 2:4). *we have a greater claim on David.* The grounds for this assertion may be that the Lord had chosen David to reign in the place of Saul (see 3:17–18; 5:2).
20:1–25 The last threat to David's reign overcome.
20:1 *troublemaker.* See note on Dt 13:13. *Benjamite.* Tribal jealousy still simmered over the transfer of the royal house from Benjamin (Saul's tribe) to Judah. *there.* In Gilgal (19:40). *We have no share in David.* Sheba appeals to the Israelite suspicion that David favored his own tribe (Judah) over the other tribes (see 1Ki 12:16). *Jesse's son.* See note on 1Sa 20:27,30–31.
20:2 *all the men of Israel.* Those referred to in 19:41–43.
20:3 *ten concubines.* See notes on 15:16; 16:22.
20:4 *Amasa.* See notes on 17:25; 19:13. David bypasses Joab.
20:6 *Abishai.* David bypasses Joab a second time (see v. 7). *your master's men.* "Joab's men" (v. 7).
20:7 *Joab's men.* See 18:2. It becomes clear that Joab also accompanied the soldiers and, though not in command (by the king's order), he was obviously the leader recognized by the soldiers (see vv. 7,11,15). *Kerethites and Pelethites.* See note on 8:18. *mighty warriors.* See 23:8–39. Once more in a time of crisis David depended mainly on the small force of professionals (many of them non-Israelite) who made up his private army.
20:8 *Gibeon.* See note on 2:12. *Amasa came.* Apparently with some troops (see v. 11 and note).
20:10 *into his belly.* See 2:23; 3:27. For the second time Joab commits murder to secure his position as commander of David's army (see 1Ki 2:5–6). *Joab and his brother Abishai.* In defiance of David's order, Joab reassumes command on his own initiative (see v. 23).
20:11 *Whoever favors Joab, and whoever is for David.* To dispel any idea that Joab was aligned with Sheba's conspiracy, an appeal is made to Amasa's troops to support Joab if they are truly loyal to David.

Amasa stopped, he dragged him from the road into a field and threw a garment over him. 13 After Amasa had been removed from the road, everyone went on with Joab to pursue Sheba son of Bikri.

14 Sheba passed through all the tribes of Israel to Abel Beth Maakah and through the entire region of the Bikrites,[a][l] who gathered together and followed him. 15 All the troops with Joab came and besieged Sheba in Abel Beth Maakah.[m] They built a siege ramp[n] up to the city, and it stood against the outer fortifications. While they were battering the wall to bring it down, 16 a wise woman[o] called from the city, "Listen! Listen! Tell Joab to come here so I can speak to him." 17 He went toward her, and she asked, "Are you Joab?"

"I am," he answered.

She said, "Listen to what your servant has to say."

"I'm listening," he said.

18 She continued, "Long ago they used to say, 'Get your answer at Abel,' and that settled it. 19 We are the peaceful[p] and faithful in Israel. You are trying to destroy a city that is a mother in Israel. Why do you want to swallow up the LORD's inheritance?"[q]

20 "Far be it from me!" Joab replied, "Far be it from me to swallow up or destroy! 21 That is not the case. A man named Sheba son of Bikri, from the hill country of Ephraim, has lifted up his hand against the king, against David. Hand over this one man, and I'll withdraw from the city."

The woman said to Joab, "His head[r] will be thrown to you from the wall."

22 Then the woman went to all the people with her wise advice,[s] and they cut off the head of Sheba son of Bikri and threw it to Joab. So he sounded the trumpet, and his men dispersed from the city, each returning to his home. And Joab went back to the king in Jerusalem.

David's Officials

23 Joab[t] was over Israel's entire army; Benaiah son of Jehoiada was over the Kerethites and Pelethites; 24 Adoniram[b][u] was in charge of forced labor; Jehoshaphat[v] son of Ahilud was recorder; 25 Sheva was secretary; Zadok[w] and Abiathar were priests; 26 and Ira the Jairite[c] was David's priest.

The Gibeonites Avenged

21 During the reign of David, there was a famine[x] for three successive years; so David sought[y] the face of the LORD. The LORD said, "It is on account of Saul and his blood-stained house; it is because he put the Gibeonites to death."

20:14 [l] Nu 21:16 **20:15** [m] 1Ki 15:20; 2Ki 15:29 [n] Isa 37:33; Jer 6:6; 32:24 **20:16** [o] 2Sa 14:2 **20:19** [p] S Dt 2:26 [q] S 1Sa 26:19 **20:21** [r] S 2Sa 4:8 **20:22** [s] Ecc 9:13 **20:23** [t] S 2Sa 2:28; 8:16-18; 24:2 **20:24** [u] 1Ki 4:6; 5:14; 12:18; 2Ch 10:18 [v] S 2Sa 8:16 **20:25** [w] S 1Sa 2:35; S 2Sa 8:17 **21:1** [x] S Ge 12:10; S Dt 32:24 [y] S Ex 32:11

[a] *14* See Septuagint and Vulgate; Hebrew *Berites*.
[b] *24* Some Septuagint manuscripts (see also 1 Kings 4:6 and 5:14); Hebrew *Adoram*
[c] *26* Hebrew; some Septuagint manuscripts and Syriac (see also 23:38) *Ithrite*

20:14 *Abel Beth Maakah.* Located to the north of Dan (see 1Ki 15:20; 2Ch 16:4 and NIV text note). Sheba's strategy was to gather as many volunteers for his revolt as possible, but he was obviously afraid to assemble his ragtag army anywhere within close reach of David's warriors.
20:18 *Get your answer at Abel.* The city was famous for the wisdom of its inhabitants.
20:19 *a mother in Israel.* A town that produced faithful Israelites — cities were commonly personified as women (see Jer 50:12; Gal 4:26). *the LORD's inheritance.* See note on 1Sa 10:1.
20:21 *hill country of Ephraim.* Either Sheba, a Benjamite (see v. 1), lived in the tribal territory of Ephraim or this was the designation of a geographic, rather than a strictly tribal, region.
20:22 *Joab went back to the king in Jerusalem.* See notes on vv. 7,10.
20:23 – 26 These royal officials apparently served David during most of his reign (see 8:15 – 18).
20:23 *Joab was over Israel's entire army.* Though in some disfavor, he held this position until he participated in Adonijah's conspiracy (1Ki 1:7; 2:28 – 35). *Kerethites and Pelethites.* See note on 8:18.
20:24 *Adoniram was in charge of forced labor.* A position not established in the early years of David's reign (see 8:15 – 16). Adoniram must have been a late appointee of David since he continued to serve under Solomon (1Ki 4:6; 5:14) and was eventually killed in the early days of the reign of Rehoboam (1Ki 12:18). *forced labor.* Labor usually performed by prisoners of war from defeated nations (see 12:31 and note; 1Ki 9:15, 20 – 21). *recorder.* See note on 8:16.
20:25 *Sheva.* See note on 8:17 ("Seraiah"). *secretary.* See note on 8:17. *Zadok and Abiathar.* See note on 8:17.
20:26 *Jairite.* A reference either to Jair of the tribe of Manasseh or to an inhabitant of one of the settlements known as Havvoth Jair (Nu 32:41; 1Ki 4:13). *priest.* See note on 8:18.
21:1 — 24:25 This concluding section forms an appendix to 1,2 Samuel and contains additional materials (without concern for chronology) relating to David's reign. Its topical arrangement is striking in that it employs the literary pattern *a-b-c/c'-b'-a'*, frequently found elsewhere in OT literature (cf., e.g., Ps 25 and its introduction; 45; cf. also Isa 6:10 and note). The first and last units (21:1 – 14; 24:1 – 25) are narratives of two events in which David had to deal with God's wrath against Israel (the first occasioned by an act of Saul, the second by his own). The second and fifth units (21:15 – 22; 23:8 – 39) are accounts of David's warriors (the second much longer than the first). At the center (22:1 — 23:7) are two of David's poems (the first much longer than the second), one of which celebrates David's victories as warrior-king, while the other recalls his role as psalmist (see note on 1Sa 16:14 — 17:58). King David's triumph song in ch. 22 and Hannah's song in 1Sa 2:1 – 10 form a literary frame around the main body of 1,2 Samuel (see note on 1Sa 2:1) and poetically highlight its central themes.
21:1 – 14 This event appears to have occurred after David's kindness was extended to Mephibosheth (ch. 9) and before Absalom's rebellion (16:7 – 8; 18:28; see note on 16:8).
21:1 *he put the Gibeonites to death.* Saul's action against the Gibeonites is not related elsewhere but appears to have been instituted early in his reign, motivated by an excessive nationalism. Perhaps tribalism was also involved, since the Gibeonites occupied territory partly assigned to Benjamin,

[2]The king summoned the Gibeonites[z] and spoke to them. (Now the Gibeonites were not a part of Israel but were survivors of the Amorites; the Israelites had sworn to spare them, but Saul in his zeal for Israel and Judah had tried to annihilate them.) [3]David asked the Gibeonites, "What shall I do for you? How shall I make atonement so that you will bless the LORD's inheritance?"[a]

[4]The Gibeonites answered him, "We have no right to demand silver or gold from Saul or his family, nor do we have the right to put anyone in Israel to death."[b]

"What do you want me to do for you?" David asked.

[5]They answered the king, "As for the man who destroyed us and plotted against us so that we have been decimated and have no place anywhere in Israel, [6]let seven of his male descendants be given to us to be killed and their bodies exposed[c] before the LORD at Gibeah of Saul—the LORD's chosen[d] one."

So the king said, "I will give them to you."

[7]The king spared Mephibosheth[e] son of Jonathan, the son of Saul, because of the oath[f] before the LORD between David and Jonathan son of Saul. [8]But the king took Armoni and Mephibosheth, the two sons of Aiah's daughter Rizpah,[g] whom she had borne to Saul, together with the five sons of Saul's daughter Merab,[a] whom she had borne to Adriel son of Barzillai the Meholathite.[h] [9]He handed them over to the Gibeonites, who killed them and exposed their bodies on a hill before the LORD. All seven of them fell together; they were put to death[i] during the first days of the harvest, just as the barley harvest was beginning.[j]

[10]Rizpah daughter of Aiah took sackcloth and spread it out for herself on a rock. From the beginning of the harvest till the rain poured down from the heavens on the bodies, she did not let the birds touch them by day or the wild animals by night.[k] [11]When David was told what Aiah's daughter Rizpah, Saul's concubine, had done, [12]he went and took the bones of Saul[l] and his son Jonathan from the citizens of Jabesh Gilead.[m] (They had stolen their bodies from the public square at Beth Shan,[n] where the Philistines had hung[o] them after they struck Saul down on Gilboa.)[p] [13]David brought the bones of Saul and his son Jonathan from there, and the bones of those who had been killed and exposed were gathered up.

[14]They buried the bones of Saul and his son Jonathan in the tomb of Saul's father Kish, at Zela[q] in Benjamin, and did everything the king commanded. After that,[r] God answered prayer[s] in behalf of the land.[t]

Wars Against the Philistines

21:15-22pp — 1Ch 20:4-8

[15]Once again there was a battle between the Philistines[u] and Israel. David went down with his men to fight against the Philistines, and he became exhausted. [16]And Ishbi-Benob, one of the descendants of Rapha, whose bronze spearhead weighed

21:2 [z]S Jos 9:15 **21:3** [a]S 1Sa 26:19 **21:4** [b]Nu 35:33-34 **21:6** [c]Nu 25:4 [d]S 1Sa 10:24 **21:7** [e]2Sa 4:4 [f]S 1Sa 18:3; S 2Sa 9:7 **21:8** [g]2Sa 3:7 [h]1Sa 18:19 **21:9** [i]S 2Sa 16:8 [j]S Ru 1:22 **21:10** [k]S Ge 40:19; S 1Sa 17:44 **21:12** [l]1Sa 31:11-13 [m]S Jdg 21:8; S 1Sa 11:1 [n]S Jos 17:11 [o]1Sa 31:10 [p]S 1Sa 28:4 **21:14** [q]Jos 18:28 [r]Jos 7:26 [s]2Sa 24:25 [t]1Ch 8:34 **21:15** [u]S 2Sa 5:25

[a] *8* Two Hebrew manuscripts, some Septuagint manuscripts and Syriac (see also 1 Samuel 18:19); most Hebrew and Septuagint manuscripts *Michal*

---

and Saul's great-grandfather was known as the "father of Gibeon" (1Ch 8:29; 9:35).

21:2 *Amorites.* A comprehensive name sometimes used to designate all the pre-Israelite inhabitants of Canaan (Ge 15:16; Jos 24:18; Jdg 6:10; Am 2:10). More precisely, the Gibeonites were called Hivites (Jos 9:7; 11:19). *the Israelites had sworn to spare them.* A pledge sworn in the name of the Lord (see Jos 9:15,18–21 and note on 9:15). *tried to annihilate them.* The reason Saul was unsuccessful is not known.

21:3 *bless.* Since the oath sworn to them in the Lord's name had been violated, they could rightly call down his curse on the land. *the LORD's inheritance.* See note on 1Sa 10:1.

21:5 *the man.* Saul. *no place anywhere in Israel.* Those who escaped Saul's attack had been driven from their towns and lands (see 4:2–3).

21:6 *seven.* Because it would represent a full number (seven symbolized completeness)—though many more Gibeonites had been slain. *Gibeah.* The place of Saul's residence (see 1Sa 10:26).

21:7 *oath before the LORD between David and Jonathan.* See 9:1–13; 1Sa 18:3; 20:15 and note.

21:8 *Rizpah.* See 3:7. *Merab.* See 1Sa 18:19. *Barzillai the Meholathite.* Not to be confused with Barzillai the Gileadite (17:27; 19:31).

21:9 *All seven of them fell together.* This nearly extinguished the house of Saul, which God had rejected (see 1Sa 13:13–14; 15:23–26). In 1Ch 8:29–39; 9:35–44 no descendants of Saul are listed other than from the line of Jonathan. *barley harvest was beginning.* About the middle of April (see note on Ru 1:22).

21:10 *sackcloth.* See note on Ge 37:34. *rain poured down.* An indication that the famine was caused by drought and evidence that the judgment on Israel for breaking the oath sworn to the Gibeonites (see v. 1) was now over.

21:12–14 *bones of Saul and his son Jonathan.* See 1Sa 31:11–13. David's final act toward Saul and Jonathan was a deed of deep respect for the king he had honored and the friend he had loved (see 1:19 and note).

21:14 *God answered prayer in behalf of the land.* Concludes the first unit of the *a-b-c/c'-b'-a'* literary structure that characterizes the last four chapters of 2 Samuel, just as its echo in 24:25 concludes the last unit (see note on 21:1—24:25).

21:15–21 These four Philistine episodes (vv. 15–17,18,19, 20–21) cannot be chronologically located with any certainty (see note on 21:1—24:25). Each involves a heroic accomplishment by one of David's mighty men, resulting in the death of a descendant of Rapha (see v. 22).

21:16,18,20,22 *Rapha.* The ancestor of at least one group of Rephaites (see 1Ch 20:4,8). In calling the four formidable enemy warriors referred to in this series "descendants of Rapha"

three hundred shekels[a] and who was
armed with a new sword, said he would
kill David. 17 But Abishai[v] son of Zeruiah
came to David's rescue; he struck the Philistine down and killed him. Then David's men swore to him, saying, "Never again will you go out with us to battle, so that the lamp[w] of Israel will not be extinguished.[x]"
18 In the course of time, there was another battle with the Philistines, at Gob. At that time Sibbekai[y] the Hushathite killed Saph, one of the descendants of Rapha.
19 In another battle with the Philistines at Gob, Elhanan son of Jair[b] the Bethlehemite killed the brother of[c] Goliath the Gittite,[z] who had a spear with a shaft like a weaver's rod.[a]
20 In still another battle, which took place at Gath, there was a huge man with six fingers on each hand and six toes on each foot—twenty-four in all. He also was descended from Rapha.
21 When he taunted[b] Israel, Jonathan son of Shimeah,[c] David's brother, killed him.
22 These four were descendants of Rapha in Gath, and they fell at the hands of David and his men.

David's Song of Praise

22:1-51pp — Ps 18:1-50

22 David sang[d] to the LORD the words of this song when the LORD delivered him from the hand of all his enemies and from the hand of Saul.
2 He said:

"The LORD is my rock,[e] my fortress[f] and
my deliverer;[g]
3 my God is my rock, in whom I take
refuge,[h]
my shield[d][i] and the horn[e][j] of my
salvation.
He is my stronghold,[k] my refuge and
my savior—
from violent people you save me.

4 "I called to the LORD, who is worthy[l] of
praise,
and have been saved from my
enemies.
5 The waves[m] of death swirled about me;
the torrents of destruction
overwhelmed me.
6 The cords of the grave[n] coiled
around me;
the snares of death confronted me.
7 "In my distress[o] I called[p] to the LORD;
I called out to my God.
From his temple he heard my voice;
my cry came to his ears.
8 The earth[q] trembled and quaked,[r]
the foundations[s] of the heavens[f]
shook;

21:17 [v] 2Sa 20:6 [w] 1Ki 11:36; 15:4; 2Ki 8:19; 2Ch 21:7; Ps 132:17 [x] 2Sa 18:3 **21:18** [y] 1Ch 11:29; 27:11 **21:19** [z] S 1Sa 17:4 [a] S 1Sa 17:7 **21:21** [b] S 1Sa 17:10 [c] S 1Sa 16:9 **22:1** [d] S Ex 15:1 **22:2** [e] S 1Sa 2:2 [f] Ps 31:3; 91:2 [g] Ps 144:2 **22:3** [h] S Dt 23:15; S 32:37; Ps 14:6; 31:2; 59:16; 71:7; 91:2; 94:22; Pr 10:29; Isa 25:4; Jer 16:19; Joel 3:16 [i] S Ge 15:1 [j] S Dt 33:17; S Lk 1:69 [k] Ps 9:9; 52:7 **22:4** [l] Ps 48:1; 96:4; 145:3 **22:5** [m] Ps 69:14-15; Jnh 2:3 **22:6** [n] Ps 116:3; Ac 2:24 **22:7** [o] Ge 35:3; S Jdg 2:15; 2Ch 15:4; Ps 4:1; 77:2; 120:1; Isa 26:16 [p] Ps 34:6, 15; 116:4 **22:8** [q] Jdg 5:4; Ps 97:4 [r] S Ex 19:18; S Jdg 5:4; Ps 68:8; 77:18; Jer 10:10 [s] Job 9:6; 26:11; Ps 75:3

[a] *16* That is, about 7 1/2 pounds or about 3.5 kilograms
[b] *19* See 1 Chron. 20:5; Hebrew *Jaare-Oregim.*
[c] *19* See 1 Chron. 20:5; Hebrew does not have *the brother of.*
[d] *3* Or *sovereign*
[e] *3* *Horn* here symbolizes strength.
[f] *8* Hebrew; Vulgate and Syriac (see also Psalm 18:7) *mountains*

(v. 22), the writer most likely identifies them as giants (see v. 20; Dt 2:10–11,20–21). In that case, they may have been related to the Anakites (see Nu 13:28,32–33; Jos 11:21–22). The list of the ten peoples of Canaan in Ge 15:19–21 mentions Rephaites but not Anakites, though the Anakites (but not Rephaites) figure significantly in the accounts of the conquest (Dt 9:2; Jos 14:12,15; Jdg 1:20).

21:17 *Abishai.* See note on 1Sa 26:6. *so that the lamp of Israel will not be extinguished.* A striking metaphor depicting Israel's dependence on David for its security and continuing existence as a nation—its national hope (see 22:29; 23:3–4; 1Ki 11:36 and note; cf. 2Sa 22:29; 23:3–4).

21:18–19 *Gob.* Mentioned nowhere else in the OT, it may have been in the near vicinity of Gezer, where 1Ch 20:4 locates this same battle. On the other hand, many Hebrew manuscripts read "Nob," a well-known town northeast of Jerusalem (see 1Sa 21:1 and note). In that case, the text nicely echoes the proper name Ishbi-Benob (v. 16), which apparently means "inhabitant of Nob."

21:19 *Elhanan ... killed the brother of Goliath.* See NIV text note. Since it is clear from 1Sa 17 that David killed Goliath, an early copyist probably misread the Hebrew for "Lahmi the brother of" (see 1Ch 20:5) as "the Bethlehemite" (in Hebrew the word for "killed" stands first in the clause). *Jair.* See NIV text note. The Hebrew for "Oregim" occurs also at the end of the verse, where it is translated "weaver's." An early copyist probably inserted it in the name by mistake, since 1Ch 20:5 reads "Jair" (apparently correctly) instead of "Jaare-Oregim."

21:21 *taunted Israel.* As Goliath had done (see 1Sa 17:10,25). *Shimeah.* Also called Shammah (1Sa 16:9; 17:13).

22:1–51 For the relationship of this song to Hannah's song in the overall literary structure of 1 and 2 Samuel, see notes on 1Sa 2:1–10, especially on 2:1. David's song is preserved also as Ps 18 (see notes on that psalm). Besides an introduction (vv. 2–4) and conclusion (vv. 47–51), the song consists of three major sections: The first describes David's deliverance from mortal danger at the hands of his enemies (vv. 5–20); the second sets forth the moral grounds for God's saving help (vv. 21–30); the third recounts the help that the Lord gave him (vv. 31–46). The song was probably composed shortly after David's victories over foreign enemies (8:1–14) and before his sins against Bathsheba and Uriah (11:2–4,14–17; compare vv. 21–25 with 1Ki 15:5).

22:1 *from ... all his enemies.* See 8:1–14. *from ... Saul.* See 1Sa 18–27.

22:2 *rock.* A figure particularly appropriate to David's experience (see vv. 3,32,47; 23:3; cf. Dt 32:4,15,18,31; Ps 28:1; 31:2; 61:2; 78:35; 89:26; 94:22; 95:1). He had often taken refuge among the rocks of the desert (1Sa 23:25; 24:2), but he realized that true security was found only in the Lord. *fortress.* The Hebrew for this word occurs in 5:17; 23:14; 1Sa 22:4–5; 24:22, referring to one or more strongholds where David sought refuge.

22:3 *my shield.* See v. 31; Ge 15:1 and note. *horn.* See NIV text note; Dt 33:17; Jer 48:25.

22:5 *waves of death.* In vv. 5–6 David depicts his experiences in poetic figures of mortal danger.

22:6 *grave.* See notes on Ps 30:3; Jnh 2:2 ("realm of the dead").

22:7 *his temple.* Heaven, where the Lord is enthroned as King (see Ps 11:4; Isa 6:1 and notes; see also Jnh 2:7).

22:8–16 See note on Ps 18:7–15.

they trembled because he was angry.
9 Smoke rose from his nostrils;
consuming fire[t] came from his mouth,
burning coals[u] blazed out of it.
10 He parted the heavens and came down;
dark clouds[v] were under his feet.
11 He mounted the cherubim[w] and flew;
he soared[a] on the wings of the wind.[x]
12 He made darkness[y] his canopy around him —
the dark[b] rain clouds of the sky.
13 Out of the brightness of his presence
bolts of lightning[z] blazed forth.
14 The LORD thundered[a] from heaven;
the voice of the Most High resounded.
15 He shot his arrows[b] and scattered the enemy,
with great bolts of lightning he routed them.
16 The valleys of the sea were exposed
and the foundations of the earth laid bare
at the rebuke[c] of the LORD,
at the blast[d] of breath from his nostrils.

17 "He reached down from on high[e] and took hold of me;
he drew[f] me out of deep waters.
18 He rescued[g] me from my powerful enemy,
from my foes, who were too strong for me.
19 They confronted me in the day of my disaster,
but the LORD was my support.[h]
20 He brought me out into a spacious[i] place;
he rescued[j] me because he delighted[k] in me.[l]

21 "The LORD has dealt with me according to my righteousness;[m]
according to the cleanness[n] of my hands[o] he has rewarded me.
22 For I have kept[p] the ways of the LORD;
I am not guilty of turning from my God.
23 All his laws are before me;[q]
I have not turned[r] away from his decrees.
24 I have been blameless[s] before him
and have kept myself from sin.
25 The LORD has rewarded me according to my righteousness,[t]
according to my cleanness[c] in his sight.

26 "To the faithful you show yourself faithful,
to the blameless you show yourself blameless,
27 to the pure[u] you show yourself pure,
but to the devious you show yourself shrewd.[v]
28 You save the humble,[w]
but your eyes are on the haughty[x] to bring them low.[y]
29 You, LORD, are my lamp;[z]
the LORD turns my darkness into light.
30 With your help I can advance against a troop[d];
with my God I can scale a wall.

31 "As for God, his way is perfect:[a]
The LORD's word is flawless;[b]
he shields[c] all who take refuge in him.
32 For who is God besides the LORD?
And who is the Rock[d] except our God?[e]

[a] *11* Many Hebrew manuscripts (see also Psalm 18:10); most Hebrew manuscripts *appeared* [b] *12* Septuagint (see also Psalm 18:11); Hebrew *massed* [c] *25* Hebrew; Septuagint and Vulgate (see also Psalm 18:24) *to the cleanness of my hands* [d] *30* Or *can run through a barricade*

22:9 [t]Ps 50:3; 97:3; Heb 12:29; S Rev 11:5 [u]Isa 6:6; Eze 1:13; 10:2 **22:10** [v]S Ex 19:9; Lev 16:2; S Dt 33:26; 1Ki 8:12; Job 26:9; Ps 104:3; Isa 19:1; Jer 4:13; Na 1:3 **22:11** [w]S Ge 3:24; S Ex 25:22 [x]Ps 104:3 **22:12** [y]S Ex 19:9 **22:13** [z]Job 37:3; Ps 77:18 **22:14** [a]S 1Sa 2:10 **22:15** [b]S Dt 32:23 **22:16** [c]Ps 6:1; 50:8,21; 106:9; Na 1:4 [d]S Ex 14:21; Isa 30:33; 40:24 **22:17** [e]Ps 144:7 [f]Ex 2:10 **22:18** [g]Lk 1:71 **22:19** [h]Ps 23:4 **22:20** [i]Job 36:16; Ps 31:8 [j]Ps 118:5 [k]Ps 22:8; Isa 42:1; Mt 12:18 [l]S 2Sa 15:26 **22:21** [m]S 1Sa 26:23 [n]Ps 26:6 [o]Job 17:9; 22:30; 42:7-8; Ps 24:4 **22:22** [p]Ge 18:19; Ps 128:1; Pr 8:32 **22:23** [q]Dt 6:4-9; Ps 119:30-32 [r]Ps 119:102 **22:24** [s]S Ge 6:9; Eph 1:4 **22:25** [t]S 1Sa 26:23 **22:27** [u]Mt 5:8 [v]Lev 26:23-24 **22:28** [w]S Ex 3:8; 1Sa 2:8-9; Ps 72:12-13 [x]Ps 131:1; Pr 30:13; Da 4:31; Zep 3:11 [y]Isa 2:12,17; 5:15; S Lk 1:51 **22:29** [z]Ps 27:1; Isa 2:5; Mic 7:8; Rev 21:23; 22:5 **22:31** [a]S Dt 32:4; Mt 5:48 [b]Ps 12:6; 119:140; Pr 30:5-6 [c]S Ge 15:1 **22:32** [d]S 1Sa 2:2 [e]S 2Sa 7:22

22:9 *Smoke rose from his nostrils.* See note on Ps 18:8.
22:10 *parted the heavens and came down.* See Isa 64:1 and note.
22:11 *mounted the cherubim and flew.* See notes on 1Sa 4:4; Ge 3:24; Ps 18:10; Eze 1:5.
22:14 *The LORD thundered.* The reference to thunder as the voice of God is common in the OT (see Ps 29; Job 37:2 – 5). Thunder is particularly suited to expressing God's power and majesty.
22:17 *He reached down from on high.* In vv. 17 – 20 David describes his deliverance, initially in figurative terms (v. 17; cf. v. 5) and subsequently in more literal language (vv. 18 – 20).
22:20 *spacious place.* See note on Ps 18:19. *delighted in.* The Hebrew underlying this expression is used in 15:26 ("pleased with"); Ps 22:8 (cf. Mt 3:17, "with ... well pleased") and expresses the idea of the sovereign good pleasure and favor of God toward his anointed one (v. 51).
22:21,25 *according to my righteousness.* See 1Ki 15:5. In vv. 21 – 25 David refers to the Lord's deliverances as a reward for his own righteousness. While these statements may give the impression of self-righteous boasting and a meritorious basis for divine favor, they should be understood in their context as: (1) David's desire to please the Lord in his service as the Lord's anointed (see note on v. 51); (2) his recognition that the Lord rewards those who faithfully seek to serve him.
22:26 – 30 See notes on Ps 18:25 – 29.
22:29 *You ... are my lamp.* The Lord causes David's life and undertakings to flourish (see Job 18:5 – 6; 21:17; see also note on Ps 27:1).
22:31 *his way is perfect.* The remainder of the song (vv. 31 – 51) accentuates David's praise to God for his deliverances.
22:32,47 *Rock.* See note on v. 2.

33 It is God who arms me with strength[a]
and keeps my way secure.
34 He makes my feet like the feet of a deer;[f]
he causes me to stand on the
heights.[g]
35 He trains my hands[h] for battle;
my arms can bend a bow[i] of bronze.
36 You make your saving help my shield;[j]
your help has made[b] me great.
37 You provide a broad path[k] for my feet,
so that my ankles do not give way.

38 "I pursued my enemies and crushed
them;
I did not turn back till they were
destroyed.
39 I crushed[l] them completely, and they
could not rise;
they fell beneath my feet.
40 You armed me with strength for battle;
you humbled my adversaries
before me.[m]
41 You made my enemies turn their
backs[n] in flight,
and I destroyed my foes.
42 They cried for help,[o] but there was no
one to save them —[p]
to the LORD, but he did not answer.[q]
43 I beat them as fine as the dust[r] of the
earth;
I pounded and trampled[s] them like
mud[t] in the streets.

44 "You have delivered[u] me from the
attacks of the peoples;
you have preserved[v] me as the head
of nations.
People[w] I did not know now serve me,
45 foreigners cower[x] before me;
as soon as they hear of me, they
obey me.[y]
46 They all lose heart;
they come trembling[c][z] from their
strongholds.

47 "The LORD lives! Praise be to my Rock!
Exalted[a] be my God, the Rock, my
Savior![b]
48 He is the God who avenges[c] me,[d]
who puts the nations under me,

22:34 [f] Isa 35:6; Hab 3:19 [g] S Dt 32:13 **22:35** [h] Ps 144:1 [i] Ps 7:12; 11:2; Zec 9:13 **22:36** [j] Eph 6:16 **22:37** [k] Pr 4:11 **22:39** [l] Ps 44:5; 110:6; Mal 4:3 **22:40** [m] S Jos 10:24; S 1Ki 5:3 **22:41** [n] S Ex 23:27 **22:42** [o] Isa 1:15 [p] Ps 50:22 [q] S 1Sa 14:37 **22:43** [r] 1Ki 20:10; 2Ki 13:7; Isa 41:2; Am 1:3 [s] Ps 7:5; Isa 41:25; Mic 7:10; Zec 10:5 [t] Isa 5:25; 10:6; 22:5; Mic 7:10 **22:44** [u] S Ex 11:3; S 2Sa 3:1 [v] Dt 28:13 [w] S 2Sa 8:1-14; Isa 55:3-5 **22:45** [x] Ps 66:3; 81:15 [y] S Dt 33:29 **22:46** [z] Mic 7:17 **22:47** [a] S Ex 15:2 [b] Dt 32:15; Ps 18:31; 89:26; 95:1 **22:48** [c] S Nu 31:3 [d] Ps 144:2 **22:49** [e] Ps 140:1,4 [f] Ps 27:6 **22:50** [g] Ps 9:11; 47:6; 68:4 [h] Ro 15:9* **22:51** [i] Ps 21:1; 144:9-10 [j] 1Sa 16:13; Ps 89:20; Ac 13:23 [k] S 2Sa 7:13 [l] Ps 89:24,29 **23:1** [m] S Ex 11:3; Ps 78:70-71; 89:27 [n] 1Sa 2:10,35; Ps 18:50; 20:6; 84:9; Isa 45:1; Hab 3:13

49 who sets me free from my enemies.[e]
You exalted me[f] above my foes;
from a violent man you rescued me.
50 Therefore I will praise you, LORD,
among the nations;
I will sing the praises[g] of your
name.[h]

51 "He gives his king great victories;[i]
he shows unfailing kindness to his
anointed,[j]
to David[k] and his descendants
forever."[l]

David's Last Words

23 These are the last words of David:

"The inspired utterance of David son
of Jesse,
the utterance of the man exalted[m] by
the Most High,
the man anointed[n] by the God of Jacob,
the hero of Israel's songs:

2 "The Spirit[o] of the LORD spoke
through me;
his word was on my tongue.
3 The God of Israel spoke,
the Rock[p] of Israel said to me:
'When one rules over people in
righteousness,[q]
when he rules in the fear[r] of God,[s]
4 he is like the light[t] of morning[u] at
sunrise[v]
on a cloudless morning,
like the brightness after rain[w]
that brings grass from the earth.'

5 "If my house were not right with God,
surely he would not have made with
me an everlasting covenant,[x]

[a] 33 Dead Sea Scrolls, some Septuagint manuscripts, Vulgate and Syriac (see also Psalm 18:32); Masoretic Text *who is my strong refuge* [b] 36 Dead Sea Scrolls; Masoretic Text *shield; / you stoop down to make* [c] 46 Some Septuagint manuscripts and Vulgate (see also Psalm 18:45); Masoretic Text *they arm themselves*

23:2 [o] Mt 22:43; Mk 12:36; 2Pe 1:21 **23:3** [p] Dt 32:4; S 1Sa 2:2; Ps 18:31 [q] Ps 72:2 [r] S Ge 42:18 [s] Isa 11:1-5 **23:4** [t] Jn 1:5 [u] Ps 119:147; 130:6; Pr 4:18 [v] S Jdg 5:31; Mt 13:43 [w] S Dt 32:2 **23:5** [x] S Ge 9:16; Ps 89:29

22:34 See Hab 3:19 and note.
22:47 *The LORD lives!* See note on Ps 18:46.
22:50 *I will praise you, LORD, among the nations.* For Paul's reference to this vow, see Ro 15:9.
22:51 *his king ... his anointed.* See notes on 1Sa 2:10; 10:25; 12:14–15. David refers to himself in the third person in a way that acknowledges the covenantal character of his kingship. It is in the context of David's official capacity as the Lord's anointed that the entire song is to be read and understood (see note on vv. 21,25). *his descendants forever.* David speaks of God's promise through Nathan (see 7:12–16).
23:1 *last words of David.* Probably to be understood as David's last poetic testimony (in the manner of his psalms), perhaps composed at the time of his final instructions and warnings to his son Solomon (see 1Ki 2:1–10).
23:2 See notes on 2Ti 3:16; 2Pe 1:20.
23:3 *Rock.* See note on 22:2; see also 1Sa 2:2 and note; Dt 32:4,15,18,30–31. *When one rules over people in righteousness.* In brief and vivid strokes David portrays the ideal theocratic king — to be fully realized only in the rule of David's greater son, Jesus Christ. This prophetic utterance complements that of 7:12–16 and anticipates those of Isa 9:7; 11:1–5; Jer 23:5–6; 33:15–16; Zec 9:9.
23:4 *like the light of morning.* See notes on Ps 27:1; 36:9.
23:5 *If my house were not right with God.* David recalls God's covenant with him and his dynasty (see 7:12–16). *everlasting covenant.* David expressly calls God's promise to him a covenant that will not be abrogated (see notes on 7:20,28; Isa 55:3; see also Ps 89:3–4,28–29,34–37; 132:11–12). *bring to fruition.* Through David's promised descendants.

arranged and secured in every part;
surely he would not bring to fruition
my salvation
and grant me my every desire.
6 But evil men are all to be cast aside
like thorns,[y]
which are not gathered with the hand.
7 Whoever touches thorns
uses a tool of iron or the shaft of a
spear;
they are burned up where they lie."

David's Mighty Warriors

23:8-39pp — 1Ch 11:10-41

8 These are the names of David's mighty
warriors:[z]
Josheb-Basshebeth,[a][a] a Tahkemonite,[b]
was chief of the Three; he raised his spear
against eight hundred men, whom he
killed[c] in one encounter.
9 Next to him was Eleazar son of Dodai[b]
the Ahohite.[c] As one of the three mighty
warriors, he was with David when they
taunted the Philistines gathered at Pas
Dammim[d] for battle. Then the Israelites
retreated, 10 but Eleazar stood his ground
and struck down the Philistines till his
hand grew tired and froze to the sword.
The LORD brought about a great victory
that day. The troops returned to Eleazar,
but only to strip the dead.
11 Next to him was Shammah son of
Agee the Hararite. When the Philistines
banded together at a place where there
was a field full of lentils, Israel's troops
fled from them. 12 But Shammah took his
stand in the middle of the field. He defended it and struck the Philistines down,
and the LORD brought about a great victory.
13 During harvest time, three of the thirty chief warriors came down to David at
the cave of Adullam,[d] while a band of
Philistines was encamped in the Valley
of Rephaim.[e] 14 At that time David was in
the stronghold,[f] and the Philistine garrison
was at Bethlehem.[g] 15 David longed for water and said, "Oh, that someone would get
me a drink of water from the well near the
gate of Bethlehem!" 16 So the three mighty
warriors broke through the Philistine lines,
drew water from the well near the gate of
Bethlehem and carried it back to David.
But he refused to drink it; instead, he
poured[h] it out before the LORD. 17 "Far be
it from me, LORD, to do this!" he said. "Is
it not the blood[i] of men who went at the
risk of their lives?" And David would not
drink it.
Such were the exploits of the three
mighty warriors.
18 Abishai[j] the brother of Joab son of
Zeruiah was chief of the Three.[e] He raised
his spear against three hundred men,
whom he killed, and so he became as famous as the Three. 19 Was he not held in
greater honor than the Three? He became
their commander, even though he was not
included among them.
20 Benaiah[k] son of Jehoiada, a valiant
fighter from Kabzeel,[l] performed great exploits. He struck down Moab's two mightiest warriors. He also went down into a pit
on a snowy day and killed a lion. 21 And he
struck down a huge Egyptian. Although
the Egyptian had a spear in his hand, Benaiah went against him with a club. He
snatched the spear from the Egyptian's
hand and killed him with his own spear.
22 Such were the exploits of Benaiah son
of Jehoiada; he too was as famous as the
three mighty warriors. 23 He was held in
greater honor than any of the Thirty, but
he was not included among the Three.
And David put him in charge of his bodyguard.

24 Among the Thirty were:
Asahel[m] the brother of Joab,

23:6 [y] Isa 5:6; 9:18; 10:17; 27:4; 33:12; Mic 7:4; Na 1:10; Mt 13:40-41 **23:8** [z] S 2Sa 17:10 [a] 1Ch 27:2 **23:9** [b] 1Ch 27:4 [c] 1Ch 8:4 **23:13** [d] S Ge 38:1; S Jos 12:15 [e] S Jos 17:15 **23:14** [f] 1Sa 22:4-5; S 2Sa 5:17 [g] Ru 1:19 **23:16** [h] S Ge 35:14 **23:17** [i] Lev 17:10-12 **23:18** [j] S 1Sa 26:6 **23:20** [k] S 2Sa 8:18; 1Ch 27:5 [l] Jos 15:21 **23:24** [m] S 2Sa 2:18

[a] 8 Hebrew; some Septuagint manuscripts suggest *Ish-Bosheth,* that is, *Esh-Baal* (see also 1 Chron. 11:11 *Jashobeam*). [b] 8 Probably a variant of *Hakmonite* (see 1 Chron. 11:11) [c] 8 Some Septuagint manuscripts (see also 1 Chron. 11:11); Hebrew and other Septuagint manuscripts *Three; it was Adino the Eznite who killed eight hundred men* [d] 9 See 1 Chron. 11:13; Hebrew *gathered there.* [e] 18 Most Hebrew manuscripts (see also 1 Chron. 11:20); two Hebrew manuscripts and Syriac *Thirty*

23:6 *evil men ... cast aside.* Godless people who have no interest in the righteous king will be destroyed (see Ps 2:8–9; 110:5–6).
23:8–39 See note on 21:1—24:25. This list of 37 (see v. 39) of David's most valiant warriors and the description of some of their exploits are paralleled in 1Ch 11:11–41. There the list is expanded by 16 names (1Ch 11:41–47).
23:8 *Three.* Two groups of three warriors (vv. 8–12 and 13–23) and one group of thirty warriors (vv. 24–39) are mentioned (see v. 39 for the total number of warriors).
23:13 *harvest time.* See 11:1 and note. The circumstances of this event suggest that it happened shortly after David had fled from Saul, when men first began to gather to his cause (see 1Sa 22:1–4), or shortly after his conquest of Jerusalem (see 2Sa 5:17–18). *three.* Probably not the same as the three mighty men of v. 9. *thirty chief warriors.* See vv. 23–24,39. *cave of Adullam.* See 1Sa 22:1. *Rephaim.* See 5:18.
23:14 *stronghold.* See note on 1Sa 22:4.
23:15–17 See note on 1Ch 11:15–19.
23:15 *Bethlehem.* David's hometown (1Sa 17:58).
23:18 *Abishai.* See 10:10,14; 18:2; see also note on 1Sa 26:6. *Three.* Presumably those referred to in vv. 13–17.
23:20 *Benaiah son of Jehoiada.* Commander of the Kerethites and Pelethites (see 8:18 and note; 20:23) and of the division of troops for the third month of the year (1Ch 27:5). He supported Solomon's succession to the throne (1Ki 1–2) and eventually replaced Joab as commander of the army (1Ki 2:35).
23:24 *Thirty.* At least 30 names are listed in vv. 24–39. Since the three of vv. 13–17 are also included in the Thirty (see

Elhanan son of Dodo from Bethlehem,
25 Shammah the Harodite,[n]
Elika the Harodite,
26 Helez[o] the Paltite,
Ira[p] son of Ikkesh from Tekoa,
27 Abiezer[q] from Anathoth,[r]
Sibbekai[a] the Hushathite,
28 Zalmon the Ahohite,
Maharai[s] the Netophathite,[t]
29 Heled[bu] son of Baanah the Netophathite,
Ithai son of Ribai from Gibeah[v] in
Benjamin,
30 Benaiah the Pirathonite,[w]
Hiddai[c] from the ravines of Gaash,[x]
31 Abi-Albon the Arbathite,
Azmaveth the Barhumite,[y]
32 Eliahba the Shaalbonite,
the sons of Jashen,
Jonathan 33 son of[d] Shammah the
Hararite,
Ahiam son of Sharar[e] the Hararite,
34 Eliphelet son of Ahasbai the Maakathite,[z]
Eliam[a] son of Ahithophel[b] the Gilonite,
35 Hezro the Carmelite,[c]
Paarai the Arbite,
36 Igal son of Nathan from Zobah,[d]
the son of Hagri,[f]
37 Zelek the Ammonite,
Naharai the Beerothite,[e] the armor-
bearer of Joab son of Zeruiah,
38 Ira the Ithrite,[f]
Gareb the Ithrite
39 and Uriah[g] the Hittite.
There were thirty-seven in all.

23:25 [n] Jdg 7:1 **23:26** [o] 1Ch 27:10 [p] 1Ch 27:9 **23:27** [q] 1Ch 27:12 [r] S Jos 21:18 **23:28** [s] 1Ch 27:13 [t] 2Ki 25:23; Ezr 2:22; Ne 7:26; Jer 40:8 **23:29** [u] 1Ch 27:15 [v] S Jos 15:57 **23:30** [w] S Jdg 12:13 [x] Jos 24:30 **23:31** [y] 2Sa 3:16 **23:34** [z] S Dt 3:14 [a] S 2Sa 11:3 [b] S 2Sa 15:12 **23:35** [c] S Jos 12:22 **23:36** [d] S 1Sa 14:47 **23:37** [e] S Jos 9:17 **23:38** [f] 1Ch 2:53 **23:39** [g] 2Sa 11:3
24:1 [h] S Jos 9:15 [i] Job 1:6; Zec 3:1 [j] S Ex 30:12; 1Ch 27:23 **24:2** [k] S 2Sa 20:23 [l] S 2Sa 3:10 [m] 2Ch 2:17; 17:14; 25:5 **24:3** [n] S 2Sa 2:18 [o] S Dt 1:11 **24:5** [p] S Jos 13:9 [q] S Nu 21:32 **24:6** [r] S Ge 10:19; Jdg 1:31 **24:7** [s] S Jos 19:29

David Enrolls the Fighting Men

24:1-17pp — 1Ch 21:1-17

24 Again[h] the anger of the LORD burned against Israel,[i] and he incited David against them, saying, "Go and
take a census of[j] Israel and Judah."
2 So the king said to Joab[k] and the army
commanders[g] with him, "Go throughout
the tribes of Israel from Dan to Beersheba[l]
and enroll[m] the fighting men, so that I may
know how many there are."
3 But Joab[n] replied to the king, "May the
LORD your God multiply the troops a hundred times over,[o] and may the eyes of my
lord the king see it. But why does my lord
the king want to do such a thing?"
4 The king's word, however, overruled
Joab and the army commanders; so they
left the presence of the king to enroll the
fighting men of Israel.
5 After crossing the Jordan, they camped
near Aroer,[p] south of the town in the gorge,
and then went through Gad and on to Jazer.[q] 6 They went to Gilead and the region
of Tahtim Hodshi, and on to Dan Jaan
and around toward Sidon.[r] 7 Then they
went toward the fortress of Tyre[s] and all

[a] 27 Some Septuagint manuscripts (see also 21:18; 1 Chron. 11:29); Hebrew *Mebunnai* [b] 29 Some Hebrew manuscripts and Vulgate (see also 1 Chron. 11:30); most Hebrew manuscripts *Heleb* [c] 30 Hebrew; some Septuagint manuscripts (see also 1 Chron. 11:32) *Hurai* [d] 33 Some Septuagint manuscripts (see also 1 Chron. 11:34); Hebrew does not have *son of.* [e] 33 Hebrew; some Septuagint manuscripts (see also 1 Chron. 11:35) *Sakar* [f] 36 Some Septuagint manuscripts (see also 1 Chron. 11:38); Hebrew *Haggadi* [g] 2 Septuagint (see also verse 4 and 1 Chron. 21:2); Hebrew *Joab the army commander*

v. 13), the total number of warriors mentioned is at least 33. 1Ch 11:41–47 lists 16 additional names for this group and apparently includes the names of replacements for vacancies when a warrior either dropped out or died. *Asahel.* See 2:18–23.

23:34 *Eliam.* Father of Bathsheba (see 11:3 and note) and son of David's counselor Ahithophel, who joined in Absalom's conspiracy (see 15:12 and note; 16:20–23; 17:1–23).

23:39 *Uriah the Hittite.* Perhaps mentioned last in this list to remind the reader of how serious David's sin against Uriah really was (see notes on 11:17; 1Ki 15:5).

24:1 *Again.* The previous occasion may have been the famine of 21:1. *the anger of the LORD burned against Israel.* The specific reason for the Lord's displeasure is not stated. Because the anger is said to be directed against Israel rather than David, some have concluded that it was occasioned by the widespread support among the people for the rebellions of Absalom and Sheba against David (see 15:12; 17:11,24–26; 18:7; 20:1–2), the divinely chosen and anointed theocratic king. This would mean that the events of this chapter are to be placed chronologically shortly after those of chs. 15–20 and so after 980 BC (see note on 15:7). *the LORD ... incited David against them.* 1Ch 21:1 says that Satan "incited" David to take the census. Although Scripture is clear that God does not cause anyone to sin (Jas 1:13–14), it is also clear that the evil acts of people and Satan are under God's sovereign control (see Ex 4:21; 7:3; 9:12; 10:1,20,27; 11:10; 14:4,8; Jos 11:20; 1Ki 22:22–23; Job 1:12; 2:6; Eze 3:20; 14:9; Ac 4:28). *take a census of Israel and Judah.* David's military census (see vv. 2–3) does not appear to have been prompted by any immediate external threat. Since he wanted to "know how many there are" (v. 2), it is evident that his action was motivated by pride in the size of the empire he had acquired, by reliance for his security on the size of the reserve of manpower he could muster in an emergency or, more likely, by both. The mere taking of a census was hardly sinful (see Nu 1:2–3; 26:2–4), but in this instance it represented an unwarranted glorying in and dependence on human power rather than the Lord (not much different from Israel's initial desire to have a king for its security; see 1Sa 8–12). The act was uncharacteristic of David (see 22:2–4,47–51; 1Sa 17:26,37, 45–47).

24:2,15 *from Dan to Beersheba.* See note on 1Sa 3:20.

24:3 *But why ... ?* David's directive does not go unchallenged. The fact that he does not answer suggests that he knew his reasons were highly questionable. In any event, Joab's challenge renders David even more guilty.

24:5–8 The military census was begun in southern Transjordan and moved northward, then west across the Jordan, moving from north to south.

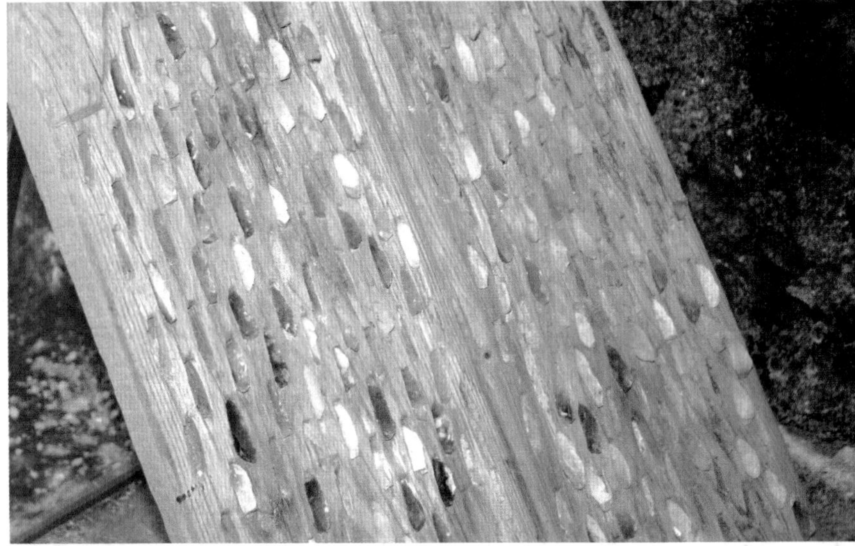

View of the bottom of a threshing sledge. Stones would be inserted into the boards, and the sledge would be dragged around the threshing floor; the stones would facilitate the process of threshing the grain.

www.HolyLandPhotos.org

the towns of the Hivites[t] and Canaanites.
Finally, they went on to Beersheba[u] in the
Negev[v] of Judah.
8 After they had gone through the entire
land, they came back to Jerusalem at the
end of nine months and twenty days.
9 Joab reported the number of the fighting men to the king: In Israel there were
eight hundred thousand able-bodied men
who could handle a sword, and in Judah
five hundred thousand.[w]
10 David was conscience-stricken[x] after
he had counted the fighting men, and he
said to the LORD, "I have sinned[y] greatly in
what I have done. Now, LORD, I beg you,
take away the guilt of your servant. I have
done a very foolish thing.[z]"
11 Before David got up the next morning, the word of the LORD had come to
Gad[a] the prophet, David's seer:[b] 12 "Go
and tell David, 'This is what the LORD
says: I am giving you three options.
Choose one of them for me to carry ou
against you.' "
13 So Gad went to David and said to him
"Shall there come on you three[a] years o
famine[c] in your land? Or three months
of fleeing from your enemies while they
pursue you? Or three days of plague[d] in
your land? Now then, think it over and
decide how I should answer the one who
sent me."
14 David said to Gad, "I am in deep distress. Let us fall into the hands of the
LORD, for his mercy[e] is great; but do not le
me fall into human hands."
15 So the LORD sent a plague on Israe
from that morning until the end of the
time designated, and seventy thousand o
the people from Dan to Beersheba died.
16 When the angel stretched out his hand
to destroy Jerusalem, the LORD relented[g] concerning the disaster and said to

24:7 [t]S Ex 3:8 [u]Ge 21:31 [v]S Dt 1:7
24:9 [w]S Nu 1:44-46
24:10 [x]S 1Sa 24:5 [y]S Nu 22:34 [z]S Nu 12:11
24:11 [a]S 1Sa 22:5 [b]1Sa 9:9
24:13 [c]Dt 28:38-42, 48; S 32:24; Eze 14:21 [d]S Ex 5:3; S 30:12; S Lev 26:25; Dt 28:21-22, 27-28, 35
24:14 [e]Ne 9:28; Ps 4:1; 51:1; 86:5; 103:8, 13; 119:132; 130:4; Isa 54:7; 55:7; Jer 33:8; 42:12; Da 9:9
24:15 [f]1Ch 27:24
24:16 [g]S Ge 6:6

[a] *13* Septuagint (see also 1 Chron. 21:12); Hebrew *seven*

24:9 *eight hundred thousand ... five hundred thousand.* These figures differ from those of 1Ch 21:5 (see notes on 1Ch 21:5–6).

24:10 *I have sinned greatly.* See note on v. 1.

24:11 *Gad the prophet, David's seer.* See notes on 1Sa 9:9; 22:5.

24:12 *Go and tell David.* See 12:1 and note. *three options.* The three alternative judgments (v. 13) were all included in the curses that Moses said would come on God's people when they failed to adhere to their covenant obligations (see Dt 28:15–25).

24:14 *not ... into human hands.* David, who knew bot God and war, knew that even in his anger God is mor merciful than humans let loose in the rampages of war (se Ps 30:5).

24:16 *angel.* Angels appear elsewhere in Scripture as instru ments of God's judgment (see Ex 33:2; 2Ki 19:35; Ps 35:5–6 78:49; Mt 13:41; Ac 12:23). *the LORD relented.* See note on 1S 15:29. *threshing floor of Araunah.* Located on Mount Moriah immediately north of David's city and overlooking it. Later would become the site of the temple (see 1Ch 21:28—22:1 2Ch 3:1). *Jebusite.* See note on 5:6.

the angel who was afflicting the people, "Enough! Withdraw your hand." The angel of the LORD[h] was then at the threshing floor of Araunah the Jebusite.
[17]When David saw the angel who was striking down the people, he said to the LORD, "I have sinned; I, the shepherd,[a] have done wrong. These are but sheep.[i] What have they done?[j] Let your hand fall on me and my family."[k]

David Builds an Altar

24:18-25pp — 1Ch 21:18-26

[18]On that day Gad went to David and said to him, "Go up and build an altar to the LORD on the threshing floor of Araunah[l] the Jebusite." [19]So David went up, as the LORD had commanded through Gad.
[20]When Araunah looked and saw the king and his officials coming toward him, he went out and bowed down before the king with his face to the ground.
[21]Araunah said, "Why has my lord the king come to his servant?"

"To buy your threshing floor," David answered, "so I can build an altar to the LORD, that the plague on the people may be stopped."[m]
[22]Araunah said to David, "Let my lord the king take whatever he wishes and offer it up. Here are oxen[n] for the burnt offering, and here are threshing sledges and ox yokes for the wood. [23]Your Majesty, Araunah[b] gives[o] all this to the king." Araunah also said to him, "May the LORD your God accept you."
[24]But the king replied to Araunah, "No, I insist on paying you for it. I will not sacrifice to the LORD my God burnt offerings that cost me nothing."[p]

So David bought the threshing floor and the oxen and paid fifty shekels[c][q] of silver for them. [25]David built an altar[r] to the LORD there and sacrificed burnt offerings and fellowship offerings. Then the LORD answered his prayer[s] in behalf of the land, and the plague on Israel was stopped.

24:16 [h]S Ge 16:7; S 19:13; S Ex 12:23; Ac 12:23 **24:17** [i]Ps 74:1; 100:3; Jer 49:20 [j]S Ge 18:23 [k]Jnh 1:12 **24:18** [l]Ge 22:2; 2Ch 3:1 **24:21** [m]Nu 16:44-50 **24:22** [n]S 1Sa 6:14 **24:23** [o]Ge 23:11 **24:24** [p]Mal 1:13-14 [q]S Ge 23:16 **24:25** [r]S 1Sa 7:17 [s]2Sa 21:14

[a] *17* Dead Sea Scrolls and Septuagint; Masoretic Text does not have *the shepherd.* [b] *23* Some Hebrew manuscripts and Septuagint; most Hebrew manuscripts *King Araunah* [c] *24* That is, about 1 1/4 pounds or about 575 grams

24:17 *Let your hand fall on me and my family.* Although the people of Israel were not without guilt (see v. 1), David assumes full blame for his own act and acknowledges his responsibility as king for the well-being of the Lord's people (see 5:2; 7:7-8).
24:19 *as the LORD had commanded.* The Lord himself appointed the atoning sacrifice in answer to David's prayer.
24:21 *To buy your threshing floor.* David does not simply expropriate the property for his royal purposes (see 1Sa 8:14). Cf. photo below.
24:22 *threshing sledges.* See Am 1:3 and note on Ru 1:22; see also photo, p. 500.
24:24 *burnt offerings.* See Lev 1:1-17 and note on 1:3. *David bought the threshing floor.* Thus the later site of the temple (see note on v. 16) became the royal property of the house of David. *and the oxen.* David's haste could not wait for oxen to be brought some distance from his own herds. *fifty shekels.* See note on 1Ch 21:25.
24:25 *fellowship offerings.* See notes on 1Sa 11:15; Lev 3:1; see also note on Lev 7:11-36. Reconciliation and restoration of covenant fellowship were obtained by the king's repentance, intercessory prayer and the offering of sacrifices. *the LORD answered his prayer in behalf of the land.* See note on 21:14.

Threshing floors were open areas where grain was initially processed. Often a threshing sledge would be dragged by an animal, while a person would stand on the sledge to thresh the grain beneath. Then the grain would be winnowed, which was a process by which the grain was tossed into the air and the chaff (inedible) would be blown away. In 2 Samuel 24:18, Gad instructs David to "build an altar to the LORD on the threshing floor of Araunah the Jebusite."

Z. Radovan/www.BibleLandPictures.com

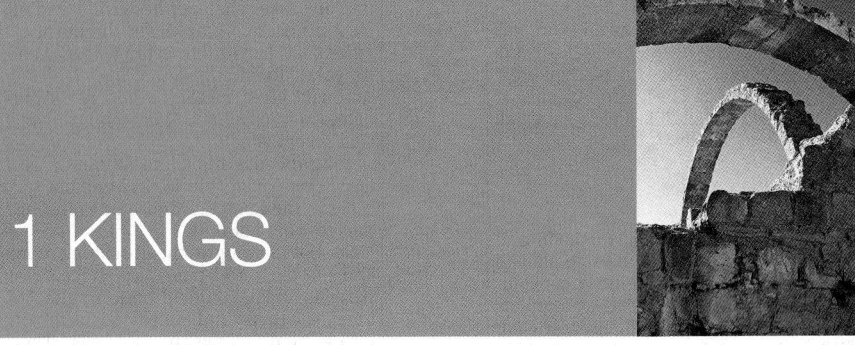

1 KINGS

INTRODUCTION

Title

1 and 2 Kings (like 1 and 2 Samuel and 1 and 2 Chronicles) are actually one literary work, called in Hebrew tradition simply "Kings." The division of this work into two books was introduced by the translators of the Septuagint (the pre-Christian Greek translation of the OT) and was subsequently followed in the Latin Vulgate (c. AD 400) and most modern versions. In 1448 the division into two sections also appeared in a Hebrew manuscript and was perpetuated in later printed editions of the Hebrew text. Both the Septuagint and the Latin Vulgate further designated Samuel and Kings in a way that emphasized the relationship of these two works (Septuagint: First, Second, Third and Fourth Book of Kingdoms; Latin Vulgate: First, Second, Third and Fourth Kings). Together, Samuel and Kings relate the whole history of the monarchy, from its rise under the ministry of Samuel to its fall at the hands of the Babylonians.

The division between 1 and 2 Kings has been made at a somewhat arbitrary and yet appropriate place, shortly after the deaths of Ahab of the northern kingdom (1Ki 22:37) and Jehoshaphat of the southern kingdom (22:50). Placing the division at this point causes the account of the reign of Ahaziah of Israel to overlap the end of 1 Kings (22:51 – 53) and the beginning of 2 Kings (ch. 1). The same is true of the narration of the ministry of Elijah, which for the most part appears in 1 Kings (chs. 17 – 19). However, his final act of judgment and the passing of his cloak to Elisha at the moment of his ascension to heaven in a whirlwind are contained in 2 Kings (1:1 — 2:17).

Author, Sources and Date

There is little conclusive evidence as to the identity of the author of 1,2 Kings. Although Jewish tradition credits Jeremiah, few today accept this as likely. Whoever the author was, it is clear that he was familiar with the book of Deuteronomy — as were many of Israel's prophets. It is also clear that he used a variety of sources in compiling his history of the monarchy. Three such sources are named: "the book of the annals of Solomon" (11:41), "the book of the annals of the kings of Israel" (14:19)

Author:
Unknown

Audience:
God's chosen people, the Israelites

Date:
Probably about 550 BC, during the Babylonian exile

Theme:
After Solomon's death, the nation is divided into the northern kingdom (Israel) and the southern kingdom (Judah).

and "the book of the annals of the kings of Judah" (14:29). It is likely that other written sources were also employed (such as those mentioned in Chronicles; see below).

Although some scholars have concluded that the three sources specifically cited in 1,2 Kings are to be viewed as official court annals from the royal archives in Jerusalem and Samaria, this is by no means certain. It seems at least questionable whether official court annals would have included details of conspiracies such as those referred to in 16:20; 2Ki 15:15. It is also questionable whether official court annals would have been readily accessible for public scrutiny, as the author clearly implies in his references to them. Such considerations have led some scholars to conclude that these sources were probably records of the reigns of the kings of Israel and Judah compiled by the succession of Israel's prophets spanning the kingdom period. 1,2 Chronicles makes reference to a number of such writings: "the records of Samuel the seer, the records of Nathan the prophet and the records of Gad the seer" (1Ch 29:29), "the prophecy of Ahijah the Shilonite" and "the visions of Iddo the seer" (2Ch 9:29), "the records of Shemaiah the prophet" (2Ch 12:15), "the annals of Jehu son of Hanani" (2Ch 20:34), "the annotations on the book of the kings" (2Ch 24:27), the "events of Uzziah's reign ... recorded by the prophet Isaiah son of Amoz" (2Ch 26:22; see also 2Ch 32:32) — and there may have been others. It is most likely, for example, that for the ministries of Elijah and Elisha the author depended on a prophetic source (perhaps from the eighth century) that had drawn up an account of those two prophets in which they were already compared with Moses and Joshua.

Some scholars place the date of composition of 1,2 Kings in the time subsequent to Jehoiachin's release from prison (562 BC; 2Ki 25:27 – 30; see also Jer 52:31 – 34; and compare 2Ki 25:1 – 12 with Jer 39:10; 52:4 – 16) and prior to the end of the Babylonian exile in 538. This position is challenged by others on the basis of statements in 1,2 Kings that speak of certain things in the preexilic period that are said to have continued in existence until "today" or "to this day" (see, e.g., 8:8, the poles used to carry the ark; 9:20 – 21, conscripted labor; 12:19, Israel in rebellion against the house of David; 2Ki 8:22, Edom in rebellion against the kingdom of Judah). From such statements it is argued that the writer must have been a person living in Judah in the preexilic period rather than in Babylon in postexilic times. If this argument is accepted, one must conclude that the original book was composed about the time of the death of Josiah and that the material pertaining to the time subsequent to his reign was added during the exile c. 550. While this "two-edition" viewpoint is possible, it rests largely on the "to this day" statements.

An alternative is to understand these statements as those of the original source used by the author rather than statements of the author himself. A comparison of 2Ch 5:9 with 1Ki 8:8 suggests that this is a legitimate conclusion. Chronicles is clearly a postexilic writing, yet the wording of the statement concerning the poles used to carry the ark ("they are still there today") is the same in Chronicles as it is in Kings. Probably the Chronicler was simply quoting his source, namely, 1Ki 8:8. There is no reason that the author of 1,2 Kings could not have done the same thing in quoting from his earlier sources. This explanation allows for positing a single author living in exile and using the source materials at his disposal (compare, e.g., 2Ki 19:1 — 20:19 with Isa 36 – 39).

Theme: Kingship and Covenant

1,2 Kings contains no explicit statement of purpose or theme. Reflection on its contents, however,

The high place at Dan, where Jeroboam set up one of the golden calves (1Ki 12:29)
Kim Walton

reveals that the author has selected and arranged his material in a manner that provides a sequel to the history found in 1,2 Samuel — a history of kingship regulated by covenant. In general, 1,2 Kings describes the history of the kings of Israel and Judah in the light of God's covenants. The guiding thesis of the book is that the welfare of Israel and her kings depended on their submission to and reliance on Israel's covenant God — their obedience to the Sinaitic covenant regulations and their faithful response to God's prophets.

It is clearly not the author's intention to present a social, political and economic history of Israel's monarchy in accordance with the principles of modern historiography. The author repeatedly refers the reader to other sources for more detailed information about the reigns of the various kings (see, e.g., 11:41; 14:19,29; 15:7,31; 16:5,14,20,27), and he gives a covenantal rather than a social or political or economic assessment of their reigns. From the standpoint of a political historian, Omri would be considered one of the more important rulers in the northern kingdom. He established a powerful dynasty and made Samaria the capital city. According to the Mesha Stele (see chart, p. xxiii), Omri was the ruler who subjugated the Moabites to the northern kingdom. Long after Omri's death, the Assyrian king Shalmaneser III referred to Jehu as the "son of Omri" (probably in accordance with their literary conventions when speaking of a later king of a realm). Yet in spite of Omri's political importance, his reign is dismissed in six verses (16:23 – 28) with the statement that he "did evil in the eyes of the LORD and sinned more than all those before him"

Together, 1 and 2 Samuel and 1 and 2 Kings relate the whole history of the monarchy, from its rise under the ministry of the prophet Samuel to its fall at the hands of the Babylonians.

(16:25). Similarly, the reign of Jeroboam II, who presided over the northern kingdom during the time of its greatest political and economic power, is treated only briefly (2Ki 14:23 – 29).

Another example of the writer's covenantal rather than merely political or economic interest can be seen in the description of the reign of Josiah of Judah. Nothing is said about the early years of his reign, but a detailed description is given of the reformation and renewal of the covenant that he promoted in his 18th year as king (2Ki 22:3 — 23:28). Nor is anything said of the motives leading Josiah to oppose Pharaoh Necho of Egypt at Megiddo, or of the major shift in geopolitical power from Assyria to Babylonia that was connected with this incident (see notes on 2Ki 23:29 – 30).

It becomes apparent, then, that the kings who receive the most attention in 1,2 Kings are those during whose reigns there was either notable deviation from or affirmation of the covenant (or significant interaction between a king and God's prophet; see below). Ahab, son of Omri, is an example of the former (16:29 — 22:39). His reign is given extensive treatment, not so much because of its extraordinary political importance but because of the serious threat to covenant fidelity and continuity that arose in the northern kingdom during his reign. Ultimately the pagan influence of Ahab's wife Jezebel through Ahab's daughter Athaliah (whether she was Jezebel's daughter is unknown) nearly led to the extermination of the dynasty of David in Judah (see 2Ki 11:1 – 3).

Manasseh (2Ki 21:1 – 18) is an example of a similar sort. Here again it is deviation from the covenant that is emphasized in the account of his reign rather than political features, such as involvement in the Assyrian-Egyptian conflict (mentioned in Assyrian records but not in 2 Kings). The extreme apostasy characterizing Manasseh's reign made exile for Judah inevitable (2Ki 21:10 – 15; 23:26 – 27; Jer 15:4).

On the positive side, Hezekiah (2Ki 18:1 — 20:21) and Josiah (2Ki 22:1 — 23:29) are given extensive treatment because of their involvement in covenant renewal. These are the only two kings given unqualified approval by the writer for their loyalty to the Lord (2Ki 18:3; 22:2). It is noteworthy that all the kings of the northern kingdom are said to have done evil in the eyes of the Lord and walked in the ways of Jeroboam, who caused Israel to sin (see, e.g., 16:26,31; 22:52; 2Ki 3:3; 10:29). It was Jeroboam who established the golden calf worship at Bethel and Dan shortly after the division of the kingdom (see 12:26 – 33; 13:1 – 6).

While the writer depicts Israel's obedience or disobedience to the Sinaitic covenant as decisive for her historical destiny, he also recognizes the far-reaching historical significance of the Davidic covenant, which promised that David's dynasty would endure forever. This is particularly noticeable in references to the "lamp" that the Lord had promised David (see 11:36 and note; 15:4; 2Ki 8:19; see also note on 2Sa 21:17). It also appears in more general references to the promise to David (8:20,25) and its consequences for specific historical developments in Judah's later history (11:12 – 13,32; 2Ki 19:34; 20:6). In addition, the writer uses the life and reign of David as a standard by which the lives of later kings are measured (see, e.g., 9:4; 11:4,6, 33,38; 14:8; 15:3,5,11; 2Ki 16:2; 18:3; 22:2).

Another prominent feature of the narratives of 1,2 Kings is the emphasis on the relationship between prophecy and fulfillment in the historical developments of the monarchy. On at least 11 occasions a prophecy is recorded that is later said to have been fulfilled (see, e.g., 2Sa 7:13 and 1Ki 8:20; 1Ki 11:29 – 39 and 1Ki 12:15; 1Ki 13 and 2Ki 23:16 – 18). The result of this emphasis is that the history of the kingdom is not presented as a chain of chance occurrences or the mere interplay of human actions but as the unfolding of Israel's historical destiny under the guidance of an omniscient and omnipotent God — Israel's covenant Lord, who rules all history in accordance with his sovereign purposes (see 8:56; 2Ki 10:10).

The author also stresses the importance of the prophets themselves in their role as official emissaries from the court of Israel's covenant Lord, the Great King to whom Israel and her king were bound in service through the covenant. The Lord sent a long succession of such prophets to call king and people back to covenant loyalty (2Ki 17:13). For the most part their warnings and exhortations fell on deaf ears. Many of these prophets are mentioned in the narratives of 1,2 Kings (see, e.g., Ahijah, 11:29 – 40; 14:5 – 18; Shemaiah, 12:22 – 24; Micaiah, 22:8 – 28; Jonah, 2Ki 14:25; Isaiah, 2Ki 19:1 – 7,20 – 34; Huldah, 2Ki 22:14 – 20), but particular attention is given to the ministries of Elijah and Elisha (1Ki 17 – 19; 2Ki 1 – 13).

Reflection on these features of 1,2 Kings suggests that it was written to explain to a people in exile that the reason for their condition of humiliation was their stubborn persistence in breaking the covenant. In bringing the exile upon his people, God, after much patience, imposed the curses of the covenant, which had stood as a warning to them from the beginning (see Lev 26:27 – 45; Dt 28:64 – 68). This is made explicit with respect to the captivity of the northern kingdom in 2Ki 17:7 – 23; 18:9 – 12, and with respect to the southern kingdom in 2Ki 21:12 – 15. The reformation under Josiah in the southern kingdom is viewed as too little, too late (see 2Ki 23:26 – 27; 24:3).

The books of Kings, then, provide a retrospective analysis of Israel's history. They explain the reasons both for the destruction of Samaria and Jerusalem and their respective kingdoms and for the bitter experience of being forced into exile. This does not mean, however, that there is no hope for the future. The writer consistently keeps the promise to David in view as a basis on which Israel in exile may look to the future with hope rather than with despair. In this connection the final four verses of 2 Kings, reporting Jehoiachin's release from prison in Babylon and his elevation to a place of honor in the court there (2Ki 25:27 – 30), take on added significance. The future remains open for a new work of the Lord in faithfulness to his promise to the house of David.

It is important to note that, although the author was undoubtedly a Judahite exile, and although the northern kingdom had been dispersed for well over a century and a half at the time of his writing, the scope of his concern was all Israel — the whole covenant people. Neither he nor the prophets (see Isa 10:20 – 21; 11:11 – 13; Jer 31; Eze 48:1 – 29; Hos 11:8 – 11; Am 9:11 – 15; Zec 9:10 – 13) viewed the division of the Israelite kingdom as a divine rejection of the ten tribes, nor did they see the earlier exile of the northern kingdom as a final exclusion of the northern tribes from Israel's future. As a matter of fact, many from the north had fled south during the Assyrian invasions, so that a significant remnant of the northern tribes lived on in the kingdom of Judah and shared in its continuing history.

Chronology

1,2 Kings presents the reader with abundant chronological data. Not only is the length of the reign of each king given, but during the period of the divided kingdom the beginning of the reign of each king is synchronized with the regnal year of the ruling king in the opposite kingdom. Often additional data, such as the age of the ruler at the time of his accession, are also provided.

By integrating Biblical data with those derived from Assyrian chronological records, the year 853 BC can be fixed as the year of Ahab's death and 841 as the year Jehu began to reign. The years in which Ahab and Jehu had contacts with Shalmaneser III of Assyria can also be given definite dates (by means of astronomical calculations based on an Assyrian reference to a solar eclipse). With these fixed points, it is then possible to work both forward and backward in the lines of the kings of Israel and Judah to give dates for each king. By the same means it can be determined that the division of the kingdom occurred in 930, that Samaria fell to the Assyrians in 722 – 721 and that Jerusalem fell to the Babylonians in 586.

The synchronistic data correlating the reigns of the kings of Israel and Judah present some knotty problems, which have long been considered nearly insoluble. In more recent times, most of these problems have been resolved in a satisfactory way through recognizing such possibilities as overlapping reigns, coregencies of sons with their fathers, differences in the time of the year in which the reign of a king officially began, and differences in the way a king's first year was reckoned (e.g., see notes on 15:33; 2Ki 8:25; see also charts, pp. 544 – 545 and p. 511).

Assyrian king Sargon II

Kim Walton, courtesy of the Oriental Institute Museum

Contents

1,2 Kings narrates the history of Israel during the period of the monarchy from the closing days of David's rule until the time of the Babylonian exile. After an extensive account of Solomon's reign, the narrative relates the division of the kingdom and then presents an interrelated account of developments within the two kingdoms. In this account, special attention is given to the ministries of Elijah and Elisha in the northern kingdom, with almost a third of the book (nearly equal to the amount of narrative given to Solomon's reign) devoted to God's efforts through his prophets to turn that kingdom away from its apostasies back to covenant faithfulness (see note on 1Ki 12:25—2Ki 17:41).

Kingship in the northern kingdom was plagued with instability and violence. Twenty rulers represented nine different dynasties during the approximately 210 years from the division of the kingdom in 930 BC to the fall of Samaria in 722–721. In the southern kingdom there were also 20 rulers, but these were all descendants of David (except Athaliah, whose usurping of the throne interrupted the sequence for a few years) and spanned a period of about 345 years from the division of the kingdom until the fall of Jerusalem in 586.

Outline

1,2 Kings can be broadly outlined by relating its contents to the major historical periods it describes and to the ministries of Elijah and Elisha.

- I. The Solomonic Era (1:1—12:24)
  - A. Solomon's Accession to the Throne (1:1—2:12)
  - B. Solomon's Throne Established (2:13–46)
  - C. Solomon's Wisdom (ch. 3)
  - D. Solomon's Reign Characterized (ch. 4)
  - E. Solomon's Building Projects (5:1—9:9)
    1. Preparation for building the temple (ch. 5)
    2. Building the temple (ch. 6)
    3. Building the palace (7:1–12)
    4. The temple furnishings (7:13–51)
    5. Dedication of the temple (ch. 8)
    6. The Lord's response and warning (9:1–9)
  - F. Solomon's Reign Characterized (9:10—10:29)
  - G. Solomon's Folly (11:1–13)
  - H. Solomon's Throne Threatened (11:14–43)
  - I. Rehoboam's Accession to the Throne (12:1–24)
- II. Israel and Judah from Jeroboam I/Rehoboam to Ahab/Asa (12:25—16:34)
  - A. Jeroboam I of Israel (12:25—14:20)
  - B. Rehoboam of Judah (14:21–31)
  - C. Abijah of Judah (15:1–8)
  - D. Asa of Judah (15:9–24)
  - E. Nadab of Israel (15:25–32)

- F. Baasha of Israel (15:33 — 16:7)
- G. Elah of Israel (16:8 – 14)
- H. Zimri of Israel (16:15 – 20)
- I. Omri of Israel (16:21 – 28)
- J. Ahab of Israel (16:29 – 34)

III. The Ministries of Elijah and Other Prophets from Ahab/Asa to Ahaziah/Jehoshaphat (chs. 17 – 22)
- A. Elijah (and Other Prophets) in the Reign of Ahab (17:1 — 22:40)
    1. Elijah and the drought (ch. 17)
    2. Elijah on Mount Carmel (ch. 18)
    3. Elijah's flight to Horeb (ch. 19)
    4. A prophet condemns Ahab for sparing Ben-Hadad (ch. 20)
    5. Elijah condemns Ahab for seizing Naboth's vineyard (ch. 21)
    6. Micaiah predicts Ahab's death; its fulfillment (22:1 – 40)
- B. Jehoshaphat of Judah (22:41 – 50)
- C. Ahaziah of Israel (22:51 – 53)

IV. The Ministries of Elijah and Elisha during the Reigns of Ahaziah and Joram (2Ki 1:1 — 8:15)
- A. Elijah in the Reign of Ahaziah (ch. 1)
- B. Elijah's Departure; Elisha's Inauguration (2:1 – 18)
- C. Elisha in the Reign of Joram (2:19 — 8:15)
    1. Elisha's initial miraculous signs (2:19 – 25)
    2. Elisha during the campaign against Moab (ch. 3)
    3. Elisha's ministry to needy ones in Israel (ch. 4)
    4. Elisha heals Naaman (ch. 5)
    5. Elisha's deliverance of one of the prophets (6:1 – 7)
    6. Elisha's deliverance of Joram from Aramean raiders (6:8 – 23)
    7. Aramean siege of Samaria lifted, as Elisha prophesied (6:24 — 7:20)
    8. The Shunammite's land restored (8:1 – 6)
    9. Elisha predicts Hazael's oppression of Israel (8:7 – 15)

V. Israel and Judah from Joram/Jehoram to the Exile of Israel (8:16 — 17:41)
- A. Jehoram of Judah (8:16 – 24)
- B. Ahaziah of Judah (8:25 – 29)
- C. Jehu's Revolt and Reign in Israel (chs. 9 – 10)
    1. Elisha orders Jehu's anointing (9:1 – 13)
    2. Jehu's assassination of Joram and Ahaziah (9:14 – 29)
    3. Jehu's execution of Jezebel (9:30 – 37)
    4. Jehu's slaughter of Ahab's family (10:1 – 17)
    5. Jehu's eradication of Baal worship (10:18 – 36)
- D. Athaliah and Joash of Judah; Repair of the Temple (chs. 11 – 12)
- E. Jehoahaz of Israel (13:1 – 9)
- F. Jehoash of Israel; Elisha's Last Prophecy (13:10 – 25)
- G. Amaziah of Judah (14:1 – 22)

  - H. Jeroboam II of Israel (14:23–29)
  - I. Azariah of Judah (15:1–7)
  - J. Zechariah of Israel (15:8–12)
  - K. Shallum of Israel (15:13–16)
  - L. Menahem of Israel (15:17–22)
  - M. Pekahiah of Israel (15:23–26)
  - N. Pekah of Israel (15:27–31)
  - O. Jotham of Judah (15:32–38)
  - P. Ahaz of Judah (ch. 16)
  - Q. Hoshea of Israel (17:1–6)
  - R. Exile of Israel; Resettlement of the Land (17:7–41)
- VI. Judah from Hezekiah to the Babylonian Exile (chs. 18–25)
  - A. Hezekiah (chs. 18–20)
    1. Hezekiah's good reign (18:1–8)
    2. The Assyrian threat and deliverance (18:9—19:37)
    3. Hezekiah's illness and alliance with Babylonia (ch. 20)
  - B. Manasseh (21:1–18)
  - C. Amon (21:19–26)
  - D. Josiah (22:1—23:30)
    1. Repair of the temple; discovery of the Book of the Law (ch. 22)
    2. Renewal of the covenant; end of Josiah's reign (23:1–30)
  - E. Jehoahaz Exiled to Egypt (23:31–35)
  - F. Jehoiakim: First Babylonian Deportation (23:36—24:7)
  - G. Jehoiachin: Second Babylonian Deportation (24:8–17)
  - H. Zedekiah: Third Babylonian Deportation (24:18—25:21)
  - I. Removal of the Remnant to Egypt (25:22–26)
  - J. Elevation of Jehoiachin in Babylon (25:27–30)

The narrative of the Solomonic era in 1Ki 1:1—12:24 is an exquisite example of literary inversion (*a-b-c-d/d′-c′-b′-a′* pattern), in this case consisting of nine sections:

a Solomon's accession to the throne (1:1—2:12)
  b Solomon's throne established (2:13–46)
    c Solomon's wisdom (ch. 3)
      d Solomon's reign characterized (ch. 4)
        e Solomon's building projects (5:1—9:9)
      d′ Solomon's reign characterized (9:10—10:29)
    c′ Solomon's folly (11:1–13)
  b′ Solomon's throne threatened (11:14–43)
a′ Rehoboam's accession to the throne (12:1–24)

Significant are the contrasts thus highlighted and the length of the centered section, which notably focuses on Solomon's building projects (see Outline above).

CHRONOLOGY OF FOREIGN KINGS

THIS IS A CHRONOLOGY OF SELECTED FOREIGN KINGS MENTIONED IN THIS STUDY BIBLE.		
ARAM	Ben-Hadad I	c. 895 – 860*
	Ben-Hadad II	c. 860 – 843
	Hazael	c. 843 – 796
	Ben-Hadad III	c. 796 – 770
	Rezin	740s – 732
ASSYRIA	Tiglath-Pileser III	745 – 727
	Shalmaneser V	727 – 722
	Sargon II	721 – 705
	Sennacherib	705 – 681
	Esarhaddon	681 – 669
	Ashurbanipal	669 – 627
BABYLONIA	Marduk-Baladan II	722 – 710, 703
	Nebuchadnezzar II	605 – 562
	Amel-Marduk	562 – 560
	Nabonidus	556 – 539
	Belshazzar (Coregency with Nabonidus)	553(?) – 539
EGYPT	Ahmose I	1550 – 1525**
	Thutmose II	1491 – 1479
	Thutmose III	1479 – 1425
	Tutankhamun	1333 – 1323
	Seti I	1289 – 1278
	Rameses II	1279 – 1212
	Merneptah	1212 – 1202
	Siamun	978 – 959
	Psusennes II	959 – 945
	Shishak I	945 – 924
	Osorkon I	924 – 889
	Shabako	716 – 702
	Shebitku	701 – 690
	Tirhakah	690 – 664
	Necho II	610 – 595
	Psammeticus II	595 – 589
	Hophra	589 – 570
PERSIA	Cyrus the Great	559 – 530
	Cambyses II	530 – 522
	Darius I the Great	522 – 486
	Xerxes (Ahasuerus)	486 – 465
	Artaxerxes I	465 – 424
	Darius II	423 – 404

*All dates are BC and are those of the kings' reigns.

**The earlier Egyptian dates assigned here are less certain than the later ones; there were also a few coregencies.

Adonijah Sets Himself Up as King

1 When King David was very old, he
could not keep warm even when they
put covers over him. 2 So his attendants
said to him, "Let us look for a young virgin to serve the king and take care of him.
She can lie beside him so that our lord the
king may keep warm."
3 Then they searched throughout Israel
for a beautiful young woman and found
Abishag,[a] a Shunammite,[b] and brought her
to the king. 4 The woman was very beautiful; she took care of the king and waited
on him, but the king had no sexual relations with her.
5 Now Adonijah,[c] whose mother was
Haggith, put himself forward and said,
"I will be king." So he got chariots[d] and
horses[a] ready, with fifty men to run ahead
of him. 6 (His father had never rebuked[e]
him by asking, "Why do you behave as
you do?" He was also very handsome and
was born next after Absalom.)
7 Adonijah conferred with Joab[f] son of
Zeruiah and with Abiathar[g] the priest, and
they gave him their support. 8 But Zadok[h]
the priest, Benaiah[i] son of Jehoiada, Nathan[j] the prophet, Shimei[k] and Rei and David's special guard[l] did not join Adonijah.
9 Adonijah then sacrificed sheep, cattle
and fattened calves at the Stone of Zo-
heleth near En Rogel.[m] He invited all his
brothers, the king's sons,[n] and all the royal
officials of Judah, 10 but he did not invite[o]
Nathan the prophet or Benaiah or the special guard or his brother Solomon.[p]
11 Then Nathan asked Bathsheba,[q] Solomon's mother, "Have you not heard that
Adonijah,[r] the son of Haggith, has become
king, and our lord David knows nothing
about it? 12 Now then, let me advise[s] you
how you can save your own life and the
life of your son Solomon. 13 Go in to King
David and say to him, 'My lord the king,
did you not swear[t] to me your servant:
"Surely Solomon your son shall be king
after me, and he will sit on my throne"?
Why then has Adonijah become king?'
14 While you are still there talking to the
king, I will come in and add my word to
what you have said."
15 So Bathsheba went to see the aged
king in his room, where Abishag[u] the Shunammite was attending him. 16 Bathsheba
bowed down, prostrating herself before
the king.
"What is it you want?" the king asked.

[a] 5 Or *charioteers*

1:3 [a] ver 15; S 2Sa 3:7; 1Ki 2:17,22 [b] S Jos 19:18 **1:5** [c] S 2Sa 3:4 [d] S 1Sa 8:11 **1:6** [e] 1Sa 3:13 **1:7** [f] S 2Sa 2:13, 18 [g] S 1Sa 22:20 **1:8** [h] S 1Sa 2:35; S 2Sa 8:17 [i] S 2Sa 8:18 [j] S 2Sa 7:2 [k] 1Ki 4:18 [l] 2Sa 23:8 **1:9** [m] S 2Sa 17:17 [n] 1Ch 29:24 **1:10** [o] ver 26 [p] S 2Sa 12:24 **1:11** [q] 2Sa 12:24 [r] S 2Sa 3:4 **1:12** [s] Pr 15:22 **1:13** [t] ver 17,30 **1:15** [u] S ver 3

1:1 — 12:24 The narrative of the Solomonic era is an exquisite example of literary inversion, in this case consisting of nine sections (see diagram, p. 510 [bottom]).
1:1 — 2:12 Solomon's accession to the throne (see note on 1:1 — 12:24).
1:1 *very old.* 2Sa 5:4 indicates that David died at about 70 years of age (cf. 1Ki 2:11).
1:2 *may keep warm.* The Jewish historian Josephus (first century AD) and the Greek physician Galen (second century AD) both refer to the ancient medical practice of using a healthy person's body to provide warmth for one who is ill.
1:3 *Shunammite.* See note on SS 6:13. Abishag came from Shunem (2Ki 4:8; Jos 19:18; 1Sa 28:4), located near the plain of Jezreel in the tribal territory of Issachar (see map, p. 557).
1:4 *had no sexual relations with her.* Significant in connection with Adonijah's request to be given Abishag as his wife after the death of David (see notes on 2:17,22).
1:5 *Adonijah.* The fourth son of David (see 2Sa 3:4), who was at this time approximately 35 years of age. It is likely that he was the oldest surviving son of David (see note on 2Sa 13:28; see also 2Sa 18:14). *put himself forward.* A unilateral attempt to usurp the throne, bypassing King David's right to designate his own successor (Adonijah must at least have known that his father favored Solomon; see v. 10). If successful, it would have thwarted God's and David's choice of Solomon (see vv. 13,17,30; 1Ch 22:9 – 10; see also note on 2Sa 12:25). *fifty men to run ahead of him.* Adonijah here follows the example of Absalom before him (see note on 2Sa 15:1).
1:6 *never rebuked him.* David appears to have been consistently negligent in disciplining his sons (see notes on 2Sa 13:21; 14:33). *very handsome.* Attractive physical appearance was an important asset to an aspirant to the throne (see 1Sa 9:2; 16:12; 2Sa 14:25).
1:7 *Joab son of Zeruiah.* See notes on 1Sa 26:6; 2Sa 2:13; 19:13; 20:10,23. Joab's alignment with Adonijah may have been motivated by a struggle for power with Benaiah (see v. 8; 2Sa 8:18; 20:23; 23:20 – 23). Joab held his position more by his standing with the army than by the favor and confidence of David (see 2:5 – 6). *Abiathar the priest.* See note on 2Sa 8:17.
1:8 *Zadok the priest.* See note on 2Sa 8:17. *Benaiah son of Jehoiada.* See note on 2Sa 23:20. *Nathan the prophet.* See 2Sa 12:1 – 25. *Shimei.* Not the Shimei of 2:8,46; 2Sa 16:5 – 8; perhaps the same as Shimei son of Ela (4:18). *Rei.* Or possibly "his friends." There is no other OT reference to Rei if taken as a proper name. *David's special guard.* See 2Sa 23:8 – 39.
1:9 *Adonijah then sacrificed.* Here also (see note on v. 5) Adonijah followed the example of Absalom (see 2Sa 15:7 – 12). *En Rogel.* Means "the spring of Rogel"; located just south of Jerusalem in the Kidron Valley. Apparently the site of a spring had some kind of symbolic significance for the business at hand (see v. 33 and note).
1:11 *Bathsheba, Solomon's mother.* The queen mother held an important and influential position in the royal court (see 2:19; 15:13; 2Ki 10:13; 2Ch 15:16). *has become king.* Although the preceding narrative does not relate the actual proclamation of Adonijah's kingship, it can be assumed (see v. 25; 2:15; cf. 2Sa 15:10).
1:12 *save your own life and the life of your son Solomon.* It was common in the ancient Near East for a usurper to liquidate all potential claimants to the throne in an attempt to secure his own position (see 15:29; 2Ki 10:11; 11:1).
1:13 *did you not swear to me . . . ?* Although 2 Samuel does not record David's oath concerning the succession of Solomon, it does suggest that Solomon was the son through whom the Lord's promise to David for an eternal dynasty would be carried forward (see note on v. 5).
1:15 *Shunammite.* See note on v. 3.

17She said to him, "My lord, you yourself swore[v] to me your servant by the LORD your God: 'Solomon your son shall be king after me, and he will sit on my throne.' 18But now Adonijah has become king, and you, my lord the king, do not know about it. 19He has sacrificed[w] great numbers of cattle, fattened calves, and sheep, and has invited all the king's sons, Abiathar the priest and Joab the commander of the army, but he has not invited Solomon your servant. 20My lord the king, the eyes of all Israel are on you, to learn from you who will sit on the throne of my lord the king after him. 21Otherwise, as soon as my lord the king is laid to rest[x] with his ancestors, I and my son Solomon will be treated as criminals."

22While she was still speaking with the king, Nathan the prophet arrived. 23And the king was told, "Nathan the prophet is here." So he went before the king and bowed with his face to the ground.

24Nathan said, "Have you, my lord the king, declared that Adonijah shall be king after you, and that he will sit on your throne? 25Today he has gone down and sacrificed great numbers of cattle, fattened calves, and sheep. He has invited all the king's sons, the commanders of the army and Abiathar the priest. Right now they are eating and drinking with him and saying, 'Long live King Adonijah!' 26But me your servant, and Zadok the priest, and Benaiah son of Jehoiada, and your servant Solomon he did not invite.[y] 27Is this something my lord the king has done without letting his servants know who should sit on the throne of my lord the king after him?"

David Makes Solomon King

1:28-53pp — 1Ch 29:21-25

28Then King David said, "Call in Bathsheba." So she came into the king's presence and stood before him.

29The king then took an oath: "As surely as the LORD lives, who has delivered me out of every trouble,[z] 30I will surely carry out this very day what I swore[a] to you by the LORD, the God of Israel: Solomon your son shall be king after me, and he will sit on my throne in my place."

31Then Bathsheba bowed down with her face to the ground, prostrating herself before the king, and said, "May my lord King David live forever!"

32King David said, "Call in Zadok[b] the priest, Nathan the prophet and Benaiah son of Jehoiada." When they came before the king, 33he said to them: "Take your lord's servants with you and have Solomon my son mount my own mule[c] and take him down to Gihon.[d] 34There have Zadok the priest and Nathan the prophet anoint[e] him king over Israel. Blow the trumpet[f] and shout, 'Long live King Solomon!' 35Then you are to go up with him, and he is to come and sit on my throne and reign in my place. I have appointed him ruler over Israel and Judah."

36Benaiah son of Jehoiada answered the king, "Amen! May the LORD, the God of my lord the king, so declare it. 37As the LORD was with my lord the king, so may he be with[g] Solomon to make his throne even greater[h] than the throne of my lord King David!"

38So Zadok[i] the priest, Nathan the prophet, Benaiah son of Jehoiada, the Kerethites[j] and the Pelethites went down and had Solomon mount King David's mule, and they escorted him to Gihon.[k] 39Zadok the priest took the horn of oil[l] from the sacred tent[m] and anointed Solomon. Then they sounded the trumpet[n] and all the people shouted,[o] "Long live King Solomon!"

1:17 [v]S ver 13 **1:19** [w]ver 9 **1:21** [x]S Ge 15:15; 1Ki 2:10 **1:26** [y]ver 10 **1:29** [z]S 2Sa 4:9 **1:30** [a]S ver 13; 1Ch 23:1 **1:32** [b]S 1Sa 2:35 **1:33** [c]Jdg 10:4; Zec 9:9 [d]ver 38; 2Ch 32:30; 33:14 **1:34** [e]S 1Sa 2:35; 10:1 [f]S 2Sa 15:10 **1:37** [g]Jos 1:5, 17 [h]ver 47 **1:38** [i]ver 8 [j]S 1Sa 30:14; S 2Sa 15:18 [k]S ver 33 **1:39** [l]S Ex 29:7; S 1Sa 10:1; 2Ki 11:12; Ps 89:20 [m]S Ex 26:1; S 27:21 [n]S 2Sa 15:10; 2Ki 11:14 [o]ver 34; Nu 23:21; Ps 47:5; Zec 9:9

1:17 *you yourself swore to me ... by the LORD your God.* An oath taken in the Lord's name was inviolable (see Ex 20:7; Lev 19:12; Jos 9:15,18,20; Jdg 11:30,35; Ecc 5:4–7).
1:21 *laid to rest with his ancestors.* A conventional expression for death (see Ge 47:30; Dt 31:16).
1:24 Nathan approached David diplomatically by raising a question that revealed the dilemma. Either David had secretly encouraged Adonijah to claim the throne and thereby had broken his oath to Bathsheba and Solomon (see v. 27), or he had been betrayed by Adonijah.
1:25 *Long live King Adonijah!* An expression of recognition and acclamation of the new king (see 1Sa 10:24; 2Sa 16:16; 2Ki 11:12).
1:31 *May my lord King David live forever!* An expression of Bathsheba's thanks in the stereotyped hyperbolic language of the court (see Ne 2:3; Da 2:4; 3:9; 5:10; 6:21).
1:33 *your lord's servants.* Presumably including the Kerethites and Pelethites (see v. 38). *my own mule.* Although crossbreeding was forbidden in the Mosaic law (Lev 19:19), mules (perhaps imported; see Eze 27:14) were used in the time of David, at least as mounts for royalty (see 2Sa 13:29 and note; 18:9). To ride on David's own mule was a public proclamation that Solomon's succession to the throne was sanctioned by David (see Ge 41:43 and first NIV text note; Est 6:7–8). *Gihon.* The site of a spring on the eastern slope of Mount Zion (see notes on v. 9; 2Sa 5:8).
1:34 *anoint him.* See notes on 1Sa 2:10; 9:16. *Blow the trumpet.* See 2Ki 9:13; 2Sa 15:10; 20:1. *Long live King Solomon!* See note on v. 25.
1:35 *Israel and Judah.* The distinction between Israel and Judah was rooted in the separate arrangements by which David became king over these two tribal units (see 2Sa 2:4; 5:3).
1:36 *Amen! May the LORD ... so declare it.* See Jer 28:6.
1:37 *even greater.* Not a deprecation of David's accomplishments, but an expression of total loyalty to David and Solomon. Benaiah shared David's own desire for his chosen successor (see vv. 47–48).
1:38 *the Kerethites and the Pelethites.* See note on 2Sa 8:18.
1:39 *Zadok ... anointed Solomon.* Kings chosen by God to rule over his people who were not in a line of dynastic succes-

40 And all the people went up after him,
playing pipes[p] and rejoicing greatly, so
that the ground shook with the sound.
41 Adonijah and all the guests who were
with him heard it as they were finishing
their feast. On hearing the sound of the
trumpet, Joab asked, "What's the meaning
of all the noise in the city?"[q]
42 Even as he was speaking, Jonathan[r]
son of Abiathar the priest arrived. Adonijah said, "Come in. A worthy man like you
must be bringing good news."[s]
43 "Not at all!" Jonathan answered. "Our
lord King David has made Solomon king.
44 The king has sent with him Zadok the
priest, Nathan the prophet, Benaiah son
of Jehoiada, the Kerethites and the Pelethites, and they have put him on the king's
mule, 45 and Zadok the priest and Nathan
the prophet have anointed him king at Gihon. From there they have gone up cheering, and the city resounds[t] with it. That's
the noise you hear. 46 Moreover, Solomon
has taken his seat[u] on the royal throne.
47 Also, the royal officials have come to
congratulate our lord King David, saying,
'May your God make Solomon's name
more famous than yours and his throne
greater[v] than yours!' And the king bowed
in worship on his bed 48 and said, 'Praise
be to the LORD, the God of Israel, who has
allowed my eyes to see a successor[w] on my
throne today.' "

49 At this, all Adonijah's guests rose in
alarm and dispersed. 50 But Adonijah, in
fear of Solomon, went and took hold of
the horns[x] of the altar. 51 Then Solomon
was told, "Adonijah is afraid of King Solomon and is clinging to the horns of the
altar. He says, 'Let King Solomon swear to
me today that he will not put his servant
to death with the sword.' "
52 Solomon replied, "If he shows himself
to be worthy, not a hair[y] of his head will
fall to the ground; but if evil is found in
him, he will die." 53 Then King Solomon
sent men, and they brought him down
from the altar. And Adonijah came and
bowed down to King Solomon, and Solomon said, "Go to your home."

David's Charge to Solomon

2:10-12pp — 1Ch 29:26-28

2 When the time drew near for David
to die,[z] he gave a charge to Solomon
his son.
2 "I am about to go the way of all the
earth,"[a] he said. "So be strong,[b] act like a
man, 3 and observe[c] what the LORD your
God requires: Walk in obedience to him,
and keep his decrees and commands, his
laws and regulations, as written in the
Law of Moses. Do this so that you may
prosper[d] in all you do and wherever you
go 4 and that the LORD may keep his promise[e] to me: 'If your descendants watch

1:40 [p] S 1Sa 10:5
1:41 [q] 2Ch 23:12-13
1:42 [r] S 2Sa 15:27,36 [s] S 2Sa 18:26
1:45 [t] ver 40
1:46 [u] S Dt 17:18
1:47 [v] ver 37
1:48 [w] 1Ki 3:6
1:50 [x] S Ex 27:2
1:52 [y] S 1Sa 14:45
2:1 [z] S Ge 27:2; S Nu 27:13
2:2 [a] Jos 23:14 [b] S Jos 1:6
2:3 [c] S Dt 4:6; S 10:12; S 17:14-20; S Jos 1:7 [d] 1Ch 22:13
2:4 [e] S 2Sa 7:13, 25; 2Ch 23:3

sion were anointed by prophets (Saul, 1Sa 9:16; David, 1Sa 16:12; Jehu, 2Ki 9). Kings who assumed office in the line of dynastic succession were anointed by priests (Solomon, here; Joash, 2Ki 11:12). The distinction seems to be that the priest worked within the established order while the prophets introduced new divine initiatives. *horn of oil.* Perhaps containing the anointing oil described in Ex 30:22 – 33. *sacred tent.* The tent David had erected in Jerusalem to house the ark (see 2Sa 6:17) rather than the tabernacle at Gibeon (see 3:4 and note; 2Ch 1:3).

1:41 *heard it.* Although Gihon may not have been visible from En Rogel, the distance was not great and the sound would carry down the Kidron Valley.

1:42 *Jonathan son of Abiathar.* See 2Sa 17:17 – 21.

1:47 *more famous.* See note on v. 37.

1:48 *successor.* In Solomon's accession to the throne David sees a fulfillment of the promise in 2Sa 7:12,16.

1:49 *dispersed.* No one wanted to be identified with Adonijah's abortive coup now that it appeared certain to fail.

1:50 *took hold of the horns of the altar.* The horns of the altar were vertical projections at each corner. The idea of seeking asylum at the altar was rooted in the Pentateuch (see Ex 21:13 – 14). The priest smeared the blood of the sacrifice on the horns of the altar (see Ex 29:12; Lev 4:7,18,25,30,34) during the sacrificial ritual. Adonijah thus seeks to place his own destiny under the protection of God.

1:52 *worthy.* One who recognizes and submits to Solomon's office and authority. *if evil is found in him.* If he shows evidence of continuing opposition to Solomon's accession to the throne.

2:1 *he gave a charge.* Moses (Dt 31:1 – 8), Joshua (Jos 23:1 – 16) and Samuel (1Sa 12:1 – 25), as representatives of the Lord's rule, had all given final instructions and admonitions shortly before their deaths.

2:2 *the way of all the earth.* To the grave (see Jos 23:14). *be strong.* See Dt 31:7,23; Jos 1:6 – 7,9,18.

2:3 *observe what the LORD your God requires.* See Ge 26:5; Lev 18:30; Dt 11:1. *Walk in obedience to him.* A characteristic expression of Deuteronomy for obedience to covenant obligations (Dt 5:33; 8:6; 10:12; 11:22; 19:9; 26:17; 28:9; 30:16). *his decrees and commands, his laws and regulations.* Four generally synonymous terms for covenant obligations (see 6:12; 8:58; 2Ki 17:37; Dt 8:11; 11:1; 26:17; 28:15,45; 30:10,16). *that you may prosper.* See Dt 29:9.

2:4 *that the LORD may keep his promise to me.* David here alludes to the covenanted promise of an everlasting dynasty given to him by God through Nathan the prophet (see notes on 2Sa 7:11 – 16). Although the covenant promise to David was unconditional, individual participation in its blessing on the part of David's royal descendants was conditioned on obedience to the obligations of the Sinaitic covenant (see 2Ch 7:17 – 22). *with all their heart and soul.* See Dt 4:29; 6:5; 10:12; 30:6. *you will never fail to have a successor on the throne of Israel.* Both Solomon and his descendants fell short of their covenant obligations. This led to the division of the kingdom and eventually to the exile of both the northern and southern kingdoms. It was only in the coming of Christ that the fallen tent of David would be restored (see notes on Am 9:11 – 15; Ac 15:16) and the promise of David's eternal dynasty ultimately fulfilled. When the nation and its king turned away from the requirements of the Sinaitic covenant, they experienced the covenant curses rather than its blessings; but in all this God remained faithful to his covenant promises to Abraham and to David (see

SOLOMON'S JERUSALEM

c. 950 BC

Solomon extended the city northward from the original site and there built his magnificent temple.

His royal residence was nearby, but its exact location is unknown.

how they live, and if they walk
faithfully[f] before me with all their
heart and soul, you will never fail
to have a successor on the throne
of Israel.'
5 "Now you yourself know what
Joab[g] son of Zeruiah did to me—
what he did to the two commanders of Israel's armies, Abner[h] son of
Ner and Amasa[i] son of Jether. He
killed them, shedding their blood
in peacetime as if in battle, and
with that blood he stained the belt
around his waist and the sandals
on his feet. 6 Deal with him according to your wisdom,[j] but do not let
his gray head go down to the grave
in peace.
7 "But show kindness[k] to the sons
of Barzillai[l] of Gilead and let them
be among those who eat at your table.[m] They stood by me when I fled
from your brother Absalom.
8 "And remember, you have with
you Shimei[n] son of Gera, the Benjamite from Bahurim, who called
down bitter curses on me the day
I went to Mahanaim.[o] When he
came down to meet me at the Jordan, I swore[p] to him by the LORD:
'I will not put you to death by the
sword.' 9 But now, do not consider him innocent. You are a man of
wisdom;[q] you will know what to do
to him. Bring his gray head down
to the grave in blood."
10 Then David rested with his ancestors and was buried[r] in the City
of David.[s] 11 He had reigned[t] forty
years over Israel—seven years in
Hebron and thirty-three in Jerusalem. 12 So Solomon sat on the
throne[u] of his father David, and his
rule was firmly established.[v]

2:4 [f] 2Ki 18:3-6; 20:3; Ps 26:1-3; 132:12
2:5 [g] S 2Sa 2:18 [h] S 1Sa 14:50; S 2Sa 3:27 [i] S 2Sa 17:25
2:6 [j] ver 9 **2:7** [k] S Ge 40:14 [l] S 2Sa 17:27; 19:31-39
[m] S 2Sa 9:7 **2:8** [n] ver 36-46; 2Sa 16:5-13 [o] S Ge 32:2
[p] 2Sa 19:18-23 **2:9** [q] ver 6 **2:10** [r] Ac 2:29 [s] S 2Sa 5:7
2:11 [t] S 2Sa 5:4,5 **2:12** [u] 1Ch 17:14; 29:23; 2Ch 9:8
[v] ver 46; 2Ch 1:1; 12:13; 17:1; 21:4

Lev 26:42–45; Isa 9:6–7; 11:1–16; 16:5; 55:3; Jer 23:5–6; 30:9; 33:17,20–22,25–26; Eze 34:23–24; 37:24–28).

2:5 *Joab son of Zeruiah.* See note on 1:7. *Abner son of Ner.* See notes on 2Sa 3:25–32. *Amasa son of Jether.* See 2Sa 20:10. *shedding their blood in peacetime.* Joab's actions were unlawful assassinations (see Dt 19:1–13; 21:1–9) and only served his own self-interest. In addition, he murdered David's son Absalom (see 2Sa 18:14–15) and participated in Adonijah's conspiracy to usurp the throne (see 1:7,19).

2:7 *sons of Barzillai.* See note on 2Sa 17:27. *eat at your table.* A position of honor that brought with it other benefits (see 18:19; 2Ki 25:29; 2Sa 9:7; 19:28; Ne 5:17).

2:8 See 2Sa 16:5–13. *Shimei son of Gera, the Benjamite.* Gera was probably the ancestor of Shimei's particular line of descent rather than his immediate father (see Ge 46:21; Jdg 3:15). See NIV text notes on Ge 10:2; Da 5:22.

2:9 *do not consider him innocent.* The Mosaic law prohibited cursing a ruler (21:10; Ex 22:28).

2:10 *rested with his ancestors.* See note on 1:21. *City of David.* See 2Sa 5:7 and note. Peter implies that David's tomb was still known in his day (Ac 2:29).

2:11 *forty years.* See 2Sa 5:4–5. David ruled c. 1010–970 BC (see Introduction to 1Samuel: Chronology).

Solomon's Throne Established

13 Now Adonijah,[w] the son of Haggith,
went to Bathsheba, Solomon's mother. Bathsheba asked him, "Do you come
peacefully?"[x]
He answered, "Yes, peacefully." 14 Then
he added, "I have something to say to you."
"You may say it," she replied.
15 "As you know," he said, "the kingdom
was mine. All Israel looked to me as their
king. But things changed, and the kingdom has gone to my brother; for it has
come to him from the LORD. 16 Now I have
one request to make of you. Do not refuse me."
"You may make it," she said.
17 So he continued, "Please ask King Solomon — he will not refuse you — to give
me Abishag[y] the Shunammite as my wife."
18 "Very well," Bathsheba replied, "I will
speak to the king for you."
19 When Bathsheba went to King Solomon to speak to him for Adonijah, the
king stood up to meet her, bowed down to
her and sat down on his throne. He had a
throne brought for the king's mother,[z] and
she sat down at his right hand.[a]
20 "I have one small request to make of
you," she said. "Do not refuse me."
The king replied, "Make it, my mother;
I will not refuse you."
21 So she said, "Let Abishag[b] the Shunammite be given in marriage to your
brother Adonijah."
22 King Solomon answered his mother,
"Why do you request Abishag[c] the Shunammite for Adonijah? You might as well
request the kingdom for him — after all,
he is my older brother[d] — yes, for him and
for Abiathar[e] the priest and Joab son of
Zeruiah!"
23 Then King Solomon swore by the
LORD: "May God deal with me, be it ever so
severely,[f] if Adonijah does not pay with his
life for this request! 24 And now, as surely
as the LORD lives — he who has established
me securely on the throne of my father
David and has founded a dynasty for me
as he promised[g] — Adonijah shall be put
to death today!" 25 So King Solomon gave
orders to Benaiah[h] son of Jehoiada, and he
struck down Adonijah and he died.[i]
26 To Abiathar[j] the priest the king said,
"Go back to your fields in Anathoth.[k] You
deserve to die, but I will not put you to
death now, because you carried the ark[l] of
the Sovereign LORD before my father David and shared all my father's hardships."[m]
27 So Solomon removed Abiathar from the
priesthood of the LORD, fulfilling[n] the word
the LORD had spoken at Shiloh about the
house of Eli.
28 When the news reached Joab, who
had conspired with Adonijah though not
with Absalom, he fled to the tent of the
LORD and took hold of the horns[o] of the altar. 29 King Solomon was told that Joab had
fled to the tent of the LORD and was beside
the altar.[p] Then Solomon ordered Benaiah[q]
son of Jehoiada, "Go, strike him down!"
30 So Benaiah entered the tent[r] of the
LORD and said to Joab, "The king says,
'Come out!'[s] "
But he answered, "No, I will die here."
Benaiah reported to the king, "This is
how Joab answered me."

2:13 [w] S 2Sa 3:4 [x] S 1Sa 16:4
2:17 [y] S 1Ki 1:3
2:19 [z] 1Ki 15:13; 2Ki 10:13; 24:15; 2Ch 15:16; Jer 13:18; 22:26; 29:2 [a] Ps 45:9
2:21 [b] 1Ki 1:3
2:22 [c] S Ge 22:24; S 1Ki 1:3 [d] 1Ch 3:2 [e] S 1Sa 22:20
2:23 [f] S Ru 1:17
2:24 [g] 2Sa 7:11
2:25 [h] S 2Sa 8:18 [i] S 2Sa 12:10
2:26 [j] S 1Sa 22:20 [k] S Jos 21:18 [l] S 2Sa 15:24 [m] S 2Sa 15:14
2:27 [n] S 1Sa 2:27-36
2:28 [o] S Ex 27:2
2:29 [p] Ex 21:14 [q] ver 25
2:30 [r] 2Ki 11:15 [s] Ex 21:14

2:13 – 46 Solomon's throne established (see note on 1:1 — 12:24).

2:13 *Adonijah, the son of Haggith.* See note on 1:5. *Do you come peacefully?* The question (see 1Sa 16:4; 2Ki 9:22) reveals Bathsheba's apprehension concerning Adonijah's intention (see 1:5).

2:15 *the kingdom was mine.* See 1:11. *All Israel looked to me as their king.* A gross exaggeration (see 1:7 – 8). *it has come to him from the LORD.* Adonijah professes to view Solomon's kingship as God's will and to have no further intentions of seeking the position for himself.

2:17 *give me Abishag the Shunammite as my wife.* Adonijah's request has the appearance of being innocent (but see note on v. 22) since Abishag had remained a virgin throughout the period of her care for David (see 1:1 – 4; Dt 22:30).

2:19 *right hand.* The position of honor (see Ps 110:1; Mt 20:21).

2:20 *one small request.* Bathsheba does not seem to have attached any great significance to Adonijah's request.

2:22 *You might as well request the kingdom for him.* Solomon immediately understood Adonijah's request as another attempt to gain the throne. Possession of the royal harem was widely regarded as signifying the right of succession to the throne (see notes on 2Sa 3:7; 12:8; 16:21). Although Abishag was a virgin, she would be regarded by the people as belonging to David's harem; so marriage to Abishag would greatly strengthen Adonijah's claim to the throne. *for Abiathar the priest and Joab son of Zeruiah.* See note on 1:7. Solomon assumes that Abiathar and Joab continue to be involved in Adonijah's treacherous schemes.

2:23 *May God deal with me, be it ever so severely.* A curse formula (see note on 1Sa 3:17).

2:24 *has founded a dynasty for me.* Solomon's son and successor, Rehoboam, was born shortly before Solomon became king (cf. 11:42; 14:21). *as he promised.* See 1Ch 22:9 – 10.

2:25 *Benaiah son of Jehoiada.* See notes on 1:7; 2Sa 23:20.

2:26 *you carried the ark.* See 2Sa 15:24 – 25,29; 1Ch 15:11 – 12. *shared all my father's hardships.* See 1Sa 22:20 – 23; 23:6 – 9; 30:7; 2Sa 17:15; 19:11.

2:27 *fulfilling the word the LORD had spoken at Shiloh about the house of Eli.* See notes on 1Sa 2:30 – 35.

2:28 *news.* Of Adonijah's death and Abiathar's banishment. *conspired with Adonijah.* See 1:7. *tent of the LORD.* See note on 1:39. *took hold of the horns of the altar.* See note on 1:50.

2:29 *strike him down!* The right of asylum was extended only to those who accidentally caused someone's death (see Ex 21:14). Solomon was completely justified in denying this right to Joab, not only for his complicity in Adonijah's conspiracy, but also for his murder of Abner and Amasa (see vv. 31 – 33). In this incident Solomon finds a suitable occasion for carrying out his father's instruction (see vv. 5 – 6).

31 Then the king commanded Benaiah,
"Do as he says. Strike him down and bury
him, and so clear me and my whole family of the guilt of the innocent blood[t] that
Joab shed. 32 The LORD will repay[u] him for
the blood he shed,[v] because without my
father David knowing it he attacked two
men and killed them with the sword. Both
of them — Abner son of Ner, commander
of Israel's army, and Amasa[w] son of Jether,
commander of Judah's army — were better[x] men and more upright than he. 33 May
the guilt of their blood rest on the head of
Joab and his descendants forever. But on
David and his descendants, his house and
his throne, may there be the LORD's peace
forever."
34 So Benaiah[y] son of Jehoiada went up
and struck down Joab[z] and killed him, and
he was buried at his home out in the country. 35 The king put Benaiah[a] son of Jehoiada over the army in Joab's position and
replaced Abiathar with Zadok[b] the priest.
36 Then the king sent for Shimei[c] and
said to him, "Build yourself a house in
Jerusalem and live there, but do not go
anywhere else. 37 The day you leave and
cross the Kidron Valley,[d] you can be sure
you will die; your blood will be on your
own head."[e]
38 Shimei answered the king, "What you
say is good. Your servant will do as my
lord the king has said." And Shimei stayed
in Jerusalem for a long time.
39 But three years later, two of Shimei's
slaves ran off to Achish[f] son of Maakah,
king of Gath, and Shimei was told, "Your
slaves are in Gath." 40 At this, he saddled
his donkey and went to Achish at Gath in
search of his slaves. So Shimei went away
and brought the slaves back from Gath.
41 When Solomon was told that Shimei had gone from Jerusalem to Gath and
had returned, 42 the king summoned Shimei and said to him, "Did I not make you
swear by the LORD and warn[g] you, 'On the
day you leave to go anywhere else, you
can be sure you will die'? At that time you
said to me, 'What you say is good. I will
obey.' 43 Why then did you not keep your
oath to the LORD and obey the command
I gave you?"
44 The king also said to Shimei, "You
know in your heart all the wrong[h] you did
to my father David. Now the LORD will repay you for your wrongdoing. 45 But King
Solomon will be blessed, and David's
throne will remain secure[i] before the LORD
forever."
46 Then the king gave the order to Benaiah[j] son of Jehoiada, and he went out and
struck Shimei[k] down and he died.
The kingdom was now established[l] in
Solomon's hands.

Solomon Asks for Wisdom

3:4-15pp — 2Ch 1:2-13

3 Solomon made an alliance with Pharaoh king of Egypt and married[m] his
daughter.[n] He brought her to the City of David[o] until he finished building his palace[p]
and the temple of the LORD, and the wall
around Jerusalem. 2 The people, however,
were still sacrificing at the high places,[q]

2:31 [t]S Dt 19:13 **2:32** [u]Jdg 9:57 [v]S Ge 4:14; S Jdg 9:24 [w]S 2Sa 17:25 [x]2Ch 21:13 **2:34** [y]ver 25 [z]S 2Sa 2:18 **2:35** [a]S 2Sa 8:18 [b]S 1Sa 2:35 **2:36** [c]S 2Sa 16:5 **2:37** [d]S 2Sa 15:23; Jn 18:1 [e]S Lev 20:9 **2:39** [f]1Sa 27:2 **2:42** [g]S 2Sa 19:23 **2:44** [h]2Sa 16:5-13 **2:45** [i]S 2Sa 7:13 **2:46** [j]S 2Sa 8:18 [k]S ver 8 [l]S ver 12 **3:1** [m]1Ki 7:8; 11:1-13 [n]1Ki 9:24; 2Ch 8:11 [o]2Sa 5:7; 1Ki 2:10 [p]S 2Sa 7:2; 1Ki 9:10 **3:2** [q]Lev 17:3-5; S 26:30; Dt 12:14;

2:32 *he attacked two men and killed them.* See 2Sa 3:27; 20:9–10. *Israel's army.* See 2Sa 2:8–9. *Judah's army.* See 2Sa 20:4.
2:34 *at his home out in the country.* The tomb of Joab's father was located near Bethlehem (see 2Sa 2:32).
2:35 *Benaiah son of Jehoiada.* See note on 2Sa 23:20. *Zadok the priest.* See notes on 1Sa 2:35; 2Sa 8:17.
2:36 *do not go anywhere else.* Confinement to Jerusalem would greatly reduce the possibility of Shimei's (see v. 8) conspiring with any remaining followers of Saul against Solomon's rule.
2:37 *Kidron Valley.* See map, p. 515.
2:39 *Achish son of Maakah, king of Gath.* Gath was a major Philistine city (see Jos 13:3; 1Sa 6:16–17). It is likely that Gath was ruled successively by Maok, Achish the elder (1Sa 27:2), Maakah and Achish the younger (here); cf. 1Sa 21:10 and note.
2:43 See v. 36 and note.
2:46 *struck Shimei down and he died.* The third execution carried out by Benaiah (see vv. 25,34). It brought to completion the tasks assigned to Solomon by David just before his death (vv. 6,9).
3:1–28 Solomon's wisdom (see note on 1:1 — 12:24).
3:1 *made an alliance with Pharaoh.* It appears likely that Solomon established his marriage alliance with Siamun, one of the last kings of the Twenty-First Egyptian Dynasty. (Siamun was pharaoh of Egypt 978–959 BC.) Such an alliance attests Egyptian recognition of the growing importance and strength of the Israelite state (see 7:8; 9:16,24). 1Ki 9:16 indicates that the pharaoh gave his daughter the Canaanite town of Gezer as a dowry at the time of her marriage to Solomon. Gezer was located near the crossing of two important trade routes. One, to the west of Gezer, went from Egypt to the north and was very important for Egypt's commercial interests. The other, to the north of Gezer, went from Jerusalem to the Mediterranean Sea and the port of Joppa and was important to Solomon as a supply line for his building projects. The marriage alliance enabled both Solomon and the pharaoh to accomplish important economic and political objectives. No precise date is given for the conclusion of the marriage alliance, though it appears to have occurred in the third or fourth year of Solomon's reign (see 2:39). Solomon began construction of the temple in his fourth year (6:1), and control of the Gezer area was important to him for the beginning of this project (see map, p. 536; see also map, p. 2520, at the end of this study Bible). *married his daughter.* Solomon had already married Rehoboam's mother, Naamah (see 14:21,31), and may have had other wives also (cf. 11:1–3). *City of David.* The Egyptian princess was given a temporary residence in the old fortress (see 2Sa 5:7 and note) until a separate palace of her own could be constructed some 20 years later (7:8; 9:10; 2Ch 8:11).
3:2 *high places.* Upon entering Canaan, the Israelites often followed the Canaanite custom of locating their altars on

because a temple had not yet been built for
the Name[r] of the LORD. 3 Solomon showed
his love[s] for the LORD by walking[t] according to the instructions[u] given him by his father David, except that he offered sacrifices and burned incense on the high places.[v]
4 The king went to Gibeon[w] to offer sacrifices, for that was the most important
high place, and Solomon offered a thousand burnt offerings on that altar. 5 At Gibeon the LORD appeared[x] to Solomon during
the night in a dream,[y] and God said, "Ask[z]
for whatever you want me to give you."
6 Solomon answered, "You have shown
great kindness to your servant, my father
David, because he was faithful[a] to you and
righteous and upright in heart. You have
continued this great kindness to him and
have given him a son[b] to sit on his throne
this very day.
7 "Now, LORD my God, you have made
your servant king in place of my father
David. But I am only a little child[c] and
do not know how to carry out my duties.
8 Your servant is here among the people
you have chosen,[d] a great people, too numerous to count or number.[e] 9 So give your
servant a discerning[f] heart to govern your
people and to distinguish[g] between right
and wrong. For who is able[h] to govern this
great people of yours?"

10 The Lord was pleased that Solomon
had asked for this. 11 So God said to him,
"Since you have asked[i] for this and not for
long life or wealth for yourself, nor have
asked for the death of your enemies but
for discernment[j] in administering justice,
12 I will do what you have asked.[k] I will
give you a wise[l] and discerning heart, so
that there will never have been anyone
like you, nor will there ever be. 13 Moreover, I will give you what you have not[m]
asked for — both wealth and honor[n] — so
that in your lifetime you will have no
equal[o] among kings. 14 And if you walk[p]
in obedience to me and keep my decrees
and commands as David your father did,
I will give you a long life."[q] 15 Then Solomon awoke[r] — and he realized it had been
a dream.[s]
He returned to Jerusalem, stood before
the ark of the Lord's covenant and sacrificed burnt offerings[t] and fellowship offerings.[u] Then he gave a feast[v] for all his
court.

A Wise Ruling

16 Now two prostitutes came to the king
and stood before him. 17 One of them said,

3:2 1Ki 15:14; 22:43 [r]S Dt 14:23 **3:3** [s]Dt 6:5; Ps 31:23; 145:20 [t]S Dt 10:12; S Jos 1:7 [u]S Dt 17:19; S 1Ki 14:8 [v]S ver 2; Lev 17:3-5; 2Ki 12:3; 15:4, 35; 16:4; 21:3 **3:4** [w]S Jos 9:3 **3:5** [x]1Ki 9:2; 11:9 [y]S Mt 27:19 [z]S Mt 7:7 **3:6** [a]S Ge 17:1 [b]1Ki 1:48 **3:7** [c]Nu 27:17; 1Ch 22:5; 29:1; Jer 1:6 **3:8** [d]S Dt 7:6 [e]S Ge 12:2; 15:5; S 1Ch 27:23 **3:9** [f]S 2Sa 14:17; Jas 1:5 [g]S Dt 1:16 [h]2Co 2:16 **3:11** [i]Jas 4:3 [j]1Ch 22:12 **3:12** [k]1Jn 5:14-15 [l]S 2Sa 14:20; 1Ki 4:29, 30, 31; 5:12; 10:23; Ecc 1:16 **3:13** [m]Mt 6:33; Eph 3:20 [n]Pr 3:1-2, 16; 8:18 [o]1Ki 10:23; 2Ch 9:22; Ne 13:26 **3:14** [p]1Ki 9:4; Ps 25:13; 101:2; 128:1; Pr 3:1-2, 16 [q]Ps 61:6 **3:15** [r]S Ge 28:16 [s]ver 5 [t]Lev 6:8-13 [u]Lev 7:11-21 [v]Est 1:3, 9; 2:18; 5:8; 6:14; 9:17; Da 5:1

high hills, probably on the old Baal sites. The question of the legitimacy of Israelite worship at these high places has long been a matter of debate. It is clear that the Israelites were forbidden to take over pagan altars and high places and use them for the worship of the Lord (Nu 33:52; Dt 7:5; 12:3). It is also clear that altars were to be built only at divinely sanctioned sites (see Ex 20:24; Dt 12:5,8,13 – 14). It is not so clear whether multiplicity of altars was totally forbidden, provided the above conditions were met (see 19:10,14; Lev 26:30 – 31; Dt 12; 1Sa 9:12). It seems, however, that these conditions were not followed even in the time of Solomon, when pagan high places were being used for the worship of the Lord. This would eventually lead to religious apostasy and syncretism and was strongly condemned (2Ki 17:7 – 18; 21:2 – 9; 23:4 – 25). *because a temple had not yet been built.* Worship at a variety of places was apparently considered normal prior to the building of the temple (see Jdg 6:24; 13:19; 1Sa 7:17; 9:12 – 13). *Name of the LORD.* See notes on Dt 12:5; Ps 5:11.

3:3 *except.* Solomon's one major fault early in his reign was inconsistency in meeting the Mosaic requirements concerning places of legitimate worship.

3:4 *Gibeon.* The Gibeonites tricked Joshua and Israel into a peace treaty at the time of the conquest of Canaan (see Jos 9:3 – 27). The city was subsequently given to the tribe of Benjamin and was set apart for the Levites (Jos 18:25; 21:17). David avenged Saul's violation of the Gibeonite treaty by the execution of seven of Saul's descendants (see 2Sa 21:1 – 9). *most important high place.* The reason for Gibeon's importance was the presence there of the tabernacle and the altar of burnt offering (see 1Ch 21:29; 2Ch 1:2 – 6). These must have been salvaged after the destruction of Shiloh by the Philistines (see note on 1Sa 7:1).

3:5 *dream.* Revelation through dreams is found elsewhere in the OT (see Ge 28:12; 31:11; 46:2; Nu 12:6; Jdg 7:13; Da 2:4; 7:1), as well as in the NT (see, e.g., Mt 1:20; 2:12,22).

3:6 *kindness.* The Hebrew for this word often refers to God's covenant favors (see notes on 2Sa 7:15; Ps 6:4). Solomon is praising the Lord for faithfulness to his promises to David (2Sa 7:8 – 16). *because.* See note on 2Sa 22:21.

3:7 *I am only a little child.* The birth of Solomon is generally placed in approximately the middle of David's 40-year reign, meaning that Solomon was about 20 years old at the beginning of his own reign (see 2:11 – 12) and lacked experience in assuming the responsibilities of his office (cf. Jer 1:6).

3:8 *great people, too numerous to count.* From the small beginnings of a single family living in Egypt (see Ge 46:26 – 27; Dt 7:7), the Israelites had increased to an extent approaching that anticipated in the promise given to Abraham (Ge 13:16; 22:17 – 18) and Jacob (Ge 32:12). See 4:20 and note.

3:9 *a discerning heart.* The phrase indicates the ability to listen patiently to all sides of an issue in order to come to true and wise decisions — a characteristic traditionally associated with a good king in the ancient Near East (cf. Isa 11:2 – 5).

3:11 *long life ... wealth ... death of your enemies.* Typical desires of ancient Near Eastern monarchs.

3:12 *never ... anyone like you.* See 4:29 – 34; 10:1 – 13.

3:13 *I will give you what you have not asked for.* Cf. Jesus' promise in Lk 12:31.

3:14 *if you walk in obedience to me ... I will give you a long life.* Echoes Dt 6:2; 17:20; 22:7. Unfortunately Solomon did not remain obedient to the covenant as his father David had (11:6), and he did not live to be much more than 60 years of age (see note on v. 7; cf. 11:42).

3:15 *ark of the Lord's covenant.* See notes on 6:19; 2Sa 6:2. *fellowship offerings.* See note on 1Sa 11:15.

3:16 *two prostitutes came to the king.* It was possible for Isra-

"Pardon me, my lord. This woman and I
live in the same house, and I had a baby
while she was there with me. 18 The third
day after my child was born, this woman
also had a baby. We were alone; there was
no one in the house but the two of us.
19 "During the night this woman's son
died because she lay on him. 20 So she got
up in the middle of the night and took my
son from my side while I your servant was
asleep. She put him by her breast and put
her dead son by my breast. 21 The next
morning, I got up to nurse my son—and
he was dead! But when I looked at him
closely in the morning light, I saw that it
wasn't the son I had borne."
22 The other woman said, "No! The living one is my son; the dead one is yours."
But the first one insisted, "No! The dead
one is yours; the living one is mine." And
so they argued before the king.
23 The king said, "This one says, 'My son
is alive and your son is dead,' while that
one says, 'No! Your son is dead and mine
is alive.'"
24 Then the king said, "Bring me a
sword." So they brought a sword for the
king. 25 He then gave an order: "Cut the
living child in two and give half to one and
half to the other."
26 The woman whose son was alive was
deeply moved[w] out of love for her son and
said to the king, "Please, my lord, give her
the living baby! Don't kill him!"
But the other said, "Neither I nor you
shall have him. Cut him in two!"
27 Then the king gave his ruling: "Give
the living baby to the first woman. Do not
kill him; she is his mother."
28 When all Israel heard the verdict the
king had given, they held the king in awe,
because they saw that he had wisdom[x]
from God to administer justice.

Solomon's Officials and Governors

4 So King Solomon ruled over all Israel.
2 And these were his chief officials:[y]

Azariah[z] son of Zadok—the priest;
3 Elihoreph and Ahijah, sons of Shisha—secretaries;[a]
Jehoshaphat[b] son of Ahilud—recorder;
4 Benaiah[c] son of Jehoiada—commander in chief;
Zadok[d] and Abiathar—priests;
5 Azariah son of Nathan—in charge of
the district governors;
Zabud son of Nathan—a priest and
adviser to the king;
6 Ahishar—palace administrator;[e]
Adoniram[f] son of Abda—in charge of
forced labor.[g]

7 Solomon had twelve district governors[h]
over all Israel, who supplied provisions for
the king and the royal household. Each
one had to provide supplies for one month
in the year. 8 These are their names:

Ben-Hur—in the hill country[i] of Ephraim;
9 Ben-Deker—in Makaz, Shaalbim,[j]
Beth Shemesh[k] and Elon Bethha-
nan;
10 Ben-Hesed—in Arubboth (Sokoh[l]

3:26 [w] Ps 102:13; Isa 49:15; 63:15; Jer 3:12; 31:20; Hos 11:8
3:28 [x] S 2Sa 14:20; Col 2:3
4:2 [y] 1Ki 12:6; Job 12:12 [z] 1Ch 6:10; 2Ch 26:17
4:3 [a] S 2Sa 8:17 [b] S 2Sa 8:16
4:4 [c] S 2Sa 8:18 [d] S 2Sa 8:17
4:6 [e] S Ge 41:40 [f] S 2Sa 20:24 [g] S Ge 49:15
4:7 [h] ver 27
4:8 [i] S Jos 24:33
4:9 [j] Jdg 1:35 [k] S Jos 15:10
4:10 [l] S Jos 15:35

elites (and others within the realm) to bypass lower judicial officials (Dt 16:18) and appeal directly before the king (see 2Ki 8:3; 2Sa 15:2).

3:17 *live in the same house.* Brothels were common in ancient Near Eastern cities.

3:25 *Cut the living child in two.* This royal command, whereby Solomon in his wisdom resolved a judicial enigma and restored a violated relationship, served the author as a narrative foil to expose more effectively the folly Solomon later displayed, which led to God's judicial cutting of the kingdom in two, giving one part to Solomon's son and one part to Jeroboam (see 11:9–13). In the prophetic literature, these two kingdoms are often compared to prostitutes (see v. 16; see also Jer 3:6–12; Eze 16:15–46; 23:3–5; Hos 1:2 and notes).

3:28 *they saw that he had wisdom from God.* This episode strikingly demonstrated that the Lord had answered Solomon's prayer for a discerning heart (vv. 9,12).

4:1–34 Solomon's reign characterized (see note on 1:1—12:24).

4:1 *ruled over all Israel.* Solomon ruled over an undivided kingdom, as his father had before him (see 2Sa 8:15).

4:2 *son.* According to 2Sa 15:27,36 and 1Ch 6:8–9, Azariah was the son of Ahimaaz and the grandson of Zadok (see note on 2:8). Apparently Zadok's son Ahimaaz had died, so that Zadok was succeeded by his grandson Azariah. *Zadok.* See 2:27,35.

4:3 *Shisha.* See note on 2Sa 8:17. *secretaries.* See note on 2Sa 8:17. *Jehoshaphat son of Ahilud.* The same person who served in David's court (see 2Sa 8:16). *recorder.* See note on 2Sa 8:16.

4:4 *Benaiah.* Replaced Joab as commander of the army (see 2:35; 2Sa 8:18). *Zadok and Abiathar.* Abiathar was banished at the beginning of Solomon's reign (2:27,35), and Zadok was succeeded by his grandson Azariah (v. 2).

4:5 *Nathan.* Either the prophet (1:11) or the son of David (2Sa 5:14). *district governors.* See vv. 7–19. *priest.* See note on 2Sa 8:18. *adviser to the king.* See note on 2Sa 15:37.

4:6 *palace administrator.* The first OT reference to an office mentioned frequently in 1,2 Kings (1Ki 16:9; 18:3; 2Ki 18:18,37; 19:2). It is likely that this official was administrator of the palace and steward of the king's properties. *Adoniram.* Served not only under Solomon, but also under David before him (2Sa 20:24) and Rehoboam after him (1Ki 12:18). *forced labor.* See notes on 9:15; 2Sa 20:24.

4:7 *Solomon had twelve district governors.* The 12 districts were not identical to tribal territories, possibly because the tribes varied greatly in agricultural productivity. But Solomon's administrative decision violated traditional tribal boundaries and probably stirred up ancient tribal loyalties, eventually contributing to the disruption of the united kingdom.

4:8 *Ben-Hur.* Hebrew *Ben* means "son of."

and all the land of Hepher[m] were
his);
11 Ben-Abinadab — in Naphoth Dor[n] (he
was married to Taphath daughter
of Solomon);
12 Baana son of Ahilud — in Taanach
and Megiddo, and in all of Beth
Shan[o] next to Zarethan[p] below Jezreel, from Beth Shan to Abel Meholah[q] across to Jokmeam;[r]
13 Ben-Geber — in Ramoth Gilead (the
settlements of Jair[s] son of Manasseh in Gilead[t] were his, as well as
the region of Argob in Bashan and
its sixty large walled cities[u] with
bronze gate bars);
14 Ahinadab son of Iddo — in Mahanaim;[v]
15 Ahimaaz[w] — in Naphtali (he had married Basemath daughter of Solomon);
16 Baana son of Hushai[x] — in Asher and
in Aloth;
17 Jehoshaphat son of Paruah — in Issachar;
18 Shimei[y] son of Ela — in Benjamin;
19 Geber son of Uri — in Gilead (the
country of Sihon[z] king of the Amorites and the country of Og[a] king of
Bashan). He was the only governor
over the district.

Solomon's Daily Provisions

20 The people of Judah and Israel were
as numerous as the sand[b] on the seashore;
they ate, they drank and they were happy.[c] 21 And Solomon ruled[d] over all the
kingdoms from the Euphrates River[e] to
the land of the Philistines, as far as the
border of Egypt.[f] These countries brought
tribute[g] and were Solomon's subjects all
his life.
22 Solomon's daily provisions[h] were thirty cors[a] of the finest flour and sixty cors[b]
of meal, 23 ten head of stall-fed cattle,
twenty of pasture-fed cattle and a hundred
sheep and goats, as well as deer, gazelles,
roebucks and choice fowl.[i] 24 For he ruled
over all the kingdoms west of the Euphrates River, from Tiphsah[j] to Gaza, and had
peace[k] on all sides. 25 During Solomon's
lifetime Judah and Israel, from Dan to Beersheba,[l] lived in safety,[m] everyone under
their own vine and under their own fig
tree.[n]
26 Solomon had four[c] thousand stalls
for chariot horses,[o] and twelve thousand
horses.[d]
27 The district governors,[p] each in his
month, supplied provisions for King Solomon and all who came to the king's table.
They saw to it that nothing was lacking.
28 They also brought to the proper place
their quotas of barley and straw for the
chariot horses and the other horses.

Solomon's Wisdom

29 God gave Solomon wisdom[q] and very
great insight, and a breadth of understanding as measureless as the sand[r] on the seashore. 30 Solomon's wisdom was greater
than the wisdom of all the people of the
East,[s] and greater than all the wisdom of
Egypt.[t] 31 He was wiser[u] than anyone else,

4:10 [m] S Jos 12:17 **4:11** [n] S Jos 11:2 **4:12** [o] S Jos 17:11 [p] S Jos 3:16 [q] S Jdg 7:22 [r] 1Ch 6:68 **4:13** [s] S Nu 32:41 [t] Nu 32:40 [u] Dt 3:4 **4:14** [v] Jos 13:26 **4:15** [w] 2Sa 15:27 **4:16** [x] S 2Sa 15:32 **4:18** [y] 1Ki 1:8 **4:19** [z] S Jos 12:2 [a] Dt 3:8-10; S Jos 12:4 **4:20** [b] S Ge 12:2; S 32:12 [c] 1Ch 22:9 **4:21** [d] 2Ch 9:26; Ezr 4:20; Ps 72:11; La 1:1 [e] S Ge 2:14; Ps 72:8 [f] S Ex 23:31 [g] S Jdg 3:15; Eze 16:13 **4:22** [h] 1Ki 10:5 **4:23** [i] Ne 5:18 **4:24** [j] 2Ki 15:16 [k] S Jos 14:15 **4:25** [l] S Jdg 20:1 [m] 1Ch 22:9; Jer 23:6; Eze 28:26; 39:26 [n] Dt 8:8; 2Ki 18:31; Ps 105:33; Isa 36:16; Jer 5:17; Joel 2:22; Mic 4:4; Zec 3:10 **4:26** [o] S Dt 17:16 **4:27** [p] ver 7 **4:29** [q] S 1Ki 3:12 [r] S Ge 32:12 **4:30** [s] S Ge 25:6; S Jdg 6:3; Da 1:20; Mt 2:1 [t] Isa 19:11; Ac 7:22 **4:31** [u] S 1Ki 3:12

[a] 22 That is, probably about 5 1/2 tons or about 5 metric tons [b] 22 That is, probably about 11 tons or about 10 metric tons [c] 26 Some Septuagint manuscripts (see also 2 Chron. 9:25); Hebrew *forty* [d] 26 Or *charioteers*

4:11 *Ben-Abinadab.* Most likely the "son of" David's brother Abinadab (see 1Sa 16:8; 17:13), making him Solomon's first cousin (he was also his son-in-law).
4:12 *Baana son of Ahilud.* Probably a brother of Jehoshaphat the recorder (v. 3).
4:16 *Baana son of Hushai.* Perhaps the son of David's trusted adviser (see notes on 2Sa 15:32,37).
4:18 *Shimei son of Ela.* Perhaps the same Shimei mentioned in 1:8.
4:20 *as numerous as the sand on the seashore.* See 3:8 and note; see also v. 29; Ge 22:17; 2Sa 17:11; Isa 10:22; Jer 33:22; Hos 1:10; cf. Ge 41:49; Jos 11:4; Jdg 7:12; Ps 78:27. *they ate, they drank and they were happy.* Judah and Israel prospered (see 5:4).
4:21 *from the Euphrates River to the land of the Philistines, as far as the border of Egypt.* The borders of Solomon's empire extended to the limits originally promised to Abraham (see note on 2Sa 8:3). However, rebellion was brewing in Edom (11:14–21) and Damascus (11:23–25). *brought tribute.* From the outset of his reign, Solomon enjoyed the submission of the peoples David had conquered (cf. note on Ps 2:1–3).
4:22 *Solomon's daily provisions.* For all his household, his palace servants and his court officials and their families.
4:24 *Tiphsah.* A city on the west bank of the Euphrates River. *Gaza.* The southernmost city of the Philistines near the Mediterranean coast.
4:25 *from Dan to Beersheba.* See note on 1Sa 3:20.
4:26 *four thousand.* See NIV text note. 1Ki 10:26 and 2Ch 1:14 indicate that Solomon had 1,400 chariots, meaning that he maintained stalls for two horses for each chariot, with places for about 1,200 reserve horses. By way of comparison, an Assyrian account of the battle of Qarqar in 853 BC (about a century after Solomon) speaks of 1,200 chariots from Damascus, 700 chariots from Hamath and 2,000 chariots from Israel (the northern kingdom). *chariot horses.* See 2Sa 15:1 and note.
4:27 *district governors.* See v. 7 and note.
4:29 *as measureless as the sand on the seashore.* See note on v. 20.
4:30 *people of the East.* The phrase is general and appears to refer to the peoples of Mesopotamia (see Ge 29:1) and Arabia (see Jer 49:28; Eze 25:4,10) — those associated with Israel's northeastern and eastern horizons, just as Egypt was the main region on her southwestern horizon. Many examples of Mesopotamian wisdom literature have been recovered (see essay, p. 786, last paragraph). *wisdom of Egypt.* See Ge 41:8; Ex 7:11; Ac 7:22. Examples of Egyptian wisdom literature are to be found in the proverbs of Ptahhotep

including Ethan the Ezrahite — wiser than Heman, Kalkol and Darda,
the sons of Mahol. And his fame
spread to all the surrounding nations. 32 He spoke three thousand
proverbs[v] and his songs[w] numbered
a thousand and five. 33 He spoke
about plant life, from the cedar of
Lebanon to the hyssop[x] that grows
out of walls. He also spoke about
animals and birds, reptiles and fish.
34 From all nations people came to
listen to Solomon's wisdom, sent
by all the kings[y] of the world, who
had heard of his wisdom.[a]

Relief from the palace of King Sargon II (721 – 705 BC) depicts the transportation of cedars by boat. King Solomon had cedar logs shipped from Lebanon for the building of the temple (1Ki 5:9).

Z. Radovan/www.BibleLandPictures.com

Preparations for Building the Temple

5:1-16pp — 2Ch 2:1-18

5[b] When Hiram[z] king of Tyre
heard that Solomon had been
anointed king to succeed his father
David, he sent his envoys to Solomon,
because he had always been on friendly
terms with David. 2 Solomon sent back this
message to Hiram:

3 "You know that because of the
wars[a] waged against my father David
from all sides, he could not build[b] a
temple for the Name of the LORD his
God until the LORD put his enemies
under his feet.[c] 4 But now the LORD my
God has given me rest[d] on every side,
and there is no adversary[e] or disaster.
5 I intend, therefore, to build a temple[f]
for the Name of the LORD my God, as
the LORD told my father David, when
he said, 'Your son whom I will put on
the throne in your place will build the
temple for my Name.'[g]
6 "So give orders that cedars[h] of
Lebanon be cut for me. My men will
work with yours, and I will pay you
for your men whatever wages you
set. You know that we have no one
so skilled in felling timber as the Sidonians."

7 When Hiram heard Solomon's message, he was greatly pleased and said,
"Praise be to the LORD[i] today, for he has
given David a wise son to rule over this
great nation."
8 So Hiram sent word to Solomon:

"I have received the message you
sent me and will do all you want
in providing the cedar and juniper
logs. 9 My men will haul them down
from Lebanon to the Mediterranean
Sea[j], and I will float them as rafts by
sea to the place you specify. There I

4:32 [v] Pr 1:1; 10:1; 25:1; Ecc 12:9 [w] Ps 78:63; SS 1:1; Eze 33:32 **4:33** [x] S Lev 14:49 **4:34** [y] 2Ch 9:23 **5:1** [z] S 2Sa 5:11 **5:3** [a] 1Ch 22:8; 28:3 [b] S 2Sa 7:5 [c] 2Sa 22:40; Ps 8:6; 110:1; S Mt 22:44; 1Co 15:25 **5:4** [d] S Jos 14:15; 1Ch 22:9; Lk 2:14 [e] 1Ki 11:14,23 **5:5** [f] S Dt 12:5; 1Ch 17:12; 1Co 3:16; Rev 21:22 [g] Dt 12:5; 2Sa 7:13 **5:6** [h] 1Ch 14:1; 22:4 **5:7** [i] 1Ki 10:9; Isa 60:6 **5:9** [j] Ezr 3:7

[a] *34* In Hebrew texts 4:21-34 is numbered 5:1-14.
[b] In Hebrew texts 5:1-18 is numbered 5:15-32.

c. 2450 BC) and Amenemope (see Introduction to Proverbs: Date; see also chart, p. xxii).
4:31 *He was wiser than anyone else.* Until Jesus came (see Lk 1:31). *Ethan the Ezrahite.* See Ps 89 title. *Heman, Kalkol and Darda.* See note on 1Ch 2:6. *his fame spread.* See, e.g., 10:1.
4:32 *three thousand proverbs.* Only some of these are preserved in the book of Proverbs.
4:33 *cedar of Lebanon.* See notes on 5:6; Jdg 9:15; Isa 9:10. *hyssop.* See note on Ex 12:22. *animals and birds, reptiles and fish.* Examples of Solomon's knowledge of these creatures are found in Pr 6:6 – 8; 26:2 – 3,11; 27:8; 28:1,15.
4:34 *all nations … all the kings of the world.* A general statement referring to the Near Eastern world (cf. Ge 41:57).
5:1 — 9:9 Solomon's building projects (see note on 1:1 — 12:24).
5:1 *Hiram king of Tyre.* Hiram ruled over Tyre c. 978 – 944 BC. He may have also served as coregent with his father, Abibaal, as early as 993. Before Solomon was born, Hiram provided timber and workmen for the building of David's palace (see 2Sa 5:11).
5:3 *he could not build a temple.* Although David was denied the privilege of building the temple, he did make plans and supply provisions for its construction (see 1Ch 22:2 – 5; 28:2; cf. also Ps 30 title and note).
5:4 *rest.* Described here as "no adversary or disaster." God's promises to his people (see Ex 33:14; Dt 25:19; Jos 1:13,15) and to David (2Sa 7:11) have now been fulfilled (see 8:56 and note), so that the Israelites are free to concentrate their strength and resources on building their Great King's royal house (see note on 2Sa 7:11).
5:5 *Name of the LORD.* See 3:2 and note. *as the LORD told my father David.* See 2Sa 7:12 – 13; 1Ch 22:8 – 10.
5:6 *So give orders.* A more detailed account of Solomon's request is found in 2Ch 2:3 – 10. *cedars of Lebanon.* Widely used in the ancient Near East in the construction of temples and palaces.
5:7 *Praise be to the LORD.* In polytheistic cultures it was common practice for the people of one nation to recognize the deities of another nation (see 10:9; 11:5) and even to ascribe certain powers to them (see 2Ki 18:25; see also 2Ch 2:12).

SOLOMON'S TEMPLE

The temple of Solomon, located near the king's palace, functioned as God's royal palace and Israel's national center of worship. The Lord said to Solomon, "I have consecrated this temple . . . by putting my Name there forever. My eyes and my heart will always be there" (1Ki 9:3). By its cosmological and royal symbolism, the sanctuary taught the absolute sovereignty of the Lord over the whole creation and his special headship over Israel.

The floor plan is a type that has a long history in Semitic religion, particularly among the West Semites. An early example of the tripartite division into portico, main hall and inner sanctuary has been found at Syrian Ebla (c. 2300 BC) and, much later but more contemporaneous with Solomon, at 'Ain Dara in north Syria (tenth century BC) and at Tell Taynat in southeast Turkey (eighth century BC). Like Solomon's, the temples at 'Ain Dara and at Tell Taynat had three divisions, had two columns supporting the entrance, and were located adjacent to the royal palace.

Many archaeological parallels can be drawn to the methods of construction used in the temple, e.g., the "dressed stone and ... cedar beams" technique described in 1Ki 6:36. Interestingly, evidence for the largest bronze-casting industry ever found in the Holy Land comes from the same locale and period as that indicated in Scripture: Zarethan in the Jordan valley c. 1000 BC.

960–586 BC

Temple source materials are subject to academic interpretation, and subsequent art reconstructions vary.

This model (p. 523) recognizes influence from the wilderness tabernacle, accepts general Near Eastern cultural diffusion, and rejects overt pagan Canaanite symbols. It uses known archaeological parallels to supplement the text and assumes interior dimensions from 1Ki 6:17–20.

will separate them and you can take
them away. And you are to grant my
wish by providing food[k] for my royal
household."

10 In this way Hiram kept Solomon supplied with all the cedar and juniper logs
he wanted, 11 and Solomon gave Hiram
twenty thousand cors[a] of wheat as food[l]
for his household, in addition to twenty thousand baths[b,c] of pressed olive oil.
Solomon continued to do this for Hiram
year after year. 12 The LORD gave Solomon
wisdom,[m] just as he had promised him.
There were peaceful relations between Hiram and Solomon, and the two of them
made a treaty.[n]
13 King Solomon conscripted laborers[o]
from all Israel—thirty thousand men.
14 He sent them off to Lebanon in shifts of
ten thousand a month, so that they spent
one month in Lebanon and two months
at home. Adoniram[p] was in charge of the
forced labor. 15 Solomon had seventy thousand carriers and eighty thousand stonecutters in the hills, 16 as well as thirty-three
hundred[d] foremen[q] who supervised the
project and directed the workers. 17 At the
king's command they removed from the
quarry[r] large blocks of high-grade stone[s] to

5:9 [k] ver 11; Eze 27:17; Ac 12:20
5:11 [l] S ver 9
5:12 [m] S 1Ki 3:12 [n] Jos 9:7; 1Ki 15:19; Am 1:9
5:13 [o] S Ge 49:15; S Lev 25:39; 1Ki 9:15
5:14 [p] S 2Sa 20:24; 1Ki 4:6; 2Ch 10:18
5:16 [q] 1Ki 9:23
5:17 [r] 1Ki 6:7 [s] 1Ch 22:2

[a] *11* That is, probably about 3,600 tons or about 3,250 metric tons [b] *11* Septuagint (see also 2 Chron. 2:10); Hebrew *twenty cors* [c] *11* That is, about 120,000 gallons or about 440,000 liters [d] *16* Hebrew; some Septuagint manuscripts (see also 2 Chron. 2:2,18) *thirty-six hundred*

5:9 *place you specify.* Joppa (2Ch 2:16; see note on 1Ki 3:1). *providing food for my royal household.* Provision of food for Hiram's court personnel appears to have covered only the cost of the wood itself. In addition, Solomon would have to provide for the wages of the Phoenician laborers (v. 6). Comparison of v. 11 with 2Ch 2:10 indicates that besides wheat and olive oil for Hiram's court, Solomon also sent barley and wine for labor costs. Hiram may have sold some of these provisions in order to pay the laborers. See also note on 9:11.

5:11 *twenty thousand cors of wheat.* See NIV text note. By way of comparison, Solomon's court received 10,950 cors of flour and 21,900 cors of meal on an annual basis (see 4:22; see also 2Ch 2:10).

5:13 *conscripted laborers.* See notes on 9:15; 2Sa 20:24. Resentment among the people toward this sort of forced labor eventually led to a civil uprising and the division of Solomon's kingdom immediately after his death (12:1–18).

5:15 *seventy thousand carriers and eighty thousand stonecutters.* Conscripted from the non-Israelite population that David had subdued and incorporated into his kingdom (see 2Ch 2:17–18). *hills.* The limestone hills of the surrounding area where the stone was quarried.

5:16 *thirty-three hundred foremen.* 1Ki 9:23 refers to 550 "chief officials ... supervising." If these are two different categories of supervisory personnel, the total is 3,850 men. 2Ch 2:2 refers to 3,600 foremen, and 2Ch 8:10 speaks of 250 supervisors, which again yields a total of 3,850 men in a supervisory capacity.

5:17 *large blocks of high-grade stone.* For the size of these stones, see 7:10. Transportation of such stones to Jerusalem would require enormous manpower.

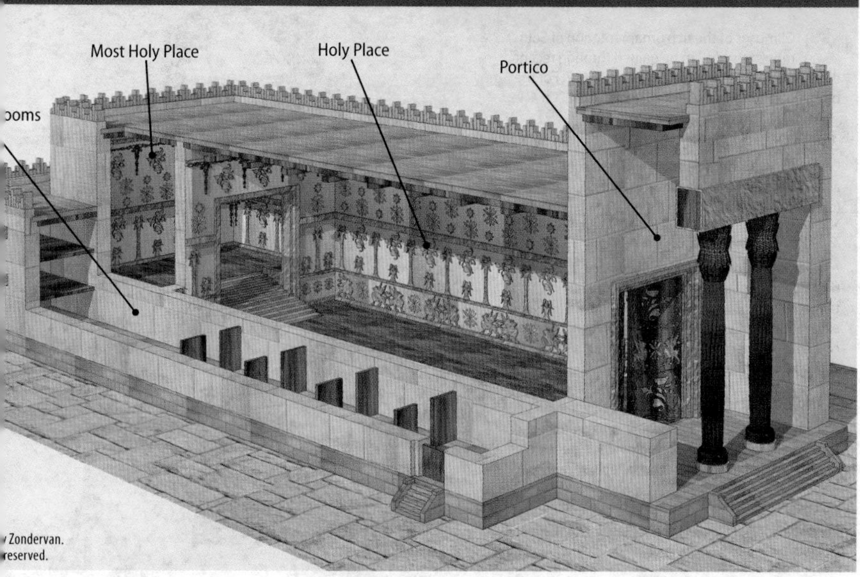

provide a foundation of dressed stone for the temple. 18The craftsmen of Solomon and Hiram[t] and workers from Byblos[u] cut and prepared the timber and stone for the building of the temple.

Solomon Builds the Temple

6:1-29pp — 2Ch 3:1-14

6 In the four hundred and eightieth[a] year after the Israelites came out of Egypt, in the fourth year of Solomon's reign over Israel, in the month of Ziv, the second month,[v] he began to build the temple of the LORD.[w]

2The temple[x] that King Solomon built for the LORD was sixty cubits long, twenty wide and thirty high.[b] 3The portico[y] at the front of the main hall of the temple extended the width of the temple, that is twenty cubits,[c] and projected ten cubits[d] from the front of the temple. 4He made narrow windows[z] high up in the temple walls. 5Against the walls of the main hall and inner sanctuary he built a structure around the building, in which there were side rooms.[a] 6The lowest floor was five cubits[e] wide, the middle floor six cubits[f] and the third floor seven.[g] He made offset ledges around the outside of the temple

5:18 [t]S 2Sa 5:11 [u]S Jos 13:5
6:1 [v]Ezr 3:8 [w]Ezr 5:11
6:2 [x]Ex 26:1
6:3 [y]Eze 40:49
6:4 [z]Eze 41:16
6:5 [a]Jer 35:2; Eze 41:5-6

[a] *1* Hebrew; Septuagint *four hundred and fortieth*
[b] *2* That is, about 90 feet long, 30 feet wide and 45 feet high or about 27 meters long, 9 meters wide and 14 meters high
[c] *3* That is, about 30 feet or about 9 meters; also in verses 16 and 20
[d] *3* That is, about 15 feet or about 4.5 meters; also in verses 23-26
[e] *6* That is, about 7 1/2 feet or about 2.3 meters; also in verses 10 and 24
[f] *6* That is, about 9 feet or about 2.7 meters
[g] *6* That is, about 11 feet or about 3.2 meters

5:18 *Byblos.* See Eze 27:9 and note.

6:1–38 See model above.

6:1 *four hundred and eightieth year ... fourth year.* Synchronizations between certain events in the reigns of later Israelite kings and Assyrian chronological records fix the fourth year of Solomon's reign at c. 966 BC (see Introduction: Chronology). If Israel's exodus is placed 480 years prior to 966, it would have occurred c. 1446 (the chronology followed in this study Bible) during the rule of the Eighteenth-Dynasty Egyptian pharaoh Thutmose III. On the basis of Ex 1:11 and certain other historical considerations, however, some have concluded that the exodus could not have occurred prior to the rule of the Nineteenth-Dynasty pharaoh Rameses II—thus not until c. 1279 (see note on Ge 47:11). This would mean that the 480 years of this verse would be understood as either a schematic (perhaps representative of 12 generations multiplied by the conventional, but not always actual, 40-year length of a generation) or aggregate figure (the combined total of a number of subsidiary time periods, which in reality were partly concurrent, examples of which are to be found in Egyptian and Mesopotamian records). See Introduction to Exodus: Chronology.

6:2 *temple that King Solomon built.* The temple was patterned after the tabernacle (and, in general, other temples of the time; see model above and accompanying text, p. 522) and was divided into three major areas: the Most Holy Place, the Holy Place and the outer courtyard. The Most Holy Place in the temple was cube-shaped, as it also was in the tabernacle. The dimensions of the temple in most instances seem to be double those of the tabernacle (see Ex 26:15–30; 36:20–34).

6:6 *offset ledges.* To avoid making holes in the temple wall, it was built with a series of ledges on which the beams for the

TEMPLE FURNISHINGS

Glimpses of the rich ornamentation of Solomon's temple can be gained through recent discoveries that illumine the text of 1Ki 6–7. For the bronze altar of burnt offering, see note on 2Ch 4:1.

1 ARK OF THE COVENANT

Cherubim with wings flanking a royal throne are attested in Egyptian, Israelite and Phoenician art (e.g., at Megiddo).

2 MOVABLE BRONZE BASIN

An extremely close parallel to the wheeled portable basins used in the courtyard of the temple has come from archaeological excavations on Cyprus. This representation combines elements from the Biblical text with the archaeological evidence.

3 INCENSE ALTAR

A stone incense altar having four horns on the corners was found at Megiddo. It provides a clear idea of the shape of the gold incense altar in the temple.

4 TABLE FOR THE BREAD OF THE PRESENCE

The table for the bread of the Presence was made of gold.

5 LAMPSTAND

Ten lampstands were in the temple, five on each side of the sanctuary (1Ki 7:49), to which were added ten tables (2Ch 4:8). Ritual sevenfold lamps have been found at several places in Israel, including Hazor and Dothan. The stand itself is modeled on bronze ones from the excavations at Megiddo.

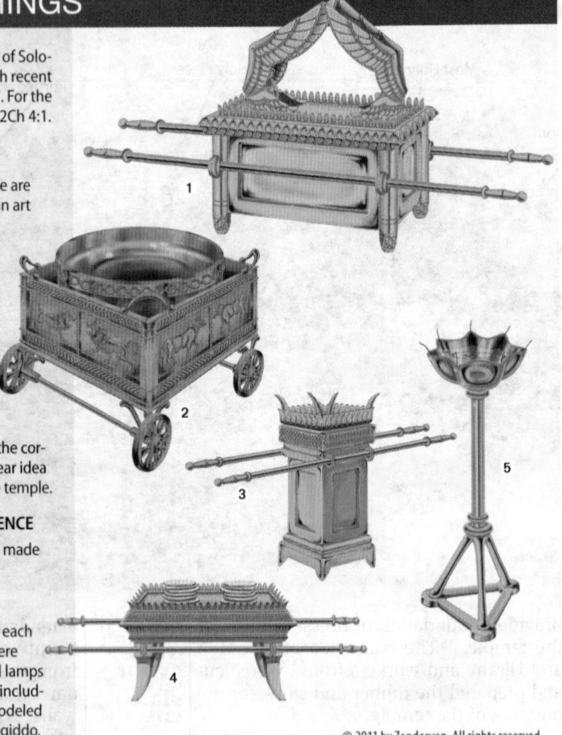

so that nothing would be inserted into the temple walls.

7 In building the temple, only blocks dressed[b] at the quarry were used, and no hammer, chisel or any other iron tool[c] was heard at the temple site while it was being built.

8 The entrance to the lowest[a] floor was on the south side of the temple; a stairway led up to the middle level and from there to the third. 9 So he built the temple and completed it, roofing it with beams and cedar[d] planks. 10 And he built the side rooms all along the temple. The height of each was five cubits, and they were attached to the temple by beams of cedar.

11 The word of the LORD came[e] to Solomon: 12 "As for this temple you are building, if you follow my decrees, observe my laws and keep all my commands[f] and obey them, I will fulfill through you the promise[g] I gave to David your father. 13 And I will live among the Israelites and will not abandon[h] my people Israel."

14 So Solomon[i] built the temple and completed[j] it. 15 He lined its interior walls with cedar boards, paneling them from the floor of the temple to the ceiling,[k] and covered the floor of the temple with planks of juniper.[l] 16 He partitioned off twenty cu-

6:7 [b] S Ex 20:25 [c] S Dt 27:5
6:9 [d] SS 1:17
6:11 [e] 1Ki 12:22; 13:20; 16:1,7; 17:2; 21:17; Jer 40:1
6:12 [f] 1Ki 11:10 [g] 2Sa 7:12-16; 1Ki 9:5
6:13 [h] S Lev 26:11; S Dt 31:6; Jn 14:18; Heb 13:5
6:14 [i] Ac 7:47 [j] 1Ch 28:20; 2Ch 5:1
6:15 [k] 1Ki 7:7 [l] Eze 41:15-16

[a] 8 Septuagint; Hebrew *middle*

three floors of side chambers rested. This accounts for the different widths of the rooms on each floor.

6:8 *entrance to the lowest floor.* Of the side chambers.

6:11 *The word of the LORD came to Solomon.* As the temple neared completion the Lord spoke to Solomon, perhaps through an unnamed prophet (but see 3:5,11–14; 9:2–9).

6:12 *if you follow my decrees ... I will fulfill through you the promise.* In words similar to those spoken by David (see 2:1–4 and notes), the Lord assures Solomon of a continuing dynasty (see 2Sa 7:12–16), but Solomon must remain faithful to the Sinaitic covenant if he is to experience personally the fulfillment of the Davidic covenant promise (see chart, p. 23).

6:13 *I will live among the Israelites.* In the temple being built (see 9:3). To avoid any apprehension among the Israelites concerning his presence with them (cf. Ps 78:60; Jer 26:6,9; see note on 1Sa 7:1), the Lord gives assurance that he will dwell in their midst (see 8:10–13; Ex 25:8; Lev 26:11).

bits at the rear of the temple with cedar boards from floor to ceiling to form within the temple an inner sanctuary, the Most Holy Place.[m] 17 The main hall in front of this room was forty cubits[a] long. 18 The inside of the temple was cedar,[n] carved with gourds and open flowers. Everything was cedar; no stone was to be seen.

19 He prepared the inner sanctuary[o] within the temple to set the ark of the covenant[p] of the LORD there. 20 The inner sanctuary[q] was twenty cubits long, twenty wide and twenty high. He overlaid the inside with pure gold, and he also overlaid the altar of cedar.[r] 21 Solomon covered the inside of the temple with pure gold, and he extended gold chains across the front of the inner sanctuary, which was overlaid with gold. 22 So he overlaid the whole interior with gold. He also overlaid with gold the altar that belonged to the inner sanctuary.

23 For the inner sanctuary he made a pair of cherubim[s] out of olive wood, each ten cubits high. 24 One wing of the first cherub was five cubits long, and the other wing five cubits—ten cubits from wing tip to wing tip. 25 The second cherub also measured ten cubits, for the two cherubim were identical in size and shape. 26 The height of each cherub was ten cubits. 27 He placed the cherubim[t] inside the innermost room of the temple, with their wings spread out. The wing of one cherub touched one wall, while the wing of the other touched the other wall, and their wings touched each other in the middle of the room. 28 He overlaid the cherubim with gold.

6:16 [m] S Ex 26:33 **6:18** [n] ver 29; Ps 74:6; Eze 41:18 **6:19** [o] 1Ki 8:6 [p] S Ex 25:10; S 1Sa 3:3 **6:20** [q] Eze 41:3-4 [r] S Ex 30:1 **6:23** [s] S Ex 37:1-9 **6:27** [t] S Ge 3:24; S Ex 25:18

29 On the walls[u] all around the temple, in both the inner and outer rooms, he carved cherubim,[v] palm trees and open flowers. 30 He also covered the floors of both the inner and outer rooms of the temple with gold.

31 For the entrance to the inner sanctuary he made doors out of olive wood that were one fifth of the width of the sanctuary. 32 And on the two olive-wood doors[w] he carved cherubim, palm trees and open flowers, and overlaid the cherubim and palm trees with hammered gold. 33 In the same way, for the entrance to the main hall he made doorframes out of olive wood that were one fourth of the width of the hall. 34 He also made two doors out of juniper wood, each having two leaves that turned in sockets. 35 He carved cherubim, palm trees and open flowers on them and overlaid them with gold hammered evenly over the carvings.

36 And he built the inner courtyard[x] of three courses[y] of dressed stone and one course of trimmed cedar beams.

37 The foundation of the temple of the LORD was laid in the fourth year, in the month of Ziv. 38 In the eleventh year in the month of Bul, the eighth month, the temple was finished in all its details[z] according to its specifications.[a] He had spent seven years building it.

Solomon Builds His Palace

7 It took Solomon thirteen years, however, to complete the construction of his palace.[b] 2 He built the Palace[c] of the Forest

6:29 [u] S ver 18 [v] ver 32,35; Eze 41:18,25 **6:32** [w] Eze 41:23 **6:36** [x] 2Ch 4:9 [y] 1Ki 7:12; Ezr 6:4 **6:38** [z] 1Ch 28:19 [a] Ex 25:9; Heb 8:5 **7:1** [b] S 2Sa 7:2

[a] *17* That is, about 60 feet or about 18 meters

6:16 *Most Holy Place.* The same terminology was used for the inner sanctuary housing the ark in the tabernacle (see Ex 26:33–34; Lev 16:2,16–17,20,23).

6:19 *ark of the covenant of the LORD.* The Ten Commandments are called the "words of the covenant" in Ex 34:28. The stone tablets on which the Ten Commandments were inscribed are called the "tablets of the covenant" in Dt 9:9. The ark in which the tablets were kept (see Ex 25:16,21; 40:20; Dt 10:1–5) is thus sometimes called the "ark of the covenant of the LORD" (see Dt 10:8; 31:9,25; Jos 3:11). Elsewhere the ark is variously designated as the "ark of the LORD" (Jos 3:13; 4:11), the "ark of the covenant law" (Ex 30:6; 31:7) and the "ark of God" (1Sa 3:3; 4:11,17,21; 5:1–2).

6:20 *pure gold.* The extensive use of gleaming gold probably symbolized the glory of God and his heavenly temple (cf. Rev 21:10–11,18,21).

6:21 *gold chains.* The curtain covering the entrance to the Most Holy Place was probably hung on these chains (see 2Ch 3:14; Mt 27:51; Heb 6:19).

6:22 *altar that belonged to the inner sanctuary.* The incense altar (see 7:48; Ex 30:1,6; 37:25–28; Heb 9:3–4 and note on 9:4).

6:23 *cherubim.* See note on Ex 25:18. They were to stand as sentries on either side of the ark (8:6–7; 2Ch 3:10–13). Two additional cherubim stood on the ark—one on each end of its atonement cover (Ex 25:17–22). *ten cubits high.* The Most Holy Place, where the cherubim stood, was 20 cubits high (v. 16).

6:29 *he carved cherubim.* Not a violation of the second commandment, which prohibited making anything to serve as a representation of God and worshiping it (see note on Ex 20:4). *palm trees and open flowers.* The depiction of cherubim and beautiful trees and flowers is reminiscent of the Garden of Eden, from which Adam and Eve had been driven as a result of sin (Ge 3:24). In a symbolic sense, readmission to the paradise of God is now to be had only by means of atonement for sin at the sanctuary (see note on Ex 26:1, "tabernacle"). Early Jewish synagogues were adorned with similar motifs.

6:36 *inner courtyard.* Suggests that there was an outer courtyard (see 8:64). 2Ch 4:9 refers to the "courtyard of the priests" (inner) and the "large court" (outer). The inner courtyard is also called the "upper courtyard" (Jer 36:10) because of its higher position on the temple mount.

6:37 *fourth year.* Of Solomon's reign (see v. 1 and note). *Ziv.* See chart, p. 113.

6:38 *eleventh year.* Of Solomon's reign (959 BC). *Bul.* See chart, p. 113.

7:1 *thirteen years.* Solomon spent almost twice as long building his own house as he did the Lord's house (see 6:38; see also Hag 1:2–4).

7:2 *Palace of the Forest of Lebanon.* Four rows of cedar pillars in

of Lebanon[d] a hundred cubits long, fifty wide and thirty high,[a] with four rows of cedar columns supporting trimmed cedar beams. 3 It was roofed with cedar above the beams that rested on the columns—forty-five beams, fifteen to a row. 4 Its windows were placed high in sets of three, facing each other. 5 All the doorways had rectangular frames; they were in the front part in sets of three, facing each other.[b]

6 He made a colonnade fifty cubits long and thirty wide.[c] In front of it was a portico, and in front of that were pillars and an overhanging roof.

7 He built the throne hall, the Hall of Justice, where he was to judge,[e] and he covered it with cedar from floor to ceiling.[d][f] 8 And the palace in which he was to live, set farther back, was similar in design. Solomon also made a palace like this hall for Pharaoh's daughter, whom he had married.[g]

9 All these structures, from the outside to the great courtyard and from foundation to eaves, were made of blocks of high-grade stone cut to size and smoothed on their inner and outer faces. 10 The foundations were laid with large stones of good quality, some measuring ten cubits[e] and some eight.[f] 11 Above were high-grade stones, cut to size, and cedar beams. 12 The great courtyard was surrounded by a wall of three courses[h] of dressed stone and one course of trimmed cedar beams, as was the inner courtyard of the temple of the LORD with its portico.

The Temple's Furnishings

7:23-26pp — 2Ch 4:2-5
7:38-51pp — 2Ch 4:6,10–5:1

13 King Solomon sent to Tyre and brought Huram,[g][i] 14 whose mother was a widow from the tribe of Naphtali and whose father was from Tyre and a skilled craftsman in bronze. Huram was filled with wisdom,[j] with understanding and with knowledge to do all kinds of bronze work. He came to King Solomon and did all[k] the work assigned to him.

15 He cast two bronze pillars,[l] each eighteen cubits high and twelve cubits in circumference.[h] 16 He also made two capitals[m] of cast bronze to set on the tops of the pillars; each capital was five cubits[i] high. 17 A network of interwoven chains adorned the capitals on top of the pillars, seven for each capital. 18 He made pomegranates in two rows[j] encircling each network to decorate the capitals on top of the pillars.[k] He did the same for each capital. 19 The capitals on top of the pillars in the portico were in the shape of lilies, four cubits[l] high. 20 On the capitals of both pillars, above the bowl-shaped part next to the network, were the two hundred pomegranates[n] in rows all around. 21 He erected the pillars at the portico of the temple. The pillar to the south he named Jakin[m] and the one to the north Boaz.[n][o] 22 The capitals on top were in the shape of lilies. And so the work on the pillars[p] was completed.

23 He made the Sea[q] of cast metal, circular in shape, measuring ten cubits from

7:2 [c] S 2Sa 7:2 [d] 1Ki 10:17; 2Ch 9:16; Isa 22:8; 37:24; Jer 22:6,23 **7:7** [e] 1Sa 7:15; Ps 122:5; Pr 20:8 [f] 1Ki 6:15 **7:8** [g] S 1Ki 3:1 **7:12** [h] S 1Ki 6:36 **7:13** [i] ver 45; 2Ch 2:13; 4:16 **7:14** [j] Ex 31:2-5; S 35:31 [k] 2Ch 4:11,16 **7:15** [l] 2Ki 11:14; 23:3; 25:17; 2Ch 3:15; 23:13; 34:31; Jer 27:19; 52:17,21; Eze 40:49 **7:16** [m] ver 20, 42; 2Ki 25:17; Jer 52:22 **7:20** [n] ver 18; 2Ch 3:16; 4:13 **7:21** [o] 2Ch 3:17 **7:22** [p] 2Ki 25:17 **7:23** [q] ver 47; 2Ki 25:13; 1Ch 18:8; 2Ch 4:18; Jer 52:17; Rev 4:6

[a] *2* That is, about 150 feet long, 75 feet wide and 45 feet high or about 45 meters long, 23 meters wide and 14 meters high [b] *5* The meaning of the Hebrew for this verse is uncertain. [c] *6* That is, about 75 feet long and 45 feet wide or about 23 meters long and 14 meters wide [d] *7* Vulgate and Syriac; Hebrew *floor* [e] *10* That is, about 15 feet or about 4.5 meters; also in verse 23 [f] *10* That is, about 12 feet or about 3.6 meters [g] *13* Hebrew *Hiram,* a variant of *Huram;* also in verses 40 and 45 [h] *15* That is, about 27 feet high and 18 feet in circumference or about 8.1 meters high and 5.4 meters in circumference [i] *16* That is, about 7 1/2 feet or about 2.3 meters; also in verse 23 [j] *18* Two Hebrew manuscripts and Septuagint; most Hebrew manuscripts *made the pillars, and there were two rows* [k] *18* Many Hebrew manuscripts and Syriac; most Hebrew manuscripts *pomegranates* [l] *19* That is, about 6 feet or about 1.8 meters; also in verse 38 [m] *21* *Jakin* probably means *he establishes.* [n] *21* *Boaz* probably means *in him is strength.*

the palace created the impression of a great forest. *a hundred cubits long, fifty wide and thirty high.* See NIV text note. Compare these measurements with those of the temple in 6:2.

7:3 *forty-five beams, fifteen to a row.* Suggests that there were three floors in the building above the main hall on the ground level. The building included storage space for weaponry (see 10:16–17).

7:6 *colonnade.* Apparently an entrance hall to the Palace of the Forest of Lebanon. Its length (50 cubits) corresponds to the width of the palace.

7:7 *throne hall.* It is not clear whether the throne hall (the Hall of Justice), Solomon's own living quarters (v. 8) and the palace for the pharaoh's daughter (v. 8) were separate buildings or locations within the Palace of the Forest of Lebanon.

7:9 *smoothed on their inner and outer faces.* The pinkish white limestone of the Holy Land is easily cut when originally quarried, but gradually hardens with exposure.

7:12 *great courtyard.* Constructed in the same way as the inner courtyard of the temple (6:36).

7:13 *King Solomon sent.* Prior to the completion of the temple and the construction of Solomon's palace (see 2Ch 2:7,13–14). *Huram.* See NIV text note. His full name is Huram-Abi (2Ch 2:13).

7:14 *widow from the tribe of Naphtali.* 2Ch 2:14 indicates that Huram-Abi's mother was from Dan. Apparently she was born in the city of Dan in northern Israel close to the tribe of Naphtali, from which her first husband came. After he died, she married a man from Tyre. *all kinds of bronze work.* Huram-Abi had a much wider range of skills as well (see 2Ch 2:7,14).

7:15 *two bronze pillars.* One was placed on each side of the main entrance to the temple (v. 21). Surely decorative, they may also have embodied a symbolism not known to us. Some believe that the pillars were freestanding, like those found at certain excavations in the Near East. Others think that they supported a roof (forming a portico to the temple) and an architrave.

7:16 *five cubits.* See 2Ki 25:17 and note.

7:21 *pillar to the south.* The temple, like the tabernacle before it, faced east (see Eze 8:16).

7:23 *Sea of cast metal.* This enormous reservoir of water cor-rim to rim and five cubits high. It took a line[r] of thirty cubits[a] to measure around it. 24 Below the rim, gourds encircled it—ten to a cubit. The gourds were cast in two rows in one piece with the Sea.

25 The Sea stood on twelve bulls,[s] three facing north, three facing west, three facing south and three facing east. The Sea rested on top of them, and their hindquarters were toward the center. 26 It was a handbreadth[b] in thickness, and its rim was like the rim of a cup, like a lily blossom. It held two thousand baths.[c]

27 He also made ten movable stands[t] of bronze; each was four cubits long, four wide and three high.[d] 28 This is how the stands were made: They had side panels attached to uprights. 29 On the panels between the uprights were lions, bulls and cherubim—and on the uprights as well. Above and below the lions and bulls were wreaths of hammered work. 30 Each stand[u] had four bronze wheels with bronze axles, and each had a basin resting on four supports, cast with wreaths on each side. 31 On the inside of the stand there was an opening that had a circular frame one cubit[e] deep. This opening was round, and with its basework it measured a cubit and a half.[f] Around its opening there was engraving. The panels of the stands were square, not round. 32 The four wheels were under the panels, and the axles of the wheels were attached to the stand. The diameter of each wheel was a cubit and a half. 33 The wheels were made like chariot wheels; the axles, rims, spokes and hubs were all of cast metal.

34 Each stand had four handles, one on each corner, projecting from the stand. 35 At the top of the stand there was a circular band half a cubit[g] deep. The supports and panels were attached to the top of the stand. 36 He engraved cherubim, lions and palm trees on the surfaces of the supports and on the panels, in every available space, with wreaths all around. 37 This is the way he made the ten stands. They were all cast in the same molds and were identical in size and shape.

38 He then made ten bronze basins,[v] each holding forty baths[h] and measuring four cubits across, one basin to go on each of the ten stands. 39 He placed five of the stands on the south side of the temple and five on the north. He placed the Sea on the south side, at the southeast corner of the temple. 40 He also made the pots[i] and shovels and sprinkling bowls.[w]

So Huram finished all the work he had undertaken for King Solomon in the temple of the LORD:

41 the two pillars;
the two bowl-shaped capitals on top of the pillars;
the two sets of network decorating the two bowl-shaped capitals on top of the pillars;
42 the four hundred pomegranates for the two sets of network (two rows of pomegranates for each network decorating the bowl-shaped capitals[x] on top of the pillars);
43 the ten stands with their ten basins;
44 the Sea and the twelve bulls under it;
45 the pots, shovels and sprinkling bowls.[y]

All these objects that Huram[z] made for King Solomon for the temple of the LORD were of burnished bronze. 46 The king had them cast in clay molds in the plain[a] of the Jordan between Sukkoth[b] and Zarethan.[c] 47 Solomon left all these things

7:23 [r] Jer 31:39; Zec 2:1 **7:25** [s] Jer 52:20 **7:27** [t] 2Ki 16:17 **7:30** [u] 2Ki 16:17 **7:38** [v] S Ex 30:18 **7:40** [w] S Ex 27:3; Jer 52:18 **7:42** [x] S ver 16 **7:45** [y] S Ex 27:3; Jer 52:18 [z] S ver 13 **7:46** [a] S Ge 13:10 [b] S Ge 33:17 [c] Jos 3:16

[a] *23* That is, about 45 feet or about 14 meters
[b] *26* That is, about 3 inches or about 7.5 centimeters
[c] *26* That is, about 12,000 gallons or about 44,000 liters; the Septuagint does not have this sentence.
[d] *27* That is, about 6 feet long and wide and about 4 1/2 feet high or about 1.8 meters long and wide and 1.4 meters high
[e] *31* That is, about 18 inches or about 45 centimeters
[f] *31* That is, about 2 1/4 feet or about 68 centimeters; also in verse 32
[g] *35* That is, about 9 inches or about 23 centimeters
[h] *38* That is, about 240 gallons or about 880 liters
[i] *40* Many Hebrew manuscripts, Septuagint, Syriac and Vulgate (see also verse 45 and 2 Chron. 4:11); many other Hebrew manuscripts *basins*

responded to the bronze basin made for the tabernacle (see Ex 30:17–21; 38:8). Its water was used by the priests for ritual cleansing (2Ch 4:6). *thirty cubits.* Technically speaking, this should be 31.416 cubits because of the ten-cubit diameter of the circular top. Thirty may be a round number here.

7:24 *ten to a cubit.* With ten gourds to a cubit it took 300 gourds to span the entire reservoir, or 600 gourds counting both rows.

7:26 *two thousand baths.* See 2Ch 4:5 and note.

7:27 *ten movable stands.* These movable bronze stands were designed to hold water basins (see v. 38) of much smaller dimensions than the bronze Sea. The water from the basins was used to wash certain prescribed parts of the animals that were slaughtered for burnt offerings (see Lev 1:9,13; 2Ch 4:6).

7:36 *He engraved cherubim, lions and palm trees.* See note on 6:29.

7:40 *pots.* See NIV text note; perhaps used for cooking meat to be eaten in connection with the fellowship offerings (see Lev 7:11–17; 22:21–23). *shovels.* Used for removing ashes from the altar. *sprinkling bowls.* For use by the priests in various rites involving the sprinkling of blood or water (see Ex 27:3).

7:41 *two sets of network.* See v. 17.

7:42 *four hundred pomegranates.* See vv. 18,20.

7:43 *ten stands with their ten basins.* See vv. 27–37.

7:44 *the Sea and the twelve bulls.* See vv. 23–26.

7:45 *pots, shovels and sprinkling bowls.* See v. 40 and note.

7:46 *Sukkoth.* Located on the east side of the Jordan (Ge 33:17; Jos 13:27; Jdg 8:4–5) just north of the Jabbok River. Excavations in this area have confirmed that Sukkoth was a center of metallurgy during the period of the monarchy. *Zarethan.* Located near Adam (see Jos 3:16) and Abel Meholah (4:12).

unweighed,[d] because there were so many;[e]
the weight of the bronze[f] was not determined.
48 Solomon also made all[g] the furnishings that were in the LORD's temple:

the golden altar;
the golden table[h] on which was the
bread of the Presence;[i]
49 the lampstands[j] of pure gold (five on
the right and five on the left, in
front of the inner sanctuary);
the gold floral work and lamps and
tongs;
50 the pure gold basins, wick trimmers,
sprinkling bowls, dishes[k] and censers;[l]
and the gold sockets for the doors of
the innermost room, the Most Holy
Place, and also for the doors of the
main hall of the temple.

51 When all the work King Solomon had
done for the temple of the LORD was finished, he brought in the things his father
David had dedicated[m] — the silver and
gold and the furnishings[n] — and he placed
them in the treasuries of the LORD's temple.

The Ark Brought to the Temple

8:1-21pp — 2Ch 5:2 – 6:11

8 Then King Solomon summoned into
his presence at Jerusalem the elders
of Israel, all the heads of the tribes and the
chiefs[o] of the Israelite families, to bring up
the ark[p] of the LORD's covenant from Zion,
the City of David.[q] 2 All the Israelites came
together to King Solomon at the time of
the festival[r] in the month of Ethanim, the
seventh month.[s]
3 When all the elders of Israel had arrived, the priests[t] took up the ark, 4 and
they brought up the ark of the LORD and
the tent of meeting[u] and all the sacred furnishings in it. The priests and Levites[v] carried them up, 5 and King Solomon and the
entire assembly of Israel that had gathered
about him were before the ark, sacrificing[w]
so many sheep and cattle that they could
not be recorded or counted.
6 The priests then brought the ark of
the LORD's covenant[x] to its place in the
inner sanctuary of the temple, the Most
Holy Place,[y] and put it beneath the wings
of the cherubim.[z] 7 The cherubim spread
their wings over the place of the ark and
overshadowed[a] the ark and its carrying
poles. 8 These poles were so long that their
ends could be seen from the Holy Place in
front of the inner sanctuary, but not from
outside the Holy Place; and they are still
there today.[b] 9 There was nothing in the
ark except the two stone tablets[c] that Moses had placed in it at Horeb, where the
LORD made a covenant with the Israelites
after they came out of Egypt.
10 When the priests withdrew from the
Holy Place, the cloud[d] filled the temple of
the LORD. 11 And the priests could not perform their service[e] because of the cloud,
for the glory[f] of the LORD filled his temple.
12 Then Solomon said, "The LORD has
said that he would dwell in a dark cloud;[g]
13 I have indeed built a magnificent temple
for you, a place for you to dwell[h] forever."
14 While the whole assembly of Israel was standing there, the king turned
around and blessed[i] them. 15 Then he said:

"Praise be to the LORD,[j] the God of
Israel, who with his own hand has
fulfilled what he promised with his
own mouth to my father David. For

7:47 [d] 1Ch 22:3; Jer 52:20 [e] Ex 36:5-7 [f] S ver 23
7:48 [g] Ex 39:32-43 [h] S Ex 25:23 [i] S Ex 25:30
7:49 [j] S Ex 25:31-38
7:50 [k] S Nu 7:14 [l] 2Ki 25:13; Jer 52:19
7:51 [m] S 2Sa 8:11 [n] 2Ki 12:13; 24:13; Jer 27:19
8:1 [o] Nu 7:2 [p] S 1Sa 3:3; Rev 11:19 [q] S 2Sa 5:7
8:2 [r] ver 65; S Lev 23:36; Ne 8:17 [s] S Lev 23:34; S Nu 29:12
8:3 [t] S Jos 3:3
8:4 [u] S Lev 17:4 [v] 1Ch 15:13
8:5 [w] S 2Sa 6:13; S 2Ch 30:24
8:6 [x] S Ex 26:33; S 2Sa 6:17; Rev 11:19 [y] S Ex 26:33 [z] S Ge 3:24; S Ex 25:18
8:7 [a] S Ex 25:20
8:8 [b] Ex 25:13-15
8:9 [c] S Ex 16:34; S 25:16; Heb 9:4
8:10 [d] S Ex 16:10; S Lev 16:2; Rev 15:8
8:11 [e] 2Ch 7:2; Rev 15:8 [f] S Ex 16:7; S 29:43
8:12 [g] S Ex 40:34; S 2Sa 22:10
8:13 [h] Ex 15:17; Ps 132:13; 135:21; Mt 23:21
8:14 [i] S Ex 39:43
8:15 [j] 1Ch 16:36; Lk 1:68

7:48 *golden altar.* See 6:22. *golden table.* The bread of the Presence was placed on this table (see Ex 25:23 – 30; 1Ch 9:32; 2Ch 13:11; 29:18). Ten such golden tables are mentioned in 1Ch 28:16 and 2Ch 4:8,19, five placed on the north and five on the south side of the temple.
7:49 *lampstands of pure gold.* Only one lampstand with seven arms had stood in the tabernacle, opposite the table for the bread of the Presence (Ex 25:31 – 40; 26:35). The ten lampstands in the temple, five on the north side and five on the south, created a lane of light in the Holy Place. *gold floral work.* See Ex 25:33. *lamps.* See Ex 25:37. *tongs.* See 2Ch 4:21; Isa 6:6.
7:50 *censers.* See 2Ki 25:15; 2Ch 4:22; Jer 52:18 – 19.
7:51 *things his father David had dedicated.* Valuable objects of silver and gold, either taken as plunder in war or received as tribute from kings seeking David's favor (see 2Sa 8:9 – 12; 1Ch 18:7 – 11; 2Ch 5:1). *treasuries of the LORD's temple.* See 15:18; 2Ki 12:18; 1Ch 9:26; 26:20 – 26; 28:12.
8:1 *bring up the ark of the LORD's covenant.* David had previously brought the ark from the house of Obed-Edom to Jerusalem (see 2Sa 6). *Zion, the City of David.* See note on 2Sa 5:7.
8:2 *festival.* It is probable that Solomon waited 11 months (see 6:38) to dedicate the temple during the Festival of Tabernacles, which was observed in the seventh month of the year (Lev 23:34; Dt 16:13 – 15). *seventh month.* Presumably in the 12th year of Solomon's reign.
8:4 *tent of meeting.* The tabernacle, which had been preserved at Gibeon (see notes on 3:4; 1Sa 7:1; see also 2Ch 5:4 – 5).
8:6 *put it beneath the wings of the cherubim.* See 6:23 – 28.
8:8 *their ends could be seen.* The carrying poles were always to remain in the gold rings of the ark (Ex 25:15). *they are still there today.* These words must be those of the original author of this description of the dedication of the temple rather than those of the final compiler of the books of Kings (see Introduction: Author, Sources and Date; see also 2Ch 5:9).
8:9 *two stone tablets.* See Ex 25:16; 40:20. *the LORD made a covenant.* See Ex 24.
8:10 *the cloud filled the temple.* Just as a visible manifestation of the presence of the Lord had descended on the tabernacle at Sinai, so now the Lord came to dwell in the temple (see Ex 40:33 – 35; Eze 10:3 – 5,18 – 19; 43:4 – 5).
8:12 *he would dwell in a dark cloud.* See Ex 19:9; 24:15,18; 33:9 – 10; 34:5; Lev 16:2; Dt 4:11; 5:22; Ps 18:10 – 11.
8:15 *what he promised.* See 2Sa 7:5 – 16.

he said, 16‘Since the day I brought my people Israel out of Egypt,[k] I have not chosen a city in any tribe of Israel to have a temple built so that my Name[l] might be there, but I have chosen[m] David[n] to rule my people Israel.’

17“My father David had it in his heart[o] to build a temple[p] for the Name of the LORD, the God of Israel. 18But the LORD said to my father David, ‘You did well to have it in your heart to build a temple for my Name. 19Nevertheless, you[q] are not the one to build the temple, but your son, your own flesh and blood—he is the one who will build the temple for my Name.’[r]

20“The LORD has kept the promise he made: I have succeeded[s] David my father and now I sit on the throne of Israel, just as the LORD promised, and I have built[t] the temple for the Name of the LORD, the God of Israel. 21I have provided a place there for the ark, in which is the covenant of the LORD that he made with our ancestors when he brought them out of Egypt.”

Solomon’s Prayer of Dedication

8:22-53pp — 2Ch 6:12-40

22Then Solomon stood before the altar of the LORD in front of the whole assembly of Israel, spread out his hands[u] toward heaven 23and said:

“LORD, the God of Israel, there is no God like[v] you in heaven above or on earth below—you who keep your covenant of love[w] with your servants who continue wholeheartedly in your way. 24You have kept your promise to your servant David my father; with your mouth you have promised and with your hand you have fulfilled it—as it is today.

25“Now LORD, the God of Israel, keep for your servant David my father the promises[x] you made to him when you said, ‘You shall never fail to have a successor to sit before me on the throne of Israel, if only your descendants are careful in all they do to walk before me faithfully as you have done.’ 26And now, God of Israel, let your word that you promised[y] your servant David my father come true.

27“But will God really dwell[z] on earth? The heavens, even the highest heaven,[a] cannot contain[b] you. How much less this temple I have built! 28Yet give attention to your servant’s prayer and his plea for mercy, LORD my God. Hear the cry and the prayer that your servant is praying in your presence this day. 29May your eyes be open[c] toward[d] this temple night and day, this place of which you said, ‘My Name[e] shall be there,’ so that you will hear the prayer your servant prays toward this place. 30Hear the supplication of your servant and of your people Israel when they pray[f] toward this place. Hear[g] from heaven, your dwelling place, and when you hear, forgive.[h]

31“When anyone wrongs their neighbor and is required to take an oath and they come and swear the oath[i] before your altar in this temple, 32then hear from heaven and act. Judge between your servants, condemning the guilty by bringing down on their heads what they have done, and vindicating the innocent by treating them in accordance with their innocence.[j]

8:16 [k]S Ex 3:10 [l]S Dt 12:5 [m]S 1Sa 9:16; S 16:1 [n]Ps 89:3-4 **8:17** [o]S 1Sa 10:7; Ac 7:46 [p]2Sa 7:27; 1Ch 22:7; Ps 26:8; 132:5 **8:19** [q]S 2Sa 7:5 [r]S 2Sa 7:13 **8:20** [s]S 2Sa 7:12 [t]1Ch 28:6 **8:22** [u]S Ex 9:29 **8:23** [v]S Ex 9:14 [w]S Dt 7:9,12; Ne 1:5; 9:32; Da 9:4 **8:25** [x]S 2Sa 7:15; 1Ch 17:23; 2Ch 1:9 **8:26** [y]S 2Sa 7:25 **8:27** [z]Ac 7:48; 17:24 [a]S Dt 10:14 [b]2Ch 2:6; Ps 139:7-16; Isa 66:1; Jer 23:24 **8:29** [c]ver 52; 2Ki 19:16; 2Ch 7:15; Ne 1:6; Ps 5:1; 31:2; 102:17; 130:2; Isa 37:17 [d]Ps 28:2; 138:2; Da 6:10 [e]S Dt 11:12; 12:11; S 2Sa 7:13 **8:30** [f]ver 47; Lev 26:40; Ne 1:6; Jer 29:12; Da 9:4 [g]ver 39; Ps 34:6 [h]S Ex 34:7,9; Lev 26:40-42; Ps 85:2 **8:31** [i]S Ex 22:11 **8:32** [j]Dt 25:1; Eze 18:20

8:16 *have not chosen a city.* See Dt 12:5 and note. *my Name.* See 3:2 and note.

8:21 *covenant of the LORD.* The two tablets containing the Ten Commandments (see Ex 25:16 and note; Heb 9:4).

8:22 *spread out his hands.* In prayer (see Ex 9:29 and note).

8:23 *no God like you.* No other god has acted in history as has the God of Israel, performing great miracles and directing the course of events so that his long-range covenant promises are fulfilled (see Ex 15:11; Dt 4:39; 7:9; Ps 86:8–10). *who keep your covenant of love.* See Dt 7:9,12 and note. *who continue … in your way.* Cf. Ex 20:6 and note.

8:24 *your promise.* See v. 15; 2Sa 7:5–16.

8:25 *if only your descendants … walk before me faithfully.* See 9:4–9; 2Ch 7:17–22; see also note on 1Ki 2:4.

8:27 *How much less this temple I have built!* With the construction of the temple and the appearance of a visible manifestation of the presence of God within its courts, the erroneous notion that God was irreversibly and exclusively bound to the temple in a way that guaranteed his assistance to Israel no matter how the people lived could very easily arise (see Jer 7:4–14; Mic 3:11). Solomon confessed that even though God had chosen to dwell among his people in a special and localized way, he far transcended being limited by anything in all creation.

8:29 *My Name.* See note on 3:2.

8:30 *pray toward this place.* When Israelites were unable to pray in the temple itself, they were to direct their prayers toward the place where God had pledged to be present among his people (see Da 6:10). *heaven, your dwelling place.* See note on v. 27.

8:31 *required to take an oath.* In cases such as default in pledges (Ex 22:10–12) or alleged adultery (Nu 5:11–31), when there was insufficient evidence to establish the legitimacy of the charge, the supposed offender was required to take an oath of innocence at the sanctuary. Such an oath, with its attendant blessings and curses, was considered a divinely given means of determining innocence or guilt since the consequences of the oath became apparent in the life of the individual either by his experiencing the blessing or the curse or by direct divine revelation through the Urim and Thummim (see Ex 28:29–30; Lev 8:8; Nu 27:21).

8:32 *hear from heaven.* It is clear that Solomon viewed the oath as an appeal to God to act and not as an automatic power that worked in a magical way.

33 "When your people Israel have
been defeated[k] by an enemy because
they have sinned[l] against you, and
when they turn back to you and give
praise to your name, praying and
making supplication to you in this
temple,[m] 34 then hear from heaven and
forgive the sin of your people Israel
and bring them back to the land you
gave to their ancestors.
35 "When the heavens are shut up
and there is no rain[n] because your
people have sinned[o] against you, and
when they pray toward this place and
give praise to your name and turn
from their sin because you have afflicted them, 36 then hear from heaven
and forgive the sin of your servants,
your people Israel. Teach[p] them the
right way[q] to live, and send rain[r] on
the land you gave your people for an
inheritance.
37 "When famine[s] or plague[t] comes
to the land, or blight[u] or mildew, locusts or grasshoppers,[v] or when an
enemy besieges them in any of their
cities, whatever disaster or disease
may come, 38 and when a prayer or
plea is made by anyone among your
people Israel — being aware of the
afflictions of their own hearts, and
spreading out their hands[w] toward
this temple — 39 then hear[x] from heav-
en, your dwelling place. Forgive[y] and
act; deal with everyone according to
all they do, since you know[z] their
hearts (for you alone know every human heart), 40 so that they will fear[a]
you all the time they live in the land[b]
you gave our ancestors.

8:33 [k]S Lev 26:17 [l]Lev 26:39 [m]Isa 37:1, 14,38 **8:35** [n]S Dt 28:24; S 2Sa 1:21 [o]Jer 5:25 **8:36** [p]S Dt 8:3; S 1Sa 12:23 [q]Ps 5:8; 27:11; 107:7; Pr 11:5; Isa 45:13; Jer 6:16; 7:23; 31:21 [r]ver 35; 1Ki 17:1; 18:1, 45; Jer 5:24; 10:3; 14:22; Zec 10:1 **8:37** [s]S Lev 26:26 [t]S Ex 30:12; S Lev 26:25 [u]S Dt 28:22 [v]S Ex 10:13; Ps 105:34 **8:38** [w]S Ex 9:29 **8:39** [x]S ver 30 [y]Ps 130:4 [z]S Jos 22:22; S Ps 44:21; Jn 2:24; S Rev 2:23 **8:40** [a]ver 39-40; Dt 6:13; Ps 103:11; 130:4 [b]S Dt 12:1

8:41 [c]S Ge 31:15; Isa 56:3, 6; 61:5 **8:42** [d]1Ki 10:1; Isa 60:3; Ac 8:27 [e]Dt 3:24 **8:43** [f]S Jos 4:24; S 1Sa 17:46 [g]Ps 102:15 [h]S Dt 28:10 **8:44** [i]1Ch 5:20; 2Ch 14:11 **8:45** [j]Ps 9:4; 140:12 **8:46** [k]Ps 130:3; 143:2; Pr 20:9;

41 "As for the foreigner[c] who does
not belong to your people Israel but
has come from a distant land because
of your name — 42 for they will hear[d]
of your great name and your mighty
hand[e] and your outstretched arm —
when they come and pray toward
this temple, 43 then hear from heaven,
your dwelling place. Do whatever the
foreigner asks of you, so that all the
peoples of the earth may know[f] your
name and fear[g] you, as do your own
people Israel, and may know that
this house I have built bears your
Name.[h]
44 "When your people go to war
against their enemies, wherever you
send them, and when they pray[i] to
the LORD toward the city you have
chosen and the temple I have built for
your Name, 45 then hear from heaven
their prayer and their plea, and uphold their cause.[j]
46 "When they sin against you — for
there is no one who does not sin[k] —
and you become angry with them and
give them over to their enemies, who
take them captive[l] to their own lands,
far away or near; 47 and if they have
a change of heart in the land where
they are held captive, and repent and
plead[m] with you in the land of their
captors and say, 'We have sinned,
we have done wrong, we have acted
wickedly';[n] 48 and if they turn back[o] to
you with all their heart[p] and soul in
the land of their enemies who took

S Ro 3:9 [l]Lev 26:33-39; S Dt 4:27; S 21:10; S 28:64; 2Ki 25:21 **8:47** [m]S ver 30; S Lev 5:5; Ezr 9:15; Ne 1:6; Jer 14:20 [n]Ezr 9:7; Ps 106:6; Jer 3:25 **8:48** [o]S Dt 4:30 [p]S Dt 4:29

8:33 *defeated by an enemy because they have sinned against you.* Defeat by enemies was listed in Dt 28:25 as one of the curses that would come on Israel if she disobeyed the covenant. Solomon's prayer reflects an awareness of the covenant obligations the Lord had placed on his people and a knowledge of the consequences that disobedience would entail.

8:34 *bring them back to the land.* A reference to prisoners taken in battle.

8:35 *no rain.* Drought was another of the covenant curses listed in Dt 28:22 – 24.

8:36 *right way to live.* In accordance with covenant obligations (see Dt 6:18; 12:25; 13:18; 1Sa 12:23).

8:37 *famine.* See Dt 32:24. *plague.* See Dt 28:21 – 22; 32:24. *locusts or grasshoppers.* See Dt 28:38,42. *an enemy besieges them in any of their cities.* See Dt 28:52. *disaster.* See Dt 28:61; 31:29; 32:23 – 25.

8:38 *aware of the afflictions of their own hearts.* Conscious of their guilt before God, with an attitude of repentance and the desire for God's forgiveness and grace (see 2Ch 6:29; Ps 38:17 – 18; Jer 17:9).

8:39 *deal with everyone according to all they do.* Not to be viewed as a request for retribution for the wrong committed (forgiveness and retribution are mutually exclusive), but as a desire for whatever discipline God in his wisdom may use to correct his people and to instruct them in the way of the covenant (see v. 40; Pr 3:11; Heb 12:5 – 15).

8:40 *fear you.* Honor and obediently serve you (see notes on Ge 20:11; Pr 1:7; see also Dt 5:29; 6:1 – 2; 8:6; 31:13; 2Ch 6:31; Ps 130:4).

8:41 *foreigner who does not belong to your people Israel.* One who comes from a foreign land to pray to Israel's God at the temple, as distinguished from a resident foreigner.

8:42 *they will hear.* See 9:9 (foreign nations generally); 10:1 (queen of Sheba); Jos 2:9 – 11 (Rahab); 1Sa 4:6 – 8 (Philistines). *your great name and your mighty hand and your outstretched arm.* God's great power, demonstrated by his interventions in the history of his people (see Dt 4:34; 5:15; 7:19; 11:2; 26:8).

8:44 *go to war ... wherever you send them.* Military initiatives undertaken with divine sanction (see, e.g., Lev 26:7; Dt 20; 21:10; 1Sa 15:3; 23:2,4; 30:8; 2Sa 5:19,24). *toward the city you have chosen.* See note on v. 30.

8:46 *no one who does not sin.* A striking acknowledgment that sin is universal (see Ps 14:1 and note; see also Ge 6:5; 8:21; Ro 3:10 – 23). *their enemies, who take them captive.* On the basis of Lev 26:33 – 45; Dt 28:64 – 68; 30:1 – 5 Solomon knew that stubborn disobedience would lead to exile from the promised land.

them captive, and pray[q] to you toward the land you gave their ancestors, toward the city you have chosen and the temple[r] I have built for your Name;[s] 49 then from heaven, your dwelling place, hear their prayer and their plea, and uphold their cause. 50 And forgive your people, who have sinned against you; forgive all the offenses they have committed against you, and cause their captors to show them mercy;[t] 51 for they are your people and your inheritance,[u] whom you brought out of Egypt, out of that iron-smelting furnace.[v]

52 "May your eyes be open[w] to your servant's plea and to the plea of your people Israel, and may you listen to them whenever they cry out to you.[x] 53 For you singled them out from all the nations of the world to be your own inheritance,[y] just as you declared through your servant Moses when you, Sovereign LORD, brought our ancestors out of Egypt."

54 When Solomon had finished all these prayers and supplications to the LORD, he rose from before the altar of the LORD, where he had been kneeling with his hands spread out toward heaven. 55 He stood and blessed[z] the whole assembly of Israel in a loud voice, saying:

56 "Praise be to the LORD, who has given rest[a] to his people Israel just as he promised. Not one word has failed of all the good promises[b] he gave through his servant Moses. 57 May the LORD our God be with us as he was with our ancestors; may he never leave us nor forsake[c] us. 58 May he turn our hearts[d] to him, to walk in obedience to him and keep the commands, decrees and laws he gave our ancestors. 59 And may these words of mine, which I have prayed before the LORD, be near to the LORD our God day and night, that he may uphold the cause of his servant and the cause of his people Israel according to each day's need, 60 so that all the peoples[e] of the earth may know that the LORD is God and that there is no other.[f] 61 And may your hearts[g] be fully committed[h] to the LORD our God, to live by his decrees and obey his commands, as at this time."

The Dedication of the Temple

8:62-66pp — 2Ch 7:1-10

62 Then the king and all Israel with him offered sacrifices[i] before the LORD. 63 Solomon offered a sacrifice of fellowship offerings to the LORD: twenty-two thousand cattle and a hundred and twenty thousand sheep and goats. So the king and all the Israelites dedicated[j] the temple of the LORD.

64 On that same day the king consecrated the middle part of the courtyard in front of the temple of the LORD, and there he offered burnt offerings, grain offerings and the fat[k] of the fellowship offerings, because the bronze altar[l] that stood before the LORD was too small to hold the burnt offerings, the grain offerings and the fat of the fellowship offerings.[m]

65 So Solomon observed the festival[n] at that time, and all Israel with him — a vast assembly, people from Lebo Hamath[o] to the Wadi of Egypt.[p] They celebrated it before the LORD our God for seven days and seven days more, fourteen days in all. 66 On the following day he sent the people away. They blessed the king and then

8:48 [q] 1Jn 1:8-10 [r] Ps 5:7; 11:4; Jnh 2:4 [s] Dt 12:11-14; Ne 1:9; Jer 23:3; 31:8
8:50 [t] 2Ki 25:28; 2Ch 30:9; Ps 106:46; Da 1:9
8:51 [u] S Ex 34:9; S Dt 9:29 [v] S Ex 1:13; Isa 48:10; Jer 11:4
8:52 [w] S ver 29 [x] Job 30:20; Ps 3:4; 22:2; 77:1; 142:1
8:53 [y] Ex 19:5; S 34:9
8:55 [z] S Ex 39:43; Nu 6:23
8:56 [a] S Ex 33:14; Dt 12:10; Heb 4:8 [b] S Jos 23:15; S Jer 29:10
8:57 [c] S Dt 4:31; S 31:6; S Mt 28:20; Heb 13:5
8:58 [d] S Jos 24:23
8:60 [e] S Jos 4:24 [f] S Dt 4:35
8:61 [g] Dt 6:5 [h] 1Ki 9:4; 11:4; 15:3, 14; 22:43; 2Ki 20:3; 1Ch 28:9; 29:19; 2Ch 16:9; 17:6; 25:2; Ps 119:80; Isa 38:3
8:62 [i] S 2Sa 6:13; 1Ch 29:21; Eze 45:17
8:63 [j] Ezr 6:16
8:64 [k] S Ex 29:13 [l] S Ex 27:1; 2Ki 16:14; 2Ch 4:1; 8:12; 15:8; Eze 43:13-17 [m] S 2Sa 6:17
8:65 [n] S ver 2 [o] S Nu 13:21 [p] S Ge 15:18

:51 *iron-smelting furnace.* See Dt 4:20 and note.

:53 *you singled them out ... to be your own inheritance.* Solo-non began his prayer with an appeal to the Davidic cove-ant (vv. 23 – 30), and he closes with an appeal to the Sinaitic ovenant (see Ex 19:5; Lev 20:24,26; Dt 7:6; 32:9).

:54 *he had been kneeling.* Cf. v. 22; see 2Ch 6:13; see also 2Sa :18; 1Ch 17:16 and note; Lk 22:41; Eph 3:14.

:56 *Praise be to the LORD.* Solomon understood this historic ay to be a testimony to God's covenant faithfulness. *rest to is people.* After the conquest of Canaan under the leader-hip of Joshua, the Lord gave the Israelites a period of rest om their enemies (Jos 11:23; 21:44; 22:4), even though iere remained much land to be possessed (Jos 13:1; Jdg 1). was only with David's victories that the rest was made dura-le and complete (see 2Sa 7:1; see also note on 1Ki 5:4). *as he romised.* See Dt 12:9 – 10. *good promises.* See Jos 21:44 – 45 nd note on 21:45.

8:58 *turn our hearts to him.* Solomon asks for a divine work of grace within his people that will enable them o be faithful to the covenant (see Dt 30:6; Ps 51:10; Php 2:13).

:59 *his servant.* The king, who, as the Lord's anointed, serves as the earthly representative of God's rule over his people (see notes on Ps 2:2,7).

8:60 *so that all ... may know.* See note on Ps 46:10.

8:63 *fellowship offerings.* Involved a communion meal (see note on 1Sa 11:15). *twenty-two thousand cattle and a hundred and twenty thousand sheep and goats.* Although these numbers may seem large, there were vast numbers of people who participated in the dedication ceremony, which lasted 14 days (see vv. 1 – 2; see also v. 65).

8:65 *Lebo Hamath.* See note on Eze 47:15. *Wadi of Egypt.* Probably Wadi el-Arish (see note on Ge 15:18). People came to Jerusalem for the dedication of the temple from nearly the entire area of Solomon's dominion (see note on 4:21). *seven days and seven days more, fourteen days in all.* It appears that the seven-day celebration for the dedication of the temple was followed by the seven-day Festival of Tabernacles (see note on v. 2), which was observed from the 15th to the 21st of the seventh month. According to Chronicles, this was followed by a final assembly on the next day, in accordance with Lev 23:33 – 36; then on the 23rd of the month the people were sent to their homes (see 2Ch 7:8 – 10).

went home, joyful and glad in heart for all the good[q] things the LORD had done for his servant David and his people Israel.

The LORD Appears to Solomon

9:1-9pp — 2Ch 7:11-22

9 When Solomon had finished[r] building the temple of the LORD and the royal palace, and had achieved all he had desired to do, 2 the LORD appeared[s] to him a second time, as he had appeared to him at Gibeon. 3 The LORD said to him:

"I have heard[t] the prayer and plea you have made before me; I have consecrated this temple, which you have built, by putting my Name[u] there forever. My eyes[v] and my heart will always be there.

4 "As for you, if you walk before me faithfully with integrity of heart[w] and uprightness, as David[x] your father did, and do all I command and observe my decrees and laws,[y] 5 I will establish[z] your royal throne over Israel forever, as I promised David your father when I said, 'You shall never fail[a] to have a successor on the throne of Israel.'

6 "But if you[a] or your descendants turn away[b] from me and do not observe the commands and decrees I have given you[a] and go off to serve other gods[c] and worship them, 7 then I will cut off Israel from the land[d] I have given them and will reject this temple I have consecrated for my Name.[e] Israel will then become a byword[f] and an object of ridicule[g] among all peoples. 8 This temple will become a heap of rubble. All[b] who pass by will be appalled[h] and will scoff and say, 'Why has the LORD done such a thing to this land and to this temple?'[i] 9 People will answer,[j] 'Because they have forsaken[k] the LORD their God, who brought their ancestors out of Egypt, and have embraced other gods, worshiping and serving them — that is why the LORD brought all this disaster[l] on them.' "

Solomon's Other Activities

9:10-28pp — 2Ch 8:1-18

10 At the end of twenty years, during which Solomon built these two buildings — the temple of the LORD and the royal palace — 11 King Solomon gave twenty towns in Galilee to Hiram king of Tyre, because Hiram had supplied him with all the cedar and juniper and gold[m] he wanted. 12 But when Hiram went from Tyre to see the towns that Solomon had given him, he was not pleased with them. 13 "What kind of towns are these you have given me, my brother?" he asked. And he called them the Land of Kabul,[c][n] a name they have to this day. 14 Now Hiram had sent to the king 120 talents[d] of gold.[o]

15 Here is the account of the forced labor King Solomon conscripted[p] to build the LORD's temple, his own palace, the terraces,[e][q] the wall of Jerusalem, and Hazor,

8:66 [q]S Ex 18:9
9:1 [r]S 2Sa 7:2
9:2 [s]S 1Ki 3:5
9:3 [t]S 1Sa 9:16; 2Ki 19:20; 20:5; Ps 10:17; 34:17 [u]S Ex 20:24; S Dt 12:5 [v]S Dt 11:12
9:4 [w]S Ge 17:1 [x]Dt 17:20; 1Ki 14:8; 15:5 [y]S 1Ki 3:14; 1Ch 28:9; Pr 4:4
9:5 [z]1Ch 22:10 [a]S 2Sa 7:15
9:6 [b]Dt 28:15; 2Sa 7:14; 2Ki 18:12; Jer 17:27; 26:4; 32:23; 44:23 [c]1Ki 11:10
9:7 [d]Lev 18:24-28; Dt 4:26; S Jos 23:13; 2Ki 17:23; Jer 24:10 [e]Dt 12:5; Jer 7:14 [f]Job 17:6; Ps 44:14; Jer 24:9; Joel 2:17 [g]S Dt 28:37; Eze 5:15
9:8 [h]S Lev 26:32 [i]S Dt 29:24; Jer 7:4-15; Mt 23:38
9:9 [j]Dt 29:25; 2Ki 22:17; Jer 5:19; 13:22; 16:11,13; 22:9 [k]S Nu 25:3; Jer 40:3; 44:23; La 4:12 [l]S Dt 31:29
9:11 [m]ver 14
9:13 [n]Jos 19:27
9:14 [o]ver 11
9:15 [p]1Ki 5:13 [q]S 2Sa 5:9 [r]Jos 11:10-11

[a] 6 The Hebrew is plural. [b] 8 See some Septuagint manuscripts, Old Latin, Syriac, Arabic and Targum; Hebrew *And though this temple is now imposing, all* [c] 13 *Kabul* sounds like the Hebrew for *good-for-nothing.* [d] 14 That is, about 4 1/2 tons or about 4 metric tons [e] 15 Or *the Millo*; also in verse 24

9:1 *When Solomon had finished.* At the earliest this would be in the 24th year (4 + 7 + 13 = 24) of Solomon's reign — 946 BC (see 6:1,37 – 38; 7:1; 9:10).
9:2 *he had appeared to him at Gibeon.* See 3:4 – 15.
9:3 *putting my Name there forever.* See notes on 3:2; 8:16. *My eyes and my heart will always be there.* See 8:29.
9:4 – 5 *if you walk before me faithfully with integrity of heart . . . I will establish your royal throne over Israel forever.* See 8:25 and note on 2:4. The Lord reemphasizes to Solomon the importance of obedience to the covenant in order to experience its blessings rather than its curses. This was particularly necessary as Solomon's kingdom grew in influence and wealth, with all the potential for covenant-breaking that prosperity brought (see Dt 8:12 – 14,17; 31:20; 32:15).
9:6 *serve other gods and worship them.* See 11:4 – 8.
9:7 *a byword and an object of ridicule among all peoples.* See the covenant curse in Dt 28:37.
9:9 *that is why the LORD brought all this disaster on them.* See Dt 29:22 – 28; Jer 22:8 – 30.
9:10 — 10:29 Solomon's reign characterized (see note on 1:1 — 12:24).
9:10 – 28 See map, p. 2520, at the end of this study Bible.
9:11 *Solomon gave twenty towns in Galilee to Hiram king of Tyre.* Comparison of vv. 10 – 14 with 5:1 – 12 suggests that during Solomon's 20 years of building activity he became more indebted to Hiram than anticipated in their original agreement (see note on 5:9), which had provided for payment for labor (5:6) and wood (5:10 – 11). From vv. 11,14 is evident that in addition to wood and labor Solomon had also acquired great quantities of gold from Hiram. It appears that Solomon gave Hiram the 20 towns in the Phoenician Galilee border area as a surety for repayment of the gold. 2Ch 8:1 – 2 indicates that at some later date when Solomon's gold reserves were increased, perhaps after the return of the expedition to Ophir (1Ki 9:26 – 28; 10:11) or the visit of the queen of Sheba (10:1 – 13), he settled his debt with Hiram and recovered the 20 towns held as collateral.
9:13 *my brother.* A term used in international diplomacy indicating a relationship of alliance between equals (see 20:32 and note; see also chart, p. 23).
9:15 *forced labor.* Non-Israelite slave labor of a permanent nature (in contrast to the temporary conscription of Israelite workmen described in 5:13 – 16). *terraces.* Probably for Solomon's expansion of Jerusalem on the ridge north from David's city (see note on 2Sa 5:9). *Hazor.* Solomon's building activity at Hazor, Megiddo and Gezer was intended to strengthen the fortifications of these ancient, strategically located towns (Solomonic gates, probably built by the same masons, have been found at all three sites). Hazor was the most important fortress in the northern Galilee area, controlling the trade route running from the Euphrates River to Egypt. *Megiddo.* Another fortress along the great north-sout

Megiddo and Gezer.[s] 16 (Pharaoh king of
Egypt had attacked and captured Gezer. He
had set it on fire. He killed its Canaanite
inhabitants and then gave it as a wedding
gift to his daughter,[t] Solomon's wife. 17 And
Solomon rebuilt Gezer.) He built up Lower
Beth Horon,[u] 18 Baalath,[v] and Tadmor[a] in
the desert, within his land, 19 as well as all
his store cities[w] and the towns for his chariots[x] and for his horses[b] — whatever he desired to build in Jerusalem, in Lebanon
and throughout all the territory he ruled.
20 There were still people left from the
Amorites, Hittites,[y] Perizzites, Hivites and
Jebusites[z] (these peoples were not Israelites). 21 Solomon conscripted the descendants[a] of all these peoples remaining in
the land — whom the Israelites could not
exterminate[c][b] — to serve as slave labor,[c]
as it is to this day. 22 But Solomon did not
make slaves[d] of any of the Israelites; they
were his fighting men, his government officials, his officers, his captains, and the
commanders of his chariots and charioteers. 23 They were also the chief officials[e]
in charge of Solomon's projects — 550 officials supervising those who did the work.
24 After Pharaoh's daughter[f] had come
up from the City of David to the palace
Solomon had built for her, he constructed
the terraces.[g]
25 Three[h] times a year Solomon sacrificed
burnt offerings and fellowship offerings on
the altar he had built for the LORD, burning
incense before the LORD along with them,
and so fulfilled the temple obligations.
26 King Solomon also built ships[i] at Ezion Geber,[j] which is near Elath[k] in Edom,
on the shore of the Red Sea.[d] 27 And Hiram sent his men — sailors[l] who knew the
sea — to serve in the fleet with Solomon's
men. 28 They sailed to Ophir[m] and brought
back 420 talents[e] of gold,[n] which they delivered to King Solomon.

The Queen of Sheba Visits Solomon

10:1-13pp — 2Ch 9:1-12

10 When the queen of Sheba[o] heard
about the fame[p] of Solomon and
his relationship to the LORD, she came to
test Solomon with hard questions.[q] 2 Arriving at Jerusalem with a very great caravan[r] — with camels carrying spices, large
quantities of gold, and precious stones —
she came to Solomon and talked with him
about all that she had on her mind. 3 Solomon answered all her questions; nothing
was too hard for the king to explain to

a 18 The Hebrew may also be read *Tamar.*
b 19 Or *charioteers* *c* 21 The Hebrew term refers to the irrevocable giving over of things or persons to the LORD, often by totally destroying them. *d* 26 Or *the Sea of Reeds* *e* 28 That is, about 16 tons or about 14 metric tons

9:15 [s]S Jos 10:33 **9:16** [t]1Ki 3:1; Ps 45:12; 68:29; 72:10 **9:17** [u]S Jos 10:10 **9:18** [v]S Jos 19:44 **9:19** [w]S Ex 1:11 [x]S Dt 17:16; 1Ki 4:26; 2Ch 1:14; 9:25 **9:20** [y]S Nu 13:29 [z]S Jos 11:3 **9:21** [a]S Ge 9:25-26 [b]S Jos 15:63 [c]S Ge 49:15; S Ex 1:11; S Dt 20:11 **9:22** [d]S Lev 25:39 **9:23** [e]1Ki 5:16 **9:24** [f]S 1Ki 3:1 [g]2Sa 5:9; 1Ki 11:27 **9:25** [h]S Ex 23:14 **9:26** [i]1Ki 10:22; 22:48; 2Ch 20:37; Isa 2:16 [j]S Nu 33:35 [k]2Ki 14:22; 16:6 **9:27** [l]Eze 27:8 **9:28** [m]S Ge 10:29 [n]ver 14; 1Ki 10:10, 11, 14, 21; 2Ch 1:15; Ecc 2:8 **10:1** [o]S Ge 10:7, 28; S 25:3; Mt 12:42; Lk 11:31 [p]Eze 16:14 [q]S Nu 12:8; S Jdg 14:12 **10:2** [r]S Ge 24:10

ade route; it commanded the pass through the Carmel nge from the plain of Jezreel to the coastal plain of Sharon. *ezer.* See note on 3:1.

:16 *Pharaoh.* See note on 3:1. *killed its Canaanite inhabitants.* though Joshua had killed the king of Gezer at the time of e conquest (Jos 10:33; 12:12), the tribe of Ephraim had een unable to drive out its inhabitants (Jos 16:10; Jdg 1:29).

:17 *Lower Beth Horon.* Located about nine miles northwest f Jerusalem at a pass giving entrance to the Judahite high- nds and Jerusalem from the coastal plain.

18 *Baalath.* To be identified with either the Bealoth of Jos 5:24 located to the south of Hebron in the tribe of Judah or e Baalath southwest of Beth Horon in the tribe of Dan (Jos 9:44). *Tadmor.* See NIV text note; see also 2Ch 8:4; Eze 47:19.

19 *towns for his chariots and … horses.* These towns are not entioned by name but must have been strategically lo- ted throughout the land. Although Solomon was a man of eace (see NIV text note on 1Ch 22:9), he was fully prepared r war (cf. Dt 17:16 – 17 and note).

:20 *Amorites … Jebusites.* See Dt 7:1; 20:17; see also notes on e 10:15 – 18; 13:7; 15:16; 23:9; Jos 5:1; Jdg 3:3; 6:10; 2Sa 21:2.

22 *Solomon did not make slaves of any of the Israelites.* See ote on v. 15.

23 *550 officials supervising.* See note on 5:16.

25 *Three times a year.* On the occasion of the three impor- nt annual festivals: the Festival of Unleavened Bread, the stival of Weeks, and the Festival of Tabernacles (see Ex 3:14 – 17; 2Ch 8:13).

26 *ships.* Used in a large trading business that brought eat wealth to Solomon's court (see v. 28; 10:11). *Ezion Ge- er.* Located at the northern tip of the Gulf of Aqaba (see 2:48; Nu 33:35; Dt 2:8; see also map, p. 117). *Red Sea.* The Hebrew for this term, normally read as *Yam Suph* ("sea of reeds"; see NIV text note), refers to the body of water through which the Israelites passed at the time of the exodus (see notes on Ex 13:18; 14:2). It can also be read, however, as *Yam Soph* ("sea of land's end"), a more likely reading when referring to the "Red Sea," and especially (as here) to its eastern arm (the Gulf of Aqaba).

9:28 *Ophir.* A source for gold (2Ch 8:18; Job 28:16; Ps 45:9; Isa 13:12), almugwood and precious stones (10:11), and silver, ivory, apes and baboons (10:22). Such a place is attested on a Hebrew ostracon (see note on Jer 34:7) that dates perhaps to the eighth century BC. It contains this note: "Gold of Ophir for Beth Horon — 30 shekels." However, Ophir's location is disputed. If it was located in Arabia, as seems most likely, it was probably a trading center for goods from farther east, as well as from east Africa. But the three-year voyages of Solomon's merchant vessels (10:22) suggest a more distant location than the Arabian coast.

10:1 *Sheba.* Archaeological evidence suggests that Sheba is to be identified with a mercantile kingdom (Saba) that flourished in southwest Arabia (see notes on Ge 10:28; Joel 3:8) c. 900 – 450 BC. It profited from the sea trade of India and east Africa by transporting luxury commodities north to Damascus and Gaza on caravan routes through the Arabian Desert. It is possible that Solomon's fleet of ships threatened Sheba's continued dominance of this trading business. *fame of Solomon.* See 4:31. *his relationship to the LORD.* The queen of Sheba recognized a connection between the wisdom of Solomon and the God he served. Jesus used her example to condemn the people of his own day who had not recognized that "something greater than Solomon" was in their midst (Mt 12:42; Lk 11:31).

her. 4 When the queen of Sheba saw all the
wisdom of Solomon and the palace he had
built, 5 the food on his table,[s] the seating of
his officials, the attending servants in their
robes, his cupbearers, and the burnt offerings he made at[a] the temple of the LORD,
she was overwhelmed.
6 She said to the king, "The report I
heard in my own country about your
achievements and your wisdom is true.
7 But I did not believe[t] these things until I
came and saw with my own eyes. Indeed,
not even half was told me; in wisdom and
wealth[u] you have far exceeded the report I
heard. 8 How happy your people must be!
How happy your officials, who continually
stand before you and hear[v] your wisdom!
9 Praise[w] be to the LORD your God, who has
delighted in you and placed you on the
throne of Israel. Because of the LORD's eternal love[x] for Israel, he has made you king
to maintain justice[y] and righteousness."
10 And she gave the king 120 talents[b] of
gold,[z] large quantities of spices, and precious stones. Never again were so many
spices brought in as those the queen of
Sheba gave to King Solomon.
11 (Hiram's ships brought gold from
Ophir;[a] and from there they brought great
cargoes of almugwood[c] and precious
stones. 12 The king used the almugwood
to make supports[d] for the temple of the
LORD and for the royal palace, and to
make harps and lyres for the musicians.
So much almugwood has never been imported or seen since that day.)
13 King Solomon gave the queen of Sheba all she desired and asked for, besides
what he had given her out of his royal
bounty. Then she left and returned with
her retinue to her own country.

Solomon's Splendor

10:14-29pp — 2Ch 1:14-17; 9:13-28

14 The weight of the gold[b] that Solomon
received yearly was 666 talents,[e] 15 not including the revenues from merchants and
traders and from all the Arabian kings and
the governors of the territories.
16 King Solomon made two hundred
large shields[c] of hammered gold; six
hundred shekels[f] of gold went into each
shield. 17 He also made three hundred
small shields of hammered gold, with
three minas[g] of gold in each shield. The
king put them in the Palace of the Forest
of Lebanon.[d]
18 Then the king made a great throne
covered with ivory and overlaid with fine
gold. 19 The throne had six steps, and its
back had a rounded top. On both sides o
the seat were armrests, with a lion stand
ing beside each of them. 20 Twelve lion
stood on the six steps, one at either en
of each step. Nothing like it had ever bee
made for any other kingdom. 21 All Kin
Solomon's goblets were gold, and all th
household articles in the Palace of the For
est of Lebanon were pure gold.[e] Nothin
was made of silver, because silver wa
considered of little value in Solomon'
days. 22 The king had a fleet of tradin
ships[h][f] at sea along with the ships[g] of Hi
ram. Once every three years it returned
carrying gold, silver and ivory, and ape
and baboons.
23 King Solomon was greater in riches
and wisdom[i] than all the other kings c
the earth. 24 The whole world sought au
dience with Solomon to hear the wisdon
God had put in his heart. 25 Year after yea
everyone who came brought a gift[k] — a

10:5 [s] 1Ki 4:22 **10:7** [t] S Ge 45:26 [u] 1Ch 29:25 **10:8** [v] Pr 8:34 **10:9** [w] S 1Ki 5:7; S Isa 42:10 [x] S Dt 7:8 [y] Ps 11:7; 33:5; 72:2; 99:4; 103:6 **10:10** [z] S 1Ki 9:28; Isa 60:6 **10:11** [a] S Ge 10:29 **10:14** [b] S 1Ki 9:28 **10:16** [c] S 2Sa 8:7 **10:17** [d] S 1Ki 7:2 **10:21** [e] Isa 60:17 **10:22** [f] S 1Ki 9:26 [g] 1Ki 9:27; Ps 48:7; Isa 2:16; 23:1, 14; 60:6,9 **10:23** [h] 1Ki 3:13; Mt 6:29 [i] S 1Ki 3:12; Mt 12:42 **10:24** [j] S 2Sa 14:20 **10:25** [k] S 1Sa 10:27

[a] 5 Or *the ascent by which he went up to* [b] 10 That i about 4 1/2 tons or about 4 metric tons [c] 11 Probabl a variant of *algumwood*; also in verse 12 [d] 12 The meaning of the Hebrew for this word is uncertain. [e] 14 That is, about 25 tons or about 23 metric tons [f] 16 That is, about 15 pounds or about 6.9 kilograms; also in verse 29 [g] 17 That is, about 3 3/4 pounds or about 1.7 kilograms; or perhaps reference is to double minas, that is, about 7 1/2 pounds or about 3.5 kilograms. [h] 22 Hebrew *of ships of Tarshish*

10:9 *Praise be to the LORD your God.* The queen of Sheba's confession is beautifully worded and reflects a profound understanding of Israel's covenant relationship with the Lord. However, it does not necessarily imply anything more than her recognition of the Lord as Israel's national God, in conformity with the ideas of polytheistic paganism (see note on 5:7; see also 2Ch 2:12; Da 3:28 – 29). There is no confession that Solomon's God has become her God to the exclusion of all others.
10:10 *120 talents of gold.* See notes on 9:11,28.
10:11 *Hiram's ships.* See 9:26 – 28. Hiram had supplied the wood, the sailors and the expertise in construction that Israel lacked. *almugwood.* Perhaps juniper; see NIV text note and 2Ch 9:10 – 11. It was apparently available from Lebanon as well as Ophir (2Ch 2:8).
10:13 *all she desired and asked for.* The exchange of gifts between Solomon and the queen may have signified the effecting of a trade agreement (see note on v. 1). There is no basis for the idea sometimes suggested that she desired offspring fathered by Solomon and left Jerusalem carryir his child.
10:15 *revenues from … Arabian kings.* Tribute for passage their caravans through Israelite territory. *governors of the te ritories.* Perhaps those of 4:7 – 19.
10:16 *large shields.* Rectangular shields that afford maximum protection (in distinction from the small round shields). These gold shields were probably not i tended for battle but for ceremonial use, symbolizing Israe wealth and glory. They were probably made of wood overla with gold. Shishak of Egypt carried them off as plunder in t fifth regnal year of Solomon's son Rehoboam (see 14:25 – 2 Ancient Greek sources also refer to gold shields.
10:17 *Palace of the Forest of Lebanon.* See 7:2 and note.
10:22 *fleet of trading ships.* See NIV text note; 2Ch 9:21. Th same fleet is referred to in v. 11; 9:26 – 28. "Ships of Tarshis are not necessarily ships that sail to Tarshish (see note on J 1:3) but can designate large trading vessels.

ticles of silver and gold, robes, weapons
and spices, and horses and mules.
26 Solomon accumulated chariots and
horses;[l] he had fourteen hundred chariots and twelve thousand horses,[a] which
he kept in the chariot cities and also with
him in Jerusalem. 27 The king made silver
as common[m] in Jerusalem as stones,[n] and
cedar as plentiful as sycamore-fig[o] trees
in the foothills. 28 Solomon's horses were
imported from Egypt and from Kue[b]—the
royal merchants purchased them from
Kue at the current price. 29 They imported
a chariot from Egypt for six hundred shekels of silver, and a horse for a hundred and
fifty.[c] They also exported them to all the
kings of the Hittites[p] and of the Arameans.

Solomon's Wives

11 King Solomon, however, loved
many foreign women[q] besides
Pharaoh's daughter—Moabites, Ammonites,[r] Edomites, Sidonians and Hittites.
2 They were from nations about which the
LORD had told the Israelites, "You must not
intermarry[s] with them, because they will
surely turn your hearts after their gods."
Nevertheless, Solomon held fast to them
in love. 3 He had seven hundred wives of
royal birth and three hundred concubines,[t]
and his wives led him astray.[u] 4 As Solomon grew old, his wives turned his heart
after other gods,[v] and his heart was not
fully devoted[w] to the LORD his God, as the
heart of David his father had been. 5 He
followed Ashtoreth[x] the goddess of the Sidonians, and Molek[y] the detestable god of
the Ammonites. 6 So Solomon did evil[z] in
the eyes of the LORD; he did not follow the
LORD completely, as David his father had
done.
7 On a hill east[a] of Jerusalem, Solomon
built a high place for Chemosh[b] the detestable god of Moab, and for Molek[c] the
detestable god of the Ammonites. 8 He did
the same for all his foreign wives, who
burned incense and offered sacrifices to
their gods.
9 The LORD became angry with Solomon
because his heart had turned away from
the LORD, the God of Israel, who had appeared[d] to him twice. 10 Although he had
forbidden Solomon to follow other gods,[e]
Solomon did not keep the LORD's command.[f] 11 So the LORD said to Solomon,
"Since this is your attitude and you have
not kept my covenant and my decrees,[g]
which I commanded you, I will most certainly tear[h] the kingdom away from you
and give it to one of your subordinates.
12 Nevertheless, for the sake of David[i]
your father, I will not do it during your
lifetime. I will tear it out of the hand of
your son. 13 Yet I will not tear the whole
kingdom from him, but will give him one
tribe[j] for the sake[k] of David my servant

10:26 [l] S Dt 17:16 **10:27** [m] Dt 17:17 [n] Job 27:16; Isa 60:17 [o] 1Ch 27:28; Am 7:14 **10:29** [p] S Nu 13:29 **11:1** [q] S ver 3; S Ex 34:16 [r] 1Ki 14:21,31 **11:2** [s] S Ex 34:16; 1Ki 16:31 **11:3** [t] S Ge 22:24; S Est 2:14 [u] ver 1; Dt 17:17; Ne 13:26; Pr 31:3 **11:4** [v] S Ex 34:16 [w] S 1Ki 8:61; S 1Ch 29:19 **11:5** [x] S Jdg 2:13 [y] ver 7; S Lev 18:21; Isa 57:9; Zep 1:5 **11:6** [z] S Dt 4:25 **11:7** [a] 2Ki 23:13 [b] S Nu 21:29 [c] S Lev 18:21; 20:2-5; Ac 7:43 **11:9** [d] S 1Ki 3:5 **11:10** [e] S 1Ki 9:6 [f] 1Ki 6:12 **11:11** [g] S Lev 18:4 [h] ver 31; S 1Sa 15:27; 2Ki 17:21; Mt 21:43 **11:12** [i] Ps 89:33 **11:13** [j] 1Ki 12:20 [k] S 2Sa 7:15

[a] 26 Or *charioteers* [b] 28 Probably *Cilicia* [c] 29 That is, about 3 3/4 pounds or about 1.7 kilograms

10:26 *chariots and horses.* See note on 4:26. Accumulation of horses by the king was forbidden in the Mosaic law (Dt 17:16).
10:27 *sycamore-fig trees.* See note on Am 7:14.
10:29 *imported ... exported.* Through his agents (v. 28) Solomon was the middleman in a lucrative trading business. *Hittites.* See note on Ge 10:15. *Arameans.* See notes on Ge 10:22; Dt 26:5; 1Ch 18:5.
11:1–13 Solomon's folly—counterpoint to his wisdom (see ch. 3 and note on 1:1—12:24).
11:1 *loved many foreign women.* Many of Solomon's marriages were no doubt for the purpose of sealing international relationships with various kingdoms, large and small—a common practice in the ancient Near East. But this violated not only Dt 17:17 with respect to the multiplicity of wives, but also the prohibition against taking wives from the pagan peoples among whom Israel settled (see Ex 34:16; Dt 7:1–3; Jos 23:12–13; Ezr 9:2; 10:2–3; Ne 13:23–27). *Moabites.* See note on Ge 19:36–38. *Ammonites.* See note on Ge 19:36–38; see also 14:21; Dt 23:3. *Edomites.* See notes on Ge 25:26; 36:1; Am 1:11; 9:12; see also Dt 23:7–8. *Sidonians.* See 16:31. *Hittites.* See note on Ge 10:15.
11:2 *they will surely turn your hearts after their gods.* As indeed they did (v. 4). An example in Israel's earlier history is found in Nu 25:1–15.
11:3 *seven hundred ... three hundred.* Cf. SS 6:8, but see note there. *concubines.* See note on Ge 25:6.
11:4 *his wives turned his heart after other gods.* As the Lord had warned (v. 2). *his heart was not fully devoted to the LORD.* See 8:61. The atmosphere of paganism and idolatry introduced into Solomon's court by his foreign wives gradually led Solomon into syncretistic religious practices.
11:5 *Ashtoreth.* See v. 33; 14:15; 2Ki 23:13; see also notes on Jdg 2:13; 1Sa 7:3. *Molek.* See 2Sa 12:30 and NIV text note there. Molek and Milkom are alternative names for the same pagan deity and are forms of a Semitic word for "king." Worship of this god not only severely jeopardized the continued recognition of the absolute kingship of the Lord over his people but also involved (on rare occasions) the abomination of child sacrifice (see 2Ki 16:3; 17:17; 21:6; Lev 18:21 and note; 20:2–5; see also notes on Ge 15:16; Jdg 10:6). The names Ashtoreth and Molek have been given the vowel pattern of Hebrew *bosheth* ("shameful thing"). *Bosheth* is often substituted as a degrading name for Baal (see notes on Jdg 6:32; Jer 7:31).
11:6 *as David his father had done.* Although David committed grievous sins, he was repentant, and he was never involved in idolatrous worship.
11:7 *high place.* See note on 3:2. *Chemosh.* See note on 2Ki 3:27.
11:9 *appeared to him twice.* See 3:4–5; 9:1–9.
11:11 *not kept my covenant.* Solomon had broken the most basic demands of the covenant (see Ex 20:2–5) and thereby severely undermined the entire covenant relationship between God and his people.
11:12 *for the sake of David your father.* Because of David's unwavering loyalty to the Lord and God's covenant with him (see 2Sa 7:11–16).
11:13 *one tribe.* Judah (see note on vv. 31–32; see also

THE DIVIDED KINGDOM

930–586 BC

The division of Solomon's kingdom had geographical and political causes, with roots reaching back to earlier tribal rivalries. Israel was closer to Phoenician cities and major trade routes than Judah, whose heartland was a plateau-like ridge higher than the district around Samaria.

The Aramean wars were fierce and destructive contests between the kingdom of Damascus and Israel during the greater part of the ninth century. These so-called Aramean-Ephraimitic wars ended with the conquests of Jeroboam II and an era of great prosperity for Israel.

The campaigns of Tiglath-Pileser III of Assyria were enormously destructive, following a celebrated pattern of siege warfare. By 732 BC the northern kingdom was tributary to the Assyrians.

1 The final capture and destruction of Samaria took place in 722/721 BC after a long siege. The surviving inhabitants were exiled to distant places in the Assyrian Empire, and new settlers were brought to Samaria.

2 The Benjamite frontier was an issue that brought Judah and Israel into conflict early in their history. After a struggle between Asa and Baasha, the border was finally fixed south of Bethel in the territory of Benjamin.

The role of Mesha, king of Moab, was first that of a vassal and then a rebel, as both the Bible and the Mesha stele make clear.

Periods of expansion and contraction characterized the two kingdoms during the period 930–722 BC. Judah was to some extent protected by its geography, but Israel was forced to develop an efficient standing army with substantial chariotry to defend against frequent attacks. Assyrian records mention that Ahab of Israel provided 2,000 chariots—by far the largest contingent in the anti-Assyrian alliance—in the battle of Qarqar in 853 BC.

3 Judah's prosperity was intermittent and depended in large part on control of the trade routes to Egypt and the "Red Sea." Border fortresses in the Judahite desert guarded the approaches from Edom. The "front door" of Judah was through Lachish and from there up to Hebron and Jerusalem. The capital was besieged many times, most forcefully by the Assyrians in 701 BC and by the Babylonians in 597 and 586, leading to the destruction of Jerusalem by Nebuchadnezzar and marking the end of the monarchy.

An impressive devotion to the Davidic dynastic line characterized the southern kingdom and helped to maintain stability, in contrast to the more mercurial northern kingdom.

ınd for the sake of Jerusalem, which I
ıave chosen."[l]

ɔolomon's Adversaries

[14]Then the LORD raised up against Sol-
ımon an adversary,[m] Hadad the Edom-
te, from the royal line of Edom. [15]Earli-
r when David was fighting with Edom,
oab the commander of the army, who
ıad gone up to bury the dead, had struck
lown all the men in Edom.[n] [16]Joab and all
he Israelites stayed there for six months,
ıntil they had destroyed all the men in
ˈdom. [17]But Hadad, still only a boy, fled
ɔ Egypt with some Edomite officials who
ıad served his father. [18]They set out from
Aidian and went to Paran.[o] Then taking
eople from Paran with them, they went
ɔ Egypt, to Pharaoh king of Egypt, who
ave Hadad a house and land and provid-
d him with food.

[19]Pharaoh was so pleased with Hadad
ıat he gave him a sister of his own wife,
ueen Tahpenes, in marriage. [20]The sister
f Tahpenes bore him a son named Genu-
ath, whom Tahpenes brought up in the
ɔyal palace. There Genubath lived with
haraoh's own children.

[21]While he was in Egypt, Hadad heard
ıat David rested with his ancestors and
ıat Joab the commander of the army was
lso dead. Then Hadad said to Pharaoh,
Let me go, that I may return to my own
ɔuntry."

[22]"What have you lacked here that you
ant to go back to your own country?"
haraoh asked.

"Nothing," Hadad replied, "but do let
me go!"

[23]And God raised up against Solomon
another adversary,[p] Rezon son of Eliada,
who had fled from his master, Hadadezer[q]
king of Zobah. [24]When David destroyed
Zobah's army, Rezon gathered a band of
men around him and became their leader; they went to Damascus,[r] where they
settled and took control. [25]Rezon was Israel's adversary as long as Solomon lived,
adding to the trouble caused by Hadad.
So Rezon ruled in Aram[s] and was hostile
toward Israel.

Jeroboam Rebels Against Solomon

[26]Also, Jeroboam son of Nebat rebelled[t]
against the king. He was one of Solomon's
officials, an Ephraimite from Zeredah, and
his mother was a widow named Zeruah.

[27]Here is the account of how he rebelled
against the king: Solomon had built the
terraces[a][u] and had filled in the gap in the
wall of the city of David his father. [28]Now
Jeroboam was a man of standing,[v] and
when Solomon saw how well[w] the young
man did his work, he put him in charge
of the whole labor force of the tribes of
Joseph.

[29]About that time Jeroboam was going
out of Jerusalem, and Ahijah[x] the prophet
of Shiloh met him on the way, wearing a
new cloak. The two of them were alone
out in the country, [30]and Ahijah took hold
of the new cloak he was wearing and tore[y]
it into twelve pieces. [31]Then he said to

11:13 [l]Dt 12:11 **11:14** [m]S 1Ki 5:4 **11:15** [n]1Ch 18:12 **11:18** [o]Nu 10:12 **11:23** [p]S 1Ki 5:4 [q]S 2Sa 8:3 **11:24** [r]S 2Sa 8:5 **11:25** [s]S Ge 10:22; S 2Sa 10:19 **11:26** [t]2Ch 13:6 **11:27** [u]S 1Ki 9:24 **11:28** [v]S Ru 2:1 [w]S Ge 39:4; Pr 22:29 **11:29** [x]1Ki 12:15; 14:2; 2Ch 9:29; 10:15 **11:30** [y]1Sa 15:27

[a] *27* Or *the Millo*

:20). *for the sake of Jerusalem, which I have chosen.* Now at Jerusalem contained the temple built by David's son in cordance with 2Sa 7:13, the destiny of Jerusalem and the ıvidic dynasty were closely linked (see 2Ki 19:34; 21:7–8; Ps ʒ2). The temple represented God's royal palace, where his rthly throne was situated and where he had pledged to be esent as Israel's Great King (9:3).

:14–43 Solomon's throne threatened (see note on 1:1—:24).

:14 *Hadad.* The name of a Semitic storm god (see notes Jdg 2:13; Zec 12:11) that was also taken by many Arıean (see 15:18; 20:1 and note) and Edomite kings (see Ge :35,39) as their royal name.

:15 *David was fighting with Edom.* See 2Sa 8:13–14; see so map, p. 536.

:16 *all the Israelites ... all the men in Edom.* All those, on th sides, who took part in the campaign.

:17 *only a boy.* Probably in his early teens.

:18 *Midian.* At this time Midianites inhabited a region on e eastern borders of Moab and Edom. *Paran.* A desert area utheast of Kadesh in the central area of the Sinai peninsula e Nu 10:12; 12:16; 13:3). *Pharaoh king of Egypt.* See note 3:1. *gave Hadad a house and land and ... food.* In a time of ael's growing strength it was in Egypt's interest to befriend ɔse who would harass Israel and keep her power in check.

:21 *Let me go.* It appears that Hadad returned to Edom durg the early days of Solomon's reign.

11:22 *What have you lacked here ... ?* Because Egypt had by this time established relatively good relations with Israel (see note on 3:1), the pharaoh was reluctant to see Hadad return to Edom and provoke trouble with Solomon.

11:23 *Zobah.* "In the vicinity of Hamath" (1Ch 18:3; see note on 2Sa 8:3; see also maps, p. 478; p. 2520 at the end of this study Bible).

11:24 *Rezon gathered a band of men ... and became their leader.* As David had done (1Sa 22:1–2), and Jephthah before him (Jdg 11:3). *they went to Damascus, where they settled and took control.* Presumably this took place in the early part of Solomon's reign (see 2Sa 8:6 for the situation in Damascus during the time of David). It is likely that Solomon's expedition (2Ch 8:3) against Hamath Zobah (the kingdom formerly ruled by Hadadezer, 2Sa 8:3–6) was provoked by opposition led by Rezon. Even though Solomon was able to retain control of the territory north of Damascus to the Euphrates (4:21,24), he was not able to drive Rezon from Damascus itself.

11:26 *rebelled against the king.* See note on v. 40.

11:27 *terraces.* See 9:15 and note.

11:28 *whole labor force of the tribes of Joseph.* See 5:13–18. Jeroboam's supervision of the conscripted laborers from the tribes of Ephraim and Manasseh made him aware of the smoldering discontent among the people over Solomon's policies (see 12:4 and note).

Jeroboam, "Take ten pieces for yourself,
for this is what the LORD, the God of Israel,
says: 'See, I am going to tear[z] the kingdom
out of Solomon's hand and give you ten
tribes. 32 But for the sake[a] of my servant David and the city of Jerusalem, which I have
chosen out of all the tribes of Israel, he will
have one tribe. 33 I will do this because they
have[a] forsaken me and worshiped[b] Ashtoreth the goddess of the Sidonians, Chemosh the god of the Moabites, and Molek
the god of the Ammonites, and have not
walked[c] in obedience to me, nor done what
is right in my eyes, nor kept my decrees[d]
and laws as David, Solomon's father, did.
34 " 'But I will not take the whole kingdom out of Solomon's hand; I have made
him ruler all the days of his life for the
sake of David my servant, whom I chose
and who obeyed my commands and decrees. 35 I will take the kingdom from his
son's hands and give you ten tribes. 36 I
will give one tribe[e] to his son so that David my servant may always have a lamp[f]
before me in Jerusalem, the city where I
chose to put my Name. 37 However, as for
you, I will take you, and you will rule[g]
over all that your heart desires;[h] you will
be king over Israel. 38 If you do whatever
I command you and walk in obedience to
me and do what is right[i] in my eyes by
obeying my decrees[j] and commands, as
David my servant did, I will be with you.
I will build you a dynasty[k] as enduring as
the one I built for David and will give Israel to you. 39 I will humble David's descendants because of this, but not forever.' "
40 Solomon tried to kill Jeroboam, but
Jeroboam fled[l] to Egypt, to Shishak[m] the
king, and stayed there until Solomon's
death.

11:31 [z] S ver 11; S 1Sa 15:27 **11:32** [a] S 2Sa 7:15 **11:33** [b] S Jdg 2:13 [c] 2Ki 21:22 [d] 1Ki 3:3 **11:36** [e] 1Ki 12:17 [f] S 2Sa 21:17 **11:37** [g] 1Ki 14:7 [h] 2Sa 3:21 **11:38** [i] S Dt 12:25; S 2Sa 8:15 [j] S Dt 17:19 [k] S Ex 1:21 **11:40** [l] 1Ki 12:2; 2Ch 10:2 [m] 2Ch 12:2 **11:43** [n] Mt 1:7 **12:1** [o] ver 25; S Ge 12:6; Jos 24:32

Solomon's Death

11:41-43pp — 2Ch 9:29-31

41 As for the other events of Solomon's
reign — all he did and the wisdom he displayed — are they not written in the book
of the annals of Solomon? 42 Solomon
reigned in Jerusalem over all Israel forty
years. 43 Then he rested with his ancestors
and was buried in the city of David his
father. And Rehoboam[n] his son succeeded
him as king.

Israel Rebels Against Rehoboam

12:1-24pp — 2Ch 10:1-11:4

12 Rehoboam went to Shechem,[o] for
all Israel had gone there to make
him king. 2 When Jeroboam son of Nebat

[a] 33 Hebrew; Septuagint, Vulgate and Syriac *because he has*

11:31 – 32 *ten tribes . . . one tribe.* The tradition of considering the ten northern tribes as a unit distinct from the southern tribes (Judah and Simeon — Levi received no territorial inheritance; see Jos 21) goes back to the period of the judges (see Jdg 5:13 – 18). The reason, no doubt, was the continuing presence of a non-Israelite corridor (Jerusalem, Gibeonite league, Gezer) that separated the two Israelite regions (see map, p. 536; see also map, p. 2519, at the end of this study Bible). Political division along the same line during the early years of David's reign and the different arrangements that brought the southern and northern segments under David's rule (see 2Sa 2:4; 5:3) reinforced this sense of division. With the conquest of Jerusalem by David (2Sa 5:6 – 7) and the pharaoh's gift of Gezer to Solomon's wife (9:16 – 17), all Israel was for the first time territorially united. In the division here announced, the "one tribe" refers to the area dominated by Judah (but including Simeon; see Jos 19:1 – 9), and the "ten tribes" refers to the region that came under David's rule at the later date. For how Benjamin relates to these tribal divisions, see note on 12:21.

11:33 *forsaken me.* See vv. 5 – 7. *have not walked in obedience to me.* See vv. 1 – 2; 3:14.

11:34 *I have made him ruler all the days of his life.* See vv. 12 – 13.

11:35 *from his son's hands.* From Rehoboam (see 12:1 – 24).

11:36 *a lamp before me in Jerusalem.* Symbolizes the continuance of the Davidic dynasty in the city where God had chosen to cause his Name to dwell (see v. 13 and note). In a number of passages, the burning or snuffing out of one's lamp signifies the flourishing or ceasing of one's life (Job 18:6; 21:17; Pr 13:9; 20:20; 24:20). Here (and in 15:4; 2Ki 8:19; 2Ch 21:7; Ps 132:17) the same figure is applied to David's dynasty (see especially Ps 132:17, where "set up a lamp for my anointed" is parallel to "make a horn grow for David"). In David's royal sons his "lamp" continues to burn before the Lord in Jerusalem.

11:37 *Israel.* The northern ten tribes.

11:38 *If you do whatever I command you . . . I will be with you.* Jeroboam was placed under the same covenant obligations as David and Solomon before him (see 2:3 – 4; 3:14; 6:12 – 13)

11:39 *humble David's descendants.* The division of the kingdom considerably reduced the status and power of the house of David. *not forever.* Anticipates a restoration (announced also in the Messianic prophecies of Jer 30:9; Eze 34:23; 37:15 – 28; Hos 3:5; Am 9:11 – 12) in which the nation is reunited under the rule of the house of David.

11:40 *Solomon tried to kill Jeroboam.* Jeroboam, perhaps indifferent to the timing announced by Ahijah (vv. 34 – 35), may have made an abortive attempt to wrest the kingdom from Solomon (see v. 26). *Shishak the king.* See 14:25 – 26 and note on 14:25. This first Egyptian pharaoh to be mentioned by name in the OT was the Libyan founder of the Twenty-Second Dynasty, and he ruled from 945 to 924 BC. Solomon's marriage ties were with the previous dynasty (see note on 3:1).

11:41 *annals of Solomon.* A written source concerning Solomon's life and administration, which was used by the writer of 1,2 Kings (see Introduction: Author, Sources and Date; see also 15:7,23).

11:43 *rested with his ancestors.* See note on 1:21.

12:1 – 24 Rehoboam's accession to the throne (see note on 1:1 — 12:24).

12:1 *Shechem.* A city of great historical significance located in the hill country of northern Ephraim (see Ge 12:6; 33:18 – 20; Jos 8:30 – 35 and note on 8:30; see also Jos 20:7; 21:21; 24:1 – 33). *all Israel.* That is, representatives of the northern tribes (see v. 16). The fact that David became king over the northern tribes on the basis of a covenant (see 2Sa 5:3) suggests that their act of submission was to

heard this (he was still in Egypt, where
he had fled[p] from King Solomon), he returned from[a] Egypt. 3So they sent for Jeroboam, and he and the whole assembly of
Israel went to Rehoboam and said to him:
4"Your father put a heavy yoke[q] on us, but
now lighten the harsh labor and the heavy
yoke he put on us, and we will serve you."
5Rehoboam answered, "Go away for
three days and then come back to me." So
the people went away.
6Then King Rehoboam consulted the
elders[r] who had served his father Solomon during his lifetime. "How would you
advise me to answer these people?" he
asked.
7They replied, "If today you will be a
servant to these people and serve them
and give them a favorable answer,[s] they
will always be your servants."
8But Rehoboam rejected[t] the advice the
elders gave him and consulted the young
men who had grown up with him and
were serving him. 9He asked them, "What
is your advice? How should we answer
these people who say to me, 'Lighten the
yoke your father put on us'?"
10The young men who had grown up
with him replied, "These people have said
to you, 'Your father put a heavy yoke on
us, but make our yoke lighter.' Now tell
them, 'My little finger is thicker than my
father's waist. 11My father laid on you a
heavy yoke; I will make it even heavier.
My father scourged you with whips; I will
scourge you with scorpions.' "
12Three days later Jeroboam and all
the people returned to Rehoboam, as the
king had said, "Come back to me in three
days." 13The king answered the people
harshly. Rejecting the advice given him

12:2 [p]S 1Ki 11:40
12:4 [q]S 1Sa 8:11-18; 1Ki 4:20-28
12:6 [r]S 1Ki 4:2
12:7 [s]Pr 15:1
12:8 [t]Lev 19:32

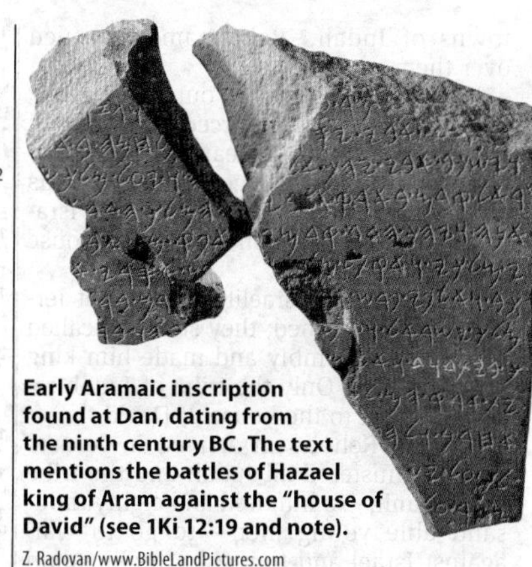

Early Aramaic inscription found at Dan, dating from the ninth century BC. The text mentions the battles of Hazael king of Aram against the "house of David" (see 1Ki 12:19 and note).

Z. Radovan/www.BibleLandPictures.com

by the elders, 14he followed the advice
of the young men and said, "My father
made your yoke heavy; I will make it even
heavier. My father scourged[u] you with
whips; I will scourge you with scorpions."
15So the king did not listen to the people,
for this turn of events was from the LORD,[v]
to fulfill the word the LORD had spoken to
Jeroboam son of Nebat through Ahijah[w]
the Shilonite.
16When all Israel saw that the king refused to listen to them, they answered the
king:

"What share[x] do we have in David,
what part in Jesse's son?
To your tents, Israel![y]
Look after your own house, David!"

So the Israelites went home.[z] 17But as
for the Israelites who were living in the

12:14 [u]Ex 1:14
12:15 [v]S Dt 2:30; 2Ch 25:20 [w]S 1Ki 11:29
12:16 [x]S Ge 31:14 [y]S 2Sa 20:1 [z]Isa 7:17

[a] 2 Or *he remained in*

be renewed with each new king and that it was subject to negotiation.

12:2 *heard this.* Heard about the death of Solomon (11:43). *returned from Egypt.* See 2Ch 10:2.

12:4 *put a heavy yoke on us.* See notes on Jer 27:2; Eze 34:27. Smoldering discontent with Solomon's heavy taxation and conscription of labor and military forces flared up into strong expression (see 4:7, 22–23,27–28; 5:13–14; 9:22; see also notes on 9:15; 11:28). Conditions had progressively worsened since the early days of Solomon's rule (see 4:20).

12:6 *elders who had served his father Solomon.* Officials of Solomon's government such as Adoniram (4:6) and the district governors (4:7–19).

12:7 Authority in the kingdom of God is for service, not for personal aggrandizement.

12:8 *young men.* Young in comparison to the officials who had served Solomon. Rehoboam was 41 years old when he became king (14:21). *serving him.* Apparently Rehoboam had quickly established new administrative positions for friends and associates of his own generation.

12:10 *My little finger is thicker than my father's waist.* A proverb claiming that Rehoboam's weakest measures will be far stronger than his father's strongest measures.

12:11 *scorpions.* Metal-spiked leather lashes. Not only will governmental burdens on the people be increased, but the punishment for not complying with the government's directives will also be intensified.

12:14 *followed the advice of the young men.* Rehoboam's answer reflects a despotic spirit completely contrary to the covenantal character of Israelite kingship (see Dt 17:14–20; see also note on 1Sa 10:25).

12:15 *this turn of events was from the LORD.* See Ru 2:3 and note. By this statement the writer of Kings does not condone either the foolish act of Rehoboam or the revolutionary spirit of the northern tribes, but he reminds the reader that all these things occurred to bring about the divinely announced punishment on the house of David for Solomon's idolatry and breach of the covenant (11:9–13). For the relationship between divine sovereignty over all things and human responsibility for evil acts, see note on 2Sa 24:1. *the word the LORD had spoken to Jeroboam … through Ahijah.* See 11:29–39.

12:16 *all Israel.* The northern tribes (see note on v. 1). *David.* The Davidic dynasty (see 2Sa 20:1 for an earlier expression of the same sentiment).

12:17 *Israelites who were living in the towns of Judah.* People

towns of Judah,[a] Rehoboam still ruled
over them.
18 King Rehoboam sent out Adoniram,[ab]
who was in charge of forced labor, but all
Israel stoned him to death.[c] King Rehoboam, however, managed to get into his
chariot and escape to Jerusalem. 19 So Israel has been in rebellion against the house
of David[d] to this day.
20 When all the Israelites heard that Jeroboam had returned, they sent and called
him to the assembly and made him king
over all Israel. Only the tribe of Judah remained loyal to the house of David.[e]
21 When Rehoboam arrived in Jerusalem, he mustered all Judah and the tribe
of Benjamin — a hundred and eighty thousand able young men — to go to war[f]
against Israel and to regain the kingdom
for Rehoboam son of Solomon.
22 But this word of God came to Shemaiah[g] the man of God:[h] 23 "Say to Rehoboam
son of Solomon king of Judah, to all Judah and Benjamin, and to the rest of the
people, 24 'This is what the LORD says: Do
not go up to fight against your brothers,
the Israelites. Go home, every one of you,
for this is my doing.' " So they obeyed the
word of the LORD and went home again, as
the LORD had ordered.

Golden Calves at Bethel and Dan

25 Then Jeroboam fortified Shechem[i]
in the hill country of Ephraim and lived
there. From there he went out and built
up Peniel.[bj]
26 Jeroboam thought to himself, "The
kingdom will now likely revert to the
house of David. 27 If these people go up to
offer sacrifices at the temple of the LORD
in Jerusalem,[k] they will again give their
allegiance to their lord, Rehoboam king
of Judah. They will kill me and return to
King Rehoboam."
28 After seeking advice, the king made
two golden calves.[l] He said to the people,
"It is too much for you to go up to Jerusalem. Here are your gods, Israel, who
brought you up out of Egypt."[m] 29 One he
set up in Bethel,[n] and the other in Dan.[o]
30 And this thing became a sin;[p] the peo-

12:17 [a] 1Ki 11:13,36
12:18 [b] S 2Sa 20:24 [c] S Jos 7:25
12:19 [d] 2Ki 17:21
12:20 [e] 1Ki 11:13,32; Eze 37:16
12:21 [f] 1Ki 14:30; 15:6,16; 2Ch 11:1
12:22 [g] 2Ch 12:5-7 [h] S Dt 33:1; 2Ki 4:7
12:25 [i] S ver 1 [j] S Jdg 8:8,17
12:27 [k] Dt 12:5-6
12:28 [l] S Ex 32:4; S 2Ch 11:15 [m] S Ex 32:8
12:29 [n] S Ge 12:8; S Jos 7:2 [o] Jdg 18:27-31; Am 8:14
12:30 [p] 1Ki 13:34; 14:16; 15:26, 30; 16:2; 2Ki 3:3; 10:29; 13:2; 17:21

[a] *18* Some Septuagint manuscripts and Syriac (see also 4:6 and 5:14); Hebrew *Adoram* [b] *25* Hebrew *Penuel,* a variant of *Peniel*

originally from the northern tribes who had settled in Judah. They were later to be joined by others from the north who desired to serve the Lord and worship at the temple (see 2Ch 11:16–17).

12:18 *Adoniram, who was in charge of forced labor.* He had served in the same capacity under both David (see 2Sa 20:24 and note) and Solomon (1Ki 4:6; 5:14).

12:19 *house of David.* An early non-Biblical reference to the "house of David" was found in 1993 on a fragment of a stele at Tell Dan (see photo, p. 539). The reading "house of David" is clear, but two other names had to be partially restored. If the restorations are correct, the king of Damascus (probably Hazael) is boasting of victories over "Joram son of Ahab, king of Israel" and "Ahaziah son of Jehoram, king of the house of David." Since Joram ruled over Israel 852–841 BC and Ahaziah over Judah in 841, this would date the inscription to 841 or shortly after — less than a century and a half after David's reign (1010–970). *this day.* See Introduction: Author, Sources and Date.

12:20–24 The kingdom is divided (see map, p. 536; see also chart, pp. 544–545, and note on 12:25—2Ki 17:41).

12:21 *tribe of Benjamin.* Although the bulk of Benjamin was aligned with the northern tribes (see note on 11:31–32), the area around Jerusalem remained under Rehoboam's control (as did the Gibeonite cities and Gezer). The northern boundary of Judah must have reached almost to Bethel (12 miles north of Jerusalem) — which Abijah, Rehoboam's son, even held for a short while (see 2Ch 13:19). *a hundred and eighty thousand able young men.* Probably includes all support personnel, together with those who would actually be committed to battle.

12:22 *Shemaiah.* Wrote a history of Rehoboam's reign (2Ch 12:15). Another of his prophecies is recorded in 2Ch 12:5–8. *man of God.* A common way of referring to a prophet (see, e.g., 13:1; Dt 18:18; 33:1; 1Sa 2:27; 9:9–10).

12:23 *rest of the people.* See note on v. 17.

12:24 *went home again.* Although full-scale civil war was averted, intermittent skirmishes and battles between Israel and Judah continued throughout the reigns of Rehoboam, Abijah and Asa, until political instability in Israel after the death of Baasha finally brought the conflict to a halt. Asa's son Jehoshaphat entered into an alliance with Ahab and sealed the relationship by the marriage of his son Jehoram to Ahab's daughter Athaliah (see 14:30; 15:6,16; 22:2,44; 2Ki 8:18).

12:25—2Ki 17:41 The period of the two kingdoms (see note on 12:20–24). In this large central section of 1,2 Kings major attention is given to the northern kingdom (of 839 verses only 157 are devoted to the Davidic kings of Judah) — to the acts of its kings and the prophetic activities related to them. It was in the north that the emerging kingdom of God was most at risk, the movement toward apostasy more powerful, and the Lord's struggle for the hearts of his people more intense. In the face of apostatizing kings, with their puppet priests and prophets, the only faithful representatives of God's rule were the prophets he raised up, especially Elijah and Elisha (see Introduction: Contents). Through their ministries the Lord was uniquely present among his people, not through the unfaithful kings and their paid religious functionaries. In the southern kingdom he was uniquely present among his people primarily through his own presence and his priests at the temple in Jerusalem.

12:25 *Peniel.* A town in Transjordan (see Ge 32:31; Jdg 8:9,17) of strategic importance for defense against the Arameans of Damascus (see 11:23–25) and the Ammonites.

12:26 *revert to the house of David.* Jeroboam did not have confidence in the divine promise given to him through Ahijah (see 11:38) and thus took action that forfeited the theocratic basis for his kingship.

12:28 *two golden calves.* Pagan gods of the Arameans and Canaanites were often represented as standing on calves or bulls as symbols of their strength and fertility (see note on Jdg 2:13). *Here are your gods, Israel, who brought you up out of Egypt.* Like Aaron (Ex 32:4–5), Jeroboam attempted to combine the pagan calf symbol with the worship of the Lord, though he attempted no physical representation of the Lord — no "god" stood on the backs of his bulls.

12:29 *Bethel.* Located about 12 miles north of Jerusalem close to the border of Ephraim but within the territory of Benjamin (Jos 18:11–13,22). Bethel held a promi-

ple came to worship the one at Bethel and
went as far as Dan to worship the other.[a]
31 Jeroboam built shrines[q] on high places and appointed priests[r] from all sorts
of people, even though they were not Levites. 32 He instituted a festival on the fifteenth day of the eighth[s] month, like the
festival held in Judah, and offered sacrifices on the altar. This he did in Bethel,[t] sacrificing to the calves he had made. And at
Bethel he also installed priests at the high
places he had made. 33 On the fifteenth day
of the eighth month, a month of his own
choosing, he offered sacrifices on the altar
he had built at Bethel.[u] So he instituted
the festival for the Israelites and went up
to the altar to make offerings.

The Man of God From Judah

13 By the word of the LORD a man of
God[v] came from Judah to Bethel,[w]
as Jeroboam was standing by the altar
to make an offering. 2 By the word of the
LORD he cried out against the altar: "Altar,
altar! This is what the LORD says: 'A son
named Josiah[x] will be born to the house of
David. On you he will sacrifice the priests
of the high places[y] who make offerings
here, and human bones will be burned
on you.'" 3 That same day the man of God
gave a sign:[z] "This is the sign the LORD has
declared: The altar will be split apart and
the ashes on it will be poured out."
4 When King Jeroboam heard what the
man of God cried out against the altar at
Bethel, he stretched out his hand from
the altar and said, "Seize him!" But the
hand he stretched out toward the man
shriveled up, so that he could not pull it
back. 5 Also, the altar was split apart and
its ashes poured out according to the sign
given by the man of God by the word of
the LORD.
6 Then the king said to the man of God,
"Intercede[a] with the LORD your God and
pray for me that my hand may be restored." So the man of God interceded
with the LORD, and the king's hand was
restored and became as it was before.
7 The king said to the man of God,
"Come home with me for a meal, and I
will give you a gift."[b]
8 But the man of God answered the king,
"Even if you were to give me half your
possessions,[c] I would not go with you, nor
would I eat bread[d] or drink water here.
9 For I was commanded by the word of the
LORD: 'You must not eat bread or drink water or return by the way you came.'" 10 So
he took another road and did not return by
the way he had come to Bethel.
11 Now there was a certain old prophet living in Bethel, whose sons came and
told him all that the man of God had done
there that day. They also told their father what he had said to the king. 12 Their

12:31 [q]S Lev 26:30; 1Ki 13:32; 2Ki 17:29 [r]S Ex 29:9; 1Ki 13:33; 2Ki 17:32; 2Ch 11:14-15; 13:9 **12:32** [s]S Nu 29:12 [t]2Ki 10:29 **12:33** [u]2Ki 23:15; Am 7:13 **13:1** [v]S Dt 33:1; S Jdg 13:6 [w]Am 7:13 **13:2** [x]2Ki 23:15-16, 20; 2Ch 34:5 [y]S Lev 26:30 **13:3** [z]S Ge 24:14; S Ex 4:8; S Jn 2:11 **13:6** [a]S Ge 20:7; S Nu 11:2; S Jer 37:3; Ac 8:24 **13:7** [b]S 1Sa 9:7 **13:8** [c]Nu 22:18 [d]ver 16

[a] *30* Probable reading of the original Hebrew text; Masoretic Text *people went to the one as far as Dan*

ent place in the history of Israel's worship of the Lord (see Ge 12:8; 28:11–19; 35:6–7; Jdg 20:26–28; 1Sa 7:16). *Dan.* Located in the far north of the land near Mount Hermon. A similarly paganized worship was practiced here during the period of the judges (Jdg 18:30–31). A raised platform ("high place") and shrine found by archaeologists at Dan may be the ones built by Jeroboam I and used by his successors (see v. 30–31; Jdg 18:7 and note; see also photo, p. 504).

12:30 *this thing became a sin.* Jeroboam's royal policy promoted violation of the second commandment (Ex 20:4–6). It inevitably led to Israel's violation of the first commandment also (Ex 20:3) and opened the door for the entrance of fully pagan practices into Israel's religious rites (especially in the time of Ahab; see 16:29–34). Jeroboam foolishly abandoned religious principle for political expediency and in so doing forfeited the promise given him by the prophet Ahijah (see 11:38).

12:31 *Jeroboam built shrines on high places.* See note on 3:2. *not Levites.* Many of the priests and Levites of the northern kingdom migrated to Judah because Jeroboam bypassed them when appointing priests in the north (see 2Ch 11:13–16).

12:32 *festival held in Judah.* Apparently the Festival of Tabernacles, observed in Judah on the 15th to the 21st of the seventh month (see 8:2; Lev 23:34). *offered sacrifices on the altar.* Jeroboam overstepped the limits of his prerogatives as king and assumed the role of a priest (see 2Ch 26:16–21).

13:1 *man of God.* See note on 12:22. *from Judah to Bethel.* God sent a prophet from the southern kingdom to Bethel in the northern kingdom. Possibly he did this to emphasize that the divinely appointed political division (11:11,29–39; 12:15,24) was not intended to establish rival religious systems in the two kingdoms. Two centuries later the prophet Amos from Tekoa in Judah also went to Bethel in the northern kingdom to pronounce God's judgment on Jeroboam II (Am 7:10–17).

13:2 *Josiah.* A prophetic announcement of the rule of King Josiah, who came to the throne in Judah nearly 300 years after the division of the kingdom. *will sacrifice the priests of the high places.* Fulfilled in 2Ki 23:15–20.

13:3 *sign.* The immediate fulfillment of a short-term prediction would serve to authenticate the reliability of the longer-term prediction (see Dt 18:21–22 and note).

13:5 *its ashes poured out.* Visibly demonstrating God's power to fulfill the words of the prophet (see note on v. 3) and providing a clear sign to Jeroboam that his offering was unacceptable to the Lord (see Lev 6:10–11).

13:6 *your God.* Should not be taken as implying that Jeroboam no longer considered the Lord as his own God (cf. 2:3; Ge 27:20) but as suggesting his recognition that the prophet had a privileged access to God. *king's hand was restored.* The Lord's gracious response to Jeroboam's request is to be seen as an additional sign (see v. 3) given to confirm the word of the prophet and to move Jeroboam to repentance.

13:7 *Come home with me.* Jeroboam attempted to renew his prestige in the eyes of the people by creating the impression that there was no fundamental break between himself and the prophetic order (see 1Sa 15:30 for a similar situation).

13:9 *You must not.* The prophet's refusal of Jeroboam's invitation rested on a previously given divine command. It underscored God's extreme displeasure with the apostate worship at Bethel.

father asked them, "Which way did he go?" And his sons showed him which road the man of God from Judah had taken. 13 So he said to his sons, "Saddle the donkey for me." And when they had saddled the donkey for him, he mounted it 14 and rode after the man of God. He found him sitting under an oak tree and asked, "Are you the man of God who came from Judah?"

"I am," he replied.

15 So the prophet said to him, "Come home with me and eat."

16 The man of God said, "I cannot turn back and go with you, nor can I eat bread[e] or drink water with you in this place. 17 I have been told by the word of the LORD: 'You must not eat bread or drink water there or return by the way you came.' "

18 The old prophet answered, "I too am a prophet, as you are. And an angel said to me by the word of the LORD:[f] 'Bring him back with you to your house so that he may eat bread and drink water.' " (But he was lying[g] to him.) 19 So the man of God returned with him and ate and drank in his house.

20 While they were sitting at the table, the word of the LORD came to the old prophet who had brought him back. 21 He cried out to the man of God who had come from Judah, "This is what the LORD says: 'You have defied[h] the word of the LORD and have not kept the command the LORD your God gave you. 22 You came back and ate bread and drank water in the place where he told you not to eat or drink. Therefore your body will not be buried in the tomb of your ancestors.' "

23 When the man of God had finished eating and drinking, the prophet who had brought him back saddled his donkey for him. 24 As he went on his way, a lion[i] met him on the road and killed him, and his body was left lying on the road, with both the donkey and the lion standing beside it. 25 Some people who passed by saw the body lying there, with the lion standing beside the body, and they went and reported it in the city where the old prophet lived.

26 When the prophet who had brought him back from his journey heard of it, he said, "It is the man of God who defied[j] the word of the LORD. The LORD has given him over to the lion, which has mauled him and killed him, as the word of the LORD had warned him."

27 The prophet said to his sons, "Saddle the donkey for me," and they did so. 28 Then he went out and found the body lying on the road, with the donkey and the lion standing beside it. The lion had neither eaten the body nor mauled the donkey. 29 So the prophet picked up the body of the man of God, laid it on the donkey, and brought it back to his own city to mourn for him and bury him. 30 Then he laid the body in his own tomb,[k] and they mourned over him and said, "Alas, my brother!"[l]

31 After burying him, he said to his sons, "When I die, bury me in the grave where the man of God is buried; lay my bones[m] beside his bones. 32 For the message he declared by the word of the LORD against the altar in Bethel and against all the shrines on the high places[n] in the towns of Samaria[o] will certainly come true."[p]

33 Even after this, Jeroboam did not change his evil ways,[q] but once more appointed priests for the high places from all sorts[r] of people. Anyone who wanted to become a priest he consecrated for

13:16 [e] ver 8 **13:18** [f] 1Ki 22:6, 12; 2Ch 35:21; Isa 36:10 [g] S Ge 19:14; S Dt 13:3 **13:21** [h] ver 26; S 1Sa 13:14; 1Ki 20:35 **13:24** [i] 1Ki 20:36 **13:26** [j] S ver 21 **13:30** [k] 2Ki 23:17 [l] Jer 22:18 **13:31** [m] 2Ki 23:18 **13:32** [n] S Lev 26:30; S 1Ki 12:31 [o] 1Ki 16:24, 28; 20:1; 2Ki 10:1; 15:13 [p] 2Ki 23:16 **13:33** [q] 1Ki 15:26 [r] S 1Ki 12:31

13:18 *I too am a prophet, as you are.* A half-truth. It is likely that the old prophet in Bethel had faithfully proclaimed the word of the Lord in former days, but those days had long since passed.
13:19 *the man of God returned with him.* Neither the old prophet's lie nor his own need justified disobedience to the direct and explicit command of the Lord. His public action in this matter undermined respect for the divine authority of all he had said at Bethel.
13:20 *the word of the LORD came to the old prophet.* The fundamental distinction between a true and a false prophecy here becomes apparent. The false prophecy arises from one's own imagination (Jer 23:16; Eze 13:2,7), while the true prophecy is from God (Ex 4:16; Dt 18:18; Jer 1:9; 2Pe 1:21).
13:22 *your body will not be buried in the tomb of your ancestors.* The man of God from Judah will die far from his own home and family burial plot.
13:24 *killed him.* A stern warning to Jeroboam that God takes his word very seriously. *the donkey and the lion standing beside it.* The remarkable fact that the donkey did not run and the lion did not attack the donkey or disturb the man's body (v. 28) clearly stamped the incident as a divine judgment. This additional miracle was reported in Bethel (v. 25) and provided yet another sign authenticating the message that the man of God from Judah had delivered at Jeroboam's altar. But Jeroboam was still not moved to repentance (v. 33).
13:30 *laid the body in his own tomb.* See v. 22. The old prophet did the only thing left for him to do in order to make amends for his deliberate and fatal deception.
13:31 *grave where the man of God is buried.* The old prophet chose in this way to identify himself with the message that the man of God from Judah had given at Bethel.
13:32 *Samaria.* As the capital of the northern kingdom, Samaria is used to designate the entire territory of the northern ten tribes (see note on 16:24). However, Samaria was not established until about 50 years after this (16:23–24). The use of the name here reflects the perspective of the author of Kings (see note on Ge 14:14 for a similar instance of the use of a place-name — Dan — of later origin than the historical incident with which it is connected).
13:33 *appointed priests ... from all sorts of people.* See 12:31 and note.

the high places. 34 This was the sin[s] of the
house of Jeroboam that led to its downfall
and to its destruction[t] from the face of the
earth.

Ahijah's Prophecy Against Jeroboam

14 At that time Abijah son of Jeroboam became ill, 2 and Jeroboam said
to his wife, "Go, disguise yourself, so you
won't be recognized as the wife of Jeroboam. Then go to Shiloh. Ahijah[u] the prophet is there — the one who told me I would
be king over this people. 3 Take ten loaves
of bread[v] with you, some cakes and a jar
of honey, and go to him. He will tell you
what will happen to the boy." 4 So Jeroboam's wife did what he said and went to
Ahijah's house in Shiloh.

Now Ahijah could not see; his sight was
gone because of his age. 5 But the LORD had
told Ahijah, "Jeroboam's wife is coming
to ask you about her son, for he is ill, and
you are to give her such and such an answer. When she arrives, she will pretend
to be someone else."

6 So when Ahijah heard the sound of
her footsteps at the door, he said, "Come
in, wife of Jeroboam. Why this pretense?[w]
I have been sent to you with bad news.
7 Go, tell Jeroboam that this is what the
LORD, the God of Israel, says:[x] 'I raised you
up from among the people and appointed
you ruler[y] over my people Israel. 8 I tore[z]
the kingdom away from the house of David and gave it to you, but you have not

13:34 [s]S 1Ki 12:30 [t]1Ki 14:10; 15:29; 2Ki 9:9; Jer 35:17; Am 7:9
14:2 [u]S 1Ki 11:29
14:3 [v]S 1Sa 9:7
14:6 [w]S 1Sa 28:12
14:7 [x]1Ki 15:29 [y]1Ki 11:37
14:8 [z]S 1Sa 15:27 [a]S 2Sa 8:15; 1Ki 3:3; 15:5; 2Ki 14:3; 15:3, 34; 16:2; 18:3; 20:3; 22:2
14:9 [b]1Ki 16:30, 33; 21:25; 2Ki 21:9,11; 24:3 [c]1Ki 16:2 [d]S Ex 20:4; S 32:4; 2Ch 11:15 [e]Dt 32:16; 1Ki 16:2; Ps 78:58; Jer 7:18; 8:19; 32:32; 44:3; Eze 8:17; 16:26 [f]Ne 9:26; Ps 50:17; Jer 2:27; 32:33; Eze 23:35
14:10 [g]S Jos 23:15; S 1Ki 13:34 [h]S Dt 32:36; 2Ki 9:8-9 [i]1Sa 12:25; 15:26; 1Ki 15:29; Hos 13:11
14:11 [j]1Ki 16:4; 21:24 [k]S Ge 40:19; S Dt 28:26

been like my servant David, who kept my
commands and followed me with all his
heart, doing only what was right[a] in my
eyes. 9 You have done more evil[b] than all
who lived before you.[c] You have made for
yourself other gods, idols[d] made of metal;
you have aroused[e] my anger and turned
your back on me.[f]

10 'Because of this, I am going to bring
disaster[g] on the house of Jeroboam. I will
cut off from Jeroboam every last male in
Israel — slave or free.[a][h] I will burn up the
house of Jeroboam as one burns dung, until it is all gone.[i] 11 Dogs[j] will eat those belonging to Jeroboam who die in the city,
and the birds[k] will feed on those who die
in the country. The LORD has spoken!'

12 "As for you, go back home. When you
set foot in your city, the boy will die. 13 All
Israel will mourn for him and bury him.
He is the only one belonging to Jeroboam
who will be buried, because he is the only
one in the house of Jeroboam in whom
the LORD, the God of Israel, has found anything good.[l]

14 "The LORD will raise up for himself a
king over Israel who will cut off the family
of Jeroboam. Even now this is beginning
to happen.[b] 15 And the LORD will strike Israel, so that it will be like a reed swaying
in the water. He will uproot[m] Israel from

[a] 10 Or *Israel — every ruler or leader*
[b] 14 The meaning of the Hebrew for this sentence is uncertain.

14:13 [l]2Ch 12:12; 19:3 **14:15** [m]S Dt 29:28; S 2Ch 7:20

13:34 *sin.* The sin in 12:30 was the establishment of a paganized worship; here it is persistence in this worship with all its attendant evils.

14:1 *At that time.* Probably indicating a time not far removed from the event narrated in ch. 13. *Abijah.* Means "My (divine) Father is the LORD," suggesting that Jeroboam, at least to some degree, desired to be regarded as a worshiper of the Lord.

14:2 *disguise yourself.* Jeroboam's attempt to mislead the prophet Ahijah into giving a favorable prophecy concerning the sick boy indicates (1) his consciousness of his own guilt, (2) his superstition that prophecy worked in a magical way and (3) his confused but real respect for the power of the Lord's prophet. *Shiloh.* See note on 1Sa 1:3. *who told me I would be king over this people.* See 11:29 – 39.

14:5 *the LORD had told Ahijah.* See 1Sa 9:15 – 17; 2Ki 6:32 for other examples of divine revelation concerning an imminent visit.

14:6 *Come in, wife of Jeroboam.* Ahijah's recognition of the woman and his knowledge of the purpose of her visit served to authenticate his message as truly being the word of the Lord.

14:7 – 8 *raised you up ... appointed you ruler ... tore the kingdom away.* Jeroboam is first reminded of the gracious acts of the Lord in his behalf (see 11:26,30 – 38).

14:8 *you have not been like my servant David.* Jeroboam had not responded to God's gracious acts and had ignored the requirements given when Ahijah told him he would become king (see 11:38).

14:9 *all who lived before you.* Jeroboam's wickedness surpassed that of Saul, David and Solomon in that he implemented a paganized system of worship for the entire populace of the northern kingdom. *other gods.* See notes on 12:28,30.

14:10 *slave or free.* Without exception (see 21:21; 2Ki 9:8; 14:26), but see NIV text note.

14:11 *birds will feed on those who die in the country.* See note on 16:4. The covenant curse of Dt 28:26 is applied to Jeroboam's male descendants, none of whom will receive an honorable burial.

14:12 *boy.* The Hebrew for this word allows for wide latitude in age (the same term is used for the young advisers of Rehoboam; see 12:8 and note). *will die.* Although the death of Abijah was a severe disappointment to Jeroboam and his wife, it was an act of God's mercy to the prince, sparing him the disgrace and suffering that were to come on his father's house (see Isa 57:1 – 2).

14:13 *All Israel will mourn for him and bury him.* Perhaps an indication that Abijah was the crown prince, and was well known and loved by the people. *buried.* He alone of Jeroboam's descendants would receive an honorable burial.

14:14 *a king ... who will cut off the family of Jeroboam.* Ahijah looked beyond the brief reign of Nadab, Jeroboam's son (15:25 – 26), to the revolt of Baasha (15:27 — 16:7).

14:15 *like a reed swaying in the water.* Descriptive of the instability of the royal house in the northern kingdom, which was to be characterized by assassinations and revolts (see 15:27 – 28; 16:16; 2Ki 9:24; 15:10,14,25,30). *He will uproot*

RULERS OF THE DIVIDED KINGDOM OF ISRAEL AND JUDAH

DATA AND DATES IN ORDER OF SEQUENCE						
	SCRIPTURE	KINGS	SYNCHRONISM OR CORRELATION	LENGTH OF REIGN	HISTORICAL DATA	DATES
1.	*1Ki 12:1–24* *1Ki 14:21–31*	***Rehoboam** (Judah)*		*17 years*		*930-913*
2.	1Ki 12:25—14:20	**Jeroboam I** (Israel)		22 years		930-909
3.	*1Ki 15:1–8*	***Abijah** (Judah)*	*18th of Jeroboam*	*3 years*		*913-910*
4.	*1Ki 15:9–24*	***Asa** (Judah)*	*20th of Jeroboam*	*41 years*		*910-869*
5.	1Ki 15:25–31	**Nadab** (Israel)	2nd of Asa	2 years		909-908
6.	1Ki 15:32—16:7	**Baasha** (Israel)	3rd of Asa	24 years		908-886
7.	1Ki 16:8–14	**Elah** (Israel)	26th of Asa	2 years		886-885
8.	1Ki 16:15–20	**Zimri** (Israel)	27th of Asa	7days		885
9.	1Ki 16:21–22	**Tibni** (Israel)			Overlap with Omri	885-880
10.	1Ki 16:23–28	**Omri** (Israel)	27th of Asa 31st of Asa	 12 years	Made king by the people Overlap with Tibni Official reign = 11 actual years Sole reign	885 885-880 885-874 880-874
11.	1Ki 16:29—22:40	**Ahab** (Israel)	38th of Asa	22 years	Official reign = 21 actual years	874-853
12.	*1Ki 22:41–50*	***Jehoshaphat** (Judah)*	 *4th of Ahab*	 *25 years*	*Coregency with Asa* *Official reign* *Sole reign* *Has Jehoram as regent*	*872-869* *872-848* *869-853* *853-848*
13.	1Ki 22:51— 2Ki 1:18	**Ahaziah** (Israel)	17th of Jehoshaphat	2 years	Official reign = 1 year actual reign	853-852
14.	2Ki 1:17 2Ki 3:1—8:15	**Joram** (Israel)	2nd of Jehoram 18th of Jehoshaphat	 12 years	 Official reign = 11 actual years	852 852-841
15.	*2Ki 8:16–24*	***Jehoram** (Judah)*	*5th of Joram*	 *8 years*	*Coregency with Jehoshaphat* *Sole reign* *Official reign = 7 actual years*	*853-848* *848-841* *848-841*
16.	*2Ki 8:25–29* *2Ki 9:29*	***Ahaziah** (Judah)*	*12th of Joram* *11th of Joram*	*1 year*	*Nonaccession-year reckoning* *Accession-year reckoning*	*841* *841*
17.	2Ki 9:30—10:36	**Jehu** (Israel)		28 years		841-814
18.	*2Ki 11*	***Athaliah** (Judah)*		*7 years*		*841-835*
19.	*2Ki 12*	***Joash** (Judah)*	*7th of Jehu*	*40 years*		*835-796*
20.	2Ki 13:1–9	**Jehoahaz** (Israel)	23rd of Joash	17 years		814-798
21.	2Ki 13:10–25	**Jehoash** (Israel)	37th of Joash	16 years		798-782

*Italics denote rulers of **Judah**.* Non-italic type denotes rulers of **Israel**.

SCRIPTURE	KINGS	SYNCHRONISM OR CORRELATION	LENGTH OF REIGN	HISTORICAL DATA	DATES
22. *2Ki 14:1–22*	***Amaziah** (Judah)*	*2nd of Jehoash*	*29 years*	*Overlap with Azariah*	*796-767 792-767*
23. 2Ki 14:23–29	**Jeroboam II** (Israel)	15th of Amaziah	41 years	Coregency with Jehoash Total reign Sole reign	793-782 793-753 782-753
24. *2Ki 15:1–7*	***Azariah** (Judah) (= **Uzziah**)*	*27th of Jeroboam*	*52 years*	*Overlap with Amaziah Total reign Sole reign*	*792-767 792-740 767-750*
25. 2Ki 15:8–12	**Zechariah** (Israel)	38th of Azariah	6 months		753
26. 2Ki 15:13–15	**Shallum** (Israel)	39th of Azariah	1 month		752
27. 2Ki 15:16–22	**Menahem** (Israel)	39th of Azariah	10 years	Ruled in Samaria	752-742
28. 2Ki 15:23–26	**Pekahiah** (Israel)	50th of Azariah	2 years		742-740
29. 2Ki 15:27–31	**Pekah** (Israel)	52nd of Azariah	20 years	In Gilead; overlapping years Total reign Sole reign	752-740 752-732 740-732
30. *2Ki 15:32–38 2Ki 15:30*	***Jotham** (Judah)*	*2nd of Pekah*	*16 years*	*Coregency with Azariah Official reign Reign to his 20th year*	*750-740 750-735 750-732*
31. *2Ki 16*	***Ahaz** (Judah)*	*17th of Pekah*	*16 years*	*Total reign From 20th of Jotham*	*735-715 735 732-715*
32. 2Ki 15:30 2Ki 17	**Hoshea** (Israel)	12th of Ahaz	9 years	20th of Jotham	732 732-722
33. 2Ki 18:1—20:21	***Hezekiah** (Judah)*	3rd of Hoshea	29 years	Coregency with Ahaz	715-686 729-715
34. *2Ki 21:1–18*	***Manasseh** (Judah)*		*55 years*	*Coregency with Hezekiah Total reign*	*697-686 697-642*
35. *2Ki 21:19–26*	***Amon** (Judah)*		*2 years*		*642-640*
36. *2Ki 22:1—23:30*	***Josiah** (Judah)*		*31 years*		*640-609*
37. *2Ki 23:31–33*	***Jehoahaz** (Judah)*		*3 months*		*609*
38. *2Ki 23:34—24:7*	***Jehoiakim** (Judah)*		*11 years*		*609-598*
39. *2Ki 24:8–17*	***Jehoiachin** (Judah)*		*3 months*		*598-597*
40. *2Ki 24:18—25:26*	***Zedekiah** (Judah)*		*11 years*		*597-586*

Adapted from *The Mysterious Numbers of the Hebrew Kings* by Edwin R. Thiele. ©1983 by Zondervan. Used by permission.

this good land that he gave to their ancestors and scatter them beyond the Euphrates River, because they aroused[n] the LORD's
anger by making Asherah[o] poles.[a] 16 And
he will give Israel up because of the sins[p]
Jeroboam has committed and has caused
Israel to commit."
17 Then Jeroboam's wife got up and
left and went to Tirzah.[q] As soon as she
stepped over the threshold of the house,
the boy died. 18 They buried him, and all
Israel mourned for him, as the LORD had
said through his servant the prophet Ahijah.
19 The other events of Jeroboam's reign,
his wars and how he ruled, are written in
the book of the annals of the kings of Israel. 20 He reigned for twenty-two years and
then rested with his ancestors. And Nadab
his son succeeded him as king.

Rehoboam King of Judah

14:21,25-31pp — 2Ch 12:9-16

21 Rehoboam son of Solomon was king
in Judah. He was forty-one years old when
he became king, and he reigned seventeen years in Jerusalem, the city the LORD
had chosen out of all the tribes of Israel
in which to put his Name. His mother's
name was Naamah; she was an Ammonite.[r]
22 Judah[s] did evil in the eyes of the LORD.
By the sins they committed they stirred up
his jealous anger[t] more than those who
were before them had done. 23 They also
set up for themselves high places, sacred stones[u] and Asherah poles[v] on every
high hill and under every spreading tree.[w]
24 There were even male shrine prostitutes[x]
in the land; the people engaged in all the
detestable[y] practices of the nations the
LORD had driven out before the Israelites.
25 In the fifth year of King Rehoboam,
Shishak king of Egypt attacked[z] Jerusalem. 26 He carried off the treasures of the
temple[a] of the LORD and the treasures of
the royal palace. He took everything, including all the gold shields[b] Solomon had
made. 27 So King Rehoboam made bronze
shields to replace them and assigned these
to the commanders of the guard on duty at
the entrance to the royal palace.[c] 28 Whenever the king went to the LORD's temple,
the guards bore the shields, and afterward
they returned them to the guardroom.
29 As for the other events of Rehoboam's
reign, and all he did, are they not written in the book of the annals of the kings
of Judah? 30 There was continual warfare[d]
between Rehoboam and Jeroboam. 31 And
Rehoboam rested with his ancestors and
was buried with them in the City of David.

14:15 [n] Jer 44:3 [o] S Dt 12:3 **14:16** [p] S 1Ki 12:30; S 15:26 **14:17** [q] S Jos 12:24; S 1Ki 15:33 **14:21** [r] S 1Ki 11:1 **14:22** [s] 2Ki 17:19; 2Ch 12:1 [t] Dt 32:21; Ps 78:58; Jer 44:3; S 1Co 10:22 **14:23** [u] S Ex 23:24; Dt 16:22; Hos 10:1 [v] S Dt 12:3 [w] S Dt 12:2; Eze 6:13 **14:24** [x] S Dt 23:17 [y] 1Ki 11:5-7; 2Ki 21:2; Ezr 9:11; Pr 21:27; Isa 1:13; Jer 16:18; 32:35; 44:4 **14:25** [z] 2Ch 12:2 **14:26** [a] 1Ki 15:15,18 [b] S 2Sa 8:7 **14:27** [c] 2Ki 11:5 **14:30** [d] 2Sa 3:1; S 1Ki 12:21

[a] 15 That is, wooden symbols of the goddess Asherah; here and elsewhere in 1 Kings

Israel. See 2Ki 17:22–23 for the fulfillment of this prophecy; see also the list of curses for covenant breaking found in Dt 28:63–64; 29:25–28. *Asherah poles.* See NIV text note. Ahijah perceived that Jeroboam's use of golden bulls in worship would inevitably lead to the adoption of other elements of Canaanite nature religion. The goddess Asherah was the consort of El, and the Asherah poles were wooden symbols of her (see notes on Ex 34:13; Jdg 2:13).

14:16 *sins Jeroboam has committed.* See 12:26–33; 13:33–34. *caused Israel to commit.* A phrase repeated often in 1,2 Kings (e.g., 15:26; 16:2,13,19,26).

14:17 *Tirzah.* Used by the kings of Israel as the royal city until Omri purchased and built up Samaria to serve that purpose (16:24). It is probably modern Tell el-Far'ah, about seven miles north of Shechem (see note on SS 6:4).

14:19 *his wars.* See v. 30; 15:6; 2Ch 13:2–20. *annals of the kings of Israel.* A record of the reigns of the kings of the northern kingdom used by the author of 1,2 Kings and apparently accessible to those interested in further details of the history of the reigns of Israelite kings. It is not to be confused with the canonical book of 1,2 Chronicles, which was written later than 1,2 Kings and contains the history of the reigns of the kings of Judah only (see Introduction: Author, Sources and Date).

14:20 *twenty-two years.* 930–909 BC. *rested with his ancestors.* See note on 1:21. *Nadab.* See 15:25–32.

14:21 *seventeen years.* 930–913 BC. *city the LORD had chosen ... to put his Name.* See 9:3; Ps 132:13.

14:22 *Judah did evil in the eyes of the LORD.* The reign of Rehoboam is described in greater detail in 2Ch 11–12. The priests and Levites who immigrated to Judah from the north led the country to follow the way of David and Solomon for the first three years of Rehoboam's reign (see 12:24; 2Ch 11:17). In later years Rehoboam and the people of Judah turned away from the Lord (2Ch 12:1).

14:23 *high places.* See note on 3:2. *sacred stones.* Stone pillars, bearing a religious significance, that were placed next to the altars. The use of such pillars was common among the Canaanites but was explicitly forbidden to the Israelites in the Mosaic law (Ex 23:24; Lev 26:1; Dt 16:21–22). It is likely that the pillars were intended to be representations of the deity (2Ki 3:2). For legitimate uses of stone pillars, see Ge 28:18; 31:45; Ex 24:4. *Asherah poles.* See note on v. 15.

14:24 *male shrine prostitutes.* Ritual prostitution was an important feature of Canaanite fertility religion. The Israelites had been warned by Moses not to engage in this abominable practice (see Dt 23:17–18; see also 1Ki 15:12; 2Ki 23:7; Hos 4:14).

14:25 *fifth year of King Rehoboam.* 926 BC. *Shishak.* See note on 11:40. *attacked Jerusalem.* Shishak's invasion is described in more detail in 2Ch 12:2–4 (see note on 12:2) and is also attested in a victory inscription found on the walls of the temple of Amun in Thebes, where more than 150 towns that Shishak plundered are listed. 2Ch 12:5–8 indicates that fear of the impending invasion led to a temporary reformation in Judah.

14:26 *gold shields Solomon had made.* See note on 10:16.

14:27 *bronze shields.* The reduced realm could not match the great wealth Solomon had accumulated in Jerusalem (see 10:21,23,27).

14:29 *annals of the kings of Judah.* A record of the reigns of the kings of Judah similar to the one for the kings of the northern kingdom (see note on v. 19; see also Introduction: Author, Sources and Date).

14:30 *continual warfare.* See notes on v. 19; 12:24.

14:31 *rested with his ancestors.* See note on 1:21.

His mother's name was Naamah; she was
an Ammonite.[e] And Abijah[a] his son succeeded him as king.

Abijah King of Judah

15:1-2,6-8pp — 2Ch 13:1-2,22–14:1

15 In the eighteenth year of the reign
of Jeroboam son of Nebat, Abijah[b]
became king of Judah, 2and he reigned in
Jerusalem three years. His mother's name
was Maakah[f] daughter of Abishalom.[c]
3He committed all the sins his father
had done before him; his heart was not
fully devoted[g] to the LORD his God, as the
heart of David his forefather had been.
4Nevertheless, for David's sake the LORD
his God gave him a lamp[h] in Jerusalem
by raising up a son to succeed him and
by making Jerusalem strong. 5For David
had done what was right in the eyes of the
LORD and had not failed to keep[i] any of the
LORD's commands all the days of his life —
except in the case of Uriah[j] the Hittite.
6There was war[k] between Abijah[d] and
Jeroboam throughout Abijah's lifetime.
7As for the other events of Abijah's reign,
and all he did, are they not written in the
book of the annals of the kings of Judah?
There was war between Abijah and Jeroboam. 8And Abijah rested with his ancestors and was buried in the City of David.
And Asa his son succeeded him as king.

14:31 [e]S 1Ki 11:1 **15:2** [f]ver 10, 13; 2Ch 11:20 **15:3** [g]S 1Ki 8:61 **15:4** [h]S 2Sa 21:17 **15:5** [i]S Dt 5:32; S 1Ki 9:4 [j]2Sa 11:2-27; 12:9 **15:6** [k]ver 16, 32; S 1Ki 12:21; 2Ch 16:9 **15:10** [l]S ver 2 **15:11** [m]1Ki 9:4 **15:12** [n]1Ki 14:24 [o]2Ch 15:8 **15:13** [p]S ver 2 [q]S 1Ki 2:19 [r]S Ex 34:13 **15:14** [s]2Ch 14:5; 17:6 [t]S 1Ki 8:61 **15:15** [u]S 2Sa 8:11 **15:16** [v]S ver 6; S 1Ki 12:21

Asa King of Judah

15:9-22pp — 2Ch 14:2-3; 15:16–16:6
15:23-24pp — 2Ch 16:11–17:1

9In the twentieth year of Jeroboam king
of Israel, Asa became king of Judah, 10and
he reigned in Jerusalem forty-one years.
His grandmother's name was Maakah[l]
daughter of Abishalom.
11Asa did what was right in the eyes of
the LORD, as his father David[m] had done.
12He expelled the male shrine prostitutes[n]
from the land and got rid of all the idols[o]
his ancestors had made. 13He even deposed his grandmother Maakah[p] from
her position as queen mother,[q] because
she had made a repulsive image for the
worship of Asherah. Asa cut it down[r] and
burned it in the Kidron Valley. 14Although
he did not remove[s] the high places, Asa's
heart was fully committed[t] to the LORD all
his life. 15He brought into the temple of
the LORD the silver and gold and the articles that he and his father had dedicated.[u]
16There was war[v] between Asa and Baasha king of Israel throughout their reigns.

[a] *31* Some Hebrew manuscripts and Septuagint (see also 2 Chron. 12:16); most Hebrew manuscripts *Abijam* [b] *1* Some Hebrew manuscripts and Septuagint (see also 2 Chron. 12:16); most Hebrew manuscripts *Abijam*; also in verses 7 and 8 [c] *2* A variant of *Absalom*; also in verse 10 [d] *6* Some Hebrew manuscripts and Syriac *Abijam* (that is, Abijah); most Hebrew manuscripts *Rehoboam*

15:1 *eighteenth year of the reign of Jeroboam.* The first of numerous synchronisms in 1,2 Kings between the reigns of the kings in the north and those in Judah (see, e.g., vv. 9,25,33; 16:8,15,29; see also chart, pp. 544–545, and Introduction: Chronology). *Abijah.* See note on 14:1. Both Rehoboam and Jeroboam had sons by this name.
15:2 *three years.* 913–910 BC. *Maakah daughter of Abishalom.* See NIV text note. Abijah's mother is said to be a daughter of Uriel of Gibeah in 2Ch 13:2. It is likely that Maakah was the granddaughter of Absalom and the daughter of a marriage between Tamar (Absalom's daughter; see 2Sa 14:27) and Uriel. Absalom's mother was also named Maakah (2Sa 3:3).
15:3 *sins his father had done.* See 14:22–24. *not fully devoted to the LORD his God, as ... David his forefather had been.* Although David fell into grievous sin, his heart was never divided between serving the Lord and serving the nature deities of the Canaanites.
15:4 *lamp in Jerusalem.* See note on 11:36.
15:5 *Uriah the Hittite.* See 2Sa 11. David's sin against Uriah the Hittite was so heinous and destructive to David's legacy that the author of Kings found it necessary to mention it here.
15:6 *Abijah.* See NIV text note; see also note on 12:24.
15:7 *other events of Abijah's reign.* See 2Ch 13. *annals of the kings of Judah.* See note on 14:29. *war between Abijah and Jeroboam.* Cf. v. 6; 14:30. From 2Ch 13 it is clear that the chronic hostile relations of preceding years flared into serious combat in which Abijah defeated Jeroboam and took several towns from him, including Bethel (2Ch 13:19).
15:8 *rested with his ancestors.* See note on 1:21.
15:9 *twentieth year of Jeroboam.* 910 BC (see note on 14:20).
15:10 *forty-one years.* 910–869 BC. *Maakah daughter of Abishalom.* See note on v. 2.
15:12 *male shrine prostitutes.* See note on 14:24. *got rid of all the idols his ancestors had made.* See 14:23. *idols.* See note on Lev 26:30.
15:13 *deposed his grandmother Maakah.* 2Ch 14:1—15:16 indicates a progression in Asa's reform over a period of years. Although Asa had destroyed pagan idols and altars early in his reign (2Ch 14:2–3), it was not until after a victory over Zerah the Cushite (2Ch 14:8–15) that Asa responded to the message of the prophet Azariah, son of Oded, by calling for a covenant renewal assembly in Jerusalem in the 15th year of his reign (2Ch 15:10). After this assembly Asa deposed his grandmother Maakah because of her idolatry (2Ch 15:16). *made a repulsive image for the worship of Asherah.* See note on 14:15. It appears that Maakah's action was a deliberate attempt to counter Asa's reform. *Kidron Valley.* See note on Isa 22:7 and map, p. 515. For similar use of the Kidron Valley during reform efforts by kings of Judah, see 2Ki 23:4, 6,12 (King Josiah) and 2Ch 29:16; 30:14 (King Hezekiah).
15:14 *did not remove the high places.* The reference here and in 2Ch 15:17 is to those high places where the Lord was worshiped (for the question of legitimacy of worship of the Lord at high places, see note on 3:2). When 2Ch 14:3 indicates that Asa removed the high places, it should probably be taken as a reference to the high places that were centers of pagan Canaanite worship (see 2Ch 17:6; 20:33 for the same distinction). This same statement of qualified approval that is made of Asa is made of five other kings of Judah prior to the time of Hezekiah (Jehoshaphat, 22:43; Joash, 2Ki 12:3; Amaziah, 2Ki 14:4; Azariah, 2Ki 15:4; Jotham, 2Ki 15:35). *fully committed to the LORD.* See note on v. 3.
15:15 *silver and gold and the articles.* Most likely consisting of war plunder that Abijah had taken from Jeroboam (2Ch 13) and that Asa acquired from Zerah the Cushite (2Ch 14:8–15).
15:16 *war between Asa and Baasha ... throughout their reigns.*

17 Baasha king of Israel went up against Judah and fortified Ramah[w] to prevent anyone from leaving or entering the territory
of Asa king of Judah.
18 Asa then took all the silver and gold
that was left in the treasuries of the LORD's
temple[x] and of his own palace. He entrusted it to his officials and sent[y] them to
Ben-Hadad[z] son of Tabrimmon, the son of
Hezion, the king of Aram, who was ruling
in Damascus. 19 "Let there be a treaty[a] between me and you," he said, "as there was
between my father and your father. See, I
am sending you a gift of silver and gold.
Now break your treaty with Baasha king
of Israel so he will withdraw from me."
20 Ben-Hadad agreed with King Asa and
sent the commanders of his forces against
the towns of Israel. He conquered[b] Ijon,
Dan, Abel Beth Maakah and all Kinnereth
in addition to Naphtali. 21 When Baasha
heard this, he stopped building Ramah[c]
and withdrew to Tirzah.[d] 22 Then King Asa
issued an order to all Judah—no one was
exempt—and they carried away from Ramah[e] the stones and timber Baasha had
been using there. With them King Asa[f]
built up Geba[g] in Benjamin, and also Mizpah.[h]
23 As for all the other events of Asa's
reign, all his achievements, all he did and
the cities he built, are they not written in

15:17 [w] S Jos 18:25 **15:18** [x] S 1Ki 14:26 [y] 2Ki 12:18; 16:8; 18:14-16, 15; Joel 3:5 [z] ver 18-20; 1Ki 20:1; 2Ki 6:24; 13:3; Jer 49:27 **15:19** [a] S Ex 23:32; S 1Ki 5:12 **15:20** [b] 1Ki 20:34 **15:21** [c] S Jos 18:25 [d] 1Ki 16:15-17 **15:22** [e] ver 17 [f] ver 9-24; Jer 41:9 [g] S Jos 18:24; 2Ki 23:8 [h] S Jos 11:3

15:24 [i] Mt 1:8 **15:26** [j] S Dt 4:25 [k] S 1Ki 12:30 **15:27** [l] 1Ki 14:14 [m] S Jos 19:44 **15:29** [n] S 1Ki 13:34 **15:30** [o] S 1Ki 12:30 [p] 1Ki 16:26; 2Ki 3:3; 14:24; 15:28; 21:16

the book of the annals of the kings of Judah? In his old age, however, his feet became diseased. 24 Then Asa rested with his
ancestors and was buried with them in the
city of his father David. And Jehoshaphat
his son succeeded him as king.

Nadab King of Israel

25 Nadab son of Jeroboam became king
of Israel in the second year of Asa king
of Judah, and he reigned over Israel two
years. 26 He did evil[j] in the eyes of the LORD,
following the ways of his father[k] and committing the same sin his father had caused
Israel to commit.
27 Baasha son of Ahijah from the tribe
of Issachar plotted against him, and he
struck him down[l] at Gibbethon,[m] a Philistine town, while Nadab and all Israel were
besieging it. 28 Baasha killed Nadab in the
third year of Asa king of Judah and succeeded him as king.
29 As soon as he began to reign, he
killed Jeroboam's whole family.[n] He did
not leave Jeroboam anyone that breathed,
but destroyed them all, according to the
word of the LORD given through his servant Ahijah the Shilonite. 30 This happened
because of the sins[o] Jeroboam had committed and had caused[p] Israel to commit,
and because he aroused the anger of the
LORD, the God of Israel.

A reference to the chronic hostile relations that had existed ever since the division of the kingdom, rather than to full-scale combat (see notes on v. 7; 12:24; see also 2Ch 15:19).

15:17 *fortified Ramah.* Baasha had recaptured the territory previously taken from Jeroboam by Abijah (see note on v. 7; see also 2Ch 13:19) since Ramah was located south of Bethel and only about five miles north of Jerusalem. *prevent anyone from leaving or entering the territory of Asa.* See 2Ch 15:9–10.

15:18 *silver and gold that was left.* That which remained after the plundering of Jerusalem by Shishak of Egypt (see 14:25). *Hezion.* It is not clear whether Hezion is to be identified with Rezon of Damascus (see 11:23–25) or regarded as the founder of a new dynasty.

15:19 *treaty ... between my father and your father.* A reference to a previously unmentioned treaty between Abijah and Tabrimmon of Aram. When Tabrimmon died, Baasha succeeded in establishing a treaty with his successor Ben-Hadad. Asa saw no hope for success against Baasha without the assistance provided by a renewal of the old treaty with Aram. Although his plan seemed to be successful, it was condemned by Hanani the prophet as a foolish act and a denial of reliance on the Lord (see 2Ch 16:7–10). The true theocratic king was never to fear his enemies but to trust in the God of the covenant for security and protection (see note on 1Sa 17:11). Ahaz was later to follow Asa's bad example and seek Assyria's help when he was attacked by Israel and Aram (see 2Ki 16:5–9; Isa 7).

15:20 *Naphtali.* The cities that Ben-Hadad conquered in Naphtali were of particular importance because the major trade routes from Damascus going west to Tyre and southwest through the plain of Jezreel to the coastal plain and Egypt transversed this area. This same territory was later seized by the Assyrian ruler Tiglath-Pileser III (2Ki 15:29).

15:21 *Tirzah.* See note on 14:17; see also map, p. 536.

15:22 *order to all Judah.* Asa's action is reminiscent of the labor force conscripted by Solomon (5:13–14; 11:28). *Geba .. Mizpah.* Asa established two border fortresses to check Baasha's desire to expand his territory southward. Geba was east of Ramah, and Mizpah was southwest of Ramah.

15:23 *other events of Asa's reign.* See 2Ch 14:2—16:14. *annals of the kings of Judah.* See note on 14:29. *feet became diseased.* See 2Ch 16:12.

15:24 *rested with his ancestors.* See note on 1:21. *Jehoshaphat his son succeeded him.* For the reign of Jehoshaphat, see 22:41–50; 2Ch 17:1—21:1.

15:25 *second year of Asa.* See note on v. 1. The second year of Asa of Judah corresponded to the 22nd and last year of Jeroboam of Israel (see v. 9; 14:20). *two years.* 909–908 BC.

15:26 *same sin his father had caused Israel to commit.* Jeroboam's sin (see note on 14:16). Although Abijah of Judah occupied Bethel during the reign of Jeroboam (see note on v. 7), it is probable that the paganized worship Jeroboam initiated was continued elsewhere until control of Bethel was regained by Baasha.

15:27 *Gibbethon.* A town located between Jerusalem and Joppa (probably a few miles west of Gezer) in the territory originally assigned to Dan (Jos 19:43–45). This Levitical city (Jos 21:23) probably fell into Philistine hands at the time of the Philistine expansion in the period of the judges (see map, p. 536).

15:28 *third year of Asa.* 908 BC (see note on v. 10). It is likely that Baasha was a commander in Nadab's army and was able to secure the support of the military for his revolt.

15:29 *the word ... given through ... Ahijah.* See 14:10–11.

15:30 *sins Jeroboam had committed and had caused Israel to commit.* See note on 14:16.

31 As for the other events of Nadab's
reign, and all he did, are they not written in the book of the annals[q] of the kings
of Israel? 32 There was war[r] between Asa
and Baasha king of Israel throughout their
reigns.

Baasha King of Israel

33 In the third year of Asa king of Judah,
Baasha son of Ahijah became king of all
Israel in Tirzah,[s] and he reigned twenty-
four years. 34 He did evil[t] in the eyes of the
LORD, following the ways of Jeroboam and
committing the same sin Jeroboam had
caused Israel to commit.

16 Then the word of the LORD came
to Jehu[u] son of Hanani[v] concerning
Baasha: 2 "I lifted you up from the dust[w]
and appointed you ruler[x] over my people
Israel, but you followed the ways of Jeroboam and caused[y] my people Israel to sin
and to arouse my anger by their sins. 3 So
I am about to wipe out Baasha[z] and his
house,[a] and I will make your house like
that of Jeroboam son of Nebat. 4 Dogs[b] will
eat those belonging to Baasha who die in
the city, and birds[c] will feed on those who
die in the country."

5 As for the other events of Baasha's
reign, what he did and his achievements,
are they not written in the book of the annals[d] of the kings of Israel? 6 Baasha rested with his ancestors and was buried in
Tirzah.[e] And Elah his son succeeded him
as king.

7 Moreover, the word of the LORD came[f]
through the prophet Jehu[g] son of Hanani
to Baasha and his house, because of all
the evil he had done in the eyes of the
LORD, arousing his anger by the things he
did, becoming like the house of Jeroboam—and also because he destroyed it.

Elah King of Israel

8 In the twenty-sixth year of Asa king of
Judah, Elah son of Baasha became king of
Israel, and he reigned in Tirzah two years.
9 Zimri, one of his officials, who had
command of half his chariots, plotted
against him. Elah was in Tirzah at the
time, getting drunk[h] in the home of Arza,
the palace administrator[i] at Tirzah. 10 Zimri
came in, struck him down and killed him
in the twenty-seventh year of Asa king of
Judah. Then he succeeded him as king.[j]

11 As soon as he began to reign and was
seated on the throne, he killed off Baasha's whole family.[k] He did not spare a
single male, whether relative or friend.
12 So Zimri destroyed the whole family of
Baasha, in accordance with the word of
the LORD spoken against Baasha through
the prophet Jehu— 13 because of all the
sins Baasha and his son Elah had committed and had caused Israel to commit, so
that they aroused the anger of the LORD,
the God of Israel, by their worthless idols.[l]

14 As for the other events of Elah's reign,
and all he did, are they not written in the
book of the annals of the kings of Israel?

15:31 [q] 1Ki 11:41
15:32 [r] S ver 6
15:33 [s] 1Ki 14:17; 16:6, 23; 2Ki 15:14; SS 6:4
15:34 [t] ver 26
16:1 [u] ver 7; 2Ch 19:2; 20:34 [v] 2Ch 16:7
16:2 [w] 1Sa 2:8 [x] S 1Ki 14:7-9 [y] S 1Ki 12:30
16:3 [z] 2Ki 9:9 [a] ver 11; 1Ki 21:22
16:4 [b] S 1Ki 14:11 [c] S Ge 40:19
16:5 [d] 1Ki 15:31
16:6 [e] S 1Ki 15:33
16:7 [f] S 1Ki 6:11 [g] S ver 1
16:9 [h] 1Ki 20:12, 16; Pr 31:4-5 [i] 1Ki 18:3
16:10 [j] 2Ki 9:31
16:11 [k] S ver 3
16:13 [l] S Dt 32:21

15:31 *annals of the kings of Israel.* See note on 14:19.
15:32 *war ... throughout their reigns.* See note on v. 16. The demise of Jeroboam's dynasty did not improve relations between the two kingdoms.
15:33 *third year of Asa.* 908 BC (see note on v. 10). *Tirzah.* See note on 14:17. *twenty-four years.* 908–886 BC. His official years were counted as 24, though his actual years were 23 (see 16:8; see also Introduction: Chronology).
15:34 *same sin Jeroboam had caused Israel to commit.* See note on 14:16. The assessment of Baasha's reign indicates no improvement over the reign of Nadab, whom he replaced (see v. 26).
16:1 *Jehu.* Like his father before him (see 2Ch 16:7–10), Jehu brought God's word of condemnation to a king. Much as the man of God from Judah (see note on 13:1) and later the prophet Amos, he was sent from the south to a northern king. His ministry continued for about 50 years until the reign of Jehoshaphat of Judah (2Ch 19:2; 20:34).
16:2 *I lifted you up from the dust.* Cf. 14:7. *followed the ways of Jeroboam.* See note on 14:16.
16:3 *wipe out Baasha and his house.* Cf. 14:10 (the house of Jeroboam); 21:21 (the house of Omri and Ahab).
16:4 Identical to the prophecy against Jeroboam's dynasty in 14:11.
16:5 *his achievements.* For the purposes of the writer of Kings (see Introduction: Theme), it was not necessary to list any of Baasha's achievements. He may have been a very successful ruler from a military-political point of view. *annals of the kings of Israel.* See note on 14:19.
16:6 *rested with his ancestors.* See note on 1:21.
16:7 *evil he had done ... like the house of Jeroboam.* See v. 2; 15:34. *he destroyed it.* Although Baasha fulfilled God's purpose (14:10,14) in destroying the house of Jeroboam, he remained responsible for this violent and unlawful act (cf. Ge 50:20; Isa 10:5–7,12).
16:8 *twenty-sixth year of Asa.* 886 BC (see note on 15:10; see also Introduction: Chronology). *two years.* 886–885 BC.
16:9 *getting drunk.* The fact that Elah was carousing at Tirzah while the army was laying siege to Gibbethon (v. 15) indicates that he had little perception of his responsibilities as king.
16:10 *twenty-seventh year of Asa.* 885 BC.
16:11 *killed off Baasha's whole family.* See 15:29; 2Ki 10:1–7; 11:1. *friend.* Probably the chief adviser to the king (see note on 2Sa 15:37).
16:12 *word of the LORD ... through the prophet Jehu.* See vv. 1–4. Zimri did not consciously decide to fulfill Jehu's prophecy, but unwittingly he became the instrument by which Jehu's prediction was fulfilled (see note on v. 7) when he conspired against Elah and destroyed the dynasty of Baasha.
16:13 *sins Baasha and his son Elah had committed.* See 15:34. *worthless idols.* A reference to all the paganism in Israel's religious observances, including the use of the golden calves in worship (see 12:28; 14:9).
16:14 *annals of the kings of Israel.* See note on 14:19.

Zimri King of Israel

15 In the twenty-seventh year of Asa king of Judah, Zimri reigned in Tirzah seven days. The army was encamped near Gibbethon,[m] a Philistine town. 16 When the Israelites in the camp heard that Zimri had plotted against the king and murdered him, they proclaimed Omri, the commander of the army, king over Israel that very day there in the camp. 17 Then Omri and all the Israelites with him withdrew from Gibbethon and laid siege to Tirzah. 18 When Zimri saw that the city was taken, he went into the citadel of the royal palace and set the palace on fire around him. So he died, 19 because of the sins he had committed, doing evil in the eyes of the LORD and following the ways of Jeroboam and committing the same sin Jeroboam had caused Israel to commit.

20 As for the other events of Zimri's reign, and the rebellion he carried out, are they not written in the book of the annals of the kings of Israel?

Omri King of Israel

21 Then the people of Israel were split into two factions; half supported Tibni son of Ginath for king, and the other half supported Omri. 22 But Omri's followers proved stronger than those of Tibni son of Ginath. So Tibni died and Omri became king.

23 In the thirty-first year of Asa king of Judah, Omri became king of Israel, and he reigned twelve years, six of them in Tirzah. 24 He bought the hill of Samaria from Shemer for two talents[a] of silver and built a city on the hill, calling it Samaria,[o] after Shemer, the name of the former owner of the hill.

25 But Omri did evil[p] in the eyes of the LORD and sinned more than all those before him. 26 He followed completely the ways of Jeroboam son of Nebat, committing the same sin Jeroboam had caused[q] Israel to commit, so that they aroused the anger of the LORD, the God of Israel, by their worthless idols.[r]

27 As for the other events of Omri's reign, what he did and the things he achieved, are they not written in the book of the annals of the kings of Israel? 28 Omri rested with his ancestors and was buried in Samaria.[s] And Ahab his son succeeded him as king.

Ahab Becomes King of Israel

29 In the thirty-eighth year of Asa king of Judah, Ahab son of Omri became king of Israel, and he reigned in Samaria over Israel twenty-two years. 30 Ahab son of Omri did more[t] evil in the eyes of the LORD than any of those before him. 31 He not only considered it trivial to commit the sins of

16:15 [m] S Jos 19:44
16:23 [n] S Jos 12:24; S 1Ki 15:33
16:24 [o] S 1Ki 13:32; S Mt 10:5
16:25 [p] ver 25-26; S Dt 4:25; Mic 6:16
16:26 [q] S 1Ki 15:30 [r] S Dt 32:21
16:28 [s] S 1Ki 13:32
16:30 [t] S 1Ki 14:9

[a] *24* That is, about 150 pounds or about 68 kilograms

16:15 *twenty-seventh year of Asa.* 885 BC (see notes on 15:1,10). *Gibbethon.* See notes on v. 9; 15:27.
16:16 *plotted against the king and murdered him.* See vv. 9–12. *Omri, the commander of the army.* He held a higher rank than Zimri did under Elah (v. 9).
16:17 *Tirzah.* The royal residence (see vv. 8–10; see also note on 14:17).
16:19 *ways of Jeroboam.* See note on 14:16.
16:20 *annals of the kings of Israel.* See note on 14:19.
16:22 *Tibni died.* It is not clear whether Tibni's death was due to natural causes or the result of the military struggle for control of the land.
16:23 *thirty-first year of Asa.* 880 BC (see note on 15:10; see also Introduction: Chronology). *became king.* Became sole king. The struggle for control of the northern kingdom between Omri and Tibni lasted four years (compare this verse with v. 15). *twelve years.* 885–874. The 12 years of Omri's reign include the four years of struggle between Omri and Tibni (cf. vv. 15,29). *Tirzah.* See note on 14:17. Omri had been able to capture Tirzah in a matter of days (vv. 15–19).
16:24 *Samaria.* Seven miles northwest of Shechem, Samaria rose about 300 feet above the surrounding fertile valleys (referred to as a "wreath" in Isa 28:1). The original owner may have been persuaded to sell his property (see 21:3) on the condition that the city be named after him (cf. Ru 4:5). The site provided an ideal location for a nearly impregnable capital city for the northern kingdom (see 20:1–21; 2Ki 6:25; 18:9–10). With the establishment of this royal city, the kings of the north came to possess a royal citadel-city like that of the Davidic dynasty (see 2Sa 5:6–12). Archaeologists have discovered that Omri and Ahab also adorned it with magnificent structures to rival those Solomon had erected in Jerusalem. From this time on, the northern kingdom could be designated by the name of the royal city, just as the southern kingdom could be designated by its capital, Jerusalem (see, e.g., 21:1; Isa 10:10; Am 6:1).
16:25 *sinned more than all.* Omri's alliance with Ethbaal of Tyre and Sidon (Omri's son Ahab married Ethbaal's daughter Jezebel to seal the alliance) led to widespread Baal worship in the northern kingdom (vv. 31–33) and eventually to the near extinction of the Davidic line in the southern kingdom (see 2Ki 11; see also note on 2Ki 8:18). This marriage alliance must have been established in the early year of Omri's reign (see note on v. 23), perhaps to strengthen his hand against Tibni (see vv. 21–22).
16:26 *same sin Jeroboam had caused Israel to commit.* See 12:26–33; see also note on 14:16. *worthless idols.* See note on v. 13.
16:27 *things he achieved.* Omri's military and political accomplishments were not of importance for the purposes of the writer of Kings (see Introduction: Theme). Apart from establishing Samaria as the capital of the northern kingdom, about all that is known of him from the Biblical account is that he organized a governmental structure in the northern kingdom that was in place during the rule of his son, Ahab (see 20:14–15). Omri's dynasty, however, endured for over 40 years. A century and a half later (732 BC) Tiglath-Pileser III of Assyria referred to Israel as the "house of Omri" in his annals. *annals of the kings of Israel.* See note on 14:19.
16:28 *rested with his ancestors.* See note on 1:21.
16:29 *thirty-eighth year of Asa.* 874 BC (see notes on 15:9–10). *twenty-two years.* 874–853 BC.
16:30 *more evil … than any.* Omri sinned more than those before him (see v. 25), and Ahab sinned more than his father had. Evil became progressively worse in the royal house of the northern kingdom. Nearly a

Jeroboam son of Nebat, but he also married[u] Jezebel daughter[v] of Ethbaal king of
the Sidonians, and began to serve Baal[w]
and worship him. 32 He set up an altar[x] for
Baal in the temple[y] of Baal that he built
in Samaria. 33 Ahab also made an Asherah
pole[z] and did more[a] to arouse the anger of
the LORD, the God of Israel, than did all the
kings of Israel before him.
34 In Ahab's time, Hiel of Bethel rebuilt
Jericho. He laid its foundations at the cost
of his firstborn son Abiram, and he set up
its gates at the cost of his youngest son
Segub, in accordance with the word of the
LORD spoken by Joshua son of Nun.[b]

Elijah Announces a Great Drought

17 Now Elijah[c] the Tishbite, from Tishbe[a] in Gilead,[d] said to Ahab, "As
the LORD, the God of Israel, lives, whom I
serve, there will be neither dew nor rain[e]
in the next few years except at my word."

Elijah Fed by Ravens

2 Then the word of the LORD came to Elijah: 3 "Leave here, turn eastward and hide[f]
in the Kerith Ravine, east of the Jordan.
4 You will drink from the brook, and I have
directed the ravens[g] to supply you with
food there."
5 So he did what the LORD had told him.
He went to the Kerith Ravine, east of the
Jordan, and stayed there. 6 The ravens
brought him bread and meat in the morning[h] and bread and meat in the evening,
and he drank from the brook.

Elijah and the Widow at Zarephath

7 Some time later the brook dried up

16:31 [u] S 1Ki 11:2 [v] S Jdg 3:6; 2Ki 9:34 [w] S Jdg 2:11 **16:32** [x] S Jdg 6:28 [y] 2Ki 10:21,27; 11:18; Jer 43:12 **16:33** [z] S Jdg 3:7; 2Ki 13:6 [a] S 1Ki 14:9; 21:25 **16:34** [b] Jos 6:26 **17:1** [c] Mal 4:5; Mt 11:14; 17:3 [d] Jdg 12:4 [e] S Dt 11:17; S 28:24; S 2Sa 1:21; S 1Ki 8:36; Job 12:15; S Lk 4:25 **17:3** [f] 1Ki 18:4, 10; Jer 36:19,26 **17:4** [g] S Ge 8:7 **17:6** [h] Ex 16:8

[a] 1 Or *Tishbite, of the settlers*

---

third of the narrative material in 1,2 Kings concerns the 34-year period of the reigns of Ahab and his two sons, Ahaziah and Joram. In this period the struggle between the kingdom of God (championed especially by Elijah and Elisha) and the kingdom of Satan was especially intense.

16:31 *married Jezebel daughter of Ethbaal.* The first-century Jewish historian Josephus refers to Ethbaal as a king-priest who ruled over Tyre and Sidon for 32 years. Ahab had already married Jezebel during the reign of his father (see note on v. 25). *Baal.* Perhaps Melqart, the local manifestation of Baal in Tyre, whose worship was brought to Israel by Jezebel. It is probable that Ahab participated in the worship of this deity at the time of his marriage. The names of Ahab's sons (Ahaziah, "The LORD grasps"; Joram, "The LORD is exalted") suggest that Ahab did not intend to replace the worship of the Lord with the worship of Baal but to worship both deities in a syncretistic way.

16:32 *temple of Baal that he built in Samaria.* Ahab imported the Phoenician Baal worship of his wife Jezebel into the northern kingdom by constructing a temple of Baal in Samaria, just as Solomon had erected the temple of the Lord in Jerusalem. This pagan temple and its sacred stone (see note on 14:23) were later destroyed by Jehu (2Ki 10:21–27).

16:33 *Asherah pole.* See note on 14:15. *than did all the kings of Israel.* See note on v. 30. Ahab elevated the worship of Baal to an official status in the northern kingdom at the beginning of his reign.

16:34 *rebuilt Jericho.* Does not mean that Jericho had remained uninhabited since its destruction by Joshua (see Jos 18:21; Jdg 1:16; 3:13; 2Sa 10:5), but that it had remained an unwalled town or village. During the rule of Ahab, Hiel fortified the city by reconstructing its walls and gates (see 9:17 for a similar use of "rebuilt"). This violated God's intention that the ruins of Jericho be a perpetual reminder that Israel had received the land of Canaan from God's hand as a gift of grace. Accordingly, Hiel suffered the curse Joshua had pronounced (Jos 6:26).

17:1—2Ki 8:15 The ministries of Elijah and Elisha and other prophets from Ahab/Asa to Joram/Jehoshaphat—during one of the greatest religious crises in the history of the kingdom of Israel.

17:1 *Elijah.* Elijah's name (meaning "The LORD is my God") was the essence of his message (18:21,39). He was sent to oppose vigorously, by word and action, both Baal worship and those who engaged in it. *from Tishbe in Gilead.* See NIV text note. Gilead was in the northern Transjordan area. The precise location of Tishbe is unknown, but see map, p. 557; see also map, p. 2522, at the end of this study Bible. *whom I serve.* Lit. "before whom I stand," a technical expression indicating one who stands in the service of a king. Kings and priests in Israel were anointed to serve as official representatives of the Lord, Israel's Great King, leading Israel in the way of faithfulness to the Lord and channeling his covenantal care and blessings to them. Since the days of Jeroboam the northern kingdom had not had such a priest (12:31), and its kings had all been unfaithful. Now, in the great crisis brought on by Ahab's promotion of Baal worship, the Lord sent Elijah (and after him Elisha) to serve as his representative (instead of king and priest), much as he had sent Moses long ago. The author of Kings highlights many parallels between the ministries of Elijah and Moses. *neither dew nor rain.* The drought was not only a divine judgment on a nation that had turned to idolatry but also a demonstration that even though Baal was considered the god of fertility and lord of the rain clouds, he was powerless to give rain (cf. Lev 26:3–4; Jer 14:22; Hos 2:5,8; Zec 10:1 and notes).

17:3 *Leave here.* With this command God withdrew his prophet from his land and people to leave them isolated from his word and blessings. The absence of the prophet confirmed and intensified the judgment. *Kerith Ravine, east of the Jordan.* Perhaps a gorge leading into the Jordan Valley (see map, p. 557; see also map, p. 2522, at the end of this study Bible).

17:4 *ravens to supply you with food there.* The Lord's faithful servant Elijah was miraculously sustained beyond the Jordan (like Israel in the wilderness in the time of Moses) while Israel in the promised land was going hungry—a clear testimony against Israel's reliance on Baal. The fact that Elijah was sustained in a miraculous way while not living among his own people demonstrated that the word of God was not dependent on the people, but the people were dependent on the word of God. *ravens.* Lived mainly on the carcasses of birds and animals they found in the fields and on the leftovers of wild kills. Since they normally fed on these where they found them, a flock of circling ravens would suggest to an observer only the presence of a dead body, thus keeping Elijah's hiding place secure. And the fact that birds of such habit here served as carriers of food heightens the miraculous element.

17:6 *meat.* Since the ravens themselves were not to be eaten (Lev 11:15; Dt 14:14) and the meat they normally ate was also forbidden food (Lev 7:24; Dt 14:21; Eze 4:14), the kind

ANCIENT NEAR EASTERN DEITIES

PALESTINIAN DEITIES IN SCRIPTURE

DEITY	COUNTRY	POSITION	REFERENCE
Baal	Canaan	Storm god	1Ki 16:31; 18:18–46
Ashtoreth (Astarte)	Canaan	Mother-goddess; love; fertility	Jdg 2:13; 10:6; 1Sa 12:10; 1Ki 11:5
Chemosh	Moab	National god of war	Nu 21:29; Jdg 11:24; 1Ki 11:7,33; Jer 48:7
Molek (Malkam, Milkom)	Ammon	National god	Jer 49:1; Zep 1:5
Dagon	Philistia	National god of grain	Jdg 16:23;1Sa 5:2–7

MESOPOTAMIAN DEITIES IN SCRIPTURE

DEITY	COUNTRY	POSITION	REFERENCE
Marduk	Babylonia	Chief god	Jer 50:2
Bel	Babylonia	Another name for Marduk	Isa 46:1; Jer 50:2; 51:44
Nebo (Nabu)	Babylonia	Son of Marduk	Isa 46:1
Queen of Heaven	Babylonia	Another name for Ishtar (same as Ashtoreth)	Jer 7:18; 44:17–25
Tammuz (Dumuzi)	Sumer	Fertility god	Eze 8:14

MAJOR DEITIES NOT IN SCRIPTURE

EGYPT	MESOPOTAMIA	CANAAN-ARAM-HATTI
Osiris — death	Anu — head of pantheon (officially recognized gods)	El — head of Canaanite pantheon
Isis — life	Enlil — storm	Anath — love and war
Horus — sun	Ea/Enki — fresh water and subterranean water	Mot — death, sterility
Hathor — mother-goddess	Sin (Nanna) — moon	Adad — Aramean storm god
Ra (Re) — sun	Ishtar — sex, fertility	Teshub — Hittite storm god
Seth — evil storm	Ninurta — war	Hannahanna — Hittite mother-goddess
Ptah — artists; Memphite creator	Tiamat — salt water	Arinna — Hittite sun goddess

Deities of these civilizations, particularly Egypt, vary as to attributes and rank, depending on the time period and the areas of the country. The ones listed are basic.

because there had been no rain in the
land. 8Then the word of the LORD came
to him: 9"Go at once to Zarephath[i] in the
region of Sidon and stay there. I have directed a widow[j] there to supply you with
food." 10So he went to Zarephath. When
he came to the town gate, a widow was
there gathering sticks. He called to her and

17:9 [i] Ob 1:20 [j] Lk 4:26

of "meat" referred to and its source remain mysterious. *in the morning ... in the evening.* To eat meat every day, to say nothing of twice a day, was not common fare for common people. Among them meat was reserved for special occasions. Kings, on the other hand, seem to have had meat daily on their table (see 1Ki 4:23). It appears, then, that Yahweh's servant Elijah is here depicted as eating at King Yahweh's table (see Ex 29:38–41; Nu 28:4–8; cf. 2Ki 4:42 and note; see also 1Ki 18:19, where Elijah speaks of the "prophets ... who eat at Jezebel's table") while apostate Israel goes hungry.

17:9 *Zarephath in the region of Sidon.* A coastal town located between Tyre and Sidon in the territory ruled by Jezebel's father Ethbaal (16:31). Elijah is commanded to go and reside in the heart of the very land from which the Baal worship now being promoted in Israel had come. *I have directed a widow there to supply you with food.* Elijah, as the bearer of God's word, was now to be sustained by human hands, but they were the hands of a poor widow facing starvation (v. 12). She was, moreover, from outside the circle of God's own people (cf. Lk 4:25–26) — in fact, she was from the pagan nation that at that time (much like Egypt earlier and Babylon later) represented the forces arrayed against God's kingdom.

17:10 *So he went.* Elijah's reliance on the Lord demonstrated the faith in the Lord that Israel should have been living by.

asked, "Would you bring me a little water
in a jar so I may have a drink?"[k] 11As she
was going to get it, he called, "And bring
me, please, a piece of bread."
12"As surely as the LORD your God lives,"
she replied, "I don't have any bread — only
a handful of flour in a jar and a little olive
oil[l] in a jug. I am gathering a few sticks
to take home and make a meal for myself
and my son, that we may eat it — and die."
13Elijah said to her, "Don't be afraid.
Go home and do as you have said. But
first make a small loaf of bread for me
from what you have and bring it to me,
and then make something for yourself and
your son. 14For this is what the LORD, the
God of Israel, says: 'The jar of flour will
not be used up and the jug of oil will not
run dry until the day the LORD sends rain[m]
on the land.' "
15She went away and did as Elijah had
told her. So there was food every day for
Elijah and for the woman and her family.
16For the jar of flour was not used up and
the jug of oil did not run dry, in keeping
with the word of the LORD spoken by Elijah.
17Some time later the son of the woman who owned the house became ill. He
grew worse and worse, and finally stopped
breathing. 18She said to Elijah, "What do
you have against me, man of God? Did you
come to remind me of my sin[n] and kill my
son?"
19"Give me your son," Elijah replied.
He took him from her arms, carried him
to the upper room where he was staying,
and laid him on his bed. 20Then he cried[o]
out to the LORD, "LORD my God, have you
brought tragedy even on this widow I am
staying with, by causing her son to die?"
21Then he stretched[p] himself out on the
boy three times and cried out to the LORD,
"LORD my God, let this boy's life return to
him!"
22The LORD heard Elijah's cry, and the
boy's life returned to him, and he lived.
23Elijah picked up the child and carried
him down from the room into the house.
He gave him to his mother[q] and said,
"Look, your son is alive!"
24Then the woman said to Elijah, "Now
I know[r] that you are a man of God[s] and
that the word of the LORD from your mouth
is the truth."[t]

Elijah and Obadiah

18 After a long time, in the third[u] year,
the word of the LORD came to Elijah: "Go and present[v] yourself to Ahab,
and I will send rain[w] on the land." 2So Elijah went to present himself to Ahab.
Now the famine was severe[x] in Samaria,
3and Ahab had summoned Obadiah, his

17:10 [k]S Ge 24:17; Jn 4:7 **17:12** [l]2Ki 4:2 **17:14** [m]ver 1 **17:18** [n]Lk 5:8 **17:20** [o]2Ki 4:33 **17:21** [p]2Ki 4:34; Ac 20:10 **17:23** [q]Heb 11:35 **17:24** [r]Jn 16:30 [s]ver 18 [t]1Ki 22:16; Ps 119:43; Jn 17:17 **18:1** [u]1Ki 17:1; Lk 4:25 [v]ver 15 [w]S Dt 28:12 **18:2** [x]S Lev 26:26

17:12 *As surely as the LORD your God lives.* Her oath in the name of the Lord was either an accommodation to Elijah, whom she recognized as an Israelite (see notes on 5:7; 10:9), or a genuine expression of previous knowledge of and commitment to the God of Israel.

17:13 *first make a small loaf of bread for me ... then make something for yourself and your son.* As a prophet, Elijah's words are the command of the Lord. The widow is asked to give all she has to sustain the bearer of the word of God. The demand to give her all is in essence the demand of the covenant that Israel had broken.

17:14 *what the LORD, the God of Israel, says.* Elijah can tell the widow "Don't be afraid" (v. 13) because the demand of the covenant is not given without the promise of the covenant. The Lord does not ask more than he promises to give.

17:15 *did as Elijah had told her.* By an act of faith the woman received the promised blessing. Israel had forsaken the covenant and followed Baal and Asherah in search of prosperity. Now in the midst of a pagan kingdom a widow realized that trustful obedience to the word of God is the way that leads to life.

17:16 *jar of flour was not used up.* God miraculously provided for this non-Israelite who, in an act of faith in the Lord's word, had laid her life on the line. He gave her "manna" from heaven even while he was withholding food from his unfaithful people in the promised land. The warning of Dt 32:21 was being fulfilled (cf. Ro 10:19; 11:11,14).

17:18 *Did you come to remind me of my sin and kill my son?* The widow concluded that Elijah's presence in her house had called God's attention to her sin, and that the death of her son was a divine punishment for this sin. Although her sense of guilt seems to have been influenced by pagan ideas, both she and Elijah are confronted with the question: Why did the God who promised life bring death instead?

17:21 *stretched himself out on the boy three times.* The apparent intent of this physical contact was to transfer the bodily warmth and energy of the prophet to the child. Elijah's prayer, however, makes it clear that he expected the life of the child to return as an answer to prayer, not as a result of bodily contact. *let this boy's life return to him.* Moved by a faith like that of Abraham (Ro 4:17; Heb 11:19), Elijah prayed for the child's return to life so that the veracity and trustworthiness of God's word might be demonstrated.

17:22 *the boy's life returned to him.* The first instance of raising the dead recorded in Scripture. This non-Israelite widow was granted the supreme covenant blessing, the gift of life rescued from the power of death. This blessing came in the person of her son, the only hope for a widow in ancient society (see 2Ki 4:14; Ru 1:11–12; 4:15–17; Lk 7:12).

17:24 *you are a man of God.* See note on 1Sa 2:27. The widow had addressed Elijah as a man of God previously (v. 18), but now she knew in a much more experiential way that he truly was a prophet of the Lord (see note on 12:22). *the word of the LORD from your mouth is the truth.* God used this experience to convince the Phoenician widow that his word was completely reliable. Her confession was one that the Lord's own people in Israel had failed to make.

18:1 *third year.* Apparently of the drought. Later Jewish tradition indicates that the drought lasted three and a half years (cf. Lk 4:25; Jas 5:17), but that probably represents a symbolic number for a drought cut short (half of seven years; see Ge 41:27; 2Ki 8:1). *present yourself to Ahab, and I will send rain on the land.* Elijah's return is not occasioned by repentance in Israel but by the command of the Lord, who in his sovereign grace determined to reveal himself anew to his people.

palace administrator.[y] (Obadiah was a devout believer[z] in the LORD. 4 While Jezebel[a] was killing off the LORD's prophets, Obadiah had taken a hundred prophets and hidden[b] them in two caves, fifty in each, and had supplied[c] them with food and water.) 5 Ahab had said to Obadiah, "Go through the land to all the springs[d] and valleys. Maybe we can find some grass to keep the horses and mules alive so we will not have to kill any of our animals."[e] 6 So they divided the land they were to cover, Ahab going in one direction and Obadiah in another.

7 As Obadiah was walking along, Elijah met him. Obadiah recognized[f] him, bowed down to the ground, and said, "Is it really you, my lord Elijah?"

8 "Yes," he replied. "Go tell your master, 'Elijah is here.' "

9 "What have I done wrong," asked Obadiah, "that you are handing your servant over to Ahab to be put to death? 10 As surely as the LORD your God lives, there is not a nation or kingdom where my master has not sent someone to look[g] for you. And whenever a nation or kingdom claimed you were not there, he made them swear they could not find you. 11 But now you tell me to go to my master and say, 'Elijah is here.' 12 I don't know where the Spirit[h] of the LORD may carry you when I leave you. If I go and tell Ahab and he doesn't find you, he will kill me. Yet I your servant have worshiped the LORD since my youth. 13 Haven't you heard, my lord, what I did while Jezebel was killing the prophets of the LORD? I hid a hundred of the LORD's prophets in two caves, fifty in each, and supplied them with food and water. 14 And now you tell me to go to my master and say, 'Elijah is here.' He will kill me!"

15 Elijah said, "As the LORD Almighty lives, whom I serve, I will surely present[i] myself to Ahab today."

Elijah on Mount Carmel

16 So Obadiah went to meet Ahab and told him, and Ahab went to meet Elijah. 17 When he saw Elijah, he said to him, "Is that you, you troubler[j] of Israel?"

18 "I have not made trouble for Israel," Elijah replied. "But you[k] and your father's family have. You have abandoned[l] the LORD's commands and have followed the Baals. 19 Now summon[m] the people from all over Israel to meet me on Mount Carmel.[n] And bring the four hundred and fifty prophets of Baal and the four hundred prophets of Asherah, who eat at Jezebel's table."[o]

20 So Ahab sent word throughout all Israel and assembled the prophets on Mount Carmel.[p] 21 Elijah went before the people and said, "How long will you waver[q] between two opinions? If the LORD[r] is God, follow him; but if Baal is God, follow him."

But the people said nothing.

22 Then Elijah said to them, "I am the only one of the LORD's prophets left,[s] but Baal has four hundred and fifty prophets.[t] 23 Get two bulls for us. Let Baal's prophets choose one for themselves, and let them cut it into pieces and put it on the wood but not set fire to it. I will prepare the other bull and put it on the wood but not set fire to it. 24 Then you call[u] on the name of your god, and I will call on the name

18:3 [y] 1Ki 16:9 [z] Ne 7:2 **18:4** [a] 1Ki 21:23; 2Ki 9:7 [b] S 1Ki 17:3; Isa 16:3; 25:4; 32:2; Ob 1:14 [c] Jer 26:24 **18:5** [d] Jer 14:3 [e] S Ge 47:4 **18:7** [f] 2Ki 1:8; Zec 13:4 **18:10** [g] S 1Ki 17:3 **18:12** [h] 2Ki 2:16; Eze 3:14; Ac 8:39 **18:15** [i] ver 1 **18:17** [j] Jos 7:25; 1Sa 14:29; 1Ki 21:20; Jer 38:4 **18:18** [k] 1Ki 16:31, 33; 21:25 [l] S Dt 31:16 **18:19** [m] 2Ki 10:19 [n] S Jos 19:26 [o] 2Ki 9:22 **18:20** [p] 2Ki 2:25; 4:25 **18:21** [q] Jos 24:15; 2Ki 17:41; Ps 119:113; Mt 6:24 [r] ver 39; Ps 100:3; 118:27 **18:22** [s] 1Ki 19:10 [t] Jer 2:8; 23:13 **18:24** [u] S 1Sa 7:8

18:3 *Obadiah.* A common OT name, meaning "servant of the LORD." *his palace administrator.* See note on 4:6.

18:5 The famine did not move Ahab to repentance (contrast Ahab's response to the famine with that of David years earlier, 2Sa 21:1). But when his military strength seemed to be jeopardized, he scoured the land for food and water (see 10:26; according to the annals of the Assyrian ruler Shalmaneser III, Ahab could bring 2,000 chariots against him).

18:8 *tell your master, 'Elijah is here.'* This action would publicly identify Obadiah with Elijah in contrast to his previous clandestine support of the prophets sought by Jezebel (see vv. 4,13).

18:12 *I don't know where the Spirit of the LORD may carry you.* Elijah's disappearance earlier and now his sudden reappearance suggested to Obadiah that God's Spirit was miraculously transporting the prophet about (see 2Ki 2:16; cf. Eze 3:12 and note).

18:13 *Jezebel was killing the prophets.* Possibly in an attempt to please Baal so he would send rain. *prophets of the LORD.* Probably members of the communities of "prophets" that had sprung up in Israel during this time of apostasy (see note on 20:35).

18:17 *you troubler of Israel.* Ahab holds Elijah responsible for the drought and charges him with a crime against the state worthy of death (see also Jos 7:25).

18:18 *You have abandoned the LORD's commands and have followed the Baals.* The source of Israel's trouble was not Elijah or even the drought, but Ahab's breach of covenantal loyalty.

18:19 *Mount Carmel.* A high ridge next to the Mediterranean Sea, where the effects of the drought would be least apparent (see Am 1:2) and the power of Baal to nurture life would seem to be strongest. *prophets of Baal … prophets of Asherah.* See v. 29 and note. *Asherah.* See note on 14:15. *eat at Jezebel's table.* See note on 2:7.

18:21 *waver.* The Hebrew for this word is the same as that used for "danced" in v. 26 (see note there). Elijah speaks with biting irony: In her religious ambivalence Israel is but engaging in a wild and futile religious "dance." *If the LORD is God, follow him; but if Baal is God, follow him.* Elijah placed a clear choice before the people. He drew a sharp contrast between the worship of the Lord and that of Baal to eliminate the apostate idea that people could worship both deities.

18:22 *only one … left.* At least the only one to stand boldly and publicly against the king and the prophets of Baal (but see v. 4; 19:10,14; 20:13,28,35; 22:6,8; cf. 19:18 and note; Ro 11:4).

18:24 *I will call … who answers.* See note on Ps 118:5. *The god who answers by fire — he is God.* Both the Lord and Baal were said to ride the thunderstorm as their divine chariot (see Ps 104:3 and note); thunder was their voice (see Ps 29:3 – 9 and

of the LORD.[v] The god who answers by
fire[w]—he is God."
Then all the people said, "What you say
is good."
25 Elijah said to the prophets of Baal,
"Choose one of the bulls and prepare it
first, since there are so many of you. Call
on the name of your god, but do not light
the fire." 26 So they took the bull given
them and prepared it.
Then they called[x] on the name of Baal
from morning till noon. "Baal, answer
us!" they shouted. But there was no response;[y] no one answered. And they
danced around the altar they had made.
27 At noon Elijah began to taunt them.
"Shout louder!" he said. "Surely he is a
god! Perhaps he is deep in thought, or
busy, or traveling. Maybe he is sleeping
and must be awakened."[z] 28 So they shouted louder and slashed[a] themselves with
swords and spears, as was their custom,
until their blood flowed. 29 Midday passed,
and they continued their frantic prophesying until the time for the evening sacrifice.[b] But there was no response, no one
answered, no one paid attention.[c]
30 Then Elijah said to all the people,
"Come here to me." They came to him,
and he repaired the altar[d] of the LORD,
which had been torn down. 31 Elijah took
twelve stones, one for each of the tribes
descended from Jacob, to whom the word
of the LORD had come, saying, "Your name
shall be Israel."[e] 32 With the stones he built
an altar in the name[f] of the LORD, and he
dug a trench around it large enough to
hold two seahs[a] of seed. 33 He arranged[g]
the wood, cut the bull into pieces and laid
it on the wood. Then he said to them, "Fill
four large jars with water and pour it on
the offering and on the wood."
34 "Do it again," he said, and they did
it again.
"Do it a third time," he ordered, and
they did it the third time. 35 The water ran
down around the altar and even filled the
trench.
36 At the time[h] of sacrifice, the prophet
Elijah stepped forward and prayed: "LORD,
the God of Abraham,[i] Isaac and Israel, let
it be known[j] today that you are God in Israel and that I am your servant and have
done all these things at your command.[k]
37 Answer me, LORD, answer me, so these
people will know[l] that you, LORD, are God,
and that you are turning their hearts back
again."
38 Then the fire[m] of the LORD fell and
burned up the sacrifice, the wood, the
stones and the soil, and also licked up the
water in the trench.
39 When all the people saw this, they
fell prostrate[n] and cried, "The LORD—he
is God! The LORD—he is God!"[o]
40 Then Elijah commanded them, "Seize
the prophets of Baal. Don't let anyone get
away!" They seized them, and Elijah had
them brought down to the Kishon Valley[p]
and slaughtered[q] there.
41 And Elijah said to Ahab, "Go, eat and
drink, for there is the sound of a heavy
rain." 42 So Ahab went off to eat and drink,
but Elijah climbed to the top of Carmel,

a 32 That is, probably about 24 pounds or about 11 kilograms

18:24 [v]S Ge 4:26 [w]S ver 38; S Ex 19:18; S Lev 9:24 **18:26** [x]Isa 44:17; 45:20 [y]Ps 115:4-5; 135:16; Isa 41:26,28; 46:7; Jer 10:5; 1Co 8:4; 12:2 **18:27** [z]Hab 2:19 **18:28** [a]S Lev 19:28 **18:29** [b]S Ex 29:41 [c]2Ki 19:12; Isa 16:12; Jer 10:5 **18:30** [d]1Ki 19:10 **18:31** [e]S Ge 17:5; 2Ki 17:34 **18:32** [f]S Dt 18:7; Col 3:17 **18:33** [g]S Ge 22:9 **18:36** [h]S Ex 29:39, 41 [i]S Ge 24:12; S Ex 4:5; Mt 22:32 [j]S Jos 4:24; S 1Sa 17:46; S Ps 46:10 [k]Nu 16:28 **18:37** [l]S Jos 4:24 **18:38** [m]ver 24; S Ex 19:18; S Lev 9:24; 2Ki 1:10; 1Ch 21:26; 2Ch 7:1; Job 1:16 **18:39** [n]S Lev 9:24 [o]S ver 24; S Ps 46:10 **18:40** [p]S Jdg 4:7 [q]S Ex 22:20; S Dt 17:12; S 2Ki 11:18

note) and lightning ("fire") their weapon (see Ps 18:14 and note). Elijah's challenge is direct. Cf. Lev 9:24.
18:26 *danced around the altar.* The ecstatic dance was part of the pagan ritual intended to arouse the deity to perform some desired action (see note on v. 21).
18:27 *deep in thought ... sleeping.* Elijah ridicules, but as he does he shows knowledge of the Baal myths that depict the gods as having very human characteristics. *busy.* Perhaps a euphemism for relieving himself.
18:28 *until their blood flowed.* Self-inflicted wounds (causing blood to flow) were symbolic of self-sacrifice as an extreme method of arousing the deity to action. Such mutilation of the body was strictly forbidden in the Mosaic law (Lev 19:28; Dt 14:1).
18:29 *frantic prophesying.* Indicative of ecstatic raving, in which the ritual reached its climax (see notes on 1Sa 10:5; 18:10). *time for the evening sacrifice.* See Ex 29:38–41; Nu 28:3–8. *no response.* Dramatic demonstration of Baal's impotence (see Ps 115:5–8; 135:15–18; Jer 10:5).
18:30 *altar of the LORD, which had been torn down.* It is possible that the altar had been built by people of the northern ten tribes after the division of the kingdom (see note on 3:2) and that it had been destroyed by the agents of Jezebel (vv. 4,13; 19:10,14).
18:31 *twelve stones, one for each of the tribes.* In this way Elijah called attention to the covenant unity of Israel as the people of God in spite of her political division. What was about to happen concerned the entire nation, not just the northern ten tribes.
18:33 *water.* By drenching the whole installation Elijah showed to all that he was using no tricks.
18:36 *prayed.* Elijah's simple but earnest prayer stands in sharp contrast to the frantic shouts and "dancing" and self-mutilation of the Baal prophets. *God of Abraham, Isaac and Israel.* An appeal to the Lord to remember his ancient covenant with the patriarchs, and to Israel to remember all that the Lord has done for her since the days of her ancestors.
18:38 *fire of the LORD fell.* See note on v. 24.
18:40 *Kishon Valley.* The Kishon River flows below Mount Carmel (see map, p. 2522, at the end of this study Bible). *slaughtered there.* Elijah, acting on the authority of the Lord, who sent him, carried out the sentence pronounced in the Mosaic law for prophets of pagan deities (Dt 13:13–18; 17:2–5).
18:41 *sound of a heavy rain.* Now that Baal worship has been struck a devastating blow, there is the promise of rain (see 17:1). Significantly, Ahab takes no action—either to carry out the Mosaic sentence or to halt Elijah. He still wavers between two opinions (see v. 21 and note).
18:42 *Elijah ... bent down to the ground and put his face between his knees.* Now that the people had confessed that the

bent down to the ground and put his face
between his knees.[r]
43 "Go and look toward the sea," he told
his servant. And he went up and looked.
"There is nothing there," he said.
Seven times Elijah said, "Go back."
44 The seventh time[s] the servant reported, "A cloud[t] as small as a man's hand is
rising from the sea."
So Elijah said, "Go and tell Ahab, 'Hitch
up your chariot and go down before the
rain stops you.' "
45 Meanwhile, the sky grew black with
clouds, the wind rose, a heavy rain[u]
started falling and Ahab rode off to Jezreel.[v] 46 The power[w] of the LORD came on Elijah and, tucking his cloak into his belt,[x] he
ran ahead of Ahab all the way to Jezreel.

Elijah Flees to Horeb

19 Now Ahab told Jezebel[y] everything
Elijah had done and how he had
killed[z] all the prophets with the sword. 2 So
Jezebel sent a messenger to Elijah to say,
"May the gods deal with me, be it ever so
severely,[a] if by this time tomorrow I do not
make your life like that of one of them."[b]
3 Elijah was afraid[a] and ran[c] for his life.[d]
When he came to Beersheba[e] in Judah,
he left his servant there, 4 while he himself went a day's journey into the wilderness. He came to a broom bush,[f] sat down
under it and prayed that he might die. "I
have had enough, LORD," he said. "Take
my life;[g] I am no better than my ancestors." 5 Then he lay down under the bush
and fell asleep.[h]
All at once an angel[i] touched him and
said, "Get up and eat." 6 He looked around,
and there by his head was some bread
baked over hot coals, and a jar of water. He ate and drank and then lay down
again.
7 The angel of the LORD came back a second time and touched him and said, "Get
up and eat, for the journey is too much
for you." 8 So he got up and ate and drank.
Strengthened by that food, he traveled forty[j] days and forty nights until he reached
Horeb,[k] the mountain of God. 9 There he
went into a cave[l] and spent the night.

The LORD Appears to Elijah

And the word of the LORD came to him:
"What are you doing here, Elijah?"[m]
10 He replied, "I have been very zealous[n] for the LORD God Almighty. The Israelites have rejected your covenant,[o] torn
down your altars,[p] and put your prophets
to death with the sword. I am the only
one left,[q] and now they are trying to kill
me too."
11 The LORD said, "Go out and stand on
the mountain[r] in the presence of the LORD,
for the LORD is about to pass by."[s]

18:42 [r] S 1Sa 12:17; Jas 5:18 **18:44** [s] S Jos 6:15 [t] Lk 12:54 **18:45** [u] S 1Ki 8:36; Job 37:13 [v] S 1Sa 29:1; S Hos 1:4 **18:46** [w] S Jdg 3:10; S 1Sa 11:6; Lk 1:35; 4:14 [x] 2Ki 4:29; 9:1 **19:1** [y] 1Ki 16:31 [z] S Ex 22:20 **19:2** [a] S Ru 1:17 [b] Ps 13:4; Jer 20:10; 26:21; 36:26 **19:3** [c] S Ge 31:21 [d] S Ge 19:17 [e] S Jos 19:2 **19:4** [f] Job 30:4 [g] S Nu 11:15; Job 6:9; 7:16; 10:1; Ps 69:19; Jer 20:18; Jnh 4:8 **19:5** [h] Ge 28:11 [i] S Ge 16:7 **19:8** [j] Ex 24:18; Mt 4:2 [k] S Ex 3:1 **19:9** [l] S Ex 33:22 [m] S Ge 3:9 **19:10** [n] S Nu 25:13; Ac 22:3; Gal 4:18 [o] S Dt 31:16 [p] 1Ki 18:30 [q] 1Ki 18:4,22; Jer 5:11; 9:2; Ro 11:3* **19:11** [r] Ex 34:2; Mt 17:1-3 [s] Ex 33:19

[a] 3 Or *Elijah saw*

Lord alone is God, Elijah prayed for the covenant curse to be lifted (see note on 17:1) by the coming of rain (see 8:35; 2Ch 7:13–14).

18:43 *Seven times.* The number symbolic of completeness (see note on Ge 5:5).

18:44 *rising from the sea.* Appearing on the western horizon above the Mediterranean.

18:46 *ran ahead of Ahab all the way to Jezreel.* Divinely energized by extraordinary strength, Elijah ran before Ahab's chariot to Jezreel (a distance of about 16 miles). This dramatic scene, with the Lord's prophet running before the king and the Lord himself racing behind him riding his mighty thundercloud chariot (see note on v. 24), served as a powerful appeal to Ahab to break once for all with Baal and henceforth to rule as the servant of the Lord.

19:1 *Jezebel.* Ahab's wife and a worshiper of Melqart, the local manifestion of Baal in Tyre, Phoenicia (see notes on 16:25, 31–32; 18:13).

19:2 *May the gods deal with me, be it ever so severely.* A curse formula (see note on 1Sa 3:17). *them.* The dead prophets of Baal (v. 1).

19:3 *Elijah was afraid and ran for his life.* In spite of Elijah's great triumph in the trial on Mount Carmel and the dramatic demonstration that his God is the Lord of heaven and earth and the source of Israel's blessings, Jezebel is undaunted. Hers is no empty threat, and Ahab has shown that he is either unwilling or unable to restrain her. So Elijah knows that one of the main sources of Israel's present apostasy is still spewing out its poison and that his own life is in danger. *Beersheba.* The southernmost city in Judah (see notes on Ge 21:31; Am 5:5; see also Jdg 20:1).

19:4 *broom bush.* A desert shrub, sometimes large enough to offer some shade. *prayed that he might die.* Cf. Jnh 4:3,8. Elijah concluded that his work was fruitless and consequently that life was not worth living. He had lost his confidence in the triumph of the kingdom of God and was withdrawing from the arena of conflict.

19:7 *angel of the LORD.* See note on Ge 16:7. God in his mercy provided sustenance and rest for his discouraged servant. *the journey is too much for you.* Evidently Elijah had already determined to go to Mount Horeb, where God had established his covenant with his people. There is no indication that the Lord had instructed him to do this as he had previously directed him to go to Kerith (17:2–3) and to Zarephath (17:8–9) and to meet Ahab (18:1).

19:8 *forty days and forty nights.* Sustained by the Lord as Moses had been for the same length of time on Mount Sinai (Ex 24:18; 34:28) and as Jesus would be in the wilderness (Mt 4:2,11). *Horeb, the mountain of God.* Probably an alternative name for Mount Sinai (see Ex 3:1; 19:1–3), located in the desert apparently about 250 miles south of Beersheba.

19:9 *What are you doing here, Elijah?* The question implies that Elijah had come to Sinai for his own misguided reasons and not because the Lord had sent him.

19:10 Elijah did not give a direct answer to the Lord's question but implied that the work the Lord had begun centuries earlier with the establishment of the Sinaitic covenant had now come to nothing. Whereas Moses had interceded for Israel when they sinned with the golden calf (Ex 32:11–13), Elijah condemned the Israelites for breaking the covenant, and bitterly complained over the fruitlessness of his own work. *only one left.* See note on 18:22.

LIVES OF **ELIJAH AND ELISHA**

The life-and-death struggle with Baalism, acute in Elijah's day, intensified under Elisha and culminated in bloody purges of the priests of Baal. Ahab's line was overthrown, and reforms were promulgated by Jehu.

Elijah's rugged figure became a model of the ideal prophet in Israel. Jesus fulfilled 40 days and nights of desert fasting, as Elijah had done; many believed he was a reincarnated Elijah (see 1Ki 19:8; Mt 4:2; 16:14 and notes).

Elisha also became a model for the prophets. Jesus' miracle of feeding the 5,000 was similar to Elisha's feeding 100 men with 20 barley loaves.

ELIJAH

Elijah of Tishbe was instrumental in Israel's reaction to Baalism. Jezebel of Tyre was symbolic of the nation's corruption.

1 Fed by ravens

2 Miracle of the widow's jar of oil

3 After the triumph on Mount Carmel, Elijah ordered the people to slaughter the prophets of Baal.

4 Elijah was so discouraged that he wanted to die. Fleeing to Sinai, he was told to anoint a new generation of political and religious leaders.

5 At Naboth's vineyard in Jezreel, God's servant confronted Jezebel's puppet, the king.

ELISHA

Elisha, like Elijah, performed miracles and was called "the chariots and horsemen of Israel" (2Ki 13:14).

1 Born west of the Jordan, the prophet frequented shrines at Mount Carmel and Gilgal. Dothan, a flourishing town in this period, was probably his residence.

2 Spring healed

3 Jeered by youths

4 Elisha journeyed from Mount Carmel to Shunem to raise a child from the dead, as Elijah had done at Zarephath.

5 Vision of chariots of fire

6 Elisha and his servant anointed Hazael and Jehu, completing Elijah's commission at Horeb.

Then a great and powerful wind[t] tore the mountains apart and shattered[u] the rocks before the LORD, but the LORD was not in the wind. After the wind there was an earthquake, but the LORD was not in the earthquake. 12 After the earthquake came a fire,[v] but the LORD was not in the fire. And after the fire came a gentle whisper.[w] 13 When Elijah heard it, he pulled his cloak over his face[x] and went out and stood at the mouth of the cave.

Then a voice said to him, "What are you doing here, Elijah?"

14 He replied, "I have been very zealous for the LORD God Almighty. The Israelites have rejected your covenant, torn down your altars, and put your prophets to death with the sword. I am the only one left,[y] and now they are trying to kill me too."

15 The LORD said to him, "Go back the way you came, and go to the Desert of Damascus. When you get there, anoint Hazael[z] king over Aram. 16 Also, anoint[a] Jehu son of Nimshi king over Israel, and anoint Elisha[b] son of Shaphat from Abel Meholah[c] to succeed you as prophet. 17 Jehu will put to death any who escape the sword of Hazael,[d] and Elisha will put to death any who escape the sword of Jehu.[e] 18 Yet I reserve[f] seven thousand in Israel—all whose knees have not bowed down to Baal and whose mouths have not kissed[g] him."

19:11 [t] S Ex 14:21; S 2Ki 2:1 [u] Na 1:6 **19:12** [v] S Ex 3:2 [w] ver 11; S 1Sa 14:6; Job 4:16; Zec 4:6; 2Co 12:9 **19:13** [x] Ex 3:6 **19:14** [y] 1Ki 18:22; Ro 11:3* **19:15** [z] 2Ki 8:7-15 **19:16** [a] 2Ki 9:1-3,6 [b] ver 21; 2Ki 2:1; 3:11 [c] S Jdg 7:22 **19:17** [d] 2Ki 8:12,29; 10:32; 12:17; 13:3,7,22; Am 1:4 [e] Jer 48:44 **19:18** [f] Ro 11:4* [g] Hos 13:2 **19:19** [h] S Ge 41:42; 2Ki 2:8,14 **19:20** [i] Lk 9:61 **19:21** [j] S 1Sa 6:14 [k] S ver 16 **20:1** [l] S 1Ki 15:18

The Call of Elisha

19 So Elijah went from there and found Elisha son of Shaphat. He was plowing with twelve yoke of oxen, and he himself was driving the twelfth pair. Elijah went up to him and threw his cloak[h] around him. 20 Elisha then left his oxen and ran after Elijah. "Let me kiss my father and mother goodbye,"[i] he said, "and then I will come with you."

"Go back," Elijah replied. "What have I done to you?"

21 So Elisha left him and went back. He took his yoke of oxen[j] and slaughtered them. He burned the plowing equipment to cook the meat and gave it to the people, and they ate. Then he set out to follow Elijah and became his servant.[k]

Ben-Hadad Attacks Samaria

20 Now Ben-Hadad[l] king of Aram mustered his entire army. Accompanied by thirty-two kings with their

19:12 *gentle whisper.* In the symbolism of these occurrences (vv. 11–12) the Lord appears to be telling Elijah that although his servant's indictment of Israel was a call for God to judge his people with windstorm, earthquake and fire, it was not God's will to do so now. Elijah must return to continue God's mission to his people, and Elisha is to carry it on for another generation (v. 16).
19:13 *What are you doing here, Elijah?* After demonstrating his presence in the gentle whisper rather than in the wind, earthquake or fire, the Lord gave Elijah an opportunity to revise the answer he had previously given to the same question (vv. 9–10).
19:14 Elijah's unrevised answer demonstrated that he did not understand the significance of the divine revelation he had just witnessed.
19:15 *The LORD said to him.* Giving instructions to Elijah that revealed his sovereign power over people and nations. Even though Israel would experience divine judgment through Hazael, Jehu and Elisha, God would continue to preserve a remnant faithful to himself among the people. *go to the Desert of Damascus.* Apparently Elijah is to go back by way of the road east of the Dead Sea and the Jordan. As it turns out, all three anointings take place east of the Jordan, though it is Elisha who effects the anointing of the two kings. *anoint.* Appears to mean here no more than "designate as divinely appointed." This anointing was actually done by Elijah's successor Elisha (see 2Ki 8:7–15). *Hazael.* Subsequently became a serious threat to Israel during the reigns of Joram, Jehu and Jehoahaz (see 2Ki 8:28–29; 10:32–33; 12:17–18; 13:3,22). There are references to him on ivory fragments from Arslan Tash (north Syria) and Nimrud (Assyria). Tiglath-Pileser III, king of Assyria, called Damascus (Aram) the "House of Hazael."
19:16 *anoint Jehu.* Jehu was a military commander under Ahab and Joram, Ahab's son (2Ki 9:5–6). He was anointed king over Israel by a "man from the company of the prophets" at the instruction of Elisha (2Ki 9:1–16), with the mandate to destroy the house of Ahab. *Elisha.* As with Elijah (see note on 17:1), Elisha's name (meaning "God is salvation" or "God saves") was the essence of his ministry. His name evokes memory of Joshua ("The LORD saves"). Elijah is given someone to finish his work, just as Moses was, and Elisha channels the covenant blessings to the faithful in Israel just as Joshua brought Israel into the promised land (see the account of Elisha's ministry in 2Ki 2:19—8:15; 9:1–3; 13:14–20). In the NT John the Baptist ("Elijah," Mt 11:14; 17:12–13) was followed by Jesus ("Joshua"; see NIV text note on Mt 1:21) to complete God's saving work. *son of Shaphat.* Shaphat means "He judges," which is also in accordance with Elisha's ministry. *Abel Meholah.* See map, p. 557.
19:17 *Jehu will put to death any who escape the sword of Hazael.* See 2Ki 9:24. *Elisha will put to death any who escape the sword of Jehu.* How this may have been fulfilled we are not told, but see 2Ki 2:24; 8:1 (see also Hos 6:5).
19:18 *seven thousand.* A round number, no doubt symbolic of the fullness or completeness of the divinely preserved godly remnant (Ro 11:2–4). In any case Elijah had been mistaken in his conclusion that he alone had remained faithful (see vv. 10,14; 18:22 and note). *not kissed him.* See Hos 13:2.
19:19 *threw his cloak around him.* Thus designating Elisha as his successor (see note on v. 16).
19:21 *slaughtered them ... burned the plowing equipment.* Elisha's break with his past vocation was complete, though he obviously came from a wealthy family. *servant.* In Hebrew the same designation as used for Joshua's relationship to Moses ("aide," Ex 24:13; 33:11).
20:1 *Ben-Hadad king of Aram.* Chronological considerations suggest that this was Ben-Hadad II (see note on 2Ki 8:7), either a son or a grandson of Ben-Hadad I, who had begun to rule Aram as early as 895 BC (see notes on 15:9–10,18–20,33). The events of this chapter span parts of

horses and chariots, he went up and besieged Samaria[m] and attacked it. 2 He sent messengers into the city to Ahab king of Israel, saying, "This is what Ben-Hadad says: 3 'Your silver and gold are mine, and the best of your wives and children are mine.' "

4 The king of Israel answered, "Just as you say, my lord the king. I and all I have are yours."

5 The messengers came again and said, "This is what Ben-Hadad says: 'I sent to demand your silver and gold, your wives and your children. 6 But about this time tomorrow I am going to send my officials to search your palace and the houses of your officials. They will seize everything you value and carry it away.' "

7 The king of Israel summoned all the elders[n] of the land and said to them, "See how this man is looking for trouble![o] When he sent for my wives and my children, my silver and my gold, I did not refuse him."

8 The elders and the people all answered, "Don't listen to him or agree to his demands."

9 So he replied to Ben-Hadad's messengers, "Tell my lord the king, 'Your servant will do all you demanded the first time, but this demand I cannot meet.' " They left and took the answer back to Ben-Hadad.

10 Then Ben-Hadad sent another message to Ahab: "May the gods deal with me, be it ever so severely, if enough dust[p] remains in Samaria to give each of my men a handful."

11 The king of Israel answered, "Tell him: 'One who puts on his armor should not boast[q] like one who takes it off.' "

12 Ben-Hadad heard this message while he and the kings were drinking[r] in their tents,[a] and he ordered his men: "Prepare to attack." So they prepared to attack the city.

Ahab Defeats Ben-Hadad

13 Meanwhile a prophet[s] came to Ahab king of Israel and announced, "This is what the LORD says: 'Do you see this vast army? I will give it into your hand today, and then you will know[t] that I am the LORD.' "

14 "But who will do this?" asked Ahab.

The prophet replied, "This is what the LORD says: 'The junior officers under the provincial commanders will do it.' "

"And who will start[u] the battle?" he asked.

The prophet answered, "You will."

15 So Ahab summoned the 232 junior officers under the provincial commanders. Then he assembled the rest of the Israelites, 7,000 in all. 16 They set out at noon while Ben-Hadad and the 32 kings allied with him were in their tents getting drunk.[v] 17 The junior officers under the provincial commanders went out first.

Now Ben-Hadad had dispatched scouts, who reported, "Men are advancing from Samaria."

18 He said, "If they have come out for peace, take them alive; if they have come out for war, take them alive."

19 The junior officers under the provincial commanders marched out of the city with the army behind them 20 and each one struck down his opponent. At that, the Arameans fled, with the Israelites in pursuit. But Ben-Hadad king of Aram escaped on horseback with some of his horsemen. 21 The king of Israel advanced

20:1 m S 1Ki 13:32
20:7 n 1Sa 11:3 o 2Ki 5:7
20:10 p S 2Sa 22:43
20:11 q Pr 27:1; Jer 9:23; Am 2:14
20:12 r S 1Ki 16:9
20:13 s S Jdg 6:8 t S Ex 6:7
20:14 u S Jdg 1:1
20:16 v S 1Ki 16:9

[a] 12 Or *in Sukkoth*; also in verse 16

two years (see vv. 22–26), followed by three years of peace between Israel and Aram (see 22:1). Ahab died at the conclusion of the three years of peace in a battle against the Arameans (22:37) in 853. This means that the events of this chapter are to be dated c. 857. *thirty-two kings.* Tribal chieftains or city-state kings who were vassals of Ben-Hadad II (ruled c. 860–843). *Samaria.* See note on 16:24.

20:4 *I and all I have are yours.* Ahab's submission to Ben-Hadad's demand suggests that Israel saw little hope for the possibility of a military victory over the Aramean forces. The negotiated settlement would end the siege on Samaria, spare Ahab's life and avoid the plundering of the city.

20:6 *I am going to send my officials to search your palace and the houses of your officials.* Ben-Hadad's new demand required the surrender of the city to his forces.

20:9 *this demand I cannot meet.* Ahab replied in language conceding Ben-Hadad's superiority ("my lord the king, 'Your servant …'") but was adamant in refusing to surrender the city.

20:10 *May the gods deal with me, be it ever so severely.* A curse formula (see note on 1Sa 3:17).

20:11 *One who puts on his armor should not boast like one who takes it off.* A saying similar to the familiar "Don't count your chickens before they hatch."

20:13 *you will know that I am the LORD.* Although Ahab had not sought God's help in the crisis confronting the city, the Lord graciously chose to reveal himself yet another time (see 18:36–37) to the king and people, this time through a deliverance.

20:14 *junior officers under the provincial commanders.* See note on 16:27. Organizational details of the provincial government of the northern kingdom are unknown.

20:15 *232 junior officers … 7,000 in all.* Not a large military force (though a significant number for a city under siege) but one of fitting size for demonstrating that the imminent victory was from the Lord rather than from Israel's own military superiority (cf. Jdg 7:2).

20:20 *each one struck down his opponent.* Apparently they were met by a small advance force like their own (see 2Sa 2:15–16). *escaped on horseback with some of his horsemen.* Since fighting on horseback did not come until later, reference must be to chariot horses and charioteers. After their defeat, the Arameans seem to have withdrawn to Damascus.

and overpowered the horses and chariots
and inflicted heavy losses on the Arameans.
22 Afterward, the prophet[w] came to the
king of Israel and said, "Strengthen your
position and see what must be done, because next spring[x] the king of Aram will
attack you again."
23 Meanwhile, the officials of the king
of Aram advised him, "Their gods are
gods[y] of the hills. That is why they were
too strong for us. But if we fight them
on the plains, surely we will be stronger
than they. 24 Do this: Remove all the kings
from their commands and replace them
with other officers. 25 You must also raise
an army like the one you lost—horse for
horse and chariot for chariot—so we can
fight Israel on the plains. Then surely we
will be stronger than they." He agreed with
them and acted accordingly.
26 The next spring[z] Ben-Hadad mustered
the Arameans and went up to Aphek[a] to
fight against Israel. 27 When the Israelites
were also mustered and given provisions,
they marched out to meet them. The Israelites camped opposite them like two
small flocks of goats, while the Arameans
covered the countryside.[b]
28 The man of God came up and told the
king of Israel, "This is what the LORD says:
'Because the Arameans think the LORD is
a god of the hills and not a god[c] of the
valleys, I will deliver this vast army into
your hands, and you will know[d] that I am
the LORD.' "

20:22 [w] S Jdg 6:8 [x] S 2Sa 11:1 **20:23** [y] ver 28; Isa 36:20; Ro 1:21-23 **20:26** [z] S 2Sa 11:1 [a] ver 30; S 1Sa 4:1; 2Ki 13:17 **20:27** [b] Jdg 6:6; S 1Sa 13:6 **20:28** [c] S ver 23 [d] S Ex 6:7; Jer 16:19-21 **20:30** [e] S ver 26 [f] Ps 62:4; Isa 26:21; 30:13 [g] 1Ki 22:25 **20:31** [h] Job 41:3 [i] S Ge 37:34 **20:34** [j] 1Ki 15:20 [k] S Ge 10:22 [l] 2Sa 8:6 [m] S Ge 14:15; Jer 49:23-27 [n] S Ex 23:32

29 For seven days they camped opposite
each other, and on the seventh day the
battle was joined. The Israelites inflicted a hundred thousand casualties on the
Aramean foot soldiers in one day. 30 The
rest of them escaped to the city of Aphek,[e]
where the wall collapsed[f] on twenty-
seven thousand of them. And Ben-
Hadad fled to the city and hid[g] in an inner
room.
31 His officials said to him, "Look, we
have heard that the kings of Israel are merciful.[h] Let us go to the king of Israel with
sackcloth[i] around our waists and ropes
around our heads. Perhaps he will spare
your life."
32 Wearing sackcloth around their waists
and ropes around their heads, they went
to the king of Israel and said, "Your servant Ben-Hadad says: 'Please let me live.' "
The king answered, "Is he still alive? He
is my brother."
33 The men took this as a good sign and
were quick to pick up his word. "Yes, your
brother Ben-Hadad!" they said.
"Go and get him," the king said. When
Ben-Hadad came out, Ahab had him come
up into his chariot.
34 "I will return the cities[j] my father
took from your father," Ben-Hadad[k] offered. "You may set up your own market
areas[l] in Damascus,[m] as my father did in Samaria."
Ahab said, "On the basis of a treaty[n] I
will set you free." So he made a treaty with
him, and let him go.

20:22 *the king of Aram will attack you again.* The anonymous prophet (see v. 13) warned Ahab against undue self-confidence. The prophet's announcement of an impending renewed attack by Ben-Hadad should have driven Ahab to more complete reliance on the God who had revealed himself on Mount Carmel and in the recent military victory.

20:23 *gods of the hills.* An expression of the pagan idea that a deity's power extended only over the limited area of his particular jurisdiction. *That is why they were too strong for us.* The Arameans believed that the outcome of military conflicts depended on the relative strength of the gods of the opposing forces rather than on the inherent strength of the two armies. For this reason, their strategy was to fight the next battle in a way that advantageously maximized the supposed strengths and weaknesses of the deities involved.

20:26 *Aphek.* Presumably the Aphek located a few miles east of the Sea of Galilee (see map, p. 557). The battle apparently took place in the Jordan Valley near the juncture of the Yarmuk and Jordan rivers (see map, p. 594).

20:28 *man of God.* Apparently the same prophet mentioned in vv. 13,22. *you will know that I am the LORD.* See note on v. 13. God will again demonstrate that he is the sovereign ruler over all nature and history and that the pagan nature deities are powerless before him.

20:29 *a hundred thousand casualties.* For the problem of apparently excessive numbers of people in Biblical narrative, see Introduction to Numbers: Special Problem.

20:30 *wall collapsed.* The God of Israel not only gave Israel's army a victory in battle but also caused an additional disaster to fall on the Aramean army. *twenty-seven thousand.* See note on v. 29.

20:31 *kings of Israel are merciful.* The Arameans recognized that Israel's kings were different from, e.g., the ruthless Assyrian kings. *sackcloth . . . ropes.* Perhaps here symbolic of humility and submission.

20:32 *Your servant.* In the diplomatic language of the time, Ben-Hadad acknowledged his inferiority and subordination to Ahab by designating himself Ahab's servant (see note on v. 9). *my brother.* Ahab disregarded Ben-Hadad's concession and responded in terminology used by rulers who considered themselves equals (see 9:13 and note). In doing this, Ahab gave much more than Ben-Hadad had asked or expected.

20:33 *come up into his chariot.* Not the treatment normally accorded a defeated military opponent.

20:34 *cities my father took from your father.* Perhaps Ramoth Gilead (see 22:3) along with some of the cities Ben-Hadad I had taken from Baasha (15:20) at an even earlier time. *your own market areas.* Outlets for engaging in the lucrative international trade—a distinct economic advantage; usually such privileges were a jealously guarded local monopoly. *made a treaty with him, and let him go.* A parity treaty (a peace treaty between equals) that included among its provisions the political and trade agreements proposed by Ben-Hadad. In all this, the Lord was not consulted.

A Prophet Condemns Ahab

35 By the word of the LORD one of the company of the prophets[o] said to his companion, "Strike me with your weapon," but he refused.[p]

36 So the prophet said, "Because you have not obeyed the LORD, as soon as you leave me a lion[q] will kill you." And after the man went away, a lion found him and killed him.

37 The prophet found another man and said, "Strike me, please." So the man struck him and wounded him. 38 Then the prophet went and stood by the road waiting for the king. He disguised himself with his headband down over his eyes. 39 As the king passed by, the prophet called out to him, "Your servant went into the thick of the battle, and someone came to me with a captive and said, 'Guard this man. If he is missing, it will be your life for his life,[r] or you must pay a talent[a] of silver.' 40 While your servant was busy here and there, the man disappeared."

"That is your sentence,"[s] the king of Israel said. "You have pronounced it yourself."

41 Then the prophet quickly removed the headband from his eyes, and the king of Israel recognized him as one of the prophets. 42 He said to the king, "This is what the LORD says: 'You[t] have set free a man I had determined should die.[b][u] Therefore it is your life for his life,[v] your people for his people.' " 43 Sullen and angry,[w] the king of Israel went to his palace in Samaria.

Naboth's Vineyard

21 Some time later there was an incident involving a vineyard belonging to Naboth[x] the Jezreelite. The vineyard was in Jezreel,[y] close to the palace of Ahab king of Samaria. 2 Ahab said to Naboth, "Let me have your vineyard to use for a vegetable garden, since it is close to my palace. In exchange I will give you a better vineyard or, if you prefer, I will pay you whatever it is worth."

3 But Naboth replied, "The LORD forbid that I should give you the inheritance[z] of my ancestors."

4 So Ahab went home, sullen and angry[a] because Naboth the Jezreelite had said, "I will not give you the inheritance of my ancestors." He lay on his bed sulking and refused[b] to eat.

5 His wife Jezebel came in and asked him, "Why are you so sullen? Why won't you eat?"

6 He answered her, "Because I said to Naboth the Jezreelite, 'Sell me your vineyard; or if you prefer, I will give you another vineyard in its place.' But he said, 'I will not give you my vineyard.' "

7 Jezebel his wife said, "Is this how you act as king over Israel? Get up and eat!

20:35 [o] S 1Sa 10:5; Am 7:14 [p] S 1Ki 13:21 **20:36** [q] 1Ki 13:24 **20:39** [r] S Jos 2:14 **20:40** [s] 2Sa 12:5; S 14:13 **20:42** [t] S 2Sa 12:7 [u] Jer 48:10 [v] S Jos 2:14 **20:43** [w] 1Ki 21:4 **21:1** [x] 2Ki 9:21 [y] S 1Sa 29:1; 2Ki 10:1 **21:3** [z] S Lev 25:23 **21:4** [a] 1Ki 20:43 [b] 1Sa 28:23

[a] *39* That is, about 75 pounds or about 34 kilograms
[b] *42* The Hebrew term refers to the irrevocable giving over of things or persons to the LORD, often by totally destroying them.

20:35 *company of the prophets.* See 2Ki 2:3,5,7,15; 4:1,38; 5:22; 6:1; 9:1. This phrase is traditionally rendered "sons of the prophets," but the Hebrew for "sons" here refers to members of a group, not to male children. Companies of prophets were apparently religious communities that sprang up in the face of general indifference and apostasy for the purpose of mutual edification and the cultivation of the experience of God. It seems likely that they were known as prophets because their religious practices (sometimes ecstatic) were called prophesying (see 18:29; Nu 11:25–27; 1Sa 10:5–6, 10–11; 18:10; 19:20–24)—to be distinguished from "prophet" in the sense of one bringing ("prophesying") a word from the Lord. The relationship of the Lord's great prophets (such as Samuel, Elijah and Elisha) to these communities was understandably a close one, the Lord's prophets probably being viewed as their spiritual mentors.
20:36 *as soon as you leave me a lion will kill you.* A penalty reminiscent of what happened to the man of God from Judah (13:23–24).
20:39 *talent.* See NIV text note. Because few soldiers could have paid such a large sum, it would appear to Ahab that the man's life was at stake.
20:40 *That is your sentence.* Ahab refused to grant clemency. Little did he know that he was pronouncing his own death sentence (cf. the similar technique used by Nathan the prophet, 2Sa 12:1–12).
20:42 *a man I had determined should die.* See NIV text note and notes on Lev 27:28; Jos 6:17. It is not clear whether Ahab violated a previous revelation or erred by simply neglecting to inquire of the Lord before releasing Ben-Hadad. In any case, the Lord had given Ben-Hadad into Ahab's hand (see v. 28), and Ahab was responsible to the Lord for his custody. *your life for his life, your people for his people.* Because Ahab sinned in his official capacity as king, the sentence fell not only on Ahab personally but also on the people of the northern kingdom. Ahab died in battle against the Arameans (22:29–39), and Israel was severely humiliated by them during the reigns of Jehu and Jehoahaz (2Ki 10:32; 13:3).
21:1 *close to the palace of Ahab.* Ahab maintained a residence in Jezreel, in addition to his official palace in Samaria (see 18:45; 2Ki 9:30). *Samaria.* The entire northern kingdom is here represented by its capital city (see note on 16:24).
21:2 *Let me have your vineyard.* Because royal power in Israel was limited by covenantal law (see Dt 17:14–20; 1Sa 10:25), Ahab was unable simply to confiscate privately held land, as was customary with Canaanite kings (see note on v. 7; see also 1Sa 8:9–17).
21:3 Naboth's refusal to dispose of his land was based on the conviction that the land was the Lord's, that he had granted a perpetual lease to each Israelite family and that this lease was to be jealously preserved as the family's permanent inheritance in the promised land.
21:7 *Is this how you act as king over Israel?* A sarcastic remark of incredulity spoken by one accustomed to the despotic practices of the Phoenician and Canaanite kings, who would not hesitate a moment to use their power to satisfy personal interests (contrast the attitude and practice of Samuel in the exercise of his civil power, 1Sa 12:3–4).

Cheer up. I'll get you the vineyard[c] of Naboth the Jezreelite."
8 So she wrote letters[d] in Ahab's name,
placed his seal[e] on them, and sent them
to the elders and nobles who lived in Naboth's city with him. 9 In those letters she
wrote:

"Proclaim a day of fasting and seat
Naboth in a prominent place among
the people. 10 But seat two scoundrels[f]
opposite him and have them bring
charges that he has cursed[g] both God
and the king. Then take him out and
stone him to death."

11 So the elders and nobles who lived
in Naboth's city did as Jezebel directed
in the letters she had written to them.
12 They proclaimed a fast[h] and seated Naboth in a prominent place among the people. 13 Then two scoundrels came and sat
opposite him and brought charges against
Naboth before the people, saying, "Naboth has cursed both God and the king."
So they took him outside the city and
stoned him to death.[i] 14 Then they sent
word to Jezebel: "Naboth has been stoned
to death."
15 As soon as Jezebel heard that Naboth had been stoned to death, she said to
Ahab, "Get up and take possession of the
vineyard[j] of Naboth the Jezreelite that he
refused to sell you. He is no longer alive,
but dead." 16 When Ahab heard that Naboth was dead, he got up and went down
to take possession of Naboth's vineyard.
17 Then the word of the LORD came to
Elijah the Tishbite: 18 "Go down to meet
Ahab king of Israel, who rules in Samaria.
He is now in Naboth's vineyard, where he
has gone to take possession of it. 19 Say
to him, 'This is what the LORD says: Have
you not murdered a man and seized his
property?'[k] Then say to him, 'This is what
the LORD says: In the place where dogs
licked up Naboth's blood,[l] dogs[m] will lick
up your blood—yes, yours!'"
20 Ahab said to Elijah, "So you have
found me, my enemy!"[n]
"I have found you," he answered, "because you have sold[o] yourself to do evil
in the eyes of the LORD. 21 He says, 'I am
going to bring disaster on you. I will wipe
out your descendants and cut off from
Ahab every last male[p] in Israel—slave
or free.[a][q] 22 I will make your house[r] like
that of Jeroboam son of Nebat and that of
Baasha son of Ahijah, because you have
aroused my anger and have caused Israel
to sin.'[s]
23 "And also concerning Jezebel the LORD
says: 'Dogs[t] will devour Jezebel by the
wall of[b] Jezreel.'
24 "Dogs[u] will eat those belonging to
Ahab who die in the city, and the birds[v]
will feed on those who die in the country."
25 (There was never[w] anyone like Ahab,
who sold himself to do evil in the eyes of
the LORD, urged on by Jezebel his wife.
26 He behaved in the vilest manner by going after idols, like the Amorites[x] the LORD
drove out before Israel.)
27 When Ahab heard these words, he
tore his clothes, put on sackcloth[y] and fasted. He lay in sackcloth and went around
meekly.[z]
28 Then the word of the LORD came to
Elijah the Tishbite: 29 "Have you noticed
how Ahab has humbled himself before
me? Because he has humbled[a] himself, I
will not bring this disaster in his day,[b] but
I will bring it on his house in the days of
his son."[c]

21:7 [c] S 1Sa 8:14
21:8 [d] 2Sa 11:14 [e] S Ge 38:18
21:10 [f] S Dt 13:13; Ac 6:11 [g] S Ex 22:28; Lev 24:15-16
21:12 [h] Isa 58:4
21:13 [i] S Lev 24:16
21:15 [j] S 1Sa 8:14
21:19 [k] Job 24:6; 31:39 [l] 2Ki 9:26; Ps 9:12; Isa 14:20 [m] 1Ki 22:38; Ps 68:23; Jer 15:3
21:20 [n] S 1Ki 18:17 [o] 2Ki 17:17; Ro 7:14
21:21 [p] Jdg 9:5; 2Ki 10:7 [q] S Dt 32:36
21:22 [r] 1Ki 16:3 [s] S 1Ki 12:30
21:23 [t] 2Ki 9:10, 34-36
21:24 [u] 1Ki 14:11 [v] S Ge 40:19; S Dt 28:26
21:25 [w] S 1Ki 14:9; S 16:33
21:26 [x] S Ge 15:16
21:27 [y] S Ge 37:34; S Jer 4:8 [z] Isa 38:15
21:29 [a] S Ex 10:3 [b] S Ex 32:14; 2Ki 22:20 [c] Ex 20:5; 2Ki 9:26; 10:6-10

[a] 21 Or *Israel—every ruler or leader* [b] 23 Most Hebrew manuscripts; a few Hebrew manuscripts, Vulgate and Syriac (see also 2 Kings 9:26) *the plot of ground at*

21:9 *Proclaim a day of fasting.* Jezebel attempted to create the impression that a disaster threatened the people that could be averted only if they would humble themselves before the Lord and remove any person whose sin had brought God's judgment on them (cf. Jdg 20:26; 1Sa 7:5–6; 2Ch 20:2–4).
21:10 *two.* Mosaic law required two witnesses for capital offenses (Nu 35:30; Dt 17:6; 19:15). *scoundrels.* See note on Dt 13:13 ("troublemakers"). *have them bring charges.* The entire scenario was designed to give an appearance of legitimate judicial procedure (see Ex 20:16; 23:7; Lev 19:16). *he has cursed both God and the king.* For this the Mosaic law prescribed death by stoning (Lev 24:15–16).
21:13 *outside the city.* In accordance with Mosaic law (Lev 24:14; Nu 15:35–36). Naboth was stoned to death on his own field (compare v. 19 with 2Ki 9:21,26), and his sons were stoned with him (see 2Ki 9:26; cf. the case of Achan, Jos 7:24–25), thus also eliminating his heirs.
21:19 *Have you not murdered a man and seized his property?* Ahab's willing compliance with Jezebel's scheme made him guilty of murder and theft. *In the place where dogs licked up Naboth's blood, dogs will lick up your blood.* Ahab's subsequent repentance (v. 29) occasioned the postponement of certain aspects of this prophecy until the time of his son Joram, whose body was thrown on the field of Naboth (2Ki 9:25–26). Ahab himself was killed in battle at Ramoth Gilead (22:29–37), and his body was brought to Samaria, where the dogs licked the blood being washed from his chariot (22:38).
21:21 *slave or free.* See note on 14:10.
21:22 *like that of Jeroboam.* See 14:10; 15:28–30. *that of Baasha.* See 16:3–4,11–13.
21:24 See notes on 14:11; 16:4.
21:25 *urged on by Jezebel.* See 16:31; 18:4; 19:1–2; 21:7.
21:26 *idols.* See note on Lev 26:30. *Amorites.* Here a designation for the entire pre-Israelite population of Canaan (see Ge 15:16; Dt 1:7).
21:27 *sackcloth.* See note on Ge 37:34.
21:29 *Because . . . , I will not bring this disaster.* See Jnh 3:10 and note. *in the days of his son.* The judgment was postponed but not rescinded (see note on v. 19).

ᴍicaiah Prophesies Against ᴀhab

2:1-28pp — 2Ch 18:1-27

22 For three years there was
no war between Aram
nd Israel. 2But in the third year
ehoshaphat king of Judah went
own to see the king of Israel.
The king of Israel had said to
is officials, "Don't you know
hat Ramoth Gilead[d] belongs to
s and yet we are doing noth-
ng to retake it from the king of
ram?"
4So he asked Jehoshaphat,
Will you go with me to fight[e]
gainst Ramoth Gilead?"
Jehoshaphat replied to the
ing of Israel, "I am as you are,
ny people as your people, my
orses as your horses." 5But Je-
oshaphat also said to the king
f Israel, "First seek the counsel[f]
f the LORD."
6So the king of Israel brought
ogether the prophets — about
our hundred men — and asked
hem, "Shall I go to war against
amoth Gilead, or shall I re-
ain?"
"Go,"[g] they answered, "for the
ord will give it into the king's hand."[h]
7But Jehoshaphat asked, "Is there no
onger a prophet[i] of the LORD here whom
ve can inquire[j] of?"
8The king of Israel answered Jehoshaphat, "There is still one prophet through
whom we can inquire of the LORD, but I
hate[k] him because he never prophesies

A depiction of Elijah confronting Jezebel and Ahab (1Ki 21:17–24), by Frederic Leighton

Jezebel and Ahab Met by Elijah, c.1862–3, Leighton, Frederic (1830–96)/© Scarborough Borough Council, North Yorkshire, UK/The Bridgeman Art Library

22:3 [d]S Dt 4:43 **22:4** [e]2Ki 3:7 **22:5** [f]Ex 33:7; 2Ki 3:11; Job 38:2; Ps 32:8; 73:24; 107:11 **22:6** [g]S Jdg 18:6 [h]S 1Ki 13:18 **22:7** [i]Dt 18:15; 2Ki 3:11; 5:8 [j]S Nu 27:21; 2Ki 3:11 **22:8** [k]Am 5:10

22:1 *three years.* See note on 20:1. *no war between Aram and Israel.* The annals of the Assyrian ruler Shalmaneser III (859 – 824 BC) record the participation of both "Ahab the Israelite" and Hadadezer (Ben-Hadad) of Damascus in a coalition of 12 rulers that fought against Assyrian forces at Qarqar on the Orontes River in 853. According to the Assyrian records, Ahab contributed 2,000 chariots and 10,000 foot soldiers to the allied forces. Assyrian claims of victory appear exaggerated since they withdrew and did not venture westward again for four or five years.
22:2 *Jehoshaphat king of Judah went down to see the king of Israel.* Perhaps to congratulate him on the success of the western alliance against the Assyrian threat (see notes on 1; 2Ch 18:2).
22:3 *Ramoth Gilead.* Located near the Yarmuk River in Transjordan; an Israelite city since the days of Moses (see 4:13; Dt 43; Jos 20:8). *belongs to us.* Israel could lay claim to Ramoth Gilead also by virtue of the treaty concluded with Ben-Hadad a few years earlier (see 20:34), the provisions of which he had apparently failed to honor.
22:4 *he asked Jehoshaphat.* Ironically, the king whom Ahab asked to go with him to battle to secure his victory bore the name Jehoshaphat, which means "The LORD judges/rules." Little did he realize — and he would not believe — that the judging Lord would "go with" him into the battle to guide a certain arrow. Significantly, in this episode the king of Israel is named only once, and that by the Lord in the heavenly court scene (v. 20). But the narrator bombards the reader with the fateful name Jehoshaphat 12 times. And then there is Micaiah ("Who is like the LORD?" [v. 8]), and there is Zedekiah ("The LORD is righteous" [v. 11]). Even though Ahab had just been allied with the Arameans against the Assyrians, now that the Assyrian threat was over he did not hesitate to seize an opportunity to free Ramoth Gilead from Aramean control. *I am as you are, my people as your people, my horses as your horses.* In this alliance Jehoshaphat completely reversed the policy of his father, Asa, who had entered into an alliance with the Arameans against Baasha of the northern kingdom (see 15:17 – 23). Of the two allies, only Jehosphaphat realized that the two Israelite kings had actually to do with two other kings: the king of Aram and the King sitting on the heavenly throne (see v. 19). Jehoshaphat was later to be condemned by the prophet Jehu (2Ch 19:2) for violating the Lord's will by joining forces with Ahab.
22:5 *First seek the counsel of the LORD.* Jehoshaphat hesitated to proceed with the planned action without the assurance of the Lord's favor (see 1Sa 23:1 – 4; 2Sa 2:1).
22:6 *prophets.* No doubt associated with the paganized worship at Bethel (see notes on 12:28 – 29), they exercised their "office" by proclaiming messages designed to please the king (see Am 7:10 – 13).
22:7 *Is there no longer a prophet of the LORD here ...?* Jehoshaphat recognized that the 400 prophets were not to be relied on (see Eze 13:2 – 3) and asked for consultation with a true prophet of the Lord.
22:8 *never prophesies anything good.* Ahab's assessment of a

anything good[l] about me, but always bad.
He is Micaiah son of Imlah."
"The king should not say such a thing,"
Jehoshaphat replied.
9 So the king of Israel called one of his
officials and said, "Bring Micaiah son of
Imlah at once."
10 Dressed in their royal robes, the king
of Israel and Jehoshaphat king of Judah
were sitting on their thrones at the threshing floor[m] by the entrance of the gate of
Samaria, with all the prophets prophesying before them. 11 Now Zedekiah[n] son of
Kenaanah had made iron horns[o] and he
declared, "This is what the LORD says:
'With these you will gore the Arameans
until they are destroyed.' "
12 All the other prophets were prophesying the same thing. "Attack Ramoth Gilead
and be victorious," they said, "for the LORD
will give it into the king's hand."
13 The messenger who had gone to summon Micaiah said to him, "Look, the other
prophets without exception are predicting
success for the king. Let your word agree
with theirs, and speak favorably."[p]
14 But Micaiah said, "As surely as the
LORD lives, I can tell him only what the
LORD tells me."[q]
15 When he arrived, the king asked him,
"Micaiah, shall we go to war against Ramoth Gilead, or not?"
"Attack and be victorious," he answered, "for the LORD will give it into the
king's hand."
16 The king said to him, "How many
times must I make you swear to tell m
nothing but the truth in the name of th
LORD?"
17 Then Micaiah answered, "I saw all Is
rael scattered[r] on the hills like sheep with
out a shepherd,[s] and the LORD said, 'Thes
people have no master. Let each one g
home in peace.' "
18 The king of Israel said to Jehoshaphat
"Didn't I tell you that he never prophesie
anything good about me, but only bad?"
19 Micaiah continued, "Therefore hea
the word of the LORD: I saw the LORD sit
ting on his throne[t] with all the multitudes
of heaven standing around him on hi
right and on his left. 20 And the LORD said
'Who will entice Ahab into attacking Ra
moth Gilead and going to his death there?
"One suggested this, and another that
21 Finally, a spirit came forward, stood be
fore the LORD and said, 'I will entice him
22 " 'By what means?' the LORD asked.
" 'I will go out and be a deceiving[v] spiri
in the mouths of all his prophets,' he said
" 'You will succeed in enticing him,' sai
the LORD. 'Go and do it.'
23 "So now the LORD has put a deceiving
spirit in the mouths of all these prophets
of yours. The LORD has decreed disaster
for you."
24 Then Zedekiah[z] son of Kenaana
went up and slapped[a] Micaiah in the face
"Which way did the spirit from[a] the LOR
go when he went from me to speak[b] t
you?" he asked.

22:8 [l] ver 13; Isa 5:20; 30:10; Jer 23:17 **22:10** [m] S Jdg 6:37 **22:11** [n] ver 24 [o] Dt 33:17; Jer 27:2; 28:10; Zec 1:18-21 **22:13** [p] S ver 8 **22:14** [q] S Nu 22:18; S 1Sa 3:17 **22:17** [r] S Ge 11:4; Na 3:18 [s] Nu 27:17; Isa 13:14; S Mt 9:36 **22:19** [t] Ps 47:8; Isa 6:1; 63:15; Eze 1:26; Da 7:9 [u] Job 1:6; 15:8; 38:7; Ps 103:20-21; 148:2; Jer 23:18,22; Lk 2:13 **22:22** [v] S Jdg 9:23; 2Th 2:11 **22:23** [w] S Dt 13:3 [x] Eze 14:9 [y] S Dt 31:29 **22:24** [z] ver 11 [a] Ac 23:2 [b] Job 26:4

[a] 24 Or *Spirit of*

prophet depended on whether his message was favorable to him (see 18:17; 21:20).

22:10 A pause in the action to describe a scene on earth (kings in royal splendor on their thrones surrounded by Ahab's minions and confidently planning a campaign of conquest), a scene that will shortly be outmatched by the description of a scene in heaven (Israel's Great King on his throne surrounded by his heavenly host and planning his campaign against King Ahab [vv. 19–23]). By reporting that Ahab and Jehoshaphat were sitting "at the threshing floor [where sheaves are crushed (Mic 4:12) and grain is winnowed (Jer 15:7)] by the entrance of the gate [where courts sit in judgment (Dt 21:19; Ru 4:1,11)] of Samaria," the author hints with biting irony at the outcome of Ahab's grand design.

22:11 *Zedekiah.* Evidently the spokesman for the 400 prophets. *iron horns.* A symbol of power (see Dt 33:17).

22:13 *Let your word agree with theirs.* A bit of advice reflecting the view that all prophets were merely self-serving.

22:15 *we.* A subtle shift (see v. 6) that seeks a favorable response by including Jehoshaphat as a cosponsor of the enterprise. *Attack ... for the LORD will give it into the king's hand.* Micaiah sarcastically mimics the 400 false prophets (see v. 12).

22:16 *tell me nothing but the truth.* Micaiah apparently betrayed his lack of seriousness, and Ahab immediately recognized this.

22:17 *like sheep without a shepherd ... These people have no master.* Using the imagery of shepherd and sheep (see Nu 27:16–17; Zec 13:7; Mt 9:36; 26:31), Micaiah depicts Ahab death in the upcoming battle.

22:19 *I saw the LORD sitting on his throne.* A true proph was one who had, as it were, been made privy to wh had transpired in God's heavenly throne room and so cou truthfully declare what God intended to do (see Isa 6:1; J 23:16–22). Micaiah's description of the heavenly scene pu the earthly scene into which he had been brought (see v. 1 and note) in its true light—a powerful portrayal of where th true power lies and of the folly of human pretensions.

22:23 *the LORD has put a deceiving spirit in the mouths of these prophets.* Some view the deceiving spirit as Satan one of his agents. Others have suggested a spirit of Go who undertakes the task of a deceiving spirit (but see 1S 15:29). Still others understand the deceiving spirit as a sym bolic picture of the power of the lie. The Lord had given th 400 prophets over to the power of the lie because they d not love the truth and had chosen to speak out of their ow hearts (see Jer 14:14; 23:16, 26; Eze 13:2–3,17; see also no on 2Sa 24:1; cf. 2Th 2:9–12 and note on 2:11). King Aha who was content to live by a lie and hated the prophet wh spoke the truth, was fittingly lured by God to his executic through a lie he wanted to believe (see also Nu 11:18–20; 18:25–26; Eze 14:9 and note).

22:24 *Which way did the spirit from the LORD go when he we from me to speak to you?* By this sarcastic question Zedekia suggests that one prophet can be a liar just as well as ar other.

25Micaiah replied, “You will find out on
he day you go to hide[c] in an inner room.”
26The king of Israel then ordered, “Take
Aicaiah and send him back to Amon the
uler of the city and to Joash the king’s
on 27and say, ‘This is what the king says:
’ut this fellow in prison[d] and give him
othing but bread and water until I return
afely.’ ”
28Micaiah declared, “If you ever return
afely, the LORD has not spoken[e] through
ne.” Then he added, “Mark my words, all
’ou people!”

hab Killed at Ramoth Gilead

2:29-36pp — 2Ch 18:28-34

29So the king of Israel and Jehoshaphat
ing of Judah went up to Ramoth Gilead.
)The king of Israel said to Jehoshaphat,
I will enter the battle in disguise,[f] but you
vear your royal robes.” So the king of Isra-
l disguised himself and went into battle.
31Now the king of Aram[g] had ordered
is thirty-two chariot commanders, “Do
ot fight with anyone, small or great, ex-
ept the king[h] of Israel.” 32When the char-
ot commanders saw Jehoshaphat, they
hought, “Surely this is the king of Israel.”
o they turned to attack him, but when
ehoshaphat cried out, 33the chariot com-
ıanders saw that he was not the king of
srael and stopped pursuing him.
34But someone drew his bow[i] at ran-
om and hit the king of Israel between
he sections of his armor. The king told
is chariot driver, “Wheel around and get
ıe out of the fighting. I’ve been wound-
d.” 35All day long the battle raged, and
ıe king was propped up in his chariot

22:25 [c]1Ki 20:30 **22:27** [d]2Ch 16:10; Jer 20:2; 26:21; 37:15; Heb 11:36 **22:28** [e]S Dt 18:22 **22:30** [f]S 1Sa 28:8 **22:31** [g]S Ge 10:22; S 2Sa 10:19 [h]S 2Sa 17:2 **22:34** [i]2Ki 9:24; 2Ch 35:23 **22:36** [j]2Ki 14:12 **22:38** [k]S 1Ki 21:19 **22:39** [l]2Ch 9:17; Ps 45:8; Am 3:15 **22:43** [m]S 1Ki 8:61; 2Ch 17:3 [n]S 1Ki 3:2

facing the Arameans. The blood from his
wound ran onto the floor of the chariot,
and that evening he died. 36As the sun
was setting, a cry spread through the
army: “Every man to his town. Every man
to his land!”[j]
37So the king died and was brought
to Samaria, and they buried him there.
38They washed the chariot at a pool in Samaria (where the prostitutes bathed),[a] and
the dogs[k] licked up his blood, as the word
of the LORD had declared.
39As for the other events of Ahab’s
reign, including all he did, the palace he
built and adorned with ivory,[l] and the cities he fortified, are they not written in the
book of the annals of the kings of Israel? 40Ahab rested with his ancestors. And
Ahaziah his son succeeded him as king.

Jehoshaphat King of Judah

22:41-50pp — 2Ch 20:31 – 21:1

41Jehoshaphat son of Asa became king
of Judah in the fourth year of Ahab king of
Israel. 42Jehoshaphat was thirty-five years
old when he became king, and he reigned
in Jerusalem twenty-five years. His mother’s name was Azubah daughter of Shilhi. 43In everything he followed the ways
of his father Asa[m] and did not stray from
them; he did what was right in the eyes of
the LORD. The high places,[n] however, were
not removed, and the people continued to
offer sacrifices and burn incense there.[b]
44Jehoshaphat was also at peace with the
king of Israel.

[a] 38 Or *Samaria and cleaned the weapons* [b] 43 In Hebrew texts this sentence (22:43b) is numbered 22:44, and 22:44-53 is numbered 22:45-54.

2:25 *hide in an inner room.* Where Zedekiah will seek refuge f. 20:30). This will vindicate Micaiah’s prophetic authority.
2:26 *king’s son.* Probably a royal official (see note on Jer 6:26).
2:27 *This is what the king says.* Ahab speaks his royal word gainst the Lord’s prophet because he trusts the (false) divine ord proclaimed by his paid prophet (see v. 11).
2:30 *The king of Israel said.* Ahab still thought he was in ɔntrol. *disguise.* By this strategy he thought he could direct ttention away from himself and so minimize any chance for lfillment of Micaiah’s prediction. The king who loved the lie ıought he could escape the truth by living a lie.
2:31 *except the king of Israel.* If the leader was killed or cap-ıred, ancient armies usually fell apart (cf. vv. 35 – 36).
2:34 *drew his bow at random.* The heavenly King aimed e arrow. *chariot driver.* A war chariot normally carried two en — a fighter and a driver. Sometimes, it appears, there ere three men, but the third seems to have been an officer ho commanded a chariot unit (see 9:22; 2Ki 9:25; Ex 14:7; 5:4, where these officers are called lit. “the third”).
2:35 *that evening he died.* Fulfilling Micaiah’s prophecy v. 17,28).
2:38 *as the word of the LORD had declared.* A partial fulfill-ıent of Elijah’s prophecy concerning Ahab’s death (see note n 21:19).

22:39 *the palace he built and adorned with ivory.* Excavators of Samaria have found ivory inlays in the ruins of some of the buildings dating from this period of Israel’s history. Ahab’s use of ivory is indicative of the realm’s economic prosperity during his reign. *cities he fortified.* Excavators have found evidence that Ahab strengthened the fortifications of Megiddo and Hazor. *annals of the kings of Israel.* See note on 14:19.
22:40 *rested with his ancestors.* See note on 1:21. *Ahaziah his son succeeded him.* For the reign of Ahaziah, see vv. 51 – 53; 2Ki 1.
22:41 *Jehoshaphat ... became king of Judah in the fourth year of Ahab.* Appears to refer to the beginning of Jehoshaphat’s reign as sole king in 869 BC (see notes on v. 42; 16:29; see also Introduction: Chronology).
22:42 *twenty-five years.* 872 – 848 BC. The full span of Jehoshaphat’s reign dates from the 39th year of King Asa, when he became coregent with his father (see note on 15:10; see also 2Ch 16:12).
22:43 *The high places, however, were not removed.* See notes on 3:2; 15:14.
22:44 *king.* Probably to be understood in the collective sense and as including Ahab, Ahaziah and Joram, all of whom ruled in the north during the reign of Jehoshaphat in the south (see note on v. 4).

[45]As for the other events of Jehoshaphat's reign, the things he achieved and
his military exploits, are they not written
in the book of the annals of the kings of
Judah? [46]He rid the land of the rest of the
male shrine prostitutes[o] who remained
there even after the reign of his father Asa.
[47]There was then no king[p] in Edom; a provincial governor ruled.
[48]Now Jehoshaphat built a fleet of trading ships[a][q] to go to Ophir for gold, but
they never set sail—they were wrecked at
Ezion Geber.[r] [49]At that time Ahaziah son
of Ahab said to Jehoshaphat, "Let my men
sail with yours," but Jehoshaphat refused.
[50]Then Jehoshaphat rested with his ancestors and was buried with them in the
city of David his father. And Jehoram hi
son succeeded him as king.

22:46 [o]S Dt 23:17
22:47 [p]1Ki 11:14-18; 2Ki 3:9; 8:20
22:48 [q]S 1Ki 9:26 [r]S Nu 33:35
22:52 [s]1Ki 15:26
22:53 [t]S Jdg 2:11 [u]1Ki 21:25

Ahaziah King of Israel

[51]Ahaziah son of Ahab became kin
of Israel in Samaria in the seventeent
year of Jehoshaphat king of Judah, an
he reigned over Israel two years. [52]He di
evil[s] in the eyes of the LORD, because h
followed the ways of his father and moth
er and of Jeroboam son of Nebat, wh
caused Israel to sin. [53]He served and wo
shiped Baal[t] and aroused the anger of th
LORD, the God of Israel, just as his fathe
had done.

[a] 48 Hebrew *of ships of Tarshish*

22:45 *military exploits.* See 2Ki 3; 2Ch 17:11; 20. *annals of the kings of Judah.* See note on 14:29.
22:46 *male shrine prostitutes.* See note on 14:24.
22:47 *no king in Edom.* Suggests that Edom was subject to Judah (see 2Sa 8:14; 2Ki 8:20).
22:48 *Ophir.* See note on 9:28. *wrecked at Ezion Geber.* The destruction of the trading ships was a judgment of God on Jehoshaphat for entering into an alliance with Ahaziah of the northern kingdom (see 2Ch 20:35–37).
22:50 *rested with his ancestors.* See note on 1:21. *Jehoram h son succeeded him.* For the reign of Jehoram, see 2Ki 8:16–2 2Ch 21.
22:51 *seventeenth year of Jehoshaphat.* 853 BC (see notes o vv. 41–42). *two years.* 853–852 (see note on 2Ki 1:17).
22:52 *ways of his father and mother.* See 16:30–33. *and Jeroboam.* See 12:28–33.

2 KINGS

INTRODUCTION

See Introduction to 1 Kings.

Outline

Below is an outline for 2 Kings. For an outline of both 1 and 2 Kings, see Introduction to 1 Kings: Outline.

- IV. The Ministries of Elijah and Elisha during the Reigns of Ahaziah and Joram (1:1 — 8:15)
  - A. Elijah in the Reign of Ahaziah (ch. 1)
  - B. Elijah's Departure; Elisha's Inauguration (2:1 – 18)
  - C. Elisha in the Reign of Joram (2:19 — 8:15)
    1. Elisha's initial miraculous signs (2:19 – 25)
    2. Elisha during the campaign against Moab (ch. 3)
    3. Elisha's ministry to needy ones in Israel (ch. 4)
    4. Elisha heals Naaman (ch. 5)
    5. Elisha's deliverance of one of the prophets (6:1 – 7)
    6. Elisha's deliverance of Joram from Aramean raiders (6:8 – 23)
    7. Aramean siege of Samaria lifted, as Elisha prophesied (6:24 — 7:20)
    8. The Shunammite's land restored (8:1 – 6)
    9. Elisha predicts Hazael's oppression of Israel (8:7 – 15)
- V. Israel and Judah from Joram/Jehoram to the Exile of Israel (8:16 — 17:41)
  - A. Jehoram of Judah (8:16 – 24)
  - B. Ahaziah of Judah (8:25 – 29)
  - C. Jehu's Revolt and Reign in Israel (chs. 9 – 10)
    1. Elisha orders Jehu's anointing (9:1 – 13)
    2. Jehu's assassination of Joram and Ahaziah (9:14 – 29)
    3. Jehu's execution of Jezebel (9:30 – 37)
    4. Jehu's slaughter of Ahab's family (10:1 – 17)
    5. Jehu's eradication of Baal worship (10:18 – 36)
  - D. Athaliah and Joash of Judah; Repair of the Temple (chs. 11 – 12)
  - E. Jehoahaz of Israel (13:1 – 9)
  - F. Jehoash of Israel; Elisha's Last Prophecy (13:10 – 25)
  - G. Amaziah of Judah (14:1 – 22)
  - H. Jeroboam II of Israel (14:23 – 29)

I. Azariah of Judah (15:1 – 7)
J. Zechariah of Israel (15:8 – 12)
K. Shallum of Israel (15:13 – 16)
L. Menahem of Israel (15:17 – 22)
M. Pekahiah of Israel (15:23 – 26)
N. Pekah of Israel (15:27 – 31)
O. Jotham of Judah (15:32 – 38)
P. Ahaz of Judah (ch. 16)
Q. Hoshea of Israel (17:1 – 6)
R. Exile of Israel; Resettlement of the Land (17:7 – 41)

VI. Judah from Hezekiah to the Babylonian Exile (chs. 18 – 25)
A. Hezekiah (chs. 18 – 20)
1. Hezekiah's good reign (18:1 – 8)
2. The Assyrian threat and deliverance (18:9 — 19:37)
3. Hezekiah's illness and alliance with Babylonia (ch. 20)
B. Manasseh (21:1 – 18)
C. Amon (21:19 – 26)
D. Josiah (22:1 — 23:30)
1. Repair of the temple; discovery of the Book of the Law (ch. 22)
2. Renewal of the covenant; end of Josiah's reign (23:1 – 30)
E. Jehoahaz Exiled to Egypt (23:31 – 35)
F. Jehoiakim: First Babylonian Deportation (23:36 — 24:7)
G. Jehoiachin: Second Babylonian Deportation (24:8 – 17)
H. Zedekiah: Third Babylonian Deportation (24:18 — 25:21)
I. Removal of the Remnant to Egypt (25:22 – 26)
J. Elevation of Jehoiachin in Babylon (25:27 – 30)

Wall relief depicting Assyrian king Sennacherib's siege of Lachish (2Ki 18:13 – 14)

Caryn Reeder, courtesy of the British Muesum

[T]he LORD's Judgment on Ahaziah

1 After Ahab's death, Moab[a] rebelled
against Israel. 2 Now Ahaziah had fall-
[e]n through the lattice of his upper room
[i]n Samaria and injured himself. So he sent
[m]essengers,[b] saying to them, "Go and con-
[s]ult Baal-Zebub,[c] the god of Ekron,[d] to see
[i]f I will recover[e] from this injury."
3 But the angel[f] of the LORD said to Eli-
[j]ah[g] the Tishbite, "Go up and meet the
[m]essengers of the king of Samaria and
[a]sk them, 'Is it because there is no God
[i]n Israel[h] that you are going off to consult
[B]aal-Zebub, the god of Ekron?' 4 Therefore
[t]his is what the LORD says: 'You will not
[l]eave[i] the bed you are lying on. You will
[c]ertainly die!'" So Elijah went.
5 When the messengers returned to the
[k]ing, he asked them, "Why have you
[c]ome back?"
6 "A man came to meet us," they replied.
And he said to us, 'Go back to the king
[w]ho sent you and tell him, "This is what
[t]he LORD says: Is it because there is no God
[i]n Israel that you are sending messengers
[t]o consult Baal-Zebub, the god of Ekron?
[T]herefore you will not leave[j] the bed you
[a]re lying on. You will certainly die!"'"
7 The king asked them, "What kind of
[m]an was it who came to meet you and
[t]old you this?"
8 They replied, "He had a garment of
hair[a][k] and had a leather belt around his
waist."
The king said, "That was Elijah the
Tishbite."
9 Then he sent[l] to Elijah a captain[m] with
his company of fifty men. The captain
went up to Elijah, who was sitting on the
top of a hill, and said to him, "Man of
God, the king says, 'Come down!'"
10 Elijah answered the captain, "If I am
a man of God, may fire come down from
heaven and consume you and your fifty
men!" Then fire[n] fell from heaven and
consumed the captain and his men.
11 At this the king sent to Elijah another captain with his fifty men. The captain
said to him, "Man of God, this is what the
king says, 'Come down at once!'"
12 "If I am a man of God," Elijah replied,
"may fire come down from heaven and
consume you and your fifty men!" Then
the fire of God fell from heaven and consumed him and his fifty men.
13 So the king sent a third captain with
his fifty men. This third captain went up
and fell on his knees before Elijah. "Man
of God," he begged, "please have respect
for my life[o] and the lives of these fifty
men, your servants! 14 See, fire has fallen

1:1 [a] S Ge 19:37; 2Ki 3:5 **1:2** [b] ver 16 [c] S Mk 3:22 [d] 1Sa 6:2; Isa 2:6; 14:29 [e] S Jdg 18:5 **1:3** [f] ver 15 [g] 1Ki 17:1 [h] S 1Sa 28:8 **1:4** [i] ver 6, 16; Ps 41:8 **1:6** [j] S ver 4 **1:8** [k] S 1Ki 18:7; Mt 3:4; Mk 1:6 **1:9** [l] 2Ki 6:14 [m] Ex 18:25; Isa 3:3 **1:10** [n] S 1Ki 18:38; S Rev 11:5; S 13:13 **1:13** [o] Ps 72:14

[a] 8 Or *He was a hairy man*

1:1 *After Ahab's death.* See 1Ki 22:37; see also Jos 1:1; Jdg 1:1; 2Sa 1:1 and notes. *Moab rebelled.* Moab had [b]een brought into subjection by David (see 2Sa 8:2), but [w]hen the northern and Transjordan tribes rebelled and [m]ade Jeroboam their king, political domination of Moab [p]robably also shifted to the northern kingdom. An inscrip[ti]on of Mesha king of Moab (see chart, p. xxiii) indicates that [d]uring the reign of Omri's "son" (probably a reference to his [g]randson Joram, not to Ahab) the Moabites were able to free [t]he area of Medeba from Israelite control (see map, p. 478).
1:2 *Baal-Zebub.* See note on Jdg 10:6. *Ekron.* The northern[m]ost of the five major Philistine cities (see Jos 13:3; 1Sa 5:10 [a]nd notes). *if I will recover.* Ahaziah appears to have feared [t]hat his injury would be fatal. He turned to the pagan deity [f]or a revelatory message, not for healing.
1:3 *angel of the LORD.* See 1Ki 19:7; see also note on Ge 16:7. [T]he Lord usually spoke directly to the consciousness of the [p]rophet (1Ki 17:2,8; 18:1; 19:9; 21:17). Perhaps the means [o]f revelation was changed in this instance to heighten the [c]ontrast between the messengers of Ahaziah (vv. 2–3,5) and [t]he angel (which means "messenger") of the Lord. *Elijah the* [T]*ishbite.* See note on 1Ki 17:1. *king of Samaria.* See note on [1]Ki 21:1.
1:4 *You will certainly die!* Ahaziah will receive the message [h]e sought, but it will come from the Lord through Elijah, not [f]rom Baal-Zebub.
1:5 *Why have you come back?* Ahaziah realized the messen[g]ers could not have traveled so quickly to Ekron and back.
1:8 *garment of hair.* Elijah's cloak (1Ki 19:19) was probably [o]f sheepskin or camel's hair, tied with a simple leather strap [(c]f. Mt 3:4). His dress contrasted sharply with the fine linen [c]lothing (see Jer 13:1) of his wealthy contemporaries and [c]onstituted a protest against the materialistic attitudes of [t]he king and the upper classes (cf. Mt 11:7–8; Lk 7:24–25). *That was Elijah the Tishbite.* Ahaziah was familiar with Elijah's appearance because of the prophet's many encounters with Ahab, his father.
1:9 *he sent to Elijah a captain with his company of fifty men.* The pagan people of that time thought that the magical power of curses could be nullified either by forcing the pronouncer of the curse to retract his statement or by killing him so that his curse would go with him to the netherworld. It appears that Ahaziah shared this view and desired to take Elijah prisoner in order to counteract the pronouncement of his death. *Man of God, the king says, 'Come down!'* Ahaziah attempted to place the prophet under the authority of the king. This constituted a violation of the covenant nature of Israelite kingship, in which the king's actions were always to be placed under the scrutiny and authority of the word of the Lord spoken by his prophets (see notes on 1Sa 10:25; 12:23).
1:10 *fire fell from heaven and consumed the captain and his men.* Another link between the ministries of Elijah and Moses (see Lev 10:2; Nu 16:35). At stake in this incident was the question of who was sovereign in Israel. Would Ahaziah recognize that the king in Israel was only a vice-regent under the authority and kingship of the Lord, or would he exercise despotic power, like pagan kings (see notes on 1Sa 12:14–15)? At Mount Carmel the Lord had revealed himself and authenticated his prophet by fire from heaven (see 1Ki 18:38–39). Now this previous revelation is confirmed to Ahaziah.
1:11 *the king sent to Elijah another captain.* Ahaziah refused to submit to the word of the Lord in spite of the dramatic revelation of God's power.
1:13 *fell on his knees before Elijah.* The third captain, recognizing that Elijah was the bearer of the word of the Lord, feared for his life and bowed before him with a humble request.

from heaven and consumed the first two
captains and all their men. But now have
respect for my life!"
15 The angel[p] of the LORD said to Elijah,
"Go down with him; do not be afraid[q] of
him." So Elijah got up and went down
with him to the king.
16 He told the king, "This is what the
LORD says: Is it because there is no God
in Israel for you to consult that you have
sent messengers[r] to consult Baal-Zebub,
the god of Ekron? Because you have done
this, you will never leave[s] the bed you are
lying on. You will certainly die!" 17 So he
died,[t] according to the word of the LORD
that Elijah had spoken.
Because Ahaziah had no son, Joram[a u]
succeeded him as king in the second year
of Jehoram son of Jehoshaphat king of Judah. 18 As for all the other events of Ahaziah's reign, and what he did, are they not
written in the book of the annals of the
kings of Israel?

Elijah Taken Up to Heaven

2 When the LORD was about to take[v]
Elijah up to heaven in a whirlwind,[w]
Elijah and Elisha[x] were on their way from
Gilgal.[y] 2 Elijah said to Elisha, "Stay here;[z]
the LORD has sent me to Bethel."
But Elisha said, "As surely as the LORD
lives and as you live, I will not leave you."[a]
So they went down to Bethel.
3 The company[b] of the prophets at Bethel came out to Elisha and asked, "Do you
know that the LORD is going to take your
master from you today?"
"Yes, I know," Elisha replied, "so be
quiet."
4 Then Elijah said to him, "Stay here,
Elisha; the LORD has sent me to Jericho.[c]"
And he replied, "As surely as the LORD
lives and as you live, I will not leave you."
So they went to Jericho.
5 The company[d] of the prophets at Jericho went up to Elisha and asked him, "Do
you know that the LORD is going to take
your master from you today?"
"Yes, I know," he replied, "so be quiet."
6 Then Elijah said to him, "Stay here;[e]
the LORD has sent me to the Jordan."[f]
And he replied, "As surely as the LORD
lives and as you live, I will not leave you."[g]
So the two of them walked on.
7 Fifty men from the company of the
prophets went and stood at a distance,
facing the place where Elijah and Elisha
had stopped at the Jordan. 8 Elijah took his
cloak,[h] rolled it up and struck[i] the water
with it. The water divided[j] to the right and
to the left, and the two of them crossed
over on dry[k] ground.
9 When they had crossed, Elijah said to
Elisha, "Tell me, what can I do for you before I am taken from you?"
"Let me inherit a double[l] portion of your
spirit,"[m] Elisha replied.
10 "You have asked a difficult thing," Elijah said, "yet if you see me when I am tak-
en from you, it will be yours—otherwise,
it will not."
11 As they were walking along and talking together, suddenly a chariot of fire[n]

1:15 [p] ver 3 [q] Isa 51:12; 57:11; Jer 1:17; Eze 2:6 **1:16** [r] S ver 2 [s] ver 4 **1:17** [t] 2Ki 8:15; Jer 20:6; 28:17 [u] 2Ki 3:1; 8:16 **2:1** [v] S Ge 5:24 [w] ver 11; 1Ki 19:11; Isa 5:28; 66:15; Jer 4:13; Na 1:3 [x] S 1Ki 19:16, 21 [y] S Dt 11:30; 2Ki 4:38 **2:2** [z] ver 6 [a] Ru 1:16 **2:3** [b] S 1Sa 10:5 **2:4** [c] Jos 3:16 **2:5** [d] ver 3 **2:6** [e] ver 2 [f] Jos 3:15 [g] Ru 1:16 **2:8** [h] S 1Ki 19:19 [i] ver 14 [j] S Ex 14:21 [k] Ex 14:22,29 **2:9** [l] S Dt 21:17 [m] S Nu 11:17 **2:11** [n] 2Ki 6:17; Ps 68:17; 104:3, 4; Isa 66:15; Hab 3:8; Zec 6:1

[a] 17 Hebrew *Jehoram,* a variant of *Joram*

1:15 *The angel of the LORD said to Elijah.* See note on v. 3.
1:17 *died, according to the word of the LORD.* In the end Ahaziah was punished for turning away from the God of Israel to a pagan deity, and the word of the Lord was shown to be both reliable and beyond the power of the king to annul. *Joram.* Ahaziah's younger brother (see 3:1; 1Ki 22:51). *second year of Jehoram son of Jehoshaphat.* Jehoram's reign overlapped that of his father, Jehoshaphat, from 853 to 848 BC (see note on 8:16). The reference here is to the second year of that coregency. The 18th year of Jehoshaphat (3:1) is therefore the same as the second year of Jehoram's coregency (852).
1:18 *annals of the kings of Israel.* See note on 1Ki 14:19.
2:1 *Gilgal.* Probably not the well-known town west of the Jordan River, since they "went down" from it to Bethel (v. 2; see also 4:38); rather, it is more likely the Gilgal located some eight miles north of Bethel.
2:2 *I will not leave you.* Elisha was aware that Elijah's ministry was almost finished and that his departure was near (v. 5). He was determined to accompany him until the moment the Lord took him. His commitment to Elijah and to Elijah's ministry was unfailing (see v. 9; 1Ki 19:21).
2:3 *company.* See note on 1Ki 20:35. During the days of Elijah and Elisha, companies of prophets were located at Bethel (here), Jericho (v. 5) and Gilgal (4:38). It appears that Elijah journeyed by divine instruction to Gilgal (v. 1), Bethel (v. 2) and Jericho (v. 4) for a last meeting with each of these companies.
2:7 *Fifty men.* Israel's heavenly King could also muster 50 companies of 50 men (see 1:9,11,13; 2:16–17; 1Ki 18:4). The present company of 50 men were to witness the miracle by which Elijah and Elisha crossed the river.
2:8 *Elijah took his cloak ... and struck the water with it.* Elijah used his cloak much as Moses had used his staff at the time of Israel's passage through the "Red Sea" (see Ex 14:16,21,26).
2:9 *Let me inherit a double portion.* Elisha was not expressing a desire for a ministry twice as great as Elijah's, but he was using terms derived from inheritance law to express his desire to carry on Elijah's ministry. Inheritance law assigned a double portion of a father's possessions to the firstborn son (see Dt 21:17 and note).
2:10 *difficult thing.* Although Elijah had previously been told to anoint Elisha as his successor (1Ki 19:16,19–21), Elijah's response clearly showed that the issue rested solely with the Lord's sovereign good pleasure. *if you see me ... it will be yours—otherwise, it will not.* Elijah left the answer to Elisha's request in the Lord's hands.
2:11 *chariot of fire and horses of fire.* The Lord's heavenly host has accompanied and supported Elijah's ministry (as it had that of Moses; see Ex 15:1–10), and now at his departure Elisha is allowed to see it (cf. 6:17). *Elijah went up to heaven in a whirlwind.* Elijah, like Enoch before him (see Ge 5:24 and note), was "taken" (vv. 9–10) to heaven bodily without experiencing death; like Moses (Dt 34:4–6), he was outside the promised land when he was taken away.

and horses of fire appeared and separated
the two of them, and Elijah went up to
heaven[o] in a whirlwind.[p] 12 Elisha saw this
and cried out, "My father! My father! The
chariots[q] and horsemen of Israel!" And Elisha saw him no more. Then he took hold
of his garment and tore[r] it in two.
13 Elisha then picked up Elijah's cloak
that had fallen from him and went back
and stood on the bank of the Jordan. 14 He
took the cloak[s] that had fallen from Elijah
and struck[t] the water with it. "Where now
is the LORD, the God of Elijah?" he asked.
When he struck the water, it divided to the
right and to the left, and he crossed over.
15 The company[u] of the prophets from
Jericho, who were watching, said, "The
spirit[v] of Elijah is resting on Elisha." And
they went to meet him and bowed to the
ground before him. 16 "Look," they said,
"we your servants have fifty able men. Let
them go and look for your master. Perhaps
the Spirit[w] of the LORD has picked him up[x]
and set him down on some mountain or
in some valley."
"No," Elisha replied, "do not send
them."
17 But they persisted until he was too
embarrassed[y] to refuse. So he said, "Send
them." And they sent fifty men, who

2:11 [o] S Ge 5:24 [p] S ver 1
2:12 [q] 2Ki 6:17; 13:14 [r] S Ge 37:29
2:14 [s] S 1Ki 19:19 [t] ver 8
2:15 [u] S 1Sa 10:5 [v] S Nu 11:17
2:16 [w] S 1Ki 18:12 [x] Ac 8:39
2:17 [y] S Jdg 3:25
2:21 [z] S Ex 15:25; 2Ki 4:41; 6:6
2:22 [a] Ex 15:25
2:23 [b] S Ex 22:28; 2Ch 30:10; 36:16; Job 19:18; Ps 31:18
2:24 [c] S Ge 4:11 [d] S Dt 18:19

searched for three days but did not find
him. 18 When they returned to Elisha, who
was staying in Jericho, he said to them,
"Didn't I tell you not to go?"

Healing of the Water

19 The people of the city said to Elisha,
"Look, our lord, this town is well situated,
as you can see, but the water is bad and
the land is unproductive."
20 "Bring me a new bowl," he said, "and
put salt in it." So they brought it to him.
21 Then he went out to the spring and
threw[z] the salt into it, saying, "This is
what the LORD says: 'I have healed this
water. Never again will it cause death or
make the land unproductive.' " 22 And the
water has remained pure[a] to this day, according to the word Elisha had spoken.

Elisha Is Jeered

23 From there Elisha went up to Bethel.
As he was walking along the road, some
boys came out of the town and jeered[b] at
him. "Get out of here, baldy!" they said.
"Get out of here, baldy!" 24 He turned
around, looked at them and called down a
curse[c] on them in the name[d] of the LORD.
Then two bears came out of the woods
and mauled forty-two of the boys. 25 And

2:12 *chariots and horsemen of Israel!* Elisha depicted Elijah as embodying the true strength of the nation. He, rather than the apostate king, is the Lord's representative. The same description was later used of Elisha (see 13:14 and note). *tore it.* See Ge 44:13 and note.

2:13 *Elisha ... picked up Elijah's cloak.* See note on v. 8. Possession of Elijah's cloak symbolized Elisha's succession to Elijah's ministry (see 1Ki 19:19).

2:14 *When he struck the water, it divided.* See v. 8. The Lord authenticated Elisha's succession to Elijah's ministry and demonstrated that the same divine power that had accompanied Elijah's ministry was now operative in the ministry of Elisha. In crossing the Jordan as Joshua had before him, Elisha is shown to be Elijah's "Joshua" (Elisha and Joshua are very similar names, Elisha meaning "God saves" and Joshua "The LORD saves").

2:15 *bowed to the ground before him.* Indicated their recognition of Elisha's succession to Elijah's position. Elisha was now the Lord's official representative in this time of royal apostasy.

2:16 *Perhaps the Spirit of the LORD has picked him up and set him down.* Obadiah expressed the same idea years earlier (see 1Ki 18:12). *do not send them.* Elisha knew their search would be fruitless.

2:17 *too embarrassed.* The same Hebrew word is used in Jdg 3:25 ("to the point of embarrassment"). Under pressure to allow the prophets to send men to look for Elijah, Elisha no longer had the heart to say no. *Send them.* When the company of prophets refused to be satisfied with Elisha's answer, he permitted them to go so that the authority and truth of his words would be confirmed to them.

2:19 *city.* Evidently Jericho (see v. 18). *the water is bad and the land is unproductive.* The inhabitants of Jericho were experiencing the effects of the covenant curse (contrast Dt 28:15–18 with Ex 23:25–26; Lev 26:9; Dt 28:1–4). See 1Ki 16:34; Jos 6:26.

2:20 *new bowl.* That which was to be used in the service of the Lord was to be undefiled by profane use (see Lev 1:3,10; Nu 19:2; Dt 21:3; 1Sa 6:7). *put salt in it.* Elisha may have used salt because of its known preservative qualities, but it is more likely that he used it to symbolize the covenant faithfulness of the Lord (see note on Nu 18:19; see also 2Ch 13:5).

2:21 *I have healed this water.* Any idea of a magical effect of the salt in the purification of the water is excluded by the explicit statement that the Lord himself healed (purified) the water. In this symbolic way Elisha was able, as the first act of his ministry, to proclaim to the people that in spite of their disobedience the Lord was merciful and was still reaching out to them in his grace (see 13:23).

2:23 *Get out of here.* Since Bethel was the royal religious center of the northern kings (1Ki 12:29; Am 7:13) and Elijah and Elisha were known to frequent Samaria (perhaps even as their main residence; see note on 5:3), the youths from Bethel no doubt assumed that Elisha was going up to Samaria to continue Elijah's struggle against royal apostasy. *baldy!* Baldness was uncommon among the ancient Jews, and luxuriant hair seems to have been viewed as a sign of strength and vigor (see note on 2Sa 14:26). By calling Elisha "baldy," the youths from Bethel expressed that city's utter disdain for the Lord's representative, who, they felt, had no power.

2:24 *called down a curse on them in the name of the LORD.* Elisha pronounced a curse similar to the covenant curse of Lev 26:21–22. The result gave warning of the judgment that would come on the entire nation should it persist in disobedience and apostasy (see 2Ch 36:16). Thus Elisha's first acts were indicative of his ministry that would follow: God's covenant blessings would come to those who looked to him (vv. 19–22), but God's covenant curses would fall on those who turned away from him (cf. 1Ki 19:17 and note).

he went on to Mount Carmel[e] and from there returned to Samaria.

Moab Revolts

3 Joram[a][f] son of Ahab became king of Israel in Samaria in the eighteenth year of Jehoshaphat king of Judah, and he reigned twelve years. 2 He did evil[g] in the eyes of the LORD, but not as his father[h] and mother had done. He got rid of the sacred stone[i] of Baal that his father had made. 3 Nevertheless he clung to the sins[j] of Jeroboam son of Nebat, which he had caused Israel to commit; he did not turn away from them.

4 Now Mesha king of Moab[k] raised sheep, and he had to pay the king of Israel a tribute of a hundred thousand lambs[l] and the wool of a hundred thousand rams. 5 But after Ahab died, the king of Moab rebelled[m] against the king of Israel. 6 So at that time King Joram set out from Samaria and mobilized all Israel. 7 He also sent this message to Jehoshaphat king of Judah: "The king of Moab has rebelled against me. Will you go with me to fight[n] against Moab?"

"I will go with you," he replied. "I am as you are, my people as your people, my horses as your horses."

8 "By what route shall we attack?" he asked.

"Through the Desert of Edom," he answered.

9 So the king of Israel set out with the king of Judah and the king of Edom.[o] After a roundabout march of seven days, the army had no more water for themselves or for the animals with them.

10 "What!" exclaimed the king of Israel. "Has the LORD called us three kings together only to deliver us into the hands of Moab?"

11 But Jehoshaphat asked, "Is there no prophet of the LORD here, through whom we may inquire[p] of the LORD?"

An officer of the king of Israel answered, "Elisha[q] son of Shaphat is here. He used to pour water on the hands of Elijah.[b][r]"

12 Jehoshaphat said, "The word[s] of the LORD is with him." So the king of Israel and Jehoshaphat and the king of Edom went down to him.

13 Elisha said to the king of Israel, "Why do you want to involve me? Go to the prophets of your father and the prophets of your mother."

"No," the king of Israel answered, "because it was the LORD who called us three kings together to deliver us into the hands of Moab."

14 Elisha said, "As surely as the LORD Almighty lives, whom I serve, if I did not have respect for the presence of Jehoshaphat king of Judah, I would not pay any attention to you. 15 But now bring me a harpist."[t]

While the harpist was playing, the hand[u] of the LORD came on Elisha 16 and he

2:25 [e] S 1Ki 18:20
3:1 [f] S 2Ki 1:17
3:2 [g] 1Ki 15:26 [h] 1Ki 16:30-32 [i] S Ex 23:24
3:3 [j] S 1Ki 12:28-32
3:4 [k] S Ge 19:37; 2Ki 1:1 [l] Ezr 7:17; Isa 16:1
3:5 [m] S 2Ki 1:1
3:7 [n] 1Ki 22:4
3:9 [o] S 1Ki 22:47
3:11 [p] S Ge 25:22; S 1Ki 22:5 [q] S Ge 20:7 [r] S 1Ki 19:16
3:12 [s] S Nu 11:17
3:15 [t] S 1Sa 10:5 [u] Jer 15:17; Eze 1:3

[a] *1* Hebrew *Jehoram,* a variant of *Joram;* also in verse 6
[b] *11* That is, he was Elijah's personal servant.

3:1 *Joram son of Ahab became king ... in the eighteenth year of Jehoshaphat.* See note on 1:17. *twelve years.* 852–841 BC.
3:2 *not as his father and mother had done.* Not as Ahab (see notes on 1Ki 16:30–34) and Jezebel (see 1Ki 18:4; 19:1–2; 21:7–15). *sacred stone of Baal that his father had made.* Apparently a reference to the stone representation of the male deity (see note on 1Ki 14:23) that Ahab placed in the temple he had constructed for Jezebel in Samaria (see 1Ki 16:32–33). From 10:27 it appears that this stone was later reinstated, perhaps by Jezebel, then destroyed by Jehu.
3:3 *sins of Jeroboam ... he had caused Israel to commit.* See note on 1Ki 14:16.
3:4 *Mesha king of Moab.* See note on 1:1. *a hundred thousand lambs and the wool of a hundred thousand rams.* The heavy annual tribute (see Isa 16:1) that Israel required from the Moabites as a vassal state.
3:5 *king of Moab rebelled.* See note on 1:1.
3:7 *Will you go with me to fight against Moab?* Joram wished to attack Moab from the rear (v. 8), but to do that his army had to pass through Judah. *I am as you are, my people as your people, my horses as your horses.* See 1Ki 22:4. Jehoshaphat had already been condemned by prophets of the Lord for his alliance with the northern kings Ahab (see 2Ch 18:1; 19:1–2) and Ahaziah (2Ch 20:35–37), yet he agreed to join with Joram against Moab. Perhaps he was disturbed by the potential danger to Judah posed by the growing strength of Moab (see 2Ch 20), and he may have considered Joram less evil than his predecessors (see v. 2).
3:8 *Through the Desert of Edom.* This route of attack took the armies of Israel and Judah south of the Dead Sea, enabling them to circumvent the fortifications of Moab's northern frontier and to avoid the possibility of a rearguard action against them by the Arameans of Damascus. The Edomites, who were subject to Judah, were in no position to resist the movement of Israel's army through their territory.
3:9 *king of Edom.* Although here designated a king, he was in reality a governor appointed by Jehoshaphat (see 8:20; 1Ki 22:47).
3:11 *Is there no prophet of the LORD here ... ?* See 1Ki 22:7. Only after the apparent failure of their own strategies did the three rulers seek the word of the Lord (v. 12). *Elisha son of Shaphat is here.* Since Elijah is reported to have sent a letter to Jehoshaphat's son Jehoram after his father's death (2Ch 21:12–15), it seems that Elisha accompanied the armies on this campaign as the representative of the aged Elijah. The event is narrated here after the account of Elisha's initiation as Elijah's successor and the two events that foreshadowed the character of his ministry. Following this introduction to Elisha's ministry, the present episode is topically associated with the series of Elisha's acts that now occupies the narrative.
3:13 *Go to the prophets of your father and ... mother.* See 1Ki 22:6.
3:14 *if I did not have respect for ... Jehoshaphat ... I would not pay any attention to you.* Joram will share in the blessing of the word of God only because of his association with Jehoshaphat.
3:15 *bring me a harpist.* To create a disposition conducive to receiving the word of the Lord. *hand of the LORD.* See note on Eze 1:3.

said, "This is what the LORD says: I will fill
this valley with pools of water. 17For this
is what the LORD says: You will see neither wind nor rain, yet this valley will be
filled with water,[v] and you, your cattle and
your other animals will drink. 18This is an
easy[w] thing in the eyes of the LORD; he will
also deliver Moab into your hands. 19You
will overthrow every fortified city and every major town. You will cut down every
good tree, stop up all the springs, and ruin
every good field with stones."
20The next morning, about the time[x] for
offering the sacrifice, there it was—water
flowing from the direction of Edom! And
the land was filled with water.[y]
21Now all the Moabites had heard that
the kings had come to fight against them;
so every man, young and old, who could
bear arms was called up and stationed on
the border. 22When they got up early in
the morning, the sun was shining on the
water. To the Moabites across the way, the
water looked red—like blood. 23"That's
blood!" they said. "Those kings must have
fought and slaughtered each other. Now to
the plunder, Moab!"
24But when the Moabites came to the
camp of Israel, the Israelites rose up and
fought them until they fled. And the Israelites invaded the land and slaughtered
the Moabites. 25They destroyed the towns,
and each man threw a stone on every good
field until it was covered. They stopped up
all the springs and cut down every good
tree. Only Kir Hareseth[z] was left with its
stones in place, but men armed with slings
surrounded it and attacked it.
26When the king of Moab saw that the
battle had gone against him, he took with
him seven hundred swordsmen to break
through to the king of Edom, but they
failed. 27Then he took his firstborn[a] son,
who was to succeed him as king, and offered him as a sacrifice on the city wall.
The fury against Israel was great; they
withdrew and returned to their own land.

3:17 [v]Ps 107:35; Isa 12:3; 32:2; 35:6; 41:18; 65:13
3:18 [w]S Ge 18:14; 2Ki 20:10; Isa 49:6; Jer 32:17,27; Mk 10:27
3:20 [x]S Ex 29:41 [y]S Ex 17:6
3:25 [z]Isa 15:1; 16:7; Jer 48:31, 36
3:27 [a]S Dt 12:31; 2Ki 16:3; 21:6; 2Ch 28:3; Ps 106:38; Jer 19:4-5; Mic 6:7
4:1 [b]S 1Sa 10:5 [c]S Ex 22:26; Lev 25:39-43; Ne 5:3-5; Job 22:6; 24:9
4:2 [d]S 1Ki 17:12
4:7 [e]S 1Ki 12:22
4:8 [f]S Jos 19:18

The Widow's Olive Oil

4 The wife of a man from the company[b] of the prophets cried out to Elisha,
"Your servant my husband is dead, and
you know that he revered the LORD. But
now his creditor[c] is coming to take my two
boys as his slaves."
2Elisha replied to her, "How can I help
you? Tell me, what do you have in your
house?"
"Your servant has nothing there at all,"
she said, "except a small jar of olive oil."[d]
3Elisha said, "Go around and ask all
your neighbors for empty jars. Don't ask
for just a few. 4Then go inside and shut
the door behind you and your sons. Pour
oil into all the jars, and as each is filled,
put it to one side."
5She left him and shut the door behind
her and her sons. They brought the jars to
her and she kept pouring. 6When all the
jars were full, she said to her son, "Bring
me another one."
But he replied, "There is not a jar left."
Then the oil stopped flowing.
7She went and told the man of God,[e]
and he said, "Go, sell the oil and pay your
debts. You and your sons can live on what
is left."

The Shunammite's Son Restored to Life

8One day Elisha went to Shunem.[f] And
a well-to-do woman was there, who urged

3:16 *this valley.* The Israelite armies were encamped in the broad valley (the Arabah) between the highlands of Moab on the east and those of Judah on the west, just south of the Dead Sea.

3:17 *will be filled with water.* The word of the Lord contained a promise and a directive. The Lord will graciously provide for his people, but they must respond to his word in faith and obedience (v. 16).

3:19 The two armies will devastate the rebellious country.

3:20 *time for offering.* See Ex 29:38–39; Nu 28:3–4. *water flowing from the direction of Edom.* Flash floods in the distant mountains of Edom caused water to flow north through the broad, usually dry, valley that sloped toward the Dead Sea (see note on v. 16).

3:23 *Those kings must have ... slaughtered each other.* The Moabites would have good reason to suspect that an internal conflict had arisen between the parties of an alliance whose members had previously been mutually hostile.

3:25 *Kir Hareseth.* The capital city of Moab (see Isa 16:7,11; Jer 48:31,36), usually identified with present-day Kerak, located about 11 miles east of the Dead Sea and 15 miles south of the Arnon River (see map, p. 557).

3:26 *break through to the king of Edom.* A desperate attempt by the king of Moab to induce Edom to turn against Israel and Judah.

3:27 *offered him as a sacrifice on the city wall.* King Mesha offered his oldest son, the crown prince, as a burnt offering (see 16:3; Jer 7:31) to the Moabite god Chemosh (see 1Ki 11:7; Nu 21:29; Jer 48:46) in an attempt to induce the deity to come to his aid. *The fury against Israel was great.* It seems that just when total victory appeared to be in Israel's grasp, God's displeasure with the Ahab dynasty showed itself in some way that caused the Israelite kings to give up the campaign.

4:1 *company of the prophets.* See notes on 2:3; 1Ki 20:35. *take my two boys as his slaves.* Servitude as a means of debt payment by labor was permitted in the Mosaic law (Ex 21:1–2; Lev 25:39–41; Dt 15:1–11). It appears that the practice was much abused (see Ne 5:5,8; Am 2:6; 8:6), even though the law limited the term of such bondage and required that those so held be treated as hired workers.

4:4 *shut the door behind you and your sons.* The impending miracle was not intended to be a public sensation but to demonstrate privately God's mercy and grace to this widow (cf. Ps 68:5). She did not hesitate to respond to the instructions of the Lord's prophet in faith and obedience.

4:8 *Shunem.* See note on 1Ki 1:3.

him to stay for a meal. So whenever he
came by, he stopped there to eat. 9 She
said to her husband, "I know that this
man who often comes our way is a holy
man of God. 10 Let's make a small room on
the roof and put in it a bed and a table,
a chair and a lamp for him. Then he can
stay[g] there whenever he comes to us."
11 One day when Elisha came, he went
up to his room and lay down there. 12 He
said to his servant Gehazi, "Call the Shunammite."[h] So he called her, and she stood
before him. 13 Elisha said to him, "Tell her,
'You have gone to all this trouble for us.
Now what can be done for you? Can we
speak on your behalf to the king or the
commander of the army?' "
She replied, "I have a home among my
own people."
14 "What can be done for her?" Elisha
asked.
Gehazi said, "She has no son, and her
husband is old."
15 Then Elisha said, "Call her." So he
called her, and she stood in the doorway.
16 "About this time[i] next year," Elisha said,
"you will hold a son in your arms."
"No, my lord!" she objected. "Please,
man of God, don't mislead your servant!"
17 But the woman became pregnant,
and the next year about that same time
she gave birth to a son, just as Elisha had
told her.
18 The child grew, and one day he went
out to his father, who was with the reapers.[j] 19 He said to his father, "My head! My
head!"
His father told a servant, "Carry him to
his mother." 20 After the servant had lifted
him up and carried him to his mother, the
boy sat on her lap until noon, and then he
died. 21 She went up and laid him on the
bed[k] of the man of God, then shut the door
and went out.
22 She called her husband and said,
"Please send me one of the servants and
a donkey so I can go to the man of God
quickly and return."
23 "Why go to him today?" he asked.
"It's not the New Moon[l] or the Sabbath."
"That's all right," she said.
24 She saddled the donkey and said to
her servant, "Lead on; don't slow down
for me unless I tell you." 25 So she set out
and came to the man of God at Mount Carmel.[m]
When he saw her in the distance, the
man of God said to his servant Gehazi,
"Look! There's the Shunammite! 26 Run to
meet her and ask her, 'Are you all right?
Is your husband all right? Is your child all
right?' "
"Everything is all right," she said.
27 When she reached the man of God at
the mountain, she took hold of his feet.
Gehazi came over to push her away, but
the man of God said, "Leave her alone!
She is in bitter distress,[n] but the LORD has
hidden it from me and has not told me
why."
28 "Did I ask you for a son, my lord?"
she said. "Didn't I tell you, 'Don't raise
my hopes'?"
29 Elisha said to Gehazi, "Tuck your
cloak into your belt,[o] take my staff[p] in
your hand and run. Don't greet anyone
you meet, and if anyone greets you, do not
answer. Lay my staff on the boy's face."

4:10 [g] Mt 10:41; S Ro 12:13 **4:12** [h] 2Ki 8:1 **4:16** [i] S Ge 18:10 **4:18** [j] S Ru 2:3 **4:21** [k] ver 32 **4:23** [l] S Nu 10:10; 1Ch 23:31; Ps 81:3 **4:25** [m] S 1Ki 18:20 **4:27** [n] 1Sa 1:15 **4:29** [o] S 1Ki 18:46 [p] S Ex 4:2

4:9 *holy man of God.* The woman recognized that Elisha was a person set apart to the Lord's work in a very special sense (see note on Ex 3:5). Nowhere else in the OT is the term "holy" applied to a prophet.

4:10 *he can stay there whenever he comes to us.* By her hospitality the woman was able to assist in sustaining the proclamation of God's word through Elisha.

4:12 *Gehazi.* Referred to here for the first time; he appears to have served Elisha in some of the same ways as Elisha had served Elijah, though the two men were of drastically different character (see 5:19–27; 6:15).

4:13 *I have a home among my own people.* The Shunammite woman felt secure and content in the community of her own family and tribe, and she had no need or desire for favors from high government officials.

4:14 *She has no son, and her husband is old.* A great disappointment because it meant that the family's name would cease and its land and possessions would pass on to others. It was also a great threat to this young wife's future in that she faced the likelihood of many years as a widow with no provider or protector—children were a widow's only social security in old age (see 8:1–6; see also note on 1Ki 17:22).

4:16 *About this time next year.* See Ge 17:21; 18:14. *man of God, don't mislead your servant!* The woman's response revealed the depths of her desire for a son and her fear of disappointment more than it showed a lack of confidence in the word of Elisha.

4:17 *just as Elisha had told her.* The trustworthiness of Elisha's word was confirmed, and the birth of the son was shown to be the result of God's gracious intervention in her behalf.

4:20 *he died.* The child, given as an evidence of God's grace and the reliability of his word, was suddenly taken from the woman in a severe test of her faith. Her subsequent actions demonstrate the strength of her faith in the face of great calamity.

4:21 *laid him on the bed of the man of God.* In this way the woman concealed the child's death from the rest of the household while she went to seek the prophet at whose word the child had been born.

4:23 *Why go to him today?* The question suggests that it was not uncommon for the woman to go to Elisha but that on this occasion the timing of her visit was unusual.

4:26 *Everything is all right.* The woman was determined to share her distress with no one but the prophet from whom she had received the promise of the birth of her son.

4:28 *Didn't I tell you, 'Don't raise my hopes'?* The woman struggled with the question of why the Lord would take from her that which she had been given as a special demonstration of his grace and the trustworthiness of his word.

4:29 *Lay my staff on the boy's face.* It appears that Elisha ex-

30 But the child's mother said, "As surely
as the LORD lives and as you live, I will not
leave you." So he got up and followed her.
31 Gehazi went on ahead and laid the
staff on the boy's face, but there was no
sound or response. So Gehazi went back
to meet Elisha and told him, "The boy has
not awakened."
32 When Elisha reached the house, there
was the boy lying dead on his couch.[q]
33 He went in, shut the door on the two of
them and prayed[r] to the LORD. 34 Then he
got on the bed and lay on the boy, mouth
to mouth, eyes to eyes, hands to hands. As
he stretched[s] himself out on him, the boy's
body grew warm. 35 Elisha turned away
and walked back and forth in the room
and then got on the bed and stretched out
on him once more. The boy sneezed seven
times[t] and opened his eyes.[u]
36 Elisha summoned Gehazi and said,
"Call the Shunammite." And he did. When
she came, he said, "Take your son."[v] 37 She
came in, fell at his feet and bowed to the
ground. Then she took her son and went
out.

Death in the Pot

38 Elisha returned to Gilgal[w] and there
was a famine[x] in that region. While the
company of the prophets was meeting
with him, he said to his servant, "Put on
the large pot and cook some stew for these
prophets."
39 One of them went out into the fields
to gather herbs and found a wild vine and
picked as many of its gourds as his garment could hold. When he returned, he
cut them up into the pot of stew, though
no one knew what they were. 40 The stew
was poured out for the men, but as they
began to eat it, they cried out, "Man of
God, there is death in the pot!" And they
could not eat it.
41 Elisha said, "Get some flour." He put it
into the pot and said, "Serve it to the people to eat." And there was nothing harmful
in the pot.[y]

Feeding of a Hundred

42 A man came from Baal Shalishah,[z]
bringing the man of God twenty loaves[a]
of barley bread[b] baked from the first ripe
grain, along with some heads of new
grain. "Give it to the people to eat," Elisha said.
43 "How can I set this before a hundred
men?" his servant asked.
But Elisha answered, "Give it to the
people to eat.[c] For this is what the LORD
says: 'They will eat and have some left
over.[d]'" 44 Then he set it before them, and
they ate and had some left over, according
to the word of the LORD.

Naaman Healed of Leprosy

5 Now Naaman was commander of the
army of the king of Aram.[e] He was a
great man in the sight of his master and
highly regarded, because through him the
LORD had given victory to Aram. He was a
valiant soldier, but he had leprosy.[a][f]
2 Now bands of raiders[g] from Aram had
gone out and had taken captive a young

4:32 [q] ver 21 **4:33** [r] 1Ki 17:20; Mt 6:6 **4:34** [s] 1Ki 17:21; Ac 20:10 **4:35** [t] S Jos 6:15 [u] 2Ki 8:5 **4:36** [v] Heb 11:35 **4:38** [w] S 2Ki 2:1 [x] S Lev 26:26; 2Ki 8:1 **4:41** [y] S Ex 15:25; S 2Ki 2:21 **4:42** [z] 1Sa 9:4 [a] Mt 14:17; 15:36 [b] S 1Sa 9:7 **4:43** [c] Lk 9:13 [d] Mt 14:20; Jn 6:12 **5:1** [e] S Ge 10:22; S 2Sa 10:19 [f] S Ex 4:6; S Nu 12:10; Lk 4:27 **5:2** [g] 2Ki 6:23; 13:20; 24:2

[a] *1* The Hebrew for *leprosy* was used for various diseases affecting the skin; also in verses 3, 6, 7, 11 and 27.

pected the Lord to restore the boy's life when the staff was placed on him. This does not suggest that Elisha attributed magical power to the staff but that he viewed it as a representation of his own presence and a symbol of divine power (see note on 2:8; cf. Ex 14:16; Ac 19:12).

4:30 *I will not leave you.* The woman was not convinced that Gehazi's mission would be successful and insisted that Elisha himself accompany her to Shunem.

4:33 *shut the door on the two of them and prayed.* Just as Elijah had done in a similar situation years before (see 1Ki 17:20–22), Elisha first turned to the Lord in earnest prayer for restoration of life to the dead child. His prayer is clear evidence that his subsequent actions were not intended as a magical means of restoring life.

4:34 *lay on the boy.* See note on 1Ki 17:21. Perhaps Elisha was familiar with the earlier similar action of Elijah.

4:37 *fell at his feet and bowed to the ground.* The woman gratefully acknowledged the special favor granted to her by the Lord through Elisha, and silently reaffirmed the verbal confession of the widow of Zarephath (see 1Ki 17:24).

4:38 *Gilgal.* See note on 2:1. *famine in that region.* Perhaps the same famine mentioned in 8:1. Famine was a covenant curse (see Lev 26:19–20,26; Dt 28:18,23–24; 1Ki 8:36–37) and evidence of God's anger with his people's disobedience to their covenant obligations. *company of the prophets.* See note on 2:3.

4:41 *flour.* The flour itself did not make the stew edible (see 2:21 and note). It was simply a means by which the Lord provided for those who were faithful to the covenant, at a time when others suffered under the covenant curse.

4:42 *first ripe grain.* Instead of bringing the firstfruits of the new harvest (see Lev 2:14; 23:15–17; Dt 18:3–5) to the apostate priests at Bethel and Dan (see 1Ki 12:28–31), godly people in the northern kingdom may have contributed their offerings for the sustenance of Elisha and those associated with him (see note on v. 23). Thus they looked upon Elisha rather than the apostate king and priests as the true representative of their covenant Lord.

4:43 *the LORD says.* The bread was multiplied at the word of the Lord through Elisha apart from any intermediate means (contrast v. 41; 2:20; cf. Mk 6:35–43 and note on 6:43).

5:1 *king of Aram.* Probably Ben-Hadad II (see notes on 8:7; 13:3; 1Ki 20:1). *the LORD had given victory to Aram.* Probably a reference to an otherwise undocumented Aramean victory over the Assyrians in the aftermath of the battle of Qarqar in 853 BC (see note on 1Ki 22:1). In the narrator's theological perspective, this victory is attributable to the sovereignty of the God of Israel, who is seen as the ruler and controller of the destinies of all nations, not just that of Israel (see Eze 30:24; Am 2:1–3; 9:7).

5:2 *bands of raiders from Aram.* Although Israel had concluded a peace treaty with the Arameans during

girl from Israel, and she served Naaman's
wife. 3 She said to her mistress, "If only
my master would see the prophet[h] who is
in Samaria! He would cure him of his leprosy."
4 Naaman went to his master and told
him what the girl from Israel had said.
5 "By all means, go," the king of Aram replied. "I will send a letter to the king of
Israel." So Naaman left, taking with him
ten talents[a] of silver, six thousand shekels[b]
of gold and ten sets of clothing.[i] 6 The letter that he took to the king of Israel read:
"With this letter I am sending my servant
Naaman to you so that you may cure him
of his leprosy."
7 As soon as the king of Israel read the
letter,[j] he tore his robes and said, "Am I
God?[k] Can I kill and bring back to life?[l]
Why does this fellow send someone to me
to be cured of his leprosy? See how he is
trying to pick a quarrel[m] with me!"
8 When Elisha the man of God heard
that the king of Israel had torn his robes,
he sent him this message: "Why have you
torn your robes? Have the man come to me
and he will know that there is a prophet[n]
in Israel." 9 So Naaman went with his horses and chariots and stopped at the door of
Elisha's house. 10 Elisha sent a messenger
to say to him, "Go, wash[o] yourself seven
times[p] in the Jordan, and your flesh will be
restored and you will be cleansed."
11 But Naaman went away angry and
said, "I thought that he would surely
come out to me and stand and call on the
name of the LORD his God, wave his hand[q]
over the spot and cure me of my leprosy.
12 Are not Abana and Pharpar, the rivers
of Damascus, better than all the waters[r]
of Israel? Couldn't I wash in them and be
cleansed?" So he turned and went off in
a rage.[s]
13 Naaman's servants went to him and
said, "My father,[t] if the prophet had told
you to do some great thing, would you not
have done it? How much more, then, when
he tells you, 'Wash and be cleansed'!"
14 So he went down and dipped himself
in the Jordan seven times,[u] as the man
of God had told him, and his flesh was
restored[v] and became clean like that of a
young boy.[w]
15 Then Naaman and all his attendants
went back to the man of God[x]. He stood
before him and said, "Now I know[y] that

5:3 [h] S Ge 20:7 **5:5** [i] ver 22; S Ge 24:53; Jdg 14:12; S 1Sa 9:7 **5:7** [j] 2Ki 19:14 [k] S Ge 30:2 [l] S Dt 32:39 [m] 1Ki 20:7 **5:8** [n] S 1Ki 22:7 **5:10** [o] Jn 9:7 [p] S Ge 33:3; S Lev 14:7 **5:11** [q] S Ex 7:19 **5:12** [r] Isa 8:6 [s] Pr 14:17,29; 19:11; 29:11 **5:13** [t] 2Ki 6:21; 13:14 **5:14** [u] S Ge 33:3; S Lev 14:7; S Jos 6:15 [v] S Ex 4:7 [w] Job 33:25 **5:15** [x] S Jos 2:11 [y] S Jos 4:24; S 1Sa 17:46

[a] 5 That is, about 750 pounds or about 340 kilograms
[b] 5 That is, about 150 pounds or about 69 kilograms

---

the reign of Ahab (see 1Ki 20:34), minor border skirmishes continued between the two states in the aftermath of the battle for control of Ramoth Gilead, in which Ahab had been killed (see note on 1Ki 22:4; see also 1Ki 22:35). *young girl from Israel.* In sharp contrast to the Israelite king in Samaria, this young girl held captive in Damascus was very much aware of God's saving presence with his people through his servant Elisha, and she selflessly shared that knowledge with her Aramean captors.

5:3 *prophet who is in Samaria.* Elisha, who maintained a residence in Samaria (see v. 9; 2:25; 6:19).

5:5 *I will send a letter to the king of Israel.* The border skirmishes had not nullified the official peace between the two nations as established by treaty. The king of Israel was Joram (see 1:17; 3:1; 9:24). *ten talents of silver.* See NIV text note. An idea of the relative value of this amount of silver can be seen by comparing it with the price Omri paid for the hill of Samaria (see 1Ki 16:24).

5:6 *so that you may cure him of his leprosy.* Ben-Hadad (king of Aram) assumed that the prophet described by the Israelite slave girl was subject to the authority of the king and that his services could be bought with a sufficiently large gift. He thought he could buy with worldly wealth one of the chief blessings of God's saving presence among his people.

5:7 *he is trying to pick a quarrel with me!* Joram concluded that the entire incident was an attempt by Ben-Hadad to create a pretext for a declaration of war. So blind was the king to God's saving presence through Elisha that he could think only of international intrigue.

5:8 *Why have you torn your robes?* Elisha chided Joram for his fear (see note on 1Sa 17:11) and for his failure to consult the Lord's prophet (see 3:13–14 for evidence of the tension that existed between Joram and Elisha).

5:9 *with his horses and chariots.* This proud pagan would command the healing by his lordly presence.

5:10 *wash yourself seven times in the Jordan.* The instruction is designed to demonstrate to Naaman that healing would come by the power of the God of Israel, but only if he obeyed the word of the Lord's prophet. The prophet himself was not a healer. Ritual washings were practiced among Eastern religions as a purification rite, and the number seven was generally known as a symbol of completeness. Naaman was to wash in the muddy waters of the Jordan River, demonstrating that there was no natural connection between the washing and the desired healing. Perhaps it also suggested that one needed to pass through the Jordan, as Israel had done, in order to obtain healing from the God of Israel (see notes on Jos 3:1—4:24; 3:10).

5:11 *wave his hand over the spot and cure me of my leprosy.* Naaman expected to be healed by the magical technique of the prophet rather than by the power of God operative in connection with his own obedient response to God's word.

5:12 *Abana and Pharpar.* The Abana was termed the Golden River by the Greeks. It is usually identified with the Barada River of today, rising in the Anti-Lebanon mountains and flowing through the city of Damascus. The Pharpar River flows east from Mount Hermon just to the south of Damascus (see map, p. 1707).

5:14 *his flesh was restored and became clean like that of a young boy.* Physically he was reborn (see also v. 15 and note). As he obeyed God's word, Naaman received the gift of God's grace. Naaman is here a sign to disobedient Israel that God's blessing is found only in the path of trustful obedience. When his own people turn away from covenant faithfulness, God will raise up those who will follow his word from outside the covenant nation (see notes on 1Ki 17:9–24; see also Mt 8:10–12; Lk 4:27).

5:15 *no God in all the world except in Israel.* Naaman's confession put to shame the Israelites who continued to waver in their opinion on whether Baal and the Lord (Yahweh) were both gods or whether Yahweh alone was God (see note on 1Ki 18:21).

there is no God in all the world except in
Israel. So please accept a gift[z] from your
servant."
16 The prophet answered, "As surely as
the LORD lives, whom I serve, I will not accept a thing." And even though Naaman
urged him, he refused.[a]
17 "If you will not," said Naaman,
"please let me, your servant, be given as
much earth[b] as a pair of mules can carry, for your servant will never again make
burnt offerings and sacrifices to any other
god but the LORD. 18 But may the LORD forgive your servant for this one thing: When
my master enters the temple of Rimmon to
bow down and he is leaning[c] on my arm
and I have to bow there also — when I
bow down in the temple of Rimmon, may
the LORD forgive your servant for this."
19 "Go in peace,"[d] Elisha said.
After Naaman had traveled some distance, 20 Gehazi, the servant of Elisha the
man of God, said to himself, "My master
was too easy on Naaman, this Aramean-
an, by not accepting from him what he
brought. As surely as the LORD[e] lives, I
will run after him and get something from
him."
21 So Gehazi hurried after Naaman.
When Naaman saw him running toward
him, he got down from the chariot to meet
him. "Is everything all right?" he asked.
22 "Everything is all right," Gehazi answered. "My master sent me to say, 'Two
young men from the company of the
prophets have just come to me from the
hill country of Ephraim. Please give them
a talent[a] of silver and two sets of clothing.' "[f]
23 "By all means, take two talents," said
Naaman. He urged Gehazi to accept them,
and then tied up the two talents of silver
in two bags, with two sets of clothing. He
gave them to two of his servants, and they
carried them ahead of Gehazi. 24 When Gehazi came to the hill, he took the things
from the servants and put them away in
the house. He sent the men away and they
left.
25 When he went in and stood before his
master, Elisha asked him, "Where have
you been, Gehazi?"
"Your servant didn't go anywhere," Gehazi answered.
26 But Elisha said to him, "Was not my
spirit with you when the man got down
from his chariot to meet you? Is this the
time[g] to take money or to accept clothes —
or olive groves and vineyards, or flocks
and herds, or male and female slaves?[h]
27 Naaman's leprosy[i] will cling to you and
to your descendants forever." Then Gehazi[j] went from Elisha's presence and his
skin was leprous — it had become as white
as snow.[k]

An Axhead Floats

6 The company[l] of the prophets said
to Elisha, "Look, the place where we
meet with you is too small for us. 2 Let us
go to the Jordan, where each of us can get
a pole; and let us build a place there for
us to meet."
And he said, "Go."
3 Then one of them said, "Won't you
please come with your servants?"
"I will," Elisha replied. 4 And he went
with them.
They went to the Jordan and began

5:15 [z] S 1Sa 9:7 **5:16** [a] ver 20, 26; Ge 14:23; Da 5:17 **5:17** [b] Ex 20:24 **5:18** [c] 2Ki 7:2 **5:19** [d] 1Sa 1:17; S Ac 15:33 **5:20** [e] Ex 20:7 **5:22** [f] S ver 5; S Ge 45:22 **5:26** [g] S ver 16 [h] Jer 45:5 **5:27** [i] S Nu 12:10 [j] Col 3:5 [k] S Ex 4:6 **6:1** [l] S 1Sa 10:5

[a] *22* That is, about 75 pounds or about 34 kilograms

5:16 *I will not accept a thing.* Elisha did not seek monetary gain for proclaiming the word of the Lord (see Mt 10:8). Naaman was healed solely by divine grace, not by the power of Elisha.

5:17 *let me ... be given as much earth as a pair of mules can carry.* In the ancient world it was commonly thought that a deity could be worshiped only on the soil of the nation to which he was bound (see v. 15). For this reason Naaman wanted to take Israelite soil with him in order to have a place in Damascus for the worship of the Lord.

5:18 *my master.* Ben-Hadad, king of Aram. *Rimmon.* Also known as Hadad (and in Canaan and Phoenicia as Baal), this Aramean deity was the god of storm ("Rimmon" means "thunderer") and war. The two names were sometimes combined (see note on Zec 12:11).

5:19 *Go in peace.* Elisha did not directly address Naaman's problem of conscience (v. 18), but commended him to the leading and grace of God as he returned to his pagan environment and official responsibilities.

5:20 *As surely as the LORD lives.* An oath formula (see note on 1Sa 14:39,45).

5:22 *company of the prophets.* See note on 2:3. *Please give them a talent of silver and two sets of clothing.* Gehazi deceived Naaman in order to satisfy his desire for material gain. The evil of his lie was compounded in that it obscured the gracious character of the Lord's work in Naaman's healing and blurred the distinction between Elisha's function as a true prophet of the Lord and the self-serving actions of false prophets and pagan soothsayers.

5:24 *house.* Of Elisha (see v. 9).

5:26 *Is this the time to take money ... ?* Gehazi sought to use the grace of God granted to another individual for his own material advantage. This was equivalent to making merchandise of God's grace (see note on 2Co 2:17). "Money" here and elsewhere in 2 Kings refers to gold or silver in various weights, not to coins, which were a later invention. *clothes ... female slaves.* Evidently what Gehazi secretly hoped to acquire with the two talents of silver (see note on v. 5).

5:27 *leprosy.* See NIV text note on v. 1. *to you and to your descendants forever.* For the extension of punishment to the children of an offender of God's law, see Ex 20:5 and note; see also note on Jos 7:24. *white as snow.* See Ex 4:6.

6:1 *company of the prophets.* See note on 2:3.

6:2 *a place there for us to meet.* Referring to some type of assembly hall. It is implied in 4:1 – 7 that there were separate dwellings for the members of the prophetic companies to live in (see note on 1Sa 19:18).

to cut down trees. 5As one of them was
cutting down a tree, the iron axhead fell
into the water. "Oh no, my lord!" he cried
out. "It was borrowed!"
6The man of God asked, "Where did it
fall?" When he showed him the place, Elisha cut a stick and threw[m] it there, and
made the iron float. 7"Lift it out," he said.
Then the man reached out his hand and
took it.

Elisha Traps Blinded Arameans

8Now the king of Aram was at war with
Israel. After conferring with his officers,
he said, "I will set up my camp in such
and such a place."
9The man of God sent word to the king[n]
of Israel: "Beware of passing that place,
because the Arameans are going down
there." 10So the king of Israel checked on
the place indicated by the man of God.
Time and again Elisha warned[o] the king,
so that he was on his guard in such places.
11This enraged the king of Aram. He
summoned his officers and demanded of
them, "Tell me! Which of us is on the side
of the king of Israel?"
12"None of us, my lord the king[p]," said
one of his officers, "but Elisha, the prophet
who is in Israel, tells the king of Israel the
very words you speak in your bedroom."
13"Go, find out where he is," the king
ordered, "so I can send men and capture
him." The report came back: "He is in Dothan."[q] 14Then he sent[r] horses and chariots and a strong force there. They went by
night and surrounded the city.
15When the servant of the man of God
got up and went out early the next morning, an army with horses and chariots had
surrounded the city. "Oh no, my lord!
What shall we do?" the servant asked.
16"Don't be afraid,"[s] the prophet answered. "Those who are with us are more[t]
than those who are with them."
17And Elisha prayed, "Open his eyes,
LORD, so that he may see." Then the LORD
opened the servant's eyes, and he looked
and saw the hills full of horses and chariots[u] of fire all around Elisha.
18As the enemy came down toward him,
Elisha prayed to the LORD, "Strike this
army with blindness."[v] So he struck them
with blindness, as Elisha had asked.
19Elisha told them, "This is not the road
and this is not the city. Follow me, and I
will lead you to the man you are looking
for." And he led them to Samaria.
20After they entered the city, Elisha said,
"LORD, open the eyes of these men so they
can see." Then the LORD opened their eyes
and they looked, and there they were, inside Samaria.
21When the king of Israel saw them,
he asked Elisha, "Shall I kill them, my father?[w] Shall I kill them?"
22"Do not kill them," he answered.
"Would you kill those you have captured[x]
with your own sword or bow? Set food

6:6 [m] S Ex 15:25; S 2Ki 2:21 **6:9** [n] ver 12 **6:10** [o] Jer 11:18 **6:12** [p] ver 9
6:13 [q] Ge 37:17 **6:14** [r] 2Ki 1:9 **6:16** [s] S Ge 15:1 [t] 2Ch 32:7; Ps 55:18; Ro 8:31; 1Jn 4:4 **6:17** [u] S 2Ki 2:11,12 **6:18** [v] Ge 19:11; Ac 13:11 **6:21** [w] S 2Ki 5:13 **6:22** [x] S Dt 20:11; 2Ch 28:8-15

6:5 *It was borrowed.* At that time an iron axhead was a costly tool, too expensive for the members of the prophetic company to purchase. Having lost it, the borrower faced the prospect of having to work off the value as a bondservant.

6:6 *Elisha cut a stick and threw it there, and made the iron float.* The Lord demonstrated here his concern for the welfare of his faithful ones.

6:8 *king of Aram.* Probably Ben-Hadad II (see note on 5:1). *war with Israel.* A reference to border clashes rather than full-scale hostility (see v. 23; see also note on 5:2). Some indication of Israelite weakness and Aramean strength is seen in the ability of the Arameans to send forces to Dothan (only about 11 miles north of Samaria) without apparent difficulty (see vv. 13–14).

6:9 *man of God.* Elisha (see v. 10). *king of Israel.* Probably Joram (see 1:17; 3:1; 9:24).

6:11 *Which of us is on the side of the king of Israel?* Repeated evidence that Israel possessed advance knowledge of Aramean military plans led the king of Aram to suspect that there was a traitor among his top officials.

6:12 *king of Israel.* Joram (see 3:1).

6:13 *capture him.* The king of Aram thought he could eliminate Elisha's influence by denying him contact with Israel's king. *Dothan.* Located on a hill about halfway between Jezreel and Samaria, where the main royal residences were (see 1:2; 3:1; 8:29; 9:15; 10:1; 1Ki 21:1).

6:16 *Those who are with us are more than those who are with them.* Elisha knew that there was greater strength in the unseen reality of the hosts of heaven than in the visible reality of the Aramean forces (see 2Ch 32:7–8; Ps 34:7; 1Jn 4:4).

6:17 *saw the hills full of horses and chariots.* In response to Elisha's prayer, his servant was able to see the protecting might of the heavenly hosts gathered about Elisha (see Ge 32:1–2; Ps 34:7; 91:11–12; Mt 18:10; 26:53; see also note on 2Ki 2:11).

6:18 *Strike this army with blindness.* Elisha had prayed for the eyes of his servant to be opened to the unseen reality of the heavenly hosts; now he prays for the eyes of the Aramean soldiers to be closed to earthly reality (see Ge 19:11).

6:19 *This is not the road and this is not the city.* Elisha's statement led the Aramean soldiers to believe that they were being directed to the city where Elisha could be found. Technically this statement was not an untruth, since Elisha accompanied them to Samaria, but it was a means of deceiving the Aramean soldiers into a trap inside Samaria, the fortress-like capital city of the northern kingdom (see Ex 1:19–20; Jos 2:6; 1Sa 16:1–2 for other instances of deception recorded in the OT).

6:20 *there they were, inside Samaria.* The power of the Lord operative through Elisha turned the intended captors into captives.

6:21 *king of Israel.* Joram (see note on v. 9).

6:22 *Do not kill them.* In reality the Aramean soldiers had been taken captive by the power of the Lord, not by Joram's military prowess. The Lord's purpose was to demonstrate to them and their king and to the Israelites and their king that Israel's national security ultimately was grounded in the Lord, not in military forces or strategies.

and water before them so that they may
eat and drink and then go back to their
master." 23 So he prepared a great feast for
them, and after they had finished eating
and drinking, he sent them away, and they
returned to their master. So the bands[y]
from Aram stopped raiding Israel's territory.

Famine in Besieged Samaria

24 Some time later, Ben-Hadad[z] king
of Aram mobilized his entire army and
marched up and laid siege[a] to Samaria.
25 There was a great famine[b] in the city;
the siege lasted so long that a donkey's
head sold for eighty shekels[a] of silver, and
a quarter of a cab[b] of seed pods[c][c] for five
shekels.[d]
26 As the king of Israel was passing by
on the wall, a woman cried to him, "Help
me, my lord the king!"
27 The king replied, "If the LORD does not
help you, where can I get help for you?
From the threshing floor? From the winepress?" 28 Then he asked her, "What's the
matter?"
She answered, "This woman said to me,
'Give up your son so we may eat him today, and tomorrow we'll eat my son.' 29 So
we cooked my son and ate[d] him. The next
day I said to her, 'Give up your son so we
may eat him,' but she had hidden him."
30 When the king heard the woman's
words, he tore[e] his robes. As he went
along the wall, the people looked, and
they saw that, under his robes, he had
sackcloth[f] on his body. 31 He said, "May
God deal with me, be it ever so severely, if
the head of Elisha son of Shaphat remains
on his shoulders today!"
32 Now Elisha was sitting in his house,
and the elders[g] were sitting with him.
The king sent a messenger ahead, but
before he arrived, Elisha said to the elders, "Don't you see how this murderer[h]
is sending someone to cut off my head?[i]
Look, when the messenger comes, shut
the door and hold it shut against him. Is
not the sound of his master's footsteps behind him?" 33 While he was still talking to
them, the messenger came down to him.
The king said, "This disaster is from the
LORD. Why should I wait[j] for the LORD any
longer?"

7 Elisha replied, "Hear the word of the
LORD. This is what the LORD says:
About this time tomorrow, a seah[e] of the
finest flour will sell for a shekel[f] and two
seahs[g] of barley for a shekel[k] at the gate
of Samaria."
2 The officer on whose arm the king was
leaning[l] said to the man of God, "Look,
even if the LORD should open the floodgates[m] of the heavens, could this happen?"
"You will see it with your own eyes,"
answered Elisha, "but you will not eat[n]
any of it!"

The Siege Lifted

3 Now there were four men with leprosy[h][o] at the entrance of the city gate. They
said to each other, "Why stay here until we die? 4 If we say, 'We'll go into the

6:23 [y] S 2Ki 5:2 **6:24** [z] S 1Ki 15:18; 2Ki 8:7 [a] Dt 28:52 **6:25** [b] S Lev 26:26; S Ru 1:1 [c] Isa 36:12 **6:29** [d] S Lev 26:29; Dt 28:53-55 **6:30** [e] 2Ki 18:37; Isa 22:15 [f] S Ge 37:34

6:32 [g] Eze 8:1; 14:1; 20:1 [h] 1Ki 18:4 [i] ver 31 **6:33** [j] Lev 24:11; Job 2:9; 14:14; Isa 40:31 **7:1** [k] ver 16 **7:2** [l] 2Ki 5:18 [m] ver 19; Ge 7:11; Ps 78:23; Mal 3:10 [n] ver 17 **7:3** [o] Lev 13:45-46; Nu 5:1-4

[a] *25* That is, about 2 pounds or about 920 grams [b] *25* That is, probably about 1/4 pound or about 100 grams [c] *25* Or *of doves' dung* [d] *25* That is, about 2 ounces or about 58 grams [e] *1* That is, probably about 12 pounds or about 5.5 kilograms of flour; also in verses 16 and 18 [f] *1* That is, about 2/5 ounce or about 12 grams; also in verses 16 and 18 [g] *1* That is, probably about 20 pounds or about 9 kilograms of barley; also in verses 16 and 18 [h] *3* The Hebrew for *leprosy* was used for various diseases affecting the skin; also in verse 8.

6:23 *bands from Aram stopped raiding Israel's territory.* See notes on v. 8; 5:2. Temporarily the Arameans recognized the futility of opposition to the power of the God of Israel.

6:24 *Ben-Hadad.* The same Ben-Hadad II who had besieged Samaria on a previous occasion (see note on 1Ki 20:1). This siege is probably to be dated c. 850 BC.

6:25 *donkey's head.* According to Pentateuchal law the donkey was unclean and not to be eaten (see Lev 11:2–7; Dt 14:4–8). The severity of the famine caused the inhabitants of Samaria not only to disregard the laws of uncleanness but also to place a high value on the least edible part of the donkey. *eighty shekels of silver.* See NIV text note; see also note on 5:5.

6:27 *If the LORD does not help you, where can I get help for you?* Joram correctly recognized his own inability to assist the woman if the Lord himself did not act in Israel's behalf, but he wrongly implied that the Lord was to be blamed for a situation brought on by Israel's own disobedience and idolatry.

6:28 *tomorrow we'll eat my son.* The sins of the king and people were so great that the covenant curses of Lev 26:29 and Dt 28:53,57 were being inflicted (cf. La 4:10).

6:30 *tore his robes.* More an expression of anger toward Elisha and the Lord (see v. 31) than one of repentance and sorrow for the sins that had provoked the covenant curse. *sackcloth.* A coarse cloth usually worn as a sign of mourning (see notes on Ge 37:34; Rev 11:3).

6:31 *May God deal with me, be it ever so severely.* A curse formula (see note on 1Sa 3:17). *if the head of Elisha ... remains on his shoulders today!* Joram considered Elisha in some way responsible for the conditions in the city. Cf. Ahab's attitude toward Elijah (1Ki 18:10,16–17; 21:20).

6:32 *elders.* Leaders of the city (see notes on Ex 3:16; 2Sa 3:17). They sit with Elisha rather than with the king.

6:33 *Why should I wait for the LORD any longer?* Joram felt himself deceived by Elisha and abandoned by the Lord, whom he blamed for the disastrous conditions in the city.

7:1 *a seah of the finest flour will sell for a shekel.* See NIV text notes. This was about double the normal cost of flour, but a phenomenal improvement over the highly inflated prices the famine had caused.

7:2 *floodgates of the heavens.* See v. 19; Ge 8:2; Isa 24:18.

7:3 *entrance of the city gate.* Pentateuchal law excluded persons with defiling skin diseases from residence in the community (Lev 13:46; Nu 5:2–3).

city' — the famine is there, and we will die. And if we stay here, we will die. So let's go over to the camp of the Arameans and surrender. If they spare us, we live; if they kill us, then we die."

5 At dusk they got up and went to the camp of the Arameans. When they reached the edge of the camp, no one was there, 6 for the Lord had caused the Arameans to hear the sound[p] of chariots and horses and a great army, so that they said to one another, "Look, the king of Israel has hired[q] the Hittite[r] and Egyptian kings to attack us!" 7 So they got up and fled[s] in the dusk and abandoned their tents and their horses and donkeys. They left the camp as it was and ran for their lives.

8 The men who had leprosy[t] reached the edge of the camp, entered one of the tents and ate and drank. Then they took silver, gold and clothes, and went off and hid them. They returned and entered another tent and took some things from it and hid them also.

9 Then they said to each other, "What we're doing is not right. This is a day of good news and we are keeping it to ourselves. If we wait until daylight, punishment will overtake us. Let's go at once and report this to the royal palace."

10 So they went and called out to the city gatekeepers and told them, "We went into the Aramean camp and no one was there — not a sound of anyone — only tethered horses and donkeys, and the tents left just as they were." 11 The gatekeepers shouted the news, and it was reported within the palace.

12 The king got up in the night and said to his officers, "I will tell you what the Arameans have done to us. They know we are starving; so they have left the camp to hide[u] in the countryside, thinking, 'They will surely come out, and then we will take them alive and get into the city.' "

13 One of his officers answered, "Have some men take five of the horses that are left in the city. Their plight will be like that of all the Israelites left here — yes, they will only be like all these Israelites who are doomed. So let us send them to find out what happened."

14 So they selected two chariots with their horses, and the king sent them after the Aramean army. He commanded the drivers, "Go and find out what has happened." 15 They followed them as far as the Jordan, and they found the whole road strewn with the clothing and equipment the Arameans had thrown away in their headlong flight.[v] So the messengers returned and reported to the king. 16 Then the people went out and plundered[w] the camp of the Arameans. So a seah of the finest flour sold for a shekel, and two seahs of barley sold for a shekel,[x] as the LORD had said.

17 Now the king had put the officer on whose arm he leaned in charge of the gate, and the people trampled him in the gateway, and he died,[y] just as the man of God had foretold when the king came down to his house. 18 It happened as the man of God had said to the king: "About this time tomorrow, a seah of the finest flour will sell for a shekel and two seahs of barley for a shekel at the gate of Samaria."

19 The officer had said to the man of God, "Look, even if the LORD should open the floodgates[z] of the heavens, could this happen?" The man of God had replied, "You will see it with your own eyes, but you will not eat any of it!" 20 And that is exactly what happened to him, for the people trampled him in the gateway, and he died.

The Shunammite's Land Restored

8 Now Elisha had said to the woman[a] whose son he had restored to life, "Go away with your family and stay for a while wherever you can, because the LORD has decreed a famine[b] in the land that will last seven years."[c] 2 The woman proceeded to do as the man of God said. She and her family went away and stayed in the land of the Philistines seven years.

3 At the end of the seven years she came

7:6 [p] S Ex 14:24; Eze 1:24 [q] 2Sa 10:6; Jer 46:21 [r] S Nu 13:29 **7:7** [s] Jdg 7:21; Ps 48:4-6; Pr 28:1; Isa 30:17 **7:8** [t] Isa 33:23; 35:6 **7:12** [u] Jos 8:4

7:15 [v] Job 27:22 **7:16** [w] Isa 33:4, 23 [x] ver 1 **7:17** [y] S ver 2 **7:19** [z] S ver 2 **8:1** [a] 2Ki 4:8-37 [b] S Lev 26:26; S Dt 28:22; S Ru 1:1 [c] S Ge 12:10

7:6 *the Lord had caused the Arameans to hear the sound.* See 2Sa 5:24 and note. *Hittite ... kings.* Kings of small city-states ruled by dynasties of Hittite origin, which had arisen in northern Aram after the fall of the Hittite Empire c. 1200 BC.

7:9 Fear of punishment can be a valid motive for changing one's behavior.

7:12 *what the Arameans have done to us.* Joram's unbelief caused him to conclude that the report of the four leprous men was part of an Aramean war strategy rather than an evidence of the fulfillment of Elisha's prophecy (see v. 1).

7:16-20 *as the LORD had said ... as the man of God had foretold ... as the man of God had said ... that is exactly what happened to him.* Emphasizing the trustworthiness of the prophetic word spoken by Elisha. In the fulfillment of Elisha's prophecy Israel was reminded that deliverance from her enemies was a gift of God's grace and that rejection of God's word provoked the wrath of divine judgment.

8:1 *the LORD has decreed a famine.* The famine should have been perceived by the people of the northern kingdom as a covenant curse sent on them because of their sin (see note on 4:38). *seven years.* It is not clear whether this famine began before or after the Aramean siege of Samaria (see 4:38; 6:24 — 7:20).

8:2 *She and her family went away.* Elisha's instruction enabled this godly woman and her family to escape the privations of the famine.

back from the land of the Philistines and
went to appeal to the king for her house
and land. 4The king was talking to Gehazi, the servant of the man of God, and had
said, "Tell me about all the great things
Elisha has done." 5Just as Gehazi was telling the king how Elisha had restored[d] the
dead to life, the woman whose son Elisha
had brought back to life came to appeal to
the king for her house and land.

Gehazi said, "This is the woman, my
lord the king, and this is her son whom
Elisha restored to life." 6The king asked
the woman about it, and she told him.

Then he assigned an official to her case
and said to him, "Give back everything
that belonged to her, including all the income from her land from the day she left
the country until now."

Hazael Murders Ben-Hadad

7Elisha went to Damascus,[e] and Ben-
Hadad[f] king of Aram was ill. When the
king was told, "The man of God has come
all the way up here," 8he said to Hazael,[g] "Take a gift[h] with you and go to meet
the man of God. Consult[i] the LORD through
him; ask him, 'Will I recover from this illness?' "

9Hazael went to meet Elisha, taking
with him as a gift forty camel-loads of all
the finest wares of Damascus. He went in
and stood before him, and said, "Your son
Ben-Hadad king of Aram has sent me to
ask, 'Will I recover from this illness?' "

8:5 [d] 2Ki 4:35
8:7 [e] S 2Sa 8:5 [f] S 2Ki 6:24
8:8 [g] 1Ki 19:15 [h] S Ge 32:20; S 1Sa 9:7 [i] S Jdg 18:5
8:10 [j] Isa 38:1
8:11 [k] S Jdg 3:25 [l] Lk 19:41
8:12 [m] S 1Ki 19:17 [n] Ps 137:9; Isa 13:16; Hos 13:16; Na 3:10; Lk 19:44 [o] S Ge 34:29 [p] 2Ki 15:16; Am 1:13
8:13 [q] S 1Sa 17:43; S 2Sa 3:8 [r] 1Ki 19:15
8:15 [s] S 2Ki 1:17
8:16 [t] S 2Ki 1:17 [u] 2Ch 21:1-4

10Elisha answered, "Go and say to him,
'You will certainly recover.'[j] Nevertheless,[a]
the LORD has revealed to me that he will in
fact die." 11He stared at him with a fixed
gaze until Hazael was embarrassed.[k] Then
the man of God began to weep.[l]

12"Why is my lord weeping?" asked
Hazael.

"Because I know the harm[m] you will do
to the Israelites," he answered. "You will
set fire to their fortified places, kill their
young men with the sword, dash[n] their little children[o] to the ground, and rip open[p]
their pregnant women."

13Hazael said, "How could your servant,
a mere dog,[q] accomplish such a feat?"

"The LORD has shown me that you will
become king[r] of Aram," answered Elisha.

14Then Hazael left Elisha and returned
to his master. When Ben-Hadad asked,
"What did Elisha say to you?" Hazael replied, "He told me that you would certainly recover." 15But the next day he took a
thick cloth, soaked it in water and spread
it over the king's face, so that he died.[s]
Then Hazael succeeded him as king.

Jehoram King of Judah

8:16-24pp — 2Ch 21:5-10,20

16In the fifth year of Joram[t] son of Ahab
king of Israel, when Jehoshaphat was king
of Judah, Jehoram[u] son of Jehoshaphat

[a] *10* The Hebrew may also be read *Go and say, 'You will certainly not recover,' for.*

8:3 *went to ... the king.* See note on 1Ki 3:16. *appeal ... for her house and land.* Either someone had illegally occupied the woman's property during her absence, or it had fallen to the domain of the king by virtue of its abandonment.

8:4 *Tell me about all the great things Elisha has done.* The king's lack of familiarity with Elisha's ministry is perhaps an indication that this incident occurred in the early days of the reign of Jehu rather than in the time of Joram, who had had numerous contacts with Elisha (see 3:13–14; 5:7–10; 6:10–23; 6:24—7:20). But see note on 5:7.

8:6 *Give back everything that belonged to her.* The widow and her son were living examples of the Lord's provision and blessing for those who were obedient to the word of the Lord through his prophets.

8:7 *Elisha went to Damascus.* The time had come for Elisha to carry out one of the three tasks originally given to Elijah at Mount Horeb (see notes on 1Ki 19:15–16). The annals of the Assyrian ruler Shalmaneser III record Assyrian victories over Ben-Hadad II (Hadadezer) of Damascus in 846 BC and Hazael of Damascus in 842. Elisha's visit to Damascus is to be dated c. 843.

8:8 *Consult the LORD through him.* In a reversal of the situation described in 1:1–4, a pagan king seeks a message from Israel's God. *Will I recover ... ?* The question is the same as that of Ahaziah in 1:2.

8:9 *forty camel-loads of all the finest wares of Damascus.* Damascus was the center for trade between Egypt, Asia Minor and Mesopotamia. Ben-Hadad evidently thought a generous gift would favorably influence Elisha's message (cf. Naaman's gift in 5:5). *Your son Ben-Hadad.* Use of father-son terminology is a tacit acknowledgment by Ben-Hadad of Elisha's superiority (see 6:21; 1Sa 25:8).

8:10 *You will certainly recover.* An assertion that Ben-Hadad's illness was not terminal. *in fact die.* By the hand of Hazael (vv. 14–15).

8:12 *harm you will do to the Israelites.* The Lord gave Elisha a clear picture of the severity of the judgment he was about to send on Israel by the hand of Hazael (see 9:14–16; 10:32; 12:17–18; 13:3,22). *rip open their pregnant women.* This vicious act was often carried out by victorious armies at that time (see 15:16; Hos 13:16; Am 1:13). Such an atrocity likely was intended to make sure that no male children would be born to provide a remnant of the conquered people, which could rise up again and reclaim the land. Elisha's words do not sanction such acts but simply describe Hazael's future attacks on Israel.

8:13 *How could your servant, a mere dog, accomplish such a feat?* See 2Sa 9:8 and note. Hazael did not show repulsion at these violent acts but saw no possibility to gain the power necessary to accomplish them. *you will become king of Aram.* Elisha's prophecy suggests that Hazael was not a legitimate successor to Ben-Hadad. In an Assyrian inscription Hazael is designated "the son of a nobody" (i.e., a commoner) who usurped the throne.

8:15 *died.* Elisha's prophecy of Hazael's kingship did not legitimize the assassination. Hazael's murder of Ben-Hadad, as well as his future acts of violence against Israel, were wicked acts arising out of his own sinful heart (see Isa 10:5–19). He was followed by a son he named Ben-Hadad III (13:24).

8:16 *fifth year of Joram.* 848 BC. Jehoram had been coregent

began his reign as king of Judah. 17He was
thirty-two years old when he became king,
and he reigned in Jerusalem eight years.
18He followed the ways of the kings of Israel, as the house of Ahab had done, for
he married a daughter[v] of Ahab. He did
evil in the eyes of the LORD. 19Neverthe-
less, for the sake of his servant David, the
LORD was not willing to destroy[w] Judah.
He had promised to maintain a lamp[x] for
David and his descendants forever.
20In the time of Jehoram, Edom rebelled
against Judah and set up its own king.[y]
21So Jehoram[a] went to Zair with all his
chariots. The Edomites surrounded him
and his chariot commanders, but he rose
up and broke through by night; his army,
however, fled back home. 22To this day
Edom has been in rebellion[z] against Judah. Libnah[a] revolted at the same time.
23As for the other events of Jehoram's
reign, and all he did, are they not written
in the book of the annals of the kings of
Judah? 24Jehoram rested with his ancestors and was buried with them in the City
of David. And Ahaziah his son succeeded
him as king.

Ahaziah King of Judah

8:25-29pp — 2Ch 22:1-6

25In the twelfth[b] year of Joram son of
Ahab king of Israel, Ahaziah son of Jehoram king of Judah began to reign. 26Aha-
ziah was twenty-two years old when he
became king, and he reigned in Jerusalem
one year. His mother's name was Athaliah,[c] a granddaughter of Omri[d] king of Israel. 27He followed the ways of the house of
Ahab[e] and did evil[f] in the eyes of the LORD,
as the house of Ahab had done, for he was
related by marriage to Ahab's family.
28Ahaziah went with Joram son of Ahab
to war against Hazael king of Aram at Ramoth Gilead.[g] The Arameans wounded Joram; 29so King Joram returned to Jezreel[h]
to recover from the wounds the Arameans
had inflicted on him at Ramoth[b] in his battle with Hazael[i] king of Aram.
Then Ahaziah[j] son of Jehoram king of
Judah went down to Jezreel to see Joram
son of Ahab, because he had been wounded.

Jehu Anointed King of Israel

9 The prophet Elisha summoned a man
from the company[k] of the prophets
and said to him, "Tuck your cloak into
your belt,[l] take this flask of olive oil[m] with
you and go to Ramoth Gilead.[n] 2When you
get there, look for Jehu son of Jehoshaphat, the son of Nimshi. Go to him, get
him away from his companions and take
him into an inner room. 3Then take the
flask and pour the oil[o] on his head and declare, 'This is what the LORD says: I anoint
you king over Israel.' Then open the door
and run; don't delay!"
4So the young prophet went to Ramoth
Gilead. 5When he arrived, he found the
army officers sitting together. "I have a
message for you, commander," he said.
"For which of us?" asked Jehu.

8:18 [v] ver 26; 2Ki 11:1 **8:19** [w] S Ge 6:13 [x] S 2Sa 21:17; Rev 21:23 **8:20** [y] S 1Ki 22:47 **8:22** [z] Ge 27:40 [a] S Nu 33:20; Jos 21:13; 2Ki 19:8 **8:25** [b] 2Ki 9:29 **8:26** [c] S ver 18 [d] 1Ki 16:23
8:27 [e] 1Ki 16:30 [f] 1Ki 15:26 **8:28** [g] S Dt 4:43; 2Ki 9:1,14 **8:29** [h] 1Ki 21:29; 2Ki 9:21 [i] 1Ki 19:15,17 [j] 2Ki 10:13 **9:1** [k] S 1Sa 10:5 [l] S 1Ki 18:46 [m] S 1Sa 10:1 [n] S 2Ki 8:28 **9:3** [o] 1Ki 19:16

[a] 21 Hebrew *Joram,* a variant of *Jehoram;* also in verses 23 and 24 [b] 29 Hebrew *Ramah,* a variant of *Ramoth*

with his father since 853 (see note on 1:17), but he now began his reign as sole king.
8:17 *reigned in Jerusalem eight years.* Jehoram's sole reign is to be dated 848 – 841 BC.
8:18 *as the house of Ahab had done.* Jehoram introduced Baal worship in Judah, as Ahab had done in the northern kingdom (see 11:18). Baal worship now spread to the southern kingdom at the same time it was being restricted in the northern kingdom by Ahab's son Joram (see 3:1 – 2). *married a daughter of Ahab.* Jehoram's wife was Athaliah, a daughter of Ahab but probably not of Jezebel (see v. 26; 2Ch 18:1). Athaliah's influence on Jehoram paralleled that of Jezebel on Ahab (see 1Ki 16:31; 18:4; 19:1 – 2; 2Ch 21:6).
8:19 *lamp for David.* See note on 1Ki 11:36; see also Ps 132:17. The Lord spared Judah and its royal house the judgment he brought on the house of Ahab because of the covenant he had made with David (see 2Sa 7:16,29; 2Ch 21:7).
8:20 *set up its own king.* Previously Edom had been subject to Judah and had been ruled by a deputy (see note on 3:9; see also 1Ki 22:47).
8:22 *To this day.* Until the time of the writing of the account of Jehoram's reign used by the author of 1,2 Kings (see Introduction to 1 Kings: Author, Sources and Date; see also note on 1Ki 8:8). Later, Amaziah of Judah was able to inflict a serious defeat on Edom (14:7), and his successor Azariah regained control of the trade route to Elath through Edomite territory (14:22; 2Ch 26:2). *Libnah revolted at the same time.* Libnah appears to have been located close to the Philistine border near Lachish (see 19:8). It is likely that this revolt was connected with that of the Philistines and Arabs described in 2Ch 21:16 – 17.
8:23 *other events of Jehoram's reign.* See 2Ch 21:4 – 20. *annals of the kings of Judah.* See note on 1Ki 14:29.
8:24 *rested with his ancestors.* See notes on 1Ki 1:21; 2Ch 21:20.
8:25 *twelfth year of Joram.* 841 BC. In 9:29 the first year of Joram's reign was counted as his accession year and his second year as the first year of his reign, whereas here his accession year was counted as the first year of his reign (see Introduction to 1 Kings: Chronology).
8:26 *twenty-two years old when he became king.* See note on 2Ch 22:2. *Athaliah.* See note on v. 18.
8:27 *ways of the house of Ahab.* See 2Ch 22:3 – 5.
8:28 *Ahaziah went with Joram ... to war against Hazael ... at Ramoth Gilead.* As Jehoshaphat had joined Ahab in battle against the Arameans at Ramoth Gilead (1Ki 22), so now Ahaziah joined his uncle Joram in a similar venture. On the previous occasion Ahab met his death (1Ki 22:37). On this occasion Joram was wounded and, while recuperating in Jezreel (see note on 1Ki 21:1), both he and his nephew Ahaziah were assassinated by Jehu (see 9:14 – 28). *Hazael.* See note on 1Ki 19:15. He reigned 843 – 796 BC.
9:1 *company of the prophets.* See note on 2:3.
9:3 *I anoint you king.* See notes on 1Sa 2:10; 9:16; 1Ki 19:16.

"For you, commander," he replied.
[6]Jehu got up and went into the house.
Then the prophet poured the oil[p] on Jehu's
head and declared, "This is what the LORD,
the God of Israel, says: 'I anoint you king
over the LORD's people Israel. [7]You are to
destroy the house of Ahab your master,
and I will avenge[q] the blood of my servants[r] the prophets and the blood of all
the LORD's servants shed by Jezebel.[s] [8]The
whole house[t] of Ahab will perish. I will
cut off from Ahab every last male[u] in Israel—slave or free.[a] [9]I will make the house
of Ahab like the house of Jeroboam[v] son
of Nebat and like the house of Baasha[w]
son of Ahijah. [10]As for Jezebel, dogs[x] will
devour her on the plot of ground at Jezreel, and no one will bury her.'" Then he
opened the door and ran.
[11]When Jehu went out to his fellow officers, one of them asked him, "Is everything all right? Why did this maniac[y] come
to you?"

"You know the man and the sort of things he says," Jehu replied.

[12]"That's not true!" they said. "Tell us."

Jehu said, "Here is what he told me: 'This is what the LORD says: I anoint you king over Israel.'"

[13]They quickly took their cloaks and
spread[z] them under him on the bare steps.
Then they blew the trumpet[a] and shouted,
"Jehu is king!"

9:6 [p]1Ki 19:16 9:7 [q]S Ge 4:24; S Rev 6:10 [r]S Dt 32:43 [s]S 1Ki 18:4 9:8 [t]2Ki 10:17 [u]S 1Sa 25:22 9:9 [v]S 1Ki 13:34; S 14:10 [w]1Ki 16:3 9:10 [x]S 1Ki 21:23 9:11 [y]S 1Sa 10:11; S Jn 10:20 9:13 [z]Mt 21:8; Lk 19:36 [a]S 2Sa 15:10 9:14 [b]S Dt 4:43; S 2Ki 8:28 9:15 [c]S 2Ki 8:29 9:16 [d]2Ch 22:7 9:17 [e]S 1Sa 14:16; Isa 21:6 [f]S 1Sa 16:4

Jehu Kills Joram and Ahaziah

9:21-29pp — 2Ch 22:7-9

[14]So Jehu son of Jehoshaphat, the son
of Nimshi, conspired against Joram. (Now
Joram and all Israel had been defending
Ramoth Gilead[b] against Hazael king of
Aram, [15]but King Joram[b] had returned to
Jezreel to recover[c] from the wounds the
Arameans had inflicted on him in the battle with Hazael king of Aram.) Jehu said,
"If you desire to make me king, don't let
anyone slip out of the city to go and tell
the news in Jezreel." [16]Then he got into
his chariot and rode to Jezreel, because
Joram was resting there and Ahaziah[d] king
of Judah had gone down to see him.
[17]When the lookout[e] standing on the
tower in Jezreel saw Jehu's troops approaching, he called out, "I see some
troops coming."

"Get a horseman," Joram ordered. "Send him to meet them and ask, 'Do you come in peace?[f]'"

[a] 8 Or *Israel—every ruler or leader* [b] 15 Hebrew *Jehoram,* a variant of *Joram;* also in verses 17 and 21-24

9:7 *destroy the house of Ahab.* Jehu learned that he was the divinely appointed agent to inflict the judgment Elijah had pronounced many years earlier in his own hearing against the house of Ahab (see vv. 25–26; 1Ki 21:21–24). *blood of all the LORD's servants shed by Jezebel.* See 1Ki 18:4; 21:13.
9:8 *slave or free.* See note on 1Ki 14:10.
9:9 *like the house of Jeroboam.* See 1Ki 14:7–11; 15:27–30. *like the house of Baasha.* See 1Ki 16:1–4, 8–12. Elijah had spoken the same words to Ahab years before (see 1Ki 21:21–24).
9:11 *this maniac.* The epithet betrays a scornful attitude on the part of the military officers of the northern kingdom toward members of the prophetic companies. Cf 1Sa 21:13–15.
9:15 *Jezreel.* About 45 miles from Ramoth Gilead. Joram apparently had a summer palace there (see 1Ki 21:1 and note; see also map, p. 557). *don't let anyone ... go and tell the news in Jezreel.* For the success of Jehu's revolt and to avoid a civil conflict, it was important to take Joram totally by surprise.
9:16 *Ahaziah ... had gone down to see him.* See 8:29.

Black obelisk of Assyrian king Shalmaneser III depicting Israelite king Jehu paying tribute (see note on 2Ki 10:34)

Todd Bolen/www.BiblePlaces.com

18 The horseman rode off to meet Jehu and said, "This is what the king says: 'Do you come in peace?' "

"What do you have to do with peace?" Jehu replied. "Fall in behind me."

The lookout reported, "The messenger has reached them, but he isn't coming back."

19 So the king sent out a second horseman. When he came to them he said, "This is what the king says: 'Do you come in peace?' "

Jehu replied, "What do you have to do with peace? Fall in behind me."

20 The lookout reported, "He has reached them, but he isn't coming back either. The driving is like[g] that of Jehu son of Nimshi—he drives like a maniac."

21 "Hitch up my chariot," Joram ordered. And when it was hitched up, Joram king of Israel and Ahaziah king of Judah rode out, each in his own chariot, to meet Jehu. They met him at the plot of ground that had belonged to Naboth[h] the Jezreelite. 22 When Joram saw Jehu he asked, "Have you come in peace, Jehu?"

"How can there be peace," Jehu replied, "as long as all the idolatry and witchcraft of your mother Jezebel[i] abound?"

23 Joram turned about and fled, calling out to Ahaziah, "Treachery,[j] Ahaziah!"

24 Then Jehu drew his bow[k] and shot Joram between the shoulders. The arrow pierced his heart and he slumped down in his chariot. 25 Jehu said to Bidkar, his chariot officer, "Pick him up and throw him on the field that belonged to Naboth the Jezreelite. Remember how you and I were riding together in chariots behind Ahab his father when the LORD spoke this prophecy[l] against him: 26 'Yesterday I saw the blood of Naboth[m] and the blood of his sons, declares the LORD, and I will surely make you pay for it on this plot of ground, declares the LORD.'[a] Now then, pick him up and throw him on that plot, in accordance with the word of the LORD."[n]

27 When Ahaziah king of Judah saw what had happened, he fled up the road to Beth Haggan.[b] Jehu chased him, shouting, "Kill him too!" They wounded him in his chariot on the way up to Gur near Ibleam,[o] but he escaped to Megiddo[p] and died there. 28 His servants took him by chariot[q] to Jerusalem and buried him with his ancestors in his tomb in the City of David. 29 (In the eleventh[r] year of Joram son of Ahab, Ahaziah had become king of Judah.)

9:20 [g] 2Sa 18:27
9:21 [h] 1Ki 21:1-7,15-19
9:22 [i] 1Ki 18:19; Rev 2:20
9:23 [j] 2Ki 11:14
9:24 [k] S 1Ki 22:34
9:25 [l] 1Ki 21:19-22,24-29
9:26 [m] S 1Ki 21:19 [n] S 1Ki 21:29
9:27 [o] S Jdg 1:27 [p] 2Ki 23:29
9:28 [q] 2Ki 14:20; 23:30
9:29 [r] 2Ki 8:25
9:30 [s] Jer 4:30; Eze 23:40
9:31 [t] 1Ki 16:9-10
9:33 [u] Ps 7:5
9:34 [v] S 1Ki 16:31
9:36 [w] Ps 68:23; Jer 15:3 [x] S 1Ki 21:23
9:37 [y] Ps 83:10; Isa 5:25; Jer 8:2; 9:22; 16:4; 25:33; Zep 1:17
10:1 [z] S 1Ki 13:32 [a] S Jdg 8:30

Jezebel Killed

30 Then Jehu went to Jezreel. When Jezebel heard about it, she put on eye makeup,[s] arranged her hair and looked out of a window. 31 As Jehu entered the gate, she asked, "Have you come in peace, you Zimri,[t] you murderer of your master?"[c]

32 He looked up at the window and called out, "Who is on my side? Who?" Two or three eunuchs looked down at him. 33 "Throw her down!" Jehu said. So they threw her down, and some of her blood spattered the wall and the horses as they trampled her underfoot.[u]

34 Jehu went in and ate and drank. "Take care of that cursed woman," he said, "and bury her, for she was a king's daughter."[v] 35 But when they went out to bury her, they found nothing except her skull, her feet and her hands. 36 They went back and told Jehu, who said, "This is the word of the LORD that he spoke through his servant Elijah the Tishbite: On the plot of ground at Jezreel dogs[w] will devour Jezebel's flesh.[d][x] 37 Jezebel's body will be like dung[y] on the ground in the plot at Jezreel, so that no one will be able to say, 'This is Jezebel.' "

Ahab's Family Killed

10 Now there were in Samaria[z] seventy sons[a] of the house of Ahab. So Jehu wrote letters and sent them to Samar-

[a] 26 See 1 Kings 21:19. [b] 27 Or *fled by way of the garden house* [c] 31 Or *"Was there peace for Zimri, who murdered his master?"* [d] 36 See 1 Kings 21:23.

9:21 *plot of ground that had belonged to Naboth.* See notes on 1Ki 21:2–3,13,19.
9:22 *idolatry and witchcraft.* Both punishable by death (see Dt 13; 18:10–12).
9:25 *chariot officer.* See note on 1Ki 22:34.
9:26 *in accordance with the word of the LORD.* Jehu saw himself providentially placed in the position of fulfilling the prophecy of Elijah given years before (see 1Ki 21:18–24). Even though Ahab's own blood was not shed on Naboth's field (see 1Ki 21:29 and note), Jehu saw in Joram's death the fulfillment of Elijah's prophecy (see note on 1Ki 21:19).
9:27 *escaped to Megiddo and died there.* It may be questioned whether Jehu was justified in extending the purge of Ahab's house (see Hos 1:4) to the descendants of the house of David through Ahab's daughter Athaliah (see 8:18,26).
9:31 *Zimri, you murderer of your master.* In bitter sarcasm Jezebel called Jehu by the name Zimri. About 45 years earlier Zimri had seized the throne from Elah by assassination and then had destroyed the whole house of Baasha. He ruled, however, for only seven days before Omri seized power (see 1Ki 16:8–20).
9:36 *the word of the LORD that he spoke through his servant Elijah.* In the manner of Jezebel's death the word of the Lord was confirmed—the word she had defied during her life (see 1Ki 21:23).
10:1 *Samaria.* In order to consolidate his coup and establish control of the northern kingdom, Jehu still faced the formidable problems of taking the nearly impregnable fortress of Samaria (see note on 1Ki 16:24) and then of completing the destruction of Ahab's house. *seventy sons of the house of*

ia: to the officials of Jezreel,[a][b] to the elders
and to the guardians[c] of Ahab's children.
He said, 2"You have your master's sons
with you and you have chariots and horses, a fortified city and weapons. Now as
soon as this letter reaches you, 3choose
the best and most worthy of your master's
sons and set him on his father's throne.
Then fight for your master's house."
4But they were terrified and said, "If two
kings could not resist him, how can we?"
5So the palace administrator, the city
governor, the elders and the guardians
sent this message to Jehu: "We are your
servants[d] and we will do anything you say.
We will not appoint anyone as king; you
do whatever you think best."
6Then Jehu wrote them a second letter,
saying, "If you are on my side and will
obey me, take the heads of your master's
sons and come to me in Jezreel by this
time tomorrow."
Now the royal princes, seventy of them,
were with the leading men of the city,
who were rearing them. 7When the letter
arrived, these men took the princes and
slaughtered all seventy[e] of them. They put
their heads[f] in baskets and sent them to
Jehu in Jezreel. 8When the messenger arrived, he told Jehu, "They have brought
the heads of the princes."
Then Jehu ordered, "Put them in two
piles at the entrance of the city gate until
morning."
9The next morning Jehu went out.
He stood before all the people and said,
"You are innocent. It was I who conspired
against my master and killed him, but
who killed all these? 10Know, then, that
not a word the LORD has spoken against
the house of Ahab will fail. The LORD has
done what he announced[g] through his
servant Elijah."[h] 11So Jehu[i] killed everyone in Jezreel who remained of the house
of Ahab, as well as all his chief men, his
close friends and his priests, leaving him
no survivor.[j]
12Jehu then set out and went toward
Samaria. At Beth Eked of the Shepherds,
13he met some relatives of Ahaziah king of
Judah and asked, "Who are you?"
They said, "We are relatives of Ahaziah,[k] and we have come down to greet
the families of the king and of the queen
mother.[l]"
14"Take them alive!" he ordered. So they
took them alive and slaughtered them by
the well of Beth Eked—forty-two of them.
He left no survivor.[m]
15After he left there, he came upon Jehonadab[n] son of Rekab,[o] who was on his
way to meet him. Jehu greeted him and
said, "Are you in accord with me, as I am
with you?"
"I am," Jehonadab answered.

10:1 [b]S 1Ki 21:1 [c]ver 5
10:5 [d]Jos 9:8
10:7 [e]S 1Ki 21:21 [f]S 2Sa 4:8
10:10 [g]2Ki 9:7-10 [h]S 1Ki 21:29
10:11 [i]Hos 1:4 [j]ver 14; Job 18:19; Mal 4:1
10:13 [k]2Ki 8:24, 29; 2Ch 22:8 [l]S 1Ki 2:19
10:14 [m]S ver 11
10:15 [n]Jer 35:6, 14-19 [o]1Ch 2:55; Jer 35:2

[a] *1* Hebrew; some Septuagint manuscripts and Vulgate *of the city*

Ahab. The 70 could include both sons and grandsons. *officials.* Officers appointed by the king (see 1Ki 4:1–6). *elders.* Local leaders by virtue of their position in the tribal and family structure (see notes on Ex 3:16; 2Sa 3:17). *guardians of Ahab's children.* Those entrusted with the care and upbringing of the princes in the royal family.

10:3 *fight for your master's house.* Jehu's strategy was to induce the leaders of Samaria into submission to his rule by bluffing a military confrontation.

10:4 *terrified.* The leaders of Samaria were completely intimidated by Jehu's challenge. *two kings.* Joram and Ahaziah (see 9:24,27).

10:5 *palace administrator.* See note on 1Ki 4:6. *city governor.* Probably an official, appointed by the king, who served as commander of the militia of the capital city. *the elders and the guardians.* See notes on these in v. 1.

10:6 *take the heads of your master's sons and come to me.* The wording of Jehu's command contains what appears to be a deliberate ambiguity. The "heads of your master's sons" could be understood as a reference to the leading figures among the 70 descendants of Ahab, such as the crown prince and several other sons of special ability and standing. On the other hand, the expression could be taken as a reference to the literal heads of all 70 princes.

10:7 *slaughtered all seventy.* The leaders of the city understood the communique in the literal sense, as Jehu most certainly had hoped they would. *put their heads in baskets and sent them to Jehu.* The leaders of Samaria did not carry the heads of the princes to Jezreel themselves as they had been ordered to do by Jehu (see v. 6). It is likely that they feared for their lives.

10:8 *Put them in two piles at the entrance of the city gate.* This gruesome procedure imitated the barbaric practice of the Assyrian rulers Ashurnasirpal and Shalmaneser III, whose reigns were characterized by acts of terror.

10:9 *It was I who ... killed him.* Jehu openly confessed his own part in the overthrow of the government of Joram. *who killed all these?* Because of the ambiguous communique Jehu sent to the leaders of Samaria (see note on v. 6), he can now deny any personal responsibility for the slaughter of the 70 sons of Ahab and can lay the blame for it on the leaders of Samaria.

10:10 *what he announced through his servant Elijah.* See 1Ki 21:20–24,29. Jehu implies a divine sanction not only for what had already been done but also for his intent to continue the purge of Ahab's house and associates.

10:11 *all his chief men, his close friends and his priests.* Jehu went beyond the responsibility given to him (see 9:7; Hos 1:4) and acted solely on grounds of political self-interest. Jehu himself had been in the service of Ahab (see 9:25).

10:13 *relatives of Ahaziah.* See 2Ch 21:17. *families of the king and of the queen mother.* Members of the royal family from Judah who had not yet heard of the deaths of Joram and Jezebel.

10:15 *Jehonadab son of Rekab.* Jehonadab was the leader of a conservative movement among the Israelites that was characterized by strong opposition to Baalism, as well as to various practices of a settled agricultural society, including the building of houses, the sowing of crops and the use of wine. His followers still adhered to these principles over 200 years later and were known as Rekabites (see Jer 35:6–10).

"If so," said Jehu, "give me your hand."[p] So he did, and Jehu helped him up into the chariot. 16 Jehu said, "Come with me and see my zeal[q] for the LORD." Then he had him ride along in his chariot.

17 When Jehu came to Samaria, he killed all who were left there of Ahab's family;[r] he destroyed them, according to the word of the LORD spoken to Elijah.

Servants of Baal Killed

18 Then Jehu brought all the people together and said to them, "Ahab served[s] Baal a little; Jehu will serve him much. 19 Now summon[t] all the prophets of Baal, all his servants and all his priests. See that no one is missing, because I am going to hold a great sacrifice for Baal. Anyone who fails to come will no longer live." But Jehu was acting deceptively in order to destroy the servants of Baal.

20 Jehu said, "Call an assembly[u] in honor of Baal." So they proclaimed it. 21 Then he sent word throughout Israel, and all the servants of Baal came; not one stayed away. They crowded into the temple of Baal until it was full from one end to the other. 22 And Jehu said to the keeper of the wardrobe, "Bring robes for all the servants of Baal." So he brought out robes for them.

23 Then Jehu and Jehonadab son of Rekab went into the temple of Baal. Jehu said to the servants of Baal, "Look around and see that no one who serves the LORD is here with you—only servants of Baal." 24 So they went in to make sacrifices and burnt offerings. Now Jehu had posted eighty men outside with this warning: "If one of you lets any of the men I am placing in your hands escape, it will be your life for his life."[v]

25 As soon as Jehu had finished making the burnt offering, he ordered the guards and officers: "Go in and kill[w] them; let no one escape."[x] So they cut them down with the sword. The guards and officers threw the bodies out and then entered the inner shrine of the temple of Baal. 26 They brought the sacred stone[y] out of the temple of Baal and burned it. 27 They demolished the sacred stone of Baal and tore down the temple[z] of Baal, and people have used it for a latrine to this day.

28 So Jehu[a] destroyed Baal worship in Israel. 29 However, he did not turn away from the sins[b] of Jeroboam son of Nebat, which he had caused Israel to commit—the worship of the golden calves[c] at Bethel[d] and Dan.

30 The LORD said to Jehu, "Because you have done well in accomplishing what is right in my eyes and have done to the house of Ahab all I had in mind to do, your descendants will sit on the throne of Israel to the fourth generation."[e] 31 Yet Jehu was not careful[f] to keep the law of the LORD, the God of Israel, with all his heart. He did not turn away from the sins[g] of Jeroboam, which he had caused Israel to commit.

32 In those days the LORD began to reduce[h] the size of Israel. Hazael[i] overpowered the Israelites throughout their territory 33 east of the Jordan in all the land of Gilead (the region of Gad, Reuben and Manasseh), from Aroer[j] by the Arnon[k] Gorge through Gilead to Bashan.

34 As for the other events of Jehu's reign, all he did, and all his achievements, are

10:15 [p] Ezr 10:19; Eze 17:18
10:16 [q] S Nu 25:13
10:17 [r] 2Ki 9:8
10:18 [s] S Jdg 2:11
10:19 [t] 1Ki 18:19
10:20 [u] S Ex 32:5
10:24 [v] S Jos 2:14
10:25 [w] S Ex 22:20; S 2Ki 11:18 [x] S 1Ki 18:40
10:26 [y] S Ex 23:24
10:27 [z] S 1Ki 16:32
10:28 [a] 1Ki 19:17
10:29 [b] S 1Ki 12:30 [c] S Ex 32:4 [d] 1Ki 12:32
10:30 [e] 2Ki 15:12
10:31 [f] Dt 4:9; Pr 4:23 [g] 1Ki 12:30
10:32 [h] 2Ki 13:25; Ps 107:39 [i] S 1Ki 19:17
10:33 [j] S Nu 32:34; Dt 2:36; Jdg 11:26; Isa 17:2 [k] S Nu 21:13

10:16 *had him ride along.* Public association with Jehonadab gave Jehu added credentials among the rural populace as a follower of the Lord.

10:18 *Ahab served Baal a little; Jehu will serve him much.* After settling in Samaria, Jehu gave the appearance of having previously appealed to the word of the Lord as a mere political maneuver.

10:19 *will no longer live.* Jehu's reputation made this no idle threat.

10:26 *burned it.* May refer to the Asherah pole (see note on 1Ki 14:15) that usually accompanied a sacred stone (see 1Ki 16:32–33).

10:27 *sacred stone of Baal.* See note on 1Ki 14:23. *to this day.* See note on 8:22.

10:29 *sins of Jeroboam ... he had caused Israel to commit.* See 1Ki 12:26–32; 13:33–34; 14:16.

10:30 *Because you have done ... to the house of Ahab all I had in mind.* Jehu was the Lord's instrument to bring judgment on the house of Ahab, for which he was commended. But he was later condemned by the prophet Hosea for the killing of all Ahab's associates, as well as Ahaziah of Judah and the 42 Judahite princes—the "massacre at Jezreel" (Hos 1:4). *fourth generation.* The restriction of this blessing to four generations is reflective of the qualified approval given to Jehu's reign. Nevertheless, his dynasty survived longer than any other dynasty of the northern kingdom, lasting nearly 100 years. It included the reigns of Jehoahaz, Jehoash, Jeroboam II and Zechariah (see note on 15:12).

10:31 *was not careful to keep the law of the LORD ... with all his heart.* Jehu seems to have been driven more by a political desire to secure his own position on the throne of the northern kingdom than by a desire to serve the Lord. In this he was guilty of using God's judgment on the house of Ahab to serve his self-interest.

10:32 *the LORD began to reduce the size of Israel.* The climax of the covenant curses enumerated in Lev 26 and Dt 28 was Israel's expulsion from Canaan. During the rule of Jehu the northern kingdom experienced the beginnings of this curse (see 17:7–18 for its full realization).

10:33 All of Transjordan was lost to Hazael and the Arameans of Damascus.

10:34 *other events of Jehu's reign.* The Black Obelisk of the Assyrian ruler Shalmaneser III informs us that Jehu paid tribute to the Assyrians shortly after coming to the throne of the northern kingdom in 841 BC. In the Assyrian inscription Jehu is called the "son of Omri," but this may simply be Shalmaneser's way of identifying Jehu with Samaria (or Israel). There is no reference to this payment of tribute in the

they not written in the book of the annals[l]
of the kings of Israel?
35 Jehu rested with his ancestors and
was buried in Samaria. And Jehoahaz his
son succeeded him as king. 36 The time
that Jehu reigned over Israel in Samaria
was twenty-eight years.

Athaliah and Joash

11:1-21pp — 2Ch 22:10-23:21

11 When Athaliah[m] the mother of
Ahaziah saw that her son was
dead, she proceeded to destroy the whole
royal family. 2 But Jehosheba, the daughter of King Jehoram[a] and sister of Ahaziah, took Joash[n] son of Ahaziah and stole
him away from among the royal princes,
who were about to be murdered. She put
him and his nurse in a bedroom to hide
him from Athaliah; so he was not killed.[o]
3 He remained hidden with his nurse at the
temple of the LORD for six years while Athaliah ruled the land.
4 In the seventh year Jehoiada sent for
the commanders of units of a hundred,
the Carites[p] and the guards and had them
brought to him at the temple of the LORD.
He made a covenant with them and put
them under oath at the temple of the
LORD. Then he showed them the king's
son. 5 He commanded them, saying, "This
is what you are to do: You who are in the
three companies that are going on duty
on the Sabbath[q] — a third of you guarding
the royal palace,[r] 6 a third at the Sur Gate,
and a third at the gate behind the guard,
who take turns guarding the temple —
7 and you who are in the other two companies that normally go off Sabbath duty
are all to guard the temple for the king.
8 Station yourselves around the king, each
of you with weapon in hand. Anyone who
approaches your ranks[b] is to be put to
death. Stay close to the king wherever he
goes."
9 The commanders of units of a hundred
did just as Jehoiada the priest ordered.
Each one took his men — those who were
going on duty on the Sabbath and those
who were going off duty — and came to
Jehoiada the priest. 10 Then he gave the
commanders the spears and shields[s] that
had belonged to King David and that were
in the temple of the LORD. 11 The guards,
each with weapon in hand, stationed
themselves around the king — near the altar and the temple, from the south side to
the north side of the temple.
12 Jehoiada brought out the king's son
and put the crown on him; he presented
him with a copy of the covenant[t] and proclaimed him king. They anointed[u] him,
and the people clapped their hands[v] and
shouted, "Long live the king!"[w]
13 When Athaliah heard the noise made
by the guards and the people, she went to
the people at the temple of the LORD. 14 She
looked and there was the king, standing
by the pillar,[x] as the custom was. The officers and the trumpeters were beside the
king, and all the people of the land were
rejoicing and blowing trumpets.[y] Then

10:34 [l] 1Ki 15:31
11:1 [m] S 2Ki 8:18
11:2 [n] 2Ki 12:1 [o] S Jdg 9:5
11:4 [p] ver 19
11:5 [q] 1Ch 9:25 [r] 1Ki 14:27
11:10 [s] S 2Sa 8:7
11:12 [t] Ex 25:16; 2Ki 23:3 [u] S 1Sa 9:16; S 1Ki 1:39 [v] Ps 47:1; 98:8; Isa 55:12 [w] S 1Sa 10:24
11:14 [x] S 1Ki 7:15 [y] S 1Ki 1:39

[a] 2 Hebrew *Joram,* a variant of *Jehoram*
[b] 8 Or *approaches the precincts*

Biblical narratives of Jehu's reign (see photo, p. 583). *annals of the kings of Israel.* See note on 1Ki 14:19.

10:35 *rested with his ancestors.* See note on 1Ki 1:21. *Jehoahaz his son succeeded him.* For the reign of Jehoahaz, see 13:1–9.

10:36 *twenty-eight years.* 841–814 BC.

11:1 *Athaliah.* See note on 8:18. *her son was dead.* See 9:27. *destroy the whole royal family.* To secure the throne in Judah for herself. By this time the royal family in Judah had already been reduced to a mere remnant. Jehoram, the late husband of Athaliah and the father of Ahaziah, had killed all his brothers when he succeeded his father Jehoshaphat on the throne (see 2Ch 21:4). Jehu had slain another 42 members of the royal house of Judah, perhaps including many of the sons of Jehoram's brothers (10:12–14; 2Ch 22:8–9), and the brothers of Ahaziah had been killed by marauding Arabs (2Ch 22:1). It is likely that Athaliah's purge focused primarily on the children of Ahaziah, i.e., her own grandchildren. Ahaziah had died at the young age of 22 (see 8:26). This attempt to completely destroy the house of David was an attack on God's redemptive plan — a plan that centered in the Messiah, which the Davidic covenant promised (see notes on 2Sa 7:11,16; 1Ki 8:25).

11:2 *daughter of King Jehoram and sister of Ahaziah.* It is likely that Jehosheba was the daughter of Jehoram by a wife other than Athaliah, and thus she was a half sister of Ahaziah. She was married to the high priest Jehoiada (see 2Ch 22:11). *him and his nurse.* The child was not more than a year old and had not yet been weaned (see vv. 3,21).

11:4 *seventh year.* Of Athaliah's rule. *commanders of units of a hundred.* 2Ch 23:1 lists the names of five commanders, all native Israelites. *Carites.* Mercenary soldiers from Caria in southwest Asia Minor who served as royal bodyguards. *had them brought to him at the temple.* 2Ch 23:2 includes the Levites and family leaders of Judah in the conspiracy.

11:10 *shields that had belonged to King David and that were in the temple.* David had taken gold shields as plunder in his battle with Hadadezer and then dedicated them to the Lord (see 2Sa 8:7–11). The temple and palace were plundered by Shishak, king of Egypt, during Rehoboam's reign (see 1Ki 14:26). Apparently David's shields had been hidden and were not taken.

11:12 *covenant.* Probably either (1) the Ten Commandments or (2) the entire Sinaitic covenant or (3) a document dealing more specifically with the covenant responsibilities of the king (see Dt 17:14–20; see also note on 1Sa 10:25). The third option is most likely. *anointed him.* See notes on 1Sa 2:10; 9:16; 1Ki 1:39. *Long live the king!* See note on Ps 62:4.

11:14 *pillar.* Apparently one of the two bronze pillars of the portico of the temple, named Jakin and Boaz (see 23:3; 1Ki 7:15–22; 2Ch 23:13). *all the people of the land.* It is likely that Jehoiada had chosen to stage his coup on a Sabbath during one of the major religious festivals, when many from the realm who were loyal to the Lord would be in Jerusalem.

Athaliah tore[z] her robes and called out,
"Treason! Treason!"[a]
15 Jehoiada the priest ordered the commanders of units of a hundred, who were
in charge of the troops: "Bring her out
between the ranks[a] and put to the sword
anyone who follows her." For the priest
had said, "She must not be put to death
in the temple[b] of the LORD." 16 So they
seized her as she reached the place where
the horses enter[c] the palace grounds, and
there she was put to death.[d]
17 Jehoiada then made a covenant[e] between the LORD and the king and people
that they would be the LORD's people. He
also made a covenant between the king
and the people.[f] 18 All the people of the
land went to the temple[g] of Baal and tore
it down. They smashed[h] the altars and
idols to pieces and killed Mattan the priest[i]
of Baal in front of the altars.
Then Jehoiada the priest posted guards
at the temple of the LORD. 19 He took with
him the commanders of hundreds, the
Carites,[j] the guards and all the people of
the land, and together they brought the
king down from the temple of the LORD
and went into the palace, entering by
way of the gate of the guards. The king
then took his place on the royal throne.
20 All the people of the land rejoiced,[k]
and the city was calm, because Athaliah had been slain with the sword at the
palace.
21 Joash[b] was seven years old when he
began to reign.[c]

11:14 [z] S Ge 37:29 [a] 2Ki 9:23 **11:15** [b] 1Ki 2:30 **11:16** [c] Ne 3:28; Jer 31:40 [d] S Ge 4:14 **11:17** [e] S Ex 24:8; 2Sa 5:3; 2Ch 15:12; 23:3; 29:10; 34:31; Ezr 10:3 [f] 2Ki 23:3; Jer 34:8 **11:18** [g] S 1Ki 16:32 [h] S Dt 12:3 [i] 1Ki 18:40; 2Ki 10:25; 23:20 **11:19** [j] ver 4 **11:20** [k] Pr 11:10; 28:12; 29:2

Joash Repairs the Temple

12:1-21pp — 2Ch 24:1-14; 24:23-27

12[d] In the seventh year of Jehu, Joash[e][l] became king, and he reigned
in Jerusalem forty years. His mother's
name was Zibiah; she was from Beersheba. 2 Joash did what was right[m] in the
eyes of the LORD all the years Jehoiada the
priest instructed him. 3 The high places,[n]
however, were not removed; the people
continued to offer sacrifices and burn incense there.
4 Joash said to the priests, "Collect[o] all
the money that is brought as sacred offerings[p] to the temple of the LORD — the
money collected in the census,[q] the money received from personal vows and the
money brought voluntarily[r] to the temple. 5 Let every priest receive the money
from one of the treasurers, then use it to
repair[s] whatever damage is found in the
temple."
6 But by the twenty-third year of King
Joash the priests still had not repaired the
temple. 7 Therefore King Joash summoned
Jehoiada the priest and the other priests
and asked them, "Why aren't you repairing the damage done to the temple? Take
no more money from your treasurers, but
hand it over for repairing the temple."
8 The priests agreed that they would not
collect any more money from the people

12:1 [l] 2Ki 11:2 **12:2** [m] S Dt 12:25; S 2Sa 8:15 **12:3** [n] S 1Ki 3:3; S 2Ki 18:4 **12:4** [o] 2Ki 22:4 [p] Nu 18:19 [q] S Ex 30:12 [r] S Ex 25:2; S 35:29 **12:5** [s] 2Ki 22:5

[a] *15* Or *out from the precincts* [b] *21* Hebrew *Jehoash,* a variant of *Joash* [c] *21* In Hebrew texts this verse (11:21) is numbered 12:1. [d] In Hebrew texts 12:1-21 is numbered 12:2-22. [e] *1* Hebrew *Jehoash,* a variant of *Joash;* also in verses 2, 4, 6, 7 and 18

11:15 *not be put to death in the temple.* So as not to defile God's holy house (see Ex 21:14 and note).
11:17 *covenant between the LORD and the king and people that they would be the LORD's people.* A renewal of the Sinaitic covenant, by which Israel had been constituted as the Lord's people (see Ex 19:5 – 6; Dt 4:20). The years of apostasy, involving both the royal house and the people of Judah, necessitated a renewal of allegiance to the Lord at the time of an important new beginning for the southern kingdom (see notes on 1Sa 11:14 – 15; 12:14 – 15,24 – 25). *covenant between the king and the people.* Defined responsibilities and mutual obligations of king and people that were compatible with Israel's covenant relationship with the Lord (see notes on 1Sa 10:25; 2Sa 5:3).
11:18 *idols.* Stone pillars (see note on 1Ki 14:23) and Asherah poles (see note on 1Ki 14:15).
11:19 *commanders of hundreds, the Carites, the guards.* See note on v. 4.
11:21 See v. 3. The Lord had preserved a lamp for David in Jerusalem (see 1Ki 11:36).
12:1 *seventh year of Jehu.* 835 BC (see note on 10:36). *forty years.* 835 – 796.
12:2 *all the years Jehoiada the priest instructed him.* After Jehoiada died, Joash turned away from the Lord (see 2Ch 24:17 – 27).
12:3 *high places . . . were not removed.* These were high places where the Lord was worshiped rather than pagan deities (see note on 1Ki 15:14). They were nevertheless potential sources for the entrance of pagan practices into Israel's worship (see note on 1Ki 3:2).
12:4 *money . . . brought as sacred offerings to the temple.* The money was derived from three different sources: (1) *money collected in the census.* At the age of 20, Israelite youths were required to register for military service and to make an offering of half a shekel (see note on 5:26) for use in the service of the central sanctuary (see Ex 30:11 – 16; 38:25 – 26). (2) *money received from personal vows.* Various types of vows and their equivalence in monetary assessments are described in Lev 27:1 – 25. (3) *money brought voluntarily to the temple.* For voluntary offerings, see Lev 22:18 – 23; Dt 16:10.
12:5 *treasurers.* Temple functionaries who handled financial matters for the priests relative to the people's sacrifices and offerings. *whatever damage is found in the temple.* Construction of the temple had been completed 124 years before the beginning of the reign of Joash (see notes on v. 1; 1Ki 6:38). In addition to deterioration due to age, it had fallen into disrepair and abuse during the rule of Athaliah (see 2Ch 24:7).
12:6 *twenty-third year of King Joash.* Joash may have instituted his plan for restoration of the temple a few years before the 23rd year of his reign. Now at age 30 he asserts his royal authority and takes charge of the temple repairs.
12:7 *Take no more money from your treasurers.* The proceeds from the sources of revenue mentioned in v. 4 were no longer to be given to the priests.
12:8 *priests agreed.* Apparently a compromise was reached:

and that they would not repair the temple
themselves.
9 Jehoiada the priest took a chest and
bored a hole in its lid. He placed it beside
the altar, on the right side as one enters the
temple of the LORD. The priests who guarded the entrance[t] put into the chest all the
money[u] that was brought to the temple of
the LORD. 10 Whenever they saw that there
was a large amount of money in the chest,
the royal secretary[v] and the high priest
came, counted the money that had been
brought into the temple of the LORD and
put it into bags. 11 When the amount had
been determined, they gave the money to
the men appointed to supervise the work
on the temple. With it they paid those who
worked on the temple of the LORD—the
carpenters and builders, 12 the masons and
stonecutters.[w] They purchased timber and
blocks of dressed stone for the repair of
the temple of the LORD, and met all the
other expenses of restoring the temple.
13 The money brought into the temple
was not spent for making silver basins,
wick trimmers, sprinkling bowls, trumpets
or any other articles of gold[x] or silver for
the temple of the LORD; 14 it was paid to the
workers, who used it to repair the temple.
15 They did not require an accounting from
those to whom they gave the money to
pay the workers, because they acted with
complete honesty.[y] 16 The money from the
guilt offerings[z] and sin offerings[a][a] was not
brought into the temple of the LORD; it belonged[b] to the priests.
17 About this time Hazael[c] king of Aram
went up and attacked Gath and captured
it. Then he turned to attack Jerusalem.
18 But Joash king of Judah took all the
sacred objects dedicated by his predecessors—Jehoshaphat, Jehoram and Ahaziah, the kings of Judah—and the gifts he
himself had dedicated and all the gold
found in the treasuries of the temple of
the LORD and of the royal palace, and he
sent[d] them to Hazael king of Aram, who
then withdrew[e] from Jerusalem.
19 As for the other events of the reign of
Joash, and all he did, are they not written in the book of the annals of the kings
of Judah? 20 His officials[f] conspired against
him and assassinated[g] him at Beth Millo,[h]
on the road down to Silla. 21 The officials
who murdered him were Jozabad son of
Shimeath and Jehozabad son of Shomer.
He died and was buried with his ancestors
in the City of David. And Amaziah his son
succeeded him as king.

Jehoahaz King of Israel

13 In the twenty-third year of Joash
son of Ahaziah king of Judah, Jehoahaz son of Jehu became king of Israel in Samaria, and he reigned seventeen
years. 2 He did evil[i] in the eyes of the LORD

12:9 [t] 2Ki 25:18; Jer 35:4; 52:24 [u] Mk 12:41; Lk 21:1 **12:10** [v] S 2Sa 8:17 **12:12** [w] 2Ki 22:5-6 **12:13** [x] S 1Ki 7:48-51 **12:15** [y] 2Ki 22:7; 1Co 4:2 **12:16** [z] Lev 5:14-19 [a] Lev 4:1-35 [b] S Lev 7:7 **12:17** [c] 2Ki 8:12 **12:18** [d] S 1Ki 15:18; S 2Ch 21:16-17 [e] 1Ki 15:21; 2Ki 15:20; 19:36 **12:20** [f] 2Ki 14:5 [g] 2Ki 14:19; 15:10,14,25, 30; 21:23; 25:25 [h] Jdg 9:6 **13:2** [i] 1Ki 12:26-33

[a] 16 Or *purification offerings*

The priests would no longer take the money received from the people, but neither would they pay for the temple repairs from the money they had already received.
12:9 *priests who guarded the entrance.* Three high-ranking priests charged with protecting the temple from unlawful (profane) entry (see 25:18; Jer 52:24). *put into the chest all the money.* When the people were assured that all their offerings would be used for the temple restoration, they responded with greater generosity. See 22:3–7 for continuation (or renewal) of this practice in the reign of Josiah.
12:10 *royal secretary.* See note on 2Sa 8:17. Joash arranges for direct royal supervision of the temple's monetary affairs.
12:11 *men appointed.* The whole matter is taken out of the hands of the priests.
12:13 *articles of gold or silver for the temple.* All the money was initially designated for the restoration of the temple. When the restoration was completed, additional funds were used for the acquisition of silver and gold articles for use in the temple service (see 2Ch 24:14).
12:16 *money from the guilt offerings.* See Lev 5:16; 6:5; Nu 5:7–10 for references to priestly income in connection with the bringing of a guilt offering.
12:17 *About this time.* These events must have taken place toward the end of Joash's reign. From 2Ch 24:17–24 it is clear that the Aramean attack was occasioned by Joash's turning away from the Lord after Jehoiada's death. Joash's apostasy reached its climax in the stoning of Jehoiada's son Zechariah (2Ch 24:22). Probably because of Joash's earlier zeal for the temple, the author of Kings did not choose to relate these matters. *Hazael.* See 8:7–15; 10:32–33; 13:3,22; see also note on 1Ki 19:15. *Gath.* One of the major Philistine cities (see Jos 13:3) that David had conquered (1Ch 18:1) and that continued to be subject to Judah during the reign of Rehoboam (2Ch 11:8). In the latter years of the reign of Joash of Judah (835–796 BC) and during the reign of Jehoahaz of Israel (814–798; see 13:3,7), the Arameans had virtually overrun the northern kingdom, enabling them to advance against the Philistines and the kingdom of Judah with little resistance. *he turned to attack Jerusalem.* See 2Ch 24:23–24.
12:18 *sacred objects ... gold ... he sent them to Hazael.* Years earlier, Asa had sought to secure assistance from the Arameans with a similar gift (see 1Ki 15:18).
12:19 *annals of the kings of Judah.* See note on 1Ki 14:29. A fuller account of the reign of Joash is also found in 2Ch 22:10—24:27.
12:20 *conspired against him.* The conspiracy was aroused in response to Joash's murder of Zechariah, son of Jehoiada (see 2Ch 24:25). *Beth Millo.* Beth means "house"; for the meaning of Millo see note on Jdg 9:6. Here the reference may be to a building (perhaps a kind of barracks) built on the "Millo" in the old City of David (see 2Sa 5:9 and note; 1Ki 11:27). Perhaps the king was staying there temporarily with his troops at the time of his assassination; Chronicles says he was killed "in his bed" (2Ch 24:25).
12:21 *officials.* Sons of Ammonite and Moabite mothers (2Ch 24:26), suggesting that they may have been mercenary military officers whose services could have been bought by others. *buried with his ancestors.* But see 2Ch 24:25. *Amaziah his son succeeded him.* For the reign of Amaziah, see 14:1–22.
13:1 *twenty-third year of Joash.* 814 BC (see note on 12:1; see also Introduction to 1 Kings: Chronology). *seventeen years.* 814–798.

by following the sins of Jeroboam son of
Nebat, which he had caused Israel to commit, and he did not turn away from them.
3So the LORD's anger[j] burned against Israel, and for a long time he kept them under the power[k] of Hazael king of Aram and
Ben-Hadad[l] his son.
4Then Jehoahaz sought[m] the LORD's favor, and the LORD listened to him, for he
saw[n] how severely the king of Aram was
oppressing[o] Israel. 5The LORD provided
a deliverer[p] for Israel, and they escaped
from the power of Aram. So the Israelites
lived in their own homes as they had before. 6But they did not turn away from the
sins[q] of the house of Jeroboam, which he
had caused Israel to commit; they continued in them. Also, the Asherah pole[a][r] remained standing in Samaria.
7Nothing had been left[s] of the army of
Jehoahaz except fifty horsemen, ten chariots and ten thousand foot soldiers, for the
king of Aram had destroyed the rest and
made them like the dust[t] at threshing time.
8As for the other events of the reign of
Jehoahaz, all he did and his achievements,
are they not written in the book of the annals of the kings of Israel? 9Jehoahaz rested with his ancestors and was buried in
Samaria. And Jehoash[b] his son succeeded
him as king.

Jehoash King of Israel

10In the thirty-seventh year of Joash
king of Judah, Jehoash son of Jehoahaz
became king of Israel in Samaria, and he
reigned sixteen years. 11He did evil in the
eyes of the LORD and did not turn away
from any of the sins of Jeroboam son of
Nebat, which he had caused Israel to commit; he continued in them.
12As for the other events of the reign of
Jehoash, all he did and his achievements,
including his war against Amaziah[u] king of
Judah, are they not written in the book of
the annals[v] of the kings of Israel? 13Jehoash
rested with his ancestors, and Jeroboam[w]
succeeded him on the throne. Jehoash was
buried in Samaria with the kings of Israel.
14Now Elisha had been suffering from the
illness from which he died. Jehoash king of
Israel went down to see him and wept over
him. "My father! My father!" he cried. "The
chariots[x] and horsemen of Israel!"
15Elisha said, "Get a bow and some arrows,"[y] and he did so. 16"Take the bow in
your hands," he said to the king of Israel. When he had taken it, Elisha put his
hands on the king's hands.
17"Open the east window," he said, and
he opened it. "Shoot!"[z] Elisha said, and
he shot. "The LORD's arrow of victory, the
arrow of victory over Aram!" Elisha declared. "You will completely destroy the
Arameans at Aphek."[a]
18Then he said, "Take the arrows,"
and the king took them. Elisha told him,
"Strike the ground." He struck it three
times and stopped. 19The man of God was

13:3 [j]S Dt 31:17 [k]S 1Ki 19:17 [l]ver 24
13:4 [m]S Dt 4:29 [n]S Dt 26:7 [o]S Nu 10:9; 2Sa 7:10
13:5 [p]S Ge 45:7; S Dt 28:29; S Jdg 2:18
13:6 [q]1Ki 12:30 [r]S 1Ki 16:33
13:7 [s]2Ki 10:32-33 [t]S 2Sa 22:43
13:12 [u]2Ki 14:15 [v]1Ki 15:31
13:13 [w]2Ki 14:23; Hos 1:1
13:14 [x]S 2Ki 2:12
13:15 [y]1Sa 20:20
13:17 [z]Jos 8:18 [a]S 1Ki 20:26

[a] 6 That is, a wooden symbol of the goddess Asherah; here and elsewhere in 2 Kings [b] 9 Hebrew *Joash,* a variant of *Jehoash;* also in verses 12-14 and 25

13:2 *sins of Jeroboam.* See 1Ki 12:26–32; 13:33–34; 14:16.
13:3 *Hazael.* See notes on 8:12,13,15; 10:33; 1 Ki 19:15. *Ben-Hadad.* See v. 24. Ben-Hadad III reigned c. 796–770 BC.
13:4 *the LORD listened to him.* Although deliverance did not come during the lifetime of Jehoahaz (see v. 22), the Lord was merciful to his people in spite of their sin, because of his covenant with Abraham, Isaac and Jacob (v. 23).
13:5 *deliverer for Israel.* Probably (1) the Assyrian ruler Adad-nirari III (810–783 BC), whose attacks on the Arameans of Damascus in 806 and 804 enabled the Israelites to break Aramean control over Israelite territory (see v. 25; 14:25); or (2) Jehoash, son of Jehoahaz (vv. 17,19,25); or (3) Jeroboam II, who was able to extend Israel's boundaries far to the north (see 14:25,27) after the Assyrians had broken the military power of the Arameans.
13:6 *Asherah pole remained standing.* This idol had been set up by Ahab (see 1Ki 16:33) and had either escaped destruction by Jehu when he purged Baal worship from Samaria (see 10:27–28) or been reintroduced during the reign of Jehoahaz.
13:7 *ten chariots.* In effect, a very small police force. Cf. the 2,000 chariots that Ahab was able to deploy against the Assyrians at the battle of Qarqar in 853 BC (see note on 1Ki 22:1). *ten thousand foot soldiers.* At the battle of Qarqar Ahab had supplied 10,000 foot soldiers to the coalition of forces opposing the Assyrians. At that time this would have represented only a contingent of Israel's army, while now it represented the entire Israelite infantry. In 857 Ahab had inflicted 100,000 casualties on the Aramean foot soldiers in one day (see 1Ki 20:29).
13:8 *annals of the kings of Israel.* See note on 1Ki 14:19.
13:9 *rested with his ancestors.* See note on 1Ki 1:21.
13:10 *thirty-seventh year of Joash.* 798 BC (see note on 12:1). *sixteen years.* 798–782.
13:11 *sins of Jeroboam.* See 1Ki 12:26–32; 13:33–34; 14:16.
13:12 *war against Amaziah.* See 14:8–14; 2Ch 25:17–24. *annals of the kings of Israel.* See note on 1Ki 14:19.
13:13 *rested with his ancestors.* See note on 1Ki 1:21. *Jeroboam succeeded him.* For the reign of Jeroboam II, see 14:23–29.
13:14 *Elisha had been suffering.* Ch. 9 contains the last previous reference to Elisha. Since Jehu had been anointed in 841 BC (see note on 10:36) and Jehoash began to reign in 798 (see note on v. 10), there is at least a 43-year period in which we are told nothing of Elisha's activities. Based on Elisha's relationship with Elijah, he must have been born prior to 880 and have lived to be more than 80 years of age. *The chariots and horsemen of Israel!* An expression of recognition by Jehoash that Elisha was of greater significance for Israel's military success than Israel's military forces were (see notes on 2:12; 6:13,16–23).
13:16 *put his hands on the king's hands.* By this symbolic act Elisha indicated that Jehoash was to engage the Arameans in battle with the Lord's blessing on him.
13:17 *east window.* Faced Transjordan, which was controlled by the Arameans (see 10:32–33). *Aphek.* About 60 years earlier Ahab had won a decisive victory at Aphek over the Arameans and Ben-Hadad II (see 1Ki 20:26–30 and note on 20:26).
13:18 *struck it three times and stopped.* The moderately en-

angry with him and said, "You should
have struck the ground five or six times;
then you would have defeated Aram and
completely destroyed it. But now you will
defeat it only three times."[b]
20 Elisha died and was buried.
Now Moabite raiders[c] used to enter the
country every spring. 21 Once while some
Israelites were burying a man, suddenly
they saw a band of raiders; so they threw
the man's body into Elisha's tomb. When
the body touched Elisha's bones, the man
came to life[d] and stood up on his feet.
22 Hazael king of Aram oppressed[e] Israel
throughout the reign of Jehoahaz. 23 But
the LORD was gracious to them and had
compassion and showed concern for them
because of his covenant[f] with Abraham,
Isaac and Jacob. To this day he has been
unwilling to destroy[g] them or banish them
from his presence.[h]
24 Hazael king of Aram died, and Ben-
Hadad[i] his son succeeded him as king.
25 Then Jehoash son of Jehoahaz recaptured from Ben-Hadad son of Hazael the
towns he had taken in battle from his father Jehoahaz. Three times[j] Jehoash defeated him, and so he recovered[k] the Israelite towns.

Amaziah King of Judah

14:1-7pp — 2Ch 25:1-4,11-12
14:8-22pp — 2Ch 25:17-26:2

14 In the second year of Jehoash[a] son
of Jehoahaz king of Israel, Amaziah son of Joash king of Judah began
to reign. 2 He was twenty-five years old
when he became king, and he reigned in
Jerusalem twenty-nine years. His mother's name was Jehoaddan; she was from
Jerusalem. 3 He did what was right in the
eyes of the LORD, but not as his father David had done. In everything he followed
the example of his father Joash. 4 The high
places,[l] however, were not removed; the
people continued to offer sacrifices and
burn incense there.
5 After the kingdom was firmly in his
grasp, he executed[m] the officials[n] who had
murdered his father the king. 6 Yet he did
not put the children of the assassins to
death, in accordance with what is written
in the Book of the Law[o] of Moses where
the LORD commanded: "Parents are not to
be put to death for their children, nor children put to death for their parents; each
will die for their own sin."[b][p]
7 He was the one who defeated ten thousand Edomites in the Valley of Salt[q] and
captured Sela[r] in battle, calling it Joktheel,
the name it has to this day.
8 Then Amaziah sent messengers to Jehoash son of Jehoahaz, the son of Jehu,
king of Israel, with the challenge: "Come,
let us face each other in battle."
9 But Jehoash king of Israel replied to
Amaziah king of Judah: "A thistle[s] in Lebanon sent a message to a cedar in Lebanon, 'Give your daughter to my son in
marriage.' Then a wild beast in Lebanon

13:19 [b] ver 25 **13:20** [c] S 2Ki 5:2 **13:21** [d] Mt 27:52 **13:22** [e] S 1Ki 19:17 **13:23** [f] S Ex 2:24 [g] S Dt 29:20 [h] S Ex 33:15; 2Ki 17:18; 24:3,20 **13:24** [i] ver 3 **13:25** [j] ver 18, 19 [k] S 2Ki 10:32

14:4 [l] 2Ki 12:3 **14:5** [m] 2Ki 21:24 [n] 2Ki 12:20 **14:6** [o] S Dt 28:61 [p] S Nu 26:11; Job 21:20; Jer 31:30; 44:3; Eze 18:4,20 **14:7** [q] S 2Sa 8:13 [r] S Jdg 1:36 **14:9** [s] Jdg 9:8-15

[a] *1* Hebrew *Joash,* a variant of *Jehoash;* also in verses 13, 23 and 27 [b] *6* Deut. 24:16

thusiastic response to Elisha's directive reflected insufficient zeal for accomplishing the announced task.

13:19 *defeat it only three times.* Jehoash's moderate enthusiasm in striking the ground with arrows symbolized the moderate success he would have against the Arameans. It would be left for Jeroboam II, son of Jehoash, to gain complete victory over them (see 14:25,28).

13:21 *When the body touched Elisha's bones, the man came to life.* The life-giving power of the God Elisha represented is demonstrated once again in this last OT reference to Elisha (for previous demonstrations of this power, see 4:32 – 37 and 1Ki 17:17 – 24; for Elijah's departure to heaven without dying, see 2:11 – 12).

13:23 *To this day.* Until the time of the writing of the source from which the author derived this account (see note on 1Ki 8:8; see also Introduction to 1 Kings: Author, Sources and Date). *unwilling to destroy them or banish them.* In his mercy and grace the Lord was long-suffering toward his people and refrained from full implementation of the covenant curse of exile from Canaan (see note on 10:32). This postponement of judgment provided Israel with the opportunity to repent and return to covenant faithfulness.

13:24 *Ben-Hadad.* See note on v. 3.

13:25 *towns he had taken … from … Jehoahaz.* Probably towns west of the Jordan, since the area east of the Jordan had been lost already in the time of Jehu (see 10:32 – 33). It was not until the time of Jeroboam II that the area east of the Jordan was fully recovered for Israel (see 14:25). *Three times.* In fulfillment of Elisha's prophecy (v. 19).

14:1 *second year of Jehoash.* 796 BC (see note on 13:10).

14:2 *twenty-nine years.* 796 – 767. Amaziah's 29-year reign included a 24-year coregency with his son Azariah (see notes on v. 21; 15:1 – 2).

14:3 *not as his father David.* Amaziah did not remain completely free from involvement with the worship of pagan deities (see 2Ch 25:14 – 16). His loyalty to the Lord fell short of that of Asa and Jehoshaphat before him (see 1Ki 15:11,14; 22:43; see also 1Ki 9:4; 11:4).

14:4 *high places, however, were not removed.* See note on 1Ki 15:14.

14:7 *defeated ten thousand Edomites.* Amaziah was able to regain temporarily (see 2Ch 28:17) some of Judah's control over the Edomites, which had been lost during the reign of Jehoram (see 8:20 – 22). *Valley of Salt.* The same battlefield on which David had defeated the Edomites (see 2Sa 8:13; 1Ch 18:12; Ps 60 title), generally identified with the Arabah directly south of the Dead Sea. *Sela.* See notes on Isa 16:1; Ob 3. *to this day.* Until the time of the writing of the account of Amaziah's reign used by the author (see note on 1Ki 8:8; see also Introduction to 1 Kings: Author, Sources and Date).

14:8 *let us face each other in battle.* A challenge amounting to a declaration of war. Perhaps it was provoked by the hostile actions of mercenary troops from the northern kingdom after their dismissal from the Judahite army (see 2Ch 25:10,13) and by the refusal of Jehoash to establish a marriage alliance with Amaziah (see v. 9).

14:9 *Jehoash … replied.* For his reply Jehoash used a fable (see Jdg 9:8 – 15) in which he represented himself as a strong

came along and trampled the thistle underfoot. [10]You have indeed defeated Edom
and now you are arrogant.[t] Glory in your
victory, but stay at home! Why ask for
trouble and cause your own downfall and
that of Judah also?"
[11]Amaziah, however, would not listen,
so Jehoash king of Israel attacked. He and
Amaziah king of Judah faced each other
at Beth Shemesh[u] in Judah. [12]Judah was
routed by Israel, and every man fled to his
home.[v] [13]Jehoash king of Israel captured
Amaziah king of Judah, the son of Joash,
the son of Ahaziah, at Beth Shemesh.
Then Jehoash went to Jerusalem and
broke down the wall[w] of Jerusalem from
the Ephraim Gate[x] to the Corner Gate[y]—a
section about four hundred cubits long.[a]
[14]He took all the gold and silver and all
the articles found in the temple of the
LORD and in the treasuries of the royal palace. He also took hostages and returned
to Samaria.
[15]As for the other events of the reign
of Jehoash, what he did and his achievements, including his war[z] against Amaziah
king of Judah, are they not written in the
book of the annals of the kings of Israel?
[16]Jehoash rested with his ancestors and
was buried in Samaria with the kings of
Israel. And Jeroboam his son succeeded
him as king.
[17]Amaziah son of Joash king of Judah
lived for fifteen years after the death of Jehoash son of Jehoahaz king of Israel. [18]As
for the other events of Amaziah's reign,
are they not written in the book of the annals of the kings of Judah?
[19]They conspired[a] against him in Jerusalem, and he fled to Lachish,[b] but they sent
men after him to Lachish and killed him
there. [20]He was brought back by horse[c]
and was buried in Jerusalem with his ancestors, in the City of David.
[21]Then all the people of Judah took Azariah,[b][d] who was sixteen years old, and
made him king in place of his father Amaziah. [22]He was the one who rebuilt Elath[e]
and restored it to Judah after Amaziah
rested with his ancestors.

Jeroboam II King of Israel

[23]In the fifteenth year of Amaziah son
of Joash king of Judah, Jeroboam[f] son
of Jehoash king of Israel became king in
Samaria, and he reigned forty-one years.
[24]He did evil in the eyes of the LORD and
did not turn away from any of the sins
of Jeroboam son of Nebat, which he had
caused Israel to commit.[g] [25]He was the
one who restored the boundaries of Israel
from Lebo Hamath[h] to the Dead Sea,[c][i] in
accordance with the word of the LORD, the

14:10 [t] 2Ch 26:16; 32:25 **14:11** [u] S Jos 15:10 **14:12** [v] 1Ki 22:36 **14:13** [w] 1Ki 3:1; 2Ch 33:14; 36:19; Jer 39:2 [x] Ne 8:16; 12:39 [y] 2Ch 26:9; Jer 31:38; Zec 14:10 **14:15** [z] 2Ki 13:12 **14:19** [a] S 2Ki 12:20 [b] S Jos 10:3 **14:20** [c] S 2Ki 9:28 **14:21** [d] 2Ki 15:1; 2Ch 26:23; Isa 1:1; Hos 1:1; Am 1:1 **14:22** [e] S 1Ki 9:26 **14:23** [f] S 2Ki 13:13; 1Ch 5:17; Am 1:1; 7:10 **14:24** [g] S 1Ki 15:30 **14:25** [h] S Nu 13:21 [i] Dt 3:17

[a] 13 That is, about 600 feet or about 180 meters
[b] 21 Also called *Uzziah*
[c] 25 Hebrew *the Sea of the Arabah*

---

cedar and Amaziah as an insignificant thistle that could easily be trampled underfoot.
14:11 *would not listen.* See 2Ch 25:20. *Beth Shemesh.* A town about 15 miles west of Jerusalem (see Jos 15:10; 1Sa 6:9 and note).
14:13 *Jehoash ... captured Amaziah.* It is likely that Amaziah was taken back to the northern kingdom as a prisoner, where he remained until being released to return to Judah after the death of Jehoash (see vv. 15–16; see also note on v. 21). *Ephraim Gate to the Corner Gate.* The Corner Gate (see Jer 31:38; Zec 14:10) was at the northwest corner of the wall around Jerusalem. The Ephraim Gate was on the north side of Jerusalem (see Ne 12:39), 600 feet east of the Corner Gate. This northwestern section of the wall of Jerusalem was the point at which the city was most vulnerable to attack.
14:14 *gold and silver and all the articles found in the temple ... and ... the royal palace.* The value of the plundered articles was probably not great, because Joash had previously stripped the temple and palace to pay tribute to Hazael of Damascus (see 12:17–18). *took hostages.* The hostages were probably intended to secure additional payments of tribute in view of the meager plunder taken in battle.
14:15 *annals of the kings of Israel.* See note on 1Ki 14:19.
14:16 *rested with his ancestors.* See 13:12–13; see also note on 1Ki 1:21.
14:17 *lived for fifteen years after the death of Jehoash.* Jehoash died in 782 BC and Amaziah in 767.
14:18 *annals of the kings of Judah.* See note on 1Ki 14:29.
14:19 *conspired against him.* 2Ch 25:27 connects the conspiracy against Amaziah with his turning away from the Lord, but it did not serve the purpose of the author of Kings to note this. *Lachish.* A fortress city in southern Judah 15 miles west of Hebron, presently known as Tell ed-Duweir (see 18:14; 2Ch 11:9).
14:21 *Then all the people of Judah took Azariah, who was.* Or "Now all the people of Judah had taken Azariah, when he was." See NIV text note and 15:13. *made him king in place of his father Amaziah.* It is likely that this occurred after Amaziah had been taken prisoner by Jehoash (see v. 13). Thus Azariah's reign substantially overlapped that of his father, Amaziah (see notes on v. 2; 15:2).
14:22 *rebuilt Elath and restored it to Judah.* Azariah extended the subjection of the Edomites begun by his father (see v. 7) and reestablished Israelite control over the important port city on the Gulf of Aqaba (see 1Ki 9:26). A royal seal inscribed "belonging to Jotham" (see 15:32) found near the site of ancient Elath attests Judahite presence there during this period. *rested with his ancestors.* See note on 1Ki 1:21.
14:23 *fifteenth year of Amaziah.* 782 BC (see note on v. 2). This was the beginning of Jeroboam's sole reign. He had previously served as coregent with his father, Jehoash. *forty-one years.* 793–753 (including the coregency with his father).
14:24 *sins of Jeroboam.* See 1Ki 12:26–32; 13:33–34; 14:16; Am 3:13–14; 4:4–5; 5:4–6; 7:10–17.
14:25 *from Lebo Hamath.* See note on Eze 47:15. Jeroboam II was able to free the northern kingdom from the oppression it had suffered at the hands of Hazael and Ben-Hadad (see 10:32; 12:17; 13:3,22,25). He also extended Israelite political control over the Arameans of Damascus, an undertaking that had been begun by his father, Jehoash (see 13:25). Assyrian pressure on the Arameans, including attacks on Damascus by Shalmaneser IV in 773 BC and Ashur-Dan III in 772, had weakened the Arameans enough to enable

God of Israel, spoken through his servant
Jonah[j] son of Amittai, the prophet from
Gath Hepher.
26 The LORD had seen how bitterly everyone in Israel, whether slave or free,[k]
was suffering;[a][l] there was no one to help
them.[m] 27 And since the LORD had not said
he would blot out[n] the name of Israel from
under heaven, he saved[o] them by the hand
of Jeroboam son of Jehoash.
28 As for the other events of Jeroboam's
reign, all he did, and his military achievements, including how he recovered for Israel both Damascus[p] and Hamath,[q] which
had belonged to Judah, are they not written in the book of the annals[r] of the kings
of Israel? 29 Jeroboam rested with his ancestors, the kings of Israel. And Zechariah
his son succeeded him as king.

Azariah King of Judah

15:1-7pp — 2Ch 26:3-4,21-23

15 In the twenty-seventh year of Jeroboam king of Israel, Azariah[b][s] son
of Amaziah king of Judah began to reign.
2 He was sixteen years old when he became king, and he reigned in Jerusalem
fifty-two years. His mother's name was
Jekoliah; she was from Jerusalem. 3 He did
what was right[t] in the eyes of the LORD,
just as his father Amaziah had done. 4 The
high places, however, were not removed;
the people continued to offer sacrifices
and burn incense there.

14:25 [j] Jnh 1:1; Mt 12:39
14:26 [k] Dt 32:36 [l] 2Ki 13:4 [m] Ps 18:41; 22:11; 72:12; 107:12; Isa 63:5; La 1:7
14:27 [n] S Dt 29:20 [o] S Jdg 6:14
14:28 [p] S 2Sa 8:5 [q] S 2Sa 8:9 [r] 1Ki 15:31
15:1 [s] S ver 32; S 2Ki 14:21
15:3 [t] S 1Ki 14:8
15:5 [u] S Ge 12:17 [v] Lev 13:46 [w] ver 7,32; 2Ch 27:1; Mic 1:1 [x] S Ge 41:40
15:7 [y] Isa 6:1; 14:28 [z] S ver 5
15:9 [a] 1Ki 15:26
15:10 [b] S 2Ki 12:20
15:11 [c] 1Ki 15:31

5 The LORD afflicted[u] the king with leprosy[c] until the day he died, and he lived in a
separate house.[d][v] Jotham[w] the king's son
had charge of the palace[x] and governed
the people of the land.
6 As for the other events of Azariah's
reign, and all he did, are they not written
in the book of the annals of the kings of
Judah? 7 Azariah rested[y] with his ancestors and was buried near them in the City
of David. And Jotham[z] his son succeeded
him as king.

Zechariah King of Israel

8 In the thirty-eighth year of Azariah
king of Judah, Zechariah son of Jeroboam
became king of Israel in Samaria, and he
reigned six months. 9 He did evil[a] in the
eyes of the LORD, as his predecessors had
done. He did not turn away from the sins
of Jeroboam son of Nebat, which he had
caused Israel to commit.
10 Shallum son of Jabesh conspired
against Zechariah. He attacked him in
front of the people,[e] assassinated[b] him
and succeeded him as king. 11 The other
events of Zechariah's reign are written
in the book of the annals[c] of the kings of
Israel. 12 So the word of the LORD spoken

[a] 26 Or *Israel was suffering. They were without a ruler or leader, and* [b] 1 Also called *Uzziah;* also in verses 6, 7, 8, 17, 23 and 27 [c] 5 The Hebrew for *leprosy* was used for various diseases affecting the skin. [d] 5 Or *in a house where he was relieved of responsibilities* [e] 10 Hebrew; some Septuagint manuscripts *in Ibleam*

Jeroboam II to gain the upper hand over them. Meanwhile, Assyria also became too weak to suppress Jeroboam's expansion. *Dead Sea.* See NIV text note. According to Am 6:14 the southern limit of Jeroboam's kingdom in Transjordan was the "valley of the Arabah" — probably to be connected with the Valley of Salt (see note on v. 7). If so, Jeroboam had also subdued Moab and the Ammonites. *word of the LORD ... spoken through ... Jonah.* Not found in the book of Jonah. However, mention of the prophet here helps to date his ministry. *Gath Hepher.* Located in the tribe of Zebulun, northeast of Nazareth (see Jos 19:13).

14:26 *slave or free.* See NIV text note; see also note on 1Ki 14:10. *suffering.* At the hands of the Arameans (see 10:32 – 33; 13:3 – 7), the Moabites (13:20) and the Ammonites (Am 1:13).

14:27 *had not said.* The sin of the Israelites had not yet reached its full measure, and the Lord mercifully extended to the nation an additional period of grace in which there was opportunity to repent (see note on 13:23). Persistence in apostasy, however, would bring certain judgment (see Am 4:2 – 3; 6:14). *saved them by the hand of Jeroboam.* See note on 13:5.

14:28 *all he did.* During Jeroboam's reign the northern kingdom enjoyed greater material prosperity than at any time since the rule of David and Solomon. Unfortunately, it was also a time of religious formalism and apostasy, as well as social injustice (see the books of Amos and Hosea, who prophesied during Jeroboam's reign). *Damascus and Hamath.* See note on v. 25. *annals of the kings of Israel.* See note on 1Ki 14:19.

14:29 *rested with his ancestors.* See note on 1Ki 1:21. *Zechariah his son succeeded him.* For the reign of Zechariah, see 15:8 – 12.

15:1 *twenty-seventh year of Jeroboam.* 767 BC, based on dating the beginning of Jeroboam's coregency with Jehoash in 793 (see note on 14:23). *Azariah ... began to reign.* He began his sole reign, after a 24-year coregency with his father, Amaziah (see notes on v. 2; 14:2,21). (His actual years were one less than his official years.)

15:2 *fifty-two years.* 792 – 740 BC (but he was coregent with his father, Amaziah, 792 – 767). See note on v. 1.

15:3 *as his father Amaziah had done.* See note on 14:3.

15:4 *high places, however, were not removed.* See 14:4; see also note on 1Ki 15:14.

15:5 *afflicted the king with leprosy.* See NIV text note; a punishment for usurping the priestly function of burning incense on the altar in the temple (see 2Ch 26:16 – 21; cf. Lev 13:46). *had charge of the palace and governed the people of the land.* Jotham ruled for his father for the remainder of Azariah's life (750 – 740 BC; see note on v. 33).

15:6 *all he did.* A more detailed account of Azariah's accomplishments is found in 2Ch 26:1 – 15. *annals of the kings of Judah.* See note on 1Ki 14:29.

15:7 *rested with his ancestors.* See note on 1Ki 1:21. *Jotham his son succeeded him.* For the reign of Jotham, see vv. 32 – 38.

15:8 *thirty-eighth year of Azariah.* 753 BC (see note on v. 2).

15:9 *sins of Jeroboam.* See 1Ki 12:26 – 32; 13:33 – 34; 14:16.

15:11 *annals of the kings of Israel.* See note on 1Ki 14:19.

15:12 *word of the LORD ... was fulfilled.* See NIV text note. With the downfall of Jehu's dynasty, the northern kingdom entered a period of political instability (see Hos 1:4).

ASSYRIAN CAMPAIGNS AGAINST ISRAEL AND JUDAH

The Assyrian invasions of the eighth century BC were the most traumatic political events in the entire history of Israel.

The brutal Assyrian style of warfare relied on massive armies, superbly equipped with the world's first great siege machines manipulated by an efficient corps of engineers.

Psychological terror, however, was Assyria's most effective weapon. It was ruthlessly applied, with corpses impaled on stakes, severed heads stacked in heaps, and captives skinned alive.

The shock of bloody military sieges on both Israel and Judah was profound. The prophets did not fail to speak out against their horror, while at the same time pleading with the people to see God's hand in history, to recognize spiritual causes in the present punishment.

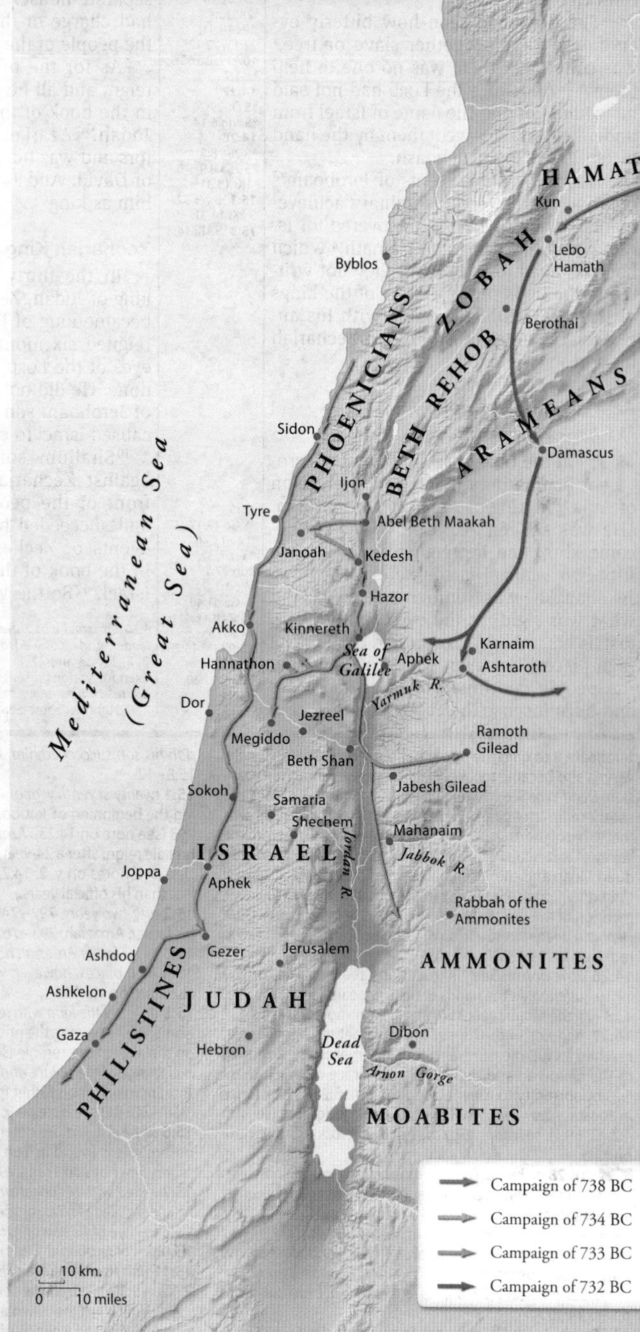

1. CAMPAIGNS OF TIGLATH-PILESER III (738–732 BC)

King Tiglath-Pileser of Assyria (745–727 BC) proved to be a vigorous campaigner, first exacting tribute from Menahem and then annexing Hamath, Philistia, Galilee, Gilead and Damascus (738–732 BC) during the reign of Pekah.

The ferocious onslaught against the northern tribes left only central Israel and the capital city of Samaria intact.

By this time Israel was a tiny nation wracked by pro- and anti-Assyrian factions, multiple assassinations, hypocrisy, arrogance and fear.

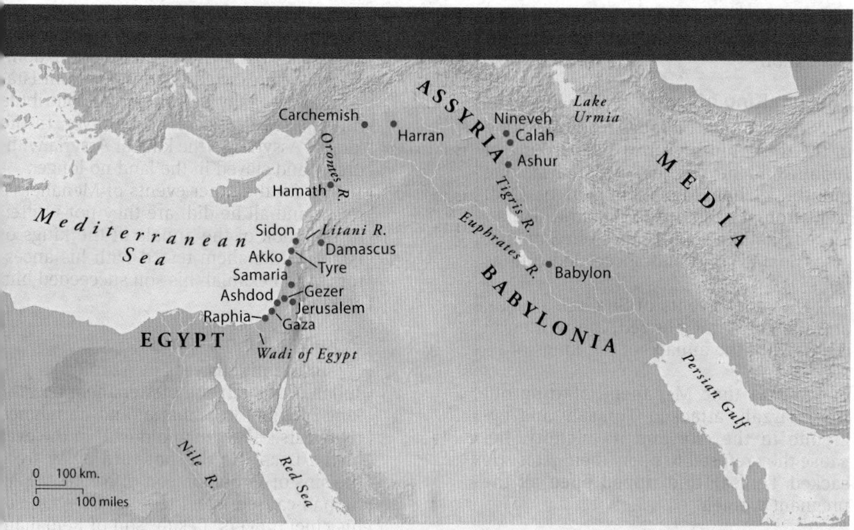

2. CAMPAIGN OF SHALMANESER V (725–722 BC)

The last king of Israel, Hoshea, conspired with Egypt and withheld the annual tribute to the Assyrians. A protracted three-year siege conducted by Shalmaneser and concluded by Sargon II saw the end of the Israelite kingdom in 722–721 BC.

At that time, according to Assyrian annals, "I [Sargon] besieged and conquered Samaria, led away as plunder 27,290 inhabitants . . . I installed over [those remaining] an officer of mine and imposed upon them the tribute of the former king."

3. SENNACHERIB'S CAMPAIGN AGAINST JUDAH (701 BC)

In the 14th year of Hezekiah, the Assyrians finally attacked Judah. The Prism of Sennacherib calls Hezekiah "overbearing and proud," indicating that he was part of Philistia's and Egypt's effort to rebel against Assyria.

A battle in the plain of Eltekeh was won by Assyria; the Egyptian and Cushite charioteers fled. Lachish was besieged and taken. Sennacherib's annals note: "As for Hezekiah the Jew, he did not submit to my yoke. I laid siege to 46 of his strong cities, walled forts and the countless small villages in their vicinity, and conquered them by means of well-tamped earth ramps and battering-rams brought near to the walls combined with the attack by foot-soldiers, using mines, breaches and sapper work. I drove out 200,150 people, young and old, male and female, horses, mules, donkeys, camels, large and small cattle beyond counting, and considered them plunder. Himself I made a prisoner in Jerusalem, his royal residence, like a bird in a cage."

Nowhere, however, does the boastful Assyrian king record the disaster mentioned in 2Ki 19:35-36; 2Ch 32:21; Isa 37:36-37.

to Jehu was fulfilled:[d] "Your descendants
will sit on the throne of Israel to the fourth
generation."[a]

Shallum King of Israel

13 Shallum son of Jabesh became king
in the thirty-ninth year of Uzziah king of
Judah, and he reigned in Samaria[e] one
month. 14 Then Menahem son of Gadi
went from Tirzah[f] up to Samaria. He attacked Shallum son of Jabesh in Samaria,
assassinated[g] him and succeeded him as
king.
15 The other events of Shallum's reign,
and the conspiracy he led, are written in
the book of the annals[h] of the kings of Israel.
16 At that time Menahem, starting out
from Tirzah, attacked Tiphsah[i] and everyone in the city and its vicinity, because they refused to open[j] their gates. He
sacked Tiphsah and ripped open all the
pregnant women.

Menahem King of Israel

17 In the thirty-ninth year of Azariah
king of Judah, Menahem son of Gadi became king of Israel, and he reigned in Samaria ten years. 18 He did evil[k] in the eyes
of the LORD. During his entire reign he did
not turn away from the sins of Jeroboam
son of Nebat, which he had caused Israel
to commit.
19 Then Pul[b][l] king of Assyria invaded the
land, and Menahem gave him a thousand
talents[c] of silver to gain his support and
strengthen his own hold on the kingdom.
20 Menahem exacted this money from Israel. Every wealthy person had to contribute
fifty shekels[d] of silver to be given to the
king of Assyria. So the king of Assyria withdrew[m] and stayed in the land no longer.
21 As for the other events of Menahem's
reign, and all he did, are they not written
in the book of the annals of the kings of
Israel? 22 Menahem rested with his ancestors. And Pekahiah his son succeeded him
as king.

Pekahiah King of Israel

23 In the fiftieth year of Azariah king of
Judah, Pekahiah son of Menahem became
king of Israel in Samaria, and he reigned
two years. 24 Pekahiah did evil[n] in the eyes
of the LORD. He did not turn away from
the sins of Jeroboam son of Nebat, which
he had caused Israel to commit. 25 One of
his chief officers, Pekah[o] son of Remaliah,
conspired against him. Taking fifty men
of Gilead with him, he assassinated[p] Pekahiah, along with Argob and Arieh, in the
citadel of the royal palace at Samaria. So
Pekah killed Pekahiah and succeeded him
as king.
26 The other events of Pekahiah's reign

15:12 [d] 2Ki 10:30 **15:13** [e] S 1Ki 13:32 **15:14** [f] S 1Ki 15:33 [g] S 2Ki 12:20 **15:15** [h] 1Ki 15:31 **15:16** [i] 1Ki 4:24 [j] S 2Ki 8:12; S Hos 13:16 **15:18** [k] 1Ki 15:26 **15:19** [l] 1Ch 5:6, 26 **15:20** [m] S 2Ki 12:18 **15:24** [n] 1Ki 15:26 **15:25** [o] 2Ch 28:6; Isa 7:1 [p] S 2Ki 12:20

[a] *12* 2 Kings 10:30 [b] *19* Also called *Tiglath-Pileser* [c] *19* That is, about 38 tons or about 34 metric tons [d] *20* That is, about 1 1/4 pounds or about 575 grams

The remaining five kings of the northern kingdom were all assassinated, with the exception of Menahem, who reigned ten years, and Hoshea, who was imprisoned by the Assyrians. From the strength and wealth of the reign of Jeroboam II, the decline and fall of the northern kingdom was swift.

15:13 *thirty-ninth year of Uzziah.* 752 BC (see note on v. 2). Uzziah is another name for Azariah (see NIV text note on 14:21).

15:14 *Menahem . . . went from Tirzah up to Samaria.* It is likely that Menahem was the commander of a military garrison at Tirzah, the former capital of the northern kingdom (see 1Ki 14:17; 15:21,33). *succeeded him.* For the reign of Menahem, see vv. 17–22.

15:15 *annals of the kings of Israel.* See note on 1Ki 14:19.

15:16 *Tiphsah.* There was a Tiphsah located far to the north of Hamath (see 14:25) on the Euphrates River (see 1Ki 4:24). It is unlikely that this was the city intended. Some interpreters prefer the reading "Tappuah" of the Septuagint (the pre-Christian Greek translation of the OT). Tappuah was a city on the border between Ephraim and Manasseh (Jos 16:8; 17:7–8). Perhaps there was a Tiphsah in Israel not otherwise mentioned. *ripped open all the pregnant women.* See 8:12 and note.

15:17 *thirty-ninth year of Azariah.* 752 BC (see note on v. 2). *ten years.* 752–742.

15:18 *sins of Jeroboam.* See 1Ki 12:26–32; 13:33–34; 14:16.

15:19 *Pul.* The Babylonian name (see 1Ch 5:26) of the Assyrian ruler Tiglath-Pileser III (745–727 BC; see NIV text note). *invaded the land.* Assyrian annals of Tiglath-Pileser III indicate that he marched west with his army in 743 and took tribute from, among others, Carchemish, Hamath, Tyre, Byblos, Damascus, and Menahem of Samaria (see map, p. 594; see also maps, pp. 2522, 2523, at the end of this study Bible). *thousand talents.* See NIV text note. This was an enormous sum of money. For the relative value of a talent of silver see note on 5:5. *gain his support and strengthen his own hold.* It appears that as a usurper Menahem still felt insecure on the throne. The opposition to his rule may have come from those following the leadership of Pekah, who favored an alliance with the Arameans of Damascus in order to resist the Assyrian threat (see note on v. 27). Hosea denounced the policy of seeking aid from the Assyrians and predicted that it would fail (Hos 5:13–15).

15:20 *fifty shekels.* See NIV text note. A simple calculation reveals that it would require approximately 60,000 men of means to provide the 1,000 talents of tribute. This gives some indication of the prosperity the northern kingdom had enjoyed during the reign of Jeroboam II.

15:21 *annals of the kings of Israel.* See note on 1Ki 14:19.

15:22 *rested with his ancestors.* See note on 1Ki 1:21.

15:23 *fiftieth year of Azariah.* 742 BC (see note on v. 2). *two years.* 742–740.

15:24 *sins of Jeroboam.* See 1Ki 12:26–32; 13:33–34; 14:16.

15:25 *One of his chief officers.* Pekah was probably the ranking official in the Transjordan provinces, but his allegiance to Menahem and Pekahiah may well have been more apparent than real (see note on v. 27). *conspired against him.* Differences over foreign policy probably played an important role in fomenting Pekah's revolution. Pekahiah undoubtedly followed the policy of his father Menahem in seeking Assyrian friendship (see v. 20). Pekah advocated friendly relations with the Arameans of Damascus in order to counter potential Assyrian aggression (see 16:1–9; Isa 7:1–2,4–6).

ınd all he did, are written in the book of
he annals of the kings of Israel.

ʔekah King of Israel

27 In the fifty-second year of Azariah
ɛing of Judah, Pekah[q] son of Remaliah[r]
ɔecame king of Israel in Samaria, and he
eigned twenty years. 28 He did evil in the
ʼyes of the LORD. He did not turn away
rom the sins of Jeroboam son of Nebat,
vhich he had caused Israel to commit.
29 In the time of Pekah king of Israel, Tig-
ath-Pileser[s] king of Assyria came and took
ion,[t] Abel Beth Maakah, Janoah, Kedesh
nd Hazor. He took Gilead and Galilee, in-
luding all the land of Naphtali,[u] and de-
ɔorted[v] the people to Assyria. 30 Then Ho-
hea[w] son of Elah conspired against Pekah
on of Remaliah. He attacked and assas-
inated[x] him, and then succeeded him as
ing in the twentieth year of Jotham son
f Uzziah.
31 As for the other events of Pekah's reign,
nd all he did, are they not written in the
ɔook of the annals[y] of the kings of Israel?

otham King of Judah

5:33-38pp — 2Ch 27:1-4,7-9

32 In the second year of Pekah son of
emaliah king of Israel, Jotham[z] son of
ɪzziah king of Judah began to reign. 33 He
was twenty-five years old when he became king, and he reigned in Jerusalem
sixteen years. His mother's name was Jerusha daughter of Zadok. 34 He did what
was right[a] in the eyes of the LORD, just as
his father Uzziah had done. 35 The high
places,[b] however, were not removed; the
people continued to offer sacrifices and
burn incense there. Jotham rebuilt the Upper Gate[c] of the temple of the LORD.
36 As for the other events of Jotham's
reign, and what he did, are they not written in the book of the annals of the kings
of Judah? 37 (In those days the LORD began
to send Rezin[d] king of Aram and Pekah
son of Remaliah against Judah.) 38 Jotham
rested with his ancestors and was buried
with them in the City of David, the city
of his father. And Ahaz his son succeeded
him as king.

Ahaz King of Judah

16:1-20pp — 2Ch 28:1-27

16 In the seventeenth year of Pekah son of Remaliah, Ahaz[e] son
of Jotham king of Judah began to reign.
2 Ahaz was twenty years old when he became king, and he reigned in Jerusalem
sixteen years. Unlike David his father, he
did not do what was right[f] in the eyes of
the LORD his God. 3 He followed the ways

15:27 [q] 2Ch 28:6; Isa 7:1 [r] Isa 7:4
15:29 [s] 2Ki 16:7; 17:6; 1Ch 5:26; 2Ch 28:20; Jer 50:17 [t] 1Ki 15:20 [u] 2Ki 16:9; 17:24; 2Ch 16:4; Isa 7:9; 9:1; 10:9, 10; 28:1; 36:19; 37:18 [v] 2Ki 24:14-16; 1Ch 5:22; Isa 14:6, 17; 36:17; 45:13
15:30 [w] 2Ki 17:1 [x] S 2Ki 12:20
15:31 [y] 1Ki 15:31
15:32 [z] ver 1, S 5; 1Ch 5:17; Isa 1:1; Hos 1:1
15:34 [a] S 1Ki 14:8
15:35 [b] 2Ki 12:3 [c] S Ge 23:10; 2Ch 23:20
15:37 [d] 2Ki 16:5; Isa 7:1; 8:6; 9:11
16:1 [e] Isa 1:1; 7:1; 14:28; Hos 1:1; Mic 1:1
16:2 [f] S 1Ki 14:8

5:26 *annals of the kings of Israel.* See note on 1Ki 14:19.
5:27 *fifty-second year of Azariah.* 740 BC (see note on v. 2). *venty years.* 752 – 732, based on the assumptions (which the ata seem to require) that Pekah had established in Transjor-an virtually a rival government to that of Menahem when enahem assassinated Shallum (see notes on vv. 17,19,25) nd that the number of regnal years given here includes this eriod of rival rule.
5:28 *sins of Jeroboam.* See 1Ki 12:26 – 32; 13:33 – 34; 14:16.
5:29 *Tiglath-Pileser king of Assyria came.* See note on v. 19; e also map, p. 594. The historical background for this attack found in 16:5 – 9; 2Ch 28:16 – 21; Isa 7:1 – 17. *Ijon ... Naphta-* Over 150 years earlier Ben-Hadad I of Damascus had taken is same territory from the northern kingdom in response an appeal by a king of Judah (see notes on 1Ki 15:19 – 20). *eported the people to Assyria.* See 1Ch 5:26. The forced exile Israelites from their homeland was a fulfillment of the cov-nant curse (see note on 10:32).
15:30 *Hoshea ... conspired against Pekah.* Hoshea probably represented the faction in the northern king-om that favored cooperation with Assyria rather than resis-nce. In one of his annals Tiglath-Pileser III claims to have aced Hoshea on the throne of the northern kingdom and have taken ten talents of gold and 1,000 talents of silver as ibute from him. *twentieth year of Jotham.* 732 BC (see notes n vv. 32 – 33). Reference is to his 20th official year, which was s 19th actual year.
5:31 *annals of the kings of Israel.* See note on 1Ki 14:19.
5:32 *second year of Pekah.* 750 BC (see note on v. 27).
5:33 *sixteen years.* 750 – 735 BC. Jotham was coregent with s father 750 – 740 (see note on v. 5). Jotham's reign was in me sense terminated in 735, and his son Ahaz took over. owever, Jotham continued to live until at least 732 (see otes on vv. 30,37).
15:34 *as his father Uzziah had done.* See note on v. 3; see also 2Ch 27:2.
15:35 *high places, however, were not removed.* See v. 4; see also note on 1Ki 15:14. *Upper Gate of the temple.* See 2Ch 23:20; Jer 20:2; Eze 9:2. Additional information on Jotham's building activities is given in 2Ch 27:3 – 4.
15:36 *other events of Jotham's reign.* See 2Ch 27:1 – 6. *annals of the kings of Judah.* See note on 1Ki 14:29.
15:37 This parenthetical statement concerning Jotham's reign supports the idea of an overlap between the reigns of Jotham and Ahaz (see note on v. 33), since 16:5 – 12; 2Ch 28:5 – 21; Isa 7:1 – 17 all place the major effort of Rezin and Pekah in the time of Ahaz.
15:38 *rested with his ancestors.* See note on 1Ki 1:21.
16:1 *seventeenth year of Pekah.* 735 BC (see note on 15:27). The reign of Ahaz apparently overlapped that of Jotham, with Ahaz serving as a senior partner beginning in 735 (see notes on 15:33,37; see also notes on 16:2; 17:1; cf. chart, p. 545). *Ahaz son of Jotham king of Judah.* In 1996 a clay seal impression reading "Belonging to Ahaz (son of) Jotham king of Judah" came to light. Written in the ancient Hebrew script used during the divided monarchy, it is the first authen-tic seal inscription that can be attributed to a king of Judah.
16:2 *twenty years old when he became king.* Perhaps the age at which Ahaz became a senior coregent with his father, Jo-tham, in 735 BC (see note on v. 1). Otherwise, according to the ages and dates provided, Ahaz would have been 11 or 12 instead of 14 or 15 years old when his son Hezekiah was born (cf. 18:1 – 2). *sixteen years.* The synchronizations of the reigns of Ahaz and Hezekiah of Judah with those of Pekah and Hoshea of the northern kingdom present some apparent chronological difficulties (see notes on v. 1; 17:1; 18:1,9 – 10). It seems best to take the 16 years specified here as the num-ber of years Ahaz reigned after the death of Jotham, thus

of the kings of Israel[g] and even sacrificed
his son[h] in the fire, engaging in the detestable[i] practices of the nations the LORD
had driven out before the Israelites. 4He
offered sacrifices and burned incense[j] at
the high places, on the hilltops and under
every spreading tree.[k]
5Then Rezin[l] king of Aram and Pekah
son of Remaliah king of Israel marched up
to fight against Jerusalem and besieged
Ahaz, but they could not overpower him.
6At that time, Rezin[m] king of Aram recovered Elath[n] for Aram by driving out the
people of Judah. Edomites then moved
into Elath and have lived there to this day.
7Ahaz sent messengers to say to Tiglath-Pileser[o] king of Assyria, "I am your
servant and vassal. Come up and save[p] me
out of the hand of the king of Aram and of
the king of Israel, who are attacking me."
8And Ahaz took the silver and gold found
in the temple of the LORD and in the treasuries of the royal palace and sent it as a
gift[q] to the king of Assyria. 9The king of
Assyria complied by attacking Damascus[r]
and capturing it. He deported its inhabitants to Kir[s] and put Rezin to death.

16:3 g 2Ki 17:19 h S Lev 18:21; S 2Ki 3:27 i S Lev 18:3; S Dt 9:4 **16:4** j 2Ki 22:17; 23:5 k Dt 12:2; Eze 6:13 **16:5** l S 2Ki 15:37 **16:6** m Isa 9:12 n S 1Ki 9:26 **16:7** o S 2Ki 15:29 p Isa 2:6; 10:20; Jer 2:18; 3:1; Eze 16:28; 23:5; Hos 10:6 **16:8** q S 1Ki 15:18; 2Ki 12:18 **16:9** r S Ge 14:15; S 2Ki 15:29 s Isa 22:6; Am 1:5; 9:7 **16:10** t ver 11, 15,16; Isa 8:2 **16:12** u 2Ch 26:16 **16:13** v Lev 6:8-13 w Lev 6:14-23 x S Ex 29:40 y Lev 7:11-21 **16:14** z S Ex 20:24; S 40:6; S 1Ki 8:64

10Then King Ahaz went to Damascus to
meet Tiglath-Pileser king of Assyria. He
saw an altar in Damascus and sent to Uriah[t] the priest a sketch of the altar, with
detailed plans for its construction. 11So
Uriah the priest built an altar in accordance with all the plans that King Ahaz
had sent from Damascus and finished it
before King Ahaz returned. 12When the
king came back from Damascus and saw
the altar, he approached it and presented
offerings[a][u] on it. 13He offered up his burnt
offering[v] and grain offering,[w] poured out
his drink offering,[x] and splashed the blood
of his fellowship offerings[y] against the altar. 14As for the bronze altar[z] that stood
before the LORD, he brought it from the
front of the temple—from between the
new altar and the temple of the LORD—
and put it on the north side of the new
altar.
15King Ahaz then gave these orders to
Uriah the priest: "On the large new altar,
offer the morning[a] burnt offering and the

a 12 Or *and went up*

16:15 a Ex 29:38-41

732–715 (see notes on 15:30,33). The beginning of his reign appears to be dated in a variety of ways in the Biblical text: (1) in 744/743, which presupposes a coregency with his grandfather Azariah at the tender age of 11 or 12 (see 17:1); (2) in 735, when he became senior coregent with Jotham (see v. 1); and (3) in 732, when he began his sole reign after the death of Jotham. *Unlike David his father.* Ahaz does not even receive the qualified approval given to Amaziah (14:3), Azariah (15:3) and Jotham (15:34).

16:3 *ways of the kings of Israel.* It is unlikely that Ahaz adhered to the calf worship introduced by Jeroboam I at Bethel and Dan (see 1Ki 12:26–32; 13:33–34; 14:16). The reference here is probably to Baal worship in the spirit of Ahab (see notes on 1Ki 16:31–33; see also 2Ch 28:2). *sacrificed his son.* Israel had been warned by Moses not to engage in this pagan rite (see Lev 18:21; Dt 18:10). In Israel the firstborn son in each household was to be consecrated to the Lord and redeemed by a payment of five shekels to the priests (see Ex 13:1,11–13; Nu 18:16). See also 3:27; 17:17; 21:6; 23:10; 2Ch 28:3; Jer 7:31; 32:35.

16:4 *high places.* See 15:4,35; see also note on 1Ki 15:14. These high places appear to be those assimilated from pagan Baal worship and used by those who worshiped Baal even while also worshiping the Lord. *under every spreading tree.* Large trees were viewed as symbols of fertility by the pre-Israelite inhabitants of Canaan. Immoral pagan rites were performed at shrines located under such trees. Contrary to the explicit prohibition of the Mosaic covenant, the Israelites adopted this pagan custom (see 17:10; 1Ki 14:23; Dt 12:2; Jer 2:20; 3:6; 17:2; Eze 6:13; 20:28; Hos 4:13–14).

16:5 *Rezin ... and Pekah ... marched up to fight against Jerusalem.* See notes on 15:25,37. *could not overpower.* See Isa 7:1–17; 2Ch 28:5–21. Rezin and Pekah desired to replace Ahaz on the throne of the southern kingdom with the son of Tabeel in order to gain another ally in their anti-Assyrian political policy (see notes on 15:19,25). The Lord delivered Judah and Ahaz from this threat in spite of their wickedness because of the promises of the Davidic covenant (see 1Ki 11:36; 2Sa 7:13; Isa 7:3–7,14).

16:6 *Rezin king of Aram recovered Elath.* See note on 14:22. *Edomites then moved into Elath.* See 2Ch 28:17. The Philistines also took this opportunity to avenge previous defeats (compare 2Ch 26:5–7 with 2Ch 28:18). *to this day.* See note on 1Ki 8:8.

16:7 *Tiglath-Pileser.* See notes on 15:19,29. *your servant and vassal.* Ahaz preferred to seek security for Judah by means of a treaty with Assyria rather than by obedience to the Lord and trust in his promises (see Ex 23:22; Isa 7:10–16).

16:8 *silver and gold found in the temple.* The temple treasure must have been restored to some degree by Jotham (see 12:18; 14:14). The name "Jehoahaz of Judah" (Ahaz) appears on an inscription of Tiglath-Pileser that contains a list of rulers (including those of the Philistines, Ammonites, Moabites and Edomites) who brought tribute to him in 734 BC.

16:9 *attacking Damascus and capturing it.* In 732 BC Tiglath-Pileser III moved against Damascus and destroyed it (see the prophecies of Isa 7:16; Am 1:3–5). *deported its inhabitants to Kir.* The Arameans were sent back to the place from which they had come (Am 9:7) in fulfillment of the prophecy of Amos (Am 1:5). The location of Kir is unknown, though it is mentioned in connection with Elam in Isa 22:6.

16:10 *Ahaz went to Damascus to meet Tiglath-Pileser.* As a vassal king to express his gratitude and loyalty to the victorious Assyrian ruler. *altar in Damascus.* Perhaps that of the god Rimmon (see 5:18; 2Ch 28:23), but more likely a royal altar of Tiglath-Pileser. Ahaz's reproduction of such an altar would have been a further sign of submission to the Assyrians.

16:13 *burnt offering ... grain offering ... drink offering ... fellowship offerings.* See chart, p. 164. With the exception of the drink offering, these same sacrifices were offered at the dedication of the temple (1Ki 8:64).

16:14 *north side of the new altar.* Ahaz removed the bronze altar of burnt offering from its prominent place in front of the temple and gave it a place alongside the stone altar.

16:15 *large new altar.* Even though fire from heaven had inaugurated and sanctioned the use of the bronze altar for the worship of the Lord (see 2Ch 7:1), Ahaz now re-

ːvening grain offering, the king's burnt of-
ːering and his grain offering, and the burnt
›ffering of all the people of the land, and
:heir grain offering and their drink offer-
ng. Splash against this altar the blood of
ıll the burnt offerings and sacrifices. But I
vill use the bronze altar for seeking guid-
ınce."[b] 16 And Uriah the priest did just as
ﾐing Ahaz had ordered.
17 King Ahaz cut off the side panels
ınd removed the basins from the mov-
ıble stands. He removed the Sea from the
›ronze bulls that supported it and set it on
ı stone base.[c] 18 He took away the Sabbath
:anopy[a] that had been built at the temple
ınd removed the royal entryway outside
he temple of the LORD, in deference to the
:ing of Assyria.[d]
19 As for the other events of the reign of
\haz, and what he did, are they not writ-
en in the book of the annals of the kings
›f Judah? 20 Ahaz rested[e] with his ances-
ors and was buried with them in the City
›f David. And Hezekiah his son succeeded
ıim as king.

·oshea Last King of Israel

7:3-7pp — 2Ki 18:9-12

17 In the twelfth year of Ahaz king of
Judah, Hoshea[f] son of Elah became
king of Israel in Samaria, and he reigned
nine years. 2 He did evil[g] in the eyes of the
LORD, but not like the kings of Israel who
preceded him.
3 Shalmaneser[h] king of Assyria came
up to attack Hoshea, who had been Shalmaneser's vassal and had paid him tribute.[i] 4 But the king of Assyria discovered
that Hoshea was a traitor, for he had sent
envoys to So[b] king of Egypt,[j] and he no
longer paid tribute to the king of Assyria, as he had done year by year. Therefore Shalmaneser seized him and put him
in prison.[k] 5 The king of Assyria invaded
the entire land, marched against Samaria
and laid siege[l] to it for three years. 6 In the
ninth year of Hoshea, the king of Assyria[m]
captured Samaria[n] and deported[o] the Israelites to Assyria. He settled them in Halah,
in Gozan[p] on the Habor River and in the
towns of the Medes.

Israel Exiled Because of Sin

7 All this took place because the Israelites had sinned[q] against the LORD their
God, who had brought them up out of
Egypt[r] from under the power of Pharaoh
king of Egypt. They worshiped other gods

16:15 [b] 1Sa 9:9 **16:17** [c] 1Ki 7:27 **16:18** [d] Eze 16:28 **16:20** [e] Isa 14:28 **17:1** [f] 2Ki 15:30 **17:2** [g] S Dt 4:25 **17:3** [h] Hos 10:14 [i] S Jdg 3:15 **17:4** [j] Ps 146:3; Isa 30:1,7; 36:6; Jer 2:36; Hos 12:1 [k] Hos 13:10 **17:5** [l] Hos 13:16 **17:6** [m] ver 20; S 2Ki 15:29; Isa 42:24 [n] Isa 10:9 [o] S Dt 4:27; S 24:1; S 2Ki 15:29; Am 7:17 [p] 1Ch 5:26 **17:7** [q] S Jos 7:11 [r] Ex 14:15-31

[a] 18 Or *the dais of his throne* (see Septuagint) [b] 4 *So* is probably an abbreviation for *Osorkon.*

·laced it with an altar built on the pattern of the pagan altar ·om Damascus. Although the bronze altar was quite large ›ee 2Ch 4:1), the new altar was larger. *morning burnt offering.* ee 3:20; Ex 29:38 – 39; Nu 28:3 – 4. *evening grain offering.* See ote on 1Ki 18:29. *king's burnt offering and his grain offering.* here is no other reference to these special offerings of the ·ing in the OT, with the possible exception of Ezekiel's depic- on of the offerings of a future prince (Eze 46:12). *I will use ıe bronze altar for seeking guidance.* Seeking omens by the xamination of the livers and other organ materials of sacri- ced animals is well attested in ancient Near Eastern texts. ·ere Ahaz states his intention to follow an Assyrian divina- on technique in an attempt to secure the Lord's guidance.

6:17 *side panels and ... basins from the movable stands.* See ·Ki 7:27 – 39. *removed the Sea from the bronze bulls.* See 1Ki :23 – 26. Perhaps the bronze was needed for tribute required y Tiglath-Pileser III.

6:18 *in deference to the king of Assyria.* As a vassal of Tiglath- ·ileser, Ahaz was forced to relinquish some of the symbols of is own royal power.

16:19 *other events of the reign of Ahaz.* See 2Ch 28, where, among other things, it is said that Ahaz went › far as to "shut the doors of the ... temple" (2Ch 28:24). *an- als of the kings of Judah.* See note on 1Ki 14:29.

6:20 *rested with his ancestors.* See note on 1Ki 1:21; see also ·Ch 28:27. *Hezekiah his son succeeded him.* For the reign of ezekiah, see 18:1 — 20:21.

7:1 *twelfth year of Ahaz.* 732 BC (see note on 15:30), on the ›ssumption that Ahaz began a coregency with Azariah in 44/743 (see notes on 16:1 – 2). *nine years.* 732 – 722 (see In- ·oduction to 1 Kings: Chronology); cf. note on 15:30.

7:3 *Shalmaneser.* Hoshea had become a vassal to Assyria ·nder the rule of Tiglath-Pileser III (see note on 15:30). The ·tter was succeeded on the Assyrian throne by Shalmane- ·er V, who ruled 727 – 722 BC (see chart, p. 511).

17:5 *three years.* 725 – 722 BC. Samaria was a strongly fortified city and extremely difficult to subdue (see note on 1Ki 16:24).

17:6 *ninth year of Hoshea.* 722 BC (see note on v. 1). *king of Assyria captured Samaria.* In the winter (December) of 722 – 721 Shalmaneser V died (possibly by assassination), and the Assyrian throne was seized by Sargon II (721 – 705). In his annals Sargon lays claim to the capture of Samaria at the beginning of his reign, but it was hardly more than a mopping-up operation. *deported the Israelites.* Because the northern kingdom refused to be obedient to its covenant obligations, the Lord brought on its citizens the judgment pronounced already by Ahijah during the reign of the northern kingdom's first king, Jeroboam I (see note on 1Ki 14:15). In his annals Sargon II claims to have deported 27,290 Israelites. He then settled other captured people in the vacated towns of the northern kingdom (see v. 24). *Gozan on the Habor River.* Gozan was an Assyrian provincial capital located on a tributary (the Habor) of the Euphrates River. *towns of the Medes.* Towns located in the area south of the Caspian Sea and northeast of the Tigris River.

17:7 – 23 A theological explanation for the downfall of the northern kingdom (see map and accompanying text, p. 600). Israel had repeatedly spurned the Lord's gracious acts, had refused to heed the prophets' warnings of impending judgment (vv. 13 – 14,23) and had failed to keep her covenant obligations (v. 15). The result was the implementation of the covenant curse precisely as it had been presented to the Israelites by Moses before they entered Canaan (Dt 28:49 – 68; 32:1 – 47).

17:7 *brought them up out of Egypt.* The deliverance from Egypt was the fundamental redemptive event in Israel's history. She owed her very existence as a nation to this gracious and mighty act of the Lord (see Ex 20:2; Dt 5:15; 26:8; Jos 24:5 – 7,17; Jdg 10:11; 1Sa 12:6; Ne 9:9 – 13; Mic 6:4). *worshiped other gods.* A violation of the most basic obligation

EXILE OF THE NORTHERN KINGDOM

The mass deportation policy of the Assyrians was a companion piece to the brutal and calculated terror initiated by Ashurnasirpal and followed by all his successors. It was intended to forestall revolts but, like all Draconian measures, it merely spread misery and engendered hatred. In the end, it hastened the disintegration of the Assyrian Empire.

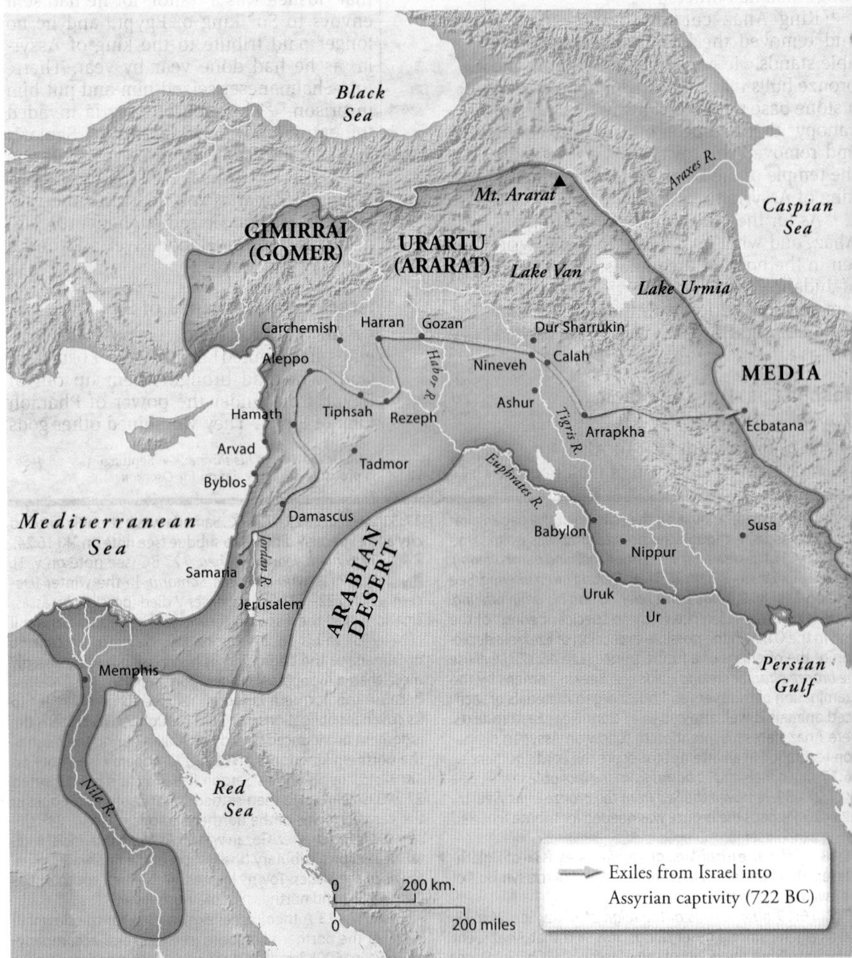

There is some evidence that Israel experienced its first deportations under Tiglath-Pileser III (745–727 BC), a cruelty repeated by Sargon II (721–705 BC) at the time of the fall of Samaria. The latter king's inscriptions boast of carrying away 27,290 inhabitants of the city "as plunder." According to 2Ki 17:6, they were sent to Assyria, to Halah, to Gozan on the Habor River, and apparently to the eastern frontiers of the empire (to the towns of the Medes, most probably somewhere in the vicinity of Ecbatana, the modern Hamadan).

The sequel is provided by the inscriptions of Sargon: "The Arabs who live far away in the desert, who know neither overseers nor officials, and who had not yet brought their tribute to any king, I deported . . . and settled them in Samaria."

Much mythology has developed around the theme of the so-called ten lost tribes of Israel. A close examination of Assyrian records reveals that the deportations approximated only a limited percentage of the population, usually consisting of noble families. Agricultural workers, no doubt the majority, were deliberately left to care for the crops (cf. the Babylonian practice, 2Ki 24:14; 25:12).

and followed the practices of the nations[s]
he LORD had driven out before them, as
vell as the practices that the kings of Is-
ael had introduced. 9 The Israelites secret-
y did things against the LORD their God
hat were not right. From watchtower to
ortified city[t] they built themselves high
laces in all their towns. 10 They set up sa-
red stones[u] and Asherah poles[v] on every
igh hill and under every spreading tree.[w]
At every high place they burned incense,
s the nations whom the LORD had driven
ut before them had done. They did wick-
d things that aroused the LORD's anger.
2 They worshiped idols,[x] though the LORD
ad said, "You shall not do this."[a] 13 The
ORD warned[y] Israel and Judah through all
is prophets and seers:[z] "Turn from your
vil ways.[a] Observe my commands and de-
rees, in accordance with the entire Law
hat I commanded your ancestors to obey
nd that I delivered to you through my ser-
ants the prophets."[b]
14 But they would not listen and were
s stiff-necked[c] as their ancestors, who
id not trust in the LORD their God.
They rejected his decrees and the cov-
nant[d] he had made with their ancestors
nd the statutes he had warned them to
eep. They followed worthless idols[e] and
hemselves became worthless.[f] They imi-
ated the nations[g] around them although
he LORD had ordered them, "Do not do
s they do."
16 They forsook all the commands of the
LORD their God and made for themselves
two idols cast in the shape of calves,[h] and
an Asherah[i] pole. They bowed down to
all the starry hosts,[j] and they worshiped
Baal.[k] 17 They sacrificed[l] their sons and
daughters in the fire. They practiced divination and sought omens[m] and sold[n] themselves to do evil in the eyes of the LORD,
arousing his anger.
18 So the LORD was very angry with Israel and removed them from his presence.[o]
Only the tribe of Judah was left, 19 and
even Judah did not keep the commands
of the LORD their God. They followed the
practices Israel had introduced.[p] 20 Therefore the LORD rejected all the people of Israel; he afflicted them and gave them into
the hands of plunderers,[q] until he thrust
them from his presence.[r]
21 When he tore[s] Israel away from the
house of David, they made Jeroboam son
of Nebat their king.[t] Jeroboam enticed
Israel away from following the LORD and
caused them to commit a great sin.[u] 22 The
Israelites persisted in all the sins of Jeroboam and did not turn away from them
23 until the LORD removed them from his
presence,[v] as he had warned[w] through all
his servants the prophets. So the people

17:8 [s]S Ex 34:15; S Lev 18:3; S Dt 9:4 **17:9** [t]2Ki 18:8 **17:10** [u]S Ex 23:24 [v]Ex 34:13; Isa 17:8; Mic 5:14 [w]S Dt 12:2 **17:12** [x]S Ex 20:4 **17:13** [y]S Jdg 6:8; S 2Ch 7:14; S Job 34:33; Eze 3:17-19 [z]S 1Sa 9:9 [a]Jer 4:1; 18:11; 23:22; 25:5; 35:15; 36:3; Zec 1:4 [b]Mt 23:34 **17:14** [c]S Ex 32:9; Ac 7:51 **17:15** [d]S Lev 26:11; Dt 29:25; Jdg 2:20; 1Ki 11:11; 2Ki 18:12; Ps 78:10; Eze 5:6; Mal 2:10 [e]S Dt 32:21; Hos 11:2; Ro 1:21-23 [f]Jer 2:5 [g]S Dt 12:4 **17:16** [h]S Ex 32:4 [i]S Dt 16:21 [j]S Ge 2:1; Isa 40:26; Jer 19:13 [k]S Jdg 2:11

[a] *12* Exodus 20:4,5

17:17 [l]S Dt 12:31; 18:10-12; 2Ki 16:3; Eze 16:21 [m]S Lev 19:26 [n]S 1Ki 21:20; Ro 7:14 **17:18** [o]S Ge 4:14; S Ex 33:15; S 2Ki 13:23; 2Th 1:9 **17:19** [p]2Ki 16:3; Jer 3:6-10; Eze 23:13 **17:20** [q]S ver 6 [r]Jer 7:15; 15:1 **17:21** [s]S 1Sa 15:27; S 1Ki 11:11 [t]1Ki 12:20 [u]S 1Ki 12:30 **17:23** [v]Eze 39:23-24 [w]S Jdg 6:8

Israel's covenant with the Lord (see v. 35; Dt 5:7; 6:14; Jos :14–16,20; Jer 1:16; 2:5–6; 25:6; 35:15).

7:8 *practices of the nations.* See Dt 18:9; Jdg 2:12–13. *prac- :es that the kings of Israel had introduced.* See, e.g., 10:31 ehu); 14:24 (Jeroboam II); 1Ki 12:28–33 (Jeroboam I); :25–26 (Omri); 16:30–34 (Ahab).

7:9 *high places in all their towns.* See 14:4; 15:4,35; see also otes on 16:4; 1Ki 3:2; 15:14.

7:10 *sacred stones.* See note on 1Ki 14:23. *Asherah poles.* See ote on 1Ki 14:15. *on every high hill and under every spreading ee.* See 16:4; 1Ki 14:23; Jer 2:20; 3:6,13; 17:2.

:11 *wicked things.* Perhaps a reference to ritual prostitution ee note on 1Ki 14:24; see also Hos 4:13–14).

:12 *idols.* See note on Lev 26:30. *You shall not do this.* See V text note; see also Ex 23:13; Lev 26:1; Dt 5:6–10.

17:13 *warned Israel and Judah through all his prophets.* Israel not only violated the requirements of the Sinaitic venant but also spurned the words of prophets the Lord d graciously sent to call his people back to the covenant ee, e.g., 1Ki 13:1–3; 14:6–16; Jdg 6:8–10; 1Sa 3:19–21, as ell as the ministries of Elijah, Elisha, Amos and Hosea). *seers.* e note on 1Sa 9:9.

:14 *stiff-necked.* A figure derived from the obstinate resis- nce of an ox to being placed under a yoke (see Dt 10:16; Jer 20; 7:26; 17:23; 19:15; Hos 4:16).

:15 *followed worthless idols.* See Dt 32:21; Jer 2:5; 8:19; 10:8; :22; 51:18.

:16 *two idols cast in the shape of calves.* The golden calves Bethel and Dan (see 1Ki 12:28–30). *Asherah pole.* See note 1Ki 14:15. *all the starry hosts.* Israel had been commanded not to worship the stars like her pagan neighbors (see Dt 4:19; 17:3). Although this form of idolatry is not mentioned previously in 1,2 Kings, the prophet Amos apparently alludes to its practice in the northern kingdom during the reign of Jeroboam II (see note on Am 5:26). It was later introduced in the southern kingdom during the reign of Manasseh (see 21:3,5) and abolished during the reformation of Josiah (see 23:4–5,12; see also Eze 8:16).

17:17 *sacrificed their sons and daughters.* See note on 16:3. *practiced divination and sought omens.* Such practices were forbidden in the Mosaic covenant (see note on 16:15; see also Lev 19:26; Dt 18:10 and note on 18:9).

17:18 *removed them from his presence.* The exile of the northern kingdom (see v. 6; 23:27; see also map, p. 600). *Only the tribe of Judah was left.* The southern kingdom included elements of the tribes of Simeon and Benjamin, but Judah was the only tribe in the south to retain its complete integrity (see notes on 1Ki 11:31–32; see also note on 2Ki 19:4).

17:20 *afflicted them and gave them into the hands of plunderers.* See 10:32–33; 13:3,20; 24:2; 2Ch 21:16; 28:18; Am 1:13.

17:21 *tore Israel away from the house of David.* See 1Ki 11:11, 31; 12:24. It was the Lord's will for the kingdom to be divided, but the division came to the nation as a punishment for its sins. *Jeroboam … caused them to commit a great sin.* See 1Ki 12:26–32; 13:33–34; see also note on Ge 20:9.

17:23 *warned through all his servants the prophets.* See 1Ki 14:15–16; Hos 10:1–7; 11:5; Am 5:27. *exile in Assyria … still there.* See maps and accompanying texts, pp. 594–595, 600.

of Israel were taken from their homeland[x] into exile in Assyria, and they are still there.

Samaria Resettled

24 The king of Assyria[y] brought people from Babylon, Kuthah, Avva, Hamath and Sepharvaim[z] and settled them in the towns of Samaria to replace the Israelites. They took over Samaria and lived in its towns. 25 When they first lived there, they did not worship the LORD; so he sent lions[a] among them and they killed some of the people. 26 It was reported to the king of Assyria: "The people you deported and resettled in the towns of Samaria do not know what the god of that country requires. He has sent lions among them, which are killing them off, because the people do not know what he requires."

27 Then the king of Assyria gave this order: "Have one of the priests you took captive from Samaria go back to live there and teach the people what the god of the land requires." 28 So one of the priests who had been exiled from Samaria came to live in Bethel and taught them how to worship the LORD.

29 Nevertheless, each national group made its own gods in the several towns[b] where they settled, and set them up in the shrines[c] the people of Samaria had made at the high places.[d] 30 The people from Babylon made Sukkoth Benoth, those from Kuthah made Nergal, and those from Hamath made Ashima; 31 the Avvites made Nibhaz and Tartak, and the Sepharvites burned their children in the fire as sacrifices to Adrammelek[e] and Anammelek, the gods of Sepharvaim.[f] 32 They worshiped the LORD, but they also appointed all sorts[g] of their own people to officiate for them as priests in the shrines at the high places. 33 They worshiped the LORD, but they also served their own gods in accordance with the customs of the nations from which they had been brought.

34 To this day they persist in their former practices. They neither worship the LORD nor adhere to the decrees and regulations, the laws and commands that the LORD gave the descendants of Jacob, whom he named Israel.[h] 35 When the LORD made a covenant with the Israelites, he commanded them: "Do not worship[i] any other gods or bow down to them, serve them or sacrifice to them.[j] 36 But the LORD, who brought you up out of Egypt with mighty power and outstretched arm,[k] is the one you must worship. To him you shall bow down and to him offer sacrifices. 37 You must always be careful[l] to keep the decrees[m] and regulations, the laws and commands he wrote for you. Do not worship other gods. 38 Do not forget[n] the covenant I have made with you, and do not worship other gods. 39 Rather, worship the LORD your God; it is he who will deliver you from the hand of all your enemies."

17:23 [x] S 1Ki 9:7
17:24 [y] 2Ki 19:37; Ezr 4:2, 10; Isa 37:38 [z] ver 31; S 2Ki 15:29; 18:34; Isa 36:19; 37:13; Am 6:2
17:25 [a] S Ge 37:20; Isa 5:29; 15:9; Jer 50:17
17:29 [b] Jer 2:28; 11:13 [c] S Lev 26:30; S 1Ki 12:31 [d] Mic 4:5
17:31 [e] 2Ki 19:37 [f] S ver 24
17:32 [g] S 1Ki 12:31
17:34 [h] S Ge 17:5; S 1Ki 18:31
17:35 [i] S Ex 20:5 [j] S Ex 20:3
17:36 [k] S Ex 3:20; Ps 136:12
17:37 [l] Dt 5:32 [m] S Lev 19:37
17:38 [n] S Dt 6:12

17:24 *king of Assyria.* Primarily Sargon II (721–705 BC), though later Assyrian rulers, including Esarhaddon (681–669) and Ashurbanipal (669–627), settled additional non-Israelites in Samaria (see Ezr 4:2,9–10). *Babylon, Kuthah.* Babylon and Kuthah (located about eight miles northeast of Babylon) were forced to submit to Assyrian rule by Sargon II in 709. *Avva.* Probably the same as Ivvah (see 18:34; 19:13). Its association with Hamath and Arpad suggests a location somewhere in Aram (Syria). *Hamath.* Located on the Orontes River (see 14:25; 18:34; see also note on Eze 47:15). In 720 Sargon II made the kingdom of Hamath into an Assyrian province. *Sepharvaim.* See note on Isa 36:19. *Samaria.* Here a designation for the entire northern kingdom (see note on 1Ki 13:32).

17:25 *did not worship the LORD.* They worshiped their own national deities. *sent lions among them.* Lions had always been present in Canaan (see 1Ki 13:24; 20:36; Jdg 14:5; 1Sa 17:34; Am 3:12). In the aftermath of the disruption and depopulation caused by the conflict with the Assyrians, the lions greatly increased in number (see Ex 23:29). This was viewed by the inhabitants of the land and the writer of Kings as a punishment from the Lord (see Lev 26:21–22).

17:26 *king of Assyria.* Sargon II. *what the god of that country requires.* According to the religious ideas of that time, each regional deity required special ritual observances, which, if ignored or violated, would bring disaster on the land.

17:27 *one of the priests.* Probably a priest of the religion Jeroboam I established in the northern kingdom (see 1Ki 12:31 and note).

17:28 *came to live in Bethel.* Bethel continued to be the center for the apostate form of Yahweh worship that had been promoted in the northern kingdom since the time of Jeroboam (see notes on 1Ki 12:28–30).

17:29 *people of Samaria.* The mixed population of the former territory of the northern kingdom. These people of mixed ancestry eventually came to be known as Samaritans. In later times the Samaritans rejected the idolatry of their polytheistic origins and followed the teachings of Moses, including monotheism. In NT times Jesus testified to a Samaritan woman (Jn 4:4–26), and many Samaritans were converted under the ministry of Philip (Ac 8:4–25).

17:32 *officiate for them as priests.* See note on 1Ki 12:31.

17:33 *They worshiped the LORD, but they also served their own gods.* A classic statement of a syncretistic (mixed) religion.

17:34 *To this day.* Until the time of the writing of 1,2 Kings. *worship the LORD.* Here used in the sense of faithful worship. In vv. 32–33 "worship the LORD" refers to a paganized worship.

17:35 *Do not worship any other gods.* The Mosaic covenant demanded exclusive worship of the Lord (Ex 20:5; Dt 5:9). This was the "first and greatest commandment" (Mt 22:38), and it was to distinguish Israel from all other peoples.

17:36 *the LORD, who brought you up out of Egypt ... you must worship.* Here, as in v. 7 (see note there), the deliverance from Egypt is cited as the gracious act of the Lord par excellence that entitled him to exclusive claim on Israel's loyalty.

17:39 *will deliver you from ... all your enemies.* See Ex 23:22; Dt 20:1–4; 23:14.

40 They would not listen, however, but
persisted in their former practices. 41 Even
while these people were worshiping the
LORD,[o] they were serving their idols. To
this day their children and grandchildren
continue to do as their ancestors did.

Hezekiah King of Judah

18:2-4pp — 2Ch 29:1-2; 31:1
18:5-7pp — 2Ch 31:20-21
18:9-12pp — 2Ki 17:3-7

18 In the third year of Hoshea son of
Elah king of Israel, Hezekiah[p] son
of Ahaz king of Judah began to reign. 2 He
was twenty-five years old when he became king, and he reigned in Jerusalem
twenty-nine years.[q] His mother's name
was Abijah[a] daughter of Zechariah. 3 He
did what was right[r] in the eyes of the
LORD, just as his father David[s] had done.
4 He removed[t] the high places,[u] smashed
the sacred stones[v] and cut down the Asherah poles. He broke into pieces the bronze
snake[w] Moses had made, for up to that
time the Israelites had been burning incense to it. (It was called Nehushtan.[b])
5 Hezekiah trusted[x] in the LORD, the
God of Israel. There was no one like him
among all the kings of Judah, either before him or after him. 6 He held fast[y] to
the LORD and did not stop following him;
he kept the commands the LORD had given
Moses. 7 And the LORD was with him; he
was successful[z] in whatever he undertook.
He rebelled[a] against the king of Assyria
and did not serve him. 8 From watchtower to fortified city,[b] he defeated the Philistines, as far as Gaza and its territory.
9 In King Hezekiah's fourth year,[c] which
was the seventh year of Hoshea son of
Elah king of Israel, Shalmaneser king of
Assyria marched against Samaria and laid
siege to it. 10 At the end of three years the
Assyrians took it. So Samaria was captured in Hezekiah's sixth year, which was
the ninth year of Hoshea king of Israel.
11 The king[d] of Assyria deported Israel to
Assyria and settled them in Halah, in Gozan on the Habor River and in towns of
the Medes.[e] 12 This happened because they
had not obeyed the LORD their God, but
had violated his covenant[f] — all that Moses the servant of the LORD commanded.[g]
They neither listened to the commands[h]
nor carried them out.
13 In the fourteenth year[i] of King Hezekiah's reign, Sennacherib king of Assyria
attacked all the fortified cities of Judah[j]

[a] 2 Hebrew *Abi,* a variant of *Abijah* [b] 4 *Nehushtan* sounds like the Hebrew for both *bronze* and *snake.*

17:41 [o] S 1Ki 18:21; Ezr 4:2; Mt 6:24
18:1 [p] Isa 1:1; Hos 1:1; Mic 1:1
18:2 [q] ver 13; Isa 38:5
18:3 [r] S 1Ki 14:8 [s] Isa 38:5
18:4 [t] 2Ch 31:1; Isa 36:7 [u] 2Ki 12:3; 21:3 [v] S Ex 23:24 [w] Nu 21:9
18:5 [x] ver 19; S 1Sa 7:3; 2Ki 19:10; Ps 21:7; 125:1; Pr 3:26
18:6 [y] Dt 10:20; S Dt 6:18
18:7 [z] S Ge 39:3; S Job 22:25 [a] 2Ki 24:1; Ezr 4:19; Isa 36:5
18:8 [b] 2Ki 17:9
18:9 [c] Isa 1:1; 36:1
18:11 [d] Isa 37:12 [e] Eze 16:39; 23:9
18:12 [f] S 2Ki 17:15 [g] 2Ki 21:8; Da 9:6,10 [h] S 1Ki 9:6
18:13 [i] S ver 2 [j] Isa 1:7; Mic 1:9

17:41 *To this day.* See note on v. 34.

18:1 *third year of Hoshea ... Hezekiah ... began to reign.* 729 BC (see 17:1). Hezekiah was coregent with his father Ahaz from 729 to 715 (see notes on 16:2; Isa 36:1). *Hezekiah son of Ahaz king of Judah.* In 1998 a clay impression of a royal stamp seal came to light that reads "Belonging to Hezekiah (son of) Ahaz king of Judah." It is one of only two such royal Judahite seals known (see note on 14:22).

18:2 *became king.* Became sole king of Judah. *twenty-nine years.* 715–686 BC. See also 2Ch 29–32 and Isa 36–39 for a description of the events of his reign, including a more detailed account of the reformation he led (2Ch 29–31). One of his first acts was to reopen the temple, which had been closed by his father, Ahaz (see note on 16:19; see also 2Ch 29:3).

18:3 *right ... as his father David.* Hezekiah is one of the few kings who is compared favorably with David. The others are Asa (1Ki 15:11), Jehoshaphat (1Ki 22:43) and Josiah (2Ki 22:2). A qualification is introduced, however, with both Asa and Jehoshaphat: They did not remove the high places (see 1Ki 15:14; 22:43).

18:4 *removed the high places.* Hezekiah was not the first king to destroy high places (see notes on 1Ki 3:2; 15:14), but he was the first to destroy high places dedicated to the worship of the Lord (see 12:3; 14:4; 15:4,35; 17:9; 1Ki 22:43). This became known even to the Assyrian king, Sennacherib (see v. 22). *sacred stones.* See 3:2; 10:26–27; 17:10; see also note on 1Ki 14:23. *Asherah poles.* See 13:6; 17:10,16; 1Ki 16:23; see also note on 1Ki 14:15. *Israelites had been burning incense to it.* It is unlikely that the "bronze snake" had been an object of worship all through the centuries of Israel's existence as a nation. Perhaps the idolatrous significance attached to it occurred during the reign of Hezekiah's father, Ahaz (see ch. 16). Snake worship of various types was common among ancient Near Eastern peoples. See note on Nu 21:8–9.

18:5 *no one like him ... either before him or after him.* A difference of emphasis is to be seen in this statement when compared to that of 23:25. Hezekiah's uniqueness is to be found in his trust in the Lord, while Josiah's uniqueness is to be found in his scrupulous observance of the Mosaic law.

18:7 *rebelled against the king of Assyria.* Judah had become a vassal to Assyria under Ahaz (see 16:7) — which required at least formal recognition of Assyrian deities. Hezekiah reversed the policy of his father, Ahaz, and sought independence from Assyrian dominance. It is likely that sometime shortly after 705 BC, when Sennacherib replaced Sargon II on the Assyrian throne, Hezekiah refused to pay the annual tribute due the Assyrians.

18:8 *defeated the Philistines.* In a reversal of the conditions existing during the time of Ahaz, in which the Philistines captured Judahite cities in the hill country and Negev (see 2Ch 28:18), Hezekiah was able once again to subdue the Philistines. Probably Hezekiah tried to coerce the Philistines into joining his anti-Assyrian policy. In one of his annals Sennacherib tells of forcing Hezekiah to release Padi, king of the Philistine city of Ekron, whom Hezekiah held prisoner in Jerusalem. This occurred in connection with Sennacherib's military campaign in 701 BC.

18:9 *Hezekiah's fourth year.* 725 BC, the fourth year of Hezekiah's coregency with Ahaz (see notes on v. 1; 17:1). *Shalmaneser.* See note on 17:3.

18:10 *three years.* See note on 17:5. *ninth year of Hoshea.* See note on 17:6.

18:11 *king of Assyria deported Israel.* See note on 17:6.

18:12 *violated his covenant.* See 17:7–23.

18:13 *fourteenth year.* Of Hezekiah's sole reign: 701 BC (see note on v. 2). *Sennacherib ... attacked.* See map, p. 595. Verses 13–16 correspond very closely with Sennacherib's own account of his 701 campaign against Phoenicia,

and captured them. 14 So Hezekiah king
of Judah sent this message to the king of
Assyria at Lachish:[k] "I have done wrong.[l]
Withdraw from me, and I will pay whatever you demand of me." The king of Assyria exacted from Hezekiah king of Judah
three hundred talents[a] of silver and thirty
talents[b] of gold. 15 So Hezekiah gave[m] him
all the silver that was found in the temple
of the LORD and in the treasuries of the
royal palace.
16 At this time Hezekiah king of Judah
stripped off the gold with which he had
covered the doors[n] and doorposts of the
temple of the LORD, and gave it to the king
of Assyria.

Sennacherib Threatens Jerusalem

18:13, 17-37pp — Isa 36:1-22
18:17-35pp — 2Ch 32:9-19

17 The king of Assyria sent his supreme
commander,[o] his chief officer and his field
commander with a large army, from Lachish to King Hezekiah at Jerusalem. They
came up to Jerusalem and stopped at the
aqueduct of the Upper Pool,[p] on the road
to the Washerman's Field. 18 They called
for the king; and Eliakim[q] son of Hilkiah
the palace administrator, Shebna[r] the secretary, and Joah son of Asaph the recorder
went out to them.
19 The field commander said to them,
"Tell Hezekiah:

"'This is what the great king, the
king of Assyria, says: On what are
you basing this confidence[s] of yours?
20 You say you have the counsel and
the might for war — but you speak
only empty words. On whom are you
depending, that you rebel against me?
21 Look, I know you are depending on
Egypt,[t] that splintered reed of a staff,[u]
which pierces the hand of anyone
who leans on it! Such is Pharaoh king
of Egypt to all who depend on him.
22 But if you say to me, "We are depending on the LORD our God" — isn't
he the one whose high places and altars Hezekiah removed, saying to Judah and Jerusalem, "You must worship before this altar in Jerusalem"?
23 "'Come now, make a bargain with
my master, the king of Assyria: I will
give you two thousand horses — if you
can put riders on them! 24 How can
you repulse one officer[v] of the least of
my master's officials, even though you
are depending on Egypt for chariots
and horsemen[c]? 25 Furthermore, have I
come to attack and destroy this place
without word from the LORD?[w] The
LORD himself told me to march against
this country and destroy it.'"

26 Then Eliakim son of Hilkiah, and Shebna and Joah said to the field commander,
"Please speak to your servants in Aramaic,
since we understand it. Don't speak to us
in Hebrew in the hearing of the people on
the wall."
27 But the commander replied, "Was it
only to your master and you that my master sent me to say these things, and not to
the people sitting on the wall — who, like

18:14 [k] 2Ki 19:8 [l] Isa 24:5; 33:8 **18:15** [m] S 1Ki 15:18; Isa 39:2 **18:16** [n] 2Ch 29:3 **18:17** [o] Isa 20:1 [p] 2Ki 20:20; 2Ch 32:4, 30; Ne 2:14; Isa 22:9 **18:18** [q] 2Ki 19:2; Isa 22:20; 36:3, 11,22; 37:2 [r] ver 26,37; Isa 22:15 **18:19** [s] S ver 5; S Job 4:6 **18:21** [t] Isa 20:5; 31:1; Eze 29:6 [u] 2Ki 24:7; Isa 20:6; 30:5,7; Jer 25:19; 37:7; 46:2 **18:24** [v] Isa 10:8 **18:25** [w] 2Ki 19:6,22; 24:3; 2Ch 35:21 **18:26** [x] Ezr 4:7

[a] 14 That is, about 11 tons or about 10 metric tons
[b] 14 That is, about 1 ton or about 1 metric ton
[c] 24 Or *charioteers*

Judah and Egypt. *captured them.* In his annals, Sennacherib claims to have captured 46 of Hezekiah's fortified cities, as well as numerous open villages, and to have taken 200,150 of the people captive. He says he made Hezekiah "a prisoner in Jerusalem his royal residence, like a bird in a cage," but he does not say he took Jerusalem (see 19:35 – 36).

18:14 *Lachish.* See notes on 14:19; Isa 36:2; see also photo, p. 568. *three hundred talents of silver and thirty talents of gold.* See NIV text notes. The Assyrian and Biblical reports of the amount of tribute paid by Hezekiah to Sennacherib agree with respect to the 30 talents of gold, but Sennacherib claims to have received 800 talents of silver rather than the 300 specified in the Biblical text.

18:15 *silver . . . in the temple . . . and in the treasuries of the royal palace.* See 12:10,18; 14:14; 16:8; 1Ki 7:51; 14:26; 15:18.

18:17 — 19:37 See Isa 36 – 37; cf. 2Ch 32.

18:17 *aqueduct . . . Field.* See note on Isa 7:3. It is ironic that the Assyrian officials demand Judah's surrender on the very spot where Isaiah had warned Ahaz to trust in the Lord rather than in an alliance with Assyria for deliverance from the threat against him from Aram and the northern kingdom of Israel (see 16:5 – 10; Isa 7:1 – 17).

18:18 *palace administrator.* See note on 1Ki 4:6. *secretary.* See note on 2Sa 8:17. *recorder.* See note on 2Sa 8:16.

18:19 *great king.* A frequently used title of the Assyrian rulers — and occasionally of the Lord (Ps 47:2; 48:2; 95:3; Mal 1:14; Mt 5:35). *says.* The following address is a masterpiece of calculated intimidation and psychological warfare designed to destroy the morale of the inhabitants of Jerusalem (see vv. 26 – 27; cf. note on Jos 6:5).

18:21 *depending on Egypt.* See 19:9; Isa 30:1 – 5; 31:1 – 3.

18:22 *isn't he the one whose high places and altars Hezekiah removed . . . ?* The Assyrians cleverly attempted to drive a wedge between Hezekiah and the people. They attempted to exploit any resentment that may have existed among those who opposed Hezekiah's reformation and his destruction of the high places (see note on v. 4).

18:23 *if you can put riders on them!* With this sarcastic taunt the Assyrians undoubtedly accurately suggest that the Judahites were so weak in military personnel that they could not even take advantage of such a generous offer. In contrast with the Assyrians, the army of Judah at the time consisted largely of foot soldiers. The city under siege would have contained few chariots, and it is not known whether the Israelites ever employed mounted men in combat.

18:26 *Aramaic.* Had become the international language of the Near East, known and used by those engaged in diplomacy and commerce. It is surprising that the Assyrian officials were able to speak the Hebrew dialect of the common people of Judah (see 2Ch 32:18).

18:27 *people sitting on the wall.* The Assyrian strategy was to negotiate in the hearing of the people in order to demoraliz

you, will have to eat their own excrement
and drink their own urine?"
28 Then the commander stood and called
out in Hebrew, "Hear the word of the great
king, the king of Assyria! 29 This is what
the king says: Do not let Hezekiah deceive[y] you. He cannot deliver you from my
hand. 30 Do not let Hezekiah persuade you
to trust in the LORD when he says, 'The
LORD will surely deliver us; this city will
not be given into the hand of the king of
Assyria.'
31 "Do not listen to Hezekiah. This is
what the king of Assyria says: Make peace
with me and come out to me. Then each
of you will eat fruit from your own vine
and fig tree[z] and drink water from your
own cistern,[a] 32 until I come and take you
to a land like your own—a land of grain
and new wine, a land of bread and vineyards, a land of olive trees and honey.
Choose life[b] and not death!
"Do not listen to Hezekiah, for he is
misleading you when he says, 'The LORD
will deliver us.' 33 Has the god[c] of any nation ever delivered his land from the hand
of the king of Assyria? 34 Where are the
gods of Hamath[d] and Arpad?[e] Where are
the gods of Sepharvaim, Hena and Ivvah?
Have they rescued Samaria from my hand?
35 Who of all the gods of these countries
has been able to save his land from me?
How then can the LORD deliver Jerusalem
from my hand?"[f]
36 But the people remained silent and
said nothing in reply, because the king
had commanded, "Do not answer him."
37 Then Eliakim[g] son of Hilkiah the palace administrator, Shebna the secretary,
and Joah son of Asaph the recorder went
to Hezekiah, with their clothes torn,[h] and
told him what the field commander had
said.

18:29 [y] 2Ki 19:10 **18:31** [z] S Nu 13:23; S 1Ki 4:25 [a] Jer 14:3; La 4:4 **18:32** [b] Dt 30:19 **18:33** [c] 2Ki 19:12 **18:34** [d] S 2Ki 17:24; S Jer 49:23 [e] Isa 10:9 **18:35** [f] Ps 2:1-2 **18:37** [g] S ver 18; Isa 33:7; 36:3, 22 [h] S 2Ki 6:30 **19:1** [i] S Ge 37:34; S Nu 14:6 **19:2** [j] S 2Ki 18:18 [k] Jer 19:1 [l] S Ge 37:34 [m] Isa 1:1 **19:3** [n] Hos 13:13 **19:4** [o] S 1Sa 17:26 [p] 2Sa 16:12 [q] S Ge 45:7; S Jer 37:3 **19:6** [r] S Dt 3:2; S Jos 1:9

Jerusalem's Deliverance Foretold

19:1-13pp — Isa 37:1-13

19 When King Hezekiah heard this,
he tore[i] his clothes and put on
sackcloth and went into the temple of
the LORD. 2 He sent Eliakim[j] the palace administrator, Shebna the secretary and the
leading priests,[k] all wearing sackcloth,[l] to
the prophet Isaiah[m] son of Amoz. 3 They
told him, "This is what Hezekiah says:
This day is a day of distress and rebuke
and disgrace, as when children come
to the moment[n] of birth and there is no
strength to deliver them. 4 It may be that
the LORD your God will hear all the words
of the field commander, whom his master,
the king of Assyria, has sent to ridicule[o]
the living God, and that he will rebuke[p]
him for the words the LORD your God has
heard. Therefore pray for the remnant[q]
that still survives."
5 When King Hezekiah's officials came
to Isaiah, 6 Isaiah said to them, "Tell your
master, 'This is what the LORD says: Do
not be afraid[r] of what you have heard—

them and turn them against Hezekiah. *eat their own excrement and drink their own urine.* A vivid portrayal of the potential hardship of a prolonged siege.

18:29 *the king says.* The Assyrian officials now address their remarks directly to the populace rather than to the officials of Hezekiah, as in vv. 19–27. *Do not let Hezekiah deceive you.* Here and in vv. 30–31 the people are urged three times to turn against Hezekiah.

18:30 *this city will not be given into the hand of the king of Assyria.* Hezekiah could say this on the basis of God's promise to him (see 20:6; see also note on Isa 38:6).

18:31 *eat fruit from your own vine and fig tree and drink water from your own cistern.* Depicting peaceful and prosperous times (see 1Ki 4:25; Mic 4:4; Zec 3:10).

18:32 *until I come and take you to a land like your own.* Ultimately surrender meant deportation, but Sennacherib pictured it as something desirable. *Choose life and not death!* The alternatives depicted for the people are: (1) Trust in the Lord and Hezekiah and die, or (2) trust in the Assyrians and enjoy prosperity and peace. These words directly contradict the alternatives placed before Israel by Moses in Dt 30:15–20.

18:33–35 *Has the god of any nation ever delivered his land from the hand of the king of Assyria?… How then can the LORD deliver Jerusalem from my hand?* The flaw in the Assyrian reasoning was to equate the one true and living God with the no-gods (Dt 32:21) of the pagan peoples the Assyrians had defeated (see 19:4,6; 2Ch 32:13–19; Isa 10:9–11).

18:34 *Hamath.* See notes on 14:25; 17:24. *Arpad.* A city located near Hamath and taken by the Assyrians in 740 BC (see 19:13; Isa 10:9; Jer 49:23). *Ivvah.* See note on 17:24.

18:36 *because the king had commanded, "Do not answer him."* The Assyrian attempt to stir up a popular revolt against the leadership and authority of Hezekiah had failed.

18:37 *clothes torn.* An expression of great emotion (see 6:30; 1Ki 21:27). Perhaps in this instance it was motivated by the Assyrian blasphemy against the true God (see 19:4,6; Mt 26:65; Mk 14:63–64).

19:1 *sackcloth.* See note on 6:30.

19:2 *palace administrator.* See note on 1Ki 4:6. *secretary.* See note on 2Sa 8:17. *leading priests.* Probably the oldest members of various priestly families (see Jer 19:1). The crisis involved not only the city of Jerusalem but also the temple. *prophet Isaiah.* The first reference to Isaiah in the book of Kings, though he had been active in the reigns of Uzziah, Jotham and Ahaz (see Isa 1:1).

19:3 *as when children come to the moment of birth and there is no strength to deliver them.* Depicts the critical nature of the threat facing the city.

19:4 *living God.* In contrast to the no-gods of 18:33–35. See 1Sa 17:26,36,45 for another example of ridiculing the living and true God. *pray.* Intercessory prayer was an important aspect of the ministry of the prophets (see, e.g., the intercession of Moses and Samuel: Ex 32:31–32; 33:12–17; Nu 14:13–19; 1Sa 7:8–9; 12:19,23; Ps 99:6; Jer 15:1). *remnant.* Those left in Judah after Sennacherib's capture of many towns and numerous people (see note on 18:13; cf. Isa 10:28–32). Archaeological evidence reveals that many Israelites fled the northern kingdom during the Assyrian assaults and settled in Judah, so that the nation of Judah became the remnant of all Israel.

those words with which the underlings
of the king of Assyria have blasphemed[s]
me. 7 Listen! When he hears a certain report,[t] I will make him want to return to his
own country, and there I will have him cut
down with the sword.[u]' "
8 When the field commander heard that
the king of Assyria had left Lachish,[v] he
withdrew and found the king fighting
against Libnah.[w]
9 Now Sennacherib received a report
that Tirhakah, the king of Cush,[a] was
marching out to fight against him. So he
again sent messengers to Hezekiah with
this word: 10 "Say to Hezekiah king of Judah: Do not let the god you depend[x] on deceive[y] you when he says, 'Jerusalem will
not be given into the hands of the king
of Assyria.' 11 Surely you have heard what
the kings of Assyria have done to all the
countries, destroying them completely.
And will you be delivered? 12 Did the gods
of the nations that were destroyed by my
predecessors deliver[z] them—the gods of
Gozan,[a] Harran,[b] Rezeph and the people
of Eden who were in Tel Assar? 13 Where is
the king of Hamath or the king of Arpad?
Where are the kings of Lair, Sepharvaim,
Hena and Ivvah?"[c]

Hezekiah's Prayer

19:14-19pp — Isa 37:14-20

14 Hezekiah received the letter[d] from the
messengers and read it. Then he went up
to the temple of the LORD and spread it out
before the LORD. 15 And Hezekiah prayed
to the LORD: "LORD, the God of Israel, enthroned between the cherubim,[e] you alone[f]
are God over all the kingdoms of the earth.
You have made heaven and earth. 16 Give
ear,[g] LORD, and hear;[h] open your eyes,[i]
LORD, and see; listen to the words Sennacherib has sent to ridicule the living God.
17 "It is true, LORD, that the Assyrian
kings have laid waste these nations and
their lands. 18 They have thrown their gods
into the fire and destroyed them, for they
were not gods[j] but only wood and stone,
fashioned by human hands.[k] 19 Now, LORD
our God, deliver[l] us from his hand, so that
all the kingdoms[m] of the earth may know[n]
that you alone, LORD, are God."

Isaiah Prophesies Sennacherib's Fall

19:20-37pp — Isa 37:21-38
19:35-37pp — 2Ch 32:20-21

20 Then Isaiah son of Amoz sent a message to Hezekiah: "This is what the LORD,
the God of Israel, says: I have heard[o] your
prayer concerning Sennacherib king of Assyria. 21 This is the word that the LORD has
spoken against[p] him:

" 'Virgin Daughter[q] Zion
despises[r] you and mocks[s] you.
Daughter Jerusalem
tosses her head[t] as you flee.
22 Who is it you have ridiculed and
blasphemed?[u]
Against whom have you raised your
voice
and lifted your eyes in pride?
Against the Holy One[v] of Israel!
23 By your messengers
you have ridiculed the Lord.
And you have said,[w]
"With my many chariots[x]
I have ascended the heights of the
mountains,
the utmost heights of Lebanon.
I have cut down[y] its tallest cedars,
the choicest of its junipers.

[a] 9 That is, the upper Nile region

19:6 [s] S 2Ki 18:25 **19:7** [t] S Ex 14:24; Jer 51:46 [u] ver 37; 2Ch 32:21; Isa 10:12 **19:8** [v] 2Ki 18:14 [w] S Nu 33:20; S 2Ki 8:22 **19:10** [x] S 2Ki 18:5 [y] 2Ki 18:29 **19:12** [z] 2Ki 18:33; 2Ch 32:17 [a] 2Ki 17:6 [b] S Ge 11:31 **19:13** [c] Isa 10:9-11; Jer 49:23 **19:14** [d] 2Ki 5:7 **19:15** [e] S Ge 3:24; S Ex 25:22 [f] S Ge 1:1; S Jos 2:11 **19:16** [g] Ps 31:2; 71:2; 88:2; 102:2 [h] S 1Ki 8:29 [i] S Ex 3:16 **19:18** [j] Isa 44:9-11; Jer 10:3-10 [k] Dt 4:28; Ps 115:4; Ac 17:29 **19:19** [l] 1Sa 12:10; Job 6:23; Ps 3:7; 71:4 [m] S 1Ki 8:43; 1Ch 16:8 [n] S Jos 4:24; S 1Sa 17:46 **19:20** [o] S 1Ki 9:3 **19:21** [p] Isa 10:5; 33:1 [q] Isa 47:1; Jer 14:17; 18:13; 31:4; 46:11; La 2:13; Am 5:2 [r] Ps 53:5 [s] Pr 1:26; 3:34 [t] Job 16:4; Ps 44:14; 64:8; 109:25; Jer 18:16 **19:22** [u] S 2Ki 18:25 [v] Lev 19:2; 1Sa 2:2; Job 6:10; Ps 16:10; 22:3; 71:22; 78:41; 89:18; Isa 1:4; 6:3; 57:15; Hos 11:9 **19:23** [w] Isa 10:18; Jer 21:14; Eze 20:47 [x] Ps 20:7; Jer 50:37 [y] Isa 10:34; 14:8; 33:9; Eze 31:3

19:7 *report.* Some interpreters link this report with the challenge to Sennacherib from Tirhakah of Egypt (v. 9). Others regard it as disturbing information from Sennacherib's homeland. *make him want to return.* Because of a spirit of insecurity and fear. *cut down with the sword.* See v. 37. Here the eventual murder of Sennacherib is connected with his blasphemy against the living God.
19:8 *Libnah.* See note on 8:22.
19:9 *Tirhakah.* See note on Isa 37:9. *Cush.* See NIV text note.
19:12 *Gozan.* See note on 17:6. *Harran.* See note on Ge 11:31. It is not known just when Harran was taken by the Assyrians. *Rezeph.* Located south of the Euphrates River and northeast of Hamath. *Eden.* A district along the Euphrates River south of Harran (see Eze 27:23; Am 1:5), not to be confused with the Garden of Eden. It was incorporated into the Assyrian Empire by Shalmaneser III in 855 BC.
19:13 *Hamath ... Ivvah.* See note on 17:24.
19:14 *letter.* See 2Ch 32:17.
19:15 *enthroned between the cherubim.* See notes on Ex 25:18; 1Sa 4:4. *you alone are God.* See v. 19; Dt 4:35,39; see also 2Ki 18:33–35; Isa 43:11 and notes.
19:18 *fashioned by human hands.* For the foolishness and futility of idolatry, see Ps 115:3–8; 135:15–18; Isa 2:20 40:19–20; 41:7; 44:9–20.
19:19 *that all the kingdoms of the earth may know.* Hezekiah recognizes that the Lord's reputation is at stake in the welfare of his covenant people (see 1Sa 12:22; see also Jos 7:9; 2Sa 7:23; Ps 23:3; Eze 5:13; 6:7 and notes).
19:20 *heard your prayer.* On this occasion Isaiah's message to Hezekiah was unsolicited by the king (contrast v. 2).
19:21–28 The arrogance of the Assyrians and their ridicule of the Israelites and their God are countered with a derisive pronouncement of judgment (cf. Ps 2) on the misconceived Assyrian pride (see Isa 10:5–34).
19:21 *Virgin Daughter Zion ... Daughter Jerusalem.* In Hebrew poetry (mainly) a conventional way of referring to a royal city, a nation or a people when these are personified as a woman, found often in the prophetic literature, with special concentration in Lamentations.
19:22 *Holy One of Israel.* A designation of the God of Israel characteristic of Isaiah (see Lev 11:44; Isa 1:4 and notes).
19:23 *Lebanon ... its tallest cedars.* See note on 1Ki 5:6.

I have reached its remotest parts,
 the finest of its forests.
24 I have dug wells in foreign lands
 and drunk the water there.
With the soles of my feet
 I have dried up all the streams of
 Egypt."

25 " 'Have you not heard?[z]
 Long ago I ordained it.
In days of old I planned[a] it;
 now I have brought it to pass,
that you have turned fortified cities
 into piles of stone.[b]
26 Their people, drained of power,[c]
 are dismayed[d] and put to shame.
They are like plants in the field,
 like tender green shoots,[e]
like grass sprouting on the roof,
 scorched[f] before it grows up.
27 " 'But I know[g] where you are
 and when you come and go
 and how you rage against me.
28 Because you rage against me
 and because your insolence has
 reached my ears,
I will put my hook[h] in your nose
 and my bit[i] in your mouth,
and I will make you return[j]
 by the way you came.'

29 "This will be the sign[k] for you, Hezekiah:

"This year you will eat what grows by
 itself,[l]
 and the second year what springs
 from that.
But in the third year sow and reap,
 plant vineyards[m] and eat their fruit.

30 Once more a remnant[n] of the kingdom
 of Judah
 will take root[o] below and bear fruit
 above.
31 For out of Jerusalem will come a
 remnant,[p]
 and out of Mount Zion a band of
 survivors.[q]

"The zeal[r] of the LORD Almighty will accomplish this.

32 "Therefore this is what the LORD says
concerning the king of Assyria:

" 'He will not enter this city
 or shoot an arrow here.
He will not come before it with shield
 or build a siege ramp against it.
33 By the way that he came he will
 return;[s]
 he will not enter this city,
 declares the LORD.
34 I will defend[t] this city and save it,
 for my sake and for the sake of
 David[u] my servant.' "

35 That night the angel of the LORD[v]
went out and put to death a hundred and
eighty-five thousand in the Assyrian camp.
When the people got up the next morning—there were all the dead bodies![w] 36 So
Sennacherib king of Assyria broke camp
and withdrew.[x] He returned to Nineveh[y]
and stayed there.

37 One day, while he was worshiping
in the temple of his god Nisrok, his sons
Adrammelek[z] and Sharezer killed him
with the sword,[a] and they escaped to the
land of Ararat.[b] And Esarhaddon[c] his son
succeeded him as king.

19:25 [z] Isa 40:21, 28 [a] Isa 22:11 [b] Mic 1:6
19:26 [c] Isa 13:7; Eze 7:17; Zep 3:16 [d] Ps 6:10; 71:24; 83:17; Isa 41:23; Jer 8:9 [e] Isa 4:2; 11:1; 53:2; Jer 23:5 [f] Job 8:12; Ps 37:2; 129:6
19:27 [g] Ps 139:1-4
19:28 [h] 2Ch 33:11; Eze 19:9; 29:4; 38:4; Am 4:2 [i] Isa 30:28 [j] ver 33
19:29 [k] S Ex 7:9; S Dt 13:2; Lk 2:12 [l] Lev 25:5 [m] Ps 107:37; Isa 65:21; Am 9:14
19:30 [n] S Ge 45:7 [o] Isa 5:24; 11:1; 27:6; Eze 17:22; Am 2:9
19:31 [p] S Ge 45:7 [q] Isa 66:19; Zep 2:9; Zec 14:16 [r] Isa 9:7
19:33 [s] ver 28
19:34 [t] 2Ki 20:6 [u] S 2Sa 7:15
19:35 [v] S Ge 19:13; S Ex 12:23 [w] Job 24:24; Isa 17:14; 41:12; Na 3:3
19:36 [x] S 2Ki 12:18 [y] S Ge 10:11
19:37 [z] 2Ki 17:31 [a] S ver 7 [b] S Ge 8:4 [c] S 2Ki 17:24

19:24 *dried up all the streams of Egypt.* A presumptuous boast for one who had not even conquered Egypt.

19:25 *I ordained it ... now I have brought it to pass.* The God of Israel is the ruler of all nations and history. The Assyrians attributed their victories to their own military superiority. However, Isaiah said that God alone ordained these victories (see Isa 10:5–19; cf. Eze 30:24–26).

19:28 *hook in your nose.* At the top of an Assyrian obelisk an Assyrian king (probably Esarhaddon, 681–669 BC) is pictured holding ropes attached to rings in the noses of four of his enemies. Here Isaiah portrays the same thing happening to Sennacherib (see note on Isa 37:29; cf. Eze 38:4; Am 4:2).

19:29 *This year you will eat what grows by itself.* Sennacherib had apparently either destroyed or confiscated the entire harvest that had been sown the previous fall. The people would only have use of the later, second growth that came from seeds dropped from the previous year's harvest (see Lev 25:5). This suggests that Sennacherib came to Judah in March or April, about the time of harvest. *the second year what springs from that.* Sennacherib's departure would be too late in the fall for new crops to be planted for the coming year. In the Holy Land, crops are normally sown in September and October. *in the third year sow and reap.* The routine times for sowing and harvesting could be observed in the following year. The third year is likely a reference to the third year of harvests detrimentally affected by the Assyrian presence.

19:30–31 *remnant.* See note on v. 4. For use of the term "remnant" as a designation for those who will participate in the future unfolding of God's redemptive program, see Isa 11:11,16; 28:5; Mic 4:7; Ro 11:5.

19:32 *not enter this city.* Sennacherib, who was presently at Libnah (see v. 8; see also note on 8:22), would not be able to carry out his threats against Jerusalem (see note on 18:13).

19:34 *for the sake of David my servant.* See note on 1Ki 11:13.

19:35 *angel of the LORD.* See note on Ge 16:7. *a hundred and eighty-five thousand.* See Isa 37:36 and note.

19:36 *Nineveh.* The capital of the Assyrian Empire.

19:37 *his sons Adrammelek and Sharezer.* Ancient records refer to the murder of Sennacherib by an unnamed son in the 23rd year of Sennacherib's reign. *Ararat.* See note on Ge 8:4. *Esarhaddon his son succeeded him.* And reigned 681–669 BC (see chart, p. 511). Assyrian inscriptions speak of a struggle among Sennacherib's sons for the right of succession to the Assyrian throne. Sennacherib's designation of Esarhaddon as heir apparent, even though he was younger than several of his brothers, may have sparked the abortive attempt at a coup by Adrammelek and Sharezer.

Hezekiah's Illness

20:1-11pp — 2Ch 32:24-26; Isa 38:1-8

20 In those days Hezekiah became ill and was at the point of death. The prophet Isaiah son of Amoz went to him and said, "This is what the LORD says: Put your house in order, because you are going to die; you will not recover."

2 Hezekiah turned his face to the wall and prayed to the LORD, 3 "Remember,[d] LORD, how I have walked[e] before you faithfully[f] and with wholehearted devotion and have done what is good in your eyes." And Hezekiah wept bitterly.

4 Before Isaiah had left the middle court, the word of the LORD came to him: 5 "Go back and tell Hezekiah, the ruler of my people, 'This is what the LORD, the God of your father David, says: I have heard[g] your prayer and seen your tears;[h] I will heal you. On the third day from now you will go up to the temple of the LORD. 6 I will add fifteen years to your life. And I will deliver you and this city from the hand of the king of Assyria. I will defend[i] this city for my sake and for the sake of my servant David.' "

7 Then Isaiah said, "Prepare a poultice of figs." They did so and applied it to the boil,[j] and he recovered.

8 Hezekiah had asked Isaiah, "What will be the sign that the LORD will heal me and that I will go up to the temple of the LORD on the third day from now?"

9 Isaiah answered, "This is the LORD's sign[k] to you that the LORD will do what he has promised: Shall the shadow go forward ten steps, or shall it go back ten steps?"

10 "It is a simple[l] matter for the shadow to go forward ten steps," said Hezekiah. "Rather, have it go back ten steps."

11 Then the prophet Isaiah called on the LORD, and the LORD made the shadow go back[m] the ten steps it had gone down on the stairway of Ahaz.

20:3 [d] S Ge 8:1; Ne 1:8; 5:19; 13:14 [e] S Ge 5:22 [f] S 1Ki 2:4; 2Ch 31:20 **20:5** [g] S 1Ki 9:3 [h] Ps 6:6,8; 39:12; 56:8 **20:6** [i] S 2Ki 19:34; S 1Ch 17:19 **20:7** [j] S Ex 9:9 **20:9** [k] S Dt 13:2; Jer 44:29 **20:10** [l] S 2Ki 3:18 **20:11** [m] Jos 10:13; 2Ch 32:31

Envoys From Babylon

20:12-19pp — Isa 39:1-8
20:20-21pp — 2Ch 32:32-33

12 At that time Marduk-Baladan son of Baladan king of Babylon sent Hezekiah letters and a gift, because he had heard of Hezekiah's illness. 13 Hezekiah received the envoys and showed them all that was in his storehouses — the silver, the gold, the spices and the fine olive oil — his armory and everything found among his treasures. There was nothing in his palace or in all his kingdom that Hezekiah did not show them.

14 Then Isaiah the prophet went to King Hezekiah and asked, "What did those men say, and where did they come from?"

20:1 *In those days.* Hezekiah's illness (vv. 1–11), as well as his reception of envoys from Babylon (vv. 12–19), must have preceded the Assyrian campaign in 701 BC (see v. 6; see also notes on vv. 12–13). Babylonian records indicate that Marduk-Baladan (v. 12) died in Elam after being expelled from Babylon in 703. *Put your house in order.* Arrangements of a testamentary nature needed to be made, especially with respect to throne succession. *you are going to die.* Assuming that Hezekiah was 25 years old in 715 when he began his sole reign (see 18:2) and that his illness occurred a little more than 15 years prior to his death (see note on v. 6), he would have been 37 or 38 years old at this time.

20:3 *walked before you faithfully ... and have done what is good.* Hezekiah's prayer is not an appeal for divine favor that is based on good works, but it expresses the realization that the Lord graciously favors those who earnestly serve him (see note on 2Sa 22:21).

20:5 *I will heal you.* God is the one who sovereignly ordains all that comes to pass (Ps 139:16; Eph 1:11). Hezekiah's petition and God's response demonstrate that (1) divine sovereignty does not make prayer inappropriate but, on the contrary, establishes it, and (2) both prayer and the divine response to prayer are to be included in one's conception of God's sovereign plan (see 1Ki 21:29; Eze 33:13–16).

20:6 *add fifteen years to your life.* Hezekiah died in 686 BC. The beginning of the extension of his life is thus to be placed no later than 701. *for my sake and for the sake of my servant David.* See 19:34; see also note on 1Ki 11:13.

20:7 *poultice.* The Lord healed Hezekiah (see v. 5), but divine healing does not necessarily exclude the use of known remedies.

20:9 *steps.* See v. 11 (see also note on Isa 38:8).

20:10 *simple matter ... go forward.* Because that was the natural direction of the shadow's movement. Hezekiah chose the more difficult movement to make sure the sign was from the Lord.

20:11 *stairway of Ahaz.* Possibly refers to one leading to his house or to some kind of instrument used to measure time.

20:12 *Marduk-Baladan.* Means "[The god] Marduk has given me a male heir." He ruled in Babylon c. 722–710 BC before being forced to submit to Assyrian domination by Sargon II of Assyria. Sometime after Sargon's death in 705, Marduk-Baladan briefly reestablished Babylonian independence and ruled in Babylon until Sennacherib forced him to flee in 703 (see note on v. 1). *sent Hezekiah letters and a gift.* It is likely that Marduk-Baladan was attempting to draw Hezekiah into an alliance against Assyria. Although Hezekiah rejected the pro-Assyrian policies of his father, Ahaz (see 16:7), and rebelled against Assyria (see 18:7), he erred in seeking to strengthen Israel's security by friendship with Babylon and Egypt (see 2Ch 32:31; Isa 30–31; see also notes on 1Sa 17:11; 1Ki 15:19).

20:13 *received the envoys and showed them all.* Hezekiah's reception of the delegation from Babylon was overly hospitable. Perhaps it was an attempt to bolster Judah's security by impressing the Babylonians with the wealth and power of his kingdom as a basis for mutual cooperation against the Assyrians. In principle this was a denial of the covenantal nature of the royal office in Israel (see note on 2Sa 24:1). *silver ... olive oil.* The presence of these treasures in Jerusalem is evidence that this incident occurred before the payment of tribute to Sennacherib in 701 BC (see 18:15–16).

20:14 *What did those men say ... ?* Hezekiah gave no response

"From a distant land," Hezekiah replied.
"They came from Babylon."
15 The prophet asked, "What did they
see in your palace?"
"They saw everything in my palace,"
Hezekiah said. "There is nothing among
my treasures that I did not show them."
16 Then Isaiah said to Hezekiah, "Hear
the word of the LORD: 17 The time will surely come when everything in your palace,
and all that your predecessors have stored
up until this day, will be carried off to Babylon.[n] Nothing will be left, says the LORD.
18 And some of your descendants,[o] your
own flesh and blood who will be born to
you, will be taken away, and they will become eunuchs in the palace of the king of
Babylon."[p]
19 "The word of the LORD you have spoken is good," Hezekiah replied. For he
thought, "Will there not be peace and security in my lifetime?"
20 As for the other events of Hezekiah's
reign, all his achievements and how he
made the pool[q] and the tunnel[r] by which
he brought water into the city, are they not
written in the book of the annals of the
kings of Judah? 21 Hezekiah rested with his
ancestors. And Manasseh his son succeeded him as king.

20:17 [n] 2Ki 24:13; 2Ch 36:10; Jer 20:5; 27:22; 52:17-23 **20:18** [o] 2Ki 24:15; Da 1:3 [p] Mic 4:10 **20:20** [q] S 2Ki 18:17 [r] S 2Sa 5:8

to Isaiah's question concerning the diplomatic purpose of the Babylonian envoys.

20:17 *carried off to Babylon.* Hezekiah's reception of the Babylonians would bring the exact opposite of what he desired and expected. Isaiah's prediction of Babylonian exile at least 115 years before it happened is all the more remarkable because, when he spoke, it appeared that Assyria rather than Babylonia was the world power from whom Judah had the most to fear.

20:18 *some of your descendants ... will be taken away.* Hezekiah's own son Manasseh was taken by the Assyrians and held prisoner for a while in Babylon (see 2Ch 33:11); later, many more from the house of David were to follow (see 24:15; 25:7; Da 1:3).

20:19 *word ... is good.* Although it is possible to understand Hezekiah's statement as a selfish expression of relief that he himself would not experience the announced adversity, it seems better to take it as a humble acceptance of the Lord's judgment (see 2Ch 32:26) and as gratefulness for the intervening time of peace that the Lord in his mercy was granting to his people.

20:20 *the pool and the tunnel.* See Jn 9:7 and note. Hezekiah built a tunnel from the Gihon spring (see 1Ki 1:33,38) to a cistern (2Ch 32:30) inside the city's walls (see map, p. 2525, at the end of this study Bible). This greatly reduced Jerusalem's vulnerability to siege by guaranteeing a continuing water supply. In 1880 an inscription (the Siloam Inscription; see photos below) was found in the rock wall near the southern exit of this tunnel, describing the method of its construction. The tunnel, cut through solid rock, is about 1,750 feet long; its height varies from 4 feet to 12 feet and it averages 2 feet in width. *annals of the kings of Judah.* See note on 1Ki 14:29.

20:21 *rested with his ancestors.* See note on 1Ki 1:21.

HEZEKIAH'S TUNNEL AND WATER PROJECTS

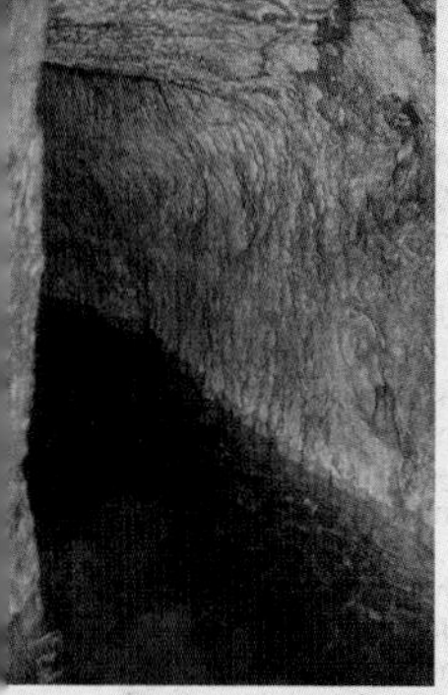

Hezekiah's tunnel
© 1995 Phoenix Data Systems

Jerusalem's water supply was vulnerable to enemy attack, since it lay outside the city wall and was limited in scope for an area of its size. Hezekiah sought to secure it from attack and siege. The Gihon spring lay in the valley just east of David's city. It was joined by aqueducts and a tunnel of about 1,750 feet in length to other locations, including the Pool of Siloam (see 2Ki 20:20 and note).

The tunnel has an inscription near its southern exit that details the arduous digging task. It describes two teams working toward each other, following a somewhat circuitous route. "When there were still 3 cubits to be excavated, there were the sounds of a man calling to his companion. On the day of the (completed) excavation, the stone-hewers struck out, each toward his opposite number, pick toward pick."*

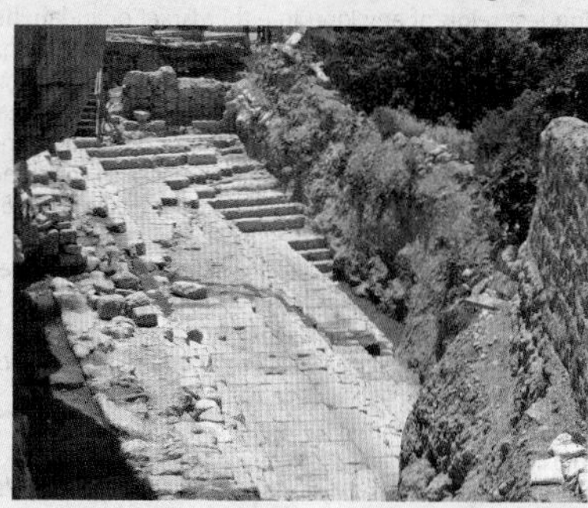

The northeast corner of the Pool of Siloam, which is located at the southern end of the City of David
www.HolyLandPhotos.org

W. W. Hallo and K. L. Younger, eds., *The Context of Scripture* (Leiden: Brill, 1997), 2:28; personal translation.

Manasseh King of Judah

21:1-10pp — 2Ch 33:1-10
21:17-18pp — 2Ch 33:18-20

21 Manasseh was twelve years old
when he became king, and he
reigned in Jerusalem fifty-five years. His
mother's name was Hephzibah.[s] 2He did
evil[t] in the eyes of the LORD, following
the detestable practices[u] of the nations
the LORD had driven out before the Israelites. 3He rebuilt the high places[v] his father
Hezekiah had destroyed; he also erected altars to Baal[w] and made an Asherah
pole,[x] as Ahab king of Israel had done. He
bowed down to all the starry hosts[y] and
worshiped them. 4He built altars[z] in the
temple of the LORD, of which the LORD had
said, "In Jerusalem I will put my Name."[a]
5In the two courts[b] of the temple of the
LORD, he built altars to all the starry hosts.
6He sacrificed his own son[c] in the fire,
practiced divination,[d] sought omens, and
consulted mediums and spiritists.[e] He did
much evil in the eyes of the LORD, arousing[f] his anger.
7He took the carved Asherah pole[g] he
had made and put it in the temple,[h] of
which the LORD had said to David and to
his son Solomon, "In this temple and in
Jerusalem, which I have chosen out of all
the tribes of Israel, I will put my Name[i]
forever. 8I will not again[j] make the feet of
the Israelites wander from the land I gave
their ancestors, if only they will be careful
to do everything I commanded them and
will keep the whole Law that my servant
Moses[k] gave them." 9But the people did
not listen. Manasseh led them astray, so
that they did more evil[l] than the nations[m]
the LORD had destroyed before the Israelites.
10The LORD said through his servants the
prophets: 11"Manasseh king of Judah has
committed these detestable sins. He has
done more evil[n] than the Amorites[o] who
preceded him and has led Judah into sin
with his idols.[p] 12Therefore this is what the
LORD, the God of Israel, says: I am going
to bring such disaster[q] on Jerusalem and
Judah that the ears of everyone who hears
of it will tingle.[r] 13I will stretch out over
Jerusalem the measuring line used against
Samaria and the plumb line[s] used against
the house of Ahab. I will wipe[t] out Jerusalem as one wipes a dish, wiping it and
turning it upside down. 14I will forsake[u]
the remnant[v] of my inheritance and give
them into the hands of enemies. They will
be looted and plundered by all their enemies; 15they have done evil[w] in my eyes
and have aroused[x] my anger from the day
their ancestors came out of Egypt until
this day."
16Moreover, Manasseh also shed so
much innocent blood[y] that he filled Jerusalem from end to end — besides the sin
that he had caused Judah[z] to commit, so
that they did evil in the eyes of the LORD.
17As for the other events of Manasseh's

21:1 [s]Isa 62:4 **21:2** [t]ver 16; S Dt 4:25; Jer 15:4 [u]Dt 9:4; S 18:9; S 1Ki 14:24; 2Ki 16:3 **21:3** [v]S 1Ki 3:3; S 2Ki 18:4 [w]S Jdg 6:28 [x]S Dt 16:21 [y]S Ge 2:1; Dt 17:3; Jer 19:13 **21:4** [z]Isa 66:4; Jer 4:1; 7:30; 23:11; 32:34; Eze 23:39 [a]S Ex 20:24; S 2Sa 7:13 **21:5** [b]1Ki 7:12; 2Ki 23:12 **21:6** [c]S Lev 18:21; S Dt 18:10; S 2Ki 3:27 [d]Dt 18:14 [e]S Lev 19:31 [f]2Ki 23:26 **21:7** [g]Dt 16:21; 2Ki 23:4 [h]S Lev 15:31 [i]S Ex 20:24; S 2Sa 7:13 **21:8** [j]S 2Sa 7:10 [k]S 2Ki 18:12 **21:9** [l]S 1Ki 14:9; Eze 5:7 [m]Dt 9:4 **21:11** [n]S 1Ki 14:9 [o]S Ge 15:16 [p]Eze 18:12 **21:12** [q]2Ki 23:26; 24:3; Jer 15:4; Eze 7:5 [r]S 1Sa 3:11 **21:13** [s]Isa 28:17; 34:11; La 2:8; Am 7:7-9 [t]2Ki 23:27 **21:14** [u]Ps 78:58-60; Jer 12:7; 23:33 [v]2Ki 19:4; Ezr 9:8; Ne 1:2; Isa 1:9; 10:21; Jer 6:9; 40:15; 42:2; 44:7,28; 50:20; Mic 2:12 **21:15** [w]S Ex 32:22 [x]Jer 25:7 **21:16** [y]2Ki 24:4; Job 22:14; Ps 10:11; 94:7; 106:38; Isa 29:15; 47:10; 59:3,7; Jer 2:34; 7:6; 19:4; 22:17; La 4:13; Eze 7:23; 8:12; 9:9; 22:3-4; Hos 4:2; Zep 1:12 [z]S ver 2,11

21:1 *twelve years old.* Thus Manasseh was born c. 709 BC. *fifty-five years.* 697 – 642 BC, including a ten-year coregency (697 – 686) with Hezekiah. This was the longest reign of any king in either Israel or Judah; he was arguably the most wicked of them all. The name Manasseh has been found on a contemporary seal reading "Belonging to Manasseh Son of the King." If this is the same Manasseh, the seal was probably used by him during the coregency.

21:2 *detestable practices.* Manasseh reversed the religious policies of his father, Hezekiah (see 18:3 – 5), and reverted to those of Ahaz (see 16:3).

21:3 *high places ... Hezekiah had destroyed.* See note on 18:4; see also 2Ch 31:1. *Asherah pole.* See 1Ki 14:15, 23; 15:13; 16:33. *as Ahab.* Manasseh was the Ahab of Judah (see 1Ki 16:30 – 33). *bowed down to all the starry hosts.* See note on 17:16.

21:4 *In Jerusalem I will put my Name.* See 1Ki 8:16; 9:3 and notes.

21:6 *sacrificed his own son.* See note on 16:3; see also 17:17; cf. 3:27 and note. *practiced divination, sought omens.* See notes on 16:15; 17:17. *consulted mediums and spiritists.* See Lev 19:31; Dt 18:11; 1Sa 28:3,7 – 9 and notes.

21:7 *carved Asherah pole.* See note on 1Ki 14:15. *David.* See 2Sa 7:13. *Solomon.* See 1Ki 9:3. *chosen out of all the tribes.* See 1Ki 11:13,32,36.

21:9 *nations the LORD had destroyed.* See 1Ki 14:24; Dt 12:29 – 31; 31:3.

21:10 *his servants the prophets.* See 2Ch 33:10,18.

21:11 *more evil than the Amorites.* See note on 1Ki 21:26 *idols.* See note on Lev 26:30.

21:12 *disaster on Jerusalem.* Fulfilled in the final destruction of the city by the Babylonians in 586 BC (see ch. 25). *ears of everyone ... will tingle.* See Jer 19:3 and note.

21:13 *measuring line ... plumb line.* Instruments normally associated with construction are used here as symbols of destruction (see Isa 34:11; Am 7:7 – 9, 17).

21:14 *I will forsake.* In the sense of giving over to judgment (see Jer 12:7), not in the sense of abrogation of the covenant (see 1Sa 12:22; Isa 43:1 – 7). *remnant of my inheritance.* Upon the destruction of the northern kingdom, Judah had become the remnant of the Lord's inheritance (see 1Ki 8:51; Dt 4:20; 1Sa 10:1; Ps 28:9; see also note on 2Ki 19:4).

21:15 The history of Israel was a history of covenant breaking. With the reign of Manasseh the cup of God's wrath overflowed, and the judgment of exile (see note on 17:7 – 23) became inevitable (see 24:1 – 4).

21:16 *innocent blood.* A reference to godly people who were martyred for opposition to Manasseh's evil practices (see vv. 10 – 11). According to a Jewish tradition (*The Ascension of Isaiah* — not otherwise substantiated), Isaiah was sawed in two during Manasseh's reign (see Introduction to Isaiah: Author; cf. Heb 11:37 and note).

21:17 *other events of Manasseh's reign.* See 2Ch 33:12 – 19. *annals of the kings of Judah.* See note on 1Ki 14:29.

reign, and all he did, including the sin he
committed, are they not written in the
book of the annals of the kings of Judah?
18 Manasseh rested with his ancestors and
was buried in his palace garden,[a] the garden of Uzza. And Amon his son succeeded
him as king.

Amon King of Judah

21:19-24pp — 2Ch 33:21-25

19 Amon was twenty-two years old when
he became king, and he reigned in Jerusalem two years. His mother's name was
Meshullemeth daughter of Haruz; she was
from Jotbah. 20 He did evil[b] in the eyes
of the LORD, as his father Manasseh had
done. 21 He followed completely the ways
of his father, worshiping the idols his father had worshiped, and bowing down to
them. 22 He forsook[c] the LORD, the God of
his ancestors, and did not walk[d] in obedience to him.
23 Amon's officials conspired against
him and assassinated[e] the king in his palace. 24 Then the people of the land killed[f]
all who had plotted against King Amon,
and they made Josiah[g] his son king in his
place.
25 As for the other events of Amon's
reign, and what he did, are they not written in the book of the annals of the kings
of Judah? 26 He was buried in his tomb in
the garden[h] of Uzza. And Josiah his son
succeeded him as king.

The Book of the Law Found

22:1-20pp — 2Ch 34:1-2,8-28

22 Josiah[i] was eight years old when
he became king, and he reigned in
Jerusalem thirty-one years. His mother's
name was Jedidah daughter of Adaiah;
she was from Bozkath.[j] 2 He did what was
right[k] in the eyes of the LORD and followed
completely the ways of his father David,
not turning aside to the right[l] or to the left.
3 In the eighteenth year of his reign, King
Josiah sent the secretary, Shaphan[m] son of
Azaliah, the son of Meshullam, to the temple of the LORD. He said: 4 "Go up to Hilkiah[n] the high priest and have him get ready
the money that has been brought into the
temple of the LORD, which the doorkeepers have collected[o] from the people. 5 Have
them entrust it to the men appointed to supervise the work on the temple. And have
these men pay the workers who repair[p]
the temple of the LORD — 6 the carpenters,
the builders and the masons. Also have
them purchase timber and dressed stone
to repair the temple.[q] 7 But they need not
account for the money entrusted to them,
because they are honest in their dealings."[r]
8 Hilkiah the high priest said to Shaphan
the secretary, "I have found the Book of
the Law[s] in the temple of the LORD." He
gave it to Shaphan, who read it. 9 Then
Shaphan the secretary went to the king
and reported to him: "Your officials have
paid out the money that was in the temple
of the LORD and have entrusted it to the
workers and supervisors at the temple."
10 Then Shaphan the secretary informed
the king, "Hilkiah the priest has given me
a book." And Shaphan read from it in the
presence of the king.[t]
11 When the king heard the words of the
Book of the Law,[u] he tore his robes. 12 He
gave these orders to Hilkiah the priest,

21:18 [a] ver 26; Est 1:5; 7:7 **21:20** [b] 1Ki 15:26 **21:22** [c] S 1Sa 8:8 [d] 1Ki 11:33 **21:23** [e] S 2Ki 12:20 **21:24** [f] 2Ki 14:5 [g] 2Ch 33:21; Zep 1:1 **21:26** [h] S ver 18 **22:1** [i] Jer 1:2; 25:3 [j] Jos 15:39 **22:2** [k] S Dt 17:19; S 1Ki 14:8 [l] S Dt 5:32 **22:3** [m] 2Ch 34:20; Jer 39:14 **22:4** [n] Ezr 7:1 [o] 2Ki 12:4-5 **22:5** [p] 2Ki 12:5, 11-14 **22:6** [q] 2Ki 12:11-12 **22:7** [r] S 2Ki 12:15 **22:8** [s] S Dt 28:61; S 31:24; Gal 3:10 **22:10** [t] Jer 36:21 **22:11** [u] ver 8

21:18 *rested with his ancestors.* See note on 1Ki 1:21. *Uzza.* Probably a shortened form of Uzziah (see NIV text note on 14:21; see also 2Ch 26:1 and note).

21:19 *two years.* 642 – 640 BC. *Jotbah.* Some identify it with the Jotbathah of Nu 33:33 – 34 and Dt 10:7, near Ezion Geber. Others, including the church father Jerome, have located it in Judah.

21:20 *did evil.* Amon did not share in the change of heart that characterized his father, Manasseh, in the last days of his life (see 2Ch 33:12 – 19). He must have restored the idolatrous practices that Manasseh abolished because these were again in existence in the time of Josiah (see 23:5 – 7,12).

21:23 *conspired against him.* Whether this palace revolt was motivated by religious or political considerations is not known.

21:24 *people of the land.* The citizenry in general (see 11:14,18; 14:21; 23:30).

21:25 *annals of the kings of Judah.* See note on 1Ki 14:29.

21:26 *Uzza.* See note on v. 18.

22:1 *thirty-one years.* 640 – 609 BC (see note on 21:19). *Bozkath.* Located in Judah in the vicinity of Lachish (see Jos 15:39).

22:2 *ways of his father David.* See note on 18:3. Josiah was the last godly king of the Davidic line prior to the exile. Jeremiah, who prophesied during the reign of Josiah (see Jer 1:2), spoke highly of him (Jer 22:15 – 16). Zephaniah also prophesied in the early days of his reign (Zep 1:1).

22:3 *eighteenth year.* 622 BC. Josiah was then 26 years old (see v. 1). He had begun to serve the Lord faithfully at the age of 16 (the 8th year of his reign, 2Ch 34:3). When he was 20 years old (the 12th year of his reign, 2Ch 34:3), he had already begun to purge the land of its idolatrous practices. *secretary, Shaphan.* See note on 2Sa 8:17. Two additional individuals are mentioned as accompanying Shaphan in 2Ch 34:8.

22:4 *Hilkiah.* Father of Azariah and grandfather of Seraiah, the high priest executed at the time of the destruction of Jerusalem by the Babylonians (see 25:18 – 21). It is unlikely that this Hilkiah was also the father of Jeremiah (see Jer 1:1). *money ... the doorkeepers have collected.* Josiah used the method devised by Joash for collecting funds for the restoration of the temple (see 12:1 – 16; 2Ch 34:9).

22:5 *men appointed to supervise.* See 2Ch 34:12 – 13.

22:8 *Book of the Law.* Some interpreters hold that this refers to a copy of the entire Pentateuch, while others understand it as a reference to a copy of part or all of Deuteronomy alone (see Dt 31:24,26; 2Ch 34:14).

22:11 *tore his robes.* See notes on 18:37; Jos 7:6; contrast Josiah's reaction with that of Jehoiakim to the

Ahikam[v] son of Shaphan, Akbor son of
Micaiah, Shaphan the secretary and Asaiah the king's attendant:[w] 13“Go and inquire[x] of the LORD for me and for the people and for all Judah about what is written
in this book that has been found. Great is
the LORD's anger[y] that burns against us because those who have gone before us have
not obeyed the words of this book; they
have not acted in accordance with all that
is written there concerning us.”
14Hilkiah the priest, Ahikam, Akbor,
Shaphan and Asaiah went to speak to the
prophet[z] Huldah, who was the wife of
Shallum son of Tikvah, the son of Harhas,
keeper of the wardrobe. She lived in Jerusalem, in the New Quarter.
15She said to them, “This is what the
LORD, the God of Israel, says: Tell the man
who sent you to me, 16‘This is what the
LORD says: I am going to bring disaster[a]
on this place and its people, according to
everything written in the book[b] the king
of Judah has read. 17Because they have
forsaken[c] me and burned incense to other gods and aroused my anger by all the
idols their hands have made,[a] my anger
will burn against this place and will not be
quenched.’ 18Tell the king of Judah, who
sent you to inquire[d] of the LORD, ‘This is
what the LORD, the God of Israel, says concerning the words you heard: 19Because
your heart was responsive and you humbled[e] yourself before the LORD when you
heard what I have spoken against this
place and its people—that they would become a curse[b][f] and be laid waste[g]—and
because you tore your robes and wept in

22:12 [v]2Ki 25:22; Jer 26:24; 39:14 [w]1Sa 8:14
22:13 [x]S Ge 25:22; S 1Sa 9:9 [y]Dt 29:24-28; S 31:17; Isa 5:25; 42:25; Am 2:4
22:14 [z]S Ex 15:20
22:16 [a]S Dt 31:29; S Jos 23:15; Jer 6:19; 11:11; 18:11; 35:17 [b]Da 9:11
22:17 [c]S 1Ki 9:9
22:18 [d]Jer 21:2; 37:3,7
22:19 [e]S Ex 10:3; Isa 57:15; 61:1; Mic 6:8 [f]Jer 24:9; 25:18; 26:6 [g]Lev 26:31
22:20 [h]Isa 47:11; 57:1; Jer 18:11 [i]S 1Ki 21:29
23:2 [j]S Dt 31:11 [k]S Ex 24:7
23:3 [l]S 1Ki 7:15 [m]S 2Ki 11:12 [n]S Dt 13:4
23:4 [o]2Ki 25:18; Jer 35:4 [p]S 2Ki 21:7

my presence, I also have heard you, declares the LORD. 20Therefore I will gather
you to your ancestors, and you will be
buried in peace.[h] Your eyes[i] will not see
all the disaster I am going to bring on this
place.’ ”
So they took her answer back to the
king.

Josiah Renews the Covenant

23:1-3pp — 2Ch 34:29-32
23:4-20Ref — 2Ch 34:3-7,33
23:21-23pp — 2Ch 35:1,18-19
23:28-30pp — 2Ch 35:20–36:1

23 Then the king called together all
the elders of Judah and Jerusalem.
2He went up to the temple of the LORD
with the people of Judah, the inhabitants
of Jerusalem, the priests and the prophets—all the people from the least to the
greatest. He read[j] in their hearing all the
words of the Book of the Covenant,[k] which
had been found in the temple of the LORD.
3The king stood by the pillar[l] and renewed
the covenant[m] in the presence of the
LORD—to follow[n] the LORD and keep his
commands, statutes and decrees with all
his heart and all his soul, thus confirming
the words of the covenant written in this
book. Then all the people pledged themselves to the covenant.
4The king ordered Hilkiah the high
priest, the priests next in rank and the
doorkeepers[o] to remove[p] from the temple of the LORD all the articles made for

[a] 17 Or *by everything they have done* [b] 19 That is, their names would be used in cursing (see Jer. 29:22); or, others would see that they are cursed.

words of the scroll written by Jeremiah (see Jer 36:24). Perhaps the covenant curses of Lev 26 and/or Dt 28, climaxing with the threat of exile, were the statements that especially disturbed Josiah.

22:12 *Ahikam son of Shaphan.* This official's name has been found on a seal impression dating to the time of Jeremiah. Ahikam was the father of Gedaliah, who was later to be appointed governor of Judah by Nebuchadnezzar (see 25:22; Jer 39:14). He was also the protector of Jeremiah when his life was threatened during the reign of Jehoiakim (see Jer 26:24). *Akbor.* His son Elnathan is mentioned in 24:8; Jer 26:22; 36:12. *Shaphan the secretary.* See note on v. 3.

22:14 *prophet Huldah.* For other female prophets see notes on Ex 15:20; Jdg 4:4. *Shallum ... keeper of the wardrobe.* Perhaps the same Shallum who was the uncle of Jeremiah (see Jer 32:7). *New Quarter.* A section of the city probably located in a newly developed area between the first and second walls in the northwest part of Jerusalem (see 2Ch 33:14; 34:22; Ne 11:9 and note; Zep 1:10).

22:16 *this place.* Jerusalem.

22:19 *your heart was responsive.* See v. 11.

22:20 *gather you to your ancestors.* See note on 1Ki 1:21. *you will be buried in peace.* This prediction refers to Josiah's death before God's judgment on Jerusalem through Nebuchadnezzar and so is not contradicted by his death in battle with Pharaoh Necho of Egypt (see 23:29–30). Josiah was assured that the final judgment on Judah and Jerusalem would not come in his own days.

23:1 *elders.* See note on 10:1.

23:2 *Book of the Covenant.* Although this designation is used in Ex 24:7 with reference to the contents of Ex 20–23, it is here applied to either all or part of the book of Deuteronomy or the entire Mosaic law. Whatever else the scroll contained, it clearly included the covenant curses of Lev 26 and/or Dt 28 (see notes on v. 21; 22:8,11).

23:3 *pillar.* See note on 11:14. *renewed the covenant.* Josiah carries out the function of covenant mediator; cf. Moses (Ex 24:3–8; Deuteronomy), Joshua (Jos 24), Samuel (1Sa 11:14—12:25) and Jehoiada (2Ki 11:17). *follow the LORD.* See notes on 1Sa 12:14,20. *pledged themselves to the covenant.* It is likely that some sort of ratification rite was performed, in which the people participated and pledged by oath to be loyal to their covenant obligations. Whether this was done symbolically (see Jer 34:18) or verbally (see Dt 27:11–26) is not clear.

23:4 *doorkeepers.* See 12:9. *Baal and Asherah.* See note on 1Ki 14:15. *starry hosts.* See note on 17:16. *Kidron Valley.* See note on Isa 22:7 and map, p. 515; see also 1Ki 15:13 and note. *took the ashes to Bethel.* See vv. 15–16. Bethel was located just over the border between Judah and the former northern kingdom in territory nominally under Assyrian control. With a decline in Assyrian power, Josiah was able to exert his own

Baal and Asherah and all the starry hosts.
He burned them outside Jerusalem in the
fields of the Kidron Valley and took the
ashes to Bethel. 5He did away with the
idolatrous priests appointed by the kings
of Judah to burn incense on the high places of the towns of Judah and on those
around Jerusalem—those who burned
incense[q] to Baal, to the sun and moon,
to the constellations and to all the starry hosts.[r] 6He took the Asherah pole from
the temple of the LORD to the Kidron Valley[s] outside Jerusalem and burned it there.
He ground it to powder[t] and scattered the
dust over the graves[u] of the common people.[v] 7He also tore down the quarters of
the male shrine prostitutes[w] that were in
the temple of the LORD, the quarters where
women did weaving for Asherah.
8Josiah brought all the priests from the
towns of Judah and desecrated the high
places, from Geba[x] to Beersheba, where
the priests had burned incense. He broke
down the gateway at the entrance of the
Gate of Joshua, the city governor, which
was on the left of the city gate. 9Although
the priests of the high places did not serve[y]
at the altar of the LORD in Jerusalem, they
ate unleavened bread with their fellow
priests.
10He desecrated Topheth,[z] which was
in the Valley of Ben Hinnom,[a] so no one
could use it to sacrifice their son[b] or
daughter in the fire to Molek. 11He removed from the entrance to the temple of
the LORD the horses that the kings of Judah[c] had dedicated to the sun. They were
in the court[a] near the room of an official
named Nathan-Melek. Josiah then burned
the chariots dedicated to the sun.[d]
12He pulled down[e] the altars the kings
of Judah had erected on the roof[f] near
the upper room of Ahaz, and the altars
Manasseh had built in the two courts[g] of
the temple of the LORD. He removed them
from there, smashed them to pieces and
threw the rubble into the Kidron Valley.[h]
13The king also desecrated the high places
that were east of Jerusalem on the south
of the Hill of Corruption—the ones Solomon[i] king of Israel had built for Ashtoreth
the vile goddess of the Sidonians, for Chemosh the vile god of Moab, and for Molek
the detestable[j] god of the people of Ammon.[k] 14Josiah smashed[l] the sacred stones
and cut down the Asherah poles and covered the sites with human bones.[m]
15Even the altar[n] at Bethel, the high
place made by Jeroboam[o] son of Nebat,
who had caused Israel to sin—even that
altar and high place he demolished. He
burned the high place and ground it to
powder, and burned the Asherah pole
also. 16Then Josiah[p] looked around, and
when he saw the tombs that were there
on the hillside, he had the bones removed
from them and burned on the altar to defile it, in accordance[q] with the word of the
LORD proclaimed by the man of God who
foretold these things.
17The king asked, "What is that tombstone I see?"
The people of the city said, "It marks
the tomb of the man of God who came

23:5 [q]S 2Ki 16:4 [r]Jer 8:2; 43:13 **23:6** [s]Jer 31:40 [t]S Ex 32:20 [u]S Nu 19:16 [v]Jer 26:23 **23:7** [w]S Ge 38:21; 1Ki 14:24; Eze 16:16 **23:8** [x]S Jos 18:24; S 1Ki 15:22 **23:9** [y]Eze 44:10-14 **23:10** [z]Isa 30:33; Jer 7:31,32; 19:6 [a]S Jos 15:8 [b]S Lev 18:21; S Dt 18:10 **23:11** [c]ver 5, 19; Ne 9:34; Jer 44:9 [d]S Dt 4:19 **23:12** [e]2Ch 33:15 [f]Jer 19:13; Zep 1:5 [g]S 2Ki 21:5 [h]S 2Sa 15:23 **23:13** [i]1Ki 11:7 [j]S Dt 27:15 [k]Jer 11:13 **23:14** [l]S Ex 23:24 [m]S Nu 19:16; S Ps 53:5 **23:15** [n]S Jos 7:2; 1Ki 13:1-3 [o]S 1Ki 12:33 **23:16** [p]S 1Ki 13:2 [q]1Ki 13:32

[a] *11* The meaning of the Hebrew for this word is uncertain.

influence in the north. He apparently deposited the ashes at Bethel in order to desecrate (see note on v. 14) the very place where golden calf worship had originally polluted the land (see notes on 1Ki 12:28–30).

23:5 *idolatrous priests.* See Hos 10:5; Zep 1:4. *kings of Judah.* A reference to Manasseh and Amon, and perhaps to Ahaz before them. *high places.* See note on 18:4.

23:6 *Asherah pole.* See note on 1Ki 14:15. The Asherah poles destroyed by Hezekiah (18:4) were reintroduced by Manasseh (21:7). When Manasseh turned to the Lord, it is likely that he too got rid of the Asherah poles (see 2Ch 33:15) and that they were then again reintroduced by Amon (2Ki 21:21; 2Ch 33:22). *scattered the dust over the graves of the common people.* Intended as a defilement of the goddess, not as a desecration of the graves of the poor (see Jer 26:23).

23:7 *male shrine prostitutes.* See note on 1Ki 14:24.

23:8 *desecrated the high places.* See note on 18:4. *Geba to Beersheba.* Geba was on the northern border of the southern kingdom (see 1Ki 15:22), and Beersheba was on its southern border (see note on 1Sa 3:20).

23:9 *ate unleavened bread with their fellow priests.* Although not permitted to serve at the temple altar, these priests were to be sustained by a share of the priestly provisions (see Lev 2:10; 6:16–18). They occupied a status similar to that of priests with physical defects (see Lev 21:16–23).

23:10 *Topheth … Molek.* See note on 1Ki 11:5. Topheth was an area in the Valley of Hinnom where altars used for child sacrifice were located (see Isa 30:33; Jer 7:31; 19:5–6 and notes). *sacrifice their son or daughter.* See 17:17; 21:6; see also note on 16:3.

23:11 *horses … dedicated to the sun.* If live, the horses may have been used to pull chariots bearing images of a sun-god in religious processions. Small images of horses have recently been found in a pagan shrine just outside one of the ancient walls of Jerusalem. *Nathan-Melek.* Perhaps the official in charge of the chariots.

23:12 *altars … on the roof.* Altars dedicated to the worship of all the starry hosts (see Jer 19:13; Zep 1:5)—erected by Ahaz (2Ki 16:3–4,10–16), Manasseh (21:3) and Amon (21:21–22).

23:13 *high places … Solomon … had built.* See note on 1Ki 11:5.

23:14 *covered the sites with human bones.* The bones would defile these sites and make them unsuitable for pagan use in the future (see Nu 19:16).

23:15 *altar at Bethel.* See 1Ki 12:32–33. Nothing is said of the golden calf, which undoubtedly had been sent to Assyria as tribute at the time of the captivity of the northern kingdom (see Hos 10:5–6).

23:16 *tombs.* Of the priests of the Bethel sanctuary (see 1Ki 13:2). *burned on the altar to defile it.* See notes on vv. 6,14. *the man of God who foretold these things.* See 1Ki 13:1–2,32.

NEBUCHADNEZZAR'S CAMPAIGNS AGAINST JUDAH

605–586 BC

Events in Judah moved swiftly following the death of Josiah. Pharaoh Necho pressed his advantage by deporting Jehoahaz, the new ruler, and appointing a second son of Josiah, Jehoiakim, as king.

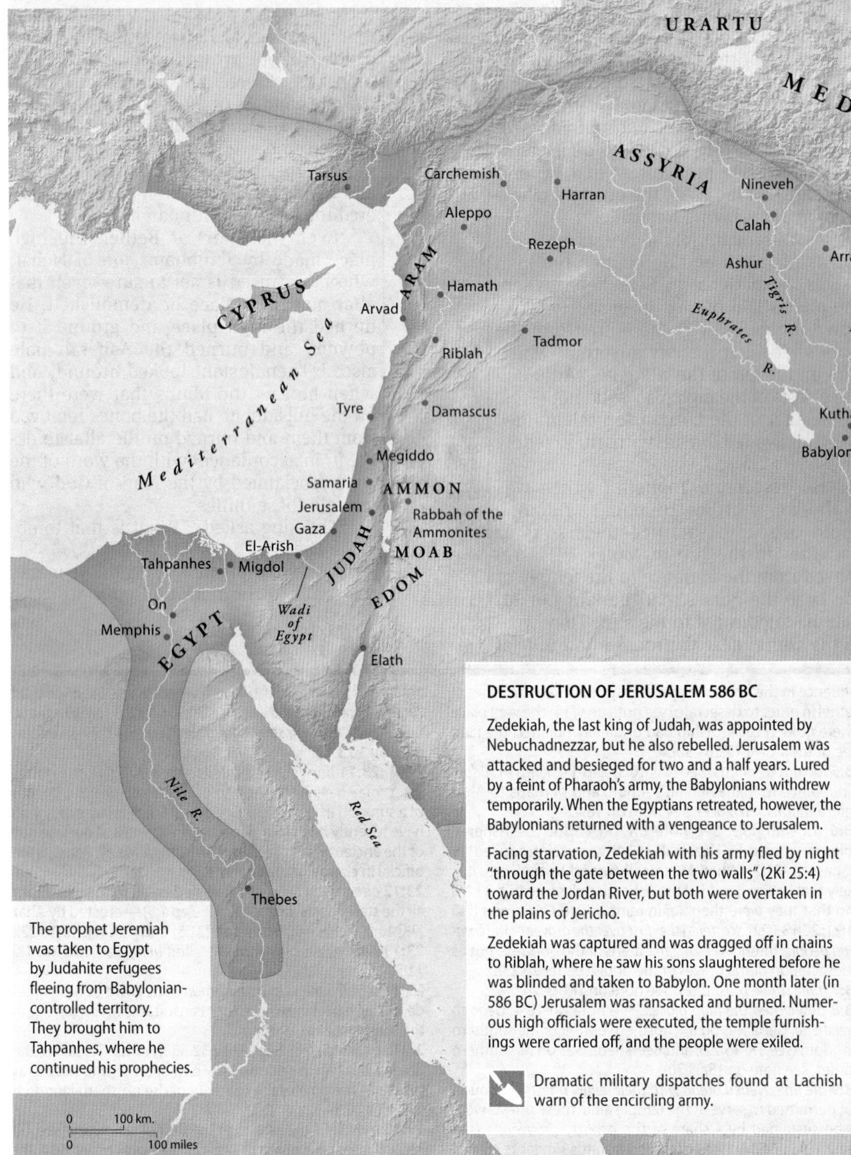

The prophet Jeremiah was taken to Egypt by Judahite refugees fleeing from Babylonian-controlled territory. They brought him to Tahpanhes, where he continued his prophecies.

DESTRUCTION OF JERUSALEM 586 BC

Zedekiah, the last king of Judah, was appointed by Nebuchadnezzar, but he also rebelled. Jerusalem was attacked and besieged for two and a half years. Lured by a feint of Pharaoh's army, the Babylonians withdrew temporarily. When the Egyptians retreated, however, the Babylonians returned with a vengeance to Jerusalem.

Facing starvation, Zedekiah with his army fled by night "through the gate between the two walls" (2Ki 25:4) toward the Jordan River, but both were overtaken in the plains of Jericho.

Zedekiah was captured and was dragged off in chains to Riblah, where he saw his sons slaughtered before he was blinded and taken to Babylon. One month later (in 586 BC) Jerusalem was ransacked and burned. Numerous high officials were executed, the temple furnishings were carried off, and the people were exiled.

Dramatic military dispatches found at Lachish warn of the encircling army.

:haldeans (Kaldu), as the Neo-Babylonians were called, had rtant connections at Ur and Harran, centers of worship of the n-god Sin. They also developed the trade routes across North a, where Tema was particularly important, becoming the ence of Nabonidus during the last days of the kingdom (see map, 23).

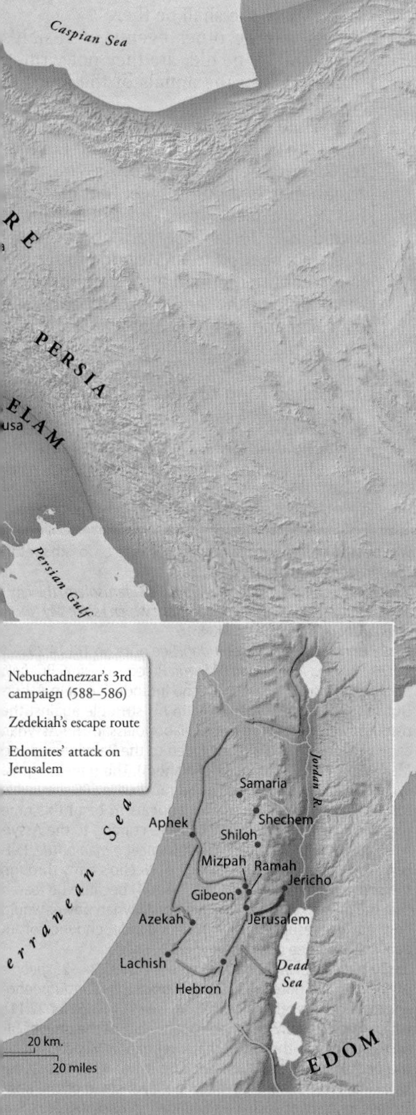

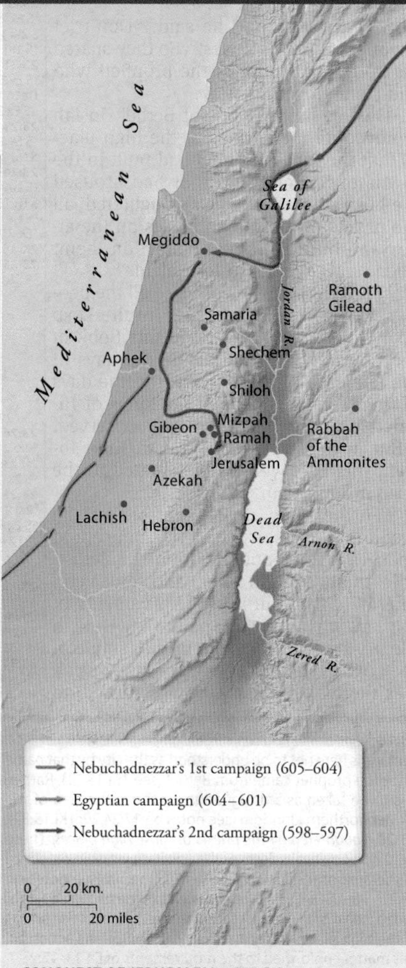

CONQUEST OF JERUSALEM c. 597 BC

Soon a stronger power appeared in the north in the person of Nebuchadnezzar, king of the Chaldeans (Neo-Babylonians), who determined to follow the fierce policies of his Assyrian predecessors.

The tribute of Jehoiakim was paid at a distance when he heard of Nebuchadnezzar's approach. After three years as a Babylonian vassal, he rebelled, bringing a rapid response in the form of small-scale raids from Babylonians, Arameans, Moabites and Ammonites (c. 602 BC). Finally, Nebuchadnezzar's forces controlled all of the coastal territory north of the Wadi of Egypt.

When 18-year-old Jehoiachin had ruled just three months (597 BC), the main Babylonian army struck, capturing Jerusalem and exiling the king as a captive in Babylon. Ten thousand persons were deported.

from Judah and pronounced against the
altar of Bethel the very things you have
done to it."
18 "Leave it alone," he said. "Don't let
anyone disturb his bones[r]." So they spared
his bones and those of the prophet[s] who
had come from Samaria.
19 Just as he had done at Bethel, Josiah
removed all the shrines at the high places that the kings of Israel had built in the
towns of Samaria and that had aroused
the LORD's anger. 20 Josiah slaughtered[t] all
the priests of those high places on the altars and burned human bones[u] on them.
Then he went back to Jerusalem.
21 The king gave this order to all the people: "Celebrate the Passover[v] to the LORD
your God, as it is written in this Book of
the Covenant."[w] 22 Neither in the days of
the judges who led Israel nor in the days
of the kings of Israel and the kings of Judah had any such Passover been observed.
23 But in the eighteenth year of King Josiah, this Passover was celebrated to the
LORD in Jerusalem.[x]
24 Furthermore, Josiah got rid of the
mediums and spiritists,[y] the household
gods,[z] the idols and all the other detestable[a] things seen in Judah and Jerusalem.
This he did to fulfill the requirements of
the law written in the book that Hilkiah
the priest had discovered in the temple of
the LORD. 25 Neither before nor after Josiah
was there a king like him who turned[b] to
the LORD as he did — with all his heart and
with all his soul and with all his strength,
in accordance with all the Law of Moses.[c]
26 Nevertheless, the LORD did not turn
away from the heat of his fierce anger,[d]
which burned against Judah because of all
that Manasseh[e] had done to arouse his anger. 27 So the LORD said, "I will remove[f] Judah also from my presence[g] as I removed
Israel, and I will reject[h] Jerusalem, the city
I chose, and this temple, about which I
said, 'My Name shall be there.'[a]"
28 As for the other events of Josiah's
reign, and all he did, are they not written
in the book of the annals of the kings of
Judah?
29 While Josiah was king, Pharaoh Necho[i] king of Egypt went up to the Euphrates River to help the king of Assyria. King
Josiah marched out to meet him in battle,
but Necho faced him and killed him at
Megiddo.[j] 30 Josiah's servants brought his
body in a chariot[k] from Megiddo to Jerusalem and buried him in his own tomb. And
the people of the land took Jehoahaz son
of Josiah and anointed him and made him
king in place of his father.

Jehoahaz King of Judah

23:31-34pp — 2Ch 36:2-4

31 Jehoahaz[l] was twenty-three years old
when he became king, and he reigned in Je-

23:18 [r] 1Ki 13:31 [s] 1Ki 13:29 **23:20** [t] S Ex 22:20; S 2Ki 11:18 [u] S 1Ki 13:2 **23:21** [v] S Ex 12:11; Dt 16:1-8 [w] S Ex 24:7 **23:23** [x] S Ex 12:11; S Nu 28:16 **23:24** [y] S Lev 19:31; S Dt 18:11 [z] S Ge 31:19 [a] Dt 7:26; 2Ki 16:3 **23:25** [b] S 1Sa 7:3 [c] Jer 22:15 **23:26** [d] 2Ki 21:6; Jer 23:20; 30:24 [e] S 2Ki 21:12 **23:27** [f] 2Ki 21:13 [g] S Ex 33:15; 2Ki 24:3 [h] Jer 27:10; 32:31 **23:29** [i] ver 33-35; Jer 46:2 [j] 2Ki 9:27 **23:30** [k] S 2Ki 9:28 **23:31** [l] 1Ch 3:15; Jer 22:11

[a] *27* 1 Kings 8:29

23:18 *prophet who had come from Samaria.* See 1Ki 13:31 – 32. Samaria is here not to be understood as the city by that name since the prophet came from Bethel (see 1Ki 13:11). Rather, it is to be taken as a designation for the entire area of the former northern kingdom (see notes on 17:24,29; 1Ki 13:32).
23:20 *slaughtered all the priests of those high places.* These were non-Levitical priests of the apostate worship practiced in the area of the former northern kingdom (see notes on 17:27 – 28,33 – 34). They were treated like the pagan priests of Judah (see v. 5) in contrast to Josiah's treatment of the priests at the high places in Judah (see vv. 8 – 9). Josiah's actions in this matter conformed to the requirements of Dt 13; 17:2 – 7.
23:21 *Celebrate the Passover.* A more complete description of this observance is found in 2Ch 35:1 – 19. *as it is written in this Book of the Covenant.* See note on v. 2. This appears to refer to Dt 16:1 – 8, where the Passover is described in a communal setting at a sanctuary (see Ex 23:15 – 17; 34:23 – 24; Lev 23:4 – 14) rather than in the family setting of Ex 12:1 – 14,43 – 49.
23:22 The uniqueness of Josiah's Passover celebration seems to be in the fact that all the Passover lambs were slaughtered exclusively by the Levites (see 2Ch 35:1 – 19; cf. 2Ch 30:2 – 3,17 – 20 for the Passover observed in the time of Hezekiah).
23:23 *eighteenth year.* See note on 22:3.
23:24 *household gods.* See note on Ge 31:19. *idols.* See Lev 26:30. *requirements of the law.* See notes on v. 2; 22:8.
23:25 *was there a king like him.* See note on 18:5. *with all his heart . . . soul and . . . strength.* See Dt 6:5.
23:26 *Nevertheless, the LORD did not turn away from the heat of his fierce anger.* The judgment against Judah and Jerusalem was postponed but not rescinded because of Josiah's reformation (see notes on 21:15; 22:20).
23:27 *as I removed Israel.* See 17:18 – 23. *Jerusalem, the city I chose.* See 21:4,7,13. *this temple, about which I said, 'My Name shall be there.'* See note on 1Ki 8:16.
23:28 *annals of the kings of Judah.* See note on 1Ki 14:29.
23:29 *Pharaoh Necho king of Egypt.* Ruled 610 – 595 BC. *help the king of Assyria.* Pharaoh Necho intended to help Ashur-Uballit II, the last Assyrian king, in his struggle against the rising power of Babylon under Nabopolassar. The Assyrian capital, Nineveh, had already fallen to the Babylonians and Medes in 612 (see the book of Nahum). The remaining Assyrian forces had regrouped at Harran, but in 609 they were forced west of the Euphrates. It appears to be at this time that the Egyptians under Necho were coming to the Assyrians' aid. *King Josiah marched out to meet him in battle.* Perhaps Josiah opposed the passage of Necho's army through the pass at Megiddo (see 2Ch 35:20 – 24) because he feared that the growth of either Egyptian or Assyrian power would have adverse results for the continued independence of Judah. *Megiddo.* See note on Jdg 5:19.
23:30 *buried him in his own tomb.* See 2Ch 35:24 – 25. *people of the land.* See note on 21:24. *Jehoahaz son of Josiah.* Jehoahaz's name was originally Shallum (see 1Ch 3:15; Jer 22:11), which was probably changed to Jehoahaz at the time of his accession to the throne. Perhaps Jehoahaz was chosen by the people over Jehoiakim because it was known that Jehoiakim favored a pro-Egyptian policy instead of the anti-Egyptian policy of Josiah and Jehoahaz. *anointed him.* See note on 1Sa 9:16.

rusalem three months. His mother's name
was Hamutal[m] daughter of Jeremiah; she
was from Libnah. 32 He did evil[n] in the eyes
of the LORD, just as his predecessors had
done. 33 Pharaoh Necho put him in chains
at Riblah[o] in the land of Hamath[p] so that he
might not reign in Jerusalem, and he imposed on Judah a levy of a hundred talents[a]
of silver and a talent[b] of gold. 34 Pharaoh
Necho made Eliakim[q] son of Josiah king
in place of his father Josiah and changed
Eliakim's name to Jehoiakim. But he took
Jehoahaz and carried him off to Egypt, and
there he died.[r] 35 Jehoiakim paid Pharaoh
Necho the silver and gold he demanded.
In order to do so, he taxed the land and
exacted the silver and gold from the people
of the land according to their assessments.[s]

Jehoiakim King of Judah

23:36 – 24:6pp — 2Ch 36:5-8

36 Jehoiakim[t] was twenty-five years old
when he became king, and he reigned
in Jerusalem eleven years. His mother's
name was Zebidah daughter of Pedaiah;
she was from Rumah. 37 And he did evil[u]
in the eyes of the LORD, just as his predecessors had done.

23:31 [m] 2Ki 24:18 **23:32** [n] 1Ki 15:26 **23:33** [o] S Nu 34:11 [p] 1Ki 8:65 **23:34** [q] 2Ki 24:6; 1Ch 3:15; 2Ch 36:5-8; Jer 1:3 [r] Jer 22:12 **23:35** [s] Jer 2:16 **23:36** [t] Jer 26:1 **23:37** [u] 1Ki 15:26

24:1 [v] ver 10; 2Ki 25:11; Ezr 5:12; Jer 4:7; 25:1,9; 39:1; 40:1; 50:17; 52:15; Eze 32:2; Da 1:1; 7:4 [w] Jer 35:11 [x] S 2Ki 18:7 **24:2** [y] Jer 5:15; Hab 1:6 [z] Jer 35:11 [a] S 2Ki 5:2 [b] Isa 28:18-19 [c] Jer 12:7-9; 25:1; 26:1; 36:1; Eze 23:23; Da 1:2 **24:3** [d] S 2Ki 18:25 [e] 2Ki 13:23 [f] S 1Ki 14:9; S 2Ki 21:12; Jer 15:4

24 During Jehoiakim's reign, Nebuchadnezzar[v] king of Babylon invaded[w] the land, and Jehoiakim became his
vassal for three years. But then he turned
against Nebuchadnezzar and rebelled.[x]
2 The LORD sent Babylonian,[c][y] Aramean,[z]
Moabite and Ammonite raiders[a] against
him to destroy[b] Judah, in accordance with
the word of the LORD proclaimed by his servants the prophets.[c] 3 Surely these things
happened to Judah according to the LORD's
command,[d] in order to remove them from
his presence[e] because of the sins of Manasseh[f] and all he had done, 4 including
the shedding of innocent blood.[g] For he
had filled Jerusalem with innocent blood,
and the LORD was not willing to forgive.[h]
5 As for the other events of Jehoiakim's
reign,[i] and all he did, are they not written
in the book of the annals of the kings of
Judah? 6 Jehoiakim rested[j] with his ancestors. And Jehoiachin[k] his son succeeded
him as king.

[a] 33 That is, about 3 3/4 tons or about 3.4 metric tons
[b] 33 That is, about 75 pounds or about 34 kilograms
[c] 2 Or *Chaldean*

24:4 [g] S 2Ki 21:16; Jer 22:3 [h] S Ex 23:21; La 3:42 **24:5** [i] Jer 22:18-19 **24:6** [j] Jer 22:19; 36:30 [k] 1Ch 3:16; Jer 22:24,28; Eze 19:1

23:31 *three months.* In 609 BC. *Jeremiah.* Not the prophet (see Jer 15:17; 16:2 and notes). *Libnah.* See note on 8:22.

23:32 *evil … as his predecessors.* See 16:3; 21:2,21; Eze 19:3 and note.

23:33 *in chains at Riblah.* By either deception or overt force the Egyptians were able to take Jehoahaz captive and impose tribute on Judah (see 2Ch 36:3). Jehoahaz was imprisoned at Necho's military headquarters, established at Riblah on the Orontes River. Nebuchadnezzar was later to make his headquarters at the same place (see 25:6,20).

23:34 *Eliakim son of Josiah.* Eliakim was an older brother of Jehoahaz (see 1Ch 3:15). Perhaps he had been bypassed earlier as a successor to Josiah because of a pro-Egyptian political stance. *changed Eliakim's name to Jehoiakim.* The meaning of these two names is similar (Eliakim, "God has established"; Jehoiakim, "Yahweh has established"). Perhaps Necho wanted to use the name change to imply that his actions were sanctioned by Yahweh, the God of Judah (see 18:25; 2Ch 35:21). In any case, the change in name indicated that Jehoiakim was subject to Necho's authority. *took Jehoahaz … to Egypt, and there he died.* See 2Ch 36:4; Jer 22:10 – 12.

23:35 *from the people of the land.* The tribute for Necho was raised by a graduated tax placed on the very people who had supported the kingship of Jehoahaz (see v. 30 and note on 21:24). Menahem of the northern kingdom had used a similar method of raising funds for tribute (see 15:20).

23:36 *eleven years.* 609 – 598 BC.

23:37 *did evil in the eyes of the LORD.* Jehoiakim was responsible for the murder of the prophet Uriah from Kiriath Jearim (Jer 26:20 – 24), and his rule was characterized by dishonesty, oppression and injustice (see Jer 22:13 – 19). He reintroduced idolatrous worship in the temple (see Eze 8:5 – 17) and refused to accept the word of the Lord through Jeremiah (see Jer 36). *his predecessors.* Manasseh (21:1 – 18) and Amon (21:19 – 26).

24:1 *Nebuchadnezzar.* Means "Nabu [a god], protect my son/boundary!" He was the son of Nabopolassar (see note on 23:29) and the most powerful king of the Neo-Babylonian Empire (612 – 539 BC), reigning 605 – 562 (see Da 1 – 4; see also chart, p. 511). *invaded the land.* In 605 Nebuchadnezzar, the crown prince and commander of the Babylonian army, defeated Pharaoh Necho and the Egyptians at the battle of Carchemish and again at Hamath (see 23:29; Jer 46:2). These victories had far-reaching implications in the geopolitical power structure of the eastern Mediterranean world. Nebuchadnezzar went on to conquer all of the "Hatti-land," which, according to Babylonian records, included the "city of Judah." Daniel was among the Judahite hostages taken at this time (see Da 1:1). Perhaps as early as Sept. 6, 605, Nebuchadnezzar acceded to the Babylonian throne upon the death of his father. *three years.* Probably 604 – 602. In 604 Nebuchadnezzar returned to the west and took tribute from "all the kings of Hatti-land." It is likely that Jehoiakim was included among these kings. *turned against Nebuchadnezzar and rebelled.* In 601 Nebuchadnezzar again marched west against Egypt and was repulsed by strong Egyptian resistance. This may have encouraged Jehoiakim's rebellion, even though Jeremiah had warned against it (see Jer 27:9 – 11).

24:2 *Babylonian, Aramean, Moabite and Ammonite raiders against him.* Reaction to Jehoiakim's rebellion was swift. Babylonian troops, perhaps garrisoned in Aram, along with troops of other loyal vassals, were sent to put down the Judahite rebellion.

24:3 *sins of Manasseh.* See 21:11 – 12; 23:26 – 27; Jer 15:3 – 4.

24:4 *innocent blood.* See note on 21:16. *not willing to forgive.* See 22:17.

24:5 *annals of the kings of Judah.* See note on 1Ki 14:29.

24:6 *rested with his ancestors.* See note on 1Ki 1:21. Jehoiakim died shortly before Jerusalem fell to the Babylonian siege (see vv. 8 – 12). Whether his death was due to natural causes or political intrigue is not indicated.

7 The king of Egypt[l] did not march out from his own country again, because the king of Babylon[m] had taken all his territory, from the Wadi of Egypt to the Euphrates River.

Jehoiachin King of Judah

24:8-17pp — 2Ch 36:9-10

8 Jehoiachin[n] was eighteen years old when he became king, and he reigned in Jerusalem three months. His mother's name was Nehushta[o] daughter of Elnathan; she was from Jerusalem. 9 He did evil[p] in the eyes of the LORD, just as his father had done.

10 At that time the officers of Nebuchadnezzar[q] king of Babylon advanced on Jerusalem and laid siege to it, 11 and Nebuchadnezzar himself came up to the city while his officers were besieging it. 12 Jehoiachin king of Judah, his mother, his attendants, his nobles and his officials all surrendered[r] to him.

In the eighth year of the reign of the king of Babylon, he took Jehoiachin prisoner. 13 As the LORD had declared,[s] Nebuchadnezzar removed the treasures[t] from the temple of the LORD and from the royal palace, and cut up the gold articles[u] that Solomon[v] king of Israel had made for the temple of the LORD. 14 He carried all Jerusalem into exile:[w] all the officers and fighting men,[x] and all the skilled workers and artisans — a total of ten thousand. Only the poorest[y] people of the land were left.

15 Nebuchadnezzar took Jehoiachin[z] captive to Babylon. He also took from Jerusalem to Babylon the king's mother,[a] his wives, his officials and the prominent people[b] of the land. 16 The king of Babylon also deported to Babylon the entire force of seven thousand fighting men, strong and fit for war, and a thousand skilled workers and artisans.[c] 17 He made Mattaniah, Jehoiachin's uncle, king in his place and changed his name to Zedekiah.[d]

Zedekiah King of Judah

24:18-20pp — 2Ch 36:11-16; Jer 52:1-3

18 Zedekiah[e] was twenty-one years old when he became king, and he reigned in Jerusalem eleven years. His mother's name was Hamutal[f] daughter of Jeremiah; she was from Libnah. 19 He did evil[g] in the eyes of the LORD, just as Jehoiakim had done. 20 It was because of the LORD's anger that all this happened to Jerusalem and Judah, and in the end he thrust[h] them from his presence.[i]

The Fall of Jerusalem

25:1-12pp — Jer 39:1-10
25:1-21pp — 2Ch 36:17-20; Jer 52:4-27
25:22-26pp — Jer 40:7-9; 41:1-3, 16-18

Now Zedekiah rebelled against the king of Babylon.

25 So in the ninth[j] year of Zedekiah's reign, on the tenth day of the tenth month, Nebuchadnezzar[k] king of Babylon marched against Jerusalem with his whole army. He encamped outside the city and

24:7 [l]S Ge 15:18; S 2Ki 18:21; S Jer 46:25 [m]Jer 1:14; 25:9; 46:24 **24:8** [n]1Ch 3:16; Jer 22:24; 37:1 [o]ver 15; Jer 13:18; 22:26; 29:2 **24:9** [p]1Ki 15:26 **24:10** [q]S ver 1 **24:12** [r]2Ki 25:27; Jer 13:18; 22:24-30; 24:1; 29:2 **24:13** [s]2Ki 20:17 [t]2Ki 25:15; Isa 39:6; 42:22 [u]2Ki 25:14; Ezr 1:7; Isa 39:6; Jer 15:13; 17:3; 20:5; 27:16; 28:3; Eze 7:21; Da 1:2; 5:2, 23; Zep 1:13 [v]S 1Ki 7:51 **24:14** [w]S Dt 28:36; S 2Ch 36:20; S Mt 1:11 [x]Isa 3:1-3 [y]Dt 15:11; 2Ki 25:12; Job 5:16; Ps 9:18; Jer 40:7; 52:16 **24:15** [z]S 2Ki 20:18; Eze 19:9 [a]S ver 8; S 1Ki 2:19 [b]Est 2:6; Isa 39:7; La 2:9; Eze 1:2; 17:12-14; Da 1:3 **24:16** [c]Ezr 2:1; Jer 24:1 **24:17** [d]1Ch 3:15; 2Ch 36:11; Jer 1:3; 37:1; 52:1; Eze 17:13 **24:18** [e]1Ch 3:16; Jer 39:1 [f]2Ki 23:31 **24:19** [g]1Ki 15:26; Jer 37:2 **24:20** [h]Dt 4:26; 29:27 [i]S Ex 33:15; S 2Ki 13:23 **25:1** [j]Jer 32:1 [k]Jer 21:2; 34:1-7

24:7 *The king of Egypt did not march out from his own country again.* This was due to the Egyptian defeat at Carchemish (see Jer 46:2) in 605 BC, and it explains why Jehoiakim received no help from Egypt in his rebellion against the Babylonians. *Wadi of Egypt.* See note on 1Ki 8:65.

24:8 *three months.* Babylonian records place this capture of Jerusalem by Nebuchadnezzar on Mar. 16, 597 BC. This means that the three-month and ten-day reign (see 2Ch 36:9 – 10) of Jehoiachin began in December, 598.

24:9 *as his father.* See 23:37; Jer 22:20 – 30.

24:12 *eighth year.* April, 597 BC (see 2Ch 36:10; see also note on Jer 52:28, where a different system of dating is reflected).

24:13 *As the LORD had declared.* See 20:13,17.

24:14 *ten thousand.* This figure may include the 7,000 fighting men and 1,000 craftsmen mentioned in v. 16 (see note on Jer 52:28, where a different number of captives is mentioned).

24:15 *Jehoiachin captive to Babylon.* Fulfilling Jeremiah's prophecy (Jer 22:24 – 27; see 2Ki 25:27 – 30).

24:17 *Mattaniah, Jehoiachin's uncle.* Mattaniah was a son of Josiah (see 1Ch 3:15; Jer 1:3) and brother of Jehoiachin's father, Jehoiakim. *changed his name to Zedekiah.* Mattaniah's name (meaning "gift of Yahweh") was changed to Zedekiah ("righteousness of Yahweh"). Perhaps Nebuchadnezzar wanted to imply that his actions against Jerusalem and Jehoiachin were just. In any case, the name change signified subjection to Nebuchadnezzar (see note on 23:34).

24:18 *eleven years.* 597 – 586 BC. *Jeremiah.* See note on 23:31. *Libnah.* See note on 8:22.

24:19 *did evil ... as Jehoiakim.* See note on 23:37. During Zedekiah's reign idolatrous practices continued to increase in Jerusalem (see 2Ch 36:14; Eze 8 – 11). He was a weak and indecisive ruler (see Jer 38:5,19) who refused to heed the word of the Lord given through Jeremiah (2Ch 36:12).

24:20 *Zedekiah rebelled.* Most interpreters link Zedekiah's revolt with the succession to the Egyptian throne in 589 BC of the ambitious pharaoh Hophra (see Jer 44:30 and note). Zedekiah had sworn allegiance to Nebuchadnezzar (Eze 17:13), had sent envoys to Babylon (see Jer 29:3) and had made a personal visit (see Jer 51:59). However, he seems to have capitulated to the seductive propaganda of the anti-Babylonian and pro-Egyptian faction in Jerusalem (see Jer 37:5; Eze 17:15 – 16) in a tragically miscalculated effort to gain independence from Babylonia.

25:1 *ninth year ... tenth day ... tenth month.* Jan. 15, 588 BC (see Jer 39:1; 52:4; Eze 24:1 – 2). *Nebuchadnezzar ... marched against Jerusalem.* Earlier, Nebuchadnezzar had subdued all the fortified cities in Judah except Lachish and Azekah (see Jer 34:7). A number of Hebrew inscriptions on potsherds were found at Lachish in 1935 and 1938. These Lachish ostraca (or letters; see chart, p. xxiii) describe conditions at Lachish and Azekah during the Babylonian siege.

EXILE OF THE SOUTHERN KINGDOM

Knowledge about the destiny of the captives from Israel and Judah is sparse in the period following the capture of Samaria and the later destruction of Jerusalem.

Assyrians and Babylonians treated their subject peoples essentially the same: overwhelming military force used in a manner inspiring psychological terror, along with mass deportations and heavy tribute.

Three deportations are mentioned in Jer 52:28-30, the largest one consisting of 3,023 Jews who were taken to Babylon along with King Jehoiachin in 597 BC.

After the destruction of Jerusalem by Nebuzaradan, the commander of the Babylonian army, hundreds of exiles were taken to Riblah in the land of Hamath, where, in addition to Zedekiah's sons, at least 61 were executed.

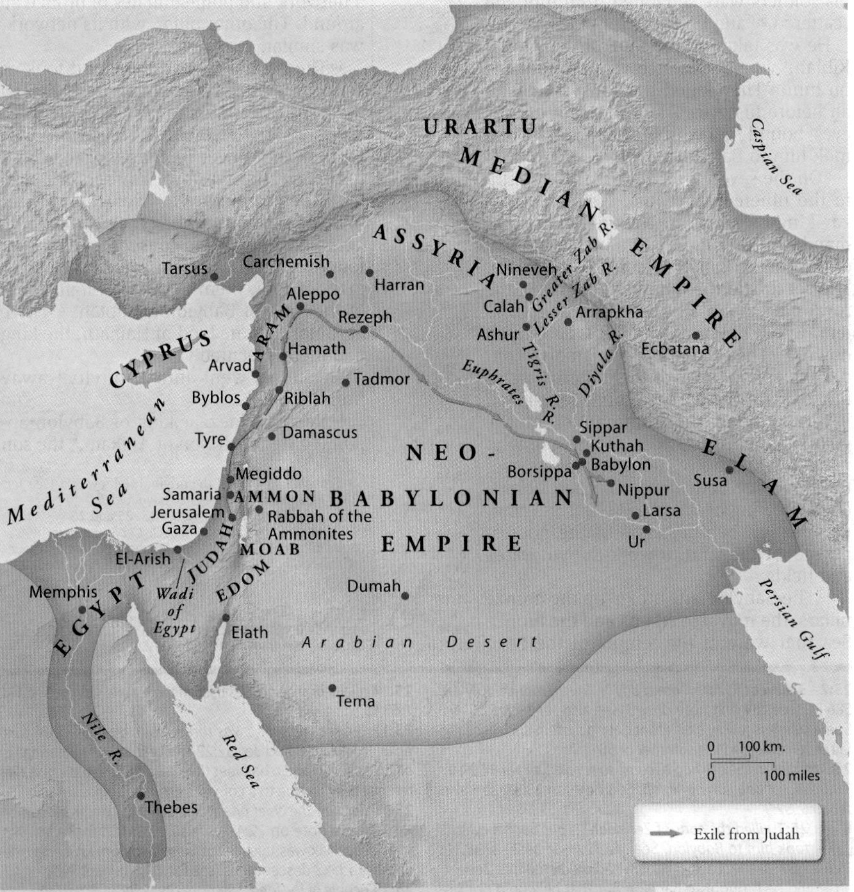

Clay tablets from the fifth century BC called the Murashu archives have been found at Nippur. They document the commercial transactions with Jewish families who remained in Mesopotamia following Ezra's return to Jerusalem.

Eze 1:1-3 and 3:15 indicate that other captives were placed at Tel Aviv and at the Kebar River, both probably in the locale of Nippur, as were other villages mentioned in Ezr 2:59; 8:15,17; Ne 7:61.

Jehoiachin and his family were kept in Babylon, where clay ration receipts bearing his name and the names of his sons have been found.

built siege works[l] all around it. 2 The city
was kept under siege until the eleventh
year of King Zedekiah.
3 By the ninth day of the fourth[a] month
the famine[m] in the city had become so severe that there was no food for the people to eat. 4 Then the city wall was broken through,[n] and the whole army fled at
night through the gate between the two
walls near the king's garden, though the
Babylonians[b] were surrounding[o] the city.
They fled toward the Arabah,[c] 5 but the
Babylonian[d] army pursued the king and
overtook him in the plains of Jericho. All
his soldiers were separated from him and
scattered,[p] 6 and he was captured.[q]
He was taken to the king of Babylon at
Riblah,[r] where sentence was pronounced
on him. 7 They killed the sons of Zedekiah before his eyes. Then they put out his
eyes, bound him with bronze shackles and
took him to Babylon.[s]
8 On the seventh day of the fifth month,
in the nineteenth year of Nebuchadnezzar king of Babylon, Nebuzaradan commander of the imperial guard, an official
of the king of Babylon, came to Jerusalem.
9 He set fire[t] to the temple of the LORD, the
royal palace and all the houses of Jerusalem. Every important building he burned
down.[u] 10 The whole Babylonian army under the commander of the imperial guard
broke down the walls[v] around Jerusalem.
11 Nebuzaradan the commander of the
guard carried into exile[w] the people who
remained in the city, along with the rest of
the populace and those who had deserted to the king of Babylon.[x] 12 But the commander left behind some of the poorest
people[y] of the land to work the vineyards
and fields.
13 The Babylonians broke[z] up the bronze
pillars, the movable stands and the bronze
Sea that were at the temple of the LORD
and they carried the bronze to Babylon.
14 They also took away the pots, shovels,
wick trimmers, dishes[a] and all the bronze
articles[b] used in the temple service. 15 The
commander of the imperial guard took
away the censers and sprinkling bowls—
all that were made of pure gold or silver.[c]
16 The bronze from the two pillars, the
Sea and the movable stands, which Solomon had made for the temple of the
LORD, was more than could be weighed.
17 Each pillar[d] was eighteen cubits[e] high.
The bronze capital on top of one pillar was
three cubits[f] high and was decorated with
a network and pomegranates of bronze all
around. The other pillar, with its network,
was similar.
18 The commander of the guard took as
prisoners Seraiah[e] the chief priest, Zephaniah[f] the priest next in rank and the three
doorkeepers.[g] 19 Of those still in the city,
he took the officer in charge of the fighting men, and five royal advisers. He also
took the secretary who was chief officer
in charge of conscripting the people of the
land and sixty of the conscripts who were
found in the city. 20 Nebuzaradan the commander took them all and brought them
to the king of Babylon at Riblah. 21 There
at Riblah,[h] in the land of Hamath, the king
had them executed.[i]
So Judah went into captivity,[j] away
from her land.[k]
22 Nebuchadnezzar king of Babylon appointed Gedaliah[l] son of Ahikam,[m] the son

[a] 3 Probable reading of the original Hebrew text (see Jer. 52:6); Masoretic Text does not have *fourth.*
[b] 4 Or *Chaldeans*; also in verses 13, 25 and 26
[c] 4 Or *the Jordan Valley*
[d] 5 Or *Chaldean*; also in verses 10 and 24
[e] 17 That is, about 27 feet or about 8.1 meters
[f] 17 That is, about 4 1/2 feet or about 1.4 meters

25:1 [l] Isa 23:13; 29:3; Jer 4:16-17; 32:2; 33:4; Eze 21:22; 24:2 **25:3** [m] S Lev 26:26; Isa 22:2; Jer 14:18; 37:21; La 2:20; 4:9 **25:4** [n] Job 30:14; Ps 144:14; Jer 50:15; 51:44,58; Eze 33:21 [o] Jer 4:17; 6:3 **25:5** [p] S Lev 26:36; Eze 12:14; 17:21 **25:6** [q] Isa 22:3; Jer 38:23 [r] S Nu 34:11 **25:7** [s] S Dt 28:36; Jer 21:7; 32:4-5; 34:3,21; Eze 12:11; 19:9; 40:1 **25:9** [t] Isa 60:7; 63:15,18; 64:11 [u] S Dt 13:16; Ne 1:3; Ps 74:3-8; 79:1; Jer 2:15; 17:27; 21:10; 26:6,18; La 4:11; Am 2:5; Mic 3:12 **25:10** [v] Ne 1:3; Jer 50:15 **25:11** [w] S Lev 26:44; 2Ki 24:14 [x] S Dt 28:36; S 2Ki 24:1 **25:12** [y] S 2Ki 24:14 **25:13** [z] S 1Ki 7:50 **25:14** [a] S Nu 7:14 [b] S 2Ki 24:13; Ezr 1:7 **25:15** [c] S 2Ki 24:13; Jer 15:13; 20:5; 27:16-22 **25:17** [d] 1Ki 7:15-22 **25:18** [e] ver 18-21; 1Ch 6:14; Ezr 7:1; Ne 11:11 [f] Jer 21:1; 29:25; 37:3 [g] S 2Ki 12:9; S 23:4 **25:21** [h] S Nu 34:11 [i] Jer 34:21 [j] S 1Ki 8:46 [k] S Ge 12:7; S Jos 23:13 **25:22** [l] Jer 39:14; 40:5,7; 41:18 [m] S 2Ki 22:12

25:2–3 *eleventh year ... ninth day ... fourth month.* July 18, 586 BC (see NIV text note on v. 3; see also Jer 39:2; 52:5–7). Some scholars follow a different dating system and place the fall of Jerusalem in the summer of 587.
25:3 *famine in the city had become so severe.* See Jer 38:2–9.
25:6 *king of Babylon at Riblah.* See note on 23:33; see also Jer 39:5; 52:9.
25:7 *killed the sons of Zedekiah ... put out his eyes ... took him to Babylon.* See Jer 32:4–5; 34:2–3; 38:18; 39:6–7; 52:10–11. Ezekiel (12:13) had predicted that Zedekiah would be brought to Babylon but that he would not see it. Zedekiah could have spared his own life and prevented the destruction of Jerusalem if he had listened to Jeremiah (see Jer 38:14–28).
25:8–21 See map and accompanying text, p. 619.
25:8 *seventh day ... fifth month ... nineteenth year.* Aug. 14, 586 BC (see Jer 52:12 and note).
25:9 *set fire to the temple.* See 2Ch 36:19; Jer 39:8; 52:13.
25:13 *bronze pillars.* See 1Ki 7:15–22. *movable stands.* See 1Ki 7:27–39. *bronze Sea.* See 1Ki 7:23–26.
25:14 *all the bronze articles used in the temple service.* See 1Ki 7:40,45.
25:17 *bronze capital ... was three cubits high.* See NIV text note. In 1Ki 7:16 and Jer 52:22 the height of the capital is given as seven and a half feet (five cubits). The two-cubit difference may be due to a copyist's error.
25:18 *Seraiah the chief priest.* Seraiah was the grandson of Hilkiah (see note on 22:4; see also 22:8; 1Ch 6:13–14). His son Jehozadak was taken captive to Babylon. Ezra was one of Jehozadak's descendants (see Ezr 7:1).
25:19 *people of the land.* See note on 21:24.
25:20 *brought them to the king of Babylon at Riblah.* See v. 6 and note.
25:21 *Judah went into captivity, away from her land.* See maps and accompanying texts, pp. 614–615, 619. Judah's exile from Canaan fulfilled the prediction of judgment given during the reign of Manasseh (see 23:27). Exile was the direst of the covenant curses (see Lev 26:33; Dt 28:36; see also Jer 25:8–11).
25:22 *Gedaliah.* See note on 22:12. Gedaliah shared Jeremi-

of Shaphan, to be over the people he had
left behind in Judah. 23 When all the army
officers and their men heard that the king
of Babylon had appointed Gedaliah as
governor, they came to Gedaliah at Mizpah—Ishmael son of Nethaniah, Johanan
son of Kareah, Seraiah son of Tanhumeth
the Netophathite, Jaazaniah the son of the
Maakathite, and their men. 24 Gedaliah
took an oath to reassure them and their
men. "Do not be afraid of the Babylonian
officials," he said. "Settle down in the land
and serve the king of Babylon, and it will
go well with you."
25 In the seventh month, however, Ishmael son of Nethaniah, the son of Elishama, who was of royal blood, came with
ten men and assassinated[n] Gedaliah and
also the men of Judah and the Babylonians who were with him at Mizpah.[o] 26 At
this, all the people from the least to the
greatest, together with the army officers,
fled to Egypt[p] for fear of the Babylonians.

Jehoiachin Released

25:27-30pp — Jer 52:31-34

27 In the thirty-seventh year of the exile
of Jehoiachin king of Judah, in the year
Awel-Marduk became king of Babylon, he
released Jehoiachin[q] king of Judah from
prison. He did this on the twenty-seventh day of the twelfth month. 28 He spoke
kindly[r] to him and gave him a seat of hon-
or[s] higher than those of the other kings
who were with him in Babylon. 29 So Jehoiachin put aside his prison clothes and
for the rest of his life ate regularly at the
king's table.[t] 30 Day by day the king gave
Jehoiachin a regular allowance as long as
he lived.[u]

25:25 [n]S 2Ki 12:20 [o]Zec 7:5
25:26 [p]Isa 30:2; Jer 43:7
25:27 [q]S 2Ki 24:12
25:28 [r]S 1Ki 8:50 [s]Ezr 5:5; 7:6, 28; 9:9; Ne 2:1; Da 2:48
25:29 [t]S 2Sa 9:7
25:30 [u]Ge 43:34; Est 2:9; 9:22; Jer 28:4

---

ah's nonresistance approach to the Babylonians (see v. 24) and won their confidence as a trustworthy governor of Judah (see Jer 41:10).

25:23 *Mizpah.* Had been a town of important political significance in the time just before the establishment of the monarchy (see note on 1Sa 7:5). Jeremiah found Gedaliah there (see Jer 40:1–6). *Ishmael son of Nethaniah.* Verse 25 gives a fuller genealogy. Elishama, Ishmael's grandfather, was the royal secretary under Jehoiakim (Jer 36:12). *Jaazaniah.* In 1932 an agate seal was found at Tell en-Nasbeh (Mizpah) bearing the name of Jaazaniah (perhaps the man mentioned here) with the inscription: "Belonging to Jaazaniah the servant of the king."

25:24 Gedaliah urged submission to the Babylonians as the judgment of God. He advocated the restoration of the normal pursuits of a peacetime society (see Jer 27). A similar message had been given by Jeremiah to the captives taken to Babylon in 597 BC (see Jer 29:4–7).

25:25 *seventh month.* October, 586 BC. *assassinated Gedaliah.* A more complete account of the assassination of Gedaliah is given in Jer 40:13—41:15. Ishmael appears to have had personal designs on the throne, to have resented Gedaliah's ready submission to the Babylonians and to have been manipulated by the Ammonites, who also chafed under Babylonian domination (see Jer 40:14; 41:10,15).

25:26 *fled to Egypt.* Pharaoh Hophra was then ruler in Egypt (see note on 24:20).

25:27 *thirty-seventh year ... twenty-seventh day ... twelfth month.* Mar. 22, 561 BC. *in the year Awel-Marduk became king of Babylon.* In 561 (some scholars place Awel-Marduk's succession to the throne in October, 562; see note on 24:1). His name means "man of (the god) Marduk." *released Jehoiachin king of Judah from prison.* Babylonian administrative tablets (see chart, p. xxiii), recording the payment of rations in oil and barley to prisoners held in Babylon, mention Jehoiachin, king of Judah, and five of his sons (cf. 24:15). No reason is given for Jehoiachin's release. Perhaps it was part of a general amnesty proclaimed at the beginning of Awel-Marduk's reign.

25:28 *spoke kindly to him and gave him a seat of honor.* The book of Kings ends on a hopeful note. The judgment of exile will not destroy the people of Israel or the line of David. God's promise concerning David's house remains (see 2Sa 7:14–16).

1 CHRONICLES

INTRODUCTION

Title

The Hebrew title of 1 and 2 Chronicles (*dibre hayyamim*) can be translated "the events (or annals) of the days (or years)." The same phrase occurs in references to sources used by the author or compiler of Kings (translated "annals" in, e.g., 1Ki 14:19,29; 15:7,23,31; 16:5,14,20,27; 22:45). The Septuagint (the pre-Christian Greek translation of the OT) refers to the book as "the things omitted," indicating that its translators regarded it as a supplement to Samuel and Kings. Jerome (AD 347 – 420), translator of the Latin Vulgate, suggested that a more appropriate title would be "chronicle of the whole sacred history." Luther took over this suggestion in his German version, and others have followed him. Chronicles was first divided into two books by the Septuagint translators.

Author, Date and Sources

According to ancient Jewish tradition, Ezra wrote Chronicles, Ezra and Nehemiah (see Introduction to Ezra: Literary Form and Authorship), but this cannot be established with certainty. A growing consensus dates Chronicles in the latter half of the fifth century BC, thus possibly within Ezra's lifetime. And it must be acknowledged that the author, if not Ezra himself, at least shared many basic concerns with that reforming priest — though Chronicles is not so narrowly priestly in its perspective as was long affirmed.

Some believe the text contains evidence here and there of later expansions after the basic work had been composed. While editorial revisions are not unlikely, all specific proposals regarding them remain tentative.

In his recounting of history long past, the Chronicler relied on many written sources. About half his work was taken from Samuel and Kings; he also drew on the Pentateuch, Judges, Ruth, Psalms, Isaiah, Jeremiah, Lamentations and Zechariah (though he used texts of these books that varied somewhat from those that have been preserved in the later standardized Hebrew texts). And there are frequent references to still other

a quick look

Author:
Unknown; possibly Ezra

Audience:
The people of Judah who had returned from exile in Babylonia

Date:
Between 450 and 400 BC

Theme:
1 Chronicles begins with Israel's genealogical records from Adam to King Saul and then focuses more extensively on an idealized portrait of King David's reign.

sources: "the book of the kings of Israel" (9:1; 2Ch 20:34; cf. 2Ch 33:18), "the book of the annals of King David" (27:24), "the book of the kings of Judah and Israel" or "... of Israel and Judah" (2Ch 16:11; 25:26; 27:7; 28:26; 32:32; 35:27; 36:8), "the annotations on the book of the kings" (2Ch 24:27). It is unclear whether these all refer to the same source or to different sources and what their relationship is to Samuel and Kings or to the royal annals referred to in Kings. In addition, the author cites a number of prophetic writings: those of "Samuel the seer" (29:29), "Nathan the prophet" (29:29; 2Ch 9:29), "Gad the seer" (29:29), "Ahijah the Shilonite" (2Ch 9:29), "Iddo the seer" (2Ch 9:29; 12:15; 13:22), "Shemaiah the prophet" (2Ch 12:15), "the prophet Isaiah" (2Ch 26:22), "the seers" (2Ch 33:19). All these he used, often with only minor changes, to tell his own story of the past. He did not invent, but he did select, arrange and integrate his sources to compose a narrative sermon for postexilic Israel as she struggled to reorient herself as the people of God in a new situation.

Purpose and Themes

Just as the author of Kings had organized and interpreted the data of Israel's history to address the needs of the exiled community, so the Chronicler wrote for the restored community. The burning issue was the question of continuity with the past: Is God still interested in us? Are his covenants still in force? Now that we have no Davidic king and are subject to Persia, do God's promises to David still have meaning for us? After the great judgment (the dethroning of the house of David, the destruction of the nation, of Jerusalem and of the temple, and the exile to Babylonia), what is our relationship to Israel of old? Several elements go into the Chronicler's answer:

(1) Continuity with the past is signified by the temple in Jerusalem, rebuilt by the Lord's sovereign influence over a Persian imperial edict (2Ch 36:22–23). For a generation that had no independent political status and no Davidic king, the author takes great pains to show that the temple of the Lord and its service (including its book of prayer and praise, an early edition of the Psalms) are supreme gifts of God given to Israel through the Davidic dynasty. For that reason his account of the reigns of David and Solomon is largely devoted to David's preparation for and Solomon's building of the temple and to David's instructions for the temple service (with the counsel of Gad the seer and Nathan the prophet, 2Ch 29:25, and also of the Levites Asaph, Heman and Jeduthun, 2Ch 35:15). See also the Chronicler's accounts of the reigns of Asa, Jehoshaphat, Joash, Hezekiah and Josiah. The temple of the Lord in the ancient holy city and its service (including the Psalms) were the chief legacy left to the restored community by the house of David.

(2) The value of this legacy is highlighted by the author's emphasis on God's furtherance of his gracious purposes toward Israel through his sovereign acts of election: (a) of the tribe of Levi to serve before the ark of the covenant (15:2; see 23:24–32), (b) of David to be king over Israel (28:4; 2Ch 6:6), (c) of Solomon his son to be king and to build the temple (28:5–6,10; 29:1), (d) of Jerusalem (2Ch 6:6,34,38; 12:13; 33:7) and (e) of the temple (2Ch 7:12,16; 33:7) to be the place where God's Name (see Dt 12:5; Ps 5:11 and notes) would be present among his people. These divine acts give assurance to postexilic Israel that her rebuilt temple in Jerusalem and its continuing service mark her as God's people, whose election has not been annulled.

(3) In addition to the temple, Israel has the law and the prophets as a major focus of her covenant life under the leadership of the house of David. Neither the Davidic kings nor the temple had in themselves assured Israel's security and blessing. All had been conditional on Israel's and the

The author of 1 and 2 Chronicles wrote for the restored community. The burning issue was the question of continuity with the past: Is God still interested in us?

king's faithfulness to the law (28:7; 2Ch 6:16; 7:17; 12:1; 33:8). In the Chronicler's account, a primary feature of the reign of every faithful Davidic king was his attempt to bring about compliance with the law: David (6:49; 15:13,15; 16:40; 22:11 – 13; 29:19), Asa (2Ch 14:4; 15:12 – 14), Jehoshaphat (2Ch 17:3 – 9; 19:8 – 10), Joash (2Ch 24:6,9), Hezekiah (2Ch 29:10,31; 30:15 – 16; 31:3 – 4,21), Josiah (2Ch 34:19 – 21,29 – 33; 35:6,12,26). And to heed God's prophetic word was no less crucial. The faithful kings, such as David, Asa, Jehoshaphat, Hezekiah and Josiah — and even Rehoboam (2Ch 11:4; 12:6) and Amaziah (2Ch 25:7 – 10) — honored it; the unfaithful kings disregarded it to their destruction (Jehoram, 2Ch 21:12 – 19; Joash, 2Ch 24:19 – 25; Amaziah, 2Ch 25:15 – 16,20; Manasseh, 2Ch 33:10 – 11; see 36:15 – 16). Chronicles, in fact, notes the ministries of more prophets than do Samuel and Kings. Jehoshaphat's word to Israel expresses the Chronicler's view succinctly: "Have faith in the LORD your God and you will be upheld; have faith in his prophets and you will be successful" (2Ch 20:20). In the Chronicler's account of Israel's years under the kings, her response to the law and the prophets was more decisive for her destiny than the reigns of kings.

Thus the law and the prophets, like the temple, are more crucial to Israel's continuing relationship with the Lord than the presence or absence of a king, the reigns of the Davidic kings themselves being testimony.

(4) The Chronicler further underscores the importance of obedience to the law and the prophets by emphasizing the theme of immediate retribution. See the express statements of David (28:9), of the Lord (2Ch 7:14) and of the prophets (2Ch 12:5; 15:2,7; 16:7,9; 19:2 – 3; 21:14 – 15; 24:20; 25:15 – 16; 28:9; 34:24 – 28). In writing his accounts of individual reigns, the author never tires of demonstrating how sin always brings judgment in the form of disaster (usually either illness or defeat in war), whereas repentance, obedience and trust yield peace, victory and prosperity.

(5) Clearly the author of Chronicles wished to sustain Israel's hope for the promised Messiah, son of David, in accordance with the Davidic covenant (2Sa 7) and the assurances of the prophets, including those near to him (Haggai, Zechariah and Malachi). He was careful to recall the Lord's pledge to David (1Ch 17) and to follow this with many references back to it (see especially his account of Solomon's reign and also 2Ch 13:5; 21:7; 23:3). But perhaps even more indicative are his idealized depictions of David, Solomon, Asa, Jehoshaphat, Hezekiah and Josiah. While not portrayed as flawless, these Davidic kings are presented as prime examples of the Messianic ideal, i.e., as royal servants of the Lord whose reigns promoted godliness and covenant faithfulness in Israel. They were crowned with God's favor toward his people in the concrete forms of victories, deliverances and prosperity. They sat, moreover, on the "throne of the LORD" (29:23; see 28:5; 2Ch 9:8) and ruled over the Lord's kingdom (17:14; 2Ch 13:8). Thus they served as types, foreshadowing the "David" to come, of whom the prophets had spoken, and their remembrance nurtured hope in the face of much discouragement (see the book of Malachi). See further the next section ("Portrait of David and Solomon").

(6) Yet another major theme of the Chronicler's history is his concern with "all Israel" (see, e.g., 9:1; 11:1 – 4; 12:38 – 40; 16:1 – 3; 18:14; 21:1 – 5; 28:1 – 8; 29:21 – 26; 2Ch 1:1 – 3; 7:8 – 10; 9:30; 10:1 – 3,16; 12:1; 18:16; 28:23; 29:24; 30:1 – 13,23 – 27; 34:6 – 9,33). As a matter of fact, he viewed the restored community as the remnant of all Israel, both north and south (9:2 – 3). This was more than a theological conceit. His narrative makes frequent note of movements of godly people from Israel to Judah for specifically religious reasons. The first were Levites in the time of Rehoboam (2Ch

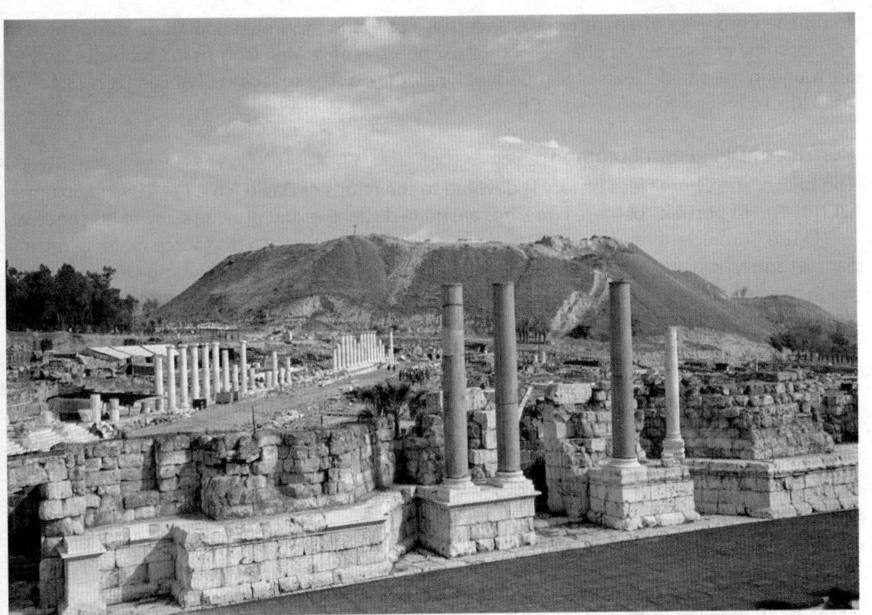

Beth Shan is the location of the temple of Dagon mentioned in 1 Chronicles 10:10. The Philistine and Israelite cities were at the top of this tell (mound in the background).

11:14). In the reign of Asa others followed from Ephraim and Manasseh (2Ch 15:9). Shortly after the Assyrian destruction of the northern kingdom, many from that devastated land resettled in Judah at Hezekiah's invitation (2Ch 30). Presumably not all who came for Hezekiah's great Passover celebration remained, but archaeology has shown a sudden large increase in population in the region around Jerusalem at this time, and the Chronicler specifically mentions "people of Israel ... who lived in the towns of Judah" (2Ch 31:6). He also speaks of "the people of Manasseh, Ephraim and the entire remnant of Israel" who joined with "the people of Judah and Benjamin and the inhabitants of Jerusalem" in restoring the temple in the days of Josiah (2Ch 34:9). These were also present at Josiah's Passover (2Ch 35:17 – 18). So the kingdom of "Judah" had absorbed many from the northern kingdom through the years, and the Chronicler viewed it as the remnant of all Israel from the time of Samaria's fall.

(7) The genealogies also demonstrate continuity with the past. To the question "Is God still interested in us?" the Chronicler answers, "He has always been." God's grace and love for the restored community did not begin with David or the conquest or the exodus — but with creation (1:1). For the genealogies, see pp. 627 – 628.

(8) The Chronicler often introduces speeches not found in Samuel and Kings, using them to convey some of his main emphases. Of the 165 speeches of varying lengths in Chronicles, only 95 are found in the parallel texts of Samuel and Kings. Cf., e.g., the speeches of Abijah (2Ch 13:4–12), Asa (2Ch 14:11) and Jehoshaphat (2Ch 20:5–12).

Portrait of David and Solomon

The bulk of the Chronicler's history is devoted to the reigns of David (chs. 11–29) and Solomon (2Ch 1–9). His portraits of these two kings are quite distinctive and provide a key to his concerns:

(1) The Chronicler has idealized David and Solomon. Anything in his source material (mainly Samuel and Kings) that might tarnish his picture of them is omitted. He makes no reference to the wars between Saul's house and David, the negotiations with Abner, or the murders of Abner and Ish-Bosheth (2Sa 1–4). The Chronicler presents David as being immediately anointed king over all Israel after the death of Saul (ch. 11) and enjoying the total support of the people (11:10—12:40; see note on 3:1–9). Subsequent difficulties for David are also not recounted. No mention is made of David's sin with Bathsheba, the crime and death of Amnon, the fratricide by Absalom and his plot against his father, the flight of David from Jerusalem, the rebellions of Sheba and Shimei, and other incidents that might diminish the glory of David's reign (2Sa 11–20). David is presented without blemish, apart from the incident of the census (the Chronicler had a special purpose for including it; see ch. 21 and notes).

The Chronicler handles Solomon similarly. Solomon is specifically named in a divine prophecy as David's successor (17:4–14; 22:7–10; 28:6). His accession to the throne is announced publicly by David and is greeted with the unanimous support of all Israel (chs. 28–29). No mention is made of the bedridden David, who must overturn the attempted coup by Adonijah at the last moment to secure the throne for Solomon. Nor is there mention that the military commander Joab and the high priest Abiathar supported Adonijah's attempt (1Ki 1). Solomon's execution of those who had wronged David (1Ki 2) is also omitted. The accession of Solomon is without competition or detracting incident. The account of his reign is devoted almost wholly to the building of the temple (2Ch 2–8), and no reference to his failures is included. No mention is made of his idolatry, his foreign wives or the rebellions against his rule (1Ki 11). Even the blame for the schism is removed from Solomon (1Ki 11:26–40; 12:1–4) and placed on the scheming of Jeroboam. Solomon's image in Chronicles is such that he can be paired with David in the most favorable light (2Ch 11:17).

The David and Solomon of the Chronicler, then, must be seen not only as the David and Solomon of history, but also as typifying the Messianic king of the Chronicler's expectation.

(2) Not only is there idealization of David and Solomon, but the author also appears to consciously adopt the account of the succession of Moses and Joshua as a model for the succession of David and Solomon:

(a) Both David and Moses fail to attain their goals—one to build the temple and the other to enter the promised land. In both cases the divine prohibition is related to the appointment of a successor (1Ch 22:5–13; 28:2–8; Dt 1:37–38; 31:2–8).

(b) Both Solomon and Joshua bring the people of God into rest (22:8–9; Jos 11:23; 21:44).

(c) There are a number of verbal parallels in the appointments of Solomon and Joshua (compare 22:11–13,16; 28:7–10,20; 2Ch 1:1 with Dt 31:5–8,23; Jos 1:5,7–9).

(d) There are both private and public announcements of the appointment of the successors: private (22:6; Dt 31:23); public (28:8; Dt 31:7 — both "in the presence/sight of all Israel").
(e) Both enjoy the immediate and wholehearted support of the people (29:23 – 24; Dt 34:9; Jos 1:16 – 18).
(f) It is twice reported that God "exalted" or "made … great" Solomon and Joshua (29:25; 2Ch 1:1; Jos 3:7; 4:14).

The Chronicler also uses other models from Pentateuchal history in his portrayal of David and Solomon. Like Moses, David received the plans for the temple from God (28:11 – 19; Ex 25:9) and called on the people to bring voluntary offerings for its construction (29:1 – 9; Ex 25:1 – 7). Solomon's relationship to Huram-Abi, the craftsman from Tyre (2Ch 2:13 – 14), echoes the role of Bezalel and Oholiab in the building of the tabernacle (Ex 35:30 — 36:7). See note on 2Ch 1:5.

Genealogies

Analysis of genealogies, both inside and outside the Bible, has disclosed that they serve a variety of functions (with different principles governing the lists), that they vary in form (some being segmented, others linear) and depth (number of generations listed), and that they are often fluid (subject to change).

There are three general areas in which genealogies function: (1) the familial or domestic, (2) the legal-political, and (3) the religious. (1) In the domestic area an individual's social status, privileges and obligations may be reflected in his placement in the lineage (see 7:14 – 19); the rights of the firstborn son and the secondary status of the children of concubines are examples from the Bible. (2) In the political sphere genealogies substantiate claims to hereditary office or settle competing claims when the office is contested. Land organization and territorial groupings of social units may also be determined by genealogical reckoning — e.g., the division of the land among the 12 tribes. In Israel military levies also proceeded along genealogical lines; several of the genealogies in 1 Chronicles reflect military conscription (5:1 – 26; 7:1 – 12,30 – 40; 8:1 – 40). (3) Genealogies function in the religious sphere primarily by establishing membership among the priests and Levites (6:1 – 30; 9:10 – 34; Ne 7:61 – 65).

Music was a significant part of life in the ancient Near East. The Bible mentions several instruments, five of which are listed in 1 Chronicles 15:28 (several more are mentioned in Ps 150:3 – 5; Da 3:5).

Karyn Reeder, courtesy of the British Museum

As to form, some genealogical lists trace several lines of descent (segmented genealogies), while others are devoted to a single line (linear genealogies).

Comparison of genealogical lists of the same tribal or family line often brings to light surprising differences. This fluidity of the lists may reflect variation in function. But sometimes changes in the status or relations of social structures are reflected in genealogies by changes in the relationships of names in the genealogy (see notes on 1:35 – 42; 6:22,27) or by the addition of names or segments to a lineage (see notes on 5:11 – 22; 6:27; 7:6 – 12). The most common type of fluidity in Biblical genealogies is telescoping, the omission of names from the list. Unimportant names are left out in order to relate an individual to a prominent ancestor, or possibly to achieve the desired number of names in the genealogy. Some Biblical genealogies, for example, omit names to achieve multiples of 7: For the period from David to the exile Matthew gives 14 generations (2 times 7), while Luke gives 21 (3 times 7), and the same authors give similar multiples of 7 for the period from the exile to Jesus (Mt 1:1 – 17; Lk 3:23 – 38).

The genealogies of Chronicles show variation in all these properties; the arrangements often reflect the purpose for which the genealogies were composed prior to their being adopted by the Chronicler as part of his record.

Outline

- I. Genealogies: Creation to Restoration (1Ch 1 – 9)
  - A. The Patriarchs (ch. 1)
  - B. The 12 Sons of Jacob/Israel (2:1 – 2)
  - C. The Family of Judah (2:3 — 4:23)
  - D. The Sons of Simeon (4:24 – 43)
  - E. Reuben, Gad and the Half-Tribe of Manasseh (ch. 5)
  - F. Levi and Families (ch. 6)
  - G. Issachar, Benjamin, Naphtali, Manasseh, Ephraim and Asher (chs. 7 – 9)
- II. The Reign of David (1Ch 10 – 29)
  - A. Death of Saul (ch. 10)
  - B. Capture of Jerusalem; David's Power Base (chs. 11 – 12)
  - C. Return of the Ark; Establishment of David's Kingdom (chs. 13 – 16)
  - D. Dynastic Promise (ch. 17)
  - E. David's Conquests (chs. 18 – 20)
  - F. The Census (ch. 21)
  - G. Preparations for the Temple (ch. 22)
  - H. Organization of the Temple Service (chs. 23 – 26)
  - I. Administrative Structures of the Kingdom (ch. 27)
  - J. David's Final Preparations for Succession and the Temple (28:1 — 29:20)
  - K. Accession of Solomon; Death of David (29:21 – 30)
- III. The Reign of Solomon (2Ch 1 – 9)
  - A. The Gift of Wisdom (ch. 1)
  - B. Building the Temple (2:1 — 5:1)
  - C. Dedication of the Temple (5:2 — 7:22)
  - D. Solomon's Other Activities (ch. 8)
  - E. Solomon's Wisdom, Splendor and Death (ch. 9)

- IV. The Schism, and the History of the Kings of Judah (2Ch 10–36)
  - A. Rehoboam (chs. 10–12)
  - B. Abijah (13:1—14:1)
  - C. Asa (14:2—16:14)
  - D. Jehoshaphat (17:1—21:3)
  - E. Jehoram (21:4–20)
  - F. Ahaziah (22:1–9)
  - G. Joash (22:10—24:27)
  - H. Amaziah (ch. 25)
  - I. Uzziah (ch. 26)
  - J. Jotham (ch. 27)
  - K. Ahaz (ch. 28)
  - L. Hezekiah (chs. 29–32)
  - M. Manasseh (33:1–20)
  - N. Amon (33:21–25)
  - O. Josiah (34:1—36:1)
  - P. Josiah's Successors (36:2–14)
  - Q. Exile and Restoration (36:15–23)

Historical Records From Adam to Abraham

To Noah's Sons

1 Adam,[a] Seth, Enosh, 2 Kenan,[b] Mahalalel,[c] Jared,[d] 3 Enoch,[e] Methuselah,[f]
Lamech,[g] Noah.[h]

4 The sons of Noah:[a][i]
Shem, Ham and Japheth.[j]

The Japhethites

1:5-7pp — Ge 10:2-5

5 The sons[b] of Japheth:
Gomer, Magog, Madai, Javan, Tubal, Meshek and Tiras.
6 The sons of Gomer:
Ashkenaz, Riphath[c] and Togarmah.
7 The sons of Javan:
Elishah, Tarshish, the Kittites and the Rodanites.

The Hamites

1:8-16pp — Ge 10:6-20

8 The sons of Ham:
Cush, Egypt, Put and Canaan.
9 The sons of Cush:
Seba, Havilah, Sabta, Raamah and Sabteka.
The sons of Raamah:
Sheba and Dedan.
10 Cush was the father[d] of
Nimrod, who became a mighty warrior on earth.
11 Egypt was the father of
the Ludites, Anamites, Lehabites,
Naphtuhites, 12 Pathrusites, Kaslu-
hites (from whom the Philistines came) and Caphtorites.
13 Canaan was the father of
Sidon his firstborn,[e] and of the Hittites, 14 Jebusites, Amorites, Girgashites, 15 Hivites, Arkites, Sinites,
16 Arvadites, Zemarites and Hamathites.

The Semites

1:17-23pp — Ge 10:21-31; 11:10-27

17 The sons of Shem:
Elam, Ashur, Arphaxad, Lud and Aram.
The sons of Aram:[f]
Uz, Hul, Gether and Meshek.
18 Arphaxad was the father of Shelah,
and Shelah the father of Eber.
19 Two sons were born to Eber:
One was named Peleg,[g] because in his time the earth was divided; his brother was named Joktan.
20 Joktan was the father of
Almodad, Sheleph, Hazarmaveth,
Jerah, 21 Hadoram, Uzal, Diklah,
22 Obal,[h] Abimael, Sheba, 23 Ophir,

1:1 [a]Ge 5:1-32; Lk 3:36-38 **1:2** [b]S Ge 5:9 [c]S Ge 5:12 [d]S Ge 5:15 **1:3** [e]S Ge 5:18; Jude 1:14 [f]S Ge 5:21 [g]S Ge 5:25 [h]S Ge 5:29 **1:4** [i]Ge 6:10; 10:1 [j]S Ge 5:32

[a] *4* Septuagint; Hebrew does not have this line. [b] *5* *Sons* may mean *descendants* or *successors* or *nations;* also in verses 6-9, 17 and 23. [c] *6* Many Hebrew manuscripts and Vulgate (see also Septuagint and Gen. 10:3); most Hebrew manuscripts *Diphath* [d] *10* *Father* may mean *ancestor* or *predecessor* or *founder;* also in verses 11, 13, 18 and 20. [e] *13* Or *of the Sidonians, the foremost* [f] *17* One Hebrew manuscript and some Septuagint manuscripts (see also Gen. 10:23); most Hebrew manuscripts do not have this line. [g] *19* *Peleg* means *division.* [h] *22* Some Hebrew manuscripts and Syriac (see also Gen. 10:28); most Hebrew manuscripts *Ebal*

1:1 — 9:44 The genealogies succinctly show the restored community's continuity with the past. The great deeds of God in Israel's behalf prior to the rise of David are passed over in silence, but the genealogies serve as a skeleton of history to show that the Israel of the restoration stands at the center of the divine purpose from the beginning (from Adam, v. 1). And the genealogies also serve the very practical purpose of legitimizing the present. They provide the framework by which the ethnic and religious purity of the people can be maintained. They also establish the continuing line of royal succession and the legitimacy of the priests for the postexilic temple service. See Introduction: Genealogies.

1:1 — 2:1 The Chronicler here covers the period from Adam to Jacob, and the materials are drawn almost entirely from Genesis. The subsidiary lines of descent are presented first: Japheth and Ham (vv. 5 – 16) are given before Shem (vv. 17 – 27), the sons of Shem other than those in Abraham's ancestry (vv. 17 – 23) before that line (vv. 24 – 27), the sons of Abraham's concubines (vv. 28 – 33) before Isaac's line (v. 34), the descendants of Esau and the Edomite ruling houses (vv. 35 – 54) before the sons of Israel/Jacob (2:1). In each case the elect lineage is given last. Several features of this genealogy are striking when compared with non-Biblical materials. The genealogy begins without an introduction. Two sections of the genealogy have no kinship terms and are only lists of names: the first 13 names (vv. 1 – 4; see note on v. 4) and vv. 24 – 27. In vv. 5 – 16 (and following v. 27) kinship terms are used. Both segmented (those tracing several lines of descent) and linear (those tracing a single line) genealogies are included. This identical structure is found in a copy of the Assyrian King List: There is no introduction, and the scribe has drawn lines across the tablet, dividing it into four sections, two of which are lists of names without kinship terms, alternating with two lists in which relations are specified; both segmented and linear genealogies are used. This suggests that the Chronicler was following a known literary pattern for his composition.

1:1 – 4 From creation to the flood. This list is taken from Ge 5:1 – 32 (see notes there). The omission of Cain and Abel demonstrates the Chronicler's interest in the chosen line (see Ge 4:17 – 25).

1:4 *The sons of Noah.* Not found in the Hebrew text (see NIV text note); this omission parallels the Assyrian King List (see note on 1:1 — 2:1). The Chronicler's readers would have known that these were the sons of Noah and would not have needed the kinship notice; the Septuagint (the pre-Christian Greek translation of the OT) and most modern translations insert the phrase to clarify the relationship.

1:5 – 23 This genealogy is drawn from the table of nations in Ge 10:2 – 29 (see notes there). The arrangement is primarily geographical and cultural rather than biological. Omitting the Philistines (v. 12) as a parenthesis, a total of 70 nations is achieved: Japheth, 14; Ham, 30; Shem, 26 (see note on Ge 10:2) — an example of a genealogy telescoped to attain multiples of 7 (see Introduction: Genealogies).

Havilah and Jobab. All these were
sons of Joktan.
[24]Shem,[k] Arphaxad,[a] Shelah,
[25]Eber, Peleg, Reu,
[26]Serug, Nahor, Terah
[27]and Abram (that is, Abraham).

The Family of Abraham

[28]The sons of Abraham:
Isaac and Ishmael.

Descendants of Hagar

1:29-31pp — Ge 25:12-16

[29]These were their descendants:
Nebaioth the firstborn of Ishmael,
Kedar, Adbeel, Mibsam, [30]Mishma,
Dumah, Massa, Hadad, Tema, [31]Je-
tur, Naphish and Kedemah. These
were the sons of Ishmael.

Descendants of Keturah

1:32-33pp — Ge 25:1-4

[32]The sons born to Keturah, Abraham's
concubine:[l]
Zimran, Jokshan, Medan, Midian,
Ishbak and Shuah.
The sons of Jokshan:
Sheba and Dedan.[m]
[33]The sons of Midian:
Ephah, Epher, Hanok, Abida and
Eldaah.
All these were descendants of Ketu-
rah.

Descendants of Sarah

1:35-37pp — Ge 36:10-14

[34]Abraham[n] was the father of Isaac.[o]
The sons of Isaac:
Esau and Israel.[p]

Esau's Sons

[35]The sons of Esau:[q]
Eliphaz, Reuel,[r] Jeush, Jalam and
Korah.
[36]The sons of Eliphaz:
Teman, Omar, Zepho,[b] Gatam and
Kenaz;
by Timna: Amalek.[c][s]
[37]The sons of Reuel:[t]
Nahath, Zerah, Shammah and Miz-
zah.

The People of Seir in Edom

1:38-42pp — Ge 36:20-28

[38]The sons of Seir:
Lotan, Shobal, Zibeon, Anah, Di-
shon, Ezer and Dishan.
[39]The sons of Lotan:
Hori and Homam. Timna was Lo-
tan's sister.
[40]The sons of Shobal:
Alvan,[d] Manahath, Ebal, Shepho
and Onam.
The sons of Zibeon:
Aiah and Anah.[u]
[41]The son of Anah:
Dishon.
The sons of Dishon:
Hemdan,[e] Eshban, Ithran and Ke-
ran.
[42]The sons of Ezer:
Bilhan, Zaavan and Akan.[f]
The sons of Dishan[g]:
Uz and Aran.

The Rulers of Edom

1:43-54pp — Ge 36:31-43

[43]These were the kings who reigned
in Edom before any Israelite king
reigned:
Bela son of Beor, whose city was
named Dinhabah.
[44]When Bela died, Jobab son of Zerah from Bozrah succeeded him as
king.
[45]When Jobab died, Husham from the
land of the Temanites[v] succeeded
him as king.

1:24 [k]S Ge 10:21-25; Lk 3:34-36 **1:32** [l]S Ge 22:24 [m]S Ge 10:7 **1:34** [n]Lk 3:34 [o]Mt 1:2; Ac 7:8 [p]S Ge 17:5 **1:35** [q]Ge 36:19 [r]S Ge 36:4 **1:36** [s]S Ex 17:14 **1:37** [t]Ge 36:17 **1:40** [u]S Ge 36:2 **1:45** [v]S Ge 36:11

[a] *24* Hebrew; some Septuagint manuscripts *Arphaxad, Cainan* (see also note at Gen. 11:10) [b] *36* Many Hebrew manuscripts, some Septuagint manuscripts and Syriac (see also Gen. 36:11); most Hebrew manuscripts *Zephi* [c] *36* Some Septuagint manuscripts (see also Gen. 36:12); Hebrew *Gatam, Kenaz, Timna and Amalek* [d] *40* Many Hebrew manuscripts and some Septuagint manuscripts (see also Gen. 36:23); most Hebrew manuscripts *Alian* [e] *41* Many Hebrew manuscripts and some Septuagint manuscripts (see also Gen. 36:26); most Hebrew manuscripts *Hamran* [f] *42* Many Hebrew and Septuagint manuscripts (see also Gen. 36:27); most Hebrew manuscripts *Zaavan, Jaakan* [g] *42* See Gen. 36:28; Hebrew *Dishon,* a variant of *Dishan*

1:24–27 See notes on 1:1—2:1; Ge 11:10–26.
1:28–34 See notes on Ge 25:1–18.
1:35–42 See Ge 36:10–28 and notes.
1:36 *sons of Eliphaz.* These correspond to Ge 36:11–12, but with one difficulty: The Hebrew text of Chronicles (see second NIV text note on this verse) lists Timna as a son of Eliphaz, while Ge 36:12 designates Timna as the concubine of Eliphaz and mother of Amalek. The NIV follows the Septuagint (the pre-Christian Greek translation of the OT), which regarded Timna as the mother of Amalek, not as the son of Eliphaz. According to this solution, the Hebrew text is here in error, or perhaps the Chronicler has once again omitted kinship terminology (see notes on v. 4 and 1:1—2:1). Alternatively, some regard this as an example of genealogical fluidity (see Introduction: Genealogies): Since the name Timna also became the name of a chiefdom in Edom (v. 51; Ge 36:40), during the course of time Timna was moved in the Edomite genealogies to the position of a son of Eliphaz and brother of Amalek.
1:43–54 See Ge 36:31–43. The Chronicler continues with extensive coverage of Edom. This is striking in contrast to his omission of the line of Cain and the brief treatment of the line of Ishmael. It probably reflects the fact that the Edomites were important in the Chronicler's own day (see 18:11–13; 2Ch 8:17; 21:8; 25:20; 28:17).

46 When Husham died, Hadad son of
Bedad, who defeated Midian in the
country of Moab, succeeded him as
king. His city was named Avith.
47 When Hadad died, Samlah from Mas-
rekah succeeded him as king.
48 When Samlah died, Shaul from Rehoboth on the river[a] succeeded him
as king.
49 When Shaul died, Baal-Hanan son of
Akbor succeeded him as king.
50 When Baal-Hanan died, Hadad succeeded him as king. His city was
named Pau,[b] and his wife's name
was Mehetabel daughter of Matred,
the daughter of Me-Zahab. 51 Hadad
also died.

The chiefs of Edom were:
Timna, Alvah, Jetheth, 52 Oholibamah, Elah, Pinon, 53 Kenaz, Teman,
Mibzar, 54 Magdiel and Iram. These
were the chiefs of Edom.

Israel's Sons

2:1-2pp — Ge 35:23-26

2 These were the sons of Israel:
Reuben, Simeon, Levi, Judah, Issachar, Zebulun, 2 Dan, Joseph, Benjamin, Naphtali, Gad and Asher.

Judah

2:5-15pp — Ru 4:18-22; Mt 1:3-6

To Hezron's Sons

3 The sons of Judah:[w]
Er, Onan and Shelah.[x] These three
were born to him by a Canaanite
woman, the daughter of Shua.[y] Er,
Judah's firstborn, was wicked in
the LORD's sight; so the LORD put
him to death.[z] 4 Judah's daughter-
in-law[a] Tamar[b] bore Perez[c] and Zerah to Judah. He had five sons in
all.

5 The sons of Perez:[d]
Hezron[e] and Hamul.
6 The sons of Zerah:
Zimri, Ethan, Heman, Kalkol and
Darda[c] — five in all.
7 The son of Karmi:
Achar,[d][f] who brought trouble on Israel by violating the ban on taking
devoted things.[e][g]
8 The son of Ethan:
Azariah.
9 The sons born to Hezron[h] were:
Jerahmeel, Ram and Caleb.[f]

From Ram Son of Hezron

10 Ram[i] was the father of
Amminadab[j], and Amminadab the

2:3 [w] S Ge 29:35; 38:2-10
[x] S Ge 38:5
[y] S Ge 38:2
[z] S Nu 26:19
2:4 [a] S Ge 11:31
[b] Ge 38:11-30
[c] S Ge 38:29
2:5 [d] S Ge 46:12
[e] Nu 26:21
2:7 [f] S Jos 7:1
[g] S Jos 6:18
2:9 [h] S Nu 26:21
2:10 [i] Lk 3:32-33 [j] S Ex 6:23

[a] *48* Possibly the Euphrates [b] *50* Many Hebrew manuscripts, some Septuagint manuscripts, Vulgate and Syriac (see also Gen. 36:39); most Hebrew manuscripts *Pai* [c] *6* Many Hebrew manuscripts, some Septuagint manuscripts and Syriac (see also 1 Kings 4:31); most Hebrew manuscripts *Dara* [d] *7* *Achar* means *trouble*; *Achar* is called *Achan* in Joshua. [e] *7* The Hebrew term refers to the irrevocable giving over of things or persons to the LORD, often by totally destroying them. [f] *9* Hebrew *Kelubai*, a variant of *Caleb*

2:1-2 Although there are numerous lists of the 12 tribes in the OT, only four are given in genealogical form: (1) Ge 29:31 — 30:24; 35:16-20; (2) Ge 35:22-26; (3) Ge 46:8-27; (4) here. Other lists of the tribes are found in 12:24-37; 27:16-22; Ex 1:2-5; Dt 27:12-13; 33; Eze 48:31-34. In other lists the tribe of Levi is omitted, and the number 12 is achieved by dividing Joseph into the tribes of Ephraim and Manasseh (Nu 1:5-15; 1:20-43; 2:3-31; 7:12-83; 10:14-28; 13:4-15; 26:5-51). In this passage the Chronicler appears to follow Ge 35:22-26 except for the position of the tribe of Dan, which is found in seventh instead of ninth place. The list here does not set the order in which the Chronicler will take up the tribes; rather, he moves immediately to his major concern with the house of David and the tribe of Judah (2:3 — 4:23), even though Judah is fourth in the genealogy. In the lists of these chapters, the Chronicler maintains the number 12, but with the following names: Judah, Simeon, Reuben, Gad, half of Manasseh, Levi, Issachar, Benjamin, Naphtali, Ephraim, Manasseh and Asher. Zebulun and Dan are omitted.
2:3-9 The lineage of Judah is traced to Hezron's sons (v. 9), whose descendants are given in 2:10 — 3:24. Of Judah's five sons, the first two (Er and Onan) died as the result of sin recorded in Ge 38. The lineage of the third son, Shelah, is taken up in 4:21; this section focuses on the remaining two (see Ge 46:12; Nu 26:19-22).
2:6 *Ethan, Heman, Kalkol and Darda.* Not immediate descendants of Zerah; rather, they are from the later period of the reign of Solomon (1Ki 4:31). A Heman and an Ethan were David's musicians (see 15:19; Ps 88-89 titles), but whether these are the same individuals is uncertain. If they are the same, the fact that in 6:33-42 and 15:19 Heman and Ethan are assigned to the tribe of Levi may be another example of genealogical fluidity, where these men's musical skills brought them into the Levitical lineage. Or the reverse may have occurred: As Levites associated with Judah, they were brought into that lineage.
2:7 *Achar.* The change from Achan to Achar (meaning "trouble"; see NIV text note) is probably a play on words reflecting the trouble he brought to Israel (see Jos 7; see also note on Hos 2:15).
2:10 — 3:24 That the Chronicler's primary concern in the genealogy of Judah is with the line of David is seen in his arrangement of this section's material as an inversion:

Descendants of Ram (David's ancestry), 2:10-17
  Descendants of Caleb, 2:18-24
    Descendants of Jerahmeel, 2:25-33
    Supplementary material on Jerahmeel, 2:34-41
  Supplementary material on Caleb, 2:42-55
Supplementary material on Ram (David's descendants), ch. 3

The Chronicler has structured this central portion of the Judah genealogy to highlight the Davidic ancestry and descent, which frame this section and emphasize the position of David — in line with the Chronicler's interests in the historical portions that follow (see note on 4:1-23).
2:10-17 Verses 10-12 are a linear genealogy from Ram to Jesse; then Jesse's lineage is segmented, reminiscent of 1Sa 16:1-13. The source for most of the material is Ru 4:19-22. In 1Sa 16:10-13 David was the eighth of Jesse's sons to ap-

father of Nahshon,[k] the leader of
the people of Judah. 11 Nahshon
was the father of Salmon,[a] Salmon
the father of Boaz, 12 Boaz[l] the father of Obed and Obed the father
of Jesse.[m]
13 Jesse[n] was the father of
Eliab[o] his firstborn; the second son
was Abinadab, the third Shimea,
14 the fourth Nethanel, the fifth
Raddai, 15 the sixth Ozem and the
seventh David. 16 Their sisters were
Zeruiah[p] and Abigail. Zeruiah's[q]
three sons were Abishai, Joab[r] and
Asahel. 17 Abigail was the mother of
Amasa,[s] whose father was Jether
the Ishmaelite.

Caleb Son of Hezron

18 Caleb son of Hezron had children by
his wife Azubah (and by Jerioth).
These were her sons: Jesher, Shobab and Ardon. 19 When Azubah
died, Caleb[t] married Ephrath, who
bore him Hur. 20 Hur was the father
of Uri, and Uri the father of Bezalel.[u]
21 Later, Hezron, when he was sixty
years old, married the daughter
of Makir the father of Gilead.[v] He
made love to her, and she bore him
Segub. 22 Segub was the father of
Jair, who controlled twenty-three
towns in Gilead. 23 (But Geshur and
Aram captured Havvoth Jair,[bw] as
well as Kenath[x] with its surrounding settlements—sixty towns.) All
these were descendants of Makir
the father of Gilead.

24 After Hezron died in Caleb Ephrathah, Abijah the wife of Hezron
bore him Ashhur[y] the father[c] of Tekoa.

Jerahmeel Son of Hezron

25 The sons of Jerahmeel the firstborn of
Hezron:
Ram his firstborn, Bunah, Oren,
Ozem and[d] Ahijah. 26 Jerahmeel had another wife, whose name
was Atarah; she was the mother of
Onam.
27 The sons of Ram the firstborn of Jerahmeel:
Maaz, Jamin and Eker.
28 The sons of Onam:
Shammai and Jada.
The sons of Shammai:
Nadab and Abishur.
29 Abishur's wife was named Abihail,
who bore him Ahban and Molid.
30 The sons of Nadab:
Seled and Appaim. Seled died without children.
31 The son of Appaim:
Ishi, who was the father of Sheshan.
Sheshan was the father of Ahlai.
32 The sons of Jada, Shammai's brother:
Jether and Jonathan. Jether died
without children.
33 The sons of Jonathan:
Peleth and Zaza.
These were the descendants of Jerahmeel.
34 Sheshan had no sons—only daughters.
He had an Egyptian servant named
Jarha. 35 Sheshan gave his daughter in marriage to his servant Jarha,
and she bore him Attai.
36 Attai was the father of Nathan,
Nathan the father of Zabad,[z]
37 Zabad the father of Ephlal,
Ephlal the father of Obed,
38 Obed the father of Jehu,
Jehu the father of Azariah,
39 Azariah the father of Helez,
Helez the father of Eleasah,
40 Eleasah the father of Sismai,
Sismai the father of Shallum,
41 Shallum the father of Jekamiah,
and Jekamiah the father of Elishama.

2:10 [k] S Nu 1:7
2:12 [l] S Ru 2:1 [m] S Ru 4:17
2:13 [n] S Ru 4:17 [o] S 1Sa 16:6
2:16 [p] 1Sa 26:6 [q] 2Sa 2:18 [r] S 2Sa 2:13
2:17 [s] 2Sa 17:25
2:19 [t] ver 42,50
2:20 [u] S Ex 31:2
2:21 [v] S Nu 27:1
2:23 [w] S Nu 32:41; Dt 3:14 [x] Nu 32:42
2:24 [y] 1Ch 4:5
2:36 [z] 1Ch 11:41

[a] *11* Septuagint (see also Ruth 4:21); Hebrew *Salma* [b] *23* Or *captured the settlements of Jair* [c] *24* Father may mean *civic leader* or *military leader*; also in verses 42, 45, 49-52 and possibly elsewhere. [d] *25* Or *Oren and Ozem, by*

pear before Samuel; in this passage only seven are named, enabling David to occupy the favored place of the seventh son (v. 15; see Introduction: Genealogies). David was the half-uncle of his famous warriors Abishai, Joab, Asahel and Amasa (11:6,20,26; 2Sa 2:13,18; 17:25; 19:13).

2:18–24 For the Chronicler the important name in this genealogy of the Calebites is Bezalel (v. 20), the wise master craftsman who supervised the building of the tabernacle (Ex 31:1–5). He is mentioned in the Bible only in Exodus and Chronicles. The Chronicler may be using Bezalel and Oholiab (Ex 31:6) as a model for his portrait of Solomon and Huram-Abi in the building of the temple (see note on 2Ch 1:5). By inserting a reference to the builder of the tabernacle next to the genealogy of David in vv. 10–17, the Chronicler characteristically juxtaposes the themes of king and temple—so important to his historical narrative.

2:25–33 This section is identified as a separate entity from the supplementary material by its opening and closing formulas: "The sons of Jerahmeel" (v. 25) and "These were the descendants of Jerahmeel" (v. 33). Verses 25–41 are the only genealogical materials on the Jerahmeelites in the Bible. 1Sa 27:10 and 30:27–29 place their settlements in the Negev.

2:34–41 Supplementary material on the line of Sheshan (v. 31); it is a linear genealogy to a depth of 13 generations. The generation of Elishama (v. 41) would be the 23rd since Judah, if there has been no telescoping in this lineage. If no names are omitted, Elishama would likely be contemporary with David, though we know nothing of him.

The Clans of Caleb

42 The sons of Caleb[a] the brother of Jerahmeel:
Mesha his firstborn, who was the
father of Ziph, and his son Mareshah,[a] who was the father of Hebron.
43 The sons of Hebron:
Korah, Tappuah, Rekem and Shema.
44 Shema was the father of Raham,
and Raham the father of Jorkeam.
Rekem was the father of Shammai.
45 The son of Shammai was Maon[b],
and Maon was the father of Beth
Zur.[c]
46 Caleb's concubine Ephah was the
mother of Haran, Moza and Gazez.
Haran was the father of Gazez.
47 The sons of Jahdai:
Regem, Jotham, Geshan, Pelet,
Ephah and Shaaph.
48 Caleb's concubine Maakah was the
mother of Sheber and Tirhanah.
49 She also gave birth to Shaaph the
father of Madmannah[d] and to Sheva the father of Makbenah and Gib-
ea. Caleb's daughter was Aksah.[e]
50 These were the descendants of
Caleb.

The sons of Hur[f] the firstborn of Ephrathah:
Shobal the father of Kiriath Jearim,[g] 51 Salma the father of Bethlehem, and Hareph the father of Beth
Gader.
52 The descendants of Shobal the father
of Kiriath Jearim were:
Haroeh, half the Manahathites,
53 and the clans of Kiriath Jearim:
the Ithrites,[h] Puthites, Shumath-
ites and Mishraites. From these descended the Zorathites and Eshtao-
lites.
54 The descendants of Salma:
Bethlehem, the Netophathites,[i] At-
roth Beth Joab, half the Manahathites, the Zorites, 55 and the clans of
scribes[b] who lived at Jabez: the Tirathites, Shimeathites and Sucathites. These are the Kenites[j] who
came from Hammath,[k] the father
of the Rekabites.[c][l]

2:42 [a] S ver 19
2:45 [b] S Jos 15:55 [c] S Jos 15:58
2:49 [d] Jos 15:31 [e] Jos 15:16
2:50 [f] 1Ch 4:4 [g] S ver 19
2:53 [h] 2Sa 23:38
2:54 [i] Ezr 2:22; Ne 7:26; 12:28
2:55 [j] S Ge 15:19; S Jdg 4:11 [k] Jos 19:35 [l] 2Ki 10:15,23; Jer 35:2-19
3:1 [m] 1Ch 14:3; 28:5 [n] S 1Sa 25:43 [o] S Jos 15:56 [p] S 1Sa 25:42
3:2 [q] 1Ki 2:22
3:4 [r] S 2Sa 5:4; 1Ch 29:27 [s] S 2Sa 5:5
3:5 [t] 2Sa 11:3

The Sons of David

3:1-4pp — 2Sa 3:2-5
3:5-8pp — 2Sa 5:14-16; 1Ch 14:4-7

3 These were the sons of David[m] born to
him in Hebron:
The firstborn was Amnon the son
of Ahinoam[n] of Jezreel;[o]
the second, Daniel the son of Abigail[p] of Carmel;
2 the third, Absalom the son of Maakah daughter of Talmai king of Geshur;
the fourth, Adonijah[q] the son of
Haggith;
3 the fifth, Shephatiah the son of Abital;
and the sixth, Ithream, by his wife
Eglah.
4 These six were born to David in
Hebron,[r] where he reigned seven
years and six months.[s]
David reigned in Jerusalem thirty-three
years, 5 and these were the children born
to him there:
Shammua,[d] Shobab, Nathan and
Solomon. These four were by Bathsheba[e][t] daughter of Ammiel. 6 There
were also Ibhar, Elishua,[f] Eliphelet,
7 Nogah, Nepheg, Japhia, 8 Elishama, Eliada and Eliphelet — nine in
all. 9 All these were the sons of Da-

[a] *42* The meaning of the Hebrew for this phrase is uncertain. [b] *55* Or *of the Sopherites* [c] *55* Or *father of Beth Rekab* [d] *5* Hebrew *Shimea,* a variant of *Shammua* [e] *5* One Hebrew manuscript and Vulgate (see also Septuagint and 2 Samuel 11:3); most Hebrew manuscripts *Bathshua* [f] *6* Two Hebrew manuscripts (see also 2 Samuel 5:15 and 1 Chron. 14:5); most Hebrew manuscripts *Elishama*

2:42 – 55 The same opening and closing formulas noted in vv. 25,33 occur in vv. 42,50a: "The sons of Caleb . . . These were the descendants of Caleb." The list in this section is a mixture of personal names and place-names; the phrase "father of" must often be understood as "founder of" or "leader of" a city (see NIV text notes on 1:10; 4:4).

2:50b – 55 Resumes the genealogy of Hur (v. 20). The same formulas for identifying the genealogical sections in vv. 25,33 and in vv. 42,50a are used in v. 50b and 4:4: "The sons of Hur . . . These were the descendants of Hur." The presence of these formulas suggests that this section and 4:1 – 4 were once a unit; the Chronicler has inserted his record of the Davidic descent (ch. 3) into the middle of this other genealogy, apparently to balance the sections of his material (see notes on 2:10 — 3:24; 4:1 – 23). Otherwise the disruption of the genealogy of Hur may have already occurred in the Chronicler's sources.

2:55 *Tirathites, Shimeathites and Sucathites.* May refer to three families, as translated here, or possibly to three different classes of scribes, perhaps those who (1) read, (2) copied and (3) checked the work. *Kenites.* Originally a foreign people, many of the Kenites were incorporated into Judah (see Nu 10:29 – 32; Jdg 1:16; 4:11).

3:1 – 24 See note on 2:10 — 3:24.

3:1 – 9 This list of David's children is largely drawn from 2Sa 3:2 – 5; 5:13 – 16; 13:1 (see notes there). The sons born in Jerusalem are repeated in 1Ch 14:3 – 7. The name Eliphelet occurs twice (vv. 6,8); in 14:5,7 two spellings of the name are given (only one son having this name is mentioned in 2Sa 5:14 – 16). The reference to David's seven-year rule in Hebron (v. 4) is repeated in 29:27, though the Chronicler does not deal with this period in his narrative. The references to Absalom, Tamar, Adonijah, Amnon and Bathsheba all recall unhappy incidents in the life of David, incidents the Chronicler has omitted from his later narrative (see 2Sa 11 – 15; 17 – 18; 1Ki 1).

vid, besides his sons by his concubines. And Tamar[u] was their sister.[v]

The Kings of Judah

10 Solomon's son was Rehoboam,[w]
Abijah[x] his son,
Asa[y] his son,
Jehoshaphat[z] his son,
11 Jehoram[aa] his son,
Ahaziah[b] his son,
Joash[c] his son,
12 Amaziah[d] his son,
Azariah[e] his son,
Jotham[f] his son,
13 Ahaz[g] his son,
Hezekiah[h] his son,
Manasseh[i] his son,
14 Amon[j] his son,
Josiah[k] his son.
15 The sons of Josiah:
Johanan the firstborn,
Jehoiakim[l] the second son,
Zedekiah[m] the third,
Shallum[n] the fourth.
16 The successors of Jehoiakim:
Jehoiachin[bo] his son,
and Zedekiah.[p]

The Royal Line After the Exile

17 The descendants of Jehoiachin the
captive:

3:9 [u]S 2Sa 13:1 [v]1Ch 14:4 **3:10** [w]1Ki 14:21-31; 2Ch 12:16 [x]1Ki 15:1-8; 2Ch 13:1 [y]1Ki 15:9-24 [z]2Ch 17:1-21:3 **3:11** [a]2Ki 8:16-24; 2Ch 21:1 [b]2Ki 8:25-10:14; 2Ch 22:1-10 [c]2Ki 11:1-12:21; 2Ch 22:11-24:27 **3:12** [d]2Ki 14:1-22; 2Ch 25:1-28 [e]2Ki 15:1-7; 2Ch 26:1-23 [f]2Ki 15:32-38; 2Ch 27:1; Isa 1:1; Hos 1:1; Mic 1:1 **3:13** [g]2Ki 16:1-20; 2Ch 28:1; Isa 7:1 [h]2Ki 18:1-20:21; 2Ch 29:1; Isa 1:1; Jer 26:19; Hos 1:1; Mic 1:1 [i]2Ki 21:1-18; 2Ch 33:1 **3:14** [j]2Ki 21:19-26; 2Ch 33:21; Zep 1:1 [k]2Ki 22:1; 2Ch 34:1; Jer 1:2; 3:6; 25:3 **3:15** [l]S 2Ki 23:34 [m]Jer 37:1 [n]S 2Ki 23:31 **3:16** [o]S 2Ki 24:6,8

Shealtiel[q] his son, 18 Malkiram, Pedaiah, Shenazzar,[r] Jekamiah, Hosh-
ama and Nedabiah.[s]
19 The sons of Pedaiah:
Zerubbabel[t] and Shimei.
The sons of Zerubbabel:
Meshullam and Hananiah.
Shelomith was their sister.
20 There were also five others:
Hashubah, Ohel, Berekiah, Hasadi-
ah and Jushab-Hesed.
21 The descendants of Hananiah:
Pelatiah and Jeshaiah, and the sons
of Rephaiah, of Arnan, of Obadiah
and of Shekaniah.
22 The descendants of Shekaniah:
Shemaiah and his sons:
Hattush,[u] Igal, Bariah, Neariah and
Shaphat — six in all.
23 The sons of Neariah:
Elioenai, Hizkiah and Azrikam —
three in all.
24 The sons of Elioenai:
Hodaviah, Eliashib, Pelaiah, Akkub, Johanan, Delaiah and Ana-
ni — seven in all.

[a] *11* Hebrew *Joram,* a variant of *Jehoram*
[b] *16* Hebrew *Jeconiah,* a variant of *Jehoiachin;* also in verse 17

[p]S 2Ki 24:18 **3:17** [q]Ezr 3:2 **3:18** [r]Ezr 1:8; 5:14 [s]Jer 22:30 **3:19** [t]Ezr 2:2; 3:2; 5:2; Ne 7:7; 12:1; Hag 1:1; 2:2; Zec 4:6 **3:22** [u]Ezr 8:2-3

3:10 *Rehoboam.* See 2Ch 10 – 12 and note on 11:1 – 23. *Abijah.* See note on 2Ch 13:1 — 14:1. *Asa.* See note on 2Ch 14:2 — 16:14. *Jehoshaphat.* See note on 2Ch 17:1 — 21:3.
3:11 *Jehoram.* See 2Ch 21. *Ahaziah.* See note on 2Ch 22:1 – 9. *Joash.* See note on 2Ch 23:1 — 24:27.
3:12 *Amaziah.* See note on 2Ch 25:1 – 28. *Azariah.* Also called Uzziah (see note on 2Ch 26:1 – 23). *Jotham.* See 2Ch 27; see also 2Ki 15:32 – 38 and notes.
3:13 *Ahaz.* See 2Ch 28:1 – 27 and notes. *Hezekiah.* See note on 2Ch 29:1 — 32:13. *Manasseh.* See note on 2Ch 33:1 – 20.
3:14 *Amon.* See note on 2Ch 33:21 – 25. *Josiah.* See note on 2Ch 34:1 — 36:1.
3:15 *Johanan the firstborn.* Not mentioned elsewhere and may have died before Josiah. The genealogy is segmented at this point, instead of linear as in vv. 10 – 14. Since Josiah's other three sons would all occupy the throne, the succession was not uniformly father to son. Shallum/Jehoahaz (2Ch 36:2 – 4; 2Ki 23:30 – 35) was replaced by Jehoiakim (2Ch 36:5 – 8; 2Ki 23:34 — 24:6); Jehoiakim was succeeded by his son Jehoiachin (2Ch 36:9 – 10; 2Ki 24:8 – 16). After Jehoiachin was taken captive to Babylon by Nebuchadnezzar, Josiah's son Zedekiah became the last king of Judah (2Ch 36:11 – 14; 2Ki 24:17 — 25:7).
3:17 – 20 Seven sons are attributed to Jehoiachin, but not one succeeded him (see notes on v. 15; Jer 22:30). Tablets found in Babylon dating from the 10th to the 35th year of Nebuchadnezzar (595 – 570 BC) and listing deliveries of rations mention Jehoiachin and five sons, as well as other Judahites held in Babylon. Jehoiachin received similar largess from Nebuchadnezzar's successor, Awel-Marduk (562 – 560 BC; see 2Ki 25:27 – 30; Jer 52:31 – 34).
3:18 *Shenazzar.* May be another spelling of the name Sheshbazzar. If so, the treasures of the temple were consigned to his care for return to Judah (Ezr 1:11). He also served for a short time as the first governor of the returnees and made an initial attempt at rebuilding the temple (Ezr 5:14 – 16). Little is known of him; he soon disappeared from the scene and was overshadowed by his nephew Zerubbabel, who assumes such importance in Ezra, Haggai and Zechariah. But see note on Ezr 1:8.
3:19 *Pedaiah.* Other texts name Shealtiel (v. 17) as Zerubbabel's father (Ezr 3:2,8; Ne 12:1; Hag 1:1,12,14; 2:2,23). Suggestions offered to resolve this difficulty are: (1) Shealtiel may have died early, and Pedaiah became the head of the family. (2) Pedaiah may have married the childless widow of Shealtiel; Zerubbabel would then be regarded as the son of Shealtiel according to the law of levirate marriage (Dt 25:5 – 6). In Lk 3:27 Neri instead of Jehoiachin (v. 17) is identified as the father of Shealtiel. Suggestions similar to those above could be made in this instance as well. It is also interesting to note that the genealogies of Jesus in Mt 1 and Lk 3 both trace his descent to Zerubbabel, but none of the names subsequent to Zerubbabel (v. 19 – 24) is found in the NT genealogies.
3:20 *five others.* May have been sons of Zerubbabel, but no kinship terms are provided. Since the sons of Hananiah (v. 19) are specified in v. 21, they could also be the sons of Meshullam (v. 19).
3:21 *sons of Rephaiah … Shekaniah.* Probably other Davidic families at the time of Zerubbabel (v. 19) or Pelatiah and Jeshaiah. If they are understood as contemporary with Zerubbabel, his genealogy was carried only two generations (his sons and grandsons) and a date for Chronicles as early as 450 BC is possible (see Introduction: Author, Date and Sources).
3:22 *six.* Shemaiah appears to have five sons, but the total is given as six. Either one of the six names is missing, or Shemaiah is to be understood as the brother of the five persons named (in which case there should be a semicolon after "sons" instead of a colon) — all six then being sons of Shekaniah.

Other Clans of Judah

4 The descendants of Judah:[v]
Perez, Hezron,[w] Karmi, Hur and
Shobal.
2 Reaiah son of Shobal was the father
of Jahath, and Jahath the father of
Ahumai and Lahad. These were the
clans of the Zorathites.
3 These were the sons[a] of Etam:
Jezreel, Ishma and Idbash. Their
sister was named Hazzelelponi.
4 Penuel was the father of Gedor,
and Ezer the father of Hushah.
These were the descendants of Hur,[x]
the firstborn of Ephrathah and father[b] of Bethlehem.[y]
5 Ashhur[z] the father of Tekoa had two
wives, Helah and Naarah.
6 Naarah bore him Ahuzzam, Hepher,
Temeni and Haahashtari. These
were the descendants of Naarah.
7 The sons of Helah:
Zereth, Zohar, Ethnan, 8 and Koz,
who was the father of Anub and
Hazzobebah and of the clans of
Aharhel son of Harum.

9 Jabez was more honorable than his
brothers. His mother had named him Jabez,[c] saying, "I gave birth to him in pain."
10 Jabez cried out to the God of Israel, "Oh,
that you would bless me and enlarge my
territory! Let your hand be with me, and
keep me from harm so that I will be free
from pain." And God granted his request.

11 Kelub, Shuhah's brother, was the father of Mehir, who was the father
of Eshton. 12 Eshton was the father
of Beth Rapha, Paseah and Tehin-
nah the father of Ir Nahash.[d] These
were the men of Rekah.

4:1 [v] S Ge 29:35; S 1Ch 2:3 [w] Nu 26:21
4:4 [x] 1Ch 2:50 [y] Ru 1:19
4:5 [z] 1Ch 2:24
4:13 [a] S Jos 15:17
4:17 [b] S Ex 15:20
4:18 [c] S Jos 15:34
4:19 [d] S Jos 15:44 [e] S Dt 3:14

13 The sons of Kenaz:
Othniel[a] and Seraiah.
The sons of Othniel:
Hathath and Meonothai.[e] 14 Meonothai was the father of Ophrah.
Seraiah was the father of Joab,
the father of Ge Harashim.[f] It was
called this because its people were
skilled workers.
15 The sons of Caleb son of Jephunneh:
Iru, Elah and Naam.
The son of Elah:
Kenaz.
16 The sons of Jehallelel:
Ziph, Ziphah, Tiria and Asarel.
17 The sons of Ezrah:
Jether, Mered, Epher and Jalon.
One of Mered's wives gave birth
to Miriam,[b] Shammai and Ishbah
the father of Eshtemoa. 18 (His wife
from the tribe of Judah gave birth
to Jered the father of Gedor, Heber
the father of Soko, and Jekuthiel
the father of Zanoah.[c]) These were
the children of Pharaoh's daughter
Bithiah, whom Mered had married.
19 The sons of Hodiah's wife, the sister
of Naham:
the father of Keilah[d] the Garmite,
and Eshtemoa the Maakathite.[e]
20 The sons of Shimon:
Amnon, Rinnah, Ben-Hanan and
Tilon.
The descendants of Ishi:
Zoheth and Ben-Zoheth.

[a] *3* Some Septuagint manuscripts (see also Vulgate); Hebrew *father* [b] *4* *Father* may mean *civic leader* or *military leader*; also in verses 12, 14, 17, 18 and possibly elsewhere. [c] *9* *Jabez* sounds like the Hebrew for *pain.* [d] *12* Or *of the city of Nahash* [e] *13* Some Septuagint manuscripts and Vulgate; Hebrew does not have *and Meonothai.* [f] *14* *Ge Harashim* means *valley of skilled workers.*

4:1–23 None of the genealogies of Judah in this section appears elsewhere in Scripture. Although the section may have the appearance of miscellaneous notes, the careful shaping of the Chronicler is evident in light of the overall inverted structure of the genealogies of Judah:

2:3	Shelah
2:4–8	Perez
2:9—3:24	Hezron
4:1–20	Perez
4:21–23	Shelah

This balancing of the material in inverse order shows the centrality of the section of the lineage of Hezron and the house of David; the same balancing in inverse order is observed within the Hezron section (see note on 2:10—3:24). The record of Judah's oldest surviving son, Shelah, frames the entire genealogy of Judah. There are 15 fragmentary genealogies in this section, with two to six generations in each.
4:1–2 The descendants of Judah here are not brothers; rather, the genealogy is linear.
4:1 *Karmi.* Either a scribal confusion or an alternative name for Caleb (2:9); the confusion may have been induced by 2:7.
4:2 *Reaiah.* A variant of Haroeh (2:52).
4:5–8 Supplementary to 2:24.
4:9–10 The practice of inserting short historical notes into genealogical records is amply attested in non-Biblical genealogical texts from the ancient Near East, as well as in other Biblical genealogies (Ge 4:19–24; 10:8–12).
4:13 *Othniel.* The first of Israel's judges (Jos 15:17; Jdg 1:13; 3:9–11).
4:14 *Ge Harashim ... skilled workers.* See NIV text note; see also note on Ne 11:35.
4:16–20 This portion of the genealogy is from preexilic times; several of the places named were not included in the province of Judah in the restoration period (e.g., Ziph and Eshtemoa).
4:17 *One of Mered's wives.* The pharaoh's daughter (v. 18). Mered is otherwise unknown; the fact that he married a daughter of a pharaoh suggests his prominence. The event may be associated with the fortunes of Israel in Egypt under Joseph.

21 The sons of Shelah[f] son of Judah:
Er the father of Lekah, Laadah the father of Mareshah and the clans of the linen workers at Beth Ashbea, 22 Jokim, the men of Kozeba, and Joash and Saraph, who ruled in Moab and Jashubi Lehem. (These records are from ancient times.) 23 They were the potters who lived at Netaim and Gederah; they stayed there and worked for the king.

Simeon

4:28-33pp — Jos 19:2-10

24 The descendants of Simeon:[g]
Nemuel, Jamin, Jarib,[h] Zerah and Shaul;
25 Shallum was Shaul's son, Mibsam his son and Mishma his son.

26 The descendants of Mishma:
Hammuel his son, Zakkur his son and Shimei his son.

27 Shimei had sixteen sons and six daughters, but his brothers did not have many children; so their entire clan did not become as numerous as the people of Judah. 28 They lived in Beersheba,[i] Moladah,[j] Hazar Shual, 29 Bilhah, Ezem,[k] Tolad, 30 Bethuel, Hormah,[l] Ziklag,[m] 31 Beth Markaboth, Hazar Susim, Beth Biri and Shaaraim.[n] These were their towns until the reign of David. 32 Their surrounding villages were Etam, Ain,[o] Rimmon, Token and Ashan[p] — five towns — 33 and all the villages around these towns as far as Baalath.[a] These were their settlements. And they kept a genealogical record.

34 Meshobab, Jamlech, Joshah son of Amaziah, 35 Joel, Jehu son of Joshibiah, the son of Seraiah, the son of Asiel, 36 also Elioenai, Jaakobah, Jeshohaiah, Asaiah, Adiel, Jesimiel, Benaiah, 37 and Ziza son of Shiphi, the son of Allon, the son of Jedaiah, the son of Shimri, the son of Shemaiah.

38 The men listed above by name were leaders of their clans. Their families increased greatly, 39 and they went to the outskirts of Gedor[q] to the east of the valley in search of pasture for their flocks. 40 They found rich, good pasture, and the land was spacious, peaceful and quiet.[r] Some Hamites had lived there formerly.

41 The men whose names were listed came in the days of Hezekiah king of Judah. They attacked the Hamites in their dwellings and also the Meunites[s] who were there and completely destroyed[b] them, as is evident to this day. Then they settled in their place, because there was pasture for their flocks. 42 And five hundred of these Simeonites, led by Pelatiah, Neariah, Rephaiah and Uzziel, the sons of Ishi, invaded the hill country of Seir.[t] 43 They killed the remaining Amalekites[u] who had escaped, and they have lived there to this day.

Reuben

5 The sons of Reuben[v] the firstborn of Israel (he was the firstborn, but when he defiled his father's marriage bed,[w] his rights as firstborn were given to the sons of Joseph[x] son of Israel;[y] so he could not be listed in the genealogical record in accordance with his birthright,[z] 2 and though Judah[a] was the strongest of his brothers and a ruler[b] came from him, the rights of the firstborn[c] belonged to Joseph) — 3 the sons of Reuben[d] the firstborn of Israel:

4:21 [f] S Ge 38:5
4:24 [g] S Ge 29:33 [h] Nu 26:12
4:28 [i] S Ge 21:14 [j] S Jos 15:26
4:29 [k] S Jos 15:29
4:30 [l] S Nu 14:45 [m] S Jos 15:31
4:31 [n] S Jos 15:36
4:32 [o] S Nu 34:11 [p] S Jos 15:42
4:39 [q] S Jos 15:58
4:40 [r] Jdg 18:7-10
4:41 [s] 2Ch 20:1; 26:7
4:42 [t] S Ge 14:6
4:43 [u] S Ge 14:7; Est 3:1; 9:16
5:1 [v] S Ge 29:32 [w] Ge 35:22; 49:4 [x] S Ge 48:16, 22; S 49:26 [y] Ge 48:5 [z] 1Ch 26:10
5:2 [a] S Ge 49:10, 12 [b] S 1Sa 9:16; S 12:12; S 2Sa 6:21; 1Ch 11:2; S 2Ch 7:18; Mt 2:6 [c] S Ge 25:31
5:3 [d] S Ge 29:32; 46:9; Ex 6:14; Nu 26:5-11

[a] *33* Some Septuagint manuscripts (see also Joshua 19:8); Hebrew *Baal* [b] *41* The Hebrew term refers to the irrevocable giving over of things or persons to the LORD, often by totally destroying them.

4:21,23 This section accurately reflects a feature of ancient Near Eastern society. Clans were often associated not only with particular localities but also with special trades or guilds, such as linen workers (v. 21), potters (v. 23), royal patronage (v. 23) and scribes (2:55).

4:24 – 43 The genealogy of Simeon is also found in Ge 46:10; Ex 6:15; Nu 26:12 – 13. Simeon settled in part of the territory of Judah; the list of occupied towns should be compared with Jos 15:26 – 32,42; 19:2 – 7. Since Simeon occupied areas allotted to Judah, this tribe was politically incorporated into Judah and appears to have lost much of its own identity in history (see Ge 34:24 – 31; 49:5 – 7; see also notes on Ge 34:25; 49:7). Geographical and historical notes are inserted in the genealogy (see note on vv. 9 – 10). Apparently two genealogies are included here: vv. 24 – 33 — ending with the formula, "they kept a genealogical record" — and vv. 34 – 43. Overpopulation (v. 38) caused them to expand toward Gedor and east toward Edom at the time of Hezekiah (vv. 39 – 43). The long hostility between Israel and Amalek surfaced once again (v. 43; cf. Ex 17:8 – 16; Dt 25:17 – 19; 1Sa 15; see Introduction to Esther: Purpose, Themes and Literary Features).

5:1 – 26 The genealogical records of the tribes east of the Jordan: Reuben, Gad and half of Manasseh (see Nu 32:33 – 42). The Chronicler's concern with "all Israel" includes incorporating the genealogical records of these tribes that were no longer significant entities in Israel's life in the restoration period, having been swept away in the Assyrian conquests.

5:1 – 10 The necessity of explaining why the birthright of the firstborn did not remain with Reuben (see Ge 35:22; 49:4 for Reuben's sin) interrupts the initial statement (v. 1), which is then repeated after the explanation (v. 3). The parenthetical material (vv. 1 – 2) shows the writer's partiality for Judah, even though Joseph received the double portion (Ephraim and Manasseh) of the firstborn. The Hebrew term translated "ruler" (v. 2) is used of David in 11:2; 17:7; 2Sa 5:2; 6:21; 7:8. The use of military titles (vv. 6 – 7) and a battle account (v. 10) suggest that this genealogy may have functioned in military organization (see Introduction: Genealogies). The source for some of this material on Reuben is Nu 26:5 – 11. The Chronicler has omitted reference to Eliab and his three sons, who perished in the rebellion of Korah (see Nu 26:8 – 10) and so were not relevant to his purpose.

Hanok, Pallu,[e] Hezron[f] and Karmi.
4 The descendants of Joel:
Shemaiah his son, Gog his son,
Shimei his son, 5 Micah his son,
Reaiah his son, Baal his son,
6 and Beerah his son, whom Tiglath-Pileser[a][g] king of Assyria took into exile. Beerah was a leader of the Reubenites.
7 Their relatives by clans,[h] listed according to their genealogical records:
Jeiel the chief, Zechariah, 8 and
Bela son of Azaz, the son of Shema, the son of Joel. They settled in the area from Aroer[i] to Nebo[j] and
Baal Meon.[k] 9 To the east they occupied the land up to the edge of the desert that extends to the Euphrates[l] River, because their livestock had increased in Gilead.[m]

10 During Saul's reign they waged war against the Hagrites[n], who were defeated at their hands; they occupied the dwellings of the Hagrites throughout the entire region east of Gilead.

Gad

11 The Gadites[o] lived next to them in Bashan, as far as Salekah:[p]
12 Joel was the chief, Shapham the second, then Janai and Shaphat, in Bashan.
13 Their relatives, by families, were:
Michael, Meshullam, Sheba, Jorai, Jakan, Zia and Eber—seven in all.
14 These were the sons of Abihail son of Huri, the son of Jaroah, the son of Gilead, the son of Michael, the son of Jeshishai, the son of Jahdo, the son of Buz.
15 Ahi son of Abdiel, the son of Guni, was head of their family.
16 The Gadites lived in Gilead, in Bashan and its outlying villages, and on all the pasturelands of Sharon as far as they extended.
17 All these were entered in the genealogical records during the reigns of Jotham[q] king of Judah and Jeroboam[r] king of Israel.

5:3 [e]S Nu 26:5 [f]S Nu 26:6 5:6 [g]ver 26; S 2Ki 15:19; 16:10; 2Ch 28:20 5:7 [h]Jos 13:15-23 5:8 [i]S Nu 32:34; Jdg 11:26 [j]S Nu 32:3 [k]S Jos 13:17 5:9 [l]S Ge 2:14 [m]S Nu 32:26 5:10 [n]ver 22; 1Ch 27:31 5:11 [o]S Ge 30:11; S Nu 1:25; S Jos 13:24-28 [p]S Dt 3:10

King of Assyria Tiglath-Pileser III, who "took the Reubenites, the Gadites and the half-tribe of Manasseh into exile" (1Ch 5:26)

Kim Walton, courtesy of the British Museum

18 The Reubenites, the Gadites and the half-tribe of Manasseh had 44,760 men ready for military service[s]—able-bodied men who could handle shield and sword, who could use a bow, and who were trained for battle. 19 They waged war against the Hagrites, Jetur,[t] Naphish and Nodab. 20 They were helped[u] in fighting them, and God delivered the Hagrites and all their allies into their hands, because they cried[v] out to him during the battle. He answered their prayers, because they trusted[w] in him. 21 They seized the livestock of the Hagrites—fifty thousand camels, two hundred fifty thousand sheep and two thousand donkeys. They also took one hundred thousand people captive, 22 and many others fell slain, because the battle[x] was God's. And they occupied the land until the exile.[y]

The Half-Tribe of Manasseh

23 The people of the half-tribe of Manasseh[z] were numerous; they settled in the land from Bashan to Baal Hermon, that is, to Senir (Mount Hermon).[a]

5:17 [q]S 2Ki 15:32 [r]S 2Ki 14:23 5:18 [s]S Nu 1:3 5:19 [t]Ge 25:15 5:20 [u]Ps 37:40; 46:5; 54:4 [v]1Ki 8:44; 2Ch 6:34; 13:14; 14:11; Ps 20:7-9; 22:5; 107:6 [w]Ps 26:1; Isa 26:3; Da 6:23 5:22 [x]S Dt 20:4; 2Ch 32:8 [y]S ver 10; S 2Ki 15:29 5:23 [z]1Ch 7:14 [a]S Dt 3:8,9; SS 4:8

[a] 6 Hebrew *Tilgath-Pilneser*, a variant of *Tiglath-Pileser*; also in verse 26

5:6 *Tiglath-Pileser.* This Assyrian king (745–727 BC; see chart, p. 511) attacked Israel (v. 26; 2Ki 15:29) and also imposed tribute on Ahaz of Judah (2Ch 28:19–20; 2Ki 16:7–10).
5:10 *Hagrites.* See vv. 19–22. Named among the enemies of Israel (Ps 83:6), this tribe is apparently associated with Hagar, the mother of Ishmael (Ge 16), but see note on Ps 83:6.
5:11–22 The materials in this list for the tribe of Gad have no parallels in the Bible. The other genealogies of Gad are organized around his seven sons (Ge 46:16; Nu 26:15–18); here four names are given, none found in the other lists. The Chronicler states (v. 17) that these records came from the period of Jotham of Judah (750–732 BC) and Jeroboam of Israel (793–753). The presence of military titles and narratives (vv. 12,18–22) suggests that this genealogy originated as part of a military census. The territory of Gad is delineated in Dt 3:12.
5:18–22 The first example of the Chronicler's theme of immediate retribution (see Introduction: Purpose and Themes). Success in warfare is attributed to their crying out to God (v. 20; cf. 2Ch 6:24–25,34–39; 12:7–12; 13:13–16; 14:9–15; 18:31; 20:1–30; 32:1–23).
5:23–26 Manasseh is treated further in 7:14–19; the half-tribe that settled east of the Jordan River is dealt with here since it shared the same fate as Reuben and Gad, and possibly also so that the Chronicler could keep the total of 12 for his tribal genealogies (see note on 2:1–2). Again immediate retribution is apparent: Just as trust in God can bring victory (vv. 18–22), so also defeat comes to the unfaithful (vv. 25–26).

24 These were the heads of their families: Epher, Ishi, Eliel, Azriel, Jeremiah,
Hodaviah and Jahdiel. They were brave
warriors, famous men, and heads of their
families. 25 But they were unfaithful[b] to
the God of their ancestors and prostituted[c]
themselves to the gods of the peoples of
the land, whom God had destroyed before
them. 26 So the God of Israel stirred up the
spirit[d] of Pul[e] king of Assyria (that is, Tiglath-Pileser[f] king of Assyria), who took the
Reubenites, the Gadites and the half-tribe
of Manasseh into exile. He took them to
Halah,[g] Habor, Hara and the river of Gozan, where they are to this day.

Levi

6[a] The sons of Levi:[h]
Gershon, Kohath and Merari.
2 The sons of Kohath:
Amram, Izhar, Hebron and Uzziel.[i]
3 The children of Amram:
Aaron, Moses and Miriam.[j]
The sons of Aaron:
Nadab, Abihu,[k] Eleazar[l] and Ithamar.[m]
4 Eleazar was the father of Phinehas,[n]
Phinehas the father of Abishua,
5 Abishua the father of Bukki,
Bukki the father of Uzzi,
6 Uzzi the father of Zerahiah,
Zerahiah the father of Meraioth,
7 Meraioth the father of Amariah,
Amariah the father of Ahitub,
8 Ahitub the father of Zadok,[o]
Zadok the father of Ahimaaz,
9 Ahimaaz the father of Azariah,
Azariah the father of Johanan,
10 Johanan the father of Azariah[p] (it was he who served as priest in the temple Solomon built in Jerusalem),
11 Azariah the father of Amariah,
Amariah the father of Ahitub,
12 Ahitub the father of Zadok,
Zadok the father of Shallum,
13 Shallum the father of Hilkiah,[q]
Hilkiah the father of Azariah,
14 Azariah the father of Seraiah,[r]
and Seraiah the father of Jozadak.[b]
15 Jozadak[s] was deported when the LORD sent Judah and Jerusalem into exile by the hand of Nebuchadnezzar.

16 The sons of Levi:[t]
Gershon,[c] Kohath and Merari.[u]
17 These are the names of the sons of Gershon:
Libni and Shimei.[v]
18 The sons of Kohath:
Amram, Izhar, Hebron and Uzziel.[w]
19 The sons of Merari:[x]
Mahli and Mushi.[y]
These are the clans of the Levites listed according to their fathers:
20 Of Gershon:

5:25 [b] Dt 32:15-18; 1Ch 9:1; 10:13; 2Ch 12:2; 26:16; 28:19; 29:6; 30:7; 36:14 [c] S Ex 34:15; S Lev 18:3 **5:26** [d] Isa 37:7 [e] S 2Ki 15:19 [f] S ver 6; S 2Ki 15:29 [g] 2Ki 17:6 **6:1** [h] S Ge 29:34; S Nu 3:17 **6:2** [i] S Ex 6:18 **6:3** [j] S Ex 15:20 [k] S Lev 10:1; S 10:1-20:2 [l] Lev 10:6 [m] S Ex 6:23 **6:4** [n] Ezr 7:5 **6:8** [o] S 2Sa 8:17; S 1Ch 12:28; S Ezr 7:2 **6:10** [p] S 1Ki 4:2 **6:13** [q] 2Ki 22:1-20; 2Ch 34:9; 35:8 **6:14** [r] S 2Ki 25:18; S Ezr 2:2 **6:15** [s] Ne 12:1; Hag 1:1,14; 2:2,4; Zec 6:11 **6:16** [t] S Ge 29:34; S Nu 3:17-20 [u] S Nu 26:57 **6:17** [v] S Ex 6:17 **6:18** [w] S Ex 6:18 **6:19** [x] S Ge 46:11; 1Ch 23:21; 24:26 [y] S Ex 6:19

[a] In Hebrew texts 6:1-15 is numbered 5:27-41, and 6:16-81 is numbered 6:1-66. [b] *14* Hebrew *Jehozadak*, a variant of *Jozadak*; also in verse 15 [c] *16* Hebrew *Gershom*, a variant of *Gershon*; also in verses 17, 20, 43, 62 and 71

The use of the retributive theme in these two accounts argues for the unity of the genealogies with the historical portions of Chronicles. The list of names given here is not properly a genealogy but a list of clans. Since they are described as brave warriors in connection with a battle report (vv. 24–26), this section too is likely derived from records of military conscription (see note on vv. 1–10; see also 2Ki 15:19,29; 17:6; 18:11).

5:25 *were unfaithful ... prostituted themselves.* See Ex 34:15 and note.

5:26 *Pul.* Tiglath-Pileser's throne name in Babylon (see photo, p. 638).

6:1–81 This chapter is devoted to a series of lists, all pertaining to the tribe of Levi. The first section (vv. 1–15) records the line of the high priests down to the exile; the clans of Levi follow (vv. 16–30). David's appointees as temple musicians came from the three clans of Levi: Gershon, Kohath and Merari (vv. 31–47). The generations between Aaron and Ahimaaz are given a separate listing (vv. 49–53), reinforcing the separate duties of priests and Levites (see note on Ex 32:26). The listing of the Levitical possessions among the tribes concludes the chapter (vv. 54–81).

6:1–3 A short segmented genealogy narrows the descendants of Levi to the lineage of Eleazar, in whose line the high priests are presented in linear form (vv. 4–15). The sons of Levi (v. 1) always appear in this order, based on age (v. 16; Ge 46:11; Ex 6:16; Nu 3:17; 26:57). Of Aaron's four sons (v. 3), the first two died as a result of sacrilege (Lev 10:1–2; Nu 26:61); succeeding generations of priests would trace their lineage to either Eleazar or Ithamar.

6:4–15 This list of high priests from the time of Eleazar to the exile has been sharply telescoped. The following high priests known from the OT are not mentioned: Jehoiada (2Ki 12:2), Uriah (2Ki 16:10–16), possibly two other Azariahs (2Ch 26:17, 20; 31:10–13), Eli (1Sa 1:9; 14:3) and Abiathar (see 2Sa 8:17 and note). The list is repeated with some variation in Ezr 7:1–5 (see notes there).

6:8 *Ahitub the father of Zadok.* This Zadok was one of David's two priests (18:16; 2Sa 8:17). When David's other priest, Abiathar (see note on vv. 4–15), supported the rebellion of Adonijah, Zadok supported Solomon (1Ki 1). After the expulsion of Abiathar (1Ki 2:26–27), Zadok alone held the office (1Ch 29:22), which continued in his line (1Ki 4:2). The Ahitub mentioned here should not be confused with the priest who was the grandson of Eli (1Sa 14:3) and grandfather of Abiathar (1Sa 22:20); the line of Zadok replaced the line of Eli (1Sa 2:27–36; 1Ki 2:26–27). For the importance of the line of Zadok, see Eze 40:46; 43:19; 44:15; 48:11. Ezra was concerned to trace his own priestly lineage to this house (Ezr 7:1–5).

6:13 *Hilkiah.* Discovered the Book of the Law in the temple during the reign of Josiah (2Ki 22; 2Ch 34).

6:14 *Seraiah.* Executed by the Babylonians after the conquest of Jerusalem in 586 BC (2Ki 25:18–21). *Jozadak.* See NIV text note; father of Joshua (see note on Ezr 2:2), the high priest in the first generation of the restoration period (see Hag 1:1; 2:2; Zec 3:1 and note; 6:11; see also Ezr 3:2; 5:2; 10:18).

6:16–19a Repeated from Ex 6:16–19; Nu 3:17–20; 26:57–61.

Libni his son, Jahath his son,
Zimmah his son, 21 Joah his son,
Iddo his son, Zerah his son
and Jeatherai his son.
22 The descendants of Kohath:
Amminadab his son, Korah[z] his son,
Assir his son, 23 Elkanah his son,
Ebiasaph his son, Assir his son,
24 Tahath his son, Uriel[a] his son,
Uzziah his son and Shaul his son.
25 The descendants of Elkanah:
Amasai, Ahimoth,
26 Elkanah his son,[a] Zophai his son,
Nahath his son, 27 Eliab his son,
Jeroham his son, Elkanah[b] his son
and Samuel[c] his son.[b]
28 The sons of Samuel:
Joel[c][d] the firstborn
and Abijah the second son.
29 The descendants of Merari:
Mahli, Libni his son,
Shimei his son, Uzzah his son,
30 Shimea his son, Haggiah his son
and Asaiah his son.

The Temple Musicians

6:54-80pp — Jos 21:4-39

31 These are the men[e] David put in charge
of the music[f] in the house of the LORD after
the ark came to rest there. 32 They ministered with music before the tabernacle, the
tent of meeting, until Solomon built the
temple of the LORD in Jerusalem. They performed their duties according to the regulations laid down for them.
33 Here are the men who served, together with their sons:
From the Kohathites:
Heman,[g] the musician,
the son of Joel,[h] the son of Samuel,
34 the son of Elkanah,[i] the son of Jeroham,
the son of Eliel, the son of Toah,
35 the son of Zuph, the son of Elkanah,
the son of Mahath, the son of Amasai,
36 the son of Elkanah, the son of Joel,
the son of Azariah, the son of Zephaniah,
37 the son of Tahath, the son of Assir,
the son of Ebiasaph, the son of Korah,[j]
38 the son of Izhar,[k] the son of Kohath,
the son of Levi, the son of Israel;
39 and Heman's associate Asaph,[l] who served at his right hand:
Asaph son of Berekiah, the son of Shimea,[m]
40 the son of Michael, the son of Baaseiah,[d]
the son of Malkijah, 41 the son of Ethni,
the son of Zerah, the son of Adaiah,
42 the son of Ethan, the son of Zimmah,
the son of Shimei, 43 the son of Jahath,
the son of Gershon, the son of Levi;
44 and from their associates, the Merarites,[n] at his left hand:
Ethan son of Kishi, the son of Abdi,
the son of Malluk, 45 the son of Hashabiah,
the son of Amaziah, the son of Hilkiah,
46 the son of Amzi, the son of Bani,

6:22 [z] S Ex 6:24
6:24 [a] 1Ch 15:5
6:27 [b] S 1Sa 1:1 [c] S 1Sa 1:20
6:28 [d] ver 33; 1Sa 8:2
6:31 [e] 1Ch 25:1; 2Ch 29:25-26; Ne 12:45 [f] 1Ch 9:33; 15:19; Ezr 3:10; Ps 68:25
6:33 [g] 1Ki 4:31; 1Ch 15:17; 25:1 [h] S ver 28
6:34 [i] S 1Sa 1:1
6:37 [j] S Ex 6:24
6:38 [k] Ex 6:21
6:39 [l] 1Ch 25:1, 9; 2Ch 29:13; Ne 11:17 [m] 1Ch 15:17
6:44 [n] 1Ch 15:17

[a] *26* Some Hebrew manuscripts, Septuagint and Syriac; most Hebrew manuscripts *Ahimoth* [26]*and Elkanah. The sons of Elkanah:* [b] *27* Some Septuagint manuscripts (see also 1 Samuel 1:19,20 and 1 Chron. 6:33,34); Hebrew does not have *and Samuel his son.* [c] *28* Some Septuagint manuscripts and Syriac (see also 1 Samuel 8:2 and 1 Chron. 6:33); Hebrew does not have *Joel.* [d] *40* Most Hebrew manuscripts; some Hebrew manuscripts, one Septuagint manuscript and Syriac *Maaseiah*

6:22–23 *Assir ... Elkanah ... Ebiasaph.* Ex 6:24 names these men as sons of Korah, but here they are presented in the form ordinarily used for a linear genealogy of successive generations (see vv. 20–21, 25–26, 29–30). Either this is another example of genealogical fluidity or one must understand "his son" as referring to Kohath and not to the immediately preceding name.

6:22 *Amminadab.* The almost parallel genealogy later in this chapter lists Izhar in the place of Amminadab — who is nowhere else listed as a son of Kohath, while every other list includes Izhar (vv. 2,37–38; Ex 6:18,21). Either Amminadab is an otherwise unattested alternative name of Izhar, or he is an otherwise unknown son. Or this may be another example of genealogical fluidity in which the Levites are linked with the tribe of Judah and the lineage of David (see Ru 4:18–22; see also Mt 1:4; Lk 3:33) in view of Aaron's marriage to the daughter of Amminadab of Judah (Ex 6:23; see 1Ch 2:10).

6:24 *Uriel.* Possibly the one who led the Kohathites in David's day (15:5).

6:26–27 *Zophai ... Nahath ... Eliab.* Apparently variant names for Zuph, Toah and Eliel (vv. 34–35).

6:27 *Samuel.* His lineage is also given in 1Sa 1:1, where his family is identified as Ephraimite (see note there). Either this is an example of genealogical fluidity, in which Samuel's involvement in the tabernacle (1Sa 3) and performance of priestly duties (9:22; 1Sa 2:18; 3:1) resulted in his incorporation into the Levites, or the term "Ephraimite" is to be understood as a place of residence, not as a statement of lineage.

6:31–48 Each of the three Levitical clans contributed musicians for the temple: Heman from the family of Kohath, Asaph from Gershon, and Ethan (also called Jeduthun) from Merari. The Chronicler makes frequent reference to the appointment of the musical guilds by David (15:16,27; 25:1–31; 2Ch 29:25–26; see Ne 12:45–47). The frequent mention of the role of the Levites has led many to assume that the author was a member of the musicians. Non-Biblical literature also attests to guilds of singers and musicians in Canaanite temples. This genealogy appears to function as a means of legitimizing the Levites of the restoration period (Ezr 2:40–41; Ne 7:43–44; 10:9–13, 28–29; 11:15–18; 12:24–47).

the son of Shemer, 47 the son of
Mahli,
the son of Mushi, the son of Merari,
the son of Levi.

48 Their fellow Levites[o] were assigned
to all the other duties of the tabernacle,
the house of God. 49 But Aaron and his descendants were the ones who presented
offerings on the altar[p] of burnt offering
and on the altar of incense[q] in connection
with all that was done in the Most Holy
Place, making atonement for Israel, in accordance with all that Moses the servant
of God had commanded.

50 These were the descendants of Aaron:
Eleazar his son, Phinehas his son,
Abishua his son, 51 Bukki his son,
Uzzi his son, Zerahiah his son,
52 Meraioth his son, Amariah his son,
Ahitub his son, 53 Zadok[r] his son
and Ahimaaz his son.

54 These were the locations of their settlements[s] allotted as their territory (they
were assigned to the descendants of Aaron who were from the Kohathite clan, because the first lot was for them):
55 They were given Hebron in Judah
with its surrounding pasturelands.
56 But the fields and villages around
the city were given to Caleb son of
Jephunneh.[t]
57 So the descendants of Aaron were
given Hebron (a city of refuge), and
Libnah,[a][u] Jattir,[v] Eshtemoa, 58 Hilen,
Debir,[w] 59 Ashan,[x] Juttah[b] and Beth
Shemesh, together with their pasturelands. 60 And from the tribe of Benjamin they were given Gibeon,[c] Geba,
Alemeth and Anathoth,[y] together
with their pasturelands.
The total number of towns distributed among the Kohathite clans came
to thirteen.
61 The rest of Kohath's descendants were
allotted ten towns from the clans of half
the tribe of Manasseh.
62 The descendants of Gershon, clan by
clan, were allotted thirteen towns from the
tribes of Issachar, Asher and Naphtali, and
from the part of the tribe of Manasseh that
is in Bashan.
63 The descendants of Merari, clan by
clan, were allotted twelve towns from the
tribes of Reuben, Gad and Zebulun.
64 So the Israelites gave the Levites these

6:48 [o] 1Ch 23:32
6:49 [p] Ex 27:1-8 [q] S Ex 30:1-7, 10; 2Ch 26:18
6:53 [r] S 2Sa 8:17
6:54 [s] S Nu 31:10
6:56 [t] S Jos 14:13; S 15:13
6:57 [u] S Nu 33:20 [v] S Jos 15:48
6:58 [w] S Jos 10:3
6:59 [x] S Jos 15:42
6:60 [y] Jer 1:1
6:64 [z] Nu 35:1-8
6:67 [a] S Jos 10:33
6:68 [b] 1Ki 4:12 [c] S Jos 10:10
6:69 [d] S Jos 10:12 [e] S Jos 19:45
6:71 [f] 1Ch 23:7 [g] S Jos 20:8
6:72 [h] S Jos 19:12
6:74 [i] S Jos 19:28
6:75 [j] Jos 19:34 [k] S Nu 13:21
6:76 [l] Jos 19:28 [m] S Nu 32:37
6:78 [n] S Jos 20:8
6:79 [o] S Dt 2:26
6:80 [p] Jos 20:8 [q] S Ge 32:2
6:81 [r] S Nu 21:32 [s] 2Ch 11:14

towns[z] and their pasturelands. 65 From the
tribes of Judah, Simeon and Benjamin
they allotted the previously named towns.
66 Some of the Kohathite clans were giv-
en as their territory towns from the tribe
of Ephraim.
67 In the hill country of Ephraim
they were given Shechem (a city of
refuge), and Gezer,[d][a] 68 Jokmeam,[b]
Beth Horon,[c] 69 Aijalon[d] and Gath
Rimmon,[e] together with their pasturelands.
70 And from half the tribe of Manasseh the Israelites gave Aner and Bile-
am, together with their pasturelands,
to the rest of the Kohathite clans.

71 The Gershonites[f] received the following:
From the clan of the half-tribe of Manasseh
they received Golan in Bashan[g] and
also Ashtaroth, together with their
pasturelands;
72 from the tribe of Issachar
they received Kedesh, Daberath,[h]
73 Ramoth and Anem, together with
their pasturelands;
74 from the tribe of Asher
they received Mashal, Abdon,[i]
75 Hukok[j] and Rehob,[k] together with
their pasturelands;
76 and from the tribe of Naphtali
they received Kedesh in Galilee,
Hammon[l] and Kiriathaim,[m] together with their pasturelands.

77 The Merarites (the rest of the Levites)
received the following:
From the tribe of Zebulun
they received Jokneam, Kartah,[e]
Rimmono and Tabor, together with
their pasturelands;
78 from the tribe of Reuben across the
Jordan east of Jericho
they received Bezer[n] in the wilderness, Jahzah, 79 Kedemoth[o] and
Mephaath, together with their pasturelands;
80 and from the tribe of Gad
they received Ramoth in Gilead,[p]
Mahanaim,[q] 81 Heshbon and Jazer,[r]
together with their pasturelands.[s]

[a] *57* See Joshua 21:13; Hebrew *given the cities of refuge: Hebron, Libnah.* [b] *59* Syriac (see also Septuagint and Joshua 21:16); Hebrew does not have *Juttah.* [c] *60* See Joshua 21:17; Hebrew does not have *Gibeon.* [d] *67* See Joshua 21:21; Hebrew *given the cities of refuge: Shechem, Gezer.* [e] *77* See Septuagint and Joshua 21:34; Hebrew does not have *Jokneam, Kartah.*

6:49–53 Repeats vv. 4–8 but presumably serves a different function: to legitimize the line of Zadok, which is traced down to Solomon's time, as the only Levitical division authorized to offer sacrifices.

6:54–81 This list of Levitical possessions is taken from Jos 21 with only minor differences (see notes there). The Levites, who were given no block of territory of their own, were distributed throughout Israel.

Issachar

7 The sons of Issachar:[t]
Tola, Puah,[u] Jashub and Shimron—
four in all.
2 The sons of Tola:
Uzzi, Rephaiah, Jeriel, Jahmai, Ibsam and Samuel—heads of their families. During the reign of David, the descendants of Tola listed as fighting men in their genealogy numbered 22,600.
3 The son of Uzzi:
Izrahiah.
The sons of Izrahiah:
Michael, Obadiah, Joel and Ishiah.
All five of them were chiefs. 4 According to their family genealogy, they had 36,000 men ready for battle, for they had many wives and children.
5 The relatives who were fighting men belonging to all the clans of Issachar, as listed in their genealogy, were 87,000 in all.

Benjamin

6 Three sons of Benjamin:[v]
Bela, Beker and Jediael.
7 The sons of Bela:
Ezbon, Uzzi, Uzziel, Jerimoth and Iri, heads of families—five in all. Their genealogical record listed 22,034 fighting men.
8 The sons of Beker:
Zemirah, Joash, Eliezer, Elioenai, Omri, Jeremoth, Abijah, Anathoth and Alemeth. All these were the
sons of Beker. 9 Their genealogical record listed the heads of families and 20,200 fighting men.
10 The son of Jediael:
Bilhan.
The sons of Bilhan:
Jeush, Benjamin, Ehud, Kenaanah, Zethan, Tarshish and Ahishahar.
11 All these sons of Jediael were heads of families. There were 17,200 fighting men ready to go out to war.
12 The Shuppites and Huppites were the descendants of Ir, and the Hushites[a] the descendants of Aher.

Naphtali

13 The sons of Naphtali:[w]
Jahziel, Guni, Jezer and Shillem[b]—the descendants of Bilhah.

Manasseh

14 The descendants of Manasseh:[x]
Asriel was his descendant through his Aramean concubine. She gave birth to Makir the father of Gilead.[y]
15 Makir took a wife from among the Huppites and Shuppites. His sister's name was Maakah.
Another descendant was named Zelophehad,[z] who had only daughters.
16 Makir's wife Maakah gave birth to a son and named him Peresh. His brother was named Sheresh, and his sons were Ulam and Rakem.
17 The son of Ulam:
Bedan.
These were the sons of Gilead[a] son of Makir, the son of Manasseh.
18 His sister Hammoleketh gave birth to Ishhod, Abiezer[b] and Mahlah.
19 The sons of Shemida[c] were:
Ahian, Shechem, Likhi and Aniam.

Ephraim

20 The descendants of Ephraim:[d]
Shuthelah, Bered his son,

7:1 [t] S Ge 30:18 [u] S Ge 46:13 7:6 [v] S Nu 26:38 7:13 [w] S Ge 30:8 7:14 [x] S Ge 41:51; S Jos 17:1; 1Ch 5:23 [y] S Nu 26:30 7:15 [z] S Nu 26:33; 36:1-12 7:17 [a] S Nu 26:30 7:18 [b] S Jos 17:2 7:19 [c] Jos 17:2 7:20 [d] S Ge 41:52; S Nu 1:33

[a] *12* Or *Ir. The sons of Dan: Hushim,* (see Gen. 46:23); Hebrew does not have *The sons of Dan.* [b] *13* Some Hebrew and Septuagint manuscripts (see also Gen. 46:24 and Num. 26:49); most Hebrew manuscripts *Shallum*

7:1–5 Parts of the genealogy of Issachar are taken from Ge 46:13; Nu 1:28; 26:23–25, though many of the names are otherwise unattested. This list of the clans appears to come from a military muster (vv. 2,4–5) from the time of David (v. 2), perhaps reflecting the census of ch. 21 and 2Sa 24.
7:6–12 There is considerable fluidity among the Biblical sources listing the sons of Benjamin. This list gives three sons; Ge 46:21 records ten; Nu 26:38–39 and 1Ch 8:1–2 both list five (the only name appearing in all these sources is Bela, the firstborn). The variations reflect different origins and functions for these genealogies. The list here appears to function in the military sphere (vv. 7,9,11).
7:13 Repeats Ge 46:24; Nu 26:48–50. *descendants of Bilhah.* Dan and Naphtali were the actual "sons" of Jacob's concubine Bilhah (Ge 30:3–8), so Naphtali's sons are Bilhah's "descendants."
7:14–19 See note on 5:23–26. The sources for this genealogy are Nu 26:29–34; Jos 17:1–18. The daughters of Zelophehad (v. 15) prompted the rulings on the inheritance rights of women (Nu 26:29–34; 27:1–11; 36:1–12; Jos 17:3–4). Of the 13 different clans of the tribe of Manasseh known from these genealogies, seven are mentioned in the Samaria ostraca (about 65 inscribed potsherds containing records of deliveries of wine, oil, barley and other commodities in the eighth century BC). The prominence of women in this genealogy is unusual; this suggests that it may have functioned in the domestic sphere, perhaps as a statement of the social status of the various clans of Manasseh (see Introduction: Genealogies).
7:20–29 The source for part of the genealogy of Ephraim is Nu 26:35. If Rephah (v. 25) is the grandson of Ephraim, ten generations are recorded from Ephraim to Joshua, a number that fits very well the 400-year interval when Israel was in Egypt. Joshua's Ephraimite ancestry is also mentioned in Nu 13:8 (where he is called "Hoshea"; see Nu 13:16). The raid against Gath (vv. 21–22) must have taken place well before the conquest of Canaan and must have originated in Egypt. The list of settlements (vv. 28–29) summarizes Jos 16–17.

Tahath his son, Eleadah his son,
Tahath his son, 21 Zabad his son
and Shuthelah his son.
Ezer and Elead were killed by the
native-born men of Gath, when they
went down to seize their livestock.
22 Their father Ephraim mourned for
them many days, and his relatives
came to comfort him. 23 Then he
made love to his wife again, and she
became pregnant and gave birth to a
son. He named him Beriah,[a] because
there had been misfortune in his family. 24 His daughter was Sheerah, who
built Lower and Upper Beth Horon[e] as
well as Uzzen Sheerah.

25 Rephah was his son, Resheph his
son,[b]
Telah his son, Tahan his son,
26 Ladan his son, Ammihud his son,
Elishama his son, 27 Nun his son
and Joshua his son.

28 Their lands and settlements included
Bethel and its surrounding villages, Naa-
ran to the east, Gezer[f] and its villages to
the west, and Shechem and its villages all
the way to Ayyah and its villages. 29 Along
the borders of Manasseh were Beth Shan,[g]
Taanach, Megiddo and Dor,[h] together with
their villages. The descendants of Joseph
son of Israel lived in these towns.

Asher

30 The sons of Asher:[i]
Imnah, Ishvah, Ishvi and Beriah.
Their sister was Serah.
31 The sons of Beriah:
Heber and Malkiel, who was the father of Birzaith.
32 Heber was the father of Japhlet, Shomer and Hotham and of their sister Shua.
33 The sons of Japhlet:
Pasak, Bimhal and Ashvath.
These were Japhlet's sons.
34 The sons of Shomer:
Ahi, Rohgah,[c] Hubbah and Aram.
35 The sons of his brother Helem:
Zophah, Imna, Shelesh and Amal.
36 The sons of Zophah:
Suah, Harnepher, Shual, Beri, Imrah, 37 Bezer, Hod, Shamma, Shil-
shah, Ithran[d] and Beera.
38 The sons of Jether:
Jephunneh, Pispah and Ara.
39 The sons of Ulla:
Arah, Hanniel and Rizia.
40 All these were descendants of Asher—heads of families, choice men, brave
warriors and outstanding leaders. The
number of men ready for battle, as listed
in their genealogy, was 26,000.

The Genealogy of Saul the Benjamite

8:28-38pp — 1Ch 9:34-44

8 Benjamin[j] was the father of Bela his
firstborn,
Ashbel the second son, Aharah the
third,
2 Nohah the fourth and Rapha the
fifth.
3 The sons of Bela were:
Addar,[k] Gera, Abihud,[e] 4 Abishua,
Naaman, Ahoah,[l] 5 Gera, Shephu-
phan and Huram.
6 These were the descendants of
Ehud,[m] who were heads of families
of those living in Geba and were
deported to Manahath:
7 Naaman, Ahijah, and Gera, who
deported them and who was the father of Uzza and Ahihud.
8 Sons were born to Shaharaim in
Moab after he had divorced his
wives Hushim and Baara. 9 By his
wife Hodesh he had Jobab, Zib-
ia, Mesha, Malkam, 10 Jeuz, Sakia
and Mirmah. These were his sons,
heads of families. 11 By Hushim he
had Abitub and Elpaal.
12 The sons of Elpaal:
Eber, Misham, Shemed (who built
Ono[n] and Lod with its surrounding villages), 13 and Beriah and
Shema, who were heads of families of those living in Aijalon[o] and
who drove out the inhabitants of
Gath.[p]
14 Ahio, Shashak, Jeremoth, 15 Zebadiah, Arad, Eder, 16 Michael, Ishpah
and Joha were the sons of Beriah.

7:24 [e] S Jos 10:10 **7:28** [f] Jos 10:33 **7:29** [g] S Jos 17:11 [h] S Jos 11:2 **7:30** [i] S Nu 1:40

8:1 [j] S Ge 46:21 **8:3** [k] S Ge 46:21 **8:4** [l] 2Sa 23:9 **8:6** [m] Jdg 3:12-30 **8:12** [n] Ezr 2:33; Ne 6:2; 7:37; 11:35 **8:13** [o] S Jos 10:12 [p] S Jos 11:22

[a] *23* *Beriah* sounds like the Hebrew for *misfortune.* [b] *25* Some Septuagint manuscripts; Hebrew does not have *his son.* [c] *34* Or *of his brother Shomer: Rohgah* [d] *37* Possibly a variant of *Jether* [e] *3* Or *Gera the father of Ehud*

7:30-40 The genealogy of Asher follows Ge 46:17 for the first three generations; it is also parallel to Nu 26:44-46, except that the name Ishvah (v. 30) is missing there. This genealogy too reflects a military function (v. 40).

8:1-40 The inclusion of a second and even more extensive genealogy of Benjamin (see note on 7:6-12) reflects both the importance of this tribe and the Chronicler's interest in Saul. Judah, Simeon and part of Benjamin had composed the southern kingdom (1Ki 12:1-21), and their territory largely comprised the restoration province of Judah in the Chronicler's own time. The genealogy of Benjamin is more extensive than that of all the other tribes except Judah and Levi. The Chronicler is also concerned with the genealogy of Saul (vv. 29-38) in order to set the stage for the historical narrative that begins with the end of his reign (ch. 10); Saul's genealogy is repeated in 9:35-44. Several references suggest that this genealogy also originated in the military sphere (vv. 6,10,13,28,40).

8:1-5 Cf. the lists in 7:6-12; Ge 46:21-22; Nu 26:38-41.

8:6-27 Unique to Chronicles.

17 Zebadiah, Meshullam, Hizki, Heber,
18 Ishmerai, Izliah and Jobab were
the sons of Elpaal.
19 Jakim, Zikri, Zabdi, 20 Elienai, Zillethai, Eliel, 21 Adaiah, Beraiah and
Shimrath were the sons of Shimei.
22 Ishpan, Eber, Eliel, 23 Abdon, Zikri,
Hanan, 24 Hananiah, Elam, Antho-
thijah, 25 Iphdeiah and Penuel were
the sons of Shashak.
26 Shamsherai, Shehariah, Athaliah,
27 Jaareshiah, Elijah and Zikri were
the sons of Jeroham.
28 All these were heads of families, chiefs
as listed in their genealogy, and they lived
in Jerusalem.

29 Jeiel[a] the father[b] of Gibeon lived in
Gibeon.[q]
His wife's name was Maakah,
30 and his firstborn son was Abdon,
followed by Zur, Kish, Baal, Ner,[c]
Nadab, 31 Gedor, Ahio, Zeker 32 and
Mikloth, who was the father of
Shimeah. They too lived near their
relatives in Jerusalem.
33 Ner[r] was the father of Kish,[s] Kish the
father of Saul[t], and Saul the father
of Jonathan, Malki-Shua, Abinadab
and Esh-Baal.[d u]
34 The son of Jonathan:[v]
Merib-Baal,[e w] who was the father
of Micah.
35 The sons of Micah:
Pithon, Melek, Tarea and Ahaz.
36 Ahaz was the father of Jehoaddah, Jehoaddah was the father of
Alemeth, Azmaveth and Zimri,
and Zimri was the father of Moza.
37 Moza was the father of Binea; Ra-
phah was his son, Eleasah his son
and Azel his son.
38 Azel had six sons, and these were
their names:
Azrikam, Bokeru, Ishmael, Sheari-
ah, Obadiah and Hanan. All these
were the sons of Azel.
39 The sons of his brother Eshek:
Ulam his firstborn, Jeush the second son and Eliphelet the third.
40 The sons of Ulam were brave
warriors who could handle the
bow. They had many sons and
grandsons — 150 in all.
All these were the descendants of
Benjamin.[x]

9 All Israel[y] was listed in the genealogies recorded in the book of the kings
of Israel and Judah. They were taken captive to Babylon[z] because of their unfaithfulness.[a]

The People in Jerusalem

9:1-17pp — Ne 11:3-19

2 Now the first to resettle on their own
property in their own towns[b] were some
Israelites, priests, Levites and temple servants.[c]
3 Those from Judah, from Benjamin, and
from Ephraim and Manasseh who lived in
Jerusalem were:
4 Uthai son of Ammihud, the son of
Omri, the son of Imri, the son of
Bani, a descendant of Perez son of
Judah.[d]
5 Of the Shelanites[f]:
Asaiah the firstborn and his sons.
6 Of the Zerahites:
Jeuel.
The people from Judah numbered
690.
7 Of the Benjamites:
Sallu son of Meshullam, the son of
Hodaviah, the son of Hassenuah;
8 Ibneiah son of Jeroham; Elah son
of Uzzi, the son of Mikri; and Meshullam son of Shephatiah, the son
of Reuel, the son of Ibnijah.
9 The people from Benjamin, as listed in their genealogy, numbered

8:29 [q] S Jos 9:3 **8:33** [r] S 1Sa 28:19 [s] S 1Sa 9:1 [t] 1Sa 14:49 [u] S 2Sa 2:8 **8:34** [v] S 2Sa 9:12 [w] S 2Sa 4:4; S 21:7-14 **8:40** [x] S Nu 26:38 **9:1** [y] 1Ch 11:1, 10; 12:38; 14:8; 15:3, 28; 18:14; 19:17; 21:5; 28:4, 8; 29:21, 23; 2Ch 1:2; 5:3; 7:8; 10:3, 16; 12:1; 13:4, 15; 18:16; 24:5; 28:23; 29:24; 30:1 [z] S Dt 21:10 [a] S 1Ch 5:25 **9:2** [b] Jos 9:27; Ezr 2:70 [c] Ezr 2:43, 58; 8:20; Ne 7:60 **9:4** [d] S Ge 38:29; 46:12

[a] *29* Some Septuagint manuscripts (see also 9:35); Hebrew does not have *Jeiel.* [b] *29* *Father* may mean *civic leader* or *military leader.* [c] *30* Some Septuagint manuscripts (see also 9:36); Hebrew does not have *Ner.* [d] *33* Also known as *Ish-Bosheth* [e] *34* Also known as *Mephibosheth* [f] *5* See Num. 26:20; Hebrew *Shilonites.*

8:29 – 38 Essentially the same as the list in 9:35 – 44.

8:33 For the sons of Saul, see 1Sa 14:49; 31:2. *Jonathan.* The firstborn and the best known of the sons of Saul, both for his military prowess and for his friendship with David (1Sa 13 – 14; 18:1 – 4; 19:1 – 7; 20:1 – 42; 23:16 – 18; 2Sa 21:13 – 14). *Esh-Baal.* See NIV text note; see also note on 2Sa 2:8.

8:34 *Merib-Baal.* See NIV text note; see also note on 2Sa 4:4.

9:1 *All Israel.* The Chronicler's concern with "all Israel" is one key to why he included the genealogies (see Introduction: Purpose and Themes). *book of the kings of Israel.* See Introduction: Author, Date and Sources.

9:2 – 34 This list of the members of the restored community reflects the Chronicler's concern with the institutions of his own day, especially the legitimacy of officeholders. He lists laity ("Israelites," v. 2) in vv. 3 – 9, priests in vv. 10 – 13 and Levites in vv. 14 – 34. He mentions a fourth class of returnees — the temple servants (v. 2) — but does not give them separate listing in the material that follows. They may originally have been foreigners who were incorporated into the Levites (Jos 9:23; Ezr 8:20) and so are not listed apart from that tribe. A similar office is known in the temple at ancient Ugarit. The list here is related to the one in Ne 11, but less than half the names are the same in the two lists.

9:3 *Ephraim and Manasseh.* Again reflecting his concern with "all Israel," the Chronicler shows that the returnees were not only from Judah and Benjamin but also from the northern tribes.

9:4 – 6 See 2:3 – 6; 4:21. The returnees of Judah are traced to Judah's sons Perez, Zerah and Shelah (see Nu 26:20).

956. All these men were heads of
their families.
10 Of the priests:
Jedaiah; Jehoiarib; Jakin;
11 Azariah son of Hilkiah, the son of
Meshullam, the son of Zadok, the
son of Meraioth, the son of Ahitub,
the official in charge of the house
of God;
12 Adaiah son of Jeroham, the son of
Pashhur,[e] the son of Malkijah; and
Maasai son of Adiel, the son of Jah-
zerah, the son of Meshullam, the
son of Meshillemith, the son of Immer.
13 The priests, who were heads of
families, numbered 1,760. They
were able men, responsible for
ministering in the house of God.
14 Of the Levites:
Shemaiah son of Hasshub, the son
of Azrikam, the son of Hashabiah,
a Merarite; 15 Bakbakkar, Heresh,
Galal and Mattaniah[f] son of Mika,
the son of Zikri, the son of Asaph;
16 Obadiah son of Shemaiah, the
son of Galal, the son of Jeduthun;
and Berekiah son of Asa, the son of
Elkanah, who lived in the villages
of the Netophathites.[g]
17 The gatekeepers:[h]
Shallum, Akkub, Talmon, Ahiman
and their fellow Levites, Shallum
their chief 18 being stationed at the
King's Gate[i] on the east, up to the
present time. These were the gatekeepers belonging to the camp of
the Levites. 19 Shallum[j] son of Kore,
the son of Ebiasaph, the son of
Korah, and his fellow gatekeepers from his family (the Korahites)
were responsible for guarding the
thresholds of the tent just as their
ancestors had been responsible for
guarding the entrance to the dwelling of the LORD. 20 In earlier times
Phinehas[k] son of Eleazar was the
official in charge of the gatekeepers, and the LORD was with him.

9:12 [e] Ezr 2:38; 10:22; Ne 10:3; Jer 21:1; 38:1
9:15 [f] 2Ch 20:14; Ne 11:22
9:16 [g] Ne 12:28
9:17 [h] ver 22; 1Ch 26:1; 2Ch 8:14; 31:14; Ezr 2:42; Ne 7:45
9:18 [i] 1Ch 26:14; Eze 43:1; 46:1
9:19 [j] Jer 35:4
9:20 [k] Nu 25:7-13
9:21 [l] 1Ch 26:2, 14
9:22 [m] S ver 17 [n] S 1Sa 9:9
9:25 [o] 2Ki 11:5
9:26 [p] 1Ch 26:22
9:27 [q] S Nu 3:38 [r] Isa 22:22
9:29 [s] S Nu 3:28; 1Ch 23:29
9:30 [t] S Ex 30:23-25
9:32 [u] Lev 24:5-8; 1Ch 23:29; 2Ch 13:11
9:33 [v] S 1Ch 6:31; 25:1-31; S 2Ch 5:12 [w] Ps 134:1

21 Zechariah[l] son of Meshelemiah
was the gatekeeper at the entrance
to the tent of meeting.
22 Altogether, those chosen to be gatekeepers[m] at the thresholds numbered
212. They were registered by genealogy
in their villages. The gatekeepers had
been assigned to their positions of trust
by David and Samuel the seer.[n] 23 They
and their descendants were in charge
of guarding the gates of the house of
the LORD — the house called the tent of
meeting. 24 The gatekeepers were on the
four sides: east, west, north and south.
25 Their fellow Levites in their villages
had to come from time to time and share
their duties for seven-day[o] periods. 26 But
the four principal gatekeepers, who were
Levites, were entrusted with the responsibility for the rooms and treasuries[p] in the
house of God. 27 They would spend the
night stationed around the house of God,[q]
because they had to guard it; and they
had charge of the key[r] for opening it each
morning.
28 Some of them were in charge of the
articles used in the temple service; they
counted them when they were brought
in and when they were taken out. 29 Others were assigned to take care of the furnishings and all the other articles of the
sanctuary,[s] as well as the special flour and
wine, and the olive oil, incense and spices.
30 But some[t] of the priests took care of mixing the spices. 31 A Levite named Mattithiah, the firstborn son of Shallum the Korahite, was entrusted with the responsibility
for baking the offering bread. 32 Some of
the Kohathites, their fellow Levites, were
in charge of preparing for every Sabbath
the bread set out on the table.[u]
33 Those who were musicians,[v] heads of
Levite families, stayed in the rooms of the
temple and were exempt from other duties because they were responsible for the
work day and night.[w]
34 All these were heads of Levite families, chiefs as listed in their genealogy, and
they lived in Jerusalem.

9:10 – 13 The list of priests is essentially the same as that in Ne 11:10 – 14. Since it is tied to the list of priests earlier in the genealogies (6:1 – 15,50 – 53), contemporary Israel's continuity with her past is shown.
9:15 – 16 *Asaph . . . Jeduthun.* Leaders of musical groups (6:39; 16:41). Later the Chronicler also lists the musicians (ch. 25) before the gatekeepers (ch. 26).
9:16 *Netophathites.* See note on Ne 12:28.
9:17 – 21 The Chronicler gives the names of four gatekeepers, while Ne 11:19 mentions only two. The chief of the gatekeepers had the honor of responsibility for the gate used by the king (Eze 46:1 – 2). The gatekeepers are also listed in ch. 26; Ezr 2:42. These officers traced their origin to Phinehas (v. 20; 6:4; Nu 3:32; 25:6 – 13).
9:22 – 27 Twenty-four guard stations were manned in three shifts around the clock; 72 men would be needed for each week. With a total of 212 men, each would have a tour of duty approximately every three weeks (26:12 – 18).
9:28 – 34 The Levites not only were responsible for the temple precincts and for opening the gates in the morning but also had charge of the chambers and supply rooms (23:28; 26:20 – 29), as well as the implements, supplies and furnishings (28:13 – 18; Ezr 1:9 – 11). In addition, they were responsible for the preparation of baked goods (Ex 25:30; Lev 2:5 – 7; 7:9). The priests alone prepared the perfumed anointing oil and spices (Ex 30:23 – 33).

The Genealogy of Saul

9:34-44pp — 1Ch 8:28-38

[35]Jeiel[x] the father[a] of Gibeon lived in
Gibeon.
His wife's name was Maakah,
[36]and his firstborn son was Abdon,
followed by Zur, Kish, Baal, Ner,
Nadab, [37]Gedor, Ahio, Zechariah
and Mikloth. [38]Mikloth was the
father of Shimeam. They too lived
near their relatives in Jerusalem.
[39]Ner[y] was the father of Kish,[z] Kish the
father of Saul, and Saul the father
of Jonathan,[a] Malki-Shua, Abinadab and Esh-Baal.[bb]
[40]The son of Jonathan:
Merib-Baal,[cc] who was the father of
Micah.
[41]The sons of Micah:
Pithon, Melek, Tahrea and Ahaz.[d]
[42]Ahaz was the father of Jadah, Jadah[e] was the father of Alemeth,
Azmaveth and Zimri, and Zimri
was the father of Moza. [43]Moza
was the father of Binea; Rephaiah
was his son, Eleasah his son and
Azel his son.
[44]Azel had six sons, and these were
their names:
Azrikam, Bokeru, Ishmael, Shea-
riah, Obadiah and Hanan. These
were the sons of Azel.

Saul Takes His Life

10:1-12pp — 1Sa 31:1-13; 2Sa 1:4-12

10 Now the Philistines fought against
Israel; the Israelites fled before
them, and many fell dead on Mount Gilboa. [2]The Philistines were in hot pursuit
of Saul and his sons, and they killed his
sons Jonathan, Abinadab and Malki-Shua.
[3]The fighting grew fierce around Saul,
and when the archers overtook him, they
wounded him.
[4]Saul said to his armor-bearer, "Draw
your sword and run me through, or these
uncircumcised fellows will come and
abuse me."
But his armor-bearer was terrified and
would not do it; so Saul took his own sword
and fell on it. [5]When the armor-bearer saw
that Saul was dead, he too fell on his sword
and died. [6]So Saul and his three sons died,
and all his house died together.
[7]When all the Israelites in the valley
saw that the army had fled and that Saul
and his sons had died, they abandoned
their towns and fled. And the Philistines
came and occupied them.
[8]The next day, when the Philistines
came to strip the dead, they found Saul
and his sons fallen on Mount Gilboa.
[9]They stripped him and took his head and
his armor, and sent messengers throughout the land of the Philistines to proclaim
the news among their idols and their people. [10]They put his armor in the temple
of their gods and hung up his head in the
temple of Dagon.[d]
[11]When all the inhabitants of Jabesh
Gilead[e] heard what the Philistines had
done to Saul, [12]all their valiant men went
and took the bodies of Saul and his sons
and brought them to Jabesh. Then they
buried their bones under the great tree in
Jabesh, and they fasted seven days.
[13]Saul died[f] because he was unfaithful[g]
to the LORD; he did not keep[h] the word of
the LORD and even consulted a medium[i]
for guidance, [14]and did not inquire of the
LORD. So the LORD put him to death and
turned[j] the kingdom[k] over to David son of
Jesse.

David Becomes King Over Israel

11:1-3pp — 2Sa 5:1-3

11 All Israel[l] came together to David at Hebron[m] and said, "We are
your own flesh and blood. [2]In the past,
even while Saul was king, you were the
one who led Israel on their military campaigns.[n] And the LORD your God said to
you, 'You will shepherd[o] my people Israel,
and you will become their ruler.[p]' "

9:35 [x]1Ch 8:29 **9:39** [y]S 1Ch 8:33 [z]S 1Sa 9:1 [a]1Sa 13:22 [b]S 2Sa 2:8 **9:40** [c]S 2Sa 4:4 **10:10** [d]S Jdg 16:23 **10:11** [e]S Jdg 21:8 **10:13** [f]S 2Sa 1:1 [g]S 1Ch 5:25 [h]S 1Sa 13:13 [i]S Lev 19:31; S 20:6; Dt 18:9-14 **10:14** [j]1Ch 12:23 [k]S 1Sa 13:14 **11:1** [l]S 1Ch 9:1 [m]S Ge 13:18; S 23:19 **11:2** [n]S 1Sa 18:5, 16 [o]Ps 78:71; Mt 2:6 [p]S 1Ch 5:2

[a] 35 *Father* may mean *civic leader* or *military leader.* [b] 39 Also known as *Ish-Bosheth* [c] 40 Also known as *Mephibosheth* [d] 41 Vulgate and Syriac (see also Septuagint and 8:35); Hebrew does not have *and Ahaz.* [e] 42 Some Hebrew manuscripts and Septuagint (see also 8:36); most Hebrew manuscripts *Jarah, Jarah*

9:35-44 The genealogy of Saul is duplicated here (see 8:29-38) as a transition to the short account of his reign that begins the Chronicler's narration (ch. 10).
10:1-14 This brief account of Saul's death introduces the reign of David, one of the Chronicler's major interests (see Introduction: Purpose and Themes; Portrait of David and Solomon).
10:2 For the strategy of pursuing the king in battle, see note on 1Ki 22:31.
10:6 *his three sons.* See v. 2 (Ish-Bosheth survived; see note on 1Sa 31:2). *all his house.* His three sons and his chief officials (his official "house"), not all his descendants (see 8:33-34 and notes; 1Sa 31:6).
10:13-14 These verses are not paralleled in the Samuel account; they were put here by the Chronicler in line with his concern with immediate retribution (see Introduction: Purpose and Themes). Seeking mediums was forbidden (Dt 18:9-14) and brought death to Saul. The Chronicler is obviously writing to an audience already familiar with Samuel and Kings, and he frequently assumes that knowledge. Here the consultation with the medium at Endor is alluded to (see 1Sa 28), but the Chronicler does not recount the incident.
11:1—2Ch 9:31 See Introduction: Portrait of David and Solomon.
11:1-3 The material here parallels that in 2Sa 5:1-3 but is recast by the Chronicler in accordance with his emphasis on

3 When all the elders of Israel had come
to King David at Hebron, he made a cov-
enant with them at Hebron before the
LORD, and they anointed[q] David king over
Israel, as the LORD had promised through
Samuel.

David Conquers Jerusalem

11:4-9pp — 2Sa 5:6-10

4 David and all the Israelites marched to
Jerusalem (that is, Jebus). The Jebusites[r]
who lived there 5 said to David, "You will
not get in here." Nevertheless, David captured the fortress of Zion — which is the
City of David.
6 David had said, "Whoever leads the
attack on the Jebusites will become commander-in-chief." Joab[s] son of Zeruiah
went up first, and so he received the command.
7 David then took up residence in the
fortress, and so it was called the City of
David. 8 He built up the city around it,
from the terraces[a][t] to the surrounding
wall, while Joab restored the rest of the
city. 9 And David became more and more
powerful,[u] because the LORD Almighty was
with him.

David's Mighty Warriors

11:10-41pp — 2Sa 23:8-39

10 These were the chiefs of David's
mighty warriors — they, together with all
Israel,[v] gave his kingship strong support
to extend it over the whole land, as the
LORD had promised[w] — 11 this is the list of
David's mighty warriors:[x]
Jashobeam,[b] a Hakmonite, was chief of
the officers[c]; he raised his spear against
three hundred men, whom he killed in
one encounter.
12 Next to him was Eleazar son of Dodai
the Ahohite, one of the three mighty warriors. 13 He was with David at Pas Dammim when the Philistines gathered there
for battle. At a place where there was a
field full of barley, the troops fled from the
Philistines. 14 But they took their stand in
the middle of the field. They defended it
and struck the Philistines down, and the
LORD brought about a great victory.[y]
15 Three of the thirty chiefs came down to
David to the rock at the cave of Adullam,
while a band of Philistines was encamped
in the Valley[z] of Rephaim. 16 At that time
David was in the stronghold,[a] and the Philistine garrison was at Bethlehem. 17 David
longed for water and said, "Oh, that someone would get me a drink of water from the
well near the gate of Bethlehem!" 18 So the
Three broke through the Philistine lines,
drew water from the well near the gate of
Bethlehem and carried it back to David. But
he refused to drink it; instead, he poured[b] it
out to the LORD. 19 "God forbid that I should
do this!" he said. "Should I drink the blood
of these men who went at the risk of their
lives?" Because they risked their lives to
bring it back, David would not drink it.
Such were the exploits of the three
mighty warriors.
20 Abishai[c] the brother of Joab was chief
of the Three. He raised his spear against
three hundred men, whom he killed, and
so he became as famous as the Three. 21 He
was doubly honored above the Three and
became their commander, even though he
was not included among them.
22 Benaiah son of Jehoiada, a valiant
fighter from Kabzeel,[d] performed great exploits. He struck down Moab's two mightiest warriors. He also went down into a pit
on a snowy day and killed a lion.[e] 23 And
he struck down an Egyptian who was five
cubits[d] tall. Although the Egyptian had a
spear like a weaver's rod[f] in his hand, Benaiah went against him with a club. He
snatched the spear from the Egyptian's
hand and killed him with his own spear.
24 Such were the exploits of Benaiah son
of Jehoiada; he too was as famous as the
three mighty warriors. 25 He was held in
greater honor than any of the Thirty, but
he was not included among the Three. And
David put him in charge of his bodyguard.

11:3 [q] 1Sa 16:1-13
11:4 [r] S Ge 10:16; S 15:18-21; S Jos 3:10; S 15:8
11:6 [s] S 2Sa 2:13
11:8 [t] S 2Sa 5:9; 2Ch 32:5
11:9 [u] Est 9:4
11:10 [v] ver 1 [w] ver 3; 1Ch 12:23
11:11 [x] S 2Sa 17:10
11:14 [y] S Ex 14:30; S 1Sa 11:13
11:15 [z] 1Ch 14:9; Isa 17:5
11:16 [a] S 2Sa 5:17
11:18 [b] S Dt 12:16
11:20 [c] S 1Sa 26:6
11:22 [d] S Jos 15:21 [e] 1Sa 17:36
11:23 [f] S 1Sa 17:7

[a] 8 Or *the Millo* [b] 11 Possibly a variant of *Jashob-Baal* [c] 11 Or *Thirty*; some Septuagint manuscripts *Three* (see also 2 Samuel 23:8) [d] 23 That is, about 7 feet 6 inches or about 2.3 meters

the popular support given David by "all Israel" (v. 1). While the Chronicler twice mentions the seven-year reign at Hebron before the death of Ish-Bosheth and the covenant with the northern tribes (3:4; 29:27), these incidents are bypassed in the narrative portion of the book. Most striking is the elimination at this point of the information in 2Sa 5:4 – 5. Rather, the Chronicler paints a picture of immediate accession over "all Israel," followed by the immediate conquest of Jerusalem (see Introduction: Portrait of David and Solomon). The author once again assumes the reader's knowledge of the parallel account.

11:4 – 9 See 2Sa 5:6 – 10 and notes. The "all Israel" theme appears in v. 4 ("all the Israelites") as a substitute for "the king and his men" (2Sa 5:6).

11:10 – 41a See 2Sa 23:8 – 39 and notes. In the Samuel account this list of David's mighty warriors is given near the end of his reign. The Chronicler has moved the list to the beginning of his reign and has greatly expanded it (11:41b — 12:40), again as part of his emphasis on the broad support of "all Israel" for the kingship of David (v. 10).

11:11 *three hundred.* Actually 800 (see 2Sa 23:8), 300 here apparently being a copyist's mistake, perhaps influenced by the same number in v. 20.

11:15 – 19 David recognizes that he is not worthy of such devotion and makes the water a drink offering to the Lord (see Ge 35:14; 2Ki 16:13; Jer 7:18; Hos 9:4).

11:22 *Benaiah ... killed a lion.* See photo, p. 648.

26 The mighty warriors were:
Asahel[g] the brother of Joab,
Elhanan son of Dodo from Bethlehem,
27 Shammoth[h] the Harorite,
Helez the Pelonite,
28 Ira son of Ikkesh from Tekoa,
Abiezer[i] from Anathoth,
29 Sibbekai[j] the Hushathite,
Ilai the Ahohite,
30 Maharai the Netophathite,
Heled son of Baanah the Netophathite,
31 Ithai son of Ribai from Gibeah in Benjamin,
Benaiah[k] the Pirathonite,[l]
32 Hurai from the ravines of Gaash,
Abiel the Arbathite,
33 Azmaveth the Baharumite,
Eliahba the Shaalbonite,
34 the sons of Hashem the Gizonite,
Jonathan son of Shagee the Hararite,
35 Ahiam son of Sakar the Hararite,
Eliphal son of Ur,
36 Hepher the Mekerathite,
Ahijah the Pelonite,
37 Hezro the Carmelite,
Naarai son of Ezbai,
38 Joel the brother of Nathan,
Mibhar son of Hagri,
39 Zelek the Ammonite,
Naharai the Berothite, the armor-bearer of Joab son of Zeruiah,
40 Ira the Ithrite,
Gareb the Ithrite,
41 Uriah[m] the Hittite,
Zabad[n] son of Ahlai,
42 Adina son of Shiza the Reubenite, who was chief of the Reubenites, and the thirty with him,
43 Hanan son of Maakah,
Joshaphat the Mithnite,
44 Uzzia the Ashterathite,[o]
Shama and Jeiel the sons of Hotham the Aroerite,
45 Jediael son of Shimri,
his brother Joha the Tizite,
46 Eliel the Mahavite,
Jeribai and Joshaviah the sons of Elnaam,
Ithmah the Moabite,
47 Eliel, Obed and Jaasiel the Mezobaite.

Killing a lion in the ancient Near East made a person a hero. Here Ashurbanipal is stabbing a lion with a sword. In 1 Chronicles 11:22, Benaiah, one of David's mighty men, is described as a "valiant fighter," and "he also went down into a pit on a snowy day and killed a lion."

11:26 [g] S 2Sa 2:18 **11:27** [h] 1Ch 27:8 **11:28** [i] 1Ch 27:12 **11:29** [j] S 2Sa 21:18 **11:31** [k] 1Ch 27:14 [l] S Jdg 12:13 **11:41** [m] 2Sa 11:6 [n] 1Ch 2:36 **11:44** [o] S Dt 1:4

Warriors Join David

12 These were the men who came
to David at Ziklag,[p] while he was
banished from the presence of Saul son of
Kish (they were among the warriors who
helped him in battle; 2 they were armed
with bows and were able to shoot arrows
or to sling stones right-handed or left-handed;[q] they were relatives of Saul[r] from
the tribe of Benjamin):

3 Ahiezer their chief and Joash the sons of Shemaah the Gibeathite; Jeziel and Pelet the sons of Azmaveth; Berakah, Jehu the Anathothite,
4 and
Ishmaiah the Gibeonite, a mighty warrior among the Thirty, who was a leader of the Thirty; Jeremiah, Jahaziel, Johanan, Jozabad the Gederathite,[a][s]
5 Eluzai, Jerimoth, Bealiah, Shemariah and Shephatiah the Haruphite;
6 Elkanah, Ishiah, Azarel, Joezer and Jashobeam the Korahites;
7 and Joelah and Zebadiah the sons of Jeroham from Gedor.[t]

8 Some Gadites[u] defected to David at his stronghold in the wilderness. They were brave warriors, ready for battle and able to handle the shield and spear. Their faces

12:1 [p] S Jos 15:31 **12:2** [q] S Jdg 3:15 [r] S 2Sa 3:19 **12:4** [s] Jos 15:36 **12:7** [t] S Jos 15:58 **12:8** [u] S Ge 30:11

[a] 4 In Hebrew texts the second half of this verse (*Jeremiah . . . Gederathite*) is numbered 12:5, and 12:5-40 is numbered 12:6-41.

11:41b—12:40 See note on vv. 10–41a. The list in 2Sa 23 ends with Uriah the Hittite (2Sa 11); the source for the additional names is not known. The emphasis continues to be on the support of "all Israel"—even Saul's own relatives recognized the legitimacy of David's kingship before Saul's death (12:1–7,16–18, 23,29).

12:1 The Chronicler assumes the reader's knowledge of the events at Ziklag (1Sa 27); see vv. 19–20.

12:8–15 The warriors of Gad were from Transjordan. Melting snows to the north would have brought the Jordan to flood stage in the first month (March-April) at the time of their crossing (v. 15). The most appropriate time for this incident

were the faces of lions,[v] and they were as
swift as gazelles[w] in the mountains.
9 Ezer was the chief,
Obadiah the second in command, Eliab the third,
10 Mishmannah the fourth, Jeremiah the
fifth,
11 Attai the sixth, Eliel the seventh,
12 Johanan the eighth, Elzabad the
ninth,
13 Jeremiah the tenth and Makbannai
the eleventh.
14 These Gadites were army commanders; the least was a match for a hundred,[x]
and the greatest for a thousand.[y] 15 It was
they who crossed the Jordan in the first
month when it was overflowing all its
banks,[z] and they put to flight everyone
living in the valleys, to the east and to the
west.
16 Other Benjamites[a] and some men
from Judah also came to David in his
stronghold. 17 David went out to meet
them and said to them, "If you have
come to me in peace to help me, I am
ready for you to join me. But if you have
come to betray me to my enemies when
my hands are free from violence, may
the God of our ancestors see it and judge
you."
18 Then the Spirit[b] came on Amasai,[c]
chief of the Thirty, and he said:

"We are yours, David!
We are with you, son of Jesse!
Success,[d] success to you,
and success to those who help you,
for your God will help you."

So David received them and made them
leaders of his raiding bands.
19 Some of the tribe of Manasseh defected to David when he went with the
Philistines to fight against Saul. (He and
his men did not help the Philistines because, after consultation, their rulers
sent him away. They said, "It will cost
us our heads if he deserts to his master
Saul.")[e] 20 When David went to Ziklag,[f]
these were the men of Manasseh who
defected to him: Adnah, Jozabad, Jediael, Michael, Jozabad, Elihu and Zillethai,
leaders of units of a thousand in Manasseh. 21 They helped David against raiding
bands, for all of them were brave warriors, and they were commanders in his
army. 22 Day after day men came to help
David, until he had a great army, like the
army of God.[a]

Others Join David at Hebron

23 These are the numbers of the men
armed for battle who came to David at
Hebron[g] to turn[h] Saul's kingdom over to
him, as the LORD had said:[i]
24 from Judah, carrying shield and
spear — 6,800 armed for battle;
25 from Simeon, warriors ready for battle — 7,100;
26 from Levi — 4,600, 27 including Jehoiada, leader of the family of Aaron,
with 3,700 men, 28 and Zadok,[j] a
brave young warrior, with 22 officers from his family;
29 from Benjamin,[k] Saul's tribe — 3,000,
most[l] of whom had remained loyal
to Saul's house until then;
30 from Ephraim, brave warriors, famous in their own clans — 20,800;
31 from half the tribe of Manasseh, designated by name to come and make
David king — 18,000;
32 from Issachar, men who understood
the times and knew what Israel
should do[m] — 200 chiefs, with all
their relatives under their command;
33 from Zebulun, experienced soldiers
prepared for battle with every type
of weapon, to help David with undivided loyalty — 50,000;
34 from Naphtali — 1,000 officers, together with 37,000 men carrying
shields and spears;
35 from Dan, ready for battle — 28,600;

12:8 [v] 2Sa 17:10 [w] S 2Sa 2:18 **12:14** [x] S Lev 26:8 [y] S Dt 32:30 **12:15** [z] S Jos 3:15 **12:16** [a] S 2Sa 3:19 **12:18** [b] S Jdg 3:10; 1Ch 28:12; 2Ch 15:1; 20:14; 24:20 [c] S 2Sa 17:25 [d] 1Sa 25:5-6 **12:19** [e] 1Sa 29:2-11 **12:20** [f] S 1Sa 27:6
12:23 [g] 2Sa 2:3-4 [h] 1Ch 10:14 [i] S 1Sa 16:1; 1Ch 11:10 **12:28** [j] 1Ch 6:8; 15:11; 16:39; 27:17 **12:29** [k] S 2Sa 3:19 [l] 2Sa 2:8-9 **12:32** [m] Est 1:13

[a] 22 Or *a great and mighty army*

would have been in the period of David's wandering in the region of the Dead Sea (1Sa 23:14; 24:1; 25:1; 26:1).

12:23 – 37 The emphasis remains on "all Israel" (v. 38). Though 13 tribes are named, they are grouped in order to maintain the traditional number of 12 (see note on 2:1 – 2). The northernmost tribes and those east of the Jordan River send the largest number of men (vv. 33 – 37), reinforcing the degree of support that David enjoyed not only in Judah and Benjamin but throughout the other tribes as well. The numbers in this section seem quite high. Essentially two approaches are followed on this question: (1) It is possible to explain the numbers so that a lower figure is actually attained. The Hebrew word for "thousand" may represent a unit of a tribe, each having its own commander (13:1; see Nu 31:14,48,52,54). In this case the numbers would be read not as a total figure, but as representative commanders. For example, the 6,800 from Judah (v. 24) would be read either as six commanders of 1,000 and eight commanders of 100 (see 13:1), or possibly as six commanders of thousands and 800 men (see Introduction to Numbers: Special Problem). Reducing the numbers in this fashion fits well with 13:1 and with the list of commanders alone found for Zadok's family (v. 28) and the tribe of Issachar (v. 32). Taking the numbers as straight totals would require the presence of 340,800 persons in Hebron for a feast at the same time. (2) Another approach is to allow the numbers to stand and to view them as hyperbole on the part of the Chronicler to achieve a number "like the army of God" (v. 22). This approach would fit well with the Chronicler's glorification of David and with the banquet scene that follows.

36 from Asher, experienced soldiers prepared for battle—40,000;
37 and from east of the Jordan, from Reuben, Gad and the half-tribe of Manasseh, armed with every type of weapon—120,000.
38 All these were fighting men who volunteered to serve in the ranks. They came
to Hebron fully determined to make David
king over all Israel.[n] All the rest of the Israelites were also of one mind to make David king. 39 The men spent three days there
with David, eating and drinking,[o] for their
families had supplied provisions for them.
40 Also, their neighbors from as far away
as Issachar, Zebulun and Naphtali came
bringing food on donkeys, camels, mules
and oxen. There were plentiful supplies[p]
of flour, fig cakes, raisin[q] cakes, wine, olive oil, cattle and sheep, for there was joy[r]
in Israel.

Bringing Back the Ark

13:1-14pp — 2Sa 6:1-11

13 David conferred with each of his officers, the commanders of thousands and commanders of hundreds. 2 He
then said to the whole assembly of Israel,
"If it seems good to you and if it is the will
of the LORD our God, let us send word far
and wide to the rest of our people throughout the territories of Israel, and also to the
priests and Levites who are with them in
their towns and pasturelands, to come and
join us. 3 Let us bring the ark of our God
back to us,[s] for we did not inquire[t] of[a]
it[b] during the reign of Saul." 4 The whole
assembly agreed to do this, because it
seemed right to all the people.
5 So David assembled all Israel,[u] from the
Shihor River[v] in Egypt to Lebo Hamath,[w]
to bring the ark of God from Kiriath Jearim.[x] 6 David and all Israel went to Baalah[y]
of Judah (Kiriath Jearim) to bring up from
there the ark of God the LORD, who is enthroned between the cherubim[z]—the ark
that is called by the Name.
7 They moved the ark of God from Abinadab's[a] house on a new cart, with Uzzah
and Ahio guiding it. 8 David and all the Israelites were celebrating with all their might
before God, with songs and with harps,
lyres, timbrels, cymbals and trumpets.[b]
9 When they came to the threshing floor
of Kidon, Uzzah reached out his hand to
steady the ark, because the oxen stumbled. 10 The LORD's anger[c] burned against
Uzzah, and he struck him down[d] because
he had put his hand on the ark. So he died
there before God.
11 Then David was angry because the
LORD's wrath had broken out against Uzzah, and to this day that place is called
Perez Uzzah.[ce]
12 David was afraid of God that day and
asked, "How can I ever bring the ark of
God to me?" 13 He did not take the ark to
be with him in the City of David. Instead,
he took it to the house of Obed-Edom[f] the
Gittite. 14 The ark of God remained with

[a] 3 Or *we neglected* [b] 3 Or *him* [c] 11 *Perez Uzzah* means *outbreak against Uzzah.*

12:38 [n] S 1Ch 9:1 **12:39** [o] 2Sa 3:20; Isa 25:6-8 **12:40** [p] S 2Sa 16:1; 17:29 [q] 1Sa 25:18 [r] 1Ch 29:22 **13:3** [s] 1Sa 7:1-2 [t] 2Ch 1:5 **13:5** [u] 1Ch 11:1; 15:3 [v] S Jos 13:3 [w] S Nu 13:21 [x] S 1Sa 7:2 **13:6** [y] S Jos 15:9 [z] S Ex 25:22; 2Ki 19:15 **13:7** [a] S 1Sa 7:1 **13:8** [b] 1Ch 15:16,19, 24; 2Ch 5:12; Ps 92:3 **13:10** [c] 1Ch 15:13,15 [d] S Lev 10:2 **13:11** [e] 1Ch 15:13; Ps 7:11 **13:13** [f] 1Ch 15:18,24; 16:38; 26:4-5, 15

12:38–40 The Chronicler's portrait of David is influenced by his Messianic expectations (see Introduction: Purpose and Themes). In the presence of a third of a million people (see note on vv. 23–37) David's coronation banquet typifies the future Messianic feast (Isa 25:6–8). The imagery of the Messianic banquet became prominent in the intertestamental literature (*Apocalypse of Baruch* 29:4–8; *Enoch* 62:14) and in the NT (see Mt 8:11–12 and Lk 13:28–30; Mt 22:1–10 and Lk 14:16–24; see also Mt 25:1–13; Lk 22:28–30; Rev 19:7–9). The Lord's Supper anticipates that coming banquet (Mt 26:29; Mk 14:25; Lk 22:15–18; 1Co 11:23–26).

13:1–14 See 2Sa 6:1–11 and notes. The author abandons the chronological order as given in 2Sa 5–6 and puts the transfer of the ark first, delaying his account of the palace building and the Philistine campaign until later (ch. 14). This is in accordance with his portrayal of David; David's concern with the ark was expressed immediately upon his accession—his consultation with the leaders appears to be set in the context of the coronation banquet (12:38–40).

13:1–4 These verses are not found in Samuel and reflect the Chronicler's own concerns with "all Israel." The semi-military expedition to retrieve the ark in 2Sa 6:1 is here broadened by consultation with and support from the whole assembly of Israel, "throughout the territories" (v. 2), including the priests and Levites—an important point for the Chronicler since only they are allowed to move the ark (15:2,13; 23:25–27; Dt 10:8).

13:3 *we did not inquire of it during the reign of Saul.* 1Sa 14:18 may be an exception (but see note there).

13:5–6 The emphasis remains on the united action of "all Israel." Israelites came to participate in this venture all the way from Lebo Hamath in the north and from the Shihor River in the south.

13:5 *Shihor.* An Egyptian term meaning "the pool of Horus." It appears to be a part of the Nile or one of the major canals of the Nile (see Jos 13:3; Isa 23:3; Jer 2:18 and notes).

13:6 *Baalah.* The Canaanite name for Kiriath Jearim, also known as Kiriath Baal (Jos 18:14). The Chronicler assumes that his readers are familiar with the account of how the ark came to be at Kiriath Jearim (1Sa 6:1—7:1). *the Name.* See Ex 23:21 and note.

13:7 *Uzzah and Ahio.* Sons or descendants of Abinadab (2Sa 6:3).

13:10 *because he had put his hand on the ark.* The ark was to be moved only by Levites, who carried it with poles inserted through rings in the sides of the ark (Ex 25:12–15). None of the holy things was to be touched, on penalty of death (Nu 4:15). These strictures were observed in the second and successful attempt to move the ark to Jerusalem (15:1–15). It cannot be known whether Uzzah and Ahio were Levites—the Samuel account does not mention the presence of Levites, but the Chronicler's careful inclusion of Levites in this expedition suggests that they were present (see note on vv. 1–4). In any case, the ark should not have been moved on a cart (as done by the Philistines, 1Sa 6) or touched.

13:13 *Obed-Edom.* Perhaps the same man mentioned in 15:18,21,24. In 26:4 God's blessing on Obed-Edom includes

the family of Obed-Edom in his house for
three months, and the LORD blessed his
household[g] and everything he had.

David's House and Family

14:1-7pp — 2Sa 5:11-16; 1Ch 3:5-8

14 Now Hiram king of Tyre sent messengers to David, along with cedar logs,[h] stonemasons and carpenters to
build a palace for him. 2And David knew
that the LORD had established him as king
over Israel and that his kingdom had been
highly exalted[i] for the sake of his people
Israel.
3In Jerusalem David took more wives
and became the father of more sons[j] and
daughters. 4These are the names of the
children born to him there:[k] Shammua,
Shobab, Nathan, Solomon, 5Ibhar, Elishua, Elpelet, 6Nogah, Nepheg, Japhia,
7Elishama, Beeliada[a] and Eliphelet.

David Defeats the Philistines

14:8-17pp — 2Sa 5:17-25

8When the Philistines heard that David had been anointed king over all Israel,[l] they went up in full force to search for
him, but David heard about it and went
out to meet them. 9Now the Philistines
had come and raided the Valley[m] of Rephaim; 10so David inquired of God: "Shall I
go and attack the Philistines? Will you deliver them into my hands?"
The LORD answered him, "Go, I will deliver them into your hands."
11So David and his men went up to Baal
Perazim,[n] and there he defeated them. He
said, "As waters break out, God has broken out against my enemies by my hand."
So that place was called Baal Perazim.[b]
12The Philistines had abandoned their
gods there, and David gave orders to burn[o]
them in the fire.[p]
13Once more the Philistines raided the
valley;[q] 14so David inquired of God again,
and God answered him, "Do not go directly after them, but circle around them and
attack them in front of the poplar trees.
15As soon as you hear the sound of marching in the tops of the poplar trees, move
out to battle, because that will mean God
has gone out in front of you to strike the
Philistine army." 16So David did as God
commanded him, and they struck down
the Philistine army, all the way from Gibeon[r] to Gezer.[s]
17So David's fame[t] spread throughout
every land, and the LORD made all the nations fear[u] him.

The Ark Brought to Jerusalem

15:25–16:3pp — 2Sa 6:12-19

15 After David had constructed buildings for himself in the City of David, he prepared[v] a place for the ark of
God and pitched[w] a tent for it. 2Then David said, "No one but the Levites[x] may carry[y] the ark of God, because the LORD chose
them to carry the ark of the LORD and to
minister[z] before him forever."

[a] 7 A variant of *Eliada* [b] 11 *Baal Perazim* means *the lord who breaks out.*

13:14 [g]S 2Sa 6:11 **14:1** [h]S 1Ki 5:6; 1Ch 17:6; 22:4; 2Ch 2:3; Ezr 3:7; Hag 1:8 **14:2** [i]S Nu 24:7; S Dt 26:19 **14:3** [j]S 1Ch 3:1 **14:4** [k]S 1Ch 3:9 **14:8** [l]1Ch 11:1 **14:9** [m]ver 13; S Jos 15:8; S 1Ch 11:15 **14:11** [n]Ps 94:16; Isa 28:21 **14:12** [o]S Ex 32:20 [p]S Jos 7:15 **14:13** [q]S ver 9 **14:16** [r]S Jos 9:3 [s]Jos 10:33 **14:17** [t]S Jos 6:27 [u]Ex 15:14-16; S Dt 2:25; Ps 2:1-12 **15:1** [v]Ps 132:1-18 [w]S 2Sa 6:17; 1Ch 16:1; 17:1 **15:2** [x]S Nu 3:6; 4:15; Dt 10:8; 31:25; 2Ch 5:5 [y]S Dt 31:9 [z]1Ch 16:4; 23:13; 2Ch 29:11; 31:2; Ps 134:1; 135:2

numerous sons. This reference also establishes that Obed-Edom was a Levite and that the ark was properly left in his care.

14:1 – 17 The Chronicler backtracks to pick up material from 2Sa 5 deferred to this point (see note on 13:1 – 14). The three-month period that the ark remained with Obed-Edom (13:14) was filled with incidents showing God's blessing on David: the building of his royal house (vv. 1 – 2), his large family (vv. 3 – 7) and his success in warfare (vv. 8 – 16) — all because of the Lord's blessing (vv. 2,17).

14:1 – 2 See 2Sa 5:11 – 12 and notes.

14:1 *Hiram.* Later provided materials and labor for building the temple (2Ch 2). His mention here implies international recognition of David as king over Israel and a treaty between David and Hiram.

14:3 – 7 See 3:1 – 9 and note; 2Sa 5:13 – 16. David's children born in Hebron are omitted (3:1 – 4; 2Sa 3:2 – 5; see note on 11:1 – 3).

14:7 *Beeliada.* Eliada (see NIV text note) in 3:8; 2Sa 5:16.

14:8 – 12 See 2Sa 5:17 – 21 and notes.

14:11 *break out ... Perazim.* The Hebrew underlying the name of this place where the Lord broke out against the Philistines is the same as that underlying the word used in 13:11 when the Lord broke out against Uzzah (see NIV text notes there and here).

14:12 *gave orders to burn them.* 2Sa 5:21 does not mention burning but says that David and his men carried the idols away. Many have seen here an intentional change on the part of the Chronicler in order to bring David's actions into strict conformity with the law, which required that pagan idols be burned (Dt 7:5,25). However, some Septuagint (the pre-Christian Greek translation of the OT) manuscripts of Samuel agree with Chronicles that David burned the idols. This would indicate that the Chronicler was not innovating for theological reasons but was carefully reproducing the Hebrew text he had before him, which differed from the Masoretic (later Hebrew) text of Samuel.

14:13 – 16 See 2Sa 5:22 – 25 and notes.

14:17 *the LORD made all the nations fear him.* Here and elsewhere the Chronicler uses an expression that refers to an incapacitating terror brought on by the sense that the awesome power of God is present in behalf of his people (see Ex 15:16). Thus David is seen by the nations as the very representative of God (similarly Asa, 2Ch 14:14; Jehoshaphat, 2Ch 17:10; 20:29).

15:1 — 16:3 This account of the successful attempt to move the ark to Jerusalem is greatly expanded over the material in 2 Samuel. Only 15:25 — 16:3 has a parallel (2Sa 6:12 – 19); the rest of the material is unique to the Chronicler and reflects his own interests, especially in the Levites and worship musicians (vv. 3 – 24; see Introduction: Purpose and Themes). Ps 132 should also be read in connection with this account.

15:1 *constructed buildings for himself.* See 14:1 – 2 and note on 13:1 – 14.

15:2 – 3 See note on 13:10.

3 David assembled all Israel[a] in Jerusalem to bring up the ark of the LORD to the place he had prepared for it. 4 He called together the descendants of Aaron and the Levites:[b]

5 From the descendants of Kohath,
Uriel[c] the leader and 120 relatives;
6 from the descendants of Merari,
Asaiah the leader and 220 relatives;
7 from the descendants of Gershon,[a]
Joel the leader and 130 relatives;
8 from the descendants of Elizaphan,[d]
Shemaiah the leader and 200 relatives;
9 from the descendants of Hebron,[e]
Eliel the leader and 80 relatives;
10 from the descendants of Uzziel,
Amminadab the leader and 112 relatives.

11 Then David summoned Zadok[f] and Abiathar[g] the priests, and Uriel, Asaiah, Joel, Shemaiah, Eliel and Amminadab the Levites. 12 He said to them, "You are the heads of the Levitical families; you and your fellow Levites are to consecrate[h] yourselves and bring up the ark of the LORD, the God of Israel, to the place I have prepared for it. 13 It was because you, the Levites,[i] did not bring it up the first time that the LORD our God broke out in anger against us.[j] We did not inquire of him about how to do it in the prescribed way.[k]" 14 So the priests and Levites consecrated themselves in order to bring up the ark of the LORD, the God of Israel. 15 And the Levites carried the ark of God with the poles on their shoulders, as Moses had commanded[l] in accordance with the word of the LORD.[m]

16 David[n] told the leaders of the Levites[o] to appoint their fellow Levites as musicians[p] to make a joyful sound with musical instruments: lyres, harps and cymbals.[q]

17 So the Levites appointed Heman[r] son of Joel; from his relatives, Asaph[s] son of Berekiah; and from their relatives the Merarites,[t] Ethan son of Kushaiah; 18 and with them their relatives next in rank: Zechariah,[b] Jaaziel, Shemiramoth, Jehiel, Unni, Eliab, Benaiah, Maaseiah, Mattithiah, Eliphelehu, Mikneiah, Obed-Edom[u] and Jeiel,[c] the gatekeepers.

19 The musicians Heman,[v] Asaph and Ethan were to sound the bronze cymbals; 20 Zechariah, Jaaziel,[d] Shemiramoth, Jehiel, Unni, Eliab, Maaseiah and Benaiah were to play the lyres according to *alamoth*,[e] 21 and Mattithiah, Eliphelehu, Mikneiah, Obed-Edom, Jeiel and Azaziah were to play the harps, directing according to *sheminith*.[e] 22 Kenaniah the head Levite was in charge of the singing; that was his responsibility because he was skillful at it.

23 Berekiah and Elkanah were to be doorkeepers for the ark. 24 Shebaniah, Joshaphat, Nethanel, Amasai, Zechariah, Benaiah and Eliezer the priests were

15:3 [a] S 1Ch 13:5
15:4 [b] S Nu 3:17-20
15:5 [c] 1Ch 6:24
15:8 [d] S Ex 6:22
15:9 [e] Ex 6:18
15:11 [f] S 1Ch 12:28 [g] S 1Sa 22:20
15:12 [h] S Ex 29:1; 30:19-21, 30; 40:31-32; S Lev 11:44
15:13 [i] 1Ki 8:4 [j] S 1Ch 13:7-10 [k] S Lev 5:10
15:15 [l] S Ex 25:14 [m] 2Sa 6:7
15:16 [n] 1Ch 6:31 [o] 2Ch 7:6 [p] Ezr 2:41; Ne 11:23; Ps 68:25 [q] S 1Ch 13:8; 23:5; 2Ch 29:26; Ne 12:27,36; Job 21:12; Ps 150:5; Am 6:5
15:17 [r] S 1Ch 6:33 [s] 1Ch 6:39 [t] 1Ch 6:44
15:18 [u] S 2Sa 6:10; 1Ch 26:4-5
15:19 [v] 1Ch 16:41; 25:6

[a] 7 Hebrew *Gershom*, a variant of *Gershon* [b] 18 Three Hebrew manuscripts and most Septuagint manuscripts (see also verse 20 and 16:5); most Hebrew manuscripts *Zechariah son and* or *Zechariah, Ben and* [c] 18 Hebrew; Septuagint (see also verse 21) *Jeiel and Azaziah* [d] 20 See verse 18; Hebrew *Aziel*, a variant of *Jaaziel*. [e] 20,21 Probably a musical term

15:4–10 The three clans of Levi are represented (Kohath, Merari and Gershon), as well as three distinct subgroups within Kohath (Elizaphan, Hebron and Uzziel)—862 in all.
15:12 *consecrate yourselves.* Through ritual washings and avoidance of ceremonial defilement (Ex 29:1–37; 30:19–21; 40:31–32; Lev 8:5–35).
15:13–15 The Chronicler provides the explanation for the failure in the first attempt to move the ark, an explanation not found in the Samuel account (see note on 13:10).
15:18,21,24 *Obed-Edom.* See note on 13:13.
15:24 *priests were to blow trumpets.* See 16:6; Nu 10:1–10.

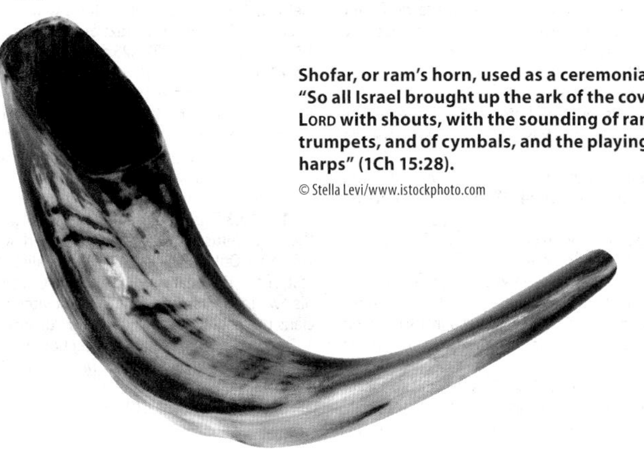

Shofar, or ram's horn, used as a ceremonial trumpet. "So all Israel brought up the ark of the covenant of the LORD with shouts, with the sounding of rams' horns and trumpets, and of cymbals, and the playing of lyres and harps" (1Ch 15:28).

to blow trumpets[w] before the ark of God.
Obed-Edom and Jehiah were also to be
doorkeepers for the ark.
25 So David and the elders of Israel and
the commanders of units of a thousand
went to bring up the ark[x] of the covenant
of the LORD from the house of Obed-Edom,
with rejoicing. 26 Because God had helped
the Levites who were carrying the ark of
the covenant of the LORD, seven bulls and
seven rams[y] were sacrificed. 27 Now David
was clothed in a robe of fine linen, as were
all the Levites who were carrying the ark,
and as were the musicians, and Kenaniah, who was in charge of the singing of
the choirs. David also wore a linen ephod.[z]
28 So all Israel[a] brought up the ark of the
covenant of the LORD with shouts,[b] with
the sounding of rams' horns[c] and trumpets, and of cymbals, and the playing of
lyres and harps.
29 As the ark of the covenant of the LORD
was entering the City of David, Michal
daughter of Saul watched from a window.
And when she saw King David dancing
and celebrating, she despised him in her
heart.

Ministering Before the Ark

16:8-22pp — Ps 105:1-15
16:23-33pp — Ps 96:1-13
16:34-36pp — Ps 106:1,47-48

16 They brought the ark of God and
set it inside the tent that David had
pitched[d] for it, and they presented burnt
offerings and fellowship offerings before
God. 2 After David had finished sacrificing
the burnt offerings and fellowship offerings, he blessed[e] the people in the name of
the LORD. 3 Then he gave a loaf of bread, a
cake of dates and a cake of raisins[f] to each
Israelite man and woman.
4 He appointed some of the Levites to
minister[g] before the ark of the LORD, to extol,[a] thank, and praise the LORD, the God
of Israel: 5 Asaph was the chief, and next
to him in rank were Zechariah, then Jaaziel,[b] Shemiramoth, Jehiel, Mattithiah, Eliab, Benaiah, Obed-Edom and Jeiel. They
were to play the lyres and harps, Asaph
was to sound the cymbals, 6 and Benaiah
and Jahaziel the priests were to blow the
trumpets regularly before the ark of the
covenant of God.
7 That day David first appointed Asaph
and his associates to give praise[h] to the
LORD in this manner:

8 Give praise[i] to the LORD, proclaim his
name;
make known among the nations[j]
what he has done.
9 Sing to him, sing praise[k] to him;
tell of all his wonderful acts.
10 Glory in his holy name;[l]
let the hearts of those who seek the
LORD rejoice.
11 Look to the LORD and his strength;
seek[m] his face always.
12 Remember[n] the wonders[o] he has done,
his miracles,[p] and the judgments he
pronounced,
13 you his servants, the descendants of
Israel,
his chosen ones, the children of
Jacob.
14 He is the LORD our God;
his judgments[q] are in all the earth.
15 He remembers[c][r] his covenant forever,
the promise he made, for a thousand
generations,
16 the covenant[s] he made with Abraham,
the oath he swore to Isaac.
17 He confirmed it to Jacob[t] as a decree,

15:24 [w] 2Ch 5:12; 7:6; 29:26 **15:25** [x] 2Ch 1:4; 5:2; Jer 3:16 **15:26** [y] Nu 23:1-4,29 **15:27** [z] S 1Sa 2:18 **15:28** [a] S 1Ch 9:1 [b] S 1Ki 1:39; Zec 4:7 [c] S Ex 19:13 **16:1** [d] S 1Ch 15:1 **16:2** [e] S Ex 39:43; Nu 6:23-27 **16:3** [f] Isa 16:7 **16:4** [g] S 1Ch 15:2 **16:7** [h] Ps 47:7 **16:8** [i] ver 34; Ps 107:1; 118:1; 136:1 [j] S 2Ki 19:19 **16:9** [k] S Ex 15:1; Ps 7:17 **16:10** [l] Ps 8:1; 29:2; 66:2 **16:11** [m] ver 10; 1Ch 28:9; 2Ch 7:14; 14:4; 15:2,12; 16:12; 18:4; 20:4; 34:3; Ps 24:6; 27:8; 105:4; 119:2, 58; Pr 8:17 **16:12** [n] Ps 77:11 [o] S Dt 4:34 [p] Ps 78:43 **16:14** [q] Isa 4:4; 26:9 **16:15** [r] S Ge 8:1; Ps 98:3; 111:5; 115:12; 136:23 **16:16** [s] S Ge 12:7; S 15:18; 22:16-18 **16:17** [t] Ge 35:9-12

[a] 4 Or *petition*; or *invoke* [b] 5 See 15:18,20; Hebrew *Jeiel*, possibly another name for *Jaaziel*. [c] 15 Some Septuagint manuscripts (see also Psalm 105:8); Hebrew *Remember*

15:27 Both 2Sa 6:14 and the Chronicler mention David's wearing a linen ephod, a garment worn by priests (1Sa 2:18; 22:18). The Chronicler adds, however, that David (as well as the rest of the Levites in the procession) was wearing a robe of fine linen, further associating him with the dress of the priestly functionaries. Apparently the Chronicler viewed David as a priest-king, a kind of Messianic figure (see Ps 110; Zec 6:9–15).

15:29 Parallel to 2Sa 6:16, but the Chronicler omits the remainder of this incident recorded there (2Sa 6:20–23). Some interpreters regard this omission as part of the Chronicler's positive view of David, so that a possibly unseemly account is omitted. On the other hand, it is equally plausible that the Chronicler here simply assumes the reader's knowledge of the other account (see notes on 10:13–14; 11:1–3; 12:1; 13:6).

16:1–3 David is further associated with the priests in his supervision of the sacrifices and his exercising the priestly prerogative of blessing the people (Nu 6:22–27; see note on 15:27 above). The baked goods provided by David were for the sacrificial meal following the fellowship offerings (Lev 3:1–17; 7:11–21,28–36).

16:4 *to extol, thank, and praise the LORD.* If the NIV text note ("petition") represents the correct translation (cf. "petition" in Ps 38 title and Ps 70 title), then the three words may refer to the three main types of psalms: (1) lament and/or petition, (2) thanksgiving and (3) praise (see Introduction to Psalms: Psalm Types; see also note on Col 3:16).

16:8–36 Similar to various parts of the book of Psalms (for vv. 8–22, see Ps 105:1–15; for vv. 23–33, Ps 96; for vv. 34–36, Ps 106:1,47–48). This psalm is not found in the Samuel account. The use of the lengthy historical portion from Ps 105 emphasizing the promises to Abraham would be particularly relevant to the Chronicler's postexilic audience, for whom the faithfulness of God was a fresh reality in their return to the land. The citation from Ps 106 would also be of immediate relevance to the Chronicler's audience as those who had been gathered and delivered from the nations (v. 35).

to Israel as an everlasting covenant:
18 "To you I will give the land of Canaan[u]
as the portion you will inherit."

19 When they were but few in number,[v]
few indeed, and strangers in it,
20 they[a] wandered[w] from nation to nation,
from one kingdom to another.
21 He allowed no one to oppress them;
for their sake he rebuked kings:[x]
22 "Do not touch my anointed ones;
do my prophets[y] no harm."

23 Sing to the LORD, all the earth;
proclaim his salvation day after day.
24 Declare his glory[z] among the nations,
his marvelous deeds among all
peoples.

25 For great is the LORD and most worthy
of praise;[a]
he is to be feared[b] above all gods.[c]
26 For all the gods of the nations are
idols,
but the LORD made the heavens.[d]
27 Splendor and majesty are before him;
strength and joy are in his dwelling
place.

28 Ascribe to the LORD, all you families of
nations,
ascribe to the LORD glory and
strength.[e]
29 Ascribe to the LORD the glory due his
name;[f]
bring an offering and come before
him.
Worship the LORD in the splendor of
his[b] holiness.[g]
30 Tremble[h] before him, all the earth!
The world is firmly established; it
cannot be moved.[i]

31 Let the heavens rejoice, let the earth be
glad;[j]
let them say among the nations,
"The LORD reigns![k]"
32 Let the sea resound, and all that is
in it;[l]
let the fields be jubilant, and
everything in them!
33 Let the trees[m] of the forest sing,
let them sing for joy before the LORD,
for he comes to judge[n] the earth.

34 Give thanks[o] to the LORD, for he is
good;[p]
his love endures forever.[q]

16:18 [u]Ge 13:14-17 **16:19** [v]Dt 7:7 **16:20** [w]S Ge 20:13 **16:21** [x]Ge 12:17; S 20:3; Ex 7:15-18; Ps 9:5 **16:22** [y]S Ge 20:7 **16:24** [z]Isa 42:12; 66:19 **16:25** [a]Ps 18:3; 48:1 [b]Ps 76:7; 89:7 [c]Ex 18:11; Dt 32:39; 2Ch 2:5; Ps 135:5; Isa 40:25 **16:26** [d]Ps 8:3; 102:25 **16:28** [e]Ps 29:1-2 **16:29** [f]Ps 8:1 [g]2Ch 20:21; Ps 29:1-2 **16:30** [h]Ps 2:11; 33:8; 76:8; 99:1; 114:7 [i]Ps 93:1 **16:31** [j]Isa 44:23; 49:13 [k]Ps 9:7; 47:8; 93:1; 97:1; 99:1; 146:10; Isa 52:7; La 5:19 **16:32** [l]Ex 20:11; Isa 42:10 **16:33** [m]Isa 14:8; 55:12 [n]1Sa 2:10; Ps 7:8; 96:10; 98:9; 110:6; Isa 2:4 **16:34** [o]S ver 8; Ps 105:1; Isa 12:4 [p]Ps 25:7; 34:8; 100:5; 135:3; 145:9; Na 1:7 [q]2Ch 5:13; 7:3; Ezr 3:11; Ps 136:1-26; Jer 33:11 **16:35** [r]Dt 32:15; Ps 18:46; 38:22; Mic 7:7 **16:36** [s]S 1Ki 8:15; Ps 72:18-19 **16:37** [t]2Ch 8:14 **16:38** [u]S 1Ch 13:13; 26:4-5 [v]1Ch 26:10 **16:39** [w]S 1Sa 2:35; S 2Sa 8:17; S 1Ch 12:28 [x]S Jos 9:3; 2Ch 1:3 **16:40** [y]S Ex 29:38; Nu 28:1-8 **16:41** [z]S 1Ch 15:19

35 Cry out, "Save us, God our Savior;[r]
gather us and deliver us from the
nations,
that we may give thanks to your holy
name,
and glory in your praise."
36 Praise be to the LORD, the God of
Israel,[s]
from everlasting to everlasting.

Then all the people said "Amen" and
"Praise the LORD."

37 David left Asaph and his associates
before the ark of the covenant of the LORD
to minister there regularly, according to
each day's requirements.[t] 38 He also left
Obed-Edom[u] and his sixty-eight associates to minister with them. Obed-Edom
son of Jeduthun, and also Hosah,[v] were
gatekeepers.
39 David left Zadok[w] the priest and his
fellow priests before the tabernacle of the
LORD at the high place in Gibeon[x] 40 to present burnt offerings to the LORD on the
altar of burnt offering regularly, morning and evening, in accordance with everything written in the Law[y] of the LORD,
which he had given Israel. 41 With them
were Heman[z] and Jeduthun and the rest
of those chosen and designated by name
to give thanks to the LORD, "for his love
endures forever." 42 Heman and Jeduthun
were responsible for the sounding of the
trumpets and cymbals and for the playing
of the other instruments for sacred song.[a]
The sons of Jeduthun[b] were stationed at
the gate.
43 Then all the people left, each for their
own home, and David returned home to
bless his family.

God's Promise to David

17:1-15pp — 2Sa 7:1-17

17 After David was settled in his palace, he said to Nathan the proph-
et, "Here I am, living in a house of cedar,
while the ark of the covenant of the LORD
is under a tent.[c]"
2 Nathan replied to David, "Whatever

[a] *18-20* One Hebrew manuscript, Septuagint and Vulgate (see also Psalm 105:12); most Hebrew manuscripts *inherit, / [19]though you are but few in number, / few indeed, and strangers in it." / [20]They* [b] *29* Or LORD *with the splendor of*

16:42 [a]2Ch 7:6 [b]1Ch 25:3 **17:1** [c]S 1Ch 15:1

16:29 *splendor of his holiness.* See 2Ch 20:21; see also Ps 29:2 and note; 96:9; 110:3.
16:39 *tabernacle ... in Gibeon.* The tabernacle remained at Gibeon until Solomon's construction of the temple in Jerusalem (2Ch 1:13; 5:5), when it was stored within the temple. The existence of these two shrines — the tabernacle and the temporary structure for the ark in Jerusalem (v. 1) — accounts for the two high priests: Zadok serving in Gibeon and Abiathar in Jerusalem (18:16; 27:34; see note on 6:8).
16:42 *sounding of the trumpets.* See Nu 10:1 – 10.
17:1 – 27 See 2Sa 7 and notes.
17:1,10 In these verses the Chronicler omits the statement that David had rest from his enemies (2Sa 7:1,11). Several factors may be at work in this omission: (1) The account of Da-

you have mind,[d] do it, for God is with
you."
3 But that night the word of God came to
Nathan, saying:

4 "Go and tell my servant David,
'This is what the LORD says: You[e]
are not the one to build me a house
to dwell in. 5 I have not dwelt in a
house from the day I brought Israel
up out of Egypt to this day. I have
moved from one tent site to another,
from one dwelling place to another.
6 Wherever I have moved with all the
Israelites, did I ever say to any of their
leaders[a] whom I commanded to shepherd my people, "Why have you not
built me a house of cedar?[f]" '
7 "Now then, tell my servant David, 'This is what the LORD Almighty
says: I took you from the pasture,
from tending the flock, and appointed you ruler[g] over my people Israel.
8 I have been with you wherever you
have gone, and I have cut off all your
enemies from before you. Now I will
make your name like the names of
the greatest men on earth. 9 And I will
provide a place for my people Israel
and will plant them so that they can
have a home of their own and no longer be disturbed. Wicked people will
not oppress them anymore, as they
did at the beginning 10 and have done
ever since the time I appointed leaders[h] over my people Israel. I will also
subdue all your enemies.
" 'I declare to you that the LORD
will build a house for you: 11 When
your days are over and you go to be
with your ancestors, I will raise up
your offspring to succeed you, one of
your own sons, and I will establish
his kingdom. 12 He is the one who will
build[i] a house for me, and I will establish his throne forever.[j] 13 I will be
his father,[k] and he will be my son.[l]
I will never take my love away from
him, as I took it away from your predecessor. 14 I will set him over my
house and my kingdom forever; his
throne[m] will be established forever.[n]' "

15 Nathan reported to David all the
words of this entire revelation.

David's Prayer

17:16-27pp — 2Sa 7:18-29

16 Then King David went in and sat before the LORD, and he said:

"Who am I, LORD God, and what
is my family, that you have brought
me this far? 17 And as if this were not
enough in your sight, my God, you
have spoken about the future of the
house of your servant. You, LORD
God, have looked on me as though I
were the most exalted of men.
18 "What more can David say to you
for honoring your servant? For you
know your servant, 19 LORD. For the
sake[o] of your servant and according
to your will, you have done this great
thing and made known all these great
promises.[p]
20 "There is no one like you, LORD,
and there is no God but you,[q] as we
have heard with our own ears. 21 And
who is like your people Israel — the
one nation on earth whose God went
out to redeem[r] a people for himself,
and to make a name for yourself, and
to perform great and awesome wonders by driving out nations from before your people, whom you redeemed
from Egypt? 22 You made your people
Israel your very own forever,[s] and you,
LORD, have become their God.

17:2 [d] 1Ch 22:7; 28:2; 2Ch 6:7 **17:4** [e] 1Ch 22:10; 28:3 **17:6** [f] S 1Ch 14:1 **17:7** [g] S 2Sa 6:21 **17:10** [h] S Jdg 2:16 **17:12** [i] S 1Ki 5:5 [j] 1Ch 22:10; 2Ch 7:18; 13:5 **17:13** [k] 2Co 6:18 [l] 1Ch 28:6; Lk 1:32; Heb 1:5* **17:14** [m] S 1Ki 2:12; 1Ch 28:5; 29:23; 2Ch 9:8 [n] Ps 132:11; Jer 33:17 **17:19** [o] 2Sa 7:16-17; 2Ki 20:6; Isa 9:7; 37:35; 55:3 [p] S 2Sa 7:25 **17:20** [q] S Ex 8:10; S 9:14; S 15:11; Isa 44:6; 46:9 **17:21** [r] S Ex 6:6 **17:22** [s] Ex 19:5-6

[a] 6 Traditionally *judges*; also in verse 10

---

vid's major wars is yet to come (chs. 18 – 20). Chronologically, this passage should follow the account of the wars (v. 8), but the author has placed it here to continue his concern with the ark and the building of the temple (vv. 4 – 6,12). (2) The Chronicler also views David as a man of war through most of his life (22:6 – 8), in contrast to Solomon, who is the man of "peace and rest" (22:9) and who will build the temple (22:10). For the Chronicler, David has rest from enemies only late in his life (22:18). (3) As part of his concern to parallel David and Solomon to Moses and Joshua, Solomon (like Joshua) brings the people to rest from enemies (see Introduction: Portrait of David and Solomon).

17:12 – 14 Though in this context these words refer to Solomon, the NT applies them to Jesus (Mk 1:11; Lk 1:32 – 33; Heb 1:5).

17:13 The Chronicler omits from his source (2Sa 7:14) any reference to "punish him with a rod" or "floggings" as discipline for Solomon. This omission reflects his idealization of Solomon as a Messianic figure, for whom such punishment would not be appropriate (see Introduction: Portrait of David and Solomon).

17:14 The Chronicler introduces his own concerns by the changes in the pronouns found in his source (2Sa 7:16); instead of "your house and your kingdom," the Chronicler reads "my house and my kingdom." This same emphasis on theocracy (God's rule) is found in several other passages unique to Chronicles (28:5 – 6; 29:23; 2Ch 1:11; 9:8; 13:4 – 8).

17:16 *sat.* Aside from its parallel in 2Sa 7:18, the only other reference in the OT to sitting as a posture for prayer is 1Ki 19:4. Three other postures for prayer are mentioned in Scripture: (1) lying prostrate (Dt 9:25 – 26; Mt 26:39); (2) standing (1Sa 1:26; Mt 6:5; Mk 11:25; Lk 18:11); (3) kneeling (Da 6:10; Lk 22:41; Ac 9:40; 20:36; 21:5; Eph 3:14).

17:21 – 22 The references to the exodus from Egypt would remind the Chronicler's audience of the second great exodus, the release of the restoration community from the period of Babylonian exile.

23 “And now, LORD, let the promise[t] you have made concerning your
servant and his house be established
forever. Do as you promised, 24 so that
it will be established and that your
name will be great forever. Then people will say, ‘The LORD Almighty, the
God over Israel, is Israel’s God!’ And
the house of your servant David will
be established before you.
25 “You, my God, have revealed to
your servant that you will build a
house for him. So your servant has
found courage to pray to you. 26 You,
LORD, are God! You have promised
these good things to your servant.
27 Now you have been pleased to bless
the house of your servant, that it may
continue forever in your sight;[u] for
you, LORD, have blessed it, and it will
be blessed forever.”

David’s Victories

18:1-13pp — 2Sa 8:1-14

18 In the course of time, David defeated the Philistines and subdued
them, and he took Gath and its surrounding villages from the control of the Philistines.
2 David also defeated the Moabites,[v] and
they became subject to him and brought
him tribute.
3 Moreover, David defeated Hadadezer
king of Zobah,[w] in the vicinity of Hamath,
when he went to set up his monument at[a]
the Euphrates River.[x] 4 David captured a
thousand of his chariots, seven thousand
charioteers and twenty thousand foot soldiers. He hamstrung[y] all but a hundred of
the chariot horses.
5 When the Arameans of Damascus[z]
came to help Hadadezer king of Zobah,
David struck down twenty-two thousand
of them. 6 He put garrisons in the Aramean
kingdom of Damascus, and the Arameans
became subject to him and brought him
tribute. The LORD gave David victory wherever he went.
7 David took the gold shields carried
by the officers of Hadadezer and brought
them to Jerusalem. 8 From Tebah[b] and
Kun, towns that belonged to Hadadezer,
David took a great quantity of bronze,
which Solomon used to make the bronze
Sea,[a] the pillars and various bronze articles.
9 When Tou king of Hamath heard that
David had defeated the entire army of
Hadadezer king of Zobah, 10 he sent his
son Hadoram to King David to greet him
and congratulate him on his victory in battle over Hadadezer, who had been at war
with Tou. Hadoram brought all kinds of
articles of gold, of silver and of bronze.
11 King David dedicated these articles to
the LORD, as he had done with the silver
and gold he had taken from all these nations: Edom[b] and Moab, the Ammonites
and the Philistines, and Amalek.[c]
12 Abishai son of Zeruiah struck down
eighteen thousand Edomites[d] in the Valley
of Salt. 13 He put garrisons in Edom, and
all the Edomites became subject to David.
The LORD gave David victory wherever he
went.

David’s Officials

18:14-17pp — 2Sa 8:15-18

14 David reigned[e] over all Israel,[f] doing
what was just and right for all his people.
15 Joab[g] son of Zeruiah was over the army;
Jehoshaphat son of Ahilud was recorder;
16 Zadok[h] son of Ahitub and Ahimelek[c][i]

17:23 [t] S 1Ki 8:25 **17:27** [u] Ps 16:11; 21:6 **18:2** [v] S Nu 21:29 **18:3** [w] 1Ch 19:6 [x] S Ge 2:14 **18:4** [y] S Ge 49:6 **18:5** [z] 2Ki 16:9 **18:8** [a] S 1Ki 7:23; 2Ch 4:2-5 **18:11** [b] S Nu 24:18 [c] Nu 24:20 **18:12** [d] 1Ki 11:15 **18:14** [e] 1Ch 29:26 [f] 1Ch 11:1 **18:15** [g] 2Sa 5:6-8 **18:16** [h] 1Ch 6:8 [i] 1Ch 24:6

[a] 3 Or *to restore his control over* [b] 8 Hebrew *Tibhath,* a variant of *Tebah* [c] 16 Some Hebrew manuscripts, Vulgate and Syriac (see also 2 Samuel 8:17); most Hebrew manuscripts *Abimelek*

18:1 — 20:8 The accounts of David’s wars serve to show the blessing of God on his reign; God keeps his promise to subdue David’s enemies (17:10). These accounts are also particularly relevant to a theme developed in the postexilic prophets: that the silver and gold of the nations would flow to Jerusalem; the tribute of enemy peoples builds the temple of God (18:7 – 8,11; 22:2 – 5,14 – 15; cf. Hag 2:1 – 9,20 – 23; Zec 2:7 – 13; 6:9 – 15; 14:12 – 14). While this passage of Chronicles portrays God’s blessing on David, it simultaneously explains the Chronicler’s report later (22:6 – 8; 28:3) that David could not build the temple because he was a man of war. The material in these chapters essentially follows the Chronicler’s source in 2 Samuel. The major differences are not changes the Chronicler introduces into the text, but items he chooses not to deal with — in particular 2Sa 9; 11:2 — 12:25, where accounts not compatible with his portrait of David occur.

18:1 - 13 See 2Sa 8:1 - 14 and notes.

18:2 The Chronicler omits the harsh treatment of the Moabites recorded in 2Sa 8:2, perhaps so that no unnecessary cruelty or brutality would tarnish his portrait of David.

18:5 *Arameans.* Mentioned also among the enemies of Saul (1Sa 14:47, “Zobah”). By the time of David they were united north (Zobah) and south (Beth Rehob, 2Sa 10:6) under Hadadezer. They persisted as a foe of Israel for two centuries until they fell to Assyria shortly before the northern kingdom likewise fell (2Ki 16:7 – 9). See note on Dt 26:5.

18:8 *Tebah and Kun.* Located in the valley between the Lebanon and Anti-Lebanon mountain ranges. *which Solomon used to make … various bronze articles.* See 2Ch 4:2 – 5,18.

18:12 *Abishai.* 2Sa 8:13 speaks only of David (see 1Ki 11:15 – 16; Ps 60 title).

18:15 - 17 The titles and duties of these officers at David’s court appear to be modeled on the organization of Egyptian functionaries serving the pharaoh.

18:15 For the account of how Joab attained his position over the army, see 11:4 – 6; 2Sa 5:6 – 8.

18:16 *Zadok … Ahimelek son of Abiathar.* See notes on 6:8; 16:39; 2Sa 8:17.

son of Abiathar were priests; Shavsha was
secretary; 17Benaiah son of Jehoiada was
over the Kerethites and Pelethites;[j] and David's sons were chief officials at the king's
side.

David Defeats the Ammonites

19:1-19pp — 2Sa 10:1-19

19 In the course of time, Nahash
king of the Ammonites[k] died, and
his son succeeded him as king. 2David
thought, "I will show kindness to Hanun
son of Nahash, because his father showed
kindness to me." So David sent a delegation to express his sympathy to Hanun
concerning his father.

When David's envoys came to Hanun in
the land of the Ammonites to express sympathy to him, 3the Ammonite commanders said to Hanun, "Do you think David is
honoring your father by sending envoys
to you to express sympathy? Haven't his
envoys come to you only to explore and
spy out[l] the country and overthrow it?"
4So Hanun seized David's envoys, shaved
them, cut off their garments at the buttocks, and sent them away.

5When someone came and told David
about the men, he sent messengers to
meet them, for they were greatly humiliated. The king said, "Stay at Jericho till your
beards have grown, and then come back."

6When the Ammonites realized that
they had become obnoxious[m] to David,
Hanun and the Ammonites sent a thousand talents[a] of silver to hire chariots and
charioteers from Aram Naharaim,[b] Aram
Maakah and Zobah.[n] 7They hired thirty-
two thousand chariots and charioteers,
as well as the king of Maakah with his
troops, who came and camped near Medeba,[o] while the Ammonites were mustered
from their towns and moved out for battle.

18:17 [j]S 1Sa 30:14; S 2Sa 15:18
19:1 [k]S Ge 19:38; Jdg 10:17-11:33; 2Ch 20:1-2; Zep 2:8-11
19:3 [l]S Nu 21:32
19:6 [m]S Ge 34:30 [n]S 1Ch 18:3
19:7 [o]S Nu 21:30
19:11 [p]S 1Sa 26:6
19:17 [q]S 1Ch 9:1

8On hearing this, David sent Joab out
with the entire army of fighting men. 9The
Ammonites came out and drew up in battle formation at the entrance to their city,
while the kings who had come were by
themselves in the open country.

10Joab saw that there were battle lines
in front of him and behind him; so he
selected some of the best troops in Israel and deployed them against the Arameans. 11He put the rest of the men under
the command of Abishai[p] his brother, and
they were deployed against the Ammonites. 12Joab said, "If the Arameans are too
strong for me, then you are to rescue me;
but if the Ammonites are too strong for
you, then I will rescue you. 13Be strong,
and let us fight bravely for our people and
the cities of our God. The LORD will do
what is good in his sight."

14Then Joab and the troops with him
advanced to fight the Arameans, and they
fled before him. 15When the Ammonites
realized that the Arameans were fleeing,
they too fled before his brother Abishai
and went inside the city. So Joab went
back to Jerusalem.

16After the Arameans saw that they had
been routed by Israel, they sent messengers and had Arameans brought from beyond the Euphrates River, with Shophak
the commander of Hadadezer's army leading them.

17When David was told of this, he gathered all Israel[q] and crossed the Jordan; he
advanced against them and formed his
battle lines opposite them. David formed
his lines to meet the Arameans in battle,
and they fought against him. 18But they
fled before Israel, and David killed seven
thousand of their charioteers and forty

[a] *6* That is, about 38 tons or about 34 metric tons
[b] *6* That is, Northwest Mesopotamia

18:17 *Kerethites and Pelethites.* A group of foreign mercenaries who constituted part of the royal bodyguard (2Sa 8:18; 20:23; see note on 1Sa 30:14). They remained loyal to David at the time of the rebellions of Absalom (2Sa 15:18) and Sheba (2Sa 20:7) and supported the succession of Solomon against his rival Adonijah (1Ki 1:38,44). *chief officials.* The earlier narrative at this point uses the Hebrew term ordinarily translated "priests" (see 2Sa 8:18 and note). The Chronicler has used a term for civil service instead of sacral service. Two approaches to this passage are usually followed: (1) Some interpreters see here an attempt by the Chronicler to keep the priesthood restricted to the Levitical line as part of his larger concern with legitimacy of religious institutions in his own day. (2) Others argue that the Hebrew term used in 2Sa 8:18 could earlier have had a broader meaning than "priest" and could be used of some other types of officials (cf. 2Sa 20:26; 1Ki 4:5). The Chronicler used an equivalent term, since by his day the Hebrew term for "priest" was restricted to priestly functionaries.

19:1 — 20:3 The Chronicler follows 2Sa 10–12 closely (see notes there), apart from his omission of the account of David's sin with Bathsheba (11:2 — 12:25). The Ammonites were a traditional enemy of Israel (2Ch 20:1–2,23; 27:5; Jdg 3:13; 10:7–9; 10:17 — 11:33; 1Sa 11:1–13; 14:47; 2Ki 10:32–33; Jer 49:1–6; Zep 2:8–11). Even during the postexilic period Tobiah the Ammonite troubled Jerusalem (Ne 2:19; 4:3,7; 6:1,12,14; 13:4–9).

19:1 *Nahash.* Possibly the same as Saul's foe (1Sa 11:1), or perhaps his descendant.

19:6 *Aram Naharaim, Aram Maakah and Zobah.* 2Sa 10:6 also mentions Beth Rehob and Tob. All these states were north and northeast of Israel and formed a solid block from the region of Lake Huleh through the Anti-Lebanon mountains to beyond the Euphrates.

19:7 *Medeba.* A town in Moab apparently in the hands of the Ammonites.

19:9 *their city.* The capital city, Rabbah, to which Joab would lay siege the following year (20:1–3).

19:18 *seven thousand.* 2Sa 10:18 has 700, which may be a copyist's mistake.

thousand of their foot soldiers. He also
killed Shophak the commander of their
army.
19 When the vassals of Hadadezer saw
that they had been routed by Israel, they
made peace with David and became subject to him.
So the Arameans were not willing to
help the Ammonites anymore.

The Capture of Rabbah

20:1-3pp — 2Sa 11:1; 12:29-31

20 In the spring, at the time when
kings go off to war, Joab led out
the armed forces. He laid waste the land
of the Ammonites and went to Rabbah[r]
and besieged it, but David remained in Jerusalem. Joab attacked Rabbah and left it
in ruins.[s] 2 David took the crown from the
head of their king[a] — its weight was found
to be a talent[b] of gold, and it was set with
precious stones — and it was placed on
David's head. He took a great quantity of
plunder from the city 3 and brought out the
people who were there, consigning them
to labor with saws and with iron picks and
axes.[t] David did this to all the Ammonite
towns. Then David and his entire army returned to Jerusalem.

War With the Philistines

20:4-8pp — 2Sa 21:15-22

4 In the course of time, war broke out
with the Philistines, at Gezer.[u] At that time
Sibbekai the Hushathite killed Sippai, one
of the descendants of the Rephaites,[v] and
the Philistines were subjugated.
5 In another battle with the Philistines,
Elhanan son of Jair killed Lahmi the brother of Goliath the Gittite, who had a spear
with a shaft like a weaver's rod.[w]
6 In still another battle, which took place
at Gath, there was a huge man with six
fingers on each hand and six toes on each
foot — twenty-four in all. He also was descended from Rapha. 7 When he taunted
Israel, Jonathan son of Shimea, David's
brother, killed him.
8 These were descendants of Rapha in
Gath, and they fell at the hands of David
and his men.

David Counts the Fighting Men

21:1-26pp — 2Sa 24:1-25

21 Satan[x] rose up against Israel and
incited David to take a census[y] of
Israel. 2 So David said to Joab and the commanders of the troops, "Go and count[z] the
Israelites from Beersheba to Dan. Then report back to me so that I may know how
many there are."
3 But Joab replied, "May the LORD multiply his troops a hundred times over.[a] My
lord the king, are they not all my lord's
subjects? Why does my lord want to do
this? Why should he bring guilt on Israel?"
4 The king's word, however, overruled
Joab; so Joab left and went throughout
Israel and then came back to Jerusalem.
5 Joab reported the number of the fighting
men to David: In all Israel[b] there were one
million one hundred thousand men who
could handle a sword, including four hundred and seventy thousand in Judah.
6 But Joab did not include Levi and
Benjamin in the numbering, because the

20:1 [r] S Dt 3:11 [s] Am 1:13-15 **20:3** [t] S Dt 29:11 **20:4** [u] Jos 10:33 [v] S Ge 14:5 **20:5** [w] S 1Sa 17:7 **21:1** [x] S 2Ch 18:21; S Ps 109:6 [y] 2Ch 14:8; 25:5 **21:2** [z] 1Ch 27:23-24 **21:3** [a] S Dt 1:11 **21:5** [b] S 1Ch 9:1

[a] *2* Or *of Milkom,* that is, Molek [b] *2* That is, about 75 pounds or about 34 kilograms

20:1 *when kings go off to war.* Immediately following the spring harvest when there was some relaxation of agricultural labors and when armies on the move could live off the land. *Rabbah.* See note on 19:9. Rabbah is the site of modern Amman, Jordan.
20:2-3 The Chronicler assumes that the reader is familiar with 2Sa 12:26-29; he does not offer an explanation of how David, who had remained in Jerusalem (v. 1), came to be at Rabbah.
20:4 *Sibbekai.* See 11:29; 27:11. *Rephaites.* Ancient people known for their large size (see Ge 14:5; Dt 2:10-11; see also note on 2Sa 21:16).
20:5 See note on 2Sa 21:19. *weaver's rod.* See 11:23; 1Sa 17:7.
20:6 *Rapha.* See note on 2Sa 21:16.
21:1—22:1 See 2Sa 24 and notes. Although the story of David's census is quite similar in both narratives, the two accounts function differently. In Samuel the account belongs to the appendix (2Sa 21-24), which begins and ends with accounts of the Lord's anger against Israel during the reign of David because of actions by her kings (in ch. 21, an act of Saul; in ch. 24, an act of David). See note on 2Sa 21:1—24:25. The Chronicler appears to include it in order to account for the purchase of the ground on which the temple would be built. The additional material in Chronicles that is not found in Samuel (21:28—22:1) makes this interest clear. The census is the preface to David's preparations for the temple (chs. 22-29).
21:1 See note on 2Sa 24:1. *Satan.* See NIV text notes on Job 1:6; Zec 3:1; see also notes on Mt 16:23; 2Co 4:4; 1Th 3:5; 1Jn 3:8.
21:4 The Chronicler abridges the more extensive account of Joab's itinerary found in 2Sa 24:4-8; he does not mention that the census required nine months and 20 days (2Sa 24:8).
21:5 *In all Israel ... one million one hundred thousand men ... including four hundred and seventy thousand in Judah.* 2Sa 24:9 has 800,000 in Israel and 500,000 (which could be a round number for 470,000) in Judah. The reason for the difference is unclear. Perhaps it is to be related to the unofficial and incomplete nature of the census (see 27:23-24), with the differing figures representing the inclusion or exclusion of certain unspecified groupings among the people (see v. 6). Or perhaps it is simply due to a copyist's mistake. The NIV relieves the problem somewhat by translating the conjunction here as "including" instead of "and." See note on 12:23-37; see also Introduction to Numbers: Special Problem.
21:6 The Chronicler adds the note that Joab exempted Levi and Benjamin from the counting. This additional note reflects the Chronicler's concern with the Levites and with the worship of Israel. The tabernacle in Gibeon and the ark in Jerusalem both fell within the borders of Benjamin.

king's command was repulsive to him.
7 This command was also evil in the sight
of God; so he punished Israel.
8 Then David said to God, "I have sinned
greatly by doing this. Now, I beg you, take
away the guilt of your servant. I have done
a very foolish thing."
9 The LORD said to Gad,[c] David's seer,[d]
10 "Go and tell David, 'This is what the
LORD says: I am giving you three options.
Choose one of them for me to carry out
against you.'"
11 So Gad went to David and said to
him, "This is what the LORD says: 'Take
your choice: 12 three years of famine,[e]
three months of being swept away[a] before
your enemies, with their swords overtaking you, or three days of the sword[f] of the
LORD[g]—days of plague in the land, with
the angel of the LORD ravaging every part
of Israel.' Now then, decide how I should
answer the one who sent me."
13 David said to Gad, "I am in deep distress. Let me fall into the hands of the
LORD, for his mercy[h] is very great; but do
not let me fall into human hands."
14 So the LORD sent a plague on Israel,
and seventy thousand men of Israel fell
dead.[i] 15 And God sent an angel[j] to destroy
Jerusalem.[k] But as the angel was doing so,
the LORD saw it and relented[l] concerning
the disaster and said to the angel who was
destroying[m] the people, "Enough! Withdraw your hand." The angel of the LORD
was then standing at the threshing floor
of Araunah[b] the Jebusite.
16 David looked up and saw the angel
of the LORD standing between heaven and
earth, with a drawn sword in his hand extended over Jerusalem. Then David and
the elders, clothed in sackcloth, fell facedown.[n]
17 David said to God, "Was it not I who
ordered the fighting men to be counted?
I, the shepherd,[c] have sinned and done
wrong. These are but sheep.[o] What have
they done? LORD my God, let your hand
fall on me and my family,[p] but do not let
this plague remain on your people."

David Builds an Altar

18 Then the angel of the LORD ordered
Gad to tell David to go up and build an
altar to the LORD on the threshing floor[q]
of Araunah the Jebusite. 19 So David went
up in obedience to the word that Gad had
spoken in the name of the LORD.
20 While Araunah was threshing wheat,[r]
he turned and saw the angel; his four
sons who were with him hid themselves.
21 Then David approached, and when
Araunah looked and saw him, he left the
threshing floor and bowed down before
David with his face to the ground.
22 David said to him, "Let me have the
site of your threshing floor so I can build
an altar to the LORD, that the plague on the
people may be stopped. Sell it to me at the
full price."
23 Araunah said to David, "Take it! Let
my lord the king do whatever pleases him.
Look, I will give the oxen for the burnt
offerings, the threshing sledges for the
wood, and the wheat for the grain offering. I will give all this."
24 But King David replied to Araunah,
"No, I insist on paying the full price. I
will not take for the LORD what is yours,
or sacrifice a burnt offering that costs me
nothing."
25 So David paid Araunah six hundred
shekels[d] of gold for the site. 26 David built
an altar to the LORD there and sacrificed
burnt offerings and fellowship offerings.
He called on the LORD, and the LORD answered him with fire[s] from heaven on the
altar of burnt offering.
27 Then the LORD spoke to the angel, and
he put his sword back into its sheath. 28 At
that time, when David saw that the LORD
had answered him on the threshing floor
of Araunah the Jebusite, he offered sacrifices there. 29 The tabernacle of the LORD,
which Moses had made in the wilderness,
and the altar of burnt offering were at that
time on the high place at Gibeon.[t] 30 But
David could not go before it to inquire of
God, because he was afraid of the sword
of the angel of the LORD.

21:9 [c] S 1Sa 22:5 [d] S 1Sa 9:9
21:12 [e] S Dt 32:24 [f] Eze 30:25 [g] S Ge 19:13
21:13 [h] Ps 6:4; 86:15; 130:4,7
21:14 [i] 1Ch 27:24
21:15 [j] S Ge 32:1 [k] Ps 125:2 [l] S Ge 6:6; S Ex 32:14 [m] S Ge 19:13
21:16 [n] S Nu 14:5; S Jos 7:6
21:17 [o] S 2Sa 7:8 [p] Jnh 1:12
21:18 [q] 2Ch 3:1
21:20 [r] S Jdg 6:11
21:26 [s] S Ex 19:18; S Jdg 6:21
21:29 [t] S Jos 9:3

[a] *12* Hebrew; Septuagint and Vulgate (see also 2 Samuel 24:13) *of fleeing* [b] *15* Hebrew *Ornan*, a variant of *Araunah*; also in verses 18-28 [c] *17* Probable reading of the original Hebrew text (see 2 Samuel 24:17 and note); Masoretic Text does not have *the shepherd*. [d] *25* That is, about 15 pounds or about 6.9 kilograms

21:9 *Gad.* A longtime friend of David, having been with him when he was a fugitive from Saul (1Sa 22:3–5; cf. 1Ch 29:29; 2Ch 29:25).

21:12 *three years of famine.* See NIV text note on 2Sa 24:13.

21:20–21 The Chronicler reports that Araunah was threshing wheat as the king approached—information not found in 2Sa 24:20. However, Josephus and a fragmentary text of Samuel from Qumran both mention this information.

21:25 *six hundred shekels of gold.* 2Sa 24:24 says 50 shekels of silver were paid for the threshing floor and oxen. The difference has been explained by some as the Chronicler's attempt to glorify David and the temple by inflating the price. However, the difference is more likely explained by the Chronicler's statement that this was the price for the "site," i.e., for a much larger area than the threshing floor alone.

21:26 *fire from heaven.* Underscores the divine approval and the sanctity of the site (see 2Ch 7:1; Lev 9:24; 1Ki 18:37–38).

21:28—22:1 This material is not found in 2Sa 24. It reflects the Chronicler's main concern in reporting this narrative (see note on 21:1—22:1).

21:30 *it.* The tabernacle.

22 Then David said, "The house of the
LORD God[u] is to be here, and also
the altar of burnt offering for Israel."

Preparations for the Temple

2 So David gave orders to assemble the
foreigners[v] residing in Israel, and from
among them he appointed stonecutters[w]
to prepare dressed stone for building
the house of God. 3 He provided a large
amount of iron to make nails for the doors
of the gateways and for the fittings, and
more bronze than could be weighed.[x] 4 He
also provided more cedar logs[y] than could
be counted, for the Sidonians and Tyrians had brought large numbers of them to
David.
5 David said, "My son Solomon is
young[z] and inexperienced, and the house
to be built for the LORD should be of great
magnificence and fame and splendor[a] in
the sight of all the nations. Therefore I
will make preparations for it." So David
made extensive preparations before his
death.
6 Then he called for his son Solomon
and charged him to build[b] a house for the
LORD, the God of Israel. 7 David said to Solomon: "My son, I had it in my heart[c] to
build[d] a house for the Name[e] of the LORD
my God. 8 But this word of the LORD came
to me: 'You have shed much blood and
have fought many wars.[f] You are not to
build a house for my Name,[g] because you
have shed much blood on the earth in my
sight. 9 But you will have a son who will
be a man of peace[h] and rest,[i] and I will
give him rest from all his enemies on every side. His name will be Solomon,[a][j] and
I will grant Israel peace and quiet[k] during
his reign. 10 He is the one who will build a
house for my Name.[l] He will be my son,[m]
and I will be his father. And I will establish[n] the throne of his kingdom over Israel
forever.'[o]
11 "Now, my son, the LORD be with[p] you,
and may you have success and build the
house of the LORD your God, as he said
you would. 12 May the LORD give you discretion and understanding[q] when he puts
you in command over Israel, so that you
may keep the law of the LORD your God.
13 Then you will have success[r] if you are
careful to observe the decrees and laws[s]
that the LORD gave Moses for Israel. Be
strong and courageous.[t] Do not be afraid
or discouraged.
14 "I have taken great pains to provide
for the temple of the LORD a hundred thousand talents[b] of gold, a million talents[c]
of silver, quantities of bronze and iron
too great to be weighed, and wood and
stone. And you may add to them.[u] 15 You
have many workers: stonecutters, masons
and carpenters,[v] as well as those skilled
in every kind of work 16 in gold and silver, bronze and iron—craftsmen[w] beyond
number. Now begin the work, and the
LORD be with you."
17 Then David ordered[x] all the leaders of
Israel to help his son Solomon. 18 He said
to them, "Is not the LORD your God with
you? And has he not granted you rest[y] on
every side?[z] For he has given the inhabitants of the land into my hands, and the
land is subject to the LORD and to his people. 19 Now devote your heart and soul to
seeking the LORD your God.[a] Begin to build
the sanctuary of the LORD God, so that you
may bring the ark of the covenant of the
LORD and the sacred articles belonging to
God into the temple that will be built for
the Name of the LORD."

22:1 [u] S Ge 28:17 **22:2** [v] S Ex 1:11; S Dt 20:11; 2Ch 8:10; S Isa 56:6 [w] 1Ki 5:17-18; Ezr 3:7 **22:3** [x] S 1Ki 7:47; 1Ch 29:2-5 **22:4** [y] S 1Ki 5:6 **22:5** [z] S 1Ki 3:7; 1Ch 29:1 [a] 2Ch 2:5 **22:6** [b] Ac 7:47 **22:7** [c] S 1Ch 17:2 [d] S 1Ki 8:17 [e] Dt 12:5, 11 **22:8** [f] S 1Ki 5:3 [g] 1Ch 28:3 **22:9** [h] S Jos 14:15; S 1Ki 5:4 [i] ver 18; 1Ch 23:25; 2Ch 14:6, 7; 15:15; 20:30; 36:21 [j] S 2Sa 12:24; S 1Ch 23:1 [k] 1Ki 4:20 **22:10** [l] S 1Ch 17:12 [m] S 2Sa 7:13 [n] 1Ki 9:5 [o] S 2Sa 7:14; S 1Ch 17:4; 2Ch 6:15 **22:11** [p] S 1Sa 16:18; S 18:12 **22:12** [q] 1Ki 3:9-12 **22:13** [r] 1Ki 2:3 [s] 1Ch 28:7 [t] S Dt 31:6 **22:14** [u] 1Ch 29:2-5, 19 **22:15** [v] Ezr 3:7 **22:16** [w] 2Ch 2:7 **22:17** [x] 1Ch 28:1-6 **22:18** [y] S ver 9 [z] 2Sa 7:1 **22:19** [a] 2Ch 7:14

a 9 *Solomon* sounds like and may be derived from the Hebrew for *peace.* *b* 14 That is, about 3,750 tons or about 3,400 metric tons *c* 14 That is, about 37,500 tons or about 34,000 metric tons

22:1—29:30 This material is unique to Chronicles and displays some of the Chronicler's most characteristic interests: the preparations for the building of the temple, the legitimacy of the priests and Levites, and the royal succession. The chapters portray a theocratic Messianic kingdom as it existed under David and Solomon.
22:1 David dedicates this property (21:18–30) as the site for the temple (see vv. 2–6; see also note on Ps 30 title).
22:2–19 Solomon's appointment to succeed David was twofold: (1) a private audience, with David and some leaders in attendance (vv. 17–19), and (2) a public announcement to the people (ch. 28), similar to when Joshua succeeded Moses (see Introduction: Portrait of David and Solomon).
22:2 *foreigners … stonecutters.* 2Sa 20:24 confirms the use of forced labor by David but does not specify that these laborers were foreigners, not Israelites. Solomon used Israelites in conscripted labor (1Ki 5:13–18; 9:15–23; 11:28), but the Chronicler mentions only his use of foreigners (2Ch 8:7–10). Though they were personally free, foreigners were without political rights and could be easily exploited. The OT frequently warns that they were not to be oppressed (Ex 22:21; 23:9; Lev 19:33; Dt 24:14; Jer 7:6; Zec 7:10). Isaiah predicts the participation of foreigners in the building of Jerusalem's walls in the future (Isa 60:10–12).
22:3 *bronze.* See note on 18:8.
22:5 *young.* Solomon's age at the time of his accession is not known with certainty. He came to the throne in 970 BC and was likely born c. 990.
22:7 *house for the Name.* See 1Ki 3:2 and note.
22:8–9 See note on 17:1. In 1Ki 5:3 Solomon explains that David could not build the temple because he was too busy with wars. The Chronicler's nuance is slightly different—not just that wars took so much of his time but that David was in some sense defiled by them because of the bloodshed. A pun on Solomon's name is woven into the divine prophetic message (see NIV text note on v. 9).
22:10 See note on 17:12–14.
22:12–13 See Introduction: Portrait of David and Solomon.
22:19 *bring the ark … into the temple.* See 2Ch 5:2–7.

The Levites

23 When David was old and full of
years, he made his son Solomon[b]
king over Israel.[c]
2 He also gathered together all the leaders of Israel, as well as the priests and
Levites. 3 The Levites thirty years old or
more[d] were counted,[e] and the total number of men was thirty-eight thousand.[f]
David said, "Of these, twenty-four thousand are to be in charge[g] of the work[h] of
the temple of the LORD and six thousand
are to be officials and judges.[i] 5 Four thousand are to be gatekeepers and four thousand are to praise the LORD with the musical instruments[j] I have provided for that
purpose."[k]
6 David separated[l] the Levites into divisions corresponding to the sons of Levi:[m]
Gershon, Kohath and Merari.

Gershonites

Belonging to the Gershonites:[n]
Ladan and Shimei.
8 The sons of Ladan:
Jehiel the first, Zetham and Joel—
three in all.
9 The sons of Shimei:
Shelomoth, Haziel and Haran—
three in all.
These were the heads of the families of Ladan.
10 And the sons of Shimei:
Jahath, Ziza,[a] Jeush and Beriah.
These were the sons of Shimei—
four in all.
11 Jahath was the first and Ziza the
second, but Jeush and Beriah did
not have many sons; so they were
counted as one family with one assignment.

Kohathites

The sons of Kohath:[o]
Amram, Izhar, Hebron and Uzziel—four in all.
13 The sons of Amram:[p]
Aaron and Moses.
Aaron was set apart,[q] he and his descendants forever, to consecrate the
most holy things, to offer sacrifices
before the LORD, to minister[r] before
him and to pronounce blessings[s]
in his name forever. 14 The sons of
Moses the man[t] of God were counted as part of the tribe of Levi.
15 The sons of Moses:
Gershom and Eliezer.[u]
16 The descendants of Gershom:[v]
Shubael was the first.
17 The descendants of Eliezer:
Rehabiah[w] was the first.
Eliezer had no other sons, but the
sons of Rehabiah were very numerous.
18 The sons of Izhar:
Shelomith[x] was the first.
19 The sons of Hebron:[y]
Jeriah the first, Amariah the second, Jahaziel the third and Jekameam the fourth.
20 The sons of Uzziel:
Micah the first and Ishiah the second.

Merarites

21 The sons of Merari:[z]
Mahli and Mushi.[a]
The sons of Mahli:
Eleazar and Kish.
22 Eleazar died without having sons:
he had only daughters. Their cousins, the sons of Kish, married
them.[b]
23 The sons of Mushi:
Mahli, Eder and Jerimoth—three
in all.
24 These were the descendants of Levi
by their families—the heads of families as they were registered under their
names and counted individually, that is,
the workers twenty years old or more[c] who
served in the temple of the LORD. 25 For

23:1 [b] 1Ch 22:9; 28:5; 2Ch 1:8 [c] S 1Ki 1:30; 1Ch 29:28 **23:3** [d] Nu 8:24 [e] 1Ch 21:7 [f] Nu 4:3-49 **23:4** [g] Ezr 3:8 [h] 2Ch 34:13; Ne 4:10 [i] 1Ch 26:29; 2Ch 19:8; Eze 44:24 **23:5** [j] S 1Ch 15:16; Ps 92:3 [k] Ne 12:45 **23:6** [l] 2Ch 8:14; 23:18; 29:25 [m] S Nu 3:17; 1Ch 24:20 **23:7** [n] 1Ch 6:71 **23:12** [o] S Ge 46:11; S Ex 6:18 **23:13** [p] Ex 6:20 [q] Ex 30:7-10 [r] S 1Ch 15:2 [s] S Nu 6:23 **23:14** [t] Dt 33:1 **23:15** [u] Ex 18:4 **23:16** [v] 1Ch 26:24-28 **23:17** [w] 1Ch 24:21 **23:18** [x] 1Ch 26:25 **23:19** [y] 1Ch 24:23; 26:31 **23:21** [z] S 1Ch 6:19 [a] S Ex 6:19 **23:22** [b] Nu 36:8 **23:24** [c] S Nu 4:3

[a] *10* One Hebrew manuscript, Septuagint and Vulgate (see also verse 11); most Hebrew manuscripts *Zina*

23:1—27:34 David's preparations for the temple were not restricted to amassing materials for the building; he also arranged for its administration and its worship. Unique to Chronicles (see note on 22:1—29:30), these details of the organization of the theocracy (God's kingdom) were of vital concern in the Chronicler's own day. Characteristically for the Chronicler, details about religious and sacred matters (chs. 23–26) take precedence over those that are civil and secular (ch. 27). David's arrangements provided the basis and authority for the practices of the restored community.
23:1 *made his son Solomon king.* The account of Solomon's succession is resumed in chs. 28–29. The Chronicler omits the accounts of disputed succession and bloody consolidation recorded in 1Ki 1–2 (see note on 28:1—29:30) since these would not be in accord with his overall portrait of David and Solomon (see Introduction: Portrait of David and Solomon).
23:2–5 The Levites were not counted in the census that had provoked the wrath of God (21:6–7).
23:3 *Levites thirty years old or more.* The census of Levites was made first in accordance with the Mosaic prescription (Nu 4:1–3). Apparently soon after this count, David instructed that the age be lowered to 20 years (vv. 24,27); a similar adjustment to age 25 had been made under Moses (Nu 8:23–24, but see note on 8:24).
23:6 *Gershon, Kohath and Merari.* The Levites were organized by their three clans (ch. 6; Ex 6:16–19; Nu 3). This list parallels those in 6:16–30; 24:20–30.
23:24,27 *twenty years old or more.* See note on v. 3.

David had said, "Since the LORD, the God
of Israel, has granted rest[d] to his people
and has come to dwell in Jerusalem forever, 26the Levites no longer need to carry the
tabernacle or any of the articles used in its
service."[e] 27According to the last instructions of David, the Levites were counted
from those twenty years old or more.

28The duty of the Levites was to help
Aaron's descendants in the service of the
temple of the LORD: to be in charge of the
courtyards, the side rooms, the purification[f] of all sacred things and the performance of other duties at the house of God.
29They were in charge of the bread set out
on the table,[g] the special flour for the grain
offerings,[h] the thin loaves made without
yeast, the baking and the mixing, and
all measurements of quantity and size.[i]
30They were also to stand every morning
to thank and praise the LORD. They were
to do the same in the evening[j] 31and whenever burnt offerings were presented to the
LORD on the Sabbaths, at the New Moon[k]
feasts and at the appointed festivals.[l] They
were to serve before the LORD regularly in
the proper number and in the way prescribed for them.

32And so the Levites[m] carried out their
responsibilities for the tent of meeting,[n] for
the Holy Place and, under their relatives
the descendants of Aaron, for the service
of the temple of the LORD.[o]

The Divisions of Priests

24 These were the divisions[p] of the descendants of Aaron:[q]

The sons of Aaron were Nadab, Abihu, Eleazar and Ithamar.[r] 2But Nadab and
Abihu died before their father did,[s] and
they had no sons; so Eleazar and Ithamar served as the priests. 3With the help
of Zadok[t] a descendant of Eleazar and
Ahimelek a descendant of Ithamar, David separated them into divisions for their
appointed order of ministering. 4A larger
number of leaders were found among Eleazar's descendants than among Ithamar's,
and they were divided accordingly: sixteen
heads of families from Eleazar's descendants and eight heads of families from Ithamar's descendants. 5They divided them
impartially by casting lots,[u] for there were
officials of the sanctuary and officials of
God among the descendants of both Eleazar and Ithamar.

6The scribe Shemaiah son of Nethanel,
a Levite, recorded their names in the presence of the king and of the officials: Zadok
the priest, Ahimelek[v] son of Abiathar and
the heads of families of the priests and of
the Levites—one family being taken from
Eleazar and then one from Ithamar.

7The first lot fell to Jehoiarib,
the second to Jedaiah,[w]
8the third to Harim,[x]
the fourth to Seorim,
9the fifth to Malkijah,
the sixth to Mijamin,
10the seventh to Hakkoz,
the eighth to Abijah,[y]
11the ninth to Jeshua,
the tenth to Shekaniah,
12the eleventh to Eliashib,
the twelfth to Jakim,
13the thirteenth to Huppah,
the fourteenth to Jeshebeab,
14the fifteenth to Bilgah,
the sixteenth to Immer,[z]
15the seventeenth to Hezir,[a]
the eighteenth to Happizzez,
16the nineteenth to Pethahiah,
the twentieth to Jehezkel,
17the twenty-first to Jakin,
the twenty-second to Gamul,
18the twenty-third to Delaiah
and the twenty-fourth to Maaziah.

19This was their appointed order of ministering when they entered the temple of

23:25 [d] S 1Ch 22:9
23:26 [e] Nu 4:5, 15; 7:9; Dt 10:8
23:28 [f] 2Ch 29:15; Ne 13:9; Mal 3:3
23:29 [g] S Ex 25:30 [h] Lev 2:4-7; 6:20-23 [i] Lev 19:35-36; S 1Ch 9:29,32
23:30 [j] S 1Ch 9:33; Ps 134:1
23:31 [k] S 2Ki 4:23 [l] Nu 28:9-29:39; Isa 1:13-14; Col 2:16
23:32 [m] 1Ch 6:48 [n] Nu 3:6-8,38 [o] 2Ch 23:18; 31:2; Eze 44:14
24:1 [p] 1Ch 23:6; 28:13; 2Ch 5:11; 8:14; 23:8; 31:2; 35:4,5; Ezr 6:18 [q] Nu 3:2-4 [r] S Ex 6:23
24:2 [s] Lev 10:1-2
24:3 [t] S 2Sa 8:17
24:5 [u] ver 31; 1Ch 25:8; 26:13
24:6 [v] 1Ch 18:16
24:7 [w] Ezr 2:36; Ne 12:6
24:8 [x] Ezr 2:39; 10:21; Ne 10:5
24:10 [y] Ne 12:4, 17; Lk 1:5
24:14 [z] Ezr 2:37; 10:20; Jer 20:1
24:15 [a] Ne 10:20

23:28–32 See note on 9:28–34. The function of the Levites was to assist the priests. In addition to the care of the precincts and implements, baked goods and music (mentioned as Levitical duties in 9:22–34), the Chronicler adds details on the role of the Levites assisting in sacrifices.
23:30 *morning ... evening.* See Ex 29:38–41; Nu 28:3–8.
24:1–19 There are several lists of priests from the postexilic period (see 6:3–15; 9:10–13; Ezr 2:36–39; Ne 10:1–8; 11:10–12; 12:1–7,12–21).
24:2 *Nadab and Abihu died.* The Chronicler alludes to the events recorded in Lev 10:1–3 (see note on 1Ch 6:1–3).
24:3 *Zadok ... Ahimelek.* Zadok and Abiathar had served as David's high priests. Here, late in David's life, Abiathar's son Ahimelek appears to have taken over some of his father's duties (see note on 6:8), but see note on 2Sa 8:17.
24:4 *sixteen ... eight.* A total of 24 divisions were selected by lot. This would allow either for service in monthly shifts, as was done by priests in Egyptian mortuary temples, or for two-week shifts once each year as found in NT times. For the names of these divisions, see vv. 7–18. The names of the first, second, fourth, ninth and twenty-fourth divisions also occur in a Dead Sea scroll, and the name of the eighth appears in Lk 1:5. See essay, pp. 1574–1575; see also note on Ne 12:7.
24:5 *casting lots.* See notes on Ex 28:30; Jos 7:14; Ne 11:1; Pr 16:33; Jnh 1:7; Ac 1:26.
24:7 *Jehoiarib.* Mattathias, father of the Maccabees, was a member of the Jehoiarib division (in the Apocrypha, see 1 Maccabees 2:1).
24:10 *Abijah.* Zechariah, the father of John the Baptist, "belonged to the priestly division of Abijah" (Lk 1:5).
24:15 *Hezir.* The division from the family of Hezir was prominent in intertestamental times; the name appears on one of the large tombs in the Kidron Valley, east of Jerusalem.

the LORD, according to the regulations prescribed for them by their ancestor Aaron,
as the LORD, the God of Israel, had commanded him.

The Rest of the Levites

20 As for the rest of the descendants of
Levi:[b]
from the sons of Amram: Shubael;
from the sons of Shubael: Jehdeiah.
21 As for Rehabiah,[c] from his sons:
Ishiah was the first.
22 From the Izharites: Shelomoth;
from the sons of Shelomoth: Jahath.
23 The sons of Hebron:[d] Jeriah the first,[a]
Amariah the second, Jahaziel the third and Jekameam the fourth.
24 The son of Uzziel: Micah;
from the sons of Micah: Shamir.
25 The brother of Micah: Ishiah;
from the sons of Ishiah: Zechariah.
26 The sons of Merari:[e] Mahli and Mushi.
The son of Jaaziah: Beno.
27 The sons of Merari:
from Jaaziah: Beno, Shoham, Zakkur and Ibri.
28 From Mahli: Eleazar, who had no sons.
29 From Kish: the son of Kish:
Jerahmeel.
30 And the sons of Mushi: Mahli, Eder and Jerimoth.

These were the Levites, according to
their families.
31 They also cast lots,[f] just
as their relatives the descendants of Aaron
did, in the presence of King David and of
Zadok, Ahimelek, and the heads of families of the priests and of the Levites. The
families of the oldest brother were treated
the same as those of the youngest.

24:20 [b]S 1Ch 23:6 **24:21** [c]1Ch 23:17 **24:23** [d]S 1Ch 23:19 **24:26** [e]S 1Ch 6:19 **24:31** [f]S ver 5

The Musicians

25 David, together with the commanders of the army, set apart some of the sons of Asaph,[g] Heman[h] and Jeduthun[i] for the ministry of prophesying,[j] accompanied by harps, lyres and cymbals.[k] Here is the list of the men[l] who performed this service:[m]

2 From the sons of Asaph:
Zakkur, Joseph, Nethaniah and Asarelah. The sons of Asaph were under the supervision of Asaph, who prophesied under the king's supervision.
3 As for Jeduthun, from his sons:[n]
Gedaliah, Zeri, Jeshaiah, Shimei,[b] Hashabiah and Mattithiah, six in all, under the supervision of their father Jeduthun, who prophesied, using the harp[o] in thanking and praising the LORD.
4 As for Heman, from his sons:
Bukkiah, Mattaniah, Uzziel, Shubael and Jerimoth; Hananiah, Hanani,
Eliathah, Giddalti and Romamti-Ezer;
Joshbekashah, Mallothi, Hothir and
Mahazioth.
5 (All these were sons of
Heman the king's seer. They were given him through the promises of God to exalt him. God gave Heman fourteen sons and three daughters.)

6 All these men were under the supervision of their father[p] for the music of the temple of the LORD, with cymbals, lyres and harps, for the ministry at the house of God.
Asaph, Jeduthun and Heman[q] were under the supervision of the king.[r]
7 Along
with their relatives—all of them trained

25:1 [g]S 1Ch 6:39 [h]S 1Ch 6:33 [i]1Ch 16:41, 42; Ne 11:17 [j]S 1Sa 10:5; 2Ki 3:15 [k]S 1Ch 15:16 [l]S 1Ch 6:31 [m]2Ch 5:12; 8:14; 34:12; 35:15; Ezr 3:10 **25:3** [n]1Ch 16:41-42 [o]S Ge 4:21; Ps 33:2 **25:6** [p]S 1Ch 15:16 [q]S 1Ch 15:19 [r]2Ch 23:18; 29:25

[a] 23 Two Hebrew manuscripts and some Septuagint manuscripts (see also 23:19); most Hebrew manuscripts *The sons of Jeriah:* [b] 3 One Hebrew manuscript and some Septuagint manuscripts (see also verse 17); most Hebrew manuscripts do not have *Shimei.*

24:20-31 This list supplements 23:7-23 by extending some of the family lines mentioned there.
25:1 *commanders of the army.* David often sought the counsel of military leaders (11:10; 12:32; 28:1), even in religious matters (13:1; 15:25). *set apart some.* David's organizing of the temple musicians may reflect his overall interest in music (1Sa 16:23; 18:10; 19:9; 2Sa 1:17-27; 6:5,14). *Asaph, Heman and Jeduthun.* See notes on 6:31-48; Ps 39 title. *ministry of prophesying.* While there are several passages in Chronicles, largely in portions unique to these books, where temple personnel are said to have issued prophetic messages (Jahaziel, a Levite descended from Asaph, 2Ch 20:14-17; Zechariah, a priest, 2Ch 24:19-20), and while three of the leading Levites are referred to as David's seers (Heman, 1Ch 25:5; Asaph, 2Ch 29:30; Jeduthun/Ethan, 35:15), reference to "prophesying" here appears clearly to refer to the musical contribution of the Levites, with instruments and song, to the liturgy of temple worship (as initially appointed by David; see 1Ch 6:31-46; 15:16-22; 16:7-38; cf. 2Ch 29:30; 35:15). The Chronicler associates this ministry on the part of the Levites with the "prophesying" stirred up by the Spirit of God in the elders appointed by Moses in the wilderness (see Nu 11:25-27 and note on 11:25) and in the band of prophets with which Samuel was associated (see 1Sa 10:5-11 and note on 10:5; 19:20-24). For a similar use of the term "prophesying," but now by "the prophets of Baal," see 1Ki 18:29 and note. The Chronicler's association of priests and Levites with prophesying may reflect postexilic interest in the prophet-priest-king figure of Messianic expectation: In Chronicles, not only do priests and Levites prophesy, but kings also function as priests (see notes on 15:27; 16:1-3). *harps ... cymbals.* See photos, pp. 627, 843.
25:5 *king's seer.* Heman, as well as Asaph and Jeduthun/Ethan (see note on v. 1), may be called seers because David consulted them for guidance when he organized the temple liturgy (see 15:16-22; 2Ch 35:15). *fourteen sons and three daughters.* Numerous progeny are a sign of divine blessing (see Job 1:2; 42:13). This is specifically stated for Heman as the result of the promises of God to exalt him. See 3:1-9; 14:2-7; 26:4-5; 2Ch 11:18-21; 13:21; 21:2; 24:3.

and skilled in music for the LORD—they numbered 288. [8]Young and old alike, teacher as well as student, cast lots[s] for their duties.

[9]The first lot, which was for Asaph,[t] fell to Joseph,
his sons and relatives[a] 12[b]
the second to Gedaliah,
him and his relatives and sons 12
[10]the third to Zakkur,
his sons and relatives 12
[11]the fourth to Izri,[c]
his sons and relatives 12
[12]the fifth to Nethaniah,
his sons and relatives 12
[13]the sixth to Bukkiah,
his sons and relatives 12
[14]the seventh to Jesarelah,[d]
his sons and relatives 12
[15]the eighth to Jeshaiah,
his sons and relatives 12
[16]the ninth to Mattaniah,
his sons and relatives 12
[17]the tenth to Shimei,
his sons and relatives 12
[18]the eleventh to Azarel,[e]
his sons and relatives 12
[19]the twelfth to Hashabiah,
his sons and relatives 12
[20]the thirteenth to Shubael,
his sons and relatives 12
[21]the fourteenth to Mattithiah,
his sons and relatives 12
[22]the fifteenth to Jerimoth,
his sons and relatives 12
[23]the sixteenth to Hananiah,
his sons and relatives 12
[24]the seventeenth to Joshbekashah,
his sons and relatives 12
[25]the eighteenth to Hanani,
his sons and relatives 12
[26]the nineteenth to Mallothi,
his sons and relatives 12
[27]the twentieth to Eliathah,
his sons and relatives 12
[28]the twenty-first to Hothir,
his sons and relatives 12
[29]the twenty-second to Giddalti,
his sons and relatives 12
[30]the twenty-third to Mahazioth,
his sons and relatives 12
[31]the twenty-fourth to Romamti-Ezer,
his sons and relatives 12.[u]

25:8 [s]1Ch 26:13 **25:9** [t]S 1Ch 6:39 **25:31** [u]S 1Ch 9:33

The Gatekeepers

26 The divisions of the gatekeepers:[v]

From the Korahites: Meshelemiah son of Kore, one of the sons of Asaph.
[2]Meshelemiah had sons:
Zechariah[w] the firstborn,
Jediael the second,
Zebadiah the third,
Jathniel the fourth,
[3]Elam the fifth,
Jehohanan the sixth
and Eliehoenai the seventh.
[4]Obed-Edom also had sons:
Shemaiah the firstborn,
Jehozabad the second,
Joah the third,
Sakar the fourth,
Nethanel the fifth,
[5]Ammiel the sixth,
Issachar the seventh
and Peullethai the eighth.
(For God had blessed Obed-Edom.[x])

[6]Obed-Edom's son Shemaiah also had sons, who were leaders in their father's family because they were very capable men. [7]The sons of Shemaiah: Othni, Rephael, Obed and Elzabad; his relatives Elihu and Semakiah were also able men. [8]All these were descendants of Obed-Edom; they and their sons and their relatives were capable men with the strength to do the work—descendants of Obed-Edom, 62 in all.
[9]Meshelemiah had sons and relatives, who were able men—18 in all.

[10]Hosah the Merarite had sons: Shimri the first (although he was not the firstborn, his father had appointed him the first),[y] [11]Hilkiah the second, Tabaliah the third and Zechariah the fourth. The sons and relatives of Hosah were 13 in all.
[12]These divisions of the gatekeepers, through their leaders, had duties for ministering[z] in the temple of the LORD, just as their relatives had. [13]Lots[a] were cast for each gate, according to their families, young and old alike.

26:1 [v]S 1Ch 9:17 **26:2** [w]S 1Ch 9:21 **26:5** [x]S 2Sa 6:10; S 1Ch 13:13; S 16:38 **26:10** [y]Dt 21:16; 1Ch 5:1 **26:12** [z]1Ch 9:22 **26:13** [a]S 1Ch 24:5,31; 25:8

[a] 9 See Septuagint; Hebrew does not have *his sons and relatives.* [b] 9 See the total in verse 7; Hebrew does not have *twelve.* [c] 11 A variant of *Zeri* [d] 14 A variant of *Asarelah* [e] 18 A variant of *Uzziel*

26:1–19 The most extensive of the Chronicler's lists of gatekeepers (see 9:17–27; 16:37–38). A list of gatekeepers in the postexilic period is found in Ezr 2:42; Ne 7:45.
26:1 *Asaph.* This name appears to be an abbreviation of Ebiasaph (6:23; 9:19); he should not be confused with the temple musician (25:1–2,6).
26:4–5 Numerous sons are again a sign of divine blessing (see note on 25:5).
26:4 *Obed-Edom.* Had cared for the ark when it was left at his house (see note on 13:13).
26:12 *duties.* Elaborated in 9:22–29.

14 The lot for the East Gate[b] fell to Shel-
›miah.[a] Then lots were cast for his son
Zechariah,[c] a wise counselor, and the lot
or the North Gate fell to him. 15 The lot
'or the South Gate fell to Obed-Edom,[d] and
he lot for the storehouse fell to his sons.
6 The lots for the West Gate and the Shal-
eketh Gate on the upper road fell to Shup-
›im and Hosah.
Guard was alongside of guard: 17 There
vere six Levites a day on the east, four a
lay on the north, four a day on the south
ind two at a time at the storehouse. 18 As
or the court[b] to the west, there were four
it the road and two at the court[b] itself.
19 These were the divisions of the gatekeepers who were descendants of Korah
ind Merari.[e]

he Treasurers and Other Officials

20 Their fellow Levites[f] were[c] in charge
f the treasuries of the house of God and
he treasuries for the dedicated things.[g]
21 The descendants of Ladan, who were
Gershonites through Ladan and who were
ieads of families belonging to Ladan the
Gershonite,[h] were Jehieli, 22 the sons of Je-
iieli, Zetham and his brother Joel. They
vere in charge of the treasuries[i] of the
emple of the LORD.
23 From the Amramites, the Izharites,
he Hebronites and the Uzzielites:[j]

4 Shubael,[k] a descendant of Gershom
son of Moses, was the official in
charge of the treasuries. 25 His relatives through Eliezer: Rehabiah
his son, Jeshaiah his son, Joram
his son, Zikri his son and Shelomith[l] his son. 26 Shelomith and his
relatives were in charge of all the
treasuries for the things dedicated[m] by King David, by the heads of
families who were the commanders
of thousands and commanders of
hundreds, and by the other army
commanders. 27 Some of the plunder taken in battle they dedicated
for the repair of the temple of the
LORD. 28 And everything dedicated
by Samuel the seer[n] and by Saul
son of Kish, Abner son of Ner and
Joab son of Zeruiah, and all the
other dedicated things were in the
care of Shelomith and his relatives.
29 From the Izharites: Kenaniah and his
sons were assigned duties away
from the temple, as officials and
judges[o] over Israel.
30 From the Hebronites: Hashabiah[p]
and his relatives — seventeen hundred able men — were responsible
in Israel west of the Jordan for all
the work of the LORD and for the
king's service. 31 As for the Hebronites,[q] Jeriah was their chief according to the genealogical records of
their families. In the fortieth[r] year
of David's reign a search was made
in the records, and capable men
among the Hebronites were found
at Jazer in Gilead. 32 Jeriah had
twenty-seven hundred relatives,
who were able men and heads of
families, and King David put them
in charge of the Reubenites, the
Gadites and the half-tribe of Manasseh for every matter pertaining
to God and for the affairs of the
king.

Army Divisions

27 This is the list of the Israelites —
heads of families, commanders of
thousands and commanders of hundreds,

26:14 [b] S 1Ch 9:18 [c] S 1Ch 9:21
26:15 [d] S 1Ch 13:13; 2Ch 25:24
26:19 [e] 2Ch 35:15; Ne 7:1; Eze 44:11
26:20 [f] 2Ch 24:5 [g] 1Ch 28:12
26:21 [h] 1Ch 23:7; 29:8
26:22 [i] 1Ch 9:26
26:23 [j] S Nu 3:27
26:24 [k] 1Ch 23:16
26:25 [l] 1Ch 23:18
26:26 [m] S 2Sa 8:11
26:28 [n] S 1Sa 9:9
26:29 [o] Dt 17:8-13; S 1Ch 23:4
26:30 [p] 1Ch 27:17
26:31 [q] S 1Ch 23:19 [r] S 2Sa 5:4

[a] *14* A variant of *Meshelemiah* [b] *18* The meaning of the Hebrew for this word is uncertain.
[c] *20* Septuagint; Hebrew *As for the Levites, Ahijah was*

:14 *East Gate.* The main entrance; it had six guard posts, as pposed to four at the other gates (v. 17).
:15 *South Gate.* Apparently the southern gate would be e main one used by the king, and this assignment prob- bly reflects a particular honor for Obed-Edom (see notes on :4 – 5; see also Eze 46:1 – 10).
:16 *Shalleketh Gate.* The only reference to a gate by this ame; presumably it was on the western side. The Chroni- er writes to an audience familiar with these topographical etails.
26:20 *treasuries of the house of God.* The Levites in charge of these treasuries received the offerings of e people and cared for the valuable temple equipment :28 – 29). *treasuries for the dedicated things.* Contained the under from warfare (vv. 27 – 28). Texts from Mesopotamian mples confirm the presence of temple officers who served assayers to handle and refine the precious metals received revenue and offerings. The procedure with reference to e offerings of the people may be seen in the reign of Joash Ch 24:4 – 14; 2Ki 12:4 – 16). Numerous passages reflect on the wealth collected in the temple (see, e.g., 29:1 – 9; 2Ch 4:1 – 22; 34:9 – 11; 36:7,10,18 – 19; 1Ki 14:25 – 28; 15:15,18; 2Ki 12:4 – 18; 14:14; 16:8; 25:13 – 17).
26:26 *things dedicated by King David.* See note on 18:1 — 20:8; see also 2Ch 5:1.
26:27 *plunder taken in battle they dedicated.* Cf. Ge 14:17 – 20.
26:29 – 32 These verses designate the 6,000 officials and judges (23:4) who would work outside Jerusalem; they are drawn from two subclans of Kohath (6:18). Dt 17:8 – 13 envis- ages a judicial function for the priests and Levites (see 2Ch 19:4 – 11).
26:30,32 *for all the work of the LORD and for the king's service . . . for every matter pertaining to God and for the affairs of the king.* In the theocracy (kingdom of God) there is no division between secular and sacred, no tension in serving God and the king (cf. Mt 22:15 – 22; Lk 16:10 – 13; Ro 13:1 – 7; 1Ti 2:1 – 4; 1Pe 2:13 – 17).
26:31 *fortieth year.* The last year of David's reign.
27:1 – 15 The names of the commanders of David's army are the same as those found in the list of his mighty warriors (see

and their officers, who served the king in
all that concerned the army divisions that
were on duty month by month throughout
the year. Each division consisted of 24,000
men.

2 In charge of the first division, for the
first month, was Jashobeam[s] son of
Zabdiel. There were 24,000 men in
his division. 3 He was a descendant of
Perez and chief of all the army officers for the first month.
4 In charge of the division for the second
month was Dodai[t] the Ahohite; Mikloth was the leader of his division.
There were 24,000 men in his division.
5 The third army commander, for the
third month, was Benaiah[u] son of Jehoiada the priest. He was chief and
there were 24,000 men in his division.
6 This was the Benaiah who was a
mighty warrior among the Thirty and
was over the Thirty. His son Ammiz-
abad was in charge of his division.
7 The fourth, for the fourth month, was
Asahel[v] the brother of Joab; his son
Zebadiah was his successor. There
were 24,000 men in his division.
8 The fifth, for the fifth month, was the
commander Shamhuth[w] the Izrahite.
There were 24,000 men in his division.
9 The sixth, for the sixth month, was Ira[x]
the son of Ikkesh the Tekoite. There
were 24,000 men in his division.
10 The seventh, for the seventh month,
was Helez[y] the Pelonite, an Ephraimite. There were 24,000 men in his division.
11 The eighth, for the eighth month, was
Sibbekai[z] the Hushathite, a Zerahite.
There were 24,000 men in his division.

27:2 [s] 2Sa 23:8
27:4 [t] S 2Sa 23:9
27:5 [u] S 2Sa 23:20
27:7 [v] S 2Sa 2:18
27:8 [w] 1Ch 11:27
27:9 [x] 2Sa 23:26
27:10 [y] 2Sa 23:26
27:11 [z] S 2Sa 21:18
27:12 [a] 2Sa 23:27
27:13 [b] 2Sa 23:28
27:14 [c] S 1Ch 11:31
27:15 [d] 2Sa 23:29 [e] S Jos 15:17
27:17 [f] 1Ch 26:30 [g] S 2Sa 8:17; S 1Ch 12:28
27:23 [h] S 2Sa 24:1; 1Ch 21:2-5

12 The ninth, for the ninth month, was
Abiezer[a] the Anathothite, a Benjamite. There were 24,000 men in his
division.
13 The tenth, for the tenth month, was Maharai[b] the Netophathite, a Zerahite.
There were 24,000 men in his division.
14 The eleventh, for the eleventh month,
was Benaiah[c] the Pirathonite, an
Ephraimite. There were 24,000 men
in his division.
15 The twelfth, for the twelfth month, was
Heldai[d] the Netophathite, from the
family of Othniel.[e] There were 24,000
men in his division.

Leaders of the Tribes

16 The leaders of the tribes of Israel:

over the Reubenites: Eliezer son of
Zikri;
over the Simeonites: Shephatiah son
of Maakah;
17 over Levi: Hashabiah[f] son of Kemuel;
over Aaron: Zadok;[g]
18 over Judah: Elihu, a brother of David;
over Issachar: Omri son of Michael;
19 over Zebulun: Ishmaiah son of Obadiah;
over Naphtali: Jerimoth son of Azriel;
20 over the Ephraimites: Hoshea son of
Azaziah;
over half the tribe of Manasseh: Joel
son of Pedaiah;
21 over the half-tribe of Manasseh in Gilead: Iddo son of Zechariah;
over Benjamin: Jaasiel son of Abner;
22 over Dan: Azarel son of Jeroham.
These were the leaders of the tribes of
Israel.

23 David did not take the number of the
men twenty years old or less,[h] because the

11:11–47; see also 2Sa 23:8–39 and notes). Those who had served David while he fled from Saul became commanders in the regular army.
27:1 *24,000.* See note on 12:23–37. Although a national militia consisting of 12 units of 24,000 each (a total of 288,000) is not unreasonable, the stress in this passage on unit commanders and divisions suggests that here too the Hebrew word for "1,000" should perhaps be taken as the designation of a military unit. To designate a division as "1,000" would be to give the upper limit of the number of men in such a unit, though such units would ordinarily not have a full complement of men. If this approach is followed, the figures in the following verses would be read as "24 units" instead of 24,000.
27:2 *Jashobeam.* See 11:11.
27:4 *Dodai.* See 11:12.
27:5 *Benaiah.* See 11:22–25; 18:17.
27:7 *Asahel.* See 11:26; 2Sa 2:18–23.
27:9–15 The remainder of the commanders were selected from among the Thirty (see 11:25 and the names listed in 11:27–31).
27:16–22 The Chronicler's interest in "all Israel" appears in this list of officers who were over the 12 tribes (see Introduction: Purpose and Themes). The number is kept at 12 by omitting Gad and Asher (see note on 2:1–2).
27:17 *Zadok.* See note on 6:8; see also 12:28; 16:39.
27:18 *Elihu.* Not named elsewhere among the brothers of David. Perhaps he is the unnamed son from the list in 2:10–17 (see note there). Elihu could also be a variant of the name of Jesse's oldest son, Eliab, or the term "brother" could be taken in the sense of "relative," in which case Elihu would be a more distant relative.
27:21 *Abner.* A relative of King Saul (see 26:28; 1Sa 14:50–51; 17:55–58; 26:5–16; 2Sa 2:8—4:1).
27:23–24 *number.* Refers to the census narrative in ch. 21 (2Sa 24).
27:23 *twenty years old or less.* The figures reported in ch. 21 and 2Sa 24 were the numbers of those older than 20 years. *promised to make Israel as numerous as the stars.* The patriarchal promises of numerous descendants (Ge 12:2; 13:16; 15:5; 22:17) appear to have been the basis for the objections of Joab (v. 24) to the taking of a census (21:3; 2Sa 24:3).

LORD had promised to make Israel as numerous as the stars[i] in the sky. 24 Joab son
of Zeruiah began to count the men but did
not finish. God's wrath came on Israel on
account of this numbering,[j] and the number was not entered in the book[a] of the
annals of King David.

The King's Overseers

25 Azmaveth son of Adiel was in charge
of the royal storehouses.
Jonathan son of Uzziah was in charge
of the storehouses in the outlying districts,
in the towns, the villages and the watch-
towers.
26 Ezri son of Kelub was in charge of the
workers who farmed the land.
27 Shimei the Ramathite was in charge of
the vineyards.
Zabdi the Shiphmite was in charge of
the produce of the vineyards for the wine
vats.
28 Baal-Hanan the Gederite was in
charge of the olive and sycamore-fig[k] trees
in the western foothills.
Joash was in charge of the supplies of
olive oil.
29 Shitrai the Sharonite was in charge of
the herds grazing in Sharon.[l]
Shaphat son of Adlai was in charge of
the herds in the valleys.
30 Obil the Ishmaelite was in charge of
the camels.
Jehdeiah the Meronothite was in charge
of the donkeys.
31 Jaziz the Hagrite[m] was in charge of the
flocks.
All these were the officials in charge of
King David's property.

32 Jonathan, David's uncle, was a counselor, a man of insight and a scribe. Jehiel son of Hakmoni took care of the king's
sons.
33 Ahithophel[n] was the king's counselor.
Hushai[o] the Arkite was the king's confidant. 34 Ahithophel was succeeded by Jehoiada son of Benaiah and by Abiathar.[p]
Joab[q] was the commander of the royal
army.

David's Plans for the Temple

28 David summoned[r] all the officials[s]
of Israel to assemble at Jerusalem:
the officers over the tribes, the commanders of the divisions in the service of the
king, the commanders of thousands and
commanders of hundreds, and the officials
in charge of all the property and livestock
belonging to the king and his sons, together with the palace officials, the warriors
and all the brave fighting men.
2 King David rose to his feet and said:
"Listen to me, my fellow Israelites, my
people. I had it in my heart[t] to build a
house as a place of rest[u] for the ark of the
covenant of the LORD, for the footstool[v] of
our God, and I made plans to build it.[w]
3 But God said to me,[x] 'You are not to build
a house for my Name,[y] because you are a
warrior and have shed blood.'[z]
4 "Yet the LORD, the God of Israel, chose
me[a] from my whole family[b] to be king over
Israel forever. He chose Judah[c] as leader,
and from the tribe of Judah he chose my
family, and from my father's sons he was
pleased to make me king over all Israel.[d]
5 Of all my sons—and the LORD has given
me many[e]—he has chosen my son Solomon[f] to sit on the throne[g] of the kingdom of

27:23 [i] S Ge 12:2 **27:24** [j] S 2Sa 24:15; 1Ch 21:14 **27:28** [k] S 1Ki 10:27 **27:29** [l] SS 2:1; Isa 33:9; 35:2; 65:10 **27:31** [m] S 1Ch 5:10 **27:33** [n] S 2Sa 15:12 [o] S 2Sa 15:37 **27:34** [p] S 1Sa 22:20 [q] S 2Sa 2:13 **28:1** [r] 1Ch 22:17 [s] 1Ch 27:1-31; 29:6 **28:2** [t] S 1Sa 10:7; S 1Ch 17:2 [u] 2Ch 6:41 [v] Ps 99:5; 132:7; Isa 60:13 [w] Ps 132:1-5 **28:3** [x] S 2Sa 7:5 [y] 1Ch 22:8 [z] S 1Ki 5:3; S 1Ch 17:4 **28:4** [a] 2Ch 6:6 [b] 1Sa 16:1-13 [c] S Ge 49:10; Nu 24:17-19 [d] 1Ch 11:1 **28:5** [e] S 1Ch 3:1 [f] S 2Sa 12:24; S 1Ch 23:1 [g] S 1Ch 17:14

[a] *24* Septuagint; Hebrew *number*

27:24 *did not finish.* Joab did not count those under age 20, nor did he include the tribes of Levi and Benjamin (21:6). *book of the annals of King David.* See Introduction: Author, Date and Sources.

27:25–31 A list of the administrators of David's property (v. 31). The large cities of the ancient Near East had three basic economic sectors: (1) royal, (2) temple and (3) private. There is no evidence of direct taxation during the reign of David; his court appears to have been financed by extensive landholdings, commerce, plunder from his many wars, and tribute from subjugated kingdoms.

27:27 *wine vats.* See note on Hag 2:16.

27:32–34 A list of David's cabinet members, supplementary to that in 18:14–17.

27:33 *Ahithophel.* Was replaced after he committed suicide, following his support of Absalom's rebellion (2Sa 15:12,31–37; 16:20—17:23).

27:34 *Benaiah.* See v. 5.

28:1—29:30 The account of the transition from the reign of David to that of Solomon is one of the clearest demonstrations of the Chronicler's idealization of their reigns when it is compared with the succession narrative in 1Ki 1–2. The Chronicler makes no mention of the infirmities of the aged David (1Ki 1:1–4), the rebellion of Adonijah and the king's sons (1Ki 1:5–10), the court intrigue to secure Solomon's succession (1Ki 1:11–31) or David's charge to Solomon to punish his enemies after his death (1Ki 2:1–9). His selection of material presents a transition of power that is smooth and peaceful and receives the support of "all Israel" (29:25), the officials and the people (28:1–2; 29:6–9,21–25). Instead of the bedridden David who sends others to anoint Solomon (1Ki 1:32–35), David himself is present and in charge of the ceremonies (see 23:1 and note).

28:1 The assembly is composed largely of the groups named in ch. 27. This public announcement (v. 5) follows the private announcement of Solomon's succession in ch. 22 (see note on 22:2–19).

28:3 *you are a warrior and have shed blood.* See note on 22:8–9.

28:5 *chosen my son Solomon.* See vv. 6,10; 29:1. These are the only uses in the OT of the Hebrew verb for "chosen" with reference to any king after David (see Introduction: Purpose and Themes). The Chronicler's application of this term to Solomon is consistent with his depiction of that king. *kingdom of the LORD.* See note on 17:14.

the LORD over Israel. 6He said to me: 'Solomon your son is the one who will build[h]
my house and my courts, for I have chosen
him to be my son,[i] and I will be his father.
7I will establish his kingdom forever if he is
unswerving in carrying out my commands
and laws,[j] as is being done at this time.'
8"So now I charge you in the sight of
all Israel[k] and of the assembly of the LORD,
and in the hearing of our God: Be careful
to follow all the commands[l] of the LORD
your God, that you may possess this good
land and pass it on as an inheritance to
your descendants forever.[m]
9"And you, my son Solomon, acknowledge the God of your father, and serve him
with wholehearted devotion[n] and with a
willing mind, for the LORD searches every heart[o] and understands every desire
and every thought. If you seek him,[p] he
will be found by you; but if you forsake[q]
him, he will reject[r] you forever. 10Consider
now, for the LORD has chosen you to build
a house as the sanctuary. Be strong and
do the work."

11Then David gave his son Solomon
the plans[s] for the portico of the temple,
its buildings, its storerooms, its upper
parts, its inner rooms and the place of
atonement. 12He gave him the plans of all
that the Spirit[t] had put in his mind for the
courts of the temple of the LORD and all
the surrounding rooms, for the treasuries
of the temple of God and for the treasuries
for the dedicated things.[u] 13He gave him
instructions for the divisions[v] of the priests
and Levites, and for all the work of serving in the temple of the LORD, as well as
for all the articles to be used in its service.
14He designated the weight of gold for
all the gold articles to be used in various
kinds of service, and the weight of silver
for all the silver articles to be used in various kinds of service: 15the weight of gold
for the gold lampstands[w] and their lamps,
with the weight for each lampstand and
its lamps; and the weight of silver for each
silver lampstand and its lamps, according to the use of each lampstand; 16the
weight of gold for each table[x] for conse-

28:6 [h] 1Ki 8:20 [i] S 2Sa 7:13; S 1Ch 17:13
28:7 [j] 1Ch 22:13
28:8 [k] S 1Ch 9:1 [l] Dt 6:1 [m] Dt 4:1; S 17:14-20
28:9 [n] S 1Ch 29:19 [o] S 1Sa 2:3; 2Ch 6:30; Ps 7:9 [p] S 1Ch 16:11; S Ps 40:16 [q] S Dt 4:31; S Jos 24:20; S 2Ch 7:19; 15:2 [r] 1Ki 9:7; Ps 44:23; 74:1; 77:7
28:11 [s] S Ex 25:9; Ac 7:44; Heb 8:5
28:12 [t] S 1Ch 12:18 [u] 1Ch 26:20
28:13 [v] S 1Ch 24:1
28:15 [w] Ex 25:31
28:16 [x] S Ex 25:23

28:6 *my son.* See 17:12–14 and note; see also 22:10.
28:8–9 See Introduction: Portrait of David and Solomon.
28:11 *portico.* See model, p. 523.
28:12 David provides Solomon with the plans for the temple. This reflects the Chronicler's modeling David after Moses: Just as Moses received the plans for the tabernacle from God (Ex 25–30), so also David received the plans for the temple from God. Cf. photo below.

Third-century painting of Solomon's temple at Dura Europos (in modern Syria). David made the plans for the temple (1Ch 28), but the construction was completed during Solomon's reign.

Z. Radovan/www.BibleLandPictures.com

crated bread; the weight of silver for the silver tables; 17 the weight of pure gold for the forks, sprinkling bowls[y] and pitchers; the weight of gold for each gold dish; the weight of silver for each silver dish; 18 and the weight of the refined gold for the altar of incense.[z] He also gave him the plan for the chariot,[a] that is, the cherubim of gold that spread their wings and overshadow[b] the ark of the covenant of the LORD.

19 "All this," David said, "I have in writing as a result of the LORD's hand on me, and he enabled me to understand all the details[c] of the plan.[d]"

20 David also said to Solomon his son, "Be strong and courageous,[e] and do the work. Do not be afraid or discouraged, for the LORD God, my God, is with you. He will not fail you or forsake[f] you until all the work for the service of the temple of the LORD is finished.[g] 21 The divisions of the priests and Levites are ready for all the work on the temple of God, and every willing person skilled[h] in any craft will help you in all the work. The officials and all the people will obey your every command."

Gifts for Building the Temple

29 Then King David said to the whole assembly: "My son Solomon, the one whom God has chosen, is young and inexperienced.[i] The task is great, because this palatial structure is not for man but for the LORD God. 2 With all my resources I have provided for the temple of my God—gold[j] for the gold work, silver for the silver, bronze for the bronze, iron for the iron and wood for the wood, as well as onyx for the settings, turquoise,[a][k] stones of various colors, and all kinds of fine stone and marble—all of these in large quantities.[l] 3 Besides, in my devotion to the temple of my God I now give my personal treasures of gold and silver for the temple of my God, over and above everything I have provided[m] for this holy temple: 4 three thousand talents[b] of gold (gold of Ophir)[n] and seven thousand talents[c] of refined silver,[o] for the overlaying of the walls of the buildings, 5 for the gold work and the silver work, and for all the work to be done by the craftsmen. Now, who is willing to consecrate themselves to the LORD today?"

6 Then the leaders of families, the officers of the tribes of Israel, the commanders of thousands and commanders of hundreds, and the officials[p] in charge of the king's work gave willingly.[q] 7 They[r] gave toward the work on the temple of God five thousand talents[d] and ten thousand darics[e] of gold, ten thousand talents[f] of silver, eighteen thousand talents[g] of bronze and a hundred thousand talents[h] of iron. 8 Anyone who had precious stones[s] gave them to the treasury of the temple of the LORD in the custody of Jehiel the Gershonite.[t] 9 The people rejoiced at the willing response of their leaders, for they had given freely and wholeheartedly[u] to the LORD. David the king also rejoiced greatly.

David's Prayer

10 David praised the LORD in the presence of the whole assembly, saying,

"Praise be to you, LORD,
the God of our father Israel,
from everlasting to everlasting.
11 Yours, LORD, is the greatness and the power[v]
and the glory and the majesty and the splendor,
for everything in heaven and earth is yours.[w]
Yours, LORD, is the kingdom;
you are exalted as head over all.[x]
12 Wealth and honor[y] come from you;
you are the ruler[z] of all things.
In your hands are strength and power
to exalt and give strength to all.
13 Now, our God, we give you thanks,
and praise your glorious name.

14 "But who am I, and who are my people, that we should be able to give as

28:17 [y] S Ex 27:3 **28:18** [z] Ex 30:1-10 [a] S Ex 25:22 [b] S Ex 25:20 **28:19** [c] 1Ki 6:38 [d] S Ex 25:9 **28:20** [e] S Dt 31:6; 1Ch 22:13; 2Ch 19:11; Hag 2:4 [f] S Dt 4:31; S Jos 24:20 [g] S 1Ki 6:14; 2Ch 7:11 **28:21** [h] Ex 35:25-36:5 **29:1** [i] 1Ki 3:7; 1Ch 22:5; 2Ch 13:7 **29:2** [j] ver 7, 14, 16; Ezr 1:4; 6:5; Hag 2:8 [k] Isa 54:11 [l] 1Ch 22:2-5 **29:3** [m] 2Ch 24:10; 31:3; 35:8 **29:4** [n] S Ge 10:29 [o] 1Ch 22:14 **29:6** [p] 1Ch 27:1; S 28:1 [q] ver 9; Ex 25:1-8; 35:20-29; 36:2; 2Ch 24:10; Ezr 7:15 **29:7** [r] S Ex 25:2; Ne 7:70-71 **29:8** [s] Ex 35:27 [t] S 1Ch 26:21 **29:9** [u] 1Ki 8:61 **29:11** [v] Ps 24:8; 59:17; 62:11 [w] Ps 89:11 [x] Rev 5:12-13 **29:12** [y] 2Ch 1:12; 32:27; Ezr 7:27; Ecc 5:19 [z] 2Ch 20:6

[a] 2 The meaning of the Hebrew for this word is uncertain. [b] 4 That is, about 110 tons or about 100 metric tons [c] 4 That is, about 260 tons or about 235 metric tons [d] 7 That is, about 190 tons or about 170 metric tons [e] 7 That is, about 185 pounds or about 84 kilograms [f] 7 That is, about 380 tons or about 340 metric tons [g] 7 That is, about 675 tons or about 610 metric tons [h] 7 That is, about 3,800 tons or about 3,400 metric tons

---

28:18 *chariot.* Probably God's mobile throne (see note on Ps 18:10).
28:19 *I have in writing as a result of the LORD's hand on me.* The Chronicler may intend no more than the ordinary process of inspiration whereby David wrote under divine influence. On the other hand, he may imply a parallel with Moses, who also received documents from the hand of the Lord (Ex 25:40; 27:8; 31:18; 32:16).
28:20 See Introduction: Portrait of David and Solomon.
29:1 *chosen.* See note on 28:5. *young.* See note on 22:5.
29:2-9 After donating his personal fortune to the construction of the temple, David appeals to the people for their voluntary gifts. The Chronicler again appears to be modeling his account of David on events from the life of Moses (Ex 25:1-8; 35:4-9,20-29). The willing response of the people aided the building of both tabernacle and temple.
29:7 *darics.* See NIV text note. The daric was a Persian gold coin, apparently named for Darius I (522-486 BC), in whose reign it first appears (see Ezr 8:27). Since the Chronicler's readers were familiar with it, he could use it as an up-to-date standard of value for an earlier treasure of gold.
29:10-11 See note on Mt 6:13.

generously as this?[a] Everything comes
from you, and we have given you only
what comes from your hand.[b] 15 We are
foreigners and strangers[c] in your sight, as
were all our ancestors. Our days on earth
are like a shadow,[d] without hope. 16 LORD
our God, all this abundance that we have
provided for building you a temple for
your Holy Name comes from your hand,
and all of it belongs to you. 17 I know,
my God, that you test the heart[e] and are
pleased with integrity. All these things I
have given willingly and with honest intent. And now I have seen with joy how
willingly your people who are here have
given to you.[f] 18 LORD, the God of our fathers Abraham, Isaac and Israel, keep
these desires and thoughts in the hearts of
your people forever, and keep their hearts
loyal to you. 19 And give my son Solomon
the wholehearted devotion[g] to keep your
commands, statutes and decrees[h] and to
do everything to build the palatial structure for which I have provided."[i]
20 Then David said to the whole assembly, "Praise the LORD your God." So they
all praised the LORD, the God of their fathers; they bowed down, prostrating themselves before the LORD and the king.

Solomon Acknowledged as King

29:21-25pp — 1Ki 1:28-53

21 The next day they made sacrifices to
the LORD and presented burnt offerings to
him:[j] a thousand bulls, a thousand rams
and a thousand male lambs, together with
their drink offerings, and other sacrifices
in abundance for all Israel.[k] 22 They ate and
drank with great joy[l] in the presence of the
LORD that day.
Then they acknowledged Solomon son
of David as king a second time, anointing
him before the LORD to be ruler and Zadok[m] to be priest. 23 So Solomon sat[n] on
the throne[o] of the LORD as king in place
of his father David. He prospered and all
Israel obeyed him. 24 All the officers and
warriors, as well as all of King David's
sons,[p] pledged their submission to King
Solomon.
25 The LORD highly exalted[q] Solomon in
the sight of all Israel and bestowed on him
royal splendor[r] such as no king over Israel
ever had before.[s]

The Death of David

29:26-28pp — 1Ki 2:10-12

26 David son of Jesse was king[t] over all
Israel.[u] 27 He ruled over Israel forty years —
seven in Hebron[v] and thirty-three in Jerusalem.[w] 28 He died[x] at a good old age, having enjoyed long life, wealth and honor.
His son Solomon succeeded him as king.[y]
29 As for the events of King David's
reign, from beginning to end, they are
written in the records of Samuel the seer,[z]
the records of Nathan[a] the prophet and the
records of Gad[b] the seer, 30 together with
the details of his reign and power, and the
circumstances that surrounded him and
Israel and the kingdoms of all the other
lands.

29:14 [a]Ps 8:4; 144:3 [b]S ver 2 **29:15** [c]S Ge 17:8; S 23:4; Ps 39:12; S Heb 11:13 [d]Job 7:6; 8:9; 14:2; 32:7; Ps 102:11; 144:4; Ecc 6:12 **29:17** [e]Ps 139:23; Pr 15:11; 17:3; Jer 11:20; 17:10 [f]1Ch 28:9; Ps 15:1-5; Pr 11:20 **29:19** [g]S 1Ki 8:61; 11:4; 1Ch 28:9; Isa 38:3 [h]Ps 72:1 [i]S 1Ch 22:14 **29:21** [j]S 1Ki 8:62 [k]1Ch 11:1 **29:22** [l]1Ch 12:40 [m]S 1Sa 2:35 **29:23** [n]S Dt 17:18 [o]S 1Ki 2:12; S 1Ch 17:14 **29:24** [p]1Ki 1:9 **29:25** [q]S Jos 3:7 [r]1Ki 10:7; 2Ch 1:1,12 [s]Ecc 2:9 **29:26** [t]1Ch 18:14 [u]1Ch 11:1 **29:27** [v]S Ge 23:19 [w]2Sa 5:4-5; S 1Ch 3:4 **29:28** [x]S Ge 15:15; Ac 13:36 [y]S 1Ch 23:1 **29:29** [z]S 1Sa 9:9 [a]S 2Sa 7:2 [b]S 1Sa 22:5

29:22 *ate and drank.* See 12:38 – 40 and note. The anointing of both Solomon and Zadok portrays the harmony between them (see Zec 4:14; 6:13 and notes). *second time.* Perhaps the first time was Solomon's anointing, recorded in 1Ki 1:32 – 36 but omitted by the Chronicler (see note on 28:1 — 29:30). However, the phrase "second time" is missing in the Septuagint (the pre-Christian Greek translation of the OT), suggesting that it may have been an addition to the Hebrew text of this passage by an ancient scribe after the Septuagint had already been translated, in order to harmonize the Chronicles account with Kings. Multiple anointings are found in the cases of both Saul (1Sa 10:1,24; 11:14 – 15) and David (1Sa 16:13; 2Sa 2:4; 5:3).

29:24 *all ... pledged their submission.* But compare the rebellion of Adonijah, in which the officers and sons of the king had assisted the attempted coup (1Ki 1:9,19,25). Again the Chronicler has bypassed a negative event that would tarnish his image of David and Solomon.

29:25 *all Israel.* See 11:1,10; 12:38 – 40; see also Introduction: Purpose and Themes.

29:27 See note on 3:1 – 9.

29:28 *long life, wealth and honor.* As a feature of the Chronicler's theme of immediate retribution (see Introduction: Purpose and Themes), the righteous enjoy these blessings (cf. Ps 128; Pr 3:2,4, 9 – 10,16,22,33 – 35).

29:29 See Introduction: Author, Date and Sources.

29:30 *kingdoms of all the other lands.* Those immediately surrounding David's kingdom.

2 CHRONICLES

INTRODUCTION

See Introduction to 1 Chronicles.

The Building of the Temple in 2 Chronicles

The Chronicler has used the Pentateuchal history as a model for his account of the reigns of David and Solomon. Similarly, the Pentateuchal record of the building of the tabernacle affects his account of the building of the temple:

(1) The building of the tabernacle was entrusted to Bezalel and Oholiab (Ex 35:30—36:7), and they provide the Chronicler's model for the relationship of Solomon and Huram-Abi (2Ch 2:13). It is significant that the only references to Bezalel outside the book of Exodus are in Chronicles (1Ch 2:20; 2Ch 1:5).

Solomon is the new Bezalel: (a) Both Solomon and Bezalel are designated by name for their tasks by God; they are the only workers on their projects to be chosen by name (Ex 31:2; 35:30—36:2; 38:22–23; 1Ch 28:6). (b) Both are from the tribe of Judah (Ex 31:2; 35:30; 1Ch 2:20; 3:10). (c) Both receive the Spirit to endow them with wisdom (Ex 31:3; 35:30–31; 2Ch 1:1–13), and Solomon's vision at Gibeon (2Ch 1:3–13) dominates the preface to the account of the temple construction (2Ch 2–7). (d) Both build a bronze altar for the sanctuary (2Ch 1:5; 4:1; 7:7)—significantly, the bronze altar is not mentioned in the summary list of Huram-Abi's work (4:12–16). (e) Both make the sanctuary furnishings (Ex 31:1–10; 37:10–29; 2Ch 4:19–22).

Similarly, Huram-Abi becomes the new Oholiab: (a) In the account of the temple building in Kings, Huram-Abi is not mentioned until after the story of the main construction of temple and palace has been told (1Ki 7:13–45); in Chronicles he is introduced as being involved in the building work from the beginning (2Ch 2:13), just as Oholiab worked on the tabernacle from the beginning (Ex 31:6). (b) Kings speaks only of Huram-Abi's skill in casting bronze (1Ki 7:14); in Chronicles, however, his list of skills is the same as Oholiab's (Ex 31:1–6; 35:30—36:2;

a quick look

Author:
Unknown; possibly Ezra

Audience:
The people of Judah who had returned from exile in Babylonia

Date:
Between 450 and 400 BC

Theme:
2 Chronicles covers the period from the beginning of Solomon's reign (970 BC) to the Babylonian exile (586 BC), presenting an idealized history of the southern kingdom of Judah.

The author of 1 and 2 Chronicles has used the Pentateuchal history as a model for his account of the reigns of David and Solomon.

38:22 – 23; 2Ch 2:14). (c) Kings reports that the mother of Huram-Abi was a widow from the tribe of Naphtali (1Ki 7:14); Chronicles, however, states that she was a widow from the tribe of Dan (2Ch 2:14), thus giving Huram-Abi the same ancestry as Oholiab (Ex 31:6; 35:34; 38:23). See note on 2Ch 2:13.

(2) The plans for both tabernacle and temple are given by God (Ex 25:1 — 30:37; see Ex 25:9,40; 27:8; see also 1Ch 28:11 – 19 — not mentioned in Samuel and Kings).

(3) The spoils of war are used as building materials for both tabernacle and temple (Ex 3:21 – 22; 12:35 – 36; see 1Ch 18:6 – 11 — not mentioned in Samuel and Kings).

(4) The people contribute willingly and generously for both structures (Ex 25:1 – 7; 36:3 – 7; see 1Ch 29:1 – 9 — not mentioned in Samuel and Kings).

(5) The glory cloud appears at the dedication of both structures (Ex 40:34 – 35; 2Ch 7:1 – 3).

Outline

- III. The Reign of Solomon (2Ch 1 – 9)
  - A. The Gift of Wisdom (ch. 1)
  - B. Building the Temple (2:1 — 5:1)
  - C. Dedication of the Temple (5:2 — 7:22)
  - D. Solomon's Other Activities (ch. 8)
  - E. Solomon's Wisdom, Splendor and Death (ch. 9)
- IV. The Schism, and the History of the Kings of Judah (2Ch 10 – 36)
  - A. Rehoboam (chs. 10 – 12)
  - B. Abijah (13:1 — 14:1)
  - C. Asa (14:2 — 16:14)
  - D. Jehoshaphat (17:1 — 21:3)
  - E. Jehoram (21:4–20)
  - F. Ahaziah (22:1 – 9)
  - G. Joash (22:10 — 24:27)
  - H. Amaziah (ch. 25)
  - I. Uzziah (ch. 26)
  - J. Jotham (ch. 27)
  - K. Ahaz (ch. 28)
  - L. Hezekiah (chs. 29 – 32)
  - M. Manasseh (33:1 – 20)
  - N. Amon (33:21 – 25)
  - O. Josiah (34:1 — 36:1)
  - P. Josiah's Successors (36:2 – 14)
  - Q. Exile and Restoration (36:15 – 23)

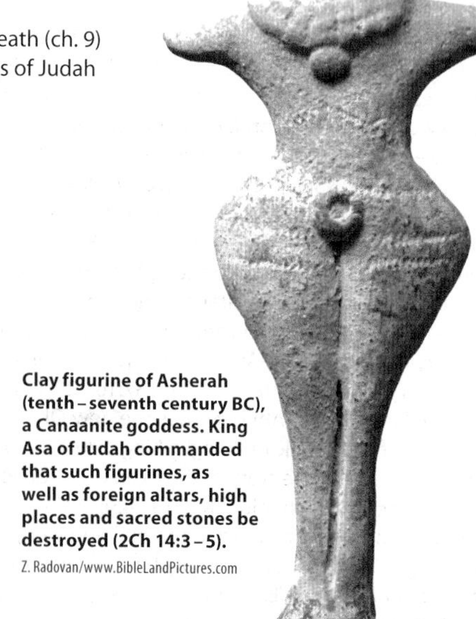

Clay figurine of Asherah (tenth – seventh century BC), a Canaanite goddess. King Asa of Judah commanded that such figurines, as well as foreign altars, high places and sacred stones be destroyed (2Ch 14:3 – 5).

Z. Radovan/www.BibleLandPictures.com

Solomon Asks for Wisdom

1:2-13pp — 1Ki 3:4-15
1:14-17pp — 1Ki 10:26-29; 2Ch 9:25-28

1 Solomon son of David established[a] himself firmly over his kingdom, for the LORD his God was with[b] him and made him exceedingly great.[c]

2 Then Solomon spoke to all Israel[d] — to the commanders of thousands and commanders of hundreds, to the judges and to all the leaders in Israel, the heads of families — 3 and Solomon and the whole assembly went to the high place at Gibeon,[e] for God's tent of meeting[f] was there, which Moses[g] the LORD's servant had made in the wilderness. 4 Now David had brought up the ark[h] of God from Kiriath Jearim to the place he had prepared for it, because he had pitched a tent[i] for it in Jerusalem. 5 But the bronze altar[j] that Bezalel[k] son of Uri, the son of Hur, had made was in Gibeon in front of the tabernacle of the LORD; so Solomon and the assembly inquired[l] of him there. 6 Solomon went up to the bronze altar before the LORD in the tent of meeting and offered a thousand burnt offerings on it.

7 That night God appeared[m] to Solomon and said to him, "Ask for whatever you want me to give you."

8 Solomon answered God, "You have shown great kindness to David my father and have made me[n] king in his place. 9 Now, LORD God, let your promise[o] to my father David be confirmed, for you have made me king over a people who are as numerous as the dust of the earth.[p] 10 Give me wisdom and knowledge, that I may lead[q] this people, for who is able to govern this great people of yours?"

11 God said to Solomon, "Since this is your heart's desire and you have not asked for wealth,[r] possessions or honor, nor for the death of your enemies, and since you have not asked for a long life but for wisdom and knowledge to govern my people over whom I have made you king, 12 therefore wisdom and knowledge will be given you. And I will also give you wealth, possessions and honor,[s] such as no king who was before you ever had and none after you will have.[t]"

13 Then Solomon went to Jerusalem from the high place at Gibeon, from before the tent of meeting. And he reigned over Israel.

14 Solomon accumulated chariots[u] and horses; he had fourteen hundred chariots and twelve thousand horses,[a] which he kept in the chariot cities and also with him in Jerusalem. 15 The king made silver and gold[v] as common in Jerusalem as stones, and cedar as plentiful as sycamore-fig trees in the foothills. 16 Solomon's horses were imported from Egypt and from Kue[b] — the royal merchants purchased them from Kue at the current price. 17 They imported a chariot[w] from Egypt for six hundred shekels[c] of silver, and a horse for a hundred and fifty.[d] They also exported them to all the kings of the Hittites and of the Arameans.

Preparations for Building the Temple

2:1-18pp — 1Ki 5:1-16

2[e] Solomon gave orders to build a temple[x] for the Name of the LORD and a royal palace for himself.[y] 2 He conscripted

1:1 [a] S 1Ki 2:12, 26; S 2Ch 12:1 [b] S Ge 21:22; S 39:2; S Nu 14:43 [c] S 1Ch 29:25 **1:2** [d] S 1Ch 9:1 **1:3** [e] S Jos 9:3 [f] S Lev 17:4 [g] Ex 40:18 **1:4** [h] S 1Ch 15:25 [i] 2Sa 6:17 **1:5** [j] Ex 38:2 [k] S Ex 31:2 [l] 1Ch 13:3 **1:7** [m] 2Ch 7:12 **1:8** [n] S 1Ch 23:1 **1:9** [o] S 2Sa 7:25; S 1Ki 8:25 [p] S Ge 12:2 **1:10** [q] Nu 27:17; 2Sa 5:2; Pr 8:15-16 **1:11** [r] S Dt 17:17 **1:12** [s] S 1Ch 29:12 [t] S 1Ch 29:25; 2Ch 9:22; Ne 13:26 **1:14** [u] S 1Sa 8:11; S 1Ki 9:19 **1:15** [v] S 1Ki 9:28; Isa 60:5 **1:17** [w] SS 1:9 **2:1** [x] S Dt 12:5 [y] Ecc 2:4

[a] 14 Or *charioteers* [b] 16 Probably Cilicia [c] 17 That is, about 15 pounds or about 6.9 kilograms [d] 17 That is, about 3 3/4 pounds or about 1.7 kilograms [e] In Hebrew texts 2:1 is numbered 1:18, and 2:2-18 is numbered 2:1-17.

1:1 — 9:31 The account of the reign of Solomon is primarily devoted to his building of the temple (chs. 2 – 7); his endowment with wisdom is mainly to facilitate the building work. Much of the material in Kings that does not bear on building the temple is omitted by the Chronicler; e.g., he does not mention the judgment between the prostitutes (1Ki 3:16 – 28) or the building of the royal palace (1Ki 7:1 – 12).

1:1 *established himself.* This expression, or a variation of it, is common in Chronicles (12:13; 13:7 – 8,21; 15:8; 16:9; 17:1; 21:4; 23:1; 25:11; 27:6; 32:5; 1Ch 11:10; 19:13). Here and in 21:4 it includes the elimination of enemies and rivals to the throne (see 1Ki 2, especially v. 46).

1:2 – 13 See 1Ki 3:4 – 15 and notes. Verses 2 – 6 are largely unique to Chronicles and show some of the writer's concerns: (1) The support of "all Israel" (v. 2) is emphasized (see Introduction to 1 Chronicles: Purpose and Themes). (2) While the writer of Kings is somewhat apologetic about Solomon's visit to a high place (1Ki 3:3), the Chronicler adds the note that this was the location of the tabernacle made by Moses in the wilderness (v. 3), bringing Solomon's action into line with the provisions of the law (Lev 17:8 – 9).

1:5 *Bezalel.* See Introduction: The Building of the Temple in Chronicles. It is specifically in connection with his offering on the altar built by Bezalel (Ex 31:1 – 11; 38:1 – 2) that Solomon receives the wisdom from God to reign. In the account that follows, Solomon devotes his gift of wisdom primarily to building the temple, just as Bezalel had been gifted by God to serve as the master craftsman of the tabernacle.

1:9 *numerous as the dust.* In provisional fulfillment of the promise to Abraham (Ge 13:16; 22:17; see note on 1Ch 27:23; cf. Ge 28:14).

1:14 – 17 The Chronicler does not include the material in 1Ki 3:16 — 4:34. He moves rather to the account of Solomon's wealth in 1Ki 10:26 – 29; part of this material is repeated in 2Ch 9:25 – 28. Recounting Solomon's wealth at this point shows the fulfillment of God's promise (v. 12).

1:15 *sycamore-fig trees.* See note on Am 7:14.

1:16 – 17 *imported . . . exported.* See note on 1Ki 10:29.

1:17 *Hittites.* See note on Ge 10:15. *Arameans.* See notes on 1Ch 18:5; Dt 26:5.

2:1 *palace.* Although the Chronicler frequently mentions the palace Solomon built (7:11; 8:1; 9:11), he gives no details of its construction (see 1Ki 7:1 – 12).

70,000 men as carriers and 80,000 as
stonecutters in the hills and 3,600 as foremen over them.[z]
3 Solomon sent this message to Hiram[a][a]
king of Tyre:

"Send me cedar logs[b] as you did
for my father David when you sent
him cedar to build a palace to live in.
4 Now I am about to build a temple[c]
for the Name of the LORD my God and
to dedicate it to him for burning fragrant incense[d] before him, for setting
out the consecrated bread[e] regularly,
and for making burnt offerings[f] every
morning and evening and on the Sabbaths,[g] at the New Moons[h] and at the
appointed festivals of the LORD our
God. This is a lasting ordinance for
Israel.
5 "The temple I am going to build
will be great,[i] because our God is
greater than all other gods.[j] 6 But who
is able to build a temple for him,
since the heavens, even the highest
heavens, cannot contain him?[k] Who
then am I[l] to build a temple for him,
except as a place to burn sacrifices
before him?
7 "Send me, therefore, a man skilled
to work in gold and silver, bronze
and iron, and in purple, crimson and
blue yarn, and experienced in the art
of engraving, to work in Judah and
Jerusalem with my skilled workers,[m]
whom my father David provided.
8 "Send me also cedar, juniper and
algum[b] logs from Lebanon, for I know
that your servants are skilled in cutting timber there. My servants will
work with yours 9 to provide me with
plenty of lumber, because the temple
I build must be large and magnificent.
10 I will give your servants, the woodsmen who cut the timber, twenty thousand cors[c] of ground wheat, twenty
thousand cors[d] of barley, twenty thousand baths[e] of wine and twenty thousand baths of olive oil.[n]"

11 Hiram king of Tyre replied by letter to
Solomon:

"Because the LORD loves[o] his people, he has made you their king."

12 And Hiram added:

"Praise be to the LORD, the God of
Israel, who made heaven and earth![p]
He has given King David a wise son,
endowed with intelligence and discernment, who will build a temple
for the LORD and a palace for himself.
13 "I am sending you Huram-Abi,[q]
a man of great skill, 14 whose mother was from Dan[r] and whose father
was from Tyre. He is trained[s] to work
in gold and silver, bronze and iron,
stone and wood, and with purple and
blue[t] and crimson yarn and fine lin-
en. He is experienced in all kinds of
engraving and can execute any design
given to him. He will work with your
skilled workers and with those of my
lord, David your father.
15 "Now let my lord send his servants the wheat and barley and the
olive oil[u] and wine he promised,
16 and we will cut all the logs from
Lebanon that you need and will float
them as rafts by sea down to Joppa.[v]
You can then take them up to Jerusalem."

17 Solomon took a census of all the foreigners[w] residing in Israel, after the cen-

2:2 [z] 2Ch 10:4 **2:3** [a] S 2Sa 5:11 [b] S 1Ch 14:1 **2:4** [c] S Dt 12:5 [d] S Ex 30:7 [e] Ex 25:30 [f] Ex 29:42; 2Ch 13:11; 29:28 [g] S Lev 23:38 [h] S Nu 28:14 **2:5** [i] 1Ch 22:5 [j] S Ex 12:12; S 1Ch 16:25 **2:6** [k] S 1Ki 8:27; Jer 23:24 [l] S Ex 3:11 **2:7** [m] S Ex 35:31; 1Ch 22:16 **2:10** [n] Ezr 3:7 **2:11** [o] 1Ki 10:9; 2Ch 9:8 **2:12** [p] Ne 9:6; Ps 8:3; 33:6; 96:5; 102:25; 146:6 **2:13** [q] S 1Ki 7:13 **2:14** [r] S Ex 31:6 [s] S Ex 35:31 [t] Ex 35:35 **2:15** [u] Ezr 3:7 **2:16** [v] S Jos 19:46; Jnh 1:3 **2:17** [w] 1Ch 22:2

[a] *3* Hebrew *Huram,* a variant of *Hiram;* also in verses 11 and 12 [b] *8* Probably a variant of *almug* [c] *10* That is, probably about 3,600 tons or about 3,200 metric tons of wheat [d] *10* That is, probably about 3,000 tons or about 2,700 metric tons of barley [e] *10* That is, about 120,000 gallons or about 440,000 liters

2:2 See vv. 17–18 and note.

2:3–10 The Chronicler's theological interests appear in his handling of Solomon's correspondence with Hiram of Tyre. In the Kings account the correspondence was initiated by Hiram (1Ki 5:1). The Chronicler omits this (and also the material in 1Ki 5:3–5) but adds his own material, reflecting his concerns with the temple worship in vv. 3–7.

2:4 See 1Ch 23:28–32 and note.

2:7 See Introduction: The Building of the Temple in Chronicles. In the Kings account Solomon's request for a master craftsman is found late in the narrative (1Ki 7:13); to carry out his parallel between Oholiab and Huram-Abi, the Chronicler includes it in the initial correspondence. Furthermore, here and in vv. 13–14 the list of Huram-Abi's skills is expanded and matches that of Bezalel and Oholiab (Kings is concerned only with casting bronze).

2:10 The payment here differs from that reported in 1Ki 5:11, but the texts speak of two different payments: In Kings the payment is an annual sum delivered to the royal household of Hiram, while Chronicles speaks of one payment to "the woodsmen who cut the timber." The goods paid are also not identical; the oil specified in Kings is of a finer quality.

2:11–16 See 1Ki 5:7–9; 7:13–14 and notes.

2:13 *Huram-Abi.* See note on v. 7. Kings reports that the ancestry of Huram-Abi was through a widow of Naphtali (1Ki 7:14); Chronicles strengthens the parallel between Huram-Abi and Oholiab by assigning Huram-Abi Danite ancestry. These statements are not necessarily contradictory: (1) The mother's ancestry may have been Danite, though she lived in the territory of Naphtali; or (2) her parents may have been from Dan and Naphtali, allowing her descent to be reckoned to either. The Danites had been previously associated with the Phoenicians (Jdg 18:7).

2:17–18 See 1Ki 5:13–18 and notes. The Chronicler specifies that this levy of forced laborers was from foreigners living among the Israelites, not from the Israelites themselves. This is not stated in the parallel passage in Kings, though 1Ki 9:20–22 confirms that foreign laborers were used (see 8:8).

sus[x] his father David had taken; and they were found to be 153,600. 18 He assigned[y] 70,000 of them to be carriers and 80,000 to be stonecutters in the hills, with 3,600 foremen over them to keep the people working.

Solomon Builds the Temple

3:1-14pp — 1Ki 6:1-29

3 Then Solomon began to build[z] the temple of the LORD[a] in Jerusalem on Mount Moriah, where the LORD had appeared to his father David. It was on the threshing floor of Araunah[ab] the Jebusite, the place provided by David. 2 He began building on the second day of the second month in the fourth year of his reign.[c]

3 The foundation Solomon laid for building the temple of God was sixty cubits long and twenty cubits wide[bd] (using the cubit of the old standard). 4 The portico at the front of the temple was twenty cubits[c] long across the width of the building and twenty[d] cubits high.

He overlaid the inside with pure gold. 5 He paneled the main hall with juniper and covered it with fine gold and decorated it with palm tree[e] and chain designs. 6 He adorned the temple with precious stones. And the gold he used was gold of Parvaim. 7 He overlaid the ceiling beams, doorframes, walls and doors of the temple with gold, and he carved cherubim[f] on the walls.

8 He built the Most Holy Place,[g] its length corresponding to the width of the temple — twenty cubits long and twenty cubits wide. He overlaid the inside with six hundred talents[e] of fine gold. 9 The gold nails[h] weighed fifty shekels.[f] He also overlaid the upper parts with gold.

10 For the Most Holy Place he made a pair[i] of sculptured cherubim and overlaid them with gold. 11 The total wingspan of the cherubim was twenty cubits. One wing of the first cherub was five cubits[g] long and touched the temple wall, while its other wing, also five cubits long, touched the wing of the other cherub. 12 Similarly one wing of the second cherub was five cubits long and touched the other temple wall, and its other wing, also five cubits long, touched the wing of the first cherub. 13 The wings of these cherubim[j] extended twenty cubits. They stood on their feet, facing the main hall.[h]

14 He made the curtain[k] of blue, purple and crimson yarn and fine linen, with cherubim[l] worked into it.

15 For the front of the temple he made two pillars,[m] which together were thirty-five cubits[i] long, each with a capital[n] five cubits high. 16 He made interwoven chains[jo] and put them on top of the pillars. He also made a hundred pomegranates[p] and attached them to the chains. 17 He

2:17 [x] S 2Sa 24:2
2:18 [y] 1Ch 22:2; 2Ch 8:8
3:1 [z] Ac 7:47 [a] S Ge 28:17 [b] S 2Sa 24:18
3:2 [c] Ezr 5:11
3:3 [d] Eze 41:2
3:5 [e] Eze 40:16
3:7 [f] Ge 3:24; Eze 41:18
3:8 [g] S Ex 26:33
3:9 [h] Ex 26:32
3:10 [i] Ex 25:18
3:13 [j] S Ex 25:18
3:14 [k] S Ex 26:31,33 [l] Ge 3:24
3:15 [m] S 1Ki 7:15; Rev 3:12 [n] 1Ki 7:22
3:16 [o] 1Ki 7:17 [p] S 1Ki 7:20

[a] *1* Hebrew *Ornan,* a variant of *Araunah* [b] *3* That is, about 90 feet long and 30 feet wide or about 27 meters long and 9 meters wide [c] *4* That is, about 30 feet or about 9 meters; also in verses 8, 11 and 13 [d] *4* Some Septuagint and Syriac manuscripts; Hebrew *and a hundred and twenty* [e] *8* That is, about 23 tons or about 21 metric tons [f] *9* That is, about 1 1/4 pounds or about 575 grams [g] *11* That is, about 7 1/2 feet or about 2.3 meters; also in verse 15 [h] *13* Or *facing inward* [i] *15* That is, about 53 feet or about 16 meters [j] *16* Or possibly *made chains in the inner sanctuary*; the meaning of the Hebrew for this phrase is uncertain.

2:18 *3,600 foremen.* See v. 2. The number given in 1Ki 5:16 is 3,300; however, some manuscripts of the Septuagint (the pre-Christian Greek translation of the OT) also have 3,600. The Chronicler may have been following a different text of Kings from the traditional Hebrew text at this point (but see note on 1Ki 5:16).

3:1 – 17 The Chronicler has considerably curtailed the description of the temple's construction found in Kings, omitting completely 1Ki 6:4 – 20. This abridgment probably indicates that the Chronicler's audience was familiar with the details of the earlier history and that the temple of the restoration period was less elaborate than the original Solomonic structure (Hag 2:3). On the other hand, the Chronicler goes into more detail on the furnishings and implements (3:6 – 9; 4:1,6 – 9).

3:1 *Mount Moriah.* The only passage in the OT where Mount Zion is identified with Mount Moriah, the place where Abraham was commanded to offer Isaac (Ge 22:2,14). *place provided by David.* See 1Ch 21:18 — 22:5.

3:2 *second month in the fourth year.* In the spring of 966 BC (see note on 1Ki 6:1).

3:3 *cubit of the old standard.* About three inches longer than the common cubit, which was c. 18 inches (see Eze 40:5 and note).

3:4 *portico.* See model, p. 523. *overlaid.* Or "inlaid," which would imply that the entire interior was not covered with gold leaf but that designs (palm trees, chains) were inlaid with gold leaf (v. 5).

3:6 *Parvaim.* Designates either the source of the gold (perhaps southeast Arabia) or a particular quality of fine gold.

3:7 *cherubim.* See vv. 10 – 14; see also notes on Ge 3:24; Eze 1:5.

3:8 *twenty cubits long and twenty cubits wide.* It was also 20 cubits high (1Ki 6:20), making the dimensions of the Most Holy Place a perfect cube, as also in the tabernacle. In the new Jerusalem there is no temple (Rev 21:22); rather, the whole city is in the shape of a cube (Rev 21:16), for the whole city becomes "the Most Holy Place."

3:9 *gold nails.* The fact that gold is a soft metal would make it unlikely that nails were made of this substance. It is probable that this small amount (only 1 1/4 pounds; see NIV text note) represents gold leaf or sheeting used to gild the nail heads.

3:10 – 13 See 1Ki 6:23 – 27 and notes.

3:14 *curtain.* Also separated the two rooms of the tabernacle (Ex 26:31). Wooden doors could also be closed across the opening (4:22; 1Ki 6:31 – 32; cf. Mt 27:51; Heb 9:8).

3:15 *together were thirty-five cubits long.* The NIV supplies the word "together" in an attempt to harmonize this measurement with the 18 cubits (each) in 1Ki 7:15; 2Ki 25:17 (see note there); Jer 52:21 (though the Septuagint, the pre-Christian Greek translation of the OT, at Jer 52:21 has 35). Alternatively, 35 may be the result of a copyist's mistake.

erected the pillars in the front of the temple, one to the south and one to the north.
The one to the south he named Jakin[a] and
the one to the north Boaz.[b]

The Temple's Furnishings

4:2-6,10–5:1pp — 1Ki 7:23-26,38-51

4 He made a bronze altar[q] twenty cubits
long, twenty cubits wide and ten cubits
high.[c] 2 He made the Sea[r] of cast metal, circular in shape, measuring ten cubits from
rim to rim and five cubits[d] high. It took a
line of thirty cubits[e] to measure around it.
3 Below the rim, figures of bulls encircled
it—ten to a cubit.[f] The bulls were cast in
two rows in one piece with the Sea.
4 The Sea stood on twelve bulls, three
facing north, three facing west, three facing south and three facing east.[s] The Sea
rested on top of them, and their hindquarters were toward the center. 5 It was a
handbreadth[g] in thickness, and its rim was
like the rim of a cup, like a lily blossom. It
held three thousand baths.[h]
6 He then made ten basins[t] for washing
and placed five on the south side and five
on the north. In them the things to be used
for the burnt offerings[u] were rinsed, but
the Sea was to be used by the priests for
washing.
7 He made ten gold lampstands[v] according to the specifications[w] for them and
placed them in the temple, five on the
south side and five on the north.
8 He made ten tables[x] and placed them
in the temple, five on the south side and
five on the north. He also made a hundred
gold sprinkling bowls.[y]
9 He made the courtyard[z] of the priests,
and the large court and the doors for the
court, and overlaid the doors with bronze.
10 He placed the Sea on the south side, at
the southeast corner.

4:1 [q] S Ex 20:24; S 40:6; S 1Ki 8:64
4:2 [r] Rev 4:6; 15:2
4:4 [s] Nu 2:3-25; Eze 48:30-34; Rev 21:13
4:6 [t] S Ex 30:18 [u] Ne 13:5,9; Eze 40:38
4:7 [v] S Ex 25:31 [w] Ex 25:40
4:8 [x] S Ex 25:23 [y] S Nu 4:14
4:9 [z] 1Ki 6:36; 2Ch 33:5

11 And Huram also made the pots and
shovels and sprinkling bowls.
So Huram finished[a] the work he had undertaken for King Solomon in the temple
of God:

12 the two pillars;
the two bowl-shaped capitals on top
of the pillars;
the two sets of network decorating
the two bowl-shaped capitals on
top of the pillars;
13 the four hundred pomegranates for
the two sets of network (two rows
of pomegranates for each network,
decorating the bowl-shaped capitals on top of the pillars);
14 the stands[b] with their basins;
15 the Sea and the twelve bulls under it;
16 the pots, shovels, meat forks and all
related articles.

All the objects that Huram-Abi[c] made for
King Solomon for the temple of the LORD
were of polished bronze. 17 The king had
them cast in clay molds in the plain of the
Jordan between Sukkoth[d] and Zarethan.[i]
18 All these things that Solomon made
amounted to so much that the weight of
the bronze[e] could not be calculated.
19 Solomon also made all the furnishings
that were in God's temple:

the golden altar;
the tables[f] on which was the bread of
the Presence;

4:11 [a] 1Ki 7:14
4:14 [b] 1Ki 7:27-30
4:16 [c] S 1Ki 7:13
4:17 [d] S Ge 33:17
4:18 [e] S 1Ki 7:23
4:19 [f] S Ex 25:23,30

[a] *17 Jakin* probably means *he establishes.* [b] *17 Boaz* probably means *in him is strength.* [c] *1* That is, about 30 feet long and wide and 15 feet high or about 9 meters long and wide and 4.5 meters high [d] *2* That is, about 7 1/2 feet or about 2.3 meters [e] *2* That is, about 45 feet or about 14 meters [f] *3* That is, about 18 inches or about 45 centimeters [g] *5* That is, about 3 inches or about 7.5 centimeters [h] *5* That is, about 18,000 gallons or about 66,000 liters [i] *17* Hebrew *Zeredatha,* a variant of *Zarethan*

3:17 *pillars.* Remains of such pillars have been found in the excavations of numerous temples in the Holy Land. Cf. Rev 3:12. *Jakin ... Boaz.* See NIV text notes.

4:1 *bronze altar.* The parallel text in Kings does not mention the main altar of the temple described here (1Ki 7:22–23), though several other passages in Kings do refer to it (1Ki 8:64; 9:25; 2Ki 16:14). The main altar of Solomon's temple was similar to the altar with steps that is described in Eze 43:13–17.

4:2 *Sea of cast metal.* A larger reservoir of water that replaced the bronze basin of the tabernacle (Ex 30:18); it was used by the priests for their ceremonial washing (v. 6; Ex 30:21). The NT views these rituals as foreshadowing the cleansing provided by Christ (Titus 3:5; Heb 9:11–14). In the temple of Ezekiel, the Sea, which was on the south side in front of the temple (v. 10), has been replaced by a life-giving river that flows from the south side of the temple (Eze 47:1–12; cf. Joel 3:18; Zec 14:8; Jn 4:9–15; Rev 22:1–2).

4:3 *bulls.* 1Ki 7:24 has "gourds." The Hebrew for the two words is very similar, so the difference may be due to a copyist's mistake.

4:4 *twelve bulls.* Possibly symbolic of the 12 tribes, which also encamped three on each side of the tabernacle during the wilderness journeys (Nu 2; cf. Eze 48:30–35).

4:5 *three thousand baths.* 1Ki 7:26 has 2,000 baths. The Hebrew for these figures could easily have been misread by the ancient scribes.

4:6 *ten basins.* See 1Ki 7:38–39.

4:7 *ten gold lampstands.* Instead of one, as in the tabernacle (Ex 25:31–40). *specifications.* See 1Ch 28:15. These lamps were not necessarily of the same shape as those described in Ex 25:31–40 but could have resembled the style depicted in Zec 4:2–6.

4:8 *ten tables.* Instead of one, as in the tabernacle (Ex 25:23–30; 40:4; Lev 24:5–9; 1Sa 21:1–6; Eze 41:22; Heb 9:2; cf. 2Ch 13:11; 29:18).

4:11–16 See 1Ki 7:40–45.

4:11 *sprinkling bowls.* See notes on Ex 27:3; 1Ki 7:40.

4:17–22 See 1Ki 7:46–50 and notes.

4:17 *clay molds.* The clay of the Jordan plain was used to make molds for these bronze castings. *Sukkoth and Zarethan.* See note on 1Ki 7:46.

DAVID AND SOLOMON'S EMPIRE

Euphrates R.
Orontes R.
Tiphsah
HAMATH
Hamath
Qatna
Tadmor
Lebo Hamath
Byblos
Mediterranean Sea
Litani R.
Sidon
Tyre
Dan
Hazor
Sea of Galilee
Akko
Ashtaroth
Megiddo
Ramoth Gilead
Beth Shan
Jordan R.
Shechem
Gezer
Gibeah
Jerusalem
Dead Sea
Beersheba
Raphia
Kir Hareseth
Wadi of Egypt
Tamar
Kadesh (Barnea)
Ezion Geber
Gulf of Aqaba

David and Solomon's empire
Solomon's expansion

0 40 km.
0 40 miles

Ivory pomegranate, possibly from an ornament in Solomon's temple. The inscription reads, "Belonging to the temple of the LORD, holy to the priests." There were hundreds of pomegranates decorating Solomon's temple (2Ch 4:13).

Z. Radovan/www.BibleLandPictures.com

20 the lampstands[g] of pure gold with their lamps, to burn in front of the inner sanctuary as prescribed;
21 the gold floral work and lamps and tongs (they were solid gold);
22 the pure gold wick trimmers, sprinkling bowls, dishes[h] and censers;[i] and the gold doors of the temple: the inner doors to the Most Holy Place and the doors of the main hall.

5 When all the work Solomon had done for the temple of the LORD was finished,[j] he brought in the things his father David had dedicated[k]—the silver and gold and all the furnishings—and he placed them in the treasuries of God's temple.

4:20 [g] Ex 25:31 **4:22** [h] S Nu 7:14 [i] S Lev 10:1 **5:1** [j] S 1Ki 6:14 [k] S 2Sa 8:11

The Ark Brought to the Temple

5:2–6:11pp — 1Ki 8:1-21

2 Then Solomon summoned to Jerusalem the elders of Israel, all the heads of the tribes and the chiefs of the Israelite families, to bring up the ark[l] of the LORD's covenant from Zion, the City of David.
3 And all the Israelites[m] came together to the king at the time of the festival in the seventh month.
4 When all the elders of Israel had arrived, the Levites took up the ark,
5 and they brought up the ark and the tent of meeting and all the sacred furnishings in it. The Levitical priests[n] carried them up;
6 and King Solomon and the entire assembly of Israel that had gathered about him were before the ark, sacrificing so many sheep and cattle that they could not be recorded or counted.
7 The priests then brought the ark[o] of the LORD's covenant to its place in the inner sanctuary of the temple, the Most Holy Place, and put it beneath the wings of the cherubim.
8 The cherubim[p] spread their wings over the place of the ark and covered the ark and its carrying poles.
9 These poles were so long that their ends, extending from the ark, could be seen from in front of the inner sanctuary, but not from outside the Holy Place; and they are still there today.
10 There was nothing in the ark except[q] the two tablets[r] that Moses had placed in it at Horeb, where the LORD made a covenant with the Israelites after they came out of Egypt.
11 The priests then withdrew from the Holy Place. All the priests who were there had consecrated themselves, regardless of their divisions.[s]
12 All the Levites who were musicians[t]—Asaph, Heman, Jeduthun and their sons and relatives—stood on the east side of the altar, dressed in fine linen and playing cymbals, harps and lyres. They were accompanied by 120 priests sounding trumpets.[u]
13 The trumpeters and musicians joined in unison to give praise and thanks to the LORD. Accompanied by trumpets, cymbals and other instruments, the singers raised their voices in praise to the LORD and sang:

5:2 [l] S Nu 3:31; S 1Ch 15:25 **5:3** [m] S 1Ch 9:1 **5:5** [n] S Nu 3:31; S 1Ch 15:2 **5:7** [o] Rev 11:19 **5:8** [p] S Ge 3:24 **5:10** [q] Heb 9:4 [r] S Ex 16:34; S Dt 10:2 **5:11** [s] S 1Ch 24:1 **5:12** [t] 1Ki 10:12; 1Ch 9:33; S 25:1; Ps 68:25 [u] S 1Ch 13:8

5:1 *things his father David had dedicated.* See notes on 1Ch 18:1—20:8; 22:2-16; 29:2-5; see also 1Ch 26:26 and note.
5:2-14 See 1Ki 8:1-11 and notes.
5:2 *ark.* Had been in a tent provided for it 40 years earlier when David brought it to Jerusalem (1Ch 15:1—16:6).
5:3 *festival in the seventh month.* The Festival of Tabernacles. The month is designated by its Canaanite name, Ethanim, in 1Ki 8:2; the Hebrew name is Tishri. According to 1Ki 6:38 the temple was completed in the eighth month of Solomon's 11th year, i.e., September-October, 959 BC. This celebration of dedication probably took place 11 months after the completion of the work (see note on 1Ki 8:2).
5:5 *brought up ... the tent of meeting.* The tabernacle had been at Gibeon (see 1:13; see also note on 1Ch 16:39).
5:6 Cf. David's bringing of the ark to Jerusalem (1Ch 15:26; 16:1-3).
5:9 *still there today.* See note on 1Ki 8:8; see also 8:8; 10:19; 20:26; 21:10; 35:25; 1Ch 4:41,43; 5:26; 13:11; 17:5.
5:10 *two tablets.* See Ex 31:18 and note; see also Ex 32:15-16. The ark had earlier contained also the gold jar of manna (Ex 16:32-34) and Aaron's staff (Nu 17:10-11; Heb 9:4). These items were presumably lost, perhaps while the ark was in Philistine hands.
5:12 *fine linen.* See 1Ch 15:27 and note.

"He is good;
his love endures forever."[v]

Then the temple of the LORD was filled
with the cloud,[w] 14 and the priests could
not perform[x] their service because of the
cloud,[y] for the glory[z] of the LORD filled the
temple of God.

6 Then Solomon said, "The LORD has
said that he would dwell in a dark
cloud;[a] 2 I have built a magnificent temple
for you, a place for you to dwell forever.[b]"
3 While the whole assembly of Isra-
el was standing there, the king turned
around and blessed them. 4 Then he said:

"Praise be to the LORD, the God of
Israel, who with his hands has fulfilled what he promised with his
mouth to my father David. For he
said, 5 'Since the day I brought my
people out of Egypt, I have not chosen a city in any tribe of Israel to have
a temple built so that my Name might
be there, nor have I chosen anyone to
be ruler over my people Israel. 6 But
now I have chosen Jerusalem[c] for my
Name[d] to be there, and I have chosen
David[e] to rule my people Israel.'
7 "My father David had it in his
heart[f] to build a temple for the Name
of the LORD, the God of Israel. 8 But
the LORD said to my father David,
'You did well to have it in your heart
to build a temple for my Name. 9 Nevertheless, you are not the one to build
the temple, but your son, your own
flesh and blood—he is the one who
will build the temple for my Name.'
10 "The LORD has kept the promise
he made. I have succeeded David my
father and now I sit on the throne of
Israel, just as the LORD promised, and
I have built the temple for the Name
of the LORD, the God of Israel. 11 There
I have placed the ark, in which is the
covenant[g] of the LORD that he made
with the people of Israel."

Solomon's Prayer of Dedication

6:12-40pp — 1Ki 8:22-53
6:41-42pp — Ps 132:8-10

12 Then Solomon stood before the altar
of the LORD in front of the whole assembly
of Israel and spread out his hands. 13 Now
he had made a bronze platform,[h] five cubits long, five cubits wide and three cubits
high,[a] and had placed it in the center of
the outer court. He stood on the platform
and then knelt down[i] before the whole assembly of Israel and spread out his hands
toward heaven. 14 He said:

"LORD, the God of Israel, there is
no God like you[j] in heaven or on
earth—you who keep your covenant
of love[k] with your servants who continue wholeheartedly in your way.
15 You have kept your promise to your
servant David my father; with your
mouth you have promised[l] and with
your hand you have fulfilled it—as
it is today.
16 "Now, LORD, the God of Israel,
keep for your servant David my father the promises you made to him
when you said, 'You shall never fail[m]
to have a successor to sit before me
on the throne of Israel, if only your
descendants are careful in all they do
to walk before me according to my
law,[n] as you have done.' 17 And now,
LORD, the God of Israel, let your word
that you promised your servant David
come true.
18 "But will God really dwell[o] on
earth with humans? The heavens,[p]
even the highest heavens, cannot
contain you. How much less this temple I have built! 19 Yet, LORD my God,
give attention to your servant's prayer
and his plea for mercy. Hear the cry
and the prayer that your servant is
praying in your presence. 20 May your
eyes[q] be open toward this temple day
and night, this place of which you
said you would put your Name[r] there.
May you hear[s] the prayer your servant prays toward this place. 21 Hear
the supplications of your servant and
of your people Israel when they pray
toward this place. Hear from heaven,
your dwelling place; and when you
hear, forgive.[t]
22 "When anyone wrongs their

5:13 [v] S 1Ch 16:34, 41; 2Ch 7:3; 20:21; Ezr 3:11; Ps 100:5; 106:1; 107:1; 118:1; 136:1; Jer 33:11 [w] S Ex 40:34 **5:14** [x] Ex 40:35; Rev 15:8 [y] Ex 19:16 [z] S Ex 29:43; S 40:35 **6:1** [a] S Ex 19:9 **6:2** [b] Ezr 6:12; 7:15; Ps 135:21 **6:6** [c] S Dt 12:5; S Isa 14:1 [d] S Ex 20:24 [e] S 1Ch 28:4 **6:7** [f] S 1Sa 10:7; S 1Ch 17:2; Ac 7:46 **6:11** [g] S Dt 10:2; Ps 25:10; 50:5 **6:13** [h] Ne 8:4 [i] Ps 95:6 **6:14** [j] S Ex 8:10; 15:11 [k] S Dt 7:9 **6:15** [l] S 1Ch 22:10 **6:16** [m] S 2Sa 7:13, 15; 2Ch 23:3 [n] Ps 132:12 **6:18** [o] S Rev 21:3 [p] Ps 11:4; Isa 40:22; 66:1 **6:20** [q] S Ex 3:16; Ps 34:15 [r] Dt 12:11 [s] 2Ch 7:14; 30:20 **6:21** [t] Ps 51:1; Isa 33:24; 40:2; 43:25; 44:22; 55:7; Mic 7:18

[a] *13* That is, about 7 1/2 feet long and wide and 4 1/2 feet high or about 2.3 meters long and wide and 1.4 meters high

5:14 *cloud ... glory of the LORD.* Cf. 7:1–3. The glory cloud represented the presence of God. It had guided Israel out of Egypt and through the wilderness and was present above the tabernacle (see Ex 13:21–22 and note on 13:21; 40:34–38 and note on 40:34; cf. Eze 43:1–5; Hag 2:9; Zec 1:16; 2:10; 8:3).
6:1–11 See notes on 1Ki 8:12–21.
6:8–9 Cf. David's speech in 1Ch 28:2–3.
6:12–21 See notes on 1Ki 8:22–30.
6:13 Not in 1Ki 8. Some think that the Chronicler may have wished to clarify the fact that Solomon was not "before the altar" (v. 12) exercising priestly duties. On the other hand, the verse may have been dropped from Kings by a copying error.
6:14 *who keep your covenant of love.* See 1Ki 8:23 and note.
6:18 Cf. 2:6.
6:22–39 See notes on 1Ki 8:31–46.
6:22–23 See Ex 22:10–11; Lev 6:3–5.

neighbor and is required to take an oath[u] and they come and swear the oath before your altar in this temple, 23 then hear from heaven and act. Judge between your servants, condemning[v] the guilty and bringing down on their heads what they have done, and vindicating the innocent by treating them in accordance with their innocence.

24 "When your people Israel have been defeated[w] by an enemy because they have sinned against you and when they turn back and give praise to your name, praying and making supplication before you in this temple, 25 then hear from heaven and forgive the sin of your people Israel and bring them back to the land you gave to them and their ancestors.

26 "When the heavens are shut up and there is no rain[x] because your people have sinned against you, and when they pray toward this place and give praise to your name and turn from their sin because you have afflicted them, 27 then hear from heaven and forgive[y] the sin of your servants, your people Israel. Teach them the right way to live, and send rain on the land you gave your people for an inheritance.

28 "When famine[z] or plague comes to the land, or blight or mildew, locusts or grasshoppers, or when enemies besiege them in any of their cities, whatever disaster or disease may come, 29 and when a prayer or plea is made by anyone among your people Israel—being aware of their afflictions and pains, and spreading out their hands toward this temple—30 then hear from heaven, your dwelling place. Forgive,[a] and deal with everyone according to all they do, since you know their hearts (for you alone know the human heart),[b] 31 so that they will fear you[c] and walk in obedience to you all the time they live in the land you gave our ancestors.

32 "As for the foreigner who does not belong to your people Israel but has come[d] from a distant land because of your great name and your mighty hand[e] and your outstretched arm—when they come and pray toward this temple, 33 then hear from heaven, your dwelling place. Do whatever the foreigner[f] asks of you, so that all the peoples of the earth may know your name and fear you, as do your own people Israel, and may know that this house I have built bears your Name.

34 "When your people go to war against their enemies,[g] wherever you send them, and when they pray[h] to you toward this city you have chosen and the temple I have built for your Name, 35 then hear from heaven their prayer and their plea, and uphold their cause.

36 "When they sin against you—for there is no one who does not sin[i]—and you become angry with them and give them over to the enemy, who takes them captive[j] to a land far away or near; 37 and if they have a change of heart[k] in the land where they are held captive, and repent and plead with you in the land of their captivity and say, 'We have sinned, we have done wrong and acted wickedly'; 38 and if they turn back to you with all their heart and soul in the land of their captivity where they were taken, and pray toward the land you gave their ancestors, toward the city you have chosen and toward the temple I have built for your Name; 39 then from heaven, your dwelling place, hear their prayer and their pleas, and uphold their cause. And forgive[l] your people, who have sinned against you.

40 "Now, my God, may your eyes be open and your ears attentive[m] to the prayers offered in this place.

41 "Now arise,[n] LORD God, and come
to your resting place,[o]
you and the ark of your might.
May your priests,[p] LORD God, be
clothed with salvation,
may your faithful people rejoice
in your goodness.[q]

6:22 [u]S Ex 22:11 **6:23** [v]Isa 3:11; 65:6; S Mt 16:27 **6:24** [w]S Lev 26:17 **6:26** [x]Lev 26:19; S Dt 11:17; 28:24; S 2Sa 1:21 **6:27** [y]ver 30, 39; 2Ch 7:14 **6:28** [z]2Ch 20:9 **6:30** [a]S ver 27 [b]S 1Sa 2:3; Ps 7:9; 44:21; Pr 16:2; 17:3 **6:31** [c]S Dt 6:13; Ps 34:7,9; 103:11,13; Pr 8:13

6:32 [d]2Ch 9:6 [e]S Ex 3:19,20 **6:33** [f]S Ex 12:43 **6:34** [g]Dt 28:7 [h]S 1Ch 5:20 **6:36** [i]S 1Ki 8:46; Job 11:12; 15:14; Ps 143:2; Ecc 7:20; Jer 9:5; 13:23; 17:9; S Ro 3:9; Eph 2:3 [j]S Lev 26:44 **6:37** [k]1Ki 8:48; 2Ch 7:14; 12:6, 12; 30:11; 33:12,19,23; 34:27; 36:12; Isa 58:3; Jer 24:7; 29:13 **6:39** [l]S ver 27; 2Ch 30:9 **6:40** [m]S 1Ki 8:29, 52; 2Ch 7:15; Ne 1:6,11; Ps 17:1,6; 116:1; 130:2; Isa 37:17 **6:41** [n]Ps 3:7; 7:6; 59:4; Isa 33:10 [o]1Ch 28:2 [p]Ps 132:16 [q]Ps 13:6; 27:13; 116:12; 142:7

6:24–25 See Lev 26:17,23; Dt 28:25,36–37,48–57, 64; Jos 7:11–12.

6:26–27 See Lev 26:19; Dt 11:10–15; 28:18,22–24.

6:28–31 See Lev 26:16,20,25–26; Dt 28:20–22,27–28,35,42.

6:32–33 The prophets also envisaged the Gentiles coming to Jerusalem to worship the Lord (Isa 2:3; 56:6–8; Mic 4:2; Zec 8:20–23; 14:16–21; cf. Ps 87).

6:34–35 See Lev 26:7–8; Dt 28:6–7. The Chronicler repeatedly demonstrates God's answer to prayer in time of battle (ch. 13; 14:9–15; 18:31; 20:1–29; 25:5–13; 32:20–22).

6:36 *no one who does not sin.* See Jer 13:23; Ro 3:23. *captive to a land far away.* See 36:15–20; Lev 26:33,44–45; Dt 28:49–52; 2Ki 17:7–20; 25:1–21.

6:40–42 The Chronicler replaces the ending of Solomon's prayer in Kings (1Ki 8:50–53) with Ps 132:8–10, a psalm that deals with bringing the ark to the temple, the theme of this section in Chronicles (5:2–14). The prayer in Kings ends with an appeal to the exodus deliverance under Moses, while in Chronicles the appeal is on the basis of the eternal promises to David.

42 LORD God, do not reject your
anointed one.[r]
Remember the great love[s]
promised to David your
servant."

The Dedication of the Temple

7:1-10pp — 1Ki 8:62-66

7 When Solomon finished praying, fire[t]
came down from heaven and consumed the burnt offering and the sacrifices, and the glory of the LORD filled[u] the
temple.[v] 2 The priests could not enter[w] the
temple of the LORD because the glory[x] of
the LORD filled it. 3 When all the Israelites
saw the fire coming down and the glory
of the LORD above the temple, they knelt
on the pavement with their faces to the
ground, and they worshiped and gave
thanks to the LORD, saying,

"He is good;
his love endures forever."[y]

4 Then the king and all the people offered
sacrifices before the LORD. 5 And King Solomon offered a sacrifice of twenty-two
thousand head of cattle and a hundred
and twenty thousand sheep and goats. So
the king and all the people dedicated the
temple of God. 6 The priests took their positions, as did the Levites[z] with the LORD's
musical instruments,[a] which King David
had made for praising the LORD and which
were used when he gave thanks, saying,
"His love endures forever." Opposite the
Levites, the priests blew their trumpets,
and all the Israelites were standing.
7 Solomon consecrated the middle part
of the courtyard in front of the temple of
the LORD, and there he offered burnt offerings and the fat[b] of the fellowship offerings, because the bronze altar he had
made could not hold the burnt offerings,
the grain offerings and the fat portions.

8 So Solomon observed the festival[c] at
that time for seven days, and all Israel[d]
with him — a vast assembly, people from
Lebo Hamath[e] to the Wadi of Egypt.[f] 9 On
the eighth day they held an assembly, for
they had celebrated[g] the dedication of the
altar for seven days and the festival[h] for
seven days more. 10 On the twenty-third
day of the seventh month he sent the people to their homes, joyful and glad in heart
for the good things the LORD had done for
David and Solomon and for his people Israel.

The LORD Appears to Solomon

7:11-22pp — 1Ki 9:1-9

11 When Solomon had finished[i] the temple of the LORD and the royal palace, and
had succeeded in carrying out all he had
in mind to do in the temple of the LORD
and in his own palace, 12 the LORD appeared[j] to him at night and said:

"I have heard your prayer and have
chosen[k] this place for myself[l] as a
temple for sacrifices.
13 "When I shut up the heavens so
that there is no rain,[m] or command
locusts to devour the land or send
a plague among my people, 14 if my
people, who are called by my name,[n]
will humble[o] themselves and pray
and seek my face[p] and turn[q] from
their wicked ways, then I will hear[r]
from heaven, and I will forgive[s] their
sin and will heal[t] their land. 15 Now
my eyes will be open and my ears attentive to the prayers offered in this
place.[u] 16 I have chosen[v] and consecrated this temple so that my Name
may be there forever. My eyes and my
heart will always be there.
17 "As for you, if you walk before me
faithfully[w] as David your father did,
and do all I command, and observe

6:42 [r] Ps 2:2 [s] Ps 89:24,28
7:1 [t] S Ex 19:18; S Lev 9:24; S 1Ki 18:38 [u] S Ex 16:10 [v] Ps 26:8
7:2 [w] S 1Ki 8:11 [x] S Ex 29:43; S 40:35
7:3 [y] S 1Ch 16:34; 2Ch 5:13; Ezr 3:11
7:6 [z] 1Ch 15:16 [a] S 1Ch 15:24
7:7 [b] S Ex 29:13
7:8 [c] 2Ch 30:26; Ne 8:17 [d] S 1Ch 9:1 [e] S Nu 13:21 [f] S Ge 15:18
7:9 [g] 2Ch 30:23 [h] S Lev 23:36
7:11 [i] S 1Ch 28:20
7:12 [j] 2Ch 1:7 [k] Dt 12:11 [l] S Dt 12:5
7:13 [m] S Dt 11:17; Am 4:7
7:14 [n] S Nu 6:27 [o] S Ex 10:3; S Lev 26:41; S 2Ch 6:37 [p] S 1Ch 16:11 [q] S 2Ki 17:13; Isa 55:7; Eze 18:32; Zec 1:4 [r] S 2Ch 6:20 [s] S 2Ch 6:27 [t] S Ex 15:26; 2Ch 30:20; Ps 60:2; Isa 30:26; 53:5; 57:18; Jer 33:6; Mal 4:2
7:15 [u] S 1Ki 8:29; S 2Ch 6:40; Ne 1:6
7:16 [v] S Dt 12:5; 2Ch 33:7
7:17 [w] S 1Ki 9:4

7:1-22 See 1Ki 8:54—9:9 and notes.
7:1-3 Not found in 1Ki 8. The addition of the fire descending from heaven to consume the sacrifices provides the same sign of divine acceptance given at the dedication of the tabernacle (Lev 9:23-24) and at David's offering on the threshing floor of Araunah the Jebusite (1Ch 21:26; cf. 1Ki 18:38). While vv. 1-3 are unique to Chronicles, the Chronicler has omitted Solomon's blessing of the congregation (1Ki 8:55-61).
7:1 *glory of the LORD.* See 5:14 and note.
7:3 *He is good … forever.* See v. 6; 5:13.
7:6 The verse is unique to Chronicles and reflects the author's overall interest in the Levites, especially the musicians (cf. 29:26-27; see note on 1Ch 6:31-48). *all the Israelites.* See Introduction to 1 Chronicles: Purpose and Themes.
7:8 *festival.* Tabernacles (see note on v. 9). *from Lebo Hamath to the Wadi of Egypt.* Not only were the patriarchal promises of descendants provisionally fulfilled under David and Solomon (see 1:9; 1Ch 27:23-24 and notes), but also the promises of land (Ge 15:18-21). *Lebo Hamath.* See note on Eze 47:15. *Wadi of Egypt.* See note on Eze 47:19.
7:9 *eighth day.* The final day of the Festival of Tabernacles (see 5:3 and note; Lev 23:36; Nu 29:35). *seven days … seven days.* The dedication had run from the 8th to the 14th day of the month, and the Festival of Tabernacles from the 15th to the 22nd day. The Day of Atonement was on the 10th day of the 7th month (Lev 16; cf. 1Ki 8:65-66).
7:12 *appeared to him.* The second time God appeared to Solomon; the first was at Gibeon (1:3-13; 1Ki 9:2). *your prayer.* See 6:14-42.
7:13-15 Unique to Chronicles. These verses illustrate the writer's emphasis on immediate retribution (see Introduction to 1 Chronicles: Purpose and Themes). The Chronicler subsequently portrays the kings in a way that demonstrates this principle (see v. 22).
7:14 See, e.g., 12:6-7,12.
7:17-18 See 1Ki 9:4-5. Such words as these reinforced ancient Israel's Messianic hopes.

my decrees[x] and laws, 18 I will establish your royal throne, as I covenanted[y] with David your father when I
said, 'You shall never fail to have a
successor[z] to rule over Israel.'[a]
19 "But if you[a] turn away[b] and forsake[c] the decrees and commands I
have given you[a] and go off to serve
other gods and worship them, 20 then
I will uproot[d] Israel from my land,[e]
which I have given them, and will
reject this temple I have consecrated
for my Name. I will make it a byword
and an object of ridicule[f] among all
peoples. 21 This temple will become a
heap of rubble. All[b] who pass by will
be appalled[g] and say,[h] 'Why has the
LORD done such a thing to this land
and to this temple?' 22 People will answer, 'Because they have forsaken
the LORD, the God of their ancestors,
who brought them out of Egypt, and
have embraced other gods, worshiping and serving them[i]—that is why
he brought all this disaster on them.' "

Solomon's Other Activities

8:1-18pp — 1Ki 9:10-28

8 At the end of twenty years, during
which Solomon built the temple of
the LORD and his own palace,[j] 2 Solomon
rebuilt the villages that Hiram[c] had given
him, and settled Israelites in them. 3 Solomon then went to Hamath Zobah and
captured it. 4 He also built up Tadmor in
the desert and all the store cities he had
built in Hamath.[k] 5 He rebuilt Upper Beth
Horon[l] and Lower Beth Horon as fortified
cities, with walls and with gates and bars,
6 as well as Baalath[m] and all his store cities,
and all the cities for his chariots and for
his horses[d]—whatever he desired to build
in Jerusalem, in Lebanon and throughout
all the territory he ruled.

7 There were still people left from the
Hittites, Amorites, Perizzites, Hivites and
Jebusites[n] (these people were not Israelites). 8 Solomon conscripted[o] the descendants of all these people remaining in the
land—whom the Israelites had not destroyed—to serve as slave labor, as it is
to this day. 9 But Solomon did not make
slaves of the Israelites for his work; they
were his fighting men, commanders of his
captains, and commanders of his chariots
and charioteers. 10 They were also King
Solomon's chief officials—two hundred
and fifty officials supervising the men.
11 Solomon brought Pharaoh's daughter[p]
up from the City of David to the palace
he had built for her, for he said, "My wife
must not live in the palace of David king
of Israel, because the places the ark of the
LORD has entered are holy."
12 On the altar[q] of the LORD that he had
built in front of the portico, Solomon sacrificed burnt offerings to the LORD, 13 according to the daily requirement[r] for offerings
commanded by Moses for the Sabbaths,[s]
the New Moons[t] and the three[u] annual festivals—the Festival of Unleavened Bread,[v]
the Festival of Weeks[w] and the Festival of
Tabernacles.[x] 14 In keeping with the ordinance of his father David, he appointed
the divisions[y] of the priests for their duties, and the Levites[z] to lead the praise
and to assist the priests according to each
day's requirement. He also appointed the
gatekeepers[a] by divisions for the various
gates, because this was what David the
man of God[b] had ordered.[c] 15 They did not
deviate from the king's commands to the
priests or to the Levites in any matter, including that of the treasuries.

7:17 [x]S Lev 19:37
7:18 [y]Isa 9:7; Jer 33:17,21 [z]S 1Ch 5:2; Isa 55:4; Mic 5:2 [a]S 2Sa 7:13; S 1Ch 17:12; 2Ch 13:5; 23:3
7:19 [b]S Dt 28:15 [c]S 1Ch 28:9; 2Ch 12:1; 24:18; Jer 9:13; 11:8
7:20 [d]S Dt 29:28 [e]1Ki 14:15; Jer 12:14; 16:13; 50:11 [f]S Dt 28:37
7:21 [g]Jer 19:8 [h]Dt 29:24
7:22 [i]Jer 16:11
8:1 [j]S 2Sa 7:2
8:4 [k]S 2Sa 8:9
8:5 [l]S Jos 10:10
8:6 [m]S Jos 19:44
8:7 [n]S Ge 10:16; S 15:18-21; Ezr 9:1
8:8 [o]S 2Ch 2:18
8:11 [p]S 1Ki 3:1
8:12 [q]S 1Ki 8:64; 2Ch 15:8
8:13 [r]S Ex 29:38 [s]Nu 28:9 [t]S Nu 10:10 [u]S Ex 23:14 [v]S Ex 12:17; Nu 28:16-25 [w]S Ex 23:16 [x]Nu 29:12-38; Ne 8:17
8:14 [y]S 1Ch 24:1 [z]S 1Ch 25:1 [a]S 1Ch 9:17 [b]Ne 12:24,36 [c]S 1Ch 23:6; Ne 12:45

[a] 19 The Hebrew is plural. [b] 21 See some Septuagint manuscripts, Old Latin, Syriac, Arabic and Targum; Hebrew *And though this temple is now so imposing, all* [c] 2 Hebrew *Huram,* a variant of *Hiram;* also in verse 18 [d] 6 Or *charioteers*

7:19 – 22 See 1Ki 9:6 – 9.
8:1 – 18 See 1Ki 9:10 – 18 and notes. Verses 13 – 16 are unique to Chronicles and underscore the Chronicler's concern to show continuity with the past and his association of David with Moses (see Introduction to 1 Chronicles: Purpose and Themes).
8:1 – 2 In 1 Ki 9:10 – 14 the cities were given to Hiram by Solomon, whereas in Chronicles the reverse is true. Perhaps as part of his effort to idealize Solomon, the Chronicler does not record the fact that Hiram found these cities unacceptable payment (1Ki 9:11 – 13); he mentions only the sequel to the story, the return of the cities to Solomon and their subsequent improvement. They may also have served as a kind of collateral against the money owed Hiram, who returned them when the debt was satisfied (see note on 1Ki 9:11). The Chronicler also says nothing about the pharaoh's gift of Gezer to Solomon (1Ki 9:16).
8:3 – 4 The Chronicler records an additional military campaign to the north, not mentioned in Kings. David had also campaigned in the north against Zobah (1Ch 18:3 – 9; 19:6; 2Sa 8:3 – 12; 10:6 – 8; cf. 1Ki 11:23 – 24).
8:5 The two Beth Horons were situated on a strategic road from the coastal plain to the area just north of Jerusalem (see map, p. 595).
8:7 *not Israelites.* See 2:17; 1Ch 22:2; 1Ki 9:21.
8:8 *to this day.* See note on 5:9.
8:11 *holy.* Both 1Ki 9:24 and Chronicles record the transfer of the pharaoh's daughter to special quarters, but only Chronicles adds the reason: Not only the temple but also David's palace was regarded as holy, because of the presence of the ark (see note on Lev 11:44).
8:12 – 16 In line with his overall interests, the Chronicler elaborates on the sacrificial and temple provisions made by Solomon. While 1Ki 9:25 mentions only the sacrifices at the three annual festivals, the Chronicler adds the offerings on Sabbaths and New Moons to conform these provisions fully to Mosaic instructions (Lev 23:1 – 37; Nu 28 – 29).

16 All Solomon's work was carried out, from the day the foundation of the temple of the LORD was laid until its completion. So the temple of the LORD was finished.

17 Then Solomon went to Ezion Geber and Elath on the coast of Edom. 18 And Hiram sent him ships commanded by his own men, sailors who knew the sea. These, with Solomon's men, sailed to Ophir and brought back four hundred and fifty talents[a] of gold,[d] which they delivered to King Solomon.

The Queen of Sheba Visits Solomon

9:1-12pp — 1Ki 10:1-13

9 When the queen of Sheba[e] heard of Solomon's fame, she came to Jerusalem to test him with hard questions. Arriving with a very great caravan — with camels carrying spices, large quantities of gold, and precious stones — she came to Solomon and talked with him about all she had on her mind. 2 Solomon answered all her questions; nothing was too hard for him to explain to her. 3 When the queen of Sheba saw the wisdom of Solomon,[f] as well as the palace he had built, 4 the food on his table, the seating of his officials, the attending servants in their robes, the cupbearers in their robes and the burnt offerings he made at[b] the temple of the LORD, she was overwhelmed.

5 She said to the king, "The report I heard in my own country about your achievements and your wisdom is true. 6 But I did not believe what they said until I came[g] and saw with my own eyes. Indeed, not even half the greatness of your wisdom was told me; you have far exceeded the report I heard. 7 How happy your people must be! How happy your officials, who continually stand before you and hear your wisdom! 8 Praise be to the LORD your God, who has delighted in you and placed you on his throne[h] as king to rule for the LORD your God. Because of the love of your God for Israel and his desire to uphold them forever, he has made you king[i] over them, to maintain justice and righteousness."

9 Then she gave the king 120 talents[c] of gold,[j] large quantities of spices, and precious stones. There had never been such spices as those the queen of Sheba gave to King Solomon.

10 (The servants of Hiram and the servants of Solomon brought gold from Ophir;[k] they also brought algumwood[d] and precious stones. 11 The king used the algumwood to make steps for the temple of the LORD and for the royal palace, and to make harps and lyres for the musicians. Nothing like them had ever been seen in Judah.)

12 King Solomon gave the queen of Sheba all she desired and asked for; he gave her more than she had brought to him. Then she left and returned with her retinue to her own country.

Solomon's Splendor

9:13-28pp — 1Ki 10:14-29; 2Ch 1:14-17

13 The weight of the gold that Solomon received yearly was 666 talents,[e] 14 not including the revenues brought in by merchants and traders. Also all the kings of Arabia[l] and the governors of the territories brought gold and silver to Solomon.

15 King Solomon made two hundred large shields of hammered gold; six hundred shekels[f] of hammered gold went into each shield. 16 He also made three hundred small shields[m] of hammered gold, with three hundred shekels[g] of gold in each shield. The king put them in the Palace of the Forest of Lebanon.[n]

17 Then the king made a great throne covered with ivory[o] and overlaid with pure gold. 18 The throne had six steps, and a footstool of gold was attached to it. On both sides of the seat were armrests, with a lion standing beside each of them. 19 Twelve lions stood on the six steps, one at either end of each step. Nothing like it had ever been made for any other kingdom.

8:18 [d] 2Ch 9:9 **9:1** [e] S Ge 10:7; Eze 23:42; Mt 12:42; Lk 11:31 **9:3** [f] 1Ki 5:12 **9:6** [g] 2Ch 6:32 **9:8** [h] S 1Ki 2:12; S 1Ch 17:14; 2Ch 13:8 [i] 2Ch 2:11 **9:9** [j] 2Ch 8:18 **9:10** [k] 2Ch 8:18 **9:14** [l] 2Ch 17:11; Isa 21:13; Jer 25:24; Eze 27:21; 30:5 **9:16** [m] 2Ch 12:9 [n] S 1Ki 7:2 **9:17** [o] S 1Ki 22:39

[a] 18 That is, about 17 tons or about 15 metric tons
[b] 4 Or *and the ascent by which he went up to*
[c] 9 That is, about 4 1/2 tons or about 4 metric tons
[d] 10 Probably a variant of *almugwood*
[e] 13 That is, about 25 tons or about 23 metric tons
[f] 15 That is, about 15 pounds or about 6.9 kilograms
[g] 16 That is, about 7 1/2 pounds or about 3.5 kilograms

8:17–18 See 1Ki 9:26–28. This joint venture between Solomon and Hiram secured for these kings the lucrative trade routes through the Mediterranean to the south Arabian peninsula; Solomon became the middleman between these economic spheres.
8:17 *Ezion Geber and Elath.* See note on Dt 2:8.
8:18 *Hiram sent him ships.* Presumably ships built in Phoenicia and assembled at the port of Ezion Geber after being shipped overland (see 9:21).
9:1–12 See 1Ki 10:1–13 and notes. The visit of the queen of Sheba portrays the fulfillment of God's promise to give Solomon wisdom and wealth (1:12). Although the themes of Solomon's wisdom and wealth are here put to the fore, a major motive for the queen's visit may have been commercial, perhaps prompted by Solomon's naval operations toward south Arabia (8:17–18).
9:1 *Sheba.* See note on 1Ki 10:1; see also Job 1:15; 6:19; Ps 72:10,15; Isa 60:6; Jer 6:20; Eze 27:22; 38:13; Joel 3:8.
9:8 *his throne.* The most significant variation from the account of the queen's visit in 1 Kings (10:9) is found here. The queen's speech becomes the vehicle for the Chronicler's conviction that the throne of Israel is the throne of God, for whom the king ruled (see 13:18; see also note on 1Ch 17:14).
9:16,20 *Palace of the Forest of Lebanon.* The royal palace in Jerusalem (cf. note on 1Ki 7:2).

20All King Solomon's goblets were gold,
and all the household articles in the Palace
of the Forest of Lebanon were pure gold.
Nothing was made of silver, because silver
was considered of little value in Solomon's
day. 21The king had a fleet of trading ships[a]
manned by Hiram's[b] servants. Once every
three years it returned, carrying gold, silver
and ivory, and apes and baboons.
22King Solomon was greater in riches
and wisdom than all the other kings of the
earth.[p] 23All the kings[q] of the earth sought
audience with Solomon to hear the wisdom
God had put in his heart. 24Year after year,
everyone who came brought a gift[r]—articles of silver and gold, and robes, weapons
and spices, and horses and mules.
25Solomon had four thousand stalls for
horses and chariots,[s] and twelve thousand
horses,[c] which he kept in the chariot cities and also with him in Jerusalem. 26He
ruled[t] over all the kings from the Euphrates River[u] to the land of the Philistines,
as far as the border of Egypt.[v] 27The king
made silver as common in Jerusalem as
stones, and cedar as plentiful as sycamore-
fig trees in the foothills. 28Solomon's horses were imported from Egypt and from all
other countries.

Solomon's Death

9:29-31pp — 1Ki 11:41-43

29As for the other events of Solomon's
reign, from beginning to end, are they
not written in the records of Nathan[w] the
prophet, in the prophecy of Ahijah[x] the
Shilonite and in the visions of Iddo the
seer concerning Jeroboam[y] son of Nebat?
30Solomon reigned in Jerusalem over all
Israel forty years. 31Then he rested with
his ancestors and was buried in the city of
David[z] his father. And Rehoboam his son
succeeded him as king.

Israel Rebels Against Rehoboam

10:1 – 11:4pp — 1Ki 12:1-24

10 Rehoboam went to Shechem, for
all Israel had gone there to make
him king. 2When Jeroboam[a] son of Nebat heard this (he was in Egypt, where he
had fled[b] from King Solomon), he returned
from Egypt. 3So they sent for Jeroboam,
and he and all Israel[c] went to Rehoboam
and said to him: 4"Your father put a heavy
yoke on us,[d] but now lighten the harsh labor and the heavy yoke he put on us, and
we will serve you."
5Rehoboam answered, "Come back to
me in three days." So the people went
away.
6Then King Rehoboam consulted the
elders[e] who had served his father Solomon during his lifetime. "How would you
advise me to answer these people?" he
asked.
7They replied, "If you will be kind to
these people and please them and give
them a favorable answer,[f] they will always
be your servants."
8But Rehoboam rejected[g] the advice the
elders[h] gave him and consulted the young
men who had grown up with him and
were serving him. 9He asked them, "What
is your advice? How should we answer
these people who say to me, 'Lighten the
yoke your father put on us'?"
10The young men who had grown up
with him replied, "The people have said
to you, 'Your father put a heavy yoke on
us, but make our yoke lighter.' Now tell
them, 'My little finger is thicker than my
father's waist. 11My father laid on you a
heavy yoke; I will make it even heavier.
My father scourged you with whips; I will
scourge you with scorpions.'"
12Three days later Jeroboam and all
the people returned to Rehoboam, as the
king had said, "Come back to me in three
days." 13The king answered them harshly. Rejecting the advice of the elders, 14he
followed the advice of the young men and
said, "My father made your yoke heavy;
I will make it even heavier. My father

9:22 [p]S 1Ki 3:13; S 2Ch 1:12 **9:23** [q]1Ki 4:34 **9:24** [r]2Ch 32:23; Ps 45:12; 68:29; 72:10; Isa 18:7 **9:25** [s]S 1Sa 8:11 **9:26** [t]S 1Ki 4:21 [u]Ps 72:8-9 [v]Ge 15:18-21 **9:29** [w]S 2Sa 7:2 [x]S 1Ki 11:29 [y]2Ch 10:2 **9:31** [z]1Ki 2:10

10:2 [a]S 2Ch 9:29 [b]S 1Ki 11:40 **10:3** [c]S 1Ch 9:1 **10:4** [d]2Ch 2:2 **10:6** [e]Job 8:8-9; 12:12; 15:10; 32:7 **10:7** [f]Pr 15:1 **10:8** [g]S 2Sa 17:14 [h]Pr 13:20

[a] 21 Hebrew *of ships that could go to Tarshish*
[b] 21 Hebrew *Huram*, a variant of *Hiram*
[c] 25 Or *charioteers*

9:26 See 7:8 and note.
9:27 See 1:15.
9:28 The Chronicler omits the accounts of Solomon's wives and the rebellions at the end of his reign (1Ki 11:1 – 40), both of which would detract from his uniformly positive portrayal of Solomon. *horses ... Egypt.* See note on 1:16 – 17.
9:29 – 31 See 1Ki 11:41 – 43.
10:1 — 36:23 The material covering the divided monarchy in Chronicles is considerably shorter than that in Kings: 27 chapters compared to 36 (1Ki 12 – 2Ki 25). Moreover, about half of this material is unique to Chronicles and shows no dependence on Kings. The most obvious reason for this is that the Chronicler has written a history of the Davidic dynasty in Judah; the history of the northern kingdom is passed over in silence except where it impinges on that of Judah. At least two considerations prompt this treatment of the divided kingdom: (1) The Chronicler is concerned to trace God's faithfulness to his promise to give David an unbroken line of descent on the throne of Israel. (2) At the time of the Chronicler the restored community was confined to the returnees of the kingdom of Judah, who were actually the remnant of all Israel (see Introduction to 1 Chronicles: Purpose and Themes).
10:1 – 19 See 1Ki 12:1 – 20 and notes. Somewhat in line with his idealization of Solomon, the Chronicler places most of the blame for the schism on the rebellious Jeroboam (cf. 13:6 – 7).
10:1 *Rehoboam.* Reigned 930 – 913 BC.
10:2 *Jeroboam.* Reigned 930 – 909 BC; his second mention in Chronicles (see 9:29). The Chronicler assumes the reader's familiarity with 1Ki 11:26 – 40.

scourged you with whips; I will scourge
you with scorpions." 15So the king did not
listen to the people, for this turn of events
was from God,[i] to fulfill the word the LORD
had spoken to Jeroboam son of Nebat
through Ahijah the Shilonite.[j]
16When all Israel[k] saw that the king refused to listen to them, they answered the
king:

"What share do we have in David,[l]
what part in Jesse's son?
To your tents, Israel!
Look after your own house, David!"

So all the Israelites went home. 17But as
for the Israelites who were living in the
towns of Judah, Rehoboam still ruled over
them.
18King Rehoboam sent out Adoniram,[a][m]
who was in charge of forced labor, but the
Israelites stoned him to death. King Rehoboam, however, managed to get into his
chariot and escape to Jerusalem. 19So Israel has been in rebellion against the house
of David to this day.

11 When Rehoboam arrived in Jerusalem,[n] he mustered Judah and Benjamin—a hundred and eighty thousand
able young men—to go to war against
Israel and to regain the kingdom for Rehoboam.
2But this word of the LORD came to Shemaiah[o] the man of God: 3"Say to Rehoboam
son of Solomon king of Judah and to all Israel in Judah and Benjamin, 4'This is what
the LORD says: Do not go up to fight against
your fellow Israelites.[p] Go home, every
one of you, for this is my doing.'" So they
obeyed the words of the LORD and turned
back from marching against Jeroboam.

Rehoboam Fortifies Judah

5Rehoboam lived in Jerusalem and built
up towns for defense in Judah: 6Bethle-
hem, Etam, Tekoa, 7Beth Zur, Soko, Adullam, 8Gath, Mareshah, Ziph, 9Adoraim,
Lachish, Azekah, 10Zorah, Aijalon and Hebron. These were fortified cities[q] in Judah
and Benjamin. 11He strengthened their defenses and put commanders in them, with
supplies of food, olive oil and wine. 12He
put shields and spears in all the cities,
and made them very strong. So Judah and
Benjamin were his.
13The priests and Levites from all their
districts throughout Israel sided with him.
14The Levites[r] even abandoned their pasturelands and property[s] and came to Judah and Jerusalem, because Jeroboam
and his sons had rejected them as priests
of the LORD 15when he appointed[t] his own
priests[u] for the high places and for the
goat[v] and calf[w] idols he had made. 16Those
from every tribe of Israel[x] who set their
hearts on seeking the LORD, the God of
Israel, followed the Levites to Jerusalem
to offer sacrifices to the LORD, the God of
their ancestors. 17They strengthened[y] the
kingdom of Judah and supported Rehoboam son of Solomon three years, following
the ways of David and Solomon during
this time.

Rehoboam's Family

18Rehoboam married Mahalath, who
was the daughter of David's son Jerimoth
and of Abihail, the daughter of Jesse's
son Eliab. 19She bore him sons: Jeush,
Shemariah and Zaham. 20Then he married

[a] 18 Hebrew *Hadoram,* a variant of *Adoniram*

10:15 [i] 2Ch 11:4; 25:16-20 [j] S 1Ki 11:29 **10:16** [k] S 1Ch 9:1 [l] S 2Sa 20:1 **10:18** [m] S 2Sa 20:24; S 1Ki 5:14 **11:1** [n] S 1Ki 12:21 **11:2** [o] S 1Ki 12:22; 2Ch 12:5-7,15 **11:4** [p] 2Ch 28:8-11

11:10 [q] S Jos 10:20; 2Ch 12:4; 17:2, 19; 21:3 **11:14** [r] S Nu 35:2-5 [s] 1Ch 6:81 **11:15** [t] S 1Ki 13:33 [u] S 1Ki 12:31 [v] Lev 17:7 [w] 1Ki 12:28; 2Ch 13:8 **11:16** [x] 2Ch 15:9 **11:17** [y] 2Ch 12:1

10:15 *Ahijah.* The Chronicler assumes the reader's familiarity with 1Ki 11:29–33.
10:18 *Adoniram ... in charge of forced labor.* Had held the same office under Solomon (see 1Ki 4:6 and note; 5:14).
10:19 *to this day.* See note on 5:9.
11:1–23 Verses 1–4 are parallel to 1Ki 12:21–24; vv. 5–23 are largely unique to Chronicles. The Chronicler's account of Rehoboam is a good example of his emphasis on immediate retribution (see Introduction to 1 Chronicles: Purpose and Themes). Ch. 11 traces the rewards for obedience to the command of God (vv. 1–4): Rehoboam enjoys prosperity and power (vv. 5–12), popular support (vv. 13–17) and progeny (vv. 18–23). Ch. 12 demonstrates the reverse: Disobedience brings judgment.
11:2 *Shemaiah.* The function of the prophets as guardians of the theocracy (God's kingdom) is prominent in Chronicles; most of Judah's kings are portrayed as receiving advice from prophets (see Introduction to 1 Chronicles: Purpose and Themes).
11:3 *all Israel in Judah and Benjamin.* A variation from the wording found in 1Ki 12:23, in accordance with the Chronicler's interest in "all Israel."
11:4 *my doing.* See 10:15.
11:5–10 This list of cities is not found in Kings. Rehoboam fortified his eastern, western and southern borders, but not the north, perhaps demonstrating his hope of reunification of the kingdoms, as well as the threat of invasion from Egypt.
11:13–17 The Chronicler assumes the reader's familiarity with 1Ki 12:26–33. This material is unique to Chronicles and reflects the author's concern both with the temple and its personnel and with showing that the kingdom of Judah was the remnant of all Israel.
11:14 *pasturelands and property.* See 1Ch 6:54–80; Lev 25:32–34; Nu 35:1–5; see also Introduction to 1 Chronicles: Purpose and Themes.
11:15 *goat and calf idols.* The account in Kings mentions only the golden calves. For the worship of goat idols, see Lev 17:7.
11:17 *three years.* See note on 12:2. *ways of David and Solomon.* Characteristic of the Chronicler's idealization of Solomon; contrast the portrait of Solomon in 1Ki 11:1–13.
11:18–22 The report on the size of Rehoboam's family is placed here as part of the Chronicler's effort to show God's blessing on his obedience (see note on 11:1–23). The material is not in chronological sequence with the surrounding context but summarizes events throughout his reign. The Chronicler uses numerous progeny as a sign of divine blessing (see 13:21; see also notes on 21:2; 1Ch 25:5).

Maakah[z] daughter of Absalom, who bore
him Abijah,[a] Attai, Ziza and Shelomith.
21 Rehoboam loved Maakah daughter of
Absalom more than any of his other wives
and concubines. In all, he had eighteen
wives[b] and sixty concubines, twenty-eight
sons and sixty daughters.
22 Rehoboam appointed Abijah[c] son of
Maakah as crown prince among his brothers, in order to make him king. 23 He acted wisely, dispersing some of his sons
throughout the districts of Judah and Benjamin, and to all the fortified cities. He
gave them abundant provisions[d] and took
many wives for them.

Shishak Attacks Jerusalem

12:9-16pp — 1Ki 14:21, 25-31

12 After Rehoboam's position as king
was established[e] and he had be-
come strong,[f] he and all Israel[a][g] with him
abandoned[h] the law of the LORD. 2 Because
they had been unfaithful[i] to the LORD,
Shishak[j] king of Egypt attacked Jerusalem in the fifth year of King Rehoboam.
3 With twelve hundred chariots and sixty
thousand horsemen and the innumerable
troops of Libyans,[k] Sukkites and Cushites[b][l] that came with him from Egypt, 4 he
captured the fortified cities[m] of Judah and
came as far as Jerusalem.
5 Then the prophet Shemaiah[n] came to
Rehoboam and to the leaders of Judah who
had assembled in Jerusalem for fear of Shishak, and he said to them, "This is what
the LORD says, 'You have abandoned me;
therefore, I now abandon[o] you to Shishak.' "
6 The leaders of Israel and the king humbled[p] themselves and said, "The LORD is
just."[q]
7 When the LORD saw that they humbled themselves, this word of the LORD
came to Shemaiah: "Since they have humbled themselves, I will not destroy them
but will soon give them deliverance.[r] My
wrath[s] will not be poured out on Jerusalem through Shishak. 8 They will, however,
become subject[t] to him, so that they may
learn the difference between serving me
and serving the kings of other lands."
9 When Shishak king of Egypt attacked
Jerusalem, he carried off the treasures of
the temple of the LORD and the treasures
of the royal palace. He took everything,
including the gold shields[u] Solomon had
made. 10 So King Rehoboam made bronze
shields to replace them and assigned these
to the commanders of the guard on duty at
the entrance to the royal palace. 11 Whenever the king went to the LORD's temple,
the guards went with him, bearing the
shields, and afterward they returned them
to the guardroom.
12 Because Rehoboam humbled[v] himself,
the LORD's anger turned from him, and he
was not totally destroyed. Indeed, there
was some good[w] in Judah.
13 King Rehoboam established[x] himself
firmly in Jerusalem and continued as king.
He was forty-one years old when he became king, and he reigned seventeen years
in Jerusalem, the city the LORD had chosen out of all the tribes of Israel in which
to put his Name.[y] His mother's name was
Naamah; she was an Ammonite. 14 He did
evil because he had not set his heart on
seeking the LORD.
15 As for the events of Rehoboam's reign,

11:20 [z]S 1Ki 15:2 [a]2Ch 12:16; 13:2 **11:21** [b]S Dt 17:17 **11:22** [c]Dt 21:15-17 **11:23** [d]2Ch 21:3 **12:1** [e]ver 13; 2Ch 1:1 [f]2Ch 11:17 [g]S 1Ch 9:1 [h]S 2Ch 7:19 **12:2** [i]1Ki 14:22-24; S 1Ch 5:25 [j]1Ki 11:40 **12:3** [k]Da 11:43 [l]S Ge 10:6; 2Ch 14:9; 16:8; Isa 18:2; Am 9:7; Na 3:9 **12:4** [m]S 2Ch 11:10 **12:5** [n]2Ch 11:2 [o]S Dt 28:15 **12:6** [p]S Lev 26:41; S 2Ch 6:37 [q]Ex 9:27; Ezr 9:15; Ps 11:7; 116:5; Da 9:14 **12:7** [r]Ps 78:38 [s]Dt 9:19; Ps 69:24; Jer 7:20; 42:18; Eze 5:13 **12:8** [t]Dt 28:48 **12:9** [u]2Ch 9:16 **12:12** [v]S 2Ch 6:37 [w]S 1Ki 14:13; 2Ch 19:3 **12:13** [x]S ver 1; S 1Ki 2:12 [y]S Ex 20:24; Dt 12:5

[a] *1* That is, Judah, as frequently in 2 Chronicles
[b] *3* That is, people from the upper Nile region

11:20 *Maakah daughter of Absalom.* See note on 1Ki 15:2. She was likely the granddaughter of Absalom, through his daughter Tamar (2Sa 14:27; 18:18), who was married to Uriel (2Ch 13:2).

11:21 – 22 These verses explain why the eldest son was not appointed Rehoboam's successor.

11:23 *dispersing some of his sons.* Rehoboam may have sought to secure the succession of Abijah by assigning other sons to outlying posts, perhaps to avoid the difficulties faced by David, whose sons at court (Absalom and Adonijah) had attempted to seize power.

12:1 – 14 See note on 11:1 – 23. Whereas obedience to the prophetic word (11:1 – 4) had brought blessing (11:5 – 23), now the prophet comes to announce judgment for disobedience (see 1Ki 14:25 – 28). While the writer of Kings also reports the attack of Shishak, the Chronicler alone adds the rationale that the invasion was because of forsaking the commands of God (vv. 1 – 2,5).

12:1 *all Israel.* Used in a variety of ways in 2 Chronicles: (1) of both kingdoms (9:30), (2) of the northern kingdom (10:16; 11:13) or (3) of the southern kingdom alone (as here; 11:3). See also Introduction to 1 Chronicles: Purpose and Themes, 6. *abandoned.* The opposite of "seeking the LORD" (v. 14); see v. 5; see also note on 24:18,20,24.

12:2 *Shishak.* Founder of the Twenty-Second Dynasty of Egypt, he ruled c. 945 – 924 BC. The Bible mentions this invasion only as it affected Jerusalem, but Shishak's own inscription on the wall of the temple of Amun at Karnak (Thebes) indicates that his armies also swept as far north as Megiddo (see photo, p. 687). *fifth year.* 925 BC. The Chronicler often introduces chronological notes not found in Kings (e.g., 11:17; 15:10,19; 16:1,12 – 13; 17:7; 21:20; 24:15,17,23; 26:16; 27:5,8; 29:3; 34:3; 36:21). These become a vehicle for his emphasis on immediate retribution by dividing the reigns of individual kings into cycles of obedience-blessing and disobedience-punishment. This sequence is clear for Rehoboam: Three years of obedience and blessing (11:17) are followed by rebellion, presumably in the fourth year (12:1), and punishment in the fifth (here).

12:3 *Sukkites.* Probably a group of mercenary soldiers of Libyan origin who are known from Egyptian texts.

12:5 See notes on vv. 1 – 14; v. 1.

12:6 – 7 See v. 12. The Chronicler has in mind God's promise in 7:14.

12:13 *seventeen years.* See note on 10:1.

from beginning to end, are they not written in the records of Shemaiah[z] the prophet and of Iddo the seer that deal with genealogies? There was continual warfare
between Rehoboam and Jeroboam. 16Re-
hoboam[a] rested with his ancestors and
was buried in the City of David. And Abijah[b] his son succeeded him as king.

Abijah King of Judah

13:1-2,22–14:1pp — 1Ki 15:1-2,6-8

13 In the eighteenth year of the reign
of Jeroboam, Abijah became king
of Judah, 2and he reigned in Jerusalem
three years. His mother's name was Maakah,[a][c] a daughter[b] of Uriel of Gibeah.
There was war between Abijah[d] and Jeroboam.[e] 3Abijah went into battle with an
army of four hundred thousand able fighting men, and Jeroboam drew up a battle
line against him with eight hundred thousand able troops.
4Abijah stood on Mount Zemaraim,[f]
in the hill country of Ephraim, and said,
"Jeroboam and all Israel,[g] listen to me!
5Don't you know that the LORD, the God
of Israel, has given the kingship of Israel
to David and his descendants forever[h] by
a covenant of salt?[i] 6Yet Jeroboam son of
Nebat, an official of Solomon son of David, rebelled[j] against his master. 7Some

12:15 [z]S 2Ch 11:2
12:16 [a]S 1Ch 3:10 [b]S 2Ch 11:20
13:2 [c]2Ch 15:16 [d]S 2Ch 11:20
[e]1Ki 15:6
13:4 [f]Jos 18:22 [g]1Ch 11:1
13:5 [h]S 2Sa 7:13; S 1Ch 17:12 [i]S Lev 2:13
13:6 [j]1Ki 11:26

[a] 2 Most Septuagint manuscripts and Syriac (see also 11:20 and 1 Kings 15:2); Hebrew *Micaiah*
[b] 2 Or *granddaughter*

12:15-16 See 1Ki 14:29-31.

13:1—14:1 The Chronicler's account of Abijah's reign is about three times longer than that in 1Ki 15:1-8, largely due to Abijah's lengthy speech (13:4-12; see note on 28:1-27). The most striking difference in the accounts of Abijah's reign in Kings and in Chronicles is the evaluation given in each: Kings offers a negative evaluation (1Ki 15:3), for which there was no doubt warrant, while the assessment in Chronicles is positive, in view of what the Chronicler is able to report of him. The kings' reigns, like the lives of common people, were often a mixture of good and evil.

13:2 *three years.* 913-910 BC. *Maakah.* See note on 11:20.

13:3 *four hundred thousand ... eight hundred thousand.* Surprisingly large figures but in line with those in 1Ch 21:5 (see note there; see also Introduction to Numbers: Special Problem).

13:4 *Mount Zemaraim.* The town of Zemaraim was in the territory of Benjamin (Jos 18:22); presumably the battle was along the common border of Benjamin and Israel. *all Israel.* See note on 12:1; here and in v. 15 the reference is to the northern kingdom.

13:5 See 7:17-18; 1Ch 17:13-14. *covenant of salt.* See notes on Nu 18:19; 2Ki 2:20.

13:6 See note on 10:1-19.

13:7 Not all in the northern kingdom are rebuked, only the leadership—a subtle appeal to those in the north who had been led into rebellion. *scoundrels.* See note on Dt 13:13. *young and indecisive.* Cf. 1Ch 22:5; 29:1. Rehoboam was 41 years old at the time of the schism (12:13).

Cartouches (oblong hieroglyphs of conquered towns) along the wall of the Karnak temple describe Shishak's military campaign in Canaan. Shishak's attack on Jerusalem is recorded in 2 Chronicles 12:2-4.

Todd Bolen/www.BiblePlaces.com

worthless scoundrels[k] gathered around
him and opposed Rehoboam son of Solomon when he was young and indecisive[l]
and not strong enough to resist them.
8 “And now you plan to resist the kingdom of the LORD, which is in the hands
of David’s descendants.[m] You are indeed
a vast army and have with you[n] the gold-
en calves[o] that Jeroboam made to be your
gods. 9 But didn’t you drive out the priests[p]
of the LORD,[q] the sons of Aaron, and the
Levites, and make priests of your own as
the peoples of other lands do? Whoever
comes to consecrate himself with a young
bull[r] and seven rams[s] may become a priest
of what are not gods.[t]
10 “As for us, the LORD is our God, and
we have not forsaken him. The priests
who serve the LORD are sons of Aaron, and
the Levites assist them. 11 Every morning
and evening[u] they present burnt offerings
and fragrant incense[v] to the LORD. They set
out the bread on the ceremonially clean
table[w] and light the lamps[x] on the gold
lampstand every evening. We are observing the requirements of the LORD our God.
But you have forsaken him. 12 God is with
us; he is our leader. His priests with their
trumpets will sound the battle cry against
you.[y] People of Israel, do not fight against
the LORD,[z] the God of your ancestors, for
you will not succeed.”[a]
13 Now Jeroboam had sent troops around
to the rear, so that while he was in front
of Judah the ambush[b] was behind them.
14 Judah turned and saw that they were being attacked at both front and rear. Then
they cried out[c] to the LORD. The priests
blew their trumpets 15 and the men of Judah raised the battle cry. At the sound of
their battle cry, God routed Jeroboam and
all Israel[d] before Abijah and Judah. 16 The
Israelites fled before Judah, and God delivered[e] them into their hands. 17 Abijah and
his troops inflicted heavy losses on them,
so that there were five hundred thousand
casualties among Israel’s able men. 18 The
Israelites were subdued on that occasion,
and the people of Judah were victorious
because they relied[f] on the LORD, the God
of their ancestors.
19 Abijah pursued Jeroboam and took
from him the towns of Bethel, Jeshanah
and Ephron, with their surrounding villages. 20 Jeroboam did not regain power
during the time of Abijah. And the LORD
struck him down and he died.
21 But Abijah grew in strength. He married fourteen wives and had twenty-two
sons and sixteen daughters.
22 The other events of Abijah’s reign,
what he did and what he said, are written
in the annotations of the prophet Iddo.
14 [a] And Abijah rested with his ancestors and was buried in the City of
David. Asa his son succeeded him as king,
and in his days the country was at peace
for ten years.

Asa King of Judah

14:2-3pp — 1Ki 15:11-12

2 Asa did what was good and right in the
eyes of the LORD his God.[g] 3 He removed
the foreign altars[h] and the high places,
smashed the sacred stones[i] and cut down
the Asherah poles.[b][j] 4 He commanded Judah to seek the LORD,[k] the God of their
ancestors, and to obey his laws and commands. 5 He removed the high places[l] and
incense altars[m] in every town in Judah,
and the kingdom was at peace under him.

13:7 [k] S Jdg 9:4 [l] S 1Ch 29:1 **13:8** [m] S 2Ch 9:8 [n] 1Sa 4:3 [o] S Ex 32:4; S 2Ch 11:15 **13:9** [p] S 1Ki 12:31 [q] 2Ch 11:14-15 [r] Ex 29:35-36 [s] S Ex 29:31 [t] Jer 2:11; Gal 4:8 **13:11** [u] S Ex 29:39; S 2Ch 2:4 [v] S Ex 25:6 [w] S 1Ch 9:32 [x] S Ex 25:37 **13:12** [y] S Nu 10:8-9 [z] S Jdg 2:15; Ac 5:39 [a] Job 9:4; Pr 21:30; 29:1 **13:13** [b] Jos 8:9; 2Ch 20:22 **13:14** [c] S 1Ch 5:20; 2Ch 14:11; 18:31 **13:15** [d] S 1Ch 9:1 **13:16** [e] 2Ch 16:8 **13:18** [f] 2Ch 14:11; 16:7; Ps 22:5 **14:2** [g] 2Ch 21:12 **14:3** [h] S Jdg 2:2 [i] S Ex 23:24 [j] S Ex 34:13 **14:4** [k] S 1Ch 16:11 **14:5** [l] S 1Ki 15:14 [m] Isa 27:9; Eze 6:4

[a] In Hebrew texts 14:1 is numbered 13:23, and 14:2-15 is numbered 14:1-14. [b] 3 That is, wooden symbols of the goddess Asherah; here and elsewhere in 2 Chronicles

13:8 *kingdom of the LORD.* The house of David represents the kingdom of God (see 9:8 and note).
13:9 See 1Ki 12:25 – 33. *consecrate himself.* Cf. Ex 29:1.
13:10 – 12 The Chronicler’s concern with acceptable worship focuses on the legitimate priests and the observance of prescribed worship (cf. 1Ch 23:28 – 31).
13:21 See note on 11:18 – 22.
14:1 *peace for ten years.* For the Chronicler peace and prosperity go hand in hand with righteous rule. This first decade of Asa’s reign (910 – 900 BC) preceded the invasion by Zerah (14:9 – 15) and was followed by 20 more years of peace, from the 15th (15:10) to the 35th years (15:19). Contrast this account with the statement that there was war between Asa and Baasha throughout their reigns (see 1Ki 15:16 and note). The tensions between the two kingdoms may have accounted for Asa’s fortifications (14:7 – 8), though actual combat was likely confined to raids until the major campaign was launched in Asa’s 36th year (16:1). See 15:8 and note.
14:2 — 16:14 The account of Asa’s reign (910 – 869 BC) here is greatly expanded over the one in 1Ki 15:9 – 24. The expansions characteristically express the Chronicler’s view concerning the relationship between obedience and blessing, disobedience and punishment. The author introduces chronological notes into his account to divide Asa’s reign into three periods (see note on 12:2): (1) For ten years Asa did what was right and prospered (14:1 – 7), and an invasion by a powerful Cushite force was repulsed because he called on the Lord (14:8 – 15). (2) There followed further reforms (15:1 – 9) and a covenant renewal in Asa’s 15th year (15:10 – 18), and so he enjoyed peace until his 35th year (15:19). (3) But then came a change: When confronted by an invasion from the northern kingdom of Israel in his 36th year (16:1), he hired Aramean reinforcements, rather than trusting in the Lord (16:2 – 6), and imprisoned the prophet who rebuked him (16:7 – 10). In his 39th year he was afflicted with a disease (16:12) but still steadfastly refused to seek the Lord. In his 41st year he died (16:13).
14:3 *sacred stones.* See note on 1Ki 14:23. *Asherah poles.* See note on Ex 34:13.
14:5 *removed the high places.* 1Ki 15:14 states that Asa did not remove the high places. This difficulty is best resolved by the

6He built up the fortified cities of Judah,
since the land was at peace. No one was
at war with him during those years, for the
LORD gave him rest.[n]
7"Let us build up these towns," he said
to Judah, "and put walls around them,
with towers, gates and bars. The land is
still ours, because we have sought the
LORD our God; we sought him and he has
given us rest[o] on every side." So they built
and prospered.
8Asa had an army of three hundred
thousand[p] men from Judah, equipped
with large shields and with spears, and
two hundred and eighty thousand from
Benjamin, armed with small shields and
with bows. All these were brave fighting
men.
9Zerah the Cushite[q] marched out against
them with an army of thousands upon
thousands and three hundred chariots,
and came as far as Mareshah.[r] 10Asa went
out to meet him, and they took up battle
positions in the Valley of Zephathah near
Mareshah.
11Then Asa called[s] to the LORD his God
and said, "LORD, there is no one like you
to help the powerless against the mighty.
Help us,[t] LORD our God, for we rely[u] on
you, and in your name[v] we have come
against this vast army. LORD, you are our
God; do not let mere mortals prevail[w]
against you."
12The LORD struck down[x] the Cushites
before Asa and Judah. The Cushites fled,
13and Asa and his army pursued them
as far as Gerar.[y] Such a great number of
Cushites fell that they could not recover;
they were crushed[z] before the LORD and
his forces. The men of Judah carried off
a large amount of plunder.[a] 14They destroyed all the villages around Gerar, for
the terror[b] of the LORD had fallen on them.
They looted all these villages, since there
was much plunder there. 15They also attacked the camps of the herders and carried off droves of sheep and goats and
camels. Then they returned to Jerusalem.

Asa's Reform

15:16-19pp — 1Ki 15:13-16

15 The Spirit of God came on[c] Azariah
son of Oded. 2He went out to meet
Asa and said to him, "Listen to me, Asa
and all Judah and Benjamin. The LORD is
with you[d] when you are with him.[e] If you
seek[f] him, he will be found by you, but
if you forsake him, he will forsake you.[g]
3For a long time Israel was without the
true God, without a priest to teach[h] and
without the law.[i] 4But in their distress they
turned to the LORD, the God of Israel, and
sought him,[j] and he was found by them.
5In those days it was not safe to travel
about,[k] for all the inhabitants of the lands
were in great turmoil. 6One nation was being crushed by another and one city by
another,[l] because God was troubling them
with every kind of distress. 7But as for
you, be strong[m] and do not give up, for
your work will be rewarded."[n]
8When Asa heard these words and the
prophecy of Azariah son of[a] Oded the
prophet, he took courage. He removed the
detestable idols[o] from the whole land of
Judah and Benjamin and from the towns
he had captured[p] in the hills of Ephraim.
He repaired the altar[q] of the LORD that was
in front of the portico of the LORD's temple.
9Then he assembled all Judah and
Benjamin and the people from Ephraim, Manasseh and Simeon who had settled among them, for large numbers[r] had
come over to him from Israel when they
saw that the LORD his God was with him.
10They assembled at Jerusalem in the

[a] 8 Vulgate and Syriac (see also Septuagint and verse 1); Hebrew does not have *Azariah son of.*

14:6 [n] S 1Ch 22:9 **14:7** [o] S 1Ch 22:9 **14:8** [p] S 1Ch 21:1 **14:9** [q] S 2Ch 12:3 [r] S Ge 10:8-9; 2Ch 11:8; 24:24 **14:11** [s] S 1Ki 8:44; S 2Ch 13:14; 25:8 [t] Ps 60:11-12; 79:9 [u] S 2Ch 13:18 [v] S 1Sa 17:45 [w] Ps 9:19 **14:12** [x] 1Ki 8:45 **14:13** [y] Ge 10:19 [z] 2Sa 22:38; Ne 9:24; Ps 44:2, 19; 135:10 [a] 2Ch 15:11, 18 **14:14** [b] S Ge 35:5; S Dt 2:25; 11:25

15:1 [c] S Nu 11:25, 26 **15:2** [d] 2Ch 20:17 [e] Jas 4:8 [f] 2Ch 7:14; Ps 78:34; Isa 45:19; 55:6; Jer 29:13; Hos 3:5 [g] S Dt 31:17; S 1Ch 28:9 **15:3** [h] S Lev 10:11 [i] La 2:9; Am 8:11 **15:4** [j] S Dt 4:29 **15:5** [k] S Jdg 5:6; 19:20; Zec 8:10 **15:6** [l] Isa 19:2; Mt 24:7; Mk 13:8; Lk 21:10 **15:7** [m] Jos 1:7, 9 [n] 1Sa 24:19; Ps 18:20; 58:11; Pr 14:14; Jer 31:16 **15:8** [o] 1Ki 15:12 [p] 2Ch 17:2 [q] S 1Ki 8:64; S 2Ch 8:12 **15:9** [r] 2Ch 11:16-17

Chronicler's own statement in 15:17, which is properly parallel to 1Ki 15:14: Early in his reign Asa did attempt to remove the high places, but pagan worship was extremely resilient, and ultimately his efforts were unsuccessful (15:17). Statements that the high places both were and were not removed are also found in the reign of Jehoshaphat (17:6; 20:33). Cf. Dt 12:2 – 3.

14:7 *rest on every side.* See note on 20:30.

14:9 *Zerah.* Probably a general leading Egyptian forces in the service of Pharaoh Osorkon I. The invasion appears to have been an attempt to duplicate the attack of Shishak 30 years earlier (12:1 – 12), but the results against Asa were quite different. *Cushite.* See vv. 12 – 13. The Cushites were natives of Nubia, the region that borders Egypt on the south — not to be confused with modern Ethiopia (Abyssinia). See also note on Isa 18:1.

14:10 *Valley of Zephathah.* Marked the entrance to a road leading to the hills of Judah and Jerusalem. *Mareshah.* Earlier fortified by Rehoboam (11:8) to protect the route mentioned here.

14:13 *Gerar.* See note on Ge 20:1. *plunder.* Much of which (v. 14) made its way to the storehouses of the temple (15:18; see note on 1Ch 18:1 — 20:8).

14:14 *terror of the LORD.* See note on 1Ch 14:17.

15:1 – 19 This chapter appears to recount a second stage in the reforms introduced by Asa, beginning with the victory over Zerah and encouraged by the preaching of Azariah (v. 1).

15:3 *priest to teach.* The duties of the priests were not only to officiate at the altar but also to teach the law (see 17:7 – 9; Lev 10:11; Dt 17:9 – 11).

15:8 *towns he had captured in … Ephraim.* A tacit admission that there had been some fighting between Baasha and Asa prior to Asa's 36th year (16:1); see 17:1.

15:9 *large numbers had come over to him.* Cf. the defection from the northern kingdom that also occurred under Rehoboam (11:13 – 17).

third month[s] of the fifteenth year of Asa's
reign. 11 At that time they sacrificed to the
LORD seven hundred head of cattle and
seven thousand sheep and goats from the
plunder[t] they had brought back. 12 They
entered into a covenant[u] to seek the LORD,[v]
the God of their ancestors, with all their
heart and soul. 13 All who would not seek
the LORD, the God of Israel, were to be put
to death,[w] whether small or great, man or
woman. 14 They took an oath to the LORD
with loud acclamation, with shouting and
with trumpets and horns. 15 All Judah rejoiced about the oath because they had
sworn it wholeheartedly. They sought
God[x] eagerly, and he was found by them.
So the LORD gave them rest[y] on every side.
16 King Asa also deposed his grandmother Maakah[z] from her position as queen
mother,[a] because she had made a repulsive image for the worship of Asherah.[b]
Asa cut it down, broke it up and burned
it in the Kidron Valley.[c] 17 Although he did
not remove the high places from Israel,
Asa's heart was fully committed to the
LORD all his life. 18 He brought into the temple of God the silver and gold and the articles that he and his father had dedicated.[d]
19 There was no more war until the thir-
ty-fifth year of Asa's reign.

Asa's Last Years

16:1-6pp — 1Ki 15:17-22
16:11 – 17:1pp — 1Ki 15:23-24

16 In the thirty-sixth year of Asa's
reign Baasha[e] king of Israel went
up against Judah and fortified Ramah to
prevent anyone from leaving or entering
the territory of Asa king of Judah.
2 Asa then took the silver and gold out of
the treasuries of the LORD's temple and of
his own palace and sent it to Ben-Hadad
king of Aram, who was ruling in Damascus.[f] 3 "Let there be a treaty[g] between me
and you," he said, "as there was between
my father and your father. See, I am sending you silver and gold. Now break your
treaty with Baasha king of Israel so he will
withdraw from me."
4 Ben-Hadad agreed with King Asa and
sent the commanders of his forces against
the towns of Israel. They conquered Ijon,
Dan, Abel Maim[a] and all the store cities
of Naphtali.[h] 5 When Baasha heard this, he
stopped building Ramah and abandoned
his work. 6 Then King Asa brought all the
men of Judah, and they carried away from
Ramah the stones and timber Baasha had
been using. With them he built up Geba
and Mizpah.[i]
7 At that time Hanani[j] the seer came to
Asa king of Judah and said to him: "Because you relied[k] on the king of Aram and
not on the LORD your God, the army of
the king of Aram has escaped from your
hand. 8 Were not the Cushites[b][l] and Libyans a mighty army with great numbers[m]
of chariots and horsemen[c]? Yet when you
relied on the LORD, he delivered[n] them
into your hand. 9 For the eyes[o] of the LORD
range throughout the earth to strengthen
those whose hearts are fully committed to
him. You have done a foolish[p] thing, and
from now on you will be at war.[q]"
10 Asa was angry with the seer because
of this; he was so enraged that he put him
in prison.[r] At the same time Asa brutally
oppressed some of the people.
11 The events of Asa's reign, from beginning to end, are written in the book of the
kings of Judah and Israel. 12 In the thirty-
ninth year of his reign Asa was afflicted[s]
with a disease in his feet. Though his disease was severe, even in his illness he did

15:10 [s] S Lev 23:15-21 **15:11** [t] S 2Ch 14:13 **15:12** [u] S 2Ki 11:17 [v] S 1Ch 16:11 **15:13** [w] S Ex 22:20; Dt 13:9-16 **15:15** [x] Dt 4:29 [y] S 1Ch 22:9 **15:16** [z] 2Ch 13:2 [a] S 1Ki 2:19 [b] S Ex 34:13 [c] S 2Sa 15:23 **15:18** [d] S 2Ch 14:13 **16:1** [e] 2Ki 9:9; Jer 41:9

16:2 [f] 2Ch 19:1-20:37; 22:1-9 **16:3** [g] 2Ch 20:35; 25:7 **16:4** [h] S 2Ki 15:29 **16:6** [i] Jer 41:9 **16:7** [j] 1Ki 16:1 [k] S 2Ch 13:18 **16:8** [l] S Ge 10:6, 8-9; S 2Ch 12:3 [m] 2Ch 24:24 [n] 2Ch 13:16 **16:9** [o] Job 24:23; Ps 33:13-15; Pr 15:3; Jer 16:17; Zec 3:9; 4:10 [p] 1Sa 13:13 [q] S 1Ki 15:6; 2Ch 19:2; 25:7; 28:16-21 **16:10** [r] S 1Ki 22:27 **16:12** [s] 2Ch 21:18; 26:19; Ps 103:3

[a] *4* Also known as *Abel Beth Maakah* [b] *8* That is, people from the upper Nile region [c] *8* Or *charioteers*

15:10 *third month of the fifteenth year.* Spring, 895 BC, the year after Zerah's invasion (v. 19). The Festival of Weeks (or Pentecost) was held in the third month (Lev 23:15 – 21) and may have been the occasion for this assembly.
15:12 *covenant.* A renewal of the covenant made at Sinai, similar to the covenant renewals on the plain of Moab (Dt 29:1), at Mount Ebal (Jos 8:30 – 35), at Shechem (Jos 24:25) and at Gilgal (1Sa 11:14; see note there). Later the priest Jehoiada (23:16), as well as Hezekiah (29:10) and Josiah (34:31), would also lead in renewals of the covenant — events of primary significance in the view of the Chronicler.
15:13 *would not seek the LORD.* Would turn to other gods. *were to be put to death.* In accordance with basic covenant law (Ex 22:20; Dt 13:6 – 9).
15:15 *rest.* See note on 20:30.
15:16 *Asherah.* See note on Ex 34:13; see also photo, p. 672. *Kidron Valley.* Just east of Jerusalem (see note on Isa 22:7 and map, p. 515; see also 1Ki 15:13 and note).
15:17 *did not remove the high places.* See 14:5 and note.
16:1 *thirty-sixth year of Asa's reign Baasha.* According to Kings, Baasha ruled for 24 years and was succeeded by Elah in the 26th year of Asa (1Ki 15:33; 16:8). Obviously Baasha could not have been alive in the 36th year of Asa, where this passage places him — he had been dead for a decade. The action described here is not dated in 1Ki 15:17. Perhaps the Chronicler's dates here and in 15:19 are the result of a copyist's error (possibly for an original 25th and 26th).
16:2 – 9 Hiring foreign troops brought Asa into a foreign alliance, which showed lack of trust in the Lord. Other examples of condemned foreign alliances are found in the reigns of Jehoshaphat (20:35 – 37), Ahaziah (22:1 – 9) and Ahaz (28:16 – 21). By hiring Ben-Hadad to the north, Asa opened a two-front war for Baasha and forced him to withdraw.
16:3 *treaty ... between my father and your father.* See note on 1Ki 15:19.
16:9 *eyes of the LORD range throughout the earth.* Asserted also in Zec 4:10.
16:11 *book of the kings of Judah and Israel.* See Introduction to 1 Chronicles: Author, Date and Sources.
16:12 *disease in his feet.* For other examples of disease as

not seek[t] help from the LORD,[u] but only
from the physicians. 13 Then in the forty-
first year of his reign Asa died and rested with his ancestors. 14 They buried him
in the tomb that he had cut out for himself[v] in the City of David. They laid him
on a bier covered with spices and various
blended perfumes,[w] and they made a huge
fire[x] in his honor.

Jehoshaphat King of Judah

17 Jehoshaphat his son succeeded
him as king and strengthened[y] himself against Israel. 2 He stationed troops in
all the fortified cities[z] of Judah and put
garrisons in Judah and in the towns of
Ephraim that his father Asa had captured.[a]
3 The LORD was with Jehoshaphat because he followed the ways of his father
David[b] before him. He did not consult the
Baals 4 but sought[c] the God of his father
and followed his commands rather than
the practices of Israel. 5 The LORD established the kingdom under his control; and
all Judah brought gifts[d] to Jehoshaphat, so
that he had great wealth and honor.[e] 6 His
heart was devoted[f] to the ways of the LORD;
furthermore, he removed the high places[g]
and the Asherah poles[h] from Judah.[i]
7 In the third year of his reign he sent
his officials Ben-Hail, Obadiah, Zechariah, Nethanel and Micaiah to teach[j] in the
towns of Judah. 8 With them were certain
Levites[k] — Shemaiah, Nethaniah, Zebadiah, Asahel, Shemiramoth, Jehonathan,
Adonijah, Tobijah and Tob-Adonijah —
and the priests Elishama and Jehoram.
9 They taught throughout Judah, taking
with them the Book of the Law[l] of the
LORD; they went around to all the towns of
Judah and taught the people.

16:12 [t] 2Ch 7:14 [u] Jer 17:5-6
16:14 [v] S Ge 50:5 [w] S Ge 50:2 [x] 2Ch 21:19; Jer 34:5
17:1 [y] S 1Ki 2:12
17:2 [z] S 2Ch 11:10 [a] 2Ch 15:8
17:3 [b] S 1Ki 22:43
17:4 [c] 2Ch 22:9
17:5 [d] S 1Sa 10:27 [e] 2Ch 18:1
17:6 [f] S 1Ki 8:61 [g] S 1Ki 15:14; 2Ch 19:3; 20:33 [h] S Ex 34:13 [i] 2Ch 21:12
17:7 [j] S Lev 10:11; Dt 6:4-9; 2Ch 19:4-11; 35:3; Ne 8:7; Mal 2:7
17:8 [k] 2Ch 19:8; Ne 8:7-8; Hos 4:6
17:9 [l] S Dt 28:61
17:10 [m] S Ge 35:5; S Dt 2:25
17:11 [n] S 2Ch 9:14 [o] 2Ch 21:16
17:14 [p] S 2Sa 24:2
17:16 [q] S Jdg 5:9
17:17 [r] S Nu 1:36
17:19 [s] S 2Ch 11:10 [t] 2Ch 25:5
18:1 [u] 2Ch 17:5 [v] 2Ch 19:1-3; 22:3 [w] 2Ch 21:6

10 The fear[m] of the LORD fell on all the
kingdoms of the lands surrounding Judah, so that they did not go to war against
Jehoshaphat. 11 Some Philistines brought
Jehoshaphat gifts and silver as tribute,
and the Arabs[n] brought him flocks:[o] seven
thousand seven hundred rams and seven
thousand seven hundred goats.
12 Jehoshaphat became more and more
powerful; he built forts and store cities
in Judah 13 and had large supplies in the
towns of Judah. He also kept experienced
fighting men in Jerusalem. 14 Their enroll-
ment[p] by families was as follows:

From Judah, commanders of units of 1,000:
Adnah the commander, with 300,000 fighting men;
15 next, Jehohanan the commander, with 280,000;
16 next, Amasiah son of Zikri, who volunteered[q] himself for the service of the LORD, with 200,000.
17 From Benjamin:[r]
Eliada, a valiant soldier, with 200,000 men armed with bows and shields;
18 next, Jehozabad, with 180,000 men armed for battle.

19 These were the men who served the
king, besides those he stationed in the fortified cities[s] throughout Judah.[t]

Micaiah Prophesies Against Ahab

18:1-27pp — 1Ki 22:1-28

18 Now Jehoshaphat had great wealth
and honor,[u] and he allied[v] himself
with Ahab[w] by marriage. 2 Some years later he went down to see Ahab in Samaria.
Ahab slaughtered many sheep and cattle

punishment for sin, see 21:16–20; 26:16–23; Ac 12:23. Cf. 2Ki 15:5. *did not seek help from the LORD, but only from the physicians.* Contrast King Hezekiah (Isa 38); cf. Jer 17:5–8; Jas 5:14–16.

17:1—21:3 The Chronicler's account of Jehoshaphat's reign is more than twice as long as that in Kings, where the interest in Ahab and Elijah overshadows the space allotted to Jehoshaphat (1Ki 22:1–46). The Chronicler has also used Jehoshaphat's reign to emphasize immediate retribution. This theme is specifically announced in 19:10 and is illustrated in the blessing of Jehoshaphat's obedient faith and in the reproof for his wrongdoing (19:2–3; 20:35–37). Jehoshaphat reigned 872–848 BC, from 872 to 869 likely as coregent with his father Asa (see 20:31 and note). The details of his reign may not be in chronological order; the teaching mission of 17:7–9 may have been part of the reforms noted in 19:4–11.

17:2 *cities of Judah … towns of Ephraim.* See note on 15:8. Abijah (13:19), Asa (15:8) and now Jehoshaphat had managed to hold these cities; they would be lost under Amaziah (25:17–24).

17:6 *removed the high places.* Just as his father Asa had attempted to remove the high places, only to have them be restored (14:5; 15:17), so also Jehoshaphat removed them initially, only to have them revive and persist (20:33; cf. 1Ki 22:43). But see notes on 1Ki 3:2; 15:14. *Asherah poles.* See NIV text note on 14:3 and note on Ex 34:13.

17:7–9 This incident may be part of the reform more fully detailed in 19:4–11. In the theocracy (God's kingdom), the law of the Lord was supposed to be an integral part of the law of the land; the king and his officials, as well as the priests and prophets, were representatives of the Lord's kingship over his people.

17:7 *third year.* Perhaps the first year of his sole reign after a coregency of three years with his father Asa (see 20:31 and note).

17:9 *Book of the Law of the LORD.* See 34:14–15; Jos 8:31,34; 23:6; see also notes on Jos 1:8; 2Ki 22:8; Ne 8:1.

17:10–11 See note on 1Ch 18:1—20:8.

17:10 *fear of the LORD.* See note on 1Ch 14:17.

17:14–18 *300,000 … 280,000 … 200,000 … 200,000 … 180,000.* See notes on 1Ch 12:23–37; 27:1.

18:1—19:3 See 1Ki 22:1–40 and notes. In conformity with his interest in the southern kingdom and Jehoshaphat, the Chronicler omits elaboration on the death of Ahab and his succession (1Ki 22:36–40) and adds the material on the

for him and the people with him and urged him to attack Ramoth Gilead. 3 Ahab king of Israel asked Jehoshaphat king of Judah, "Will you go with me against Ramoth Gilead?"

Jehoshaphat replied, "I am as you are, and my people as your people; we will join you in the war." 4 But Jehoshaphat also said to the king of Israel, "First seek the counsel of the LORD."

5 So the king of Israel brought together the prophets—four hundred men—and asked them, "Shall we go to war against Ramoth Gilead, or shall I not?"

"Go," they answered, "for God will give it into the king's hand."

6 But Jehoshaphat asked, "Is there no longer a prophet of the LORD here whom we can inquire of?"

7 The king of Israel answered Jehoshaphat, "There is still one prophet through whom we can inquire of the LORD, but I hate him because he never prophesies anything good about me, but always bad. He is Micaiah son of Imlah."

"The king should not say such a thing," Jehoshaphat replied.

8 So the king of Israel called one of his officials and said, "Bring Micaiah son of Imlah at once."

9 Dressed in their royal robes, the king of Israel and Jehoshaphat king of Judah were sitting on their thrones at the threshing floor by the entrance of the gate of Samaria, with all the prophets prophesying before them. 10 Now Zedekiah son of Kenaanah had made iron horns, and he declared, "This is what the LORD says: 'With these you will gore the Arameans until they are destroyed.' "

11 All the other prophets were prophesying the same thing. "Attack Ramoth Gilead[x] and be victorious," they said, "for the LORD will give it into the king's hand."

12 The messenger who had gone to summon Micaiah said to him, "Look, the other prophets without exception are predicting success for the king. Let your word agree with theirs, and speak favorably."

13 But Micaiah said, "As surely as the LORD lives, I can tell him only what my God says."[y]

18:11 [x]2Ch 22:5 **18:13** [y]Nu 22:18, 20,35

18:16 [z]S 1Ch 9:1 [a]S Nu 27:17 **18:18** [b]Da 7:9 **18:21** [c]1Ch 21:1; Job 1:6; Zec 3:1; Jn 8:44 **18:22** [d]Job 12:16; Eze 14:9 **18:23** [e]Ac 23:2 **18:26** [f]Heb 11:36

14 When he arrived, the king asked him, "Micaiah, shall we go to war against Ramoth Gilead, or shall I not?"

"Attack and be victorious," he answered, "for they will be given into your hand."

15 The king said to him, "How many times must I make you swear to tell me nothing but the truth in the name of the LORD?"

16 Then Micaiah answered, "I saw all Israel[z] scattered on the hills like sheep without a shepherd,[a] and the LORD said, 'These people have no master. Let each one go home in peace.' "

17 The king of Israel said to Jehoshaphat, "Didn't I tell you that he never prophesies anything good about me, but only bad?"

18 Micaiah continued, "Therefore hear the word of the LORD: I saw the LORD sitting on his throne[b] with all the multitudes of heaven standing on his right and on his left. 19 And the LORD said, 'Who will entice Ahab king of Israel into attacking Ramoth Gilead and going to his death there?'

"One suggested this, and another that. 20 Finally, a spirit came forward, stood before the LORD and said, 'I will entice him.'

" 'By what means?' the LORD asked.

21 " 'I will go and be a deceiving spirit in the mouths of all his prophets,' he said.

" 'You will succeed in enticing him,' said the LORD. 'Go and do it.'

22 "So now the LORD has put a deceiving spirit in the mouths of these prophets of yours.[d] The LORD has decreed disaster for you."

23 Then Zedekiah son of Kenaanah went up and slapped[e] Micaiah in the face. "Which way did the spirit from[a] the LORD go when he went from me to speak to you?" he asked.

24 Micaiah replied, "You will find out on the day you go to hide in an inner room."

25 The king of Israel then ordered, "Take Micaiah and send him back to Amon the ruler of the city and to Joash the king's son, 26 and say, 'This is what the king says: Put this fellow in prison[f] and give him nothing but bread and water until I return safely.' "

[a] *23* Or *Spirit of*

prophetic condemnation of Jehoshaphat's involvement (19:1–3).

18:1 Not found in 1Ki 22. The verse enhances the status of Jehoshaphat by mentioning the blessing of wealth for his fidelity, and also sets the stage for an entangling foreign alliance condemned by the prophet in 19:2–3. *allied himself with Ahab by marriage.* This marriage alliance to Athaliah, daughter of Ahab, resulted later in an attempt to exterminate the Davidic line (22:10—23:21).

18:2 The Chronicler further enhances the status of Jehoshaphat by noting the large number of animals Ahab slaughtered in his honor, a note not found in 1Ki 22. *urged him.* Also not found in the parallel text. The Hebrew for this verb is often used in the sense of inciting to evil (e.g., 1Ch 21:1) and may express the Chronicler's attitude toward Jehoshaphat's involvement. *Ramoth Gilead.* See notes on 22:5; 1Ki 22:3; see also map, p. 677.

18:4 *seek the counsel of the LORD.* This request fits the Chronicler's overall positive portrait of Jehoshaphat.

18:10 *Arameans.* See notes on 1Ch 18:5; Dt 26:5.

18:22 *deceiving spirit.* See note on 1Ki 22:23.

27 Micaiah declared, "If you ever return
safely, the LORD has not spoken through
me." Then he added, "Mark my words, all
you people!"

Ahab Killed at Ramoth Gilead

18:28-34pp — 1Ki 22:29-36

28 So the king of Israel and Jehoshaphat
king of Judah went up to Ramoth Gilead.
29 The king of Israel said to Jehoshaphat,
"I will enter the battle in disguise, but you
wear your royal robes." So the king of Israel disguised[g] himself and went into battle.
30 Now the king of Aram had ordered his
chariot commanders, "Do not fight with
anyone, small or great, except the king of
Israel." 31 When the chariot commanders
saw Jehoshaphat, they thought, "This is
the king of Israel." So they turned to attack
him, but Jehoshaphat cried out,[h] and the
LORD helped him. God drew them away
from him, 32 for when the chariot commanders saw that he was not the king of
Israel, they stopped pursuing him.
33 But someone drew his bow at random and hit the king of Israel between the
breastplate and the scale armor. The king
told the chariot driver, "Wheel around
and get me out of the fighting. I've been
wounded." 34 All day long the battle raged,
and the king of Israel propped himself up
in his chariot facing the Arameans until
evening. Then at sunset he died.[i]

19 When Jehoshaphat king of Judah
returned safely to his palace in Jerusalem, 2 Jehu[j] the seer, the son of Hanani, went out to meet him and said to the
king, "Should you help the wicked[k] and
love[a] those who hate the LORD?[l] Because
of this, the wrath[m] of the LORD is on you.
3 There is, however, some good[n] in you,
for you have rid the land of the Asherah
poles[o] and have set your heart on seeking
God.[p]"

Jehoshaphat Appoints Judges

4 Jehoshaphat lived in Jerusalem, and he
went out again among the people from Beersheba to the hill country of Ephraim and
turned them back to the LORD, the God of
their ancestors. 5 He appointed judges[q] in the
land, in each of the fortified cities of Judah.
6 He told them, "Consider carefully what
you do,[r] because you are not judging for
mere mortals[s] but for the LORD, who is with
you whenever you give a verdict. 7 Now let
the fear of the LORD be on you. Judge carefully, for with the LORD our God there is no
injustice[t] or partiality[u] or bribery."
8 In Jerusalem also, Jehoshaphat appointed some of the Levites,[v] priests[w] and
heads of Israelite families to administer[x]
the law of the LORD and to settle disputes.
And they lived in Jerusalem. 9 He gave
them these orders: "You must serve faithfully and wholeheartedly in the fear of
the LORD. 10 In every case that comes before you from your people who live in the
cities — whether bloodshed or other concerns of the law, commands, decrees or
regulations — you are to warn them not to
sin against the LORD;[y] otherwise his wrath
will come on you and your people. Do
this, and you will not sin.
11 "Amariah the chief priest will be over
you in any matter concerning the LORD,
and Zebadiah son of Ishmael, the leader
of the tribe of Judah, will be over you in
any matter concerning the king, and the
Levites will serve as officials before you.
Act with courage,[z] and may the LORD be
with those who do well."

Jehoshaphat Defeats Moab and Ammon

20 After this, the Moabites[a] and Ammonites with some of the Meu-
nites[bb] came to wage war against Jehoshaphat.

[a] 2 *Or and make alliances with* [b] 1 Some Septuagint manuscripts; Hebrew *Ammonites*

18:29 [g] S 1Sa 28:8 **18:31** [h] S 2Ch 13:14 **18:34** [i] 2Ch 22:5 **19:2** [j] S 1Ki 16:1 [k] S 2Ch 16:2-9 [l] Ps 139:21-22 [m] 2Ch 24:18; 32:25; Ps 7:11 **19:3** [n] S 1Ki 14:13 [o] S 2Ch 17:6 [p] S 2Ch 18:1; 20:35; 25:7 **19:5** [q] S Ge 47:6; S Ex 18:26 **19:6** [r] S Lev 19:15 [s] Dt 16:18-20; 17:8-13 **19:7** [t] S Ge 18:25; S Job 8:3 [u] S Ex 18:16; Dt 10:17; Job 13:10; 32:21; 34:19 **19:8** [v] S 1Ch 23:4 [w] Eze 44:24 [x] 2Ch 17:8-9 **19:10** [y] Dt 17:8-13 **19:11** [z] S 1Ch 28:20 **20:1** [a] Ps 83:6 [b] S 1Ch 4:41

18:29 The fact that Ahab directs Jehoshaphat into battle in royal regalia, thus making Jehoshaphat the logical target for attack, is consistent with Israel's dominant position at this time.

19:1 – 3 Not found in 1Ki 22.

19:2 *Should you help the wicked ... ?* Jehu's father, Hanani, had earlier given Jehoshaphat's father, Asa, the same warning (see 16:7 – 9). Jehoshaphat later committed the same sin again and suffered for it (20:35 – 37).

19:3 *Asherah poles.* See NIV text note on 14:3 and note on Ex 34:13.

19:4 *Jehoshaphat ... went ... among the people.* The king traveled throughout the realm personally to promote religious reformation.

19:5 *appointed judges.* The name Jehoshaphat (meaning "The LORD judges") is appropriate for the king who instituted this judicial reform. The arrangement of the courts under Jehoshaphat (vv. 5 – 11) would be of particular interest to the Chronicler's audience in the postexilic period, when the courts of the restored community would have their own existence and structure legitimized by this precedent.

19:6 Cf. Dt 16:18 – 20; 17:8 – 13.

19:7 *let the fear of the LORD be on you.* Let a terrifying sense of God's presence restrain you from any injustice (see note on 1Ch 14:17).

19:8 *Levites, priests ... to administer the law.* See note on 1Ch 26:29 – 32. One effect of this judicial reform appears to be the bringing of the traditional system of justice administered by the elders of the city under closer royal and priestly supervision.

19:11 *any matter concerning the LORD ... any matter concerning the king.* This division into the affairs of religion and the affairs of the king reflects the postexilic structure of the Chronicler's day. Cf. the anointing of Solomon and Zadok (1Ch 29:22) and the administration of the postexilic community by Zerubbabel, a Davidic descendant, and Joshua, the high priest (Zec 4:14; 6:9 – 15).

20:1 – 30 This episode held special interest for the Chronicler since the restored community was being harassed by the descendants of these same peoples (see Ne 2:19; 4:1 – 3,7 – 9; 6:1 – 4; 13). He uses it to encourage his

En Gedi is located on the western side of the Dead Sea. In 2 Chronicles 20:2, some people warn Jehoshaphat that a vast enemy army has already come as far as En Gedi.

Todd Bolen/www.BiblePlaces.com

[2]Some people came and told Jehoshaphat, "A vast army[c] is coming against you
from Edom,[a] from the other side of the
Dead Sea. It is already in Hazezon Tamar[d]"
(that is, En Gedi).[e] [3]Alarmed, Jehoshaphat
resolved to inquire of the LORD, and he
proclaimed a fast[f] for all Judah. [4]The people of Judah[g] came together to seek help
from the LORD; indeed, they came from every town in Judah to seek him.
[5]Then Jehoshaphat stood up in the assembly of Judah and Jerusalem at the
temple of the LORD in the front of the new
courtyard [6]and said:

"LORD, the God of our ancestors,[h]
are you not the God who is in heav-
en?[i] You rule over all the kingdoms[j]
of the nations. Power and might are
in your hand, and no one can withstand you.[k] [7]Our God, did you not
drive out the inhabitants of this land[l]
before your people Israel and give it
forever to the descendants of Abraham your friend?[m] [8]They have lived
in it and have built in it a sanctuary[n]

20:2 [c]2Ch 24:24 [d]S Ge 14:7 [e]S 1Sa 23:29; SS 1:14 **20:3** [f]1Sa 7:6; Ezr 8:23; Ne 1:4; Est 4:16; Isa 58:6; Jer 36:9; Da 9:3; Joel 1:14; 2:15; Jnh 3:5,7 **20:4** [g]Jer 36:6 **20:6** [h]Mt 6:9 [i]Dt 4:39 [j]1Ch 29:11-12 [k]2Ch 25:8; Job 25:2; 41:10; 42:2; Isa 14:27; Jer 32:27; 49:19 **20:7** [l]S Ge 12:7 [m]Isa 41:8; Jas 2:23 **20:8** [n]2Ch 6:20

[a] *2* One Hebrew manuscript; most Hebrew manuscripts, Septuagint and Vulgate *Aram*

contemporaries to trust in the Lord and his prophets, as Jehoshaphat, son of David, had exhorted (v. 20; see note there). The account is significantly structured. Apart from the outer frame, which highlights the reversal of circumstances (vv. 1–4,28–30), it falls into three divisions: (1) Jehoshaphat's prayer (vv. 5–13), (2) the Lord's response (vv. 14–19) and (3) the great victory (vv. 20–27). At the center of each is its crucial statement, and these are all linked by a key word: v. 9, "we will *stand* in your presence before this temple"; v. 17, "*stand firm* and see the deliverance the LORD will give you"; v. 23, "The Ammonites and Moabites rose up (lit. '*stood up*') against the men from Mount Seir to destroy ... them."

20:1 *Meunites.* A people from the region of Mount Seir in Edom (26:7; 1Ch 4:41; cf. 2Ch 20:10,22–23).

20:2 *Edom.* See NIV text note. Since the Arameans are well to the north and not mentioned among the attackers named in v. 1, the NIV has followed the reading "Edom." The difference between "Aram" and "Edom" in Hebrew is only one letter which is very similar in shape and was often confused in the process of copying manuscripts. *En Gedi.* See photo above.

20:5–12 Jehoshaphat's prayer shows him to be a true theocratic king, a worthy son of David and type (foreshadowing) of the awaited Messiah (see Introduction to 1 Chronicles: Purpose and Themes).

20:7 *Abraham your friend.* See Isa 41:8; Jas 2:23 and note.

for your Name, saying, 9'If calamity
comes upon us, whether the sword
of judgment, or plague or famine,[o]
we will stand in your presence before
this temple that bears your Name and
will cry out to you in our distress, and
you will hear us and save us.'

10"But now here are men from Ammon, Moab and Mount Seir, whose
territory you would not allow Israel to
invade when they came from Egypt;[p]
so they turned away from them and
did not destroy them. 11See how they
are repaying us by coming to drive us
out of the possession[q] you gave us as
an inheritance. 12Our God, will you
not judge them?[r] For we have no power to face this vast army that is attacking us. We do not know what to do,
but our eyes are on you.[s]"

13All the men of Judah, with their wives
and children and little ones, stood there
before the LORD.

14Then the Spirit[t] of the LORD came on
Jahaziel son of Zechariah, the son of Benaiah, the son of Jeiel, the son of Mattaniah,[u] a Levite and descendant of Asaph, as
he stood in the assembly.

15He said: "Listen, King Jehoshaphat
and all who live in Judah and Jerusalem!
This is what the LORD says to you: 'Do not
be afraid or discouraged[v] because of this
vast army. For the battle[w] is not yours, but
God's. 16Tomorrow march down against
them. They will be climbing up by the Pass
of Ziz, and you will find them at the end
of the gorge in the Desert of Jeruel. 17You
will not have to fight this battle. Take up
your positions; stand firm and see[x] the deliverance the LORD will give you, Judah
and Jerusalem. Do not be afraid; do not
be discouraged. Go out to face them tomorrow, and the LORD will be with you.' "

18Jehoshaphat bowed down[y] with his
face to the ground, and all the people of
Judah and Jerusalem fell down in worship
before the LORD. 19Then some Levites from
the Kohathites and Korahites stood up and
praised the LORD, the God of Israel, with a
very loud voice.

20Early in the morning they left for the
Desert of Tekoa. As they set out, Jehoshaphat stood and said, "Listen to me, Judah
and people of Jerusalem! Have faith[z] in
the LORD your God and you will be upheld;
have faith in his prophets and you will be
successful.[a]" 21After consulting the people,
Jehoshaphat appointed men to sing to the
LORD and to praise him for the splendor of
his[a] holiness[b] as they went out at the head
of the army, saying:

"Give thanks to the LORD,
for his love endures forever."[c]

22As they began to sing and praise, the
LORD set ambushes[d] against the men of
Ammon and Moab and Mount Seir who
were invading Judah, and they were defeated. 23The Ammonites[e] and Moabites
rose up against the men from Mount Seir[f]
to destroy and annihilate them. After they
finished slaughtering the men from Seir,
they helped to destroy one another.[g]

24When the men of Judah came to the
place that overlooks the desert and looked
toward the vast army, they saw only dead
bodies lying on the ground; no one had escaped. 25So Jehoshaphat and his men went
to carry off their plunder, and they found
among them a great amount of equipment and clothing[b] and also articles of
value—more than they could take away.
There was so much plunder that it took
three days to collect it. 26On the fourth day
they assembled in the Valley of Berakah,
where they praised the LORD. This is why it
is called the Valley of Berakah[c] to this day.

27Then, led by Jehoshaphat, all the men
of Judah and Jerusalem returned joyfully
to Jerusalem, for the LORD had given them
cause to rejoice over their enemies. 28They
entered Jerusalem and went to the temple of the LORD with harps and lyres and
trumpets.

29The fear[h] of God came on all the surrounding kingdoms when they heard how
the LORD had fought[i] against the enemies
of Israel. 30And the kingdom of Jehoshaphat was at peace, for his God had given
him rest[j] on every side.

20:9 [o]S 2Ch 6:28 **20:10** [p]Nu 20:14-21; Dt 2:4-6,9, 18-19 **20:11** [q]Ps 83:1-12 **20:12** [r]Jdg 11:27 [s]Ps 25:15; Isa 30:15; 45:22; Mic 7:7 **20:14** [t]S 1Ch 12:18 [u]S 1Ch 9:15 **20:15** [v]2Ch 32:7 [w]S 1Sa 17:47; Ps 91:8 **20:17** [x]S Ex 14:13 **20:18** [y]S Ge 24:26; 2Ch 29:29 **20:20** [z]Isa 7:9 [a]S Ge 39:3; Pr 16:3 **20:21** [b]S 1Ch 16:29 [c]S 2Ch 5:13; Ps 136:1 **20:22** [d]S 2Ch 13:13 **20:23** [e]S Ge 19:38 [f]2Ch 21:8 [g]S Jdg 7:22; 1Sa 14:20; Eze 38:21 **20:29** [h]S Ge 35:5; S Dt 2:25 [i]S Ex 14:14 **20:30** [j]S 1Ch 22:9

[a] *21* *Or him with the splendor of* [b] *25* Some Hebrew manuscripts and Vulgate; most Hebrew manuscripts *corpses* [c] *26* *Berakah* means *praise.*

20:9 An apparent reference to Solomon's prayer and the divine promise of response (6:14–42; 7:12–22).
20:15 See Ex 14:13–14 and note on 14:14.
20:16 *Pass of Ziz.* Began seven miles north of En Gedi and wound inland, emerging west of Tekoa. *Jeruel.* Southeast of Tekoa.
20:19 *Levites.* The Chronicler's interest in the priests and Levites is apparent throughout the account (vv. 14,21–22,28).
20:20 *Have faith in the LORD your God and ... in his prophets.* A particularly apt word for the Chronicler's contemporaries to hear from this son of David—at a time when their only hope for the future lay with the Lord and the reassuring words of his prophets.
20:21 *splendor of his holiness.* See note on 1Ch 16:29.
20:22 *ambushes.* Their nature is indicated in v. 23: Israel's foes destroyed each other in the confusion of battle, similar to the victory under Gideon (Jdg 7:22).
20:26 *to this day.* See note on 5:9.
20:29 *The fear of God.* See note on 1Ch 14:17.
20:30 *rest on every side.* Rest from enemies is part of God's blessing for obedience in Chronicles (14:5–7; 15:15; 1Ch 22:8–9,18). Righteous kings have victory in

The End of Jehoshaphat's Reign

20:31 – 21:1pp — 1Ki 22:41-50

31 So Jehoshaphat reigned over Judah.
He was thirty-five years old when he became king of Judah, and he reigned in
Jerusalem twenty-five years. His mother's name was Azubah daughter of Shilhi.
32 He followed the ways of his father Asa
and did not stray from them; he did what
was right in the eyes of the LORD. 33 The
high places,[k] however, were not removed,
and the people still had not set their hearts
on the God of their ancestors.
34 The other events of Jehoshaphat's
reign, from beginning to end, are written in the annals of Jehu[l] son of Hanani, which are recorded in the book of the
kings of Israel.
35 Later, Jehoshaphat king of Judah
made an alliance[m] with Ahaziah king of
Israel, whose ways were wicked.[n] 36 He
agreed with him to construct a fleet of
trading ships.[a] After these were built at
Ezion Geber, 37 Eliezer son of Dodavahu
of Mareshah prophesied against Jehoshaphat, saying, "Because you have made
an alliance with Ahaziah, the LORD will
destroy what you have made." The ships[o]
were wrecked and were not able to set sail
to trade.[b]
21 Then Jehoshaphat rested with his
ancestors and was buried with
them in the City of David. And Jehoram[p]
his son succeeded him as king. 2 Jehoram's
brothers, the sons of Jehoshaphat, were
Azariah, Jehiel, Zechariah, Azariahu, Michael and Shephatiah. All these were sons
of Jehoshaphat king of Israel.[c] 3 Their father had given them many gifts[q] of silver
and gold and articles of value, as well as
fortified cities[r] in Judah, but he had given
the kingdom to Jehoram because he was
his firstborn son.

20:33 [k]S 2Ch 17:6 **20:34** [l]S 1Ki 16:1 **20:35** [m]S 2Ch 16:3 [n]S 2Ch 19:1-3 **20:37** [o]S 1Ki 9:26 **21:1** [p]S 1Ch 3:11

Jehoram King of Judah

21:5-10,20pp — 2Ki 8:16-24

4 When Jehoram established[s] himself
firmly over his father's kingdom, he put
all his brothers[t] to the sword along with
some of the officials of Israel. 5 Jehoram
was thirty-two years old when he became
king, and he reigned in Jerusalem eight
years. 6 He followed the ways of the kings
of Israel,[u] as the house of Ahab had done,
for he married a daughter of Ahab.[v] He
did evil in the eyes of the LORD. 7 Nevertheless, because of the covenant the LORD
had made with David,[w] the LORD was not
willing to destroy the house of David.[x] He
had promised to maintain a lamp[y] for him
and his descendants forever.
8 In the time of Jehoram, Edom[z] rebelled
against Judah and set up its own king. 9 So
Jehoram went there with his officers and
all his chariots. The Edomites surrounded him and his chariot commanders, but
he rose up and broke through by night.
10 To this day Edom has been in rebellion
against Judah.
Libnah[a] revolted at the same time, because Jehoram had forsaken the LORD, the

21:3 [q]2Ch 11:23 [r]S 2Ch 11:10 **21:4** [s]S 1Ki 2:12 [t]Jdg 9:5 **21:6** [u]1Ki 12:28-30 [v]2Ch 18:1; 22:3 **21:7** [w]S 2Sa 7:13 [x]S 2Sa 7:15; 2Ch 23:3 [y]S 2Sa 21:17 **21:8** [z]2Ch 20:22-23 **21:10** [a]S Nu 33:20

[a] 36 Hebrew *of ships that could go to Tarshish*
[b] 37 Hebrew *sail for Tarshish*
[c] 2 That is, Judah, as frequently in 2 Chronicles

warfare (Abijah, Asa, Jehoshaphat, Uzziah, Hezekiah), while wicked rulers experience defeat (Jehoram, Ahaz, Joash, Zedekiah).

20:31 *twenty-five years.* The book of Kings reports 22 (18 in 2Ki 3:1 and 4 more in 8:16). These figures are reconciled by suggesting a coregency with his father, Asa, for three years, probably due to the severity of his father's illness and the need to arrange for a secure succession (16:10 – 14). The book of Kings speaks only of his years of sole reign after his father's death.

20:33 *high places ... were not removed.* See note on 17:6.

20:34 *Jehu son of Hanani.* See note on 19:2.

20:35 – 37 See 1Ki 22:48 – 49. The lucrative maritime trade through the Gulf of Aqaba no doubt tempted Jehoshaphat to enter into this improper alliance (see 19:2 and note). Solomon's earlier alliance for the same purpose had been with a non-Israelite king (8:17 – 18).

20:35 *Ahaziah.* Reigned 853 – 852 BC (see 1Ki 22:51 — 2Ki 1:18 for the account of his reign).

21:2 *sons of Jehoshaphat.* The Chronicler shows the blessing of God on Jehoshaphat by mentioning his large family, particularly his seven sons (see 11:18 – 22; 1Ch 25:5 and notes). Jehoshaphat's large number of sons is in striking contrast to the wicked Jehoram who, after murdering his brothers (v. 4), is left with only one son (v. 17). Jehoram's wife, Athaliah, would later perform a similar slaughter (22:10).

21:3 Cf. the similar actions of Rehoboam (11:23).

21:4 – 20 See 2Ki 8:16 – 24 and notes.

21:4 This bloody assassination of all potential rivals is not reported in Kings, but it fits the pattern of the northern kings (see v. 6). The princes of Israel were probably leading men in the southern kingdom who opposed having a king married to a daughter of Ahab. For this use of "Israel," see note on 12:1.

21:5 *eight years.* 848 – 841 BC. The period 853 – 848 was probably a coregency of Jehoram with his father, Jehoshaphat — Jehoshaphat's 18th year was also Jehoram's second year (cf. 2Ki 1:17; 3:1).

21:6 *married a daughter of Ahab.* Probably the marriage referred to in 18:1, used to cement the alliance between Jehoshaphat and Ahab. Such political marriages were common. Many of Solomon's marriages sealed international relationships (see note on 1Ki 11:1), as did Ahab's marriage to Jezebel.

21:8 – 10 The pious Jehoshaphat had enjoyed victory over Edom (20:1 – 30), while the wicked Jehoram is defeated in his attempt to keep Edom in subjection to Judah (see note on 20:30).

21:10 *To this day.* See note on 5:9. *Libnah.* Located between Judah and Philistia. *because Jehoram had forsaken the LORD.* Not found in 2Ki 8:22. The Chronicler introduces this judgment as an indication of immediate retribution (see notes on 12:1 – 14; 12:2; see also Introduction to 1 Chronicles: Purpose and Themes).

God of his ancestors. 11He had also built
high places on the hills of Judah and had
caused the people of Jerusalem to prostitute themselves and had led Judah astray.
12Jehoram received a letter from Elijah[b]
the prophet, which said:

"This is what the LORD, the God of
your father[c] David, says: 'You have
not followed the ways of your father
Jehoshaphat or of Asa[d] king of Judah.
13But you have followed the ways of
the kings of Israel, and you have led
Judah and the people of Jerusalem
to prostitute themselves, just as the
house of Ahab did.[e] You have also
murdered your own brothers, members of your own family, men who
were better[f] than you. 14So now the
LORD is about to strike your people,
your sons, your wives and everything
that is yours, with a heavy blow.
15You yourself will be very ill with a
lingering disease[g] of the bowels, until the disease causes your bowels to
come out.'"

16The LORD aroused against Jehoram
the hostility of the Philistines and of
the Arabs[h] who lived near the Cushites.
17They attacked Judah, invaded it and carried off all the goods found in the king's
palace, together with his sons and wives.
Not a son was left to him except Ahaziah,[a]
the youngest.[i]
18After all this, the LORD afflicted Jehoram with an incurable disease of the bowels. 19In the course of time, at the end of
the second year, his bowels came out because of the disease, and he died in great
pain. His people made no funeral fire in
his honor,[j] as they had for his predecessors.
20Jehoram was thirty-two years old
when he became king, and he reigned in
Jerusalem eight years. He passed away,
to no one's regret, and was buried[k] in the
City of David, but not in the tombs of the
kings.

Ahaziah King of Judah

22:1-6pp — 2Ki 8:25-29
22:7-9pp — 2Ki 9:21-29

22 The people[l] of Jerusalem[m] made
Ahaziah, Jehoram's youngest son,
king in his place, since the raiders,[n] who
came with the Arabs into the camp, had
killed all the older sons. So Ahaziah son
of Jehoram king of Judah began to reign.
2Ahaziah was twenty-two[b] years old
when he became king, and he reigned in
Jerusalem one year. His mother's name
was Athaliah, a granddaughter of Omri.
3He too followed[o] the ways of the house
of Ahab,[p] for his mother encouraged him
to act wickedly. 4He did evil in the eyes of
the LORD, as the house of Ahab had done,
for after his father's death they became his
advisers, to his undoing. 5He also followed
their counsel when he went with Joram[c]
son of Ahab king of Israel to wage war
against Hazael king of Aram at Ramoth
Gilead.[q] The Arameans wounded Joram;

21:12 [b] 2Ki 1:16-17 [c] 2Ch 17:3-6 [d] 2Ch 14:2
21:13 [e] 1Ki 16:29-33 [f] 1Ki 2:32
21:15 [g] S Nu 12:10
21:16 [h] 2Ch 17:10-11; 22:1; 26:7
21:17 [i] 2Ki 12:18; 2Ch 22:1; Joel 3:5
21:19 [j] S 2Ch 16:14
21:20 [k] 2Ch 24:25; 28:27; 33:20
22:1 [l] 2Ch 33:25; 36:1 [m] 2Ch 23:20-21; 26:1 [n] S 2Ch 21:16-17
22:3 [o] S 2Ch 18:1 [p] S 2Ch 21:6
22:5 [q] 2Ch 18:11,34

[a] 17 Hebrew *Jehoahaz,* a variant of *Ahaziah*
[b] 2 Some Septuagint manuscripts and Syriac (see also 2 Kings 8:26); Hebrew *forty-two*
[c] 5 Hebrew *Jehoram,* a variant of *Joram;* also in verses 6 and 7

21:11 *prostitute themselves.* See Ex 34:15 and note.
21:12 – 20a Not found in the parallel text in 2Ki 8.
21:12 – 15 This reference to a letter from Elijah is the only mention in Chronicles of that prophet, to whom the books of Kings give so much attention (1Ki 17 – 2Ki 2). Elijah's letter specifically announces the immediate consequences of Jehoram's disobedience — further defeat in war, which will cost Jehoram his wives and sons; and disease, which will lead to his death (see note on 16:12). Cf. also the foot disease of Asa (16:12 – 14) and the leprosy of Uzziah (26:16 – 23). The book of Kings does not mention the nature of Jehoram's death. Some have argued that this letter could not be authentic because, they claim, Elijah was taken to heaven before Jehoram became king. But this is not a necessary conclusion (see 2Ki 1:17; see also note on 2Ki 3:11). Elijah may well have been taken to heaven as late as 848 BC.
21:16 *Cushites.* See note on 14:9; see also NIV text note on 16:8.
21:20 *eight years.* See note on v. 5. *not in the tombs of the kings.* Only the Chronicler mentions the refusal of the people to accord Jehoram the customary burial honors of a tomb with the other kings of Judah (cf. 24:25).
22:1 – 9 The Chronicler's account of Ahaziah's reign is much shorter than the parallel in 2Ki 8:24 — 9:29, probably due to the fact that the Kings account focuses on the rebellion of Jehu and the downfall of the dynasty of Omri (see 2Ki 8:26; see also 1Ki 16:21 – 28) — events in the northern kingdom, in which the Chronicler is not interested. The Chronicler's account again shows his interest in immediate retribution: Ahaziah's personal wickedness and his involvement in a foreign alliance result in immediate judgment and a reign of only one year (see note on 16:2 – 9; see also Introduction to 1 Chronicles: Purpose and Themes).
22:1 *had killed all the older sons.* Emphasizes divine retribution: Jehoram, who murdered all his brothers, had to watch the death of his own sons (21:4,13,16 – 17).
22:2 *twenty-two.* See NIV text note. The Hebrew reading of "42" would make Ahaziah older than his father (21:20). *one year.* 841 BC.
22:3 – 4 The great influence of the dynasty of Omri in Judah is indicated by the power of Athaliah and the presence of advisers from the northern kingdom (see note on 18:29).
22:5 *went with Joram ... to wage war.* An action similar to that for which Jehoshaphat had been rebuked (see 19:2 and note). *Hazael.* Had been anointed by Elisha; he later killed his master in a coup to seize the throne (2Ki 8:13 – 15; cf. 1Ki 19:15 and note). *Ramoth Gilead.* Located in the Transjordan border area between Israel and Aram. More than ten years earlier Jehoshaphat had participated with Ahab in a battle there that cost Ahab his life (ch. 18; 1Ki 22).

6 so he returned to Jezreel to recover from
the wounds they had inflicted on him at
Ramoth[a] in his battle with Hazael[r] king of
Aram.

Then Ahaziah[b] son of Jehoram king of
Judah went down to Jezreel to see Joram
son of Ahab because he had been wounded.

7 Through Ahaziah's[s] visit to Joram, God
brought about Ahaziah's downfall. When
Ahaziah arrived, he went out with Joram
to meet Jehu son of Nimshi, whom the
LORD had anointed to destroy the house
of Ahab. 8 While Jehu was executing judgment on the house of Ahab,[t] he found the
officials of Judah and the sons of Ahaziah's relatives, who had been attending
Ahaziah, and he killed them. 9 He then
went in search of Ahaziah, and his men
captured him while he was hiding[u] in Samaria. He was brought to Jehu and put to
death. They buried him, for they said, "He
was a son of Jehoshaphat, who sought[v]
the LORD with all his heart." So there was
no one in the house of Ahaziah powerful
enough to retain the kingdom.

Athaliah and Joash

22:10–23:21pp — 2Ki 11:1-21

10 When Athaliah the mother of Ahaziah saw that her son was dead, she proceeded to destroy the whole royal family
of the house of Judah. 11 But Jehosheba,[c]
the daughter of King Jehoram, took Joash
son of Ahaziah and stole him away from
among the royal princes who were about
to be murdered and put him and his nurse
in a bedroom. Because Jehosheba,[c] the
daughter of King Jehoram and wife of the
priest Jehoiada, was Ahaziah's sister, she
hid the child from Athaliah so she could
not kill him. 12 He remained hidden with
them at the temple of God for six years
while Athaliah ruled the land.

23 In the seventh year Jehoiada
showed his strength. He made a
covenant with the commanders of units of
a hundred: Azariah son of Jeroham, Ishmael son of Jehohanan, Azariah son of
Obed, Maaseiah son of Adaiah, and Elishaphat son of Zikri. 2 They went throughout Judah and gathered the Levites[w] and
the heads of Israelite families from all the
towns. When they came to Jerusalem,
3 the whole assembly made a covenant[x]
with the king at the temple of God.

Jehoiada said to them, "The king's son
shall reign, as the LORD promised concerning the descendants of David.[y] 4 Now
this is what you are to do: A third of you
priests and Levites who are going on duty

22:6 [r] 1Ki 19:15; 2Ki 8:13-15 **22:7** [s] 2Ki 9:16 **22:8** [t] S 2Ki 10:13 **22:9** [u] S Jdg 9:5 [v] 2Ch 17:4 **23:2** [w] S Nu 35:2-5 **23:3** [x] S 2Ki 11:17 [y] S 2Sa 7:12; S 1Ki 2:4; S 2Ch 6:16; S 7:18; S 21:7

[a] 6 Hebrew *Ramah*, a variant of *Ramoth* [b] 6 Some Hebrew manuscripts, Septuagint, Vulgate and Syriac (see also 2 Kings 8:29); most Hebrew manuscripts *Azariah* [c] 11 Hebrew *Jehoshabeath*, a variant of *Jehosheba*

22:6 *returned to Jezreel.* Joram apparently recovered Ramoth Gilead and left Jehu in charge (2Ki 8:28—9:28). *Jezreel.* See maps, pp. 557, 594.

22:7 *God brought about Ahaziah's downfall.* The Chronicler assumes that the reader is familiar with the account of Jehu's anointing and the additional details of the coup, which resulted in the deaths of Joram and Ahaziah (2Ki 8:28—9:28). While the writer of Kings primarily portrays the end of the dynasty of Omri as a result of the judgment of God (1Ki 21:20-29; 2Ki 9:24—10:17), the Chronicler notes that the assassination of Ahaziah was also brought about by God.

22:9 The account of Ahaziah's death appears to be somewhat different in the two histories (cf. 2Ki 9:21-27; 10:12-14). Since the writer of Chronicles presumes the reader's familiarity with the other account (see note on v. 7), it is best to take the details of Chronicles as supplementary to Kings, not contradictory, though it is difficult to know the precise sequence and location of events. Apart from the Chronicler's statement that Ahaziah received a decent burial because of his father's piety rather than his own, the apparent differences in the two accounts do not appear to be theologically motivated.

22:10-12 See 2Ki 11:1-3. In the history of Judah, Athaliah represents the only break in the continuity of the Davidic dynasty; she is the only queen of Judah to rule in her own name (841-835 BC). Her attempt to wipe out the royal family repeated the action of her husband, Jehoram (21:4). It threatened the continuity of the Davidic dynasty, and if she had succeeded, Judah may have been claimed by the dynasty of Omri in the north since Athaliah was from that dynasty and had no living son and heir.

22:11 *wife of the priest Jehoiada.* Not noted in Kings.

23:1—24:27 See 2Ki 11:4—12:21 and notes. The Chronicler divides the reign of Joash (835-796 BC) into three parts: (1) the recovery of the throne for the house of David (ch. 23); (2) Joash and Jehoiada—the good years (24:1-16); and (3) Joash alone—the bad years (24:17-27). The last section is largely unique to Chronicles and further develops the theme of immediate retribution: Once again chronological notes provide the framework for cycles of obedience and disobedience (24:15-17,23; see notes on 12:2; 14:2—16:14).

23:1-21 See 2Ki 11:4-20. The Chronicler has followed his source rather closely but has introduced material reflecting his own concerns in three areas: (1) The account in Kings has more to say about the participation of the military in the coup; the Chronicler adds material emphasizing the presence of temple officials and their role (vv. 2,6,8,13,18-19). (2) The Chronicler stresses the widespread popular support for the coup by mentioning the presence of large groups of people, such as "all the people" or "the whole assembly" (vv. 3,5-6, 8,10,16-17). (3) The Chronicler shows additional concern for the sanctity of the temple area by inserting notes showing the steps taken to ensure that only qualified personnel enter the temple precincts (vv. 5-6,19).

23:1 *Azariah ... Elishaphat.* The Chronicler names the commanders, which was not done in Kings, but he does not mention the Carites, mercenaries who served as a royal guard (see note on 2Ki 11:4). Verse 20 exhibits the same omission (cf. 2Ki 11:19). The Chronicler's motive may have been his concern that only authorized persons enter the temple precincts.

23:2 *the Levites and the heads of Israelite families.* Reflects both the Chronicler's concerns with the temple personnel and the widespread support for the coup against Athaliah.

23:3 *as the LORD promised.* See 2Sa 7:11-16.

on the Sabbath are to keep watch at the doors, 5 a third of you at the royal palace and a third at the Foundation Gate, and all the others are to be in the courtyards of the temple of the LORD. 6 No one is to enter the temple of the LORD except the priests and Levites on duty; they may enter because they are consecrated, but all the others are to observe[z] the LORD's command not to enter.[a] 7 The Levites are to station themselves around the king, each with weapon in hand. Anyone who enters the temple is to be put to death. Stay close to the king wherever he goes."

8 The Levites and all the men of Judah did just as Jehoiada the priest ordered.[a] Each one took his men — those who were going on duty on the Sabbath and those who were going off duty — for Jehoiada the priest had not released any of the divisions.[b] 9 Then he gave the commanders of units of a hundred the spears and the large and small shields that had belonged to King David and that were in the temple of God. 10 He stationed all the men, each with his weapon in his hand, around the king — near the altar and the temple, from the south side to the north side of the temple.

11 Jehoiada and his sons brought out the king's son and put the crown on him; they presented him with a copy[c] of the covenant and proclaimed him king. They anointed him and shouted, "Long live the king!"

12 When Athaliah heard the noise of the people running and cheering the king, she went to them at the temple of the LORD. 13 She looked, and there was the king,[d] standing by his pillar[e] at the entrance. The officers and the trumpeters were beside the king, and all the people of the land were rejoicing and blowing trumpets, and musicians with their instruments were leading the praises. Then Athaliah tore her robes and shouted, "Treason! Treason!"

14 Jehoiada the priest sent out the commanders of units of a hundred, who were in charge of the troops, and said to them: "Bring her out between the ranks[b] and put to the sword anyone who follows her." For the priest had said, "Do not put her to death at the temple of the LORD." 15 So they seized her as she reached the entrance of the Horse Gate[f] on the palace grounds, and there they put her to death.

16 Jehoiada then made a covenant[g] that he, the people and the king[c] would be the LORD's people. 17 All the people went to the temple of Baal and tore it down. They smashed the altars and idols and killed[h] Mattan the priest of Baal in front of the altars.

18 Then Jehoiada placed the oversight of the temple of the LORD in the hands of the Levitical priests,[i] to whom David had made assignments in the temple,[j] to present the burnt offerings of the LORD as written in the Law of Moses, with rejoicing and singing, as David had ordered. 19 He also stationed gatekeepers[k] at the gates of the LORD's temple so that no one who was in any way unclean might enter.

20 He took with him the commanders of hundreds, the nobles, the rulers of the people and all the people of the land and brought the king down from the temple of the LORD. They went into the palace through the Upper Gate[l] and seated the king on the royal throne. 21 All the people of the land rejoiced, and the city was calm, because Athaliah had been slain with the sword.[m]

Joash Repairs the Temple

24:1-14pp — 2Ki 12:1-16
24:23-27pp — 2Ki 12:17-21

24 Joash was seven years old when he became king, and he reigned in Jerusalem forty years. His mother's name was Zibiah; she was from Beersheba. 2 Joash did what was right in the eyes of the LORD[n] all the years of Jehoiada the priest. 3 Jehoiada chose two wives for him, and he had sons and daughters.

4 Some time later Joash decided to restore the temple of the LORD. 5 He called

23:6 [z] Zec 3:7 **23:8** [a] 2Ki 11:9 [b] S 1Ch 24:1 **23:11** [c] Dt 17:18 **23:13** [d] 1Ki 1:41 [e] S 1Ki 7:15 **23:15** [f] Jer 31:40 **23:16** [g] 2Ch 29:10; 34:31; Ne 9:38 **23:17** [h] Dt 13:6-9 **23:18** [i] S 1Ch 23:28-32 [j] S 1Ch 23:6; S 25:6 **23:19** [k] 1Ch 9:22 **23:20** [l] S 2Ki 15:35 **23:21** [m] S 2Ch 22:1 **24:2** [n] 2Ch 25:2; 26:5

[a] 6 Or *are to stand guard where the LORD has assigned them* [b] 14 Or *out from the precincts* [c] 16 Or *covenant between the LORD and the people and the king that they* (see 2 Kings 11:17)

23:11 *copy of the covenant.* May refer to the covenant sworn by the assembly (vv. 1,3; cf. v. 16) or to the law of God, by which the king was to rule (see Dt 17:18–20). See note on 2Ki 11:12. *Long live the king!* See note on Ps 62:4.
23:13 *musicians with their instruments.* The Chronicler adds a word (not found in 2Ki 11:14) about the presence of Levitical musicians, who were leading the praises (see note on 1Ch 6:31–48).
23:18–19 The Chronicler adds information on the temple ritual and the guards at the gates (see note on vv. 1–21).
23:20 See note on v. 1.
24:1–14 See 2Ki 12:1–17 and notes.
24:1 *forty years.* 835–796 BC.
24:2 Provides the outline for the Chronicler's treatment of Joash — the good years while Jehoiada was alive (vv. 1–16), and the turn to evil after his death (vv. 17–27). See note on 25:2.
24:3 Another expression of the Chronicler's conviction that large families represent the blessing of God (see v. 27; see also note on 1Ch 25:5).
24:4 *restore the temple.* The vandalism and atrocities of Athaliah (v. 7) required the refurbishing of the temple.
24:5 The writer of 2 Kings speaks of three different sources of revenue (2Ki 12:4–5), whereas the Chronicler mentions only

together the priests and Levites and said to
them, "Go to the towns of Judah and collect the money[o] due annually from all Israel,[p] to repair the temple of your God. Do it
now." But the Levites[q] did not act at once.
[6]Therefore the king summoned Jehoiada the chief priest and said to him, "Why
haven't you required the Levites to bring
in from Judah and Jerusalem the tax imposed by Moses the servant of the LORD
and by the assembly of Israel for the tent
of the covenant law?"[r]
[7]Now the sons of that wicked woman
Athaliah had broken into the temple of
God and had used even its sacred objects
for the Baals.
[8]At the king's command, a chest was
made and placed outside, at the gate of the
temple of the LORD. [9]A proclamation was
then issued in Judah and Jerusalem that
they should bring to the LORD the tax that
Moses the servant of God had required of
Israel in the wilderness. [10]All the officials
and all the people brought their contributions gladly,[s] dropping them into the chest
until it was full. [11]Whenever the chest was
brought in by the Levites to the king's officials and they saw that there was a large
amount of money, the royal secretary and
the officer of the chief priest would come
and empty the chest and carry it back to
its place. They did this regularly and collected a great amount of money. [12]The
king and Jehoiada gave it to those who
carried out the work required for the temple of the LORD. They hired[t] masons and
carpenters to restore the LORD's temple,
and also workers in iron and bronze to repair the temple.
[13]The men in charge of the work were
diligent, and the repairs progressed under them. They rebuilt the temple of God
according to its original design and reinforced it. [14]When they had finished, they
brought the rest of the money to the king
and Jehoiada, and with it were made arti-

24:5 [o]S Ex 30:16; Ne 10:32-33; Mt 17:24 [p]1Ch 11:1 [q]S 1Ch 26:20
24:6 [r]S Ex 38:21
24:10 [s]S Ex 25:2; S 1Ch 29:3,6,9
24:12 [t]2Ch 34:11
24:18 [u]S Jos 24:20; S 2Ch 7:19 [v]S Ex 34:13; 2Ch 33:3; Jer 17:2 [w]S 2Ch 19:2
24:19 [x]S Nu 11:29; Jer 7:25; Zec 1:4
24:20 [y]S Jdg 3:10; S 1Ch 12:18 [z]Mt 23:35; Lk 11:51 [a]Nu 14:41 [b]S Dt 31:17
24:21 [c]S Jos 7:25 [d]Jer 26:21 [e]Jer 20:2
24:22 [f]S Ge 9:5
24:23 [g]2Ki 12:17-18

cles for the LORD's temple: articles for the
service and for the burnt offerings, and
also dishes and other objects of gold and
silver. As long as Jehoiada lived, burnt offerings were presented continually in the
temple of the LORD.
[15]Now Jehoiada was old and full of
years, and he died at the age of a hundred and thirty. [16]He was buried with the
kings in the City of David, because of the
good he had done in Israel for God and
his temple.

The Wickedness of Joash

[17]After the death of Jehoiada, the officials of Judah came and paid homage to
the king, and he listened to them. [18]They
abandoned[u] the temple of the LORD, the
God of their ancestors, and worshiped
Asherah poles and idols.[v] Because of
their guilt, God's anger[w] came on Judah
and Jerusalem. [19]Although the LORD sent
prophets to the people to bring them back
to him, and though they testified against
them, they would not listen.[x]
[20]Then the Spirit[y] of God came on Zechariah[z] son of Jehoiada the priest. He stood
before the people and said, "This is what
God says: 'Why do you disobey the LORD's
commands? You will not prosper.[a] Because
you have forsaken the LORD, he has forsak-
en[b] you.' "
[21]But they plotted against him, and
by order of the king they stoned[c] him to
death[d] in the courtyard of the LORD's temple.[e] [22]King Joash did not remember the
kindness Zechariah's father Jehoiada had
shown him but killed his son, who said as
he lay dying, "May the LORD see this and
call you to account."[f]
[23]At the turn of the year,[a] the army of
Aram marched against Joash; it invaded
Judah and Jerusalem and killed all the
leaders of the people.[g] They sent all the
plunder to their king in Damascus. [24]Al-

[a] *23* Probably in the spring

the census tax (see Ex 30:14; 38:26; Mt 17:24). The reason for the tardiness of the priests is not stated (see 2Ki 12:6–8). The writer of Kings notes that the audience with the priests takes place in the 23rd year of Joash's reign, when he is presumably no longer the ward of Jehoiada. Resistance on the part of the priests to the reassignment of the temple revenues for repair work may be the underlying cause.

24:8 *chest.* Mesopotamian texts speak of a similar offering box placed in temples. Representatives of both the king and the temple officials administered temple revenues (see note on 1Ch 26:20).

24:14 See 2Ki 12:13–14. *As long as Jehoiada lived.* An additional note on the part of the Chronicler to introduce the turn to the worse in the reign of Joash upon Jehoiada's death (vv. 15–16).

24:15–22 This section is unique to the Chronicler and shows his emphasis on immediate retribution (see note on 23:1—24:27). After a period of righteous rule until the death of Jehoiada, Joash turns to idolatry and murders Jehoiada's son. In the following year he is invaded and defeated by Aram because Judah, under his leadership, "had forsaken the LORD" (v. 24).

24:18,20,24 *abandoned ... forsaken ... forsaken ... forsaken.* The Hebrew word is the same in these verses; it is a verb frequently used by the Chronicler to denote the reason for divine punishment (see note on 12:1; see also 7:19,22; 12:5; 13:10–11; 15:2; 21:10; 24:18,20,24; 28:6; 29:6; 34:25; 1Ch 28:9,20).

24:19 *Although the LORD sent prophets.* Israel's failure to heed the Lord's prophets ultimately led to her destruction (see 36:16; cf. 20:20; see also Introduction to 1 Chronicles: Purpose and Themes).

24:20–21 *Zechariah ... they stoned him to death in the courtyard.* See note on Mt 23:35.

though the Aramean army had come with
only a few men,[h] the LORD delivered into
their hands a much larger army.[i] Because
Judah had forsaken the LORD, the God of
their ancestors, judgment was executed on
Joash. 25 When the Arameans withdrew,
they left Joash severely wounded. His officials conspired against him for murdering
the son of Jehoiada the priest, and they
killed him in his bed. So he died and was
buried[j] in the City of David, but not in the
tombs of the kings.

26 Those who conspired against him
were Zabad,[a] son of Shimeath an Ammonite woman, and Jehozabad, son of Shim-
rith[b][k] a Moabite woman.[l] 27 The account
of his sons, the many prophecies about
him, and the record of the restoration of
the temple of God are written in the annotations on the book of the kings. And
Amaziah his son succeeded him as king.

Amaziah King of Judah

25:1-4pp — 2Ki 14:1-6
25:11-12pp — 2Ki 14:7
25:17-28pp — 2Ki 14:8-20

25 Amaziah was twenty-five years
old when he became king, and he
reigned in Jerusalem twenty-nine years.
His mother's name was Jehoaddan; she
was from Jerusalem. 2 He did what was
right in the eyes of the LORD, but not
wholeheartedly.[m] 3 After the kingdom was
firmly in his control, he executed the officials who had murdered his father the
king. 4 Yet he did not put their children to
death, but acted in accordance with what
is written in the Law, in the Book of Moses,[n] where the LORD commanded: "Parents shall not be put to death for their children, nor children be put to death for their
parents; each will die for their own sin."[c][o]

24:24 [h] S 2Ch 14:9; 16:8; 20:2,12 [i] Lev 26:23-25; Dt 28:25
24:25 [j] S 2Ch 21:20
24:26 [k] 2Ki 12:21 [l] S Ru 1:4
25:2 [m] S 1Ki 8:61; S 2Ch 24:2
25:4 [n] S Dt 28:61 [o] S Nu 26:11
25:5 [p] S 2Sa 24:2 [q] S Ex 30:14 [r] S 1Ch 21:1; 2Ch 17:14-19
25:7 [s] S 2Ch 16:2-9; S 19:1-3
25:8 [t] S 2Ch 14:11; S 20:6
25:9 [u] Dt 8:18; Pr 10:22
25:10 [v] ver 13
25:12 [w] Ps 141:6; Ob 1:3

5 Amaziah called the people of Judah
together and assigned them according to
their families to commanders of thousands
and commanders of hundreds for all Judah and Benjamin. He then mustered[p]
those twenty years old[q] or more and found
that there were three hundred thousand
men fit for military service,[r] able to handle
the spear and shield. 6 He also hired a hundred thousand fighting men from Israel for
a hundred talents[d] of silver.

7 But a man of God came to him and
said, "Your Majesty, these troops from
Israel[s] must not march with you, for the
LORD is not with Israel — not with any of
the people of Ephraim. 8 Even if you go
and fight courageously in battle, God will
overthrow you before the enemy, for God
has the power to help or to overthrow."[t]

9 Amaziah asked the man of God, "But
what about the hundred talents I paid for
these Israelite troops?"

The man of God replied, "The LORD can
give you much more than that."[u]

10 So Amaziah dismissed the troops who
had come to him from Ephraim and sent
them home. They were furious with Judah
and left for home in a great rage.[v]

11 Amaziah then marshaled his strength
and led his army to the Valley of Salt,
where he killed ten thousand men of Seir.
12 The army of Judah also captured ten
thousand men alive, took them to the top
of a cliff and threw them down so that all
were dashed to pieces.[w]

13 Meanwhile the troops that Amaziah
had sent back and had not allowed to take
part in the war raided towns belonging to
Judah from Samaria to Beth Horon. They

[a] 26 A variant of *Jozabad* [b] 26 A variant of *Shomer* [c] 4 Deut. 24:16 [d] 6 That is, about 3 3/4 tons or about 3.4 metric tons; also in verse 9

24:24 *only a few men.* Just as God had helped the small army of Judah against overwhelming odds when the king and people were faithful to him (14:8 – 9; 20:2,12), so now in their unfaithfulness they are defeated by a much smaller force of invaders (see note on 20:30).
24:25 *for murdering ... they killed him.* Only the Chronicler mentions that this assassination was revenge for the murder of Zechariah. *not in the tombs of the kings.* Burial in the tombs of the kings was an honor accorded to Jehoiada (v. 16) but withheld from his rebellious ward, Joash (see note on 21:20).
24:26 *an Ammonite ... a Moabite.* Information not given in Kings but important to the Chronicler (see note on 20:1 – 30).
24:27 *annotations on the book of the kings.* See Introduction to 1 Chronicles: Author, Date and Sources.
25:1 – 28 Typically, the Chronicler divides the reign of Amaziah into two parts: (1) the good years, marked by obedience, divine blessing and victory (vv. 1 – 13), and (2) the bad years of idolatry, defeat and regicide (vv. 14 – 28). See 2Ki 14:1 – 20 and notes.
25:1 *twenty-nine years.* 796 – 767 BC.
25:2 The Chronicler does not indicate that Amaziah failed to remove the high places, which continued to be used as places for sacrifice by the people (see 2Ki 14:4). Also compare 24:2 with 2Ki 12:2 – 4, and 26:4 with 2Ki 15:3 – 4. The writer appears to be motivated by his outline, which covered the good years first and then the reversion to evil. Negative comments about these kings are held to the second half of the account of their reigns, whereas in Kings the summary judgment about their reigns and the high places is given immediately.
25:5 – 16 An expansion of 2Ki 14:7. The book of Kings mentions the successful war with Edom only as a prelude to Amaziah's challenge to Jehoash, but the Chronicler sets it in the framework of his emphasis on immediate retribution: Obedience brings victory over Edom, while the subsequent idolatry (vv. 14 – 16) brings defeat in the campaign against Israel. By expanding his account the Chronicler gives the theological reason for both the victory over Edom and the defeat before Israel.
25:7 *troops from Israel must not march with you.* Another instance of the Chronicler's condemnation of alliances that imply lack of trust in the Lord (see notes on 16:2 – 9; 22:5). Cf. other prophetic speeches that call on the people to trust in God (20:15 – 17,20; 32:7 – 8).
25:13 This may be the inciting incident for the later war with

killed three thousand people and carried off great quantities of plunder.

14 When Amaziah returned from slaughtering the Edomites, he brought back the gods of the people of Seir. He set them up as his own gods,[x] bowed down to them and burned sacrifices to them. 15 The anger of the LORD burned against Amaziah, and he sent a prophet to him, who said, "Why do you consult this people's gods, which could not save[y] their own people from your hand?"

16 While he was still speaking, the king said to him, "Have we appointed you an adviser to the king? Stop! Why be struck down?"

So the prophet stopped but said, "I know that God has determined to destroy you, because you have done this and have not listened to my counsel."

17 After Amaziah king of Judah consulted his advisers, he sent this challenge to Jehoash[a] son of Jehoahaz, the son of Jehu, king of Israel: "Come, let us face each other in battle."

18 But Jehoash king of Israel replied to Amaziah king of Judah: "A thistle[z] in Lebanon sent a message to a cedar in Lebanon, 'Give your daughter to my son in marriage.' Then a wild beast in Lebanon came along and trampled the thistle underfoot. 19 You say to yourself that you have defeated Edom, and now you are arrogant and proud. But stay at home! Why ask for trouble and cause your own downfall and that of Judah also?"

20 Amaziah, however, would not listen, for God so worked that he might deliver them into the hands of Jehoash, because they sought the gods of Edom.[a] 21 So Jehoash king of Israel attacked. He and Amaziah king of Judah faced each other at Beth Shemesh in Judah. 22 Judah was routed by Israel, and every man fled to his home.

25:14 [x] Ex 20:3; 2Ch 28:23; Isa 44:15
25:15 [y] Isa 36:20
25:18 [z] Jdg 9:8-15
25:20 [a] S 2Ch 10:15
25:23 [b] 2Ki 14:13; Ne 8:16; 12:39 [c] 2Ch 26:9; Jer 31:38
25:24 [d] S 1Ch 26:15
25:27 [e] S Jos 10:3
26:1 [f] S 2Ch 22:1

23 Jehoash king of Israel captured Amaziah king of Judah, the son of Joash, the son of Ahaziah,[b] at Beth Shemesh. Then Jehoash brought him to Jerusalem and broke down the wall of Jerusalem from the Ephraim Gate[b] to the Corner Gate[c]—a section about four hundred cubits[c] long. 24 He took all the gold and silver and all the articles found in the temple of God that had been in the care of Obed-Edom,[d] together with the palace treasures and the hostages, and returned to Samaria.

25 Amaziah son of Joash king of Judah lived for fifteen years after the death of Jehoash son of Jehoahaz king of Israel. 26 As for the other events of Amaziah's reign, from beginning to end, are they not written in the book of the kings of Judah and Israel? 27 From the time that Amaziah turned away from following the LORD, they conspired against him in Jerusalem and he fled to Lachish[e], but they sent men after him to Lachish and killed him there. 28 He was brought back by horse and was buried with his ancestors in the City of Judah.[d]

Uzziah King of Judah

26:1-4pp — 2Ki 14:21-22; 15:1-3
26:21-23pp — 2Ki 15:5-7

26 Then all the people of Judah[f] took Uzziah,[e] who was sixteen years old, and made him king in place of his father Amaziah. 2 He was the one who rebuilt Elath and restored it to Judah after Amaziah rested with his ancestors.

3 Uzziah was sixteen years old when he became king, and he reigned in Jerusalem

[a] *17* Hebrew *Joash,* a variant of *Jehoash;* also in verses 18, 21, 23 and 25 [b] *23* Hebrew *Jehoahaz,* a variant of *Ahaziah* [c] *23* That is, about 600 feet or about 180 meters [d] *28* Most Hebrew manuscripts; some Hebrew manuscripts, Septuagint, Vulgate and Syriac (see also 2 Kings 14:20) *David* [e] *1* Also called *Azariah*

---

the north. *Samaria.* A town by this name in the southern kingdom is not otherwise known. The reference may be a copyist's error.

25:14-25 The Chronicler's account of the war with the north is close to the parallel in 2Ki 14:8-14, except for some additions in line with his theme of immediate retribution. The Chronicler mentions Amaziah's foolish idolatry and the prophetic speech of judgment, neither of which is found in Kings. He also adds notes in vv. 20,27 to emphasize that the idolatry of Amaziah was being punished.

25:18 Cf. the parable in Jdg 9:7-15.

25:23 *Ephraim Gate to the Corner Gate.* Both gates were located in the northern wall of the city, the Ephraim Gate at the northwest and the Corner Gate at the northeast.

25:24 The family of Obed-Edom was the Levitical family into whose care the temple storehouse had been entrusted (1Ch 26:15; cf. 2Sa 6:10 and note).

25:27 See note on vv. 14-25.

25:28 *City of Judah.* A later name for the City of David (2Ki 14:20).

26:1-23 See 2Ki 15:1-7 and notes. The Chronicler characteristically divides his account of Uzziah's reign into two parts: the good years, then the bad; cf. his treatment of Uzziah's father, Amaziah, and his grandfather Joash (see notes on 24:2; 25:1-28). The Chronicler elaborates on the blessings and divine help that flowed from Uzziah's obedience and fidelity (vv. 4-15), whereas the author of Kings only alludes to his fidelity (2Ki 15:3). Where Kings only mentions Uzziah's leprosy (2Ki 15:5), the Chronicler gives additional details to show that the disease was a result of unfaithfulness (vv. 16-21). Under Uzziah and his contemporary in the north, Jeroboam II, the borders of Israel and Judah briefly reached the extent they had attained under David and Solomon (vv. 6-8; 2Ki 14:25). In part, this flourishing of the two kingdoms was facilitated by the removal of the Aramean threat by Assyria under Adadnirari III (802 BC), following which Assyria herself went into a period of weakness.

26:1 *Uzziah.* See NIV text note (see also, e.g., 2Ki 15:6-7; 1Ch 3:12). It is likely that Uzziah was a throne name, while Azariah was his personal name.

fifty-two years. His mother's name was
Jekoliah; she was from Jerusalem. 4He
did what was right in the eyes of the LORD,
just as his father Amaziah had done. 5He
sought God during the days of Zechariah,
who instructed him in the fear[a] of God.[g]
As long as he sought the LORD, God gave
him success.[h]
6He went to war against the Philistines[i]
and broke down the walls of Gath, Jabneh
and Ashdod.[j] He then rebuilt towns near
Ashdod and elsewhere among the Philistines. 7God helped him against the Philistines and against the Arabs[k] who lived in
Gur Baal and against the Meunites.[l] 8The
Ammonites[m] brought tribute to Uzziah,
and his fame spread as far as the border
of Egypt, because he had become very
powerful.
9Uzziah built towers in Jerusalem at the
Corner Gate,[n] at the Valley Gate[o] and at the
angle of the wall, and he fortified them.
10He also built towers in the wilderness
and dug many cisterns, because he had
much livestock in the foothills and in the
plain. He had people working his fields
and vineyards in the hills and in the fertile
lands, for he loved the soil.
11Uzziah had a well-trained army, ready
to go out by divisions according to their
numbers as mustered by Jeiel the secretary and Maaseiah the officer under the
direction of Hananiah, one of the royal officials. 12The total number of family
leaders over the fighting men was 2,600.
13Under their command was an army of
307,500 men trained for war, a powerful
force to support the king against his enemies. 14Uzziah provided shields, spears,
helmets, coats of armor, bows and slingstones for the entire army.[p] 15In Jerusalem
he made devices invented for use on the
towers and on the corner defenses so that
soldiers could shoot arrows and hurl large
stones from the walls. His fame spread far
and wide, for he was greatly helped until
he became powerful.
16But after Uzziah became powerful,
his pride[q] led to his downfall.[r] He was unfaithful[s] to the LORD his God, and entered
the temple of the LORD to burn incense[t] on
the altar of incense. 17Azariah[u] the priest
with eighty other courageous priests of the
LORD followed him in. 18They confronted
King Uzziah and said, "It is not right for
you, Uzziah, to burn incense to the LORD.
That is for the priests,[v] the descendants[w]
of Aaron,[x] who have been consecrated to
burn incense.[y] Leave the sanctuary, for
you have been unfaithful; and you will not
be honored by the LORD God."
19Uzziah, who had a censer in his
hand ready to burn incense, became angry. While he was raging at the priests in
their presence before the incense altar in
the LORD's temple, leprosy[b][z] broke out on
his forehead. 20When Azariah the chief
priest and all the other priests looked at
him, they saw that he had leprosy on his
forehead, so they hurried him out. Indeed,
he himself was eager to leave, because the
LORD had afflicted him.
21King Uzziah had leprosy until the day
he died. He lived in a separate house[c][a]—
leprous, and banned from the temple of
the LORD. Jotham his son had charge of
the palace and governed the people of the
land.
22The other events of Uzziah's reign,
from beginning to end, are recorded by
the prophet Isaiah[b] son of Amoz. 23Uzziah[c]

26:5 [g]S 2Ch 24:2 [h]2Ch 27:6
26:6 [i]Isa 2:6; 11:14; 14:29; Jer 25:20 [j]Am 1:8; 3:9
26:7 [k]S 2Ch 21:16 [l]2Ch 20:1
26:8 [m]S Ge 19:38
26:9 [n]S 2Ki 14:13; S 2Ch 25:23 [o]Ne 2:13; 3:13
26:14 [p]Jer 46:4
26:16 [q]S 2Ki 14:10 [r]Dt 32:15 [s]S 1Ch 5:25 [t]2Ki 16:12
26:17 [u]S 1Ki 4:2
26:18 [v]Nu 16:39 [w]Nu 18:1-7 [x]S Ex 30:7 [y]S 1Ch 6:49
26:19 [z]S Nu 12:10
26:21 [a]S Ex 4:6; Lev 13:46; S 14:8; Nu 5:2; S 19:12
26:22 [b]2Ki 15:1; Isa 1:1; 6:1
26:23 [c]Isa 1:1; 6:1

[a] *5* Many Hebrew manuscripts, Septuagint and Syriac; other Hebrew manuscripts *vision* [b] *19* The Hebrew for *leprosy* was used for various diseases affecting the skin; also in verses 20, 21 and 23. [c] *21* Or *in a house where he was relieved of responsibilities*

26:3 *fifty-two years.* 792–740 BC, including a coregency with Amaziah from 792 to 767.
26:4 The Chronicler constructs his account of Uzziah's reign to give it the same outline as that for Amaziah and Joash (see note on vv. 1–23). He also once again bypasses the statement in the parallel account that the king did not remove the high places (2Ki 15:4), just as he does in the accounts of the other two kings (see note on 25:2).
26:5 *days of Zechariah.* The author again uses chronological notes to portray the cycles of blessing and judgment associated with the individual king's response to God's commands (see note on 12:2).
26:6–8 Uzziah's conquests were toward the southeast and the southwest; Israel's powerful Jeroboam II was in control to the north of Judah.
26:7 *Meunites.* See note on 20:1.
26:9 *Corner Gate … Valley Gate.* Found at the northeast and southwest portions of the walls. *fortified.* This construction along the wall of Jerusalem may reflect, in part, repair of the damage done by Jehoash during the reign of Amaziah (25:23).
26:10 *towers … cisterns.* Towers and cisterns have been found in several excavations (Qumran, Gibeah, Beersheba). A seal bearing Uzziah's name has been found in a cistern at Tell Beit Mirsim.
26:11 *Uzziah had a well-trained army.* Tiglath-Pileser III of Assyria states that he was opposed in his advance toward the west (743 BC) by a coalition headed by "Azriau of Yaudi," perhaps Azariah (Uzziah) of Judah.
26:15 *devices … shoot arrows and hurl large stones.* Perhaps defensive constructions to protect those shooting arrows and hurling stones from the tops of the walls.
26:16 *after Uzziah became powerful.* See note on v. 5.
26:19 *leprosy.* See NIV text note; see also note on Lev 13:2; for disease as a punishment for sin, see notes on 16:12; 21:12–15.
26:21 *Uzziah … died.* See Isa 6:1 and note. *separate house.* See NIV text note; the same phrase in the Canaanite texts from Ugarit suggests a kind of quarantine or separation.
26:22 *recorded by … Isaiah.* Not a reference to the canonical book but to some other work no longer in existence.

rested with his ancestors and was buried near them in a cemetery that belonged to the kings, for people said, "He had leprosy." And Jotham his son succeeded him as king.[d]

Jotham King of Judah

27:1-4,7-9pp — 2Ki 15:33-38

27 Jotham[e] was twenty-five years old when he became king, and he reigned in Jerusalem sixteen years. His mother's name was Jerusha daughter of Zadok. 2 He did what was right in the eyes of the LORD, just as his father Uzziah had done, but unlike him he did not enter the temple of the LORD. The people, however, continued their corrupt practices. 3 Jotham rebuilt the Upper Gate of the temple of the LORD and did extensive work on the wall at the hill of Ophel.[f] 4 He built towns in the hill country of Judah and forts and towers in the wooded areas.

5 Jotham waged war against the king of the Ammonites[g] and conquered them. That year the Ammonites paid him a hundred talents[a] of silver, ten thousand cors[b] of wheat and ten thousand cors[c] of barley. The Ammonites brought him the same amount also in the second and third years.

6 Jotham grew powerful[h] because he walked steadfastly before the LORD his God.

7 The other events in Jotham's reign, including all his wars and the other things he did, are written in the book of the kings of Israel and Judah. 8 He was twenty-five years old when he became king, and he reigned in Jerusalem sixteen years. 9 Jotham rested with his ancestors and was buried in the City of David. And Ahaz his son succeeded him as king.

Ahaz King of Judah

28:1-27pp — 2Ki 16:1-20

28 Ahaz[i] was twenty years old when he became king, and he reigned in Jerusalem sixteen years. Unlike David his father, he did not do what was right in the eyes of the LORD. 2 He followed the ways of the kings of Israel and also made idols[j] for worshiping the Baals. 3 He burned sacrifices in the Valley of Ben Hinnom[k] and sacrificed his children[l] in the fire, engaging in the detestable[m] practices of the nations the LORD had driven out before the Israelites. 4 He offered sacrifices and burned incense at the high places, on the hilltops and under every spreading tree.

5 Therefore the LORD his God delivered him into the hands of the king of Aram.[n] The Arameans defeated him and took many of his people as prisoners and brought them to Damascus.

He was also given into the hands of the king of Israel, who inflicted heavy casualties on him. 6 In one day Pekah[o] son of Remaliah killed a hundred and twenty thousand soldiers in Judah[p] — because Judah had forsaken the LORD, the God of their ancestors. 7 Zikri, an Ephraimite warrior, killed Maaseiah the king's son, Az-

26:23 [d] S 2Ki 14:21; Am 1:1
27:1 [e] S 2Ki 15:5,32; S 1Ch 3:12
27:3 [f] 2Ch 33:14; Ne 3:26
27:5 [g] S Ge 19:38
27:6 [h] 2Ch 26:5
28:1 [i] S 1Ch 3:13; Isa 1:1
28:2 [j] Ex 34:17
28:3 [k] S Jos 15:8 [l] S Lev 18:21; S 2Ki 3:27; Eze 20:26 [m] S Dt 18:9; 2Ch 33:2
28:5 [n] Isa 7:1
28:6 [o] S 2Ki 15:25,27 [p] ver 8; Isa 9:21; 11:13

[a] 5 That is, about 3 3/4 tons or about 3.4 metric tons
[b] 5 That is, probably about 1,800 tons or about 1,600 metric tons of wheat
[c] 5 That is, probably about 1,500 tons or about 1,350 metric tons of barley

---

26:23 *buried … in a cemetery that belonged to the kings.* Cf. 2Ki 15:7. Apparently due to his leprosy, Uzziah was buried in a cemetery belonging to the kings, though not in the tombs of the kings.

27:1 – 9 See 2Ki 15:32 – 38 and notes.

27:1 *sixteen years.* 750 – 735 BC, including a coregency with Uzziah (750 – 740). His reign also overlapped that of his successor, Ahaz, from 735 to 732.

27:2 *did not enter the temple.* The Chronicler commends Jotham for not making the same error Uzziah did (26:16). *corrupt practices.* Appears to refer to the flourishing high places (2Ki 15:35).

27:3 – 6 Unique to the Chronicler and an elaboration of his thesis that fidelity to God's commands brings blessing: in construction, military victory and prosperity — all "because he walked steadfastly before the LORD" (v. 6). Judah's relationship with the Ammonites held particular interest for the Chronicler (see notes on 20:1 – 30; 24:26).

27:7 *all his wars.* See, e.g., 2Ki 15:37.

28:1 – 27 See 2Ki 16:1 – 20 and notes, though only the introduction and conclusion in the two accounts are strictly parallel. The reign of Ahaz is the only one for which the Chronicler does not mention a single redeeming feature. In his account the Chronicler appears to adopt explicit parallels from the speech of Abijah condemning the northern kingdom (ch. 13) in order to show that under Ahaz the southern kingdom had sunk to the same depths of apostasy. Judah's religious fidelity, of which Abijah had boasted, was completely overthrown under Ahaz.

28:1 *sixteen years.* 732 – 715 BC, not including the coregency with Jotham (735 – 732).

28:2 *made idols.* Cf. 13:8. *Baals.* See notes on Jdg 2:11,13.

28:3 *Valley of Ben Hinnom.* See 33:6; see also notes on Ne 11:30; Jer 7:31. Josiah put an end to the pagan practices observed there (2Ki 23:10). *sacrificed his children.* See Lev 20:1 – 5; Jer 7:31 – 32. 2Ki 16:3 has the singular "son." Some have regarded the plural as a deliberate inflation on the part of the Chronicler to heighten the wickedness of Ahaz. However, some manuscripts of the Septuagint (the pre-Christian Greek translation of the OT) also have a plural in 2Ki 16:3, suggesting that the Chronicler faithfully copied the text before him.

28:5 Cf. 13:16 – 17. *God delivered him into the hands of.* According to the Chronicler's view on immediate retribution, defeat in war is one of the results of disobedience (see note on 20:30). *also given into the hands of the king of Israel.* 2Ki 16:5 – 6 and Isa 7 make it clear that Rezin (king of Aram) and Pekah acted together against Judah. The Chronicler has chosen either to treat them separately or to report on two different episodes of the Aram-Israel coalition.

28:6 *Pekah.* Reigned over the northern kingdom 752 – 732 BC (see 2Ki 15:27 – 31). *had forsaken the LORD.* The same charge Abijah made against the northern kingdom (13:11).

rikam the officer in charge of the palace, and Elkanah, second to the king. 8The men of Israel took captive from their fellow Israelites who were from Judah[q] two hundred thousand wives, sons and daughters. They also took a great deal of plunder, which they carried back to Samaria.[r]

9But a prophet of the LORD named Oded was there, and he went out to meet the army when it returned to Samaria. He said to them, "Because the LORD, the God of your ancestors, was angry[s] with Judah, he gave them into your hand. But you have slaughtered them in a rage that reaches to heaven.[t] 10And now you intend to make the men and women of Judah and Jerusalem your slaves.[u] But aren't you also guilty of sins against the LORD your God? 11Now listen to me! Send back your fellow Israelites you have taken as prisoners, for the LORD's fierce anger rests on you.[v]"

12Then some of the leaders in Ephraim—Azariah son of Jehohanan, Berekiah son of Meshillemoth, Jehizkiah son of Shallum, and Amasa son of Hadlai—confronted those who were arriving from the war. 13"You must not bring those prisoners here," they said, "or we will be guilty before the LORD. Do you intend to add to our sin and guilt? For our guilt is already great, and his fierce anger rests on Israel."

14So the soldiers gave up the prisoners and plunder in the presence of the officials and all the assembly. 15The men designated by name took the prisoners, and from the plunder they clothed all who were naked. They provided them with clothes and sandals, food and drink,[w] and healing balm. All those who were weak they put on donkeys. So they took them back to their fellow Israelites at Jericho, the City of Palms,[x] and returned to Samaria.[y]

16At that time King Ahaz sent to the kings[a] of Assyria[z] for help. 17The Edomites[a] had again come and attacked Judah and carried away prisoners,[b] 18while the Philistines[c] had raided towns in the foothills and in the Negev of Judah. They captured and occupied Beth Shemesh, Aijalon[d] and Gederoth,[e] as well as Soko,[f] Timnah[g] and Gimzo, with their surrounding villages. 19The LORD had humbled Judah because of Ahaz king of Israel,[b] for he had promoted wickedness in Judah and had been most unfaithful[h] to the LORD. 20Tiglath-Pileser[c][i] king of Assyria[j] came to him, but he gave him trouble[k] instead of help.[l] 21Ahaz[m] took some of the things from the temple of the LORD and from the royal palace and from the officials and presented them to the king of Assyria, but that did not help him.[n]

22In his time of trouble King Ahaz became even more unfaithful[o] to the LORD. 23He offered sacrifices to the gods[p] of Damascus, who had defeated him; for he thought, "Since the gods of the kings of Aram have helped them, I will sacrifice to them so they will help me."[q] But they were his downfall and the downfall of all Israel.[r]

24Ahaz gathered together the furnishings[s] from the temple of God[t] and cut them in pieces. He shut the doors[u] of the LORD's temple and set up altars[v] at every street corner in Jerusalem. 25In every town in Judah he built high places to burn sacrifices to other gods and aroused the anger of the LORD, the God of his ancestors.

26The other events of his reign and all his ways, from beginning to end, are written in the book of the kings of Judah and Israel. 27Ahaz rested[w] with his ancestors

[a] *16* Most Hebrew manuscripts; one Hebrew manuscript, Septuagint and Vulgate (see also 2 Kings 16:7) *king*
[b] *19* That is, Judah, as frequently in 2 Chronicles
[c] *20* Hebrew *Tilgath-Pilneser,* a variant of *Tiglath-Pileser*

28:8 [q] Dt 28:25-41 [r] 2Ch 29:9
28:9 [s] Isa 10:6; 47:6; Zec 1:15 [t] Ezr 9:6; Rev 18:5
28:10 [u] Lev 25:39-46
28:11 [v] 2Ch 11:4
28:15 [w] 2Ki 6:22; Pr 25:21-22 [x] S Dt 34:3; S Jdg 1:16 [y] Lk 10:25-37
28:16 [z] S 2Ki 16:7; Eze 23:12
28:17 [a] Ps 137:7; Isa 34:5; 63:1; Jer 25:21; Eze 16:57; 25:12; Am 1:11 [b] 2Ch 29:9
28:18 [c] Isa 9:12; 11:14; Jer 25:20; Eze 16:27, 57; 25:15 [d] S Jos 10:12 [e] Jos 15:41 [f] S 1Sa 17:1 [g] S Ge 38:12
28:19 [h] S 1Ch 5:25
28:20 [i] S 2Ki 15:29; S 1Ch 5:6 [j] Isa 7:17; 8:7; 10:5-6; 36:1 [k] Isa 10:20 [l] S 2Ki 16:7
28:21 [m] S 2Ch 16:2-9 [n] Jer 2:36
28:22 [o] Jer 5:3; 15:7; 17:23
28:23 [p] S 2Ch 25:14 [q] Isa 10:20; Jer 44:17-18 [r] 1Ch 11:1; Jer 18:15
28:24 [s] 2Ch 29:19 [t] S 2Ki 16:18 [u] Mal 1:10 [v] 2Ch 30:14
28:27 [w] Isa 14:28-32

28:9–15 The kindness of the northern captors to their captives from Judah, especially as recorded in vv. 14–15, may be the background for Jesus' parable of the Good Samaritan (Lk 10:25–37). Oded's attitude to the north is shown by his willingness to call them "fellow Israelites" (v. 11). In this case, too, the record of ch. 13 has been reversed: The northern tribes are more righteous than the south.

28:17–18 *Edomites … attacked Judah … Philistines had raided.* Foreign alliances (v. 16) led to further defeats for Ahaz (see note on 16:2–9).

28:19 *The LORD had humbled Judah because of Ahaz.* The same formula used to describe the defeat of the northern tribes in 13:18, though under Ahaz it is Judah that is subdued.

28:20 *Tiglath-Pileser.* King of Assyria 745–727 BC (see 1Ch 5:26 and note). *trouble instead of help.* Appears on the surface to contradict the statement in 2Ki 16:9 that Tiglath-Pileser III responded to Ahaz's request by attacking and capturing Damascus, exiling its population and killing Rezin. The Chronicler assumes the reader's familiarity with the other account and knows of the temporary respite for Judah gained by Assyrian intervention against Damascus and the northern kingdom of Israel. But he focuses on the long-range results, in which Judah herself was reduced to vassalage to Assyria.

28:22–23 The Chronicler assumes the reader's familiarity with Ahaz's trip to Damascus and his copying of the altar and practices there (2Ki 16:10–16).

28:24–25 Additional details on Ahaz's alterations are found in 2Ki 16:17–18. The Chronicler also adds details in his description of Hezekiah's reforming activities to correct some of the abuses under Ahaz: Not only had the doors been shut, but also the lamps were put out and offerings were not made at the sanctuary (29:7); the altar and utensils were desecrated, and the table for the consecrated bread was neglected (29:18–19). It is precisely these accoutrements of proper temple service about which Abijah had boasted when he proclaimed the faithfulness of Judah, in contrast to that of the northern kingdom (13:11). Now these furnishings are lacking under Ahaz and make the southern kingdom just like the north (see note on vv. 1–27).

and was buried[x] in the city of Jerusalem,
but he was not placed in the tombs of the
kings of Israel. And Hezekiah his son succeeded him as king.

Hezekiah Purifies the Temple

29:1-2pp — 2Ki 18:2-3

29 Hezekiah[y] was twenty-five years
old when he became king, and he
reigned in Jerusalem twenty-nine years.
His mother's name was Abijah daughter
of Zechariah. 2He did what was right in
the eyes of the LORD, just as his father David[z] had done.
3In the first month of the first year of his
reign, he opened the doors of the temple of
the LORD and repaired[a] them. 4He brought
in the priests and the Levites, assembled
them in the square on the east side 5and
said: "Listen to me, Levites! Consecrate[b]
yourselves now and consecrate the temple of the LORD, the God of your ancestors.
Remove all defilement from the sanctuary.
6Our parents[c] were unfaithful;[d] they did
evil in the eyes of the LORD our God and
forsook him. They turned their faces away
from the LORD's dwelling place and turned
their backs on him. 7They also shut the
doors of the portico and put out the lamps.
They did not burn incense[e] or present any
burnt offerings at the sanctuary to the God
of Israel. 8Therefore, the anger of the LORD
has fallen on Judah and Jerusalem; he has
made them an object of dread and horror[f]
and scorn,[g] as you can see with your own
eyes. 9This is why our fathers have fall-
en by the sword and why our sons and
daughters and our wives are in captivity.[h] 10Now I intend to make a covenant[i]
with the LORD, the God of Israel, so that
his fierce anger[j] will turn away from us.
11My sons, do not be negligent now, for
the LORD has chosen you to stand before
him and serve him,[k] to minister[l] before
him and to burn incense."
12Then these Levites[m] set to work:
from the Kohathites,
Mahath son of Amasai and Joel son
of Azariah;
from the Merarites,
Kish son of Abdi and Azariah son
of Jehallelel;
from the Gershonites,
Joah son of Zimmah and Eden[n] son
of Joah;
13from the descendants of Elizaphan,[o]
Shimri and Jeiel;
from the descendants of Asaph,[p]
Zechariah and Mattaniah;
14from the descendants of Heman,
Jehiel and Shimei;
from the descendants of Jeduthun,
Shemaiah and Uzziel.
15When they had assembled their fellow
Levites and consecrated themselves, they
went in to purify[q] the temple of the LORD,
as the king had ordered, following the
word of the LORD. 16The priests went into
the sanctuary of the LORD to purify it. They
brought out to the courtyard of the LORD's
temple everything unclean that they found
in the temple of the LORD. The Levites took
it and carried it out to the Kidron Valley.[r]
17They began the consecration on the first

28:27 [x]S 2Ch 21:20 **29:1** [y]S 1Ch 3:13 **29:2** [z]2Ch 34:2 **29:3** [a]2Ki 18:16 **29:5** [b]S Lev 11:44; Ne 13:9 **29:6** [c]Ezr 9:7; Ps 106:6-47; Jer 2:27; 18:17; Eze 23:35; Da 9:5-6 [d]S 1Ch 5:25 **29:7** [e]S Ex 30:7 **29:8** [f]S Dt 28:25 [g]S Lev 26:32; Jer 18:16; 19:8; 25:9,18 **29:9** [h]2Ch 28:5-8,17 **29:10** [i]S 2Ki 11:17; S 2Ch 23:16 [j]S Nu 25:4; 2Ch 30:8; Ezr 10:14 **29:11** [k]S Nu 3:6; 8:6,14 [l]S 1Ch 15:2 **29:12** [m]S Nu 3:17-20 [n]2Ch 31:15 **29:13** [o]S Ex 6:22 [p]S 1Ch 6:39 **29:15** [q]S 1Ch 23:28; S Isa 1:25 **29:16** [r]S 2Sa 15:23

28:27 *not placed in the tombs of the kings.* The third king whose wickedness resulted in the loss of this honor at death. The others were Jehoram (21:20) and Joash (24:25). Uzziah's sin and leprosy brought the same result, though it is not reported in exactly the same terms (26:23). Cf. also Manasseh (33:20).

29:1 — 32:33 The Chronicler devotes more attention to Hezekiah than to any other post-Solomonic king. Although the parallel text (2Ki 18 – 20) has about the same amount of material, only about a fourth of the total relates the same or similar material; only a few verses are strict literary parallels (29:1 – 2; 32:32 – 33). In Kings preeminence among the post-Solomonic kings is given to Josiah (2Ki 22 – 23; cf. 1Ki 13:2), and the record of Hezekiah is primarily devoted to his confrontation with Sennacherib of Assyria. By contrast, the Chronicler highlights almost exclusively Hezekiah's religious reform and his devotion to matters of ceremony and ritual. The parallel passage (2Ki 18:1 – 6) touches the religious reform only briefly. The numerous parallels in these chapters with the account of Solomon's reign suggest that the Chronicler viewed Hezekiah as a second Solomon in his Passover celebration (ch. 30), his arrangements for worship (29:7,18,35; 31:2 – 3), his wealth (32:27 – 29), the honor accorded him by the Gentiles (32:23) and the extent of his dominion (30:25; cf. similarly Pr 25:1 and note).

29:1 *twenty-nine years.* 715 – 686 BC (but see note on Isa 36:1), including a 15-year extension of life granted by God (2Ki 20:6) but not mentioned by the Chronicler.

29:3 — 30:27 Not found in Kings.

29:3 *first year.* 715 BC, another example of the Chronicler's practice of introducing chronological materials into his narrative (see note on 12:2). *opened the doors of the temple.* Necessary after the actions of Ahaz (28:24). *repaired them.* The repairs to the doors included new gold overlay (2Ki 18:16).

29:5 - 11 Hezekiah's speech demonstrates again the Chronicler's convictions about the coherence of action and effect: The sins of the past bring difficulty and judgment, but renewed fidelity brings relief.

29:7 Hezekiah reinstitutes these temple arrangements — following the pattern of Solomon (2:4; 4:7).

29:8 *object of dread and horror and scorn.* Echoes the language of the prophets, especially Jeremiah (see Jer 19:8; 25:9,18; 29:18; 51:37). Reference is to the Assyrian devastation of the northern kingdom and much of Judah.

29:12 *Kohathites ... Merarites ... Gershonites.* The three clans of Levi (1Ch 6:1).

29:13 - 14 *Asaph ... Heman ... Jeduthun.* Founders of the three families of Levitical musicians (1Ch 6:31 – 48; 25:1 – 31).

29:13 *Elizaphan.* A leader of the Kohathites (Nu 3:30), whose family had achieved status almost as a subclan (see 1Ch 15:8 and note on 15:4 – 10).

29:16 *Kidron Valley.* See note on Isa 22:7 and maps, pp. 515, 748; see also 1Ki 15:13 and note.

lay of the first month, and by the eighth
lay of the month they reached the porti-
:o of the LORD. For eight more days they
:onsecrated the temple of the LORD itself,
inishing on the sixteenth day of the first
nonth.

[18]Then they went in to King Hezekiah
ınd reported: "We have purified the en-
ire temple of the LORD, the altar of burnt
offering with all its utensils, and the ta-
ole for setting out the consecrated bread,
with all its articles. [19]We have prepared
ınd consecrated all the articles[s] that King
Ahaz removed in his unfaithfulness while
ıe was king. They are now in front of the
LORD's altar."

[20]Early the next morning King Hezeki-
h gathered the city officials together and
went up to the temple of the LORD. [21]They
brought seven bulls, seven rams, seven
male lambs and seven male goats[t] as a sin
offering[a][u] for the kingdom, for the sanctuary and for Judah. The king commanded
he priests, the descendants of Aaron, to
offer these on the altar of the LORD. [22]So
hey slaughtered the bulls, and the priests
ook the blood and splashed it against the
ıltar; next they slaughtered the rams and
splashed their blood against the altar; then
hey slaughtered the lambs and splashed
heir blood[v] against the altar. [23]The goats[w]
or the sin offering were brought before
he king and the assembly, and they laid
heir hands[x] on them. [24]The priests then
laughtered the goats and presented their
blood on the altar for a sin offering to
ıtone[y] for all Israel, because the king had
ordered the burnt offering and the sin of-
ering for all Israel.[z]

[25]He stationed the Levites in the temple
of the LORD with cymbals, harps and lyres
n the way prescribed by David[a] and Gad[b]
he king's seer and Nathan the prophet;
his was commanded by the LORD through
his prophets. [26]So the Levites stood ready
with David's instruments,[c] and the priests
with their trumpets.[d]

[27]Hezekiah gave the order to sacrifice
he burnt offering on the altar. As the of-
ering began, singing to the LORD began
also, accompanied by trumpets and the
instruments[e] of David king of Israel. [28]The
whole assembly bowed in worship, while
the musicians played and the trumpets
sounded. All this continued until the sacrifice of the burnt offering[f] was completed.

[29]When the offerings were finished,
the king and everyone present with him
knelt down and worshiped.[g] [30]King Hezekiah and his officials ordered the Levites
to praise the LORD with the words of David and of Asaph the seer. So they sang
praises with gladness and bowed down
and worshiped.

[31]Then Hezekiah said, "You have now
dedicated yourselves to the LORD. Come
and bring sacrifices[h] and thank offerings
to the temple of the LORD." So the assembly brought sacrifices and thank offerings,
and all whose hearts were willing[i] brought
burnt offerings.

[32]The number of burnt offerings[j] the assembly brought was seventy bulls, a hundred rams and two hundred male lambs—
all of them for burnt offerings to the LORD.
[33]The animals consecrated as sacrifices
amounted to six hundred bulls and three
thousand sheep and goats. [34]The priests,
however, were too few to skin all the burnt
offerings;[k] so their relatives the Levites
helped them until the task was finished
and until other priests had been consecrated,[l] for the Levites had been more
conscientious in consecrating themselves
than the priests had been. [35]There were
burnt offerings in abundance, together
with the fat[m] of the fellowship offerings[n]
and the drink offerings[o] that accompanied
the burnt offerings.

So the service of the temple of the LORD
was reestablished. [36]Hezekiah and all the
people rejoiced at what God had brought
about for his people, because it was done
so quickly.[p]

Hezekiah Celebrates the Passover

30 Hezekiah sent word to all Israel[q]
and Judah and also wrote letters to

29:19 [s]2Ch 28:24 **29:21** [t]Ezr 6:17; 8:35 [u]S Lev 4:13-14 **29:22** [v]S Lev 4:18; Nu 18:17 **29:23** [w]S Lev 16:5 [x]Lev 4:15 **29:24** [y]S Ex 29:36; Lev 4:26 [z]1Ch 11:1; Ezr 8:35 **29:25** [a]S 1Ch 25:6; 28:19 [b]S 1Sa 22:5 **29:26** [c]S 1Ch 15:16 [d]S 1Ch 15:24 **29:27** [e]S 1Sa 16:16 **29:28** [f]S 2Ch 2:4 **29:29** [g]S 2Ch 20:18 **29:31** [h]Heb 13:15-16 [i]S Ex 25:2; 35:22 **29:32** [j]Lev 1:1-17 **29:34** [k]Eze 44:11 [l]2Ch 30:3, 15 **29:35** [m]S Ge 4:4; S Ex 29:13 [n]Lev 7:11-21 [o]S Ge 35:14 **29:36** [p]2Ch 35:8 **30:1** [q]S 1Ch 9:1

[a] *21* Or *purification offering*; also in verses 23 and 24

9:18 These actions under Hezekiah mirror those of Solomon (2:4).
9:21 *sin offering.* See Lev 4:1—5:13 and chart, p. 164.
9:22 *splashed their blood.* See Lev 17:6; Nu 18:17.
9:23 *laid their hands on them.* See Lev 4:13–15; 8:14–15;
lu 8:12.
9:25 *Gad … Nathan.* See 1Sa 22:5 and note; 2Sa 7; 12.
9:26 *David's instruments.* See 1Ch 23:5.
9:35 *burnt offerings in abundance … fellowship offerings …
rink offerings.* Reminiscent of the dedication of the temple
ınder Solomon (7:4–6). For the laws regarding the fellow-
hip offerings, see Lev 3; 7:11–21; for the drink offerings, see
lu 15:1–12. *service of the temple of the LORD was reestablished.*
Similar to the formula used in 8:16 with reference to Solomon's work.

30:1–27 Unique to the Chronicler; cf. the famous Passover celebration under Josiah (35:1–19; 2Ki 23:21–23). Hezekiah allowed two deviations from the law (Ex 12; Dt 16:1–8) in this observance: (1) the date in the second month (v. 2) and (2) exemption from some ritual requirements (vv. 18–19).

30:1 *all Israel and Judah.* See Introduction to 1 Chronicles: Purpose and Themes. With the northern kingdom now ended as the result of the Assyrian invasion and deportation (which surprisingly is not mentioned), the Chronicler shows "all Israel" once again united around the Davidic king and the temple (see vv. 5,18–19,25).

Ephraim and Manasseh,[r] inviting them to come to the temple of the LORD in Jerusalem and celebrate the Passover[s] to the LORD, the God of Israel. 2 The king and his officials and the whole assembly in Jerusalem decided to celebrate[t] the Passover in the second month. 3 They had not been able to celebrate it at the regular time because not enough priests had consecrated[u] themselves and the people had not assembled in Jerusalem. 4 The plan seemed right both to the king and to the whole assembly. 5 They decided to send a proclamation throughout Israel, from Beersheba to Dan,[v] calling the people to come to Jerusalem and celebrate the Passover to the LORD, the God of Israel. It had not been celebrated in large numbers according to what was written.

6 At the king's command, couriers went throughout Israel and Judah with letters from the king and from his officials, which read:

"People of Israel, return to the LORD, the God of Abraham, Isaac and Israel, that he may return to you who are left, who have escaped from the hand of the kings of Assyria. 7 Do not be like your parents[w] and your fellow Israelites, who were unfaithful[x] to the LORD, the God of their ancestors, so that he made them an object of horror,[y] as you see. 8 Do not be stiff-necked,[z] as your ancestors were; submit to the LORD. Come to his sanctuary, which he has consecrated forever. Serve the LORD your God, so that his fierce anger[a] will turn away from you. 9 If you return[b] to the LORD, then your fellow Israelites and your children will be shown compassion[c] by their captors and will return to this land, for the LORD your God is gracious and compassionate.[d] He will not turn his face from you if you return to him."

10 The couriers went from town to town in Ephraim and Manasseh, as far as Zebulun, but people scorned and ridiculed them. 11 Nevertheless, some from Asher, Manasseh and Zebulun humbled[f] themselves and went to Jerusalem.[g] 12 Also in Judah the hand of God was on the people to give them unity[h] of mind to carry out what the king and his officials had ordered, following the word of the LORD.

13 A very large crowd of people assembled in Jerusalem to celebrate the Festival of Unleavened Bread[i] in the second month. 14 They removed the altars[j] in Jerusalem and cleared away the incense altars and threw them into the Kidron Valley.[k]

15 They slaughtered the Passover lamb on the fourteenth day of the second month. The priests and the Levites were ashamed and consecrated[l] themselves and brought burnt offerings to the temple of the LORD. 16 Then they took up their regular positions[m] as prescribed in the Law of Moses the man of God. The priests splashed against the altar the blood handed to them by the Levites. 17 Since many in the crowd had not consecrated themselves, the Levites had to kill[n] the Passover lambs for all those who were not ceremonially clean and could not consecrate their lambs[a] to the LORD. 18 Although most of the many people who came from Ephraim, Manasseh, Issachar and Zebulun

30:1 [r] S Ge 41:52 [s] S Ex 12:11; S Nu 28:16
30:2 [t] Nu 9:10
30:3 [u] Nu 9:6-13; S 2Ch 29:34
30:5 [v] S Jdg 20:1
30:7 [w] Ps 78:8, 57; 106:6; Jer 11:10; Eze 20:18 [x] S 1Ch 5:25 [y] S Dt 28:25
30:8 [z] S Ex 32:9 [a] S Nu 25:4; S 2Ch 29:10
30:9 [b] Dt 30:2-5; Isa 1:16; 55:7; Jer 25:5; Eze 33:11 [c] S Ex 3:21; S 1Ki 8:50 [d] S Ex 22:27; S Dt 4:31; S 2Ch 6:39; Mic 7:18
30:10 [e] 2Ch 36:16
30:11 [f] S 2Ch 6:37 [g] ver 25
30:12 [h] Jer 32:39; Eze 11:19
30:13 [i] S Nu 28:16
30:14 [j] 2Ch 28:24 [k] S 2Sa 15:23
30:15 [l] S 2Ch 29:34
30:16 [m] 2Ch 35:10
30:17 [n] 2Ch 35:11; Ezr 6:20

[a] 17 Or *consecrate themselves*

30:2 *second month.* After the division of the kingdom, Jeroboam deferred the sacral calendar of the northern kingdom by one month (1Ki 12:32), possibly to further wean the subjects in the north away from devotion to Jerusalem. By delaying the celebration of Passover one month, Hezekiah not only allows time for the priests to consecrate themselves (v. 3) and for the people to gather (vv. 3,13) but also achieves unity between the kingdoms on the date of the Passover for the first time since the schism more than two centuries earlier. Delaying the date reflects Hezekiah's concern to involve "all Israel." For the first time since Solomon the entire nation observes Passover together, reflecting the Chronicler's view that Hezekiah is a second Solomon. Passover was prescribed for the 14th day of the first month (Ex 12:2,6; Dt 16:1–8) but could not be celebrated at that time due to the defilement of the temple and the purification rites under way (29:3,17). For celebration of Passover by the restored community shortly after the dedication of the rebuilt temple, see Ezr 6:16–22.
30:5 *large numbers.* Another comparison with the time of Solomon (see v. 26). At the time of its inception, Passover was primarily a family observance (Ex 12). It later became a national celebration at the temple (v. 8; see Dt 16:1–8).
30:8 *Come to his sanctuary.* Passover was one of three annual festivals requiring attendance at the temple (see Nu 28:9—29:39).
30:9 *shown compassion by their captors.* In Solomon's prayer in 6:39 the Chronicler omitted the phrase found in the parallel account (1Ki 8:50) that their conquerors would "show them mercy." Here the phrase is found in the speech of Hezekiah, again portraying him as a second Solomon (see Lev 26:40–42). *will return to this land.* Those who repent will have hope of return, even those from the Assyrian captivity.
30:14 *Kidron Valley.* See 29:16 and note.
30:15 *The priests and the Levites ... consecrated themselves.* The reproach previously directed against the priests (v. 3; 29:34) is here broadened to include also the Levites—an exhortation to the priests and Levites of the restored community to be faithful.
30:17 *Levites had to kill the Passover lambs.* See Ex 12:6; Dt 16:6. According to the law the heads of families were to slay the Passover sacrifice. The Levites perhaps acted for the recent arrivals from the northern kingdom who were not ceremonially clean. Cf. Jn 11:55.
30:18–19 Faith and obedience take precedence over ritual (see note on Isa 1:11–15; cf. Mk 7:1–23; Jn 7:22–23; 9:14–16).

ad not purified themselves,[o] yet they ate
he Passover, contrary to what was writ-
en. But Hezekiah prayed for them, say-
ng, “May the LORD, who is good, pardon
veryone 19 who sets their heart on seeking
od—the LORD, the God of their ances-
ors—even if they are not clean accord-
ng to the rules of the sanctuary.” 20 And
he LORD heard[p] Hezekiah and healed[q] the
eople.[r]
21 The Israelites who were present in
erusalem celebrated the Festival of Un-
eavened Bread[s] for seven days with great
ejoicing, while the Levites and priests
raised the LORD every day with resound-
ng instruments dedicated to the LORD.[a]
22 Hezekiah spoke encouragingly to all
he Levites, who showed good under-
tanding of the service of the LORD. For
he seven days they ate their assigned por-
ion and offered fellowship offerings and
raised[b] the LORD, the God of their ances-
ors.
23 The whole assembly then agreed to
elebrate[t] the festival seven more days;
o for another seven days they celebrated
oyfully. 24 Hezekiah king of Judah provid-
d[u] a thousand bulls and seven thousand
heep and goats for the assembly, and the
fficials provided them with a thousand
ulls and ten thousand sheep and goats. A
reat number of priests consecrated them-
elves. 25 The entire assembly of Judah re-
oiced, along with the priests and Levites
nd all who had assembled from Israel[v],
ncluding the foreigners who had come
rom Israel and also those who resided in
udah. 26 There was great joy in Jerusalem,
or since the days of Solomon[w] son of Daid king of Israel there had been nothing
ke this in Jerusalem. 27 The priests and
he Levites stood to bless[x] the people, and
od heard them, for their prayer reached
eaven, his holy dwelling place.

30:18 [o]Ex 12:43-49; Nu 9:6-10 **30:20** [p]S 2Ch 6:20 [q]S 2Ch 7:14; Mal 4:2 [r]Jas 5:16 **30:21** [s]Ex 12:15,17; 13:6 **30:23** [t]2Ch 7:9 **30:24** [u]1Ki 8:5; 2Ch 35:7; Ezr 6:17; 8:35 **30:25** [v]ver 11 **30:26** [w]S 2Ch 7:8 **30:27** [x]S Ex 39:43

31:1 [y]S 2Ki 18:4; 2Ch 32:12; Isa 36:7 **31:2** [z]S 2Ch 29:9 [a]S 1Ch 24:1 [b]S 1Ch 15:2 [c]Ps 7:17; 9:2; 47:6; 71:22 [d]S 1Ch 23:28-32 **31:3** [e]S 1Ch 29:3; 2Ch 35:7; Eze 45:17 [f]Nu 28:1-29:40 **31:4** [g]S Nu 18:8; S Dt 18:8; Ne 13:10 **31:5** [h]S Nu 18:12, 24; Ne 13:12; Eze 44:30 [i]Dt 12:17 **31:6** [j]S Lev 27:30; Ne 13:10-12 [k]S Ru 3:7 **31:7** [l]Ex 23:16

31 When all this had ended, the Israelites who were there went out to
the towns of Judah, smashed the sacred
stones and cut down[y] the Asherah poles.
They destroyed the high places and the
altars throughout Judah and Benjamin
and in Ephraim and Manasseh. After they
had destroyed all of them, the Israelites
returned to their own towns and to their
own property.

Contributions for Worship

31:20-21pp — 2Ki 18:5-7

2 Hezekiah[z] assigned the priests and Levites to divisions[a]—each of them according to their duties as priests or Levites—to
offer burnt offerings and fellowship offerings, to minister,[b] to give thanks and to
sing praises[c] at the gates of the LORD’s
dwelling.[d] 3 The king contributed[e] from his
own possessions for the morning and evening burnt offerings and for the burnt offerings on the Sabbaths, at the New Moons
and at the appointed festivals as written
in the Law of the LORD.[f] 4 He ordered the
people living in Jerusalem to give the portion[g] due the priests and Levites so they
could devote themselves to the Law of the
LORD. 5 As soon as the order went out, the
Israelites generously gave the firstfruits[h]
of their grain, new wine,[i] olive oil and
honey and all that the fields produced.
They brought a great amount, a tithe of
everything. 6 The people of Israel and Judah who lived in the towns of Judah also
brought a tithe[j] of their herds and flocks
and a tithe of the holy things dedicated to
the LORD their God, and they piled them
in heaps.[k] 7 They began doing this in the
third month and finished in the seventh
month.[l] 8 When Hezekiah and his officials

[a] *21* *Or priests sang to the LORD every day, accompanied by the LORD’s instruments of praise* [b] *22* *Or and confessed their sins to*

0:20 The response to Hezekiah’s prayer recalls the prayer f Solomon (7:14).

0:23 *another seven days.* The festival was observed for two veeks, just as the observance of the dedication of Solomon’s emple had been (7:8–9).

0:26 *since the days of Solomon.* An explicit indication of the hronicler’s modeling of the reign of Hezekiah after that of olomon (see note on 29:1—32:33).

0:27 *prayer reached heaven, his holy dwelling place.* Another cho of Solomon’s dedication prayer (6:21,30,33,39).

1:1–21 Apart from the first verse, which parallels 2Ki 18:4, ne material of this chapter is unique to the Chronicler, vhose interest in the Levites and the temple predominates. ezekiah’s efforts to ensure the material support of the Le-ites (v. 4) probably had relevance to the postexilic audience or whom the Chronicler wrote.

1:1 *the Israelites ... the Israelites.* Lit. “all Israel ... all the Israel-es.” The Chronicler’s interest in “all Israel” as united under Hez-kiah is again apparent. *sacred stones.* See note on 1Ki 14:23. *sherah poles.* See NIV text note on 14:3 and note on Ex 34:13.

31:2 Echoes 8:14. The Chronicler continues to model Hezekiah as a second Solomon (see notes on 29:7,18).

31:3 *king contributed.* The king’s giving from his own wealth prompted a generous response from the people, as it had also under David (1Ch 29:3–9).

31:5–6 See Dt 12:5–19; 14:22–27. The grain, new wine and olive oil had to be brought to the temple (Dt 12:17). Those coming from a distance, however, could bring the value of their offerings and purchase them on arrival (Dt 14:24). Only those who actually lived in Judah brought the tithe of their herds and flocks, a difficult procedure for those who lived farther away. For the restored community’s commitment to bring their firstfruits, tithes and offerings, see Ne 10:35–39. For their failure to do so, see Ne 13:10–13; Mal 3:8–10.

31:7 *third month.* May–June, the time of the Festival of Pentecost and the grain harvest. *seventh month.* September–October, the time of the Festival of Tabernacles and the fruit and vine harvest (see Ex 23:16).

came and saw the heaps, they praised the LORD and blessed[m] his people Israel.

9 Hezekiah asked the priests and Levites about the heaps; 10 and Azariah the chief priest, from the family of Zadok,[n] answered, "Since the people began to bring their contributions to the temple of the LORD, we have had enough to eat and plenty to spare, because the LORD has blessed his people, and this great amount is left over."[o]

11 Hezekiah gave orders to prepare storerooms in the temple of the LORD, and this was done. 12 Then they faithfully brought in the contributions, tithes and dedicated gifts. Konaniah,[p] a Levite, was the overseer in charge of these things, and his brother Shimei was next in rank. 13 Jehiel, Azaziah, Nahath, Asahel, Jerimoth, Jozabad,[q] Eliel, Ismakiah, Mahath and Benaiah were assistants of Konaniah and Shimei his brother. All these served by appointment of King Hezekiah and Azariah the official in charge of the temple of God.

14 Kore son of Imnah the Levite, keeper of the East Gate, was in charge of the freewill offerings given to God, distributing the contributions made to the LORD and also the consecrated gifts. 15 Eden,[r] Miniamin, Jeshua, Shemaiah, Amariah and Shekaniah assisted him faithfully in the towns[s] of the priests, distributing to their fellow priests according to their divisions, old and young alike.

16 In addition, they distributed to the males three years old or more whose names were in the genealogical records[t]—all who would enter the temple of the LORD to perform the daily duties of their various tasks, according to their responsibilities and their divisions. 17 And they distributed to the priests enrolled by their families in the genealogical records and likewise to the Levites twenty years old or more, according to their responsibilities and their divisions. 18 They included all the little ones, the wives, and the sons and daughters of the whole community listed in these genealogical records. For they were faithful in consecrating themselves.

19 As for the priests, the descendants of Aaron, who lived on the farmlands around their towns or in any other towns,[u] men were designated by name to distribut portions to every male among them an to all who were recorded in the genealc gies of the Levites.

20 This is what Hezekiah did through out Judah, doing what was good and righ and faithful[v] before the LORD his God. 21 I everything that he undertook in the se vice of God's temple and in obedience t the law and the commands, he sought hi God and worked wholeheartedly. And s he prospered.[w]

31:8 [m]Ps 144:13-15 **31:10** [n]S 2Sa 8:17 [o]S Ex 36:5; Eze 44:30; Mal 3:10-12 **31:12** [p]2Ch 35:9 **31:13** [q]2Ch 35:9 **31:15** [r]2Ch 29:12 [s]Jos 21:9-19 **31:16** [t]1Ch 23:3 **31:19** [u]S Nu 35:2-5 **31:20** [v]S 2Ki 20:3 **31:21** [w]S Dt 29:9 **32:1** [x]Isa 36:1; 37:9,17,37 **32:2** [y]Isa 22:7; Jer 1:15 **32:4** [z]S 2Ki 18:17; Isa 22:9,11; Na 3:14 **32:5** [a]Isa 22:10 [b]S 1Ch 11:8 [c]Isa 22:8 **32:7** [d]S Dt 31:6 [e]2Ch 20:15 [f]S Nu 14:9; 2Ki 6:16 **32:8** [g]Job 40:9; Isa 52:10; Jer 17:5; 32:21 [h]S Dt 3:22; S 1Sa 17:45 [i]S 1Ch 5:22; Ps 20:7; Isa 28:6

Sennacherib Threatens Jerusalem

32:9-19pp — 2Ki 18:17-35; Isa 36:2-20
32:20-21pp — 2Ki 19:35-37; Isa 37:36-38

32 After all that Hezekiah had so faitł fully done, Sennacherib[x] king c Assyria came and invaded Judah. He lai siege to the fortified cities, thinking to co quer them for himself. 2 When Hezekia saw that Sennacherib had come and th he intended to wage war against Jerus lem,[y] 3 he consulted with his officials an military staff about blocking off the wate from the springs outside the city, and the helped him. 4 They gathered a large grou of people who blocked all the spring and the stream that flowed through th land. "Why should the kings[a] of Assyri come and find plenty of water?" they sai 5 Then he worked hard repairing all th broken sections of the wall[a] and buildin towers on it. He built another wall ou side that one and reinforced the terraces of the City of David. He also made larg numbers of weapons[c] and shields.

6 He appointed military officers over th people and assembled them before hi in the square at the city gate and encou aged them with these words: 7 "Be stron and courageous.[d] Do not be afraid or di couraged[e] because of the king of Assyri and the vast army with him, for there i a greater power with us than with him 8 With him is only the arm of flesh,[g] bu with us[h] is the LORD our God to help u and to fight our battles."[i] And the peop gained confidence from what Hezekia the king of Judah said.

[a] 4 Hebrew; Septuagint and Syriac *king* [b] 5 Or *the Millo*

31:16 *three years.* Although no ancient versions or manuscripts disagree with this figure, it may represent a copyist's error for "30 years," the age at which duties were assigned in the temple (1Ch 23:3).

31:20–21 Another brief indication of the Chronicler's emphasis on immediate retribution: Not only does disobedience bring immediate chastening, but obedience and seeking God bring prosperity.

32:1–23 The record of Sennacherib's invasion is much more detailed in 2 Kings and Isaiah (see note on 29:1—32:33).

32:1 The Chronicler omits the date of the invasion (701 B Hezekiah's 14th year; see 2Ki 18:13; Isa 36:1; see also cha p. 511).

32:2–8 Normal preparations for invasion.

32:3–4 See v. 30.

32:9 The Chronicler omits 2Ki 18:14–16, which records Hez kiah's suit for peace with its accompanying bribe strippe from the temple treasures. These acts were apparently o of accord with the Chronicler's portrait of Hezekiah. He als omits 2Ki 18:17b–18.

[9]Later, when Sennacherib king of Assyr-
ı and all his forces were laying siege to
achish,[j] he sent his officers to Jerusalem
'ith this message for Hezekiah king of Ju-
ah and for all the people of Judah who
'ere there:

[10]"This is what Sennacherib king of
Assyria says: On what are you basing
your confidence,[k] that you remain in
Jerusalem under siege? [11]When Hezekiah says, 'The LORD our God will
save us from the hand of the king of
Assyria,' he is misleading[l] you, to let
you die of hunger and thirst. [12]Did
not Hezekiah himself remove this
god's high places and altars, saying
to Judah and Jerusalem, 'You must
worship before one altar[m] and burn
sacrifices on it'?

[13]"Do you not know what I and my
predecessors have done to all the peoples of the other lands? Were the gods
of those nations ever able to deliver
their land from my hand?[n] [14]Who of
all the gods of these nations that my
predecessors destroyed has been able
to save his people from me? How
then can your god deliver you from
my hand? [15]Now do not let Hezekiah deceive[o] you and mislead you like
this. Do not believe him, for no god of
any nation or kingdom has been able
to deliver[p] his people from my hand
or the hand of my predecessors.[q] How
much less will your god deliver you
from my hand!"

[16]Sennacherib's officers spoke further
against the LORD God and against his servant Hezekiah. [17]The king also wrote letters[r] ridiculing[s] the LORD, the God of Israel,
and saying this against him: "Just as the
gods[t] of the peoples of the other lands did
not rescue their people from my hand, so
the god of Hezekiah will not rescue his
people from my hand." [18]Then they called
out in Hebrew to the people of Jerusalem

32:9 [j]S Jos 10:3, 31 **32:10** [k]Eze 29:16 **32:11** [l]Isa 37:10 **32:12** [m]S 2Ch 31:1 **32:13** [n]ver 15 **32:15** [o]Isa 37:10 [p]Da 3:15 [q]Ex 5:2 **32:17** [r]Isa 37:14 [s]Ps 74:22; Isa 37:4, 17 [t]S 2Ki 19:12

:10 The Chronicler omits 2Ki 18:20 – 21 (and Isa 36:5 – 6), ›ntaining a portion of the Assyrian commander's speech diculing Hezekiah and the citizens of Jerusalem for trust- g in Egypt and the pharaoh. This, too, may be theologically otivated, in light of the Chronicler's attitude toward foreign iances (see note on 16:2 – 9). The same concern with for- gn alliances is also likely the reason for the omission of the aterial in 2Ki 18:23 – 27 (and Isa 36:8 – 12), where mention is again made of the hope of Egyptian intervention (see 2Ki 19:9 for the incursion of Tirhakah).

32:16 *spoke further.* The Chronicler appears to assume his reader's familiarity with the longer account of the Assyrian taunts found in Kings and Isaiah.

32:18 *called out in Hebrew.* Assumes knowledge of the fuller story (2Ki 18:26 – 28; Isa 36:11 – 13).

nnacherib watching over the exile of Lachish. These scenes were found in Sennacherib's palace in ineveh (seventh century BC).

adovan/www.BibleLandPictures.com

who were on the wall, to terrify them and
make them afraid in order to capture the
city. 19 They spoke about the God of Jerusalem as they did about the gods of the
other peoples of the world — the work of
human hands.[u]
20 King Hezekiah and the prophet Isaiah
son of Amoz cried out in prayer[v] to heaven
about this. 21 And the LORD sent an angel,[w]
who annihilated all the fighting men and
the commanders and officers in the camp
of the Assyrian king. So he withdrew to
his own land in disgrace. And when he
went into the temple of his god, some of
his sons, his own flesh and blood, cut him
down with the sword.[x]
22 So the LORD saved Hezekiah and the
people of Jerusalem from the hand of
Sennacherib king of Assyria and from the
hand of all others. He took care of them[a]
on every side. 23 Many brought offerings
to Jerusalem for the LORD and valuable
gifts[y] for Hezekiah king of Judah. From
then on he was highly regarded by all the
nations.

Hezekiah's Pride, Success and Death

32:24-33pp — 2Ki 20:1-21; Isa 37:21-38; 38:1-8

24 In those days Hezekiah became ill
and was at the point of death. He prayed
to the LORD, who answered him and gave
him a miraculous sign.[z] 25 But Hezekiah's
heart was proud[a] and he did not respond
to the kindness shown him; therefore the
LORD's wrath[b] was on him and on Judah
and Jerusalem. 26 Then Hezekiah repented[c]
of the pride of his heart, as did the people
of Jerusalem; therefore the LORD's wrath
did not come on them during the days of
Hezekiah.[d]

32:19 [u] Ps 115:4-8; Isa 2:8; 17:8; 37:19; Jer 1:16
32:20 [v] Isa 1:15; 37:15
32:21 [w] S Ge 19:13 [x] S 2Ki 19:7; Isa 37:7, 38; Jer 41:2
32:23 [y] S 1Sa 10:27; S 2Ch 9:24; Ps 68:18, 29; 76:11; Isa 16:1; 18:7; 45:14; Zep 3:10; Zec 14:16-17
32:24 [z] ver 31
32:25 [a] S 2Ki 14:10 [b] S 2Ch 19:2
32:26 [c] Jer 26:18-19 [d] 2Ch 34:27, 28; Isa 39:8
32:27 [e] S 1Ch 29:12; S 2Ch 9:24
32:29 [f] Isa 39:2
32:30 [g] S 2Ki 18:17 [h] S 1Ki 1:33 [i] S 2Sa 5:8
32:31 [j] Isa 13:1; 39:1 [k] S ver 24; Isa 38:7 [l] S Ge 22:1; Dt 8:16
33:1 [m] S 1Ch 3:13
33:2 [n] Jer 15:4

27 Hezekiah had very great wealth an
honor,[e] and he made treasuries for his si
ver and gold and for his precious stone
spices, shields and all kinds of valuable
28 He also made buildings to store the ha
vest of grain, new wine and olive oil; an
he made stalls for various kinds of cattl
and pens for the flocks. 29 He built village
and acquired great numbers of flocks an
herds, for God had given him very grea
riches.[f]
30 It was Hezekiah who blocked[g] the up
per outlet of the Gihon[h] spring and cha
neled[i] the water down to the west side
the City of David. He succeeded in every
thing he undertook. 31 But when envoy
were sent by the rulers of Babylon[j] to as
him about the miraculous sign[k] that ha
occurred in the land, God left him to tes
him and to know everything that was i
his heart.
32 The other events of Hezekiah's reig
and his acts of devotion are written in th
vision of the prophet Isaiah son of Amo
in the book of the kings of Judah and I
rael. 33 Hezekiah rested with his ance
tors and was buried on the hill where th
tombs of David's descendants are. All J
dah and the people of Jerusalem honore
him when he died. And Manasseh his so
succeeded him as king.

Manasseh King of Judah

33:1-10pp — 2Ki 21:1-10
33:18-20pp — 2Ki 21:17-18

33 Manasseh[m] was twelve years o
when he became king, and h
reigned in Jerusalem fifty-five year
2 He did evil in the eyes of the LORD,[n] fo

[a] 22 Hebrew; Septuagint and Vulgate *He gave them res*

32:20 This brief reference to the prayers of Hezekiah and Isaiah abridges the much longer narrative in 2Ki 19:1 – 34 (and Isa 37:1 – 35).

32:21 See 2Ki 19:35 – 37; Isa 37:36 – 38. The Chronicler and the parallel accounts telescope events somewhat: Sennacherib's invasion of Judah was in 701 BC, while his death at the hand of his sons was in 681.

32:23 *highly regarded by all the nations.* Another effort to compare Hezekiah with Solomon (see 9:23 – 24).

32:24 The Chronicler again abridges the narrative in 2Ki 20:1 – 11 (and Isa 38:1 – 8), assuming the reader's familiarity with the role of Isaiah and the miraculous sign of the shadow reversing ten steps.

32:25 – 30 Not found in the parallel texts.

32:25 – 26 *proud … pride.* The Chronicler does not specify the nature of Hezekiah's pride (however, see v. 31; 2Ki 20:12 – 13; Isa 39:1 – 2). Even for a second Solomon like Hezekiah, disobedience brings anger from the Lord.

32:27 – 29 The Chronicler likens Hezekiah to Solomon also by recounting his wealth (9:13 – 14).

32:30 See vv. 2 – 4; 2Ki 20:20.

32:31 See v. 25. The Chronicler assumes the reader's knowledge of the fuller account in 2Ki 20:12 – 19 (and Isa 39:1 – 8). The envoys from Babylon were apparently interested in joi efforts against the Assyrians, hoping to open two fron against them simultaneously.

33:1 – 20 See 2Ki 21:1 – 18 and notes. Manasseh h the longest reign of any of the kings of Judah, a total 55 years (v. 1). The emphasis in the two accounts differs: Wh both histories report at length the evil done in Manasse reign, only the Chronicler mentions his journey to Babyl and his repentance and restoration to rule. For the writer Kings, the picture is only a bad one in which Manasseh cou be considered almost single-handedly the cause of the ex (2Ki 21:10 – 15; 23:26). Some interpreters regard the reco of Manasseh's repentance in Chronicles as motivated by t author's emphasis on immediate retribution: Length of rei is viewed as a blessing for obedience, so that the Chronic deliberately records some good in Manasseh as a ground his long reign. However, it must be noted that length of rei is not elsewhere used by the Chronicler as an indication divine blessing. The usual indicators for such blessing in account are peace and prosperity, building projects, succe in warfare and large families.

33:1 *fifty-five years.* 697 – 642 BC.

ɔwing the detestable[o] practices of the
ıations the LORD had driven out before
he Israelites. 3He rebuilt the high places
is father Hezekiah had demolished; he
lso erected altars to the Baals and made
ısherah poles.[p] He bowed down[q] to all
he starry hosts and worshiped them. 4He
uilt altars in the temple of the LORD, of
vhich the LORD had said, "My Name[r] will
emain in Jerusalem forever." 5In both
ourts of the temple of the LORD,[s] he built
ltars to all the starry hosts. 6He sacri-
ced his children[t] in the fire in the Valley
f Ben Hinnom, practiced divination and
itchcraft, sought omens, and consulted
ıediums[u] and spiritists.[v] He did much
vil in the eyes of the LORD, arousing his
nger.
7He took the image he had made and
ut it in God's temple,[w] of which God had
aid to David and to his son Solomon,
In this temple and in Jerusalem, which
have chosen out of all the tribes of Is-
ıel, I will put my Name forever. 8I will
ot again make the feet of the Israelites
ave the land[x] I assigned to your ances-
ırs, if only they will be careful to do ev-
rything I commanded them concerning
l the laws, decrees and regulations given
ırough Moses." 9But Manasseh led Ju-
ah and the people of Jerusalem astray,
ɔ that they did more evil than the na-
ons the LORD had destroyed before the
raelites.[y]
10The LORD spoke to Manasseh and his
eople, but they paid no attention. 11So
e LORD brought against them the army
ɔmmanders of the king of Assyria, who
ɔok Manasseh prisoner,[z] put a hook[a] in
is nose, bound him with bronze shack-
s[b] and took him to Babylon. 12In his dis-
ess he sought the favor of the LORD his
od and humbled[c] himself greatly before
the God of his ancestors. 13And when he
prayed to him, the LORD was moved by his
entreaty and listened to his plea; so he
brought him back to Jerusalem and to his
kingdom. Then Manasseh knew that the
LORD is God.
14Afterward he rebuilt the outer wall
of the City of David, west of the Gihon[d]
spring in the valley, as far as the entrance
of the Fish Gate[e] and encircling the hill of
Ophel;[f] he also made it much higher. He
stationed military commanders in all the
fortified cities in Judah.
15He got rid of the foreign gods and
removed[g] the image from the temple of
the LORD, as well as all the altars he had
built on the temple hill and in Jerusalem; and he threw them out of the city.
16Then he restored the altar of the LORD
and sacrificed fellowship offerings and
thank offerings[h] on it, and told Judah to
serve the LORD, the God of Israel. 17The
people, however, continued to sacrifice at
the high places, but only to the LORD their
God.
18The other events of Manasseh's
reign, including his prayer to his God
and the words the seers spoke to him in
the name of the LORD, the God of Israel,
are written in the annals of the kings of
Israel.[a] 19His prayer and how God was
moved by his entreaty, as well as all his
sins and unfaithfulness, and the sites
where he built high places and set up
Asherah poles and idols before he humbled[i] himself—all these are written in the
records of the seers.[b][j] 20Manasseh rested
with his ancestors and was buried[k] in his
palace. And Amon his son succeeded him
as king.

33:2 [o] S Dt 18:9 **33:3** [p] Dt 16:21-22; S 2Ch 24:18 [q] Dt 17:3 **33:4** [r] 2Ch 7:16 **33:5** [s] S 2Ch 4:9 **33:6** [t] S Lev 18:21; S Dt 18:10 [u] S Ex 22:18; S Lev 19:31 [v] S 1Sa 28:13 **33:7** [w] S 2Ch 7:16 **33:8** [x] S 2Sa 7:10 **33:9** [y] Jer 15:4; Eze 5:7 **33:11** [z] S Dt 28:36 [a] S 2Ki 19:28; Isa 37:29; Eze 29:4; 38:4; Am 4:2 [b] Ps 149:8 **33:12** [c] S 2Ch 6:37 **33:14** [d] S 1Ki 1:33 [e] Ne 3:3; 12:39; Zep 1:10 [f] 2Ch 27:3; Ne 3:26 **33:15** [g] 2Ki 23:12 **33:16** [h] Lev 7:11-18 **33:19** [i] S 2Ch 6:37 [j] 2Ki 21:17 **33:20** [k] 2Ki 21:18; S 2Ch 21:20

[a] *18* That is, Judah, as frequently in 2 Chronicles
[b] *19* One Hebrew manuscript and Septuagint; most Hebrew manuscripts *of Hozai*

:3,19 *Asherah poles.* See note on Ex 34:13.
:4 *My Name will remain in Jerusalem forever.* See 1Ki 3:2 and ›te; 9:3; Ps 132:13–14.
:6 *sacrificed his children … Valley of Ben Hinnom.* See 28:3 ıd note.
:10 See note on vv. 1–20. The Chronicler abridges what e Lord said to Manasseh and the people through the ophets; the fuller record is found in 2Ki 21:10–15.
33:11–17 Unique to the Chronicler, showing his stress on immediate retribution: Manasseh's ʼil brings invasion and defeat, while his repentance brings storation to rule.
33:11 *took him to Babylon.* In extant non-Biblical records there is no reference as yet to Manasseh being ken to Babylon by an Assyrian king. Esarhaddon (681–669 :) lists him among 22 kings required to forward materials r his building projects, and Ashurbanipal (669–627) names m as one of a number of vassals supporting his campaign ainst Egypt. The fact that an Assyrian king would have him ken to Babylon suggests that this incident may have taken ace during the rebellion of Shamash-Shum-Ukin against his brother and overlord Ashurbanipal. This rebellion lasted from 652 to 648, and Manasseh may have joined or at least have been suspected of assisting in the Babylonian defection from Assyria. Manasseh may have been found innocent, or he may have been pardoned on the basis of a renewed pledge of loyalty. Egypt had also bolted from the Assyrian yoke under the new Twenty-Sixth Dynasty, and the return of Manasseh to rule may reflect the Assyrian need of a vassal near the border of Egypt.
33:12 The language is reminiscent of Solomon's prayer (7:14).
33:14 *rebuilt the outer wall.* For the Chronicler such building programs are a sign of divine blessing (8:1–6; 11:5–12; 14:6–7; 26:9–10,14–15; 32:1–5, 27–30; 1Ch 11:7–9; 15:1).
33:15–16 Whatever the precise nature of Manasseh's reforms, Josiah would later still need to remove "the altars Manasseh had built in the two courts of the temple" (2Ki 23:12).
33:20 *buried in his palace.* Cf. 2Ki 21:18. His burial in the palace garden makes Manasseh the fifth king the Chronicler names who was not buried in the tombs of the kings (see note on 28:27).

Amon King of Judah

33:21-25pp — 2Ki 21:19-24

21 Amon[l] was twenty-two years old
when he became king, and he reigned in
Jerusalem two years. 22 He did evil in the
eyes of the LORD, as his father Manasseh
had done. Amon worshiped and offered
sacrifices to all the idols Manasseh had
made. 23 But unlike his father Manasseh,
he did not humble[m] himself before the
LORD; Amon increased his guilt.
24 Amon's officials conspired against
him and assassinated him in his palace.
25 Then the people[n] of the land killed all
who had plotted against King Amon, and
they made Josiah his son king in his place.

Josiah's Reforms

34:1-2pp — 2Ki 22:1-2
34:3-7Ref — 2Ki 23:4-20
34:8-13pp — 2Ki 22:3-7

34 Josiah[o] was eight years old when
he became king,[p] and he reigned in
Jerusalem thirty-one years. 2 He did what
was right in the eyes of the LORD and followed the ways of his father David,[q] not
turning aside to the right or to the left.
3 In the eighth year of his reign, while
he was still young, he began to seek the
God[r] of his father David. In his twelfth
year he began to purge Judah and Jerusalem of high places, Asherah poles and
idols. 4 Under his direction the altars of
the Baals were torn down; he cut to piec
es the incense altars that were abov
them, and smashed the Asherah poles
and the idols. These he broke to piece
and scattered over the graves of those wh
had sacrificed to them.[t] 5 He burned[u] th
bones of the priests on their altars, and s
he purged Judah and Jerusalem. 6 In th
towns of Manasseh, Ephraim and Sime
on, as far as Naphtali, and in the ruin
around them, 7 he tore down the altars an
the Asherah poles and crushed the idols t
powder[v] and cut to pieces all the incens
altars throughout Israel. Then he wen
back to Jerusalem.
8 In the eighteenth year of Josiah's reigr
to purify the land and the temple, he ser
Shaphan son of Azaliah and Maaseiah th
ruler of the city, with Joah son of Joaha
the recorder, to repair the temple of th
LORD his God.
9 They went to Hilkiah[w] the high pries
and gave him the money that had bee
brought into the temple of God, whic
the Levites who were the gatekeepers ha
collected from the people of Manassel
Ephraim and the entire remnant of Isr
el and from all the people of Judah an
Benjamin and the inhabitants of Jerus
lem. 10 Then they entrusted it to the me
appointed to supervise the work on th
LORD's temple. These men paid the wor
ers who repaired and restored the templ
11 They also gave money[x] to the carpente

33:21 [l] S 1Ch 3:14 **33:23** [m] S Ex 10:3; 2Ch 7:14; Ps 18:27; 147:6; Pr 3:34 **33:25** [n] S 2Ch 22:1 **34:1** [o] S 1Ch 3:14 [p] Zep 1:1 **34:2** [q] 2Ch 29:2 **34:3** [r] S 1Ch 16:11 **34:4** [s] S Ex 34:13 [t] Ex 32:20; S Lev 26:30; 2Ki 23:11; Mic 1:5 **34:5** [u] S 1Ki 13:2 **34:7** [v] S Ex 32:20 **34:9** [w] S 1Ch 6:13 **34:11** [x] 2Ch 24:12

33:21 – 25 See 2Ki 21:19 – 26. The Chronicler's account of the reign of Amon (642 – 640 BC) is quite similar to that in Kings, apart from (1) the additional note that Amon was not repentant like his father, Manasseh, a note based on a passage unique to the Chronicler (vv. 12 – 13), and (2) the absence of the death formula.

34:1 — 36:1 See 2Ki 22:1 — 23:30 and notes. Both accounts of Josiah's reign are about the same length and treat the same subjects, but with considerable variation in emphasis. Both deal with three different aspects of Josiah's reform: (1) the removal of foreign religions, (2) the finding of the Book of the Law and the covenant renewal that followed and (3) the celebration of Passover. On the second item the two histories are quite similar. On the first item the writer of Kings goes to great lengths (2Ki 23:4 – 20), while the Chronicler summarizes it only briefly (34:3 – 7,33). The account of the Passover is greatly expanded in Chronicles (35:1 – 19), while only alluded to in 2 Kings (23:21 – 23). Not only are these items treated at different lengths, but the order is also changed. In Kings the finding of the Book of the Law in the temple in Josiah's 18th year is the first incident mentioned. The writer appears to have organized his material geographically, i.e., beginning with the temple and spreading through the city, then into the rest of the nation. The Chronicler, on the other hand, has arranged the incidents in order of their occurrence and has characteristically introduced a number of chronological notes into the text: 34:3 (two notes without parallel in Kings); 34:8 (see 2Ki 22:3); 35:19 (see 2Ki 23:23; see also note on 2Ch 12:2). Chronicles makes it clear that the reform began in Josiah's 12th year (34:3), six years before the discovery of the Book of the Law.

34:1 – 2 See 2Ki 22:1 – 2.

34:1 *thirty-one years.* 640 – 609 BC.

34:3 – 7 The writer of Kings covers this aspect of Josia reform in much greater detail (2Ki 23:4 – 20). He also dela his account of the removal of pagan religions until after th discovery of the Book of the Law, while the Chronicler plac it before.

34:3 Some interpreters have sought to tie the events of J siah's 8th (v. 3), 12th (v. 3) and 18th (v. 8) years to stages the progressive decline and fall of the Assyrian Empire, whi had dominated the area for about two centuries. The demi of Assyrian control over Aram and Israel undoubtedly faci tated and encouraged Josiah's reassertion of Davidic autho ity over former Assyrian provinces (vv. 6 – 7). However, o must not undercut religious motives in Josiah's reforms. one does, the reform is reduced to a mere political rebellic *Asherah poles.* See note on Ex 34:13.

34:6 *Manasseh, Ephraim and Simeon, as far as Naphta* The Chronicler's concern for "all Israel" (see Introduction 1 Chronicles: Purpose and Themes) is apparent in his recor ing the involvement of the northern tribes in Josiah's refor (see also vv. 9,21,33). The Chronicler again shows all Isra united under a Davidic king, just as he did under Hezeki (see note on 30:1). *Simeon.* Some Simeonites must have m grated from Judah to the north.

34:7 *throughout Israel.* Defined by the list of tribes in v. 6.

34:8 – 21 See 2Ki 22:3 – 13 and notes.

34:9 *Manasseh, Ephraim and the entire remnant of Isra* Again as part of his concern with "all Israel," the Chronic notes that worshipers from the north also brought gifts the temple (not explicitly indicated in 2Ki 22:4).

34:10 – 13 Cf. 24:8 – 12.

and builders to purchase dressed stone, and timber for joists and beams for the buildings that the kings of Judah had allowed to fall into ruin.[y]

12The workers labored faithfully.[z] Over them to direct them were Jahath and Obadiah, Levites descended from Merari, and Zechariah and Meshullam, descended from Kohath. The Levites—all who were skilled in playing musical instruments—[a] 13had charge of the laborers[b] and supervised all the workers from job to job. Some of the Levites were secretaries, scribes and gatekeepers.

The Book of the Law Found

34:14-28pp — 2Ki 22:8-20
34:29-32pp — 2Ki 23:1-3

14While they were bringing out the money that had been taken into the temple of the LORD, Hilkiah the priest found the Book of the Law of the LORD that had been given through Moses. 15Hilkiah said to Shaphan the secretary, "I have found the Book of the Law[c] in the temple of the LORD." He gave it to Shaphan.

16Then Shaphan took the book to the king and reported to him: "Your officials are doing everything that has been committed to them. 17They have paid out the money that was in the temple of the LORD and have entrusted it to the supervisors and workers." 18Then Shaphan the secretary informed the king, "Hilkiah the priest has given me a book." And Shaphan read from it in the presence of the king.

19When the king heard the words of the Law,[d] he tore[e] his robes. 20He gave these orders to Hilkiah, Ahikam son of Shaphan[f], Abdon son of Micah,[a] Shaphan the secretary and Asaiah the king's attendant: 21"Go and inquire of the LORD for me and for the remnant in Israel and Judah about what is written in this book that has been found. Great is the LORD's anger that is poured out[g] on us because those who have gone before us have not kept the word of the LORD; they have not acted in accordance with all that is written in this book."

22Hilkiah and those the king had sent with him[b] went to speak to the prophet[h] Huldah, who was the wife of Shallum son of Tokhath,[c] the son of Hasrah,[d] keeper of the wardrobe. She lived in Jerusalem, in the New Quarter.

23She said to them, "This is what the LORD, the God of Israel, says: Tell the man who sent you to me, 24'This is what the LORD says: I am going to bring disaster[i] on this place and its people[j]—all the curses[k] written in the book that has been read in the presence of the king of Judah. 25Because they have forsaken me[l] and burned incense to other gods and aroused my anger by all that their hands have made,[e] my anger will be poured out on this place and will not be quenched.' 26Tell the king of Judah, who sent you to inquire of the LORD, 'This is what the LORD, the God of Israel, says concerning the words you heard: 27Because your heart was responsive[m] and you humbled[n] yourself before God when you heard what he spoke against this place and its people, and because you humbled yourself before me and tore your robes and wept in my presence, I have heard you, declares the LORD. 28Now I will gather you to your ancestors,[o] and you will be buried in peace. Your eyes will not see all the disaster I am going to bring on this place and on those who live here.'"[p]

So they took her answer back to the king.

29Then the king called together all the elders of Judah and Jerusalem. 30He went up to the temple of the LORD[q] with the people of Judah, the inhabitants of Jerusalem, the priests and the Levites—all the people from the least to the greatest. He read in their hearing all the words of the Book of the Covenant, which had been found in the temple of the LORD. 31The king stood by his pillar[r] and renewed the covenant[s] in the presence of the LORD—to follow[t] the LORD and keep his commands, statutes and decrees with all his heart and all his soul, and to obey the words of the covenant written in this book.

32Then he had everyone in Jerusalem and Benjamin pledge themselves to it; the people of Jerusalem did this in accordance with the covenant of God, the God of their ancestors.

33Josiah removed all the detestable[u] idols from all the territory belonging to the Israelites, and he had all who were present in Israel serve the LORD their God. As long as he lived, they did not fail to follow the LORD, the God of their ancestors.

34:11 [y] 2Ch 33:4-7
34:12 [z] 2Ki 12:15 [a] S 1Ch 25:1
34:13 [b] S 1Ch 23:4
34:15 [c] S 2Ki 22:8; Ezr 7:6; Ne 8:1
34:19 [d] Dt 28:3-68 [e] Isa 36:22; 37:1
34:20 [f] S 2Ki 22:3
34:21 [g] La 2:4; 4:11; Eze 36:18
34:22 [h] S Ex 15:20; Ne 6:14
34:24 [i] Pr 16:4; Isa 3:9; Jer 40:2; 42:10; 44:2, 11 [j] 2Ch 36:14-20 [k] Dt 28:15-68
34:25 [l] 2Ch 33:3-6; Jer 22:9
34:27 [m] S 2Ch 32:26 [n] S Ex 10:3; S 2Ch 6:37
34:28 [o] 2Ch 35:20-25 [p] S 2Ch 32:26
34:30 [q] S 2Ki 23:2
34:31 [r] S 1Ki 7:15 [s] S 2Ki 11:17; S 2Ch 23:16 [t] S Dt 13:4
34:33 [u] S Dt 18:9

[a] *20* Also called *Akbor son of Micaiah*
[b] *22* One Hebrew manuscript, Vulgate and Syriac; most Hebrew manuscripts do not have *had sent with him.*
[c] *22* Also called *Tikvah* [d] *22* Also called *Harhas*
[e] *25* Or *by everything they have done*

34:14 *Book of the Law of the LORD.* See note on 17:9.
34:22–28 See 2Ki 22:14–20 and notes.
34:22 *prophet Huldah.* See note on 2Ki 22:14.
34:28 *will be buried in peace.* See the death and burial account (35:20–25).
34:29–31 See 2Ki 23:1–3 and notes.
34:30 *the priests and the Levites.* Cf. 2Ki 23:2, which has "the priests and the prophets."
34:33 *all the territory belonging to the Israelites ... all who were present in Israel.* See note on v. 6.

Josiah Celebrates the Passover

35:1,18-19pp — 2Ki 23:21-23

35 Josiah celebrated the Passover[v] to the LORD in Jerusalem, and the Passover lamb was slaughtered on the fourteenth day of the first month. 2 He appointed the priests to their duties and encouraged them in the service of the LORD's temple. 3 He said to the Levites, who instructed[w] all Israel and who had been consecrated to the LORD: "Put the sacred ark in the temple that Solomon son of David king of Israel built. It is not to be carried about on your shoulders. Now serve the LORD your God and his people Israel. 4 Prepare yourselves by families in your divisions,[x] according to the instructions written by David king of Israel and by his son Solomon.

5 "Stand in the holy place with a group of Levites for each subdivision of the families of your fellow Israelites, the lay people. 6 Slaughter the Passover lambs, consecrate yourselves[y] and prepare the lambs for your fellow Israelites, doing what the LORD commanded through Moses."

7 Josiah provided for all the lay people who were there a total of thirty thousand lambs and goats for the Passover offerings,[z] and also three thousand cattle — all from the king's own possessions.[a]

8 His officials also contributed[b] voluntarily to the people and the priests and Levites. Hilkiah,[c] Zechariah and Jehiel, the officials in charge of God's temple, gave the priests twenty-six hundred Passover offerings and three hundred cattle. 9 Also Konaniah[d] along with Shemaiah and Nethanel, his brothers, and Hashabiah, Jeiel and Jozabad,[e] the leaders of the Levites, provided five thousand Passover offerings and five hundred head of cattle for the Levites.

10 The service was arranged and the priests stood in their places with the Levites in their divisions[f] as the king had ordered.[g] 11 The Passover lambs were slaughtered,[h] and the priests splashed against the altar the blood handed to them, while the Levites skinned the animals. 12 They set aside the burnt offerings to give them to the subdivisions of the families of the people to offer to the LORD, as it is written in the Book of Moses. They did the same with the cattle. 13 They roasted the Passover animals over the fire as prescribed,[i] and boiled the holy offerings in pots, caldrons and pans and served them quickly to all the people. 14 After this, they made preparations for themselves and for the priests, because the priests, the descendants of Aaron, were sacrificing the burnt offerings and the fat portions[j] until nightfall. So the Levites made preparations for themselves and for the Aaronic priests.

15 The musicians,[k] the descendants of Asaph, were in the places prescribed by David, Asaph, Heman and Jeduthun the king's seer. The gatekeepers at each gate did not need to leave their posts, because their fellow Levites made the preparations for them.

16 So at that time the entire service of the LORD was carried out for the celebration of the Passover and the offering of burnt offerings on the altar of the LORD, as King Josiah had ordered. 17 The Israelites who were present celebrated the Passover at that time and observed the Festival of Unleavened Bread for seven days. 18 The Passover had not been observed like this in Israel since the days of the prophet Samuel; and none of the kings of Israel had ever celebrated such a Passover as did Josiah, with the priests, the Levites and all Judah and Israel who were there with the people of Jerusalem. 19 This Passover was celebrated in the eighteenth year of Josiah's reign.

The Death of Josiah

35:20–36:1pp — 2Ki 23:28-30

20 After all this, when Josiah had set the temple in order, Necho king of Egypt went up to fight at Carchemish[l] on the Euphrates,[m] and Josiah marched out to meet him in battle. 21 But Necho sent messengers to

35:1 [v] Ex 12:1-30; S Nu 28:16
35:3 [w] S 2Ch 17:7
35:4 [x] ver 10; S 1Ch 24:1; Ezr 6:18
35:6 [y] S Lev 11:44
35:7 [z] S 2Ch 30:24 [a] S 2Ch 31:3
35:8 [b] S 1Ch 29:3; 2Ch 29:31-36 [c] S 1Ch 6:13
35:9 [d] 2Ch 31:12 [e] 2Ch 31:13
35:10 [f] S ver 4 [g] 2Ch 30:16
35:11 [h] S 2Ch 30:17
35:13 [i] Ex 12:2-11
35:14 [j] S Ex 29:13
35:15 [k] S 1Ch 25:1; S 26:12-19; 2Ch 29:30; Ne 12:46; Ps 68:25
35:20 [l] Isa 10:9; Jer 46:2 [m] S Ge 2:14

35:1 – 19 The Chronicler gives much more extensive coverage to Josiah's Passover celebration than is found in the brief allusion in Kings (2Ki 23:21 – 23).
35:1 *first month.* The traditional month; contrast the Passover of Hezekiah (see note on 30:2).
35:3 *Put the sacred ark in the temple.* Implies that it had been removed, perhaps for protection during the evil reigns of Manasseh and Amon, who preceded Josiah.
35:4 *David ... Solomon.* The Chronicler specifically parallels David and Solomon in three cases: 7:10 (contrast 1Ki 8:66, where only David is mentioned); 11:17; and here. This tendency reflects his glorification and idealization of both (see Introduction to 1 Chronicles: Portrait of David and Solomon).
35:7 – 9 The emphasis in Chronicles on voluntary and joyful giving (24:8 – 14; 29:31 – 36; 31:3 – 21; 1Ch 29:3 – 9) presumably had direct relevance to the postexilic readers for whom the Chronicler wrote.
35:18 *since the days of the prophet Samuel.* Instead of "in the days of the judges" (2Ki 23:22). This is the Chronicler's way of highlighting the importance of the prophets (see Introduction to 1 Chronicles: Purpose and Themes, 3).
35:19 *eighteenth year.* The same year as the discovery of the Book of the Law (34:8,14).
35:20 – 27 See 2Ki 23:28 – 30. In 609 BC Pharaoh Necho "went up to the Euphrates River to help the king of Assyria" (2Ki 23:29) against the Babylonians.
35:21 – 22 Unique to the Chronicler, showing his view on retribution once again: Josiah's death in battle comes as a result of his disobedience to the word of God as heard even in the mouth of the pagan pharaoh.

him, saying, "What quarrel is there, king
of Judah, between you and me? It is not
you I am attacking at this time, but the
house with which I am at war. God has
told[n] me to hurry; so stop opposing God,
who is with me, or he will destroy you."
22 Josiah, however, would not turn away
from him, but disguised[o] himself to engage
him in battle. He would not listen to what
Necho had said at God's command but
went to fight him on the plain of Megiddo.
23 Archers[p] shot King Josiah, and he told
his officers, "Take me away; I am badly wounded." 24 So they took him out of
his chariot, put him in his other chariot
and brought him to Jerusalem, where he
died. He was buried in the tombs of his
ancestors, and all Judah and Jerusalem
mourned for him.
25 Jeremiah composed laments for Josiah, and to this day all the male and female singers commemorate Josiah in the
laments.[q] These became a tradition in Israel and are written in the Laments.[r]
26 The other events of Josiah's reign and
his acts of devotion in accordance with
what is written in the Law of the LORD—
27 all the events, from beginning to end, are
written in the book of the kings of Israel

36 and Judah. 1 And the people[s] of the
land took Jehoahaz son of Josiah
and made him king in Jerusalem in place
of his father.

Jehoahaz King of Judah

36:2-4pp — 2Ki 23:31-34

2 Jehoahaz[a] was twenty-three years old
when he became king, and he reigned
in Jerusalem three months. 3 The king of
Egypt dethroned him in Jerusalem and
imposed on Judah a levy of a hundred talents[b] of silver and a talent[c] of gold. 4 The
king of Egypt made Eliakim, a brother of
Jehoahaz, king over Judah and Jerusalem
and changed Eliakim's name to Jehoiakim. But Necho[t] took Eliakim's brother
Jehoahaz and carried him off to Egypt.[u]

Jehoiakim King of Judah

36:5-8pp — 2Ki 23:36 – 24:6

5 Jehoiakim[v] was twenty-five years old
when he became king, and he reigned in
Jerusalem eleven years. He did evil in the
eyes of the LORD his God. 6 Nebuchadnezzar[w] king of Babylon attacked him and
bound him with bronze shackles to take
him to Babylon.[x] 7 Nebuchadnezzar also
took to Babylon articles from the temple
of the LORD and put them in his temple[d]
there.[y]
8 The other events of Jehoiakim's reign,
the detestable things he did and all that
was found against him, are written in the
book of the kings of Israel and Judah. And
Jehoiachin his son succeeded him as king.

Jehoiachin King of Judah

36:9-10pp — 2Ki 24:8-17

9 Jehoiachin[z] was eighteen[e] years old
when he became king, and he reigned
in Jerusalem three months and ten days.
He did evil in the eyes of the LORD. 10 In

35:21 [n] S 1Ki 13:18; S 2Ki 18:25 **35:22** [o] S 1Sa 28:8 **35:23** [p] S 1Ki 22:34 **35:25** [q] S Ge 50:10; Jer 22:10,15-16 [r] 2Ch 34:28 **36:1** [s] S 2Ch 22:1
36:4 [t] Jer 22:10-12 [u] Eze 19:4 **36:5** [v] Jer 22:18; 25:1; 26:1; 35:1; 36:1; 45:1; 46:2 **36:6** [w] Jer 25:9; 27:6; Eze 29:18 [x] Eze 19:9; Da 1:1 **36:7** [y] ver 18; Ezr 1:7; Jer 27:16; Da 1:2 **36:9** [z] Jer 22:24-28; 24:1; 27:20; 29:21; 52:31

[a] 2 Hebrew *Joahaz,* a variant of *Jehoahaz;* also in verse 4 [b] 3 That is, about 3 3/4 tons or about 3.4 metric tons [c] 3 That is, about 75 pounds or about 34 kilograms [d] 7 Or *palace* [e] 9 One Hebrew manuscript, some Septuagint manuscripts and Syriac (see also 2 Kings 24:8); most Hebrew manuscripts *eight*

35:21 *house with which I am at war.* A reference to the Babylonians; Nabopolassar was on the throne of Babylon, while his son Nebuchadnezzar was commanding the armies in the field. Nebuchadnezzar would succeed his father after another battle at Carchemish against Egypt in 605 BC. Josiah may have been an ally of Babylon (see 32:31; 33:11 and notes).
35:22 *disguised himself.* Cf. Ahab and Jehoshaphat (see 18:29 and note). *plain of Megiddo.* See note on Jdg 5:19.
35:24b – 25 Unique to Chronicles.
35:25 *Jeremiah composed laments for Josiah.* Jeremiah held Josiah in high esteem (Jer 22:15 – 16). The statement that he composed laments is one of the reasons the book of Lamentations has been traditionally associated with him. *to this day.* See note on 5:9.
36:2 – 14 Josiah is the only king of Judah to be succeeded by three of his sons (Jehoahaz, Jehoiakim and Zedekiah). The Chronicler's account of the reigns of the remaining kings of Judah is quite brief.
36:2 See 2Ki 23:31 – 35. With the death of Josiah at the hands of Pharaoh Necho, Judah slipped into a period of Egyptian domination (vv. 3 – 4). *three months.* In 609 BC. Necho's assertion of authority over Judah ended the brief 20 years of Judahite independence under Josiah. The Chronicler makes no moral judgment on this brief reign, though the author of Kings does (2Ki 23:32).
36:4 Just as Necho took Jehoahaz into captivity and replaced him with Eliakim, whose name he changed to Jehoiakim, so also Nebuchadnezzar would later take Jehoiachin to Babylon, replacing him with Mattaniah, whose name he changed to Zedekiah (2Ki 24:15 – 17). Each conqueror wanted to place his own man on the throne; the change of name implied authority over him.
36:5 – 8 See 2Ki 23:36 — 24:7. Jehoiakim persecuted the prophets and is the object of scathing denunciation by Jeremiah (Jer 25 – 26; 36). After the Egyptian defeat at Carchemish (Jer 46:2) in 605 BC, Jehoiakim transferred allegiance to Nebuchadnezzar of Babylon. When he later rebelled and again allied himself with Egypt, Nebuchadnezzar sent a punitive army against him. But Jehoiakim died before the army arrived, and Nebuchadnezzar took his son Jehoiachin into captivity.
36:5 *eleven years.* 609 – 598 BC.
36:6 *Nebuchadnezzar … attacked him.* See chart, p. 511.
36:9 – 10 See 2Ki 24:8 – 17; see also Jer 22:24 – 28; 24:1; 29:2; 52:31. Although Jehoiachin was taken into captivity (597 BC) with a large retinue, including the queen mother and high officials, and was succeeded by Zedekiah, the exiles continued to date in terms of their reign (Jer 52:31; Eze 1:2; cf. Est 2:5 – 6).
36:9 *three months and ten days.* 598 – 597 BC.

the spring, King Nebuchadnezzar sent for
him and brought him to Babylon,[a] together with articles of value from the temple
of the LORD, and he made Jehoiachin's uncle,[a] Zedekiah, king over Judah and Jerusalem.

Zedekiah King of Judah

36:11-16pp — 2Ki 24:18-20; Jer 52:1-3

11 Zedekiah[b] was twenty-one years old
when he became king, and he reigned in
Jerusalem eleven years. 12 He did evil in the
eyes of the LORD[c] his God and did not humble[d] himself before Jeremiah the prophet,
who spoke the word of the LORD. 13 He also
rebelled against King Nebuchadnezzar,
who had made him take an oath[e] in God's
name. He became stiff-necked[f] and hardened his heart and would not turn to the
LORD, the God of Israel. 14 Furthermore, all
the leaders of the priests and the people
became more and more unfaithful,[g] following all the detestable practices of the nations and defiling the temple of the LORD,
which he had consecrated in Jerusalem.

The Fall of Jerusalem

36:17-20pp — 2Ki 25:1-21; Jer 52:4-27
36:22-23pp — Ezr 1:1-3

15 The LORD, the God of their ancestors,
sent word to them through his messengers[h] again and again,[i] because he had
pity on his people and on his dwelling
place. 16 But they mocked God's messengers, despised his words and scoffed[j] at his
prophets until the wrath[k] of the LORD was
aroused against his people and there was
no remedy.[l] 17 He brought up against them
the king of the Babylonians,[bm] who killed
their young men with the sword in the
sanctuary, and did not spare young men[n]
or young women, the elderly or the infirm.[o] God gave them all into the hands of
Nebuchadnezzar.[p] 18 He carried to Babylon
all the articles[q] from the temple of God,
both large and small, and the treasures of
the LORD's temple and the treasures of the
king and his officials. 19 They set fire[r] to
God's temple[s] and broke down the wall[t]
of Jerusalem; they burned all the palaces
and destroyed[u] everything of value there.[v]
20 He carried into exile[w] to Babylon the
remnant, who escaped from the sword,
and they became servants[x] to him and
his successors until the kingdom of Persia
came to power. 21 The land enjoyed its sabbath rests;[y] all the time of its desolation it
rested,[z] until the seventy years[a] were completed in fulfillment of the word of the
LORD spoken by Jeremiah.
22 In the first year of Cyrus[b] king of Persia, in order to fulfill the word of the LORD
spoken by Jeremiah, the LORD moved the
heart of Cyrus king of Persia to make a
proclamation throughout his realm and
also to put it in writing:

23 "This is what Cyrus king of Persia
says:
" 'The LORD, the God of heaven,
has given me all the kingdoms of the
earth and he has appointed[c] me to
build a temple for him at Jerusalem in
Judah. Any of his people among you
may go up, and may the LORD their
God be with them.' "

36:10 [a] ver 18; S 2Ki 20:17; Ezr 1:7; Isa 52:11; Jer 14:18; 21:7; 22:25; 24:1; 27:16, 20, 22; 29:1; 34:21; 40:1; Eze 17:12; Da 5:2 **36:11** [b] S 2Ki 24:17; Jer 27:1; 28:1; 34:2; 37:1; 39:1 **36:12** [c] Jer 37:1-39:18 [d] S Dt 8:3; 2Ch 7:14; Jer 44:10 **36:13** [e] Eze 17:13 [f] S Ex 32:9; S Dt 9:27 **36:14** [g] S 1Ch 5:25 **36:15** [h] Isa 5:4; 44:26; Jer 7:25; Hag 1:13; Zec 1:4; Mal 2:7; 3:1; S Mt 5:12 [i] Jer 7:13, 25; 11:7; 25:3-4; 35:14, 15; 44:4-6 **36:16** [j] S 2Ki 2:23; Job 8:2; Isa 28:14, 22; 29:20; 57:4; Jer 5:13; 43:2; Mic 2:11 [k] Ezr 5:12; Pr 1:30-31; Jer 44:3 [l] Ne 9:30; Pr 29:1; Jer 7:26; 20:8; 25:4; 30:12; Da 9:6; Zec 1:2 **36:17** [m] S Ge 10:10 [n] Jer 6:11; 9:21; 18:21; 44:7 [o] S Dt 32:25; Jer 51:22 [p] Ezr 5:12; Jer 32:28; La 2:21; Eze 9:6; 23:47

[a] *10* Hebrew *brother,* that is, relative (see 2 Kings 24:17)
[b] *17* Or *Chaldeans*

36:18 [q] S ver 7; S ver 10; Jer 27:20 **36:19** [r] Jer 11:16; 17:27; 21:10, 14; 22:7; 32:29; 39:8; La 4:11; Eze 20:47; Am 2:5; Zec 11:1 [s] 1Ki 9:8-9 [t] S 2Ki 14:13 [u] La 2:6 [v] Ps 79:1-3 **36:20** [w] S Lev 26:44; S 2Ki 24:14; Ezr 2:1; Ne 7:6 [x] Jer 27:7 **36:21** [y] S Lev 25:4 [z] S 1Ch 22:9 [a] Jer 1:1; 25:11; 27:22; 29:10; 40:1; Da 9:2; Zec 1:12; 7:5 **36:22** [b] Isa 44:28; 45:1, 13; Da 1:21; 6:28; 10:1 **36:23** [c] S Jdg 4:10

36:11 – 14 See 2Ki 24:18 – 20; Jer 52:1 – 3. Verses 13b – 14 are unique to the Chronicler (cf. Jer 1:3; 21:1 – 7; 24:8; 27:1 – 15; 32:1 – 5; 34:1 – 7,21; 37:1 — 39:7). Zedekiah succumbed to the temptation to look to Egypt for help and rebelled against Nebuchadnezzar. Babylonian reaction was swift. Jerusalem was besieged (Jer 21:3 – 7) in 588 BC and held out for over two years before being destroyed in the summer of 586.
36:11 *eleven years.* 597 – 586 BC.
36:15 – 16 See 24:19 and note.
36:20 – 21 The conclusions of the two Biblical histories are interestingly different: (1) The author(s) of Kings had sought to show why the exile occurred and had traced the sad history of Israel's disobedience to the exile. With the state at an end, the author(s) could still show God's faithfulness to his promises to David (2Ki 25:27 – 30) by reporting the favor bestowed on his descendants. (2) The Chronicler, whose vantage point was after the exile, was able to look back on the exile not only as judgment but also as containing hope for the future. For him the purified remnant had returned to a purified land (vv. 22 – 23), and a new era of hope was beginning. The exile was not judgment alone, but also blessing, for it allowed the land to catch up on its sabbath rests (Lev 26:40 – 45). And God had remembered his covenant (Lev 26:45) and restored his people to the land (see note on vv. 22 – 23).
36:22 – 23 Not found in Kings. It is repeated at the beginning of Ezra (1:1 – 3), which resumes the history at the point where Chronicles ends — indicating that Chronicles and Ezra may have been written by the same author. See the prophecy of Jeremiah (Jer 25:1 – 14; cf. Da 9). Cyrus also issued decrees for other captive peoples, allowing them to return to their lands. Under God's sovereignty, this effort by a Persian king to win the favor of peoples treated harshly by the Babylonians also inaugurated the restoration period. See notes on Ezr 1:1 – 4.
36:22 *Cyrus king of Persia.* See chart, p. 511.
36:23 *God of heaven.* See note on Ezr 1:2.

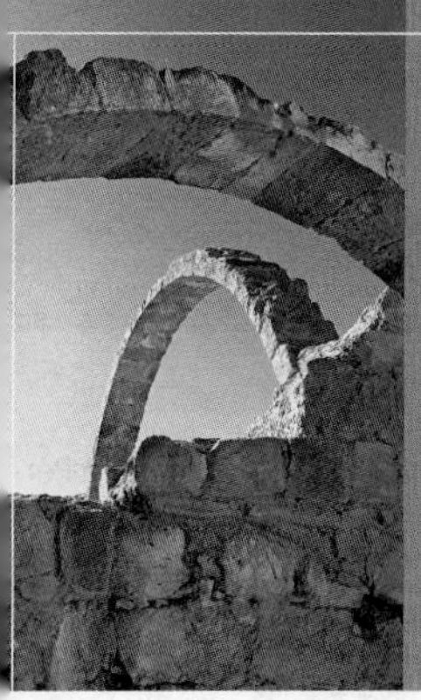

EZRA

INTRODUCTION

Ezra and Nehemiah

Although the caption to Ne 1:1, "The words of Nehemiah son of Hakaliah," indicates that Ezra and Nehemiah were originally two separate compositions, they were combined as one very early. Josephus (c. AD 37 – 100) and the Jewish Talmud refer to the book of Ezra but not to a separate book of Nehemiah. The oldest manuscripts of the Septuagint (the pre-Christian Greek translation of the OT) also treat Ezra and Nehemiah as one book, calling it Esdras B (Esdras A is an Apocryphal work).

Origen (c. AD 185 – 253) is the first writer known to distinguish between two books, which he called 1 Ezra and 2 Ezra. In translating the Latin Vulgate (c. AD 390 – 405), Jerome called Nehemiah the second book of Esdrae (Ezra). The English translations by Wycliffe (1382) and Coverdale (1535) called Ezra "I Esdras" and Nehemiah "II Esdras." The same separation first appeared in a Hebrew manuscript in 1448.

a quick look

Author:
Unknown; probably Ezra

Audience:
The people of Judah who had returned from exile in Babylonia

Date:
Sometime after 440 BC

Theme:
A remnant of the Israelites, who had been exiled to Babylonia, return to Judah and Jerusalem to rebuild the temple under God's direction.

Literary Form and Authorship

As in the closely related books of 1 and 2 Chronicles, one notes the prominence of various lists in Ezra and Nehemiah, which have evidently been obtained from official sources. Included are lists of (1) the temple articles (Ezr 1:9 – 11), (2) the returned exiles (Ezr 2, which is virtually the same as Ne 7:6 – 73), (3) the genealogy of Ezra (Ezr 7:1 – 5), (4) the heads of the clans (8:1 – 14), (5) those involved in mixed marriages (10:18 – 43), (6) those who helped rebuild the wall (Ne 3), (7) those who sealed the covenant (Ne 10:1 – 27), (8) residents of Jerusalem and other towns (Ne 11:3 – 36) and (9) priests and Levites (Ne 12:1 – 26).

Also included in Ezra are seven official documents or letters (all in Aramaic except the first, which is in Hebrew): (1) the decree of Cyrus (1:2 – 4), (2) the accusation of Rehum and others against the Jews (4:11 – 16), (3) the reply of Artaxerxes I (4:17 – 22), (4) the report from Tattenai (5:7 – 17), (5) the memorandum of Cyrus's decree (6:2b – 5), (6) Darius's reply to Tattenai (6:6 – 12) and (7) the authorization given by Artaxerxes I

Ezra and Nehemiah relate how God's covenant people were restored from Babylonian exile to the covenant land as a people under God's rule.

to Ezra (7:12 – 26). The documents are similar to contemporary non-Biblical documents of the Persian period.

Certain materials in Ezra are first-person extracts from his memoirs: 7:27 – 28; 8:1 – 34; 9. Other sections are written in the third person: 7:1 – 26; 10; see also Ne 8. Linguistic analysis has shown that the first-person and third-person extracts resemble each other, making it likely that the same author wrote both.

Most scholars conclude that the author/compiler of Ezra and Nehemiah was also the author of 1,2 Chronicles. This viewpoint is based on certain characteristics common to both Chronicles and Ezra-Nehemiah. The verses at the end of 2 Chronicles (2Ch 36:22 – 33) and at the beginning of Ezra (1:1 – 3a) are virtually identical. Both Chronicles and Ezra-Nehemiah exhibit a fondness for lists, for the description of religious festivals and for such phrases as "heads of families" and "the house of God." Especially striking in these books is the prominence of Levites and temple personnel. The words for "singer," "gatekeeper" and "temple servants" are used almost exclusively in Ezra-Nehemiah and Chronicles. See Introduction to 1 Chronicles: Author, Date and Sources.

Date

The Ezra memoirs (see note on 7:28) may be dated sometime after 440 BC and the Nehemiah memoirs sometime after 430. These were then combined with other materials somewhat later. See Introduction to 1 Chronicles: Author, Date and Sources.

The Order of Ezra and Nehemiah

According to the traditional view, Ezra arrived in Jerusalem in the seventh year (Ezr 7:8) of Artaxerxes I (458 BC), followed by Nehemiah, who arrived in the king's 20th year (444; Ne 2:1,11).

Some have proposed a reverse order in which Nehemiah arrived in 444 BC, while Ezra arrived in the seventh year of Artaxerxes II (398). By amending "seventh" (Ezr 7:8) to either "27th" or "37th," others place Ezra's arrival after Nehemiah's but still maintain that they were contemporaries.

These alternative views, however, present more problems than the traditional position. As the text stands, Ezra arrived before Nehemiah, and they are found together in Ne 8:9 (at the reading of the Law) and Ne 12:26,36 (at the dedication of the wall). See chart, p. 726; see also notes on Ne 1:1; 2:1.

Languages

Ezra and Nehemiah were written in a form of late Hebrew with the exception of Ezr 4:8 — 6:18; 7:12 – 26, which were written in Aramaic, the language of international diplomacy during the Persian period. Of these 67 Aramaic verses, 52 are in records or letters. Ezra evidently found these documents in Aramaic and copied them, inserting connecting verses in Aramaic.

Major Theological Themes

The books of Ezra and Nehemiah relate how God's covenant people were restored from Babylonian exile to the covenant land as a people under God's rule even while continuing under Gentile rule. The major theological themes of this account are:

(1) The restoration of Israel from exile was God's doing. He moved the hearts of Persian emperors and of the repatriates and those who supported them, raised up prophets to prod and support the repatriates, protected them on the way and delivered them from their opponents, stirred up Ezra and Nehemiah to perform their separate ministries, and prospered the rebuilding of the temple and Jerusalem.

(2) The restoration of the covenant community was complete — even though political independence was not attained. "All Israel" was repatriated through a representative remnant; the temple was rebuilt and its services (daily sacrifices, priestly ministries, Levitical praise, annual festivals) revived in accordance with the Law of Moses and the regulations instituted by David; the Law was reestablished as regulative for the life of the community; the "holy city" (Jerusalem) was rebuilt and inhabited; the people were purged; the covenant was renewed.

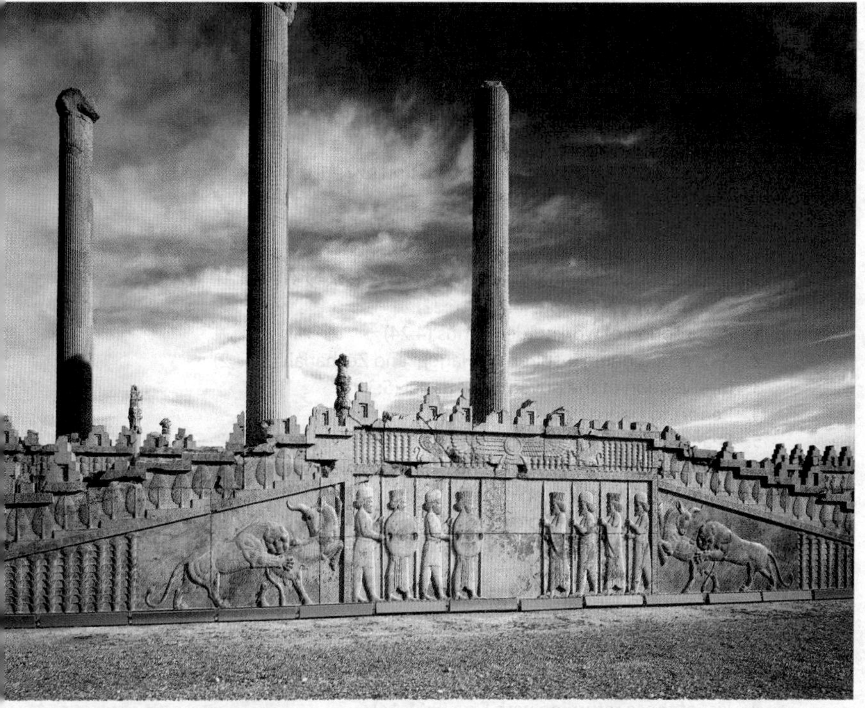

Detailed carving on the eastern stairs of the audience hall at Persepolis. It is believed that Cyrus the Great chose the site of Persepolis, Darius the Great built the foundations and great palaces, and construction was completed during the reign of Xerxes. All three kings play a role in the book of Ezra.

(3) Just as God used the world powers to judge his people, so he used them to restore his people to their land; imperial action and authority directly and indirectly initiated, protected and sustained every aspect of the restoration.

(4) Israel's restoration evoked fierce opposition, but that opposition was thwarted at every turn.

(5) The restored community was a chastened people, yet they were also in need of frequent rebuke and reformation. The Israelites remained a wayward people. They still awaited the "new covenant," of which Jeremiah had spoken (31:31–34), and the renewal to be effected by God's Spirit, as announced by Joel (2:28–32) and Ezekiel (36:16—37:14).

Outline

- I. First Return from Exile and Rebuilding of the Temple (chs. 1–6)
  - A. First Return of the Exiles (ch. 1)
    1. The edict of Cyrus (1:1–4)
    2. The return under Sheshbazzar (1:5–11)
  - B. List of Returning Exiles (ch. 2)
  - C. Revival of Temple Worship (ch. 3)
    1. The rebuilding of the altar (3:1–3)
    2. The Festival of Tabernacles (3:4–6)
    3. The beginning of temple reconstruction (3:7–13)
  - D. Opposition to Rebuilding (4:1–23)
    1. Opposition during the reign of Cyrus (4:1–5)
    2. Opposition during the reign of Xerxes (4:6)
    3. Opposition during the reign of Artaxerxes (4:7–23)
  - E. Completion of the Temple (4:24—6:22)
    1. Resumption of work under Darius (4:24)
    2. A new beginning inspired by Haggai and Zechariah (5:1–2)
    3. Intervention of the governor, Tattenai (5:3–5)
    4. Report to Darius (5:6–17)
    5. Search for the decree of Cyrus (6:1–5)
    6. Darius's order for the rebuilding of the temple (6:6–12)
    7. Completion of the temple (6:13–15)
    8. Dedication of the temple (6:16–18)
    9. Celebration of Passover (6:19–22)
- II. Ezra's Return and Reforms (chs. 7–10)
  - A. Ezra's Return to Jerusalem (chs. 7–8)
    1. Introduction (7:1–10)
    2. The authorization by Artaxerxes (7:11–26)
    3. Ezra's doxology (7:27–28)
    4. List of those returning with Ezra (8:1–14)
    5. The search for Levites (8:15–20)
    6. Prayer and fasting (8:21–23)

   7. The assignment of the sacred articles (8:24 – 30)
   8. The journey and arrival in Jerusalem (8:31 – 36)
- B. Ezra's Reforms (chs. 9 – 10)
   1. The offense of mixed marriages (9:1 – 5)
   2. Ezra's confession and prayer (9:6 – 15)
   3. The people's response (10:1 – 4)
   4. The calling of a public assembly (10:5 – 15)
   5. Investigation of the offenders (10:16 – 17)
   6. The list of offenders (10:18 – 43)
   7. The dissolution of mixed marriages (10:44)

Cyrus Helps the Exiles to Return

1:1-3pp — 2Ch 36:22-23

1 In the first year of Cyrus king of Persia, in order to fulfill the word of
the LORD spoken by Jeremiah,[a] the LORD
moved the heart[b] of Cyrus king of Persia to
make a proclamation throughout his realm
and also to put it in writing:

2 "This is what Cyrus king of Persia
says:
" 'The LORD, the God of heaven,
has given me all the kingdoms of the
earth and he has appointed[c] me to
build[d] a temple for him at Jerusalem
in Judah. 3 Any of his people among
you may go up to Jerusalem in Judah
and build the temple of the LORD, the
God of Israel, the God who is in Jerusalem, and may their God be with
them. 4 And in any locality where survivors[e] may now be living, the people
are to provide them with silver and
gold,[f] with goods and livestock, and
with freewill offerings[g] for the temple
of God[h] in Jerusalem.' "[i]

5 Then the family heads of Judah and
Benjamin,[j] and the priests and Levites —
everyone whose heart God had moved[k] —
prepared to go up and build the house[l] of
the LORD in Jerusalem. 6 All their neighbors
assisted them with articles of silver and
gold,[m] with goods and livestock, and with
valuable gifts, in addition to all the freewill offerings.

1:1 [a] Jer 25:11-12; 29:10-14; Zec 1:12-16 [b] Ezr 6:22; 7:27 **1:2** [c] S Jdg 4:10; Ps 72:11; Isa 41:2,25; 44:28; 45:13; 46:11; 49:7, 23; 60:3,10 [d] Hag 1:2 **1:4** [e] Isa 10:20-22 [f] S Ex 3:22 [g] Nu 15:3; Ps 50:14; 54:6; 116:17 [h] Ps 72:8-11; Rev 21:24 [i] Ezr 3:7; 4:3; 5:13; 6:3,14 **1:5** [j] 2Ch 11:1, 3,10,12,23; 15:2,8-9; 25:5; 31:1; 34:9; Ezr 4:1; 10:9; Ne 11:4; 12:34 [k] ver 1; Ex 35:20-22; 2Ch 36:22; Hag 1:14; S Php 2:13 [l] Ps 127:1 **1:6** [m] S Ex 3:22

1:1 – 3a Virtually identical with the last two verses of 2 Chronicles. This fact has been used to argue that Chronicles and Ezra-Nehemiah were written and/or edited by the same person, the so-called Chronicler. However, the repetition may have been a device of the author of Chronicles (or less probably of Ezra) to dovetail the narratives chronologically.

1:1 *first year.* Of the reign of Cyrus over Babylon, beginning in March, 538 BC, after he captured Babylon in October, 539. Cyrus, the founder of the Persian Empire, reigned over the Persians from 559 until 530 (see chart, p. 511). Isa 44:28; 45:1 speak of him as the Lord's "shepherd" and his "anointed." *to fulfill the word of the LORD spoken by Jeremiah.* Jeremiah prophesied a 70-year Babylonian exile (Jer 25:11 – 12; 29:10). The first deportation began in 605, the third year of Jehoiakim (see Da 1:1 and note); in 538, approximately 70 years later, the people began to return.

1:2 – 4 This oral proclamation of Cyrus's decree was written in Hebrew, the language of the Israelite captives, in contrast to the copy of the decree in 6:3 – 5, which was an Aramaic memorandum for the archives.

1:2 *God of heaven.* A Persian title for God. Of the 22 OT occurrences of the phrase, 17 occur in Ezra, Nehemiah and Daniel. *temple ... at Jerusalem.* Jerusalem and the house of God are prominent subjects in Ezra and Nehemiah.

1:3 Cyrus instituted the policy of placating the gods of his subject peoples instead of carrying off their idols as the Assyrians and the Babylonians had done earlier. His generosity to the Jews was paralleled by his benevolence to the Babylonians. Cf. photo, p. 721.

1:4 *any locality where survivors may now be living, the people.* Probably designates the many Jews who did not wish to leave Mesopotamia. *freewill offerings.* A key to the restoration of God's temple and its services (see 2:68; 3:5; 8:28).

1:5 *family heads.* In ancient times families were extended families — more like clans than modern nuclear families. The authority figure was the patriarch, who was the "family head." See 10:16; see also 2:59; Ne 7:61; 10:34. *Judah and Benjamin.* The two main tribes of the kingdom of Judah, which the Babylonians had exiled. *Levites.* See Introduction to Leviticus: Title.

RETURN FROM EXILE

Restoration of the Jewish exiles began under Cyrus (559–530 BC), who allowed them to return to Judah with the captured temple treasures. The temple was consecrated in 516 BC by official permission of Darius I (522–486).

Ezra won the approval of Artaxerxes I (465–424 BC) to return with additional exiles and to promote obedience to the law; Nehemiah, to rebuild the walls of Jerusalem.

Babylon and vicinity long retained a large and prosperous Jewish community, as clay tablets from the Murashu archives at Nippur testify.

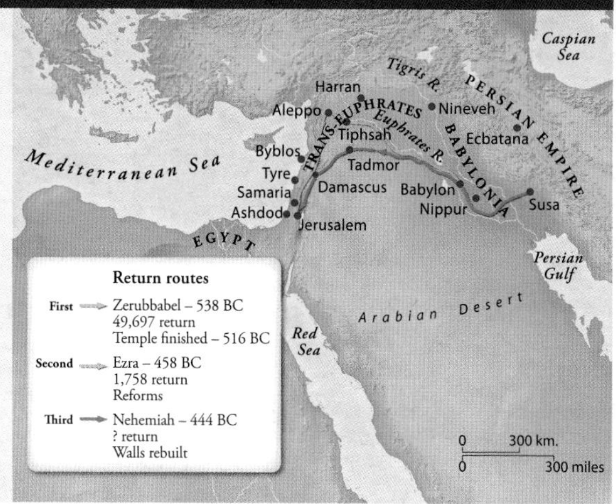

7 Moreover, King Cyrus brought out the
articles belonging to the temple of the
LORD, which Nebuchadnezzar had carried
away from Jerusalem and had placed in
the temple of his god.[a][n] 8 Cyrus king of Persia had them brought by Mithredath the
treasurer, who counted them out to Sheshbazzar[o] the prince of Judah.
9 This was the inventory:

gold dishes	30
silver dishes	1,000
silver pans[b]	29
10 gold bowls	30
matching silver bowls	410
other articles	1,000

11 In all, there were 5,400 articles of
gold and of silver. Sheshbazzar brought
all these along with the exiles when they
came up from Babylon to Jerusalem.

The List of the Exiles Who Returned

2:1-70pp — Ne 7:6-73

2 Now these are the people of the province who came up from the captivity of the exiles,[p] whom Nebuchadnezzar
king of Babylon[q] had taken captive to
Babylon (they returned to Jerusalem and
Judah, each to their own town,[r] 2 in company with Zerubbabel,[s] Joshua,[t] Nehemiah, Seraiah,[u] Reelaiah, Mordecai, Bilshan,
Mispar, Bigvai, Rehum and Baanah):

The list of the men of the people of Israel:

3 the descendants of Parosh[v]	2,172
4 of Shephatiah	372
5 of Arah	775
6 of Pahath-Moab (through the line of Jeshua and Joab)	2,812
7 of Elam	1,254
8 of Zattu	945
9 of Zakkai	760
10 of Bani	642
11 of Bebai	623
12 of Azgad	1,222
13 of Adonikam[w]	666
14 of Bigvai	2,056
15 of Adin	454

[a] 7 Or *gods* [b] 9 The meaning of the Hebrew for this word is uncertain.

1:7 [n] S 2Ki 24:13; S 2Ch 36:7, 10; Ezr 5:14; 6:5; Jer 52:17-19 **1:8** [o] S 1Ch 3:18 **2:1** [p] S 2Ch 36:20 [q] S 2Ki 24:16; 25:12 [r] ver 70; 1Ch 9:2; Ne 7:73; 11:3 **2:2** [s] S 1Ch 3:19; Mt 1:12; Lk 3:27 [t] Ezr 3:2; 5:2; 10:18; Ne 12:1, 8; Hag 1:1, 12; 2:4; Zec 3:1-10; 6:9-15 [u] 1Ch 6:14; Ne 10:2; 11:11; 12:1 **2:3** [v] Ezr 8:3; 10:25; Ne 3:25 **2:13** [w] Ezr 8:13

1:7 It was the custom for conquerors to carry off the images of the gods of conquered cities. Since the Jews did not have an image of the Lord (see note on Ex 20:4), Nebuchadnezzar (see chart, p. 511) carried away only the temple articles.

1:8 *Mithredath.* A Persian name meaning "given by/to Mithra," a Persian god who became popular among Roman soldiers in the second century AD. *Sheshbazzar.* A Babylonian name meaning either "Sin, protect the father" or "Shamash/Shashu, protect the father." Sin was the moon-god, and Shamash (Shashu is a variant) was the sun-god. In spite of his Babylonian name, Sheshbazzar was probably a Jewish official who served as a deputy governor of Judah under the satrap in Samaria (see 5:14). Some believe that Sheshbazzar and Zerubbabel were the same person and give the following reasons: (1) Both were governors (5:14; Hag 1:1; 2:2). (2) Both are said to have laid the foundation of the temple (3:2–8; 5:16; Hag 1:14–15; Zec 4:6–10). (3) Jews in Babylon were often given "official" Babylonian names (cf. Da 1:7). (4) Josephus (*Antiquities*, 11.1.3) seems to identify Sheshbazzar with Zerubbabel.

Others point out, however, that the Apocrypha distinguishes between the two men (1 Esdras 6:18). Furthermore, it is likely that Sheshbazzar was an elderly man at the time of the return, while Zerubbabel was probably a younger contemporary. Sheshbazzar also may have been viewed as the official governor, while Zerubbabel served as the popular leader (3:8–11). Whereas the high priest Joshua is associated with Zerubbabel, no priest is associated with Sheshbazzar. Although Sheshbazzar presided over the foundation of the temple in 536 BC, so little was accomplished that Zerubbabel had to preside over a second foundation some 16 years later (see Hag 1:14–15; Zec 4:6–10).

Still others hold that Sheshbazzar is to be identified with Shenazzar (1Ch 3:18), the fourth son of King Jehoiachin. Zerubbabel would then have been Sheshbazzar's nephew (compare 3:2 with 1Ch 3:17–18).

1:9–11 When Assyrian and Babylonian conquerors carried off plunder, their scribes made a careful inventory of all the goods seized. The total of the figures in vv. 9–10 adds up to 2,499 rather than the 5,400 of v. 11. It may be that only the larger and more valuable vessels were specified.

1:11 We are not told anything about the details of Sheshbazzar's journey, which probably took place in 537 BC. Judging from Ezra's later journey (7:8–9), the trip took about four months. See map, p. 2523, at the end of this study Bible; see also map, p. 724.

2:1–70 The list of returning exiles in ch. 2 almost exactly parallels the list in Ne 7:6–73 (see also 1 Esdras 5:4–46 in the Apocrypha). The list of localities indicates that people retained the memories of their homes and that exiles from a wide background of tribes, villages and towns returned. In comparing the list here with that in Ne 7, one notes many differences in the names and numbers listed. About 20 percent of the numbers, e.g., are not the same in Ezra and Nehemiah. Many of these differences may be explained, however, by assuming that a cipher notation was used with vertical strokes for units and horizontal strokes for tens, which led to copying errors.

2:1 *province.* Probably Judah (cf. 5:8, where the Aramaic word for "province" is translated "district"; see also Ne 1:3).

2:2 *Zerubbabel.* See notes on 3:2; 5:2. *Joshua.* Means "The LORD saves." The Greek form is "Jesus" (see NIV text note on Mt 1:21). This Joshua is the same as the Joshua of Hag 1:1, the son of the high priest Jozadak (see Ezr 3:2), who was taken into exile (1Ch 6:15). *Nehemiah.* Not the Nehemiah of the book by that name. *Mordecai.* A Babylonian name based on that of Marduk, the god of Babylon (cf. Jer 50:2). Esther's cousin had the same name (see Est 2:5 and note).

2:3 *Parosh.* Means "flea" (Israelites were often named after insects and animals). Other members of this family, as well as of several other families named in vv. 6–14, returned with Ezra (8:3–14).

2:5 *Arah.* Probably means "wild ox." Since the name is rare in the OT and has been found in documents from Mesopotamia, it may have been adopted during the exile.

2:6 *Pahath-Moab.* Means "governor of Moab" and may have once designated an official title.

2:12 *Azgad.* Cf. 8:12; means "Gad is strong." It is a reference

CHRONOLOGY: EZRA–NEHEMIAH

Dates below are given according to a Nisan-to-Nisan Jewish calendar (see chart, p. 113).
Roman numerals represent months; Arabic numerals represent days.

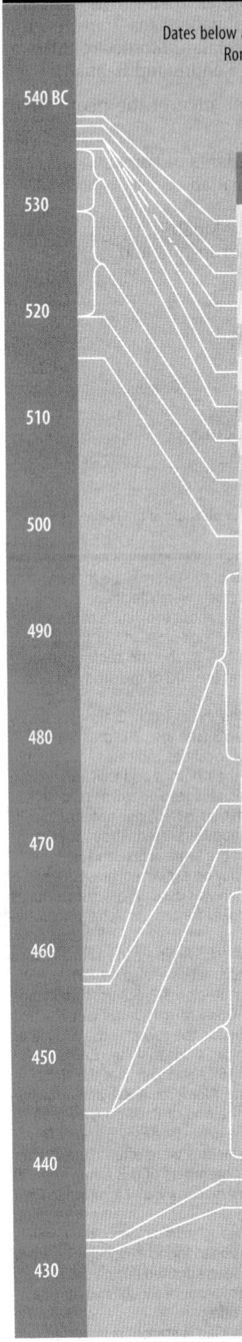

540 BC, 530, 520, 510, 500, 490, 480, 470, 460, 450, 440, 430

YEAR	MONTH	DAY	EVENT	REFERENCE
539 BC	Oct.	12	Capture of Babylon	Da 5:30
538 537	Mar. to Mar.	24 11	Cyrus's first year	Ezr 1:1–4
537(?)			Return under Sheshbazzar	Ezr 1:11
537	VII		Building of altar	Ezr 3:1
536	II		Work on temple begun	Ezr 3:8
536–530			Opposition during Cyrus's reign	Ezr 4:1–5
530–520			Work on temple ceased	Ezr 4:24
520	VI = Sept.	24 21	Work on temple renewed under Darius	Ezr 5:2; Hag 1:14
516	XII = Mar.	3 12	Temple completed	Ezr 6:15
458	I = Apr.	1 8	Ezra departs from Babylon	Ezr 7:6–9
	V = Aug.	1 4	Ezra arrives in Jerusalem	Ezr 7:8–9
	IX = Dec.	20 19	People assemble	Ezr 10:9
	X = Dec.	1 29	Committee begins investigation	Ezr 10:16
457	I = Mar.	1 27	Committee ends investigation	Ezr 10:17
445 444	Apr. to Apr.	13 2	20th year of Artaxerxes I	Ne 1:1
444	I = Mar.–Apr.		Nehemiah approaches the king	Ne 2:1
	Aug.(?)		Nehemiah arrives in Jerusalem	Ne 2:11
	VI = Oct.	25 2	Completion of wall	Ne 6:15
	VII = Oct. to Nov.	8 5	Public assembly	Ne 7:73—8:1
	VII = Oct.	15-22 22-28	Festival of Tabernacles	Ne 8:14
	VII = Oct.	24 30	Day of Fasting	Ne 9:1
433 432	Apr. to Apr.	1 19	32nd year of Artaxerxes; Nehemiah's recall and return	Ne 5:14; 13:6

16 of Ater (through Hezekiah) 98
17 of Bezai 323
18 of Jorah 112
19 of Hashum 223
20 of Gibbar 95

21 the men of Bethlehem[x] 123
22 of Netophah 56
23 of Anathoth 128
24 of Azmaveth 42
25 of Kiriath Jearim,[a] Kephirah and Beeroth 743
26 of Ramah[y] and Geba 621
27 of Mikmash 122
28 of Bethel and Ai[z] 223
29 of Nebo 52
30 of Magbish 156
31 of the other Elam 1,254
32 of Harim 320
33 of Lod, Hadid and Ono 725
34 of Jericho[a] 345
35 of Senaah 3,630

36 The priests:

the descendants of Jedaiah[b] (through the family of Jeshua) 973
37 of Immer[c] 1,052
38 of Pashhur[d] 1,247
39 of Harim[e] 1,017

40 The Levites:[f]

the descendants of Jeshua[g] and Kadmiel (of the line of Hodaviah) 74

41 The musicians:[h]

the descendants of Asaph 128

42 The gatekeepers[i] of the temple:

the descendants of
Shallum, Ater, Talmon,
Akkub, Hatita and Shobai 139

43 The temple servants:[j]

the descendants of
Ziha, Hasupha, Tabbaoth,
44 Keros, Siaha, Padon,
45 Lebanah, Hagabah, Akkub,
46 Hagab, Shalmai, Hanan,
47 Giddel, Gahar, Reaiah,
48 Rezin, Nekoda, Gazzam,
49 Uzza, Paseah, Besai,
50 Asnah, Meunim, Nephusim,
51 Bakbuk, Hakupha, Harhur,
52 Bazluth, Mehida, Harsha,
53 Barkos, Sisera, Temah,
54 Neziah and Hatipha

55 The descendants of the servants of Solomon:

the descendants of
Sotai, Hassophereth, Peruda,
56 Jaala, Darkon, Giddel,
57 Shephatiah, Hattil,
Pokereth-Hazzebaim and Ami

58 The temple servants[k] and the descendants of the servants of Solomon 392

59 The following came up from the
towns of Tel Melah, Tel Harsha, Ke-
rub, Addon and Immer, but they

2:21 [x] Mic 5:2
2:26 [y] S Jos 18:25
2:28 [z] S Ge 12:8
2:34 [a] 1Ki 16:34; 2Ch 28:15
2:36 [b] S 1Ch 24:7
2:37 [c] S 1Ch 24:14
2:38 [d] S 1Ch 9:12
2:39 [e] S 1Ch 24:8
2:40 [f] Ge 29:34; Nu 3:9; Dt 18:6-7; 1Ch 16:4; Ezr 7:7; 8:15; Ne 12:24 [g] Ezr 3:9
2:41 [h] S 1Ch 15:16
2:42 [i] 1Sa 3:15; S 1Ch 9:17
2:43 [j] S 1Ch 9:2; Ne 11:21
2:58 [k] S 1Ch 9:2

[a] 25 See Septuagint (see also Neh. 7:29); Hebrew *Kiriath Arim.*

either to Gad (the god of fortune, referred to in Isa 65:11) or to the Transjordanian tribe of Gad.

2:16 *Ater.* Means "left-handed," as in Jdg 3:15; 20:16.

2:21–35 Whereas the names in vv. 3–20 are of families, vv. 21–35 present a series of villages and towns, many of which were in Benjamite territory north of Jerusalem. It is significant that there are no references to towns in the Negev, south of Judah. When Nebuchadnezzar overran Judah in 597 BC (Jer 13:19), the Edomites (see the book of Obadiah) took advantage of the situation and occupied that area.

2:23 *Anathoth.* See note on Jer 1:1.

2:28 *Bethel.* See note on Ge 12:8. Towns such as Bethel, Mizpah, Gibeon and Gibeah seem to have escaped the Babylonian assault. Bethel, however, was destroyed in the transition between the Babylonian and Persian periods. Archaeological excavations reveal that there was a small town on the site in Ezra's day. *Ai.* See note on Jos 7:2.

2:31 See v. 7.

2:33 *Lod.* Modern Lydda (see note on Ne 6:2).

2:35 *Senaah.* The largest number of returnees—3,630 (3,930 in Ne 7:38)—is associated with Senaah. It has therefore been suggested that they did not come from a specific locality or family but represented the poorer and lower classes of people, as inferred from the meaning of the name ("the hated one").

2:36–39 Four clans of priests numbering 4,289, about a tenth of the total.

2:40 *Levites.* See Introduction to Leviticus: Title. *74.* The number of Levites who returned was relatively small (cf. 8:15). Since the Levites had been entrusted with the menial tasks of temple service, many of them may have found a more comfortable way of life in exile.

2:41 *Asaph.* One of the three Levites appointed by David over the temple singers (1Ch 25:1; 2Ch 5:12; 35:15), whose duties are detailed in 1Ch 15:16–24.

2:42 *gatekeepers.* Usually Levites (1Ch 9:26; 2Ch 23:4; 35:15; Ne 12:25; 13:22). They are mentioned 16 times in Ezra-Nehemiah and 19 times in Chronicles. Their primary function was to tend the doors and gates of the temple (1Ch 9:17–27) and to perform other menial tasks (1Ch 9:28–32; 2Ch 31:14).

2:43–58 The temple servants and the descendants of Solomon's servants together numbered 392 (v. 58), which was more than the total of the Levites, singers and gatekeepers together (vv. 40–42).

2:46 *Hanan.* Means "(God) is gracious." The verb "to be gracious" and its derivatives are the components of numerous personal names in the OT—e.g., Johanan ("The LORD is gracious"; see 8:12), which has given us the English name John (see note on Mk 1:4).

2:55,58 *descendants of the servants of Solomon.* The phrase occurs only here and in Ne 7:57,60; 11:3. These may be the descendants of the Canaanites whom Solomon enslaved (1Ki 9:20–21).

2:59–63 Individuals who lacked evidence of their ancestry.

2:59 *towns.* Places in Mesopotamia where the Jews were settled by their Babylonian captors. *Tel Melah.*

could not show that their families
were descended[l] from Israel:

60 The descendants of
Delaiah, Tobiah and Nekoda 652

61 And from among the priests:

The descendants of
Hobaiah, Hakkoz and Barzillai
(a man who had married
a daughter of Barzillai the
Gileadite[m] and was called by
that name).

62 These searched for their family records, but they could not find them and
so were excluded from the priesthood[n]
as unclean. 63 The governor ordered
them not to eat any of the most sacred
food[o] until there was a priest ministering with the Urim and Thummim.[p]

64 The whole company numbered
42,360, 65 besides their 7,337 male and
female slaves; and they also had 200
male and female singers.[q] 66 They had
736 horses,[r] 245 mules, 67 435 camels
and 6,720 donkeys.

68 When they arrived at the house of the
LORD in Jerusalem, some of the heads of
the families[s] gave freewill offerings toward
the rebuilding of the house of God on its
site. 69 According to their ability they gave
to the treasury for this work 61,000 darics[a] of gold, 5,000 minas[b] of silver and 100
priestly garments.

70 The priests, the Levites, the musicians, the gatekeepers and the temple servants settled in their own towns, along
with some of the other people, and the
rest of the Israelites settled in their towns.[t]

Rebuilding the Altar

3 When the seventh month came and
the Israelites had settled in their
towns,[u] the people assembled[v] together
as one in Jerusalem. 2 Then Joshua[w] son
of Jozadak[x] and his fellow priests and Zerubbabel son of Shealtiel[y] and his associates began to build the altar of the God
of Israel to sacrifice burnt offerings on it,
in accordance with what is written in the
Law of Moses[z] the man of God. 3 Despite
their fear[a] of the peoples around them,
they built the altar on its foundation and
sacrificed burnt offerings on it to the LORD,
both the morning and evening sacrifices.[b]
4 Then in accordance with what is written,
they celebrated the Festival of Tabernacles[c]
with the required number of burnt offerings prescribed for each day. 5 After that,

2:59 [l] S Nu 1:18 **2:61** [m] S 2Sa 17:27 **2:62** [n] Nu 3:10; 16:39-40 **2:63** [o] Lev 2:3, 10 [p] S Ex 28:30 **2:65** [q] S 2Sa 19:35 **2:66** [r] Isa 66:20 **2:68** [s] S Ex 25:2 **2:70** [t] S ver 1; S 1Ch 9:2; Ne 11:3-4 **3:1** [u] Ne 7:73 [v] S Lev 23:24 **3:2** [w] S Ezr 2:2 [x] Hag 1:1; Zec 6:11 [y] 1Ch 3:17 [z] S Ex 20:24; Dt 12:5-6 **3:3** [a] Ezr 4:4; Da 9:25 [b] S Ex 29:39; Nu 28:1-8 **3:4** [c] S Ex 23:16; Nu 29:12-38; Ne 8:14-18; Zec 14:16-19

[a] 69 That is, about 1,100 pounds or about 500 kilograms
[b] 69 That is, about 3 tons or about 2.8 metric tons

Means "mound of salt," possibly a mound on which salt had been scattered (see Jdg 9:45 and note). The Hebrew word *tel* designates a hill-like mound (see note on Jos 11:13) formed by the remains of a ruined city. The Jewish exiles had been settled along the Kebar River (Eze 1:1), perhaps near Nippur, a city in southern Mesopotamia that was the stronghold of rebels. The Jews had probably been settled on the mounds of ruined cities that had been depopulated by the Babylonians.
2:63 *governor.* Probably either Sheshbazzar or Zerubbabel (see note on 1:8). *Urim and Thummim.* See note on Ex 28:30.
2:64 *42,360.* Considerably more than the sum of the other figures given:

Categories	*Ezra*	*Nehemiah*	*1 Esdras*
Men of Israel	24,144	25,406	25,947
Priests	4,289	4,289	5,288
Levites, musicians, gatekeepers	341	360	341
Temple servants, descendants of Solomon's servants	392	392	372
Men of unproven origin	652	642	652
Totals	29,818	31,089	32,600

It is difficult to account for the difference of about 10,000–12,000. The figure may refer to an unspecified 10,000–12,000 women and/or children, and it doubtless includes the priests of unproven origin referred to in vv. 61–63. Some suggest that the groups explicitly counted were returnees from Judah and Benjamin, while the remainder were from other tribes.
2:65 *male and female slaves.* The ratio of slaves to others (one to six) is relatively high. The fact that so many returned with their masters speaks highly of the benevolent treatment of servants by the Jews. *singers.* The male and female musicians listed here may be secular singers who sang at social events such as weddings and funerals (2Ch 35:25), as distinct from the temple singers (or musicians) of v. 41, who were all male.
2:66 *horses.* Perhaps a donation from Cyrus for the nobility. *mules.* See 1Ki 1:33 and note.
2:67 *donkeys.* Were used to carry loads, women or children. Sheep, goats and cattle are not mentioned. They would have slowed the caravan.
2:68 *arrived ... Jerusalem.* For the route of the return from exile, see map, p. 2523, at the end of this study Bible; see also map, p. 724.
2:69 The parallel passage (Ne 7:70–72) gives a fuller description than the account in Ezra. In Ezra the gifts come from the heads of the families (v. 68), while in Nehemiah the gifts are credited to three sources: the governor, the heads of the families, and the rest of the people. *darics.* See note on 1Ch 29:7. Some believe that the coin intended was the Greek *drachma,* a silver coin. *minas.* In the sexagesimal system (based on the number 60) that originated in Mesopotamia, there were 60 shekels in a mina and 60 minas in a talent. A shekel, which was about two-fifths of an ounce of silver, was the average wage for a month's work. Thus a mina would be the equivalent of five years' wages, and a talent would be 300 years' wages.
2:70 Later, Nehemiah (11:1–2) would be compelled to move people by lot to reinforce the population of Jerusalem.
3:1 *seventh month.* Tishri (September-October), about three months after the arrival of the exiles in Judah (in 537 BC). Tishri was one of the most sacred months of the Jewish year (see Lev 23:23–43 and notes).
3:2 *Joshua ... Zerubbabel.* The priest takes precedence over the civil leader in view of the nature of the occasion (contrast 3:8; 4:3; 5:2; Hag 1:1).
3:4 *Festival of Tabernacles.* See Lev 23:33–43 and notes.

ZERUBBABEL'S TEMPLE

Construction of the second temple was started in 536 BC on the Solomonic foundations leveled a half-century earlier by the Babylonians. People who remembered the earlier temple wept at the comparison (Ezr 3:12). Not until 516 BC, the 6th year of the Persian emperor Darius I (522–486), was the temple finally completed at the urging of Haggai and Zechariah (Ezr 6:13–15).

Archaeological evidence confirms that the Persian period in the Holy Land was a comparatively impoverished one in terms of material culture. Later Aramaic documents from Elephantine in Upper Egypt illustrate the official process of gaining permission to construct a Jewish place of worship and the opposition engendered by such a project.

Of the temple and its construction, little is known. Consequently, all art reconstructions of it are tentative. Among the few contemporary buildings, the Persian palace at Lachish and the Tobiad monument at Iraq al-Amir may be compared in terms of technique.

Unlike the more famous structures razed in 586 BC and AD 70, the temple begun by Zerubbabel suffered no major hostile destruction, but was gradually repaired and reconstructed over a long period of time. Eventually it was replaced entirely by Herod's magnificent edifice.

hey presented the regular burnt offerings,
he New Moon[d] sacrifices and the sacri-
ices for all the appointed sacred festivals
of the LORD,[e] as well as those brought as
reewill offerings to the LORD. 6On the first
lay of the seventh month they began to
offer burnt offerings to the LORD, though
he foundation of the LORD's temple had
not yet been laid.

Rebuilding the Temple

7Then they gave money to the masons
and carpenters,[f] and gave food and drink
and olive oil to the people of Sidon and
Tyre, so that they would bring cedar logs[g]
by sea from Lebanon[h] to Joppa, as authorized by Cyrus[i] king of Persia.

8In the second month[j] of the second
year after their arrival at the house of God
in Jerusalem, Zerubbabel[k] son of Shealtiel,
Joshua son of Jozadak and the rest of the
people (the priests and the Levites and all
who had returned from the captivity to Jerusalem) began the work. They appointed
Levites twenty[l] years old and older to supervise the building of the house of the
LORD. 9Joshua[m] and his sons and brothers
and Kadmiel and his sons (descendants of
Hodaviah[a]) and the sons of Henadad and
their sons and brothers — all Levites —
joined together in supervising those working on the house of God.

3:5 [d] S Nu 28:3, 11,14; Col 2:16 [e] Lev 23:1-44; S Nu 29:39
3:7 [f] 1Ch 22:15 [g] S 1Ch 14:1 [h] Isa 35:2; 60:13 [i] S Ezr 1:2-4
3:8 [j] 1Ki 6:1 [k] Zec 4:9 [l] S Nu 4:3
3:9 [m] Ezr 2:40

[a] 9 Hebrew *Yehudah,* a variant of *Hodaviah*

3:5 *New Moon.* See note on 1Sa 20:5. *appointed sacred festivals.* See note on Lev 23:2. *freewill offerings.* See note on 1:4. It s noteworthy that the restoration of the sacrifices preceded the erection of the temple itself.

3:7 *cedar logs.* As in the case of the first temple, the Phoenicians cooperated by sending timber and workers (1Ki 5:6–12).

3:8 *second month.* The same month (April-May) in which Solomon had begun his temple (1Ki 6:1). *second year.* Since the Jews probably returned to Judah in the spring of 537 BC, the second year would be the spring of 536. *twenty years old.* In earlier times the lower age limit for Levites was 30 (Nu 4:3) or 25 years (Nu 8:24). It was later reduced to 20 (1Ch 23:24,27; 2Ch 31:17), probably because there were so few Levites.

10 When the builders laid[n] the foundation of the temple of the LORD, the priests
in their vestments and with trumpets,[o]
and the Levites (the sons of Asaph) with
cymbals, took their places to praise[p] the
LORD, as prescribed by David[q] king of Israel.[r] 11 With praise and thanksgiving they
sang to the LORD:

"He is good;
his love toward Israel endures
forever."[s]

And all the people gave a great shout[t] of
praise to the LORD, because the foundation[u] of the house of the LORD was laid.
12 But many of the older priests and Levites
and family heads, who had seen the former temple,[v] wept[w] aloud when they saw
the foundation of this temple being laid,
while many others shouted for joy. 13 No
one could distinguish the sound of the
shouts of joy[x] from the sound of weeping,
because the people made so much noise.
And the sound was heard far away.

Opposition to the Rebuilding

4 When the enemies of Judah and
Benjamin heard that the exiles were
building[y] a temple for the LORD, the God
of Israel, 2 they came to Zerubbabel and to
the heads of the families and said, "Let us
help you build because, like you, we seek
your God and have been sacrificing to him
since the time of Esarhaddon[z] king of Assyria, who brought us here."[a]

3 But Zerubbabel, Joshua and the rest
of the heads of the families of Israel answered, "You have no part with us in
building a temple to our God. We alone
will build it for the LORD, the God of Israel, as King Cyrus, the king of Persia, commanded us."[b]

4 Then the peoples around them set out
to discourage the people of Judah and
make them afraid to go on building.[a][c]
5 They bribed officials to work against
them and frustrate their plans during the
entire reign of Cyrus king of Persia and
down to the reign of Darius king of Persia.

Later Opposition Under Xerxes and Artaxerxes

6 At the beginning of the reign of Xerxes,[b][d] they lodged an accusation against
the people of Judah and Jerusalem.[e]
7 And in the days of Artaxerxes[f] king of
Persia, Bishlam, Mithredath, Tabeel and
the rest of his associates wrote a letter
to Artaxerxes. The letter was written in
Aramaic script and in the Aramaic[g] language.[c,d]
8 Rehum the commanding officer and
Shimshai the secretary wrote a letter
against Jerusalem to Artaxerxes the king
as follows:

9 Rehum the commanding officer and
Shimshai the secretary, together with

3:10 [n] Ezr 5:16; 6:3; Hag 2:15 [o] S Nu 10:2; S 2Sa 6:5; 1Ch 16:6; 2Ch 5:13; Ne 12:35 [p] S 1Ch 25:1 [q] S 1Ch 6:31 [r] Zec 6:12 **3:11** [s] 1Ch 16:34, 41; S 2Ch 7:3; Ps 30:5; 107:1; 118:1; 138:8 [t] S Jos 6:5, 10 [u] Hag 2:18; Zec 4:9; 8:9 **3:12** [v] Hag 2:3, 9 [w] Jer 31:9; 50:4 **3:13** [x] Job 8:21; 33:26; Ps 27:6; 42:4; Isa 16:9; Jer 48:33 **4:1** [y] Ne 2:20 **4:2** [z] S 2Ki 17:24 [a] S 2Ki 17:41 **4:3** [b] Ezr 1:1-4 **4:4** [c] S Ezr 3:3 **4:6** [d] Est 1:1; Da 9:1 [e] Est 3:13; 9:5 **4:7** [f] Ezr 7:1; Ne 2:1 [g] 2Ki 18:26; Isa 36:11; Da 1:4; 2:4

[a] 4 Or *and troubled them as they built* [b] 6 Hebrew *Ahasuerus* [c] 7 Or *written in Aramaic and translated* [d] 7 The text of 4:8 – 6:18 is in Aramaic.

3:10 *trumpets.* Made of hammered silver (see Nu 10:2 and note). According to Josephus (*Antiquities*, 3.12.6), the trumpet was "in length a little short of a cubit; it is a narrow tube, slightly thicker than a flute." With the possible exception of their use at the coronation of Joash (2Ki 11:14; 2Ch 23:13), the trumpets were always blown by priests. They were most often used on joyous occasions, such as here and at the dedication of the rebuilt walls of Jerusalem (Ne 12:35; cf. 2Ch 5:13; Ps 98:6). *cymbals.* The Hebrew for this word occurs 13 times in the OT, all in Chronicles except here and Ne 12:27.
3:11 *sang.* May mean "sang responsively," referring to antiphonal singing by a choir divided into two groups. *He is good . . . endures forever.* See introduction to Ps 136.
3:13 *shouts of joy . . . sound of weeping.* The people of Israel were accustomed to showing their emotions in visible and audible ways (10:1; Ne 1:4; 8:9). The same God who had permitted judgment had now brought them back and would enable them to complete the project. A Babylonian cornerstone reads: "I started the work weeping, I finished it rejoicing." Cf. Ps 126:5 – 6.
4:1 – 23 A summary of various attempts to thwart the efforts of the Jews. In vv. 1 – 5 the author describes events in the reign of Cyrus (559 – 530 BC), in v. 6 the reign of Xerxes (486 – 465) and in vv. 7 – 23 the reign of Artaxerxes I (465 – 424). He then reverts in v. 24 to the time of Darius I (522 – 486), during whose reign the temple was completed (see 5:1 – 2; 6:13 – 15; Haggai; Zec 1:1 – 17; 4:9).
4:1 *enemies.* The people who offered their "help" (v. 2) were from Samaria. *Judah and Benjamin.* See notes on 1:5; 1Ki 12:21.
4:2 After the fall of Samaria in 722 – 721 BC, the Assyrian kings brought in people from Mesopotamia and Aram (modern Syria). These people served their own gods but also took up the worship of the Lord as the god of the land (2Ki 17:24 – 41). *Esarhaddon.* See note on 2Ki 19:37; see also chart, p. 511.
4:4 *make them afraid.* The Hebrew for this verb often describes the fear aroused in a battle situation (Jdg 20:41; 2Sa 4:1; 2Ch 32:18).
4:5 *bribed.* Cf. the hiring of Balaam (Dt 23:4 – 5; Ne 13:2) and the hiring of a prophet to intimidate Nehemiah (Ne 6:12 – 13). *Darius king of Persia.* See chart, p. 511.
4:6 *Xerxes.* See the book of Esther; see also chart, p. 511. When Darius died in 486 BC, Egypt rebelled, and Xerxes, the son of Darius, had to march west to suppress the revolt.
4:7 *Artaxerxes.* Three Persian kings bore this name Artaxerxes I (465 – 424 BC), II (404 – 358) and III (358 – 338). The king here is Artaxerxes I (see chart, p. 511). *Mithredath.* See 1:8 and note. *Tabeel.* An Aramaic name (see Isa 7:6 and note). *wrote a letter.* Near Eastern kings employed an elaborate system of informers and spies. Egyptian sources speak of the "ears and eyes" of the pharaoh. Sargon II of Assyria had agents in Urartu whom he ordered: "Write me whatever you see and hear." The King's Eye and the King's Ear were two officials who reported to the Persian monarch.
4:8 — 6:18 For this passage the author draws upon Aramaic documents; a further Aramaic section is 7:12 – 26.
4:8 *commanding officer.* An official who had the role of a chancellor or commissioner. Perhaps Rehum dictated, and Shimshai wrote the letter in Aramaic. (Alternatively, Shims

the rest of their associates[h] — the
judges, officials and administrators
over the people from Persia, Uruk[i]
and Babylon, the Elamites of Susa,[j]
10 and the other people whom the
great and honorable Ashurbanipal[k]
deported and settled in the city of
Samaria and elsewhere in Trans-Euphrates.[l]

11 (This is a copy of the letter they sent
him.)

To King Artaxerxes,

From your servants in Trans-Euphrates:

12 The king should know that the
people who came up to us from you
have gone to Jerusalem and are rebuilding that rebellious and wicked
city. They are restoring the walls and
repairing the foundations.[m]
13 Furthermore, the king should
know that if this city is built and its
walls are restored, no more taxes, tribute or duty[n] will be paid, and eventually the royal revenues will suffer.[a]
14 Now since we are under obligation
to the palace and it is not proper for
us to see the king dishonored, we are
sending this message to inform the
king, 15 so that a search may be made
in the archives[o] of your predecessors.
In these records you will find that this
city is a rebellious city, troublesome
to kings and provinces, a place with
a long history of sedition. That is why
this city was destroyed.[p] 16 We inform
the king that if this city is built and
its walls are restored, you will be left
with nothing in Trans-Euphrates.

17 The king sent this reply:

To Rehum the commanding officer,
Shimshai the secretary and the rest of
their associates living in Samaria and
elsewhere in Trans-Euphrates:[q]

Greetings.

18 The letter you sent us has been
read and translated in my presence.
19 I issued an order and a search was
made, and it was found that this city
has a long history of revolt[r] against
kings and has been a place of rebellion and sedition. 20 Jerusalem has
had powerful kings ruling over the
whole of Trans-Euphrates,[s] and taxes,
tribute and duty were paid to them.
21 Now issue an order to these men to
stop work, so that this city will not

4:9 [h] ver 23; Ezr 5:6; 6:6, 13 [i] Ge 10:10 [j] Ne 1:1; Est 1:2; Da 8:2
4:10 [k] S 2Ki 17:24 [l] ver 17; Ne 4:2
4:12 [m] Ezr 5:3,9
4:13 [n] Ezr 7:24; Ne 5:4
4:15 [o] Ezr 5:17; 6:1 [p] Est 3:8
4:17 [q] S ver 10
4:19 [r] S 2Ki 18:7
4:20 [s] Ge 15:18-21; S Ex 23:31; S Jos 1:4; S 1Ki 4:21; 1Ch 18:3; Ps 72:8-11

[a] *13* The meaning of the Aramaic for this clause is uncertain.

ai may have been a high official rather than a scribe.) The etter would then be read in a Persian translation in the pres- nce of the king (v. 18). According to Herodotus (3.128), royal cribes were attached to each governor to report directly to he Persian king.

:9 *associates.* See vv. 17,23; 5:3,6; 6:6 ("other officials"); 6:13.)ne of the striking characteristics of Persian bureaucracy was hat each responsibility was shared among colleagues. *Uruk.* ee note on Ge 10:10. *Babylon.* During the reign of the Assyr- an king Ashurbanipal (669 – 627 BC) a major revolt had taken lace (652 – 648), involving Shamash-Shum-Ukin, the brother f the king and the ruler over Babylonia. After a long siege hamash-Shum-Ukin hurled himself into the flames. Doubt- ess these men of Babylon and the other cities mentioned vere the descendants of the rebels, whom the Assyrians de- orted to the west. *Susa.* See note on Est 1:2; the major city of lam (in southwest Iran). Because of Susa's part in the revolt, shurbanipal brutally destroyed it in 640 (two centuries be- ore Rehum's letter).

4:10 *Ashurbanipal.* The last great Assyrian king (see chart, p. 511), famed for his library at Nineveh. He is not amed elsewhere in the OT, but he is probably the king who eed Manasseh from exile (2Ch 33:11 – 13). *deported.* Ashur- anipal may be the unnamed Assyrian king who brought eople to Samaria, according to 2Ki 17:24. It is characteristic f such deportations that the descendants of populations hat had been removed from their homelands nearly two enturies earlier should still stress their origins. *Samaria.* The nurder of Amon, king of Judah (642 – 640 BC; see 2Ki 21:23; Ch 33:24), was probably the result of an anti-Assyrian move- nent inspired by the revolt in Elam and Babylonia. The Assyr- ans may then have deported the rebellious Samaritans and eplaced them with the rebellious Elamites and Babylonians. *Trans-Euphrates.* Lit. "beyond the River," i.e., the Euphrates River. From Israel's point of view the land "beyond the River" was Mesopotamia (Jos 24:2 – 3,14 – 15; 2Sa 10:16). From the Mesopotamian point of view the land "beyond the River" extended from the Euphrates to Gaza (1Ki 4:24).

4:12 *people.* Lit. "Jews" or "Judahites" (see note on Zec 8:23). *restoring the walls and repairing the foundations.* As Isaiah had foretold (see Isa 58:12 and note).

4:13 Most of the gold and silver coins that came into Persia's treasury were melted down to be stored as bullion. Very little of the taxes returned to benefit the provinces.

4:14 *we are under obligation to the palace.* Lit. "we eat the salt of the palace." Salt was made a royal monopoly by the Ptolemies in Egypt, and perhaps by the Persians as well.

4:15 *archives.* See 5:17; 6:1 and note; Est 2:23; 6:1 – 2. There were several repositories of such documents at the major capitals. These royal archives preserved documents for centuries. In the third century BC the Babylonian priest Berossus made use of the Babylonian Chronicles in his history of Babylon, which covered events from the Assyrian to the Hellenistic (beginning with Alexander's conquest of Babylon in 330 BC) eras.

4:18 *read.* Since the king probably could not read Aramaic, he would have had the document read to him. *translated.* From Aramaic into Persian (see NIV text notes on v. 7; Ne 8:8).

4:19 *rebellion.* There is some truth in the accusation. Jerusalem had rebelled against the Assyrians in 701 BC (2Ki 18:7) and against the Babylonians in 600 and 589 (2Ki 24:1,20).

4:21 – 23 As a result of the intervention of the provincial authorities, Artaxerxes I (see v. 11 and note on v. 7) ordered that the Jews stop rebuilding the walls of Jerusalem (see note on Ne 1:3). The events of vv. 7 – 23 probably occurred prior to 444 BC. The forcible destruction of these recently rebuilt

be rebuilt until I so order. 22 Be careful not to neglect this matter. Why let this threat grow, to the detriment of the royal interests?[t]

23 As soon as the copy of the letter of King Artaxerxes was read to Rehum and Shimshai the secretary and their associates,[u] they went immediately to the Jews in Jerusalem and compelled them by force to stop.

24 Thus the work on the house of God in Jerusalem came to a standstill until the second year of the reign of Darius[v] king of Persia.

Tattenai's Letter to Darius

5 Now Haggai[w] the prophet and Zechariah[x] the prophet, a descendant of Iddo, prophesied[y] to the Jews in Judah and Jerusalem in the name of the God of Israel, who was over them. 2 Then Zerubbabel[z] son of Shealtiel and Joshua[a] son of Jozadak set to work[b] to rebuild the house of God in Jerusalem. And the prophets of God were with them, supporting them.

3 At that time Tattenai,[c] governor of Trans-Euphrates, and Shethar-Bozenai[d] and their associates went to them and asked, "Who authorized you to rebuild this temple and to finish it?"[e] 4 They[a] also asked, "What are the names of those who are constructing this building?" 5 But the eye of their God[f] was watching over the elders of the Jews, and they were not stopped until a report could go to Darius and his written reply be received.

6 This is a copy of the letter that Tattenai, governor of Trans-Euphrates, and Shethar-Bozenai and their associates, the officials of Trans-Euphrates, sent to King Darius. 7 The report they sent him read as follows:

To King Darius:

Cordial greetings.

8 The king should know that we went to the district of Judah, to the temple of the great God. The people are building it with large stones and placing the timbers in the walls. The work[g] is being carried on with diligence and is making rapid progress under their direction.

9 We questioned the elders and asked them, "Who authorized you to rebuild this temple and to finish it?"[h] 10 We also asked them their names, so that we could write down the names of their leaders for your information.

11 This is the answer they gave us:

"We are the servants of the God of heaven and earth, and we are rebuilding the temple[i] that was built many years ago, one that a great king of Israel built and finished. 12 But because our ancestors angered[j] the God of heaven, he gave them into the hands of Nebuchadnezzar the Chaldean, king of Babylon, who destroyed this temple and deported the people to Babylon.[k]

13 "However, in the first year of Cyrus king of Babylon, King Cyrus issued a decree[l] to rebuild this house of God. 14 He even removed from the temple[b] of Babylon the gold and sil-

4:22 [t] Da 6:2 **4:23** [u] S ver 9 **4:24** [v] Ne 2:1-8; Da 9:25; Hag 1:1,15; Zec 1:1 **5:1** [w] Ezr 6:14; Hag 1:1,3, 12; 2:1,10,20 [x] Zec 1:1; 7:1 [y] Hag 1:14-2:9; Zec 4:9-10; 8:9 **5:2** [z] S 1Ch 3:19; Hag 1:14; 2:21; Zec 4:6-10 [a] S Ezr 2:2 [b] ver 8; Hag 2:2-5 **5:3** [c] Ezr 6:6 [d] Ezr 6:6 [e] S Ezr 4:12 **5:5** [f] S 2Ki 25:28; Ezr 7:6,9, 28; 8:18,22, 31; Ne 2:8, 18; Ps 33:18; Isa 66:14 **5:8** [g] S ver 2 **5:9** [h] S Ezr 4:12 **5:11** [i] 1Ki 6:1; 2Ch 3:1-2 **5:12** [j] S 2Ch 36:16 [k] S Dt 21:10; S 28:36; S 2Ki 24:1; S Jer 1:3 **5:13** [l] S Ezr 1:2-4

[a] *4* See Septuagint; Aramaic *We.* [b] *14* Or *palace*

---

walls rather than the destruction by Nebuchadnezzar would then be the basis of the report made to Nehemiah (Ne 1:3).

4:24 After this long digression describing the opposition to Jewish efforts, the writer returns to his original subject of the rebuilding of the temple (vv. 1–5). *second year of the reign of Darius.* According to Persian reckoning, the second regnal year of Darius I began on Nisan 1 (Apr. 3), 520 BC, and lasted until Feb. 21, 519. In that year the prophet Haggai (Hag 1:1–5) exhorted Zerubbabel to begin rebuilding the temple on the first day of the sixth month (Aug. 29). Work began on the temple on the 24th day of the month, Sept. 21 (Hag 1:15). During his first two years Darius had to establish his right to the throne by fighting numerous rebels, as recounted in his famous Behistun (Bisitun) inscription. It was only after the stabilization of the Persian Empire that efforts to rebuild the temple could be permitted.

5:1 *Haggai ... Zechariah.* Beginning on Aug. 29, 520 BC (see Hag 1:1 and note), and continuing until Dec. 18 (see Hag 2:1,10,20 and notes), the prophet Haggai delivered a series of messages to stir up the people to resume work on the temple. Two months after Haggai's first speech, Zechariah began to prophesy (see Zec 1:1 and note; see also Introduction to Zechariah: Dates).

5:2 *Zerubbabel.* A Babylonian name meaning "offspring of Babylon," referring to his birth in exile. He was the son of Shealtiel and the grandson of Jehoi achin (1Ch 3:17), the next-to-last king of Judah. Zerubbabe was the last of the Davidic line to be entrusted with politica authority by the occupying powers. He was also an ancesto of Jesus (Mt 1:12–13; Lk 3:27). *Joshua.* See note on 2:2.

5:3 *Tattenai.* Probably a Babylonian name. *Shethar-Bozena* Perhaps a Persian official.

5:5 *not stopped.* The Persian governor gave the Jews the ben efit of the doubt by not stopping the work while the inquir was proceeding.

5:6–7 *sent to King Darius ... sent him.* Texts found i the royal city of Persepolis vividly confirm that suc inquiries were sent directly to the king himself, revealing th close attention he paid to minute details.

5:8 *timbers.* The Hebrew word may refer to interior panelin (1Ki 6:15–18) or to logs alternating with the brick or ston layers in the walls (see note on 6:4).

5:11 *great king of Israel.* According to 1Ki 6:1 Solomon bega building the temple in the fourth year of his reign (966 BC The project lasted seven years (1Ki 6:38).

5:12 *Chaldean.* The Akkadian word means "conqueror." Th origin of the Chaldeans is obscure. Led by Nebuchadnezzar father, Nabopolassar, they overthrew the Assyrians and es tablished the Neo-Babylonian Empire (612–539 BC).

ver articles of the house of God,
which Nebuchadnezzar had taken
from the temple in Jerusalem and
brought to the temple[a] in Babylon.[m]
Then King Cyrus gave them to a man
named Sheshbazzar,[n] whom he had
appointed governor, 15 and he told
him, 'Take these articles and go and
deposit them in the temple in Jerusalem. And rebuild the house of God
on its site.'
16 "So this Sheshbazzar came and
laid the foundations of the house of
God[o] in Jerusalem. From that day to
the present it has been under construction but is not yet finished."
17 Now if it pleases the king, let a
search be made in the royal archives[p]
of Babylon to see if King Cyrus did
in fact issue a decree to rebuild this
house of God in Jerusalem. Then let
the king send us his decision in this
matter.

The Decree of Darius

6 King Darius then issued an order, and
they searched in the archives[q] stored
in the treasury at Babylon. 2 A scroll was
found in the citadel of Ecbatana in the
province of Media, and this was written
on it:

Memorandum:

3 In the first year of King Cyrus, the
king issued a decree concerning the
temple of God in Jerusalem:

Let the temple be rebuilt as a
place to present sacrifices, and let its
foundations be laid.[r] It is to be sixty cubits[b] high and sixty cubits wide,
4 with three courses[s] of large stones
and one of timbers. The costs are to
be paid by the royal treasury.[t] 5 Also,
the gold[u] and silver articles of the
house of God, which Nebuchadnezzar took from the temple in Jerusalem
and brought to Babylon, are to be returned to their places in the temple in
Jerusalem; they are to be deposited in
the house of God.[v]

6 Now then, Tattenai,[w] governor of
Trans-Euphrates, and Shethar-Bozenai[x] and you other officials of that
province, stay away from there. 7 Do
not interfere with the work on this
temple of God. Let the governor of
the Jews and the Jewish elders rebuild this house of God on its site.
8 Moreover, I hereby decree what
you are to do for these elders of the
Jews in the construction of this house
of God:

Their expenses are to be fully paid
out of the royal treasury,[y] from the
revenues[z] of Trans-Euphrates, so that
the work will not stop. 9 Whatever
is needed — young bulls, rams, male
lambs for burnt offerings[a] to the God
of heaven, and wheat, salt, wine and
olive oil, as requested by the priests
in Jerusalem — must be given them

5:14 [m] Ezr 1:7 [n] S 1Ch 3:18
5:16 [o] S Ezr 3:10
5:17 [p] S Ezr 4:15
6:1 [q] S Ezr 4:15
6:3 [r] S Ezr 3:10; Hag 2:3
6:4 [s] S 1Ki 6:36 [t] ver 8; Ezr 7:20
6:5 [u] S 1Ch 29:2 [v] S Ezr 1:7
6:6 [w] Ezr 5:3 [x] Ezr 5:3
6:8 [y] S ver 4 [z] S 1Sa 9:20
6:9 [a] Lev 1:3,10

[a] 14 Or *palace* [b] 3 That is, about 90 feet or about 27 meters

5:14 *Sheshbazzar ... governor.* See note on 1:8.

6:1 *archives ... in the treasury at Babylon.* Many documents have also been found in the so-called "treasury" area of Persepolis (see map, p. 774).

6:2 *Ecbatana.* One of the four capitals (along with Babylon, Persepolis and Susa) of the Persian Empire. It is located in what is today the Iranian city of Hamadan. This is the only reference to the site in the OT, though there are numerous references in the Apocryphal books (Judith 1:1 – 4; Tobit 3:7; 7:1; 14:12 – 14; 2 Maccabees 9:3). *Media.* The homeland of the Medes in northwestern Iran. The Medes were an Indo-European tribe related to the Persians. After the rise of Cyrus in 550 BC, they became subordinate to the Persians. The name of the area was retained as late as the NT era (cf. Ac 2:9).

6:3 – 5 Compare this Aramaic memorandum of the decree of Cyrus with the Hebrew version in 1:2 – 4. The Aramaic is written in a more sober administrative style, without any reference to the Lord (Yahweh). A similar memorandum dealing with permission to rebuild the Jewish temple at Elephantine in Upper Egypt was found among fifth-century BC Aramaic papyri recovered at that site.

6:3 *sixty cubits high and sixty cubits wide.* See NIV text note. These dimensions, which differ from those of Solomon's temple (see NIV text note on 1Ki 6:2), are probably not specifications of the temple as built but of the outer limits of a building the Persians were willing to subsidize. The second temple was not as grandiose as the first (3:12; Hag 2:3).

6:4 *large stones ... timbers.* See 5:8. The same kind of construction is mentioned in 1Ki 6:36; 7:12. Such a design was possibly intended to cushion the building against earthquake shocks. *costs are to be paid by the royal treasury.* In 1973 archaeologists discovered at Xanthos in southwest Turkey a temple foundation charter from the late Persian period that provides some striking parallels with this decree of Cyrus. As in Ezra, amounts of sacrifices, names of priests and the responsibility for the upkeep of the temple are specified. The Persian king seems to have known details of the temple. See also notes on v. 8; 7:20.

6:8 *paid out of the royal treasury.* It was a consistent policy of Persian kings to help restore sanctuaries in their empire. For example, a memorandum concerning the rebuilding of the Jewish temple at Elephantine was written by the Persian governors of Judah and Samaria. Also from non-Biblical sources we learn that Cyrus repaired temples at Uruk and Ur. Cambyses, successor to Cyrus, gave funds for the temple at Sais in Egypt. The temple of Amun in the Khargah Oasis was rebuilt by order of Darius.

6:9 That the Persian monarchs were interested in the details of foreign religions is shown clearly by the ordinances of Cambyses and Darius I, regulating the temples and priests in Egypt. On the authority of Darius II (423 – 404 BC) a letter was written to the Jews at Elephantine concerning the keeping of the Festival of Unleavened Bread.

daily without fail, 10 so that they may
offer sacrifices pleasing to the God of
heaven and pray for the well-being of
the king and his sons.[b]
11 Furthermore, I decree that if anyone defies this edict, a beam is to
be pulled from their house and they
are to be impaled[c] on it. And for this
crime their house is to be made a
pile of rubble.[d] 12 May God, who has
caused his Name to dwell there,[e]
overthrow any king or people who
lifts a hand to change this decree or
to destroy this temple in Jerusalem.
I Darius[f] have decreed it. Let it be
carried out with diligence.

Completion and Dedication of the Temple

13 Then, because of the decree King
Darius had sent, Tattenai, governor of
Trans-Euphrates, and Shethar-Bozenai
and their associates[g] carried it out with
diligence. 14 So the elders of the Jews continued to build and prosper under the
preaching[h] of Haggai the prophet and
Zechariah, a descendant of Iddo. They
finished building the temple according to
the command of the God of Israel and the
decrees of Cyrus,[i] Darius[j] and Artaxerxes,[k]
kings of Persia. 15 The temple was completed on the third day of the month Adar, in
the sixth year of the reign of King Darius.[l]
16 Then the people of Israel—the priests,
the Levites and the rest of the exiles—
celebrated the dedication[m] of the house
of God with joy. 17 For the dedication of
this house of God they offered[n] a hundred
bulls, two hundred rams, four hundred
male lambs and, as a sin offering[a] for all
Israel, twelve male goats, one for each of
the tribes of Israel. 18 And they installed
the priests in their divisions[o] and the Levites in their groups[p] for the service of God
at Jerusalem, according to what is written
in the Book of Moses.[q]

The Passover

19 On the fourteenth day of the first
month, the exiles celebrated the Passover.[r] 20 The priests and Levites had purified themselves and were all ceremonially
clean. The Levites slaughtered[s] the Pass-

6:10 [b] Ezr 7:23; 1Ti 2:1-2 **6:11** [c] S Dt 21:22-23; Est 2:23; 5:14; 9:14 [d] Ezr 7:26; Da 2:5; 3:29 **6:12** [e] S Ex 20:24; S Dt 12:5; S 2Ch 6:2 [f] ver 14 **6:13** [g] S Ezr 4:9 **6:14** [h] S Ezr 5:1 [i] S Ezr 1:1-4 [j] ver 12 [k] Ezr 7:1; Ne 2:1 **6:15** [l] Zec 1:1; 4:9 **6:16** [m] S 1Ki 8:63 **6:17** [n] S 2Sa 6:13; S 2Ch 29:21; S 30:24 **6:18** [o] S 2Ch 35:4; Lk 1:5 [p] S 1Ch 24:1 [q] Nu 3:6-9; 8:9-11; 18:1-32 **6:19** [r] S Ex 12:11; S Nu 28:16 **6:20** [s] S 2Ch 30:15, 17; 35:11

[a] 17 Or *purification offering*

6:10 *pray for the well-being of the king and his sons.* In the inscription on the Cyrus Cylinder (made of baked clay), the king asks: "May all the gods whom I have resettled in their sacred cities ask Bel and Nebo daily for a long life for me." The Jews of Elephantine offered to pray for the Persian governor of Judah. The daily synagogue services included a prayer for the royal family (cf. 1Ti 2:1–2).

6:11 *if anyone defies this edict.* It was customary at the end of decrees and treaties to append a long list of curses against anyone who might disregard them. *impaled.* According to Herodotus (3.159), Darius I impaled 3,000 Babylonians when he took the city of Babylon. See note on Est 2:23.

6:12 *May God ... overthrow any king or people.* At the end of his famous Behistun (Bisitun) inscription Darius I warned: "If you see this inscription or these sculptures, and destroy them and do not protect them as long as you have strength, may Ahuramazda strike you, and may you not have a family, and what you do ... may Ahuramazda utterly destroy." *caused his Name to dwell.* See note on Dt 12:5.

6:13–14 Work on the temple had made little progress, not only because of opposition but also because of the preoccupation of the returnees with their own homes (Hag 1:2–9). Because they had placed their own interests first (cf. Mt 6:33), God sent them famine as a judgment (Hag 1:5–6,10–11). Spurred on by the preaching of Haggai and Zechariah, and under the leadership of Zerubbabel and Joshua, a new effort was begun (Hag 1:12–15).

6:14 *Artaxerxes.* The reference to him seems out of place, because he did not contribute to rebuilding the temple. He may have been inserted here since he contributed to the work of the temple at a later date under Ezra (7:21–24).

6:15 *temple was completed.* On Mar. 12, 516 BC, almost 70 years after its destruction. The renewed work on the temple had begun on Sept. 21, 520 (Hag 1:15), and sustained effort had continued for almost three and a half years. According to Hag 2:3, the older members who could remember the splendor of Solomon's temple were disappointed when they saw the smaller size of Zerubbabel's temple (cf. Ezr 3:12). Yet in the long run the second temple, though not as grand as the first, enjoyed a much longer life. The general plan of the second temple was similar to that of Solomon's, but the Most Holy Place was left empty because the ark of the covenant had been lost through the Babylonian conquest. According to Josephus (*Wars*, 5.5.5), on the Day of Atonement the high priest placed his censer on the slab of stone that marked the former location of the ark. The Holy Place was furnished with a table for the bread of the Presence, the incense altar, and one lampstand (Josephus, *Against Apion*, 2.8; in the Apocrypha, cf. 1 Maccabees 1:21–22; 4:49–51) instead of Solomon's ten (1Ki 7:49).

6:16 *exiles ... dedication.* Cf. the dedication of Solomon's temple (1Ki 8). The leaders of those who returned from exile were responsible for the completion of the temple. "Dedication" translates the Aramaic word *ḥanukkah.* The Jewish holiday in December that celebrates the recapture of the temple from the Seleucids and its rededication (165 BC) is also known as Hanukkah (see Jn 10:22 and NIV text note).

6:17 *hundred ... two hundred ... four hundred.* The number of animals sacrificed was small in comparison with similar services in the reigns of Solomon (1Ki 8:5,63), Hezekiah (2Ch 30:24) and Josiah (2Ch 35:7), when thousands rather than hundreds were offered.

6:18 *divisions.* The priests were separated into 24 divisions (1Ch 24:1–19), each of which served at the temple for a week at a time (cf. Lk 1:5,8). In 1962 fragments of a synagogue inscription listing the 24 divisions were found at Caesarea. *written in the Book of Moses.* Perhaps referring to such passages as Ex 29; Lev 8; Nu 3; 8:5–26; 18.

6:19 *fourteenth day ... first month ... Passover.* The date would have been about Apr. 21, 516 BC. For the origin and meaning of the Passover and the Festival of Unleavened Bread (v. 22) see Ex 12:1–30 and notes.

6:20 *purified themselves ... ceremonially clean.* See note on Lev 4:12. Priests and Levites had to be ceremonially clean to fulfill their ritual functions.

over lamb for all the exiles, for their relatives the priests and for themselves. 21 So
the Israelites who had returned from the
exile ate it, together with all who had separated themselves[t] from the unclean practices[u] of their Gentile neighbors in order to
seek the LORD,[v] the God of Israel. 22 For sev-
en days they celebrated with joy the Festival of Unleavened Bread,[w] because the
LORD had filled them with joy by changing
the attitude[x] of the king of Assyria so that
he assisted them in the work on the house
of God, the God of Israel.

Ezra Comes to Jerusalem

7 After these things, during the reign of
Artaxerxes[y] king of Persia, Ezra son
of Seraiah,[z] the son of Azariah, the son of
Hilkiah,[a] 2 the son of Shallum, the son of
Zadok,[b] the son of Ahitub,[c] 3 the son of Amariah, the son of Azariah, the son of Meraioth, 4 the son of Zerahiah, the son of Uzzi,
the son of Bukki, 5 the son of Abishua, the
son of Phinehas,[d] the son of Eleazar, the
son of Aaron the chief priest— 6 this Ezra[e]
came up from Babylon. He was a teacher
well versed in the Law of Moses, which
the LORD, the God of Israel, had given. The
king had granted[f] him everything he asked,
for the hand of the LORD his God was on
him.[g] 7 Some of the Israelites, including
priests, Levites, musicians, gatekeepers
and temple servants, also came up to Jerusalem in the seventh year of King Artaxerxes.[h]

8 Ezra arrived in Jerusalem in the fifth
month of the seventh year of the king. 9 He
had begun his journey from Babylon on
the first day of the first month, and he arrived in Jerusalem on the first day of the
fifth month, for the gracious hand of his
God was on him.[i] 10 For Ezra had devoted
himself to the study and observance of the
Law of the LORD, and to teaching[j] its decrees and laws in Israel.

King Artaxerxes' Letter to Ezra

11 This is a copy of the letter King Artaxerxes had given to Ezra the priest, a
teacher of the Law, a man learned in matters concerning the commands and decrees of the LORD for Israel:

12 Artaxerxes, king of kings,[k]

6:21 [t] Ezr 9:1; Ne 9:2 [u] S Dt 18:9; Eze 36:25 [v] 1Ch 22:19; Ps 14:2 **6:22** [w] S Ex 12:17 [x] S Ezr 1:1 **7:1** [y] S Ezr 4:7; S 6:14 [z] S 2Ki 25:18 [a] 2Ki 22:4 **7:2** [b] 1Ki 1:8; 2:35; 1Ch 6:8; Eze 40:46; 43:19; 44:15 [c] Ne 11:11 **7:5** [d] 1Ch 6:4 **7:6** [e] Ne 12:36 [f] S 2Ki 25:28 [g] S Ezr 5:5; S Isa 41:20 **7:7** [h] Ezr 8:1 **7:9** [i] ver 6 **7:10** [j] S Dt 33:10 **7:12** [k] Eze 26:7; Da 2:37

6:21 *with all who had separated themselves.* The returning ex-les were willing to accept those who separated themselves from the paganism of the foreigners who had been intro-duced into the area by the Assyrians.

6:22 *king of Assyria.* A surprising title for Darius, the Persian king. But even after the fall of Nineveh in 612 BC, the term "Assyria" continued to be used for former territories the As-syrians had occupied. Persian kings adopted a variety of titles, including "king of Babylon" (cf. 5:13; Ne 13:6).

7:1–5 The genealogy of Ezra given here lists 16 ancestors back to Aaron, the brother of Moses.

7:1 *After these things.* The events of the preceding chapter concluded with the completion of the temple in 516 BC. *Artaxerxes.* The identity of the king mentioned in this chapter has been disputed. If this was Artaxerxes I, which seems likely, Ezra would have arrived in Judah in 458, and there would be a gap of almost 60 years between the events of ch. 6 and those of ch. 7. The only recorded event during this interval is the opposition to the rebuilding of Jerusalem in the reign of Xerxes (486–465) in 4:6. *Ezra.* Perhaps a short-ened form of Azariah ("The LORD helps"), a name that occurs twice in the list of his ancestors. The Greek form is Esdras, as in the Apocrypha. *Seraiah.* Means "The LORD is prince." The high priest under Zedekiah, he was killed by Nebuchadnez-zar in 586 (2Ki 25:18–21), some 128 years before Ezra's ar-rival. He was therefore the ancestor rather than the father of Ezra; "son" often means "descendant" (see 1Ch 6:14–15). *Hilkiah.* Means "My portion is the LORD." He was the high priest under Josiah (2Ki 22:4).

7:2 *Zadok.* Means "righteous." He was a priest under David (2Sa 8:17). Solomon appointed Zadok as high priest in place of Abiathar, who supported the rebel Adonijah (1Ki 1:7–8; 2:35). Ezekiel regarded the Zadok-ites as free from idolatry (Eze 44:15). They held the office of high priest until 171 BC. The Sadducees may have been named after Zadok, and the Qumran community (see essay, pp. 1575–1576) looked for the restoration of the Zadokite priesthood. *Ahitub.* Probably means "My (divine) brother is good." He was actually the grandfather of Zadok (Ne 11:11).

7:5 *Eleazar.* Means "God helps."

7:6 *teacher.* Lit. "scribe" (see Ne 8:1,4,9,13; 12:26,36). Earlier, scribes served kings as secretaries, such as Shaphan under Josiah (2Ki 22:3, where the Hebrew word for "scribe" is trans-lated "secretary"). Other scribes took dictation—such as Bar-uch, who wrote down what Jeremiah spoke (Jer 36:32). From the exilic period on, the "scribes" were scholars who studied and taught the Scriptures ("scribes" is rendered "teachers of the law" in the NT; see notes on Mt 2:4; Lk 5:17). In the NT period they, among others, were addressed as "rabbis" (cf. Mt 23:7). *well versed.* The Hebrew for this phrase is translated "skillful" in Ps 45:1 and "skilled" in Pr 22:29. *hand of the LORD.* For this striking description of God's power and favor, cf. also vv. 9,28; 8:18,22,31; Ne 2:8,18.

7:7–9 *seventh year ... first day of the first month ... first day of the fifth month.* Ezra began his journey on the first of Nisan (Apr. 8, 458 BC) and arrived in Jerusalem on the first of Av (Aug. 4, 458). The journey took four months, including an 11-day delay indicated by the comparison of v. 9 with 8:31. The spring was the most auspicious time for such journeys; most armies went on campaigns at that time of the year (see 2Sa 11:1 and note). Although the actual distance between Babylon and Jerusalem is about 500 miles, the travelers had to cover a total of about 900 miles, going northwest along the Euphrates River and then south. The relatively slow pace was caused by the presence of the elderly and the children. See map, p. 2523, at the end of this study Bible; see also map, p. 724.

7:10 *study ... observance ... teaching.* See Ne 8.

7:11 *letter.* Many regard the letter of Artaxerxes I as the be-ginning point of Daniel's first 69 "sevens" (Da 9:24–27). Oth-ers regard the commission of Nehemiah by the same king as the starting point of this prophecy (Ne 1:1,11; 2:1–8). By using either a solar calendar with the former date (458 BC) or a lunar calendar with the latter date (444), one can arrive remarkably close to the date of Jesus' public ministry.

7:12 *king of kings.* The phrase was originally used by Assyr-ian kings, since their empires incorporated many kingdoms. It was then used by the later Babylonian (Eze 26:7; Da 2:37)

To Ezra the priest, teacher of the Law
of the God of heaven:

Greetings.

13 Now I decree that any of the Israelites in my kingdom, including
priests and Levites, who volunteer
to go to Jerusalem with you, may
go. 14 You are sent by the king and
his seven advisers[l] to inquire about
Judah and Jerusalem with regard to
the Law of your God, which is in
your hand. 15 Moreover, you are to
take with you the silver and gold that
the king and his advisers have freely
given[m] to the God of Israel, whose
dwelling[n] is in Jerusalem, 16 together with all the silver and gold[o] you
may obtain from the province of
Babylon, as well as the freewill offerings of the people and priests for
the temple of their God in Jerusalem.[p] 17 With this money be sure to
buy bulls, rams and male lambs,[q] together with their grain offerings and
drink offerings,[r] and sacrifice[s] them
on the altar of the temple of your
God in Jerusalem.

18 You and your fellow Israelites
may then do whatever seems best
with the rest of the silver and gold, in
accordance with the will of your God.
19 Deliver[t] to the God of Jerusalem all
the articles entrusted to you for worship in the temple of your God. 20 And
anything else needed for the temple
of your God that you are responsible
to supply, you may provide from the
royal treasury.[u]

21 Now I, King Artaxerxes, decree that all the treasurers of
Trans-Euphrates are to provide with
diligence whatever Ezra the priest,
the teacher of the Law of the God of
heaven, may ask of you— 22 up to a
hundred talents[a] of silver, a hundred
cors[b] of wheat, a hundred baths[c] of
wine, a hundred baths[c] of olive oil,
and salt without limit. 23 Whatever
the God of heaven has prescribed, let
it be done with diligence for the temple of the God of heaven. Why should
his wrath fall on the realm of the
king and of his sons?[v] 24 You are also
to know that you have no authority
to impose taxes, tribute or duty[w] on
any of the priests, Levites, musicians,
gatekeepers, temple servants or other
workers at this house of God.[x]

25 And you, Ezra, in accordance
with the wisdom of your God, which
you possess, appoint[y] magistrates and
judges to administer justice to all the
people of Trans-Euphrates—all who
know the laws of your God. And you
are to teach[z] any who do not know
them. 26 Whoever does not obey the

7:14 [l] Est 1:14
7:15 [m] S 1Ch 29:6 [n] S Dt 12:5; S 2Ch 6:2
7:16 [o] S Ex 3:22 [p] Zec 6:10
7:17 [q] S 2Ki 3:4 [r] Nu 15:5-12 [s] Dt 12:5-11
7:19 [t] Ezr 5:14; Jer 27:22
7:20 [u] S Ezr 6:4
7:23 [v] S Ezr 6:10
7:24 [w] S Ezr 4:13 [x] Ezr 8:36
7:25 [y] S Ex 18:21,26 [z] S Lev 10:11

[a] *22* That is, about 3 3/4 tons or about 3.4 metric tons [b] *22* That is, probably about 18 tons or about 16 metric tons [c] *22* That is, about 600 gallons or about 2,200 liters

and Persian kings. Cf. 1Ti 6:15; Rev 17:14; 19:16. See NIV text note on v. 26.

7:13 *Israelites.* It is noteworthy that "Israel" is used rather than "Judah." It was Ezra's aim to make one Israel of all who returned. The markedly Jewish coloring of this decree may have resulted from the king's use of Jewish officials, quite possibly Ezra himself, to help him compose it.

7:14 *seven advisers.* Cf. Est 1:14, which refers to the seven nobles who "had special access to the king." This corresponds with Persian practice as reported by the early Greek historians Herodotus and Xenophon. *Law of your God.* Perhaps the complete Pentateuch (the five books of Moses; see v. 6).

7:15 *silver and gold.* Cf. Hag 2:8. *freely given.* The Persian treasury had ample funds, and benevolence was a well-attested policy of Persian kings.

7:16 *offerings of the people.* The custom of sending gifts to Jerusalem from the Jews who lived outside the Holy Land continued until the Jewish-Roman War (AD 66–73), when the Romans forced the Jews to send such contributions to the temple of Jupiter instead (Josephus, *Antiquities*, 18.9.1; *Wars*, 7.6.6). There are close parallels to such directives in the contemporary letters from the Jewish garrison at Elephantine in Egypt, including a papyrus in which Darius II ordered: "Let grain offering, incense and burnt offering be offered" on Yahweh's altar "in your name."

7:20 *provide from the royal treasury.* Texts from the treasury at Persepolis also record the disbursement of supplies and funds from the royal purse.

7:22 *hundred talents.* An enormous amount (see NIV text note). *hundred cors.* The total was relatively small (see NIV text note). The wheat would be used in grain offerings. *salt without limit.* See note on 4:14. A close parallel is the benefaction of Antiochus III as recorded by Josephus (*Antiquities*, 12.3.3): "In the first place we have decided, on account of their piety, to furnish for their sacrifices an allowance of sacrificial animals, wine, oil and frankincense to the value of 20,000 pieces of silver, and sacred artabae of fine flour in accordance with their native law, and 1,460 medimni of wheat and 375 medimni of salt."

7:23 *wrath fall on the realm of the king.* Egypt had rebelled against the Persians in 460 BC and had expelled the Persians with the help of the Athenians in 459. In 458, when Ezra traveled to Jerusalem, the Persians were involved in suppressing this revolt. *his sons.* We do not know how many sons the king had at this time, but he ultimately had 18, according to Ctesias (a Greek physician who wrote an extensive history of Persia).

7:24 *no ... taxes ... or duty on any of the priests ... temple servants.* Priests and other temple personnel were often given exemptions from enforced labor or taxes. A close parallel is found in the Gadates Inscription of Darius I to a governor in western Turkey, granting exemptions to the priests of Apollo. Antiochus III granted similar exemptions to the Jews: "The priests, the scribes of the temple and the temple singers shall be relieved from the poll tax, the crown tax and the salt tax that they pay" (Josephus, *Antiquities*, 12.3.3).

7:26 *Whoever does not obey ... must surely be punished.* The extensive powers given to Ezra are striking and ex-law of your God and the law of the king must surely be punished by death, banishment, confiscation of property, or imprisonment.[a][a]

[27]Praise be to the LORD, the God of our
ancestors, who has put it into the king's
heart[b] to bring honor[c] to the house of the
LORD in Jerusalem in this way [28]and who
has extended his good favor[d] to me before
the king and his advisers and all the king's
powerful officials. Because the hand of the
LORD my God was on me,[e] I took courage
and gathered leaders from Israel to go up
with me.

List of the Family Heads Returning With Ezra

8 These are the family heads and those registered with them who came up with me from Babylon during the reign of King Artaxerxes:[f]

[2]of the descendants of Phinehas, Gershom;
of the descendants of Ithamar, Daniel;
of the descendants of David, Hattush
[3]of the descendants of Shekaniah;[g]

of the descendants of Parosh,[h] Zechariah, and with him were registered 150 men;

[4]of the descendants of Pahath-Moab,[i] Eliehoenai son of Zerahiah, and with him 200 men;

[5]of the descendants of Zattu,[b] Shekaniah son of Jahaziel, and with him 300 men;

[6]of the descendants of Adin,[j] Ebed son of Jonathan, and with him 50 men;

[7]of the descendants of Elam, Jeshaiah son of Athaliah, and with him 70 men;

[8]of the descendants of Shephatiah, Zebadiah son of Michael, and with him 80 men;

[9]of the descendants of Joab, Obadiah son of Jehiel, and with him 218 men;

[10]of the descendants of Bani,[c] Shelomith son of Josiphiah, and with him 160 men;

[11]of the descendants of Bebai, Zechariah son of Bebai, and with him 28 men;

[12]of the descendants of Azgad, Johanan son of Hakkatan, and with him 110 men;

[13]of the descendants of Adonikam,[k] the last ones, whose names were Eliphelet, Jeuel and Shemaiah, and with them 60 men;

[14]of the descendants of Bigvai, Uthai and Zakkur, and with them 70 men.

The Return to Jerusalem

[15]I assembled them at the canal that flows toward Ahava,[l] and we camped there three days. When I checked among the

7:26 [a]S Ezr 6:11 **7:27** [b]S Ezr 1:1 [c]S 1Ch 29:12 **7:28** [d]S 2Ki 25:28 [e]S Ezr 5:5 **8:1** [f]Ezr 7:7 **8:3** [g]1Ch 3:22 [h]S Ezr 2:3 **8:4** [i]Ezr 2:6 **8:6** [j]Ezr 2:15; Ne 7:20; 10:16 **8:13** [k]Ezr 2:13 **8:15** [l]ver 21,31

[a] *26* The text of 7:12-26 is in Aramaic. [b] *5* Some Septuagint manuscripts (also 1 Esdras 8:32); Hebrew does not have *Zattu.* [c] *10* Some Septuagint manuscripts (also 1 Esdras 8:36); Hebrew does not have *Bani.*

end to secular fields. Perhaps the implementation of these provisions involved Ezra in a great deal of traveling, which would explain the silence about his activities between his arrival and the arrival of Nehemiah 13 years later. A close parallel to the king's commission of Ezra may be found in an earlier commission by Darius I, who sent Udjahorresnet, a priest and scholar, back to Egypt. He ordered the codification of the Egyptian laws by the chief men of Egypt—a task that took from 518 to 503 BC. See NIV text note.

7:28 *me.* The first occurrence of the first person for Ezra—a trait that characterizes the Ezra memoirs, which begin in v. 27 and continue to the end of ch. 9.

8:1–21 In vv. 1–14 Ezra lists those who accompanied him on his return from Mesopotamia, including the descendants of 15 individuals. The figures of the men given total 1,496, in addition to the individuals named. There were also women and children (see note on v. 21). About 40 Levites (vv. 18–19) are also included, as are 220 "temple servants" (v. 20).

8:2 *Gershom.* For the meaning of the name see NIV text note on Ex 2:22. *Ithamar.* Also the name of the fourth son of Aaron (Ex 6:23).

8:3 *Zechariah.* Cf. v. 11. The name means "The LORD remembers"; it was the name of about 30 individuals mentioned in the Bible, including both the OT prophet and the father of John the Baptist (Lk 1:5–67).

8:4 *Eliehoenai.* Means "On the LORD are my eyes"; the name occurs only here and in 1Ch 26:3. Cf. Ps 25:15.

8:6 *Ebed.* May be a shortened form of Obadiah (cf. v. 9), meaning "servant of the LORD." *Jonathan.* Means "The LORD gives"; it was the name of 15 OT individuals.

8:7 *Athaliah.* The father of Jeshaiah. Athaliah was also the name of a famous queen, daughter of Ahab (2Ki 11).

8:8 *Michael.* Means "Who is like God?" It was the name of ten other Biblical personages, including the archangel (Da 10:13; Jude 9; Rev 12:7).

8:10 *Shelomith.* Although it is a feminine form (see also note on SS 6:13), it is often a man's name, as here. The Greek equivalent is Salome.

8:12 *Azgad.* See note on 2:12. *Johanan.* See note on 2:46.

8:15 *canal that flows toward Ahava.* Probably flows into either the Euphrates or the Tigris at a place not far from Babylon (the Kebar "River" in Eze 1:1 was also a canal; see note there). *three days.* Perhaps from the 9th to the 12th day of Nisan; the journey began on the 12th (see v. 31). *no Levites.* Since they were entrusted with many menial tasks, they may have found a more comfortable way of life in exile. A rabbinic midrash (comment) on Ps 137 relates the legend that Levites were in the caravan but were not qualified to officiate because when Nebuchadnezzar had ordered them to sing for him the songs of Zion "they refused and bit off the ends of their fingers, so that they could not play on the harps." In the Hellenistic era (following Alexander's conquest of the Holy Land in 333 BC) the role of the Levites declined sharply, though the Temple Scroll among the Dead Sea Scrolls from Qumran (see essay, pp. 1574–1575) assigns important roles to them.

people and the priests, I found no Levites[m] there. 16 So I summoned Eliezer, Ariel, Shemaiah, Elnathan, Jarib, Elnathan, Nathan, Zechariah and Meshullam, who were leaders, and Joiarib and Elnathan, who were men of learning, 17 and I ordered them to go to Iddo, the leader in Kasiphia. I told them what to say to Iddo and his fellow Levites, the temple servants[n] in Kasiphia, so that they might bring attendants to us for the house of our God. 18 Because the gracious hand of our God was on us,[o] they brought us Sherebiah,[p] a capable man, from the descendants of Mahli son of Levi, the son of Israel, and Sherebiah's sons and brothers, 18 in all; 19 and Hashabiah, together with Jeshaiah from the descendants of Merari, and his brothers and nephews, 20 in all. 20 They also brought 220 of the temple servants[q]—a body that David and the officials had established to assist the Levites. All were registered by name.

21 There, by the Ahava Canal,[r] I proclaimed a fast, so that we might humble ourselves before our God and ask him for a safe journey[s] for us and our children, with all our possessions. 22 I was ashamed to ask the king for soldiers[t] and horsemen to protect us from enemies on the road, because we had told the king, "The gracious hand of our God is on everyone[u] who looks to him, but his great anger is against all who forsake him.[v]" 23 So we fasted[w] and petitioned our God about this, and he answered our prayer.

24 Then I set apart twelve of the leading priests, namely, Sherebiah,[x] Hashabiah and ten of their brothers, 25 and I weighed out[y] to them the offering of silver and gold and the articles that the king, his advisers, his officials and all Israel present there had donated for the house of our God. 26 I weighed out to them 650 talents[a] of silver, silver articles weighing 100 talents,[b] 100 talents[b] of gold, 27 20 bowls of gold valued at 1,000 darics,[c] and two fine articles of polished bronze, as precious as gold.

28 I said to them, "You as well as these articles are consecrated to the LORD.[z] The silver and gold are a freewill offering to the LORD, the God of your ancestors. 29 Guard them carefully until you weigh them out in the chambers of the house of the LORD in Jerusalem before the leading priests and the Levites and the family heads of Israel." 30 Then the priests and Levites received the silver and gold and sacred articles that had been weighed out to be taken to the house of our God in Jerusalem.

31 On the twelfth day of the first month we set out from the Ahava Canal[a] to go to Jerusalem. The hand of our God was on us,[b] and he protected us from enemies and bandits along the way. 32 So we arrived in Jerusalem, where we rested three days.[c]

33 On the fourth day, in the house of our God, we weighed out[d] the silver and gold and the sacred articles into the hands of Meremoth[e] son of Uriah, the priest. Eleazar son of Phinehas was with him, and so were the Levites Jozabad[f] son of Jeshua and Noadiah son of Binnui.[g] 34 Everything was accounted for by number and weight, and the entire weight was recorded at that time.

35 Then the exiles who had returned from captivity sacrificed burnt offerings to

8:15 [m] S Ezr 2:40 **8:17** [n] Ezr 2:43 **8:18** [o] S Ezr 5:5 [p] ver 24 **8:20** [q] S 1Ch 9:2 **8:21** [r] S ver 15 [s] Ps 5:8; 27:11; 107:7 **8:22** [t] Ne 2:9; Jer 41:16 [u] S Ezr 5:5 [v] S Dt 31:17 **8:23** [w] S 2Ch 20:3; Ac 14:23 **8:24** [x] ver 18 **8:25** [y] ver 33

8:28 [z] S Lev 21:6; 22:2-3 **8:31** [a] S ver 15 [b] S Ezr 5:5 **8:32** [c] S Ge 40:13 **8:33** [d] ver 25 [e] Ne 3:4,21 [f] Ne 11:16 [g] Ne 3:24

[a] 26 That is, about 24 tons or about 22 metric tons
[b] 26 That is, about 3 3/4 tons or about 3.4 metric tons
[c] 27 That is, about 19 pounds or about 8.4 kilograms

8:16 *Ariel.* Means "lion of God" or "altar hearth" or possibly "City of God" (see note on Isa 29:1–2,7). It occurs only here as a personal name. *Meshullam.* Some assume that he is the same as the Meshullam who opposed the marriage reforms (10:15).
8:17 *Kasiphia.* Some have located it at the site that was later to become the Parthian capital of Ctesiphon on the Tigris River, north of Babylon.
8:18–19 *18 ... 20.* Only about 40 Levites from two families were found who were willing to join Ezra's caravan.
8:20 *temple servants.* See note on 2:43–57.
8:21 *safe journey.* Lit. "straight way"—unimpeded by obstacles and dangers (see v. 31; cf. Pr 3:6). *possessions.* The vast treasures they were carrying with them offered a tempting bait for robbers.
8:22 *I was ashamed.* Scripture speaks often of unholy shame (Jer 48:13; 49:23; Mic 3:7) and on occasion, as here, of holy shame. Ezra was quick to blush with such shame (see also 9:6). Having proclaimed his faith in God's ability to protect the caravan, he was embarrassed to ask for human protection. Grave dangers faced travelers going the great distance between Mesopotamia and the Holy Land. Some 13 years later Nehemiah was accompanied by an armed escort. The difference, however, does not mean that Nehemiah was a man of lesser faith (see note on Ne 2:9).
8:23 *fasted and petitioned.* For the association of fasting and prayer, see 2Sa 12:16; Ne 1:4; Da 9:3; Mt 17:21; Ac 14:23.
8:26 *650 talents ... 100 talents.* Enormous sums, worth millions of dollars today. See also note on 7:22.
8:27 *darics.* See NIV text note. The word occurs only here and in 2:69; 1Ch 29:7; Ne 7:70. *polished.* This kind of bronze may have been a bright yellow (the Hebrew for "yellow" in Lev 13:30,32,36 is related to the Hebrew for "polished" here) alloy of copper, which resembles gold and was highly prized in ancient times.
8:31 *twelfth day.* See notes on v. 15; 7:7–9.
8:32 *rested three days.* Nehemiah also took a similar rest period after his arrival in Jerusalem (Ne 2:11).
8:33 *Meremoth son of Uriah.* Probably the same as the man who repaired two sections of the wall (Ne 3:4,21).
8:34 *recorded.* According to Babylonian practice (e.g., in the Code of Hammurapi; see chart, p. xxii), almost every transaction, including sales and marriages, had to be recorded in writing. Ezra may have had to send back to Artaxerxes a signed certification of the delivery of the treasures.
8:35 *sacrificed.* Except for the identical number of male goats, the offerings here were far fewer than those presented by the

he God of Israel: twelve bulls[h] for all Is-
ael,[i] ninety-six rams, seventy-seven male
ambs and, as a sin offering,[a] twelve male
;oats.[j] All this was a burnt offering to the
.ORD. 36 They also delivered the king's or-
lers[k] to the royal satraps and to the gov-
ɹrnors of Trans-Euphrates,[l] who then gave
ıssistance to the people and to the house
of God.[m]

:zra's Prayer About Intermarriage

9 After these things had been done, the
leaders came to me and said, "The
ɪeople of Israel, including the priests and
he Levites, have not kept themselves sep-
rate[n] from the neighboring peoples with
heir detestable practices, like those of
he Canaanites, Hittites, Perizzites, Jebu-
ites,[o] Ammonites,[p] Moabites,[q] Egyptians
nd Amorites.[r] 2 They have taken some of
heir daughters[s] as wives for themselves
nd their sons, and have mingled[t] the holy
ace[u] with the peoples around them. And
he leaders and officials have led the way
n this unfaithfulness."[v]
3 When I heard this, I tore[w] my tunic and
loak, pulled hair from my head and beard
nd sat down appalled.[x] 4 Then everyone
who trembled[y] at the words of the God of
Israel gathered around me because of this
unfaithfulness of the exiles. And I sat there
appalled[z] until the evening sacrifice.
5 Then, at the evening sacrifice,[a] I rose
from my self-abasement, with my tunic
and cloak torn, and fell on my knees with
my hands[b] spread out to the LORD my God
6 and prayed:

"I am too ashamed[c] and disgraced,
my God, to lift up my face to you,
because our sins are higher than our
heads and our guilt has reached to the
heavens.[d] 7 From the days of our ancestors[e] until now, our guilt has been
great. Because of our sins, we and our
kings and our priests have been subjected to the sword[f] and captivity,[g] to
pillage and humiliation[h] at the hand
of foreign kings, as it is today.
8 "But now, for a brief moment, the
LORD our God has been gracious[i] in
leaving us a remnant[j] and giving us

8:35 [h] S Lev 1:3 [i] S 2Ch 29:24 [j] S 2Ch 29:21; S 30:24 **8:36** [k] Ezr 7:21-24 [l] Ne 2:7 [m] Est 9:3 **9:1** [n] S Ezr 6:21 [o] S Ge 10:16; S Jos 15:8 [p] Ge 19:38 [q] S Ge 19:37 [r] Ex 13:5; 23:28; Dt 20:17; S Jos 3:10; S Jdg 3:5; 1Ki 9:20; S 2Ch 8:7; Ne 9:8 **9:2** [s] S Ex 34:16; S Ru 1:4 [t] Ps 106:35 [u] S Ex 22:31; S Lev 27:30; S Dt 14:2 [v] Ezr 10:2 **9:3** [w] S Nu 14:6 [x] S Ex 32:19; S 33:4 **9:4** [y] Ezr 10:3; Ps 119:120; Isa 66:2,5 [z] Ne 1:4; Ps 119:136; Da 10:2 **9:5** [a] S Ex 29:41 [b] Ne 8:6; Ps 28:2; 134:2 **9:6** [c] Jer 31:19 [d] S 2Ch 28:9; Job 42:6; Ps 38:4; Isa 59:12; Jer 3:25; 14:20; Rev 18:5 **9:7** [e] S 2Ch 29:6 [f] Eze 21:1-32 [g] S Dt 28:64 [h] S Dt 28:37 **9:8** [i] Ps 25:16; 67:1; 119:58; Isa 33:2 [j] S Ge 45:7

[a] 35 Or *purification offering*

ɜturnees under Zerubbabel (6:17), who brought with him a ır greater number of families.

9:1 *After these things had been done ... have not kept themselves separate.* Ezra had reached Jerusalem in the fth month (7:9). The measures dealing with the problem of ıtermarriage were announced in the ninth month (10:9), or ɪur months after his arrival. Those who brought Ezra's atten-on to the problem were probably the ordinary members f the community rather than the leaders, who were them-elves guilty (v. 2). Malachi, who prophesied about the same me as Ezra's mission, indicates that some Jews had broken ɪeir marriages to marry daughters of a foreign god (Mal :10–16), perhaps the daughters of influential landholders. ne of the reasons for such intermarriages may have been ɪe shortage of returning Jewish women who were avail-ble. What happened to a Jewish community that was lax ɔncerning intermarriage can be seen in the example of the ephantine settlement in Egypt, which was contemporary ɪith Ezra and Nehemiah. There the Jews who married pagan pouses expressed their devotion to pagan gods in addition ɔ the Lord. The Elephantine community was gradually as-milated and disappeared. *neighboring peoples.* The eight ɾoups mentioned are representative of the original inhabi-ınts of Canaan before the Israelite conquest (see note on Ex :8). Only the Ammonites, Moabites and Egyptians were still ɪving there in the postexilic period (cf. 2Ch 8:7–8). *Canaan-es.* See note on Ge 10:6. *Hittites.* See note on Ge 10:15. *Per-zites.* See note on Ge 13:7. *Jebusites.* See note on Ge 10:16. *mmonites, Moabites.* See note on Ge 19:36–38. *Amorites.* ee note on Ge 10:16.

9:2 *holy race.* The Hebrew for this phrase is translated "holy seed" in Isa 6:13. *led the way.* In the wrong direc-on (see 10:18). *unfaithfulness.* See 10:6; Jos 22:16; Da 9:7. arrying those who did not belong to the Lord was an act f infidelity for the people of Israel (cf. Dt 7:1–6; 1Co 7:39 nd notes).

:3 *tore my tunic and cloak.* A common way to express grief or distress (see v. 5; Ge 37:29,34; Jos 7:6; Jdg 11:35; 2Sa 13:19; 2Ch 34:27; Est 4:1; Job 1:20; Isa 36:22; Jer 41:5; Mt 26:65). *pulled hair from my head and beard.* Unique in the Bible. Elsewhere we read about the shaving of one's head and/or beard (Job 1:20; Jer 41:5; 47:5; Eze 7:18; Am 8:10). When Nehemiah was confronted with the same problem of intermarriage, instead of pulling out his own hair he pulled out the hair of the offending parties (Ne 13:25).

9:4 *everyone who trembled.* Cf. Ex 19:16; Isa 66:2; Heb 12:21. *appalled.* See v. 3; cf. Da 4:19; 8:27. *evening sacrifice.* See Ex 12:6. The informants had probably visited Ezra in the morning, so that he must have sat appalled for many hours. The time of the evening sacrifice, usually about 3:00 p.m., was also the appointed time for prayer and confession (Ac 3:1).

9:5–15 See similar prayers in Ne 9:5–37; Da 9:3–19 (see also notes there).

9:5 *self-abasement.* The Hebrew for this word later meant "fasting." See note on Lev 16:29,31. *fell on my knees.* Cf. 1Ki 8:54; Ps 95:6; Da 6:10. *with my hands spread out.* See note on Ex 9:29.

9:6 *ashamed and disgraced.* See 8:22 and note; Lk 18:13. Ezra felt both an inner shame before God and an outward humiliation before people for his own sins and the sins of his people. The two Hebrew verbs often occur together; see Ps 35:4; Isa 45:16; Jer 31:19 ("ashamed and humiliated"). *our sins ... our guilt.* Cf. also vv. 7,13,15; 10:10,19; 1Ch 21:3; 2Ch 24:18; Ps 38:4. *has reached to the heavens.* But God's love is more than a match for our guilt (Ps 103:11–12).

9:7 *From the days of our ancestors.* Israelites were conscious of their corporate solidarity with their ancestors. *sword.* Cf. Ne 4:13. In Eze 21 "the sword of the king of Babylon" (21:19) is described as an instrument of divine judgment. *humiliation.* Cf. Da 9:7–8; 2Ch 32:21.

9:8 *remnant.* See Ge 45:7; Isa 1:9; 10:20–22; Ro 11:5 and notes. *firm place.* Lit. "nail" or "peg," like a nail driven into a wall (see Isa 22:23 and note) or a tent peg driven into the ground (Isa 33:20; 54:2). *light to our eyes.* An increase in light

a firm place[ak] in his sanctuary, and
so our God gives light to our eyes[l]
and a little relief in our bondage.
9Though we are slaves,[m] our God has
not forsaken us in our bondage. He
has shown us kindness[n] in the sight
of the kings of Persia: He has granted
us new life to rebuild the house of our
God and repair its ruins,[o] and he has
given us a wall of protection in Judah
and Jerusalem.
10"But now, our God, what can we
say after this? For we have forsaken
the commands[p] 11you gave through
your servants the prophets when you
said: 'The land you are entering[q] to
possess is a land polluted[r] by the corruption of its peoples. By their detestable practices[s] they have filled it with
their impurity from one end to the
other. 12Therefore, do not give your
daughters in marriage to their sons or
take their daughters for your sons. Do
not seek a treaty of friendship with
them[t] at any time, that you may be
strong[u] and eat the good things[v] of the
land and leave it to your children as
an everlasting inheritance.'[w]
13"What has happened to us is a
result of our evil[x] deeds and our great
guilt, and yet, our God, you have punished us less than our sins deserved[y]
and have given us a remnant like
this. 14Shall we then break your commands again and intermarry[z] with the
peoples who commit such detestable
practices? Would you not be angry
enough with us to destroy us,[a] leaving
us no remnant[b] or survivor? 15LORD,
the God of Israel, you are righteous![c]
We are left this day as a remnant.
Here we are before you in our guilt,
though because of it not one of us can
stand[d] in your presence.[e]"

9:8 [k]Ecc 12:11; Isa 22:23 [l]Ps 13:3; 19:8 **9:9** [m]S Ex 1:14; Ne 9:36 [n]S 2Ki 25:28; Ps 106:46 [o]Ps 69:35; Isa 43:1; 44:26; 48:20; 52:9; 63:9; Jer 32:44; Zec 1:16-17 **9:10** [p]Dt 11:8; Isa 1:19-20 **9:11** [q]Dt 4:5 [r]S Lev 18:25-28 [s]S Dt 9:4; S 18:9; S 1Ki 14:24 **9:12** [t]S Ex 34:15 [u]Dt 11:8 [v]S Ge 45:18 [w]Ps 103:17; Eze 37:25; Joel 3:20 **9:13** [x]S Ex 32:22 [y]Job 11:6; 15:5; 22:5; 33:27; Ps 103:10 **9:14** [z]Ne 13:27

[a]S Dt 9:8 [b]Dt 9:14 **9:15** [c]S Ge 18:25; S 2Ch 12:6; Ne 9:8; Ps 51:4; 129:4; 145:17; Isa 24:16; Jer 12:1; 23:6; 33:16; La 1:18; Da 9:7; Zep 3:5 [d]Ps 76:7; 130:3; Mal 3:2 [e]S 1Ki 8:47 **10:1** [f]2Ch 20:9; Da 9:20 [g]S Nu 25:6 **10:2** [h]ver 26 [i]S Ezr 9:2 [j]Dt 30:8-10

The People's Confession of Sin

10 While Ezra was praying and con
fessing,[f] weeping[g] and throwing
himself down before the house of God,
a large crowd of Israelites—men, wom-
en and children—gathered around him.
They too wept bitterly. 2Then Shekaniah
son of Jehiel, one of the descendants of
Elam,[h] said to Ezra, "We have been unfaithful[i] to our God by marrying foreign
women from the peoples around us. But
in spite of this, there is still hope for Israel.[j] 3Now let us make a covenant[k] before
our God to send away[l] all these women
and their children, in accordance with the
counsel of my lord and of those who fear
the commands of our God. Let it be done
according to the Law. 4Rise up; this matter
is in your hands. We will support you, so
take courage and do it."
5So Ezra rose up and put the leading
priests and Levites and all Israel under
oath[m] to do what had been suggested. And
they took the oath. 6Then Ezra withdrew
from before the house of God and went
to the room of Jehohanan son of Eliashib.

[a] 8 Or *a foothold*

10:3 [k]S 2Ki 11:17 [l]S Ex 34:16 **10:5** [m]Ne 5:12; 13:25

means vitality and joy (Ps 13:3; 19:8; Ecc 8:1; see note on Ps 6:7; cf. also note on Ps 27:1).

9:9 *kings of Persia.* The Achaemenid Persian kings were favorably disposed to the Jews: Cyrus the Great (559–530 BC) gave them permission to return (see 1:1 and note); his son Cambyses (530–522), though not named in the Bible, also favored the Jews, as we learn from Elephantine papyri; Darius I (522–486) renewed the decree of Cyrus (ch. 6); his son Xerxes (486–465) granted privileges and protection to Jews (Est 8–10); his son Artaxerxes I (465–424) gave authorizations to Ezra (ch. 7) and to Nehemiah (Ne 2). *repair its ruins.* Isaiah had prophesied that the Lord would restore Jerusalem's ruins (Isa 44:26), which would burst into singing (Isa 52:9; cf. 58:12; 61:4). *wall of protection.* Used of a city wall only in Mic 7:11. The use here is metaphorical (cf. Zec 2:4–5).

9:11–12 The references are not to a single OT passage but to several passages, such as Dt 11:8–9; Isa 1:19; Eze 37:25.

9:11 *your servants the prophets.* See notes on Jer 7:25; Zec 1:6. *corruption.* Of Canaanite idolatry and the immoral practices associated with it (Lev 18:3; 2Ch 29:5; La 1:17; Eze 7:20; 36:17). The degrading practices and beliefs of the Canaanites are described in texts from ancient Ugarit (see chart, p. xxiv).

9:14 *be angry.* God's anger came upon the Israelites because they had violated his covenant with them (Dt 7:4; 11:16–17; 29:26–28; Jos 23:16; Jdg 2:20).

9:15 *you are righteous.* See note on Ps 4:1. *our guilt.* A proper sense of God's holiness makes us aware of our unworthiness. See Isa 6:1–5; Lk 5:8. For comparable passages of national lament, see Ps 44; 60; 74; 79–80; 83; 85; 90; 108; 126; 129; 137.

10:1 *weeping.* Not silently but out loud (see 3:13 and note Ne 1:4; Joel 2:12). *throwing himself down.* The prophets and other leaders used object lessons, even bizarre actions, to attract people's attention (Isa 7:3; 8:1–4,18; Jer 13:1–11; 19; 27:2–12; Eze 4:1—5:4).

10:2 Ezra, as a wise teacher, waited for his audience to draw their own conclusions about what should be done. *Shekaniah.* Perhaps his father, Jehiel, is the Jehiel mentioned in v. 26 since he was also of the family of Elam. If so, Shekaniah was doubtless grieved that his father had married a non-Jewish woman. Six members of the clan of Elam were involved in intermarriage (v. 26).

10:3 *women and their children.* Mothers were given custody of their children when marriages were dissolved. When Hagar was dismissed, Ishmael was sent with her (Ge 21:14). In Babylonia divorced women were granted their children and had to wait for them to grow up before remarrying, according to the Code of Hammurapi (see chart, p. xxii). In Greece, however, children from broken homes remained with their fathers.

10:4 *Rise up.* Cf. David's exhortation (1Ch 22:16).

10:6 *room.* Such temple chambers were used as storerooms

Vhile he was there, he ate no food and
lrank no water,[n] because he continued to
nourn over the unfaithfulness of the ex-
les.
7 A proclamation was then issued
hroughout Judah and Jerusalem for all
he exiles to assemble in Jerusalem. 8 Any-
ne who failed to appear within three
lays would forfeit all his property, in ac-
ordance with the decision of the officials
nd elders, and would himself be expelled
rom the assembly of the exiles.

9 Within the three days, all the men of
udah and Benjamin[o] had gathered in Je-
usalem. And on the twentieth day of the
inth month, all the people were sitting in
he square before the house of God, great-
y distressed by the occasion and because
f the rain. 10 Then Ezra[p] the priest stood
p and said to them, "You have been un-
aithful; you have married foreign women,
dding to Israel's guilt.[q] 11 Now honor[a] the
ORD, the God of your ancestors, and do his
vill. Separate yourselves from the peoples
round you and from your foreign wives."[r]
12 The whole assembly responded with a
oud voice:[s] "You are right! We must do as
ou say. 13 But there are many people here
nd it is the rainy season; so we cannot
tand outside. Besides, this matter cannot
e taken care of in a day or two, because
ve have sinned greatly in this thing. 14 Let
ur officials act for the whole assembly.
hen let everyone in our towns who has
narried a foreign woman come at a set
time, along with the elders and judges[t] of
each town, until the fierce anger[u] of our
God in this matter is turned away from
us." 15 Only Jonathan son of Asahel and
Jahzeiah son of Tikvah, supported by Meshullam and Shabbethai[v] the Levite, opposed this.
16 So the exiles did as was proposed.
Ezra the priest selected men who were
family heads, one from each family division, and all of them designated by name.
On the first day of the tenth month they
sat down to investigate the cases, 17 and
by the first day of the first month they finished dealing with all the men who had
married foreign women.

10:6 [n]S Ex 34:28; Dt 9:18; Ps 102:4; Jnh 3:7 **10:9** [o]S Ezr 1:5 **10:10** [p]Ezr 7:21 [q]2Ch 28:13 **10:11** [r]S Dt 24:1; Mal 2:10-16 **10:12** [s]S Jos 6:5 **10:14** [t]Dt 16:18 [u]S Nu 25:4; S 2Ch 29:10 **10:15** [v]Ne 11:16 **10:18** [w]S Jdg 3:6 [x]S Ezr 2:2 **10:19** [y]S 2Ki 10:15 [z]S Lev 5:15; 6:6 **10:20** [a]S 1Ch 24:14 **10:21** [b]S 1Ch 24:8

Those Guilty of Intermarriage

18 Among the descendants of the priests,
the following had married foreign
women:[w]

From the descendants of Joshua[x] son
of Jozadak, and his brothers: Maaseiah, Eliezer, Jarib and Gedaliah.
19 (They all gave their hands[y] in
pledge to put away their wives, and
for their guilt they each presented a
ram from the flock as a guilt offering.)[z]
20 From the descendants of Immer:[a]
Hanani and Zebadiah.
21 From the descendants of Harim:[b]
Maaseiah, Elijah, Shemaiah, Jehiel
and Uzziah.

[a] *11* Or *Now make confession to*

:29; Ne 13:4 – 5). *ate no food and drank no water.* Complete sting from both food and drink was rare. Moses did it twice x 34:28; Dt 9:18), and the Ninevites also did it (Jnh 3:7). Ordinarily, fasting involved abstaining only from eating (1Sa 7; 2Sa 3:35). *mourn.* The Hebrew for this word describes the reaction of those aware of the threat of deserved dgment (Ex 33:4; Nu 14:39).

10:7 – 8 While Ezra continued to fast and pray, the officials and elders ordered all the exiles to assemble Jerusalem. Although Ezra had been invested with great uthority (7:25 – 26), he used it sparingly and influenced the eople by his example.

0:8 *within three days.* Since the territory of Judah had been uch reduced, the most distant people would not be more an 50 miles from Jerusalem. The borders were Bethel in the orth, Beersheba in the south, Jericho in the east and Ono in e west (cf. Ne 7:26 – 38; 11:25 – 35). *forfeit.* The Hebrew for is word means "to ban from profane use and to devote to e Lord," either by destruction (see Ex 22:20; Dt 13:12 – 18 nd NIV text notes) or by giving it to the Lord's treasury (cf. ev 27:28; Jos 6:19; 7:1 – 15).

0:9,16 – 17 See chart, p. 726.

0:9 *Judah and Benjamin.* See note on 1:5. *square.* Either the uter court of the temple or the open space before the Water ate (Ne 8:1). *rain.* The Hebrew for this word is a plural of tensity, indicating torrential rains. The ninth month, Kislev lovember-December), is in the middle of the "rainy season" . 13), which begins with light showers in October and lasts mid-April. December and January are also cold months, with temperatures in the 50s and even 40s in Jerusalem. The people shivered not only because they were drenched but perhaps also because they sensed divine displeasure in the heavy rains (see 1Sa 12:17 – 18; Eze 13:11,13).

10:10 *adding to Israel's guilt.* See Ex 9:34; Jdg 3:12; 4:1; 2Ch 28:13. The sins and failures of the exiles were great enough, but they added insult to injury by marrying pagan women.

10:11 *Separate yourselves.* See Nu 16:21; 2Co 6:14.

10:12 *with a loud voice.* See Ne 9:4.

10:14 *elders and judges of each town.* See Dt 16:18; 19:12; 21:3,19; Ru 4:2.

10:15 Perhaps these four men opposed the measure because they wanted to protect themselves or their relatives, or they may have viewed it as being too harsh. *Tikvah.* Means "hope" (found elsewhere only in 2Ki 22:14). *Meshullam.* See note on 8:16. If he is the Meshullam of v. 29, he himself had married a pagan wife.

10:16 – 17 The committee completed its work in three months, discovering that about 110 men were guilty of marrying pagan wives.

10:18 – 22 See 2:36 – 39.

10:19 *gave their hands.* For the symbolic use of the hands in making commitments or pledges, cf. notes on Ge 14:22; Pr 6:1. *ram.* Guilt offerings were to be made for sins committed unintentionally (Lev 5:14 – 19) as well as intentionally (Lev 6:1 – 7), and a ram was the appropriate offering in either case (Lev 5:15; 6:6).

22 From the descendants of Pashhur:[c]
Elioenai, Maaseiah, Ishmael, Nethanel, Jozabad and Elasah.

23 Among the Levites:[d]

Jozabad, Shimei, Kelaiah (that is, Kelita), Pethahiah, Judah and Eliezer.

24 From the musicians:
Eliashib.[e]
From the gatekeepers:
Shallum, Telem and Uri.

25 And among the other Israelites:

From the descendants of Parosh:[f]
Ramiah, Izziah, Malkijah, Mijamin, Eleazar, Malkijah and Benaiah.
26 From the descendants of Elam:[g]
Mattaniah, Zechariah, Jehiel, Abdi, Jeremoth and Elijah.
27 From the descendants of Zattu:
Elioenai, Eliashib, Mattaniah, Jeremoth, Zabad and Aziza.
28 From the descendants of Bebai:
Jehohanan, Hananiah, Zabbai and Athlai.
29 From the descendants of Bani:
Meshullam, Malluk, Adaiah, Jashub, Sheal and Jeremoth.
30 From the descendants of Pahath-Moab:
Adna, Kelal, Benaiah, Maaseiah, Mattaniah, Bezalel, Binnui and Manasseh.
31 From the descendants of Harim:
Eliezer, Ishijah, Malkijah, Shemaiah, Shimeon,
32 Benjamin, Malluk and Shemariah.
33 From the descendants of Hashum:
Mattenai, Mattattah, Zabad, Eliphelet, Jeremai, Manasseh and Shimei.
34 From the descendants of Bani:
Maadai, Amram, Uel,
35 Benaiah, Bedeiah, Keluhi,
36 Vaniah, Meremoth, Eliashib,
37 Mattaniah, Mattenai and Jaasu.
38 From the descendants of Binnui:[a]
Shimei,
39 Shelemiah, Nathan, Adaiah,
40 Maknadebai, Shashai, Sharai,
41 Azarel, Shelemiah, Shemariah,
42 Shallum, Amariah and Joseph.
43 From the descendants of Nebo:
Jeiel, Mattithiah, Zabad, Zebina, Jaddai, Joel and Benaiah.

44 All these had married foreign women and some of them had children by these wives.[b]

10:22 [c] S 1Ch 9:12
10:23 [d] Ne 8:7; 9:4
10:24 [e] Ne 3:1; 12:10; 13:7,28
10:25 [f] S Ezr 2:3
10:26 [g] S ver 2

[a] *37,38* See Septuagint (also 1 Esdras 9:34); Hebrew *Jaasu* [38] *and Bani and Binnui,* [b] *44* Or *and they sent them away with their children*

10:24 It is striking that only one musician and three gatekeepers were involved. No temple servants (2:43 – 54) or descendants of Solomon's servants (2:55 – 57) sinned through intermarriage.
10:25 – 43 See 2:3 – 20.
10:30 *Bezalel.* Cf. Ex 31:2.
10:31 *Shimeon.* The Hebrew for this name is the same as that for Simeon, Jacob's second son (see NIV text note on Ge 29:33). In Greek the name became Simon (e.g., Mt 4:18).
10:43 *Nebo.* The Hebrew equivalent of the name of the Babylonian god Nabu (see Isa 46:1 and note); found only here as a personal name.
10:44 Some of the marriages had produced children, but this was not accepted as a reason for halting the divorce proceedings. See NIV text note.

NEHEMIAH

INTRODUCTION

See Introduction to Ezra.

Outline

- I. Nehemiah's First Administration (chs. 1 – 12)
  - A. Nehemiah's Response to the Situation in Jerusalem (ch. 1)
    1. News of the plight of Jerusalem (1:1 – 4)
    2. Nehemiah's prayer (1:5 – 11)
  - B. Nehemiah's Journey to Jerusalem (2:1 – 10)
    1. The king's permission (2:1 – 8)
    2. The journey itself (2:9 – 10)
  - C. Nehemiah's First Actions upon Arrival (2:11 – 20)
    1. His nocturnal inspection of the walls (2:11 – 16)
    2. His exhortation to rebuild (2:17 – 18)
    3. His response to opposition (2:19 – 20)
  - D. List of the Builders of the Wall (ch. 3)
    1. The northern section (3:1 – 7)
    2. The western section (3:8 – 13)
    3. The southern section (3:14)
    4. The eastern section (3:15 – 32)
  - E. Opposition to Rebuilding the Wall (ch. 4)
    1. The derision of Sanballat and Tobiah (4:1 – 5)
    2. The threat of attack (4:6 – 15)
    3. Rebuilding the wall (4:16 – 23)
  - F. Social and Economic Problems (ch. 5)
    1. The complaints of the poor (5:1 – 5)
    2. The cancellation of debts (5:6 – 13)
    3. Nehemiah's unselfish example (5:14 – 19)
  - G. The Wall Rebuilt Despite Opposition (ch. 6)
    1. Attempts to snare Nehemiah (6:1 – 9)
    2. The hiring of false prophets (6:10 – 14)
    3. The completion of the wall (6:15 – 19)

a quick look

Author:
Unknown; possibly Ezra appropriating Nehemiah's memoirs

Audience:
The people of Judah who had returned from exile in Babylonia

Date:
Sometime after 430 BC

Theme:
Nehemiah travels from Susa in Elam to Jerusalem in Judah to lead the Jews in rebuilding the city walls.

Achaemenid tombs at Naqsh-i-Rustam, Iran, from left to right: Darius I, Xerxes I, Artaxerxes I. Nehemiah was the cupbearer for Artaxerxes and was sent by him to Jerusalem to help rebuild the city walls (Ne 2).

H. List of Exiles (7:1 – 73a)
  1. Provisions for the protection of Jerusalem (7:1 – 3)
  2. Nehemiah's discovery of the list of returnees (7:4 – 5)
  3. The returnees delineated (7:6 – 72)
  4. Settlement of the exiles (7:73a)

I. Ezra's Preaching and the Outbreak of Revival (7:73b — 10:39)
  1. The public explanation of the Scriptures (7:73b — 8:12)
  2. The Festival of Tabernacles (8:13 – 18)
  3. A day of fasting, confession and prayer (9:1 – 37)
  4. A binding agreement (9:38)
  5. A list of those who sealed the agreement (10:1 – 29)
  6. Provisions of the agreement (10:30 – 39)

J. New Residents of Judah and Jerusalem (ch. 11)
  1. New residents for Jerusalem (11:1 – 24)
     a. Introductory remarks (11:1 – 4a)
     b. Residents from Judah (11:4b – 6)
     c. From Benjamin (11:7 – 9)
     d. From the priests (11:10 – 14)
     e. From the Levites (11:15 – 18)
     f. From the temple staff (11:19 – 24)

2. New residents for Judah (11:25 – 36)
    a. Places settled by people from Judah (11:25 – 30)
    b. Places settled by people from Benjamin (11:31 – 35)
    c. Transfer of Levites from Judah to Benjamin (11:36)
K. Lists of Priests and the Dedication of the Wall (ch. 12)
    1. Priests and Levites from the first return (12:1 – 9)
    2. High priests and Levites since Joiakim (12:10 – 26)
    3. Dedication of the wall of Jerusalem (12:27 – 43)
    4. Regulation of the temple offerings and services (12:44 – 47)

II. Nehemiah's Second Administration (ch. 13)
A. Abuses during His Absence (13:1 – 5)
    1. Mixed marriages (13:1 – 3)
    2. Tobiah's occupation of the temple quarters (13:4 – 5)
B. Nehemiah's Return (13:6 – 9)
    1. His arrival (13:6 – 7)
    2. His expulsion of Tobiah (13:8 – 9)
C. Reorganization and Reforms (13:10 – 31)
    1. Offerings for the temple staff (13:10 – 14)
    2. Abuse of the Sabbath (13:15 – 22)
    3. Mixed marriages (13:23 – 29)
    4. Provisions of wood and firstfruits (13:30 – 31)

Nehemiah's Prayer

1 The words of Nehemiah son of Hakaliah:

In the month of Kislev[a] in the twentieth
year, while I was in the citadel of Susa,[b]
2 Hanani,[c] one of my brothers, came from
Judah with some other men, and I questioned them about the Jewish remnant[d]
that had survived the exile, and also about
Jerusalem.
3 They said to me, "Those who survived
the exile and are back in the province are
in great trouble and disgrace. The wall of
Jerusalem is broken down, and its gates
have been burned with fire.[e]"
4 When I heard these things, I sat down
and wept.[f] For some days I mourned and
fasted[g] and prayed before the God of heav-
en. 5 Then I said:

"LORD, the God of heaven, the great
and awesome God,[h] who keeps his
covenant of love[i] with those who love
him and keep his commandments,
6 let your ear be attentive and your
eyes open to hear[j] the prayer[k] your
servant is praying before you day and
night for your servants, the people of
Israel. I confess[l] the sins we Israelites,
including myself and my father's family, have committed against you. 7 We
have acted very wickedly[m] toward

1:1 [a] Zec 7:1 [b] S Ezr 4:9; S Est 2:8 **1:2** [c] Ne 7:2 [d] S 2Ki 21:14; Ne 7:6; Jer 52:28 **1:3** [e] S Lev 26:31; 2Ki 25:10; Ne 2:3, 13, 17; Isa 22:9; Jer 39:8; 52:14; La 2:9 **1:4** [f] Ps 137:1 [g] S 2Ch 20:3; S Ezr 9:4; Da 9:3 **1:5** [h] S Dt 7:21; Ne 4:14 [i] S Dt 7:9; S 1Ki 8:23; Da 9:4 **1:6** [j] S 1Ki 8:29; S 2Ch 7:15 [k] S 1Ki 8:30 [l] S 1Ki 8:47 **1:7** [m] Ps 106:6

1:1 *The words of.* Originally an introduction to the title of a separate composition (see Jer 1:1; Am 1:1), though the books of Ezra and Nehemiah appear as a single work from earliest times (see Introduction to Ezra: Ezra and Nehemiah). *Nehemiah.* Means "The LORD comforts." *Kislev ... twentieth year.* November-December, 445 BC. See chart, p. 726. *Susa.* See note on Ezr 4:9.

1:2 *Hanani.* Probably a shortened form of Hananiah, which means "The LORD is gracious." *one of my brothers.* See 7:2. The Elephantine papyri (see chart, p. xxii) mention a Hananiah who was the head of Jewish affairs in Jerusalem. Many believe that he is to be identified with Nehemiah's brother and that he may have governed between Nehemiah's first and second terms. *Jewish remnant.* See Ezr 9:8 and notes on Ge 45:7; 2Ki 19:30–31; Isa 1:9; 10:20–22; Zec 8:23.

1:3 *province.* See note on Ezr 2:1. *wall of Jerusalem is broken down.* The lack of a city wall meant that the people were defenseless against their enemies. Thucydides (1.89) describes the comparable condition of Athens after its devastation by the Persians in 480–479 BC. Excavations at Jerusalem during 1961–67 revealed that the lack of a wall on the eastern slopes also meant the disintegration of the terraces there. When Nebuchadnezzar assaulted Jerusalem in 586, he battered and broke down the walls around it (2Ki 25:10). But most interpreters do not believe that Nehemiah's distress was caused by Nebuchadnezzar's destruction but by the episode of Ezr 4:7–23. The Jews had attempted to rebuild the walls earlier in the reign of Artaxerxes I, but after the protest of Rehum and Shimshai the king ordered the Jews to desist. See note on Ezr 4:21–23.

1:4 *sat down.* Cf. Ezr 9:3; Job 2:13. *wept.* See 8:9; Ezr 3:13 and note; 10:1; Est 8:3. *mourned.* See Ezr 10:6; Da 10:2. *fasted and prayed.* See note on Ezr 8:23. During the exile, fasting became a common practice, including solemn fasts to commemorate the fall of Jerusalem and the murder of Gedaliah (see note on Zec 8:19; see also Est 4:16; Da 9:3; 10:3; Zec 7:3–7). *God of heaven.* See note on Ezr 1:2.

1:5 *who keeps his covenant of love.* See 9:32; see also Dt 7:9,12 and note. *who love him and keep his commandments.* See Da 9:4; Ex 20:6 and note.

1:6 *praying before you day and night.* Cf. Ps 42:3; 88:1; Jer 9:1; 14:17; La 2:18; Lk 2:37; 1Th 3:10; 1Ti 5:5; 2Ti 1:3. *sins ... myself and my father's family.* Nehemiah does not exclude himself or members of his own family in his confession of sins. A true sense of the awesome holiness of God reveals the depths of our own sinfulness (Isa 6:1–5; Lk 5:8).

THE MURASHU TEXTS AND THE ELEPHANTINE PAPYRI

Two collections of valuable documents illuminate the lives of Jews living in the Diaspora (the dispersion) during the Persian era: the Murashu cuneiform texts from Mesopotamia and the Elephantine papyri from Egypt.

Murashu and Sons were wealthy bankers and brokers who loaned almost everything at a price. About 700 of the cuneiform texts from their archives, which span the period from 454 to 404 BC, have now been published. In documents like these, theophoric names with various forms of the name *Yahweh* (Yah, Yeho, Yahu, Ya, Yama) may be recognized as Jewish. Among 2,500 individuals mentioned in the texts, about 70 (approximately 3 percent) are likely Jews. Jews were found in 28 of 200 settlements in the region around Nippur in southern Mesopotamia.

Aramaic papyri from a Jewish military garrison serving the Persians, on the island of Elephantine near Aswan, shed valuable light on a Jewish community in Egypt from 495 to 398 BC. About 40 of the 95 Jewish names from Elephantine contain some form of the name *Yahweh*. The letters reveal that Egyptians had destroyed the Jewish temple in their area. The papyri reveal the incidence of mixed marriages, which led to syncretistic practices. One papyrus names the sons of Sanballat, thus confirming that Nehemiah's opponent was indeed the governor of Samaria.

you. We have not obeyed the commands, decrees and laws you gave
your servant Moses.
8 "Remember[n] the instruction you
gave your servant Moses, saying, 'If
you are unfaithful, I will scatter[o] you
among the nations, 9 but if you return
to me and obey my commands, then
even if your exiled people are at the
farthest horizon, I will gather[p] them
from there and bring them to the
place I have chosen as a dwelling for
my Name.'[q]
10 "They are your servants and your
people, whom you redeemed by your
great strength and your mighty hand.[r]
11 Lord, let your ear be attentive[s] to
the prayer of this your servant and
to the prayer of your servants who
delight in revering your name. Give
your servant success today by granting him favor[t] in the presence of this
man."

I was cupbearer[u] to the king.

Artaxerxes Sends Nehemiah to Jerusalem

2 In the month of Nisan in the twentieth
year of King Artaxerxes,[v] when wine
was brought for him, I took the wine and
gave it to the king. I had not been sad in
his presence before, 2 so the king asked
me, "Why does your face look so sad
when you are not ill? This can be nothing
but sadness of heart."
I was very much afraid, 3 but I said to
the king, "May the king live forever![w] Why
should my face not look sad when the
city[x] where my ancestors are buried lies in
ruins, and its gates have been destroyed
by fire?[y]"
4 The king said to me, "What is it you
want?"
Then I prayed to the God of heaven,
5 and I answered the king, "If it pleases the
king and if your servant has found favor
in his sight, let him send me to the city in
Judah where my ancestors are buried so
that I can rebuild it."
6 Then the king[z], with the queen sitting
beside him, asked me, "How long will
your journey take, and when will you get
back?" It pleased the king to send me; so
I set a time.
7 I also said to him, "If it pleases the
king, may I have letters to the governors of
Trans-Euphrates,[a] so that they will provide
me safe-conduct until I arrive in Judah?
8 And may I have a letter to Asaph, keeper of the royal park, so he will give me

1:8 [n] S Ge 8:1; S 2Ki 20:3; Ne 4:14; 5:19; 6:14; 13:22, 29, 31 [o] S Lev 26:33 **1:9** [p] S Dt 30:4; Ps 106:47; 107:3; Isa 11:12; 56:8; Jer 42:12; Eze 11:17 [q] S 1Ki 8:48; Jer 29:14; Eze 11:17; 20:34-38; 36:24-38; Mic 2:12 **1:10** [r] S Ex 32:11; Isa 51:9-11 **1:11** [s] S 2Ch 6:40 [t] S Ex 3:21 [u] S Ge 40:1 **2:1** [v] S Ezr 4:7; S 6:14 **2:3** [w] 1Ki 1:31; Da 2:4; 3:9; 5:10; 6:6, 21 [x] Ps 137:6 [y] S Ne 1:3 **2:6** [z] Ne 5:14; 13:6 **2:7** [a] S Ezr 8:36

1:7 *commands, decrees and laws.* See note on Ge 26:5. *laws you gave ... Moses.* For the prominence of the Mosaic law in Ezra and Nehemiah, see Ezr 3:2; 6:18; 7:6; Ne 1:8; 8:1,14; 9:14; 10:29; 13:1.

1:8 *Remember.* See notes on 13:31; Ge 8:1; a key word in the book (4:14; 5:19; 6:14; 13:14, 22,29,31). *unfaithful ... scatter.* Dispersion was the inescapable consequence of the people's unfaithfulness. By the NT period there were still more Jews in the Diaspora (dispersion) than in the Holy Land.

1:9 *I will gather them.* See Dt 30:1 – 5; a frequent promise, especially in the Prophets (e.g., Isa 11:12; Jer 23:3; 31:8 – 10; Eze 20:34,41; 36:24; Mic 2:12). *chosen as a dwelling for my Name.* See Dt 12:5 and note; Ps 132:13.

1:10 *your people ... you redeemed.* Although they had sinned and failed, they were still God's people by virtue of his redeeming them (see Dt 4:34; 9:29).

1:11 *Give your servant success today.* Cf. Ge 24:12. *cupbearer.* Lit. "one who gives (someone) something to drink." The Hebrew for this word occurs 11 other times in the OT in the sense of "cupbearer" (Ge 40:1,2,5,9,13,20,21,23; 41:9; 1Ki 10:5; 2Ch 9:4). According to the Greek historian Xenophon (*Cyropaedia*, 1.3.9), one of the cupbearer's duties was to choose and taste the king's wine to make certain that it was not poisoned (see 2:1). Thus Nehemiah had to be a man who enjoyed the unreserved confidence of the king. The need for trustworthy court attendants is underscored by the intrigues that characterized the Achaemenid court of Persia. Xerxes, the father of Artaxerxes I, was killed in his own bedchamber by a courtier.

2:1 *Nisan ... twentieth year.* March-April, 444 BC (see chart, p. 726). *King Artaxerxes.* See chart, p. 511. *sad in his presence.* No matter what one's personal problems were, the king's servants were expected to keep their feelings to themselves and to display a cheerful disposition before him.

2:3 *May the king live forever!* A common form of address to kings (cf. note on Ps 62:4). *city.* Nehemiah does not mention Jerusalem by name (see v. 5); he may have wished to arouse the king's sympathy by stressing first the desecration of ancestral tombs.

2:4 *prayed.* Before turning to answer the king, Nehemiah utters a brief, spontaneous prayer to God. One of Nehemiah's striking characteristics is his frequent recourse to prayer (1:4; 4:4,9; 5:19; 6:9,14; 13:14,22,29,31).

2:6 *queen.* The Hebrew for this word is used only here and in Ps 45:9 ("royal bride"). It is a loanword from Akkadian and means lit. "(woman) of the palace." The Aramaic equivalent is found only in Da 5:2 – 3,23, where it is translated "wives." Ctesias, a Greek who lived at the Achaemenid court, informs us that the name of Artaxerxes' queen was Damaspia and that he had at least three concubines. Like Esther (Est 5), Damaspia may have used her influence with the king. The Achaemenid court was notorious for the great influence exercised by the royal women. Especially domineering was Amestris, the cruel wife of Xerxes and mother of Artaxerxes I. *How long will your journey take ... ?* Nehemiah probably asked for a brief leave of absence, which he then had extended. We can infer from 5:14 that he spent 12 years on his first term as governor of Judah. In the 32nd year of Artaxerxes, Nehemiah returned to report to the king and then came back to Judah for a second term (13:6 – 7). See photo, p. 744.

2:7 *letters ... provide me safe-conduct.* A contemporary document from Arsames, the satrap of Egypt who was at the Persian court, to one of his officers who was returning to Egypt orders Persian officials to provide him with food and drink on the stages of his journey. *Trans-Euphrates.* See note on Ezr 4:10.

2:8 *park.* The Hebrew for this word is *pardes*, a loanword from Old Persian meaning "enclosure," a pleasant retreat. The word occurs elsewhere in the OT only in Ecc 2:5 ("parks") and SS 4:13 ("orchard"). In the Septuagint (the pre-Christian Greek

JERUSALEM OF THE **RETURNING EXILES**

AFTER 458 BC

A smaller city was rebuilt, with new walls higher on the eastern hill. Temple worship was restored in a rebuilt temple on the former site. Rebuilding on the western hill did not occur until later.

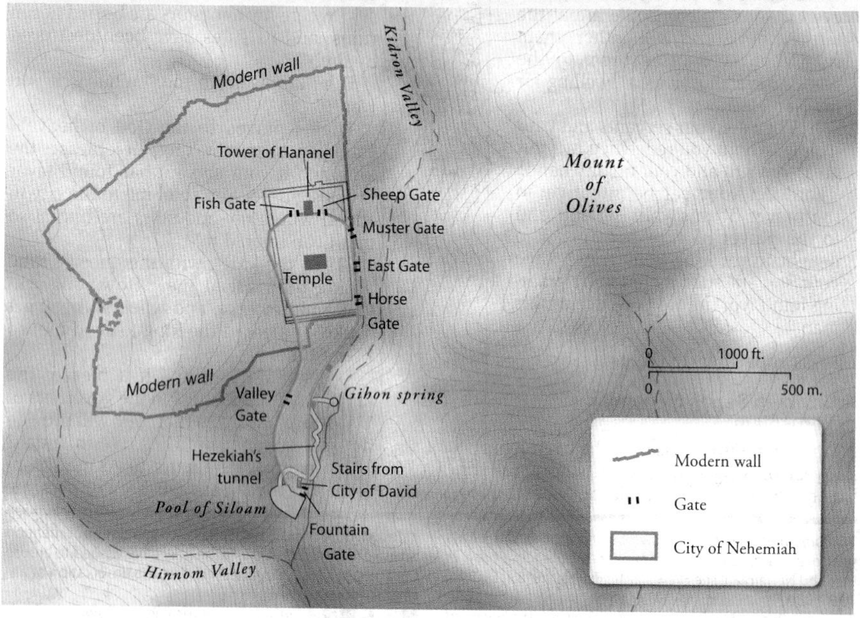

timber to make beams for the gates of the
citadel[b] by the temple and for the city wall
and for the residence I will occupy?" And
because the gracious hand of my God was
on me,[c] the king granted my requests.[d] 9So
I went to the governors of Trans-Euphrates
and gave them the king's letters. The king
had also sent army officers and cavalry[e]
with me.
10When Sanballat[f] the Horonite and Tobiah[g] the Ammonite official heard about
this, they were very much disturbed that
someone had come to promote the welfare
of the Israelites.[h]

2:8 [b]Ne 7:2 [c]S Ezr 5:5 [d]S Ezr 4:24
2:9 [e]S Ezr 8:22
2:10 [f]ver 19; Ne 4:1,7; 6:1-2, 5,12,14; 13:28 [g]Ne 4:3; 13:4-7 [h]Est 10:3

---

translation of the OT) the Greek transliteration *paradeisos* is used here. In the period between the OT and the NT, the word acquired the sense of the abode of the blessed dead, i.e., "paradise." It appears three times in the NT (Lk 23:43; 2Co 12:4; Rev 2:7). As to the location of the "royal park," some believe that it was in Lebanon, which was famed for its forests of cedars and other coniferous trees (see notes on Jdg 9:15; Ezr 3:7). But a more plausible suggestion is that it should be identified with Solomon's gardens at Etham, about six miles south of Jerusalem (see Josephus, *Antiquities*, 8.7.3). For city gates, costly imported cedars from Lebanon would not be used but rather indigenous oak, poplar or terebinth (Hos 4:13). *citadel.* Probably refers to the fortress north of the temple, the forerunner of the Antonia fortress built by Herod the Great (Josephus, *Antiquities*, 15.11.4; see Ac 21:34,37; 22:24).
2:9 *army officers and cavalry.* In striking contrast to Ezra (see note on Ezr 8:22), Nehemiah was accompanied by an armed escort since he was officially Judah's governor.

2:10 *Sanballat.* A Babylonian name, meaning "Sin (the moon-god) has given life." *Horonite.* Identifies him as coming from (1) Hauran (Eze 47:16,18), east of the Sea of Galilee; (2) Horonaim, in Moab (Jer 48:34); or, most probably, (3) either Upper or Lower Beth Horon, two key cities about 11 miles northwest of Jerusalem, which guarded the main road to Jerusalem (Jos 10:10; 16:3,5; 1 Maccabees 3:16; 7:39). Sanballat was the chief political opponent of Nehemiah (v. 19; 4:1,7; 6:1–2,5,12,14; 13:28). He held the position of governor over Samaria (cf. 4:1–2). An Elephantine papyrus letter of the late fifth century BC to Bagohi (Bigvai), governor of Judah, refers to "Delaiah and Shelemiah, the sons of Sanballat, governor of Samaria." In 1962 a fourth-century BC papyrus listing the name Sanballat, probably a descendant of Nehemiah's contemporary, was found in a cave north of Jericho. *Tobiah.* Means "The LORD is good." He was probably a worshiper of the Lord (Yahweh), as indicated not only by his name but also by that of his son Jehohanan (6:17–18), meaning "The LORD is gracious." Jehohanan was married to the daughter of Meshullam, son of Berekiah, the leader of one of the groups repairing the wall (3:4,30; 6:18). Tobiah also had a close relationship with Eliashib the priest (13:4–7).

Nehemiah Inspects Jerusalem's Walls

11 I went to Jerusalem, and after staying there three days[i] 12 I set out during the
night with a few others. I had not told anyone what my God had put in my heart to
do for Jerusalem. There were no mounts
with me except the one I was riding on.
13 By night I went out through the Valley Gate[j] toward the Jackal[a] Well and the
Dung Gate,[k] examining the walls[l] of Jerusalem, which had been broken down, and
its gates, which had been destroyed by
fire. 14 Then I moved on toward the Fountain Gate[m] and the King's Pool,[n] but there
was not enough room for my mount to
get through; 15 so I went up the valley by
night, examining the wall. Finally, I turned
back and reentered through the Valley
Gate. 16 The officials did not know where I
had gone or what I was doing, because as
yet I had said nothing to the Jews or the
priests or nobles or officials or any others
who would be doing the work.
17 Then I said to them, "You see the
trouble we are in: Jerusalem lies in ruins,
and its gates have been burned with fire.[o]
Come, let us rebuild the wall[p] of Jerusalem, and we will no longer be in disgrace.[q]" 18 I also told them about the gracious hand of my God on me[r] and what
the king had said to me.
They replied, "Let us start rebuilding."
So they began this good work.
19 But when Sanballat[s] the Horonite, Tobiah the Ammonite official and Geshem[t]
the Arab heard about it, they mocked
and ridiculed us.[u] "What is this you are
doing?" they asked. "Are you rebelling
against the king?"
20 I answered them by saying, "The God
of heaven will give us success. We his servants will start rebuilding,[v] but as for you,
you have no share[w] in Jerusalem or any
claim or historic right to it."

Builders of the Wall

3 Eliashib[x] the high priest and his fellow priests went to work and rebuilt[y]
the Sheep Gate.[z] They dedicated it and set

2:11 [i]S Ge 40:13 **2:13** [j]S 2Ch 26:9 [k]Ne 3:13; 12:31 [l]S Ne 1:3 **2:14** [m]Ne 3:15; 12:37 [n]S 2Ki 18:17 **2:17** [o]S Ne 1:3 [p]Ps 102:16; Isa 30:13; 58:12 [q]Eze 5:14 **2:18** [r]S Ezr 5:5 **2:19** [s]S ver 10 [t]Ne 6:1,2,6 [u]Ps 44:13-16 **2:20** [v]Ezr 4:1 [w]Ezr 4:3; Ac 8:21 **3:1** [x]S Ezr 10:24 [y]Isa 58:12 [z]ver 32; Ne 12:39; Jn 5:2

[a] 13 Or *Serpent* or *Fig*

Ammonite. See Ezr 9:1; see also note on Ge 19:36–38. Tobiah was probably governor of Transjordan under the Persians. In later generations a prominent family bearing the name of Tobiah was sometimes associated with the region of Ammon in non-Biblical texts. *very much disturbed.* The reasons for the opposition of Sanballat and Tobiah were not basically religious but political. The authority of the Samaritan governor in particular was threatened by Nehemiah's arrival.

2:11 *three days.* See note on Ezr 8:32.

2:12 Nehemiah was cautious and discreet as he inspected the city's fortifications. *one I was riding on.* Probably a mule or donkey.

2:13 Nehemiah did not make a complete circuit of the walls but only of the southern area (see map, p. 748). Jerusalem was always attacked from the north because it was most vulnerable there, so the walls had probably been completely destroyed in that part of the city. *Valley Gate.* See 3:13. According to 2Ch 26:9 Uzziah fortified towers in the west wall, which overlooked the central valley between the Hinnom and Kidron Valleys. Excavations in 1927–28 uncovered the remains of a gate from the Persian period, which has been identified as the Valley Gate. *Jackal Well.* Many interpreters suggest that this was En Rogel (Jos 15:7–8; 18:16; 2Sa 17:17; 1Ki 1:9), a well situated at the junction of the Hinnom and Kidron Valleys, 250 yards south of the southeast ridge of Jerusalem (see map, p. 748). Others suggest that it was the Pool of Siloam (see map, p. 748). *Dung Gate.* Perhaps the gate leading to the rubbish dump in the Hinnom Valley (cf. 3:13–14; 12:31; 2Ki 23:10). It was situated about 500 yards south of the Valley Gate (3:13).

2:14 *Fountain Gate.* Possibly in the southeast wall facing toward En Rogel (see 3:15; 12:37). *King's Pool.* Hezekiah may have diverted the overflow from his Siloam tunnel (cf. 2Ki 20:20; 2Ch 32:30) to irrigate the royal gardens (2Ki 25:4) located outside the city walls at the junction of the Kidron and Hinnom Valleys. The King's Pool was probably therefore the Pool of Siloam (3:15) or the adjacent Birket el-Hamra. *not enough room.* Possibly because of the collapse of the supporting terraces (cf. 2Sa 5:9; 1Ki 9:15,24) on the east side of the city.

2:15 *valley.* The Kidron.

2:16 *nobles.* The Hebrew root for this word means "free" (see 4:14,19; 5:7; 6:17; 7:5; 13:17; see also note on 3:5).

2:17 *ruins.* The condition of the walls and gates of the city since their destruction by Nebuchadnezzar in 586 BC, in spite of abortive attempts to rebuild them. The leaders and people had evidently become reconciled to this sad state of affairs. It took an outsider to assess the situation and to rally them to renewed efforts.

2:18 *my God ... and ... the king.* Nehemiah could personally attest that God was alive and active in his behalf and that he (Nehemiah) had come with royal sanction and authority.

2:19 *Sanballat ... Tobiah.* See note on v. 10. *Geshem.* Inscriptions from Dedan in northwest Arabia and from Tell el-Maskhutah near Ismailia in Egypt bear the name Geshem, who may have been in charge of a north Arabian confederacy that controlled vast areas from northeast Egypt to northern Arabia, including the southern part of the Holy Land. Geshem may have been opposed to Nehemiah's development of an independent kingdom because he feared that it might interfere with his lucrative spice trade. *Arab.* See 2Ch 9:14; Isa 21:13; Jer 25:24. Arabs became dominant in Transjordan from the Assyrian to the Persian periods. Sargon II of Assyria resettled some Arabs in Samaria in 715 BC. Early Greek and Roman sources reveal that the Arabs enjoyed a favored status under the Persians.

3:1–32 One of the most important chapters in the OT for determining the topography of Jerusalem (see map, p. 2525, at the end of this study Bible; see also map, p. 748). The narrative begins at the Sheep Gate (northeast corner of the city) and proceeds in a counterclockwise direction around the wall. About 40 key men are named as participants in the reconstruction of about 45 sections. The towns listed as the homes of the builders may have represented the administrative centers of the province of Judah. Ten gates are named: (1) Sheep Gate (v. 1), (2) Fish Gate (v. 3), (3) Jeshanah Gate (v. 6), (4) Valley Gate (v. 13), (5) Dung Gate (v. 14), (6) Fountain Gate (v. 15), (7) Water Gate (v. 26), (8) Horse Gate (v. 28), (9) East Gate (v. 29), (10) Inspection Gate (v. 31). The account

its doors in place, building as far as the Tower of the Hundred, which they dedicated, and as far as the Tower of Hananel.[a] 2 The men of Jericho[b] built the adjoining section, and Zakkur son of Imri built next to them.

3 The Fish Gate[c] was rebuilt by the sons of Hassenaah. They laid its beams and put its doors and bolts and bars in place. 4 Meremoth[d] son of Uriah, the son of Hakkoz, repaired the next section. Next to him Meshullam son of Berekiah, the son of Meshezabel, made repairs, and next to him Zadok son of Baana also made repairs. 5 The next section was repaired by the men of Tekoa,[e] but their nobles would not put their shoulders to the work under their supervisors.[a]

6 The Jeshanah[b] Gate[f] was repaired by Joiada son of Paseah and Meshullam son of Besodeiah. They laid its beams and put its doors with their bolts and bars in place. 7 Next to them, repairs were made by men from Gibeon[g] and Mizpah — Melatiah of Gibeon and Jadon of Meronoth — places under the authority of the governor of Trans-Euphrates. 8 Uzziel son of Harhaiah, one of the goldsmiths, repaired the next section; and Hananiah, one of the perfume-makers, made repairs next to that. They restored Jerusalem as far as the Broad Wall.[h] 9 Rephaiah son of Hur, ruler of a half-district of Jerusalem, repaired the next section. 10 Adjoining this, Jedaiah son of Harumaph made repairs opposite his house, and Hattush son of Hashabneiah made repairs next to him. 11 Malkijah son of Harim and Hasshub son of Pahath-Moab repaired another section and the Tower of the Ovens.[i] 12 Shallum son of Hallohesh, ruler of a half-district of Jerusalem, repaired the next section with the help of his daughters.

13 The Valley Gate[j] was repaired by Hanun and the residents of Zanoah.[k] They rebuilt it and put its doors with their bolts and bars in place. They also repaired a thousand cubits[c] of the wall as far as the Dung Gate.[l]

14 The Dung Gate was repaired by Malkijah son of Rekab, ruler of the district of Beth Hakkerem.[m] He rebuilt it and put its doors with their bolts and bars in place.

15 The Fountain Gate was repaired by Shallun son of Kol-Hozeh, ruler of the

3:1 [a] Ne 12:39; Ps 48:12; Jer 31:38; Zec 14:10 **3:2** [b] Ne 7:36 **3:3** [c] S 2Ch 33:14 **3:4** [d] S Ezr 8:33 **3:5** [e] ver 27; S 2Sa 14:2 **3:6** [f] Ne 12:39 **3:7** [g] S Jos 9:3 **3:8** [h] Ne 12:38 **3:11** [i] Ne 12:38 **3:13** [j] S 2Ch 26:9 [k] S Jos 15:34 [l] S Ne 2:13 **3:14** [m] Jer 6:1

[a] *5* Or *their Lord* or *the governor* [b] *6* Or *Old* [c] *13* That is, about 1,500 feet or about 450 meters

suggests that most of the rebuilding was concerned with the gates, where the enemy's assaults were always concentrated. Not all the sections of the walls or buildings in Jerusalem were in the same state of disrepair. A selective policy of destruction seems to be indicated by 2Ki 25:9.

3:1 *Eliashib the high priest.* It was fitting that the high priest should set the example. Among the ancient Sumerians the king himself would carry bricks for the building of a temple. *Sheep Gate.* See v. 32; 12:39. It was known in NT times (Jn 5:2) as located near the Bethesda Pool (in the northeast corner of Jerusalem). Even today a sheep market is held periodically near this area. The Sheep Gate may have replaced the earlier Benjamin Gate (Jer 37:13; 38:7; Zec 14:10). *Tower of the Hundred.* See 12:39. "Hundred" may refer to (1) its height (100 cubits), (2) the number of its steps or (3) a military unit (cf. Dt 1:15). *Tower of Hananel.* The towers were associated with the "citadel by the temple" (2:8) in protecting the vulnerable northern approaches to the city.

3:3 *Fish Gate.* See 12:39. During the days of the first temple, it was one of Jerusalem's main entrances (2Ch 33:14; Zep 1:10). Merchants brought fish from either Tyre or the Sea of Galilee to the fish market (13:16) through this entrance, which was located in the north wall of the city (see note on Zep 1:10).

3:4 *Meremoth.* See note on Ezr 8:33. *Meshullam.* Repaired a second section (v. 30). Nehemiah complained that Meshullam had given his daughter in marriage to a son of Tobiah (see 6:17 – 18 and note on 2:10).

3:5 *Tekoa.* A small town about 6 miles south of Bethlehem and 11 miles from Jerusalem. It was the hometown of the prophet Amos. *nobles.* The Hebrew for this word is different from that in 2:16 (see note there) and means "mighty" or "magnificent" (see 10:29; 2Ch 23:20; Jer 14:3). These aristocrats disdained manual labor. *shoulders.* Lit. "back of the neck." The expression is drawn from the imagery of oxen that refuse to yield to the yoke (Jer 27:12).

3:6 *Jeshanah Gate.* In the northwest corner. It may be another name for the Gate of Ephraim (see 12:39), which otherwise is not mentioned in ch. 3.

3:8 *goldsmiths.* See vv. 31 – 32. *perfume-makers.* See 1Sa 8:13. *Broad Wall.* See 12:38. In 1970 – 71 archaeological excavations in Jerusalem uncovered such a wall west of the temple area. It is dated to the early seventh century BC and was probably built by Hezekiah (2Ch 32:5). The expansion to and beyond the Broad Wall may have become necessary because of the influx of refugees fleeing from the fall of Samaria in 722 – 721.

3:10 *Jedaiah ... made repairs opposite his house.* See vv. 23,28 – 30. It made sense to have him and others repair the sections of the wall nearest their homes.

3:11 *Tower of the Ovens.* It was on the western wall, perhaps in the same location as one built by Uzziah (2Ch 26:9). The ovens may have been those situated in the "street of the bakers" (Jer 37:21).

3:12 *daughters.* A unique OT reference to women working on the wall. When the Athenians attempted to rebuild their walls after the Persians had destroyed them, it was decreed that "the whole population of the city — men, women and children — should take part in the wall-building" (Thucydides, 1.90.3).

3:13 *Valley Gate.* See note on 2:13. *a thousand cubits.* An extraordinary length (see NIV text note); probably most of the section was relatively intact. *Dung Gate.* See note on 2:13.

3:14 *Beth Hakkerem.* Means "house of the vineyard." It was a fire-signal point (Jer 6:1) and is identified with Ramat Rahel, two miles south of Jerusalem. It may have been the residence of a district governor in the Persian period.

3:15 *Fountain Gate.* See note on 2:14. *Pool of Siloam.* See NIV text note; perhaps the Lower Pool of Isa 22:9 (see note on Isa 8:6). *King's Garden.* See note on 2:14. *City of David.* See 12:37; see also 2Sa 5:7 and note.

district of Mizpah. He rebuilt it, roofing it
over and putting its doors and bolts and
bars in place. He also repaired the wall of
the Pool of Siloam,[a][n] by the King's Garden, as far as the steps going down from
the City of David. 16 Beyond him, Nehemiah son of Azbuk, ruler of a half-district of
Beth Zur,[o] made repairs up to a point opposite the tombs[b][p] of David, as far as the
artificial pool and the House of the Heroes.
17 Next to him, the repairs were made
by the Levites under Rehum son of Bani.
Beside him, Hashabiah, ruler of half the
district of Keilah,[q] carried out repairs for
his district. 18 Next to him, the repairs were
made by their fellow Levites under Binnui[c]
son of Henadad, ruler of the other half-district of Keilah. 19 Next to him, Ezer son of
Jeshua, ruler of Mizpah, repaired another
section, from a point facing the ascent to
the armory as far as the angle of the wall.
20 Next to him, Baruch son of Zabbai zealously repaired another section, from the
angle to the entrance of the house of Eliashib the high priest. 21 Next to him, Meremoth[r] son of Uriah, the son of Hakkoz, repaired another section, from the entrance
of Eliashib's house to the end of it.
22 The repairs next to him were made by
the priests from the surrounding region.
23 Beyond them, Benjamin and Hasshub
made repairs in front of their house; and
next to them, Azariah son of Maaseiah,
the son of Ananiah, made repairs beside
his house. 24 Next to him, Binnui[s] son of
Henadad repaired another section, from
Azariah's house to the angle and the corner, 25 and Palal son of Uzai worked opposite the angle and the tower projecting
from the upper palace near the court of
the guard.[t] Next to him, Pedaiah son of
Parosh[u] 26 and the temple servants[v] living
on the hill of Ophel[w] made repairs up to
a point opposite the Water Gate[x] toward
the east and the projecting tower. 27 Next
to them, the men of Tekoa[y] repaired another section, from the great projecting tower[z]
to the wall of Ophel.

28 Above the Horse Gate,[a] the priests
made repairs, each in front of his own
house. 29 Next to them, Zadok son of Immer made repairs opposite his house.
Next to him, Shemaiah son of Shekaniah,
the guard at the East Gate, made repairs.
30 Next to him, Hananiah son of Shelemiah, and Hanun, the sixth son of Zalaph,
repaired another section. Next to them,
Meshullam son of Berekiah made repairs
opposite his living quarters. 31 Next to him,
Malkijah, one of the goldsmiths, made repairs as far as the house of the temple
servants and the merchants, opposite the
Inspection Gate, and as far as the room
above the corner; 32 and between the room
above the corner and the Sheep Gate[b] the
goldsmiths and merchants made repairs.

Opposition to the Rebuilding

4 [d] When Sanballat[c] heard that we were
rebuilding the wall, he became angry
and was greatly incensed. He ridiculed the
Jews, 2 and in the presence of his associates[d] and the army of Samaria, he said,
"What are those feeble Jews doing? Will

3:15 [n] Isa 8:6; Jn 9:7
3:16 [o] S Jos 15:58 [p] Ac 2:29
3:17 [q] S Jos 15:44
3:21 [r] S Ezr 8:33
3:24 [s] S Ezr 8:33
3:25 [t] Jer 32:2; 37:21; 39:14 [u] S Ezr 2:3
3:26 [v] Ne 7:46; 11:21 [w] S 2Ch 33:14 [x] Ne 8:1,3,16; 12:37
3:27 [y] S ver 5 [z] Ps 48:12
3:28 [a] S 2Ki 11:16
3:32 [b] S ver 1; Jn 5:2
4:1 [c] S Ne 2:10
4:2 [d] S Ezr 4:9-10

[a] *15* Hebrew *Shelah,* a variant of *Shiloah,* that is, Siloam [b] *16* Hebrew; Septuagint, some Vulgate manuscripts and Syriac *tomb* [c] *18* Two Hebrew manuscripts and Syriac (see also Septuagint and verse 24); most Hebrew manuscripts *Bavvai* [d] In Hebrew texts 4:1-6 is numbered 3:33-38, and 4:7-23 is numbered 4:1-17.

3:16 *Beth Zur.* A district capital, 13 miles south of Jerusalem. Excavations in 1931 and 1957 revealed that occupation was sparse during the early Persian period but was resumed in the fifth century BC. *tombs of David.* Cf. 2:5. David was buried in the city area (1Ki 2:10; 2Ch 21:20; 32:33; Ac 2:29). The so-called Tomb of David on Mount Zion, venerated today by Jewish pilgrims, is in the Coenaculum building, erected in the fourteenth century AD. Such a site for David's tomb is mentioned no earlier than the ninth century AD. *House of the Heroes.* May have been the house of David's mighty warriors (see 2Sa 23:8 – 39), which perhaps served later as the barracks or armory.
3:17 – 18 *Keilah.* Located about 15 miles southwest of Jerusalem, it played an important role in David's early history (1Sa 23:1 – 13).
3:19 *armory.* See note on v. 16. *angle.* See 2Ch 26:9.
3:20 – 21 The residences of the high priest and his fellow priests were located inside the city along the eastern wall.
3:25 *upper palace.* Perhaps the old palace of David (see 12:37). Like Solomon's palace, it would have had a guardhouse (Jer 32:2).
3:26 *Ophel.* See v. 27. The word means "swelling" or "bulge," hence a (fortified) "hill" (as in Mic 4:8; see NIV text note there), specifically the northern part of the southeastern hill of Jerusalem, which formed the original City of David, just south of the temple area (2Ch 27:3). *Water Gate.* So called because it led to the main source of Jerusalem's water, the Gihon spring. It must have opened onto a large area, for the reading of the Law took place there (8:1,3,16; 12:37). *projecting tower.* Perhaps the large tower whose ruins were discovered by archaeologists on the crest of the Ophel hill in 1923 – 25. Excavations at the base of the tower in 1978 revealed a level dating to the Persian era.
3:27 *men of Tekoa.* The common people of Tekoa did double duty, whereas the nobles of Tekoa shirked their responsibility (see note on v. 5).
3:28 *Horse Gate.* Where Athaliah was slain (2Ch 23:15). It may have been the easternmost point in the city wall — a gate through which one could reach the Kidron Valley (Jer 31:40).
3:29 *East Gate.* May have been the predecessor of the present Golden Gate (see note on Eze 44:2).
3:31 *goldsmiths.* See v. 8. *Inspection Gate.* In the northern part of the eastern wall.
3:32 *Sheep Gate.* Back to the point of departure (see v. 1).
4:1 *Jews.* See note on Zec 8:23.
4:2 *he said.* Disputes between rival Persian governors were frequent. Sanballat asked several derisive questions to taunt the Jews and to discourage them in their efforts. *burned.* Fire

they restore their wall? Will they offer sacrifices? Will they finish in a day? Can they bring the stones back to life from those heaps of rubble[e]—burned as they are?"

3 Tobiah[f] the Ammonite, who was at his side, said, "What they are building—even a fox climbing up on it would break down their wall of stones!"[g]

4 Hear us, our God, for we are despised.[h] Turn their insults back on their own heads. Give them over as plunder in a land of captivity. 5 Do not cover up their guilt[i] or blot out their sins from your sight,[j] for they have thrown insults in the face of[a] the builders.

6 So we rebuilt the wall till all of it reached half its height, for the people worked with all their heart.

7 But when Sanballat, Tobiah,[k] the Arabs, the Ammonites and the people of Ashdod heard that the repairs to Jerusalem's walls had gone ahead and that the gaps were being closed, they were very angry. 8 They all plotted together[l] to come and fight against Jerusalem and stir up trouble against it. 9 But we prayed to our God and posted a guard day and night to meet this threat.

10 Meanwhile, the people in Judah said, "The strength of the laborers[m] is giving out, and there is so much rubble that we cannot rebuild the wall."

11 Also our enemies said, "Before they know it or see us, we will be right there among them and will kill them and put an end to the work."

12 Then the Jews who lived near them came and told us ten times over, "Wherever you turn, they will attack us."

13 Therefore I stationed some of the people behind the lowest points of the wall at the exposed places, posting them by families, with their swords, spears and bows. 14 After I looked things over, I stood up and said to the nobles, the officials and the rest of the people, "Don't be afraid[n] of them. Remember[o] the Lord, who is great and awesome,[p] and fight[q] for your families, your sons and your daughters, your wives and your homes."

15 When our enemies heard that we were aware of their plot and that God had frustrated it,[r] we all returned to the wall, each to our own work.

16 From that day on, half of my men did the work, while the other half were equipped with spears, shields, bows and armor. The officers posted themselves behind all the people of Judah 17 who were building the wall. Those who carried materials did their work with one hand and held a weapon[s] in the other, 18 and each of the builders wore his sword at his side as he worked. But the man who sounded the trumpet[t] stayed with me.

19 Then I said to the nobles, the officials and the rest of the people, "The work is extensive and spread out, and we are widely separated from each other along the wall. 20 Wherever you hear the sound of the trumpet,[u] join us there. Our God will fight[v] for us!"

21 So we continued the work with half the men holding spears, from the first light of dawn till the stars came out. 22 At that time I also said to the people, "Have every man and his helper stay inside Jerusalem at night, so they can serve us as guards by night and as workers by day." 23 Nei-

4:2 [e] Ps 79:1; Jer 26:18 **4:3** [f] S Ne 2:10 [g] Job 13:12; 15:3 **4:4** [h] Ps 44:13; 123:3-4; Jer 33:24 **4:5** [i] Isa 2:9; La 1:22 [j] 2Ki 14:27; Ps 51:1; 69:27-28; 109:14; Jer 18:23 **4:7** [k] S Ne 2:10 **4:8** [l] Ps 2:2; 83:1-18 **4:10** [m] S 1Ch 23:4 **4:14** [n] S Ge 28:15; S Dt 1:29 [o] S Ne 1:8 [p] S Ne 1:5 [q] S 2Sa 10:12 **4:15** [r] S 2Sa 17:14; Job 5:12 **4:17** [s] Ps 149:6 **4:18** [t] S Nu 10:2 **4:20** [u] Eze 33:3 [v] S Ex 14:14; S Dt 20:4; Jos 10:14

[a] 5 Or *have aroused your anger before*

---

had damaged the stones, which were probably limestone, and had caused many of them to crack and crumble.

4:4–5 As in the so-called imprecatory psalms (see note on Ps 5:10), Nehemiah does not himself take action against his opponents but calls down on them redress from God. In v. 5 Nehemiah's prayer echoes the language of Jer 18:23.

4:7 *Ashdod.* See note on Isa 20:1. It became a district capital under Persian rule.

4:9 *prayed … posted a guard.* Prayer and watchfulness blend faith and action and also emphasize both the divine side and the human side (see notes on Jas 2:14–26).

4:10 *giving out.* The picture is of workers staggering under the weight of their load and ready to fall at any step.

4:11 *our enemies said.* Either Nehemiah had friendly informants, or the enemy was spreading unsettling rumors.

4:12 *ten times over.* Many times.

4:13 *lowest points … exposed places.* Nehemiah posted men conspicuously in the areas that were the most vulnerable along the wall.

4:14 *Don't be afraid of them. Remember the Lord.* See note on 1:8. The best way to dispel fear is to remember the Lord, who alone is to be feared (see Dt 3:22; 20:3; 31:6; Ps 56:3–4).

4:16 *shields.* Made primarily of wood or wickerwork and therefore combustible (Eze 39:9). *armor.* The Hebrew for this word designated primarily a breastplate of metal or a coat of mail (see 2Ch 18:33).

4:17 *work with one hand … weapon in the other.* Means either that the workers carried their materials with one hand and their weapons with the other or simply that the weapons were kept close at hand.

4:18 *trumpet.* See note on Isa 18:3; see also Jos 6:4, 6,8,13.

4:20 *Our God will fight for us!* See Jos 5:13–15 and notes; 10:14,42; Jdg 4:14; 20:35; 2Sa 5:24; see also essay, p. 308.

4:21 *till the stars came out.* Indicates the earnestness of their efforts, since the usual time to stop working was at sunset (Dt 24:15; Mt 20:8).

4:22 *guards by night.* Even men from outside Jerusalem stayed in the city at night so that some of them could serve as sentries.

4:23 See NIV text note. Although the precise meaning of the end of the verse is not clear, the implication is that constant preparedness was the rule. According to Josephus (*Antiquities,* 11.5.8), Nehemiah "himself made the rounds of the city by night, never tiring either through work or lack of food and sleep, neither of which he took for pleasure but as a necessity."

ther I nor my brothers nor my men nor
the guards with me took off our clothes;
each had his weapon, even when he went
for water.[a]

Nehemiah Helps the Poor

5 Now the men and their wives raised a
great outcry against their fellow Jews.
2Some were saying, "We and our sons and
daughters are numerous; in order for us
to eat and stay alive, we must get grain."
3Others were saying, "We are mortgaging our fields,[w] our vineyards and our
homes to get grain during the famine."[x]
4Still others were saying, "We have had
to borrow money to pay the king's tax[y] on
our fields and vineyards. 5Although we are
of the same flesh and blood[z] as our fellow Jews and though our children are as
good as theirs, yet we have to subject our
sons and daughters to slavery.[a] Some of
our daughters have already been enslaved,
but we are powerless, because our fields
and our vineyards belong to others."[b]

6When I heard their outcry and these
charges, I was very angry. 7I pondered
them in my mind and then accused the
nobles and officials. I told them, "You are
charging your own people interest!"[c] So
I called together a large meeting to deal
with them 8and said: "As far as possible,
we have bought[d] back our fellow Jews
who were sold to the Gentiles. Now you
are selling your own people, only for them
to be sold back to us!" They kept quiet,
because they could find nothing to say.[e]
9So I continued, "What you are doing
is not right. Shouldn't you walk in the
fear of our God to avoid the reproach[f] of
our Gentile enemies? 10I and my brothers
and my men are also lending the people
money and grain. But let us stop charging interest![g] 11Give back to them immediately their fields, vineyards, olive groves
and houses, and also the interest[h] you are

5:3 [w] Ps 109:11 [x] Ge 47:23
5:4 [y] S Ezr 4:13
5:5 [z] S Ge 29:14 [a] Lev 25:39-43, 47; S 2Ki 4:1; Isa 50:1 [b] Dt 15:7-11; S 2Ki 4:1
5:7 [c] Ex 22:25-27; S Lev 25:35-37; Dt 23:19-20; 24:10-13
5:8 [d] Lev 25:47 [e] Jer 34:8
5:9 [f] Isa 52:5
5:10 [g] S Ex 22:25
5:11 [h] Isa 58:6

[a] 23 The meaning of the Hebrew for this clause is uncertain.

5:1–19 During his major effort to rebuild the walls of Jerusalem, Nehemiah confronted a socioeconomic crisis that had deep moral implications. Since the building of the wall took only 52 days (6:15), it is surprising that Nehemiah called a "large meeting" (v. 7) in the midst of such a project. Perhaps the pressures created by the rebuilding program brought to light problems that had long been simmering and that had to be dealt with before work could proceed. Among the classes affected by the crisis were (1) the landless, who were short of food (v. 2); (2) the landowners, who were compelled to mortgage their properties (v. 3); and (3) those forced to borrow money at exorbitant interest rates and sell their children into slavery (vv. 4–5).

5:1 *wives.* The situation was so serious that the wives joined in the protest as they ran short of funds and supplies to feed their families. They complained not against the foreign authorities but against their own countrymen who were taking advantage of their poorer neighbors at a time when all were needed for the defense of the country.

5:2 *grain.* About six to seven bushels would be needed for a man to feed his family for a month.

5:3 *mortgaging.* Even those who had property were forced to mortgage it, benefiting the wealthy few (cf. Isa 5:8). In times of economic stress the rich got richer and the poor got poorer. *famine.* The economic situation was aggravated by the natural conditions that had produced a famine. Some 75 years earlier the prophet Haggai had referred to a time of drought, when food was insufficient (Hag 1:5–11). Such times of distress were considered to be expressions of God's judgment (Isa 51:19; Jer 14:13–18; Am 4:6). Famines were common in Canaan. They occurred in the times of Abraham (Ge 12:10), Isaac (Ge 26:1), Joseph (Ge 41:27,54), Ruth (Ru 1:1), David (2Sa 21:1), Elijah (1Ki 18:2), Elisha (2Ki 4:38) and Claudius (Ac 11:28).

5:4 *tax.* It is estimated that the Persian king collected the equivalent of 20 million darics (see NIV text note on Ezr 8:27) a year in taxes. Little was ever returned to benefit the provinces, because most of it was melted down and stored as bullion. Alexander the Great found at Susa alone 9,000 talents (about 340 tons) of coined gold and 40,000 talents (about 1,500 tons) of silver stored as bullion. As coined money was increasingly taken out of circulation by taxes, poverty increased dramatically. The acquisition of land by the Persians and its removal from production also contributed to produce a 50 percent rise in prices during the Persian period.

5:5 *slavery.* In times of economic distress families would borrow funds, using family members as collateral. If a man could not repay the loan and its interest, his children, his wife, or even the man himself could be sold into bondage. An Israelite who fell into debt, however, would serve his creditor as a "hired worker" (Lev 25:39–40). He was to be released in the seventh year (Dt 15:12–18), unless he chose to stay voluntarily. During the seven-year famine in Egypt, Joseph was approached by people who asked him to accept their land and their bodies in exchange for food (Ge 47:18–19). The irony for the Israelites was that at least as exiles in Mesopotamia their families were together, but now, because of dire economic necessity, their children were being sold into slavery.

5:6 *I was very angry.* Sometimes it becomes necessary to express righteous indignation against social injustice (cf. Mk 11:15–18; Eph 4:26).

5:7 *interest.* See notes on Ex 22:25–27; Lev 25:36; Dt 23:20. Josephus (*Antiquities*, 4.8.25) explains: "Let it not be permitted to lend upon usury to any Hebrew either meat or drink; for it is not just to draw a revenue from the misfortunes of a fellow countryman."

5:8 *fellow Jews who were sold.* Impoverished fellow Jews could be hired as servants, but they were not to be sold as slaves (Lev 25:39–42). *to the Gentiles.* The sale of fellow Hebrews as slaves to foreigners was forbidden (Ex 21:8). *kept quiet.* Their guilt was so obvious that they had no rebuttal or excuse (cf. Jn 8:7–10).

5:9 *not right.* Failure to treat others, especially fellow believers, with compassion is an insult to our Maker and a blot on our testimony (cf. Pr 14:31; 1Pe 2:12–15).

5:10 *let us stop charging interest!* The OT condemns the greed that seeks to profit from the misfortune of others (Ps 119:36; Isa 56:9–12; 57:17; Jer 6:13; 8:10; 22:13–17; Eze 22:12–13; 33:31). In view of the economic crisis facing his people, Nehemiah urges the creditors to relinquish their rights to repayment with interest.

charging them — one percent of the money, grain, new wine and olive oil.”
12 “We will give it back,” they said. “And
we will not demand anything more from
them. We will do as you say.”
Then I summoned the priests and made
the nobles and officials take an oath[i] to do
what they had promised. 13 I also shook[j]
out the folds of my robe and said, “In this
way may God shake out of their house and
possessions anyone who does not keep
this promise. So may such a person be
shaken out and emptied!”
At this the whole assembly said,
“Amen,”[k] and praised the LORD. And the
people did as they had promised.
14 Moreover, from the twentieth year of
King Artaxerxes,[l] when I was appointed
to be their governor[m] in the land of Judah, until his thirty-second year — twelve
years — neither I nor my brothers ate the
food allotted to the governor. 15 But the
earlier governors — those preceding me —
placed a heavy burden on the people and
took forty shekels[a] of silver from them in
addition to food and wine. Their assistants
also lorded it over the people. But out of
reverence for God[n] I did not act like that.
16 Instead,[o] I devoted myself to the work
on this wall. All my men were assembled
there for the work; we[b] did not acquire
any land.
17 Furthermore, a hundred and fifty Jews
and officials ate at my table, as well as
those who came to us from the surrounding nations. 18 Each day one ox, six choice
sheep and some poultry[p] were prepared
for me, and every ten days an abundant
supply of wine of all kinds. In spite of all
this, I never demanded the food allotted to
the governor, because the demands were
heavy on these people.
19 Remember[q] me with favor, my God,
for all I have done for these people.

Further Opposition to the Rebuilding

6 When word came to Sanballat, Tobiah,[r] Geshem[s] the Arab and the rest of
our enemies that I had rebuilt the wall and
not a gap was left in it — though up to that
time I had not set the doors in the gates —
2 Sanballat and Geshem sent me this message: “Come, let us meet together in one
of the villages[c] on the plain of Ono.[t]”
But they were scheming to harm me;
3 so I sent messengers to them with this

5:12 [i] S Ezr 10:5
5:13 [j] S Mt 10:14 [k] Dt 27:15-26
5:14 [l] S Ne 2:6 [m] Ge 42:6; Ezr 6:7; Jer 40:7; Hag 1:1
5:15 [n] S Ge 20:11
5:16 [o] 2Th 3:7-10
5:18 [p] 1Ki 4:23
5:19 [q] S Ge 8:1; S 2Ki 20:3; S Ne 1:8
6:1 [r] Ne 2:10 [s] S Ne 2:19
6:2 [t] S 1Ch 8:12

[a] *15* That is, about 1 pound or about 460 grams
[b] *16* Most Hebrew manuscripts; some Hebrew manuscripts, Septuagint, Vulgate and Syriac *I*
[c] *2* Or *in Kephirim*

5:11 *one percent.* Perhaps one percent per month, an annual interest rate of 12 percent. *grain, new wine and olive oil.* See notes on 10:37; Dt 7:13.

5:13 *shook out the folds of my robe.* Symbolizing the solemnity of an oath and reinforcing the attendant curses for its nonfulfillment. *Amen.* See 8:6; Nu 5:22; see also note on Dt 27:15.

5:14 *thirty-second year.* From Apr. 1, 433 BC, to Apr. 19, 432. Nehemiah served his first term as governor for 12 years before being recalled to court (13:6), after which he returned to Jerusalem (13:7) for a second term whose length cannot be determined. *food allotted to the governor.* See v. 18. Provincial governors normally assessed the people in their provinces for their support. But Nehemiah, like Paul (1Co 9; 2Th 3:8–9), sacrificed even what was normally his in order to serve as an example to the people.

5:15 *governors.* The Hebrew for this word is used of Sheshbazzar (Ezr 5:14) and Zerubbabel (Hag 1:1,14; 2:2), as well as of various Persian officials (Ezr 5:3,6; 6:6–7,13; 8:36; Ne 2:7,9; 3:7). Nehemiah was not referring here to men of the caliber of Zerubbabel. Some believe that Judah did not have governors before Nehemiah and that the reference here is to governors of Samaria. But new archaeological evidence, in the form of seals and seal impressions, confirms the reference to the previous governors of Judah. *heavy burden.* It was customary Persian practice to exempt temple personnel from taxation, which increased the burden on lay people. *assistants.* If the governors themselves used extortion, their underlings often proved even more oppressive (cf. Mt 18:21–35; 20:25–28). *reverence for God.* Those in high positions are in danger of abusing their authority over their subordinates if they forget that they themselves are servants of a superior "Master in heaven" (Col 4:1; cf. Ge 39:9; 2Co 5:11).

5:16 *did not acquire any land.* Nehemiah's behavior as governor was guided by principles of service rather than by opportunism.

5:17 *ate at my table.* As part of his social responsibility, a ruler or governor was expected to entertain lavishly. A text found at Nimrud has Ashurnasirpal II feeding 69,574 guests at a banquet for ten days. When Solomon dedicated the temple, he sacrificed 22,000 cattle and 120,000 sheep and goats and held a great festival for the assembly for 14 days (1Ki 8:62–65). We are not told how many he fed (cf. 1Ki 4:27).

5:18 *Each day.* The meat listed here would provide one meal for 600–800 persons, including the 150 Jews and officials of v. 17. Cf. Solomon's provisions for one day (1Ki 4:22–23). *choice sheep.* Cf. Mal 1:8. *poultry.* Chickens were domesticated in the Indus River Valley by 2000 BC and were brought to Egypt by the time of Thutmose III (fifteenth century BC). They were known in Mesopotamia and in Greece by the eighth century. The earliest inscriptional evidence of poultry in the land of Canaan is the seal of Jaazaniah (dated c. 600 BC), which depicts a fighting rooster.

5:19 *Remember me.* See note on 1:8; cf. Heb 6:10. Perhaps Nehemiah's memoirs (see Introduction to Ezra: Literary Form and Authorship) were inscribed as a memorial that was set up in the temple. A striking parallel to Nehemiah's prayer is found in a prayer of Nebuchadnezzar: "O Marduk, my lord, do remember my deeds favorably as good [deeds]; may (these) my good deeds be always before your mind."

6:1 *Sanballat, Tobiah, Geshem.* See notes on 2:10,19.

6:2 *Ono.* Located about seven miles southeast of Joppa near Lod (modern Lydda), in the westernmost area settled by the returning Jews (Ne 7:37; 11:35). It may have been proposed as neutral territory, but Nehemiah recognized the invitation as a trap (cf. Ge 4:8; Jer 41:1–3).

6:3 Nehemiah's sharp reply may seem like a haughty response to a reasonable invitation, but he correctly discerned the insincerity of his enemies. He refused to be

'eply: "I am carrying on a great project
ınd cannot go down. Why should the
vork stop while I leave it and go down to
/ou?" 4 Four times they sent me the same
nessage, and each time I gave them the
ıame answer.
5 Then, the fifth time, Sanballat[u] sent his
ıide to me with the same message, and in
ıis hand was an unsealed letter 6 in which
vas written:

"It is reported among the nations—
and Geshem[a v] says it is true—that
you and the Jews are plotting to revolt, and therefore you are building the wall. Moreover, according to
these reports you are about to become
their king 7 and have even appointed
prophets to make this proclamation
about you in Jerusalem: 'There is a
king in Judah!' Now this report will
get back to the king; so come, let us
meet together."

8 I sent him this reply: "Nothing like
vhat you are saying is happening; you are
ust making it up out of your head."
9 They were all trying to frighten us,
hinking, "Their hands will get too weak
or the work, and it will not be completed."
But I prayed, "Now strengthen my
ıands."
10 One day I went to the house of Shemaah son of Delaiah, the son of Mehetabel,
vho was shut in at his home. He said, "Let
us meet in the house of God, inside the
temple[w], and let us close the temple doors,
because men are coming to kill you—by
night they are coming to kill you."
11 But I said, "Should a man like me run
away? Or should someone like me go into
the temple to save his life? I will not go!"
12 I realized that God had not sent him,
but that he had prophesied against me[x]
because Tobiah and Sanballat[y] had hired
him. 13 He had been hired to intimidate me
so that I would commit a sin by doing this,
and then they would give me a bad name
to discredit me.[z]
14 Remember[a] Tobiah and Sanballat,[b] my
God, because of what they have done; remember also the prophet[c] Noadiah and
how she and the rest of the prophets[d] have
been trying to intimidate me. 15 So the wall
was completed on the twenty-fifth of Elul,
in fifty-two days.

Opposition to the Completed Wall

16 When all our enemies heard about
this, all the surrounding nations were
afraid and lost their self-confidence, because they realized that this work had
been done with the help of our God.
17 Also, in those days the nobles of Judah were sending many letters to Tobiah,
and replies from Tobiah kept coming to
them. 18 For many in Judah were under

6:5 [u] S Ne 2:10
6:6 [v] S Ne 2:19
6:10 [w] Nu 18:7
6:12 [x] Eze 13:22-23 [y] S Ne 2:10
6:13 [z] Jer 20:10
6:14 [a] S Ne 1:8 [b] S Ne 2:10 [c] S Ex 15:20; Eze 13:17-23; S Ac 21:9; Rev 2:20 [d] Jer 23:9-40; Zec 13:2-3

[a] 6 Hebrew *Gashmu*, a variant of *Geshem*

listracted by matters that would divert his energies from ebuilding Jerusalem's wall.

:4 *Four times.* Nehemiah's foes were persistent, but he was qually persistent in resisting them.

6:5 *unsealed letter.* During this period a letter was ordinarily written on a papyrus or leather sheet, which was olled up, tied with a string and sealed with a clay bulla (seal npression) to guarantee the letter's authenticity. Sanbalat apparently wanted the contents of his letter to be made nown to the public at large.

6:6 *their king.* The Persian kings did not tolerate the claims of pretenders to kingship, as can be seen from he Behistun (Bisitun) inscription of Darius I. In NT times the Roman emperor was likewise suspicious of any unauthorized laims to royalty (Jn 19:12; cf. Mt 2:1–13).

:8 Nehemiah does not mince words. He calls the report a lie. le may have sent his own messenger to the Persian king to ssure him of his loyalty.

6:9 *hands will get ... weak.* Figurative language to express the idea of discouragement. The Hebrew for this hrase is used also in Ezr 4:4; Jer 38:4, as well as on an ostraon from Lachish dated c. 588 BC.

:10 *Shemaiah ... was shut in.* Perhaps as a symbolic action o indicate that his own life was in danger and to suggest hat both Nehemiah and he must flee to the temple (for ther symbolic actions, see 1Ki 22:11; Isa 20:2–4; Jer 27:2–7; 28:10–11; Eze 4:1–17; 12:3–11; Ac 21:11). Since Shemaiah ad access to the temple, he may have been a priest. He was learly a friend of Tobiah (cf. v. 12) and therefore Nehemiah's nemy. It was at least credible for Shemaiah to propose that Nehemiah take refuge in the temple area at the altar of asylum (see Ex 21:13–14 and notes), but not in the "house of God," the temple building itself.

6:11 Even if the threat against his life was real, Nehemiah was not a coward who would run into hiding. Nor would he transgress the law to save his life. As a layman, he was not permitted to enter the sanctuary (Nu 18:7). When King Uzziah entered the temple to burn incense, he was punished by being afflicted with leprosy (2Ch 26:16–21).

6:12 The fact that Shemaiah proposed a course of action contrary to God's word revealed him as a false prophet (cf. Dt 18:20; Isa 8:19–20; see note on Dt 13:1–5).

6:13 If Nehemiah had wavered in the face of the threat against him, his leadership would have been discredited and morale among the people would have plummeted.

6:14 *Remember.* See note on 1:8. *prophet.* See note on Ex 15:20.

6:15 *twenty-fifth of Elul.* Oct. 2, 444 BC. *fifty-two days.* The walls that lay in ruins for nearly a century and a half were rebuilt in less than two months once the people were galvanized into action by Nehemiah's leadership. Archaeological investigations have shown that the circumference of the wall in Nehemiah's day was much reduced. Josephus states (*Antiquities*, 11.5.8) that the rebuilding of the wall took two years and four months, but he is doubtless including such additional tasks as further strengthening of various sections, embellishing and beautifying, and the like. The dedication of the wall is described in 12:27–47.

6:17–18 Tobiah was related to an influential family in Ju-

oath to him, since he was son-in-law to
Shekaniah son of Arah, and his son Jehohanan had married the daughter of Meshullam son of Berekiah. 19 Moreover, they
kept reporting to me his good deeds and
then telling him what I said. And Tobiah
sent letters to intimidate me.

7 After the wall had been rebuilt and I
had set the doors in place, the gatekeepers,[e] the musicians[f] and the Levites[g]
were appointed. 2 I put in charge of Jerusalem my brother Hanani,[h] along with
Hananiah[i] the commander of the citadel,[j]
because he was a man of integrity and
feared[k] God more than most people do.
3 I said to them, "The gates of Jerusalem
are not to be opened until the sun is hot.
While the gatekeepers are still on duty,
have them shut the doors and bar them.
Also appoint residents of Jerusalem as
guards, some at their posts and some near
their own houses."

The List of the Exiles Who Returned

7:6-73pp — Ezr 2:1-70

4 Now the city was large and spacious,
but there were few people in it,[l] and the
houses had not yet been rebuilt. 5 So my
God put it into my heart to assemble the
nobles, the officials and the common people for registration by families. I found the
genealogical record of those who had been
the first to return. This is what I found
written there:

6 These are the people of the province who came up from the captivity
of the exiles[m] whom Nebuchadnezzar king of Babylon had taken captive (they returned to Jerusalem and
Judah, each to his own town, 7 in
company with Zerubbabel,[n] Joshua,
Nehemiah, Azariah, Raamiah, Naha-
mani, Mordecai, Bilshan, Mispereth,
Bigvai, Nehum and Baanah):

The list of the men of Israel:

8 the descendants of Parosh 2,172
9 of Shephatiah 372
10 of Arah 652
11 of Pahath-Moab (through the line of Jeshua and Joab) 2,818
12 of Elam 1,254
13 of Zattu 845
14 of Zakkai 760
15 of Binnui 648
16 of Bebai 628
17 of Azgad 2,322
18 of Adonikam 667
19 of Bigvai 2,067
20 of Adin[o] 655
21 of Ater (through Hezekiah) 98
22 of Hashum 328
23 of Bezai 324
24 of Hariph 112
25 of Gibeon 95

26 the men of Bethlehem and Netophah[p] 188
27 of Anathoth[q] 128
28 of Beth Azmaveth 42
29 of Kiriath Jearim, Kephirah[r] and Beeroth[s] 743
30 of Ramah and Geba 621
31 of Mikmash 122
32 of Bethel and Ai[t] 123
33 of the other Nebo 52
34 of the other Elam 1,254
35 of Harim 320
36 of Jericho[u] 345
37 of Lod, Hadid and Ono[v] 721
38 of Senaah 3,930

39 The priests:

the descendants of Jedaiah (through the family of Jeshua) 973
40 of Immer 1,052
41 of Pashhur 1,247
42 of Harim 1,017

43 The Levites:

the descendants of Jeshua (through Kadmiel through the line of Hodaviah) 74

44 The musicians:[w]

the descendants of Asaph 148

45 The gatekeepers:[x]

the descendants of Shallum, Ater, Talmon, Akkub, Hatita and Shobai 138

46 The temple servants:[y]

the descendants of
Ziha, Hasupha, Tabbaoth,
47 Keros, Sia, Padon,
48 Lebana, Hagaba, Shalmai,
49 Hanan, Giddel, Gahar,

7:1 [e] 1Ch 9:27; S 26:12-19 [f] Ps 68:25 [g] Ne 8:9
7:2 [h] Ne 1:2 [i] Ne 10:23 [j] Ne 2:8 [k] 1Ki 18:3
7:4 [l] Ne 11:1
7:6 [m] S 2Ch 36:20; S Ne 1:2
7:7 [n] S 1Ch 3:19
7:20 [o] S Ezr 8:6
7:26 [p] S 2Sa 23:28; S 1Ch 2:54
7:27 [q] S Jos 21:18
7:29 [r] S Jos 18:26 [s] S Jos 18:25
7:32 [t] S Ge 12:8
7:36 [u] Ne 3:2
7:37 [v] S 1Ch 8:12
7:44 [w] Ne 11:23
7:45 [x] S 1Ch 9:17
7:46 [y] S Ne 3:26

dah, since his son Jehohanan was married to the daughter of Meshullam, who had helped repair the wall of Jerusalem (3:4,30).

7:2 *in charge of Jerusalem.* Over Rephaiah and Shallum, who were over sections of the city (3:9,12). *Hanani.* See note on 1:2. *citadel.* See notes on 2:8; 3:1.

7:3 *until the sun is hot.* Normally the gates would be opened at dawn, but their opening was to be delayed until the su was high in the heavens to prevent the enemy from making surprise attack before most of the people were up.

7:6–73 Essentially the same as Ezr 2. See notes there for th nature of the list and the reasons for the numerous variatior in names and numbers between the two lists.

7:43 *74.* See note on Ezr 2:40.

50 Reaiah, Rezin, Nekoda,
51 Gazzam, Uzza, Paseah,
52 Besai, Meunim, Nephusim,
53 Bakbuk, Hakupha, Harhur,
54 Bazluth, Mehida, Harsha,
55 Barkos, Sisera, Temah,
56 Neziah and Hatipha

57 The descendants of the servants of
Solomon:

the descendants of
Sotai, Sophereth, Perida,
58 Jaala, Darkon, Giddel,
59 Shephatiah, Hattil,
Pokereth-Hazzebaim and Amon

60 The temple servants and the
descendants of the servants
of Solomon[z] 392

61 The following came up from the
towns of Tel Melah, Tel Harsha, Ke-
rub, Addon and Immer, but they
could not show that their families
were descended from Israel:

62 the descendants of
Delaiah, Tobiah and Nekoda 642

63 And from among the priests:
the descendants of
Hobaiah, Hakkoz and Barzillai
(a man who had married a
daughter of Barzillai the Gileadite
and was called by that name).
64 These searched for their family records, but they could not find
them and so were excluded from the
priesthood as unclean. 65 The governor, therefore, ordered them not to
eat any of the most sacred food until
there should be a priest ministering
with the Urim and Thummim.[a]

66 The whole company numbered
42,360, 67 besides their 7,337 male
and female slaves; and they also had
245 male and female singers. 68 There
were 736 horses, 245 mules,[a] 69 435
camels and 6,720 donkeys.

70 Some of the heads of the families
contributed to the work. The governor gave to the treasury 1,000 darics[b]
of gold, 50 bowls and 530 garments
for priests. 71 Some of the heads of the
families[b] gave to the treasury for the
work 20,000 darics[c] of gold and 2,200
minas[d] of silver. 72 The total given by
the rest of the people was 20,000 darics of gold, 2,000 minas[e] of silver and
67 garments for priests.[c]
73 The priests, the Levites, the gatekeepers, the musicians and the temple servants,[d] along with certain of
the people and the rest of the Israelites, settled in their own towns.[e]

Ezra Reads the Law

When the seventh month came and the
8 Israelites had settled in their towns,[f]
1 all the people came together as one
in the square before the Water Gate.[g] They
told Ezra the teacher of the Law to bring
out the Book of the Law of Moses,[h] which
the LORD had commanded for Israel.
2 So on the first day of the seventh
month[i] Ezra the priest brought the Law[j]
before the assembly, which was made up
of men and women and all who were able
to understand. 3 He read it aloud from daybreak till noon as he faced the square before the Water Gate[k] in the presence of the
men, women and others who could understand. And all the people listened attentively to the Book of the Law.
4 Ezra the teacher of the Law stood on a
high wooden platform[l] built for the occasion. Beside him on his right stood Mattithiah, Shema, Anaiah, Uriah, Hilkiah and
Maaseiah; and on his left were Pedaiah,
Mishael, Malkijah, Hashum, Hashbadda-
nah, Zechariah and Meshullam.

7:60 [z] S 1Ch 9:2
7:65 [a] S Ex 28:30
7:71 [b] S 1Ch 29:7
7:72 [c] S Ex 25:2
7:73 [d] Ne 1:10; Ps 34:22; 103:21; 113:1; 135:1 [e] S Ezr 3:1; Ne 11:1 [f] Ezr 3:1
8:1 [g] S Ne 3:26 [h] S Dt 28:61; S 2Ch 34:15
8:2 [i] Lev 23:23-25; Nu 29:1-6 [j] S Dt 31:11
8:3 [k] S Ne 3:26
8:4 [l] 2Ch 6:13

[a] *68* Some Hebrew manuscripts (see also Ezra 2:66); most Hebrew manuscripts do not have this verse.
[b] *70* That is, about 19 pounds or about 8.4 kilograms
[c] *71* That is, about 375 pounds or about 170 kilograms; also in verse 72
[d] *71* That is, about 1 1/3 tons or about 1.2 metric tons
[e] *72* That is, about 1 1/4 tons or about 1.1 metric tons

:57,60 *descendants of the servants of Solomon.* See note on zr 2:55,58.
:70 *darics.* See note on Ezr 2:69.
:73 *settled in their own towns.* See note on Ezr 2:70. *seventh nonth.* October-November, 444 BC.
:1–18 The reading from "the Book of the Law of Moses" by zra is the first reference to Ezra in almost 13 years since his rrival in 458 BC.
:1 *all the people came together.* See Ezr 3:1, which also re-ers to an assembly called in the seventh month (Tishri), the eginning of the civil year (see chart, p. 113). *square before he Water Gate.* See vv. 3,16; see also notes on 3:26; Ezr 10:9. quares were normally located near a city gate (2Ch 32:6). *eacher of the Law.* See note on Ezr 7:6. *Book of the Law of Aoses.* Cf. vv. 2–3,5,8–9, 13–15,18. Several views have been proposed concerning the extent of this Book: (1) the laws of Exodus and Leviticus, (2) the laws of Deuteronomy, (3) the entire Pentateuch. See notes on Jos 1:8; 2Ki 22:8.
8:2 *first day of the seventh month.* Oct. 8, 444 BC; the New Year's Day of the civil calendar (see note on Lev 23:24), celebrated as the Festival of Trumpets (Nu 29:1–6), with cessation of labor and a sacred assembly. *women.* See 10:28. Women did not usually participate in assemblies (see note on Ex 10:11) but were brought, together with children, on such solemn occasions (Dt 31:12; Jos 8:35; 2Ki 23:2).
8:3 *read it aloud.* See Ex 24:7; Ac 8:30 and note; 1Ti 4:13; Rev 1:3. *from daybreak till noon.* The people evidently stood (vv. 5,7) for five or six hours, listening attentively to the reading and explanation (vv. 7–8,12) of the Scriptures.

5 Ezra opened the book. All the people could see him because he was standing[m] above them; and as he opened it, the people all stood up. 6 Ezra praised the LORD, the great God; and all the people lifted their hands[n] and responded, "Amen! Amen!" Then they bowed down and worshiped the LORD with their faces to the ground.

7 The Levites[o]—Jeshua, Bani, Sherebiah, Jamin, Akkub, Shabbethai, Hodiah, Maaseiah, Kelita, Azariah, Jozabad, Hanan and Pelaiah—instructed[p] the people in the Law while the people were standing there. 8 They read from the Book of the Law of God, making it clear[a] and giving the meaning so that the people understood what was being read.

9 Then Nehemiah the governor, Ezra the priest and teacher of the Law, and the Levites[q] who were instructing the people said to them all, "This day is holy to the LORD your God. Do not mourn or weep."[r] For all the people had been weeping as they listened to the words of the Law.

10 Nehemiah said, "Go and enjoy choice food and sweet drinks, and send some to those who have nothing[s] prepared. This day is holy to our Lord. Do not grieve, for the joy[t] of the LORD is your strength."

11 The Levites calmed all the people, saying, "Be still, for this is a holy day. Do not grieve."

12 Then all the people went away to eat and drink, to send portions of food and to celebrate with great joy,[u] because they now understood the words that had been made known to them.

13 On the second day of the month, the heads of all the families, along with the priests and the Levites, gathered around Ezra the teacher to give attention to the words of the Law. 14 They found written in the Law, which the LORD had commanded through Moses, that the Israelites were to live in temporary shelters[v] during the festival of the seventh month 15 and that they should proclaim this word and spread it throughout their towns and in Jerusalem: "Go out into the hill country and bring back branches from olive and wild olive trees, and from myrtles, palms and shade trees, to make temporary shelters"—as it is written.[b]

16 So the people went out and brought back branches and built themselves temporary shelters on their own roofs, in their courtyards, in the courts of the house of God and in the square by the Water Gate[w] and the one by the Gate of Ephraim.[x] 17 The whole company that had returned

8:5 [m] Jdg 3:20 **8:6** [n] S Ezr 9:5; 1Ti 2:8 **8:7** [o] S Ezr 10:23 [p] S Lev 10:11; S 2Ch 17:7 **8:9** [q] Ne 7:1,65,70 [r] Dt 12:7,12; 16:14-15 **8:10** [s] 1Sa 25:8; S 2Sa 6:19; Est 9:22; Lk 14:12-14 [t] S Lev 23:40; S Dt 12:18; 16:11,14-15 **8:12** [u] Est 9:22 **8:14** [v] S Ex 23:16 **8:16** [w] S Ne 3:26 [x] S 2Ch 25:23

[a] 8 Or *God, translating it* [b] 15 See Lev. 23:37-40.

8:5 *book.* Scroll (see note on Ex 17:14). *people all stood up.* The rabbis deduced from this verse that the congregation should stand for the reading of the Torah. It is customary in Eastern Orthodox churches for the congregation to stand throughout the service.

8:6 *lifted their hands.* See Ex 9:29 and note; Ps 28:2; 134:2; 1Ti 2:8. *Amen! Amen!* See notes on Dt 27:15; Ro 1:25. The repetition conveys the intensity of feeling behind the affirmation (for other repetitions see Ge 22:11 and note; cf. 2Ki 11:14; Lk 23:21). *worshiped.* In its original sense the Hebrew for this verb meant "to prostrate oneself on the ground," as the frequently accompanying phrase "to the ground" indicates. Private acts of worship often involved prostration "to the ground," as in the case of Abraham's servant (Ge 24:52), Moses (Ex 34:8), Joshua (Jos 5:14) and Job (Job 1:20). There are three cases of spontaneous communal worship in Exodus (4:31; 12:27; 33:10). In 2Ch 20:18 Jehoshaphat and the people "fell down in worship before the LORD" when they heard his promise of victory.

8:7 *instructed.* See v. 8; Ezr 7:6,10 and note on 7:6.

8:8 *read.* See note on v. 3. *making it clear.* Rabbinic tradition understands the Hebrew for this expression as referring to translation from Hebrew into an Aramaic Targum (see NIV text note). But there is no evidence of Targums (free Aramaic translations of OT books or passages) from such an early date. The earliest extensive Targum is one on Job dated c. 150–100 BC (from Qumran).Targums exist for every book of the OT except Daniel and Ezra-Nehemiah. *understood.* See v. 12.

8:9 *Nehemiah ... Ezra.* An explicit reference showing that they were contemporaries (see 12:26,36). *Do not mourn.* See Ezr 10:6 and note; Est 9:22; Isa 57:18–19; Jer 31:13. *weep.* See 1:4; Ezr 3:13 and note; 10:1. *weeping as they listened.* Out of remorse for their own failures and those of their ancestors.

8:10 *choice food.* Delicious, festive food prepared with much fat. The fat of sacrificial animals was offered to God as the tastiest element of the burnt offering (Lev 1:8,12), the fellowship offering (Lev 3:9–10), the sin offering (Lev 4:8–10) and the guilt offering (Lev 7:3–4; see chart, p. 164). The fat was not to be eaten in these cases. *send some to those who have nothing.* It was customary for God's people to remember the less fortunate on joyous occasions (2Sa 6:19; Est 9:22; contrast 1Co 11:20–22; Jas 2:14–16).

8:14 *temporary shelters.* See notes on Ex 23:16; Lev 23:34,42; Jn 7:37.

8:15 *myrtles.* Evergreen bushes with a pleasing scent (Isa 41:19; 55:13; Zec 1:8,10–11). *palms.* The date palm was common around Jericho (Dt 34:3; 2Ch 28:15). *shade trees.* Cf. Eze 6:13; 20:28. Later Jewish celebrations of the Festival of Tabernacles include waving the *lulav* (made of branches of palms, myrtles and willows) with the right hand and holding branches of the *ethrog* (a citrus native to Canaan) in the left.

8:16 *courts of the house of God.* See note on 13:7. The temple that Ezekiel saw in his visions had an outer and an inner court (see model, p. 1399). Ezekiel's temple was to some extent patterned after Solomon's, which had an inner court of priests and an outer court (1Ki 6:36; 7:12; 2Ki 21:5; 23:12; 2Ch 4:9; 33:5). The temple of the NT era had a court of the Gentiles and an inner court, which was subdivided into courts of the women, of Israel and of the priests. The Temple Scroll from Qumran has God setting forth in detail an ideal temple. Columns 40–46 describe the outer court as follows: "On the roof of the third story are columns for the constructing of booths for the Festival of Tabernacles, to be occupied by the elders, tribal chieftains, and commanders of thousands and hundreds." *Gate of Ephraim.* A gate of the oldest rampart of Jerusalem (see note on 3:6; see also 2Ki 14:13). It was restored by Nehemiah (12:39).

rom exile built temporary shelters and
ived in them.[y] From the days of Joshua
on of Nun until that day, the Israelites
ad not celebrated[z] it like this. And their
oy was very great.
[18]Day after day, from the first day to
he last, Ezra read[a] from the Book of the
aw[b] of God. They celebrated the festival
or seven days, and on the eighth day, in
ccordance with the regulation,[c] there was
n assembly.[d]

The Israelites Confess Their Sins

9 On the twenty-fourth day of the same
month, the Israelites gathered togeth-
r, fasting and wearing sackcloth and puting dust on their heads.[e] [2]Those of Israel-
te descent had separated themselves from
ll foreigners.[f] They stood in their places
nd confessed their sins and the sins of
heir ancestors.[g] [3]They stood where they
vere and read from the Book of the Law
f the LORD their God for a quarter of the
ay, and spent another quarter in confes-
ion and in worshiping the LORD their God.
Standing on the stairs of the Levites[h] were
eshua, Bani, Kadmiel, Shebaniah, Bunni,
herebiah, Bani and Kenani. They cried
ut with loud voices to the LORD their God.
And the Levites—Jeshua, Kadmiel, Bani,
Iashabneiah, Sherebiah, Hodiah, Sheba-
iah and Pethahiah—said: "Stand up and
raise the LORD your God,[i] who is from
verlasting to everlasting.[a]"

"Blessed be your glorious name,[j]
and may it be exalted above all blessing and praise. [6]You alone are the
LORD.[k] You made the heavens,[l] even
the highest heavens, and all their
starry host,[m] the earth[n] and all that
is on it, the seas[o] and all that is in
them.[p] You give life to everything,
and the multitudes of heaven[q] worship you.
[7]"You are the LORD God, who chose
Abram[r] and brought him out of Ur of
the Chaldeans[s] and named him Abraham.[t] [8]You found his heart faithful to
you, and you made a covenant with
him to give to his descendants the
land of the Canaanites, Hittites, Amorites, Perizzites, Jebusites and Girgashites.[u] You have kept your promise[v]
because you are righteous.[w]
[9]"You saw the suffering of our ancestors in Egypt;[x] you heard their cry
at the Red Sea.[b][y] [10]You sent signs[z] and
wonders[a] against Pharaoh, against all
his officials and all the people of his
land, for you knew how arrogantly the Egyptians treated them. You
made a name[b] for yourself,[c] which remains to this day. [11]You divided the
sea before them,[d] so that they passed
through it on dry ground, but you
hurled their pursuers into the depths,[e]
like a stone into mighty waters.[f] [12]By
day[g] you led[h] them with a pillar of
cloud,[i] and by night with a pillar of
fire to give them light on the way they
were to take.
[13]"You came down on Mount Sinai;[j]
you spoke[k] to them from heaven.[l] You
gave them regulations and laws that
are just[m] and right, and decrees and
commands that are good.[n] [14]You made
known to them your holy Sabbath[o]
and gave them commands, decrees
and laws through your servant Moses. [15]In their hunger you gave them
bread from heaven[p] and in their thirst

8:17 [y]Hos 12:9 [z]S 1Ki 8:2; S 2Ch 7:8; S 8:13 **8:18** [a]Dt 31:11; S 33:10 [b]S Dt 28:61 [c]S Lev 23:36, 40; S Ezr 3:4 [d]S Lev 23:36 **9:1** [e]Lev 26:40-45; S Jos 7:6; 2Ch 7:14-16 **9:2** [f]S Ezr 6:21; Ne 10:28; 13:3, 30 [g]S Lev 26:40; S Ezr 10:11; Ps 106:6 **9:4** [h]S Ezr 10:23 **9:5** [i]Ps 78:4 [j]S 2Sa 7:26 **9:6** [k]S Dt 6:4 [l]S Ex 8:19 [m]Isa 40:26; 45:12 [n]S Ge 1:1; Isa 37:16 [o]Ps 95:5; 146:6; Jnh 1:9 [p]Dt 10:14; Ac 4:24; Rev 10:6 [q]Ps 103:20; 148:2 **9:7** [r]S Ge 16:11 [s]S Ge 11:28 [t]S Ge 17:5 **9:8** [u]S Ge 15:18-21; S Ezr 9:1 [v]S Jos 21:45 [w]Ge 15:6; S Ezr 9:15 **9:9** [x]Ex 2:23-25; 3:7 [y]Ex 14:10-30 **9:10** [z]S Ex 10:1; Ps 74:9 [a]S Ex 3:20; S 6:6 [b]Jer 32:20; Da 9:15 [c]S Nu 6:27 **9:11** [d]Ps 78:13 [e]S Ex 14:28 [f]Ex 15:4-5, 10; Heb 11:29 **9:12** [g]S Dt 1:33 [h]S Ex 15:13 [i]S Ex 13:21 **9:13** [j]S Ex 19:11 [k]S Ex 19:19 [l]S Ex 20:22 [m]Ps 119:137 [n]S Ex 20:1; Dt 4:7-8 **9:14** [o]S Ge 2:3; Ex 20:8-11 **9:15** [p]S Ex 16:4; Ps 78:24-25; Jn 6:31

[a] 5 Or *God for ever and ever* [b] 9 Or *the Sea of Reeds*

:17 *From the days of Joshua ... until that day.* The phrase does ot mean that the Festival of Tabernacles had not been celbrated since Joshua's time, because such celebrations took lace after the dedication of Solomon's temple (2Ch 7:8–10) nd after the return of the exiles (Ezr 3:4). Apparently what s meant is that the festival had not been celebrated before vith such great joy (cf. 2Ch 30:26; 35:18).
:18 *assembly.* See Nu 29:35.
9:1–37 The ninth chapters of Ezra, Nehemiah and Daniel are devoted to confessions of national sin and o prayers for God's grace.
:1 *twenty-fourth day.* Oct. 30, 444 BC; a day of penance in the pirit of the Day of Atonement, which was held on the tenth lay (Lev 16:29–30). *fasting ... sackcloth ... dust.* See notes on ie 37:34; Ezr 8:23; 10:6; Joel 1:13–14.
:3 *quarter of the day.* About three hours.
9:5–37 One of the most beautiful prayers outside the Psalms, it reviews God's grace and power (1) in cretion (v. 6), (2) in the Abrahamic covenant (vv. 7–8), (3) in gypt and at the "Red Sea" (vv. 9–11), (4) in the wilderness nd at Sinai (vv. 12–21), (5) during the conquest of Canaan (vv. 22–25), (6) through the judges (vv. 26–28), (7) through the prophets (vv. 29–31) and (8) in the present situation (vv. 32–37). Cf. Ps 78; 105–106. See similar prayers in Ezr 9:5–15; Da 9:3–19 (see also note there).
9:6 *You alone are the LORD.* Though not in the words of Dt 6:4, which expresses the central monotheistic conviction of Israel's faith, the prayer begins with a similar affirmation (cf. 2Ki 19:15; Ps 86:10). *highest heavens.* See Dt 10:14; 1Ki 8:27; 2Ch 2:6; Ps 148:4. *multitudes of heaven worship you.* See Ps 89:5–7.
9:7 *Ur of the Chaldeans.* See note on Ge 11:28. *named him Abraham.* See note on Ge 17:5.
9:8 *faithful.* Compare Ro 4:16–22 with Jas 2:21–23. *made a covenant with him.* See note on Ge 15:18. *Canaanites ... Girgashites.* See notes on Ge 10:6,15–18; 13:7; Ex 3:8; Ezr 9:1.
9:9 *Red Sea.* See notes on Ex 13:18; 14:2.
9:11 *divided the sea.* See Ex 14:21–22; 1Co 10:1.
9:14 *holy Sabbath.* According to the rabbis, "the Sabbath outweighs all the commandments of the Torah." See 10:31–33; 13:15–22.
9:15 *bread from heaven.* See note on Ex 16:4. *water from the*

you brought them water from the
rock;[q] you told them to go in and take
possession of the land you had sworn
with uplifted hand[r] to give them.[s]
16 "But they, our ancestors, became arrogant and stiff-necked,[t] and
they did not obey your commands.[u]
17 They refused to listen and failed
to remember[v] the miracles[w] you performed among them. They became
stiff-necked[x] and in their rebellion
appointed a leader in order to return
to their slavery.[y] But you are a forgiving God,[z] gracious and compassionate,[a] slow to anger[b] and abounding
in love.[c] Therefore you did not desert them,[d] 18 even when they cast for
themselves an image of a calf[e] and
said, 'This is your god, who brought
you up out of Egypt,' or when they
committed awful blasphemies.[f]
19 "Because of your great compassion you did not abandon[g] them in
the wilderness. By day the pillar of
cloud[h] did not fail to guide them on
their path, nor the pillar of fire by
night to shine on the way they were
to take. 20 You gave your good Spirit[i] to
instruct[j] them. You did not withhold
your manna[k] from their mouths, and
you gave them water[l] for their thirst.
21 For forty years[m] you sustained them
in the wilderness; they lacked nothing,[n] their clothes did not wear out
nor did their feet become swollen.[o]
22 "You gave them kingdoms and
nations, allotting to them even the
remotest frontiers. They took over
the country of Sihon[a][p] king of Heshbon and the country of Og king of
Bashan.[q] 23 You made their children
as numerous as the stars in the sky,[r]
and you brought them into the land
that you told their parents to enter
and possess. 24 Their children went in
and took possession of the land.[s] You
subdued[t] before them the Canaanites,
who lived in the land; you gave the
Canaanites into their hands, along
with their kings and the peoples of
the land, to deal with them as they
pleased. 25 They captured fortified cities and fertile land;[u] they took possession of houses filled with all kinds of
good things,[v] wells already dug, vineyards, olive groves and fruit trees in
abundance. They ate to the full and
were well-nourished;[w] they reveled in
your great goodness.[x]
26 "But they were disobedient and
rebelled against you; they turned their
backs on your law.[y] They killed[z] your
prophets,[a] who had warned them in
order to turn them back to you; they
committed awful blasphemies.[b] 27 So
you delivered them into the hands of
their enemies,[c] who oppressed them.
But when they were oppressed they
cried out to you. From heaven you
heard them, and in your great compassion[d] you gave them deliverers,[e]
who rescued them from the hand of
their enemies.
28 "But as soon as they were at rest,
they again did what was evil in your
sight.[f] Then you abandoned them to
the hand of their enemies so that they
ruled over them. And when they cried
out to you again, you heard from
heaven, and in your compassion[g] you
delivered them[h] time after time.
29 "You warned[i] them in order to
turn them back to your law, but they
became arrogant[j] and disobeyed your

9:15 [q] Ex 17:6; Nu 20:7-13 [r] S Ge 14:22 [s] Dt 1:8,21 **9:16** [t] S Ex 32:9; Jer 7:26; 17:23; 19:15 [u] Dt 1:26-33; 31:29 **9:17** [v] Jdg 8:34; Ps 78:42 [w] Ps 77:11; 78:12; 105:5; 106:7 [x] Jer 7:26; 19:15 [y] Nu 14:1-4 [z] Ps 130:4; Da 9:9 [a] S Dt 4:31 [b] S Ex 34:6; Ps 103:8; Na 1:3 [c] S Ex 22:27; Nu 14:17-19; Ps 86:15 [d] Ps 78:11; Eze 5:6 **9:18** [e] S Ex 32:4 [f] S Ex 20:23 **9:19** [g] Ex 13:22 [h] S Ex 13:21 **9:20** [i] Nu 9:17; 11:17; Isa 63:11, 14; Hag 2:5; Zec 4:6 [j] Ps 23:3; 143:10 [k] S Ex 16:15 [l] Ex 17:6 **9:21** [m] S Ex 16:35 [n] S Dt 2:7 [o] S Dt 8:4 **9:22** [p] S Nu 21:21 [q] S Nu 21:33; Dt 2:26-3:11 **9:23** [r] S Ge 12:2; S Lev 26:9; S Nu 10:36 **9:24** [s] S Jos 11:23 [t] S Jdg 4:23; S 2Ch 14:13 **9:25** [u] S Dt 11:11 [v] S Ex 18:9 [w] Dt 6:10-12 [x] Dt 8:8-11; 32:12-15; Ps 23:6; 25:7; 69:16 **9:26** [y] S 1Ki 14:9; Jer 44:10 [z] S Jos 7:25 [a] Jer 2:30; 26:8; Mt 21:35-36; 23:29-36: Ac 7:52 [b] S Jdg 2:12-13 **9:27** [c] S Nu 25:17; S Jdg 2:14 [d] Ps 51:1; 103:8; 106:45; 119:156 [e] S Jdg 3:9 **9:28** [f] S Ex 32:22; S Jdg 2:17 [g] S 2Sa 24:14 [h] Ps 22:4; 106:43; 136:24 **9:29** [i] S Jdg 6:8 [j] ver 16-17; Ps 5:5; Isa 2:11; Jer 43:2

[a] *22* One Hebrew manuscript and Septuagint; most Hebrew manuscripts *Sihon, that is, the country of the*

rock. See note on Ex 17:6. *sworn with uplifted hand.* See Ge 14:22 and note; 22:15–17; Ex 6:8; Eze 20:6; 47:14.
9:16 *stiff-necked.* See vv. 17,29; see also notes on 3:5; Ex 32:9.
9:17 *appointed a leader.* Their intention to do so is recorded in Nu 14:4. *gracious … abounding in love.* See note on Ex 34:6–7.
9:18 *blasphemies.* See v. 26; Ex 32:4; Eze 35:12.
9:19 *compassion.* See vv. 27–28.
9:20 *Spirit to instruct.* See Ex 31:3.
9:21 *clothes did not wear out.* Evidence of the special providence of God (see Dt 8:4; 29:5; contrast Jos 9:13). *swollen.* Or "blistered"; the Hebrew for this word occurs only here and in Dt 8:4.
9:22 *Sihon … Og.* See Nu 21:21–35.
9:23 *numerous as the stars.* See notes on Ge 13:16; 15:5; 22:17.
9:25 See Dt 6:10–12 and note; Jos 24:13. *fertile.* See v. 35; cf. Nu 14:7; Dt 8:7; Jos 23:13. *wells already dug.* Because of the lack of rainfall during much of the year, almost every house had its own well or cistern in which to store water from the rainy seasons (2Ki 18:31; Pr 5:15). By 1200 BC the technique of waterproofing cisterns was developed, permitting greater occupation of the central hills of Judah. *vineyards, olive groves and fruit trees.* Cf. Dt 8:8. The Egyptian story of Sinuhe (c. 2000 BC) describes Canaan as follows: "Figs were in it, and grapes. It had more wine than water. Plentiful was its honey, abundant its olives. Every (kind of) fruit was on its trees." See note on Ex 3:8. *well-nourished.* Elsewhere the Hebrew for this word always implies physical fullness and spiritual insensitivity.
9:26–28 See note on Jdg 2:6—3:6.
9:26 *turned their backs on your law.* Totally disregarded God's law (cf. Ps 50:17; Jer 2:27; 32:33; Eze 23:35). *killed your prophets.* See 1Ki 18:4,13; 19:10,14; 2Ch 24:20–21; Jer 2:30; 26:20–23; cf. Lk 11:50–51; Heb 11:32,36–38.
9:27 *deliverers.* See Introduction to Judges: Title.

commands. They sinned against your
ordinances, of which you said, 'The
person who obeys them will live by
them.'[k] Stubbornly they turned their
backs[l] on you, became stiff-necked[m]
and refused to listen.[n] 30 For many
years you were patient with them. By
your Spirit you warned them through
your prophets.[o] Yet they paid no attention, so you gave them into the
hands of the neighboring peoples.[p]
31 But in your great mercy you did
not put an end[q] to them or abandon
them, for you are a gracious and merciful[r] God.

32 "Now therefore, our God, the
great God, mighty[s] and awesome,[t]
who keeps his covenant of love,[u] do
not let all this hardship seem trifling
in your eyes—the hardship[v] that has
come on us, on our kings and leaders,
on our priests and prophets, on our
ancestors and all your people, from
the days of the kings of Assyria until today. 33 In all that has happened
to us, you have remained righteous;[w]
you have acted faithfully, while we
acted wickedly.[x] 34 Our kings,[y] our
leaders, our priests and our ancestors[z] did not follow your law; they did
not pay attention to your commands
or the statutes you warned them to
keep. 35 Even while they were in their
kingdom, enjoying your great goodness[a] to them in the spacious and
fertile land you gave them, they did
not serve you[b] or turn from their evil
ways.

36 "But see, we are slaves[c] today,
slaves in the land you gave our ancestors so they could eat its fruit and
the other good things it produces.
37 Because of our sins, its abundant
harvest goes to the kings you have
placed over us. They rule over our
bodies and our cattle as they please.
We are in great distress.[d]

The Agreement of the People

38 "In view of all this, we are making
a binding agreement,[e] putting it in writing,[f] and our leaders, our Levites and our
priests are affixing their seals to it."[a]

9:29 [k]S Dt 30:16 [l]S 1Sa 8:3 [m]Jer 19:15 [n]Zec 7:11-12 **9:30** [o]2Ki 17:13-18; S 2Ch 36:16 [p]Jer 16:11; Zec 7:12 **9:31** [q]Isa 48:9; 65:9 [r]S Dt 4:31 **9:32** [s]Job 9:19; Ps 24:8; 89:8; 93:4 [t]S Dt 7:21 [u]S Dt 7:9; S 1Ki 8:23; Da 9:4 [v]S Ex 18:8 **9:33** [w]S Ge 18:25 [x]Jer 44:3; Da 9:7-8,14 **9:34** [y]S 2Ki 23:11 [z]Jer 44:17 **9:35** [a]Isa 63:7 [b]Dt 28:45-48 **9:36** [c]S Ezr 9:9 **9:37** [d]Dt 28:33; La 5:5 **9:38** [e]S 2Ch 23:16

[f]Isa 44:5 **10:2** [g]S Ezr 2:2 **10:3** [h]S 1Ch 9:12 **10:5** [i]S 1Ch 24:8 **10:8** [j]Ne 12:1 **10:9** [k]Ne 12:1 **10:16** [l]S Ezr 8:6 **10:20** [m]1Ch 24:15 **10:23** [n]S Ne 7:2 **10:28** [o]Ps 135:1 [p]2Ch 6:26; S Ne 9:2

10

[b] Those who sealed it were:

Nehemiah the governor, the son of Hakaliah.

Zedekiah, 2 Seraiah,[g] Azariah, Jeremiah,
3 Pashhur,[h] Amariah, Malkijah,
4 Hattush, Shebaniah, Malluk,
5 Harim,[i] Meremoth, Obadiah,
6 Daniel, Ginnethon, Baruch,
7 Meshullam, Abijah, Mijamin,
8 Maaziah, Bilgai and Shemaiah.
These were the priests.[j]

9 The Levites:[k]

Jeshua son of Azaniah, Binnui of the sons of Henadad, Kadmiel,
10 and their associates: Shebaniah,
Hodiah, Kelita, Pelaiah, Hanan,
11 Mika, Rehob, Hashabiah,
12 Zakkur, Sherebiah, Shebaniah,
13 Hodiah, Bani and Beninu.

14 The leaders of the people:

Parosh, Pahath-Moab, Elam, Zattu, Bani,
15 Bunni, Azgad, Bebai,
16 Adonijah, Bigvai, Adin,[l]
17 Ater, Hezekiah, Azzur,
18 Hodiah, Hashum, Bezai,
19 Hariph, Anathoth, Nebai,
20 Magpiash, Meshullam, Hezir,[m]
21 Meshezabel, Zadok, Jaddua,
22 Pelatiah, Hanan, Anaiah,
23 Hoshea, Hananiah,[n] Hasshub,
24 Hallohesh, Pilha, Shobek,
25 Rehum, Hashabnah, Maaseiah,
26 Ahiah, Hanan, Anan,
27 Malluk, Harim and Baanah.

28 "The rest of the people—priests,
Levites, gatekeepers, musicians, temple servants[o] and all who separated
themselves from the neighboring peoples[p] for the sake of the Law of God,

[a] 38 In Hebrew texts this verse (9:38) is numbered 10:1.
[b] In Hebrew texts 10:1-39 is numbered 10:2-40.

9:29 *The person who obeys them will live by them.* See note on Lev 18:5. *Stubbornly they turned their backs.* See Zec 7:11; cf. the similar expressions in v. 16; 3:5; Hos 4:16.
9:32 *who keeps his covenant of love.* See 1:5; see also Dt 7:9,12 and note. *kings of Assyria.* Including Tiglath-Pileser III, also known as Pul (1Ch 5:26); Shalmaneser V (2Ki 18:9); Sargon II (Isa 20:1); Sennacherib (2Ki 18:13); Esarhaddon (Ezr 4:2); and Ashurbanipal (Ezr 4:10). See chart, p. 511.
9:37 *rule over our bodies.* See 1Sa 8:11–13. The Persian rulers drafted their subjects into military service. Some Jews may have accompanied Xerxes on his invasion of Greece in 480 BC.
10:1–27 A legal list, bearing the official seal and containing a roster of 84 names.
10:2–8 About half of these names occur again in 12:1–7.
10:9–13 Most of these names appear also in the lists of Levites in 8:7; 9:4–5.
10:14–27 Almost half of the names in this category are also found in the lists of 7:6–63; Ezr 2:1–61.
10:28 *The rest of the people.* Those who did not affix their seals to the agreement (cf. 9:38—10:1). *Levites.* See Introduction to Leviticus: Title. *gatekeepers.* See note on Ezr 2:42. *wives ... sons and daughters.* See note on 8:2.

together with their wives and all their
sons and daughters who are able to
understand— 29 all these now join
their fellow Israelites the nobles, and
bind themselves with a curse and an
oath[q] to follow the Law of God giv-
en through Moses the servant of God
and to obey carefully all the commands, regulations and decrees of the
LORD our Lord.
30 "We promise not to give our
daughters in marriage to the peoples
around us or take their daughters for
our sons.[r]
31 "When the neighboring peoples
bring merchandise or grain to sell on
the Sabbath,[s] we will not buy from
them on the Sabbath or on any holy
day. Every seventh year we will forgo
working the land[t] and will cancel all
debts.[u]
32 "We assume the responsibility for
carrying out the commands to give a
third of a shekel[a] each year for the
service of the house of our God: 33 for
the bread set out on the table;[v] for the
regular grain offerings and burnt offerings; for the offerings on the Sabbaths, at the New Moon[w] feasts and
at the appointed festivals; for the holy
offerings; for sin offerings[b] to make
atonement for Israel; and for all the
duties of the house of our God.[x]
34 "We—the priests, the Levites
and the people—have cast lots[y] to
determine when each of our families
is to bring to the house of our God at
set times each year a contribution of
wood[z] to burn on the altar of the LORD
our God, as it is written in the Law.
35 "We also assume responsibility
for bringing to the house of the LORD
each year the firstfruits[a] of our crops
and of every fruit tree.[b]
36 "As it is also written in the Law,
we will bring the firstborn[c] of our
sons and of our cattle, of our herds
and of our flocks to the house of our
God, to the priests ministering there.[d]
37 "Moreover, we will bring to the
storerooms of the house of our God,
to the priests, the first of our ground
meal, of our grain offerings, of the
fruit of all our trees and of our new
wine and olive oil.[e] And we will bring
a tithe[f] of our crops to the Levites,[g] for
it is the Levites who collect the tithes
in all the towns where we work.[h] 38 A
priest descended from Aaron is to accompany the Levites when they receive the tithes, and the Levites are
to bring a tenth of the tithes[i] up to the
house of our God, to the storerooms
of the treasury. 39 The people of Israel, including the Levites, are to bring
their contributions of grain, new wine
and olive oil to the storerooms, where
the articles for the sanctuary and for
the ministering priests, the gatekeepers and the musicians are also kept.
"We will not neglect the house of
our God."[j]

The New Residents of Jerusalem

11:3-19pp — 1Ch 9:1-17

11 Now the leaders of the people settled in Jerusalem. The rest of the

10:29 [q] S Nu 5:21; Ps 119:106 **10:30** [r] S Ex 34:16; Ne 13:23 **10:31** [s] Ne 13:16, 18; Jer 17:27; Eze 23:38; Am 8:5 [t] S Ex 23:11; Lev 25:1-7 [u] S Dt 15:1 **10:33** [v] Lev 24:6 [w] Nu 10:10; Ps 81:3; Isa 1:14 [x] S 2Ch 24:5 **10:34** [y] S Lev 16:8 [z] Ne 13:31

10:35 [a] S Ex 22:29; S Nu 18:12 [b] Dt 26:1-11 **10:36** [c] S Ex 13:2; S Nu 18:14-16 [d] Ne 13:31 **10:37** [e] S Nu 18:12 [f] S Lev 27:30; S Nu 18:21 [g] Dt 14:22-29 [h] Eze 44:30 **10:38** [i] Nu 18:26 **10:39** [j] Ne 13:11,12

[a] 32 That is, about 1/8 ounce or about 4 grams
[b] 33 Or *purification offerings*

10:31 – 33 Perhaps a code drawn up by Nehemiah to correct the abuses listed in 13:15 – 22.
10:31 *sell on the Sabbath.* Though Ex 20:8 – 11; Dt 5:12 – 15 do not explicitly prohibit trading on the Sabbath, see Jer 17:19 – 27; Am 8:5 and note. *seventh year … forgo working the land … cancel all debts.* See note on Lev 25:4. The Romans misrepresented the Sabbath and the sabbath year as caused by laziness. According to Tacitus, the Jews "were led by the charms of indolence to give over the seventh year as well to inactivity."
10:32 *third of a shekel.* Ex 30:13 – 14 speaks of a "half shekel" as "an offering to the LORD" from each man who was 20 years old or more as a symbolic ransom. Later Joash used the annual contributions for the repair of the temple (2Ch 24:4 – 14). In the NT period Jewish men from everywhere sent an offering of a half shekel (actually two drachmas, its equivalent; see Josephus, *Antiquities*, 3.8.2) for the temple in Jerusalem (Mt 17:24). The pledge of a third of a shekel in Nehemiah's time may have been due to economic circumstances.
10:33 *bread.* See note on Lev 24:8.
10:34 *cast lots.* See notes on 11:1; Jnh 1:7. *contribution of wood.* Though there is no specific reference to a wood offering in the Pentateuch, the perpetual burning of fire on the sanctuary altar (Lev 6:12 – 13) would have required a continual supply of wood. Josephus mentions "the festival of wood offering" on the 14th day of the fifth month (Av). The Jewish Mishnah (rabbinic interpretations and applications of Pentateuchal laws) lists nine times when certain families brought wood and stipulates that all kinds of wood were suitable, except the vine and the olive. The Temple Scroll from Qumran describes the celebration of a wood offering festival for six days following a new olive oil festival.
10:35 *firstfruits.* Brought to the sanctuary to support the priests and Levites (see Ex 23:19 and note; Nu 18:13; Dt 26:1 – 11; Eze 44:30).
10:36 *firstborn.* See note on Ex 13:13.
10:37 *storerooms.* Chambers in the courts of the temple were used as storage rooms for silver, gold and sacred articles (cf. vv. 38 – 39; 12:44; 13:4 – 5,9; Ezr 8:28 – 30). *new wine.* See note on Dt 7:13. Though the Hebrew for this term can refer to freshly pressed grape juice (Isa 65:8; Mic 6:15), it can also be used of intoxicating wine (Hos 4:11). *tithe.* See notes on Ge 14:20; 28:22; Lev 27:30; Am 4:4. *Levites.* Tithes were meant for their support (13:12 – 13; Nu 18:21 – 32).
10:39 See 13:11. *We will not neglect.* Haggai (Hag 1:4 – 9) had accused the people of neglecting the temple.

people cast lots to bring one out of every ten of them to live in Jerusalem,[k] the
holy city,[l] while the remaining nine were
to stay in their own towns.[m] 2 The people
commended all who volunteered to live in
Jerusalem.
3 These are the provincial leaders who
settled in Jerusalem (now some Israelites,
priests, Levites, temple servants and descendants of Solomon's servants lived in
the towns of Judah, each on their own
property in the various towns,[n] 4 while other people from both Judah and Benjamin[o]
lived in Jerusalem):[p]

From the descendants of Judah:

Athaiah son of Uzziah, the son of
Zechariah, the son of Amariah, the
son of Shephatiah, the son of Mahalalel, a descendant of Perez; 5 and Maaseiah son of Baruch, the son of Kol-
Hozeh, the son of Hazaiah, the son
of Adaiah, the son of Joiarib, the son
of Zechariah, a descendant of Shelah. 6 The descendants of Perez who
lived in Jerusalem totaled 468 men of
standing.

7 From the descendants of Benjamin:

Sallu son of Meshullam, the son of
Joed, the son of Pedaiah, the son of
Kolaiah, the son of Maaseiah, the son
of Ithiel, the son of Jeshaiah, 8 and his
followers, Gabbai and Sallai—928
men. 9 Joel son of Zikri was their chief
officer, and Judah son of Hassenuah
was over the New Quarter of the city.

10 From the priests:

Jedaiah; the son of Joiarib; Jakin;
11 Seraiah[q] son of Hilkiah, the son of
Meshullam, the son of Zadok, the son
of Meraioth, the son of Ahitub,[r] the
official in charge of the house of God,
12 and their associates, who carried on
work for the temple—822 men; Adaiah son of Jeroham, the son of Pelali-
ah, the son of Amzi, the son of Zechariah, the son of Pashhur, the son of
Malkijah, 13 and his associates, who
were heads of families—242 men;
Amashsai son of Azarel, the son of
Ahzai, the son of Meshillemoth, the
son of Immer, 14 and his[a] associates,
who were men of standing—128.
Their chief officer was Zabdiel son of
Haggedolim.

15 From the Levites:

Shemaiah son of Hasshub, the son
of Azrikam, the son of Hashabiah,
the son of Bunni; 16 Shabbethai[s] and
Jozabad,[t] two of the heads of the Levites, who had charge of the outside
work of the house of God; 17 Mattaniah[u] son of Mika, the son of Zabdi,
the son of Asaph,[v] the director who
led in thanksgiving and prayer; Bakbukiah, second among his associates;
and Abda son of Shammua, the son
of Galal, the son of Jeduthun.[w] 18 The
Levites in the holy city[x] totaled 284.

19 The gatekeepers:

Akkub, Talmon and their associates,
who kept watch at the gates—172
men.

20 The rest of the Israelites, with the
priests and Levites, were in all the towns
of Judah, each on their ancestral property.
21 The temple servants[y] lived on the hill
of Ophel, and Ziha and Gishpa were in
charge of them.
22 The chief officer of the Levites in

11:1 [k] Ne 7:4 [l] Isa 48:2; 52:1; 64:10; Zec 14:20-21 [m] S Ne 7:73 **11:3** [n] S Ezr 2:1 **11:4** [o] S Ezr 1:5 [p] S Ezr 2:70 **11:11** [q] S 2Ki 25:18; S Ezr 2:2 [r] S Ezr 7:2 **11:16** [s] Ezr 10:15 [t] S Ezr 8:33 **11:17** [u] S 1Ch 9:15; Ne 12:8 [v] 2Ch 5:12 [w] S 1Ch 25:1 **11:18** [x] S Rev 21:2 **11:21** [y] S Ezr 2:43; S Ne 3:26

[a] 14 Most Septuagint manuscripts; Hebrew *their*

11:1 *cast lots.* See 10:34. Lots were usually made out of small stones or pieces of wood. Sometimes arrows were used (Eze 21:21). *one out of every ten of them to live in Jerusalem.* Josephus (*Antiquities*, 11.5.8) asserts: "But Nehemiah, seeing that the city had a small population, urged the priests and Levites to leave the countryside and move to the city and remain there, for he had prepared houses for them at his own expense." The practice of redistributing populations was also used to establish Greek and Hellenistic cities. It involved the forcible transfer from rural settlements to urban centers. Tiberias on the Sea of Galilee was populated with Gentiles by such a process by Herod Antipas in AD 18. *holy city.* See Isa 48:2 and note; Da 9:24; Mt 4:5; 27:53; Rev 11:2; cf. Joel 3:17.
11:2 In addition to those chosen by lot (v. 1), some volunteered out of a sense of duty. But evidently most preferred to stay in their hometowns.
11:3–19 A census roster that parallels 1Ch 9:2–21, a list of the first residents in Jerusalem after the return from Babylonia. About half the names in the two lists are the same.
11:8 *928.* The men of Benjamin provided twice as many men as Judah (v. 6) to live in and protect the city of Jerusalem.
11:9 *New Quarter.* See 2Ki 22:14 and note; 2Ch 34:22; Zep 1:10. Like the "market district" (Zep 1:11), which was probably the Tyropoeon Valley area, the New Quarter was a new suburb in north Jerusalem (see map, p. 2525, at the end of this study Bible). Excavations indicate that the city had spread outside the walls in this direction by the late eighth century BC before the so-called Broad Wall was built c. 700 by Hezekiah (see note on 3:8).
11:16 *outside work.* Duties outside the temple (cf. 1Ch 26:29) but connected with it.
11:17 *Asaph.* See note on Ezr 2:41; see also titles of Ps 50; 73–83. *Jeduthun.* See 1Ch 16:42; 25:1,3; 2Ch 5:12; titles of Ps 39; 62; 77.
11:18 *284.* The relatively small number of Levites, compared with 1,192 priests (the total of 822, 242 and 128 in vv. 12–13), is striking (see note on Ezr 2:40).
11:20 *ancestral property.* Inalienable hereditary possessions—including land, buildings and movable goods—acquired by either conquest or inheritance (Ge 31:14; Nu 18:21; 27:7; 34:2; 36:3; 1Ki 21:1–4).
11:21 *Ophel.* See note on 3:26.

Jerusalem was Uzzi son of Bani, the son of
Hashabiah, the son of Mattaniah,[z] the son
of Mika. Uzzi was one of Asaph's descendants, who were the musicians responsible for the service of the house of God.
23 The musicians[a] were under the king's orders, which regulated their daily activity.
24 Pethahiah son of Meshezabel, one of
the descendants of Zerah[b] son of Judah,
was the king's agent in all affairs relating
to the people.
25 As for the villages with their fields,
some of the people of Judah lived in Kiriath Arba[c] and its surrounding settlements,
in Dibon[d] and its settlements, in Jekabzeel
and its villages, 26 in Jeshua, in Moladah,[e]
in Beth Pelet,[f] 27 in Hazar Shual,[g] in Beersheba[h] and its settlements, 28 in Ziklag,[i] in
Mekonah and its settlements, 29 in En Rimmon, in Zorah,[j] in Jarmuth,[k] 30 Zanoah,[l]
Adullam[m] and their villages, in Lachish[n]
and its fields, and in Azekah[o] and its settlements. So they were living all the way
from Beersheba[p] to the Valley of Hinnom.
31 The descendants of the Benjamites
from Geba[q] lived in Mikmash,[r] Aija, Bethel[s] and its settlements, 32 in Anathoth,[t]
Nob[u] and Ananiah, 33 in Hazor,[v] Ramah[w]
and Gittaim,[x] 34 in Hadid, Zeboim[y] and Ne-
ballat, 35 in Lod and Ono,[z] and in Ge Harashim.
36 Some of the divisions of the Levites of
Judah settled in Benjamin.

11:22 [z] S 1Ch 9:15 **11:23** [a] S 1Ch 15:16; Ne 7:44 **11:24** [b] S Ge 38:30 **11:25** [c] S Ge 35:27 [d] S Nu 21:30 **11:26** [e] Jos 15:26 [f] Jos 15:27 **11:27** [g] Jos 15:28 [h] S Ge 21:14 **11:28** [i] S 1Sa 27:6 **11:29** [j] Jos 15:33 [k] S Jos 10:3; S 15:35 **11:30** [l] Jos 15:34 [m] Jos 15:35 [n] S Jos 10:3; 15:39 [o] S Jos 10:10 [p] Jos 15:28 **11:31** [q] Jos 21:17; Isa 10:29 [r] S 1Sa 13:2 [s] S Jos 12:9 **11:32** [t] Jos 21:18; Isa 10:30; Jer 1:1 [u] S 1Sa 21:1 **11:33** [v] S Jos 11:1 [w] S Jos 18:25 [x] 2Sa 4:3 **11:34** [y] 1Sa 13:18

Priests and Levites

12 These were the priests[a] and Levites[b] who returned with Zerubbabel[c] son of Shealtiel[d] and with Joshua:[e]
Seraiah,[f] Jeremiah, Ezra,
2 Amariah, Malluk, Hattush,
3 Shekaniah, Rehum, Meremoth,
4 Iddo,[g] Ginnethon,[a] Abijah,[h]
5 Mijamin,[b] Moadiah, Bilgah,
6 Shemaiah, Joiarib, Jedaiah,[i]
7 Sallu, Amok, Hilkiah and Jedaiah.
These were the leaders of the priests and
their associates in the days of Joshua.
8 The Levites were Jeshua,[j] Binnui, Kadmiel, Sherebiah, Judah, and also Mattaniah,[k] who, together with his associates,
was in charge of the songs of thanksgiving. 9 Bakbukiah and Unni, their associates, stood opposite them in the services.

[a] 4 Many Hebrew manuscripts and Vulgate (see also verse 16); most Hebrew manuscripts *Ginnethoi*
[b] 5 A variant of *Miniamin*

11:35 [z] S 1Ch 8:12 **12:1** [a] Ne 10:1-8 [b] Ne 10:9 [c] S 1Ch 3:19; Ezr 3:2; Zec 4:6-10 [d] Ezr 3:2 [e] S Ezr 2:2 [f] S Ezr 2:2 **12:4** [g] ver 16; Zec 1:1 [h] S 1Ch 24:10; Lk 1:5 **12:6** [i] S 1Ch 24:7 **12:8** [j] S Ezr 2:2 [k] S Ne 11:17

11:23 *king's orders ... regulated.* David had regulated the services of the Levites, including the musicians (1Ch 25). The Persian king Darius I gave a royal stipend so that the Jewish elders might "pray for the well-being of the king and his sons" (Ezr 6:10). Artaxerxes I may have done much the same for the Levite choir.

11:25 – 30 An important list, corresponding to earlier lists of towns in Judah. All these names also appear in Jos 15 with the exception of Dibon, Jekabzeel (but see Kabzeel in Jos 15:21), Jeshua, Mekonah and En Rimmon (but see Ain and Rimmon in Jos 15:32). The list, however, is not comprehensive, since a number of towns listed in ch. 3; Ezr 2:21 – 22 are lacking. No Judean coins have been found outside the area designated by vv. 25 – 30.

11:25 *Kiriath Arba.* See note on Ge 23:2. In the Hellenistic era it fell to the Idumeans, together with other Judean towns.

11:26 *Moladah.* Near Beersheba; later occupied by the Idumeans. *Beth Pelet.* Means "house of refuge," a site near Beersheba.

11:27 *Beersheba.* See note and NIV text note on Ge 21:31. Archaeological excavations reveal that the city was destroyed by Sennacherib in 701 BC and only resettled in the Persian period.

11:28 *Ziklag.* Given to David by Achish, king of Gath (1Sa 27:6), and taken by the Amalekites (1Sa 30:1); see Jos 15:31.

11:29 *En Rimmon.* Means "spring of the pomegranate," probably Khirbet Umm er-Ramamin, nine miles north-northeast of Beersheba (see Jos 15:32). *Zorah.* See note on Jdg 13:2. *Jarmuth.* Eight miles north-northeast of Eleutheropolis (Beit Jibrin), it was one of five Canaanite cities in the south that attempted to halt Joshua's invasion (Jos 10:3 – 5).

11:30 *Zanoah.* A village in the Shephelah district of low hills between Judah and Philistia. The residents of Zanoah repaired the Valley Gate (3:13). The site has been identified with Khirbet Zanu, three miles south-southeast of Beth Shemesh. *Adullam.* See note on Ge 38:1. *Lachish.* See Jos 10:3; see also notes on Isa 36:2; Mic 1:13. *Azekah.* See note on Jer 34:7. *Hinnom.* The valley west and south of Jerusalem; Gehenna in the NT (see notes on Isa 66:24; Rev 19:20).

11:31 – 35 Most of the Benjamite towns listed here appear also in 7:26 – 38; Ezr 2:23 – 35.

11:31 *Geba.* See 12:29; see also note on 1Sa 13:3. *Mikmash.* See note on 1Sa 13:2. *Aija.* An alternative name for Ai (see note on Jos 7:2). *Bethel.* See notes on Ge 12:8; Jos 7:2; Ezr 2:28; Am 4:4.

11:32 *Anathoth.* See note on Jer 1:1. *Nob.* See note on 1Sa 21:1. *Ananiah.* Probably Bethany, meaning "house of Ananiah" (see note on Mt 21:17).

11:34 *Hadid.* Three to four miles northeast of Lod (see 7:37; Ezr 2:33).

11:35 *Lod.* See note on Ezr 2:33. *Ono.* See note on 6:2. *Ge Harashim.* See 1Ch 4:14 and note; the broad valley between Lod and Ono. The name may preserve the ancient memory that the Philistines in that area were blacksmiths (1Sa 13:19 – 20).

12:1 *Zerubbabel son of Shealtiel.* See Ezr 3:2,8; 5:2; see also note on Hag 1:1. *Joshua.* Returned from Babylonian exile in 538/537 BC (see vv. 10,26; 7:7; Ezr 2:2 and note; Hag 1:1; Zec 3:1 and note). *Ezra.* Not the Ezra of the book, who was the leader of the exiles who returned 80 years later.

12:7 *leaders of the priests.* The rotation of 24 priestly divisions was established at the time of David (see 1Ch 24:3,7 – 19 and note on 24:4). Twenty-two heads of priestly houses are mentioned in vv. 1 – 7. Inscriptions listing the 24 divisions of the priests probably hung in many synagogues in the Holy Land. So far, only fragments of two such inscriptions have been recovered — from Ashkelon in the 1920s and from Caesarea in the 1960s (dated to the third and fourth centuries AD).

12:9 *opposite them.* See v. 24; Ezr 3:11 and note; cf. 2Ch 7:6. The singing was antiphonal, with two sections of

10 Joshua was the father of Joiakim, Joiakim the father of Eliashib,[l] Eliashib the
father of Joiada, 11 Joiada the father of Jonathan, and Jonathan the father of Jaddua.
12 In the days of Joiakim, these were the
heads of the priestly families:
of Seraiah's family, Meraiah;
of Jeremiah's, Hananiah;
13 of Ezra's, Meshullam;
of Amariah's, Jehohanan;
14 of Malluk's, Jonathan;
of Shekaniah's,[a] Joseph;
15 of Harim's, Adna;
of Meremoth's,[b] Helkai;
16 of Iddo's,[m] Zechariah;
of Ginnethon's, Meshullam;
17 of Abijah's,[n] Zikri;
of Miniamin's and of Moadiah's, Piltai;
18 of Bilgah's, Shammua;
of Shemaiah's, Jehonathan;
19 of Joiarib's, Mattenai;
of Jedaiah's, Uzzi;
20 of Sallu's, Kallai;
of Amok's, Eber;
21 of Hilkiah's, Hashabiah;
of Jedaiah's, Nethanel.
22 The family heads of the Levites in the
days of Eliashib, Joiada, Johanan and Jaddua, as well as those of the priests, were
recorded in the reign of Darius the Persian.
23 The family heads among the descendants of Levi up to the time of Johanan
son of Eliashib were recorded in the book
of the annals. 24 And the leaders of the Levites[o] were Hashabiah, Sherebiah, Jeshua
son of Kadmiel, and their associates, who
stood opposite them to give praise and
thanksgiving, one section responding to
the other, as prescribed by David the man
of God.[p]
25 Mattaniah, Bakbukiah, Obadiah, Meshullam, Talmon and Akkub were gatekeepers who guarded the storerooms at
the gates. 26 They served in the days of Joiakim son of Joshua, the son of Jozadak,
and in the days of Nehemiah the governor
and of Ezra the priest, the teacher of the
Law.

12:10 [l]S Ezr 10:24; Ne 3:20
12:16 [m]S ver 4
12:17 [n]S 1Ch 24:10
12:24 [o]S Ezr 2:40
[p]S 2Ch 8:14
12:27 [q]Dt 20:5
[r]S 2Sa 6:5
[s]S 1Ch 15:16, 28; 25:6; Ps 92:3
12:28 [t]S 1Ch 2:54; 9:16
12:30 [u]Ex 19:10; Job 1:5

Dedication of the Wall of Jerusalem

27 At the dedication[q] of the wall of Jerusalem, the Levites were sought out from
where they lived and were brought to Jerusalem to celebrate joyfully the dedication with songs of thanksgiving and with
the music of cymbals,[r] harps and lyres.[s]
28 The musicians also were brought together from the region around Jerusalem — from the villages of the Netophathites,[t] 29 from Beth Gilgal, and from the
area of Geba and Azmaveth, for the musicians had built villages for themselves
around Jerusalem. 30 When the priests and
Levites had purified themselves ceremonially, they purified the people,[u] the gates
and the wall.
31 I had the leaders of Judah go up on
top of[c] the wall. I also assigned two large
choirs to give thanks. One was to proceed

[a] *14* Very many Hebrew manuscripts, some Septuagint manuscripts and Syriac (see also verse 3); most Hebrew manuscripts *Shebaniah's* [b] *15* Some Septuagint manuscripts (see also verse 3); Hebrew *Meraioth's* [c] *31* Or *go alongside*

---

the choir standing opposite each other. *services.* The Hebrew for this word (*Mishmarot*) is the title of a work from Qumran, which discusses in detail the rotation of the priestly families' service in the temple according to the sect's solar calendar and synchronized with the conventional lunar calendar.

12:10 *Joshua.* See note on v. 1. *Joiakim.* See vv. 12,26. *Eliashib.* See vv. 22 – 23; the high priest who assisted in rebuilding the wall (3:1,20 – 21; 13:28). A priest named Eliashib was guilty of defiling the temple by assigning rooms to Tobiah the Ammonite (13:4,7). It is not known whether this Eliashib was the same as the high priest.

12:11 *Jonathan.* Since v. 22 mentions a Johanan after Joiada and before Jaddua, and v. 23 identifies Johanan as "son" of Eliashib, some believe that "Jonathan" is an error for "Johanan." Further complicating the identification are attempts to identify this high priest with a "Johanan" mentioned in the Elephantine papyri and in Josephus (*Antiquities,* 11.7.1). Such an identification, however, is disputable.

12:12 – 21 All but one (Hattush, v. 2) of the 22 priestly families listed in vv. 1 – 7 are repeated (Rehum, v. 3, is a variant of Harim, v. 15; Mijamin, v. 5, is a variant of Miniamin, v. 17) in this later list, which dates to the time of Joiakim (v. 12), high priest in the late sixth and/or early fifth centuries BC.

12:22 *Darius the Persian.* Probably Darius II Nothus (423 – 404 BC).

12:23 *book of the annals.* Cf. 7:5. This may have been the official temple chronicle, containing various lists and records. Cf. the annals of the Persian kings (Ezr 4:15; Est 2:23; 6:1; 10:2); cf. also the "book of the annals of the kings," mentioned frequently in 1, 2 Kings.

12:26 *Nehemiah … Ezra.* See note on 8:9.

12:27 *dedication.* See note on Ezr 6:16. *cymbals.* See note on Ezr 3:10. Cymbals were used in religious ceremonies (1Ch 16:42; 25:1; 2Ch 5:12; 29:25). Ancient examples have been found at Beth Shemesh and Tell Abu Hawam. *harps.* See note on Ge 31:27; used mainly in religious ceremonies (1Sa 10:5; 2Sa 6:5; Ps 150:3). Ancient harps have been reconstructed from information derived from the remains of harps at Ur, pictures of harps, and cuneiform texts describing in detail the tuning of harps. *lyres.* Had strings of the same length but of different diameters and tensions (see 1Ch 15:16; Da 3:5).

12:28 *Netophathites.* From Netophah, a town near Bethlehem (7:26).

12:29 *Beth Gilgal.* Perhaps the Gilgal near Jericho (see note on Jos 4:19), or the Gilgal of Elijah (2Ki 2:1), about seven miles north of Bethel.

12:30 *purified.* See note on Lev 4:12. The Levites are said to have purified all that was sacred in the temple (1Ch 23:28) and the temple itself (2Ch 29:15) during times of revival. Ritual purity was intended to teach God's holiness and moral purity (Lev 16:30).

12:31 *two large choirs.* See note on v. 38. The two great processions probably started from the area of the Valley Gate

on top of[a] the wall to the right, toward
the Dung Gate.[v] 32 Hoshaiah and half the
leaders of Judah followed them, 33 along
with Azariah, Ezra, Meshullam, 34 Judah,
Benjamin,[w] Shemaiah, Jeremiah, 35 as well
as some priests with trumpets,[x] and also
Zechariah son of Jonathan, the son of
Shemaiah, the son of Mattaniah, the son
of Micaiah, the son of Zakkur, the son of
Asaph, 36 and his associates — Shemaiah,
Azarel, Milalai, Gilalai, Maai, Nethanel,
Judah and Hanani — with musical instruments[y] prescribed by David the man of
God.[z] Ezra[a] the teacher of the Law led the
procession. 37 At the Fountain Gate[b] they
continued directly up the steps of the City
of David on the ascent to the wall and
passed above the site of David's palace to
the Water Gate[c] on the east.

38 The second choir proceeded in the opposite direction. I followed them on top
of[b] the wall, together with half the people — past the Tower of the Ovens[d] to the
Broad Wall,[e] 39 over the Gate of Ephraim,[f]
the Jeshanah[c] Gate,[g] the Fish Gate,[h] the
Tower of Hananel[i] and the Tower of the
Hundred,[j] as far as the Sheep Gate.[k] At the
Gate of the Guard they stopped.

40 The two choirs that gave thanks then
took their places in the house of God; so
did I, together with half the officials, 41 as
well as the priests — Eliakim, Maaseiah,
Miniamin, Micaiah, Elioenai, Zechariah and Hananiah with their trumpets —
42 and also Maaseiah, Shemaiah, Eleazar,
Uzzi, Jehohanan, Malkijah, Elam and
Ezer. The choirs sang under the direction
of Jezrahiah. 43 And on that day they offered great sacrifices, rejoicing because
God had given them great joy. The wom-
en and children also rejoiced. The sound
of rejoicing in Jerusalem could be heard
far away.

44 At that time men were appointed to be
in charge of the storerooms[l] for the contributions, firstfruits and tithes.[m] From the
fields around the towns they were to bring
into the storerooms the portions required
by the Law for the priests and the Levites,
for Judah was pleased with the ministering priests and Levites.[n] 45 They performed
the service of their God and the service
of purification, as did also the musicians
and gatekeepers, according to the commands of David[o] and his son Solomon.[p]
46 For long ago, in the days of David and
Asaph,[q] there had been directors for the
musicians and for the songs of praise[r] and
thanksgiving to God. 47 So in the days of
Zerubbabel and of Nehemiah, all Israel
contributed the daily portions for the musicians and the gatekeepers. They also set
aside the portion for the other Levites, and
the Levites set aside the portion for the descendants of Aaron.[s]

Nehemiah's Final Reforms

13 On that day the Book of Moses was
read aloud in the hearing of the
people and there it was found written that
no Ammonite or Moabite should ever be
admitted into the assembly of God,[t] 2 because they had not met the Israelites with
food and water but had hired Balaam[u] to
call a curse down on them.[v] (Our God,
however, turned the curse into a blessing.)[w] 3 When the people heard this law,
they excluded from Israel all who were of
foreign descent.[x]

4 Before this, Eliashib the priest had
been put in charge of the storerooms[y] of
the house of our God. He was closely associated with Tobiah,[z] 5 and he had provided him with a large room formerly used
to store the grain offerings and incense

12:31 [v] Ne 2:13 **12:34** [w] S Ezr 1:5 **12:35** [x] S Ezr 3:10 **12:36** [y] S 1Ch 15:16 [z] S 2Ch 8:14 [a] Ezr 7:6 **12:37** [b] S Ne 2:14 [c] S Ne 3:26 **12:38** [d] Ne 3:11 [e] Ne 3:8 **12:39** [f] S 2Ki 14:13 [g] Ne 3:6 [h] S 2Ch 33:14 [i] S Ne 3:1 [j] Ne 3:1 [k] S Ne 3:1 **12:44** [l] Ne 13:4, 13 [m] S Lev 27:30 [n] S Dt 18:8 **12:45** [o] S 2Ch 8:14 [p] S 1Ch 6:31; 23:5 **12:46** [q] S 2Ch 35:15 [r] 2Ch 29:27; Ps 137:4 **12:47** [s] S Dt 18:8 **13:1** [t] ver 23; Dt 23:3 **13:2** [u] Nu 22:3-11 [v] S Nu 23:7; S Dt 23:3 [w] S Nu 23:11; Dt 23:4-5 **13:3** [x] ver 23; S Ne 9:2 **13:4** [y] S Ne 12:44 [z] Ne 2:10

[a] 31 Or *proceed alongside* [b] 38 Or *them alongside* [c] 39 Or *Old*

(2:13,15; 3:13) near the center of the western section of the wall. The first procession, led by Ezra (v. 36), moved in a counterclockwise direction upon the wall; the second, with Nehemiah (v. 38), moved in a clockwise direction. Both met between the Water Gate (v. 37) and the Gate of the Guard (v. 39), then entered the temple area. Cf. Ps 48:12–13. *to the right.* Or "to the south." Semites oriented themselves facing east, so the right hand represented the south (see Jos 17:7; 1Sa 23:24; Job 23:9). *Dung Gate.* See note on 2:13.

12:35 *trumpets.* See note on Ezr 3:10. Each choir had priests blowing trumpets, as well as Levites playing other musical instruments. *Asaph.* See note on 11:17.

12:36 *Ezra the teacher of the Law.* See notes on Ezr 7:1,6.

12:37 *Fountain Gate.* See note on 2:14. *City of David.* See 3:15; see also note on 2Sa 5:7. *Water Gate.* See note on 3:26.

12:38 *choir.* Lit. "thanks," i.e., "thanksgiving choir" (see v. 40). *Tower of the Ovens.* See note on 3:11. *Broad Wall.* See note on 3:8.

12:39 *Gate of Ephraim.* See notes on 3:6; 8:16. *Jeshanah Gate.* See note on 3:6. *Fish Gate.* See note on 3:3. *Tower of Hananel ... Tower of the Hundred ... Sheep Gate.* See note on 3:1. *Gate of the Guard.* Cf. Jer 32:2.

12:43 *God had given them great joy.* See 1Ch 29:9. *women.* See 8:2; Ex 15:20 and notes. *heard far away.* See note on Ezr 3:13; cf. 1Ki 1:40; 2Ki 11:13.

12:44 *Judah was pleased.* The people cheerfully contributed their offerings to support the priests and Levites (cf. 2Co 9:7). *ministering.* See Dt 10:8.

12:46 *Asaph.* See note on 11:17.

12:47 *Zerubbabel.* See Ezr 1:2 and note. *contributed.* The Hebrew for this verb implies continued giving.

13:1–2 See Dt 23:3–6.

13:2 *Balaam.* See notes on Nu 22:5,8.

13:4 *Eliashib.* See note on 12:10. *Tobiah.* See note on 2:10.

13:5 *provided him with a large room.* During Nehemiah's absence from the city to return to the Persian king's court, Tobiah, one of his archenemies, had used his influence with Eliashib to gain entrance into a chamber ordinarily set aside for the storage of tithes and other offerings (see 10:37 and note; cf. Nu 18:21–32; Dt 14:28–29; 26:12–15). Elsewhere

and temple articles, and also the tithes[a] of
grain, new wine and olive oil prescribed
for the Levites, musicians and gatekeepers, as well as the contributions for the
priests.
6 But while all this was going on, I was
not in Jerusalem, for in the thirty-second
year of Artaxerxes[b] king of Babylon I had
returned to the king. Some time later I
asked his permission 7 and came back to
Jerusalem. Here I learned about the evil
thing Eliashib[c] had done in providing Tobiah[d] a room in the courts of the house of
God. 8 I was greatly displeased and threw
all Tobiah's household goods out of the
room.[e] 9 I gave orders to purify the rooms,[f]
and then I put back into them the equipment of the house of God, with the grain
offerings and the incense.[g]
10 I also learned that the portions assigned to the Levites had not been given to
them,[h] and that all the Levites and musicians responsible for the service had gone
back to their own fields.[i] 11 So I rebuked
the officials and asked them, "Why is the
house of God neglected?"[j] Then I called
them together and stationed them at their
posts.
12 All Judah brought the tithes[k] of grain,
new wine and olive oil into the storerooms.[l] 13 I put Shelemiah the priest, Zadok the scribe, and a Levite named Pedaiah in charge of the storerooms and made
Hanan son of Zakkur, the son of Mattaniah, their assistant, because they were
considered trustworthy. They were made
responsible for distributing the supplies to
their fellow Levites.[m]
14 Remember[n] me for this, my God, and
do not blot out what I have so faithfully done for the house of my God and its
services.
15 In those days I saw people in Judah
treading winepresses on the Sabbath and
bringing in grain and loading it on donkeys, together with wine, grapes, figs and
all other kinds of loads. And they were
bringing all this into Jerusalem on the
Sabbath.[o] Therefore I warned them against
selling food on that day. 16 People from
Tyre who lived in Jerusalem were bringing
in fish and all kinds of merchandise and
selling them in Jerusalem on the Sabbath[p]
to the people of Judah. 17 I rebuked the
nobles of Judah and said to them, "What
is this wicked thing you are doing—desecrating the Sabbath day? 18 Didn't your
ancestors do the same things, so that our
God brought all this calamity on us and on
this city?[q] Now you are stirring up more
wrath against Israel by desecrating the
Sabbath."[r]
19 When evening shadows fell on the

13:5 [a] S Lev 27:30; S Nu 18:21 **13:6** [b] S Ne 2:6 **13:7** [c] S Ezr 10:24 [d] S Ne 2:10 **13:8** [e] Mt 21:12-13; Mk 11:15-17; Lk 19:45-46; Jn 2:13-16 **13:9** [f] S 1Ch 23:28; S 2Ch 29:5 [g] S Lev 2:1 **13:10** [h] S Dt 12:19 [i] S 2Ch 31:4 **13:11** [j] S Ne 10:37-39; Hag 1:1-9; Mal 3:8-9 **13:12** [k] S 2Ch 31:6 [l] S Dt 18:8; 1Ki 7:51; S 2Ch 31:5; S Ne 10:37-39; Mal 3:10 **13:13** [m] S Ne 12:44; Ac 6:1-5 **13:14** [n] S Ge 8:1; S 2Ki 20:3 **13:15** [o] Ex 20:8-11; S 34:21; Dt 5:12-15 **13:16** [p] S Ne 10:31 **13:18** [q] Jer 44:23 [r] S Ne 10:31

---

we read of the chamber of Meshullam (3:30) and of Jehohanan (Ezr 10:6).

13:6 *thirty-second year of Artaxerxes.* See note on 5:14. *king of Babylon.* The title was assumed by Cyrus after his conquest of Babylon (see Ezr 5:13) and was adopted by subsequent Achaemenid (Persian) kings.

13:7 *came back to Jerusalem.* Nehemiah's second term must have ended before 407 BC, when Bagohi (Bigvai) was governor of Judah according to the Elephantine papyri. Some have suggested that after Nehemiah's first term he was succeeded by his brother Hanani (see note on 1:2). *courts.* See note on 8:16. Zerubbabel's temple had two courtyards (Zec 3:7; cf. Isa 62:9).

13:8 *displeased … threw.* Nehemiah expressed his indignation by taking action (cf. vv. 24–25; 5:6–7). Contrast the reaction of Ezra, who "sat down appalled" (Ezr 9:3). Nehemiah's action reminds us of Christ's expulsion of the money changers from the temple area (Mt 21:12–13).

13:9 *rooms.* Though only a single chamber was mentioned in vv. 5–8, additional rooms were involved. A parallel to the occupation and desecration of the temple by Tobiah comes from a century earlier in Egypt, where Greek mercenaries had occupied the temple of Neith at Sais. Upon the appeal of the Egyptian priest Udjahorresnet, the Persian king had the squatters driven out and the temple's ceremonies, processions and revenues restored: "And His Majesty commanded that all the foreigners who had settled in the temple of Neith should be driven out and that all their houses and all their superfluities that were in this temple should be thrown down, and that all their own baggage should be carried for them outside the wall of this temple."

13:10 Nehemiah was apparently correcting an abuse of long standing. Strictly speaking, the Levites had no holdings (Nu 18:20,23–24; Dt 14:29; 18:1), but some may have had private income (Dt 18:8). Therefore the Levites were dependent on the faithful support of the people. This may explain the reluctance of great numbers of Levites to return from exile (see Ezr 8:15–20). For the complaints of those who found little material advantage in serving the Lord, see Mal 2:17; 3:13–15.

13:11 *neglected.* See note on 10:39.

13:12 *tithes.* See 12:44. Temples in Mesopotamia also levied tithes for the support of their personnel.

13:13 Of the four treasurers, one was a priest, one a Levite, one a scribe and one a layman of rank. *trustworthy.* Nehemiah appointed honest men to make sure that supplies were distributed equitably, just as the church appointed deacons for this purpose (Ac 6:1–5).

13:15 *treading winepresses.* See notes on Isa 5:2; 16:10. *Sabbath.* The temptation to violate the Sabbath rest was especially characteristic of non-Jewish merchants (see 10:31; Isa 56:1–8). On the other hand, the high regard that many had for the Sabbath was expressed by parents who called their children Shabbethai (see 8:7; 11:16; Ezr 10:15).

13:16 *Tyre.* See note on Isa 23:1. *fish.* Most of the fish exported by the Tyrians (Eze 26:4–5,14) was dried, smoked or salted. Fish, much of it from the Sea of Galilee, was an important part of the Israelites' diet (Lev 11:9; Nu 11:5; Mt 15:34; Lk 24:42; Jn 21:5–13). It was sold at the market near the Fish Gate (see note on 3:3).

13:17–18 *desecrating the Sabbath.* Cf. Ex 16:28–29; Nu 15:32–36; Isa 58:13–14; Jer 17:19–27; Am 8:5,7–8. "Desecrating" means turning what is sacred into common use and so profaning it (see Mal 2:10–11).

13:17 *rebuked the nobles.* Because they were the leaders.

gates of Jerusalem before the Sabbath,[s]
I ordered the doors to be shut and not
opened until the Sabbath was over. I stationed some of my own men at the gates
so that no load could be brought in on
the Sabbath day. 20 Once or twice the merchants and sellers of all kinds of goods
spent the night outside Jerusalem. 21 But
I warned them and said, "Why do you
spend the night by the wall? If you do this
again, I will arrest you." From that time
on they no longer came on the Sabbath.
22 Then I commanded the Levites to purify
themselves and go and guard the gates in
order to keep the Sabbath day holy.

Remember[t] me for this also, my God,
and show mercy to me according to your
great love.

23 Moreover, in those days I saw men
of Judah who had married[u] women from
Ashdod, Ammon and Moab.[v] 24 Half of
their children spoke the language of Ashdod or the language of one of the other
peoples, and did not know how to speak
the language[w] of Judah. 25 I rebuked them
and called curses down on them. I beat
some of the men and pulled out their hair.
I made them take an oath[x] in God's name
and said: "You are not to give your daughters in marriage to their sons, nor are you
to take their daughters in marriage for your
sons or for yourselves.[y] 26 Was it not because of marriages like these that Solomon
king of Israel sinned? Among the many nations there was no king like him.[z] He was
loved by his God,[a] and God made him king
over all Israel, but even he was led into sin
by foreign women.[b] 27 Must we hear now
that you too are doing all this terrible wickedness and are being unfaithful to our God
by marrying[c] foreign women?"

28 One of the sons of Joiada son of Eliashib[d] the high priest was son-in-law to
Sanballat[e] the Horonite. And I drove him
away from me.

29 Remember[f] them, my God, because
they defiled the priestly office and the
covenant of the priesthood and of the Levites.[g]

30 So I purified the priests and the Levites of everything foreign,[h] and assigned
them duties, each to his own task. 31 I also
made provision for contributions of wood[i]
at designated times, and for the firstfruits.[j]

Remember[k] me with favor, my God.

13:19 [s] Lev 23:32 **13:22** [t] S Ge 8:1; S Ne 1:8 **13:23** [u] Ezr 9:1-2; Mal 2:11 [v] ver 1; S ver 1, S 3; Ex 34:16; S Ru 1:4; S Ne 10:30 **13:24** [w] Est 1:22; 3:12; 8:9 **13:25** [x] S Ezr 10:5 [y] S Ex 34:16 **13:26** [z] S 1Ki 3:13; S 2Ch 1:12 [a] 2Sa 12:25 [b] S Ex 34:16; S 1Ki 11:3 **13:27** [c] Ezr 9:14 **13:28** [d] S Ezr 10:24 [e] S Ne 2:10 **13:29** [f] S Ne 1:8 [g] S Nu 3:12 **13:30** [h] S Ne 9:2 **13:31** [i] Ne 10:34 [j] Ne 10:35-36 [k] S Ge 8:1; S Ne 1:8

13:19 *When evening shadows fell on the gates.* Before sunset, when the Sabbath began. The Israelites, like the Babylonians, counted their days from sunset to sunset (the Egyptians reckoned theirs from dawn to dawn). The precise moment when the Sabbath began was heralded by the blowing of a trumpet by a priest. According to the Jewish Mishnah, on the eve of the Sabbath they used to blow three blasts to cause the people to cease from work and three to mark the break between the sacred and the profane. Josephus (*Wars*, 4.9.12) speaks of the location on the parapet of the temple where a priest blew the trumpet. Excavators at the temple mount recovered a stone from the southwest corner of the parapet with the inscription "for the place of the blowing [of the trumpet]."

13:22 *Remember me.* See note on 1:8.

13:23 Ezra had dealt with the same problem of intermarriage some 25 years before (see note on Ezr 9:1). *Ashdod.* See 4:7; Isa 20:1 and notes. *Ammon and Moab.* See note on Ge 19:36–38.

13:24 The Israelites recognized other people as foreigners by their languages (see Dt 3:9; Jdg 12:6; Ps 114:1; Isa 33:19; Eze 3:5–6).

13:25 *pulled out their hair.* See Ezr 9:3; Isa 50:6 and notes. *You are not to give.* Nehemiah's action was designed to prevent future intermarriages, whereas Ezra dissolved the existing unions.

13:26 *Solomon.* Israel's outstanding king in terms of wealth and political achievements (1Ki 3:13; 2Ch 1:12). Solomon began his reign by humbly asking for wisdom from the Lord (1Ki 3:5–9). *he was led into sin.* In later years his foreign wives led him to worship other gods, so that he built a high place for Chemosh, the god of the Moabites (1Ki 11:7).

13:28 *son-in-law to Sanballat.* According to Lev 21:14 the high priest was not to marry a foreigner. The expulsion of Joiada's son followed either this special ban or the general prohibition against intermarriage. The union described in this verse was especially rankling to Nehemiah in the light of Sanballat's enmity (see 2:10). Josephus (*Antiquities*, 11.7.2) records that an almost identical episode, involving a marriage between the daughter of a Sanballat of Samaria and the brother of the Jewish high priest, took place a little over a century later in the time of Alexander the Great.

13:30 *duties.* Or "divisions," referring to the assignment of particular duties to groups of priests and Levites, possibly on a rotating basis (see note on 12:9).

13:31 *wood.* See 10:34 and note. *Remember me with favor.* The last recorded words of Nehemiah recapitulate a theme running through the final chapter (vv. 14,22; see note on 1:8). His motive throughout his ministry was to please and to serve his divine Sovereign.

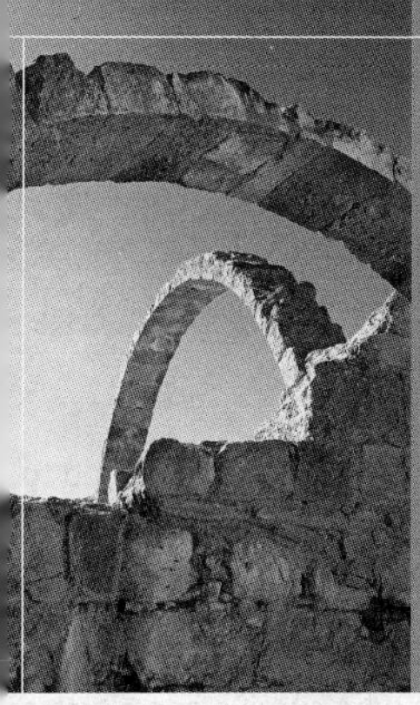

ESTHER

INTRODUCTION

Author and Date

Although we do not know who wrote the book of Esther, from internal evidence it is possible to make some inferences about the author and the date of composition. It is clear that the author was a Jew, both from his emphasis on the origin of a Jewish festival and from the Jewish nationalism that permeates the story. The author's knowledge of Persian customs, the setting of the story in the city of Susa and the absence of any reference to conditions or circumstances in the land of Judah suggest that he was a resident of a Persian city. The earliest date for the book would be shortly after the events narrated, i.e., c. 460 BC (before Ezra's return to Jerusalem; see note on 8:12). Internal evidence also suggests that the festival of Purim had been observed for some time prior to the actual writing of the book (9:19) and that Xerxes had already died (see 10:2 and note). Several scholars have dated the book later than 330 BC; the absence of Greek words and the style of the author's Hebrew dialect, however, suggest that the book must have been written before the Persian Empire fell to Greece in 331.

Purpose, Themes and Literary Features

The author's central purpose was to record the institution of the annual festival of Purim and to keep alive for later generations the memory of the great deliverance of the Jewish people during the reign of Xerxes. The book accounts for both the initiation of that observance and the obligation for its perpetual commemoration (see 3:7; 9:26–32; see also chart, pp. 188–189).

Throughout much of the story the author calls to mind the ongoing conflict between Israel and the Amalekites (see notes on 2:5; 3:1–6; 9:5–10), a conflict that began during the exodus (Ex 17:8–16; Dt 25:17–19) and continued through Israel's history (1Sa 15; 1Ch 4:43; and, of course, Esther). As the first to attack Israel after its deliverance from Egypt, the Amalekites were viewed—and the author of Esther views them—as the epitome of all the powers of the world arrayed against God's people (see Nu 24:20; 1Sa 15:2–3; 28:18). Now that

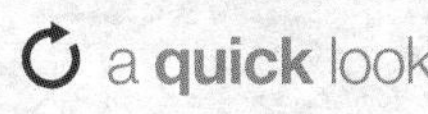

Author:
Unknown

Audience:
The Jewish people

Date:
Sometime after 460 BC

Theme:
The book of Esther describes how the Jews of Persia are saved from certain destruction through divine providence.

The future existence of God's chosen people and ultimately the appearance of the Redeemer-Messiah are jeopardized by Haman's edict to destroy the Jews.

Israel has been released from captivity, Haman's edict is the final major effort in the OT period to destroy them.

Closely associated with the conflict with the Amalekites is the rest that is promised to the people of God (see Dt 25:19). With Haman's defeat the Jews enjoy rest from their enemies (9:16,22).

The author also draws upon the remnant motif that recurs throughout the Bible (natural disasters, disease, warfare or other calamities threaten God's people; those who survive constitute a remnant). Events in the Persian city of Susa threatened the continuity of God's purposes in redemptive history. The future existence of God's chosen people, and ultimately the appearance of the Redeemer-Messiah, were jeopardized by Haman's edict to destroy the Jews. The author of Esther patterned much of his material on the events of the Joseph story (see notes on 2:3 – 4,9,21 – 23; 3:4; 4:14; 6:1,8,14; 8:6), in which the remnant motif is also central to the narrative (see Ge 45:7 and note).

Feasting is another prominent theme in Esther, as shown in the outline at the end of the Introduction. Banquets provide the setting for important plot developments. There are ten banquets: (1) 1:3 – 4, (2) 1:5 – 8, (3) 1:9, (4) 2:18, (5) 3:15, (6) 5:5 – 6, (7) 7:1 – 10, (8) 8:17, (9) 9:17 and (10) 9:18. The three pairs of banquets that mark the beginning, middle and end of the story are particularly prominent: the two banquets given by Xerxes, the two prepared by Esther and the double celebration of Purim.

Recording duplications appears to be one of the favorite compositional techniques of the writer. In addition to the three groups of banquets that come in pairs, there are two lists of the king's servants (1:10,14), two reports that Esther concealed her identity (2:10,20), two gatherings of women (2:8,19), two fasts (4:3,16), two consultations of Haman with his wife and friends (5:14; 6:13), two unscheduled appearances of Esther before

Persian archers on glazed brick from the Achaemenid palace in Susa (sixth century BC)

Z. Radovan/www.BibleLandPictures.com

Painting by Bernardo Cavallino of Esther approaching King Xerxes

the king (5:2; 8:3), two investitures for Mordecai (6:10 – 11; 8:15), two coverings of Haman's face (6:12; 7:8), two royal edicts (3:12 – 15; 8:1 – 14), two references to the subsiding of the king's anger (2:1; 7:10), two references to the irrevocability of the Persian laws (1:19; 8:8), two days for the Jews to take vengeance (9:5 – 12,13 – 15) and two letters instituting the commemoration of Purim (9:20 – 28,29 – 32).

An outstanding feature of this book — one that has given rise to considerable discussion — is the complete absence of any explicit reference to God, worship, prayer or sacrifice. This "secularity" has produced many detractors who have judged the book to be of little religious value. However, it appears that the author has deliberately refrained from mentioning God or any religious activity as a literary device to heighten the fact that it is God who controls and directs all the seemingly insignificant coincidences (see, e.g., note on 6:1) that make up the plot and issue in deliverance for the Jews. God's sovereign rule is assumed at every point (see notes on 4:12 – 16; 6:1), an assumption made all the more effective by the total absence of reference to him. It becomes clear to the careful reader that Israel's Great King exercises his providential and sovereign control over all the vicissitudes of his beleaguered covenant people.

Outline

I. The Feasts of Xerxes (1:1 — 2:18)
   A. Vashti Deposed (ch. 1)
   B. Esther Made Queen (2:1 – 18)
II. The Feasts of Esther (2:19 — 7:10)
   A. Mordecai Uncovers a Plot (2:19 – 23)
   B. Haman's Plot (ch. 3)
   C. Mordecai Persuades Esther to Help (ch. 4)
   D. Esther's Request to the King: Her First Banquet (5:1 – 8)
   E. A Sleepless Night (5:9 — 6:14)
   F. Haman Hanged: Esther's Second Banquet (ch. 7)
III. The Feasts of Purim (chs. 8 – 10)
   A. The King's Edict in Behalf of the Jews (ch. 8)
   B. The Institution of Purim (ch. 9)
   C. The Promotion of Mordecai (ch. 10)

Queen Vashti Deposed

1 This is what happened during the
time of Xerxes,[a][a] the Xerxes who ruled
over 127 provinces[b] stretching from India to Cush[b]:[c] 2 At that time King Xerxes
reigned from his royal throne in the citadel
of Susa,[d] 3 and in the third year of his reign
he gave a banquet[e] for all his nobles and
officials. The military leaders of Persia and
Media, the princes, and the nobles of the
provinces were present.
4 For a full 180 days he displayed the
vast wealth of his kingdom and the splendor and glory of his majesty. 5 When these
days were over, the king gave a banquet,
lasting seven days,[f] in the enclosed garden[g] of the king's palace, for all the people
from the least to the greatest who were
in the citadel of Susa. 6 The garden had
hangings of white and blue linen, fastened
with cords of white linen and purple material to silver rings on marble pillars.
There were couches[h] of gold and silver on
a mosaic pavement of porphyry, marble,
mother-of-pearl and other costly stones.
7 Wine was served in goblets of gold, each
one different from the other, and the royal
wine was abundant, in keeping with the
king's liberality.[i] 8 By the king's command
each guest was allowed to drink with no
restrictions, for the king instructed all the
wine stewards to serve each man what he
wished.
9 Queen Vashti also gave a banquet[j] for
the women in the royal palace of King Xerxes.
10 On the seventh day, when King Xerxes
was in high spirits[k] from wine,[l] he commanded the seven eunuchs who served
him — Mehuman, Biztha, Harbona,[m] Big-
tha, Abagtha, Zethar and Karkas — 11 to
bring[n] before him Queen Vashti, wearing
her royal crown, in order to display her
beauty[o] to the people and nobles, for she
was lovely to look at. 12 But when the attendants delivered the king's command,
Queen Vashti refused to come. Then the
king became furious and burned with anger.[p]
13 Since it was customary for the king
to consult experts in matters of law and
justice, he spoke with the wise men who
understood the times[q] 14 and were closest
to the king — Karshena, Shethar, Admatha,
Tarshish, Meres, Marsena and Memukan,
the seven nobles[r] of Persia and Media who
had special access to the king and were
highest in the kingdom.
15 "According to law, what must be done
to Queen Vashti?" he asked. "She has not
obeyed the command of King Xerxes that
the eunuchs have taken to her."
16 Then Memukan replied in the presence of the king and the nobles, "Queen
Vashti has done wrong, not only against
the king but also against all the nobles and
the peoples of all the provinces of King
Xerxes. 17 For the queen's conduct will
become known to all the women, and so
they will despise their husbands and say,
'King Xerxes commanded Queen Vashti
to be brought before him, but she would
not come.' 18 This very day the Persian and
Median women of the nobility who have
heard about the queen's conduct will respond to all the king's nobles in the same
way. There will be no end of disrespect
and discord.[s]

1:1 [a] S Ezr 4:6 [b] Est 9:30; Da 3:2; 6:1 [c] Est 8:9 **1:2** [d] S Ezr 4:9; S Est 2:8 **1:3** [e] S 1Ki 3:15 **1:5** [f] Jdg 14:17 [g] S 2Ki 21:18 **1:6** [h] Est 7:8; Eze 23:41; Am 3:12; 6:4 **1:7** [i] Est 2:18; Da 5:2 **1:9** [j] S 1Ki 3:15 **1:10** [k] S Jdg 16:25; S Ru 3:7 [l] S Ge 14:18; Est 3:15; 5:6; 7:2; Pr 31:4-7; Da 5:1-4 [m] Est 7:9 **1:11** [n] SS 2:4 [o] Ps 45:11; Eze 16:14 **1:12** [p] Ge 39:19; Est 2:21; 7:7; Pr 19:12 **1:13** [q] 1Ch 12:32 **1:14** [r] Ezr 7:14 **1:18** [s] Pr 19:13; 27:15

[a] *1* Hebrew *Ahasuerus*; here and throughout Esther
[b] *1* That is, the upper Nile region

1:1 *Xerxes.* A transliteration of the Greek form of the Persian name Khshayarshan (see NIV text note). Xerxes succeeded his father Darius and ruled 486 – 465 BC (see chart, p. 511). *127 provinces.* See 8:9. The Greek historian Herodotus (3.89) records that Xerxes' father Darius had organized the empire into 20 satrapies. (Satraps, the rulers of the satrapies, are mentioned in 3:12; 8:9; 9:3.) The provinces were smaller administrative units.

1:2 *citadel of Susa.* The fortified acropolis and palace complex; it is distinguished from the surrounding city in 3:15; 8:14 – 15. Several archaeological investigations have been made at the site since the mid-nineteenth century. Xerxes had made extensive renovations in the palace structures. *Susa.* The winter residence of the Persian kings (see note on Ezr 4:9). The three other capitals were Ecbatana (see Ezr 6:2 and note), Babylon and Persepolis. One of Daniel's visions was set in Susa (Da 8:2); Nehemiah also served there (Ne 1:1).

1:3 – 4 The year (483 – 482 BC), the persons in attendance and the length of the meeting suggest that the purpose of the gathering may have been to plan for the disastrous campaigns of 482 – 479 against Greece. Herodotus (7.8) possibly describes this assembly.

1:3 *banquet.* Feasting is a prominent theme in Esther (see Introduction: Purpose, Themes and Literary Features).

1:5 – 6 The excavations at Susa have unearthed a text in which Xerxes' father Darius describes in some detail the building of his palace. Xerxes continued the work his father had begun.

1:9 *Queen Vashti.* Deposed in 484/483 BC; Esther became queen in 479/478 (2:16 – 17). The Greek historians call Xerxes' queen Amestris; they record her influence during the early part of his reign and as queen mother during the following reign of her son Artaxerxes (Ezr 7:1,7,11 – 12,21; 8:1; Ne 2:1; 5:14; 13:6) until the time of her own death c. 424. Artaxerxes came to the throne when he was 18 years old; therefore he was born c. 484/483, approximately at the time when Vashti was deposed. Since he was the third son of Amestris, the name Amestris cannot be identified with Esther and perhaps could be viewed as a Greek version of the name Vashti. Comparatively little is known of the late portions of Xerxes' reign, nor is it possible to determine the subsequent events of the life of Esther. Apparently after Esther's death or her fall from favor, Vashti was able to reassert her power and to exercise a controlling influence over her son.

1:12 *refused to come.* We are not told why.

1:13 – 14 Ezr 7:14 and the Greek historian Herodotus indicate that seven men functioned as the immediate advisers to the king.

PERSIAN EMPIRE

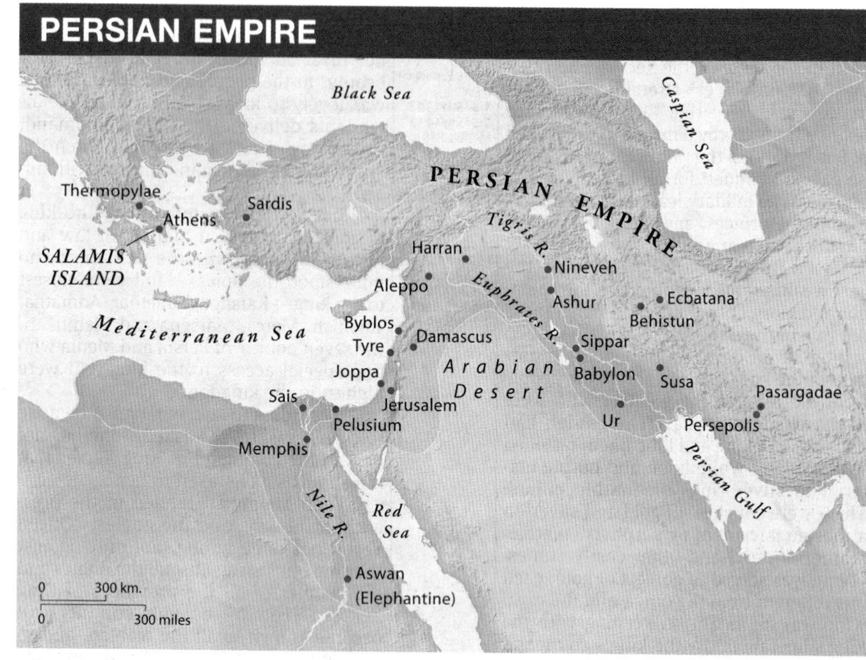

19 "Therefore, if it pleases the king,[t] let
him issue a royal decree and let it be written in the laws of Persia and Media, which
cannot be repealed,[u] that Vashti is never
again to enter the presence of King Xerxes. Also let the king give her royal position to someone else who is better than
she. 20 Then when the king's edict is proclaimed throughout all his vast realm, all
the women will respect their husbands,
from the least to the greatest."
21 The king and his nobles were pleased
with this advice, so the king did as Memukan proposed. 22 He sent dispatches to all
parts of the kingdom, to each province in
its own script and to each people in their
own language,[v] proclaiming that every
man should be ruler over his own household, using his native tongue.

1:19 [t] Ecc 8:4 [u] Est 8:8; Da 6:8, 12 **1:22** [v] S Ne 13:24 **2:1** [w] Est 7:10

Esther Made Queen

2 Later when King Xerxes' fury had
subsided,[w] he remembered Vashti and
what she had done and what he had decreed about her. 2 Then the king's personal attendants proposed, "Let a search be
made for beautiful young virgins for the
king. 3 Let the king appoint commissioners in every province of his realm to bring
all these beautiful young women into the
harem at the citadel of Susa. Let them be
placed under the care of Hegai, the king's
eunuch, who is in charge of the wom-
en; and let beauty treatments be given to
them. 4 Then let the young woman who
pleases the king be queen instead of Vashti." This advice appealed to the king, and
he followed it.
5 Now there was in the citadel of Susa

1:19 *cannot be repealed.* The irrevocability of Persian laws is mentioned in 8:8 and Da 6:8,12. *never again to enter.* The punishment corresponds to the crime: Since Vashti refused to appear before the king, it is decreed that she never appear before him again. Furthermore, from this point on she is no longer given the title "Queen" in the book of Esther.
1:22 *proclaiming … tongue.* Referring to the practice in ethnically mixed marriages of using the husband's native language as a sign of his rule in the home (see Ne 13:23–25).
2:1 *Later.* Esther was taken to Xerxes "in the seventh year of his reign" (v. 16), i.e., in December, 479 BC, or January, 478. The Greek wars intervened before a new queen was sought (see note on 1:3–4).
2:2 *virgins for the king.* To add to his harem.
2:3–4 The phraseology here is similar to that in Ge 41:34–37. This and numerous other parallels suggest that the author of Esther modeled his work after the Joseph story (see Introduction: Purpose, Themes and Literary Features). Both accounts are set in the courts of foreign monarchs and portray Israelite heroes who rise to prominence and provide the means by which their people are saved (see notes on vv. 9,21–23; 3:4; 4:14; 6:1,8,14; 8:6).
2:5 *in the citadel of Susa a Jew.* As far back as the fall of the northern kingdom in 722–721 BC, Israelites had been exiled among the cities of the Medes (2Ki 17:6). After the conquest of Babylon by King Cyrus of Persia in

a Jew of the tribe of Benjamin, named
Mordecai son of Jair, the son of Shimei,
the son of Kish,[x] 6who had been carried
into exile from Jerusalem by Nebuchadnezzar king of Babylon, among those
taken captive with Jehoiachin[a][y] king of
Judah.[z] 7Mordecai had a cousin named
Hadassah, whom he had brought up because she had neither father nor mother.
This young woman, who was also known
as Esther,[a] had a lovely figure[b] and was
beautiful. Mordecai had taken her as his
own daughter when her father and mother died.
8When the king's order and edict had
been proclaimed, many young women
were brought to the citadel of Susa[c] and
put under the care of Hegai. Esther also
was taken to the king's palace and entrusted to Hegai, who had charge of the harem.
9She pleased him and won his favor.[d] Immediately he provided her with her beauty
treatments and special food.[e] He assigned
to her seven female attendants selected
from the king's palace and moved her and
her attendants into the best place in the
harem.
10Esther had not revealed her nationality
and family background, because Mordecai
had forbidden her to do so.[f] 11Every day he
walked back and forth near the courtyard
of the harem to find out how Esther was
and what was happening to her.
12Before a young woman's turn came to
go in to King Xerxes, she had to complete
twelve months of beauty treatments prescribed for the women, six months with
oil of myrrh and six with perfumes[g] and
cosmetics. 13And this is how she would
go to the king: Anything she wanted was
given her to take with her from the harem
to the king's palace. 14In the evening she
would go there and in the morning return
to another part of the harem to the care of
Shaashgaz, the king's eunuch who was in
charge of the concubines.[h] She would not
return to the king unless he was pleased
with her and summoned her by name.[i]
15When the turn came for Esther (the
young woman Mordecai had adopted, the
daughter of his uncle Abihail[j]) to go to the
king,[k] she asked for nothing other than
what Hegai, the king's eunuch who was
in charge of the harem, suggested. And
Esther won the favor[l] of everyone who
saw her. 16She was taken to King Xerxes
in the royal residence in the tenth month,
the month of Tebeth, in the seventh year
of his reign.
17Now the king was attracted to Esther
more than to any of the other women, and
she won his favor and approval more than
any of the other virgins. So he set a royal
crown on her head and made her queen[m]
instead of Vashti. 18And the king gave a
great banquet,[n] Esther's banquet, for all

2:5 [x]S 1Sa 9:1 **2:6** [y]S 2Ki 24:6, 15 [z]Da 1:1-5; 5:13 **2:7** [a]Ge 41:45 [b]S Ge 39:6 **2:8** [c]Ne 1:1; Est 1:2; Da 8:2 **2:9** [d]S Ge 39:21 [e]S Ge 37:3; 1Sa 9:22-24; S 2Ki 25:30; Est 9:19; Eze 16:9-13; Da 1:5 **2:10** [f]ver 20 **2:12** [g]Pr 27:9; SS 1:3; Isa 3:24 **2:14** [h]1Ki 11:3; SS 6:8; Da 5:2 [i]Est 4:11 **2:15** [j]Est 9:29 [k]Ps 45:14 [l]S Ge 18:3; S 30:27; Est 5:8; 7:3; 8:5 **2:17** [m]Eze 16:9-13 **2:18** [n]S 1Ki 3:15

[a] 6 Hebrew *Jeconiah,* a variant of *Jehoiachin*

539, some of the Jewish population taken there by the Babylonians (605–586) probably moved eastward into the cities of Medo-Persia. Only 50,000 returned to Israel in the restoration of 538/537 (Ezr 2:64–65). The presence of a large Jewish population in Medo-Persia is confirmed by the discovery of an archive of texts in Nippur (southern Mesopotamia) from the period of Artaxerxes I (465–424) and Darius II (424–405). This archive contains the names of about 100 Jews who lived in that city. Some had attained positions of importance and wealth (see essay, p. 746, and charts, pp. xxii, xxiv). Similar Jewish populations are probable in many other Medo-Persian cities. *Mordecai.* The name is derived from that of the Babylonian deity Marduk. There are numerous examples in the Bible of Israelites having double names—a Hebrew name and a "Gentile" name. Mordecai likely had a Hebrew name, as did Esther (v. 7), Daniel and his friends (Da 1:6–7), Joseph (Ge 41:45) and others, but the text does not mention Mordecai's Hebrew name. A cuneiform tablet from Borsippa near Babylon mentions a scribe by the name of Mardukaya; he was an accountant or minister at the court of Susa in the early years of Xerxes. Many interpreters identify him with Mordecai. *son of Jair, the son of Shimei, the son of Kish.* The persons named could be immediate ancestors, in which case Mordecai would be the great-grandson of a Kish who was among the exiles with Jehoiachin in 597 BC. It is more likely, however, that the names refer to remote ancestors in the tribe of Benjamin (see 2Sa 16:5 for Shimei, 1Sa 9:1 for Kish). This association with the tribe and family of King Saul sets the stage for the ongoing conflict between Israel and the Amalekites (see notes on 3:1–6). If the names are those of remote ancestors, the clause "who had been carried into exile" (v. 6) would not apply to Mordecai, who would have been over 100 years old in that case; rather, it would have to be taken as an elliptical construction in the sense of "whose family had been carried into exile."

2:6 *carried into exile.* In 597 BC. *Jehoiachin king of Judah.* See 2Ki 24:8–17; 2Ch 36:9–10.

2:7 *Hadassah.* Esther's Hebrew name, meaning "myrtle." The name Esther is likely derived from the Persian word for "star," though some derive it from the name of the Babylonian goddess Ishtar (see note on Jer 7:18).

2:8 *Esther also was taken.* Neither she nor Mordecai would have had any choice in the matter (cf. 2Sa 11:4).

2:9 *special food.* Unlike Daniel and his friends (Da 1:5–10), Esther does not observe the dietary laws, perhaps in part to conceal her Jewish identity (vv. 10,20). Giving such portions is a sign of special favor (1Sa 9:22–24; 2Ki 25:29–30; Da 1:5–10; negatively, Jer 13:25); in the Joseph narrative cf. Ge 43:34 and note. The motif of giving portions appears later as a practice in observing Purim (9:19,22).

2:10 The fact that Esther concealed her identity is reported twice—here and in v. 20 (for the author's use of duplications, see Introduction: Purpose, Themes and Literary Features).

2:14 *to another part of the harem.* To the chambers of the concubines.

2:16 *tenth month … seventh year.* December, 479 BC, or January, 478 (see notes on 1:3–4; 2:1). Esther's tenure as queen continued through the events of the book, i.e., through 473 (see 3:7 and note; see also 8:9–13; 9:1). She may have died or fallen from favor shortly thereafter (see note on 1:9).

his nobles and officials.[o] He proclaimed a holiday throughout the provinces and distributed gifts with royal liberality.[p]

Mordecai Uncovers a Conspiracy

19 When the virgins were assembled a second time, Mordecai was sitting at the king's gate.[q] 20 But Esther had kept secret her family background and nationality just as Mordecai had told her to do, for she continued to follow Mordecai's instructions as she had done when he was bringing her up.[r]

21 During the time Mordecai was sitting at the king's gate, Bigthana[a] and Teresh, two of the king's officers[s] who guarded the doorway, became angry[t] and conspired to assassinate King Xerxes. 22 But Mordecai found out about the plot and told Queen Esther, who in turn reported it to the king, giving credit to Mordecai. 23 And when the report was investigated and found to be true, the two officials were impaled[u] on poles. All this was recorded in the book of the annals[v] in the presence of the king.[w]

Haman's Plot to Destroy the Jews

3 After these events, King Xerxes honored Haman son of Hammedatha, the Agagite,[x] elevating him and giving him a seat of honor higher than that of all the other nobles. 2 All the royal officials at the king's gate knelt down and paid honor to Haman, for the king had commanded this concerning him. But Mordecai would not kneel down or pay him honor.

3 Then the royal officials at the king's gate asked Mordecai, "Why do you disobey the king's command?"[y] 4 Day after day they spoke to him but he refused to comply.[z] Therefore they told Haman about it to see whether Mordecai's behavior would be tolerated, for he had told them he was a Jew.

5 When Haman saw that Mordecai would not kneel down or pay him honor, he was enraged.[a] 6 Yet having learned who Mordecai's people were, he scorned the idea of killing only Mordecai. Instead Haman looked for a way[b] to destroy[c] all

[a] 21 Hebrew *Bigthan*, a variant of *Bigthana*

2:18 [o] S Ge 40:20 [p] S Est 1:7 **2:19** [q] Est 4:2; 5:13 **2:20** [r] ver 10 **2:21** [s] S Ge 40:2 [t] S Est 1:12; 3:5; 5:9; 7:7 **2:23** [u] S Ge 40:19; S Dt 21:22-23; Ps 7:14-16; Pr 26:27; Ecc 10:8 [v] Est 6:1; 10:2 [w] Est 6:2

3:1 [x] S Ex 17:8-16; S Nu 24:7; Dt 25:17-19; 1Sa 14:48 **3:3** [y] Est 5:9; Da 3:12 **3:4** [z] Ge 39:10 **3:5** [a] S Est 2:21 **3:6** [b] Pr 16:25 [c] Ps 74:8; 83:4

2:18 *holiday.* The Hebrew for this word, unique to this verse, may imply a remission of taxes, an emancipation of slaves, a cancellation of debts or a remission of obligatory military service.

2:19 See Introduction: Purpose, Themes and Literary Features. The enlargement of the harem apparently continued unabated. Perhaps there is a causal connection between the second gathering of women and the assassination plot (vv. 21–23); some have suggested that it reflects palace intrigue in support of the deposed Vashti. *king's gate.* The gateway of an ancient city was its major commercial and legal center. Markets were held in the gateway; the court sat there to transact its business (see Dt 21:18–20; Jos 20:4; Ru 4:1–11; Ps 69:12). A king might hold an audience at the gate (see 2Sa 19:8; 1Ki 22:10). Daniel was at the king's gate (NIV "royal court") as ruler over all Babylon (Da 2:48–49). Mordecai's sitting at the king's gate confirms his holding a high position in the civil service of the empire (see note on v. 5). From this vantage point he might overhear plans for the murder of the king.

2:21–23 Another point of comparison with the Joseph narrative is the involvement of two chamberlains (Ge 40:1–3; see note on vv. 3–4).

2:23 *impaled on poles.* The Persian form of execution, as is confirmed in pictures and statues from the ancient Near East and in the comments of the Greek historian Herodotus (3.125,129; 4.43). According to Herodotus (3.159) Darius I impaled 3,000 Babylonians when he took Babylon, an act that Darius himself recorded in his Behistun (Bisitun) inscription. In Israelite and Canaanite practice, hanging was an exhibition of the corpse and not the means of execution itself (Dt 21:22–23; Jos 8:29; 10:26; 1Sa 31:8–10; 2Sa 4:12). The sons of Haman were killed by the sword, and then their corpses were displayed on poles (9:5–14). The execution of the pharaoh's chief baker in the Joseph narrative was similar (Ge 40:19). *annals.* The concern of the author of Esther with rhetorical symmetry is seen in the fact that the annals are mentioned in the beginning (here), middle (6:1) and end (10:2) of the narrative. The episode dealing with the plot of Bigthana and Teresh is a good example of the many "coincidences" in the book that later take on crucial significance for the story, showing God's providence at work (see 6:2 and note; see also Introduction: Purpose, Themes and Literary Features, last paragraph).

3:1 *After these events.* Four years have elapsed since Esther's selection as queen (v. 7; 2:16–17). *son of Hammedatha, the Agagite.* There is some debate about the ancestry of Haman. The name Hammedatha appears to be Persian and probably refers to an immediate ancestor. The title "Agagite" could refer to some other immediate ancestor or to an unknown place; however, it is far more likely that it refers to Agag, king of Amalek (1Sa 15:20). The Amalekites had attacked Israel after she fled from Egypt (Ex 17:8–16; 1Sa 15:2); for this reason the Lord would "be at war against the Amalekites from generation to generation" (Ex 17:16). Israel was not to forget but must "blot out the name of Amalek from under heaven" (Dt 25:19). Saul's attack on Amalek (1Sa 15) resulted in the death of most, though not all (1Ch 4:42–43), of King Agag's people and later in the death of the king himself. Centuries after the battle led by the Benjamite Saul, the Benjamite Mordecai (see note on 2:5) continues the war with the Amalekites. *elevating him.* The fact that no reason is given for the promotion of Haman provides an ironic contrast between the unrewarded merit of Mordecai (2:21–23; see 6:3) and the unmerited reward of Haman.

3:2–6 Obedience to the second commandment (Ex 20:4–5) is not the issue in Mordecai's refusal to bow down to Haman, for Israelites were willing to bow down to kings (see 1Sa 24:8; 2Sa 14:4; 1Ki 1:16) and to other persons (see Ge 23:7; 33:3; 44:14). Only the long-standing enmity between Israel and Amalek accounts both for Mordecai's refusal and for Haman's intent to destroy all the Jews (vv. 5–6). The threat against the Jews "throughout the whole kingdom" (v. 6) is a threat against the ultimate issue of redemptive history (see Introduction: Purpose, Themes and Literary Features).

3:4 Compare the phraseology with that in the Joseph story (Ge 39:10).

Mordecai's people, the Jews,[d] throughout
the whole kingdom of Xerxes.
7 In the twelfth year of King Xerxes, in
the first month, the month of Nisan, the
pur[e] (that is, the lot[f]) was cast in the presence of Haman to select a day and month.
And the lot fell on[a] the twelfth month, the
month of Adar.[g]
8 Then Haman said to King Xerxes,
"There is a certain people dispersed
among the peoples in all the provinces of
your kingdom who keep themselves separate. Their customs[h] are different from
those of all other people, and they do not
obey[i] the king's laws; it is not in the king's
best interest to tolerate them.[j] 9 If it pleases
the king, let a decree be issued to destroy
them, and I will give ten thousand talents[b]
of silver to the king's administrators for
the royal treasury."[k]
10 So the king took his signet ring[l] from
his finger and gave it to Haman son of
Hammedatha, the Agagite, the enemy of
the Jews. 11 "Keep the money," the king
said to Haman, "and do with the people
as you please."
12 Then on the thirteenth day of the first
month the royal secretaries were summoned. They wrote out in the script of
each province and in the language[m] of
each people all Haman's orders to the
king's satraps, the governors of the various provinces and the nobles of the various peoples. These were written in the
name of King Xerxes himself and sealed[n]
with his own ring. 13 Dispatches were sent
by couriers to all the king's provinces with
the order to destroy, kill and annihilate all
the Jews[o] — young and old, women and
children — on a single day, the thirteenth
day of the twelfth month, the month of
Adar,[p] and to plunder[q] their goods. 14 A
copy of the text of the edict was to be issued as law in every province and made
known to the people of every nationality
so they would be ready for that day.[r]
15 The couriers went out, spurred on by
the king's command, and the edict was issued in the citadel of Susa.[s] The king and
Haman sat down to drink,[t] but the city of
Susa was bewildered.[u]

Mordecai Persuades Esther to Help

4 When Mordecai learned of all that had
been done, he tore his clothes,[v] put on
sackcloth and ashes,[w] and went out into
the city, wailing[x] loudly and bitterly. 2 But
he went only as far as the king's gate,[y]
because no one clothed in sackcloth was
allowed to enter it. 3 In every province
to which the edict and order of the king
came, there was great mourning among
the Jews, with fasting, weeping and wailing. Many lay in sackcloth and ashes.
4 When Esther's eunuchs and female
attendants came and told her about Mordecai, she was in great distress. She sent
clothes for him to put on instead of his
sackcloth, but he would not accept them.
5 Then Esther summoned Hathak, one of
the king's eunuchs assigned to attend her,

3:6 [d] Est 9:24
3:7 [e] Est 9:24, 26 [f] S Lev 16:8; S 1Sa 10:21 [g] ver 13; Est 9:19
3:8 [h] Ac 16:20-21 [i] Jer 29:7; Da 6:13 [j] Ezr 4:15
3:9 [k] Est 7:4
3:10 [l] S Ge 41:42
3:12 [m] S Ne 13:24 [n] S Ge 38:18
3:13 [o] S 1Sa 15:3; S Ezr 4:6 [p] S ver 7 [q] Est 8:11; 9:10
3:14 [r] Est 8:8; 9:1
3:15 [s] Est 8:14 [t] S Est 1:10 [u] Est 8:15
4:1 [v] S Nu 14:6 [w] S 2Sa 13:19; Eze 27:30-31 [x] S Ex 11:6; Ps 30:11
4:2 [y] S Est 2:19

[a] 7 Septuagint; Hebrew does not have *And the lot fell on.* [b] 9 That is, about 375 tons or about 340 metric tons

3:7 *twelfth year ... first month.* April or May, 474 BC, the fifth year of Esther's reign. *pur.* See 9:24,26. This word is found in Akkadian texts with the meaning "lot" (as here). The celebration known as Purim takes its name from the plural of this noun (see 9:26). There is irony in the fact that the month of the Jews' celebration of the Passover deliverance from Egypt is also the month that Haman begins plotting their destruction (Ex 12:2–11). *twelfth month.* An 11-month delay is contemplated between the securing of the decree and the execution of it in the month Adar (February-March).
3:8 *a certain people.* The name of the people Haman wishes to destroy is slyly omitted in this blend of the true and the false: The Jews did have their own customs and laws, but they were not disobedient to the king (Jer 29:7). *dispersed.* See 8:11,17; 9:2,12,16,19–20,28.
3:9 *ten thousand talents.* Herodotus (3.95) records that the annual income of the Persian Empire was 15,000 talents. If this figure is correct, Haman offers two-thirds of that amount — a huge sum. Presumably the money would have come from the plundered wealth of the victims of the decree. Verse 13 implies that those who would take part in the massacre were to be allowed to keep the plunder, perhaps adding financial incentive to the execution of the decree since Xerxes disavows taking the money (v. 11). On the other hand, 4:7 may imply that the king had planned on collecting some of the money (see also 7:4 and note). *king's administrators.* This phrase may represent the title of revenue officers who would bring the money to the treasury, or it could refer to those who carry out the decree. The Amalekites had once before plundered Israel (1Sa 14:48); Haman plans a recurrence.
3:10 *took his signet ring ... and gave it to Haman.* Authorizing Haman to put the king's seal on the royal decree (v. 12). *enemy of the Jews.* An epithet also applied to Haman later in the book (8:1; 9:10; cf. also 7:6; 9:24).
3:12 *thirteenth day ... first month.* In the 12th year of Xerxes's reign (v. 7), i.e., Apr. 17, 474 BC.
3:13 Haman's decree against Israel mandates virtually the same destruction that had earlier been decreed against Amalek (1Sa 15:3). *thirteenth day ... twelfth month.* Mar. 7, 473 BC (see 8:12).
3:15 Haman and the king will drink together again in the story when the fate of the Jews is once again being decided (7:1–2), but then it will be at the dissolution of their relationship and the reversal of the decree here celebrated. The celebration here is in sharp contrast to the fasting and mourning of the Jews (4:1–3,16).
4:2 *king's gate.* See note on 2:19.
4:3 See note on 3:15. The prominence of feasting throughout the book of Esther sets the fasts of vv. 3,16 in sharp relief; a pair of fasts matches the prominent pairs of banquets (see Introduction: Purpose, Themes and Literary Features; see also note on 9:31; cf. note on Joel 1:14).
4:5–15 The fact that the dialogue of Esther and Mordecai

and ordered him to find out what was
troubling Mordecai and why.
6 So Hathak went out to Mordecai in
the open square of the city in front of
the king's gate. 7 Mordecai told him everything that had happened to him, including the exact amount of money Haman had promised to pay into the royal
treasury for the destruction of the Jews.[z]
8 He also gave him a copy of the text of
the edict for their annihilation, which had
been published in Susa, to show to Esther
and explain it to her, and he told him to
instruct her to go into the king's presence
to beg for mercy and plead with him for
her people.
9 Hathak went back and reported to Esther what Mordecai had said. 10 Then she
instructed him to say to Mordecai, 11 "All
the king's officials and the people of the
royal provinces know that for any man or
woman who approaches the king in the
inner court without being summoned[a] the
king has but one law:[b] that they be put
to death unless the king extends the gold
scepter[c] to them and spares their lives. But
thirty days have passed since I was called
to go to the king."
12 When Esther's words were reported
to Mordecai, 13 he sent back this answer:
"Do not think that because you are in the
king's house you alone of all the Jews will
escape. 14 For if you remain silent[d] at this
time, relief[e] and deliverance[f] for the Jews
will arise from another place, but you and
your father's family will perish. And who
knows but that you have come to your
royal position for such a time as this?"[g]
15 Then Esther sent this reply to Mordecai: 16 "Go, gather together all the Jews
who are in Susa, and fast[h] for me. Do not
eat or drink for three days, night or day.
I and my attendants will fast as you do.
When this is done, I will go to the king,
even though it is against the law. And if I
perish, I perish."[i]
17 So Mordecai went away and carried
out all of Esther's instructions.

4:7 [z] Est 7:4 **4:11** [a] Est 2:14 [b] Da 2:9 [c] Est 5:1, 2; 8:4; Ps 125:3 **4:14** [d] Job 34:29; Ps 28:1; 35:22; Ecc 3:7; Isa 42:14; 57:11; 62:1; 64:12; Am 5:13 [e] Est 9:16,22 [f] S Ge 45:7; S Dt 28:29 [g] S Ge 50:20 **4:16** [h] S 2Ch 20:3; Est 9:31 [i] S Ge 43:14

Esther's Request to the King

5 On the third day Esther put on her royal robes[j] and stood in the inner court
of the palace, in front of the king's[k] hall.
The king was sitting on his royal throne
in the hall, facing the entrance. 2 When he
saw Queen Esther standing in the court,
he was pleased with her and held out to
her the gold scepter that was in his hand.
So Esther approached and touched the tip
of the scepter.[l]
3 Then the king asked, "What is it,
Queen Esther? What is your request? Even
up to half the kingdom,[m] it will be given
you."
4 "If it pleases the king," replied Esther,
"let the king, together with Haman, come
today to a banquet I have prepared for
him."
5 "Bring Haman at once," the king said,
"so that we may do what Esther asks."
So the king and Haman went to the banquet Esther had prepared. 6 As they were
drinking wine,[n] the king again asked Esther, "Now what is your petition? It will
be given you. And what is your request?
Even up to half the kingdom,[o] it will be
granted."[p]
7 Esther replied, "My petition and my request is this: 8 If the king regards me with
favor[q] and if it pleases the king to grant
my petition and fulfill my request, let the
king and Haman come tomorrow to the
banquet[r] I will prepare for them. Then I
will answer the king's question."

5:1 [j] Eze 16:13 [k] Pr 21:1 **5:2** [l] S Est 4:11 **5:3** [m] Est 7:2; Da 5:16; Mk 6:23 **5:6** [n] S Est 1:10 [o] Da 5:16; Mk 6:23 [p] Est 9:12 **5:8** [q] S Est 2:15 [r] S 1Ki 3:15

---

is mediated by Hathak reflects the prohibition against Mordecai's entering the royal citadel dressed in mourning (v. 2).

4:7 See note on 3:9. That Mordecai is aware of the amount Haman promised to the king is a reminder of his high position in the bureaucracy at Susa (2:21–23; see also note on 2:5).

4:11 Herodotus (3.118,140) also notes that anyone approaching the Persian king unsummoned would be killed unless the king gave immediate pardon.

4:12–16 The themes of the book of Esther are most clearly expressed in this passage. Mordecai's confidence that the Jews would be delivered is based on God's sovereignty in working out his purposes and fulfilling his promises. Their deliverance will come, even if through some means other than Esther. Yet that sovereignty is not fatalistic: Unless Esther exercises her individual responsibility, she and her family will perish. Cf. Mt 26:24; Ac 2:23 for similar treatments of the relationship between divine sovereignty and human responsibility.

4:14 *from another place.* As close as the book comes to an explicit reference to God (see Introduction: Purpose, Themes and Literary Features). In Jewish tradition, "the Place" is one of the surrogates used for God's name. *such a time as this.* Cf. Ge 45:5–7 in the Joseph narrative.

4:16 *fast.* See note on v. 3. Prayer, which usually accompanied such fasting, was presumably a part of this fast as well (see Jdg 20:26–27; 1Sa 7:6; 2Sa 12:16; Ezr 8:21–23; Ne 9:1–3; Isa 58:3–4; Jer 14:12; Joel 1:14; 2:12–17; Jnh 3:7–8). The omission of any reference to prayer or to God is consistent with the author's intention; absence of any distinctively religious concepts or vocabulary is a rhetorical device used to heighten the fact that it is indeed God who has been active in the whole narrative (see Introduction: Purpose, Themes and Literary Features). *if I perish, I perish.* Esther's defining moment. Cf. the similar formulation in the Joseph narrative (Ge 43:14).

5:2 An example of divine providence influencing a king, as in Pr 21:1 (see note there).

5:6–7 One can only speculate regarding Esther's reasons for delaying her answer to the king's question until he had asked it a third time (vv. 3,6; 7:2). The author uses these delays as plot retardation devices that sustain the tension and permit the introduction of new material on Haman's self-aggrandizement (vv. 11–12) and Mordecai's reward (6:6–11).

Haman's Rage Against Mordecai

9 Haman went out that day happy and in high spirits. But when he saw Mordecai at the king's gate and observed that he neither rose nor showed fear in his presence, he was filled with rage[s] against Mordecai.[t] 10 Nevertheless, Haman restrained himself and went home.

Calling together his friends and Zeresh,[u] his wife, 11 Haman boasted[v] to them about his vast wealth, his many sons,[w] and all the ways the king had honored him and how he had elevated him above the other nobles and officials. 12 "And that's not all," Haman added. "I'm the only person[x] Queen Esther invited to accompany the king to the banquet she gave. And she has invited me along with the king tomorrow. 13 But all this gives me no satisfaction as long as I see that Jew Mordecai sitting at the king's gate.[y]"

14 His wife Zeresh and all his friends said to him, "Have a pole set up, reaching to a height of fifty cubits,[a][z] and ask the king in the morning to have Mordecai impaled[a] on it. Then go with the king to the banquet and enjoy yourself." This suggestion delighted Haman, and he had the pole set up.

Mordecai Honored

6 That night the king could not sleep;[b] so he ordered the book of the chronicles,[c] the record of his reign, to be brought in and read to him. 2 It was found recorded there that Mordecai had exposed Bigthana and Teresh, two of the king's officers who guarded the doorway, who had conspired to assassinate King Xerxes.[d]

3 "What honor and recognition has Mordecai received for this?" the king asked.

"Nothing has been done for him,"[e] his attendants answered.

4 The king said, "Who is in the court?" Now Haman had just entered the outer court of the palace to speak to the king about impaling Mordecai on the pole he had set up for him.

5 His attendants answered, "Haman is standing in the court."

"Bring him in," the king ordered.

6 When Haman entered, the king asked him, "What should be done for the man the king delights to honor?"

Now Haman thought to himself, "Who is there that the king would rather honor than me?" 7 So he answered the king, "For the man the king delights to honor, 8 have them bring a royal robe[f] the king has worn and a horse[g] the king has ridden, one with a royal crest placed on its head. 9 Then let the robe and horse be entrusted to one of the king's most noble princes. Let them robe the man the king delights to honor, and lead him on the horse through the city streets, proclaiming before him, 'This is what is done for the man the king delights to honor!'[h] "

10 "Go at once," the king commanded Haman. "Get the robe and the horse and do just as you have suggested for Mordecai the Jew, who sits at the king's gate. Do not neglect anything you have recommended."

11 So Haman got[i] the robe and the horse. He robed Mordecai, and led him on horseback through the city streets, proclaiming

5:9 [s]S Est 2:21; Pr 14:17 [t]S Est 3:3,5 **5:10** [u]Est 6:13 **5:11** [v]Pr 13:16 [w]Est 9:7-10,13 **5:12** [x]Job 22:29; Pr 16:18; 29:23 **5:13** [y]S Est 2:19 **5:14** [z]Est 7:9 [a]S Ezr 6:11 **6:1** [b]Da 2:1; 6:18 [c]S Est 2:23 **6:2** [d]Est 2:21-23 **6:3** [e]Ecc 9:13-16 **6:8** [f]S Ge 41:42; S Isa 52:1 [g]1Ki 1:33 **6:9** [h]Ge 41:43 **6:11** [i]S Ge 41:42

[a] *14* That is, about 75 feet or about 23 meters

5:9 Haman's rage is kindled when Mordecai does not rise in his presence—an ironic contrast to his earlier refusal to bow (3:2–5).

5:11 *many sons.* Haman had ten sons (9:7–10). Herodotus (1.136) reports that the Persians prized a large number of sons second only to valor in battle; the Persian king sent gifts to the subject with the most sons (cf. Ps 127:3–5).

5:12–13 See Pr 16:18; 29:23.

5:13 *that Jew Mordecai.* See notes on 6:10; 7:6.

5:14 *height of fifty cubits.* Perhaps hyperbolic (see NIV text note). Some, however, suggest that the pole (see 2:23 and note) was set up atop another structure to achieve this height, e.g., the city wall (see 1Sa 31:10). *impaled.* See note on 2:23.

6:1 This verse marks the literary center of the narrative. When things could not look worse, a series of seemingly trivial coincidences marks a critical turn that brings resolution to the story. The king's inability to sleep, his requesting the reading of the annals, the reading of the passage reporting Mordecai's past kindness (v. 2), Haman's preparations in the early hours of the morning (5:14), his sudden entry into the outer court (6:5) and his assumption that he was the man the king wished to honor (v. 6)—all are events testifying to the sovereignty of God over the events of the narrative. Circumstances that seemed incidental earlier in the narrative take on crucial significance later. Just as in the Joseph story (Ge 41:1–45), the hero's personal fortunes are reversed because of the monarch's disturbed sleep (cf. Da 2:1; 6:18).

6:2 The scribe was reading from the annals that recorded events five years earlier (compare 3:7 with 2:16; see 2:23 and note).

6:4–6 Again, the irony is evident: Just as Haman had withheld from the king the identity of the "certain people" (see 3:8 and note), so now the king unintentionally keeps from Haman the identity of the "man the king delights to honor" (v. 6).

6:8 *royal robe the king has worn.* See 8:15; see also Introduction: Purpose, Themes and Literary Features. Cf. in the Joseph story Ge 41:41–43. Great significance was attached to the king's garment in ancient times; wearing his garments was a sign of unique favor (1Sa 18:4). To wear another's garments was to partake of his power, stature, honor or sanctity (2Ki 2:13–14; Isa 61:3,10; Zec 3:3–7; cf. Mk 5:27–28). Haman's suggestion is not only a great honor to the recipient but is also considerably flattering to the king: Wearing his garment was chosen instead of wealth.

6:10 *Mordecai the Jew.* An ironic echo of Haman's sarcastic epithet "that Jew Mordecai" (5:13; see also note on 7:6).

before him, "This is what is done for the
man the king delights to honor!"
12 Afterward Mordecai returned to the
king's gate. But Haman rushed home,
with his head covered[j] in grief, 13 and told
Zeresh[k] his wife and all his friends everything that had happened to him.
His advisers and his wife Zeresh said to
him, "Since Mordecai, before whom your
downfall[l] has started, is of Jewish origin,
you cannot stand against him — you will
surely come to ruin!"[m] 14 While they were
still talking with him, the king's eunuchs
arrived and hurried Haman away to the
banquet[n] Esther had prepared.

Haman Impaled

7 So the king and Haman went to Queen
Esther's banquet,[o] 2 and as they were
drinking wine[p] on the second day, the king
again asked, "Queen Esther, what is your
petition? It will be given you. What is your
request? Even up to half the kingdom,[q] it
will be granted.[r]"
3 Then Queen Esther answered, "If I
have found favor[s] with you, Your Majesty,
and if it pleases you, grant me my life —
this is my petition. And spare my people —
this is my request. 4 For I and my people
have been sold to be destroyed, killed and
annihilated.[t] If we had merely been sold as
male and female slaves, I would have kept
quiet, because no such distress would justify disturbing the king.[a]"
5 King Xerxes asked Queen Esther, "Who
is he? Where is he — the man who has
dared to do such a thing?"
6 Esther said, "An adversary and enemy!
This vile Haman!"
Then Haman was terrified before the
king and queen. 7 The king got up in a
rage,[u] left his wine and went out into the
palace garden.[v] But Haman, realizing that
the king had already decided his fate,[w]
stayed behind to beg Queen Esther for his
life.
8 Just as the king returned from the palace garden to the banquet hall, Haman
was falling on the couch[x] where Esther
was reclining.[y]
The king exclaimed, "Will he even mo-
lest the queen while she is with me in the
house?"[z]
As soon as the word left the king's
mouth, they covered Haman's face.[a] 9 Then
Harbona,[b] one of the eunuchs attending
the king, said, "A pole reaching to a height
of fifty cubits[b][c] stands by Haman's house.
He had it set up for Mordecai, who spoke
up to help the king."
The king said, "Impale him on it!"[d] 10 So
they impaled[e] Haman[f] on the pole[g] he had
set up for Mordecai.[h] Then the king's fury
subsided.[i]

The King's Edict in Behalf of the Jews

8 That same day King Xerxes gave
Queen Esther the estate of Haman,[j]
the enemy of the Jews. And Mordecai
came into the presence of the king, for Esther had told how he was related to her.
2 The king took off his signet ring,[k] which
he had reclaimed from Haman, and presented it to Mordecai. And Esther appointed him over Haman's estate.[l]

6:12 [j] 2Sa 15:30; Est 7:8; Jer 14:3, 4; Mic 3:7 **6:13** [k] Est 5:10 [l] Ps 57:6; Pr 26:27; 28:18 [m] Est 7:7 **6:14** [n] S 1Ki 3:15 **7:1** [o] Ge 40:20-22; Mt 22:1-14 **7:2** [p] S Est 1:10 [q] S Est 5:3 [r] Est 9:12 **7:3** [s] S Est 2:15 **7:4** [t] Est 3:9; S 4:7 **7:7** [u] S Ge 34:7; S Est 1:12; Pr 19:12; 20:1-2 [v] S 2Ki 21:18 [w] Est 6:13 **7:8** [x] S Est 1:6 [y] Ge 39:14; Jn 13:23 [z] S Ge 34:7 [a] S Est 6:12 **7:9** [b] Est 1:10 [c] Est 5:14 [d] S Dt 21:22-23; Ps 7:14-16; 9:16; Pr 11:5-6; S 26:27; S Mt 7:2 **7:10** [e] Ge 40:22 [f] Pr 10:28 [g] Est 9:25 [h] Da 6:24 [i] Est 2:1 **8:1** [j] Pr 22:22-23 **8:2** [k] S Ge 24:22; S 41:42 [l] S Ge 41:41; Pr 13:22; 14:35; Da 2:48

[a] 4 Or *quiet, but the compensation our adversary offers cannot be compared with the loss the king would suffer*
[b] 9 That is, about 75 feet or about 23 meters

6:13 *his wife and all his friends.* See 5:14; see also Introduction: Purpose, Themes and Literary Features.
6:14 Guests were usually escorted to feasts (see in the Joseph narrative Ge 43:15 – 26; cf. Mt 22:1 – 14).
7:2 See 5:3,6; see also note on 5:6 – 7.
7:3 *found favor with you.* See 2:15,17.
7:4 *sold.* Esther refers to the bribe Haman offered to the king (3:9; 4:7); she also paraphrases Haman's edict (3:13). *because no such distress ... king.* See NIV text note. The statement probably means either (1) that the affliction of the Jews would be less injurious to the king if slavery was all that was involved, or (2) that Esther would not trouble the king if slavery was the only issue.
7:6 *This vile Haman!* Esther's biting words are a rhetorical counterpoint to Haman's sneering characterization of Mordecai as "that Jew Mordecai" (5:13; see also note on 6:10).
7:7 *went out.* The king's leaving the room sets the stage for the final twist that would seal Haman's fate.
7:8 *falling on the couch where Esther was reclining.* Meals were customarily taken reclining on a couch (see Am 6:4,7; Jn 13:23 and note). It is ironic that Haman, who became angry when the Jew Mordecai would not bow down (which set the whole story in motion), now falls before the Jewess Esther (see 6:13). *covered Haman's face.* See 6:12; see also Introduction: Purpose, Themes and Literary Features.
7:9 Before this moment there is no evidence that Esther had known of Mordecai's triumph earlier in the day (6:1 – 11); she has pleaded for the life of her people. Harbona's reference to the pole (see 2:23 and note) in effect introduces a second charge against Haman — his attempt to kill the king's benefactor.
7:10 *impaled Haman on the pole he had set up for Mordecai.* John Calvin said, "Man falls as God's providence ordains, but he falls by his own fault." See 9:1,25 and note on 9:1; Job 4:8; Ps 7:15 – 16; Pr 26:27 and note; Jer 50:15,29; Eze 9:10; 16:43; Ob 15 and note; cf. Gal 6:7 – 8 . *subsided.* See 2:1; see also Introduction: Purpose, Themes and Literary Features.
8:1 – 17 By echoing much of the phraseology of 3:1 — 4:3, the author emphasizes how the tables were turned.
8:1 *gave Queen Esther the estate of Haman.* Herodotus (3.128 – 129) and Josephus (*Antiquities*, 11.17) confirm that the property of a traitor reverted to the crown; Xerxes presents Haman's wealth (5:11) to Esther.
8:2 Cf. 3:10 – 11, where the king's offer of his ring includes Haman's keeping the money; here Mordecai receives the office and the estate of Haman.
8:3 – 6 Esther and Mordecai are secure (7:4 — 8:2), but the irrevocable decree is still a threat to the rest of the Jews.

3Esther again pleaded with the king,
falling at his feet and weeping. She begged
him to put an end to the evil plan of Haman the Agagite,[m] which he had devised
against the Jews. 4Then the king extended
the gold scepter[n] to Esther and she arose
and stood before him.
5"If it pleases the king," she said, "and
if he regards me with favor[o] and thinks it
the right thing to do, and if he is pleased
with me, let an order be written overruling
the dispatches that Haman son of Hammedatha, the Agagite, devised and wrote to
destroy the Jews in all the king's provinces. 6For how can I bear to see disaster fall
on my people? How can I bear to see the
destruction of my family?"[p]
7King Xerxes replied to Queen Esther
and to Mordecai the Jew, "Because Haman attacked the Jews, I have given his
estate to Esther, and they have impaled[q]
him on the pole he set up. 8Now write
another decree[r] in the king's name in behalf of the Jews as seems best to you, and
seal[s] it with the king's signet ring[t]—for no
document written in the king's name and
sealed with his ring can be revoked."[u]
9At once the royal secretaries were
summoned—on the twenty-third day
of the third month, the month of Sivan.
They wrote out all Mordecai's orders to
the Jews, and to the satraps, governors
and nobles of the 127 provinces stretching from India to Cush.[a][v] These orders
were written in the script of each province and the language of each people and
also to the Jews in their own script and
language.[w] 10Mordecai wrote in the name
of King Xerxes, sealed the dispatches with
the king's signet ring, and sent them by
mounted couriers, who rode fast horses
especially bred for the king.
11The king's edict granted the Jews in
every city the right to assemble and protect themselves; to destroy, kill and annihilate the armed men of any nationality
or province who might attack them and
their women and children,[b] and to plunder[x] the property of their enemies. 12The
day appointed for the Jews to do this in
all the provinces of King Xerxes was the
thirteenth day of the twelfth month, the
month of Adar.[y] 13A copy of the text of
the edict was to be issued as law in every province and made known to the people of every nationality so that the Jews
would be ready on that day[z] to avenge
themselves on their enemies.
14The couriers, riding the royal horses,

8:3 [m]S Ex 17:8-16 **8:4** [n]S Est 4:11 **8:5** [o]S Est 2:15 **8:6** [p]Ge 44:34 **8:7** [q]S Dt 21:22-23 **8:8** [r]S Est 3:12-14 [s]S Ge 38:18 [t]S Ge 41:42 [u]S Est 1:19; Da 6:15 **8:9** [v]Est 1:1 [w]S Ne 13:24 **8:11** [x]S Ge 14:23; S Est 3:13; 9:10, 15, 16 **8:12** [y]Est 3:13; 9:1 **8:13** [z]Est 3:14

[a] *9* That is, the upper Nile region [b] *11* *Or province, together with their women and children, who might attack them;*

8:3 *Agagite.* See note on 3:1.
8:5 *favor.* See 4:11; 5:2.
8:6 Cf. the Joseph story (Ge 44:34).
8:8 *write another decree.* See 1:19 and note; see also Introduction: Purpose, Themes and Literary Features. The dilemma is the same as the one that confronted Darius the Mede in Daniel (Da 6:8,12,15). The solution is to issue another decree (cf. Da 6:25–27) that in effect counters the original decree of Haman (3:12; cf. Da 6:7–9) without formally revoking it (see note on 9:2–3).
8:9–13 The phraseology is taken from the parallel in 3:12–14. The extent of the destruction mandated is virtually the same as that earlier decreed against Amalek (see note on 3:13).
8:9 *twenty-third day … third month.* In Xerxes's 12th year, i.e., June 25, 474 BC, two months and ten days after the proclamation of Haman's edict (see note on 3:12).
8:12 *thirteenth day … twelfth month.* Mar. 7, 473 BC (see 3:13 and note). Some 15 years after this first Purim, Ezra would lead his expedition to Jerusalem in 458 BC (Ezr 7:9).
8:14–17 The phraseology is taken from 3:15—4:3.

CHIASTIC STRUCTURE OF REVERSALS IN ESTHER

3:10	the king gives Haman his ring	8:2	the king gives Mordecai the same ring
3:12	Haman summons the king's secretaries	8:9	Mordecai summons the king's secretaries
3:12	letters written, sealed with ring	8:10	letters written, sealed with the same ring
3:13	the Jews, even women and children, are to be killed on one day	8:11	in self-defense, the Jews can kill their enemies in one day
3:14	Haman's decree publicly displayed as law	8:13	Mordecai's decree publicly displayed as law
3:15	couriers go out in haste	8:14	couriers go out in haste
3:15	the city of Susa is bewildered	8:15	the city of Susa rejoices
4:1	Mordecai wears sackcloth and ashes	8:15	Mordecai wears royal robes
4:1	Mordecai goes through the city wailing loudly	6:11	Mordecai led through the city in honor
5:14	Zeresh advises Mordecai's death	6:13	Zeresh predicts Haman's ruin

went out, spurred on by the king's command, and the edict was issued in the citadel of Susa.[a]

The Triumph of the Jews

15 When Mordecai[b] left the king's presence, he was wearing royal garments of blue and white, a large crown of gold[c] and a purple robe of fine linen.[d] And the city of Susa held a joyous celebration.[e] 16 For the Jews it was a time of happiness and joy,[f] gladness and honor.[g] 17 In every province and in every city to which the edict of the king came, there was joy[h] and gladness among the Jews, with feasting and celebrating. And many people of other nationalities became Jews because fear[i] of the Jews had seized them.[j]

9 On the thirteenth day of the twelfth month, the month of Adar,[k] the edict commanded by the king was to be carried out. On this day the enemies of the Jews had hoped to overpower them, but now the tables were turned and the Jews got the upper hand[l] over those who hated them.[m] 2 The Jews assembled in their cities[n] in all the provinces of King Xerxes to attack those determined to destroy them. No one could stand against them,[o] because the people of all the other nationalities were afraid of them. 3 And all the nobles of the provinces, the satraps, the governors and the king's administrators helped the Jews,[p] because fear of Mordecai had seized them.[q] 4 Mordecai[r] was prominent[s] in the palace; his reputation spread throughout the provinces, and he became more and more powerful.[t]

5 The Jews struck down all their enemies with the sword, killing and destroying them,[u] and they did what they pleased to those who hated them. 6 In the citadel of Susa, the Jews killed and destroyed five hundred men. 7 They also killed Parshandatha, Dalphon, Aspatha, 8 Poratha, Adalia, Aridatha, 9 Parmashta, Arisai, Aridai and Vaizatha, 10 the ten sons[v] of Haman son of Hammedatha, the enemy of the Jews.[w] But they did not lay their hands on the plunder.[x]

11 The number of those killed in the citadel of Susa was reported to the king that same day. 12 The king said to Queen Esther, "The Jews have killed and destroyed five hundred men and the ten sons of Haman in the citadel of Susa. What have they done in the rest of the king's provinces? Now what is your petition? It will be given you. What is your request? It will also be granted."[y]

13 "If it pleases the king," Esther answered, "give the Jews in Susa permission to carry out this day's edict tomorrow also, and let Haman's ten sons[z] be impaled[a] on poles."

14 So the king commanded that this be done. An edict was issued in Susa, and they impaled[b] the ten sons of Haman. 15 The Jews in Susa came together on the fourteenth day of the month of Adar, and they put to death in Susa three hundred men, but they did not lay their hands on the plunder.[c]

16 Meanwhile, the remainder of the Jews who were in the king's provinces also assembled to protect themselves and get relief[d] from their enemies.[e] They killed seventy-five thousand of them[f] but did not lay their hands on the plunder.[g] 17 This happened on the thirteenth day of the month of Adar, and on the fourteenth they rested and made it a day of feasting[h] and joy.

18 The Jews in Susa, however, had assembled on the thirteenth and fourteenth,

8:14 [a] Est 3:15
8:15 [b] Est 9:4; 10:2 [c] S 2Sa 12:30 [d] S Ge 41:42 [e] Est 3:15
8:16 [f] Ps 97:10-12 [g] Est 4:1-3; Ps 112:4; Jer 29:4-7
8:17 [h] Ps 35:27; 45:15; 51:8; Pr 11:10 [i] S Ex 15:14, 16; Dt 11:25; Da 6:26 [j] Est 9:3
9:1 [k] S Est 8:12 [l] Jer 29:4-7 [m] S Est 3:12-14; Pr 22:22-23
9:2 [n] S Ge 22:17 [o] Ps 35:26; 40:14; 70:2; 71:13,24
9:3 [p] S Ezr 8:36 [q] Est 8:17
9:4 [r] S Est 8:15 [s] S Ex 11:3 [t] S 2Sa 3:1; 1Ch 11:9
9:5 [u] Dt 25:17-19; S 1Sa 15:3; S Ezr 4:6
9:10 [v] S Est 5:11; Ps 127:3-5 [w] S 1Sa 15:33 [x] S Ge 14:23; S 1Sa 14:32; S Est 3:13
9:12 [y] Est 5:6; 7:2
9:13 [z] S Est 5:11 [a] S Dt 21:22-23
9:14 [b] S Ezr 6:11
9:15 [c] S Ge 14:23; S Est 8:11
9:16 [d] S Est 4:14 [e] Dt 25:19 [f] S 1Ch 4:43 [g] S Est 8:11
9:17 [h] S 1Ki 3:15

8:15 *royal garments.* See note on 6:8; Mordecai's second investiture (see 6:7–11; see also Introduction: Purpose, Themes and Literary Features).

9:1 The Jews carry out the edict of Mordecai eight months and 20 days later (see 8:9). *tables were turned.* The statement that the opposite happened points to the author's concern with literary symmetry: He balances most of the details from the first half of the story with their explicit reversal in the second half (see note on 8:1–17 and chart, p. 781).

9:2–3 An illustration of Ge 12:3. Confronted with two conflicting edicts issued in the king's name—the edict of Haman (see 3:12) and the edict of Mordecai (see 8:7–14)—the governors follow the edict of the current regime.

9:3 Just as "people of other nationalities" were seized by "fear of the Jews" (8:17), so also the government officials of Persia were seized by "fear of Mordecai."

9:5–10 The Jews attend to the unfinished business of blotting out the name and memory of the Amalekites (Ex 17:14–16; Dt 25:17–19; see notes on 3:1–6). This incident is presented as the antithesis of 1Sa 15: The narrator is emphatic that the Jews did not take plunder, in spite of the king's permission to do so (8:11). Seizing the plunder centuries earlier in the battle against Amalek had cost Saul his kingship (1Sa 15:17–19,23); here, not taking the plunder brings royal power to Mordecai, as well as grateful recognition by his people (vv. 20–23). See vv. 15–16; cf. Ge 14:22—15:1.

9:12 See 5:3,6; 7:2.

9:13–14 *impaled ... impaled.* See vv. 7–10 and note on 2:23.

9:13 *Susa.* The city, not the citadel (vv. 11–12; see note on 1:2).

9:15–16 See note on vv. 5–10.

9:16,22 *relief from their enemies.* Closely associated with the vengeance on its enemies is the rest promised to Israel (Dt 25:19). The defeat of Haman brings rest to the Jews (see Introduction: Purpose, Themes and Literary Features; cf. 1Ch 22:6–10; Ps 95:7–11; Isa 32:18; Heb 3:7–4:11).

9:18–19 The author accounts for the tradition of observing Purim on two different days: It is observed on the 14th in most towns, but the Jews of Susa observed it on the 15th. Today it is observed on the 14th except in Jerusalem, where it is observed on the 15th.

9:20 *Mordecai recorded these events.* Some take this as indi-

and then on the fifteenth they rested and made it a day of feasting and joy.

[19]That is why rural Jews—those living in villages—observe the fourteenth of the month of Adar[i] as a day of joy and feasting, a day for giving presents to each other.[j]

Purim Established

[20]Mordecai recorded these events, and he sent letters to all the Jews throughout the provinces of King Xerxes, near and far, [21]to have them celebrate annually the fourteenth and fifteenth days of the month of Adar [22]as the time when the Jews got relief[k] from their enemies, and as the month when their sorrow was turned into joy and their mourning into a day of celebration.[l] He wrote them to observe the days as days of feasting and joy and giving presents of food[m] to one another and gifts to the poor.[n]

[23]So the Jews agreed to continue the celebration they had begun, doing what Mordecai had written to them. [24]For Haman son of Hammedatha, the Agagite,[o] the enemy of all the Jews, had plotted against the Jews to destroy them and had cast the *pur*[p] (that is, the lot[q]) for their ruin and destruction.[r] [25]But when the plot came to the king's attention,[a] he issued written orders that the evil scheme Haman had devised against the Jews should come back onto his own head,[s] and that he and his sons should be impaled[t] on poles.[u] [26](Therefore these days were called Purim, from the word *pur*.[v]) Because of everything written in this letter and because of what they had seen and what had happened to them, [27]the Jews took it on themselves to establish the custom that they and their descendants and all who join them should without fail observe these two days every year, in the way prescribed and at the time appointed. [28]These days should be remembered and observed in every generation by every family, and in every province and in every city. And these days of Purim should never fail to be celebrated by the Jews—nor should the memory of these days die out among their descendants.

[29]So Queen Esther, daughter of Abihail,[w] along with Mordecai the Jew, wrote with full authority to confirm this second letter concerning Purim. [30]And Mordecai sent letters to all the Jews in the 127 provinces[x] of Xerxes' kingdom—words of goodwill and assurance— [31]to establish these days of Purim at their designated times, as Mordecai the Jew and Queen Esther had decreed for them, and as they had established for themselves and their descendants in regard to their times of fasting[y] and lamentation.[z] [32]Esther's decree confirmed these regulations about Purim, and it was written down in the records.

The Greatness of Mordecai

10 King Xerxes imposed tribute throughout the empire, to its distant shores.[a] [2]And all his acts of power and might, together with a full account of the greatness of Mordecai,[b] whom the king had promoted,[c] are they not written in the book of the annals[d] of the kings of Media and Persia? [3]Mordecai the Jew was second[e] in rank[f] to King Xerxes,[g] preeminent among the Jews, and held in high esteem by his many fellow Jews, because he worked for the good of his people and spoke up for the welfare of all the Jews.[h]

9:19 [i]S Est 3:7 [j]Dt 16:11, 14; S Est 2:9; Rev 11:10 **9:22** [k]S Est 4:14 [l]Ne 8:12; Ps 30:11-12 [m]S 2Ki 25:30 [n]S Ne 8:10 **9:24** [o]S Ex 17:8-16 [p]S Est 3:7 [q]S Lev 16:8 [r]Est 3:6 **9:25** [s]Ps 7:16 [t]S Dt 21:22-23 [u]Est 7:10 **9:26** [v]S Est 3:7

9:29 [w]Est 2:15 **9:30** [x]S Est 1:1 **9:31** [y]S Est 4:16 [z]Est 4:1-3 **10:1** [a]Ps 72:10; 97:1 **10:2** [b]S Est 8:15 [c]S Ge 41:44 [d]S Est 2:23 **10:3** [e]Da 5:7 [f]Ge 41:43 [g]Ge 41:40 [h]Ne 2:10; Jer 29:4-7; Da 6:3

[a] 25 Or *when Esther came before the king*

---

cating that Mordecai wrote the book of Esther; however, the more natural understanding is that he recorded the events in the letters he sent.

9:22 *presents of food.* See note on 2:9; cf. Ne 8:10,12.

9:24,26 *pur.* See note on 3:7.

9:25 *come back onto his own head.* See notes on v. 1; Pr 26:27.

9:31 *fasting.* See notes on 4:3,16. No date is assigned for this fast. Jews traditionally observe the 13th of Adar, Haman's propitious day (see 3:7,13), as a fast ("the fast of Esther") before the celebration of Purim. These three days of victory celebration on the 13th–15th days of Adar rhetorically balance the three days of Esther's fasting prior to interceding with the king (4:16).

10:1–2 The reference to this taxation may represent material in the author's source, to which he directs the reader for additional information and confirmation (see note on 2:23).

10:2 This verse indicates that the book of Esther was written after the death of Xerxes (cf. 1Ki 11:41; 14:19,29 and often in 1,2 Kings).

THE BOOKS OF POETRY

The books of poetry vary in literary form and content, but in general they contain some of the world's most enduring poetic achievements, not only in sacred Scripture, but also in all of ancient literature. They cover a wide variety of functions, from wisdom literature (see essay, p. 786) to the liturgical and personal prayers, hymns and worship of Israel (Psalms). Other than some narrative elements present at the beginning and end of Job and in Ecclesiastes, these books are almost entirely composed of poetry. Ancient Hebrew poetry employed a number of formulas and unique structures that require different interpretive approaches from those of Hebrew narrative. These beautiful, passionate and often deeply personal writings are a reflection of the hearts of the writers and of the heart of God. For their theology, see Introductions to Job, Psalms, Proverbs, Ecclesiastes and Song of Songs.

WISDOM LITERATURE

An ancient tradition among the Jews divided the collection of their holy books into three major divisions: the Law (Pentateuch), the Prophets (Former and Latter) and the Writings. Included within the third division are Psalms and Wisdom materials such as Job, Proverbs and Ecclesiastes (also some psalms and probably the Song of Songs — see introduction to that book: Interpretation).

This wisdom literature is usually associated with the sages, who are mentioned along with priests and prophets as an important force in Israelite society (see, e.g., Jer 18:18 and note). These gifted persons were recognized as possessing wide knowledge of the created world (see 1Ki 4:29 – 34), special insight into human affairs (as exemplified by proverbs) and exceptionally good judgment regarding courses of action to be followed to attain success in various enterprises (see 2Sa 16:15 – 23). In general, priests and prophets dealt with religious and moral concerns (proclaiming, teaching, interpreting and applying God's word to his people), whereas the sages generally focused more on the practical aspects of how life should be guided in the created order of things (Proverbs) and on the intellectual challenges that arise from the ambiguities of human experience (Job, Ecclesiastes).

זה שלמה המלך העושה משפט משתי

Hebrew manuscript (c. AD 1280) shows Solomon seated on his throne. Solomon is usually associated with wisdom literature such as Proverbs, Ecclesiastes and Song of Songs.

Z. Radovan/www.BibleLandPictures.com

Israel's sages reflected on life in light of God's special revelations to his people, but for their unique contribution to understanding how people ought to live in God's world they drew heavily on human experience of the created order. In this they learned much from the sages and wisdom traditions of other peoples. Comparison of their writings with those of their neighbors discloses their acquaintance with the larger intellectual world of the ancient Near East but also the distinctive perspective they brought to their reflections on the human condition.

JOB

INTRODUCTION

Author

Although most of the book consists of the words of Job and his friends, Job himself was not the author. We may be sure that the author was an Israelite, since he (not Job or his friends) frequently uses the Israelite covenant name for God (Yahweh; NIV "the LORD"). In the prologue (chs. 1 – 2), divine discourses (38:1 — 42:6) and epilogue (42:7 – 17), "LORD" occurs a total of 25 times, while in the rest of the book (chs. 3 – 37) it appears only once (12:9).

This unknown author probably had access to a tradition (oral or written) about an ancient righteous man who endured great suffering with remarkable "perseverance" (Jas 5:11; see note there) and without turning against God (see Eze 14:14,20), a tradition he put to use for his own purposes. While the author preserves much of the archaic and non-Israelite flavor in the language of Job and his friends, he also reveals his own style as a writer of wisdom literature. The book's profound insights, its literary structures and the quality of its rhetoric all display the author's genius.

a quick look

Author:
Unknown

Audience:
God's people

Date:
Unknown, though Job himself probably lived during the patriarchal period

Theme:
This wisdom book deals with the question of whether God is a God of justice in the light of all of life's perplexities, such as human suffering.

Date

Two dates are involved: (1) that of Job himself and (2) that of the composition of the book. The latter could be dated anytime from the reign of Solomon to the time of Israel's exile in Babylonia. Although the author was an Israelite, he mentions nothing of Israel's history. He had an account of a non-Israelite sage, Job (1:1), who probably lived in the second millennium BC (2000 – 1000). Like the Hebrew patriarchs, Job lived more than 100 years (42:16). Like them, his wealth was measured in livestock and servants (1:3), and like them he acted as priest for his family (1:5). The raiding of Sabean (1:15) and Chaldean (1:17) tribes fits the second millennium, as does the mention of the *keśiṭah*, "a piece of silver," in 42:11 (see Ge 33:19; Jos 24:32). The discovery of a Targum (Aramaic paraphrase) on

Job was a great man with thousands of animals, including sheep, camels, oxen and donkeys. The animals and servants were the first things taken from Job (1:14–17).

Job dating to the first or second century BC (the earliest written Targum yet discovered) makes a very late date for composition highly unlikely.

Language and Text

In many places Job is difficult to translate because of its many unusual words and its style. For that reason, modern translations frequently differ widely. Even the pre-Christian translator(s) of Job into Greek (the Septuagint) seem(s) often to have been perplexed. The Septuagint of Job is about 400 lines shorter than the accepted Hebrew text, and it may be that the translator(s) simply omitted lines he (they) did not understand. The early Syriac (Peshitta), Aramaic (Targum) and Latin (Vulgate) translators had similar difficulties.

Setting and Perspective

While it may be that the author intended his book to be a contribution to an ongoing high-level discussion of major theological issues in an exclusive company of learned scholars, it seems more likely that he intended his story to be told to godly sufferers who, like Job, were struggling with the crisis of faith brought on by prolonged, bitter suffering. He seems to sit too close to the suffering — to be more the sympathetic and compassionate pastor than the detached theologian or philosopher. He has heard what the learned theologians of his day have been saying about the ways of God and what brings on suffering, and he lets their voices be heard. And he knows that the godly sufferers of his day have also heard the "wisdom" of the learned and have internalized it as the wisdom of the ages. But he also knows what "miserable" comfort (16:2) that so-called wisdom gives — that it only rubs salt in the wounds and creates a stumbling block for faith. Against that wisdom he has no rational arguments to marshal. But he has a story to tell that challenges it at its very roots and speaks to the struggling faith of the sufferer. In effect he says to the godly sufferer,

"Forget the logical arguments spun out by those who sit together at their ease and discuss the ways of God, and forget those voices in your own heart that are little more than echoes of their pronouncements. Let me tell you a story."

Theological Theme and Message

When good people suffer, the human spirit struggles to understand. Throughout recorded history people have asked: If God is almighty and is truly good, how can he allow such an outrage? The way this question has often been put leaves open three possibilities: (1) God is not almighty after all; (2) God is not just; (3) humans may be innocent. In ancient Israel, however, it was indisputable that God is almighty, that he is perfectly just and that no human is pure in his sight. These three assumptions were also fundamental to the theology of Job and his friends. Simple logic then dictated the conclusion: Every person's suffering is indicative of the measure of their guilt in the eyes of God.

But what thus appeared to be theologically self-evident and unassailable in the abstract was often in radical tension with actual human experience. There were those whose godliness was genuine, whose moral character was upright and who had kept themselves from great transgression, but who nonetheless were made to suffer bitterly (see, e.g., Ps 73). In the speeches of Job 3–37, we hear on the one hand the flawless logic but wounding thrusts of those who insisted on the traditional theology and on the other hand the writhing of soul of the righteous sufferer (see note on 5:27).

The author of the book of Job broke out of the tight, logical mold of the traditional orthodox theology of his day. He saw that it led to a dead end—that it had no way to cope with the suffering of godly people. Instead of logical arguments, he tells a story. And in his story he shifts the angle of perspective. All around him, among theologians and common people alike, were those who attempted to solve the "God problem" in the face of human suffering at the expense of humans (they must all deserve what they get). The author of Job, on the other hand, gave encouragement to godly sufferers by showing them that their suffering provided an occasion like no other for exemplifying what true godliness is for human beings.

He begins by introducing a third party into the equation. The relationship between God and humans is not exclusive and closed. Among God's creatures there is the great adversary (see chs. 1–2). Incapable of contending with God hand to hand, he is bent on frustrating God's creation enterprise centered on God's relationship with the creature that bears his image. As tempter he seeks to alienate humans from God (see Ge 3; Mt 4:1); as accuser (one of the names by which he is called, *śaṭan*, means "accuser" or "adversary" [see note on 1:6]) he seeks to alienate God from humans (see Zec 3:1; Rev 12:9–10). His all-consuming purpose is to drive a wedge between God and humans to effect an alienation that cannot be reconciled.

When God calls up the name of Job before the accuser and testifies to his righteousness, Satan attempts with one crafty thrust both to assail God's beloved and to show up God as a fool. He charges that Job's godliness is mere self-serving; he is righteous only because it pays (see 1:9 and note). If God will only let Satan tempt Job by breaking the link between righteousness and blessing, he will expose this man and all righteous people as the frauds they really are.

The adversary is sure he has found an opening to accomplish his purpose in the very structure of creation. Humans are totally dependent on God for their lives and well-being. That fact can

When good people suffer, the human spirit struggles to understand. Throughout recorded history people have asked: How can this be? If God is almighty and "holds the whole world in his hands," and if he is truly good, how can he allow such an outrage?

occasion one of humankind's greatest temptations: to love the gifts rather than the Giver, to try to please God merely for the sake of his benefits, to be "religious" and "good" only because it pays. If he is right — if the godliness of the righteous can be shown to be evil — then a chasm of alienation stands between God and human beings that cannot be bridged. Then even the godliest among them would be shown to be ungodly. God's whole enterprise in creation and redemption would be shown to be radically flawed, and God can only sweep it all away in awful judgment.

The accusation, once raised, cannot be ignored; it strikes too deeply into the very structure of creation. So God lets the adversary have his way with Job (within specified limits). From this comes Job's profound anguish, robbed as he is of every sign of God's favor so that God becomes for him the great enigma. And his righteousness is also assailed on earth through the logic of the orthodox theology of his friends. Alone, he agonizes. But he knows in the depths of his heart that his godliness has been authentic and that someday he will be vindicated (see 13:18; 14:13 – 17; 16:19; 19:25 – 27). And in spite of all, though he may curse the day of his birth (ch. 3) and chide God for treating him unjustly (9:28 – 35), he will not curse God (as his wife, the human nearest his heart, proposed [see 2:9] and as Satan said he would [see notes on 1:11 – 12; 2:10; 3:3; 9:2 – 3]).

So the adversary is silenced, and God's delight in the godly is vindicated. Robbed of every sign of God's favor, Job refuses to repudiate his Maker. Godly Job, dependent creature that he is, passes the supreme test occasioned by his creaturely condition and the adversary's accusation.

This first test of Job's godliness inescapably involves a second that challenges his godliness at a level no less deep than the first. For the test that sprang from Satan's accusation to be real, Job had to be kept in the dark about what is taking place in God's council chamber. But Job belongs to a race of creatures endowed with wisdom, understanding and insight (something of their godlikeness) that cannot rest until it knows and understands all it can about the creation and the ways of God. Job's friends confidently assume that the logic of their theology can account for all of God's ways. However, Job's experience makes bitterly clear to him that their "wisdom" cannot fathom the truth of his situation. Yet Job's wisdom is also at a loss to understand. So when the dialogue between Job and his three "wise" friends finally stalemates, the author introduces a poetic essay on wisdom (ch. 28) that exposes the limits of all human wisdom (see note on 28:1 – 28). Standing as it does at a major juncture between the dialogue (chs. 3 – 27) and the final, major speeches (chs. 29 – 37), this authorial commentary on what has been going on in the stalemated dialogue anticipates God's final word to Job.

In the end the adversary is silenced. Job's friends are silenced. Job is silenced. But God is not. And when he speaks, it is to the godly Job that he speaks, resulting in the silence of regret for hasty words in days of suffering and the silence of repose in the ways of the Almighty (see 38:1 — 42:6). Furthermore, as his heavenly friend, God hears Job's intercessions for his associates (42:7 – 10a) and restores Job's blessed state (42:10b – 17).

In summary, the author's pastoral word to godly sufferers is that God treasures their righteousness above all else. And Satan knows that if he is to thwart the all-encompassing purpose of God he must assail the godly righteousness of human beings (see 1:21 – 22; 2:9 – 10; 23:8,10; cf. Ge 15:6; Hab 2:4). At stake in the suffering of the truly godly is the outcome of the titanic struggle between the great adversary and God. At the same time the author gently reminds the godly sufferer that true, godly wisdom is to reverently love God more than all his gifts and to trust the wise goodness of God even though his ways are often beyond the power of human wisdom to fathom (see Isa 55:8 – 9). So here is presented a profound, but painfully practical, drama that wrestles with the wisdom and justice of the Great King's rule (a "theodicy"; cf. chart, p. xxii ["Babylonian Theodicy"]). Righteous sufferers must trust in, acknowledge, serve and submit to the omniscient and omnipotent Sovereign, realizing that some suffering is the result of unseen, spiritual conflicts between the kingdom of God and the kingdom of Satan — between the power of light and the power of darkness (cf. Eph 6:10 – 18; Col 1:12 – 13 and notes). Even though God's people may not always understand why God acts the way he does, they should rest in the assurance of knowing he understands.

***Job and His Friends*, by Gustave Dore (1832-1883)**
Gustave Dore

Literary Form and Structure

Like some other ancient compositions (cf., e.g., the Code of Hammurapi; see chart, p. xxii), the book of Job has a sandwich literary structure: prologue (prose), main body (poetry), and epilogue (prose), revealing a creative composition, not an arbitrary compilation. Some of Job's words are lament (cf. ch. 3 and many shorter poems in his speeches), but the form of lament is unique to Job and often unlike the regular format of most lament psalms (except Ps 88). Much of the book takes the form of legal disputation. Although the friends come to console him, they end up arguing over the reason for Job's suffering. The argument breaks down in ch. 27, and Job then proceeds to make his final appeal to God for vindication (chs. 29 – 31). The wisdom poem in ch. 28 appears to be the words of the author, who sees the failure of the dispute as evidence of a lack of wisdom. So in praise of true wisdom he centers his structural apex between the three cycles of dialogue-dispute (chs. 3 – 27) and the three monologues: Job's (chs. 29 – 31), Elihu's (chs. 32 – 37) and God's (38:1 — 42:6). Job's monologue turns directly to God for a legal decision: that he is innocent of the charges his counselors have leveled against him. Elihu's monologue — another human perspective on why people suffer — rebukes Job but moves beyond the punishment theme to the value of divine chastening and God's redemptive purpose in it. God's monologue gives the divine perspective: Job is not condemned, but neither is a logical or legal answer given to why Job has suffered. That remains a mystery to Job, though the readers are ready for Job's restoration in the epilogue because they have had the heavenly vantage point of the prologue all along. So the literary structure and the theological significance of the book are beautifully tied together.

Outline

I. Prologue (chs. 1 – 2)
  A. Job's Happiness (1:1 – 5)
  B. Job's Testing (1:6 — 2:13)
    1. Satan's first accusation (1:6 – 12)
    2. Job's faith despite loss of family and property (1:13 – 22)
    3. Satan's second accusation (2:1 – 6)
    4. Job's faith during personal suffering (2:7 – 10)
    5. The coming of the three friends (2:11 – 13)
II. Dialogue-Dispute (chs. 3 – 27)
  A. Job's Opening Lament (ch. 3)
  B. First Cycle of Speeches (chs. 4 – 14)
    1. Eliphaz (chs. 4 – 5)
    2. Job's reply (chs. 6 – 7)
    3. Bildad (ch. 8)
    4. Job's reply (chs. 9 – 10)
    5. Zophar (ch. 11)
    6. Job's reply (chs. 12 – 14)
  C. Second Cycle of Speeches (chs. 15 – 21)
    1. Eliphaz (ch. 15)
    2. Job's reply (chs. 16 – 17)
    3. Bildad (ch. 18)
    4. Job's reply (ch. 19)
    5. Zophar (ch. 20)
    6. Job's reply (ch. 21)
  D. Third Cycle of Speeches (chs. 22 – 26)
    1. Eliphaz (ch. 22)
    2. Job's reply (chs. 23 – 24)
    3. Bildad (ch. 25)
    4. Job's reply (ch. 26)
  E. Job's Closing Discourse (ch. 27)
III. Interlude on Wisdom (ch. 28)
IV. Monologues (29:1 — 42:6)
  A. Job's Call for Vindication (chs. 29 – 31)
    1. His past honor and blessing (ch. 29)
    2. His present dishonor and suffering (ch. 30)
    3. His protestations of innocence and final oath (ch. 31)

- B. Elihu's Speeches (chs. 32 – 37)
  1. Introduction (32:1 – 5)
  2. The speeches themselves (32:6 — 37:24)
     - a. First speech (32:6 — 33:33)
     - b. Second speech (ch. 34)
     - c. Third speech (ch. 35)
     - d. Fourth speech (chs. 36 – 37)
- C. Divine Discourses (38:1 — 42:6)
  1. God's first discourse (38:1 — 40:2)
  2. Job's response (40:3 – 5)
  3. God's second discourse (40:6 — 41:34)
  4. Job's repentance (42:1 – 6)

V. Epilogue (42:7 – 17)
- A. God's Verdict (42:7 – 9)
- B. Job's Restoration (42:10 – 17)

Prologue

1 In the land of Uz[a] there lived a man whose name was Job.[b] This man was blameless[c] and upright;[d] he feared God[e] and shunned evil.[f] 2 He had seven sons[g] and three daughters,[h] 3 and he owned seven thousand sheep, three thousand camels, five hundred yoke of oxen and five hundred donkeys,[i] and had a large number of servants.[j] He was the greatest man[k] among all the people of the East.[l]

4 His sons used to hold feasts[m] in their homes on their birthdays, and they would invite their three sisters to eat and drink with them. 5 When a period of feasting had run its course, Job would make arrangements for them to be purified.[n] Early in the morning he would sacrifice a burnt offering[o] for each of them, thinking, "Perhaps my children have sinned[p] and cursed God[q] in their hearts." This was Job's regular custom.

6 One day the angels[a][r] came to present themselves before the LORD, and Satan[b][s] also came with them.[t] 7 The LORD said to Satan, "Where have you come from?"

Satan answered the LORD, "From roaming throughout the earth, going back and forth on it."[u]

8 Then the LORD said to Satan, "Have you considered my servant Job?[v] There is no one on earth like him; he is blameless and upright, a man who fears God[w] and shuns evil."[x]

9 "Does Job fear God for nothing?"[y] Satan replied. 10 "Have you not put a hedge[z] around him and his household and everything he has?[a] You have blessed the work of his hands, so that his flocks and herds are spread throughout the land.[b] 11 But now stretch out your hand and strike everything he has,[c] and he will surely curse you to your face."[d]

12 The LORD said to Satan, "Very well, then, everything he has[e] is in your power, but on the man himself do not lay a finger."[f]

Then Satan went out from the presence of the LORD.

13 One day when Job's sons and daughters[g] were feasting[h] and drinking wine at the oldest brother's house, 14 a messenger came to Job and said, "The oxen were plowing and the donkeys were grazing nearby, 15 and the Sabeans[j] attacked and made off with them. They put the servants to the sword, and I am the only one who has escaped to tell you!"

[a] 6 Hebrew *the sons of God* [b] 6 Hebrew *satan* means *adversary.*

1:1 [a]S Ge 10:23 [b]Eze 14:14, 20; Jas 5:11 [c]S Ge 6:9; S Job 23:10 [d]Job 23:7; Ps 11:7; 107:42; Pr 21:29; Mic 7:2 [e]S Ge 22:12 [f]ver 8; S Dt 4:6; Job 2:3; 1Th 5:22 **1:2** [g]S Ru 4:15 [h]ver 13,18; Job 42:13; Ps 127:3; 144:12 **1:3** [i]S Ge 13:2 [j]S Ge 12:16 [k]ver 8; Job 29:25 [l]S Ge 25:6; Job 42:10; Ps 103:10 **1:4** [m]ver 13,18 **1:5** [n]S Ne 12:30 [o]S Ge 8:20 [p]Job 8:4 [q]1Ki 21:10,13; Ps 10:3; 74:10 **1:6** [r]S 1Ki 22:19; *fn* Ge 6:2 [s]S 2Sa 24:1; S 2Ch 18:21; S Ps 109:6; Lk 22:31 [t]Job 2:1 **1:7** [u]S Ge 3:1; 1Pe 5:8 **1:8** [v]S Jos 1:7 [w]Ps 25:12; 112:1; 128:4 [x]S ver 1; S Ex 20:20

1:9 [y]1Ti 6:5 **1:10** [z]S 1Sa 25:16 [a]ver 12; Job 2:4; Ps 34:7 [b]ver 3; Job 8:7; 29:6; 42:12,17 **1:11** [c]Job 19:21; Lk 22:31 [d]Lev 24:11; Job 2:5; Isa 3:8; 65:3; Rev 12:9-10 **1:12** [e]S ver 10 [f]Job 2:6; 1Co 10:13 **1:13** [g]S ver 2 [h]S ver 4 **1:14** [i]Ge 36:24 **1:15** [j]S Ge 10:7; S Job 9:24

1:1 *land of Uz.* A large territory east of the Jordan Valley (see v. 3), which included Edom in the south (see Ge 36:28; La 4:21) and Aram in the north (see Ge 10:23; 22:21; see also note on 1Ch 18:5). *blameless and upright.* Spiritually and morally upright (see note on Ps 26:1). This does not mean that Job was sinless. He later defends his moral integrity but also admits he is a sinner (see 6:24; 7:21 and note). *feared God.* See 28:28; Pr 3:7 and note; see also note on Ge 20:11.

1:2 *seven.* An ideal number, signifying completeness (see notes on 42:13; Ru 4:15).

1:3 *seven thousand sheep.* See note on 42:12; see also photo, p. 788. Job's enormous wealth was in livestock, not land (see Ge 12:16 and note; 13:2; 26:14). *camels.* See note on Ge 12:16. *donkeys.* The Hebrew for this word is feminine in form. Donkeys that produced offspring were very valuable. *people of the East.* The Hebrew for this phrase is translated "eastern peoples" in Ge 29:1; Jdg 6:3 (see note there).

1:5 *period of feasting.* On special occasions, feasts might last a week (see Ge 29:27; Jdg 14:12). *purified.* Made ceremonially clean in preparation for the sacrifices he offered for his children (see Ex 19:10,14, where the Hebrew for this verb is translated "consecrate"). *he would sacrifice.* Before the ceremonial laws of Moses were introduced, the father of the household acted as priest (see Ge 15:9–10).

1:6 *angels came to present themselves.* See NIV text note here and on 2:1; 38:7. They came as members of the heavenly council who stand in the presence of God (see 1Ki 22:19 and note; Ps 89:5–7; Jer 23:18,22 and note on 23:18). *Satan.* Lit. "the accuser" or "the adversary" (see NIV text note; see also Rev 12:10 and note). In Job the Hebrew for this word is always preceded by the definite article. In the Hebrew of 1Ch 21:1 the article is not used, because "Satan" had become a proper name by that time.

1:7 *The LORD.* That is, Yahweh, the Israelite covenant name for God (see Introduction: Author; see also note on Ge 2:4).

1:8 *Have you considered … Job?* The Lord, not Satan, initiates the dialogue that leads to the testing of Job. He holds up Job as one against whom "the accuser" can lodge no accusation. *my servant.* See 42:7–8 and note; a designation for one who stands in a special relationship with God and is loyal in service (e.g., Moses, Nu 12:7; David, 2Sa 7:5; see Isa 42:1 and note; 52:13; 53:11).

1:9 "The accuser" boldly accuses the man God commends. He charges that the righteousness of Job in which God expresses such delight is actually self-serving. This is the heart of Satan's attack on both God and his faithful servant.

1:10 *hedge.* Symbolizes protection (see Isa 5:5; contrast Job 3:23).

1:11 *stretch out your hand and strike.* See 4:5. *he will … curse you.* But Job never did curse God (see v. 12; 2:9–10 and notes). *curse.* See note on Ge 12:3.

1:12 Satan, the accuser, is given power to afflict (v. 12a) but is kept on a leash (v. 12b). In all the evil he effects among human beings (vv. 15,17) or in nature (vv. 16,19), Satan is under God's power (compare 1Ch 21:1 with 2Sa 24:1; see 1Sa 16:14 and note; 2Sa 24:16; 1Co 5:5 and note; 2Co 12:7; Heb 2:14). The contest, however, is not a sham. Will Job curse God to his face? If Job does not, the accuser will be proven false and God's delight in Job will be vindicated.

1:15 *Sabeans.* Probably south Arabians from Sheba, whose descendants became wealthy traders in spices, gold and precious stones (see the account of the queen of Sheba in 1Ki 10:1–13; see also Ps 72:10,15; Isa 60:6; Jer 6:20; Eze 27:2

[16]While he was still speaking, another messenger came and said, "The fire of
God fell from the heavens[k] and burned up
the sheep and the servants,[l] and I am the
only one who has escaped to tell you!"
[17]While he was still speaking, another messenger came and said, "The Chaldeans[m] formed three raiding parties and
swept down on your camels and made off
with them. They put the servants to the
sword, and I am the only one who has escaped to tell you!"
[18]While he was still speaking, yet another messenger came and said, "Your sons
and daughters[n] were feasting[o] and drinking wine at the oldest brother's house,
[19]when suddenly a mighty wind[p] swept in
from the desert and struck the four corners of the house. It collapsed on them
and they are dead,[q] and I am the only one
who has escaped to tell you!"[r]
[20]At this, Job got up and tore his robe[s]
and shaved his head.[t] Then he fell to the
ground in worship[u] [21]and said:

"Naked I came from my mother's
womb,
and naked I will depart.[a][v]
The LORD gave and the LORD has taken
away;[w]
may the name of the LORD be
praised."[x]

[22]In all this, Job did not sin by charging
God with wrongdoing.[y]

2 On another day the angels[b][z] came to
present themselves before the LORD,
and Satan also came with them[a] to present
himself before him. [2]And the LORD said to
Satan, "Where have you come from?"
Satan answered the LORD, "From roaming throughout the earth, going back and
forth on it."[b]
[3]Then the LORD said to Satan, "Have you
considered my servant Job? There is no
one on earth like him; he is blameless and
upright, a man who fears God and shuns
evil.[c] And he still maintains his integrity,[d]
though you incited me against him to ruin
him without any reason."[e]
[4]"Skin for skin!" Satan replied. "A man
will give all he has[f] for his own life. [5]But
now stretch out your hand and strike his
flesh and bones,[g] and he will surely curse
you to your face."[h]
[6]The LORD said to Satan, "Very well,

[a] 21 Or *will return there* [b] 1 Hebrew *the sons of God*

1:16 [k]S 1Ki 18:38; 2Ki 1:12; Job 20:26 [l]S Ge 18:17; S Lev 10:2; S Nu 11:1-3 **1:17** [m]S Ge 11:28, 31; S Job 9:24 **1:18** [n]S ver 2 [o]S ver 4 **1:19** [p]Ps 11:6; Isa 5:28; 21:1; Jer 4:11; 13:24; 18:17; Eze 17:10; Hos 13:15; Mt 7:25 [q]Job 16:7; 19:13-15 [r]Eze 24:26 **1:20** [s]S Ge 37:29; S Mk 14:63 [t]Isa 3:24; 15:2; 22:12; Jer 7:29; 16:6; Eze 27:31; 29:18; Mic 1:16 [u]1Pe 5:6 **1:21** [v]Ecc 5:15; 1Ti 6:7 [w]Ru 1:21; 1Sa 2:7 [x]S Jdg 10:15; Job 2:10; Ecc 7:14; Jer 40:2; S Eph 5:20; 1Th 5:18; Jas 5:11 **1:22** [y]Job 2:10; Ps 39:1; Pr 10:19; 13:3; Isa 53:7; Ro 9:20 **2:1** [z]*fn* Ge 6:2 [a]S Job 1:6 **2:2** [b]S Ge 3:1 **2:3** [c]S Ex 20:20; S Job 1:1, 8 [d]Job 6:29; 13:18; 27:6; 31:6; 32:1; 40:8 [e]Job 9:17; Ps 44:17 **2:4** [f]S Job 1:10 **2:5** [g]Job 16:8; 19:20; 33:21; Ps 102:5; La 4:8 [h]S Ex 20:7; S Job 1:11

Lamashtu, a demon from Mesopotamian mythology, is portrayed here as the large figure in the lower center while the sick person just above its head is accompanied by physicians on either side. In the ancient Near East, illnesses like Job's were often met with both magic and religion—a combination of incantations and medical treatments.

Joel 3:8). Job 6:19 calls the Sabeans "traveling merchants" and associates them with Tema (about 350 miles southeast of Jerusalem).
1:16 *fire of God.* Lightning (see Nu 11:1 and note; 1Ki 18:38; 2Ki 1:12).
1:17 *Chaldeans.* A people who were nomadic until c. 1000 BC, when they settled in southern Mesopotamia and later became the nucleus of Nebuchadnezzar's Neo-Babylonian Empire (see note on Ezr 5:12).
1:19 *mighty wind.* Tornado.
1:20 *At this, Job got up.* He is silent until his children are killed. *tore his robe and shaved his head.* In mourning (see notes on Ge 37:34; Isa 15:2).
1:21 *depart.* See NIV text note; see also Ge 2:7; 3:19 and note. *The LORD gave and the LORD has taken away.* Job's faith leads him to see the sovereign God's hand at work, and that gives him repose even in the face of calamity.
2:1–3 Except for the final sentence, this passage is almost identical to 1:6–8. He who accused Job of having a deceitful motive is now shown to have a deceitful motive himself: to discredit the Lord through Job.
2:3 *you incited me.* God cannot be stirred up to do things against his will. Though it is not always clear how, everything that happens is part of his divine purpose (see 42:2 and note).
2:4 *Skin for skin!* Probably a proverbial statement equivalent to our "quid pro quo" (this for that).
2:5 *strike his flesh and bones.* See 1:11–12; cf. Ge 2:23; Lk 24:39. *he will . . . curse you.* See note on 1:11.

then, he is in your hands;[i] but you must
spare his life."[j]
7 So Satan went out from the presence
of the LORD and afflicted Job with painful sores from the soles of his feet to the
crown of his head.[k] 8 Then Job took a piece
of broken pottery and scraped himself
with it as he sat among the ashes.[l]
9 His wife said to him, "Are you still
maintaining your integrity?[m] Curse God
and die!"[n]
10 He replied, "You are talking like a foolish[a] woman. Shall we accept good from
God, and not trouble?"[o]
In all this, Job did not sin in what he
said.[p]

11 When Job's three friends, Eliphaz the
Temanite,[q] Bildad the Shuhite[r] and Zophar
the Naamathite,[s] heard about all the troubles that had come upon him, they set
out from their homes and met together by
agreement to go and sympathize with him
and comfort him.[t] 12 When they saw him
from a distance, they could hardly recognize him;[u] they began to weep aloud,[v] and
they tore their robes[w] and sprinkled dust on
their heads.[x] 13 Then they sat on the ground[y]
with him for seven days and seven nights.[z]
No one said a word to him,[a] because they
saw how great his suffering was.

Job Speaks

3 After this, Job opened his mouth and
cursed the day of his birth.[b] 2 He said:

3 "May the day of my birth perish,
and the night that said, 'A boy is
conceived!'[c]
4 That day—may it turn to darkness;
may God above not care about it;
may no light shine on it.
5 May gloom and utter darkness[d] claim it
once more;
may a cloud settle over it;
may blackness overwhelm it.
6 That night—may thick darkness[e]
seize it;
may it not be included among the
days of the year
nor be entered in any of the months.
7 May that night be barren;
may no shout of joy[f] be heard in it.
8 May those who curse days[b] curse that
day,[g]
those who are ready to rouse
Leviathan.[h]
9 May its morning stars become dark;
may it wait for daylight in vain
and not see the first rays of dawn,[i]
10 for it did not shut the doors of the
womb on me
to hide trouble from my eyes.

[a] 10 The Hebrew word rendered *foolish* denotes moral deficiency. [b] 8 Or *curse the sea*

2:6 [i] 2Co 12:7 [j] S Job 1:12 **2:7** [k] S Dt 28:35; S Job 16:16 **2:8** [l] Ge 18:27; Est 4:3; Job 16:15; 19:9; 30:19; 42:6; Ps 7:5; Isa 58:5; 61:3; Jer 6:26; La 3:29; Eze 26:16; Jnh 3:5-8,6; Mt 11:21 **2:9** [m] Job 6:29; 13:15; 27:5; 33:9; 35:2; 1Th 5:8 [n] S Ex 20:7; S 2Ki 6:33 **2:10** [o] S Job 1:21; S Ecc 2:24; La 3:38 [p] S Job 1:22; S 6:24; Jas 1:12; 5:11 **2:11** [q] S Ge 36:11 [r] S Ge 25:2 [s] Job 11:1; 20:1 [t] S Ge 37:35; S Job 6:10; Jn 11:19 **2:12** [u] Job 17:7; Isa 52:14 [v] S 2Sa 15:23 [w] S Ge 37:29; S Mk 14:63 [x] S Jos 7:6; S 2Sa 1:2 **2:13** [y] Isa 3:26; 47:1; Jer 48:18; La 2:10; Eze 26:16; Jnh 3:6; Hag 2:22 [z] S Ge 50:10 [a] Pr 17:28; Isa 23:2; 47:5

3:1 [b] Jer 15:10; 20:14 **3:3** [c] ver 11,16; Job 10:18-19; Ecc 4:2; 6:3; Jer 20:14-18; Mt 26:24 **3:5** [d] Job 10:21,22; 34:22; 38:17; Ps 23:4; 44:19; 88:12; Jer 2:6; 13:16 **3:6** [e] Job 23:17; 30:26 **3:7** [f] Ps 20:5; 33:3; 65:13; Isa 26:19; Jer 51:48 **3:8** [g] Job 10:18; Jer 20:14 [h] S Ge 1:21; Job 41:1,8,10,25; Ps 74:14; 104:26 **3:9** [i] Job 41:18; Hab 3:4

2:6 *spare his life.* Satan is still limited by God. If Job should die, neither God nor Job could be vindicated.

2:7 The precise nature of Job's sickness is uncertain, but its symptoms were painful festering sores over the whole body (7:5), nightmares (7:14), scabs that peeled and became black (30:28,30), disfigurement and a revolting appearance (2:12; 19:19), bad breath (19:17), excessive thinness (17:7; 19:20), fever (30:30) and pain day and night (30:17). *sores.* The Hebrew for this word is translated "boils" in Ex 9:9; Lev 13:18; 2Ki 20:7. Cf. photo, p. 795.

2:8 *ashes.* Symbolic of mourning (see 42:6; Est 4:3; cf. Jnh 3:6, which speaks of sitting in dust).

2:9 *Curse God.* The Hebrew for this expression here and in 1:5 employs a euphemism (lit. "Bless God"). *and die.* Since nothing but death is left for Job, his wife wants him to provoke God to administer the final stroke due to all who curse him (Lev 24:10–16).

2:10 *Shall we accept good from God, and not trouble?* A key theme of the book: Trouble and suffering are not merely punishment for sin; for God's people they may serve as a trial (as here) or as a discipline that culminates in spiritual gain (see note on 5:17–26; see also Dt 8:5; 2Sa 7:14; Ps 94:12; Pr 3:11–12; 1Co 11:32; Heb 12:5–11 and notes). Job's reply to his wife silences "the accuser," who is not heard from again. And true to his word here, Job refuses to turn his back on God throughout the long struggle that follows. He faces God with questions, complaints, accusations and appeals, but he continues to face him—and never curses him, as Satan said he would (v. 5; 1:11 [see note there]).

2:11 *Eliphaz.* An Edomite name (see note on Ge 36:11). *Temanite.* Teman was a village in Edom, south of the Dead Sea (see Ge 36:11; Jer 49:7; Eze 25:13; Am 1:12; Ob 9 and notes). *Shuhite.* Bildad may have been a descendant of Shuah, the youngest son of Abraham and Keturah (Ge 25:2).

2:12 *could hardly recognize him.* Cf. Isa 52:14; 53:3. *tore their robes and sprinkled dust on their heads.* Visible signs of mourning (see note on 1:20).

2:13 *sat on the ground with him.* See Eze 3:15; possibly an expression of sympathy or shock. *seven.* The number of completeness (see 1:2; Ge 50:10; 1Sa 31:13 and note; see also note on Ru 4:15). *No one said a word to him.* A wiser response than their later speeches would prove to be (see 16:2–3). See photo, p. 791.

3:1–26 Job's first speech is addressed to no one in particular. In it he simply gives expression to the depths of his suffering.

3:3 *May the day of my birth perish.* Job's very existence, which has been a joy to him because of God's favor, is now his intolerable burden. He is as close as he will ever come to cursing God, but he does not do it (see Jer 20:14–18 and note).

3:4 *may it turn to darkness.* God had said in Ge 1:3, "Let there be light." Job, using similar language, would negate God's creative act.

3:8 *those who curse days.* Eastern soothsayers, like Balaam (see Nu 22–24), who pronounced curses on people, objects and days (see note on Ge 12:3). *Leviathan.* Using vivid, figurative language, Job wishes that "those who curse days" would arouse the sea monster Leviathan (see note on Isa 27:1) to swallow the day and night of his birth (see v. 3).

11 "Why did I not perish at birth,
and die as I came from the womb?[j]
12 Why were there knees to receive me[k]
and breasts that I might be nursed?
13 For now I would be lying down[l] in
peace;
I would be asleep and at rest[m]
14 with kings and rulers of the earth,[n]
who built for themselves places now
lying in ruins,[o]
15 with princes[p] who had gold,
who filled their houses with silver.[q]
16 Or why was I not hidden away in the
ground like a stillborn child,[r]
like an infant who never saw the
light of day?[s]
17 There the wicked cease from turmoil,[t]
and there the weary are at rest.[u]
18 Captives[v] also enjoy their ease;
they no longer hear the slave
driver's[w] shout.[x]
19 The small and the great are there,[y]
and the slaves are freed from their
owners.

20 "Why is light given to those in
misery,
and life to the bitter of soul,[z]
21 to those who long for death that does
not come,[a]
who search for it more than for
hidden treasure,[b]
22 who are filled with gladness
and rejoice when they reach the
grave?[c]
23 Why is life given to a man
whose way is hidden,[d]
whom God has hedged in?[e]
24 For sighing[f] has become my daily
food;[g]
my groans[h] pour out like water.[i]
25 What I feared has come upon me;
what I dreaded[j] has happened
to me.[k]
26 I have no peace,[l] no quietness;
I have no rest,[m] but only turmoil."[n]

3:11 [j]S ver 3 **3:12** [k]S Ge 48:12; Isa 66:12 **3:13** [l]Job 17:13; 30:23 [m]ver 17; Job 7:8-10, 21; 10:22; 13:19; 14:10-12; 19:27; 21:13, 23; 27:19; Ps 139:11; Isa 8:22 **3:14** [n]Job 9:24; 12:17; Isa 14:9; Eze 32:28-32 [o]Job 15:28; Jer 51:37; Na 3:7 **3:15** [p]Job 12:21; Isa 45:1 [q]Job 15:29; 20:10; 27:17; Ps 49:16-17; Pr 13:22; 28:8; Ecc 2:26; Isa 2:7; Zep 1:11 **3:16** [r]Ps 58:8; Ecc 4:3; 6:3 [s]S ver 3; Ps 71:6 **3:17** [t]ver 26; Job 30:26; Ecc 4:2; Isa 14:3 [u]S ver 13 **3:18** [v]Isa 51:14 [w]S Ge 15:13 [x]Job 39:7 **3:19** [y]Job 9:22; 17:16; 21:33; 24:24; 30:23; Ecc 12:5 **3:20** [z]S 1Sa 1:10; Eze 27:30-31 **3:21** [a]Rev 9:6 [b]Ps 119:127; Pr 2:4 **3:22** [c]Job 7:16; Ecc 4:3; Jer 8:3 **3:23** [d]Pr 4:19; Isa 59:10; Jer 13:16; 23:12 [e]Job 6:4; 16:13; 19:6, 8, 12; Ps 88:8; La 2:4; 3:7; Hos 2:6 **3:24** [f]Ps 5:1; 38:9; Isa 35:10 [g]Job 6:7; 33:20; Ps 107:18 [h]Ps 22:1; 32:3; 38:8 [i]1Sa 1:15; Job 30:16; Ps 6:6; 22:14; 42:3, 4; 80:5; Isa 53:12; La 2:12 **3:25** [j]Job 7:9; 9:28; 30:15; Hos 13:3 [k]S Ge 42:36 **3:26** [l]Isa 48:22; Jn 14:27 [m]Job 7:4, 14; Ps 6:6; Da 4:5; Mt 11:28 [n]S ver 17; S Job 10:18; S 19:8 **4:1** [o]S Ge 36:11; Job 15:1; 22:1 **4:2** [p]Job 32:20; Jer 4:19; 20:9 **4:3** [q]Dt 32:2; Job 29:23; Hos 6:3 [r]Job 26:2; Ps 71:9; Isa 13:7; 35:3; Zep 3:16; Heb 12:12 **4:4** [s]Job 16:5; 29:16, 25; Isa 1:17 [t]Job 29:11, 15; Isa 35:3; Jer 31:8; Heb 12:12 **4:5** [u]S Jos 1:9 [v]Ru 1:13; Job 1:11; 19:21; 30:21; Ps 38:2; Isa 53:4 [w]Job 6:14; Pr 24:10 **4:6** [x]2Ki 18:19; Ps 27:3; 71:5; Pr 3:26 [y]S Ge 6:9 **4:7** [z]Job 5:11; 36:7; Ps 41:12; 2Pe 2:9 [a]Job 8:20; Ps 37:25; 91:9-10; Pr 12:21; 19:23 **4:8** [b]Job 5:3; 15:17 [c]Jdg 14:18; Job 5:6; 15:35; Ps 7:14; Isa 59:4 [d]Ps 7:15; 9:15; Pr 11:18; 22:8; Isa 17:11; Hos 8:7; 10:13; Gal 6:7-8 **4:9** [e]S Ex 15:10; S Job 41:21; 2Th 2:8 [f]S Lev 26:38; Job 40:13; Isa 25:7 **4:10** [g]Ps 22:13 [h]Ps 17:12; 22:21; Pr 28:15 [i]Job 5:15; 29:17; 36:6; 38:15; Ps 35:10; 58:6

Eliphaz

4 Then Eliphaz the Temanite[o] replied:

2 "If someone ventures a word with you,
will you be impatient?
But who can keep from speaking?[p]
3 Think how you have instructed many,[q]
how you have strengthened feeble
hands.[r]
4 Your words have supported those who
stumbled;[s]
you have strengthened faltering
knees.[t]
5 But now trouble comes to you, and
you are discouraged;[u]
it strikes[v] you, and you are
dismayed.[w]
6 Should not your piety be your
confidence[x]
and your blameless[y] ways your hope?

7 "Consider now: Who, being innocent,
has ever perished?[z]
Where were the upright ever
destroyed?[a]
8 As I have observed,[b] those who plow
evil[c]
and those who sow trouble reap it.[d]
9 At the breath of God[e] they perish;
at the blast of his anger they are no
more.[f]
10 The lions may roar[g] and growl,
yet the teeth of the great lions[h] are
broken.[i]

3:11–12,16,20–23 A series of rhetorical questions.
3:16 Since in fact his birth had taken place, the next possibility would have been a stillbirth. He would then have lived only in the grave (or Sheol), which he envisions as a place of peace and rest (vv. 13–19; see note on Ge 37:35). Such a situation would be much better than his present intolerable condition, in which he can find neither peace nor rest (v. 26).
3:18 *slave driver's shout.* As in Egypt (see Ex 5:13–14).
3:23 *whom God has hedged in.* God, who had put a hedge of protection around him (see 1:10 and note), has now, he feels, hemmed him in with turmoil (see v. 26).
4:1 *Eliphaz the Temanite.* See note on 2:11. Teman was an Edomite town noted for wisdom (see Jer 49:7). The speeches of Job's three friends contain elements of truth, but they must be carefully interpreted in context. The problem is not so much with what the friends knew but with what they did not know: God's high purpose in allowing Satan to buffet Job.
4:2 *ventures a word.* Eliphaz seems to be genuinely concerned with Job's well-being and offers a complimentary word (vv. 3–4). *impatient.* See note on 9:2–3.
4:5 *strikes you.* See 1:11; 2:5; 19:21.
4:6–7 Eliphaz counsels Job to be confident that his piety will count with God, that though God is now chastening him for some sin, it is to a good end (see v. 17; 5:17), and he can be assured that God will not destroy him along with the wicked.
4:6 *piety.* Lit. "fear (of God)" (see note on 1:1). The word is used only by Eliphaz (see 15:4; 22:4).
4:7–9 If Job is truly innocent, he will not be destroyed.
4:8–11 Just as the strongest lions eventually die (vv. 10–11), so the wicked are eventually destroyed (vv. 8–9).
4:8 *those who sow trouble reap it.* Cf. Gal 6:7–8 and notes.
4:9 *blast of his anger.* See Ex 15:7–8. God's judgment is fearfully severe.

11 The lion perishes for lack of prey,[j]
and the cubs of the lioness are scattered.[k]

12 "A word[l] was secretly brought to me,
my ears caught a whisper[m] of it.[n]
13 Amid disquieting dreams in the night,
when deep sleep falls on people,[o]
14 fear and trembling[p] seized me
and made all my bones shake.[q]
15 A spirit glided past my face,
and the hair on my body stood on end.[r]
16 It stopped,
but I could not tell what it was.
A form stood before my eyes,
and I heard a hushed voice:[s]
17 'Can a mortal be more righteous than God?[t]
Can even a strong man be more pure than his Maker?[u]
18 If God places no trust in his servants,[v]
if he charges his angels with error,[w]
19 how much more those who live in houses of clay,[x]
whose foundations[y] are in the dust,[z]
who are crushed[a] more readily than a moth![b]
20 Between dawn and dusk they are broken to pieces;
unnoticed, they perish forever.[c]
21 Are not the cords of their tent pulled up,[d]
so that they die[e] without wisdom?'[f]

5 "Call if you will, but who will answer you?[g]
To which of the holy ones[h] will you turn?
2 Resentment[i] kills a fool,
and envy slays the simple.[j]
3 I myself have seen[k] a fool taking root,[l]
but suddenly[m] his house was cursed.[n]
4 His children[o] are far from safety,[p]
crushed in court[q] without a defender.[r]
5 The hungry consume his harvest,[s]
taking it even from among thorns,
and the thirsty pant after his wealth.
6 For hardship does not spring from the soil,
nor does trouble sprout from the ground.[t]
7 Yet man is born to trouble[u]
as surely as sparks fly upward.

8 "But if I were you, I would appeal to God;
I would lay my cause before him.[v]
9 He performs wonders[w] that cannot be fathomed,[x]
miracles that cannot be counted.[y]
10 He provides rain for the earth;[z]
he sends water on the countryside.[a]
11 The lowly he sets on high,[b]
and those who mourn[c] are lifted[d] to safety.
12 He thwarts the plans[e] of the crafty,
so that their hands achieve no success.[f]
13 He catches the wise[g] in their craftiness,[h]

4:11 [j] Dt 28:41; Job 27:14; 29:17; Ps 34:10; 58:6; Pr 30:14 [k] Job 5:4 **4:12** [l] ver 17-21; Job 32:13; Jer 9:23 [m] Job 26:14 [n] Job 33:14 **4:13** [o] Job 33:15 **4:14** [p] Job 21:6; Ps 48:6; 55:5; 119:120, 161; Jer 5:22; Hab 3:16; S 2Co 7:15 [q] Jer 23:9; Da 10:8; Hab 3:16 **4:15** [r] Da 5:6; 7:15, 28; 10:8; Mt 14:26 **4:16** [s] S 1Ki 19:12 **4:17** [t] Job 9:2; 13:18; Ps 143:2 [u] Job 8:3; 10:3; 14:4; 15:14; 21:14; 25:4; 31:15; 32:22; 35:10; 36:3, 13; 37:23; 40:19; Ps 18:26; 51:5; 119:73; Pr 20:9; Ecc 7:20; Isa 51:13; Mal 2:10; Ac 17:24 **4:18** [v] Heb 1:14 [w] Job 15:15; 21:22; 25:5 **4:19** [x] Job 10:9; 33:6; Isa 64:8; Ro 9:21; 2Co 4:7; 5:1 [y] Job 22:16 [z] S Ge 2:7 [a] Job 5:4 [b] Job 7:17; 15:16; 17:14; 25:6; Ps 22:6; Isa 41:14 **4:20** [c] Job 14:2, 20; 15:33; 20:7; 24:24; Ps 89:47; 90:5-6; Jas 4:14 **4:21** [d] Job 8:22; Isa 38:12 [e] Jn 8:24 [f] Job 18:21; 36:12; Pr 5:23; Jer 9:3 **5:1** [g] Hab 1:2 [h] Job 15:15; Ps 89:5, 7 **5:2** [i] Job 21:15; 36:13 [j] Pr 12:16; Gal 5:26 **5:3** [k] S Job 4:8 [l] Ps 37:35; Isa 40:24; Jer 12:2; Eze 17:6 [m] Pr 6:15 [n] Job 24:18; Ps 37:22, 35-36; 109:9-10; Pr 3:33 **5:4** [o] Job 20:10; 27:14 [p] S Job 4:11 [q] Job 4:19; Am 5:12 [r] Ps 109:12; Isa 9:17; 1Jn 2:1 **5:5** [s] Lev 26:16; S Jdg 2:15; Job 20:18; 31:8; Mic 6:15 **5:6** [t] S Job 4:8 **5:7** [u] S Ge 3:17; Job 10:17; 15:35; Ps 51:5; 58:3; 90:10; Pr 22:8 **5:8** [v] Job 8:5; 11:13; 13:3, 15; 23:4; 40:1; Ps 35:23; 50:15; Jer 12:1; 1Co 4:4 **5:9** [w] Ps 78:4; 111:2 [x] Dt 29:29; Job 9:4, 10; 11:7; 25:2; 26:14; 33:12; 36:5, 22, 26; 37:5, 14, 16, 23; 42:3; Ps 40:5; 71:17; 72:18; 86:10; 131:1; 139:6, 17; 145:3; Isa 40:28; Ro 11:33 [y] Ps 71:15 **5:10** [z] Mt 5:45 [a] S Lev 26:4; Job 36:28; 37:6, 13; 38:28, 34; Ps 135:7; Jer 14:22 **5:11** [b] S 1Sa 2:7-8; S Job 4:7; Ps 75:7; 113:7-8 [c] Isa 61:2; Mt 5:4; Ro 12:15 [d] S Mt 23:12; Jas 4:10 **5:12** [e] Ne 4:15; Ps 33:10; Isa 8:10; 19:3; Jer 19:7 [f] Job 12:23; Ps 78:59; 140:8 **5:13** [g] Job 37:24; Isa 29:14; 44:25; Jer 8:8; 18:18; 51:57 [h] Job 15:5; Ps 36:3; Lk 20:23; 1Co 3:19*; 2Co 11:3; Eph 4:14

4:12–21 Eliphaz tells of a hair-raising (see v. 15), mystical experience mediated through a dream (see v. 13), through which he claims to have received divine revelation and on which he bases his advice to Job.
4:13 *Amid ... dreams ... when deep sleep falls on people.* Eliphaz's words are echoed by Elihu in 33:15.
4:14 *all my bones shake.* A sign of great distress (see Jer 23:9; Hab 3:16).
4:17–21 All mortals are sinful; therefore God has a right to punish them. Job should be thankful for the correction God is giving him (see 5:17–26 and note).
4:18–19 See 15:15–16.
4:18 *servants.* Angels.
4:19 *houses of clay.* Bodies made of dust (see 10:9; 33:6; see also note on Ge 2:7). *moth.* A symbol of fragility (cf. 27:18).
4:20 *Between dawn and dusk.* A vivid picture of the shortness of life.
4:21 *tent.* A temporary home, like the human body (see 2Co 5:1,4; 2Pe 1:13 and notes). *without wisdom.* Needlessly and senselessly (see v. 20).
5:1 *To which ... will you turn?* To plead your case with God. The idea of a mediator, someone to arbitrate between God and Job, is an important motif in the book (see 9:33; 16:19–20 and notes; see also note and NIV text note on 19:25). *holy ones.* Holy angels, the "sons of God" in the prologue (see NIV text notes on 1:6; 2:1).
5:2 Without mentioning him, Eliphaz implies that Job is resentful against God and that harm will follow. *fool.* One who pays no attention to God (see NIV text notes on 2:10; Pr 1:7).
5:3 *a fool taking root.* A wicked man prospering like a tree taking root (see Ps 1:3).
5:6 Unlike a weed, trouble must be sown and cultivated.
5:7 *man is born to trouble.* Proof that no one is righteous in the eyes of God (see notes on 4:17–21; 13:28—14:1). Job should stop behaving like a fool (see vv. 1–6) and should humble himself. Then God would bless, and injustice would shut its mouth (see v. 16). *sparks.* Lit. "sons of Resheph." In Canaanite mythology, Resheph was a god of plague and destruction. "(Sons of) Resheph" is used as a poetic image in the OT for fire (SS 8:6), bolts of lightning (Ps 78:48) and pestilence (Dt 32:24; Hab 3:5).
5:9 Repeated in 9:10.
5:13 Quoted in part in 1Co 3:19 (the only clear quotation of Job in the NT).

and the schemes of the wily are
swept away.[i]
14 Darkness[j] comes upon them in the
daytime;
at noon they grope as in the night.[k]
15 He saves the needy[l] from the sword in
their mouth;
he saves them from the clutches of
the powerful.[m]
16 So the poor[n] have hope,
and injustice shuts its mouth.[o]

17 "Blessed is the one whom God
corrects;[p]
so do not despise the discipline[q] of
the Almighty.[a][r]
18 For he wounds, but he also binds up;[s]
he injures, but his hands also heal.[t]
19 From six calamities he will rescue[u]
you;
in seven no harm will touch you.[v]
20 In famine[w] he will deliver you from
death,
and in battle from the stroke of the
sword.[x]
21 You will be protected from the lash of
the tongue,[y]
and need not fear[z] when destruction
comes.[a]
22 You will laugh[b] at destruction and
famine,[c]
and need not fear the wild animals.[d]
23 For you will have a covenant[e] with the
stones[f] of the field,
and the wild animals will be at
peace with you.[g]
24 You will know that your tent is
secure;[h]
you will take stock of your property
and find nothing missing.[i]
25 You will know that your children will
be many,[j]
and your descendants like the grass
of the earth.[k]
26 You will come to the grave in full
vigor,[l]
like sheaves gathered in season.[m]

27 "We have examined this, and it is true.
So hear it[n] and apply it to yourself."[o]

Job 6

6 Then Job replied:

2 "If only my anguish could be weighed
and all my misery be placed on the
scales![p]
3 It would surely outweigh the sand[q] of
the seas—
no wonder my words have been
impetuous.[r]
4 The arrows[s] of the Almighty[t] are in me,[u]
my spirit drinks[v] in their poison;[w]
God's terrors[x] are marshaled
against me.[y]
5 Does a wild donkey[z] bray[a] when it has
grass,
or an ox bellow when it has fodder?[b]
6 Is tasteless food eaten without salt,
or is there flavor in the sap of the
mallow[b]?[c]
7 I refuse to touch it;
such food makes me ill.[d]

8 "Oh, that I might have my request,
that God would grant what I hope
for,[e]

[a] *17* Hebrew *Shaddai*; here and throughout Job
[b] *6* The meaning of the Hebrew for this phrase is uncertain.

5:13 [i] Job 9:4; 18:7; Pr 21:30; 29:6; Jer 8:9 **5:14** [j] Job 15:22, 30; 18:6,18; 20:26; 22:11; 27:20; Isa 8:22; Jn 12:35 [k] S Dt 28:29; S Job 18:5; Am 8:9 **5:15** [l] S Ex 22:23; Job 8:6; 22:27; 33:26; 36:15 [m] S Job 4:10; S 31:22 **5:16** [n] Job 20:19; 31:16; Pr 17:5; 22:22; Isa 11:4; 41:17; 61:1 [o] Ps 63:11; 107:42; Ro 3:19 **5:17** [p] Dt 8:5; Job 33:19; 36:10; Zep 3:7; Jas 1:12 [q] Ps 94:12; Pr 3:11; Jer 31:18 [r] S Ge 17:1; S Job 15:11; Heb 12:5-11 **5:18** [s] Ps 147:3; Isa 57:15; 61:1; Hos 6:1 [t] S Dt 32:39 **5:19** [u] Da 3:17; 6:16 [v] Ps 34:19; 91:10; Pr 3:25-26; 24:15-16 **5:20** [w] ver 22; Ps 33:19; 37:19 [x] Ps 22:20; 91:7; 140:7; 144:10; Jer 39:18 **5:21** [y] Ps 12:2-4; 31:20 [z] Ps 23:4; 27:1; 91:5 [a] ver 15 **5:22** [b] Job 8:21; 39:7,18,22; 41:29 [c] S ver 20 [d] S Lev 25:18; Ps 91:13; Hos 2:18; Mk 1:13 **5:23** [e] Isa 28:15; Hos 2:18 [f] 2Ki 3:19, 25; Ps 91:12; Mt 13:8 [g] Job 40:20; Isa 11:6-9; 65:25; Eze 34:25 **5:24** [h] Job 12:6; 21:9 [i] Job 8:6; 22:23 **5:25** [j] Dt 28:4; Ps 112:2 [k] Ps 72:16; Isa 44:3-4; 48:19 **5:26** [l] S Ge 15:15; S Dt 11:21; S Ecc 8:13 [m] Pr 3:21-26 **5:27** [n] Job 32:10, 17 [o] Job 8:5; 11:13; 22:27 **6:2** [p] Job 31:6; Pr 11:1; Da 5:27 **6:3** [q] 1Ki 4:29; Pr 27:3 [r] ver 11, 26; Job 7:11; 16:6; 21:4; 23:2 **6:4** [s] S Dt 32:23; Ps 38:2 [t] S Ge 17:1 [u] Job 7:20; 16:12,13; 19:12; La 3:12 [v] Job 21:20 [w] S Dt 32:32; Job 30:21; 34:6; Jer 15:18; 30:12 [x] Job 9:34; 13:21; 18:11; 23:6; 27:20; 30:15; 33:16 [y] S Job 3:23; Ps 88:15-18 **6:5** [z] S Ge 16:12 [a] Job 30:7 [b] Job 24:6; Isa 30:24 **6:6** [c] Job 33:20; Ps 107:18 **6:7** [d] S Job 3:24 **6:8** [e] Job 14:13

5:17–26 While the preceding hymn (vv. 8–16) spoke of God's goodness and justice, this poem celebrates the blessedness of the one whom God disciplines (see Pr 1:2,7; 3:11–12 and note; 5:12 and note; 23:13,23). Eliphaz believed that discipline is temporary and is followed by healing (v. 18), and that those who are good will always be rescued. But with Job's wealth gone and his children dead, these words about security (v. 24) and children (v. 25) must have seemed cruel and hollow to him.
5:17 *Almighty.* The first of 31 times that the Hebrew word *Shaddai* is used in Job (see note on Ge 17:1).
5:18–19 See Hos 6:1–2.
5:19 *six ... seven.* See 33:29; 40:5; Pr 6:16 and note; 30:15,18,21,29; Ecc 11:2; Am 1:3,6,9,11,13 and note on 1:3; 2:1,4,6; Mic 5:5 and note. Normally, such number patterns are not to be taken literally but are a poetic way of saying "many."
5:23 *covenant with the stones.* A figurative way of saying that stones will "be at peace with you" and will not ruin the crops (see 2Ki 3:19; Isa 5:2; Mt 13:5).
5:25 *like the grass of the earth.* As numerous as blades of grass (see note on Ge 13:16).
5:26 Eliphaz's prediction was more accurate than he realized (see 42:16–17).
5:27 *apply it to yourself.* Eliphaz's conclusion: Job must turn from unrighteousness (4:7) and resentment against God (v. 2) to humility (v. 11) and the acceptance of God's righteous discipline (v. 17). Eliphaz's purpose is to offer theological comfort and counsel to Job (2:11), but instead he wounds him with false accusation.
6:2–3 Job appeals for a sympathetic understanding of the harsh words he spoke in ch. 3.
6:4 *arrows of the Almighty.* Job shares Eliphaz's "orthodox" theology and believes that God is aiming his arrows of judgment at him—though he does not know why (see 7:20 and note; 16:12–13; see also La 3:12; cf. Dt 32:23; Ps 7:13; 38:2).
6:5–6 Job claims the right to bray and bellow, since he has been wounded by God and offered tasteless food (words) by his friends.
6:8–9 Job repeats the anguished thoughts of 3:20–26.

9 that God would be willing to crush[f] me,
to let loose his hand and cut off my life![g]
10 Then I would still have this consolation[h] —
my joy in unrelenting pain[i] —
that I had not denied the words[j] of the Holy One.[k]

11 "What strength do I have, that I should still hope?
What prospects, that I should be patient?[l]
12 Do I have the strength of stone?
Is my flesh bronze?[m]
13 Do I have any power to help myself,[n]
now that success has been driven from me?

14 "Anyone who withholds kindness from a friend[o]
forsakes the fear of the Almighty.[p]
15 But my brothers are as undependable as intermittent streams,[q]
as the streams that overflow
16 when darkened by thawing ice
and swollen with melting snow,[r]
17 but that stop flowing in the dry season,
and in the heat[s] vanish from their channels.
18 Caravans turn aside from their routes;
they go off into the wasteland and perish.
19 The caravans of Tema[t] look for water,
the traveling merchants of Sheba[u] look in hope.
20 They are distressed, because they had been confident;
they arrive there, only to be disappointed.[v]
21 Now you too have proved to be of no help;
you see something dreadful and are afraid.[w]
22 Have I ever said, 'Give something on my behalf,
pay a ransom[x] for me from your wealth,[y]
23 deliver me from the hand of the enemy,
rescue me from the clutches of the ruthless'?[z]

24 "Teach me, and I will be quiet;[a]
show me where I have been wrong.[b]
25 How painful are honest words![c]
But what do your arguments prove?
26 Do you mean to correct what I say,
and treat my desperate words as wind?[d]
27 You would even cast lots[e] for the fatherless[f]
and barter away your friend.

28 "But now be so kind as to look at me.
Would I lie to your face?[g]
29 Relent, do not be unjust;[h]
reconsider, for my integrity[i] is at stake.[a][j]
30 Is there any wickedness on my lips?[k]
Can my mouth not discern[l] malice?

7 "Do not mortals have hard service[m] on earth?[n]
Are not their days like those of hired laborers?[o]
2 Like a slave longing for the evening shadows,[p]
or a hired laborer waiting to be paid,[q]
3 so I have been allotted months of futility,
and nights of misery have been assigned to me.[r]
4 When I lie down I think, 'How long before I get up?'[s]
The night drags on, and I toss and turn until dawn.[t]
5 My body is clothed with worms[u] and scabs,
my skin is broken and festering.[v]

6 "My days are swifter than a weaver's shuttle,[w]
and they come to an end without hope.[x]

[a] 29 Or *my righteousness still stands*

6:9 [f] Job 19:2 [g] S Nu 11:15; S Ps 31:22 **6:10** [h] S Job 2:11; 15:11; Ps 94:19 [i] Ps 38:17; Jer 4:19; 45:3 [j] Job 22:22; 23:12; Ps 119:102; Mk 8:38 [k] S Lev 11:44; S 2Ki 19:22; S Isa 31:1 **6:11** [l] S ver 3 **6:12** [m] Job 26:2 **6:13** [n] Job 26:2 **6:14** [o] Job 12:4; 17:2,6; 19:19, 21; 21:3; 30:1, 10; Ps 38:11; 69:20; 1Jn 3:17 [p] S Ge 17:1 **6:15** [q] Job 13:4; 16:2; 21:34; Ps 22:1; 38:11; Jer 15:18 **6:16** [r] Ps 147:18 **6:17** [s] Job 24:19 **6:19** [t] S Ge 25:15 [u] S Ge 10:7,28 **6:20** [v] Jer 14:3; Joel 1:11 **6:21** [w] Ps 38:11 **6:22** [x] S Nu 35:31; Job 33:24; Ps 49:7 [y] Jer 15:10 **6:23** [z] S 2Ki 19:19 **6:24** [a] S Job 2:10; 33:33; Ps 39:1; 141:3; Pr 10:19; 11:12; 17:27; Ecc 5:2 [b] Job 19:4 **6:25** [c] Ecc 12:11; Isa 22:23 **6:26** [d] S ver 3; S Ge 41:6; Job 8:2; 15:3; 16:3; Jer 5:13 **6:27** [e] Eze 24:6; Joel 3:3; Ob 1:11; Na 3:10 [f] S Ex 22:22,24; Job 31:17,21; Isa 10:2 **6:28** [g] Job 9:15; 24:25; 27:4; 32:10; 33:1,3; 34:6; 36:3,4 **6:29** [h] Job 19:6; 27:2; 40:8; Isa 40:27 [i] S Job 2:3 [j] Job 9:21; 10:7; 11:2; 12:4; 23:7,10; 33:9,32; 34:5,36; 35:2; 42:6; Ps 66:10; Zec 13:9 **6:30** [k] Job 27:4 [l] Job 12:11 **7:1** [m] Job 14:14; Isa 40:2 [n] S Job 5:7 [o] S Lev 25:50 **7:2** [p] Job 14:1; Ecc 2:23 [q] S Lev 19:13; S Job 14:6 **7:3** [r] Job 16:7; Ps 6:6; 42:3; 56:8; Ecc 4:1; Isa 16:9; Jer 9:1; La 1:2,16 **7:4** [s] Dt 28:67 [t] ver 13-14 **7:5** [u] Job 17:14; 21:26; 24:20; 25:6; Isa 14:11 [v] S Dt 28:35 **7:6** [w] Job 9:25; Ps 39:5; Isa 38:12 [x] Job 13:15; 14:19; 17:11,15; 19:10; Ps 37:4; 52:9

6:10 *Then.* In the afterlife, Job would have the joy of knowing that he had remained true to God.
6:11–13 With no human resources left, Job considers his condition hopeless.
6:11 *patient.* See note on 9:2–3.
6:14–17 Job needs spiritual help, but his friends are proving to be undependable (cf. Gal 6:1).
6:15 *brothers.* By calling his friends his "brothers," Job makes their callousness stand out more sharply.
6:19 *Tema.* See note on Isa 21:14. *Sheba.* See note on 1:15.
6:22–23 Job has not asked them for anything except what will cost them nothing: their friendship and counsel.
6:25 *honest words.* Job is referring to his own words.
6:26 *wind.* See 8:2.
6:27 In addition to dishonesty, Job accuses his friends of heartless cruelty.
6:29 Job softens his tone, pleading that his friends take back their false accusations.
7:1–21 Having replied to Eliphaz, Job now addresses his complaint toward God.
7:1 *hard service.* See 14:14. The Hebrew for this expression sometimes implies military service. It is also used in reference to the Babylonian exile (see Isa 40:2 and note).
7:2 *evening shadows.* End of the workday.
7:5 See note on 2:7.
7:6 *weaver's shuttle.* See photo, p. 801.

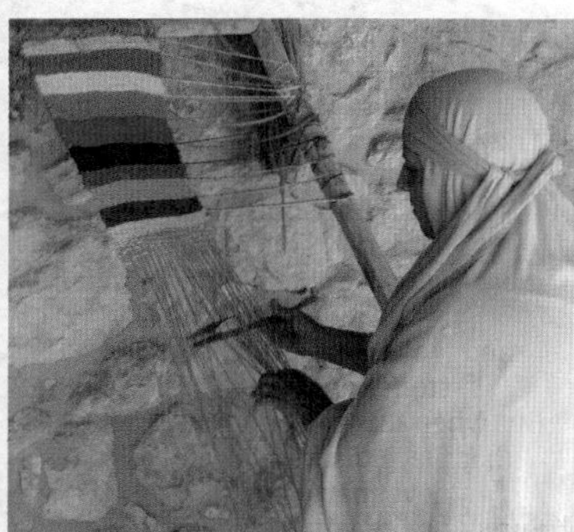

"My days are swifter than a weaver's shuttle" (Job 7:6).

Todd Bolen/www.BiblePlaces.com. Used by permission of Nazareth Village, www. nazarethvillage.com

7 Remember, O God, that my life is but a
breath;[y]
my eyes will never see happiness
again.[z]
8 The eye that now sees me will see me
no longer;
you will look for me, but I will be no
more.[a]
9 As a cloud vanishes[b] and is gone,
so one who goes down to the grave[c]
does not return.[d]
10 He will never come to his house
again;
his place[e] will know him no more.[f]

11 "Therefore I will not keep silent;[g]
I will speak out in the anguish[h] of
my spirit,
I will complain[i] in the bitterness of
my soul.[j]
12 Am I the sea,[k] or the monster of the
deep,[l]
that you put me under guard?[m]
13 When I think my bed will comfort me
and my couch will ease my
complaint,[n]
14 even then you frighten me with dreams
and terrify[o] me with visions,[p]
15 so that I prefer strangling and death,[q]
rather than this body of mine.[r]
16 I despise my life;[s] I would not live
forever.[t]
Let me alone;[u] my days have no
meaning.[v]
17 "What is mankind that you make so
much of them,
that you give them so much
attention,[w]
18 that you examine them every morning[x]
and test them[y] every moment?[z]
19 Will you never look away from me,[a]
or let me alone even for an instant?[b]
20 If I have sinned, what have I done to you,[c]
you who see everything we do?
Why have you made me your target?[d]
Have I become a burden to you?[a][e]
21 Why do you not pardon my offenses
and forgive my sins?[f]
For I will soon lie down in the dust;[g]
you will search for me, but I will be
no more."[h]

[a] *20* A few manuscripts of the Masoretic Text, an ancient Hebrew scribal tradition and Septuagint; most manuscripts of the Masoretic Text *I have become a burden to myself.*

7:7 [y] ver 16; Ge 27:46; Ps 39:4, 5, 11; 62:9; 78:39; 89:47; 144:4; Ecc 7:15; S Jas 4:14 [z] Job 10:20 **7:8** [a] S Job 3:13; 8:18; 15:29; 20:7, 9, 21; 27:17; Ps 37:36; 103:16; Isa 41:12; Jn 16:16; Ac 20:25 **7:9** [b] S Job 3:25 [c] S Job 3:13; 11:8; 14:13; 17:16; 26:6; 38:17; Am 9:2 [d] 2Sa 12:23 **7:10** [e] Job 18:21; 21:18; 27:21, 23; Ps 58:9; Jer 18:17; 19:8 [f] S ver 8; Ps 37:10; 104:35 **7:11** [g] Job 9:35; 13:13; Ps 22:2; 40:9 [h] Job 10:1; Ps 6:3; Isa 38:15, 17 [i] ver 13; Job 9:27; 21:4; 23:2 [j] S 1Sa 1:10; S Job 6:3 **7:12** [k] Job 38:8-11 [l] S Ge 1:21 [m] ver 20; Isa 1:14 **7:13** [n] S ver 11 **7:14** [o] Job 9:34 [p] S Ge 41:8; S Job 3:26 **7:15** [q] 1Ki 19:4; Jnh 4:3 [r] Job 6:9; Rev 9:6 **7:16** [s] S 1Ki 19:4; Job 9:21 [t] S Job 3:22 [u] ver 19; Job 10:20; Ps 39:13 [v] S ver 7 **7:17** [w] S Job 4:19; 22:2; Ps 8:4; 144:3; Heb 2:6 **7:18** [x] Ps 73:14 [y] Job 23:10; Ps 139:23 [z] Job 14:3; Ps 17:3; 26:2; 66:10; 139:1-6; 143:2 **7:19** [a] S ver 16 [b] Job 9:18; 13:26; 14:6; 27:2; Ps 139:7 **7:20** [c] Job 35:6; Jer 7:19 [d] S Job 6:4 [e] S ver 12 **7:21** [f] Job 9:28; 10:14; 16:6; Ps 119:120; Isa 43:25; Jer 31:34; Heb 1:3 [g] S Ge 3:19; Job 10:9; 34:15; Ps 7:5; 22:15; 90:3; 104:29 [h] S ver 8; S Job 3:13

7:7 *my life is but a breath.* As a chronic sufferer he has lost all sense of purpose in life (see v. 3; see also Ps 144:3–4). He does not anticipate healing and sees death as his only escape.

7:8 *you will look … no more.* See v. 21.

7:9 *one who goes down to the grave does not return.* Such statements are based on common observation and are not meant to dogmatize about what happens after death. Mesopotamian descriptions of the netherworld refer to it similarly as the "place of no return" (10:21; see note there). For the OT perspective on life after death, see Ps 6:5 and note.

7:11 *not keep silent.* Job is determined to cry out against the apparent injustice of God, who, it seems, will not leave him alone (vv. 17–20). *speak out in … anguish.* See Jer 4:19. *bitterness of … soul.* See 10:1 and note; 21:25; 27:2.

7:12 *the sea, or the monster of the deep.* See 3:8 and NIV text note. The fearsome sea monster was a symbol of chaos (see Ps 74:13–14 and note; Isa 27:1 and note; 51:9), and Job objects to being treated like it.

7:13–15 Job thinks that even the nightmares that disturb his sleep are from God.

7:16 *I despise my life.* See note on 9:21.

7:17 *What is mankind that you make so much of them …?* See Ps 144:3; cf. Ps 8:4–8, where the answer is given that humanity is created in God's image to have dominion over the world (see notes on Ge 1:26–28; Ps 8:6–8). Job's words (vv. 18–21) are a parody on this theme—as if God's only interest in people is to scrutinize them unmercifully and take quick offense at their slightest fault.

7:19 *even for an instant.* Lit. "long enough for me to swallow my saliva."

7:20 *If I have sinned, what have I done to you … ?* I have not been perfect, but what terrible sin have I committed that deserves this kind of suffering? *you who see everything we do.* The Hebrew for this clause is used in a favorable sense in Isa 27:3, but here Job complains that God is too critical (cf. v. 12). *made me your target.* See note on 6:4. *burden to you.* See NIV text note. Ancient Hebrew scribes report that a change in the text had been made from "you" to "myself" because the reading "you" involved too presumptuous a questioning of God's justice.

7:21 *offenses … sins.* Job confesses that he is a sinner, but he cannot understand why God refuses to forgive him. *lie down in the dust.* Of the netherworld, as in Mesopotamian descriptions of it (see note on v. 9).

Bildad

8 Then Bildad the Shuhite[i] replied:

2 "How long will you say such things?[j]
Your words are a blustering wind.[k]
3 Does God pervert justice?[l]
Does the Almighty pervert what is right?[m]
4 When your children sinned against him,
he gave them over to the penalty of their sin.[n]
5 But if you will seek God earnestly
and plead[o] with the Almighty,[p]
6 if you are pure and upright,
even now he will rouse himself on your behalf[q]
and restore you to your prosperous state.[r]
7 Your beginnings will seem humble,
so prosperous[s] will your future be.[t]

8 "Ask the former generation[u]
and find out what their ancestors learned,
9 for we were born only yesterday and know nothing,[v]
and our days on earth are but a shadow.[w]
10 Will they not instruct[x] you and tell you?
Will they not bring forth words from their understanding?[y]
11 Can papyrus grow tall where there is no marsh?[z]
Can reeds[a] thrive without water?
12 While still growing and uncut,
they wither more quickly than grass.[b]
13 Such is the destiny[c] of all who forget God;[d]
so perishes the hope of the godless.[e]
14 What they trust in is fragile[a];
what they rely on is a spider's web.[f]
15 They lean on the web,[g] but it gives way;
they cling to it, but it does not hold.[h]
16 They are like a well-watered plant in the sunshine,
spreading its shoots[i] over the garden;[j]
17 it entwines its roots around a pile of rocks
and looks for a place among the stones.
18 But when it is torn from its spot,
that place disowns[k] it and says, 'I never saw you.'[l]
19 Surely its life withers[m] away,
and[b] from the soil other plants grow.[n]

20 "Surely God does not reject one who is blameless[o]
or strengthen the hands of evildoers.[p]
21 He will yet fill your mouth with laughter[q]
and your lips with shouts of joy.[r]
22 Your enemies will be clothed in shame,[s]
and the tents[t] of the wicked will be no more."[u]

Job

9 Then Job replied:

2 "Indeed, I know that this is true.
But how can mere mortals prove their innocence before God?[v]

[a] *14* The meaning of the Hebrew for this word is uncertain. [b] *19* Or *Surely all the joy it has / is that*

8:1 [i] S Ge 25:2; Job 18:1; 25:1 **8:2** [j] Job 11:2; 18:2 [k] S 2Ch 36:16; S Job 6:26 **8:3** [l] S Job 4:17; 34:12; Isa 29:15; Ro 3:5 [m] S Ge 18:25; S Jer 12:1 **8:4** [n] Job 1:19 **8:5** [o] Job 9:15 [p] S Job 5:8,27 **8:6** [q] S Job 5:15; 22:27; 33:26; 34:28; Isa 58:9; 65:24 [r] S Job 5:24 **8:7** [s] Job 21:13; 22:21; 36:11; Ps 25:13 [t] S Job 1:10; Jer 29:11; 31:17 **8:8** [u] S Dt 32:7; S Ps 71:18 **8:9** [v] S Ge 47:9 [w] S 1Ch 29:15; S 2Ch 10:6; S Ps 39:6 **8:10** [x] Pr 1:8 [y] Pr 2:1-2; 4:1 **8:11** [z] Job 40:21 [a] S Ex 2:3; Isa 19:6; 35:7 **8:12** [b] ver 19; S 2Ki 19:26; Job 18:16; 20:5; Ps 90:5-6; 102:11; Isa 34:4; 40:7,24 **8:13** [c] Ps 37:38; 73:17 [d] Ps 9:17; 50:22; Isa 51:13; Jer 17:6 [e] Job 6:9; 11:20; 13:16; 15:34; 20:5; 27:8; 34:30; Ps 37:1-2; 112:10; Pr 10:28; 11:7; Jer 15:9 **8:14** [f] ver 15; Job 27:18; Isa 59:5 **8:15** [g] S ver 14 [h] Ps 49:11; Mt 7:26-27 **8:16** [i] Ps 80:11; Isa 16:8 [j] Ps 37:35; Jer 11:16 **8:18** [k] Job 20:9; Ps 103:16 [l] S Job 7:8; S 14:20 **8:19** [m] S ver 12; S Job 15:30 [n] Ps 119:90; Ecc 1:4 **8:20** [o] Job 1:1 [p] S Ge 18:25 **8:21** [q] S Job 5:22 [r] S Ezr 3:13; Job 35:10; Ps 47:5; 107:22; 118:15; 126:2; 132:16; Isa 35:6 **8:22** [s] Job 27:7; Ps 6:10; 35:26; 44:7; 53:5; 71:13; 86:17; 109:29; 132:18; Eze 7:27; 26:16 [t] S Job 4:21 [u] S 1Sa 8:3; Job 18:6, 14,21; 21:28; 27:8,18; 34:26; 36:6; 38:13; Ps 52:5; Pr 14:11 **9:2** [v] S Job 4:17; Ro 3:20

8:2 *How long ... ?* See 18:2. In contrast to the older Eliphaz, Bildad is impatient.
8:3 *Does God pervert justice?* But Job has not yet blatantly accused God of injustice.
8:5–6 Bildad reasons as follows: God cannot be unjust, so Job and his family must be suffering as a result of sinfulness. Job should plead for mercy, and if he has been upright, God will restore him.
8:6 *if you are pure and upright.* We know God's verdict about Job (see 1:8; 2:3), but Bildad is confident that Job is a hypocrite (see v. 13).
8:7 See v. 21. Bildad spoke more accurately than he realized (see 42:10–17).
8:8 *Ask the former generation.* Eliphaz appealed to revelation from the spirit world (see 4:12–21), while Bildad appeals to the accumulated wisdom of tradition.
8:9 *our days ... are but a shadow.* A common motif in wisdom literature (see 14:2 and note; 1Ch 29:15; Ps 102:11; 144:4; Ecc 6:12; 8:13).
8:11–19 A practical wisdom poem, giving words of instruction learned from the "former generation" and "their ancestors" (v. 8). It is introduced in v. 10 and applied to Job in vv. 20–22.
8:20 Bildad is blunt about Job's being an evildoer, whereas Eliphaz had resorted to insinuation (see 4:7–9).
8:21 See note on v. 7.
8:22 *clothed in.* See note on Ps 109:29.
9:2–3 Job does not believe he is sinless (see note on 1:1), but he wishes to have his day in court so he can prove he is innocent of the kind of sin that deserves the suffering he endures. In his despair he voices awful complaints against God (see vv. 16–20,22–24,29–35; 10:1–7,13–17). Yet he does not abandon God or curse him (see 10:2,8–12; see also Introduction: Theological Theme and Message), as Satan said he would (see 1:11 and note; 2:5; cf. 2:9). Ch. 42 implies that Job persevered, but chs. 9–10 show that he did so with impatience (see 4:2; 6:11; 21:4). Cf. Jas 5:11, which speaks of Job's perseverance, not (as traditionally) his patience.

3 Though they wished to dispute with him,[w]
they could not answer him one time out of a thousand.[x]
4 His wisdom[y] is profound, his power is vast.[z]
Who has resisted[a] him and come out unscathed?[b]
5 He moves mountains[c] without their knowing it
and overturns them in his anger.[d]
6 He shakes the earth[e] from its place
and makes its pillars tremble.[f]
7 He speaks to the sun and it does not shine;[g]
he seals off the light of the stars.[h]
8 He alone stretches out the heavens[i]
and treads on the waves of the sea.[j]
9 He is the Maker[k] of the Bear[a] and Orion,
the Pleiades and the constellations of the south.[l]
10 He performs wonders[m] that cannot be fathomed,
miracles that cannot be counted.[n]
11 When he passes me, I cannot see him;
when he goes by, I cannot perceive him.[o]
12 If he snatches away, who can stop him?[p]
Who can say to him, 'What are you doing?'[q]
13 God does not restrain his anger;[r]
even the cohorts of Rahab[s] cowered at his feet.

14 "How then can I dispute with him?
How can I find words to argue with him?[t]
15 Though I were innocent, I could not answer him;[u]
I could only plead[v] with my Judge[w] for mercy.[x]
16 Even if I summoned him and he responded,
I do not believe he would give me a hearing.[y]
17 He would crush me[z] with a storm[a]
and multiply[b] my wounds for no reason.[c]
18 He would not let me catch my breath
but would overwhelm me with misery.[d]
19 If it is a matter of strength, he is mighty![e]
And if it is a matter of justice, who can challenge him[b]?[f]
20 Even if I were innocent, my mouth would condemn me;
if I were blameless, it would pronounce me guilty.[g]

21 "Although I am blameless,[h]
I have no concern for myself;[i]
I despise my own life.[j]
22 It is all the same; that is why I say,
'He destroys both the blameless and the wicked.'[k]
23 When a scourge[l] brings sudden death,
he mocks the despair of the innocent.[m]
24 When a land falls into the hands of the wicked,[n]

[a] 9 Or *of Leo* [b] 19 See Septuagint; Hebrew *me.*

9:3 [w] ver 32; Job 40:5 [x] ver 12,14,29, 32; Job 10:2; 12:14; 13:9, 14; 22:4; 23:7, 13; 37:19; 40:2; Ps 44:21; Isa 14:24 **9:4** [y] Job 11:6; 28:12,20,23; 38:36; Ps 51:6; Pr 2:6; Ecc 2:26 [z] ver 19; S Job 5:9; 12:13,16; 23:6; 24:22; 26:12; 30:18; Ps 93:4; 95:3; Pr 8:14; Isa 40:26; 63:1; Da 2:20; 4:35 [a] Jer 50:24 [b] S 2Ch 13:12; S Job 5:13 **9:5** [c] Mt 17:20 [d] Ps 18:7; 46:2-3; Isa 13:13; Mic 1:4 **9:6** [e] S Ex 19:18; Isa 2:21; 13:13; 24:18-20; Am 8:8; Heb 12:26 [f] S 2Sa 22:8; Job 26:14; 36:29; 37:4-5; Ps 75:3; Hab 3:4 **9:7** [g] Isa 34:4; Jer 4:28; Joel 2:2,10,31; 3:15; Zep 1:15; Zec 14:6 [h] Isa 13:10; Jer 4:23; Eze 32:8 **9:8** [i] S Ge 1:1, 8; S Isa 48:13 [j] Job 38:16; Ps 77:19; Pr 8:28; Hab 3:15; Mt 14:25; Mk 6:48; Jn 6:19 **9:9** [k] Job 32:22; 40:15,19 [l] S Ge 1:16 **9:10** [m] Dt 6:22; Ps 72:18; 136:4; Jer 32:20 [n] S Job 5:9 **9:11** [o] Job 23:8-9; 35:14 **9:12** [p] Nu 23:20; Job 11:10; Isa 14:27; 43:13 [q] S ver 3; S Dt 32:39; Isa 29:16; 45:9; Da 2:21; 4:32; Ro 9:20 **9:13** [r] Nu 14:18; Job 10:15; Ps 78:38; Isa 3:11; 6:5; 48:9 [s] Job 26:12; Ps 87:4; 89:10; Isa 30:7; 51:9 **9:14** [t] S ver 3 **9:15** [u] Job 10:15; 13:19; 34:5-6; 40:5; 42:7 [v] Job 8:5 [w] S Ge 18:25; 1Sa 24:12; Ps 50:6; 96:13 [x] ver 20,29; Job 15:6; 23:4; 40:2 **9:16** [y] Job 13:22; Ro 9:20-21 **9:17** [z] Job 16:12; 30:16; Ps 10:10; Isa 38:13 [a] Job 30:22; Ps 83:15; Jnh 1:4 [b] Job 16:14 [c] S Job 2:3 **9:18** [d] S Job 7:19; S 10:1 **9:19** [e] S ver 4; S Ne 9:32 [f] ver 33; Jer 49:19 **9:20** [g] S ver 15 **9:21** [h] S Ge 6:9; Job 34:6,7 [i] ver 14; S Job 6:29; 10:1; 13:13 [j] S Nu 11:15; S Job 7:16 **9:22** [k] S Job 3:19; 10:8; Ecc 9:2,3; Eze 21:3 **9:23** [l] Heb 11:36 [m] Job 24:1,12; Ps 64:4; Hab 1:3; 1Pe 1:7 **9:24** [n] Job 1:15,17; 10:3; 16:11; 21:16; 22:18; 27:2; 40:8; Ps 73:3

:3 *dispute.* See v. 14. Job's speech is filled with the imagery of the courtroom: "answer him" (vv. 3,15,32), "argue with him" (v. 14), "innocent ... plead ... Judge" (v. 15), "summoned" (v. 16), "pronounce me guilty" (v. 20), "judges" (v. 24), "court" (v. 32), "charges ... against me" (10:2), "witnesses" (10:17). Job argues his innocence, but he feels that because God is so great there is no use in contending with him (v. 14). Job's innocence does him no good (v. 15).

9:5–10 A beautiful hymn about God's greatness. But Job is not blessed by it, for he does not see that God's power is controlled by goodness and justice.

:6 For the metaphor of the earth resting on a foundation, see 38:6; 1Sa 2:8 and note; Ps 24:2 and note; 75:3; 104:5.

9:8 *stretches out the heavens.* Either (1) creates the heavens (see Isa 44:24), or perhaps (2) causes the dawn to spread, like someone stretching out a tent (see Ps 104:2). *treads on the waves.* Canaanite texts describe the goddess Asherah as walking on the sea (or sea-god) to subdue it. Similarly, God "treads on the waves" to control the raging sea.

:9 *Bear ... Orion ... Pleiades.* These three constellations are mentioned again in 38:31–32, and the last two are mentioned in Am 5:8 (see note there). Despite their limited knowledge of astronomy, the ancient Israelites were awed by the fact that God had created the constellations.

9:10 The same words are spoken by Eliphaz in 5:9.

9:12 *who can stop him?* Job argues that God has an unchallengeable, sovereign freedom that works to accomplish everything he pleases.

9:13 *Rahab.* A mythical sea monster (see 26:12), elsewhere used as symbolic of Egypt (see Isa 30:7 and note). See 3:8; 7:12 and notes. The name Rahab in Jos 2 is from a different Hebrew root.

9:15 Job believes that his only recourse before the lofty majesty of God is to throw himself on God's mercy.

9:17 Job does not know that God has allowed Satan to crush him for a high purpose.

9:20 *my mouth would condemn me.* See 15:6.

9:21 *I despise my own life.* See 7:16; words of despairing resignation that would be partially echoed in Job's final outpouring of repentance (see 42:6 and note).

9:22–24 God has become Job's great enigma. Job describes a phantom God—one who does not exist,

he blindfolds its judges.[o]
If it is not he, then who is it?[p]

25 "My days are swifter than a runner;[q]
they fly away without a glimpse of joy.[r]
26 They skim past[s] like boats of papyrus,[t]
like eagles swooping down on their prey.[u]
27 If I say, 'I will forget my complaint,[v]
I will change my expression, and smile,'
28 I still dread[w] all my sufferings,
for I know you will not hold me innocent.[x]
29 Since I am already found guilty,
why should I struggle in vain?[y]
30 Even if I washed myself with soap[z]
and my hands[a] with cleansing powder,[b]
31 you would plunge me into a slime pit[c]
so that even my clothes would detest me.[d]

32 "He is not a mere mortal[e] like me that I might answer him,[f]
that we might confront each other in court.[g]
33 If only there were someone to mediate between us,[h]
someone to bring us together,[i]
34 someone to remove God's rod from me,[j]
so that his terror would frighten me no more.[k]
35 Then I would speak up without fear of him,[l]
but as it now stands with me, I cannot.[m]

10 "I loathe my very life;[n]
therefore I will give free rein to my complaint
and speak out in the bitterness of my soul.[o]
2 I say to God:[p] Do not declare me guilty,
but tell me what charges[q] you have against me.[r]
3 Does it please you to oppress me,[s]
to spurn the work of your hands,[t]
while you smile on the plans of the wicked?[u]
4 Do you have eyes of flesh?
Do you see as a mortal sees?[v]
5 Are your days like those of a mortal
or your years like those of a strong man,[w]
6 that you must search out my faults
and probe after my sin[x]—
7 though you know that I am not guilty[y]
and that no one can rescue me from your hand?[z]

8 "Your hands shaped[a] me and made me.
Will you now turn and destroy me?[b]
9 Remember that you molded me like clay.[c]
Will you now turn me to dust again?[d]
10 Did you not pour me out like milk
and curdle me like cheese,
11 clothe me with skin and flesh
and knit me together[e] with bones and sinews?

9:24 [o]S Job 3:14; 12:6; 19:7; 21:7; 24:23; 31:35; 35:15; Ps 73:12; Ecc 8:11; Jer 12:1; La 3:9 [p]Job 12:9; 13:1; 24:12; Isa 41:20 **9:25** [q]S Job 7:6 [r]Job 7:7; 10:20 **9:26** [s]Job 24:18; Ps 46:3 [t]Isa 18:2 [u]Job 39:29; Hab 1:8 **9:27** [v]S Job 7:11 **9:28** [w]S Job 3:25 [x]S Ex 34:7; S Job 7:21 **9:29** [y]S ver 3, S 15; Ps 37:33 **9:30** [z]Mal 3:2 [a]Job 17:9; 31:7; Isa 1:15 [b]Job 14:4,17; 33:9; Isa 1:18; Jer 2:22; Hos 13:12 **9:31** [c]Ps 35:7; 40:2; 51:9; Jer 2:22; Na 3:6; Mal 2:3 [d]S Job 7:20; 34:9; 35:3; Ps 73:13 **9:32** [e]S Nu 23:19 [f]S ver 3; Ro 9:20 [g]Ps 143:2; Ecc 6:10 **9:33** [h]S 1Sa 2:25 [i]S ver 19 **9:34** [j]Job 21:9; Ps 39:10; 73:5 [k]S Job 6:4; 7:14; 33:7; Ps 32:4 **9:35** [l]S Job 7:11 [m]Job 7:15; 13:21 **10:1** [n]S Nu 11:15; S 1Ki 19:4 [o]S 1Sa 1:10; S Job 7:11; 9:18,21 **10:2** [p]Job 13:3; 40:1 [q]Isa 3:13; Hos 4:1; 5:1; 12:2; Mic 6:2; Ro 8:33 [r]S Job 9:3 **10:3** [s]S Job 9:22; 16:9,14; 19:6,21; 22:10; 30:13,21; 31:23; 34:6 [t]ver 8; Ge 1:26; S Job 4:17; 14:15; 34:19; Ps 8:6; 95:6; 100:3; 138:8; 149:2; Isa 60:21; 64:8 [u]S Job 9:24 **10:4** [v]1Sa 16:7; Job 11:11; 14:16; 24:23; 28:24; 31:4; 34:21; 41:11; Ps 11:4; 33:15; 119:168; 139:12; Pr 5:21; 15:3; Jer 11:20-23; 16:17 **10:5** [w]Job 36:26; Ps 39:5; 90:2,4; 102:24; 2Pe 3:8 **10:6** [x]Job 14:16 **10:7** [y]ver 15; S Job 6:29; 11:4; 16:17; 27:5,6; 31:6; 32:1 [z]S Dt 32:39 **10:8** [a]Ge 2:7 [b]S ver 3; S 2Sa 14:14; S Job 30:15 **10:9** [c]S Job 4:19; Isa 29:16 [d]S Ge 2:7; S Job 7:21 **10:11** [e]Ps 139:13,15

---

except in Job's mind. The God of the Bible is not morally indifferent (cf. God's words in 38:2; 40:2 and Job's response in 42:3).

9:24 *blindfolds its judges.* Statues of Lady Justice are blindfolded, implying that she will judge impartially. But Job's accusation against God is that he has blindfolded the judges so that they see neither guilt nor innocence.

9:26 *boats of papyrus.* See note on Ex 2:3.

9:28 *you will not hold me innocent.* Job wants to stand before God as an innocent man—not sinless, but innocent of any sin commensurate with his suffering.

9:29 *already found guilty.* As appears from the bitter suffering he is enduring.

9:30 *cleansing powder.* A vegetable alkali used as a cleansing agent (see Jer 2:22). The Hebrew underlying this word is translated "soap" in Mal 3:2.

9:33 *someone to mediate between us.* See note on 5:1. God is so immense that Job feels he needs someone who can help him, someone who can argue his case in court. Job's call is not directly predicting the mediatorship of Christ, for Job is not looking for one to forgive him but for one who can testify to his innocence (see 16:18–21; 19:25–26 and notes).

9:34 See 13:21. *God's rod.* Symbolic of divine judgment and wrath (see, e.g., Ps 89:30–37; La 3:1 and notes).

10:1 *I loathe my very life.* See note on 9:21. *bitterness of my soul.* Because Job is so bitter, his mind has conjured up a false picture of God.

10:3 Job imagines that God is angry with him, an innocent man (see 9:28 and note), and that he takes delight in the wicked. Such words are a reminder that the sickroom is not the place to argue theology (see 2:13 and note); in times of severe suffering, people may say things that require a response of love and understanding. Job himself will eventually repent (see 42:6 and note), and God will forgive.

10:8–17 Job continues to question God as if he were his adversary in court. He wants to know how God, who so wonderfully formed him in the womb, could all the while have planned (see v. 13) to punish him—even though he may be innocent.

10:8–11 A poetic description of God making a baby in the womb (see Ps 139:13–16 and notes).

10:8 See Ps 119:73.

10:9 *molded me like clay.* See note on 4:19; see also photo, p. 805. *turn me to dust.* See note on Ge 3:19.

10:10 *like milk ... like cheese.* As semen poured into the womb produces an embryo.

"Your hands shaped me and made me. Will you now turn and destroy me? Remember that you molded me like clay. Will you now turn me to dust again?" (Job 10:8 – 9).

12 You gave me life[f] and showed me
kindness,[g]
and in your providence[h] watched
over[i] my spirit.

13 "But this is what you concealed in
your heart,
and I know that this was in your
mind:[j]
14 If I sinned, you would be watching me[k]
and would not let my offense go
unpunished.[l]
15 If I am guilty[m] — woe to me![n]
Even if I am innocent, I cannot lift
my head,[o]
for I am full of shame
and drowned in[a] my affliction.[p]

10:12 [f]S Ge 2:7 [g]S Ge 24:12 [h]S Ge 45:5 [i]1Pe 2:25 **10:13** [j]Job 23:13; Ps 115:3 **10:14** [k]Job 13:27 [l]S Ex 34:7; S Job 7:21 **10:15** [m]S ver 7 [n]S Job 9:13 [o]S Job 9:15 [p]Ps 25:16 **10:16** [q]S 1Sa 17:34; Ps 7:2; Isa 38:13; Jer 5:6; 25:38; La 3:10; Hos 5:14; 13:7 [r]Job 5:9; Isa 28:21; 29:14; 65:7 **10:17** [s]1Ki 21:10; Job 16:8 [t]Ru 1:21 [u]S Job 5:7 **10:18** [v]S Job 3:8; S Ps 22:9 [w]Job 3:26; Ecc 4:2; 7:1 **10:19** [x]S Job 3:3; Jer 15:10 **10:20** [y]Job 14:1; Ecc 6:12 [z]S Job 7:7 [a]S Job 7:16 [b]S Job 9:25 **10:21** [c]S 2Sa 12:23; S Job 3:13; 16:22; Ps 39:13; Ecc 12:5 [d]S Job 3:5 **10:22** [e]S Job 3:5 [f]S 1Sa 2:9; S Job 3:13 **11:1** [g]S Job 2:11 **11:2** [h]S Job 8:2; S 16:3 [i]S Ge 41:6; S Job 6:29 **11:3** [j]Eph 4:29; 5:4 [k]Job 12:4; 16:10; 17:2; 21:3; 30:1; Ps 1:1 **11:4** [l]Job 9:21 [m]S Job 10:7 **11:5** [n]Ex 20:19; Job 23:5; 32:13; 38:1 **11:6** [o]S Job 9:4; 1Co 2:10

16 If I hold my head high, you stalk me
like a lion[q]
and again display your awesome
power against me.[r]
17 You bring new witnesses against me[s]
and increase your anger toward me;[t]
your forces come against me wave
upon wave.[u]

18 "Why then did you bring me out of the
womb?[v]
I wish I had died before any eye
saw me.[w]
19 If only I had never come into being,
or had been carried straight from the
womb to the grave![x]
20 Are not my few days[y] almost over?[z]
Turn away from me[a] so I can have a
moment's joy[b]
21 before I go to the place of no return,[c]
to the land of gloom and utter
darkness,[d]
22 to the land of deepest night,
of utter darkness[e] and disorder,
where even the light is like
darkness."[f]

Zophar

11 Then Zophar the Naamathite[g] replied:

2 "Are all these words to go
unanswered?[h]
Is this talker to be vindicated?[i]
3 Will your idle talk[j] reduce others to
silence?
Will no one rebuke you when you
mock?[k]
4 You say to God, 'My beliefs are
flawless[l]
and I am pure[m] in your sight.'
5 Oh, how I wish that God would
speak,[n]
that he would open his lips against
you
6 and disclose to you the secrets of
wisdom,[o]
for true wisdom has two sides.

[a] 15 Or *and aware of*

10:15 – 16 Job says that whether he is guilty or innocent, the all-powerful God will not treat him justly.

10:17 *witnesses against me.* See note on 9:3.

10:18 – 22 See notes on ch. 3.

10:21 *place of no return.* See note on 7:9. *land of gloom and utter darkness.* See 38:17. Ancient Mesopotamian documents refer to the netherworld as the "house of darkness" (see note on Ecc 12:5).

11:1 – 20 Like Eliphaz (see 4:7 – 11) and Bildad (see 8:3 – 6), Zophar claims that Job's sins have caused his troubles.

11:2 – 3 Zophar's failure to put himself in Job's place before condemning him shows a lack of compassion. Job has sincerely challenged what he perceives to be God's unjust actions (see 9:14 – 24), but he has not mocked God, as Zophar accuses him of having done.

11:4 *I am pure.* In 10:7,15 Job had disclaimed being guilty, and in 9:21 he said he was "blameless," the word God used to describe him in 1:8; 2:3. Zophar, however, implies that Job was claiming purity, but Job nowhere makes such a claim.

11:5 Zophar thought God should speak against Job, but eventually God spoke against Zophar himself (see 42:7 – 9 and notes).

11:6 *true wisdom has two sides.* OT wisdom literature (especially Proverbs) makes abundant use of the term *mashal* ("proverb," "riddle," "parable"), which often had a hidden as well as an obvious meaning. Zophar thinks Job is shallow and lacks an understanding of the true nature of God (see vv. 7 – 9).

Know this: God has even forgotten
some of your sin.[p]

7 "Can you fathom[q] the mysteries of God?
Can you probe the limits of the
Almighty?
8 They are higher[r] than the heavens[s]
above — what can you do?
They are deeper than the depths
below[t] — what can you know?[u]
9 Their measure[v] is longer than the earth
and wider than the sea.[w]

10 "If he comes along and confines you in
prison
and convenes a court, who can
oppose him?[x]
11 Surely he recognizes deceivers;
and when he sees evil, does he not
take note?[y]
12 But the witless can no more become
wise
than a wild donkey's colt[z] can be
born human.[a][a]

13 "Yet if you devote your heart[b] to him
and stretch out your hands[c] to him,[d]
14 if you put away[e] the sin that is in your
hand
and allow no evil[f] to dwell in your
tent,[g]
15 then, free of fault, you will lift up your
face;[h]
you will stand firm[i] and without
fear.[j]
16 You will surely forget your trouble,[k]
recalling it only as waters gone by.[l]
17 Life will be brighter than noonday,[m]
and darkness will become like
morning.[n]
18 You will be secure, because there is
hope;
you will look about you and take
your rest[o] in safety.[p]
19 You will lie down, with no one to make
you afraid,[q]
and many will court your favor.[r]
20 But the eyes of the wicked will fail,[s]
and escape will elude them;[t]
their hope will become a dying
gasp."[u]

Job

12 Then Job replied:

2 "Doubtless you are the only people
who matter,
and wisdom will die with you![v]
3 But I have a mind as well as you;
I am not inferior to you.
Who does not know all these
things?[w]

4 "I have become a laughingstock[x] to my
friends,[y]
though I called on God and he
answered[z] —
a mere laughingstock, though
righteous and blameless![a]
5 Those who are at ease have contempt[b]
for misfortune
as the fate of those whose feet are
slipping.[c]
6 The tents of marauders are
undisturbed,[d]
and those who provoke God are
secure[e] —
those God has in his hand.[b]

[a] 12 Or *wild donkey can be born tame* [b] 6 Or *those whose god is in their own hand*

11:6 [p]S Ezr 9:13; S Job 15:5 **11:7** [q]S Job 5:9; Ecc 3:11 **11:8** [r]Eph 3:18 [s]S Ge 15:5; Job 22:12; 25:2; Ps 57:10; Isa 55:9 [t]S Job 7:9 [u]Job 15:13,25; 33:13; 40:2; Ps 139:8 **11:9** [v]Eph 3:19-20 [w]Job 22:12; 35:5; 36:26; 37:5,23; Isa 40:26 **11:10** [x]S Job 9:12; Rev 3:7 **11:11** [y]S Job 10:4; 31:37; 34:11,25; 36:7; Ps 10:14 **11:12** [z]S Ge 16:12 [a]S 2Ch 6:36 **11:13** [b]1Sa 7:3; Ps 78:8 [c]S Ex 9:29 [d]S Job 5:8,27 **11:14** [e]S Jos 24:14 [f]Ps 101:4 [g]Job 22:23 **11:15** [h]Job 22:26 [i]S 1Sa 2:9; Ps 20:8; 37:23; 40:2; 119:5; Eph 6:14 [j]S Ge 4:7; S Ps 3:6 **11:16** [k]Isa 26:16; 37:3; 65:16 [l]Jos 7:5; Job 22:11; Ps 58:7; 112:10; Eze 21:7 **11:17** [m]Job 22:28; Ps 37:6; Isa 58:8,10; 62:1 [n]Job 17:12; 18:6; 29:3; Ps 18:28; 112:4; 119:105; Isa 5:20; Jn 8:12 **11:18** [o]Ps 3:5; 4:8; 127:2; Ecc 5:12 [p]S Lev 26:6; Pr 3:24; Isa 11:10; 14:3; 28:12; 30:15; 32:18; Zec 3:10 **11:19** [q]S Lev 26:6 [r]Isa 45:14 **11:20** [s]Dt 28:65; Job 17:5 [t]Job 12:10; 18:18; 27:22; 34:22; 36:6; Ps 139:11-12; Jer 11:11; 23:24; 25:35; Am 2:14; 9:2-3 [u]S Job 8:13 **12:2** [v]Job 15:8; 17:10 **12:3** [w]Job 13:2; 15:9 **12:4** [x]S Ge 38:23 [y]S Job 6:14; S 11:3; S 16:10; S 19:14 [z]Ps 91:15 [a]S Ge 6:9; S Job 6:29; S 15:16 **12:5** [b]Ps 123:4 [c]Ps 17:5; 37:31; 38:16; 66:9; 73:2; 94:18 **12:6** [d]S Job 5:24 [e]S Job 9:24

11:7 Unwittingly, Zophar anticipates the Lord's discourses in 38:1 — 42:6.

11:8 – 9 In the same way that Zophar speaks of the height, depth, length and width of God's knowledge, Paul speaks of Christ's love (Eph 3:18).

11:8 *what can you do?* Can you climb into the heavens and explore God's knowledge?

11:11 – 12 *deceivers ... the witless.* Zophar claims that it would take a miracle to change Job.

11:12 The NIV text note contrasts two related but utterly different Biblical animals — the wild donkey and the domestic donkey. Then the point would be that a witless man can no more become wise than a wild donkey can be born as a domestic one.

11:13 – 20 Zophar assumes that Job's problems are rooted in his sin; all Job has to do is to repent, and then his life will become blessed and happy. But God nowhere guarantees a life "brighter than noonday" (v. 17) simply because we are his children. He has higher purposes for us than our physical prosperity, or people courting our favor (v. 19). Zophar's philosophy is in conflict with Ps 73.

11:13 *stretch out your hands to him.* To pray for help (see Ex 9:29; 17:11 and notes; Ps 28:2; 44:20; 77:2; 88:9; 141:2; 143:6; Isa 1:15; 1Ti 2:8).

11:15 *free of fault, you will lift up your face.* Zophar echoes Job's thought in 10:15.

11:20 Bildad ended his speech in a similar way (see 8:22).

12:1 — 14:22 As before, Job's reply is divided into two parts: He speaks to his three friends (12:2 — 13:19), then to God (13:20 — 14:22).

12:2 For the first time, Job reacts with sarcasm to the harshness of his counselors (see v. 20).

12:3 *Who does not know ... ?* See v. 9. The advice of Job's friends is trivial and commonplace.

12:4 *God ... answered.* In the days before his suffering began (contrast 9:16).

12:5 The prosperous despise those who, like Job, have trouble.

12:6 Such statements (see 9:21 – 24) irked the counselors and made them brand Job as a man whose feet were slipping (see v. 5).

7 "But ask the animals, and they will
teach you,[f]
or the birds in the sky,[g] and they will
tell you;[h]
8 or speak to the earth, and it will teach
you,
or let the fish in the sea inform
you.
9 Which of all these does not know[i]
that the hand of the LORD has done
this?[j]
10 In his hand is the life[k] of every creature
and the breath of all mankind.[l]
11 Does not the ear test words
as the tongue tastes food?[m]
12 Is not wisdom found among the aged?[n]
Does not long life bring
understanding?[o]

13 "To God belong wisdom[p] and power;[q]
counsel and understanding are his.[r]
14 What he tears down[s] cannot be
rebuilt;[t]
those he imprisons cannot be
released.[u]
15 If he holds back the waters,[v] there is
drought;[w]
if he lets them loose, they devastate
the land.[x]
16 To him belong strength and insight;[y]
both deceived and deceiver are his.[z]
17 He leads rulers away stripped[a]
and makes fools of judges.[b]
18 He takes off the shackles[c] put on by
kings
and ties a loincloth[a] around their
waist.[d]
19 He leads priests away stripped[e]
and overthrows officials long
established.[f]
20 He silences the lips of trusted advisers
and takes away the discernment of
elders.[g]
21 He pours contempt on nobles[h]
and disarms the mighty.[i]

12:7 [f] Job 35:11 *fn* [g] Mt 6:26 [h] Job 18:3; Ro 1:20 **12:9** [i] Isa 1:3 [j] S Job 9:24 **12:10** [k] Da 5:23 [l] S Ge 2:7; S Nu 16:22; S Job 11:20; Ac 17:28 **12:11** [m] Job 34:3 **12:12** [n] S 1Ki 4:2; Job 15:10 [o] ver 20; Job 17:4; 32:7, 9; 34:4, 10 **12:13** [p] Pr 21:30; Isa 45:9 [q] S Job 9:4; S Jer 32:19; 1Co 1:24 [r] S Nu 23:19; 1Ki 3:12; Job 32:8; 38:36; Pr 2:6; Isa 40:13-14; Da 1:17 **12:14** [s] Job 16:9; 19:10 [t] Dt 13:16; Ps 127:1; Isa 24:20; 25:2; Eze 26:14 [u] S Job 9:3; Isa 22:22; Rev 3:7 **12:15** [v] Job 28:25; Isa 40:12 [w] S Dt 28:22; S 1Ki 17:1 [x] S Ge 7:24 **12:16** [y] S Job 9:4 [z] 2Ch 18:22; Job 13:7, 9; 27:4; Ro 2:11 **12:17** [a] ver 19; Job 19:9; Isa 20:4 [b] S Job 3:14; 1Co 1:20 **12:18** [c] Ps 107:14; 116:16; Na 1:13 [d] ver 21; Job 34:18; Ps 107:40; Isa 5:27; 40:23

22 He reveals the deep things of darkness[j]
and brings utter darkness[k] into the
light.[l]
23 He makes nations great, and destroys
them;[m]
he enlarges nations,[n] and disperses
them.[o]
24 He deprives the leaders of the earth of
their reason;[p]
he makes them wander in a trackless
waste.[q]
25 They grope in darkness with no light;[r]
he makes them stagger like
drunkards.[s]

13 "My eyes have seen all this,[t]
my ears have heard and
understood it.
2 What you know, I also know;
I am not inferior to you.[u]
3 But I desire to speak to the Almighty[v]
and to argue my case with God.[w]
4 You, however, smear me with lies;[x]
you are worthless physicians,[y] all of
you![z]
5 If only you would be altogether silent![a]
For you, that would be wisdom.[b]
6 Hear now my argument;
listen to the pleas of my lips.[c]
7 Will you speak wickedly on God's
behalf?
Will you speak deceitfully for him?[d]
8 Will you show him partiality?[e]
Will you argue the case for God?

[a] 18 Or *shackles of kings / and ties a belt*

12:19 [e] S ver 17 [f] S Dt 24:15; S Job 9:24; 14:20; 22:8; 24:12, 22; 34:20, 28; 35:9; Isa 2:22; 31:8; 40:17, 23; Jer 25:18; Da 2:21, 34; Lk 1:52 **12:20** [g] S ver 12, 24; Da 4:33-34 **12:21** [h] S ver 18; S Isa 34:12 [i] S Job 3:15 **12:22** [j] 1Co 4:5 [k] Job 3:5 [l] Ps 139:12; Da 2:22 **12:23** [m] Ps 2:1; 46:6; Isa 13:4; Jer 25:9 [n] S Ex 34:24; Ps 107:38; Isa 9:3; 26:15; 54:3 [o] S Job 5:12; Ac 17:26 **12:24** [p] S ver 20 [q] Ps 107:40 **12:25** [r] S Dt 28:29; Job 18:6; 21:17; 29:3 [s] Ps 107:27; Isa 24:20 **13:1** [t] S Job 9:24 **13:2** [u] S Job 12:3 **13:3** [v] Job 5:17; 40:2 [w] S Job 5:8; 9:14-20; S 10:2 **13:4** [x] Ps 119:69; Isa 9:15; Jer 23:32 [y] Jer 8:22 [z] S Job 6:15 **13:5** [a] ver 13; S Jdg 18:19 [b] Pr 17:28 **13:6** [c] Job 33:1; 36:4 **13:7** [d] S Job 12:16; S 16:17 **13:8** [e] S Lev 19:15

12:7–12 Job appeals to all creation to testify that God does what he pleases.
12:9 *that the hand of the LORD has done this.* An echo of Isa 41:20. *LORD.* The only place in Job's and his friends' speeches (chs. 3–37) where the divine name "LORD" (Hebrew *Yahweh*) is used (see Introduction: Author).
12:11 Echoed by Elihu in 34:3. Cf. 6:6, where Job says that Eliphaz's words are like "tasteless food."
12:12 Job sarcastically chides his counselors for being elders and yet lacking in true wisdom.
12:13–25 The theme of this section is stated in v. 13: God is sovereign in the created world, and especially in history. The rest of the poem dwells on the negative aspects of God's power and wisdom—e.g., the destructive forces of nature (vv. 14–15), how judges become fools (v. 17), how priests become humiliated (v. 19), how trusted advisers are silenced and elders deprived of good sense (v. 20). Contrast the claim of Eliphaz that God always uses his power in ways that make sense (5:10–16).
12:20 See note on v. 2.
12:21a,24b The Hebrew text of these lines is repeated verbatim in Ps 107:40 (see note there).
12:22 God knows even plans conceived and held in secret.
12:25 *grope in darkness.* Job concludes this section with a parody of Eliphaz's confident assertion in 5:14.
13:1–12 Job feels that his counselors have become completely untrustworthy (see v. 12). He calls them quacks (see v. 4; see also 16:2 and note) and accuses them of showing partiality to God through their false accusations (see vv. 7–8). Someday God will examine them and punish them (see vv. 9–11).
13:1 *all this.* God's sovereign actions as described in ch. 12.
13:2 See 15:9. *I am not inferior to you.* See 12:3 and note.
13:5 See v. 13. The friends' earlier silence may have ministered to Job (see 2:13 and note); his current retort is intended as sarcasm (cf. Pr 17:28).

9 Would it turn out well if he examined
you?[f]
Could you deceive him as you might
deceive a mortal?[g]
10 He would surely call you to account
if you secretly showed partiality.[h]
11 Would not his splendor[i] terrify you?
Would not the dread of him fall on
you?[j]
12 Your maxims are proverbs of ashes;
your defenses are defenses of clay.[k]

13 "Keep silent[l] and let me speak;[m]
then let come to me what may.[n]
14 Why do I put myself in jeopardy
and take my life in my hands?[o]
15 Though he slay me, yet will I hope[p] in
him;[q]
I will surely[a] defend my ways to his
face.[r]
16 Indeed, this will turn out for my
deliverance,[s]
for no godless[t] person would dare
come before him![u]
17 Listen carefully to what I say;[v]
let my words ring in your ears.
18 Now that I have prepared my case,[w]
I know I will be vindicated.[x]
19 Can anyone bring charges against me?[y]
If so, I will be silent[z] and die.[a]

20 "Only grant me these two things,
God,
and then I will not hide from you:
21 Withdraw your hand[b] far from me,
and stop frightening me with your
terrors.[c]
22 Then summon me and I will answer,[d]
or let me speak, and you reply to
me.[e]
23 How many wrongs and sins have I
committed?[f]
Show me my offense and my sin.[g]
24 Why do you hide your face[h]
and consider me your enemy?[i]

13:9 [f] S Job 9:3 [g] S Job 12:16; Gal 6:7 **13:10** [h] S Lev 19:15; S 2Ch 19:7 **13:11** [i] Job 31:23 [j] S Ex 3:6 **13:12** [k] S Ne 4:2-3 **13:13** [l] S ver 5 [m] S Job 7:11 [n] S Job 9:21 **13:14** [o] S Jdg 9:17 **13:15** [p] S Job 7:6 [q] Ps 23:4; 27:1; Pr 14:32; Isa 12:2; Da 3:28 [r] S Job 5:8; 27:5 **13:16** [s] Ps 30:5; Isa 12:1; 54:7-8; Hos 14:4; Php 1:19 [t] S Job 8:13 [u] S Ge 3:8 **13:17** [v] Job 21:2 **13:18** [w] S ver 3; Job 23:4; 37:19 [x] S Job 2:3; S 9:21 **13:19** [y] Job 40:4; Isa 50:8; Ro 8:33 [z] S Job 9:15 [a] S Job 3:13; 10:8 **13:21** [b] S Ex 9:3; Heb 10:31 [c] S Job 6:4 **13:22** [d] Job 9:35; 14:15 [e] S Job 9:16 **13:23** [f] S 1Sa 26:18 [g] Job 7:21; 9:21; 14:17; 33:9 **13:24** [h] S Dt 32:20 [i] Job 16:9; 19:11; 33:10; Ps 88:14-15; Jer 30:14; La 2:5 **13:25** [j] Job 19:2 [k] Lev 26:36 [l] Job 19:22, 28 [m] Job 21:18; Ps 1:4; 35:5; 83:13; Isa 17:13; 42:3; 43:17; Hos 13:3 **13:26** [n] Job 18:7; 20:11; 21:23; Ps 25:7 **13:27** [o] S Ge 40:15; Job 33:11; Jer 20:2; Ac 16:24 [p] Job 10:14 **13:28** [q] Ps 102:26; Mk 2:21 [r] S Dt 28:35; Ps 39:11; Isa 50:9; 51:8; Hos 5:12; Jas 5:2 **14:1** [s] Job 15:14; Mt 11:11 [t] S Job 10:20 [u] S Ge 3:17; S Job 7:2

Relief of shackled captives being driven from a city by Assyrians (700 BC). Job describes feeling as though he is in shackles (Job 13:27).

Z. Radovan/www.BibleLandPictures.com

25 Will you torment[j] a windblown
leaf?[k]
Will you chase[l] after dry chaff?[m]
26 For you write down bitter things
against me
and make me reap the sins of my
youth.[n]
27 You fasten my feet in shackles;[o]
you keep close watch on all my
paths[p]
by putting marks on the soles of my
feet.

28 "So man wastes away like something
rotten,
like a garment[q] eaten by moths.[r]

14 "Mortals, born of woman,[s]
are of few days[t] and full of
trouble.[u]

[a] 15 Or *He will surely slay me; I have no hope — / yet I will*

13:12 *defenses.* Arguments in their defense of God's judgment.

13:15 See NIV text note. Both readings state that no matter what happens, Job intends to seek vindication from God and believes that he will receive it (see v. 18).

13:16 *turn out for my deliverance.* See Php 1:19 (perhaps Paul was reflecting on Job's experience).

13:17 Job asks his friends to listen to what he is going to say to God in 13:20 — 14:22.

13:20 *two things.* Job wants God (1) to withdraw his hand of punishment (v. 21) and (2) to start communicating with him (v. 22).

13:21 See 9:34.

13:23 Job's words are based on the counselors' point that suffering always implies sinfulness. He does not yet understand that God has a higher purpose in his suffering. *wrongs ... sins ... offense.* The three most important Hebrew terms for sin lie behind these translations (see Ex 34:7; see also notes on Ps 32:5; 51:1 – 2; Isa 59:12).

13:24 *hide your face.* Withhold your blessing (see note on Ps 13:1).

13:25 *windblown leaf ... dry chaff.* See note on Ps 1:4.

13:26 *write down ... things against me.* See Ps 130:3; Hos 13:12; contrast 1Co 13:5. *sins of my youth.* Since Job feels that he is not presently guilty of a sinful life, God must still be holding the sins of his youth against him.

13:27 *You fasten ... my paths.* Elihu later quotes Job's words (see 33:11). *marks on the soles of my feet.* The Babylonian Code of Hammurapi (see chart, p. xxii) attests to the practice of putting marks on slaves. Job feels that he is being harassed by a God who has taken him captive and is tormenting him (see v. 25; see also photo above).

13:28 — 14:1 The introduction to ch. 14, expressing the pessimistic theme that the legacy of human beings is trouble and their destiny is death.

13:28 *garment eaten by moths.* See Mt 6:19 – 20 and notes; Lk 12:33.

14:1 See 5:7 and note.

[2]They spring up like flowers[v] and wither
away;[w]
like fleeting shadows,[x] they do not
endure.[y]
[3]Do you fix your eye on them?[z]
Will you bring them[a] before you for
judgment?[a]
[4]Who can bring what is pure[b] from the
impure?[c]
No one![d]
[5]A person's days are determined;[e]
you have decreed the number of his
months[f]
and have set limits he cannot
exceed.[g]
[6]So look away from him and let him
alone,[h]
till he has put in his time like a hired
laborer.[i]

[7]"At least there is hope for a tree:[j]
If it is cut down, it will sprout
again,
and its new shoots[k] will not fail.[l]
[8]Its roots may grow old in the ground
and its stump[m] die in the soil,
[9]yet at the scent of water[n] it will bud
and put forth shoots like a plant.[o]
[10]But a man dies and is laid low;[p]
he breathes his last and is no more.[q]
[11]As the water of a lake dries up
or a riverbed becomes parched and
dry,[r]
[12]so he lies down and does not rise;[s]
till the heavens are no more,[t] people
will not awake
or be roused from their sleep.[u]

[13]"If only you would hide me in the
grave[v]
and conceal me till your anger has
passed![w]
If only you would set me a time
and then remember[x] me![y]
[14]If someone dies, will they live again?
All the days of my hard service[z]
I will wait for my renewal[b][a] to come.

14:2 [v]Ps 103:15; S Jas 1:10 [w]Ps 37:2; 90:5-6; Isa 40:6-8 [x]Job 8:9; Ps 39:4; 102:11; 109:23; 144:4; Ecc 6:12 [y]S Job 4:20; Ps 49:12
14:3 [z]Ps 8:4; 144:3 [a]S Job 7:18
14:4 [b]Ps 51:10 [c]S Job 4:17; Eph 2:1-3 [d]S Job 9:30; Jn 3:6; Ro 5:12; 7:14
14:5 [e]Job 24:1; Ps 31:15; 139:16 [f]Job 21:21; Ps 39:4; 90:12 [g]Ac 17:26
14:6 [h]S Job 7:19 [i]Job 7:1, 2; Ps 39:13; Isa 16:14; 21:16
14:7 [j]Job 19:10; 24:20; Ps 52:5 [k]Isa 11:1; 53:2; 60:21 [l]Isa 6:13
14:8 [m]Isa 6:13; 11:1; 53:2
14:9 [n]Job 29:19; Ps 1:3; Jer 17:8; Eze 31:7 [o]Lev 26:4; Eze 34:27; Zec 10:1
14:10 [p]ver 12 [q]S Job 10:21; 13:19
14:11 [r]S 2Sa 14:14
14:12 [s]ver 10 [t]Ps 102:26; Rev 20:11; 21:1 [u]Ac 3:21
14:13 [v]S Job 7:9 [w]Ps 30:5; Isa 26:20; 54:7 [x]S Ge 8:1 [y]Job 6:8
14:14 [z]S Job 7:1 [a]S 2Ki 6:33
14:15 [b]S Job 13:22 [c]S Job 10:3

[15]You will call and I will answer you;[b]
you will long for the creature your
hands have made.[c]
[16]Surely then you will count my steps[d]
but not keep track of my sin.[e]
[17]My offenses will be sealed[f] up in a
bag;[g]
you will cover over my sin.[h]

[18]"But as a mountain erodes and
crumbles[i]
and as a rock is moved from its
place,[j]
[19]as water wears away stones
and torrents[k] wash away the soil,[l]
so you destroy a person's hope.[m]
[20]You overpower them once for all, and
they are gone;[n]
you change their countenance and
send them away.[o]
[21]If their children are honored, they do
not know it;
if their offspring are brought low,
they do not see it.[p]
[22]They feel but the pain of their own
bodies[q]
and mourn only for themselves.[r]"

Eliphaz

15 Then Eliphaz the Temanite[s] replied:

[2]"Would a wise person answer with
empty notions
or fill their belly with the hot east
wind?[t]
[3]Would they argue with useless words,
with speeches that have no value?[u]
[4]But you even undermine piety
and hinder devotion to God.[v]

[a] 3 Septuagint, Vulgate and Syriac; Hebrew *me*
[b] 14 Or *release*

14:16 [d]S Job 10:4; Ps 139:1-3; Pr 5:21; Jer 16:17; 32:19 [e]Job 10:6; 1Co 13:5 **14:17** [f]Jer 32:10 [g]S Dt 32:34 [h]S Job 9:30; S 13:23 **14:18** [i]Eze 38:20 [j]Job 18:4 **14:19** [k]Eze 13:13 [l]S Ge 7:23 [m]S Job 7:6 **14:20** [n]S Job 4:20 [o]S Job 7:10; 8:18; S 12:19; 27:19; Jas 1:10 **14:21** [p]Job 21:21; Ecc 9:5; Isa 63:16 **14:22** [q]Ps 38:7; Isa 21:3; Jer 4:19 [r]Job 21:21 **15:1** [s]S Job 4:1 **15:2** [t]S Ge 41:6 **15:3** [u]S Ne 4:2-3; S Job 6:26 **15:4** [v]Job 25:6

14:2–6 A symmetrical poem centered around v. 4 (v. 2 corresponds to v. 5, and v. 3 to v. 6). Job complains to God: Given the insignificance of humans and their inherent impurity, why do you take them so seriously (see 13:25)?
14:2 *They … wither away.* Life at best is brief and fragile (see 8:9; Ps 37:2; Isa 40:7,24; cf. Jas 1:10). *like fleeting shadows.* See note on 8:9.
14:7–12 People are like a flower that lives its short life and is gone (v. 2), not like a tree that revives even after it has been cut down.
14:7 *sprout.* The Hebrew root underlying this word is translated "renewal" in v. 14.
14:13–17 Job's spirit now appears to rise above the despair engendered by his rotting body. Although resurrection in the fullest sense is not taught here, Job is saying that if God so desires he is able to hide Job in the grave, then raise him back to life at a time when the divine anger is past.
14:14 *hard service.* See note on 7:1.
14:18–22 Job's pessimism arises not from skepticism about the possibility of resurrection from the dead but rather from God's apparent unwillingness to do something immediately for a person like him, whose life has become a nightmare of pain and mourning.
15:1–6 Up to this point Eliphaz has been the most sympathetic of the three counselors, but now he has run out of patience with Job and denounces him more severely than before.
15:2 *empty.* The Hebrew for this word is translated "long-winded" in 16:3, where Job hurls Eliphaz's charges back at him. *hot east wind.* The sirocco that blows in from the desert (see 27:21; 38:24; see also notes on Ge 41:6; Jer 4:11).
15:4 *piety.* See note on 4:6.

5 Your sin[w] prompts your mouth;[x]
you adopt the tongue of the crafty.[y]
6 Your own mouth condemns you, not
mine;
your own lips testify against you.[z]

7 "Are you the first man ever born?[a]
Were you brought forth before the
hills?[b]
8 Do you listen in on God's council?[c]
Do you have a monopoly on
wisdom?[d]
9 What do you know that we do not
know?
What insights do you have that we
do not have?[e]
10 The gray-haired and the aged[f] are on
our side,
men even older than your father.[g]
11 Are God's consolations[h] not enough for
you,
words[i] spoken gently to you?[j]
12 Why has your heart[k] carried you away,
and why do your eyes flash,
13 so that you vent your rage[l] against God
and pour out such words[m] from your
mouth?[n]

14 "What are mortals, that they could be
pure,
or those born of woman,[o] that they
could be righteous?[p]
15 If God places no trust in his holy
ones,[q]
if even the heavens are not pure in
his eyes,[r]
16 how much less mortals, who are vile
and corrupt,[s]
who drink up evil[t] like water![u]

17 "Listen to me and I will explain to
you;
let me tell you what I have seen,[v]
18 what the wise have declared,
hiding nothing received from their
ancestors[w]
19 (to whom alone the land[x] was given
when no foreigners moved among
them):
20 All his days the wicked man suffers
torment,[y]
the ruthless man through all the
years stored up for him.[z]
21 Terrifying sounds fill his ears;[a]
when all seems well, marauders
attack him.[b]
22 He despairs of escaping the realm of
darkness;[c]
he is marked for the sword.[d]
23 He wanders about[e] for food like a
vulture;[f]
he knows the day of darkness[g] is at
hand.[h]
24 Distress and anguish[i] fill him with
terror;[j]
troubles overwhelm him, like a king[k]
poised to attack,
25 because he shakes his fist[l] at God
and vaunts himself against the
Almighty,[m]
26 defiantly charging against him
with a thick, strong shield.[n]

27 "Though his face is covered with fat
and his waist bulges with flesh,[o]
28 he will inhabit ruined towns
and houses where no one lives,[p]
houses crumbling to rubble.[q]
29 He will no longer be rich and his
wealth will not endure,[r]
nor will his possessions spread over
the land.[s]

15:5 [w] Job 11:6; 22:5 [x] Pr 16:23 [y] S Job 5:13 **15:6** [z] S Job 9:15; 18:7; Ps 10:2; S Mt 12:37; Lk 19:22 **15:7** [a] Job 38:21 [b] S 1Sa 2:8; Ps 90:2; Pr 8:25 **15:8** [c] Job 29:4; Isa 9:6; 40:13; 41:28; Jer 23:18; Ro 11:34; 1Co 2:11 [d] S Job 12:2 **15:9** [e] S Job 12:3 **15:10** [f] S Job 12:12 [g] S 2Ch 10:6 **15:11** [h] S Ge 37:35; S Job 6:10; 2Co 1:3-4 [i] Zec 1:13 [j] S Dt 8:3; S 32:39; S Job 5:17; 22:22; 23:12; 36:16; Ps 119:11,72; Jer 15:16 **15:12** [k] Job 11:13; 36:13 **15:13** [l] Pr 29:11; Da 11:30 [m] Ps 94:4 [n] S Job 11:8; 22:5; 32:3 **15:14** [o] S Job 14:1 [p] S 2Ch 6:36; S Job 4:17 **15:15** [q] S Job 5:1 [r] S Job 4:18 **15:16** [s] S Lev 5:2; S Job 4:19; Ps 14:1 [t] Job 20:12 [u] Job 12:4; 34:7; Pr 19:28 **15:17** [v] S Job 4:8 **15:18** [w] S Dt 32:7 **15:19** [x] Ge 12:1; Job 22:8

15:20 [y] ver 24; Isa 8:22; 50:11; 66:24 [z] Job 24:1; 27:13-23; Isa 2:12; Jer 46:10; Ob 1:15; Zep 1:7 **15:21** [a] ver 24; S 1Sa 3:11; Job 18:11; 20:25; Jer 6:25; 20:3 [b] Job 22:10; 27:20; Isa 13:3; Jer 51:25,53, 56; 1Th 5:3 **15:22** [c] ver 23; S Job 5:14; 24:17; 38:15; Ps 91:5; SS 3:8 [d] Job 16:13; 18:19; 19:29; 20:24; 27:14; 33:18; 36:12; Pr 7:23; Isa 1:20; Jer 44:27; Hos 9:13; Am 5:19 **15:23** [e] Ps 109:10 [f] Pr 30:17; Eze 39:17; Mt 24:28; Lk 17:37 [g] S ver 22 [h] Job 18:12 **15:24** [i] Isa 8:22; 9:1 [j] S ver 20 [k] Job 18:14 **15:25** [l] Ps 44:16; Isa 10:32; 37:23 [m] S Job 11:8; 35:12; 36:9; 40:8; Ps 2:2-3; 73:9; 75:5; Pr 21:30; Isa 3:16; 45:9 **15:26** [n] Jer 44:16 **15:27** [o] S Jdg 3:17 **15:28** [p] Isa 5:9 [q] S Job 3:14 **15:29** [r] S Job 3:15; S 7:8 [s] Isa 5:8

15:5 See Mt 15:11,17–18.
15:6 *mouth condemns you.* See 9:20.
15:7–10 Eliphaz says that Job presumes to be wise enough to sit among the members of God's council in heaven (see note on 1:6), when in reality he is no wiser than ordinary elders and sages on earth.
15:10 In ancient times, wisdom was associated with advanced age (cf. 32:6–9).
15:11–13 Eliphaz chides Job for replying in rage to his friends' attempts to console him with gentle words, which Eliphaz believes come from God himself (v. 11). But Eliphaz has been guilty of cruel insinuation (ch. 5), and the other two counselors have been even more malicious. Genuine words of comfort for Job have been few indeed (see 4:2–6).
15:14–16 See 25:4–6. Eliphaz repeats what he had already said in 4:17–19, perhaps because he thought the earlier words had come to him through divine revelation (see note on 4:12–21).
15:14 *born of woman.* An echo of Job's words in 14:1.
15:15 *holy ones.* Angels (see note on 5:1).
15:16 *drink up evil like water.* See Elihu's description of Job in 34:7.
15:17–26 Eliphaz now bolsters his earlier advice with traditional wisdom: The wicked can never escape the suffering they deserve.
15:19 *no foreigners moved among them.* Corrupting the community's traditions.
15:20–35 A poem on the fate of the wicked (see 8:11–19). Eliphaz continues with a variety of figures: belligerent sinners who attack God (vv. 24–26); fat, rich wicked people who finally get what they deserve (vv. 27–32); grapevines stripped before the fruit is ripe (v. 33a); olive trees shedding their blossoms (v. 33b). As long as Eliphaz rejects Job's insistence that the wicked go on prospering, he does not have to wrestle with the disturbing corollary: the mystery of why the innocent sometimes suffer.
15:23,30 *darkness.* Death, characterized by the journey to the netherworld (see note on 10:21).

[30]He will not escape the darkness;[t]
a flame[u] will wither his shoots,[v]
and the breath of God's mouth[w] will carry him away.[x]
[31]Let him not deceive[y] himself by trusting what is worthless,[z]
for he will get nothing in return.[a]
[32]Before his time[b] he will wither,[c]
and his branches will not flourish.[d]
[33]He will be like a vine stripped of its unripe grapes,[e]
like an olive tree shedding its blossoms.[f]
[34]For the company of the godless[g] will be barren,
and fire will consume[h] the tents of those who love bribes.[i]
[35]They conceive trouble[j] and give birth to evil;[k]
their womb fashions deceit."

Job 16

16 Then Job replied:

[2]"I have heard many things like these;
you are miserable comforters,[l] all of you![m]
[3]Will your long-winded speeches never end?[n]
What ails you that you keep on arguing?[o]
[4]I also could speak like you,
if you were in my place;
I could make fine speeches against you
and shake my head[p] at you.
[5]But my mouth would encourage you;
comfort[q] from my lips would bring you relief.[r]

[6]"Yet if I speak, my pain is not relieved;
and if I refrain, it does not go away.[s]
[7]Surely, God, you have worn me out;[t]
you have devastated my entire household.[u]
[8]You have shriveled me up — and it has become a witness;
my gauntness[v] rises up and testifies against me.[w]
[9]God assails me and tears[x] me in his anger[y]
and gnashes his teeth at me;[z]
my opponent fastens on me his piercing eyes.[a]
[10]People open their mouths[b] to jeer at me;[c]
they strike my cheek[d] in scorn
and unite together against me.[e]
[11]God has turned me over to the ungodly
and thrown me into the clutches of the wicked.[f]
[12]All was well with me, but he shattered me;
he seized me by the neck and crushed me.[g]
He has made me his target;[h]
[13] his archers surround me.[i]
Without pity, he pierces[j] my kidneys
and spills my gall on the ground.
[14]Again and again[k] he bursts upon me;
he rushes at me like a warrior.[l]

[15]"I have sewed sackcloth[m] over my skin
and buried my brow in the dust.[n]
[16]My face is red with weeping,[o]
dark shadows ring my eyes;[p]
[17]yet my hands have been free of violence[q]
and my prayer is pure.[r]

[18]"Earth, do not cover my blood;[s]
may my cry[t] never be laid to rest![u]
[19]Even now my witness[v] is in heaven;[w]
my advocate is on high.[x]

15:30 [t]S Job 5:14 [u]ver 34; Job 16:7; 20:26; 22:20; 31:12 [v]ver 32; Job 8:19; 18:16; 29:19; Hos 9:1-16; Mal 4:1 [w]S Ex 15:10 [x]Isa 40:23-24 **15:31** [y]Job 31:5; Pr 1:16; 6:18; Isa 44:20; 59:7; Mic 2:11; S Mk 13:5; Jas 1:16 [z]Isa 30:12; 47:10; 59:4; Jer 7:4,8; S Mt 6:19 [a]Job 20:7; 22:13; 27:9; 35:13; Pr 15:29; Isa 1:15; Jer 11:11; Mic 3:4 **15:32** [b]Ecc 7:17 [c]Job 22:16; 36:14; Ps 55:23; 109:8; Pr 10:27 [d]S ver 30 **15:33** [e]Hab 3:17 [f]S Job 4:20 **15:34** [g]S Job 8:13 [h]S ver 30; Heb 10:27 [i]S Ex 23:8; S 1Sa 8:3 **15:35** [j]S Job 5:7 [k]S Job 4:8; S Isa 29:20; Gal 6:7; Jas 1:15 **16:2** [l]Ps 69:20 [m]S Job 6:15 **16:3** [n]Job 11:2; 18:2 [o]S Job 6:26 **16:4** [p]S 2Ki 19:21; Ps 22:7; Isa 37:22; Jer 48:27; La 2:15; Zep 2:15; S Mt 27:39 **16:5** [q]Job 29:25 [r]S Ge 37:35 **16:6** [s]S Job 6:3; S 7:21 **16:7** [t]S Jdg 8:5; S Job 7:3 [u]S Job 1:19 **16:8** [v]Job 17:7; 19:20; 33:21; Ps 6:7; 22:17; 88:9; 102:5; 109:24; La 5:17 [w]S Job 10:17 **16:9** [x]S Job 12:14; Hos 6:1 [y]S Job 9:5; 18:4; 19:11 [z]Job 30:21; Ps 35:16; 37:12; 112:10; La 2:16; Ac 7:54 [a]S Job 13:24 **16:10** [b]Ps 22:13; 35:21 [c]Job 12:4; 19:18; 21:3; 30:1,9; Ps 22:13; 69:12; 119:51 [d]Isa 50:6; La 3:30; Mic 5:1; Ac 23:2 [e]ver 7; S Job 11:3; 19:12; 30:12; Ps 27:3; 35:15; Ac 7:57 **16:11** [f]S Job 9:24 **16:12** [g]S Job 9:17 [h]S Job 6:4; La 3:12 **16:13** [i]S Job 3:23 [j]Job 20:24; Pr 7:23; La 3:13 **16:14** [k]Job 9:17 [l]S Job 10:3; Joel 2:7 **16:15** [m]S Ge 37:34 [n]S Job 2:8 **16:16** [o]ver 20; Ps 6:6 [p]Job 2:7; 17:7; 30:17,30; 33:19; Isa 52:14 **16:17** [q]Isa 55:7; 59:6; Jer 18:11; Jnh 3:8 [r]S Job 6:28; S 10:7; 13:7; Isa 53:9; Zep 3:13 **16:18** [s]S Ge 4:10; Isa 26:21 [t]Ps 5:2; 18:6; 102:1; 119:169 [u]Job 19:24; Ps 66:18-19; Heb 11:4 **16:19** [v]S Ge 31:50; S Ro 1:9; 1Th 2:5 [w]Job 22:12; 42:2 [x]Job 19:27; 21:17; 25:2; 27:13; 31:2; Ps 113:5; Isa 33:5; 57:15; 58:4; 66:1; Mk 11:10

15:35 *They conceive trouble and give birth to evil.* See Isa 59:4 and note. Once initiated, sinful thoughts develop quickly into evil acts (cf. Jas 1:15 and note).

16:2–5 Helpful advice is usually brief and encouraging, not lengthy and judgmental.

16:2 *miserable comforters.* See note on 13:1–12. Job would eventually be comforted, but not by his three friends (see 42:11).

16:3 *long-winded.* See note on 15:2.

16:4 *shake ... head.* A gesture of insult and scorn (see Ps 22:7; Jer 48:27; Mt 27:39).

16:9 The figure here is graphic and disturbing: God, like a ferocious lion (see 10:16), attacks and tears at Job's flesh.

16:10–14 Job sees himself as God's target and views his situation as the reverse of Eliphaz's description in 15:25–26.

16:12 *All was well ... but he shattered me.* See 2:3 and note. *made me his target.* See note on 6:4.

16:15–17 Job summarizes his misery: Though innocent, he continues to suffer.

16:15 *sackcloth ... dust.* Signs of mourning (see notes on Ge 37:34; Jnh 3:5–6).

16:18–21 Verse 18 (see v. 22; 17:1) indicates that Job does not think he will live long enough to be vindicated before his peers. His only hope is that in heaven he has a friend (v. 20), a holy one (see 5:1), who will be his "witness," his "advocate," his "intercessor," one who will plead with God on his behalf (v. 21; see 5:1; 9:33 and notes).

16:18 *blood ... cry.* Job felt that his blood, like Abel's (see Ge 4:10 and note), was innocent and would therefore cry out from the ground after his death.

20 My intercessor[y] is my friend[a][z]
as my eyes pour out[a] tears[b] to God;
21 on behalf of a man he pleads[c] with God
as one pleads for a friend.

22 "Only a few years will pass
before I take the path of no return.[d]

17 1 My spirit[e] is broken,
my days are cut short,[f]
the grave awaits me.[g]
2 Surely mockers[h] surround me;[i]
my eyes must dwell on their
hostility.

3 "Give me, O God, the pledge you
demand.[j]
Who else will put up security[k] for
me?[l]
4 You have closed their minds to
understanding;[m]
therefore you will not let them
triumph.
5 If anyone denounces their friends for
reward,[n]
the eyes of their children will fail.[o]

6 "God has made me a byword[p] to
everyone,[q]
a man in whose face people spit.[r]
7 My eyes have grown dim with grief;[s]
my whole frame is but a shadow.[t]
8 The upright are appalled at this;
the innocent are aroused[u] against the
ungodly.
9 Nevertheless, the righteous[v] will hold
to their ways,
and those with clean hands[w] will
grow stronger.[x]

10 "But come on, all of you, try again!
I will not find a wise man among
you.[y]
11 My days have passed,[z] my plans are
shattered.
Yet the desires of my heart[a]
12 turn night into day;[b]
in the face of the darkness light is
near.[c]
13 If the only home I hope for is the
grave,[d]
if I spread out my bed[e] in the realm
of darkness,[f]
14 if I say to corruption,[g] 'You are my
father,'
and to the worm,[h] 'My mother' or
'My sister,'
15 where then is my hope —[i]
who can see any hope for me?[j]
16 Will it go down to the gates of death?[k]
Will we descend together into the
dust?"[l]

Bildad

18 Then Bildad the Shuhite[m] replied:

2 "When will you end these speeches?[n]
Be sensible, and then we can talk.
3 Why are we regarded as cattle[o]
and considered stupid in your sight?[p]
4 You who tear yourself[q] to pieces in
your anger,[r]
is the earth to be abandoned for
your sake?
Or must the rocks be moved from
their place?[s]

5 "The lamp of a wicked man is snuffed
out;[t]
the flame of his fire stops burning.[u]

[a] 20 Or *My friends treat me with scorn*

16:20 [y] S Ro 8:34 [z] Jn 15:15 [a] La 2:19 [b] S ver 16 **16:21** [c] 1Ki 8:45; Ps 9:4; 140:12 **16:22** [d] S Job 10:21 **17:1** [e] Ps 143:4 [f] Isa 38:12 [g] Ps 88:3-4; Ecc 12:1-7 **17:2** [h] S Job 11:3 [i] S Job 6:14; Ps 22:7; 119:51; Jer 20:7; La 3:14 **17:3** [j] Ps 35:27; 119:122 [k] Pr 6:1 [l] Ps 35:2; 40:17; Isa 38:14 **17:4** [m] S Job 12:12 **17:5** [n] S Ex 22:15 [o] S Job 11:20 **17:6** [p] S 1Ki 9:7; Job 30:9; Jer 15:4 [q] S ver 2 [r] S Nu 12:14 **17:7** [s] S Job 16:8 [t] S Job 2:12; S 16:16 **17:8** [u] S Ex 4:14 **17:9** [v] Pr 4:18 [w] S 2Sa 22:21; S Job 9:30 [x] S 1Sa 2:4; Ps 84:7 **17:10** [y] S Job 12:2 **17:11** [z] ver 15; Isa 38:10 [a] S Job 7:6 **17:12** [b] Isa 50:11 [c] Job 5:17-26; S 11:17 **17:13** [d] S 2Sa 14:14; S Job 3:13 [e] Ps 139:8 [f] Ps 88:18 **17:14** [g] Job 13:28; 30:28, 30; Ps 16:10; 49:9 [h] S Job 4:19; S 7:5 **17:15** [i] S Job 7:6 [j] Ps 31:22; La 3:18; Eze 37:11 **17:16** [k] S Job 7:9; 33:28; Ps 9:13; 30:3; 107:18; Isa 38:10, 17; Jnh 2:6 [l] S Ge 2:7; S Job 3:19; 20:11; 21:26 **18:1** [m] S Job 8:1 **18:2** [n] S Job 8:2; S 16:3 **18:3** [o] S Job 12:7 [p] Ps 73:22 **18:4** [q] Job 13:14 [r] S Job 16:9 [s] Job 14:18 **18:5** [t] Job 21:17; 35:15; Pr 13:9; 20:20; 24:20; Jer 25:10; Mt 25:8; Jn 8:12 [u] S Job 5:14; 12:25; 24:17; 38:15

16:20 *intercessor.* The Hebrew for this word is translated "messenger" in 33:23 (see note on 33:23 – 28).
16:22 *Only a few years will pass.* Job does not expect his death immediately. *path of no return.* Path to the netherworld (see notes on 7:9; 10:21; see also 17:1).
17:1 *the grave awaits me.* See note on vv. 10 – 16.
17:3 *Give me ... the pledge you demand.* Job is asking God for a guarantee that he is right, that he is not guilty of sins that deserve punishment (as his counselors have said).
17:4 *their minds.* Those of his three friends.
17:5 Job quotes a proverb to counter the false accusations of his friends.
17:6 – 9 The guarantee Job asked for (v. 3) is not provided, so he feels that God is responsible for making him an object of scorn. If the tone of vv. 8 – 9 is intended as sarcastic (as v. 10 would seem to indicate), the so-called "upright" and "innocent" (v. 8) are the three counselors.
17:6 *byword.* See 30:9; an object of scorn and ridicule (see the covenant curse in Dt 28:37). *in whose face people spit.* See 30:10; see also Isa 50:6 and note; Mt 27:30.
17:7 *frame is but a shadow.* See note on 2:7.
17:10 – 16 Zophar had promised that Job's repentance would turn his darkness into light (11:17). Job now makes a parody on such advice (vv. 12 – 16). His only hope is the grave (see v. 1), which will not be as his home had been (vv. 13 – 15).
17:13 *home.* See Ecc 12:5 and note. *darkness.* The netherworld (see 10:21; 18:18 and notes).
17:14 In the grave, one's family consists only of decomposition and maggots.
17:15 *where ... is my hope ... ?* See 14:19.
17:16 *gates of death.* See 38:17; Mt 16:18. In Mesopotamian literature, all who entered the netherworld passed through a series of seven gates. *dust.* See note on 7:21.
18:1 – 4 Bildad resents what he perceives to be a belittling attitude. He considers Job's emotional reaction as self-centered and irrational.
18:5 – 21 Another poem on the fate of the wicked (see 8:11 – 19; 15:20 – 35). Bildad wants to convince Job that he is wrong when he claims that the righteous suffer and the wicked prosper. Bildad is absolutely certain that every wicked person gets paid in full, in this life, for his wicked deeds.
18:5 *The lamp of a wicked man is snuffed out.* See 21:17; Pr 13:9 and note. Life, symbolized by light, is extinguished.

6 The light in his tent[v] becomes dark;[w]
the lamp beside him goes out.[x]
7 The vigor[y] of his step is weakened;[z]
his own schemes[a] throw him down.[b]
8 His feet thrust him into a net;[c]
he wanders into its mesh.
9 A trap seizes him by the heel;
a snare[d] holds him fast.[e]
10 A noose[f] is hidden for him on the ground;
a trap[g] lies in his path.[h]
11 Terrors[i] startle him on every side[j]
and dog[k] his every step.
12 Calamity[l] is hungry[m] for him;
disaster[n] is ready for him when he falls.[o]
13 It eats away parts of his skin;[p]
death's firstborn devours his limbs.[q]
14 He is torn from the security of his tent[r]
and marched off to the king[s] of terrors.[t]
15 Fire resides[a] in his tent;[u]
burning sulfur[v] is scattered over his dwelling.
16 His roots dry up below[w]
and his branches wither above.[x]
17 The memory of him perishes from the earth;[y]
he has no name[z] in the land.[a]
18 He is driven from light into the realm of darkness[b]
and is banished[c] from the world.[d]
19 He has no offspring[e] or descendants[f] among his people,
no survivor[g] where once he lived.[h]
20 People of the west are appalled[i] at his fate;[j]
those of the east are seized with horror.
21 Surely such is the dwelling[k] of an evil man;[l]
such is the place[m] of one who does not know God."[n]

18:6 [v]S Job 8:22 [w]S Job 5:14 [x]S Job 11:17; S 12:25 **18:7** [y]S Job 13:26 [z]Ps 18:36; Pr 4:12 [a]S Job 5:13 [b]S Job 15:6 **18:8** [c]Job 19:6; Ps 9:15; 10:9; 35:7; 57:6; 66:11; 140:5; La 1:13; Mic 7:2; Hab 1:15 **18:9** [d]Job 22:10; 30:12; Isa 24:18; Jer 48:44; Am 5:19 [e]Pr 5:22 **18:10** [f]Pr 7:22; Isa 51:20 [g]S 1Sa 28:9 [h]Ps 140:5 **18:11** [i]ver 14; S Job 6:4; 20:25; 24:17; Ps 55:4; 88:15; Isa 28:19; Jer 15:8; La 2:22 [j]S Job 15:21; Ps 31:13 [k]ver 18; Job 20:8; Isa 22:18 **18:12** [l]Job 21:17 [m]Isa 8:21; 9:20; 65:13 [n]Job 31:3 [o]Job 15:23 **18:13** [p]Nu 12:12 [q]Zec 14:12 **18:14** [r]S Job 8:22 [s]Job 15:24 [t]S ver 11 **18:15** [u]ver 18; Job 20:26 [v]S Ge 19:24 **18:16** [w]Isa 5:24; Hos 5:12; Am 2:9 [x]S Ge 27:28; S Job 8:12; S 15:30 **18:17** [y]S Dt 32:26 [z]Dt 9:14; Ps 9:5; 69:28; Pr 10:7; Isa 14:22 [a]Job 24:20; Ps 34:16; Pr 2:22; 10:7; Isa 49:15 **18:18** [b]S Job 5:14 [c]S ver 11 [d]S Job 11:20; 30:8 **18:19** [e]Ps 37:28; Isa 1:4; 14:20; Jer 22:30 [f]Ps 21:10; 109:13; Isa 14:22 [g]S 2Ki 10:11; S Eze 17:8 [h]Job 27:14-15 **18:20** [i]Ps 22:6-7; Isa 52:14; 53:2-3; Eze 27:35 [j]Ps 37:13; Jer 46:21; 50:27,31; Eze 7:7 **18:21** [k]Job 21:28 [l]Isa 57:20 [m]S Job 7:10 [n]S Job 4:21; 1Th 4:5 **19:2** [o]Job 13:25 [p]Job 6:9 **19:3** [q]S Ge 31:7 [r]Job 20:3 **19:4** [s]Job 6:24 **19:5** [t]Ps 35:26; 38:16; 55:12 **19:6** [u]S Job 6:29 [v]S Job 18:8 [w]S Job 10:3 **19:7** [x]Job 30:20; Ps 22:2 [y]Job 30:24, 28; 31:35; Ps 5:2 [z]S Job 9:24; Hab 1:2-4 **19:8** [a]La 3:7; Hos 2:6 [b]Job 3:26; 23:17; 30:26; Ecc 6:4; Isa 59:9; Jer 8:15; 14:19; La 3:2 **19:9** [c]S Job 12:17 [d]Ge 43:28; Ex 12:42; Ps 15:4; 50:23; Pr 14:31 [e]S Job 2:8; 29:14; Ps 89:39,44; La 5:16 **19:10** [f]S Job 12:14 [g]S Job 7:6 [h]S Job 14:7 **19:11** [i]Job 16:9 [j]S Job 13:24

Job

19 Then Job replied:

2 "How long will you torment[o] me
and crush[p] me with words?
3 Ten times[q] now you have reproached[r] me;
shamelessly you attack me.
4 If it is true that I have gone astray,
my error[s] remains my concern alone.
5 If indeed you would exalt yourselves above me[t]
and use my humiliation against me,
6 then know that God has wronged me[u]
and drawn his net[v] around me.[w]

7 "Though I cry, 'Violence!' I get no response;[x]
though I call for help,[y] there is no justice.[z]
8 He has blocked my way so I cannot pass;[a]
he has shrouded my paths in darkness.[b]
9 He has stripped[c] me of my honor[d]
and removed the crown from my head.[e]
10 He tears me down[f] on every side till I am gone;
he uproots my hope[g] like a tree.[h]
11 His anger[i] burns against me;
he counts me among his enemies.[j]

[a] 15 Or *Nothing he had remains*

18:13 *death's firstborn.* Probably a deadly disease (cf. 5:7 and note).

18:14 *king of terrors.* A vivid figure of speech referring to death (or the realm of the dead), which is personified in v. 13. Canaanite literature pictured death (or the grave) as the devouring god Mot. Isaiah reverses the figure and envisions the Lord as swallowing up death forever (see Isa 25:8 and note; see also 1Co 15:54).

18:15 *burning sulfur.* Reminiscent of the destruction of Sodom and Gomorrah (see Ge 19:24 and note).

18:16 *roots … and … branches.* Figurative for descendants (see, e.g., Isa 11:1,10) and/or ancestors (see, e.g., Jdg 5:14; Isa 14:29). See also Am 2:9 and note.

18:17 *memory of him perishes.* Apparently, for Bildad, the only retribution beyond death is having one's memory (name) cut off by not leaving any heirs (see v. 19).

18:18 *darkness.* The netherworld (see 10:21 and note; 17:13).

18:21 *evil man … does not know God.* Having no intimate knowledge of God is synonymous with being wicked (see Hos 4:1–2,6).

19:3 *Ten times.* Several times. Ten is often used as a round number (see, e.g., Ge 31:41; 1Sa 1:8).

19:4 *my concern alone.* Job's friends have no right to interfere or to behave as if they were God (see v. 22).

19:6 *wronged.* Cf. 40:8 and note. The Hebrew for this verb is twice translated "pervert" in 8:3 (see note there), where Bildad denied that God perverts justice. But Job, struggling with the enigma of his suffering, can only conclude that God is his enemy, though in fact he is his friend who delights in him (see 1:8; 2:3). Job's true enemy, of course, is Satan, the accuser (see notes on 1:6,12). *drawn his net.* The wicked may get themselves into trouble, as Bildad had pointed out (see 18:8–10), but Job here attributes his suffering to God.

19:7 *I cry, 'Violence!'* See Hab 1:2–4 and notes.

19:8–12 In Job's mind, God is at war with him (see 16:10–14 and note).

19:10 *uproots my hope like a tree.* Unlike 14:7–9, where Job had used as a symbol of hope a tree that is cut down but later sprouts again. See also 24:20.

12 His troops advance in force;[k]
they build a siege ramp[l] against me
and encamp around my tent.[m]

13 "He has alienated my family[n] from me;
my acquaintances are completely
estranged from me.[o]
14 My relatives have gone away;
my closest friends[p] have forgotten me.
15 My guests[q] and my female servants[r]
count me a foreigner;
they look on me as on a stranger.
16 I summon my servant, but he does not
answer,
though I beg him with my own
mouth.
17 My breath is offensive to my wife;
I am loathsome[s] to my own family.
18 Even the little boys[t] scorn me;
when I appear, they ridicule me.[u]
19 All my intimate friends[v] detest me;[w]
those I love have turned against me.[x]
20 I am nothing but skin and bones;[y]
I have escaped only by the skin of
my teeth.[a]

21 "Have pity on me, my friends,[z] have pity,
for the hand of God has struck[a] me.
22 Why do you pursue[b] me as God does?[c]
Will you never get enough of my
flesh?[d]

23 "Oh, that my words were recorded,
that they were written on a scroll,[e]
24 that they were inscribed with an iron
tool[f] on[b] lead,
or engraved in rock forever![g]

25 I know that my redeemer[c][h] lives,[i]
and that in the end he will stand on
the earth.[d]
26 And after my skin has been destroyed,
yet[e] in[f] my flesh I will see God;[j]
27 I myself will see him
with my own eyes[k]—I, and not
another.
How my heart yearns[l] within me!

28 "If you say, 'How we will hound[m] him,
since the root of the trouble lies in
him,[g]'
29 you should fear the sword yourselves;
for wrath will bring punishment by
the sword,[n]
and then you will know that there is
judgment.[h]"[o]

Zophar

20 Then Zophar the Naamathite[p] replied:

2 "My troubled thoughts prompt me to
answer
because I am greatly disturbed.[q]

[a] 20 Or *only by my gums* [b] 24 Or *and* [c] 25 Or *vindicator* [d] 25 Or *on my grave* [e] 26 Or *And after I awake, / though this body has been destroyed, / then* [f] 26 Or *destroyed, / apart from* [g] 28 Many Hebrew manuscripts, Septuagint and Vulgate; most Hebrew manuscripts *me* [h] 29 Or *sword, / that you may come to know the Almighty*

19:12 [k] S Job 16:13 [l] S Job 16:10 [m] S Job 3:23 **19:13** [n] Ps 69:8 [o] ver 19; Job 16:7; 42:11; Ps 31:11; 38:11; 88:8 **19:14** [p] ver 19; S 2Sa 15:12; Job 12:4; 16:20; Ps 88:18; Jer 20:10; 38:22 **19:15** [q] Ge 14:14 [r] Ecc 2:7 **19:17** [s] Ps 38:5 **19:18** [t] S 2Ki 2:23 [u] S Job 16:10 **19:19** [v] S ver 14; S Job 6:14; Ps 55:12-13 [w] Job 30:10 [x] S ver 13; Jn 13:18 **19:20** [y] S Job 2:5 **19:21** [z] S Job 6:14 [a] S Jdg 2:15; S Job 4:5; S 10:3; La 3:1 **19:22** [b] S Job 13:25 [c] ver 6 [d] S 2Ch 28:9; Ps 14:4; 27:2; 69:26; Pr 30:14; Isa 53:4 **19:23** [e] S Ex 17:14; S Ps 40:7; S Isa 8:1 **19:24** [f] Jer 17:1 [g] S Job 16:18 **19:25** [h] S Ex 6:6; S Lev 25:25; Ps 68:5; 78:35; Pr 23:11; Isa 41:14; 43:14; 44:6,24; 47:4; 48:17; 49:26; 54:5; 59:20; 60:16 [i] S 1Sa 14:39; Job 16:19 **19:26** [j] S Nu 12:8; S Mt 5:8; 1Co 13:12; 1Jn 3:2 **19:27** [k] Lk 2:30 [l] Ps 42:1; 63:1; 84:2 **19:28** [m] S Job 13:25 **19:29** [n] Job 15:22 [o] Job 27:13-23; Ps 1:5; 9:7; 58:11; Ecc 3:17; 11:9; 12:14 **20:1** [p] S Job 2:11 **20:2** [q] Ps 42:5; La 1:20

19:12 *siege ramp.* See 30:12.

19:13–19 See Jer 12:6 and note. Very little in life hurts more than rejection by one's family and friends. Job's children are gone, and his wife, brothers, friends and servants find him repulsive.

19:17 *breath is offensive.* See note on 2:7.

19:18 *little boys scorn me.* An intolerable insult in a patriarchal society, where one's elders were to be honored and respected (see Ex 20:12 and note).

19:20 *skin and bones.* See note on 2:7. *skin of my teeth.* The NIV text note understands the phrase to imply that even Job's teeth are gone.

19:21 *hand of God has struck me.* See note on v. 6; see also 1:11; 2:4–6.

19:23–27 Probably the best-known and most-loved passage in the book of Job, reaching a high point in Job's understanding of his own situation and of his relationship to God. Its position between two sections in which Job pleads with (vv. 21–22) and then warns (vv. 28–29) his friends causes it to stand out even more boldly.

19:23 *my words.* Job wishes that his complaint and defense were recorded, so that even after his death they would endure until he is finally vindicated. *scroll.* See note on Ex 17:14.

19:24 *iron.* See also 20:24; 28:2; 40:18; 41:27. Iron did not come into common use in the ancient Near East until the twelfth century BC, though limited use of iron in the region is attested at least as early as 2000 BC.

19:25 *I know that my redeemer lives.* This staunch confession of faith has been appropriated by generations of Christians, especially through the medium of Handel's *The Messiah.* But these celebrate redemption from guilt and judgment; Job had something else in mind. Although in other contexts he desires a "vindicator" (see NIV text note; see also Pr 23:11 and note) as an advocate in heaven who would plead with God on his behalf (see 9:33–34; 16:18–21 and notes; see also note on 5:1), here the "redeemer" seems to be none other than God himself (see note on Ru 2:20). Job expresses confidence that ultimately God will vindicate his faithful servants in the face of all false accusations. *in the end.* Lit. "afterward" (after Job's life has ended). *he will stand.* To defend and vindicate me (see 42:7–10 and notes).

19:26 *my skin has been destroyed.* Job senses that the ravages of his disease will eventually bring about his death. *I will see God.* He is absolutely certain, however, that death is not the end of existence and that someday he will stand in the presence of his divine "redeemer" (v. 25) and see him with his own eyes (see v. 27; see also Mt 5:8; 1Jn 3:2). See note on 42:5.

19:28 *hound.* The Hebrew for this verb is translated "pursue" in v. 22. It serves as a clue that Job's tirade against the counselors is being resumed after the intervening section (vv. 23–27).

20:1–29 Yet another poem on the fate of the wicked as held by the traditional theology of Job's friends (see 8:11–19; 15:20–35; 18:5–21).

20:2–3 Zophar takes Job's words, especially his closing words in 19:28–29, as a personal affront. Job has dared to

3 I hear a rebuke[r] that dishonors me,
and my understanding inspires me
to reply.

4 "Surely you know how it has been
from of old,[s]
ever since mankind[a] was placed on
the earth,
5 that the mirth of the wicked[t] is brief,
the joy of the godless[u] lasts but a
moment.[v]
6 Though the pride[w] of the godless
person reaches to the heavens[x]
and his head touches the clouds,[y]
7 he will perish forever,[z] like his own
dung;
those who have seen him will say,
'Where is he?'[a]
8 Like a dream[b] he flies away,[c] no more
to be found,
banished[d] like a vision of the night.[e]
9 The eye that saw him will not see him
again;
his place will look on him no more.[f]
10 His children[g] must make amends to the
poor;
his own hands must give back his
wealth.[h]
11 The youthful vigor[i] that fills his bones[j]
will lie with him in the dust.[k]

12 "Though evil[l] is sweet in his mouth
and he hides it under his tongue,[m]
13 though he cannot bear to let it go
and lets it linger in his mouth,[n]
14 yet his food will turn sour in his
stomach;[o]
it will become the venom of
serpents[p] within him.
15 He will spit out the riches[q] he
swallowed;
God will make his stomach vomit[r]
them up.
16 He will suck the poison[s] of serpents;
the fangs of an adder will kill him.[t]
17 He will not enjoy the streams,
the rivers[u] flowing with honey[v] and
cream.[w]

20:3 [r]Job 19:3 **20:4** [s]Dt 4:32; S 32:7 **20:5** [t]Ps 94:3 [u]S Job 8:13 [v]S Job 8:12; Ps 37:35-36; 73:19 **20:6** [w]Job 33:17; Isa 16:6 [x]S Ge 11:4 [y]Isa 14:13-14; Ob 1:3-4 **20:7** [z]S Job 4:20 [a]S Job 7:8; S 14:20 **20:8** [b]Ps 73:20; Ecc 5:3 [c]Ps 90:10; Ecc 6:12; 12:7 [d]S Job 18:11 [e]Job 27:20; 34:20; Ps 90:5; Isa 17:14; 29:7 **20:9** [f]S Job 7:8 **20:10** [g]S Job 5:4 [h]ver 15, 18, 20; S Job 3:15; 31:8 **20:11** [i]S Job 13:26 [j]Job 21:24 [k]S Job 17:16 **20:12** [l]S Job 15:16 [m]Ps 10:7; 140:3 **20:13** [n]S Nu 11:18-20 **20:14** [o]Pr 20:17; Jer 2:19; 4:18; Rev 10:9 [p]S Nu 21:6 **20:15** [q]S ver 10 [r]S Lev 18:25 **20:16** [s]S Dt 32:32 [t]Dt 32:24 **20:17** [u]Ps 36:8 [v]Dt 32:13 [w]Dt 32:14; Job 29:6

20:18 [x]S ver 10; S Job 5:5 [y]Ps 109:11 **20:19** [z]S Job 5:16; Ps 10:2; 94:6; 109:16 [a]S Dt 15:11; 24:14; Job 24:4, 14; 35:9; Pr 14:31;

18 What he toiled for he must give back
uneaten;[x]
he will not enjoy the profit from his
trading.[y]
19 For he has oppressed the poor[z] and left
them destitute;[a]
he has seized houses[b] he did not
build.

20 "Surely he will have no respite from
his craving;[c]
he cannot save himself by his
treasure.[d]
21 Nothing is left for him to devour;
his prosperity will not endure.[e]
22 In the midst of his plenty, distress will
overtake him;[f]
the full force of misery will come
upon him.[g]
23 When he has filled his belly,[h]
God will vent his burning anger[i]
against him
and rain down his blows on him.[j]
24 Though he flees[k] from an iron weapon,
a bronze-tipped arrow pierces him.[l]
25 He pulls it out of his back,
the gleaming point out of his liver.
Terrors[m] will come over him;[n]
26 total darkness[o] lies in wait for his
treasures.
A fire[p] unfanned will consume him[q]
and devour what is left in his tent.[r]
27 The heavens will expose his guilt;
the earth will rise up against him.[s]
28 A flood will carry off his house,[t]
rushing waters[b] on the day of God's
wrath.[u]

[a] 4 Or *Adam* [b] 28 Or *The possessions in his house will be carried off, / washed away*

28:28; Am 8:4 [b]Isa 5:8 **20:20** [c]Ecc 5:12-14 [d]S ver 10; Pr 11:4; Zep 1:18; Lk 12:15 **20:21** [e]S Job 7:8 **20:22** [f]S Jdg 2:15; Lk 12:16-20 [g]ver 29; Job 21:17, 30; 31:2-3 **20:23** [h]S Nu 11:18-20 [i]La 4:11; Eze 5:13; 6:12 [j]ver 14; Ps 78:30-31 **20:24** [k]Isa 24:18; Jer 46:21; 48:44 [l]S Job 15:22 **20:25** [m]S Job 18:11 [n]S Job 15:21; Ps 88:15-16 **20:26** [o]S Job 5:14 [p]S Job 1:16 [q]Job 15:34; 26:6; 28:22; 31:12; Ps 21:9 [r]S Job 18:15 **20:27** [s]S Dt 31:28 **20:28** [t]Dt 28:31; Mt 7:26-27 [u]ver 29; Nu 14:28-32; Job 21:17, 20, 30; 40:11; Ps 60:3; 75:8; Pr 16:4; Isa 24:18; 51:17; Am 5:18; Jn 3:36; Ro 1:18; Eph 5:6

assert that on Zophar's theory of retribution Zophar himself is due for punishment.

20:4–11 Zophar is proud that he is a healthy and prosperous man, for, in his view, that in itself is proof of his goodness and righteousness. But the joy and vigor of the wicked will always be brief and elusive (see Ps 73:18–20 and note).

20:6 *pride … reaches to the heavens.* See Ge 11:4 and note.

20:7 *dung.* A symbol of what is temporary and worthless (see 1Ki 14:10).

20:10,19 Oppression of the poor is the mark of the truly wicked (see, e.g., Am 2:6–8 and notes; 8:4–8). On this subject, Job had no quarrel with Zophar (see 31:16–23).

20:11 *dust.* See note on 7:21.

20:12–15 The wicked deeds of evil people are like tasty food that pleases their palates but turns sour in their stomachs.

20:15 *riches he swallowed.* After taking what belonged to the poor (see note on vv. 10,19).

20:17 *honey and cream.* See 29:6 and note; cf. Dt 6:3 and note.

20:18 *What he toiled for … he will not enjoy.* A common theme in wisdom literature (see, e.g., Ecc 2:18–23).

20:20–25 Although the wicked may fill their bellies, when God vents his anger against them there will be nothing for them to eat.

20:24 *iron.* See note on 19:24.

20:26 *darkness.* See note on 10:21.

20:27 See Dt 30:19 and note.

20:28 *flood … rushing waters.* Caused by intermittent streams that can overflow and cause extensive damage during the rainy season (see 6:15–16).

29 Such is the fate God allots the wicked,
the heritage appointed for them by God."[v]

Job

21

Then Job replied:

2 "Listen carefully to my words;[w]
let this be the consolation you give me.[x]
3 Bear with me while I speak,
and after I have spoken, mock on.[y]

4 "Is my complaint[z] directed to a human being?
Why should I not be impatient?[a]
5 Look at me and be appalled;
clap your hand over your mouth.[b]
6 When I think about this, I am terrified;[c]
trembling seizes my body.[d]
7 Why do the wicked live on,
growing old and increasing in power?[e]
8 They see their children established around them,
their offspring before their eyes.[f]
9 Their homes are safe and free from fear;[g]
the rod of God is not on them.[h]
10 Their bulls never fail to breed;
their cows calve and do not miscarry.[i]
11 They send forth their children as a flock;[j]
their little ones dance about.
12 They sing to the music of timbrel and lyre;[k]
they make merry to the sound of the pipe.[l]
13 They spend their years in prosperity[m]
and go down to the grave[n] in peace.[a][o]
14 Yet they say to God, 'Leave us alone![p]
We have no desire to know your ways.[q]
15 Who is the Almighty, that we should serve him?
What would we gain by praying to him?'[r]
16 But their prosperity is not in their own hands,
so I stand aloof from the plans of the wicked.[s]

17 "Yet how often is the lamp of the wicked snuffed out?[t]
How often does calamity[u] come upon them,
the fate God allots in his anger?[v]
18 How often are they like straw before the wind,
like chaff[w] swept away[x] by a gale?[y]
19 It is said, 'God stores up the punishment of the wicked for their children.'[z]
Let him repay the wicked, so that they themselves will experience it![a]
20 Let their own eyes see their destruction;[b]
let them drink[c] the cup of the wrath of the Almighty.[d]
21 For what do they care about the families they leave behind[e]
when their allotted months[f] come to an end?[g]

22 "Can anyone teach knowledge to God,[h]
since he judges even the highest?[i]
23 One person dies in full vigor,[j]
completely secure and at ease,[k]

[a] 13 Or *in an instant*

20:29 [v] S ver 22; S Job 15:20; 22:5; 31:2; 36:17; Jer 13:25; Rev 21:8 **21:2** [w] S Job 13:17 [x] ver 34 **21:3** [y] S Job 6:14; S 11:3; S 16:10 **21:4** [z] S Job 7:11 [a] S Job 6:3 **21:5** [b] S Jdg 18:19; Job 29:9; 40:4 **21:6** [c] S Ge 45:3 [d] S Job 4:14 **21:7** [e] ver 13; S Job 9:24; 12:19; Ps 37:1; 73:3; Ecc 7:15; 8:14; Hab 1:13; Mal 3:15 **21:8** [f] Ps 17:14; Mal 3:15 **21:9** [g] S Job 5:24 [h] S Job 9:34 **21:10** [i] Ex 23:26 **21:11** [j] Ps 78:52; 107:41 **21:12** [k] Ps 33:2 [l] S Ge 4:21; S 1Ch 15:16; Ps 71:22; 81:2; 108:2; Isa 5:12; Mt 11:17 **21:13** [m] S ver 7; S Job 8:7; Ps 10:1-12; 94:3 [n] Job 24:19; Ps 49:14; Isa 14:15 [o] S Job 3:13 **21:14** [p] S Job 4:17; 22:17; Isa 30:11 [q] S Dt 32:15; S 1Sa 15:11; Ps 95:10; Pr 1:29; Jer 2:20,31 **21:15** [r] S Job 5:2; 34:9; 35:3; Ps 73:13; 139:20; Isa 48:5; Jer 9:6; 44:17 **21:16** [s] Job 22:18; Ps 1:1; 26:5; 36:1 **21:17** [t] S Job 18:5 [u] Job 18:12 [v] S Job 20:22,28 **21:18** [w] S Job 13:25 [x] S Ge 19:15; S Job 7:10; Pr 10:25 [y] S Ge 7:23 **21:19** [z] Ex 20:5; Jer 31:29; Eze 18:2; Jn 9:2 [a] Jer 25:14; 50:29; 51:6,24,56 **21:20** [b] S Ex 32:33; Nu 16:22; S 2Ki 14:6; Jer 42:16 [c] Job 6:4 [d] S Job 20:28; Jer 25:15; Rev 14:10 **21:21** [e] Job 14:22 [f] S Job 14:5 [g] S Job 14:21; Ecc 9:5-6 **21:22** [h] Job 35:11; 36:22; 39:17; Ps 94:12; Isa 40:13-14; Jer 32:33; Ro 11:34 [i] S Job 4:18; Ps 82:1; 86:8; 135:5 **21:23** [j] S Ge 15:15; S Job 13:26 [k] S Job 3:13

20:29 Like Bildad in 18:21 (see note there), Zophar concludes his speech with a summary statement in which he claims that all he has said is in accord with God's plans for judging sinners. *Such is the fate God allots the wicked.* Repeated almost verbatim by Job in 27:13.
21:2 *consolation you give me.* See v. 34 ("you console me"), which, with v. 2, frames Job's reply to Zophar.
21:4 *Is my complaint directed to a human being?* No, says Job, I am complaining to God, because he is responsible for my condition—at least Job so perceived it. *impatient.* See note on 9:2–3.
21:5 *Look at me.* Job addresses his three friends.
21:6 *this.* His complaint to God. *I am terrified.* To contemplate the morally upside-down situation in which the wicked flourish.
21:7–15 Job's counselors have elaborated on the fate of the wicked (see 8:11–19; 15:20–35; 18:5–21; ch. 20), but Job insists that experience shows just the reverse of what his friends have said. The wicked, who want to know nothing of God's ways and who even consider prayer a useless exercise (vv. 14–15), flourish in all they do. Far from dying prematurely, as Zophar assumed concerning them (see 20:11), they live long and increase in power (v. 7). Bildad's claim that the wicked have no offspring or descendants (see 18:19) Job flatly denies (vv. 8,11).
21:9 *rod of God.* See note on 9:34.
21:13 *peace.* The Hebrew root underlying this word is translated "those who live quietly" in Ps 35:20.
21:16 See 22:18. Job disavows the unholy "plans of the wicked" and knows that God is in control (see v. 17), but such knowledge makes God all the more of an enigma to him.
21:17 *lamp of the wicked snuffed out.* See 18:5 and note.
21:18 *straw … chaff.* See 13:25; see also note on Ps 1:4.
21:20 *drink … wrath of the Almighty.* See note on Isa 51:17.
21:22 *Can anyone teach … God … ?* See Isa 40:14. On the contrary, God is the one who does the teaching (see 35:11; 36:22; chs. 38–41).

[24]well nourished[l] in body,[a]
bones[m] rich with marrow.[n]
[25]Another dies in bitterness of soul,[o]
never having enjoyed anything good.
[26]Side by side they lie in the dust,[p]
and worms[q] cover them both.[r]

[27]"I know full well what you are thinking,
the schemes by which you would wrong me.
[28]You say, 'Where now is the house of the great,[s]
the tents where the wicked lived?'[t]
[29]Have you never questioned those who travel?
Have you paid no regard to their accounts—
[30]that the wicked are spared from the day of calamity,[u]
that they are delivered from[b] the day of wrath?[v]
[31]Who denounces their conduct to their face?
Who repays them for what they have done?[w]
[32]They are carried to the grave,
and watch is kept over their tombs.[x]
[33]The soil in the valley is sweet to them;[y]
everyone follows after them,
and a countless throng goes[c] before them.[z]

[34]"So how can you console me[a] with your nonsense?
Nothing is left of your answers but falsehood!"[b]

Eliphaz

22 Then Eliphaz the Temanite[c] replied:

[2]"Can a man be of benefit to God?[d]
Can even a wise person benefit him?[e]
[3]What pleasure[f] would it give the Almighty if you were righteous?[g]
What would he gain if your ways were blameless?[h]

[4]"Is it for your piety that he rebukes you
and brings charges against you?[i]
[5]Is not your wickedness great?
Are not your sins[j] endless?[k]
[6]You demanded security[l] from your relatives for no reason;[m]
you stripped people of their clothing, leaving them naked.[n]
[7]You gave no water[o] to the weary
and you withheld food from the hungry,[p]
[8]though you were a powerful man, owning land[q]—
an honored man,[r] living on it.[s]
[9]And you sent widows[t] away empty-handed[u]
and broke the strength of the fatherless.[v]
[10]That is why snares[w] are all around you,[x]
why sudden peril terrifies you,[y]
[11]why it is so dark[z] you cannot see,
and why a flood of water covers you.[a]

[12]"Is not God in the heights of heaven?[b]
And see how lofty are the highest stars!

21:24 [l]Ps 73:4 [m]Job 20:11 [n]Pr 3:8 **21:25** [o]S Job 10:1 **21:26** [p]S Job 17:16 [q]S Job 7:5 [r]Job 24:20; Ecc 9:2-3; Isa 14:11 **21:28** [s]Job 1:3; 12:21; 29:25; 31:37 [t]S Job 8:22 **21:30** [u]Job 31:3 [v]S Job 20:22, 28; S Isa 5:30; Ro 2:5; 2Pe 2:9 **21:31** [w]Job 34:11; Ps 62:12; Pr 24:11-12; Isa 59:18 **21:32** [x]Isa 14:18 **21:33** [y]Job 3:22 [z]S Job 3:19 **21:34** [a]ver 2 [b]S Job 6:15; 8:20 **22:1** [c]S Job 4:1 **22:2** [d]Lk 17:10 [e]S Job 7:17 **22:3** [f]Isa 1:11; Hag 1:8 [g]Ps 143:2 [h]Job 35:7; Pr 9:12 **22:4** [i]S Job 9:3; 19:29; Ps 143:2; Isa 3:14; Eze 20:35 **22:5** [j]S Ezr 9:13; S Job 15:5 [k]S Job 15:13; S 20:29; 29:17 **22:6** [l]S Ex 22:26 [m]S 2Ki 4:1 [n]S Ex 22:27; Dt 24:12-13 **22:7** [o]Mt 10:42 [p]ver 9; Job 29:12; 31:17,21, 31; Isa 58:7, 10; Eze 18:7; Mt 25:42

[a] *24* The meaning of the Hebrew for this word is uncertain. [b] *30* Or *wicked are reserved for the day of calamity, / that they are brought forth to* [c] *33* Or *them, / as a countless throng went*

22:8 [q]S Job 15:19 [r]Isa 3:3; 5:13; 9:15 [s]S Job 12:19 **22:9** [t]Job 29:13; 31:16; Ps 146:9 [u]Job 24:3, 21; Isa 10:2; Lk 1:53 [v]S ver 7; S Job 6:27; S Isa 1:17 **22:10** [w]S Job 18:9 [x]S Job 10:3 [y]S Job 15:21 **22:11** [z]S Job 5:14 [a]S Ge 7:23; Job 36:28; 38:34, 37; Ps 69:1-2; 124:4-5; Isa 58:10-11; La 3:54 **22:12** [b]S Job 11:8; S 16:19

21:26 *dust.* See note on 7:21.
21:34 *how can you console me . . . ?* See 16:2 and note.
22:1—26:14 The third cycle of speeches, unlike the first (chs. 4–14) and second (chs. 15–21), is truncated and abbreviated. Bildad's speech is very brief (25:1–6), and Zophar does not speak at all. The dialogue between Job and his friends comes to an end because the friends cannot convince Job of his guilt—Job cannot acknowledge what is not true.
22:1 *Eliphaz the Temanite.* See note on 4:1.
22:2–4 Eliphaz's odd reasoning is as follows: All things have their origin in God. So when people give back what God has given them, that does not enhance God in any way. Indeed, God is indifferent to human goodness, because goodness is expected of them. It is when people become wicked that God is aroused (v. 4).
22:4 *piety.* See note on 4:6. *brings charges against.* See note on 9:3.
22:5–11 In his earlier speeches, Eliphaz was the least caustic and at first even offered consolation (4:6; 5:17). But despite what he said in 4:3–4, Eliphaz now reprimands Job for gross social sins against the needy, who are naked and hungry (vv. 6–7), and against widows and the fatherless (v. 9). The only proof Eliphaz has for Job's alleged wickedness is his present suffering (vv. 10–11). In ch. 29 Job emphatically denies the kind of behavior of which Eliphaz accuses him.
22:6 *demanded security . . . stripped people of their clothing.* Sins condemned by the prophets (see, e.g., Am 2:8 and note).
22:9 *widows . . . fatherless.* See 24:3; Isa 1:17 and note; Jas 1:27. *strength.* Lit. "arm" (as in 38:15).
22:10 *snares.* See 19:6 and note.
22:11 *dark . . . flood of water.* Two common figures of trouble and distress (see Ps 42:7; Isa 8:7–8 and notes; 8:22; 43:2).
22:12–20 Eliphaz finally appears to support the argument of Bildad and Zophar, who were fully convinced that Job was a wicked man. Eliphaz makes a severe accusation: Job follows the path of the ungodly (v. 15), who defy God's power and say, "What can the Almighty do to us?" (v. 17; see vv. 13–14). They even have contempt for God's goodness (v. 18).

13 Yet you say, 'What does God know?[c]
Does he judge through such
darkness?[d]
14 Thick clouds[e] veil him, so he does not
see us[f]
as he goes about in the vaulted
heavens.'[g]
15 Will you keep to the old path
that the wicked[h] have trod?[i]
16 They were carried off before their
time,[j]
their foundations[k] washed away by a
flood.[l]
17 They said to God, 'Leave us alone!
What can the Almighty do to us?'[m]
18 Yet it was he who filled their houses
with good things,[n]
so I stand aloof from the plans of the
wicked.[o]
19 The righteous see their ruin and
rejoice;[p]
the innocent mock[q] them, saying,
20 'Surely our foes are destroyed,[r]
and fire[s] devours their wealth.'

21 "Submit to God and be at peace[t] with
him;[u]
in this way prosperity will come to
you.[v]
22 Accept instruction from his mouth[w]
and lay up his words[x] in your
heart.[y]
23 If you return[z] to the Almighty, you will
be restored:[a]
If you remove wickedness far from
your tent[b]
24 and assign your nuggets[c] to the dust,
your gold[d] of Ophir[e] to the rocks in
the ravines,[f]
25 then the Almighty will be your gold,[g]
the choicest silver for you.[h]
26 Surely then you will find delight in the
Almighty[i]
and will lift up your face[j] to God.[k]
27 You will pray to him,[l] and he will hear
you,[m]
and you will fulfill your vows.[n]
28 What you decide on will be done,[o]
and light[p] will shine on your ways.[q]
29 When people are brought low[r] and you
say, 'Lift them up!'
then he will save the downcast.[s]
30 He will deliver even one who is not
innocent,[t]
who will be delivered through the
cleanness of your hands."[u]

Job

23 Then Job replied:

2 "Even today my complaint[v] is bitter;[w]
his hand[a] is heavy in spite of[b] my
groaning.[x]
3 If only I knew where to find him;
if only I could go to his dwelling![y]
4 I would state my case[z] before him
and fill my mouth with arguments.[a]
5 I would find out what he would
answer me,[b]
and consider what he would say to
me.
6 Would he vigorously oppose me?[c]
No, he would not press charges
against me.[d]
7 There the upright[e] can establish their
innocence before him,[f]
and there I would be delivered
forever from my judge.[g]

8 "But if I go to the east, he is not there;
if I go to the west, I do not find him.
9 When he is at work in the north, I do
not see him;

[a] 2 Septuagint and Syriac; Hebrew / *the hand on me*
[b] 2 Or *heavy on me in*

22:13 [c] ver 14; Ps 10:11; 59:7; 64:5; 73:11; 94:7; Isa 29:15; Eze 9:9; Zep 1:12 [d] Ps 139:11; Eze 8:12; Eph 6:12 **22:14** [e] Job 26:9; Ps 97:2; 105:39 [f] S ver 13; S 2Ki 21:16 [g] Job 37:18; Ps 18:11; Pr 8:27; Isa 40:22; Jer 23:23-24 **22:15** [h] Job 23:10; 34:36 [i] Job 34:8; Ps 1:1; 50:18 **22:16** [j] S Job 15:32 [k] S Job 4:19 [l] S Ge 7:23; Mt 7:26-27 **22:17** [m] Job 21:15 **22:18** [n] S Job 12:6 [o] S Job 21:16 **22:19** [p] Ps 5:11; 9:2; 32:11; 58:10; 64:10; 97:12; 107:42 [q] Job 21:3; Ps 52:6 **22:20** [r] Ps 18:39 [s] S Job 15:30 **22:21** [t] Isa 26:3, 12; 27:5; Ro 5:1 [u] S Ge 17:1; Jer 9:24 [v] S Job 8:7; Ps 34:8-10; Pr 3:10; 1Pe 5:6 **22:22** [w] S Dt 8:3 [x] S Job 6:10 [y] S Job 15:11; 28:23; Ps 37:31; 40:8; Pr 2:6; Eze 3:10 **22:23** [z] Isa 31:6; 44:22; 55:7; 59:20; Jer 3:14, 22; Eze 18:32; Zec 1:3; Mal 3:7 [a] S Job 5:24; Isa 19:22; Ac 20:32 [b] Job 11:14 **22:24** [c] Job 28:6 [d] Ps 19:10 [e] S Ge 10:29 [f] S Job 1:10; 31:25; Isa 2:20; 30:22; 31:7; 40:19-20; Mt 6:19 **22:25** [g] Job 31:24; Ps 49:6; 52:7; Pr 11:28 [h] 2Ki 18:7; Isa 33:6; Mt 6:20-21 **22:26** [i] Job 27:10; Ps 2:8; 16:6; 37:4; Isa 58:14; 61:10 [j] Job 11:15 [k] Job 11:17; 33:26; Ps 27:6; 100:1 **22:27** [l] S Job 5:27 [m] S Job 5:15; S Ps 86:7; S Isa 30:19 [n] S Nu 30:2 **22:28** [o] Ps 103:11; 145:19 [p] Job 33:28; Ps 97:11; Pr 4:18 [q] S Job 11:17 **22:29** [r] S Est 5:12 [s] Ps 18:27; S Mt 23:12 **22:30** [t] Isa 1:18; Ro 4:5 [u] S 2Sa 22:21 **23:2** [v] S Job 7:11 [w] S 1Sa 1:10; S Job 6:3 [x] Ps 6:6; 32:4; Jer 45:3; Eze 21:7 **23:3** [y] Dt 4:29 **23:4** [z] S Job 13:18 [a] S Job 9:15 **23:5** [b] S Job 11:5 **23:6** [c] S Job 9:4 [d] S Job 6:4 **23:7** [e] S Job 1:1 [f] S Ge 3:8; S Job 9:3; 13:3 [g] S Job 6:29

22:18 See 21:16 and note.

22:21 – 30 Eliphaz makes one last attempt to reach Job. In many ways it is a commendable call to repentance: Submit to God (v. 21), lay up God's words in your heart (v. 22), return to the Almighty and forsake wickedness (v. 23), find your delight in God rather than in gold (vv. 24 – 26), pray and obey (v. 27) and become concerned about sinners (vv. 29 – 30). But Eliphaz's advice assumes (1) that Job is a very wicked man and (2) that Job's major concern is the return of his prosperity (see v. 21). Job had already made it clear in 19:25 – 27 that he deeply yearned to see God and be his friend.

22:22 See Job's response in 23:12. *lay up his words in your heart.* The author of Ps 119 speaks similarly about the written word God gave Israel (Ps 119:11; see Pr 2:1 and note).

22:24 *gold of Ophir.* The finest gold (see 28:16; see also notes on 1Ki 9:28; 10:11; Ps 45:9; Isa 13:12).

22:28 *light will shine on your ways.* Through obedience to the word of God (see vv. 22,27; 29:3; cf. Ps 119:105).

22:30 *cleanness of your hands.* See note on Ps 24:4.

23:2 *my complaint.* See 21:4 and note. *his hand is heavy.* See NIV text notes; 33:7 and note; see also note on 1Sa 5:6.

23:3 *where to find him.* See note on vv. 8 – 9.

23:6 *not press charges against me.* Job is seeking a fair trial. In 9:14 – 20 Job was fearful he could not find words to argue with God. Now he is confident that if God would give him a hearing, he would be acquitted (see 13:13 – 19; see also Ps 17:1 – 3; 26:1 – 3 and notes).

23:8 – 9 *east . . . west . . . north . . . south.* Whatever direction Job went, he could not find God (contrast Ps 139:7 – 10).

23:8,10 *I do not find him . . . But he knows the way that I take.* Job is frustrated over his apparent inability to have an audience with God, who knows that he is an upright man. Job is here answering Eliphaz's admoni-

when he turns to the south, I catch
no glimpse of him.[h]
10 But he knows the way that I take;[i]
when he has tested me,[j] I will come
forth as gold.[k]
11 My feet have closely followed his
steps;[l]
I have kept to his way without
turning aside.[m]
12 I have not departed from the
commands of his lips;[n]
I have treasured the words of his
mouth more than my daily
bread.[o]

13 "But he stands alone, and who can
oppose him?[p]
He does whatever he pleases.[q]
14 He carries out his decree against me,
and many such plans he still has in
store.[r]
15 That is why I am terrified before him;[s]
when I think of all this, I fear him.[t]
16 God has made my heart faint;[u]
the Almighty[v] has terrified me.[w]
17 Yet I am not silenced by the darkness,[x]
by the thick darkness that covers my
face.

24 "Why does the Almighty not set
times[y] for judgment?[z]
Why must those who know him look
in vain for such days?[a]
2 There are those who move boundary
stones;[b]
they pasture flocks they have
stolen.[c]
3 They drive away the orphan's donkey
and take the widow's ox in pledge.[d]
4 They thrust the needy[e] from the
path
and force all the poor[f] of the land
into hiding.[g]
5 Like wild donkeys[h] in the desert,
the poor go about their labor[i] of
foraging food;
the wasteland[j] provides food for
their children.
6 They gather fodder[k] in the fields
and glean in the vineyards[l] of the
wicked.[m]
7 Lacking clothes, they spend the night
naked;
they have nothing to cover
themselves in the cold.[n]
8 They are drenched[o] by mountain rains
and hug[p] the rocks for lack of shelter.[q]
9 The fatherless[r] child is snatched[s] from
the breast;
the infant of the poor is seized[t] for a
debt.[u]
10 Lacking clothes, they go about naked;[v]
they carry the sheaves,[w] but still go
hungry.
11 They crush olives among the terraces[a];
they tread the winepresses,[x] yet
suffer thirst.[y]
12 The groans of the dying rise from the
city,
and the souls of the wounded cry
out for help.[z]
But God charges no one with
wrongdoing.[a]

13 "There are those who rebel against the
light,[b]

[a] *11* The meaning of the Hebrew for this word is uncertain.

23:9 [h]S Job 9:11 **23:10** [i]Job 1:1; 27:6; 31:6; 36:7; Ps 7:9; 11:5; 34:15; 37:18; 94:11; 119:168; 146:8 [j]S Job 7:18; Ps 139:1-3 [k]S Job 6:29; S 22:15; S Ps 12:6; 1Pe 1:7 **23:11** [l]Ps 17:5 [m]Job 31:7; Ps 40:4; 44:18; 119:51,59,157; 125:5; Jer 11:20 **23:12** [n]S Job 6:10 [o]S Job 15:11; Mt 4:4; Jn 4:32, 34 **23:13** [p]S Job 9:3 [q]S Job 10:13; Isa 55:11 **23:14** [r]1Th 3:3; 1Pe 4:12 **23:15** [s]S Ge 45:3 [t]S Jos 24:14; Ps 34:9; 36:1; 111:10; Pr 1:7; Ecc 3:14; 12:13; 2Co 5:11 **23:16** [u]S Dt 20:3 [v]Job 27:2 [w]S Ex 3:6; Rev 6:16 **23:17** [x]S Job 3:6; S 19:8 **24:1** [y]S Job 14:5 [z]S Job 9:23; 2Pe 3:7 [a]S Job 15:20; Ac 1:7 **24:2** [b]S Dt 19:14 [c]Ex 20:15; Dt 28:31 **24:3** [d]S Job 6:27; S 22:9 **24:4** [e]Job 29:16; 31:19 [f]Job 29:12; 30:25; Ps 12:5; 41:1; 82:3,4; Isa 11:4 [g]S Job 20:19; S Pr 28:12 **24:5** [h]S Ge 16:12 [i]Ps 104:23 [j]Job 30:3 **24:6** [k]S Job 6:5 [l]ver 18 [m]Ru 2:22; S 1Ki 21:19 **24:7** [n]S Ex 22:27 **24:8** [o]Da 4:25,33 [p]La 4:5 [q]S Jdg 6:2 **24:9** [r]S Dt 24:17 [s]Job 29:17 [t]Ps 14:4; Pr 30:14; Isa 3:14; 10:1-2; Eze 18:12 [u]S Lev 25:47; S 2Ki 4:1 **24:10** [v]Dt 24:12-13 [w]S Lev 19:9 **24:11** [x]Isa 5:2; 16:10; Hag 2:16 [y]Mic 6:15 **24:12** [z]S Job 12:19; 30:28; Ps 5:2; 22:24; 39:12; 119:147; Isa 30:19; Jer 50:46; 51:52,54; Eze 26:15; Rev 6:10 [a]S Job 9:23 **24:13** [b]ver 16; Job 38:15; Jn 3:19-20; 1Th 5:4-5

---

tion beginning in 22:21: "Submit to God and ... prosperity will come." Job replies that this is what he has always done (vv. 11–12). He treasures God's words more than his daily food. He admits that God is testing him—not to purge away his sinful dross but to show that Job is pure gold (see Ps 119:11,101,168; 1Pe 1:7 and note).

23:12 Job's response to the advice offered by Eliphaz in 22:22. *words ... more than my daily bread.* See Dt 8:3; Mt 4:4 and notes.

23:13 *he stands alone.* Lit. "he is one (unique)." Though Job is not an Israelite, he worships the one true God—there is no other (see Dt 6:4 and note). *He does whatever he pleases.* He is sovereign (see Ps 115:3; 135:6 and notes; see also Lk 10:21).

23:15 *I am terrified.* See note on 21:6. A part of Job's faith is the recognition that God does what he pleases. By contrast, the counselors tried to make God predictable.

23:17 *I am not silenced by the darkness.* Job responds to Eliphaz's accusation in 22:11 (see note there).

24:1–12 Job describes the terrible injustice that often exists in the world. Robbery of both the haves (see v. 2) and the have-nots (see vv. 3–4) is equally obnoxious to him. But perhaps his suffering has enabled him to empathize with the poor, who must forage for food (v. 5) and "glean in the vineyards of the wicked" (v. 6). The scene he depicts is heartrending: The naked shiver in the cold of night (vv. 7–8), fatherless infants are "snatched from the breast" (v. 9), field hands harvest food but go hungry (v. 10), vineyard workers make wine but suffer thirst (v. 11; see photos, p. 820), groans rise from the dying and wounded (v. 12). Job cannot understand why God is silent and indifferent (vv. 1,12) in the face of such misery, but the fact that God waits disproves the counselors' theory of suffering. Job is no more out of God's favor as one of the victims than the criminal in vv. 13–17 is in God's favor because of God's inaction.

24:1 See note on vv. 21–24.

24:2 *move boundary stones.* A serious crime in ancient times (see note on Dt 19:14).

24:3 *orphan's ... widow's.* See 22:9; Isa 1:17 and note; Jas 1:27.

24:5 *wild donkeys.* See 39:5–8.

24:6 *glean.* See note on Ru 1:22.

24:7,10 Job implicitly denies the accusation of Eliphaz (see 22:6).

24:13–17 A description of those who cause the suffering depicted in vv. 2–12: the murderer (v. 14), the adulterer (v. 15),

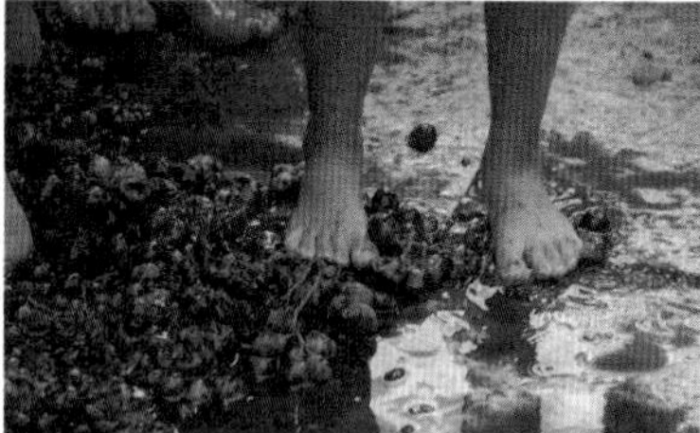

An ancient winepress was a flat area (right) where grapes would be placed after harvesting. Here people would tread on them (above; see Job 24:11). The juice of the grapes would flow down into a vat (right), later to be processed into wine.

Todd Bolen/www.BiblePlaces.com

who do not know its ways
or stay in its paths.[c]
14 When daylight is gone, the murderer rises up,
kills[d] the poor and needy,[e]
and in the night steals forth like a thief.[f]
15 The eye of the adulterer[g] watches for dusk;[h]
he thinks, 'No eye will see me,'[i]
and he keeps his face concealed.
16 In the dark, thieves break into houses,[j]
but by day they shut themselves in;
they want nothing to do with the light.[k]
17 For all of them, midnight is their morning;
they make friends with the terrors[l] of darkness.[m]

18 "Yet they are foam[n] on the surface of the water;[o]
their portion of the land is cursed,[p]
so that no one goes to the vineyards.[q]
19 As heat and drought snatch away the melted snow,[r]
so the grave[s] snatches away those who have sinned.
20 The womb forgets them,
the worm[t] feasts on them;[u]
the wicked are no longer remembered[v]
but are broken like a tree.[w]
21 They prey on the barren and childless woman,
and to the widow they show no kindness.[x]
22 But God drags away the mighty by his power;[y]
though they become established,[z]
they have no assurance of life.[a]
23 He may let them rest in a feeling of security,[b]
but his eyes[c] are on their ways.[d]
24 For a little while they are exalted,
and then they are gone;[e]
they are brought low and gathered up like all others;[f]
they are cut off like heads of grain.[g]

25 "If this is not so, who can prove me false
and reduce my words to nothing?"[h]

Bildad

25 Then Bildad the Shuhite[i] replied:

2 "Dominion and awe belong to God;[j]
he establishes order in the heights of heaven.[k]
3 Can his forces be numbered?
On whom does his light not rise?[l]

24:13 [c] Job 17:12; 38:20; Ps 18:28; Isa 5:20; Eph 5:8-14 **24:14** [d] Isa 3:15; Mic 3:3 [e] S Job 20:19; Ps 37:32 [f] Ps 10:9 **24:15** [g] Job 31:9, 27; Pr 1:10 [h] Pr 7:8-9 [i] Ps 10:11 **24:16** [j] S Ex 22:2; Mt 6:19 [k] S ver 13 **24:17** [l] S Job 18:11 [m] S Job 15:22; S 18:5 **24:18** [n] S Job 9:26; Jude 1:13 [o] Job 22:16; Isa 57:20 [p] S Job 5:3 [q] ver 6 **24:19** [r] Job 6:17 [s] S Job 21:13 **24:20** [t] S Job 7:5 [u] S Job 21:26 [v] S Job 18:17 [w] S Job 14:7; Ps 31:12; Da 4:14 **24:21** [x] S Job 22:9 **24:22** [y] S Job 9:4 [z] S Job 12:19 [a] Dt 28:66; Mt 6:27; Jas 4:14 **24:23** [b] S Job 9:24; Am 6:1 [c] S 2Ch 16:9 [d] S Job 10:4 **24:24** [e] S 2Ki 19:35; S Job 4:20; Ps 37:10; 83:13; Isa 5:24; 17:13; 40:24; 41:2, 15 [f] S Job 3:19 [g] Isa 17:5 **24:25** [h] S Job 6:28; S 16:17 **25:1** [i] S Job 8:1 **25:2** [j] S Job 9:4; Ps 47:9; 89:18; Zec 9:7; Rev 1:6 [k] S 2Ch 20:6; S Job 11:8; S 16:19 **25:3** [l] Mt 5:45; Jas 1:17

the robber (v. 16). Darkness is their element, the medium in which they thrive (see vv. 14–17; Jn 3:19; Ro 1:21).

24:18–20 Job seems to agree with the counselors here. But it is also legitimate to translate the verses as Job's call for redress against evildoers: "May their portion of the land be cursed . . . / may the grave snatch away . . . / May the womb forget them, / may the worm feast on them; / may the wicked be no longer remembered / but be broken like a tree."

24:20 *worm feasts on them.* See 21:26; Isa 14:11; 66:24 and note; Mk 9:48 and note. *broken like a tree.* See note on 19:10.

24:21–24 By way of summary, Job says that God judges the wicked, but he does so in his own good time. Job wishes, however, that God would give the righteous the satisfaction of seeing it happen (v. 1).

25:1–6 See note on 22:1—26:14. Bildad adds nothing new here, and Zophar, who had already admitted how disturbed he was (see 20:2), does not even comment.

25:2 *establishes order in the heights of heaven.* He who establishes order in heaven is sovereign over all creation.

25:3 *his forces.* Angels. *his light.* The sun.

[4]How then can a mortal be righteous
before God?
How can one born of woman be
pure?[m]
[5]If even the moon[n] is not bright
and the stars are not pure in his eyes,[o]
[6]how much less a mortal, who is but a
maggot —
a human being,[p] who is only a
worm!"[q]

Job 26

Then Job replied:

[2]"How you have helped the powerless![r]
How you have saved the arm that is
feeble![s]
[3]What advice you have offered to one
without wisdom!
And what great insight[t] you have
displayed!
[4]Who has helped you utter these words?
And whose spirit spoke from your
mouth?[u]

[5]"The dead are in deep anguish,[v]
those beneath the waters and all that
live in them.
[6]The realm of the dead[w] is naked before
God;
Destruction[a][x] lies uncovered.[y]
[7]He spreads out the northern skies[z] over
empty space;
he suspends the earth over nothing.[a]
[8]He wraps up the waters[b] in his clouds,[c]
yet the clouds do not burst under
their weight.
[9]He covers the face of the full moon,
spreading his clouds[d] over it.
[10]He marks out the horizon on the face
of the waters[e]
for a boundary between light and
darkness.[f]
[11]The pillars of the heavens quake,[g]
aghast at his rebuke.
[12]By his power he churned up the
sea;[h]
by his wisdom[i] he cut Rahab[j] to
pieces.
[13]By his breath the skies[k] became fair;
his hand pierced the gliding serpent.[l]
[14]And these are but the outer fringe of
his works;
how faint the whisper[m] we hear of
him![n]
Who then can understand the
thunder of his power?"[o]

Job's Final Word to His Friends

27

And Job continued his discourse:[p]

[2]"As surely as God lives, who has
denied me justice,[q]
the Almighty,[r] who has made my life
bitter,[s]
[3]as long as I have life within me,
the breath of God[t] in my nostrils,
[4]my lips will not say anything wicked,
and my tongue will not utter lies.[u]
[5]I will never admit you are in the right;
till I die, I will not deny my
integrity.[v]

[a] 6 Hebrew *Abaddon*

25:4 [m]S Job 4:17 **25:5** [n]Job 31:26 [o]S Job 4:18 **25:6** [p]Ps 80:17; 144:3; Eze 2:1 [q]S Job 4:19; S 7:5 **26:2** [r]Job 6:12 [s]S Job 4:3 **26:3** [t]Job 34:35 **26:4** [u]1Ki 22:24 **26:5** [v]Ps 88:10; Isa 14:9; 26:14 **26:6** [w]Ps 139:8 [x]S Job 20:26; S Rev 9:11 [y]Job 10:22; 11:8; 38:17; 41:11; Ps 139:11-12; Pr 15:11; S Heb 4:13 **26:7** [z]Job 9:8 [a]Job 38:6; Ps 104:5; Pr 3:19-20; 8:27; Isa 40:22 **26:8** [b]Pr 30:4 [c]S Ge 1:2; Job 36:27; 37:11; Ps 147:8 **26:9** [d]S 2Sa 22:10; S Job 22:14 **26:10** [e]Pr 8:27, 29; Isa 40:22 [f]S Ge 1:4; S Job 28:3; 38:8-11 **26:11** [g]S 2Sa 22:8 **26:12** [h]S Ex 14:21 [i]Job 12:13 [j]S Job 9:13 **26:13** [k]Job 9:8 [l]Isa 27:1 **26:14** [m]Job 4:12 [n]Job 42:5; Hab 3:2; 1Co 13:12 [o]S Job 9:6

27:1 [p]Job 29:1 **27:2** [q]S Job 6:29; S 9:24; Isa 45:9; 49:4, 14 [r]Job 23:16 [s]S 1Sa 1:10; S Job 7:19; S 10:1 **27:3** [t]S Ge 2:7; Job 32:8; 33:4; 34:14; S Ps 144:4 **27:4** [u]S Job 6:28; S 12:16; S 16:17 **27:5** [v]S Job 2:9; S 10:7; S 32:2

:5:4 – 6 Bildad echoes Eliphaz's earlier statements about hu-
nan depravity (4:17 – 19; 15:14 – 16).
:6:2 – 4 With biting sarcasm, Job responds to Bildad alone
the Hebrew for the words "you" and "your" in these verses is
ingular rather than plural), indicating that Eliphaz and Zohar have already been silenced.
6:2 *saved the arm that is feeble.* See 4:3 – 4; Isa 35:3; Heb
2:12.
:6:5 – 14 Job's highly figurative description of the vast power
f God — the theme also of Bildad's final speech (ch. 25).
:6:5 *The dead.* The Hebrew for this expression is translated
spirits of the dead" in Pr 2:18, "spirits of the departed" in
sa 14:9 and "spirits" in Isa 26:14. The term is used figura-
ively of the deceased who inhabit the netherworld (see
:13 – 15,17 – 19; see also note on 3:16). *waters.* Part of the
vorld inhabited by living beings, and therefore above the
etherworld.
:6:6 *The realm of the dead.* Personified elsewhere as the "king
of terrors" (18:14; see note there). *Destruction.* See NIV text
note; see also 28:22; 31:12; Pr 15:11 and NIV text notes. In Rev
:11, Abaddon is the name of the "angel of the Abyss."
:6:7 See 37:18. *He.* God. *suspends the earth over nothing.* Per-
aps Job's way of acknowledging that the landmasses are
nade secure only by God's sustaining power.
:6:12 *churned up the sea.* See Isa 51:15; Jer 31:35. *Rahab.* See
ote on 9:13.

26:13 *gliding serpent.* A description of the sea monster Leviathan (see notes on 3:8; Isa 27:1).

26:14 *these are but the outer fringe of his works.* What God has revealed of his dominion over natural and supernatural forces amounts to no more than a whisper. Job is impressed with the severely limited character of human understanding. Zophar had chided Job about his inability to fathom the mysteries of God (11:7 – 9), but the knowledge possessed by Job's friends was not superior to that of Job himself (see 12:3; 13:2). *thunder of his power.* If it is difficult for us to comprehend the little that we know about God, how much more impossible it would be to understand the full extent of his might!

27:1 – 23 The dialogue-dispute section of the book begins with Job's opening lament (ch. 3), continues with the three cycles of speeches (chs. 4 – 14; 15 – 21; 22 – 26) and concludes with Job's closing discourse (ch. 27), in which he reasserts his own innocence (vv. 2 – 6) and eloquently describes the ultimate fate of the wicked (vv. 13 – 23).

27:2 *As surely as God lives.* The most solemn of oaths (see note on Ge 42:15). Job's faith in God continued despite his perception of denied justice.

27:5 *you.* The Hebrew for this word is plural. In his summary statement, Job once again speaks to his three friends as a group.

6 I will maintain my innocence[w] and
never let go of it;
my conscience[x] will not reproach me
as long as I live.[y]

7 "May my enemy be like the wicked,[z]
my adversary[a] like the unjust!
8 For what hope have the godless[b] when
they are cut off,
when God takes away their life?[c]
9 Does God listen to their cry
when distress comes upon them?[d]
10 Will they find delight in the Almighty?[e]
Will they call on God at all times?

11 "I will teach you about the power of
God;
the ways[f] of the Almighty I will not
conceal.[g]
12 You have all seen this yourselves.
Why then this meaningless talk?

13 "Here is the fate God allots to the
wicked,
the heritage a ruthless man receives
from the Almighty:[h]
14 However many his children,[i] their fate
is the sword;[j]
his offspring will never have enough
to eat.[k]
15 The plague will bury those who
survive him,
and their widows will not weep for
them.[l]
16 Though he heaps up silver like dust[m]
and clothes like piles of clay,[n]
17 what he lays up[o] the righteous will
wear,[p]
and the innocent will divide his
silver.[q]
18 The house[r] he builds is like a moth's
cocoon,[s]
like a hut[t] made by a watchman.
19 He lies down wealthy, but will do so
no more;[u]
when he opens his eyes, all is gone.[v]
20 Terrors[w] overtake him like a flood;[x]
a tempest snatches him away in the
night.[y]
21 The east wind[z] carries him off, and he
is gone;[a]
it sweeps him out of his place.[b]
22 It hurls itself against him without
mercy[c]
as he flees headlong[d] from its
power.[e]
23 It claps its hands[f] in derision
and hisses him out of his place."[g]

Interlude: Where Wisdom Is Found

28 There is a mine for silver
and a place where gold is refined.[h]
2 Iron is taken from the earth,
and copper is smelted from ore.[i]
3 Mortals put an end to the darkness;[j]
they search out the farthest recesses
for ore in the blackest darkness.[k]
4 Far from human dwellings they cut a
shaft,[l]
in places untouched by human feet;
far from other people they dangle
and sway.
5 The earth, from which food comes,[m]
is transformed below as by fire;
6 lapis lazuli[n] comes from its rocks,
and its dust contains nuggets of
gold.[o]
7 No bird of prey knows that hidden
path,
no falcon's eye has seen it.[p]

27:6 [w] Job 29:14; Ps 119:121; 132:9; Isa 59:17; 61:10 [x] S Ac 23:1; Ro 2:15 [y] S Job 2:3; S 10:7; S 23:10; S 34:17 **27:7** [z] S Job 8:22 [a] Job 31:35 **27:8** [b] S Job 8:13 [c] S Nu 16:22; S Job 8:22; S 11:20; Lk 12:20 **27:9** [d] S Dt 1:45; S 1Sa 8:18; S Job 15:31 **27:10** [e] S Job 22:26 **27:11** [f] Job 36:23 [g] ver 13 **27:13** [h] S Job 16:19; S 20:29 **27:14** [i] S Job 5:4 [j] S Job 15:22; S La 2:22 [k] S Job 4:11 **27:15** [l] Ps 78:64 **27:16** [m] S 1Ki 10:27 [n] Zec 9:3 **27:17** [o] Ps 39:6; 49:10; Ecc 2:26 [p] S Job 7:8; Pr 13:22; 28:8; Ecc 2:26 [q] Ex 3:22; S Job 3:15 **27:18** [r] S Job 8:22 [s] S Job 8:14 [t] Isa 1:8; 24:20 **27:19** [u] S Job 3:13; S 7:8 [v] S Job 14:20 **27:20** [w] S Job 6:4 [x] S Job 15:21 [y] S Job 20:8 **27:21** [z] Job 38:24; Jer 13:24; 22:22 [a] Job 30:22 [b] S Job 7:10 **27:22** [c] Jer 13:14; Eze 5:11; 24:14 [d] 2Ki 7:15 [e] S Job 11:20 **27:23** [f] S Nu 24:10; Na 3:19 [g] S Job 7:10 **28:1** [h] Ps 12:6; 66:10; Jer 9:7; Da 11:35; Mal 3:3 **28:2** [i] Dt 8:9 **28:3** [j] Ecc 1:13; 7:25; 8:17 [k] S Job 26:10; 38:19 **28:4** [l] ver 10; 2Sa 5:8 **28:5** [m] Ge 1:29; Ps 104:14; 145:15 **28:6** [n] ver 16; SS 5:14; Isa 54:11 [o] S Job 22:24 **28:7** [p] ver 21

27:6 *maintain my innocence.* God had spoken similarly of Job (see 2:3).
27:7 *May my enemy be like the wicked.* Job evidently calls for his "friends" ("my enemy ... adversary"), who had falsely accused him of being wicked, to be treated as though they themselves were wicked (cf. Ps 109:6–15; 137:8–9).
27:11 *I will teach you.* Job is about to remind his counselors about an issue on which they all agree: that the truly wicked deserve God's wrath (vv. 13–23). The three friends had falsely put Job in that category.
27:13–23 A poem that dramatizes the effect of Job's earlier call for redress (v. 7).
27:13 Job echoes the words of Zophar in 20:29 (see note there).
27:18 *cocoon ... hut.* Symbols of fragility (see note on 4:19; Isa 1:8 and note; 24:20).
27:21 *east wind.* See note on 15:2.
28:1–28 Job's friends' application of traditional wisdom to human suffering has been even more unsatisfactory than Job's untraditional response. Both attempts to penetrate the mystery have failed, and the dialogue has come to a stalemate. Therefore the author of the book inserts a striking wisdom poem that answers the question, "Where can wisdom be found?" (v. 12; see v. 20). The poem consists of three parts: (1) Humans find precious stones and metals by digging into the deep bowels of the earth (vv. 1–11); (2) but wisdom, the dearest treasure of all, is not found there and it cannot be bought with precious stones or metals dug from the earth (vv. 12–19); (3) wisdom is found only in God (vv. 20–27). And God tells human beings that true wisdom for them is to "fear ... the Lord ... and to shun evil" (v. 28). This chapter, then, anticipates the theme of God's speeches (38:1—42:6) and echoes the assessment of Job that God had given at the beginning (see 1:1,8 and notes; see also Introduction: Theological Theme and Message).
28:1–11 A fascinating, lyrical description of ancient mining techniques.
28:2 *Iron.* See note on 19:24.
28:3 *put an end to the darkness.* By using an artificial source of light, such as a torch or lamp.
28:4 *dangle and sway.* Mining, then as now, is difficult and dangerous work. People will hazard everything to dig up the earth's treasures.
28:6 *lapis lazuli.* See v. 16; see also notes on SS 5:14; Isa 54:11

8 Proud beasts[q] do not set foot on it,
and no lion prowls there.[r]
9 People assault the flinty rock[s] with their hands
and lay bare the roots of the mountains.[t]
10 They tunnel through the rock;[u]
their eyes see all its treasures.[v]
11 They search[a] the sources of the rivers[w]
and bring hidden things[x] to light.

12 But where can wisdom be found?[y]
Where does understanding dwell?[z]
13 No mortal comprehends its worth;[a]
it cannot be found in the land of the living.[b]
14 The deep[c] says, "It is not in me";
the sea[d] says, "It is not with me."
15 It cannot be bought with the finest gold,
nor can its price be weighed out in silver.[e]
16 It cannot be bought with the gold of Ophir,[f]
with precious onyx or lapis lazuli.[g]
17 Neither gold nor crystal can compare with it,[h]
nor can it be had for jewels of gold.[i]
18 Coral[j] and jasper[k] are not worthy of mention;
the price of wisdom is beyond rubies.[l]
19 The topaz[m] of Cush[n] cannot compare with it;
it cannot be bought with pure gold.[o]

20 Where then does wisdom come from?
Where does understanding dwell?[p]
21 It is hidden from the eyes of every living thing,
concealed even from the birds in the sky.[q]
22 Destruction[b][r] and Death[s] say,
"Only a rumor of it has reached our ears."
23 God understands the way to it
and he alone[t] knows where it dwells,[u]
24 for he views the ends of the earth[v]
and sees everything under the heavens.[w]
25 When he established the force of the wind
and measured out the waters,[x]
26 when he made a decree for the rain[y]
and a path for the thunderstorm,[z]
27 then he looked at wisdom and appraised it;
he confirmed it and tested it.[a]
28 And he said to the human race,
"The fear of the Lord—that is wisdom,
and to shun evil[b] is understanding."[c]

28:8 [q] Job 41:34 [r] Isa 35:9 **28:9** [s] S Dt 8:15 [t] Jnh 2:6 **28:10** [u] S ver 4 [v] Pr 2:4 **28:11** [w] S Ge 7:11 [x] Isa 48:6; Jer 33:3 **28:12** [y] ver 28; Pr 1:20; 3:13-20; 8:1; 9:1-3; Ecc 7:24 [z] ver 20,23 **28:13** [a] Pr 3:15; Mt 13:44-46 [b] Dt 29:29; Ps 27:13; 52:5; 116:9; 142:5; Isa 38:11; Jer 11:19; Eze 26:20; 32:24 **28:14** [c] Ps 42:7; Ro 10:7 [d] Dt 30:13 **28:15** [e] ver 17; Pr 3:13-14; 8:10-11; 16:16; Ac 8:20 **28:16** [f] S Ge 10:29 [g] S ver 6; S Ex 24:10 **28:17** [h] Ps 119:72; Pr 8:10 [i] S ver 15 **28:18** [j] Eze 27:16 [k] Rev 21:11 [l] Pr 3:15; 8:11 **28:19** [m] Ex 28:17 [n] Isa 11:11 [o] Pr 3:14-15; 8:10-11,19 **28:20** [p] S Job 9:4 **28:21** [q] ver 7 **28:22** [r] S Job 20:26; S Rev 9:11 [s] Pr 8:32-36 **28:23** [t] Ecc 3:11; 8:17 [u] S Job 9:4; S 22:22; Pr 8:22-31

Job's Final Defense

29 Job continued his discourse:[d]

2 "How I long for the months gone by,[e]
for the days when God watched over me,[f]
3 when his lamp shone on my head
and by his light I walked through darkness![g]
4 Oh, for the days when I was in my prime,
when God's intimate friendship[h] blessed my house,[i]
5 when the Almighty was still with me
and my children[j] were around me,[k]

[a] *11* Septuagint, Aquila and Vulgate; Hebrew *They dam up* [b] *22* Hebrew *Abaddon*

28:24 [v] Job 36:32; 37:3; 38:18,24,35; Ps 33:13-14; 66:7; Isa 11:12 [w] S Jos 3:11; S Job 10:4; S Heb 4:13 **28:25** [x] S Job 12:15; 38:8-11 **28:26** [y] Job 36:28; 37:6; Jer 51:16 [z] Job 36:33; 37:3,8,11; 38:25,27; Ps 65:12; 104:14; 147:8; Isa 35:7 **28:27** [a] Pr 3:19; 8:22-31 **28:28** [b] Ps 11:5; 97:10; Pr 3:7; 8:13 [c] S Ex 20:20; S Dt 4:6; S Job 37:24 **29:1** [d] Job 27:1 **29:2** [e] S Ge 31:30 [f] Jer 1:12; 31:28; 44:27 **29:3** [g] S Job 11:17; S 12:25 **29:4** [h] S Job 15:8 [i] Ps 25:14; Pr 3:32 **29:5** [j] Ps 127:3-5; 128:3 [k] Ru 4:1

28:9 *roots of the mountains.* A poetic expression emphasizing great depth (cf. Jnh 2:6).

28:10 *tunnel through the rock.* An eighth-century BC inscription found at Jerusalem's Pool of Siloam testifies to the sophistication of ancient tunneling technology.

28:12 The questions, repeated almost verbatim in v. 20, are answered in v. 28.

28:16 *gold of Ophir.* See 22:24 and note.

28:18 *the price of wisdom is beyond rubies.* Cf. the value of a "wife of noble character" (Pr 31:10), who fears the Lord (Pr 31:30) and is therefore wise (see v. 28).

28:19 *Cush.* The upper Nile region, south of Egypt.

28:21 *hidden ... from the birds.* As are precious stones and metals (see v. 7).

28:22 *Destruction and Death.* See note on 26:6.

28:25–27 Wisdom has been with God from the time of creation itself (see Pr 8:22–31 and notes).

28:28 *fear of the Lord ... shun evil.* See the description of Job's character in 1:1,8; 2:3. *that is wisdom.* "The fear of the LORD is the beginning of wisdom" (Ps 111:10; Pr 9:10; see Pr 1:7).

29:1—31:40 Job submits his final defense in a three-part summation: Part one (ch. 29) is a nostalgic review of his former happiness, wealth and honor; part two (ch. 30) is a lament over the loss of everything, especially his honor; part three (ch. 31) is a final protestation of his innocence.

29:1–25 A classic example of Semitic rhetoric, using the following symmetrical pattern: blessing (vv. 2–6), honor (vv. 7–10), benevolence (vv. 11–17), blessing (vv. 18–20), honor (vv. 21–25).

29:2–6 Words charged with emotion. In earlier days, God had been Job's friend and companion.

29:3 *by his light I walked.* See note on 22:28.

29:4 *when God's intimate friendship blessed my house.* Lit. "when God's council was by my tent." The clause evokes a situation similar to that in Ge 18, where God and two members of his heavenly council eat and drink at Abraham's tent—and there God discloses to his friend the imminent birth of the promised son and God's intentions concerning Sodom and Gomorrah.

29:5 *my children were around me.* See 1:2 and note.

[6]when my path was drenched with
cream[l]
and the rock[m] poured out for me
streams of olive oil.[n]

[7]"When I went to the gate[o] of the city
and took my seat in the public
square,
[8]the young men saw me and stepped
aside[p]
and the old men rose to their feet;[q]
[9]the chief men refrained from speaking[r]
and covered their mouths with their
hands;[s]
[10]the voices of the nobles were hushed,[t]
and their tongues stuck to the roof of
their mouths.[u]
[11]Whoever heard me spoke well of me,
and those who saw me
commended me,[v]
[12]because I rescued the poor[w] who cried
for help,
and the fatherless[x] who had none to
assist them.[y]
[13]The one who was dying blessed me;[z]
I made the widow's[a] heart sing.
[14]I put on righteousness[b] as my clothing;
justice was my robe and my turban.[c]
[15]I was eyes[d] to the blind
and feet to the lame.[e]
[16]I was a father to the needy;[f]
I took up the case[g] of the stranger.[h]
[17]I broke the fangs of the wicked
and snatched the victims[i] from their
teeth.[j]

[18]"I thought, 'I will die in my own
house,
my days as numerous as the grains
of sand.[k]
[19]My roots will reach to the water,[l]
and the dew will lie all night on my
branches.[m]
[20]My glory will not fade;[n]
the bow[o] will be ever new in my
hand.'[p]

[21]"People listened to me expectantly,
waiting in silence for my counsel.[q]
[22]After I had spoken, they spoke no
more;[r]
my words fell gently on their ears.[s]
[23]They waited for me as for showers
and drank in my words as the spring
rain.[t]
[24]When I smiled at them, they scarcely
believed it;
the light of my face[u] was precious to
them.[a][v]
[25]I chose the way for them and sat as
their chief;[w]
I dwelt as a king[x] among his troops;
I was like one who comforts
mourners.[y]

30 "But now they mock me,[z]
men younger than I,
whose fathers I would have disdained
to put with my sheep dogs.[a]
[2]Of what use was the strength of their
hands to me,
since their vigor had gone from
them?
[3]Haggard from want and hunger,
they roamed[b] the parched land[b]
in desolate wastelands[c] at night.[d]
[4]In the brush they gathered salt herbs,[e]
and their food[c] was the root of the
broom bush.[f]
[5]They were banished from human
society,
shouted at as if they were thieves.
[6]They were forced to live in the dry
stream beds,
among the rocks and in holes in the
ground.[g]
[7]They brayed[h] among the bushes[i]
and huddled in the undergrowth.
[8]A base and nameless brood,[j]
they were driven out of the land.[k]

[a] 24 The meaning of the Hebrew for this clause is uncertain. [b] 3 Or *gnawed* [c] 4 Or *fuel*

29:6 [l]S Job 20:17 [m]Ps 81:16 [n]Ge 49:20; S Dt 32:13 **29:7** [o]ver 21; Job 5:4; 31:21; Jer 20:2; 38:7 **29:8** [p]1Ti 5:1 [q]S Lev 19:32 **29:9** [r]ver 21; Job 31:21 [s]S Jdg 18:19; Job 40:4; Pr 30:32 **29:10** [t]ver 22 [u]Ps 137:6 **29:11** [v]S Job 4:4; Heb 11:4 **29:12** [w]S Job 24:4 [x]S Dt 24:17; Job 31:17, 21 [y]Ps 72:12; Pr 21:13 **29:13** [z]Job 31:20 [a]S Dt 10:18; S Job 22:9 **29:14** [b]S 2Sa 8:15; S Job 27:6; Eph 4:24; 6:14 [c]S Job 19:9 **29:15** [d]Nu 10:31 [e]S Job 4:4 **29:16** [f]S Job 24:4 [g]Ex 18:26 [h]S Job 4:4; Pr 22:22-23 **29:17** [i]Job 24:9 [j]S Job 4:10, 11; S Ps 3:7 **29:18** [k]Ps 1:1-3; 15:5; 16:8; 30:6; 62:2; 139:18; Pr 3:1-2 **29:19** [l]S Nu 24:6; S Job 14:9 [m]S Ge 27:8; S Job 15:30; S Ps 133:3 **29:20** [n]Ps 92:14 [o]Job 30:11; Ps 18:34; Isa 38:12 [p]Ge 49:24 **29:21** [q]S ver 7, S 9 **29:22** [r]ver 10 [s]Dt 32:2 **29:23** [t]S Job 4:3

29:24 [u]S Nu 6:25 [v]Pr 16:14, 15 **29:25** [w]S Job 21:28 [x]S Job 1:3 [y]S Job 4:4 **30:1** [z]S Job 6:14; S 11:3; S Ps 119:21 [a]Isa 56:10 **30:3** [b]Isa 8:21 [c]Job 24:5 [d]Jer 17:6 **30:4** [e]Job 39:6 [f]S 1Ki 19:4 **30:6** [g]Isa 2:19; Hos 10:8 **30:7** [h]Job 6:5 [i]Job 39:5-6 **30:8** [j]S Jdg 9:4 [k]S Job 18:18

29:6 *cream ... olive oil.* Symbols of richness and luxury (see 20:17; Eze 16:19).
29:7 *gate of the city.* Where the most important business was conducted and the most significant legal cases were tried (see note on Ru 4:1). *took my seat.* As a city elder, a member of the ruling council (see note on Ge 19:1).
29:12–13 *I rescued ... the fatherless ... I made the widow's heart sing.* Implicitly responding to Eliphaz's accusation in 22:9 (see note on 22:5–11), Job expresses his concern for the helpless and unfortunate (see 24:9; 31:16–18, 21).
29:14 *I put on righteousness ... justice was my robe.* For similar imagery, see Ps 132:9,16; Isa 59:17; 61:10; Ro 13:14; Eph 4:24; 6:14,17 and notes; see also note on Ps 109:29.
29:18 *I thought.* Job muses on what might have been the course of his life.
29:21–25 Job's counsel was valued (vv. 21–23), his approval sought (v. 24) and his civic leadership accepted with gratitude (v. 25).
30:1–31 In contrast to the positive notes of blessing and honor sounded in ch. 29, Job now bemoans the suffering and dishonor he has been forced to undergo. God has heaped overwhelming terrors on him (v. 15). His final, forlorn lament (see v. 31) over his condition shows that his rage has not yet subsided.
30:1,9 *now ... mock me.* Earlier both young and old had deferred to him (see 29:8–11,21–25).
30:4 *salt herbs.* Probably saltwort, which grows in otherwise infertile areas, including the regions where Job and his friends lived. Cf. 39:6. *broom bush.* A large shrub that grows in the deserts of the Middle East (see 1Ki 19:4; Ps 120:4 and notes).

9 "And now those young men mock me[l]
in song;[m]
I have become a byword[n] among
them.
10 They detest me[o] and keep their
distance;
they do not hesitate to spit in my
face.[p]
11 Now that God has unstrung my bow[q]
and afflicted me,[r]
they throw off restraint[s] in my
presence.
12 On my right[t] the tribe[a] attacks;
they lay snares[u] for my feet,[v]
they build their siege ramps
against me.[w]
13 They break up my road;[x]
they succeed in destroying me.[y]
'No one can help him,' they say.
14 They advance as through a gaping
breach;[z]
amid the ruins they come rolling in.
15 Terrors[a] overwhelm me;[b]
my dignity is driven away as by the
wind,
my safety vanishes like a cloud.[c]

16 "And now my life ebbs away;[d]
days of suffering grip me.[e]
17 Night pierces my bones;
my gnawing pains never rest.[f]
18 In his great power[g] God becomes like
clothing to me[b];
he binds me like the neck of my
garment.
19 He throws me into the mud,[h]
and I am reduced to dust and ashes.[i]

20 "I cry out to you,[j] God, but you do not
answer;[k]
I stand up, but you merely look at me.
21 You turn on me ruthlessly;[l]
with the might of your hand[m] you
attack me.[n]
22 You snatch me up and drive me before
the wind;[o]
you toss me about in the storm.[p]
23 I know you will bring me down to
death,[q]
to the place appointed for all the
living.[r]

24 "Surely no one lays a hand on a
broken man[s]
when he cries for help in his distress.[t]
25 Have I not wept for those in trouble?[u]
Has not my soul grieved for the
poor?[v]
26 Yet when I hoped for good, evil came;
when I looked for light, then came
darkness.[w]
27 The churning inside me never stops;[x]
days of suffering confront me.[y]
28 I go about blackened,[z] but not by the
sun;
I stand up in the assembly and cry
for help.[a]
29 I have become a brother of jackals,[b]
a companion of owls.[c]
30 My skin grows black[d] and peels;[e]
my body burns with fever.[f]
31 My lyre is tuned to mourning,[g]
and my pipe[h] to the sound of wailing.

31 "I made a covenant with my eyes[i]
not to look lustfully at a young
woman.[j]

[a] 12 The meaning of the Hebrew for this word is uncertain. [b] 18 Hebrew; Septuagint *power he grasps my clothing*

30:9 [l]S Job 16:10; Ps 69:11 [m]Job 12:4; La 3:14,63 [n]S Job 17:6 **30:10** [o]Job 19:19 [p]S Dt 25:9; Mt 26:67 **30:11** [q]S Job 29:20 [r]S Ge 12:17; S Ru 1:21 [s]Job 41:13; Ps 32:9 **30:12** [t]Ps 109:6; Zec 3:1 [u]S Job 18:9 [v]Ps 140:4-5 [w]S Job 16:10 **30:13** [x]Isa 3:12 [y]S Job 10:3 **30:14** [z]S 2Ki 25:4 **30:15** [a]S Job 6:4 [b]S Ex 3:6; Job 10:8; 31:2-3,23; Ps 55:4-5 [c]S Job 3:25 **30:16** [d]S Job 3:24 [e]ver 27; S Job 9:17 **30:17** [f]S Dt 28:35; S Job 16:16 **30:18** [g]S Job 9:4 **30:19** [h]Ps 40:2; 69:2,14; 130:1; Jer 38:6,22 [i]S Ge 3:19; S Job 2:8 **30:20** [j]S 1Ki 8:52; Ps 34:17; Pr 2:3; Mic 4:9 [k]S Job 19:7; La 3:8 **30:21** [l]Jer 6:23; 30:14; 50:42 [m]Isa 9:12; 14:26; 31:3; Eze 6:14 [n]S Job 4:5; S 6:4; S 10:3 **30:22** [o]Job 27:21; Jude 1:12 [p]S Job 9:17 **30:23** [q]S 2Sa 14:14; S Job 3:13; S 10:3 [r]S Job 3:19 **30:24** [s]Ps 145:14; Isa 42:3; 57:15 [t]S Job 19:7 **30:25** [u]Lk 19:41; Php 3:18 [v]S Job 24:4; Ps 35:13-14; Ro 12:15 **30:26** [w]S Job 3:6,17; S 19:8; S Ps 82:5; S Jer 4:23 **30:27** [x]Ps 38:8; La 2:11 [y]S ver 16 **30:28** [z]S Job 17:14; La 4:8 [a]S Job 19:7; S 24:12 **30:29** [b]Ps 44:19; Isa 34:13; Jer 9:11 [c]Ps 102:6; Mic 1:8 **30:30** [d]S Job 17:14 [e]La 3:4; 4:8 [f]S Dt 28:35; S Job 16:16; Ps 102:3; La 1:13; 5:10 **30:31** [g]S Ge 8:8; Ps 137:2; Isa 16:11; 24:8; Eze 26:13 [h]S Ge 4:21 **31:1** [i]Pr 4:25; 17:24; 2Pe 2:14 [j]Ex 20:14, 17; Dt 5:18; Mt 5:28

30:9 *those young men mock me.* See v. 1 and note on vv. 1,9. *byword.* See note on 17:6.
30:11 *God has unstrung my bow.* In contrast to 29:20, where Job was confident that his bow would be new and strong.
30:12 *siege ramps.* See 19:12.
30:14 *breach.* In a city wall.
30:15 *driven ... as by the wind.* See v. 22.
30:17 *gnawing pains.* See note on 2:7.
30:18 *neck of my garment.* Tight-fitting collar.
30:19 *dust and ashes.* Symbolic of humiliation and insignificance (see note on Ge 18:27). Job would someday use "dust and ashes" to symbolize repentance (42:6).
30:20 – 23 Job now shifts his thoughts away from human beings and toward God. He accuses God of abusing his power by attacking him despite his pleas for mercy.
30:24 Job feels that he has been treated unjustly, whether by God or by humans.
30:26 Cf. Isa 5:2,7.
30:28 *blackened.* See v. 30; see also note on 2:7.
30:29 *brother of jackals ... companion of owls.* The prophet Micah uses similar imagery of himself in Mic 1:8.
30:30 *fever.* See note on 2:7.
31:1 – 40 The climactic section of Job's three-part summation (see note on 29:1—31:40). It is negative in the sense that Job denies all the sins listed, but it has the positive purpose of attesting loyalty to God as his sovereign Lord. In the strongest legal terms, using a series of self-maledictory oaths, Job completes his defense. No more can be said (v. 40). He now affixes his signature to the document (v. 35), and the burden of proof that he is a wretched sinner rests with God. Job's call for vindication had reached a climax in 27:2 – 6. Now he amplifies that statement with the details of his godly life. Each of seven disavowals (vv. 5 – 7,9,13,16 – 21,24 – 27,29 – 34, 38 – 39) is accompanied by an oath that calls for the punishment the offense deserves (vv. 8,10 – 12,14 – 15,22 – 23,28,40 [but see notes on vv. 14,34]). The principle at work is the so-called law of retaliation (see Ex 21:23 – 25; Lev 24:20 and notes).
31:1 – 12 Job begins with sins of the heart, especially sexual lust (vv. 1 – 4), cheating in business (vv. 5 – 8) and marital infidelity (vv. 9 – 12).
31:1 *look lustfully at a young woman.* To do so is to sin (see Mt 5:28; 2Pe 2:14 and notes).

[2] For what is our lot[k] from God above,
our heritage from the Almighty on high?[l]
[3] Is it not ruin[m] for the wicked,
disaster[n] for those who do wrong?[o]
[4] Does he not see my ways[p]
and count my every step?[q]

[5] "If I have walked with falsehood
or my foot has hurried after deceit[r] —
[6] let God weigh me[s] in honest scales[t]
and he will know that I am blameless[u] —
[7] if my steps have turned from the path,[v]
if my heart has been led by my eyes,
or if my hands[w] have been defiled,[x]
[8] then may others eat what I have sown,[y]
and may my crops be uprooted.[z]

[9] "If my heart has been enticed[a] by a woman,[b]
or if I have lurked at my neighbor's door,
[10] then may my wife grind[c] another man's grain,
and may other men sleep with her.[d]
[11] For that would have been wicked,[e]
a sin to be judged.[f]
[12] It is a fire[g] that burns to Destruction[a];[h]
it would have uprooted my harvest.[i]

[13] "If I have denied justice to any of my servants,[j]
whether male or female,
when they had a grievance against me,[k]
[14] what will I do when God confronts me?[l]
What will I answer when called to account?[m]
[15] Did not he who made me in the womb make them?[n]
Did not the same one form us both within our mothers?[o]

[16] "If I have denied the desires of the poor[p]
or let the eyes of the widow[q] grow weary,[r]
[17] if I have kept my bread to myself,
not sharing it with the fatherless[s] —
[18] but from my youth I reared them as a father would,
and from my birth I guided the widow[t] —
[19] if I have seen anyone perishing for lack of clothing,[u]
or the needy[v] without garments,
[20] and their hearts did not bless me[w]
for warming them with the fleece[x] from my sheep,
[21] if I have raised my hand against the fatherless,[y]
knowing that I had influence in court,[z]

[a] 12 Hebrew *Abaddon*

31:2 [k] Nu 26:55; Ps 11:6; 16:5; 50:18; Ecc 3:22; 5:19; 9:9 [l] S Job 16:19; S 20:29 **31:3** [m] S Job 21:30 [n] Job 18:12 [o] Job 34:22; Ro 2:9 **31:4** [p] 2Ch 16:9; Ps 139:3; Da 4:37; 5:23 [q] S ver 14; S Job 10:4 **31:5** [r] S Job 15:31 **31:6** [s] Ps 139:23 [t] S Lev 19:36; S Job 6:2 [u] S Ge 6:9; S Job 2:3; S 23:10 **31:7** [v] S Job 23:11 [w] S Job 9:30 [x] Ps 7:3 **31:8** [y] S Job 5:5; S 20:10; Jn 4:37 [z] ver 12; Mic 6:15 **31:9** [a] S Dt 11:16; S Job 24:15; Jas 1:14 [b] Pr 5:3; 7:5 **31:10** [c] S Jdg 16:21 [d] Dt 28:30 **31:11** [e] Pr 6:32-33 [f] S Ge 38:24; S Ex 21:12; Jn 8:4-5 **31:12** [g] S Job 15:30 [h] S Job 26:6 [i] S ver 8 **31:13** [j] S Dt 5:14 [k] Ex 21:2-11; Lev 25:39-46; Dt 24:14-15 **31:14** [l] Job 33:5 [m] ver 4, 37; Ps 10:13, 15; 94:7; Isa 10:3; Jer 5:31; Hos 9:7; Mic 7:4; Col 4:1 **31:15** [n] S Job 4:17; Pr 22:2 [o] S Job 10:3; Eph 6:9 **31:16** [p] S Lev 25:17; S Job 5:16 [q] S Job 22:9; Jas 1:27 [r] Job 22:7 **31:17** [s] S Job 6:27; S 22:7 **31:18** [t] Isa 51:18 **31:19** [u] Job 22:6; Isa 58:7 [v] S Job 24:4 **31:20** [w] Job 29:13 [x] Jdg 6:37 **31:21** [y] S Job 22:7; Jas 1:27 [z] S Job 29:7, 9

31:4 Echoed by Elihu in 34:21.
31:6 *God weigh me in honest scales.* See photo below; see also 6:2; Pr 16:11 and note; 21:2; 24:12; Am 8:5; Mic 6:11. *blameless.* Does not imply sinless perfection (see note on 1:1).
31:12 *Destruction.* See note on 26:6.
31:13 – 23 Job reveals genuine understanding concerning matters of social justice: Human equality is based on creation (vv. 13 – 15), compassion toward those in need is essential (vv. 16 – 20), and power and influence must not be abused (vv. 21 – 23).
31:14 *what will I do . . . ?* Or "*then* what will I do . . . ?"
31:16 – 17 *widow . . . fatherless.* See note on 29:12 – 13.

Detail from a black basalt obelisk from Nimrud (883 – 859 BC) depicting the weighing of tribute from foreign lands. Job 31:6 urges, "Let God weigh me in honest scales."

Z. Radovan/www.BibleLandPictures.com

22 then let my arm fall from the shoulder,
let it be broken off at the joint.[a]
23 For I dreaded destruction from God,[b]
and for fear of his splendor[c] I could
not do such things.[d]

24 "If I have put my trust in gold[e]
or said to pure gold, 'You are my
security,'[f]
25 if I have rejoiced over my great
wealth,[g]
the fortune my hands had gained,[h]
26 if I have regarded the sun[i] in its
radiance
or the moon[j] moving in splendor,
27 so that my heart was secretly enticed[k]
and my hand offered them a kiss of
homage,[l]
28 then these also would be sins to be
judged,[m]
for I would have been unfaithful to
God on high.[n]

29 "If I have rejoiced at my enemy's
misfortune[o]
or gloated over the trouble that came
to him[p]—
30 I have not allowed my mouth to sin
by invoking a curse against their
life[q]—
31 if those of my household have never
said,
'Who has not been filled with Job's
meat?'[r]—
32 but no stranger had to spend the night
in the street,
for my door was always open to the
traveler[s]—
33 if I have concealed[t] my sin as people
do,[a]
by hiding[u] my guilt in my heart
34 because I so feared the crowd[v]
and so dreaded the contempt of the
clans
that I kept silent[w] and would not go
outside—

35 ("Oh, that I had someone to hear me![x]
I sign now my defense—let the
Almighty answer me;
let my accuser[y] put his indictment in
writing.
36 Surely I would wear it on my
shoulder,[z]
I would put it on like a crown.[a]
37 I would give him an account of my
every step;[b]
I would present it to him as to a
ruler.[c])—

38 "if my land cries out against me[d]
and all its furrows are wet[e] with
tears,
39 if I have devoured its yield without
payment[f]
or broken the spirit of its tenants,[g]
40 then let briers[h] come up instead of
wheat
and stinkweed[i] instead of barley."

The words of Job are ended.[j]

Elihu

32 So these three men stopped answering Job,[k] because he was righteous in his own eyes.[l] 2 But Elihu son of
Barakel the Buzite,[m] of the family of Ram,

[a] 33 Or *as Adam did*

31:22 [a] Nu 15:30; Job 5:15; 38:15; Ps 10:15; 37:17; 137:5 **31:23** [b] S Job 10:3; S 30:15 [c] Job 13:11 [d] S Ge 20:11 **31:24** [e] S Job 22:25 [f] Mt 6:24; Lk 12:15 **31:25** [g] S Ge 12:16; Ps 49:6; 52:7; 62:10; Isa 10:14 [h] S Job 22:24; Eze 28:5; Lk 12:20-21 **31:26** [i] S Ge 1:16 [j] Job 25:5 **31:27** [k] S Dt 11:16; S Job 24:15; Jas 1:14 [l] Jer 8:2; 16:11 **31:28** [m] S Ge 38:24; Dt 17:2-7 [n] S Nu 11:20; Eze 8:16 **31:29** [o] S Nu 14:1; Ps 35:15; Ob 1:12; Mt 5:44 [p] Pr 17:5; 24:17-18 **31:30** [q] Job 5:3; Ro 12:14 **31:31** [r] S Job 22:7 **31:32** [s] Ge 19:2-3; Jdg 19:20; Mt 25:35; S Ro 12:13 **31:33** [t] Ps 32:5; Pr 28:13 [u] S Ge 3:8 **31:34** [v] Ex 23:2 [w] Ps 32:3; 39:2 **31:35** [x] S Job 9:24; 30:28 [y] Job 27:7 **31:36** [z] S Ex 28:12 [a] Job 29:14 **31:37** [b] S ver 14; S Job 11:11 [c] S Job 21:28 **31:38** [d] S Ge 4:10 [e] Ps 65:10 **31:39** [f] S 1Ki 21:19 [g] S Lev 19:13; Jas 5:4 **31:40** [h] S Ge 3:18; Mt 13:7 [i] Zep 2:9; Mt 13:26 [j] Ps 72:20; Jer 51:64 **32:1** [k] ver 15 [l] S Job 2:3; S 10:7 **32:2** [m] S Ge 22:21

31:24–28 Covetous greed (vv. 24–25) and idolatry (vv. 26–27) are equally reprehensible in the eyes of God (v. 28; see Mt 6:19–21 and notes; Col 3:5).
31:25 *my great wealth.* See 1:3 and note; see also 1:10.
31:26–28 The sun and moon are not to be objects of worship (see note on Ge 1:16; see also Dt 4:19; 17:3; Eze 8:16–17).
31:27 *kiss.* An ancient gesture of worship (see 1Ki 19:18; Hos 13:2 and note).
31:29–32 The sin of gloating over one's enemy was condemned by Moses (see Ex 23:4–5 and note) and by Christ (see Mt 5:43–47).
31:33–34 A strong denial of hypocrisy.
31:33 *as people do.* See NIV text note and Ge 3:8–10; Hos 6:7 and note.
31:34 This disavowal (see note on 31:1–40) lacks a following "then"; instead, it is followed by a parenthetical section and another "if" (v. 38).
31:35–37 Job's final call for justice. His signature endorses every word of the oaths he has just taken.
31:35 *someone to hear me.* See notes on 5:1; 9:33; 16:18–21; 19:25. *let the Almighty answer me.* See note on 38:1. *accuser.* The Hebrew for this word is not the same as that for "Satan" (see note on 1:6). Here Job's accuser is either (1) a human adversary (perhaps one of the three friends) or (2) God himself. In any event, Job assumes that accusations have been lodged against him before the court of heaven to which God has responded with judgments.
31:36 *shoulder.* Inscriptions were sometimes worn on the shoulder as a perpetual reminder of their importance (see Ex 28:12).
31:38–40 A climactic oath that completes an earlier theme and creates a unique emphasis. Job calls for a curse on his land if he has not been fully committed to social justice (see also vv. 13–15).
31:40 *The words of Job are ended.* His complaints and arguments are now over. He will make only brief statements of contrition (see 40:3–5; 42:1–6 and notes) following the divine discourses.
32:1—37:24 A fourth counselor, named Elihu and younger than the other three (32:4,6–7,9), has been standing on the sidelines, giving deference to age and listening to the dialogue-dispute. But now he declares himself ready to show that both Job and the three other counselors are in the wrong. The author introduces Elihu's four poetic speeches (32:6—33:33; ch. 34; ch. 35; chs. 36–37) with a short prose preface (32:1–5).
32:1 *righteous in his own eyes.* Job insisted on his innocence in spite of the terrible suffering that he was experiencing.

became very angry with Job for justifying
himself[n] rather than God.[o] 3 He was also
angry with the three friends,[p] because they
had found no way to refute Job,[q] and yet
had condemned him.[a r] 4 Now Elihu had
waited before speaking to Job because
they were older than he.[s] 5 But when he
saw that the three men had nothing more
to say, his anger was aroused.

6 So Elihu son of Barakel the Buzite said:

"I am young in years,
and you are old;[t]
that is why I was fearful,
not daring to tell you what I know.
7 I thought, 'Age should speak;
advanced years should teach wisdom.'[u]
8 But it is the spirit[b v] in a person,
the breath of the Almighty,[w] that gives them understanding.[x]
9 It is not only the old[c] who are wise,[y]
not only the aged[z] who understand what is right.[a]

10 "Therefore I say: Listen to me;[b]
I too will tell you what I know.[c]
11 I waited while you spoke,
I listened to your reasoning;
while you were searching for words,
12 I gave you my full attention.
But not one of you has proved Job wrong;
none of you has answered his arguments.[d]
13 Do not say, 'We have found wisdom;[e]
let God, not a man, refute[f] him.'
14 But Job has not marshaled his words against me,[g]
and I will not answer him with your arguments.

15 "They are dismayed and have no more to say;
words have failed them.[h]
16 Must I wait, now that they are silent,
now that they stand there with no reply?
17 I too will have my say;
I too will tell what I know.[i]
18 For I am full of words,
and the spirit[j] within me compels me;[k]
19 inside I am like bottled-up wine,
like new wineskins ready to burst.[l]
20 I must speak and find relief;
I must open my lips and reply.[m]
21 I will show no partiality,[n]
nor will I flatter anyone;[o]
22 for if I were skilled in flattery,
my Maker[p] would soon take me away.[q]

33 "But now, Job, listen[r] to my words;
pay attention to everything I say.[s]
2 I am about to open my mouth;
my words are on the tip of my tongue.
3 My words come from an upright heart;[t]
my lips sincerely speak what I know.[u]
4 The Spirit[v] of God has made me;[w]
the breath of the Almighty[x] gives me life.[y]
5 Answer me[z] then, if you can;
stand up[a] and argue your case before me.[b]

[a] 3 Masoretic Text; an ancient Hebrew scribal tradition *Job, and so had condemned God* [b] 8 Or *Spirit*; also in verse 18 [c] 9 Or *many*; or *great*

32:2 [n] ver 1 [o] S Job 13:19; 27:5; 30:21; 35:2 **32:3** [p] Job 42:7 [q] ver 12-13 [r] S Job 15:13 **32:4** [s] S Lev 19:32 **32:6** [t] Job 15:10 **32:7** [u] S 1Ch 29:15; S 2Ch 10:6 **32:8** [v] ver 18 [w] S Job 27:3 [x] S Job 12:13; S Ps 119:34; Jas 1:5 **32:9** [y] 1Co 1:26 [z] Ps 119:100 [a] S Job 12:12, 20; Lk 2:47; 1Ti 4:12 **32:10** [b] Job 33:1, 31, 33; 34:2, 16; 37:2, 14; Ps 34:11 [c] S Job 5:27 **32:12** [d] ver 3 **32:13** [e] S Job 4:12; S Ecc 9:11 [f] S Job 11:5 **32:14** [g] Job 23:4 **32:15** [h] ver 1 **32:17** [i] S Job 5:27; 33:3; 36:4 **32:18** [j] ver 8 [k] Ac 4:20; 1Co 9:16; 2Co 5:14 **32:19** [l] Jer 20:9; Am 3:8; Mt 9:17 **32:20** [m] S Job 4:2; S Jer 6:11 **32:21** [n] S Lev 19:15; S 2Ch 19:7; S Job 13:10; Mt 22:16 [o] Pr 29:5; 1Th 2:5 **32:22** [p] S Job 4:17; S 9:9 [q] Ps 12:2-4 **33:1** [r] Job 32:10 [s] S Job 6:28; S 13:6 **33:3** [t] 1Ki 3:6; Ps 7:10; 11:2; 64:10 [u] S Job 6:28 **33:4** [v] S Ge 1:2 [w] Job 10:3 [x] S Job 27:3 [y] S Nu 16:22; S Job 12:10 **33:5** [z] ver 32 [a] Job 13:18 [b] S Job 31:14

32:2–3 *angry.* Elihu considers Job's emphasis on vindicating himself rather than God reprehensible, but he also believes that the friends' inability to refute Job was tantamount to condemning God (see NIV text note on v. 3).

32:2 *Elihu.* Means "He is my God." Elihu's speeches in some ways anticipate the divine word out of the storm (38:1—42:6). *Buzite.* An inhabitant of Buz, a desert region in the east (see Jer 25:23).

32:6,10,17 *tell ... what I know.* The impetuous Elihu is eager to share his knowledge and assumes that he can communicate it effectively (see note on 36:4).

32:6 *young ... fearful.* See Jer 1:6–8; 1Ti 4:12; 2Ti 1:7 and notes.

32:8 *breath of the Almighty.* See 33:4.

32:14 *I will not answer him with your arguments.* Elihu feels that something important has been left out and, where the wisdom of age has failed, he by the Spirit of God (see NIV text note on v. 8) has the understanding to supply the right answers.

32:15–22 Elihu delivers a soliloquy to himself, but it is also for the benefit of those who may be listening.

32:15–16 *words have failed them ... they stand there with no reply.* See v. 5. The breakdown of the third cycle in the dialogue-dispute cut short Bildad's last word and left Zophar without a third speech (see note on 22:1—26:14).

32:18 *I am full of words.* Elihu's speeches continue unabated through ch. 37. He has a genuine contribution to make, however, to the problems Job is facing. At the same time, he does not stoop to false accusation about Job's earlier life but usually confines his criticism of Job to quotations from Job himself. This is perhaps the reason that God, in the epilogue, does not condemn Elihu along with Job's three friends (see 42:7–9 and note).

32:19 *new wineskins ready to burst.* Old wineskins might be expected to crack or break (see Mt 9:17 and note), but not new ones. Elihu is obviously eager to speak.

33:1–33 Elihu turns to Job and speaks directly to him. Unlike the three friends, he addresses Job by name (vv. 1,31; 37:14).

33:1 *pay attention to everything I say.* He is thoroughly convinced of the importance and wisdom of the advice he is about to give (see vv. 31,33).

33:4 *Spirit of God has made me.* See Ge 1:2 and note. *breath of the Almighty.* See 32:8. *gives me life.* See 27:3; see also Ge 2:7 and note.

33:5 *Answer me.* He opens and closes his speech (see v. 32) with the same plea. *if you can.* His attitude of superiority shows through.

6 I am the same as you in God's sight;[c]
I too am a piece of clay.[d]
7 No fear of me should alarm you,
nor should my hand be heavy on
you.[e]

8 "But you have said in my hearing—
I heard the very words—
9 'I am pure,[f] I have done no wrong;[g]
I am clean and free from sin.[h]
10 Yet God has found fault with me;
he considers me his enemy.[i]
11 He fastens my feet in shackles;[j]
he keeps close watch on all my
paths.'[k]

12 "But I tell you, in this you are not right,
for God is greater than any mortal.[l]
13 Why do you complain to him[m]
that he responds to no one's words[a]?[n]
14 For God does speak[o]—now one way,
now another[p]—
though no one perceives it.[q]
15 In a dream,[r] in a vision[s] of the night,[t]
when deep sleep[u] falls on people
as they slumber in their beds,
16 he may speak[v] in their ears
and terrify them[w] with warnings,[x]
17 to turn them from wrongdoing
and keep them from pride,[y]
18 to preserve them from the pit,[z]
their lives from perishing by the
sword.[b][a]

19 "Or someone may be chastened[b] on a
bed of pain[c]
with constant distress in their
bones,[d]

33:6 [c]Ac 14:15; Jas 5:17 [d]S Job 4:19 **33:7** [e]S Job 9:34; 2Co 2:4 **33:9** [f]S Job 10:7 [g]S Job 9:30; S 13:23 [h]S Job 2:9 **33:10** [i]S Job 13:24 **33:11** [j]S Job 13:27 [k]Job 14:16; Pr 3:6; Isa 30:21 **33:12** [l]S Job 5:9; Ps 8:4; 50:21; Ecc 7:20; Isa 55:8-9 **33:13** [m]Job 40:2; Isa 45:9 [n]S Job 11:8 **33:14** [o]Ps 62:11 [p]ver 29 [q]Job 4:12 **33:15** [r]S Ge 20:3; Job 4:13; S Mt 27:19 [s]Ac 16:9 [t]S Ge 15:1; Da 2:19 [u]S Ge 2:21 **33:16** [v]Job 36:10, 15 [w]S Job 6:4 [x]Ps 88:15-16 **33:17** [y]S Job 20:6 **33:18** [z]ver 22, 24, 28, 30; Ps 28:1; 30:9; 69:15; 88:6; 103:4; Pr 1:12; Isa 14:15; 38:17; Jnh 2:6; Zec 9:11 [a]S Job 15:22; Mt 26:52

20 so that their body finds food[e] repulsive
and their soul loathes the choicest
meal.[f]
21 Their flesh wastes away to nothing,
and their bones,[g] once hidden, now
stick out.[h]
22 They draw near to the pit,[i]
and their life to the messengers of
death.[c][j]
23 Yet if there is an angel at their side,
a messenger,[k] one out of a thousand,
sent to tell them how to be upright,[l]
24 and he is gracious to that person and
says to God,
'Spare them from going down to the
pit;[m]
I have found a ransom for them[n]—
25 let their flesh be renewed[o] like a
child's;
let them be restored as in the days of
their youth'[p]—
26 then that person can pray to God and
find favor with him,[q]
they will see God's face and shout
for joy;[r]
he will restore them to full well-
being.[s]

[a] 13 Or *that he does not answer for any of his actions*
[b] 18 Or *from crossing the river*
[c] 22 Or *to the place of the dead*

33:19 [b]S Job 5:17 [c]S Ge 17:1; S Dt 8:5; 2Co 12:7-10; Jas 1:3 [d]S Job 16:16; Ps 6:2; 38:3; Isa 38:13 **33:20** [e]Ps 102:4; 107:18 [f]S Job 3:24; S 6:6 **33:21** [g]S Job 2:5 [h]S Job 16:8 **33:22** [i]S ver 18 [j]Job 38:17; Ps 9:13; 88:3; 107:18; 116:3 **33:23** [k]Gal 3:19; Heb 8:6; 9:15 [l]Job 36:9-10; Mic 6:8 **33:24** [m]S ver 18 [n]S Job 6:22 **33:25** [o]Ps 103:5 [p]2Ki 5:14 **33:26** [q]S Job 5:15; Pr 8:35; 12:2; 18:22; Lk 2:52 [r]S Ezr 3:13; S Job 22:26 [s]Ps 13:5; 50:15; 51:12; 1Jn 1:9

33:6 *I . . . am a piece of clay.* See note on 4:19.
33:7 *hand . . . heavy on.* The idiom is elsewhere used only of God (see 23:2 and NIV text notes; see also note on 1Sa 5:6).
33:8 *But you have said.* Elihu's method is to quote Job (vv. 9–11; 34:5–6,9; 35:2–3) and then show him where and how he is wrong. The quotations are not always verbatim, which indicates that Elihu is content simply to repeat the substance of Job's arguments.
33:11 Elihu quotes Job's words almost verbatim here (see 13:27).
33:12 *you are not right.* Elihu feels that Job needs to be corrected. Certainly Job's perception of God as his enemy (see v. 10; 13:24; 19:11) is wrong, but Elihu is also offended by what he considers Job's claim to purity (see v. 9). Job, however, had never claimed to be "pure . . . and free from sin" (v. 9), though some of his words were also understood that way by Eliphaz (see 15:14–16). Job admits being a sinner (7:21; 13:26) but disclaims the outrageous sins for which he thinks he is being punished. His complaints about God's silence (see v. 13) are also an offense to Elihu. He imputes to Job the blanket statement that God never speaks to human beings, whereas Job's point is that God is silent in his present experience.
33:15 *In a dream . . . when deep sleep falls on people.* Elihu echoes Eliphaz (see 4:13).
33:18 *pit.* A metaphor for the grave (see vv. 22,24,28,30), as often in the Psalms. *perishing by the sword.* See 36:12. The reading in the NIV text note on both verses refers to the figurative waterway between the land of the living and the realm of the dead. The Hebrew for "river" here is *shelaḥ* (from a root that means "to send") and sometimes means "water channel" (see Ne 3:15 and NIV text note), a conduit through which water is "sent" (see Jn 9:7 and note) by a spring. The "river" therefore is the figurative means of passage between this world and the next.
33:19 *chastened on a bed of pain.* Dreams and visions (see v. 15) are not the only ways in which God speaks. He can talk to us in ways that we do not perceive (see v. 14). Elihu rightly states that God speaks to humans in order to turn them from sin. But he overlooks Job's reason for wanting an audience with God: to find out what sins he is being accused of (see 13:22–23).
33:23–28 After emphasizing the importance of the chastening aspect of suffering, a point mentioned only briefly by Eliphaz (see 5:17; see also note on 5:17–26), Elihu now moves on to the possibility of deliverance and restoration based on a mediator (see note on 5:1). He further allows for God's gracious response of forgiveness where sincere repentance is present (vv. 27–28). But Elihu is still ignorant of the true nature of Job's relationship to God, known only in the divine council (chs. 1–2).
33:24 *Spare them from going down to the pit.* See Isa 38:17 and note. *ransom.* See Ps 49:7–9 and note.
33:25 *flesh be renewed like a child's . . . restored.* Similar phrases are used in 2Ki 5:14 with reference to healing from leprosy.
33:26 *see God's face.* Not literally (see note on Ge 16:13).

27 And they will go to others and say,
'I have sinned,[t] I have perverted
what is right,[u]
but I did not get what I deserved.[v]
28 God has delivered[w] me from going
down to the pit,[x]
and I shall live to enjoy the light of
life.'[y]

29 "God does all these things to a
person[z]—
twice, even three times[a]—
30 to turn them back[b] from the pit,[c]
that the light of life[d] may shine on
them.[e]

31 "Pay attention, Job, and listen[f] to me;[g]
be silent,[h] and I will speak.
32 If you have anything to say, answer
me;[i]
speak up, for I want to vindicate
you.[j]
33 But if not, then listen to me;[k]
be silent,[l] and I will teach you
wisdom.[m]"

34

Then Elihu said:

2 "Hear my words, you wise men;
listen to me,[n] you men of learning.
3 For the ear tests words
as the tongue tastes food.[o]
4 Let us discern for ourselves what is
right;[p]
let us learn together what is good.[q]

5 "Job says, 'I am innocent,[r]
but God denies me justice.[s]
6 Although I am right,
I am considered a liar;[t]
although I am guiltless,[u]
his arrow inflicts an incurable wound.'[v]
7 Is there anyone like Job,
who drinks scorn like water?[w]
8 He keeps company with evildoers;
he associates with the wicked.[x]
9 For he says, 'There is no profit
in trying to please God.'[y]

10 "So listen to me,[z] you men of
understanding.[a]
Far be it from God to do evil,[b]
from the Almighty to do wrong.[c]
11 He repays everyone for what they have
done;[d]
he brings on them what their
conduct deserves.[e]
12 It is unthinkable that God would do
wrong,[f]
that the Almighty would pervert
justice.[g]
13 Who appointed[h] him over the earth?
Who put him in charge of the whole
world?[i]
14 If it were his intention
and he withdrew his spirit[a][j] and
breath,[k]
15 all humanity would perish[l] together
and mankind would return to the
dust.[m]

[a] 14 Or *Spirit*

33:27 [t]S Nu 22:34 [u]Lk 15:21 [v]S Ezr 9:13; Ps 22:27; 51:13; Ro 6:21; Jas 2:13 **33:28** [w]S Ex 15:13; Ps 34:22; 107:20 [x]S ver 18; S Job 17:16 [y]S Job 22:28 **33:29** [z]Ps 139:16; Pr 16:9; 20:24; Jer 10:23; 1Co 12:6; Eph 1:11; Php 2:13 [a]ver 14 **33:30** [b]Jas 5:19 [c]S ver 18 [d]Ps 49:19; 56:13; 116:9; Isa 53:11 [e]Isa 60:1; Eph 5:14 **33:31** [f]Jer 23:18 [g]S Job 32:10 [h]ver 33 **33:32** [i]ver 5 [j]S Job 6:29; 35:2 **33:33** [k]S Job 32:10 [l]ver 31 [m]S Job 6:24; Pr 10:8,10,19 **34:2** [n]S Job 32:10 **34:3** [o]Job 12:11 **34:4** [p]S Job 12:12; Heb 5:14 [q]1Th 5:21 **34:5** [r]S Job 10:7 [s]S Job 6:29 **34:6** [t]S Job 6:28 [u]S Job 9:21 [v]S Job 6:4; S 10:3; S Jer 10:19 **34:7** [w]S Job 9:21; S 15:16 **34:8** [x]S Job 22:15 **34:9** [y]S Job 9:29-31; S 21:15 **34:10** [z]Job 32:10 [a]ver 16; S Job 12:12 [b]S Ge 18:25 [c]ver 12; Dt 32:4; Job 8:3; 36:23; Ps 92:15; Ro 3:5; 9:14 **34:11** [d]S Job 21:31; S Mt 16:27 [e]Jer 17:10; 32:19; Eze 33:20 **34:12** [f]S ver 10; Titus 1:2; Heb 6:18 [g]S Job 8:3; Ps 9:16; Col 3:25; 2Th 1:6 **34:13** [h]Heb 1:2 [i]Job 36:23; 38:4,6; Isa 40:14 **34:14** [j]S Ge 6:3 [k]S Nu 16:22; S Job 27:3 **34:15** [l]S Ge 6:13; La 3:22; Mal 3:6; Jn 3:16 [m]S Ge 2:7; S Job 7:21; 9:22; Ps 90:10

33:29 *twice … three times.* See note on 5:19.

33:30 *to turn them back from the pit.* Elihu teaches that God's apparent harshness in chastening human beings is in reality an act of love, since they are never punished in this life in keeping with what they fully deserve (see v. 27). *light of life.* Spiritual well-being (see Ps 49:19; see also Ps 27:1 and note). In some contexts, the phrase refers to resurrection (see note on Isa 53:11).

33:32 *I want to vindicate you.* But this will happen, Elihu insists, only if Job repents.

34:1 – 37 The second of Elihu's four speeches (see note on 32:1 — 37:24), divided into three sections: (1) addressed to a group of wise men (vv. 2 – 15), doubtless including the three friends; (2) addressed to Job (vv. 16 – 33); (3) addressed to himself (vv. 34 – 37), as in 32:15 – 22 (see note there).

34:2,10 *listen to me.* Although it is possible that Elihu is overly impressed with his own wisdom, it is more likely that he considered himself a messenger of God (see 32:8,18 and NIV text note on 32:8), especially in the light of his humble attitude in v. 4.

34:2 *wise men … men of learning.* Also referred to as "men of understanding" (vv. 10,34).

34:3 Elihu echoes the words of Job in 12:11 (see note there).

34:5,9 *Job says … For he says.* Elihu again quotes Job and then goes on to defend God's justice against what he considers to be Job's false theology (e.g., 9:14 – 24; 16:11 – 17; 19:7; 21:17 – 18; 24:1 – 12; 27:2). The substance of the quotation in v. 5 is accurate (cf. 12:4; 13:18; 27:6), and much of v. 6 represents Job fairly (see 21:34; 27:5; see also 6:4 and note) — though Job had never claimed to be completely guiltless. Verse 9 is not a direct quotation from Job, who had only imagined the wicked saying something similar (see 21:15). But perhaps Elihu derives it from Job's repeated statement that God treats the righteous and the wicked in the same way (cf. 9:22; 21:17; 24:1 – 12), leading to the conclusion that it does not pay to please God.

34:7 *drinks scorn like water.* See Eliphaz's description of humans in 15:16.

34:10 *Far be it from God to do evil.* See Ge 18:25 and note. Elihu's concern that Job was making God the author of evil is commendable. Job, in his frustration, has come perilously close to charging God with wrongdoing (12:4 – 6; 24:1 – 12). He has suggested that this is the only conclusion he can reach on the basis of his knowledge and experience (9:24).

34:11 See Ecc 12:14; Ro 2:6 – 11; 2Co 5:10 and notes.

34:13 – 15 Elihu is zealous for God's glory as the sovereign Sustainer who demonstrates his grace every moment by granting life and breath to human beings.

34:15 *return to the dust.* See Ecc 12:7; see also Ge 3:19 and note.

16 "If you have understanding,[n] hear
this;
listen to what I say.[o]
17 Can someone who hates justice
govern?[p]
Will you condemn the just and
mighty One?[q]
18 Is he not the One who says to kings,
'You are worthless,'
and to nobles,[r] 'You are wicked,'[s]
19 who shows no partiality[t] to princes
and does not favor the rich over the
poor,[u]
for they are all the work of his
hands?[v]
20 They die in an instant, in the middle of
the night;[w]
the people are shaken and they pass
away;
the mighty are removed without
human hand.[x]

21 "His eyes are on the ways of mortals;[y]
he sees their every step.[z]
22 There is no deep shadow,[a] no utter
darkness,[b]
where evildoers can hide.[c]
23 God has no need to examine people
further,[d]
that they should come before him
for judgment.[e]
24 Without inquiry he shatters[f] the
mighty[g]
and sets up others in their place.[h]
25 Because he takes note of their deeds,[i]
he overthrows them in the night[j] and
they are crushed.[k]
26 He punishes them for their wickedness[l]
where everyone can see them,
27 because they turned from following
him[m]
and had no regard for any of his
ways.[n]
28 They caused the cry of the poor to
come before him,
so that he heard the cry of the
needy.[o]
29 But if he remains silent,[p] who can
condemn him?[q]
If he hides his face,[r] who can see
him?
Yet he is over individual and nation
alike,[s]
30 to keep the godless[t] from ruling,[u]
from laying snares for the people.[v]

31 "Suppose someone says to God,
'I am guilty[w] but will offend no
more.
32 Teach me what I cannot see;[x]
if I have done wrong, I will not do
so again.'[y]
33 Should God then reward you on your
terms,
when you refuse to repent?[z]
You must decide, not I;
so tell me what you know.

34 "Men of understanding declare,
wise men who hear me say to me,
35 'Job speaks without knowledge;[a]
his words lack insight.'[b]
36 Oh, that Job might be tested to the
utmost
for answering like a wicked man![c]
37 To his sin he adds rebellion;
scornfully he claps his hands[d]
among us
and multiplies his words[e] against
God."[f]

35

Then Elihu said:

2 "Do you think this is just?
You say, 'I am in the right,[g] not God.'[h]
3 Yet you ask him, 'What profit is it
to me,[a]
and what do I gain by not sinning?'[i]

4 "I would like to reply to you
and to your friends with you.

[a] 3 Or *you*

34:16 [n] S ver 10 [o] S Job 32:10 **34:17** [p] ver 30; 2Sa 23:3-4; Pr 20:8, 26; 24:23-25; 28:28 [q] ver 29; S Job 10:7; 40:8; Ro 3:5-6 **34:18** [r] S Job 12:18 [s] Ex 22:28; Isa 40:24 **34:19** [t] S Job 13:10; S Ac 10:34 [u] S Lev 19:15; Jas 2:5 [v] S Job 10:3 **34:20** [w] ver 25; S Ex 11:4; S Job 20:8 [x] S Job 12:19 **34:21** [y] Jer 32:19 [z] S Job 14:16; Pr 15:3; S Heb 4:13 **34:22** [a] S Job 3:5 [b] Ps 74:20 [c] S Ge 3:8; S Job 11:20 **34:23** [d] Ps 11:4 [e] Job 11:11 **34:24** [f] Isa 8:9; 9:4; Jer 51:20; Da 2:34 [g] Job 12:19 [h] Da 2:21 **34:25** [i] S Job 11:11 [j] S ver 20 [k] Pr 5:21-23 **34:26** [l] S Ge 6:5; S Job 8:22; S 28:24; Ps 9:5; Jer 44:5 **34:27** [m] Ps 14:3 [n] S 1Sa 15:11 **34:28** [o] S Ex 22:23; S Job 5:15; S 12:19 **34:29** [p] Ps 28:1; 83:1; 109:1 [q] S ver 17; Ro 8:34 [r] Ps 13:1 [s] Ps 83:18; 97:9 **34:30** [t] S Job 8:13 [u] S ver 17 [v] Ps 25:15; 31:4; 91:3; 124:7; 140:5; Pr 29:2-12 **34:31** [w] Ps 51:5; Lk 15:21; Ro 7:24; 1Jn 1:8, 10 **34:32** [x] Ex 33:13; Job 35:11; 38:36; Ps 15:2; 25:4; 27:11; 51:6; 86:11; 139:23-24; 143:8 [y] Job 33:27; S Lk 19:8 **34:33** [z] S 2Ki 17:13; Job 33:23; 36:10, 15, 18, 21; 41:11; 42:6; Pr 17:23; Jnh 3:8 **34:35** [a] Job 35:16; 38:2; 42:3 [b] Job 26:3 **34:36** [c] S Job 6:29; S 22:15 **34:37** [d] S Job 27:23 [e] Job 35:16 [f] Job 23:2 **35:2** [g] S Job 33:32 [h] S Job 2:9; S 32:2 **35:3** [i] S Job 9:29-31; S 21:15

34:16 *hear ... listen.* The Hebrew for these verbs is singular, addressed to Job. Elihu is concerned that Job's attitude about God's justice be corrected (see v. 17), so he stresses God's impartial rule as Lord of all, especially in meting out justice to the wicked in high places (see vv. 18–20).

34:18 *worthless.* See note on Dt 13:13.

34:21–28 God's omniscience guarantees that he will not make any mistakes when he punishes evildoers. It is not necessary for him to set times to examine people for judgment (see v. 23; contrast 24:1).

34:21 Elihu echoes the words of Job in 31:4.

34:29 *if he remains silent, who can condemn him?* Elihu attempts to answer Job's complaint about God's silence (ch. 23). God watches over people and nations to see that right is done (vv. 29–30).

34:31–33 First indirectly (vv. 31–32) and then more directly (v. 33), Elihu condemns Job and calls for his repentance.

34:35 *Job speaks without knowledge.* A motif in the first discourse of the Lord (see 38:2 and note) and the final response of Job (see 42:3).

35:1–16 Elihu's third speech (see note on 32:1—37:24), addressed to Job.

35:2 *in the right.* The Hebrew for this phrase is translated "vindicated" in Job's statement in 13:18. Elihu thinks that it is unjust and inconsistent for Job to expect vindication from God and at the same time imply that God does not care whether we are righteous (see v. 3). But allowance must be made for a person to express their feelings. The psalmist who thirsted for God (Ps 42:1–2) also questioned why God had forgotten him (Ps 42:9) and rejected him (Ps 43:2).

5 Look up at the heavens[j] and see;
gaze at the clouds so high above you.[k]
6 If you sin, how does that affect him?
If your sins are many, what does that do to him?[l]
7 If you are righteous, what do you give to him,[m]
or what does he receive[n] from your hand?[o]
8 Your wickedness only affects humans like yourself,[p]
and your righteousness only other people.[q]

9 "People cry out[r] under a load of oppression;[s]
they plead for relief from the arm of the powerful.[t]
10 But no one says, 'Where is God my Maker,[u]
who gives songs[v] in the night,[w]
11 who teaches[x] us[y] more than he teaches[a] the beasts of the earth
and makes us wiser than[b] the birds in the sky?'
12 He does not answer[z] when people cry out
because of the arrogance[a] of the wicked.[b]
13 Indeed, God does not listen to their empty plea;
the Almighty pays no attention to it.[c]
14 How much less, then, will he listen
when you say that you do not see him,[d]
that your case[e] is before him
and you must wait for him,[f]
15 and further, that his anger never punishes[g]
and he does not take the least notice of wickedness.[c][h]
16 So Job opens his mouth with empty talk;[i]
without knowledge he multiplies words."[j]

36

Elihu continued:

2 "Bear with me a little longer and I will show you
that there is more to be said in God's behalf.
3 I get my knowledge from afar;[k]
I will ascribe justice to my Maker.[l]
4 Be assured that my words are not false;[m]
one who has perfect knowledge[n] is with you.[o]

5 "God is mighty,[p] but despises no one;[q]
he is mighty, and firm in his purpose.[r]
6 He does not keep the wicked alive[s]
but gives the afflicted their rights.[t]
7 He does not take his eyes off the righteous;[u]
he enthrones them with kings[v]
and exalts them forever.[w]
8 But if people are bound in chains,[x]
held fast by cords of affliction,[y]
9 he tells them what they have done—
that they have sinned arrogantly.[z]
10 He makes them listen[a] to correction[b]
and commands them to repent of their evil.[c]

[a] *10,11* Or *night, / [11]who teaches us by* [b] *11* Or *us wise by* [c] *15* Symmachus, Theodotion and Vulgate; the meaning of the Hebrew for this word is uncertain.

35:5 [j] S Ge 15:5; S Dt 10:14 [k] S Job 11:7-9; Ps 19:1-4 **35:6** [l] S Job 7:20 **35:7** [m] Ro 11:35 [n] 1Co 4:7 [o] S Job 22:2-3; Lk 17:10 **35:8** [p] Eze 18:24 [q] Eze 18:5-9; Zec 7:9-10 **35:9** [r] Ex 2:23 [s] S Job 20:19 [t] S Job 5:15; S 12:19 **35:10** [u] S Job 4:17 [v] S Job 8:21 [w] Ps 42:8; 77:6; 119:62; 149:5; Ac 16:25 **35:11** [x] S Job 21:22; Lk 12:24 [y] Job 12:7 **35:12** [z] S 1Sa 8:18 [a] S Job 15:25 [b] Ps 66:18 **35:13** [c] S Dt 1:45; S 1Sa 8:18; S Job 15:31; S Pr 15:8 **35:14** [d] S Job 9:11 [e] Ps 37:6 [f] Job 31:35 **35:15** [g] S Job 9:24 [h] S Job 18:5; Ps 10:11; Hos 7:2; Am 8:7 **35:16** [i] Titus 1:10 [j] S Job 34:35, 37; 1Co 4:20; Jude 1:10 **36:3** [k] S Job 6:28 [l] S Job 4:17 **36:4** [m] S Job 6:28; S 13:6 [n] Job 37:5, 16, 23 [o] S Job 32:17 **36:5** [p] S Job 9:4 [q] Ps 5:2; 22:24; 31:22; 69:33; 102:17; 103:10 [r] S Nu 23:19; Ro 11:29 **36:6** [s] S Job 34:26 [t] S Job 4:10 **36:7** [u] S Job 11:11; Ps 11:5; 33:18; 34:15; Mt 6:18 [v] Ps 113:8; Isa 22:23 [w] S 1Sa 2:7-8; S Job 4:7 **36:8** [x] S 2Sa 3:34; 2Ki 23:33; Ps 107:10, 14 [y] ver 10, 15, 21; Ps 119:67, 71 **36:9** [z] S Job 15:25 **36:10** [a] S Job 33:16 [b] S Job 5:17 [c] S ver 8; S Jdg 6:8; S Job 34:33; 1Th 5:22

35:5 *Look up at the heavens and see.* Elihu asserts that God is so far above human beings that there is really nothing they can do, good or bad, that will affect God's essential nature (see v. 6).

35:9 *People cry out … they plead for relief.* Elihu states that those like Job who pray for help when suffering innocently never seem to get around to trusting the justice and goodness of their Maker, who is also the author of wisdom and joy (see vv. 10–11). Such failure is a sign of arrogance (see v. 12), so Job's complaint against God's justice and about God's silence is meaningless talk (see vv. 13–16).

35:10–11 *God … gives songs … teaches … makes us wiser.* God chooses to condescend, to reach out to people in love.

35:12 The verse is difficult. A comma after the first line would change the meaning and make more sense of the verse in context: Since the wicked are arrogant, God does not listen (see v. 13). Job himself shares their arrogance. He too receives no answer, because he does not ask rightly (see v. 14).

35:16 *without knowledge.* See 38:2 and note. *multiplies words.* "Against God" (34:37).

36:1—37:24 Elihu's fourth and final (see 36:2) speech (see note on 32:1—37:24), addressed for the most part to Job (but see note on 37:2).

36:2–4 Elihu desires to strengthen the case for God's goodness and justice.

36:4 *perfect knowledge.* Here Elihu applies the phrase to himself, while in 37:16 he applies it to God—thus appearing to make himself equal to God. But the Hebrew for "knowledge" is not quite the same here as in 37:16. Elihu is probably referring to his ability as a communicator; i.e., he claims perfection in the knowledge of speech (see note on 32:6,10,17).

36:5 God's power assures the fulfillment of his purpose.

36:6–9 A classic statement of God's justice in rewarding the righteous and punishing sinners (in contrast to what Job has been claiming). In v. 7 Elihu perhaps has in mind Job's complaint that God will not leave him alone (see 7:17–19), and in v. 9 he may be thinking of Job's charge that God will not present his indictment against him (see 31:35–36).

36:10 *makes them listen to correction.* Elihu states that God uses trouble to gain people's attention.

[11] If they obey and serve him,[d]
they will spend the rest of their days
in prosperity[e]
and their years in contentment.[f]
[12] But if they do not listen,
they will perish by the sword[a][g]
and die without knowledge.[h]

[13] "The godless in heart[i] harbor
resentment;[j]
even when he fetters them, they do
not cry for help.[k]
[14] They die in their youth,[l]
among male prostitutes of the
shrines.[m]
[15] But those who suffer[n] he delivers in
their suffering;[o]
he speaks[p] to them in their
affliction.[q]

[16] "He is wooing[r] you from the jaws of
distress
to a spacious place[s] free from
restriction,[t]
to the comfort of your table[u] laden
with choice food.[v]
[17] But now you are laden with the
judgment due the wicked;[w]
judgment and justice have taken
hold of you.[x]
[18] Be careful that no one entices you by
riches;
do not let a large bribe[y] turn you
aside.[z]
[19] Would your wealth[a] or even all your
mighty efforts
sustain you so you would not be in
distress?
[20] Do not long for the night,[b]
to drag people away from their
homes.[b]
[21] Beware of turning to evil,[c]
which you seem to prefer to
affliction.[d]

[22] "God is exalted in his power.[e]
Who is a teacher like him?[f]
[23] Who has prescribed his ways[g] for him,[h]
or said to him, 'You have done
wrong'?[i]
[24] Remember to extol his work,[j]
which people have praised in song.[k]
[25] All humanity has seen it;[l]
mortals gaze on it from afar.
[26] How great is God—beyond our
understanding![m]
The number of his years is past
finding out.[n]

[27] "He draws up the drops of water,[o]
which distill as rain to the streams[c];[p]
[28] the clouds pour down their moisture
and abundant showers[q] fall on
mankind.[r]
[29] Who can understand how he spreads
out the clouds,
how he thunders[s] from his pavilion?[t]
[30] See how he scatters his lightning[u]
about him,
bathing the depths of the sea.[v]
[31] This is the way he governs[d] the
nations[w]
and provides food[x] in abundance.[y]
[32] He fills his hands with lightning
and commands it to strike its mark.[z]
[33] His thunder announces the coming
storm;[a]
even the cattle make known its
approach.[e][b]

37 "At this my heart pounds[c]
and leaps from its place.

36:11 [d] S Lev 26:33; Dt 28:1; Isa 1:19; Hag 1:12 [e] S Dt 30:15; S Job 8:7 [f] S Ex 8:22; S Dt 8:1; Jn 14:21; 1Ti 4:8 **36:12** [g] S Lev 26:38; S Job 15:22 [h] S Job 4:21; Eph 4:18 **36:13** [i] S Job 15:12; Ro 2:5 [j] S Job 5:2 [k] S Job 4:17; Am 4:11 **36:14** [l] S Job 15:32 [m] S Dt 23:17 **36:15** [n] S Job 5:15 [o] 2Co 12:10 [p] S Job 33:16 [q] S ver 8; S Job 34:33 **36:16** [r] Hos 2:14 [s] S 2Sa 22:20; Ps 18:19 [t] Ps 118:5 [u] Ps 23:5; 78:19 [v] S Ge 17:1; S Job 15:11 **36:17** [w] S Job 20:29 [x] Job 22:11 **36:18** [y] S Ex 23:8; Am 5:12 [z] S Job 34:33 **36:19** [a] Ps 49:6; Jer 9:23 **36:20** [b] Job 34:20, 25 **36:21** [c] S Job 34:33; Ps 66:18 [d] S ver 8; Heb 11:25 **36:22** [e] S Job 5:9; S 9:4 [f] S Job 21:22; S Ro 11:34 **36:23** [g] Job 27:11 [h] S Job 34:13; Ro 11:33 [i] S Ge 18:25; S Job 34:10 **36:24** [j] 1Ch 16:24; Ps 35:27; 92:5; 111:2; 138:5; 145:10 [k] S Ex 15:1; Rev 15:3 **36:25** [l] Ro 1:20 **36:26** [m] S Job 5:9; 1Co 13:12 [n] S Ge 21:33; S Job 10:5; Heb 1:12 **36:27** [o] S Job 26:8 [p] S 2Sa 1:21; Job 28:26; 38:28; Isa 55:10 **36:28** [q] Ps 65:10; 72:6; Joel 2:23 [r] S Job 5:10; S 22:11; S 28:26; Mt 5:45 **36:29** [s] Ps 29:3; Jer 10:13 [t] S Job 9:6; 37:16; Ps 18:7-15; 19:4, 5; 104:2; Pr 8:28; Isa 40:22 **36:30** [u] Ex 19:16; Job 37:11, 15; Ps 18:12, 14; 97:4; Jer 10:13; Hab 3:11 [v] Ps 68:22; Isa 51:10 **36:31** [w] Dt 28:23-24; 1Ki 17:1; Job 37:13; Am 4:7-8 [x] Ps 145:15 [y] Ps 104:14-15, 27-28; Isa 30:23; Ac 14:17 **36:32** [z] S Job 28:24; 37:12, 15; Ps 18:14; 29:7-9 **36:33** [a] Job 37:5; 40:9 [b] S Job 28:26 **37:1** [c] Ps 38:10; Isa 15:5; Jer 4:19; Hab 3:16

[a] 12 Or *will cross the river* [b] 20 The meaning of the Hebrew for verses 18-20 is uncertain. [c] 27 Or *distill from the mist as rain* [d] 31 Or *nourishes* [e] 33 Or *announces his coming— / the One zealous against evil*

36:12 See NIV text note (see also note on 33:18).
36:13–15 Elihu understands that the basic spiritual need of human beings stems from their hardness of heart—their refusal to yield to God, to cry out to God in their distress (see Ps 107:6 and note), or to hear the voice of God in their suffering.
36:14 *male prostitutes of the shrines.* See note on 1Ki 14:24.
36:16–21 Elihu warns Job to respond to God's discipline by turning away from evil (see v. 21). Verse 16 shows that he still views Job as a man for whom there is hope.
36:16 *He is wooing you.* With tender compassion, God brings his people back to himself (see Hos 2:14 and note).
36:21 *Beware of turning to evil.* Elihu's evaluation of Job is the opposite of God's (see 1:8 and note; 2:3).
36:22–33 Elihu anticipates some of God's statements in the discourses of chs. 38–41.
36:24 *his work, which people have praised in song.* See, e.g., notes on Ex 15:1–18; Jdg 5:1–31.
36:26 *beyond our understanding.* See 37:5. That God's ways and thoughts are infinitely higher than ours is an important theme in chs. 38–41 (see also Isa 55:8–9; Ro 11:33–36).
36:30 *bathing.* That is, in light.
36:31 *governs.* The NIV text note understands the verse to mean that the Lord "nourishes" the nations with the showers mentioned in vv. 27–30.
37:1–13 A continuation of Elihu's hymnic description of God's marvels exhibited in the earth's atmosphere, beginning in 36:27. His heart pounds at the awesome display (see v. 1). The passage reveals a sophisticated observation of atmospheric conditions and their effects: the evaporation and distillation of water for rain (see 36:27 and NIV text note),

2 Listen![d] Listen to the roar of his voice,[e]
to the rumbling that comes from his mouth.[f]
3 He unleashes his lightning[g] beneath the whole heaven
and sends it to the ends of the earth.[h]
4 After that comes the sound of his roar;
he thunders[i] with his majestic voice.[j]
When his voice resounds,
he holds nothing back.
5 God's voice thunders[k] in marvelous ways;[l]
he does great things beyond our understanding.[m]
6 He says to the snow,[n] 'Fall on the earth,'
and to the rain shower, 'Be a mighty downpour.'[o]
7 So that everyone he has made may know his work,[p]
he stops all people from their labor.[a][q]
8 The animals take cover;[r]
they remain in their dens.[s]
9 The tempest comes out from its chamber,[t]
the cold from the driving winds.[u]
10 The breath of God produces ice,
and the broad waters become frozen.[v]
11 He loads the clouds with moisture;[w]
he scatters his lightning[x] through them.[y]
12 At his direction they swirl around
over the face of the whole earth
to do whatever he commands them.[z]
13 He brings the clouds to punish people,[a]
or to water his earth and show his love.[b]

14 "Listen[c] to this, Job;
stop and consider God's wonders.[d]
15 Do you know how God controls the clouds
and makes his lightning[e] flash?[f]
16 Do you know how the clouds hang poised,[g]
those wonders of him who has perfect knowledge?[h]
17 You who swelter in your clothes
when the land lies hushed under the south wind,[i]
18 can you join him in spreading out the skies,[j]
hard as a mirror of cast bronze?[k]

19 "Tell us what we should say to him;[l]
we cannot draw up our case[m]
because of our darkness.[n]
20 Should he be told that I want to speak?
Would anyone ask to be swallowed up?
21 Now no one can look at the sun,[o]
bright as it is in the skies
after the wind has swept them clean.
22 Out of the north he comes in golden splendor;[p]
God comes in awesome majesty.[q]
23 The Almighty is beyond our reach and exalted in power;[r]
in his justice[s] and great righteousness, he does not oppress.[t]
24 Therefore, people revere him,[u]
for does he not have regard for all the wise[v] in heart?[b]"

The LORD Speaks

38 Then the LORD spoke to Job[w] out of the storm.[x] He said:

[a] 7 Or *work, / he fills all people with fear by his power*
[b] 24 Or *for he does not have regard for any who think they are wise.*

37:2 [d] S Job 32:10 [e] ver 5 [f] Ps 18:13; 29:3-9 **37:3** [g] S 2Sa 22:13; Ps 18:14 [h] S Job 36:32; Mt 24:27; Lk 17:24 **37:4** [i] S 1Sa 2:10 [j] S Ex 20:19 **37:5** [k] S 1Sa 2:10; Jn 12:29 [l] S Job 36:33 [m] S Job 5:9; S 11:7-9; S 36:4 **37:6** [n] Dt 28:12; Job 38:22 [o] S Ge 7:4; S Job 5:10; S 28:26 **37:7** [p] Ps 109:27 [q] Ps 104:19-23; 111:2 **37:8** [r] S Job 28:26 [s] Job 38:40; Ps 104:22 **37:9** [t] Ps 50:3 [u] Ps 147:17 **37:10** [v] Job 38:29-30; Ps 147:17 **37:11** [w] S Job 26:8 [x] S Job 36:30 [y] S Job 28:26 **37:12** [z] S ver 3; Ps 147:16; 148:8 **37:13** [a] S Ge 7:4; Ex 9:22-23; S 1Sa 12:17 [b] S 1Ki 18:45; S Job 5:10; S 36:31; 38:27 **37:14** [c] S Job 32:10 [d] S Job 5:9 **37:15** [e] S Job 36:30 [f] S Job 36:32 **37:16** [g] S Job 36:29 [h] S Job 5:9; S 36:4 **37:17** [i] Ac 27:13 **37:18** [j] S Ge 1:1, 8; S Job 22:14 [k] Dt 28:23 **37:19** [l] Ro 8:26 [m] S Job 13:18 [n] S Job 9:3 **37:21** [o] S Jdg 5:31; Ac 22:11; 26:13 **37:22** [p] Ps 19:5 [q] Ex 24:17 **37:23** [r] S Job 5:9; S 36:4; Ro 11:33; 1Ti 6:16 [s] S Job 8:3 [t] S Job 4:17; Ps 44:1; Isa 63:9; Jer 25:5; La 3:33; Eze 18:23, 32 **37:24** [u] S Ge 22:12; Job 28:28; Ecc 12:13; Mic 6:8; Mt 10:28 [v] S Job 5:13; Eph 5:15 **38:1** [w] S Job 11:5 [x] S Ex 14:21; S 1Sa 2:10; Job 40:6; Isa 21:1; Eze 1:4

the clouds as holders of moisture (see 36:28; 37:11) and the cyclonic behavior of clouds (see v. 12). Such forces originate from God's command and always perform his will for humankind, whether for good or for ill (v. 13).
37:2 *Listen.* The Hebrew for this verb is plural, indicating that others (including the three friends) besides Job are being addressed here (see note on 36:1 — 37:24). *roar of his voice … rumbling.* Thunder (see v. 4; see also introduction to Ps 29).
37:5 *beyond our understanding.* See note on 36:26.
37:10 *breath of God.* Here a metaphor for a chilling wind.
37:14 – 18 Elihu challenges Job to ponder God's power over the elements. The question format is also used in the divine discourses (chs. 38 – 41).
37:16 *perfect knowledge.* See note on 36:4.
37:18 See 26:7.
37:19 *we cannot draw up our case.* Job had dared to sign his defense and call for an audience with God (see 31:35). For this Elihu seeks to shame him. But he softens his tone by including himself as one equally vulnerable to God's majesty.
37:22 *Out of the north he comes.* See note on Ps 48:2. *God comes.* Elihu prepares Job for the appearance of God in the storm (chs. 38 – 41).
37:24 *revere.* Fear (see 28:28; Ge 20:11 and notes).
38:1 — 42:6 The theophany (appearance of God) to Job, consisting of two discourses by the Lord (38:1 — 40:2; 40:6 — 41:34), each of which receives a brief response from Job (40:3 – 5; 42:1 – 6).
38:1 *the LORD.* The Israelite covenant name for God (see Introduction: Author). *storm.* See 40:6. Elihu had imagined the appearance of the divine presence as a display of "golden splendor" and "awesome majesty" (37:22). He also had anticipated the storm or whirlwind (see note on 37:22), from which Job would hear the voice of God. Job had said, "Let the Almighty answer me" (31:35). Now God speaks to Job, but not to give Job the justification of his ways that Job had been demanding. Out of the awesome majesty of the thunderstorm, he reminds Job that the wisdom that directs the Creator's ways is beyond the reach of human

[2] "Who is this that obscures my plans[y]
with words without knowledge?[z]
[3] Brace yourself like a man;
I will question you,
and you shall answer me.[a]

[4] "Where were you when I laid the
earth's foundation?[b]
Tell me, if you understand.[c]
[5] Who marked off its dimensions?[d]
Surely you know!
Who stretched a measuring line[e]
across it?
[6] On what were its footings set,[f]
or who laid its cornerstone[g]—
[7] while the morning stars[h] sang together[i]
and all the angels[a][j] shouted for joy?[k]

[8] "Who shut up the sea behind doors[l]
when it burst forth from the womb,[m]
[9] when I made the clouds its garment
and wrapped it in thick darkness,[n]
[10] when I fixed limits for it[o]
and set its doors and bars in place,[p]
[11] when I said, 'This far you may come
and no farther;[q]
here is where your proud waves
halt'?[r]

[12] "Have you ever given orders to the
morning,[s]
or shown the dawn its place,[t]
[13] that it might take the earth by the
edges
and shake the wicked[u] out of it?[v]
[14] The earth takes shape like clay under a
seal;[w]
its features stand out like those of a
garment.
[15] The wicked are denied their light,[x]
and their upraised arm is broken.[y]

38:2 [y]S 1Ki 22:5; Isa 40:13 [z]S Job 34:35; Mk 10:38; 1Ti 1:7 **38:3** [a]Job 40:7; 42:4; Mk 11:29 **38:4** [b]S ver 5; S Ge 1:1; S 1Sa 2:8 [c]ver 18; S Job 34:13; Pr 30:4 **38:5** [d]ver 4; Ps 102:25; Pr 8:29; Isa 40:12; 48:13; Jer 31:37 [e]Jer 31:39; Zec 1:16; 4:9-10 **38:6** [f]Pr 8:25 [g]S Job 26:7 **38:7** [h]S Ge 1:16 [i]Ps 19:1-4; 148:2-3 [j]S 1Ki 22:19 [k]S Dt 16:15 **38:8** [l]ver 11; Ps 33:7; Pr 8:29; Jer 5:22 [m]S Ge 1:9-10 **38:9** [n]S Ge 1:2 **38:10** [o]S Job 28:25; Ps 33:7; 104:9; Isa 40:12 [p]Ne 3:3; Job 7:12; 26:10 **38:11** [q]S ver 8 [r]Ps 65:7; 89:9; 104:6-9 **38:12** [s]Ps 57:8 [t]Ps 74:16; Am 5:8 **38:13** [u]Ps 104:35 [v]S Job 8:22 **38:14** [w]Ex 28:11 **38:15** [x]S Dt 28:29; S Job 15:22; S 18:5 [y]S Ge 17:14; S Job 4:10; S 31:22

[16] "Have you journeyed to the springs of
the sea
or walked in the recesses of the
deep?[z]
[17] Have the gates of death[a] been shown to
you?
Have you seen the gates of the
deepest darkness?[b]
[18] Have you comprehended the vast
expanses of the earth?[c]
Tell me, if you know all this.[d]

[19] "What is the way to the abode of light?
And where does darkness reside?[e]
[20] Can you take them to their places?
Do you know the paths[f] to their
dwellings?
[21] Surely you know, for you were already
born![g]
You have lived so many years!

[22] "Have you entered the storehouses of
the snow[h]
or seen the storehouses[i] of the
hail,[j]
[23] which I reserve for times of trouble,[k]
for days of war and battle?[l]
[24] What is the way to the place where the
lightning is dispersed,[m]
or the place where the east winds[n]
are scattered over the earth?[o]
[25] Who cuts a channel for the torrents of
rain,
and a path for the thunderstorm,[p]

[a] 7 Hebrew *the sons of God*

38:16 [z]S Ge 1:7; S Job 9:8 **38:17** [a]S Job 33:22; Mt 16:18; Rev 1:18 [b]S Job 7:9 **38:18** [c]S Job 28:24; Isa 40:12 [d]S ver 4 **38:19** [e]S Ge 1:4; S Job 28:3; Ps 139:11-12 **38:20** [f]S Job 24:13 **38:21** [g]Job 15:7 **38:22** [h]S Job 37:6 [i]S Dt 28:12 [j]Ps 105:32; 147:17 **38:23** [k]Ps 27:5; Isa 28:17; 30:30; Eze 13:11 [l]Ex 9:26; Jos 10:11; Eze 13:13; Rev 16:21 **38:24** [m]S Job 28:24 [n]S Job 27:21 [o]Jer 10:13; 51:16 **38:25** [p]Job 28:26

understanding—that humanity's almost godlike wisdom should not presume to match God's wisdom or take its measure (cf. Isa 55:8–9).

38:2 See 35:16. In 42:3 Job echoes the Lord's words. God states that Job's complaining and raging against him are unjustified and proceed from limited understanding.

38:3 Repeated in 40:7 (see also 42:4). The format of God's response is to ply Job with rhetorical questions, to each of which Job must plead ignorance. God says nothing about Job's suffering, nor does he address Job's problem about divine justice. Job gets neither a bill of indictment nor a verdict of innocence. But, more important, God does not humiliate or condemn him—which surely would have been the case if the counselors had been right. So by implication Job is vindicated, and later his vindication is directly affirmed (see 42:7–9 and note). The divine discourses, then, succeed in bringing Job to complete faith in God's wisdom and goodness without his receiving a direct answer to his questions.

38:4–38 Inanimate creation testifies to God's sovereignty and power (the earth, vv. 4–7,18; the sea, vv. 8–11,16; the sun, vv. 12–15; the netherworld, v. 17; light and darkness, vv. 19–20; the weather, vv. 22–30,34–38; the constellations, vv. 31–33). See note on 38:39—39:30.

38:4–5 See the similar questions of Agur and the similar irony in his demand for a response (Pr 30:4; see Isa 40:12 and note).

38:7 See Ps 148:2–3 and note on Ps 65:13. When the earth was created, the angels were there to sing the praises of the Creator, but Job was not (see vv. 4–5). He should therefore not expect to be able to understand even lesser aspects of God's plans for the world and for humankind. *angels.* See NIV text notes here and on 1:6; 2:1.

38:10–11 See Ps 33:7 and note; Jer 5:22.

38:11 *when I said.* God the Father controls the sea by speaking to it, as does God the Son (see Mk 4:41 and note; Lk 8:24–25).

38:12–13 The arrival of the dawn sends the wicked scurrying for cover.

38:14 *clay under a seal.* Either a cylinder seal (see note on Ge 38:18) or a stamp seal.

38:15 *their light.* The night is when the wicked are active (see Jn 3:19; for the imagery, cf. Lk 11:35). *upraised arm is broken.* See 22:9 and note.

38:16 *springs of the sea.* See Ge 7:11; 8:2.

38:17 *gates of death.* See note on 17:16; see also 26:5–6.

38:22–23 *hail ... for days of war.* See, e.g., Jos 10:11; Isa 28:2 and notes.

38:24 *east winds.* See note on 15:2.

26 to water[q] a land where no one lives,
an uninhabited desert,[r]
27 to satisfy a desolate wasteland
and make it sprout with grass?[s]
28 Does the rain have a father?[t]
Who fathers the drops of dew?
29 From whose womb comes the ice?
Who gives birth to the frost from the heavens[u]
30 when the waters become hard as stone,
when the surface of the deep is frozen?[v]

31 "Can you bind the chains[a] of the Pleiades?
Can you loosen Orion's belt?[w]
32 Can you bring forth the constellations[x] in their seasons[b]
or lead out the Bear[c] with its cubs?[y]
33 Do you know the laws[z] of the heavens?[a]
Can you set up God's[d] dominion over the earth?

34 "Can you raise your voice to the clouds
and cover yourself with a flood of water?[b]
35 Do you send the lightning bolts on their way?[c]
Do they report to you, 'Here we are'?
36 Who gives the ibis wisdom[e][d]
or gives the rooster understanding?[f][e]
37 Who has the wisdom to count the clouds?
Who can tip over the water jars[f] of the heavens[g]
38 when the dust becomes hard[h]
and the clods of earth stick together?[i]

39 "Do you hunt the prey for the lioness
and satisfy the hunger of the lions[j]
40 when they crouch in their dens[k]
or lie in wait in a thicket?[l]
41 Who provides food[m] for the raven[n]
when its young cry out to God
and wander about for lack of food?[o]

39 "Do you know when the mountain goats[p] give birth?
Do you watch when the doe bears her fawn?[q]
2 Do you count the months till they bear?
Do you know the time they give birth?[r]
3 They crouch down and bring forth their young;
their labor pains are ended.
4 Their young thrive and grow strong in the wilds;
they leave and do not return.

5 "Who let the wild donkey[s] go free?
Who untied its ropes?
6 I gave it the wasteland[t] as its home,
the salt flats[u] as its habitat.[v]
7 It laughs[w] at the commotion in the town;
it does not hear a driver's shout.[x]
8 It ranges the hills[y] for its pasture
and searches for any green thing.

9 "Will the wild ox[z] consent to serve you?[a]
Will it stay by your manger[b] at night?
10 Can you hold it to the furrow with a harness?[c]
Will it till the valleys behind you?
11 Will you rely on it for its great strength?[d]
Will you leave your heavy work to it?
12 Can you trust it to haul in your grain
and bring it to your threshing floor?

13 "The wings of the ostrich flap joyfully,
though they cannot compare
with the wings and feathers of the stork.[e]
14 She lays her eggs on the ground
and lets them warm in the sand,
15 unmindful that a foot may crush them,
that some wild animal may trample them.[f]

[a] *31* Septuagint; Hebrew *beauty* [b] *32* Or *the morning star in its season* [c] *32* Or *out Leo* [d] *33* Or *their* [e] *36* That is, wisdom about the flooding of the Nile [f] *36* That is, understanding of when to crow; the meaning of the Hebrew for this verse is uncertain.

38:26 [q] Job 36:27 [r] Ps 84:6; 107:35; Isa 41:18 **38:27** [s] S Job 28:26; S 37:13; S Ps 104:14 **38:28** [t] S 2Sa 1:21; S Job 5:10 **38:29** [u] Ps 147:16-17 **38:30** [v] Job 37:10 **38:31** [w] Job 9:9; Am 5:8 **38:32** [x] 2Ki 23:5; Isa 13:10; 40:26; 45:12; Jer 19:13 [y] S Ge 1:16 **38:33** [z] Ps 148:6; Jer 31:36 [a] S Ge 1:16 **38:34** [b] S Job 5:10; S 22:11 **38:35** [c] S Job 36:32 **38:36** [d] S Job 9:4; S 34:32; Jas 1:5 [e] S Job 12:13 **38:37** [f] S Jos 3:16 [g] S Job 22:11 **38:38** [h] S Lev 26:19 [i] 1Ki 18:45 **38:39** [j] S Ge 49:9 **38:40** [k] S Job 37:8 [l] S Ge 49:9 **38:41** [m] S Ge 1:30 [n] S Ge 8:7; Lk 12:24 [o] Ps 147:9; S Mt 6:26 **39:1** [p] S Dt 14:5 [q] Ge 49:21 **39:2** [r] S Ge 31:7-9 **39:5** [s] S Ge 16:12 **39:6** [t] Job 24:5; Ps 107:34; Jer 2:24 [u] Job 30:4 [v] Job 30:7; Jer 14:6; 17:6 **39:7** [w] S Job 5:22 [x] Job 3:18 **39:8** [y] Isa 32:20 **39:9** [z] S Nu 23:22 [a] S Ex 21:6 [b] S Ge 42:27 **39:10** [c] Job 41:13; Ps 32:9 **39:11** [d] ver 19; Job 40:16; 41:12,22; Ps 147:10 **39:13** [e] Zec 5:9 **39:15** [f] 2Ki 14:9

38:31 – 32 *Pleiades … Orion's … Bear.* See note on 9:9.
38:36 *ibis … rooster.* Two birds whose habits were sometimes observed by people who wished to forecast the weather. The words serve as a transition to the next major section of the first divine discourse.
38:39 — 39:30 Animate creation testifies to God's sovereignty, power and loving care (the lion, 38:39 – 40; the raven, 38:41; the mountain goat, 39:1 – 4; the wild donkey, vv. 5 – 8; the wild ox, vv. 9 – 12; the ostrich, vv. 13 – 18; the horse, vv. 19 – 25; the hawk, v. 26; the eagle, vv. 27 – 30). See note on 38:4 – 38.
38:41 *provides food for the raven.* God cares for and feeds all the birds, of which the raven is representative (e.g., compare Lk 12:24 with Mt 6:26).
39:5 *wild donkey.* See 24:5; see also the description of Ishmael in Ge 16:12 and note there.
39:9 – 12 As there was an implied contrast between the wild donkey and the domestic donkey (see v. 7), here there is a more explicit contrast between the wild ox and the domestic ox.
39:11 *great strength.* In the OT, the wild ox (the now virtually extinct aurochs) often symbolizes strength (see, e.g., Nu 23:22 and note; 24:8; Dt 33:17; Ps 22:21 and note; 29:6). Next to the elephant and rhinoceros, the wild ox was the largest and most powerful land animal of the OT world.
39:13 – 18 This stanza is unique in the discourses, because in it the Lord asks Job no questions.
39:13 *wings and feathers of the stork.* A stork's wings were particularly impressive (see Zec 5:9).

16 She treats her young harshly,[g] as if
they were not hers;
she cares not that her labor was in
vain,
17 for God did not endow her with
wisdom
or give her a share of good sense.[h]
18 Yet when she spreads her feathers to
run,
she laughs[i] at horse and rider.

19 "Do you give the horse its strength[j]
or clothe its neck with a flowing
mane?
20 Do you make it leap like a locust,[k]
striking terror[l] with its proud
snorting?[m]
21 It paws fiercely, rejoicing in its
strength,[n]
and charges into the fray.[o]
22 It laughs[p] at fear, afraid of nothing;
it does not shy away from the sword.
23 The quiver[q] rattles against its side,
along with the flashing spear[r] and
lance.
24 In frenzied excitement it eats up the
ground;
it cannot stand still when the
trumpet sounds.[s]
5 At the blast of the trumpet[t] it snorts,
'Aha!'
It catches the scent of battle from
afar,
the shout of commanders and the
battle cry.[u]

6 "Does the hawk take flight by your
wisdom
and spread its wings toward the
south?[v]
7 Does the eagle soar at your command
and build its nest on high?[w]
8 It dwells on a cliff and stays there at
night;
a rocky crag[x] is its stronghold.

39:16 [g] ver 17; La 4:3
39:17 [h] S ver 16; S Job 21:22
39:18 [i] S Job 5:22
39:19 [j] S ver 11
39:20 [k] Joel 2:4-5; Rev 9:7 [l] Job 41:25 [m] Jer 8:16
39:21 [n] ver 11 [o] Jer 8:6
39:22 [p] S Job 5:22
39:23 [q] Isa 5:28; Jer 5:16 [r] Na 3:3
39:24 [s] Nu 10:9; Jer 4:5, 19; Eze 7:14; Am 3:6
39:25 [t] Jos 6:5 [u] Jer 8:6; Am 1:14; 2:2
39:26 [v] Jer 8:7
39:27 [w] Jer 49:16; Ob 1:4; Hab 2:9
39:28 [x] Jer 49:16; Ob 1:3
39:29 [y] S Job 9:26
39:30 [z] Mt 24:28; Lk 17:37
40:1 [a] S Job 5:8; S 10:2
40:2 [b] S Job 13:3 [c] S Job 9:15; S 11:8; S 33:13; Ro 9:20 [d] S Job 9:3
40:4 [e] Job 42:6 [f] S Jdg 18:19; S Job 29:9
40:5 [g] S Job 9:3 [h] S Job 9:15
40:6 [i] S Ex 14:21; S Job 38:1
40:7 [j] S Job 38:3
40:8 [k] S Job 15:25; S 27:2; Ro 3:3 [l] S Job 2:3; S 34:17
40:9 [m] S 2Ch 32:8; S Ps 98:1 [n] Isa 6:8; Eze 10:5

29 From there it looks for food;[y]
its eyes detect it from afar.
30 Its young ones feast on blood,
and where the slain are, there it is."[z]

40 The LORD said to Job:[a]

2 "Will the one who contends with the
Almighty[b] correct him?[c]
Let him who accuses God answer
him!"[d]

3 Then Job answered the LORD:

4 "I am unworthy[e]—how can I reply to
you?
I put my hand over my mouth.[f]
5 I spoke once, but I have no answer[g]—
twice, but I will say no more."[h]

6 Then the LORD spoke to Job out of the
storm:[i]

7 "Brace yourself like a man;
I will question you,
and you shall answer me.[j]
8 "Would you discredit my justice?[k]
Would you condemn me to justify
yourself?[l]
9 Do you have an arm like God's,[m]
and can your voice[n] thunder like his?[o]
10 Then adorn yourself with glory and
splendor,
and clothe yourself in honor and
majesty.[p]
11 Unleash the fury of your wrath,[q]
look at all who are proud and bring
them low,[r]
12 look at all who are proud[s] and humble
them,[t]
crush[u] the wicked where they stand.

[o] S Ex 20:19; S Job 36:33 **40:10** [p] Ps 29:1-2; 45:3; 93:1; 96:6; 104:1; 145:5 **40:11** [q] S Job 20:28; Ps 7:11; Isa 5:25; 9:12, 19; 10:5; 13:3, 5; 30:27; 42:25; 51:20; Jer 7:20; Na 1:6; Zep 1:18 [r] Ps 18:27; Isa 2:11, 12, 17; 23:9; 24:10; 25:12; 26:5; 32:19 **40:12** [s] Ps 10:4; Isa 25:11; Jer 48:29; 49:16; Zep 2:10 [t] S 1Sa 2:7; S Ps 52:5; 1Pe 5:5 [u] Ps 60:12; Isa 22:5; 28:3; 63:2-3, 6; Da 5:20; Mic 5:8; 7:10; Zec 10:5; Mal 4:3

9:18 *horse and rider.* Forms a transition to the next paragraph.
9:19–25 The horse is the only domestic animal in the iscourses. This fact, though unexpected, serves the Lord's urpose, since it is specifically the war horse that is in view.
9:20 *like a locust.* Horses and locusts are compared also in er 51:27; Rev 9:7; cf. Joel 2:4 and note.
9:26 *hawk.* The sparrow hawk, though not resident to the oly Land, stops there in its migration south for the winter.
9:27 *eagle.* Or possibly "vulture" (see v. 30).
0:1–2 The conclusion of the first divine discourse. Once gain, God challenges Job to answer him.
0:3–5 Job, duly chastened, is unwilling to speak another 'ord of complaint.
0:4 *unworthy.* The Hebrew for this word can also mean mall" or "insignificant."
0:5 *once ... twice.* See note on 5:19.
0:6 See 38:1 and note.
0:7 Repeated from 38:3 (see note there).
40:8–14 The prologue to the second divine discourse, which ends at 41:34. Unlike the first discourse, God here addresses the issues of his own justice and Job's futile attempt at self-justification. In chs. 21 and 24 Job had complained about God's indifference toward the evil actions of the wicked. Here the Lord asserts his ability and determination to administer justice—a matter over which Job has no control. Therefore by implication Job is admonished to leave all this, including his own vindication (see v. 14), under God's control (see v. 9).
40:8 *Would you condemn me to justify yourself?* In 19:6, Job had said, "God has wronged me."
40:10 *clothe yourself in honor and majesty.* The same Hebrew underlying this clause describes God in Ps 104:1: "you are clothed with splendor and majesty." The Lord here challenges Job to take on the appearance of deity—if he can. *clothe yourself in.* See note on Ps 109:29.
40:11–12 See Isa 13:11, where the Lord describes himself as doing these things.

13 Bury them all in the dust together;[v]
shroud their faces in the grave.[w]
14 Then I myself will admit to you
that your own right hand can save
you.[x]

15 "Look at Behemoth,
which I made[y] along with you
and which feeds on grass like
an ox.[z]
16 What strength[a] it has in its loins,
what power in the muscles of its
belly![b]
17 Its tail sways like a cedar;
the sinews of its thighs are close-
knit.[c]
18 Its bones are tubes of bronze,
its limbs[d] like rods of iron.[e]
19 It ranks first among the works of God,[f]
yet its Maker[g] can approach it with
his sword.[h]
20 The hills bring it their produce,[i]
and all the wild animals play[j]
nearby.[k]
21 Under the lotus plants it lies,
hidden among the reeds[l] in the
marsh.[m]
22 The lotuses conceal it in their
shadow;
the poplars by the stream[n]
surround it.
23 A raging river[o] does not alarm it;
it is secure, though the Jordan[p]
should surge against its mouth.
24 Can anyone capture it by the eyes,
or trap it and pierce its nose?[q]

41 [a] "Can you pull in Leviathan[r] with
a fishhook[s]
or tie down its tongue with a rope?
2 Can you put a cord through its nose[t]
or pierce its jaw with a hook?[u]
3 Will it keep begging you for mercy?[v]
Will it speak to you with gentle
words?
4 Will it make an agreement with you
for you to take it as your slave for
life?[w]

40:13 [v] Nu 16:31-34 [w] S Job 4:9
40:14 [x] Ex 15:6, 12; Ps 18:35; 20:6; 48:10; 60:5; 108:6; Isa 41:10; 63:5
40:15 [y] S Job 9:9 [z] Isa 11:7; 65:25
40:16 [a] S Job 39:11 [b] Job 41:9
40:17 [c] Job 41:15
40:18 [d] Job 41:12 [e] Isa 11:4; 49:2
40:19 [f] Job 41:33; Ps 40:5; 139:14; Isa 27:1 [g] S Job 4:17; S 9:9 [h] S Ge 3:24
40:20 [i] Ps 104:14 [j] Ps 104:26 [k] S Job 5:23
40:21 [l] S Ge 41:2; Ps 68:30; Isa 35:7 [m] Job 8:11
40:22 [n] Ps 1:3; Isa 44:4
40:23 [o] Isa 8:7; 11:15 [p] S Jos 3:1
40:24 [q] 2Ki 19:28; Job 41:2,7,26; Isa 37:29
41:1 [r] S Job 3:8 [s] Am 4:2
41:2 [t] S Job 40:24 [u] Eze 19:4
41:3 [v] 1Ki 20:31
41:4 [w] S Ex 21:6
41:7 [x] S Job 40:24
41:8 [y] S Job 3:8
41:9 [z] Job 40:16
41:10 [a] S Job 3:8 [b] S 2Ch 20:6; S Isa 46:5; Jer 50:44; Rev 6:17
41:11 [c] S Job 34:33; Ro 11:35 [d] Ps 24:1; 50:12; S Jos 3:11; S Job 10:4; Ac 4:24; 1Co 10:26

5 Can you make a pet of it like a bird
or put it on a leash for the young
women in your house?
6 Will traders barter for it?
Will they divide it up among the
merchants?
7 Can you fill its hide with harpoons
or its head with fishing spears?[x]
8 If you lay a hand on it,
you will remember the struggle and
never do it again![y]
9 Any hope of subduing it is false;
the mere sight of it is overpowering.[z]
10 No one is fierce enough to rouse it.[a]
Who then is able to stand
against me?[b]
11 Who has a claim against me that I
must pay?[c]
Everything under heaven belongs
to me.[d]

12 "I will not fail to speak of Leviathan's
limbs,[e]
its strength[f] and its graceful form.
13 Who can strip off its outer coat?
Who can penetrate its double coat of
armor[b]?[g]
14 Who dares open the doors of its
mouth,[h]
ringed about with fearsome teeth?
15 Its back has[c] rows of shields
tightly sealed together;[i]
16 each is so close to the next
that no air can pass between.
17 They are joined fast to one another;
they cling together and cannot be
parted.
18 Its snorting throws out flashes of
light;
its eyes are like the rays of dawn.[j]
19 Flames[k] stream from its mouth;
sparks of fire shoot out.

[a] In Hebrew texts 41:1-8 is numbered 40:25-32, and 41:9-34 is numbered 41:1-26. [b] *13* Septuagint; Hebrew *double bridle* [c] *15* Or *Its pride is its*

41:12 [e] Job 40:18 [f] S Job 39:11 **41:13** [g] S Job 30:11; S 39:10 **41:14** [h] Ps 22:13 **41:15** [i] Job 40:17 **41:18** [j] S Job 3:9 **41:19** [k] Da 10:6

40:13 *dust.* See note on 7:21.
40:14 *your own right hand can save you.* Contrast Ps 49:7–9 (see note there).
40:15–24 The first of two poems (ch. 41 constitutes the second) in this discourse, each describing a huge beast and resuming the animal theme of ch. 39.
40:15 *Behemoth.* The word is Hebrew and means "beast par excellence," referring to a large land animal. Much of the language used to describe it in vv. 16–24 is highly poetic and hyperbolic. *which I made.* It is one of God's creatures, not a mythical being.
40:18 *iron.* See note on 19:24.
40:19 *first among the works of God.* The Hebrew underlying this phrase is translated "first of his works" in Pr 8:22 with reference to the creation of wisdom (see Pr 8:12). Here the descriptive phrase stresses the importance of Behemoth as an example of a huge animal under the control of a sovereign God.
40:21–23 *reeds in the marsh ... poplars ... Jordan.* The area described is probably the Huleh region, north of the Sea of Galilee.
40:24 The proposal to capture Behemoth forms a transition to the similar proposal concerning Leviathan in 41:1.
41:1–34 The second of two poems in the Lord's final discourse (see note on 40:15–24).
41:1 *Leviathan.* Its description in this chapter indicates that it is even more terrifying than Behemoth in ch. 40.
41:10 Leviathan is mighty, but God is infinitely more powerful.
41:11 Alluded to by Paul in Ro 11:35.
41:14–15 *doors of its mouth ... fearsome teeth ... back has rows of shields.* Similar to those of a crocodile.
41:18–21 Exaggerated poetic imagery (hyperbole).

20 Smoke pours from its nostrils[l]
as from a boiling pot over burning reeds.
21 Its breath[m] sets coals ablaze,
and flames dart from its mouth.[n]
22 Strength[o] resides in its neck;
dismay goes before it.
23 The folds of its flesh are tightly joined;
they are firm and immovable.
24 Its chest is hard as rock,
hard as a lower millstone.[p]
25 When it rises up, the mighty are terrified;[q]
they retreat before its thrashing.[r]
26 The sword that reaches it has no effect,
nor does the spear or the dart or the javelin.[s]
27 Iron it treats like straw[t]
and bronze like rotten wood.
28 Arrows do not make it flee;[u]
slingstones are like chaff to it.
29 A club seems to it but a piece of straw;[v]
it laughs[w] at the rattling of the lance.
30 Its undersides are jagged potsherds,
leaving a trail in the mud like a threshing sledge.[x]
31 It makes the depths churn like a boiling caldron[y]
and stirs up the sea like a pot of ointment.[z]
32 It leaves a glistening wake behind it;
one would think the deep had white hair.
33 Nothing on earth is its equal[a] —
a creature without fear.
34 It looks down on all that are haughty;[b]
it is king over all that are proud.[c]"

Job

42

Then Job replied to the LORD:

2 "I know that you can do all things;[d]
no purpose of yours can be thwarted.[e]
3 You asked, 'Who is this that obscures my plans without knowledge?'[f]
Surely I spoke of things I did not understand,
things too wonderful for me to know.[g]

4 "You said, 'Listen now, and I will speak;
I will question you,
and you shall answer me.'[h]
5 My ears had heard of you[i]
but now my eyes have seen you.[j]
6 Therefore I despise myself[k]
and repent[l] in dust and ashes."[m]

Epilogue

7 After the LORD had said these things
to Job[n], he said to Eliphaz the Temanite, "I am angry with you and your two
friends,[o] because you have not spoken the
truth about me, as my servant Job has.[p]
8 So now take seven bulls and seven rams[q]
and go to my servant Job[r] and sacrifice a
burnt offering[s] for yourselves. My servant
Job will pray for you, and I will accept
his prayer[t] and not deal with you according to your folly.[u] You have not spoken the
truth about me, as my servant Job has."[v]
9 So Eliphaz the Temanite, Bildad the Shuhite and Zophar the Naamathite[w] did what
the LORD told them; and the LORD accepted
Job's prayer.[x]
10 After Job had prayed for his friends,
the LORD restored his fortunes[y] and gave
him twice as much as he had before.[z] 11 All
his brothers and sisters and everyone who
had known him before[a] came and ate with
him in his house. They comforted and
consoled him over all the trouble the LORD

41:20 [l] Ps 18:8 **41:21** [m] S Job 4:9; Isa 11:4; 40:7 [n] Ps 18:8; Isa 10:17; 30:27; 33:14; 66:14-16; Jer 4:4 **41:22** [o] S Job 39:11 **41:24** [p] Mt 18:6 **41:25** [q] Job 39:20 [r] S Job 3:8 **41:26** [s] S Jos 8:18; S Job 40:24 **41:27** [t] ver 29 **41:28** [u] Ps 91:5 **41:29** [v] ver 27 [w] S Job 5:22 **41:30** [x] Isa 28:27; 41:15; Am 1:3 **41:31** [y] 1Sa 2:14 [z] Eze 32:2 **41:33** [a] S Job 40:19 **41:34** [b] Ps 18:27; 101:5; 131:1; Pr 6:17; 21:4; 30:13 [c] Job 28:8 **42:2** [d] S Ge 18:14; S Mt 19:26 [e] S 2Ch 20:6; S Job 16:19; Ac 4:28; Eph 1:11 **42:3** [f] S Job 34:35 [g] S Job 5:9 **42:4** [h] S Job 38:3 **42:5** [i] S Job 26:14; Ro 10:17 [j] Jdg 13:22; Isa 6:5; S Mt 5:8; Lk 2:30; Eph 1:17-18 **42:6** [k] Job 40:4; Eze 6:9; Ro 12:3 [l] S Job 34:33 [m] S Ex 10:3; S Ezr 9:6; S Job 2:8; S 6:29 **42:7** [n] S Jos 1:7 [o] Job 32:3 [p] ver 8; S Job 9:15 **42:8** [q] Nu 23:1,29; Eze 45:23 [r] Job 1:8 [s] S Ge 8:20 [t] Jas 5:15-16; 1Jn 5:16 [u] Ge 20:7; Job 22:30 [v] S ver 7 **42:9** [w] Job 2:11 [x] S Ge 19:21; S 20:17; Eze 14:14 **42:10** [y] Dt 30:3; Ps 14:7 [z] S Job 1:3; Ps 85:1-3; 126:5-6; Php 2:8-9; Jas 5:11 **42:11** [a] S Job 19:13

1:27 *Iron.* See note on 19:24.
1:30 *jagged potsherds.* Broken pottery fragments.
1:34 *king over all that are proud.* The Lord alone can humble ...ch creatures. Job cannot be expected to do so, though God ...hallenges him to attempt it — if he so desires (see 40:11 – 12 ...nd note).
2:1 – 6 Job's last words are his response to the Lord's second ...iscourse.
42:2 Job finally sees that God and his purposes are supreme.
2:3 *You asked.* Job quotes the Lord's words in 38:2.
2:4 *You said.* Job quotes the Lord's words in 38:3; 40:7.
42:5 Job — and his three friends and Elihu — had only heard about God, but now Job has seen God (see Isa ...5) with the eyes of faith and spiritual understanding. He ...an therefore accept God's ways with him (see v. 2) — which ...clude suffering. *my eyes have seen you.* A down payment on ...e hope expressed in 19:26 (see note there).
42:6 *I despise myself.* See note on 9:21. To his humility (see 40:4 – 5) Job adds repentance for the presumptuous words he had spoken to God. *dust and ashes.* See 30:19 and note.
42:7 – 9 Despite Job's mistakes in word and attitude while he suffered, he is now commended and the counselors are rebuked. Why? Because even in his rage, even when he challenged God, he was determined to speak honestly before him. The counselors, on the other hand, mouthed many correct theological statements, but without a living knowledge of the God they claimed to honor. Job spoke *to* God; they only spoke *about* God. Even worse, their spiritual arrogance caused them to claim knowledge they did not possess. They presumed to know why Job was suffering.
42:7 – 8 *my servant Job.* The phrase is used four times in these two verses (see note on 1:8).
42:10 Job's prayer for those who had abused him is a touching OT illustration of the high Christian virtue our Lord taught in Mt 5:44 (see note on Ps 35:13 – 14). Job's prayer marked the turning point back to prosperity for him. *restored his fortunes.* See Ps 14:7.

had brought on him,[b] and each one gave him a piece of silver[a] and a gold ring.
12 The LORD blessed the latter part of Job's life more than the former part. He had fourteen thousand sheep, six thousand camels, a thousand yoke of oxen and a thousand donkeys.
13 And he also had seven sons and three daughters.
14 The first daughter he named Jemimah, the second Keziah and the third Keren-Happuch.
15 Nowhere in all the land were there found women as beautiful as Job's daughters, and their father granted them an inheritance along with their brothers.
16 After this, Job lived a hundred and forty years; he saw his children and their children to the fourth generation.
17 And so Job died, an old man and full of years.[c]

42:11 [b] S Ge 37:35
42:17 [c] S Ge 15:15

[a] *11* Hebrew *him a kesitah;* a kesitah was a unit of money of unknown weight and value.

42:11 Contrast 16:2; 19:13. *piece of silver.* The Hebrew for this phrase (see NIV text note) is found elsewhere in the OT only in Ge 33:19 (see note there); Jos 24:32. *gold ring.* See photo below.

42:12–16 The cosmic contest with Satan, the accuser, is now over, and Job is restored. No longer is there a reason for Job to experience suffering—unless he was sinful and deserved it, which is not the case. God does not allow us to suffer for no reason, and even though the reason may be hidden in the mystery of his divine purpose (see Isa 55:8–9)—never for us to know in this life—we must trust in him as the God who does only what is right (see Ge 18:25; Ps 119:121; Eze 18:5 and notes).

42:12 The number of animals is in each case twice as many (see v. 10) as Job had owned before (see 1:3).

42:13 *seven sons and three daughters.* To replace the children he had lost earlier (see 1:2,18–19).

42:14 Strikingly, only the names of the daughters are given. *Jemimah.* Means "dove." *Keziah.* Means "cinnamon." *Keren Happuch.* Means "container of antimony," a highly prized eye shadow (see note on Jer 4:30).

42:15 *granted them an inheritance along with their brothers.* Cf. Zelophehad's daughters (Nu 27:1–11; ch. 36; see notes there).

42:16 *lived a hundred and forty years.* The longevity of a true patriarch (see note on Ex 6:16). *he saw ... to the fourth generation.* See Ge 50:23 and note.

42:17 *an old man and full of years.* See 5:26; Ge 25:8 and notes.

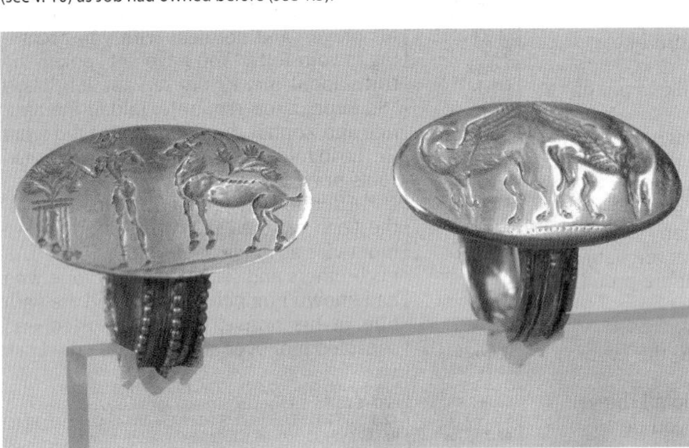

Two gold rings from Mycenae (1500 BC). After Job's trials, God restored his wealth. "All his brothers and sisters and everyone who had known him before came and ate with him in his house. They comforted and consoled him over all the trouble the LORD had brought on him, and each one gave him a piece of silver and a gold ring" (Job 42:11).

Two rings from Mycenae by National Archaeological Museum, Athens, Greece Bernard Cox/The Bridgeman Art Library

PSALMS

NTRODUCTION

Title

'he titles "Psalms" and "Psalter" come from the Septuagint (the pre-Christian Greek translation of he OT), where they originally referred to stringed instruments (such as harp, lyre and lute), then to ongs sung with their accompaniment. The traditional Hebrew title is *tehillim* (meaning "praises"; ee note on Ps 145 title), even though many of the psalms are *tephilloth* (meaning "prayers"). In act, one of the first collections included in the book is titled the prayers of David son of Jesse" (72:20).

Collection, Arrangement and Date

'he Psalter is a collection of collections and represents the fi- al stage in a process that spanned centuries. It was put into s final form by postexilic temple personnel, who complet- d it probably in the fourth century BC. As such, it has often een called the prayer book of the second (Zerubbabel's and lerod's) temple and was used in the synagogues as well. But it more than a treasury of prayers and hymns for liturgical and rivate use on chosen occasions. Both the scope of its subject natter and the arrangement of the whole collection strongly uggest that this collection was viewed by its final editors as a ook of instruction in the faith and in full-orbed godliness — hus a guide for the life of faith in accordance with the Law, the 'rophets and the Writings (see chart, pp. 852 – 855). By the first entury AD it was referred to as the "Book of Psalms" (Lk 20:42; c 1:20). At that time Psalms appears also to have been used as title for the entire section of the Hebrew OT canon more com- ionly known as the Writings (see Lk 24:44 and note).

Many collections preceded this final compilation of the salms. In fact, the formation of psalters probably goes back the early days of the first (Solomon's) temple (or even to the me of David), when the temple liturgy began to take shape. eference has already been made to "the prayers of David."

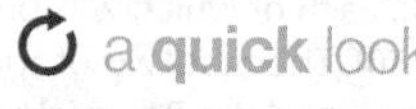

a quick look

Authors:
David, Asaph, the Sons of Korah, Solomon, Heman, Ethan, Moses and unknown authors

Audience:
God's people

Date:
Between the time of Moses (probably about 1440 BC) and the time following the Babylonian exile (after 538 BC)

Theme:
The book of Psalms contains ancient Israel's favorite hymns and prayers, which were used in their worship of the Lord, the Great King.

Additional collections expressly referred to in the present Psalter titles are: (1) the songs and/or psalms "of the Sons of Korah" (Ps 42–49; 84–85; 87–88), (2) the psalms and/or songs "of Asaph" (Ps 50; 73–83) and (3) the songs "of ascents" (Ps 120–134).

Other evidence points to further compilations. Ps 1–41 (Book I) make frequent use of the divine name Yahweh ("the LORD"), while Ps 42–72 (Book II) make frequent use of Elohim ("God"). The reason for the Elohim collection in distinction from the Yahweh collection remains a matter of speculation. Moreover, Ps 93–100 appear to be a traditional collection (see "The LORD reigns" in 93:1; 96:10; 97:1; 99:1). Other apparent groupings include Ps 111–118 (a series of Hallelujah psalms; see introduction to Ps 113–118), Ps 138–145 (all of which include "of David" in their titles) and Ps 146–150 (each of which begins and ends with "Praise the LORD"; see NIV text note on 111:1). Whether the "Great Hallel" (Ps 120–136) was already a recognized unit is not known.

In its final edition, the Psalter contained 150 psalms. On this the Septuagint (the pre-Christian Greek translation of the OT) and Hebrew texts agree, though they arrive at this number differently. The Septuagint has an extra psalm at the end (but not numbered separately as Ps 151); it also unites Ps 9–10 (see NIV text note on Ps 9) and Ps 114–115 and divides Ps 116 and Ps 147 each into two psalms. Strangely, both the Septuagint and Hebrew texts number Ps 42–43 as two psalms though they were evidently originally one (see NIV text note on Ps 42).

In its final form the Psalter was divided into five Books (Ps 1–41; 42–72; 73–89; 90–106; 107–150), each of which was provided with a concluding doxology (see 41:13; 72:18–19; 89:52; 106:48; 150). The first two of these Books were probably preexilic. The division of the remaining psalms into three Books, thus attaining the number five, was possibly in imitation of the five books of Moses (otherwise known simply as the Law). At least one of these divisions (between Ps 106–107) seems arbitrary (see introduction to Ps 107). In spite of this five-book division, the Psalter was clearly thought of as a whole, with an introduction (Ps 1–2) and a conclusion (Ps 146–150). Notes throughout the Psalms give additional indications of conscious arrangement (see also chart, pp. 852–855).

Authorship and Titles (or Superscriptions)

Of the 150 psalms, only 34 lack superscriptions of any kind (only 17 in the Septuagint, the pre-Christian Greek translation of the OT). These so-called "orphan" psalms are found mainly in Books III–V, where they tend to occur in clusters: Ps 91; 93–97; 99; 104–107; 111–119; 135–137; 146–150. (In Books I–II, only Ps 1–2; 10; 33; 43; 71 lack titles, and Ps 10 and 43 are actually continuations of the preceding psalms.)

The contents of the superscriptions vary but fall into a few broad categories: (1) author, (2) name of collection, (3) type of psalm, (4) musical notations, (5) liturgical notations and (6) brief indications of occasion for composition. For details, see notes on the titles of the various psalms.

Students of the Psalms are not agreed on the antiquity and reliability of these superscriptions. That many of them are at least preexilic appears evident from the fact that the Septuagint translators were sometimes unclear as to their meaning. Furthermore, the practice of attaching titles, including the name of the author, is ancient. On the other hand, comparison between the Septuagint and the Hebrew texts shows that the content of some titles was still subject to change well into the postexilic period. Most discussion centers on categories 1 and 6 above.

As for the superscriptions regarding occasion of composition, many of these brief notations of events read as if they had been taken from 1,2 Samuel. Moreover, they are sometimes not easily correlated with the content of the psalms they head. The suspicion therefore arises that they are later attempts to fit the psalms into the real-life events of history. But then why the limited number of such notations, and why the apparent mismatches? The arguments cut both ways.

Regarding authorship, opinions are even more divided. The notations themselves are ambiguous since the Hebrew phraseology used, meaning in general "belonging to," can also be taken in the sense of "concerning" or "for the use of" or "dedicated to." The name may refer to the title of a collection of psalms that had been gathered under a certain name (as "Of Asaph" or "Of the Sons of Korah"). To complicate matters, there is evidence within the Psalter that at least some of the psalms were subjected to editorial revision in the course of their transmission. As for Davidic authorship, there can be little doubt that the Psalter contains psalms composed by that noted singer and musician and that there was at one time a "Davidic" psalter. This, however, may have also included psalms written concerning David, or concerning one of the later Davidic kings, or even psalms written in the manner of those he authored. It is also true that the tradition as to which psalms are "Davidic" remains somewhat indefinite, and some "Davidic" psalms seem clearly to reflect later situations (see, e.g., Ps 30 title — but see also note there; and see introduction to Ps 69 and note on Ps 122 title). Moreover, "David" is sometimes used elsewhere in the OT as a collective for the kings of his dynasty, and this could also be true in some of the psalm titles.

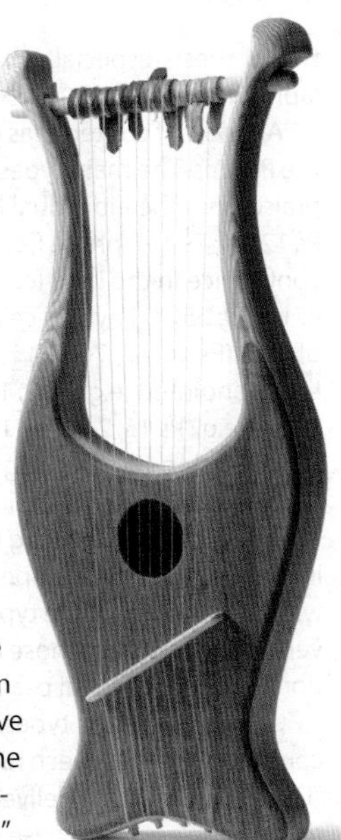

Model of a lyre

The word *Selah* is found in 39 psalms, all but two of which (Ps 140; 143, both "Davidic") are in Books I – III. It is also found in Hab 3, a psalm-like poem. Suggestions as to its meaning abound, but honesty must confess ignorance. Most likely it is a liturgical notation. The common suggestions that it calls for a brief musical interlude or for a brief liturgical response by the congregation are plausible but unproven (the former may be supported by the Septuagint rendering). In some instances its present placement in the Hebrew text is highly questionable. It is found in the NIV only in the text notes.

Psalm Types

Hebrew superscriptions to the Psalms acquaint us with an ancient system of classification: (1) *mizmor* ("psalm"); (2) *shiggaion* (see note on Ps 7 title); (3) *miktam* (see note on Ps 16 title); (4) *shir* ("song"); (5) *maśkil* (see note on Ps 32 title); (6) *tephillah* ("prayer"); (7) *tehillah* ("praise"); (8) *lehazkir* ("for being remembered" — i.e., before God, a petition); (9) *letodah* ("for praising" or "for giving thanks"); (10) *lelammed* ("for teaching"); and (11) *shir yedidoth* ("song of loves" — i.e., a wedding song). The meaning of many of these terms, however, is uncertain. In addition, some titles contain two of these (especially *mizmor* and *shir*), indicating that the types are diversely based and overlapping.

Analysis of content has given rise to a different classification that has proven useful for study of the Psalms. The main types that can be identified are: (1) prayers of the individual (e.g., Ps 3 – 7); (2) praise from the individual for God's saving help (e.g., Ps 30; 34); (3) prayers of the community (e.g., Ps 12; 44; 79); (4) praise from the community for God's saving help (e.g., Ps 66; 75); (5) confessions of confidence in the Lord (e.g., Ps 11; 16; 52); (6) hymns in praise of God's majesty and virtues (e.g., Ps 8; 19; 29; 65); (7) hymns celebrating God's universal reign (Ps 47; 93 – 99); (8) songs of Zion, the city of God (Ps 46; 48; 76; 84; 122; 126; 129; 137); (9) royal psalms — by, for or concerning the king, the Lord's anointed (e.g., Ps 2; 18; 20; 45; 72; 89; 110); (10) pilgrimage songs (Ps 120 – 134); (11) liturgical songs (e.g., Ps 15; 24; 68); (12) didactic (instructional) songs (e.g., Ps 1; 34; 37; 73; 112; 119; 128; 133); (13) salvation-history songs (e.g., Ps 78; 103; 105 – 107; 135 – 136).

This classification also involves some overlapping. For example, "prayers of the individual" may include prayers of the king (in his special capacity as king) or even prayers of the community speaking in the collective first person singular. Nevertheless, it is helpful to study a psalm in conjunction with others of the same type. Attempts to fix specific liturgical settings for each type have not been very convincing. For those psalms about which something can be said in this regard, see introductions to the individual psalms.

Of all these psalm types, the prayers (both of the individual and of the community) are the most complex. Several speech functions are combined to form these appeals to God: (1) address to God: "LORD," "my God," "my deliverer"; (2) initial appeal: "Arise," "Answer me," "Help," "Save me"; (3) description of distress: "Many rise up against me," "The wicked advance against me," "I am in distress"; (4) complaint against God: "Why have you forsaken me?" "How long will you hide your face from me?"; (5) petition: "Do not be far from me," "Vindicate me"; (6) motivation for God to hear: "for I take refuge in you," "for your name's sake"; (7) accusation against the adversary: "[Their] mouths are full of lies," "Ruthless people are trying to kill me" ("the wicked" are often quoted); (8) call for judicial redress: "Let the wicked be put to shame," "Call the evildoer to account for his wickedness"; (9) claims of innocence: "[They] hate me without reason"; (10) confessions of sin: "I have sinned against you," "I confess my iniquity"; (11) professions of trust: "You, LORD, are a shield around me," "You will answer me"; (12) vows to praise God for deliverance: "I will sing of your strength," "I sing praise to you — I whom you have delivered"; (13) calls to praise God: "Glorify the LORD with me," "Sing praise to the Lord"; (14) motivations for praise: "for you have delivered me," "[for] the LORD hears the needy."

Though not all these appear in every prayer, they all belong to the conventions of prayer in the Psalter, with petition itself being only one (usually brief) element among the rest. On the whole they reflect the then-current conventions of a court trial, the psalmists presenting their cases before the heavenly King/Judge. When beset by wicked adversaries, the petitioners appeal to God for a hearing, describe their situation, plead their innocence ("righteousness"), lodge their accusations against their adversaries, and appeal for deliverance and judicial redress. When suffering at the hands of God (when God is their adversary), they confess their guilt and plead for mercy. Attention to these various speech functions and their role in the psalmists' judicial appeals to the heavenly Judge will significantly aid the reader's understanding of these psalms.

It should be noted that reference to "penitential" and "imprecatory" psalms as distinct psalm

Musicians in the palace of the Hittite king Barekup (eighth century BC). The psalms were originally intended to be sung, and several of them (e.g., Ps 150:3–5) mention instruments such as the harp, lute, lyre, trumpet, timbrel, horn and cymbals.

Z. Radovan/www.BibleLandPictures.com

types has no basis in the Psalter collection itself. The former ("penitential") refers to an early Christian selection of seven psalms (6; 32; 38; 51; 102; 130; 143) for liturgical expressions of penitence; the latter ("imprecatory") is based on a misconstrual of one of the speech functions found in the prayers. What are actually appeals to the heavenly Judge for judicial redress (function 8 noted on the previous page) are taken to be curses ("imprecation" means "curse") pronounced by the psalmists on their adversaries. See note on 5:10.

Literary Features

The Psalter is poetry from first to last, even though it contains many prayers and not all OT prayers were poetic (see 1Ki 8:23–53; Ezr 9:6–15; Ne 9:5–37; Da 9:4–19)—nor, for that matter, was all praise poetic (see 1Ki 8:15–21). The psalms are impassioned, vivid and concrete; they are rich in images, in simile and metaphor. Assonance, alliteration and wordplays abound in the Hebrew text. Effective use of repetition and the piling up of synonyms and complements to fill out the picture

The Psalter was put into its final form by postexilic temple personnel, who completed it probably in the fourth century BC. It has often been called the prayer book of the second (Zerubbabel's and Herod's) temple and was used in synagogues as well.

are characteristic. Key words frequently highlight major themes in prayer or song. Enclosure (repetition of a significant word or phrase from the beginning that recurs at the end) frequently wraps up a composition or a unit within it. The notes on the structure of the individual psalms often call attention to literary frames within which the psalm has been set.

Hebrew poetry lacks rhyme and regular meter. Its most distinctive and pervasive feature is parallelism. Most poetic lines are composed of two (sometimes three) balanced segments (the balance is often loose, with the second segment commonly somewhat shorter than the first). The second segment either echoes (synonymous parallelism), contrasts (antithetic parallelism) or syntactically completes (synthetic parallelism) the first. These three types are generalizations and are not wholly adequate to describe the rich variety that the creativity of the poets has achieved within the basic two-segment line structure. When the second or third segment of a poetic line repeats, echoes or overlaps the content of the preceding segment, it usually intensifies or more sharply focuses the thought or its expression. They can serve, however, as rough distinctions that will assist the reader. In the NIV the second and third segments of a line are slightly indented relative to the first. See chart, p. 859.

Determining where the Hebrew poetic lines or line segments begin or end (scanning) is sometimes an uncertain matter. Even the Septuagint (the pre-Christian Greek translation of the OT) at times scans the lines differently from the way the Hebrew texts now available to us do. It is therefore not surprising that modern translations occasionally differ.

A related problem is the extremely concise, often elliptical, writing style of the Hebrew poets. The syntactical connection of words must at times be inferred simply from context. Where more than one possibility presents itself, translators are confronted with ambiguity. They are not always sure with which line segment a border word or phrase is to be read.

The stanza structure of Hebrew poetry is also a matter of dispute. Occasionally, recurring refrains mark off stanzas, as in Ps 42–43; 57. In Ps 110 two balanced stanzas are divided by their introductory prophecies (see also introduction to Ps 132), while Ps 119 devotes eight lines to each letter of the Hebrew alphabet. For the most part, however, no such obvious indicators are present. The NIV has used spaces to mark off poetic paragraphs (called "stanzas" in the notes). Usually this could be done with some confidence, and the reader is advised to be guided by them. But there are a few places where these divisions are questionable—and are challenged in the notes.

Close study of the Psalms discloses that the authors often composed with an overall design in mind. This is true of the alphabetic acrostics, in which the poet devoted to each letter of the Hebrew alphabet one line segment (as in Ps 111–112), a single line (as in Ps 25; 34; 145), two lines (as in Ps 37) or eight lines (as in Ps 119). In addition Ps 33; 38; 103 have 22 lines each, no doubt because of the number of letters in the Hebrew alphabet (see Introduction to Lamentations: Literary Features). The oft-voiced notion that this device was used as a memory aid seems culturally prejudiced and probably unwarranted. Actually, people of that time were able to memorize far more readily than most people today. It is much more likely that the alphabet—which was invented as a simple system of symbols capable of representing in writing the rich and complex patterns of human speech and therefore of inscribing all that can be put into words (one of the greatest intellectual achievements of all time)—commended itself as a framework on which to hang significant phrases.

Other forms were also used. Ps 44 is a prayer fashioned after the design of a ziggurat (a Babylonian stepped pyramid; see note on Ge 11:4). A sense of symmetry is pervasive. There are psalms that devote the same number of lines to each stanza (e.g., Ps 12; 41), or do so with variation only in the introductory or concluding stanza (e.g., Ps 38; 83; 94). Others match the opening and closing stanzas and balance the ones between (e.g., Ps 33; 86). A particularly interesting device is to place a key thematic line at the very center, sometimes constructing the whole or part of the poem around that center (see note on 6:6). Still other design features are pointed out in the notes. The authors of the psalms crafted their compositions very carefully. They were heirs of an ancient art (in many details showing that they had inherited a poetic tradition that goes back hundreds of years), and they developed it to a state of high sophistication. Their works are best appreciated when carefully studied and pondered.

Theology: Introduction

The Psalter is for the most part a book of prayer and praise. In it faith speaks *to* God in prayer and *about* God in praise. But there are also psalms that are explicitly didactic (instructional) in form and purpose (teaching the way of godliness). As noted above (Collection, Arrangement and Date), the manner in which the whole collection has been arranged suggests that one of its main purposes was instruction in the life of faith, a faith formed and nurtured by the Law, the Prophets and the Writings. Accordingly, the Psalter is theologically rich. Its theology is, however, not abstract or systematic but doxological, confessional and practical. So a summation of that theology impoverishes it by translating it into an objective mode.

Furthermore, any summation faces a still greater problem. The Psalter is a large collection of independent pieces of many kinds, serving different purposes and composed over the course of many centuries. Not only must a brief summary of its theology be selective and incomplete; it will also of necessity be somewhat artificial. It will suggest that each psalm reflects or at least presupposes the theology outlined, that there is no theological tension or progression within the Psalter. Manifestly this is not so.

Still, the final editors of the Psalter were obviously not eclectic in their selection. They knew that many voices from many times spoke here, but none that in their judgment was incompatible with the Law and the Prophets. No doubt they also assumed that each psalm was to be understood in the light of the collection as a whole. That assumption we may share. Hence something, after all, can be said concerning seven major theological themes that, while admittedly a bit artificial, need not seriously distort and can be helpful to the student of the Psalms.

Theology: Major Themes

(1) At the core of the theology of the Psalter is the conviction that the gravitational center of life (of right human understanding, trust, hope, service, morality, adoration), but also of history and of the whole creation (heaven and earth), is *God* (Yahweh, "the LORD"; see Dt 6:4 and note). He is *the Great King* over all, the One to whom all things are subject. He created all things and preserves them; they are the robe of glory with which he has clothed himself. Because he ordered them, they have a well-defined and true identity (no chaos there). Because he maintains them, they are sustained and kept secure from disruption, confusion or annihilation. Because he alone

is the sovereign God, they are governed by one hand and held in the service of one divine purpose. Under God creation is a cosmos — an orderly and systematic whole. What we distinguish as "nature" and history had for the psalmists one Lord, under whose rule all things worked together. Through the creation the Great King's majestic glory is displayed. He is good (wise, righteous, faithful, amazingly benevolent and merciful — evoking trust), and he is great (his knowledge, thoughts and works are beyond human comprehension — evoking reverent awe). By his good and lordly rule he is shown to be the Holy One.

(2) As the Great King by right of creation and enduring, absolute sovereignty, *he ultimately will not tolerate any worldly power that opposes, denies or ignores him.* He will come to rule the nations so that all will be compelled to acknowledge him. This expectation is no doubt the root and broadest scope of the psalmists' long view of the future. Because the Lord is the Great King beyond all challenge, *his righteous and peaceful kingdom will come, overwhelming all opposition* and purging the creation of all rebellion against his rule — such will be the ultimate outcome of history.

(3) As the Great King on whom all creatures depend, *he opposes the proud, those who rely on their own resources (and/or the gods they have contrived) to work out their own destiny.* These are the ones who ruthlessly wield whatever power they possess to attain worldly wealth, status and security — who are a law to themselves and exploit others as they will. In the Psalter, this kind of pride is the root of all evil. Those who embrace it, though they may seem to prosper, will be brought down to death, their final end. The humble, the poor and needy, those who acknowledge their dependence on the Lord in all things — these are the ones in whom God delights. Hence the "fear of the LORD" — i.e., humble trust in and obedience to the Lord — is the "beginning" of all wisdom (111:10). Ultimately, those who embrace it will inherit the earth. Not even death can hinder their seeing the face of God.

The psalmists' hope for the future — the future of God and his kingdom and the future of the godly — was firm, though somewhat generalized. None of the psalmists gives expression to a two-age vision of the future (the present evil age giving way to a new age of righteousness and peace on the other side of a great eschatological divide). Such a view began to appear in the intertestamental literature — a view that had been foreshadowed by Daniel (see especially 12:2 – 3) and by Isaiah (see 65:17 – 25; 66:22 – 24) — and it later received full expression in the teaching of Jesus and the apostles. But this revelation was only a fuller development consistent with the hopes the psalmists lived by.

(4) Because God is the Great King, *he is the ultimate Executor of justice among humans (to avenge oneself is an act of the proud).* God is the court of appeal when persons are threatened or wronged — especially when no earthly court that he has established has jurisdiction (as in the case of international conflicts) or is able to judge (as when one is wronged by public slander) or is willing to act (out of fear or corruption). *He is the mighty and faithful Defender of the defenseless and the wronged.* He knows every deed and the secrets of every heart. There is no escaping his scrutiny. No false testimony will mislead him in judgment. And he hears the pleas brought to him. As the good and faithful Judge, he delivers those who are oppressed or wrongfully attacked and redresses the wrongs committed against them (see note on 5:10). This is the unwavering conviction that accounts for the psalmists' impatient complaints when they boldly, yet as poor and needy, cry to him, "Why, LORD (have you not yet delivered me)?" "How long, LORD (before you act)?"

(5) As the Great King over all the earth, *the Lord has chosen the Israelites to be his servant people, his inheritance among the nations.* He has delivered them by mighty acts out of the hands of the world powers, has given them a land of their own (territory that he took from other nations to be his own inheritance in the earth) *and has united them with himself in covenant as the initial embodiment of his redeemed kingdom.* Thus both their destiny and his honor came to be bound up with this relationship. *To them he also gave his word of revelation*, which testified of him, made specific his promises and proclaimed his will. By God's covenant, Israel was to live among the nations, loyal only to her heavenly King. She was to trust solely in his protection, hope in his promises, live in accordance with his will and worship him exclusively. She was to sing his praises to the whole world — which in a special sense revealed Israel's anticipatory role in the evangelization of the nations.

(6) As the Great King, Israel's covenant Lord, *God chose David to be his royal representative on earth.* In this capacity, David was the Lord's servant — i.e., a member of the Great King's administration. The Lord himself anointed him and adopted him as his royal "son" to rule in his name. Through him God made his people secure in the promised land and subdued all the powers that threatened them. What is more, *he covenanted to preserve the Davidic dynasty.* Henceforth the kingdom of God on earth, while not dependent on the house of David, was linked to it by God's decision and commitment. In its continuity and strength lay Israel's security and hope as she faced a hostile world. And since the Davidic kings were God's royal representatives in the earth, in concept seated at God's right hand (110:1), the scope of their rule was potentially worldwide (see Ps 2).

A shepherd leads his sheep.

The Lord's anointed, however, was more than a warrior king. He was to be endowed by God to govern his people with godlike righteousness: to deliver the oppressed, defend the defenseless, suppress the wicked and thus bless the nation with internal peace and prosperity. He was also an intercessor with God in behalf of the nation, the builder and maintainer of the temple (as God's earthly palace and the nation's house of prayer) and the foremost voice calling the nation to worship the Lord. It is perhaps with a view to these last duties that he is declared to be not only king, but also priest (see Ps 110 and notes).

(7) As the Great King, Israel's covenant Lord, *God* (who had chosen David and his dynasty to be his royal representatives) *also chose Jerusalem (the City of David) as his own royal city, the earthly seat of his throne. Thus Jerusalem (Zion) became the earthly capital (and symbol) of the kingdom of God. There in his palace (the temple) he sat enthroned among his people.* There his people could meet with him to bring their prayers and praise and to see his power and glory. From there he brought salvation, dispensed blessings and judged the nations. And with him as the city's great Defender, Jerusalem was the secure citadel of the kingdom of God, the hope and joy of God's people.

God's goodwill and faithfulness toward his people were most strikingly symbolized by his pledged presence among them at his temple in Jerusalem, the "city of the Great King" (48:2). But no manifestation of his benevolence was greater than his readiness to forgive the sins of those who humbly confessed them and whose hearts showed him that their repentance was genuine and their professions of loyalty to him had integrity. As they anguished over their own sinfulness, the psalmists remembered the ancient testimony of their covenant Lord: I am Yahweh ("the LORD"), "the compassionate and gracious God, slow to anger, abounding in love and faithfulness, maintaining love to thousands, and forgiving wickedness, rebellion and sin" (Ex 34:6 – 7). Only so did they dare to submit to him as his people, to "fear" him (see 130:3 – 4).

Theology: Summary, Messianic Import and Conclusion

Unquestionably the supreme kingship of Yahweh (in which he displays his transcendent greatness and goodness) is the most basic metaphor and most pervasive theological concept in the Psalter — as in the OT generally. It provides the fundamental perspective in which people are to view themselves, the whole creation, events in nature and history, and the future. All creation is Yahweh's one kingdom. To be a creature in the world is to be a part of his kingdom and under his rule. To be a human being in the world is to be dependent on and responsible to him. To proudly deny that fact is the root of all wickedness — the wickedness that now pervades the world.

God's election of Israel and subsequently of David and Zion, together with the giving of his word, represent the renewed inbreaking of God's righteous kingdom into this world of rebellion and evil. It initiates the great divide between the righteous nation and the wicked nations, and on a deeper level between the righteous and the wicked, a more significant distinction that cuts even through Israel. In the end this divine enterprise will triumph. Human pride will be humbled, and wrongs will be redressed. The humble will be given the whole earth to possess, and the righteous and peaceful kingdom of God will come to full realization. These theological themes, of course, have profound religious and moral implications. Of these, too, the psalmists spoke.

One question that ought yet to be addressed is: Do the Psalms speak of the Christ? Yes, in a variety of ways — but not as the Prophets do. The Psalter was never numbered among the Prophets.

On the other hand, when the Psalter was being given its final form, what the psalms said about the Lord and his ways with his people, about the Lord and his ways with the nations, about the Lord and his ways with the righteous and the wicked, and what the psalmists said about the Lord's anointed, his temple and his holy city—all this was understood in light of the prophetic literature (both Former and Latter Prophets). Relative to these matters, the Psalter and the Prophets were mutually reinforcing and interpretive.

When the Psalms speak of the king on David's throne, they speak of the king who is being crowned (as in Ps 2; 72; 110—though some think 110 is an exception) or is reigning (as in Ps 45) at the time. They proclaim his status as the Lord's anointed and declare what the Lord will accomplish through him and his dynasty. Thus they also speak of the sons of David to come—and in the exile and the postexilic era, when there was no reigning king, they spoke to Israel only of the great Son of David whom the prophets had announced as the one in whom God's covenant with David would yet be fulfilled. So the NT quotes these psalms as testimonies to Christ, which in their unique way they are. In him they are truly fulfilled.

When in the Psalms righteous sufferers—who are "righteous" because they are innocent, not having provoked or wronged their adversaries, and because they are among the "humble" who trust in the Lord—cry out to God in their distress (as in Ps 22; 69), they give voice to the sufferings of God's servants in a hostile and evil world.

These cries became the prayers of God's oppressed people, and as such they were taken up into Israel's book of prayers. When Christ came in the flesh, he identified himself with God's "humble" people in the world. He became for them God's righteous servant par excellence, and he shared their sufferings at the hands of the wicked. Thus these prayers became his prayers also—uniquely his prayers. In him the suffering and deliverance of which these prayers speak are fulfilled (though they continue to be the prayers also of those who take up their cross and follow him).

Similarly, in speaking of God's covenant people, of the city of God and of the temple in which God dwells, the Psalms ultimately speak of Christ's church. The Psalter is not only the prayer book of the second temple; it is also the enduring prayer book of the people of God. Now, however, it must be used in the light of the new era of redemption that dawned with the first coming of the Messiah and that will be consummated at his second coming.

THE DESIGN AND MESSAGE OF THE PSALTER

THE PSALMS EXHIBIT NUMEROUS STRUCTURAL FEATURES THAT CONTRIBUTE TO THEIR OVERALL THEME: INSTRUCTION IN THE GODLY LIFE UNDER THE REIGN OF GOD

BOOK I

Ps 1–2 Introduction, framed by two *'ashre* ("Blessed is/are") declarations
1 Evokes instructions of *Torah* [Law] and *Ḥokmah* [Wisdom]
2 Evokes Former and Latter Prophets (Yahweh and his anointed, Israel's only hope in the turmoil of history)

Thus 1. The Psalter must be read in the context of the rest of the OT canon.
2. As the portal to the temple of the Psalter, these two psalms teach that those who would appropriate the prayers and praises of the Psalter must fit the profile of the framing declarations; their lives must be shaped by Law and godly Wisdom, and they must "take refuge" in Yahweh and his anointed—the two basic components of "the fear of Yahweh."

Ps 3–14

64 lines

3 Plea for deliverance from foes
4 Plea for relief in time of drought
5 Plea for deliverance from foes
6 Plea for healing
7 Plea for deliverance from foes
8 Praise of the Creator (the glory of God bestowed on humans)

64 lines

9 Plea for deliverance from hostile nations
10 Plea for deliverance from the wicked
11 Trust in Yahweh's righteous rule
12 Plea for help in an ungodly time
13 Plea for deliverance from serious illness and enemies
14 The folly of humankind ("The LORD looks down . . . to see . . . All have turned away")

Ps 15–24

15 Who has access to the temple?
16 Confession of trust in Yahweh
17 Plea for deliverance from foes
18 Royal praise for deliverance
19 Yahweh's glory in Creation and Torah
(The summer sun moving across the face of the sky from east to west)
20–21 Prayer for king's victory; praise for victory
22 Plea for deliverance from foes
23 Confession of trust in Yahweh
24 Who may ascend the holy hill?

Ps 25–33

25 Alphabetic acrostic (22 verses long)
Prayer for covenant mercies
26 Prayer of a "blameless" person
27 Appeal against false accusers
"Be strong and take heart
and wait for the LORD."
28 Prayer of one going "down to the pit"
29 Praise of the King of creation
(The winter thunderstorm moving across the face of the sky from west to east)
30 Praise of one spared from going "down to the pit"
31 Appeal against false accusers
"Be strong and take heart,
all you who hope in the LORD."
32 Blessedness of a penitent person
33 Twenty-two verses long
Praise for God's good rule

Ps 34–37

34 Alphabetic acrostic
Instruction in godly wisdom
35 Appeal against malicious slanderers
36 Appeal against threats of godless, wicked people
37 Alphabetic acrostic
Instruction in godly wisdom

Ps 38–41

38 Prayer for relief from serious illness and enemies: a confession of sin
39 Prayer for relief from serious illness and enemies: a confession of sin
40 Prayer for relief from troubles (serious illness?) and enemies: a confession of sin
41 Prayer for relief from serious illness and enemies: a confession of sin
40:4 ***'Ashre*** "Blessed is the one who trusts in the LORD."
41:1 ***'Ashre*** "Blessed are those who have regard for the weak."

THE DESIGN AND MESSAGE OF THE PSALTER

BOOK II

Ps 42–45 Three prayers with a royal psalm attached (see Ps 69–72)
42 Prayer of individual ("Why have you forgotten me" in the face of the oppression of enemies?)
43 Continuation of Ps 42
44 Prayer of the community ("Why do you hide your face and forget our . . . oppression?")
45 Song in praise of the king on a day of his glory (wedding to a foreign princess)
(" . . . ride forth . . . in the cause of truth, humility and justice")
("Your throne . . . will last for ever and ever")

Ps 46–48 In celebration of the security of Zion
46 Zion's security
47 Zion's Great King triumphant over all nations
48 Zion's security

Ps 49–53 The proper posture before God
49 The folly of those who "trust in their wealth and boast of their great riches"
50 God calls his people to account
51 Humble prayer for forgiveness and cleansing
52 The folly of the one who "trusted in his great wealth" and those who "boast of evil"
53 The folly of those who live as if there is no God (repeat of Ps 14)

Ps 54–60 Seven prayers at the center of Book II
54 Prayer of individual for help against enemies
55 Prayer for help: a conspiracy in Jerusalem ("they prowl about on its walls")
("words. . . are drawn **swords**")
56 Prayer for help against enemies
57 Prayer for deliverance from enemies
("tongues are sharp **swords**")
58 Prayer for the heavenly Judge to set right what human rulers have not
59 Prayer for help: enemies surround Jerusalem ("They . . . prowl about the city")
("spew . . . words from their lips . . . sharp as **swords**")
60 Prayer of community for help after suffering devastating defeat
("You have rejected us" and "no longer go out with our armies")

Ps 61–64 Four royal prayers with interweaving themes
61 Appeal for restoration to God's presence ("rock," "refuge," "strong tower," "in the shelter of your wings")
62 Appeal for deliverance from arrogant foes ("rock," "fortress," "mighty rock," "refuge"; "You reward everyone according to what they have done")
63 Appeal for God's refreshing presence when threatened by enemies ("sing in the shadow of your wings"; "Those who want to kill me . . . will go down to the depths of the earth")
64 Appeal for God's protection against conspirators ("The righteous will rejoice in the LORD and will take refuge in him")

Ps 65–68 God's "awesome and righteous deeds" evoke the praise of "all. . . the earth"
65 God's blessing the earth into fruitfulness is highlighted ("the hope of all the ends of the earth")
66 God's saving acts on behalf of Israel are highlighted ("Shout for joy to God, all the earth!")
67 God's blessing the earth into fruitfulness is highlighted ("all the peoples praise . . . all the ends of the earth . . . fear")
68 God's saving acts in behalf of Israel are highlighted ("kings . . . bring you gifts . . . Sing to God, you kingdoms of the earth")

Ps 69–72 Three prayers with a royal psalm attached (see Ps 42–45)
69 A king's prayer for deliverance when under vicious attack
70 A short prayer (repeat of Ps 40; see introduction to Ps 71)
71 A king's prayer for God's help in old age when under attack
72 A prayer that the king be specially gifted to rule justly
(". . . endure . . . through all generations")
(". . . all nations . . . be blessed through him")

THE DESIGN AND MESSAGE OF THE PSALTER

BOOK III

MADE UP OF THREE GROUPS OF SIX PSALMS (73–78), FIVE PSALMS (79–83), SIX PSALMS (84–89)

Ps 73–78

73 Instruction based on individual experience
74 Communal prayer: God has "rejected" his people
75 Praise to God: His "Name is near," and he cuts off the horns of the wicked but causes the "horns of the righteous" to be "lifted up"

78 Instruction based on communal experience
77 Individual prayer: God has rejected him
76 Celebration: God's "name is great" in Israel; he "breaks the spirit of [enemy] rulers"

Ps 79–83

79 Communal prayer: when invaded by fierce enemies
80 Prayer for God to restore his people after they have been ravaged by enemies

83 Communal prayer: when attacked by coalition of enemies
82 Prayer for God to judge the wicked rulers of the earth

81 Exhortation to Israel: "If Israel would only follow my ways, how quickly I would subdue their enemies"

Ps 84–89

84 Expression of yearning for "the courts of the LORD" and prayer for God to "look with favor" on "our shield," "your anointed"

85 Prayer for God to "restore" his people from some situation of distress
86 Individual prayer for God's help when under attack by enemies

89 Prayer for God to rescue his people, to remember his covenant with David
88 Individual prayer for God to remove his wrath and deliver from death

87 Song celebrating God's special love for Zion and care for its citizens

BOOKS IV AND V

Ps 90–100 Eleven psalms framed by "Lord [Adonai] . . . our dwelling place throughout all generations" (90:1) and "The LORD [Yahweh] . . . his love . . . faithfulness continues through all generations" (100:5)

90 Plaintive prayer concerning the mortality of those who have long had the Lord as their "dwelling place"
91 Assurances for those who make the Most High their "dwelling" place (v. 9; cf. v. 1): "With long life I will satisfy" them (v. 16)
92 Celebration of Yahweh's righteous rule and its result (what the "senseless. . . do not know"): "evildoers. . . will be destroyed forever" but "the righteous. . . will still bear fruit in old age"
93 Celebration of the invincible reign of Yahweh
94 Appeal to Yahweh to deal judicially with those who perpetrate injustices and oppression: "Take notice, you senseless ones among the people"
95 Call for the delivered covenant community to joyfully worship Yahweh their God (and warning not to repeat earlier rebelliousness)
96 Call to all nations to worshipfully celebrate the universal reign of Yahweh
97 Joyful celebration of Yahweh's universal reign—whose throne is founded on "righteousness and justice"
98 Call to all nations to worshipfully praise Yahweh for his saving acts in behalf of Israel
99 Joyful celebration of Yahweh's universal reign, especially for what he has done for Israel
100 Concluding exhortation to worshipfully praise Yahweh, Israel's Maker and "good" Shepherd-King

THE DESIGN AND MESSAGE OF THE PSALTER

BOOKS IV AND V (CONT.)

Ps 101–110 A "little psalter" framed by two royal psalms

101 A royal pledge to reign righteously
102 Individual lament
103 Praise of Yahweh for his "great...love"
104 Praise of Yahweh the Creator
105 Recital of Israel's saving history
106 Recital of Israel's history of rebellion
107 Call for praise of Yahweh who hears cries of distress
108 Praise of Yahweh for his "great...love"
109 Individual lament
110 Prophecies concerning the Messianic King-Priest

Ps 111–119 The "Egyptian Hallel" framed by 111/112 and 119

111/112 Formal and thematic twins: Righteous God (111:3) and God-fearing persons, "who find great delight in his [God's] commands" (112:1)

Egyptian Hallel
113
114
115
116
117
118

Psalms used in Israel's great annual festivals

119 Prayer of one who finds "delight" in God's "commands" (v. 35)

Ps 120–137 Songs of ascents plus two appendices

120–134 The Songs of Ascents
135–136 Hymns traditionally associated by the Jews with the songs of ascents
137 Song of love for Zion by one returned from Babylonian exile (brings closure to the preceding collection)

Ps 138–145 Eight psalms assigned to David: prayers framed by praise

138 Praise of Yahweh: "When I called, you answered"; "May all the kings . . . praise you . . . for [your] glory"
139 Acknowledgment of total nakedness before the omniscient and omnipresent God
140–144 Five prayers for deliverance from:
140: evildoers, "the violent...the wicked"
141: evildoers
142: pursuers who "are too strong for me"
143: enemies
144: foreigners
145 (Acrostic) Praise of Yahweh, "the King": who "is near to all who call on him"; "All your works . . . tell of the glory of your kingdom . . . so that all . . . may know of . . . the glorious splendor of your kingdom"

Ps 146–150 Five Hallelujah psalms that serve as the concluding doxology for the entire Psalter (see Introduction: Collection, Arrangement and Date)

MESSIANIC PSALMS

PSALM	SUBJECT	MESSIANIC	NT PROOF	FURTHER (CONTEXTUAL) EVIDENCE
Christ spoken of in the third person				
Ps 8	Humiliation and glory	Ps 8:4b–8	Heb 2:5–10; 1Co 15:27	All things are under their feet (Ps 8:6). In him humanity's role as ruler over other creatures comes to fulfillment.
Ps 72	Rule	Ps 72:6–17	Heb 2:5–10; 1Co 15:27	Transition to the future (Ps 72:5). His reign is forever (v. 7). Territory (v. 8). All worship him (vv. 9–11).
Ps 89	Of David	Ps 89:3–4, 28–29, 34–36	Ac 2:30	David's line is eternal (Ps 89:4, 29, 36–37).
Ps 109	Judas cursed	Ps 109:6–19	Ac 1:16–20	Adversaries (pl.) in Ps 109:4–5 shift in v. 6 to one preeminent betrayer. The plural is resumed in v. 20.
Ps 132	Of David	Ps 132:11–12	Ac 2:30	David's line is eternal (Ps 132:12).
Christ addressed in the second person				
Ps 45	Throne forever	Ps 45:6–7	Heb 1:8–9	He is deity (Ps 45:6), yet not the Father (Ps 45:7).
Ps 102	Eternity	Ps 102:25–27	Heb 1:10–12	Address to Yahweh (Ps 102:1–22); to El, a change (Ps 102:24), applied to Christ.
Ps 110	Ascension and priesthood	Ps 110:1–7	Mt 22:43–45; Ac 2:33–35; Heb 1:13; 5:6–10; 6:20; 7:24	He is David's Lord (Ps 110:1). Eternal priest (Ps 110:4).
Christ speaks in the first person				
Ps 2	Kiss the Son	Ps 2:1–11	Ac 4:25–28; 13:33; Heb 1:5; 5:5	The speaker is God's only Son (Ps 2:7).
Ps 16	No decay	Ps 16:10	Ac 2:24–31; 13:35–37	He possesses more than David — no decay (Ps 16:10).
Ps 22	Passion	Ps 22:1–31	Mt 27:35–46; Jn 19:23–25; Heb 2:12	Not seeing decay cannot apply to David; nor pierced hands and feet (Ps 22:16); nor lots cast for his garments (Ps 22:18).
Ps 40	Incarnation	Ps 40:6–8	Heb 10:5–10	Praises in Ps 40:1–5 are interrupted by a descriptive section (vv. 6–8). David did not always delight to do God's will, but Christ did (v. 8).
Ps 69	Judas cursed	Ps 69:25	Ac 1:16–20	The specific "deserted" place lies between generalizations in Ps 69:24 and 26, narrowed down to Judas.

BOOK I

Psalms 1–41

Psalm 1

[1]Blessed is the one[a]
who does not walk[b] in step with the wicked[c]
or stand in the way[d] that sinners take[e]
or sit[f] in the company of mockers,[g]
[2]but whose delight[h] is in the law of the LORD,[i]
and who meditates[j] on his law day and night.
[3]That person is like a tree[k] planted by streams[l] of water,[m]
which yields its fruit[n] in season
and whose leaf[o] does not wither—
whatever they do prospers.[p]
[4]Not so the wicked!
They are like chaff[q]
that the wind blows away.
[5]Therefore the wicked will not stand[r] in the judgment,[s]
nor sinners in the assembly[t] of the righteous.
[6]For the LORD watches over[u] the way of the righteous,
but the way of the wicked leads to destruction.[v]

Psalm 2

[1]Why do the nations conspire[a]
and the peoples plot[w] in vain?

[a] *1* Hebrew; Septuagint *rage*

1:1 [a]S Dt 33:29; Ps 40:4; 128:4 [b]Ps 89:15 [c]S Job 21:16; Ps 10:2-11 [d]S Ge 49:6 [e]Ps 26:9; 37:38; 51:13; 104:35 [f]Ps 26:4 [g]S Job 11:3; Pr 1:22; Isa 28:14; Hos 7:5 **1:2** [h]Ps 112:1; 119:16, 35; Ro 7:22 [i]Ps 19:7; 119:1; Eze 11:20; 18:17 [j]S Ge 24:63 **1:3** [k]Ps 52:8; 92:12; 128:3; Jer 11:16; Zec 4:3 [l]Ps 46:4; 65:9; Isa 33:21; Jer 31:9 [m]S Nu 24:6; S Job 14:9; S Eze 17:5 [n]Ps 92:14; Eze 47:12 [o]Isa 1:30; 64:6 [p]S Ge 39:3 **1:4** [q]S Job 13:25; Isa 40:24; Jer 13:24 **1:5** [r]Ps 5:5 [s]S Job 19:29 [t]Ps 26:12; 35:18; 82:1; 89:5; 107:32; 111:1; 149:1 **1:6** [u]Ps 37:18; 121:5; 145:20; Na 1:7 [v]S Lev 26:38; Ps 9:6 **2:1** [w]Ps 21:11; 83:5; Pr 24:2

Ps 1–2 These two "orphan" psalms (having no title) are bound together by framing clauses ("Blessed is the one ... whose delight is in the law of the LORD"; "Blessed are all who take refuge in him") that highlight their function as the introduction to the whole Psalter. Together they point on the one hand to God's law and to the instruction of the wisdom teachers (Ps 1) and on the other hand to a central theme in the Prophets, both Former and Latter, namely, what Yahweh has committed himself to accomplish for and through his anointed king from the house of David (Ps 2). As the port of entry into the Psalter, these two psalms make clear that those who would find their own voice in the Psalms and so would appropriate them as testimonies to their own faith must fit the profile of those called "blessed" here. See also note on Ps 40–41.

Ps 1 Godly wisdom here declares the final outcome of the two "ways": "the way that sinners take" (v. 1) and "the way of the righteous" (v. 6). See 34:19–22; Ps 37; see also essay, p. 786. The psalmist develops three contrasts that set the righteous apart from the wicked: (1) as to their "way" of life (vv. 1–2); (2) as to the life condition they experience ("like a tree," "like chaff," vv. 3–4); and, climactically, (3) as to God's judgment on their different ways (vv. 5–6). As part of the introduction to the Psalter, this psalm reminds the reader (1) that those of whom the Psalms speak (using various terms) as the people of God must be characterized by delight in God's revealed will—those who stubbornly choose the way of sinners have no place among them (v. 5; see Ps 15; 24)—and (2) that the godly piety that speaks in the Psalms is a faithful response to God's written directives for life—which is the path that leads to blessedness. For a prime indicator of the psalm's central theme, cf. the first and last words, which frame the whole ("Blessed ... destruction").

1:1 Speaks progressively of association with the ungodly and participation in their ungodly ways. *Blessed.* The happy condition of those who revere the Lord and do his will (see 94:12; 112:1; 119:1–2; 128:1; Pr 29:18; cf. Ps 41:1; 106:3; Pr 14:21; Isa 56:2) and who put their trust in him (see 40:4; 84:5,12; 144:15; 146:5; Pr 16:20; Isa 30:18; Jer 17:7; cf. Ps 2:12; 34:8). Reference is not first of all to health and wealth but to the assurance and experience that they live under the guardianship and faithful care of the gracious Lord of life. The Psalter begins by proclaiming the blessedness of the godly and ends by calling all living things to praise God in his earthly and heavenly sanctuaries (Ps 150). *walk in step with the wicked.* Order one's life according to the deliberations and advice of the wicked (see Pr 1:10–19). *stand.* Position oneself. *sinners.* Those for whom wickedness is habitual—a way of life (see v. 5). *sit.* Settle oneself. *mockers.* Those who ridicule God and defiantly reject his law (see Pr 1:22 and note).

1:2 *meditates on his law.* Seeking guidance for life in God's law rather than in the deliberations of the wicked. *day and night.* See Jos 1:8.

1:3 *like a tree ... does not wither.* See Jer 17:8; a simile of the blessedness of the righteous. Such a tree withstands the buffeting of the winds and, flourishing, it blesses people and animals with its unfailing fruit and shade.

1:4 *like chaff ... blows away.* A simile of the wretchedness of the wicked. Chaff is carried away by the lightest wind, and its removal brings about cleansing by extracting what is utterly useless (see note on Ru 1:22).

1:5 *will not stand in the judgment.* Will not be able to withstand God's wrath when he judges (see 76:7; 130:3; Ezr 9:15; Na 1:6 and note; Mal 3:2; Mt 25:31–46; Rev 6:17). *assembly.* The worshiping assembly at God's sanctuary (as in 22:25; 26:12; 35:18; 40:9–10; 111:1; 149:1; see Ps 15; 24). *righteous.* One of several terms in the OT for God's people; it presents them as those who honor God and order their lives in all things according to his will.

1:6 *way ... way.* What is here said of the two ways applies by implication also to those who choose them (see 37:20).

Ps 2 Peter and John ascribed this psalm to David in Ac 4:25—possibly in accordance with the Jewish practice of honoring David as the primary author of the Psalter. A royal psalm, it was originally composed for the coronation of Davidic kings in light of the Lord's covenant with David (see 2Sa 7). As the second half of a two-part introduction to the Psalms, it proclaims the blessedness of all who acknowledge the lordship of God and his anointed and "take refuge in him" (v. 12; see introductions to Ps 1–2 and Ps 1; see also note on 1:1). This psalm is frequently quoted in the NT, where it is applied to Christ as the great Son of David and God's Anointed.

Four balanced stanzas of three verses each are divided at the center (v. 7a) by a short prose line that serves as a thematic hinge. Stanzas two and three contain messages from the heavenly King that warrant the warning to the "kings" (v. 10) whose rebellion (v. 2) is the focus of the first stanza.

2:1–3 The nations rebel. In the ancient Near East the coronation of a new king was often the occasion for the revolt of peoples and kings who had been subject to the crown. The newly anointed king is here pictured as ruler over an empire.

2:1–2 For a NT application, see Ac 4:25–28.

2:1 *Why ... ?* A rhetorical question that implies "How dare they!"

[2]The kings[x] of the earth rise up
and the rulers band together
against the LORD and against his
anointed,[y] saying,
[3]"Let us break their chains[z]
and throw off their shackles."[a]

[4]The One enthroned[b] in heaven laughs;[c]
the Lord scoffs at them.
[5]He rebukes them in his anger[d]
and terrifies them in his wrath,[e]
saying,
[6]"I have installed my king[f]
on Zion,[g] my holy mountain.[h]"

[7]I will proclaim the LORD's decree:

He said to me, "You are my son;[i]
today I have become your father.[j]
[8]Ask me,
and I will make the nations[k] your
inheritance,[l]
the ends of the earth[m] your possession.
[9]You will break them with a rod of iron[a];[n]
you will dash them to pieces[o] like
pottery.[p]"

[10]Therefore, you kings, be wise;[q]
be warned, you rulers[r] of the earth.
[11]Serve the LORD with fear[s]
and celebrate his rule[t] with
trembling.[u]
[12]Kiss his son,[v] or he will be
angry
and your way will lead to your
destruction,
for his wrath[w] can flare up in a
moment.
Blessed[x] are all who take refuge[y] in
him.

Psalm 3[b]

A psalm of David. When he fled
from his son Absalom.[z]

[1]LORD, how many are my foes!
How many rise up against me!
[2]Many are saying of me,
"God will not deliver him."[a][c]

2:2 [x]Ps 48:4 [y]S 1Sa 9:16; Jn 1:41; Ac 4:25-26* **2:3** [z]S Job 36:8 [a]S 2Sa 3:34 **2:4** [b]Isa 37:16; 40:22; 66:1 [c]Ps 37:13; Pr 1:26 **2:5** [d]Ps 6:1; 27:9; 38:1 [e]Ps 21:9; 79:6; 90:7; 110:5 **2:6** [f]Ps 10:16; 24:10 [g]2Ki 19:31; Ps 9:11; 48:2, 11; 78:68; 110:2; 133:3 [h]S Ex 15:17 **2:7** [i]S Mt 3:17; S 4:3 [j]S 2Sa 7:14; Ac 13:33*; Heb 1:5*; 5:5* **2:8** [k]Rev 2:26 [l]S Job 22:26; Mt 21:38 [m]Ps 22:27; 67:7 **2:9** [n]S Ge 49:10; Rev 12:5 [o]S Ex 15:6 [p]Isa 30:14; Jer 19:10; Rev 2:27*; 19:15 **2:10** [q]Pr 27:11 [r]Ps 141:6; Pr 8:15; Am 2:3 **2:11** [s]Ps 103:11 [t]Ps 9:2; 35:9; 104:34; Isa 61:10 [u]S 1Ch 16:30 **2:12** [v]ver 7 [w]S Dt 9:8; Rev 6:16 [x]Ps 84:12 [y]Ps 5:11; 34:8; 64:10 **3:Title** [z]2Sa 15:14 **3:2** [a]Ps 22:8; 71:11; Isa 36:15; 37:20

[a] 9 Or *will rule them with an iron scepter* (see Septuagint and Syriac) [b] In Hebrew texts 3:1-8 is numbered 3:2-9. [c] 2 The Hebrew has *Selah* (a word of uncertain meaning) here and at the end of verses 4 and 8.

2:2 *LORD ... his anointed.* To rebel against the Lord's anointed is also to rebel against the One who anointed him. *anointed.* Refers to the Davidic king and is ultimately fulfilled in Christ. The English word "Messiah" comes from the Hebrew word for "anointed one," and the English word "Christ" from the Greek word for "anointed one" (see NIV text note on Mt 1:1).

2:4–6 The Lord mocks the rebels. With derisive laughter the Lord meets the confederacy of rebellious world powers with the sovereign declaration that it is he who has established the Davidic king in his own royal city of Zion (Jerusalem).

2:4 See 59:8.

2:5 *anger ... wrath.* God's anger is always an expression of his righteousness (see 7:11; see also note on 4:1).

2:6 *holy mountain.* The site of the Jerusalem temple (see 2Ch 33:15); see also 3:4; 15:1; 43:3; 99:9.

2:7–9 The Lord's anointed proclaims the Lord's coronation decree. For NT application to Jesus' resurrection, see Ac 13:33; to his superiority over angels, see Heb 1:5; to his appointment as high priest, see Heb 5:5.

2:7 *son ... father.* In the ancient Near East the relationship between a great king and one of his subject kings, who ruled by his authority and owed him allegiance, was expressed not only by the words "lord" and "servant" but also by "father" and "son." The Davidic king was the Lord's "servant" and his "son" (2Sa 7:5,14; cf. chart, p. 23).

2:8 *your inheritance.* Your domain—just as the promised land was the Lord's "inheritance" (Ex 15:17; see Jos 22:19; Ps 28:9; 79:1; 82:8). *ends of the earth.* Ultimately the rule of the Lord's anointed will extend as far as the rule of God himself.

2:9 According to Rev 12:5; 19:15–16 this word will be fulfilled in the triumphant reign of Christ; in Rev 2:26–27 Christ declares that he will appoint those who remain faithful to him to share in his subjugating rule over the nations. *dash them to pieces like pottery.* See Jer 19:11.

2:10–12 The rebellious rulers are warned.

2:11 *celebrate his rule.* Hail the Lord as King with joy. *trembling.* Awe and reverence.

2:12 *Kiss.* As a sign of submission (see 1Sa 10:1; 1Ki 19:18; Hos 13:2; see also note on Ge 41:40). Submission to an Assyrian king was expressed by kissing his feet. *he ... his ... him.* Most likely the reference is to "the LORD" (v. 11), who anointed his "son." *your way will lead to your destruction.* See 1:6 and note. *Blessed.* See 1:1 and note. *take refuge.* See 5:11; 34:8; 64:10; cf. 104:18.

Ps 3–14 A group of 12 psalms composed of ten prayers (but see introduction to Ps 11), divided into two groups of five (Ps 3–7; 9–13), each of which has appended to it a sixth that characterizes the human condition (Ps 8; 14). For the sharp contrast between these two characterizations and how their complementary depictions of humankind bear on the collection of prayers to which they have been attached, see introductions to Ps 8; 14.

Ps 3 Though threatened by many foes, the psalmist prays confidently to the Lord. Ps 3 and 4 are linked by references to glory (see v. 3; 4:2) and to David's sleep at night (see v. 5; 4:8). In v. 5 David speaks of the assurance of his waking in the morning because the Lord will keep him while he sleeps; in 4:8 he speaks of the inner quietness with which he goes to sleep because of the Lord's care. This juxtaposition of prayers with references to waking (morning) and sleeping (evening) at the beginning of the Psalter suggests that God's faithful care sustains the godly day and night whatever the need or circumstances.

3 title *When he fled.* See 2Sa 15:13—17:22. References to events in David's life stand in the superscriptions of 13 psalms (3; 7; 18; 34; 51; 52; 54; 56; 57; 59; 60; 63; 142), all but one (Ps 142) in Books I and II. See Introduction: Authorship and Titles (or Superscriptions).

3:1–2 David's need: threatened by many foes.

3:2 See 22:7–8; 71:10–11. The psalmists frequently quote their wicked oppressors in order to portray how they mock (see note on 1:1) God and his servants (see note on 10:11). For *Selah*, see NIV text note; see also Introduction: Authorship and Titles (or Superscriptions), last paragraph.

TYPES OF HEBREW **PARALLELISM**

TYPE	CHARACTERISTIC	EXAMPLE
I. Synonymous	Repetition of same thought	
Identical	Each element is synonymous	Ps 24:1 The earth is the LORD's, and everything in it, the world, and all who live in it.
Similar	Each element is similar	Ps 19:2 Day after day they pour forth speech; night after night they reveal knowledge.
Incomplete	Second element of previous line is repeated	Jer 17:9 The heart is deceitful above all things and beyond cure. Who can understand it?
Continued	Second element is repeated and built upon	Ps 24:5 They will receive blessing from the LORD, and vindication from God their Savior.
II. Antithetic	Parallel by contrast (by use of the opposite)	Ps 1:6 For the LORD watches over the way of the righteous, but the way of the wicked leads to destruction.
III. Synthetic	Building on a thought	
Completion	Completes a thought	Ps 2:6 I have installed my king on Zion, my holy mountain.
Comparison	Draws an analogy	Pr 15:17 Better a small serving of vegetables with love than a fattened calf with hatred.
Reason	Gives a reason	Pr 26:4 Do not answer a fool according to his folly, or you yourself will be just like him.
Conceptual	Use of theme element	Ps 1:1 Blessed is the one who does not walk in step with the wicked or stand in the way that sinners take or sit in the company of mockers.
IV. Climactic	Builds on same word or phrase	Ps 29:1 Ascribe to the LORD, you heavenly beings, ascribe to the LORD glory and strength.
V. Emblematic	Use of simile or metaphor	Ps 42:1 As the deer pants for streams of water, so my soul pants for you, my God. Pr 25:25 Like cold water to a weary soul is good news from a distant land.

[3]But you, LORD, are a shield[b]
around me,
my glory, the One who lifts my head
high.[c]
[4]I call out to the LORD,[d]
and he answers me from his holy
mountain.[e]

[5]I lie down and sleep;[f]
I wake again,[g] because the LORD
sustains me.
[6]I will not fear[h] though tens of
thousands
assail me on every side.[i]

[7]Arise,[j] LORD!
Deliver me,[k] my God!
Strike[l] all my enemies on the
jaw;
break the teeth[m] of the
wicked.

[8]From the LORD comes deliverance.[n]
May your blessing[o] be on your
people.

3:3 [b]S Ge 15:1 [c]Ps 27:6 **3:4** [d]S Job 30:20 [e]Ps 2:6 **3:5** [f]S Lev 26:6 [g]Ps 17:15; 139:18 **3:6** [h]Job 11:15; Ps 23:4; 27:3 [i]Ps 118:11 **3:7** [j]S 2Ch 6:41 [k]Ps 6:4; 7:1; 59:1; 109:21; 119:153; Isa 25:9; 33:22; 35:4; 36:15; 37:20; Jer 42:11; Mt 6:13 [l]Job 16:10 [m]Job 29:17; Ps 57:4; Pr 30:14; La 3:16 **3:8** [n]Ps 27:1; 37:39; 62:1; Isa 43:3, 11; 44:6, 8; 45:21; Hos 13:4; Jnh 2:9; Rev 7:10 [o]Nu 6:23; Ps 29:11; 129:8

Psalm 4[a]

For the director of music. With stringed instruments. A psalm of David.

[1]Answer me[p] when I call to you,
my righteous God.
Give me relief from my distress;[q]
have mercy[r] on me and hear my
prayer.[s]

[2]How long will you people turn my
glory[t] into shame?[u]
How long will you love delusions
and seek false gods[b]?[cv]
[3]Know that the LORD has set apart his
faithful servant[w] for himself;
the LORD hears[x] when I call to him.

[a] In Hebrew texts 4:1-8 is numbered 4:2-9.
[b] 2 Or *seek lies* [c] 2 The Hebrew has *Selah* (a word of uncertain meaning) here and at the end of verse 4.

4:1 [p]Ps 13:3; 27:7; 69:16; 86:7; 102:2 [q]S Ge 32:7; S Jdg 2:15 [r]Ps 30:10 [s]Ps 17:6; 54:2; 84:8; 88:2 **4:2** [t]Ex 16:7; 1Sa 4:21 [u]2Ki 19:26; Job 8:22; Ps 35:26 [v]Jdg 2:17; Ps 31:6; 40:4; Jer 13:25; 16:19; Am 2:4 **4:3** [w]Ps 12:1; 30:4; 31:23; 79:2; Mic 7:2; 1Ti 4:7; 2Pe 3:11 [x]Ps 6:8; Mic 7:7

3:3–4 David's confidence in God, who does not fail to answer his prayers.
3:3 *shield.* That the king is a shield (protector) of his people was a common concept in ancient Israel (see NIV text notes on 7:10; 47:9; 59:11; 84:9; 89:18; Ge 15:1). That the Lord is the shield of his people is frequently asserted (see 84:11; 91:4; 115:9–11; Dt 33:29; Pr 30:5) or claimed (see 18:2,30; 28:7; 33:20; 119:114; 144:2). *my glory.* David rejoices in the Lord as his provider and protector, who has raised him to a position of honor. *lifts my head high.* In victory over his enemies (see 110:7).
3:4 *I call out … he answers.* See note on 118:5. *holy mountain.* The place of the Lord's sanctuary, the earthly counterpart of his heavenly throne room (see note on 2:6).
3:5–6 David's sense of security.
3:5 Even while David's own watchfulness is surrendered to sleep, the watchful Lord preserves him (see 4:8).
3:7–8 David's prayer.
3:7 *Arise … Deliver.* Hebrew idiom frequently prefaces an imperative calling for immediate action with a call to "arise" (see Ex 12:31, "Up!"; Dt 2:13; Jdg 7:9, "Get up"). In poetry the two imperatives of the idiom are often distributed between the two halves of the Hebrew poetic line. Hence David's prayer is: "Arise (and) deliver me." *LORD … my God.* That is, "LORD my God"; the two elements of a compound divine name are also frequently distributed between the two halves of a poetic line. *break the teeth.* Probably comparing the enemies to wild animals (see note on 7:2).
3:8 *From the LORD comes deliverance.* A common feature in the prayers of the Psalter is a concluding expression of confidence that the prayer will be or has been heard (as in 6:8–10; 7:10–17; 10:16–18; 12:7; 13:5–6 and often elsewhere; see note on 12:5–6). Here David's confidence becomes a testimony to God's people. *May your blessing be on your people.* See 25:22; 28:8–9; 51:18. Those anointed by God to rule in Israel stood before the heavenly King as his servants, responsible for the well-being of his people.
Ps 4 A prayer for relief from the threat of slanderers who falsely blame the king for some calamity (possibly a drought; see v. 7) that has stricken the nation, thereby undermining his public standing (his "glory," v. 2) and endangering the very security of his throne. Those spreading falsehoods (see v. 2 and note) appear to have looked to the king, rather than to the Lord, to preserve the nation from all disasters. See introductions to Ps 3 and 5 for links with those psalms.
4 title *For the director of music.* Probably a liturgical notation, indicating either that the psalm was to be added to the collection of works to be used by the director of music in Israel's worship services or that when the psalm was used in the temple worship it was to be spoken by the leader of the Levitical choir—or by the choir itself (see 1Ch 23:5,30; 25; Ne 11:17). In this liturgical activity the Levites functioned as representatives of the worshiping congregation. Following their lead, the people probably responded with "Amen" and "Praise the LORD" (Hallelujah); see 1Ch 16:36; Ne 5:13; cf. 1Co 14:16; Rev 5:14; 7:12; 19:4. *With stringed instruments.* See Ps 6; 54; 55; 61; 67; 76 titles (cf. Hab 3:19 and note). This is a liturgical notation, indicating that the Levites were to accompany the psalm with harp and lyre (see 1Ch 23:5; 25:1,3,6; cf. Ps 33:2; 43:4; 71:22; see also notes on Ps 39; 42 titles).
4:1 Initial request to be heard. *Answer me when I call.* See note on 118:5. *righteous.* Very often the "righteousness" of God in the Psalms (and frequently elsewhere in the OT) refers to the faithfulness with which he acts. This faithfulness is in full accordance with his commitments to his people and with his status as the divine King—to whom the powerless may look for protection, the oppressed for redress and the needy for help. *Give me relief.* Lit. "Make a spacious place for me" (see 18:19 and note). *my distress.* The threat of being publicly discredited by the slander of those who blame him for the nation's troubles.
4:2–3 David challenges those who have turned on him and warns them that the Lord will hear his prayer for deliverance from their attacks (see note on 5:9).
4:2 *How long … ?* See Introduction: Theology: Major Themes, 4; see also note on 6:3. *turn my glory into shame.* That is, through slander rob David of the public honor he had enjoyed under the Lord's blessing and care (see 3:3 and note) and bring him into public disrepute. *delusions.* Rumors and accusations that were void of any truth. *false gods.* Or, more likely here, "lies," as indicated in the NIV text note (see 5:6 and note on 5:9). For *Selah*, see NIV text note and note on 3:2.
4:3 *his faithful servant.* Hebrew *ḥasid*, which occurs 26 times in the Psalms (once of God: 145:17, "faithful"; cf. 18:25) and is usually rendered (in the plural) in

4 Tremble and[a] do not sin;[y]
when you are on your beds,[z]
search your hearts and be silent.
5 Offer the sacrifices of the righteous
and trust in the LORD.[a]

6 Many, LORD, are asking, "Who will
bring us prosperity?"
Let the light of your face shine on us.[b]
7 Fill my heart[c] with joy[d]
when their grain and new wine[e]
abound.

8 In peace[f] I will lie down and sleep,[g]
for you alone, LORD,
make me dwell in safety.[h]

Psalm 5[b]

For the director of music. For pipes.
A psalm of David.

1 Listen[i] to my words, LORD,
consider my lament.[j]
2 Hear my cry for help,[k]
my King and my God,[l]
for to you I pray.

3 In the morning,[m] LORD, you hear my
voice;
in the morning I lay my requests
before you
and wait expectantly.[n]
4 For you are not a God who is pleased
with wickedness;
with you, evil people[o] are not
welcome.
5 The arrogant[p] cannot stand[q]
in your presence.
You hate[r] all who do wrong;
6 you destroy those who tell lies.[s]
The bloodthirsty and deceitful
you, LORD, detest.
7 But I, by your great love,
can come into your house;
in reverence[t] I bow down[u]
toward your holy temple.[v]

8 Lead me, LORD, in your
righteousness[w]
because of my enemies—
make your way straight[x]
before me.
9 Not a word from their mouth can be
trusted;
their heart is filled with malice.
Their throat is an open grave;[y]
with their tongues they tell lies.[z]

4:4 [y] Eph 4:26* [z] Ps 63:6; Da 2:28 **4:5** [a] Ps 31:6; 115:9; Pr 3:5; 28:26; Isa 26:4; Jn 14:1 **4:6** [b] Nu 6:25 **4:7** [c] Ac 14:17 [d] Isa 9:3; 35:10; 65:14, 18 [e] S Ge 27:28; S Dt 28:51 **4:8** [f] S Nu 6:26; S Job 11:18 [g] S Lev 26:6 [h] S Dt 33:28; S Jer 32:37 **5:1** [i] S 1Ki 8:29; Ps 17:1; 40:1; 116:2; Da 9:18 [j] Ps 38:9; Isa 35:10; 51:11 **5:2** [k] S Job 19:7; S 24:12; S 36:5 [l] Ps 44:4; 68:24; 84:3 **5:3** [m] Isa 28:19; 50:4; Jer 21:12; Eze 46:13; Zep 3:5 [n] Ps 62:1; 119:81; 130:5; Hab 2:1; Ro 8:19 **5:4** [o] Ps 1:5; 11:5; 104:35; Pr 2:22 **5:5** [p] 2Ki 19:32; Ps 73:3; 75:4; Isa 33:19; 37:33 [q] Ps 1:5 [r] Ps 45:7; 101:3; 119:104; Pr 8:13 **5:6** [s] Pr 19:22; S Jn 8:44; Ac 5:3; Rev 21:8 **5:7** [t] Dt 13:4; Jer 44:10; Da 6:26 [u] S 2Sa 12:16; Ps 138:2 [v] S 1Ki 8:48 **5:8** [w] Ps 23:3; 31:1; 71:2; 85:13; 89:16; Pr 8:20 [x] S 1Ki 8:36; Jn 1:23 **5:9** [y] Jer 5:16; Lk 11:44 [z] Ps 12:2; 28:3; 36:3; Pr 15:4; Jer 9:8; Ro 3:13*

[a] 4 Or *In your anger* (see Septuagint) [b] In Hebrew texts 5:1-12 is numbered 5:2-13.

the NIV as "faithful (servants/people)." It is one of several Hebrew words for God's people, referring to them as people who are or should be devoted to God and faithful to him (see note on 1Sa 2:9).

4:4–5 An exhortation not to give way to anger or fear and go looking for a scapegoat (the king) on whom to lay blame for their present troubles, but to search their own hearts and put their trust in the Lord.

4:4 *Tremble and do not sin.* Paul uses these words in a different context (see Eph 4:26 and note; see also NIV text note here).

4:6 In the face of widespread uncertainty, David prays for the Lord to bless. *Who ... ?* Because of the slanders being spread, many are looking for another leader to replace the king. *will bring us prosperity.* See 34:10; 84:11; 85:12; 103:5; 107:9; cf. 16:2; Jas 1:17. *Let ... your face shine on.* David appeals to the Lord to restore the well-being of the nation—employing a common expression for favor (see note on 13:1), reminiscent of the Aaronic benediction (see Nu 6:24–26 and notes).

4:7–8 David's confidence (see note on 3:8).

4:7 *heart.* In Biblical language the center of the human spirit, from which spring emotions, thoughts, motivations, courage and action—"everything you do flows from it" (Pr 4:23).

4:8 *In peace.* Without anxiety. *I will lie down and sleep.* See 3:5 and note.

Ps 5 This morning prayer, perhaps offered at the time of the morning sacrifice, is the psalmist's cry for help when his enemies spread malicious lies to destroy him. For the structure, see stanza divisions in notes.

5 title *For the director of music.* See note on Ps 4 title. *pipes.* The Hebrew for this word occurs only here; meaning uncertain.

5:1–2 Initial appeal to be heard.

5:2 *King.* See Introduction: Theology: Major Themes.

5:3–7 Seven lines (in the Hebrew text) in which the psalmist declares that he prays to God "in the morning" "toward your holy temple" because he can be confident of God's dealings toward the wicked.

5:3 *In the morning.* See introduction to Ps 57; cf. Jer 21:12 and note.

5:5 *The arrogant.* See note on 31:23.

5:6 *tell lies.* Destroy others by slander or false testimony (see v. 9 and note).

5:7 *great love.* See note on 6:4.

5:8–11 Seven lines (in Hebrew) in which the psalmist pleads his case against his enemies, who seek to destroy him through slander.

5:8 *Lead me.* As a shepherd (see 23:3). *righteousness.* See note on 4:1. *make your way straight.* May the way down which you lead me be straight, level and smooth, free from obstacles and temptations. The psalmist prays that God will so direct him that his enemies will have no grounds for their malicious accusations (see 25:4; 27:11; 139:24; 143:8–10).

5:9–10 Accusation and call for judicial action (both are common elements in the prayers of the Psalter when the psalmist is under threat or attack from human adversaries).

5:9 *word from their mouth.* The most frequent weapon used against the psalmists is the tongue (for a striking example, see Ps 12; see also note on 10:7). The psalmists experienced that the tongue is as deadly as swords and arrows (see 55:21; 57:4; 59:7; 64:3–4; cf. Pr 12:18; 25:18). Perhaps appeals to God against those who maliciously wield the tongue are frequent in the Psalms because only in God's courtroom can a person experience redress for such attacks. *heart.* See note on 4:7. *throat ... grave.* See note on 49:14. *they tell lies.* For the plots and intrigues of enemies, usually involving lies to discredit the king and bring him down, see Ps 17; 25; 27–28; 31; 35; 41; 52; 54–57; 59; 63–64; 71; 86; 109;

10 Declare them guilty, O God!
Let their intrigues be their downfall.
Banish them for their many sins,[a]
for they have rebelled[b] against you.
11 But let all who take refuge in you be glad;
let them ever sing for joy.[c]
Spread your protection over them,
that those who love your name[d] may
rejoice in you.[e]

12 Surely, LORD, you bless the righteous;[f]
you surround them[g] with your favor
as with a shield.[h]

Psalm 6[a]

For the director of music. With stringed instruments. According to *sheminith.*[b] A psalm of David.

1 LORD, do not rebuke me in your anger[i]
or discipline me in your wrath.
2 Have mercy on me,[j] LORD, for I am
faint;[k]
heal me,[l] LORD, for my bones are in
agony.[m]
3 My soul is in deep anguish.[n]
How long,[o] LORD, how long?

4 Turn,[p] LORD, and deliver me;
save me because of your unfailing
love.[q]
5 Among the dead no one proclaims
your name.
Who praises you from the
grave?[r]

5:10 [a] La 1:5 [b] Ps 78:40; 106:7; 107:11; La 3:42 **5:11** [c] Ps 33:1; 81:1; 90:14; 92:4; 95:1; 145:7 [d] Ps 69:36; 119:132 [e] S Job 22:19 **5:12** [f] Ps 112:2 [g] Ps 32:7 [h] S Ge 15:1 **6:1** [i] S Ps 2:5 **6:2** [j] Ps 4:1; 26:11; Jer 3:12; 12:15; 31:20 [k] Ps 61:2; 77:3; 142:3; Isa 40:31; Jer 8:18; Eze 21:7 [l] S Nu 12:13 [m] Ps 22:14; 31:10; 32:3; 38:3; 42:10; 102:3 **6:3** [n] S Job 7:11; Ps 31:7; 38:8; 55:4; S Jn 12:27; Ro 9:2; 2Co 2:4 [o] 1Sa 1:14; 1Ki 18:21; Ps 4:2; 89:46; Isa 6:11; Jer 4:14; Hab 1:2; Zec 1:12 **6:4** [p] Ps 25:16; 31:2; 69:16; 71:2; 86:16; 88:2; 102:2; 119:132 [q] Ps 13:5; 31:16; 77:8; 85:7; 119:41; Isa 54:8,10 **6:5** [r] Ps 30:9; 88:10-12; 115:17; Ecc 9:10; Isa 38:18

[a] In Hebrew texts 6:1-10 is numbered 6:2-11.
[b] Title: Probably a musical term

140–141 — all psalms ascribed to David. Frequently such attacks came when the king was "low" and seemingly abandoned by God (as in Ps 25; 35; 41; 71; 86; 109). In that case he was viewed as no longer fit to be king — God was no longer with him (and so he could no longer secure the safety of the nation; see 1Sa 8:20; 11:12; 12:12; 25:28; 2Sa 3:18; 7:9–11). In any event, he was an easy prey (see 3:2; 22:7–8; 71:11). See note on 86:17. See also Paul's use of this verse in Ro 3:13.

5:10 The presence of so-called imprecations (curses) in the Psalms has occasioned endless discussion and has caused many Christians to wince, in view of Jesus' instructions to turn the other cheek and to pray for one's enemies (see Mt 5:39,44), as well as his own example on the cross (see Lk 23:34). Actually, these "imprecations" are not that at all; rather, they are appeals to God to redress wrongs perpetrated against the psalmists by imposing penalties commensurate with the violence done (see 28:4) — in accordance also with God's norm for judicial action in human courts (see Dt 25:1–3; see also 2Th 1:6; Rev 6:10; 19:2). The psalmists knew that those who have been wronged are not to avenge that wrong by their own hand but are to leave redress to the Lord, who says, "It is mine to avenge; I will repay" (Dt 32:35; see Pr 20:22; Ro 12:19). Therefore they appeal their cases to the divine Judge (see Jer 15:15). *Banish them.* From God's presence, thus from the source of blessing and life (see Ge 3:23). *rebelled against you.* By their attacks on the psalmist.

5:11 The psalmist expands his prayer to include all the godly (see note on 3:8). *your name.* The name of the Lord is the manifestation of his character (see notes on Ex 3:14–15; 34:6–7). It has no separate existence apart from the Lord but is synonymous with the Lord himself in his gracious manifestation and accessibility to his people. Hence the Jerusalem temple is the earthly residence of his Name among his people (see 74:7; Dt 12:5,11 and note on 12:5; 2Sa 7:13; Da 9:18–19), and his people can pray to him by calling on his name (see 79:6; 80:18; 99:6; 105:1; 116:4,13,17). The name of the Lord protects (see 20:1; Pr 18:10); the Lord saves by his name (see 54:1); and his saving acts testify that his name is near (see 52:9). Accordingly, the godly "trust in" his name (20:7; 33:21), "hope in" his name (52:9), "sing the praises of" his name (7:17; 9:2; 18:49) and "rejoice in" his name (89:16). Both the "love" and the "fear" that belong alone to God are similarly directed toward his name (love: 69:36; 119:132; fear: 61:5; 86:11; 102:15).

5:12 A concluding profession of confidence that God will surely protect the innocent. See note on 3:8. *righteous.* See note on 1:5.

Ps 6 A prayer in time of severe illness, an occasion seized upon by David's enemies to vent their animosity. The stanza structure is symmetrical: three verses, two verses, two verses, three verses. In early Christian liturgical tradition Ps 6 was numbered with the seven penitential psalms (the others: Ps 32; 38; 51; 102; 130; 143).

6 title See note on Ps 4 title. *According to.* Represents a Hebrew preposition of varied usage (also found in the titles of Ps 8; 12; 46; 53; 81; 84; 88). *sheminith.* Occurs also in Ps 12 title and in 1Ch 15:21. It perhaps refers to an eight-stringed instrument (see NIV text note).

6:1–3 Initial appeal for mercy. Though the Lord has sent him illness to chasten him for his sin (see 32:3–5; 38:1–8,17–18), David asks that God would not in anger impose the full measure of the penalty for sin, for then death must come (see v. 5; see also 130:3).

6:1 Ps 38 begins similarly. *rebuke . . . discipline.* That is, rebuke-and-discipline (see 39:11; see also note on 3:7). *anger . . . wrath.* See note on 2:5.

6:2 *bones.* As the inner skeleton, they here represent the whole body.

6:3 *soul.* Not a spiritual aspect in distinction from the physical, nor the psalmist's "inner" being in distinction from his "outer" being, but his very self as a living, conscious, personal being. Its use in conjunction with "bones" (also in 35:9–10: "soul" and "whole being") did not for the Hebrew writer involve reference to two distinct entities but constituted for him two ways of referring to himself, as is the case also in the combination "soul" and "body" (31:9). *How long . . . how long?* See Introduction: Theology: Major Themes, 4. Such language of impatience and complaint is found frequently in the prayers of the Psalter (usually "how long?" or "when?" or "why?"). It expresses the anguish of relief not (yet) granted and exhibits the boldness with which the psalmists wrestled with God on the basis of their relationship with him and their conviction concerning his righteousness (see note on 4:1).

6:4–5 Earnest prayer for deliverance from death.

6:4 *unfailing love.* The Hebrew for this phrase denotes a strong sense of goodwill, especially such as can be relied upon in times of need. Appeal to God's "(unfailing) love" (sometimes rendered "kindness" or "mercy" [see Jos 2:12; Hos 6:6 and notes]) is frequent in the OT since it summarizes all that the Lord covenanted to show to Israel (see Dt 7:9,12), as well as to David and his dynasty (see 89:24,28,33,49; 2Sa 7:15; Isa 55:3).

6:5 David urges that God's praise is at stake. It is the living, not the dead, who remember God's

[6]I am worn out[s] from my groaning.[t]

All night long I flood my bed with
weeping[u]
and drench my couch with tears.[v]
[7]My eyes grow weak[w] with sorrow;
they fail because of all my foes.

[8]Away from me,[x] all you who do evil,[y]
for the LORD has heard my weeping.
[9]The LORD has heard my cry for mercy;[z]
the LORD accepts my prayer.
[10]All my enemies will be overwhelmed
with shame and anguish;[a]
they will turn back and suddenly be
put to shame.[b]

Psalm 7[a]

A *shiggaion*[bc] of David, which he sang to the LORD concerning Cush, a Benjamite.

[1]LORD my God, I take refuge[d] in you;
save and deliver me[e] from all who
pursue me,[f]
[2]or they will tear me apart like a lion[g]
and rip me to pieces with no one to
rescue[h] me.

[3]LORD my God, if I have done this
and there is guilt on my hands[i]—
[4]if I have repaid my ally with evil
or without cause[j] have robbed my
foe—
[5]then let my enemy pursue and
overtake[k] me;
let him trample my life to the
ground[l]
and make me sleep in the
dust.[cm]

[6]Arise,[n] LORD, in your anger;
rise up against the rage of my
enemies.[o]
Awake,[p] my God; decree
justice.
[7]Let the assembled peoples gather
around you,
while you sit enthroned over them
on high.[q]
[8] Let the LORD judge[r] the peoples.
Vindicate me, LORD, according to my
righteousness,[s]
according to my integrity,[t] O Most
High.[u]

[a] In Hebrew texts 7:1-17 is numbered 7:2-18. [b] Title: Probably a literary or musical term [c] 5 The Hebrew has *Selah* (a word of uncertain meaning) here.

6:6 [s]S Jdg 8:5 [t]S Job 3:24; S 23:2; Ps 12:5; 77:3; 102:5; La 1:8,11,21, 22 [u]S Job 16:16 [v]S Job 7:3; Lk 7:38; Ac 20:19 **6:7** [w]S Job 16:8; Ps 31:9; 69:3; 119:82; Isa 38:14 **6:8** [x]Ps 119:115; 139:19 [y]Ps 5:5; S Mt 7:23 **6:9** [z]Ps 28:6; 116:1 **6:10** [a]S 2Ki 19:26 [b]Ps 40:14 **7:Title** [c]Hab 3:1 **7:1** [d]Ps 2:12; 11:1; 31:1 [e]S Ps 3:7 [f]Ps 31:15; 119:86,157, 161 **7:2** [g]S Ge 49:9; Rev 4:7 [h]Ps 3:2; 71:11 **7:3** [i]Isa 59:3 **7:4** [j]Ps 35:7,19; Pr 24:28 **7:5** [k]S Ex 15:9 [l]S 2Sa 22:43; 2Ki 9:33; Isa 10:6; La 3:16 [m]S Job 7:21 **7:6** [n]S 2Ch 6:41 [o]Ps 138:7 [p]Ps 35:23; 44:23 **7:7** [q]Ps 68:18 **7:8** [r]S 1Ch 16:33 [s]S 1Sa 26:23; Ps 18:20 [t]S Ge 20:5 [u]S Ge 3:5; S Nu 24:16; S Mk 5:7

---

mercies and celebrate his deliverances. The Israelites usually viewed death as they saw it—the very opposite of life. And resurrection was not yet a part of their communal experience with God. The grave brought no escape from God (see 139:8), but just how they viewed the condition of the godly dead is not clear. (Non-Biblical documents from the ancient Near East indicate a general conception that immortality was reserved for the gods but that the dead continued to have some kind of shadowy existence in the dismal netherworld.) The OT writers knew that human beings were created for life, that God's will for his people was life and that he had power over death. They also knew that death was everyone's lot, and at its proper time the godly rested in God and accepted it with equanimity (see Ge 15:15; 25:8; 47:30; 49:33; 1Ki 2:2). Death could even be a blessing for the righteous, affording escape from the greater evil that would overtake the living (see 2Ki 22:20; Isa 57:1–2). Furthermore, the death of the righteous was reputedly better than that of the wicked (see Nu 23:10). It seems clear that there was even an awareness that death (as observed) was not the end of hope for the righteous, that God had more in store for them (see especially 16:9–11; 17:15; 49:14–15; 73:24; see also note on Ge 5:24).

6:6–7 Anguish at night because of the prolongation of the illness and the barbs of the enemies.

6:6 *I am worn out from my groaning.* The very center of the poem—thus underscoring the pathos of this prayer. This literary device—of placing a key thematic line at the very center of the psalm—was frequently used (see notes on 8:4; 14:4; 34:8–14; 42:8; 47:5–6; 48:8; 54:4; 55:15; 63:6; introduction to Ps 69; 71:14; 74:12; 82:5; 86:9; 97:7; introductions to Ps 101 and 106; 113:5; introduction to Ps 138; 141:5; see also Introduction: Literary Features).

6:7 *eyes grow weak … fail.* In the vivid language of the OT the eyes are dimmed by failing strength (see 38:10; 1Sa 14:27,29 and NIV text note on v. 27; Jer 14:6), by grief (often associated with affliction: 31:9; 88:9; Job 17:7; La 2:11) and by longings unsatisfied or hope deferred (see 69:3; 119:82,123; Dt 28:32; Isa 38:14). *because of all my foes.* See note on 5:9.

6:8–10 Concluding expression of buoyant confidence (see note on 3:8).

6:10 At David's restoration, his enemies will be disgraced.

Ps 7 An appeal to the Lord's court of justice when enemies attack.

7 title *shiggaion.* See NIV text note. The word occurs only here (but see its plural in Hab 3:1). *Cush.* Not otherwise known, but as a Benjamite he was probably a supporter of Saul. Hence the title evokes Saul's determined attempts on David's life. See Introduction: Authorship and Titles (or Superscriptions).

7:1–2 Initial summation of David's appeal.

7:2 *like a lion.* As a young shepherd, David had been attacked by lions (see 1Sa 17:34–35). But it is also a convention in the Psalms to liken the attack of enemies to that of ferocious animals, especially the lion (see 10:9; 17:12; 22:12–13,16,20–21; 35:17; 57:4; 58:6; 124:6).

7:3–5 David pleads his own innocence; he has given his enemy no cause to attack him.

7:5 *me.* Lit. "my glory," a way of referring to the core of one's being (see 16:9; 30:12; 57:8; 108:1 and notes). For *Selah,* see NIV text note and note on 3:2.

7:6–9 An appeal to the Judge of all the earth to execute his judgment over all peoples, and particularly to adjudicate David's cause.

7:6 *Arise … rise up.* See note on 3:7. *anger.* See v. 11 and note on 2:5. *Awake.* The Lord does not sleep (see 121:4) while evil triumphs and the oppressed cry to him in vain (as they do to Baal; see 1Ki 18:27). But the psalmists' language of urgent prayer vividly expresses their anguished impatience with God's inaction in the face of their great need (see 80:2; see also 78:65; Isa 51:9).

7:8 *my righteousness.* See vv. 3–5. *my integrity.* See note on 15:2.

[9]Bring to an end the violence of the wicked
and make the righteous secure—[v]
you, the righteous God[w]
who probes minds and hearts.[x]

[10]My shield[a][y] is God Most High,
who saves the upright in heart.[z]
[11]God is a righteous judge,[a]
a God who displays his wrath[b] every day.
[12]If he does not relent,[c]
he[b] will sharpen his sword;[d]
he will bend and string his bow.[e]
[13]He has prepared his deadly weapons;
he makes ready his flaming arrows.[f]

[14]Whoever is pregnant with evil
conceives trouble and gives birth[g] to disillusionment.
[15]Whoever digs a hole and scoops it out
falls into the pit[h] they have made.[i]
[16]The trouble they cause recoils on them;
their violence comes down on their own heads.

[17]I will give thanks to the LORD because of his righteousness;[j]
I will sing the praises[k] of the name of the LORD Most High.[l]

Psalm 8[c]

For the director of music.
According to *gittith*.[d] A psalm of David.

[1]LORD, our Lord,
how majestic is your name[m] in all the earth!

You have set your glory[n]
in the heavens.[o]
[2]Through the praise of children and infants
you have established a stronghold[p]
against your enemies,
to silence the foe[q] and the avenger.
[3]When I consider your heavens,[r]
the work of your fingers,[s]
the moon and the stars,[t]
which you have set in place,

7:9 [v]Ps 37:23; 40:2 [w]Jer 11:20 [x]S 1Ch 28:9; Ps 26:2; Rev 2:23 **7:10** [y]Ps 3:3 [z]S Job 33:3 **7:11** [a]S Ge 18:25; Ps 9:8; 67:4; 75:2; 96:13; 98:9; Isa 11:4; Jer 11:20 [b]S Dt 9:8 **7:12** [c]Eze 3:19; 33:9 [d]S Dt 32:41 [e]S 2Sa 22:35; Ps 21:12; Isa 5:28; 13:18 **7:13** [f]Ps 11:2; 18:14; 64:3 **7:14** [g]Isa 59:4; Jas 1:15 **7:15** [h]Ps 35:7, 8; 40:2; 94:13; Pr 26:27 [i]S Job 4:8 **7:17** [j]Ps 5:8 [k]S 2Ch 31:2; Ro 15:11; Heb 2:12 [l]S Ge 14:18 **8:1** [m]S 1Ch 16:10 [n]S Ex 15:11; Lk 2:9 [o]Ps 57:5; 108:5; 113:4; 148:13; Hab 3:3 **8:2** [p]Mt 21:16* [q]Ps 143:12 **8:3** [r]S Ge 15:5; S Dt 10:14 [s]S Ex 8:19; S 1Ch 16:26; S 2Ch 2:12; Ps 102:25 [t]S Ge 1:16; 1Co 15:41

[a] 10 Or *sovereign* [b] 12 Or *If anyone does not repent, / God* [c] In Hebrew texts 8:1-9 is numbered 8:2-10. [d] Title: Probably a musical term

7:9 *the righteous.* See note on 1:5. *righteous God.* See note on 4:1. *minds and hearts.* Lit. "hearts and kidneys." The Israelites used the words as virtual synonyms (but "heart" most often) to refer to the innermost center of one's conscious life (see note on 4:7). To "search mind and heart" was a conventional expression for God's examination of one's hidden character and motives (see Jer 11:20; 17:10; 20:12; Rev 2:23 and note).
7:10–13 David's confidence that his prayer will be heard (see note on 3:8).
7:10 *shield.* See note on 3:3. *heart.* See note on 4:7.
7:11 *every day.* God's judgments are not all kept in store for some future day.
7:12–13 *sword ... bow ... flaming arrows.* The weapons of the heavenly Warrior King used in defense of his people (see Ex 15:3 and note) but also in judgment.
7:12 *his bow.* See note on Ge 9:13.
7:14–16 David comforts himself with the common wisdom that under God's rule "crime does not pay."
7:15 *digs a hole.* A metaphor from the hunt; pits were used to trap animals (see 9:15 and note).
7:16 *recoils on them.* See note on Pr 26:27.
7:17 A vow to praise God. Many prayers in the Psalter include such vows in anticipation of the expected answer to prayer. They reflect Israel's religious consciousness that praise must follow deliverance as surely as prayer springs from need—if God is to be truly honored. Such praise was usually offered with thank offerings and involved celebrating God's saving act in the presence of those assembled at the temple (see 50:14–15,23; see also note on 9:1). *name of the LORD.* See note on 5:11. *Most High.* See note on Ge 14:19.
Ps 8 In praise of the Creator (not of human beings—as is evident from the doxology that encloses it, vv. 1,9; see also note on 9:1) out of wonder over his sovereign ordering of the creation. Ge 1 (particularly vv. 26–28) clearly provides the lenses, but David speaks out of his present experience of reality. Two matters especially impressed him: (1) the glory of God reflected in the starry heavens, and (2) the astonishing condescension of God to be mindful of puny mortals, to crown them with glory almost godlike and to grant them lordly power over his other creatures. At this juncture in the Psalter this psalm surprises. After five psalms (and 64 Hebrew poetic lines—following Ps 1–2, which introduce the Psalter; see introduction to Ps 1–2) in which the psalmists have called on Yahweh to deal with human perversity, this psalm's praise of Yahweh for his astounding endowment of the human race with royal "glory and honor" (v. 5) serves as a striking and unexpected counterpoint. Its placement here highlights the glory (God's gift) and disgrace (humanity's own doing) that characterize human beings and the corresponding range of differences in God's dealings with them. And after five more psalms (and 64 poetic lines), this psalm in turn receives a counterpoint (see introduction to Ps 14; see also chart, p. 852, and introduction to Ps 3–14).
8 title *For the director of music.* See note on Ps 4 title. *According to.* See note on Ps 6 title. *gittith.* See Ps 81; 84 titles. The Hebrew word perhaps refers to either a winepress ("song of the winepress") or the Philistine city of Gath ("Gittite lyre or music"; see 2Sa 15:18).
8:1a *name.* See note on 5:11.
8:1b–2 The mighty God, whose glory is displayed across the face of the heavens, appoints (and evokes) the praise of little children to silence the dark powers arrayed against him (for a NT application, see Mt 21:16).
8:2 *avenger.* See 44:16; one who strikes back in malicious revenge deprives God of a prerogative that is his alone (see 9:11–12; Dt 32:35 and note).
8:3–5 The vastness and majesty of the heavens as the handiwork of God (see 19:1–6; 104:19–23) evoke wonder for what their Maker has done for human beings, who are here today and gone tomorrow (see 144:3–4). (See Job 7:17–21 for Job's complaint that God takes humans too seriously.)
8:3 *fingers.* See note on Ex 8:19; see also photo, p. 865.

4 what is mankind that you are mindful
of them,
human beings that you care for
them?[a][u]

Babylonian boundary stone. A seated person, perhaps a priest, is worshiping the four main Babylonian deities: Ishtar, the goddess of love and fertility, symbolized by the star; the moon-god Sin; the sun-god Shamash; and the goddess Ishara, symbolized by the scorpion. The author of Psalm 8 recognizes the Lord as the creator of "the moon and the stars" (8:3).

Z. Radovan/www.BibleLandPictures.com

5 You have made them[b] a little lower
than the angels[c][v]
and crowned them[b] with glory and
honor.[w]
6 You made them rulers[x] over the works
of your hands;[y]
you put everything under their[d]
feet:[z]
7 all flocks and herds,[a]
and the animals of the wild,[b]
8 the birds in the sky,
and the fish in the sea,[c]
all that swim the paths of the seas.

9 LORD, our Lord,
how majestic is your name in all the
earth![d]

Psalm 9[e,f]

For the director of music. To the tune of "The Death of the Son." A psalm of David.

1 I will give thanks to you, LORD, with all
my heart;[e]
I will tell of all your wonderful
deeds.[f]
2 I will be glad and rejoice[g] in you;
I will sing the praises[h] of your name,[i]
O Most High.

8:4 [u]S 1Ch 29:14
8:5 [v]S Ge 1:26 [w]Ps 21:5; 103:4
8:6 [x]S Ge 1:28 [y]S Job 10:3; Ps 19:1; 102:25; 145:10; Isa 26:12; 29:23; 45:11; Heb 1:10 [z]S 1Ki 5:3; 1Co 15:25, 27*; Eph 1:22; Heb 2:6-8*
8:7 [a]Ge 13:5; 26:14 [b]S Ge 2:19
8:8 [c]Ge 1:26
8:9 [d]ver 1
9:1 [e]Ps 86:12; 111:1; 119:2, 10, 145; 138:1 [f]S Dt 4:34
9:2 [g]S Job 22:19; Ps 14:7; 31:7; 70:4; 97:8; 126:3; Pr 23:15; Isa 25:9; Jer 30:19; Joel 2:21; Zep 3:14; S Mt 5:12; Rev 19:7 [h]S 2Ch 31:2 [i]Ps 92:1

[a] 4 Or *what is a human being that you are mindful of him, / a son of man that you care for him?* [b] 5 Or *him* [c] 5 Or *than God* [d] 6 Or *made him ruler . . . ; / . . . his* [e] Psalms 9 and 10 may originally have been a single acrostic poem in which alternating lines began with the successive letters of the Hebrew alphabet. In the Septuagint they constitute one psalm. [f] In Hebrew texts 9:1-20 is numbered 9:2-21.

8:4–6 Heb 2:6–8, quoting the Septuagint (the pre-Christian Greek translation of the OT), applies these verses to Jesus, who as the incarnate Son of God is both the representative human being and the one in whom humanity's appointed destiny will be fully realized. The author of Hebrews thus makes use of the eschatological implications of these words in his testimony to Christ. Paul does the same with v. 6 in 1Co 15:27 (see also Eph 1:22 and note).

8:4 *what . . . ?* The Hebrew for this word is translated "how" in vv. 1,9 and begins the line that serves as the center of the psalm (see note on 6:6). *are mindful of.* Lit. "remember" (see note on Ge 8:1). *human beings.* See NIV text note. "Son of man" is a literal translation of a Hebrew phrase commonly used to refer to a human being (see 80:17; 144:3; see also note on Eze 2:1 and NIV text note there).

8:5 *angels.* The exalted creatures that surround God in his heavenly realm (as, e.g., in Isa 6:2); but see NIV text note.

8:6–8 See Ge 1:26–27. The power to exercise rule over some of God's creatures is even now a part of humanity's "glory and honor" (v. 5). The full realization of that potential—and vocation—belongs to humanity's appointed destiny (the eschatological import drawn on by Paul and the author of Hebrews; see note on vv. 4–6). But this power—and vocation—to rule is not absolute or independent. It is participation, but not as an equal, in God's rule; and it is a gift, not a right.

8:9 Repeated verbatim from v. 1a (see note there).

Ps 9 That Ps 9 and 10 were sometimes viewed (or used) as one psalm is known from the Septuagint (the pre-Christian Greek translation of the OT; see NIV text note). Whether they were originally composed as one psalm is not known, though a number of indicators point in that direction. Ps 10 is the only psalm from Ps 3 to 32 that has no superscription, and the Hebrew text of the two psalms together appears to reflect an incomplete (or broken) acrostic structure. The first letter of each verse or pair of verses tends to follow the order of the Hebrew alphabet near the beginning of Ps 9 and again near the end of Ps 10. The thoughts also tend to be developed in two-verse units throughout. Ps 9 is predominantly praise (by the king) for God's deliverance from hostile nations. It concludes with a short prayer for God's continuing righteous judgments (see v. 4) on the haughty nations. For other lengthy prefaces to prayer, see Ps 40; 44; 89. Ps 10 is predominantly prayer against the unscrupulous people within the realm. The attacks of "the wicked" (9:5; 10:4), whether from within or from without, on the godly community are equally threatening to true Israel. Praise of God's past deliverances is often an integral part of prayer in the Psalter (see 3:3–4,8 and notes; 25:6; 40:1–5), as also in other ancient Near Eastern prayers. Probably Ps 9–10 came to be separated for the purpose of separate liturgical use, as did Ps 42–43 (see introduction there).

9 title *For the director of music.* See note on Ps 4 title. *To the tune of.* See titles of Ps 22; 45; 56–60; 69; 75; 80; see also NIV text note on Ps 88 title. Nothing more is known of the apparent tune titles.

9:1–2 Initial announcement of praise.

9:1 *heart.* See note on 4:7. *tell of.* The praise of God in the Psalter is rarely a private matter between the psalmist and the Lord. It is usually a public (at the temple)

3 My enemies turn back;
they stumble and perish before
you.
4 For you have upheld my right[j] and
my cause,[k]
sitting enthroned[l] as the righteous
judge.[m]
5 You have rebuked the nations[n] and
destroyed the wicked;
you have blotted out their name[o] for
ever and ever.
6 Endless ruin has overtaken my
enemies,
you have uprooted their cities;[p]
even the memory of them[q] has
perished.

7 The LORD reigns forever;[r]
he has established his throne[s] for
judgment.
8 He rules the world in righteousness[t]
and judges the peoples with
equity.[u]
9 The LORD is a refuge[v] for the
oppressed,[w]
a stronghold in times of trouble.[x]
10 Those who know your name[y] trust in
you,
for you, LORD, have never forsaken[z]
those who seek you.[a]

11 Sing the praises[b] of the LORD,
enthroned in Zion;[c]
proclaim among the nations[d] what
he has done.[e]
12 For he who avenges blood[f]
remembers;
he does not ignore the cries of the
afflicted.[g]

13 LORD, see how my enemies[h] persecute
me!
Have mercy[i] and lift me up from
the gates of death,[j]
14 that I may declare your praises[k]
in the gates of Daughter
Zion,[l]
and there rejoice in your
salvation.[m]

15 The nations have fallen into the
pit they have dug;[n]
their feet are caught in the net
they have hidden.[o]
16 The LORD is known by his acts of
justice;
the wicked are ensnared by the
work of their hands.[a] [p]
17 The wicked go down to the realm of
the dead,[q]
all the nations that forget God.[r]

[a] *16* The Hebrew has *Higgaion* and *Selah* (words of uncertain meaning) here; *Selah* occurs also at the end of verse 20.

9:4 [j] S 1Ki 8:45 [k] S Job 16:21 [l] Ps 11:4; 47:8; Isa 6:1 [m] Ps 7:11; 67:4; 98:9; 1Pe 2:23 **9:5** [n] Ge 20:7; S 37:10; S 1Ch 16:21; Ps 59:5; 105:14; Isa 26:14; 66:15 [o] S Job 18:17 **9:6** [p] S Dt 29:28; Jer 2:3; 46:1-51:58; Zep 2:8-10 [q] Ps 34:16; 109:15; Ecc 9:5; Isa 14:22; 26:14 **9:7** [r] S 1Ch 16:31; Rev 19:6 [s] Ps 11:4; 47:8; 93:2; Isa 6:1; 66:1 **9:8** [t] S ver 4; Ps 7:11 [u] Ps 11:7; 45:6; 72:2 **9:9** [v] S Dt 33:27; S 2Sa 22:3 [w] Ps 10:18; 74:21 [x] Ps 32:7; 121:7 **9:10** [y] Ps 91:14 [z] S Ge 28:15; S Dt 4:31; Ps 22:1; 37:25; 71:11; Isa 49:14; Jer 15:18; Heb 13:5 [a] Ps 70:4 **9:11** [b] Ps 7:17 [c] S Ps 2:6 [d] Ps 18:49; 44:11; 57:9; 106:27; Isa 24:13; Eze 20:23; 1Ti 3:16 [e] Ps 105:1 **9:12** [f] S 2Sa 4:11 [g] ver 18; Ps 10:17; 22:24; 72:4; Isa 49:13 **9:13** [h] Nu 10:9; Ps 3:7; 18:3 [i] Ps 6:2; 41:4; 51:1; 86:3, 16; 119:132 [j] S Job 17:16; Mt 16:18 **9:14** [k] Ps 51:15; 1Pe 2:9 [l] 2Ki 19:21; Isa 1:8; 10:32; 37:22; 62:11; Jer 4:31; 6:2; La 1:6; Mic 1:13; Zep 3:14; Zec 2:10; Mt 21:5; Jn 12:15 [m] Ps 13:5; 35:9; 50:23; 51:12 **9:15** [n] S Job 4:8; Ps 35:7 [o] Ps 35:8; 57:6 **9:16** [p] Pr 5:22 **9:17** [q] S Nu 16:30; Pr 5:5 [r] S Job 8:13

celebration of God's holy virtues or of his saving acts or gracious bestowal of blessings. In his praise the psalmist proclaims to the assembled throng God's glorious attributes or his righteous (see note on 4:1) deeds (see, e.g., 22:22–31; 56:12–13; 61:8; 65:1; 69:30–33). To this is usually added a call to praise God, summoning all who hear to take up the praise—to acknowledge and joyfully celebrate God's glory, his goodness and all his righteous acts. This aspect of praise in the Psalms has rightly been called the OT anticipation of NT evangelism. *wonderful deeds.* God's saving acts, sometimes involving miracles and sometimes not, but always involving the manifestation of God's sovereign lordship over events. Here reference is to the destruction of the enemies celebrated in this psalm.

9:2,10 *your name.* See note on 5:11.

9:2 *Most High.* See note on Ge 14:19.

9:3–6 In destroying the enemies, God has redressed the wrongs committed by them against David (and Israel).

9:4 *enthroned.* See note on v. 7.

9:5 *blotted out their name.* As if from a register of all living persons written on a papyrus scroll (see Nu 5:23; see also Dt 9:14; 25:19; 29:20; 2Ki 14:27).

9:7–10 Celebration of the righteous rule of God (see note on 4:1; see also Ps 93; 96–99), which evokes trust on the part of those who look to the Lord.

9:7 *his throne.* In heaven (see 11:4). See also v. 4.

9:8 See Ac 17:31.

9:10 *Those who know your name.* Those who acknowledge in their hearts who the Lord is and also live out that acknowledgment (see 91:14; see also note on 5:11).

9:11–12 A call to the assembly at the temple to take up the praise of God for his righteous judgments (see note on v. 1).

9:11 *enthroned in Zion.* God's heavenly throne (see v. 7) has its counterpart on earth in his temple at Jerusalem, from which center he rules the world (see 2:6; 3:4 and notes; 20:2). For God's election of Zion as the seat of his rule, see 132:13; see also Introduction: Theology: Major Themes, 7.

9:12 *he who avenges blood.* See Dt 32:41,43.

9:13–14 Perhaps a recollection of David's prayer ("the cries of the afflicted," v. 12), which the Lord has now answered.

9:13 *gates of death.* See Job 17:16 and note.

9:14 *declare.* See notes on v. 1; 7:17. *gates.* Having been thrust down by the attacks of his enemies to "the gates of death" (v. 13), David prayed to be lifted up so he could celebrate his deliverance (see note on v. 1) in "the gates of … Zion." *Daughter Zion.* A personification of Jerusalem (see note on 2Ki 19:21).

9:15–18 Under the Lord's just rule, those who wickedly attack others bring destruction on themselves (see 7:14–16 and note), and their end will be the grave. But those who are attacked ("the needy," v. 18) will not trust in the Lord in vain.

9:15 *pit … dug … net … hidden.* In the Psalter, imagery drawn from the hunt is frequently (in 14 psalms) employed to depict the cunning attacks of enemies who sought to destroy by hidden means or surprise attacks, the tongue being the most common weapon (see 5:9 and note). In ancient times hunters used snares, traps, nets and pits, often in combination, and always involving concealment. See note on Pr 26:27.

9:16 For *Selah*, see NIV text note and note on 3:2.

9:17 *forget.* Take no account of.

18 But God will never forget the needy;
the hope[s] of the afflicted[t] will never perish.
19 Arise,[u] LORD, do not let mortals triumph;[v]
let the nations be judged[w] in your presence.
20 Strike them with terror,[x] LORD;
let the nations know they are only mortal.[y]

Psalm 10[a]

1 Why, LORD, do you stand far off?[z]
Why do you hide yourself[a] in times of trouble?

2 In his arrogance the wicked man hunts down the weak,[b]
who are caught in the schemes he devises.
3 He boasts[c] about the cravings of his heart;
he blesses the greedy and reviles the LORD.[d]
4 In his pride the wicked man does not seek him;
in all his thoughts there is no room for God.[e]
5 His ways are always prosperous;
your laws are rejected by[b] him;
he sneers at all his enemies.
6 He says to himself, "Nothing will ever shake me."
He swears, "No one will ever do me harm."[f]

7 His mouth is full[g] of lies and threats;[h]
trouble and evil are under his tongue.[i]
8 He lies in wait[j] near the villages;
from ambush he murders the innocent.[k]
His eyes watch in secret for his victims;
9 like a lion in cover he lies in wait.
He lies in wait to catch the helpless;[l]
he catches the helpless and drags them off in his net.[m]
10 His victims are crushed,[n] they collapse;
they fall under his strength.
11 He says to himself, "God will never notice;[o]
he covers his face and never sees."[p]

12 Arise,[q] LORD! Lift up your hand,[r] O God.
Do not forget the helpless.[s]
13 Why does the wicked man revile God?[t]
Why does he say to himself,
"He won't call me to account"?[u]
14 But you, God, see the trouble[v] of the afflicted;
you consider their grief and take it in hand.
The victims commit themselves to you;[w]
you are the helper[x] of the fatherless.
15 Break the arm of the wicked man;[y]
call the evildoer to account for his wickedness
that would not otherwise be found out.

9:18 [s] Ps 25:3; 39:7; 71:5; Pr 23:18; Jer 14:8 [t] ver 12; Ps 74:19 **9:19** [u] Ps 3:7 [v] 2Ch 14:11 [w] Ps 110:6; Isa 2:4; Joel 3:12 **9:20** [x] S Ge 35:5; Ps 31:13; Isa 13:8; Lk 21:26 [y] Ps 62:9; Isa 31:3; Eze 28:2 **10:1** [z] Ps 22:1, 11; 35:22; 38:21; 71:12 [a] Ps 13:1 **10:2** [b] ver 9; S Job 20:19 **10:3** [c] Ps 49:6; 94:4; Jer 48:30 [d] S Job 1:5 **10:4** [e] Ps 36:1 **10:6** [f] Rev 18:7 **10:7** [g] Ro 3:14* [h] Ps 73:8; 119:134; Ecc 4:1; Isa 30:12 [i] S Job 20:12 **10:8** [j] Ps 37:32; 59:3; 71:10; Pr 1:11; Jer 5:26; Mic 7:2 [k] Hos 6:9 **10:9** [l] S ver 2 [m] S Job 18:8 **10:10** [n] S Job 9:17 **10:11** [o] Job 22:13; Ps 42:9; 77:9 [p] S Job 22:14 **10:12** [q] Ps 3:7 [r] Ps 17:7; 20:6; 106:26; Isa 26:11; Mic 5:9 [s] Ps 9:12 **10:13** [t] ver 3 [u] S Job 31:14 **10:14** [v] ver 7; Ps 22:11 [w] Ps 37:5 [x] S Dt 33:29 **10:15** [y] S Job 31:22

[a] Psalms 9 and 10 may originally have been a single acrostic poem in which alternating lines began with the successive letters of the Hebrew alphabet. In the Septuagint they constitute one psalm. [b] 5 See Septuagint; Hebrew / *they are haughty, and your laws are far from*

9:18 *God will never forget.* Those who forget God will come to nothing, but the needy and afflicted will not be forgotten by God (see v. 12). *needy ... afflicted.* In this psalm David and Israel are counted among them because of the threat from the enemies.
9:19–20 A prayer at the conclusion of praise, asking that the Lord may ever rule over the nations as he has done in the event here celebrated—that those who "forget God" (v. 17) may know that they are only weak mortals, not gods, and cannot withstand the God of Israel (see 10:18).
9:19 *Arise.* See note on 3:7.
Ps 10 A prayer for rescue from the attacks of unscrupulous people—containing a classic OT portrayal of "the wicked" (v. 4). See introduction to Ps 9.
10:1 See note on 6:3.
10:2–11 Accusation lodged against the oppressors (see note on 5:9–10). Here the psalmist launches into a characterization of oppressors in general. Their deeds betray the arrogance (see vv. 2–5—so long as they prosper, v. 5) with which they defy God (see vv. 3–4,13; see especially their words in vv. 6,11,13). They greedily seek to glut their unrestrained appetites (see v. 3) by victimizing others, taking account of neither God (see v. 4) nor his law (see v. 5).
10:2 *hunts ... caught.* The psalmists often use imagery from the hunt (see vv. 8–9 and note on v. 9).
10:3 *heart.* See note on 4:7.
10:4 The wicked do not consider that they have God to contend with (see note on v. 11; see also 14:1; 36:1; 53:1).
10:6 See vv. 11,13 and note on 3:2. *to himself.* Lit. "in his heart" (also in vv. 11,13); see note on 4:7. *shake me.* Take away my well-being, destroy my security.
10:7 *lies and threats.* The two most common weapons of the tongue in Israel's experience (see note on 5:9). *lies.* Slander and false testimony for malicious purposes (see, e.g., 1Ki 21:8–15).
10:9 See note on 7:2. *lies in wait.* The imagery shifts from the lion to the hunter (see note on 9:15).
10:11 See note on 3:2. The arrogance with which the wicked speak (see 17:10), especially their easy dismissal of God's knowledge of their evil acts and his unfailing prosecution of their malicious deeds, is frequently noted by the psalmists (see v. 13; 12:4; 42:3,10; 59:7; 64:5; 71:11; 73:11; 94:7; 115:2; see also Isa 29:15; Eze 8:12).
10:12–15 Prayer that God will call the wicked to account.
10:12 *Arise.* See note on 3:7. *forget.* See 9:18. *helpless.* Those at the mercy of the oppressors (see v. 9).
10:13 *Why ... ? Why ... ?* See note on 6:3.
10:14 Appeal to God's righteous rule (see 5:4–6).
10:15 *Break the arm.* Destroy the power to oppress. *call the evildoer to account.* Humble such arrogance (see v. 13) with your righteous judgment.

16 The LORD is King for ever and ever;[z]
the nations[a] will perish from his land.
17 You, LORD, hear the desire of the afflicted;[b]
you encourage them, and you listen to their cry,[c]
18 defending the fatherless[d] and the oppressed,[e]
so that mere earthly mortals
will never again strike terror.

Psalm 11

For the director of music. Of David.

1 In the LORD I take refuge.[f]
How then can you say to me:
"Flee[g] like a bird to your mountain.[h]
2 For look, the wicked bend their bows;[i]
they set their arrows[j] against the strings
to shoot from the shadows[k]
at the upright in heart.[l]
3 When the foundations[m] are being destroyed,
what can the righteous do?"

4 The LORD is in his holy temple;[n]
the LORD is on his heavenly throne.[o]
He observes everyone on earth;[p]
his eyes examine[q] them.
5 The LORD examines the righteous,[r]
but the wicked, those who love violence,
he hates with a passion.[s]
6 On the wicked he will rain
fiery coals and burning sulfur;[t]
a scorching wind[u] will be their lot.

7 For the LORD is righteous,[v]
he loves justice;[w]
the upright[x] will see his face.[y]

Psalm 12[a]

For the director of music. According to *sheminith*.[b] A psalm of David.

1 Help, LORD, for no one is faithful anymore;[z]
those who are loyal have vanished from the human race.
2 Everyone lies[a] to their neighbor;
they flatter with their lips
but harbor deception in their hearts.[b]

3 May the LORD silence all flattering lips[c]
and every boastful tongue—[d]

10:16 [z]S Ex 15:18 [a]S Dt 8:20 **10:17** [b]S Ps 9:12 [c]S Ex 22:23 **10:18** [d]S Dt 24:17; Ps 146:9 [e]S Ps 9:9 **11:1** [f]S Ps 7:1 [g]S Ge 14:10 [h]Ps 50:11 **11:2** [i]S 2Sa 22:35 [j]S Ps 7:13; S 58:7 [k]Ps 10:8 [l]S Job 33:3; Ps 7:10 **11:3** [m]Ps 18:15; 82:5; Isa 24:18 **11:4** [n]S 1Ki 8:48; Ps 18:6; 27:4; Jnh 2:7; Mic 1:2; Hab 2:20 [o]S 2Ch 6:18; S Ps 9:7; Mt 5:34; 23:22; S Rev 4:2 [p]Pr 15:3 [q]Ps 33:18; 66:7 **11:5** [r]S Dt 7:13; S Job 23:10 [s]S Job 28:28; Ps 5:5; 45:7; Isa 1:14 **11:6** [t]S Ge 19:24; S Rev 9:17 [u]S Ge 41:6; S Job 1:19 **11:7** [v]S 2Ch 12:6; S Ezr 9:15; 2Ti 4:8 [w]S Ps 9:8; 33:5; 99:4; Isa 28:17; 30:18; 56:1; 61:8; Jer 9:24 [x]S Job 1:1; Lk 23:50 [y]Ps 17:15; 140:13 **12:1** [z]Isa 57:1; Mic 7:2 **12:2** [a]Ps 5:6; 34:13; 141:3; Pr 6:19; 12:17; 13:3; Isa 32:7 [b]S Ps 5:9; Ro 16:18 **12:3** [c]Pr 26:28; 28:23 [d]Ps 73:9; Da 7:8; Jas 3:5; Rev 13:5

[a] In Hebrew texts 12:1-8 is numbered 12:2-9.
[b] Title: Probably a musical term

10:16–18 The psalmist's confidence in the righteous reign of the Lord (see note on 3:8). Reference to the nations (v. 16) and to the humbling of proud humans (see v. 18; see also 9:19–20) suggests links with Ps 9. As the conclusion to Ps 10, this stanza expands the vision of God's just rule to its universal scope and sets the purging of the Lord's land of all nations that do not acknowledge him (see v. 16) alongside God's judicial dealing with the wicked oppressors.
10:18 *mere earthly mortals.* Who are not God and so constitute no ultimate threat (see 49:12,20; 56:4,11; 62:9; 78:39; 103:14–16; 118:6,8–9; 144:4; Isa 31:3; Jer 17:5).
Ps 11 A confession of confident trust in the Lord's righteous rule, at a time when wicked adversaries seem to have the upper hand. Two four-line stanzas (in the Hebrew text: vv. 1–3,4–6) are followed by a climactic profession of confident faith (v. 7).
11 title *For the director of music.* See note on Ps 4 title.
11:1–3 David testifies of his unshakable trust in the Lord (his refuge) to apprehensive people around him. These people, seeing the power and underhandedness of the enemy (they "shoot from the shadows," v. 2), fear that the foundations (v. 3) are crumbling and that flight to a mountain refuge is the only recourse. David dismisses their fearful advice with disdain.
11:2 It is not clear whether those who wield the bows and arrows are archers or false accusers (see 57:4; 64:3–4; see also note on 5:9). *heart.* See note on 4:7.
11:3 *foundations.* Of the world order (see 82:5). To those who counsel flight, the powerful upsurge of evil appears to indicate that the righteous can no longer count on a world order in which good triumphs over evil. *righteous.* See note on 1:5.
11:4–7 Reply to the fearful: The Lord is still securely on his heavenly throne. And the righteous Lord (see v. 7) discerns the righteous (see v. 5) to give them a place in his presence (see v. 7), while his judgment will "rain" (v. 6) on the wicked.
11:4 *The LORD is in his holy temple.* Repeated verbatim in Hab 2:20. Here reference is to his heavenly temple.
11:6 Perhaps recalling God's judgment on Sodom and Gomorrah (see Ge 19:24,28; see also Rev 14:10 and note; 20:10; 21:8). *their lot.* Lit. "the portion of their cup" (see 75:8 and note on 16:5).
11:7 *righteous.* See note on 4:1. *the upright.* Those concerning whom the fearful despaired (see v. 2). *see his face.* The Hebrew for "see the king's face" was an expression denoting access to the king (see Ge 43:3,5; 44:23,26; 2Sa 3:13, "come into my presence"; 14:24,28,32). Sometimes it referred to those who served before the king (see 2Ki 25:19, "royal advisers"; Est 1:14, those "who had special access to the king"). Here David speaks of special freedom of access before the heavenly King. Reference is no doubt to his presence at God's earthly temple, but ultimate access to the heavenly temple may also be implied (see 16:11; 17:15; see also 23:6; 140:13).
Ps 12 A prayer for help when it seems that everyone is faithless and every tongue false (see Mic 7:1–7). The psalm is composed of four couplets (vv. 1–2,3–4,5–6,7–8), framed by references to the prevailing evil in the "human race" (vv. 1,8).
12 title *For the director of music.* See note on Ps 4 title. *According to sheminith.* See note on Ps 6 title.
12:1–2 Initial appeal, with description of the cause of distress.
12:1 *faithful.* See note on 4:3. *those who are loyal.* Those who maintain moral integrity.
12:2 See 5:9 and note.
12:3–4 The prayer.
12:3 *silence.* Put an end to. *boastful.* See note on 10:2–11.

4 those who say,
"By our tongues we will prevail;[e]
our own lips will defend us — who is
lord over us?"

5 "Because the poor are plundered[f] and
the needy groan,[g]
I will now arise,[h]" says the LORD.
"I will protect them[i] from those who
malign them."
6 And the words of the LORD are flawless,[j]
like silver purified[k] in a crucible,[l]
like gold[a] refined seven times.

7 You, LORD, will keep the needy safe[m]
and will protect us forever from the
wicked,[n]
8 who freely strut[o] about
when what is vile is honored by the
human race.

Psalm 13[b]

For the director of music. A psalm of David.

1 How long,[p] LORD? Will you forget me[q]
forever?
How long will you hide your face[r]
from me?
2 How long must I wrestle with my
thoughts[s]
and day after day have sorrow in my
heart?
How long will my enemy triumph
over me?[t]

3 Look on me[u] and answer,[v] LORD my
God.
Give light to my eyes,[w] or I will sleep
in death,[x]
4 and my enemy will say, "I have
overcome him,[y]"
and my foes will rejoice when I fall.[z]

5 But I trust in your unfailing love;[a]
my heart rejoices in your salvation.[b]
6 I will sing[c] the LORD's praise,
for he has been good to me.

Psalm 14

14:1-7pp — Ps 53:1-6

For the director of music. Of David.

1 The fool[c] says in his heart,
"There is no God."[d]
They are corrupt, their deeds are
vile;
there is no one who does good.

12:4 [e]Pr 18:21; Jas 3:6 **12:5** [f]Ps 44:24; 62:10; 72:14; 73:8; Ecc 4:1; 5:8; Isa 3:15; 5:7; 30:12; 59:13; Ac 7:34 [g]S Ps 6:6 [h]Ps 3:7 [i]Ps 34:6; 35:10 **12:6** [j]S 2Sa 22:31; Ps 18:30 [k]S Job 23:10; S 28:1; Isa 48:10; Zec 13:9 [l]Ps 119:140 **12:7** [m]Ps 16:1; 27:5 [n]Ps 37:28; Jn 17:12 **12:8** [o]Ps 55:10-11 **13:1** [p]Ps 6:3 [q]Ps 42:9; La 5:20 [r]S Dt 31:17; S Ps 22:24; S Isa 8:17; S 54:9 **13:2** [s]Ps 42:4; 55:2; 139:23; Isa 33:18; Da 7:28 [t]Ps 94:3 **13:3** [u]Ps 9:12; 25:18; 31:7; 35:23; 59:4; 80:14; 107:41; 119:50,153 [v]S Ps 4:1 [w]S Ezr 9:8 [x]Ps 76:5; 90:5; Jer 51:39

[a] *6* Probable reading of the original Hebrew text; Masoretic Text *earth* [b] In Hebrew texts 13:1-6 is numbered 13:2-6. [c] *1* The Hebrew words rendered *fool* in Psalms denote one who is morally deficient.

13:4 [y]S 1Ki 19:2; Ps 25:2 [z]Ps 38:16; 118:13 **13:5** [a]S Ps 6:4 [b]S Job 33:26; Ps 9:14; Isa 25:9; 33:2 **13:6** [c]S Ex 15:1; Ps 7:17 **14:1** [d]Ps 10:4

12:4 See notes on 3:2; 10:11.
12:5-6 A reassuring word from the Lord. Such words of assurance following prayer in the Psalms were perhaps spoken by a priest (see 1Sa 1:17) or a prophet (see 51:8 and note; 2Sa 12:13).
12:5 *I will now arise.* See Isa 33:10.
12:6 *words of the LORD.* Set in sharp contrast to the boastful words of the adversaries; they are as flawless as thoroughly refined silver. *crucible.* In the metallurgy of the ancient Near East, heating in special furnaces was used to extract silver and gold from crushed ore and to remove the dross (base metals such as copper, tin, iron, bronze and lead). This process provided vivid metaphors for many of Israel's poets (see 66:10; Pr 17:3; 27:21; Isa 1:22a,25; 48:10; Jer 6:27-30; 9:7; Eze 22:17-22; Zec 13:9; Mal 3:3). *seven.* Signifies fullness or completeness — here thoroughness of refining.
12:7-8 Concluding expression of confidence (see note on 3:8).
12:7 *the wicked.* The enemies of v. 5.
12:8 David is confident, even though at the present time the wicked think they have the upper hand (see vv. 1-4).
Ps 13 A cry to the Lord for deliverance from a serious illness that threatens to be fatal (see v. 3), which would give David's enemies just what they wanted. See introduction to Ps 6. The psalm is composed of three couplets of graduated diminishing length (in Hebrew) to form (probably deliberately) a rhetorical pyramid capped with a ringing profession of faith and a vow to praise God (vv. 5-6).
13 title *For the director of music.* See note on Ps 4 title.
13:1-2 An anguished complaint concerning a prolonged, serious illness.
13:1 *How long ... ?* See note on 6:3. *forget.* Ignore. *hide your face.* For use in combination with "forget," see 44:24. In moments of need the psalmists frequently ask God why he hides his face (see 30:7; 44:24; 88:14), or they plead with him not to do so (see 27:9; 69:17; 102:2; 143:7). When he does hide his face, those who depend on him can only despair (see 30:7; 104:29). When his face shines on a person, blessing and deliverance come (see 4:6 and note; 31:16; 44:3; 67:1; 80:3,7,19; 119:135; see also Nu 6:25 and note).
13:2 *heart.* See note on 4:7.
13:3-4 Appeal for deliverance from death.
13:3 *Give light to my eyes.* Restore me (see note on 6:7).
13:4 See notes on 3:2; 5:9. *fall.* Referring to death (as in 18:38; 82:7; 106:26; Jdg 5:27; 2Sa 1:19; Job 18:12).
13:5-6 Concluding expression of confidence (see note on 3:8).
13:5 *unfailing love.* See note on 6:4. *heart.* See note on 4:7. *rejoices.* It is David who will rejoice, not his enemies.
13:6 *I will sing the LORD's praise.* See note on 7:17. *he has been good to me.* See 119:68; 136:1; 1 Ch 16:34.
Ps 14 A testimony concerning the moral folly of those who live as if there were no God and therefore feel free to cruelly prey on others who are at their mercy (Ps 53 is a somewhat revised duplicate). In its depiction of their godless arrogance, it has links with Ps 10; 12 (see also 28:3-5). And it shares with Ps 11 the conviction that the righteous Lord is on his heavenly throne. This psalm brings to closure the collection of prayers that began with Ps 3 (for the next grouping of psalms, see introduction to Ps 15-24). Five psalms (and 64 Hebrew poetic lines) after Ps 8's surprising evocation of humanity's "glory and honor" (8:5), this psalm highlights people's disgrace (see introduction to Ps 8). In this it serves as a counterpoint to that earlier recollection of humanity's high dignity and thereby exposes more sharply the depth of their disgrace — from which the petitioners in this and the preceding psalms have suffered.
14 title *For the director of music.* See note on Ps 4 title.
14:1-3 Characterization of the wicked. For Paul's use of these verses in a different context, see Ro 3:10-12.

14:1 *The fool.* See NIV text note. The Hebrew word is *nabal*; for its meaning, see 1Sa 25:25; 2Sa 13:13; Isa

[2]The LORD looks down from heaven[e]
on all mankind
to see if there are any who
understand,[f]
any who seek God.[g]
[3]All have turned away,[h] all have become
corrupt;[i]
there is no one who does good,[j]
not even one.[k]

[4]Do all these evildoers know nothing?[l]

They devour my people[m] as though
eating bread;
they never call on the LORD.[n]
[5]But there they are, overwhelmed with
dread,
for God is present in the company of
the righteous.
[6]You evildoers frustrate the plans of the
poor,
but the LORD is their refuge.[o]

[7]Oh, that salvation for Israel would
come out of Zion![p]
When the LORD restores[q] his
people,
let Jacob rejoice and Israel be
glad!

14:2 [e]Job 41:34; Ps 85:11; 102:19; La 3:50 [f]Ps 92:6 [g]S Ezr 6:21 **14:3** [h]S 1Sa 8:3; 1Ti 5:15 [i]2Pe 2:7 [j]1Ki 8:46; Ps 143:2; Ecc 7:20 [k]Ro 3:10-12* **14:4** [l]Ps 82:5; Jer 4:22 [m]Ps 27:2; Mic 3:3 [n]Ps 79:6; Isa 64:7; 65:1; Jer 10:25; Hos 7:7 **14:6** [o]S 2Sa 22:3 **14:7** [p]Ps 2:6 [q]S Dt 30:3; S Jer 48:47

15:1 [r]Ex 29:46; Ps 23:6; 27:4; 61:4 [s]Ex 25:8; 1Ch 22:19; Ps 20:2; 78:69; 150:1 [t]S Ex 15:17 **15:2** [u]S Ge 6:9; S Ps 18:32; Eph 1:4; S 1Th 3:13; Titus 1:6 [v]Pr 16:13; Isa 45:19;

Psalm 15

A psalm of David.

[1]LORD, who may dwell[r] in your sacred
tent?[s]
Who may live on your holy mountain?[t]

[2]The one whose walk is blameless,[u]
who does what is righteous,
who speaks the truth[v] from their
heart;
[3]whose tongue utters no slander,[w]
who does no wrong to a neighbor,
and casts no slur on others;
[4]who despises a vile person
but honors[x] those who fear the LORD;
who keeps an oath[y] even when it hurts,
and does not change their mind;
[5]who lends money to the poor without
interest;[z]
who does not accept a bribe[a] against
the innocent.

Whoever does these things
will never be shaken.[b]

Jer 7:28; 9:5; Zec 8:3,16; Ro 9:1; S Eph 4:25 **15:3** [w]S Lev 19:16 **15:4** [x]S Job 19:9; Ac 28:10 [y]S Dt 23:21; S Jos 9:18; Mt 5:33 **15:5** [z]S Ex 22:25 [a]S Ex 18:21; S 1Sa 8:3; Ac 24:26 [b]S Job 29:18; Ps 21:7; 112:6; Ac 2:25; Heb 12:28; 2Pe 1:10

32:5–7 (in Proverbs "fool" renders two other Hebrew words; see NIV text notes on Pr 1:4,7). *says.* See note on 3:2. *heart.* See note on 4:7. *no God.* A practical atheism (see 10:4,6,11,13; 36:1; see also note on 10:4). *no one who does good.* Context limits the scope of this assertion—and the assertion in v. 3—to the "fool" who takes no account of God and does not hesitate to show his malice toward "the company of the righteous" (v. 5)—as in 9:19–20; 10:2–11,13,18; 12:1–4,7–8 (this is also the situation that Ps 11 describes). In other psalms the psalmists do include themselves among those who are not righteous in God's eyes (see 130:3; 143:2; see also 1Ki 8:46; Job 9:2; Ecc 7:20).

14:2 *The LORD.* Emphatically contrasted with "the fool" (v. 1). *looks down from heaven.* See 33:13–14. *who seek God.* To "seek God" authentically is to "seek" what is morally "good" (Am 5:14–15); it is to "seek justice" in all human relationships (Isa 1:17). See also Ps 15.

14:3 *turned away.* From God and goodness.

14:4–6 The folly of the wicked exposed.

14:4 *Do all these evildoers know nothing?* In Hebrew the centered line of the psalm (see note on 6:6), containing the hinge on which the psalm's thematic development turns. *devour … never call on the LORD.* Renewed characterization of the wicked: They live by the violence of their own hands and do not rely on the Lord (see 10:2–4).

14:5 Even God's mighty defense of the righteous teaches the wicked nothing. *righteous.* See note on 1:5.

14:6 *poor.* Those who lack the resources to defend themselves. The same Hebrew word is rendered "weak" in 10:2 and "helpless" in 10:9,12. *refuge.* See note on 2:12.

14:7 The psalmist longs for Israel's complete deliverance from her enemies—which will come when God deals with the wicked in defense of their victims. For a similar expansion of scope, see 10:16–18 and note. *Zion.* See note on 9:11. *Jacob … Israel.* Synonyms (see Ge 32:28).

Ps 15–24 Ps 15 and its distinctive counterpart, Ps 24, frame a cluster of psalms that have been arranged in a concentric pattern with Ps 19 serving as the hinge (for the thematic links between Ps 16 and 23, Ps 17 and 22, and Ps 18 and 20–21, see introductions to those psalms). The framing psalms (15; 24) are thematically linked by their evocation of the high majesty of God and their insistence on moral purity "without [which] no one will see the Lord" (Heb 12:14). At the center Ps 19 uniquely combines a celebration of the divine majesty as displayed in the creation and an exposition of how moral purity is attained through God's law, forgiveness and shepherding care. Together, these three psalms (15; 19; 24) provide instructive words concerning the petitioners heard in the enclosed psalms, offer a counterpoint to Ps 14, and reinforce the instruction of Ps 1.

Ps 15 Instruction concerning those who wish to have access to God at his temple (see 24:3–6; Isa 33:14–16). See also introduction to Ps 15–24.

15:1 *dwell … live on.* Not as a priest but as God's welcome guest in his holy, royal house, the temple (see 23:6; 27:4–6; 61:4; 84:10; 2Sa 12:20). *holy mountain.* See note on 2:6.

15:2–5 Not sacrifices or ritual purity (as among the religions of the ancient Near East) but moral righteousness gives access to the Lord, the God of Israel (see the basic covenantal law: Ex 20:1–17; see also Isa 1:10–17; 33:14–16; 58:6–10; Jer 7:2–7; Eze 18:5–9; Hos 6:6; Am 5:14–15,21–24; Mic 6:6–8; Zec 7:9–10; 8:16–17).

15:2 *The one … righteous.* A summary introduction to the list that follows. *blameless.* That is, uniting loyalty to God and faithfulness to his covenant directives. See Ge 17:1 and note; see also how the Hebrew word is used in 18:23; 37:18; 84:11; 101:2,6; 119:1,80; Jos 24:14 ("all faithfulness"); Jdg 9:16,19 ("honorably") and how a closely related word is used in Ps 7:8 ("integrity"). *righteous.* See note on 1:5. *heart.* See note on 4:7.

15:3 *tongue.* See note on 5:9.

15:4 *despises a vile person.* Or "despises those repudiated" by God—because they have become an offense to him. *those who fear the LORD.* Those who honor God and order their lives in accordance with his will (see note on Ge 20:11) because of their reverence for him.

15:5 *interest.* See note on Ex 22:25–27. *be shaken.* See note on 10:6.

Psalm 16

A *miktam*[a] of David.

[1]Keep me safe,[c] my God,
for in you I take refuge.[d]

[2]I say to the LORD, "You are my Lord;[e]
apart from you I have no good
thing."[f]
[3]I say of the holy people[g] who are in the
land,[h]
"They are the noble ones in whom is
all my delight."
[4]Those who run after other gods[i] will
suffer[j] more and more.
I will not pour out libations of blood
to such gods
or take up their names[k] on my lips.

[5]LORD, you alone are my portion[l] and
my cup;[m]
you make my lot[n] secure.
[6]The boundary lines[o] have fallen for me
in pleasant places;
surely I have a delightful
inheritance.[p]
[7]I will praise the LORD, who
counsels me;[q]
even at night[r] my heart instructs me.

16:1 [c]S Ps 12:7 [d]Ps 2:12 **16:2** [e]Ps 31:14; 118:28; 140:6 [f]Ps 73:25 **16:3** [g]Dt 33:3; Ps 30:4; 85:8; Da 7:18; Ac 9:13; Ro 1:7 [h]Ps 101:6 **16:4** [i]Ex 18:11; 20:3; S Dt 8:19; S 31:20 [j]Ps 32:10; Pr 23:29 [k]S Ex 23:13 **16:5** [l]S Lev 2:2 [m]Ps 23:5; 75:8; 116:13; Isa 51:17; La 4:21; Eze 23:32-34; Hab 2:16 [n]S Job 31:2 **16:6** [o]S Dt 19:14; Ps 104:9; Pr 8:29; Jer 5:22 [p]S Job 22:26 **16:7** [q]Ps 73:24; Pr 15:22; Isa 11:2 [r]Job 35:10; Ps 42:8; 77:6

16:8 [s]1Ki 2:19; 1Ch 6:39; Ps 73:23 [t]Ps 15:5 **16:9** [u]Ps 4:7; 13:5; 28:7;

[8]I keep my eyes always on the LORD.
With him at my right hand,[s] I will
not be shaken.[t]

[9]Therefore my heart is glad[u] and my
tongue rejoices;
my body also will rest secure,[v]
[10]because you will not abandon me to
the realm of the dead,[w]
nor will you let your faithful[b] one[x]
see decay.[y]
[11]You make known to me the path of
life;[z]
you will fill me with joy in your
presence,[a]
with eternal pleasures[b] at your right
hand.[c]

Psalm 17

A prayer of David.

[1]Hear me,[d] LORD, my plea is just;
listen to my cry.[e]

[a] Title: Probably a literary or musical term
[b] 10 Or *holy*

30:11 [v]S Dt 33:28 **16:10** [w]S Nu 16:30; Ps 30:3; 31:17; 86:13; Hos 13:14 [x]S 2Ki 19:22 [y]S Job 17:14; Ac 2:31; 13:35* **16:11** [z]Ps 139:24; Mt 7:14 [a]Ac 2:25-28* [b]Ps 21:6 [c]Ps 80:17 **17:1** [d]Ps 30:10; 64:1; 80:1; 140:6 [e]Ps 5:2; 39:12; 142:6; 143:1

's 16 A prayer for safekeeping (v. 1 — the petition element n prayer psalms is often relatively short; see 3:7; 22:19 – 21; 4:23 – 26), pleading for the Lord's protection against the hreat of death. In accordance with its dominant theme, it ould also be called a psalm of trust. In this regard it has close hematic links with Ps 23 (compare 16:2 with 23:1; 16:5 with 3:5; 16:7 – 8 with 23:4; 16:11 with 23:6). Together these two salms underscore faith/trust as the second essential characeristic (alongside conformity to God's law; see introduction o Ps 15 – 24) of those who bring their prayers to God (see ntroduction to Ps 1 – 2; see also note on 34:8 – 14).
6 title *miktam.* The term remains unexplained, though it lways stands in the superscription of Davidic prayers occaioned by great danger (see Ps 56 – 60).
6:1 The petition and the basis for it. The rest of the psalm laborates on the latter element.
16:2 – 4 The Lord is David's one and only good thing (see 73:25,28); David will have nothing to do with the couneerfeit gods to whom others pour out their libations (see 4:2).
6:3 See Ps 101.
6:4 *suffer more and more.* In contrast with David's good "poron" (v. 5; see note on 11:6), which affords him much joy (see 3:18 – 26). *libations of blood.* Blood of sacrifices poured on ltars. *take up their names.* Appeal to or worship them (see os 23:7).
6:5 – 6 Joy over the inheritance received from the Lord. Daid refers to what the Lord bestowed on his people in the romised land, either to the gift of fields there (see Nu 16:14) r to the Lord himself (as in 73:26; 119:57; 142:5; La 3:24), who vas the inheritance of the priests (see Nu 18:20) and the Leites (see Dt 10:9).
16:5 *cup.* A metaphor referring to what the host offers his guests to drink. To the godly the Lord offers a cup f blessing (see 23:5) or salvation (see 116:13); he makes the vicked drink from a cup of wrath (see Jer 25:15; Rev 14:10; 6:19). *secure.* Just as each Israelite's family inheritance in the romised land was to be secure (see Lev 25; Nu 36:7).
16:7 – 8 Praise of the Lord who counsels and keeps.
16:7 *counsels.* Shows the way that leads to life (see v. 11). *heart.* Lit. "kidneys" (see note on 7:9). The reference here is probably to conscience.
16:8 *With him at my right hand.* As sustainer and protector (see 73:23; 109:31; 110:5; 121:5); complemented by the reference to the Lord's right hand in v. 11. *not be shaken.* See note on 10:6.
16:9 – 11 Describes the joy of the total security that God's faithful care provides. David speaks of himself and of the life he enjoys by the gracious provision and care of God. The Lord, in whom the psalmist takes refuge, wills life for him (hence he makes known to him the path of life, v. 11) and will not abandon him to the grave, even though "flesh and ... heart ... fail" (73:26). But implicit in these words of assurance (if not actually explicit) is the confidence that, with the Lord as his refuge, even the grave cannot rob him of life (see 17:15; 73:24; see also note on 11:7). If this could be said of David — and of all those godly Israelites who made David's prayer their own — how much more of David's promised Son! So Peter quotes vv. 8 – 11 and declares that with these words David prophesied of Christ and his resurrection (Ac 2:25 – 28; see Paul's similar use of v. 10b in Ac 13:35). See also note on 6:5.
16:9 *heart.* See note on 4:7. *tongue.* Lit. "glory" (see note on 7:5).
16:10 *faithful one.* Hebrew *ḥasid* (see note on 4:3). Reference is first of all to David, but the psalm is ultimately fulfilled in Christ (see note on vv. 9 – 11).
16:11 *path of life.* See Pr 15:24. *your right hand.* See note on v. 8.
Ps 17 David appeals to the Lord as Judge when he is under attack by ungodly foes. The circumstances evoked and the petition to which they gave rise show considerable affinity with Ps 22 (see introduction to Ps 15 – 24). The psalm reflects many of the Hebrew conventions of lodging a judicial appeal before the king.
17 title *A prayer.* See titles of Ps 86; 90; 102; 142; see also 72:20.
17:1 – 2 The initial appeal for justice.

Hear[f] my prayer —
it does not rise from deceitful lips.[g]
2 Let my vindication[h] come from you;
may your eyes see what is right.[i]

3 Though you probe my heart,[j]
though you examine me at night and test me,[k]
you will find that I have planned no evil;[l]
my mouth has not transgressed.[m]
4 Though people tried to bribe me,
I have kept myself from the ways of the violent
through what your lips have commanded.
5 My steps have held to your paths;[n]
my feet have not stumbled.[o]

6 I call on you, my God, for you will answer me;[p]
turn your ear to me[q] and hear my prayer.[r]
7 Show me the wonders of your great love,[s]
you who save by your right hand[t]
those who take refuge[u] in you from their foes.
8 Keep me[v] as the apple of your eye;[w]
hide me[x] in the shadow of your wings[y]
9 from the wicked who are out to destroy me,
from my mortal enemies who surround me.[z]

10 They close up their callous hearts,[a]
and their mouths speak with arrogance.[b]
11 They have tracked me down, they now surround me,[c]
with eyes alert, to throw me to the ground.
12 They are like a lion[d] hungry for prey,[e]
like a fierce lion crouching in cover.

13 Rise up,[f] LORD, confront them, bring them down;[g]
with your sword rescue me from the wicked.
14 By your hand save me from such people, LORD,
from those of this world[h] whose reward is in this life.[i]
May what you have stored up for the wicked fill their bellies;
may their children gorge themselves on it,
and may there be leftovers[j] for their little ones.

15 As for me, I will be vindicated and will see your face;
when I awake,[k] I will be satisfied with seeing your likeness.[l]

Psalm 18[a]

18:Title – 50pp — 2Sa 22:1-51

For the director of music. Of David the servant of the LORD. He sang to the LORD the words of this song when the LORD delivered him from the hand of all his enemies and from the hand of Saul. He said:

1 I love you, LORD, my strength.[m]

2 The LORD is my rock,[n] my fortress[o] and my deliverer;[p]

[a] In Hebrew texts 18:1-50 is numbered 18:2-51.

17:1 [f] S Ps 5:1 [g] Isa 29:13 **17:2** [h] Ps 24:5; 26:1; Isa 46:13; 50:8-9; 54:17 [i] Ps 99:4 **17:3** [j] Ps 139:1; Jer 12:3 [k] S Job 7:18 [l] Job 23:10; Jer 50:20 [m] Ps 39:1 **17:5** [n] Job 23:11; Ps 44:18; 119:133 [o] Dt 32:35; Ps 73:2; 121:3 **17:6** [p] Ps 86:7 [q] Ps 116:2 [r] S Ps 4:1 **17:7** [s] Ps 31:21; 69:13; 106:45; 107:43; 117:2 [t] S Ps 10:12 [u] Ps 2:12 **17:8** [v] S Nu 6:24 [w] S Dt 32:10; Pr 7:2 [x] Ps 27:5; 31:20; 32:7 [y] Ru 2:12; Ps 36:7; 63:7; Isa 34:15 **17:9** [z] Ps 109:3 **17:10** [a] Ps 73:7; 119:70; Isa 6:10 [b] S 1Sa 2:3 **17:11** [c] Ps 88:17 **17:12** [d] Ps 7:2; Jer 5:6; 12:8; La 3:10 [e] S Ge 49:9 **17:13** [f] S Nu 10:35 [g] Ps 35:8; 55:23; 73:18 **17:14** [h] Lk 16:8 [i] Ps 49:17; Lk 16:25 [j] Isa 2:7; 57:17 **17:15** [k] S Ps 3:5 [l] S Nu 12:8; S Mt 5:8; 1Jn 3:2 **18:1** [m] S Ex 15:2; S Dt 33:29; S 1Sa 2:10; Ps 22:19; 28:7; 59:9; 81:1; Isa 12:2; 49:5; Jer 16:19 **18:2** [n] S Ex 33:22 [o] Ps 28:8; 31:2,3; Isa 17:10; Jer 16:19 [p] Ps 40:17

17:1 *plea.* For justice. His case is truly "just," not a clever misrepresentation by deceitful lips (for a similar situation, see 1Sa 24:15).

17:3 – 5 David's claim of innocence in support of the rightness of his case. He is not guilty of the ungodly ways of his attackers — let God examine him (cf. 139:23 – 24).

17:3 *heart.* See note on 4:7.

17:4 *what your lips have commanded.* God's revealed will, by which he has made known the "paths" (v. 5) that people are to follow.

17:6 – 9 The petition: what David wants the Lord to do for him — motivated by David's trust in him ("for you will answer me," v. 6) and the Lord's unfailing righteousness (see v. 7).

17:6 *I call . . . you will answer.* See note on 118:5.

17:7 *wonders.* See note on 9:1. *great love.* See note on 6:4.

17:8 *apple of your eye.* See note on Dt 32:10. *shadow.* A conventional Hebrew metaphor for protection against oppression — as shade protects from the oppressive heat of the hot desert sun. Kings were spoken of as the "shade" of those dependent on them for protection (as in Nu 14:9, "protection" — lit. "shade"; La 4:20, "shadow"; Eze 31:6,12,17). Similarly, the Lord is the protective "shade" of his people (see 91:1; 121:5; Isa 25:4; 49:2; 51:16). *wings.* Metaphor for the protective outreach of God's power (see 36:7; 57:1; 61:4; 63:7; 91:4; Ru 2:12; see also Mt 23:37).

17:10 – 12 The accusation lodged against the vicious adversaries (see note on 5:9 – 10).

17:10 *mouths.* See note on 5:9. *speak with arrogance.* See note on 10:11.

17:12 *lion.* See note on 7:2.

17:13 – 14 Petition: how David wants the Lord to deal with the two parties in the conflict.

17:13 *Rise up.* See note on 3:7. *bring them down.* See note on 5:10. *your sword.* See 7:12 – 13 and note.

17:14 *such people.* See 9:19 – 20; 10:18; 12:1 – 4,8; 14:1 – 3.

17:15 Concluding confession of confidence (see note on 3:8). *will be vindicated.* The righteous Judge (see note on 4:1) will acknowledge and vindicate the innocence (righteousness) of the petitioner. *see your face.* See note on 11:7. *when I awake.* From the night of death (see note on 11:7) — in radical contrast to the destiny of "those of this world" (v. 14; see notes on 6:5; 16:9 – 11). *seeing your likeness.* As Moses the servant of the Lord had seen it (see Nu 12:8).

Ps 18 This song of David occurs also (with minor variations) in 2Sa 22 (see notes there). In its structure, apart from the introduction (vv. 1 – 3) and the conclusion (vv. 46 – 50), the song is composed of three major divisions: (1) the Lord's deliverance of David from his mortal enemies in answer to his cry for help (vv. 4 – 19); (2) the moral grounds for the Lord's saving help (vv. 20 – 29); (3) the Lord's help recounted

my God is my rock, in whom I take
refuge,[q]
my shield[a][r] and the horn[b] of my
salvation,[s] my stronghold.

3 I called to the LORD, who is worthy of
praise,[t]
and I have been saved from my
enemies.[u]
4 The cords of death[v] entangled me;
the torrents[w] of destruction
overwhelmed me.
5 The cords of the grave coiled
around me;
the snares of death[x] confronted me.
6 In my distress[y] I called to the LORD;[z]
I cried to my God for help.
From his temple he heard my voice;[a]
my cry came[b] before him, into his
ears.
7 The earth trembled[c] and quaked,[d]
and the foundations of the
mountains shook;[e]
they trembled because he was
angry.[f]
8 Smoke rose from his nostrils;[g]
consuming fire[h] came from his
mouth,
burning coals[i] blazed out of it.
9 He parted the heavens and came
down;[j]
dark clouds[k] were under his feet.
10 He mounted the cherubim[l] and flew;
he soared[m] on the wings of the
wind.[n]

18:2 [q] Ps 2:12; 9:9; 94:22 [r] S Ge 15:1; Ps 28:7; 84:9; 119:114; 144:2 [s] S 1Sa 2:1; S Lk 1:69 **18:3** [t] S 1Ch 16:25 [u] S Ps 9:13 **18:4** [v] Ps 116:3 [w] Ps 93:4; 124:4; Isa 5:30; 17:12; Jer 6:23; 51:42, 55; Eze 43:2 **18:5** [x] Pr 13:14 **18:6** [y] S Dt 4:30 [z] Ps 30:2; 99:6; 102:2; 120:1 [a] Ps 66:19; 116:1 [b] S Job 16:18 **18:7** [c] Ps 97:4; Isa 5:25; 64:3 [d] S Jdg 5:4 [e] S Jdg 5:5 [f] S Job 9:5; Jer 10:10 **18:8** [g] S Job 41:20 [h] S Ex 15:7; S 19:18; S Job 41:21; Ps 50:3; 97:3; Da 7:10 [i] Pr 25:22; Ro 12:20 **18:9** [j] S Ge 11:5; S Ps 57:3 [k] S Ex 20:21; S Dt 33:26; S Ps 104:3 **18:10** [l] S Ge 3:24; Eze 10:18 [m] S Dt 33:26 [n] Ps 104:3 **18:11** [o] S Ex 19:9; S Dt 4:11

11 He made darkness his covering,[o] his
canopy[p] around him—
the dark rain clouds of the sky.
12 Out of the brightness of his presence[q]
clouds advanced,
with hailstones[r] and bolts of
lightning.[s]
13 The LORD thundered[t] from heaven;
the voice of the Most High
resounded.[c]
14 He shot his arrows[u] and scattered
the enemy,
with great bolts of lightning[v] he
routed them.[w]
15 The valleys of the sea were exposed
and the foundations[x] of the earth
laid bare
at your rebuke,[y] LORD,
at the blast of breath from your
nostrils.[z]

16 He reached down from on high
and took hold of me;
he drew me out of deep
waters.[a]
17 He rescued me from my powerful
enemy,[b]

[a] 2 Or *sovereign* [b] 2 *Horn* here symbolizes strength.
[c] 13 Some Hebrew manuscripts and Septuagint (see also 2 Samuel 22:14); most Hebrew manuscripts *resounded, / amid hailstones and bolts of lightning*

[p] S Job 22:14; Isa 4:5; Jer 43:10 **18:12** [q] Ps 104:2 [r] S Jos 10:11 [s] S Job 36:30 **18:13** [t] S Ex 9:23; S 1Sa 2:10 **18:14** [u] S Dt 32:23 [v] S Job 36:30; Rev 4:5 [w] S Jdg 4:15 **18:15** [x] S Ps 11:3 [y] Ps 76:6; 104:7; 106:9; Isa 50:2 [z] S Ex 15:8 **18:16** [a] Ex 15:5; Ps 69:2; Pr 18:4; 20:5 **18:17** [b] ver 48; Ps 38:19; 59:1; 143:9

(vv. 30–45). David's celebration of God's saving help in answer to prayer when under threat from powerful enemies receives its counterpart in the two closely related psalms (Ps 20–21; see introductions to those psalms and introduction to Ps 15–24).

18 title *For the director of music.* See note on Ps 4 title. *servant of the LORD.* See 78:70; 89:3,20,39; 132:10; 144:10. The title designates David in his royal office as, in effect, an official in the Lord's own kingly rule over his people (see 2Sa 7:5)—as were Moses (see Ex 14:31 and note), Joshua (see Jos 24:29) and the prophets (Elijah, 2Ki 9:36; Jonah, 2Ki 14:25; Isaiah, Isa 20:3; Daniel, Da 6:20). *song.* See note on Ps 30 title. *when the LORD delivered him.* It is possible that David composed his song shortly after his victories over his foreign enemies (2Sa 8:1–14), but it may have been later in his life.

18:1–3 A prelude of praise.

18:1 Does not occur in 2Sa 22. *I love you.* From an unusual Hebrew expression that emphasizes the fervor of David's love. *my strength.* My source of strength.

18:2 *rock … rock.* The translation of two different Hebrew words. "Rock" is a common poetic figure for God (or the gods: Dt 32:31,37; Isa 44:8), symbolizing his unfailing (see Isa 26:4) strength as a fortress refuge (see vv. 31,46; 31:2–3; 42:9; 62:7; 71:3; 94:22; Isa 17:10) or as deliverer (see 19:14; 62:2; 78:35; 89:26; 95:1; Dt 32:15). It is a figure particularly appropriate for David's experience (see 1Sa 23:14,25; 24:2,22; 26:20), for the Lord was his true security. *fortress.* See note on 2Sa 22:2. *shield.* See note on 3:3. *horn.* See NIV text note; Dt 33:17; Jer 48:25.

18:4–6 God heard his cry for help.

18:4–5 David depicts his experiences in poetic figures of mortal danger.

18:4 *cords.* 2Sa 22:5 has "waves." *torrents of destruction.* See note on 30:1.

18:5 *cords of the grave … snares of death.* See 116:3. He had, as it were, been snared by death (personified) and bound as a prisoner of the grave (see Job 36:8). See also note on 30:3.

18:6 *temple.* God's heavenly abode, where he sits enthroned (see 11:4; 113:5; Isa 6:1; 40:22).

18:7–15 The Lord came to the aid of his servant—depicted as a fearful theophany (divine manifestation) of the heavenly Warrior descending in wrathful attack upon David's enemies (see 5:4–5; 68:1–8; 77:16–19; Mic 1:3–4; Na 1:2–6; Hab 3:3–15). He sweeps down upon them like a fierce thunderstorm (see Jos 10:11; Jdg 5:20–22; 1Sa 2:10; 7:10; 2Sa 5:24; Isa 29:6).

18:8 God's fierce majesty is portrayed in terms similar to those applied to the awesome Leviathan (Job 41:19–21).

18:9 *parted the heavens and came down.* See Isa 64:1 and note.

18:10 *cherubim.* Symbols of royalty (see 80:1; 99:1; see also notes on Ge 3:24; Ex 25:18). In Eze 1 and 10, cherubim appear as the bearers of the throne-chariot of God.

18:13 *voice.* For thunder as the voice of God, see Ps 29; Job 37:2–5. *Most High.* See note on Ge 14:19.

18:14 *arrows.* For shafts of lightning as the arrows of God, see 77:17; 144:6; Hab 3:11; see also note on Ge 9:13, and photo, p. 874.

18:15 Perhaps recalls the great deed of the heavenly Warrior when he defeated Israel's enemy at the "Red Sea" (see Ex 15:1–12).

18:16–19 The deliverance.

18:16 *deep waters.* See note on 32:6.

Plaque of a storm-god shows him on top of a horned animal, holding a weapon in his right hand and bolts of lightning in his left. It was common for people in the ancient world to connect natural phenomena with their gods. Psalm 18:14 also describes Israel's God as being God of the storms: The Lord "shot his arrows and scattered the enemy, with great bolts of lightning he routed them."

Kim Walton, courtesy of the Oriental Institute Museum

from my foes, who were too strong
for me.[c]
18 They confronted me in the day of my
disaster,[d]
but the LORD was my support.[e]
19 He brought me out into a spacious
place;[f]
he rescued me because he delighted
in me.[g]
20 The LORD has dealt with me according
to my righteousness;[h]
according to the cleanness of my
hands[i] he has rewarded me.[j]
21 For I have kept the ways of the LORD;[k]
I am not guilty of turning[l] from my
God.
22 All his laws are before me;[m]
I have not turned away from his
decrees.
23 I have been blameless[n] before him
and have kept myself from sin.
24 The LORD has rewarded me according
to my righteousness,[o]
according to the cleanness of my
hands in his sight.
25 To the faithful[p] you show yourself
faithful,[q]
to the blameless you show yourself
blameless,
26 to the pure[r] you show yourself pure,
but to the devious you show yourself
shrewd.[s]
27 You save the humble[t]
but bring low those whose eyes are
haughty.[u]
28 You, LORD, keep my lamp[v] burning;
my God turns my darkness into
light.[w]
29 With your help[x] I can advance against
a troop[a];
with my God I can scale a wall.
30 As for God, his way is perfect:[y]
The LORD's word is flawless;[z]
he shields[a] all who take refuge[b] in
him.

18:17 [c] S Jdg 18:26 **18:18** [d] Pr 1:27; 16:4; Jer 17:17; 40:2; Ob 1:13 [e] Ps 20:2; Isa 3:1 **18:19** [f] Ps 31:8 [g] S Nu 14:8 **18:20** [h] S 1Sa 26:23 [i] Job 22:30; Ps 24:4 [j] S Ru 2:12; S 2Ch 15:7; 1Co 3:8 **18:21** [k] 2Ch 34:33; Ps 37:34; 119:2; Pr 8:32; 23:26 [l] Ps 119:102 **18:22** [m] Ps 119:30 **18:23** [n] S Ge 6:9 **18:24** [o] S 1Sa 26:23 **18:25** [p] Ps 31:23; 37:28; 50:5; Pr 2:8 [q] Ps 25:10; 40:11; 89:24; 146:6 **18:26** [r] Pr 15:26; Mt 5:8; Php 1:10; 1Ti 5:22; Titus 1:15; 1Jn 3:3 [s] Pr 3:34; Mt 10:16; Lk 16:8 **18:27** [t] S 2Ch 33:23; S Mt 23:12 [u] S Job 41:34; S Ps 10:5; Pr 3:33-34 **18:28** [v] 1Ki 11:36; Ps 132:17 [w] Job 29:3; Ps 97:11; 112:4; Jn 1:5; S Ac 26:18; 2Co 4:6; 2Pe 1:19 **18:29** [x] ver 32, 39; Isa 45:5; Heb 11:34

[a] 29 Or *can run through a barricade*

18:30 [y] S Dt 32:4 [z] S Ps 12:6; Pr 30:5 [a] Ps 3:3 [b] Ps 2:12

18:19 *spacious place.* See 4:1 and note. He is free to roam unconfined by the threats and dangers that had hemmed him in (vv. 4–6,16–18). To be afflicted or oppressed is like being bound by fetters (Job 36:8,13). To be delivered is to be set free (Job 36:16). *delighted in me.* God was pleased with David as "a man after his own heart" (1Sa 13:14; see also 1Sa 15:28; 1Ki 14:8; 15:5; Ac 13:22), a man with whom he had made a covenant assuring him of an enduring dynasty (2Sa 7). The thought is further elaborated in vv. 20–29.

18:20–24 David's righteousness rewarded. David's assertion of his righteousness (like that of Samuel, 1Sa 12:3; Hezekiah, 2Ki 20:3; Job, Job 13:23; 27:6; 31; see also Ps 17:3–5; 26; 44:17–18; 101) is not a pretentious boast of sinless perfection (see 51:5). Rather, it is a claim that, in contrast to his enemies, he has devoted himself heart and life to the service of the Lord, that his has been a godliness with integrity—itself the fruit of God's gracious working in his heart (see 51:10–12).

18:20,24 *my righteousness.* See notes on 1:5; 2Sa 22:21,25. *rewarded me.* As a king benevolently rewards those who loyally serve him.

18:21 *ways of the LORD.* See 25:4 and note.

18:23 *blameless.* See note on 15:2.

18:25–29 Because God responds to people in accordance with their ways (see Job 34:11; Pr 3:34), David has experienced the Lord's favor.

18:26 *devious.* Deviating from the straight path of truth and righteousness. *shrewd.* God responds to their perverse dealings thrust for thrust, like a wrestler countering his opponent (see 1Ki 22:23 and note; see also note on Jdg 11:35).

18:27 The thought of this verse fits well with David's and Saul's reversals of status (see 1Sa 16:13–14 and note). It also echoes the central theme of Hannah's song (1Sa 2:1–10), which the author of Samuel uses to highlight a major thesis of his account of the ways of God as he brings about his kingdom. *eyes ... haughty.* See Pr 6:17 and note.

18:28 *keep my lamp burning.* God causes his life, his undertakings and his dynasty to flourish (see especially Job 18:5–6; 21:17). *light.* See note on 27:1.

18:30–36 By God's blessing David the king has thrived.

18:30 *is perfect.* Does not fail—and so, because of his blessing, David's way has not failed (see v. 32). *The LORD's word.* While the reference is general, it applies especially to God's

31 For who is God besides the LORD?[c]
And who is the Rock[d] except our God?
32 It is God who arms me with strength[e]
and keeps my way secure.[f]
33 He makes my feet like the feet of a deer;[g]
he causes me to stand on the heights.[h]
34 He trains my hands for battle;[i]
my arms can bend a bow of bronze.
35 You make your saving help my shield,
and your right hand sustains[j] me;
your help has made me great.
36 You provide a broad path[k] for my feet,
so that my ankles do not give way.[l]

37 I pursued my enemies[m] and overtook them;
I did not turn back till they were destroyed.
38 I crushed them[n] so that they could not rise;[o]
they fell beneath my feet.[p]
39 You armed me with strength[q] for battle;
you humbled my adversaries[r] before me.
40 You made my enemies turn their backs[s] in flight,
and I destroyed[t] my foes.
41 They cried for help, but there was no one to save them[u]—
to the LORD, but he did not answer.[v]
42 I beat them as fine as windblown dust;[w]
I trampled them[a] like mud in the streets.
43 You have delivered me from the attacks of the people;
you have made me the head of nations.[x]
People I did not know[y] now serve me,
44 foreigners[z] cower before me;
as soon as they hear of me, they obey me.
45 They all lose heart;[a]
they come trembling[b] from their strongholds.[c]

46 The LORD lives![d] Praise be to my Rock![e]
Exalted be God[f] my Savior![g]
47 He is the God who avenges[h] me,
who subdues nations[i] under me,
48 who saves[j] me from my enemies.[k]
You exalted me above my foes;
from a violent man[l] you rescued me.
49 Therefore I will praise you, LORD,
among the nations;[m]
I will sing[n] the praises of your name.[o]
50 He gives his king great victories;
he shows unfailing love to his anointed,[p]
to David[q] and to his descendants forever.[r]

Psalm 19[b]

For the director of music.
A psalm of David.

1 The heavens[s] declare[t] the glory of God;[u]
the skies[v] proclaim the work of his hands.[w]

[a] 42 Many Hebrew manuscripts, Septuagint, Syriac and Targum (see also 2 Samuel 22:43); Masoretic Text *I poured them out* [b] In Hebrew texts 19:1-14 is numbered 19:2-15.

18:31 [c] S Dt 4:35; 32:39; Ps 35:10; 86:8; 89:6; Isa 44:6,8; 45:5,6,14, 18,21; 46:9 [d] S Ge 49:24 **18:32** [e] S ver 29; 1Pe 5:10 [f] S Ps 15:2; 19:13; Heb 10:14; Jas 3:2 **18:33** [g] Ps 42:1; Pr 5:19; Isa 35:6; Hab 3:19 [h] S Dt 32:13 **18:34** [i] Ps 144:1 **18:35** [j] Ps 3:5; 37:5,17; 41:3; 51:12; 54:4; 55:22; 119:116; Isa 41:4,10,13; 43:2; 46:4 **18:36** [k] Ps 31:8 [l] S Job 18:7; Ps 66:9 **18:37** [m] S Lev 26:7 **18:38** [n] Ps 68:21; 110:6 [o] Ps 36:12; 140:10; Isa 26:14 [p] Ps 47:3 **18:39** [q] ver 32; Isa 45:5,24 [r] ver 47; Ps 47:3; 144:2 **18:40** [s] S Jos 7:12 [t] ver 37 **18:41** [u] S 2Ki 14:26; Ps 50:22 [v] S 1Sa 8:18; S 14:37; Jer 11:11 **18:42** [w] S Dt 9:21; S Isa 2:22 **18:43** [x] 2Sa 8:1-14 [y] Isa 55:5 **18:44** [z] Ps 54:3; 144:7,11; Isa 25:5 **18:45** [a] S 1Sa 17:32; 2Co 4:1; Heb 12:3 [b] Isa 66:2; Hos 3:5; 11:10 [c] Ps 9:9; Mic 7:17 **18:46** [d] S Jos 3:10; S 1Sa 14:39; 2Co 13:4 [e] ver 31; Ex 33:22 [f] Ps 21:13; 35:27; 40:16; 108:5 [g] S 1Ch 16:35; S Lk 1:47 **18:47** [h] S Ge 4:24 [i] S ver 39; S Jdg 4:23 **18:48** [j] Ps 7:10; 37:40; Da 3:17 [k] S ver 17 [l] Ps 140:1 **18:49** [m] S Ps 9:11 [n] Ps 7:17; 9:2; 101:1; 108:1; 146:2 [o] Ro 15:9* **18:50** [p] S 2Sa 23:1 [q] Ps 144:10 [r] Ps 89:4 **19:1** [s] Ps 89:5; Isa 40:22 [t] Ps 50:6; 148:3; Ro 1:19 [u] Ps 4:2; 8:1; 97:6; Isa 6:3 [v] S Ge 1:8 [w] S Ps 8:6; S 103:22

promise to David (see 2Sa 7:8–16). *flawless.* See note on 12:6. *shields.* See note on 3:3.

18:37–42 With God's help David has crushed all his foes.

18:43–45 God has made David the head of nations (see 2Sa 5; 8; 10)—he who had been, it seemed, on the brink of death (see vv. 4–5 and note on v. 5), sinking into the depths (see v. 16).

18:43 *attacks of the people.* All the threats he had endured from his own people in the days of Saul, and perhaps also in the time of Absalom's rebellion. *People I did not know.* Those with whom he had had no previous relationship.

18:46–50 Concluding doxology.

18:46 *The LORD lives!* God's interventions and blessings in David's behalf have shown him to be the living God (see Dt 5:26).

18:47 *avenges me.* Redresses the wrongs committed against me (see Dt 32:41 and note on 32:35).

18:49 David vows to praise the Lord among the nations (see note on 9:1). *name.* See note on 5:11.

18:50 *his king . . . his anointed.* David views himself as the Lord's chosen and anointed king (see 1Sa 16:13; see also notes on 1Sa 10:25; 12:14–15). *shows unfailing love.* David's final words recall the Lord's covenant with him (see 2Sa 7:8–16). The whole song is to be understood in the context of David's official capacity and the Lord's covenant with him. What David claims in this grand conclusion—as, indeed, in the whole psalm—has been and is being fulfilled in Jesus Christ, David's great descendant.

Ps 19 A hymn extolling the majestic "glory of God" (v. 1) as displayed in the heavens, especially in the brilliant summer sun as it moves across a cloudless sky from east to west (see vv. 1–6; see also introduction to Ps 29), and "the law of the LORD" (v. 7), which blesses the lives of those who heed it (see vv. 7–13). An attached prayer (vv. 12–13) asks God to provide what his law cannot: forgiveness for "hidden faults" and a shepherd's care that preserves from "willful sins." Placed next to Ps 18, this psalm completes the cycle of praise—for the Lord's saving acts, for his glory reflected in creation and for his life-nurturing law. Placed at the center of Ps 15–24, it powerfully reinforces the themes of the two framing psalms (see introduction to Ps 15–24) and reminds all who would enter Yahweh's presence that they must come as those who have seen with their eyes his glory on display in the creation and who have in their hearts a deep devotion to his law.

19 title *For the director of music.* See note on Ps 4 title.

2 Day after day they pour forth speech;
night after night they reveal knowledge.[x]
3 They have no speech, they use no words;
no sound is heard from them.
4 Yet their voice[a] goes out into all the earth,
their words to the ends of the world.[y]
In the heavens God has pitched a tent[z] for the sun.[a]
5 It is like a bridegroom[b] coming out of his chamber,[c]
like a champion[d] rejoicing to run his course.
6 It rises at one end of the heavens[e]
and makes its circuit to the other;[f]
nothing is deprived of its warmth.

7 The law of the LORD[g] is perfect,[h]
refreshing the soul.[i]
The statutes of the LORD are trustworthy,[j]
making wise the simple.[k]
8 The precepts of the LORD are right,[l]
giving joy[m] to the heart.
The commands of the LORD are radiant,
giving light to the eyes.[n]
9 The fear of the LORD[o] is pure,
enduring forever.
The decrees of the LORD are firm,
and all of them are righteous.[p]

10 They are more precious than gold,[q]
than much pure gold;
they are sweeter than honey,[r]
than honey from the honeycomb.[s]
11 By them your servant is warned;
in keeping them there is great reward.
12 But who can discern their own errors?
Forgive my hidden faults.[t]
13 Keep your servant also from willful sins;[u]
may they not rule over me.[v]
Then I will be blameless,[w]
innocent of great transgression.

14 May these words of my mouth and this meditation of my heart
be pleasing[x] in your sight,
LORD, my Rock[y] and my Redeemer.[z]

Psalm 20[b]

For the director of music.
A psalm of David.

1 May the LORD answer you when you are in distress;[a]
may the name of the God of Jacob[b] protect you.[c]
2 May he send you help[d] from the sanctuary[e]
and grant you support[f] from Zion.[g]

[a] 4 Septuagint, Jerome and Syriac; Hebrew *measuring line* [b] In Hebrew texts 20:1-9 is numbered 20:2-10.

19:2 [x] Ps 74:16 **19:4** [y] Ro 10:18* [z] S Job 36:29; Ps 104:2 [a] S Jdg 5:31 **19:5** [b] Joel 2:16 [c] S Job 36:29 [d] 1Sa 17:4 **19:6** [e] Dt 30:4 [f] Ps 113:3; Ecc 1:5 **19:7** [g] S Ps 1:2 [h] Ps 119:142; Jas 1:25 [i] Ps 23:3 [j] Ps 93:5; 111:7; 119:138,144 [k] S Dt 4:6; Ps 119:130 **19:8** [l] Ps 33:4; 119:128 [m] Ps 119:14 [n] S Ezr 9:8; Ps 38:10 **19:9** [o] Ps 34:11; 111:10; Pr 1:7; Ecc 12:13; Isa 33:6 [p] Ps 119:138, 142 **19:10** [q] S Job 22:24; Ps 119:72; Pr 8:10 [r] Ps 119:103; SS 4:11; Eze 3:3 [s] S 1Sa 14:27 **19:12** [t] Ps 51:2; 90:8; Ecc 12:14 **19:13** [u] S Nu 15:30 [v] Ps 119:133 [w] S Ge 6:9; S Ps 18:32 **19:14** [x] Ps 104:34 [y] Ps 18:31 [z] S Ex 6:6; S Job 19:25 **20:1** [a] Ps 4:1 [b] Ex 3:6; Ps 46:7,11 [c] Ps 59:1; 69:29; 91:14 **20:2** [d] Ps 30:10; 33:20; 37:40; 40:17; 54:4; 118:7 [e] S Nu 3:28 [f] S Ps 18:18 [g] Ps 2:6; 128:5; 134:3; 135:21

19:1 – 4a The silent heavens speak, declaring the glory of their Maker to all who are on the earth (see 148:3). The heavenly lights are not divine (see Ge 1:16 and note; Dt 4:19; 17:3), nor do they control or disclose anyone's destiny (see Isa 47:13; Jer 10:2; Da 4:7). Their glory testifies to the righteousness and faithfulness of the Lord who created them (see 50:6; 89:5 – 8; 97:6; see also Ro 1:19 – 20).

19:4 Interpreting this heavenly proclamation eschatologically in the light of Christ, Paul applies this verse to the proclamation of the gospel in his own day (see Ro 10:18). He thus associates these two universal proclamations.

19:4b – 6 The heavens are the divinely pitched "tent" for the lordly sun — widely worshiped in the ancient Near East (cf. Dt 4:19; 17:3; 2Ki 23:5,11; Jer 8:2; Eze 8:16), but here, as in 136:7 – 8; Ge 1:16, a mere creature of God. Of the created realm, the sun is the supreme metaphor of the glory of God (see 84:11; Isa 60:19 – 20), as it makes its daily triumphant sweep across the whole extent of the heavens and pours out its warmth on every creature.

19:7 – 9 Stately, rhythmic celebration of the life-nurturing effects of the Lord's revealed law (see Ps 119).

19:7 *trustworthy.* God's laws are "trustworthy" (see also 111:7; 119:86) or "firm" (19:9) or "true" (119:142,151,160) in the sense that they faithfully represent God's righteous will (119:138,160), they endure generation after generation (they "stand firm," 93:5; see also 119:91,152,160), and they truly fulfill their purpose in the lives of those who honor them (see the effects noted here; see also 119:43,93,98 – 100,165) — they can be trusted. *the simple.* The childlike, those whose understanding and judgment have not yet matured (see 119:98 – 100; Pr 1:4; cf. also 2Ti 3:15; Heb 5:13 – 14).

19:8 *heart.* See note on 4:7.

19:9 *fear of the LORD.* The sum of what the law requires (see note on 15:4).

19:10 – 11 The matchless worth of God's law and its rich value for life (see Dt 5:33).

19:10 *sweeter than honey.* By contrast, those who abandon the law turn justice into bitterness (see Am 5:7; 6:12).

19:12 – 13 Humanity's moral consciousness remains flawed; hence people err without realizing it and have reason to seek pardon for "hidden faults" (v. 12; see Lev 5:2 – 4). "Willful sins" (v. 13), however, are open rebellion; they are the "great transgression" (v. 13) that leads to being cut off from God's people (see Nu 15:30 – 31).

19:14 The psalmist presents this hymn as a praise offering to the Lord. *heart.* See note on 4:7. *Rock . . . Redeemer.* See 78:35. *Rock.* See notes on 18:2; Ge 49:24. *Redeemer.* See notes on Ex 6:6; Isa 41:14.

Ps 20 A liturgy of prayer for the king just before he goes out to battle against a threatening force (see 2Ch 20:1 – 30). Ps 20 – 21 serve as the counterpart of Ps 18 in the arrangement of Ps 15 – 24 (see introduction to Ps 15 – 24); in Ps 18 we hear the voice of the king, while in Ps 20 – 21 we hear the voices of the people.

20 title *For the director of music.* See note on Ps 4 title.

20:1 – 5 The people (perhaps his assembled army) address the king, adding their prayers to his prayer for victory.

20:1 *answer you.* Hear your prayers, offered in the present distress, accompanied by "sacrifices" (v. 3); see v. 9. *name.* See vv. 5,7; see also note on 5:11. *Jacob.* See note on 14:7. *protect you.* Lit. "raise you to a high, secure place."

20:2 *Zion.* See note on 9:11.

3 May he remember[h] all your sacrifices
and accept your burnt offerings.[a][i]
4 May he give you the desire of your heart[j]
and make all your plans succeed.[k]
5 May we shout for joy[l] over your victory
and lift up our banners[m] in the name of our God.

May the LORD grant all your requests.[n]

6 Now this I know:
The LORD gives victory to his anointed.[o]
He answers him from his heavenly sanctuary
with the victorious power of his right hand.[p]
7 Some trust in chariots[q] and some in horses,[r]
but we trust in the name of the LORD our God.[s]
8 They are brought to their knees and fall,[t]
but we rise up[u] and stand firm.[v]
9 LORD, give victory to the king!
Answer us[w] when we call!

Psalm 21[b]

For the director of music.
A psalm of David.

1 The king rejoices in your strength, LORD.[x]
How great is his joy in the victories you give![y]
2 You have granted him his heart's desire[z]
and have not withheld the request of his lips.[a]
3 You came to greet him with rich blessings
and placed a crown of pure gold[a] on his head.[b]
4 He asked you for life, and you gave it to him—
length of days, for ever and ever.[c]
5 Through the victories[d] you gave, his glory is great;
you have bestowed on him splendor and majesty.[e]
6 Surely you have granted him unending blessings
and made him glad with the joy[f] of your presence.[g]
7 For the king trusts in the LORD;[h]
through the unfailing love[i] of the Most High[j]
he will not be shaken.[k]

8 Your hand will lay hold[l] on all your enemies;
your right hand will seize your foes.
9 When you appear for battle,
you will burn them up as in a blazing furnace.
The LORD will swallow them up in his wrath,
and his fire will consume them.[m]

[a] 3,2 The Hebrew has *Selah* (a word of uncertain meaning) here. [b] In Hebrew texts 21:1-13 is numbered 21:2-14.

20:3 [h] Ac 10:4 [i] S Dt 33:11 **20:4** [j] Ps 21:2; 37:4; 145:16, 19; Isa 26:8; Eze 24:25; Ro 10:1 [k] Ps 140:8; Pr 16:3; Da 11:17 **20:5** [l] S Job 3:7 [m] S Nu 1:52; Ps 60:4; Isa 5:26; 11:10, 12; 13:2; 30:17; 49:22; 62:10; Jer 50:2; 51:12, 27 [n] 1Sa 1:17 **20:6** [o] S 2Sa 23:1; Ps 28:8 [p] S Job 40:14; Hab 3:13 **20:7** [q] S 2Ki 19:23 [r] S Dt 17:16; Ps 33:17; 147:10; Pr 21:31; Isa 31:1; 36:8,9 [s] S 2Ch 32:8 **20:8** [t] Ps 27:2; Isa 40:30; Jer 46:6; 50:32 [u] Mic 7:8 [v] S Job 11:15; Ps 37:23; Pr 10:25; Isa 7:9 **20:9** [w] Ps 17:6 **21:1** [x] S 1Sa 2:10 [y] S 2Sa 22:51 **21:2** [z] S Ps 20:4 **21:3** [a] S 2Sa 12:30; Rev 14:14 [b] Zec 6:11 **21:4** [c] Ps 10:16; 45:17; 48:14; 133:3 **21:5** [d] ver 1; Ps 18:50; 44:4 [e] S Ps 8:5; 45:3; 93:1; 96:6; 104:1 **21:6** [f] Ps 43:4; 126:3 [g] S 1Ch 17:27 **21:7** [h] S 2Ki 18:5 [i] Ps 6:4 [j] Ge 14:18 [k] S Ps 15:5; S 55:22 **21:8** [l] Isa 10:10 **21:9** [m] S Dt 32:22; Ps 50:3; Jer 15:14

20:3 For *Selah*, see NIV text note and note on 3:2.

20:4 *heart.* See note on 4:7.

20:5 *May we shout ... name of our God.* See note on 5:11. *banners.* Probably the troop standards around which the units rallied.

20:6 A participant in the liturgy (perhaps a Levite; see 2Ch 20:14) announces assurance that the king's prayer will be heard. *his anointed.* The king appointed by the Lord to rule in his name (see 2:2 and note).

20:7–8 The army's confession of trust in the Lord rather than in a chariot corps (cf. 33:16–17)—the enemy perhaps came reinforced by such a prized corps. See David's similar confession of confidence when he faced Goliath (1Sa 17:45–47).

20:9 The army's concluding petition. *Answer ... when.* See note on v. 1. The psalm ends as it began.

Ps 21 A psalm of praise for victories granted to the king. It is thus linked with Ps 20, but whether both were occasioned by the same events is unknown. Here the people's praise follows that of the king (see v. 1); there (Ps 20) the people's prayer was added to the king's. In its structure, the psalm is framed by vv. 1,13 ("in your strength, LORD" is in both verses). See introduction to Ps 20; see also introduction to Ps 15–24.

21 title *For the director of music.* See note on Ps 4 title.

21:2–6 The people celebrate the Lord's many favors to the king: all "his heart's desire" (v. 2). Verse 2 announces the theme; vv. 3–5 develop the theme; v. 6 climactically summarizes the theme.

21:2 *heart's.* See note on 4:7. For *Selah*, see NIV text note and note on 3:2.

21:3 *came to greet him.* Back from the battles. *placed a crown ... on his head.* Exchanged the warrior's helmet for the ceremonial emblem of royalty—possibly the captured crown of the defeated king (see 2Sa 12:30).

21:4 The king's life has been spared—to live "for ever and ever" (see 1Ki 1:31; Da 2:4; 3:9; see also 1Sa 10:24; 1Ki 1:25,34,39).

21:5 *glory ... splendor and majesty.* See 45:3; like that of his heavenly Overlord (see 96:3).

21:6 *unending blessings.* Either (1) blessings of enduring value or (2) an unending flow of blessings. *your presence.* Your favor, which is the supreme cause of joy because it is the greatest blessing and the wellspring of all other blessings.

21:7 A participant in the liturgy (perhaps a priest or Levite) proclaims the king's trust in the Lord and the reason for his security. *LORD ... Most High.* That is, "LORD Most High" (see 7:17; see also note on 3:7). *unfailing love.* See note on 6:4. *Most High.* See note on Ge 14:19. *shaken.* See note on 10:6.

21:8–12 The people hail the future victories of their triumphant king. Verse 8 announces the theme; vv. 9–11 develop the theme; v. 12 summarizes the theme.

21:9 *The LORD ... in his wrath.* Credits the king's victories to the Lord's wrath (see note on 2:5).

10 You will destroy their descendants
from the earth,
their posterity from mankind.[n]
11 Though they plot evil[o] against you
and devise wicked schemes,[p] they
cannot succeed.
12 You will make them turn their backs[q]
when you aim at them with drawn
bow.

13 Be exalted[r] in your strength, LORD;[s]
we will sing and praise your might.

Psalm 22[a]

For the director of music. To the tune of "The Doe of the Morning." A psalm of David.

1 My God, my God, why have you
forsaken me?[t]
Why are you so far[u] from saving me,
so far from my cries of anguish?[v]
2 My God, I cry out by day, but you do
not answer,[w]
by night,[x] but I find no rest.[b]

3 Yet you are enthroned as the Holy One;[y]
you are the one Israel praises.[c][z]
4 In you our ancestors put their trust;
they trusted and you delivered
them.[a]
5 To you they cried out[b] and were saved;
in you they trusted[c] and were not
put to shame.[d]

6 But I am a worm[e] and not a man,
scorned by everyone,[f] despised[g] by
the people.
7 All who see me mock me;[h]
they hurl insults,[i] shaking their
heads.[j]

8 "He trusts in the LORD," they say,
"let the LORD rescue him.[k]
Let him deliver him,[l]
since he delights[m] in him."

9 Yet you brought me out of the womb;[n]
you made me trust[o] in you, even at
my mother's breast.
10 From birth[p] I was cast on you;
from my mother's womb you have
been my God.

11 Do not be far from me,[q]
for trouble is near[r]
and there is no one to help.[s]

12 Many bulls[t] surround me;[u]
strong bulls of Bashan[v] encircle me.
13 Roaring lions[w] that tear their prey[x]
open their mouths wide[y] against me.
14 I am poured out like water,
and all my bones are out of joint.[z]
My heart has turned to wax;[a]
it has melted[b] within me.
15 My mouth[d] is dried up like a potsherd,[c]
and my tongue sticks to the roof of
my mouth;[d]
you lay me in the dust[e] of death.

[a] In Hebrew texts 22:1-31 is numbered 22:2-32.
[b] 2 Or *night, and am not silent* [c] 3 Or *Yet you are holy, / enthroned on the praises of Israel*
[d] 15 Probable reading of the original Hebrew text; Masoretic Text *strength*

21:10 [n]Dt 28:18 **21:11** [o]Ps 2:1 [p]Job 10:3; Ps 10:2; 26:10; 37:7 **21:12** [q]S Ex 23:27 **21:13** [r]S Ps 18:46 [s]Ps 18:1 **22:1** [t]S Job 6:15; S Ps 9:10; Mt 27:46*; Mk 15:34* [u]Ps 10:1 [v]S Job 3:24 **22:2** [w]S Job 19:7 [x]Ps 42:3; 88:1 **22:3** [y]S 2Ki 19:22; Ps 71:22; S Mk 1:24 [z]S Ex 15:2; Ps 148:14 **22:4** [a]Ps 78:53; 107:6 **22:5** [b]S 1Ch 5:20 [c]Isa 8:17; 25:9; 26:3; 30:18 [d]S 2Ch 13:18; Ps 25:3; 31:17; 71:1; Isa 49:23; Ro 9:33 **22:6** [e]S Job 4:19 [f]S 2Sa 12:14; Ps 31:11; 64:8; 69:19; 109:25 [g]Ps 119:141; Isa 49:7; 53:3; 60:14; Mal 2:9; Mt 16:21 **22:7** [h]S Job 17:2; Ps 35:16; 69:12; 74:18; Mt 27:41; Mk 15:31; Lk 23:36 [i]Mt 27:39, 44; Mk 15:32; Lk 23:39 [j]Mk 15:29

22:8 [k]Ps 91:14 [l]S Ps 3:2 [m]S 2Sa 22:20; S Mt 3:17; 27:43 **22:9** [n]Job 10:18; Ps 71:6 [o]Ps 78:7; Na 1:7 **22:10** [p]Ps 71:6; Isa 46:3; 49:1 **22:11** [q]ver 19; S Ps 10:1 [r]S Ps 10:14 [s]S 2Ki 14:26; S Isa 41:28 **22:12** [t]Ps 68:30 [u]Ps 17:9; 27:6; 49:5; 109:3; 140:9 [v]Dt 32:14; Isa 2:13; Eze 27:6; 39:18; Am 4:1 **22:13** [w]ver 21; Eze 22:25; Zep 3:3 [x]S Ge 49:9 [y]La 3:46 **22:14** [z]S Ps 6:2 [a]Job 23:16; Ps 68:2; 97:5; Mic 1:4 [b]Jos 7:5; Ps 107:26; Da 5:6 **22:15** [c]Isa 45:9 [d]Ps 137:6; La 4:4; Eze 3:26; Jn 19:28 [e]S Job 7:21; Ps 104:29

21:10 The king's royal enemies will be left with no descendants to rise up against him again.
21:12 *with drawn bow.* See note on Ge 9:13.
21:13 Conclusion—and return to the beginning: Lord, assert your strength, in which "the king rejoices" (v. 1; see also v. 7, "trusts"), and we will ever "praise your might."
Ps 22 The anguished prayer of David as a godly sufferer victimized by the vicious and prolonged attacks of enemies whom he has not provoked and from whom the Lord has not (yet) delivered him. In the arrangement of Ps 15–24, this psalm serves as the counterpart of Ps 17 (see introduction to Ps 17; see also introduction to Ps 15–24). The prayer is in many ways similar to Ps 69, but it contains no calls for redress (see note on 5:10) such as are found in 69:22–28. No other psalm fitted quite so aptly the circumstances of Jesus at his crucifixion. Hence on the cross he quoted from it (see Mt 27:46 and parallels), and the Gospel writers, especially Matthew and John, frequently alluded to it (as they did to Ps 69) in their accounts of Christ's passion (Mt 27:35,39,43; Jn 19:23–24,28). They saw in the passion of Jesus the fulfillment of this cry of the righteous sufferer. The author of Hebrews placed the words of v. 22 on Jesus' lips (see Heb 2:12 and note). No psalm is quoted more frequently in the NT.
22 title See notes on Ps 4; 9 titles.
22:1 *why . . . ? Why . . . ?* See note on 6:3.
22:1a Quoted by Jesus (see Mt 27:46; Mk 15:34 and notes).
22:2 *I cry . . . you do not answer.* See note on 118:5.
22:3–5 Recollection of what the Lord has been for Israel (see note on vv. 9–10).
22:3 *enthroned.* See note on 9:11. *Holy One.* See Lev 11:44 and note. *the one Israel praises.* For his saving acts in her behalf (see 148:14; Dt 10:21; Jer 17:14).
22:6 *a worm and not a man.* See Job 25:6; Isa 41:14; 52:14.
22:7 *hurl insults, shaking their heads.* See Mt 27:39; Mk 15:29; see also note on 5:9.
22:8 Quoted in part in Mt 27:43; see note on 3:2.
22:9–10 Recollection of what the Lord has been for him (see note on vv. 3–5).
22:12–18 The psalmist's deep distress. In vv. 12–13,16–18 he uses four figures to portray the attacks of his enemies; in vv. 14–15 he describes his inner sense of powerlessness under their fierce attacks.
22:12–13,16 *bulls . . . lions . . . Dogs.* Metaphors for the enemies (see note on 7:2).
22:12 *Bashan.* Noted for its good pasturage, and hence for the size and vigor of its animals (see Dt 32:14; Eze 39:18 and note; Am 4:1).
22:14 *bones . . . heart.* See note on 102:4. *heart.* See note on 4:7.
22:15 See Jn 19:28 and note. *dust of death.* See v. 29; see also Job 7:21 and note.

16 Dogs[f] surround me,
a pack of villains encircles me;
they pierce[a][g] my hands and my feet.
17 All my bones are on display;
people stare[h] and gloat over me.[i]
18 They divide my clothes among them
and cast lots[j] for my garment.[k]

19 But you, LORD, do not be far from me.[l]
You are my strength;[m] come quickly[n]
to help me.[o]
20 Deliver me from the sword,[p]
my precious life[q] from the power of
the dogs.[r]
21 Rescue me from the mouth of the
lions;[s]
save me from the horns of the wild
oxen.[t]

22 I will declare your name to my people;
in the assembly[u] I will praise you.[v]
23 You who fear the LORD, praise him![w]
All you descendants of Jacob, honor
him![x]
Revere him,[y] all you descendants of
Israel!
24 For he has not despised[z] or scorned
the suffering of the afflicted one;[a]
he has not hidden his face[b] from him
but has listened to his cry for help.[c]

25 From you comes the theme of my
praise in the great assembly;[d]
before those who fear you[b] I will
fulfill my vows.[e]
26 The poor will eat[f] and be satisfied;
those who seek the LORD will praise
him —[g]
may your hearts live forever!

22:16 [f]Php 3:2 [g]Isa 51:9; 53:5; Zec 12:10; Jn 20:25 **22:17** [h]Lk 23:35 [i]Ps 25:2; 30:1; 35:19; 38:16; La 2:17; Mic 7:8 **22:18** [j]S Lev 16:8; Mt 27:35*; Mk 15:24; Lk 23:34; Jn 19:24* [k]Mk 9:12 **22:19** [l]S ver 11 [m]S Ps 18:1 [n]Ps 38:22; 70:5; 141:1 [o]Ps 40:13 **22:20** [p]S Job 5:20; Ps 37:14 [q]Ps 35:17 [r]Php 3:2 **22:21** [s]S ver 13; S Job 4:10 [t]ver 12; S Nu 23:22 **22:22** [u]Ps 26:12; 40:9, 10; 68:26 [v]Ps 35:18; Heb 2:12* **22:23** [w]Ps 33:2; 66:8; 86:12; 103:1; 106:1; 113:1; 117:1; 135:19 [x]Ps 50:15; Isa 24:15; 25:3; 49:23; 60:9; Jer 3:17 [y]S Dt 14:23; Ps 33:8 **22:24** [z]Ps 102:17 [a]S Ps 9:12 [b]Ps 13:1; 27:9; 69:17; 102:2; 143:7 [c]S Job 24:12; S 36:5: Heb 5:7

27 All the ends of the earth[h]
will remember and turn to the LORD,
and all the families of the nations
will bow down before him,[i]
28 for dominion belongs to the LORD[j]
and he rules over the nations.

29 All the rich[k] of the earth will feast and
worship;[l]
all who go down to the dust[m] will
kneel before him —
those who cannot keep themselves
alive.[n]
30 Posterity[o] will serve him;
future generations[p] will be told about
the Lord.
31 They will proclaim his righteousness,[q]
declaring to a people yet unborn:[r]
He has done it![s]

Psalm 23

A psalm of David.

1 The LORD is my shepherd,[t] I lack
nothing.[u]
2 He makes me lie down in green
pastures,
he leads me beside quiet waters,[v]

[a] *16* Dead Sea Scrolls and some manuscripts of the Masoretic Text, Septuagint and Syriac; most manuscripts of the Masoretic Text *me, / like a lion* [b] *25* Hebrew *him*

22:25 [d]Ps 26:12; 35:18; 40:9; 82:1 [e]S Nu 30:2 **22:26** [f]Ps 107:9 [g]Ps 40:16 **22:27** [h]S Ps 2:8 [i]Ps 86:9; 102:22; Da 7:27; Mic 4:1 **22:28** [j]Ps 47:7-8; Zec 14:9 **22:29** [k]Ps 45:12 [l]Ps 95:6; 96:9; 99:5; Isa 27:13; 49:7; 66:23; Zec 14:16 [m]Isa 26:19 [n]Ps 89:48 **22:30** [o]Isa 53:10; 54:3; 61:9; 66:22 [p]Ps 102:18 **22:31** [q]S Ps 5:8; 40:9 [r]Ps 71:18; 78:6; 102:18 [s]Lk 18:31; 24:44 **23:1** [t]S Ge 48:15; S Ps 28:9; S Jn 10:11 [u]Ps 34:9, 10; 84:11; 107:9; Php 4:19 **23:2** [v]Ps 36:8; 46:4; Rev 7:17

22:16 *pierce my hands and my feet.* The "dogs" wound his limbs as he seeks to ward off their attacks. But see also v. 20 and note on vv. 20 – 21; Isa 53:5; Zec 12:10; Jn 19:34,37.
22:17 *All my bones are on display.* The figure is probably that of one attacked by highway robbers or enemy soldiers, who strip him of his garments (see v. 18; see also note on vv. 20 – 21).
22:18 See introduction to this psalm; see also Jn 19:23 – 24.
22:20 – 21 The psalmist's prayer recalls in reverse order the four figures by which he portrayed his attackers in vv. 12 – 13,16 – 18: "sword," "dogs," "lions," "wild oxen." Here "sword" refers back to the scene described in vv. 16 – 18, and thus many interpret it as an attack by robbers or enemy soldiers, though "sword" is often used figuratively of any violent death.
22:21 *wild oxen.* The aurochs, the wild ancestor of domestic cattle.
22:22 – 31 Vows to praise the Lord when the Lord's sure deliverance comes (see note on 7:17). The vows proper appear in vv. 22,25. Verses 23 – 24 anticipate the calls to praise God that will accompany the psalmist's praise (see note on 9:1). Verses 26 – 31 describe the expanding company of those who will take up the praise — a worldwide company of persons from every station in life and continuing through the generations. No psalm or prophecy contains a grander vision of the scope of the throng of worshipers who will join in the praise of God's saving acts.
22:22 See Heb 2:12 and note. *name.* See note on 5:11.
22:23 *fear the LORD.* See v. 25; see also note on 15:4.
22:25 *assembly.* See note on 1:5.
22:26 *will eat and be satisfied.* As they share in the ceremonial festival of praise (see Lev 7:11 – 27).
22:27 *All the ends of the earth.* They too will be told of God's saving acts (see 18:49 and note on 9:1). The good news that the God of Israel hears the prayers of his people and saves them will move them to turn from their idols to the true God (cf. 1Th 1:9).
22:28 The rule of the God of Israel is universal, and the nations will come to recognize that fact through what he does in behalf of his people (see Ps 47; Ge 12:2 – 3; see also Dt 32:21; Ro 10:19; 11:13 – 14).
22:29 *All the rich … all who go down to the dust.* The most prosperous and those on the brink of death, and all those whose life situation falls in between these two extremes. *dust.* See v. 15; see also Job 7:21 and note.
22:31 *righteousness.* See note on 4:1.
Ps 23 A profession of joyful trust in the Lord as the good Shepherd-King. In the arrangement of Ps 15 – 24 it serves as the counterpart of Ps 16, with which it is thematically linked (see introduction to Ps 16; see also introduction to Ps 15 – 24). The psalm may have accompanied a festival of praise at "the house of the LORD" (v. 6) following a deliverance, such as is contemplated in 22:25 – 31 (see note on 7:17). The basic theme of the psalm is announced in v. 1a. Verses 1b – 3

3 he refreshes my soul.[w]
He guides me[x] along the right
paths[y]
for his name's sake.[z]
4 Even though I walk
through the darkest valley,[a][a]
I will fear no evil,[b]
for you are with me;[c]
your rod and your staff,
they comfort me.

5 You prepare a table[d] before me
in the presence of my enemies.

[a] 4 Or *the valley of the shadow of death*

23:3 [w] S Ps 19:7 [x] Ps 25:9; 73:24; Isa 42:16 [y] S Ps 5:8 [z] Ps 25:11; 31:3; 79:9; 106:8; 109:21; 143:11 **23:4** [a] S Job 3:5; Ps 107:14 [b] Ps 3:6; 27:1 [c] Ps 16:8; Isa 43:2 **23:5** [d] S Job 36:16

develop the theme by affirming the psalmist's total security under the Shepherd-King's care. Verse 4 elaborates on this theme by focusing on the Shepherd's protection in times of great danger and distress. Verse 5 describes the psalmist's privileged position as an honored guest at the Shepherd-King's table. In v. 6 the psalmist professes his full confidence for the future — a confidence grounded in the Shepherd-King's faithful covenant love. The psalm is framed by its first and last lines, each of which refers to "the LORD."

23:1 *shepherd.* A widely used metaphor for kings in the ancient Near East, and also in Israel (see 78:70 – 72; 2Sa 5:2; Isa 44:28; Jer 3:15; 23:1 – 4; Mic 5:4; see also Jer 2:8 and note). For the Lord as the shepherd of Israel, see 28:9; 79:13; 80:1; 95:7; 100:3; Ge 48:15; Isa 40:11; Jer 17:16; 31:10; 50:19; Eze 34:11 – 16. Here David the king acknowledges that the Lord is his Shepherd-King. For Jesus as the shepherd of his people, see Jn 10:11,14; Heb 13:20; 1Pe 5:4; Rev 7:17. *lack nothing.* On the contrary, he will enjoy "goodness" all his life (v. 6).

23:2 *lie down.* For flocks lying down in contented and secure rest, see Isa 14:30; 17:2; Jer 33:12; Eze 34:14 – 15; Zep 2:7; 3:13. *green pastures.* Metaphor for all that makes life flourish (see Eze 34:14; Jn 10:9). *leads me.* Like a shepherd (see Isa 40:11). *quiet waters.* Lit. "waters of resting places," i.e., restful waters — waters that provide refreshment and well-being (see Isa 49:10). See essay and photo below.

23:3 *refreshes my soul.* Revives me, refreshes my spirit (see 19:7; Ru 4:15; Pr 25:13; La 1:16). *guides me along the right paths.* See photo, p. 849. As a shepherd leads his sheep (see 77:20; 78:72) in paths that offer safety and well-being, so David's Shepherd-King guides him in ways that cause him to be secure and prosperous. For this meaning of "right," see Pr 8:18 ("prosperity"); 21:21 ("prosperity"); Isa 48:18; see also Pr 8:20 – 21. It is possible that "right paths" intentionally bears a double meaning, namely, that it also refers to paths that conform the psalmist's life to God's moral will (cf. Pr 4:11 and note). *for his name's sake.* The prosperity of the Lord's servant brings honor to the Lord's name (see 1Ki 8:41 – 42; Isa 48:9; Jer 14:21; Eze 20:9,14,22).

23:4 *the darkest valley.* A metaphor for circumstances of greatest peril (see 107:10 and note). See also NIV text note. *with me.* See 16:8 and note; see also Dt 31:6,8; Mt 28:20. *rod.* Instrument of authority (as in 2:9; 45:6; Ex 21:20; 2Sa 7:14; Job 9:34); used also by shepherds for counting, guiding, rescuing and protecting sheep (see Lev 27:32; Eze 20:37). *staff.* Instrument of support (as in Ex 21:19; Jdg 6:21; 2Ki 4:29; Zec 8:4). *comfort me.* Reassure me (as in 71:21; 86:17; Ru 2:13; Isa 12:1; 40:1; 49:13).

23:5 The heavenly Shepherd-King receives David at his table as his vassal king and takes him under his protection. In the ancient Near East, covenants were often concluded with a meal expressive of the bond of friendship (see 41:9; Ge 31:54; Ob 7); in the case of vassal treaties or covenants, the vassal was present as the guest of the overlord (see Ex 24:8 – 12). *anoint my head with oil.* Customary treatment of an honored guest at a banquet (see Lk 7:46; see also 2Sa 12:20; Ecc 9:8; Da 10:3). *cup.* Of the Lord's banquet (see note on 16:5).

GOD AS **SHEPHERD**

When describing the authority and care exercised by a deity or a king who represents the gods, the metaphor of a shepherd was natural in the ancient Near East. Marduk was the chief god in Babylonia for much of its history, and a standard hymn of praise concludes by extolling his care for the weak like a benevolent shepherd. A hymn to Shamash, the Mesopotamian sun-god, states: "You shepherd all living creatures together, you are their herdsman, above and below."

Hammurapi (c. 1750 BC), who wrote that he received kingship from the gods, claims that he fulfilled his royal duty as a shepherd by providing the people with "pastures and watering places," having "settled them in peaceful abodes." Another text affirming the role of Ashurbanipal (c. 650 BC) reports that he was appointed as shepherd to overthrow enemies. The image not only suggested protection; it was an affirmation of the authority to rule (2Sa 5:2; 1Ch 11:2).

Thus the metaphor of shepherd was a royal one, with connotations of strong leadership but tender care. One ancient Sumerian wisdom text offers a particularly good parallel to Psalm 23: "A man's personal god is a shepherd who finds pasturage for him. Let him lead him like sheep to the grass they can eat." For the psalmist, there is but one shepherd, his personal God, Yahweh (Ge 48:15).

Pharaoh Amunhotep I with ruler's shepherd crook

You anoint my head with oil;[e]
my cup[f] overflows.
6 Surely your goodness and love[g] will
follow me
all the days of my life,
and I will dwell in the house of the LORD
forever.

Psalm 24

Of David. A psalm.

1 The earth is the LORD's,[h] and
everything in it,
the world, and all who live in it;[i]
2 for he founded it on the seas
and established it on the waters.[j]

3 Who may ascend the mountain[k] of the
LORD?
Who may stand in his holy place?[l]
4 The one who has clean hands[m] and a
pure heart,[n]
who does not trust in an idol[o]
or swear by a false god.[a]

5 They will receive blessing[p] from the
LORD
and vindication[q] from God their
Savior.
6 Such is the generation of those who
seek him,
who seek your face,[r] God of Jacob.[b,c]

7 Lift up your heads, you gates;[s]
be lifted up, you ancient doors,
that the King[t] of glory[u] may come in.[v]
8 Who is this King of glory?
The LORD strong and mighty,[w]
the LORD mighty in battle.[x]
9 Lift up your heads, you gates;
lift them up, you ancient doors,
that the King of glory may come in.
10 Who is he, this King of glory?
The LORD Almighty[y]—
he is the King of glory.

Psalm 25[d]

Of David.

1 In you, LORD my God,
I put my trust.[z]

23:5 [e]Ps 45:7; 92:10; Lk 7:46 [f]S Ps 16:5 **23:6** [g]S Ne 9:25 **24:1** [h]S Ex 9:29; Job 41:11 [i]1Co 10:26* **24:2** [j]S Ge 1:6; Ps 104:3; 2Pe 3:5 **24:3** [k]Ps 2:6 [l]Ps 15:1; 65:4 **24:4** [m]S 2Sa 22:21 [n]Ps 51:10; 73:1; Mt 5:8 [o]Eze 18:15 **24:5** [p]Dt 11:26 [q]Ps 17:2 **24:6** [r]Ps 27:8; 105:4; 119:58; Hos 5:15 **24:7** [s]Ps 118:19, 20; Isa 26:2; 60:11, 18; 62:10 [t]Ps 44:4; 74:12 [u]Ps 29:3; Ac 7:2; 1Co 2:8 [v]Zec 9:9; Mt 21:5 **24:8** [w]S 1Ch 29:11; Ps 89:13; Jer 50:34; Eph 6:10 [x]Ex 15:3, 6; Dt 4:34 **24:10** [y]S 1Sa 1:11

[a] 4 Or *swear falsely* [b] 6 Two Hebrew manuscripts and Syriac (see also Septuagint); most Hebrew manuscripts *face, Jacob* [c] 6 The Hebrew has *Selah* (a word of uncertain meaning) here and at the end of verse 10. [d] This psalm is an acrostic poem, the verses of which begin with the successive letters of the Hebrew alphabet.

25:1 [z]Ps 86:4; 143:8

23:6 *goodness and love.* Both frequently refer to covenant benefits (see note on 6:4); here they are personified (see 25:21; 43:3; 79:8; 89:14). *follow.* Lit. "pursue"—usually with hostile intent. However, rather than having enemies ever in pursuit of him (see 1Sa 23:25; 24:14; 26:18,20), David will have the goodness and unfailing love of his Shepherd-King attending him. *dwell in the house of the LORD.* See note on 15:1. *forever.* The Hebrew for this word suggests "throughout the years," as in Pr 28:16 ("enjoy a long reign"). But see also notes on 11:7; 16:9–11.

Ps 24 A processional liturgy (see Ps 47; 68; 118; 132) celebrating the Lord's entrance into Zion—composed either for the occasion when David brought the ark to Jerusalem (see 2Sa 6) or for a festival commemorating the event. Together with Ps 15 it frames the intervening collection of psalms and with that psalm sharply delineates those who may approach God in prayer and "dwell in the house of the LORD" (23:6; see introduction to Ps 15–24). The church has long used this psalm in celebration of Christ's ascension into the heavenly Jerusalem—and into the sanctuary on high (see introduction to Ps 47).

24:1–2 The prelude (perhaps spoken by a Levite), proclaiming the Lord as the Creator, Sustainer and Possessor of the whole world (see 19:1–4) and therefore worthy of worship and reverent loyalty as "the King of glory" (vv. 7–10; see Ps 29; 33:6–11; 89:5–18; 93; 95:3–5; 96; 104).

24:1 *The earth ... everything in it.* For Paul's use of this declaration, see 1Co 10:25–26.

24:2 An echo of Ge 1:1–10. *founded ... established.* A metaphor taken from the founding of a city (see Jos 6:26; 1Ki 16:24; Isa 14:32) or of a temple (see 1Ki 5:17; 6:37; Ezr 3:6–12; Isa 44:28; Hag 2:18; Zec 4:9; 8:9). Like a temple, the earth was depicted as having foundations (see 18:15; 82:5; 1Sa 2:8; Pr 8:29; Isa 24:18) and pillars (see 75:3; Job 9:6). In the ancient Near East, temples were thought of as microcosms of the created world, so language applicable to a temple could readily be applied to the earth (see note on Ex 26:1). *on.* Or "above" (see 104:5–9; Ge 1:9; 7:11; 49:25; Ex 20:4; Dt 33:13).

24:3–6 Instruction concerning those who may enter the sanctuary (probably spoken by a priest). See 15:1–5a.

24:3 *mountain of the LORD.* See 2:6 and note.

24:4 *clean hands.* Guiltless actions. *pure heart.* Right attitudes and motives (see 51:10; 73:1). Jesus said that the "pure in heart ... will see God" (Mt 5:8). *heart.* See note on 4:7. *trust in.* Or "worship" (see 25:1–2; 86:4; 143:8). *by a false god.* Cf. Isa 19:18; Jer 7:9; Zep 1:5. But see NIV text note. If the latter is the sense, reference is probably to perjury (for the same concern see Ex 20:16 and note; Lev 19:12; Jer 5:2; 7:9; Zec 5:4; Mal 3:5).

24:5 *vindication.* That is, the fruits of vindication, such as righteous treatment from a faithful God; hence, here a synonym of "blessing" (see 23:3 and note).

24:6 *generation.* Or "company," as in 14:5 (those who share a common characteristic); see also 112:2; Pr 30:11–14 and notes on Ps 73:15; 78:8. *Jacob.* See note on 14:7. For *Selah,* see NIV text note and note on 3:2.

24:7–10 Heralding the approach of the King of glory (perhaps spoken by the king at the head of the assembled Israelites, with responses by the keepers of the gates). The Lord's arrival at his sanctuary in Zion completes his march from Egypt. "The LORD Almighty" (v. 10), "the LORD mighty in battle" (v. 8; see Ex 15:1–18), has triumphed over all his enemies and comes now in victory to his own city (see Ps 46; 48; 76; 87), his "resting place" (132:8,14; see 68:7–8; Jdg 5:4–5; Hab 3:3–7). Henceforth Jerusalem is the royal city of the kingdom of God (see note on 9:11).

24:7 *Lift up your heads ... be lifted up.* In jubilant reception of the victorious King of glory (see 3:3; 27:6; 110:7). *gates.* Reference could be to the gates of either the city or the sanctuary. *doors.* A synonym for "gates," not in this case the doors of the gates (as in Jdg 16:3; 1Sa 21:13). The gates are personified for dramatic effect, as in Isa 14:31.

24:10 *LORD Almighty.* See note on 1Sa 1:3. Here it stands in climactic position.

Ps 25–33 A group of nine psalms containing an unusual (even for the Psalter) concentration of pleas for mercy or

2 I trust in you;[a]
do not let me be put to shame,
nor let my enemies triumph over me.
3 No one who hopes in you
will ever be put to shame,[b]
but shame will come on those
who are treacherous[c] without cause.

4 Show me your ways, LORD,
teach me your paths.[d]
5 Guide me in your truth[e] and teach me,
for you are God my Savior,[f]
and my hope is in you[g] all day long.
6 Remember, LORD, your great mercy and
love,[h]
for they are from of old.
7 Do not remember the sins of my youth[i]
and my rebellious ways;[j]
according to your love[k] remember me,
for you, LORD, are good.[l]

8 Good and upright[m] is the LORD;
therefore he instructs[n] sinners in his
ways.
9 He guides[o] the humble in what is right
and teaches them[p] his way.
10 All the ways of the LORD are loving and
faithful[q]
toward those who keep the demands
of his covenant.[r]
11 For the sake of your name,[s] LORD,
forgive[t] my iniquity,[u] though it is
great.

12 Who, then, are those who fear the
LORD?[v]
He will instruct them in the ways[w]
they should choose.[a]
13 They will spend their days in
prosperity,[x]
and their descendants will inherit
the land.[y]
14 The LORD confides[z] in those who fear
him;
he makes his covenant known[a] to
them.
15 My eyes are ever on the LORD,[b]
for only he will release my feet from
the snare.[c]

16 Turn to me[d] and be gracious
to me,[e]
for I am lonely[f] and afflicted.

[a] 12 Or *ways he chooses*

25:2 [a] Ps 31:6; 143:8 **25:3** [b] S Ps 22:5; S Isa 29:22 [c] Isa 24:16; Hab 1:13; Zep 3:4; 2Ti 3:4 **25:4** [d] S Job 34:32 **25:5** [e] Ps 31:3; 43:3; Jn 16:13 [f] Ps 24:5 [g] ver 3; Ps 33:20; 39:7; 42:5; 71:5; 130:7; 131:3 **25:6** [h] Ps 5:7; 98:3; Isa 63:7, 15; Jer 31:20; Hos 11:8 **25:7** [i] Job 13:26; Isa 54:4; Jer 3:25; 31:19; 32:30; Eze 16:22,60; 23:3; 2Ti 2:22 [j] S Ex 23:21; Ps 107:17 [k] Ps 6:4; 51:1; 69:16; 109:26; 119:124 [l] S 1Ch 16:34; Ps 34:8; 73:1 **25:8** [m] Ps 92:15; Isa 26:7 [n] Ps 32:8; Isa 28:26 **25:9** [o] S Ps 23:3 [p] ver 4; Ps 27:11 **25:10** [q] S Ps 18:25 [r] Ps 103:18; 132:12 **25:11** [s] S Ex 9:16; Ps 31:3; 79:9; Jer 14:7 [t] S Ex 34:9 [u] S Ex 32:30; S Ps 78:38 **25:12** [v] S Job 1:8 [w] ver 8 **25:13** [x] S Dt 30:15; S 1Ki 3:14; S Job 8:7 [y] S Nu 14:24; Mt 5:5 **25:14** [z] Pr 3:32 [a] Ge 17:2; Jn 7:17 **25:15** [b] S 2Ch 20:12; Ps 123:2; Heb 12:2 [c] S Job 34:30; S Ps 119:110 **25:16** [d] S Ps 6:4 [e] S Nu 6:25 [f] Ps 68:6

grace (see 25:16; 26:11; 27:7; 28:2; 30:8,10; 31:9) accompanied by professions of trust (see 25:2; 26:1; 27:3; 28:7; 31:6,14; 32:10; 33:21) and appeals to or celebrations of Yahweh's unfailing love (see 25:6–7,10; 26:3; 31:7,16,21; 32:10; 33:5,18,22). The series begins with an alphabetic acrostic prayer for God's saving help (Ps 25; see NIV text note) and culminates in a 22-verse (the number of letters in the Hebrew alphabet) hymn of praise for Yahweh's sovereign rule and saving help (Ps 33). (For thematic links between these two psalms, see note on 25:3.) This prayer and hymn frame a concentrically arranged cluster that hinges on Ps 29 (for thematic links between Ps 26 and 32, 27 and 31, and 28 and 30, see introductions to those psalms). For the significance of Ps 29 as a hinge, see introduction to that psalm.

Ps 25 David prays for God's covenant mercies when suffering affliction for sins and when enemies seize the occasion to attack, perhaps by trying to discredit the king through false accusations (see note on 5:9). Appealing to God's covenant benevolence (his mercy, love, goodness, uprightness, faithfulness and grace; see vv. 6–8,10,16) and to his own reliance on the Lord (see vv. 1,5,15,20–21), he prays for deliverance from his enemies (see vv. 2,19), for guidance in God's will (see vv. 4–5,21; see also vv. 8–10,12), for the forgiveness of his sins (see vv. 7,11,18) and for relief from his affliction (see vv. 2,16–18,20). These are related: God's forgiveness will express itself in removing his affliction, and then his enemies will no longer have occasion to slander him. And with God guiding him in "his way" (v. 9)—i.e., in "the demands of his covenant" (v. 10)—he will no longer wander into "rebellious ways" (v. 7). This psalm is linked with Ps 24 by its reference to putting one's trust in the true "God" (v. 1) instead of a "false god" (24:4).

25:1–3 Prayer for relief from distress or illness and the slander of David's enemies that it occasions.

25:3 *hopes.* The three references to hoping in God occurring here (vv. 3,5,21) are echoed by three references to "hope" in 33:18,20,22 (by means of closely related Hebrew synonyms). *without cause.* David has given no cause for the hostility of his adversaries.

25:4–7 Prayer for guidance and pardon.

25:4 *your ways ... your paths.* Metaphors for "the demands of his covenant" (v. 10; see Dt 8:6; 10:12–13; 26:17; 30:16; Jos 22:5; see also vv. 8–9; 18:21; 51:13; 81:13; 95:10; 119:3,15; 128:1 and note on 119:29).

25:5 *your truth.* Here synonymous for "your ways" and "your paths" (see note on v. 4; see also note on 19:7).

25:6–7 *Remember ... Do not remember.* Remember your long-standing ("from of old") "mercy and love," but do not remember my long-standing sins (those "of my youth").

25:7 *love.* See v. 10 and note on 6:4.

25:8–15 Confidence in the Lord's covenant favors. In this context of prayer for pardon, David implicitly identifies himself with "sinners" (v. 8), as well as with the "humble" (v. 9)—those who keep God's covenant (see vv. 10,14) and those who fear the Lord (see vv. 12,14). As sinner he is in need of forgiveness; as humble servant of the Lord he hopefully awaits God's pardon and guidance in covenant faithfulness.

25:9 *humble.* Those who acknowledge that they are without resources.

25:10 *ways of the LORD.* The Lord's benevolent dealings (see 103:7; 138:5) with those who are true to his ways (see note on v. 4).

25:11 *For the sake of your name.* See note on 23:3; see also 1Jn 2:12. *name.* See note on 5:11.

25:12 *fear the LORD.* See notes on 15:4; 34:8–14; Pr 1:7; Lk 12:5.

25:13 *inherit the land.* Retain their family portion in the promised land (see 37:9,11,18,22,29,34; 69:36; Isa 60:21).

25:14 *confides.* Takes them into his confidence, as friends (see Ge 18:17–19; Job 29:4). *fear.* See note on 15:4.

25:15 *snare.* Set by the enemies (v. 2; see note on 9:15).

25:16–21 Prayer for relief from distress (probably illness) and related attacks of his enemies.

17 Relieve the troubles[g] of my heart
and free me from my anguish.[h]
18 Look on my affliction[i] and my
distress[j]
and take away all my sins.[k]
19 See how numerous are my enemies[l]
and how fiercely they hate me![m]

20 Guard my life[n] and rescue me;[o]
do not let me be put to shame,[p]
for I take refuge[q] in you.
21 May integrity[r] and uprightness[s]
protect me,
because my hope, LORD,[a] is in you.[t]

22 Deliver Israel,[u] O God,
from all their troubles!

Psalm 26

Of David.

1 Vindicate me,[v] LORD,
for I have led a blameless life;[w]
I have trusted[x] in the LORD
and have not faltered.[y]
2 Test me,[z] LORD, and try me,
examine my heart and my mind;[a]
3 for I have always been mindful of your
unfailing love[b]
and have lived[c] in reliance on your
faithfulness.[d]
4 I do not sit[e] with the deceitful,
nor do I associate with hypocrites.[f]
5 I abhor[g] the assembly of evildoers
and refuse to sit with the wicked.
6 I wash my hands in innocence,[h]
and go about your altar, LORD,
7 proclaiming aloud your praise[i]
and telling of all your wonderful
deeds.[j]

8 LORD, I love[k] the house where you live,
the place where your glory dwells.[l]
9 Do not take away my soul along with
sinners,
my life with those who are
bloodthirsty,[m]
10 in whose hands are wicked schemes,[n]
whose right hands are full of bribes.[o]
11 I lead a blameless life;
deliver me[p] and be merciful to me.

12 My feet stand on level ground;[q]
in the great congregation[r] I will
praise the LORD.

[a] *21* Septuagint; Hebrew does not have *LORD*.

25:17 [g] 1Ki 1:29; Ps 34:6, 17; 40:12; 54:7; 116:3 [h] Ps 6:3; 39:2 **25:18** [i] S Ps 13:3; Ro 12:12 [j] S 2Sa 16:12 [k] Ps 103:3 **25:19** [l] Ps 3:1; 9:13 [m] Ps 35:19; 38:19; 69:4 **25:20** [n] Ps 86:2 [o] Ps 17:13; 22:21; 43:1; 71:2; 116:4; 140:1; 142:6; 144:11 [p] ver 3 [q] Ps 2:12 **25:21** [r] S Ge 20:5; Pr 10:9 [s] 1Ki 9:4; Ps 85:10; 111:8; Isa 60:17; Mal 2:6 [t] ver 3 **25:22** [u] Ps 130:8; Lk 24:21 **26:1** [v] S 1Sa 24:15 [w] Ps 15:2; Pr 20:7 [x] Ps 22:4; 40:4; Isa 12:2; 25:9; Jer 17:7; Da 3:28 [y] 2Ki 20:3; Heb 10:23 **26:2** [z] Ps 66:10 [a] S Dt 6:6; S Ps 7:9; Jer 11:20; 20:12; Eze 11:5

26:3 [b] Ps 6:4 [c] S 1Ki 2:4 [d] Ps 40:11; 43:3; 86:11; 119:30 **26:4** [e] Ps 1:1 [f] Ps 28:3; Mt 6:2 **26:5** [g] Ps 139:21 **26:6** [h] Ps 73:13; Mt 27:24 **26:7** [i] Isa 42:12; 60:6 [j] S Jos 3:5; Ps 9:1 **26:8** [k] Ps 122:6; Isa 66:10 [l] S Ex 29:43; 2Ch 7:1; Ps 96:6 **26:9** [m] Ps 5:6; 28:3; 55:23; 139:19; Pr 29:10 **26:10** [n] S Ps 21:11 [o] S Job 36:18; S Isa 1:23; S Eze 22:12 **26:11** [p] Ps 31:5; 69:18; 119:134; Titus 2:14 **26:12** [q] Ps 27:11; 40:2; 143:10; Isa 26:7; 40:3-4; 45:13; Zec 4:7; Lk 6:17 [r] S Ps 22:25

25:17 *heart.* See note on 4:7.

25:21 *integrity and uprightness.* Personified virtues (see 23:6 and note). Pardon is not enough; David prays that God will enable him to live a life of unmarred moral rectitude—even as God is "good and upright" (v. 8; see 51:10–12). *integrity.* See note on 15:2.

25:22 A concluding prayer in behalf of all God's people (see 3:8 and note).

Ps 26 A prayer for God's discerning mercies—to spare his faithful and godly servant from the death that overtakes the wicked and ungodly. This prayer for vindication (v. 1) because the psalmist has led "a blameless life" (v. 11) and has refused "to sit with the wicked" (v. 5) has its counterpoint (in the concentric arrangement of Ps 25–33; see introduction to Ps 25–33) in Ps 32, which celebrates the blessedness of those who have confessed their sins and been forgiven. The king's prayer for vindication suggests that he is threatened by the "deceitful" (v. 4) and "bloodthirsty" (v. 9) to whom he refers (as in Ps 23; 25; 27–28). This psalm is linked with Ps 27–28 (see also Ps 23–24) by the theme of the Lord's house: Here David's "love" (v. 8) for the temple (or tabernacle) testifies to the authenticity of his piety; in Ps 27 the Lord's temple is David's sanctuary from his enemies; in Ps 28 David directs his cry for help to the Lord's throne room ("your Most Holy Place," 28:2) in the temple. Three thematically important verbs ("lived," v. 3; "sit," vv. 4–5; "stand," v. 12) recall the three thematic verbs of 1:1.

26:1–8 An appeal for God to take account of David's moral integrity, his unwavering trust and his genuine delight in the Lord—not a boast of self-righteousness, such as that of the Pharisee (Lk 18:9–14).

26:1 *blameless life.* A claim of moral integrity (see vv. 2–5; see also note on 15:2). *trusted.* Obedience and trust are the two sides of godliness, as the Abraham story exemplifies (see Ge 12:4 and note; 22:12; see also Ps 34:8–14 and note).

26:2 *heart … mind.* See note on 7:9.

26:3 *your unfailing love … your faithfulness.* That is, your unfailing love-and-faithfulness (see 40:10). David keeps his eye steadfastly on the Lord's great love (see note on 6:4) and faithfulness (see 25:10), which are pledged to those "who keep the demands of his covenant" (25:10). *lived in reliance on.* In order to receive the covenant benefits.

26:4–5 *sit with.* David refuses to settle in or associate himself with that company he describes as "deceitful," "hypocrites," "evildoers," "wicked" (see 1:1 and note; see also Ps 101).

26:4 *hypocrites.* Context may suggest those who deal fraudulently—or people like those described in Pr 6:12–14.

26:6 *wash my hands in innocence.* Reference appears to be to a ritual claiming innocence. "Clean hands and a pure heart" are requisite for those who come to God (see 24:4 and note). *go about your altar.* To vocally celebrate God's saving acts beside his altar was a public act of devotion in which one also invited all the assembled worshipers to praise the Lord (see 43:3–4).

26:7 *your praise.* See note on 9:1.

26:8 *where your glory dwells.* Cf. note on Eze 1:1–28. The presence of God's glory signaled the presence of God himself (see Ex 24:16; 33:22). His glory dwelling in the tabernacle (see Ex 40:34 and note) and later the temple (see 1Ki 8:11) assured Israel of the Lord's holy, yet gracious, presence among them. Jn 1:14 announces that same presence in the Word who became flesh and who "made his dwelling among us."

26:9–11 An appeal that God will not bring on David the end (death) that awaits the wicked.

26:9 *soul.* See note on 6:3.

26:11 *lead a blameless life.* A return to the appeal with which David began (see v. 1).

26:12 A concluding confession of confidence (see note on 3:8) and a vow to praise God (see note on 7:17). *level ground.* Where the going is smooth and free from the danger of

Psalm 27

Of David.

[1]The LORD is my light[s] and my
salvation[t]—
whom shall I fear?
The LORD is the stronghold[u] of my life—
of whom shall I be afraid?[v]

[2]When the wicked advance against me
to devour[a] me,
it is my enemies and my foes
who will stumble and fall.[w]
[3]Though an army besiege me,
my heart will not fear;[x]
though war break out against me,
even then I will be confident.[y]

[4]One thing[z] I ask from the LORD,
this only do I seek:
that I may dwell in the house of the
LORD
all the days of my life,[a]
to gaze on the beauty of the LORD
and to seek him in his temple.
[5]For in the day of trouble[b]
he will keep me safe[c] in his dwelling;
he will hide me[d] in the shelter of his
sacred tent
and set me high upon a rock.[e]

[6]Then my head will be exalted[f]
above the enemies who
surround me;[g]
at his sacred tent I will sacrifice[h] with
shouts of joy;[i]
I will sing[j] and make music[k] to the
LORD.

[7]Hear my voice[l] when I call, LORD;
be merciful to me and answer me.[m]
[8]My heart says of you, "Seek his face![n]"
Your face, LORD, I will seek.
[9]Do not hide your face[o] from me,
do not turn your servant away in
anger;[p]
you have been my helper.[q]
Do not reject me or forsake[r] me,
God my Savior.[s]
[10]Though my father and mother forsake me,
the LORD will receive me.
[11]Teach me your way,[t] LORD;
lead me in a straight path[u]
because of my oppressors.[v]
[12]Do not turn me over to the desire of
my foes,
for false witnesses[w] rise up
against me,
spouting malicious accusations.

[13]I remain confident of this:
I will see the goodness of the LORD[x]
in the land of the living.[y]
[14]Wait[z] for the LORD;
be strong[a] and take heart
and wait for the LORD.

[a] 2 Or *slander*

27:1 [s]S 2Sa 22:29 [t]S Ex 15:2; S Ps 3:8 [u]Ps 9:9 [v]S Job 13:15; Ps 56:4,11; 118:6 **27:2** [w]Ps 9:3; S 20:8; 37:24; Da 11:19; Ro 11:11 **27:3** [x]S Ge 4:7; S Ps 3:6 [y]S Job 4:6 **27:4** [z]Lk 10:42 [a]Ps 23:6; 61:4 **27:5** [b]S Job 38:23 [c]S Ps 12:7 [d]S Ps 17:8 [e]Ps 40:2 **27:6** [f]2Sa 22:49; Ps 3:3; 18:48 [g]S Ps 22:12 [h]Ps 50:14; 54:6; 107:22; 116:17 [i]S Ezr 3:13; S Job 22:26 [j]S Ex 15:1 [k]Ps 33:2; 92:1; 147:7; S Eph 5:19 **27:7** [l]Ps 5:3; 18:6; 55:17; 119:149; 130:2; Isa 28:23 [m]S Ps 4:1 **27:8** [n]S 1Ch 16:11 **27:9** [o]S Dt 31:17; S Ps 22:24 [p]S Ps 2:5 [q]S Ge 49:25; S Dt 33:29 [r]S Dt 4:31; Ps 37:28; 119:8; Isa 41:17; 62:12; Jer 14:9 [s]Ps 18:46 **27:11** [t]S Ex 33:13 [u]S Ezr 8:21; Ps 5:8 [v]Ps 72:4; 78:42; 106:10; Jer 21:12 **27:12** [w]S Dt 19:16; S Mt 26:60; Ac 6:13; 1Co 15:15 **27:13** [x]Ex 33:19; S 2Ch 6:41; Ps 23:6; 31:19; 145:7 [y]S Job 28:13 **27:14** [z]Ps 33:20; 130:5,6; Isa 8:17; 30:18; Hab 2:3; Zep 3:8; Ac 1:4 [a]S Dt 1:21; S Jdg 5:21; S Eph 6:10

falling (see 143:10; Isa 40:4; 42:16). *congregation.* See note on 1:5 ("assembly"). *praise.* See note on 9:1.

Ps 27 David's triumphantly confident prayer to God to deliver him from all those who conspire to bring him down. The prayer presupposes the Lord's covenant with David (see 2Sa 7). Faith's soliloquy (in two stanzas: vv. 1–3,4–6), which publicly testifies to the king's confident reliance on the Lord, introduces the prayer of vv. 7–12. The conclusion (vv. 13–14) echoes the confidence of vv. 1–6 and adds faith's dialogue with itself—faith exhorting faith to wait patiently for that which is sure, though not yet seen (see Ps 42–43; Heb 11:1). See further the introduction to Ps 26. In the concentric arrangement of Ps 25–33 (see introduction to Ps 25–33), Ps 27 stands in counterpoint with Ps 31, a similar confident prayer for Yahweh's saving help as the psalmist's refuge when under attack. In both, the adversaries try to destroy the psalmist by spreading lies. Both psalms speak of keeping "safe" in Yahweh's "dwelling" (27:5; 31:20) and of hiding in the "shelter" of Yahweh's "sacred tent" (27:5) or "presence" (31:20). Both conclude with an exhortation to "be strong and take heart" out of hope in the Lord. In addition, they share other significant vocabulary—e.g., reference to the "goodness"/"good things" of Yahweh (27:13; 31:19).

27:1–3 The king's security in the Lord in the face of all that his enemies can do (see Ps 2).

27:1 *light.* Often symbolizes well-being (see 97:11; Job 18:5–6; 22:28; 29:3; Pr 13:9; La 3:2) or life and salvation (see 18:28; Isa 9:2; 49:6; 58:8; 59:9; Jer 13:16; Am 5:18–20). To say "The LORD is my light" is to confess confidence in him as the source of these benefits (see Isa 10:17; 60:1–2,19–20; Mic 7:8–9; cf. also note on Col 1:12). *my salvation.* "My Savior" (v. 9).

27:2 *devour me.* See 7:2 and note.

27:3 *heart.* See note on 4:7.

27:4–6 The Lord's temple (or tabernacle) is the king's stronghold—because the Lord himself is his "stronghold" (v. 1; see notes on 9:11; 18:2).

27:4 *dwell in.* See note on 15:1. *beauty of the LORD.* His unfailing benevolence (see 90:17: "favor of the Lord").

27:5 *shelter of his sacred tent.* See 31:20; 32:7; 61:4; 91:1.

27:6 *I will sacrifice.* See note on 7:17. *I will sing.* See note on 9:1.

27:7–12 Prayer for deliverance from treacherous enemies. Their chief weapon is false charges intent on discrediting the king (see note on 5:9).

27:7 *I call ... answer me.* See note on 118:5.

27:9 *hide your face.* See note on 13:1. *anger.* See note on 2:5. *you have been my helper.* Or "be my helper." *Do not ... forsake me.* See Dt 31:6 and note.

27:10 *the LORD will receive me.* Or "may the LORD receive me."

27:11 *Teach me your way.* Only those who know and do the Lord's will can expect to receive favorable response to their prayers (see Ps 24–26; see also 2Sa 7:14). *lead me in a straight path.* See 5:8 and note.

27:13–14 Concluding note of confidence (see note on 3:8).

27:13 *goodness of the LORD.* The "good" things promised in the Lord's covenant with David (see 2Sa 7:28; see also 31:19 and note). *land of the living.* This life.

27:14 *Wait for the LORD.* Faith encouraging faith (see 42:5,11; 43:5; 62:5).

Psalm 28

Of David.

1 To you, LORD, I call;
you are my Rock,
do not turn a deaf ear[b] to me.
For if you remain silent,[c]
I will be like those who go down to the pit.[d]
2 Hear my cry for mercy[e]
as I call to you for help,
as I lift up my hands[f]
toward your Most Holy Place.[g]

3 Do not drag me away with the wicked,
with those who do evil,
who speak cordially with their neighbors
but harbor malice in their hearts.[h]
4 Repay them for their deeds
and for their evil work;
repay them for what their hands have done[i]
and bring back on them what they deserve.[j]

5 Because they have no regard for the deeds of the LORD
and what his hands have done,[k]
he will tear them down
and never build them up again.

6 Praise be to the LORD,[l]
for he has heard my cry for mercy.[m]
7 The LORD is my strength[n] and my shield;
my heart trusts[o] in him, and he helps me.
My heart leaps for joy,[p]
and with my song I praise him.[q]

8 The LORD is the strength[r] of his people,
a fortress of salvation[s] for his anointed one.[t]
9 Save your people[u] and bless your inheritance;[v]
be their shepherd[w] and carry them[x] forever.

Psalm 29

A psalm of David.

1 Ascribe to the LORD,[y] you heavenly beings,[z]
ascribe to the LORD glory[a] and strength.

28:1 [b] S Dt 1:45 [c] S Est 4:14 [d] S Job 33:18 **28:2** [e] Ps 17:1; 61:1; 116:1; 130:2; 142:1; 143:1 [f] S Ezr 9:5; Ps 63:4; 141:2; La 2:19; 1Ti 2:8 [g] Ps 5:7; 11:4 **28:3** [h] Ps 12:2; S 26:4; 55:21; Jer 9:8 **28:4** [i] Ps 62:12; 2Ti 4:14; Rev 22:12 [j] La 3:64; Rev 18:6 **28:5** [k] Isa 5:12 **28:6** [l] S Ge 24:27; 2Co 1:3; Eph 1:3; 1Pe 1:3 [m] ver 2 **28:7** [n] S Ps 18:1 [o] Ps 13:5; 112:7; Isa 26:3 [p] S Dt 16:15; S Ps 16:9 [q] Ps 33:3; 40:3; 69:30; 144:9; 149:1 **28:8** [r] Ps 18:1 [s] S Ex 15:2; Ps 27:1; Hab 3:13 [t] S Ps 20:6 **28:9** [u] 1Ch 16:35; Ps 106:47; 118:25 [v] S Ex 34:9 [w] 1Ch 11:2; S Ps 23:1; 78:52,71; 80:1; Isa 40:11; Jer 31:10; Eze 34:12-16, 23,31; Mic 7:14 [x] S Dt 1:31; 32:11; Isa 46:3; 63:9 **29:1** [y] ver 2; 1Ch 16:28 [z] S 2Sa 1:19; Ps 103:20; Isa 10:13 [a] Ps 8:1

Ps 28 A prayer for deliverance from deadly peril at the hands of malicious and God-defying enemies. As with Ps 25, the prayer ends with intercession for all the people of the Lord (see 3:8 and note). Reference in the last verse to the Lord as the shepherd of his people connects this psalm with Ps 23. However, in the concentric arrangement of Ps 25–33 (see introduction to Ps 25–33) it is linked more closely with Ps 30. In Ps 28 the psalmist cries to Yahweh "for mercy" (vv. 2,6) when about to go "down to the pit" (v. 1); in Ps 30 the psalmist praises Yahweh for having heard his cry "for mercy" (vv. 8,11) and sparing him from going "down to the pit" (v. 3). These two psalms are also linked by other significant language: cf. 28:1 and 30:8 ("To you, LORD, I call[ed]"); 28:2 and 30:2 ("call[ed] to you for help"); 28:7 ("he helps me") and 30:10 ("be my help").
28:1–2 Initial appeal to be heard.
28:1 *Rock.* See note on 18:2. *remain silent.* Do not act in my behalf. *pit.* Metaphor for the grave (see note on 30:1).
28:2 *lift up my hands.* In worship and prayer (see 63:4; 134:2; 141:2). *Most Holy Place.* The inner sanctuary of the temple (see 1Ki 6:5), where the ark of the covenant stood (see 1Ki 8:6–8); it was God's throne room on earth.
28:3–5 Prayer for the Lord, enthroned in the temple, to deliver his servant and deal in judgment with those who harbor malice toward the king and God's people and defy God himself.
28:3 *harbor malice.* See note on 5:9. *hearts.* See note on 4:7.
28:4 *Repay them.* See note on 5:10; see also Mt 16:27; 2Ti 4:14; Rev 20:12–13; 22:12.
28:5 This expression of confidence climaxes the prayer and prepares for the shift to praise in vv. 6–7. *deeds of the LORD.* His redemption of Israel, the establishment of Israel as his kingdom (by covenant, Ex 19–24), and the appointment of the house of David (also by covenant, 2Sa 7) as his earthly regent over his people. *what his hands have done.* By "what their hands have done" (v. 4), "the wicked" (v. 3) show that they do not acknowledge Israel and David's regency as the work of God's hands. *he will tear.* Or "may he tear."
28:6–7 Joyful praise, in confidence of being heard (see note on 3:8).
28:7 *shield.* See note on 3:3. *heart.* See note on 4:7.
28:8–9 The Lord and his people (see note on 3:8).
28:8 *people ... anointed one.* These constitute a unity (see note on 2:2).
28:9 *Save ... bless.* God's two primary acts by which he effects his people's well-being: He saves from time to time as circumstances require; he blesses day by day to make their lives and labors fruitful. *your inheritance.* See Dt 9:29. *shepherd.* See introduction; see also 80:1; Isa 40:11; Jer 31:10; Eze 34; Mic 5:4 and note on Ps 23:1. The answer to this prayer—the last, full answer—has come in the ministry of the "good shepherd" (Jn 10:11,14).
Ps 29 A hymn in praise of the King of creation, whose glory is trumpeted by the thunderclaps that rumble through the cloudy mass of winter's rainstorms as they rise above the Mediterranean ("the mighty waters," v. 3), and move from west to east across the face of the sky, sweeping over the Lebanon range (vv. 5–6) and reaching the wilds of (northern) Kadesh on the upper reaches of the Orontes River (v. 8). The glory of the Lord is not only visible in the creation (19:1–6; see introduction to that psalm; see also Ps 104); it is also audible in creation's most awesome voice. (The most powerful forces experienced by the ancients were earthquakes, the raging sea, and heavy thunderstorms.) This hymn to Yahweh ("the LORD") served also as a testimony and protest against the worship of the Canaanite god Baal, who was thought to be the divine power present in the thunderstorm (cf. 31:6). Its placement marks it as the hinge psalm in the concentric arrangement of Ps 25–33 (see introduction to Ps 25–33), a placement and function similar to that of Ps 19 (see introduction to Ps 15–24). In the midst of prayer and praise, it reminds

[2]Ascribe to the LORD the glory due
his name;
worship the LORD in the splendor
of his[a] holiness.[b]

[3]The voice[c] of the LORD is over the
waters;
the God of glory[d] thunders,[e]
the LORD thunders over the
mighty waters.[f]
[4]The voice of the LORD is powerful;[g]
the voice of the LORD is majestic.
[5]The voice of the LORD breaks the
cedars;
the LORD breaks in pieces the
cedars of Lebanon.[h]
[6]He makes Lebanon leap[i] like a calf,
Sirion[bj] like a young wild ox.[k]
[7]The voice of the LORD strikes
with flashes of lightning.[l]
[8]The voice of the LORD shakes the
desert;
the LORD shakes the Desert of
Kadesh.[m]
[9]The voice of the LORD twists the
oaks[cn]
and strips the forests bare.
And in his temple all cry, "Glory!"[o]

[10]The LORD sits enthroned over the
flood;[p]
the LORD is enthroned as King
forever.[q]
[11]The LORD gives strength to his people;[r]
the LORD blesses his people with
peace.[s]

Cedar trees are still common in modern Lebanon today. Psalm 29:5 boasts of the Lord's glory and strength: "The voice of the LORD breaks the cedars; the LORD breaks in pieces the cedars of Lebanon."

Psalm 30[d]

A psalm. A song. For the dedication
of the temple.[e] Of David.

[1]I will exalt[t] you, LORD,
for you lifted me out of the depths[u]
and did not let my enemies gloat
over me.[v]

[a] 2 Or *LORD with the splendor of* [b] 6 That is, Mount Hermon [c] 9 Or *LORD makes the deer give birth* [d] In Hebrew texts 30:1-12 is numbered 30:2-13. [e] Title: Or *palace*

29:2 [b]S 1Ch 16:29; Ps 96:7-9 **29:3** [c]Job 37:5 [d]S Ps 24:7; Ac 7:2 [e]S 1Sa 2:10; Ps 18:13; 46:6; 68:33; 77:17; Jer 10:13; 25:30; Joel 2:11; Am 1:2 [f]S Ex 15:10 **29:4** [g]Ps 68:33 **29:5** [h]S Jdg 9:15 **29:6** [i]Ps 114:4 [j]Dt 3:9 [k]S Nu 23:22; Job 39:9; Ps 92:10 **29:7** [l]Eze 1:14; Rev 8:5 **29:8** [m]Nu 13:26; S 20:1 **29:9** [n]Isa 2:13; Eze 27:6; Am 2:9 [o]Ps 26:8 **29:10** [p]Ge 6:17 [q]S Ex 15:18 **29:11** [r]S Ps 18:1; 28:8; 68:35 [s]S Lev 26:6; S Nu 6:26 **30:1** [t]S Ex 15:2 [u]Job 11:8; Ps 63:9; 107:26; Pr 9:18; Isa 14:15 [v]S Ps 22:17

those who meditate on the psalms and use them as their own that the One with whom they have to do is the mighty Lord over all that is. All creation displays his power and glory, evoking awe and praise (vv. 1–2), but his gracious ways with his people (v. 11) also invite confident prayer in every need.

In its structure a two-verse introduction and a two-verse conclusion enclose a seven-verse stanza. In both the introduction and the conclusion the name Yahweh ("the LORD") is sounded four times; in the body of the psalm it is heard ten times. "The voice of the LORD" is repeated seven times in vv. 3–9—the seven thunders of God. (The number seven often signifies completeness in the Bible.)

29:1–2 A summons to all beings in the divine realm (see note on v. 1) to worship the Lord—adapted from a conventional call to praise in the liturgy of the temple (see 96:7–9; 1Ch 16:28–29).

29:1 *heavenly beings.* Lit. "sons of god(s)." Perhaps reference is to the angelic host (see 103:20; 148:2; Job 1:6 and NIV text note; 2:1 and NIV text note; Isa 6:2) or possibly to all those foolishly thought to be gods—as in Ps 97 (see 97:7), which has several thematic links with this psalm. The Lord alone must be acknowledged as the divine King.

29:2 *name.* See note on 5:11. *in the splendor of his holiness.* A rather literal translation of a difficult Hebrew phrase (see NIV text note; see also 96:9; 110:3; 1Ch 16:29; 2Ch 20:21). It is uncertain whether it describes God himself or the sanctuary or the (priestly) garb the worshipers are to wear when they approach God. The use of an almost identical Hebrew phrase in 110:3 (translated "in holy splendor") seems to support the last alternative, but the Hebrew text and the context of 2Ch 20:21 favor "in the splendor of his holiness."

29:3–9 Praise of the Lord, whose voice is the crashing thunder (see 68:4,33). The sound and fury of creation's awesome displays of power proclaim the glory of Israel's God.

29:5 *cedars of Lebanon.* The most majestic and highly prized trees of the Middle East (see SS 5:15 and note; see also photo above).

29:6 *leap.* See 114:4 and note.

29:9 *temple.* A primary thematic link with Ps 23–28. Reference may be to the temple in Jerusalem or to God's heavenly temple, where he sits enthroned (see 2:4; 11:4; 113:5; Isa 6:1; 40:22) as the Lord of all creation. But perhaps it is the creation itself that here is named God's temple (see note on 24:2). Then the "all" (those who cry "Glory!") is absolutely all—all creation shouts his praise (cf. 150:6). *Glory!* See note on 26:8.

29:10–11 The Lord's absolute and everlasting rule is committed to his people's complete salvation and unmixed blessedness—the crowning comfort in a world where threatening tides seem to make everything uncertain.

29:10 *enthroned over the flood.* As the One who by his word brought the ordered creation out of the formless "deep" (Ge 1:2,6–10).

Ps 30 A song of praise publicly celebrating the Lord's deliverance from the threat of death, probably brought on by illness ("you healed me," v. 2; see note on 7:17). For its relationship to Ps 28, see introduction to that psalm. The psalm is framed by commitments to praise (see vv. 1,12).

30 title *A song.* See titles of Ps 18; 45–46; 48; 65–68; 75–76; 83;

2 LORD my God, I called to you for help,[w]
and you healed me.[x]
3 You, LORD, brought me up from the
realm of the dead;[y]
you spared me from going down to
the pit.[z]
4 Sing[a] the praises of the LORD, you his
faithful people;[b]
praise his holy name.[c]
5 For his anger[d] lasts only a moment,[e]
but his favor lasts a lifetime;[f]
weeping[g] may stay for the night,
but rejoicing comes in the morning.[h]
6 When I felt secure, I said,
"I will never be shaken."[i]
7 LORD, when you favored me,
you made my royal mountain[a] stand
firm;
but when you hid your face,[j]
I was dismayed.

8 To you, LORD, I called;
to the Lord I cried for mercy:
9 "What is gained if I am silenced,
if I go down to the pit?[k]
Will the dust praise you?
Will it proclaim your faithfulness?[l]
10 Hear,[m] LORD, and be merciful to me;[n]
LORD, be my help.[o]"

11 You turned my wailing[p] into dancing;[q]
you removed my sackcloth[r] and
clothed me with joy,[s]
12 that my heart may sing your praises
and not be silent.
LORD my God, I will praise[t] you
forever.[u]

Psalm 31[b]

31:1-4pp — Ps 71:1-3

For the director of music.
A psalm of David.

1 In you, LORD, I have taken refuge;[v]
let me never be put to shame;
deliver me in your righteousness.[w]

30:2 [w] Ps 5:2; 88:13 [x] S Nu 12:13 **30:3** [y] S Ps 16:10; S 56:13 [z] Ps 28:1; 55:23; 69:15; 86:13; 143:7; Pr 1:12; Isa 38:17; Jnh 2:6 **30:4** [a] Ps 33:1; 47:7; 68:4 [b] S Ps 16:3 [c] Ex 3:15; Ps 33:21; 103:1; 145:21 **30:5** [d] Ps 103:9 [e] S Job 14:13 [f] S Ezr 3:11 [g] 2Sa 15:30; Ps 6:6; 126:6; Jer 31:16 [h] 2Co 4:17 **30:6** [i] S Job 29:18 **30:7** [j] S Dt 31:17 **30:9** [k] S Job 33:18; Isa 38:18 [l] S Ps 6:5; 88:11 **30:10** [m] S Ps 17:1 [n] Ps 4:1 [o] S Ps 20:2

[a] *7* That is, Mount Zion [b] In Hebrew texts 31:1-24 is numbered 31:2-25.

30:11 [p] S Est 4:1 [q] S Ex 15:20 [r] S 2Sa 3:31; S Ps 35:13 [s] S Dt 16:15; S Ps 16:9 **30:12** [t] Ps 35:18; 75:1; 118:21; Rev 11:17 [u] Ps 44:8; 52:9 **31:1** [v] S Ps 7:1 [w] Ps 5:8

87–88; 92; 108—all psalms of praise except 83; 88. In addition there are the songs "of ascents" (Ps 120–134). *For the dedication of the temple. Of David.* If "Of David" indicates authorship, the most probable occasion for the psalm is recorded in 1Ch 21:1—22:6. In 1Ch 22:1–6 David dedicated both property and building materials for the temple, and he may well have intended that Ps 30 be used at the dedication of the temple itself. If this is the case, vv. 2–3 would refer to David's predicament in 1Ch 21:17–30. The "favor" of v. 5 would be an echo of the "mercy" of 1Ch 21:13, and v. 6 would refer to his sin of misplaced trust in a large, superior army (see 1Ch 21:1–8). Later, the psalm came to be applied to the exile experience of Israel. In Jewish liturgical practice dating from Talmudic times it is chanted at Hanukkah, the festival that celebrates the rededication of the temple by Judas Maccabeus (165 BC) after its desecration by Antiochus Epiphanes (168). In such communal use, the "I" of the psalm becomes the collective "person" of Israel—a common mode of speaking in the OT.

30:1–3 Introductory announcement of the occasion for praise.

30:1 *lifted me out of the depths.* The vivid imagery that associates distress with "the depths"—so expressive of universal human experience—is common in OT poetry (see 69:2,15; 71:20; 88:6; 130:1; La 3:55; Jnh 2:2). The depths are often linked, as here, with Sheol ("the realm of the dead," v. 3) and "the pit" (v. 3), together with a cluster of related associations: silence (see 31:17; 94:17; 115:17; 1Sa 2:9), darkness (see 88:6,12; 143:3; Job 10:21–22; 17:13; Ecc 6:4; La 3:6), destruction (see v. 9; 18:4; 55:23, "decay"; 88:11; Isa 38:17; Hos 13:14), dust (see v. 9; 7:5; 22:15,29; Job 17:16; 40:13; Isa 26:19; 29:4), mire (see 40:2; 69:2,14), slime (see 40:2) and mud (see 40:2; Job 30:19). See also note on 49:14. *my enemies gloat over me.* See introduction to Ps 6.

30:3 *realm of the dead.* Figurative of a "brink-of-death" experience, as in 18:5; Jnh 2:2. *pit.* See note on 28:1.

30:4–5 Call to the gathered worshipers to take up the praise of God (see note on 9:1).

30:4 *faithful people.* See note on 4:3. *name.* Lit. "memorial" or "name of renown" (see 97:12; 135:13; Isa 26:8; Hos 12:5). The Hebrew evokes Ex 3:15 and refers to the name around which clustered memories of all that God had done, especially in Israel's history.

30:5 *anger.* See note on 2:5. *lasts only a moment.* See Isa 54:7. *stay for the night.* The figure is that of a guest lodging for only one night.

30:6–10 Expanded recollection of the Lord's gracious deliverance.

30:6–7 In his security he had grown arrogant, forgetful of who had made his "mountain stand firm," but the Lord reminded him.

30:6 *never be shaken.* He spoke as do the wicked (see 10:6), hence lost the blessing of the righteous (see 15:5). *shaken.* See note on 10:6.

30:7 *made my royal mountain stand firm.* Reference may be to David's security in his mountain fortress, Zion; or that mountain fortress may here serve as a metaphor for David's state as a vigorous and victorious king, the "mountain" on which he sat with such secure confidence in God. *hid your face.* See note on 13:1.

30:8–10 Shattered strength swept away all self-reliance; at the brink of death his cries for God's mercy rose.

30:9 See note on 6:5. *your faithfulness.* To your covenant.

30:11–12 God answered—and David vows to prolong his praise forever (see note on 7:17). Dancing and joy replace wailing and sackcloth, so that songs of praise, not silence, may attend the acts of God.

30:11 *sackcloth.* A coarse, black fabric (see Isa 50:3; Rev 11:3 and note) woven of goat hair and commonly used for making sacks. It was worn as a symbol of mourning (see 35:13; 69:11 and note on Ge 37:34).

30:12 *heart.* Lit. "glory" (see note on 7:5).

Ps 31 A prayer for deliverance when confronted by a conspiracy so powerful and pervasive that all David's friends abandoned him. According to Lk 23:46, Jesus on the cross applied Ps 31:5 to his own circumstances; thus those who share in his sufferings at the hands of anti-Christian forces are encouraged to hear and use this psalm in a new light (see Ac 7:59; 1Pe 4:19). No psalm expresses a more sturdy trust in the Lord when powerful human forces threaten. The heart of the prayer itself is found in vv. 9–18, which are

[2]Turn your ear to me,[x]
come quickly to my rescue;[y]
be my rock of refuge,[z]
a strong fortress to save me.
[3]Since you are my rock and my fortress,[a]
for the sake of your name[b] lead and guide me.
[4]Keep me free from the trap[c] that is set for me,
for you are my refuge.[d]
[5]Into your hands I commit my spirit;[e]
deliver me, LORD, my faithful God.[f]

[6]I hate those who cling to worthless idols;[g]
as for me, I trust in the LORD.[h]
[7]I will be glad and rejoice in your love,
for you saw my affliction[i]
and knew the anguish[j] of my soul.
[8]You have not given me into the hands[k] of the enemy
but have set my feet in a spacious place.[l]

[9]Be merciful to me, LORD, for I am in distress;[m]
my eyes grow weak with sorrow,[n]
my soul and body[o] with grief.
[10]My life is consumed by anguish[p]
and my years by groaning;[q]
my strength fails[r] because of my affliction,[a][s]
and my bones grow weak.[t]
[11]Because of all my enemies,[u]
I am the utter contempt[v] of my neighbors[w]
and an object of dread to my closest friends—
those who see me on the street flee from me.
[12]I am forgotten as though I were dead;[x]
I have become like broken pottery.
[13]For I hear many whispering,[y]
"Terror on every side!"[z]
They conspire against me[a]
and plot to take my life.[b]

[14]But I trust[c] in you, LORD;
I say, "You are my God."
[15]My times[d] are in your hands;
deliver me from the hands of my enemies,
from those who pursue me.
[16]Let your face shine[e] on your servant;
save me in your unfailing love.[f]
[17]Let me not be put to shame,[g] LORD,
for I have cried out to you;
but let the wicked be put to shame
and be silent[h] in the realm of the dead.
[18]Let their lying lips[i] be silenced,
for with pride and contempt
they speak arrogantly[j] against the righteous.

[19]How abundant are the good things[k]
that you have stored up for those who fear you,

[a] *10* Or *guilt*

31:2 [x]S Ps 6:4 [y]S Ex 2:17 [z]S 2Sa 22:3; S Ps 18:2 **31:3** [a]S Ps 18:2 [b]S Ps 23:3 **31:4** [c]S 1Sa 28:9; S Job 18:10 [d]Ps 9:9 **31:5** [e]Lk 23:46; Ac 7:59 [f]Isa 45:19; 65:16 **31:6** [g]S Dt 32:21 [h]S Ps 4:5 **31:7** [i]S Ps 13:3 [j]S Ps 25:17; Lk 22:44 **31:8** [k]S Dt 32:30 [l]S 2Sa 22:20 **31:9** [m]Ps 4:1 [n]Ps 6:7 [o]Ps 63:1 **31:10** [p]ver 7 [q]Ps 6:6 [r]Ps 22:15; 32:4; 38:10; 73:26 [s]Ps 25:18 [t]S Ps 6:2 **31:11** [u]Dt 30:7; Ps 3:7; 25:19; 102:8 [v]S Ps 22:6 [w]Ps 38:11 **31:12** [x]Ps 28:1; 88:4 **31:13** [y]S Lev 19:16; Ps 50:20 [z]S Job 18:11; Isa 13:8; Jer 6:25; 20:3, 10; 46:5; 49:5; La 2:22 [a]Ps 41:7; 56:6; 71:10; 83:3 [b]S Ge 37:18; S Mt 12:14 **31:14** [c]Ps 4:5 **31:15** [d]S Job 14:5 **31:16** [e]S Nu 6:25 [f]S Ps 6:4 **31:17** [g]S Ps 22:5 [h]1Sa 2:9; Ps 94:17; 115:17 **31:18** [i]Ps 120:2; Pr 10:18; 26:24 [j]S 1Sa 2:3; Jude 1:15 **31:19** [k]S Ps 27:13; Ro 11:22

both preceded and followed by nine Hebrew poetic lines—stanzas that resound with the theme of trust (see v. 14). Verse 13, at the center of the psalm, expresses most clearly the prayer's occasion. For the linkage of this psalm with Ps 27, see introduction to that psalm.

31 title *For the director of music.* See note on Ps 4 title.

31:1–5 Initial appeal to the Lord, the faithful refuge.

31:1 *righteousness.* See note on 4:1.

31:2 *rock.* See note on 18:2.

31:3 *for the sake of your name.* God's honor is at stake in the safety of his servant now under attack (see note on 23:3). *name.* See note on 5:11. *lead and guide.* As a shepherd (see 23:2–3 and notes).

31:4 *trap that is set for me.* By his enemies (see v. 11; see also note on 9:15).

31:5 *Into your hands I commit my spirit.* The climactic expression of trust in the Lord—echoed by Jesus in Lk 23:46. *commit.* Lit. "deposit" (as in Jer 36:20, "put"), here in the very hands of God, thus entrusting to God's care (see Lev 6:4; 1Ki 14:27). *my spirit.* His very life. *faithful God.* The trustworthy God (see note on 30:9).

31:6–8 Confession of loyal trust in the Lord, whose past mercies to David when enemies threatened are joyfully recalled.

31:6 *hate.* Refuse to be associated with. *who cling to worthless idols.* See Jnh 2:8. *cling to.* Lit. "watch" (expectantly for the help of; see 59:9 and note).

31:7 *love.* See vv. 16,21; see also note on 6:4. *soul.* See note on 6:3.

31:8 *spacious place.* See note on 18:19.

31:9–13 The distress described: He is utterly drained physically and emotionally (see vv. 9–10; see also 22:14–15); all his friends have abandoned him like a piece of broken pottery (see vv. 11–12); and all this because the conspiracy against him is so strong (v. 13).

31:9 *eyes grow weak.* See note on 13:3. *soul.* See note on 6:3.

31:10 *bones.* See note on 6:2.

31:11–12 Abandonment by friends was a common experience at a time when God seemed to have withdrawn his favor (see 38:11; 41:9; 69:8; 88:8,18; Job 19:13–19; Jer 12:6; 15:17).

31:13 *many whispering.* See note on 5:9. *Terror on every side!* See notes on Jer 6:25; 20:3.

31:14–18 His trust in the Lord is unwavering; his defense against his powerful enemies is his reliance on God's faithfulness and discerning judgment.

31:14 Cf. v. 22.

31:15 *My times are in your hands.* All the events and circumstances of life are in the hands of the Lord, "my God" (v. 14).

31:16 *face shine.* See note on 13:1.

31:17–18 *but let the wicked … be silenced.* See note on 5:10.

31:18 *lying lips.* See note on 5:9. *righteous.* See note on 1:5.

31:19–20 Confident anticipation of God's saving help (see note on 3:8).

31:19 *stored up.* David deposits his life in the hands of God to share in the covenant benefits that God has stored up for his faithful servants ("good things," Ex 18:9; Nu 10:29,32; Dt 26:11; Jos 23:15; Ne 9:25; Isa 63:7; Jer 33:9; see

that you bestow in the sight of all,[l]
on those who take refuge[m] in you.
20 In the shelter[n] of your presence you hide[o] them
from all human intrigues;[p]
you keep them safe in your dwelling
from accusing tongues.

21 Praise be to the LORD,[q]
for he showed me the wonders of his love[r]
when I was in a city under siege.[s]
22 In my alarm[t] I said,
"I am cut off[u] from your sight!"
Yet you heard my cry[v] for mercy
when I called to you for help.

23 Love the LORD, all his faithful people![w]
The LORD preserves those who are true to him,[x]
but the proud he pays back[y] in full.
24 Be strong and take heart,[z]
all you who hope in the LORD.

Psalm 32

Of David. A *maskil*.[a]

1 Blessed is the one
whose transgressions are forgiven,
whose sins are covered.[a]
2 Blessed is the one
whose sin the LORD does not count against them[b]
and in whose spirit is no deceit.[c]

3 When I kept silent,[d]
my bones wasted away[e]
through my groaning[f] all day long.
4 For day and night
your hand was heavy[g] on me;
my strength was sapped[h]
as in the heat of summer.[b]

5 Then I acknowledged my sin to you
and did not cover up my iniquity.[i]
I said, "I will confess[j]
my transgressions[k] to the LORD."
And you forgave
the guilt of my sin.[l]

6 Therefore let all the faithful pray to you
while you may be found;[m]
surely the rising[n] of the mighty waters[o]
will not reach them.[p]

31:19 [l] Ps 23:5 [m] Ps 2:12 **31:20** [n] Ps 55:8 [o] S Ps 17:8 [p] S Ge 37:18 **31:21** [q] Ps 28:6 [r] S Ps 17:7 [s] 1Sa 23:7 **31:22** [t] Ps 116:11 [u] Job 6:9; 17:1; Ps 37:9; 88:5; Isa 38:12 [v] Ps 6:9; 66:19; 116:1; 145:19 **31:23** [w] S Ps 4:3 [x] S Ps 18:25; Rev 2:10 [y] Dt 32:41; Ps 94:2 **31:24** [z] Ps 27:14 **32:1** [a] Ps 85:2; 103:3 **32:2** [b] S Ro 4:7-8* [c] Jn 1:47; Rev 14:5 **32:3** [d] S Job 31:34 [e] Ps 31:10 [f] S Job 3:24; Ps 6:6 **32:4** [g] 1Sa 5:6; S Job 9:34; Ps 38:2; 39:10 [h] Ps 22:15 **32:5** [i] Job 31:33 [j] Pr 28:13 [k] Ps 103:12 [l] S Lev 26:40; 1Jn 1:9 **32:6** [m] Ps 69:13; Isa 55:6 [n] Ps 69:1 [o] S Ex 15:10 [p] Isa 43:2

[a] Title: Probably a literary or musical term [b] 4 The Hebrew has *Selah* (a word of uncertain meaning) here and at the end of verses 5 and 7.

Jos 21:45; 23:14, "good promises"; 2Ch 6:41; Ne 9:25,35; Ps 27:13, "goodness"; Jer 31:12,14, "bounty"). *fear.* See note on 15:4. *bestow in the sight of all.* Thus showing the Lord's approval of and his standing with his faithful servants, in contrast to the accusations of their adversaries (see 86:17).
31:20 *shelter of your presence.* See note on 27:5. *accusing tongues.* See "whispering" (v. 13) and "lying lips" (v. 18).
31:21–22 Praise anticipating deliverance (see note on 12:5–6).
31:21 *city under siege.* Metaphor for the threat he had experienced.
31:22 *cut off from your sight.* See note on 13:1.
31:23–24 Praise culminates by encouraging the people of God (see 62:8).
31:23 *faithful people.* See note on 4:3. *those … true to him.* Those who maintain moral integrity and faithfulness to the Lord. *the proud.* Those who refuse to live in humble reliance on the Lord. They arrogantly try to make their way in the world either as a law to themselves (see, e.g., v. 18; 10:2–11; 73:6; 94:2–7; Dt 8:14; Isa 2:17; Eze 28:2,5; Hos 13:6) or by relying on false gods (see Jer 13:9–10). Hence "the proud" is often equivalent to "the wicked."
Ps 32 A grateful testimony of joy for God's gift of forgiveness toward those who with integrity confess their sins and are receptive to God's rule in their lives. The psalm appears to be a liturgical dialogue between David and God in the presence of the worshipers at the sanctuary. In vv. 1–2 and again in v. 11 David speaks to the assembly; in vv. 3–7 he speaks to God (in their hearing); in vv. 8–10 he is addressed by one of the Lord's priests (but see note on vv. 8–10). In traditional Christian usage, the psalm has been numbered among the penitential psalms (see introduction to Ps 6). Its placement in the concentric arrangement of Ps 25–33 (see introduction to Ps 25–33) suggests that the editors of the Psalter intended it to stand in counterpoint to Ps 26 (see introduction to that psalm).
32 title *maskil.* Occurs also in the titles of Ps 42; 44–45; 52–55; 74; 78; 88–89; 142. The Hebrew word may indicate that these psalms contain instruction in godliness (see 14:2; 53:2, "any who understand"; 41:1, "those who have regard"; but see also 47:7, where it is rendered "psalm").
32:1–2 Exuberant proclamation of the happy state of those who experience God's forgiveness. *Blessed … Blessed.* See note on 1:1. Repetition underscores. *are forgiven … are covered … does not count against them.* Repetition with variation emphasizes and illumines. For Paul's use of these verses, see Ro 4:6–8.
32:2 *in whose spirit is no deceit.* Only those honest with God receive pardon.
32:3–5 Testimony to a personal experience of God's pardon. God's heavy hand, pressing down "day and night" on the stubborn silence of unacknowledged sin, filled life with groaning, but full confession brought blessed relief. Neither the sin nor the form of suffering is identified, other than that the latter was physically and psychologically devastating. But it would be uncharacteristic of the Psalms to speak of mere emotional disturbance brought on by suppressed guilt. Some affliction, perhaps illness, was most likely the instrument of God's discipline (see Ps 38).
32:4 *strength was sapped.* Under God's heavy hand of discipline David wilted like a plant in the heat of summer. For *Selah*, see NIV text note and note on 3:2.
32:5 Again repetition is used (see note on vv. 1–2). *sin … iniquity … transgressions.* See 51:1–2; the three most common OT words for evil thoughts and actions (see Isa 59:12). *confess.* See Ps 51; 2Sa 12:13.
32:6–7 A chastened confession that life is secure only with God.
32:6 Though addressed to God as confession, it is also intended for the ears of the fellow worshipers. He admonishes them to "seek the LORD while he may be found … while he is near" (Isa 55:6) and not to foolishly provoke his

[7]You are my hiding place;[q]
you will protect me from trouble[r]
and surround me with songs of deliverance.[s]

[8]I will instruct[t] you and teach you[u] in the way you should go;
I will counsel you with my loving eye on[v] you.
[9]Do not be like the horse or the mule,
which have no understanding
but must be controlled by bit and bridle[w]
or they will not come to you.
[10]Many are the woes of the wicked,[x]
but the LORD's unfailing love
surrounds the one who trusts[y] in him.

[11]Rejoice in the LORD[z] and be glad, you righteous;
sing, all you who are upright in heart!

32:7 [q]S Jdg 9:35 [r]S Ps 9:9 [s]S Jdg 5:1 **32:8** [t]S Ps 25:8 [u]Ps 34:11 [v]Ps 33:18 **32:9** [w]S Job 30:11; S 39:10; Jas 3:3 **32:10** [x]Ro 2:9 [y]Ps 4:5; Pr 16:20 **32:11** [z]Ps 64:10

33:1 [a]S Ps 5:11; S 101:1 [b]Ps 147:1 [c]Ps 11:7 **33:2** [d]S Ge 4:21; 1Co 14:7; Rev 5:8 [e]Ps 92:3; 144:9 **33:3** [f]Ps 40:3; Isa 42:10; S Rev 5:9 [g]S Job 3:7; Ps 35:27; 47:1 **33:4** [h]S Ps 19:8 [i]Ps 119:142; Rev 19:9; 22:6 [j]Ps 18:25; 25:10 **33:5** [k]Ps 11:7 [l]Ps 6:4

Psalm 33

[1]Sing joyfully[a] to the LORD, you righteous;
it is fitting[b] for the upright[c] to praise him.
[2]Praise the LORD with the harp;[d]
make music to him on the ten-stringed lyre.[e]
[3]Sing to him a new song;[f]
play skillfully, and shout for joy.[g]

[4]For the word of the LORD is right[h] and true;[i]
he is faithful[j] in all he does.
[5]The LORD loves righteousness and justice;[k]
the earth is full of his unfailing love.[l]

withdrawal—and the coming near of his heavy hand—as David had done. A God who forgives is a God to whom one can entrust and devote one's life (see 130:4). *faithful.* See note on 4:3. *mighty waters.* Powerful imagery for threatening forces or circumstances. This and related imagery was borrowed from ancient Near Eastern creation myths. In many of these a primal mass of chaotic waters (their threatening and destructive forces were often depicted as a many-headed monster of the deep; see 74:13–14 and note) had to be subdued by the creator-god before he could fashion the world and/or rule as the divine king over the earth. Though in these myths the chaotic waters were subdued when the present world was created, they remained a constant threat to the security and well-being of the present order in the earth (the realm of dry land that is the normal habitat for people and animals). Hence by association they were linked with anything that in human experience endangered or troubled that order. They were also associated with the sea, whose angry waves seemed determined at times to engulf the land. Since in Canaanite mythology Sea and Death were the two great enemies of Baal ("lord" of earth), imagery drawn from both realms was used by OT poets, sometimes side by side, to depict threats and distress (see 18:4–5,16; 42:7; 65:7; 74:12–14; 77:16,19; 89:9–10; 93:3–4; 124:4–5; 144:7–8; Job 7:12; 26:12; 38:8–11; Isa 5:30; 8:7–8; 17:12–14; 51:9–10; Jer 5:22; 47:2; 51:55; Hab 3:8–10; see also note on SS 8:7). For imagery associated with the realm of death, see notes on 30:1; 49:14.

32:7 *surround me with songs of deliverance.* Because of your help, I will be surrounded by people celebrating your acts of deliverance, as I bring my thank offerings to you (see notes on 7:17; 9:1; see also 35:27; 51:8).

32:8–10 A priestly word of godly instruction, either to David (do not be foolish toward God again) or to those who have just been exhorted to trust in the Lord (to trust add obedience). Some believe that the psalmist himself here turns to others to warn them against the ways into which he has fallen (see 51:13 and note).

32:9 God's servants must be wiser than beasts, more open to God's will than horses and mules are to the will of their masters (see Isa 1:3).

32:10 *unfailing love.* See note on 6:4.

32:11 A final word to the assembled worshipers—let the praise of God resound (see note on 9:1). See also note on 1:5. *Rejoice in the LORD.* Cf. Php 4:4 and note. *heart.* See note on 4:7.

Ps 33 A liturgy in praise of the Lord, the sovereign God of Israel—a counterpoint to the acrostic prayer of Ps 25. These two psalms frame the intervening psalms (see introduction to Ps 25–33). In the Psalms, calls to praise (as in vv. 1–3) and motivations for praise (as in vv. 4–19) belong to the language of praise (see note on 9:1). Most likely the voices of the Levitical choir (see 1Ch 16:7–36; 25:1) are heard in this psalm. Perhaps the choir leader spoke in vv. 1–3, the choir in vv. 4–19, and the people responded with the words of vv. 20–22. The original occasion is unknown, but reference to a "new song" (see note on v. 3) suggests a national deliverance, such as Judah experienced in the time of Jehoshaphat (see 2Ch 20) or Hezekiah (see 2Ki 19); see vv. 10–11,16–17. Along with Ps 1–2; 10 (but see introduction to Ps 9), this is one of only four psalms in Book I without a superscription.

Although structurally not an alphabetic acrostic like the psalm that follows it, the length of the psalm (22 verses) has been determined by the length of the Hebrew alphabet (22 letters); see Ps 38; 103; La 5. The body of the psalm is framed by a three-verse introduction (call to praise) and a three-verse conclusion (response to praise). In vv. 4–19 are heard the praise of the Lord, developed in two parts of eight verses each (vv. 4–11,12–19). In the first of these a four-verse stanza (vv. 6–9) has been inserted between the two halves of the main stanza (vv. 4–5,10–11) to reinforce its theme. A similar use of this poetic device can be found in Ps 77 (see introduction to that psalm and note on 77:16–19).

33:1–3 The call to praise. Cf. Eph 5:19.

33:1 *righteous.* The assembly of worshipers (see note on 1:5).

33:3 *new song.* Celebrating God's saving act, as in 40:3; 96:1; 98:1; 144:9; 149:1; see Isa 42:10; Rev 5:9; 14:3; see also note on 7:17.

33:4–19 The praise, in two eight-verse parts.

33:4–11 Under the Lord's rule by his sovereign "word" (v. 4) his "plans" for his people "stand firm" (v. 11), even as the creation order "stood firm" (v. 9) because it was ordered by his sovereign "word" (v. 6). Hence his chosen people are the blessed nation (see vv. 12–19).

33:4 *word.* God's royal word, by which he governs all things (see 107:20; 147:15,18). *right and true.* Not chaotic, devious or erratic. Under the Lord's rule, order and goodness are present in the creation.

33:5 *loves.* Delights in doing. *righteousness and justice.* See

6 By the word[m] of the LORD the heavens
were made,[n]
their starry host[o] by the breath of his
mouth.
7 He gathers the waters[p] of the sea into
jars[a];[q]
he puts the deep into storehouses.
8 Let all the earth fear the LORD;[r]
let all the people of the world[s] revere
him.[t]
9 For he spoke, and it came to be;
he commanded,[u] and it stood firm.

10 The LORD foils[v] the plans[w] of the
nations;[x]
he thwarts the purposes of the
peoples.
11 But the plans of the LORD stand firm[y]
forever,
the purposes[z] of his heart through all
generations.

12 Blessed is the nation whose God is the
LORD,[a]
the people he chose[b] for his
inheritance.[c]
13 From heaven the LORD looks down[d]
and sees all mankind;[e]
14 from his dwelling place[f] he watches
all who live on earth—
15 he who forms[g] the hearts of all,
who considers everything they do.[h]

16 No king is saved by the size of his
army;[i]
no warrior escapes by his great
strength.
17 A horse[j] is a vain hope for deliverance;
despite all its great strength it cannot
save.
18 But the eyes[k] of the LORD are on those
who fear him,
on those whose hope is in his
unfailing love,[l]
19 to deliver them from death[m]
and keep them alive in famine.[n]

20 We wait[o] in hope for the LORD;
he is our help and our shield.
21 In him our hearts rejoice,[p]
for we trust in his holy name.[q]
22 May your unfailing love[r] be with us,
LORD,
even as we put our hope in you.

Psalm 34[b,c]

Of David. When he pretended to be
insane[s] before Abimelek, who
drove him away, and he left.

1 I will extol the LORD at all times;[t]
his praise will always be on my lips.

[a] 7 Or *sea as into a heap* [b] This psalm is an acrostic poem, the verses of which begin with the successive letters of the Hebrew alphabet. [c] In Hebrew texts 34:1-22 is numbered 34:2-23.

33:6 [m] S Ge 1:3; Heb 11:3 [n] S Ex 8:19; S 2Ch 2:12 [o] S Ge 1:16 **33:7** [p] S Ge 1:10 [q] S Jos 3:16 **33:8** [r] S Dt 6:13; Ps 2:11 [s] Ps 49:1; Isa 18:3; Mic 1:2 [t] S Dt 14:23 **33:9** [u] Ps 148:5 **33:10** [v] Isa 44:25 [w] S Job 5:12 [x] Ps 2:1 **33:11** [y] S Nu 23:19 [z] Jer 51:12, 29 **33:12** [a] Ps 144:15 [b] S Ex 8:22; Dt 7:6; Ps 4:3; 65:4; 84:4 [c] S Ex 34:9 **33:13** [d] Ps 53:2; 102:19 [e] Job 28:24; Ps 11:4; 14:2; S Heb 4:13 **33:14** [f] S Lev 15:31; 1Ki 8:39 **33:15** [g] Job 10:8; Ps 119:73 [h] S Job 10:4; Jer 32:19 **33:16** [i] 1Sa 14:6 **33:17** [j] S Ps 20:7 **33:18** [k] S Ex 3:16; S Ps 11:4; 1Pe 3:12 [l] S Ps 6:4 **33:19** [m] Ps 56:13; Ac 12:11 [n] S Job 5:20 **33:20** [o] S Ps 27:14 **33:21** [p] S 1Sa 2:1; S Joel 2:23 [q] S Ps 30:4; S 99:3 **33:22** [r] Ps 6:4 **34:Title** [s] 1Sa 21:13 **34:1** [t] Ps 71:6; S Eph 5:20; 1Th 5:18

note on 4:1. *his unfailing love.* Here, his goodness to all his creatures (see 36:5–9; 104:27–28; see also note on 6:4).
33:6 *word.* God's creating word (see v. 9; 104:7; 119:89; Ge 1; Job 38:8–11; Heb 11:3).
33:7 *into jars … storehouses.* Like a householder storing up olive oil and grain (see 104:9; Ge 1:9–10; Job 38:8–11; Pr 8:29; Jer 5:22).
33:8 *all the earth … all the people.* Not only Israel, but all humankind, for all experience the goodness of his sovereign rule (see note on 9:1)—but he foils all their contrary designs (vv. 10–11). *fear the LORD.* See v. 18; see also note on 15:4.
33:11 *heart.* See note on 4:7.
33:12–19 Israel is safe and secure under God's protective rule.
33:12 *Blessed.* See note on 1:1. *people he chose for his inheritance.* Israel (see Dt 7:6–9; 9:29).
33:16 *king.* Nation (see v. 12) and king constitute an organic social unit (see 28:8 and note).
33:17 See Pr 21:31 and note.
33:18–19 This concluding couplet of the second eight-verse unit of praise contrasts with the concluding couplet of the first (vv. 10–11); both are climactic, and together they voice the heart of the praise.
33:18,22 *unfailing love.* Here, his covenant favor toward Israel (see note on 6:4).
33:20–22 The people's response: faith's commitment expressed in confession (vv. 20–21) and petition (v. 22).
33:20 *shield.* See note on 3:3.
33:21 *hearts.* See note on 4:7. *name.* See note on 5:11.
Ps 34–37 This small grouping of four psalms is framed by two alphabetic acrostics that contain wisdom-like instruction (see essay, p. 786) in godliness and related warnings concerning the fate of the wicked—instruction and warnings that reinforce key themes in the two enclosed prayers (Ps 35–36).
Ps 34 An alphabetic acrostic that begins with praise of the Lord for deliverance in answer to prayer (vv. 1–7), then shifts to wisdom-like instruction. This shift is unusual in the Psalter (but see also Ps 92); more commonly, praise of the Lord leads to a call to praise, as in v. 3 (see note on 9:1). Together with Ps 37 it frames the two intervening psalms (see introduction to Ps 34–37). The structure of Ps 34 is somewhat complex, yet it is strikingly effective. Following an introduction of three verses, the poem's themes are developed in stanzas of four verses (4–7), seven verses (8–14), four verses (15–18) and four verses (19–22). For further details, see following notes.
34 title The superscription assigns this psalm to the occasion in David's life (see note on Ps 3 title) narrated in 1Sa 21:10–15—but note "Abimelek" rather than "Achish" (perhaps Abimelek was a traditional dynastic name or title for Philistine kings; see Ge 20; 21:22–34; 26). Not all agree with this tradition, however; some feel that it is more likely that early Hebrew editors of the Psalms linked 1Sa 21 with Ps 34 on the basis of word association (the Hebrew for "pretended to be insane," 1Sa 21:13, comes from the same root as the Hebrew used here for "Taste," v. 8).
34:1–7 Praise for the Lord's deliverance in answer to prayer.
34:1–3 Commitment to continual praise of the Lord—so that the godly who are afflicted may be encouraged (v. 2; see also the instruction that follows in vv. 8–22).

2 I will glory[u] in the LORD;
let the afflicted hear and rejoice.[v]
3 Glorify the LORD[w] with me;
let us exalt[x] his name together.

4 I sought the LORD,[y] and he answered me;
he delivered[z] me from all my fears.
5 Those who look to him are radiant;[a]
their faces are never covered with shame.[b]
6 This poor man called, and the LORD heard him;
he saved him out of all his troubles.[c]
7 The angel of the LORD[d] encamps around those who fear him,
and he delivers[e] them.

8 Taste and see that the LORD is good;[f]
blessed is the one who takes refuge[g] in him.
9 Fear the LORD,[h] you his holy people,
for those who fear him lack nothing.[i]
10 The lions may grow weak and hungry,
but those who seek the LORD lack no good thing.[j]
11 Come, my children, listen[k] to me;
I will teach you[l] the fear of the LORD.[m]
12 Whoever of you loves life[n]
and desires to see many good days,
13 keep your tongue[o] from evil
and your lips from telling lies.[p]
14 Turn from evil and do good;[q]
seek peace[r] and pursue it.

15 The eyes of the LORD[s] are on the righteous,[t]
and his ears are attentive[u] to their cry;
16 but the face of the LORD is against[v] those who do evil,[w]
to blot out their name[x] from the earth.

17 The righteous cry out, and the LORD hears[y] them;
he delivers them from all their troubles.
18 The LORD is close[z] to the brokenhearted[a]
and saves those who are crushed in spirit.

19 The righteous person may have many troubles,[b]
but the LORD delivers him from them all;[c]

34:2 [u] Ps 44:8; Jer 9:24; 1Co 1:31 [v] Ps 69:32; 107:42; 119:74 **34:3** [w] Ps 63:3; 86:12; Da 4:37; Jn 17:1; Ro 15:6 [x] S Ex 15:2 **34:4** [y] S Ex 32:11; Ps 77:2 [z] ver 17; Ps 18:43; 22:4; 56:13; 86:13 **34:5** [a] S Ex 34:29 [b] Ps 25:3; 44:15; 69:7; 83:16 **34:6** [c] S Ps 25:17 **34:7** [d] S Ge 32:1; S Da 3:28; S Mt 18:10 [e] Ps 22:4; 37:40; 41:1; 97:10; Isa 31:5; Ac 12:11 **34:8** [f] Heb 6:5; 1Pe 2:3 [g] S Ps 2:12 **34:9** [h] S Dt 6:13; Rev 14:7 [i] S Ps 23:1 **34:10** [j] S Ps 23:1 **34:11** [k] Ps 66:16 [l] S Ps 32:8 [m] S Ps 19:9 **34:12** [n] Ecc 3:13 **34:13** [o] Ps 39:1; 141:3; Pr 13:3; 21:23; Jas 1:26 [p] S Ps 12:2; 1Pe 2:22 **34:14** [q] Ps 37:27; Isa 1:17; 3Jn 1:11 [r] S Ro 14:19 **34:15** [s] Ps 33:18 [t] S Job 23:10; S 36:7 [u] Mal 3:16; S Jn 9:31 **34:16** [v] Lev 17:10; Jer 23:30 [w] 1Pe 3:10-12* [x] S Ex 17:14; Ps 9:6 **34:17** [y] Ps 145:19 **34:18** [z] Dt 4:7; Ps 119:151; 145:18; Isa 50:8 [a] Ps 51:17; 109:16; 147:3; Isa 61:1 **34:19** [b] ver 17; Ps 25:17 [c] S Job 5:19; 2Ti 3:11

34:2 *glory in the LORD.* That is, give the Lord all the praise.
34:3 *name.* See note on 5:11.
34:4 – 7 The occasion: God's saving answer to prayer. The theme is developed in alternating lines — an *a-b/a-b* pattern (note the shift from first-person singular references to third-person plural references — what Yahweh has done for the psalmist he will do for all those who "fear him," v. 7). For thematic links with vv. 15 – 18, see note on those verses.
34:5 *radiant.* With joy (see Isa 60:5).
34:6 *poor.* Here, as often in the Psalms, "poor" characterizes not necessarily one who has no possessions but one who is (and recognizes that he is) without resources to effect his own deliverance (or secure his own life, safety or well-being) — and so is dependent on God.
34:7 *angel of the LORD.* God's heavenly representative, his "messenger," sent to effect his will on earth (see 35:5 – 6; see also note on Ge 16:7). *encamps around.* The line speaks of the security with which the Lord surrounds his people, individually and collectively; it does not necessarily teach a doctrine of individual "guardian angels." *those who fear him.* Those described in vv. 8 – 14 (see note on 25:12).
34:8 – 14 Instruction in "the fear of the LORD." These verses are thematically linked, with a title line (v. 11) at the center — Hebrew authors often centered key lines (see note on 6:6). Note the pattern of the imperatives: "taste" (v. 8), "fear" (v. 9), "come" (v. 11), "keep" (v. 13), "turn" (v. 14). A symmetrical development of the theme "good" dominates the stanza: Because the Lord is "good" (v. 8), those who trust in him will lack nothing "good" (v. 10); but in order to experience "good days" (v. 12) they must shun evil and "do good" (v. 14). To trust and obey — that is "the fear of the LORD." On the instruction of this stanza, see Ps 37. For Peter's use of vv. 12 – 16, see 1Pe 3:8 – 12.
34:8 *blessed.* See note on 1:1.
34:9 *Fear the LORD.* See v. 11; see also note on 15:4. *holy people.* See notes on Ex 3:5; Lev 11:44; Ro 6:22; 1Co 1:2; 1Pe 1:16.
34:10 *those who seek the LORD lack no good thing.* See 84:11; see also introduction to Ps 23 and note on 23:1; cf. Am 5:4 and note.
34:11 *Come, my children.* Conventional language of the wisdom teachers (see Introduction to Proverbs: Purpose and Teaching).
34:13 See 15:2 – 3; Jas 3:5 – 10. For the tongue as a weapon, see note on 5:9.
34:14 *Turn from evil and do good.* A key link with Ps 37 (see 37:27). *seek peace.* See 37:37; 120:7; Pr 12:20; Zec 8:19 (also Zec 8:16 – 17); Mt 5:9; Ro 12:18; 1Co 7:15; 2Co 13:11; 1Th 5:13; Heb 12:14; Jas 3:17 – 18.
34:15 – 18 Assurance that the Lord hears the prayers of the righteous. He so thoroughly thwarts those who do evil that they are forgotten (v. 16). As in vv. 4 – 7, which these verses structurally balance, the theme is developed in alternating lines (in an *a-b/a-b* pattern). Furthermore, the corresponding lines of these two balanced stanzas are thematically, and sometimes even verbally, linked (cf. vv. 4 and 15, vv. 5 and 16, vv. 6 and 17, vv. 7 and 18); godly instruction is patterned after the praise. And these two stanzas, each of which has four Hebrew poetic lines, frame the intervening seven-line stanza (vv. 8 – 14).
34:15 *righteous.* See vv. 8 – 14; see also note on 1:5.
34:16 *face of the LORD.* See note on 13:1.
34:17 – 18 See especially 51:17.
34:19 – 22 Assurance that the Lord is the unfailing deliverer of the righteous — and that he holds the wicked accountable for their hostility toward the righteous (see v. 21). Here, too, an *a-b/a-b* thematic pattern appears to be employed (note the contrast expressed in vv. 19,21 and the reinforcement of v. 20 found in v. 22).

20 he protects all his bones,
not one of them will be broken.[d]
21 Evil will slay the wicked;[e]
the foes of the righteous will be condemned.
22 The LORD will rescue[f] his servants;
no one who takes refuge[g] in him will be condemned.

Psalm 35

Of David.

1 Contend,[h] LORD, with those who contend with me;
fight[i] against those who fight against me.
2 Take up shield[j] and armor;
arise[k] and come to my aid.[l]
3 Brandish spear[m] and javelin[a][n]
against those who pursue me.
Say to me,
"I am your salvation.[o]"

4 May those who seek my life[p]
be disgraced[q] and put to shame;[r]
may those who plot my ruin
be turned back[s] in dismay.
5 May they be like chaff[t] before the wind,
with the angel of the LORD[u] driving them away;
6 may their path be dark and slippery,
with the angel of the LORD pursuing them.
7 Since they hid their net[v] for me without cause[w]
and without cause dug a pit[x] for me,
8 may ruin overtake them by surprise—[y]
may the net they hid entangle them,
may they fall into the pit,[z] to their ruin.
9 Then my soul will rejoice[a] in the LORD
and delight in his salvation.[b]
10 My whole being will exclaim,
"Who is like you,[c] LORD?
You rescue the poor from those too strong[d] for them,
the poor and needy[e] from those who rob them."

11 Ruthless witnesses[f] come forward;
they question me on things I know nothing about.
12 They repay me evil for good[g]
and leave me like one bereaved.
13 Yet when they were ill, I put on sackcloth[h]
and humbled myself with fasting.[i]

34:20 [d] Jn 19:36* **34:21** [e] Ps 7:9; 9:16; 11:5; 37:20; 73:27; 94:23; 106:43; 112:10; 140:11; Pr 14:32; 24:16 **34:22** [f] S Ex 6:6; S 15:13; Lk 1:68; Rev 14:3 [g] Ps 2:12 **35:1** [h] S 1Sa 24:15 [i] S Ex 14:14 **35:2** [j] Ps 3:3 [k] Ps 3:7 [l] S Ge 50:24; S Job 17:3 **35:3** [m] S Nu 25:7 [n] S Jos 8:18 [o] Ps 27:1 **35:4** [p] Ps 38:12; 40:14; Jer 4:30 [q] Ps 69:6, 19; 70:2; 83:17; Isa 45:16; Mal 2:9 [r] Ps 25:3 [s] Ps 129:5 **35:5** [t] S Job 13:25; Ps 1:4 [u] Ps 34:7 **35:7** [v] S Job 18:8 [w] S Ps 7:4 [x] S Job 9:31; S Ps 7:15; S 55:23 **35:8** [y] Isa 47:11; 1Th 5:3 [z] S Ps 7:15 **35:9** [a] S Ps 2:11; S Lk 1:47 [b] Ps 9:14; 13:5; 27:1

[a] 3 Or *and block the way*

35:10 [c] S Ex 9:14; S Ps 18:31; 113:5 [d] Ps 18:17 [e] Ps 12:5; 37:14; 74:21; 86:1; 109:16; 140:12; Isa 41:17 **35:11** [f] S Ex 23:1; S Mt 26:60 **35:12** [g] Ps 38:20; 109:5; Pr 17:13; Jer 18:20 **35:13** [h] S 2Sa 3:31; 1Ki 20:31; Ps 30:11; 69:11 [i] Job 30:25; Ps 69:10; 109:24

34:20 *all his bones.* His whole being (see note on 6:2). *not one of them will be broken.* Perhaps John's Gospel applies this word to Jesus (see NIV text note on Jn 19:36)—as the one above all others who could be called "righteous" (v. 19).
34:21–22 *condemned.* Dealt with as guilty (cf. Jer 2:3; Hos 10:2).
34:22 *who takes refuge in him.* See 2:12.
Ps 35 An appeal to the heavenly King, as divine Warrior and Judge, to come to the defense of "his servant" (v. 27) who is being maliciously slandered by those toward whom he had shown only the most tender friendship. The attack seems to have been occasioned by some "distress" (v. 26) that had overtaken the king (see vv. 15,19,21,25), perhaps an illness (see v. 13; see also introduction to Ps 6). Ps 35 exemplifies such a "cry" (34:15) to the Lord in expectation of vindication as that spoken of in 34:15–22—except that here the author does not expressly identify himself as one of the "righteous" (34:21); he appeals to the Lord rather as an innocent victim of an unmotivated attack. This psalm has been paired with Ps 36 and placed between the two acrostic wisdom psalms (34 and 37; see introduction to Ps 34–37). Together they evoke terror among people who have "no fear of God" (36:1) but also testify to the security of those who fear the Lord (cf. 34:7) and trust him (cf. 37:3,5), relying on his love (36:5,7,11) and righteousness (35:24,28; 36:6,10).

Regarding structure, two stanzas at the beginning, having four Hebrew poetic lines each (vv. 1–3,4–6), are balanced by two four-line stanzas at the end (vv. 22–25,26–27—for thematic links between the beginning and the end, see notes on these stanzas). At the center a seven-line stanza (vv. 11–16)—flanked by two Hebrew five-line stanzas (vv. 7–10 and vv. 17–21; see following notes)—sets forth the psalmist's chief indictment against his adversaries. A final line (v. 28) brings the psalm to a close with a vow to praise God (see note on 7:17).
35:1–3 Appeal for help to the Lord as Warrior-King (see Ex 15:1–18), David's Overlord. For links with vv. 22–25, see note on those verses.
35:2 *shield and armor.* For defense. For the Lord himself as the psalmists' "shield," see 3:3; 7:10; 18:2,30; 28:7; 33:20; 59:11; 84:9,11; 89:18; 115:9–11; 119:114; 144:2. *arise.* See note on 3:7.
35:3 *spear and javelin.* For attack (but see NIV text note on "javelin"). For the Lord wielding a spear, see Hab 3:11.
35:4–6 Appeal to the Lord to deal with the attackers by frustrating all their efforts and totally disabling them. For links with vv. 26–27, see note on those verses.
35:4 *plot my ruin.* See note on 5:9.
35:5–6 *angel of the LORD.* See 34:7 and note.
35:5 *like chaff.* See note on 1:4.
35:7–10 Appeal to the Lord to match the attackers' violent intent with his saving act (see note on 5:10)—which the psalmist will celebrate with praise (see note on 7:17).
35:7–8 *hid their net ... dug a pit ... net they hid ... fall into the pit.* See 9:15 and note.
35:9 *soul.* See note on 6:3.
35:10 *poor and needy.* See 34:6 and note.
35:11–16 The accusation: They repaid my friendship with malicious slander. This accusation stands at the center of the psalm (see note on 6:6).
35:13–14 The psalmist provides a living example of Jesus' later command to "pray for those who persecute you" (Mt 5:44)—as do Job (Job 42:7–10; see note on 42:10) and Jesus himself (Lk 23:34).
35:13 *sackcloth.* See note on 30:11. *fasting.* An act of mourning (see 69:10).

When my prayers returned to me
unanswered,
14 I went about mourning[j]
as though for my friend or brother.
I bowed my head in grief
as though weeping for my mother.
15 But when I stumbled, they gathered in
glee;[k]
assailants gathered against me
without my knowledge.
They slandered[l] me without ceasing.
16 Like the ungodly they maliciously
mocked;[a][m]
they gnashed their teeth[n] at me.

17 How long,[o] Lord, will you look on?
Rescue me from their ravages,
my precious life[p] from these lions.[q]
18 I will give you thanks in the great
assembly;[r]
among the throngs[s] I will praise
you.[t]
19 Do not let those gloat over me
who are my enemies[u] without cause;
do not let those who hate me without
reason[v]
maliciously wink the eye.[w]
20 They do not speak peaceably,
but devise false accusations[x]
against those who live quietly in the
land.
21 They sneer[y] at me and say, "Aha! Aha![z]
With our own eyes we have seen it."

22 LORD, you have seen[a] this; do not be
silent.
Do not be far[b] from me, Lord.
23 Awake,[c] and rise[d] to my defense!
Contend[e] for me, my God and Lord.
24 Vindicate me in your righteousness,
LORD my God;
do not let them gloat[f] over me.
25 Do not let them think, "Aha,[g] just what
we wanted!"
or say, "We have swallowed
him up."[h]

26 May all who gloat[i] over my distress[j]
be put to shame[k] and confusion;
may all who exalt themselves over me[l]
be clothed with shame and disgrace.
27 May those who delight in my
vindication[m]
shout for joy[n] and gladness;
may they always say, "The LORD be
exalted,
who delights[o] in the well-being of
his servant."[p]

28 My tongue will proclaim your
righteousness,[q]
your praises all day long.[r]

Psalm 36[b]

For the director of music. Of David
the servant of the LORD.

1 I have a message from God in my heart
concerning the sinfulness of the
wicked:[c][s]
There is no fear[t] of God
before their eyes.[u]

35:14 [j]Ps 38:6; 42:9; 43:2 **35:15** [k]S Job 31:29 [l]S Job 16:10 **35:16** [m]S Ps 22:7; Mk 10:34 [n]S Job 16:9; Mk 9:18; Ac 7:54 **35:17** [o]Ps 6:3 [p]Ps 22:20 [q]Ps 22:21; 57:4; 58:6 **35:18** [r]S Ps 22:25 [s]Ps 42:4; 109:30 [t]S Ps 22:22 **35:19** [u]Ps 9:13 [v]ver 7; Ps 38:19; 69:4; Jn 15:25* [w]Pr 6:13; 10:10 **35:20** [x]Ps 38:12; 55:21; Jer 9:8; Mic 6:12 **35:21** [y]S Job 16:10 [z]Ps 40:15; 70:3; Eze 25:3 **35:22** [a]Ex 3:7; Ps 10:14 [b]S Ps 10:1 **35:23** [c]S Ps 7:6; 80:2 [d]Ps 17:13 [e]S 1Sa 24:15 **35:24** [f]Ps 22:17 **35:25** [g]ver 21 [h]Ps 124:3; Pr 1:12; La 2:16 **35:26** [i]Ps 22:17 [j]Ps 4:1 [k]S Job 8:22; Ps 109:29; Mic 7:10 [l]Job 19:5; Ps 38:16 **35:27** [m]Ps 9:4 [n]Ps 20:5; S 33:3 [o]Ps 147:11; 149:4 [p]S Job 17:3 **35:28** [q]Ps 5:8; 51:14 [r]Ps 71:15,24; 72:15 **36:1** [s]S Job 21:16 [t]Jer 2:19; 36:16,24 [u]S Job 23:15; Ro 3:18*

[a] 16 Septuagint; Hebrew may mean *Like an ungodly circle of mockers,* [b] In Hebrew texts 36:1-12 is numbered 36:2-13. [c] 1 Or *A message from God: The transgression of the wicked / resides in their hearts.*

35:15 *stumbled.* Not morally. He was brought low by circumstances (see 9:3; 27:2; 37:24; 56:13; 119:165).
35:16 *gnashed their teeth.* In malice (see 37:12; La 2:16).
35:17–21 Renewed appeal for God's saving help, accompanied by a vow to praise God (v. 18; see note on 7:17). This five-line stanza and the five-line stanza in vv. 7–10 frame the central accusation.
35:17 *How long ... ?* See note on 6:3. *lions.* See note on 7:2.
35:18 *assembly.* See note on 1:5.
35:19 *enemies without cause.* See vv. 11–17; an experience frequently reflected also elsewhere in the Psalter (see 38:19; 69:4; 109:3; 119:78,86,161). See also La 3:52. *hate me without reason.* See 69:4. It is not known which of these passages is referred to in Jn 15:25. Both psalms reflect circumstances applicable also to Jesus' experience (but see introduction to Ps 69).
35:21 *Aha! Aha!* See v. 25; see also note on 3:2.
35:22–25 A return to the opening appeal (vv. 1–3) for God to arouse himself, take up the psalmist's cause and "contend" (v. 23) with those attacking him.
35:22 *do not be silent.* Do not remain inactive (see 28:1 and note; 83:1; 109:1).
35:23 *Awake.* See note on 7:6. *rise.* See note on 3:7.
35:24 *righteousness.* See note on 4:1.
35:25 *swallowed.* See 124:3.
35:26–27 Again (see vv. 4–6) an appeal for God to bring "shame" and "disgrace" on the adversaries. For both form and substance, cf. 40:14–16.
35:26 *who gloat over my distress.* In Hebrew, a verbal echo of "who plot my ruin" (v. 4). *clothed with.* See note on 109:29.
35:27 May all who are faithful supporters of the Lord's "servant" (here no doubt equivalent to his "anointed"; see note on 2:2) have reason to rejoice and praise the Lord.
35:28 A concluding vow to praise God (see note on 7:17). *righteousness.* See note on 4:1.
Ps 36 A prayer for God's unfailing protection, as the psalmist reflects on the godlessness of the wicked and the goodness of God. For this psalm's relationship with Ps 35, see introduction to Ps 34–37. Structurally—though different from the scansion in the NIV—a short couplet (v. 1) introduces a series of four stanzas of three Hebrew poetic lines each (vv. 2–4, 5–7a,7b–9,10–12). In later Jewish practice, vv. 7–10 became part of the morning prayer.
36 title *For the director of music.* See note on Ps 4 title. *servant of the LORD.* His royal servant (see notes on Ps 18 title; 35:27; see also 2Sa 7:20).
36:1 *message from God.* Usually reserved for words of revelation from God, such as those spoken by the prophets. Here reference is to an insight, perhaps coming like a flash, into the true character of the wicked. *heart.* See note on 4:7. *no fear of God.* Such as the psalmist calls for in Ps 34 and (implicitly) in Ps 37. See 55:19; Ge 20:11 and note. They

[2] In their own eyes they flatter
 themselves
 too much to detect or hate their sin.[v]
[3] The words of their mouths[w] are wicked
 and deceitful;[x]
 they fail to act wisely[y] or do good.[z]
[4] Even on their beds they plot evil;[a]
 they commit themselves to a sinful
 course[b]
 and do not reject what is wrong.[c]
[5] Your love, LORD, reaches to the
 heavens,
 your faithfulness[d] to the skies.[e]
[6] Your righteousness[f] is like the highest
 mountains,[g]
 your justice like the great deep.[h]
 You, LORD, preserve both people and
 animals.[i]
[7] How priceless is your unfailing love,
 O God![j]
 People take refuge in the shadow of
 your wings.[k]
[8] They feast on the abundance of your
 house;[l]
 you give them drink from your river[m]
 of delights.[n]
[9] For with you is the fountain of life;[o]
 in your light[p] we see light.
[10] Continue your love[q] to those who
 know you,[r]
 your righteousness to the upright in
 heart.[s]
[11] May the foot of the proud not come
 against me,
 nor the hand of the wicked[t] drive me
 away.
[12] See how the evildoers lie fallen—
 thrown down, not able to rise![u]

Psalm 37[a]

Of David.

[1] Do not fret because of those who are
 evil
 or be envious[v] of those who do
 wrong;[w]

[a] This psalm is an acrostic poem, the stanzas of which begin with the successive letters of the Hebrew alphabet.

36:2 [v] Dt 29:19 **36:3** [w] Ps 10:7 [x] S Job 5:13; Ps 5:6,9; 43:1; 144:8,11; Isa 44:20 [y] Ps 94:8 [z] Jer 4:22; 13:23; Am 3:10 **36:4** [a] Pr 4:16 [b] Isa 65:2 [c] Ps 52:3; Ro 12:9 **36:5** [d] Ps 89:1; 119:90 [e] Ps 57:10; 71:19; 89:2; 103:11; 108:4 **36:6** [f] Ps 5:8 [g] Ps 68:15 [h] S Ge 1:2; S 7:11 [i] Ne 9:6; Ps 104:14; 145:16 **36:7** [j] Ps 6:4 [k] S Ru 2:12; S Ps 17:8; 57:1; 91:4 **36:8** [l] Ps 65:4; Isa 25:6; Jer 31:12,14 [m] Job 20:17; Rev 22:1 [n] S Ps 23:2; 63:5 **36:9** [o] Ps 87:7; Pr 10:11; 16:22; Jer 2:13 [p] Ps 4:6; 27:1; 76:4; 104:2; Isa 2:5; 9:2; 60:1,19; Jn 1:4; 1Pe 2:9 **36:10** [q] Jer 31:3 [r] Jer 9:24; 22:16 [s] Ps 7:10; 11:2; 94:15; 125:4 **36:11** [t] Ps 71:4; 140:4 **36:12** [u] S Ps 18:38 **37:1** [v] Pr 3:31; 23:17-18 [w] Ps 73:3; Pr 24:19

take no account of his all-seeing eye, his righteous judgment and his power to deal with them (see note on 10:11). For Paul's use of this verse, see Ro 3:18.

36:2–4 The wicked characterized (see also 10:2–11 and notes; see also introduction to Ps 37).

36:2 *flatter themselves.* Not in self-righteousness but out of the smug, conceited notion that they are accountable to no one.

36:3 *words of their mouths.* See note on 5:9. *are ... deceitful.* See 35:20. *fail to act wisely.* See 94:8–11; Pr 2:9–11. *fail to ... do good.* In contrast to the wise and godly person (see 34:14; 37:3,27; see also note on 34:8–14).

36:4 *on their beds.* Where one's thoughts are free to range and to set the course for the activities of the day. The wicked do not meditate on God's law "day and night" (1:2; see 119:55). On the other hand, the hearts of the godly instruct them at night (see 16:7); they commune at night with God (see 42:8), think of him (see 63:6) and reflect on his promises (see 119:148). *plot evil.* See 34:14; 37:27; cf. Mic 2:1.

36:5–7a The trustworthiness of the Lord.

36:5 *love ... faithfulness.* That is, love-and-faithfulness (as in 57:3; 61:7; 85:10; 86:15; 89:14; 115:1; 138:2; Pr 3:3; 14:22; 16:6; 20:28; see note on 3:7). *reaches to the heavens ... to the skies.* Encompasses all the realms of creaturely existence (see 57:10; 108:4).

36:6 *righteousness ... justice.* That is, righteousness-and-justice (as in 33:5; 37:6; 89:14; 97:2; Hos 2:19; see also Isa 9:7; 33:5; Jer 9:24). *righteousness.* See note on 4:1. *like the highest mountains ... great deep.* As high as the mountains, as deep as the sea.

36:7a *unfailing love.* See v. 5; see also note on 6:4.

36:7b–9 The Lord's benevolence toward all his creatures (see 33:4–5).

36:7b *shadow of your wings.* See 17:8 and note.

36:8 *feast ... drink.* Life-giving food and water. *house.* Here, God's whole estate or realm—i.e., the earth, from which springs the abundance of food for all living things (see note on 24:2). *river.* The "channel" (Job 38:25) by which God brings forth the rain out of his "storehouses" (33:7; see Job 38:8–11,22,37; Jer 10:13) in his "upper chambers" (104:13; see 65:9; Isa 30:25 and the references to "blessings" from heaven in Ge 49:25; Dt 33:23). This vivid imagery, depicting God's control over, and gift of, the waters from heaven, which feed the rivers and streams of earth to give life and health wherever they flow, is the source of the symbol of "the river of the water of life" that flows from the temple of God (Rev 22:1–2; see also Eze 47:1–12). *of delights.* Furnishing many sources of joy.

36:9 The climax and summation of vv. 5–9. *fountain of life.* See Jer 2:13; 17:13. Ultimately, for sinners, God provides the water of life through Jesus Christ (Jn 4:10,14). *your light.* See 27:1 and note. *see.* Experience, have, enjoy, as in 16:10; 27:13; 34:8,12; 49:9,19; 89:48; 90:15; 106:5 ("enjoy"); Job 9:25 ("glimpse"); 42:5; Ecc 1:16 ("experienced"); 3:13 ("find"); 6:6 ("enjoy"); Isa 53:10; La 3:1. *light.* Life in its fullness as it was created to be. For the association of light with life, see 49:19; 56:13; Job 3:20; 33:28,30; Isa 53:11.

36:10–12 The prayer: Your "love" (v. 5) and "righteousness" (v. 6), which you display in all creation—show these to all who know (acknowledge) you and are upright (the people of God). But keep the wicked, "foot" and "hand," from success against me (the king; see note on 33:16).

36:10 *love.* See note on 6:4. *those who know you.* See 9:10 and note. *righteousness.* See note on 4:1.

36:11 *proud.* See note on 31:23.

36:12 Confidence (see note on 3:8). *lie fallen.* Perhaps in death (see note on 13:4).

Ps 37 Instruction in godly wisdom. (For other "wisdom" psalms, see 34:8–22; 49; 112; others closely related are Ps 1; 73; 91; 92:6–9,12–15; 111; 119; 127–128; 133; see also essay, p. 786.) This psalm's dominant theme is related to the contrast between the wicked and the righteous reflected in Ps 36. The central issue addressed is: Who will "inherit the land" (vv. 9,11,22,29), i.e., live on to enjoy the blessings of the Lord in the promised land? Will the wicked, who plot (v. 12), scheme (vv. 7,32), default on debts (v. 21), use raw power to gain advantage (v. 14) and seem thereby to flourish (vv. 7,16,35)? Or will the righteous, who trust in the Lord (vv. 3,5,7,34) and are humble (v. 11),

2 for like the grass they will soon wither,[x]
like green plants they will soon die away.[y]

3 Trust in the LORD and do good;
dwell in the land[z] and enjoy safe pasture.[a]
4 Take delight[b] in the LORD,
and he will give you the desires of your heart.[c]

5 Commit your way to the LORD;
trust in him[d] and he will do this:
6 He will make your righteous reward[e] shine like the dawn,[f]
your vindication like the noonday sun.

7 Be still[g] before the LORD
and wait patiently[h] for him;
do not fret[i] when people succeed in their ways,[j]
when they carry out their wicked schemes.[k]

8 Refrain from anger[l] and turn from wrath;
do not fret[m]—it leads only to evil.
9 For those who are evil will be destroyed,[n]
but those who hope[o] in the LORD will inherit the land.[p]

10 A little while, and the wicked will be no more;[q]
though you look for them, they will not be found.
11 But the meek will inherit the land[r]
and enjoy peace and prosperity.[s]

12 The wicked plot[t] against the righteous
and gnash their teeth[u] at them;
13 but the Lord laughs at the wicked,
for he knows their day is coming.[v]

14 The wicked draw the sword[w]
and bend the bow[x]
to bring down the poor and needy,[y]
to slay those whose ways are upright.
15 But their swords will pierce their own hearts,[z]
and their bows will be broken.[a]

16 Better the little that the righteous have
than the wealth[b] of many wicked;
17 for the power of the wicked will be broken,[c]
but the LORD upholds[d] the righteous.

37:2 [x]S 2Ki 19:26; Job 14:2; Ps 102:4; Isa 40:7 [y]ver 38; Ps 90:6; 92:7; Jas 1:10 **37:3** [z]Dt 30:20 [a]Eze 34:14; Jn 10:9 **37:4** [b]S Job 27:10 [c]S Job 7:6; Ps 21:2; 145:19; Mt 6:33 **37:5** [d]Ps 4:5 **37:6** [e]Ps 18:24; 103:17; 112:3 [f]S Job 11:17 **37:7** [g]S Ex 14:14; S Isa 41:1 [h]S Ps 27:14; 40:1; 130:5; Isa 38:13; Hab 3:16; Ro 8:25 [i]ver 1 [j]Jer 12:1 [k]Ps 21:11; 26:10; 119:150 **37:8** [l]Eph 4:31; Col 3:8 [m]ver 1 **37:9** [n]S Ps 31:22; 101:8; 118:10; Pr 2:22 [o]Isa 25:9; 26:8; 40:31; 49:23; 51:5 [p]ver 22; Ps 25:13; Isa 49:8; 57:13; Mt 5:5

37:10 [q]S Job 7:10; Eze 27:36 **37:11** [r]S Nu 14:24; Mt 5:5 [s]S Lev 26:6; S Nu 6:26 **37:12** [t]Ps 2:1; 31:13 [u]S Job 16:9; Ps 35:16; 112:10 **37:13** [v]1Sa 26:10; Eze 12:23 **37:14** [w]S Ps 22:20 [x]Ps 11:2 [y]S Ps 35:10 **37:15** [z]S Ps 9:16 [a]S 1Sa 2:4; Ps 46:9; Jer 49:35 **37:16** [b]Pr 15:16; 16:8 **37:17** [c]Job 38:15; Ps 10:15 [d]Ps 41:12; 140:12; 145:14; 146:7

---

blameless (vv. 18,37), generous (vv. 21,26), upright (v. 37) and peaceful (v. 37), and from whose mouth is heard the moral wisdom that reflects meditation on God's law (vv. 30–31)? For a similar characterization of the wicked, see 10:2–11; 73:4–12. For a similar characterization of the righteous, see Ps 112. For a similar statement concerning the transitoriness of the wicked, see Ps 49; 73:18–20.

Structurally, in this alphabetic acrostic, two verses are devoted to each letter of the alphabet, though with some irregularity. The main theme is developed in vv. 1–11, then further elaborated in the rest of the psalm. The whole is framed by statements contrasting the brief career of the wicked (vv. 1–2) and the Lord's sustaining help of the righteous (vv. 39–40). For this psalm's relationship to Ps 34–36, see introduction to Ps 34–37.

37:1–2 See v. 7; Ps 73.

37:1 Almost identical to Pr 24:19.

37:2 See note on v. 20.

37:3 See 34:8–14 and note.

37:4 *heart.* See note on 4:7.

37:5 *Commit.* See 1Pe 5:7.

37:6 *your righteous reward.* That is, the prosperity and well-being that God will bestow in accordance with "your" faithful reliance on him (cf. v. 9; see Pr 8:18; 21:21 ["prosperity"] for this sense of the Hebrew word; see also Isa 48:18). *righteous reward … vindication.* That is, righteous reward-and-vindication (see note on 36:6). *your vindication.* See 35:27 and note; see also Isa 54:17. The close Hebrew synonyms here rendered "righteous reward" and "vindication" both refer to manifestations of God's favor on those he pleases to bless or deliver, as in Isa 59:9 (where these terms are linked with "light") and 59:11 (where "justice" [or "vindication"] is linked with "deliverance"). Accordingly, "your righteous reward" and "your vindication" in this verse have direct links with "your (God's) righteousness" and "your (God's) justice" in 36:6.

37:8 *anger … wrath.* Evidence of fretting over the wicked's prosperity, gained to the disadvantage of and even at the expense of the righteous.

37:9 *hope in.* See v. 34. *inherit the land.* Receive from the Lord secure entitlement (for them and their children) to the promised land as the created and redeemed sphere and bountiful source of provision for the life of God's people. Those who hope in the Lord—i.e., trustfully look to him to bestow life and its blessings as a gift—will inherit the land, not those who apart from God and by evil means try to take possession of it and its wealth (see vv. 11,22,29; cf. Jos 7).

37:10 *A little while.* Shortness of time is here a figure for certainty of event (see 58:9; Job 20:5–11; Hag 2:6).

37:11 See Mt 5:5 and note. *meek.* Those who humbly acknowledge their dependence on the goodness and grace of God and betray no arrogance toward others. *peace and prosperity.* Unmixed blessedness.

37:12 *righteous.* See note on 1:5. *gnash their teeth.* See 35:16 and note.

37:13 *Lord laughs.* See 2:4. *knows their day is coming.* Strikingly, the psalmist nowhere speaks of God's active involvement in bringing the wicked down—though he hints at it in v. 22. The certainty that the life of the wicked will be "destroyed" is frequently asserted (vv. 9,22,28,34,38; cf. vv. 2,8,10,15,17,20,36,38)—and the Lord also knows it—but God's positive action is here reserved for his care for and protection of the righteous. *their day.* The time when each will be "destroyed," as in 1Sa 26:10 ("his time," lit. "his day"); Job 18:20 ("his fate").

37:14–15 *sword … bow … swords … bows.* See 64:3–4,7–8; Pr 30:14 and note on Ps 5:9.

37:14 *poor and needy.* See 34:6 and note.

37:15 *pierce … hearts.* See 45:5.

37:16–17 *righteous.* See note on 1:5.

18 The blameless spend their days under
the LORD's care,[e]
and their inheritance will endure
forever.[f]
19 In times of disaster they will not wither;
in days of famine they will enjoy
plenty.

20 But the wicked will perish:[g]
Though the LORD's enemies are like
the flowers of the field,
they will be consumed, they will go
up in smoke.[h]

21 The wicked borrow and do not repay,
but the righteous give generously;[i]
22 those the LORD blesses will inherit the
land,
but those he curses[j] will be
destroyed.[k]

23 The LORD makes firm the steps[l]
of the one who delights[m] in him;
24 though he may stumble, he will not
fall,[n]
for the LORD upholds[o] him with his
hand.

25 I was young and now I am old,
yet I have never seen the righteous
forsaken[p]
or their children begging[q] bread.
26 They are always generous and lend
freely;[r]
their children will be a blessing.[a][s]

27 Turn from evil and do good;[t]
then you will dwell in the land
forever.[u]
28 For the LORD loves the just
and will not forsake his faithful ones.[v]

Wrongdoers will be completely
destroyed[b];
the offspring of the wicked will
perish.[w]
29 The righteous will inherit the land[x]
and dwell in it forever.[y]

30 The mouths of the righteous utter
wisdom,[z]
and their tongues speak what is just.

31 The law of their God is in their hearts;[a]
their feet do not slip.[b]

32 The wicked lie in wait[c] for the
righteous,[d]
intent on putting them to death;
33 but the LORD will not leave them in the
power of the wicked
or let them be condemned[e] when
brought to trial.[f]

34 Hope in the LORD[g]
and keep his way.[h]
He will exalt you to inherit the land;
when the wicked are destroyed,[i] you
will see[j] it.

35 I have seen a wicked and ruthless
man
flourishing[k] like a luxuriant native
tree,
36 but he soon passed away and was no
more;
though I looked for him, he could
not be found.[l]

37 Consider the blameless,[m] observe the
upright;[n]
a future awaits those who seek
peace.[c][o]
38 But all sinners[p] will be destroyed;[q]
there will be no future[d] for the
wicked.[r]

39 The salvation[s] of the righteous comes
from the LORD;
he is their stronghold in time of
trouble.[t]
40 The LORD helps[u] them and delivers[v]
them;
he delivers them from the wicked
and saves[w] them,
because they take refuge[x] in him.

37:18 [e]S Job 23:10; Ps 44:21 [f]ver 27,29 **37:20** [g]S Ps 34:21 [h]Ps 68:2; 102:3; Isa 51:6 **37:21** [i]S Lev 25:35; Ps 112:5 **37:22** [j]S Job 5:3 [k]ver 9 **37:23** [l]S Job 11:15; S Ps 7:9; 66:9 [m]S Nu 14:8; Ps 147:11 **37:24** [n]S Ps 13:4; 27:2; 38:17; 55:22; 119:165; Pr 3:23; 10:9 [o]2Ch 9:8; Ps 41:12; 145:14 **37:25** [p]ver 28; S Ge 15:1; Heb 13:5 [q]Ps 111:5; 145:15; Mk 10:46 **37:26** [r]S Lev 25:35 [s]Dt 28:4; Ps 112:2 **37:27** [t]Ps 34:14; 3Jn 1:11 [u]S Nu 24:21 **37:28** [v]S Dt 7:6; S Ps 18:25; S 97:10 [w]S Ge 17:14; S Dt 32:26; Pr 2:22 **37:29** [x]ver 9; Pr 2:21 [y]Isa 34:17 **37:30** [z]Ps 49:3; Pr 10:13 **37:31** [a]S Dt 6:6; S Job 22:22 [b]S Dt 32:35 **37:32** [c]S Ps 10:8 [d]Ps 11:5 **37:33** [e]Job 32:3; Ps 34:22; 79:11 [f]2Pe 2:9 **37:34** [g]Ps 27:14 [h]S Ps 18:21 [i]ver 9 [j]Ps 52:6 **37:35** [k]S Job 5:3 **37:36** [l]ver 10; Pr 12:7; Isa 41:12; Da 11:19 **37:37** [m]ver 18; S Ge 6:9; Ps 18:25 [n]Ps 11:7 [o]Isa 57:1-2 **37:38** [p]S Ps 1:1 [q]S ver 2; Ps 73:19 [r]ver 9 **37:39** [s]S Ps 3:8 [t]S Ps 9:9 **37:40** [u]S 1Ch 5:20; S Ps 20:2 [v]S Ps 34:7 [w]S Ps 18:48 [x]Ps 2:12

[a] *26* Or *freely; / the names of their children will be used in blessings* (see Gen. 48:20); or *freely; / others will see that their children are blessed* [b] *28* See Septuagint; Hebrew *They will be protected forever* [c] *37* Or *upright; / those who seek peace will have posterity* [d] *38* Or *posterity*

37:18 *blameless.* See v. 37; see also 15:2 and note. *under the LORD's care.* See 1:6 ("the LORD watches over").
37:20 *like the flowers.* Cf. v. 2; 90:5–6; 92:7; 102:11; 103:15–16; Job 14:2 and note; Isa 40:6–7; see Jas 1:10–11.
37:21 Or "The wicked must borrow and cannot repay,/but the righteous are able to give generously" (see Dt 15:6; 28:12,44).
37:24 See Pr 24:16.
37:26 See note on v. 21.
37:27 *Turn from evil and do good.* See 34:14 and note.
37:28 *faithful ones.* See note on 4:3.
37:29 *dwell in it forever.* They and their children and children's children, in contrast to the wicked (see v. 28).
37:30 *wisdom.* See 119:98,130; Dt 4:6.
37:31 *hearts.* See note on 4:7. *do not slip.* From the right path (see 17:5).
37:32 *lie in wait.* See 10:8–9; see also note on 7:2. *intent on putting them to death.* Attempting to seize by false charges at court (see v. 33) the very livelihood of their intended victims.
37:34 See v. 9.
37:35–36 Cf. vv. 25–26.
37:37–38 The great contrast: hope for the "upright," no hope for the "wicked."
37:39–40 *the righteous ... them.* They are not at the mercy of the wicked: The Lord is their refuge, and in spite of all that the wicked do the Lord makes secure their inheritance in the promised land.

Psalm 38[a]

A psalm of David. A petition.

[1] LORD, do not rebuke me in your anger
or discipline me in your wrath.[y]
[2] Your arrows[z] have pierced me,
and your hand has come down
on me.
[3] Because of your wrath there is no
health[a] in my body;
there is no soundness in my bones[b]
because of my sin.
[4] My guilt has overwhelmed[c] me
like a burden too heavy to bear.[d]

[5] My wounds[e] fester and are loathsome[f]
because of my sinful folly.[g]
[6] I am bowed down[h] and brought very
low;
all day long I go about mourning.[i]
[7] My back is filled with searing pain;[j]
there is no health[k] in my body.
[8] I am feeble and utterly crushed;[l]
I groan[m] in anguish of heart.[n]

[9] All my longings[o] lie open before you,
Lord;
my sighing[p] is not hidden from
you.
[10] My heart pounds,[q] my strength
fails[r] me;
even the light has gone from my
eyes.[s]
[11] My friends and companions avoid me
because of my wounds;[t]
my neighbors stay far away.
[12] Those who want to kill me set their
traps,[u]
those who would harm me talk of
my ruin;[v]
all day long they scheme and lie.[w]

[13] I am like the deaf, who cannot hear,[x]
like the mute, who cannot speak;
[14] I have become like one who does not
hear,
whose mouth can offer no reply.
[15] LORD, I wait[y] for you;
you will answer,[z] Lord my God.
[16] For I said, "Do not let them gloat[a]
or exalt themselves over me when
my feet slip."[b]

[17] For I am about to fall,[c]
and my pain[d] is ever with me.
[18] I confess my iniquity;[e]
I am troubled by my sin.
[19] Many have become my enemies[f]
without cause[b];
those who hate me[g] without reason[h]
are numerous.
[20] Those who repay my good with evil[i]
lodge accusations[j] against me,
though I seek only to do what is
good.

[21] LORD, do not forsake me;[k]
do not be far[l] from me, my God.
[22] Come quickly[m] to help me,[n]
my Lord and my Savior.[o]

[a] In Hebrew texts 38:1-22 is numbered 38:2-23.
[b] *19* One Dead Sea Scrolls manuscript; Masoretic Text *my vigorous enemies*

38:1 [y]Ps 6:1 **38:2** [z]S Job 6:4 **38:3** [a]Pr 3:8; 4:22 [b]S Job 33:19 **38:4** [c]Ps 40:12; 65:3 [d]S Nu 11:14; S Ezr 9:6; Lk 11:46 **38:5** [e]ver 11; Ps 147:3 [f]Job 19:17 [g]Ps 69:5; Pr 5:23; 12:23; 13:16; Ecc 10:3 **38:6** [h]Ps 57:6; 145:14; 146:8 [i]S Ps 35:14 **38:7** [j]S Job 14:22 [k]ver 3 **38:8** [l]Ps 34:18; Pr 17:22 [m]S Ps 6:6; 22:1; Pr 5:11 [n]S Ps 6:3 **38:9** [o]Ps 119:20; 143:7 [p]S Job 3:24 **38:10** [q]S Job 37:1 [r]S Ps 31:10 [s]S Ps 6:7; S 19:8; 88:9 **38:11** [t]S ver 5 **38:12** [u]Ps 31:4; 140:5; 141:9 [v]Ps 35:4; 41:5 [w]S Ps 35:20 **38:13** [x]Ps 115:6; 135:17; Isa 43:8; Mk 7:37 **38:15** [y]Ps 27:14 [z]Ps 17:6 **38:16** [a]S Ps 22:17 [b]S Dt 32:35 **38:17** [c]S Ps 37:24 [d]ver 7; S Job 6:10 **38:18** [e]S Lev 26:40 **38:19** [f]S Ps 18:17 [g]S Ps 25:19 [h]S Ps 35:19 **38:20** [i]S Ge 44:4; 1Jn 3:12 [j]Ps 54:5; 59:10; 119:23 **38:21** [k]Ps 27:9; 71:18; 119:8 [l]S Ps 10:1; S 22:11; 35:22; 71:12 **38:22** [m]S Ps 22:19 [n]Ps 40:13 [o]S 1Ch 16:35

Ps 38–41 The final four psalms of Book I are all linked by common central themes (see introductions to these psalms). One of these themes is confession of sin, which is found elsewhere in Book I only in Ps 25; 32 (see introductions to those psalms). Significantly, following a wisdom psalm (37), the first reference to sin here characterizes it as "folly" (38:5).
Ps 38 An urgent appeal for relief from a severe and painful illness, God's "rebuke" for a sin David has committed. Neither the specific occasion nor the illness can be identified. David's suffering is aggravated by the withdrawal of his friends (see v. 11) and the unwarranted efforts of his enemies to seize this opportunity to bring him down (vv. 12,16,19–20). In traditional Christian usage, this is one of seven penitential psalms (see introduction to Ps 6). Like Ps 33 (see introductory note on its structure), its length (22 verses) is based on the number of letters in the Hebrew alphabet. The psalm is composed of five stanzas of four verses each, with a two-verse conclusion.
38 title *A petition.* Occurs elsewhere only in the title of Ps 70.
38:1–4 Plea for relief from the Lord's rebuke.
38:1 *rebuke … discipline.* That is, rebuke-and-discipline (see 39:11; see also note on 3:7). *anger … wrath.* See note on 2:5.
38:2 *arrows.* A vivid metaphor for God's blows (see Job 6:4; 34:6; La 3:12; Eze 5:16; see also note on Ge 9:13). *your hand has come down on me.* See 32:4 and note on 32:3–5.
38:3 *bones.* See note on 6:2.
38:4 *burden.* Not only a psychological "burden of guilt" but the heavy burden of suffering described in vv. 5–8.
38:5–8 The devastating physical and psychological effects of his illness.
38:8 *heart.* See note on 4:7.
38:9–12 Renewed appeal, with further elaboration of his troubles: his illness (v. 10), abandonment by his friends (v. 11) and the hostility of his enemies (v. 12).
38:10 *light has gone from my eyes.* See note on 13:3.
38:11 See note on 31:11–12.
38:12 See note on 5:9. *set their traps.* See note on 9:15.
38:13–16 Let the Lord answer (v. 15) my enemies. Like a deaf-mute, David will not reply to his enemies (vv. 13–14); he waits for the Lord to act in his behalf (vv. 15–16). See 1Sa 25:32–39; 2Sa 16:10,12.
38:16 *when my feet slip.* When he experiences a personal blow to health or circumstance—here referring to his illness (see 66:9; 94:18; 121:3).
38:17–20 As health declines, the vigor of his many enemies increases.
38:17 *about to fall.* Death seems near (see note on 13:4). *fall.* In Hebrew, a verbal link with 35:15 ("stumbled").
38:18 See vv. 3–4; Ps 32.
38:19–20 He has sinned against the Lord, but he is innocent of any wrong against those attacking him (see note on 35:19).
38:20 *repay my good.* See 35:12–14. *lodge accusations against.* Accuse (falsely), as in 71:13; 109:4,20,29; Zec 3:1. *good.* Morally good (see 34:14).
38:21–22 In conclusion, a renewed appeal.

Psalm 39[a]

For the director of music. For Jeduthun.
A psalm of David.

[1] I said, "I will watch my ways[p]
and keep my tongue from sin;[q]
I will put a muzzle on my mouth[r]
while in the presence of the
wicked."
[2] So I remained utterly silent,[s]
not even saying anything good.
But my anguish[t] increased;
3 my heart grew hot[u] within me.
While I meditated,[v] the fire[w] burned;
then I spoke with my tongue:

[4] "Show me, LORD, my life's end
and the number of my days;[x]
let me know how fleeting[y] my life is.[z]
[5] You have made my days[a] a mere
handbreadth;
the span of my years is as nothing
before you.
Everyone is but a breath,[b]
even those who seem secure.[b]

[6] "Surely everyone goes around[c] like a
mere phantom;[d]
in vain they rush about,[e] heaping up
wealth[f]
without knowing whose it will
finally be.[g]

[7] "But now, Lord, what do I look for?
My hope is in you.[h]
[8] Save me[i] from all my transgressions;[j]
do not make me the scorn[k] of
fools.

39:1 [p] 1Ki 2:4; Ps 119:9, 59; Pr 20:11 [q] S Job 1:22; Ps 34:13; Jas 3:2 [r] S Job 6:24; Jas 1:26 **39:2** [s] ver 9; S Job 31:34; Ps 77:4 [t] Ps 6:3; S 25:17; 31:10 **39:3** [u] Lk 24:32 [v] Ps 1:2; 48:9; 77:12; 119:15 [w] Jer 5:14; 20:9; 23:29 **39:4** [x] S Job 14:5 [y] S Job 14:2 [z] S Ge 47:9; S Job 7:7 **39:5** [a] S Job 10:20; Ps 89:45; 102:23 [b] S Job 7:7; Ps 62:9 **39:6** [c] Jas 1:11 [d] Job 8:9; Ps 102:11; Ecc 6:12; S Jas 4:14 [e] Ps 127:2 [f] S Job 27:17 [g] Lk 12:20 **39:7** [h] S Ps 9:18; S 25:5 **39:8** [i] Ps 6:4; 51:14 [j] Ps 32:1; 51:1; Isa 53:5,8,10 [k] S Dt 28:37; Ps 69:7; 79:4; Isa 43:28; Da 9:16 **39:9** [l] S ver 2 [m] Ps 38:13 [n] Isa 38:15 **39:10** [o] 2Ch 21:14; Eze 7:9; 24:16 [p] S Ex 9:3 **39:11** [q] S Dt 28:20;

[9] I was silent;[l] I would not open my
mouth,[m]
for you are the one who has done
this.[n]
[10] Remove your scourge from me;
I am overcome by the blow[o] of your
hand.[p]
[11] When you rebuke[q] and discipline[r]
anyone for their sin,
you consume[s] their wealth like a
moth[t]—
surely everyone is but a breath.[u]

[12] "Hear my prayer, LORD,
listen to my cry for help;[v]
do not be deaf[w] to my weeping.[x]
I dwell with you as a foreigner,[y]
a stranger,[z] as all my ancestors were.[a]
[13] Look away from me, that I may enjoy
life again
before I depart and am no more."[b]

Psalm 40[c]

40:13-17pp — Ps 70:1-5

For the director of music.
Of David. A psalm.

[1] I waited patiently[c] for the LORD;
he turned to me and heard my cry.[d]

[a] In Hebrew texts 39:1-13 is numbered 39:2-14.
[b] 5 The Hebrew has *Selah* (a word of uncertain meaning) here and at the end of verse 11.
[c] In Hebrew texts 40:1-17 is numbered 40:2-18.

Isa 66:15; Eze 5:15; 2Pe 2:16 [r] Ps 94:10; Isa 26:16 [s] Ps 90:7 [t] S Job 13:28; S Isa 51:8; Lk 12:33; S Jas 5:2 [u] S Job 7:7 **39:12** [v] S Ps 17:1 [w] S Dt 1:45 [x] S 2Ki 20:5 [y] Lev 25:23 [z] S Ge 23:4; S Heb 11:13 [a] S Ge 47:9; S 1Ch 29:15 **39:13** [b] S Job 10:21 **40:1** [c] S Ps 37:7 [d] Ps 6:9; S 31:22; 34:15; 116:1; 145:19

Ps 39 David's poignant prayer when deeply troubled by the fragility of human life. He is reminded of this by the present illness through which God is rebuking him (vv. 10–11) for his "transgressions" (v. 8). Ps 38 speaks of silence before the enemy, Ps 39 of silence before God. Both are prayers in times of illness (God's "rebuke," v. 11; 38:1); both acknowledge sin, and both express deep trust in God. See introduction to Ps 40. In addition, this psalm has many links with Ps 90; see also Ps 49. The psalm's structure is symmetrical: The first two stanzas of five and three Hebrew poetic lines are balanced by the last two stanzas of five and three lines. At the center (v. 6; see note on 6:6) stands a wisdom observation that places David's situation in the broader context of a widespread human condition (see note on v. 6).

39 title *For the director of music.* See note on Ps 4 title. *Jeduthun.* One of David's three choir leaders (1Ch 16:41–42; 25:1,6; 2Ch 5:12; called his "seer" in 2Ch 35:15). Jeduthun is probably also the Ethan of 1Ch 6:44; 15:19; if so, he represented the family of Merari, even as Asaph did the family of Gershon and Heman the family of Kohath, the three sons of Levi (see 1Ch 6:16,33,39,43–44). See titles of Ps 62; 77; 89.

39:1–3 Introduction: Having determined to keep silent, he could finally no longer suppress his anguish.

39:1 He had kept a muzzle on his mouth for fear that rebellious words would escape in the hearing of the wicked (see Ps 73).

39:2–3 Suppressed anguish only intensified the agony (see Jer 20:9).

39:4–5 A prayer for understanding and patient acceptance of the brief span of human life.

39:4 *how fleeting my life is.* See 78:39 and note on 37:20.

39:5 *as nothing before you.* See 90:4. *but a breath.* See v. 11; 62:9; 144:4. For *Selah*, see NIV text note and note on 3:2.

39:6 Could almost serve as a summary of Ecclesiastes.

39:7–11 A modest prayer: Only grant me relief from your present rebuke.

39:8 *Save me.* As from an enemy. *scorn of fools.* If the Lord does not restore him, he will be mocked (see 22:7–8; 69:6–12) by godless fools (see 14:1).

39:10 *blow of your hand.* See 32:4; 38:2.

39:11 *rebuke and discipline.* See 6:1; 38:1. *but a breath.* See note on v. 5.

39:12–13 The modest prayer repeated even more modestly.

39:12 *a foreigner, a stranger.* He lives this life before God only as a pilgrim passing through (cf. Heb 11:13 and note).

39:13 *Look away from me.* See Job 7:17–19; 10:20–21; 14:6. *enjoy life again.* See Job 9:27; 10:20. *am no more.* Here there is no glimpse of what lies beyond the horizon of death (see note on 6:5).

Ps 40–41 Book I of the Psalter closes with two psalms containing "Blessed are those [or "is the one"] who" statements (40:4; 41:1), thus balancing the two psalms with which the Book begins (1:1; 2:12). In this way, the whole of Book I is framed by declarations of the blessedness of those who "delight ... in the law of the LORD" (1:2), who "take refuge

[2]He lifted me out of the slimy pit,[e]
out of the mud[f] and mire;[g]
he set my feet[h] on a rock[i]
and gave me a firm place to stand.
[3]He put a new song[j] in my mouth,
a hymn of praise to our God.
Many will see and fear the LORD[k]
and put their trust[l] in him.

[4]Blessed is the one[m]
who trusts in the LORD,[n]
who does not look to the proud,[o]
to those who turn aside to false
gods.[a][p]
[5]Many, LORD my God,
are the wonders[q] you have done,
the things you planned for us.
None can compare[r] with you;
were I to speak and tell of your
deeds,
they would be too many[s] to declare.

[6]Sacrifice and offering you did not
desire—[t]
but my ears you have opened[b]—[u]
burnt offerings[v] and sin offerings[c]
you did not require.
[7]Then I said, "Here I am, I have
come—
it is written about me in the scroll.[d][w]

[8]I desire to do your will,[x] my God;[y]
your law is within my heart."[z]

[9]I proclaim your saving acts[a] in the
great assembly;[b]
I do not seal my lips, LORD,
as you know.[c]
[10]I do not hide your righteousness in my
heart;
I speak of your faithfulness[d] and
your saving help.
I do not conceal your love and your
faithfulness
from the great assembly.[e]

[11]Do not withhold your mercy[f] from me,
LORD;
may your love[g] and faithfulness[h]
always protect[i] me.
[12]For troubles[j] without number
surround me;
my sins have overtaken me, and I
cannot see.[k]

[a] *4* Or *to lies* [b] *6* Hebrew; some Septuagint manuscripts *but a body you have prepared for me* [c] *6* Or *purification offerings* [d] *7* Or *come / with the scroll written for me*

40:2 [e]S Job 9:31; S Ps 7:15 [f]S Job 30:19 [g]Ps 69:14 [h]Ps 31:8 [i]Ps 27:5 **40:3** [j]S Ps 28:7; S 96:1; Rev 5:9 [k]Ps 52:6; 64:9 [l]S Ex 14:31 **40:4** [m]Ps 34:8 [n]Ps 84:12 [o]Ps 101:5; 138:6; Pr 3:34; 16:5; Isa 65:5; 1Pe 5:5 [p]S Dt 31:20; S Ps 4:2; S 26:1 **40:5** [q]S Dt 4:34; Ps 75:1; 105:5; 136:4 [r]Ps 139:18 [s]Ps 71:15; 139:17 **40:6** [t]S 1Sa 15:22; Jer 6:20; Am 5:22 [u]Ex 21:6 [v]Ps 50:8; 51:16; Isa 1:11; Hos 6:6 **40:7** [w]Job 19:23; Jer 36:2; 45:1; Eze 2:9; Zec 5:1 **40:8** [x]S Mt 26:39 [y]Heb 10:5-7* [z]S Dt 6:6; S Job 22:22; Ro 7:22 **40:9** [a]S Ps 22:31 [b]S Ps 22:25 [c]S Jos 22:22 **40:10** [d]Ps 89:1 [e]S Ps 22:22 **40:11** [f]Zec 1:12 [g]Pr 20:28 [h]S Ps 26:3 [i]Ps 61:7 **40:12** [j]S Ps 25:17 [k]Ps 38:4; 65:3

in him" (2:12), who do "not look to the proud" but make the Lord their trust (40:4) and who have "regard for the weak" (41:1)—a concise instruction in godliness. See introduction to Ps 1–2.

Ps 40 A prayer for help when troubles abound. The causes of distress are not specified, but David acknowledges that they are occasioned by his sin (see v. 12), as in Ps 38–39; 41 (see introductions to Ps 39; 41). They are aggravated by the gloating of his enemies, a theme also present in Ps 38–39; 41 (see introduction to Ps 38). The prayer begins with praise of God for his past mercies (vv. 1–5: two stanzas of five Hebrew poetic lines each) and a testimony to the king's own faithfulness to the Lord (vv. 6–10: two three-line stanzas). These form the grounds for his present appeal for help (vv. 11–17: two five-line stanzas and a concluding couplet; note the structural centering of vv. 6–10). For other lengthy prefaces to prayer, see Ps 44; 89. Ps 70 is a somewhat revised duplicate of vv. 13–17 of this psalm.

40 title *For the director of music.* See note on Ps 4 title.

40:1–5 Praise of the Lord for past mercies (see introduction to Ps 9).

40:1–3 David's experience of God's past help in time of trouble, which moved him to praise and others to faith (see notes on 7:17; 9:1).

40:2 See 30:1 and note.

40:3 *new song.* See note on 33:3. *Many will see.* As a result of David's praise (see 18:49; 22:22–31; see also note on 9:1). *fear.* See notes on 15:4; 25:12; 34:8–14; Pr 1:7; Lk 12:5.

40:4–5 The Lord's benevolence to others: to all who trust in the Lord (v. 4), and to his people Israel (v. 5).

40:4 See Jer 17:7; praise of the Lord for the blessedness of those who trust in him (see 32:1–2; 146:5). *Blessed.* See note on 1:1. *proud.* See note on 31:23.

40:5 *wonders.* See note on 9:1. *planned.* God's actions in behalf of Israel are according to his predetermined purpose (see Isa 25:1; 46:10–11).

40:6–8 David's commitment to God's will. Heb 10:5–10 applies these verses to Christ (see notes there).

40:6 *did not desire ... not require.* More important is obedience (see 1Sa 15:22), especially to God's moral law (see Isa 1:10–17; Am 5:21–24; Mic 6:6–8)—i.e., the ten basic commandments of his covenant (see Ex 20:3–17; Dt 5:7–21). *ears ... opened.* Ears made able and eager to hear God's law (see Pr 28:9; Isa 48:8; 50:4–5).

40:7 *Here I am, I have come.* Probably refers to David's commitment to the Lord at the time of his enthronement. *it is written about me in the scroll.* Some take this to be a reference to a prophecy, perhaps Dt 17:14–15. The context, however, strongly suggests that the "scroll" refers to the personal copy of the law that the king is to "write for himself" (Dt 17:18) at the time of his enthronement to serve as the covenant charter of his administration (see Dt 17:18–20; 2Ki 11:12; cf. 1Ki 2:3; see also NIV text note).

40:8 *I desire.* Whatever is in full accord with God's "desire" (v. 6)—a claim that frames the stanza.

40:9–10 David's life is filled with praise, proclaiming God's faithful and loving acts in behalf of his people (cf. 85:10–11). This, too, God desires more than animal sacrifices (see 50:7–15,23).

40:9 *proclaim.* See 68:11; 96:2; as good tidings (see 1Ki 1:42; Isa 40:9; 41:27; 52:7; 61:1). *in the great assembly.* See notes on 1:5; 9:1. *not seal my lips.* He is not silent about God's praise (see 38:13–16; 39:1 and notes).

40:10 *heart.* See note on 4:7. *your love and your faithfulness.* See note on 26:3.

40:11–17 The prayer for help.

40:11–13 David's plea for deliverance from his troubles.

40:11 *your love and faithfulness.* Which he has been proclaiming to all at the temple (see v. 10 and note).

40:12 *sins have overtaken me.* In the form of the "troubles without number" that burden him (see Ps 38–39 and their

They are more than the hairs of my
head,[l]
and my heart fails[m] within me.
13 Be pleased to save me, LORD;
come quickly, LORD, to help me.[n]
14 May all who want to take my life[o]
be put to shame and confusion;[p]
may all who desire my ruin[q]
be turned back in disgrace.
15 May those who say to me, "Aha!
Aha!"[r]
be appalled at their own shame.
16 But may all who seek you[s]
rejoice and be glad[t] in you;
may those who long for your saving
help always say,
"The LORD is great!"[u]
17 But as for me, I am poor and needy;[v]
may the Lord think[w] of me.
You are my help[x] and my deliverer;[y]
you are my God, do not delay.[z]

Psalm 41[a]

For the director of music.
A psalm of David.

1 Blessed[a] are those who have regard for
the weak;[b]
the LORD delivers them in times of
trouble.[c]
2 The LORD protects[d] and preserves
them —[e]
they are counted among the blessed
in the land —[f]
he does not give them over to the
desire of their foes.[g]

40:12 [l]Ps 69:4 [m]Ps 73:26 **40:13** [n]Ps 22:19; 38:22 **40:14** [o]S 1Sa 20:1 [p]S Est 9:2; Ps 35:26 [q]S Ps 35:4 **40:15** [r]S Ps 35:21 **40:16** [s]Dt 4:29; 1Ch 28:9; Ps 9:10; 119:2 [t]Ps 9:2 [u]Ps 35:27 **40:17** [v]Ps 86:1; 109:22 [w]Ps 144:3 [x]S Ps 20:2 [y]S Ps 18:2 [z]Ps 119:60 **41:1** [a]S Dt 14:29 [b]S Job 24:4 [c]Ps 25:17 **41:2** [d]Ps 12:5; 32:7 [e]Ezr 9:9; Ps 71:20; 119:88, 159; 138:7; 143:11 [f]Ps 37:22 [g]S Dt 6:24 **41:3** [h]Ps 6:6 [i]2Sa 13:5; 2Ki 1:4 **41:4** [j]Ps 6:2; S 9:13 [k]S Dt 32:39 [l]Ps 51:4 **41:5** [m]S Ps 38:12 **41:6** [n]Ps 12:2; 101:7; Mt 5:11 [o]Pr 26:24 [p]S Lev 19:16 **41:7** [q]Ps 71:10 **41:8** [r]S 2Ki 1:4 **41:9** [s]S 2Sa 15:12; S Job 19:14 [t]Nu 30:2; Job 19:19; Ps 55:20; 89:34; Mt 26:23; Lk 22:21; Jn 13:18* **41:10** [u]ver 4 [v]Ps 3:3; 9:13 [w]S 2Sa 3:39

3 The LORD sustains them on their
sickbed[h]
and restores them from their bed of
illness.[i]
4 I said, "Have mercy[j] on me, LORD;
heal[k] me, for I have sinned[l] against
you."
5 My enemies say of me in malice,
"When will he die and his name
perish?[m]"
6 When one of them comes to
see me,
he speaks falsely,[n] while his heart
gathers slander;[o]
then he goes out and spreads[p] it
around.
7 All my enemies whisper together[q]
against me;
they imagine the worst for me,
saying,
8 "A vile disease has afflicted him;
he will never get up[r] from the place
where he lies."
9 Even my close friend,[s]
someone I trusted,
one who shared my bread,
has turned[b] against me.[t]
10 But may you have mercy[u] on me,
LORD;
raise me up,[v] that I may repay[w]
them.

[a] In Hebrew texts 41:1-13 is numbered 41:2-14.
[b] 9 Hebrew *has lifted up his heel*

introductions). *cannot see.* See note on 13:3. *more than the hairs of my head.* See Mt 10:30; Lk 12:7. *heart.* See note on 4:7.
40:14–16 Prayer for God's saving help to confound David's adversaries and move the godly to praise. For harassment by enemies in times of trouble, see 38:12; 39:8; 41:5,7 and often in the Psalms (see note on 5:9). For both form and substance, see 35:26–27.
40:14 *shame … confusion … disgrace.* David asks that those who have wished to put him to public shame be put to shame themselves (see note on 5:10).
40:15 *Aha! Aha!* See note on 3:2.
40:17 *poor and needy.* In need of God's help (see note on 34:6).
Ps 41 David's prayer for mercy when seriously ill. He acknowledges that his illness is related to his sin (v. 4). See introductions to Ps 38–40. His enemies greet the prospect of his death with malicious glee (see note on 5:9), and even his "close friend" (v. 9) betrays his friendship (see note on 31:11–12). This psalm concludes a collection of four psalms connected by common themes and, together with Ps 40, forms the conclusion to Book I (see introduction to Ps 40–41). (Book I begins and ends with a "Blessed" psalm.) In its structure, the psalm is very symmetrical, composed of four stanzas of three verses each. The first and fourth stanzas frame the prayer with expressions of confidence; stanzas two and three elaborate the prayer. Verse 13 is actually not part of the psalm but the doxology that closes Book I (see note on v. 13).

41 title *For the director of music.* See note on Ps 4 title.
41:1–3 Confidence that the Lord will restore.
41:1 *Blessed are those who have regard for the weak.* True of all, but especially of a king, whose duty it is to defend the powerless (see 72:2,4,12–14; 82:3–4; Pr 29:14; 31:8–9; Isa 11:4; Jer 22:16). *Blessed.* See note on 1:1.
41:4–6 Prayer for God to show mercy and to heal.
41:4 *sinned.* See note on 32:3–5.
41:5 *When will he die … ?* See note on 3:2. *his name perish.* See note on 9:5.
41:6 *see me.* Visit me in my sickness. *speaks falsely.* Speaks as if he were my friend. *heart.* See note on 4:7.
41:7–9 His enemies and his friend.
41:9 *close friend … who shared my bread.* One who shared the king's table — i.e., was an honored, as well as trusted, friend (see note on 31:11–12). Reference may be to one who had sealed his friendship by a covenant (see note on 23:5). For Jesus' use of this verse in application to himself, see Jn 13:18. In fulfilling the role of his royal ancestor as God's anointed king over Israel, the great Son of David also experienced the hostility of others and the betrayal of a trusted associate and thus fulfilled his forefather's lament.
41:10–12 Prayer, with confidence.
41:10 *that I may repay them.* That I (as king) may call them to account.

11 I know that you are pleased with me,[x]
for my enemy does not triumph
over me.[y]
12 Because of my integrity[z] you uphold me[a]
and set me in your presence forever.[b]

13 Praise[c] be to the LORD, the God of
Israel,[d]
from everlasting to everlasting.
Amen and Amen.[e]

BOOK II

Psalms 42–72

Psalm 42[a,b]

For the director of music.
A *maskil*[c] of the Sons of Korah.

1 As the deer[f] pants for streams of
water,[g]
so my soul pants[h] for you, my God.
2 My soul thirsts[i] for God, for the living
God.[j]
When can I go[k] and meet with God?
3 My tears[l] have been my food
day and night,
while people say to me all day long,
"Where is your God?"[m]
4 These things I remember
as I pour out my soul:[n]
how I used to go to the house of God[o]
under the protection of the Mighty
One[d]
with shouts of joy[p] and praise[q]
among the festive throng.[r]

41:11 [x]S Nu 14:8 [y]Ps 25:2 **41:12** [z]S Ps 25:21 [a]Ps 18:35; S 37:17; 63:8 [b]S Job 4:7; Ps 21:6; 61:7 **41:13** [c]S Ge 24:27 [d]Ps 72:18 [e]Ps 72:19; 89:52; 106:48 **42:1** [f]S Ps 18:33 [g]S Dt 10:7 [h]S Job 19:27; Ps 119:131; Joel 1:20 **42:2** [i]Ps 63:1; 143:6 [j]S Jos 3:10; S 1Sa 14:39; S Mt 16:16; Ro 9:26 [k]Ps 43:4; 84:7 **42:3** [l]S Job 3:24 [m]ver 10; Ps 79:10; 115:2; Joel 2:17; Mic 7:10 **42:4** [n]S 1Sa 1:15 [o]Ps 55:14; 122:1; Isa 2:2; 30:29 [p]S Ezr 3:13 [q]S Jos 6:5; Ps 95:2; 100:4; 147:7; Jnh 2:9 [r]Ps 35:18; 109:30

[a] In many Hebrew manuscripts Psalms 42 and 43 constitute one psalm. [b] In Hebrew texts 42:1-11 is numbered 42:2-12. [c] Title: Probably a literary or musical term [d] 4 See Septuagint and Syriac; the meaning of the Hebrew for this line is uncertain.

41:12 *my integrity.* See note on 15:2. *set.* Establish. *in your presence.* As the royal servant of Israel's heavenly King. (For the idiom see 101:7; 1Sa 16:22, "in my service"; 1Ki 10:8, "before you"; 17:1, "whom I serve.") *forever.* Never to be rejected (see 2Sa 7:15–16).

41:13 The doxology with which the worshiping community is to respond to the contents of Book I (see 72:18–19; 89:52; 106:48; 150).

Ps 42–45 Book II of the Psalter begins with three prayers (but see introduction to Ps 42–43) and an attached royal psalm in perfect balance with the ending of Book II (see introduction to Ps 69–72). These prayers contain certain key words found elsewhere in Book II only in Ps 69–71—and in the cluster of seven psalms placed at the center of this Book (see introduction to Ps 54–60). Although Ps 42–43 is the prayer of an individual and Ps 44 a prayer of the community, the two have much in common. Central to both is the cry, "Why, God?" (42:9; 43:2; 44:23–24)—why have you forgotten me/us (42:9; 44:24) and rejected me/us (43:2; 44:23) in the face of the oppression of our enemies (42:9; 44:24)? But that "Why?" (see note on 6:3), so expressive of the tension faith experiences in the face of such circumstances as the psalmists describe, is not faith's last word. Just here—and that in the first of these two introductory psalms—faith responds with its own reassuring refrain, "hope in God" (42:5,11; 43:5), because his "love" will not fail (42:8; 44:26).

Following the communal cry of anguish over God's apparently unprovoked abandonment of his people to the pillage and ridicule of foreign peoples (Ps 44), the editors of the Psalter have pointed its readers to the Lord's anointed as he is depicted in an honorific song on one of the high days of his reign. In this song two relevant themes loom large: (1) the king's responsibility to uphold justice within the realm and to protect the people from external enemies and (2) the assurance of his enjoying God's favor so that his kingdom flourishes under his rule and his dynasty is stable and enduring—of which the glory of his wedding to a foreign princess is a token. This placement of Ps 45 hints at a Messianic reading of the psalm on the part of the Psalter's editors. See further the introduction to Ps 45 and the introduction to Ps 69–72.

Ps 42–43 A prayer for deliverance from being "oppressed by the enemy" (42:9; 43:2) and for restoration to the presence of God at his temple. That these two psalms form a single prayer (though they are counted as two psalms also in the Septuagint, the pre-Christian Greek translation of the OT [but see NIV text note]) is evident from its unique structure (see below) and the development of common themes. Ps 43 may have come to be separated from Ps 42 for a particular liturgical purpose (see introduction to Ps 9). The speaker may have been a leading member of the Korahites, whose normal duties involved him in the liturgical activities of the temple (see especially 42:4 and note on Ps 42 title). It may be that the "unfaithful nation" (43:1) referred to was the Arameans of Damascus and that the author had been taken captive by the Arameans during one of their incursions into Judah, such as that of Hazael (see 2Ki 12:17–18). (This attack by Hazael affected especially the area in which the Korahites, descendants of Kohath, had been assigned cities; see Jos 21:4,9–19.) See also notes below. This psalm begins Book II of the Psalter (see introduction to Ps 42–45), a collection that is distinguished from Book I primarily by the fact that the Hebrew word for "God" (*Elohim*) predominates, whereas in the first book the Hebrew word for "the LORD" (*Yahweh*) predominates.

Structurally, the three stanzas of this psalm are symmetrical (each contains four verses), and each is followed by the same refrain (42:5,11; 43:5). The middle stanza, however, has at its center (see note on 6:6) an additional verse (42:8) that interrupts the developing thought and injects a note of confidence, such as comes to expression also in the threefold refrain. Apart from the refrains, the prayer is framed by an expression of longing for God's presence (42:1) and a vow to praise God at his altar (43:4; see note there). For other psalms with recurring refrains, see Ps 46; 49; 59; 80; 107.

42 title *For the director of music.* See note on Ps 4 title. *maskil.* See note on Ps 32 title. *of the Sons of Korah.* Or "for the Sons of Korah"; see "For Jeduthun" in Ps 39 title. "Sons of Korah" refers to the Levitical choir made up of the descendants of Korah appointed by David to serve in the temple liturgy. The Korahites represented the Levitical family of Kohath, son of Levi. Their leader in the days of David was Heman (see Ps 88 title)—just as Asaph led the choir of the Gershonites and Jeduthun (Ethan) the choir of the Merarites (see 1Ch 6:31–47 and note on Ps 39 title). This is the first of a collection of seven psalms ascribed to the "Sons of Korah" (Ps 42–49); four more occur in Book III (Ps 84–85; 87–88).

42:1–4 Longing to be with God at the temple.

42:1 *deer pants for ... water.* Because its life depends on

5 Why, my soul, are you downcast?[s]
Why so disturbed[t] within me?
Put your hope in God,[u]
for I will yet praise[v] him,
my Savior[w] and my God.[x]

6 My soul is downcast within me;
therefore I will remember[y] you
from the land of the Jordan,[z]
the heights of Hermon[a]—from
Mount Mizar.
7 Deep calls to deep[b]
in the roar of your waterfalls;
all your waves and breakers
have swept over me.[c]

8 By day the LORD directs his love,[d]
at night[e] his song[f] is with me—
a prayer to the God of my life.[g]

9 I say to God my Rock,[h]
"Why have you forgotten[i] me?
Why must I go about mourning,[j]
oppressed[k] by the enemy?"[l]
10 My bones suffer mortal agony[m]
as my foes taunt[n] me,
saying to me all day long,
"Where is your God?"[o]

11 Why, my soul, are you downcast?
Why so disturbed within me?
Put your hope in God,
for I will yet praise him,
my Savior and my God.[p]

Psalm 43[a]

1 Vindicate me, my God,
and plead my cause[q]
against an unfaithful nation.
Rescue me[r] from those who are
deceitful and wicked.[s]
2 You are God my stronghold.
Why have you rejected[t] me?
Why must I go about mourning,[u]
oppressed by the enemy?[v]
3 Send me your light[w] and your faithful
care,[x]
let them lead me;[y]
let them bring me to your holy mountain,[z]
to the place where you dwell.[a]
4 Then I will go[b] to the altar[c] of God,
to God, my joy[d] and my delight.[e]
I will praise you with the lyre,[f]
O God, my God.

[a] In many Hebrew manuscripts Psalms 42 and 43 constitute one psalm.

42:5 [s] Ps 38:6; 77:3; La 3:20; Mt 26:38 [t] S Job 20:2 [u] S Ps 25:5; S 71:14 [v] Ps 9:1 [w] Ps 18:46 [x] ver 11; Ps 43:5 **42:6** [y] Ps 63:6; 77:11 [z] Ge 13:10; S Nu 13:29 [a] S Dt 3:8; S 4:48 **42:7** [b] S Ge 1:2; S 7:11 [c] Ps 69:2; Jnh 2:3 **42:8** [d] Ps 57:3 [e] S Ps 16:7 [f] Ps 77:6 [g] Ps 133:3; Ecc 5:18; 8:15 **42:9** [h] Ps 18:31 [i] S Ps 10:11 [j] S Ps 35:14 [k] Job 20:19; Ps 43:2; 106:42 [l] Ps 9:13; 43:2 **42:10** [m] S Ps 6:2 [n] Dt 32:27; Ps 44:16; 89:51; 102:8; 119:42 [o] S ver 3 **42:11** [p] ver 5; Ps 43:5 **43:1** [q] S Jdg 6:31 [r] S Ps 25:20 [s] S Ps 36:3; 109:2 **43:2** [t] Ps 44:9; 74:1; 88:14; 89:38 [u] S Ps 35:14 [v] S Ps 42:9 **43:3** [w] Ps 27:1 [x] S Ps 26:3 [y] S Ps 25:5 [z] Ps 2:6 [a] S 2Sa 15:25 **43:4** [b] S Ps 42:2 [c] Ps 26:6; 84:3 [d] S Ps 21:6 [e] Ps 16:3 [f] S Ge 4:21

water—especially when being pressed by hunters, as the psalmist was by his oppressors. *soul.* See note on 6:3.

42:2 *My soul thirsts for God.* See 63:1; cf. Isa 55:1 and note; Mt 5:6. *living God.* See Dt 5:26. *When . . . ?* Circumstances (see v. 9; 43:1–2) now prevent him from being at the temple. *meet with God.* Enter his presence to commune with him (see Ex 19:17; 29:42–43; 30:6,36).

42:3 *day and night.* See vv. 8,10. *Where is your God?* See notes on 3:2; 10:11.

42:4 *soul.* See note on 6:3.

42:5 The refrain: faith encouraging faith (see 27:13–14 and introduction to Ps 27). *praise him.* For his saving help (see notes on 7:17; 9:1; see also 43:4).

42:6–10 The cause and depth of the trouble of his soul.

42:6 *soul is downcast.* See vv. 5,11; 43:5. *therefore I will remember you.* As he remembers (v. 4) in his exile the joy of his past intimacy with God, so now in his exile he remembers God and painfully wonders (vv. 7,9–10), yet not without hope (v. 8). (But some believe that the clause should be rendered "because I remember you.") *from the land . . . from Mount Mizar.* Probably indicating that the author speaks from exile outside the contemporary boundaries of Israel and Judah. Some think the author locates himself at Mount Mizar (a small peak or village, not otherwise known) on the flanks of Mount Hermon somewhere near the headwaters of the Jordan. Others translate the Hebrew for "from" as "far from" and understand "the land of the Jordan" to refer to the promised land (which lies along the Jordan and from which the author was separated). The mention of "the heights of Hermon" may then be a reference to the high peak that marked the northern border of the land (see Dt 3:8; Jos 11:17; 13:11; 1Ch 5:23) and looked down upon it (see 133:3; SS 4:8). Some have suggested that "Mount Mizar" is an additional reference to "the heights of Hermon," calling that high peak the "little mountain" (literal translation) in comparison with Mount Zion (see 68:15–16).

42:7 *Deep calls . . . your waterfalls.* Often taken to be an allusion to the cascading waters of the upper Jordan as they rush down from Mount Hermon. It is more likely, however, that this is a literary allusion to the "waterfalls" by which the waters from God's storehouse of water above (see note on 36:8)—the "deep" above—pour down into the streams and rivers that empty into the seas—the "deep" below. It pictures the great distress the author suffers, and the imagery is continued in the following reference to God's "waves and breakers" sweeping over him (see 69:1–2; 88:7; Jnh 2:3,5; see also note on 32:6). God's hand is involved in the psalmist's suffering, at least to the extent that he has allowed this catastrophe. He seems to the psalmist to have "forgotten" (v. 9)—to have "rejected" (43:2)—him. But he makes no link between this and any sin in his life (see Ps 44; 77).

42:8 The center: confession of hope in all the trouble. That is, "Day-and-night [cf. v. 3] the LORD directs his love . . . his song is with me" (see note on 3:7). *the LORD.* Only here at the center in this psalm (see introduction). *directs his love.* Sends forth his love, like a messenger to do his will (see 43:3). *love.* See note on 6:4. *his song.* A song concerning him. *prayer.* Praise and prayer belong together in the thought of the psalmist.

42:9 Echoed in 43:2. *Rock.* See note on 18:2. *Why . . . ? Why . . . ?* See note on 6:3 and introduction to Ps 42–45.

42:10 See v. 3. *bones.* See note on 6:2.

43:1–4 Prayer for deliverance from the enemy and for restoration to God's presence.

43:1 A plea in the language of the court (see introduction to Ps 17).

43:2 Echoes 42:9.

43:3 *your light and your faithful care.* Personified as God's messengers who work out (1) his salvation (light; see note on 27:1) and (2) his faithful care in behalf of his own (see 26:3; 30:9; 40:10). May these guide me back to your temple. *holy mountain.* See note on 2:6.

43:4 See note on 7:17. *to the altar.* See 26:6 and note.

[5]Why, my soul, are you downcast?
Why so disturbed within me?
Put your hope in God,
for I will yet praise him,
my Savior and my God.[g]

Psalm 44[a]

For the director of music.
Of the Sons of Korah. A *maskil.*[b]

[1]We have heard it with our ears,[h]
O God;
our ancestors have told us[i]
what you did in their days,
in days long ago.[j]
[2]With your hand you drove out[k] the
nations
and planted[l] our ancestors;
you crushed[m] the peoples
and made our ancestors flourish.[n]
[3]It was not by their sword[o] that they
won the land,
nor did their arm bring them victory;
it was your right hand,[p] your arm,[q]
and the light[r] of your face, for you
loved[s] them.

[4]You are my King[t] and my God,[u]
who decrees[c] victories[v] for Jacob.
[5]Through you we push back[w] our
enemies;
through your name we trample[x] our
foes.
[6]I put no trust in my bow,[y]
my sword does not bring me victory;
[7]but you give us victory[z] over our
enemies,
you put our adversaries to shame.[a]
[8]In God we make our boast[b] all day
long,[c]
and we will praise your name
forever.[d][d]

[9]But now you have rejected[e] and
humbled us;[f]
you no longer go out with our
armies.[g]
[10]You made us retreat[h] before the enemy,
and our adversaries have
plundered[i] us.
[11]You gave us up to be devoured like
sheep[j]
and have scattered us among the
nations.[k]
[12]You sold your people for a pittance,[l]
gaining nothing from their sale.

[13]You have made us a reproach[m] to our
neighbors,[n]
the scorn[o] and derision[p] of those
around us.
[14]You have made us a byword[q] among
the nations;
the peoples shake their heads[r] at us.
[15]I live in disgrace[s] all day long,
and my face is covered with
shame[t]
[16]at the taunts[u] of those who reproach
and revile[v] me,
because of the enemy, who is bent
on revenge.[w]

[17]All this came upon us,
though we had not forgotten[x] you;
we had not been false to your
covenant.

43:5 [g]S Ps 42:6 **44:1** [h]2Sa 7:22; 1Ch 17:20; Jer 26:11 [i]S Jdg 6:13 [j]S Dt 32:7; S Job 37:23 **44:2** [k]S Jos 3:10; Ac 7:45 [l]S Ex 15:17; S Isa 60:21 [m]S Jdg 4:23; S 2Ch 14:13 [n]Ps 80:9; Jer 32:23 **44:3** [o]Jos 24:12 [p]Ps 78:54 [q]Ex 15:16; Ps 77:15; 79:11; 89:10; 98:1; Isa 40:10; 52:10; 63:5 [r]Ps 89:15 [s]S Dt 4:37 **44:4** [t]S Ps 24:7 [u]Ps 5:2 [v]S Ps 21:5 **44:5** [w]S Jos 23:5 [x]Ps 60:12; 108:13 **44:6** [y]Ge 48:22; Hos 1:7 **44:7** [z]S Dt 20:4 [a]S Job 8:22 **44:8** [b]S Ps 34:2; 1Co 1:31; 2Co 10:17 [c]Ps 52:1 [d]S Ps 30:12 **44:9** [e]S Ps 43:2 [f]S Dt 8:3; S 31:17; Ps 107:39; Isa 5:15 [g]S Jos 7:12; Ps 108:11 **44:10** [h]S Lev 26:17 [i]S Jdg 2:14 **44:11** [j]ver 22; Jer 12:3 [k]S Lev 26:33; S Ps 9:11; Eze 6:8; Zec 2:6 **44:12** [l]S Dt 32:30; Isa 52:3; Jer 15:13; 50:1; 52:3

[a] In Hebrew texts 44:1-26 is numbered 44:2-27.
[b] Title: Probably a literary or musical term
[c] 4 Septuagint, Aquila and Syriac; Hebrew *King, O God; / command*
[d] 8 The Hebrew has *Selah* (a word of uncertain meaning) here.

44:13 [m]S 2Ch 29:8; Isa 30:3; Jer 25:9; 42:18; 44:8 [n]Ps 79:4; 80:6; 89:41 [o]S Dt 28:37; S Mic 2:6 [p]Eze 23:32 **44:14** [q]S 1Ki 9:7 [r]S 2Ki 19:21 **44:15** [s]Ge 30:23; 2Ch 32:21; Ps 35:26 [t]S Ps 34:5 **44:16** [u]S Ps 42:10 [v]Ps 10:13; 55:3; 74:10 [w]S 1Sa 18:25; S Jer 11:19; Ro 12:19 **44:17** [x]S Dt 6:12; S 32:18; Ps 119:16,61, 153,176; Pr 3:1

Ps 44 Israel's cry for help after suffering a devastating defeat at the hand of an enemy. The psalm probably relates to an experience of the kingdom of Judah (which as a nation did not break covenant with the Lord until late in her history), perhaps during the reign of Jehoshaphat or Hezekiah.

Structurally, three thematic developments rise one upon the other as the psalm advances to the prayer in the closing verses. First there is praise of the Lord for past victories (vv. 1–8), second a description of the present defeat and its consequences (vv. 9–16), third a plea of innocence (vv. 17–22), then finally the prayer (vv. 23–26). Each of the themes (recalling of past mercies, description of the present distress and claim of covenant loyalty) in its own way functions as a ground for the appeal for help (see Ps 40 and its introduction; see also the lengthy prefaces to prayer in Ps 40; 89). For the thematic links between Ps 44 and 42–43 and the function of these psalms in the arrangement of Book II, see introduction to Ps 42–45.

44 title See note on Ps 42 title.

44:1–8 Praise to God for past victories: (1) those by which Israel became established in the land (vv. 1–3) and (2) those by which Israel has been kept secure in the land (vv. 4–8).

44:1 See 78:3.

44:3 *light of your face.* See notes on 4:6; 13:1.

44:4 *my.* Here and elsewhere in this psalm the first-person singular pronoun refers to the nation corporately (see note on Ps 30 title). *Jacob.* See note on 14:7.

44:5,8 *your name.* See v. 20; see also note on 5:11.

44:8 *In God we make our boast.* That is, we give God all the praise. For *Selah*, see NIV text note and note on 3:2.

44:9–16 But now you have forsaken us: (1) You have caused us to suffer defeat (vv. 9–12); (2) you have shamed us before our enemies (vv. 13–16).

44:11 *gave us up to be devoured like sheep.* Have not protected us as our Shepherd-King (see v. 4 and note on 23:1).

44:12 *sold your people.* Like chattel no longer valued (see Dt 32:30; Jdg 2:14). *for a pittance.* For nothing of value (see Isa 52:3; Jer 15:13; cf. Isa 43:3–4).

44:14 *shake their heads.* In scorn (see 64:8).

44:16 *bent on revenge.* See 8:2 and note.

44:17–22 And we have not been disloyal to you: (1) We have not been untrue to your covenant (vv. 17–19); (2) you are our witness that we have not turned to another god (vv. 20–22).

44:17 *your covenant.* See Ex 19–24.

[18] Our hearts had not turned[y] back;
our feet had not strayed from your path.
[19] But you crushed[z] us and made us a haunt for jackals;[a]
you covered us over with deep darkness.[b]
[20] If we had forgotten[c] the name of our God
or spread out our hands to a foreign god,[d]
[21] would not God have discovered it,
since he knows the secrets of the heart?[e]
[22] Yet for your sake we face death all day long;
we are considered as sheep[f] to be slaughtered.[g]
[23] Awake,[h] Lord! Why do you sleep?[i]
Rouse yourself![j] Do not reject us forever.[k]
[24] Why do you hide your face[l]
and forget[m] our misery and oppression?[n]
[25] We are brought down to the dust;[o]
our bodies cling to the ground.

44:18 [y] Ps 119:51,157 **44:19** [z] S 2Ch 14:13; Ps 51:8 [a] S Job 30:29; S Isa 34:13 [b] S Job 3:5 **44:20** [c] S Dt 32:18; S Jdg 3:7 [d] S Ex 20:3; Isa 43:12; Jer 5:19 **44:21** [e] S 1Sa 16:7; 1Ki 8:39; Pr 15:11; Jer 12:3; 17:10 **44:22** [f] S ver 11 [g] Isa 53:7; Jer 11:19; 12:3; Ro 8:36* **44:23** [h] S Ps 7:6 [i] Ps 78:65 [j] Ps 59:5 [k] Ps 74:1; 77:7 **44:24** [l] S Dt 32:20; Ps 13:1 [m] La 5:20 [n] S Dt 26:7 **44:25** [o] Ps 119:25 **44:26** [p] S Nu 10:35; S Ps 12:5; 102:13 [q] Ps 26:11

[26] Rise up[p] and help us;
rescue[q] us because of your unfailing love.[r]

Psalm 45[a]

For the director of music. To the tune of "Lilies." Of the Sons of Korah. A *maskil*.[b] A wedding song.[s]

[1] My heart is stirred by a noble theme
as I recite my verses for the king;
my tongue is the pen of a skillful writer.
[2] You are the most excellent of men
and your lips have been anointed with grace,[t]
since God has blessed you forever.[u]
[3] Gird your sword[v] on your side, you mighty one;[w]
clothe yourself with splendor and majesty.[x]

[a] In Hebrew texts 45:1-17 is numbered 45:2-18.
[b] Title: Probably a literary or musical term

[r] Ps 6:4 **45:Title** [s] SS 1:1 **45:2** [t] Lk 4:22 [u] Ps 21:6 **45:3** [v] S Dt 32:41; Ps 149:6; Rev 1:16 [w] S 2Sa 1:19 [x] S Job 40:10; S Ps 21:5

44:18 *hearts.* See note on 4:7. *your path.* The way marked out in God's covenant (see note on 5:8).
44:19 *you crushed us.* But that cannot be used as evidence that we have been disloyal. *haunt for jackals.* A desolate place, uninhabited by people (see Isa 13:22; Jer 9:11). *deep darkness.* The absence of all that was associated with the metaphor "light" (see notes on 30:1; 36:9).
44:20 *spread out our hands.* Prayed (see Ex 9:29 and note).
44:22 *Yet.* Or "As a matter of fact" or "As you, God, know." From the time of her stay in Egypt (see Ex 1), Israel has suffered the hostility of the nations because of her relationship with the Lord (see Mt 10:34). For Paul's application of this verse to the Christian community in the light of Christ's death and resurrection, see Ro 8:36.
44:23–26 The appeal for help: (1) awake to our need (vv. 23–24); (2) arise to our help (vv. 25–26; see introduction to Ps 16).
44:23 *Awake.* See note on 7:6. *Why . . . ?* See note on 6:3 and introduction to Ps 42–45.
44:24 *hide your face.* See note on 13:1.
44:25 *brought down to the dust.* About to sink into death (see 22:29 and note; see also note on 30:1). In Hebrew there is a verbal link with the refrain, "Why, my soul, are you downcast?" in Ps 42–43.
44:26 *Rise up and help.* See 46:1,5; see also note on 3:7. *unfailing love.* See note on 6:4; see also 42:8 and note.
Ps 45 A song in praise of the king on his wedding day (see title; see also introduction to Ps 42–45). He undoubtedly belonged to David's dynasty, and the song was probably used at more than one royal wedding. Since the bride is a foreign princess (see vv. 10,12), the wedding reflects the king's standing as a figure of international significance (see note on v. 9). Accordingly he is addressed as one whose reign is to be characterized by victories over the nations (vv. 3–5; cf. Ps 2; 110). As a royal son of David, he is a type (foreshadowing) of Christ. After the exile this psalm was applied to the Messiah, the promised Son of David who would sit on David's throne (for the application of vv. 6–7 to Christ, see Heb 1:8–9). The superscription implies that it was composed and sung by a member of the Levitical temple choir. As a word from one of the temple personnel, the song was no doubt received as a word from the temple—and from the One who sat enthroned there.

In its structure, the song is framed by vv. 1,17, while vv. 2,16 constitute a secondary frame within them—all addressed to the king. The body of the song falls into two parts: (1) words addressed to the king (vv. 3–9) and (2) words addressed to the royal bride (vv. 10–15). These in turn each contain two parts, reflecting a similar pattern: (1) (a) exhortations to the king (vv. 3–5), (b) the glory of the king (vv. 6–9); (2) (a) exhortations to the bride (vv. 10–12), (b) the glory of the bride (vv. 13–15).
45 title *For the director of music.* See note on Ps 4 title. *To the tune of.* See note on Ps 9 title. *Lilies.* See Ps 69 title. "Lilies" may be an abbreviated form of "The Lily (Lilies) of the Covenant" found in the titles of Ps 60; 80. *Of the Sons of Korah.* See note on Ps 42 title. *maskil.* See note on Ps 32 title. *song.* See note on Ps 30 title.
45:1 See v. 17, where the speaker pledges (perhaps by means of this song) to perpetuate the king's memory throughout the generations and awaken the praise of the nations. *heart.* See note on 4:7.
45:2 *most excellent of men.* One who excels in manly traits and beauty, as a king should (see 1Sa 9:2; 16:18)—but he is so far beyond ordinary men as to be almost godlike (see note on v. 6). *lips . . . anointed with grace.* See Pr 22:11; Ecc 10:12; cf. Isa 50:4; Lk 4:22; see also v. 16, where it is suggested that such a king will be perpetuated in his sons. *forever.* See note on v. 6.
45:3–5 Go forth with your sword victoriously in the service of all that is right, and clothe yourself thereby with glory—make your reign adorn you more truly than the wedding garb with which you are now arrayed (v. 8).
45:3 *clothe yourself with.* See note on 109:29. *splendor and majesty.* See 21:5 and note.

Bronze and silver scepter-head found in the sacred area at Dan (ninth century BC). Psalm 45:6 reads, "Your throne, O God, will last for ever and ever; a scepter of justice will be the scepter of your kingdom."

Z. Radovan/www.BibleLandPictures.com

4 In your majesty ride forth victoriously[y]
in the cause of truth, humility and justice;[z]
let your right hand[a] achieve awesome deeds.[b]
5 Let your sharp arrows[c] pierce the hearts[d] of the king's enemies;[e]
let the nations fall beneath your feet.
6 Your throne, O God,[a] will last for ever and ever;[f]
a scepter of justice will be the scepter of your kingdom.
7 You love righteousness[g] and hate wickedness;[h]
therefore God, your God, has set you above your companions
by anointing[i] you with the oil of joy.[j]
8 All your robes are fragrant[k] with myrrh[l] and aloes[m] and cassia;[n]
from palaces adorned with ivory[o]
the music of the strings[p] makes you glad.
9 Daughters of kings[q] are among your honored women;
at your right hand[r] is the royal bride[s] in gold of Ophir.[t]

10 Listen, daughter,[u] and pay careful attention:[v]
Forget your people[w] and your father's house.
11 Let the king be enthralled by your beauty;[x]
honor[y] him, for he is your lord.[z]
12 The city of Tyre[a] will come with a gift,[b][b]
people of wealth will seek your favor.
13 All glorious[c] is the princess within her chamber;
her gown is interwoven with gold.[d]
14 In embroidered garments[e] she is led to the king;[f]
her virgin companions[g] follow her—
those brought to be with her.
15 Led in with joy and gladness,[h]
they enter the palace of the king.

16 Your sons will take the place of your fathers;
you will make them princes[i] throughout the land.

45:4 [y] Rev 6:2 [z] Zep 2:3 [a] Ps 21:8 [b] S Dt 4:34; Ps 65:5; 66:3 **45:5** [c] S Dt 32:23 [d] S Nu 24:8 [e] Ps 9:13; 92:9 **45:6** [f] S Ge 21:33; La 5:19 **45:7** [g] Ps 33:5 [h] S Ps 11:5 [i] Ps 2:2; Isa 45:1; 61:1; Zec 4:14 [j] S Ps 23:5; Heb 1:8-9* **45:8** [k] Pr 27:9; SS 1:3; 4:10 [l] S Ge 37:25 [m] S Nu 24:6; Jn 19:39 [n] S Ex 30:24 [o] S 1Ki 22:39 [p] Ps 144:9; 150:4; Isa 38:20 **45:9** [q] SS 6:8 [r] 1Ki 2:19 [s] Isa 62:5 [t] S Ge 10:29 **45:10** [u] Ru 1:11 [v] Jer 5:1 [w] Ru 1:16 **45:11** [x] S Est 1:11; S La 2:15 [y] Eph 5:33 [z] 1Pe 3:6 **45:12** [a] S Jos 19:29 [b] S 1Ki 9:16; S 2Ch 9:24 **45:13** [c] Isa 61:10 [d] Ex 39:3 **45:14** [e] S Jdg 5:30 [f] Est 2:15 [g] SS 1:3 **45:15** [h] S Est 8:17 **45:16** [i] 1Sa 2:8; Ps 68:27; 113:8

[a] *6* Here the king is addressed as God's representative.
[b] *12* Or *A Tyrian robe is among the gifts*

45:4 *justice.* See notes on 37:6; Zec 7:9; see also Introduction to Amos: Theological Theme and Message. *awesome deeds.* See 66:5; 106:22; 145:6.
45:5 *nations fall beneath your feet.* See 2:8–9; 110:1–2,5–6.
45:6–9 The glory of the king's reign: justice and righteousness (see Ps 72).
45:6 *O God.* Possibly the king's throne is called God's throne because he is God's appointed regent. But it is also possible that the king himself is addressed as "god." The Davidic king (the "LORD's anointed," 2Sa 19:21), because of his special relationship with God, was called at his enthronement the "son" of God (see 2:7; 2Sa 7:14; 1Ch 28:6; cf. Ps 89:27). In this psalm, which praises the king and especially extols his "splendor and majesty" (v. 3), it is not unthinkable that he was called "god" as a title of honor (cf. Isa 9:6). Such a description of the Davidic king attains its fullest meaning when applied to Christ, as the author of Hebrews does (Heb 1:8–9). (The pharaohs of Egypt were sometimes addressed as "my god" by their vassal kings in Canaan, as evidenced by the Amarna letters; see chart, p. xxii.) *for ever and ever.* See vv. 2,17. Such was the language used with respect to kings (see note on 21:4). It here gains added significance in the light of God's covenant with David (see 89:4,29,36; 132:12; 2Sa 7:16). In Christ, the Son of David, it is fulfilled.
45:7 *companions.* The noble guests of the king, perhaps from other lands. *oil of joy.* God has anointed him with a more delightful oil than the aromatic oils with which his head and body were anointed on his wedding day—namely, with joy (see 23:5; Isa 61:3).
45:8–9 The glory of the king's wedding.
45:8 *myrrh.* See notes on Ge 37:25; SS 1:13. *aloes.* See note on SS 4:14. *cassia.* See note on Ex 25:6. *palaces adorned with ivory.* See 1Ki 22:39; Am 3:15; 6:4.
45:9 *Daughters of kings.* Whether members of his royal harem (see 1Ki 11:1–3) or guests at his wedding, they represent international recognition of the king. *in gold of Ophir.* Adorned with jewels of finest gold (see notes on Ge 10:29; 1Ki 9:28) and all the finery associated with it.
45:10–12 The word to the royal bride.
45:10–11 Be totally loyal to your adoring king.
45:12 *city of Tyre.* Lit. "Daughter (of) Tyre," a personification of the city of Tyre (see note on 2Ki 19:21). The king of Tyre was the first foreign ruler to recognize the Davidic dynasty (see 2Sa 5:11), and Solomon maintained close relations with that city-state (see 1Ki 5; 9:10–14,26–28). As a great trading center on the Mediterranean coast, Tyre was world renowned for its wealth (see Isa 23; Eze 26:1—28:19). *people of wealth.* Such as those from your homeland. *seek your favor.* Desire to be in your good graces as the wife of this king. These honors will be yours if you faithfully honor your royal husband.
45:13–15 The royal bride's glory.
45:14 *virgin companions.* She too has "companions" (see v. 7), perhaps her permanent attendants.
45:16 *Your.* The king's. *take the place of your fathers.* As the family line continues (dynastic succession). Perhaps it is also hinted that they will surpass the fathers in honor (see note on v. 2). *land.* Or "earth."

17 I will perpetuate your memory through
all generations;[j]
therefore the nations will praise you[k]
for ever and ever.[l]

Psalm 46[a]

For the director of music.
Of the Sons of Korah.
According to *alamoth.*[b] A song.

1 God is our refuge[m] and strength,[n]
an ever-present[o] help[p] in trouble.[q]
2 Therefore we will not fear,[r] though the
earth give way[s]
and the mountains fall[t] into the
heart of the sea,[u]
3 though its waters roar[v] and foam[w]
and the mountains quake[x] with their
surging.[c]

4 There is a river[y] whose streams[z] make
glad the city of God,[a]
the holy place where the Most High[b]
dwells.[c]
5 God is within her,[d] she will not fall;[e]
God will help[f] her at break of day.
6 Nations[g] are in uproar,[h] kingdoms[i] fall;
he lifts his voice,[j] the earth melts.[k]

7 The LORD Almighty[l] is with us;[m]
the God of Jacob[n] is our fortress.[o]

8 Come and see what the LORD has done,[p]
the desolations[q] he has brought on
the earth.
9 He makes wars[r] cease
to the ends of the earth.
He breaks the bow[s] and shatters the
spear;
he burns the shields[d] with fire.[t]

[a] In Hebrew texts 46:1-11 is numbered 46:2-12. [b] Title: Probably a musical term [c] 3 The Hebrew has *Selah* (a word of uncertain meaning) here and at the end of verses 7 and 11. [d] 9 Or *chariots*

45:17 [j]S Ex 3:15; Ps 33:11; 119:90; 135:13 [k]Ps 138:4 [l]S Ps 21:4; Rev 22:5 **46:1** [m]Ps 9:9; 37:39; 61:3; 73:26; 91:2,9; 142:5; Isa 33:16; Jer 16:19; 17:17; Joel 3:16; Na 1:7 [n]Ps 18:1 [o]Ps 34:18; La 3:57 [p]Ps 18:6; Lk 1:54 [q]S Dt 4:30; Ps 25:17 **46:2** [r]S Ge 4:7; Ps 3:6 [s]Ps 82:5; Isa 13:13; 24:1, 19,20; Jer 4:23; Da 11:19; Am 8:14; S Rev 6:14 [t]ver 6; Ps 18:7; 97:5; Isa 54:10; Am 9:5; Mic 1:4; Na 1:5; Hab 3:6 [u]Ex 15:8 **46:3** [v]Ps 93:3; Isa 17:13; Jer 5:22; Eze 1:24; Rev 19:6 [w]S Job 9:26 [x]S Jdg 5:5 **46:4** [y]S Ge 2:10; Rev 22:1 [z]S Ps 1:3 [a]Ps 48:1,8; 87:3; 101:8; Rev 3:12 [b]Ge 14:18 [c]S 2Sa 15:25 **46:5** [d]Dt 23:14; S Ps 26:8; Isa 12:6; Zec 2:5 [e]Ps 125:1 [f]S 1Ch 5:20 **46:6** [g]S Job 12:23 [h]Ps 74:23; Isa 5:30; 17:12 [i]Ps 68:32; 102:22; Isa 13:4,13; 23:11; Eze 26:18; Mt 4:8 [j]S Ps 29:3; Isa 33:3 [k]S ver 2 **46:7** [l]S 1Sa 1:11 [m]S Ge 21:22 [n]S Ps 20:1 [o]ver 11; Ps 18:2 **46:8** [p]Ps 66:5 [q]Isa 17:9; 64:10; Da 9:26; Lk 21:20 **46:9** [r]Isa 2:4 [s]S Ps 37:15; S Isa 22:6 [t]Isa 9:5; Eze 39:9; Hos 2:18

45:17 See note on v. 1. *for ever and ever.* See note on v. 6.
Ps 46–48 Following the cluster of psalms that introduce Book II of the Psalter (see introduction to Ps 42–45), the next thematically related cluster of psalms all express confidence in the security of God's people in the midst of a threatening world. Ps 46 and 48 focus on the security of Jerusalem, "the city of [our] God" (46:4; 48:1), and Ps 47 on the worldwide reign of "the great King" (47:2), whose royal city Jerusalem is (48:2).
Ps 46 A celebration of the security of Jerusalem as the city of God (the inspiration of Martin Luther's great hymn "A Mighty Fortress Is Our God"; see vv. 7,11). Thematically, this psalm is closely related to Ps 48 (see also Ps 76; 87), while Ps 47 celebrates God's victorious reign over all the earth (see introduction to Ps 46–48). It probably predates the exile. However, as a song concerning the "city of God" (v. 4), the royal city of his kingdom on earth (see Ps 48), it remained for Israel a song of hope celebrating the certain triumph of God's kingdom. It was originally liturgical and sung at the temple: The citizens of Jerusalem (or the Levitical choir in their stead) apparently sang the opening stanza (vv. 1–3) and the responses (vv. 7,11), while the Levitical leader of the liturgy probably sang the second and third stanzas (vv. 4–6,8–10). In its structure, apart from the refrains (vv. 7,11), the psalm is composed of three symmetrical stanzas, each containing three verses. For other psalms with recurring refrains, see introduction to Ps 42–43.
46 title *For the director of music.* See note on Ps 4 title. *Of the Sons of Korah.* See note on Ps 42 title. *According to.* See note on Ps 6 title. *alamoth.* See NIV text note. Since the Hebrew word appears to mean "young women," the phrase "According to *alamoth*" may refer to the "young women playing the timbrels" who accompanied the singers as the liturgical procession made its way to the temple (68:25). *A song.* See note on Ps 30 title.
46:1–3 A triumphant confession of fearless trust in God, though the continents break up and sink beneath the surging waters of the seas—i.e., though the creation itself may seem to become uncreated (see 104:6–9; Ge 1:9–10) and all may appear to be going down before the onslaught of the primeval deep. The described upheaval is probably imagery for great threats to Israel's existence (see note on 32:6), especially from her enemies (see vv. 6,8–10; 65:5–8).
46:3 For *Selah,* see NIV text note and note on 3:2.
46:4–6 A description of blessed Zion—a comforting declaration of God's mighty, sustaining presence in his city.
46:4 *river.* Jerusalem had no river, unlike Thebes (Na 3:8), Damascus (2Ki 5:12), Nineveh (Na 2:6,8) or Babylon (137:1)—yet she had a "river." Here the "river" of 36:8 (see note there) serves as a metaphor for the continual outpouring of the sustaining and refreshing blessings of God, which make the city of God like the Garden of Eden (see v. 5; Ge 2:10; Isa 33:21; 51:3; cf. also Eze 31:4–9). *city of God.* See v. 5; see especially Ps 48. *God … Most High.* That is, God Most High (see 57:2; see also note on 3:7). *Most High.* See note on Ge 14:19. *dwells.* See note on 9:11.
46:5 *at break of day.* Or "as dawn approaches"—i.e., when attacks against cities were likely to be launched. His help brings on the dawn of deliverance, dispelling the night of danger (see 44:19 and note; cf. Isa 37:36 for an example).
46:6 *Nations … fall.* Because of God's victory (see vv. 8–9; 48:4–7). *in uproar.* See v. 3 and note on vv. 1–3; see also 2:1–3; Rev 11:18. *lifts his voice.* See 2:5; 9:5; Jer 25:30; Am 1:2; see also 104:7. God's thunder is evoked (see introduction to Ps 29), the thunder of his wrath (see 18:13; Isa 2:10). *earth melts.* As though struck by lightning (see 97:4–5).
46:7 The people's glad response (also v. 11). *LORD Almighty.* See note on 1Sa 1:3. *Jacob.* See note on 14:7.
46:8–10 A declaration of the blessed effects of God's triumph over the nations.
46:8 *Come and see.* An invitation to see God's victories in the world (see 48:8 and note). *the LORD.* Emphatic because of its rare use in Book II of the Psalter. *on the earth.* Among the hostile nations.
46:9 No more attacks against his city. The verse probably speaks of universal peace (see note on 65:6–7). *breaks … shatters … burns.* See 76:3; see also 1Sa 2:4. For the Messiah's universal victory over Israel's enemies, see Isa 9:2–7.

10 He says, "Be still, and know that I am God;[u]
I will be exalted[v] among the nations,
I will be exalted in the earth."

11 The LORD Almighty is with us;
the God of Jacob[w] is our fortress.[x]

Psalm 47[a]

For the director of music.
Of the Sons of Korah. A psalm.

1 Clap your hands,[y] all you nations;
shout to God with cries of joy.[z]

2 For the LORD Most High[a] is awesome,[b]
the great King[c] over all the earth.
3 He subdued[d] nations under us,
peoples under our feet.
4 He chose our inheritance[e] for us,
the pride of Jacob,[f] whom he loved.[b]

5 God has ascended[g] amid shouts of joy,[h]
the LORD amid the sounding of trumpets.[i]
6 Sing praises[j] to God, sing praises;
sing praises to our King, sing praises.

7 For God is the King of all the earth;[k]
sing to him a psalm[l] of praise.

8 God reigns[m] over the nations;
God is seated on his holy throne.[n]
9 The nobles of the nations assemble
as the people of the God of Abraham,
for the kings[c] of the earth belong to God;[o]
he is greatly exalted.[p]

Psalm 48[d]

A song.
A psalm of the Sons of Korah.

1 Great is the LORD,[q] and most worthy of praise,[r]
in the city of our God,[s] his holy mountain.[t]

[a] In Hebrew texts 47:1-9 is numbered 47:2-10.
[b] *4* The Hebrew has *Selah* (a word of uncertain meaning) here.
[c] *9* Or *shields*
[d] In Hebrew texts 48:1-14 is numbered 48:2-15.

46:10 [u] Dt 4:35; 1Ki 18:36, 39; Ps 100:3; Isa 37:16, 20; 43:11; 45:21; Eze 36:23 [v] Ps 18:46; Isa 2:11 **46:11** [w] S Ps 20:1 [x] S ver 7 **47:1** [y] S 2Ki 11:12 [z] S Ps 33:3 **47:2** [a] Ge 14:18 [b] S Dt 7:21 [c] Ps 2:6; 48:2; 95:3; Mt 5:35 **47:3** [d] Ps 18:39, 47; Isa 14:6 **47:4** [e] Ps 2:8; 16:6; 78:55; 1Pe 1:4 [f] Am 6:8; 8:7 **47:5** [g] Ps 68:18; Eph 4:8 [h] S Job 8:21; S Ps 106:5 [i] S Nu 10:2; S 2Sa 6:15 **47:6** [j] S 2Sa 22:50 **47:7** [k] Zec 14:9 [l] 1Ch 16:7; Col 3:16 **47:8** [m] S 1Ch 16:31 [n] S 1Ki 22:19; S Ps 9:4; Rev 4:9 **47:9** [o] S Job 25:2 [p] Ps 46:10; 97:9 **48:1** [q] Ps 86:10; 96:4; 99:2; 135:5; 147:5; Jer 10:6 [r] S 2Sa 22:4; S 1Ch 16:25; Ps 18:3 [s] S Ps 46:4 [t] S Dt 33:19; Ps 2:6; 87:1; Isa 11:9; 32:16; Jer 31:23; Da 9:16; Mic 4:1; Zec 8:3

46:10 *He says.* God's voice breaks through as he addresses the nations (see v. 6) — the climax. *Be still.* Here, the Hebrew for this phrase probably means "Enough!" as in 1Sa 15:16. *know.* Acknowledge. *I will be exalted … in the earth.* God's mighty acts in behalf of his people will bring him universal recognition, a major theme in the Psalter (see 22:27; 47:9; 57:5,11; 64:9; 65:8; 66:1 – 7; 67:2 – 5,7; 77:14; 86:9; 98:2 – 3; 99:2 – 3; 102:15) and elsewhere in the OT (see Ex 7:5; 14:4,18; Lev 26:45; Nu 14:15; 1Sa 17:46; 1Ki 8:41 – 43; 2Ki 19:19; Isa 2:2 – 3; 11:10; 25:3; 49:6 – 7; 51:5; 52:10; 60:1 – 14; 62:1 – 2; Jer 16:19; Eze 20:41; 28:25; 36:23; Hab 2:14). This has proven to be supremely true of God's climactic saving act in the birth, life, death, resurrection and glorification of Jesus Christ — yet to be brought to complete fruition at his return.
46:11 See note on v. 7.
Ps 47 Celebration of the universal reign of Israel's God: a testimony to the nations. This psalm belongs to a group of hymns to the Great King found elsewhere clustered in Ps 92 – 100. Here it serves to link Ps 46 and 48, identifying the God who reigns in Zion as "the great King over all the earth" (v. 2; see v. 7; 48:2; see also introduction to Ps 46 – 48). It dates from the period of the monarchy and was composed for use in the temple liturgy on one of the high festival days. The specific setting is perhaps the Festival of Tabernacles (see Lev 23:34), which was also the festival for which Solomon waited to dedicate the temple (see 1Ki 8:2). A liturgical procession is presupposed (v. 5), similar to that indicated in Ps 24; 68. Later Jewish usage employed this psalm in the synagogue liturgy for *Rosh Hashanah* (the New Year festival). The Christian church has appropriately employed it in the celebration of Christ's ascension (see v. 5). Structurally, an introductory call to praise (v. 1) is followed by three stanzas of three Hebrew poetic lines each (vv. 2 – 4,5 – 7,8 – 9) devoted to the praise of which God is worthy as "the King of all the earth" (v. 7).
47 title See note on Ps 42 title.
47:1 – 4 The nations are called to rejoice in the God of Israel, the Lord over all the earth — OT anticipation of the evangelization of the nations (see notes on v. 9; 9:1).
47:1 *Clap your hands.* As at the enthronement of a king (see 2Ki 11:12; see also 98:8) or at other times of rejoicing (see Isa 55:12). *cries of joy.* See 1Ki 1:40; 2Ki 11:14.
47:2 – 3 The Lord of all the earth has shaped the destiny of his people Israel (see 105:6; 135:4; Ex 9:29; 15:1 – 18; 19:5 – 6; Dt 7:6; 14:2; Isa 41:8).
47:2 *LORD Most High is awesome.* See 68:35; 89:7; 99:3; 111:9; cf. note on 45:4. *Most High.* See note on Ge 14:19. *great King.* A title often used by the imperial rulers of Assyria (see note on 2Ki 18:19).
47:3 See 2Sa 5:17 – 25; 8:1 – 14; 10.
47:4 *inheritance.* The promised land (see Ge 12:7; 17:8; Ex 3:8; Dt 1:8; Jer 3:18). *pride.* That in which Jacob took supreme delight. *Jacob.* See note on 14:7. For *Selah*, see NIV text note and note on 3:2.
47:5 – 6 The center of the poem (see note on 6:6). These verses portray the liturgical ascension of God to the temple — perhaps represented by the processional bearing of the ark into the temple. The ark is symbolic of God's throne; the temple is the earthly symbol of his heavenly palace (see Ps 24; 68).
47:5 *shouts of joy … sounding of trumpets.* See note on v. 1. *trumpets.* The ram's horn, here announcing the presence of God as King (see 98:6; Ex 19:16,19; Jos 6:4).
47:7 – 9 The liturgical enthronement of God as world ruler.
47:7 *God is the King of all the earth.* See 2Sa 15:10; 2Ki 9:13; Isa 52:7. *psalm.* Hebrew *maskil*; see note on Ps 32 title.
47:8 *seated on his holy throne.* In the Most Holy Place of the temple, where he takes the reins of world rule into his hands (see Jer 17:12). This verse is frequently echoed in Revelation (see Rev 4:9,10; 5:1,7,13; 6:16; 7:10,15; 19:4).
47:9 The nations acknowledge the God of Israel to be the Great King — anticipated as the final effect of God's rule (see note on 46:10). *as the people of the God of Abraham.* Thus the promises to Abraham will be fulfilled (see Ge 12:2 – 3 and note; 17:4 – 6; 22:17 – 18). *kings.* See NIV text note; see also note on 3:3; cf. Isa 2:2; 56:7.
Ps 48 A celebration of the security of Zion (as viewed with the eyes of faith) in that it is the city of the Great King (see in-

2 Beautiful[u] in its loftiness,
the joy of the whole earth,
like the heights of Zaphon[av] is Mount Zion,[w]
the city of the Great King.[x]
3 God is in her citadels;[y]
he has shown himself to be her fortress.[z]

4 When the kings joined forces,
when they advanced together,[a]
5 they saw her and were astounded;
they fled in terror.[b]
6 Trembling seized[c] them there,
pain like that of a woman in labor.[d]
7 You destroyed them like ships of Tarshish[e]
shattered by an east wind.[f]

8 As we have heard,
so we have seen
in the city of the LORD Almighty,
in the city of our God:
God makes her secure
forever.[bg]

9 Within your temple, O God,
we meditate[h] on your unfailing love.[i]
10 Like your name,[j] O God,
your praise reaches to the ends of the earth;[k]
your right hand is filled with righteousness.
11 Mount Zion rejoices,
the villages of Judah are glad
because of your judgments.[l]

12 Walk about Zion, go around her,
count her towers,[m]
13 consider well her ramparts,[n]
view her citadels,[o]
that you may tell of them
to the next generation.[p]

14 For this God is our God for ever and ever;
he will be our guide[q] even to the end.

Psalm 49[c]

For the director of music.
Of the Sons of Korah. A psalm.

1 Hear[r] this, all you peoples;[s]
listen, all who live in this world,[t]

48:2 [u]Ps 50:2; La 2:15; Eze 16:14 [v]S Jos 13:27 [w]S Ps 2:6 [x]Mt 5:35 **48:3** [y]ver 13; Ps 122:7 [z]Ps 18:2 **48:4** [a]2Sa 10:1-19 **48:5** [b]Ex 15:16; Isa 13:8; Jer 46:5; Da 5:9 **48:6** [c]S Job 4:14 [d]S Ge 3:16 **48:7** [e]S Ge 10:4; S 1Ki 10:22; 22:48 [f]S Ge 41:6 **48:8** [g]Jer 23:6; Zec 8:13; 14:11 **48:9** [h]S Ps 39:3 [i]Ps 6:4 **48:10** [j]S Ex 6:3; S Jos 7:9 [k]1Sa 2:10; Ps 22:27; 65:5; 98:3; 100:1; Isa 11:12; 24:16; 42:10; 49:6 **48:11** [l]Ps 97:8 **48:12** [m]S Ne 3:1 **48:13** [n]2Sa 20:15; Isa 26:1; La 2:8; Hab 2:1 [o]S ver 3 [p]Ps 71:18; 78:6; 109:13 **48:14** [q]Ps 25:5; 73:24; Pr 6:22; Isa 49:10; 57:18; 58:11 **49:1** [r]Isa 1:2 [s]Ps 78:1 [t]S Ps 33:8

[a] *2 Zaphon* was the most sacred mountain of the Canaanites. [b] *8* The Hebrew has *Selah* (a word of uncertain meaning) here. [c] In Hebrew texts 49:1-20 is numbered 49:2-21.

roductions to Ps 46–47; see also introduction to Ps 46–48). t may have been sung by the Levitical choir on behalf of the assembled worshipers at the temple. Structure and theme are beautifully matched. The first and last verses combine to frame the whole with a comforting confession concerning Zion's God. The center, v. 8 (see note on 6:6), summarizes the main theme of the body of the psalm. Four stanzas (having a symmetrical pattern in Hebrew: three lines, four lines, four ines, three lines) develop the theme: (1) the beauty of Zion as God's impregnable citadel (vv. 2–3); (2) the futility of all enemy attacks (vv. 4–7); (3) Zion's joy over God's saving acts vv. 9–11)—related to the second stanza; (4) Zion as impregnable citadel (vv. 12–13)—related to the first stanza. Regularly distributed between the four main stanzas are allusions to the four primary directions (see notes on vv. 2,7,10,13)—suggesting that the city is secure from all points of attack.
48 title *song.* See note on Ps 30 title. *of the Sons of Korah.* See note on Ps 42 title.
48:1 *in the city of our God, his holy mountain.* See 46:4. *our God.* Occurs in this psalm only here, in the center (v. 8) and at the end (v. 14). *holy mountain.* See 43:3; see also note on 2:6.
48:2–3 Describes the lofty impregnability of Mount Zion.
48:2 *Beautiful.* Its loftiness and secure position are its beauty (see note on 27:4). *loftiness.* Although not the highest ridge in its environment, in its significance as the mountain of God it is the "highest" mountain in the world (see 68:15–16 and note; Isa 2:2). *joy of the whole earth.* Perhaps referring to admiration from other nations, like that expressed by the queen of Sheba (see 1Ki 10:1–13). *Zaphon.* See NIV text note. Mount Zaphon in the far north was for the Phoenicians the sacred residence of El, the chief of their gods—as Mount Olympus was the mountain citadel of Zeus for the Greeks. *Great King.* See note on 47:2.
48:3 God himself, not her walls, was Zion's defense, a fact on which the next stanza elaborates (see note on vv. 12–13; see also Zec 2:5 and note). *her citadels.* See v. 13.
48:4–7 The futile attacks of hostile nations—they fled in panic when they saw that the Great King was in Zion. Such events as the destruction of the confederacy in the days of Jehoshaphat (see 2Ch 20) or the slaughter of the Assyrians in the time of Hezekiah (see 2Ki 19:35–36) may have been in the psalmist's mind.
48:7 *ships of Tarshish.* Great merchant ships of the Mediterranean (see 1Ki 10:22 and note). *shattered by an east wind.* See Ac 27:14; see also 1Ki 22:48. *east.* See introduction above.
48:8 The central verse and theme (see note on 6:6). *heard ... seen.* "Seen" is climactic, as in Job 42:5. They had heard because "our ancestors have told us what you did in their days" (44:1; see 78:3), but now in the liturgical experience of God at his temple they have "seen" how secure the city of God is. *LORD Almighty.* See note on 1Sa 1:3. *our God.* See note on v. 1. For *Selah*, see NIV text note and note on 3:2.
48:9–11 The worshipers meditate at the temple with joy because of God's mighty acts in Zion's behalf.
48:9 *Within your temple.* In the temple courts. *unfailing love.* See note on 6:4. As is clear from vv. 10–11, reference here is to God's saving acts by which he has expressed his covenant love for his people (see 31:21; 40:9–10).
48:10 *name.* See note on 5:11. *reaches.* From the temple to the ends of the earth (see 9:11; 22:27). *right hand.* In Hebrew idiom a subtle reference to the south. *righteousness.* Righteous acts (see 40:9–10 and note; see also note on 4:1).
48:11 *judgments.* God's righteous judgments, by which he has acted in defense of Zion.
48:12–13 The people contemplate Zion's defense, viewed from the perspective of what they have "seen" (v. 8) at the temple. The strength of Zion's "towers," "ramparts" and "citadels" is the presence of God.
48:13 *next generation.* Lit. "the generation behind"; in Hebrew idiom "behind" is a subtle reference to the west.
48:14 *our God.* See note on v. 1. *guide.* The great Shepherd-King (see notes on 23:1,3). *the end.* Lit. "death."
Ps 49–53 This cluster of psalms presents a striking contrast that brings the Psalter's call for godliness into

[2]both low and high,[u]
rich and poor alike:
[3]My mouth will speak words of wisdom;[v]
the meditation of my heart will give you understanding.[w]
[4]I will turn my ear to a proverb;[x]
with the harp[y] I will expound my riddle:[z]

[5]Why should I fear[a] when evil days come,
when wicked deceivers surround me—
[6]those who trust in their wealth[b]
and boast[c] of their great riches?[d]
[7]No one can redeem the life of another
or give to God a ransom for them—
[8]the ransom[e] for a life is costly,
no payment is ever enough—[f]
[9]so that they should live on[g] forever
and not see decay.[h]
[10]For all can see that the wise die,[i]
that the foolish and the senseless[j]
also perish,
leaving their wealth[k] to others.[l]
[11]Their tombs[m] will remain their houses[a]
forever,
their dwellings for endless generations,[n]
though they had[b] named[o] lands after themselves.

[12]People, despite their wealth, do not endure;[p]
they are like the beasts that perish.[q]

[13]This is the fate of those who trust in themselves,[r]
and of their followers, who approve their sayings.[c]

49:2 [u] Ps 62:9 **49:3** [v] S Ps 37:30 [w] Ps 119:130 **49:4** [x] Ps 78:2; Pr 1:6; Eze 12:22; 16:44; 18:2-3; Lk 4:23 [y] S 1Sa 16:16; Ps 33:2 [z] S Nu 12:8 **49:5** [a] Ps 23:4; 27:1 **49:6** [b] S Job 22:25; Ps 73:12; Jer 48:7 [c] S Ps 10:3 [d] S Job 36:19 **49:8** [e] S Nu 35:31 [f] Mt 16:26 **49:9** [g] Ps 22:29; 89:48 [h] Ps 16:10 **49:10** [i] Ecc 2:16 [j] Ps 92:6; 94:8 [k] S Job 27:17 [l] Ecc 2:18,21; Lk 12:20 **49:11** [m] Mk 5:3; Lk 8:27 [n] Ps 106:31 [o] S Dt 3:14 **49:12** [p] S Job 14:2 [q] ver 20; 2Pe 2:12 **49:13** [r] Lk 12:20

[a] *11* Septuagint and Syriac; Hebrew *In their thoughts their houses will remain* [b] *11* Or *generations, / for they have* [c] *13* The Hebrew has *Selah* (a word of uncertain meaning) here and at the end of verse 15.

---

sharp focus. On the one hand, we meet two psalms that face each other: (1) as God's summons to his people to come before him and hear his verdict concerning their lives (Ps 50) and (2) as a penitent's humble prayer for forgiveness and cleansing (Ps 51). On the other hand, these are bracketed by two psalms (49; 52) that denounce those who trust in their wealth (49:6; 52:7) and make their "boast" either in that wealth (49:6) or in the "evil" practices by which they obtained it (52:1). These descriptions of the ungodly are found nowhere else in the Psalter. In the first of these framing psalms, such people are characterized as "foolish" and "senseless" (49:10). So it is appropriate that this four-psalm segment of the Psalter has appended to it in climax a somewhat revised repetition of Ps 14 with its denunciation of the fools whose thoughts and ways are God-less. Placed immediately after Ps 46–48, these five psalms serve as a stern reminder that only those who put their trust in the Lord have reason to celebrate the security of "the city of our God" (48:1,8; see introduction to Ps 46–48).

Ps 49 A wisdom word concerning rich fools who proudly rely on their great wealth and on themselves to assure their welfare and security in the world (see Ps 52 and introduction to Ps 49–53). The Levitical author knows what it is to be without wealth (see Nu 18:21–24; Dt 14:27–29) and has observed the attitudes of many of the rich (see vv. 5–6). He has seen through their folly, however, and offers his wisdom for all to hear (vv. 1–2), so that those who are awed by the rich may be freed from their spell. Inescapable death is the destiny and undoing of such "foolish and ... senseless" (49:10) people, and in the end the "upright will prevail over them" (v. 14). As elsewhere (see note on structure in the introduction to Ps 33), the author has composed a poem of 22 Hebrew lines, in accordance with the number of letters in the Hebrew alphabet. The thematic structure is symmetrical: Following a four-line introduction (vv. 1–4), the instruction proper is developed in two balanced stanzas of eight lines each (vv. 5–11,13–19) with appended refrains (vv. 12,20). For other psalms with recurring refrains, see introduction to Ps 42–43. The date of this psalm may well be postexilic. See introduction to Ps 37.

49 title See note on Ps 42 title.

49:1–4 Introduction.

49:1–2 More like the address of the prophets (see 1Ki 22:28; Isa 34:1; Mic 1:2) than that of the wisdom teachers (see 34:11; Pr 1:8,10; 2:1).

49:3 See Mt 12:34. *wisdom.* See essay, p. 786. *heart.* See note on 4:7.

49:4 *turn my ear.* The wisdom he is about to speak first had to be "heard" by him—all true wisdom is from God (see Job 28). *proverb ... riddle.* The two Hebrew words for these nouns were used to refer to insightful pieces of instruction that were artfully crafted (see 78:2 ["parable," "things from of old"]; Pr 1:6; Eze 17:2 ["allegory," "parable"]). *with the harp.* Another hint of the author's sense of inspiration (see 1Sa 10:5–6; 2Ki 3:15).

49:5–11 Those of little means or power need not be unsettled when surrounded by rich fools who threaten and strut; death is their destiny.

49:6 *who trust in their wealth.* See 52:7. *boast of.* Or "boast in," i.e., openly proclaim that they rely on their wealth to preserve them in a happy condition (see 52:1 and note).

49:7–9 Wealth cannot buy escape from death—not even one's family "redeemer" can accomplish it (cf. Ex 21:30; Lev 25:47–49). Only God himself can redeem a life from the grave (see v. 15 and note).

49:10 Any who have "eyes in their heads" (Ecc 2:14) can see that even the wise die (see Ecc 7:2; 9:5) and leave their wealth to others (see Ecc 2:18,21). How much more the fool (see 73:18–20; 92:6–7)! See also 52:5; 89:48; Job 30:23; Ecc 2:14–16. *wise ... foolish ... senseless.* Essentially the "righteous" and the "wicked" of Ps 37. *wealth.* Often gotten by devious means that their foolish wisdom had contrived (vv. 5,12; see also 52:1–4,7). *to others.* But not to their children (see note on 37:29; see also 39:6; Lk 12:20–21).

49:11 Though they lavish wealth on their tombs and try at least to perpetuate their memory by putting their names to their large landholdings (see Nu 32:41) as an enduring memorial, they only suffer the bitter irony of having their graves as their "eternal home" (Ecc 12:5). Cf. the psalmist's hope in v. 15.

49:12 Their epitaph (see note on 10:18; see also Ecc 3:19; 7:2) and the psalm's refrain.

49:13–19 The final end of these rich fools and of the righteous—so why should any stand in awe of the rich?

49:13 *in themselves.* As those who have "succeeded" (see v. 6). For *Selah,* see NIV text note and note on 3:2.

14 They are like sheep and are destined[s]
to die;[t]
death will be their shepherd
(but the upright will prevail[u] over
them in the morning).
Their forms will decay in the
grave,
far from their princely mansions.
15 But God will redeem me from the
realm of the dead;[v]
he will surely take me to himself.[w]
16 Do not be overawed when others grow
rich,
when the splendor of their houses
increases;
17 for they will take nothing[x] with them
when they die,
their splendor will not descend with
them.[y]
18 Though while they live they count
themselves blessed—[z]
and people praise you when you
prosper—
19 they will join those who have gone
before them,[a]
who will never again see the light[b] of
life.
20 People who have wealth but lack
understanding[c]
are like the beasts that perish.[d]

Psalm 50

A psalm of Asaph.

1 The Mighty One, God, the LORD,[e]
speaks and summons the earth
from the rising of the sun to where it
sets.[f]
2 From Zion,[g] perfect in beauty,[h]
God shines forth.[i]
3 Our God comes[j]
and will not be silent;[k]
a fire devours[l] before him,[m]
and around him a tempest[n] rages.
4 He summons the heavens above,
and the earth,[o] that he may judge his
people:[p]

49:14 [s]Jer 43:11; Eze 31:14 [t]Nu 16:30; S Job 21:13; Ps 9:17; 55:15 [u]Isa 14:2; Da 7:18; 1Co 6:2 **49:15** [v]Ps 56:13; Hos 13:14 [w]S Ge 5:24 **49:17** [x]1Ti 6:7 [y]S Ps 17:14 **49:18** [z]Ps 10:6; Lk 12:19 **49:19** [a]S Ge 15:15 [b]S Job 33:30 **49:20** [c]Pr 16:16 [d]S ver 12 **50:1** [e]Jos 22:22 [f]Ps 113:3 **50:2** [g]Ps 2:6 [h]S Ps 48:2; S La 2:15 [i]S Dt 33:2 **50:3** [j]Ps 96:13 [k]ver 21; Isa 42:14; 64:12; 65:6 [l]S Lev 10:2 [m]S Ps 18:8 [n]Job 37:9; Ps 83:15; 107:25; 147:18; Isa 29:6; 30:28; Jnh 1:4; Na 1:3 **50:4** [o]Dt 4:26; 31:28; Isa 1:2 [p]Heb 10:30

49:14 *like sheep.* Death is already their shepherd, guiding them to the grave. *death will be their shepherd.* For the imagery of death (or the grave) as an insatiable monster feeding on its victims, see 69:15; 141:7; Pr 1:12; 27:20; 30:15–16; Isa 5:14; Jnh 2:2 ("deep"; lit. "belly"); Hab 2:5. The imagery is borrowed from Canaanite mythology, which so depicts the god Mot ("Death"). As one Canaanite document reads, "Do not approach divine Mot, or he will put you like a lamb into his mouth." *prevail over.* See Lev 26:17; Isa 14:2; in contrast to the situation referred to in v. 5. *in the morning.* See vv. 15,19 and notes on 6:5; 11:7; 16:9–11; 17:15. But see also introduction to Ps 57.

49:15 See note on vv. 7–9. *redeem … from the realm of the dead.* Cf. v. 11. While the psalmist may here refer to saving (for a while) from the universal prospect of death (as in Job 5:20; see 116:8), the context strongly suggests that he, as one of the upright, speaks of his final destiny. Perhaps the thought is of being conveyed into the presence of God in his heavenly temple, analogous to the later Jewish thought of being conveyed to "Abraham's side" (Lk 16:22; see notes on 6:5; 11:7; 16:9–11; 17:15). *take me to himself.* See 73:24; Ge 5:24 and notes.

49:16 *their houses.* Their whole estates (see Ex 20:17).

49:17 *take nothing with them when they die.* See 1Ti 6:7.

49:19 *light of life.* See notes on 27:1; 36:9; see also Isa 53:11.

49:20 The last word. See note on v. 12.

Ps 50 The Lord calls his covenant people to account. For this psalm's place in the arrangement of the Psalter, see introduction to Ps 49–53. The psalm appears to have been composed for a temple liturgy in which Israel reaffirms her commitment to God's covenant. A leader of the Levitical choir addresses Israel on behalf of the Lord (see Ps 15; 24, either of which may have been spoken earlier in the same liturgy). This liturgy was possibly related to the Festival of Tabernacles (see Dt 31:9–13; see also introduction to Ps 47). In its rebuke of a false understanding of sacrifice, the psalm has affinity with the prophecies of Amos, Micah and Isaiah and so may date from the late eighth and/or early seventh centuries BC. Others find a closer relationship with the reformation of Josiah (2Ki 22:1—23:25) and the ministry of Jeremiah. Structurally, the psalm has three parts: (1) the announcement of the coming of Israel's covenant Lord to call his people to account (vv. 1–6); (2) the Lord's words of correction for those of honest intent (vv. 7–15); (3) his sharp rebuke of "the wicked" among them (vv. 16–23).

50 title A traditional ascription of the psalm to Asaph; or it may mean "for Asaph" (see "For Jeduthun" in Ps 39 title) or for the descendants of Asaph who functioned in his place. This psalm may have been separated from the other psalms of Asaph (73–83) in order to be paired with Ps 51 in the cluster of Ps 49–53. Asaph was one of David's three choir leaders (see note on Ps 39 title).

50:1–6 The Lord "comes" (v. 3) in the temple worship to correct and rebuke his people: Israel must know that the God of Zion is the God of Sinai (see Ex 19:16–20).

50:1 *The Mighty One, God, the LORD.* A sequence found elsewhere only in Jos 22:22 (see note there). Ps 50 is noteworthy for its use of numerous names and titles for God (seven in all: three in v. 1, four in the rest of the psalm; see notes on vv. 6,14,21–22). *the earth.* See "the heavens … the earth" (v. 4) and "the heavens" (v. 6). When Moses renewed the covenant between the Lord and Israel on the plains of Moab, he called upon the heavens and the earth to serve as third-party witnesses to the covenant (Dt 30:19; 31:28). The Lord now summons these (vv. 1–4) to testify that his present word to his people is in complete accord with that covenant (see Isa 1:2). God's relationship with his people has the whole creation as its context, and for that reason the whole creation is a party of interest to that relationship (see Ge 1–3; see also Jer 12:4; Ro 8:22 and notes). Cf. Mic 6:1–2 and note.

50:2 *perfect in beauty.* Because God resides there (cf. Eze 27:3–4,11; 28:12). *shines forth.* Manifests his glory as he comes to act (see 80:1; 94:1; Dt 33:2; cf. Eze 28:7,17), now calling his people to account but not yet announcing judgment as in Isa 1 or Mic 1.

50:3 *comes.* From his enthronement between the cherubim (see 80:1; 99:1; see also 1Sa 4:4; 2Sa 6:2; 2Ki 19:15) in the Most Holy Place of the temple (see note on 28:2; see also Isa 26:21; Mic 1:3). *will not be silent.* No longer (see v. 21) will he let their sins go unrebuked. *fire … tempest.* See Ex 19:16,18.

50:4 *judge.* Call them to account in accordance with his covenant.

[5]"Gather to me this consecrated people,[q]
who made a covenant[r] with me by sacrifice."
[6]And the heavens proclaim[s] his righteousness,
for he is a God of justice.[a,b][t]

[7]"Listen, my people, and I will speak;
I will testify[u] against you, Israel:
I am God, your God.[v]
[8]I bring no charges[w] against you concerning your sacrifices
or concerning your burnt offerings,[x] which are ever before me.
[9]I have no need of a bull[y] from your stall
or of goats[z] from your pens,[a]
[10]for every animal of the forest[b] is mine,
and the cattle on a thousand hills.[c]
[11]I know every bird[d] in the mountains,
and the insects in the fields[e] are mine.
[12]If I were hungry I would not tell you,
for the world[f] is mine, and all that is in it.[g]
[13]Do I eat the flesh of bulls
or drink the blood of goats?

[14]"Sacrifice thank offerings[h] to God,
fulfill your vows[i] to the Most High,[j]
[15]and call[k] on me in the day of trouble;[l]
I will deliver[m] you, and you will honor[n] me."

[16]But to the wicked person, God says:

"What right have you to recite my laws
or take my covenant[o] on your lips?[p]
[17]You hate[q] my instruction
and cast my words behind[r] you.
[18]When you see a thief, you join[s] with him;
you throw in your lot with adulterers.[t]
[19]You use your mouth for evil
and harness your tongue to deceit.[u]
[20]You sit and testify against your brother[v]
and slander your own mother's son.
[21]When you did these things and I kept silent,[w]
you thought I was exactly[c] like you.
But I now arraign[x] you
and set my accusations[y] before you.

[22]"Consider this, you who forget God,[z]
or I will tear you to pieces, with no one to rescue you:[a]
[23]Those who sacrifice thank offerings honor me,
and to the blameless[d] I will show my salvation.[b]"

50:5 [q]S Dt 7:6; S Ps 18:25 [r]Ex 24:7; S 2Ch 6:11 **50:6** [s]S Ps 19:1 [t]S Ge 16:5; S Job 9:15 **50:7** [u]Heb 2:4 [v]Ex 20:2; Ps 48:14 **50:8** [w]S 2Sa 22:16 [x]S Ps 40:6 **50:9** [y]S Lev 1:5 [z]S Lev 16:5 [a]S Nu 32:16 **50:10** [b]Ps 104:20; Isa 56:9; Mic 5:8 [c]Ps 104:24 **50:11** [d]Mt 6:26 [e]Ps 8:7; 80:13 **50:12** [f]Ex 19:5 [g]Dt 10:14; S Jos 3:11; Ps 24:1; 1Co 10:26 **50:14** [h]S Ezr 1:4; S Ps 27:6 [i]S Nu 30:2; S Ps 66:13; 76:11 [j]Ps 7:8 **50:15** [k]Ps 4:1; 81:7; Isa 55:6; 58:9; Zec 13:9 [l]Ps 69:17; 86:7; 107:6; 142:2; Jas 5:13 [m]Ps 3:7 [n]S Ps 22:23 **50:16** [o]Ps 25:10 [p]Isa 29:13 **50:17** [q]Pr 1:22 [r]S 1Ki 14:9 **50:18** [s]Ro 1:32; 1Ti 5:22 [t]S Job 22:15 **50:19** [u]Ps 10:7; 36:3; 52:2; 101:7 **50:20** [v]Mt 10:21 **50:21** [w]Isa 42:14; 57:11; 62:1; 64:12 [x]Ps 6:1; S 18:15; 76:6; 104:7; Isa 50:2 [y]Ps 85:5; Isa 57:16 **50:22** [z]S Job 8:13; S Isa 17:10 [a]S Dt 32:39; Mic 5:8 **50:23** [b]S Ps 9:14; 91:16; 98:3; Isa 52:10

[a] *6* With a different word division of the Hebrew; Masoretic Text *for God himself is judge* [b] *6* The Hebrew has *Selah* (a word of uncertain meaning) here. [c] *21* Or *thought the 'I AM' was* [d] *23* Probable reading of the original Hebrew text; the meaning of the Masoretic Text for this phrase is uncertain.

50:5 *consecrated people.* See note on 4:3. *by sacrifice.* Sacrifices were a part of the ritual that sealed the covenant (see Ex 24:4–8 and note on 24:6) and continued to be an integral part of Israel's expression of covenant commitment to the Lord.
50:6 *proclaim.* See note on v. 1. *righteousness.* See note on 4:1. *God of justice.* See notes on 89:14; Ge 18:25; Zec 7:9; see also Introduction to Amos: Theological Theme and Message. For *Selah*, see NIV text note and note on 3:2.
50:7–15 The Lord corrects his people.
50:7 *my people ... your God.* "Our God" (v. 3) and "your God" (here) reflect the covenant bond (see Zec 8:8 and note). *I am God, your God.* See Ex 19:3–6; Lev 19:2–4,10,25,31,34,36; 20:7,24; 22:33; 23:22.
50:8–13 Israel had not failed to bring enough sacrifices (v. 8), but she was ever tempted to think that sacrifices were of first importance to God, as though he were dependent on them. This notion was widespread among Israel's pagan neighbors. See note on 40:6.
50:10 *thousand.* Used here figuratively for a very large number.
50:12 *the world ... in it.* See 24:1 and note.
50:14–15 God wants Israel to acknowledge her dependence on him by giving thank offerings for his mercies (v. 14) and by praying to him in times of need (v. 15; see 116:17–19). Those who do so may expect God's gracious answer to their prayers (stated more directly in v. 23). God also desires obedience to his moral law (see vv. 16–21 and note on 40:6).
50:14 *thank offerings.* See Lev 7:12–13 and note on Ps 7:17. *God ... Most High.* That is, God Most High (see 57:2 and note on 3:7). *fulfill.* See note on Ecc 5:6. *your vows.* Vows that accompanied prayer in times of need, usually involving thank offerings (see 66:13–15), always involving praise of the Lord for his answer to prayer (see note on 7:17). See also Heb 13:15. *Most High.* See note on v. 1; see also note on Ge 14:19.
50:15 *honor me.* With praise in the fulfillment of the vows (see v. 23)—and, implicitly, with obedience to his covenant law (see following verses).
50:16–23 The Lord's rebuke of the wicked.
50:16 *recite my laws.* Apparently a part of the liturgy of covenant commitment.
50:17 *You hate my instruction.* They formally participate in the holy ritual but reject God's law as the rule for life outside the ritual.
50:19 *use your mouth for evil.* See note on 5:9.
50:21 God's merciful and patient silence is distorted by the wicked into bad and self-serving theology (see Ecc 8:11; Isa 42:14; 57:11). *thought I was exactly.* See NIV text note; Ex 3:14 and note (see also note on v. 1). *set my accusations before you.* Confront you with the particulars of my indictment.
50:22 *God.* A relatively rare word for "God" (Hebrew *Eloah*), though common in Job. See note on v. 1.
50:23 See note on vv. 14–15.

Psalm 51[a]

For the director of music.
A psalm of David. When the prophet Nathan came to him after David had committed adultery with Bathsheba.[c]

"Cleanse me with hyssop, and I will be clean; wash me, and I will be whiter than snow" (Ps 51:7).

Baker Photo Archive

[1] Have mercy[d] on me, O God,
according to your unfailing love;[e]
according to your great compassion[f]
blot out[g] my transgressions.[h]
[2] Wash away[i] all my iniquity
and cleanse[j] me from my sin.

[3] For I know my transgressions,
and my sin is always before me.[k]
[4] Against you, you only, have I sinned[l]
and done what is evil in your sight;[m]
so you are right in your verdict
and justified when you judge.[n]
[5] Surely I was sinful[o] at birth,[p]
sinful from the time my mother conceived me.
[6] Yet you desired faithfulness even in the womb;
you taught me wisdom[q] in that secret place.[r]

[7] Cleanse[s] me with hyssop,[t] and I will be clean;
wash me, and I will be whiter than snow.[u]
[8] Let me hear joy and gladness;[v]
let the bones[w] you have crushed rejoice.

[a] In Hebrew texts 51:1-19 is numbered 51:3-21.

51:Title [c] 2Sa 11:4; 12:1 **51:1** [d] S 2Sa 24:14; S Ps 9:13 [e] S Ps 25:7; S 119:88 [f] S Ne 9:27; Ps 86:15; Isa 63:7 [g] S 2Sa 12:13; S 2Ch 6:21; S Ne 4:5; Ac 3:19 [h] S Ps 39:8 **51:2** [i] S Ru 3:3; Jer 2:22; 13:27; Ac 22:16; 1Jn 1:9 [j] Pr 20:30; Isa 4:4; Eze 36:25; Zec 13:1; Mt 23:25-26; Heb 9:14 **51:3** [k] Isa 59:12 **51:4** [l] S 1Sa 15:24 [m] S Ge 20:6; Lk 15:21 [n] Ro 3:4* **51:5** [o] S Lev 5:2 [p] S Job 5:7 **51:6** [q] Ps 119:66; 143:10 [r] S Job 9:4; S 34:32 **51:7** [s] Isa 4:4; Eze 36:25; Zec 13:1 [t] S Ex 12:22; S Nu 19:6; Heb 9:19 [u] Isa 1:18; 43:25; 44:22 **51:8** [v] Isa 35:10; Jer 33:11; Joel 1:16 [w] S Ex 12:46

Ps 51 David's humble prayer for forgiveness and cleansing. As the prayer of a contrite sinner, it represents a proper response to the Lord's confrontation of his people in Ps 50 (compare v. 16 with 50:8–15; see also introduction to Ps 49–53). This psalm has many points of contact with Ps 25. In traditional Christian usage it is one of seven penitential psalms (see introduction to Ps 6). The psalm is constructed symmetrically: A two-verse introduction balances a two-verse conclusion, and the enclosed four stanzas in Hebrew consist of five lines, three lines, three lines and five lines, respectively. The whole is framed by David's prayer for himself (vv. 1–2) and for Zion (vv. 18–19). The well-being of the king and the city stand and fall together (see 28:8 and note on 3:8).

51 title *For the director of music.* See note on Ps 4 title. *When.* For the event referred to, see 2Sa 11:1—12:25; see also note on Ps 3 title.

51:1–2 Opening prayer for pardon (see Lk 18:13). Note the piling up of synonyms: mercy, unfailing love, great compassion; blot out, wash, cleanse; transgressions, iniquity, sin (for this last triad, see note on 32:5).

51:1 *unfailing love.* See note on 6:4. *blot out.* See v. 9. The image is that of a papyrus scroll (see note on 9:5) on which God had recorded David's deeds. The blotting out of sins pictures forgiveness (Jer 18:23; see Isa 43:25). For the imagery of God's keeping records of the events in his realm in the way that earthly kings do, see 56:8 and note; 87:6; 130:3; 139:16 and note; Ne 13:14; Da 7:10; see also Ex 32:32–33.

51:2 See v. 7. *Wash.* As a filthy garment. *cleanse me.* Make me clean in your sight (see Lev 11:32).

51:3–6 Confession of sin (cf. Pr 28:13; 1Jn 1:9).

51:3 *before me.* On my mind.

51:4 *Against you … only.* David acknowledges that his sin was preeminently against God (see 2Sa 12:13; cf. Ge 20:6; 39:9; Lk 15:18). He had violated specific covenant stipulations (Ex 20:13–14,17). *when you judge.* As the Lord did through Nathan the prophet (2Sa 12:7–12). For a NT application, see Ro 3:4.

51:5 He cannot plead that this sin was a rare aberration in his life; it sprang from what he is and has been from birth (see 58:3; Ge 8:21; 1Ki 8:46 and note; cf. Jn 9:34; Eph 2:3). The apparently similar statements in Job 14:4; 15:14; 25:4–6 rise from a different motivation.

51:6 The great contrast: He has acted absolutely contrary to what God desires and to what God has been teaching him. But it is just this "desire" of God and this teaching of God that are his hope—what he pleads for in vv. 7,10. *faithfulness.* Moral integrity. *womb.* See 139:13–16 and notes. *wisdom.* Those who give themselves over to sin are fools; those who have God's law in their hearts are wise (see 37:30–31).

51:7–9 Renewed prayer for pardon (see note on vv. 1–2).

51:7 *Cleanse me.* Lit. "Un-sin me." *hyssop.* Used in ritual cleansing; see note on Ex 12:22; see also photo above. *be clean.* The Hebrew root for this phrase is the same as that for "cleanse" in v. 2. *whiter than snow.* Like a filthy garment, he needs washing (see note on v. 2); but if God washes him, he will be so pure that there is no figurative word that can describe him (see Isa 1:18; Da 7:9; Rev 7:14; 19:14).

51:8 *Let me hear joy.* Let me be surrounded by joy (see 32:7 and note; see also 35:27), or let me hear a prophetic message of forgiveness that will result in joy—from the assurance of sins forgiven (see 2Sa 12:13). *bones.* See note on 6:2.

9 Hide your face from my sins[x]
and blot out[y] all my iniquity.

10 Create in me a pure heart,[z] O God,
and renew a steadfast spirit
within me.[a]
11 Do not cast me[b] from your presence[c]
or take your Holy Spirit[d] from me.
12 Restore to me the joy of your
salvation[e]
and grant me a willing spirit,[f] to
sustain me.[g]

13 Then I will teach transgressors your
ways,[h]
so that sinners[i] will turn back to
you.[j]
14 Deliver me[k] from the guilt of
bloodshed,[l] O God,
you who are God my Savior,[m]
and my tongue will sing of your
righteousness.[n]
15 Open my lips, Lord,[o]
and my mouth will declare your
praise.
16 You do not delight in sacrifice,[p] or I
would bring it;
you do not take pleasure in burnt
offerings.
17 My sacrifice,[q] O God, is[a] a broken
spirit;
a broken and contrite heart[r]
you, God, will not despise.

18 May it please you to prosper Zion,[s]
to build up the walls of Jerusalem.[t]
19 Then you will delight in the sacrifices
of the righteous,[u]
in burnt offerings[v] offered whole;
then bulls[w] will be offered on your
altar.

Psalm 52[b]

For the director of music. A *maskil*[c] of David. When Doeg the Edomite[x] had gone to Saul and told him: "David has gone to the house of Ahimelek."

1 Why do you boast of evil, you mighty
hero?
Why do you boast[y] all day long,[z]
you who are a disgrace in the eyes of
God?
2 You who practice deceit,[a]
your tongue plots destruction;[b]
it is like a sharpened razor.[c]
3 You love evil[d] rather than good,
falsehood[e] rather than speaking the
truth.[d]

[a] 17 Or *The sacrifices of God are* [b] In Hebrew texts 52:1-9 is numbered 52:3-11. [c] Title: Probably a literary or musical term [d] 3 The Hebrew has *Selah* (a word of uncertain meaning) here and at the end of verse 5.

51:9 [x] Jer 16:17; Zec 4:10 [y] S 2Sa 12:13 **51:10** [z] S Ps 24:4; 78:37; Mt 5:8; Ac 15:9 [a] Eze 18:31; 36:26 **51:11** [b] Ps 27:9; 71:9; 138:8 [c] S Ge 4:14; S Ex 33:15 [d] Ps 106:33; Isa 63:10; Eph 4:30 **51:12** [e] S Job 33:26 [f] Ps 110:3 [g] S Ps 18:35 **51:13** [h] S Ex 33:13; Ac 9:21-22 [i] S Ps 1:1 [j] S Job 33:27 **51:14** [k] S Ps 39:8 [l] S 2Sa 12:9 [m] Ps 25:5; 68:20; 88:1 [n] S Ps 5:8; 35:28; 71:15 **51:15** [o] Ex 4:15 **51:16** [p] S 1Sa 15:22 **51:17** [q] Pr 15:8; Hag 2:14 [r] Mt 11:29 **51:18** [s] Ps 102:16; 147:2; Isa 14:32; 51:3; Zec 1:16-17 [t] Ps 69:35; Isa 44:26 **51:19** [u] Dt 33:19 [v] Ps 66:13; 96:8; Jer 17:26 [w] Ps 66:15 **52:Title** [x] 1Sa 21:7; 22:9 **52:1** [y] Ps 10:3; 94:4 [z] Ps 44:8 **52:2** [a] S Ps 50:19 [b] Ps 5:9 [c] S Nu 6:5 **52:3** [d] Ex 10:10; 1Sa 12:25; Am 5:14-15; Jn 3:20 [e] Ps 58:3; Jer 9:5; Rev 21:8

51:9 *Hide your face.* From what is "always before me" (v. 3). *blot out.* See note on v. 1.

51:10–12 Prayer for purity—for a pure heart, a steadfast spirit of faithfulness and a willing spirit of service. These can be his only if God does not reject him and take his Holy Spirit from him. If granted, the joy of God's salvation will return to gladden his troubled soul.

51:10 *Create.* As something new, which cannot emerge from what now is (see v. 5) and which only God can fashion (see Ge 1:1 and note; Isa 65:17; Jer 31:22). *heart.* See note on 4:7.

51:11 The two requests are essentially one (see 139:7; Eze 39:29). David's prayer recalls the rejection of Saul (see 1Sa 16:1,14; 2Sa 7:15) and pleads for God not to take away his Spirit, by which he had equipped and qualified him for his royal office (see 1Sa 16:13; cf. 2Sa 23:1–2). *Holy Spirit.* The phrase is found elsewhere in the OT only in Isa 63:10–11. By his Spirit, God effected his purposes in creation (see 104:30; Ge 1:2; Job 33:4) and redemption (see Isa 32:15; 44:3; 63:11,14; Hag 2:5), equipped his servants for their appointed tasks (see Ex 31:3; Nu 11:29; Jdg 3:10; 1Sa 10:6; 16:13; Isa 11:2; 42:1), inspired his prophets (see Nu 24:2–3; 2Sa 23:2; Ne 9:30; Isa 59:21; 61:1; Eze 11:5; Mic 3:8; Zec 7:12) and directed their ministries (see 1Ki 18:12; 2Ki 2:16; Isa 48:16; Eze 2:2; 3:14). And it is by his Spirit that God gives his people a "new heart and ... a new spirit" to live by his will (see Eze 36:26–27; see also Jer 24:7; 32:39; Eze 11:19; 18:31).

51:13–17 The vow to praise God (see note on 7:17).

51:13 His praise for God's forgiveness and purification will be accompanied by instruction for "transgressors" and "sinners," whose waywardness he himself had been guilty of (see v. 3). He commits himself to go from praise of God to instruction of others, as did the author of Ps 34 (see also note on 32:8–10). *your ways.* See 25:4 and note.

51:14 If God will only forgive, praise will follow. *righteousness.* See note on 4:1.

51:15 *Open my lips.* By granting the forgiveness and cleansing I seek.

51:16 See note on 40:6.

51:17 *broken spirit; a broken and contrite heart.* What pleases God more than sacrifices is a humble heart that looks to him when troubles crush and penitently pleads for mercy when sin has been committed (see 50:7–15 and notes; see also 34:17–18).

51:18–19 Prayer for Zion (see note on 3:8).

51:19 *sacrifices of the righteous.* Such as are pleasing to God; here, sacrifices accompanied by praise for God's mercies (see 50:14–15 and notes).

Ps 52 Fearless confidence in God when under attack by an arrogant and evil enemy. David stands in the presence of God and from the high tower of that refuge hurls his denunciation (much like the prophetic denunciation in Isa 22:15–19) into the face of his attacker. Though not a wisdom psalm, it has much in common with Ps 49 (see introduction to Ps 49–53; see also introduction to Ps 49). The extended depiction of David's enemy forms a sharp contrast with the spirit of Ps 51. See also David's denunciation of Goliath (1Sa 17:45–47).

52 title *For the director of music.* See note on Ps 4 title. *maskil.* See note on Ps 32 title. *When.* See note on Ps 3 title. For the event referred to, see 1Sa 22:9–10.

52:1–4 The enemy castigated.

52:1 *Why ... ?* By what right? See 50:16; Isa 3:15. *boast.* By act as well as by word (see 75:4–5). *mighty hero.* In his own estimation (see Isa 22:17).

52:2 *your tongue.* See v. 4; see also note on 5:9.

52:3 Your whole moral sense is perverted. *love.* Prefer. For *Selah*, see NIV text note and note on 3:2.

[4] You love every harmful word,
you deceitful tongue![f]

[5] Surely God will bring you down to
everlasting ruin:
He will snatch you up and pluck[g]
you from your tent;
he will uproot[h] you from the land of
the living.[i]

[6] The righteous will see and fear;
they will laugh[j] at you, saying,

[7] "Here now is the man
who did not make God his
stronghold[k]
but trusted in his great wealth[l]
and grew strong by destroying
others!"

[8] But I am like an olive tree[m]
flourishing in the house of God;
I trust[n] in God's unfailing love
for ever and ever.

[9] For what you have done I will always
praise you[o]
in the presence of your faithful
people.[p]
And I will hope in your name,[q]
for your name is good.[r]

Psalm 53[a]

53:1-6pp — Ps 14:1-7

For the director of music. According to *mahalath.*[b] A *maskil*[c] of David.

[1] The fool[s] says in his heart,
"There is no God."[t]
They are corrupt, and their ways are
vile;
there is no one who does good.

[2] God looks down from heaven[u]
on all mankind
to see if there are any who
understand,[v]
any who seek God.[w]

[3] Everyone has turned away, all have
become corrupt;
there is no one who does good,
not even one.[x]

[4] Do all these evildoers know nothing?

They devour my people as though
eating bread;
they never call on God.

[5] But there they are, overwhelmed with
dread,
where there was nothing to dread.[y]
God scattered the bones[z] of those who
attacked you;
you put them to shame,[b] for God
despised them.[c]

[6] Oh, that salvation for Israel would
come out of Zion!
When God restores his people,
let Jacob rejoice and Israel be glad!

Psalm 54[d]

For the director of music.
With stringed instruments. A *maskil*[c]
of David. When the Ziphites[d]
had gone to Saul and said,
"Is not David hiding among us?"

[1] Save me[e], O God, by your name;[f]
vindicate me by your might.[g]

52:4 [f]Ps 5:9; 10:7; 109:2; 120:2, 3; Pr 10:31; 12:19 **52:5** [g]S Dt 29:28; S Job 40:12; Isa 22:19; Eze 17:24 [h]S Dt 28:63 [i]S Job 28:13 **52:6** [j]S Job 22:19 **52:7** [k]S 2Sa 22:3 [l]S Ps 49:6; S Pr 11:28; Mk 10:23 **52:8** [m]S Ps 1:3; S Rev 11:4 [n]Ps 6:4; 13:5 **52:9** [o]S Ps 30:12 [p]S Dt 7:6; Ps 16:3 [q]S Job 7:6; Ps 25:3 [r]Ps 54:6 **53:1** [s]Ps 74:22; 107:17; Pr 10:23 [t]Ps 10:4 **53:2** [u]S Ps 33:13 [v]Ps 82:5; Jer 4:22; 8:8 [w]2Ch 15:2 **53:3** [x]Ro 3:10-12* **53:5** [y]S Lev 26:17 [z]2Ki 23:14; Ps 141:7; Jer 8:1; Eze 6:5 [a]2Ki 17:20 [b]S Job 8:22 [c]Jer 6:30; 14:19; La 5:22 **54:Title** [d]1Sa 23:19; 26:1 **54:1** [e]S 1Sa 24:15 [f]Ps 20:1 [g]2Ch 20:6

[a] In Hebrew texts 53:1-6 is numbered 53:2-7. [b] Title: Probably a musical term [c] Title: Probably a literary or musical term [d] In Hebrew texts 54:1-7 is numbered 54:3-9.

2:4 *tongue.* See note on v. 2.
2:5–7 The enemy's end announced (implicitly a prayer): God will slay you, and the righteous will mock you.
2:5 Note the triple imagery: "bring you down," "snatch you up," "uproot you." The arrogant enemy will meet the same end as the rich fools of Ps 49. *from your tent.* See Job 18:14. *uproot you.* Contrast v. 8.
2:6 *righteous.* See note on 1:5. *fear.* Learn from your downfall (see 40:3 and note).
2:7 See Ps 49.
2:8–9 David's security is God.
2:8 *like an olive tree.* Which lives for hundreds of years. *flourishing.* See 1:3. It will not be uprooted (see v. 5). *in the house of God.* Olive trees were not planted in the temple courts, but David had access to God's temple as his refuge (see 15:1; 3:6; 27:4; 61:4 and note), where he was kept safe (see 27:5 and note). *unfailing love.* See note on 6:4.
2:9 A vow to praise God (see note on 7:17). *faithful people.* See note on 4:3. *name.* See note on 5:11.
Ps 53 A testimony concerning the folly of the wicked, a somewhat revised duplicate of Ps 14; see introduction there. The main difference between the two psalms is that here the word "God" is used instead of "the LORD"; see also note on v. 5.) The original psalm may have been revised in the light of an event such as is narrated in 2Ch 20. Here it also serves as a further commentary on the kind of arrogant fool denounced in Ps 49; 52 (see introduction to Ps 49–53).
53 title *For the director of music.* See note on Ps 4 title. *According to.* See note on Ps 6 title. *mahalath.* Possibly the name of a tune (see note on Ps 9 title). The Hebrew appears to be the word for "suffering" or "sickness" (see Ps 88 title and NIV text note there). Perhaps the Hebrew phrase indicates here that the psalm is to be used in a time of affliction, when the godless mock (see Ps 102; see also note on 5:9). *maskil.* See note on Ps 32 title.
53:1–4 See notes on 14:1–4.
53:5 Differs considerably from 14:5–6, though the basic thought remains the same: God overwhelms the godless who attack his people. Here the verbs are in the past tense (perhaps to express the certainty of their downfall). *where there was nothing to dread.* They fell victim to fear when, humanly speaking, they were not even threatened. God's curse fell on them rather than on Israel (see Lev 26:36–37; see also Jdg 7:21; 2Ki 3:22–23; 7:6–7; Pr 28:1). *scattered the bones.* Over the battlefield of their defeat, their bodies left unburied like something loathsome (see Isa 14:18–20; Jer 8:2 and note). *God despised them.* As they had despised him.
53:6 See note on 14:7.
Ps 54–60 A cluster of seven prayers framed by a prayer of an individual (Ps 54) and a prayer of the community (Ps 60;

2 Hear my prayer, O God;[h]
listen to the words of my mouth.

3 Arrogant foes are attacking me;[i]
ruthless people[j] are trying to
kill me[k]—
people without regard for God.[a][l]

4 Surely God is my help;[m]
the Lord is the one who
sustains me.[n]

5 Let evil recoil[o] on those who
slander me;
in your faithfulness[p] destroy them.

6 I will sacrifice a freewill offering[q] to
you;
I will praise[r] your name, LORD, for it
is good.[s]

7 You have delivered me[t] from all my
troubles,
and my eyes have looked in triumph
on my foes.[u]

Psalm 55[b]

For the director of music.
With stringed instruments. A *maskil*[c]
of David.

1 Listen to my prayer, O God,
do not ignore my plea;[v]
2 hear me and answer me.[w]
My thoughts trouble me and I am
distraught[x]
3 because of what my enemy is
saying,
because of the threats of the
wicked;
for they bring down suffering on me[y]
and assail[z] me in their anger.[a]

4 My heart is in anguish[b] within me;
the terrors[c] of death have fallen
on me.
5 Fear and trembling[d] have beset me;
horror[e] has overwhelmed me.
6 I said, "Oh, that I had the wings of a
dove!
I would fly away and be at rest.
7 I would flee far away
and stay in the desert;[d][f]
8 I would hurry to my place of
shelter,[g]
far from the tempest and storm.[h]"

54:2 [h]S Ps 4:1; 5:1; 55:1 **54:3** [i]Ps 86:14 [j]Ps 18:48; 140:1,4,11 [k]S 1Sa 20:1 [l]Ps 36:1 **54:4** [m]S 1Ch 5:20; S Ps 20:2 [n]S Ps 18:35 **54:5** [o]S Dt 32:35; Ps 94:23; Pr 24:12 [p]Ps 89:49; Isa 42:3 **54:6** [q]S Lev 7:12, 16; S Ezr 1:4; S Ps 27:6 [r]Ps 44:8; 69:30; 138:2; 142:7; 145:1 [s]Ps 52:9 **54:7** [t]Ps 34:6 [u]Ps 59:10; 92:11; 112:8; 118:7 **55:1** [v]Ps 27:9; La 3:56 **55:2** [w]Ps 4:1 [x]1Sa 1:15-16; Ps 77:3; 86:6-7; 142:2 **55:3** [y]S 2Sa 16:6-8; Ps 17:9; 143:3 [z]S Ps 44:16 [a]Ps 71:11 **55:4** [b]S Ps 6:3 [c]S Job 18:11 **55:5** [d]S Job 4:14; S 2Co 7:15 [e]Dt 28:67; Isa 21:4; Jer 46:5; 49:5; Eze 7:18 **55:7** [f]1Sa 23:14 **55:8** [g]Ps 31:20 [h]Ps 77:18; Isa 4:6; 25:4; 28:2; 29:6; 32:2

[a] *3* The Hebrew has *Selah* (a word of uncertain meaning) here. [b] In Hebrew texts 55:1-23 is numbered 55:2-24. [c] Title: Probably a literary or musical term [d] *7* The Hebrew has *Selah* (a word of uncertain meaning) here and in the middle of verse 19.

see introduction to Ps 42–45). The psalm that introduces this cluster (Ps 54) is a seven-verse poem that is paradigmatic in its structure (see introduction to this psalm below). The psalm that concludes it echoes the key complaint of Ps 44, namely, that God has "rejected" his people and no longer goes out "with our armies" (44:9; 60:10). At the center is Ps 57, a prayer of 14 Hebrew lines—structurally a double seven—with a refrain that appeals to God to "be exalted" (vv. 5,11) above all creation through his saving acts. For the links between Ps 55 and 59, see introductions to those psalms; for the contrast between Ps 56 and 58, see introductions to those psalms.

Ps 54 A prayer for deliverance from enemies who want to have David killed. The prayer is short, like those of Ps 3; 4; 13; yet it is one of the most typical prayers of the Psalter, containing the main speech functions found in these prayers (see Introduction: Psalm Types). Completely symmetrical, the prayer is framed by David's cry for vindication (v. 1) and his statement of assurance that he will look in triumph on his foes (v. 7). A confession of confidence (v. 4) centers the prayer (see 42:8 and note on 6:6). The opening stanza has two verses, like the conclusion (and both refer to "your name"), while vv. 3,5 each form a separate element in the prayer. On the seven-verse structure, see introduction to Ps 29.

54 title *For the director of music.* See note on Ps 4 title. *With stringed instruments.* See note on Ps 4 title. *maskil.* See note on Ps 32 title. *When.* For the event referred to, see 1Sa 23:19; see also note on Ps 3 title.

54:1–2 Prayer for God to judge his case (see Ps 17).

54:1 *name.* See v. 6; see also note on 5:11.

54:3 The case against his enemies. *without regard for God.* Like those of Ps 53. For *Selah*, see NIV text note and note on 3:2.

54:4 A confession of confidence at the center of the prayer (see 42:8 and note).

54:5 The call for redress (see note on 5:10).

54:6 The vow to praise God (see note on 7:17). *name.* See v. 1 and note.

54:7 Assurance of being heard (see note on 3:8).

Ps 55 A prayer for God's help when threatened by a powerful conspiracy in Jerusalem under the leadership of a former friend. (Ps 59 is also a prayer for God's help against powerful foes who "prowl about" [55:10; 59:6,14] the city to achieve their evil ends and whose primary weapon is the mouth; see introduction to Ps 54–60.) The situation described is like that of Absalom's conspiracy against the king (see 25:15–17): The city is in turmoil; danger is everywhere; there is uncertainty as to who can be trusted; rumors, false reports and slander are circulating freely. Under such circumstances David longs for a quiet retreat to escape it all (vv. 6–8). That being out of the question, he casts his cares on the Lord, whom he knows he can trust. In its structure, the prayer is framed by a plea for help (v. 1) and a simple confession of faith: "I trust in you" (v. 23); at the center (v. 15) stands the heart of the prayer. On either side of the center, 12 Hebrew lines link it with the introduction and conclusion, and each of these dozen lines is divided into a similar stanza pattern: five lines, three lines, four lines.

55 title *For the director of music.* See note on Ps 4 title. *With stringed instruments.* See note on Ps 4 title. *maskil.* See note on Ps 32 title.

55:1–3 Initial appeal for God to hear.

55:4–8 His heart's anguish.

55:4–5 Danger is everywhere (see 31:13), a danger so great that it is as if death itself were stalking him (see 18:4–5; 116:3).

55:4 *heart.* See note on 4:7. *terrors of death.* See 1Sa 5:11; 15:32; 28:5; Job 18:14.

55:6–8 He longs for a quiet retreat, away from treacherous and conniving people (see similarly Jer 9:2–6).

55:7 For *Selah*, see NIV text note and note on 3:2.

9 Lord, confuse the wicked, confound
their words,[i]
for I see violence and strife[j] in the
city.[k]
10 Day and night they prowl[l] about on its
walls;
malice and abuse are within it.
11 Destructive forces[m] are at work in the
city;
threats and lies[n] never leave its
streets.

12 If an enemy were insulting me,
I could endure it;
if a foe were rising against me,
I could hide.
13 But it is you, a man like myself,
my companion, my close friend,[o]
14 with whom I once enjoyed sweet
fellowship[p]
at the house of God,[q]
as we walked about
among the worshipers.

15 Let death take my enemies by surprise;[r]
let them go down alive to the realm
of the dead,[s]
for evil finds lodging among them.

16 As for me, I call to God,
and the LORD saves me.
17 Evening,[t] morning[u] and noon[v]
I cry out in distress,
and he hears my voice.
18 He rescues me unharmed
from the battle waged against me,
even though many oppose me.

55:9 [i]Ge 11:9; Ac 2:4 [j]Ps 11:5; Isa 59:6; Jer 6:7; Eze 7:11; Hab 1:3 [k]Ge 4:17 **55:10** [l]1Pe 5:8 **55:11** [m]Ps 5:9 [n]Ps 10:7 **55:13** [o]S 2Sa 15:12 **55:14** [p]Ac 1:16-17 [q]Ps 42:4 **55:15** [r]Ps 64:7; Pr 6:15; Isa 29:5; 47:9, 11; 1Th 5:3 [s]S Ps 49:14 **55:17** [t]Ps 141:2; Ac 3:1; 10:3,30 [u]Ps 5:3; 88:13; 92:2 [v]Ac 10:9 **55:19** [w]S Ex 15:18; Dt 33:27; Ps 29:10 [x]Ps 78:59 [y]Ps 36:1; 64:4 **55:20** [z]Ps 7:4 [a]S Ps 41:9 **55:21** [b]Ps 12:2 [c]Pr 5:3; 6:24 [d]Ps 57:4; 59:7; 64:3; Pr 12:18; Rev 1:16 **55:22** [e]S Ps 18:35; Mt 6:25-34; 1Pe 5:7 [f]Ps 15:5; 21:7; 37:24; 112:6 **55:23** [g]Ps 9:15; S 30:3; 73:18; 94:13; Isa 14:15; Eze 28:8; S Lk 8:31 [h]Ps 5:6 [i]S Job 15:32 [j]Ps 11:1; 25:2; 56:3

19 God, who is enthroned from of old,[w]
who does not change—
he will hear[x] them and humble them,
because they have no fear of God.[y]

20 My companion attacks his friends;[z]
he violates his covenant.[a]
21 His talk is smooth as butter,[b]
yet war is in his heart;
his words are more soothing than oil,[c]
yet they are drawn swords.[d]

22 Cast your cares on the LORD
and he will sustain you;[e]
he will never let
the righteous be shaken.[f]
23 But you, God, will bring down the
wicked
into the pit[g] of decay;
the bloodthirsty and deceitful[h]
will not live out half their days.[i]

But as for me, I trust in you.[j]

Psalm 56[a]

For the director of music. To the tune of "A Dove on Distant Oaks." Of David. A *miktam*.[b] When the Philistines had seized him in Gath.

1 Be merciful to me,[k] my God,
for my enemies are in hot pursuit;[l]
all day long they press their attack.[m]

[a] In Hebrew texts 56:1-13 is numbered 56:2-14.
[b] Title: Probably a literary or musical term

56:1 [k]Ps 6:2 [l]Ps 57:1-3 [m]Ps 17:9

5:9 – 11 Prayer for God to foil the plots of his enemies. **5:9** *confuse ... confound their words.* Paralyze the conspira-rs with conflicting designs, as at Babel (Ge 11:5 – 9; see 2Sa ':1 – 14). *the city.* See v. 11; Jerusalem.
5:10 *malice and abuse.* Like watchmen on the walls (see 27:1; 130:6; SS 5:7).
5:11 *threats and lies.* Like watchmen who patrol the city reets (see SS 3:3).
5:12 – 14 The insults and plots of an enemy can be en-ıred — but those of a treacherous friend?
5:13 *my companion, my close friend.* See v. 20; see also 41:9 d note.
:14 *at the house of God.* Their ties of friendship had been bond hallowed by common commitment to the Lord and aled by its public display in the presence of God and the orshipers at the temple.
5:15 The centered (see note on 6:6) prayer for redress (see te on 5:10). *Let death take my enemies.* The conspirators ere seeking his death. *alive to the realm of the dead.* May ey go to the grave before life has run its normal course (see 23; Nu 16:29 – 33; Pr 1:12; Isa 5:14).
5:16 – 19 Assurance of being heard (see note on 3:8).
:17 *Evening, morning and noon I cry out.* Cf. Da 6:10.
5:18 *rescues.* See Isa 50:2; Jer 31:11 and note.
55:19 He who is the eternal King will deal with those who never change in their ways and show "no fear of od" (see 36:1 and note; see also Ps 14; 53).
5:20 – 21 Further sorrowful (or angry) reflection over the achery of his former friend.
55:20 *his friends.* Lit. "those at peace with him" (see 7:4).
55:21 See 28:3; Pr 5:3 – 4; see also note on 5:9. *heart.* See note on 4:7.
55:22 – 23 Once more, assurance of being heard.
55:22 A testimony to all who are assembled at the temple. 1Pe 5:7 echoes this assurance. *righteous.* See note on 1:5.
55:23 *pit of decay.* The grave (see note on 30:1). *not live out half their days.* See note on v. 15.
Ps 56 A prayer for help when the psalmist is attacked by enemies and his very life is threatened. It is marked by consoling trust in the face of unsettling fear. Structurally, the prayer falls into two balanced halves of seven Hebrew lines each, as does Ps 57 (see introduction to that psalm). The structure of each half is the same (two lines, two lines, three lines) with a refrain at the center of each (on the use of refrains, see introduction to Ps 42 – 43). The whole is framed by an urgent appeal to God (vv. 1 – 2) and a word of confident assurance (vv. 12 – 13). This confidence in God's defense and deliverance stands in sharp contrast to the failure of wicked earthly rulers referred to in Ps 58.
56 title *For the director of music.* See note on Ps 4 title. *To the tune of.* See note on Ps 9 title. *miktam.* See note on Ps 16 title. *When.* See note on Ps 3 title. For the event referred to, see 1Sa 21:10 – 15; see also Ps 34 title and note. *had seized.* Or "were about to seize."
56:1 – 2 Initial appeal for God's help.
56:2 *their pride.* Confident in their position of strength, Da-

[2]My adversaries pursue me all day
long;[n]
in their pride many are
attacking me.[o]

[3]When I am afraid,[p] I put my trust
in you.[q]
4 In God, whose word I praise—[r]
in God I trust and am not afraid.[s]
What can mere mortals do to me?[t]

[5]All day long they twist my words;[u]
all their schemes are for my ruin.
[6]They conspire,[v] they lurk,
they watch my steps,[w]
hoping to take my life.[x]
[7]Because of their wickedness do not[a] let
them escape;[y]
in your anger, God, bring the nations
down.[z]

[8]Record my misery;
list my tears on your scroll[b][a]—
are they not in your record?[b]
[9]Then my enemies will turn back[c]
when I call for help.[d]
By this I will know that God is
for me.[e]

[10]In God, whose word I praise,
in the LORD, whose word I praise—
[11]in God I trust and am not afraid.
What can man do to me?

[12]I am under vows[f] to you, my God;
I will present my thank offerings
to you.

56:2 [n]Ps 35:25; 124:3 [o]Ps 35:1 **56:3** [p]Ps 55:4-5 [q]S Ps 55:23 **56:4** [r]ver 10 [s]S Ps 27:1 [t]Ps 118:6; Mt 10:28; Heb 13:6 **56:5** [u]Ps 41:7; 2Pe 3:16 **56:6** [v]Ps 59:3; 94:21; Mk 3:6 [w]Ps 17:11 [x]Ps 71:10 **56:7** [y]Pr 19:5; Eze 17:15; Ro 2:3; Heb 12:25 [z]Ps 36:12; 55:23 **56:8** [a]S 2Ki 20:5 [b]Isa 4:3; Da 7:10; 12:1; Mal 3:16 **56:9** [c]Ps 9:3 [d]Ps 102:2 [e]S Nu 14:8; S Dt 31:6; Ro 8:31 **56:12** [f]Ps 50:14 **56:13** [g]Ps 30:3; 33:19; 49:15; 86:13; 107:20; 116:8 [h]S Job 33:30 **57:Title** [i]1Sa 22:1; 24:3; Ps 142 Title **57:1** [j]Ps 2:12; 9:9; 34:22 [k]S Ru 2:12; S Mt 23:37 [l]Isa 26:20 **57:2** [m]Ps 138:8 **57:3** [n]Ps 18:9, 16; 69:14; 142:6; 144:5,7 [o]Ps 56:1 [p]Ps 25:10; 40:11; 115:1 **57:4** [q]S Ps 35:17

[13]For you have delivered me from death[g]
and my feet from stumbling,
that I may walk before God
in the light of life.[h]

Psalm 57[c]

57:7-11pp — Ps 108:1-5

For the director of music. To the tune of "Do Not Destroy." Of David. A *miktam.*[d] When he had fled from Saul into the cave.[i]

[1]Have mercy on me, my God, have
mercy on me,
for in you I take refuge.[j]
I will take refuge in the shadow of your
wings[k]
until the disaster has passed.[l]

[2]I cry out to God Most High,
to God, who vindicates me.[m]
[3]He sends from heaven and saves me,[n]
rebuking those who hotly pursue
me—[e][o]
God sends forth his love and his
faithfulness.[p]

[4]I am in the midst of lions;[q]
I am forced to dwell among ravenous
beasts—

[a] 7 Probable reading of the original Hebrew text; Masoretic Text does not have *do not.* [b] 8 Or *misery; / put my tears in your wineskin* [c] In Hebrew texts 57:1-11 is numbered 57:2-12. [d] Title: Probably a literary or musical term [e] 3 The Hebrew has *Selah* (a word of uncertain meaning) here and at the end of verse 6.

---

vid's enemies take no account of his God (see notes on 3:2; 5:9; 10:11).

56:3–4 See vv. 10–11; confession of trust in the face of fear.

56:4 *word.* God's reassuring promise that he will be the God of his people and will come to their aid when they appeal to him (see 50:15; 91:15; see also 119:74,81; 130:5). *mortals.* Lit. "flesh"—i.e., human feebleness compared with God's power (see note on 10:18).

56:5–7 Accusation and call for redress (see note on 5:9–10).

56:5 *twist my words.* See notes on 3:2; 5:9; 10:11.

56:7 See note on 5:10. *anger.* See note on 2:5.

56:8–9 Appeal for God to take special note of the psalmist's troubles.

56:8 *Record ... list ... on your scroll.* Record my troubles in your heavenly royal records as matters calling for your action (see note on 51:1).

56:9 If God takes such note of his tears that he records them in his book, he will surely respond to David's call for help.

56:10–11 Renewed confession of trust in the face of fear (see vv. 3–4).

56:12–13 Assurance of being heard (see note on 3:8).

56:12 *I am under vows.* Speaking as if his prayer has already been heard, David acknowledges that now he must keep the vows he made to God when he was in trouble (see 66:14 and note on 7:17).

56:13 *stumbling.* See note on 35:15. *before God.* See note on 11:7. *light of life.* The full blessedness of life (see note on 36:9).

Ps 57 A prayer for deliverance when threatened by fierce enemies (it has many links with Ps 56). The psalm appears to reflect the imagery of the night of danger followed by the morning of salvation (v. 8: "I will awaken the dawn"). For other instances of these associations, see 30:5; 46:5; 59:6,14,16; 63:1,6; 90:14. Verses 7–11 are used again in 108:1–5. Structurally, the prayer is made up of two balanced halves, each having seven Hebrew lines and each composed of three couplets and a refrain (see introduction to Ps 56; see also introduction to Ps 54). For the placement of this psalm in the arrangement of Book II of the Psalter see introduction to Ps 42–45; see also introduction to Ps 54–60.

57 title See note on Ps 56 title. *Do Not Destroy.* See Ps 58; 59; 75 titles. *When.* For the event referred to, see 1Sa 24:1–3; see also Ps 142 title.

57:1–5 The prayer.

57:1 Initial cry for God's merciful help. *shadow of your wings.* See note on 17:8.

57:2–3 Confidence of being heard.

57:2 *Most High.* See note on Ge 14:19. *who vindicates me.* See 138:8. But the Hebrew can also be translated "who makes an end of troubles for me" (see 7:9).

57:3 *He sends.* God sends his love and faithfulness (here personified) as his messengers from heaven to save his servant (see note on 43:3). *his love and his faithfulness.* See note on 26:3. *love.* See note on 6:4.

57:4 The threatening situation. *I am forced to dwell.* Like a sheep among lions. *ravenous beasts.* The psalmists often compare their enemies to ferocious beasts (see note on 7:2). (The use of the metaphor here has no connection with the description of Saul and Jonathan in 2Sa 1:23.) *tongues.* See note on 5:9.

men whose teeth are spears and
arrows,
whose tongues are sharp swords.[r]

5 Be exalted, O God, above the heavens;
let your glory be over all the earth.[s]

6 They spread a net for my feet[t]—
I was bowed down[u] in distress.
They dug a pit[v] in my path—
but they have fallen into it
themselves.[w]

7 My heart, O God, is steadfast,
my heart is steadfast;[x]
I will sing and make music.
8 Awake, my soul!
Awake, harp and lyre![y]
I will awaken the dawn.

9 I will praise you, Lord, among the
nations;
I will sing of you among the peoples.
10 For great is your love, reaching to the
heavens;
your faithfulness reaches to the
skies.[z]

57:4 [r]S Ps 55:21; Pr 30:14 **57:5** [s]ver 11; Ps 108:5 **57:6** [t]Ps 10:9; 31:4; 140:5 [u]S Ps 38:6; 145:14 [v]S Ps 9:15 [w]S Est 6:13; Ps 7:15; Pr 28:10; Ecc 10:8 **57:7** [x]Ps 112:7 **57:8** [y]Ps 33:2; 149:3; 150:3 **57:10** [z]S Ps 36:5

57:11 [a]S Ps 8:1; 113:4 [b]S ver 5 **58:1** [c]Ps 82:2 **58:2** [d]Mt 15:19 [e]Ps 94:20; Isa 10:1; Lk 6:38 **58:4** [f]S Nu 21:6 **58:5** [g]Ps 81:11 [h]Ecc 10:11; Jer 8:17

11 Be exalted, O God, above the heavens;[a]
let your glory be over all the earth.[b]

Psalm 58[a]

For the director of music.
To the tune of "Do Not Destroy."
Of David. A *miktam*.[b]

1 Do you rulers indeed speak justly?[c]
Do you judge people with equity?
2 No, in your heart you devise injustice,[d]
and your hands mete out violence
on the earth.[e]

3 Even from birth the wicked go astray;
from the womb they are wayward,
spreading lies.
4 Their venom is like the venom of a snake,[f]
like that of a cobra that has stopped
its ears,
5 that will not heed[g] the tune of the
charmer,[h]
however skillful the enchanter
may be.

[a] In Hebrew texts 58:1-11 is numbered 58:2-12.
[b] Title: Probably a literary or musical term

7:5 A prayer for God to show his exalted power and glory roughout his creation by coming to his servant's rescue ee 7:6–7; 21:13; 46:10; 59:5,8; 113:4–9; cf. Ex 14:4; Isa 26:15; :23; 59:19; see also note on Ps 46:10).

57:6–11 Praise for God's saving help—confidently anticipating the desired deliverance. For such a sudden transition from prayer to assurance, see note on 3:8.

:6 The threat and its outcome: The enemies suffer the camity they plotted. *net ... pit.* They hunted him as if he were a ld beast, but the "lions" (v. 4) themselves were caught (see 15; 9:15 and notes).

:7 All cause for fear has been removed. *heart.* See note on . *is steadfast.* Feels secure (see 112:7).

57:8 *Awake ... Awake.* Greet with joy the dawn of the day of deliverance (see Isa 51:9,17; 52:1). *soul.* Lit. "glo-" (see note on 7:5). *harp and lyre.* Instruments (here personi-d) to accompany the praise of the Lord at his temple in lebration of deliverance (see 71:22; 81:2 and note on Ps 4 e). *awaken the dawn.* With joyful cries proclaiming God's ving act. (Dawn, too, is here personified—the Canaanites en deified it.)

:9–10 The vow to praise God (see notes on 7:17; 9:1).

:10 *love ... faithfulness.* That is, love-and-faithfulness (see 3 and note on 36:5; see also note on 3:7). *love.* See note on . *reaching to the heavens ... to the skies.* See note on 36:5.

:11 The refrain (see v. 5), but now as praise (see 18:46; 30:1; :3; 35:27; 40:16; 70:4; 92:8; 97:9; 99:2; 113:4; 148:13).

Ps 58 A prayer for God, the supreme Judge, to set right human affairs, judging those rulers who corrupt juse and championing the cause of the righteous. (The psalm as applied by the early church to Jesus' trial before the Sandrin; see Mt 26:57–68 and parallels.) Concern for the just e of judicial power is pervasive throughout the OT. This was e primary agency in the administrative structures of the cient Near East for the protection of the innocent (usually e poor and powerless) against the assaults of unscrupulous ople (usually the rich and powerful). Israelite society was ubled with the corruption of this judicial power from the ys of Samuel to the end of the monarchy (see, e.g., 1Sa ; Isa 1:23; 5:23; 10:1–2; Eze 22:6,12; Am 5:7,10–13; Mic 3:1–3,9–11; 7:2). Even in David's time all was not well (see 2Sa 15:1–4). For the central concern of this psalm, see Ps 82. In the arrangement of the Psalter, Ps 58 stands in counterpoint to Ps 56 (see introduction to that psalm).

Structurally, the psalm is framed by a rhetorical address to the wicked judges (vv. 1–2) and by a reassuring word to "the righteous" (vv. 9–11). The frame emphasizes the fact that those who do not judge uprightly (v. 1) will be judged by God (v. 11). Between the framing verses, two three-verse stanzas flesh out the theme: Verses 3–5 elaborate on the ways of the wicked rulers, and vv. 6–8 call for their disablement and removal.

58 title *For the director of music.* See note on Ps 4 title. *To the tune of.* See note on Ps 9 title. *Do Not Destroy.* See Ps 57; 59; 75 titles. *miktam.* See note on Ps 16 title.

58:1–5 Accusation against the wicked judges.

58:1–2 Direct challenge to the wicked rulers: Their mouths, hearts and hands are united in the pursuit of injustice.

58:1 *rulers.* Lit. "gods" (see Ps 82:1 and note; see also introduction to Ps 82), a title applied to those whose administrative positions called upon them to act as earthly representatives of God's heavenly court (see NIV text notes on Ex 21:6; 22:8–9; see also Dt 1:17; 2Ch 19:6 and note on Ps 45:6). *speak justly.* Make just judicial pronouncements.

58:2 *heart.* See note on 4:7. *mete out violence.* Issue decisions that result in cruel injustice.

58:3–5 The depth and stubbornness of the rulers' wickedness.

58:3 *from birth ... from the womb.* Their corrupt ways are not sporadic; they act in accordance with their nature (see 51:5). Here reference is to "the wicked"; the author does not make a general statement about all people, as is the case in Ge 6:5; 8:21; Job 14:4; 15:14–16; 25:4–6. *the wicked.* Most probably a characterization of the rulers. For a description of the wicked in general, see Ps 10. *spreading lies.* They have never been concerned for the truth (see Jn 8:44).

58:4 *venom.* What issues from their mouths is as cruel and deadly as the venom of snakes (see 140:3; Mt 23:33; Jas 3:8). *stopped its ears.* They are incorrigible; nothing—neither appeals nor threats—will move them.

[6]Break the teeth in their mouths,
O God;[i]
LORD, tear out the fangs of those
lions![j]
[7]Let them vanish like water that flows
away;[k]
when they draw the bow, let their
arrows fall short.[l]
[8]May they be like a slug that
melts away as it moves
along,[m]
like a stillborn child[n] that never sees
the sun.

[9]Before your pots can feel the heat of
the thorns[o]—
whether they be green or
dry—the wicked will be
swept away.[a][p]
[10]The righteous will be glad[q] when they
are avenged,[r]
when they dip their feet in the blood
of the wicked.[s]
[11]Then people will say,
"Surely the righteous still are
rewarded;[t]
surely there is a God who judges the
earth."[u]

58:6 [i]Ps 3:7 [j]S Job 4:10 **58:7** [k]S Lev 26:36; S Job 11:16 [l]Ps 11:2; 57:4; 64:3 **58:8** [m]Isa 13:7 [n]S Job 3:16 **58:9** [o]Ps 118:12; Ecc 7:6 [p]S Job 7:10; S 21:18 **58:10** [q]S Job 22:19 [r]Dt 32:35; Ps 7:9; 91:8; Jer 11:20; Ro 12:17-21 [s]Ps 68:23 **58:11** [t]S Ge 15:1; S Ps 128:2; Lk 6:23 [u]S Ge 18:25

59:Title [v]1Sa 19:11 **59:1** [w]Ps 143:9 [x]S Ps 20:1 **59:2** [y]Ps 14:4; 36:12; 53:4; 92:7; 94:16 [z]S Ps 26:9; 139:19; Pr 29:10 **59:3** [a]S Ps 56:6 **59:4** [b]Ps 119:3 [c]Mt 5:11

Psalm 59[b]

For the director of music.
To the tune of "Do Not Destroy." Of David.
A *miktam*.[c] When Saul had sent men to watc
David's house[v] in order to kill him.

[1]Deliver me from my enemies, O God;[w]
be my fortress against those who are
attacking me.[x]
[2]Deliver me from evildoers[y]
and save me from those who are
after my blood.[z]

[3]See how they lie in wait for me!
Fierce men conspire[a] against me
for no offense or sin of mine,
LORD.
[4]I have done no wrong,[b] yet they are
ready to attack me.[c]
Arise to help me; look on my
plight![d]
[5]You, LORD God Almighty,
you who are the God of Israel,[e]

[a] 9 The meaning of the Hebrew for this verse is uncertain. [b] In Hebrew texts 59:1-17 is numbered 59:2-18. [c] Title: Probably a literary or musical term

[d]S Ps 13:3 **59:5** [e]Ps 69:6; 80:4; 84:8

58:6–8 Appeal for God to defang the wicked rulers and purge the land of such perverse judges. The author uses imagery drawn from conventional curses of the ancient Near East (see notes on 5:10; Ge 12:3).
58:6 Let the weapons of their mouths (see 57:4) be broken and torn out. *lions.* See note on 7:2.
58:7 *water that flows away.* And is absorbed by the ground. *arrows.* Malicious pronouncements (see 57:4—but the Hebrew of the whole clause is obscure).
58:8 *slug.* That appears to dry up to nothing as it moves over a stone in the hot sun.
58:9–11 Assurance that God will surely judge them (see note on 3:8).
58:9 See NIV text note. The verse may be speaking picturesquely of the speed of God's judgment—speed probably signifying here the inescapable certainty of his judgment (see note on 37:10; see also Lk 18:7–8). *thorns.* Twigs from wild thornbushes were used as fuel for quick heat (see 118:12; Ecc 7:6). *swept away.* As by a storm—God's storm (see Job 27:21).
58:10 *righteous.* Here a judicial term for those who are in the right but who have been wronged (see note on 1:5). *when they are avenged.* When the wrongs committed against them are redressed. *dip their feet in the blood.* Vivid imagery borrowed from the literary conventions of the ancient Near East (see 68:23). Its origin is the exaggerated language of triumphant reports of victory on the battlefield.
58:11 The climax: When God has judged the unjust "gods" (see note on v. 1), all people will see that right ultimately triumphs under God's just rule (see note on 46:10; see also Ps 93; 96–99). No more will people despair, like those in Mal 3:15.
Ps 59 A prayer for deliverance when endangered by enemy attacks (for links with Ps 55, see introduction to that psalm; see also introduction to Ps 54–60). If originally composed by David under the circumstances noted in the superscription, it must have been revised for use by one of David's royal sons when Jerusalem was under siege by a hostile force made up of troops from many nations— as when Hezekiah was besieged by the Assyrians (see 2K 18:19). (Some, however, ascribe it to Nehemiah; see Ne 4 The enemy weapon most prominent is the tongue, attackin with slander and curses (see note on 5:9). In this psalm, to the imagery of the night of danger (vv. 6,14), followed by th morning of deliverance (v. 16), is evoked (see introductio to Ps 57).
Regarding the structure, each of the two closely balance halves of the psalm (vv. 1–9,10–17) concludes with an al most identical refrain (vv. 9,17), preceded by a stanza tha begins with a like characterization of the enemies (vv. 6,14 The first half of the psalm is predominantly prayer, the sec ond half predominantly assurance of deliverance. The whol is framed by a cry for God to be the psalmist's "fortress" (v. 1 and a joyful confession that God is indeed his "fortress (v. 17).
59 title See note on Ps 56 title. *Do Not Destroy.* See Ps 57; 58 75 titles. *When.* For the event referred to, see 1Sa 19:11.
59:1–2 The cry for deliverance.
59:1 *be my fortress.* Lit. "raise me to a high, secure place."
59:2 *evildoers … those who are after my blood.* Com mon characterizations of those who attack the psalm ists out of malice.
59:3–5 By slander (v. 10) and lies (v. 12) the enemies seek t justify their attacks, but the psalmist protests his innocenc and pleads with God to judge those who wrong him (se 58:11).
59:3 *lie in wait.* See 10:8–9 and note on 7:2.
59:4 *Arise.* See note on 3:7.
59:5 *LORD God Almighty.* See note on 1Sa 1:3. *God of Israe* This appeal to the Lord as the God of Israel to punish the na tions makes clear that the attack on the psalmist involves a attack by the nations on Israel. *rouse yourself.* See note on 7:6 *punish … show no mercy.* See note on 5:10. *traitors.* Whethe Israelites had joined in the attack is not clear; the Hebrev indicates only that the enemies were treacherous. For *Selah* see NIV text note and note on 3:2.

rouse yourself[f] to punish all the
nations;[g]
show no mercy to wicked traitors.[a][h]

6 They return at evening,
snarling like dogs,[i]
and prowl about the city.
7 See what they spew from their
mouths[j]—
the words from their lips are sharp
as swords,[k]
and they think, "Who can hear us?"[l]
8 But you laugh at them, LORD;[m]
you scoff at all those nations.[n]

9 You are my strength,[o] I watch for you;
you, God, are my fortress,[p]
my God on whom I can rely.
10 God will go before me
and will let me gloat over those who
slander me.
11 But do not kill them, Lord our shield,[b][q]
or my people will forget.[r]
In your might uproot them
and bring them down.[s]
12 For the sins of their mouths,[t]
for the words of their lips,[u]
let them be caught in their pride.[v]
For the curses and lies they utter,
13 consume them in your wrath,
consume them till they are no
more.[w]
Then it will be known to the ends of
the earth
that God rules over Jacob.[x]

14 They return at evening,
snarling like dogs,
and prowl about the city.
15 They wander about for food[y]
and howl if not satisfied.
16 But I will sing[z] of your strength,[a]
in the morning[b] I will sing of your
love;[c]
for you are my fortress,[d]
my refuge in times of trouble.[e]

17 You are my strength, I sing praise to
you;
you, God, are my fortress,
my God on whom I can rely.[f]

59:5 [f] S Ps 44:23 [g] S Ps 9:5; S Isa 10:3 [h] Jer 18:23 **59:6** [i] ver 14; Ps 22:16 **59:7** [j] Ps 94:4; Pr 10:32; 12:23; 15:2, 28 [k] S Ps 55:21 [l] S Job 22:13 **59:8** [m] Ps 37:13; Pr 1:26 [n] Ps 2:4 **59:9** [o] S Ps 18:1 [p] Ps 9:9; 18:2; 62:2; 71:3 **59:11** [q] Ps 3:3; 84:9 [r] Dt 4:9; 6:12 [s] Ps 89:10; 106:27; 144:6; Isa 33:3 **59:12** [t] Ps 10:7 [u] Ps 64:8; Pr 10:14; 12:13 [v] Isa 2:12; 5:15; Zep 3:11 **59:13** [w] Ps 104:35 [x] Ps 83:18 **59:15** [y] Job 15:23 **59:16** [z] Ps 108:1 [a] S 1Sa 2:10 [b] Ps 5:3; 88:13 [c] Ps 101:1 [d] S 2Sa 22:3 [e] S Dt 4:30 **59:17** [f] ver 10 **60:Title** [g] 2Sa 8:13 **60:1** [h] 2Sa 5:20; Ps 44:9 [i] Ps 79:5 [j] Ps 80:3

Psalm 60[c]

60:5-12pp — Ps 108:6-13

For the director of music. To the tune of "The Lily of the Covenant." A *miktam*[d] of David. For teaching. When he fought Aram Naharaim[e] and Aram Zobah,[f] and when Joab returned and struck down twelve thousand Edomites in the Valley of Salt.[g]

1 You have rejected us,[h] God, and burst
upon us;
you have been angry[i]—now
restore us![j]

[a] *5* The Hebrew has *Selah* (a word of uncertain meaning) here and at the end of verse 13. [b] *11* Or *sovereign* [c] In Hebrew texts 60:1-12 is numbered 60:3-14. [d] Title: Probably a literary or musical term [e] Title: That is, Arameans of Northwest Mesopotamia [f] Title: That is, Arameans of central Syria

:6 – 8 Confidence: Surely God mocks such a pack of "dogs" e 22:16 – 17).
:6 *about the city.* The enemies besiege the city like dogs at ght on the prowl for food (see vv. 14 – 15).
:7 *words from their lips are sharp as swords.* Their "curses d lies" (v. 12). For the imagery, see 57:4; see also note on . *they think.* See note on 3:2.
:9 *watch.* Hebrew *shamar* (see note on v. 17). This verb used similarly in 31:6; Jnh 2:8 ("cling to"); the basic idea pears to be to "look to expectantly" for help. The psalm- watches as one who longingly waits for the morning (of vation); see 130:6.
:10 – 13 The prayer renewed. Confident that the Lord will ar his prayer (v. 10) and will punish the nations (v. 5), the almist prays that God will not sweep them away suddenly t will prolong their punishment so that Israel ("my people," 1) will not forget God's acts of salvation, as they had done often before (see 78:11; 106:13). Nevertheless, the psalm- asks God not to allow the enemies to escape the full con- quences of their malice (vv. 12 – 13).
:10 *rely.* See note on 6:4. *slander.* See note on 5:9.
:11 *shield.* See note on 3:3. *uproot them.* Like vagabonds, h no place to settle (see Ge 4:12; 2Sa 15:20; La 4:15) and ving to hunt for food (like dogs, v. 15; see 109:10; Am 4:8).
:12 See note on v. 7. *caught in their pride.* Let the pride h which they treacherously attack the Lord's servant and people be the trap that catches them. *curses and lies.* See 7; Ge 12:3 and notes.
:13 *Then it will be known.* When God has thus dealt with Is- l's enemies, all the world will acknowledge that the Judge of all the earth (see 58:11) is the God of Israel. *Jacob.* See note on 14:7.
59:14 – 16 Assurance of being heard (see note on 3:8). Just as God mocks the defiant pack of "dogs" (vv. 6 – 8), so the psalmist will sing for joy at God's triumph over them.
59:16 *strength … love … fortress.* See the refrain (vv. 9,17). *morning.* See introduction.
59:17 The vow to praise God (see note on 7:17). *sing.* Hebrew *zamar* (see note on v. 9). The play on words in the refrain marks an advance from looking to God for help in the night of danger to singing in the morning of salvation (cf. 57:8 and note; cf. also 30:5).
Ps 60 A national prayer for God's help after suffering a severe blow by a foreign nation, presumably Edom (see v. 9). The prayer leader may have been the king (the "me" in v. 9), as in 2Ch 20. The lament that God has "rejected" (vv. 1,10) his people and no longer goes out "with our armies" (v. 10) links the psalm with Ps 44 (see 44:9; see also introduction to Ps 54 – 60). Verses 5 – 12 appear again in 108:6 – 13. As for its structure, the prayer transitions from lament to confidence. The stanza divisions are given in the notes below.
60 title See note on Ps 56 title. *The Lily of the Covenant.* See Ps 80 title and note on Ps 45 title. *For teaching.* Only here in the psalm titles. For other songs that Israel was to learn, see Dt 31:19,21; 2Sa 1:18. That it was intended for a variety of uses, especially to convey confidence in times of national threat, is illustrated by its use in Ps 108. *When.* For the events referred to, see 2Sa 8; 1Ch 18 (perhaps also 2Sa 10). If the tradition that assigns the prayer to these events is correct, it must be supposed that our knowledge of the events is incomplete,

[2] You have shaken the land[k] and torn it
open;
mend its fractures,[l] for it is
quaking.
[3] You have shown your people desperate
times;[m]
you have given us wine that makes
us stagger.[n]
[4] But for those who fear you, you have
raised a banner[o]
to be unfurled against the bow.[a]

[5] Save us and help us with your right
hand,[p]
that those you love[q] may be
delivered.
[6] God has spoken from his
sanctuary:
"In triumph I will parcel out
Shechem[r]
and measure off the Valley of
Sukkoth.[s]
[7] Gilead[t] is mine, and Manasseh is
mine;
Ephraim[u] is my helmet,
Judah[v] is my scepter.[w]

60:2 [k] Ps 18:7 [l] S 2Ch 7:14
60:3 [m] Ps 71:20 [n] Ps 75:8; Isa 29:9; 51:17; 63:6; Jer 25:16; Zec 12:2; Rev 14:10
60:4 [o] Isa 5:26; 11:10,12; 18:3
60:5 [p] S Job 40:14 [q] S Dt 33:12
60:6 [r] S Ge 12:6 [s] S Ge 33:17
60:7 [t] Jos 13:31 [u] S Ge 41:52 [v] S Nu 34:19 [w] S Ge 49:10

[a] *4* The Hebrew has *Selah* (a word of uncertain meaning) here.

since these accounts do not mention Edom. The Israelite war against Edom at this time of great northern battles may have been occasioned by an Edomite attack undertaken to try to capitalize on Israel's preoccupation elsewhere, an attack in which Edom succeeded in overrunning the garrisons that guarded Judah's southern borders.

60:1 – 3 Lament over God's rejection of his people (see 44:9 – 16; 89:38 – 45) and prayer for restoration.

60:1 *rejected us.* At least momentarily (see 30:5). Defeat by the enemy is interpreted as a sign of God's anger (though no reason for that anger is noted, and the bond between Israel and God is not broken). *burst upon.* Like a flood (see 2Sa 5:20).

60:2 *shaken the land.* As by a devastating earthquake — such as was occasionally experienced in ancient Canaan.

60:3 *wine that makes us stagger.* God has made them drink from the cup of his wrath rather than from his cup of blessing and salvation (see note on 16:5).

60:4 – 8 A plea for help, grounded in reasons for confidence. The petition (v. 5) is followed by a reassuring message from the Lord (vv. 6 – 8) — perhaps recalling an already ancient word from the time of the conquest. If so, it may have been preserved in the "Book of the Wars of the LORD" (Nu 21:14). In any event, the Lord is depicted as Israel's triumphant Warrior-King (see Ex 15:3,13 – 18).

60:4 *those who fear you.* Your people, in distinction from the nations (see 61:5; see also note on Ge 20:11). *banner.* Possibly the reassuring word from God recited in vv. 6 – 8 (see Ex 17:15). *bow.* The enemy armed with bows. For *Selah*, see NIV text note and note on 3:2.

60:5 *those you love.* The Hebrew for this expression is here a word of special endearment, as in 127:2; 2Sa 12:25; Jer 11:15.

60:6 *parcel out … measure off.* Divide his conquered territory among his servant people who were with him in the battles. *Shechem … Sukkoth.* Cities representative of the territory west and east of the Jordan taken over by the Lord and Israel (see Ge 33:17 – 18; 1Ki 12:25). See map on this page.

60:7 Israel is the Lord's kingdom — the land conquered and his people established within it. *Gilead … Manasseh.* Half of Manasseh was established in Gilead, east of the Jordan, and half of it west of the Jordan just north of Ephraim (see Jos 13:29 – 31; 17:5 – 11). This once again showed that the Lord's kingdom included territory both east and west of the Jordan. *Ephraim … Judah.* The two leading tribes of Israel, the one representative of the Rachel tribes (Ephraim) in the north, the other of the Leah tribes (Judah) in the south; see Ge 48:13 – 20; 49:8 – 12; Nu 2:3,18

CITIES AND REGIONS IN PSALM 60

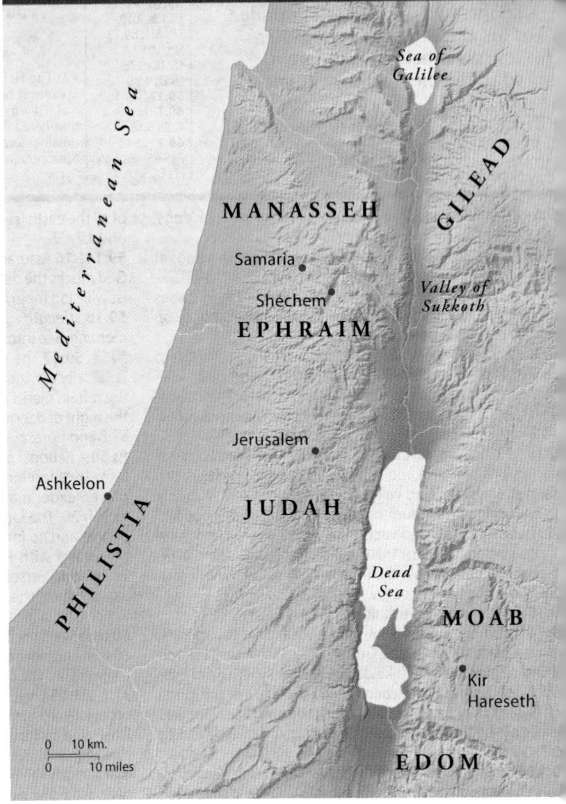

8 Moab is my washbasin,
on Edom I toss my sandal;
over Philistia I shout in triumph.[x]"

9 Who will bring me to the fortified city?
Who will lead me to Edom?
10 Is it not you, God, you who have now rejected us
and no longer go out with our armies?[y]
11 Give us aid against the enemy,
for human help is worthless.[z]
12 With God we will gain the victory,
and he will trample down our enemies.[a]

Psalm 61[a]

For the director of music.
With stringed instruments. Of David.

1 Hear my cry, O God;[b]
listen to my prayer.[c]

2 From the ends of the earth I call to you,
I call as my heart grows faint;[d]
lead me to the rock[e] that is higher than I.
3 For you have been my refuge,[f]
a strong tower against the foe.[g]

4 I long to dwell[h] in your tent forever
and take refuge in the shelter of your wings.[b][i]
5 For you, God, have heard my vows;[j]
you have given me the heritage of those who fear your name.[k]

6 Increase the days of the king's life,[l]
his years for many generations.[m]
7 May he be enthroned in God's presence forever;[n]
appoint your love and faithfulness to protect him.[o]

60:8 [x] S 2Sa 8:1 **60:10** [y] S Jos 7:12 **60:11** [z] Ps 146:3; Pr 3:5 **60:12** [a] S Job 40:12; Ps 44:5 **61:1** [b] Ps 64:1 [c] Ps 4:1; 86:6 **61:2** [d] S Ps 6:2 [e] Ps 18:2; 31:2; 94:22 **61:3** [f] Ps 9:9; S 46:1; 62:7 [g] Ps 59:9; Pr 18:10 **61:4** [h] S Ps 15:1 [i] S Dt 32:11; S Mt 23:37 **61:5** [j] S Nu 30:2; Ps 56:12 [k] S Ex 6:3; S Dt 33:9; Ne 1:11; Ps 102:15; Isa 59:19; Mt 6:9 **61:6** [l] 1Ki 3:14 [m] S Ps 21:4 **61:7** [n] S Ps 41:12; Lk 22:69; Eph 1:20; Col 3:1 [o] Ps 40:11

[a] In Hebrew texts 61:1-8 is numbered 61:2-9. [b] *4* The Hebrew has *Selah* (a word of uncertain meaning) here.

Jos 15–16. Together they represented all Israel (Isa 11:13; Zec 9:13). *helmet.* As a powerful and aggressive tribe (Dt 33:17; Jdg 7:24—8:3; 12:1), Ephraim figuratively represents the Lord's helmet. *scepter.* Called such because from Judah would come (Ge 49:10)—and had now come (1Sa 16:1–13)—the Lord's chosen earthly regent over his people (see 2Sa 7).

60:8 *Moab ... Edom ... Philistia.* Perpetual enemies on Israel's eastern, southern and western borders, respectively (see Ex 15:14–15; see also Ex 13:17; Nu 20:14–21; 22–24). *is my washbasin.* Is reduced to a household vessel in which the Lord washes his feet (Ge 18:4). The metaphor is perhaps suggested by the fact that Moab lay along the east shore of the Dead Sea. *toss my sandal.* Perhaps refers to the conventional symbolic act by which one claimed possession of land (cf. Ru 4:7 and note).

60:9–12 The closing stanza, expressing confidence of victory (see note on 3:8).

60:9 *me ... me.* Possibly referring to the king (see introduction), though the praying community may be referring to itself collectively (see note on Ps 30 title). *lead me.* As God went before his people into battle in the wilderness (Ex 13:21) and during the conquest (Ex 23:27–28; 33:2; Dt 9:3; 31:8).

60:10 *rejected.* See v. 1.

60:11 *human help.* See 108:12–13; 121:1–2; Isa 30:1–5. *help.* Lit. "salvation" (see v. 5, "save").

60:12 *gain the victory.* Lit. "do mighty things." With God's help Israel will achieve in a manner similar to that of the Lord himself (see 118:15–16) and will triumph over Edom (see Nu 24:18, "grow strong"). *trample down.* Like a victorious warrior (see Isa 14:19,25; Jer 12:10; Zec 10:5).

Ps 61–64 A series of four psalms linked together by the common theme of strong reliance on God for deliverance in the face of great—perhaps mortal—danger. Two make explicit reference to the king (Ps 61; 63), and the other two (62; 64) may also represent a royal voice, though this is disputed. All have been crafted with considerable care.

Ps 61 A prayer for restoration to God's presence. The circumstances appear to be similar to those referred to in Ps 42–43. Here, however, a king is involved (v. 6), and if the author was David, he may have composed this prayer at the time of his flight from Absalom (see 2Sa 17:21–29). For another possibility, see note on v. 2. Structurally, the prayer is framed by a cry to God (v. 1) and a vow to praise him (v. 8). The body of the psalm is composed of three couplets: vv. 2–3,4–5,6–7.

61 title See note on Ps 4 title.

61:1 Initial plea for God to hear.

61:2–3 The prayer.

61:2 *ends of the earth.* So it seemed (see 42:6). Possibly the phrase here refers to the brink of the netherworld, i.e., the grave (see 63:9); the psalmist feels himself near death. *heart.* See note on 4:7. *lead me.* See 23:2. *rock.* Secure place (see 27:5; 40:2). *higher than I.* The place of security that he seeks is beyond his reach; only God can bring him to it. Since God is often confessed by the psalmists to be their "rock of refuge" (31:2; see also 18:2; 62:2,6–7; 71:3; 94:22), it may be that God himself is that higher "rock" (the secure refuge) that the psalmist pleads for (see v. 3). Or it may be the secure refuge of God's sanctuary (see v. 4; see also 27:5).

61:3 The reason he appeals to God: God has never failed him as a refuge. *foe.* If this is a prayer when faced with death, death is the present foe (see 68:20; 141:8; Job 33:22; Isa 25:8; 28:15; Jer 9:21; Hos 13:14; see also 1Co 15:26). See note on 49:14.

61:4–5 Longing for the security of God's sanctuary (see 27:5 and note).

61:4 *dwell in.* See note on 15:1. *tent.* Residence (see 2Sa 6:17; 7:2; 1Ki 1:39; 2:28–30). *shelter of your wings.* See note on 17:8. For *Selah*, see NIV text note and note on 3:2.

61:5 The reason for his longing: Either (1) because God has been so responsive to him in the past or (2) confidence that his longing is about to be satisfied. *my vows.* The vows that accompanied his prayers (see 50:14; 66:14; see also note on 7:17). *heritage.* A place with God's people in the promised land, together with all that the Lord had promised to give and to be to his people (see 16:6; 37:18; 135:12; 136:21–22). *those who fear.* See 60:4 and note. *your name.* See note on 5:11.

61:6–7 Prayer for the king's long life. The king himself may have made this prayer—such transitions to the third person are known from the literature of the ancient Near East—or it may be the prayer of the people, perhaps voiced by a priest or Levite. Later Jewish interpretations applied these verses to the Messiah. They are fulfilled in Christ, David's great Son.

61:6 May the king live forever (see note on 45:6).

61:7 *enthroned in God's presence.* See note on 41:12. *love and faithfulness.* Personified as God's agents (see notes on 23:6; 43:3; see also note on 26:3).

[8]Then I will ever sing in praise of your
name[p]
and fulfill my vows day after day.[q]

Psalm 62[a]

For the director of music.
For Jeduthun. A psalm of David.

[1]Truly my soul finds rest[r] in God;[s]
my salvation comes from him.
[2]Truly he is my rock[t] and my salvation;[u]
he is my fortress,[v] I will never be
shaken.[w]

[3]How long will you assault me?
Would all of you throw me down—
this leaning wall,[x] this tottering
fence?
[4]Surely they intend to topple me
from my lofty place;
they take delight in lies.
With their mouths they bless,
but in their hearts they curse.[b][y]

[5]Yes, my soul, find rest in God;[z]
my hope comes from him.
[6]Truly he is my rock and my salvation;
he is my fortress, I will not be
shaken.
[7]My salvation and my honor depend on
God[c];
he is my mighty rock, my refuge.[a]
[8]Trust in him at all times, you people;[b]
pour out your hearts to him,[c]
for God is our refuge.

[9]Surely the lowborn[d] are but a breath,[e]
the highborn are but a lie.
If weighed on a balance,[f] they are
nothing;
together they are only a breath.
[10]Do not trust in extortion[g]
or put vain hope in stolen
goods;[h]
though your riches increase,
do not set your heart on them.[i]

[11]One thing God has spoken,
two things I have heard:
"Power belongs to you, God,[j]
[12]and with you, Lord, is unfailing
love";[k]
and, "You reward everyone
according to what they have
done."[l]

Psalm 63[d]

A psalm of David.
When he was in the Desert of Judah.

[1]You, God, are my God,
earnestly I seek you;
I thirst for you,[m]
my whole being longs for you,
in a dry and parched land
where there is no water.[n]

61:8 [p]S Ex 15:1; Ps 7:17; 30:4 [q]S Nu 30:2; S Dt 23:21 **62:1** [r]S Ps 5:3 [s]ver 5 **62:2** [t]Ps 18:31; 89:26 [u]S Ex 15:2 [v]S Ps 59:9 [w]S Job 29:18 **62:3** [x]Isa 30:13 **62:4** [y]Ps 28:3; 55:21 **62:5** [z]ver 1 **62:7** [a]S Ps 61:3 **62:8** [b]Ps 37:5; Isa 26:4 [c]1Sa 1:15; Ps 42:4; Mt 26:36-46 **62:9** [d]Ps 49:2 [e]S Job 7:7 [f]Isa 40:15 **62:10** [g]S Ps 12:5; 1Ti 6:17 [h]Isa 61:8; Eze 22:29; Na 3:1 [i]S Job 31:25; Mt 19:23-24; 1Ti 6:6-10 **62:11** [j]S 1Ch 29:11; Rev 19:1 **62:12** [k]Ps 86:5; 103:8; 130:7 [l]S Job 21:31; Ps 28:4; S Mt 16:27; Ro 2:6*; 1Co 3:8; Col 3:25 **63:1** [m]Ps 42:2; 84:2 [n]Ps 143:6

[a] In Hebrew texts 62:1-12 is numbered 62:2-13.
[b] *4* The Hebrew has *Selah* (a word of uncertain meaning) here and at the end of verse 8.
[c] *7* Or / *God Most High is my salvation and my honor*
[d] In Hebrew texts 63:1-11 is numbered 63:2-12.

61:8 The vow to praise God (see note on 7:17).

Ps 62 The psalmist commits himself to God when threatened by the assaults of conspirators who wish to "topple me from my lofty place" (v. 4). The author may have been a king. If it was David, the circumstances could well have been the efforts of the family of Saul to topple him. Verse 3 suggests a time of weakness and may indicate advanced age. Implicitly the psalm is an appeal to God to uphold him. No psalm surpasses it in its expression of simple trust in God (see Ps 31 and introduction to Ps 61). The psalm is composed of three parts (vv. 3–4,5–8,9–10), framed by a confession of tranquil resting in God (vv. 1–2) and the reason for such trust (vv. 11–12). The middle stanza constitutes a thematic hinge: Its first two verses (vv. 5–6) echo the opening couplet, while the last two verses (vv. 7–8) anticipate the closing couplet. The other two stanzas (vv. 3–4,9–10) speak of those who threaten.

62 title See note on Ps 39 title.

62:1–2 Profession of complete trust in God for protection.

62:1 *my soul.* See note on 6:3. *finds rest.* Lit. "is silence," i.e., is in repose.

62:2,6 *shaken.* See note on 10:6.

62:3–4 The threatening activities of the enemies.

62:3 Question to the assailants: Will you never give up? *leaning wall … tottering fence.* A metaphor for the psalmist's fragile condition: either (1) a confession that he has no strength in himself, (2) an acknowledgment that he is in a weakened condition or, perhaps, (3) a reflection on how his enemies perceive him, as a "pushover."

62:4 *lofty place.* Possibly the throne. *lies.* See note on 10:7. *bless.* For example, "Long live the king" (1Sa 10:24; 2Sa 16:16; see also 1Ki 1:25,34,39). *curse.* Call down curses (see note on Ge 12:3). For *Selah*, see NIV text note and note on 3:2.

62:5–8 Trust in God: an exhortation to himself (v. 5) and to the people (v. 8).

62:5 *find rest.* See note on v. 1; faith encouraging faith (see 27:13–14; 42:5,11; 43:5).

62:8 Exhortation to God's people (see 31:23–24). *pour out your hearts.* In earnest prayer (see La 2:19). *hearts.* See note on 4:7.

62:9–10 Humans, as a threat, are nothing (see note on 10:18).

62:9 *lowborn … highborn.* Persons of every condition. *breath … lie.* People appear to be much more than they really are (see 37:2,20; 39:5 and notes), especially the rich and powerful.

62:10 A warning to those (including those conspiring against him) who trust in their own devices to get what they want (by fair means or foul) rather than trusting in God to sustain them—a virtual summary of Ps 49. *heart.* See note on 4:7.

62:11–12 The climax: recollection of God's reassuring word to his people. *Power … unfailing love.* He is able to do all that he has promised and is committed to his people's salvation and blessedness.

62:11 *One thing … two things.* See note on Am 1:3.

62:12 *unfailing love.* See note on 6:4. *reward … according to.* See notes on Jer 17:10; 32:19.

Ps 63 A confession of longing for God and for the security his presence offers when deadly enemies threaten. That longing is vividly described by the metaphor of thirst (v. 1) and hunger (v. 5; see 42:1–2). Like Ps 62 this psalm is an implicit prayer. It is linked to that psalm also by

[2]I have seen you in the sanctuary[o]
and beheld your power and your glory.[p]
[3]Because your love is better than life,[q]
my lips will glorify you.
[4]I will praise you as long as I live,[r]
and in your name I will lift up my hands.[s]
[5]I will be fully satisfied as with the richest of foods;[t]
with singing lips my mouth will praise you.

[6]On my bed I remember you;
I think of you through the watches of the night.[u]
[7]Because you are my help,[v]
I sing in the shadow of your wings.[w]
[8]I cling to you;[x]
your right hand upholds me.[y]

[9]Those who want to kill me will be destroyed;[z]
they will go down to the depths of the earth.[a]
[10]They will be given over to the sword[b]
and become food for jackals.[c]

[11]But the king will rejoice in God;
all who swear by God will glory in him,[d]
while the mouths of liars will be silenced.[e]

63:2 [o]S Ps 15:1; 27:4; 68:24 [p]S Ex 16:7 **63:3** [q]Ps 36:7; 69:16; 106:45; 109:21 **63:4** [r]Ps 104:33; 146:2; Isa 38:20 [s]S Ps 28:2; 1Ti 2:8 **63:5** [t]S Ps 36:8; Mt 5:6 **63:6** [u]Dt 6:4-9; Ps 16:7; 119:148; Mt 14:25 **63:7** [v]Ps 27:9; 118:7 [w]S Ru 2:12 **63:8** [x]S Nu 32:12; Hos 6:3 [y]S Ps 41:12 **63:9** [z]Ps 40:14 [a]Ps 55:15; 71:20; 95:4; 139:15 **63:10** [b]Jer 18:21; Eze 35:5; Am 1:11 [c]La 5:18 **63:11** [d]Ps 21:1; Isa 19:18; 45:23; 65:16 [e]S Job 5:16; Ro 3:19 **64:1** [f]Ps 142:2 [g]Ps 140:1

Psalm 64[a]

For the director of music.
A psalm of David.

[1]Hear me, my God, as I voice my complaint;[f]
protect my life from the threat of the enemy.[g]

[a] In Hebrew texts 64:1-10 is numbered 64:2-11.

the advancement from hearing (62:11) to seeing (v. 2; see 48:8 and note). The imagery of the night of danger (v. 6) and the morning of salvation (see note on v. 1) once more occurs (see introduction to Ps 57). In the early church this psalm was prescribed for daily public prayers. In its structure, the initial expression of longing (v. 1) gives way at the end to the expectation of joy (v. 11)—the literary frame of the psalm. Verse 6 provides the key thematic link connecting vv. 1 and 11. It stands at the center between two precisely balanced stanzas (vv. 2–5,7–10), each having four verses and each made up of 27 Hebrew words. The psalmist's night meditations (v. 6) nurture his longing for God (v. 1; cf. 143:5–6) and reinforce his expectations (v. 11). For the thematic links between the two major stanzas, see following notes.

63 title See note on Ps 3 title. *When.* If this tradition is correct, the reference is probably to 2Sa 15:23–28; 16:2,14; 17:16,29 since the psalmist is referred to as king (see v. 11).

63:1 Intense longing for God in a time of need. *earnestly.* Lit. "at dawn," "in the morning." *I thirst for you.* See 42:2 and note. *dry and parched land.* A metaphor (see 143:6; Isa 32:2) for his situation of need, in which he does not taste "the richest of foods" (v. 5) supplied by the "river whose streams make glad the city of God" (46:4; see note there).

63:2–5 Comforting reflection on what he had seen in the sanctuary; it awakens joyful expectations.

63:2 See 27:4; 48:8 and notes.

63:3 *love.* See note on 6:4.

63:4 *name.* See note on 5:11. *lift up my hands.* While lifting the hands to God usually signifies prayer, it also—though rarely in Biblical reference—accompanied praise (see 134:2).

63:5 *richest of foods.* Lit. "fat and fatness" (for a similar idea, see Isa 25:6).

63:6 A centering line (see introduction to this psalm): night reflections, remembering what he had seen "in the sanctuary" (v. 2). *On my bed.* At night as he expectantly awaits the dawning of the morning of deliverance. *watches of the night.* See note on Jdg 7:19; see also 119:148; La 2:19.

63:7–10 The great contrast between "my" prospects (vv. 7–8) and theirs (vv. 9–10). As will be noted, each of these four verses has some kind of thematic link with the corresponding verse in the four-verse stanza with which it is balanced (see introduction to this psalm).

63:7 *shadow of your wings.* See note on 17:8. God's saving help brings the psalmist back to the sanctuary (see v. 2) with songs of praise.

63:8 He has experienced God's "love," which is "better than life" (v. 3).

63:9 His enemies will get what they deserve; in wanting to kill him they forfeit their own lives (see Ge 9:5; Ex 21:23; Dt 19:21; see also note on Ps 5:10). The final end of the enemies stands in sharp contrast with the psalmist's prospects, as anticipated in vv. 7–8—but also as voiced in v. 4: "I will praise," but "they will go down" to the place of silence (see v. 11). *depths.* See note on 30:1. *earth.* Here, the netherworld or grave (see note on 61:2).

63:10 *food for jackals.* Like bodies of enemies left unburied on the battlefield to add to their disgrace (see note on 53:5). Note the vivid portrayal of the contrast between the two prospects: "I will be fully satisfied as with the richest of foods" (v. 5); "they will ... become food for jackals."

63:11 The closing frame (see introduction to this psalm), in which the speaker is finally identified as the king. *all who swear by God.* Those who revere and trust God (see Dt 6:13). *mouths of liars.* Those who live by falsehood (see 5:6; 58:3; 101:7 and note on 5:9).

Ps 64 Confident prayer to God for protection when threatened by a conspiracy (see introduction to Ps 61–64). The circumstances may be similar to those reflected in Ps 62 (see introduction to that psalm), but here there is no allusion to the king's weakened condition, and it is not clear whether the conspirators come from within or outside Israel (see note on v. 2). As so often in the prayers of the Psalter, the enemy's tongue is his main weapon (see note on 5:9). The prayer is framed by an initial plea for protection from an enemy (v. 1) and a concluding call to rejoicing and praise (v. 10). Two carefully balanced stanzas spell out David's prayer and the adversaries' threat (vv. 2–4) and God's anticipated counteraction and its effect on all who hear about it (vv. 7–9). The point-counterpoint relationship of these two stanzas is highlighted by the use of key words that occur in corresponding positions in the Hebrew poetic lines—in reverse order: "doers" (v. 2), "tongues" (v. 3), "shoot ... suddenly" (v. 4), "shoot ... suddenly" (v. 7), "tongues" (v. 8), "works" (v. 9: in Hebrew the same word as for "doers" in v. 2). At the center, vv. 5–6 describe the disdainful confidence of the conspirators.

64 title See note on Ps 4 title.

64:1 Initial appeal for God to hear.

2 Hide me from the conspiracy[h] of the wicked,[i]
from the plots of evildoers.
3 They sharpen their tongues like swords[j]
and aim cruel words like deadly arrows.[k]
4 They shoot from ambush at the innocent;[l]
they shoot suddenly, without fear.[m]

5 They encourage each other in evil plans,
they talk about hiding their snares;[n]
they say, "Who will see it[a]?"[o]
6 They plot injustice and say,
"We have devised a perfect plan!"
Surely the human mind and heart are cunning.

7 But God will shoot them with his arrows;
they will suddenly be struck down.
8 He will turn their own tongues against them[p]
and bring them to ruin;
all who see them will shake their heads[q] in scorn.[r]
9 All people will fear;[s]
they will proclaim the works of God
and ponder what he has done.[t]

10 The righteous will rejoice in the LORD[u]
and take refuge in him;[v]
all the upright in heart will glory in him![w]

Psalm 65[b]

For the director of music. A psalm of David. A song.

1 Praise awaits[c] you, our God, in Zion;[x]
to you our vows will be fulfilled.[y]
2 You who answer prayer,
to you all people will come.[z]
3 When we were overwhelmed by sins,[a]
you forgave[d] our transgressions.[b]
4 Blessed are those you choose[c]
and bring near[d] to live in your courts!
We are filled with the good things of your house,[e]
of your holy temple.

[a] 5 Or *us* [b] In Hebrew texts 65:1-13 is numbered 65:2-14. [c] 1 Or *befits*; the meaning of the Hebrew for this word is uncertain. [d] 3 Or *made atonement for*

64:2 [h] S Ex 1:10 [i] Ps 56:6; 59:2 **64:3** [j] S Ps 55:21; Isa 49:2 [k] S Ps 7:13; S 58:7 **64:4** [l] S Job 9:23; Ps 10:8; 11:2 [m] S Ps 55:19 **64:5** [n] Ps 91:3; 119:110; 140:5; 141:9 [o] S Job 22:13 **64:8** [p] S Ps 59:12; Pr 18:7 [q] S 2Ki 19:21; Ps 109:25 [r] S Dt 28:37 **64:9** [s] S Ps 40:3 [t] Jer 51:10 **64:10** [u] S Job 22:19 [v] Ps 11:1; 25:20; 31:2 [w] Ps 32:11 **65:1** [x] Ps 2:6 [y] S Dt 23:21; Ps 116:18 **65:2** [z] Ps 86:9; Isa 66:23 **65:3** [a] S Ps 40:12 [b] Ps 79:9; Ro 3:25; Heb 9:14 **65:4** [c] S Ps 33:12 [d] S Nu 16:5 [e] S Ps 36:8

64:2–4 The petition and the threat.
64:2 *plots.* The Hebrew root underlying this word is the same as that for "conspire" in 2:1.
64:3 *tongues.* See note on 5:9. *swords ... deadly arrows.* See 59:7 and note.
64:4 *without fear.* They feel themselves secure from exposure and retaliation (see Ps 10 and notes on 10:6,11), but see vv. 7–8.
64:5–6 The enemies' contemptuous self-confidence.
64:5 *hiding their snares.* See note on 9:15.
64:6 *heart.* See note on 4:7. *cunning.* Lit. "deep" (see Pr 18:4; 20:5).
64:7–9 Confidence in God's righteous judgment—he will do to the adversaries what they had intended to do to David (see vv. 3–4)—and its effect on those who hear about it. For the links between this stanza and vv. 2–4, see introduction to this psalm.
64:7 *shoot ... arrows.* See note on Ge 9:13.
64:8 *shake their heads.* See 44:14.
64:9 All people will fear, proclaim and ponder how God's "works" undo and judge the doings of the "evildoers" (v. 2; see note on 46:10; see also 40:3; 58:11; 65:8).
64:10 Framing conclusion (see v. 1): "The righteous will rejoice in the LORD and take refuge in him"—take refuge and praise him. *righteous.* See note on 1:5.
Ps 65–68 Four psalms dominated by the theme of praise and linked by the shared recognition that God's "awesome" deeds evoke the wonder of "all the ends of the earth" and move (or should move) "all the earth" to join Israel in singing the praise of her God (see note on 46:10). In these four psalms, the occasions—and reasons—for this universal praise include (1) God's mighty acts in maintaining the creation order and making it fruitful so that humans are richly blessed, and (2) God's saving acts in behalf of his people. These are significantly brought together here by alternating the focus; Ps 65 and 67 speak of the former, and Ps 66 and 68 speak of the latter. Thus in this short series all of God's benevolent acts are brought into purview, and the whole human race is encompassed in the community of praise.
Ps 65 A hymn in praise of God's great goodness to his people. In answer to their prayers (1) he pardons their sins so that they continue to enjoy the "good things" that accompany their fellowship with him at his temple (vv. 1–4); (2) as the One who established the secure order of the creation, he also orders the affairs of the world so that international turbulence is put to rest and Israel is secure in her land (vv. 5–8); and (3) he turns the promised land into a veritable Garden of Eden (vv. 9–13). In all this he is hailed as "the hope" of all humankind. His wondrous deeds fill them with "awe" and move them to "songs of joy."
65 title See notes on Ps 4; 30 titles.
65:1–2 Introductory commitment to praise.
65:1 *awaits.* Or "is silent before" (see note on 62:1; see also NIV text note here). Perhaps the imagery is that of praise personified as a permanent resident of the temple, lying quietly at rest, whom the people will awaken when they come to make good their vows (see 57:8). *our vows.* Those made in conjunction with their prayers in time of need (see 66:14 and note on 7:17).
65:2 *all people.* Lit. "all flesh," perhaps referring to all God's people, as in Joel 2:28. Most interpreters believe (in light of vv. 5,8) that the reference is more universal, as in 64:9; 66:1,4,8; 67:3–5 and elsewhere. *will come.* To praise God as the (only) God who hears and graciously answers prayers.
65:3–4 The crucial act of divine mercy that opens the way for the benefits spelled out in the two remaining stanzas.
65:3 *forgave our transgressions.* Accepted the atonement sacrifices you appointed and so forgave our sins (see NIV text note; see also 32:1–2; 78:38; 79:9 and notes on Lev 16:20–22; 17:11; Heb 2:17; 9:5,7).
65:4 *Blessed.* See note on 1:1. *those you choose and bring near.* Everyone belonging to Israel as God's chosen people (see, e.g., 33:12; Dt 4:37) and whom God accepts at his temple. *live in your courts.* See note on 15:1; see also 23:6. *good things of your house.* All the blessings that flow from God's presence (see 36:8 and note).

5 You answer us with awesome and
righteous deeds,[f]
God our Savior,[g]
the hope of all the ends of the earth[h]
and of the farthest seas,[i]
6 who formed the mountains[j] by your
power,
having armed yourself with
strength,[k]
7 who stilled the roaring of the seas,[l]
the roaring of their waves,
and the turmoil of the nations.[m]
8 The whole earth is filled with awe at
your wonders;
where morning dawns, where
evening fades,
you call forth songs of joy.[n]

9 You care for the land and water it;[o]
you enrich it abundantly.[p]
The streams of God are filled with
water
to provide the people with grain,[q]
for so you have ordained it.[a]
10 You drench its furrows and level its
ridges;
you soften it with showers[r] and bless
its crops.
11 You crown the year with your bounty,[s]
and your carts overflow with
abundance.[t]
12 The grasslands of the wilderness
overflow;[u]
the hills are clothed with gladness.[v]
13 The meadows are covered with flocks[w]
and the valleys are mantled with
grain;[x]
they shout for joy and sing.[y]

Psalm 66

For the director of music.
A song. A psalm.

1 Shout for joy to God, all the earth![z]
2 Sing the glory of his name;[a]
make his praise glorious.[b]
3 Say to God, "How awesome are your
deeds![c]
So great is your power
that your enemies cringe[d] before
you.
4 All the earth bows down[e] to you;
they sing praise[f] to you,
they sing the praises of your name."[b]

[a] 9 Or *for that is how you prepare the land* [b] 4 The Hebrew has *Selah* (a word of uncertain meaning) here and at the end of verses 7 and 15.

65:5 [f] S Dt 4:34; S Ps 45:4; 106:22; Isa 64:3 [g] Ps 18:46; 68:19; 85:4 [h] S Ps 48:10 [i] Ps 107:23 **65:6** [j] Am 4:13 [k] S Ps 18:1; 93:1; Isa 51:9 **65:7** [l] Ps 89:9; 93:3-4; 107:29; S Mt 8:26 [m] Dt 32:41; Ps 2:1; 74:23; 139:20; Isa 17:12-13 **65:8** [n] Ps 100:2; 107:22; 126:2; Isa 24:16; 52:9 **65:9** [o] S Lev 26:4 [p] Ps 104:24 [q] S Ge 27:28; S Dt 32:14; Ps 104:14 **65:10** [r] S Dt 32:2; S 2Sa 1:21; S Job 36:28; Ac 14:17 **65:11** [s] S Dt 28:12; Ps 104:28; Jn 10:10 [t] Job 36:28; Ps 147:14; Lk 6:38 **65:12** [u] S Job 28:26; Joel 2:22 [v] Ps 98:8 **65:13** [w] Ps 144:13; Isa 30:23; Zec 8:12 [x] Ps 72:16 [y] Ps 98:8; Isa 14:8; 44:23; 49:13; 55:12 **66:1** [z] Ps 81:1; 84:8; 95:1; 98:4; 100:1 **66:2** [a] Ps 79:9; 86:9 [b] Isa 42:8, 12; 43:21 **66:3** [c] S Dt 7:21; S 10:21; Ps 65:5; 106:22; 111:6; 145:6 [d] S 2Sa 22:45 **66:4** [e] Ps 22:27 [f] Ps 7:17; 67:3

65:5 – 8 God, who continues to uphold the creation order, stills the nations and makes Israel secure in answer to her prayers.

65:5 *awesome ... deeds.* Acts of God such as were associated with his deliverance of Israel from Egypt and the conquest of Canaan, acts of power that made Israel's enemies cringe (see 66:3; see also 106:22; 145:6; Dt 10:21; 2Sa 7:23; Isa 64:3). *righteous deeds.* Saving acts by which God kept his covenanted promises to Israel (see note on 4:1). *hope of all.* Even if the nations of the world did not yet fully realize it.

65:6 – 7 The God of creation, who by his power brought order to the world out of the earlier chaos (see Ge 1), similarly in the redemption of his people establishes a peaceful order among nations (see Isa 2:4; 11:6 – 9; Mic 4:3 – 4) so that Israel may be at rest in the promised land (see also Ps 33; 46). God's mighty acts in redemption are often compared by OT poets with his mighty acts in creation (see 74:12 – 17; 89:9 – 18; Isa 27:1; 40:6 – 14,21 – 31; 51:9 – 11), since his power as Creator guaranteed his power as Redeemer. *formed the mountains ... stilled ... the seas.* Gave order to the whole creation (see 95:4 – 5).

65:7 *turmoil of the nations.* God's stilling the turbulence of the nations — which often threatened Israel — is compared to his taming the turbulence of the primeval waters of chaos (see notes on 32:6; 33:7).

65:8 All peoples will (ultimately) see God's saving acts in behalf of his people and will be moved to awe (see note on 46:10). And all creation will rejoice (see v. 13). *wonders.* Or "signs," referring to God's great saving acts, such as those he performed when he delivered Israel out of Egypt (Dt 4:34; see Ps 78:43; 105:27; 135:9). As "signs" they indicated that God was at work (see Jn 2:11 and note).

65:9 – 13 God blesses the promised land with all good things in answer to Israel's prayers.

65:9 *streams of God.* See note on 36:8.

65:11 *bounty.* Lit. "goodness" (see 68:10; see also 31:19 and note).

65:13 *they shout for joy and sing.* In the exuberant language of the psalmists, all creation — even its inanimate elements — joins the human chorus to celebrate the goodness of God in creation, blessing and redemption (see 89:12; 96:11 – 13; 98:8 – 9; 103:22; 145:10; 148:3 – 4,7 – 10; see also Job 38:7; Isa 44:23; 49:13; 55:12).

Ps 66 A psalm of praise for God's answer to prayer — probably delivering the psalmist from an enemy threat. He has set his personal experience of God's saving help as one of God's people in the larger context of God's help of Israel in the exodus. The praise is offered at the temple in fulfillment of a vow (vv. 13 – 14; see note on 7:17). Such praise was often climaxed by a call for others to take up the praise (see note on 9:1). Here the psalmist exuberantly begins with that call and, as often elsewhere (e.g., 67:3 – 5; 68:32; 98:4; 99:1 – 3; 100:1; 117:1), addresses it even to the far corners of the earth. This psalm is the second in a series of four (see introduction to Ps 65 – 68). It is framed by a call to praise God (vv. 1 – 2) and a declaration of the present occasion for praise (vv. 19 – 20, in Hebrew involving a play on words — the Hebrew for "praise" and "prayer" sound very much alike). The opening stanza (vv. 1 – 4) is followed by two thematic sequences having the same structure: a three-verse stanza (vv. 5 – 7,13 – 15) followed by a five-verse stanza (vv. 8 – 12,16 – 20). The first line of the first stanza of the first sequence (v. 5) begins with "Come and see"; the first line of the second stanza of the second sequence (v. 16) begins with "Come and hear."

66 title See notes on Ps 4; 30 titles.

66:1 – 4 Calling all the earth to joyful praise.

66:1 *all the earth.* See note on 65:2.

66:2 *name.* See note on 5:11.

66:3 *awesome.* See v. 5; see also note on 65:5. *cringe.* See 18:44; cf. Jos 5:1; 2Ch 20:29.

66:4 See note on 46:10. For *Selah,* see NIV text note and note on 3:2.

5 Come and see what God has done,
his awesome deeds[g] for mankind!
6 He turned the sea into dry land,[h]
they passed through[i] the waters on foot—
come, let us rejoice[j] in him.
7 He rules forever[k] by his power,
his eyes watch[l] the nations—
let not the rebellious[m] rise up against him.

8 Praise[n] our God, all peoples,
let the sound of his praise be heard;
9 he has preserved our lives[o]
and kept our feet from slipping.[p]
10 For you, God, tested[q] us;
you refined us like silver.[r]
11 You brought us into prison[s]
and laid burdens[t] on our backs.
12 You let people ride over our heads;[u]
we went through fire and water,
but you brought us to a place of abundance.[v]

13 I will come to your temple with burnt offerings[w]
and fulfill my vows[x] to you—
14 vows my lips promised and my mouth spoke
when I was in trouble.

66:5 [g] ver 3; Ps 106:22 **66:6** [h] S Ge 8:1; S Ex 14:22 [i] 1Co 10:1 [j] S Lev 23:40 **66:7** [k] S Ex 15:18; Ps 145:13 [l] S Ex 3:16; S Ps 11:4 [m] S Nu 17:10; Ps 112:10; 140:8 **66:8** [n] S Ps 22:23 **66:9** [o] Ps 30:3 [p] S Dt 32:35; S Job 12:5 **66:10** [q] S Ex 15:25 [r] S Job 6:29; S 28:1; S Ps 12:6 **66:11** [s] Ps 142:7; 146:7; Isa 42:7, 22; 61:1 [t] S Ge 3:17; S Ex 1:14; Ps 38:4; Isa 10:27 **66:12** [u] Isa 51:23 [v] Ps 18:19 **66:13** [w] S Ps 51:19 [x] Ps 22:25; 50:14; 116:14; Ecc 5:4; Jnh 2:9 **66:15** [y] S Lev 16:5; Ps 51:19 **66:16** [z] Ps 34:11 [a] Ps 71:15, 24

15 I will sacrifice fat animals to you
and an offering of rams;
I will offer bulls and goats.[y]

16 Come and hear,[z] all you who fear God;
let me tell[a] you what he has done for me.
17 I cried out to him with my mouth;
his praise was on my tongue.
18 If I had cherished sin in my heart,
the Lord would not have listened;[b]
19 but God has surely listened
and has heard[c] my prayer.
20 Praise be to God,
who has not rejected[d] my prayer
or withheld his love from me!

Psalm 67[a]

For the director of music.
With stringed instruments.
A psalm. A song.

1 May God be gracious to us and bless us
and make his face shine on us—[be]

[a] In Hebrew texts 67:1-7 is numbered 67:2-8. [b] *1* The Hebrew has *Selah* (a word of uncertain meaning) here and at the end of verse 4.

66:18 [b] S Dt 1:45; S 1Sa 8:18; Jas 4:3 **66:19** [c] S Ps 18:6 **66:20** [d] Ps 22:24 **67:1** [e] Nu 6:24-26

66:5–7 Recollection of God's deliverance of Israel at the "Red Sea" as a sign of his power to rule over the nations. The psalmist portrays his deliverance (see introduction above) both as similar to this "Red Sea" rescue in its manifestation of God's saving power (see 65:5–7 for a comparison of God's mighty saving acts with his mighty acts of creation) and as a continuation of God's same saving purposes.
66:5 *Come and see.* See introduction to this psalm. God's saving acts of old can still be "seen" at his temple, where they are continually celebrated (see 46:8; 48:8–9 and notes). *for mankind.* Specifically for his people.
66:6 *waters.* Possibly the Jordan, but more likely a parallel reference to the "Red Sea."
66:7 *rebellious.* Nations that are in revolt against God's rule (see 68:6).
66:8–12 Praise of God's deliverance of his people.
66:8 *peoples.* Here probably the grateful throng of worshipers (see 2Ch 20:27–28).
66:9 *from slipping.* See note on 38:16.
66:10 *tested ... refined.* From one point of view, times of distress constitute a testing of God's people as to their trust in and loyalty to God. The metaphor is borrowed from the technology of refining precious metals, which included heating the metals in a crucible to see if all impurities had been removed (see 12:6 and note; 17:3).
66:11–12 *You ... You.* God's rule is all-pervasive; even when enemies maliciously oppress his people, God is not a mere passive observer but has his own holy purposes in it (see Isa 45:7; Am 3:6). *prison ... burdens ... ride over.* Probably recalling the Egyptian oppression from which the exodus brought relief.
66:12 *fire and water.* Conventional metaphors for severe trials (see Isa 43:2). *to a place of abundance.* Lit. "to an overflowing" (see 23:5). God's people were brought out of a situation of distress into a situation of overflowing blessings: the promised land.
66:13–15 Announcement of fulfillment of vows: addressed to God (see note on 7:17; see also 50:14; 116:17–19).
66:13 *I.* The king.
66:16–20 Proclamation of what God has done for the psalmist—in praise of God and addressed to the worshiping congregation (cf. 34:1–7).
66:16 *Come and hear.* See introduction. *fear God.* See notes on 15:4; Ge 20:11; Pr 1:7; Lk 12:5.
66:17 *his praise.* Prayer and praise belonged together in the OT (see also Php 4:6; 1Ti 2:1).
66:20 *Praise be to God.* See v. 8. *love.* See note on 6:4.
Ps 67 A communal prayer for God's blessing. Its content, form and brevity suggest that it served as a liturgical prayer of the people at the conclusion of worship, perhaps just prior to (or immediately after) the priestly benediction (see note on v. 1). God's blessing of his people (as well as his saving acts in their behalf) will catch the attention of the nations and move them to praise him (see 65:2). This psalm is the third in a series of four having special thematic links with Ps 65 (see introduction to Ps 65–68). It has a completely symmetrical structure: Two verses at the beginning contain the prayer, while the two verses of the concluding stanza speak of the effects of God's answer. In the intervening stanza, framed by a refrain (vv. 3,5), the people seek to motivate God's answer by referring to the worldwide praise that his mercies to his people will awaken.
67 title See notes on Ps 4; 30 titles.
67:1–2 The prayer.
67:1 The heart of the prayer, anticipating (or echoing) the priestly benediction (see Nu 6:24–26 and notes). *make his face shine.* See notes on 4:6; 13:1. For *Selah*, see NIV text note and note on 3:2.

2 so that your ways may be known on
earth,
your salvation[f] among all nations.[g]
3 May the peoples praise you, God;
may all the peoples praise you.[h]
4 May the nations be glad and sing for
joy,
for you rule the peoples with equity[j]
and guide the nations of the earth.[k]
5 May the peoples praise you, God;
may all the peoples praise you.
6 The land yields its harvest;[l]
God, our God, blesses us.[m]
7 May God bless us still,
so that all the ends of the earth[n] will
fear him.[o]

Psalm 68[a]

For the director of music. Of David.
A psalm. A song.

1 May God arise,[p] may his enemies be
scattered;[q]
may his foes flee[r] before him.
2 May you blow them away like smoke—[s]
as wax melts[t] before the fire,
may the wicked perish[u] before God.
3 But may the righteous be glad
and rejoice[v] before God;
may they be happy and joyful.

4 Sing to God, sing in praise of his name,[w]
extol him who rides on the clouds[bx];
rejoice before him—his name is the
LORD.[y]
5 A father to the fatherless,[z] a defender
of widows,[a]
is God in his holy dwelling.[b]
6 God sets the lonely[c] in families,[cd]
he leads out the prisoners[e] with
singing;
but the rebellious live in a sun-
scorched land.[f]

67:2 [f]Isa 40:5; 52:10; 62:1 [g]Ps 98:2; Isa 62:2; Ac 10:35; Titus 2:11 **67:3** [h]ver 5 **67:4** [i]Ps 100:1-2 [j]S Ps 9:4; 96:10-13 [k]Ps 68:32 **67:6** [l]S Ge 8:22; S Lev 26:4; Ps 85:12; Isa 55:10; Eze 34:27; Zec 8:12 [m]S Ge 12:2 **67:7** [n]S Ps 2:8 [o]Ps 33:8 **68:1** [p]Ps 12:5; 132:8 [q]Ps 18:14; 89:10; 92:9; 144:6 [r]Nu 10:35; Isa 17:13; 21:15; 33:3 **68:2** [s]S Ps 37:20 [t]S Ps 22:14 [u]S Nu 10:35; Ps 9:3; 80:16 **68:3** [v]Ps 64:10; 97:12

[a] In Hebrew texts 68:1-35 is numbered 68:2-36.
[b] 4 Or *name, / prepare the way for him who rides through the deserts* [c] 6 Or *the desolate in a homeland*

68:4 [w]S 2Sa 22:50; Ps 7:17; S 30:4; 66:2; 96:2; 100:4; 135:3 [x]ver 33; S Ex 20:21; S Dt 33:26 [y]S Ex 6:3; Ps 83:18 **68:5** [z]Ps 10:14 [a]S Ex 22:22; S Dt 10:18 [b]S Dt 26:15; Jer 25:30 **68:6** [c]Ps 25:16 [d]Ps 113:9 [e]Ps 79:11; 102:20; 146:7; Isa 61:1; Lk 4:18 [f]Isa 35:7; 49:10; 58:11

67:2 May God's favors to his people be so obvious that all the world takes notice (see note on 46:10).

67:3–5 The motivation. Elaborating on v. 2, the people speak of the worldwide praise that will resound to God when he graciously blesses his people. Their wish is twofold: (1) that God's blessings may be so abundant that the people will be moved to praise him, and (2) that the nations may indeed add their praise to that of Israel—an appropriate expression at this climax of the liturgy of worship.

67:4 May the nations rejoice in the Lord when they see how benevolent the rule of God is (see 65:7–8; 98:4–6; 100:1).

67:6–7 The effects of God's blessing his people.

67:6 The promised land will yield its abundance (see 65:9–13).

67:7 *all the ... earth.* See 65:8 and note. *fear him.* See note on 66:16.

Ps 68 A hymn celebrating the triumphal march of Israel's God from Mount Sinai to Mount Zion. Interwoven in it is a prayer that this mighty display of God's power will be continued until all God's people are rescued and secure and all kingdoms of the earth bring tribute to and sing the praises of the God of Israel. The voice heard here is that of the worshiping community, and the psalm may originally have accompanied a liturgical procession of the people up to the temple in Jerusalem (see introductions to Ps 24; 47; 118; 132). The first half of the psalm (vv. 1–18 have 19 Hebrew poetic lines) contains many clear references to God's triumphal march from Mount Sinai (in the days of Moses) to Mount Zion (in the days of David). The events at Mount Sinai marked the birth of the kingdom of God among his people Israel; the placement of the ark of the covenant (the footstool of God's throne) in the temple in Jerusalem marked the establishment of God's redemptive kingdom among the nations of the earth, with Jerusalem as its royal city. The second half of the psalm (vv. 19–35 also have 19 Hebrew poetic lines) is framed by the cry "Praise be to the Lord/God" and looks forward with expectations of God's continuing triumphs until the redemption of his people is complete and his kingly rule is universally acknowledged with songs of praise. The early church, taking its cue from Eph 4:8–13, understood this psalm to foreshadow the resurrection, ascension and present rule of Christ and the final triumph of his church over the hostile world. Ps 68 is the last in a series of four (see introduction to Ps 65–68).

The psalm is composed of nine stanzas, with a concluding doxology. The first stanza (vv. 1–3) suggests the beginning of a liturgical procession, and the last (vv. 32–35) its conclusion, with God enthroned in his sanctuary. The seventh (vv. 24–27) speaks expressly of a procession coming into view and entering the sanctuary. In light of these clear references, the third stanza (vv. 7–10) suggests a stage in the procession recalling the wilderness journey from Sinai to the promised land, while the fifth (vv. 15–18) marks that stage in which the Lord ascends Mount Zion. On the other hand, the second stanza (vv. 4–6) reflects on the benevolence of God's rule; the fourth (vv. 11–14) recalls his victories over the kings of Canaan; the sixth (vv. 19–23) speaks reassuringly of God's future victories; and the eighth (vv. 28–31) contains prayers that God may muster his power to subdue the enemy as he had done before.

68 title See notes on Ps 4; 30 titles.

68:1–3 The start of the procession, liturgically recalling the beginning of God's march with his people in army formation from Sinai (see Nu 10:33–35).

68:1 *enemies be scattered.* See note on v. 30.

68:3 *righteous.* Israel as the committed people of God in distinction from those opposed to the coming of God's kingdom (the "wicked" of v. 2); see 1:5 and note.

68:4–6 A call to praise God for the benevolence of his rule.

68:4 *name.* See note on 5:11. *who rides on the clouds.* An epithet of Baal found in Canaanite literature is used to make the point that the Lord (Yahweh, not Baal) is the exalted One who truly makes the storm cloud his chariot (see v. 33; 18:9; 104:3; Dt 33:26; Isa 19:1; Mt 26:64).

68:5–6 God is the defender of the powerless (see 10:14; 146:7–9; 147:6; Dt 10:18).

68:6 *sets the lonely in families.* See Ex 1:21; Ru 4:14–17; 1Sa 2:5. *leads out the prisoners.* As he led Israel out of Egypt (see 69:33; 107:10,14). *rebellious.* See notes on v. 18; 66:7. *sun-scorched land.* A place utterly barren, lacking even soil for vegetation (see Eze 26:4,14).

[7] When you, God, went out[g] before your
people,
when you marched through the
wilderness,[a][h]
[8] the earth shook,[i] the heavens poured
down rain,[j]
before God, the One of Sinai,[k]
before God, the God of Israel.[l]
[9] You gave abundant showers,[m]
O God;
you refreshed your weary
inheritance.
[10] Your people settled in it,
and from your bounty,[n] God, you
provided[o] for the poor.

[11] The Lord announces the word,
and the women who proclaim it are
a mighty throng:[p]
[12] "Kings and armies flee[q] in haste;
the women at home divide the
plunder.[r]
[13] Even while you sleep among the sheep
pens,[b][s]
the wings of my dove are sheathed
with silver,
its feathers with shining gold."
[14] When the Almighty[c] scattered[t] the
kings in the land,
it was like snow fallen on Mount
Zalmon.[u]

68:7 [g] S Ex 13:21 [h] Ps 78:40; 106:14 **68:8** [i] S 2Sa 22:8 [j] S Jdg 5:4; 2Sa 21:10; Ecc 11:3 [k] S Dt 33:2 [l] S Jdg 5:5 **68:9** [m] S Dt 32:2; S Job 36:28; S Eze 34:26 **68:10** [n] S Dt 28:12 [o] Ps 65:9 **68:11** [p] Lk 2:13 **68:12** [q] Jos 10:16 [r] S Jdg 5:30 **68:13** [s] S Ge 49:14 **68:14** [t] 2Sa 22:15 [u] Jdg 9:48

68:15 [v] ver 22; Nu 21:33; Jer 22:20 [w] S Ps 36:6 **68:16** [x] Dt 12:5; S Ps 2:6; 132:13 [y] Ps 132:14 **68:17** [z] S 2Ki 2:11; Isa 66:15; Hab 3:8 [a] Da 7:10 **68:18** [b] S Ps 47:5 [c] Ps 7:7 [d] Jdg 5:12

[15] Mount Bashan,[v] majestic mountain,[w]
Mount Bashan, rugged mountain,
[16] why gaze in envy, you rugged
mountain,
at the mountain where God chooses[x]
to reign,
where the LORD himself will dwell
forever?[y]
[17] The chariots[z] of God are tens of
thousands
and thousands of thousands;[a]
the Lord has come from Sinai into
his sanctuary.[d]
[18] When you ascended[b] on high,[c]
you took many captives;[d]
you received gifts from people,[e]
even from[e] the rebellious[f]—
that you,[f] LORD God, might dwell
there.

[19] Praise be to the Lord, to God our
Savior,[g]
who daily bears our burdens.[h]

[a] 7 The Hebrew has *Selah* (a word of uncertain meaning) here and at the end of verses 19 and 32. [b] 13 Or *the campfires;* or *the saddlebags* [c] 14 Hebrew *Shaddai* [d] 17 Probable reading of the original Hebrew text; Masoretic Text *Lord is among them at Sinai in holiness* [e] 18 Or *gifts for people, / even* [f] 18 Or *they*

[e] Eph 4:8* [f] S Nu 17:10 **68:19** [g] S Ps 65:5 [h] Ps 81:6

68:7–10 Recollection of God's march through the wilderness from Sinai into the promised land (see Jdg 5:4–5; Hab 3:3–6).
68:7 For *Selah,* see NIV text note and note on 3:2.
68:8 *earth shook.* A reference to the quaking of Mount Sinai (Ex 19:18). *heavens poured down rain.* The Pentateuch preserves no tradition of rain during the wilderness wanderings, but here (and in Jdg 5:4) rain is closely associated with the quaking of the earth as a manifestation of the majesty of God. Perhaps the "thunder and lightning, with a thick cloud" over Mount Sinai (Ex 19:16) were accompanied by rain. But see also v. 9, which suggests rains that refreshed the people on their journey.
68:9 *your ... inheritance.* The people of Israel (see Dt 9:29).
68:10 *it.* Probably refers to the promised land. *bounty.* Lit. "goodness" (see 65:11 and note). *provided.* From the produce of Canaan (see Jos 5:11–12). *poor.* Israel as a people dependent on God.
68:11–14 Recollection of God's victories over the kings of Canaan.
68:11 *announces the word.* God declares beforehand that he will be victorious over the Canaanite kings (see Ex 23:22–23,27–28,31; Dt 7:10–24; 11:23–25; Jos 1:2–6). *proclaim it.* Celebrate God's victories (see Ex 15:1–21; 1Sa 18:6–7; 2Ch 20:26–28). *proclaim.* See 40:9 and note.
68:13 *sleep among the sheep pens.* Rest in camp (see Jdg 5:16; see also NIV text note). *wings of my dove are sheathed.* Israel, God's "dove" (see 74:19 and note; cf. Hos 7:11), is enriched with the silver and gold of plunder from the kings of Canaan even though she still remains in camp. This poetic hyperbole (a figure of speech that uses exaggeration for emphasis) celebrates the fact that God had defeated the kings even before Israel met them in battle (see Jos 2:8–11; 5:1; 6:16; see also 2Sa 5:24; 2Ki 7:5–7; 19:35; 2Ch 20:22–30).
68:14 *Almighty.* See NIV text note; see also note on Ge 17:1. *like snow fallen on Mount Zalmon.* A mountain near Shechem bore this name (see Jdg 9:46–48), but some identify the mountain referred to here as Jebel Druze, a dark volcanic mountain east of Bashan. Its name appears to mean "the dark one"—in distinction from the Lebanon ("the white one") range, composed of limestone—and the figure may involve the contrast of white snow scattered on "Dark Mountain." The reference may then be to abandoned weapons littering the field from which the kings have fled headlong (see 2Ki 7:15).
68:15–18 Celebration of God's ascent to Mount Zion.
68:15–16 The mountains surrounding Bashan, including the towering Mount Hermon, are portrayed as being jealous because God has chosen Mount Zion as the seat of his rule, making it the "highest" of mountains (see 48:2 and note).
68:17 *chariots of God.* God's great heavenly host, here likened to a vast chariot force (see 2Ki 6:17; Hab 3:8,15). In the time of the Roman Empire Jesus referred to God's host in terms of "legions" (Mt 26:53).
68:18 *ascended on high.* Went up to your place of enthronement on Mount Zion (see 47:5–6 and note; see also 7:7). *took many captives ... received gifts.* Like a victorious king after triumphs on the field of battle. *rebellious.* Those who had opposed the kingdom of God (see v. 6 and note on 66:7) are compelled to submit to him and bring tribute. *that you ... might dwell there.* Grammatically completes the clause, "When you ascended on high." Paul applies this verse (as translated in the Septuagint, the pre-Christian Greek translation of the OT) to the ascended Christ (see Eph 4:8–13 and notes on 4:8–9,11), thereby implying that Christ's ascension was a continuation of, and a fulfillment of, God's establishment of his kingdom in his royal city, Jerusalem (see introduction to this psalm).
68:19–23 Joyous confession of hope that God's victorious campaigns will continue until the salvation of his people is complete.
68:19 *bears our burdens.* Releases us from bearing the burdens that enslavement to our enemies would impose on us

20 Our God is a God who saves;[i]
from the Sovereign LORD comes
escape from death.[j]
21 Surely God will crush the heads[k] of his
enemies,
the hairy crowns of those who go on
in their sins.
22 The Lord says, "I will bring them from
Bashan;
I will bring them from the depths of
the sea,[l]
23 that your feet may wade in the blood
of your foes,[m]
while the tongues of your dogs[n] have
their share."

24 Your procession, God, has come into
view,
the procession of my God and King
into the sanctuary.[o]
25 In front are the singers,[p] after them the
musicians;[q]
with them are the young women
playing the timbrels.[r]
26 Praise God in the great congregation;[s]
praise the LORD in the assembly of
Israel.[t]
27 There is the little tribe[u] of Benjamin,[v]
leading them,
there the great throng of Judah's
princes,
and there the princes of Zebulun and
of Naphtali.[w]

28 Summon your power,[x] God[a];
show us your strength,[y] our God, as
you have done[z] before.
29 Because of your temple at Jerusalem
kings will bring you gifts.[a]

68:20 [i]S 1Sa 10:19 [j]Ps 56:13; Jer 45:5; Eze 6:8 **68:21** [k]Ps 74:14; 110:5; Hab 3:13 **68:22** [l]S Job 36:30; Mt 18:6 **68:23** [m]Ps 58:10 [n]S 1Ki 21:19; S 2Ki 9:36 **68:24** [o]S Ps 63:2 **68:25** [p]S 1Ch 15:16 [q]S 1Ch 6:31; S 2Ch 5:12; Rev 18:22 [r]S Ge 31:27; S Isa 5:12 **68:26** [s]S Ps 22:22; Heb 2:12 [t]S Lev 19:2 **68:27** [u]S 1Sa 9:21 [v]S Nu 34:21 [w]S Jdg 5:18 **68:28** [x]S Ex 9:16 [y]Ps 29:11 [z]Isa 26:12; 29:23; 45:11; 60:21; 64:8 **68:29** [a]S 2Ch 9:24; S 32:23 **68:30** [b]Isa 27:1; 51:9; Eze 29:3 [c]S Job 40:21 [d]Ps 22:12; Isa 34:7; Jer 50:27 [e]Ps 18:14; 89:10 [f]Ps 120:7; 140:2 **68:31** [g]Isa 19:19; 43:3; 45:14 [h]Isa 11:11; 18:1; Zep 3:10 **68:32** [i]S Ps 46:6; 67:4 [j]Ps 7:17 **68:33** [k]S Dt 33:26 [l]S Ex 9:23; S Ps 29:3 [m]Ps 29:4; Isa 30:30; 33:3; 66:6 **68:34** [n]ver 28 [o]Ps 45:3 **68:35** [p]S Dt 7:21 [q]S Ge 28:17 [r]Ps 18:1; Isa 40:29; 41:10; 50:2 [s]S Ps 29:11 [t]Ps 28:6; 66:20; 2Co 1:3 **69:1** [u]S Ps 42:7 [v]Ps 32:6; Jnh 2:5

30 Rebuke the beast[b] among the reeds,[c]
the herd of bulls[d] among the calves
of the nations.
Humbled, may the beast bring bars of
silver.
Scatter the nations[e] who delight in war.[f]
31 Envoys will come from Egypt;[g]
Cush[b][h] will submit herself to God.
32 Sing to God, you kingdoms of the
earth,[i]
sing praise[j] to the Lord,
33 to him who rides[k] across the highest
heavens, the ancient heavens,
who thunders[l] with mighty voice.[m]
34 Proclaim the power[n] of God,
whose majesty[o] is over Israel,
whose power is in the heavens.
35 You, God, are awesome[p] in your
sanctuary;[q]
the God of Israel gives power and
strength[r] to his people.[s]

Praise be to God![t]

Psalm 69[c]

For the director of music.
To the tune of "Lilies." Of David.

1 Save me, O God,
for the waters[u] have come up to my
neck.[v]

[a] *28* Many Hebrew manuscripts, Septuagint and Syriac; most Hebrew manuscripts *Your God has summoned power for you* [b] *31* That is, the upper Nile region
[c] In Hebrew texts 69:1-36 is numbered 69:2-37.

(see 81:6; Isa 9:4; 10:27). But some associate this line with such passages as 55:22; Isa 46:4.
68:20 *escape from death.* At the hand of our enemies—implicitly, perhaps, also from death itself as the last great enemy (see notes on 6:5; 11:7; 16:9–11; 17:15; 49:14–15).
68:21 As God assures the life of his people (see v. 20), so he will crush those who oppose him. *crush the heads.* See Nu 24:17; Jer 48:45–46 and note.
68:22 *them.* The enemies who fled at the victorious onward march of God and his host (see vv. 12,17). *Bashan ... depths of the sea.* The former (see also v. 15) was the high plateau east of the Jordan, the latter the Mediterranean Sea—none of the enemies will escape (see Am 9:1–4).
68:23 See note on 58:10.
68:24–27 The liturgical procession approaches the temple (see Ps 24; 47).
68:25 *young women playing the timbrels.* See note on Jer 31:4.
68:27 All Israel is represented, from little Benjamin to powerful Judah, and tribes from the north as well as the south. *Benjamin, leading.* Perhaps reflecting the fact that from the tribe of Benjamin came the first king (Saul), who began the royal victories over Israel's enemies (see 1Sa 11:11; 14:20–23).
68:28–31 Prayer for God to continue his conquest of the threatening powers.
68:28 *Summon your power.* Or, perhaps, "Command your power to act."
68:29 *Because of your temple.* Because your earthly royal house has been established in Jerusalem. *bring you gifts.* Acknowledge you by bringing tribute, as subjected kings brought tribute to their conquerors (see 2Sa 8:2,6,10; 2Ki 3:4).
68:30 *Rebuke.* See note on 76:6. *beast among the reeds.* The pharaoh (see Eze 29:3). *herd of bulls among the calves.* Powerful princes supporting the pharaoh, and the lesser princes of other nations. Egypt is singled out here as representative of the hostile nations—because of Israel's past experiences with that world power. It may also be that at the time the psalm was composed Egypt was the one great empire on Israel's immediate horizons. *Scatter the nations.* See v. 1; so that Israel may have peace (see 46:9; 48:4–7; 65:7; 76:3).
68:32–35 Climax of the liturgical procession: a call for all kingdoms to hail with praise the God of Israel as the God who reigns in heaven and has established his earthly throne in the temple in Jerusalem (see Ps 47).
68:33 See v. 4 and note. *thunders with mighty voice.* See note on 29:3–9.
68:35 *awesome.* See 45:4 and note. *gives power and strength to his people.* The Lord of all has made Israel his people (his "kingdom"; see Ex 19:5–6), and his rule among them makes them participants in his victorious power (see 29:10–11).
Ps 69–72 Book II of the Psalter closes with a cluster of three

[2]I sink in the miry depths,[w]
where there is no foothold.
I have come into the deep waters;
the floods engulf me.
[3]I am worn out calling for help;[x]
my throat is parched.
My eyes fail,[y]
looking for my God.
[4]Those who hate me[z] without reason[a]
outnumber the hairs of my head;
many are my enemies without cause,[b]
those who seek to destroy me.[c]
I am forced to restore
what I did not steal.

[5]You, God, know my folly;[d]
my guilt is not hidden from you.[e]

[6]Lord, the LORD Almighty,
may those who hope in you
not be disgraced because of me;
God of Israel,
may those who seek you
not be put to shame because
of me.
[7]For I endure scorn[f] for your sake,[g]
and shame covers my face.[h]
[8]I am a foreigner to my own family,
a stranger to my own mother's
children;[i]
[9]for zeal for your house consumes me,[j]
and the insults of those who insult
you fall on me.[k]
[10]When I weep and fast,[l]
I must endure scorn;
[11]when I put on sackcloth,[m]
people make sport of me.
[12]Those who sit at the gate[n] mock me,
and I am the song of the drunkards.[o]

[13]But I pray to you, LORD,
in the time of your favor;[p]
in your great love,[q] O God,
answer me with your sure salvation.

69:2 [w]S Job 30:19 **69:3** [x]Ps 6:6 [y]Ps 119:82 **69:4** [z]S Ps 25:19 [a]Jn 15:25* [b]S Ps 35:19; 38:19 [c]Ps 40:14; 119:95; Isa 32:7 **69:5** [d]Ps 38:5 [e]S Ps 44:21 **69:7** [f]S Ps 39:8 [g]Jer 15:15 [h]Ps 44:15 **69:8** [i]Job 19:13-15; Ps 31:11; 38:11; Isa 53:3; Jn 7:5 **69:9** [j]Jn 2:17* [k]Ps 89:50-51; Ro 15:3* **69:10** [l]S Ps 35:13 **69:11** [m]S 2Sa 3:31; S Ps 35:13 **69:12** [n]S Ge 18:1; S 23:10 [o]Job 30:9 **69:13** [p]Isa 49:8; 2Co 6:2 [q]S Ps 17:7; 51:1

prayers and an attached royal psalm — in perfect balance with its beginning (see note on Ps 42 – 45). These three prayers were originally all pleas of a king in Israel for deliverance from enemies (apparently internal) determined to do away with him. They all contain certain key words that are found elsewhere in Book II only in Ps 42 – 44 and in the seven psalms (54 – 60) placed at the center of the Book. Another link between Ps 69 – 71 and 42 – 44 is the placement of a short psalm at the center of each triad. These placements have the appearance of deliberate editorial design. In the former cluster Ps 43 has been artificially separated from 42 (see introduction to Ps 42 – 43), while in the latter cluster Ps 70 repeats (with some revision) Ps 40:13 – 17 and was probably intended to serve as an introduction to Ps 71. The attached prayer for the king (Ps 72) stands in similar relationship to Ps 69 – 71 as Ps 45 stands to Ps 42 – 44 and brings Book II to its conclusion. Thus, as with Ps 45, its placement hints at a Messianic reading of the psalm already by the editors of the Psalter (see also introduction to Ps 72). In Ps 65 – 68 all peoples on earth are drawn into the community of those praising God (see note on Ps 65 – 68). Here in Ps 69 all creation is called to join that chorus (v. 34), and Ps 72 envisions that all peoples and kings will submit to the son of David (vv. 8 – 11) and be blessed through his reign (v. 17).

Ps 69 A plea for God to have mercy and to save from a host of enemies: the prayer of a godly king when under vicious attack by a widespread conspiracy at a time when God had wounded him (see v. 26) for some sin in his life (see v. 5). If, as tradition claims, David authored the original psalm (see title), the occasion is unknown. In its present form the prayer suggests a later son of David who ruled over the southern kingdom of Judah (see v. 35). That king may have been Hezekiah (see 2Ki 18 – 20; 2Ch 29 – 32). This psalm begins a series of three prayers for deliverance when threatened by enemies (see introduction to Ps 69 – 72). Structurally, the psalm is composed of two halves of 22 Hebrew lines each. The first half (vv. 1 – 15) ends with petitions that echo the descriptions of distress at the beginning. It should also be noted that in Hebrew v. 5 stands at the center of vv. 1 – 12 and v. 29 stands at the center of vv. 22 – 36. The centering of these two verses accounts for why they both stand thematically somewhat apart from their immediate contexts (for this literary device, see note on 6:6; for the thematic relationship of these two verses, see notes below). The authors of the NT viewed this cry of a godly sufferer as foreshadowing the sufferings of Christ; no other psalm, except Ps 22, is quoted more frequently in the NT.

69 title *For the director of music.* See note on Ps 4 title. *To the tune of.* See note on Ps 9 title. *Lilies.* See note on Ps 45 title.

69:1 – 4 Description of the dire distress that evokes the psalmist's prayer.

69:1 – 2 *waters … miry depths … deep waters … floods.* Conventional imagery for great distress (see notes on 30:1; 32:6) — here the results of God's wounding (see v. 26), but especially of the attacks of the enemies (see vv. 14 – 15,29).

69:3 *throat is parched.* See 22:15. *eyes fail.* See 6:7 and note.

69:4 *without reason … without cause.* Those whom he has not wronged are pitted against him (see 35:19 and note). *outnumber the hairs of my head.* See note on 40:12. *I am forced.* An illustrative way of saying that his enemies are spreading false accusations about him (see 5:9 and note).

69:5 A confession of personal guilt — the reason why God has wounded him (see v. 26) and why he is "afflicted and in pain" (v. 29). *folly.* See NIV text note on 14:1.

69:6 – 12 Prayer that God's discipline of his godly servant may not bring disgrace on all those who trustingly look to the Lord. The author acknowledges that God's wounding of him has been occasioned by some sin in his life (but he has not sinned against those who have become his enemies). Because of his present suffering, his enemies mock his deep commitment to the Lord (see 22:6 – 8; 42:3; 79:10; 115:2; Job 2:9). Implicitly he prays that God will restore him again and vindicate his trust in him.

69:8 Even those nearest him dissociate themselves from him (see 31:11 – 12 and note).

69:9 *zeal for your house.* What was true of the author was even more true of Jesus (see Jn 2:17). *insults of those who insult you.* Those who mock God also mock his servant who trusts in him (see 74:18,22 – 23; 2Ki 18:31 – 35), as Christ also experienced (see Ro 15:3).

69:10 – 11 *weep and fast … put on sackcloth.* As tokens of humbling himself before the Lord in repentance as he prays for God to have mercy and restore him (see 35:13 and note; see also Ge 37:34; 2Sa 12:16 – 17; Joel 1:13 – 14; 2:15 – 17; Jnh 3:5).

69:12 *Those who sit at the gate … drunkards.* Everyone, from the elders of the city to the town drunks.

69:13 – 15 Though they mock, I pray to you.

69:13 *time of your favor.* When God is near to save (see 32:6 and note; see also Isa 49:8; 61:2; 2Co 6:2). *great love.* See note on 6:4.

14 Rescue me from the mire,
do not let me sink;
deliver me from those who hate me,
from the deep waters.[r]
15 Do not let the floodwaters[s] engulf me
or the depths swallow me up[t]
or the pit close its mouth over me.[u]

16 Answer me, LORD, out of the goodness of your love;[v]
in your great mercy turn to me.
17 Do not hide your face[w] from your servant;
answer me quickly,[x] for I am in trouble.[y]
18 Come near and rescue me;
deliver[z] me because of my foes.

19 You know how I am scorned,[a]
disgraced and shamed;
all my enemies are before you.
20 Scorn has broken my heart
and has left me helpless;
I looked for sympathy, but there was none,
for comforters,[b] but I found none.[c]
21 They put gall in my food
and gave me vinegar[d] for my thirst.[e]

22 May the table set before them become a snare;
may it become retribution and[a] a trap.[f]
23 May their eyes be darkened so they cannot see,
and their backs be bent forever.[g]
24 Pour out your wrath[h] on them;
let your fierce anger overtake them.
25 May their place be deserted;[i]
let there be no one to dwell in their tents.[j]
26 For they persecute those you wound
and talk about the pain of those you hurt.[k]
27 Charge them with crime upon crime;[l]
do not let them share in your salvation.[m]
28 May they be blotted out of the book of life[n]
and not be listed with the righteous.[o]

29 But as for me, afflicted and in pain —
may your salvation, God, protect me.[p]

30 I will praise God's name in song[q]
and glorify him[r] with thanksgiving.
31 This will please the LORD more than an ox,
more than a bull with its horns and hooves.[s]
32 The poor will see and be glad[t] —
you who seek God, may your hearts live![u]

[a] 22 Or *snare / and their fellowship become*

69:14 [r] ver 2; Ps 144:7 **69:15** [s] Ps 124:4-5 [t] Nu 16:33 [u] Ps 28:1 **69:16** [v] S Ps 63:3 **69:17** [w] S Ps 22:24 [x] Ps 143:7 [y] S Ps 50:15; 66:14 **69:18** [z] Ps 49:15 **69:19** [a] S Ps 22:6 **69:20** [b] Job 16:2 [c] Ps 142:4; Isa 63:5 **69:21** [d] S Nu 6:3; Mt 27:48; Mk 15:36; Lk 23:36 [e] Mt 27:34; Mk 15:23; Jn 19:28-30 **69:22** [f] S 1Sa 28:9; S Job 18:10 **69:23** [g] Ro 11:9-10* **69:24** [h] Ps 79:6; Jer 10:25 **69:25** [i] S Lev 26:43; Mt 23:38 [j] Ac 1:20* **69:26** [k] S Job 19:22; Zec 1:15 **69:27** [l] Ne 4:5 [m] Ps 109:14 **69:28** [n] Ex 32:32-33; S Lk 10:20 [o] Eze 13:9 **69:29** [p] S Ps 20:1 **69:30** [q] Ps 28:7 [r] Ps 34:3 **69:31** [s] Ps 50:9-13; 51:16 **69:32** [t] S Ps 34:2 [u] Ps 22:26

69:14–15 *mire ... deep waters ... floodwaters ... depths.* See note on vv. 1–2. The psalmists' petitions commonly echo their earlier descriptions of the distress that occasions the prayer. Here the return to the beginning marks the end of the first half of the psalmist's appeal to God.
69:15 *swallow me.* See note on 49:14. *pit.* See note on 30:1.
69:16–18 An appeal for God to hear — such as commonly begins the prayers brought together in the Psalter.
69:16 *love.* See note on 6:4.
69:17 *hide your face.* See note on 13:1.
69:19–21 In my trouble they heaped on scorn instead of bringing comfort (see 35:11–16; see also 142:4; Job 13:4; 16:2; 21:34).
69:20 *heart.* See note on 4:7.
69:21 *gall in my food ... vinegar for my thirst.* Vivid metaphors for the bitter scorn they made him eat and drink when his whole being craved the nourishment and refreshment of comfort. The authors of the Gospels, especially Matthew, suggest that the suffering expressed in this verse foreshadowed Christ's suffering on the cross (see Mt 27:34,48; Mk 15:23,36; Lk 23:36; Jn 19:29).
69:22–28 Prayer for God to redress the wrongs committed (see note on 5:10).
69:22–23 For Paul's application of these verses to the Jews who rejected the Christ, see Ro 11:9–10.
69:22 They had set his table with "gall" and "vinegar" (v. 21). *table set before them.* Reference may be to the meal accompanying the sealing of a covenant (see note on 23:5). In that case, this verse alludes to a pact uniting the enemies and calls on God to turn it against them. *become a snare ... a trap.* Note the unusual use of this imagery (see note on 9:15).
69:23 They mocked him for his "wound" (v. 26); now may they experience the same failing of the eyes (see v. 3 and note on 6:7) and bending of the back (from weakness and pain; see 38:5–8). *May ... their backs be bent.* Lit. "May ... their loins give way." "Loins" refers to the belly and lower part of the back; they were viewed as the back's center of strength (see 66:11; see also Job 40:16).
69:24 *wrath ... anger.* See note on 2:5. *overtake them.* Like a flash flood.
69:25 They sought to remove him from his place; may they be removed. Cf. Peter's application of this judgment to Judas (Ac 1:20).
69:26 The great wrong committed by his enemies against him and to which reference has repeatedly been made.
69:27 They have falsely charged him with crimes (v. 4); may their real crimes all be charged against them.
69:28 They had plotted his death; may death be their destiny. *book of life.* God's royal list of the righteous, whom he blesses with life (see 1:3; 7:9; 11:7; 34:12; 37:17,29; 55:22; 75:10; 92:12–14; 140:13). For other references to God's books see notes on 9:5; 51:1. In the NT the "book of life" refers to God's list of those destined for eternal life (see Php 4:3; Rev 3:5 and note; 13:8; 17:8; 20:12,15; 21:27; cf. Lk 10:20; Heb 12:23 and notes).
69:29 A summary renewal of the prayer just prior to the vow to praise God (see note on v. 5). *pain.* An echo of v. 26. *your salvation.* Cf. vv. 13,27. *protect me.* Lit. "raise me to a high, secure place."
69:30–33 A vow to praise God (see note on 7:17) out of assurance that the prayer will be heard (see note on 3:8).
69:30 *God's name.* See v. 36 and note on 5:11.
69:32 *poor.* See note on 34:6. *see and be glad.* See 22:26 and note. *hearts.* See note on 4:7. *live.* Bubble over with

[33]The LORD hears the needy[v]
and does not despise his captive
people.

[34]Let heaven and earth praise him,
the seas and all that move in them,[w]
[35]for God will save Zion[x]
and rebuild the cities of Judah.[y]
Then people will settle there and
possess it;
[36] the children of his servants will
inherit it,[z]
and those who love his name will
dwell there.[a]

Psalm 70[a]

70:1-5pp — Ps 40:13-17

For the director of music.
Of David. A petition.

[1]Hasten, O God, to save me;
come quickly, LORD, to help me.[b]

[2]May those who want to take my life[c]
be put to shame and confusion;
may all who desire my ruin
be turned back in disgrace.[d]
[3]May those who say to me, "Aha!
Aha!"[e]
turn back because of their shame.
[4]But may all who seek you[f]
rejoice and be glad[g] in you;
may those who long for your saving
help always say,
"The LORD is great!"[h]

[5]But as for me, I am poor and needy;[i]
come quickly to me,[j] O God.
You are my help[k] and my deliverer;[l]
LORD, do not delay.[m]

Psalm 71

71:1-3pp — Ps 31:1-4

[1]In you, LORD, I have taken refuge;[n]
let me never be put to shame.[o]
[2]In your righteousness, rescue me and
deliver me;
turn your ear[p] to me and save me.
[3]Be my rock of refuge,
to which I can always go;
give the command to save me,
for you are my rock and my fortress.[q]
[4]Deliver[r] me, my God, from the hand of
the wicked,[s]
from the grasp of those who are evil
and cruel.[t]

[5]For you have been my hope,[u] Sovereign
LORD,
my confidence[v] since my youth.
[6]From birth[w] I have relied on you;
you brought me forth from my
mother's womb.[x]
I will ever praise[y] you.
[7]I have become a sign[z] to many;
you are my strong refuge.[a]

[a] In Hebrew texts 70:1-5 is numbered 70:2-6.

69:33 [v]Ps 12:5 **69:34** [w]Ps 96:11; 98:7; Isa 44:23 **69:35** [x]Ob 1:17 [y]S Ezr 9:9; S Ps 51:18 **69:36** [z]Ps 25:13 [a]S Ps 37:29 **70:1** [b]Ps 22:19; 71:12 **70:2** [c]Ps 35:4 [d]Ps 6:10; 35:26; 71:13; 109:29; 129:5 **70:3** [e]S Ps 35:21 **70:4** [f]Ps 9:10 [g]Ps 31:6-7; 32:11; 118:24 [h]Ps 35:27 **70:5** [i]Ps 86:1; 109:22 [j]Ps 141:1 [k]Ps 30:10; 33:20 [l]Ps 18:2 [m]Ps 119:60 **71:1** [n]S Dt 23:15; Ru 2:12 [o]S Ps 22:5 **71:2** [p]S 2Ki 19:16 **71:3** [q]Ps 18:2 **71:4** [r]S 2Ki 19:19 [s]Ps 140:4 [t]S Ge 48:16 **71:5** [u]S Ps 9:18; S 25:5 [v]S Job 4:6; Jer 17:7 **71:6** [w]S Ps 22:10 [x]S Job 3:16; S Ps 22:9 [y]Ps 9:1; 34:1; 52:9; 119:164; 145:2 **71:7** [z]S Dt 28:46; Isa 8:18; 1Co 4:9 [a]S 2Sa 22:3; Ps 61:3

the joy of life, because the Lord does hear the prayers of his people in need — contrary to the mocking of scoffers.
69:34 – 36 A call for all creation to take up the praise of the Lord (see note on 9:1), a call that confidently anticipates that God will restore Judah and assure his people's inheritance in the promised land.
69:34 See 148:1 – 13; Isa 49:13.
69:35 – 36 *people ... children.* God's people and their children through the generations, specifically "those who love his name."
69:35 *Zion.* See note on 9:11.
Ps 70 An urgent prayer for God's help when threatened by enemies — a somewhat revised duplicate of 40:13 – 17 (see notes there). This is the second in a series of three such prayers; its language has many links with that of Ps 71. For this psalm's placement in the Psalter, see introduction to Ps 69 – 72; for its special relationship to Ps 71, see introduction to that psalm. The prayer is framed by pleas for God to "come quickly" with his help (vv. 1,5). The rest of the prayer focuses on the effects of God's saving help: (1) upon those "who want to take my life" (vv. 2 – 3) and (2) for those "who seek you" (v. 4).
70 title See note on Ps 4 title. *A petition.* See note on Ps 38 title.
70:4 God's deliverance of his servant will give joy to all who trust in the Lord, because they see in it the assurance of their own salvation. *The LORD is great!* Because his saving help is sure and effective (contrast v. 3).
70:5 This verse echoes most of the language of v. 1: "God," "LORD," "come quickly," "(my) help (me)."
Ps 71 A prayer for God's help in old age when enemies threaten because they see that the king's strength is waning (see note on 5:9). The psalm bears no title, but it may well be that Ps 70 was viewed by the editors of the Psalms as the introduction to Ps 71 (compare vv. 1,12 – 13 with 70:1 – 2,5), in which case the psalm is ascribed to David (in his old age; see vv. 9,18). This suggestion gains support from the fact that Ps 72 is identified as a prayer by and/or for King Solomon (see introduction to that psalm). This is the third in a series of three prayers (see introduction to Ps 69 – 72); its dominant theme is hope (see v. 14). Formally symmetrical, the psalm is composed of six stanzas, having a five-four-five, five-four-five (in Hebrew) line pattern: vv. 1 – 4 (five lines), vv. 5 – 8 (four lines), vv. 9 – 13 (five lines), vv. 15 – 18 (five lines), vv. 19 – 21 (four lines), vv. 22 – 24 (five lines). Thus each half is made up of 14 lines. At the center (v. 14; see note on 6:6) stands a confident confession of hope. The whole is framed by an appeal for help (vv. 1 – 4) and a vow to praise God in anticipation of deliverance (vv. 22 – 24). The second and fifth stanzas are linked by references to the troubles the king has experienced; stanzas three and four are linked by references to old age.
71:1 – 4 The initial appeal for God's help. Verses 1 – 3 differ only a little from 31:1 – 3a.
71:2 *your righteousness.* See vv. 15 – 16,19,24; see also note on 4:1.
71:3 *give the command to save.* In Hebrew a noteworthy verbal link with 44:4 ("who decrees victories"). The Hebrew phraseology occurs only in these two places in the OT.
71:5 – 8 A confession that the Lord has always been his hope (see vv. 14,19 – 21).
71:5 – 6 Cf. 22:10 – 11.
71:7 *sign to many.* The troubles of his life (see v. 20) have been viewed by others as holding some special significance — es-

8 My mouth[b] is filled with your praise,
declaring your splendor[c] all day long.
9 Do not cast[d] me away when I am old;[e]
do not forsake[f] me when my strength is gone.
10 For my enemies[g] speak against me;
those who wait to kill[h] me conspire[i] together.
11 They say, "God has forsaken[j] him;
pursue him and seize him,
for no one will rescue[k] him."
12 Do not be far[l] from me, my God;
come quickly, God, to help[m] me.
13 May my accusers[n] perish in shame;[o]
may those who want to harm me
be covered with scorn and disgrace.[p]
14 As for me, I will always have hope;[q]
I will praise you more and more.
15 My mouth will tell[r] of your righteous deeds,[s]
of your saving acts all day long—
though I know not how to relate them all.
16 I will come and proclaim your mighty acts,[t] Sovereign LORD;
I will proclaim your righteous deeds, yours alone.
17 Since my youth, God, you have taught[u] me,
and to this day I declare your marvelous deeds.[v]
18 Even when I am old and gray,[w]
do not forsake me, my God,
till I declare your power[x] to the next generation,
your mighty acts to all who are to come.[y]

19 Your righteousness, God, reaches to the heavens,[z]
you who have done great things.[a]
Who is like you, God?[b]
20 Though you have made me see troubles,[c]
many and bitter,
you will restore[d] my life again;
from the depths of the earth[e]
you will again bring me up.
21 You will increase my honor[f]
and comfort[g] me once more.

22 I will praise you with the harp[h]
for your faithfulness, my God;
I will sing praise to you with the lyre,[i]
Holy One of Israel.[j]
23 My lips will shout for joy[k]
when I sing praise to you—
I whom you have delivered.[l]
24 My tongue will tell of your righteous acts
all day long,[m]
for those who wanted to harm me[n]
have been put to shame and confusion.[o]

71:8 [b] ver 15; Ps 51:15; 63:5 [c] Ps 96:6; 104:1 **71:9** [d] S Ps 51:11 [e] Ps 92:14; Isa 46:4 [f] S Dt 4:31; S 31:6 **71:10** [g] Ps 3:7 [h] S Ps 10:8; 59:3; Pr 1:18 [i] S Ex 1:10; S Ps 31:13; S Mt 12:14 **71:11** [j] S Ps 9:10; Isa 40:27; 54:7; La 5:20; Mt 27:46 [k] S Ps 7:2 **71:12** [l] S Ps 38:21 [m] Ps 22:19; 38:22 **71:13** [n] Jer 18:19 [o] S Job 8:22; Ps 25:3 [p] S Ps 70:2 **71:14** [q] Ps 25:3; 42:5; 130:7; 131:3 **71:15** [r] S ver 8; S Ps 66:16 [s] S Ps 51:14 **71:16** [t] Ps 9:1; 77:12; 106:2; 118:15; 145:4 **71:17** [u] S Dt 4:5; S Jer 7:13 [v] S Job 5:9; Ps 26:7; 86:10; 96:3 **71:18** [w] Isa 46:4 [x] S Ex 9:16 [y] Job 8:8; Ps 22:30,31; 78:4; 145:4; Joel 1:3 **71:19** [z] S Ps 36:5 [a] Ps 126:2; Lk 1:49 [b] Ps 35:10; 77:13; 89:8 **71:20** [c] Ps 25:17 [d] Ps 80:3,19; 85:4; Hos 6:2 [e] S Ps 63:9 **71:21** [f] Ps 18:35 [g] Ps 23:4; 86:17; Isa 12:1; 40:1-2; 49:13; 54:10 **71:22** [h] Ps 33:2 [i] S Job 21:12; Ps 92:3; 144:9 [j] S 2Ki 19:22 **71:23** [k] Ps 20:5 [l] S Ex 15:13 **71:24** [m] S Ps 35:28 [n] ver 13 [o] S Est 9:2

pecially since the Lord has been his "strong refuge" through them all.
71:8 *My mouth is filled with your praise . . . your splendor.* Because of the Lord's faithful care, the psalmist has been moved to fulfill in his life the high purpose of God in saving and blessing his people (see Jer 13:11; 33:9).
71:9 – 13 A prayer for God's continuing help in the waning years of the psalmist's life.
71:10 *enemies speak against me.* See notes on 3:2; 5:9.
71:12 *Do not be far from me.* Cf. 22:11,19; 35:22; 38:21. *come quickly . . . to help me.* Cf. 22:19; 38:22; 40:13; 70:1; cf. also 70:5; 141:1.
71:13 A plea for redress (see note on 5:10). Key words in this closing verse of the first half of the psalm are echoed in the last verse of the second half. Similar language is found in 35:4,26; 40:14 – 15; 70:2 – 3; 83:17; 109:28 – 29.
71:14 A centered confession of unfaltering hope — providing a striking link with Ps 42 – 43 (see 42:8 and note; see also note on 6:6).
71:15 – 18 A vow to praise God, accompanying the renewal of his prayer (v. 18); see note on 7:17.
71:15 *tell . . . righteous deeds . . . saving acts.* Here one of the "righteous deeds" the psalmist vows to "tell," i.e., to recount, is God's act of deliverance in answer to the psalmist's prayer (see notes on vv. 16 – 17; 4:1).
71:16 – 17 *mighty acts . . . righteous deeds . . . marvelous deeds.* God's "mighty (marvelous) acts" in behalf of his people are expressions of his righteousness; see also his "righteous acts" (v. 24).
71:16 *come.* To the temple, where God's people assemble for worship.
71:19 – 21 A confession that the Lord is still his hope, in the face of all his troubles (see vv. 5 – 8,14).
71:19 *reaches to the heavens.* Is as expansive as all space above the earth (see also 36:5 and note). *Who is like you, God?* See Mic 7:18 and note.
71:20 *you have made me see troubles.* The "troubles" referred to are not specified. That God is somehow involved the psalmist does not question; he shares the mature and robust faith that all things are in the hands of the one sovereign God (see Dt 6:4 and note), the God to whom he turns in prayer (cf. 1Sa 16:11 – 12; Isa 45:5 – 7; Am 3:6). *restore my life again.* He who gave him life (see v. 6) will renew his life. *depths of the earth.* The realm of the dead, of which the grave is the portal (see note on 30:1).
71:22 – 24 A vow to praise in confident anticipation of God's saving help (see notes on 3:8; 7:17).
71:22 *harp . . . lyre.* See note on 57:8. *Holy One of Israel.* See 78:41; 89:18; see also 2Ki 19:22 and note.
71:24 *righteous acts.* God's saving acts in behalf of his people according to his covenant promises (see 88:12; Jdg 5:11; 1Sa 12:7 and note; Da 9:16; Mic 6:5; Rev 15:4).

Psalm 72

Of Solomon.

[1] Endow the king with your justice,[p]
O God,
the royal son with your righteousness.
[2] May he judge your people in
righteousness,[q]
your afflicted ones with justice.

[3] May the mountains bring prosperity to
the people,
the hills the fruit of righteousness.
[4] May he defend the afflicted[r] among the
people
and save the children of the needy;[s]
may he crush the oppressor.[t]
[5] May he endure[a][u] as long as the sun,
as long as the moon, through all
generations.[v]
[6] May he be like rain[w] falling on a mown
field,
like showers watering the earth.
[7] In his days may the righteous flourish[x]
and prosperity abound till the moon
is no more.

[8] May he rule from sea to sea
and from the River[b][y] to the ends of
the earth.[z]
[9] May the desert tribes bow before him
and his enemies lick the dust.
[10] May the kings of Tarshish[a] and of
distant shores[b]
bring tribute to him.
May the kings of Sheba[c] and Seba
present him gifts.[d]
[11] May all kings bow down[e] to him
and all nations serve[f] him.

[12] For he will deliver the needy who cry out,
the afflicted who have no one to
help.
[13] He will take pity[g] on the weak and the
needy
and save the needy from death.
[14] He will rescue[h] them from oppression
and violence,
for precious[i] is their blood in his sight.

[15] Long may he live!
May gold from Sheba[j] be given him.
May people ever pray for him
and bless him all day long.[k]
[16] May grain[l] abound throughout the land;
on the tops of the hills may it sway.
May the crops[m] flourish like Lebanon[n]
and thrive[c] like the grass of the
field.[o]
[17] May his name endure forever;[p]
may it continue as long as the sun.[q]

Then all nations will be blessed
through him,[d]
and they will call him blessed.[r]

[a] 5 Septuagint; Hebrew *You will be feared* [b] 8 That is, the Euphrates [c] 16 Probable reading of the original Hebrew text; Masoretic Text *Lebanon, / from the city* [d] 17 Or *will use his name in blessings* (see Gen. 48:20)

72:1 [p] S Dt 1:16; S Ps 9:8 **72:2** [q] Isa 9:7; 11:4-5; 16:5; 32:1; 59:17; 63:1; Jer 23:5; 33:15 **72:4** [r] S Ps 9:12; 76:9; Isa 49:13 [s] ver 13; Isa 11:4; 29:19; 32:7 [t] S Ps 27:11 **72:5** [u] 1Sa 13:13 [v] Ps 33:11 **72:6** [w] S Dt 32:2 **72:7** [x] Ps 92:12; Pr 14:11 **72:8** [y] S Ex 23:31; S 1Ki 4:21 [z] Zec 9:10 **72:10** [a] S Ge 10:4 [b] S Est 10:1 [c] S Ge 10:7 [d] S 1Ki 9:16; S 2Ch 9:24 **72:11** [e] S Ge 27:29 [f] S Ezr 1:2 **72:13** [g] Isa 60:10; Joel 2:18; Lk 10:33 **72:14** [h] Ps 69:18; Eze 13:23; 34:10 [i] 1Sa 26:21 **72:15** [j] S Ge 10:7 [k] S Ps 35:28 **72:16** [l] S Ge 27:28; Ps 4:7 [m] Isa 4:2; 27:6; Eze 34:27 [n] Ps 92:12; 104:16 [o] S Nu 22:4; Isa 44:4; 58:11; 66:14 **72:17** [p] S Ex 3:15 [q] Ps 89:36 [r] S Ge 12:3; Lk 1:48

Ps 72 A prayer for the king, a son of David who rules on David's throne as God's earthly regent over his people. It may have been used at the time of the king's coronation (as were Ps 2; 110). These verses express the desire of the nation that the king's reign will, as a consequence of God's endowment of his servant, be characterized by justice and righteousness, the supreme virtues of kingship. The prayer reflects the ideal concept of the king and the glorious effects of his reign. See Jeremiah's indictment of some of the last Davidic kings (e.g., Jer 22:2–3,13,15) and the prophetic announcement of the Messiah's righteous rule (see Isa 9:7; 11:4–5; Jer 23:5–6; 33:15–16; Zec 9:9). Later Jewish tradition saw in this psalm a description of the Messiah, as did the early church. The last three verses do not belong to the prayer (see notes there). For this psalm's function within Book II of the Psalter, see introduction to Ps 69–72.

72 title *Of Solomon.* Either by him or for him—of course, both may be true. This psalm was probably also used by Israel (Judah) as a prayer for later Davidic kings.

72:1 The basic prayer. *justice... righteousness.* May the king be endowed with the gift for and the love of justice and righteousness so that his reign reflects the rule of God himself. Solomon asked for the necessary wisdom so he could govern God's people justly (see 1Ki 3:9,11–12; see also Pr 16:12). *righteousness.* See note on 4:1.

72:2–7 The quality of his reign: May it be righteous, prosperous and enduring.

72:3 Righteousness in the realm will be like fertilizing rain on the land, for then the Lord will bless his people with abundance (see vv. 6–7; 5:12; 65:9–13; 133:3; Lev 25:19; Dt 28:8).

72:5 *endure as long as the sun.* See 21:4 and note.

72:6 See v. 3 and note; see also v. 7. For another vivid metaphor expressive of the significance of the Lord's anointed for the realm, see La 4:20.

72:7 *righteous.* See note on 1:5. *flourish.* Because the king supports and protects them but uses all his royal power to suppress the wicked (see Ps 101).

72:8–14 The extent of his domain (vv. 8–11) as the result of his righteous rule (vv. 12–14).

72:8 May his kingdom and authority extend to all the world (see vv. 9–11; cf. 110:2 and note). Ideally and potentially, as God's earthly regent, he possesses royal authority that extends on earth as far as God's—an expectation that is fulfilled in Christ. See Zec 9:10 and note.

72:9 May the tribes of the Arabian Desert to the east yield to him. *lick the dust.* See Mic 7:17 and note.

72:10 May the kings whose lands border the Mediterranean Sea to the west acknowledge him as overlord, as well as those who rule in south Arabia and along the eastern African coast. *Tarshish.* A distant Mediterranean seaport, perhaps as far west as modern Spain. *Sheba.* See notes on Ge 10:28; 1Ki 10:1; Joel 3:8. *Seba.* Elsewhere in the OT associated with Cush (Ge 10:7; Isa 43:3); it may refer to a region in modern Sudan, south of Egypt.

72:15–17 Concluding summation: May the king enjoy a long, prosperous, world-renowned reign—one that blesses all the nations.

72:17 *all nations.* The language recalls the promise to Abraham (see Ge 12:3; 22:18) and suggests that it will be fulfilled through the royal son of David—ultimately the Messiah.

18 Praise be to the LORD God, the God of
Israel,[s]
who alone does marvelous deeds.[t]
19 Praise be to his glorious name[u] forever;
may the whole earth be filled with
his glory.[v]
Amen and Amen.[w]

20 This concludes the prayers of David
son of Jesse.[x]

BOOK III

Psalms 73–89

Psalm 73

A psalm of Asaph.

1 Surely God is good to Israel,
to those who are pure in heart.[y]

2 But as for me, my feet had almost
slipped;[z]
I had nearly lost my foothold.[a]
3 For I envied[b] the arrogant
when I saw the prosperity of the
wicked.[c]

4 They have no struggles;
their bodies are healthy and strong.[a]
5 They are free[d] from common human
burdens;
they are not plagued by human ills.
6 Therefore pride[e] is their necklace;[f]
they clothe themselves with
violence.[g]
7 From their callous hearts[h] comes
iniquity[b];
their evil imaginations have no
limits.
8 They scoff, and speak with malice;[i]
with arrogance[j] they threaten
oppression.[k]

72:18 [s] 1Ch 29:10; Ps 41:13; 106:48; Lk 1:68 [t] S Job 5:9 **72:19** [u] S 2Sa 7:26 [v] Nu 14:21 [w] S Ps 41:13 **72:20** [x] S Ru 4:17 **73:1** [y] S Ps 24:4; Mt 5:8 **73:2** [z] S Dt 32:35 [a] Ps 69:2; Eph 4:27 **73:3** [b] Pr 3:31; 23:17; 24:1-2 [c] S Job 9:24; S 21:7; Jer 12:1; Mal 3:15 **73:5** [d] ver 12; Eze 23:42 **73:6** [e] S Lev 26:19 [f] S Ge 41:42; SS 4:9; Eze 16:11 [g] S Ge 6:11; S Pr 4:17 **73:7** [h] S Ps 17:10 **73:8** [i] Ps 41:5; Eze 25:15; Col 3:8 [j] Ps 17:10 [k] S Ps 10:7; S 12:5

[a] 4 With a different word division of the Hebrew; Masoretic Text *struggles at their death; / their bodies are healthy* [b] 7 Syriac (see also Septuagint); Hebrew *Their eyes bulge with fat*

72:18–19 A doxology at the conclusion of Book II of the Psalter (see 41:13 and note). It is the people's response, their "Amen," to the contents of Book II (see note on Ps 4 title).
72:19 *filled with his glory.* See note on 85:9.
72:20 An editorial notation. *prayers of David.* See titles of Ps 86; 142.
Ps 73–78 Book III consists of three groupings of psalms, having an overall symmetrical pattern (six psalms [73–78], five psalms [79–83], six psalms [84–89]) and at its center (Ps 81) an urgent exhortation to fundamental covenant loyalty to the Lord (see introduction to Ps 79–83, introduction to Ps 84–89 and introduction to Ps 81). The first group is framed by psalms of instruction. Ps 73 is a word of godly wisdom based on an individual's life experience, while Ps 78 is a psalm of instruction based on Israel's communal experience in its historical pilgrimage with God. Within this frame, Ps 74 (a communal prayer) is linked with Ps 77 (a prayer of an individual) by the common experience of seeming to be rejected by God (see 74:1; 77:7) and by an extended evocation of God's saving act in Israel's exodus from Egypt (see 74:13–15; 77:16–19). At the center, two psalms (75; 76) express joyful assurance that Israel's God (his "Name is near," 75:1; "in Israel his name is great," 76:1) calls the arrogant wicked to account and rescues their victims; he cuts off "the horns of all the wicked" (75:10) and breaks "the spirit of rulers" (76:12).
Ps 73 A word of godly wisdom concerning the destinies of the righteous and the wicked (see introduction to Ps 73–78). Placed at the beginning of Book III, this psalm voices the faith (confessed [v. 1], tested [vv. 2–26] and reaffirmed [vv. 27–28]) that undergirds the following collection. It serves in Book III as Ps 1–2 serve in Book I (see introduction to Ps 1–2). Here the psalmist addresses one of the most disturbing problems of the OT people of God: How is it that the wicked so often prosper while the godly suffer so much? Thematically the psalm has many links with Ps 49 (see introduction to that psalm; see also Ps 37). Its date may be as late as the postexilic era. Thematic development divides the psalm's structure into two halves of 14 verses each. Apart from the opening profession of faith (v. 1), the first half is framed by two couplets (vv. 2–3,13–14) that focus on the psalmist's condition—which is sharply contrasted with the perceived condition of the wicked (vv. 4–12). The psalm as a whole is framed by the equally sharp contrast between v. 1 and v. 27.
73 title The psalm is ascribed to Asaph, leader of one of David's three Levitical choirs (the other two leaders were Heman and Jeduthun/Ethan; these three represented the families and descendants of the three sons of Levi; see notes on Ps 39; 42; 50 titles). It begins a collection of 11 Asaphite psalms (Ps 73–83), to which Ps 50 at one time probably belonged. In view of the fact that the collection clearly contains prayers from a later date (e.g., Ps 74; 79; 83), references to Asaph in these titles must sometimes include descendants of Asaph who functioned in his place (see note on Ps 50 title). The Asaphite psalms are dominated by the theme of God's rule over his people and the nations. Apart from an introductory word of instruction (Ps 73), the collection is bracketed by prayers for God to rescue his people from foreign oppression (Ps 74; 83). The rest of the collection (Ps 75–82) appears to reflect thematic pairing: (1) The God who brings down the wicked and exalts the righteous (Ps 75) is the God and Savior of Israel (Ps 76). (2) God's saving acts in behalf of his people are remembered (Ps 77–78). (3) God is petitioned for help against the devastating attacks of Israel's enemies (Ps 79–80). (4) God is portrayed as presiding in judgment over his people (Ps 81) and over the world powers (Ps 82). This pairing, however, as is true of the whole Asaph collection, has been subsumed under another ordering principle (see introduction to Ps 73–78).
73:1–14 An almost fatal trial of faith: In the midst of many troubles a godly Israelite lets his eyes become fixed on the prosperity of the wicked.
73:1 *pure in heart.* See v. 13; see also note on 24:4. *heart.* See note on 4:7.
73:2 *feet had almost slipped.* From the path of truth and godliness (see 37:31 and note).
73:4–12 A description of the prosperous state of the wicked and the haughty self-reliance such prosperity engenders—hardly an objective account; it is rather the exaggerated picture that envious and troubled eyes perceived (see the description of the wicked in 10:2–11; cf. Job's anguished portrayal of the prosperity of the wicked in Job 21).
73:6 *pride is their necklace.* Contrast Pr 1:9; 3:3,22. *clothe themselves with.* See note on 109:29.

9 Their mouths lay claim to heaven,
and their tongues take possession of the earth.
10 Therefore their people turn to them
and drink up waters in abundance.[a]
11 They say, "How would God know?
Does the Most High know anything?"

12 This is what the wicked are like—
always free of care,[l] they go on amassing wealth.[m]

13 Surely in vain[n] I have kept my heart pure
and have washed my hands in innocence.[o]
14 All day long I have been afflicted,[p]
and every morning brings new punishments.

15 If I had spoken out like that,
I would have betrayed your children.
16 When I tried to understand[q] all this,
it troubled me deeply
17 till I entered the sanctuary[r] of God;
then I understood their final destiny.[s]

18 Surely you place them on slippery ground;[t]
you cast them down to ruin.[u]
19 How suddenly[v] are they destroyed,
completely swept away[w] by terrors!
20 They are like a dream[x] when one awakes;[y]
when you arise, Lord,
you will despise them as fantasies.[z]

21 When my heart was grieved
and my spirit embittered,
22 I was senseless[a] and ignorant;
I was a brute beast[b] before you.

23 Yet I am always with you;
you hold me by my right hand.[c]
24 You guide[d] me with your counsel,[e]
and afterward you will take me into glory.
25 Whom have I in heaven but you?[f]
And earth has nothing I desire besides you.[g]
26 My flesh and my heart[h] may fail,[i]
but God is the strength[j] of my heart
and my portion[k] forever.

27 Those who are far from you will perish;[l]
you destroy all who are unfaithful[m] to you.
28 But as for me, it is good to be near God.[n]
I have made the Sovereign LORD my refuge;[o]
I will tell of all your deeds.[p]

[a] *10* The meaning of the Hebrew for this verse is uncertain.

73:12 [l]S ver 5 [m]S Ps 49:6 **73:13** [n]S Job 9:29-31; S 21:15 [o]S Ge 44:16 **73:14** [p]ver 5 **73:16** [q]Ecc 8:17 **73:17** [r]Ex 15:17; Ps 15:1 [s]S Job 8:13; Php 3:19 **73:18** [t]S Dt 32:35; Ps 35:6 [u]S Ps 17:13 **73:19** [v]Dt 28:20; Pr 24:22; Isa 47:11 [w]S Ge 19:15 **73:20** [x]S Job 20:8 [y]Ps 78:65; Isa 29:8 [z]Pr 12:11; 28:19 **73:22** [a]Ps 49:10; 92:6; 94:8 [b]Ps 49:12, 20; Ecc 3:18; 9:12 **73:23** [c]S Ge 48:13 **73:24** [d]S Ps 48:14 [e]S 1Ki 22:5 **73:25** [f]Ps 16:2 [g]Php 3:8 **73:26** [h]Ps 84:2 [i]S Ps 31:10; 40:12 [j]Ps 18:1 [k]S Dt 32:9 **73:27** [l]S Ps 34:21 [m]S Lev 6:2; Jer 5:11; Hos 4:12; 9:1 **73:28** [n]Zep 3:2; Heb 10:22; Jas 4:8 [o]Ps 9:9 [p]Ps 26:7; 40:5

73:11 *They say.* Their speech (v. 11) and actions (v. 12) show that they live "far from" God (v. 27). *God ... Most High.* That is, God Most High (see 57:2; see also note on 3:7). *Most High.* See note on Ge 14:19.
73:13–14 The thoughts that plagued the psalmist when he compared the state of the wicked with his own troubled lot.
73:13 *heart pure.* See note on v. 1.
73:14 *punishments.* As children are punished by their parents to keep them in the right way (see Pr 3:12; 23:13–14).
73:15–28 The renewal of faith: In the temple, where God's ways are celebrated and taught, the psalmist sees the destiny God has appointed for the wicked (see v. 17).
73:15 *If I had spoken out like that.* If the psalmist had given public expression to his thoughts as embodying true insight. *your children.* Those characterized by a humble reliance on and commitment to God.
73:17 *till I entered the sanctuary.* The crucial turning point (see note on vv. 15–28).
73:18–20 Though the wicked seem to prosper, God has made their position precarious; without warning they are swept away. The psalmist does not reflect on their state after death but leaves it as his final word that the wicked fall utterly and inevitably from their state of proud prosperity (see Ps 49; cf. the final state of the godly in v. 24).
73:20 When God arouses himself as from sleep (see note on 7:6) and deals with the wicked, they vanish like the shadowy characters of a dream.
73:21 *heart.* See note on 4:7. *spirit.* Lit. "kidneys" (see note on 7:9).
73:22 *a brute beast.* As stupid as a beast (see Job 18:3).
73:23–26 Although the psalmist had (almost) fallen to the level of beastly stupidity, God has not, will not, let him go—ever!
73:24 God's counsel has overcome the psalmist's folly and will guide him through all the pitfalls of life (see 16:7; 32:8; 107:11). *take me into glory.* At the end of the believer's pilgrimage on earth (see 49:15 and note).
73:25 Though he has envied the prosperity of the wicked, he now confesses that nothing in heaven or earth is more desirable than God.
73:26 *My flesh ... heart.* My whole being (see 84:2). *heart.* See note on 4:7. *portion.* Since the psalmist was a Levite, the Lord was his portion in the promised land in that he lived by the people's tithes dedicated to the Lord (see Nu 18:21–24; Dt 10:9; 18:1–2). But here he confesses more—what every godly Israelite could confess: The Lord himself is the sustainer and preserver of the life of those who put their trust in him (see note on 16:5–6).
73:27–28 See 34:21–22; 37:18–20; Pr 24:16.
73:27 *all who are unfaithful.* Lit. "all who commit (spiritual) prostitution/adultery" (see note on Ex 34:15). Although this expression elsewhere refers to blatant idolatry (as, e.g., in Dt 31:16; Jer 2:20; Hos 2:5 [see note there]) or to political alliance with any world power rather than relying on the Lord for security (as, e.g., in Eze 16:26–29), here it refers to the reliance of the wicked on their predatory economic and political practices, the "violence" with which they accumulated their wealth at the expense of others (vv. 6–11). See Isa 1:21 and note.
73:28 *I will tell of all your deeds.* A concluding vow to praise God for all his mercies to him (see note on 7:17).

Psalm 74

A *maskil*[a] of Asaph.

[1] O God, why have you rejected[q] us
forever?[r]
Why does your anger smolder
against the sheep of your
pasture?[s]
[2] Remember the nation you purchased[t]
long ago,[u]
the people of your inheritance,[v]
whom you redeemed[w]—
Mount Zion,[x] where you dwelt.[y]
[3] Turn your steps toward these
everlasting ruins,[z]
all this destruction the enemy has
brought on the sanctuary.

[4] Your foes roared[a] in the place where
you met with us;
they set up their standards[b] as signs.
[5] They behaved like men wielding axes
to cut through a thicket of trees.[c]
[6] They smashed all the carved[d] paneling
with their axes and hatchets.
[7] They burned your sanctuary to the
ground;
they defiled[e] the dwelling place[f] of
your Name.[g]
[8] They said in their hearts, "We will
crush[h] them completely!"
They burned[i] every place where God
was worshiped in the land.

[9] We are given no signs from God;[j]
no prophets[k] are left,
and none of us knows how long this
will be.
[10] How long[l] will the enemy mock[m] you,
God?
Will the foe revile[n] your name
forever?
[11] Why do you hold back your hand,
your right hand?[o]
Take it from the folds of your
garment[p] and destroy
them!

[12] But God is my King[q] from long ago;
he brings salvation[r] on the earth.

[13] It was you who split open the sea[s] by
your power;
you broke the heads of the monster[t]
in the waters.
[14] It was you who crushed the heads of
Leviathan[u]
and gave it as food to the creatures
of the desert.[v]

[a] Title: Probably a literary or musical term

74:1 [q] S Ps 43:2 [r] S Ps 44:23 [s] Ps 79:13; 95:7; 100:3 **74:2** [t] S Ex 15:16; S 1Co 6:20 [u] S Dt 32:7 [v] S Ex 34:9 [w] S Ex 15:13; S Isa 48:20 [x] Ps 2:6 [y] Ps 43:3; 68:16; Isa 46:13; Joel 3:17,21; Ob 1:17 **74:3** [z] Isa 44:26; 52:9 **74:4** [a] La 2:7 [b] S Nu 2:2; S Jer 4:6 **74:5** [c] Jer 46:22 **74:6** [d] S 1Ki 6:18 **74:7** [e] S Lev 20:3; Ac 21:28 [f] S Lev 15:31 [g] Ps 75:1 **74:8** [h] Ps 94:5 [i] 2Ki 25:9; 2Ch 36:19; Jer 21:10; 34:22; 52:13 **74:9** [j] S Ex 4:17; S 10:1 [k] S 1Sa 3:1 **74:10** [l] Ps 6:3; 79:5; 80:4 [m] ver 22 [n] S Ps 44:16 **74:11** [o] S Ex 15:6 [p] Ne 5:13; Eze 5:3 **74:12** [q] Ps 2:6; S 24:7; 68:24 [r] Ps 27:1 **74:13** [s] S Ex 14:21 [t] Isa 27:1; 51:9; Eze 29:3; 32:2 **74:14** [u] S Job 3:8 [v] Isa 13:21; 23:13; 34:14; Jer 50:39

Ps 74 A prayer for God to come to the aid of his people and defend his cause in the face of the mocking of the enemies—the Lord's relation to his people is like that of a king to his nation. The psalm dates from the time of the exile, when Israel had been destroyed as a nation, the promised land devastated and the temple reduced to ruins (see Ps 79; La 2). Its relationship to the ministries of Jeremiah and Ezekiel is uncertain (see note on v. 9). Thematically the psalm divides into two halves of 11 verses each, with v. 12 (the center line; see note there) highlighting the primary thematic element that unifies the prayer. Verses 1–11 are framed by the "whys" of the people's complaint (vv. 1,11); the whole psalm is framed by pleas for God to "remember" (vv. 2,22). Note also that the "theys" of vv. 4–8 have their counterpoint in the "yous" of vv. 13–17 (highlighted in the Hebrew by seven emphatic pronouns)—the mighty acts of God are appealed to against the destructive and haughty deeds of the enemies. For the placement of this psalm in the Psalter and its relationship to the psalms around it, see introduction to Ps 73–78.
74 title *maskil.* See note on Ps 32 title. *Asaph.* See note on Ps 73 title.
74:1–2 Initial complaint and appeal.
74:1 *why ... ? Why ... ?* Cf. "How long ... ?" (v. 10) and "Why ... ?" (v. 11). See note on 6:3. *forever.* So it seemed, since no relief was in sight. *anger.* See note on 2:5. *sheep ... pasture.* Metaphors related to the basic figure of a king as the shepherd of his realm (see notes on 23:1; 95:7; see also 79:13; 100:3).
74:2 *purchased.* Or "acquired" or "created" (see Ex 15:16 and note). *your inheritance.* See Dt 9:29. *redeemed.* Here, as often, a synonym for "delivered." *Mount Zion.* See note on 9:11. This verse recalls the victory song of Ex 15 (see especially vv. 13–17, and compare the center verse of this psalm, v. 12, with the last verse of the song, Ex 15:18) and thus sets the stage for the other exodus recollections that follow. The Babylonian destruction of Zion seems to be the undoing of God's great victory over Egypt when he redeemed his people.
74:3–8 The Babylonians' high-handed destruction of the Lord's temple.
74:3 *Turn your steps toward.* Hurry to restore.
74:4 *standards.* Probably troop standards (see Nu 1:52; Isa 31:9; Jer 4:21). *as signs.* Signifying their triumph.
74:6 *carved paneling.* See 1Ki 6:15.
74:7 *your Name.* See note on 5:11. The NIV capitalizes "Name" when it stands for God's presence at the sanctuary (see Dt 12:5).
74:8 *They said.* See note on 10:11. *every place where God was worshiped.* Lit. "all the meeting places of God" (see v. 4). At the time of the Babylonian attacks there may have been a number of (illegitimate) places in Judah where people went to worship God (see notes on 1Ki 3:2; 2Ki 18:4).
74:9–11 The complaint and prayer renewed (see vv. 1–2).
74:9 *no signs.* As there were at the time of the exodus (see vv. 13–15; 78:43).
74:10 *mock you ... revile your name.* See v. 18; see also v. 22; 2Ki 18:32–35; Isa 37:6,23.
74:12 The center verse (center line in the Hebrew text; see note on 6:6). The whole psalm presupposes the truth confessed here: God is Israel's King, her hope and Savior; Israel is God's people (kingdom). This accounts for both the complaint and the prayer, and why the destruction of Israel brings with it the mocking of God. *my.* Communal use of the singular pronoun (see note on Ps 30 title). *from long ago.* From the days of the exodus (see Ex 3:7; 19:5–6).
74:13–17 The Lord is the mighty God of salvation and creation (see 65:6–7 and note).
74:13–14 Recollection of God's mighty acts when he delivered his people from Egypt. The imagery is borrowed from ancient Near Eastern creation

15 It was you who opened up springs[w]
and streams;
you dried up[x] the ever-flowing rivers.
16 The day is yours, and yours also the
night;
you established the sun and moon.[y]
17 It was you who set all the boundaries[z]
of the earth;
you made both summer and winter.[a]

18 Remember how the enemy has mocked
you, LORD,
how foolish people[b] have reviled
your name.
19 Do not hand over the life of your dove[c]
to wild beasts;
do not forget the lives of your
afflicted[d] people forever.
20 Have regard for your covenant,[e]
because haunts of violence fill the
dark places[f] of the land.
21 Do not let the oppressed[g] retreat in
disgrace;
may the poor and needy[h] praise your
name.
22 Rise up,[i] O God, and defend your
cause;
remember how fools[j] mock you all
day long.

23 Do not ignore the clamor[k] of your
adversaries,[l]
the uproar[m] of your enemies,[n] which
rises continually.

Psalm 75[a]

For the director of music.
To the tune of "Do Not Destroy."
A psalm of Asaph. A song.

1 We praise you, God,
we praise you, for your Name is
near;[o]
people tell of your wonderful deeds.[p]

2 You say, "I choose the appointed time;[q]
it is I who judge with equity.[r]
3 When the earth and all its people
quake,[s]
it is I who hold its pillars[t] firm.[b]
4 To the arrogant[u] I say, 'Boast no more,'[v]
and to the wicked, 'Do not lift up
your horns.[c][w]

74:15 [w] S Ex 17:6; S Nu 20:11 [x] S Ex 14:29; S Jos 2:10 **74:16** [y] S Ge 1:16; Ps 136:7-9 **74:17** [z] Dt 32:8; Ac 17:26 [a] S Ge 8:22 **74:18** [b] Dt 32:6 **74:19** [c] S Ge 8:8; S Isa 59:11 [d] S Ps 9:18 **74:20** [e] S Ge 6:18 [f] Job 34:22 **74:21** [g] Ps 9:9; 10:18; 103:6; Isa 58:10 [h] S Ps 35:10 **74:22** [i] Ps 17:13 [j] S Ps 53:1 **74:23** [k] Isa 31:4 [l] S Ps 65:7 [m] S Ps 46:6 [n] S Nu 25:17 **75:1** [o] Ps 145:18 [p] S Jos 3:5; Ps 44:1; S 71:16; 77:12; 105:2; 107:8,15; 145:5,12 **75:2** [q] S Ex 13:10 [r] S Ps 7:11 **75:3** [s] Isa 24:19 [t] 1Sa 2:8; S 2Sa 22:8 **75:4** [u] S Ps 5:5 [v] S 1Sa 2:3 [w] Zec 1:21

[a] In Hebrew texts 75:1-10 is numbered 75:2-11.
[b] *3* The Hebrew has *Selah* (a word of uncertain meaning) here.
[c] *4* *Horns* here symbolize strength; also in verses 5 and 10.

myths, in which the primeval chaotic waters were depicted as a many-headed monster that the creator-god overcame, after which he established the world order (see note on 32:6). The poet here interweaves creation and salvation themes to celebrate the fact that the God of Israel has shown by his saving acts (his opening of the "Red Sea" for his people and his destruction of the Egyptians) that he is able to overcome all hostile powers to redeem his people and establish his new order in the world. For poetic use of this imagery (1) to celebrate God's creation works, see 89:10; Job 9:13; 26:12–13; (2) to celebrate the deliverance from Egypt, see Isa 51:9; (3) to announce a future deliverance of Israel, see Isa 27:1. Echoes of the same imagery are present in the judgment announced against Egypt in Eze 29:3–5; 32:2–6.

74:15 Recollection of God's water miracles at the "Red Sea," in the wilderness and at the Jordan.

74:16–17 God is the One who established the orders of creation; he (alone) is able to effect redemption and establish his kingdom in the world against all creaturely opposition.

74:18–23 A prayer for God to defend his cause and restore his people.

74:18 See vv. 2,10. *foolish people.* The foes of v. 10 ("foe" is collective) are here called "foolish" for their contempt of God (see v. 22; see also NIV text note on 14:1).

74:19 *your dove.* Israel—probably a figure of endearment (see SS 2:14; 5:2; 6:9; see also Ps 68:13 and note). *wild beasts.* See note on 7:2.

74:20 *your covenant.* God's covenant to be the God of Israel, the one who makes his people secure and richly blessed in the promised land (see Ex 19:5–6; 23:27–31; 34:10–11; Lev 26:11–12,42,44–45; Dt 28:1–14; see also Ps 105:8–11; 106:45; 111:5,9; Isa 54:10; Jer 14:21; Eze 16:60).

74:21 *poor and needy.* See note on 34:6. *praise your name.* May they have cause to do so.

74:22 *Rise up.* See note on 3:7.

74:23 *clamor … uproar.* See 64:2.

Ps 75 A song of reassurance when arrogant worldly powers threaten Israel's security. The psalm may date from the time of the Assyrian menace (see 2Ki 18:13—19:37). See also Ps 11; 76. Thematic parallels to the song of Hannah (1Sa 2:1–10) are numerous. The worshiping congregation speaks (v. 1), perhaps led in its praise by one of the descendants of Asaph (v. 9). The psalm is framed by thanksgiving (v. 1) and praise (vv. 9–10). Two stanzas of four (Hebrew) lines each form the body of the psalm, and each stanza is composed of two couplets. The first stanza contains a reassuring word from heaven; the second contains a triumphant response from earth. For this psalm's relationship to those around it, especially to Ps 76, see introduction to Ps 73–78.

75 title *For the director of music.* See note on Ps 4 title. *To the tune of.* See note on Ps 9 title. *Do Not Destroy.* See Ps 57; 58; 59 titles. *Asaph.* See note on Ps 73 title. *song.* See note on Ps 30 title.

75:1 The congregation begins with thanksgiving in the form of praise (see 7:17; 28:7; 30:12; 35:18). *Name.* See notes on 5:11; 74:7. *wonderful deeds.* See note on 9:1.

75:2–5 A reassuring word from above: God will not fail to call the arrogant to account. It is not clear whether a new word from the Lord is heard or whether these verses recall (and perhaps summarize) earlier prophetic words (such as those of Isaiah in 2Ki 19:21–34; see notes there).

75:2 God will not fail to judge (see Ps 96; 98 and notes on 96:13; 98:9)—but in his own time.

75:3 When, because of the upsurge of evil powers, the whole moral order of the world seems to have crumbled, God still guarantees its stability (see note on 11:3). *pillars.* A figure for that which stabilizes the world order (see note on 24:2). For *Selah,* see NIV text note and note on 3:2.

75:4 *arrogant … wicked.* To the psalmists the wicked are both arrogant (see especially Ps 10 and note on 10:2–11; 73:4–12 and note; 94:4; see also note on 31:23) and foolish (see introduction to Ps 14 and note on 14:1; 74:18,22 and note on 74:18; 92:6; 94:8 and note on 94:8–11). *lift up*

[5]Do not lift your horns against heaven;
do not speak so defiantly.[x]' "

[6]No one from the east or the west
or from the desert can exalt
themselves.
[7]It is God who judges:[y]
He brings one down, he exalts another.[z]
[8]In the hand of the LORD is a cup
full of foaming wine mixed[a] with
spices;
he pours it out, and all the wicked of
the earth
drink it down to its very dregs.[b]

[9]As for me, I will declare[c] this forever;
I will sing[d] praise to the God of
Jacob,[e]
[10]who says, "I will cut off the horns of
all the wicked,
but the horns of the righteous will
be lifted up."[f]

Psalm 76[a]

For the director of music.
With stringed instruments. A psalm
of Asaph. A song.

[1]God is renowned in Judah;
in Israel his name is great.[g]
[2]His tent is in Salem,[h]
his dwelling place in Zion.[i]
[3]There he broke the flashing arrows,[j]
the shields and the swords, the
weapons of war.[b k]

[4]You are radiant with light,[l]
more majestic than mountains rich
with game.
[5]The valiant[m] lie plundered,
they sleep their last sleep;[n]
not one of the warriors
can lift his hands.
[6]At your rebuke,[o] God of Jacob,
both horse and chariot[p] lie still.

[7]It is you alone who are to be feared.[q]
Who can stand[r] before you when
you are angry?[s]
[8]From heaven you pronounced
judgment,
and the land feared[t] and was quiet—
[9]when you, God, rose up to judge,[u]
to save all the afflicted[v] of the land.

[a] In Hebrew texts 76:1-12 is numbered 76:2-13.
[b] 3 The Hebrew has *Selah* (a word of uncertain meaning) here and at the end of verse 9.

75:5 [x]S Job 15:25 **75:7** [y]S Ge 16:5; Ps 50:6; 58:11; Rev 18:8 [z]1Sa 2:7; S Job 5:11; Ps 147:6; Eze 21:26; Da 2:21 **75:8** [a]Pr 23:30 [b]Isa 51:17; Jer 25:15; Zec 12:2 **75:9** [c]Ps 40:10 [d]Ps 108:1 [e]S Ge 24:12; Ps 76:6 **75:10** [f]Ps 89:17; 92:10; 112:9; 148:14 **76:1** [g]Ps 99:3 **76:2** [h]S Ge 14:18; Heb 7:1 [i]S 2Sa 5:7; Ps 2:6 **76:3** [j]Eze 39:9 [k]Ps 46:9 **76:4** [l]S Ps 36:9 **76:5** [m]S Jdg 20:44 [n]S Ps 13:3; S Mt 9:24 **76:6** [o]S Ps 50:21 [p]S Ex 15:1 **76:7** [q]S 1Ch 16:25 [r]S Ezr 9:15; Rev 6:17 [s]Ps 2:5; Na 1:6 **76:8** [t]S 1Ch 16:30; Eze 38:20 **76:9** [u]S Ps 9:8; 58:11; 74:22; 82:8; 96:13 [v]S Ps 72:4

your horns. A figure for defiant opposition, based on the action of attacking bulls. "Horn" (see also v. 10) is a common Biblical metaphor for vigor or strength (see NIV text notes here and on 18:2).
75:5 *so defiantly.* Lit. "with a stiff/outstretched neck," a sign of defiance.
75:6–8 Triumphant echo from earth: perhaps spoken by the Levitical song leader in elaboration of the comforting word from God.
75:8 *cup.* See note on 16:5. *mixed with spices.* The spices used increased the intoxicating effect (see Pr 9:2,5 and note on 9:2; 23:29–30 and note on 23:30; SS 8:2; Isa 65:11). *drink it down.* Because God pours it out, they have no choice.
75:9 Concluding vow to praise God forever (see note on 7:17) for his righteous judgments. *me.* Probably the Levitical song leader speaking representatively for the people, but the pronoun may be a communal use of the singular, as in 74:12 (see note on Ps 30 title). *Jacob.* A synonym for Israel (see Ge 32:28 and note).
75:10 *righteous.* See notes on 1:5; Ge 7:1; Dt 6:25; 2Sa 22:21,25. *lifted up.* See v. 7; see also note on v. 4.
Ps 76 A celebration of the Lord's invincible power in defense of Jerusalem, his royal city. The psalm is thematically related to Ps 46; 48; 87 (see introduction to Ps 46). The ancient tradition may well be correct that the psalm was composed after the Lord's destruction of Sennacherib's army when it threatened Jerusalem (see 2Ki 19:35). Structurally, the opening (vv. 1–3) and closing (vv. 11–12) stanzas contain the main theme. Between them, two four-line (in Hebrew) stanzas of praise addressed to God (vv. 4–6,7–10) celebrate his awesome act of judgment. For this psalm's relationship to those around it, especially to Ps 75, see introduction to Ps 73–78.
76 title *For the director of music.* See note on Ps 4 title. *With stringed instruments.* See note on Ps 4 title. *Asaph.* See note on Ps 73 title. *song.* See note on Ps 30 title.
76:1–3 God's crushing defeat of the enemy in defense of Zion.
76:1 *is renowned.* Now especially—as a result of his marvelous act. *Israel.* Probably refers to the whole of God's covenant people. As a result of the Assyrian invasions, many displaced Israelites from the northern kingdom now resided in Judah (see introduction to Ps 80 and note on Ne 3:8).
76:2 *tent ... dwelling place.* Since the two Hebrew words for these nouns frequently refer to a lion's den, covert or lair (see 10:9; 104:22; Job 38:40; Jer 25:38; Am 3:4), it may be that the psalmist is here depicting Israel's God as a lion overpowering its prey. In that case, an alternative rendering of v. 4 should be considered (see note on that verse). *Salem.* Jerusalem, as the parallelism makes clear (see note on Ge 14:18). *Zion.* See note on 9:11.
76:3 For *Selah*, see NIV text note and note on 3:2.
76:4–10 Praise of the awesome majesty of God, whose mighty judgment evokes fearful reverence (see introduction).
76:4 *more majestic ... with game.* If the nouns in v. 2 refer to a lion's den (see note there), this line should be rendered something like "the majestic One from the mountains rich with game."
76:5–6 Perhaps echoes also God's victory over the Egyptians at the "Red Sea" (see Ex 14:28,30; 15:4–5,10).
76:6 *rebuke.* This word, when predicated of God, usually refers to either (1) the thunder of his fierce majesty, by which he wields his sovereign control over cosmic entities (see 18:15; 104:7; 106:9; Job 26:11; Isa 50:2; Na 1:4) or repulses his enemies (as here; see also 9:5; 68:30; Isa 17:13); or (2) the thunder of his wrath (see 80:16; Isa 51:20; 54:9; 66:15; Mal 2:3). *God of Jacob.* A link with Ps 75 (see 75:9 and note).
76:7 *you alone ... you.* This first line of the second four-line stanza echoes the emphatic "you" with which the first four-line stanza begins (v. 4).
76:8 *From heaven.* Though God is present in Zion (see v. 2), he sovereignly rules from heaven.

[10]Surely your wrath against mankind
brings you praise,[w]
and the survivors of your wrath are
restrained.[a]

[11]Make vows to the LORD your God and
fulfill them;[x]
let all the neighboring lands
bring gifts[y] to the One to be feared.
[12]He breaks the spirit of rulers;
he is feared by the kings of the
earth.

Psalm 77[b]

For the director of music. For Jeduthun.
Of Asaph. A psalm.

[1]I cried out to God[z] for help;
I cried out to God to hear me.
[2]When I was in distress,[a] I sought the
Lord;
at night[b] I stretched out untiring
hands,[c]
and I would not be comforted.[d]

[3]I remembered[e] you, God, and I
groaned;[f]
I meditated, and my spirit grew
faint.[c][g]
[4]You kept my eyes from closing;
I was too troubled to speak.[h]
[5]I thought about the former days,[i]
the years of long ago;
[6]I remembered my songs in the night.
My heart meditated and my spirit
asked:

[7]"Will the Lord reject forever?[j]
Will he never show his favor[k] again?
[8]Has his unfailing love[l] vanished
forever?
Has his promise[m] failed for all
time?
[9]Has God forgotten to be merciful?[n]
Has he in anger withheld his
compassion?[o]"

[10]Then I thought, "To this I will appeal:
the years when the Most High
stretched out his right hand.[p]
[11]I will remember the deeds of the
LORD;
yes, I will remember your miracles[q]
of long ago.
[12]I will consider[r] all your works
and meditate on all your mighty
deeds."[s]

[13]Your ways, God, are holy.
What god is as great as our God?[t]
[14]You are the God who performs
miracles;[u]
you display your power among the
peoples.
[15]With your mighty arm you redeemed
your people,[v]
the descendants of Jacob and
Joseph.

76:10 [w]Ex 9:16; Ro 9:17 **76:11** [x]S Lev 22:18; S Ps 50:14; Ecc 5:4-5 [y]S 2Ch 32:23 **77:1** [z]S 1Ki 8:52 **77:2** [a]S Ge 32:7; S 2Sa 22:7; S Ps 118:5 [b]Ps 6:6; 22:2; 88:1 [c]S Ex 9:29; S Job 11:13 [d]S Ge 37:35; Mt 2:18 **77:3** [e]Ps 78:35 [f]Ex 2:23; S Ps 6:6; Jer 45:3 [g]S Ps 6:2 **77:4** [h]S Ps 39:2 **77:5** [i]Dt 32:7; Ps 44:1; 143:5; Ecc 7:10 **77:7** [j]S 1Ch 28:9 [k]Ps 85:1; 102:13; 106:4 **77:8** [l]S Ps 6:4; 90:14 [m]2Pe 3:9 **77:9** [n]Ps 25:6; 40:11; 51:1 [o]Isa 49:15 **77:10** [p]S Ex 15:6 **77:11** [q]S Ne 9:17 **77:12** [r]S Ge 24:63 [s]Ps 143:5 **77:13** [t]S Ex 15:11; S Ps 71:19; 86:8 **77:14** [u]S Ex 3:20; S 34:10 **77:15** [v]S Ex 6:6

[a] 10 Or *Surely the wrath of mankind brings you praise, / and with the remainder of wrath you arm yourself*
[b] In Hebrew texts 77:1-20 is numbered 77:2-21.
[c] 3 The Hebrew has *Selah* (a word of uncertain meaning) here and at the end of verses 9 and 15.

76:10 *wrath.* See note on 2:5. *brings you praise.* When his judgments bring deliverance, those rescued praise him. If the alternative translation in the NIV text note is taken, "the wrath of mankind brings you praise" would mean that when people rise up against God's kingdom he crushes them in wrath, to his own praise as Victor and Deliverer. And "the remainder of wrath" would indicate that particular judgments do not exhaust his wrath; a remainder is left to deal with other hostile powers.

76:11 – 12 Let Israel acknowledge God's help with grateful vows; let the nations acknowledge his sovereign rule with tribute.

76:11 *Make vows … fulfill.* See note on 50:14.

76:12 *spirit of rulers.* Their bold rebelliousness.

Ps 77 Comforting reflections in a time of great distress. For the relationship of this psalm to Ps 74, see introduction to Ps 73 – 78. The interplay of verb forms in vv. 1 – 6 makes it uncertain whether the psalm is a prayer (in which case the verbs of these verses would have to be rendered in the present tense) or the recollection of a past experience (as the NIV understands it). The "distress" (v. 2) appears to be personal rather than national. Comparison of vv. 16 – 19 with Hab 3:8 – 10 suggests, but does not prove, a time late in the monarchy. The poetic development advances from anguished bewilderment (vv. 1 – 9) to comforting recollection (vv. 10 – 20). A striking and dramatic feature is the insertion of a four-verse stanza (vv. 16 – 19) between the third and fourth verses of another four-verse stanza (vv. 13 – 15,20).

77 title *For the director of music.* See note on Ps 4 title. *Jeduthun.* See note on Ps 39 title. *Asaph.* See note on Ps 73 title.

77:1 – 9 Anguished perplexity over God's apparent inaction, when he seemingly fails to respond to unceasing and urgent prayers.

77:3 – 6 Remembrance of God's past mercies intensifies the present perplexity (as also in 22:1 – 11). God's failure to act now is so troubling that the psalmist cannot sleep (cf. 3:5; 4:8) and words fail (but see vv. 10 – 20).

77:3 For *Selah,* see NIV text note and note on 3:2.

77:6 *heart.* See note on 4:7.

77:7 – 9 Though words fail (v. 4), troubled thoughts will not go away.

77:8 *unfailing love.* See note on 6:4.

77:9 *anger.* See note on 2:5.

77:10 – 20 Reassuring recollection of God's mighty acts in behalf of Israel in the exodus.

77:10 – 12 Faith's decision to look beyond the present troubles — and God's bewildering inactivity — to draw hope anew from God's saving acts of old.

77:10 *Most High.* See note on Ge 14:19.

77:11,14 *miracles.* See note on 9:1 ("wonderful deeds").

77:13 – 20 God's mighty acts in the exodus recalled.

77:13 Appears to echo Ex 15:11. *are holy.* Or "are seen in the sanctuary" (cf. 63:2).

77:15 *redeemed.* Here, as often, a synonym for "delivered" (see note on 71:23). *Joseph.* OT authors sometimes refer to the northern kingdom as "Joseph" (or "Ephraim," Joseph's son) in distinction from the southern kingdom of Judah (see 78:67; 2Sa 19:20; 1Ki 11:28; Eze 37:16,19; Am 5:6,15; 6:6; Zec 10:6). However, here and elsewhere (see 80:1; 81:5; Ob 18) Joseph — the one elevated to the position of firstborn (see Ge

[16]The waters[w] saw you, God,
the waters saw you and writhed;[x]
the very depths were convulsed.
[17]The clouds poured down water,[y]
the heavens resounded with
thunder;[z]
your arrows[a] flashed back and forth.
[18]Your thunder was heard in the
whirlwind,[b]
your lightning[c] lit up the world;
the earth trembled and quaked.[d]
[19]Your path[e] led through the sea,[f]
your way through the mighty waters,
though your footprints were not
seen.
[20]You led your people[g] like a flock[h]
by the hand of Moses and Aaron.[i]

Psalm 78

A *maskil*[a] of Asaph.

[1]My people, hear my teaching;[j]
listen to the words of my mouth.
[2]I will open my mouth with a parable;[k]
I will utter hidden things, things
from of old—
[3]things we have heard and known,
things our ancestors have told us.[l]
[4]We will not hide them from their
descendants;[m]
we will tell the next generation[n]
the praiseworthy deeds[o] of the LORD,
his power, and the wonders[p] he has
done.
[5]He decreed statutes[q] for Jacob[r]
and established the law in Israel,
which he commanded our ancestors
to teach their children,
[6]so the next generation would know
them,
even the children yet to be born,[s]
and they in turn would tell their
children.

[a] Title: Probably a literary or musical term

77:16 [w]Ex 14:21, 28; Isa 50:2; Hab 3:8 [x]Ps 114:4; Hab 3:10 **77:17** [y]S Jdg 5:4 [z]S Ex 9:23; S Ps 29:3 [a]S Dt 32:23 **77:18** [b]S Ps 55:8 [c]S 2Sa 22:13 [d]S Jdg 5:4 **77:19** [e]S Ex 14:22 [f]S Job 9:8 **77:20** [g]S Ex 13:21 [h]Ps 78:52; Isa 63:11 [i]S Ex 4:16; S Nu 33:1 **78:1** [j]Isa 51:4; 55:3 **78:2** [k]S Ps 49:4; S Mt 13:35* **78:3** [l]S Jdg 6:13 **78:4** [m]S Dt 11:19 [n]S Dt 32:7; S Ps 71:18 [o]Ps 26:7; 71:17 [p]S Job 5:9 **78:5** [q]Ps 19:7; 81:5 [r]Ps 147:19 **78:6** [s]S Ps 22:31

48:5 and note; Jos 16:1–4; 1Ch 5:2; Eze 47:13)—represents the whole of his generation and thus also all the descendants of Jacob.

77:16–19 A poetically heightened description of the majesty of God displayed when he opened a way through the "Red Sea" (see 74:13–15). Verses 16,19 speak expressly of that event; the intervening verses (vv. 17–18) evoke the majesty of God displayed in the thunderstorm and earthquake. Ex 14:19 speaks only of God's cloud, not of a thunderstorm or earthquake, but the Hebrew poets often associated either or both with the Lord's coming to effect redemption or judgment—no doubt because these were the two most fearsome displays of power known to them (see 18:12–14; 68:8; Jdg 5:4–5; Hab 3:6,10). For Christians, the display of God's power in behalf of his people now includes the resurrection of Jesus Christ from the dead (see Mt 28:2; cf. Eph 1:18–23 and note on 1:19).
77:17 *arrows.* Lightning bolts (see note on Ge 9:13).
77:20 Completes the thought of v. 15 (see introduction). *led your people.* Through the Desert of Sinai. *like a flock.* See 23:1; 74:1 and notes.

Ps 78 A salvation-history psalm, warning Israel not to repeat their sins of the past but to remember God's saving acts and marvelously persistent grace and, remembering, to keep faith with him and his covenant. Here, as elsewhere (pervasively in the OT), trust in and loyalty to God on the part of God's people are covenant matters. They do not spring from abstract principles (such as the formal structure of the God-human relationship) or from general human consciousness (such as feelings of dependence on "God" or a sense of awe in the presence of the "holy"), but they result from remembering God's mighty saving acts. Correspondingly, unfaithfulness is the more blameworthy because it contemptuously disregards all God's wonderful acts in his people's behalf (see Ps 105–106).

The psalm probably dates from the period of the divided monarchy and may have been composed about the time of the prophet Hosea (both Hosea and Isaiah speak frequently of the northern kingdom as Ephraim since it was the dominant tribe of that realm). Israel's unfaithfulness is here epitomized in the sin of Ephraim (v. 9); the psalm concludes by recalling the rejection of "Israel" (v. 59) and the abandonment of Shiloh (v. 60) but the election of Judah and Mount Zion (v. 68). Coming, as may be assumed, from the pen of an Asaphite, the psalm was no doubt a warning to worshipers at Jerusalem not to fall away after the manner of the Israelites to the north.

By placing this psalm next to Ps 77, the editors of the Psalter ranked David alongside Moses (and Aaron) as the Lord's shepherd over his people (see vv. 70–72; 77:20), who brought the exodus to its (provisionally) climactic fruition by completing the conquest of the promised land—a perspective apparently shared by the author of the psalm.

The psalm is composed of 77 (Hebrew) lines (72 numbered verses) and seven stanzas—with an 11-line introduction. After the introduction, the structure of the stanzas is symmetrical: 8 lines, 16 lines, 9 lines, 16 lines, 9 lines, 8 lines. The two sequences of 16 lines–9 lines constitute a thematic cycle, while the two 8-line stanzas frame the double cycle and underscore the contrast between the sin of Israel ("Ephraim," vv. 9–16) and the unending mercy of God to his people—mercy that is evidenced in his victory over his enemies and his election of Zion (in Judah) and David (vv. 65–72). For this psalm's relationship to Ps 73 in the arrangement of the Psalter, see introduction to Ps 73–78.
78 title *maskil.* See note on Ps 32 title. *Asaph.* See note on Ps 73 title.

78:1–8 Our children must hear what our fathers have told us, so that they may be faithful to the Lord.
78:1–2 This introduction is written in the style of a wisdom writer (see essay, p. 786; see also Ps 49:1–4).
78:2 *parable … hidden things.* While both terms had specialized uses, they apparently also became conventionalized more generally for instruction in a wide variety of forms (see note on 49:14). Mt 13:35 refers to this verse as a prophecy of Jesus' parabolic teaching. Matthew apparently perceived in this psalm a prophetic voice anticipating that of the great Prophet. The "parable" of the psalm is, however, more like the teaching of Stephen (Ac 7) than that of Jesus.

78:4–5 The Lord's saving acts and his covenant statutes—both must be taught, and in relationship, for together they remain the focal point for faith and obedience down through the generations (see vv. 7–8).
78:4 *not hide them.* See Job 15:18.
78:5 *teach their children.* See, e.g., Ex 10:2; 12:26–27; 13:8,14; Dt 4:9; 6:7,20–21.

7 Then they would put their trust in God
and would not forget[t] his deeds
but would keep his commands.[u]
8 They would not be like their
ancestors[v] —
a stubborn[w] and rebellious[x]
generation,
whose hearts were not loyal to God,
whose spirits were not faithful to
him.

9 The men of Ephraim, though armed
with bows,[y]
turned back on the day of battle;[z]
10 they did not keep God's covenant[a]
and refused to live by his law.[b]
11 They forgot what he had done,[c]
the wonders he had shown them.
12 He did miracles[d] in the sight of their
ancestors
in the land of Egypt,[e] in the region of
Zoan.[f]
13 He divided the sea[g] and led them
through;
he made the water stand up like a
wall.[h]
14 He guided them with the cloud by day
and with light from the fire all night.[i]
15 He split the rocks[j] in the wilderness
and gave them water as abundant as
the seas;
16 he brought streams out of a rocky crag
and made water flow down like
rivers.

17 But they continued to sin[k] against him,
rebelling in the wilderness against
the Most High.
18 They willfully put God to the test[l]
by demanding the food they craved.[m]
19 They spoke against God;[n]
they said, "Can God really
spread a table in the wilderness?
20 True, he struck the rock,
and water gushed out,[o]
streams flowed abundantly,
but can he also give us bread?
Can he supply meat[p] for his people?"
21 When the LORD heard them, he was
furious;
his fire broke out[q] against Jacob,
and his wrath rose against Israel,
22 for they did not believe in God
or trust[r] in his deliverance.
23 Yet he gave a command to the skies
above
and opened the doors of the
heavens;[s]
24 he rained down manna[t] for the people
to eat,
he gave them the grain of heaven.
25 Human beings ate the bread of angels;
he sent them all the food they could
eat.
26 He let loose the east wind[u] from the
heavens
and by his power made the south
wind blow.
27 He rained meat down on them like
dust,
birds[v] like sand on the seashore.

78:7 [t]S Dt 6:12 [u]S Dt 5:29 **78:8** [v]S 2Ch 30:7 [w]S Ex 32:9 [x]S Ex 23:21; S Dt 21:18; Isa 30:9; 65:2 **78:9** [y]ver 57; 1Ch 12:2; Hos 7:16 [z]S Jdg 20:39 **78:10** [a]S Jos 7:11; S 2Ki 17:15 [b]S Ex 16:28; S Jer 11:8 **78:11** [c]Ps 106:13 **78:12** [d]S Ne 9:17; Ps 106:22 [e]Ex 11:9 [f]S Nu 13:22 **78:13** [g]S Ex 14:21; Ps 66:6; 136:13 [h]S Ex 14:22; S 15:8 **78:14** [i]Ex 13:21; Ps 105:39 **78:15** [j]S Nu 20:11; 1Co 10:4 **78:17** [k]ver 32, 40; Dt 9:22; Isa 30:1; 63:10; Heb 3:16 **78:18** [l]S Ex 17:2; 1Co 10:9 [m]S Ex 15:24; Nu 11:4 **78:19** [n]Nu 21:5 **78:20** [o]S Nu 20:11; S Isa 35:6 [p]Nu 11:18 **78:21** [q]S Nu 11:1 **78:22** [r]S Dt 1:32; Heb 3:19 **78:23** [s]Ge 7:11; S 2Ki 7:2 **78:24** [t]Ex 16:4; Jn 6:31* **78:26** [u]S Nu 11:31 **78:27** [v]S Ex 16:13; Nu 11:31

78:8 *stubborn and rebellious.* Like a rebellious son (see Dt 9:6–7,24; 31:27). *generation.* Reference here is to a people with certain shared characteristics (see 24:6; Dt 32:5,20), thus not limited to the exodus generation (see vv. 9–11,56–64). *hearts.* See note on 4:7.

78:9–16 The northern kingdom has violated God's covenant, not remembering his saving acts (a message emphasized by the prophets Amos and Hosea). Israel's history with God has been a long series of rebellions on her part (vv. 9–16,32–39,56–64), beginning already in the wilderness (vv. 17–31,40–55).

78:9 *men of Ephraim.* The northern kingdom, dominated by the tribe of Ephraim (see introduction). *turned back.* Neither the tribe of Ephraim nor the northern kingdom had a reputation for cowardice or ineffectiveness in battle (see, e.g., Dt 33:17). This verse is best understood as a metaphor for Israel's betrayal of God's covenant (see v. 10), related to the figure of the "faulty bow" (v. 57).

78:12–16 A summary reference to the plagues in Egypt and to the water miracles at the "Red Sea" and in the wilderness. In the two cycles that follow (vv. 17–39,40–64), further elaboration intensifies the indictment.

78:12 See Ex 7–12. *Zoan.* A city in the northeast part of the Nile delta (see v. 43; see also Nu 13:22 and note).

78:13 See Ex 14:1—15:21.

78:15–16 See v. 20; Ex 17:6; Nu 20:8,10–11.

78:17–31 Israel's rebelliousness in the wilderness; God's marvelous provision of food—and his anger.

78:17 *continued.* Although no sin in the wilderness has yet been mentioned, the poet probably expected his readers to recall (in conjunction with the miraculous provisions of water just mentioned) how the people grumbled at Marah because of lack of water (see Ex 15:24). *Most High.* See vv. 35,56; see also note on Ge 14:19.

78:18 See Ex 16:2–3. *put God to the test.* See vv. 41,56; see also note on Ex 17:2.

78:19 *Can God really spread a table . . . ?* For a different use of the same imagery, see 23:5.

78:20 *bread . . . meat.* The poet is probably combining and compressing two episodes (Ex 16:2–3; Nu 11:4).

78:21 *wrath.* See vv. 31,49–50,58–59,62; see also note on 2:5.

78:23 *opened the doors of the heavens.* For this imagery, see Ge 7:11; 2Ki 7:2; Mal 3:10.

78:25 *bread of angels.* So called because it came down from heaven. *angels.* Lit. "mighty ones." The Hebrew word is used only here of the angels, but reference is clearly to heavenly beings (see 103:20).

78:26–28 See Ex 16:13; Nu 11:31.

78:26 *east wind . . . south wind.* Since the quail were migrating from Egypt at this time, the south wind may have carried them north and the east wind may have diverted them to the wilderness area occupied by the Israelites (the book of Numbers does not provide wind directions).

78:27 *like dust . . . like sand.* Similes for a huge number (see note on Ge 13:16).

28 He made them come down inside their
camp,
all around their tents.
29 They ate till they were gorged—[w]
he had given them what they craved.
30 But before they turned from what they
craved,
even while the food was still in their
mouths,[x]
31 God's anger rose against them;
he put to death the sturdiest[y] among
them,
cutting down the young men of
Israel.

32 In spite of all this, they kept on
sinning;[z]
in spite of his wonders,[a] they did not
believe.[b]
33 So he ended their days in futility[c]
and their years in terror.
34 Whenever God slew them, they would
seek[d] him;
they eagerly turned to him again.
35 They remembered that God was their
Rock,[e]
that God Most High was their
Redeemer.[f]
36 But then they would flatter him with
their mouths,[g]
lying to him with their tongues;
37 their hearts were not loyal[h] to him,
they were not faithful to his
covenant.
38 Yet he was merciful;[i]
he forgave[j] their iniquities[k]
and did not destroy them.
Time after time he restrained his anger[l]
and did not stir up his full wrath.
39 He remembered that they were but
flesh,[m]
a passing breeze[n] that does not
return.

40 How often they rebelled[o] against him
in the wilderness[p]
and grieved him[q] in the wasteland!

41 Again and again they put God to the
test;[r]
they vexed the Holy One of Israel.[s]
42 They did not remember[t] his power—
the day he redeemed them from the
oppressor,[u]
43 the day he displayed his signs[v] in
Egypt,
his wonders[w] in the region of Zoan.
44 He turned their river into blood;[x]
they could not drink from their
streams.
45 He sent swarms of flies[y] that devoured
them,
and frogs[z] that devastated them.
46 He gave their crops to the grasshopper,[a]
their produce to the locust.[b]
47 He destroyed their vines with hail[c]
and their sycamore-figs with sleet.
48 He gave over their cattle to the hail,
their livestock[d] to bolts of lightning.
49 He unleashed against them his hot
anger,[e]
his wrath, indignation and
hostility—
a band of destroying angels.[f]
50 He prepared a path for his anger;
he did not spare them from death
but gave them over to the plague.
51 He struck down all the firstborn of
Egypt,[g]
the firstfruits of manhood in the
tents of Ham.[h]
52 But he brought his people out like a
flock;[i]
he led them like sheep through the
wilderness.
53 He guided them safely, so they were
unafraid;
but the sea engulfed[j] their enemies.[k]
54 And so he brought them to the border
of his holy land,
to the hill country his right hand[l]
had taken.

78:29 [w]S Nu 11:20 **78:30** [x]S Nu 11:33 **78:31** [y]Isa 10:16 **78:32** [z]S ver 17 [a]ver 11 [b]ver 22 **78:33** [c]Nu 14:29,35 **78:34** [d]S Dt 4:29; Hos 5:15 **78:35** [e]S Ge 49:24 [f]S Dt 9:26 **78:36** [g]Eze 33:31 **78:37** [h]ver 8; Ac 8:21 **78:38** [i]S Ex 34:6 [j]Isa 1:25; 27:9; 48:10; Da 11:35 [k]Ps 25:11; 85:2 [l]S Job 9:13; S Isa 30:18 **78:39** [m]S Ge 6:3; S Isa 29:5 [n]S Job 7:7; Jas 4:14 **78:40** [o]S Ex 23:21 [p]Ps 95:8; 106:14 [q]Eph 4:30 **78:41** [r]S Ex 17:2 [s]S 2Ki 19:22; Ps 71:22; 89:18 **78:42** [t]S Jdg 3:7; S Ne 9:17 [u]S Ps 27:11 **78:43** [v]Ex 10:1 [w]S Ex 3:20 **78:44** [x]Ex 7:20-21; Ps 105:29 **78:45** [y]Ex 8:24; Ps 105:31 [z]S Ex 8:2,6 **78:46** [a]Na 3:15 [b]S Ex 10:13 **78:47** [c]Ex 9:23; Ps 105:32; 147:17 **78:48** [d]Ex 9:25 **78:49** [e]Ex 15:7 [f]S Ge 19:13; 1Co 10:10 **78:51** [g]S Ex 12:12; Ps 135:8 [h]Ps 105:23; 106:22 **78:52** [i]S Job 21:11; S Ps 28:9; 77:20 **78:53** [j]S Ex 14:28 [k]Ex 15:7; Ps 106:10 **78:54** [l]Ps 44:3

78:30–31 See Nu 11:33.
78:32–39 Rebelliousness, which became Israel's way of life, showed itself early in the wilderness wandering (vv. 17–31) and continued throughout that journey.
78:32 *did not believe.* That God could give them victory over the Canaanites (see Nu 14:11).
78:33 The exodus generation was condemned to die in the wilderness (see Nu 14:22–23,28–35; cf. note on Heb 3:16–19).
78:34–37 A cycle repeated frequently during the period of the judges (see note on Jdg 2:6—3:6).
78:35 *Rock.* See note on 18:2. *Redeemer.* Deliverer (see note on 71:23).
78:36 See Isa 29:13.
78:37 *hearts.* See note on 4:7.
78:38 See Ex 32:14; Nu 14:20. *forgave.* See note on 65:3.
78:39 See 103:14; see also 39:5; 62:9; 144:4 and notes.
78:40–64 The second cycle (the first is vv. 17–39).
78:40–55 Israel's rebelliousness began in the wilderness; she did not remember how she had been delivered from oppression by God's plagues upon Egypt (see v. 12). Yet he brought his people through the sea and the wilderness and established them in the promised land.
78:41 *Holy One of Israel.* See 71:22; 89:18; see also 2Ki 19:22 and note.
78:44–51 The plagues upon Egypt (see Ex 7–12): The sequence in Exodus is followed only in the first and last; the third, fifth, sixth and ninth plagues are not mentioned.
78:47 *sycamore-figs.* See note on Am 7:14.
78:49 *destroying angels.* The poet personifies God's wrath, indignation and hostility as agents of his anger.
78:51 *tents.* Dwellings. *Ham.* For the association of Ham with Egypt, see 105:23,27; 106:21–22; Ge 10:6 and note.
78:52 *like a flock.* See 77:20 and note.
78:53 *sea.* "Red Sea" (see Ex 15:1–21 and notes).
78:54 *holy land.* See note on Zec 2:12.

[55]He drove out nations[m] before them
and allotted their lands to them as
an inheritance;[n]
he settled the tribes of Israel in their
homes.

[56]But they put God to the test
and rebelled against the Most
High;
they did not keep his statutes.
[57]Like their ancestors[o] they were disloyal
and faithless,
as unreliable as a faulty bow.[p]
[58]They angered him[q] with their high
places;[r]
they aroused his jealousy with their
idols.[s]
[59]When God heard[t] them, he was
furious;[u]
he rejected Israel[v] completely.
[60]He abandoned the tabernacle of
Shiloh,[w]
the tent he had set up among
humans.[x]
[61]He sent the ark of his might[y] into
captivity,[z]
his splendor into the hands of the
enemy.
[62]He gave his people over to the sword;[a]
he was furious with his
inheritance.[b]
[63]Fire consumed[c] their young men,
and their young women had no
wedding songs;[d]
[64]their priests were put to the sword,[e]
and their widows could not weep.

[65]Then the Lord awoke as from sleep,[f]
as a warrior wakes from the stupor
of wine.
[66]He beat back his enemies;
he put them to everlasting shame.[g]
[67]Then he rejected the tents of Joseph,
he did not choose the tribe of
Ephraim;[h]
[68]but he chose the tribe of Judah,[i]
Mount Zion,[j] which he loved.
[69]He built his sanctuary[k] like the heights,
like the earth that he established
forever.
[70]He chose David[l] his servant
and took him from the sheep pens;
[71]from tending the sheep[m] he brought
him
to be the shepherd[n] of his people
Jacob,
of Israel his inheritance.
[72]And David shepherded them with
integrity of heart;[o]
with skillful hands he led them.

78:55 [m] Ps 44:2 [n] S Dt 1:38; S Jos 13:7; Ac 13:19 **78:57** [o] S 2Ch 30:7; Eze 20:27 [p] S ver 9 **78:58** [q] S Jdg 2:12 [r] S Lev 26:30 [s] Ex 20:4; S Dt 5:8; 32:21 **78:59** [t] Ps 55:19 [u] S Lev 26:28; S Nu 32:14 [v] S Dt 32:19 **78:60** [w] S Jos 18:1 [x] Eze 8:6 **78:61** [y] Ps 132:8 [z] S 1Sa 4:17 **78:62** [a] S Dt 28:25 [b] S 1Sa 10:1 **78:63** [c] S Nu 11:1 [d] S 1Ki 4:32; Jer 7:34; 16:9; 25:10 **78:64** [e] 1Sa 4:17 **78:65** [f] Ps 44:23 **78:66** [g] 1Sa 5:6 **78:67** [h] Jer 7:15; Hos 9:13; 12:1 **78:68** [i] S Nu 1:7; Ps 108:8 [j] S Ex 15:17; S Ps 68:16 **78:69** [k] S Ps 15:1 **78:70** [l] S 1Sa 16:1 **78:71** [m] S Ge 37:2 [n] S Ps 28:9 **78:72** [o] S Ge 17:1

78:55 Summarizes the story told in Joshua.
78:56–64 Rebelliousness continued to be Israel's way of life in the promised land (a recurring theme of Judges; see also 1Sa 2:12—7:2), so God rejected Israel (v. 59; see Jer 7:15).
78:57 *faulty bow.* See note on v. 9.
78:58 *high places.* See note on 1Sa 9:12. *jealousy.* God's intense reaction to disloyalty to him (see note on Ex 20:5).
78:59 *rejected Israel completely.* Abandoned her to her enemies. The psalmist does not speak of a permanent casting off of Israel, not even of the ten northern tribes (cf. note on Ro 9:1—11:36).
78:60 *Shiloh.* The center of worship since the time of Joshua (see Jos 18:1,8; 21:1–2; Jdg 18:31; 1Sa 1:3; Jer 7:12), it was located in Ephraim between Bethel and Shechem (see Jdg 21:19; see also map, p. 2521, at the end of this study Bible). Apparently it was destroyed by the Philistines when they captured the ark or shortly afterward (see note on Jer 7:12).
78:61 *his might…his splendor.* The ark is here so called because it was the sign of God's kingship in Israel and the focal point for the display of his power and glory (see 26:8; 63:2; 1Sa 4:3,21–22).
78:62,71 *his inheritance.* See Dt 9:29.
78:63 *Fire.* Often associated with the sword (see vv. 62,64) as the two primary instruments of destruction in ancient warfare. *no wedding songs.* So great was the catastrophe that both the wedding songs of the brides and the wailing of the widows (see v. 64) were silenced in the land.
78:64 *priests were put to the sword.* See 1Sa 4:11.
78:65–72 The Lord's election of Judah (instead of Ephraim) as the leading tribe in Israel (anticipated in Jacob's deathbed blessing of his sons, Ge 49:8–12), of Mount Zion (instead of Shiloh) as the place of his sanctuary (royal seat) and of David as his regent to shepherd his people.
78:65 *awoke as from sleep.* Poetic hyperbole to highlight the contrast between God's action in behalf of his people in the days of David and the preceding time of Israel's troubles (see note on 7:6).
78:66–72 The saving events noted have two focal points: (1) God's decisive victory over his enemies (thus securing his realm) and the establishment of Zion as his royal city, and (2) the appointment of David to be the shepherd of his people.
78:67 *tents of Joseph.* A figure for the tribe of Ephraim (for the figurative use of "tents," see v. 51; see also 69:25; 83:6; 84:10; 120:5; Ge 9:27; Dt 33:18; 1Ki 12:16; Job 8:22; 12:6; Hab 3:7; Mal 2:12).
78:68,70 *he chose … Mount Zion … He chose David.* See Ps 132.
78:69 *heights … earth.* The verse is subject to two interpretations: (1) The Lord built his sanctuary as impregnable as a mountain fortress and as enduring and immovable as the age-old earth, or (2) the Lord built his sanctuary as secure and enduring as the heavens and the earth (see note on 24:2) and there manifests himself as the Lord of glory (see 24:7–10; 26:8; 63:2; 96:6), even as he does in the creation (see 19:1; 29:9; 97:6).
78:70–71 See 1Sa 16:11–13; 2Sa 7:8.
78:70 *his servant.* Here an official title marking David as a member of God's royal administration (see notes on Ex 14:31; Ps 18 title; Isa 41:8–9; 42:1). For David as God's "servant," see also 89:3,20,39; 132:10; 144:20.
78:71 *shepherd.* See v. 72; see also note on 23:1.
78:72 Israel under the care of the Lord's royal shepherd from the house of David was for the prophets the hope of God's people (see Eze 34:23; 37:24; Mic 5:4—fulfilled in Jesus Christ, Mt 2:6; Jn 10:11; Rev 7:17). *shepherded.* See note on 23:1.

Psalm 79

A psalm of Asaph.

[1] O God, the nations have invaded
your inheritance;[p]
they have defiled[q] your holy
temple,
they have reduced Jerusalem to
rubble.[r]
[2] They have left the dead bodies of
your servants
as food for the birds of the
sky,[s]
the flesh of your own people
for the animals of the
wild.[t]
[3] They have poured out blood like
water
all around Jerusalem,
and there is no one to bury[u]
the dead.[v]
[4] We are objects of contempt to our
neighbors,
of scorn[w] and derision to those
around us.[x]

[5] How long,[y] LORD? Will you be angry[z]
forever?
How long will your jealousy burn
like fire?[a]
[6] Pour out your wrath[b] on the nations
that do not acknowledge[c] you,
on the kingdoms
that do not call on your name;[d]

Ancient street in Jerusalem that used to run under Robinson's Arch. The rubble in the background is from the destruction of Jerusalem in AD 70 by the Romans. "O God, the nations have invaded your inheritance; they have defiled your holy temple, they have reduced Jerusalem to rubble" (Ps 79:1).

www.HolyLandPhotos.org

[7] for they have devoured[e] Jacob
and devastated his homeland.

[8] Do not hold against us the sins of past
generations;[f]
may your mercy come quickly to
meet us,
for we are in desperate need.[g]

79:1 [p] S Ex 34:9 [q] S Lev 20:3 [r] S 2Ki 25:9; S Ne 4:2; S Isa 6:11 **79:2** [s] Rev 19:17-18 [t] S Dt 28:26; Jer 7:33 **79:3** [u] Jer 25:33; Rev 11:9 [v] Jer 16:4 **79:4** [w] S Ps 39:8; S Eze 5:14 [x] Ps 44:13; 80:6 **79:5** [y] S Ps 74:10 [z] Ps 74:1; 85:5 [a] S Dt 29:20; Ps 89:46; Zep 3:8 **79:6** [b] S Ps 2:5; 69:24; 110:5; Rev 16:1 [c] Ps 147:20; Jer 10:25 [d] S Ps 14:4 **79:7** [e] Isa 9:12; Jer 10:25 **79:8** [f] S Ge 9:25; Jer 44:21 [g] Ps 116:6; 142:6

Ps 79–83 A group of five psalms at the center of Book III that are framed by two urgent prayers of the community when the nation has been invaded by powerful enemies (for the different events alluded to, see introductions to Ps 79; 83). In the center of this group (Ps 81)—thus also at the center of Book III—stands an urgent admonition to wayward Israel, reminding God's people that only if they are faithful to the Lord, who brought them out of Egypt, will he preserve them or rescue them from the ravaging of their enemies. Bracketing this center on one side is a communal prayer for God to "restore" his "flock" and revive his once thriving "vine" that has been decimated by enemies (Ps 80) and on the other a prayer that the God who judges all kings and possesses all nations will arouse himself to "judge the earth" (Ps 82).

Ps 79 Israel's prayer for God's forgiveness and help and for his judgment on the nations that have so cruelly destroyed her, showing utter contempt for both the Lord and his people. For the relationship of this psalm to Ps 80–83 in the arrangement of the Psalter, see introduction to Ps 79–83. Like Ps 74, with which it has many thematic links, Ps 79 dates from the time of the exile. The poignancy of its appeal is heightened by its juxtaposition to Ps 77 (recalling God's saving acts under Moses) and Ps 78 (recalling God's saving acts under David), two psalms with which it is significantly linked by the shepherd-sheep figure and other thematic elements. Israel acknowledges that the Lord has used the nations to punish her for her sins, so she pleads for pardon. But she knows too that the nations have acted out of their hostility to and disdain for God and his people; that warrants her plea for God's judgment on them (see Isa 10:5–11; 47:6–7). Daniel's prayer (Da 9:4–19) contains much that is similar to the elements of penitence in this psalm.

79 title *Asaph.* See note on Ps 73 title.

79:1–4 What the nations have done: They have attacked God's own special domain, violated his temple, destroyed his royal city, slaughtered his people, degraded them in death (by withholding burial—see note on 53:5—and leaving their bodies as carrion for birds and beasts) and reduced them to the scorn of the world.

79:1 *your inheritance.* Cf. 78:62,71. Here reference is to Israel's homeland as the Lord's domain (see note on 2:8; cf. 114:2 and note). *holy temple.* See note on 78:69; see also photo above.

79:2 *your servants.* Though banished from the Lord's land for sins that cannot be denied, the exiles plead their special covenant relationship with God (see "your own people," here, and "your people, the sheep of your pasture," v. 13). *your own people.* See note on 4:3.

79:3 *poured out blood … all around Jerusalem.* Cf. 2Ki 21:16.

79:5–8 A prayer for God to relent and deal with the nations who do not acknowledge him.

79:5 *How long … ?* See note on 6:3. *angry.* See v. 6 ("wrath"); see also note on 2:5. *jealousy.* See note on 78:58. *burn like fire.* See Dt 4:24; 6:15; Zep 1:18; 3:8.

79:6–7 See Jer 10:25 and note. Perhaps the psalmist is quoting Jeremiah here.

79:6 *Pour out your wrath.* As they "poured out" (v. 3) the blood of your people. The exiles plead with God to redress the wrongs committed against them (see note on 5:10).

79:7 *devoured.* Like wild beasts (see 44:11; 74:19 and note on 7:2). *Jacob.* A synonym for Israel (see Ge 32:28).

79:8 *sins of past generations.* Israel suffered exile because of the accumulated sins of the nation (see 2Ki 17:7–23; 23:26–27; 24:3–4; Da 9:4–14), of which she did not repent

[9]Help us,[h] God our Savior,
for the glory of your name;
deliver us and forgive our sins
for your name's sake.[i]
[10]Why should the nations say,
"Where is their God?"[j]

Before our eyes, make known among
the nations
that you avenge[k] the outpoured
blood[l] of your servants.
[11]May the groans of the prisoners come
before you;
with your strong arm preserve those
condemned to die.
[12]Pay back into the laps[m] of our
neighbors seven times[n]
the contempt they have hurled at
you, Lord.
[13]Then we your people, the sheep of
your pasture,[o]
will praise you forever;[p]
from generation to generation
we will proclaim your praise.

Psalm 80[a]

For the director of music. To the tune of "The Lilies of the Covenant." Of Asaph. A psalm.

[1]Hear us, Shepherd of Israel,
you who lead Joseph like a
flock.[q]
You who sit enthroned between the
cherubim,[r]
shine forth [2]before Ephraim,
Benjamin and Manasseh.[s]
Awaken[t] your might;
come and save us.[u]

[3]Restore[v] us,[w] O God;
make your face shine on us,
that we may be saved.[x]

[4]How long,[y] LORD God Almighty,
will your anger smolder[z]
against the prayers of your
people?
[5]You have fed them with the bread of
tears;[a]
you have made them drink tears by
the bowlful.[b]
[6]You have made us an object of
derision[b] to our neighbors,
and our enemies mock us.[c]

[7]Restore us, God Almighty;
make your face shine on us,
that we may be saved.[d]

79:9 [h]S 2Ch 14:11 [i]Ps 25:11; 31:3; Jer 14:7
79:10 [j]S Ps 42:3 [k]Ps 94:1; S Rev 6:10 [l]ver 3
79:12 [m]Isa 65:6; Jer 32:18 [n]S Ge 4:15
79:13 [o]S Ps 74:1 [p]Ps 44:8
80:1 [q]Ps 77:20 [r]S Ex 25:22
80:2 [s]Nu 2:18-24 [t]S Ps 35:23 [u]Ps 54:1; 69:1; 71:2; 109:26; 116:4; 119:94
80:3 [v]S Ps 71:20; 85:4; Jer 31:18; La 5:21 [w]S Nu 6:25 [x]ver 7,19
80:4 [y]S Ps 74:10 [z]S Dt 29:20
80:5 [a]S Job 3:24 [b]Isa 30:20
80:6 [c]S Ps 79:4
80:7 [d]ver 3

[a] In Hebrew texts 80:1-19 is numbered 80:2-20.
[b] 6 Probable reading of the original Hebrew text; Masoretic Text *contention*

until the judgment of God had fallen on her. The exiles here pray that God will take notice of their penitence and not continue to hold the sins of past generations against his now repentant people. *mercy.* Here personified as God's agent sent to bring relief (see notes on 23:6; 43:3).

79:9–11 A prayer for God to help and forgive his people and to redress the violent acts of the enemies.

79:9 *for the glory of your name.* As the desolation of God's people brings reproach to God (see v. 10), so their salvation and prosperity bring him glory (see note on 23:3). *forgive.* See note on 65:3.

79:10 *Where is their God?* See note on 3:2. *avenge.* Redress (see Dt 32:35,43).

79:11 *prisoners … those condemned to die.* The exiles, as imperial captives in Babylonia (see 102:20)—not actually in prisons, but under threat of death should they seek to return to their homeland.

79:12–13 Concluding prayer and vow to praise God.

79:12 *Pay back into the laps.* See note on Jer 32:18. *seven times.* In full measure; the number seven symbolized completeness. *contempt … at you.* The enemies' violent action against Israel was above all a high-handed reviling of God (see vv. 1,10; 2Ki 19:10–12,22–23; Isa 52:5).

79:13 *sheep of your pasture.* See 23:2; 74:1 and notes; see also 77:20; 78:72; 80:1. *will praise you forever.* See note on 7:17. *from generation to generation.* See 78:4.

Ps 80 Israel's prayer for restoration when she had been ravaged by a foreign power. For the relationship of this psalm to the others in its group, see introduction to Ps 79–83. It seems likely that "Ephraim, Benjamin and Manasseh" (v. 2) here represent the northern kingdom. Recent archaeological surveys of the Holy Land have shown that Jerusalem and the surrounding countryside experienced a dramatic increase of population at this time, no doubt the result of a massive influx of displaced persons from the north fleeing the Assyrian beast. This could account for the presence of "Ephraim, Benjamin and Manasseh" at the Jerusalem sanctuary, and for a national prayer for restoration with special focus on these tribes (see notes below). The prayer has five stanzas of four (Hebrew) lines each. A recurring petition climaxes the first, second and last (for other refrains, see introduction to Ps 42–43), with a progressing urgency of appeal: "God" (v. 3); "God Almighty" (v. 7); "LORD God Almighty" (v. 19).

80 title *For the director of music.* See note on Ps 4 title. *To the tune of.* See note on Ps 9 title. *Lilies.* See note on Ps 45 title. *Asaph.* See note on Ps 73 title.

80:1–3 An appeal for God to arouse himself and go before his people again with all his glory and might as he did of old in the wilderness.

80:1 See the shepherd-flock motif in 74:1; 77:20; 78:52, 71–72; 79:13; see also 23:1–2 and notes. *Joseph.* See note on 77:15. *enthroned between the cherubim.* See note on Ex 25:18. *shine forth.* Let your glory be seen again, as in the wilderness journey (see Ex 24:16–17; 40:34–35), but now especially through your new saving act (see 102:15–16; Ex 14:4,17–18; Nu 14:22; Isa 40:5; 44:23; 60:1–2).

80:2 *before Ephraim, Benjamin and Manasseh.* March against the nations as you marched in the midst of your army from Sinai into the promised land (in that march the ark of the covenant advanced in front of the troops of these three tribes; see Nu 10:21–24; see also introduction to Ps 68). *Awaken.* See note on 7:6.

80:3 *make your face shine.* See vv. 7,19; an echo of the priestly benediction (see Nu 6:25; see also notes on 4:6; 13:1).

80:4–7 A lament over the Lord's severe punishment of his people.

80:4 *How long … ?* See note on 6:3. *LORD … Almighty.* See vv. 7,14,19; see also note on 1Sa 1:3. *anger.* See note on 2:5.

80:5 God has now given them tears to eat and tears to drink rather than "the bread of angels" and water from the rock (see 78:20,25).

8 You transplanted a vine[e] from Egypt;
you drove out[f] the nations and planted[g] it.
9 You cleared the ground for it,
and it took root and filled the land.
10 The mountains were covered with its shade,
the mighty cedars with its branches.
11 Its branches reached as far as the Sea,[a]
its shoots as far as the River.[b][h]

12 Why have you broken down its walls[i]
so that all who pass by pick its grapes?
13 Boars from the forest ravage[j] it,
and insects from the fields feed on it.
14 Return to us, God Almighty!
Look down from heaven and see![k]
Watch over this vine,
15 the root your right hand has planted,
the son[c] you have raised up for yourself.

16 Your vine is cut down, it is burned with fire;[l]
at your rebuke[m] your people perish.
17 Let your hand rest on the man at your right hand,
the son of man[n] you have raised up for yourself.

80:8 [e] Isa 5:1-2; Jer 2:21; Mt 21:33-41 [f] Ex 23:28-30; S Jos 13:6; Ac 7:45 [g] S Ex 15:17 **80:11** [h] Ps 72:8 **80:12** [i] Ps 89:40; Isa 5:5; 30:13; Jer 39:8 **80:13** [j] Jer 5:6 **80:14** [k] S Dt 26:15 **80:16** [l] Ps 79:1 [m] S Dt 28:20 **80:17** [n] S Job 25:6

80:18 [o] Ps 85:6; Isa 57:15; Hos 6:2 **81:1** [p] S Ps 66:1 **81:2** [q] S Ex 15:20 [r] Ps 92:3 [s] S Job 21:12 **81:3** [t] S Ex 19:13 [u] S Ne 10:33 **81:4** [v] ver 1 **81:5** [w] S Ex 11:4

18 Then we will not turn away from you;
revive[o] us, and we will call on your name.

19 Restore us, LORD God Almighty;
make your face shine on us,
that we may be saved.

Psalm 81[d]

For the director of music. According to *gittith*.[e] Of Asaph.

1 Sing for joy to God our strength;
shout aloud to the God of Jacob![p]
2 Begin the music, strike the timbrel,[q]
play the melodious harp[r] and lyre.[s]

3 Sound the ram's horn[t] at the New Moon,[u]
and when the moon is full, on the day of our festival;
4 this is a decree for Israel,
an ordinance of the God of Jacob.[v]
5 When God went out against Egypt,[w]
he established it as a statute for Joseph.

[a] *11* Probably the Mediterranean [b] *11* That is, the Euphrates [c] *15* Or *branch* [d] In Hebrew texts 81:1-16 is numbered 81:2-17. [e] Title: Probably a musical term

80:8–16 This use of the vine-vineyard metaphor (here to describe Israel's changed condition) is found also in the Prophets (see Isa 3:14; 5:1–7; 27:2; Jer 2:21; 12:10; Eze 17:6–8; 19:10–14; Hos 10:1; 14:7; Mic 7:1; see also Ge 49:22; Mt 20:1–16; Mk 12:1–9; Lk 20:9–16; Jn 15:1–5).
80:8–11 Israel was once God's flourishing, transplanted vine.
80:8 *transplanted ... from Egypt.* See 78:52. *drove out the nations and planted.* See 44:2.
80:9 *cleared the ground.* See Isa 5:2.
80:10 *mighty cedars.* Lit. "cedars of God" (the Hebrew word for "God" is sometimes used in the sense of "mighty"; see, e.g., note on 29:1).
80:11 *Sea ... River.* See NIV text notes; see also Ex 23:31 and note.
80:12–15 A prayer for God to renew his care for his ravaged vine.
80:12 *Why ... ?* Israel's anguished perplexity over God's abandonment (see note on 6:3). *broken down its walls.* Taken away its defenses.
80:14 *Watch over.* See Ex 3:16. But the Hebrew for this phrase may have the sense here that it has in Ru 1:6: "Come to the aid of."
80:15 *son.* Israel (see Ex 4:22–23; Hos 11:1). But "son" may sometimes be used also to refer to a vine branch (see NIV text note; see also note on Ge 49:22). That may be the case here, thus yielding the conventional pair "root and branch," a figure for the whole vine (see Job 18:16; 29:19; Eze 17:7; Mal 4:1; see also Isa 5:24; 27:6; 37:31; Eze 17:9; 31:7; Hos 9:16; Am 2:9; Ro 11:16). *raised up.* See v. 17; lit. "made vigorous."
80:16–19 Concluding prayer for restoration.
80:16 *rebuke.* See 9:5 and note on 76:6.
80:17 *Let your hand rest on.* Show your favor to (see Ezr 7:6,9,28; 8:18,22,31; Ne 2:8,18). *at.* Lit. "of." *your right hand.* Reference may be to the Davidic king as the Lord's anointed, seated in the place of honor in God's presence (see 110:1) and the one in whom the hope of the nation rested (see 2:7–9; 72:8–11; 89:21–25). But v. 15 strongly suggests another sense: that "the man" is Jacob/Israel and that he is "of" God's "right hand" in that he has been "planted" and "raised up" by him.
80:18 A vow to be loyal to God and to trust in him alone. It occurs in a place where it would be more common to find a vow to praise God (see note on 7:17).
Ps 81 A festival song. It was probably composed for use at both the New Year festival (the first day of the month, "New Moon") and the beginning of Tabernacles (the 15th day of the month, full moon); see notes below. As memorials of God's saving acts, Israel's annual religious festivals called the nation to celebration, remembrance and recommitment (see Ps 95; see also chart, pp. 188–189). For the significant placement of this psalm within Book III of the Psalter, see introduction to Ps 73–78 and introduction to Ps 79–83. The psalm falls into two main parts (vv. 1–5, 6–16).
81 title *For the director of music.* See note on Ps 4 title. *According to.* See note on Ps 6 title. *gittith.* See note on Ps 8 title. *Asaph.* See note on Ps 73 title.
81:1–5 A summons to celebrate the appointed sacred festival.
81:1 *Jacob.* A synonym for Israel (see Ge 32:28).
81:2 *timbrel.* See note on Jer 31:4. *harp and lyre.* See note on 57:8.
81:3 *ram's horn.* The ram's horn trumpet (see Ex 19:13). *our festival.* Probably the Festival of Tabernacles (see Ex 23:16; Zec 14:16 and notes), often called simply "the festival" (see, e.g., 1Ki 8:2,65).
81:4–5 *decree ... ordinance ... statute.* See the passages referred to in note on v. 3.
81:5 *When God went out against Egypt.* Some believe this indicates that the festival referred to is Passover and Unleavened Bread (see Ex 12:14,42). More likely it serves as a reference to the whole exodus period, while highlighting especially God's triumph over Egypt by which he had set his

I heard an unknown voice say:[x]

6 "I removed the burden[y] from their
shoulders;[z]
their hands were set free from the
basket.
7 In your distress you called[a] and I
rescued you,
I answered[b] you out of a
thundercloud;
I tested you at the waters of
Meribah.[ac]
8 Hear me, my people,[d] and I will warn
you—
if you would only listen to me,
Israel!
9 You shall have no foreign god[e] among
you;
you shall not worship any god other
than me.
10 I am the LORD your God,
who brought you up out of Egypt.[f]
Open[g] wide your mouth and I will
fill[h] it.

11 "But my people would not listen
to me;
Israel would not submit to me.[i]
12 So I gave them over[j] to their stubborn
hearts
to follow their own devices.

81:5 [x]Ps 114:1 **81:6** [y]S Ex 1:14 [z]Isa 9:4; 52:2 **81:7** [a]S Ex 2:23 [b]Ex 19:19 [c]S Ex 17:7; S Dt 33:8 **81:8** [d]Ps 50:7; 78:1 **81:9** [e]S Ex 20:3 **81:10** [f]S Ex 6:6; S 13:3; S 29:46 [g]Eze 2:8 [h]Ps 107:9 **81:11** [i]Ex 32:1-6 **81:12** [j]Eze 20:25; Ac 7:42; Ro 1:24

13 "If my people would only listen
to me,[k]
if Israel would only follow my ways,
14 how quickly I would subdue[l] their
enemies
and turn my hand against[m] their
foes!
15 Those who hate the LORD would
cringe[n] before him,
and their punishment would last
forever.
16 But you would be fed with the finest
of wheat;[o]
with honey from the rock I would
satisfy you."

Psalm 82

A psalm of Asaph.

1 God presides in the great assembly;
he renders judgment[p] among the
"gods":[q]

2 "How long will you[b] defend the unjust
and show partiality[r] to the wicked?[as]
3 Defend the weak and the fatherless;[t]
uphold the cause of the poor[u] and
the oppressed.

81:13 [k]S Dt 5:29 **81:14** [l]Ps 47:3 [m]Am 1:8 **81:15** [n]S 2Sa 22:45 **81:16** [o]S Dt 32:14 **82:1** [p]Ps 7:8; 58:11; Isa 3:13; 66:16; Joel 3:12 [q]S Job 21:22 **82:2** [r]Dt 1:17 [s]Ps 58:1-2; Pr 18:5 **82:3** [t]S Dt 24:17 [u]Ps 140:12; Jer 5:28; 22:16

[a] *7,2* The Hebrew has *Selah* (a word of uncertain meaning) here. [b] *2* The Hebrew is plural.

people free (see vv. 6–7). *Joseph.* See note on 77:15. *heard an unknown voice.* The "voice" is the thunder of God's judgment against Egypt (see v. 7), which the Levitical author then proceeds to interpret as to its present reference for the celebrating congregation (vv. 6–16).

81:6–10 God heard and delivered and now summons his people to loyalty.

81:6 *burden ... basket.* The forced labor to which the Israelites were subjected in Egypt (see Ex 1:11–14).

81:7 *you called and I rescued.* See Ex 3:7–10. *out of a thundercloud.* See 106:9; Ex 14:21,24; 15:8,10; see also note on 76:6. *I tested you.* See Ex 17:1–7. For *Selah*, see NIV text note and note on 3:2.

81:8–10 God heard his people in their distress (vv. 6–7); now they must listen to him.

81:9–10 See Ex 19:4–5; 20:2–4; Dt 4:15–20.

81:10 *Open wide your mouth.* Trust in the Lord alone for all of life's needs. *I will fill it.* See v. 16; as he did in the wilderness (see 78:23–29; see also 37:3–4; Dt 11:13–15; 28:1–4).

81:11–16 Israel has not listened—if only God's people would! See Eze 18:23,32; 33:11.

81:11 See 78:10,17,32,40,56; Dt 9:7,24; Jer 7:24–26.

81:12 It is God who circumcises the heart (see Dt 30:6; see also 1Ki 8:58; Jer 31:33; Eze 11:19; 36:26). Thus for God to abandon his people to their sins is the most fearful of punishments (see 78:29; Isa 6:9–10; 29:10; 63:17; cf. Ro 1:24,26,28).

81:13–16 See the promised covenant blessings outlined in Ex 23:22–27; Lev 26:3–13; Dt 7:12–26; 28:1–14.

81:13 *my ways.* See 25:4 and note.

81:16 *honey from the rock.* See note on Dt 32:13.

Ps 82 A word of judgment on unjust rulers and judges. The Levitical author of this psalm evokes a vision of God presiding over his heavenly court—analogous to the experiences of the prophets (see 1Ki 22:19–22; Isa 6:1–7; Jer 23:18, 22; see also Job 15:8). As the Great King (see introduction to Ps 47) and the Judge of all the earth (see 94:2; Ge 18:25; 1Sa 2:10) who "loves justice" (99:4) and judges the nations in righteousness (see 9:8; 96:13; 98:9), he is seen calling to account those responsible for defending the weak and oppressed on earth. An early rabbinic interpretation (see Jn 10:34–35) understood the "gods" (vv. 1,6) to be unjust rulers and judges in Israel, of whom there were many (see 1Sa 8:3; Isa 1:16–17; 3:13–15; Jer 21:12; 22:3; Eze 34:4,21; Mic 3:1–3; 7:3). Today many identify the "gods" as the kings of surrounding nations who encouraged the conceit that they were actually or virtually divine beings but who ruled with lofty disregard for justice—though honoring it as a royal ideal. Others hold that the "gods" are the divine beings in whose names the kings claimed to rule (see 95:3). In any event, rulers and judges here are confronted by their King and Judge (see Ps 58). Structurally, the words of the Levite (vv. 1,6) frame the words of God. At the very center (see note on v. 5) stands the most devastating judgment of all. For this psalm's placement in Book III of the Psalter, see introduction to Ps 79–83.

82 title See note on Ps 73 title.

82:1 *great assembly.* The assembly in the great Hall of Justice (cf. 1Ki 7:7) in heaven (see 89:5; 1Ki 22:19; Job 1:6; 2:1; Isa 6:1–4). As if in a vision, the psalmist sees the rulers and judges gathered before the Great King to give account of their administration of justice. *gods.* See v. 6. In the language of the OT—and in accordance with the conceptual world of the ancient Near East—rulers and judges, as deputies of the heavenly King, could be given the honorific title "god" (see note on 45:6; see also NIV text notes on Ex 21:6; 22:8) or be called "son of God" (see 2:7 and note).

82:2 For *Selah*, see NIV text note and note on 3:2.

82:3–4 In the OT a first-order task of kings and judges was to protect the powerless against all who would

4 Rescue the weak and the needy;
deliver them from the hand of the wicked.

5 "The 'gods' know nothing, they understand nothing.[v]
They walk about in darkness;[w]
all the foundations[x] of the earth are shaken.

6 "I said, 'You are "gods";[y]
you are all sons of the Most High.'
7 But you will die[z] like mere mortals;
you will fall like every other ruler."

8 Rise up,[a] O God, judge[b] the earth,
for all the nations are your inheritance.[c]

Psalm 83[a]

A song. A psalm of Asaph.

1 O God, do not remain silent;[d]
do not turn a deaf ear,
do not stand aloof, O God.
2 See how your enemies growl,[e]
how your foes rear their heads.[f]
3 With cunning they conspire[g] against your people;
they plot against those you cherish.[h]

4 "Come," they say, "let us destroy[i] them as a nation,[j]
so that Israel's name is remembered[k] no more."

5 With one mind they plot together;[l]
they form an alliance against you—
6 the tents of Edom[m] and the Ishmaelites,
of Moab[n] and the Hagrites,[o]
7 Byblos,[p] Ammon[q] and Amalek,[r]
Philistia,[s] with the people of Tyre.[t]
8 Even Assyria[u] has joined them
to reinforce Lot's descendants.[b][v]

9 Do to them as you did to Midian,[w]
as you did to Sisera[x] and Jabin[y] at the river Kishon,[z]
10 who perished at Endor[a]
and became like dung[b] on the ground.
11 Make their nobles like Oreb and Zeeb,[c]
all their princes like Zebah and Zalmunna,[d]
12 who said, "Let us take possession[e]
of the pasturelands of God."

[a] In Hebrew texts 83:1-18 is numbered 83:2-19.
[b] 8 The Hebrew has *Selah* (a word of uncertain meaning) here.

82:5 [v]S Ps 14:4; S 53:2 [w]Job 30:26; Isa 5:30; 8:21-22; 9:2; 59:9; 60:2; Jer 13:16; 23:12; La 3:2 [x]S Jdg 5:4; S Ps 11:3 **82:6** [y]Jn 10:34* **82:7** [z]Ps 49:12; Eze 31:14 **82:8** [a]Ps 12:5 [b]S Ps 76:9 [c]Ps 2:8 **83:1** [d]Ps 28:1; 35:22; Isa 42:14; 57:11; 62:1; 64:12 **83:2** [e]Ps 2:1; Isa 17:12 [f]Jdg 8:28 **83:3** [g]S Ex 1:10; S Ps 31:13 [h]Ps 17:14 **83:4** [i]S Est 3:6 [j]Jer 33:24 [k]Jer 11:19 **83:5** [l]Ps 2:2 **83:6** [m]Ps 137:7; Isa 34:5; Jer 49:7; Am 1:11 [n]2Ch 20:1 [o]S Ge 25:16 **83:7** [p]S Jos 13:5 [q]Ge 19:38 [r]S Ge 14:7; S Ex 17:14 [s]Ex 15:14 [t]Isa 23:3; Eze 27:3 **83:8** [u]S Ge 10:11 [v]S Dt 2:9 **83:9** [w]S Ge 25:2; Jdg 7:1-23 [x]S Jdg 4:2 [y]S Jos 11:1 [z]S Jdg 4:23-24 **83:10** [a]S 1Sa 28:7 [b]S 2Ki 9:37; Isa 5:25; Jer 8:2; 9:22; 16:4; 25:33; Zep 1:17 **83:11** [c]Jdg 7:25 [d]S Jdg 8:5 **83:12** [e]2Ch 20:11; Eze 35:10

exploit or oppress them (see 72:2,4,12–14; Pr 31:8–9; Isa 11:4; Jer 22:3,16).

82:5 *The 'gods' know ... nothing.* The center of the poem (see note on 6:6). They ought to have shared in the wisdom of God (see 1Ki 3:9; Pr 8:14–16; Isa 11:2), but they are utterly devoid of true understanding of moral issues or of the moral order that God's rule sustains (see Isa 44:18; Jer 3:15; 9:24). *foundations ... are shaken.* When such people are the wardens of justice, the whole world order crumbles (see 11:3; 75:3 and notes).

82:6 Quoted in part in Jn 10:34 (see note there). *I said.* Those who rule (or judge) do so by God's appointment (see 2:7; Isa 44:28) and thus are his representatives—whether they acknowledge him or not (see Ex 9:16; Jer 27:6; Da 2:21; 4:17,32; 5:18; Jn 19:11; Ro 13:1). *"gods" ... sons of.* See note on v. 1. *Most High.* See note on Ge 14:19.

82:7 However exalted their position, these corrupt "gods" will be brought low by the same judgment as other human beings. *fall.* See note on 13:4.

82:8 Having seen the prospect in store, the psalmist prays for God's judgment to hasten and for the perfect reign of God to come quickly to the whole world. *Rise up.* See note on 3:7. *inheritance.* Domain (see note on 79:1).

Ps 83 Israel's prayer for God to crush his enemies when the whole world—or so it seemed—was arrayed against his people. For this psalm's relationship to those around it, see introduction to Ps 79–83. The occasion may have been that reported in 2Ch 20, when Moab, Ammon, Edom and their allies were invading Judah. In any event, the psalm must date from sometime after the reign of Solomon and before the great thrust of Assyria in the time of King Menahem (see 2Ki 15:19).

Each of the two main divisions (vv. 1–8, 9–18) consists of two four-verse stanzas, with the latter division being extended by a two-verse stanza that brings the prayer to its climactic conclusion.

83 title *song.* See note on Ps 30 title. *Asaph.* See note on Ps 73 title.

83:1–4 An appeal to God to act in the face of Israel's imminent danger.

83:1 *do not remain silent.* Do not remain inactive (see 35:22; 109:1).

83:2 *growl.* In Hebrew the same verb as for "are in uproar" in 46:6 and for "snarling" in 59:6,14.

83:4 *they say.* See note on 3:2. *let us destroy them.* Israel's very existence is at stake (see v. 12).

83:5–8 The array of nations allied against Israel—threat from every quarter.

83:6 *Hagrites.* Either Ishmaelites (descendants of Hagar) or a group mentioned in Assyrian inscriptions as an Aramean confederacy (see 1Ch 5:10,18–22; 27:31).

83:7 *Byblos.* See 1Ki 5:18; Eze 27:9; an important Phoenician city. *Amalek.* See note on Ge 14:7.

83:8 *Assyria.* Since it is mentioned only as an ally of Moab and Ammon (the descendants of Lot; see note on Ge 19:36–38), Assyria, though distantly active in the region, must not yet have become a major threat in its own right. For *Selah,* see NIV text note and note on 3:2.

83:9–12 A plea for God to destroy his enemies as he did of old in the time of the judges. Those who hurl themselves against the kingdom of God to destroy it from the earth—so that the godless powers are left to shape the destiny of the world as they will—must be crushed if God's kingdom of righteousness and peace is to come and be at rest (see note on 5:10).

83:9 *as you did to Midian.* In Gideon's great victory (see Jdg 7). *as you did to Sisera and Jabin.* In Barak's defeat of the Canaanite coalition (see Jdg 4).

83:10 *Endor.* See Jos 17:11 and note; northeast of where the main battle was fought—apparently where much of the fleeing army was overtaken and decimated.

83:11 *Oreb and Zeeb ... Zebah and Zalmunna.* Leaders of the Midianite host destroyed by Gideon (see Jdg 7:25—8:21).

83:12 See v. 4.

13 Make them like tumbleweed, my God,
like chaff[f] before the wind.
14 As fire consumes the forest
or a flame sets the mountains
ablaze,[g]
15 so pursue them with your tempest[h]
and terrify them with your storm.[i]
16 Cover their faces with shame,[j] LORD,
so that they will seek your name.

17 May they ever be ashamed and
dismayed;[k]
may they perish in disgrace.[l]
18 Let them know that you, whose name
is the LORD[m] —
that you alone are the Most High[n]
over all the earth.[o]

Psalm 84[a]

For the director of music. According to *gittith*.[b] Of the Sons of Korah. A psalm.

1 How lovely is your dwelling place,[p]
LORD Almighty!
2 My soul yearns,[q] even faints,
for the courts of the LORD;
my heart and my flesh cry out
for the living God.[r]
3 Even the sparrow has found a home,
and the swallow a nest for herself,
where she may have her young —
a place near your altar,[s]
LORD Almighty,[t] my King[u] and my
God.[v]
4 Blessed are those who dwell in your
house;
they are ever praising you.[c]

5 Blessed are those whose strength[w] is in
you,
whose hearts are set on pilgrimage.[x]
6 As they pass through the Valley of
Baka,
they make it a place of springs;[y]

83:13 [f]S Job 13:25 **83:14** [g]Dt 32:22; Isa 9:18 **83:15** [h]S Ps 50:3 [i]S Job 9:17 **83:16** [j]S Ps 34:5; 109:29; 132:18 **83:17** [k]S 2Ki 19:26 [l]S Ps 35:4 **83:18** [m]S Ps 68:4 [n]Ps 7:8; 18:13 [o]S Job 34:29 **84:1** [p]S Dt 33:27; Ps 27:4; 43:3; 90:1; 132:5 **84:2** [q]S Job 19:27 [r]S Jos 3:10 **84:3** [s]S Ps 43:4 [t]Jer 44:11 [u]Ps 2:6 [v]Ps 5:2 **84:5** [w]Ps 81:1 [x]Jer 31:6 **84:6** [y]S Job 38:26

[a] In Hebrew texts 84:1-12 is numbered 84:2-13.
[b] Title: Probably a musical term
[c] *4* The Hebrew has *Selah* (a word of uncertain meaning) here and at the end of verse 8.

83:13 – 16 The plea renewed, with vivid imagery of fleeing armies and of God's fearsome power.
83:15 Imagery of the heavenly Warrior attacking his enemies out of the thunderstorm (see 18:7 – 15; 68:33; 77:17 – 18; Ex 15:7 – 10; Jos 10:11; Jdg 5:4,20 – 21; 1Sa 2:10; 7:10; Isa 29:5 – 6; 33:3). For the storm cloud as God's chariot, see 68:4 and note.
83:16 *will seek.* See note on v. 18. *name.* See note on 5:11.
83:17 – 18 The prayer's climactic conclusion.
83:18 The ultimate goal of God's warfare is not merely the security of Israel and the destruction of Israel's (and God's) enemies but the worldwide acknowledgment of the true God and of his rule, even to the point of seeking him as his people do (see v. 16; see also 40:9; 47:9; 58:11; 59:13 and notes). *Most High.* See note on Ge 14:19.
Ps 84 – 89 The first of the six psalms that make up the final group of Book III (see introduction to Ps 73 – 78) expresses yearning for fellowship with God, who dwells in his temple in Zion and from whom alone come security and blessing. References to God as "LORD Almighty" and a prayer for "our shield," the Lord's "anointed," form distinctive links with the final psalm of the group (for the former, see 84:1,3,8,12 and 89:8; for the latter, see 84:9 and 89:18,38,51). The five psalms thus introduced are four cries out of distress arranged around a central song (Ps 87) that celebrates God's special love for Zion and the care he has for all its citizens. Of these four, the first (Ps 85) and the last (Ps 89) are communal prayers, and the remaining two (Ps 86; 88) are prayers of individuals. They all make much of God's "love and faithfulness" (see 85:7,10 – 11; 86:5,13,15; 88:11; 89:1 – 2,5,8,14,24, 28,33,49) and his "saving" help (see 85:4,7,9; 86:2,16; 88:1; 89:26). And three of them share another key concept, "righteousness" (see 85:10 – 11,13; 88:12; 89:14). The two final prayers (Ps 88; 89) both end unrelieved by the usual expression of confidence that God will hear and act (see note on 3:8). However, the editors of Book III have placed them under the near shadow of Ps 87, the more distant shadow of Ps 84 and the still more distant shadow of Ps 82. From these psalms they should not be disassociated.
Ps 84 A prayer of longing for the house of the Lord. The author (presumably a Levite who normally functioned in the temple service), now barred from access to God's house (perhaps when Sennacherib was ravaging Judah; see 2Ki 18:13 – 16), gives voice to his longing for the sweet nearness to God in his temple that he had known in the past. Reference to God and his temple and to the blessedness (see vv. 4 – 5,12) of those having free access to both dominates the prayer and highlights its central themes. For its placement in the arrangement of the Psalter, see introduction to Ps 84 – 89. Whatever its origin, the psalm now voices the devotion to and reliance on God that motivate the remaining prayers of the group it introduces.

The psalm has three main divisions and a conclusion (v. 12). In the Hebrew text, a six-line unit (vv. 1 – 4) precedes and another six-line unit (vv. 8 – 11) follows a three-line reflection (vv. 5 – 7) on the blessedness of those free to make pilgrimage to Zion. Each of these six-line divisions contains three references to the "LORD," while the seventh reference (symbolizing completeness or perfection) appears in the conclusion.
84 title *For the director of music.* See note on Ps 4 title. *According to.* See note on Ps 6 title. *gittith.* See note on Ps 8 title. *Of the Sons of Korah.* See note on Ps 42 title.
84:1 – 4 A confession of deep longing for the house of the Lord.
84:1 *lovely.* The traditional rendering of the Hebrew here, but perhaps better translated "beloved" or "loved." *LORD Almighty.* See vv. 3,8,12; see also note on 1Sa 1:3.
84:2 *My soul yearns.* I yearn (see note on 6:3). *courts.* Of the temple (see v. 10; 2Ki 21:5; 23:11 – 12). *my heart . . . flesh.* My whole being (see 73:26). *heart.* See note on 4:7. *living God.* See Dt 5:26.
84:3 The psalmist envies the small birds that have such unhindered access to the temple and the altar. They are able even to build their nests for their young there — the place where Israel was to have communion with God.
84:4 – 5,12 *Blessed.* See note on 1:1.
84:4 *who dwell in your house.* See note on 15:1. For *Selah*, see NIV text note and note on 3:2.
84:5 – 7 The joyful blessedness of those who are free to make pilgrimage to Zion — them too the psalmist envies.
84:5 *those whose strength is in you.* Those who have come to know the Lord as their deliverer and the sustainer of their lives. *whose hearts are set on pilgrimage.* Lit. "in whose hearts are (the) highways," i.e., the highways the Israelites took to observe the religious festivals at Jerusalem (Zion, v. 7). *hearts.* See note on 4:7.
84:6 *As they pass.* On their way to the temple. *Baka.* Means either "weeping" or "balsam trees" (common in

the autumn[z] rains also cover it with
pools.[a]
7 They go from strength to strength,[a]
till each appears[b] before God in Zion.[c]

8 Hear my prayer,[d] LORD God Almighty;
listen to me, God of Jacob.
9 Look on our shield,[b][e] O God;
look with favor on your anointed one.[f]

10 Better is one day in your courts
than a thousand elsewhere;
I would rather be a doorkeeper[g] in the
house of my God
than dwell in the tents of the wicked.
11 For the LORD God is a sun[h] and shield;[i]
the LORD bestows favor and honor;
no good thing does he withhold[j]
from those whose walk is blameless.

12 LORD Almighty,
blessed[k] is the one who trusts in you.

Psalm 85[c]

For the director of music.
Of the Sons of Korah. A psalm.

1 You, LORD, showed favor to your land;
you restored the fortunes[l] of Jacob.
2 You forgave[m] the iniquity[n] of your
people
and covered all their sins.[d]
3 You set aside all your wrath[o]
and turned from your fierce
anger.[p]

4 Restore[q] us again, God our Savior,[r]
and put away your displeasure
toward us.
5 Will you be angry with us forever?[s]
Will you prolong your anger through
all generations?
6 Will you not revive[t] us again,
that your people may rejoice[u] in
you?
7 Show us your unfailing love,[v] LORD,
and grant us your salvation.[w]

8 I will listen to what God the LORD says;
he promises peace[x] to his people, his
faithful servants —
but let them not turn to folly.[y]

84:6 [z] Joel 2:23 **84:7** [a] S Job 17:9 [b] S Dt 16:16 [c] 1Ki 8:1 **84:8** [d] Ps 4:1 **84:9** [e] S Ps 59:11 [f] 1Sa 16:6; Ps 2:2; 18:50; 132:17 **84:10** [g] 1Ch 23:5 **84:11** [h] Isa 60:19; Jer 43:13; Rev 21:23 [i] S Ge 15:1 [j] Ps 34:10 **84:12** [k] Ps 2:12 **85:1** [l] S Dt 30:3; Ps 14:7 **85:2** [m] S Nu 14:19 [n] S Ex 32:30; S Ps 78:38 **85:3** [o] Ps 106:23; Da 9:16 [p] Ex 32:12; Dt 13:17; Ps 78:38; Jnh 3:9 **85:4** [q] S Ps 71:20 [r] S Ps 65:5 **85:5** [s] S Ps 50:21 **85:6** [t] S Ps 80:18 [u] Php 3:1 **85:7** [v] S Ps 6:4 [w] Ps 27:1 **85:8** [x] S Lev 26:6; S Isa 60:17; S Jn 14:27; 2Th 3:16 [y] Pr 26:11; 27:22

[a] 6 Or *blessings* [b] 9 Or *sovereign* [c] In Hebrew texts 85:1-13 is numbered 85:2-14. [d] 2 The Hebrew has *Selah* (a word of uncertain meaning) here.

arid valleys). *place of springs.* The joyful expectations of the pilgrims transform the difficult ways into places of refreshment. *autumn rains.* See note on Jas 5:7. Reference to these rains suggests that the psalmist had in mind especially the pilgrimage to observe the Festival of Tabernacles (see chart, pp. 188–189). *pools.* The Hebrew for this word may refer to "blessings" or to "pools" (see NIV text note); it is likely that both are intended. By God's benevolent care over his pilgrims, the vale of weeping (or balsam trees), already transformed by the glad hearts of the expectant wayfarers, is turned into a valley of praise (see 2Ch 20:26).

84:7 *from strength to strength.* Whatever the toils and hardships of the journey (see Isa 40:31). *Zion.* See 9:11 and note.

84:8–11 A prayer for the king, and its motivation: Only as God blesses the king in Jerusalem will the psalmist once more realize his great desire to return to his accustomed service in the temple (see introduction).

84:8 *LORD God Almighty ... God of Jacob.* That is, "LORD God Almighty, the God of Jacob" (see 59:5; see also note on 3:7). *Jacob.* A synonym for Israel (see Ge 32:28).

84:9 *our shield.* The king in Jerusalem (see NIV text note; see also note on 3:3). *anointed one.* God's earthly regent over his people (from David's line — perhaps Hezekiah [see introduction to this psalm]); see note on 2:2.

84:10 *doorkeeper.* Probably the psalmist's normal (and humble) service at the temple (see 2Ki 22:4). *dwell in the tents of the wicked.* Share in the life of those who do not honor the God of Zion. Perhaps reference is to the peoples imported by Sargon II (see 2Ki 17:24–33), among whom the psalmist was forced at the time to live.

84:11 *sun.* The glorious source of the light of life (see note on 27:1). *shield.* See note on 3:3. *blameless.* See 15:2; Ge 17:1 and notes.

84:12 The sum of it all (see 40:4).

Ps 85 A communal prayer for the renewal of God's mercies to his people at a time when they are once more suffering distress. Verse 12 suggests that a drought has ravaged the land and may reflect the drought with which the Lord chastened his people in the time of Haggai (see Hag 1:5–11). For this prayer's placement in the Psalter and its relationship to the psalms of its group, see introduction to Ps 84–89. Christian liturgical usage has often employed this psalm in the Christmas season. The psalm has two main divisions of seven (Hebrew) lines each: (1) the prayer (vv. 1–7); (2) a reassuring word (vv. 8–13). Each division contains a three-line stanza followed by a four-line stanza, with the corresponding stanzas of the second half answering to those of the first: Verses 1–3 speak of mercies granted, while vv. 8–9 speak of mercies soon to come; vv. 4–7 voice the prayer, and vv. 10–13 offer the blessed reassurance that the prayer will be heard.

85 title *For the director of music.* See note on Ps 4 title. *Of the Sons of Korah.* See note on Ps 42 title.

85:1–7 Prayer for the renewal of God's favor.

85:1–3 Israel begins her prayer by appealing to the Lord's past mercies, recalling how he has forgiven and restored his people before (perhaps a reference to the restoration from exile).

85:1 *restored the fortunes of Jacob.* Or "brought Jacob back from exile" (see Jer 29:14 and NIV text note there). *Jacob.* A synonym for Israel (see Ge 32:28).

85:2 For *Selah,* see NIV text note and note on 3:2.

85:3 *wrath ... anger.* See v. 5; see also note on 2:5.

85:4–7 The prayer acknowledges that the present troubles are indicative of God's displeasure. No confession of sin is expressed, but in the light of v. 3 (and possibly v. 8; see below) it is probably implicit.

85:7 *unfailing love.* See v. 10; see also note on 6:4.

85:8–13 God's reassuring answer to the prayer, conveyed through a priest or Levite, perhaps one of the Korahites (see note on 12:5–6; see also 2Ch 20:14).

85:8–9 The assurance that God will again bless his people.

85:8 *I will listen.* The speaker awaits the word from the Lord. *promises peace.* The word from the Lord perhaps takes the form of the priestly benediction (see Nu 6:22–26). *faithful servants.* See note on 4:3. *but let them not turn to folly.* And so provoke God's displeasure again. But it is also possible to

[9]Surely his salvation[z] is near those who
fear him,
that his glory[a] may dwell in our
land.

[10]Love and faithfulness[b] meet together;
righteousness[c] and peace kiss each
other.
[11]Faithfulness springs forth from the
earth,
and righteousness[d] looks down from
heaven.
[12]The LORD will indeed give what is
good,[e]
and our land will yield[f] its harvest.
[13]Righteousness goes before him
and prepares the way for his steps.

Psalm 86

A prayer of David.

[1]Hear me, LORD, and answer[g] me,
for I am poor and needy.
[2]Guard my life, for I am faithful to you;
save your servant who trusts in you.[h]
You are my God; [3]have mercy[i] on me,
Lord,
for I call[j] to you all day long.
[4]Bring joy to your servant, Lord,
for I put my trust[k] in you.

[5]You, Lord, are forgiving and good,
abounding in love[l] to all who call to
you.
[6]Hear my prayer, LORD;
listen to my cry[m] for mercy.
[7]When I am in distress,[n] I call[o] to you,
because you answer[p] me.

[8]Among the gods[q] there is none like
you,[r] Lord;
no deeds can compare with yours.
[9]All the nations you have made
will come[s] and worship[t] before you,
Lord;
they will bring glory[u] to your
name.

85:9 [z]Ps 27:1; Isa 43:3; 45:8; 46:13; 51:5; 56:1; 62:11 [a]S Ex 29:43; Isa 60:19; Hag 2:9; Zec 2:5 **85:10** [b]Ps 89:14; 115:1; Pr 3:3 [c]Ps 72:2-3; Isa 32:17 **85:11** [d]Isa 45:8 **85:12** [e]Ps 84:11; Jas 1:17 [f]Lev 26:4; S Ps 67:6; Zec 8:12 **86:1** [g]Ps 17:6 **86:2** [h]Ps 25:2; 31:14 **86:3** [i]Ps 4:1; S 9:13; 57:1 [j]Ps 88:9 **86:4** [k]Ps 46:5; 143:8 **86:5** [l]Ex 34:6; Ne 9:17; Ps 103:8; 145:8; Joel 2:13; Jnh 4:2 **86:6** [m]Ps 5:2; 17:1 **86:7** [n]Ps 27:5; S 50:15; 94:13; Hab 3:16 [o]Job 22:27; Ps 4:3; 80:18; 91:15; Isa 30:19; 58:9; 65:24; Zec 13:9 [p]Ps 3:4 **86:8** [q]S Ex 8:10; S Job 21:22 [r]S Ps 18:31 **86:9** [s]S Ps 65:2 [t]Ps 66:4; Isa 19:21; 27:13; 49:7; Zec 8:20-22; 14:16; Rev 15:4 [u]Isa 43:7; 44:23

translate the clause: "and to those who turn from folly." *folly.* See NIV text note on 14:1.

85:9 *glory.* Wherever God's saving power is displayed his glory is revealed (see 57:5 and note; 72:18–19; Ex 14:4,17–18; Nu 14:22; Isa 6:3 and note; 40:5 and note; 44:23; 66:19; Eze 39:21).

85:10–13 God's sure mercies to his people spring from his covenant love, to which in his faithfulness and righteousness he remains true, and that assures his people's welfare (peace). Cf. 40:9–10.

85:10 *Love and faithfulness ... righteousness and peace.* These expressions of God's favor toward his people are here personified (see note on 23:6), and the vivid portrayal of their meeting and embracing offers one of the most beautiful images in all Scripture of God's gracious dealings with his covenant people. *righteousness.* See vv. 11,13; see also note on 4:1. *peace.* See notes on Nu 6:26; Eze 34:25; Lk 2:14; Ro 1:7.

85:11 *Faithfulness springs forth.* As new growth springs from the earth to bless all living things with plenty. *righteousness looks down.* It shines down benevolently. (With "disaster" as subject, the Hebrew for "looks down" indicates the opposite effect: Jer 6:1, "looms.") From heaven and from earth God's covenant blessings will abound till Israel's cup overflows.

85:12 *what is good.* See 4:6 and note. *will yield its harvest.* See 67:6 and note.

85:13 *Righteousness goes before.* Again the psalmist personifies. Acting either as herald or guide, righteousness leads the way and marks the course for God's engagement in his people's behalf—and righteousness is God's perfect faithfulness to all his covenant commitments (see note on 4:1).

Ps 86 The prayer of an individual for God's help when attacked by enemies, whose fierce onslaughts betray their disdain for the Lord. Whether or not David was the author (see Introduction: Authorship and Titles [or Superscriptions]), the psalmist's identification of himself as God's "servant" (v. 2) suggests his royal status and thus his special relationship with the Lord (see 2Sa 7:5,8 and note on Ps 18 title). For the placement of this psalm in the arrangement of the Psalter, see introduction to Ps 84–89.

This carefully designed poetic prayer is composed of five stanzas, having a symmetrical verse pattern (four, three, three, three, four). The author identifies himself as the Lord's servant in the first and last stanzas, which also contain the prayer for God's mercy and deliverance from the enemy threat. The second stanza (vv. 5–7) adds a profession of assurance; the fourth stanza (vv. 11–13) adds a vow to praise God. These are linked by references to God's "love" (see note on 6:4) in vv. 5,13. The center stanza (vv. 8–10) hails the Lord as the incomparable, the only God, whom all the nations will someday worship. Verse 9 is the center verse (see note on 6:6).

86 title *prayer.* See note on Ps 17 title. *of David.* This is the only psalm in Book III (Ps 73–89) that is ascribed to David. Perhaps its placement among the Korahite psalms is in part because those who arranged the Psalter perceived a thematic link between v. 9 and 87:4.

86:1–4 Initial prayer for God to have mercy and protect the life of his servant.

86:1 *poor and needy.* See 35:10; see also 34:6 and note.

86:2 *faithful to you.* The Hebrew for this phrase is *ḥasid* (see note on 4:3). *your servant.* See vv. 4,16; see also introduction. *You are my God.* Not that David has chosen him, but that he has chosen David to be his servant (see 1Sa 13:14; 15:28; 16:12; 2Sa 7:8). David's faithfulness to God and God's commitment to him are deliberately juxtaposed.

86:5–7 In his need David prays to the Lord because he is confident that, out of his kindness and love, God answers prayer.

86:5 *love.* See vv. 13,15; see also note on 6:4.

86:7 *I call ... you answer.* See note on 118:5.

86:8–10 At the center of his prayer David gives expression to his fundamental belief (see also 115:3–7; 135:13–17 and related notes) and makes clear why he appeals to Yahweh in the surrounding stanzas.

86:9 *All the nations.* See note on 46:10. This is the center verse of the psalm (see note on 6:6) and contains the psalm's most exalted confession of faith concerning God's sovereign and universal rule. *they will bring glory.* As David vows to do (v. 12). *your name.* See vv. 11–12; see also note on 5:11.

[10] For you are great[v] and do marvelous
deeds;[w]
you alone[x] are God.
[11] Teach me your way,[y] LORD,
that I may rely on your faithfulness;[z]
give me an undivided[a] heart,
that I may fear[b] your name.
[12] I will praise you, Lord my God, with all
my heart;[c]
I will glorify your name forever.
[13] For great is your love toward me;
you have delivered me[d] from the
depths,
from the realm of the dead.[e]

[14] Arrogant foes are attacking me, O God;
ruthless people are trying to kill me—
they have no regard for you.[f]
[15] But you, Lord, are a compassionate
and gracious[g] God,
slow to anger,[h] abounding[i] in love
and faithfulness.[j]
[16] Turn to me[k] and have mercy[l] on me;
show your strength[m] in behalf of
your servant;
save me, because I serve you
just as my mother did.[n]
[17] Give me a sign[o] of your goodness,
that my enemies may see it and be
put to shame,
for you, LORD, have helped me and
comforted me.

86:10 [v] S 2Sa 7:22; S Ps 48:1 [w] S Ex 3:20; S Ps 71:17; 72:18 [x] S Dt 6:4; S Isa 43:10; Mk 12:29; 1Co 8:4 **86:11** [y] S Ex 33:13; S 1Sa 12:23; Ps 25:5 [z] S Ps 26:3 [a] Jer 24:7; 32:39; Eze 11:19; 1Co 7:35 [b] S Dt 6:24 **86:12** [c] S Ps 9:1 **86:13** [d] S Ps 34:4; 49:15; 116:8 [e] S Ps 16:10; S 56:13 **86:14** [f] Ps 54:3 **86:15** [g] S Ps 51:1; 103:8; 111:4; 116:5; 145:8 [h] Nu 14:18 [i] ver 5 [j] S Ex 34:6; S Ne 9:17; Joel 2:13 **86:16** [k] S Ps 6:4 [l] S Ps 9:13 [m] Ps 18:1 [n] Ps 116:16 **86:17** [o] S Ex 3:12; Mt 24:3; S Jn 2:11 **87:1** [p] S Ps 48:1

Psalm 87

Of the Sons of Korah.
A psalm. A song.

[1] He has founded his city on the holy
mountain.[p]
[2] The LORD loves the gates of Zion[q]
more than all the other dwellings of
Jacob.

[3] Glorious things are said of you,
city of God:[a][r]
[4] "I will record Rahab[b][s] and Babylon
among those who acknowledge
me—
Philistia[t] too, and Tyre[u], along with
Cush[c]—
and will say, 'This one was born in
Zion.' "[d][v]

[a] 3 The Hebrew has *Selah* (a word of uncertain meaning) here and at the end of verse 6. [b] 4 A poetic name for Egypt [c] 4 That is, the upper Nile region [d] 4 Or *"I will record concerning those who acknowledge me: / 'This one was born in Zion.' / Hear this, Rahab and Babylon, / and you too, Philistia, Tyre and Cush."*

87:2 [q] Ps 2:6 **87:3** [r] S Ps 46:4 **87:4** [s] S Job 9:13 [t] S 2Sa 8:1; Ps 83:7 [u] Ps 45:12; Joel 3:4 [v] Isa 19:25

86:10 *marvelous deeds.* See note on 9:1.
86:11–13 A prayer for godliness and a vow to praise God.
86:11 *Teach me ... give me.* What would be the benefit if God were to save him from his enemies but abandon him to his own waywardness? David's dependence on God is complete, and so is his devotion to God—save me from the enemy outside but also from my frailty within (see 25:5; 51:7,10 and notes). Only one who is thus devoted to God may expect God's help and will truly fulfill the vow (v. 12). *undivided heart.* See Eze 11:19 and note; see also 1Ch 12:33; 1Co 7:35. *heart.* See note on 4:7.
86:12 Vow to praise God (see note on 7:17).
86:13 David anticipates the answer to his prayer (see note on 3:8). *depths.* See note on 30:1.
86:14–17 Conclusion: the prayer renewed.
86:14 *ruthless.* The Hebrew for this word suggests also ferocity. *they have no regard for you.* In their arrogance they dismiss the heavenly Warrior, who is David's defender (see note on 10:11; see also Jer 20:11).
86:15 Echoes v. 5, but is even more similar to Ex 34:6 (see note on Ex 34:6–7).
86:16 *show your strength.* Exert your power in my behalf. *I serve you just as my mother did.* See 116:16.
86:17 *goodness.* Covenanted favors (see 27:13 and note). *may see it.* May see that you stand with me and help me (see 31:19 and note).
Ps 87 A celebration of Zion as the "city of God" (v. 3), the special object of his love and the royal city of his kingdom (see introductions to Ps 46; 48; 76). According to the ancient and consistent interpretation of Jewish and Christian interpreters alike, this psalm stands in lonely isolation in the Psalter (but see 47:9 and note) in that it foresees the ingathering of the nations into Zion as fellow citizens with Israel in the kingdom of God—after the manner of such prophetic visions as Isa 2:2–4; 19:19–25; 25:6; 45:14,22–24; 56:6–8; 60:3; 66:23; Da 7:14; Mic 4:1–3; Zec 8:23; 14:16. So interpreted, this psalm stands in sharpest possible contrast to the other Zion songs of the Psalter (see Ps 46; 48; 76; 125; 129; 137). The key to its main thrust lies in v. 4. Placed at the center of four prayers arising from deep crises—two of individuals (Ps 86; 88) and two of the community (Ps 85:89)—it offers reassurance that God will surely answer such prayers (see introduction to Ps 84–89).
87 title *Of the Sons of Korah.* See note on Ps 42 title. *song.* See note on Ps 30 title.
87:1 *He has founded his city.* The Lord himself has laid the foundations of Zion (see Isa 14:32) and of the temple as his royal house. *mountain.* The Hebrew for this word is plural, emphasizing the majesty of the holy mountain on which God's throne has been set (see 48:2; 121:1 and notes).
87:2 *loves ... more than.* As the city of his founding, his chosen seat of rule over his people, Zion is the Lord's most cherished city, even among the towns of Israel (see 9:11 and note; 78:68; 132:13–14). *Jacob.* A synonym for Israel (see Ge 32:28).
87:3 For *Selah*, see NIV text note and note on 3:2.
87:4 *I will record ... This one was born in Zion.* God will list them in his royal register (see notes on 9:5; 51:1; 69:28) as those who are native (born) citizens of his royal city, having all the privileges and enjoying all the benefits and security of such citizenship. *Rahab.* Whereas elsewhere this name is applied to the mythical monster of the deep (see 89:10; see also notes on 32:6; Job 9:13), here the reference is to Egypt (see NIV text note), as in Isa 30:7 (see note there); 51:9. The nations listed are representative of all Gentile peoples. As usually interpreted, the psalm here foresees a widespread conversion to the Lord from the peoples who from time immemorial had been hostile to him and to his kingdom (see Isa 19:21; 26:18 and note). But see third NIV text note. *Philistia too.* See Zec 9:7 and note.

5 Indeed, of Zion it will be said,
"This one and that one were born in her,
and the Most High himself will establish her."
6 The LORD will write in the register[w] of the peoples:
"This one was born in Zion."

7 As they make music[x] they will sing,
"All my fountains[y] are in you."

Psalm 88[a]

A song. A psalm of the Sons of Korah.
For the director of music.
According to *mahalath leannoth*.[b]
A *maskil*[c] of Heman the Ezrahite.

1 LORD, you are the God who saves me;[z]
day and night I cry out[a] to you.
2 May my prayer come before you;
turn your ear to my cry.

3 I am overwhelmed with troubles[b]
and my life draws near to death.[c]
4 I am counted among those who go down to the pit;[d]
I am like one without strength.[e]

87:6 [w] Ex 32:32; Ps 69:28; Isa 4:3; Mal 3:16 **87:7** [x] Ps 149:3 [y] S Ps 36:9 **88:1** [z] S Ps 51:14 [a] Ps 3:4; 22:2; Lk 18:7 **88:3** [b] Ps 6:3; 25:17 [c] S Job 33:22 **88:4** [d] S Ps 31:12 [e] Ps 18:1 **88:5** [f] S Ps 31:22 **88:6** [g] Ps 30:1; S 69:15; La 3:55; Jnh 2:3 **88:7** [h] Ps 7:11 [i] S Ps 42:7 **88:8** [j] S Job 19:13; Ps 31:11 [k] Jer 32:2; 33:1 [l] S Job 3:23 **88:9** [m] S Ps 38:10 [n] Ps 5:2 [o] Job 11:13; Ps 143:6 **88:10** [p] S Ps 6:5

5 I am set apart with the dead,
like the slain who lie in the grave,
whom you remember no more,
who are cut off[f] from your care.

6 You have put me in the lowest pit,
in the darkest depths.[g]
7 Your wrath[h] lies heavily on me;
you have overwhelmed me with all your waves.[d][i]
8 You have taken from me my closest friends[j]
and have made me repulsive to them.
I am confined[k] and cannot escape;[l]
9 my eyes[m] are dim with grief.

I call[n] to you, LORD, every day;
I spread out my hands[o] to you.
10 Do you show your wonders to the dead?
Do their spirits rise up and praise you?[p]

[a] In Hebrew texts 88:1-18 is numbered 88:2-19. [b] Title: Possibly a tune, "The Suffering of Affliction" [c] Title: Probably a literary or musical term [d] 7 The Hebrew has *Selah* (a word of uncertain meaning) here and at the end of verse 10.

87:5 *This one and that one.* Wherever they may be dispersed among the nations. *Most High.* See note on Ge 14:19.
87:7 *All my fountains.* All that refreshes them is found in the city of God, a possible allusion to God's "river of delights" (36:8) "whose streams make glad the city of God" (46:4); see notes on those passages. Alternatively, "fountains" may be a metaphor for sources; the sense of the line would then be: We all spring from you. *my.* Communal use of the singular pronoun (see note on Ps 30 title).
Ps 88 A cry out of the depths, the prayer of one on the edge of death, whose whole life has been lived, as it were, in the near vicinity of the grave (see also Ps 90). So troubled have been his years that he seems to have known only the back of God's hand (God's "wrath," v. 7), and even those nearest him have withdrawn themselves as from one with a defiling skin disease (see v. 8). No expressions of hopeful expectation (as in most prayers of the Psalter; but see Ps 44; 89) burst from these lips; the last word speaks of darkness as "my closest friend." And yet the prayer begins, "LORD, you are the God who saves me." The psalm recalls the fact that although sometimes godly persons live lives of unremitting trouble (see 73:14) they can still grasp the hope that God is Savior (see also Ps 87 and introduction to Ps 84–89). Many early church leaders interpreted this psalm as a prayer of the suffering Christ (as they did Ps 22); for that reason it became part of the Good Friday liturgy.

Structurally, the prayer ends (vv. 13–18) as it began (vv. 1–5), each section with two Hebrew poetic lines of petition (vv. 1–2, 13–14) followed by four lines describing the psalmist's distress (vv. 3–5,15–18). Between the beginning and the end are two stanzas of four lines each (vv. 6–9a,9b–12). In the first of these the psalmist expresses his recognition that what has happened to him is God's doing. In the second he appeals to God to consider the consequences if he does not deliver the petitioner from death.
88 title The psalm bears a double title, perhaps representing two different traditions. *song.* See note on Ps 30 title. *of the Sons of Korah.* See note on Ps 42 title. *For the director of music.* See note on Ps 4 title. *According to.* See note on Ps 6 title. *maskil.* See note on Ps 32 title. *Heman.* See note on Ps 39 title. *Ezrahite.* The reference appears to be to Zerah, one of Judah's sons, who is recorded as having a Heman and an Ethan (see Ps 89 title) among his sons (see 1Ch 2:6). If so, the title here represents a confusion in the tradition, arising from the similarity between these two Judahite names and those of two famous Korahite choir leaders, Heman and Ethan (Jeduthun; see note on Ps 39 title).
88:1–2 Opening appeal to the Lord as "the God who saves me."
88:3–5 Living on the brink of death. Whether the psalmist lies mortally ill or experiences some analogous trouble or peril cannot be known.
88:4 *pit.* See 28:1; 30:3,9; 143:7.
88:5 *remember no more.* From the perspective of this life, death cuts off from God's care; there is no remembering by God of the needy sufferer to rescue and restore (see 25:7; 74:2; 106:4). In his dark mood the author portrays his situation in bleakest colors (see note on 6:5; cf. Job's experiences).
88:6–9a You, God, have done this! The psalmist knows no reason for it (see v. 14; cf. Ps 44), but he knows God's hand is in it (see Ru 1:20–21; Am 3:6). That his Savior-God shows him the face of wrath deepens his anguish and helplessness. But he does not try to resolve the dark enigma; he simply pleads his case—and it is to his Savior-God that he can appeal (see v. 1).
88:6 *lowest pit ... darkest depths.* See note on 30:1.
88:7 *wrath.* See v. 16; see also note on 2:5. *all your waves.* See note on 32:6. For *Selah*, see NIV text note and note on 3:2.
88:8 *my closest friends.* See v. 18 and note on 31:11–12.
88:9 *eyes are dim.* See note on 6:7.
88:9b–12 Appeal to God to help before the psalmist sinks into "the land of oblivion" (see note on v. 5).
88:10,12 *wonders.* God's saving acts in behalf of his people (see note on 9:1).
88:10 *rise up.* In the realm of the dead (not in the resurrection); see Isa 14:9. *praise you.* See 6:5; 30:9; 115:17 and notes.

[11] Is your love declared in the grave,
your faithfulness[q] in Destruction[a]?
[12] Are your wonders known in the place of darkness,
or your righteous deeds in the land of oblivion?

[13] But I cry to you for help,[r] LORD;
in the morning[s] my prayer comes before you.[t]
[14] Why, LORD, do you reject[u] me
and hide your face[v] from me?
[15] From my youth[w] I have suffered[x] and been close to death;
I have borne your terrors[y] and am in despair.[z]
[16] Your wrath[a] has swept over me;
your terrors[b] have destroyed me.
[17] All day long they surround me like a flood;[c]
they have completely engulfed me.
[18] You have taken from me friend[d] and neighbor—
darkness is my closest friend.

Psalm 89[b]

A *maskil*[c] of Ethan the Ezrahite.

[1] I will sing[e] of the LORD's great love forever;
with my mouth I will make your faithfulness known[f]
through all generations.
[2] I will declare that your love stands firm forever,
that you have established your faithfulness in heaven itself.[g]
[3] You said, "I have made a covenant with my chosen one,
I have sworn to David my servant,
[4] 'I will establish your line forever
and make your throne firm through all generations.' "[d][h]

[5] The heavens[i] praise your wonders, LORD,
your faithfulness too, in the assembly[j] of the holy ones.
[6] For who in the skies above can compare with the LORD?
Who is like the LORD among the heavenly beings?[k]
[7] In the council[l] of the holy ones[m] God is greatly feared;
he is more awesome than all who surround him.[n]
[8] Who is like you,[o] LORD God Almighty?[p]
You, LORD, are mighty, and your faithfulness surrounds you.

[9] You rule over the surging sea;
when its waves mount up, you still them.[q]

88:11 [q] S Ps 30:9 **88:13** [r] S Ps 30:2 [s] Ps 5:3; S 55:17 [t] Ps 119:147 **88:14** [u] S Ps 43:2 [v] Ps 13:1 **88:15** [w] Ps 129:1; Jer 22:21; Eze 16:22; Hos 2:15 [x] Ps 9:12 [y] Job 6:4; S 18:11 [z] 2Co 4:8 **88:16** [a] Ps 7:11 [b] Job 6:4 **88:17** [c] Ps 124:4 **88:18** [d] ver 8; Ps 38:11 **89:1** [e] Ps 59:16 [f] S Ps 36:5; 40:10 **89:2** [g] S Ps 36:5 **89:4** [h] 2Sa 7:12-16; 1Ki 8:16; Ps 132:11-12; Isa 9:7; Eze 37:24-25; S Mt 1:1; S Lk 1:33 **89:5** [i] S Ps 19:1 [j] S Ps 1:5 **89:6** [k] S Ge 1:26; S Ex 9:14; S Ps 18:31; 113:5 **89:7** [l] Ps 111:1 [m] S Job 5:1 [n] Ps 47:2 **89:8** [o] S Ps 71:19 [p] Isa 6:3 **89:9** [q] S Ps 65:7

[a] *11* Hebrew *Abaddon* [b] In Hebrew texts 89:1-52 is numbered 89:2-53. [c] Title: Probably a literary or musical term [d] *4* The Hebrew has *Selah* (a word of uncertain meaning) here and at the end of verses 37, 45 and 48.

88:11 *love ... faithfulness.* That is, love-and-faithfulness (see note on 36:5; see also note on 3:7). *love.* See note on 6:4.
88:12 *righteous deeds.* See 71:24 and note.
88:13–14 Concluding prayer—with echoes of the initial petition in vv. 1–2.
88:13 *in the morning.* See 101:8 and note.
88:14 *Why ... ?* See note on 6:3. *hide your face.* See note on 13:1.
88:15–18 The psalmist has been no stranger to trouble; all his life he has suffered the terrors of God (cf. Ps 90).
88:17 *like a flood.* See v. 7; see also note on 32:6.
Ps 89 A prayer that mourns the downfall of the Davidic dynasty and pleads for its restoration. The bitter shock of that event (reflected in the sudden transition at v. 38) is almost unbearable—that God, the faithful and almighty One, has abandoned his anointed and made him the mockery of the nations, in seeming violation of his firm covenant with David—and it evokes from the psalmist a lament that borders on reproach. The event was probably the destruction of Jerusalem by Nebuchadnezzar in 586 BC (see vv. 38–45).

As with Ps 44 (see introduction to that psalm), a massive foundation is laid for the prayer with which the psalm concludes. An introduction (vv. 1–4) sings of God's love and faithfulness (vv. 1–2) and his covenant with David (vv. 3–4). These two themes are then jubilantly expanded in order: vv. 5–18, God's love and faithfulness; vv. 19–37, his covenant with David. Suddenly jubilation turns to lament, and the psalmist recounts in detail how God has rejected his anointed (vv. 38–45). Thus he comes to his prayer, impatient and urgent, that God will remember once more his covenant with David (vv. 46–51). (Verse 52 concludes not the psalm but Book III of the Psalter.)
89 title *maskil.* See note on Ps 32 title. *Ethan.* Jeduthun (see note on Ps 39 title). The author was no doubt a Levite (perhaps a descendant of Jeduthun) who voiced this agonizing prayer as spokesman for the nation. *Ezrahite.* See note on Ps 88 title.
89:1–2 God's love and faithfulness celebrated.
89:1 *love ... faithfulness.* See vv. 2,33,49; that is, love-and-faithfulness (see v. 14); see note on 36:5. *love.* See vv. 2,14,24,28,33,49; see also note on 6:4. It is God's love and faithfulness that appear to have failed in his rejection (see vv. 38–45) of the Davidic king. The author repeats each of these words precisely seven times (in v. 14 the Hebrew uses a different—but related—word for "faithfulness").
89:2 *in heaven itself.* God's love and faithfulness have been made sure in the highest seat of power and authority (see vv. 5–8).
89:3–4 God's covenant with David celebrated (see 2Sa 7:8–16).
89:3 *servant.* See vv. 20,39,50; here an official title (see note on 78:70).
89:4 For *Selah,* see NIV text note and note on 3:2.
89:5–8 The Lord's faithfulness and awesome power set him apart among all the powers in the heavenly realm, and they acknowledge him with praise and reverence.
89:5 *The heavens.* All beings belonging to the divine realm in the heavens. *wonders.* God's mighty acts in creation and redemption (see note on 9:1). *assembly of the holy ones.* The divine council in heaven (see v. 7; see also note on 82:1).
89:6 *heavenly beings.* Lit. "sons of god(s)" (see 29:1 and note).
89:8 LORD *... Almighty.* See note on 1Sa 1:3. *your faithfulness surrounds you.* It also surrounds this stanza (see v. 5).
89:9–13 The Lord's power as Creator—and creation's joy in him.

89:9–10 Poetic imagery borrowed from ancient Near Eastern myths of creation, here celebrating God's

[10]You crushed Rahab[r] like one of the slain;
with your strong arm you scattered[s] your enemies.
[11]The heavens are yours,[t] and yours also the earth;[u]
you founded the world and all that is in it.[v]
[12]You created the north and the south;
Tabor[w] and Hermon[x] sing for joy[y] at your name.
[13]Your arm is endowed with power;
your hand is strong, your right hand exalted.[z]

[14]Righteousness and justice are the foundation of your throne;[a]
love and faithfulness go before you.[b]
[15]Blessed are those who have learned to acclaim you,
who walk[c] in the light[d] of your presence, LORD.
[16]They rejoice in your name[e] all day long;
they celebrate your righteousness.
[17]For you are their glory and strength,[f]
and by your favor you exalt our horn.[a][g]
[18]Indeed, our shield[b][h] belongs to the LORD,
our king[i] to the Holy One of Israel.

[19]Once you spoke in a vision,
to your faithful people you said:
"I have bestowed strength on a warrior;
I have raised up a young man from among the people.
[20]I have found David[j] my servant;[k]
with my sacred oil[l] I have anointed[m] him.
[21]My hand will sustain him;
surely my arm will strengthen him.[n]
[22]The enemy will not get the better of him;[o]
the wicked will not oppress[p] him.
[23]I will crush his foes before him[q]
and strike down his adversaries.[r]
[24]My faithful love will be with him,[s]
and through my name his horn[c] will be exalted.
[25]I will set his hand over the sea,
his right hand over the rivers.[t]
[26]He will call out to me, 'You are my Father,[u]
my God, the Rock[v] my Savior.'[w]
[27]And I will appoint him to be my firstborn,[x]
the most exalted[y] of the kings[z] of the earth.
[28]I will maintain my love to him forever,
and my covenant with him will never fail.[a]
[29]I will establish his line forever,
his throne as long as the heavens endure.[b]

[30]"If his sons forsake my law
and do not follow my statutes,
[31]if they violate my decrees
and fail to keep my commands,
[32]I will punish their sin with the rod,
their iniquity with flogging;[c]
[33]but I will not take my love from him,[d]
nor will I ever betray my faithfulness.

[a] *17 Horn* here symbolizes strong one.
[b] *18* Or *sovereign*
[c] *24 Horn* here symbolizes strength.

89:10 [r]S Job 9:13 [s]S Ps 59:11; S 68:1; 92:9 **89:11** [t]S Dt 10:14; Ps 115:16 [u]1Ch 29:11; S Ps 24:1 [v]S Ge 1:1 **89:12** [w]S Jos 19:22 [x]S Dt 3:8; S 4:48 [y]Ps 98:8 **89:13** [z]S Jos 4:24 **89:14** [a]Ps 97:2 [b]Ps 85:10-11 **89:15** [c]Ps 1:1 [d]Ps 44:3 **89:16** [e]Ps 30:4; 105:3 **89:17** [f]Ps 18:1 [g]ver 24; Ps 75:10; 92:10; 112:9; 148:14 **89:18** [h]Ps 18:2 [i]Ps 47:9; Isa 16:5; 33:17, 22 **89:20** [j]Ac 13:22 [k]Ps 78:70 [l]S Ex 29:7; S 1Ki 1:39 [m]S 1Sa 2:35; S 2Sa 22:51 **89:21** [n]ver 13; Ps 18:35 **89:22** [o]S Jdg 3:15 [p]2Sa 7:10 **89:23** [q]Ps 18:40 [r]2Sa 7:9 **89:24** [s]S 2Sa 7:15 **89:25** [t]Ps 72:8 **89:26** [u]S 2Sa 7:14; S Jer 3:4; Heb 1:5 [v]S Ps 62:2 [w]S 2Sa 22:47 **89:27** [x]S Col 1:18 [y]S Nu 24:7 [z]Ps 2:6; Rev 1:5; 19:16 **89:28** [a]ver 33-34; Isa 55:3 **89:29** [b]ver 4,36 **89:32** [c]2Sa 7:14 **89:33** [d]S 2Sa 7:15

sovereign power over the primeval chaotic waters so that the creation order could be established (see Ge 1:6–10; see also notes on 65:6–7; 74:13–14).

89:10 *Rahab.* Mythical monster of the deep (see notes on 32:6; 87:4), probably another name for Leviathan (see 74:14; 104:26). The last half of this verse is probably echoed in Lk 1:51.

89:12 The parallelism indicates that the reference is to Mount Hermon (see note on Dt 3:8) in the north and Mount Tabor (see note on Jdg 4:6) in the south. *sing for joy.* See note on 65:13. *name.* See vv. 16,24; see also note on 5:11.

89:14–18 The Lord's righteousness and faithfulness in his rule in behalf of his people—and their joy in him.

89:14 Righteousness and justice are the foundation stones of God's throne (see 97:2 and note; cf. Pr 16:12; 25:5; 29:14). Love and faithfulness are personified as throne attendants that herald his royal movements (see note on 23:6). *Righteousness.* See v. 16; see also note on 4:1.

89:17 *horn.* King (see NIV text note; see also v. 18).

89:18 *Holy One of Israel.* See 71:22; 78:41; 2Ki 19:22 and note.

89:19–29 The Lord's election of David to be his regent over his people, and his everlasting covenant with him. The thought is developed by couplets: (1) introduction (v. 19); (2) I have anointed David as my servant and will sustain him (vv. 20–21); (3) I will crush all his foes (vv. 22–23); (4) I will extend his realm (vv. 24–25); (5) I will make him first among the kings (vv. 26–27); (6) I will cause his dynasty to endure forever (vv. 28–29)—a promise fulfilled in the eternal reign of Jesus Christ (see Jn 12:34).

89:19 *vision.* Reference is to the revelation to Samuel (see 1Sa 16:12) and/or to Nathan (see 2Sa 7:4–16). *faithful people.* See note on 4:3.

89:25 *sea ... rivers.* David's rule will reach from the Mediterranean Sea to the Euphrates River (see 72:8; 80:11 and note on Ex 23:31). But the author uses imagery that underscores the fact that, as his royal "son" (see v. 26) and regent, David's rule will be a reflection of God's (see vv. 9–10 and notes; also compare v. 23 with v. 10).

89:27 *firstborn.* The royal son of highest privilege and position in the kingdom of God (see 2:7–12; 45:6–9; 72:8–11; 110), thus "the most exalted of the kings of the earth" (see Rev 1:5). So the words may speak of universal rule—ultimately fulfilled in Christ.

89:29 *as long as the heavens endure.* See vv. 36–37.

89:30–37 The Lord's covenant with David and his dynasty (see note on 2Sa 7:1–29; see also chart, p. 23) was everlasting (see vv. 28–29) and unconditional—though if any of his royal descendants is unfaithful he will individually suffer under God's rod (to the detriment of the entire nation).

34 I will not violate my covenant
or alter what my lips have uttered.[e]
35 Once for all, I have sworn by my holiness —
and I will not lie to David —
36 that his line will continue forever
and his throne endure before me like the sun;[f]
37 it will be established forever like the moon,
the faithful witness in the sky."[g]

38 But you have rejected,[h] you have spurned,
you have been very angry with your anointed one.
39 You have renounced the covenant with your servant
and have defiled his crown in the dust.[i]
40 You have broken through all his walls[j]
and reduced his strongholds[k] to ruins.
41 All who pass by have plundered[l] him;
he has become the scorn of his neighbors.[m]
42 You have exalted the right hand of his foes;
you have made all his enemies rejoice.[n]
43 Indeed, you have turned back the edge of his sword
and have not supported him in battle.[o]
44 You have put an end to his splendor
and cast his throne to the ground.
45 You have cut short[p] the days of his youth;
you have covered him with a mantle of shame.[q]

89:34 [e]S Nu 23:19 89:36 [f]ver 4 89:37 [g]Jer 33:20-21 89:38 [h]1Ch 28:9; Ps 44:9; 78:59 89:39 [i]La 5:16 89:40 [j]S Ps 80:12 [k]Isa 22:5; La 2:2 89:41 [l]S Jdg 2:14 [m]S Ps 44:13 89:42 [n]Ps 13:2; 80:6 89:43 [o]Ps 44:10 89:45 [p]S Ps 39:5 [q]Ps 44:15; 109:29

89:46 [r]Ps 79:5 89:47 [s]S Ge 47:9; S Job 7:7; Ps 39:5; 1Pe 1:24 89:48 [t]S Ge 5:24; Ps 22:29 89:50 [u]Ps 69:19 89:51 [v]Ps 74:10 89:52 [w]S Ps 41:13; S 72:19 90:1 [x]S Dt 33:27; Eph 2:22; Rev 21:3

46 How long, LORD? Will you hide yourself forever?
How long will your wrath burn like fire?[r]
47 Remember how fleeting is my life.[s]
For what futility you have created all humanity!
48 Who can live and not see death,
or who can escape the power of the grave?[t]
49 Lord, where is your former great love,
which in your faithfulness you swore to David?
50 Remember, Lord, how your servant has[a] been mocked,[u]
how I bear in my heart the taunts of all the nations,
51 the taunts with which your enemies, LORD, have mocked,
with which they have mocked every step of your anointed one.[v]

52 Praise be to the LORD forever!
Amen and Amen.[w]

BOOK IV

Psalms 90–106

Psalm 90

A prayer of Moses the man of God.

1 Lord, you have been our dwelling place[x]
throughout all generations.

[a] 50 Or *your servants have*

89:38–45 God's present rejection of David's son, and all its fearful consequences — the undoing of all that had been promised and assured by covenant (see especially vv. 19–29). To fully appreciate the poignancy of this lament, cf. Ps 18.

89:46–51 The prayer, an appeal — in spite of all — to God's faithfulness to his covenant with David. In this dark hour, that remains the psalmist's hope.

89:46 *How long ... ?* See note on 6:3. *wrath.* See note on 2:5.

89:47 *how fleeting is my life.* See 37:20; 39:4–6 and notes. The shortness of human life adds urgency to the prayer. *futility.* Because humans have limited powers and are subject to death, they are dependent on God's involvement in the world (see 60:11; 90:5–6 and note; 108:12; 127:1–2; see also Job 7:1–3; Ecc 1:2 and note).

89:49 *former great love.* The love referred to in v. 1.

89:50 *Remember.* See v. 47.

89:52 A brief doxology with which the final editors concluded Book III of the Psalter (see note on 41:13).

Ps 90–100 A series of 11 psalms arranged within the frame "you have been our dwelling place throughout all generations" (90:1) and "his faithfulness continues through all generations" (100:5) — a series that begins with prayer and ends with praise. The first two of these psalms (90–91) are thematically connected (point and counterpoint); the next three (92–94) form a trilogy that serves as a transition to the final thematic cluster (95–99). At the very middle, Ps 95 anticipates the four following psalms and adds a warning for the celebrants of Yahweh's reign that echoes the warning of Moses in Dt 6:13–18. Evidently the editors of the Psalter intended readers of this group of psalms to hear echoes of the voice of Moses as interceder (Ps 90) and as admonisher (95:8–11), through which ministries (shared also by Aaron and Samuel) Israel had been blessed under the reign of the Great King, Yahweh (see 99:6–8).

Ps 90 A prayer to the everlasting God to have compassion on his servants, who through the ages have known him to be their safe haven (v. 1; see also 91:9) but who also painfully experience his wrath because of their sin and his sentence of death that cuts short their lives — a plea that through this long night of his displeasure God will teach them true wisdom (see v. 12 and note) and, in the morning after, bless them in equal measure with expressions of his love so that joy may yet fill their days and the days of their children and their daily labors may be blessed. This psalm has many links with Ps 39.

So that the melancholy depiction of the human state found here might not stand alone, the editors of the Psalter have followed it immediately with a psalm that speaks in

[2] Before the mountains were born[y]
or you brought forth the whole world,
from everlasting to everlasting[z] you are God.[a]

[3] You turn people back to dust,
saying, "Return to dust, you mortals."[b]
[4] A thousand years in your sight
are like a day that has just gone by,
or like a watch in the night.[c]
[5] Yet you sweep people away[d] in the sleep of death—
they are like the new grass of the morning:
[6] In the morning it springs up new,
but by evening it is dry and withered.[e]

[7] We are consumed by your anger
and terrified by your indignation.
[8] You have set our iniquities before you,
our secret sins[f] in the light of your presence.[g]
[9] All our days pass away under your wrath;
we finish our years with a moan.[h]
[10] Our days may come to seventy years,[i]
or eighty,[j] if our strength endures;
yet the best of them are but trouble and sorrow,[k]
for they quickly pass, and we fly away.[l]
[11] If only we knew the power of your anger!
Your wrath[m] is as great as the fear that is your due.[n]
[12] Teach us to number our days,[o]
that we may gain a heart of wisdom.[p]

[13] Relent, LORD! How long[q] will it be?
Have compassion on your servants.[r]
[14] Satisfy[s] us in the morning with your unfailing love,[t]
that we may sing for joy[u] and be glad all our days.[v]
[15] Make us glad for as many days as you have afflicted us,
for as many years as we have seen trouble.
[16] May your deeds be shown to your servants,
your splendor to their children.[w]

90:2 [y] S Job 15:7 [z] Isa 9:6; 57:15 [a] S Ge 21:33; S Job 10:5; Ps 102:24-27; Pr 8:23-26 **90:3** [b] S Ge 2:7; S Job 7:21; 34:15; 1Co 15:47 **90:4** [c] S Job 10:5; 2Pe 3:8 **90:5** [d] S Ge 19:15 **90:6** [e] Isa 40:6-8; Mt 6:30; Jas 1:10 **90:8** [f] S Ps 19:12; 2Co 4:2; Eph 5:12 [g] S Heb 4:13 **90:9** [h] Ps 78:33 **90:10** [i] Isa 23:15, 17; Jer 25:11 [j] 2Sa 19:35 [k] S Job 5:7 [l] S Job 20:8; S 34:15 **90:11** [m] Ps 7:11 [n] Ps 76:7 **90:12** [o] Ps 39:4; 139:16; Pr 16:9; 20:24 [p] Dt 32:29 **90:13** [q] Ps 6:3 [r] S Dt 32:36 **90:14** [s] Ps 103:5; 107:9; 145:16,19 [t] S Ps 77:8; 143:8 [u] S Ps 5:11 [v] Ps 31:7 **90:16** [w] Ps 44:1; Hab 3:2

counterpoint of the happy condition of those who dwell "in the shelter of the Most High" (91:1) and "make the Most High [their] dwelling" (91:9; see also 92:13). To isolate Ps 90 from this context is to distort its intended function in the Psalter collection. See also Ps 103.

Two stanzas descriptive of the human condition under God's aggrieved anger (vv. 3–6,7–10) are framed by two couplets (vv. 1–2,11–12) that, by their implicit contrasts, highlight the major polarities over which the intervening stanzas brood: (1) The Lord, who has ever been our "dwelling place" (v. 1), has shown us the power of his wrath (v. 7). (2) God is the Everlasting One (v. 2), while we must come to terms with the small number of our days (v. 12). These reflections lead to the prayer with which the psalm concludes (vv. 13–17).

90 title *A prayer.* See note on Ps 17 title. *Moses.* Tradition has assigned this psalm to Moses—perhaps because (1) it shares some language with Dt 32–33; (2) as an intercessory prayer it fits well on the lips of Moses, the great interceder for Israel (see Ex 32:11–13; 34:9; Nu 14:13–19; Dt 9:25–29; Ps 106:23; Jer 15:1; see also Ps 99:6); and (3) elsewhere only Moses asks God directly to "relent" from his anger toward Israel (v. 13; see Ex 32:12). *man of God.* A phrase normally applied in the OT to prophets (see note on 1Sa 2:27), including Moses (see, e.g., Jos 14:6).

90:1 *dwelling place.* See 91:9. The Hebrew for this phrase is translated "refuge" in 71:3. Here and in 91:9 it has the connotation of "home" or "safe haven."

90:3–6 Human beings live under God's sentence of death—"dust … to dust" (Ge 3:19).

90:4–5 *A … Yet.* Though for God 1,000 years are like a mere watch in the night (three-four hours), he cuts human life short like new grass that shows itself at dawn's light but is withered away by the hot Canaanite sun before evening falls.

90:4 *A thousand years … are like a day.* Cf. 2Pe 3:8 and note. *watch in the night.* See note on Jdg 7:19.

90:5–6 The shortness of human life frequently occupied the thoughts of Biblical writers (see 37:2,20,36; 39:5,11; 62:9; 78:39; 89:47; 102:3,11; 103:15–16; 109:23; 144:4; Job 8:9; 14:1–2; Ecc 6:12; Isa 40:6–8; Jas 1:10–11; 1Pe 1:24–25).

90:7–10 Even life's short span is filled with trouble, as God ferrets out every sin and makes the sinner feel his righteous anger.

90:7 *anger … indignation.* See vv. 9,11; see also note on 2:5.

90:8 *light of your presence.* The holy light of God that illumines the hidden corners of the heart and exposes its dark secrets.

90:10 *eighty.* Hebrew poetic convention called for 80 following 70 in parallel construction (see note on Am 1:3). *if our strength endures.* If God gives us the strength to live that long. *the best of them.* Reference is either to the best of the days or to what people prize most in their years—these are all soured by trouble and sorrow (or disappointment).

90:11–12 *If only we knew … Teach us.* No one has taken the measure of God's anger. But everyone ought to know the measure of their (few) days or they will play the arrogant fool, with no thought of their mortality or of their accountability to God (see Ps 10; 30:6; 49; 73:4–12; see also Dt 8).

90:11 *fear that is your due.* See note on 15:4.

90:12 *gain a heart of wisdom.* God's discipline humbles arrogant sinners and teaches them true wisdom (see 39; 94:12; Pr 3:1–12; Heb 12:7–11; cf. Ps 92:6–7; 94:8–10).

90:13–17 Prayer for God to be compassionate and restore the joys of life. The good hope with which such a prayer may be uttered comes to expression in Ps 91; 92; see also 94:12–14.

90:13 *Relent.* Lit. "Turn" (cf. v. 3). *How long … ?* See note on 6:3.

90:14 *in the morning.* Let there be for us a dawning of your love to relieve this long, dark night of your anger (see introduction to Ps 57). The final answer to this prayer comes with the resurrection (see Ro 5:2–5; 8:18; 2Co 4:16–18). *unfailing love.* See note on 6:4.

90:16 *deeds … splendor.* That is, deeds-of-splendor (see 111:3; see also note on 3:7). For a fuller description of such deeds, see the whole of Ps 111. *to their children.* As to past generations (v. 1).

[17] May the favor[a] of the Lord our God
rest on us;
establish the work of our hands for
us—
yes, establish the work of our
hands.[x]

Psalm 91

[1] Whoever dwells in the shelter[y] of the
Most High
will rest in the shadow[z] of the
Almighty.[b]
[2] I will say of the LORD, "He is my
refuge[a] and my fortress,[b]
my God, in whom I trust."

[3] Surely he will save you
from the fowler's snare[c]
and from the deadly pestilence.[d]
[4] He will cover you with his feathers,
and under his wings you will find
refuge;[e]
his faithfulness will be your shield[f]
and rampart.
[5] You will not fear[g] the terror of night,
nor the arrow that flies by day,
[6] nor the pestilence that stalks in the
darkness,
nor the plague that destroys at
midday.

90:17 [x] Isa 26:12
91:1 [y] S Ex 33:22 [z] Ps 63:7; Isa 49:2; La 4:20
91:2 [a] ver 9; S 2Sa 22:3; Ps 9:9 [b] S 2Sa 22:2
91:3 [c] Ps 124:7; Pr 6:5 [d] 1Ki 8:37
91:4 [e] S Ru 2:12; Ps 17:8 [f] S Dt 32:10; Ps 35:2; Isa 27:3; 31:5; Zec 12:8
91:5 [g] S Job 5:21

[a] 17 Or *beauty* [b] 1 Hebrew *Shaddai*

90:17 *favor.* See NIV text note; see also 27:4 and note. *establish.* As you only have been our security in the world (see v. 1), so also make our labors to be effective and enduring—though we are so transient.

Ps 91 A glowing testimony to the security of those who trust in God—set beside Ps 90 as a counterpoint to the dismal depiction of the human condition found there (see introduction to that psalm). It was probably written by one of the temple personnel (a priest or Levite) as a word of assurance to godly worshipers. Because the "you" of vv. 3–13 applies to any who "make the Most High your dwelling" (v. 9; see 90:1), the devil applied vv. 11–12 to Jesus (see Mt 4:6; Lk 4:10–11).

Structurally, the psalm is divided into two halves of eight verses each, with the opening couplet of the second half (vv. 9–10) echoing the theme of vv. 1–2. In the first half, the godly are assured of security from four threats (vv. 5–6)—though thousands fall (v. 7). In the second half, they are assured of triumphing over four menacing beasts (v. 13). The message of vv. 14–16 offers climactic assurance.

91:1 *shelter.* The temple (as in 27:5; 31:20; see also 23:6; 27:4), where the godly find safety under the protective wings of the Lord (see v. 4; 61:4). *Most High.* See v. 9; see also note on Ge 14:19. *shadow.* See note on 17:8. *Almighty.* See NIV text note; see also note on Ge 17:1.

91:3 *fowler's snare.* Metaphor for danger from human enemies (see 124:7; see also note on 9:15). See photo below. *pestilence.* Danger to life from disease. These two threats are further elaborated in vv. 5–6.

91:4 *with his feathers … wings.* See note on 17:8.

91:5 *terror.* As in 64:1 ("threat"), reference is to attack by enemies; thus it is paired with "arrow." These two references to threats from war are arrayed alongside "pestilence" and "plague" (v. 6), two references to mortal diseases that often

Egyptian men hunting and capturing birds with a net (Thebes, 1420–1411 BC). The psalmist declares that God will protect his people from their enemies: "Surely he will save you from the fowler's snare" (Ps 91:3).

Z. Radovan/www.BibleLandPictures.com

7 A thousand may fall at your side,
ten thousand at your right hand,
but it will not come near you.
8 You will only observe with your eyes
and see the punishment of the
wicked.[h]

9 If you say, "The LORD is my refuge,"
and you make the Most High your
dwelling,
10 no harm[i] will overtake you,
no disaster will come near your tent.
11 For he will command his angels[j]
concerning you
to guard you in all your ways;[k]
12 they will lift you up in their hands,
so that you will not strike your foot
against a stone.[l]
13 You will tread on the lion and the
cobra;
you will trample the great lion and
the serpent.[m]

14 "Because he[a] loves me," says the LORD,
"I will rescue him;
I will protect him, for he
acknowledges my name.
15 He will call on me, and I will answer
him;
I will be with him in trouble,
I will deliver him and honor him.[n]
16 With long life[o] I will satisfy him
and show him my salvation.[p]"

Psalm 92[b]

A psalm. A song. For the Sabbath day.

1 It is good to praise the LORD
and make music[q] to your name,[r]
O Most High,[s]
2 proclaiming your love in the morning[t]
and your faithfulness at night,
3 to the music of the ten-stringed lyre[u]
and the melody of the harp.[v]

4 For you make me glad by your deeds,
LORD;
I sing for joy[w] at what your hands
have done.[x]
5 How great are your works,[y] LORD,
how profound your thoughts![z]
6 Senseless people[a] do not know,
fools do not understand,
7 that though the wicked spring up like
grass

91:8 [h] Ps 37:34; S 58:10 **91:10** [i] Pr 12:21 **91:11** [j] S Ge 32:1; Heb 1:14 [k] Ps 34:7 **91:12** [l] Mt 4:6*; Lk 4:10-11* **91:13** [m] Da 6:22; Lk 10:19 **91:15** [n] S 1Sa 2:30; Jn 12:26 **91:16** [o] Dt 6:2; S Ps 21:4 [p] S Ps 50:23 **92:1** [q] S Ps 27:6 [r] S Ps 9:2; 147:1 [s] Ps 135:3 **92:2** [t] S Ps 55:17 **92:3** [u] S Ps 71:22 [v] S 1Sa 10:5; S Ne 12:27; S Ps 33:2; 81:2 **92:4** [w] S Ps 5:11; 27:6 [x] S Ps 8:6; 111:7; 143:5 **92:5** [y] S Job 36:24; Rev 15:3 [z] Ps 40:5; 139:17; Isa 28:29; 31:2; Ro 11:33 **92:6** [a] S Ps 73:22

[a] 14 That is, probably the king [b] In Hebrew texts 92:1-15 is numbered 92:2-16.

---

reached epidemic proportions. *night ... day.* At whatever time of day or night the threat may come, you will be kept safe—the time references are not specific to their respective phrases (see also v. 6).

91:7 *ten thousand.* Hebrew poetic convention called for 10,000 following 1,000 in parallel construction (see notes on 90:10; 1Sa 18:7; Am 1:3).

91:9 *dwelling.* See 90:1 and note.

91:11–12 Quoted by Satan in Mt 4:6; Lk 4:10–11.

91:11 *his angels.* See note on 34:7.

91:12 *against a stone.* On the stony trails of Canaan (see Pr 3:23).

91:13 *lion ... cobra ... great lion ... serpent.* These double references to lions and to poisonous snakes balance the double references of vv. 5–6 and complete the illustrative roster of mortal threats (see Am 5:19).

91:14–16 Employing the form of a prophetic message, the author (see introduction) supports his testimony by assuring the godly that it is confirmed by all the promises of God to those who truly love and trust him.

91:14 *protect him.* Lit. "raise him to a high, secure place." *acknowledges my name.* See 9:10 ("know your name") and note. *my name.* See note on 5:11.

91:15 *He will call ... I will answer.* See note on 118:5.

91:16 *With long life.* The climactic counterpoint to Ps 90.

Ps 92 A joyful celebration of the righteous rule of God. Its testimony to the prosperity of the righteous, "planted in the house of the LORD" (v. 13), links it thematically with Ps 91 (see introduction to that psalm), while its joy over God's righteous reign relates it to the cluster of psalms that follow (Ps 93–100; see especially Ps 94). There are, in fact, reasons to believe that the editors of the Psalter brought together Ps 92–94 as a trilogy that serves as a bridge between Ps 90–91 and 95–99 (see introductions to Ps 93; 94). Notably, God's name Yahweh ("LORD") occurs seven times in this psalm. Verses 10–11 suggest that the author may have been one of Israel's kings.

Following the introduction on praise (vv. 1–3), vv. 4–5 offer the motivation for the praise ("me," "I"), which is picked up again in vv. 10–11 ("my," "me," "My," "my," "my," "my"). Verses 6–9 expound the folly and destiny of evildoers, while vv. 12–15 expound the prosperity of the righteous. Notice also the link between v. 7 and v. 13. The NIV text offers a different analysis of the psalm's structure.

92 title *A song.* See note on Ps 30 title. *For the Sabbath day.* In the postexilic liturgy of the temple, this psalm came to be sung at the time of the morning sacrifice on the Sabbath. (The rest of the weekly schedule was: first day, Ps 24; second day, Ps 48; third day, Ps 82; fourth day, Ps 94; fifth day, Ps 81; sixth day, Ps 93.)

92:1–3 Hymnic introduction.

92:1 *LORD ... Most High.* That is, "LORD Most High" (see 7:17; see also note on 3:7). *name.* See note on 5:11. *Most High.* A link with Ps 91 (see vv. 1,9 of that psalm). For the title, see note on Ge 14:19.

92:2 *love ... faithfulness.* That is, love-and-faithfulness (see note on 36:5; see also note on 3:7). *love.* See note on 6:4. *morning ... night.* Continuously.

92:3 *lyre ... harp.* See note on 57:8. *harp.* See note on Ge 31:27.

92:4–5 Joy over God's saving acts (see vv. 10–11).

92:5 *profound.* Lit. "deep." *your thoughts.* As shown by your deeds.

92:6–9 The fatal folly of evildoers (contrast vv. 12–15).

92:6 *Senseless ... fools.* See NIV text note on 14:1; see also 49:10—and note especially 94:8–11. They do not know that the Lord rules righteously. They see the wicked flourishing but do not see the Lord or foresee the end he has appointed for them. The author thus characterizes his "wicked foes" (v. 11), whom the Lord has routed.

92:7 A condensed statement of what is expounded more fully in Ps 73 (see also 37:2; 62:9; 90:5–6 and notes).

and all evildoers flourish,
they will be destroyed
forever.[b]

8 But you, LORD, are forever exalted.

9 For surely your enemies[c], LORD,
surely your enemies will
perish;
all evildoers will be scattered.[d]
10 You have exalted my horn[a][e] like that
of a wild ox;[f]
fine oils[g] have been poured on me.
11 My eyes have seen the defeat of my
adversaries;
my ears have heard the rout of my
wicked foes.[h]

12 The righteous will flourish[i] like a
palm tree,
they will grow like a cedar of
Lebanon;[j]
13 planted in the house of the LORD,
they will flourish in the courts of
our God.[k]
14 They will still bear fruit[l] in old
age,
they will stay fresh and green,
15 proclaiming, "The LORD is upright;
he is my Rock, and there is no
wickedness in him.[m]"

92:7 [b]S Ps 37:2 **92:9** [c]S Ps 45:5 [d]S Ps 68:1; S 89:10 **92:10** [e]S Ps 89:17 [f]S Ps 29:6 [g]S Ps 23:5 **92:11** [h]S Ps 54:7; 91:8 **92:12** [i]S Ps 72:7 [j]S Ps 1:3; 52:8; Jer 17:8; Hos 14:6 **92:13** [k]Ps 135:2 **92:14** [l]S Ps 1:3; S Jn 15:2 **92:15** [m]S Job 34:10 **93:1** [n]S 1Ch 16:31; S Ps 97:1 [o]S Job 40:10; S Ps 21:5 [p]S Ps 65:6 [q]Ps 24:2; 78:69; 119:90 [r]1Ch 16:30; Ps 96:10 **93:2** [s]S 2Sa 7:16 [t]S Ge 21:33 **93:3** [u]Ps 96:11; 98:7; Isa 5:30; 17:12-13; Jer 6:23 [v]S Ps 46:3 [w]Job 9:8; Ps 107:25, 29; Isa 51:15; Jer 31:35; Hab 3:10 **93:4** [x]Ps 65:7; Jer 6:23 [y]S Ps 18:4; Jnh 1:15 [z]S Ne 9:32; S Job 9:4 **93:5** [a]Ps 29:2; 96:9 [b]Ps 5:7; 23:6 **94:1** [c]S Ge 4:24; Ro 12:19 [d]S Dt 33:2; Ps 80:1

Psalm 93

1 The LORD reigns,[n] he is robed in majesty;[o]
the LORD is robed in majesty and
armed with strength;[p]
indeed, the world is established,[q]
firm and secure.[r]
2 Your throne was established[s] long ago;
you are from all eternity.[t]

3 The seas[u] have lifted up, LORD,
the seas have lifted up their voice;[v]
the seas have lifted up their
pounding waves.[w]
4 Mightier than the thunder[x] of the great
waters,
mightier than the breakers[y] of the sea—
the LORD on high is mighty.[z]

5 Your statutes, LORD, stand firm;
holiness[a] adorns your house[b]
for endless days.

Psalm 94

1 The LORD is a God who avenges.[c]
O God who avenges, shine forth.[d]

[a] *10* *Horn* here symbolizes strength.

92:8 *forever exalted.* God's eternal exaltation assures the destruction of his enemies.
92:9 *enemies.* Here the evildoers, referred to also in v. 7.
92:10–11 Joy over God's favors (see vv. 4–5): God has made him triumphant (see 89:24) and anointed him with "the oil of joy" (45:7; see also 23:5) by giving him victory over all his enemies.
92:12–15 The secure prosperity of the righteous (contrast vv. 6–9).
92:13 *planted in the house of the LORD.* Though the wicked may "spring up like grass," their end is sure (see v. 7). But the righteous are planted in a secure place (see Ps 91) and so retain the vigor of youth into old age, rejoicing in God's just discrimination (see v. 15). *courts.* Of the temple (see 84:2,10; 2Ki 21:5; 23:11–12).
92:15 *upright ... Rock ... no wickedness in him.* See Dt 32:4 and note.
Ps 93 A hymn to the eternal, universal and invincible reign of the Lord, a theme it shares with Ps 47; 95–99. Together these hymns offer a majestic confession of faith in and hope for the kingdom of God on earth. They may all have been composed by temple personnel and spoken by them in the liturgy. Ps 93 celebrates Yahweh's secure cosmic rule that grounds his righteous and effective rule over human affairs—which is the joy (Ps 92) and the hope (Ps 94) of those who rely on him for protection against the assaults of the godless fools who live by violence. Structurally, the psalm has two short stanzas (vv. 1–2,3–4) and a conclusion (v. 5).
93:1–2 The Lord's reign, by which the creation order has been and will be secure throughout the ages, is from eternity (see Ge 1:1). Though Israel as a nation has come late on the scene, her God has been King since before the creation of the world.
93:1 *The LORD reigns.* The ultimate truth, and first article, in Israel's creed (see 96:10; 97:1; 99:1; see also Zec 14:9 and note, as well as Introduction to Psalms: Theology: Major Themes).
93:3–4 Both at and since his founding of the world, the Lord has shown himself to be mightier than all the forces of disorder that threaten his kingdom.
93:3 *seas.* Reference is to the primeval chaotic waters, tamed and assigned a place by the Lord's creative word (see 33:7; 104:7–9; Ge 1:6–10; Job 38:8–11). Implicitly they symbolize all that opposes the coming of the Lord's kingdom (see 65:6–7; 74:13–14 and notes).
93:4 The thunder of the chaotic waters is no match for the thunder of the Lord's ordering word (see 104:7).
93:5 *statutes.* He whose indisputable rule has made the world secure has given his people life directives that are stable and reliable (see 19:7)—and that they must honor (see 95:8–11). *your house.* His earthly temple—but also the heavenly. *for endless days.* Qualifies both clauses.
Ps 94 An appeal to the Lord, as "Judge of the earth" (v. 2), to redress the wrongs perpetrated against the weak by arrogant and wicked persons who occupy seats of power. The psalm has links with Ps 92 (see introductions to Ps 92; 93) but is the voice of the oppressed within Israel, seeking redress at God's throne for injustices done to them by the "fools" smugly established in the power structures of the nation. Thus it is unique within the Ps 90–100 group of psalms and stands here as representative of the many cries of the oppressed found in Books I–III of the Psalter. Following a three-verse introduction, the thought advances regularly in five stanzas of four verses each, with the main thematic shift coming at v. 12.
94:1–3 Initial appeal to God, the Judge.
94:1 *avenges.* Redresses wrongs (see note on 5:10; see also Dt 32:35,41 and note on 32:35). To avenge is the function of a king in his role as chief executive of the realm. Thus a direct conceptual link with Ps 47; 93; 95–99 is established at the outset. *shine forth.* Cf. notes on 50:2; 80:1.

[2]Rise up,[e] Judge[f] of the earth;
pay back[g] to the proud what they deserve.
[3]How long, LORD, will the wicked,
how long will the wicked be jubilant?[h]

[4]They pour out arrogant[i] words;
all the evildoers are full of boasting.[j]
[5]They crush your people,[k] LORD;
they oppress your inheritance.[l]
[6]They slay the widow[m] and the foreigner;
they murder the fatherless.[n]
[7]They say, "The LORD does not see;[o]
the God of Jacob[p] takes no notice."

[8]Take notice, you senseless ones[q] among the people;
you fools, when will you become wise?
[9]Does he who fashioned the ear not hear?
Does he who formed the eye not see?[r]
[10]Does he who disciplines[s] nations not punish?
Does he who teaches[t] mankind lack knowledge?
[11]The LORD knows all human plans;[u]
he knows that they are futile.[v]

[12]Blessed is the one you discipline,[w] LORD,
the one you teach[x] from your law;
[13]you grant them relief from days of trouble,[y]
till a pit[z] is dug for the wicked.
[14]For the LORD will not reject his people;[a]
he will never forsake his inheritance.
[15]Judgment will again be founded on righteousness,[b]
and all the upright in heart[c] will follow it.

[16]Who will rise up[d] for me against the wicked?
Who will take a stand for me against evildoers?[e]
[17]Unless the LORD had given me help,[f]
I would soon have dwelt in the silence of death.[g]
[18]When I said, "My foot is slipping,[h]"
your unfailing love, LORD, supported me.
[19]When anxiety[i] was great within me,
your consolation[j] brought me joy.

[20]Can a corrupt throne[k] be allied with you—
a throne that brings on misery by its decrees?[l]
[21]The wicked band together[m] against the righteous
and condemn the innocent[n] to death.[o]
[22]But the LORD has become my fortress,
and my God the rock[p] in whom I take refuge.[q]
[23]He will repay[r] them for their sins
and destroy[s] them for their wickedness;
the LORD our God will destroy them.

94:2 [e] S Nu 10:35 [f] S Ge 18:25; Heb 12:23; S Jas 5:9 [g] S Ps 31:23 **94:3** [h] Ps 13:2 **94:4** [i] Jer 43:2 [j] S Ps 52:1 **94:5** [k] Ps 44:2; 74:8; Isa 3:15; Jer 8:21 [l] Ps 28:9 **94:6** [m] S Dt 10:18; S Isa 1:17 [n] Dt 24:19 **94:7** [o] S Job 22:14 [p] S Ge 24:12 **94:8** [q] S Dt 32:6; S Ps 73:22 **94:9** [r] Ex 4:11; Pr 20:12 **94:10** [s] S Ps 39:11 [t] S Ex 35:34; Job 35:11; Isa 28:26 **94:11** [u] Ps 139:2; Pr 15:26; S Mt 9:4 [v] 1Co 3:20* **94:12** [w] S Job 5:17; 1Co 11:32; Heb 12:5 [x] S Dt 8:3; S 1Sa 12:23 **94:13** [y] S Ps 86:7 [z] S Ps 7:15; S 55:23 **94:14** [a] S Dt 31:6; Ps 37:28; Ro 11:2 **94:15** [b] Ps 97:2 [c] Ps 7:10; 11:2; S 36:10 **94:16** [d] Nu 10:35; Ps 17:13; Isa 14:22 [e] S Ps 59:2 **94:17** [f] Ps 124:2 [g] S Ps 31:17 **94:18** [h] S Dt 32:35; S Job 12:5 **94:19** [i] Ecc 11:10 [j] S Job 6:10 **94:20** [k] Jer 22:30; 36:30 [l] S Ps 58:2 **94:21** [m] S Ps 56:6 [n] Ps 106:38; Pr 17:15,26; 28:21; Isa 5:20,23; Mt 27:4 [o] S Ge 18:23 **94:22** [p] S Ps 61:2 [q] S 2Sa 22:3; S Ps 18:2 **94:23** [r] S Ex 32:34; S Ps 54:5 [s] Ps 9:5; 37:38; 145:20

94:2 *the proud.* See vv. 4–7 for a description of them.
94:3 *How long ...?* See note on 6:3.
94:4–7 Indictment of the wicked.
94:4 *arrogant words ... boasting.* For similar expressions of the arrogance of the wicked, see 10:2–11 and notes.
94:5 *your people ... your inheritance.* Those among them who are vulnerable (see v. 6).
94:7 *They say.* See note on 3:2. *Jacob.* A synonym for Israel (see Ge 32:28).
94:8–11 Warning to the wicked—those "senseless ... fools" (see 92:6–9; see also NIV text note on 14:1).
94:10 *disciplines.* Keeps them in line by means of punishment (see Lev 26:18; Jer 31:18). *teaches.* Gives human beings some knowledge of the creation order (see Isa 28:26).
94:11 *The LORD knows.* Contrary to their foolish supposition (see v. 7).
94:12–15 Here the focus shifts from the arrogance and folly of the wicked to the happy state of those who count themselves among the Lord's people and who live under his discipline and rely on his royal protection.
94:12 *Blessed.* See note on 1:1. *discipline ... teach.* See v. 10 and note. Here the author speaks of God's correcting and teaching his people in the ways of his law.
94:14 *people ... inheritance.* See v. 5. The Lord will not abandon the powerless among his people to the injustice of their oppressors. Paul may be echoing this verse in Ro 11:1–2.
94:15 However this difficult verse is to be translated, the author appears to say that God's righteous rule will restore justice for those who have been wrongfully treated while being themselves innocent—described as "the upright in heart" (see also v. 21). *heart.* See note on 4:7.
94:16–19 The Lord is the only sure court of appeal.
94:17 *silence of death.* See note on 30:1. Without God's help the wicked would have silenced the psalmist in the grave, but now it is the wicked for whom the pit will be dug (see v. 13).
94:18 *When I said.* When feeling about to be overwhelmed by the wicked (see note on 38:16). *love.* See note on 6:4.
94:20–23 Confidence that the Lord's justice will prevail. Cf. notes on 89:14; Zec 8:16.
94:20 *corrupt throne.* A seat of authority that works mischief. The author speaks of injustice at the center of power (cf. notes on Ne 5:6; Zec 8:16).
94:21 *righteous.* Here referring to those who have not wronged anyone—i.e., "the innocent" (see note on v. 15). For the basic concept, see note on 1:5.

Psalm 95

1 Come,[t] let us sing for joy[u] to the LORD;
let us shout aloud[v] to the Rock[w] of our salvation.
2 Let us come before him[x] with thanksgiving[y]
and extol him with music[z] and song.

3 For the LORD is the great God,[a]
the great King[b] above all gods.[c]
4 In his hand are the depths of the earth,[d]
and the mountain peaks belong to him.
5 The sea is his, for he made it,
and his hands formed the dry land.[e]

6 Come, let us bow down[f] in worship,[g]
let us kneel[h] before the LORD our Maker;[i]
7 for he is our God
and we are the people of his pasture,[j]
the flock under his care.

Today, if only you would hear his voice,
8 "Do not harden your hearts[k] as you did at Meribah,[a][l]
as you did that day at Massah[b] in the wilderness,[m]
9 where your ancestors tested[n] me;
they tried me, though they had seen what I did.
10 For forty years[o] I was angry with that generation;
I said, 'They are a people whose hearts go astray,[p]
and they have not known my ways.'[q]
11 So I declared on oath[r] in my anger,
'They shall never enter my rest.' "[s]

Psalm 96

96:1-13pp — 1Ch 16:23-33

1 Sing to the LORD[t] a new song;[u]
sing to the LORD, all the earth.

95:1 [t] Ps 34:11; 80:2 [u] S Ps 5:11 [v] Ps 81:1; Isa 44:23; Zep 3:14 [w] S 2Sa 22:47 **95:2** [x] Ps 100:2; Mic 6:6 [y] S Ps 42:4 [z] Ps 81:2; S Eph 5:19 **95:3** [a] Ps 48:1; 86:10; 145:3; 147:5 [b] S Ps 47:2 [c] Ps 96:4; 97:9 **95:4** [d] S Ps 63:9 **95:5** [e] S Ge 1:9; Ps 146:6 **95:6** [f] S 2Sa 12:16; Php 2:10 [g] S Ps 22:29 [h] 2Ch 6:13 [i] Ps 100:3; 149:2; Isa 17:7; 54:5; Da 6:10-11; Hos 8:14 **95:7** [j] S Ps 74:1 **95:8** [k] Mk 10:5; Heb 3:8 [l] S Ex 17:7; S Dt 33:8; Heb 3:15*; 4:7 [m] S Ps 78:40 **95:9** [n] S Nu 14:22; 1Co 10:9 **95:10** [o] S Ex 16:35; S Nu 14:34; Ac 7:36; Heb 3:17 [p] Ps 58:3; 119:67, 176; Pr 12:26; 16:29; Isa 53:6; Jer 31:19; 50:6; Eze 34:6 [q] S Dt 8:6 **95:11** [r] S Nu 14:23 [s] Dt 1:35; Heb 3:7-11*; 4:3* **96:1** [t] Ps 30:4 [u] Ps 33:3; S 40:3; 98:1; 144:9; 149:1; Isa 42:10; S Rev 5:9

[a] 8 *Meribah* means *quarreling.* [b] 8 *Massah* means *testing.*

Ps 95 A call to worship the Lord, spoken by a priest or Levite to the assembled Israelites at the temple. (See introduction to Ps 93.) Placed at the center of its group (Ps 90–100) and at the beginning of a series of psalms celebrating the universal reign of Israel's God (Ps 95–99), Ps 95 contains a sharp reminder that Israel's sense of security under Yahweh's rule—from which spring both her prayers (as in Ps 90; 94) and her praise (as in Ps 91–93; 95–100)—is warranted only if she shows herself to be Yahweh's loyal and obedient servant. Its function in context is similar to that of Ps 81 (see introduction to Ps 79–83).

The psalm is composed of two parts: (1) a call to praise the Lord of all the earth (vv. 1–5); (2) a call to acknowledge by submissive attitude and obedient heart the Lord's kingship over his people (vv. 6–11). Each part also has two subdivisions, the latter of which forms the climax. Cf. the structure of Ps 96.

95:1–2 The call to praise God.

95:1 *Rock of our salvation.* See note on 18:2.

95:3–5 Why Israel is to praise the Lord—because he is above all gods, and there is no corner of the universe that is not in his hand. The ancient pagan world had different gods for different peoples, different geographic areas, different cosmic regions (heaven, earth, netherworld) and different aspects of life (e.g., war, fertility, crafts).

95:4–5 *depths ... mountain peaks ... sea ... dry land.* All the world—the extremes and all that lies between and all that is in them.

95:6–11 The exhortation to submit to the Lord with obedient hearts—a bent knee is not enough. For a NT reflection on these verses in the light of the advent of Christ, see Heb 3:7—4:13.

95:6–7 The call to confess submission to the Lord by kneeling before him.

95:6 *our Maker.* Both as Creator of all things (see Ge 1) and as Israel's Redeemer, he has made them what they are: the people of the Lord in the earth (see Isa 45:9–13; 51:12–16).

95:7 *people of his pasture.* See 100:3; Jer 23:1; Eze 34:17–23. Since kings were commonly called the shepherds of their people (see notes on 23:1; 74:1), their realms could be referred to as their pastures (see 23:2; Jer 25:36; 49:20; 50:45). *if only you would hear his voice.* In the liturgy of the religious festival, possibly in some such manner as Ps 50 and/or 78. The concern expressed in what follows echoes that of Moses in Dt 6:16–19.

95:8 *Meribah ... Massah.* See NIV text notes. The leader of the liturgy reminds Israel of times of her rebellion in the wilderness (see Ex 17:7; Nu 20:13).

95:9 *me.* Official representatives of the Lord, when speaking for him, could shift to first person (see 50:5,7–15; see also note on Ge 16:7). *had seen what I did.* In Egypt and at the "Red Sea"—and his provision of food in the wilderness (see Ex 16; see also Nu 14:11).

95:10 *forty years.* The climax of Israel's rebellion came when God's people faithlessly refused to undertake the conquest of Canaan and considered returning to Egypt (see Nu 14:1–4). It was then that God condemned them to a 40-year stay in the wilderness (see Nu 14:34). *angry.* See note on 2:5. *that generation.* The (adult) Israelites who came out of Egypt and covenanted with God at Sinai (see Nu 32:13). *They are a people ... my ways.* A restatement of the Lord's word in Nu 14:11. *hearts.* See note on 4:7. *my ways.* See 25:4 and note.

95:11 *on oath.* See Nu 14:28; Dt 1:34–35. *never enter my rest.* The language of Nu 14:30 is "not one of you will enter the land," but since the promised land was also called the place where God will give his people "rest" (Jos 1:13,15; see Ex 33:14; Dt 12:10; 25:19), the two statements are equivalent. *rest.* A rich concept indicating the Israelites' possession of a place with God in the earth where they are secure from all external threats and internal calamities (see Dt 3:20; 1Ki 5:4 and notes).

Ps 96 A call to all nations to praise the Lord as the only God and to proclaim the glory of his reign throughout the world—an OT anticipation of the world mission of the NT people of God (see Mt 28:16–20). (See introductions to Ps 93; 95.) This psalm appears in slightly altered form in 1Ch 16:23–33. Here in the Psalter it is paired with Ps 98, with which it shares much in form, language and theme (compare especially their opening and closing stanzas). Each of these

[2]Sing to the LORD, praise his name;[v]
proclaim his salvation[w] day after
day.
[3]Declare his glory[x] among the nations,
his marvelous deeds[y] among all
peoples.

[4]For great is the LORD and most worthy
of praise;[z]
he is to be feared[a] above all gods.[b]
[5]For all the gods of the nations are
idols,[c]
but the LORD made the heavens.[d]
[6]Splendor and majesty[e] are before
him;
strength and glory[f] are in his
sanctuary.

[7]Ascribe to the LORD,[g] all you families of
nations,[h]
ascribe to the LORD glory and
strength.
[8]Ascribe to the LORD the glory due his
name;
bring an offering[i] and come into his
courts.[j]
[9]Worship the LORD[k] in the splendor of
his[a] holiness;[l]
tremble[m] before him, all the
earth.[n]
[10]Say among the nations, "The LORD
reigns.[o]"
The world is firmly established,[p] it
cannot be moved;[q]
he will judge[r] the peoples with
equity.[s]

[11]Let the heavens rejoice,[t] let the earth
be glad;[u]
let the sea resound, and all that is
in it.
[12]Let the fields be jubilant, and
everything in them;
let all the trees of the forest[v] sing
for joy.[w]
[13]Let all creation rejoice before the
LORD, for he comes,
he comes to judge[x] the earth.
He will judge the world in
righteousness[y]
and the peoples in his faithfulness.[z]

96:2 [v]S Ps 68:4 [w]Ps 27:1; 71:15 **96:3** [x]Ps 8:1 [y]S Ps 71:17; Rev 15:3 **96:4** [z]S Ps 48:1 [a]S Dt 28:58; S 1Ch 16:25; Ps 89:7 [b]S Ps 95:3 **96:5** [c]S Lev 19:4 [d]S Ge 1:1; S 2Ch 2:12 **96:6** [e]S Ps 21:5 [f]Ps 29:1; 89:17 **96:7** [g]Ps 29:1 [h]Ps 22:27 **96:8** [i]Ps 45:12; S 51:19; 72:10 [j]Ps 65:4; 84:10; 92:13; 100:4 **96:9** [k]Ex 23:25; Jnh 1:9 [l]S Ps 93:5 [m]S Ex 15:14; Ps 114:7 [n]Ps 33:8 **96:10** [o]Ps 97:1 [p]Ps 24:2; 78:69; 119:90 [q]S Ps 93:1 [r]Ps 58:11 [s]Ps 67:4; 98:9

[a] 9 Or *LORD with the splendor of*

96:11 [t]S Rev 12:12 [u]Ps 97:1; Isa 49:13 **96:12** [v]Isa 44:23; 55:12; Eze 17:24 [w]Ps 65:13 **96:13** [x]Rev 19:11 [y]S Ps 7:11; Ac 17:31 [z]Ps 86:11

in turn is followed by a hymn that celebrates Yahweh's reign (cf. 97:1; 99:1) and its special benefits for Israel (cf. 97:8 – 12; 99:4 – 9). This arrangement suggests that Ps 97 has been linked with 96 and Ps 99 with 98 to form a pair of thematic couplets — introduced by Ps 95.

The psalm is composed of two parts: (1) The first begins with a threefold call to all nations to "sing to the LORD" in praise of his "name" (vv. 1 – 6); (2) the second begins with a threefold call to all nations to "ascribe to the LORD glory ... the glory due his name" (vv. 7 – 13). Each part has two subdivisions, the last of which forms the climax to the whole psalm. Cf. the structure of Ps 95.

96:1 – 3 The call to all the earth to sing the praise of the Lord among the nations. Triple repetition ("Sing ... sing ... Sing") was a common feature in OT liturgical calls to worship (see vv. 7 – 9 and note; see also 103:20 – 22; 118:2 – 4; 135:1; 136:1 – 3).

96:1 *new song.* See note on 33:3. *all the earth.* See v. 9; or "all the land," in which case the call is addressed to all Israel. However, the worldwide perspective of this psalm (see especially v. 7) suggests that here the psalmist has in view broader horizons (see 97:1; 100:1 and note; 117:1; see also note on 9:1).

96:2 *name.* See v. 8; see also note on 5:11. *proclaim his salvation.* Proclaim as good news (see 40:9 and note) the Lord's saving acts in Israel's behalf (see 3:8; see also 85:9).

96:3 *glory.* See note on 85:9. *marvelous deeds.* See note on 71:16 – 17.

96:4 – 6 Why "all the earth" (v. 1) is to praise the Lord: He alone is God (see Ps 115).

96:4 *feared.* See note on 15:4.

96:5 *made the heavens.* As the Maker of the heavenly realm, in pagan eyes the abode of the gods, the Lord is greater than all the gods (see 97:7).

96:6 *Splendor and majesty ... strength and glory.* Two pairs of divine attributes personified as throne attendants whose presence before the Lord heralds the exalted nature of the one, universal King. For similar personifications, see 23:6 and note. *glory.* The Hebrew for this word here connotes radiant beauty.

96:7 – 9 The call to all nations to worship the Lord (see 29:1 – 2 and note). The two half-sentences of 29:2 have been expanded in this psalm.

96:8 *courts.* Of the temple (see 84:2,10; 2Ki 21:5; 23:11 – 12).

96:9 *splendor of his holiness.* See note on 29:2. *tremble.* In reverent awe, equivalent to "fear" (see v. 4).

96:10 – 13 The call to all nations to proclaim among the nations the righteous reign of the Lord.

96:10 *The LORD reigns.* See 93:1 and note. *The world ... with equity.* In OT perspective, the world order is one, embracing both its physical and moral aspects because both have been established by God as aspects of his one kingdom and both are upheld by his one rule. Therefore God's rule over creation and over human affairs (also his acts of creation and redemption) is often spoken of in one breath, and righteousness, faithfulness and love are equally ascribable to both. And since the creation order is secure in its goodness (see Ge 1), it often serves in OT poetry (as it does here) as a manifest assurance that God's rule over human affairs will also be "with equity," "in righteousness" and "in ... faithfulness" (v. 13; see also 9:7 – 8; 11:3; 33:4 – 11; 36:5 – 9; 57:10; 58:11; 65:6 – 7; 71:19; 74:13 – 14,16 – 17; 75:2; 82:5; 93:3 – 4; 98:9; 99:4; 119:89 – 91 and notes). *will judge.* See v. 13 and note.

96:11 – 12 Because God's kingdom is one (see v. 10 and note), all his creatures will rejoice when God's rule over humankind brings righteousness to full expression in his cosmic kingdom (see note on 65:13; see also 97:7 – 9). For the present state of the creation as it awaits the fullness of redemption, see Ro 8:21 – 22 and notes.

96:13 *comes ... comes ... will judge.* Because God reigns over all things and is the Lord of history, Israel lived in hope (as the prophets announced) of the coming of God — his future acts by which he would decisively deal with all wickedness and establish his righteousness in the earth. *righteousness.* See note on 4:1.

Psalm 97

[1] The LORD reigns,[a] let the earth be glad;[b]
let the distant shores[c] rejoice.
[2] Clouds[d] and thick darkness[e] surround him;
righteousness and justice are the
foundation of his throne.[f]
[3] Fire[g] goes before[h] him
and consumes[i] his foes on every side.
[4] His lightning[j] lights up the world;
the earth[k] sees and trembles.[l]
[5] The mountains melt[m] like wax[n] before
the LORD,
before the Lord of all the earth.[o]
[6] The heavens proclaim his
righteousness,[p]
and all peoples see his glory.[q]

[7] All who worship images[r] are put to
shame,[s]
those who boast in idols[t]—
worship him,[u] all you gods![v]

[8] Zion hears and rejoices
and the villages of Judah are glad[w]
because of your judgments,[x] LORD.
[9] For you, LORD, are the Most High[y] over
all the earth;[z]
you are exalted[a] far above all gods.
[10] Let those who love the LORD hate evil,[b]
for he guards[c] the lives of his faithful
ones[d]
and delivers[e] them from the hand of
the wicked.[f]
[11] Light shines[a][g] on the righteous[h]
and joy on the upright in heart.[i]
[12] Rejoice in the LORD,[j] you who are righteous,
and praise his holy name.[k]

Psalm 98

A psalm.

[1] Sing to the LORD[l] a new song,[m]
for he has done marvelous things;[n]

[a] 11 One Hebrew manuscript and ancient versions (see also 112:4); most Hebrew manuscripts *Light is sown*

97:1 [a]Ex 15:18; Ps 93:1; 96:10; 99:1; Isa 24:23; 52:7 [b]S Ps 96:11 [c]S Est 10:1 **97:2** [d]S Job 22:14 [e]S Ex 19:9 [f]Ps 89:14 **97:3** [g]Isa 9:19; Da 7:10; Joel 1:19; 2:3 [h]Hab 3:5 [i]S 2Sa 22:9 **97:4** [j]S Job 36:30 [k]S 2Sa 22:8 [l]S Ps 18:7; 104:32; S Rev 6:12 **97:5** [m]S Ps 46:2, 6 [n]S Ps 22:14 [o]S Jos 3:11 **97:6** [p]Ps 50:6; 98:2 [q]S Ps 19:1 **97:7** [r]S Lev 26:1 [s]Isa 42:17; Jer 10:14 [t]S Dt 5:8 [u]Heb 1:6 [v]Ex 12:12; Ps 16:4 **97:8** [w]S Ps 9:2 [x]Ps 48:11 **97:9** [y]Ps 7:8 [z]S Job 34:29 [a]S Ps 47:9 **97:10** [b]S Job 28:28; Am 5:15; Ro 12:9 [c]Ps 145:20 [d]Ps 31:23; 37:28; Pr 2:8 [e]S Ps 34:7; Da 3:28; 6:16 [f]Ps 37:40; Jer 15:21; 20:13 **97:11** [g]S Job 22:28 [h]Ps 11:5 [i]Ps 7:10 **97:12** [j]S Job 22:19; Ps 104:34; Isa 41:16; Php 4:4 [k]S Ex 3:15; S Ps 99:3 **98:1** [l]Ps 30:4 [m]S Ps 96:1 [n]Ex 15:1; Ps 96:3; Isa 12:5; Lk 1:51

Ps 97 A joyful celebration of the Lord's righteous reign over all the earth (see introductions to Ps 93; 95), with special attention to the benefits of the Lord's reign enjoyed by Israel (see introduction to Ps 96). The psalm's two main divisions (vv. 1–6,8–12—closely balanced, having 42 and 43 Hebrew words, respectively) are joined by a centered verse (v. 7; see note on 6:6) that serves as a counterpoint to the main theme. The opening verses of the two main divisions are thematically linked: v. 1, "be glad ... rejoice"; v. 8, "rejoices ... are glad"—in reverse order, a frequent stylistic device in OT poetry. The first major division is framed by references to "the earth" (v. 1) and "the heavens" (v. 6), the second by references to "Zion ... the villages of Judah" (v. 8) and the "righteous" (v. 12).

97:1–6 A testimony to the nations—that they too have seen God's majesty displayed (vv. 2–6) and ought to rejoice with Israel that the Lord reigns supreme.

97:1 *The LORD reigns.* See 93:1 and note. *earth.* See 96:1; 99:1; 117:1; see also note on 9:1. *distant shores.* Even distant lands reached by the far-ranging ships that sail the seas (see 1Ki 9:26–28; 10:22; Isa 60:9; Jnh 1:3).

97:2–6 The Lord's majestic glory revealed in the sky's awesome displays, especially in the thunderstorm (see 18:7–15 and note; see also introduction to Ps 29).

97:2 *Clouds and thick darkness.* The dark storm clouds that hide the sun and cast a veil across the sky are dramatic visual reminders that the fierce heat and brilliance (also metaphors) of God's naked glory must be veiled from creaturely eyes (see Ex 19:9; 1Ki 8:12). Thus also a curtain closed off the Most Holy Place in the tabernacle and temple (see Ex 26:33; 2Ch 3:14), veiling it in darkness. *righteousness.* See v. 6; see also note on 4:1. *foundation of his throne.* God rules by his power (see 66:7), but his reign is founded on righteousness and justice, which also the heavens proclaim (see v. 6 and note). That a throne was established by righteousness and justice was proverbial in Israel (see Pr 16:32; 25:5; 29:14; cf. Ps 9:7–8; 103:6,19 and notes).

97:3 *Fire.* Manifested in the storm cloud's lightning bolts (see v. 4), fire often signified God's judicial wrath (see, e.g., 21:9; 50:3; 83:14; Dt 4:24; 9:3; 32:22; 1Ki 19:12; Isa 10:17; 30:27,30; see also note on La 1:13).

97:4 *earth.* Here the land realm (the continents) personified.

97:6 *proclaim his righteousness.* The stable order of the heaven's vast array "speaks" (see 19:1–4); it declares that God's reign similarly upholds the moral order (see note on 96:10). *all peoples see.* Verses 2–6 have spoken of general revelation (cf. 19:1–6).

97:7 The center verse (see note on 6:6) and counterpoint of the psalm: joy to all who acknowledge the Lord; shame and disgrace to those who trust in false gods. *worship him.* With biting irony the psalm calls on all the gods that people foolishly worship to bow in worship before the Lord (see v. 9; see also 29:1 and note).

97:8–12 A declaration of Zion's joy that the Lord reigns (vv. 8–9), and a reminder that only those who hate evil have real cause to rejoice in his righteous rule (vv. 10–12).

97:8 *Zion hears.* That "the LORD reigns" (v. 1) in "righteousness" (v. 6). *judgments.* The executive and judicial acts of the Lord who reigns (v. 1) over all human affairs (see 105:7; Isa 26:9), especially his saving acts in Israel's behalf (see 48:11; 105:5; Dt 33:21).

97:9 *Most High.* See note on Ge 14:19.

97:10 *faithful ones.* See note on 4:3.

97:11 *Light.* See 27:1 and note; see also 36:9. *righteous.* See v. 12; see also note on 1:5. *heart.* See note on 4:7.

97:12 *name.* See note on 30:4.

Ps 98 A call to celebrate with joy the righteous reign of the Lord (see introductions to Ps 93; 95). Its beginning and end echo Ps 96, with which it has been paired (see introduction to Ps 96). The three stanzas progressively extend the call to ever wider circles: (1) the worshiping congregation at the temple (vv. 1–3); (2) all the peoples of the earth (vv. 4–6); (3) the whole creation (vv. 7–9). The first stanza recalls God's revelation of his righteousness (v. 2) in the past; the last stanza speaks confidently of his coming rule "in righteousness" (v. 9); the middle stanza is enclosed by the jubilant cry "Shout for joy" (vv. 4,6).

98:1–3 The call to celebrate in song God's saving acts in behalf of his people.

98:1 *new song.* See note on 33:3. *marvelous things.* See note on 9:1 ("wonderful deeds").

An ivory plaque from Megiddo (thirteenth – twelfth century BC) depicts a ruler on his cherub-flanked throne with his attendants inspecting prisoners. Psalm 99:1 describes the Lord as "enthroned between the cherubim." Verse 5 also says we are to "exalt the LORD our God and worship at his footstool" — a footstool is part of a king's throne on which he placed his feet, which can also be seen on the ivory plaque.

his right hand[o] and his holy arm[p]
have worked salvation[q] for him.
2 The LORD has made his salvation
known[r]
and revealed his righteousness[s] to
the nations.[t]
3 He has remembered[u] his love
and his faithfulness to Israel;
all the ends of the earth[v] have seen
the salvation of our God.[w]

4 Shout for joy[x] to the LORD, all the earth,
burst into jubilant song with music;
5 make music to the LORD with the
harp,[y]
with the harp and the sound of
singing,[z]
6 with trumpets[a] and the blast of the
ram's horn[b] —
shout for joy[c] before the LORD, the
King.[d]

7 Let the sea[e] resound, and everything
in it,
the world, and all who live in it.[f]

98:1 [o]S Ex 15:6 [p]S Jos 4:24; Job 40:9; Isa 51:9; 52:10; 53:1; 63:5 [q]S Ps 44:3; Isa 59:16 **98:2** [r]Isa 52:10; Lk 3:6 [s]S Ps 97:6 [t]S Ps 67:2 **98:3** [u]S 1Ch 16:15 [v]S Ge 49:10; S Ps 48:10 [w]S Ps 50:23 **98:4** [x]Ps 20:5; Isa 12:6; 44:23; 52:9; 54:1; 55:12 **98:5** [y]Ps 33:2; 92:3; 147:7 [z]Isa 51:3 **98:6** [a]S Nu 10:2; S 2Sa 6:15 [b]S Ex 19:13 [c]Ps 20:5; 100:1; Isa 12:6 [d]Ps 2:6; 47:7 **98:7** [e]S Ps 93:3 [f]S Ps 24:1

8 Let the rivers clap their hands,[g]
let the mountains[h] sing together
for joy;
9 let them sing before the LORD,
for he comes to judge the
earth.
He will judge the world in
righteousness
and the peoples with equity.[i]

Psalm 99

1 The LORD reigns,[j]
let the nations tremble;[k]
he sits enthroned[l] between the
cherubim,[m]
let the earth shake.
2 Great is the LORD[n] in Zion;[o]
he is exalted[p] over all the
nations.

98:8 [g]S 2Ki 11:12 [h]Ps 148:9; Isa 44:23; 55:12 **98:9** [i]S Ps 96:10 **99:1** [j]S 1Ch 16:31; S Ps 97:1 [k]S Ex 15:14; S 1Ch 16:30 [l]S 2Sa 6:2 [m]S Ex 25:22 **99:2** [n]S Ps 48:1 [o]Ps 2:6 [p]Ex 15:1; Ps 46:10; 97:9; 113:4; 148:13

98:2 *made … known … revealed … to the nations.* God's saving acts in behalf of his people are also his self-revelation to the nations; in this sense God is his own evangelist (see 77:14 and note on 46:10; see also Isa 52:10). *salvation … righteousness.* God's saving acts reveal his righteousness (see notes on 4:1; 71:24).
98:3 *love … faithfulness.* That is, love-and-faithfulness (see note on 36:5; see also note on 3:7). This compound expression often sums up God's covenant commitment to his people (see note on 6:4).
98:4 – 6 The call to all the earth to join in the celebration.
98:4 See 100:1. *all the earth.* The peoples of the earth (see 96:1 and note; see also 99:1).
98:5 *harp.* See note on Ge 31:27.
98:6 *trumpets.* The special long, straight trumpets of the sanctuary (referred to only here in Psalms; see notes on Nu 10:2 – 3,10). *ram's horn.* The more common trumpet (referred to also in 47:5; 81:3; 150:3; see note on Joel 2:1).
98:7 – 9 The call to the whole creation to celebrate (see note on 96:11 – 12).
98:7 *sea … world.* The two great regions of creaturely life.
98:8 *rivers … mountains.* From the rivers to the mountains, let every feature of the whole earth clap and sing (see note on 65:13).
98:9 *comes to judge.* See 96:13 and note. Israel in faith lived between the past (see vv. 1 – 3) and the future righteous (saving) acts of God. *righteousness … equity.* See 96:10 and note.
Ps 99 A hymn celebrating the Lord as the great and holy King in Zion — with special emphasis on the benefits of the Lord's reign for Israel, a feature it shares with Ps 97 (see introduction to Ps 96). In developing his theme, the poet makes striking use of the symbolic significance (completeness) of the number seven: Seven times he speaks of the "LORD," and seven times he refers to him by means of independent personal pronouns (Hebrew). (See introduction to Ps 93.)

The form is symmetrical, with four stanzas of three Hebrew poetic lines each and two main divisions (marked by a refrain) that are closely balanced, having 42 and 41 Hebrew words, respectively — a formal feature it shares with Ps 97 (see introduction to that psalm). The lesser refrain, "he is holy" (vv. 3,5, and expanded in v. 9), probably reflects a traditional, threefold liturgical rubric (see Isa 6:3; Rev 4:8; see also Ps 96:1 – 3,7 – 9 and notes for further evidence of a liturgical penchant for triple repetition). The second half of the psalm develops the theme introduced in the second stanza.

99:1 – 3 The God enthroned in Zion is ruler over all the nations — let them acknowledge him.
99:1 *The LORD reigns.* See 93:1 and note. *tremble … shake.* In reverent awe before God. *cherubim.* See 80:1; see also notes on Ex 25:18; Eze 1:5.

[3]Let them praise[q] your great and
awesome name[r]—
he is holy.[s]

[4]The King[t] is mighty, he loves
justice[u]—
you have established equity;[v]
in Jacob you have done
what is just and right.[w]
[5]Exalt[x] the LORD our God
and worship at his footstool;
he is holy.

[6]Moses[y] and Aaron[z] were among his
priests,
Samuel[a] was among those who
called on his name;
they called on the LORD
and he answered[b] them.
[7]He spoke to them from the pillar of
cloud;[c]
they kept his statutes and the
decrees he gave them.

[8]LORD our God,
you answered them;
you were to Israel a forgiving God,[d]
though you punished[e] their
misdeeds.[a]

99:3 [q]Ps 30:4; 33:21; 97:12; 103:1; 106:47; 111:9; 145:21; 148:5 [r]Ps 76:1 [s]S Ex 15:11; S Lev 11:44; Rev 4:8 **99:4** [t]Ps 2:6 [u]S 1Ki 10:9 [v]Ps 98:9 [w]S Ge 18:19; Rev 15:3 **99:5** [x]S Ex 15:2 **99:6** [y]S Ex 24:6 [z]S Ex 28:1 [a]1Sa 7:5 [b]Ps 4:3; 91:15 **99:7** [c]S Ex 13:21; S 19:9; S Nu 11:25 **99:8** [d]S Ex 22:27; S Nu 14:20 [e]S Lev 26:18 **100:1** [f]S Ps 98:6 **100:2** [g]S Dt 10:12 [h]S Ps 95:2 **100:3** [i]S 1Ki 18:21; S Ps 46:10 [j]S Job 10:3 [k]Ps 79:13; Isa 19:25; 63:8, 17-19; 64:9 [l]S 2Sa 24:17; S Ps 74:1

[9]Exalt the LORD our God
and worship at his holy mountain,
for the LORD our God is holy.

Psalm 100

A psalm. For giving grateful praise.

[1]Shout for joy[f] to the LORD, all the earth.
[2]Worship the LORD[g] with gladness;
come before him[h] with joyful songs.
[3]Know that the LORD is God.[i]
It is he who made us,[j] and we are
his[b];
we are his people,[k] the sheep of his
pasture.[l]

[4]Enter his gates with thanksgiving[m]
and his courts[n] with praise;
give thanks to him and praise his
name.[o]
[5]For the LORD is good[p] and his love
endures forever;[q]
his faithfulness[r] continues through
all generations.

[a] 8 Or *God, / an avenger of the wrongs done to them*
[b] 3 Or *and not we ourselves*

100:4 [m]S Ps 42:4 [n]S Ps 96:8 [o]Ps 116:17 **100:5** [p]S 1Ch 16:34 [q]S Ezr 3:11; Ps 106:1 [r]Ps 108:4; 119:90

99:3 *Let them praise.* As the Great King, he ought to be shown the fear (v. 1) and honor that are his due. *name.* See v. 6; see also note on 5:11. *holy.* See vv. 5,9; see also Introduction to Leviticus: Theological Themes and note on Lev 11:44.
99:4–5 The Lord has shown the quality of his rule by what he has done for Israel.
99:4 *is mighty … loves justice.* Two chief characteristics of God's reign. *established equity.* That is, created conditions in the world that embody equity—especially for Israel (see 96:10 and note). *Jacob.* A synonym for Israel (see Ge 32:28). *just and right.* Justice and righteousness, as in 97:2 (cf. 119:121; Eze 18:5 and notes). Though even the heavens proclaim God's righteousness (see 97:6 and note), it is in the whole complex of his saving acts in and for Israel that the righteousness of God's reign is especially disclosed (see 98:2 and note).
99:5 See also v. 9. For other refrains in the Psalms, see introduction to Ps 42–43. *footstool.* God's royal footstool (see 2Ch 9:18), here a metaphor linking the heavenly throne with the earthly; when God sits on his heavenly throne, his earthly throne is his footstool (here "his holy mountain," v. 9; see 132:7; 1Ch 28:2; La 2:1; see also photo, p. 968).
99:6–7 In Israel the Lord provided priestly intermediaries, who (1) were appointed to intercede with him on behalf of his faltering people (v. 6), and (2) were given knowledge of his will so they could instruct Israel (v. 7).
99:6 *Moses … Aaron … Samuel.* These three no doubt serve here as representatives of all those the Lord used as intermediaries with his people in times of great crises. *priests … who called on his name.* The priestly function of intercession is highlighted (see Ex 17:11 and note; 32:11–13,31–32; Nu 14:13–19; 21:7; 1Sa 7:5,8–9; 12:19,23; Jer 15:1). *they called … he answered.* See note on 118:5. *answered them.* See v. 8; see also the Lord's responses to the intercessions referred to in note on vv. 6–7.
99:7 *spoke to them from the pillar of cloud.* Though reference may be to all Israel ("them"), more likely the hymn recalls God's speaking with Moses (see Ex 33:9) and Aaron (see Nu 12:5–6). But that special mode of revelation in the wilderness may also be generalized here to include God's revelations to Samuel, who was called to his prophetic ministry at the sanctuary, "where the ark of God was" (1Sa 3:3; see also 1Sa 12:23). *they kept.* However imperfectly, it was in Israel that God's righteous statutes and decrees were kept because only in Israel had they been made known (see 147:19–20; Dt 4:5–8).
99:8–9 The justice and righteousness of God's rule in Israel (see v. 4) have been especially shown in the manner in which he has dealt with the nation's sins (see Ex 34:6–7; see also note on 4:1).
99:9 *holy mountain.* See v. 5 and note. *the LORD our God is holy.* Climactic expansion of the secondary refrain.
Ps 100 A call to praise the Lord. This psalm closes the series that begins with Ps 90. It has special affinity with 95:1–2,6–7; see also Ps 117. (See introduction to Ps 93.) The second main division (vv. 4–5) parallels the structure of the first (vv. 1–3), namely, a call to praise followed by a declaration of why the Lord is worthy of praise.
100 title *grateful praise.* See v. 4; see also note on 75:1. Perhaps it indicates that the psalm was to accompany a thank offering (see note on 7:17; see also Lev 7:12).
100:1 *all the earth.* Though vv. 3,5 clearly speak of God's special relationship with Israel, the call to worship goes out to the whole world, which ought to acknowledge the Lord because of what he has done for his people (see also Ps 98–99; 117).
100:3 *Know.* Acknowledge. *made us.* See 95:6 and note. *sheep of his pasture.* See 95:7 and note; see also note on 23:1.
100:4 *his gates.* The gates of the temple (see 24:7 and note). *courts.* Of the temple (see 84:2,10; 2Ki 21:5; 23:11–12).
100:5 *the LORD is good.* In that his love-and-faithfulness (see note on 36:5) are unfailing through all time (see 98:3 and note). *love.* See note on 6:4.

Psalm 101

Of David. A psalm.

1 I will sing of your love[s] and justice;
to you, LORD, I will sing praise.
2 I will be careful to lead a blameless life[t]—
when will you come to me?

I will conduct the affairs[u] of my house
with a blameless heart.
3 I will not look with approval
on anything that is vile.[v]

I hate what faithless people do;[w]
I will have no part in it.
4 The perverse of heart[x] shall be far from me;
I will have nothing to do with what is evil.

5 Whoever slanders their neighbor[y] in secret,
I will put to silence;
whoever has haughty eyes[z] and a proud heart,
I will not tolerate.

6 My eyes will be on the faithful in the land,
that they may dwell with me;
the one whose walk is blameless[a]
will minister to me.

7 No one who practices deceit
will dwell in my house;

101:1 [s] Ps 33:1; 51:14; 89:1; 145:7
101:2 [t] S Ge 17:1; Php 1:10 [u] S 1Ki 3:14
101:3 [v] Jer 16:18; Eze 11:21; Hos 9:10 [w] S Ps 5:5
101:4 [x] Pr 3:32; 6:16-19; 11:20
101:5 [y] S Ex 20:16; S Lev 19:16 [z] S Ps 10:5
101:6 [a] ver 2; Ps 119:1

Ps 101 – 110 A collection of ten psalms located between two other groups (see introductions to Ps 90 – 100; 111 – 119) and framed by two psalms that pertain to the king (the first the king's vow to pattern his reign after God's righteous rule; the last God's commitment to maintain the king — his anointed — and give him victories over all his enemies). This little psalter-within-the-Psalter is concentrically arranged. Inside the frame, Ps 102 and 109 are prayers of individuals in times of intense distress; Ps 103 and 108 praise the Lord for his "great ... love" that reaches to the heavens (103:11; 108:4); Ps 104 and 107 are complements, with 104 celebrating God's many wise and benevolent acts in creation and 107 celebrating God's "wonderful deeds" (vv. 8,15,21,24,31) for people through his lordship over creation. The remaining two are also complements, with Ps 105 reciting the history of Israel's redemption and 106 reciting the same history as a history of Israel's rebellion. This little psalter includes most of the forms and themes found in the rest of the Psalter. Its outer frame is devoted to royal psalms and its center pair to recitals of Israel's history with God. Meanwhile, its themes range from creation and God's eternal enthronement to the covenant with Abraham, Isaac and Jacob, Israel's exodus from Egypt and entrance into Canaan, her exile and restoration, and finally the ultimate triumph of the Lord's anointed. The traditional division between Books IV and V at Ps 107 was probably done by a later compiler, breaking up the collection consisting of Ps 101 – 110.

Ps 101 A king's pledge to reign righteously (see 2Ki 23:3), after the pattern of God's rule. For its relationship to Ps 110, see introduction to Ps 101 – 110. If authored by David (see title), it may have been composed before the ark of God was successfully brought into Jerusalem (see note on v. 2a; see also 2Sa 6). Only Christ, the great Son of David, has perfectly fulfilled these commitments.

Composed of seven couplets (the number of completeness), the psalm begins with a twofold introduction (vv. 1 – 3a; see notes below), followed by a five-stanza (vv. 3b – 8) elaboration of the theme of the second stanza. Of these five stanzas, the middle one (v. 6) speaks of the king's commitment to the "faithful" and "blameless," while the other four (vv. 3b – 4,5,7,8) declare his repudiation of all the "faithless" and "wicked" in the land. (For the parallel relationship of stanzas six and seven with three and four, see notes below.) The middle stanza is linked with stanzas one and two also by the catchword "blameless." (For centering in the Psalms, see note on 6:6.) The whole psalm is framed by references to the "LORD" in the first and last stanzas (see vv. 1,8). The second stanza from the end echoes two phrases found in the second stanza from the beginning ("of/in my house" [vv. 2,7] and "in my presence" [v. 7] — in Hebrew the same as for "look with approval" [v. 3]), thus forming an inner frame. For other doublets, see notes below.

101:1 – 2a Celebration of the pattern of God's reign, which the king makes the model for his own.

101:1 *love and justice.* Two of the chief qualities of God's rule (see 6:4; 99:4 and notes). For this particular combination, see Hos 12:6; Mic 6:8; cf. Zec 7:9. The present phrase is probably a shortened form of "love and faithfulness" combined with "righteousness and justice" (as in 89:14; cf. 33:5; 36:5 – 6; 48:9 – 11; Isa 16:5; Hos 2:19).

101:2a *blameless.* See vv. 2b,6; see also note on Ge 17:1. *when ... ?* Perhaps expressive of David's yearning for the presence of the ark of the Lord in his royal city as the sign of God's readiness to be with him and sustain him in his pledge to reign as he ought (see 2Sa 6 and note on 6:2). For later kings it would be a plea for divine enablement relative to the pledge given in vv. 1 – 2 (cf. Ps 72; 1Ki 3:7 – 9).

101:2b – 3a The essential commitment. *heart ... look.* In OT understanding, a person follows the dictates of the heart — the inmost being (see note on 4:7) — and/or the attractions of the eye — external influences (see 119:37; Jdg 14:1 – 2; 2Sa 11:2; 2Ki 16:10; Job 31:1; Pr 4:25; 17:24). For the combination heart-eyes, see v. 5; Nu 15:39; Job 31:7; Pr 21:4; Ecc 2:10; Jer 22:17.

101:2b *house.* Royal administration (also in v. 7).

101:3a *vile.* "Belial" (2Co 6:15) is derived from the Hebrew for this word (see note on Dt 13:13).

101:3b – 4 A repudiation of evil deeds and those who promote them (see v. 7).

101:3b *faithless.* Those who rebel against what is right (see Hos 5:2, "rebels").

101:4 *perverse.* The opposite of "blameless" (see 18:26, "devious"; see also Pr 11:20; 19:1; 28:6). A perverse heart and a deceitful tongue (see v. 7) are root and fruit (see Pr 17:20).

101:5 A pledge to remove from his presence all slanderous and all arrogant persons (see v. 8). *put to silence.* Destroy (as in 54:5; 94:23). See v. 8. *haughty eyes ... proud heart.* See vv. 2b – 3a and note; called "the unplowed field of the wicked" in Pr 21:4; cf. Ps 131:1; Isa 10:12. The arrogant tend to be ruthless (see Isa 10:12) and are a law to themselves (see note on 31:23).

101:6 A pledge to surround himself in his reign with the faithful and blameless. *My eyes will be on.* I will look with favor on (see 33:18; 34:15). *the faithful.* Those who maintain moral integrity. *minister to me.* Serve as my aide (see Ex 24:13), attendant (see Ge 39:4; 1Ki 19:21), personal servant (see 2Ki 4:43), commander and official (see 1 Ch 27:1; 2Ch 17:19; Pr 29:12).

101:7 A repudiation of all who make their way by double dealing (see vv. 3b – 4).

no one who speaks falsely
will stand in my presence.

8 Every morning[b] I will put to silence
all the wicked[c] in the land;
I will cut off every evildoer[d]
from the city of the LORD.[e]

Psalm 102[a]

A prayer of an afflicted person
who has grown weak and pours out
a lament before the LORD.

1 Hear my prayer,[f] LORD;
let my cry for help[g] come to you.
2 Do not hide your face[h] from me
when I am in distress.
Turn your ear[i] to me;
when I call, answer me quickly.

3 For my days vanish like smoke;[j]
my bones[k] burn like glowing embers.
4 My heart is blighted and withered like grass;[l]
I forget to eat my food.[m]
5 In my distress I groan aloud[n]
and am reduced to skin and bones.
6 I am like a desert owl,[o]
like an owl among the ruins.
7 I lie awake;[p] I have become
like a bird alone[q] on a roof.
8 All day long my enemies[r] taunt me;[s]
those who rail against me use my
name as a curse.[t]
9 For I eat ashes[u] as my food
and mingle my drink with tears[v]
10 because of your great wrath,[w]
for you have taken me up and
thrown me aside.
11 My days are like the evening shadow;[x]
I wither[y] away like grass.

12 But you, LORD, sit enthroned forever;[z]
your renown endures[a] through all
generations.[b]
13 You will arise[c] and have compassion[d]
on Zion,
for it is time[e] to show favor[f] to her;
the appointed time[g] has come.
14 For her stones are dear to your
servants;
her very dust moves them to pity.

[a] In Hebrew texts 102:1-28 is numbered 102:2-29.

101:8 [b] Ps 5:3; Jer 21:12 [c] Ps 75:10 [d] S 2Sa 3:39; Ps 118:10-12 [e] S Ps 46:4 **102:1** [f] Ps 4:1 [g] S Ex 2:23 **102:2** [h] S Ps 22:24 [i] S 2Ki 19:16; Ps 31:2; 88:2 **102:3** [j] S Ps 37:20; S Jas 4:14 [k] La 1:13 **102:4** [l] S Ps 37:2; 90:5-6 [m] S 1Sa 1:7; S Ezr 10:6; S Job 33:20 **102:5** [n] S Ps 6:6 **102:6** [o] S Dt 14:15-17; Job 30:29; Isa 34:11; Zep 2:14 **102:7** [p] Ps 77:4 [q] Ps 38:11 **102:8** [r] S Ps 31:11 [s] S Ps 42:10; Lk 22:63-65; 23:35-37 [t] S Ex 22:28; Isa 65:15; Jer 24:9; 25:18; 42:18; 44:12; Eze 14:8; Zec 8:13

102:9 [u] Isa 44:20 [v] Ps 6:6; 42:3; 80:5 **102:10** [w] Ps 7:11; 38:3 **102:11** [x] S 1Ch 29:15; S Job 14:2; S Ps 39:6 [y] S Job 8:12; Jas 1:10 **102:12** [z] S Ex 15:18 [a] Ps 135:13; Isa 55:13; 63:12 [b] S Ex 3:15 **102:13** [c] S Ps 44:26 [d] S Dt 32:36; S 1Ki 3:26; Isa 54:8; 60:10; Zec 10:6 [e] Ps 119:126 [f] S Ps 77:7 [g] S Ex 13:10; Da 8:19; Ac 1:7

101:8 A pledge to remove all the wicked from the Lord's kingdom (see v. 5). *Every morning.* With diligence and persistence (see Jer 21:12; Zep 3:5). It appears to have been customary for kings to hear judicial cases in the morning—when the mind is fresh and the air cool. That is when victims looked for deliverance from those oppressing them (cf. 88:13; 143:8; Isa 33:2). *city of the LORD.* See Ps 46; 48; 87; see also note on 3:4.

Ps 102 The prayer of an individual in a time of great distress. For its relationship to Ps 109 in the arrangement of the Psalter, see introduction to Ps 101–110. In early Christian worship this psalm came to be used as a penitential prayer (see introduction to Ps 6), even though it contains no explicit confession of sin.

The main body of the psalm (vv. 1–22) is developed in four stanzas (initial appeal for God to hear, vv. 1–2; description of distress, vv. 3–11; assurance that the Lord will surely hear, vv. 12–17; call for the Lord's certain deliverance to be recorded for his enduring praise, vv. 18–22), followed by a concluding recapitulation (vv. 23–28).

102 title Unique in the Psalter (no author named and no liturgical or historical notes), the title identifies only the life situation in which the prayer is to be used, and in accordance with vv. 1–11,23–24 it designates the prayer as that of an individual. In addition, vv. 12–22,28 clearly indicate national involvement in the calamity. *prayer.* See vv. 1,17. *weak.* See 61:2; 77:3; 142:3; 143:4; see also 107:5; Jnh 2:7. *lament.* The Hebrew for this word is translated "complaint" in 64:1; 142:2; Job 7:13; 9:27; 10:1; 21:4. See Introduction: Psalm Types; Introduction to Lamentations: Themes and Theology.

102:1–2 Initial appeal for God to hear.

102:2 *hide your face.* See note on 13:1. *when I call, answer me.* See note on 118:5.

102:3–11 The description of distress—a suffering so great that it withers body and spirit—brought on by a visitation of God's wrath (v. 10) and making him the mockery of his enemies (v. 8). For the framing imagery that binds this section together, see vv. 3–4 and v. 11.

102:3 *my days vanish like smoke.* See also vv. 11,23. *bones burn.* As if a fire is consuming his physical frame (see 31:10; 32:3; 42:10).

102:4 *heart.* See note on 4:7. Here "heart" is used in combination with "bones" (v. 3) to refer to the whole person (body and spirit); see 22:14; Pr 14:30; 15:30; Isa 66:14 ("and you" represents the Hebrew for "and your bones"); Jer 20:9; 23:9. *blighted.* Or "scorched" (by the hot sun); see 121:6. *withered like grass.* See v. 11; see also note on 90:5–6.

102:6 *owl.* Associated with desert areas and ruins (see Isa 34:11,15; Jer 50:39; Zep 2:14).

102:8 *enemies taunt me.* See 109:25; see also notes on 5:9; 39:8. *use my name as a curse.* They say, "May you become like that one (the one named) is."

102:9 *drink ... tears.* For tears as food and drink, see 42:3; 80:5.

102:10 *wrath.* See note on 2:5.

102:11 An echo of vv. 3–4. *shadow.* See 109:23; 144:4; Job 8:9; 14:2; Ecc 6:12. *grass.* See 37:20; 90:5–6 and notes.

102:12–17 Assurance that heaven's eternal King will surely hear the prayer of the destitute (v. 17) and restore Zion. For such expressions of assurance in the prayers of the Psalter, see note on 3:8. This six-verse stanza weaves its themes in a balanced *a-b-c/a-b-c* pattern (see notes on vv. 15–17).

102:12 *sit enthroned forever.* A central theme of the preceding collection (Ps 90–100). Because God reigns forever and remains the same (see v. 27), his mercies to those who look to him for salvation will not fail. *renown.* See note on 30:4 ("name"). For elaborate celebrations of the Lord's renown, see Ps 111; 135; 145.

102:13 This verse and v. 16 (see also v. 14) suggest that the psalmist's distress was occasioned by the Babylonian exile. *arise.* See note on 3:7. *appointed time.* The time set by God for judgment and deliverance (see 75:2; Ex 9:5; 2Sa 24:15; Da 11:27,35). Perhaps the psalmist is referring to a time announced by a prophet.

102:14 *dear to your servants.* If Zion, the city of God (see 46:4;

15 The nations will fear[h] the name of the LORD,
all the kings[i] of the earth will revere your glory.
16 For the LORD will rebuild Zion[j]
and appear in his glory.[k]
17 He will respond to the prayer[l] of the destitute;
he will not despise their plea.

18 Let this be written[m] for a future generation,
that a people not yet created[n] may praise the LORD:
19 "The LORD looked down[o] from his sanctuary on high,
from heaven he viewed the earth,
20 to hear the groans of the prisoners[p]
and release those condemned to death."
21 So the name of the LORD will be declared[q] in Zion
and his praise[r] in Jerusalem
22 when the peoples and the kingdoms
assemble to worship[s] the LORD.

23 In the course of my life[a] he broke my strength;
he cut short my days.[t]
24 So I said:
"Do not take me away, my God, in the midst of my days;
your years go on[u] through all generations.
25 In the beginning[v] you laid the foundations of the earth,
and the heavens[w] are the work of your hands.[x]
26 They will perish,[y] but you remain;
they will all wear out like a garment.
Like clothing you will change them
and they will be discarded.
27 But you remain the same,[z]
and your years will never end.[a]
28 The children of your servants[b] will live in your presence;
their descendants[c] will be established before you."

Psalm 103

Of David.

1 Praise the LORD,[d] my soul;[e]
all my inmost being, praise his holy name.[f]

[a] 23 Or *By his power*

102:15 [h] 1Ki 8:43; Ps 67:7; Isa 2:2 [i] Ps 76:12; 138:4; 148:11 **102:16** [j] S Ps 51:18 [k] Ps 8:1; Isa 60:1-2 **102:17** [l] S 1Ki 8:29; Ps 4:1; 6:9 **102:18** [m] S Ro 4:24 [n] S Ps 22:31 **102:19** [o] Ps 53:2 **102:20** [p] S Ps 68:6; S Lk 4:19 **102:21** [q] Ps 22:22 [r] Ps 9:14 **102:22** [s] S Ps 22:27; Isa 49:22-23; Zec 8:20-23 **102:23** [t] S Ps 39:5 **102:24** [u] S Ge 21:33; Job 36:26; Ps 90:2 **102:25** [v] S Ge 1:1; Heb 1:10-12* [w] S 2Ch 2:12 [x] S Ps 8:3 **102:26** [y] Isa 13:10, 13; 34:4; 51:6; Eze 32:8; Joel 2:10; Mt 24:35; 2Pe 3:7-10; Rev 20:11 **102:27** [z] S Nu 23:19; Heb 13:8; Jas 1:17 [a] Ps 9:7 **102:28** [b] Ps 69:36 [c] Ps 25:13; 89:4 **103:1** [d] Ps 28:6 [e] Ps 104:1 [f] S Ps 30:4

48:1–2,8; 87:3; 101:8; 132:13), is so loved by the Lord's servants (see Ps 126; 137), how much more is she cherished by the Lord!

102:15 *nations will fear.* See notes on 25:12; 46:10. *the name of the LORD.* An echo of reference to the Lord's "renown" (v. 12; see note on 30:4 ["name"]). Yahweh's "renown" that "endures through all generations" (v. 12) will evoke the awe of earth's most powerful inhabitants. *name.* See note on 5:11.

102:16 *will rebuild Zion.* Yahweh will "have compassion" on Zion (v. 13) by rebuilding her. *and appear in his glory.* Or "and thus appear in his glory" (see v. 15 and note on 46:10; see also Isa 40:1–5). This hope will find its fullest expression in the "new Jerusalem" (see Rev 21).

102:17 *the destitute.* Reference is to "your servants" (v. 14). *their plea.* Expressive of the pity they feel for their beloved Zion now lying in ruins (v. 14).

102:18–22 Let God's certain deliverance of his people be recorded for his continual praise (v. 8)—until that great day when the worshiping community celebrating Zion's redemption has expanded to include representatives of the "peoples" and "kingdoms" of the world (v. 22). See introduction to Ps 117; see also Rev 15:4; 21:24,26.

102:18 *written.* Only here does a psalmist call for memory to be sustained by a written record of God's saving act; usually oral transmission suffices (see 22:30; 44:1; 78:1–4). *created.* Brought into being by God's sovereign act (see 51:10; 104:30; 139:13).

102:20 *prisoners ... those condemned to death.* Perhaps prisoners of war, but more likely the exiles in Babylon (see 79:11 and note).

102:21 *praise.* See note on 9:1.

102:22 See note on 46:10; see also 47:9 and note; 96; 98; 100. The expectation here expressed may also be influenced by such prophecies as Isa 2:2–4; Mic 4:1–3.

102:23–28 Concluding recapitulation. The stanza is framed by the radical contrast expressed in vv. 23,28. That human life is cut short (v. 23) by the One whose own being spans all ages (vv. 25–27) adds to the psalmist's sense of loss on the one hand but also to his hope on the other (v. 28) and thus to the urgency of his prayer—as in 90:1–6 (see note on 90:4–5).

102:23–24a See vv. 3–11.

102:24b–27 See v. 12 and note. For a NT application of vv. 25–27 to Christ, see Heb 1:10–12 and note on 1:10.

102:26 *Like clothing.* With his first creation God clothed himself with the manifestation of his glory (see 8:1,3–4; 19:1; 29:3–9; 104:1,31; Isa 6:3; see also Job 38–41, especially 40:10). But he is more enduring than what he has made—and the first creation will give way to a new creation (see Isa 65:17; 66:22).

102:28 Because the Lord does not change (see v. 27), Israel's future is secure (see Mal 3:6). *live in your presence.* Or "dwell in the (promised) land" (see 37:3,29; see also 69:36; Isa 65:9). *established before you.* See 2Sa 7:24.

Ps 103 A salvation-history hymn, celebrating God's love and compassion toward his people. For its relationship to Ps 108 in the arrangement of the Psalter, see introduction to Ps 101–110. Calls to praise (vv. 1–2,20–22) frame the body of the hymn (vv. 3–19) and set its tone. The recital of praise falls into two unequal parts: (1) a three-verse celebration of personal benefits received (vv. 3–5) and (2) a 14-verse recollection of God's mercies to his people Israel (vv. 6–19). The major division (vv. 6–19) is composed of six couplets framed by the breakup of a seventh couplet (vv. 6,19) that describes the general character of God's reign. Thematic development divides the six framed couplets into two equal parts (vv. 7–12,13–18), of which the first celebrates God's compassion on his people as sinners, while the second sings of his compassion on them as frail mortals (see also 78:38–39). The concluding couplets of these two parts proclaim the vastness of his love (vv. 11–12) and its unending perseverance (vv. 17–18). As with the hymn found in Ps 33, the length of

2 Praise the LORD,[g] my soul,
and forget not[h] all his benefits—
3 who forgives all your sins[i]
and heals[j] all your diseases,
4 who redeems your life[k] from the pit
and crowns you with love and
compassion,[l]
5 who satisfies[m] your desires with good
things
so that your youth is renewed[n] like
the eagle's.[o]

6 The LORD works righteousness[p]
and justice for all the oppressed.[q]

7 He made known[r] his ways[s] to Moses,
his deeds[t] to the people of Israel:
8 The LORD is compassionate and
gracious,[u]
slow to anger, abounding in love.
9 He will not always accuse,
nor will he harbor his anger forever;[v]
10 he does not treat us as our sins
deserve[w]
or repay us according to our
iniquities.
11 For as high as the heavens are above
the earth,
so great is his love[x] for those who
fear him;[y]
12 as far as the east is from the west,
so far has he removed our
transgressions[z] from us.

13 As a father has compassion[a] on his
children,
so the LORD has compassion on those
who fear him;
14 for he knows how we are formed,[b]
he remembers that we are dust.[c]
15 The life of mortals is like grass,[d]
they flourish like a flower[e] of the field;
16 the wind blows[f] over it and it is gone,
and its place[g] remembers it no more.
17 But from everlasting to everlasting
the LORD's love is with those who
fear him,
and his righteousness with their
children's children[h]—
18 with those who keep his covenant[i]
and remember[j] to obey his precepts.[k]

19 The LORD has established his throne[l] in
heaven,
and his kingdom rules[m] over all.

20 Praise the LORD,[n] you his angels,[o]
you mighty ones[p] who do his bidding,[q]
who obey his word.
21 Praise the LORD, all his heavenly hosts,[r]
you his servants[s] who do his will.
22 Praise the LORD, all his works[t]
everywhere in his dominion.

Praise the LORD, my soul.[u]

103:2 [g] Ps 106:1; 117:1 [h] S Dt 6:12; Ps 77:11 **103:3** [i] S Ex 34:7 [j] S Ex 15:26; Col 3:13; 1Pe 2:24; 1Jn 1:9 **103:4** [k] Ps 34:22; 56:13; Isa 43:1 [l] S Ps 8:5; 23:6 **103:5** [m] S Ps 90:14; S 104:28 [n] Job 33:25; Ps 119:25, 93; 2Co 4:16 [o] S Ex 19:4 **103:6** [p] Ps 9:8; 65:5; Isa 9:7 [q] S Ps 74:21; S Lk 4:19 **103:7** [r] Ps 99:7; 147:19 [s] S Ex 33:13 [t] Ps 106:22 **103:8** [u] S Ex 22:27; S Ps 86:15; Mic 7:18-19; Jas 5:11 **103:9** [v] Ps 30:5; 79:5; Isa 57:16; Jer 3:5, 12; Mic 7:18 **103:10** [w] S Ezr 9:13; Ro 6:23 **103:11** [x] Ps 13:5; 57:10; 100:5; 106:45; 117:2; La 3:22; Eph 3:18 [y] S 2Ch 6:31 **103:12** [z] S 2Sa 12:13; Ro 4:7; Eph 2:5

103:13 [a] Mal 3:17; 1Jn 3:1 **103:14** [b] Ps 119:73; 139:13-15; Isa 29:16 [c] S Ge 2:7; S Ps 146:4 **103:15** [d] Ps 37:2; 90:5; 102:11; Isa 40:6 [e] S Job 14:2; Jas 1:10 **103:16** [f] Isa 40:7; Hag 1:9 [g] S Job 7:8 **103:17** [h] S Ge 48:11; S Ezr 9:12 **103:18** [i] S Dt 29:9 [j] Ps 119:52 [k] S Nu 15:40; Jn 14:15 **103:19** [l] Ps 47:8; 80:1; 113:5 [m] Ps 22:28; 66:7; Da 4:17 **103:20** [n] Ps 28:6 [o] S Ne 9:6; Lk 2:13; Heb 1:14 [p] S Ps 29:1 [q] Ps 107:25; 135:7; 148:8 **103:21** [r] S 1Ki 22:19 [s] S Ne 7:73 **103:22** [t] Ps 19:1; 67:3; 145:10; 150:6 [u] ver 1; Ps 104:1

the psalm has been determined by the number of letters in the Hebrew alphabet (see introduction to Ps 33).
103:1–2 Call to praise God, directed inward (cf. vv. 20–22).
103:1–2,22 *my soul.* A conventional Hebrew way of addressing oneself (see 104:1,35; 116:7). *soul.* See note on 6:3.
103:3–5 Recital of personal blessings received.
103:3 *forgives … heals.* See Mt 9:2,5 and parallels.
103:4 *redeems.* A synonym for "delivers" (see note on 71:23). *pit.* A metaphor for the grave (see note on 30:1). *love and compassion.* The key words of the hymn (see vv. 8,11,13,17). *love.* See vv. 8,11,17; see also note on 6:4.
103:5 *like the eagle's.* The vigor of youth is restored to match the proverbial, unflagging strength of the eagle (see Isa 40:30–31).
103:6–19 God's love and compassion toward his people.
103:6 Together with v. 19 (the second verse of a split couplet, providing the other side of the literary frame) it characterizes the reign of God, under which Israel has been so graciously blessed. *righteousness.* See v. 17; see also note on 4:1.
103:7–12 God's compassion on his people as sinners.
103:7–8 See Ex 33:13; see also note on Ex 34:6–7.
103:7 *his ways.* See 25:10 and note.
103:9 *anger.* See note on 2:5.
103:11–12 The vastness of God's love (note the spatial imagery) is supremely shown in his forgiving Israel's sins.
103:11 See 36:5–9. *so great is.* So prevails. *those who fear him.* See vv. 13,17–18; see also note on 66:16.
103:12 See Isa 1:18; 38:17; 43:25; Jer 31:34; 50:20; Mic 7:18–19.
103:13–18 God's compassion on his people as frail mortals (see 78:39).
103:13–14 In Hebrew the initial words of these two verses strikingly echo the sounds of the initial words of vv. 11–12, thereby effecting a tight literary bond between vv. 13–18 and vv. 7,12.
103:14 *we are dust.* See Ge 2:7; 3:19.
103:15–16 See note on 90:5–6.
103:17–18 The infinite temporal span of God's love (cf. the spatial imagery in vv. 11–12).
103:17 *everlasting to everlasting … their children's children.* God's love outlasts anyone's little time in this life (cf. note on 109:12).
103:18 *who keep his covenant … obey his precepts.* See 25:10; Ex 19:5 and note; 20:6 and note; Dt 4:40; 29:9.
103:19 See v. 6 and note; see also 9:4,7; 11:4; 47:2,7–8; 123:1.
103:20–22 Concluding call to praise, directed to all creatures—from the psalmist's inner self (vv. 1–2) to the creatures who serve God in heaven. A call to praise God is often the climax of praise in the Psalter (as also of the whole collection; see Ps 148–150). See note on 9:1. *Praise … Praise … Praise.* See note on 96:1–3. (The final line was probably added by the editors of the Psalter; see 104:1,35.)
103:20 *who do his bidding.* See 91:11; Heb 1:14.
103:21 *heavenly hosts.* Uniquely here and in 148:2 the Hebrew for "hosts" is masculine, and in both places the "hosts" are associated with "angels." *servants.* Translates the participle of the Hebrew verb for "minister" in 101:6 (see note there; see also note on 104:4).
103:22 *all his works.* See 65:13; 96:11–12 and notes.

Psalm 104

[1]Praise the LORD, my soul.[v]

LORD my God, you are very great;
you are clothed with splendor and majesty.[w]

[2]The LORD wraps[x] himself in light[y] as with a garment;
he stretches[z] out the heavens[a] like a tent[b]
[3] and lays the beams[c] of his upper chambers on their waters.[d]
He makes the clouds[e] his chariot[f]
and rides on the wings of the wind.[g]
[4]He makes winds his messengers,[a][h]
flames of fire[i] his servants.

[5]He set the earth[j] on its foundations;[k]
it can never be moved.
[6]You covered it[l] with the watery depths[m] as with a garment;
the waters stood[n] above the mountains.
[7]But at your rebuke[o] the waters fled,
at the sound of your thunder[p] they took to flight;
[8]they flowed over the mountains,
they went down into the valleys,
to the place you assigned[q] for them.
[9]You set a boundary[r] they cannot cross;
never again will they cover the earth.

[10]He makes springs[s] pour water into the ravines;
it flows between the mountains.
[11]They give water[t] to all the beasts of the field;
the wild donkeys[u] quench their thirst.
[12]The birds of the sky[v] nest by the waters;
they sing among the branches.[w]
[13]He waters the mountains[x] from his upper chambers;[y]
the land is satisfied by the fruit of his work.[z]
[14]He makes grass grow[a] for the cattle,
and plants for people to cultivate—
bringing forth food[b] from the earth:
[15]wine[c] that gladdens human hearts,
oil[d] to make their faces shine,
and bread that sustains[e] their hearts.

[a] 4 Or *angels*

104:1 [v]S Ps 103:22 [w]S Job 40:10 **104:2** [x]Isa 49:18; Jer 43:12 [y]Ps 18:12; 1Ti 6:16 [z]Job 9:8; Jer 51:15 [a]Job 37:18; Isa 40:22; 42:5; 44:24; Zec 12:1 [b]S Ps 19:4 **104:3** [c]Am 9:6 [d]S Ps 24:2 [e]S Dt 33:26; Isa 19:1; Na 1:3 [f]S 2Ki 2:11 [g]Ps 18:10 **104:4** [h]Ps 148:8; Heb 1:7* [i]Ge 3:24; 2Ki 2:11 **104:5** [j]Ex 31:17; Job 26:7; Ps 24:1-2; 102:25; 121:2 [k]S 1Sa 2:8 **104:6** [l]Ge 7:19 [m]S Ge 1:2 [n]2Pe 3:6 **104:7** [o]S Ps 18:15 [p]S Ex 9:23; Ps 29:3 **104:8** [q]Ps 33:7 **104:9** [r]S Ge 1:9; S Ps 16:6 **104:10** [s]Ps 107:33; Isa 41:18 **104:11** [t]ver 13 [u]S Ge 16:12; Isa 32:14; Jer 14:6 **104:12** [v]ver 17; Mt 8:20 [w]Mt 13:32 **104:13** [x]Ps 135:7; 147:8; Jer 10:13; Zec 10:1 [y]S Lev 26:4 [z]Am 9:6 **104:14** [a]S Job 38:27; Ps 147:8 [b]S Ge 1:30; S Job 28:5 **104:15** [c]S Ge 14:18; S Jdg 9:13 [d]Ps 23:5; 92:10; Lk 7:46 [e]S Dt 8:3; Mt 6:11

Ps 104 A hymn to the Creator. For its relationship to Ps 108 in the arrangement of the Psalter, see introduction to Ps 101–110. The preexilic author has adapted Ge 1 to his own quite different purpose and has subordinated its sequence somewhat to his own design (see next paragraph). Ge 1 recounts God's acts of creation as his first work at the beginning, but the poet views the created world displayed before his eyes and sings the glory of its Maker and Sustainer. The psalmist's theme is the visible creation, which he views as the radiant and stately robe with which the invisible Creator has clothed himself to display his glory.

Following his one-verse introduction, the poet designed the main body of his poem concentrically, with stanzas of three-five-nine-five-three verses. The first stanza speaks of the celestial realm above (vv. 2–4) and the fifth of the nautical realm below (vv. 24–26)—the two realms that bracket the "earth" (see note on v. 5). The second sings of the earth's solid foundations and secure boundaries (vv. 5–9) and the fourth of the orderly cycles of life on earth, governed by sun and moon (vv. 19–23). At the center a nine-verse stanza (composed of three triplets) celebrates the luxuriation of life in the earth (vv. 10–18). To the poem's main body he added a four-verse stanza that recites how God maintains life on earth (vv. 27–30), a two-verse conclusion (vv. 31–32—which together with v. 1 frames the whole), and a three-verse epilogue (vv. 33–35). The outer frame ("Praise the LORD, my soul") was probably added by the editors of the Psalter when they inserted the Book division after Ps 106—thus concluding Book IV with doxologies (see the liturgical frames added to Ps 105–106 and the similar conclusion to Book V: Ps 146–150).

104:1–2 *clothed with ... wraps himself in.* See note on 109:29.

104:1 Introduction: the theme of the hymn.

104:2–4 The celestial realm above.

104:2 *light.* Cf. the first day of creation (Ge 1:3–5). *heavens.* Cf. the second day of creation (Ge 1:6–8). *like a tent.* Over the earth and the luminaries that give it light.

104:3 *upper chambers.* Vivid imagery for the heavenly abode of God (see v. 13). In the singular, the Hebrew for this phrase usually refers to the upper-level room of a house (as in 1Ki 17:19; 2Ki 1:2). *their waters.* The waters above the "tent" (v. 2; see Ge 1:7), from which, in the imagery of the OT, God gives the rain (see v. 13; see also 36:8 and note). *clouds his chariot.* See 18:7–15; 68:4; 77:16–19 and notes.

104:4 *winds ... flames of fire.* The winds and lightning bolts of the thunderstorm, here personified as the agents of God's purposes (see 148:8; cf. 103:21; see also Heb 1:7 and note).

104:5–9 The earth realm (the spatial element) made secure. Verses 5,9 frame the stanza, highlighting its two main themes.

104:5 *earth.* Land in distinction from sky and seas, not the earth as a planet (see Ge 1:10). *foundations.* See 24:2 and note. *can never be moved.* Firmly founded (see 93:1; 96:10), it will not give way (cf. v. 9).

104:7 *rebuke.* See note on 76:6. *waters fled.* Cf. the third day of creation (Ge 1:9–13).

104:9 *set a boundary.* So that the land ("earth") will never be overwhelmed by the sea (cf. v. 5; see 33:7 and note; see also Ge 9:15).

104:10–18 The earth a flourishing garden of life—the center of the psalm and the focal point of the author's contemplation of the creation (the earth, bounded by sky, vv. 2–4, and sea, vv. 24–26). Cf. the third and sixth days of creation (Ge 1:9–13, 24–31).

104:10–12 The gift of water from below—watering the ravines of the Negev, south of Israel's heartland.

104:13–15 The gift of water from above—watering the uplands of Israel's heartland with its cultivated fields.

104:13 *upper chambers.* See v. 3 and note.

104:15 *hearts ... hearts.* See note on 4:7. *oil.* Olive oil. *make their faces shine.* As food (see 1Ki 17:12), causing a person's face to glow with health, and/or as cosmetic (see Est 2:12).

[16]The trees of the LORD[f] are well watered,
the cedars of Lebanon[g] that he
planted.
[17]There the birds[h] make their nests;
the stork has its home in the
junipers.
[18]The high mountains belong to the wild
goats;[i]
the crags are a refuge for the
hyrax.[j]

[19]He made the moon to mark the
seasons,[k]
and the sun[l] knows when to go
down.
[20]You bring darkness,[m] it becomes
night,[n]
and all the beasts of the forest[o]
prowl.
[21]The lions roar for their prey[p]
and seek their food from God.[q]
[22]The sun rises, and they steal away;
they return and lie down in their
dens.[r]
[23]Then people go out to their work,[s]
to their labor until evening.[t]

[24]How many are your works,[u] LORD!
In wisdom you made[v] them all;
the earth is full of your creatures.[w]
[25]There is the sea,[x] vast and spacious,
teeming with creatures beyond
number—
living things both large and small.[y]
[26]There the ships[z] go to and fro,
and Leviathan,[a] which you formed to
frolic[b] there.[c]
[27]All creatures look to you
to give them their food[d] at the proper
time.
[28]When you give it to them,
they gather it up;

104:16 [f]Ge 1:11 [g]S Ps 72:16 **104:17** [h]ver 12 **104:18** [i]S Dt 14:5 [j]Pr 30:26 **104:19** [k]S Ge 1:14 [l]Ps 19:6 **104:20** [m]Isa 45:7; Am 5:8 [n]Ps 74:16 [o]S Ps 50:10 **104:21** [p]Am 3:4 [q]Ps 145:15; Joel 1:20; S Mt 6:26 **104:22** [r]S Job 37:8 **104:23** [s]S Ge 3:19 [t]Jdg 19:16 **104:24** [u]Ps 40:5 [v]S Ge 1:31 [w]Ps 24:1; 50:10-11 **104:25** [x]Ps 69:34 [y]Eze 47:10 **104:26** [z]Ps 107:23; Eze 27:9; Jnh 1:3 [a]S Job 3:8; 41:1 [b]Job 40:20 [c]S Ge 1:21 **104:27** [d]Job 36:31; Ps 145:15; 147:9 **104:28** [e]Ps 103:5; 145:16; Isa 58:11 **104:29** [f]S Dt 31:17 [g]S Job 7:21 **104:30** [h]S Ge 1:2 **104:31** [i]Ex 40:35; Ps 8:1; S Ro 11:36 [j]S Ge 1:4 **104:32** [k]S Ps 97:4

when you open your hand,
they are satisfied[e] with good things.
[29]When you hide your face,[f]
they are terrified;
when you take away their breath,
they die and return to the dust.[g]
[30]When you send your Spirit,[h]
they are created,
and you renew the face of the
ground.

[31]May the glory of the LORD[i] endure
forever;
may the LORD rejoice in his works[j]—
[32]he who looks at the earth, and it
trembles,[k]
who touches the mountains,[l] and
they smoke.[m]

[33]I will sing[n] to the LORD all my life;
I will sing praise to my God as long
as I live.
[34]May my meditation be pleasing to him,
as I rejoice[o] in the LORD.
[35]But may sinners vanish[p] from the earth
and the wicked be no more.[q]
Praise the LORD, my soul.

Praise the LORD.[a][r]

Psalm 105

105:1-15pp — 1Ch 16:8-22

[1]Give praise to the LORD,[s] proclaim his
name;[t]
make known among the nations
what he has done.

[a] 35 Hebrew *Hallelu Yah*; in the Septuagint this line stands at the beginning of Psalm 105.

[l]S Ex 19:18 [m]Ps 144:5 **104:33** [n]S Ex 15:1; Ps 108:1 **104:34** [o]S Ps 2:11; 9:2; 32:11 **104:35** [p]Ps 37:38 [q]S Job 7:10 [r]Ps 28:6; 105:45; 106:48 **105:1** [s]S 1Ch 16:34 [t]Ps 80:18; 99:6; 116:13; Joel 2:32; Ac 2:21

104:16–18 Well-watered Lebanon (north of Israel's heartland), with its great trees, its hordes of birds and its alpine animals, the very epitome of God's earthly parkland (see 72:16; 2Ki 14:9; 19:23; Isa 10:34; 35:2; 40:16; 60:13; Jer 22:6; Hos 14:7).
104:19–23 The orderly cycles of life (the temporal element; see notes on vv. 2–4,5–9; see also introduction) on earth, governed by the moon and sun. Cf. the fourth day of creation (Ge 1:14–19).
104:21,23 *lions ... people.* The one (representing the animal world) lord of the night; the other lord of the day.
104:24–26 The nautical realm below (see note on vv. 19–23). Cf. the fifth day of creation (Ge 1:20–23). The realm of the sea is structurally balanced with the celestial realm (vv. 2–4) as the other boundary to the realm of earth.
104:24 A pause to recapitulate before treating the sea.
104:25 *teeming.* See Ge 1:20–21.
104:26 *Leviathan.* That fearsome mythological monster of the deep (see Job 3:8 and note) is here portrayed as nothing more than God's harmless pet playing in the ocean.
104:27–30 By God's benevolent care this zoological garden flourishes. Cf. the sixth day of creation (Ge 1:24–31).
104:29 *hide your face.* See note on 13:1.
104:30 *your Spirit.* See note on 51:11. *created.* See note on 102:18.
104:31 *glory of the LORD.* Such as is displayed in his creation (see 19:1–4a and note).
104:32 He is so much greater than his creation that with a look or a touch or a word (33:6,9) he could undo it.
104:33–35 A concluding expression of the psalmist's devotion to Yahweh (cf. NIV text note on v. 35).
104:33 A vow to praise God—here attached to a hymn of praise (see note on 7:17).
104:34 *my meditation.* The preceding hymn (see 19:14 and note).
104:35 May the earth be purged of that which alone mars it (cf. Rev 21:27). *Praise the LORD* (last occurrence). Probably belonged originally to Ps 105 (see NIV text note and 105:45; 106:1,48).
Ps 105 A salvation-history psalm, exhorting Israel to worship and trust in the Lord because of all his saving acts in fulfillment of his covenant with Abraham to give his descendants the land of Canaan. It was composed to be addressed to Israel by a Levite (see 1Ch 16:7 and compare

2 Sing to him,[u] sing praise to him;[v]
tell of all his wonderful acts.[w]
3 Glory in his holy name;[x]
let the hearts of those who seek the
Lord rejoice.
4 Look to the Lord and his strength;
seek his face[y] always.

5 Remember the wonders[z] he has done,
his miracles, and the judgments he
pronounced,[a]
6 you his servants, the descendants of
Abraham,[b]
his chosen[c] ones, the children of
Jacob.
7 He is the Lord our God;
his judgments are in all the earth.

8 He remembers his covenant[d] forever,
the promise he made, for a thousand
generations,
9 the covenant he made with Abraham,[e]
the oath he swore to Isaac.
10 He confirmed it[f] to Jacob as a decree,
to Israel as an everlasting covenant:[g]
11 "To you I will give the land of Canaan[h]
as the portion you will inherit."[i]

12 When they were but few in number,[j]
few indeed, and strangers in it,[k]
13 they wandered from nation to nation,[l]
from one kingdom to another.
14 He allowed no one to oppress[m] them;
for their sake he rebuked kings:[n]
15 "Do not touch[o] my anointed ones;
do my prophets[p] no harm."

16 He called down famine[q] on the land
and destroyed all their supplies of
food;
17 and he sent a man before them—
Joseph, sold as a slave.[r]
18 They bruised his feet with shackles,[s]
his neck was put in irons,
19 till what he foretold[t] came to pass,
till the word[u] of the Lord proved him
true.
20 The king sent and released him,
the ruler of peoples set him free.[v]
21 He made him master of his household,
ruler over all he possessed,
22 to instruct his princes[w] as he pleased
and teach his elders wisdom.[x]

23 Then Israel entered Egypt;[y]
Jacob resided[z] as a foreigner in the
land of Ham.[a]
24 The Lord made his people very fruitful;
he made them too numerous[b] for
their foes,
25 whose hearts he turned[c] to hate his
people,
to conspire[d] against his servants.

105:2 [u] Ps 30:4; 33:3; 96:1 [v] Ps 7:17; 18:49; 27:6; 59:17; 71:22; 146:2 [w] S Ps 75:1 **105:3** [x] S Ps 89:16 **105:4** [y] S Ps 24:6 **105:5** [z] S Ps 40:5 [a] S Dt 7:18 **105:6** [b] ver 42 [c] S Dt 10:15; Ps 106:5 **105:8** [d] S Ge 9:15; Ps 106:45; 111:5; Eze 16:60; S Lk 1:72 **105:9** [e] Ge 12:7; S 15:18; S 22:16-18; Lk 1:73; Gal 3:15-18 **105:10** [f] Ge 28:13-15 [g] Isa 55:3 **105:11** [h] S Ge 12:7 [i] S Nu 34:2 **105:12** [j] Dt 7:7 [k] Ge 23:4; Heb 11:9 **105:13** [l] Ge 15:13-16; Nu 32:13; 33:3-49 **105:14** [m] Ge 35:5 [n] Ge 12:17-20; S 20:3; S Ps 9:5 **105:15** [o] S Ge 26:11; S 1Sa 12:3 [p] S Ge 20:7 **105:16** [q] S Ge 12:10; S Lev 26:26; Isa 3:1; Eze 4:16 **105:17** [r] S Ge 37:28; Ac 7:9 **105:18** [s] S Ge 40:15 **105:19** [t] S Ge 12:10; 40:20-22 [u] Ge 41:40 **105:20** [v] Ge 41:14 **105:22** [w] Ge 41:43-44 [x] S Ge 41:40 **105:23** [y] Ge 46:6; Ac 7:15; 13:17 [z] Ge 47:28 [a] S Ps 78:51 **105:24** [b] Ex 1:7,9; Ac 7:17 **105:25** [c] S Ex 4:21 [d] Ex 1:6-10; Ac 7:19

vv. 1–15 with 1Ch 16:8–22) on one of Israel's annual religious festivals (see chart, pp. 188–189), possibly the Festival of Tabernacles (see Lev 23:34) but more likely the Festival of Weeks or Pentecost (see Ex 23:16; Lev 23:15–21; Nu 28:26; Dt 16:9–12; see also Dt 26:1–11). For other recitals of the same history (but for different purposes), see Ps 78; 106; Jos 24:2–13; Ne 9:7–25. For the relationship of this psalm to Ps 106 in the arrangement of the Psalter, see introduction to Ps 101–110.

The introduction is composed of seven verses in two parts: (1) an exhortation (with ten imperatives) to worship the Lord (vv. 1–4); (2) a call to remember what the Lord has done (vv. 5–7). The main body that follows is framed by two four-verse stanzas (vv. 8–11, 42–45) that summarize—as introduction and conclusion—its main theme: The Lord has remembered his covenant with Abraham (see chart, p. 23). The editors of the Psalter have added an outer frame of "Hallelujahs" (see introduction to Ps 104; see also note on 104:35).

105:1–4 The exhortation to worship Yahweh and trust in him.

105:1 *Give praise.* See note on Ps 100 title. *his name.* See v. 3; see also note on 5:11. *make known among the nations.* As an integral part of praise (see note on 9:1).

105:2 *wonderful acts.* See v. 5 ("wonders"); see also note on 9:1.

105:3,25 *hearts.* See note on 4:7.

105:5–7 Exhortation to remember God's saving acts.

105:5 *Remember.* As a motivation for and focus of worship and the basis for trust—remember how the Lord has remembered (see vv. 8–11). *judgments.* See v. 7; see also notes on 48:11; 97:8. *pronounced.* As Lord, he commands and it is done (see 7:6 ["decree justice"]; 33:9; 71:3; 78:23; 147:15,18; 148:5; Isa 5:6; 55:11; Jer 1:12; Am 9:3–4).

105:6,9 *Abraham ... Jacob ... Isaac.* While "Jacob" occurs 34 times in the Psalter, Abraham is recalled by name in Psalms only here (see also v. 42) and in 47:9. Reference to Isaac occurs in Psalms only here.

105:8–11 The Lord remembers his covenant with Abraham (see vv. 42–45).

105:8 *covenant.* The promissory covenant of Ge 15:9–21 (see chart, p. 23). This verse and v. 9 may be echoed in Lk 1:72–73. *thousand generations.* See Ex 20:6; Dt 7:9; 1Ch 16:15.

105:10 *as a decree.* As a fixed policy governing his future actions (see note on v. 45).

105:12–41 A recital of God's saving acts in Israel's behalf from the granting of the covenant (see v. 11; Ge 15:9–21) to its fulfillment (see v. 44; Jos 21:43). Cf. the recital prescribed by Moses in conjunction with the offering of firstfruits (Dt 26:1–11).

105:14–15 See Ge 20:2–7 and note on 20:7.

105:18 *shackles ... irons.* That is, shackles of iron (see 149:8; see also note on 3:7). The poet takes the freedom to use a later conventional description of prisoners (see Job 13:27; 33:11). (Shackles are not spoken of in Ge 39:20–23, and iron came into common use for them at a later time—earlier shackles were made of bronze; see Jdg 16:21.)

105:22 *instruct.* Lit. "bind," i.e., govern or control. He whose "neck" (v. 18; Hebrew *nephesh*) had been shackled was given authority to "bind" the pharaoh's princes "as he pleased" (Hebrew "with his *nephesh*"—here meaning his will). *elders.* The pharaoh's counselors, conventionally older men of wide experience and learning (see note on Ex 3:16).

105:23,27 *land of Ham.* See 78:51 and note.

105:25 *turned.* In OT perspective God's sovereign control over Israel's destiny is so complete that it governs—mysteriously—even the evil that others commit

26 He sent Moses[e] his servant,
and Aaron,[f] whom he had chosen.[g]
27 They performed[h] his signs[i] among them,
his wonders[j] in the land of Ham.
28 He sent darkness[k] and made the land dark —
for had they not rebelled against[l] his words?
29 He turned their waters into blood,[m]
causing their fish to die.[n]
30 Their land teemed with frogs,[o]
which went up into the bedrooms of their rulers.
31 He spoke,[p] and there came swarms of flies,[q]
and gnats[r] throughout their country.
32 He turned their rain into hail,[s]
with lightning throughout their land;
33 he struck down their vines[t] and fig trees[u]
and shattered the trees of their country.
34 He spoke,[v] and the locusts came,[w]
grasshoppers[x] without number;[y]
35 they ate up every green thing in their land,
ate up the produce of their soil.
36 Then he struck down all the firstborn[z] in their land,
the firstfruits of all their manhood.
37 He brought out Israel, laden with silver and gold,[a]
and from among their tribes no one faltered.
38 Egypt was glad when they left,
because dread of Israel[b] had fallen on them.

39 He spread out a cloud[c] as a covering,
and a fire to give light at night.[d]

105:26 [e]S Ex 3:10 [f]S Ex 4:16; S Nu 33:1 [g]S Nu 16:5; 17:5-8 **105:27** [h]ver 28-37; Ex 7:8-12:51 [i]S Ex 4:17; S 10:1 [j]S Ex 3:20; Da 4:3 **105:28** [k]S Ge 1:4; S Ex 10:22 [l]S Ex 7:22 **105:29** [m]S Ps 78:44 [n]Ex 7:21 **105:30** [o]S Ex 8:2,6 **105:31** [p]Ps 107:25; 148:8 [q]Ex 8:21-24; S Ps 78:45 [r]Ex 8:16-18 **105:32** [s]Ex 9:22-25; S Job 38:22; S Ps 78:47 **105:33** [t]Ps 78:47 [u]Ex 10:5,12 **105:34** [v]Ps 107:25 [w]S Ex 10:4, 12-15 [x]S 1Ki 8:37 [y]Joel 1:6 **105:36** [z]S Ex 4:23; S 12:12 **105:37** [a]S Ex 3:21,22 **105:38** [b]Ex 15:16 **105:39** [c]S Ex 13:21; 1Co 10:1 [d]S Ps 78:14

against them; hence the bold language used here (see Ex 4:21; 7:3; Jos 11:20; 2Sa 24:1; Isa 10:5–7; 37:26–27; Jer 34:22).
105:26,42 *servant.* See 78:70 and note.
105:28–36 Recital of the plagues against Egypt. In this poetic recollection seven plagues (symbolizing completeness) represent the ten plagues of Ex 7–11. Apart from omissions (the plagues of livestock disease and boils) the poet follows the order of Exodus, except that he combines the third and fourth plagues (gnats and flies) — in reverse order — to stay within the number seven. He also places the ninth plague (darkness) first in order to frame his recital with mention of the two plagues that climaxed the series (see photo below).
105:37 *laden with silver and gold.* See Ex 3:22 and note; 12:35–36.
105:39 *as a covering.* Elsewhere it is said that the cloud (symbolic of God's presence) served (1) as a guide for

Illustration of the plague of frogs from a fourteenth-century Hebrew manuscript. Psalm 105 recounts the plagues in Egypt.
Z. Radovan/www.BibleLandPictures.com

40 They asked,[e] and he brought them quail;[f]
he fed them well with the bread of heaven.[g]
41 He opened the rock,[h] and water gushed out;
it flowed like a river in the desert.

42 For he remembered his holy promise[i]
given to his servant Abraham.
43 He brought out his people with rejoicing,[j]
his chosen ones with shouts of joy;
44 he gave them the lands of the nations,[k]
and they fell heir to what others had toiled[l] for —
45 that they might keep his precepts
and observe his laws.[m]

Praise the LORD.[a][n]

Psalm 106

106:1,47-48pp — 1Ch 16:34-36

1 Praise the LORD.[b][o]

Give thanks to the LORD, for he is good;[p]
his love endures forever.[q]

2 Who can proclaim the mighty acts[r] of the LORD
or fully declare his praise?
3 Blessed are those who act justly,[s]
who always do what is right.[t]

4 Remember me,[u] LORD, when you show favor[v] to your people,
come to my aid[w] when you save them,
5 that I may enjoy the prosperity[x] of your chosen ones,[y]
that I may share in the joy[z] of your nation
and join your inheritance[a] in giving praise.

105:40 [e] Ps 78:18,24 [f] S Ex 16:13 [g] S Ex 16:4; Jn 6:31 **105:41** [h] S Nu 20:11; 1Co 10:4 **105:42** [i] Ge 12:1-3; 13:14-17; 15:13-16 **105:43** [j] Ex 15:1-18; Ps 106:12 **105:44** [k] Ex 32:13; Jos 11:16-23; 12:8; 13:6-7; Ps 111:6 [l] Dt 6:10-11; Ps 78:55 **105:45** [m] S Dt 4:40; 6:21-24; Ps 78:5-7 [n] S Ps 104:35 **106:1** [o] S Ps 22:23; S 103:2 [p] S Ps 119:68 [q] S Ezr 3:11; Ps 136:1-26; Jer 33:11 **106:2** [r] S Ps 71:16

[a] *45* Hebrew *Hallelu Yah* [b] *1* Hebrew *Hallelu Yah;* also in verse 48

106:3 [s] Ps 112:5; Hos 12:6 [t] Ps 15:2 **106:4** [u] Ps 25:6,7 [v] S Ps 77:7 [w] S Ge 50:24 **106:5** [x] S Dt 30:15; Ps 1:3 [y] S Ps 105:6 [z] Ps 20:5; 27:6; 47:5; 118:15 [a] S Ex 34:9

Israel in her wilderness journeys (see 78:14; Ex 13:21; Nu 9:17; Ne 9:12,19), (2) as a shield of darkness to protect Israel from the pursuing Egyptians (see Ex 14:19–20) and (3) as a covering for the fiery manifestations of God's glorious presence (see Ex 16:10; 24:16; 34:5; 40:34–35,38; Nu 11:25; 12:5; 16:42; Dt 31:15; 1Ki 8:11). The psalmist appears to highlight yet another function: God's protective cover over his people in the wilderness, perhaps as his shading "wings" (17:8; see note there), so that the sun would not harm them by day (see 121:5–6).

105:40 *bread of heaven.* See 78:24–25 and notes on 78:25; Jn 6:31–32.

105:41 *like a river.* Poetically heightened imagery to evoke due wonder for the event. This miracle of the wilderness wanderings concludes the recital and has been placed in climactic position as one of the most striking manifestations of God's redeeming power and benevolence (see 114:8; Isa 43:19–20; cf. Isa 50:2).

105:42–45 Concluding summary (balancing the introduction to the recital: vv. 8–11).

105:44 *gave them the lands.* See v. 11.

105:45 *precepts.* God has kept his "decree" (v. 10) so that Israel might keep his "precepts" — the Hebrew word is the same (see note on v. 5: "remember"). God's redemptive working in fulfillment of his covenant promise has as its goal the creating of a people in the earth who conform their lives to his holy will (see Isa 5:1–7).

Ps 106 A salvation-history psalm, stressing Israel's long history of rebellion and a prayer for God to once again save his people. In length, poetic style and shared themes it has much affinity with Ps 105, even while it contrasts with it by reciting the past as a history of rebellion (see Ps 78; Ne 9:5–37). See further the introduction to Ps 101–110.

In the final edited form of the Psalter, the psalm is set between two liturgical calls to praise ("Hallelujah!"). Within this outer frame stands another, also drawn from the liturgical language of praise (vv. 1b,48a; see notes there). And still a third frame (formed by two couplets devoted to prayer [vv. 4–5,47; see notes there]) encloses the main body of the psalm. Verses 2–3 are transitional. While the recital character of the central theme (as in Ps 105; see also Ps 78) controls the basic outline, attention to symmetry brings to light the carefully designed pattern of thematic development. The recital begins with 14 Hebrew poetic lines devoted to the period of the exodus and the wilderness wanderings (vv. 6–18) and ends with 14 Hebrew lines devoted to Israel's time in the promised land (vv. 34–46). The intervening verses (vv. 19–33) make up three stanzas with a six-four-six line pattern. In the two six-line stanzas, instances of Israel's engagement in idolatry in the wilderness period are recalled (the golden calf at Horeb [vv. 19–23]; the Baal of Peor in the plains of Moab [vv. 28–33]). These stanzas each end with a word about Moses: In the first, Moses intercedes for Israel and wards off God's wrath; in the second, Israel so vexes Moses that he acts rashly and loses his opportunity to enter the promised land — a most poignant contrast. At the center, a four-line stanza recalls Israel's refusal to take over the promised land and Yahweh's condemnation of that generation to die in the wilderness (see Nu 14:1–23; cf. Heb 3:16–19 and note).

106:1–5 Introduction.

106:1 *Give thanks to the LORD.* With praise (see note on Ps 100 title); a conventional, liturgical call to praise God (see 107:1; 118:1,29; 136:1). *love.* See note on 6:4.

106:2–3 Transition to the main body of the psalm — question and answer.

106:2 *Who can … ?* With integrity. *his praise.* Praise for the Lord's mighty acts (see v. 47; see also note on 9:1).

106:3 *Blessed.* See note on 1:1. *act justly … do what is right.* See note on 119:121. This verse answers the question posed in v. 2.

106:4–5 A poetic couplet, voicing the prayer of an individual (cf. v. 47).

106:4 *Remember me.* As one committed to the way of life described in v. 3. *when you show favor.* Or "with the favor you show" (see vv. 44–46). *when you save them.* Or "with your salvation." The psalmist prays that God will include him in all the mercies of his "great love" (v. 45), which he shows to his people. Thus the inner logic of the prayer seems to be completed at v. 46.

106:5 *prosperity … joy … praise.* A progressive sequence of cause and effect. *your inheritance.* See v. 40.

[6] We have sinned,[b] even as our
ancestors[c] did;
we have done wrong and acted
wickedly.[d]
[7] When our ancestors were in Egypt,
they gave no thought[e] to your
miracles;
they did not remember[f] your many
kindnesses,
and they rebelled by the sea,[g] the
Red Sea.[a]
[8] Yet he saved them[h] for his name's
sake,[i]
to make his mighty power[j] known.
[9] He rebuked[k] the Red Sea, and it
dried up;[l]
he led them through[m] the depths as
through a desert.
[10] He saved them[n] from the hand of the
foe;[o]
from the hand of the enemy he
redeemed them.[p]
[11] The waters covered[q] their adversaries;
not one of them survived.
[12] Then they believed his promises
and sang his praise.[r]

[13] But they soon forgot[s] what he had
done
and did not wait for his plan to
unfold.[t]
[14] In the desert[u] they gave in to their
craving;
in the wilderness[v] they put God to
the test.[w]
[15] So he gave them[x] what they asked for,
but sent a wasting disease[y] among
them.

[16] In the camp they grew envious[z] of
Moses
and of Aaron, who was consecrated
to the LORD.
[17] The earth opened[a] up and swallowed
Dathan;[b]
it buried the company of Abiram.[c]
[18] Fire blazed[d] among their followers;
a flame consumed the wicked.

106:6 [b]S 1Ki 8:47; S Ro 3:9 [c]S 2Ch 30:7 [d]Ne 1:7 **106:7** [e]S Jdg 3:7 [f]Ps 78:11,42 [g]Ex 14:11-12 **106:8** [h]Ex 14:30; S Ps 80:3; 107:13; Isa 25:9; Joel 2:32 [i]S Ex 9:16; S Ps 23:3 [j]S Ex 14:31 **106:9** [k]Ps 18:15; Isa 50:2 [l]S Ex 14:21; Na 1:4 [m]Ps 78:13; Isa 63:11-14 **106:10** [n]Ex 14:30; Ps 107:13 [o]S Ps 78:53 [p]Ps 78:42; 107:2; Isa 35:9; 62:12 **106:11** [q]S Ex 14:28 **106:12** [r]Ex 15:1-21; S Ps 105:43 **106:13** [s]S Ex 15:24 [t]S Ex 16:28; S Nu 27:21 **106:14** [u]S Ps 78:40 [v]S Ps 68:7 [w]S Ex 17:2; 1Co 10:9 **106:15** [x]S Ex 16:13; Ps 78:29 [y]S Nu 11:33 **106:16** [z]Nu 16:1-3 **106:17** [a]Dt 11:6 [b]S Ex 15:12 [c]S Nu 16:1 **106:18** [d]S Lev 10:2 **106:19** [e]S Ex 32:4; Ac 7:41 **106:20** [f]Jer 2:11; Ro 1:23 **106:21** [g]Ps 78:11 [h]Dt 10:21; Ps 75:1

[19] At Horeb they made a calf[e]
and worshiped an idol cast from
metal.
[20] They exchanged their glorious God[f]
for an image of a bull, which eats
grass.
[21] They forgot the God[g] who saved them,
who had done great things[h] in
Egypt,
[22] miracles in the land of Ham[i]
and awesome deeds[j] by the Red Sea.
[23] So he said he would destroy[k] them —
had not Moses, his chosen one,
stood in the breach[l] before him
to keep his wrath from destroying
them.

[24] Then they despised[m] the pleasant
land;[n]
they did not believe[o] his promise.
[25] They grumbled[p] in their tents
and did not obey the LORD.
[26] So he swore[q] to them with uplifted
hand
that he would make them fall in the
wilderness,[r]
[27] make their descendants fall among the
nations
and scatter[s] them throughout the
lands.

[28] They yoked themselves to the Baal of
Peor[t]
and ate sacrifices offered to lifeless
gods;
[29] they aroused the LORD's anger[u] by their
wicked deeds,[v]
and a plague[w] broke out among
them.
[30] But Phinehas[x] stood up and intervened,
and the plague was checked.[y]

[a] 7 Or *the Sea of Reeds*; also in verses 9 and 22

106:22 [i]S Ps 78:51 [j]S Ex 3:20; S Dt 4:34 **106:23** [k]S Ex 32:10 [l]Ex 32:11-14; S Nu 11:2; S Dt 9:19 **106:24** [m]Nu 14:30-31 [n]S Dt 8:7; S Jer 3:19 [o]S Nu 14:11; Heb 3:18-19 **106:25** [p]S Ex 15:24; Dt 1:27; 1Co 10:10 **106:26** [q]S Nu 14:23; Heb 4:3 [r]S Dt 2:14; Heb 3:17 **106:27** [s]S Lev 26:33 **106:28** [t]S Nu 23:28 **106:29** [u]Nu 25:3 [v]S Ps 64:2; 141:4 [w]S Nu 16:46; 25:8 **106:30** [x]S Ex 6:25 [y]Nu 25:8

106:6–12 Israel's rebelliousness and the Lord's mercy in the exodus event.
106:6 A general confession of sin introducing the recital. *We.* The author identifies himself with Israel in her rebellion, even as he prays for inclusion in God's mercies toward his people (see Ezr 9:6–7).
106:7,22 *miracles.* For example, the plagues against Egypt (see note on 9:1, "wonderful deeds").
106:10 *redeemed.* Here, as often, a synonym for "delivered" (see note on 71:23).
106:12 *sang his praise.* See Ex 15:1–21.
106:13–18 Israel's discontent and the Lord's judgments.
106:13–15 Discontent with the Lord's provisions (see Ex 16; Nu 11).
106:16–18 Discontent with the Lord's leadership arrangements (see Nu 16:1–35).
106:19–23 Idolatry at Horeb and Moses' intercession.
106:19 *Horeb.* See note on Ex 3:1.
106:20 *glorious God.* See 1Sa 15:29; Jer 2:11 and notes; Hos 4:7.
106:22 *land of Ham.* See 78:51 and note.
106:23 *stood in the breach.* See Ex 32:11–14,31–32. *wrath.* See note on 2:5.
106:24–27 Israel's lack of faith at the border of the promised land and the Lord's judgment (see Nu 14:1–23).
106:24 *pleasant land.* So described in Jer 3:19; 12:10; Zec 7:14; see also Dt 8:7–9; Eze 20:6.
106:26–27 *fall.* See note on 13:4.
106:27 *scatter them throughout the lands.* See Lev 26:33; Dt 28:36–37,64 and note on 28:64; Eze 20:23.
106:28–33 Idolatry at Peor — and Moses' loss.
106:28 *yoked themselves to.* See Nu 25:3,5.

31 This was credited to him[z] as
righteousness
for endless generations[a] to come.
32 By the waters of Meribah[b] they angered
the LORD,
and trouble came to Moses because
of them;
33 for they rebelled[c] against the Spirit[d] of
God,
and rash words came from Moses'
lips.[a][e]

34 They did not destroy[f] the peoples
as the LORD had commanded[g] them,
35 but they mingled[h] with the nations
and adopted their customs.
36 They worshiped their idols,[i]
which became a snare[j] to them.
37 They sacrificed their sons[k]
and their daughters to false gods.[l]
38 They shed innocent blood,
the blood of their sons[m] and
daughters,
whom they sacrificed to the idols of
Canaan,
and the land was desecrated by their
blood.
39 They defiled themselves[n] by what they
did;
by their deeds they prostituted[o]
themselves.

40 Therefore the LORD was angry[p] with his
people
and abhorred his inheritance.[q]

106:31 [z] S Ge 15:6; S Nu 25:11-13 [a] Ps 49:11 **106:32** [b] S Ex 17:7; Nu 20:2-13 **106:33** [c] S Ex 23:21; Ps 107:11 [d] S Ps 51:11; Isa 63:10 [e] Ex 17:4-7; Nu 20:8-12 **106:34** [f] S Jos 9:15; Jdg 1:27-36 [g] Ex 23:24; S Dt 2:34; 7:16; 20:17 **106:35** [h] Jdg 3:5-6; Ezr 9:1-2 **106:36** [i] S Dt 7:16 [j] S Ex 10:7 **106:37** [k] S Lev 18:21; S Dt 12:31; Eze 16:20-21 [l] S Ex 22:20; S Dt 32:17; 1Co 10:20 **106:38** [m] S Lev 18:21; S Dt 18:10; S 2Ki 3:27 **106:39** [n] S Ge 3:17; Lev 18:24; Eze 20:18 [o] S Nu 15:39 **106:40** [p] S Lev 26:28 [q] S Ex 34:9; S Dt 9:29 **106:41** [r] S Jdg 2:14

41 He gave them into the hands[r] of the
nations,
and their foes ruled over them.
42 Their enemies oppressed[s] them
and subjected them to their power.
43 Many times he delivered them,[t]
but they were bent on rebellion[u]
and they wasted away in their sin.
44 Yet he took note of their distress
when he heard their cry;[v]
45 for their sake he remembered his
covenant[w]
and out of his great love[x] he
relented.[y]
46 He caused all who held them captive
to show them mercy.[z]

47 Save us,[a] LORD our God,
and gather us[b] from the nations,
that we may give thanks[c] to your holy
name[d]
and glory in your praise.

48 Praise be to the LORD, the God of Israel,
from everlasting to everlasting.

Let all the people say, "Amen!"[e]

Praise the LORD.

[a] 33 Or *against his spirit, / and rash words came from his lips*

106:42 [s] S Jdg 4:3 **106:43** [t] S Jos 10:14; Jdg 7:1-25; S Ne 9:28; Ps 81:13-14 [u] S Jdg 2:16-19; 6:1-7 **106:44** [v] S Jdg 3:9 **106:45** [w] S Ge 9:15; Ps 105:8; S Lk 1:72 [x] S Ps 17:7; S 103:11 [y] S Ex 32:14 **106:46** [z] S Ex 3:21; S 1Ki 8:50 **106:47** [a] S Ps 28:9 [b] Ps 107:3; 147:2; Isa 11:12; 27:13; 56:8; 66:20; Jer 31:8; Eze 20:34; Mic 4:6 [c] Ps 105:1 [d] Ps 30:4; S 99:3 **106:48** [e] S Ps 41:13; S 72:19

106:31 *credited to him as righteousness.* As Abram's faith was "credited ... to him as righteousness" (Ge 15:6; see note there), so, says the psalmist, was Phinehas's priestly zeal for the Lord (see Nu 25:7–8). *for endless generations.* The psalmist refers to the "covenant of a lasting priesthood" (Nu 25:13) that the Lord granted Phinehas as a gracious reward for his zealous act. It was the granting of this promissory covenant that warranted the statement about crediting righteousness, for God's granting of a promissory covenant to Abram had followed upon his crediting Abram's faith to him as righteousness (see Ge 15:9–21). Similarly, God's promissory covenants with Noah (see Ge 9:9–17) and with David (see 2Sa 7:5–16) followed upon God's testimony to their righteousness (see Ge 7:1; 1Sa 13:14). See chart, p. 23.
106:32 *Meribah.* See note on Ex 17:7.
106:33 *against the Spirit of God.* For a literal rendering of the Hebrew, see NIV text note. The interpretation embodied in the NIV text appears warranted by Isa 63:10 (see also Ps 78:40). For the Spirit of God present and at work in the wilderness wanderings, see Ex 31:3; Nu 11:17; 24:2; Ne 9:20; Isa 63:10–14. See also note on 51:11.
106:34–39 A general description of Israel's rebelliousness in the promised land, applicable from the time of the judges to the Babylonian exile.
106:36 *became a snare to them.* See Ex 23:33; Dt 7:16; Jdg 2:3; 8:27; cf. Ex 10:7; 34:12; 1Sa 18:21; cf. also note on 9:15.
106:37 *false gods.* The Hebrew for this word occurs elsewhere in the OT only in Dt 32:17.
106:38 Cf. Jer 19:4–5. *innocent blood.* The blood of anyone not guilty of a capital crime. *desecrated.* The very land itself is defiled by the slaughter of innocents (see Nu 35:33; Jer 3:2,9).
106:39 *defiled.* See Lev 18:24; Jer 2:23; Eze 20:30–31; 22:3–4. *prostituted themselves.* See Ex 34:15 and note.
106:40–46 God's stern measures against his rebellious people (vv. 40–43), but at the same time his gracious remembering of his covenant (vv. 44–46). The judgments here recalled focus particularly on God's most severe covenant sanctions (see Lev 26:25–26,33,38–39; Dt 28:25,36–37,48–57, 64–68).
106:40 *angry.* See note on 2:5. *abhorred.* See 5:6.
106:44 *heard their cry.* See Ex 2:23; 3:7–9; Nu 20:16; Jdg 3:9,15; 4:3; 6:6–7; 10:10; 1Sa 9:16; 2Ch 20:6–12; Ne 9:27–28.
106:45 *remembered his covenant.* See 105:8,42; Ex 2:24; Lev 26:42,45. *love.* See note on 6:4.
106:46 Makes clear that the author's recital includes the Babylonian captivity (see 1Ki 8:50; 2Ch 30:9; Ezr 9:9; Jer 42:12). Although there were earlier captivities of Israelite communities, no other captive group was said to have been shown "mercy."
106:47 A communal prayer for deliverance and restoration from dispersion (see introduction and note on v. 4). *name.* See note on 5:11. *glory in.* Triumphantly celebrate. The Hebrew for this phrase is found elsewhere only in the parallel in 1Ch 16:35. *praise.* See note on 9:1.
106:48a A conventional word of praise, serving as the doxology to close the psalm and Book IV (see 41:13 and note; see also introduction to this psalm and note on v. 1).
106:48b *Let all the people say.* 1Ch 16:36 sets off the closing exclamations somewhat differently. *Amen!* See Dt 27:15 and note; 1Ch 16:36; Ne 5:13; Jer 11:5; Ro 1:25 and note; 1Co 14:16.

BOOK V

Psalms 107–150

Psalm 107

[1] Give thanks to the LORD,[f] for he is good;[g]
his love endures forever.

[2] Let the redeemed[h] of the LORD tell their
story—
those he redeemed from the hand of
the foe,
[3] those he gathered[i] from the lands,
from east and west, from north and
south.[a]

[4] Some wandered in desert[j] wastelands,
finding no way to a city[k] where they
could settle.
[5] They were hungry[l] and thirsty,[m]
and their lives ebbed away.
[6] Then they cried out[n] to the LORD in
their trouble,
and he delivered them from their
distress.
[7] He led them by a straight way[o]
to a city[p] where they could settle.
[8] Let them give thanks[q] to the LORD for
his unfailing love[r]
and his wonderful deeds[s] for
mankind,
[9] for he satisfies[t] the thirsty
and fills the hungry with good
things.[u]

[10] Some sat in darkness,[v] in utter
darkness,
prisoners suffering[w] in iron
chains,[x]
[11] because they rebelled[y] against God's
commands
and despised[z] the plans[a] of the Most
High.
[12] So he subjected them to bitter labor;
they stumbled, and there was no one
to help.[b]

107:1 [f]S 1Ch 16:8; S 2Ch 5:13 [g]S 2Ch 7:3 **107:2** [h]S Ps 106:10; S Isa 35:9 **107:3** [i]S Ne 1:9 **107:4** [j]S Jos 5:6 [k]ver 36 **107:5** [l]Ex 16:3 [m]S Ex 15:22; S 17:2 **107:6** [n]S Ex 14:10 **107:7** [o]S Ezr 8:21 [p]ver 36 **107:8** [q]Ps 105:1 [r]Ps 6:4 [s]S Ps 75:1 **107:9** [t]Ps 22:26; 63:5; Isa 58:11; Mt 5:6; Lk 1:53 [u]S Ps 23:1; Jer 31:25 **107:10** [v]ver 14; Ps 88:6; 143:3; Isa 9:2; 42:7,16; 49:9; Mic 7:9 [w]Ps 102:20; Isa 61:1 [x]S Job 36:8

[a] 3 Hebrew *north and the sea*

107:11 [y]S Ps 5:10 [z]S Nu 14:11 [a]S 1Ki 22:5; 2Ch 36:16 **107:12** [b]S 2Ki 14:26; Ps 72:12

Ps 107 A salvation-history psalm, exhorting Israel to praise the Lord for his unfailing love in that he hears the prayers of those in need and saves them (see next paragraph—on structure). It was composed for liturgical use at one of Israel's annual religious festivals. Interpretations vary widely, but the following is most likely: Having experienced anew God's mercies in her return from Babylonian exile (v. 3; see Jer 33:11), Israel is led by a Levite in celebrating God's unfailing benevolence toward those who have cried out to him in the crises of their lives. In its recitative style the psalm is closely related to Ps 104–106, and in its language to Ps 105–106. See introduction to Ps 101–110.

The introduction (vv. 1–3) and conclusion (v. 43) enclose six stanzas, of which the last two (vv. 33–38, 39–42) stand apart as an instructive supplement focusing in a more general way on reversals in fortunes—which, however, end up with God restoring the "hungry" (v. 36) and the "needy" (v. 41). Of the four remaining stanzas (marked by recurring refrains: vv. 6,13, 19,28; vv. 8,15,21,31), the first and last refer to God's deliverance of those lost in the trackless desert (vv. 4–9) and those imperiled on the boisterous sea (vv. 23–32). The two central stanzas celebrate deliverance from the punishment of foreign bondage (vv. 10–16) and from the punishment of disease (vv. 17–22). Of the concluding lines to these four stanzas, the first two (vv. 9,16) and the last two (vv. 22,32) are similar. The verse pattern of these four stanzas (six-seven-six-ten) makes deliberate use of the significant numbers seven and ten.

107:1–3 Introductory call to praise Yahweh.

107:1 A conventional, liturgical call to praise the Lord (see 106:1; 118:1,29; 136:1; Jer 33:11). *Give thanks.* See vv. 8,15,21, 31; see also note on Ps 100 title. *love.* See vv. 8,15,21,31,43; see also note on 6:4.

107:2 *redeemed.* Here, as often, a synonym for "delivered" (see note on 71:23).

107:3 *from the lands.* From the dispersion resulting from the Assyrian (see 2Ki 17:6) and Babylonian captivities (see 2Ki 24:14,16; 25:11,26; Jer 52:28–30; see also Ne 1:8; Est 8:5,9,13; Isa 11:12; 43:5–6; Eze 11:17; 20:34). *south.* Lit. "(the) sea" (see NIV text note), i.e., the west, as in Isa 49:12. But perhaps the last two letters of the Hebrew word have been lost, which if supplied yield "south."

107:4–9 Deliverance for those lost in the "desert wastelands." No reference is made to rebellion (as in the third and fourth stanzas), but since Israel had journeyed through the desert on her way to Canaan she had firsthand experience of the terrors of the desert. She was, moreover, bounded on the east by the great Arabian Desert (as on the west by the Mediterranean Sea; see vv. 23–32), across which her merchant caravans traveled.

107:4,7,36 *city where they could settle.* Lit. "city of habitation," i.e., where people live and where a steady supply of food and water makes human life secure.

107:6 *they cried out.* The author uses the same Hebrew verb in v. 28, thus linking the fifth stanza with the second. In vv. 13,19 he uses a different (but similar-sounding) Hebrew verb, linking the third and fourth stanzas. Just as Israel's history was a history of divine deliverance (see Ps 105) and a history of rebellion (see Ps 106), so also it was a history of crying out to the Lord in distress (see references in note on 106:44).

107:7 *straight way.* Direct route, clear of dangerous and difficult obstacles.

107:8 For other refrains, see introduction to Ps 42–43. *wonderful deeds.* See vv. 15,21,24,31; see also note on 9:1.

107:9 *satisfies the thirsty … fills the hungry.* See v. 5; see also 105:40–41.

107:10–16 Deliverance from the punishment of foreign bondage. God even delivers those who cry out to him when their distress is a result of his discipline for their sins (see vv. 17–20, 33–41).

107:10 *sat in darkness … utter darkness.* Vivid imagery for distress (see 18:28; Isa 5:30; 8:22; 59:9; see also note on 44:19). *prisoners.* While reference is no doubt to foreign bondage, the imagery of being bound was also used by OT poets to refer to other forms of distress (see Job 36:8; Isa 28:22; La 3:7); so the reference may be deliberately ambiguous.

107:11 *plans.* God's wise directives embodied in his words (see 73:24 and note).

107:12 *subjected them to bitter labor.* Lit. "brought down their heart with labor," i.e., a labor so burdensome it broke their spirit. *stumbled.* Their strength failed (see 31:10; 109:24; Ne 4:10; Isa 40:30; Zec 12:8).

13 Then they cried to the LORD in their
trouble,
and he saved them[c] from their
distress.
14 He brought them out of darkness,[d] the
utter darkness,[e]
and broke away their chains.[f]
15 Let them give thanks[g] to the LORD for
his unfailing love[h]
and his wonderful deeds[i] for
mankind,
16 for he breaks down gates of bronze
and cuts through bars of iron.

17 Some became fools[j] through their
rebellious ways[k]
and suffered affliction[l] because of
their iniquities.
18 They loathed all food[m]
and drew near the gates of death.[n]
19 Then they cried[o] to the LORD in their
trouble,
and he saved them[p] from their
distress.
20 He sent out his word[q] and healed
them;[r]
he rescued[s] them from the grave.[t]
21 Let them give thanks[u] to the LORD for
his unfailing love[v]
and his wonderful deeds[w] for
mankind.
22 Let them sacrifice thank offerings[x]
and tell of his works[y] with songs of
joy.[z]

23 Some went out on the sea[a] in
ships;[b]
they were merchants on the mighty
waters.

107:13 [c] S Ps 106:8 **107:14** [d] S ver 10; Isa 9:2; 42:7; 50:10; 59:9; 60:2; S Lk 1:79 [e] Ps 86:13; Isa 29:18 [f] S Job 36:8; Ps 116:16; Ac 12:7 **107:15** [g] ver 8, 21, 31; Ps 105:1 [h] Ps 6:4 [i] S Ps 75:1 **107:17** [j] S Ps 53:1 [k] S Ps 25:7 [l] S Lev 26:16; Isa 65:6-7; Jer 30:14-15; Gal 6:7-8 **107:18** [m] S Job 3:24; S 6:6 [n] S Job 17:16; S 33:22 **107:19** [o] ver 28; Ps 5:2 [p] ver 13; Ps 34:4 **107:20** [q] S Dt 32:2; Ps 147:15; Mt 8:8; Lk 7:7 [r] S Ex 15:26 [s] S Job 33:28 [t] Ps 16:10; 30:3; S 56:13 **107:21** [u] S ver 15 [v] Ps 6:4 [w] Ps 75:1 **107:22** [x] S Lev 7:12 [y] Ps 9:11; 73:28; 118:17 [z] S Job 8:21; S Ps 65:8 **107:23** [a] Isa 42:10 [b] S Ps 104:26 **107:24** [c] Ps 64:9; 111:2; 143:5

24 They saw the works of the LORD,[c]
his wonderful deeds in the deep.
25 For he spoke[d] and stirred up a tempest[e]
that lifted high the waves.[f]
26 They mounted up to the heavens and
went down to the depths;
in their peril[g] their courage melted[h]
away.
27 They reeled[i] and staggered like
drunkards;
they were at their wits' end.
28 Then they cried[j] out to the LORD in
their trouble,
and he brought them out of their
distress.[k]
29 He stilled the storm[l] to a whisper;
the waves[m] of the sea[a] were
hushed.[n]
30 They were glad when it grew calm,
and he guided them[o] to their desired
haven.
31 Let them give thanks[p] to the LORD for
his unfailing love[q]
and his wonderful deeds[r] for
mankind.
32 Let them exalt[s] him in the assembly[t] of
the people
and praise him in the council of the
elders.

33 He turned rivers into a desert,[u]
flowing springs[v] into thirsty ground,

[a] 29 Dead Sea Scrolls; Masoretic Text / *their waves*

107:25 [d] S Ps 105:31 [e] S Ps 50:3 [f] S Ps 93:3 **107:26** [g] Lk 8:23 [h] S Jos 2:11 **107:27** [i] Isa 19:14; 24:20; 28:7 **107:28** [j] S ver 19 [k] Ps 4:1; Jnh 1:6 **107:29** [l] Lk 8:24 [m] S Ps 93:3 [n] S Ps 65:7; Jnh 1:15 **107:30** [o] ver 7 **107:31** [p] S ver 15 [q] Ps 6:4 [r] Ps 75:1; 106:2 **107:32** [s] Ps 30:1; 34:3; 99:5 [t] S Ps 1:5; 22:22, 25; 26:12; 35:18 **107:33** [u] 1Ki 17:1; Ps 74:15; Isa 41:15; 42:15; 50:2 [v] S Ps 104:10

107:13 *cried to.* See note on v. 6.
107:16 Either this verse is quoted from Isa 45:2 or both verses quote an established saying. *gates of bronze.* City gates—normally of wood; here proverbially of bronze, the strongest gates then imaginable (see 1Ki 4:13; cf. Jer 1:18). *bars of iron.* Bars that secured city gates (see Dt 3:5; Jer 51:30). "Can a man break iron ... or bronze?" was a proverb of the time (Jer 15:12).
107:17–22 Deliverance from the punishment of wasting disease (see note on vv. 10–16).
107:17 *fools.* See Jer 4:22; see also NIV text note on 14:1. "Fools despise wisdom and instruction" (Pr 1:7; see v. 43). *affliction because of their iniquities.* See Lev 26:16,25; Dt 28:20–22,35,58–61.
107:18 *gates of death.* The realm of the dead was sometimes depicted as a netherworld city with a series of concentric walls and gates (seven, each inside the other, according to ancient Near Eastern mythology) to keep those descending there from returning to the land of the living (see 9:13 and note on Job 38:17; see also Mt 16:18).
107:19 *cried to.* See note on v. 6. *saved.* See v. 13 (another link between the second and third stanzas); cf. vv. 6,28.
107:20 *his word.* His command, here personified as the agent of his purpose (see 147:15,18; see also note on 23:6).
107:22 *thank offerings.* See Lev 7:12–15; 22:29–30. *tell of his works.* See note on 7:17. In their concluding lines, stanzas four and five are linked, as are stanzas two and three. *songs of joy.* See, e.g., Ps 116.
107:23–32 Deliverance from the perils of the sea (see note on vv. 4–9). Israel's merchants also braved the sea in pursuit of trade (see Ge 49:13; Jdg 5:17; 1Ki 9:26–28; 10:22).
107:23 *mighty waters.* See 29:3.
107:24 *wonderful deeds in the deep.* Since the peoples of the eastern Mediterranean coastlands associated the "mighty waters" (v. 23) of the sea with the primeval chaotic waters (see note on 32:6), the Lord's total control of them was always for Israel a cause of wonder and a sense of security. Therefore the terrifying storms that sometimes swept the Mediterranean (see Jnh 1; Ac 27) are here included among his wonderful deeds.
107:27 *they were at their wits' end.* Lit. "all their wisdom/skill was swallowed up."
107:30 *haven.* Perhaps trading center.
107:32 See v. 22. *elders.* See note on Ex 3:16.
107:33–42 A twofold instructive supplement recalling how the Lord sometimes disciplined his people by turning the fruitful land (v. 34) into a virtual desert (see 1Ki 17:1–7; 2Ki 8:1) but then restored the land again (see Ru 1:6; 1Ki 18:44–45), so that the hungry (v. 36) could live there and prosper in the midst of plenty. But then he sent powerful armies against them (such as the Assyrians, 2Ki 17:3–6, and the Babylonians, 2Ki 24:10–17; 25:1–26) that devastated the

[34] and fruitful land into a salt waste,[w]
because of the wickedness of those
who lived there.
[35] He turned the desert into pools of
water[x]
and the parched ground into flowing
springs;[y]
[36] there he brought the hungry to live,
and they founded a city where they
could settle.
[37] They sowed fields and planted
vineyards[z]
that yielded a fruitful harvest;
[38] he blessed them, and their numbers
greatly increased,[a]
and he did not let their herds
diminish.[b]
[39] Then their numbers decreased,[c] and
they were humbled[d]
by oppression, calamity and sorrow;
[40] he who pours contempt on nobles[e]
made them wander in a trackless
waste.[f]
[41] But he lifted the needy[g] out of their
affliction
and increased their families like
flocks.[h]
[42] The upright see and rejoice,[i]
but all the wicked shut their
mouths.[j]
[43] Let the one who is wise[k] heed these
things
and ponder the loving deeds[l] of the
LORD.

Psalm 108[a]

108:1-5pp — Ps 57:7-11
108:6-13pp — Ps 60:5-12

A song. A psalm of David.

[1] My heart, O God, is steadfast;[m]
I will sing[n] and make music with all
my soul.
[2] Awake, harp and lyre![o]
I will awaken the dawn.
[3] I will praise you, LORD, among the
nations;
I will sing of you among the
peoples.
[4] For great is your love,[p] higher than the
heavens;
your faithfulness[q] reaches to the
skies.
[5] Be exalted, O God, above the
heavens;[s]
let your glory be over all the earth.[t]
[6] Save us and help us with your right
hand,[u]
that those you love may be
delivered.
[7] God has spoken[v] from his sanctuary:[w]
"In triumph I will parcel out
Shechem[x]
and measure off the Valley of
Sukkoth.[y]
[8] Gilead is mine, Manasseh is mine;
Ephraim is my helmet,
Judah[z] is my scepter.
[9] Moab[a] is my washbasin,
on Edom[b] I toss my sandal;
over Philistia[c] I shout in triumph."
[10] Who will bring me to the fortified
city?
Who will lead me to Edom?
[11] Is it not you, God, you who have
rejected us
and no longer go out with our
armies?[d]
[12] Give us aid against the enemy,
for human help is worthless.[e]
[13] With God we will gain the victory,
and he will trample down[f] our
enemies.

[a] In Hebrew texts 108:1-13 is numbered 108:2-14.

107:34 [w] S Ge 13:10 **107:35** [x] S 2Ki 3:17; Ps 105:41; 126:4; Isa 43:19; 51:3 [y] S Job 38:26; S Isa 35:7 **107:37** [z] S 2Ki 19:29; S Isa 37:30 **107:38** [a] S Ge 12:2; S Dt 7:13 [b] S Ge 49:25 **107:39** [c] S 2Ki 10:32; Eze 5:12 [d] S Ps 44:9 **107:40** [e] S Job 12:18 [f] S Dt 32:10 **107:41** [g] S 1Sa 2:8; Ps 113:7-9 [h] S Job 21:11 **107:42** [i] S Job 22:19; Ps 97:10-12 [j] S Job 5:16; Ro 3:19 **107:43** [k] Jer 9:12; Hos 14:9 [l] Ps 103:11 **108:1** [m] Ps 112:7; 119:30,112 [n] S Ps 18:49 **108:2** [o] S Job 21:12 **108:4** [p] Nu 14:18; Ps 106:45 [q] S Ex 34:6 [r] S Ps 36:5 **108:5** [s] S Ps 8:1 [t] S Ps 57:5 **108:6** [u] S Job 40:14 **108:7** [v] Ps 89:35 [w] Ps 68:35; 102:19 [x] S Ge 12:6 [y] S Ge 33:17 **108:8** [z] S Ps 78:68 **108:9** [a] S Ge 19:37 [b] S 2Sa 8:13-14 [c] S 2Sa 8:1 **108:11** [d] S Ps 44:9 **108:12** [e] Ps 118:8; 146:3; Isa 10:3; 30:5; 31:3; Jer 2:36; 17:5 **108:13** [f] Ps 44:5; Isa 22:5; 63:3,6

and once more and deported its people; yet afterward he restored the needy (v. 41). But the poet generalizes upon these experiences in the manner of the wisdom teachers.
07:33 – 35 The imagery is similar to that found in Isa 35:6 – 7; 1:18; 42:15; 43:19 – 20; 50:2 and may indicate that the author as been influenced by Isaiah.
107:40 Perhaps quoted from Job 12:21,24. In their prosperity the people, led by their nobles, grow proud nd turn their backs on the God who has blessed them (see t 31:20; 32:15), so he returns them to the desert (see Dt 2:10; Hos 2:3,14).
07:41 *needy.* Those in need of help (see v. 39; see also 9:18 nd note).
07:42 Conclusion to the instruction (vv. 33 – 41); perhaps an cho of Job 5:16. *upright . . . wicked.* A frequent contrast in OT visdom literature (see Pr 2:21 – 22; 11:6 – 7; 12:6; 14:11; 15:8; 1:18,29; 29:27 — but the Hebrew for "wicked" here is shared nore often with Job).
07:43 Conclusion to the psalm. *one who is wise.* See Dt 32:29; Hos 14:9. *these things.* The instruction in vv. 33 – 42. *ponder the loving deeds of the LORD.* The theme of vv. 4 – 32, emphatically reiterated.
Ps 108 Praise of God's love, and prayer for his help against the enemies — a combination (with very slight modifications) of 57:7 – 11 and 60:5 – 12 (see notes there). For a similar composition of a new psalm by combination of portions from several psalms, see 1Ch 16:8 – 36. The celebration of the greatness of God's love (v. 4) links this psalm thematically with Ps 103 (see 103:11). See introduction to Ps 101 – 110.
108 title *song.* See note on Ps 30 title. *of David.* Both sources (Ps 57; 60) were credited to him.
108:1 – 5 Praise of God's love, possibly intended to function here as an expression of trust in God (the God of vv. 7 – 9,11), to whom appeal is to be made (vv. 6,12); see 109:1 and note. For this stanza, see notes on 57:7 – 11.
108:1 *soul.* Lit. "glory" (see note on 7:5).
108:6 – 13 Prayer for God's help against enemies (see notes on 60:5 – 12).

Psalm 109

For the director of music.
Of David. A psalm.

[1]My God, whom I praise,[g]
do not remain silent,[h]
[2]for people who are wicked and
deceitful[i]
have opened their mouths against me;
they have spoken against me with
lying tongues.[j]
[3]With words of hatred[k] they surround me;
they attack me without cause.[l]
[4]In return for my friendship they
accuse me,
but I am a man of prayer.[m]
[5]They repay me evil for good,[n]
and hatred for my friendship.

[6]Appoint someone evil to oppose my
enemy;
let an accuser[o] stand at his right hand.
[7]When he is tried, let him be found
guilty,[p]
and may his prayers condemn[q] him.
[8]May his days be few;[r]
may another take his place[s] of
leadership.
[9]May his children be fatherless
and his wife a widow.[t]
[10]May his children be wandering
beggars;[u]
may they be driven[a] from their
ruined homes.
[11]May a creditor[v] seize all he has;
may strangers plunder[w] the fruits of
his labor.[x]
[12]May no one extend kindness to him
or take pity[y] on his fatherless
children.
[13]May his descendants be cut off,[z]
their names blotted out[a] from the
next generation.
[14]May the iniquity of his fathers[b] be
remembered before the LORD;
may the sin of his mother never be
blotted out.
[15]May their sins always remain before[c]
the LORD,
that he may blot out their name[d]
from the earth.

[16]For he never thought of doing a
kindness,
but hounded to death the poor

109:1 [g]S Ex 15:2; Jer 17:14 [h]S Job 34:29 **109:2** [i]S Ps 43:1 [j]S Ps 52:4 **109:3** [k]Ps 69:4 [l]Ps 35:7; Jn 15:25 **109:4** [m]Ps 69:13; 141:5 **109:5** [n]S Ge 44:4 **109:6** [o]1Ch 21:1; Job 1:6; Zec 3:1 **109:7** [p]Ps 1:5 [q]Pr 28:9; Isa 41:24 **109:8** [r]S Job 15:32 [s]Ac 1:20* **109:9** [t]Ex 22:24; Jer 18:21 **109:10** [u]S Ge 4:12 **109:11** [v]Ne 5:3 [w]S Nu 14:3; Isa 1:7; 6:11; 36:1; La 5:2 [x]Job 20:18 **109:12** [y]S Job 5:4 **109:13** [z]Job 18:19; Ps 21:10 [a]S Nu 14:12; Ps 9:5; Pr 10:7 **109:14** [b]Ex 20:5; Nu 14:18; Isa 65:6-7; Jer 32:18 **109:15** [c]Ps 90:8 [d]S Ex 17:14; S Dt 32:26

[a] *10* Septuagint; Hebrew *sought*

Ps 109 A prayer for God to deliver from false accusers. The author speaks of his enemies in the singular in vv. 6–19 but in the plural elsewhere. Either (1) the author shifts here to a collective mode of speaking, or (2) the enemies are united under a leader whose personal animosity toward the psalmist has fired the antagonism of others and so is singled out for special attention. Traditional attempts to isolate a distinct class of psalms called "imprecatory" (and then identify Ps 109 as the climax of the series) are mistaken (see note on vv. 6–15). Thematically, this prayer has much affinity with Ps 35. Within the cluster in which it stands, its affinity is with Ps 102 (see introduction to Ps 101–110)—and it is only one line longer than that psalm.

Two (Hebrew) four-line stanzas of petition frame the whole (vv. 1–5,26–29), followed by a two-line conclusion (vv. 30–31). The remaining 20 lines fall into two main divisions of ten lines each (vv. 6–15,16–25). Of these, the second is thematically divided into two parts of five lines each, the first of which (vv. 16–20) catalogues what "he" has done, while the second (vv. 21–25) describes how "I" am suffering.

109 title See note on Ps 4 title.

109:1–5 Appeal to God to deliver David from false accusers.

109:1 *whom I praise.* The one he publicly praises as his trustworthy deliverer and defender (see 22:3 and note; see also 35:18; 74:21; 76:10; 79:13; 102:18). *silent.* (Judicially) inactive (see 28:1; 35:22; 50:3,21; 83:1).

109:2–5 The particulars of his case, which he presents before the heavenly bar of justice (see 35:11–16).

109:2 *opened their mouths against me.* See note on 5:9.

109:4 *but I am a man of prayer.* In contrast to the enemy (see vv. 16–18). The intent may be: But I have prayed for them (as in 35:13–14; see note there).

109:6–15 Appeal for judicial redress—that the Lord will deal with them in accordance with their malicious intent against him, matching punishment with crime (see note on 5:10; see also 35:4–10 and note).

109:6 *someone evil ... accuser.* The psalmist's enemy falsely accused him in order to bring him down; now let the enemy be confronted by an accuser.

109:7 *his prayers.* The petitions he offers in his defense.

109:8 *days be few.* The false accuser was no doubt seeking to effect David's death (see 1Ki 21:8–15). *another take his place of leadership.* The enemy held some official position and was perhaps plotting a coup. For a NT application of these words to Judas, see Ac 1:20.

109:10–11 May he also be deprived of all his property so that he has no inheritance to pass on to his children.

109:12 *no one extend kindness.* See v. 16. *his ... children.* The close identity of a man with his children and of children with their parents, resulting from the tightly bonded unity of the three- or four-generation households of that ancient society, is alien to the modern reader, whose sense of self is highly individualistic. But that deep, profoundly human bond accounts for the ancient legal principle of "punishing the children for the sin of the parents to the third and fourth generation" (see Ex 20:5; but see also 103:17; Ge 18:19).

109:13 Since a man lived on in his children (see previous note), the focus of judgment remains on the false accuser (see 21:10; 37:28). *names blotted out.* See note on 9:5.

109:14–15 *iniquity of his fathers ... sin of his mother ... their sins.* These verses return to the theme of vv. 7–8 (and thus form a frame around the stanza): May the indictment the accuser lodges against him include the sins of his parents (see note on v. 12).

109:15 *blot out their name.* May this slanderer be the last of his family line.

109:16–20 The ruthless character of the enemy—may he be made to suffer the due consequences (see 10:2–15; 59:12–13). Accusation of the adversary is a common feature in psalms that are appeals to the heavenly Judge (see, e.g., 5:9–10; 10:2–11; 17:10–12).

and the needy[e] and the brokenhearted.[f]
17 He loved to pronounce a curse—
may it come back on him.[g]
He found no pleasure in blessing—
may it be far from him.
18 He wore cursing[h] as his garment;
it entered into his body like water,[i]
into his bones like oil.
19 May it be like a cloak wrapped[j] about him,
like a belt tied forever around him.
20 May this be the LORD's payment[k] to my accusers,
to those who speak evil[l] of me.

21 But you, Sovereign LORD,
help me for your name's sake;[m]
out of the goodness of your love,[n]
deliver me.[o]
22 For I am poor and needy,
and my heart is wounded within me.
23 I fade away like an evening shadow;[p]
I am shaken off like a locust.
24 My knees give[q] way from fasting;[r]
my body is thin and gaunt.[s]
25 I am an object of scorn[t] to my accusers;
when they see me, they shake their heads.[u]

26 Help me,[v] LORD my God;
save me according to your unfailing love.
27 Let them know[w] that it is your hand,
that you, LORD, have done it.
28 While they curse,[x] may you bless;
may those who attack me be put to shame,
but may your servant rejoice.[y]
29 May my accusers be clothed with disgrace
and wrapped in shame[z] as in a cloak.

30 With my mouth I will greatly extol the LORD;
in the great throng[a] of worshipers I will praise him.
31 For he stands at the right hand[b] of the needy,
to save their lives from those who would condemn them.

109:16 [e]S Job 20:19; S Ps 35:10 [f]S Ps 34:18 **109:17** [g]Pr 28:27; S Mt 7:2 **109:18** [h]Ps 10:7 [i]Nu 5:22 **109:19** [j]ver 29; Ps 73:6; Eze 7:27 **109:20** [k]S Ex 32:34; Ps 54:5; 94:23; Isa 3:11; 2Ti 4:14 [l]Ps 71:10 **109:21** [m]S Ex 9:16; S Ps 23:3 [n]Ps 69:16 [o]S Ps 3:7 **109:23** [p]S Job 14:2 **109:24** [q]Heb 12:12 [r]S Ps 35:13 [s]S Job 16:8 **109:25** [t]S Ps 22:6 [u]S Job 16:4; S Mt 27:39; Mk 15:29 **109:26** [v]Ps 12:1; 119:86 **109:27** [w]S Job 37:7 **109:28** [x]S 2Sa 16:12 [y]Ps 66:4; Isa 35:10; 51:11; 54:1; 65:14 **109:29** [z]S Ps 35:26

Psalm 110

Of David. A psalm.

1 The LORD says[c] to my lord:[a]
"Sit at my right hand[d]
until I make your enemies
a footstool for your feet."[e]

[a] *1* Or *Lord*

109:30 [a]S Ps 35:18 **109:31** [b]Ps 16:8; 108:6 **110:1** [c]Mt 22:44*; Mk 12:36*; Lk 20:42*; Ac 2:34* [d]S Mk 16:19; Heb 1:13*; 12:2 [e]S Jos 10:24; S 1Ki 5:3; 1Co 15:25

109:17 *pronounce a curse.* The enemy added curses to lies (see note on Ge 12:3). *come back on him.* See note on Est 7:10.
109:18–19 *garment ... cloak wrapped.* See note on v. 29.
109:18 *into his body like water, into his bones like oil.* Pronouncing curses on others was his food and drink, as well as his clothing; he lived by such cursing (cf. Pr 4:17 and note).
109:20 *the LORD's payment.* See 54:5; 94:23; Isa 3:11; 2Ti 4:14.
109:21–25 The intensity of "my" suffering—Lord, deliver me!
109:21 *for your name's sake.* See notes on 5:11; 23:3. *love.* See v. 26; see also note on 6:4.
109:22 The psalmist's description of his situation echoes the words of v. 16. *poor and needy.* Dependent on the Lord (see note on 34:6). *heart.* See note on 4:7. *is wounded.* The Hebrew for this phrase sounds like the Hebrew for "curse" in vv. 17–18, a deliberate wordplay—while he lives by cursing, I live with deep inward pain.
109:23 *I fade away.* Apparently the psalmist suffers a life-sapping affliction, which is the occasion for his enemies to turn on him (see vv. 24–25; see also note on 5:9). *like an evening shadow.* See 102:11. *shaken off.* See Ne 5:13; Job 38:13.
109:26–29 Concluding petition, with many echoes of preceding themes.
109:28 *servant.* Perhaps identifies the psalmist as the Lord's anointed (see title; see also 78:70 and note).
109:29 *clothed with ... wrapped in.* For other uses of this imagery, see vv. 18–19; 35:26; 45:3; 73:6; 104:1–2; 132:9,16,18; Job 8:22; 29:14; 40:10; Pr 31:25; Isa 59:17; 61:3,10; Eze 7:27; 26:16; 31:15; Zec 6:13; Lk 24:19; Ro 13:14; 1Co 15:53–54; Gal 3:27; Col 3:12; 1Pe 5:5.
109:30–31 A vow to praise the Lord for his deliverance (see note on 7:17).

Ps 110 Prophecies concerning the Messianic King-Priest. This psalm (specifically its two brief prophecies, vv. 1,4) is frequently referred to in the NT testimony to Christ. Like Ps 2, it has the marks of a coronation psalm, composed for use at the enthronement of a new Davidic king. Before the Christian era, Jews already viewed it as Messianic. Because of the manner in which it has been interpreted in the NT—especially by Jesus (see Mt 22:43–45; Mk 12:36–37; Lk 20:42–44) but also by Peter (see Ac 2:34–36) and the author of Hebrews (see especially Heb 1:13; 5:6–10; 7:11–28)—Christians have generally held that this is the most directly "prophetic" of all the psalms. If so, David, speaking prophetically (see 2Sa 23:2), composed a coronation psalm for his great future Son, of whom the prophets did not speak until later. It may be, however, that David composed the psalm for the coronation of his son Solomon, that he called him "my lord" (v. 1; but see NIV text note) in view of his new status, which placed him above the aged David, and that in so doing he spoke a word that had far larger meaning than he knew at the time. This would seem to be more in accord with what we know of David from Samuel, Kings and Chronicles. For this psalm's setting in the Psalter, see introduction to Ps 101–110.

The psalm falls into two precisely balanced halves (vv. 1–3,4–7). Each of the two brief prophecies (vv. 1,4) is followed by thematically and structurally similar elaboration: As v. 4 is to v. 1, so v. 5 is to v. 2 and vv. 6–7 are to v. 3 (a poetic couplet).
110:1–3 The Lord's decree, establishing his anointed as his regent in the face of all opposition (see 2:7–12).
110:1 The first prophecy (see note on v. 4). *my lord.* My sovereign, therefore superior to David (see

[2]The LORD will extend your mighty
scepter[f] from Zion,[g] saying,
"Rule[h] in the midst of your
enemies!"
[3]Your troops will be willing
on your day of battle.
Arrayed in holy splendor,[i]
your young men will come to you
like dew from the morning's
womb.[a][j]

[4]The LORD has sworn
and will not change his mind:[k]
"You are a priest forever,[l]
in the order of Melchizedek.[m]"

[5]The Lord is at your right hand[b];[n]
he will crush kings[o] on the day of his
wrath.[p]
[6]He will judge the nations,[q] heaping up
the dead[r]
and crushing the rulers[s] of the whole
earth.
[7]He will drink from a brook along the
way,[c]
and so he will lift his head high.[t]

Psalm 111[d]

[1]Praise the LORD.[e]

I will extol the LORD[u] with all my heart[v]
in the council[w] of the upright and in
the assembly.[x]

110:2 [f]S Ge 49:10; Ps 45:6; Isa 14:5; Jer 48:17 [g]S Ps 2:6 [h]Ps 72:8 **110:3** [i]S Ex 15:11 [j]Mic 5:7 **110:4** [k]S Nu 23:19 [l]Zec 6:13; Heb 5:6*; 7:21* [m]S Ge 14:18; Heb 5:10; 7:15-17* **110:5** [n]Ps 16:8 [o]S Dt 7:24; Ps 2:12; 68:21; 76:12; Isa 60:12; Da 2:44 [p]S Ps 2:5; Ro 2:5; Rev 6:17; 11:18 **110:6** [q]S Ps 9:19 [r]Isa 5:25; 34:3; 66:24

[a] *3* The meaning of the Hebrew for this sentence is uncertain. [b] *5* Or *My lord is at your right hand, LORD* [c] *7* The meaning of the Hebrew for this clause is uncertain. [d] This psalm is an acrostic poem, the lines of which begin with the successive letters of the Hebrew alphabet. [e] *1* Hebrew *Hallelu Yah*

[s]S Ps 18:38 **110:7** [t]Ps 3:3; 27:6 **111:1** [u]Ps 34:1; 109:30; 115:18; 145:10 [v]S Ps 9:1 [w]Ps 89:7 [x]S Ps 1:5

Mt 22:44–45; Mk 12:36–37; Lk 20:42–44; Ac 2:34–35; Heb 1:13 and their contexts). *Sit.* Sit enthroned. *right hand.* The place of honor beside a king (see 45:9; 1Ki 2:19); thus he is made second in authority to God himself. NT references to Jesus' exaltation to this position are many (see Mt 26:64; Mk 14:62; 16:19; Lk 22:69; Ac 2:33; 5:31; 7:55–56; Ro 8:34; Eph 1:20; Col 3:1; Heb 1:3; 8:1; 10:12; 12:2). *enemies.* See note on 2:1–3. *footstool for your feet.* See Heb 10:12–13. Ancient kings often had themselves portrayed as placing their feet on vanquished enemies (see Jos 10:24). For a royal footstool as part of the throne, see 2Ch 9:18. For the thought here, see 1Ki 5:3. Paul applies this word to Christ in 1Co 15:25; Eph 1:22.

110:2 *extend your mighty scepter.* Expand your reign in ever widening circles until no foe remains to oppose your rule. *Zion.* David's royal city (see 2Sa 5:7,9), but also God's (see 9:11 and note), where he rules as the Great King (see Ps 46; 48; 132:13–18). The Lord's anointed is his regent over his emerging kingdom in the world.

110:3 *willing.* Lit. "freewill offerings," i.e., they will offer themselves as dedicated warriors to support you on the battlefield (see Jdg 5:2)—as the Israelites offered their treasures for the building of the tabernacle in the wilderness (see Ex 35:29; 36:3; see also Ezr 1:4; 2:68). Accordingly, Paul speaks of Christ's followers offering their bodies "as a living sacrifice" (Ro 12:1) and of himself as a "drink offering" (Php 2:17); see also 2Co 8:5. *Arrayed in holy splendor.* If the phrase is descriptive of the Lord's anointed, it depicts him as clothed in royal majesty and glory. If it speaks of the young warriors who flock to him, it apparently describes them as dressed in priestly garb, ready for participation in a holy war (see 1Sa 21:4–5; 25:28; 2Ch 13:8,12; 20:15,21; Isa 13:3–4; Jer 6:4; 51:27) and pouring into his camp morning by morning as copious as the dew (see 2Sa 17:11–12). *holy splendor.* See note on 29:2.

110:4–7 The Lord's oath, establishing his anointed as king-priest in Zion and assuring him victory over all powers that oppose him.

110:4 The second prophecy (see note on v. 1). *has sworn.* In accordance also with his sworn covenant to maintain David's royal line forever (see 89:35–37). The force of this oath is elaborated by the author of Hebrews (Heb 6:16–18; 7:20–22). *priest ... in the order of Melchizedek.* David and his royal sons, as chief representatives of the rule of God, performed many worship-focused activities, such as overseeing the ark of the covenant (see 2Sa 6:1–15, especially v. 14; 1Ki 8:1), building and overseeing the temple (see 1Ki 5–7; 2Ki 12:4–7; 22:3–7; 23:4–7; 2Ch 15:8; 24:4–12; 29:3–11; 34:8) and overseeing the work of the priests and Levites and the temple liturgy (see 1Ch 6:31; 15:11–16; 16:4–42; 23:3–31; 25:1; 2Ch 17:7–9; 19:8–11; 29:25,30; 31:2; 35:15–16; Ezr 3:10; 8:20; Ne 12:24,36,45). In all these duties they exercised authority over even the high priest. But they could not engage in those specifically priestly functions that had been assigned to the Aaronic priesthood (see 2Ch 26:16–18). In the present message the son of David is installed by God as king-priest in Zion after the manner of Melchizedek, the king-priest of God Most High at Jerusalem in the days of Abraham (see Ge 14:18,20 and notes). As such a king-priest he was appointed to a higher order of priesthood than that of Aaron and his sons. (For the union of king and priest in one person, see Zec 6:13 and note.) What this means for Christ's priesthood is the main theme of Heb 7. *forever.* Permanently and irrevocably; perhaps alluded to in Jn 12:34.

110:5 *The Lord is at your right hand.* God is near to assist you in your warfare (see v. 2; cf. 109:31). Some take these words as an address to God (see NIV text note): The Lord (David's superior son) is at your (God's) right hand (as in v. 1). *on the day of his wrath.* See 2:5 and note.

110:6 *He.* The Lord's anointed. *heaping up the dead.* Battlefield imagery (borrowed from David's victories) that depicts the victory of the Lord's anointed over all powers that oppose the kingdom of God (see 2:9; Rev 19:11–21).

110:7 *drink from a brook.* Even in the heat of battle he will find refreshment and "lift his head high" with undiminished vigor (see note on v. 3).

Ps 111–119 A cluster of nine psalms framed by unusual alphabetic acrostics (see introductions to Ps 111; 119) that enclose the "Egyptian Hallel" (see introduction to Ps 113–118). The framing psalms that enclose the celebration of redemption contained in the Hallel offer instruction in the piety that must characterize those who join in the celebration of God's saving acts in behalf of his people.

Ps 111 Praise of God for his unfailing righteousness. The psalm combines hymnic praise with wisdom instruction, as its first and last verses indicate. Close comparison with Ps 112 shows that these two psalms are twins, probably written by the same author and intended to be kept together. The two psalms are most likely postexilic. For the relationship of these psalms with those that follow, see introduction to Ps 111–119.

Structurally, both Ps 111 and Ps 112 are alphabetic acrostics (see NIV text note), but unique in that each (Hebrew) half-line

[2]Great are the works[y] of the LORD;
they are pondered by all[z] who
delight in them.
[3]Glorious and majestic are his deeds,
and his righteousness endures[a]
forever.
[4]He has caused his wonders to be
remembered;
the LORD is gracious and
compassionate.[b]
[5]He provides food[c] for those who fear
him;[d]
he remembers his covenant[e] forever.

[6]He has shown his people the power of
his works,[f]
giving them the lands of other
nations.[g]
[7]The works of his hands[h] are faithful
and just;
all his precepts are trustworthy.[i]
[8]They are established for ever[j] and
ever,
enacted in faithfulness and
uprightness.
[9]He provided redemption[k] for his
people;
he ordained his covenant forever—
holy and awesome[l] is his name.

111:2 [y]S Job 36:24; Ps 143:5; Rev 15:3 [z]Ps 64:9 **111:3** [a]Ps 112:3,9; 119:142 **111:4** [b]S Dt 4:31; S Ps 86:15 **111:5** [c]S Ge 1:30; S Ps 37:25; Mt 6:26,31-33 [d]Ps 103:11 [e]S 1Ch 16:15; S Ps 105:8 **111:6** [f]Ps 64:9; S 66:3,5 [g]S Ps 105:44 **111:7** [h]S Ps 92:4 [i]Ps 19:7; 119:128 **111:8** [j]Ps 119:89,152, 160; Isa 40:8; S Mt 5:18 **111:9** [k]Ps 34:22; S 103:4; 130:7; Lk 1:68 [l]Ps 30:4; 99:3; Lk 1:49 **111:10** [m]S Job 23:15; S Ps 19:9 [n]Dt 4:6 [o]S Dt 4:6; Ps 119:98, 104, 130 [p]Ps 28:6; 89:52 **112:1** [q]Ps 33:2; 103:1; 150:1 [r]Ps 1:1-2 [s]S Job 1:8; Ps 103:11; 115:13; 128:1 [t]S Ps 1:2; 119:14,16,47,92 **112:2** [u]Ps 25:13; 37:26; 128:2-4 **112:3** [v]S Dt 8:18 [w]S Ps 37:6; S 111:3 **112:4** [x]S Ps 18:28

[10]The fear of the LORD[m] is the beginning
of wisdom;[n]
all who follow his precepts have
good understanding.[o]
To him belongs eternal praise.[p]

Psalm 112[a]

[1]Praise the LORD.[b][q]

Blessed are those[r] who fear the LORD,[s]
who find great delight[t] in his
commands.

[2]Their children[u] will be mighty in the
land;
the generation of the upright will be
blessed.
[3]Wealth and riches[v] are in their houses,
and their righteousness endures[w]
forever.
[4]Even in darkness light dawns[x] for the
upright,

[a] This psalm is an acrostic poem, the lines of which begin with the successive letters of the Hebrew alphabet. [b] *1* Hebrew *Hallelu Yah*

advances the alphabet. Both psalms are framed by first and last verses that highlight their primary themes, and in both psalms the main body develops the theme introduced by the first verse, while the closing verse adds a counterpoint. In both psalms the main body of eight verses falls thematically into two halves of four verses each, with the corresponding verses of each half containing certain thematic links (compare, e.g., 111:2 and 111:6; also vv. 5 and 9). Corresponding verses of the two psalms also tend to share common themes (compare, e.g., 111:3–5 with 112:3–5). Both of these twin psalms are composed of the same number of Hebrew syllables.

111:1 *I will extol.* Introductory to the praise that follows in vv. 2–9. *with all my heart.* A verbal link with a recurring phrase in Ps 119 (see vv. 2,10,34,58,69,145). *council of the upright.* Probably a more intimate circle than the assembly (see 107:32 for a similar distinction) and referring to those who are truly godly—such as the "upright" of 112:2,4 (see 11:7; 33:1; 49:14; 97:11; 107:42; 140:13). *in the assembly.* See note on 9:1.

111:2–5 The stanza is framed by references to the Lord's "works" and "his covenant" (see vv. 6–9 and note).

111:2 *works of the LORD.* The hymn focuses especially on what God has done for his people. Verses 5,9 sum it up. *pondered.* Reflectively examined (see Ezr 10:16, "investigate"; Ecc 1:13, "study").

111:3 *righteousness.* As embodied in his deeds (see note on 4:1).

111:4 *wonders.* See note on 9:1. *gracious and compassionate.* See Ex 34:6–7 and note.

111:5 *provides food.* Illustrative of his bountiful provisions for the daily needs of his people (as in the Lord's prayer: "Give us today our daily bread," Mt 6:11). *fear.* See v. 10 and note. *his covenant.* The Lord remembers "forever" the covenant he "ordained ... forever" (v. 9; see also 105:8–11).

111:6–9 The stanza is framed by references to the Lord's "works" and "his covenant" (see vv. 2–5 and note).

111:7 *faithful and just.* Cf. "Glorious and majestic" (v. 3). *precepts are trustworthy.* See note on 93:5.

111:8 *They.* "The works of his hands" (v. 7). *faithfulness and uprightness.* Cf. "gracious and compassionate" (v. 4).

111:9 *provided redemption.* The other great benefit of God's deeds in behalf of his people (cf. "provides food," v. 5). *holy and awesome.* As shown by his works. *name.* See note on 5:11.

111:10 Concluding word of godly wisdom. *The fear of the LORD is the beginning of wisdom.* The classic OT statement concerning the religious basis of what it means to be wise (see Job 28:28; Pr 1:7; 9:10; see also note on 66:16). *who follow his precepts.* Lit. "who do them." The plural Hebrew pronoun refers back to "precepts" in v. 7 (see 19:7–9, where "The fear of the LORD" stands parallel to "statutes," "precepts," "commands," "decrees"; see also 112:1).

Ps 112 A eulogy to the godly—in the spirit of Ps 1 but formed after the pattern of Ps 111 and likely intended as its complement (see introduction to Ps 111).

112:1 The basic theme, developed more fully in vv. 2–9. Verse 10 states its converse. See 1:1–2; 128:1. *Blessed.* See note on 1:1. *fear the LORD.* See 66:16 and note. *delight ... commands.* A verbal and conceptual link with Ps 119 (see 119:35).

112:2–5 The stanza is framed by references to godly people's children and their generosity (see vv. 6–9 and note).

112:2 *children.* The godly bring blessing to their children and to themselves—not least in the fact that through their children they are "remembered" in the community (see v. 6; see also Dt 25:6; Ru 4:10; see further Ps 37:26; 127:3–5; 128:3 and note on 109:12). *will be mighty.* Will be persons of influence and reputation.

112:3 Cf. 111:3. *Wealth and riches.* See 1:3; 128:2. *righteousness.* See v. 9; see also note on 1:5. *endures.* It is not an occasional characteristic of their actions (see "steadfast," v. 7).

112:4 *darkness.* A metaphor for calamitous times (see 107:10 and note). *light.* See note on 27:1. *gracious and compassionate.* See 111:4; cf. Ex 34:6–7 and note. *righteous.* Cf. what is said of the Lord in 116:5; 145:8,17.

for those who are gracious and
compassionate and righteous.[y]
5 Good will come to those who are
generous and lend freely,[z]
who conduct their affairs with
justice.

6 Surely the righteous will never be
shaken;[a]
they will be remembered[b] forever.
7 They will have no fear of bad news;
their hearts are steadfast,[c] trusting in
the LORD.[d]
8 Their hearts are secure, they will have
no fear;[e]
in the end they will look in triumph
on their foes.[f]
9 They have freely scattered their gifts to
the poor,[g]
their righteousness endures[h] forever;
their horn[a] will be lifted[i] high in
honor.

10 The wicked will see[j] and be vexed,
they will gnash their teeth[k] and
waste away;[l]
the longings of the wicked will come
to nothing.[m]

112:4 [y] Ps 5:12
112:5 [z] S Ps 37:21, 26; Lk 6:35
112:6 [a] S Ps 15:5; S 55:22 [b] Pr 10:7; Ecc 2:16
112:7 [c] Ps 57:7; 108:1 [d] S Ps 28:7; 56:3-4; S Isa 12:2
112:8 [e] Ps 3:6; 27:1; 56:11; Pr 1:33; Isa 12:2 [f] S Ps 54:7
112:9 [g] Lk 19:8; Ac 9:36; 2Co 9:9* [h] S Ps 111:3 [i] S Ps 75:10
112:10 [j] Ps 86:17 [k] S Ps 37:12; S Mt 8:12 [l] S Ps 34:21 [m] S Job 8:13

113:1 [n] S Ps 22:23 [o] Ps 34:22; S 103:21; 134:1
113:2 [p] S Ps 30:4; 48:10; 145:21; 148:13; 149:3; Isa 12:4 [q] Ps 115:18; 131:3; Da 2:20 **113:3** [r] Isa 24:15; 45:6; 59:19; Mal 1:11
113:4 [s] S Ps 99:2 [t] S Ps 8:1; S 57:11 **113:5** [u] S Ex 8:10; S Ps 35:10 [v] S Ps 103:19 [w] S Job 16:19 **113:6** [x] Ps 11:4; 138:6; Isa 57:15
113:7 [y] 1Sa 2:8; Ps 35:10; 68:10; 140:12 [z] Ps 107:41

Psalm 113

1 Praise the LORD.[b][n]

Praise the LORD, you his servants;[o]
praise the name of the LORD.
2 Let the name of the LORD be praised,[p]
both now and forevermore.[q]
3 From the rising of the sun[r] to the place
where it sets,
the name of the LORD is to be
praised.

4 The LORD is exalted[s] over all the
nations,
his glory above the heavens.[t]
5 Who is like the LORD our God,[u]
the One who sits enthroned[v] on high,[w]
6 who stoops down to look[x]
on the heavens and the earth?

7 He raises the poor[y] from the dust
and lifts the needy[z] from the ash heap;

[a] 9 *Horn* here symbolizes dignity. [b] 1 Hebrew *Hallelu Yah*; also in verse 9

112:5 *Good.* Well-being and prosperity (see 34:8–14 and note). *are generous and lend freely.* See v. 9; see also 111:5.
112:6–9 The stanza is framed by reference to the righteous being "remembered" (see note on v. 2) and to their generosity (see note on vv. 2–5).
112:6 *shaken.* See note on 10:6.
112:7 Shares with 111:7 the basic theme of reliability. *hearts.* See v. 8; see also note on 4:7. *trusting.* Their trust in God will be as steadfast as their righteousness is enduring (see v. 3). For trust and obedience to God's righteous will as the sum of true godliness, see 34:8–14 and note.
112:8 *secure.* In Hebrew a verbal echo of "established" in 111:8. *will look in triumph.* "Even in darkness light dawns" (v. 4).
112:9 See 2Co 9:9 and note. *gifts to the poor.* See v. 5. *their righteousness.* Just as the Lord remembers his covenant (111:5,9), so the righteous act according to "justice" (v. 5) and "righteousness" (v. 9), two of the prime moral virtues the Lord requires of his covenant servant (see Ge 18:19; Ps 106:3; Isa 5:7; 56:1; Eze 18:5,21; 33:14,16,19; 45:9; Am 5:24; 6:12; see also 2Sa 8:15; Pr 1:3; 21:3; Jer 22:15; 32:15—sometimes rendered "just" and "right"). *lifted high in honor.* As God's name is held in holy awe (see 111:9), so the godly will be held in honor.
112:10 The counterpoint—like 111:10. *see and be vexed.* Godliness is the way to blessedness, whereas the way the wicked have chosen leads to a dead end (see 10:2–11; 107:42). *come to nothing.* See 1:4–6; see also Ps 37; Pr 10:28.
Ps 113–118 The "Egyptian Hallel," which came to be used in Jewish liturgy at the great religious festivals (Passover, Weeks, Tabernacles, Dedication, New Moon; see Lev 23; Nu 10:10; Jn 10:22; see also chart, pp. 188–189). At Passover, Ps 113 and 114 were sung before the meal (before the second cup was passed) and Ps 115–118 after the meal (when the fourth cup had been filled). For the frame within which the "Hallel" has been set, see introduction to Ps 111–119.
Ps 113 A hymn to the Lord celebrating his high majesty and his mercies to the lowly (see 138:6). It was probably composed originally for the temple liturgy. Thematically, the psalm has strong links with the song of Hannah (1Sa 2:1–15) and the song of Mary (Lk 1:46–55).

Three precisely balanced stanzas (each having three verses) give the psalm a pleasing symmetry. With seven (the number of completeness) verbs the author celebrates God's praise in stanzas two and three ("is exalted," "sits ... on high," "stoops down," "raises," "lifts," "seats," "settles")—and note the fourfold praise in the first stanza. At the center (v. 5; see note on 6:6) a rhetorical question focuses and heightens the hymnic theme.
113:1b–3 The fourfold call to praise.
113:1 *name of the LORD.* See vv. 2–3. Triple repetition was a common liturgical convention (see note on 96:1–3). *name.* See note on 5:11.
113:2 *now and forevermore.* The praise of those who truly praise the Lord cannot rest content until it fills all time—and space (v. 3).
113:3 The psalmist employs an ancient formula for indicating universal space. Canaanite Amarna letter No. 288 reads as follows: "Behold, the king, my lord, has set his name at the rising of the sun and at the setting of the sun" (see chart, p. xxii; cf. Ps 139:9 and note).
113:4–6 The Lord is enthroned on high, exalted over all creation.
113:4 See the refrain in 57:5,11. *exalted over all the nations.* And implicitly over all their gods (see 95:3; 96:4–5; 97:9; see also 47:2,7–8). Accordingly, those who receive his saving help exalt him in grateful praise (118:28)—a thematic frame to the "Hallel." *above the heavens.* Above even the most exalted aspect of the creation (see v. 6; 148:13).
113:5 The rhetorical center (see note on 6:6). *Who is like the LORD ... ?* See note on Mic 1:1. *our God.* What grace, that he has covenanted to be "our" God (see Ge 17:7; Ex 19:5–6; 20:2)!
113:7–9 The Lord exalts the lowly—the God of highest majesty does not ally himself with the high and mighty of the earth but stands with and raises up the poor and needy (see 1Sa 2:3–8; Lk 1:46–55). Cf. the deliverance celebrated in Ps 118.
113:7–8 Repeated almost verbatim from 1Sa 2:8.
113:7 *poor ... needy.* See 9:18; 34:6 and notes. *dust ... ash*

[8]he seats them[a] with princes,
with the princes of his people.
[9]He settles the childless[b] woman in her home
as a happy mother of children.

Praise the LORD.

Psalm 114

[1]When Israel came out of Egypt,[c]
Jacob from a people of foreign tongue,
[2]Judah[d] became God's sanctuary,[e]
Israel his dominion.

[3]The sea looked and fled,[f]
the Jordan turned back;[g]
[4]the mountains leaped[h] like rams,
the hills like lambs.

[5]Why was it, sea, that you fled?[i]
Why, Jordan, did you turn back?
[6]Why, mountains, did you leap like rams,
you hills, like lambs?

[7]Tremble, earth,[j] at the presence of the Lord,
at the presence of the God of Jacob,
[8]who turned the rock into a pool,
the hard rock into springs of water.[k]

Psalm 115

115:4-11pp — Ps 135:15-20

[1]Not to us, LORD, not to us
but to your name be the glory,[l]
because of your love and faithfulness.[m]

[2]Why do the nations say,
"Where is their God?"[n]
[3]Our God is in heaven;[o]
he does whatever pleases him.[p]
[4]But their idols are silver and gold,[q]
made by human hands.[r]
[5]They have mouths, but cannot speak,[s]
eyes, but cannot see.

113:8 [a]S 2Sa 9:11 **113:9** [b]S 1Sa 2:5 **114:1** [c]S Ex 13:3; S 29:46 **114:2** [d]Ps 76:1 [e]S Ex 15:17; Ps 78:68-69 **114:3** [f]Ex 14:21; Ps 77:16 [g]S Ex 15:8; S Jos 3:16 **114:4** [h]S Jdg 5:5 **114:5** [i]S Ex 14:21 **114:7** [j]S Ex 15:14; S 1Ch 16:30 **114:8** [k]S Ex 17:6; S Nu 20:11 **115:1** [l]Ps 29:2; 66:2; 96:8 [m]S Ex 34:6 **115:2** [n]S Ps 42:3 **115:3** [o]Ezr 5:11; Ne 1:4; Ps 103:19; 136:26; Mt 6:9 [p]Ps 135:6 **115:4** [q]Rev 9:20 [r]S 2Ki 19:18; S 2Ch 32:19; Jer 10:3-5; Ac 19:26 **115:5** [s]Jer 10:5

heap. Symbolic of a humble status (see Ge 18:27; 1Ki 16:2), but here probably also of extreme distress and need (see Job 30:19; 42:6; Isa 47:1; Jer 25:34).

113:9 *childless woman.* In that ancient society barrenness was the greatest disgrace and the deepest tragedy for a woman (see Ge 30:1; 1Sa 1:6–7,10); in her old age she would be as desolate as Naomi because she would have no one to sustain her (see Ru 1:11–13; see also 2Ki 4:14). *home.* Family circle. *happy mother.* Because of God's gracious provision, as in the case of Sarah (see Ge 21:2), Rebekah (see Ge 25:21), Rachel (see Ge 30:23), Hannah (see 1Sa 1:20), the Shunammite (see 2Ki 4:17) and others.

Ps 114 A hymnic celebration of the exodus, the second psalm in the "Egyptian Hallel" (see introduction to Ps 113–118). It is one of the most exquisitely fashioned songs of the Psalter. It probably dates from the period of the monarchy sometime after the division of the kingdom (see v. 2). No doubt it was composed for liturgical use at the temple during one of the annual religious festivals (see introduction to Ps 113). The theme is progressively developed through four balanced stanzas, reaching its climax in the fourth. The first two stanzas (vv. 1–4) recall the great events of the exodus; the last two (vv. 5–8) celebrate their continuing significance.

114:1–2 The great OT redemptive event.

114:1 *Israel ... Jacob.* Synonyms (see Ex 19:3). *came out of Egypt.* Recalls the exodus and all the great events of the wilderness journey.

114:2 *Judah ... Israel.* The southern and northern kingdoms, viewed here as the one people of God. *became.* The crucial event was the establishment of the covenant at Sinai, where Israel became bound to the Lord as a "kingdom of priests and a holy nation" (Ex 19:3–6). *God's.* Lit. "his." The antecedent is not expressed until the climax (v. 7). *sanctuary.* His temple, in which he took up his residence in the world — symbolized by the tabernacle, later the temple. In Ex 15:17 the promised land is similarly called God's sanctuary. *dominion.* The special realm over which he ruled as King. This, rather than the exodus itself, was the great wonder of God's grace.

114:3–4 The author evokes a fearsome scene, such as that portrayed by other poets (see 18:7–15; 68:7–8; 77:16–19; Jdg 5:4–5; Hab 3:3–10).

114:3 *sea ... Jordan.* The "Red Sea" and the Jordan River, through which the Lord brought his people — here they are personified. *looked and fled.* Saw the mighty God approach in his awesome pillar of cloud and fled.

114:4 *leaped.* The mountains and hills quaked at God's approach (see 29:6).

114:7–8 The Lord of yesterday (vv. 5–6) — "the God of Jacob" — is still with us.

114:7 *Tremble.* In awesome recognition. *earth.* All creation. *Jacob.* A synonym for Israel (see Ge 32:28).

114:8 *turned the rock into a pool.* Thus sustaining and refreshing life (see Ex 17:6; Nu 20:11).

Ps 115 This third psalm in the "Egyptian Hallel" (see introduction to Ps 113–118) offers praise to the Lord, the one true God, for his love and faithfulness toward his people. It was composed as a liturgy of praise for the temple worship. It may have been written for use at the dedication of the second temple (see Ezr 6:16) when Israel was beginning to revive after the disruption of the exile. See introduction to Ps 113. Structurally, the song advances in five movements, involving a liturgical exchange between the people and temple personnel: (1) vv. 1–8: the people; (2) vv. 9–11: Levitical choir leader (the refrain perhaps spoken by the Levitical choir); (3) vv. 12–13: the people; (4) vv. 14–15: the priests; (5) vv. 16–18: the people.

115:1–8 Praise of God's love and faithfulness toward his people, which silences the taunts of the nations.

115:1 *Not to us ... not to us.* The introductory confession of faith. Israel's existence, and now her revival, is not her own achievement. *name.* See note on 5:11. *love and faithfulness.* The most common OT expression for God's covenant benefits (see note on 26:3). *love.* See note on 6:4.

115:2 *Where is their God?* The taunt of the nations when Israel is decimated by natural disasters (see Joel 2:17) or crushed by enemies, especially when Judah is destroyed and the temple of God razed (see 3:2; 10:11 and notes; 42:3; 79:10; Mic 7:10).

115:3 *is in heaven.* Sits enthroned (see 113:5) in the "highest heavens" (v. 16). *whatever pleases him.* If Israel is decimated or destroyed, it is God's doing; it is not his failure or inability to act, nor is it the achievement of the idols the nations worship. When Israel is revived, that is also God's doing, and no other god can oppose him.

115:4–7 Whatever glory and power the false gods are thought to have (as symbolized in the images made to

[6]They have ears, but cannot hear,
noses, but cannot smell.
[7]They have hands, but cannot feel,
feet, but cannot walk,
nor can they utter a sound with their
throats.
[8]Those who make them will be like
them,
and so will all who trust in them.

[9]All you Israelites, trust[t] in the LORD—
he is their help and shield.
[10]House of Aaron,[u] trust in the LORD—
he is their help and shield.
[11]You who fear him,[v] trust in the
LORD—
he is their help and shield.

[12]The LORD remembers[w] us and will
bless us:[x]
He will bless his people Israel,
he will bless the house of Aaron,
[13]he will bless those who fear[y] the
LORD—
small and great alike.

[14]May the LORD cause you to flourish,[z]
both you and your children.
[15]May you be blessed by the LORD,
the Maker of heaven[a] and earth.

[16]The highest heavens belong to the
LORD,[b]
but the earth he has given[c] to
mankind.

[17]It is not the dead[d] who praise the LORD,
those who go down to the place of
silence;
[18]it is we who extol the LORD,[e]
both now and forevermore.[f]

Praise the LORD.[a][g]

Psalm 116

[1]I love the LORD,[h] for he heard my voice;
he heard my cry[i] for mercy.[j]
[2]Because he turned his ear[k] to me,
I will call on him as long as I live.

[3]The cords of death[l] entangled me,
the anguish of the grave came
over me;
I was overcome by distress and
sorrow.
[4]Then I called on the name[m] of the
LORD:
"LORD, save me![n]"

[5]The LORD is gracious and righteous;[o]
our God is full of compassion.[p]
[6]The LORD protects the unwary;
when I was brought low,[q] he
saved me.[r]

[7]Return to your rest,[s] my soul,
for the LORD has been good[t] to you.

115:9 [t]Ps 37:3; 62:8 **115:10** [u]Ex 30:30; Ps 118:3 **115:11** [v]Ps 22:23; 103:11; 118:4 **115:12** [w]S 1Ch 16:15 [x]S Ge 12:2 **115:13** [y]S Ps 112:1 **115:14** [z]Dt 1:11 **115:15** [a]S Ge 1:1; Ac 14:15; S Rev 10:6 **115:16** [b]S Ps 89:11 [c]S Ge 1:28; Ps 8:6-8 **115:17** [d]Ps 88:10-12 **115:18** [e]S Ps 111:1 [f]S Ps 113:2 [g]Ps 28:6; 33:2; 103:1 **116:1** [h]Ps 18:1 [i]S Ps 31:22; S 40:1 [j]S Ps 6:9; S 28:2 **116:2** [k]S Ps 5:1 **116:3** [l]S 2Sa 22:6; Ps 18:4-5 **116:4** [m]Ps 80:18; 118:5 [n]S Ps 80:2 **116:5** [o]S Ex 9:27; S 2Ch 12:6; S Ezr 9:15 [p]S Ex 22:27; S Ps 86:15 **116:6** [q]S Ps 79:8 [r]Ps 18:3; 22:5; 107:13 **116:7** [s]Ps 46:10; 62:1; 131:2; Mt 11:29 [t]Ps 13:6; 106:1; 142:7

[a] 18 Hebrew *Hallelu Yah*

represent them), they are mere figments of human imagination and utterly worthless (see 135:15–18; Isa 46:1–7).

115:8 *Those who make them.* The taunting nations (cf. v. 2). *like them.* Powerless and ineffectual. For a graphic elaboration of this truth, see Isa 44:9–20.

115:9–11 The call to trust in the Lord, not in idols (see v. 8). For triple repetition as a liturgical convention, see note on 96:1–3. For the same groupings, see 118:2–4; see also 135:19–20.

115:11 *You who fear him.* Perhaps proselytes (see 1Ki 8:41–43; Ezr 6:21; Ne 10:28).

115:12–13 The people's confession of trust.

115:14–15 The priestly blessing.

115:14 *cause you to flourish.* In numbers, wealth and strength (cf. Ecc 2:9: "became greater by far than"—lit. "increased more than").

115:16–18 The people's concluding doxology.

115:16 *highest heavens ... earth.* The heavens are the exclusive realm of the exalted, all-sovereign God; the earth is the divinely appointed place for human beings, where they live under God's rule and care, enjoy his abundant blessings (vv. 12–13) and celebrate his praise (v. 18).

115:17 *not the dead.* The dead no longer live in "the earth" (v. 16) but have descended to the silent realm below, where blessings are no longer enjoyed and hence praise is absent (see notes on 6:5; 30:1).

Ps 116 Praise of the Lord for deliverance from death. It may have been written by a king (see v. 16 and note; cf. also Hezekiah's thanksgiving, Isa 38:10–20); its language echoes many of the psalms of David. In Jewish liturgy (see introduction to Ps 113–118), the singular personal pronoun must have been used corporately (see note on Ps 30 title), and the references to "death" may have been understood as alluding to the Egyptian bondage and/or the exile.

Structurally, the psalm is so designed that the second half (vv. 10–19) mirrors the first half (vv. 1–9)—which may be why the Septuagint (the pre-Christian Greek translation of the OT) divides the psalm into two. Basically the theme is developed in a series of couplets (vv. 1–2,3–4,5–6, 8–9//10–11,13–14,15–16, 17–19—the final couplet being expanded into a triplet). Verse 7 (between the last two couplets of the first half) and v. 12 (between the first two couplets of the second half) have striking verbal and thematic links (see notes on those verses).

116:1–2 I love the Lord because he has heard and saved me (cf. 18:1).

116:2 *I will call on him.* In him I will trust, and my prayers will ever be to him. "I will call/I called" is a key thematic phrase (in Hebrew one word, and always in the same form as here), occurring twice in each half of the psalm (vv. 2,4,13,17).

116:3–4 The deadly threat (see 18:4–6).

116:3 *cords of death.* See note on 18:5.

116:5–6 Testimony to God's goodness—echoing Ex 34:6.

116:5 *gracious ... righteous ... compassion.* See 145:8,17; cf. 112:4. *our God.* The author is conscious of those about him; he is praising the Lord "in the presence of all his people" (vv. 14,18).

116:6 *unwary.* Those who are childlike in their sense of dependence on and trust in the Lord (see note on 19:7).

116:7 *rest.* A state of unthreatened well-being (cf. Jer 6:16; see 1Ki 5:4; see also note on 23:2, "quiet waters"). *my soul.* See note on 103:1–2,22. *has been good.* See v. 12 and note.

8 For you, LORD, have delivered me[u] from
death,
my eyes from tears,
my feet from stumbling,
9 that I may walk before the LORD[v]
in the land of the living.[w]

10 I trusted[x] in the LORD when I said,
"I am greatly afflicted";[y]
11 in my alarm I said,
"Everyone is a liar."[z]

12 What shall I return to the LORD
for all his goodness[a] to me?

13 I will lift up the cup of salvation
and call on the name[b] of the LORD.
14 I will fulfill my vows[c] to the LORD
in the presence of all his people.

15 Precious in the sight[d] of the LORD
is the death of his faithful servants.[e]
16 Truly I am your servant, LORD;[f]
I serve you just as my mother did;[g]
you have freed me from my
chains.[h]

17 I will sacrifice a thank offering[i] to you
and call on the name of the LORD.

18 I will fulfill my vows[j] to the LORD
in the presence of all his people,
19 in the courts[k] of the house of the
LORD—
in your midst, Jerusalem.[l]

Praise the LORD.[a]

Psalm 117

1 Praise the LORD,[m] all you nations;[n]
extol him, all you peoples.
2 For great is his love[o] toward us,
and the faithfulness of the LORD[p]
endures forever.

Praise the LORD.[a]

Psalm 118

1 Give thanks to the LORD,[q] for he is
good;[r]
his love endures forever.[s]

[a] 19,2 Hebrew *Hallelu Yah*

116:8 [u]S Ps 86:13 **116:9** [v]S Ge 5:22; Ps 56:13; 89:15 [w]S Job 28:13; Ps 27:13; Isa 38:11; Jer 11:19 **116:10** [x]2Co 4:13* [y]Ps 9:18; 72:2; S 107:17; 119:67,71,75 **116:11** [z]Jer 9:3-5; Hos 7:13; Mic 6:12; Ro 3:4 **116:12** [a]Ps 103:2; 106:1 **116:13** [b]S Ps 105:1 **116:14** [c]S Nu 30:2; S Ps 66:13 **116:15** [d]Ps 72:14 [e]S Nu 23:10 **116:16** [f]Ps 119:125; 143:12 [g]S Ps 86:16 [h]S Job 12:18 **116:17** [i]S Lev 7:12; S Ezr 1:4 **116:18** [j]ver 14; S Lev 22:18 **116:19** [k]Ps 92:13; 96:8; 100:4; 135:2 [l]Ps 102:21 **117:1** [m]S Ps 22:23; S 103:2 [n]Ro 15:11* **117:2** [o]S Ps 17:7; S 103:11 [p]Ps 119:90; 146:6 **118:1** [q]S 1Ch 16:8 [r]S 2Ch 5:13; S 7:3 [s]S Ezr 3:11

116:8–9 The deliverance experienced—a return to the theme of vv. 3–4.
116:10–11 Introduction to the second half of the psalm, an elaboration on the introduction to the first half (vv. 1–2).
116:10 *I trusted in the LORD.* The author speaks of his faith that moved him to call on the Lord when he was threatened. *I am greatly afflicted.* This and the quotation in v. 11 should perhaps be taken, together with the one in v. 4, as a brief recollection of the prayer offered when the psalmist was in distress. The threat of death from which he had been delivered was brought on by the false accusations of enemies, as in Ps 109 (see notes on 5:9; 10:7). (For another interpretation, see following note.)
116:11 *Everyone is a liar.* The heart of the accusation he had lodged against his false accusers (for examples of similar accusations, see 5:9–10; 35:11,15; 109:2–4). Others interpret these words as a declaration that all people offer but a false hope for deliverance (see 60:11; 118:8–9)—therefore the psalmist called on the Lord.
116:12 *goodness.* The Hebrew for this word occurs only here in the OT but represents the same basic root as "has been good" in v. 7. Verses 7,12, taken together, concisely focus the central movement of the psalm's theme.
116:13–14 Answer to the question in v. 12: By offering to the Lord those expressions of devotion he desires (compare vv. 13–14,17–18 with 50:14–15,23).
116:13 *cup of salvation.* Often thought to be related to the cup of the Passover meal referred to in Mt 26:27 and parallels, but far more likely the cup of wine drunk at the festal meal that climaxed a thank offering (cf. 22:26,29; Lev 7:11–21)—called the "cup of salvation" because the thank offering and its meal celebrated deliverance by the Lord. See the parallel with "sacrifice a thank offering" in the corresponding series in vv. 17–18.
116:14 *vows.* To praise the Lord (see note on 7:17).
116:15–16 Elaboration on vv. 3–4. Note the references to "death" in vv. 3,15; cf. vv. 8–9.
116:15 *Precious . . . is the death.* Not in the sense of highly valued but of that which is carefully watched over; cf. the analogous expression, "precious is their blood in his sight" (72:14). *his faithful servants.* See note on 4:3.
116:16 *your servant.* This may identify the psalmist as the Lord's anointed (see 78:70), but in any event as one devoted to the Lord (see 19:11,13). *I serve you just as my mother did.* See 86:16 and note.
116:17–19 Reiteration of the vows of vv. 13–14.
116:17 *sacrifice a thank offering.* See note on v. 13.
116:19 *courts.* Of the temple (see 84:2,10; 2Ki 21:5; 23:11–12).
Ps 117 The shortest psalm in the Psalter—and the shortest chapter in the Bible—Ps 117 is an expanded Hallelujah (cf. introduction to Ps 119). It may originally have served as the conclusion to the preceding collection of Hallelujah psalms (Ps 111–116)—of which it is the seventh. All nations and peoples are called on to praise the Lord (as in 47:1; 67:3–5; 96:7; 98:4; 100:1; see note on 9:1) for his great love and enduring faithfulness toward Israel (see Isa 12:4–6). Thus the Hallelujahs of the OT Psalter, when fully expounded, express that great truth, so often emphasized in the OT, that the destiny of all peoples is involved in what God was doing in and for his people Israel (see, e.g., 2:8–12; 47:9; 67:2; 72:17; 102:15; 110). See introduction to Ps 113–118.
117:1 Quoted in Ro 15:11 as proof that the salvation of Gentiles and the glorifying of God by Gentiles was not a divine afterthought.
117:2 The reason for the praise. *love . . . faithfulness.* That is, love-and-faithfulness (see 36:5 and note; see also note on 3:7). *love.* See note on 6:4.
Ps 118 A hymn of thanksgiving for deliverance from enemies. The setting may be that of a Davidic king leading the nation in a liturgy of thanksgiving for deliverance and victory after a hard-fought battle with a powerful confederacy of nations (cf. 2Ch 20:27–28; see note on v. 19). The speaker in vv. 5–21 is the king. As the last song of the Egyptian Hallel (Ps 113–118; see note on Ps 111–119), this psalm may have been the hymn sung by Jesus and his disciples at the conclusion of the Last Supper (see Mt 26:30 and note).
Following a liturgical call to praise (vv. 1–4), the king offers a song of thanksgiving for deliverance and victory in battle

[2]Let Israel say:[t]
"His love endures forever."[u]
[3]Let the house of Aaron say:[v]
"His love endures forever."
[4]Let those who fear the LORD[w] say:
"His love endures forever."

[5]When hard pressed,[x] I cried to the
LORD;
he brought me into a spacious
place.[y]
[6]The LORD is with me;[z] I will not be
afraid.
What can mere mortals do to me?[a]
[7]The LORD is with me; he is my
helper.[b]
I look in triumph on my enemies.[c]

[8]It is better to take refuge in the LORD[d]
than to trust in humans.[e]
[9]It is better to take refuge in the LORD
than to trust in princes.[f]
[10]All the nations surrounded me,
but in the name of the LORD I cut
them down.[g]
[11]They surrounded me[h] on every side,[i]
but in the name of the LORD I cut
them down.
[12]They swarmed around me like bees,[j]
but they were consumed as quickly
as burning thorns;[k]
in the name of the LORD I cut them
down.[l]
[13]I was pushed back and about to fall,
but the LORD helped me.[m]

118:2 [t]Ps 115:9 [u]Ps 106:1; 136:1-26 **118:3** [v]Ex 30:30; Ps 115:10 **118:4** [w]S Ps 115:11 **118:5** [x]Ps 18:6; 31:7; 77:2; 120:1 [y]ver 21; Ps 34:4; 86:7; 116:1; 138:3 **118:6** [z]S Dt 31:6; Heb 13:6* [a]S Ps 56:4 **118:7** [b]S Dt 33:29 [c]S Ps 54:7 **118:8** [d]Ps 2:12; 5:11; 9:9; 37:3; 40:4; Isa 25:4; 57:13 [e]2Ch 32:7-8; S Ps 108:12; S Isa 2:22 **118:9** [f]Ps 146:3 **118:10** [g]S Ps 37:9 **118:11** [h]Ps 88:17 [i]Ps 3:6 **118:12** [j]Dt 1:44 [k]S Ps 58:9 [l]Ps 37:9 **118:13** [m]ver 7; 2Ch 18:31; Ps 86:17 **118:14** [n]S Ex 15:2 [o]S Ps 62:2 **118:15** [p]S Job 8:21; S Ps 106:5 [q]S Ex 15:6; Ps 89:13; 108:6 [r]Lk 1:51

[14]The LORD is my strength[n] and my
defense[a];
he has become my salvation.[o]

[15]Shouts of joy[p] and victory
resound in the tents of the righteous:
"The LORD's right hand[q] has done
mighty things![r]
[16]The LORD's right hand is lifted high;
the LORD's right hand has done
mighty things!"
[17]I will not die[s] but live,
and will proclaim[t] what the LORD has
done.
[18]The LORD has chastened[u] me severely,
but he has not given me over to
death.[v]
[19]Open for me the gates[w] of the righteous;
I will enter[x] and give thanks to the
LORD.
[20]This is the gate of the LORD[y]
through which the righteous may
enter.[z]
[21]I will give you thanks, for you
answered me;[a]
you have become my salvation.[b]

[22]The stone[c] the builders rejected
has become the cornerstone;[d]

[a] 14 Or *song*

118:17 [s]Hab 1:12 [t]S Dt 32:3; Ps 64:9; 71:16; 73:28 **118:18** [u]Jer 31:18; 1Co 11:32; Heb 12:5 [v]Ps 86:13 **118:19** [w]S Ps 24:7 [x]Ps 100:4 **118:20** [y]Ps 122:1-2 [z]Ps 15:1-2; 24:3-4; Rev 22:14 **118:21** [a]S ver 5 [b]Ps 27:1 **118:22** [c]Isa 8:14 [d]Isa 17:10; 19:13; 28:16; Zec 4:7; 10:4; Mt 21:42; Mk 12:10; Lk 20:17*; S Ac 4:11*; 1Pe 2:7*

(vv. 5–21). A three-verse stanza (vv. 5–7) summarizing the main theme is followed by two seven-verse composite stanzas (vv. 8–14,15–21) of elaboration, each closing with the refrain: "has/have become my salvation." In vv. 22–27 the people rejoice over what the Lord has done. Thereafter, the king speaks his final word of praise (v. 28), and a liturgical conclusion (v. 29) repeats the opening call to praise, thus framing the whole.
118:1–4 The liturgical call to praise.
118:1 A conventional call to praise (shared in whole or in part with Ps 105–107; 136; 1Ch 16:8,34; 2Ch 20:21). *Give thanks.* See note on Ps 100 title. This, together with vv. 2–4 (except for the refrain) and 29, may have been by the same voice that speaks in vv. 5–21. *love.* See vv. 2–4,29; see also note on 6:4.
118:2–4 *Israel ... house of Aaron ... those who fear the LORD.* See 115:9–11 and note. Triple repetition is a common feature in this psalm (see note on 96:1–3).
118:4 *fear the LORD.* See note on 66:16.
118:5–21 The king's song of thanksgiving for deliverance and victory.
118:5–7 The introduction: I cried to the Lord; he answered; I need fear no one.
118:5 *I cried ... he brought me.* For the conjunction of this appeal and response elsewhere, see 3:4; 4:1; 17:6; 22:2; 27:7; 86:7; 91:15; 99:6; 102:2; 120:1; 138:3; 1Ki 18:24; Pr 21:13; Isa 65:24; Jer 33:3; Jnh 2:2—all these passages share the same Hebrew terms. *into a spacious place.* See 18:19 and note.
118:8–14 Reflection on the experience of the Lord's saving help—framed by vv. 8–9 and v. 14.
118:8–9 See 33:16–19; see also Ps 62; 146.
118:10 *in the name of the LORD.* See 1Sa 17:45. *name.* See vv. 11–12,26; see also note on 5:11.
118:12 *as burning thorns.* See 58:9 and note.
118:13 *fall.* Be killed (see vv. 17–18; see also note on 13:4).
118:14 Perhaps recalls the triumph song of Ex 15, but more likely the verse had become a widely used testimony of praise to the Lord (see Isa 12:2).
118:15–21 Celebration of the Lord's deliverance—framed by vv. 15–16 and v. 21.
118:15 *tents.* Dwellings. *righteous.* Israel as the people (ideally) committed in heart and life to the Lord (see v. 20; see also 68:3 and note). Cf. "the tents of the wicked" (84:10).
118:17 *live, and ... proclaim.* See 115:17–18; see also note on 6:5.
118:18 *chastened me.* The king acknowledges that the grave threat through which he has passed has also served God's purpose—to discipline him and teach him humble godliness (see 6:1; 38:1; 94:12; Dt 4:36; 8:5).
118:19 *Open for me.* This line suggests a liturgical procession (see v. 27) in which the king approaches the inner court of the temple at the head of the jubilant worshipers (see Ps 24; 68). *gates.* Those leading to the inner temple court. *of the righteous.* Often thought to be the name of a particular gateway, but more likely only descriptive here of the gate "through which the righteous may enter" (v. 20). It is possible that the procession began outside the city and that "the gates of the righteous" are the gates of Jerusalem, the city of God (see note on 24:7; see also Isa 26:2).
118:21 This closing verse of the thanksgiving song echoes the "Give thanks" of v. 1, the "brought me" of v. 5 and the testimony of v. 14.
118:22–27 The people's exultation.

118:22 *The stone the builders rejected.* Most likely a reference to the king (whose deliverance and victory

[23]the LORD has done this,
and it is marvelous[e] in our eyes.
[24]The LORD has done it this very day;
let us rejoice today and be glad.[f]

[25]LORD, save us![g]
LORD, grant us success!

[26]Blessed is he who comes[h] in the name
of the LORD.
From the house of the LORD we bless
you.[a][i]
[27]The LORD is God,[j]
and he has made his light shine[k]
on us.
With boughs in hand,[l] join in the festal
procession
up[b] to the horns of the altar.[m]

[28]You are my God, and I will praise you;
you are my God,[n] and I will exalt[o]
you.

[29]Give thanks to the LORD, for he is good;
his love endures forever.

[a] *26* The Hebrew is plural. [b] *27* Or *Bind the festal sacrifice with ropes / and take it*

118:23 [e]Mt 21:42*; Mk 12:11* **118:24** [f]S Ps 70:4 **118:25** [g]S Ps 28:9; 116:4 **118:26** [h]S Mt 11:3; 21:9*; 23:39*; Mk 11:9*; Lk 13:35*; 19:38*; Jn 12:13* [i]Ps 129:8 **118:27** [j]S 1Ki 18:21 [k]Ps 27:1; Isa 58:10; 60:1, 19, 20; Mal 4:2; 1Pe 2:9 [l]S Lev 23:40 [m]Ex 27:2 **118:28** [n]S Ge 28:21; S Ps 16:2; 63:1; Isa 25:1 [o]S Ex 15:2

are being celebrated), who had been looked on with disdain by the kings invading his realm — the builders of worldly empires. Others suppose that the stone refers to Israel, a nation held in contempt by the world powers. *cornerstone.* Lit. "head of the corner" — either a capstone over a door (a large stone used as a lintel), a large stone used to anchor and align the corner of a wall or the keystone of an arch (see Zec 4:7; 10:4). By a wordplay (pun) the author hints at "chief ruler" (the Hebrew word for "corner" is sometimes used as a metaphor for leader/ruler; see Isa 19:13; see also Jdg 20:2; 1Sa 14:38). This stone, disdained by the worldly powers, has become the most important stone in the structure of the new world order that God is bringing about through Israel. Jesus applied this verse (and v. 23) to himself (see Mt 21:42; Mk 12:10–11; Lk 20:17; see also Ac 4:11; Eph 2:20; 1Pe 2:7).

118:24 *The LORD has done it this very day ... rejoice.* This day of rejoicing was made possible by God's deliverance in the victory being celebrated. Others suppose a reference to Passover or the Festival of Tabernacles. *has done it.* Has made the "stone" the "cornerstone" (v. 22; see also vv. 15–17, 23).

118:25 Prayer for the Lord to continue to save and sustain his people (cf. note on Mt 21:9).

118:26 *who comes in the name of the LORD.* The one who with God's help had defeated the enemies "in the name of the LORD" (see vv. 10–12). *From the house of the LORD.* From God's very presence (see 134:3). *you.* The plural (see NIV text note) may have been used to exalt the king (the plural was often used with reference to God), whom God had so singularly blessed (see NIV text note on 1Ki 9:6). Alternatively, it may refer to those who have come with the king victoriously from the battle. The crowds who greeted Jesus at his entrance into Jerusalem as King used the words of vv. 25–26 (see Jn 12:13).

118:27 *made his light shine on us.* An echo of the priestly benediction (see Nu 6:25 and note). *With boughs ... up.* Apparently a call to complete the climax of the liturgy of a thank offering (see Lev 7:11–21), though others suggest the liturgy of the Festival of Tabernacles.

118:28 The king's closing reiteration of his vow in v. 21.

118:29 Renewal of the opening call to grateful praise (see v. 1 and note).

Four-horned altar from Ekron. Psalm 118:27 mentions "the horns of the altar."

Psalm 119[a]

א Aleph

[1] Blessed are those whose ways are
blameless,[p]
who walk[q] according to the law of
the LORD.[r]
[2] Blessed[s] are those who keep his
statutes[t]
and seek him[u] with all their
heart—[v]
[3] they do no wrong[w]
but follow his ways.[x]
[4] You have laid down precepts[y]
that are to be fully obeyed.[z]
[5] Oh, that my ways were steadfast
in obeying your decrees![a]
[6] Then I would not be put to shame[b]
when I consider all your commands.[c]
[7] I will praise you with an upright heart
as I learn your righteous laws.[d]
[8] I will obey your decrees;
do not utterly forsake me.[e]

ב Beth

[9] How can a young person stay on the
path of purity?[f]
By living according to your word.[g]

119:1 [p] S Ge 17:1; S Dt 18:13; Pr 11:20 [q] Ps 128:1 [r] S Ps 1:2 **119:2** [s] Ps 112:1; Isa 56:2 [t] ver 146; Ps 99:7 [u] S 1Ch 16:11; S Ps 40:16 [v] S Dt 10:12 **119:3** [w] S Ps 59:4; 1Jn 3:9; 5:18 [x] Ps 128:1; Jer 6:16; 7:23 **119:4** [y] Ps 103:18 [z] S ver 56; S Dt 6:17 **119:5** [a] S Lev 19:37

[a] This psalm is an acrostic poem, the stanzas of which begin with successive letters of the Hebrew alphabet; moreover, the verses of each stanza begin with the same letter of the Hebrew alphabet.

119:6 [b] ver 46,80 [c] ver 117 **119:7** [d] S Dt 4:8 **119:8** [e] S Ps 38:21 **119:9** [f] S Ps 39:1 [g] ver 65,169

Ps 119 The longest psalm in the Psalter—and the longest chapter in the Bible—is a devotional poem celebrating the word of God (cf. introduction to Ps 117). The author was an Israelite of exemplary piety who (1) was passionately devoted to the word of God as the word of life; (2) humbly acknowledged, nevertheless, the errant ways of his heart and life; (3) knew the pain—but also the fruits—of God's corrective discipline; and (4) had suffered much at the hands of those who arrogantly disregarded God's word and made him the target of their hostility, ridicule and slander. It is possible that he was a priest (see notes on vv. 23,57)—and the psalm might well be a vehicle for priestly instruction in godliness. He elaborated on the themes of 19:7–13 and interwove with them many prayers for deliverance, composing a massive alphabetic acrostic (see NIV text note) that demands patient, meditative reading. Of all the psalms, this one is the most likely to have been composed originally in writing and intended to be read rather than sung or recited. Most of its lines are addressed to God, mingling prayers with professions of devotion to God's law. Yet, as the opening verses (and perhaps also its elaborate acrostic form) make clear, it was intended for godly instruction (in the manner of Ps 1; see v. 9 and note). For its placement in the Psalter, see introduction to Ps 111–119. See also notes on 111:1; 112:1.

Whereas elsewhere in the Psalter the focus falls primarily on God's mighty acts of creation and redemption and his rule over all the world, here devotion to the word of God (and the God of the word) is the dominant theme. The author highlights two aspects of that word: (1) God's directives for life and (2) God's promises—the one calling for obedience, the other for faith (the two elements of true godliness; see 34:8–14 and note). In referring to these, he makes use of eight Hebrew terms supplied him by OT traditions: *torah*, "law"; *'edot*, "statutes"; *piqqudim*, "precepts"; *miṣwot*, "commands, commandments"; *mishpaṭim*, "laws" (all shared with 19:7–9; *mishpaṭim* is translated "decrees" in 19:9); *ḥuqqim*, "decrees"; *dabar*, "word" (sometimes in the sense of "law," sometimes in the sense of "promise"); *'imrah*, "word," but more often "promise." These terms he distributes throughout the 22 stanzas (using all eight in *He*, *Waw*, *Heth*, *Yodh*, *Kaph*, *Pe*—never using less than six), employing a different order in each stanza. It may be that the availability of these eight terms determined (in large part) for the author the decision to devote eight verses to each letter of the alphabet.

Apart from the obvious formal structure dictated by the chosen acrostic form, little need (or can) be said. It must be noted, however, that the first three and the last three verses were designed as introduction and conclusion to the whole. The former sets the tone of instruction in godly wisdom; the latter succinctly restates and summarizes the main themes. It may also be observed that the middle of the psalm has been marked by a similar three-verse introduction to the second half (see note on vv. 89–91). The following notes point out continuities of thought and possible structure within stanzas.

119:1–3 General introduction.

119:1–2 *Blessed.* See note on 1:1.

119:1 *whose ways are blameless.* This opening general description is further elaborated in the rest of the introduction, which concludes with an equally general statement: "follow his ways" (v. 3). See Ge 17:1; cf. Ge 26:5 and note. *law.* Hebrew *torah*, a collective term for God's covenant directives for his people (see Dt 4:44 and note). "Law" often came, especially later, to have a broader reference—the whole Pentateuch (see Lk 24:44 and note) or even the whole OT (see Jn 10:34; 12:34; 15:25; 1Co 14:21 and notes)—but here it is limited by the synonyms with which it is used interchangeably.

119:2 *statutes.* Hebrew *'edot*, a specifically covenantal term referring to stipulations laid down by the covenant Lord (see 25:10,"demands"; Dt 4:45,"stipulations"). *seek him with all their heart.* See Dt 4:29 and note. *heart.* See v. 7; see also note on 4:7.

119:3 *ways.* The Hebrew for this word occurs only rarely in this psalm but is common in Deuteronomy and elsewhere as a general reference to God's covenant requirements (see note on 25:4)—used here to balance "ways" in v. 1.

119:4–8 Those who obey God's law (see vv. 4–5,8) can hope for God's help (see vv. 6–8).

119:4 *precepts.* Hebrew *piqqudim*, covenant regulations laid down by the Lord (see 19:8; 111:7).

119:5 *decrees.* Hebrew *ḥuqqim*, covenant directives (see Dt 6:2; 28:15,45; 30:10,16; 1Ki 11:11), emphasizing their fixed character.

119:6 *not be put to shame.* The psalmist would not suffer poverty, sickness or humiliation at the hands of his enemies and so become the object of sneers (see vv. 31,46,80; 25:2–3,20; see also introduction to this psalm), but he would have reason to praise the Lord (see v. 7) for blessings received and deliverances granted because the Lord does not forsake him (see v. 8). *consider.* Respect, have regard for (see v. 15; 74:20). *commands.* Hebrew *miṣwot*, covenant directives (see Ex 20:6; 24:12; Dt 4:2) designated specifically as that which God has commanded.

119:7 *righteous.* One of the author's favorite characterizations of God's law (see vv. 62,75,106,123,138,144,160,164,172; see also 19:9). *laws.* Hebrew *mishpaṭim*, covenant directives (see Ex 21:1; 24:3; Dt 4:1), as the laws laid down by a ruler (king).

119:8 *not … forsake me.* To poverty, sickness or my enemies (cf. 9:10; 22:1; 27:9–10; 38:21; 71:9,11,18).

119:9 a *young person.* Indicates instruction addressed to the

10 I seek you with all my heart;[h]
do not let me stray from your
commands.[i]
11 I have hidden your word in my heart[j]
that I might not sin[k] against you.
12 Praise be[l] to you, LORD;
teach me[m] your decrees.[n]
13 With my lips I recount
all the laws that come from your
mouth.[o]
14 I rejoice in following your statutes[p]
as one rejoices in great riches.
15 I meditate on your precepts[q]
and consider your ways.
16 I delight[r] in your decrees;
I will not neglect your word.

ג Gimel

17 Be good to your servant[s] while I live,
that I may obey your word.[t]
18 Open my eyes that I may see
wonderful things in your law.
19 I am a stranger on earth;[u]
do not hide your commands from me.
20 My soul is consumed[v] with longing
for your laws[w] at all times.
21 You rebuke the arrogant,[x] who are
accursed,[y]
those who stray[z] from your
commands.

119:10 [h] S Ps 9:1 [i] ver 21,118 **119:11** [j] S Dt 6:6; S Job 22:22 [k] ver 133,165; Ps 18:22-23; 19:13; Pr 3:23; Isa 63:13 **119:12** [l] Ps 28:6 [m] Ps 143:8,10 [n] S Ex 18:20 **119:13** [o] ver 72 **119:14** [p] ver 111 **119:15** [q] ver 97,148; Ps 1:2 **119:16** [r] S Ps 112:1 **119:17** [s] Ps 13:6; 116:7 [t] ver 67; Ps 103:20 **119:19** [u] S Ge 23:4; Heb 11:13 **119:20** [v] Ps 42:2; 84:2 [w] ver 131; S Ps 63:1; Isa 26:9 **119:21** [x] ver 51; Job 30:1; Ps 5:5; Jer 20:7; 50:32; Da 4:37; Mal 3:15 [y] Dt 27:26 [z] S ver 10

22 Remove from me their scorn[a] and
contempt,
for I keep your statutes.[b]
23 Though rulers sit together and
slander me,
your servant will meditate on your
decrees.
24 Your statutes are my delight;
they are my counselors.

ד Daleth

25 I am laid low in the dust;[c]
preserve my life[d] according to your
word.[e]
26 I gave an account of my ways and you
answered me;
teach me your decrees.[f]
27 Cause me to understand the way of
your precepts,
that I may meditate on your
wonderful deeds.[g]
28 My soul is weary with sorrow;[h]
strengthen me[i] according to your
word.[j]
29 Keep me from deceitful ways;[k]
be gracious to me[l] and teach me
your law.

119:22 [a] Ps 39:8 [b] ver 2 **119:25** [c] Ps 44:25 [d] ver 50,107; Ps 143:11 [e] ver 9 **119:26** [f] Ps 25:4; 27:11; 86:11 **119:27** [g] Ps 105:2; 145:5 **119:28** [h] Ps 6:7; 116:3; Isa 51:11; Jer 45:3 [i] Ps 18:1; Isa 40:29; 41:10 [j] ver 9 **119:29** [k] Ps 26:4 [l] S Nu 6:25

young after the manner of the wisdom teachers (see 34:11; Pr 1:4; Ecc 11:9; 12:1; see also the first two paragraphs of Introduction to Proverbs: Purpose and Teaching). *purity.* Free from all moral taint (see 73:13). *word.* Hebrew *dabar*, a general designation for God's (word) revelation but here used with special reference to his law (sometimes promises).

119:10 *I seek you.* The author's devotion is first of all to the God of the law and the promises; they have meaning for him only because they are God's word of life for him. *heart.* See v. 11; see also note on 4:7.

119:11 *word.* Hebrew *'imrah*, a synonym of *dabar* ("word"; see note on v. 9; see also Dt 33:9; Pr 30:5). Except where noted, as here, "word" in this psalm is *dabar*; *'imrah* is usually translated "promise."

119:13 *recount.* Either in meditation or in liturgies of covenant commitment to the Lord (see 50:16, "recite").

119:14 *as one rejoices in great riches.* See vv. 72,111,162.

119:15 *ways.* The Hebrew for this word is a synonym of the Hebrew for "ways" in v. 3 (see 25:4 and note).

119:17–24 Devotion to God's law marks the Lord's servant but alienates him from the arrogant (v. 21) of the world.

119:17 *that I may obey.* Out of gratitude for God's care and blessing.

119:18 *wonderful things.* Usually ascribed to God's redeeming acts (see 9:1 and note)—but God's law also contains wonders (see v. 27) to contemplate, if only God opens a person's eyes.

119:19 *stranger on earth.* As a servant of the Lord, i.e., a citizen of his kingdom, the psalmist is not at home in any of the kingdoms of the world (see 39:12 and note; see also note on v. 54).

119:20 *My soul is.* I am (see vv. 28,81; see also note on 6:3).

119:21 *the arrogant.* Those who are a law to themselves, most fully described in 10:2–11 (see vv. 51,69,78,85,122; see also note on 31:23). The author has suffered much from their hostility because of his zeal for God and his law, as the next two verses and many others indicate. *accursed.* Ripe for God's judgment.

119:22 *scorn and contempt.* Of the arrogant.

119:23 *rulers.* Because the author mentions also speaking "before kings" (v. 46) and being persecuted by "rulers" (v. 161), it may be that he held some official position, such as priest (one of whose functions it would have been to teach God's law; see Lev 10:11; Ezr 7:6; Ne 8:2–8; Jer 2:8; 18:18; Mal 2:7; see also note on v. 57). The kings and rulers referred to may have been Israelite in the time of the monarchy but more likely were local rulers in the postexilic Persian imperial system. *sit.* As those securely settled in the world—not as strangers (cf. v. 19). *together and slander.* As they share their worldly counsels, they speak derisively of the one who stands apart because he delights in God's statutes and makes them his "counselors" (v. 24).

119:25–32 Whether "laid low" (v. 25) or having his understanding broadened (v. 32), he is determined to "hold fast" (v. 31) to God's word.

119:25 *laid low.* The author speaks much of his sorrow, suffering and affliction (see vv. 28,50,67, 71,75,83,92,107,143,153). It is likely that the ridicule, slander and persecution from his adversaries are usually occasioned by this suffering of God's devoted servant, who makes God's word (his law and promises) the hope of his life (see vv. 42, 51,65,69,78,85,95,110,134,141,150,154,157,161; see also notes on v. 6; 5:9; 31:11–12). *in the dust.* See 44:25 and note. *word.* Especially its promises, as also in vv. 28,37,42,49,65, 74,81,107,114,147.

119:27 *wonderful deeds.* See note on v. 18.

119:29 *deceitful ways.* Ways that seem right but lead to death (see Pr 14:12 and note)—in contrast to the ways prescribed by God's law, which are trustworthy (see

30 I have chosen[m] the way of faithfulness;[n]
I have set my heart[o] on your laws.
31 I hold fast[p] to your statutes, LORD;
do not let me be put to shame.
32 I run in the path of your commands,
for you have broadened my understanding.

ה He

33 Teach me,[q] LORD, the way of your decrees,
that I may follow it to the end.[a]
34 Give me understanding,[r] so that I may keep your law[s]
and obey it with all my heart.[t]
35 Direct me[u] in the path of your commands,[v]
for there I find delight.[w]
36 Turn my heart[x] toward your statutes
and not toward selfish gain.[y]
37 Turn my eyes away from worthless things;
preserve my life[z] according to your word.[b][a]
38 Fulfill your promise[b] to your servant,
so that you may be feared.
39 Take away the disgrace[c] I dread,
for your laws are good.
40 How I long[d] for your precepts!
In your righteousness preserve my life.[e]

ו Waw

41 May your unfailing love[f] come to me, LORD,
your salvation, according to your promise;[g]

119:30 [m] S Jos 24:22 [n] S Ps 26:3 [o] S Ps 108:1 **119:31** [p] S Dt 10:20 **119:33** [q] ver 12 **119:34** [r] ver 27, 73, 144, 169; S Job 32:8; Pr 2:6; Da 2:21; Jas 1:5 [s] S Dt 6:25 [t] ver 69 **119:35** [u] Ps 25:4-5 [v] ver 32 [w] S Ps 1:2 **119:36** [x] S Jos 24:23 [y] Eze 33:31 **119:37** [z] ver 25; Ps 71:20 [a] ver 9 **119:38** [b] S Nu 23:19 **119:39** [c] ver 22; Ps 69:9; 89:51; Isa 25:8; 51:7; 54:4 **119:40** [d] ver 20 [e] ver 25, 149, 154 **119:41** [f] S Ps 6:4 [g] ver 76, 116, 154, 170 **119:42** [h] Pr 27:11 [i] S Ps 42:10 **119:43** [j] S 1Ki 17:24 [k] ver 74, 81, 114, 147 **119:44** [l] ver 33, 34, 55; S Dt 6:25 **119:45** [m] ver 94, 155 **119:46** [n] Mt 10:18; Ac 26:1-2 [o] S ver 6 **119:47** [p] ver 77, 143; S Ps 112:1 [q] ver 97, 127, 159, 163, 165 **119:48** [r] S Ge 24:63

42 then I can answer[h] anyone who taunts me,[i]
for I trust in your word.
43 Never take your word of truth from my mouth,[j]
for I have put my hope[k] in your laws.
44 I will always obey your law,[l]
for ever and ever.
45 I will walk about in freedom,
for I have sought out your precepts.[m]
46 I will speak of your statutes before kings[n]
and will not be put to shame,[o]
47 for I delight[p] in your commands
because I love them.[q]
48 I reach out for your commands, which I love,
that I may meditate[r] on your decrees.

ז Zayin

49 Remember your word[s] to your servant,
for you have given me hope.[t]
50 My comfort in my suffering is this:
Your promise preserves my life.[u]
51 The arrogant mock me[v] unmercifully,
but I do not turn[w] from your law.
52 I remember,[x] LORD, your ancient laws,
and I find comfort in them.
53 Indignation grips me[y] because of the wicked,
who have forsaken your law.[z]
54 Your decrees are the theme of my song[a]
wherever I lodge.

[a] 33 Or *follow it for its reward* [b] 37 Two manuscripts of the Masoretic Text and Dead Sea Scrolls; most manuscripts of the Masoretic Text *life in your way*

119:49 [s] ver 9 [t] ver 43 **119:50** [u] S ver 25 **119:51** [v] S ver 21; S Job 16:10; S 17:2 [w] S Job 23:11 **119:52** [x] Ps 103:18 **119:53** [y] S Ex 32:19; S 33:4 [z] Ps 89:30 **119:54** [a] ver 172; Ps 101:1; 138:5

vv. 86,138) and true (see vv. 142,151,160). *teach me your law.* By keeping me true to your law, let me enjoy your blessings.
119:30 *way of faithfulness.* See note on v. 29.
119:31 *put to shame.* See note on v. 6.
119:32 *broadened my understanding.* See 1Ki 4:29, "breadth of understanding."
119:33–40 Prayer for instruction in God's will as he longs for his precepts.
119:34 *heart.* See v. 36; see also note on 4:7.
119:36–37 *heart ... eyes.* See 101:2b–3a and note.
119:38 *that you may be feared.* The Lord's saving acts in fulfillment of his promises contribute to the recognition that he is the true God (see 130:4; 2Sa 7:25–26; 1Ki 8:39–40; Jer 33:8–9).
119:39 *disgrace I dread.* See notes on vv. 6,25.
119:40 *righteousness.* See note on 4:1.
119:41–48 May the Lord deliver me and not take his truth from my mouth; then I will honor his law in my life and speak of it before kings, for I love his commands.
119:41 *love.* See vv. 64,76,88,124,149,159; see also note on 6:4.
119:42 *anyone who taunts me.* See note on v. 25 ("laid low"). *word.* See note on v. 25.
119:43 *word of truth from my mouth.* See v. 13 and note; see also v. 46.
119:45 *freedom.* Lit. "a wide space," i.e., unconfined by affliction or oppression (see 18:19 and note).
119:46 *before kings.* Such will be his boldness (see note on v. 23).
119:48 *I reach out for.* An act accompanying praise (as in 63:4; 134:2); so the sense may be: I praise.
119:49–56 God's word is my comfort and my guide whatever my circumstances.
119:49 *word.* See note on v. 25.
119:50–51 *in my suffering ... The arrogant mock.* See note on v. 25 ("laid low").
119:51 *arrogant.* See note on v. 21.
119:52 *ancient.* God's law is not fickle but is grounded firmly in his unchanging moral character. This is a major source of the author's comfort and one of the main reasons he cherishes the law so highly (see vv. 89,144,152,160).
119:53 *Indignation grips me.* Zeal for God's law (see vv. 136,139) awakens righteous anger against those who reject it (see vv. 113,115,158) and brings abhorrence of all that is contrary to it (see vv. 104,128,163), but it draws together those who honor it (see v. 63).
119:54 *wherever I lodge.* The sense may be that of v. 19 (see note there).

55 In the night, LORD, I remember[b] your
name,
that I may keep your law.[c]
56 This has been my practice:
I obey your precepts.[d]

ח Heth

57 You are my portion,[e] LORD;
I have promised to obey your words.[f]
58 I have sought[g] your face with all my
heart;
be gracious to me[h] according to your
promise.[i]
59 I have considered my ways[j]
and have turned my steps to your
statutes.
60 I will hasten and not delay
to obey your commands.[k]
61 Though the wicked bind me with ropes,
I will not forget[l] your law.
62 At midnight[m] I rise to give you thanks
for your righteous laws.[n]
63 I am a friend to all who fear you,[o]
to all who follow your precepts.[p]
64 The earth is filled with your love,[q]
LORD;
teach me your decrees.[r]

ט Teth

65 Do good[s] to your servant
according to your word,[t] LORD.
66 Teach me knowledge[u] and good
judgment,
for I trust your commands.
67 Before I was afflicted[v] I went astray,[w]
but now I obey your word.[x]
68 You are good,[y] and what you do is
good;
teach me your decrees.[z]

119:55 [b] ver 62, 72; Ps 1:2; 42:8; S 63:6; 77:2; Isa 26:9; Ac 16:25 [c] S ver 44
119:56 [d] ver 4, 100, 134, 168; S Nu 15:40
119:57 [e] S Dt 32:9; Jer 51:19; La 3:24 [f] ver 17, 67, 101
119:58 [g] S Dt 4:29; S 1Ch 16:11; Ps 34:4 [h] S Ge 43:29; S Ezr 9:8 [i] ver 41
119:59 [j] Jos 24:14-15; S Ps 39:1
119:60 [k] ver 115
119:61 [l] ver 83, 109, 153, 176
119:62 [m] S ver 55; Ac 16:25 [n] ver 7
119:63 [o] Ps 15:4; 101:6-7; 103:11 [p] ver 56; Ps 111:10
119:64 [q] Ps 33:5 [r] ver 12, 108
119:65 [s] ver 17; Ps 125:4; Isa 50:2; 59:1; Mic 2:7 [t] S ver 9
119:66 [u] S Ps 51:6
119:67 [v] S Ps 116:10 [w] S Ps 95:10; S Jer 8:4 [x] S ver 17
119:68 [y] Ps 100:5; 106:1; 107:1; 135:3 [z] S Ex 18:20
119:69 [a] Job 13:4; Ps 109:2

69 Though the arrogant have smeared me
with lies,[a]
I keep your precepts with all my
heart.
70 Their hearts are callous[b] and unfeeling,
but I delight in your law.
71 It was good for me to be afflicted[c]
so that I might learn your decrees.
72 The law from your mouth is more
precious to me
than thousands of pieces of silver
and gold.[d]

י Yodh

73 Your hands made me[e] and formed me;
give me understanding to learn your
commands.
74 May those who fear you rejoice[f] when
they see me,
for I have put my hope in your
word.[g]
75 I know, LORD, that your laws are
righteous,[h]
and that in faithfulness[i] you have
afflicted me.
76 May your unfailing love[j] be my
comfort,
according to your promise[k] to your
servant.
77 Let your compassion[l] come to me that I
may live,
for your law is my delight.[m]
78 May the arrogant[n] be put to shame for
wronging me without cause;[o]
but I will meditate on your precepts.

119:70 [b] S Ps 17:10; Isa 29:13; Ac 28:27 **119:71** [c] ver 67, 75 **119:72** [d] S Job 28:17; S Ps 19:10 **119:73** [e] S Ge 1:27; S Job 4:17; 10:8; Ps 138:8; 139:13-16 **119:74** [f] S Ps 34:2 [g] ver 9; Ps 130:5 **119:75** [h] ver 7, 138, 172 [i] Heb 12:5-11 **119:76** [j] Ps 6:4 [k] S ver 41 **119:77** [l] Ps 90:13; 103:13 [m] S ver 47 **119:78** [n] ver 51; Jer 50:32 [o] ver 86, 161; Ps 35:19

119:55 *name.* See note on 5:11.
119:57–64 The Lord is the psalmist's true homestead because it is God's law that fills the earth with all that makes life secure and joyous. So God's promises are his hope and God's righteous laws his delight.
119:57 *portion.* May identify the author as a priest or Levite (see 73:26 and note).
119:58 *heart.* See note on 4:7.
119:61 *bind me with ropes.* Oppress me.
119:62 *give you thanks.* See note on Ps 100 title. *righteous.* See note on v. 7.
119:63 *friend.* See note on v. 53.
119:65–72 Do good to me in accordance with your goodness, even if that means affliction, because your affliction is good for me; it teaches me knowledge and good judgment from your law.
119:65 *Do good.* Cf. v. 68; see 31:19; 86:17 and notes. *word.* See note on v. 25.
119:66 *trust.* Have confidence in; God's commands are not deceitful (see note on v. 29) or fickle (see note on v. 52).
119:67 *afflicted.* At the hands of God (see v. 71; see also note on v. 25, "laid low"). *word.* See note on v. 11.
119:69 *arrogant.* See note on v. 21.
119:70 *callous and unfeeling.* Lit. "fat as grease." Similar expressions occur also in Isa 6:10; Jer 5:28 (see also 17:10).
119:72 *than thousands … of silver and gold.* See vv. 14,57, 111,162.
119:73–80 Complete your forming of me by helping me to conform to your righteous laws so that the arrogant may be put to shame and those who fear you may rejoice with me. (The stanza has a concentric structure; compare vv. 73 and 80, 74 and 79, 75 and 78, 76 and 77.)
119:73 *understanding.* What I need to perfect the work you began when you formed me.
119:74 *fear you.* See v. 79; see also note on 34:8–14. *when they see me.* When I am perfectly formed and enjoying the blessings of the godly. *word.* See note on v. 25.
119:75 *laws.* Here the Hebrew for this word (*mishpaṭim*) may refer to God's just decisions in dealing with his servant, as the rest of the verse implies (see v. 84 and note). *you have afflicted me.* See vv. 67,71.
119:76 *unfailing love.* See note on 6:4. *my comfort.* In my affliction.
119:77 *that I may live.* And not perish in my affliction.
119:78 *the arrogant.* See note on v. 21. *be put to shame.* As they have subjected me to shame (see note on 5:10). *for wronging me.* See note on v. 25 ("laid low").

79 May those who fear you turn to me,
those who understand your statutes.[p]
80 May I wholeheartedly follow[q] your
decrees,[r]
that I may not be put to shame.[s]

כ Kaph

81 My soul faints[t] with longing for your
salvation,[u]
but I have put my hope[v] in your
word.
82 My eyes fail,[w] looking for your
promise;[x]
I say, "When will you comfort me?"
83 Though I am like a wineskin in the
smoke,
I do not forget[y] your decrees.
84 How long[z] must your servant wait?
When will you punish my
persecutors?[a]
85 The arrogant[b] dig pits[c] to trap me,
contrary to your law.
86 All your commands are trustworthy;[d]
help me,[e] for I am being persecuted[f]
without cause.[g]
87 They almost wiped me from the earth,
but I have not forsaken[h] your
precepts.
88 In your unfailing love[i] preserve my life,[j]
that I may obey the statutes[k] of your
mouth.

ל Lamedh

89 Your word, LORD, is eternal;[l]
it stands firm in the heavens.
90 Your faithfulness[m] continues through
all generations;[n]
you established the earth, and it
endures.[o]
91 Your laws endure[p] to this day,
for all things serve you.[q]
92 If your law had not been my delight,[r]
I would have perished in my
affliction.[s]
93 I will never forget[t] your precepts,
for by them you have preserved my
life.[u]
94 Save me,[v] for I am yours;
I have sought out your precepts.[w]
95 The wicked are waiting to destroy me,[x]
but I will ponder your statutes.[y]
96 To all perfection I see a limit,
but your commands are boundless.[z]

מ Mem

97 Oh, how I love your law![a]
I meditate[b] on it all day long.
98 Your commands are always with me
and make me wiser[c] than my
enemies.
99 I have more insight than all my
teachers,
for I meditate on your statutes.[d]
100 I have more understanding than the
elders,
for I obey your precepts.[e]

119:79 [p] ver 27, 125 **119:80** [q] ver 1; S 1Ki 8:61 [r] S Ge 26:5 [s] S ver 6 **119:81** [t] ver 20; Ps 84:2 [u] ver 123 [v] S ver 43 **119:82** [w] S Ps 6:7; 69:3; La 2:11 [x] ver 41, 123 **119:83** [y] S ver 61 **119:84** [z] Ps 6:3; Rev 6:10 [a] ver 51; Jer 12:3; 15:15; 20:11 **119:85** [b] ver 51 [c] Ps 35:7; 57:6; Jer 18:20,22 **119:86** [d] ver 138 [e] S Ps 109:26 [f] S Ps 7:1 [g] S ver 78 **119:87** [h] ver 150; Isa 1:4,28; 58:2; 59:13 **119:88** [i] ver 124; Ps 51:1; 109:26 [j] S Ps 41:2 [k] ver 2,100,129, 134,168 **119:89** [l] ver 111,144; S Ps 111:8; Isa 51:6; S Mt 5:18; 1Pe 1:25 **119:90** [m] S Ps 36:5 [n] S Ps 45:17 [o] S Job 8:19; Ps 148:6 **119:91** [p] Jer 33:25 [q] Ps 104:2-4; Jer 31:35 **119:92** [r] Ps 37:4; S 112:1 [s] ver 50,67 **119:93** [t] ver 83 [u] S Ps 103:5 **119:94** [v] ver 146; Ps 54:1; 116:4; Jer 17:14; 31:18; 42:11 [w] S ver 45 **119:95** [x] S Ps 69:4 [y] ver 99 **119:96** [z] Ps 19:7 **119:97** [a] S ver 47 [b] S ver 15 **119:98** [c] ver 130; S Dt 4:6; Ps 19:7; 2Ti 3:15 **119:99** [d] ver 15 **119:100** [e] S ver 56; S Dt 6:17

119:79 *turn to me.* See v. 63 and note on v. 53.
119:80 *not be put to shame.* See note on v. 6.
119:81–88 Save me from my affliction and my persecutors, according to your promises, and I will obey your statutes. This last stanza of the first half of the psalm, like the closing stanza, is dominated by prayer for God's help (see note on v. 25).
119:81 *soul.* See note on 6:3.
119:82 *My eyes fail.* See note on 6:7.
119:83 *like a wineskin in the smoke.* As a wineskin hanging in the smoke and heat above a fire becomes smudged and shriveled, so the psalmist bears the marks of his affliction.
119:84 *How long … wait?* Lit. "How (many are) the days of your servant?" That is, do not delay the punishment of my persecutors, because my life is short. *punish.* Lit. "effect justice upon" (the Hebrew for "justice" is *mishpaṭ*; see note on v. 7, "laws"; see also note on 5:10).
119:85 *The arrogant.* See note on v. 21. *dig pits.* Probably referring to slander—public accusations that the psalmist must be guilty of vile sins or he would not be suffering such affliction (see notes on 5:9; 9:15). *contrary to your law.* See Ex 20:16.
119:86 *trustworthy.* See note on v. 29 ("deceitful ways").
119:88 *love.* See note on 6:4.
119:89–91 God's sovereign and unchanging word governs and maintains all creation. (These first three verses of the second half of the psalm teach a general truth; cf. vv. 1–3.)
119:89 *Your word.* Here God's word by which he created, maintains and governs all things (see 33:4,6; 107:20; 147:15,18). *stands firm in the heavens.* The secure order of the heavens and the earth (v. 90) declares (19:1–4) the reassuring truth that God's word (his "laws," v. 91), by which he upholds and governs all things, is enduring (eternal) and trustworthy ("your faithfulness," v. 90). And that is the larger truth that confirms the confidence of the godly in the trustworthiness of God's word (his laws and promises) of special revelation (see notes on 93:5; 96:10; see also note on v. 29, "deceitful ways").
119:90 *Your faithfulness.* An indirect reference to God's word (see v. 89 and note).
119:92 *would have perished in my affliction.* Would not have learned the way of life (see v. 93) from your law (see vv. 67,71 and note on vv. 65–72).
119:95 *The wicked.* See note on v. 21 ("the arrogant"). *waiting to destroy me.* See note on v. 25 ("laid low").
119:96 *perfection.* Probably that which has been perfected in the sense of completed, given fixed bounds so that it is no longer open-ended. *boundless.* Lit. "very broad," i.e., an inexhaustible source of wise counsel for life (see vv. 97–100).
119:97–104 Meditation on God's law yields the highest wisdom.
119:98 *my enemies.* Those arrogant ones (see note on v. 21) who place confidence in worldly wisdom.
119:99 *teachers.* Merely human teachers.
119:100 *elders.* Old men, taught by experience (see note on Ex 3:16).

101 I have kept my feet[f] from every evil
path
so that I might obey your word.[g]
102 I have not departed from your laws,[h]
for you yourself have taught[i] me.
103 How sweet are your words to my taste,
sweeter than honey[j] to my mouth![k]
104 I gain understanding[l] from your
precepts;
therefore I hate every wrong path.[m]

נ Nun

105 Your word is a lamp[n] for my feet,
a light[o] on my path.
106 I have taken an oath[p] and confirmed it,
that I will follow your righteous
laws.[q]
107 I have suffered much;
preserve my life,[r] LORD, according to
your word.
108 Accept, LORD, the willing praise of my
mouth,[s]
and teach me your laws.[t]
109 Though I constantly take my life in my
hands,[u]
I will not forget[v] your law.
110 The wicked have set a snare[w] for me,
but I have not strayed[x] from your
precepts.
111 Your statutes are my heritage forever;
they are the joy of my heart.[y]
112 My heart is set[z] on keeping your
decrees
to the very end.[a][a]

ס Samekh

113 I hate double-minded people,[b]
but I love your law.[c]
114 You are my refuge and my shield;[d]
I have put my hope[e] in your word.
115 Away from me,[f] you evildoers,
that I may keep the commands of
my God!

119:101 [f]Pr 1:15 [g]S ver 57 **119:102** [h]S Dt 17:20 [i]S Dt 4:5 **119:103** [j]S Ps 19:10 [k]Pr 24:13-14 **119:104** [l]S Ps 111:10 [m]ver 128 **119:105** [n]Pr 20:27; 2Pe 1:19 [o]ver 130; Pr 6:23 **119:106** [p]S Ne 10:29 [q]ver 7 **119:107** [r]S ver 25 **119:108** [s]Ps 51:15; 63:5; 71:8; 109:30 [t]S ver 64 **119:109** [u]S Jdg 12:3 [v]S ver 61 **119:110** [w]Ps 25:15; S 64:5; Isa 8:14; Am 3:5 [x]ver 10 **119:111** [y]ver 14,162 **119:112** [z]S Ps 108:1 [a]ver 33 **119:113** [b]S 1Ki 18:21; Jas 1:8; 4:8 [c]ver 47 **119:114** [d]S Ge 15:1; S Ps 18:2 [e]S ver 43 **119:115** [f]S Ps 6:8

119:116 [g]S Ps 18:35; 41:3; 55:22; Isa 46:4 [h]S ver 41 [i]Ro 5:5 **119:117** [j]Isa 41:10; 46:4 [k]Ps 34:4 [l]ver 6 **119:118** [m]S ver 10 **119:119** [n]Isa 1:22,25; Eze 22:18, 19 [o]ver 47

First-century oil lamp. "Your word is a lamp for my feet, a light on my path" (Ps 119:105).

116 Sustain me,[g] my God, according to
your promise,[h] and I will live;
do not let my hopes be dashed.[i]
117 Uphold me,[j] and I will be delivered;[k]
I will always have regard for your
decrees.[l]
118 You reject all who stray[m] from your
decrees,
for their delusions come to nothing.
119 All the wicked of the earth you discard
like dross;[n]
therefore I love your statutes.[o]
120 My flesh trembles[p] in fear of you;[q]
I stand in awe[r] of your laws.

ע Ayin

121 I have done what is righteous and just;[s]
do not leave me to my oppressors.
122 Ensure your servant's well-being;[t]
do not let the arrogant oppress me.[u]
123 My eyes fail,[v] looking for your
salvation,[w]
looking for your righteous promise.[x]

[a] 112 *Or decrees / for their enduring reward*

119:120 [p]S Job 4:14; S Isa 64:2 [q]S Jos 24:14 [r]Jer 10:7; Hab 3:2 **119:121** [s]S 2Sa 8:15; S Job 27:6 **119:122** [t]S Job 17:3 [u]ver 21, 121,134; Ps 106:42 **119:123** [v]Isa 38:14 [w]ver 81 [x]S ver 82

119:102 *you ... have taught me.* Through your laws.
119:103 *words.* Perhaps better understood here as "laws" (see vv. 67,133,158,172 and note on v. 11).
119:104 *hate every wrong path.* See note on v. 53.
119:105 *lamp ... light.* Apart from which I could only grope about in the darkness (see photo above).
119:106 *have taken an oath and confirmed it.* Have covenanted (see Ne 10:29).
119:107 See v. 25 and note.
119:109 *take my life in my hands.* By publicly honoring God's law even in the face of threats and hostility (see especially vv. 23,46,161).
119:110 *set a snare.* See v. 85 and note.
119:111–112 *heart.* See note on 4:7.
119:111 *my heritage.* The possession I have received from God as my homestead and that from which I draw the provisions for my life (see note on vv. 57–64).
119:113 *hate double-minded people.* See v. 115; see also note on v. 53. "Double-minded" people are "unstable in all they do" (Jas 1:8).
119:114 *word.* See note on v. 25.
119:118 *reject.* Or "shake off" or "make light of." *their delusions.* Probably their deceitful ways (see note on v. 29).
119:119 *dross.* Scum removed from molten ore or metal. The Hebrew for this word is a pun on the word for "stray" in v. 118: Those who stray are treated like dross.
119:120 *My flesh trembles.* He quivers out of his deep reverence for God.
119:121–128 As your faithful servant, I pray for deliverance from my oppressors—another stanza in which prayer for deliverance is dominant (see vv. 81–88 and note; see also note on v. 25, "laid low").
119:121 *what is righteous and just.* A phrase commonly used to sum up the whole will of God for moral action (see 106:3; Ge 18:19; 2Sa 8:15; Pr 1:3; 21:3; Isa 56:1; Jer 22:15; 33:15; Eze 18:5,19,21,17; 33:14,16,19; 45:9).
119:122 The only verse in this psalm that does not have either a direct or an indirect (as in vv. 90,121,132; see note on v. 75) reference to God's word. *the arrogant.* See note on v. 21.
119:123 *My eyes fail.* See note on 6:7.

124 Deal with your servant according to
your love[y]
and teach me your decrees.[z]
125 I am your servant;[a] give me
discernment
that I may understand your statutes.[b]
126 It is time for you to act, LORD;
your law is being broken.[c]
127 Because I love your commands[d]
more than gold,[e] more than pure
gold,[f]
128 and because I consider all your
precepts right,[g]
I hate every wrong path.[h]

פ Pe

129 Your statutes are wonderful;[i]
therefore I obey them.[j]
130 The unfolding of your words gives
light;[k]
it gives understanding to the simple.[l]
131 I open my mouth and pant,[m]
longing for your commands.[n]
132 Turn to me[o] and have mercy[p] on me,
as you always do to those who love
your name.[q]
133 Direct my footsteps according to your
word;[r]
let no sin rule[s] over me.
134 Redeem me from human oppression,[t]
that I may obey your precepts.[u]
135 Make your face shine[v] on your servant
and teach me your decrees.[w]
136 Streams of tears[x] flow from my eyes,
for your law is not obeyed.[y]

צ Tsadhe

137 You are righteous,[z] LORD,
and your laws are right.[a]
138 The statutes you have laid down are
righteous;[b]
they are fully trustworthy.[c]
139 My zeal wears me out,[d]
for my enemies ignore your words.

119:124 [y]S ver 88; S Ps 25:7 [z]ver 12
119:125 [a]S Ps 116:16 [b]S ver 79
119:126 [c]S Nu 15:31
119:127 [d]S ver 47 [e]Ps 19:10 [f]S Job 3:21
119:128 [g]S Ps 19:8 [h]ver 104, 163; Ps 31:6; Pr 13:5
119:129 [i]ver 18 [j]ver 22, S 88
119:130 [k]S ver 105 [l]S Ps 19:7
119:131 [m]Ps 42:1 [n]S ver 20
119:132 [o]S Ps 6:4 [p]S 2Sa 24:14; S Ps 9:13 [q]S Ps 5:11
119:133 [r]ver 9 [s]S ver 11; S Ro 6:16
119:134 [t]S ver 122 [u]S ver 56, S 88
119:135 [v]S Nu 6:25; Ps 4:6; 67:1; 80:3 [w]ver 12
119:136 [x]Ps 6:6; Isa 22:4; Jer 9:1, 18; 13:17; 14:17; La 1:16; 3:48 [y]ver 158; Ps 106:25; Isa 42:24; Eze 9:4
119:137 [z]S Ex 9:27; S Ezr 9:15 [a]S Ne 9:13
119:138 [b]S ver 75; S Ps 19:7 [c]ver 86
119:139 [d]Ps 69:9; Jn 2:17
119:140 [e]S Jos 23:14 [f]Ps 12:6 [g]ver 47

140 Your promises[e] have been thoroughly
tested,[f]
and your servant loves them.[g]
141 Though I am lowly and despised,[h]
I do not forget your precepts.[i]
142 Your righteousness is everlasting
and your law is true.[j]
143 Trouble and distress have come
upon me,
but your commands give me
delight.[k]
144 Your statutes are always righteous;
give me understanding[l] that I may
live.

ק Qoph

145 I call with all my heart;[m] answer me,
LORD,
and I will obey your decrees.[n]
146 I call out to you; save me[o]
and I will keep your statutes.
147 I rise before dawn[p] and cry for help;
I have put my hope in your word.
148 My eyes stay open through the
watches of the night,[q]
that I may meditate on your
promises.
149 Hear my voice[r] in accordance with
your love;[s]
preserve my life,[t] LORD, according to
your laws.
150 Those who devise wicked schemes[u]
are near,
but they are far from your law.
151 Yet you are near,[v] LORD,
and all your commands are true.[w]
152 Long ago I learned from your statutes[x]
that you established them to last
forever.[y]

119:141 [h]S Ps 22:6 [i]ver 61, 134 **119:142** [j]ver 151, 160; Ps 19:7 **119:143** [k]ver 24, S 47 **119:144** [l]S ver 34 **119:145** [m]ver 10 [n]ver 22, 55 **119:146** [o]S ver 94 **119:147** [p]Ps 5:3; 57:8; 108:2 **119:148** [q]S Ps 63:6 **119:149** [r]S Ps 27:7 [s]ver 124 [t]S ver 40 **119:150** [u]S Ps 37:7 **119:151** [v]S Ps 34:18; Php 4:5 [w]S ver 142 **119:152** [x]ver 7, 73 [y]S ver 89; S Ps 111:8; Lk 21:33

119:124 *love.* See note on 6:4.
119:126 *act.* Either in defense of his servant or in judgment on the lawbreakers or both.
119:127 *more than gold.* See vv. 14,57,72,111.
119:128 *I hate every wrong path.* See note on v. 53.
119:129 *wonderful.* See v. 18 and note.
119:130 *unfolding.* Lit. "opening," here meaning (1) the revelation of your words, (2) the interpretation (see "expound," 49:4) of your words or (3) the entering of your words into the heart. *the simple.* See 19:7 and note.
119:132 *as you always do.* Lit. "as is (your) manner" (the Hebrew for "manner" is *mishpaṭ*); hence an indirect reference (see note on v. 122) to God's law (see note on v. 7).
119:134,154 *Redeem.* Here, as often, a synonym for "deliver."
119:134 *oppression.* See note on v. 25 ("laid low").
119:135 *your face shine.* See note on 13:1 ("hide your face").
119:136 See v. 53 and note.
119:137 – 144 The Lord and his laws are righteous.
119:137 *righteous.* See note on 4:1.
119:138 *trustworthy.* See v. 142; see also note on v. 29 ("deceitful ways").
119:139 *My zeal.* See note on v. 53.
119:140 *promises.* Hebrew *'imrah*; perhaps better rendered "word" here (see note on v. 11). *tested.* Lit. "refined," i.e., God's word contains nothing worthless or useless.
119:141 *lowly and despised.* Cf. v. 143; see also note on v. 25.
119:145 – 152 Save me, Lord, and I will keep your law. As the psalm draws to a close, prayer for deliverance becomes more dominant (see note on v. 25, "laid low").
119:148 *watches of the night.* See note on Jdg 7:19; see also La 2:19.
119:149 *love.* See note on 6:4. *your laws.* Or "your justice" (complementing "your love"); Hebrew *mishpaṭ* (see note on v. 75).
119:150 *far from your law.* See vv. 21,53,85,118,126,139,155, 158.
119:151 *are true.* See note on v. 29 ("deceitful ways").
119:152 *last forever.* See note on v. 52.

ר Resh

153 Look on my suffering[z] and deliver me,[a]
for I have not forgotten[b] your law.
154 Defend my cause[c] and redeem me;[d]
preserve my life[e] according to your promise.[f]
155 Salvation is far from the wicked,
for they do not seek out[g] your decrees.
156 Your compassion, LORD, is great;[h]
preserve my life[i] according to your laws.[j]
157 Many are the foes who persecute me,[k]
but I have not turned[l] from your statutes.
158 I look on the faithless with loathing,[m]
for they do not obey your word.[n]
159 See how I love your precepts;
preserve my life,[o] LORD, in accordance with your love.
160 All your words are true;
all your righteous laws are eternal.[p]

ש Sin and Shin

161 Rulers persecute me[q] without cause,
but my heart trembles[r] at your word.
162 I rejoice[s] in your promise
like one who finds great spoil.[t]
163 I hate and detest[u] falsehood
but I love your law.[v]
164 Seven times a day I praise you
for your righteous laws.[w]
165 Great peace[x] have those who love your law,
and nothing can make them stumble.[y]
166 I wait for your salvation,[z] LORD,
and I follow your commands.
167 I obey your statutes,
for I love them[a] greatly.
168 I obey your precepts[b] and your statutes,[c]
for all my ways are known[d] to you.

ת Taw

169 May my cry come[e] before you, LORD;
give me understanding[f] according to your word.[g]
170 May my supplication come[h] before you;
deliver me[i] according to your promise.[j]
171 May my lips overflow with praise,[k]
for you teach me[l] your decrees.
172 May my tongue sing[m] of your word,
for all your commands are righteous.[n]
173 May your hand be ready to help[o] me,
for I have chosen[p] your precepts.
174 I long for your salvation,[q] LORD,
and your law gives me delight.[r]
175 Let me live[s] that I may praise you,
and may your laws sustain me.
176 I have strayed like a lost sheep.[t]
Seek your servant,
for I have not forgotten[u] your commands.

Psalm 120

A song of ascents.

1 I call on the LORD[v] in my distress,[w]
and he answers me.

119:153 [z]S Ps 13:3 [a]S Ps 3:7 [b]S Ps 44:17 **119:154** [c]Ps 35:1; Jer 50:34; Mic 7:9 [d]S 1Sa 24:15 [e]ver 25 [f]S ver 41 **119:155** [g]ver 94, 118 **119:156** [h]S Ne 9:27; Jas 5:11 [i]ver 25 [j]ver 149 **119:157** [k]S Ps 7:1 [l]S Ps 44:18 **119:158** [m]ver 104; S Ex 32:19 [n]S ver 136 **119:159** [o]ver 25; S Ps 41:2 **119:160** [p]S ver 89; S Ps 111:8 **119:161** [q]ver 23, 122, 157; 1Sa 24:14-15 [r]ver 120 **119:162** [s]S ver 111 [t]1Sa 30:16; Isa 9:3; 53:12 **119:163** [u]S ver 128 [v]ver 47 **119:164** [w]ver 7, 160 **119:165** [x]Ps 37:11; Isa 26:3, 12; 27:5; 32:17; 57:19; 66:12 [y]S ver 11; S Ps 37:24; 1Jn 2:10 **119:166** [z]ver 81 **119:167** [a]ver 47 **119:168** [b]S ver 56, S 88 [c]ver 2, 22 [d]S Job 10:4; S 23:10; Ps 139:3; Pr 5:21 **119:169** [e]S Job 16:18 [f]S ver 34 [g]S ver 9 **119:170** [h]1Ki 8:30; 2Ch 6:24; Ps 28:2; 140:6; 143:1 [i]Ps 3:7; 22:20; 59:1 [j]S ver 41 **119:171** [k]Ps 51:15; 63:3 [l]Ps 94:12; Isa 2:3; Mic 4:2 **119:172** [m]Ps 51:14 [n]ver 7, S 75 **119:173** [o]Ps 37:24; 73:23; Isa 41:10 [p]S Jos 24:22 **119:174** [q]ver 166 [r]ver 16, 24 **119:175** [s]ver 116, 159; Isa 55:3 **119:176** [t]ver 10; S Ps 95:10; Jer 50:17; Eze 34:11; S Lk 15:4 [u]S Ps 44:17 **120:1** [v]S Ps 18:6 [w]S 2Sa 22:7; S Ps 118:5

119:153–160 See note on vv. 145–152.
119:155 *the wicked.* See note on v. 21 ("the arrogant").
119:156 *your laws.* See v. 149 and note.
119:158 *word.* Hebrew *'imrah* (see note on v. 11).
119:160 *All.* Lit. "The sum of" (as in 139:17). *true.* See note on v. 29 ("deceitful ways"). *eternal.* See note on v. 52.
119:161–168 See note on vv. 145–152.
119:161 *Rulers.* See note on v. 23. *heart.* See note on 4:7.
119:162 *great spoil.* See vv. 14,72,111.
119:163 *I hate.* See note on v. 53. *falsehood.* Or "that which is (ways that are) deceitful" (see v. 29 and note).
119:164 *Seven.* A number signifying completeness—he praises God throughout the day.
119:165 *Great peace.* Complete security and well-being.
119:169–176 See note on vv. 145–152.
119:171 *overflow with praise.* Because you have delivered me.
119:172 *righteous.* See note on v. 7.
119:174–176 The conclusion to the psalm.
119:176 *I have strayed.* See Isa 53:6; the clearest expression of the author's acknowledgment that, for all his devotion to God's law, he has again and again wandered into other (deceitful) ways and, like a lost sheep, must be brought back by his heavenly Shepherd. For one who has made God's law the guide and dearest treasure of his life, the last word can only be such a confession—and such a prayer.
Ps 120–137 A collection of 15 psalms (120–134), each bearing the title "song of ascents," to which has been attached Ps 135–137. Ps 120–136 have been referred to in some Jewish traditions as the "Great Hallel" (in distinction from the "Egyptian Hallel"; see introduction to Ps 113–118). Ps 137, expressive of deep devotion to Zion/Jerusalem, the city containing the great symbols of the Lord's presence with his people, brings the collection to its close. These "songs of ascents" most likely refer to the annual religious pilgrimages to Jerusalem (see 84:5–7; Ex 23:14–17; Dt 16:16; Mic 4:2; Zec 14:16 and note), which brought the singing worshipers to Mount Zion (Isa 30:29). The spirit of these songs is similar to that of Ps 84 (cf. Ps 42–43).

Each song begins with a prayer that evokes the experience of being far from home and beset by barbarians and ends with a call to praise God in the sanctuary. In the main Hebrew text tradition the middle psalm (127) is ascribed to Solomon, while four of the others (122; 124; 131; 133), two on each side of the middle, are ascribed to David. For further observations relative to arrangement within this collection, see introductions to the individual psalms.
Ps 120 The prayer of an individual for deliverance from false accusers (see 5:9 and note). The reference to "war" (v. 7) is probably metaphorical. The theme is developed in three short stanzas: The prayer uttered (vv. 1–2), the adversaries addressed (vv. 3–4), the circumstances lamented (vv. 5–7).
120 title See introduction to Ps 120–137.
120:1–2 The prayer.
120:1 *I call ... he answers.* See note on 118:5.

[2]Save me, LORD,
from lying lips[x]
and from deceitful tongues.[y]

[3]What will he do to you,
and what more besides,
you deceitful tongue?
[4]He will punish you with a warrior's
sharp arrows,[z]
with burning coals of the broom
bush.

[5]Woe to me that I dwell in Meshek,
that I live among the tents of Kedar![a]
[6]Too long have I lived
among those who hate peace.
[7]I am for peace;
but when I speak, they are for war.

Psalm 121

A song of ascents.

[1]I lift up my eyes to the mountains —
where does my help come from?
[2]My help comes from the LORD,
the Maker of heaven[b] and earth.[c]
[3]He will not let your foot slip —
he who watches over you will not
slumber;
[4]indeed, he who watches[d] over Israel
will neither slumber nor sleep.

[5]The LORD watches over[e] you —
the LORD is your shade at your right
hand;
[6]the sun[f] will not harm you by day,
nor the moon by night.

[7]The LORD will keep you from all
harm[g] —
he will watch over your life;
[8]the LORD will watch over your coming
and going
both now and forevermore.[h]

Psalm 122

A song of ascents. Of David.

[1]I rejoiced with those who said
to me,
"Let us go to the house of the
LORD."

120:2 [x]S Ps 31:18 [y]S Ps 52:4 **120:4** [z]S Dt 32:23 **120:5** [a]S Ge 25:13; Jer 2:10 **121:2** [b]S Ge 1:1 [c]S Ps 104:5; Ps 115:15
121:4 [d]Ps 127:1 **121:5** [e]S Ps 1:6 **121:6** [f]Isa 49:10 **121:7** [g]S Ps 9:9 **121:8** [h]Dt 28:6

120:2,6 *me . . . I.* Lit. "my soul" (see note on 6:3).
120:2 *lying lips . . . deceitful tongues.* See note on 5:9.
120:3 – 4 Assurance that God will act (see 6:8 – 10 and note on 3:8).
120:3 *he.* The Lord. *what more besides.* An echo of a common oath formula (see 1Sa 3:17 and note), thus suggesting the certainty and severity of God's judgment on the enemies.
120:4 *sharp arrows . . . burning coals.* As a weapon, the tongue is a sharp arrow (see Pr 25:18; Jer 9:8; see also 57:4; 64:3) and a searing fire (see Pr 16:27; Jas 3:6), and God's judgment will answer in kind (see 7:11 – 13; 11:6; 64:7). For judgment in kind, see 63:9 – 10; 64:7 – 8 and notes. *broom bush.* A desert shrub, sometimes large enough to provide shade. Charcoal made from its wood produced an especially hot and durable fire.
120:5 – 7 Complaint over prolonged harassment.
120:5 *Meshek . . . Kedar.* The former was in central Asia Minor (see note on Ge 10:2), the latter in Arabia (see note on Isa 21:16). Besieged by slanderers, the psalmist feels as though he is far from home, surrounded by barbarians.
Ps 121 A dialogue (perhaps liturgical) of confession and assurance. Its use as a pilgrimage song provides the key to its understanding. Whether the dialogue takes place in a single heart (cf. the refrain in Ps 42 – 43) or between individuals in the caravan is of no great consequence since all would share the same convictions. The comforting assurance expressed (see Ps 33) is equally appropriate for the pilgrimage to Jerusalem and for the pilgrimage of life to the "glory" into which the faithful will be received (see notes on 49:15; 73:24). The psalm is composed of four couplets, each having an introductory line, which the rest of the couplet develops. Key terms are "the LORD" and "watch over," each occurring five times.
121 title See introduction to Ps 120 – 137.
121:1 – 2 Confession of trust in the Lord.
121:1 *mountains.* Those in the vicinity of Jerusalem, of which Mount Zion is one (125:2), or, if the plural indicates majesty (as in the Hebrew in 87:1; 133:3), Mount Zion itself.
121:2 *Maker of heaven and earth.* The one true God, the King of all creation (see 124:8; 134:3; see also 33:6; 89:11 – 13; 96:4 – 5; 104:2 – 9; 136:4 – 9).
121:3 – 4 Assurance concerning the unsleeping guardian over Israel.
121:3 *not let your foot slip.* Not even where the way is treacherous. *not slumber.* Like the pagan god Baal (see 1Ki 18:27) — though sometimes he seemed to (see 44:23; 78:65).
121:4 *he who watches over Israel.* The Lord of all creation and the guardian over Israel — the One in whom the faithful may put unfaltering trust.
121:5 – 6 Assurance concerning unfailing protection.
121:5 *shade.* See 91:1 ("shadow") and note on 17:8. *at your right hand.* See 16:8 and note.
121:6 *sun . . . moon.* Here, in agreement with the "shade" metaphor, these serve as figures for all that distresses or threatens, day or night (see Isa 4:6; 25:4 – 5; 49:10; Jnh 4:8).
121:7 – 8 Assurance concerning all of life.
121:8 *your coming and going.* Lit. "your going and coming." Although the Hebrew order is like that in such military contexts as 1Sa 29:6 ("to have you serve"); 2Sa 3:25 ("your movements"), the sense here is similar to that in Dt 28:6.
Ps 122 A hymn of joy over Jerusalem (see Ps 42 – 43; 46; 48; 84; 87; 137 and the introductions to those psalms). Sung by a pilgrim in Jerusalem (very likely at one of the three annual festivals, Dt 16:16), it expresses deep joy over the city and offers a prayer for its welfare. As the third of the pilgrimage psalms (see introduction to Ps 120 – 137), it shares many dominant themes with Ps 132, the third from the end of this collection — possibly a deliberate arrangement. Structurally, a two-verse introduction locates the worshiper with the festival throng in the city of his joy, and the major themes are developed in two closely balanced stanzas of four verses each (in Hebrew the first has a total of 57 syllables, the second 60 syllables; see also introductions to Ps 127; 128; 129). References to "the house of the LORD" (vv. 1,9) frame the song.
122 title *ascents.* See introduction to Ps 120 – 137. *Of David.* This element is not present in all ancient witnesses to the text, and the content suggests a later date (see note on v. 1).
122:1 – 2 Joy for having joined the pilgrimage to Jerusalem.
122:1 *the house of the LORD.* The temple (2Sa 7:5,13; 1Ki 5:3,5; 8:10, "temple"). That Jerusalem became the city of pilgrim-

[2]Our feet are standing
in your gates, Jerusalem.

[3]Jerusalem is built like a city
that is closely compacted together.
[4]That is where the tribes go up—
the tribes of the LORD—
to praise the name of the LORD
according to the statute given to
Israel.
[5]There stand the thrones for judgment,
the thrones of the house of David.

[6]Pray for the peace of Jerusalem:
"May those who love[i] you be secure.
[7]May there be peace[j] within your walls
and security within your citadels.[k]"
[8]For the sake of my family and friends,
I will say, "Peace be within you."
[9]For the sake of the house of the LORD
our God,
I will seek your prosperity.[l]

Psalm 123

A song of ascents.

[1]I lift up my eyes to you,
to you who sit enthroned[m] in heaven.
[2]As the eyes of slaves look to the hand
of their master,
as the eyes of a female slave look to
the hand of her mistress,
so our eyes look to the LORD[n] our God,
till he shows us his mercy.

[3]Have mercy on us, LORD, have mercy
on us,
for we have endured no end of
contempt.
[4]We have endured no end
of ridicule from the arrogant,
of contempt from the proud.

Psalm 124

A song of ascents. Of David.

[1]If the LORD had not been on our
side—
let Israel say[o]—
[2]if the LORD had not been on our side
when people attacked us,
[3]they would have swallowed us alive
when their anger flared against us;
[4]the flood[p] would have engulfed us,
the torrent[q] would have swept
over us,

122:6 [i]S Ps 26:8
122:7 [j]S 1Sa 25:6 [k]S Ps 48:3
122:9 [l]Ps 128:5
123:1 [m]S Ps 68:5; Isa 6:1; 63:15
123:2 [n]S Ps 25:15
124:1 [o]Ps 129:1
124:4 [p]Ps 88:17 [q]S Ps 18:4

age before the dedication of the temple is doubtful in light of 1Ki 3:4; 8:1–11.
122:2 *gates.* Gateways.
122:3–5 Jerusalem's significance for the faithful.
122:3 *closely compacted together.* Perhaps refers to the city's well-knit construction (see Ps 48) and probably echoes the account of the construction of the tabernacle (cf. Ex 26:11, "fasten ... together as a unit"). If so, Jerusalem is being celebrated as the earthly residence of God (see note on 9:11; see also Isa 4:5).
122:4 *to praise ... the LORD.* For his saving acts in behalf of Israel and his blessings on the nation. *name.* See note on 5:11. *statute given to Israel.* See 81:3–5; Dt 16:1–17.
122:5 *There ... the thrones of the house of David.* Jerusalem is both the city of the Lord and the royal city of his chosen dynasty, through which he (ideally) protects and governs the nation (see 2:2,6–7; 89:3–4,19–37; 110; 2Sa 7:8–16 and notes). In postexilic times it remained, though now in Messianic hope, the city of David.
122:6–9 Prayers for Jerusalem's peace.
122:6 In Hebrew a beautiful wordplay tightly binds together "Pray," "peace," "Jerusalem" and "be secure." *peace.* See vv. 7–8; includes both security and prosperity. *those who love you.* The psalmist, those referred to in vv. 1,8 and all who love Jerusalem because they are devoted to the Lord and his chosen king. These constitute a loving fellowship of those who worship together, pray together and seek each other's welfare as the people of God (see Ps 133).
122:7 *walls ... citadels.* See 48:13 ("ramparts ... citadels").
122:8–9 *For the sake of ... For the sake of.* Because Jerusalem is the place supreme where God and his people meet together in fruitful communion, the psalmist vows to seek the city's peace and prosperity.
122:9 *the house of the LORD.* See v. 1 and note; the phrase provides a literary frame for the psalm.
Ps 123 A prayer of God's humble people for him to show mercy and so foil the contempt of the proud. See introduction to Ps 124. As to its structure, a one-verse introduction is followed by two brief stanzas, each developing its own theme.
123 title See introduction to Ps 120–137.
123:1 *I lift up my eyes.* The psalmist speaks as a representative member of or as spokesperson for the community—see the first-person plurals that follow. *who sit enthroned in heaven.* The same God whose earthly throne is in the temple on Mount Zion (see 122:5 and note; see also 2:4; 9:11; 11:4; 80:1; 99:1; 113:5; 132:14).
123:2 With the use of two similes drawn from domestic life, the faithful (men and women alike) present themselves as dependent and confidently reliant on God.
123:4 *the arrogant ... the proud.* Those who live by their own wits and strength (see notes on 10:2–11; 31:23) and pour contempt on those who humbly rely on the Lord. For examples, see those with whom King Hezekiah (2Ki 18:17—19:19) or Governor Nehemiah (Ne 4; 6:1–4) had to contend.
Ps 124 Israel's praise of the Lord for deliverance from powerful enemies—an appropriate sequel to Ps 123. Very likely a Levite speaks in vv. 1–5, while the worshipers answer in vv. 6–8. That it shares with Ps 129 a similar introduction and a theme focused on Zion's deliverance from powerful enemies suggests that these two psalms were arranged to frame the intervening four (see note on 125:5).
124 title *ascents.* See introduction to Ps 120–137. *Of David.* Not all ancient witnesses to the text contain this element, and both language and theme suggest a postexilic date (see note on Ps 122 title). It may have been assigned to David because of supposed echoes of Ps 18; 69.
124:1–5 Let Israel acknowledge that the Lord alone has saved her from extinction (see 20:7; 94:17).
124:2 *people attacked.* Proud and arrogant people (123:4) may attack, but the Lord is Israel's help (v. 8).
124:3 *swallowed us.* Like death (see note on 49:14). But see 69:15.
124:4–5 *flood ... torrent ... raging waters.* See 18:16; see also 32:6; 69:1–2 and notes.

5 the raging waters
would have swept us away.

6 Praise be to the LORD,
who has not let us be torn by their teeth.
7 We have escaped like a bird
from the fowler's snare;[r]
the snare has been broken,[s]
and we have escaped.
8 Our help is in the name[t] of the LORD,
the Maker of heaven[u] and earth.

Psalm 125

A song of ascents.

1 Those who trust in the LORD are like Mount Zion,[v]
which cannot be shaken[w] but endures forever.
2 As the mountains surround Jerusalem,[x]
so the LORD surrounds[y] his people
both now and forevermore.

3 The scepter[z] of the wicked will not remain[a]
over the land allotted to the righteous,
for then the righteous might use
their hands to do evil.[b]

4 LORD, do good[c] to those who are good,
to those who are upright in heart.[d]
5 But those who turn[e] to crooked ways[f]
the LORD will banish[g] with the evildoers.

Peace be on Israel.[h]

Psalm 126

A song of ascents.

1 When the LORD restored[i] the fortunes of[a] Zion,
we were like those who dreamed.[b]
2 Our mouths were filled with laughter,[j]
our tongues with songs of joy.[k]
Then it was said among the nations,
"The LORD has done great things[l] for them."
3 The LORD has done great things[m] for us,
and we are filled with joy.[n]

4 Restore our fortunes,[c][o] LORD,
like streams in the Negev.[p]
5 Those who sow with tears[q]
will reap[r] with songs of joy.[s]

[a] *1* Or *LORD brought back the captives to* [b] *1* Or *those restored to health* [c] *4* Or *Bring back our captives*

124:7 [r] S Ps 91:3 [s] Ps 25:15 **124:8** [t] S 1Sa 17:45 [u] Ge 1:1; Ps 115:15; 121:2; 134:3 **125:1** [v] Ps 48:12; Isa 33:20 [w] Ps 46:5; 48:2-5 **125:2** [x] S 1Ch 21:15 [y] Ps 32:10; Zec 2:4-5 **125:3** [z] S Est 4:11 [a] Ps 89:22; Pr 22:8; Isa 13:11; 14:5 [b] 1Sa 24:10 **125:4** [c] S Ps 119:65 [d] S Ps 36:10 **125:5** [e] S Job 23:11 [f] Pr 2:15; Isa 59:8 [g] Ps 92:7 [h] Ps 128:6; Gal 6:16 **126:1** [i] Ezr 1:1-3; Ps 85:1; Hos 6:11 **126:2** [j] S Ge 21:6 [k] S Job 8:21; S Ps 65:8 [l] S Dt 10:21; Ps 71:19; Lk 1:49 **126:3** [m] Ps 106:21; Joel 2:21,26 [n] S Ps 9:2; 16:11 **126:4** [o] S Dt 30:3 [p] S Ps 107:35; Isa 43:19; 51:3 **126:5** [q] Ps 6:6; 80:5; Jer 50:4 [r] Gal 6:9 [s] Ps 16:11; 20:5; 23:6; Isa 35:10; 51:11; 60:15; 61:7; Jer 31:6-7,12

124:6–8 Response of praise for deliverance—with a vivid enrichment of the imagery.
124:6 *torn by their teeth.* As by wild beasts (see note on 7:2).
124:7 *escaped like a bird from the fowler's snare.* A most apt figure for Israel's release from Babylonian captivity (cf. note on 9:15).
124:8 In climax, the great confession (see 121:2 and note).
Ps 125 Israel's security celebrated in testimony, prayer and benediction. The psalm is most likely postexilic and was probably spoken in the temple liturgy by a Levite. Ps 125 and 126 are thematically linked and precisely balanced, each being composed (in Hebrew) of 116 syllables. Their juxtaposition was no doubt deliberate.
125 title See introduction to Ps 120–137.
125:1–2 The solid security of God's people.
125:1 *Those who trust in the LORD.* God's "people" (v. 2) are also characterized as "the righteous" (v. 3; see note on 1:5) and "those who are good," "who are upright in heart" (v. 4). For a similar description of the "righteous," see 34:8–14 and note. *like Mount Zion.* In their security (see Ps 46; 48).
125:2 *mountains surround Jerusalem.* Though Jerusalem is not surrounded by a ring of peaks, the city is located in what OT writers called a mountainous region. *so the LORD surrounds his people.* As surely, as substantially and as immovably (see 2Ki 6:17; Zec 2:5).
125:3 Wicked rulers, whether by example or by oppression, tend to corrupt even the righteous, but the Lord will preserve his people also from this corrosive threat. *scepter of the wicked.* Probably referring to Persian rule (see Ne 9:36–37) and its invidious underlings, such as those Nehemiah had to contend with (see Ne 2:19; 4:1–3,7–8; 6:1–14,17–19; 13:7–8,28). *land allotted to the righteous.* The promised land (see 78:55).
125:4–5 To everyone as they are and do—that is God's way (see 18:25–27); thus the confident prayer (v. 4) and the equally confident assertion (v. 5).
125:4 *heart.* See note on 4:7.
125:5 *Peace be on Israel.* Perhaps a concise form of the priestly benediction (Nu 6:24–26; see notes there). This benediction has its counterpart in the prayer of 126:4–6. Its repetition at the end of Ps 128 suggests a frame around the four closely balanced psalms (made up of two pairs: 125–126; 127–128).
Ps 126 A song of joy for the restoration of the exiled community to Zion (cf. Ps 42–43; 84; 137). The psalm divides into two stanzas of four (Hebrew) lines each, with their initial lines sharing a common theme. Thematic unity is further served by repetition (cf. vv. 2–3) and other key words ("the LORD," "songs of joy," "carrying"). References to God's action (vv. 1,3) frame the first stanza, while v. 2 offers exposition. For this psalm's relationship to Ps 125, see introduction to that psalm.
126 title See introduction to Ps 120–137.
126:1–3 Joy over restoration experienced.
126:1 *restored the fortunes of.* This translation and its alternative (see NIV text note here and on v. 4) have essentially the same result. *dreamed.* The wonder and joy of the reality were so marvelous that they hardly dared believe it. It seemed more like the dreams with which they had so long been tantalized.
126:2 The twofold effect: joy for those who returned and honor for God among the nations (see note on 46:10).
126:4–6 Prayer for restoration to be completed.
126:4 *Restore our fortunes.* Either complete the repatriation of exiles (see NIV text note) or fully restore the security and prosperity of former times. *like streams in the Negev.* Which are bone-dry in summer, until the winter rains renew their flow.
126:5–6 An apt metaphorical portrayal of the joy already experienced and the joy anticipated. *with tears … weeping.* Even when sowing is accompanied by trouble or sorrow, harvest brings joy. For a related figure, see 20:5.

6 Those who go out weeping,[t]
carrying seed to sow,
will return with songs of joy,
carrying sheaves with them.

Psalm 127

A song of ascents. Of Solomon.

1 Unless the LORD builds[u] the house,
the builders labor in vain.
Unless the LORD watches[v] over the city,
the guards stand watch in vain.
2 In vain you rise early
and stay up late,
toiling for food[w] to eat—
for he grants sleep[x] to[a] those he loves.[y]
3 Children are a heritage from the LORD,
offspring a reward[z] from him.
4 Like arrows[a] in the hands of a warrior
are children born in one's youth.
5 Blessed is the man
whose quiver is full of them.[b]
They will not be put to shame
when they contend with their opponents[c] in court.[d]

126:6 [t] S Nu 25:6; S Ps 30:5 **127:1** [u] Ps 78:69 [v] Ps 121:4 **127:2** [w] S Ge 3:17 [x] S Nu 6:26; S Job 11:18 [y] S Dt 33:12; Ecc 2:25 **127:3** [z] S Ge 1:28 **127:4** [a] Ps 112:2 **127:5** [b] Ps 128:2-3 [c] S Ge 24:60 [d] S Ge 23:10

128:1 [e] Ps 103:11; S 112:1 [f] Ps 119:1-3 **128:2** [g] S Ps 58:11; 109:11; Isa 3:10 [h] S Ge 39:3; Pr 10:22 **128:3** [i] S Ge 49:22 [j] S Job 29:5 [k] Ps 52:8; 144:12 **128:4** [l] S Ps 1:1 [m] Ps 112:1 **128:5** [n] S Ps 20:2 [o] Ps 122:9 **128:6** [p] S Ge 48:11 [q] S Ps 125:5

Psalm 128

A song of ascents.

1 Blessed are all who fear the LORD,[e]
who walk in obedience to him.[f]
2 You will eat the fruit of your labor;[g]
blessings and prosperity[h] will be yours.
3 Your wife will be like a fruitful vine[i]
within your house;
your children[j] will be like olive shoots[k]
around your table.
4 Yes, this will be the blessing[l]
for the man who fears the LORD.[m]
5 May the LORD bless you from Zion;[n]
may you see the prosperity of Jerusalem[o]
all the days of your life.
6 May you live to see your children's children—[p]
peace be on Israel.[q]

[a] 2 Or *eat— / for while they sleep he provides for*

Ps 127 Godly wisdom concerning home and hearth. Its theme is timeless; it reminded the pilgrims on their way to Jerusalem that all of life's securities and blessings are gifts from God rather than their own achievements (see Dt 28:1–14). Two precisely balanced stanzas (in Hebrew having four poetic lines each, and each composed of 57 syllables) develop, respectively, two distinct but related themes. Since this psalm shares with Ps 128 the theme of domestic happiness and is structurally very similar to it, their juxtaposition appears to be deliberate.

127 title *ascents.* See introduction to Ps 120–137. *Of Solomon.* If Solomon was not the author (not all witnesses to the text ascribe it to him), it is easy to see why some thought him so.

127:1–2 It is the Lord who provides shelter, security and sustenance.

127:1 *house.* Domestic shelter. *builders.* The Hebrew for this word is a pun on that for "Children" in v. 3. *watches over.* See 121:3–8. *city.* The center of power, the refuge when enemies invade the land. *guards stand watch.* See 2Sa 13:34; 18:24–27; SS 3:3; 5:7.

127:2 *he grants sleep.* A good harvest is not the achievement of endless toil but the result of God's blessing (see Pr 10:22; Mt 6:25–34; 1Pe 5:7). *those he loves.* See especially Dt 33:12; Jer 11:15.

127:3–5 Children are God's gift and a sign of his favor.

127:3 *Children.* See note on v. 1. Children too are a gift—not the mere product of virility and fertility (see 113:9 and note; Ge 30:2). *heritage.* Emphasis here is on gift rather than possession. But perhaps more is implied. In the OT economy an Israelite's "inheritance" from the Lord was first of all property in the promised land (Nu 26:53; Jos 11:23; Jdg 2:6), which provided a sure place in the life and "rest" (Jos 1:13) of the Lord's kingdom. But without children the inheritance in the land would be lost (Nu 27:8–11), so that offspring were a heritage in a double sense. *reward from him.* Bestowed by God on one who stands in his favor because he has been faithful.

127:5 *when they contend with their opponents.* Fathers with many children have many defenders when falsely accused in court. Moreover, the very fact that they have many children as God's "reward" (v. 3) testifies to God's favor toward them (in effect, they are God-provided character witnesses; see 128:3–4). *in court.* Lit. "in the gate." For "[city/town] gate" as court, see Dt 17:5; 21:19; 22:15,24; 25:7; Ru 4:1; Isa 29:21 ("court"); Am 5:12 ("courts").

Ps 128 The blessedness of the godly man; another word of wisdom concerning hearth and home (see introduction to Ps 127). Structurally, the frame ("who fear[s] the LORD") around vv. 1–4 sets off those verses as the main body of the psalm.

128 title See introduction to Ps 120–137.

128:1–4 Blessedness affirmed.

128:1 *Blessed.* See note on 1:1. *fear the LORD.* See v. 4; see also note on 66:16.

128:2 Blessings upon labor.

128:3 A faithful and fruitful wife. *vine.* Symbol of fruitfulness (Ge 49:22)—and perhaps also of sexual charms (SS 7:8–12) and festivity (Jdg 9:13). *within your house.* She is not like the faithless wife whose "feet never stay at home" (Pr 7:11). *olive shoots.* Ever green and with the promises of both long life and productivity (of staples: wood, fruit, oil). The vine and the olive tree are frequently paired in the OT (as, e.g., in Ex 23:11). Both were especially long-lived, and they produced the wine and the oil that played such a central role in the lives of the people. *around your table.* Converting each family meal into a banquet of domestic joys.

128:5–6 The benediction pronounced—completing the scope of true blessedness: unbroken prosperity, secure relationship with God and secure national existence (the prosperity of Jerusalem entailed both), and long life.

128:5 *from Zion.* See 9:11 and note; 20:2; 135:21.

128:6 *peace be on Israel.* See 125:5 and note.

Psalm 129

A song of ascents.

[1]"They have greatly oppressed[r] me from
my youth,"[s]
let Israel say;[t]
[2]"they have greatly oppressed me from
my youth,
but they have not gained the victory[u]
over me.
[3]Plowmen have plowed my back
and made their furrows long.
[4]But the LORD is righteous;[v]
he has cut me free[w] from the cords
of the wicked."[x]

[5]May all who hate Zion[y]
be turned back in shame.[z]
[6]May they be like grass on the roof,[a]
which withers[b] before it can grow;
[7]a reaper cannot fill his hands with it,[c]
nor one who gathers fill his arms.
[8]May those who pass by not say to
them,
"The blessing of the LORD be on
you;
we bless you[d] in the name of the
LORD."

Psalm 130

A song of ascents.

[1]Out of the depths[e] I cry to you,[f] LORD;
[2] Lord, hear my voice.[g]
Let your ears be attentive[h]
to my cry for mercy.[i]

[3]If you, LORD, kept a record of sins,
Lord, who could stand?[j]
[4]But with you there is forgiveness,[k]
so that we can, with reverence, serve
you.[l]

[5]I wait for the LORD,[m] my whole being
waits,[n]
and in his word[o] I put my hope.
[6]I wait for the Lord
more than watchmen[p] wait for the
morning,
more than watchmen wait for the
morning.[q]

[7]Israel, put your hope[r] in the LORD,
for with the LORD is unfailing love[s]
and with him is full redemption.[t]
[8]He himself will redeem[u] Israel
from all their sins.[v]

Psalm 131

A song of ascents. Of David.

[1]My heart is not proud,[w] LORD,
my eyes are not haughty;[x]
I do not concern myself with great
matters[y]
or things too wonderful for me.[z]

129:1 [r]S Ex 1:13 [s]S Ps 88:15 [t]Ps 124:1 **129:2** [u]Jer 1:19; 15:20; 20:11; Mt 16:18 **129:4** [v]S Ex 9:27 [w]Ps 37:9 [x]Ps 140:5 **129:5** [y]Mic 4:11 [z]S Ps 70:2 **129:6** [a]Isa 37:27 [b]S 2Ki 19:26; Ps 102:11 **129:7** [c]S Dt 28:38; Ps 79:12 **129:8** [d]Ps 118:26 **130:1** [e]S Job 30:19; Ps 42:7; La 3:55 [f]Ps 22:2; 55:17; 142:5 **130:2** [g]S Ps 27:7; 28:2 [h]S 2Ch 6:40 [i]S Ps 28:6; 31:22; 86:6; 140:6 **130:3** [j]S 1Sa 6:20; S Ezr 9:15; Ps 143:2; Na 1:6; Rev 6:17 **130:4** [k]S Ex 34:7; S 2Sa 24:14; S Jer 31:34 [l]S 1Ki 8:40 **130:5** [m]S Ps 27:14; Isa 8:17; 26:8; 30:18; 49:23 [n]S Ps 5:3 [o]S Ps 119:74 **130:6** [p]Ps 63:6 [q]S 2Sa 23:4 **130:7** [r]S Ps 25:5; S 71:14 [s]S 1Ch 21:13 [t]S Ps 111:9; S Ro 3:24 **130:8** [u]Lk 1:68 [v]S Ex 34:7; S Mt 1:21 **131:1** [w]Ps 101:5; Isa 2:12; Ro 12:16 [x]S 2Sa 22:28; S Job 41:34 [y]Jer 45:5 [z]S Job 5:9; Ps 139:6

Ps 129 Israel's prayer for the continued withering of all her powerful enemies. The rescue celebrated (v. 4) is probably from Babylonian exile. Against the background of Ps 124–128, this prayer for the withholding of God's blessing (v. 8) is set in sharp relief. Like Ps 127, its two main stanzas (vv. 1–4,5–8a) are perfectly balanced, having a total of 59 Hebrew syllables each. Its total syllable count (127) closely matches that of Ps 130 (128 syllables). For its apparent link with Ps 124, see introduction to that psalm.
129 title See introduction to Ps 120–137.
129:1–4 The wicked oppressors have not prevailed.
129:1 *from my youth.* From the time Israel was enslaved in Egypt, she has suffered much at the hands of hostile powers.
129:2 *have not gained the victory.* Have not succeeded in their efforts to destroy Israel totally or to hold her permanently in bondage.
129:4 *righteous.* See note on 4:1.
129:5–8 May all those oppressors who have shown hatred toward Zion wither away (see Ps 137).
129:5 See note on 5:10.
129:6 *like grass on the roof.* May those who would plow the backs of Israel (see v. 3) wither like grass that sprouts on the flat, sunbaked housetops, where no plow can prepare a nurturing soil to sustain the young shoots—and so there is no harvest (v. 7).
129:8 *those who pass by.* Whoever may pass by the harvesters in the fields will exchange no joyful greetings (Ru 2:4) because the hands of the harvesters will be empty.
Ps 130 A testimony of trust in the Lord—by one who knows that even though he is a sinner, the Lord hears his cry out of the depths. This is the sixth of seven penitential psalms (see introduction to Ps 6). Composed of four couplets, the psalm further divides into two halves of two couplets each. Its total syllable count closely matches that of Ps 129 (see introduction to that psalm).
130 title See introduction to Ps 120–137.
130:1–4 A prayer for mercy and grounds for assurance.
130:1 *the depths.* As in 69:2 (see notes on 30:1; 32:6; cf. 121:1; 123:1).
130:4 *there is forgiveness.* No doubt recalling such reassuring words as Ex 34:6–7. *with reverence, serve you.* Honor, worship, trust and serve you as the one true God (see Ps 34:8–14 and note). If God were not forgiving, people could only flee from him in terror.
130:5–8 Trust in the Lord: a personal testimony, expanding into a reassuring invitation (see 131:3).
130:5 *I wait.* In hopeful expectation. *his word.* Especially his covenant promises (see 119:25,28,37,42,49,65,74,81,107,114,147).
130:6 *watchmen.* See 127:1; 2Sa 13:34; 18:24–27; SS 3:3; 5:7. *the morning.* See introduction to Ps 57; see also note on 59:9.
130:7 See 131:3. *unfailing love.* See note on 6:4.
130:8 *from all their sins.* From the root of trouble—but also from all its consequences. This greatest of all hopes has been fulfilled in Christ.
Ps 131 A confession of humble trust in the Lord—appropriately placed next to Ps 130.
131 title *ascents.* See introduction to Ps 120–137. *Of David.* See Introduction: Authorship and Titles (or Superscriptions).
131:1 *heart.* See note on 4:7. *proud ... haughty.* Pride in humanity's presumed ability to master the whole creation, design its own moral world and control its own destiny (of which Babel is the prime Biblical example; see Ge 11:1–9)

2 But I have calmed and quieted
myself,[a]
I am like a weaned child with its
mother;
like a weaned child I am content.[b]
3 Israel, put your hope[c] in the LORD
both now and forevermore.[d]

Psalm 132

132:8-10pp — 2Ch 6:41-42

A song of ascents.

1 LORD, remember David
and all his self-denial.[e]
2 He swore an oath to the LORD,
he made a vow to the Mighty One of
Jacob:[f]
3 "I will not enter my house[g]
or go to my bed,
4 I will allow no sleep to my eyes
or slumber to my eyelids,
5 till I find a place[h] for the LORD,
a dwelling for the Mighty One of
Jacob."
6 We heard it in Ephrathah,[i]
we came upon it in the fields of
Jaar:[a][j]
7 "Let us go to his dwelling place,[k]
let us worship at his footstool,[l]
saying,
8 'Arise, LORD,[m] and come to your resting
place,
you and the ark of your might.
9 May your priests be clothed with your
righteousness;[n]
may your faithful people[o] sing for
joy.' "
10 For the sake of your servant
David,
do not reject your anointed one.

131:2 [a]S Ps 116:7 [b]Mt 18:3; 1Co 13:11; 14:20 **131:3** [c]S Ps 25:5; 119:43; 130:7 [d]S Ps 113:2 **132:1** [e]1Sa 18:11; S 2Sa 15:14 **132:2** [f]S Ge 49:24; Isa 49:26; 60:16 **132:3** [g]S 2Sa 7:2,27 **132:5** [h]S 1Ki 8:17; Ac 7:46 **132:6** [i]S 1Sa 17:12 [j]S Jos 9:17; S 1Sa 7:2 **132:7** [k]S 2Sa 15:25; Ps 5:7; 122:1 [l]S 1Ch 28:2 **132:8** [m]S Nu 10:35 **132:9** [n]S Job 27:6; Isa 61:3, 10; Zec 3:4; Mal 3:3; Eph 6:14 [o]Ps 16:3; 30:4; 149:5

[a] 6 Or *heard of it in Ephrathah, / we found it in the fields of Jearim.* (See 1 Chron. 13:5,6) (And no quotation marks around verses 7-9)

is that which, more than all else, alienates humans from God (see note on 31:23). *concern myself with.* (Presume to) walk among, live among, be party to. *great matters ... too wonderful for me.* Heroic exploits or achievements to rival, if not substitute for, the mighty works of God. The focus seems to be on not claiming godlike powers (thus trusting in God for deliverance and blessing) rather than on seeking (or claiming) godlike understanding.

131:2 *weaned child.* A child of three or four who walks trustingly beside its mother.

131:3 As the psalmist, so ought all Israel (see 130:7) — for all time.

Ps 132 A prayer for God's favor on the reigning son of David and on the regime that David founded — as the structure makes clear (and see note on v. 10). Its language suggests a date early in the monarchy. The venerable belief that it was composed for the dedication of the temple may be correct (compare vv. 8 – 10 with 2Ch 6:41 – 42), but the possibility cannot be ruled out that it was used in the coronation ritual (cf. Ps 2; 72; 110). The author of Chronicles places the prayer (or a portion of it) on the lips of the king himself. As used in postexilic liturgies, it had Messianic implications.

Two verses of petition (vv. 1,10) are each followed (in Hebrew) by two four-line stanzas, all having an identical form: an introductory line followed by a three-line quotation (see the structure of these quotations). A final couplet brings the prayer to its climactic conclusion. The four stanzas, together with the final couplet, ground the prayer made in vv. 1,10. Verses 2 – 9 appeal to David's oath to the Lord to find a "place" for the Lord and to bring the ark to its "resting place," while vv. 11 – 18 appeal to the Lord's oath to David and to his election of Zion as his "resting place" (but see note on v. 10).

132 title See introduction to Ps 120 – 137.

132:1 The initial petition (see v. 10). *remember.* See 20:3; see also 1Ki 11:12 – 13; 15:4 – 5. *self-denial.* What David took on himself in his vow (vv. 2 – 5; see Nu 30:13, where the same technical term for a self-denying oath is used).

132:2 – 5 David's oath concerning a temple for the Lord is recalled.

132:2 *He swore an oath.* This prayer for David's son is grounded in the special relationship between David and the Lord, as epitomized in their mutual oaths (see vv. 11 – 12). In 2Sa 6 – 7, which narrates the events here recalled, David's oath is not mentioned. *LORD ... Mighty One of Jacob.* See v. 5; Isa 1:24; see also note on 3:7. *Jacob.* A synonym for Israel (see Ge 32:28).

132:6 – 9 Moments in the people's procession to the temple for worship are recalled.

132:6 *it ... it.* Often thought to refer to the ark (see NIV text note), but more likely it refers to the call to worship that follows (in Hebrew the pronoun is feminine, but the Hebrew for "ark" is masculine). *Ephrathah.* The region around Bethlehem, David's hometown (see Ru 4:11; Mic 5:2). *fields of Jaar.* See NIV text note; see also 2Sa 6:2 and first NIV text note there. The call to worship is depicted as emanating from David's city and the city where the ark had been since the days of Samuel (see 1Sa 7:1). The call appears to come from a time after the temple had been built — thus involving a poetic compression of events.

132:7 *footstool.* See 99:5 and note.

132:8 *Arise.* Although (in accordance with a common feature in Hebrew poetry) the Hebrew omits an introductory word, such as "saying" (which the NIV supplies at the end of v. 7 for clarity), vv. 8 – 9 are probably words on the lips of the worshipers. See introduction to Ps 24. *resting place.* As the promised land was Israel's place of rest at the end of her wanderings (see Nu 10:33; Jos 1:13; Mic 2:10), so the temple was the Lord's resting place after he had been moving about in a tent (see 2Sa 7:6; see also 1Ch 28:2). The expression may suggest that the temple was the place of God's throne (v. 14). *ark of your might.* See note on 78:61.

132:9 *clothed with.* Beyond their normal priestly garb — may their ministry be characterized by, i.e., result in, righteousness. See note on 109:29. *righteousness.* Since the corresponding word in v. 16 is "salvation," the same word used by the author of Chronicles when quoting this verse (2Ch 6:41), and since "righteousness" and "salvation" are often paralleled (40:10; 51:14; 71:15; 98:2; Isa 45:8; 46:13; 51:5 – 6; 56:1; 59:17; 60:17 – 18; 61:10; 62:1), the reference is clearly to God's righteousness that effects the salvation of his people (see note on 4:1). *faithful people.* See note on 4:3.

132:10 The second petition (see v. 1). *your servant.* See note on Ps 18 title. *do not reject.* Do not refuse his petitions (as in 1Ki 2:16 – 17,20; see 1Ki 8:59; 2Ch 6:41 – 42). If, as some have proposed, the petitions in vv. 1,10 form a frame around the

[11] The LORD swore an oath to David,[p]
a sure oath he will not revoke:
"One of your own descendants[q]
I will place on your throne.
[12] If your sons keep my covenant[r]
and the statutes I teach them,
then their sons will sit
on your throne[s] for ever and ever."

[13] For the LORD has chosen Zion,[t]
he has desired it for his dwelling,[u]
saying,
[14] "This is my resting place for ever and
ever;[v]
here I will sit enthroned,[w] for I have
desired it.
[15] I will bless her with abundant
provisions;
her poor I will satisfy with food.[x]
[16] I will clothe her priests[y] with salvation,
and her faithful people will ever sing
for joy.[z]

[17] "Here I will make a horn[a] grow[a] for
David
and set up a lamp[b] for my anointed
one.[c]
[18] I will clothe his enemies with shame,[d]
but his head will be adorned with a
radiant crown."[e]

132:11 [p] S Ps 89:3-4,35 [q] S 1Ch 17:11-14; S Mt 1:1; Lk 3:31 **132:12** [r] 2Ch 6:16; S Ps 25:10 [s] Lk 1:32; Ac 2:30 **132:13** [t] S Ex 15:17; Ps 48:1-2; S 68:16 [u] S 1Ki 8:13 **132:14** [v] ver 8; Ps 68:16 [w] S 2Sa 6:2; Ps 80:1 **132:15** [x] Ps 107:9; 147:14 **132:16** [y] S 2Ch 6:41 [z] S Job 8:21; Ps 149:5 **132:17** [a] S 1Sa 2:10; Ps 92:10; Eze 29:21; S Lk 1:69 [b] 1Ki 11:36; 2Ki 8:19; 2Ch 21:7; Ps 18:28 [c] S Ps 84:9 **132:18** [d] S Job 8:22 [e] S 2Sa 12:30 **133:1** [f] S Ge 13:8; S Ro 12:10

Psalm 133

A song of ascents. Of David.

[1] How good and pleasant it is
when God's people live together[f] in
unity![g]

[2] It is like precious oil poured on the
head,[h]
running down on the beard,
running down on Aaron's beard,
down on the collar of his robe.
[3] It is as if the dew[i] of Hermon[j]
were falling on Mount Zion.[k]
For there the LORD bestows his
blessing,[l]
even life forevermore.[m]

Psalm 134

A song of ascents.

[1] Praise the LORD, all you servants[n] of the
LORD
who minister[o] by night[p] in the house
of the LORD.

[a] *17 Horn* here symbolizes strong one, that is, king.

[g] Jn 17:11 **133:2** [h] S Ex 29:7 **133:3** [i] Job 29:19; Pr 19:12; Isa 18:4; 26:19; 45:8; Hos 14:5; Mic 5:7 [j] S Dt 3:8; S 4:48 [k] S Ex 15:17; S Ps 2:6; 74:2 [l] S Lev 25:21 [m] S Ps 21:4 **134:1** [n] S Ps 113:1; 135:1-2; Rev 19:5 [o] S Nu 16:9; S 1Ch 15:2 [p] S 1Ch 23:30

first half of the psalm, the second half offers assurance that the prayer will be heard (perhaps spoken by a priest or Levite). In any event, David's vow to provide the Lord a dwelling place, which would be for his royal sons and for Israel a house of prayer (see 1Ki 8:27–53; 9:3; 2Ch 7:15–16; Isa 56:7), is made the basis for the appeal that God will hear his anointed's prayer. *your anointed one.* See note on 2:2.

132:11–12 The Lord's covenant with David is recalled, as grounds for the prayer. These and vv. 13–18 are a poetic recollection of 1Ki 9:1–5 (see 2Ch 7:11–18).

132:11 *swore an oath.* See v. 2 and note. 2Sa 7 does not mention an oath, but elsewhere God's promise to David is called a covenant (89:3,28,34,39; 2Sa 23:5; Isa 55:3), and covenants were made on oath. *will not revoke.* See 110:4. *One of your own descendants . . . on your throne.* Peter alludes to this verse with reference to Jesus in Ac 2:30.

132:12 *covenant . . . statutes.* The stipulations of the Sinaitic covenant, which all Israelites were to keep (see 1Sa 10:25 and note; see also 1Ki 2:3–4).

132:13–16 The Lord's election of Zion recalled, as grounds for the prayer (see Introduction: Theology: Major Themes, 7).

132:13 *desired it for his dwelling.* David's and the Lord's desires harmonize (see Dt 12:5–14).

132:15 The Lord, enthroned in his resting place (see vv. 8,14), will bless the land, making it a place of rest for his people (see Dt 12:9; Jos 1:13; 1Ki 5:4 and note).

132:16 See note on v. 9.

132:17–18 Concluding word of assurance, which addresses the petition (vv. 1,10) directly and climactically.

132:17 *horn.* The Lord's anointed (see NIV text note). *grow.* Like a plant or branch. *set up a lamp for.* See note on 1Ki 11:36.

132:18 *clothe . . . with . . . adorned with.* See note on 109:29. *clothe . . . with shame.* In contrast to v. 16. *be adorned with.* Lit. "blossom"—subtly evoking the imagery: "grow" (v. 17) and blossom.

Ps 133 A song in praise of unity among the people of God. If David was the author (but see note on title), he may have been moved to write it by some such occasion as when, after many years of conflict, all Israel came to Hebron to make him king (2Sa 5:1–3). Other historical possibilities are after the influx of many refugees from the northern tribes into the kingdom of Judah during the great Assyrian invasions (see introduction to Ps 80) or the postexilic regathering of representatives of "all Israel," as reflected in Ezra and Nehemiah (see Ezr 8:25; Ne 12:47). The first and last (Hebrew) lines (vv. 1,3b) frame the whole with the song's main theme. Next to these an inner frame (lines 2,4) elaborates with two striking, complementary similes (vv. 2a,3a). The center line (v. 2b) extends the first simile.

133 title *ascents.* See introduction to Ps 120–137. *Of David.* See Introduction: Authorship and Titles (or Superscriptions); see also notes on titles of Ps 122; 124; 127.

133:1 *good and pleasant.* See 135:3; 147:1.

133:2 *like precious oil . . . on Aaron's beard . . . on the collar of his robe.* The oil of Aaron's anointing (Ex 29:7; Lev 21:10) saturated all the hair of his beard and ran down on his priestly robe, signifying his total consecration to holy service. Similarly, communal harmony sanctifies God's people.

133:3 *dew of Hermon . . . on Mount Zion.* A dew as profuse as that of Mount Hermon would make Mount Zion (or the mountains of Zion) richly fruitful (see Ge 27:28; Hag 1:10; Zec 8:12). So would communal unity make Israel richly fruitful. The two similes (vv. 2–3) are well chosen: God's blessings flowed to Israel through the priestly ministrations at the sanctuary (Ex 29:44–46; Lev 9:22–24; Nu 6:24–26)—epitomizing God's redemptive mercies—and through heaven's dew that sustained life in the fields—epitomizing God's providential mercies in the creation order. *life.* The great covenant blessing (see Dt 30:15,19–20; 32:47).

Ps 134 A liturgy of praise—a brief exchange between the worshipers, as they are about to leave the temple after the evening service, and the Levites, who kept the temple watch

2 Lift up your hands[q] in the sanctuary[r]
and praise the LORD.[s]

3 May the LORD bless you from Zion,[t]
he who is the Maker of heaven[u] and earth.

Psalm 135

135:15-20pp — Ps 115:4-11

1 Praise the LORD.[a]

Praise the name of the LORD;
praise him, you servants[v] of the LORD,
2 you who minister in the house[w] of the LORD,
in the courts[x] of the house of our God.
3 Praise the LORD, for the LORD is good;[y]
sing praise to his name,[z] for that is pleasant.[a]
4 For the LORD has chosen Jacob[b] to be his own,
Israel to be his treasured possession.[c]
5 I know that the LORD is great,[d]
that our Lord is greater than all gods.[e]
6 The LORD does whatever pleases him,[f]
in the heavens and on the earth,[g]
in the seas and all their depths.
7 He makes clouds rise from the ends of the earth;
he sends lightning with the rain[h]
and brings out the wind[i] from his storehouses.[j]

8 He struck down the firstborn[k] of Egypt,
the firstborn of people and animals.
9 He sent his signs[l] and wonders into your midst, Egypt,
against Pharaoh and all his servants.[m]
10 He struck down many[n] nations
and killed mighty kings —
11 Sihon[o] king of the Amorites,[p]
Og king of Bashan,[q]
and all the kings of Canaan[r] —
12 and he gave their land as an inheritance,[s]
an inheritance to his people Israel.

13 Your name, LORD, endures forever,[t]
your renown,[u] LORD, through all generations.
14 For the LORD will vindicate his people[v]
and have compassion on his servants.[w]

15 The idols of the nations[x] are silver and gold,
made by human hands.[y]
16 They have mouths, but cannot speak,[z]
eyes, but cannot see.
17 They have ears, but cannot hear,
nor is there breath[a] in their mouths.

a 1 Hebrew *Hallelu Yah*; also in verses 3 and 21

134:2 [q]S Ps 28:2; 1Ti 2:8 [r]Ps 15:1 [s]Ps 33:2; 103:1 **134:3** [t]S Lev 25:21; S Ps 20:2 [u]S Ps 124:8 **135:1** [v]Ne 7:73 **135:2** [w]S 1Ch 15:2; Lk 2:37 [x]S Ps 116:19 **135:3** [y]S 1Ch 16:34; S Ps 119:68 [z]S Ps 68:4 [a]S Ps 92:1; 147:1 **135:4** [b]S Dt 10:15 [c]Ex 19:5; Dt 7:6; Mal 3:17; S Titus 2:14 **135:5** [d]S Ps 48:1; 145:3 [e]S Ex 12:12; S 1Ch 16:25; S Job 21:22 **135:6** [f]Ps 115:3; Da 4:35 [g]Mt 6:10 **135:7** [h]S Job 5:10; Ps 68:9; Isa 30:23; Jer 10:13; 51:16; Joel 2:23; Zec 10:1 [i]Am 4:13 [j]S Dt 28:12 **135:8** [k]S Ex 4:23; S 12:12 **135:9** [l]S Ex 7:9 [m]Ps 136:10-15 **135:10** [n]Nu 21:21-25; Jos 24:8-11; Ps 44:2; 78:55; 136:17-21 **135:11** [o]S Nu 21:21 [p]S Nu 21:26 [q]S Nu 21:33 [r]S Jos 12:7-24; 24:12 **135:12** [s]S Dt 29:8 **135:13** [t]S Ex 3:15 [u]S Ps 102:12 **135:14** [v]S 1Sa 24:15; Heb 10:30* [w]S Dt 32:36 **135:15** [x]Ps 96:5; Rev 9:20 [y]Isa 2:8; 31:7; 37:19; 40:19; Jer 1:16; 10:5 **135:16** [z]S 1Ki 18:26 **135:17** [a]Jer 10:14; Hab 2:19

---

through the night. In the Psalter it concludes the "songs of ascents," as Ps 117 concludes a collection of Hallelujah psalms (Ps 111 – 117). Its date is probably postexilic.

134 title See introduction to Ps 120 – 137.

134:1 – 2 The departing worshipers call on the Levites to continue the praise of the Lord through the night (see 1Ch 9:33).

134:2 *Lift up your hands.* See 63:4 and note.

134:3 One of the Levites responds with a benediction on the worshipers (see note on 121:2; see also 124:8; 128:5).

Ps 135 A salvation-history psalm, calling Israel to praise the Lord — the one true God: Lord of all creation, Lord over all the nations, Israel's Redeemer. No doubt postexilic, it echoes many lines found elsewhere in the OT. It was clearly composed for the temple liturgy. For its place in the Great Hallel, see introduction to Ps 120 – 137. Framed with "Hallelujahs" (as are also Ps 146 – 150), its first and last stanzas are also calls to praise God. Recital of God's saving acts for Israel in Egypt and Canaan (vv. 8 – 12) makes up the middle of seven stanzas, while the remaining four constitute two pairs related to each other by theme and language (vv. 3 – 4,13 – 14; vv. 5 – 7,15 – 18).

135:1 – 2 Initial call to praise, addressed to priests and Levites (see 134:1 – 2).

135:1,3,13 *name.* See note on 5:11.

135:3 – 4 A central reason for Israel to praise the Lord (see vv. 13 – 14).

135:3 *that is pleasant.* See 133:1.

135:4 *Jacob.* A synonym for Israel (see Ge 32:28). *his treasured possession.* See Ex 19:5 and note.

135:5 – 7 The Lord is great, as well as good (v. 3); he is the absolute Lord in all creation (cf. the word about idols in vv. 15 – 18; see Jer 10:11 – 16; see also 115:3 and 96:5; 97:7 and notes).

135:6 *does whatever pleases him.* The idols can do nothing (vv. 16 – 17); they are themselves done (made) by their worshipers (v. 18). *heavens … earth … seas.* The three great domains of the visible creation, as the ancients viewed it (see Ge 1:8 – 10 and introduction to Ps 104).

135:7 *He makes clouds.* The Lord, not Baal or any other god, brings the life-giving rains (see Ps 29 and its introduction; see also Jer 14:22; Zec 10:1 and notes). *wind.* See 104:4; 148:8. The idols do not even have any "wind" (breath) in their mouths (v. 17). *storehouses.* See 33:7 and note; Job 38:22.

135:8 – 12 The Lord's triumph over Egypt and over the kings whose lands became Israel's inheritance, a concise recollection of Ex 7 – 14; Nu 21:21 – 35; Joshua.

135:13 – 14 See vv. 3 – 4 and note.

135:14 *vindicate.* Uphold against all attacks by the world powers both Israel's cause and her claim that the Lord is the only true God. *have compassion on.* See Ex 34:6 – 7 and note. *his servants.* His covenant people.

135:15 – 18 The powerlessness of the false gods and of those who trust in them (see vv. 5 – 7 and note; see also 115:4 – 8 and notes).

[18]Those who make them will be like
them,
and so will all who trust in them.

[19]All you Israelites, praise the LORD;[b]
house of Aaron, praise the
LORD;
[20]house of Levi, praise the LORD;
you who fear him, praise the
LORD.
[21]Praise be to the LORD from Zion,[c]
to him who dwells in Jerusalem.[d]

Praise the LORD.

Psalm 136

[1]Give thanks[e] to the LORD, for he is good.[f]
His love endures forever.[g]
[2]Give thanks[h] to the God of gods.[i]
His love endures forever.
[3]Give thanks[j] to the Lord of lords:[k]
His love endures forever.

[4]to him who alone does great
wonders,[l]
His love endures forever.
[5]who by his understanding[m] made the
heavens,[n]
His love endures forever.
[6]who spread out the earth[o] upon the
waters,[p]
His love endures forever.
[7]who made the great lights[q]—
His love endures forever.
[8]the sun to govern[r] the day,
His love endures forever.
[9]the moon and stars to govern the
night;
His love endures forever.

[10]to him who struck down the firstborn[s]
of Egypt
His love endures forever.
[11]and brought Israel out[t] from among
them
His love endures forever.
[12]with a mighty hand[u] and outstretched
arm;[v]
His love endures forever.
[13]to him who divided the Red Sea[a][w]
asunder
His love endures forever.
[14]and brought Israel through[x] the midst
of it,
His love endures forever.
[15]but swept Pharaoh and his army into
the Red Sea;[y]
His love endures forever.

[16]to him who led his people through the
wilderness;[z]
His love endures forever.

[17]to him who struck down great kings,[a]
His love endures forever.
[18]and killed mighty kings[b]—
His love endures forever.
[19]Sihon king of the Amorites[c]
His love endures forever.
[20]and Og king of Bashan[d]—
His love endures forever.
[21]and gave their land[e] as an inheritance,[f]
His love endures forever.
[22]an inheritance[g] to his servant Israel.[h]
His love endures forever.

[23]He remembered us[i] in our low estate
His love endures forever.
[24]and freed us[j] from our enemies.[k]
His love endures forever.
[25]He gives food[l] to every creature.
His love endures forever.

[26]Give thanks[m] to the God of heaven.[n]
His love endures forever.[o]

[a] *13* Or *the Sea of Reeds*; also in verse 15

135:19 [b] S Ps 22:23 **135:21** [c] Ps 128:5; 134:3 [d] S 1Ki 8:13; S 2Ch 6:2 **136:1** [e] Ps 105:1 [f] Ps 100:5; 106:1; 145:9; Jer 33:11; Na 1:7 [g] ver 2-26; S 2Ch 5:13; S Ezr 3:11; Ps 118:1-4 **136:2** [h] Ps 105:1 [i] S Dt 10:17 **136:3** [j] Ps 105:1 [k] S Dt 10:17; S 1Ti 6:15 **136:4** [l] S Ex 3:20; S Job 9:10 **136:5** [m] Pr 3:19; Jer 51:15 [n] S Ge 1:1 **136:6** [o] S Ge 1:1; Isa 42:5; Jer 10:12; 33:2 [p] S Ge 1:6 **136:7** [q] Ge 1:14, 16; Ps 74:16; Jas 1:17 **136:8** [r] S Ge 1:16 **136:10** [s] S Ex 4:23; S 12:12 **136:11** [t] S Ex 6:6; 13:3; Ps 105:43 **136:12** [u] S Ex 3:20; S Dt 5:15 [v] S Dt 9:29 **136:13** [w] S Ps 78:13 **136:14** [x] Ex 14:22; Ps 106:9 **136:15** [y] S Ex 14:27 **136:16** [z] S Ex 13:18; Ps 78:52 **136:17** [a] Nu 21:23-25; Jos 24:8-11; Ps 78:55; 135:9-12 **136:18** [b] Dt 29:7; S Jos 12:7-24

136:19 [c] Nu 21:21-25 **136:20** [d] Nu 21:33-35 **136:21** [e] Jos 12:1 [f] S Dt 1:38; S Jos 14:1 **136:22** [g] S Dt 29:8; Ps 78:55 [h] Isa 20:3; 41:8; 42:19; 43:10; 44:1,21; 45:4; 49:5-7 **136:23** [i] Ps 78:39; 103:14; 115:12 **136:24** [j] S Jos 10:14; S Ne 9:28 [k] S Dt 6:19 **136:25** [l] S Ge 1:30; S Mt 6:26 **136:26** [m] Ps 105:1 [n] S Ps 115:3 [o] S Ezr 3:11

135:19–21 Concluding call to praise, addressed to all who are assembled at the temple (see 115:9–11; 118:2–4).
135:20 *house of Levi.* Mentioned expressly only here in the Psalter (cf. 1Ch 23:4,30–31; 25:1; 2Ch 20:19,21).
135:21 *from Zion.* Not only in Zion but also from Zion—to the ends of the earth (see notes on 9:1; 22:22–31).
Ps 136 A salvation-history liturgy of praise to the Lord as Creator and as Israel's Redeemer. Its theme and many of its verses parallel much of Ps 135. Most likely a Levitical song leader led the recital, while the Levitical choir (1Ch 16:41; 2Ch 5:13; Ezr 3:11) or the worshipers (2Ch 7:3,6; 20:21) responded with the refrain (see 106:1; 107:1; 118:1–4,29). This liturgy concludes the Great Hallel (see introduction to Ps 120–137).

Following the initial call to praise God (vv. 1–3), the recital devotes six verses to God's creation acts (vv. 4–9), six to his deliverance of Israel out of Egypt (vv. 10–15), one to the wilderness journey (v. 16) and six to the conquest (vv. 17–22). The four concluding verses return to the same basic themes in reverse order: God's action in history in behalf of his people (vv. 23–24), God's action in the creation order (v. 25) and a closing call to praise God (v. 26). The echoing response (*"His love endures forever"*) occurs 26 times, the numerical value of the divine name Yahweh (when the Hebrew letters were used as numbers). This psalm is the only one that repeats the same refrain after each verse.
136:1–3,26 *Give thanks to.* Or "Praise" (see 7:17 and note).
136:2 *the God of gods.* See Dt 10:17; see also 135:5.
136:5 *by his understanding.* See Pr 3:19; Jer 10:12.
136:6 *upon the waters.* See 24:2 and note.
136:7–9 Direct echoes of Ge 1:16.
136:23–24 Probably a concluding summary of the deliverance recalled above, but may allude also to the deliverances experienced during the period of the judges and the reign of David.
136:26 *the God of heaven.* A Persian title for God (see note on Ezr 1:2) found frequently in Ezra, Nehemiah and Daniel. Its intent is similar to that of the language of vv. 2–3.

Psalm 137

[1]By the rivers of Babylon[p] we sat and
wept[q]
when we remembered Zion.[r]
[2]There on the poplars[s]
we hung our harps,[t]
[3]for there our captors[u] asked us for
songs,
our tormentors demanded[v] songs of
joy;
they said, "Sing us one of the songs
of Zion!"[w]

[4]How can we sing the songs of the
LORD[x]
while in a foreign land?

137:1 [p]Eze 1:1, 3; 3:15; 10:15 [q]Ne 1:4 [r]Isa 3:26; La 1:4 **137:2** [s]S Lev 23:40 [t]Job 30:31; Isa 24:8; Eze 26:13; Am 6:5 **137:3** [u]Ps 79:1-4; La 1:5 [v]S Job 30:9; Ps 80:6 [w]Eze 16:57; 22:4; 34:29 **137:4** [x]S Ne 12:46

137:5 [y]Isa 2:3; 56:7; 65:11; 66:20

[5]If I forget you,[y] Jerusalem,
may my right hand forget its skill.
[6]May my tongue cling to the roof[z] of my
mouth
if I do not remember[a] you,
if I do not consider Jerusalem[b]
my highest joy.

[7]Remember, LORD, what the Edomites[c]
did
on the day Jerusalem fell.[d]
"Tear it down," they cried,
"tear it down to its foundations!"[e]

137:6 [z]S Ps 22:15 [a]Ne 2:3 [b]S Dt 4:29; Jer 51:50; Eze 6:9 **137:7** [c]S Ge 25:30; S 2Ch 28:17; S Ps 83:6; La 4:21-22 [d]2Ki 25:1-10; Ob 1:11 [e]Ps 74:8

Ps 137 A plaintive song of the exile — of one who has recently returned from Babylon but in whose soul there lingers the bitter memory of the years in a foreign land and of the cruel events that led to that enforced stay. Here speaks the same deep love of Zion as that found in Ps 42–43; 46; 48; 84; 122; 126. The editors of the Psalter attached this song to the Great Hallel as a closing expression of supreme devotion to the city at the center of Israel's worship of the Lord (see introduction to Ps 120–137). The 12 poetic lines of the Hebrew song divide symmetrically into three stanzas of four lines each: the remembered sorrow and torment (vv. 1–3), an oath of total commitment to Jerusalem (vv. 4–6) and a call for retribution on Edom and Babylon (vv. 7–9).
137:1 *rivers.* The Tigris and Euphrates and the many canals associated with them. *we sat.* Again and again the thought of their forced separation from Zion brought them down to the posture of mourning (see Job 2:8,13; La 2:10).
137:2 *we hung our harps.* "The joyful harp is silent" (Isa 24:8) because the callous Babylonians demanded exotic entertainment with the joyful songs of distant Zion, while the exiles' instruments were only "tuned to mourning" (Job 30:31).
137:4–6 Only someone whose heart had disowned the Lord and his holy city, Jerusalem, could play the puppet on a Babylonian stage. But may I never play the harp again or sing another syllable if I am untrue to that beloved city!
137:7–9 Lord, remember Edom; and as for you, Babylon, I bless whoever does to you what you did to Jerusalem: a passionate call for redress from a loyal son of the ravaged city (see note on 5:10).
137:7 *Edomites.* The agelong animosity of Edom — descendants of Esau, Jacob's brother — showed its most dastardly face in Jerusalem's darkest hour. No doubt the author knew the Lord's judgments against that nation announced by the prophets (Isa 63:1–4; Jer 49:7–22; Eze 25:8,12–14; 35; Obadiah). *Tear it down.* Lit. "Strip her" — cities were conventionally portrayed as women. La 4:21 anticipates that Edom will be punished by suffering the same humiliation.

Town along the Euphrates River. Babylon was located between the Euphrates and Tigris Rivers. "By the rivers of Babylon we sat and wept when we remembered Zion" (Ps 137:1), but the "rivers" (or "streams") may have also included irrigation canals.

8 Daughter Babylon, doomed to
destruction,[f]
happy is the one who repays
you
according to what you have done
to us.
9 Happy is the one who seizes your
infants
and dashes them[g] against the rocks.

Psalm 138

Of David.

1 I will praise you, LORD, with all my
heart;
before the "gods"[h] I will sing[i] your
praise.
2 I will bow down toward your holy
temple[j]
and will praise your name[k]
for your unfailing love and your
faithfulness,[l]
for you have so exalted your solemn
decree
that it surpasses your fame.[m]
3 When I called,[n] you answered me;[o]
you greatly emboldened[p] me.

4 May all the kings of the earth[q] praise
you, LORD,
when they hear what you have
decreed.
5 May they sing[r] of the ways of the LORD,
for the glory of the LORD[s] is great.

6 Though the LORD is exalted, he looks
kindly on the lowly;[t]
though lofty, he sees them[u] from
afar.
7 Though I walk[v] in the midst of trouble,
you preserve my life.[w]
You stretch out your hand[x] against the
anger of my foes;[y]
with your right hand[z] you save me.[a]
8 The LORD will vindicate[b] me;
your love, LORD, endures forever[c]—
do not abandon[d] the works of your
hands.[e]

137:8 [f] Isa 13:1, 19; 47:1-15; Jer 25:12, 26; 50:1; 50:2-51:58 **137:9** [g] S 2Ki 8:12; S Isa 13:16; Lk 19:44 **138:1** [h] Ps 95:3; 96:4 [i] Ps 27:6; 108:1 **138:2** [j] S 1Ki 8:29; S Ps 5:7 [k] Ps 74:21; 97:12; 140:13 [l] Ps 108:4; 115:1 [m] Ps 119:9 **138:3** [n] Ps 18:6; 30:2; 99:6; 116:4 [o] S Ps 118:5 [p] Pr 28:1; S Ac 4:29 **138:4** [q] Ps 72:11; 102:15 **138:5** [r] S Ps 51:14; 71:16; 145:7 [s] Ps 21:5 **138:6** [t] S Ps 113:6 [u] S Ps 40:4; S Mt 23:12 **138:7** [v] Ps 23:4 [w] S Ps 41:2 [x] S Ex 7:5 [y] Ps 7:6 [z] Ps 20:6; 60:5; 108:6 [a] Ps 17:7, 14 **138:8** [b] Php 1:6 [c] S Ezr 3:11; Ps 100:5 [d] S Ps 51:11 [e] S Job 10:3, 8

137:8 *Daughter Babylon.* A personification of Babylon (see note on 2Ki 19:21). *doomed to destruction.* The author and those who took up this psalm surely knew of the Lord's announced judgments on this cruel destroyer (Isa 13; 47; Jer 50 – 51). In the day of the Lord's judgment Babylon was to receive what she had done to others (see Jer 50:15,29; 51:24,35,49; cf. Rev 18:5 – 6). For the principle involved, see note on Ob 15. *happy is the one who repays you.* Because a cruel international predator has been removed from the earth (see Isa 14:3 – 8 and notes; cf. Jer 51:47 – 48; Rev 19:1 – 3).
137:9 *your infants.* War was as cruel then as now; women and children were not spared (see 2Ki 8:12; 15:16; Isa 13:16,18; Hos 10:14; 13:16; Am 1:13; Na 3:10). For the final announcement of the destruction of the "Babylon" that persists in its warfare against the City of God, and the joy with which that announcement is greeted, see Rev 14:18 and note; 18:1 — 19:4.
Ps 138 – 145 A final collection of eight Davidic psalms brings the Psalter toward its close. While much in some of these psalms points to a later, even postexilic, date, they clearly stand in the tradition of psalmody of which David was the reputed father and echo the language and concerns of the earlier Davidic psalms. The collection is framed by songs of praise (Ps 138; 145). The first of these extols the greatness of the Lord's glory as displayed in his answering the prayer ("call") of the "lowly" when suffering at the hands of the proud. The last, employing a grand and intricately woven alphabetic acrostic design, extols the glorious majesty of the Lord as displayed in his benevolent care over all his creatures — especially those who "call" on him (look to him in every need). Within this frame have been placed six prayers — with certain interlocking themes that will be pointed out in the notes on the individual psalms.

This final Davidic collection contains the Psalter's two most magnificent expositions of the greatness and goodness of God, one of them (Ps 139) focusing on his relationship with an individual, the other (Ps 145) on his relationship with his whole creation.
Ps 138 A song of praise for God's saving help against threatening foes — understood by many to have been originally on the lips of a king. In some respects it is like Ps 18, though in style and scope much less grand. Two (Hebrew) four-line stanzas (vv. 1 – 3,6 – 8) develop the main theme; at the center a two-line stanza (vv. 4 – 5) expands the company of those who praise the Lord to "all the kings of the earth." The psalm shares nearly a third of its vocabulary with Ps 145.
138 title See introduction to Ps 138 – 145.
138:1 – 3 Praise for God's faithful love shown in answer to prayers for help.
138:1 *heart.* See note on 4:7. *"gods."* Either pagan kings (see vv. 4 – 5) or the "gods" they claimed to represent (see introduction to Ps 82; see also note on 82:1).
138:2 *your holy temple.* If David is in fact the author, reference is to the tent he set up for the ark (2Sa 6:17) — many psalms ascribed to David refer to the "temple" (see, e.g., 5:7; 11:4; 18:6; 27:4; see also Ps 30 title). *name.* See note on 5:11. *love and … faithfulness.* See note on 36:5. *love.* See v. 8; see also note on 6:4. *your solemn decree.* Perhaps God's command that effects his purposes in the world (see 147:15), but more likely his promises (see v. 4 and note). God's display of his love and faithfulness in his answers to prayer (v. 3) has made his name ("fame") and promises more magnificent than anything else that even kings may prize.
138:3 *I called, you answered.* See note on 118:5.
138:4 – 5 The center of the poem (see note on 6:6): a wish that all the kings of earth may come to join in praising the Lord (see note on 9:1). The verbs, however, could be read as simple futures. In that case, these verses voice a confident expectation.
138:4 *what you have decreed.* God's grand commitments either to his people or to the royal house of David (see 18:30 and note; there, too, God's word and "ways" [v. 5] are linked).
138:5 *ways of the LORD.* See 25:10 and note. God's words and his ways are in harmony, and together they display his great glory (cf. Ps 145).
138:6 – 8 A testimony to God's condescending and faithful love, concluded with a prayer.
138:6 See 113:4 – 9 and notes. *sees them from afar.* Cf. the acknowledgment of the psalmist in 139:2.
138:8 *will vindicate me.* See 57:2 and note. *do not abandon the works of your hands.* A concluding prayer that the faithfulness of God celebrated here truly "endures forever."

Psalm 139

For the director of music.
Of David. A psalm.

1 You have searched me,[f] LORD,
and you know[g] me.
2 You know when I sit and when I rise;[h]
you perceive my thoughts[i] from
afar.
3 You discern my going out[j] and my
lying down;
you are familiar with all my ways.[k]
4 Before a word is on my tongue
you, LORD, know it completely.[l]
5 You hem me in[m] behind and before,
and you lay your hand upon me.
6 Such knowledge is too wonderful
for me,[n]
too lofty[o] for me to attain.

7 Where can I go from your Spirit?
Where can I flee[p] from your
presence?
8 If I go up to the heavens,[q] you are
there;
if I make my bed[r] in the depths, you
are there.
9 If I rise on the wings of the dawn,
if I settle on the far side of the sea,
10 even there your hand will guide me,[s]
your right hand[t] will hold me fast.
11 If I say, "Surely the darkness will
hide me
and the light become night
around me,"
12 even the darkness will not be dark[u] to
you;
the night will shine like the day,
for darkness is as light to you.

13 For you created my inmost being;[v]
you knit me together[w] in my
mother's womb.[x]
14 I praise you[y] because I am fearfully and
wonderfully made;
your works are wonderful,[z]
I know that full well.
15 My frame was not hidden from you
when I was made[a] in the secret
place,
when I was woven together[b] in the
depths of the earth.[c]

139:1 [f] S Ps 17:3; Ro 8:27 [g] Ps 44:21 **139:2** [h] 2Ki 19:27 [i] Ps 94:11; Pr 24:12; Jer 12:3 **139:3** [j] 2Ki 19:27 [k] S Job 31:4 **139:4** [l] S Heb 4:13 **139:5** [m] S 1Sa 25:16; Ps 32:10; 34:7; 125:2 **139:6** [n] S Ps 131:1 [o] Ro 11:33 **139:7** [p] Jer 23:24; Jnh 1:3 **139:8** [q] Dt 30:12-15; Am 9:2-3 [r] Job 17:13 **139:10** [s] Ps 23:3 [t] Ps 108:6; Isa 41:10 **139:12** [u] Job 34:22; Da 2:22 **139:13** [v] Ps 119:73 [w] S Job 10:11 [x] Isa 44:2, 24; 46:3; 49:5; Jer 1:5 **139:14** [y] Ps 119:164; 145:10 [z] S Job 40:19 **139:15** [a] Ecc 11:5 [b] S Job 10:11 [c] S Ps 63:9

Ps 139 A prayer for God to examine the heart and see its true devotion. Like Job, the author firmly claims his loyalty to the Lord. Nowhere (outside Job) does one find expressed such profound awareness of how awesome it is to ask God to examine not only one's life but also one's soul. The thought progresses steadily in four poetic paragraphs of six verses each (vv. 1–6,7–12,13–18,19–24), and each paragraph is concluded with a couplet that elaborates on the unit's central theme. References to God's searching and knowing begin and end the prayer.
139 title *For the director of music.* See note on Ps 4 title. *Of David.* See introduction to Ps 138–145.
139:1–6 God, you know me perfectly—here no abstract doctrine of divine omniscience but far beyond David's knowledge of himself: his every action (v. 2a), his every undertaking (v. 3a) and the manner in which he pursues it (v. 3b), even his thoughts before they are fully crystallized (v. 2b) and his words before they are uttered (v. 4). See also v. 23.
139:1 *searched me … know me.* See note on vv. 23–24.
139:2 *perceive … from afar.* See the contrast in 138:8 (see also note there). *my thoughts.* Those that pertain to my wishes, desires and/or plans.
139:5–6 The psalmist's response to the fact that God knows him so well.
139:5 *You hem me in.* To keep me under scrutiny. *lay your hand upon me.* So that I do not escape you. The figures are different in Job 13:27, but the thought is much the same. *hand.* Or "hands."
139:6 *too wonderful for me.* Yours is a "wonder" knowledge, beyond my human capacity—the Hebrew term regularly applies to God's wondrous acts (see 77:11,14, "miracles"; Ex 15:11).
139:7–12 There is no hiding from God—here no abstract doctrine of divine omnipresence but an awed confession that God cannot be escaped (see Jer 23:23–24).
139:7 *your Spirit … your presence.* See 51:11 and note; Isa 63:9–10; Eze 39:29 ("face … Spirit").
139:8 *the heavens … the depths.* The two vertical extremes.
139:9 *wings of the dawn … far side of the sea.* The two horizontal extremes: east and west (the sea is the Mediterranean). Using a literary figure in which the totality is denoted by referring to its two extremes (merism), vv. 8–9 specify all spatial reality, the whole creation.
139:10 *guide me … hold me fast.* Though this language occurs in 73:23–24 to indicate God's solicitous care, it here denotes God's inescapable supervision, not unlike the thought of v. 5.
139:11–12 Just as the whole creation offers no hiding place (vv. 8–9), neither does the darkness of night (see Job 34:22).
139:13–18 God himself put David together in the womb—here no abstract doctrine of divine omnipotence but the One who ordained the span of Davd's life before he was born. God knew him so thoroughly because he made him.
139:13 *created.* The Hebrew for this verb is the same as in Ge 14:19,22; Pr 8:22 ("brought … forth"), not as in Ge 1:1,21,27. *inmost being.* Lit. "kidneys"—in Hebrew idiom, the innermost center of emotions and of moral sensitivity—that which God tests and examines when he searches (vv. 1,23) a person (see note on 7:9).
139:14 *fearfully … wonderfully … wonderful.* You know me as the One who formed me (see vv. 15–16), but I cannot begin to comprehend this creature you have fashioned. I can only look upon him with awe and wonder (see note on v. 6)—and praise you (see Ecc 11:5).
139:15 *secret place … depths of the earth.* Reference is to the womb: called "the secret place" because it normally conceals (see 2Sa 12:12), and it shares with "the depths of the earth" (see note on 30:1) associations with darkness, dampness and separation from the visible realm of life. Moreover, both phrases refer to the place of the dead (63:9; Job 14:13; Isa 44:23; 45:19), with which on one level the womb appears to have been associated: Humans come from the dust and return to the dust (90:3; Ge 3:19; Ecc 3:20; 12:7), and the womb is the "depth"-like place where they are formed (see Isa 44:2,24; 49:5; Jer 1:5).

16 Your eyes saw my unformed body;
all the days ordained[d] for me were
written in your book
before one of them came to be.
17 How precious to me are your
thoughts,[a][e] God![f]
How vast is the sum of them!
18 Were I to count them,[g]
they would outnumber the grains
of sand[h] —
when I awake,[i] I am still with
you.

19 If only you, God, would slay the
wicked![j]
Away from me,[k] you who are
bloodthirsty![l]
20 They speak of you with evil intent;
your adversaries[m] misuse your
name.[n]
21 Do I not hate those[o] who hate you,
LORD,
and abhor[p] those who are in
rebellion against you?
22 I have nothing but hatred for them;
I count them my enemies.[q]
23 Search me,[r] God, and know my
heart;[s]
test me and know my anxious
thoughts.
24 See if there is any offensive way[t]
in me,
and lead me[u] in the way
everlasting.

139:16 [d] S Job 33:29; S Ps 90:12 **139:17** [e] S Ps 92:5 [f] S Job 5:9 **139:18** [g] Ps 40:5 [h] S Job 29:18 [i] S Ps 3:5 **139:19** [j] Ps 5:6; Isa 11:4 [k] S Ps 6:8 [l] S Ps 59:2 **139:20** [m] S Ps 65:7 [n] S Dt 5:11 **139:21** [o] 2Ch 19:2; Ps 31:6; 119:113 [p] S Ps 26:5 **139:22** [q] Mt 5:43 **139:23** [r] Job 31:6 [s] S 1Sa 16:7; S 1Ch 29:17; S Ps 7:9; Pr 17:3; Jer 11:20; S Rev 2:23 **139:24** [t] Jer 25:5; 36:3 [u] Ps 5:8; 23:2; 143:10

140:1 [v] Ps 17:13; S 25:20; 59:2; 71:4; 142:6; 143:9 [w] ver 11; Ps 86:14 **140:2** [x] Ps 36:4; 52:2; Pr 6:14; 16:27; Isa 59:4; Hos 7:15 [y] S Ps 68:30 **140:3** [z] Ps 57:4 [a] Ps 58:4;

Psalm 140[b]

For the director of music.
A psalm of David.

1 Rescue me,[v] LORD, from evildoers;
protect me from the violent,[w]
2 who devise evil plans[x] in their hearts
and stir up war[y] every day.
3 They make their tongues as sharp as[z] a
serpent's;
the poison of vipers[a] is on their lips.[c]

4 Keep me safe,[b] LORD, from the hands of
the wicked;[c]
protect me from the violent,
who devise ways to trip my feet.
5 The arrogant have hidden a snare[d]
for me;
they have spread out the cords of
their net[e]
and have set traps[f] for me along my
path.

6 I say to the LORD, "You are my God."[g]
Hear, LORD, my cry for mercy.[h]
7 Sovereign LORD,[i] my strong deliverer,
you shield my head in the day of
battle.

[a] 17 Or *How amazing are your thoughts concerning me*
[b] In Hebrew texts 140:1-13 is numbered 140:2-14.
[c] 3 The Hebrew has *Selah* (a word of uncertain meaning) here and at the end of verses 5 and 8.

Ro 3:13*; Jas 3:8 **140:4** [b] Ps 141:9 [c] S Ps 36:11 **140:5** [d] S Job 34:30; S Ps 119:110 [e] S Job 18:8 [f] Job 18:9; Ps 31:4; S 38:12 **140:6** [g] S Ps 16:2 [h] S Ps 28:2,6 **140:7** [i] Ps 68:20

139:16 *all the days ordained.* The span of life and its events sovereignly determined. *your book.* The heavenly royal register of God's decisions (see note on 56:8).

139:17 – 18 The psalmist's response: God's thoughts of him are vast and precious.

139:17 *your thoughts.* As expressed in his works — and in contrast with "my thoughts" (v. 2; see note there).

139:18 *when I awake.* The sleep of exhaustion overcomes every attempt to count God's thoughts/works (see 63:6; 119:148), and waking only floods my soul once more with the sense of the presence of this God. On the other hand, reference may be to "awaking" from the sleep of death, as in Ps 17:15 (see also 2Ki 4:31; Job 14:12; Isa 26:9; Jer 51:39,57; Da 12:2). If so, the psalmist extends the sphere of God's presence to beyond the "gates of death."

139:19 – 24 David's zeal for God and his loyalty to God set him against all God's adversaries (see 5:10 and note).

139:19 *If only you … would slay the wicked!* Jealous impatience with God's patience toward the wicked — whose end will come (Isa 11:3 – 4). But the psalmist leaves it to God (see Dt 32:35 and note).

139:20 *misuse your name.* Perhaps by calling down curses on those trying to be the faithful servants of God (see note on Ge 12:3).

139:21 – 22 A declaration of loyalty that echoes the pledge required by ancient Near Eastern kings of their vassals (e.g., "With my friend you shall be friend, and with my enemy you shall be enemy," from a treaty between Mursilis II, a Hittite king, and Tette of Nuhassi, fourteenth century BC).

139:23 – 24 Examine me, see the integrity of my devotion and keep me true (see v. 1; 17:3 – 5 and notes).

139:23 *Search me … know my heart.* After David calls for redress against God's and his enemies (vv. 19 – 22), he then asks God to see if he has said or done anything offensive (vv. 23b – 24). *heart.* See note on 4:7. *anxious thoughts.* See 94:19. It is no light matter to be examined by God.

139:24 *the way everlasting.* See note on 16:9 – 11.

Ps 140 A prayer for deliverance from the plots and slander of unscrupulous enemies. It recalls Ps 58 and 64 but employs a number of words found nowhere else in the OT. Four well-balanced stanzas are followed by a two-verse conclusion. The prayer is strikingly rich in physiological allusions: heart, head, tongue, lips, hands, feet — also ears (lit. "Give ear to," v. 6) and teeth (by a wordplay on the Hebrew for "make … sharp," v. 3). See introduction to Ps 141; see also introduction to Ps 138 – 145.

140 title *For the director of music.* See note on Ps 4 title. *of David.* See note on Ps 138 title.

140:1 – 3 Rescue me from those "vipers."

140:1 *LORD.* Hebrew *Yahweh;* God's personal name occurs seven times (the number of completeness) in this psalm.

140:2 *hearts.* See note on 4:7.

140:3 *tongues.* See note on 5:9. *poison of vipers.* See 58:4 and note. For *Selah,* see NIV text note and note on 3:2.

140:4 – 5 Protect me from those proud and wicked hunters (see 10:2 – 11 and notes).

140:5 *The arrogant.* See note on 31:23. *snare … net … traps.* See 141:9 – 10.

140:6 – 8 Do not let these wicked men attain their evil designs against me.

140:6 *Hear, LORD, my cry for mercy.* A thematic and verbal link with 141:1; 142:1; 143:1.

[8] Do not grant the wicked[j] their desires, LORD;
do not let their plans succeed.
[9] Those who surround me proudly rear their heads;
may the mischief of their lips engulf them.[k]
[10] May burning coals fall on them;
may they be thrown into the fire,[l]
into miry pits, never to rise.
[11] May slanderers not be established in the land;
may disaster hunt down the violent.[m]

[12] I know that the LORD secures justice for the poor[n]
and upholds the cause[o] of the needy.[p]
[13] Surely the righteous will praise your name,[q]
and the upright will live[r] in your presence.[s]

Psalm 141

A psalm of David.

[1] I call to you, LORD, come quickly[t] to me;
hear me[u] when I call to you.
[2] May my prayer be set before you like incense;[v]
may the lifting up of my hands[w] be like the evening sacrifice.[x]

[3] Set a guard over my mouth,[y] LORD;
keep watch over the door of my lips.[z]
[4] Do not let my heart[a] be drawn to what is evil
so that I take part in wicked deeds[b]
along with those who are evildoers;
do not let me eat their delicacies.[c]

[5] Let a righteous man strike me — that is a kindness;
let him rebuke me[d] — that is oil on my head.[e]
My head will not refuse it,
for my prayer will still be against the deeds of evildoers.

[6] Their rulers will be thrown down from the cliffs,[f]
and the wicked will learn that my words were well spoken.
[7] They will say, "As one plows[g] and breaks up the earth,[h]
so our bones have been scattered at the mouth[i] of the grave."

[8] But my eyes are fixed[j] on you, Sovereign LORD;
in you I take refuge[k] — do not give me over to death.

140:8 [j]Ps 10:2-3; S 66:7 **140:9** [k]Pr 18:7 **140:10** [l]Ps 11:6; 21:9; S Mt 3:10; Lk 12:49; Rev 20:15 **140:11** [m]S Ps 34:21 **140:12** [n]S Ps 82:3 [o]S 1Ki 8:45 [p]S Ps 35:10 **140:13** [q]S Ps 138:2 [r]S Ps 11:7 [s]Ps 16:11 **141:1** [t]S Ps 22:19 [u]S Ps 4:1; 5:1-2; 27:7; 143:1 **141:2** [v]S Lk 1:9; Rev 5:8; 8:3 [w]S Ps 28:2; 63:4; 1Ti 2:8 [x]S Ex 29:39,41; 30:8 **141:3** [y]S Ps 34:13; Jas 1:26; 3:8 [z]S Ps 12:2 **141:4** [a]S Jos 24:23 [b]S Ps 106:29 [c]Pr 23:1-3 **141:5** [d]Pr 9:8; 19:25; 25:12; Ecc 7:5 [e]S Ex 29:7; Ps 23:5 **141:6** [f]S 2Ch 25:12 **141:7** [g]Ps 129:3 [h]Nu 16:32-33 [i]S Nu 16:30 **141:8** [j]Ps 123:2 [k]Ps 2:12; 11:1

140:9 – 11 Let the harm they plot against me recoil on their heads (see note on 5:10; cf. note on Pr 26:27).
140:10 *burning coals.* For the reference, see Lev. 16:12; Job 41:21; Pr 6:28; Isa 47:14; Eze 24:11. Other examples of this imagery for divine judgment may be found in Ps 18:8; 120:4; Eze 10:2. *fire ... miry pits.* This combination, together with the conjunction of fire and darkness in Job 15:30; 20:26, suggests the idea that the fire of God's judgment (see, e.g., 21:9; 97:3; Isa 1:31; 26:11; 33:14) reaches even into the realm of the dead (see Job 31:12 and note on Ps 30:1). *never to rise.* See 36:12; Isa 26:14.
140:11 *hunt down.* May the ruin these hunters (vv. 4 – 5) intended to bring on me hunt them down.
140:12 – 13 Confidence in God's just judgment (see note on 3:8).
140:12 *poor ... needy.* See notes on 9:18; 34:6.
140:13 *the righteous.* See note on 1:5. *will praise.* Having experienced God's help (see notes on 7:17; 9:1). *will live in your presence.* In contrast to the wicked (v. 10; see notes on 11:7; 16:9 – 11).
Ps 141 A prayer for deliverance from the wicked and their evil ways. The stanza structure of the first half (vv. 1 – 4: two couplets plus three couplets) is repeated in the second half (vv. 6 – 10), while at the center (v. 5) a single couplet develops a complementary theme (see note on v. 5). Like Ps 140, the prayer is profuse in its physiological allusions: hands, mouth, lips, heart, head, bones, eyes (see introduction to that psalm).
141 title See introduction to Ps 138 – 145.
141:1 – 2 Initial appeal for God to hear.
141:1 *hear me when I call.* See 140:6 and note.
141:2 *my prayer ... like incense.* See notes on Ex 30:1; Lk 1:9; Rev 5:8. *like the evening sacrifice.* See Ex 29:38 – 41; Nu 28:3 – 8. These sacrifices are frequently mentioned (see 1Ki 18:29; 2Ki 16:15; 1Ch 16:40; 2Ch 13:11; 31:3; Ezr 3:3; 9:4 – 5; Da 9:21).
141:3 – 4 A plea that God will keep him from speaking, desiring or doing what is evil.
141:4 *Do not let my heart be drawn to ... evil.* Keep me from yielding to the example and urgings of the wicked (see Pr 1:10 – 16). *heart.* See note on 4:7. *their delicacies.* Usually taken to refer to the luxuriant tables the wicked set from their unjust gains — thus a prayer that the psalmist be kept from acquiring an appetite for such unholy dainties. But the noun occurs only here, and it may refer to the pleasant sounding, but deceptive and evil, words of the wicked — thus a prayer that the psalmist be kept from taking into his mouth the talk of the wicked that corresponds with their evil way of life (cf. v. 6 and note). Words related to this noun are elsewhere used to characterize words/thoughts (see Pr 15:26; 16:21; 23:8).
141:5 The center of the poem (see note on 6:6). *Let a righteous man strike me.* The disciplining blows and rebukes of the righteous are the true "kindness" (Hebrew *ḥesed*, meaning "love" or "acts of authentic friendship"; see Pr 27:6; see also note on Ps 6:4). *oil on my head.* See note on 23:5. *My head ... deeds of evildoers.* Perhaps better: "Let my head not refuse it (this 'oil' from the righteous), for my prayer is still against their (the wicked's) evil deeds."
141:6 – 7 The destiny of the wicked. *Their rulers will be thrown down ... the wicked will learn ... They will say.* Perhaps better: "Let their rulers be thrown down ... let the wicked learn ... Let them say."
141:6 *my words.* Of commitment to righteousness, as in vv. 3 – 5. *well spoken.* Good and right.
141:8 – 10 A plea that God will deliver from the designs of the wicked.
141:8 *do not give me over to death.* As you do the wicked (see v. 7; see also 73:18 – 20,23 – 26 and notes).

9 Keep me safe[l] from the traps set by
evildoers,[m]
from the snares[n] they have laid
for me.
10 Let the wicked fall[o] into their own nets,
while I pass by in safety.[p]

Psalm 142[a]

A *maskil*[b] of David.
When he was in the cave.[q] A prayer.

1 I cry aloud[r] to the LORD;
I lift up my voice to the LORD for
mercy.[s]
2 I pour out before him my complaint;[t]
before him I tell my trouble.[u]

3 When my spirit grows faint[v] within me,
it is you who watch over my way.
In the path where I walk
people have hidden a snare for me.
4 Look and see, there is no one at my
right hand;
no one is concerned for me.
I have no refuge;[w]
no one cares[x] for my life.

5 I cry to you, LORD;
I say, "You are my refuge,[y]
my portion[z] in the land of the living."[a]

6 Listen to my cry,[b]
for I am in desperate need;[c]
rescue me[d] from those who pursue me,
for they are too strong[e] for me.
7 Set me free from my prison,[f]
that I may praise your name.[g]
Then the righteous will gather about me
because of your goodness to me.[h]

Psalm 143

A psalm of David.

1 LORD, hear my prayer,[i]
listen to my cry for mercy;[j]
in your faithfulness[k] and righteousness[l]
come to my relief.
2 Do not bring your servant into
judgment,
for no one living is righteous[m] before
you.
3 The enemy pursues me,
he crushes me to the ground;
he makes me dwell in the darkness[n]
like those long dead.[o]

[a] In Hebrew texts 142:1-7 is numbered 142:2-8.
[b] Title: Probably a literary or musical term

141:9 [l]Ps 140:4 [m]S Ps 64:5 [n]S Ps 38:12 **141:10** [o]Ps 7:15; 35:8; 57:6 [p]Ps 124:7 **142:Title** [q]1Sa 22:1; 24:3; Ps 57 Title **142:1** [r]S 1Ki 8:52; Ps 3:4 [s]Ps 30:8 **142:2** [t]Ps 64:1 [u]S Ps 50:15 **142:3** [v]Ps 6:2; 77:3; 84:2; 88:4; 143:4,7; Jer 8:18; La 1:22 **142:4** [w]Jer 25:35 [x]Jer 30:17 **142:5** [y]S Ps 46:1 [z]S Dt 32:9; Ps 16:5 [a]S Job 28:13; Ps 27:13 **142:6** [b]S Ps 17:1 [c]S Ps 79:8 [d]S Ps 25:20 [e]Jer 31:11 **142:7** [f]S Ps 66:11 [g]Ps 7:17; 9:2 [h]S 2Ch 6:41 **143:1** [i]S Ps 141:1 [j]S Ps 28:2; 130:2 [k]S Ex 34:6; Ps 89:1-2 [l]Ps 71:2 **143:2** [m]S Ps 14:3; Ro 3:10 **143:3** [n]S Ps 107:10 [o]La 3:6

141:9 *traps ... snares.* Perhaps, as usual, the plots of enemies to bring him down (as in 38:12; 64:5; 91:3; 140:5; 142:3; see note on 9:15)—note this link with Ps 140; 142.
141:10 *Let the wicked fall.* See note on 5:10. *fall into their own nets.* In Hebrew a verbal echo of 140:10 ("thrown into ... miry pits").
Ps 142 A plaintive prayer for deliverance from powerful enemies—when powerless, alone and without refuge. Much of its language echoes that of other psalms (see notes below). Apart from the introduction (vv. 1–2) and conclusion (v. 7b), the prayer (in Hebrew) is composed of two four-line stanzas (vv. 3–4,5–7a).
142 title *maskil.* See note on Ps 32 title. *of David.* See introduction to Ps 138–145. *When ... cave.* See note on Ps 57 title. *A prayer.* See note on Ps 17 title.
142:1–2 Initial appeal—using the formal third person "I cry aloud to the LORD" (as was often done when addressing kings), equivalent to: "I cry aloud to you, LORD."
142:1 Very similar to 77:1. *lift up my voice to the LORD for mercy.* See 140:6 and note.
142:2 *I pour out before him my complaint.* Very similar to language found in the title of Ps 102.
142:3–4 Description of his "desperate need" (v. 6).
142:3 *When my spirit grows faint.* Because he is overwhelmed by his situation (see 22:14–15)—a thematic and verbal link with 143:6 (see also 77:3; Ps 102 title; Jnh 2:7). *you who watch over.* And are concerned about (cf. v. 4). *hidden a snare for me.* A thematic and verbal link with 140:5; 141:9–10 (see note on 9:15).
142:4 *right hand.* Where one's helper or defender stands (see 16:8 and note). *is concerned.* In Hebrew a less common synonym of "know" (v. 3, "watch over"); see Ru 2:10,19 ("notice"). *cares for.* See Dt 11:12.
142:5–7 Prayer for rescue.
142:5 *You are my refuge.* See 71:7; Jer 17:17. *portion.* The sustainer and preserver of his life (see 73:26 and note). *in the land of the living.* See 27:13 and note; 52:5; 116:9.
142:6 *Listen to my cry.* See 17:1. *rescue me.* See 143:9; 144:7.
142:7 *prison.* Metaphor for the sense of being fettered by affliction (see note on 18:19; see also Job 36:8). *that I may praise your name.* In celebration of your saving help (see note on 7:17). *name.* See note on 5:11. *righteous.* See note on 1:5. *will gather about me.* He will no longer be alone. The conclusion expresses an expectant word of confidence (see note on 3:8). *your goodness to me.* See 13:6; 116:7.
Ps 143 A prayer for deliverance from enemies and for divine leading. This is the seventh and final penitential psalm (see introduction to Ps 6). The psalm is composed of two balanced divisions of seven Hebrew lines each (vv. 1–6,7–10) and a two-line concluding reiteration of the basic appeal of the prayer (vv. 11–12). The three middle lines (vv. 3–4) of the first division describe the psalmist's distress, while the three middle lines (vv. 8–9) of the second division express the psalmist's trust in the Lord to deliver him from his distress. Appeal to God's righteousness (vv. 1,11) and the author's self-identification as "your servant" (vv. 2,12) enclose the prayer. See also his appeal to God's faithfulness (v. 1) and unfailing love (v. 12), which together form a frequent pair (see note on 36:5). For another enclosure, see note on v. 7.
143 title See introduction to Ps 138–145.
143:1–2 Initial appeal.
143:1 *my cry for mercy.* See 140:6 and note. *righteousness.* See note on 4:1.
143:2 As he begins his prayer, he pleads that God not sit in judgment over his servant (he knows his own failings; see also v. 10) but that he focus his judicial attention on the enemy's harsh and unwarranted attacks. *your servant.* A verbal link with 144:10—which suggests why this psalm was traditionally ascribed to David (see also 78:70; 132:10 and notes).
143:3–4 The distress he suffers.
143:3 The last half of this verse appears almost verbatim in La 3:6. *in the darkness.* As one cut off from the enjoyments of life (see v. 7; see also notes on 27:1; 30:1).

[4]So my spirit grows faint within me;
my heart within me is dismayed.[p]
[5]I remember[q] the days of long ago;
I meditate[r] on all your works
and consider what your hands have done.
[6]I spread out my hands[s] to you;
I thirst for you like a parched land.[a]

[7]Answer me quickly,[t] LORD;
my spirit fails.[u]
Do not hide your face[v] from me
or I will be like those who go down to the pit.
[8]Let the morning bring me word of your unfailing love,[w]
for I have put my trust in you.
Show me the way[x] I should go,
for to you I entrust my life.[y]
[9]Rescue me[z] from my enemies,[a] LORD,
for I hide myself in you.
[10]Teach me[b] to do your will,
for you are my God;[c]
may your good Spirit
lead[d] me on level ground.[e]

[11]For your name's sake,[f] LORD, preserve my life;[g]
in your righteousness,[h] bring me out of trouble.
[12]In your unfailing love, silence my enemies;[i]
destroy all my foes,[j]
for I am your servant.[k]

143:4 [p]Ps 30:7 **143:5** [q]Ps 77:6 [r]S Ge 24:63 **143:6** [s]S Ex 9:29; S Job 11:13 **143:7** [t]S Ps 69:17 [u]S Ps 142:3 [v]S Ps 22:24; 27:9; 30:7 **143:8** [w]Ps 6:4; 90:14 [x]S Ex 33:13; S Job 34:32; Ps 27:11; 32:8 [y]Ps 25:1-2; S 86:4 **143:9** [z]S Ps 140:1 [a]S Ps 18:17; 31:15 **143:10** [b]S Ps 119:12 [c]Ps 31:14 [d]S Ne 9:20; Ps 25:4-5 [e]Ps 26:12 **143:11** [f]Ps 25:11 [g]S Ps 41:2 [h]Ps 31:1; 71:2 **143:12** [i]Ps 8:2 [j]Ps 54:5 [k]S Ps 116:16

144:1 [l]S Ge 49:24 **144:2** [m]Ps 59:9; 91:2 [n]Ps 27:1; 37:39; 43:2 [o]S Ge 15:1; S Ps 18:2 [p]S Jdg 4:23; S Ps 18:39 **144:3** [q]Heb 2:6 **144:4** [r]S Job 7:7; 27:3; Isa 2:22

Psalm 144

Of David.

[1]Praise be to the LORD my Rock,[l]
who trains my hands for war,
my fingers for battle.
[2]He is my loving God and my fortress,[m]
my stronghold[n] and my deliverer,
my shield,[o] in whom I take refuge,
who subdues peoples[b][p] under me.

[3]LORD, what are human beings[q] that you care for them,
mere mortals that you think of them?
[4]They are like a breath;[r]
their days are like a fleeting shadow.[s]

[5]Part your heavens,[t] LORD, and come down;[u]
touch the mountains, so that they smoke.[v]
[6]Send forth lightning[w] and scatter[x] the enemy;
shoot your arrows[y] and rout them.
[7]Reach down your hand from on high;[z]
deliver me and rescue me[a]

[a] 6 The Hebrew has *Selah* (a word of uncertain meaning) here. [b] 2 Many manuscripts of the Masoretic Text, Dead Sea Scrolls, Aquila, Jerome and Syriac; most manuscripts of the Masoretic Text *subdues my people*

[s]S 1Ch 29:15; S Job 14:2; S Jas 4:14 **144:5** [t]Ps 18:9; Isa 64:1 [u]S Ge 11:5; S Ps 57:3 [v]Ps 104:32 **144:6** [w]Hab 3:11; Zec 9:14 [x]S Ps 59:11; S 68:1 [y]Ps 7:12-13; 18:14 **144:7** [z]S 2Sa 22:17 [a]Ps 3:7; S 57:3

143:4 *my spirit grows faint.* See note on 142:3. *heart.* See note on 4:7.
143:5–6 Remembrance of God's past acts of deliverance encourages him in his appeal.
143:6 *spread out my hands.* In prayer (see 44:20; 88:9; Ex 9:29). *thirst for you.* See note on 63:1. For *Selah*, see NIV text note and note on 3:2.
143:7–10 The prayer.
143:7 *my spirit fails.* Or perhaps: "my spirit faints with longing," which parallels the construction in 119:81; in view of the next line the thought appears closer to that of 104:29 (where "breath" translates the same Hebrew word as that for "spirit" here). Ultimately, the failing of "my spirit" will be healed by the leading of "your good Spirit" (v. 10)—the two references enclose the prayer. *hide your face.* See note on 13:1. *the pit.* See v. 3 and note on 30:1.
143:8 *the morning.* Of salvation from the present "darkness" (v. 3; see introduction to Ps 57; see also note on 101:8). *unfailing love.* See v. 12; see also note on 6:4. *I have put my trust in you … to you I entrust my life.* See 25:1–2; see also 24:4 and note. *Show me the way.* See v. 10. Deliverance from the enemy is not enough—either for God's "servant" (vv. 2,12) or for entrance into life.
143:10 *level ground.* See note on 26:12.
143:11–12 Concluding reiteration of the prayer (see introduction). Note how "your righteousness," "your unfailing love" and "your servant" all establish links with vv. 1–2.
143:11 *For your name's sake.* See note on 23:3.
143:12 *destroy all my foes.* See note on 5:10.
Ps 144 A prayer for deliverance from treacherous enemies, composed in the mode of a royal prayer. Verses 1–10 show much affinity to Ps 18, with vv. 5–7 all appearing to be variations on lines found there (see notes below). The remaining lines of this section contain similar echoes of other psalms, and the author may have drawn directly on them. This first part of the psalm is fairly typical of the prayers of the Psalter. What follows is clearly composite: Verse 11 recapitulates the prayer of vv. 5–8; vv. 12–14 describe a people enjoying ideal conditions; v. 15 closes the psalm with an echo of 33:12. For thematic continuities, see notes below.
144 title See introduction to Ps 138–145.
144:1–2 Praise of the Lord. As the opening words of a prayer, it seems to function both as an initial appeal (see 143:1–2) and as a confession of confidence that the prayer will be heard. The unusual piling up of epithets for God echoes Ps 18 (see note on 18:2).
144:2 *my loving God.* Lit. "my unfailing love" (see note on 6:4); so called because God is the source of benevolent acts of love that David can count on—just as God can be called "my salvation" because he is the source of salvation (see 27:1; 35:3; 62:2).
144:3–4 Acknowlegment of the relative insignificance of human beings and an expression of wonder that God cares for them.
144:3 A variation of 8:4.
144:4 *breath.* See 39:4–6 and notes. *shadow.* See 102:11 and note.
144:5–8 Prayer for deliverance.
144:5 See 18:9 and note on 18:7–15; see also Isa 64:1 and note.
144:6 See 18:14 and note.
144:7 See 18:16–17 and note on 32:6.

Detail of the porch of the Caryatids on the Acropolis of Athens, Greece. Psalm 144:12 mentions daughters being "like pillars carved to adorn a palace."

Rob & Lisa Meehan

from the mighty waters,[b]
from the hands of foreigners[c]
8 whose mouths are full of lies,[d]
whose right hands[e] are deceitful.[f]

9 I will sing a new song[g] to you, my God;
on the ten-stringed lyre[h] I will make
music to you,
10 to the One who gives victory to
kings,[i]
who delivers his servant David.[j]

From the deadly sword[k] 11 deliver me;
rescue me[l] from the hands of
foreigners[m]
whose mouths are full of lies,[n]
whose right hands are deceitful.[o]

144:7 [b] Ps 69:2 [c] S Ps 18:44 **144:8** [d] Ps 12:2; 41:6 [e] Ge 14:22; Dt 32:40 [f] S Ps 36:3 **144:9** [g] S Ps 28:7; S 96:1 [h] Ps 33:2-3; S 71:22 **144:10** [i] S 2Sa 8:14 [j] Ps 18:50 [k] S Job 5:20 **144:11** [l] Ps 3:7; S 25:20 [m] S Ps 18:44 [n] Ps 41:6-7 [o] Ps 12:2; S 36:3; 106:26; Isa 44:20

12 Then our sons in their youth
will be like well-nurtured plants,[p]
and our daughters will be like pillars[q]
carved to adorn a palace.
13 Our barns will be filled[r]
with every kind of provision.
Our sheep will increase by thousands,
by tens of thousands in our fields;
14 our oxen[s] will draw heavy loads.[a]
There will be no breaching of walls,[t]
no going into captivity,
no cry of distress in our streets.[u]

[a] 14 Or *our chieftains will be firmly established*

144:12 [p] Ps 92:12-14; S 128:3 [q] SS 4:4; 7:4 **144:13** [r] Pr 3:10 **144:14** [s] Pr 14:4 [t] 2Ki 25:11 [u] Isa 24:11; Jer 14:2-3

144:8 *mouths.* See note on 5:9. *right hands.* Hands raised to swear covenant oaths of allegiance or submission (see 106:26; Ex 6:8; Dt 32:40).
144:9 – 10 Vow to praise God (see note on 7:17).
144:9 *new song.* See note on 33:3.
144:10 *his servant David.* See 143:2 and note.
144:11 Repetition of the prayer in vv. 7 – 8, apparently to serve as transition to what follows: If God will deliver his servant David, the realm will prosper and be secure.
144:12 – 15 Many believe this to be a separate prayer ("May our sons ..."), unrelated to vv. 1 – 11, but the apparently transitional function of v. 11 supports the NIV rendering.
144:12 – 14 Possibly a postexilic echo of Dt 28:3 – 8.
144:12 *daughters ... like pillars carved.* Temple columns in the shape of women were not uncommon (e.g., the caryatids on the Acropolis in Athens; see photo above).
144:14 *our oxen will draw heavy loads.* Or "our oxen will be heavy with flesh" or "our oxen will be heavy with young" (see also NIV text note).

15 Blessed is the people[v] of whom this is
true;
blessed is the people whose God is
the LORD.

Psalm 145[a]

A psalm of praise. Of David.

1 I will exalt you,[w] my God the King;[x]
I will praise your name[y] for ever and
ever.
2 Every day I will praise[z] you
and extol your name[a] for ever and
ever.
3 Great[b] is the LORD and most worthy of
praise;[c]
his greatness no one can fathom.[d]
4 One generation[e] commends your works
to another;
they tell[f] of your mighty acts.[g]
5 They speak of the glorious splendor[h] of
your majesty—
and I will meditate on your
wonderful works.[b][i]
6 They tell[j] of the power of your
awesome works—[k]
and I will proclaim[l] your great deeds.[m]
7 They celebrate your abundant
goodness[n]
and joyfully sing[o] of your
righteousness.[p]

8 The LORD is gracious and
compassionate,[q]
slow to anger and rich in love.[r]

9 The LORD is good[s] to all;
he has compassion[t] on all he has
made.
10 All your works praise you,[u] LORD;
your faithful people extol[v] you.[w]
11 They tell of the glory of your kingdom[x]
and speak of your might,[y]
12 so that all people may know of your
mighty acts[z]
and the glorious splendor of your
kingdom.[a]
13 Your kingdom is an everlasting
kingdom,[b]
and your dominion endures through
all generations.

The LORD is trustworthy[c] in all he
promises[d]
and faithful in all he does.[c]
14 The LORD upholds[e] all who fall
and lifts up all[f] who are bowed
down.[g]
15 The eyes of all look to you,
and you give them their food[h] at the
proper time.
16 You open your hand
and satisfy the desires[i] of every
living thing.

17 The LORD is righteous[j] in all his ways
and faithful in all he does.[k]
18 The LORD is near[l] to all who call on
him,[m]
to all who call on him in truth.

144:15 [v]Dt 28:3 **145:1** [w]Ps 30:1; 34:1 [x]Ps 2:6; 5:2 [y]S Ps 54:6 **145:2** [z]S Ps 71:6 [a]Ps 34:1; Isa 25:1; 26:8 **145:3** [b]S Ps 95:3 [c]S 2Sa 22:4; Ps 96:4 [d]S Job 5:9 **145:4** [e]Ps 22:30 [f]S Dt 11:19 [g]S Ps 71:16 **145:5** [h]Ps 96:6; 148:13 [i]S Ps 75:1 **145:6** [j]Ps 78:4 [k]S Ps 66:3 [l]S Dt 32:3 [m]Ps 75:1; 106:22 **145:7** [n]S Ex 18:9; S Ps 27:13 [o]S Ps 5:11; S 101:1 [p]S Ps 138:5 **145:8** [q]S Ps 86:15; 103:8 [r]S Ps 86:5 **145:9** [s]S 1Ch 16:34; S Ps 136:1; Mt 19:17; Mk 10:18 [t]Ps 103:13-14 **145:10** [u]S Ps 8:6; S 103:22; S 139:14 [v]Ps 30:4; 148:14; 149:9 [w]Ps 115:17-18 **145:11** [x]ver 12-13; S Ex 15:2; Mt 6:33 [y]Ps 21:13 **145:12** [z]S Ps 75:1; 105:1 [a]ver 11; Ps 103:19; Isa 2:10,19,21 **145:13** [b]S Ex 15:18; 1Ti 1:17; 2Pe 1:11; Rev 11:15 [c]S Dt 7:9; S 1Co 1:9 [d]S Jos 23:14 **145:14** [e]S Ps 37:17 [f]S 1Sa 2:8; Ps 146:8 [g]S Ps 38:6 **145:15** [h]S Ge 1:30; S Job 28:5; S Ps 37:25; S Mt 6:26 **145:16** [i]S Ps 90:14; S 104:28 **145:17** [j]S Ex 9:27; S Ezr 9:15 [k]ver 13 **145:18** [l]S Nu 23:21; S Ps 46:1; Php 4:5 [m]Ps 18:6; 80:18

[a] This psalm is an acrostic poem, the verses of which (including verse 13b) begin with the successive letters of the Hebrew alphabet. [b] *5* Dead Sea Scrolls and Syriac (see also Septuagint); Masoretic Text *On the glorious splendor of your majesty / and on your wonderful works I will meditate* [c] *13* One manuscript of the Masoretic Text, Dead Sea Scrolls and Syriac (see also Septuagint); most manuscripts of the Masoretic Text do not have the last two lines of verse 13.

144:15 *Blessed.* See note on 1:1. *the people of whom this is true.* Cf. 33:12; see Dt 28:3–8; 1Ki 5:4 and note.

Ps 145 A magnificent hymn to the Lord, the Great King, for his mighty acts and benevolent virtues, which are the glory of his kingly rule. It exploits to the full the traditional language of praise and, as an alphabetic acrostic, reflects the care of studied composition. This care can be seen also in the manner in which the whole is structured. Between the two-line introduction (vv. 1–2) and one-line conclusion (v. 21), four main stanzas (vv. 3–7,9–13a,13b–16,17–20) describe these divine attributes: greatness, goodness, trustworthiness, righteousness. The first two of these stanzas are each composed of five poetic lines, the last two of four lines. Centered between the first two is an additional thematic line (v. 8) echoing Ex 34:6–7. This significant theme is centered (see note on 6:6) and not elaborated here (but see 86:15; 103:8–12; 111:4–5; 116:5–6) to allow the author to remain within the 22-line limits of the Hebrew alphabet. Further, the first two stanzas (vv. 3–13a) highlight the commending, telling, celebrating, singing and extolling of the glory of the Lord's reign, while the last two (vv. 13b–20) focus on what it is he does that is worthy of praise.

145 title *praise.* Hebrew *tehillah*, occurring only here in the psalm titles, but from a plural form (*tehillim*) has come the traditional Hebrew name of the Psalter. *Of David.* See introduction to Ps 138–145.

145:1–2 Initial commitment to praise God. *name.* See v. 21, thus framing the psalm (see note on 5:11).

145:3–7 Praise of God's mighty acts, which display his greatness (v. 3) and his goodness (v. 7)—as the author underscores by framing the paragraph with these two references. For the same combination, see 86:10,17; 135:3,5.

145:4 *commends … tell.* See vv. 5–7,10–12,21; see also note on 9:1. *your works.* In creation, providence and redemption.

145:7 *righteousness.* See v. 17; see also note on 4:1.

145:8 This centered line (see introduction above) is equal in thematic importance to vv. 3,9,13b,17. It echoes the classic expositon of the divine attributes in Ex 34:6–7 (see note there).

145:9–13a Praise of God's benevolent virtues, which move all creatures to celebrate the glory of his kingdom.

145:10 *All your works praise you.* See v. 21; see also note on 65:13. *faithful people.* See note on 4:3.

145:13b–16 Praise of God's faithfulness.

145:13b,17 *faithful.* See note on 6:4.

145:17–20 Praise of God's righteousness.

145:18 *in truth.* With godly integrity.

19 He fulfills the desires[n] of those who
fear him;[o]
he hears their cry[p] and saves them.[q]
20 The LORD watches over[r] all who love
him,[s]
but all the wicked he will destroy.[t]

21 My mouth will speak[u] in praise of the
LORD.
Let every creature[v] praise his holy
name[w]
for ever and ever.

Psalm 146

1 Praise the LORD.[a]

Praise the LORD,[x] my soul.

2 I will praise the LORD all my life;[y]
I will sing praise[z] to my God as long
as I live.[a]
3 Do not put your trust in princes,[b]
in human beings,[c] who cannot save.
4 When their spirit departs, they return
to the ground;[d]
on that very day their plans come to
nothing.[e]
5 Blessed are those[f] whose help[g] is the
God of Jacob,
whose hope is in the LORD their God.

6 He is the Maker of heaven[h] and earth,
the sea, and everything in them —
he remains faithful[i] forever.

145:19 [n]S Ps 20:4 [o]S Job 22:28 [p]S Ps 31:22; S 40:1 [q]S 1Sa 10:19; Ps 7:10; 34:18 **145:20** [r]S Ps 1:6 [s]Ps 31:23; 91:14; 97:10 [t]S Ps 94:23 **145:21** [u]Ps 71:8 [v]Ps 65:2; 150:6 [w]S Ex 3:15; S Ps 30:4; S 99:3 **146:1** [x]Ps 103:1; 104:1 **146:2** [y]Ps 104:33 [z]S Ps 105:2 [a]S Ps 63:4 **146:3** [b]Ps 118:9 [c]Ps 60:11; S 108:12; Isa 2:22 **146:4** [d]S Ge 3:19; S Job 7:21; Ps 103:14; Ecc 12:7 [e]Ps 33:10; 1Co 2:6 **146:5** [f]Ps 33:18; 37:9; 119:43; 144:15; Jer 17:7 [g]Ps 70:5; 71:5; 121:2 **146:6** [h]S 2Ch 2:12; Ps 115:15; Ac 14:15; S Rev 10:6 [i]S Dt 7:9;

7 He upholds[j] the cause of the
oppressed[k]
and gives food to the hungry.[l]
The LORD sets prisoners free,[m]
8 the LORD gives sight[n] to the blind,[o]
the LORD lifts up those who are bowed
down,[p]
the LORD loves the righteous.[q]
9 The LORD watches over the foreigner[r]
and sustains the fatherless[s] and the
widow,[t]
but he frustrates the ways of the
wicked.

10 The LORD reigns[u] forever,
your God, O Zion, for all
generations.

Praise the LORD.

Psalm 147

1 Praise the LORD.[b]

How good it is to sing praises to our
God,
how pleasant[v] and fitting to praise
him![w]

[a] *1* Hebrew *Hallelu Yah*; also in verse 10 [b] *1* Hebrew *Hallelu Yah*; also in verse 20

S Ps 18:25; 108:4; 117:2 **146:7** [j]S Ps 37:17 [k]Ps 103:6 [l]Ps 107:9; 145:15 [m]S Ps 66:11; S 68:6 **146:8** [n]Pr 20:12; Isa 29:18; 32:3; 35:5; 42:7, 18-19; 43:8; Mt 11:5 [o]S Ex 4:11 [p]S Ps 38:6 [q]S Dt 7:13; S Job 23:10 **146:9** [r]S Lev 19:34 [s]S Ps 10:18 [t]S Ex 22:22; Jas 1:27 **146:10** [u]S Ge 21:33; S 1Ch 16:31; Ps 93:1; 99:1; Rev 11:15 **147:1** [v]S Ps 135:3 [w]Ps 33:1

145:21 The praise of God must continue, and every creature take it up — forever. *every creature.* Or perhaps "every human" (lit. "all flesh"; see 65:2, "all people"; but see also 150:6).

Ps 146 – 150 A final cluster of five hymns all bracketed by shouts of Hallelujah! ("Praise Yahweh!") — which may have been added by the final editors (see introductions to Ps 105 – 106; see also Ps 111 – 117). The Psalter collection begins with two psalms that address the reader and whose function is to identify those to whom the collections specifically belong (see introduction to Ps 1 – 2). Here, at the collection's end, that congregation gives voice to its final themes. They are the themes of praise — and calls to praise — of Zion's heavenly King (see 146:10; 147:12; 149:2), the Maker, Sustainer and Lord over all creation (see 146:6; 147:4,8 – 9,15 – 18; 148:5 – 6); the one sure hope of those who in their need and vulnerability look to him for help (see 146:5 – 9; 147:2 – 3,6,11,13 – 14; 149:4); the Lord of history whose commitment to his people is their security and the guarantee that, as his kingdom people (see especially 147:19 – 20), they will ultimately triumph over all the forces of this world arrayed against them (see 146:3,10; 147:2,6,10,13 – 14; 148:14; 149:4 – 9).

Ps 146 A hymn in praise of Zion's heavenly King, with special focus on his powerful and trustworthy care for Zion's citizens who look to him when oppressed, broken or vulnerable. It has many thematic links with Ps 33; 62; 145. For its placement, see introduction to Ps 146 – 150.

146:1 – 2 Initial vow to praise God — as long as life continues (see 145:21 and note on 7:17).

146:1 *Praise the LORD, my soul.* See the frames around Ps 103 – 104. *soul.* See note on 6:3.

146:3 – 4 A call to trust ultimately in the Lord rather than in any human help (see 118:10 – 11 and note; 147:10 – 11).

146:5 – 9 Encouragement to trust in the covenant God of Jacob (see note on 14:7), who as Creator is Lord over all, as the Faithful One defends the defenseless and provides for the needy, and as the Righteous One shows favor to the righteous but checks the wicked in their pursuits.

146:6 *Maker of heaven and earth.* See note on 121:2.

146:7 *upholds the cause of the oppressed.* See 9:9; 10:18; 103:6. *gives food to the hungry.* See 17:14; 34:10; 107:9; cf. Isa 49:10. *sets prisoners free.* See 68:6; 79:11; 102:20; 107:10,14; cf. Isa 42:7 and note; 61:1.

146:8 *gives sight to the blind.* See Isa 29:18; 35:5; cf. Isa 42:7; 43:8. *lifts up those who are bowed down.* See 145:14. *righteous.* See note on 1:5.

146:9 *watches over the foreigner . . . fatherless . . . widow.* See Dt 10:18; cf. Isa 1:17; 9:17 and notes; cf. also Jer 22:16; Jas 1:17. *frustrates the ways of the wicked.* Cf. 104:35; 145:20.

146:10 Concluding exultant testimony to the citizens of God's royal city. *The LORD reigns forever.* See 93:1 and note. *Zion.* See note on 9:11.

Ps 147 Praise of God, the Creator and Lord over all, for his special mercies to Israel — possibly composed for the Levitical choirs on the joyous occasion of the dedication of the rebuilt walls of Jerusalem (see Ne 12:27 – 43). Following the introduction (v. 1), two couplets in which the Lord's unique favors to Israel are celebrated (vv. 2 – 3,19 – 20) frame its main body, while at the center another couplet (vv. 10 – 11) highlights the Lord's special pleasure in those who rely finally on him rather than on any of his creatures. In the balanced stanzas that intervene (vv. 4 – 9,12 – 18), this thematic core is placed in the larger context of God's works and ways. See introduction to Ps 146 – 150.

147:1 See note on 135:3.

2 The LORD builds up Jerusalem;[x]
he gathers the exiles[y] of Israel.
3 He heals the brokenhearted[z]
and binds up their wounds.[a]
4 He determines the number of the stars[b]
and calls them each by name.
5 Great is our Lord[c] and mighty in
power;[d]
his understanding has no limit.[e]
6 The LORD sustains the humble[f]
but casts the wicked[g] to the ground.

7 Sing to the LORD[h] with grateful praise;[i]
make music[j] to our God on the
harp.[k]

8 He covers the sky with clouds;[l]
he supplies the earth with rain[m]
and makes grass grow[n] on the hills.
9 He provides food[o] for the cattle
and for the young ravens[p] when they
call.

10 His pleasure is not in the strength[q] of
the horse,[r]
nor his delight in the legs of the
warrior;
11 the LORD delights[s] in those who fear
him,[t]
who put their hope[u] in his unfailing
love.[v]

12 Extol the LORD, Jerusalem;[w]
praise your God, Zion.

13 He strengthens the bars of your gates[x]
and blesses your people[y] within you.
14 He grants peace[z] to your borders
and satisfies you[a] with the finest of
wheat.[b]

147:2 [x]S Ps 51:18 [y]S Ps 106:47 **147:3** [z]S Ps 34:18 [a]S Nu 12:13; S Job 5:18; Isa 1:6; Eze 34:16 **147:4** [b]S Ge 15:5 **147:5** [c]S Ps 48:1 [d]S Ex 14:31 [e]Ps 145:3; Isa 40:28 **147:6** [f]S 2Ch 33:23; Ps 146:8-9 [g]Ps 37:9-10; 145:20 **147:7** [h]Ps 30:4; 33:3 [i]S Ps 42:4 [j]S Ps 27:6 [k]S Ps 98:5 **147:8** [l]S Job 26:8 [m]S Dt 11:14; S 32:2; S 2Sa 1:21; S Job 5:10 [n]S Job 28:26; S Ps 104:14 **147:9** [o]S Ge 1:30; Ps 104:27-28; S Mt 6:26 [p]S Ge 8:7 **147:10** [q]S 1Sa 16:7 [r]S Job 39:11; Ps 33:16-17 **147:11** [s]S Ps 35:27 [t]Ps 33:18; 103:11 [u]Ps 119:43 [v]Ps 6:4 **147:12** [w]Ps 48:1 **147:13** [x]S Dt 33:25 [y]S Lev 25:21; Ps 128:5;

15 He sends his command[c] to the
earth;
his word runs[d] swiftly.
16 He spreads the snow[e] like wool
and scatters the frost[f] like ashes.
17 He hurls down his hail[g] like pebbles.
Who can withstand his icy blast?
18 He sends his word[h] and melts
them;
he stirs up his breezes,[i] and the
waters flow.

19 He has revealed his word[j] to Jacob,[k]
his laws and decrees[l] to Israel.
20 He has done this for no other
nation;[m]
they do not know[n] his laws.[a]

Praise the LORD.[o]

Psalm 148

1 Praise the LORD.[b][p]

Praise the LORD from the heavens;[q]
praise him in the heights above.
2 Praise him, all his angels;[r]
praise him, all his heavenly hosts.[s]
3 Praise him, sun[t] and moon;
praise him, all you shining stars.

[a] *20* Masoretic Text; Dead Sea Scrolls and Septuagint *nation; / he has not made his laws known to them*
[b] *1* Hebrew *Hallelu Yah*; also in verse 14

134:3 **147:14** [z]S Lev 26:6; S 2Sa 7:10; S Isa 48:18 [a]S Ps 132:15 [b]S Dt 32:14 **147:15** [c]Job 37:12; Ps 33:9; 148:5 [d]Isa 55:11 **147:16** [e]Ps 148:8 [f]S Job 37:12; 38:29 **147:17** [g]Ex 9:22-23; S Job 38:22; S Ps 78:47 **147:18** [h]ver 15; Ps 33:9; 107:20 [i]S Ps 50:3 **147:19** [j]S Ex 20:1; Ro 3:2 [k]Ps 78:5 [l]S Dt 33:4; Jos 1:8; 2Ki 22:8; Mal 4:4; Ro 9:4 **147:20** [m]Dt 4:7-8,32-34 [n]S Ps 79:6 [o]Ps 33:2; 103:1 **148:1** [p]Ps 33:2; 103:1 [q]Ps 19:1; 69:34; 150:1 **148:2** [r]Ps 103:20 [s]S 1Ki 22:19 **148:3** [t]S Ps 19:1

147:2 *builds up.* Refers to the postexilic rebuilding of Jerusalem. *exiles.* Translates an unusual Hebrew word found also in Isa 11:10; 56:8 — all of which speak of gathering (restoring) "the exiles of Israel."

147:3 *brokenhearted.* Such as the exiles (see Ps 137; cf. Ps 126) and those who struggled in the face of great opposition to rebuild Jerusalem's walls (Ne 2:17 – 20; 4:1 – 23).

147:4 - 6 He whose power and understanding are such that he fixes the number of (or counts) the stars and names them is able to sustain his humble ones and bring the wicked down (see 20:8; 146:9; see also Isa 40:26 – 29).

147:6 *humble.* Those who acknowledge that they are without resources to deliver or maintain themselves — those who, as God's people, put their trust in him (see 149:4; see also 22:26, "the poor"; 37:11, "the meek," and note; 69:32, "the poor"). *ground.* Probably the grave (see note on 61:2).

147:7 - 9 Israel's God is Lord of creation, the one who provides for all living things.

147:10 - 11 The central couplet (see note on 6:6), thematically linked with vv. 2 – 3 and vv. 19 – 20 (see introduction to Ps 147). Israel's God is not particularly impressed by the creaturely capacities that humans are prone to rely on (cf. 146:3 – 4 and note); it gives him delight when his people rely on him (cf. 146:5 – 9).

147:11 *fear.* See note on 34:8 – 14. *unfailing love.* See note on 6:4.

147:12 - 18 The Lord of all creation, Zion's God, secures his people's defenses and prosperity, their peace and abundant provision. The verses mention clouds and rain (v. 8); snow, frost and hail (vv. 16 – 17); icy winds and warm breezes (vv. 17 – 18) — the whole range of weather.

147:15 *his command ... his word.* Personified as messengers commissioned to carry out a divine order (see v. 18; see also notes on 23:6; 33:4; 104:4).

147:19 - 20 God's most unique gift to Israel: his redemptive word, by which he makes known his program of salvation and his holy will. These verses constitute the end frame, thematically linked with vv. 2 – 3 and vv. 10 – 11 (see introduction to Ps 147 and note on vv. 10 – 11).

Ps 148 A call to all things in all creation to praise the Lord. Whatever its original liturgical purpose, its placement here at the center of the five concluding hymns serves to complete the scope of the calls to praise with which the Psalter closes (see introduction to Ps 146 – 150). Two similarly constructed stanzas call on all creatures in the heavens (vv. 1 – 6) and all creatures beneath the heavens (vv. 7 – 14) to join in the chorus of praise (see 103:20 – 22 and note). Both stanzas end with a couplet setting forth the motivation for praise. The second of these (vv. 12 – 14), made up of extended lines, clearly constitutes the climax.

148:1 - 6 Let all creatures in the heavens praise the Lord.

148:2 *heavenly hosts.* See 103:21 and note.

148:3 *sun and moon ... shining stars.* See note on 65:13.

[4]Praise him, you highest heavens[u]
and you waters above the skies.[v]

[5]Let them praise the name[w] of the LORD,
for at his command[x] they were created,
[6]and he established them for ever and ever—
he issued a decree[y] that will never pass away.

[7]Praise the LORD[z] from the earth,
you great sea creatures[a] and all ocean depths,[b]
[8]lightning and hail,[c] snow and clouds,
stormy winds that do his bidding,[d]
[9]you mountains and all hills,[e]
fruit trees and all cedars,
[10]wild animals[f] and all cattle,
small creatures and flying birds,
[11]kings[g] of the earth and all nations,
you princes and all rulers on earth,
[12]young men and women,
old men and children.

[13]Let them praise the name of the LORD,[h]
for his name alone is exalted;
his splendor[i] is above the earth and the heavens.[j]
[14]And he has raised up for his people a horn,[a][k]
the praise[l] of all his faithful servants,[m]
of Israel, the people close to his heart.[n]

Praise the LORD.

Psalm 149

[1]Praise the LORD.[b][o]

Sing to the LORD a new song,[p]
his praise in the assembly[q] of his faithful people.

[2]Let Israel rejoice[r] in their Maker;[s]
let the people of Zion be glad in their King.[t]
[3]Let them praise his name with dancing[u]
and make music to him with timbrel and harp.[v]
[4]For the LORD takes delight[w] in his people;
he crowns the humble with victory.[x]
[5]Let his faithful people rejoice[y] in this honor
and sing for joy on their beds.[z]

[6]May the praise of God be in their mouths[a]
and a double-edged[b] sword in their hands,[c]

[a] *14 Horn* here symbolizes strength. [b] *1* Hebrew *Hallelu Yah;* also in verse 9

148:4 [u]S Dt 10:14 [v]S Ge 1:7 **148:5** [w]Ps 145:21 [x]S Ps 147:15 **148:6** [y]Jer 31:35-36; 33:25 **148:7** [z]Ps 33:2 [a]S Ge 1:21; Ps 74:13-14 [b]S Dt 33:13 **148:8** [c]S Ex 9:18; S Jos 10:11 [d]Job 37:11-12; S Ps 103:20; 147:15-18 **148:9** [e]Isa 44:23; 49:13; 55:12 **148:10** [f]Isa 43:20; Hos 2:18 **148:11** [g]S Ps 102:15 **148:13** [h]S Ps 113:2; 138:4 [i]S Ps 145:5 [j]S Ps 8:1 **148:14** [k]S 1Sa 2:1 [l]S Ex 15:2; Ps 22:3 [m]S Ps 145:10 [n]S Dt 26:19 **149:1** [o]Ps 33:2; 103:1 [p]S Ps 28:7; S 96:1; Rev 5:9 [q]S Ps 1:5 **149:2** [r]Isa 13:3; Jer 51:48 [s]S Job 10:3; Ps 95:6; Isa 44:2; 45:11; 54:5 [t]Ps 10:16; 47:6; Isa 32:1; Zec 9:9 **149:3** [u]S Ex 15:20 [v]S Ps 57:8 **149:4** [w]Ps 35:27; 147:11 [x]Ps 132:16 **149:5** [y]S Ps 132:16 [z]Job 35:10; Ps 42:8 **149:6** [a]Ps 66:17 [b]Heb 4:12; Rev 1:16 [c]Ne 4:17

148:4 *waters above the skies.* The "deep" above (see Ge 1:7; cf. "ocean depths" in v. 7; see also note on 42:7).
148:5–6 Motivation ("for," v. 5) for the heavenly creatures to praise the Lord (cf. vv. 13–14 and "for," v. 13).
148:5,13 *name of the LORD.* See note on 5:11. They are to praise the Lord because he has created them and made their existence secure.
148:7–14 Let all creatures of earth praise the Lord ("the earth and the heavens" [v. 13] are the sum of all creation; see 89:11; 113:6; 136:5–6; Ge 2:1,4).
148:7 *sea creatures and all ocean depths.* Likely with Ge 1 in mind (see Ge 1:7,10,21), the call begins with these and moves toward the human components. This and the pairs that follow employ a figure of speech that refers to all reality pertaining to the sphere to which they belong—here, all creatures great and small that belong to the realm of lakes and seas.
148:8 *his bidding.* Lit. "his word" (see 147:15 and note).
148:13–14 Climactic conclusion, with focus again on motivation for praising God (cf. vv. 5–6 and note).
148:13 *his name ... his splendor.* As shown in the glory of his creation. *is above.* The glory of the Creator is greater than the glory of the creation.
148:14 *horn.* The Lord's anointed (see NIV text note; 132:17 and note; see also notes on 2:2; Ps 18 title). It may be, however, that "horn" here represents the strength and vigor of God's people (see 92:10; 1Sa 2:1; Jer 48:25; La 2:17). In any event, reference is to God's saving acts for Israel—God is to be praised for his works in creation and redemption (see note on 65:6–7). *praise.* See 22:3 and note. *faithful servants.* See note on 4:3.
Ps 149 Praise of God for the high honor bestowed on his people Israel. Israel's unique honor has two sides: She was granted salvation (in fact and in promise), and, under the particular administration of the emerging kingdom of God put in place in the inauguration of the Sinaitic covenant (see chart, p. 23), she was armed to execute God's sentence of judgment on the world powers that have launched attacks against the kingdom of God. Under that arrangement, she served as the earthly contingent of the armies of the King of heaven (see 68:17 and note; see also Jos 5:14; 2Sa 5:23–24; 2Ch 20:15–17,22; Hab 3:3–15). This next-to-last psalm should be read in the light of the second psalm (see introduction to Ps 2; see also introduction to Ps 146–150).

Following an introductory verse, the two main themes are developed in two balanced stanzas of four verses each. References to God's "faithful people" enclose the song (see also v. 5). The common pair of synonyms, "honor" (v. 5) and "glory" (v. 9), effectively link the two stanzas (see 8:5; 21:5, "glory ... majesty"; 104:1,31, "majesty ... glory"; 145:5,12, "glorious splendor"; Isa 35:2, "glory ... splendor").
149:1 *new song.* See note on 33:3. *in the assembly.* See note on 9:1. *his faithful people.* See vv. 5,9; see also note on 4:3.
149:2–5 Let Israel rejoice in their King, who has crowned them with the honor of salvation.
149:3 *his name.* See note on 5:11.
149:4 *crowns.* Endows with splendor (see Isa 55:5; 60:9; 61:3). *humble.* Those who acknowledge that they are without resources (see 147:6 and note).
149:5 *on their beds.* The salvation (v. 4) so tangible in the daytime evokes songs in the night (see 42:8; 63:6; 77:6).
149:6–9 Let Israel praise their God, who has given them the glory of bearing the sword as his army in service (cf. Ps 137; 139:19–22; Eze 38–39; Da 2:44; 7:22,26–27; Am 9:12).

[7]to inflict vengeance[d] on the nations
and punishment[e] on the peoples,
[8]to bind their kings with fetters,[f]
their nobles with shackles of iron,[g]
[9]to carry out the sentence written
against them —[h]
this is the glory of all his faithful
people.[i]

Praise the LORD.

Psalm 150

[1]Praise the LORD.[a][j]

Praise God in his sanctuary;[k]
praise him in his mighty heavens.[l]
[2]Praise him for his acts of power;[m]
praise him for his surpassing
greatness.[n]

149:7 [d]S Nu 31:3; S Dt 32:41 [e]Ps 81:15 **149:8** [f]S 2Sa 3:34; S Isa 14:1-2 [g]2Ch 33:11 **149:9** [h]Dt 7:1; Eze 28:26 [i]S Ps 145:10 **150:1** [j]S Ps 112:1 [k]Ps 68:24-26; 73:17; 102:19 [l]S Ps 148:1 **150:2** [m]S Dt 3:24 [n]S Ex 15:7 **150:3** [o]S Nu 10:2 [p]S Ps 57:8 **150:4** [q]S Ex 15:20 [r]S Ps 45:8 [s]S Ge 4:21

[3]Praise him with the sounding of the
trumpet,[o]
praise him with the harp and
lyre,[p]
[4]praise him with timbrel and dancing,[q]
praise him with the strings[r] and
pipe,[s]
[5]praise him with the clash of
cymbals,[t]
praise him with resounding
cymbals.

[6]Let everything[u] that has breath praise
the LORD.

Praise the LORD.

[a] *1* Hebrew *Hallelu Yah;* also in verse 6

150:5 [t]S 2Sa 6:5 **150:6** [u]S Ps 103:22

149:7 *vengeance.* God's just retribution on those who have attacked his kingdom. Of this divine retribution the OT speaks often: 58:10; 79:10; 94:1; Nu 31:2; Dt 32:35,41,43; 2Ki 9:7; Isa 34:8; 35:4; 47:3; 59:17; 61:2; 63:4; Jer 46:10; 50:15, 28; 51:6,11,36; Eze 25:14,17; Mic 5:15; Na 1:2. In the NT age, however, God's people are armed with the "sword of the Spirit" for overcoming the powers arrayed against God's kingdom (see 2Co 6:7; 10:4; Eph 6:12,17; Heb 4:12); their participation in God's retribution on the world awaits the final judgment (see 1Co 6:2–3).

149:9 *sentence written.* God's firmly determined judgment (see 139:16 and note).

Ps 150 The final great Hallelujah — perhaps composed specifically to close the Psalter. See the doxologies that conclude the first four Books: 41:13; 72:18–19; 89:52; 106:48. This final call to praise God moves powerfully by stages from place to themes to orchestra to choir, framed with Hallelujahs. See introduction to Ps 146–150.

150:1 *Where* God should be praised. *his sanctuary.* At Jerusalem. *his mighty heavens.* Lit. "the vault of his power" (see 19:1, "skies"; Ge 1:6), i.e., the vault that displays or symbolizes his power or in which his power resides. Usually thought to refer to God's heavenly temple (see 11:4), it may signify the vaulted ceiling of the visible universe viewed as a cosmic temple.

150:2 *Why* God should be praised. *his acts of power.* What he does (in creation and redemption). *his surpassing greatness.* Who he is.

150:3–5 *How* God should be praised — with the whole orchestra (eight instruments: wind, string, percussion), with dancing aptly placed at the middle (see photos, pp. 627, 843, 845).

150:6 *Who* should praise God. The choir, with articulate expression, celebrates God's "acts of power" and "surpassing greatness" (v. 2). *Praise the LORD.* Hebrew *Hallelu Yah.* For another final great Hallelujah (see introduction to this psalm), see Rev 19:1–8 and note on 19:1.

PROVERBS

INTRODUCTION

Authors

Although the book begins with a title ascribing the proverbs to Solomon, it is clear from later chapters that he was not the only author of the book. Pr 22:17 refers to the "sayings of the wise," and 24:23 mentions additional "sayings of the wise." The presence of an introduction in 22:17 – 21 further indicates that these sections stem from a circle of wise men, not from Solomon himself. Ch. 30 is attributed to Agur, son of Jakeh, and 31:1 – 9 to King Lemuel, neither of whom is mentioned elsewhere. Lemuel's sayings contain several Aramaic spellings that may point to a non-Israelite background.

Most of the book, however, is closely linked with Solomon. The headings in 10:1 and 25:1 include his name, though 25:1 states that these proverbs were "compiled by the men of Hezekiah king of Judah." This indicates that a group of wise men or scribes compiled these proverbs as editors and added chs. 25 – 29 to the earlier collections. Solomon's ability to produce proverbs is specified in 1Ki 4:32, where 3,000 proverbs are attributed to him. In light of statements about his unparalleled wisdom (1Ki 4:29 – 31,34; 10:1 – 13, 23 – 24), it is quite likely that he was the source of most of Proverbs. The book contains a short prologue (1:1 – 7) and a longer epilogue (31:10 – 31), which may have been added to the other materials. It is possible that the discourses in the large opening section (1:8 — 9:18) were the work of a compiler or editor, but the similarities of ch. 6 in this section with other chapters (compare 6:1 with 11:15; 17:18; 20:16; 27:13; compare 6:14,19 with 10:12; 15:18; 16:28; 28:25; 29:22; compare 6:19 with 14:5,25; 19:5) fit a Solomonic origin equally well. The emphasis on the "fear of the LORD" (1:7) throughout the book ties the various segments together.

a **quick** look

Author:
King Solomon and other wise men

Audience:
The people of Israel

Date:
Primarily during Solomon's reign (970 – 930 BC)

Theme:
Proverbs describes the importance of living wisely and in the fear of the Lord as opposed to following the seductive path of folly.

Date

If Solomon is granted a prominent role in the book, most of Proverbs would stem from the tenth century BC, during the time of Israel's united kingdom. The peace and prosperity that characterized that era accord well with the development of reflective wisdom and the production of literary works. Moreover, several interpreters have noted that the 30 sayings of the wise in 22:17—24:22 (especially the first ten) contain similarities to the 30 sections of the Egyptian "Wisdom of Amenemope," an instructional piece that is roughly contemporary with the time of Solomon (see chart, p. xxii). Likewise, the personification of wisdom so prominent in chs. 1–9 (see 1:20 and note; 3:15–18; 8:1–36; 9:1–12) can be compared with the personification of abstract ideas in both Mesopotamian and Egyptian writings of the second millennium BC.

The role of Hezekiah's men (see 25:1) indicates that important sections of Proverbs were compiled and edited from 715 to 686 BC. This was a time of spiritual renewal led by the king, who also showed great interest in the writings of David and Asaph (see 2Ch 29:30). Perhaps it was also at this time that the sayings of Agur (ch. 30) and Lemuel (31:1–9) and the other "sayings of the wise" (22:17—24:22; 24:23–34) were added to the Solomonic collections, though it is possible that the task of compilation was not completed until after the reign of Hezekiah.

The Nature of a Proverb

The proverbs contained in this book are not to be interpreted as prophecies or their statements about effects and results as promises. For instance, 10:27 says that the years of the wicked are cut short, while the righteous live long and prosperous lives (see 3:2 and note). The righteous have abundant food (10:3), but the wicked will go hungry (13:25). While such statements are generally true, there are enough exceptions to indicate that sometimes the righteous suffer and the wicked prosper (see note on 3:2). Normally the righteous and wicked "receive their due on earth" (11:31), but at other times reward and punishment lie beyond the grave.

The Hebrew word translated "proverb" is also translated "message" (Nu 23:7,18), "taunt" (Isa 14:4) and "parable" (Eze 17:2), so its meaning is considerably broader than the English term. This may help explain the presence of the longer discourse sections in chs. 1–9. Most proverbs are short, compact statements that express truths about human behavior. Often there is repetition of a word or sound that aids memorization. In 30:33, e.g., the same Hebrew verb is translated "churning," "twisting" and "stirring up."

In the longest section of the book (10:1—22:16) most of the proverbs are two lines long, and those in chs. 10–15 almost always express a contrast. Sometimes the writer simply makes a general observation, such as "A bribe is seen as a charm by the one who gives it" (17:8; cf. 14:20), but usually he evaluates conduct: "the one who hates bribes will live" (15:27). Many proverbs, in fact, describe the consequences of a particular action or character trait: "A wise son brings joy to his father" (10:1). Since the proverbs were written primarily for instruction, they are often given in the form of commands: "Do not love sleep or you will grow poor" (20:13). Even where the imperative form is not used, the desired action is quite clear (see 14:5).

A common feature of the proverbs is the use of figurative language: "Like cold water to a weary soul / is good news from a distant land" (25:25). In ch. 25 alone there are 12 verses that begin with "like" or "as." These similes make the proverbs more vivid and powerful. Occasionally the simile is used in a humorous or sarcastic way: "Like a gold ring in a pig's snout / is a beautiful woman who shows no discretion" (11:22; cf. 26:9), or, "As a door turns on its hinges, / so a sluggard turns on his bed" (26:14). Equally effective is the use of metaphors: "The teaching of the wise is a fountain of life" (13:14), and "The soothing tongue is a tree of life" (15:4). According to 16:24, "Gracious words are a honeycomb." The figure of sowing and reaping is used in both a positive and a negative way (cf. 11:18; 22:8).

In order to develop a proper set of values, a number of proverbs use direct comparisons: "Better the poor whose walk is blameless / than the rich whose ways are perverse" (28:6). This "better ... than" pattern can be seen also in 15:16–17; 16:19,32; 17:1,12; a modified form occurs in 22:1. Another pattern found in the book is the so-called numerical proverb. Used for the first time in 6:16 (see note there), this type of saying normally has the number three in the first line and four in the second (cf. 30:15,18,21,29; see Am 1:3 and note).

The repetition of entire proverbs (compare 6:10–11 with 24:33–34; 14:12 with 16:25; 18:8 with 26:22; 20:16 with 27:13; 21:19 with 25:24) or parts of proverbs may serve a poetic purpose. A slight variation allows the writer(s) to use the same image to make a related point (as in 17:3; 27:21) or to substitute a word or two to achieve greater clarity or a different emphasis (cf. 19:1; 28:6). In 26:4–5 the same line is repeated in a seemingly contradictory way, but this was designed to make two different points (see notes there).

At times the book of Proverbs is very direct and earthy (cf. 6:6; 21:9; 25:16; 26:3). This is the nature of wisdom literature as it seeks pedagogically effective ways to illumine life situations and to guide the unwise (or not yet wise) into wise choices concerning how to shape their lives as members of the human community that lives under the scrutiny and the providential rule and care of the Creator (see essay, p. 786).

Purpose and Teaching

According to the purpose and theme of the book (1:1–7), Proverbs was written to give "prudence to those who are simple, knowledge and discretion to the young" (1:4), and to make the wise even wiser (1:5). The frequent references to "my son(s)" (1:8,10; 2:1; 3:1; 4:1; 5:1) emphasize instructing the young and guiding them in a way of life that yields rewarding ends. Acquiring wisdom and knowing how to avoid the pitfalls of folly lead to personal well-being, happy family relationships, fruitful labors and good standing in the community (see chart, p. 1030). Although Proverbs is a practical book dealing with the art of living, it bases its practical wisdom solidly on the fear of the Lord (1:7; see Ps 34:8–14 and note). Throughout the book reverence for God and reliance on him are set forth as the path to life, prosperity and security (cf. 3:5–10; 9:10–12; 14:26–27; 16:3,6–7;

Boundary marker of Eanna-shum-iddina, governor of Sealand (Babylonia, 1100 BC). Proverbs 23:10 prohibits the moving of boundary stones, which would be the equivalent of stealing land.

Caryn Reeder, courtesy of the British Muesum

18:10; 19:23; 20:22; 22:4; 28:25; 29:25). Such godly wisdom is a virtual "tree of life" (3:18; 11:30; 13:12; 15:4) that yields the happy life that God fashioned the creation to produce.

In the initial cycle of instruction (1:8—9:18) the writer urges the young man to choose the way of wisdom (that leads to life) and shun the ways of folly (that, however tempting they may be, lead to death). The author chooses two prime exemplifications of folly to give concreteness to his exhortations: (1) to get ahead in the world by exploiting (even oppressing) others, rather than by diligent and honest labor, and (2) to find sexual pleasure outside the bonds and responsibilities of marriage. Temptation to the one comes from the young man's male peers (1:10–19); temptation to the other comes from the adulterous woman (2:16–19; ch. 5; 6:20–35; ch. 7). Together, these two temptations illustrate the pervasiveness and power of the allurements to folly that the young man will face in life and must be prepared to resist (see also Literary Structure below).

The major collections of proverbs that follow (starting with ch. 10) range widely across the broad spectrum of human situations, relationships and responsibilities, offering insights, warnings, instructions and counsel, along with frequent motivations to heed them. The range and variety of these defy summation. However, an illustrative section can convey the general character, moral tone and scope of the collections. In a variety of situations and relationships the reader is exhorted to honesty, integrity, diligence, kindness, generosity, readiness to forgive, truthfulness, patience, humility, cheerfulness, loyalty, temperance, self-control and the prudent consideration of consequences that flow from attitudes, choices and/or actions. Anger is to be held in check, violence and quarrelsomeness shunned, gossip avoided, arrogance repudiated. Drunkenness, gluttony, envy and greed are all to be renounced. The poor are not to be exploited, the courts are not to be unjustly manipulated, legitimate authorities are to be honored. Parents are responsible to care for the proper instruction and discipline of their children, and children are to duly honor their parents and bring no disgrace on them. Human observation and experience have taught the wise that a certain order is in place in God's creation. To honor it leads to known positive effects; to defy it leads only to unhappy consequences. All of life is to be lived in conscious awareness of the unfailing scrutiny of the Lord of creation and in reliance on his generous providence.

Although Proverbs is more practical than theological, God's work as Creator is especially highlighted. The role of wisdom in creation is the subject of 8:22–31 (see notes there), where wisdom as an attribute of God is personified. God is called the Maker of the poor (14:31; 17:5; 22:2). He sovereignly directs the steps of people (cf. 16:9; 20:24)—even the actions of kings (21:1)—and his eyes observe all that humans do (cf. 5:21; 15:3). All history moves forward under his control (see 16:4,33 and notes).

In summary, Proverbs provides instruction on how to live wisely and successfully in the "fear of the Lord" (1:7; 9:10) under the reign of God. The fear of the Lord includes reverence for, trust in and commitment to the Lord and his will, as disclosed in his creation and as revealed in his word. Wisdom in this context, then, is basically following the benevolent King's design for human happiness within the creation order—resulting in quality of mind (1:2) and quality of life (1:3).

Literary Structure

The sectional headings found in the NIV text (also reflected in the Outline) divide the book into well-defined units. A short statement of the purpose and theme (1:1–7) opens the book, and

Although Proverbs is more practical than theological, God's work as Creator is especially highlighted, and wisdom as an attribute of God is personified.

a longer epilogue (identifiable by its subject matter and its alphabetic form, 31:10 – 31) closes it. The first nine chapters contain a series of discourses that contrast the way and benefits of wisdom with the way of the fool. Except for the sections where personified wisdom speaks (1:20; 8:1; 9:1), each discourse begins with "my son" or "my sons."

A key feature in the introductory discourses of Proverbs is the personification of both wisdom and folly as women, each of whom (by appeals and warnings on the part of Lady Wisdom, by enticements on the part of Lady Folly) seeks to persuade "simple" youths to follow her ways. These discourses are strikingly organized. Beginning (1:8 – 33) and ending (chs. 8 – 9) with direct enticements and appeals, the main body of the discourses is made up of two nicely balanced sections, one devoted to the commendation of wisdom (chs. 2 – 4) and the other to warnings against folly (chs. 5 – 7). In these discourses the young man is depicted as being enticed to folly by men who try to get ahead in the world by exploiting others (1:10 – 19) and by women who seek sexual pleasure outside the bond of marriage (ch. 5; 6:20 – 35; ch. 7). In the social structures of that day, these were the two great temptations for young men. The second especially functions here as illustrative and emblematic of the appeal of Lady Folly.

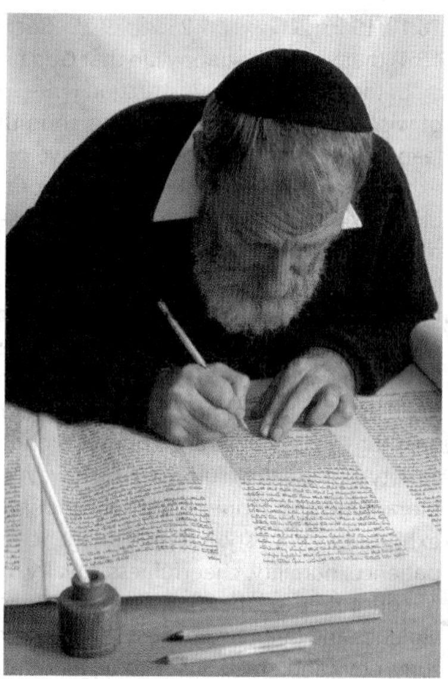

A book like Proverbs would have been given to scribes and copied over and over.

Z. Radovan/www.BibleLandPictures.com

The main collection of Solomon's proverbs in 10:1 — 22:16 consists of individual couplets, many of which express a contrast. On the surface, there does not seem to be any discernible arrangement, though occasionally two or three proverbs deal with the same subject. For example, 11:24 – 25 deals with generosity, 16:12 – 15 mentions kings, and 19:4,6 – 7 talks about friendship. However, there is growing evidence that arrangements of larger units were deliberate. Further study of this possibility is necessary. The second Solomonic collection (chs. 25 – 29) continues the pattern of two-line verses, but there are also examples of proverbs with three (25:13; 27:10,22,27) or four (25:4 – 5,21 – 22; 26:18 – 19) lines. The last five verses of ch. 27 (vv. 23 – 27) present a short discourse on the benefits of raising flocks and herds.

In the "thirty sayings" (22:20) of the wise (22:17 — 24:22) and the further sayings of 24:23 – 34, there is a prevalence of two- or three-verse units and something of a return to the style of chs. 1 – 9 (see especially 23:29 – 35). These sections have been appended to the preceding and contain some proverbs similar to those included in the foregoing collections (compare 24:6 with 11:14; 24:16 with 11:5). One finds even stronger links with chs. 1 – 9 (compare 23:27 with 2:16; 24:33 – 34 with 6:10 – 11).

At the end of the book the editor(s) has (have) attached three additional pieces, diverse in form and content: the "sayings of Agur," the "sayings of King Lemuel" and a description of "a wife of noble character." The first of these (ch. 30) is dominated by numerical proverbs (30:15,18,21,24,29; see note on 6:16). The second (31:1 – 9) is devoted exclusively to instruction for kings. The third (31:10 – 31), effectively an epilogue to the whole, is an impressive acrostic poem honoring the wife of noble character (cf. Ru 3:11 and note). She demonstrates, and thus epitomizes, many of the qualities and values identified with wisdom throughout the book. In view of the fact that Proverbs is primarily addressed to young men on the threshold of mature life, this focus on the ideal wife appears surprising. But its purpose may be twofold: (1) to offer counsel on the kind of wife a young man ought to seek, and (2) in a subtle way to advise the young man (again) to marry Lady Wisdom, thus returning to the theme of chs. 1 – 9 (as climaxed in ch. 9; compare the description of Lady Wisdom in 9:1 – 2 with the virtues of the wife in 31:10 – 31). In any event, the concluding epitomizing of wisdom in the wife of noble character forms a literary frame with the opening discourses, where wisdom is personified as a woman.

Outline

- I. Purpose and Theme (1:1 – 7)
- II. The Superiority of the Way of Wisdom (1:8 — 9:18)
  - A. Appeals and Warnings Confronting Youth (1:8 – 33)
    1. Enticements to secure happiness by violence (1:8 – 19)
    2. Warnings against rejecting wisdom (1:20 – 33)
  - B. Commendation of Wisdom (chs. 2 – 4)
    1. Benefits of accepting wisdom's instructions (ch. 2)
    2. Wisdom bestows well-being (3:1 – 20)
    3. Wisdom's instructions and benefits (3:21 – 35)
    4. Challenge to hold on to wisdom (ch. 4)
  - C. Warnings against Folly (chs. 5 – 7)
    1. Warning against adultery (ch. 5)
    2. Warning against perverse ways (6:1 – 19)
    3. Cost of committing adultery (6:20 – 35)
    4. Warning against the enticements of an adulterous woman (ch. 7)
  - D. Appeals Addressed to Youth (chs. 8 – 9)
    1. Wisdom's call (ch. 8)
    2. Invitations of wisdom and folly (ch. 9)
- III. The Main Collection of Solomon's Proverbs (10:1 — 22:16)
- IV. Thirty Sayings of the Wise (22:17 — 24:22)
- V. Further Sayings of the Wise (24:23 – 34)
- VI. Hezekiah's Collection of Solomon's Proverbs (chs. 25 – 29)
- VII. Sayings of Agur (ch. 30)
- VIII. Sayings of King Lemuel (31:1 – 9)
- IX. Epilogue: The Wife of Noble Character (31:10 – 31)

THE WISE MAN ACCORDING TO PROVERBS: AN OUTLINE

I. HIS CHARACTER

A. He Is Teachable, Not Intractable
   1. He receives and loves instruction (18:15; 19:20)
   2. He grows in wisdom (1:5; 9:9; 10:14)

B. He Is Righteous, Not Wicked
   1. He fears the Lord (1:7; 14:16; see below under relationship to the Lord)
   2. He hates what is false (13:5)
   3. He shuns evil (3:7; 14:16; 16:6)
   4. He does what is righteous (2:20)
   5. He speaks the truth (22:21)

C. He Is Humble, Not Proud (15:33)

D. He Is Self-controlled, Not Rash
   1. His temperament
      a. He is self-controlled (29:11)
      b. He has a calm spirit (17:27)
      c. He is slow to become angry (29:8,11)
   2. His actions
      a. He is cautious, not rash (19:2)
      b. He thinks before he acts (13:16; 14:8)
      c. He thinks before he speaks (12:23; 15:2)

E. He Is Forgiving, Not Vindictive
   1. He is patient (19:11)
   2. He is concerned about goodwill/peace (14:9)
   3. He forgives those who wrong him (10:12; 17:9)
   4. He is not vindictive (20:22; 24:29)

II. HIS RELATIONSHIPS

A. To the Lord
   1. He fears the Lord (9:10; 14:16; 15:33)
   2. He trusts in the Lord (3:5; 16:3,20)
   3. He is ever mindful of the Lord (3:6)
   4. He chooses the Lord's way/wisdom (8:10–11; 17:24)
   5. He submits to the Lord's discipline (1:2–3; 3:11)
   6. He confesses his sin to the Lord (28:13)

B. To His Family
   1. To his parents
      a. He respects them (17:6; contrast 30:17)
      b. He listens to them (23:22; cf. 1:8; 4:1)
      c. He seeks to bring them honor and joy
         (1) By being wise (10:1; 15:20; 29:3)
         (2) By being righteous (23:24)
         (3) By being diligent (10:5)
   2. To his wife
      a. He appreciates her
         (1) As a gift from the Lord (18:22; 19:14)
         (2) As his crowning glory (12:4; 31:10–31)
      b. He praises her (31:28)
      c. He trusts her (31:11)
      d. He is faithful to her (5:15–20)
   3. To his children
      a. He loves them (3:12; 13:24)
      b. He is concerned about them (1:8—9:18)
      c. He trains them (22:6)
         (1) Reasons for training them
            (a) Own peace of mind and joy (29:17)
            (b) Child's honor and well-being (1:8–9; 4:9; 19:18; 23:13–14)
         (2) By teaching/instructing them (1:10; chs. 5–7; 28:7; cf. 4:1–9)
         (3) By disciplining them
            (a) By verbal correction (13:1)
            (b) By physical discipline (13:24; 23:13–14)
      d. He provides for their
         (1) Physical needs (21:20; cf. 27:23–27)
         (2) Spiritual heritage (14:26; 20:7)

C. To His Friends and Neighbors
   1. To his friends
      a. He values them (27:10)
      b. He is constant to them (17:17; 18:24)
      c. He gives them counsel (27:9,17; cf. 27:6; 28:23)
   2. To his neighbors
      a. He fulfills his obligations to them (3:27–28)
      b. He strives for peace with them (3:29–30)
      c. He does not outstay his welcome (25:17)
      d. He does not deceive or mislead them (16:29; 26:18–19)

III. HIS WORDS

A. The Power and Limitations of His Words
   1. Their power
      a. The power of life and death (12:6; 13:14; 15:4; 18:21)
      b. The power to heal or to wound (11:9,11; 12:18; 15:4,30; 16:24)
   2. Their limitations
      a. Cannot substitute for deeds (14:23)
      b. Cannot alter the facts (26:23–26)
      c. Cannot compel response (29:19)

B. The Character of His Words
   1. They are honest, not false (12:22; 16:13)
   2. They are few, not many (10:19)
      a. Not boastful (27:2)
      b. Not argumentative (17:14)
      c. Not contentious (29:9)
      d. Not a slanderer
         (1) Revealing secrets (11:13; 20:19)
         (2) Spreading gossip (10:18; 26:20–22)
   3. They are calm, not emotional
      a. Rational (15:28; 17:27)
      b. Gentle and peaceful (15:1,18)
      c. Persuasive (25:15)
   4. They are apt, not untimely (15:23; 25:11)

C. The Source of His Words
   1. His heart/character (compare 4:23 with Mt 12:33–35)
      a. Positively, he is righteous (cf. 10:11; 13:14)
      b. Negatively, he is not
         (1) Proud (13:10; cf. 6:16–19)
         (2) Hateful (26:24,28)
   2. His companions (13:20; 27:17)

Purpose and Theme

1 The proverbs[a] of Solomon[b] son of David, king of Israel:[c]

[2] for gaining wisdom and instruction;
for understanding words of insight;
[3] for receiving instruction in prudent
behavior,
doing what is right and just and fair;
[4] for giving prudence to those who are
simple,[ad]
knowledge and discretion[e] to the
young—
[5] let the wise listen and add to their
learning,[f]
and let the discerning get
guidance—
[6] for understanding proverbs and
parables,[g]
the sayings and riddles[h] of the wise.[bi]

[7] The fear of the LORD[j] is the beginning
of knowledge,
but fools[c] despise wisdom[k] and
instruction.[l]

Prologue: Exhortations to Embrace Wisdom

Warning Against the Invitation of Sinful Men

[8] Listen, my son,[m] to your father's[n]
instruction
and do not forsake your mother's
teaching.[o]
[9] They are a garland to grace your
head
and a chain to adorn your neck.[p]

[10] My son, if sinful men entice[q] you,
do not give in[r] to them.[s]
[11] If they say, "Come along with us;
let's lie in wait[t] for innocent
blood,
let's ambush some harmless soul;
[12] let's swallow[u] them alive, like the
grave,
and whole, like those who go down
to the pit;[v]
[13] we will get all sorts of valuable
things
and fill our houses with plunder;
[14] cast lots with us;
we will all share the loot[w]"—
[15] my son, do not go along with
them,
do not set foot[x] on their paths;[y]
[16] for their feet rush into evil,[z]
they are swift to shed blood.[a]

a 4 The Hebrew word rendered *simple* in Proverbs denotes a person who is gullible, without moral direction and inclined to evil. *b* 6 Or *understanding a proverb, namely, a parable, / and the sayings of the wise, their riddles* *c* 7 The Hebrew words rendered *fool* in Proverbs, and often elsewhere in the Old Testament, denote a person who is morally deficient.

1:1 [a]Mt 13:3 [b]1Ki 4:29-34 [c]Pr 10:1; 25:1; Ecc 1:1 **1:4** [d]Pr 8:5 [e]Pr 8:12 **1:5** [f]Pr 9:9 **1:6** [g]S Ps 49:4; Mt 13:10-17 [h]S Nu 12:8; S Jdg 14:12 [i]Pr 22:17; 24:23 **1:7** [j]S Ex 20:20; S Job 23:15; Ps 34:4-22; S 112:1; Pr 9:10; 15:33; Isa 33:6; 50:10; 59:19 [k]S Dt 4:6; Jer 8:9 [l]Pr 8:33-36; 9:7-9; 12:1; 13:18; 15:32 **1:8** [m]ver 8-9; Pr 2:1; 3:1; 4:1; 5:1; 6:1; 7:1; 19:27; 22:17; 23:26-28 [n]Jer 35:8 [o]S Dt 21:18; Pr 6:20 **1:9** [p]Pr 3:21-22; 4:1-9 **1:10** [q]S Job 24:15 [r]Dt 13:8 [s]ver 15; Ps 1:1; Pr 16:29 **1:11** [t]S Ps 10:8 **1:12** [u]S Ps 35:25 [v]ver 16-18; S Job 33:18; S Ps 30:3 **1:14** [w]ver 19 **1:15** [x]S Ps 119:101 [y]S Ge 49:6; Pr 4:14 **1:16** [z]S Job 15:31 [a]Pr 6:18; Isa 59:7

1:1 *Solomon.* His wisdom and prolific production of proverbs and songs are mentioned in 1Ki 4:29–34 (see notes there). His name occurs again in the headings of 10:1 and 25:1. Cf. SS 1:1.
1:2–4 Verses 2–3 apply to the son; v. 4 refers to the father.
1:2 *wisdom and instruction.* The two primary virtues in the long list that articulates the purpose of the book (vv. 2–6). Repeated at the end of v. 7, the phrase thus frames the entire prologue (vv. 2–7). *wisdom.* This key term occurs more than 40 times in the book. It includes skill in living—following God's design and thus avoiding moral pitfalls. A craftsman can be called a wise (skillful) man (Ex 31:3). Proverbs urges people to get wisdom (4:5; cf. Jas 1:5 and note), for it is worth more than silver or gold (3:13–14). The NT refers to Christ as "wisdom from God" (1Co 1:30; cf. Col 2:3).
1:3 *right and just and fair.* See 2:9; Ps 119:121 and note; Php 4:8.
1:4 *prudence.* Good judgment or good sense (see 15:5; 19:25). Outside Proverbs the Hebrew word is used in the negative sense of "crafty" (Ge 3:1; see Job 5:13). *simple.* Another key word in Proverbs, occurring about 15 times. It denotes those who are easily persuaded and who "have no sense" (9:4,16), who are immature, inexperienced and naive (cf. v. 10; Ps 19:7 and notes). See NIV text note on 1:4.
1:6 *riddles.* The Hebrew for this word can sometimes refer to allegories (cf. Eze 17:2).
1:7 The theme of the book (see 9:10; 31:30; cf. Job 28:28; Ps 111:10 and note). *fear of the LORD.* A loving reverence for God that includes submission to his lordship and to the commands of his word (see Ecc 12:13 and note; see also Introduction: Purpose and Teaching). See note on Ge 20:11. *fools.* See NIV text note. "Fools" are those who "hate knowledge" (v. 22) and correction of any kind (12:1), who are "quick to quarrel" (20:3) and "give full vent" to their anger (29:11), who are complacent (1:32) and who trust in themselves (28:26) rather than in God (Ps 14:1). *despise wisdom and instruction.* See 1:2; 5:12 and notes.
1:8 A typical introduction to an instruction speech in Proverbs, evoking a domestic situation of a father preparing his son for life in the world. Here and in 6:20 and 31:1 the mother is also depicted as teacher.
1:9 *to grace … to adorn.* See 6:21. Those who follow wisdom add beauty and honor to their lives (cf. 4:9).
1:10 *entice.* The Hebrew word is related to the Hebrew noun translated "simple" (see v. 4 and note). One who is "simple" is easily enticed. See Ps 19:7 and note.
1:11 *Come along.* But the father wisely advises, "Do not go along" (v. 15). Cf. Lady Wisdom's appeal in 9:4–6. *lie in wait for … blood.* Their goal is personal enrichment by theft or oppression (vv. 13,19), even if they have to commit murder. The author uses two major enticements that confronted the young man (in that culture) as examples of the way of folly: (1) to get rich by exploiting others (here) and (2) to be drawn into illicit sexual pleasure by immoral women who fail to honor their marriage vows (5:1–6; 6:24; 7:5; cf. 2:12–19).
1:12 *swallow … like the grave.* Vivid poetic imagery for shamelessly victimizing others (cf. Ps 49:14 and note).
1:13 *valuable things.* By contrast, the book of Proverbs teaches that wisdom brings the greatest riches people could ever gain (3:13–16; 16:16; see also Job 28:12–19).
1:15 *paths.* Cf. the destructive paths of the adulterous woman in 2:18 (see note there); 7:25.
1:16 The same as the first two lines of Isa 59:7 and partially quoted in Ro 3:15. Cf. Pr 6:17–18.

17 How useless to spread a net
where every bird can see it!
18 These men lie in wait[b] for their own blood;
they ambush only themselves![c]
19 Such are the paths of all who go after ill-gotten gain;
it takes away the life of those who get it.[d]

Wisdom's Rebuke

20 Out in the open wisdom calls aloud,[e]
she raises her voice in the public square;
21 on top of the wall[a] she cries out,
at the city gate she makes her speech:

22 "How long will you who are simple[f] love your simple ways?
How long will mockers delight in mockery
and fools hate[g] knowledge?
23 Repent at my rebuke!
Then I will pour out my thoughts to you,
I will make known to you my teachings.
24 But since you refuse[h] to listen when I call[i]
and no one pays attention[j] when I stretch out my hand,
25 since you disregard all my advice
and do not accept my rebuke,
26 I in turn will laugh[k] when disaster[l] strikes you;
I will mock[m] when calamity overtakes you[n]—
27 when calamity overtakes you like a storm,
when disaster[o] sweeps over you like a whirlwind,
when distress and trouble overwhelm you.

28 "Then they will call to me but I will not answer;[p]
they will look for me but will not find me,[q]
29 since they hated knowledge
and did not choose to fear the LORD.[r]
30 Since they would not accept my advice
and spurned my rebuke,[s]
31 they will eat the fruit of their ways
and be filled with the fruit of their schemes.[t]
32 For the waywardness of the simple will kill them,
and the complacency of fools will destroy them;[u]

1:18 [b] S Ps 71:10 [c] S ver 11-12 **1:19** [d] S ver 13-14; Pr 4:14-17; 11:19 **1:20** [e] S Job 28:12; Pr 7:10-13; 9:1-3,13-15 **1:22** [f] Pr 6:32; 7:7; 8:5; 9:4,16 [g] Ps 50:17 **1:24** [h] Jer 26:5; 35:17; 36:31 [i] Isa 65:12; 66:4; Jer 7:13 [j] S 1Sa 8:19 **1:26** [k] S Ps 2:4 [l] ver 33; S Ps 59:8 [m] S 2Ki 19:21 [n] Dt 28:63 **1:27** [o] S Ps 18:18; Pr 5:12-14 **1:28** [p] S Dt 1:45; S 1Sa 8:18; S Jer 11:11 [q] S Job 27:9; Pr 8:17; Eze 8:18; Hos 5:6; Zec 7:13 **1:29** [r] S Job 21:14 **1:30** [s] ver 25 **1:31** [t] S 2Ch 36:16; Pr 14:14; Jer 6:19; 14:16; 21:14; 30:15 **1:32** [u] Pr 5:22; 15:10; Isa 66:4

[a] *21* Septuagint; Hebrew / *at noisy street corners*

1:17 *net.* Nets were used to catch birds and animals (see 6:5; 7:23; Ecc 9:12; Isa 51:20; Jer 5:26).
1:18 *ambush only themselves.* See v. 11. The wicked unintentionally spread a net for their own feet (29:6; Ps 35:8), so they are less intelligent than birds (see 7:22–23).
1:19 According to Isa 17:14, destruction is the fate of those who plunder God's people. Contrast the long life enjoyed by the "one who hates ill-gotten gain" (28:16).
1:20 *wisdom calls aloud.* Personified wisdom also calls out to the simple in 8:1–5; 9:4–6 (see note on 8:1–36). *public square.* Open area inside the gate of a fortified city (see 8:3).
1:21 *city gate.* Where the leaders of the city met to hold court (see 31:23; see also Ge 19:1; Ru 4:1; Job 29:7 and notes) and where the marketplace was located (2Ki 7:1). As a young man confronts life in its social context, two voices lure him, appeal for his allegiance and seek to shape his life: (1) the voice of wisdom (as exemplified in the instructions of the teachers of wisdom) and (2) the voice of folly (as exemplified in the sinners of vv. 10–19 and in the adulterous woman of 5:3; 6:24; 7:5). Thus in the midst of life the youth must learn to exercise discretion. Here and in chs. 8–9 wisdom makes her appeal. She speaks neither out of heaven (by special revelation, as do the prophets) nor out of the earth (through voices from the dead—necromancy; see Lev 19:31; Dt 18:11; 1Sa 28:7–19), but out of the center of the life of the city, where communal experience of the creation order (established by God's wisdom, 8:22–31) is concentrated (see, e.g., 11:10 and note). And it is there also that the godly, the truly wise, test human experience in the crucible of faith and afterward give divine wisdom a human voice in their wise instructions—as in Proverbs.
1:22 *mockers.* Those who are "proud and arrogant" (21:24); who are full of insults, hatred and strife (9:7–8; 22:10; 29:8); who resist correction (13:1; 15:12) even though they deserve flogging (19:25; 21:11).
1:23 *pour out my thoughts.* Wisdom is like a fountain. Her words constantly refresh and strengthen (see 18:4 and note).
1:24 *refuse to listen.* As Israel rejected the Lord (see Isa 1:4; 5:24; Hos 2:13; 11:2), who brought forth wisdom "as the first of his works" (8:22), and as the people of Jerusalem rejected Jesus (see Mt 23:37), the embodiment and supreme manifestation of God's wisdom (see Jn 1:1–14; 1Co 1:24; Col 1:15–17; 2:3; Heb 1:1–4 and notes). *stretch out my hand.* Cf. Isa 65:2, where God held out his hands all day long to "an obstinate people."
1:25 *disregard … advice.* Cf. 8:33.
1:26 *laugh when disaster strikes you.* Not an expression of heartlessness but a reaction to the absurdity of fools, who laugh at wisdom, choose folly and bring disaster on themselves. Cf. the Lord's response to kings who think they can rebel against him (Ps 2:4). *calamity overtakes you.* Also the fate of troublemakers and villains (6:12–15).
1:27 *like a storm.* See 10:25 and note. *distress and trouble.* See Isa 8:22.
1:28 *I will not answer.* Just as God refused to listen to Israel when the people sinned (see Dt 1:45; Isa 1:15 and note). *find me.* Those who find wisdom find life and blessing (see v. 33; 3:13; 8:17,35).
1:29 *fear the LORD.* See v. 7 and note.
1:31 *eat … be filled with the fruit.* The consequences depend on their actions (see 12:14 and note; 18:20; 31:31; Isa 3:10). "A man reaps what he sows" (Gal 6:7). *schemes.* To refuse wisdom's "advice" (v. 30) is to suffer the consequences of one's own foolish "schemes" (the Hebrew for "advice" and "schemes" is the same).
1:32 *complacency.* A false sense of security (see Isa 32:9; Am 6:1 and notes; Zep 1:12).

33 but whoever listens to me will live in
safety[v]
and be at ease, without fear of
harm."[w]

Moral Benefits of Wisdom

2 My son,[x] if you accept my words
and store up my commands within
you,
2 turning your ear to wisdom
and applying your heart to
understanding[y] —
3 indeed, if you call out for insight[z]
and cry aloud for understanding,
4 and if you look for it as for silver
and search for it as for hidden
treasure,[a]
5 then you will understand the fear of
the LORD
and find the knowledge of God.[b]
6 For the LORD gives wisdom;[c]
from his mouth come knowledge
and understanding.[d]
7 He holds success in store for the
upright,
he is a shield[e] to those whose walk
is blameless,[f]
8 for he guards the course of the
just
and protects the way of his faithful
ones.[g]

9 Then you will understand[h] what is
right and just
and fair — every good path.

1:33 [v] S Nu 24:21; S Dt 33:28; Pr 3:23 [w] S ver 21-26; S Ps 112:8
2:1 [x] S Pr 1:8
2:2 [y] Pr 22:17; 23:12
2:3 [z] Jas 1:5
2:4 [a] S Job 3:21; Mt 13:44
2:5 [b] S Dt 4:6
2:6 [c] S Job 12:13; S Ps 119:34 [d] S Job 9:4; S 22:22
2:7 [e] S Ge 15:1; Pr 30:5-6 [f] S Ge 6:9; Ps 84:11
2:8 [g] 1Sa 2:9; S Ps 18:25; S 97:10
2:9 [h] S Dt 1:16
2:10 [i] Pr 14:33
2:11 [j] Pr 4:6
2:12 [k] ver 16; Pr 3:13-18; 4:5
2:13 [l] Pr 4:19
2:14 [m] Pr 10:23; 15:21
2:15 [n] S Ps 125:5 [o] Pr 21:8
2:16 [p] Pr 5:1-6; 6:20-29; 7:5-27
2:17 [q] Mal 2:14
2:18 [r] Pr 5:5; 7:27; 9:18
2:19 [s] Pr 3:16-18; 5:8; Ecc 7:26

10 For wisdom will enter your heart,[i]
and knowledge will be pleasant to
your soul.
11 Discretion will protect you,
and understanding will guard you.[j]
12 Wisdom will save[k] you from the ways
of wicked men,
from men whose words are perverse,
13 who have left the straight paths
to walk in dark ways,[l]
14 who delight in doing wrong
and rejoice in the perverseness of
evil,[m]
15 whose paths are crooked[n]
and who are devious in their ways.[o]

16 Wisdom will save you also from the
adulterous woman,[p]
from the wayward woman with her
seductive words,
17 who has left the partner of her youth
and ignored the covenant she made
before God.[a][q]
18 Surely her house leads down to death
and her paths to the spirits of the
dead.[r]
19 None who go to her return
or attain the paths of life.[s]

20 Thus you will walk in the ways of the
good
and keep to the paths of the
righteous.

[a] 17 *Or covenant of her God*

1:33 *in safety ... at ease.* Words used of places that enjoy God's protection (see Isa 32:18; Eze 34:27).

2:1 *store up ... within you.* Just as the psalmist hid God's word in his heart to avoid sin (Ps 119:11).

2:2 *turning your ear.* Listening implies attentiveness and obedience (Isa 55:3; Jer 13:15). *heart.* See note on Ps 4:7.

2:4 *silver ... hidden treasure.* Job 28:1–11 describes ancient mining techniques, comparing mining with the search for wisdom (see Job 28:12,20).

2:5 *fear of the LORD.* See note on 1:7. *knowledge of God.* Involves having a personal relationship with God (cf. Php 3:10 and note) and knowing what he is teaching us (v. 6).

2:7 *holds ... in store.* For those who "store up" his commands (v. 1). *shield.* Associated with victory also in Ps 18:2,35; cf. Pr 30:5. See Ps 3:3 and note. *blameless.* Having spiritual and moral integrity. This does not imply sinlessness (see 19:1). See v. 21; see also Job 1:1; Ps 15:2 and notes.

2:8 *guards ... protects.* See Ps 91:3–7,11–12.

2:9–11 Those who know the Lord and the wisdom he gives will know what course of action to follow (cf. Heb 5:11–14).

2:9 *right and just and fair.* See 1:3 and note. *good path.* Cf. "right paths" in Ps 23:3 (see note there).

2:10 *pleasant to your soul.* Just as the words of the wise are "sweet to the soul" of another (see 16:24 and note; cf. 3:17).

2:11 *protect ... guard.* As God guards the faithful (v. 8).

2:12–19 Wisdom will save one from the enticements of men to follow perverse ways (vv. 12–15) and from the "seductive words" of the adulterous woman (vv. 16–19). See note on 1:11.

2:12 *words are perverse.* Cf. v. 14. The deceitfulness of human speech is also mentioned in 6:12,17; 8:13; 10:31–32; 17:20; 19:28.

2:13 *straight paths.* See 3:6 and note; 9:15. *dark ways.* People love darkness instead of light (see Jn 3:19–21; see also Job 24:14–17; Isa 29:15; Ro 13:12).

2:14 *delight ... rejoice in ... evil.* Like the sinners of 1:10–19.

2:15 *paths are crooked.* See Isa 59:7–8.

2:16 *adulterous woman ... wayward woman.* The Hebrew for these terms occurs again in 5:20 and 7:5. The terms mean lit. "stranger" and "foreigner" (cf. 5:10) because anyone other than one's own wife was to be considered off limits, like a foreigner who worshiped another god (cf. 1Ki 11:1–2). "Wayward woman/wife" is parallel to "neighbor's wife" in 6:24 and "adulterous woman" in 23:27. *seductive words.* Equal to the "smooth talk" of 6:24; 7:21. Cf. 5:3 and note.

2:17 *partner of her youth.* Her husband, whom she married when she was a young woman (cf. Isa 54:6). *covenant ... before God.* Probably the marriage covenant, spoken in God's presence (see Eze 16:8; Mal 2:14). Alternatively, the breaking of the seventh commandment (Ex 20:14) may be indicated (see NIV text note).

2:18 *leads down to death.* According to 7:27, "Her house is a highway to the grave." A life of immorality leads to the destruction and death of all who are involved (cf. 5:5; 9:18). *spirits of the dead.* See Job 26:5 and note. The deceased are in the grave (or Sheol), "the chambers of death" (7:27).

21 For the upright will live in the land,[t]
and the blameless will remain
in it;
22 but the wicked[u] will be cut off from the
land,[v]
and the unfaithful will be torn
from it.[w]

Wisdom Bestows Well-Being

3 My son,[x] do not forget my teaching,[y]
but keep my commands in your
heart,
2 for they will prolong your life many
years[z]
and bring you peace and
prosperity.[a]

3 Let love and faithfulness[b] never leave
you;
bind them around your neck,
write them on the tablet of your
heart.[c]
4 Then you will win favor and a good
name
in the sight of God and man.[d]

5 Trust in the LORD[e] with all your
heart
and lean not on your own
understanding;
6 in all your ways submit to him,
and he will make your paths[f]
straight.[a][g]

7 Do not be wise in your own eyes;[h]
fear the LORD[i] and shun evil.[j]
8 This will bring health to your body[k]
and nourishment to your bones.[l]

9 Honor the LORD with your wealth,
with the firstfruits[m] of all your
crops;
10 then your barns will be filled[n] to
overflowing,
and your vats will brim over with
new wine.[o]

11 My son,[p] do not despise the LORD's
discipline,[q]
and do not resent his rebuke,
12 because the LORD disciplines those he
loves,[r]
as a father the son he delights in.[b][s]

13 Blessed are those who find wisdom,
those who gain understanding,
14 for she is more profitable than silver
and yields better returns than
gold.[t]
15 She is more precious than rubies;[u]
nothing you desire can compare with
her.[v]

[a] 6 Or *will direct your paths* [b] 12 Hebrew; Septuagint *loves, / and he chastens everyone he accepts as his child*

2:21 [t] S Ps 37:29 **2:22** [u] S Ps 5:4 [v] S Job 18:17 [w] Dt 28:63; S 29:28; Ps 37:9, 28-29; Pr 10:30 **3:1** [x] S Pr 1:8 [y] S Ps 44:17 **3:2** [z] S Dt 11:21 [a] S Dt 5:16; S 30:15, 16; S 1Ki 3:13, 14; Pr 9:6, 10-11 **3:3** [b] S Ps 85:10 [c] S Ex 13:9; S Dt 6:6; Pr 6:21; 7:3; S 2Co 3:3 **3:4** [d] S 1Sa 2:26; Lk 2:52 **3:5** [e] S Ps 4:5 **3:6** [f] S Job 33:11; S Isa 30:11 [g] Ps 5:8; Pr 16:3; Isa 40:3; Jer 42:3 **3:7** [h] Pr 26:5, 12; Isa 5:21 [i] Ps 111:10 [j] S Ex 20:20; S Dt 4:6; S Job 1:1 **3:8** [k] S Ps 38:3; Pr 4:22 [l] Job 21:24 **3:9** [m] S Ex 22:29; Dt 26:1-15 **3:10** [n] Ps 144:13 [o] S Job 22:21; Joel 2:24; Mal 3:10-12 **3:11** [p] Pr 1:8-9 [q] S Job 5:17 **3:12** [r] Pr 13:24; Rev 3:19 [s] S Dt 8:5; S Job 5:17; Heb 12:5-6* **3:14** [t] S Job 28:15; Pr 8:19; 16:16 **3:15** [u] S Job 28:18 [v] S Job 28:17-19

2:21 *live in the land.* Abraham's descendants had been promised the land of Canaan (Ge 12:7; 17:8; Dt 4:1), and Ps 37:29 says, "The righteous will inherit the land" (see Ps 37:9,11; Mt 5:5). *blameless.* See note on v. 7.

2:22 *cut off from the land ... torn from it.* In Dt 28:63 God warned that if the people refuse to obey him, they "will be uprooted from the land." The wicked and their offspring will be cut off (Ps 37:9,28).

3:2 *prolong your life.* Fear of the Lord (19:23) brings health to the body (v. 8) and "adds length to life" (10:27; see also 9:10–11). *prosperity.* When Solomon prayed for wisdom (1Ki 3:9), God promised him riches as well as long life if he obeyed God's commands (1Ki 3:13–14). Normally the righteous are prosperous and happy (12:21), but sometimes it is the wicked who are strong and prosperous (Ps 73:3,12), temporary though that may be (Ps 37:10,20,35–36; 73:17–19). Job 1–2 also shows how disaster and death can strike a godly person (see note on vv. 11–12).

3:3 *love and faithfulness.* See Ps 26:3 and note. *bind ... neck.* Like a beautiful necklace (cf. v. 22; 1:9; 3:22). *write them on the tablet of your heart.* See 7:3; cf. Jer 31:33 and note. These instructions are not to be taken literally (see Ex 13:9; Dt 6:8–9 and notes).

3:4 *favor.* See 8:35; 12:2; Ge 6:8. *God and man.* See 1Sa 2:26; Lk 2:52; Ro 12:17 and note; 2Co 8:21.

3:5 *Trust in the LORD.* "Commit your way to the LORD" (Ps 37:5), like Israel's ancestors, who trusted in God and were rescued (Ps 22:4–5). *with all your heart.* Like Caleb (Nu 14:24; Dt 1:36; Jos 14:6–14) or the godly King Hezekiah (Isa 38:3). David challenged Solomon to serve God "with wholehearted devotion" (1Ch 28:9).

3:6 *submit to him.* Be ever mindful of God and serve him with a willing, faithful and obedient heart (see 1Ch 28:9; Hos 4:1; 6:3,6). *make your paths straight.* He will remove the obstacles from your pathway and bring you to your appointed goal (see 11:5; Isa 45:13 and note).

3:7 *fear the LORD and shun evil.* Cf. Job, who was "blameless and upright" and thus "shunned evil" (Job 1:1). See note on 1:7.

3:8 *bones.* The whole body. Elsewhere, good news and pleasant words bring health to the bones (15:30; 16:24; cf. 12:4; 14:30; 17:22).

3:9 *firstfruits.* The Israelites were required to give to the priests the first part of the olive oil, wine and grain produced each year (see Lev 23:10; Nu 18:12–13).

3:10 *filled to overflowing.* For those who bring to the Lord his tithes and offerings, God promises to pour out more blessing than they have room for (see Mal 3:10; see also Dt 28:8,12; 2Co 9:6–11). *vats.* See note on Hag 2:16.

3:11–12 A warning that the righteous are not always prosperous (see v. 2 and note). Through times of testing and affliction, God is teaching them (see 12:1; Ps 119:71). Heb 12:5–6 quotes both of these verses to encourage believers to endure hardship (Heb 12:7). "God disciplines us for our good" (Heb 12:10).

3:12 *as a father.* God disciplined his son Israel by testing the nation in the wilderness 40 years (Dt 8:2–5).

3:13–18 A poem praising wisdom that begins and ends with the word "blessed" (cf. Job 5:17).

3:14 *more profitable than silver ... gold.* The psalmist makes the same claim for the commands and precepts of the Lord (Ps 19:10; 119:72,127).

3:15–18 Wisdom is personified.

3:15 *rubies.* See 8:11; 20:15. Although rubies were the most priceless jewels in the ancient world, they are considered of less value than wisdom also in Job 28:18. The "wife of noble character" is "worth far more than rubies" (31:10; see note on 31:10–31).

[16]Long life is in her right hand;[w]
in her left hand are riches and honor.[x]
[17]Her ways are pleasant ways,
and all her paths are peace.[y]
[18]She is a tree of life[z] to those who take
hold of her;
those who hold her fast will be
blessed.[a]

[19]By wisdom[b] the LORD laid the earth's
foundations,[c]
by understanding he set the
heavens[d] in place;
[20]by his knowledge the watery depths
were divided,
and the clouds let drop the dew.

[21]My son,[e] do not let wisdom and
understanding out of your sight,[f]
preserve sound judgment and
discretion;
[22]they will be life for you,[g]
an ornament to grace your neck.[h]
[23]Then you will go on your way in
safety,[i]
and your foot will not stumble.[j]
[24]When you lie down,[k] you will not be
afraid;[l]
when you lie down, your sleep[m] will
be sweet.
[25]Have no fear of sudden disaster
or of the ruin that overtakes the
wicked,
[26]for the LORD will be at your side[n]
and will keep your foot[o] from being
snared.[p]

[27]Do not withhold good from those to
whom it is due,
when it is in your power to act.

3:16 [w]S Ge 15:15 [x]S 1Ki 3:13,14
3:17 [y]Mt 11:28-30
3:18 [z]S Ge 2:9; S Pr 10:11; S Rev 2:7 [a]S Pr 2:12; 4:3-9,8; 8:17-21
3:19 [b]S Ge 1:31; Ps 136:5-9 [c]S Job 28:25-27 [d]Pr 8:27-29
3:21 [e]Pr 1:8-9; 6:20 [f]Pr 4:20-22
3:22 [g]S Dt 30:20; Pr 4:13 [h]S Pr 1:8-9
3:23 [i]S Pr 1:33 [j]S Ps 37:24; S 119:11; Pr 4:12
3:24 [k]S Lev 26:6 [l]Ps 91:5; 112:8 [m]S Job 11:18; Jer 31:26
3:26 [n]S 2Ki 18:5; S Job 4:6 [o]S 1Sa 2:9 [p]S Job 5:19
3:28 [q]Lev 19:13; Dt 24:15; Lk 10:25-37
3:29 [r]Zec 8:17
3:31 [s]S Ps 37:1; Pr 24:1-2
3:32 [t]S Ps 101:4 [u]S Job 29:4
3:33 [v]S Job 5:3 [w]Zec 5:4 [x]Ps 37:22; Pr 14:11
3:34 [y]S 2Ki 19:21 [z]S Ps 40:4 [a]S Ps 18:25-27; S Mt 23:12; Jas 4:6*; 1Pe 5:5*
4:1 [b]S Pr 1:8 [c]Pr 19:20 [d]S Job 8:10

[28]Do not say to your neighbor,
"Come back tomorrow and I'll give
it to you"—
when you already have it with you.[q]
[29]Do not plot harm against your
neighbor,
who lives trustfully near you.[r]
[30]Do not accuse anyone for no
reason—
when they have done you no
harm.

[31]Do not envy[s] the violent
or choose any of their ways.

[32]For the LORD detests the perverse[t]
but takes the upright into his
confidence.[u]
[33]The LORD's curse[v] is on the house of
the wicked,[w]
but he blesses the home of the
righteous.[x]
[34]He mocks[y] proud mockers[z]
but shows favor to the humble[a] and
oppressed.
[35]The wise inherit honor,
but fools get only shame.

Get Wisdom at Any Cost

4 Listen, my sons,[b] to a father's
instruction;[c]
pay attention and gain
understanding.[d]
[2]I give you sound learning,
so do not forsake my teaching.
[3]For I too was a son to my father,
still tender, and cherished by my
mother.

3:16 *Long life.* See note on v. 2. *riches and honor.* See 8:18; 22:4.
3:17 *peace.* Hebrew *shalom*, translated "peace and prosperity" in v. 2 (see 16:7; Ps 119:165).
3:18 *tree of life.* Source of life. This figure of speech (see also 11:30; 13:12; 15:4) may recall the tree in the Garden of Eden (see Ge 2:9 and note; see also Introduction: Purpose and Teaching).
3:19–20 The role of wisdom in creation is described more fully in 8:22–31 (see notes there). Divine wisdom guided the Creator and now permeates the whole creation. To live by wisdom is to imitate the Lord and conform to the divinely appointed creation order.
3:19 *earth's foundations.* See 8:29. God's work in creation is compared to the construction of a building (see 1Ki 5:17; 6:37; see also Job 38:4–6; Ps 24:2 and note; 104:5; Zec 12:1). *set the heavens in place.* See Isa 42:5; 48:13 and note; 51:16.
3:20 *divided.* Or "broken open." God opened up springs and streams (see Ge 7:11; 49:25; Ps 74:15). Alternatively, though perhaps less likely, reference is to the dividing of the waters above from the waters below (see Ge 1:7; Ps 42:7 and note). *dew.* Probably also includes rain (see Dt 33:13; 2Sa 1:21).
3:22 *ornament to grace your neck.* Like a beautiful necklace (see v. 3 and note).
3:23 *in safety, and your foot will not stumble.* See v. 26; cf. 10:9.
3:24 *When you lie down, you will not be afraid.* Also listed among the covenant blessings (see Lev 26:6; Job 11:18–19; Mic 4:4; Zep 3:13; see also Pr 1:33). *your sleep will be sweet.* See 6:22; Ps 4:8.
3:25 *disaster … ruin.* The Lord shields the godly from deadly arrows and plagues (see 10:25; Ps 91:3–8; Job 5:21).
3:26 *will keep your foot from being snared.* Contrast the fate of the fool in 1:18; 7:22–23.
3:27 *not withhold good.* See Ac 9:36; Gal 6:10; 1Jn 3:17–18. *those to whom it is due.* Especially the poor and needy.
3:28 See Lk 11:5–8; Jas 2:15–16.
3:30 *Do not accuse … for no reason.* See Job 2:3.
3:31 *Do not envy.* See 23:17; 24:19; Ps 37:1,7. *the violent.* Like the sinners of 1:10–19 (cf. 16:29).
3:32 *detests.* A word that elsewhere expresses abhorrence of pagan practices (see Dt 18:9,12) and moral abuses. It is common in Proverbs (e.g., 6:16; 8:7; 11:20). *takes the upright into his confidence.* See Ge 18:17 and note; Job 29:4; Ps 25:14; Am 3:7; Jn 15:15.
3:33 This contrast is seen also in Dt 11:26–28. *The LORD's curse is on the house of the wicked.* See Jos 7:24–25; Zec 5:3–4. *blesses the home of the righteous.* See Job 42:12–14.
3:34 *mocks proud mockers.* See note on 1:26. *shows favor.* See v. 4. James and Peter both quote this verse (Jas 4:6; 1Pe 5:5).
4:3 *still tender.* Cf. David's words about Solomon, who was "young and inexperienced" (1Ch 22:5; 29:1). This is part of an autobiographical statement, such as was sometimes used by the wisdom teachers (see 24:30–34; see also the book of

4 Then he taught me, and he said to me,
"Take hold[e] of my words with all
your heart;
keep my commands, and you will
live.[f]
5 Get wisdom,[g] get understanding;
do not forget my words or turn away
from them.
6 Do not forsake wisdom, and she will
protect you;[h]
love her, and she will watch over
you.[i]
7 The beginning of wisdom is this: Get[a]
wisdom.
Though it cost all[j] you have,[b] get
understanding.[k]
8 Cherish her, and she will exalt you;
embrace her, and she will honor
you.[l]
9 She will give you a garland to grace
your head
and present you with a glorious
crown.[m]"

10 Listen, my son,[n] accept what I say,
and the years of your life will be
many.[o]
11 I instruct[p] you in the way of wisdom
and lead you along straight paths.[q]
12 When you walk, your steps will not be
hampered;
when you run, you will not stumble.[r]
13 Hold on to instruction, do not let it go;
guard it well, for it is your life.[s]
14 Do not set foot on the path of the
wicked
or walk in the way of evildoers.[t]
15 Avoid it, do not travel on it;
turn from it and go on your way.
16 For they cannot rest until they do evil;[u]
they are robbed of sleep till they
make someone stumble.
17 They eat the bread of wickedness
and drink the wine of violence.[v]

18 The path of the righteous[w] is like the
morning sun,[x]
shining ever brighter till the full light
of day.[y]
19 But the way of the wicked is like deep
darkness;[z]
they do not know what makes them
stumble.[a]

20 My son,[b] pay attention to what I say;
turn your ear to my words.[c]
21 Do not let them out of your sight,[d]
keep them within your heart;
22 for they are life to those who find them
and health to one's whole body.[e]
23 Above all else, guard[f] your heart,
for everything you do flows from it.[g]
24 Keep your mouth free of perversity;
keep corrupt talk far from your lips.
25 Let your eyes[h] look straight ahead;
fix your gaze directly before you.
26 Give careful thought to the[c] paths for
your feet[i]
and be steadfast in all your ways.
27 Do not turn to the right or the left;[j]
keep your foot from evil.

Warning Against Adultery

5 My son,[k] pay attention to my
wisdom,
turn your ear to my words[l] of
insight,

[a] 7 Or *Wisdom is supreme; therefore get*
[b] 7 Or *wisdom. / Whatever else you get*
[c] 26 Or *Make level*

4:4 [e] S 1Ki 9:4 [f] Pr 7:2 **4:5** [g] S Pr 2:12; 3:13-18 **4:6** [h] 2Th 2:10 [i] S Pr 2:11 **4:7** [j] Mt 13:44-46 [k] Pr 23:23 **4:8** [l] S Pr 3:18 **4:9** [m] S Pr 1:8-9 **4:10** [n] Ps 34:11-16; Pr 1:8-9 [o] S Dt 11:21 **4:11** [p] S 1Sa 12:23 [q] 2Sa 22:37; Ps 5:8 **4:12** [r] S Job 18:7; Pr 3:23 **4:13** [s] S Pr 3:22 **4:14** [t] Ps 1:1; S Pr 1:15 **4:16** [u] Ps 36:4; Mic 7:3 **4:17** [v] Ge 49:5; Ps 73:6; Pr 1:10-19; 14:22; Isa 59:6; Jer 22:3; Hab 1:2; Mal 2:16 **4:18** [w] Job 17:9 [x] S Job 22:28 [y] S 2Sa 23:4; Da 12:3; Mt 5:14; Jn 8:12; Php 2:15 **4:19** [z] S Pr 2:13 [a] S Dt 32:35; S Job 3:23; Pr 13:9; S Isa 8:15 **4:20** [b] Ps 34:11-16; Pr 1:8-9 [c] Pr 5:1 **4:21** [d] Pr 3:21 **4:22** [e] S Pr 3:8 **4:23** [f] S 2Ki 10:31 [g] Pr 10:11; Lk 6:45 **4:25** [h] S Job 31:1 **4:26** [i] Heb 12:13* **4:27** [j] S Lev 10:11; S Dt 5:32 **5:1** [k] S Pr 1:8 [l] Pr 4:20

Ecclesiastes). *cherished.* Deeply loved (cf. Ge 37:3; Jer 6:26 and note; Zec 12:10).

4:4 *with all your heart.* See note on 3:5.

4:6 *protect ... watch over.* The Hebrew words for these two verbs occur together also in 2:8,11. *love her.* To love wisdom is to prosper (8:21); to hate wisdom is to "love death" (8:36).

4:7 *beginning of wisdom.* See 1:7; see also NIV text note. *Though it cost all you have.* Cf. the parables of the hidden treasure and the pearl in Mt 13:44–46 (see note there).

4:9 *glorious crown.* Wreaths or crowns were worn at joyous occasions, such as weddings or feasts (see SS 3:11; Eze 16:12; 23:42; cf. 1Pe 5:4).

4:10 *years ... will be many.* See note on 3:2.

4:11 *straight paths.* Right paths (see notes on 3:6; Ps 23:3).

4:12 *you will not stumble.* Because of some obstacle or lack of light (see v. 19; 3:23; 10:9; Ps 18:36; Isa 5:27; 40:30–31).

4:14 *path of the wicked.* Cf. the destructive paths of the adulterous woman in 2:18; 7:25; see Ps 1:1; 17:4–5.

4:16 *cannot rest until they do evil.* See Ps 36:4 and note; Mic 2:1. Contrast the attitude of David, who would not sleep until he found a permanent place for God's house (Ps 132:3–5).

4:17 *eat the bread ... drink the wine.* They thrive on wickedness and violence (see 13:2; Job 15:16; cf. Ps 109:18 and note).

4:18 *path of the righteous is ... shining ever brighter.* The godly have all the guidance and protection they need (see vv. 11–12) and are able to lead others to righteousness (Da 12:3).

4:19 *deep darkness.* A dangerous path that leads to destruction (see note on 2:13; see also Isa 59:9–10; Jer 23:12; Jn 11:10; 12:35).

4:21 *heart.* See 3:1,3; see also note on Ps 4:7.

4:22 *health.* Physical, psychological and spiritual (see 3:8 and note).

4:23 *everything you do flows from it.* If we store up good things (2:1) in our hearts, our words and actions will be good. "For the mouth speaks what the heart is full of" (Mt 12:34; cf. Mk 7:14–23; Lk 6:45 and notes).

4:24 *Keep your mouth free of perversity.* See note on 2:12; see also 19:1. *corrupt talk.* See 6:12; 19:28; Eph 4:29 and note; Jas 3:6.

4:25 *look straight ahead.* Not at "worthless things" (Ps 119:37).

4:26 Heb 12:13 quotes the first half of this verse (see note there and NIV text note here).

4:27 *Do not turn to the right or the left.* A warning found also in Dt 5:32–33; 28:14; Jos 1:7. *foot from evil.* See 1:15.

[2]that you may maintain discretion
and your lips may preserve knowledge.
[3]For the lips of the adulterous woman drip honey,
and her speech is smoother than oil;[m]
[4]but in the end she is bitter as gall,[n]
sharp as a double-edged sword.
[5]Her feet go down to death;
her steps lead straight to the grave.[o]
[6]She gives no thought to the way of life;
her paths wander aimlessly, but she does not know it.[p]

[7]Now then, my sons, listen[q] to me;
do not turn aside from what I say.
[8]Keep to a path far from her,[r]
do not go near the door of her house,
[9]lest you lose your honor to others
and your dignity[a] to one who is cruel,
[10]lest strangers feast on your wealth
and your toil enrich the house of another.[s]
[11]At the end of your life you will groan,
when your flesh and body are spent.
[12]You will say, "How I hated discipline!
How my heart spurned correction![t]
[13]I would not obey my teachers
or turn my ear to my instructors.

5:3 [m]S Ps 55:21; Pr 7:5
5:4 [n]Ecc 7:26
5:5 [o]S Ps 9:17; S Pr 2:18; 7:26-27
5:6 [p]Pr 9:13; 30:20
5:7 [q]Pr 1:8-9
5:8 [r]S Pr 2:16-19; 6:20-29; 7:1-27
5:10 [s]Pr 29:3
5:12 [t]Pr 12:1
5:14 [u]Pr 1:24-27; 6:33 [v]Pr 31:3
5:18 [w]SS 4:12-15 [x]S Dt 20:7; Pr 2:17; Ecc 9:9; Mal 2:14
5:19 [y]SS 4:5; 8:14
5:21 [z]S Ps 119:168 [a]Jer 29:23 [b]S Job 10:4; S 14:16; Pr 15:3; Jer 32:19; S Heb 4:13
5:22 [c]Ps 9:16 [d]Nu 32:23; S Job 18:9; Ps 7:15-16; S Pr 1:31-32
5:23 [e]S Job 4:21; Pr 10:21 [f]Job 34:21-25; Pr 11:5

[14]And I was soon in serious trouble[u]
in the assembly of God's people."[v]

[15]Drink water from your own cistern,
running water from your own well.
[16]Should your springs overflow in the streets,
your streams of water in the public squares?
[17]Let them be yours alone,
never to be shared with strangers.
[18]May your fountain[w] be blessed,
and may you rejoice in the wife of your youth.[x]
[19]A loving doe, a graceful deer[y]—
may her breasts satisfy you always,
may you ever be intoxicated with her love.
[20]Why, my son, be intoxicated with another man's wife?
Why embrace the bosom of a wayward woman?

[21]For your ways are in full view[z] of the LORD,
and he examines[a] all your paths.[b]
[22]The evil deeds of the wicked ensnare them;[c]
the cords of their sins hold them fast.[d]
[23]For lack of discipline they will die,[e]
led astray by their own great folly.[f]

[a] 9 Or *years*

5:2 *lips may preserve knowledge.* Applied to a priest in Mal 2:7.
5:3 *lips ... drip honey.* Probably a reference to the pleasant-sounding talk (cf. 16:24) of the adulterous woman, though some explain it as kisses (cf. SS 4:11; 5:13; 7:9). *adulterous woman.* See note on 2:16. *smoother than oil.* See 2:16. Her words are soothing (see Ps 55:21) but full of flattery (Pr 26:28) and hypocrisy (see Ps 5:9 and note).
5:4 *gall.* A bitter herb (see Dt 29:18; La 3:15,19; Am 6:12). *double-edged sword.* A lethal weapon (see Jdg 3:16; see also Ps 55:21; 149:6; Heb 4:12; cf. Rev 1:16 and note).
5:5 *down to death.* Her immorality hastens her end (see note on 2:18).
5:6 *paths wander aimlessly.* See 2:15; 10:9. *does not know it.* Or "does not acknowledge it."
5:7–14 The father warns the son about the high cost of immorality.
5:8 *far from her.* See Ge 39:12; 2Ti 2:22. *door of her house.* Cf. 7:27; 9:14.
5:9 *one who is cruel.* Possibly the vengeful husband (see 6:34–35).
5:10 *strangers feast on your wealth.* Contrast the riches and honor that come to those who embrace wisdom (3:16–18). Immorality eventually reduces one to "a loaf of bread" (6:26; see note there).
5:11 *flesh and body are spent.* Possibly because of the debilitating effects of immorality (see 1Co 6:18; cf. Pr 3:8; 4:22), but more likely referring to the loss of vigor that accompanies old age.
5:12 *hated discipline ... spurned correction.* In old age he will look back and sadly acknowledge that he has played the fool (see 1:7 and note; see also 1:22,29–30).
5:13 *would not obey.* Despite the repeated urging to "listen" or "pay attention" to their instruction (cf. v. 7; 1:8; 4:1; 5:1).
5:14 *serious trouble.* Physical, financial and social. *in the assembly of God's people.* The offender was subject to "blows and disgrace" (6:33) or even death (see Lev 20:10; Dt 22:22).
5:15 *your own cistern ... your own well.* Your own wife (see SS 4:12,15). Let your own wife be your source of pleasure, as water refreshes a thirsty man. Wells and cisterns were privately owned (Jer 38:6) and of great value (2Ki 18:31).
5:16 *springs ... streams of water.* Like "cistern" and "well" in v. 15 and "fountain" in v. 18, these also refer to the wife (see SS 4:12,15). *in the public squares.* The wife may become promiscuous if the husband is unfaithful.
5:18 *wife of your youth.* Chosen by you when you were young. True joy in marital relationships comes from long and deep commitment.
5:19 *doe ... deer.* Descriptive of the wife, perhaps because of the delicate beauty of the doe's limbs (see SS 2:9). *may her breasts satisfy you always.* See SS 7:7–8. *intoxicated.* Marital love is portrayed as better than wine in SS 4:10 (cf. SS 7:9).
5:20 *Why ... ?* In light of the sheer joy found within the bonds of marriage and the "serious trouble" (v. 14) outside it, why commit adultery? *another man's wife.* See v. 3; 2:16 and note.
5:21 *in full view of the LORD.* See 15:3; Job 31:4; 34:21; Jer 16:17; 32:19. *examines all your paths.* See Job 7:18; 34:23; Ps 11:4; 26:2; 139:23; Jer 11:20; 12:3; 17:10.
5:22 *ensnare them.* See 1:18 and note; Dt 7:25; 12:30. In Ecc 7:26 the sinner is ensnared by a woman "whose heart is a trap." *cords of their sins.* See Job 36:8; Ecc 4:12; Isa 5:18; cf. Hos 11:4 and note.
5:23 The death of the fool is described in similar terms in 1:29–32; 7:21–27; cf. Job 36:12. *discipline.* See v. 12 and note.

Warnings Against Folly

6 My son,[g] if you have put up security[h]
for your neighbor,[i]
if you have shaken hands in pledge[j]
for a stranger,
2 you have been trapped by what you
said,
ensnared by the words of your
mouth.
3 So do this, my son, to free yourself,
since you have fallen into your
neighbor's hands:
Go—to the point of exhaustion—[a]
and give your neighbor no rest!
4 Allow no sleep to your eyes,
no slumber to your eyelids.[k]
5 Free yourself, like a gazelle[l] from the
hand of the hunter,[m]
like a bird from the snare of the
fowler.[n]

6 Go to the ant, you sluggard;[o]
consider its ways and be wise!
7 It has no commander,
no overseer or ruler,
8 yet it stores its provisions in summer[p]
and gathers its food at harvest.[q]

9 How long will you lie there, you
sluggard?[r]
When will you get up from your
sleep?

6:1 [g] S Pr 1:8 [h] Job 17:3 [i] Pr 17:18 [j] Pr 11:15; 22:26-27 **6:4** [k] Ps 132:4 **6:5** [l] S 2Sa 2:18 [m] Isa 13:14 [n] S Ps 91:3 **6:6** [o] ver 6-11; Pr 20:4 **6:8** [p] Pr 30:24-25 [q] Pr 10:4 **6:9** [r] Pr 24:30-34; 26:13-16 **6:10** [s] Pr 24:33; Ecc 4:5 **6:11** [t] ver 10-11; Pr 20:13; 24:30-34 **6:13** [u] S Ps 35:19; Pr 16:30 [v] Isa 58:9 **6:14** [w] S Ps 140:2 [x] ver 16-19 **6:15** [y] S Ps 55:15 [z] Job 5:3 [a] Pr 14:32; 29:1 **6:16** [b] ver 16-19; Pr 3:32; 8:13; 15:8,9,26; 16:5 **6:17** [c] S Job 41:34; S Ps 10:5 [d] Pr 12:22 [e] S Dt 19:10; Pr 1:16; Isa 1:21; 59:7; Jer 2:34; Mic 7:2

10 A little sleep, a little slumber,
a little folding of the hands to rest[s]—
11 and poverty[t] will come on you like a
thief
and scarcity like an armed man.

12 A troublemaker and a villain,
who goes about with a corrupt
mouth,
13 who winks maliciously with his eye,[u]
signals with his feet
and motions with his fingers,[v]
14 who plots evil[w] with deceit in his
heart—
he always stirs up conflict.[x]
15 Therefore disaster will overtake him in
an instant;[y]
he will suddenly[z] be destroyed—
without remedy.[a]

16 There are six things the LORD hates,[b]
seven that are detestable to him:
17 haughty eyes,[c]
a lying tongue,[d]
hands that shed innocent blood,[e]
18 a heart that devises wicked
schemes,
feet that are quick to rush into
evil,[f]

[a] 3 Or *Go and humble yourself,*

6:18 [f] S Job 15:31

6:1 *put up security ... shaken hands in pledge.* Refers to responsibility for someone else's debt (cf. 22:26) or for some other obligation. It can end in abject poverty (cf. 22:27) or even slavery if you cannot pay. For example, Judah volunteered to personally guarantee the safe return of Benjamin to Jacob (Ge 43:9), and when this seemed impossible, he had to offer himself to Joseph as a slave (Ge 44:32–33). Such an arrangement was sealed by a handshake (see 11:15; 17:18; 20:16; 22:26; cf. Job 17:3).
6:2 *trapped ... ensnared.* Cf. v. 5; see also 1:18; 5:22 and notes.
6:3 *to free yourself.* To gain release from the obligation. *fallen into your neighbor's hands.* Assumed responsibility for the neighbor's obligation. *give your neighbor no rest.* Be as persistent as the person in Lk 11:8.
6:4 *no sleep ... no slumber.* Like David in Ps 132:4.
6:5 *snare of the fowler.* See Ps 124:7.
6:6 *ant.* A creature referred to elsewhere in the Bible only in 30:25, where it stores up its food in the summer (as here; see v. 8). The ant is mentioned also in Canaanite Amarna letter 252.15–19, again in a proverbial context (see chart, p. xxii). *sluggard.* A lazy individual who refuses to work and whose desires are not met (see 10:26; 13:4; 15:19; 19:24; 20:4; 21:25; 22:13; 24:30; 26:13–16).
6:7 *no commander.* Cf. the locust in 30:27.
6:9 *How long will you lie there, you sluggard?* The sluggard's love for sleep is described also in 26:14 (see note there).
6:10–11 Repeated in 24:33–34.
6:11 *poverty ... scarcity.* Connected with too much sleep also in 10:5; 19:15; 20:13. Hard work is an antidote to poverty (see 12:11; 14:23; 28:19). *like a thief ... an armed man.* Poverty will come when it is too late to do anything about it (cf. Mt 24:43).
6:12–14 A vivid description of one who uses mouth, eyes, feet and fingers (all a person's means of communication) in devious ways to achieve the deceitful plots of the heart—here especially to spread slander to destroy someone.
6:12 *A troublemaker.* A worthless, wicked person (16:27; Jdg 19:22; 1Sa 25:25; Job 34:18). See note on Dt 13:13. *corrupt mouth.* See 2:12 and note; 19:28.
6:13 *winks ... with his eye.* To make insinuations (see 10:10; 16:30).
6:14 *plots evil.* See v. 18; 3:29; Mic 2:1. *stirs up conflict.* Through slander such people create distrust that culminates in alienation and conflict (see v. 19; 10:12; 15:18; 16:28; 28:25; 29:22).
6:15 *disaster will overtake him in an instant.* Usually a sign of God's judgment (see 1:26; 24:22 and notes; Job 34:20). *suddenly be destroyed—without remedy.* Such scoundrels will suffer the same fate they thought to bring upon others—their punishment will fit their crime (cf. Gal 6:7–8). *without remedy.* See 29:1 and note.
6:16–19 A further elaboration on the theme of vv. 12–15, explaining why "disaster will overtake" (v. 15) the scoundrel described here.
6:16 *six ... seven.* A way of handling numbers in synonymous parallelism in Hebrew poetry (see Introduction: The Nature of a Proverb). Such catalogues of items are frequent in the wisdom literature of the OT (see 30:15,18,21,29; see also Job 5:19 and note). In all such cases in Proverbs, the higher number is the operational one. *detestable.* See 3:32 and note.
6:17 *haughty eyes.* They reflect a proud heart, and God will judge them (see 21:4; 30:13; Ps 18:27; 101:5). *lying tongue.* See 2:12 and note; 12:19; 17:7; 21:6. *hands that shed innocent blood.* See 1:11 and note; see also 1:16; 28:17.
6:18 *heart that devises wicked schemes.* See 1:31; 24:2; Ge 6:5. *feet that ... rush into evil.* See 1:16 and note.

19 a false witness[g] who pours out
lies[h]
and a person who stirs up conflict
in the community.[i]

Warning Against Adultery

20 My son,[j] keep your father's command
and do not forsake your mother's
teaching.[k]
21 Bind them always on your heart;
fasten them around your neck.[l]
22 When you walk, they will guide you;
when you sleep, they will watch
over you;
when you awake, they will speak to
you.
23 For this command is a lamp,
this teaching is a light,[m]
and correction and instruction
are the way to life,[n]
24 keeping you from your neighbor's wife,
from the smooth talk of a wayward
woman.[o]
25 Do not lust in your heart after her
beauty
or let her captivate you with her
eyes.
26 For a prostitute can be had for a loaf of
bread,
but another man's wife preys on
your very life.[p]
27 Can a man scoop fire into his lap
without his clothes being burned?
28 Can a man walk on hot coals
without his feet being scorched?
29 So is he who sleeps[q] with another
man's wife;[r]
no one who touches her will go
unpunished.
30 People do not despise a thief if he
steals
to satisfy his hunger when he is
starving.

6:19 [g] S Dt 19:16 [h] S Ps 12:2 [i] ver 12-15; Pr 15:18; Zec 8:17 **6:20** [j] S Pr 3:21 [k] Pr 1:8 **6:21** [l] Dt 6:8; S Pr 3:3; 7:1-3 **6:23** [m] S Ps 119:105 [n] Pr 10:17 **6:24** [o] Ge 39:8; S Ps 55:21; Pr 2:16; 7:5 **6:26** [p] Pr 7:22-23 **6:29** [q] S Ex 20:14 [r] Pr 2:16-19; S 5:8

6:31 [s] Ex 22:1-14 **6:32** [t] S Ex 20:14 [u] Pr 7:7; 9:4, 16 **6:33** [v] Pr 5:9-14 **6:34** [w] S Nu 5:14 [x] S Ge 34:7 **6:35** [y] Job 31:9-11; SS 8:7 **7:1** [z] S Pr 1:8 **7:2** [a] Pr 4:4 **7:3** [b] S Pr 3:3 **7:5** [c] ver 21; S Job 31:9; S Pr 2:16; 6:24 **7:7** [d] S Pr 1:22; S 6:32

31 Yet if he is caught, he must pay
sevenfold,[s]
though it costs him all the wealth of
his house.
32 But a man who commits adultery[t] has
no sense;[u]
whoever does so destroys himself.
33 Blows and disgrace are his lot,
and his shame will never[v] be wiped
away.
34 For jealousy[w] arouses a husband's
fury,[x]
and he will show no mercy when he
takes revenge.
35 He will not accept any compensation;
he will refuse a bribe, however great
it is.[y]

Warning Against the Adulterous Woman

7 My son,[z] keep my words
and store up my commands within
you.
2 Keep my commands and you will
live;[a]
guard my teachings as the apple of
your eye.
3 Bind them on your fingers;
write them on the tablet of your
heart.[b]
4 Say to wisdom, "You are my sister,"
and to insight, "You are my
relative."
5 They will keep you from the adulterous
woman,
from the wayward woman with her
seductive words.[c]

6 At the window of my house
I looked down through the lattice.
7 I saw among the simple,
I noticed among the young
men,
a youth who had no sense.[d]

6:19 *false witness.* See Ex 20:16; Dt 19:16–19. Proverbs emphasizes the damage done by false witnesses (12:17–18; 25:18; see note on Ps 5:9) and the punishment they receive (see note on v. 15; see also 19:5,9; 21:28). *pours out lies.* See 14:5,25. *stirs up conflict.* See note on v. 14.
6:20 See 1:8 and note.
6:21 See 1:9 and note.
6:22 *walk.* Cf. 4:11. *when you sleep.* See note on 3:24. *watch over you.* See 4:6.
6:23 *lamp ... light.* Just as the word of God "is a lamp for my feet, a light on my path" (Ps 119:105; cf. Ps 19:8). *way to life.* See 3:22; 4:22; 10:17. Contrast the way to death for the one who hates discipline (see 5:23 and note).
6:24 See notes on 2:16; 5:3.
6:25 *Do not lust.* Jesus shows the close connection between lust and adultery (Mt 5:28; cf. Ex 20:14,17 and notes). *captivate you.* See 5:20.
6:26 *another man's wife preys on your very life.* See 2:16–18 and notes; 5:5; 7:27.
6:29 *no one ... will go unpunished.* See vv. 33–34; see also note on 5:14.
6:31 *sevenfold.* Hebrew law demanded no more than fivefold payment as a penalty for any theft (Ex 22:1–9). The number seven is here symbolic—the thief will pay in full.
6:32 *destroys himself.* See 5:14; 7:22–23 and notes.
6:33 *disgrace.* Followed Amnon's rape of Tamar (2Sa 13:13,22).
6:34 *jealousy.* Its strength is also illustrated in 27:4; SS 8:6.
7:1 See 2:1; Ps 119:11.
7:2 *apple of your eye.* See Dt 32:10 and note.
7:3 *Bind them on your fingers.* As a reminder (see 6:21; Dt 6:8). *tablet of your heart.* See 3:3; Jer 31:33 and note.
7:4 *wisdom.* As embodied in the instructions of the wisdom teacher (vv. 1–3). *my sister ... relative.* Make wisdom your most intimate companion. "Sister" may be used here in the sense of "bride" (see SS 4:9–10,12; 5:1–2).
7:5 See notes on 2:16; 5:3.
7:7 *simple.* See note on 1:4. *who had no sense.* See 6:32; 9:4,16.

[8]He was going down the street near her
corner,
walking along in the direction of her
house
[9]at twilight,[e] as the day was fading,
as the dark of night set in.

[10]Then out came a woman to meet him,
dressed like a prostitute and with
crafty intent.
[11](She is unruly[f] and defiant,
her feet never stay at home;
[12]now in the street, now in the squares,
at every corner she lurks.)[g]
[13]She took hold of him[h] and kissed him
and with a brazen face she said:[i]

[14]"Today I fulfilled my vows,
and I have food from my fellowship
offering[j] at home.
[15]So I came out to meet you;
I looked for you and have found
you!
[16]I have covered my bed
with colored linens from Egypt.
[17]I have perfumed my bed[k]
with myrrh,[l] aloes and cinnamon.
[18]Come, let's drink deeply of love till
morning;
let's enjoy ourselves with love![m]
[19]My husband is not at home;
he has gone on a long journey.
[20]He took his purse filled with money
and will not be home till full
moon."

[21]With persuasive words she led him
astray;
she seduced him with her smooth
talk.[n]

7:9 [e]Job 24:15
7:11 [f]Pr 9:13
7:12 [g]Pr 8:1-36; 23:26-28
7:13 [h]S Ge 39:12 [i]S Pr 1:20
7:14 [j]S Lev 7:11-18
7:17 [k]S Est 1:6; Isa 57:7; Eze 23:41; Am 6:4 [l]S Ge 37:25
7:18 [m]S Ge 39:7
7:21 [n]S ver 5
7:22 [o]S Job 18:10
7:23 [p]S Job 15:22; S 16:13 [q]S Pr 6:26; Ecc 7:26
7:24 [r]Pr 1:8-9; 8:32
7:25 [s]Pr 5:7-8
7:27 [t]Jdg 16:19; S Pr 2:18; Rev 22:15
8:1 [u]S Job 28:12
8:3 [v]Pr 7:6-13
8:4 [w]Isa 42:2
8:5 [x]S Pr 1:22 [y]Pr 1:4

[22]All at once he followed her
like an ox going to the slaughter,
like a deer[a] stepping into a noose[b][o]
[23]till an arrow pierces[p] his liver,
like a bird darting into a snare,
little knowing it will cost him his
life.[q]

[24]Now then, my sons, listen[r] to me;
pay attention to what I say.
[25]Do not let your heart turn to her ways
or stray into her paths.[s]
[26]Many are the victims she has brought
down;
her slain are a mighty throng.
[27]Her house is a highway to the grave,
leading down to the chambers of
death.[t]

Wisdom's Call

8 Does not wisdom call out?[u]
Does not understanding raise her
voice?
[2]At the highest point along the way,
where the paths meet, she takes her
stand;
[3]beside the gate leading into the city,
at the entrance, she cries aloud:[v]
[4]"To you, O people, I call out;[w]
I raise my voice to all mankind.
[5]You who are simple,[x] gain prudence;[y]
you who are foolish, set your hearts
on it.[c]
[6]Listen, for I have trustworthy things to
say;

[a] 22 Syriac (see also Septuagint); Hebrew *fool*
[b] 22 The meaning of the Hebrew for this line is uncertain. [c] 5 Septuagint; Hebrew *foolish, instruct your minds*

7:8 *in the direction of her house.* See 5:8.
7:9 *dark of night.* He was hoping no one would see him (see 2:13 and note).
7:10 *dressed like a prostitute.* Perhaps in a gaudy, provocative manner (see Eze 16:16) and heavily veiled (see Ge 38:14–15).
7:11 *unruly.* Applied to the woman "Folly" in 9:13 (see note there).
7:12 *she lurks.* Ready to catch her prey (see vv. 22–33).
7:13 *kissed him.* A bold greeting (see Ge 29:11).
7:14 *Today I fulfilled my vows.* An offering made as the result of a vow was one of the fellowship offerings, and the meat had to be eaten on the first or second day (see Lev 7:15–16). So the young man had an opportunity to enjoy a sumptuous feast, one that ironically had a religious significance (cf. 1Sa 1:21 and note). *fellowship offering.* Part of the meat could be eaten by the one who brought the offering and by his (or her) family (Lev 7:12–15).
7:16 *colored linens from Egypt.* Linen is associated with the wealthy in 31:22. Egyptian linen was of great value (see Isa 19:9 and note; Eze 27:7).
7:17 *myrrh, aloes and cinnamon.* Fragrant perfumes that are linked with making love (see SS 1:3; 4:14; 5:5 and notes; see also Ps 45:8).
7:18 *drink deeply of love.* Making love is compared to eating and drinking also in 9:17; 30:20; SS 4:16; 5:1. *enjoy ourselves.* See SS 4:10.
7:19 *not at home.* So he will never know (cf. 6:34–35). *long journey.* Perhaps he was a wealthy merchant.
7:20 *money.* Pieces of silver of various weights were a common medium of exchange, but not in the form of coins until a later period (see note on Ge 20:16).
7:21 *persuasive words ... smooth talk.* See notes on 2:16; 5:3; see also 6:24; 7:5. *led him astray.* Cf. 5:23.
7:22 *like an ox going to the slaughter.* Totally oblivious of the fate that awaits him. *noose.* Cf. Isa 51:20.
7:23 *pierces his liver.* The terrible fate of the wicked is similarly described in Job 20:24–25. *darting into a snare.* See notes on 1:17–18; 5:22.
7:24 See 5:7.
7:25 *her paths.* See 1:15.
7:26 *Many are the victims.* See 9:18; 23:28; Isa 5:14 and note.
7:27 *highway to the grave.* See notes on 2:18; 5:5; see also 14:12; 16:25; Mt 7:13; cf. 1Co 6:9–10.
8:1–36 Wisdom is personified (see note on 1:20) as she addresses humankind in preparation for the final plea from both "Wisdom" and "Folly" in ch. 9.
8:1 *call out ... raise her voice.* See 1:20 and note.
8:2–3 See notes on 1:20–21.
8:4 *mankind.* See v. 31 and note.
8:5 *simple ... foolish.* Both are addressed in wisdom's speech in 1:22,32. *simple, gain prudence.* See note on 1:4.
8:6 *trustworthy things ... what is right.* See Php 4:8.

I open my lips to speak what is
right.
7 My mouth speaks what is true,[z]
for my lips detest wickedness.
8 All the words of my mouth are just;
none of them is crooked or perverse.
9 To the discerning all of them are right;
they are upright to those who have
found knowledge.
10 Choose my instruction instead of silver,
knowledge rather than choice gold,[a]
11 for wisdom is more precious[b] than
rubies,
and nothing you desire can compare
with her.[c]

12 "I, wisdom, dwell together with
prudence;
I possess knowledge and discretion.[d]
13 To fear the LORD[e] is to hate evil;[f]
I hate[g] pride and arrogance,
evil behavior and perverse speech.
14 Counsel and sound judgment are mine;
I have insight, I have power.[h]
15 By me kings reign
and rulers[i] issue decrees that are
just;
16 by me princes govern,[j]
and nobles — all who rule on earth.[a]
17 I love those who love me,[k]
and those who seek me find me.[l]
18 With me are riches and honor,[m]
enduring wealth and prosperity.[n]
19 My fruit is better than fine gold;[o]
what I yield surpasses choice silver.[p]
20 I walk in the way of righteousness,[q]
along the paths of justice,

8:7 [z] Jn 8:14
8:10 [a] S Job 28:17; S Ps 19:10
8:11 [b] ver 19; S Job 28:17-19 [c] Pr 3:13-15
8:12 [d] Pr 1:4
8:13 [e] S Ge 22:12 [f] S Ex 20:20; S Job 28:28 [g] Jer 44:4
8:14 [h] S Job 9:4; Pr 21:22; Ecc 7:19
8:15 [i] S Ps 2:10
8:16 [j] S 2Ch 1:10; Pr 29:4
8:17 [k] S 1Sa 2:30; Jn 14:21-24 [l] S 1Ch 16:11; S Pr 1:28; 3:13-18; Mt 7:7-11
8:18 [m] S 1Ki 3:13 [n] S Dt 8:18
8:19 [o] S Job 28:17-19 [p] S Pr 3:13-14
8:20 [q] S Ps 5:8
8:21 [r] Pr 15:6; 24:4
8:24 [s] S Ge 7:11
8:25 [t] S Job 38:6 [u] S Job 15:7
8:26 [v] S Ps 90:2
8:27 [w] S Job 26:7 [x] S Job 22:14
8:28 [y] S Job 36:29 [z] S Ge 1:7; S Job 9:8; S 26:10
8:29 [a] S Ge 1:9; S Ps 16:6 [b] S Job 38:8 [c] S 1Sa 2:8; S Job 38:5

21 bestowing a rich inheritance on those
who love me
and making their treasuries full.[r]

22 "The LORD brought me forth as the first
of his works,[b,c]
before his deeds of old;
23 I was formed long ages ago,
at the very beginning, when the
world came to be.
24 When there were no watery depths, I
was given birth,
when there were no springs
overflowing with water;[s]
25 before the mountains were settled in
place,[t]
before the hills, I was given birth,[u]
26 before he made the world or its fields
or any of the dust of the earth.[v]
27 I was there when he set the heavens in
place,[w]
when he marked out the horizon[x] on
the face of the deep,
28 when he established the clouds above[y]
and fixed securely the fountains of
the deep,[z]
29 when he gave the sea its boundary[a]
so the waters would not overstep his
command,[b]
and when he marked out the
foundations of the earth.[c]

[a] *16* Some Hebrew manuscripts and Septuagint; other Hebrew manuscripts *all righteous rulers* [b] *22* Or *way;* or *dominion* [c] *22* Or *The LORD possessed me at the beginning of his work;* or *The LORD brought me forth at the beginning of his work*

8:7 *my lips detest wickedness.* See 3:32 and note; 12:22.
8:8 *crooked or perverse.* See Php 2:15; cf. Pr 2:15.
8:9 *To the discerning.* The wiser they are the more they appreciate words of wisdom. *who have found knowledge.* Especially the knowledge of God (see note on 2:5).
8:10 *silver ... gold.* See v. 19; 2:4; 3:14 and note.
8:11 Almost identical with 3:15 (see note there).
8:12 *dwell together with prudence.* Cf. Job 28:20. *prudence ... knowledge and discretion.* See 1:4 and note.
8:13 *To fear the LORD is to hate evil.* See 3:7 and note; 16:6. *I hate pride and arrogance.* See 16:18; 1Sa 2:3; Isa 13:11; see also Ps 10:2 – 11 and note. *evil behavior and perverse speech.* See note on 2:12; see also 6:12 – 19.
8:14 *Counsel and sound judgment ... insight ... power.* These characterize the Lord (2:6 – 7; Job 12:13,16; Isa 40:13 – 14; Ro 16:27) and the Spirit of the Lord (Isa 11:2). *Counsel.* See 1:25; 19:20. *power.* Cf. Ecc 9:16.
8:15 *By me kings reign.* See 29:4. Solomon prayed for wisdom to govern Israel (see 1Ki 3:9; 2Ch 1:10).
8:17 *I love.* I pour out my benefits on (see 4:6 and note; see also Jn 14:21). *those who seek me find me.* See 2:4 – 5; Isa 55:6; Jas 1:5. Verse 35 completes the thought: "those who find me find life."
8:18 *riches and honor.* See v. 21; 3:16; 22:4. *prosperity.* See note on 3:2; see also 21:21.
8:19 *My fruit.* Wisdom is called a "tree of life" in 3:18 (see note there). *fine gold ... choice silver.* See v. 10; Job 28:15; see also 3:14 and note.
8:20 *walk in the way.* See introduction to Ps 1; see also note on Ps 1:6. *way ... paths.* See 3:17. *justice.* See v. 15.
8:21 *bestowing a rich inheritance.* See v. 18; Zec 8:12 and note. *making their treasuries full.* See 3:10; 24:4 and notes.
8:22 – 31 A hymn describing wisdom's role in creation. Wisdom is here personified, as in 1:20 – 33; 3:13 – 18; 9:1 – 12. Therefore these verses should not be interpreted as a direct description of Christ. Yet they provide part of the background for the NT portrayal of Christ as the divine Word (Jn 1:1 – 5) and as the wisdom of God (see note on 1:24). Here, wisdom is an attribute of God involved with him in creation.
8:22 *brought ... forth.* The Hebrew for this verb is also used in Ge 4:1; 14:19,22 ("Creator"); Dt 32:6 ("Creator"). *me.* Wisdom (see 3:19 and note; Ps 104:24). *as the first of his works.* Cf. Job 40:19 and note.
8:23 *when the world came to be.* Wisdom was already there when God began to create the world (cf. Jn 1:1 and Christ's statement in Jn 17:5).
8:24 *I was given birth.* Elsewhere it is the sea (Job 38:8 – 9) and the mountains and earth that are "brought forth" (Job 15:7; Ps 90:2). *springs overflowing with water.* See Ps 104:10.
8:27 *set the heavens in place.* See 3:19 and note. *when he marked out the horizon on the face of the deep.* See Job 26:10.
8:28 *fountains of the deep.* Earth's springs and streams (see note on 3:20; cf. Ge 7:11).
8:29 *the sea its boundary.* See Ge 1:9 and note; Job 38:10 – 11; Ps 104:9. *foundations of the earth.* See note on 3:19.

30 Then I was constantly[a] at his side.[d]
I was filled with delight day after day,
rejoicing always in his presence,
31 rejoicing in his whole world
and delighting in mankind.[e]

32 "Now then, my children, listen[f] to me;
blessed are[g] those who keep my ways.[h]
33 Listen to my instruction and be wise;
do not disregard it.
34 Blessed are those who listen[i] to me,
watching daily at my doors,
waiting at my doorway.
35 For those who find me[j] find life[k]
and receive favor from the LORD.[l]
36 But those who fail to find me harm
themselves;[m]
all who hate me love death."[n]

Invitations of Wisdom and Folly

9 Wisdom has built[o] her house;
she has set up[b] its seven pillars.
2 She has prepared her meat and mixed
her wine;[p]
she has also set her table.[q]
3 She has sent out her servants, and she
calls[r]
from the highest point of the city,[s]
4 "Let all who are simple[t] come to my
house!"
To those who have no sense[u] she says,
5 "Come,[v] eat my food
and drink the wine I have mixed.[w]
6 Leave your simple ways and you will
live;[x]
walk in the way of insight."[y]

7 Whoever corrects a mocker invites
insults;
whoever rebukes the wicked incurs
abuse.[z]
8 Do not rebuke mockers[a] or they will
hate you;
rebuke the wise and they will love you.[b]
9 Instruct the wise and they will be
wiser still;
teach the righteous and they will
add to their learning.[c]

10 The fear of the LORD[d] is the beginning
of wisdom,
and knowledge of the Holy One[e] is
understanding.[f]
11 For through wisdom[c] your days will be
many,
and years will be added to your life.[g]
12 If you are wise, your wisdom will
reward you;
if you are a mocker, you alone will
suffer.

13 Folly is an unruly woman;[h]
she is simple and knows nothing.[i]
14 She sits at the door of her house,
on a seat at the highest point of the
city,[j]
15 calling out[k] to those who pass by,
who go straight on their way,

[a] 30 Or *was the artisan;* or *was a little child*
[b] 1 Septuagint, Syriac and Targum; Hebrew *has hewn out*
[c] 11 Septuagint, Syriac and Targum; Hebrew *me*

8:30 [d] Pr 3:19-20; Rev 3:14 **8:31** [e] S Job 28:25-27; 38:4-38; Ps 104:1-30; Pr 30:4; Jn 1:1-4; Col 1:15-20 **8:32** [f] S Pr 7:24 [g] Lk 11:28 [h] S 2Sa 22:22; S Ps 18:21 **8:34** [i] 1Ki 10:8 **8:35** [j] Pr 3:13-18 [k] Pr 9:6; Jn 5:39-40 [l] S Job 33:26 **8:36** [m] Pr 15:32; Isa 3:9; Jer 40:2 [n] S Job 28:22 **9:1** [o] Eph 2:20-22; 1Pe 2:5 **9:2** [p] Isa 25:6; 62:8 [q] Lk 14:16-23 **9:3** [r] S Pr 1:20; 8:1-3 [s] ver 14 **9:4** [t] S Pr 1:22 [u] ver 16; S Pr 6:32 **9:5** [v] Jn 7:37-38 [w] S Ps 42:2; 63:1; 143:6; Isa 44:3; 55:1 **9:6** [x] S Pr 8:35 [y] S Pr 3:1-2

9:7 [z] Pr 23:9; Mt 7:6 **9:8** [a] Pr 15:12 [b] Ps 141:5 **9:9** [c] Pr 1:5,7; 12:15; 13:10; 14:6; 15:31; 19:25 **9:10** [d] S Pr 1:7 [e] Ps 22:3; Pr 30:3 [f] S Dt 4:6 **9:11** [g] S Ge 15:15; S Dt 11:21; S Pr 3:1-2; 10:27

9:13 [h] Pr 7:11 [i] S Pr 5:6 **9:14** [j] ver 3; Eze 16:25 **9:15** [k] S Pr 1:20

8:30 *filled with delight . . . rejoicing.* Cf. the joyful shouts of the angels at the time of creation (Job 38:7).

8:31 *delighting in mankind.* Cf. v. 4. Humans, made in the image of God, represented the climax of creation (see Ge 1:26–28; Ps 8:5 and notes).

8:32 *blessed.* The blessings associated with gaining wisdom are given in 3:13–18; see Ps 1:1–3 and notes; 119:1–2; 128:1.

8:34 *watching daily at my doors.* Contrast the warning not to go near the door of the adulterous woman's house (5:8).

8:35 *find life.* See 1:28; 3:2; 4:22 and notes. Cf. Jn 1:4. *favor.* See 3:4; 12:2; 18:22 and note.

8:36 *all who hate me love death.* See 1:28–33; 5:12,23; 7:27 and notes.

9:1 *has built her house.* See 14:1 and note; cf. 24:3 and note; 31:10–27. Both wisdom and folly have a house to which humans are invited (see v. 14; 5:8; 7:8; 8:34). *seven pillars.* Perhaps "seven" refers symbolically to the perfection of wisdom's work.

9:2 See v. 17 and note. The banquet prepared by wisdom contrasts with the perfumed bed made ready by the adulteress in 7:17. *mixed her wine.* With spices, to make it tastier (see SS 8:2).

9:3 *she calls from the highest point of the city.* See the description of Folly in v. 14; see also 8:1–3.

9:4 The same invitation is given by Lady Folly in v. 16. *simple.* See 1:4; 8:5 and notes. *have no sense.* See 6:32; 7:7.

9:5 *Come.* Wisdom's invitation counters the enticements of sinners in 1:10–11 (see note on 1:11). *eat . . . drink.* As in v. 2, wisdom's gifts are described symbolically as a great banquet (see Isa 55:1–2 and notes; cf. Jn 6:27,35,51,55).

9:6 *Leave your simple ways.* See 1:22; see also 1:10–11 and notes. *you will live.* See v. 11; 8:35; see also note on 3:2; cf. 3:18 and note.

9:7 *Whoever corrects a mocker invites insults.* See 1:22 and note; cf. 1:30. *incurs abuse.* Cf. 1Pe 4:4.

9:8 *they will hate you.* See 15:12,32. *rebuke the wise and they will love you.* See 10:8; 17:10.

9:9 *they will be wiser still.* See 18:15; 21:11.

9:10–12 Wisdom's final words summarize the heart of the message in chs. 1–9.

9:10 *The fear of the LORD is the beginning of wisdom.* See 1:7 and note. *knowledge of the Holy One.* See 30:3; see also note on 2:5. *Holy One.* Occurs elsewhere in Proverbs only in 30:3. See note on Lev 11:44.

9:11 *years will be added to your life.* See note on 3:2; see also 3:16; 10:27; 14:27; 19:23.

9:12 *your wisdom will reward you.* Some of wisdom's rewards are given in 3:16–18; 4:22; 8:35; 14:14. *mocker.* See v. 7; see also note on 1:22. *will suffer.* See 1:26 and note; 19:29.

9:13 *Folly is an unruly woman.* "Unruly" links the personified "folly" with the adulterous woman, the wayward woman of 2:16; 7:11. *simple and knows nothing.* She lacks good judgment, prudence and the fear of the Lord (see 1:3–4,22,29; 5:6).

9:14 *sits.* Cf. wisdom's building her house (v. 1). *at the door of her house.* See v. 1 and note. *at the highest point of the city.* Cf. the position of wisdom in v. 3; 8:2.

9:15 *calling out.* Cf. the appeal of Lady Wisdom in v. 3; 8:1,4.

16 “Let all who are simple come to my
house!”
To those who have no sense[l] she says,
17 “Stolen water is sweet;
food eaten in secret is delicious![m]”
18 But little do they know that the dead
are there,
that her guests are deep in the realm
of the dead.[n]

Proverbs of Solomon

10 The proverbs[o] of Solomon:[p]

A wise son brings joy to his father,[q]
but a foolish son brings grief to his
mother.

2 Ill-gotten treasures have no lasting
value,[r]
but righteousness delivers from
death.[s]

3 The LORD does not let the righteous go
hungry,[t]
but he thwarts the craving of the
wicked.[u]

4 Lazy hands make for poverty,[v]
but diligent hands bring wealth.[w]

5 He who gathers crops in summer is a
prudent son,
but he who sleeps during harvest is
a disgraceful son.[x]

6 Blessings crown the head of the
righteous,
but violence overwhelms the mouth
of the wicked.[a][y]

7 The name of the righteous[z] is used in
blessings,[b]
but the name of the wicked[a] will
rot.[b]

8 The wise in heart accept commands,
but a chattering fool comes to ruin.[c]

9 Whoever walks in integrity[d] walks
securely,[e]
but whoever takes crooked paths
will be found out.[f]

10 Whoever winks maliciously[g] causes
grief,
and a chattering fool comes to ruin.

11 The mouth of the righteous is a
fountain of life,[h]
but the mouth of the wicked
conceals violence.[i]

12 Hatred stirs up conflict,
but love covers over all wrongs.[j]

13 Wisdom is found on the lips of the
discerning,[k]
but a rod is for the back of one who
has no sense.[l]

14 The wise store up knowledge,[m]
but the mouth of a fool invites ruin.[n]

[a] 6 Or *righteous, / but the mouth of the wicked conceals violence* [b] 7 See Gen. 48:20.

9:16 [l] S Pr 1:22 **9:17** [m] Pr 20:17 **9:18** [n] S Pr 2:18; 7:26-27 **10:1** [o] S 1Ki 4:32 [p] S Pr 1:1 [q] Pr 15:20; 17:21; 19:13; 23:22-25; 27:11; 29:3 **10:2** [r] Pr 13:11; 21:6 [s] ver 16; Pr 11:4, 19; 12:28 **10:3** [t] Mt 6:25-34 [u] Pr 13:25 **10:4** [v] Pr 6:6-8; 19:15; 24:30-34 [w] Pr 12:24; 21:5 **10:5** [x] Pr 24:30-34 **10:6** [y] ver 8, 11, 14; Pr 12:13; 13:3; Ecc 10:12 **10:7** [z] S Ps 112:6 [a] S Job 18:17; S Ps 109:13 [b] S Job 18:17; Ps 9:6 **10:8** [c] ver 14; S Job 33:33; Mt 7:24-27 **10:9** [d] S Ps 25:21 [e] S Ps 37:24 [f] Pr 28:18 **10:10** [g] S Ps 35:19 **10:11** [h] ver 27; S Pr 3:18; S 4:23; 11:30; 13:12, 14, 19; 14:27; 15:4; 16:22 [i] S ver 6 **10:12** [j] Pr 17:9; 1Co 13:4-7; 1Pe 4:8 **10:13** [k] ver 31; S Ps 37:30; Pr 15:7 [l] S Dt 25:2; Pr 14:3; 26:3 **10:14** [m] Pr 11:13; 12:23 [n] S ver 6; S Ps 59:12; S Pr 14:3; 18:6, 7; S Mt 12:37

9:16 Her invitation is identical to wisdom's (v. 4; see note on 1:21).

9:17 *Stolen water ... food eaten in secret.* The banquet prepared by Lady Folly seems poorer than the wine and meat of wisdom (v. 2). And it was stolen at that! This meal refers to stolen pleasures, exemplified by the illicit sex offered by the adulterous woman (see 7:18 and note; cf. 5:15–16). *sweet.* But see Job 20:12–15 and note.

9:18 *the dead are there ... her guests are deep in the realm of the dead.* Similar to 2:18; 5:5; 7:27 (see notes there).

10:1 *The proverbs of Solomon.* See note on 1:1; the title of a collection of individual proverbs that extends through 22:16. The numerical values of the consonants in the Hebrew word for “Solomon” total 375—the exact number of verses in 10:1—22:16; 375 of Solomon's proverbs were selected from a much larger number (cf. 1Ki 4:32). At the very center of this section is a verse that highlights one of its dominant themes (see 16:4 and note). *A wise son.* See v. 5; 15:20; 17:21,25. In later collections such a son is described as “a righteous child” (23:24) who “heeds instruction” (28:7).

10:2 *Ill-gotten treasures have no lasting value.* They are fleeting (21:6) and result in God's judgment (see v. 16; 1:19 and note; Eze 7:19). *righteousness delivers from death.* Repeated in 11:4 (see also 2:16–18; 3:2; 13:21; cf. 12:28; 21:21; Ps 1:5 and note).

10:3 *not let the righteous go hungry.* See 13:25; 28:25 and note; Ps 34:9–10; 37:19,25–26. But see note on Pr 3:2. *thwarts the craving of the wicked.* See Nu 11:34; Ps 112:10 and note.

10:4 Many proverbs praise diligence and the profit it brings, and they condemn laziness as a cause of hunger and poverty (see 6:6–11 and notes; 12:11,24,27; 13:4; 14:23; 18:9; 27:23–27; 28:19).

10:5 *sleeps during harvest.* Sleeping when there is work to be done is condemned also in 6:9–11; 19:15; 20:13. *disgraceful son.* See 17:2; 19:26; 28:7; 29:15.

10:6 *Blessings.* God's gifts and favors (see 3:13–18; 28:20; Ge 49:26; Dt 33:16). *crown.* See 11:26. *violence overwhelms the mouth of the wicked.* The trouble caused by their lips will eventually ruin them (see v. 11 and note; see also Ps 140:9; Hab 2:17; but cf. Pr 2:11).

10:7 *name of the righteous.* Their name is remembered and is “used in blessings” (see Ge 48:20; cf. 22:1 and note).

10:8 *The wise ... accept commands.* See 9:8–9. *chattering fool comes to ruin.* See vv. 10,14,18,19.

10:9 *Whoever walks in integrity walks securely.* See 2:7; 3:23; 13:6; Ps 23:4; Isa 33:15–16. *whoever takes crooked paths will be found out.* See 26:26; Lk 8:17; 1Ti 5:24–25; 2Ti 3:9.

10:10 *winks maliciously.* See note on 6:13. *chattering fool.* See v. 8.

10:11 *fountain of life.* A source of life-giving wisdom (see 13:14; 14:27; 16:22; see also Ps 37:30). *mouth of the wicked conceals violence.* Perhaps the meaning is that violence controls the mouth of the wicked (but see note on v. 6).

10:12 *stirs up conflict.* See note on 6:14. *love covers over all wrongs.* Promotes forgiveness (see 17:9). This line is quoted in Jas 5:20; 1Pe 4:8. Cf. 1Co 13:5.

10:13 *rod is for the back.* See 14:3; 19:29; 26:3.

10:14 *store up knowledge.* Rather than babbling folly—and so the wise prosper. See 2:1 and note. *invites ruin.* Quick with

15 The wealth of the rich is their fortified city,[o]
but poverty is the ruin of the poor.[p]

16 The wages of the righteous is life,[q]
but the earnings of the wicked are sin and death.[r]

17 Whoever heeds discipline shows the way to life,[s]
but whoever ignores correction leads others astray.

18 Whoever conceals hatred with lying lips[t]
and spreads slander is a fool.

19 Sin is not ended by multiplying words,
but the prudent hold their tongues.[u]

20 The tongue of the righteous is choice silver,
but the heart of the wicked is of little value.

21 The lips of the righteous nourish many,
but fools die for lack of sense.[v]

22 The blessing of the LORD[w] brings wealth,[x]
without painful toil for it.[y]

23 A fool finds pleasure in wicked schemes,[z]
but a person of understanding delights in wisdom.

24 What the wicked dread[a] will overtake them;[b]
what the righteous desire will be granted.[c]

25 When the storm has swept by, the wicked are gone,
but the righteous stand firm[d] forever.[e]

26 As vinegar to the teeth and smoke[f] to the eyes,
so are sluggards to those who send them.[g]

27 The fear of the LORD adds length to life,[h]
but the years of the wicked are cut short.[i]

28 The prospect of the righteous is joy,
but the hopes of the wicked come to nothing.[j]

29 The way of the LORD is a refuge for the blameless,
but it is the ruin of those who do evil.[k]

30 The righteous will never be uprooted,
but the wicked will not remain in the land.[l]

31 From the mouth of the righteous comes the fruit of wisdom,[m]
but a perverse tongue[n] will be silenced.

32 The lips of the righteous know what finds favor,[o]
but the mouth of the wicked only what is perverse.[p]

10:15 [o] Pr 18:11 [p] Pr 19:7 **10:16** [q] S Dt 30:15 [r] Pr 11:18-19; 15:6; S Ro 6:23 **10:17** [s] Pr 6:23; 15:5 **10:18** [t] S Ps 31:18 **10:19** [u] S Job 1:22; S 6:24; Pr 17:28; S 20:25; 21:23; Jas 1:19; 3:2-12 **10:21** [v] Pr 5:22-23; Isa 5:13; Jer 5:4; Hos 4:1, 6, 14 **10:22** [w] S Ps 128:2 [x] S Ge 13:2; S 49:25; S Dt 8:18 [y] S 2Ch 25:9 **10:23** [z] S Pr 2:14 **10:24** [a] Isa 65:7; 66:4 [b] S Ge 42:36 [c] S Ps 37:4; 145:17-19; Eze 11:8 **10:25** [d] S Ps 20:8 [e] Pr 12:3, 7; Mt 7:24-27 **10:26** [f] Isa 65:5 [g] Pr 13:17; 25:13; 26:6 **10:27** [h] S ver 11; Dt 11:9; Pr 9:10-11; 19:23; 22:4 [i] S Job 15:32 **10:28** [j] Est 7:10; S Job 8:13; Ps 112:10; Pr 11:7 **10:29** [k] Pr 21:15; Hos 14:9 **10:30** [l] Ps 37:9, 28-29; S Pr 2:20-22 **10:31** [m] S ver 13; S Pr 15:2; 31:26 [n] S Ps 52:4 **10:32** [o] Ecc 10:12 [p] S Ps 59:7

his mouth, the fool only brings ruin on himself (see vv. 8,10; 13:3).

10:15 *wealth ... is their fortified city.* Repeated in 18:11. Wealth brings friends (14:20; 19:4) and power (18:23; 22:7)—but ultimate security is found only in God (Ps 52:7–8). *poverty is the ruin of the poor.* Poverty has no security—as it has no influence (18:23) or friends (19:4,7). See v. 4 and note.
10:16 *wages of the righteous is life.* Not wealth (v. 15), but righteousness assures life (see note on 3:2; see also 3:16; 4:22). *earnings of the wicked are sin and death.* See 15:6; see also 1:13,31 and notes. "The wages of sin is death" (Ro 6:23).
10:17 *way to life.* See 6:23; 12:28 and notes. *whoever ignores correction.* See 5:12; 15:10.
10:18 *conceals hatred.* By pretending friendliness (see 26:24,26,28).
10:19 *hold their tongues.* See 11:12; 21:23; see also 13:3; Ps 5:9; 10:7; 120:4; Jas 3:2 and notes.
10:20 *choice silver.* What the righteous say has great value (see 3:14; 8:10; 25:11). *heart of the wicked.* Their thoughts and schemes (see 6:14,18).
10:21 *nourish many.* See v. 11 and note. *die for lack of sense.* See 5:23 and note; 7:7; 9:16.
10:22 *blessing of the LORD brings wealth.* Wealth is a gift from God, not a product of human attainment (see notes on v. 6; 3:10; see also 8:21; Ge 24:35; 26:12). *without painful toil for it.* Unlike the "ill-gotten treasures" of v. 2 (see note there); cf. 15:6.
10:23 *finds pleasure in wicked schemes.* See 2:14; 15:21; 26:19.
10:24 *What the wicked dread.* Calamity and distress (see 1:26–27 and notes; 3:25; Job 15:21; Isa 66:4). *what the righteous desire.* See Ps 9:18; 37:4; 145:19; Mt 5:6; 1Jn 5:14–15.
10:25 Cf. the wise man who built his house on a rock, and the foolish man who built his on the sand (Mt 7:24–27). *the wicked are gone.* See Ps 37:10; Isa 28:18. *the righteous stand firm.* Unshakable, immovable (see 3:25 and note; see also 12:3,7; 14:11; Ps 10:6 and note; 15:5; 1Co 15:58).
10:26 *vinegar.* See Ps 69:21. *sluggards.* See note on 6:6. *who send them.* As messengers (cf. 13:17 and note; 25:13; 26:6 and note) or workers.
10:27 *fear of the LORD.* See note on 1:7. *adds length to life.* See note on 3:2. *years ... are cut short.* See Job 22:16; Ps 37:36; 55:23.
10:28 *prospect of the righteous.* See v. 24 and note. *joy.* Of fulfillment (cf. 11:23). *hopes of the wicked come to nothing.* See 11:7,23.
10:29 *way of the LORD.* The way he prescribes, the life of wisdom (see Ps 27:11; 143:8; Mt 22:16; Ac 18:25). *ruin of those who do evil.* Since judgment comes to those who refuse God's way (see 21:15; 2Co 2:15–16; 2Pe 2:21 and note).
10:30 *never be uprooted.* See v. 25; 2:21 and note; 12:3; Ps 125:1. *not remain in the land.* See note on 2:22.
10:31 *perverse tongue.* See note on 2:12. *silenced.* See Ps 12:3; cf. Mt 5:29–30 and notes.

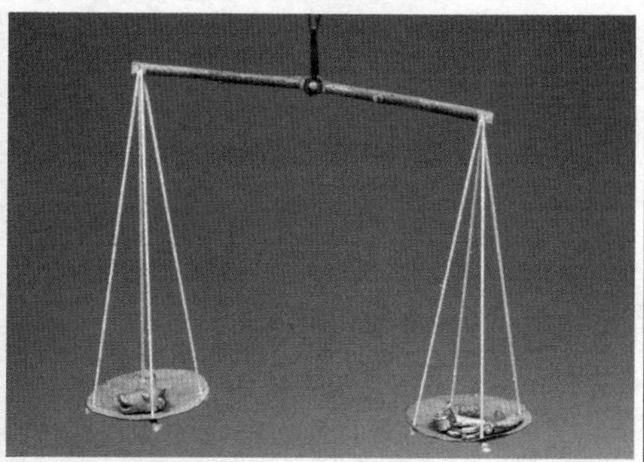

Reconstruction with original parts of a Roman period scale. "The LORD detests dishonest scales, but accurate weights find favor with him" (Pr 11:1).
Z. Radovan/www.BibleLandPictures.com

11 The LORD detests dishonest
scales,[q]
but accurate weights find favor with
him.[r]

2 When pride comes, then comes
disgrace,[s]
but with humility comes
wisdom.[t]

3 The integrity of the upright guides
them,
but the unfaithful are destroyed by
their duplicity.[u]

4 Wealth[v] is worthless in the day of
wrath,[w]
but righteousness delivers from
death.[x]

5 The righteousness of the blameless
makes their paths straight,[y]
but the wicked are brought down by
their own wickedness.[z]

6 The righteousness of the upright
delivers them,
but the unfaithful are trapped by evil
desires.[a]

7 Hopes placed in mortals die with
them;[b]
all the promise of[a] their power
comes to nothing.[c]

8 The righteous person is rescued from
trouble,
and it falls on the wicked instead.[d]

9 With their mouths the godless destroy
their neighbors,
but through knowledge the righteous
escape.[e]

10 When the righteous prosper, the city
rejoices;[f]
when the wicked perish, there are
shouts of joy.[g]

11 Through the blessing of the upright a
city is exalted,[h]
but by the mouth of the wicked it is
destroyed.[i]

12 Whoever derides their neighbor has no
sense,[j]
but the one who has understanding
holds their tongue.[k]

13 A gossip betrays a confidence,[l]
but a trustworthy person keeps a
secret.[m]

14 For lack of guidance a nation falls,[n]
but victory is won through many
advisers.[o]

[a] 7 Two Hebrew manuscripts; most Hebrew manuscripts, Vulgate, Syriac and Targum *When the wicked die, their hope perishes; / all they expected from*

11:1 [q] S Lev 19:36; Dt 25:13-16; S Job 6:2; Pr 20:10, 23 [r] Pr 16:11; Eze 45:10 **11:2** [s] Pr 16:18 [t] Pr 18:12; 29:23 **11:3** [u] ver 5; Pr 13:6 **11:4** [v] Eze 27:27 [w] S Job 20:20; S Eze 7:19 [x] S Pr 10:2 **11:5** [y] S 1Ki 8:36 [z] S ver 3; Pr 5:21-23; 13:6; 21:7 **11:6** [a] S Est 7:9 **11:7** [b] S Job 8:13 [c] S Pr 10:28 **11:8** [d] Pr 21:18 **11:9** [e] Pr 12:6; Jer 45:5 **11:10** [f] S 2Ki 11:20 [g] S Est 8:17 **11:11** [h] Pr 14:34 [i] Pr 29:8 **11:12** [j] Pr 14:21 [k] S Job 6:24 **11:13** [l] Pr 20:19 [m] S Pr 10:14 **11:14** [n] Pr 20:18 [o] S 2Sa 15:34; Pr 15:22; 24:6

11:1 *detests dishonest scales.* Similar denunciation is found in the Law (see Lev 19:35 and note) and the Prophets (Hos 12:7; Am 8:5; Mic 6:11). See also 16:11; 20:10,23. *accurate weights.* See note on 16:11. Silver was weighed on scales balanced against a stone weight. Weights with dishonest labels were used for cheating. See photo above.
11:2 *When pride comes, then comes disgrace.* Along with destruction (see 16:18; cf. the humbling of proud Assyria in Isa 10:12; cf. also Isa 14:13–15). *with humility comes wisdom.* Along with honor (see note on 15:33).
11:3 *integrity ... guides them.* Cf. the actions of Joseph in Ge 39:6–12. *unfaithful are destroyed.* See v. 6; 2:22 and note; 19:3. *duplicity.* Cf. Lk 20:23.
11:4 *day of wrath.* The day of judgment (see Isa 10:3; Zep 1:18). *righteousness delivers from death.* See 2:16–18; 3:2; 10:2; 13:21.
11:5 *blameless.* See note on 2:7. *makes their paths straight.* Enables them to reach their goals (see v. 3; 3:6 and note; 10:9).
11:6 *righteousness ... delivers them.* See vv. 3–4. *trapped.* See 5:22 and note.
11:7 For the thought in the NIV text note, see v. 23; 10:28.
11:8 *trouble ... falls on the wicked instead.* Cf. the rescue of Mordecai and the execution of Haman in Est 5:14; 7:10 (see note there).
11:9 *destroy their neighbors.* By spreading slander (cf. 10:18). *through knowledge.* Perhaps the knowledge of the schemes and distortions of the godless (cf. Jn 2:25).
11:10 *city rejoices.* See 28:12; 29:2. Thus life in the city is itself a teacher of wisdom (see note on 1:21). *shouts of joy.* Cf. the joy at the fall of Assyria (see Isa 30:32 and note; Na 3:19; cf. 2Ch 21:20).
11:11 *blessing of the upright.* Their good influence and desire for justice, as well as their prosperity (v. 10), bring honor to the city. *mouth of the wicked.* Their deceit, dishonesty and sowing of discord (see v. 9; 6:12–14 and notes).
11:12 *derides their neighbor.* Shows their contempt openly (see 10:18; 14:21). *holds their tongue.* See 10:19 and note.
11:14 See the close parallels in 15:22; 20:18; 24:6. *advisers.* See 2Sa 16:23; Isa 1:26.

15 Whoever puts up security[p] for a
stranger will surely suffer,
but whoever refuses to shake hands
in pledge is safe.[q]

16 A kindhearted woman gains honor,[r]
but ruthless men gain only
wealth.

17 Those who are kind benefit
themselves,
but the cruel bring ruin on
themselves.

18 A wicked person earns deceptive
wages,
but the one who sows righteousness
reaps a sure reward.[s]

19 Truly the righteous attain life,[t]
but whoever pursues evil finds
death.[u]

20 The LORD detests those whose hearts
are perverse,[v]
but he delights[w] in those whose
ways are blameless.[x]

21 Be sure of this: The wicked will not go
unpunished,
but those who are righteous will go
free.[y]

22 Like a gold ring in a pig's snout
is a beautiful woman who shows no
discretion.

23 The desire of the righteous ends only
in good,
but the hope of the wicked only in
wrath.

24 One person gives freely, yet gains even
more;
another withholds unduly, but
comes to poverty.

25 A generous[z] person will prosper;
whoever refreshes others will be
refreshed.[a]

26 People curse the one who hoards
grain,
but they pray God's blessing on the
one who is willing to sell.

27 Whoever seeks good finds favor,
but evil comes to one who searches
for it.[b]

28 Those who trust in their riches will
fall,[c]
but the righteous will thrive like a
green leaf.[d]

29 Whoever brings ruin on their family
will inherit only wind,
and the fool will be servant to the
wise.[e]

30 The fruit of the righteous is a tree of
life,[f]
and the one who is wise saves lives.

31 If the righteous receive their due[g] on
earth,
how much more the ungodly and the
sinner!

12 Whoever loves discipline loves
knowledge,
but whoever hates correction is
stupid.[h]

11:15 [p] S Pr 6:1 [q] Pr 17:18; 22:26-27 **11:16** [r] Pr 31:31 **11:18** [s] S Ex 1:20; S Job 4:8; Hos 10:12-13 **11:19** [t] S Dt 30:15; S Pr 10:2 [u] 1Sa 2:6; Ps 89:48; Pr 1:18-19; Ecc 7:2; Jer 43:11 **11:20** [v] Pr 3:32 [w] S Nu 14:8 [x] S 1Ch 29:17; S Ps 15:2; 101:1-4; S 119:1; Pr 12:2, 22; 15:9 **11:21** [y] Pr 16:5 **11:25** [z] 1Ch 29:17; Isa 32:8 [a] Pr 22:9; 2Co 9:6-9 **11:27** [b] Ps 7:15-16 **11:28** [c] Job 31:24-28; S Ps 49:6; S 52:7; 62:10; Jer 9:23; 48:7 [d] Ps 52:8; 92:12-14 **11:29** [e] Pr 14:19 **11:30** [f] S Ge 2:9; S Pr 10:11 **11:31** [g] Jer 25:29; 49:12; 1Pe 4:18 **12:1** [h] Pr 5:11-14; S 9:7-9; 13:1, 18; 15:5, 10, 12, 32

11:15 See note on 6:1.
11:16 Assumes that "a good name is more desirable than great riches" (22:1) and insightfully observes that a woman, if she is kindhearted, will be accorded more respect than wealthy men if they are ruthless. *kindhearted woman.* See 31:28,30.
11:17 *benefit themselves.* See Mt 5:7. *bring ruin on themselves.* See Ge 34:25–30; 49:7.
11:18 *deceptive wages.* Because they do not last (see notes on 10:2,16; see also Hag 1:6). *reaps a sure reward.* See 10:24; Gal 6:8–9; Jas 3:18.
11:19 *attain life.* See 10:16 and note; 12:28; 19:23. *finds death.* See 5:23; 21:16; Ro 6:23; Jas 1:15.
11:20 *detests those whose hearts are perverse.* See 3:32 and note; 16:5. *blameless.* See note on 2:7.
11:21 *will not go unpunished.* See 6:29. *will go free.* See Ps 118:5.
11:22 *gold ring.* Commonly worn by women on their noses (see Ge 24:47; Eze 16:12 and note). *shows no discretion.* Abigail was praised by David for her display of "good judgment" (1Sa 25:33).
11:23 See 10:24,28. *wrath.* Judgment (see v. 4; Isa 10:3; Zep 1:18; Ro 2:8–9).
11:24 Generosity is the path to blessing and further prosperity (see 3:9–10; Ecc 11:1–2 and notes; Ps 112:9; 2Co 9:6–9). By contrast, the stingy do not make friends and hurt themselves in the long run (21:13; cf. 23:6–8 and notes; see also NIV text note on 23:7).
11:25 *generous person will prosper.* "For they share their food with the poor" (22:9). "Whoever sows generously will also reap generously" (2Co 9:6; cf. Lk 6:38). *be refreshed.* See Ro 1:12 and note; 15:32.
11:26 *hoards grain.* Probably in times of scarcity to raise the price. *pray God's blessing on.* Cf. 10:6.
11:27 *Whoever seeks good finds favor.* Like the person in v. 25 (cf. Mt 7:12). *evil comes to one who searches for it.* One's wicked schemes will backfire (see v. 8; 1:18 and notes).
11:28 *Those who trust in their riches.* Usually said of the wicked (see Ps 49:6; 62:10 and note; cf. 1Ti 6:17). *like a green leaf.* See Ps 1:3 and note; Ge 49:22; Jer 17:8.
11:29 *Whoever brings ruin on their family will inherit only wind.* The inheritance of Levi and Simeon was affected because of their cruelty against Shechem (Ge 34:25–30; 49:5–7). See 15:27 and note. *servant to the wise.* As those who are evil serve the good (14:19; cf. 17:2).
11:30 *fruit of the righteous.* What the wise produce (8:18–19). *tree of life.* See note on 3:18. *saves lives.* By winning people over to wisdom and righteousness (see Da 12:3; 1Co 9:19–22; Jas 5:20).
11:31 *the righteous receive their due.* Even Moses and David were punished for their sins (see Nu 20:11–12; 2Sa 12:10 and notes). *how much more the ungodly and the sinner!* See 1:18,31 and notes; Ps 11:6; 73:18–19.
12:1 *loves discipline loves knowledge.* See 1:7; 10:17; see also 6:23 and note. *hates correction is stupid.* See 1:22; 5:12 and note.

2 Good people obtain favor from the
LORD,[i]
but he condemns those who devise
wicked schemes.[j]

3 No one can be established through
wickedness,
but the righteous cannot be
uprooted.[k]

4 A wife of noble character[l] is her
husband's crown,
but a disgraceful wife is like decay in
his bones.[m]

5 The plans of the righteous are just,
but the advice of the wicked is
deceitful.

6 The words of the wicked lie in wait for
blood,
but the speech of the upright rescues
them.[n]

7 The wicked are overthrown and are no
more,[o]
but the house of the righteous stands
firm.[p]

8 A person is praised according to their
prudence,
and one with a warped[q] mind is
despised.

9 Better to be a nobody and yet have a
servant
than pretend to be somebody and
have no food.

10 The righteous care for the needs of
their animals,[r]
but the kindest acts of the wicked
are cruel.

12:2 [i] S Job 33:26; Ps 84:11 [j] 2Sa 15:3; S Pr 11:20 **12:3** [k] S Pr 10:25 **12:4** [l] S Ru 3:11; Pr 31:10-11 [m] Pr 18:22 **12:6** [n] S Pr 11:9; 14:3 **12:7** [o] S Ps 37:36 [p] S Pr 10:25; 14:11; 15:25 **12:8** [q] Isa 19:14; 29:24 **12:10** [r] S Nu 22:29 **12:11** [s] Pr 28:19 **12:13** [t] S Ps 59:12; S Pr 10:6; 18:7 [u] Pr 21:23 **12:14** [v] Pr 13:2; 15:23; 18:20 [w] Pr 14:14 **12:15** [x] Pr 14:12; 16:2, 25 [y] S Pr 9:7-9; 19:20 **12:16** [z] S 1Sa 25:25 [a] S Job 5:2 [b] Pr 29:11 **12:17** [c] S Ps 12:2; Pr 14:5,25 **12:18** [d] S Ps 55:21; Pr 25:18 [e] Pr 15:4 **12:20** [f] S Ro 14:19 **12:21** [g] S Job 4:7

11 Those who work their land will have
abundant food,
but those who chase fantasies have
no sense.[s]

12 The wicked desire the stronghold of
evildoers,
but the root of the righteous
endures.

13 Evildoers are trapped by their sinful
talk,[t]
and so the innocent escape trouble.[u]

14 From the fruit of their lips people are
filled with good things,[v]
and the work of their hands brings
them reward.[w]

15 The way of fools seems right to them,[x]
but the wise listen to advice.[y]

16 Fools[z] show their annoyance at once,[a]
but the prudent overlook an insult.[b]

17 An honest witness tells the truth,
but a false witness tells lies.[c]

18 The words of the reckless pierce like
swords,[d]
but the tongue of the wise brings
healing.[e]

19 Truthful lips endure forever,
but a lying tongue lasts only a
moment.

20 Deceit is in the hearts of those who
plot evil,
but those who promote peace have
joy.[f]

21 No harm overtakes the righteous,[g]
but the wicked have their fill of
trouble.

12:2 *obtain favor.* See 3:4; 8:35. *condemns those who devise wicked schemes.* Cf. 14:17; Job 5:12–13; 1Co 3:19.
12:3 *No one can be established.* See 11:5. *righteous cannot be uprooted.* See 2:21; 10:25,30 and notes.
12:4 *wife of noble character.* Someone like Ruth (Ru 3:11). Such a woman is fully described in 31:10–31. *her husband's crown.* She brings him honor and joy (see 4:9 and note). *decay.* See Hab 3:16 and note. *his bones.* See note on 3:8.
12:5 *advice of the wicked is deceitful.* See 1:10–19 and notes; Ps 1:1.
12:6 *lie in wait for blood.* See note on 1:11; see also 1:16. *speech of the upright rescues them.* See 11:3–4,6,9.
12:7 See 10:25 and note.
12:8 *praised according to their prudence.* See 3:4 and note. *one with a warped mind is despised.* See Dt 32:5; Titus 3:11 and note.
12:9 *yet have a servant.* Even people of moderate means had servants (see Jdg 6:15,27). *pretend to be somebody.* Cf. 13:7.
12:10 *care for the needs of their animals.* See 27:23; Dt 25:4; Mt 12:11; see also chart, p. 287 (item 16). *kindest acts of the wicked are cruel.* Probably to both people and animals.
12:11 Repeated with slight variation in 28:19. *chase fantasies.* Scheme for making easy money.
12:12 *desire the stronghold of evildoers.* See 1:13 and note; 21:10. *root of the righteous endures.* They bear fruit, like firmly rooted trees (see vv. 3,7; 11:30; Ps 1:3; see also 10:25 and note).
12:13 *trapped by their sinful talk.* See 1:18 and note; 29:6. *the innocent escape trouble.* See 11:8–9 and notes; 21:23; 2Pe 2:9.
12:14 Those who speak wisely will reap a good harvest from their words, just as farmers enjoy the harvest of their crops (see 1:31 and note; Job 34:11).
12:15 *seems right.* But ends in death (see 1:25,30; 14:12; 16:25).
12:16 *overlook an insult.* Have good self-control (see 29:11; 2Sa 16:11–12).
12:17 *false witness tells lies.* See note on 6:19.
12:18 *The words of the reckless.* Cf. Ps 106:33. *pierce like swords.* See note on Ps 5:9. *tongue of the wise brings healing.* With soothing, comforting words (see 4:20–22; 15:4).
12:19 *lasts only a moment.* The lies will be refuted and the liar punished (see 19:9; Ps 52:4–5).
12:20 *Deceit is in the hearts.* See 6:14 and note; see also 1:31; 24:2; Ge 6:5. *hearts.* See note on Ps 4:7. *those who promote peace have joy.* "Blessed are the peacemakers" (Mt 5:9; cf. Jas 3:18 and note).
12:21 *No harm.* See 1:33 and note; 2:8; Ps 91:9–13; 121:7. *their fill of trouble.* See 1:31 and note; 11:5,8; 22:8; Job 4:8.

22 The LORD detests lying lips,[h]
but he delights[i] in people who are
trustworthy.[j]

23 The prudent keep their knowledge to
themselves,[k]
but a fool's heart blurts out folly.[l]

24 Diligent hands will rule,
but laziness ends in forced
labor.[m]

25 Anxiety weighs down the heart,[n]
but a kind word cheers it up.

26 The righteous choose their friends
carefully,
but the way of the wicked leads
them astray.[o]

27 The lazy do not roast[a] any game,
but the diligent feed on the riches of
the hunt.

28 In the way of righteousness there is
life;[p]
along that path is immortality.

13 A wise son heeds his father's
instruction,
but a mocker does not respond to
rebukes.[q]

2 From the fruit of their lips people enjoy
good things,[r]
but the unfaithful have an appetite
for violence.

3 Those who guard their lips[s] preserve
their lives,[t]
but those who speak rashly will
come to ruin.[u]

4 A sluggard's appetite is never filled,[v]
but the desires of the diligent are
fully satisfied.

5 The righteous hate what is false,[w]
but the wicked make themselves a
stench
and bring shame on themselves.

6 Righteousness guards the person of
integrity,
but wickedness overthrows the
sinner.[x]

7 One person pretends to be rich, yet has
nothing;[y]
another pretends to be poor, yet has
great wealth.[z]

8 A person's riches may ransom their life,
but the poor cannot respond to
threatening rebukes.[a]

9 The light of the righteous shines
brightly,
but the lamp of the wicked is
snuffed out.[b]

10 Where there is strife, there is pride,
but wisdom is found in those who
take advice.[c]

11 Dishonest money dwindles away,[d]
but whoever gathers money little by
little makes it grow.

12 Hope deferred makes the heart sick,
but a longing fulfilled is a tree of
life.[e]

12:22 [h] 1Ki 13:18; Pr 6:17 [i] Ps 18:19 [j] S Pr 11:20 **12:23** [k] S Pr 10:14 [l] S Ps 38:5; S 59:7; Pr 18:2 **12:24** [m] S Pr 10:4 **12:25** [n] Pr 15:13 **12:26** [o] S Ps 95:10 **12:28** [p] S Dt 30:15; S Pr 10:2 **13:1** [q] S Pr 12:1; 15:5 **13:2** [r] S Pr 12:14 **13:3** [s] S Ps 12:2; S 34:13 [t] S Pr 10:6; 21:23 [u] S Job 1:22; Pr 18:7,20-21 **13:4** [v] Pr 21:25-26 **13:5** [w] S Ps 119:128 **13:6** [x] S Pr 11:3, 5; Jer 44:5 **13:7** [y] Rev 3:17 [z] 2Co 6:10 **13:8** [a] Pr 15:16 **13:9** [b] S Job 18:5; S Pr 4:18-19 **13:10** [c] S Jdg 19:30; S Pr 9:9 **13:11** [d] S Pr 10:2 **13:12** [e] S Pr 10:11

[a] *27* The meaning of the Hebrew for this word is uncertain.

12:22 Compare the structure of this verse with that of 11:1,20. *detests.* See note on 3:32. *people who are trustworthy.* See 16:13.
12:23 *keep their knowledge to themselves.* Store up knowledge and use discretion (see 10:14 and note). *blurts out folly.* See v. 16; 13:16; 15:2,7,28; 29:11.
12:24 *Diligent hands ... laziness.* Contrasted also in 10:4 (see note there). *will rule.* Cf. 17:2. *forced labor.* See Jdg 1:28; see also note on 2Sa 20:24.
12:25 *Anxiety weighs down the heart.* See Ps 94:19. *kind word cheers it up.* See 15:23.
12:26 *choose their friends carefully.* See 13:20; 18:24; 22:24. *leads them astray.* See 5:23; 14:22.
12:27 *do not roast any game.* And are too lazy to lift the food from the dish to their mouths (19:24). *feed on the riches of the hunt.* Cf. Ecc 5:19.
12:28 See 10:2 and note. *there is life.* Cf. 3:2 and note; 11:4. *immortality.* Lit. "no death." The way or path of righteousness does not lead to death. Cf. the identification of wisdom with the "tree of life" (3:18 [see note there]; cf. 14:32).
13:1 *heeds his father's instruction.* See 1:8 and note; 4:1. *mocker does not respond to rebukes.* See 1:22; 9:7–8 and notes.
13:2 See 12:14 and note. *have an appetite for violence.* See 4:17 and note.
13:3 *Those who guard their lips preserve their lives.* "The tongue has the power of life and death" (18:21; cf. Jas 3:1–12). The ability to control the tongue is one of the clearest marks of wisdom. See 10:19 and note. *those who speak rashly will come to ruin.* See 10:14; 12:18 and note; 18:7.
13:4 *sluggard's.* See 6:6 and note. *appetite is never filled.* Is never satisfied, yet the sluggard refuses to work (see 21:25–26). *desires of the diligent are fully satisfied.* Diligence yields a profit (see 6:6; see also notes on 10:4,24).
13:5 *bring shame on themselves.* Like a lazy son (10:5; cf. 19:26).
13:6 This contrast repeats the thought of 2:21–22; 10:9; 11:3,5 (see notes there); cf. 21:12; Ps 25:21.
13:7 Both pretenses are folly and lead to folly (see 14:8 and note; see also 11:24 and note; 12:9).
13:8 *may ransom their life.* May pay off robbers or enemies (see 10:15 and note; Jer 41:8).
13:9 *light ... lamp.* Symbols of life (cf. Job 3:20). *shines brightly.* There is joy and prosperity (see note on 4:18). *lamp of the wicked is snuffed out.* Their lives will end (see 20:20; 24:20; Job 18:5; 21:17).
13:10 *pride.* See 11:2 and note.
13:11 *Dishonest money dwindles away.* Such as wealth gained by extortion (Ps 62:10) or deceit (Pr 21:6). See note on 10:2; see also Jer 17:11. *makes it grow.* See note on 10:4.
13:12 *Hope deferred makes the heart sick.* Cf. Ge 30:1. *longing fulfilled is a tree of life.* It revives and strengthens (see note on 3:18; see also 10:28; 13:19).

[13]Whoever scorns instruction will pay
for it,[f]
but whoever respects[g] a command is
rewarded.[h]

[14]The teaching of the wise is a fountain
of life,[i]
turning a person from the snares of
death.[j]

[15]Good judgment wins favor,
but the way of the unfaithful leads
to their destruction.[a]

[16]All who are prudent act with[b]
knowledge,
but fools expose[k] their folly.[l]

[17]A wicked messenger falls into trouble,[m]
but a trustworthy envoy brings
healing.[n]

[18]Whoever disregards discipline comes
to poverty and shame,[o]
but whoever heeds correction is
honored.[p]

[19]A longing fulfilled is sweet to the
soul,[q]
but fools detest turning from evil.

[20]Walk with the wise and become wise,
for a companion of fools suffers
harm.[r]

[21]Trouble pursues the sinner,[s]
but the righteous[t] are rewarded with
good things.[u]

[22]A good person leaves an inheritance
for their children's children,
but a sinner's wealth is stored up for
the righteous.[v]

13:13 [f]S Nu 15:31 [g]Ex 9:20 [h]Pr 16:20 **13:14** [i]S Pr 10:11 [j]Pr 14:27 **13:16** [k]Ecc 10:3 [l]Est 5:11; S Ps 38:5 **13:17** [m]S Pr 10:26 [n]Pr 25:13 **13:18** [o]S Pr 1:7; S 12:1 [p]Ps 141:5; Pr 25:12; Ecc 7:5 **13:19** [q]S Pr 10:11 **13:20** [r]2Ch 10:8 **13:21** [s]2Sa 3:39; Jer 40:3; 50:7; Eze 14:13; 18:4 [t]Ps 32:10 [u]Ps 25:13 **13:22** [v]S Est 8:2; S Job 27:17; Ecc 2:26 **13:24** [w]S 2Sa 7:14 [x]S Pr 3:12 [y]Pr 19:18; 22:15; 23:13-14; 29:15, 17; Eph 6:4; Heb 12:7 **13:25** [z]Pr 10:3 **14:1** [a]S Ru 3:11; Pr 24:3 **14:3** [b]S Pr 10:14; Ecc 10:12 [c]S Pr 10:13; S 12:6 **14:4** [d]Ps 144:14 **14:5** [e]S Ps 12:2; S Pr 12:17 **14:6** [f]S Pr 9:9

[23]An unplowed field produces food for
the poor,
but injustice sweeps it away.

[24]Whoever spares the rod[w] hates their
children,
but the one who loves their children
is careful to discipline[x] them.[y]

[25]The righteous eat to their hearts'
content,
but the stomach of the wicked goes
hungry.[z]

14 The wise woman builds her
house,[a]
but with her own hands the foolish
one tears hers down.

[2]Whoever fears the LORD walks
uprightly,
but those who despise him are
devious in their ways.

[3]A fool's mouth lashes out with pride,[b]
but the lips of the wise protect
them.[c]

[4]Where there are no oxen, the manger
is empty,
but from the strength of an ox[d] come
abundant harvests.

[5]An honest witness does not deceive,
but a false witness pours out lies.[e]

[6]The mocker seeks wisdom and finds
none,
but knowledge comes easily to the
discerning.[f]

[a] *15* Septuagint and Syriac; the meaning of the Hebrew for this phrase is uncertain. [b] *16* Or *prudent protect themselves through*

13:13 *Whoever scorns instruction will pay for it.* See 1:29–31; 5:12 and note. *whoever respects a command is rewarded.* With the benefits wisdom gives (see 3:2 and note; 3:16–18; 16:20; cf. 13:21).
13:14 *fountain of life.* See note on 10:11. *from the snares of death.* See notes on 1:17; 5:22; see also 7:23; 22:5.
13:15 *wins favor.* See 3:4; 8:35. *leads to their destruction.* See v. 13 and note.
13:16 See 12:23 and note.
13:17 *falls into trouble.* Perhaps by misrepresenting the sender. *brings healing.* A tactful, honest approach benefits both parties (see 25:13; cf. 12:18; 15:4).
13:18 *comes to poverty and shame.* See 5:10–12 and notes. *whoever heeds correction is honored.* See v. 1; 3:16–18; 8:35; 10:17.
13:19 *longing fulfilled.* See v. 12. *fools detest turning from evil.* Cf. their hatred of correction in 5:12.
13:20 *Walk with the wise and become wise.* So choose your friends with care (see 2:20; 12:26). *companion of fools suffers harm.* See 1:10,18; 2:12; 16:29; 22:24–25; cf. 1Co 15:33 and note.
13:21 See v. 13 and note.
13:22 *is stored up for the righteous.* Job agrees that this is often what happens to the possessions of the wicked (Job 27:16–17; cf. Pr 28:8; Ecc 2:18–21).
13:23 *injustice sweeps it away.* Probably a case of the rich and powerful oppressing the poor (see Am 2:6–7 and notes; cf. Ps 35:10).
13:24 *Whoever spares the rod hates their children.* Parents are encouraged to apply the rod of punishment to drive out folly (22:15) so that the child will not follow a path of destruction (19:18; 23:13–14). The rod and a reprimand "impart wisdom" (29:15) and promote a healthy and happy family life (29:17). Discipline is rooted in love (see 3:11–12 and note). *rod.* Probably a figure of speech for caring discipline of any kind.
13:25 States more specifically the teaching of vv. 13,18,21,23; see 10:3 and note.
14:1 *wise woman builds her house.* She is a source of strength and an example of diligence for her family (see 31:10–31). Cf. the house built by wisdom in 9:1.
14:2 *fears the LORD.* See note on 1:7.
14:3 *lips of the wise protect them.* Cf. Ecc 9:13–18.
14:4 Perhaps the thought is that people need to take good care of their oxen (the means of production) if they expect an abundant harvest (see 12:10 and note).
14:5 See note on 6:19.
14:6 *mocker.* See 1:22; Ps 1:1 and notes. *seeks wisdom and finds none.* Because of refusal to fear the Lord or accept any correction.

7 Stay away from a fool,
for you will not find knowledge on their lips.

8 The wisdom of the prudent is to give thought to their ways,[g]
but the folly of fools is deception.[h]

9 Fools mock at making amends for sin,
but goodwill is found among the upright.

10 Each heart knows its own bitterness,
and no one else can share its joy.

11 The house of the wicked will be destroyed,[i]
but the tent of the upright will flourish.[j]

12 There is a way that appears to be right,[k]
but in the end it leads to death.[l]

13 Even in laughter[m] the heart may ache,
and rejoicing may end in grief.

14 The faithless will be fully repaid for their ways,[n]
and the good rewarded for theirs.[o]

15 The simple believe anything,
but the prudent give thought to their steps.[p]

16 The wise fear the LORD and shun evil,[q]
but a fool[r] is hotheaded and yet feels secure.

17 A quick-tempered person[s] does foolish things,[t]
and the one who devises evil schemes is hated.[u]

18 The simple inherit folly,
but the prudent are crowned with knowledge.

19 Evildoers will bow down in the presence of the good,
and the wicked at the gates of the righteous.[v]

20 The poor are shunned even by their neighbors,
but the rich have many friends.[w]

21 It is a sin to despise one's neighbor,[x]
but blessed is the one who is kind to the needy.[y]

22 Do not those who plot evil go astray?[z]
But those who plan what is good find[a] love and faithfulness.

23 All hard work brings a profit,
but mere talk leads only to poverty.

24 The wealth of the wise is their crown,
but the folly of fools yields folly.[a]

25 A truthful witness saves lives,
but a false witness is deceitful.[b]

26 Whoever fears the LORD has a secure fortress,[c]
and for their children it will be a refuge.[d]

27 The fear of the LORD is a fountain of life,[e]
turning a person from the snares of death.[f]

14:8 [g] ver 15; Pr 15:28; 21:29 [h] ver 24 **14:11** [i] S Job 8:22; Pr 21:12 [j] S Ps 72:7; S Pr 3:33; S 12:7 **14:12** [k] S Pr 12:15 [l] Pr 16:25 **14:13** [m] Ecc 2:2; 7:3,6 **14:14** [n] S Pr 1:31 [o] S 2Ch 15:7; Pr 12:14 **14:15** [p] S ver 8 **14:16** [q] S Ex 20:20; Pr 22:3 [r] S 1Sa 25:25 **14:17** [s] S 2Ki 5:12 [t] ver 29; Pr 15:18; 16:28; 26:21; 28:25; 29:22 [u] S Est 5:9 **14:19** [v] Pr 11:29 **14:20** [w] Pr 19:4,7 **14:21** [x] Pr 11:12 [y] Pr 19:17 **14:22** [z] Pr 4:16-17 **14:24** [a] ver 8 **14:25** [b] S Pr 12:17 **14:26** [c] Pr 18:10 [d] Ps 9:9 **14:27** [e] S Pr 10:11 [f] Ps 18:5; Pr 13:14

[a] 22 Or *show*

14:8 *folly of fools is deception.* What fools believe to be prudent (but is really folly) does not bring success; instead, it tends toward their ruin.
14:9 *mock at making amends for sin.* Cf. 19:28. *goodwill … among the upright.* See 11:27.
14:10 *knows its own bitterness.* See 1Ki 8:38. Cf. the experience of Hannah (1Sa 1:10) and Peter (Mt 26:75). *can share its joy.* Cf. Mt 13:44; 1Pe 1:8.
14:11 See 10:25 and note.
14:12 Repeated in 16:25. *in the end it leads to death.* See 5:4,23; 7:21–27; Mt 7:13–14.
14:13 *in laughter the heart may ache.* Cf. Ezr 3:11–12. *rejoicing may end in grief.* As the death of Rachel in childbirth (Ge 35:16–18).
14:14 See 1:31; 12:14 and notes; see also 11:5,8; 18:20; 22:8; Job 4:8.
14:15 *simple.* See note on 1:4. *give thought to their steps.* See 4:26 and note; 21:29.
14:16 *fear the LORD and shun evil.* See notes on 1:7; 3:7. *hotheaded.* Cf. 21:24. *yet feels secure.* But people and nations can have a false sense of security (cf. 27:24; Jdg 18:7; Isa 32:9–13; 47:8–11; Jer 22:21; Da 8:25; 11:21,24; Am 6:1; Zec 1:15 and note).
14:17 *quick-tempered.* See v. 29; Titus 1:7. *who devises evil schemes.* Cf. 12:2; Job 5:12–13; 1Co 3:19.
14:18 *crowned with knowledge.* Adorned and blessed with knowledge (see note on 4:9; see also v. 24; 12:4; Ps 103:4).
14:19 *Evildoers will bow down.* Cf. 17:2. *at the gates of the righteous.* Perhaps to beg for a favor (cf. 1Sa 2:36).
14:20 *shunned even by their neighbors.* And sometimes by their relatives (see 19:7).
14:21 *blessed is the one who is kind to the needy.* Sharing food (22:9), lending money (28:8) and defending rights (31:9) are ways one can show kindness. Such a person "honors God" (v. 31; cf. 17:5) and "will lack nothing" (28:27). Cf. 21:13; Ps 41:1.
14:22 *plot evil.* See 3:29; 6:14,18; Mic 2:1. *go astray.* See 5:23; 12:26. *find love and faithfulness.* Receive the support and care of faithful friends (cf. 3:3; 16:6; 20:28)—perhaps God's support and care are also implied here. *love and faithfulness.* See Ps 26:3 and note.
14:23 *hard work brings a profit.* See note on 10:4; see also 21:5.
14:24 *wealth … is their crown.* The wise obtain wealth, and it adorns them like a crown (see 10:22 and note). *yields folly.* An empty inheritance (see v. 18; 3:35).
14:25 See v. 5; 12:17; see also note on 6:19.
14:26 *fears the LORD.* See 1:7; 3:7 and notes. *secure fortress … refuge.* Means either that the godliness of parents will result in blessing for themselves and their children (see 20:7) or that the fear of the Lord will be a strong tower where the children also can find refuge (see 18:10; Ps 71:7; Isa 33:6).
14:27 See note on 10:11; see also 13:14.

[28] A large population is a king's glory,
but without subjects a prince is ruined.[g]

[29] Whoever is patient has great understanding,[h]
but one who is quick-tempered displays folly.[i]

[30] A heart at peace gives life to the body,
but envy rots the bones.[j]

[31] Whoever oppresses the poor shows contempt for their Maker,[k]
but whoever is kind to the needy honors God.[l]

[32] When calamity comes, the wicked are brought down,[m]
but even in death the righteous seek refuge in God.[n]

[33] Wisdom reposes in the heart of the discerning[o]
and even among fools she lets herself be known.[a]

[34] Righteousness exalts a nation,[p]
but sin condemns any people.

[35] A king delights in a wise servant,
but a shameful servant arouses his fury.[q]

15 A gentle answer[r] turns away wrath,[s]
but a harsh word stirs up anger.

[2] The tongue of the wise adorns knowledge,[t]
but the mouth of the fool gushes folly.[u]

[3] The eyes[v] of the LORD are everywhere,[w]
keeping watch on the wicked and the good.[x]

[4] The soothing tongue[y] is a tree of life,[z]
but a perverse tongue crushes the spirit.[a]

[5] A fool spurns a parent's discipline,
but whoever heeds correction shows prudence.[b]

[6] The house of the righteous contains great treasure,[c]
but the income of the wicked brings ruin.[d]

[7] The lips of the wise spread knowledge,[e]
but the hearts of fools are not upright.

[8] The LORD detests the sacrifice[f] of the wicked,[g]
but the prayer of the upright pleases him.[h]

[9] The LORD detests the way of the wicked,[i]
but he loves those who pursue righteousness.[j]

[10] Stern discipline awaits anyone who leaves the path;
the one who hates correction will die.[k]

[11] Death and Destruction[b] lie open before the LORD[l] —
how much more do human hearts![m]

[a] 33 Hebrew; Septuagint and Syriac *discerning / but in the heart of fools she is not known* [b] 11 Hebrew *Abaddon*

14:28 [g] S 2Sa 19:7 **14:29** [h] S 2Ki 5:12; Pr 17:27 [i] S ver 17; Ecc 7:8-9 **14:30** [j] Pr 17:22 **14:31** [k] Pr 17:5 [l] S Dt 24:14; S Job 20:19; S Mt 10:42 **14:32** [m] S Ps 34:21; S Pr 6:15 [n] S Job 13:15 **14:33** [o] Pr 2:6-10 **14:34** [p] Pr 11:11 **14:35** [q] S Est 8:2; Mt 24:45-51; 25:14-30 **15:1** [r] 1Ki 12:7; 2Ch 10:7 [s] Pr 25:15 **15:2** [t] ver 7; S Pr 10:31 [u] S Ps 59:7; Ecc 10:12 **15:3** [v] S 2Ch 16:9 [w] S Job 10:4; S 31:4; S Heb 4:13 [x] S Job 34:21; Pr 5:21; Jer 16:17 **15:4** [y] S Ps 5:9 [z] S Pr 10:11 [a] Pr 12:18 **15:5** [b] S Pr 10:17; S 12:1; S 13:1 **15:6** [c] S Pr 8:21 [d] S Pr 10:16 **15:7** [e] S ver 2; S Pr 10:13 **15:8** [f] S Ps 51:17; S Isa 1:13 [g] S Pr 6:16; 21:27 [h] ver 29; Job 35:13; Pr 28:9; S Jn 9:31 **15:9** [i] S Pr 6:16 [j] S Dt 7:13; S Pr 11:20 **15:10** [k] S Pr 1:31-32; S 12:1 **15:11** [l] S Job 26:6 [m] S 1Sa 2:3; S 2Ch 6:30; S Ps 44:21; S Rev 2:23

14:29 *patient.* See 15:18; 16:32; 19:11; Jas 1:19. *quick-tempered.* See v. 17; cf. Eph 4:26.
14:30 *gives life to the body.* Cf. the healthy effects of fearing the Lord and walking in wisdom in 3:7–8,16–18. *envy rots the bones.* See note on 3:8; see also 12:4; Ps 37:7–8.
14:31 *shows contempt for their Maker.* Because God created both the rich and the poor in his image (see 17:5; 22:2; Ge 1:26 and note; Job 31:15; Jas 3:9). *kind to the needy.* See note on v. 21. *honors God.* Does God's will, and in a sense gives to God himself (see 19:17 and note; Mt 25:40; cf. Jas 2:1–3).
14:32 *wicked are brought down.* See 1:26 and note; 11:5; 24:16. *even in death the righteous seek refuge in God.* Their faith in God gives them hope beyond the grave (see 12:28; Ps 49:15 and notes).
14:33 *even among fools she lets herself be known.* Perhaps means that even fools occasionally display a bit of wisdom (cf. Ac 17:27–28; Ro 1:19–20), but see NIV text note.
14:34 *Righteousness exalts a nation.* See note on 11:11. Israel was promised prosperity and prestige if she obeyed God's laws (see Dt 28:1–14). *sin condemns any people.* The Canaanites were eventually driven out because of their terrible sin (see Ge 15:16 and note; Lev 18:24–25), and Israel later fell under the same curse (Dt 28:15–68; cf. 2Sa 12:10).
14:35 *arouses his fury.* See 16:14 and note; 19:12; Da 2:12.
15:1 *gentle answer turns away wrath.* Cf. the way Gideon calmed the anger of the men of Ephraim in Jdg 8:1–3 (cf. also Pr 15:18; Ecc 10:4). *harsh word stirs up anger.* Nabal's sarcastic response put David in a fighting mood (1Sa 25:10–13).
15:2 *gushes folly.* See vv. 7,28; 12:23; 13:16.
15:3 *eyes of the LORD are everywhere.* See 5:21; Job 31:4; 34:21; Jer 16:17; 32:19.
15:4 *soothing tongue.* See note on 12:18. *tree of life.* See note on 3:18. *perverse tongue crushes the spirit.* Especially false testimony in court (see 6:19 and note; 22:22) or slander in the community.
15:6 See 10:2,16,22 and notes. *great treasure.* See 8:18,21; 24:4; Zec 8:12 and note; see also note on 3:10.
15:8 *detests the sacrifice of the wicked.* Those whose hearts are not right with God gain nothing by offering sacrifices (see Ecc 5:1; see also Pr 21:3; Isa 1:11–15; Jer 6:20 and notes). *prayer of the upright.* See 3:32.
15:9 *who pursue righteousness.* See 21:21; 1Ti 6:11.
15:10 *the path.* The right (or "straight") path (see 2:13). *one who hates correction will die.* See 5:12,23 and notes.
15:11 *Death and Destruction.* See 27:20 and note. *lie open before the LORD.* Not even the grave, the netherworld, is inaccessible to God (see Job 26:6 and note; Ps 139:8). Therefore he knows the secrets of everyone's inmost being (cf. 1Sa 16:7 and note).

[12]Mockers resent correction,[n]
so they avoid the wise.

[13]A happy heart makes the face cheerful,[o]
but heartache crushes the spirit.[p]

[14]The discerning heart seeks knowledge,[q]
but the mouth of a fool feeds on folly.

[15]All the days of the oppressed are wretched,
but the cheerful heart has a continual feast.[r]

[16]Better a little with the fear of the LORD
than great wealth with turmoil.[s]

[17]Better a small serving of vegetables with love
than a fattened calf with hatred.[t]

[18]A hot-tempered person stirs up conflict,[u]
but the one who is patient calms a quarrel.[v]

[19]The way of the sluggard is blocked with thorns,[w]
but the path of the upright is a highway.

[20]A wise son brings joy to his father,[x]
but a foolish man despises his mother.

[21]Folly brings joy to one who has no sense,[y]
but whoever has understanding keeps a straight course.

[22]Plans fail for lack of counsel,[z]
but with many advisers[a] they succeed.[b]

[23]A person finds joy in giving an apt reply[c]—
and how good is a timely word![d]

[24]The path of life leads upward for the prudent
to keep them from going down to the realm of the dead.

[25]The LORD tears down the house of the proud,[e]
but he sets the widow's boundary stones in place.[f]

[26]The LORD detests the thoughts[g] of the wicked,[h]
but gracious words are pure[i] in his sight.

[27]The greedy bring ruin to their households,
but the one who hates bribes will live.[j]

[28]The heart of the righteous weighs its answers,[k]
but the mouth of the wicked gushes evil.[l]

[29]The LORD is far from the wicked,
but he hears the prayer of the righteous.[m]

[30]Light in a messenger's eyes brings joy to the heart,
and good news gives health to the bones.[n]

[31]Whoever heeds life-giving correction
will be at home among the wise.[o]

[32]Those who disregard discipline despise themselves,[p]

15:12 [n]S Pr 9:8; S 12:1 **15:13** [o]ver 15 [p]S Pr 12:25; 17:22; 18:14 **15:14** [q]Pr 18:15 **15:15** [r]ver 13 **15:16** [s]ver 17; Ps 37:16-17; Pr 13:8; 16:8; 17:1 **15:17** [t]S ver 16; Pr 17:1; Ecc 4:6 **15:18** [u]S Pr 6:16-19; S 14:17 [v]S Ge 13:8 **15:19** [w]Pr 22:5 **15:20** [x]S Pr 10:1 **15:21** [y]S Pr 2:14 **15:22** [z]S Ps 16:7 [a]1Ki 1:12; Pr 24:6 [b]S Pr 11:14 **15:23** [c]S Pr 12:14 [d]Pr 25:11 **15:25** [e]S Pr 12:7 [f]S Dt 19:14; Pr 23:10-11 **15:26** [g]S Ps 94:11 [h]S Pr 6:16 [i]S Ps 18:26 **15:27** [j]S Ex 23:8; S Ps 15:5; Isa 1:23; 33:15 **15:28** [k]S Pr 14:8 [l]S Ps 59:7 **15:29** [m]S ver 8; S Job 15:31; Ps 145:18-19; Isa 59:2; S Jn 9:31 **15:30** [n]Pr 25:25 **15:31** [o]S Pr 9:7-9; S 12:1 **15:32** [p]S Pr 1:7; S 12:1

15:12 See 1:30; 10:8; 13:1; 17:10. *Mockers.* See note on 1:22.
15:13 *happy heart makes the face cheerful.* Cf. 14:30. *heartache crushes the spirit.* Cf. the great sorrow of Job (Job 3) and David (Ps 51:8,10).
15:15 *cheerful heart has a continual feast.* Life is as joyful and satisfying as the days of a festival (see v. 13; 14:30; cf. Lev 23:39–41).
15:16 *fear of the LORD.* See 1:7 and note. *great wealth with turmoil.* The "ill-gotten treasures" of 10:2 (see note there).
15:17 *fattened calf.* Such meat was something of a luxury, reserved for special occasions (cf. 7:14; Mt 22:4; Lk 15:23).
15:18 *stirs up conflict.* See note on 6:14. *patient.* See 14:29; 16:32; 19:11; Jas 1:19.
15:19 *sluggard.* See note on 6:6. *blocked with thorns.* Mainly because he was too lazy to remove them (see 24:30–31; Hos 2:6). *highway.* The upright can make progress and reach their goals (see note on 3:6).
15:20 See 10:1 and note.
15:21 A variation of 10:23.
15:22 See the close parallels in 11:14; 20:18; 24:6.
15:23 *apt reply.* Cf. Isa 50:4. *how good is a timely word!* Cf. 24:26.
15:24 *leads upward.* Along the "highway" (v. 19), the "straight course" (v. 21) that leads to life. *to keep them from going down to the realm of the dead.* See note on 2:18.
15:25 *tears down the house of the proud.* See 2:22; 14:11; see also 10:25 and note. *sets the widow's boundary stones in place.* In ancient times boundary stones marked a person's property. Anyone who moved such a stone was, in effect, stealing land (see 22:28; 23:10; Job 24:2; Dt 19:14 and note).
15:26 *detests the thoughts of the wicked.* Cf. vv. 8–9. *gracious words are pure.* See 22:11; Ps 24:4 and note.
15:27 *The greedy bring ruin to their households.* See 1:19; 11:29; 28:25. Achan's whole family perished because of his greed at Jericho (see Jos 7:24 and note). *one who hates bribes will live.* See 17:8 and note; 28:16.
15:28 *weighs its answers.* Cf. 10:32; 1Pe 3:15. *gushes evil.* See v. 2; see also v. 7; 12:23.
15:29 *far from the wicked.* See 1:28 and note.
15:30 *Light in a messenger's eyes brings joy.* Cf. v. 13; 16:15; Job 29:24. *good news gives health to the bones.* See 3:8 and note; see also Php 2:19.
15:31 *Whoever heeds life-giving correction.* See 1:23; 6:23 and note.
15:32 *Those who disregard discipline despise themselves.* See note on 5:12; see also 1:7; 5:23; 8:36. *one who heeds correction.* Cf. vv. 5,31.

CHARACTER TRAITS IN PROVERBS

TRAITS TO BE PROMOTED	
avoidance of strife	20:3
compassion for animals	12:10
contentment	13:25; 14:30; 15:27
diligence	6:6–13; 12:24,27; 13:4
faithful love	20:6
faithfulness	3:5–6; 5:15–17; 25:13; 28:20
generosity	21:26; 22:9
honesty	16:11; 24:26
humility	11:2; 16:19; 25:6–7; 29:23
integrity	11:3; 25:26; 28:18
kindness to others	11:16–17
kindness to enemies	25:21–22
leadership	30:19–31
loyalty	19:22
nobility	12:4; 31:10,29
patience	15:18; 16:32
peacefulness	16:7
praiseworthiness	27:21
righteousness	4:26–27; 11:5–6,30; 12:28; 13:6; 29:2
self-control	17:27; 25:28; 29:11
strength and honor	20:29
strength in adversity	24:10
teachableness	15:31
truthfulness	12:19,22; 23:23

TRAITS TO BE AVOIDED	
anger	29:22
antisocial behavior	18:1
beauty without discretion	11:22
blaming God	19:3
dishonesty	24:28
greed	28:25
hatred	29:27
hot temper	19:19; 29:22
immorality	6:20–35
inappropriate desire	27:7
injustice	22:16
jealousy	27:4
lack of mercy	21:13
laziness	6:6–11; 18:9; 19:15; 20:4; 24:30–34; 26:13–15
maliciousness	6:27
meddling	26:17; 30:10
pride	15:5; 16:18; 21:4,24; 29:23; 30:13
quarrelsomeness	26:21
self-conceit	26:12,16
self-deceit	28:11
self-glory	25:27
self-righteousness	30:12
social disruption	19:10
stubbornness	29:1
unfaithfulness	25:19
unneighborliness	3:27–30
vengeance	24:28–29
wickedness	21:10
wicked scheming	16:30

but the one who heeds correction
gains understanding.[q]

[33] Wisdom's instruction is to fear the
LORD,[r]
and humility comes before honor.[s]

16 To humans belong the plans of the
heart,
but from the LORD comes the proper
answer of the tongue.[t]

[2] All a person's ways seem pure to
them,[u]
but motives are weighed[v] by the
LORD.[w]

[3] Commit to the LORD whatever
you do,
and he will establish your plans.[x]

[4] The LORD works out everything to its
proper end[y]—
even the wicked for a day of
disaster.[z]

[5] The LORD detests all the proud of
heart.[a]
Be sure of this: They will not go
unpunished.[b]

[6] Through love and faithfulness sin is
atoned for;
through the fear of the LORD[c] evil is
avoided.[d]

[7] When the LORD takes pleasure in
anyone's way,
he causes their enemies to make
peace[e] with them.[f]

[8] Better a little with righteousness
than much gain[g] with injustice.[h]

[9] In their hearts humans plan their
course,
but the LORD establishes their steps.[i]

[10] The lips of a king speak as an oracle,
and his mouth does not betray
justice.[j]

[11] Honest scales and balances belong to
the LORD;
all the weights in the bag are of his
making.[k]

[12] Kings detest wrongdoing,
for a throne is established through
righteousness.[l]

[13] Kings take pleasure in honest lips;
they value the one who speaks what
is right.[m]

[14] A king's wrath is a messenger of
death,[n]
but the wise will appease it.[o]

15:32 [q] S Pr 9:7-9; S 12:1; Ecc 7:5 **15:33** [r] S Pr 1:7 [s] Pr 16:18; 18:12; 22:4; 29:23; Isa 66:2 **16:1** [t] ver 9; Pr 19:21 **16:2** [u] S Pr 12:15; 30:12 [v] S 1Sa 2:3 [w] S 2Ch 6:30; Pr 20:27; 21:2; Lk 16:15 **16:3** [x] S 2Ch 20:20; S Ps 20:4; 37:5-6; S Pr 3:5-6 **16:4** [y] Ex 9:16 [z] S 2Ch 34:24; S Ps 18:18; Ro 9:22 **16:5** [a] S Ps 40:4; S Pr 6:16 [b] Pr 11:20-21 **16:6** [c] S Ge 20:11; S Ex 1:17 [d] S Ex 20:20 **16:7** [e] S Ge 39:21 [f] Ps 105:15; Jer 39:12; 40:1; 42:12; Da 1:9 **16:8** [g] S Ps 37:16 [h] S Pr 15:16; 17:1; Ecc 4:6 **16:9** [i] S ver 1; S Job 33:29; S Ps 90:12 **16:10** [j] Pr 17:7 **16:11** [k] S Pr 11:1; Eze 45:10 **16:12** [l] Pr 26:28; 25:5; 29:14; 31:5 **16:13** [m] Pr 22:11 **16:14** [n] S Ge 40:2; S Job 29:24; Pr 20:2 [o] Pr 25:15; 29:8; Ecc 10:4

15:33 *fear the LORD.* See note on 1:7. *humility comes before honor.* See 18:12; 25:6–7; Mt 23:12; Lk 14:11 and note; 18:14; 1Pe 5:6. Wisdom also comes with humility (11:2; 13:10).

16:1 *from the LORD comes the proper answer of the tongue.* Either an acknowledgment that God must give the ability to articulate and accomplish those "plans" or, more likely, that God's sovereign governance of human affairs overrides human intentions (see vv. 4,9 and notes; cf. 19:21; see also Ge 50:20 and the experience of Balaam in Nu 22–24).

16:2 *ways seem pure to them.* See 14:12 and note. *motives are weighed by the LORD.* See 21:2; 24:12 and note; Ps 139:23; 1Co 4:4–5; Heb 4:12.

16:3 *Commit.* See 1Pe 5:7. *he will establish your plans.* Your goals will be reached (see 3:5–6 and notes; Ps 1:3; 55:22; 90:17).

16:4 The middle verse of this section of Proverbs (10:1—22:16; see 10:1 and note), aptly summarizing the Lord's sovereignty over every human thought and action. The verse also occupies the central position in a series of seven verses (1–7) at the beginning of ch. 16—the middle chapter in the book of Proverbs. Each of the seven verses features the name Yahweh, again stressing his supreme position as Lord over all. *works out everything to its proper end.* God is sovereign in every life and in all of history (see Ecc 7:14; Ac 3:17–18; Ro 8:28). *the wicked for a day of disaster.* God displays his power even through the wicked (cf. Ex 9:16), and all evil will be judged (cf. Eze 38:22–23; Ro 2:5–11).

16:5 See 11:20–21.

16:6 *Through love and faithfulness sin is atoned for.* The moral quality of conduct that God desires is sometimes summed up as "love and faithfulness" (3:3; see Ps 26:3; Hos 4:1 and notes). When his people repent of sin and bring their lives into accord with his will, God forgives and withdraws his judgment (see Isa 1:18–19; 55:7; Jer 3:22; 18:7–10 and note; Eze 18:23,30–32; 33:11–12,14–16; Hos 14:1–2, 4). Thus it can be said that love and faithfulness, in a manner of speaking, atone for sin, i.e., they turn away God's wrath against it. *fear of the LORD.* See note on 1:7. *evil is avoided.* See 3:7 and note.

16:7 *causes their enemies to make peace with them.* As in the reigns of godly Asa and Jehoshaphat (2Ch 14:6–7; 17:10). *peace.* See 3:17; Ro 12:18 and notes; Heb 12:14.

16:8 See 10:2 and note.

16:9 *the LORD establishes their steps.* Verses 1,3–4 (see notes) also emphasize God's control of people's lives (see 19:21; 20:24; Ps 37:23; Jer 10:23).

16:10 *speak as an oracle.* In judging cases brought before him, a king functioned as God's representative (see Dt 1:17). Therefore he needed the divine gift of wisdom to discern between right and wrong in order to render God's judgment (see 1Ki 3:9). When he did so, his judgment was tantamount to a divine word for the people (see 2Sa 14:17; 1Ki 3:28 and notes).

16:11 See note on 11:1. *Honest scales . . . belong to the LORD.* Cf. 21:2; 24:12; Job 6:2; 31:6. *all the weights in the bag.* Merchants carried stones of different sizes with them to weigh and measure quantities of silver for payment (cf. Mic 6:11).

16:12–15 A series of four proverbs highlighting the rule of the king as chief political executive in the life of the community (cf. v. 10).

16:12 *throne is established through righteousness.* True when the king "judges the poor with fairness" (29:14), refuses to take bribes (29:4) and removes any wicked advisers (25:5). See 14:34; Dt 17:19–20; Isa 16:5; Ro 13:3–4.

16:13 *in honest lips.* Rather than in flattering lips (cf. 26:28).

16:14 *messenger of death.* Any angry king can pronounce death quickly and effectively (see 19:12; Est 7:7–10; Mt 22:7; Lk 19:27). *the wise will appease it.* Cf. Daniel's response to the rage of Nebuchadnezzar (Da 2:12–16).

15 When a king's face brightens, it means life;[p]
his favor is like a rain cloud in spring.[q]

16 How much better to get wisdom than gold,
to get insight[r] rather than silver![s]

17 The highway of the upright avoids evil;
those who guard their ways preserve their lives.[t]

18 Pride[u] goes before destruction,
a haughty spirit[v] before a fall.[w]

19 Better to be lowly in spirit along with the oppressed
than to share plunder with the proud.

20 Whoever gives heed to instruction prospers,[a][x]
and blessed is the one who trusts in the LORD.[y]

21 The wise in heart are called discerning,
and gracious words promote instruction.[b][z]

22 Prudence is a fountain of life to the prudent,[a]
but folly brings punishment to fools.

23 The hearts of the wise make their mouths prudent,[b]
and their lips promote instruction.[c][c]

24 Gracious words are a honeycomb,[d]
sweet to the soul and healing to the bones.[e]

25 There is a way that appears to be right,[f]
but in the end it leads to death.[g]

26 The appetite of laborers works for them;
their hunger drives them on.

27 A scoundrel[h] plots evil,
and on their lips it is like a scorching fire.[i]

28 A perverse person stirs up conflict,[j]
and a gossip separates close friends.[k]

29 A violent person entices their neighbor
and leads them down a path that is not good.[l]

30 Whoever winks[m] with their eye is plotting perversity;
whoever purses their lips is bent on evil.

31 Gray hair is a crown of splendor;[n]
it is attained in the way of righteousness.

32 Better a patient person than a warrior,
one with self-control than one who takes a city.

33 The lot is cast[o] into the lap,
but its every decision[p] is from the LORD.[q]

17

Better a dry crust with peace and quiet
than a house full of feasting, with strife.[r]

2 A prudent servant will rule over a disgraceful son

16:15 [p]S Ge 40:2; S Job 29:24 [q]Pr 19:12; 25:2-7 **16:16** [r]Ps 49:20 [s]S Job 28:15; S Pr 3:13-14 **16:17** [t]Pr 19:16 **16:18** [u]S 1Sa 17:42 [v]Ps 18:27; Isa 13:11; Jer 48:29 [w]S Est 5:12; Pr 11:2; S 15:33; 18:12; 29:23 **16:20** [x]Pr 13:13 [y]S Ps 32:10; 40:4; Pr 19:8; 29:25; Jer 17:7 **16:21** [z]ver 23 **16:22** [a]S Pr 10:11 **16:23** [b]Job 15:5 [c]ver 21 **16:24** [d]S 1Sa 14:27 [e]Pr 24:13-14 **16:25** [f]S Pr 12:15 [g]Est 3:6; Pr 14:12 **16:27** [h]S Ps 140:2 [i]Jas 3:6 **16:28** [j]S Pr 14:17 [k]Pr 17:9 **16:29** [l]S Pr 1:10; 12:26 **16:30** [m]S Pr 6:13 **16:31** [n]Pr 20:29 **16:33** [o]S Lev 16:8; S 1Sa 10:21; Eze 21:21 [p]1Sa 14:41 [q]Jos 7:14; Pr 18:18; 29:26; Jnh 1:7 **17:1** [r]S Pr 15:16, 17; S 16:8

[a] 20 Or *whoever speaks prudently finds what is good*
[b] 21 Or *words make a person persuasive*
[c] 23 Or *prudent / and make their lips persuasive*

16:15 *face brightens.* Cf. Nu 6:25 and note; La 4:20. *his favor is like a rain cloud in spring.* The spring rain was essential for the full development of barley and wheat; it was therefore a sign of good things to come. Cf. the "dew" of 19:12; see Ps 72:6.
16:16 See 1:13; 3:14 and notes; 8:10,19.
16:17 *highway of the upright.* See notes on 3:6; 15:19. *avoids evil.* Cf. the thorns and snares in the paths of the wicked (22:5).
16:18 See 11:2 and note; cf. 1Co 10:12.
16:19 *Better to be lowly in spirit.* See 3:34; Isa 57:15; Mt 5:3 and note. *share plunder with the proud.* See 1:13–14; Jdg 5:30.
16:20 *prospers.* See 13:13; 28:25 and notes. *blessed is the one who trusts in the LORD.* See v. 3; 3:5–6; Ps 34:8; 37:4–5; 84:12.
16:21 *gracious words promote instruction.* Cf. the last line of v. 23. "Gracious" (lit. "sweet") is expanded in v. 24. Cf. the persuasive but destructive words of the adulterous woman in 7:21.
16:22 *fountain of life.* See note on 10:11. *punishment to fools.* See 13:13 and note; see also 7:22; 13:15; 15:10.
16:23 *make their mouths prudent.* See 22:17–18.
16:24 *Gracious words are a honeycomb.* They are good for you (see 24:13–14), and they taste good (cf. 2:10; Ps 19:10). *healing to the bones.* See notes on 4:22; 12:18; 15:30. *bones.* See note on 3:8.
16:25 See 14:12 and note.
16:26 Cf. 2Th 3:10: "The one who is unwilling to work shall not eat"; see also Ecc 6:7; Eph 4:28.
16:27 *A scoundrel.* See 6:12 and note. *plots evil.* See 3:29; 6:14; Mic 2:1. *scorching fire.* Their speech is inflammatory and destructive (see Jas 3:6).
16:28 *stirs up conflict.* See note on 6:14. *gossip.* See 11:13.
16:29 See 1:10–19 and notes; cf. Ro 1:32.
16:30 *winks with their eye.* See note on 6:13. *purses their lips.* Thereby making insinuations (see note on 6:12–14).
16:31 *Gray hair is a crown of splendor.* The elderly were to receive deep respect (see Lev 19:32). *in the way of righteousness.* See 3:1–2,16.
16:32 *patient … warrior.* See 14:29; 15:18; 19:11; Jas 1:19. "Wisdom is better than weapons of war" (Ecc 9:18). *one with self-control than one who takes a city.* Although those who practice patience and self-control receive far less attention and acclaim than a warrior who takes a city, they accomplish better things.
16:33 *The lot is cast into the lap.* Here the lot may have been several pebbles held in the fold of a garment and then drawn out or shaken to the ground. It was commonly used to make decisions (see notes on Ex 28:30; Nu 26:53; Ne 11:1; Jnh 1:7; Ac 1:26; see also Ps 22:18). *every decision is from the LORD.* God, not chance, is in control (see vv. 1,3–4,9).
17:2 *A prudent servant will rule over a disgraceful son.* See 11:29 and note. *disgraceful son.* See 10:5; 19:26; 28:7; 29:15.

and will share the inheritance as one
of the family.

3 The crucible for silver and the furnace
for gold,[s]
but the LORD tests the heart.[t]

4 A wicked person listens to deceitful
lips;
a liar pays attention to a destructive
tongue.

5 Whoever mocks the poor[u] shows
contempt for their Maker;[v]
whoever gloats over disaster[w] will
not go unpunished.[x]

6 Children's children[y] are a crown to the
aged,
and parents are the pride of their
children.

7 Eloquent lips are unsuited to a godless
fool—
how much worse lying lips to a
ruler![z]

8 A bribe is seen as a charm by the one
who gives it;
they think success will come at
every turn.[a]

9 Whoever would foster love covers over
an offense,[b]
but whoever repeats the matter
separates close friends.[c]

10 A rebuke impresses a discerning
person
more than a hundred lashes a
fool.

11 Evildoers foster rebellion against God;
the messenger of death will be sent
against them.

12 Better to meet a bear robbed of her
cubs
than a fool bent on folly.[d]

13 Evil will never leave the house
of one who pays back evil[e] for
good.[f]

14 Starting a quarrel is like breaching a
dam;
so drop the matter before a dispute
breaks out.[g]

15 Acquitting the guilty and condemning
the innocent[h]—
the LORD detests them both.[i]

16 Why should fools have money in hand
to buy wisdom,
when they are not able to
understand it?[j]

17 A friend loves at all times,
and a brother is born for a time of
adversity.[k]

18 One who has no sense shakes hands in
pledge
and puts up security for a neighbor.[l]

19 Whoever loves a quarrel loves sin;
whoever builds a high gate invites
destruction.

20 One whose heart is corrupt does not
prosper;
one whose tongue is perverse falls
into trouble.

17:3 [s] Pr 27:21 [t] S 1Ch 29:17; Ps 26:2; S 139:23; 1Pe 1:7 **17:5** [u] S Job 5:16 [v] Pr 14:31 [w] S Job 31:29 [x] Eze 25:3; Ob 1:12 **17:6** [y] S Ps 128:5-6 **17:7** [z] Pr 16:10 **17:8** [a] S Ex 23:8; Pr 19:6 **17:9** [b] S Pr 10:12 [c] Pr 16:28 **17:12** [d] S 1Sa 25:25 **17:13** [e] S 1Sa 19:4 [f] S Ge 44:4; S Ps 35:12 **17:14** [g] Mt 5:25-26 **17:15** [h] S Ps 94:21; S Pr 18:5 [i] Ex 23:6-7; Isa 5:23; La 3:34-36 **17:16** [j] Pr 23:23 **17:17** [k] S 2Sa 15:21; Pr 27:10 **17:18** [l] Pr 6:1-5; S 11:15; 22:26-27

17:3 The first line of this verse is repeated in 27:21. *The crucible ... the furnace.* Silver and gold were refined to remove their impurities (see Ps 12:6 and note). *tests the heart.* See 15:11; 16:2 and notes; Jer 17:10. *heart.* See note on Ps 4:7.
17:5 *Whoever mocks the poor shows contempt for their Maker.* See 14:31 and note. *whoever gloats over disaster will not go unpunished.* The people of Edom in particular were condemned for gloating over the collapse of "brother" Jacob/Israel (Ob 10; see Eze 35:12,15; see also Pr 24:17).
17:6 *crown to the aged.* Cf. the "gray hair" of 16:31. To live to see one's grandchildren was considered a great blessing (see Ge 48:11; Ps 128:5–6). *parents are the pride of their children.* See Ge 47:7.
17:7 For the structure of this verse cf. 15:11; 19:7,10; 21:27. *lying lips to a ruler.* The right to rule depends on honesty and justice (see 12:22; 16:12–13).
17:8 *A bribe is seen as a charm.* A sad commentary on human behavior (see 18:16; 21:14; Ecc 10:19). Elsewhere, bribes are condemned (see v. 23; 15:27; 28:16; Ex 23:8; Dt 16:19; 1Sa 12:3; Ecc 7:7; Isa 1:23; Am 5:12; 1Ti 6:10).
17:9 *Whoever would foster love covers over an offense.* See 10:12 and note.
17:10 *rebuke impresses a discerning person.* See 9:8–9. *a hundred lashes a fool.* Fools deserved and received flogging (cf. 10:13; 19:25,29; 26:3; Dt 25:2–3).
17:11 *messenger of death.* See 16:14 and note; cf. the dispatching of Abishai and Joab to end Sheba's rebellion against David (2Sa 20:1–22; see 1Ki 2:25,29,46).
17:12 *bear robbed of her cubs.* Sure to attack you and rip you open (see 2Sa 17:8; Hos 13:8; cf. the raging of the fool in 29:9).
17:13 *Evil will never leave the house.* Such was the fate of David's family after his affair with Bathsheba and the murder of Uriah (see 2Sa 12:10 and note; cf. Jer 18:20–23). *one who pays back evil for good.* Like Nabal, who refused to reward David's men (1Sa 25:21; see Ps 109:5; Ro 12:17–21).
17:15 *Acquitting the guilty.* Perhaps because of a bribe (see v. 8; 24:24).
17:16 *fools have money in hand.* Perhaps to pay the fee for their schooling.
17:17 *friend loves at all times.* See 18:24; cf. David's friendship with Jonathan (2Sa 1:26; see Lev 19:18 and note; Ru 1:16; 1Co 13:4–7).
17:18 See 6:1 and note.
17:19 *Whoever loves a quarrel loves sin.* A "hot-tempered person commits many sins" (29:22). *builds a high gate.* To build strong defenses (to protect something precious) invites attacks. Some, however, render the ambiguous Hebrew as "opens his mouth wide," meaning brags too much and so "invites destruction," including his own (cf. 16:18; 29:23).
17:20 *does not prosper.* Contrast 16:20. *whose tongue is perverse.* See note on 2:12.

21 To have a fool for a child brings grief;
there is no joy for the parent of a godless fool.[m]

22 A cheerful heart is good medicine,
but a crushed[n] spirit dries up the bones.[o]

23 The wicked accept bribes[p] in secret
to pervert the course of justice.[q]

24 A discerning person keeps wisdom in view,
but a fool's eyes[r] wander to the ends of the earth.

25 A foolish son brings grief to his father
and bitterness to the mother who bore him.[s]

26 If imposing a fine on the innocent is not good,[t]
surely to flog honest officials is not right.

27 The one who has knowledge uses words with restraint,[u]
and whoever has understanding is even-tempered.[v]

28 Even fools are thought wise if they keep silent,
and discerning if they hold their tongues.[w]

18 An unfriendly person pursues selfish ends
and against all sound judgment starts quarrels.

2 Fools find no pleasure in understanding
but delight in airing their own opinions.[x]

3 When wickedness comes, so does contempt,
and with shame comes reproach.

4 The words of the mouth are deep waters,[y]
but the fountain of wisdom is a rushing stream.

5 It is not good to be partial to the wicked[z]
and so deprive the innocent of justice.[a]

6 The lips of fools bring them strife,
and their mouths invite a beating.[b]

7 The mouths of fools are their undoing,
and their lips are a snare[c] to their very lives.[d]

8 The words of a gossip are like choice morsels;
they go down to the inmost parts.[e]

9 One who is slack in his work
is brother to one who destroys.[f]

10 The name of the LORD is a fortified tower;[g]
the righteous run to it and are safe.[h]

11 The wealth of the rich is their fortified city;[i]
they imagine it a wall too high to scale.

12 Before a downfall the heart is haughty,
but humility comes before honor.[j]

13 To answer before listening—
that is folly and shame.[k]

14 The human spirit can endure in sickness,
but a crushed spirit who can bear?[l]

17:21 [m]S Pr 10:1 **17:22** [n]S Ps 38:8 [o]S Ex 12:46; Pr 14:30; S 15:13; 18:14 **17:23** [p]S Ex 18:21; S 23:8; S 1Sa 8:3 [q]S Job 34:33 **17:24** [r]S Job 31:1 **17:25** [s]S Pr 10:1 **17:26** [t]S Ps 94:21 **17:27** [u]S Job 6:24 [v]S Pr 14:29 **17:28** [w]S Job 2:13; 13:5; S Pr 10:19 **18:2** [x]S Pr 12:23 **18:4** [y]S Ps 18:16 **18:5** [z]Pr 24:23-25; 28:21 [a]S Ps 82:2; S Pr 17:15 **18:6** [b]S Pr 10:14 **18:7** [c]Ps 140:9 [d]S Ps 64:8; S Pr 10:14; S 12:13; S 13:3; Ecc 10:12 **18:8** [e]Pr 26:22 **18:9** [f]Pr 28:24 **18:10** [g]S Ps 61:3 [h]S Ps 20:1; Pr 14:26 **18:11** [i]Pr 10:15 **18:12** [j]S Pr 11:2; 15:33; S 16:18 **18:13** [k]Pr 20:25 **18:14** [l]S Pr 15:13; S 17:22

17:21 *grief … no joy.* See v. 25; 19:13.
17:22 *cheerful heart.* See 14:30; 15:13,30; 16:15. *crushed spirit dries up the bones.* See notes on 3:8; 14:30; see also 12:4; Ps 32:3.
17:23 *accept bribes.* See note on v. 8.
17:24 *wander to the ends of the earth.* Fools "chase fantasies" (12:11) and are interested in everything except wisdom (cf. Dt 30:11–14).
17:25 See v. 21. *bitterness.* See 14:10 and note.
17:26 *imposing a fine on the innocent.* See v. 15. *flog honest officials.* See v. 10 and note; cf. the beating and disgrace endured by Jeremiah (Jer 20:2; 38:1–6).
17:27 *uses words with restraint.* See 10:19. *even-tempered.* See 16:32 and note.
17:28 *fools are thought wise if they keep silent.* Cf. Job's sarcastic comment in Job 13:5 (see note there).
18:1 *pursues selfish ends.* He is quarrelsome and hot-tempered (cf. 17:14).
18:2 *airing their own opinions.* See Ecc 10:3.
18:3 *shame … reproach.* Cf. 3:35; 6:33; 10:5; 11:2; Ps 31:17.
18:4 *deep waters.* Profound or obscure (cf. 20:5). *fountain of wisdom is a rushing stream.* A wise person's words are refreshing and a source of life (see 1:23; 10:11 and notes).
18:5 *partial to the wicked.* See 17:15 and note. Favoritism of any kind was condemned in the law (see Lev 19:15; Dt 1:17; 16:19). *deprive the innocent of justice.* See 17:26; 31:5; Mal 3:5.
18:6 *bring them strife.* Fools are quick to quarrel (see 17:14,19; 20:3). *invite a beating.* By a rod on their backs (see 10:13; 19:29).
18:7 See 10:14 and note.
18:8 Repeated in 26:22. *words of a gossip are like choice morsels.* They are as pleasant as words of wisdom (cf. 16:21,23), but they promote dissension (see 11:13; 26:20). *they go down to the inmost parts.* Where they are thoroughly digested and so are carried about and live on and on.
18:9 *who is slack in his work.* See 10:4 and note.
18:10 *name of the LORD.* His "name" often equals his "person," since it expresses his nature and qualities (see Ex 3:14–15 and notes). *fortified tower.* See Ps 18:2 and note; 91:2; 144:2. *safe.* See 29:25; Ps 27:5.
18:11 *wealth … is their fortified city.* Identical to the first line in 10:15 (see note there). *wall too high to scale.* But God can bring it down (see Isa 25:12).
18:12 *humility comes before honor.* Identical to the second line in 15:33 (see note there).
18:14 See 15:13; 17:22 and notes.

15 The heart of the discerning acquires
knowledge,[m]
for the ears of the wise seek it out.

16 A gift[n] opens the way
and ushers the giver into the
presence of the great.

17 In a lawsuit the first to speak seems
right,
until someone comes forward and
cross-examines.

18 Casting the lot settles disputes[o]
and keeps strong opponents apart.

19 A brother wronged[p] is more unyielding
than a fortified city;
disputes are like the barred gates of
a citadel.

20 From the fruit of their mouth a
person's stomach is filled;
with the harvest of their lips they are
satisfied.[q]

21 The tongue has the power of life and
death,[r]
and those who love it will eat its
fruit.[s]

22 He who finds a wife finds what is
good[t]
and receives favor from the LORD.[u]

23 The poor plead for mercy,
but the rich answer harshly.

24 One who has unreliable friends soon
comes to ruin,
but there is a friend who sticks
closer than a brother.[v]

19 Better the poor whose walk is
blameless
than a fool whose lips are
perverse.[w]

2 Desire without knowledge is not
good—
how much more will hasty feet miss
the way![x]

18:15 [m]S Pr 15:14 **18:16** [n]S Ge 32:13; S 1Sa 10:4; Pr 19:6 **18:18** [o]S Pr 16:33 **18:19** [p]S 1Sa 17:28 **18:20** [q]S Pr 12:14 **18:21** [r]S Ps 12:4 [s]Pr 13:2-3; S Mt 12:37 **18:22** [t]S Pr 12:4 [u]S Job 33:26; Pr 19:14; 31:10 **18:24** [v]S 1Sa 20:42; Jn 15:13-15 **19:1** [w]Pr 28:6 **19:2** [x]Pr 29:20

19:3 [y]Ps 14:1; Pr 9:13; 24:9; Isa 32:6 [z]Jas 1:13-15 **19:4** [a]ver 7; Pr 14:20 **19:5** [b]S Ex 23:1 [c]S Ps 56:7 [d]ver 9; S Dt 19:19; Pr 21:28 **19:6** [e]Pr 29:26 [f]S Pr 17:8; S 18:16 **19:7** [g]Pr 10:15 [h]S ver 4 **19:8** [i]S Pr 16:20 **19:9** [j]S ver 5; S Dt 19:19 **19:10** [k]Pr 26:1 [l]Pr 30:21-23; Ecc 10:5-7 **19:11** [m]S 2Ki 5:12 **19:12** [n]Pr 20:2 [o]S Ps 133:3 [p]S Est 1:12; S 7:7; Ps 72:5-6; Pr 16:14-15

3 A person's own folly[y] leads to their
ruin,
yet their heart rages against the
LORD.[z]

4 Wealth attracts many friends,
but even the closest friend of the
poor person deserts them.[a]

5 A false witness[b] will not go
unpunished,[c]
and whoever pours out lies will not
go free.[d]

6 Many curry favor with a ruler,[e]
and everyone is the friend of one
who gives gifts.[f]

7 The poor are shunned by all their
relatives—
how much more do their friends
avoid them![g]
Though the poor pursue them with
pleading,
they are nowhere to be found.[a][h]

8 The one who gets wisdom loves life;
the one who cherishes
understanding will soon
prosper.[i]

9 A false witness will not go
unpunished,
and whoever pours out lies will
perish.[j]

10 It is not fitting for a fool[k] to live in
luxury—
how much worse for a slave to rule
over princes![l]

11 A person's wisdom yields patience;[m]
it is to one's glory to overlook an
offense.

12 A king's rage is like the roar of a
lion,[n]
but his favor is like dew[o] on the
grass.[p]

[a] *7* The meaning of the Hebrew for this sentence is uncertain.

18:17 A warning to judges to hear both sides of a case (cf. Dt 1:16), but applicable to many situations.
18:18 *Casting the lot settles disputes.* See 16:33 and note.
18:19 *A brother wronged.* Cf. Esau's anger because of the blessing Jacob received from Isaac (Ge 27:41).
18:20 See 12:14 and note.
18:21 *tongue has the power of life and death.* See notes on 10:19; 13:3; cf. Jas 3:6–10. *its fruit.* See v. 20.
18:22 *who finds a wife finds what is good.* See 12:4 and note; 19:14; 31:10. *receives favor from the LORD.* Identical to the second line in 8:35—where finding wisdom brings the Lord's favor.
18:24 *One who has unreliable friends soon comes to ruin.* One must choose friends carefully (see 12:26 and note; 17:17).
19:1 Almost identical to 28:6. *blameless.* See note on 2:7. *than a fool.* Even if the fool becomes rich (see 28:6).
19:2 *Desire without knowledge.* Cf. Ro 10:2 and note. *hasty.* Haste can lead to poverty (21:5) or folly (29:20). *miss the way.* Fail to achieve one's goal.
19:3 *their heart rages against the LORD.* God is blamed for one's troubles (see Ge 4:5; Isa 8:21; cf. La 3:39).
19:4 See v. 7; 14:20.
19:5,9 See 6:19 and note.
19:6 *curry favor.* Cf. Job 11:19. *friend of one who gives gifts.* Generosity (v. 4) or bribery (17:8) could be in view.
19:7 *The poor are shunned.* See v. 4; 14:20.
19:8 *loves life.* Cf. 8:35–36. *prosper.* See 13:13 and note.
19:10 *not fitting for a fool to live in luxury.* Or to have honor (26:1).
19:11 *patience.* See 14:29; 15:18; 16:32; Ecc 7:9; Jas 1:19. *overlook an offense.* See 12:16; 29:11; 2Sa 16:11–12.
19:12 See 16:14–15 and notes. *A king's rage is like the roar of a lion.* Almost identical to the first line of 20:2.

13 A foolish child is a father's ruin,[q]
and a quarrelsome wife is like
the constant dripping of a leaky
roof.[r]
14 Houses and wealth are inherited from
parents,[s]
but a prudent wife is from the LORD.[t]
15 Laziness brings on deep sleep,
and the shiftless go hungry.[u]
16 Whoever keeps commandments keeps
their life,
but whoever shows contempt for
their ways will die.[v]
17 Whoever is kind to the poor lends to
the LORD,[w]
and he will reward them for what
they have done.[x]
18 Discipline your children, for in that
there is hope;
do not be a willing party to their
death.[y]
19 A hot-tempered person must pay the
penalty;
rescue them, and you will have to do
it again.
20 Listen to advice and accept discipline,[z]
and at the end you will be counted
among the wise.[a]
21 Many are the plans in a person's heart,
but it is the LORD's purpose that
prevails.[b]
22 What a person desires is unfailing love[a];
better to be poor than a liar.
23 The fear of the LORD leads to life;
then one rests content, untouched
by trouble.[c]

19:13 [q]S Pr 10:1 [r]S Est 1:18; Pr 21:9 **19:14** [s]2Co 12:14 [t]S Pr 18:22 **19:15** [u]S Pr 10:4; 20:13 **19:16** [v]S Pr 16:17; S Ro 10:5 **19:17** [w]S Dt 24:14 [x]S Dt 24:19; Pr 14:21; 22:9; S Mt 10:42 **19:18** [y]S Pr 13:24; 23:13-14 **19:20** [z]Pr 4:1 [a]S Pr 12:15 **19:21** [b]Ps 33:11; Pr 16:9; 20:24; Isa 8:10; 14:24, 27; 31:2; 40:8; 46:10; 48:14; 55:11; Jer 44:29; La 3:37 **19:23** [c]S Job 4:7; S Pr 10:27 **19:24** [d]Pr 26:15 **19:25** [e]S Ps 141:5 [f]S Pr 9:9; 21:11 **19:26** [g]Pr 28:24 **19:27** [h]S Pr 1:8 **19:28** [i]S Job 15:16 **19:29** [j]S Dt 25:2 **20:1** [k]S Lev 10:9; Hab 2:5 [l]S 1Sa 25:36 [m]1Ki 20:16 [n]Pr 31:4 **20:2** [o]S Pr 19:12 [p]S Est 7:7; S Pr 16:14 **20:3** [q]S 1Sa 25:25 [r]S Ge 13:8 **20:4** [s]S Pr 6:6 [t]Ecc 10:18

24 A sluggard buries his hand in the dish;
he will not even bring it back to his
mouth![d]
25 Flog a mocker, and the simple will
learn prudence;
rebuke the discerning,[e] and they will
gain knowledge.[f]
26 Whoever robs their father and drives
out their mother[g]
is a child who brings shame and
disgrace.
27 Stop listening to instruction, my son,[h]
and you will stray from the words of
knowledge.
28 A corrupt witness mocks at justice,
and the mouth of the wicked gulps
down evil.[i]
29 Penalties are prepared for mockers,
and beatings for the backs of fools.[j]

20 Wine[k] is a mocker[l] and beer a
brawler;
whoever is led astray[m] by them is
not wise.[n]
2 A king's wrath strikes terror like the
roar of a lion;[o]
those who anger him forfeit their
lives.[p]
3 It is to one's honor to avoid strife,
but every fool[q] is quick to quarrel.[r]
4 Sluggards[s] do not plow in season;
so at harvest time they look but find
nothing.[t]
5 The purposes of a person's heart are
deep waters,[u]

[a] 22 Or *Greed is a person's shame*

20:5 [u]S Ps 18:16

19:13 *foolish child.* See 17:21,25. *quarrelsome wife.* Also denounced in 21:9,19; 25:24; 27:15. Stirring up dissension is condemned throughout Proverbs (see 6:14 and note).
19:14 *prudent wife.* See 12:4 and note; see also 18:22.
19:15 See 6:11; 10:4 and notes.
19:16 See 13:13; 15:10; 16:17 and notes.
19:17 *kind to the poor.* See note on 14:21; see also 14:31. *lends to the LORD.* The Lord regards it as a gift to him (cf. Mt 25:40).
19:18 *Discipline your children … not … to their death.* See note on 13:24.
19:19 *hot-tempered.* Cf. 14:16–17,29; 15:18.
19:21 See 16:1,4,9 and notes.
19:22 *desires … unfailing love.* But such loyalty is difficult to find (cf. 14:22; 20:6). *better to be poor than a liar.* See vv. 1,28; 6:12.
19:23 *fear of the LORD.* See note on 1:7. *leads to life.* See note on 10:11. *untouched by trouble.* See 3:2; 14:26 and notes.
19:24 Almost identical to 26:15. *sluggard.* See note on 6:6.
19:25 *Flog a mocker.* See v. 29; 14:3; 21:11; see also notes on 1:22; 17:10; 21:24. *the simple.* Not to be confused with the mocker (see note on 1:4).
19:26 *robs … father and drives out … mother.* Children were expected to take care of their parents when they were sick or elderly (cf. Isa 51:18). Robbing them (cf. Jdg 17:1–2) and attacking or calling down curses on them (Ex 21:15,17) were serious crimes (see note on Ex 21:17). *shame and disgrace.* See 10:5; 13:5.
19:27 See 5:1–2.
19:28 *corrupt witness.* See v. 5; see also note on 6:19. *gulps down evil.* Cf. the description of those "who drink up evil like water" (Job 15:16; see Job 34:7).
19:29 *Penalties … for mockers.* See v. 25. *beatings for the backs of fools.* See 10:13; 14:3; 26:3.
20:1 *Wine is a mocker and beer a brawler.* Those who overindulge become mockers and brawlers (see Hos 7:5 and note). Proverbs associates drunkenness with poverty (see 23:20–21 and note), strife (23:29–30) and injustice (31:4–5). *Wine … beer.* Wine is fruit alcohol; beer is grain alcohol. *led astray.* See Ge 9:21 and note; Isa 28:7.
20:2 See 16:14; 19:12 and notes.
20:3 *quick to quarrel.* See 6:14; 17:14,19; 18:6.
20:4 *Sluggards.* See note on 6:6. *but find nothing.* See 13:4; 21:25–26.
20:5 *purposes.* Or "motives" (cf. 16:1–2). *deep waters.* Cf. 18:4. *draws them out.* As if from a well.

but one who has insight draws them
out.

[6]Many claim to have unfailing love,
but a faithful person who can find?[v]

[7]The righteous lead blameless lives;[w]
blessed are their children after
them.[x]

[8]When a king sits on his throne to
judge,[y]
he winnows out all evil with his eyes.[z]

[9]Who can say, "I have kept my heart
pure;[a]
I am clean and without sin"?[b]

[10]Differing weights and differing
measures—
the LORD detests them both.[c]

[11]Even small children are known by their
actions,
so is their conduct really pure[d] and
upright?

[12]Ears that hear and eyes that see—
the LORD has made them both.[e]

[13]Do not love sleep or you will grow
poor;[f]
stay awake and you will have food
to spare.

[14]"It's no good, it's no good!" says the
buyer—
then goes off and boasts about the
purchase.

[15]Gold there is, and rubies in abundance,
but lips that speak knowledge are a
rare jewel.

[16]Take the garment of one who puts up
security for a stranger;
hold it in pledge[g] if it is done for an
outsider.[h]

[17]Food gained by fraud tastes sweet,[i]
but one ends up with a mouth full of
gravel.[j]

[18]Plans are established by seeking
advice;
so if you wage war, obtain guidance.[k]

[19]A gossip betrays a confidence;[l]
so avoid anyone who talks too
much.

[20]If someone curses their father or
mother,[m]
their lamp will be snuffed out in
pitch darkness.[n]

[21]An inheritance claimed too soon
will not be blessed at the end.

[22]Do not say, "I'll pay you back for this
wrong!"[o]
Wait for the LORD, and he will
avenge you.[p]

[23]The LORD detests differing weights,
and dishonest scales do not please
him.[q]

[24]A person's steps are directed[r] by the
LORD.[s]
How then can anyone understand
their own way?[t]

[25]It is a trap to dedicate something
rashly
and only later to consider one's
vows.[u]

[26]A wise king winnows out the wicked;
he drives the threshing wheel over
them.[v]

20:6 [v]Ps 12:1 **20:7** [w]S Ps 26:1 [x]Ps 37:25-26; 112:2 **20:8** [y]S 1Ki 7:7 [z]ver 26; Pr 25:4-5 **20:9** [a]S Job 15:14 [b]1Ki 8:46; Ecc 7:20; 1Jn 1:8 **20:10** [c]ver 23; S Pr 11:1 **20:11** [d]S Ps 39:1 **20:12** [e]S Ps 94:9 **20:13** [f]S Pr 6:11; S 19:15 **20:16** [g]S Ex 22:26 [h]Pr 27:13 **20:17** [i]Pr 9:17 [j]Job 20:14; La 3:16 **20:18** [k]Pr 11:14; 24:6 **20:19** [l]Pr 11:13 **20:20** [m]Pr 30:11 [n]Ex 21:17; S Job 18:5 **20:22** [o]Pr 24:29 [p]Isa 37:20; Jer 1:19; 42:11; Ro 12:19 **20:23** [q]S ver 10; S Dt 25:13 **20:24** [r]S Ps 90:12 [s]S Job 33:29 [t]S Pr 19:21; Jer 10:23 **20:25** [u]S Pr 10:19; 18:13; Ecc 5:2, 4-5; Jer 44:25 **20:26** [v]S ver 8

20:6 *unfailing love.* See notes on 19:22; Ps 6:4. *a faithful person who can find?* Cf. Ecc 7:28–29.
20:7 *blameless lives.* See note on 2:7. *blessed are their children.* See 13:22; see also note on 14:26.
20:8 See v. 26 and note. *winnows out all evil.* See 16:10; Ps 11:4.
20:9 *pure ... clean ... without sin.* No one is without sin (cf. Job 14:4; Ro 3:23; 1Jn 1:8,10)—but those whose sins have been forgiven have "clean hands and a pure heart" (Ps 24:4; see also 51:1–2,9–10).
20:10 See note on 11:1; cf. 16:11.
20:12 See Ex 4:11; Ps 94:8–9.
20:13 *sleep ... grow poor.* See 24:33–34.
20:14 *It's no good, it's no good!* Prices were often agreed upon by bargaining, so the buyer is questioning the quality of the article in order to buy it more cheaply.
20:15 *Gold ... rubies.* Wisdom is valued more highly than gold or rubies (3:14–15; 8:10–11).
20:16 Repeated in 27:13. See note on 6:1. *Take the garment.* A garment could be taken as security for a debt (Dt 24:10–13). Anyone who foolishly assumes responsibility for the debt of a stranger, whose reliability is unknown, or of a wayward woman, whose unreliability is known, ought to be held accountable, even to the point of taking their garment as a pledge.
20:17 *tastes sweet.* Cf. the sweet food prepared by the adulterous woman in 9:17. Zophar observes that evil is sweet in the mouth of the wicked but turns sour in their stomachs (Job 20:12–18). See note on 10:2.
20:18 *advice ... guidance.* See 15:22; Lk 14:31.
20:20 *curses their father or mother.* Punishable by death (see 19:26; Ex 21:17 and notes; Lev 20:9; cf. Pr 30:11, 17). *their lamp ... snuffed out.* They will die (see note on 13:9).
20:21 *inheritance claimed too soon will not be blessed.* Cf. 19:26; see the sad experience of the son who "squandered his wealth in wild living" (see Lk 15:12–13 and notes).
20:22 *I'll pay you back.* Vengeance was God's prerogative. He would repay the wicked for their actions (see 24:12,29; Dt 32:35; Ps 94:1 and notes). *Wait for the LORD.* See Ps 27:14 and note; 37:34.
20:23 See v. 10 and note.
20:24 See notes on 3:5–6; 16:9.
20:25 *dedicate something.* Promise to make a special gift to the Lord if he answers an earnest request (see Lev 27:1–25; 1Sa 1:11). *rashly.* See Dt 23:21; Jdg 11:30–31,34–35 and note on 11:30. When a vow was made hastily, it was sometimes not carried out (cf. Ecc 5:4–6 and note on 5:6).
20:26 See v. 8. *winnows.* See note on Ru 1:22. *threshing wheel.* The wheel of the threshing cart that separated the grain from

27 The human spirit is[a] the lamp of the
LORD[w]
that sheds light on one's inmost
being.[x]

28 Love and faithfulness keep a king safe;
through love[y] his throne is made
secure.[z]

29 The glory of young men is their
strength,
gray hair the splendor of the old.[a]

30 Blows and wounds scrub[b] away evil,
and beatings[c] purge the inmost
being.

21 In the LORD's hand the king's
heart is a stream of water
that he channels toward all who
please him.[d]

2 A person may think their own ways are
right,
but the LORD weighs the heart.[e]

3 To do what is right and just
is more acceptable to the LORD than
sacrifice.[f]

4 Haughty eyes[g] and a proud heart—
the unplowed field of the wicked—
produce sin.

5 The plans of the diligent lead to
profit[h]
as surely as haste leads to poverty.

6 A fortune made by a lying tongue
is a fleeting vapor and a deadly
snare.[b][i]

7 The violence of the wicked will drag
them away,[j]
for they refuse to do what is right.

8 The way of the guilty is devious,[k]
but the conduct of the innocent is
upright.

9 Better to live on a corner of the roof
than share a house with a
quarrelsome wife.[l]

10 The wicked crave evil;
their neighbors get no mercy from
them.

11 When a mocker is punished, the
simple gain wisdom;
by paying attention to the wise they
get knowledge.[m]

12 The Righteous One[c] takes note of the
house of the wicked
and brings the wicked to ruin.[n]

13 Whoever shuts their ears to the cry of
the poor
will also cry out[o] and not be
answered.[p]

14 A gift given in secret soothes anger,
and a bribe concealed in the cloak
pacifies great wrath.[q]

15 When justice is done, it brings joy to
the righteous
but terror to evildoers.[r]

20:27 [w] S Ps 119:105 [x] S Pr 16:2 **20:28** [y] Ps 40:11 [z] S Pr 16:12; Isa 16:5 **20:29** [a] Pr 16:31 **20:30** [b] S Ps 51:2; Pr 22:15 [c] Isa 1:5 **21:1** [d] Est 5:1; Jer 39:11-12 **21:2** [e] S Pr 16:2 **21:3** [f] S 1Sa 15:22; Isa 1:11; Mic 6:6-8 **21:4** [g] S Job 41:34 **21:5** [h] S Pr 10:4 **21:6** [i] S Pr 10:2 **21:7** [j] S Pr 11:5 **21:8** [k] S Pr 2:15 **21:9** [l] ver 19; Pr 19:13; 25:24 **21:11** [m] S Pr 19:25 **21:12** [n] S Pr 14:11 **21:13** [o] S Ex 11:6 [p] S Job 29:12 **21:14** [q] S Ge 32:20 **21:15** [r] S Pr 10:29

[a] 27 Or *A person's words are* [b] 6 Some Hebrew manuscripts, Septuagint and Vulgate; most Hebrew manuscripts *vapor for those who seek death* [c] 12 Or *The righteous person*

---

the husk (cf. Isa 28:27–28). The wicked will be separated from the righteous and duly punished.

20:27 See 27:19 and note; cf. 15:11; Heb 4:12–13 and notes.

20:28 *Love and faithfulness.* See 3:3; 14:22; Ps 26:3 and note. *keep a king safe ... secure.* Benevolence and kindness endear a king to his people and encourage them to be loyal subjects (cf. 16:12 and note).

20:29 *their strength.* Cf. Jer 9:23. *gray hair the splendor of the old.* See 16:31 and note.

20:30 *Blows and wounds scrub away evil.* Stern punishment is necessary to restrain evil. Proverbs often refers to fools whose backs are beaten (10:13; 14:3; 19:29; 26:3), but even then, because they are fools, they may not change their ways (cf. 17:10; see 27:22 and note).

21:1 *In the LORD's hand the king's heart.* God controls the lives and actions even of kings, such as Nebuchadnezzar (Da 4:31–32,35) and Cyrus (Isa 45:1–7; cf. Ezr 6:22; cf. also Ro 13:1–6 and notes). *channels toward all who please him.* Cf. 16:1,4,9 and notes.

21:2 *think their own ways are right.* See 14:12; 16:2. *weighs the heart.* See 16:2; 24:12; Job 31:6 and notes. Ancient Egyptian paintings depict a deity weighing a human heart on scales to determine whether the weight of its sins is heavier than a feather.

21:3 *what is right and just.* See note on Ps 119:121. *more acceptable ... than sacrifice.* A theme also found in the Prophets (see Isa 1:11–15 and note). See v. 27; see also note on 15:8.

21:4 *Haughty eyes.* See note on 6:17. *proud heart.* See 16:5,18.

21:5 *plans of the diligent lead to profit.* See note on 10:4. *haste.* Either rash actions (see 19:2 and note) or a desire to get rich quick (see 13:11 and note; 20:21; 28:20).

21:6 *fortune made by a lying tongue.* See note on 10:2; cf. 19:1. *fleeting vapor.* See 13:11; Ecc 1:14 and notes. *deadly snare.* Cf. 5:22; 7:23.

21:7 *violence of the wicked will drag them away.* See 1:18–19 and notes.

21:9 Repeated in 25:24. *corner of the roof.* Roofs were flat, and small rooms could be built there (see 2Ki 4:10). *quarrelsome wife.* See 19:13 and note.

21:10 *crave evil.* See 4:16; 10:23. *their neighbors get no mercy.* Cf. 14:21.

21:11 See 19:25 and note.

21:12 Cf. Job 34:17. *house of the wicked ... to ruin.* See 10:25 and note; 14:11.

21:13 *cry of the poor.* See note on 14:21; see also 28:27. *also cry out and not be answered.* See note on 1:28. Cf. the fate of the rich man (Lk 16:19–31) and the unmerciful servant (Mt 18:23–35). Contrast Ps 118:5 (see note there).

21:14 *gift ... bribe.* See note on 17:8; see also 18:16; 19:6. *soothes anger ... wrath.* Perhaps that of an offended party (see 6:34–35).

21:15 *joy to the righteous.* See 11:10 and note. *terror to evildoers.* See 10:29 and note; Ro 13:3.

16 Whoever strays from the path of
prudence
comes to rest in the company of the
dead.[s]

17 Whoever loves pleasure will become
poor;
whoever loves wine and olive oil
will never be rich.[t]

18 The wicked become a ransom[u] for the
righteous,
and the unfaithful for the upright.

19 Better to live in a desert
than with a quarrelsome and
nagging wife.[v]

20 The wise store up choice food and
olive oil,
but fools gulp theirs down.

21 Whoever pursues righteousness and
love
finds life, prosperity[a][w] and honor.[x]

22 One who is wise can go up against the
city of the mighty[y]
and pull down the stronghold in
which they trust.

23 Those who guard their mouths[z] and
their tongues
keep themselves from calamity.[a]

24 The proud and arrogant person[b]—
"Mocker" is his name—
behaves with insolent fury.

25 The craving of a sluggard will be the
death of him,[c]
because his hands refuse to
work.

26 All day long he craves for more,
but the righteous[d] give without
sparing.[e]

27 The sacrifice of the wicked is
detestable[f]—
how much more so when brought
with evil intent![g]

28 A false witness[h] will perish,[i]
but a careful listener will testify
successfully.

29 The wicked put up a bold front,
but the upright give thought to their
ways.[j]

30 There is no wisdom,[k] no insight, no
plan
that can succeed against the
LORD.[l]

31 The horse is made ready for the day
of battle,
but victory rests with the LORD.[m]

22 A good name is more desirable
than great riches;
to be esteemed is better than silver
or gold.[n]

2 Rich and poor have this in common:
The LORD is the Maker of them all.[o]

3 The prudent see danger and take
refuge,[p]
but the simple keep going and pay
the penalty.[q]

4 Humility is the fear of the LORD;
its wages are riches and honor[r] and
life.[s]

21:16 [s]Eze 18:24 **21:17** [t]Pr 23:20-21, 29-35 **21:18** [u]Pr 11:8; Isa 43:3 **21:19** [v]S ver 9 **21:21** [w]Ps 25:13 [x]Mt 5:6 **21:22** [y]S Pr 8:14 **21:23** [z]S Ps 34:13 [a]S Pr 10:19; 12:13; S 13:3 **21:24** [b]Jer 43:2 **21:25** [c]Pr 13:4 **21:26** [d]S 2Sa 17:27 [e]S Lev 25:35 **21:27** [f]S 1Ki 14:24 [g]S Pr 15:8 **21:28** [h]Isa 29:21 [i]S Pr 19:5 **21:29** [j]S Pr 14:8 **21:30** [k]S Job 12:13; S 15:25 [l]S 2Ch 13:12; S Job 5:13; Isa 8:10 **21:31** [m]Ps 33:12-19; Isa 31:1 **22:1** [n]Ecc 7:1 **22:2** [o]S Job 31:15; Pr 29:13; Mt 5:45 **22:3** [p]S Pr 14:16 [q]Pr 27:12 **22:4** [r]S Pr 15:33 [s]S Pr 10:27; Da 4:36

[a] 21 Or *righteousness*

21:16 Graphically illustrated by a man who succumbs to an adulterous woman (see 2:18 and note; 5:23; 7:22–23; 9:18).
21:17 *wine and olive oil.* Both were associated with lavish feasting (see 23:20–21; Am 6:6). Olive oil was also used in various lotions or perfumes, some of which were very expensive (Jn 12:5).
21:18 *The wicked become a ransom for the righteous.* Close to the thought of 11:8. In Isa 43:3–4 God gave three nations to Persia in exchange for Persia's willingness to release the exiles of Judah (see note on Isa 43:3).
21:19 See 19:13 and note.
21:20 *store up choice food.* See 3:10 and note; 8:21. *olive oil.* See note on v. 17; see also Dt 7:13.
21:21 *pursues righteousness.* See 15:9 and note. *finds life.* See 10:2 and note. *life, prosperity and honor.* Benefits for those who seek wisdom (see note on 3:2; see also 3:16; 8:18; cf. 22:4).
21:22 *wise ... pull down the stronghold.* Probably another way of saying, "Wisdom is better than strength" (Ecc 9:16). Cf. 24:5; cf. also 2Co 10:4, where spiritual weapons "have divine power to demolish strongholds."
21:23 See 13:3 and note; 18:21.
21:24 *"Mocker" is his name.* See note on 1:22. God mocks and punishes such a person for their "insolent fury" (cf. v. 11; 3:34; 19:25,29).
21:25 *craving of a sluggard.* See notes on 6:6; 13:4.
21:26 *give without sparing.* The righteous are prosperous, so they can share with those in need (see Ps 37:25–26; 112:9; cf. Eph 4:28).
21:27 *The sacrifice of the wicked is detestable.* See notes on v. 3; 15:8.
21:28 *false witness will perish.* See 19:5,9.
21:29 *bold front.* Cf. the behavior of the adulterous woman in 7:13.
21:30 *no plan that can succeed against the LORD.* Because he is sovereign and controls people and nations (see v. 1; 16:4,9 and notes; 19:21; 1Co 3:19–20).
21:31 *horse.* God often cautions against trusting in horses and chariots for victory (e.g., Ps 20:7; 33:16–17; Hos 1:7; cf. Dt 17:16; Isa 31:1–3). *victory rests with the LORD.* See 1Sa 17:47; Ps 3:8 and notes.
22:1 *good name.* Its value is recognized also in 3:4; 10:7; Ecc 7:1. *better than silver or gold.* Like the possession of wisdom (see 3:14 and note; 16:16).
22:2 *Maker of them all.* See 14:31 and note.
22:3 *prudent ... take refuge.* Cf. 14:8. *simple.* See note on 1:4; see also 9:16.
22:4 See 18:12. *Humility is the fear of the LORD.* Associated also in 15:33 (see note on 1:7). *riches and honor and life.* Benefits for those who seek wisdom (see note on 3:2; see also 3:16; 8:18; cf. 21:21).

REWARDS, NOT PROMISES

Proverbs often holds out the stick and the carrot to motivate people to the best type of behavior and attitudes. Those actions it characterizes as wise often are accompanied by reward, and those it characterizes as foolish are said to result in punishment. Indeed, the ultimate reward for wise behavior is life, and for foolish behavior is death.

However, these rewards and punishments are often misunderstood by modern readers, who take them as promises. The proverb form is not in the business of giving out guarantees. For instance, consider Proverbs 22:6:

Start children off on the way they should go,
and even when they are old they will
not turn from it.

This proverb provides strong motivation for a parent to provide proper education. "The way they should go" is defined by the values and principles in Proverbs. But what exactly does the second part of the proverb tell us? Again, Proverbs does not give promises; rather, it tells us the best course to a desired end, all things being equal. Of course, children are more likely to be godly if they are trained in such a way. But other factors may enter in. Perhaps the child will fall in with a bad peer group against the advice of the parents (see 1:8–19). The parents should nonetheless follow the advice of 22:6 and increase the likelihood that their children will stay on the right path.

"Menna's Lament" deals with a headstrong child who ignores his father's advice.

Kim Walton, courtesy of the Oriental Institute Museum

5 In the paths of the wicked are snares
and pitfalls,[t]
but those who would preserve their
life stay far from them.

6 Start[u] children off on the way they
should go,[v]
and even when they are old they will
not turn from it.[w]

7 The rich rule over the poor,
and the borrower is slave to the
lender.

8 Whoever sows injustice reaps
calamity,[x]
and the rod they wield in fury will
be broken.[y]

9 The generous will themselves be
blessed,[z]
for they share their food with the
poor.[a]

10 Drive out the mocker, and out goes
strife;
quarrels and insults are
ended.[b]

11 One who loves a pure heart and who
speaks with grace
will have the king for a friend.[c]

12 The eyes of the LORD keep watch over
knowledge,
but he frustrates the words of the
unfaithful.

22:5 [t]Pr 15:19
22:6 [u]S Ge 14:14 [v]Eph 6:4 [w]S Dt 6:7
22:8 [x]S Ex 1:20; S Job 4:8; Gal 6:7-8 [y]Hos 8:7
22:9 [z]S Dt 14:29 [a]S Pr 11:25; S 19:17; 28:27
22:10 [b]Pr 26:20
22:11 [c]Pr 16:13; Mt 5:8

22:5 *snares and pitfalls.* Evil (cf. 15:19). *stay far from them.* By taking the "highway of the upright" (16:17).

22:6 A proverb, not a prophecy or promise (see Introduction: The Nature of a Proverb; see also essay above). *Start children off.* Cf. Ge 18:19. Instruction (1:8) and discipline (22:15) are primarily involved. *way they should go.* The right way, the way of wisdom (see 4:11 and note). *old.* Or "grown."

22:7 *The rich.* See note on 10:15. *the borrower is slave to the lender.* One of the reasons why putting up security for someone else (v. 26) was frowned upon (cf. Ne 5:4–5).

22:8 *Whoever sows injustice reaps calamity.* See 12:21. "A man reaps what he sows" (Gal 6:7; see also Hos 8:7 and note). *rod they wield in fury.* Their ability to oppress others (see Ps 125:3 and note; Isa 14:5–6).

22:9 *The generous will … be blessed.* See note on 11:25. *share their food.* See 14:21 and note; see also Dt 15:7–11.

22:10 *Drive out the mocker.* See note on 1:22; cf. Ge 21:9–10. *out goes strife … insults.* Cf. 17:14; 18:3; 20:3.

22:11 *pure heart.* Cf. Ps 24:4. *speaks with grace.* Characteristic of the wise in Ecc 10:12. *king for a friend.* Cf. v. 29.

22:12 *The eyes of the LORD keep watch.* See 5:21; 15:3; Job 31:4; 34:21; Ps 121:3–8; Jer 16:17; Heb 4:13. *over knowledge.* God protects those who have knowledge (cf. Ps 1:6; 34:15).

13 The sluggard says, "There's a lion
outside![d]
I'll be killed in the public square!"

14 The mouth of an adulterous woman is
a deep pit;[e]
a man who is under the LORD's
wrath falls into it.[f]

15 Folly is bound up in the heart of a
child,
but the rod of discipline will drive it
far away.[g]

16 One who oppresses the poor to
increase his wealth
and one who gives gifts to the rich—
both come to poverty.

Thirty Sayings of the Wise

Saying 1

17 Pay attention[h] and turn your ear to the
sayings of the wise;[i]
apply your heart to what I teach,[j]
18 for it is pleasing when you keep them
in your heart
and have all of them ready on your
lips.
19 So that your trust may be in the
LORD,
I teach you today, even you.
20 Have I not written thirty sayings for
you,
sayings of counsel and knowledge,
21 teaching you to be honest and to speak
the truth,[k]
so that you bring back truthful
reports
to those you serve?

Saying 2

22 Do not exploit the poor[l] because
they are poor
and do not crush the needy in
court,[m]
23 for the LORD will take up their
case[n]
and will exact life for life.[o]

Saying 3

24 Do not make friends with a hot-
tempered person,
do not associate with one easily
angered,
25 or you may learn their ways
and get yourself ensnared.[p]

Saying 4

26 Do not be one who shakes hands
in pledge[q]
or puts up security for
debts;
27 if you lack the means to pay,
your very bed will be snatched
from under you.[r]

Saying 5

28 Do not move an ancient boundary
stone[s]
set up by your ancestors.

Saying 6

29 Do you see someone skilled[t] in their
work?
They will serve[u] before kings;[v]
they will not serve before officials
of low rank.

22:13 [d] Pr 26:13 **22:14** [e] S Pr 5:3-5; 23:27 [f] Ecc 7:26 **22:15** [g] S Pr 13:24; S 20:30 **22:17** [h] S Pr 1:8 [i] S Pr 1:6; 30:1; 31:1 [j] S Pr 2:2 **22:21** [k] Ecc 12:10 **22:22** [l] S Lev 25:17; S Job 5:16 [m] S Ex 23:6 **22:23** [n] S Job 29:16; Ps 140:12 [o] Est 8:1; S 9:1; Pr 23:10-11 **22:25** [p] 1Co 15:33 **22:26** [q] Pr 6:1-5 **22:27** [r] S Pr 11:15; S 17:18 **22:28** [s] S Dt 19:14 **22:29** [t] S 1Ki 11:28 [u] S Ge 41:46 [v] S Ge 39:4

---

frustrates ... the unfaithful. Overrules their plans and desires (see 16:9; 21:30 and notes).
22:13 The sluggard (see note on 6:6) creates excuses to avoid work (see 26:13).
22:14 *mouth of an adulterous woman.* Her seductive words (see note on 5:3; see also 2:16; 7:5). *deep pit.* Perhaps a well or a hunter's trap (see 5:22 and note; 7:22; 23:27).
22:15 *rod of discipline.* See note on 13:24.
22:16 *oppresses the poor.* Condemned also in 14:31; 28:3. *gives gifts to the rich.* Perhaps bribes (see 17:8 and note; 18:16; 19:6). *poverty.* See 21:5; 28:22 and note.
22:17—24:22 A new section that returns more to the style of chs. 1–9. For its relationship to the Egyptian "Wisdom of Amenemope," see Introduction: Date. Pr 22:17–21 forms the introduction to this section and is also to be numbered as the first "*Saying*"—as in Amenemope. It emphasizes the importance of wisdom (v. 17) and "knowledge" (v. 20): "Teach" (vv. 17,19) and "teaching" (v. 21) are derived from the same root as the Hebrew for "knowledge."
22:17 *Pay attention and turn your ear to.* See 4:20; 5:1. *sayings of the wise.* See 24:23; a title, like "proverbs of Solomon" in 10:1. *apply your heart to.* See 23:12; Ps 4:7 and notes; Pr 24:32. The opening saying of Amenemope begins similarly: "Give your ears, hear ... give your heart to understand."
22:18 *it is pleasing.* See 2:10; 16:24 and notes.
22:19 *that your trust may be in the LORD.* See note on 3:5.
22:20 *thirty sayings.* There are 30 units in 22:17—24:22. The separate units are marked off by numbered sayings in the NIV text. Most of them are two or three verses long, but see 22:17–21 and 23:29–35. The Egyptian "Wisdom of Amenemope" also contains 30 sections (see chart, p. xxii).
22:21 *those you serve.* Possibly parents or guardians.
22:22 *Do not exploit the poor.* See v. 16; 14:31. *do not crush the needy in court.* See Isa 1:17 and note.
22:23 *the LORD will take up their case.* See 23:11 and note; Ps 12:5; 140:12; Isa 3:13–15; Mal 3:5. *will exact life for life.* See Ex 22:21–27 and note.
22:24 *Do not make friends.* Cf. 12:26. *hot-tempered.* The characteristics of "hot-tempered" people are given in 14:16–17; 15:18; 29:22.
22:25 *may learn their ways.* "Bad company corrupts good character" (1Co 15:33). *ensnared.* See note on 5:22; see also 12:13; 13:14; 29:6.
22:26 See note on 6:1.
22:27 *your very bed will be snatched from ... you.* You will be reduced to poverty.
22:28 *ancient boundary stone.* See 15:25 and note.
22:29 *skilled in their work.* Artisans were considered to be wise (see note on 8:30; see also Ex 35:30—36:2). *serve before kings.* Like Joseph, an administrator (Ge 41:46); David, a musician (1Sa 16:21–23); and Huram, a worker in bronze (1Ki 7:13–14).

Saying 7

23 When you sit to dine with a ruler,
note well what[a] is before you,
2 and put a knife to your throat
if you are given to gluttony.
3 Do not crave his delicacies,[w]
for that food is deceptive.

Saying 8

4 Do not wear yourself out to get rich;
do not trust your own cleverness.
5 Cast but a glance at riches, and they
are gone,[x]
for they will surely sprout wings
and fly off to the sky like an eagle.[y]

Saying 9

6 Do not eat the food of a begrudging
host,
do not crave his delicacies;[z]
7 for he is the kind of person
who is always thinking about the
cost.[b]
"Eat and drink," he says to you,
but his heart is not with you.
8 You will vomit up the little you have
eaten
and will have wasted your
compliments.

Saying 10

9 Do not speak to fools,
for they will scorn your prudent
words.[a]

Saying 11

10 Do not move an ancient boundary
stone[b]
or encroach on the fields of the
fatherless,
11 for their Defender[c] is strong;[d]
he will take up their case against
you.[e]

Saying 12

12 Apply your heart to instruction[f]
and your ears to words of
knowledge.

Saying 13

13 Do not withhold discipline from a child;
if you punish them with the rod,
they will not die.
14 Punish them with the rod
and save them from death.[g]

Saying 14

15 My son, if your heart is wise,
then my heart will be glad indeed;
16 my inmost being will rejoice
when your lips speak what is right.[h]

Saying 15

17 Do not let your heart envy[i] sinners,
but always be zealous for the fear of
the LORD.
18 There is surely a future hope for you,
and your hope will not be cut off.[j]

Saying 16

19 Listen, my son,[k] and be wise,
and set your heart on the right path:
20 Do not join those who drink too much
wine[l]
or gorge themselves on meat,
21 for drunkards and gluttons become
poor,[m]
and drowsiness clothes them in rags.

23:3 [w] ver 6-8; Ps 141:4 **23:5** [x] S Mt 6:19 [y] Pr 27:24 **23:6** [z] ver 1-3; Ps 141:4 **23:9** [a] S Pr 9:7 **23:10** [b] S Dt 19:14 **23:11** [c] S Job 19:25 [d] Ps 24:8 [e] Ex 22:22-24; Pr 15:25; 22:22-23 **23:12** [f] S Pr 2:2 **23:14** [g] S Pr 13:24; S 19:18 **23:16** [h] ver 24; Pr 27:11; 29:3 **23:17** [i] S Ps 37:1; S 73:3 **23:18** [j] S Ps 9:18; 37:1-4; Pr 24:14, 19-20 **23:19** [k] Dt 4:9; Pr 28:7 **23:20** [l] Isa 5:11, 22; 56:12; Hab 2:15 **23:21** [m] S Pr 21:17

[a] *1* Or *who* [b] *7* Or *for as he thinks within himself, / so he is*; or *for as he puts on a feast, / so he is*

23:2 *gluttony.* Cf. the similar warning in vv. 20–21.

23:3 *Do not crave his delicacies.* Repeated in a different context in v. 6. *deceptive.* Perhaps the meaning is that the ruler wants to obligate you in some way, even to influence you to support a wicked scheme (cf. Ps 141:4).

23:4 *Do not wear yourself out to get rich.* The desire to get rich can ruin a person physically and spiritually. "For the love of money is a root of all kinds of evil" (1Ti 6:10; cf. 15:27; 28:20; Heb 13:5).

23:5 *riches ... are gone.* Our trust must be in God, not in riches (see Jer 17:11; Lk 12:20–21; 1Ti 6:7–10,17).

23:6 *begrudging host.* One "eager to get rich" (28:22).

23:7 See NIV text note. *his heart is not with you.* Cf. 26:24–25. *heart.* See vv. 12,15,17,19,26; Ps 4:7 and note.

23:8 *vomit.* Out of disgust at the attitude of the host.

23:9 *scorn your prudent words.* Fools "despise wisdom" (1:7) and hate knowledge and correction (1:22; 12:1). They heap abuse on one who rebukes them (9:7).

23:10 *ancient boundary stone.* See note on 15:25; see also 22:28 and photo, p. 1026. *fatherless.* Oppressing the widow and the fatherless is strongly denounced (see Isa 10:2; Jer 22:3; Zec 7:10 and note).

23:11 *Defender.* Guardian-redeemer or protector, someone who helped close relatives regain land (see Lev 25:25 and note) or who avenged their death (Nu 35:12,19). God is a "father to the fatherless, a defender of widows" (Ps 68:5). See notes on Ru 2:20; Isa 41:14; Jer 31:11; see also Jer 50:34. *will take up their case.* See Ps 12:5; 140:12; Isa 3:13–15; Mal 3:5.

23:12 *Apply your heart to.* An echo of 22:17.

23:13–14 See 13:24 and note.

23:15 See 10:1 and note; see also v. 24; 27:11; 29:3. *My son.* See 1:8 and note.

23:16 *what is right.* The Hebrew word for this phrase is translated "smoothly" in v. 31. The same lips can be blessed by producing "right" speech or cursed by savoring wine that goes down "smoothly."

23:17 *Do not ... envy sinners.* See 3:31; 24:1,19. *fear of the LORD.* See notes on 1:7; 3:7.

23:18 *future hope.* See 24:14,20; Ps 37:37; Jer 29:11.

23:19 *right path.* Cf. 4:25–26.

23:20 *Do not join.* See 1:15; 12:26 and note. *those who drink too much wine.* Drunkenness is also condemned in vv. 29–35; 20:1 (see note there); cf. Dt 21:20; Mt 24:49; Lk 21:34; Ro 13:13; Eph 5:18; 1Ti 3:3.

23:21 *gluttons.* See v. 2; 28:7; cf. Mt 11:19. *become poor.* See 21:17. *drowsiness.* Cf. the poverty that overtakes the sluggard in 6:9–11 (see notes there).

Saying 17

22 Listen to your father, who gave you life,
and do not despise your mother when she is old.[n]
23 Buy the truth and do not sell it—
wisdom, instruction and insight as well.[o]
24 The father of a righteous child has great joy;
a man who fathers a wise son rejoices in him.[p]
25 May your father and mother rejoice;
may she who gave you birth be joyful![q]

Saying 18

26 My son,[r] give me your heart
and let your eyes delight in my ways,[s]
27 for an adulterous woman is a deep pit,[t]
and a wayward wife is a narrow well.
28 Like a bandit she lies in wait[u]
and multiplies the unfaithful among men.

Saying 19

29 Who has woe? Who has sorrow?
Who has strife? Who has complaints?
Who has needless bruises? Who has bloodshot eyes?
30 Those who linger over wine,[v]
who go to sample bowls of mixed wine.
31 Do not gaze at wine when it is red,
when it sparkles in the cup,
when it goes down smoothly!
32 In the end it bites like a snake
and poisons like a viper.
33 Your eyes will see strange sights,
and your mind will imagine confusing things.
34 You will be like one sleeping on the high seas,
lying on top of the rigging.
35 "They hit me," you will say, "but I'm not hurt!
They beat me, but I don't feel it!
When will I wake up
so I can find another drink?"[w]

Saying 20

24 Do not envy[x] the wicked,
do not desire their company;
2 for their hearts plot violence,[y]
and their lips talk about making trouble.[z]

Saying 21

3 By wisdom a house is built,[a]
and through understanding it is established;
4 through knowledge its rooms are filled
with rare and beautiful treasures.[b]

Saying 22

5 The wise prevail through great power,
and those who have knowledge muster their strength.
6 Surely you need guidance to wage war,
and victory is won through many advisers.[c]

Saying 23

7 Wisdom is too high for fools;
in the assembly at the gate they must not open their mouths.

Saying 24

8 Whoever plots evil
will be known as a schemer.

23:22 [n]S Lev 19:32 **23:23** [o]Pr 4:7; 17:16 **23:24** [p]S ver 15-16 **23:25** [q]S Pr 10:1 **23:26** [r]Pr 5:1-6 [s]S Ps 18:21 **23:27** [t]S Pr 22:14 **23:28** [u]Pr 7:11-12 **23:30** [v]ver 20-21; Isa 5:11 **23:35** [w]Pr 20:1 **24:1** [x]Pr 3:31-32; 23:17-18 **24:2** [y]S Ps 2:1; Isa 32:6; 55:7-8; 59:7; 65:2; 66:18; Hos 4:1 [z]Ps 10:7 **24:3** [a]S Pr 14:1 **24:4** [b]S Pr 8:21 **24:6** [c]S Pr 11:14; S 20:18; Lk 14:31

23:22 *do not despise your mother.* Cf. 1:8; 10:1; 15:20; 30:17.
23:23 *Buy the truth ... wisdom ... insight.* See 4:5; see also 4:7 and note.
23:24–25 See v. 15; 27:11; see also 10:1 and note.
23:27 *deep pit ... narrow well.* From which it is difficult to escape. *deep pit.* See note on 22:14. *wayward wife.* See note on 2:16; see also 5:20; 7:18–20. *well.* The same metaphor is used of women in general in the Akkadian "Pessimistic Dialogue" (see chart, p. xxiv).
23:28 *lies in wait.* See 6:26; 7:12; Ecc 7:26. *multiplies the unfaithful.* Cf. 7:26.
23:29–35 A vivid description of the physical and psychological effects of drunkenness.
23:29 *Who has woe?* Cf. the woes pronounced on drunkards in Isa 5:11,22. *strife.* See 20:1 and note. *bruises.* Cf. the "beatings for the backs of fools" in 19:29.
23:30 *linger over wine.* Drink too much (see v. 20; 1Sa 25:36). *mixed wine.* Wine mixed with spices (see 9:2; Ps 75:8; Isa 5:22 and notes).
23:32 *bites like a snake.* Death will be the result (cf. Nu 21:6).
23:33 *see strange sights ... imagine confusing things.* Perhaps a reference to the delirium that afflicts the alcoholic.
23:34 *You will be like one sleeping on the high seas.* Your head will be spinning.
23:35 *They beat me, but I don't feel it!* Cf. the condition of Israel in Jer 5:3. *so I can find another drink.* Pain and misery do not prevent drunkards from repeating their folly (cf. 26:11; 27:22; Isa 56:12; Am 4:1).
24:1 *Do not envy.* See v. 19; Ps 37:1. *do not desire their company.* See 1:15; 12:26 and note; 23:20.
24:2 *plot violence.* See 1:11; 6:14; Job 15:35; Ps 5:9 and notes; 38:12.
24:3 *house.* Symbolic of the life of an individual or a family. *is built.* Cf. the similar expression in 9:1.
24:4 *rare and beautiful treasures.* Wisdom promises to bestow wealth on those who love her (8:21).
24:5 *wise ... knowledge.* An echo of 22:17–21. *prevail through great power.* See note on 21:22.
24:7 *gate.* See note on 1:21.
24:8 *plots evil.* See v. 2 and note. *schemer.* Cf. "those who devise wicked schemes" (12:2; cf. also 14:17).

9 The schemes of folly are sin,
and people detest a mocker.

Saying 25

10 If you falter in a time of trouble,
how small is your strength![d]
11 Rescue those being led away to death;
hold back those staggering toward
slaughter.[e]
12 If you say, "But we knew nothing
about this,"
does not he who weighs[f] the heart
perceive it?
Does not he who guards your life know
it?
Will he not repay[g] everyone
according to what they have
done?[h]

Saying 26

13 Eat honey, my son, for it is good;
honey from the comb is sweet to
your taste.
14 Know also that wisdom is like honey
for you:
If you find it, there is a future hope
for you,
and your hope will not be cut off.[i]

Saying 27

15 Do not lurk like a thief near the house
of the righteous,
do not plunder their dwelling place;
16 for though the righteous fall seven
times, they rise again,
but the wicked stumble when
calamity strikes.[j]

Saying 28

17 Do not gloat[k] when your enemy falls;
when they stumble, do not let your
heart rejoice,[l]
18 or the LORD will see and disapprove
and turn his wrath away from
them.[m]

Saying 29

19 Do not fret[n] because of evildoers
or be envious of the wicked,
20 for the evildoer has no future hope,
and the lamp of the wicked will be
snuffed out.[o]

Saying 30

21 Fear the LORD and the king,[p] my son,
and do not join with rebellious
officials,
22 for those two will send sudden
destruction[q] on them,
and who knows what calamities
they can bring?

Further Sayings of the Wise

23 These also are sayings of the wise:[r]

To show partiality[s] in judging is not
good:[t]
24 Whoever says to the guilty, "You are
innocent,"[u]
will be cursed by peoples and
denounced by nations.
25 But it will go well with those who
convict the guilty,
and rich blessing will come on them.

26 An honest answer
is like a kiss on the lips.

27 Put your outdoor work in order
and get your fields ready;
after that, build your house.

28 Do not testify against your neighbor
without cause[v] —
would you use your lips to mislead?

24:10 [d] S Job 4:5 **24:11** [e] Ps 82:4 **24:12** [f] S 1Sa 2:3; S Ps 139:2 [g] S Ps 54:5 [h] Job 34:11; Ps 62:12; S Mt 16:27; Ro 2:6* **24:14** [i] Ps 119:103; Pr 16:24; 23:18 **24:16** [j] S Job 5:19; S Ps 34:21 **24:17** [k] Ob 1:12 [l] S 2Sa 3:32; Mic 7:8 **24:18** [m] S Job 31:29 **24:19** [n] Ps 37:1 **24:20** [o] S Job 18:5; S Pr 23:17-18 **24:21** [p] Ro 13:1-5 **24:22** [q] S Ps 73:19 **24:23** [r] S Pr 1:6 [s] S Ex 18:16; S Lev 19:15 [t] Ps 72:2; Pr 28:21; 31:8-9; Jer 22:16 **24:24** [u] S Pr 17:15 **24:28** [v] S Ps 7:4

24:9 *schemes of folly are sin.* Cf. 1:10–19; 9:13–18. *people detest a mocker.* Because mockers are proud, insulting (9:7) and quarrelsome (22:10). See note on 1:22.
24:10 Cf. Jer 12:5; Gal 6:9.
24:11 *those being led away to death.* Perhaps the innocent condemned to die (cf. 17:15; Isa 58:6–7).
24:12 *we knew nothing about this.* See Jas 4:17. *does not he who weighs the heart perceive it?* God knows even our thoughts and motives (see 16:2; 21:2 and note; Ps 94:9–11). *repay everyone.* See v. 29; 20:22; Ps 5:10 and notes. *according to what they have done.* See Mt 16:27 and note.
24:14 *wisdom is like honey for you.* It nourishes and brings healing (see 16:24 and note). *future hope.* Contrast v. 20; see Ps 9:18; 37:37; Jer 29:11.
24:15 *lurk.* See 1:11 and note; 12:6; Ps 10:9–10.
24:16 *seven times.* Many times (see 6:16; Job 5:19 and note; cf. Pr 26:16). *rise again.* God promises to uphold and rescue the righteous (cf. Ps 34:19; 37:24; Mic 7:8). *wicked stumble.* See v. 22; 4:19; 6:15 and note; 11:3,5.
24:17 *Do not gloat.* See 17:5 and note; cf. Ps 137:7 and note.
24:19 Almost identical to Ps 37:1; see v. 1; 3:31; 23:17.
24:20 *no future hope.* For himself or his posterity (contrast v. 14; 23:18; see Ps 37:2,28,38). *lamp … will be snuffed out.* See note on 13:9.
24:21 *Fear the LORD and the king.* Submission to civil authority is also commanded in Ecc 8:2–5. 1Pe 2:17 reads, "Fear God, honor the emperor," and Ro 13:1–7 urges the same obedience (see notes there). These passages all view the king as a terror to the wicked (cf. 20:8,26).
24:22 *those two.* God and the king. *sudden destruction … calamities.* God's judgment is more common (see 6:15; 11:3,5), but the power of the king is seen in 20:8,26.
24:23–34 An appendix to 22:17—24:22, giving five additional sayings of the wise.
24:23 *partiality in judging is not good.* See 18:5 and note.
24:24 *You are innocent.* See 17:15 and note. *will be cursed by peoples.* Just as they "curse the one who hoards grain" (11:26).
24:25 *rich blessing.* See 10:6 and note; Dt 16:20.
24:26 *honest answer.* Cf. 16:13. *like a kiss.* Cf. the "gracious words" that are "sweet to the soul" in 16:24.
24:27 *get your fields ready.* Plan carefully and acquire the means as you build your house. *build your house.* See v. 3 and note.
24:28 *testify … without cause.* See 3:30; Job 2:3. *use your lips to mislead.* See 6:19 and note; 12:17; 25:18.

29 Do not say, "I'll do to them as they have done to me;
I'll pay them back for what they did."[w]

30 I went past the field of a sluggard,[x]
past the vineyard of someone who has no sense;
31 thorns had come up everywhere,
the ground was covered with weeds,
and the stone wall was in ruins.
32 I applied my heart to what I observed
and learned a lesson from what I saw:
33 A little sleep, a little slumber,
a little folding of the hands to rest[y]—
34 and poverty will come on you like a thief
and scarcity like an armed man.[z]

More Proverbs of Solomon

25 These are more proverbs[a] of Solomon, compiled by the men of Hezekiah king of Judah:[b]

2 It is the glory of God to conceal a matter;
to search out a matter is the glory of kings.[c]
3 As the heavens are high and the earth is deep,
so the hearts of kings are unsearchable.

4 Remove the dross from the silver,
and a silversmith can produce a vessel;
5 remove wicked officials from the king's presence,[d]
and his throne will be established[e] through righteousness.[f]

6 Do not exalt yourself in the king's presence,
and do not claim a place among his great men;
7 it is better for him to say to you,
"Come up here,"[g]
than for him to humiliate you before his nobles.

What you have seen with your eyes
8 do not bring[a] hastily to court,
for what will you do in the end
if your neighbor puts you to shame?[h]

9 If you take your neighbor to court,
do not betray another's confidence,
10 or the one who hears it may shame you
and the charge against you will stand.

11 Like apples[b] of gold in settings of silver[i]
is a ruling rightly given.
12 Like an earring of gold or an ornament of fine gold
is the rebuke of a wise judge to a listening ear.[j]

13 Like a snow-cooled drink at harvest time
is a trustworthy messenger to the one who sends him;

24:29 [w] Pr 20:22; Mt 5:38-41 **24:30** [x] Pr 6:6-11; 26:13-16 **24:33** [y] S Pr 6:10 **24:34** [z] S Pr 10:4; Ecc 10:18 **25:1** [a] S 1Ki 4:32 [b] S Pr 1:1 **25:2** [c] Pr 16:10-15 **25:5** [d] S Pr 20:8 [e] S 2Sa 7:13 [f] S Pr 16:12; 29:14 **25:7** [g] Lk 14:7-10 **25:8** [h] Mt 5:25-26 **25:11** [i] ver 12; Pr 15:23 **25:12** [j] S ver 11; Ps 141:5; S Pr 13:18

[a] 7,8 Or *nobles / on whom you had set your eyes.* / [8]*Do not go* [b] 11 Or possibly *apricots*

24:29 *I'll pay them back.* See v. 12. A spirit of revenge is discouraged also in 20:22 (see note there); cf. 25:21–22; Mt 5:43–45; Ro 12:17–19.
24:30 *sluggard.* See note on 6:6.
24:31 *thorns … weeds.* See 15:19 and note; cf. Isa 34:13.
24:32 *I applied my heart to.* See 22:17; 23:12 and note; Ps 4:7 and note.
24:33–34 See 6:10–11 and note on 6:11.
25:1—29:27 Another collection of Solomon's proverbs, similar to 10:1—22:16.
25:1 *proverbs of Solomon.* See notes on 1:1; 10:1. *compiled by the men of Hezekiah.* There was a great revival in the reign of Hezekiah (c. 715–686 BC), who restored the singing of hymns to its proper place (2Ch 29:30). His interest in "the words of David" corresponds to his support of this compilation of Solomon's proverbs. Solomon was the last king to rule over all Israel during the united monarchy; Hezekiah was the first king to rule over all Israel (now restricted to the southern kingdom) after the destruction of the divided monarchy's northern kingdom.
25:2–7 Appropriately enough, kings are the subject of this initial series of proverbs compiled by King Hezekiah's men to honor King Solomon.
25:2 *to conceal a matter.* God gets glory because humans cannot fully understand his universe or the way he rules it (see Dt 29:29; Job 26:14 and note; Isa 40:12–24; Ro 11:33–36). *to search out a matter.* A king gets glory if he can uncover the truth and administer justice (see 1Ki 3:9; 4:34).
25:3 *are unsearchable.* Cannot be understood—like the four things in 30:18–19. Yet God controls the hearts of kings (see note on 21:1).
25:4 *Remove the dross from the silver.* A process compared to the purification of society in general and rulers in particular in Isa 1:22–25; Eze 22:18; Zec 13:8–9; Mal 3:2–3.
25:5 *his throne will be established through righteousness.* See note on 16:12; see also 20:26.
25:6 *in the king's presence.* Probably at a feast (cf. 23:1). Jesus spoke about the place of honor at a wedding feast (Lk 14:7–11).
25:7 *Come up here.* Cf. "Friend, move up to a better place" (Lk 14:10); contrast Isa 22:15–19.
25:8 *do not bring hastily to court.* A warning about the seriousness of disputes (see 17:14) and the need to exercise caution (see 24:28).
25:9 *do not betray another's confidence.* If you do, you are a gossip (see 11:13; 20:19; cf. Ro 1:29; 2Co 12:20).
25:10 *shame you … charge against you will stand.* A good name is one of life's most valuable possessions (see 22:1 and note).
25:11 *gold … silver.* Cf. the fruit of wisdom in 8:19.
25:12 *earring of gold.* Comparable to the beautiful wreath and necklace that represent the adornment of wisdom and sound teaching (see 1:9; 3:22; 4:9). *rebuke of a wise judge.* Cf. the "life-giving correction" of 15:31.
25:13 *snow-cooled drink at harvest time.* Probably a drink cooled by snow from the mountains; it did not snow at harvest time. See 26:1; contrast 10:26. *trustworthy messenger.* See 13:17 and note.

he refreshes the spirit of his
master.[k]
14 Like clouds and wind without rain
is one who boasts of gifts never
given.
15 Through patience a ruler can be
persuaded,[l]
and a gentle tongue can break a
bone.[m]
16 If you find honey, eat just enough—
too much of it, and you will
vomit.[n]
17 Seldom set foot in your neighbor's
house—
too much of you, and they will hate
you.
18 Like a club or a sword or a sharp
arrow
is one who gives false testimony
against a neighbor.[o]
19 Like a broken tooth or a lame foot
is reliance on the unfaithful in a time
of trouble.
20 Like one who takes away a garment on
a cold day,
or like vinegar poured on a wound,
is one who sings songs to a heavy
heart.
21 If your enemy is hungry, give him food
to eat;
if he is thirsty, give him water to
drink.
22 In doing this, you will heap burning
coals[p] on his head,
and the LORD will reward you.[q]

23 Like a north wind that brings
unexpected rain
is a sly tongue—which provokes a
horrified look.
24 Better to live on a corner of the roof
than share a house with a
quarrelsome wife.[r]
25 Like cold water to a weary soul
is good news from a distant land.[s]
26 Like a muddied spring or a polluted
well
are the righteous who give way to
the wicked.
27 It is not good to eat too much honey,[t]
nor is it honorable to search out
matters that are too deep.[u]
28 Like a city whose walls are broken
through
is a person who lacks self-control.

26 Like snow in summer or rain[v] in
harvest,
honor is not fitting for a fool.[w]
2 Like a fluttering sparrow or a darting
swallow,
an undeserved curse does not come
to rest.[x]
3 A whip for the horse, a bridle for the
donkey,[y]
and a rod for the backs of fools![z]
4 Do not answer a fool according to his
folly,
or you yourself will be just like
him.[a]
5 Answer a fool according to his folly,
or he will be wise in his own eyes.[b]

25:13 [k]S Pr 10:26; 13:17 **25:15** [l]Ecc 10:4 [m]Pr 15:1 **25:16** [n]ver 27 **25:18** [o]S Pr 12:18 **25:22** [p]S Ps 18:8 [q]S 2Ch 28:15; Mt 5:44; Ro 12:20* **25:24** [r]S Pr 21:9 **25:25** [s]Pr 15:30 **25:27** [t]ver 16 [u]Pr 27:2; S Mt 23:12 **26:1** [v]S 1Sa 12:17 [w]ver 8; Pr 19:10 **26:2** [x]S Dt 23:5 **26:3** [y]Ps 32:9 [z]S Pr 10:13 **26:4** [a]ver 5; Isa 36:21 **26:5** [b]ver 4; S Pr 3:7

25:14 *clouds ... without rain.* An image applied to false teachers in Jude 12 (see note on Jude 12–13).
25:15 *Through patience a ruler can be persuaded.* Cf. 14:29. *gentle tongue.* See note on 15:1.
25:16 *honey.* See v. 27.
25:18 *club ... sword ... arrow.* Cf. Ps 57:4; Jer 9:8. *false testimony.* See note on 6:19; see also 24:28; Ex 20:16.
25:19 *broken tooth ... lame foot.* Relying on Egypt was like leaning on a splintered reed (Isa 36:6).
25:20 *sings songs to a heavy heart.* The exiles were reluctant to sing the songs of Zion (Ps 137:3–4).
25:21–22 Quoted in Ro 12:20.
25:21 Kindness to one's enemy is encouraged in 20:22; Ex 23:4–5 (see note there). *give him food ... water.* At Elisha's request, a trapped Aramean army was given a great feast and then sent home (2Ki 6:21–23; cf. 2Ch 28:15).
25:22 *heap burning coals on his head.* Horrible punishment reserved for the wicked (see Ps 140:10). Here, however, it is kindness that will hurt the enemy (cf. the broken bone of v. 15) but perhaps win him over. Alternatively, the expression may reflect an Egyptian expiation ritual, in which a guilty person, as a sign of his repentance, carried a basin of glowing coals on his head. The meaning here, then, would be that in returning good for evil—and so being kind to your enemy (see Ro 12:20)—you may cause him to repent or change. *the LORD will reward you.* Even if the enemy remains hostile (cf. 11:18; 19:17).
25:23 *north.* Perhaps northwest (cf. Lk 12:54). *sly tongue.* One that spreads slander (cf. 10:18).
25:24 Echoed from 21:9 (see note there).
25:25 *good news from a distant land.* See Ge 45:25–28.
25:26 *muddied spring.* Cf. Eze 34:18–19. *the righteous who give way.* Perhaps through bribery (cf. 17:8; 29:4; Isa 1:21–23).
25:27 *too much honey.* See v. 16.
25:28 *city whose walls are broken through.* Defenseless and disgraced (cf. Ne 1:3 and note). *person who lacks self-control.* See 16:32 and note.
26:1–12 As kings are the subject of the series of proverbs that begins ch. 25 (see note on 25:2–7), so fools are the subject at the beginning of ch. 26.
26:1 *rain in harvest.* It rarely rains in the Holy Land from June through September, but see 1Sa 12:17–18. *honor is not fitting for a fool.* See v. 8.
26:2 *undeserved curse does not come to rest.* When David was cursed by Shimei, he realized that the curse would not take effect because he was innocent of the charge of murdering members of Saul's family (2Sa 16:8,12).
26:3 *rod for the backs of fools.* See 14:3; 19:29.
26:4 *Do not answer a fool according to his folly.* Do not stoop to his level (see 23:9; Mt 7:6 and notes).
26:5 *Answer a fool according to his folly.* Sometimes folly must be plainly exposed and denounced. Thus vv. 4–5 do not contradict each other, as often claimed.

Marble sarcophagus of Thracian horseman with hunting dog (Roman, first century AD). "Like one who grabs a stray dog by the ears is someone who rushes into a quarrel not their own" (Pr 26:17). In the ancient Near East, dogs were not domesticated pets as they are today. They were used mainly for hunting or would roam outside villages as scavengers.

6 Sending a message by the hands of a fool[c]
is like cutting off one's feet or drinking poison.
7 Like the useless legs of one who is lame
is a proverb in the mouth of a fool.[d]
8 Like tying a stone in a sling
is the giving of honor to a fool.[e]
9 Like a thornbush in a drunkard's hand
is a proverb in the mouth of a fool.[f]
10 Like an archer who wounds at random
is one who hires a fool or any passer-by.

26:6 [c] S Pr 10:26 **26:7** [d] ver 9 **26:8** [e] S ver 1 **26:9** [f] ver 7

26:11 [g] 2Pe 2:22* [h] S Ps 85:8 **26:12** [i] S Pr 3:7 [j] Pr 29:20 **26:13** [k] Pr 6:6-11; 24:30-34 [l] Pr 22:13 **26:14** [m] S Pr 6:9 **26:15** [n] Pr 19:24 **26:20** [o] Pr 22:10 **26:21** [p] S Pr 14:17 **26:22** [q] Pr 18:8

11 As a dog returns to its vomit,[g]
so fools repeat their folly.[h]
12 Do you see a person wise in their own eyes?[i]
There is more hope for a fool than for them.[j]

13 A sluggard says,[k] "There's a lion in the road,
a fierce lion roaming the streets!"[l]
14 As a door turns on its hinges,
so a sluggard turns on his bed.[m]
15 A sluggard buries his hand in the dish;
he is too lazy to bring it back to his mouth.[n]
16 A sluggard is wiser in his own eyes
than seven people who answer discreetly.

17 Like one who grabs a stray dog by the ears
is someone who rushes into a quarrel not their own.

18 Like a maniac shooting
flaming arrows of death
19 is one who deceives their neighbor
and says, "I was only joking!"

20 Without wood a fire goes out;
without a gossip a quarrel dies down.[o]
21 As charcoal to embers and as wood to fire,
so is a quarrelsome person for kindling strife.[p]
22 The words of a gossip are like choice morsels;
they go down to the inmost parts.[q]

23 Like a coating of silver dross on earthenware
are fervent[a] lips with an evil heart.

[a] 23 Hebrew; Septuagint *smooth*

26:6 *Sending a message by the hands of a fool.* He will likely misrepresent the one who sends him, or in some other manner frustrate the sender's purpose (see 13:17 and note).
26:8 *Like tying a stone in a sling.* A fool with authority wields a formidable weapon, but it is useless in his hands—as useless as a stone that is tied, not placed, in a sling. *honor to a fool.* See v. 1.
26:9 Fools reciting proverbs will do as much damage to themselves and others as a drunkard wielding a thornbush.
26:10 *one who hires a fool or any passer-by.* Abimelek hired "reckless scoundrels" to help him murder his half brothers and set up a brief and ill-fated rule (Jdg 9:4–6).
26:11 *As a dog returns to its vomit.* Quoted in 2Pe 2:22 with reference to false teachers (see note there). *fools repeat their folly.* Drunkards return to their drinks (see 23:35 and note).
26:12 *wise in their own eyes.* This phrase is applied to the sluggard in v. 16 and the rich in 28:11; cf. 26:5. *There is more hope … for them.* Repeated in 29:20.
26:13–16 A series of proverbs that focuses on the sluggard (see notes on 25:2–7; 26:1–12).
26:13 See 22:13 and note.
26:14 Sluggards love to sleep and seem to be attached to their beds as a door is to its hinges.
26:15 See 19:24 and note.
26:16 *wiser in his own eyes.* See v. 12 and note. *seven.* Many (see note on 24:16).
26:17 *grabs a stray dog by the ears.* To do so is to immediately create a disturbance. See photo above.
26:18 *Like a maniac shooting.* Cf. the archer in v. 10. *flaming arrows.* Could easily ignite sheaves of grain (cf. Zec 12:6).
26:19 *I was only joking!* Explaining it as a prank is a poor excuse.
26:21 *kindling strife.* See 6:14 and note.
26:22 Identical to 18:8 (see note there).
26:23 *coating of silver dross on earthenware.* Silver dross was a cheap substance used to make pottery look different from

24 Enemies disguise themselves with their lips,[r]
but in their hearts they harbor deceit.[s]
25 Though their speech is charming,[t] do not believe them,
for seven abominations fill their hearts.[u]
26 Their malice may be concealed by deception,
but their wickedness will be exposed in the assembly.
27 Whoever digs a pit[v] will fall into it;[w]
if someone rolls a stone, it will roll back on them.[x]
28 A lying tongue hates those it hurts,
and a flattering mouth[y] works ruin.

27 Do not boast[z] about tomorrow,
for you do not know what a day may bring.[a]

2 Let someone else praise you, and not your own mouth;
an outsider, and not your own lips.[b]

3 Stone is heavy and sand[c] a burden,
but a fool's provocation is heavier than both.

4 Anger is cruel and fury overwhelming,
but who can stand before jealousy?[d]

5 Better is open rebuke
than hidden love.

6 Wounds from a friend can be trusted,
but an enemy multiplies kisses.[e]

7 One who is full loathes honey from the comb,
but to the hungry even what is bitter tastes sweet.

26:24 [r]S Ps 31:18 [s]Ps 41:6 **26:25** [t]Ps 28:3 [u]Jer 9:4-8 **26:27** [v]S Ps 7:15 [w]S Est 6:13 [x]S Est 2:23; S 7:9; Ps 35:8; 141:10; Pr 28:10; 29:6; Isa 50:11 **26:28** [y]S Ps 12:3; Pr 29:5 **27:1** [z]S 1Ki 20:11 [a]Mt 6:34; Jas 4:13-16 **27:2** [b]S Pr 25:27 **27:3** [c]S Job 6:3 **27:4** [d]S Nu 5:14 **27:6** [e]Ps 141:5; Pr 28:23

8 Like a bird that flees its nest[f]
is anyone who flees from home.
9 Perfume[g] and incense bring joy to the heart,
and the pleasantness of a friend springs from their heartfelt advice.
10 Do not forsake your friend or a friend of your family,
and do not go to your relative's house when disaster[h] strikes you—
better a neighbor nearby than a relative far away.
11 Be wise, my son, and bring joy to my heart;[i]
then I can answer anyone who treats me with contempt.[j]
12 The prudent see danger and take refuge,
but the simple keep going and pay the penalty.[k]
13 Take the garment of one who puts up security for a stranger;
hold it in pledge if it is done for an outsider.[l]
14 If anyone loudly blesses their neighbor early in the morning,
it will be taken as a curse.
15 A quarrelsome wife is like the dripping[m]
of a leaky roof in a rainstorm;
16 restraining her is like restraining the wind
or grasping oil with the hand.
17 As iron sharpens iron,
so one person sharpens another.

27:8 [f]Isa 16:2 **27:9** [g]S Est 2:12; S Ps 45:8 **27:10** [h]S Pr 17:17 **27:11** [i]S Pr 10:1; S 23:15-16 [j]S Ge 24:60 **27:12** [k]Pr 22:3 **27:13** [l]Pr 20:16 **27:15** [m]S Est 1:18

the clay it actually was. This fits the analogy in the simile very well (a false and deceptive exterior). Cf. the clean outside of the cup and dish (Lk 11:39; cf. Mt 23:27). *fervent lips with an evil heart.* The speech of an adulterous woman is seductive (see 2:16; 5:3 and notes).
26:24 *in their hearts they harbor deceit.* See 12:20.
26:25 *their speech is charming.* See Jer 9:8. *seven.* See note on v. 16. For seven things the Lord detests, see 6:16–19.
26:26 *exposed in the assembly.* See 5:14; Lk 8:17.
26:27 *Whoever digs a pit will fall into it.* "The trouble they cause recoils on them" (Ps 7:16). See 1:18 and note; 28:10; 29:6; Est 7:10 and note; Ps 7:15; Ecc 10:8–9; Ob 15 and note.
26:28 *lying tongue hates those it hurts.* See 10:18. *flattering mouth works ruin.* See 29:5; cf. 16:13.
27:1 Cf. the words of the rich fool and God's response in Lk 12:19–20; cf. also Pr 16:9; Isa 56:12; Mt 6:34; Jas 4:13–16.
27:2 *Let someone else praise you.* See 2Co 10:12,18.
27:4 *who can stand before jealousy?* See 6:34; SS 8:6.
27:5 *open rebuke.* Called "life-giving correction" in 15:31; cf. Gal 2:14.
27:6 See 28:23. *Wounds from a friend.* Called a "kindness" in Ps 141:5 (see note there). *enemy multiplies kisses.* See 5:3 and note; Mt 26:49.
27:7 *loathes honey.* Cf. 25:16,27.
27:8 *anyone who flees from home.* They have lost their security and may be vulnerable to temptation (cf. 7:21–23).
27:9 *Perfume.* See note on 21:17. *incense.* Cf. the one "perfumed with myrrh and incense" (SS 3:6). *bring joy to the heart.* See v. 11. *pleasantness of a friend.* See 16:21,24 and notes.
27:10 Do not fail a friend in need; when in need rely on friendship rather than on mere family relationships. *relative far away.* Either physically or emotionally.
27:11 *Be wise, my son.* See 10:1 and note. *then I can answer anyone who treats me with contempt.* Wise children serve as a powerful testimony that the parents who have shaped them have shown themselves to be people of worth.
27:12 *the simple.* See note on 1:4. *keep going and pay the penalty.* See 7:22–23; 9:16–18.
27:13 Identical to 20:16 (see note there).
27:14 *blesses their neighbor.* Perhaps to win the neighbor's favor (cf. Ps 12:2).
27:15 See 19:13 and note.
27:17 *sharpens another.* Develops and molds the other's character.

18 The one who guards a fig tree will eat
its fruit,[n]
and whoever protects their master
will be honored.[o]

19 As water reflects the face,
so one's life reflects the heart.[a]

20 Death and Destruction[b] are never
satisfied,[p]
and neither are human eyes.[q]

21 The crucible for silver and the furnace
for gold,[r]
but people are tested by their
praise.

22 Though you grind a fool in a mortar,
grinding them like grain with a
pestle,
you will not remove their folly from
them.

23 Be sure you know the condition of
your flocks,[s]
give careful attention to your
herds;
24 for riches do not endure forever,[t]
and a crown is not secure for all
generations.
25 When the hay is removed and new
growth appears
and the grass from the hills is
gathered in,
26 the lambs will provide you with
clothing,
and the goats with the price of a
field.
27 You will have plenty of goats' milk to
feed your family
and to nourish your female servants.

27:18 [n] 1Co 9:7 [o] Lk 19:12-27 **27:20** [p] Pr 30:15-16; Hab 2:5 [q] Ecc 1:8; 6:7 **27:21** [r] S Pr 17:3 **27:23** [s] Pr 12:10 **27:24** [t] Pr 23:5

28 The wicked flee[u] though no one
pursues,[v]
but the righteous are as bold as a
lion.[w]

2 When a country is rebellious, it has
many rulers,
but a ruler with discernment and
knowledge maintains order.

3 A ruler[c] who oppresses the poor
is like a driving rain that leaves no
crops.

4 Those who forsake instruction praise
the wicked,
but those who heed it resist them.

5 Evildoers do not understand what is
right,
but those who seek the LORD
understand it fully.

6 Better the poor whose walk is
blameless
than the rich whose ways are
perverse.[x]

7 A discerning son heeds instruction,
but a companion of gluttons
disgraces his father.[y]

8 Whoever increases wealth by taking
interest[z] or profit from the poor
amasses it for another,[a] who will be
kind to the poor.[b]

9 If anyone turns a deaf ear to my
instruction,
even their prayers are detestable.[c]

28:1 [u] S 2Ki 7:7 [v] S Lev 26:17 [w] S Ps 138:3 **28:6** [x] Pr 19:1 **28:7** [y] Pr 23:19-21 **28:8** [z] S Ex 18:21; Eze 18:8 [a] S Job 27:17 [b] S Job 3:15; Ps 112:9; Lk 14:12-14 **28:9** [c] S Ps 109:7; S Pr 15:8; S Isa 1:13

[a] 19 Or *so others reflect your heart back to you*
[b] 20 Hebrew *Abaddon*
[c] 3 Or *A poor person*

27:18 *will eat its fruit.* Cf. 2Ti 2:6. *will be honored.* See Ge 39:4; Mt 25:21; Lk 12:42–44; Jn 12:26.

27:19 *one's life reflects the heart.* And the condition of one's heart indicates one's true character (see Mt 5:8).

27:20 *Death and Destruction.* See note on Job 26:6; see also Pr 15:11. *are never satisfied.* Their appetite is insatiable (see 30:15–16; Isa 5:14; Hab 2:5). *neither are human eyes.* See Ecc 4:8.

27:21 *crucible...gold.* See 17:3; Ps 12:6 and note. *people are tested by their praise.* People must not become proud, and they must be wary of flattery (cf. 12:8; Lk 6:26).

27:22 *mortar.* A bowl (see Nu 11:8). *pestle.* A club-like tool for pounding grain in a mortar. *you will not remove their folly.* In spite of severe punishment, fools refuse to change (see note on 20:30; see also 26:11; Jer 5:3 and note).

27:23–27 A section praising the basic security afforded by agricultural pursuits—reflecting the agricultural base of the ancient economy.

27:23 *give careful attention to your herds.* Like Jacob, with Laban's flocks (Ge 31:38–40).

27:24 *riches do not endure.* See notes on 23:5; Mt 6:19. *crown is not secure.* Cf. 29:14. Even kings may lose their wealth and power (see Job 19:9; La 5:16).

27:25 *hay is removed.* This began in March or April.

27:26 *price of a field.* See 31:16.

27:27 *goats' milk.* Drunk as commonly as cows' milk (see Isa 7:21–22). *female servants.* See 31:15.

28:1 *The wicked flee.* See Lev 26:17; Ps 53:5 and notes. *bold as a lion.* Like David in 1Sa 17:46; cf. 2Sa 22:33–37.

28:2 *it has many rulers.* Israel's rebellion often brought frequent and rapid change in leadership (see 1Ki 16:8–28; 2Ki 15:8–14; 23:29—24:17). *ruler with discernment... maintains order.* A wise ruler will be successful (see 8:15–16; 16:12 and note; 24:5; 29:4).

28:3 *who oppresses the poor.* See 14:31 and note. *driving rain.* Describes the destructive power of Assyria's king in Isa 28:2 (see note there). The gentle rain is compared to a righteous king in Ps 72:6–7.

28:4 *instruction.* Either the teachings of wisdom (3:1; 7:2) or the law of Moses (Ps 119:53). *praise the wicked.* Cf. Ro 1:32 and note. *who heed it.* See v. 7; 29:18; cf. v. 9. *resist them.* See Eph 5:7,11.

28:5 *who seek the LORD.* Who fear him (see note on 1:7). *understand it fully.* They know "what is right and just and fair" (2:9).

28:6 *blameless.* See v. 18; 2:7; Ps 15:2 and notes.

28:7 *heeds instruction.* See note on v. 4. *companion of gluttons.* See 23:20–21 and notes.

28:8 *interest or profit from the poor.* Prohibited in Ex 22:25 (see notes on Ex 22:25–27; Lev 25:36; Eze 18:8). *amasses it for another.* See 13:22 and note; cf. Lk 12:20. *kind to the poor.* See 14:31 and note.

28:9 *my instruction.* See note on v. 4. *their prayers are detest-*

10 Whoever leads the upright along an evil path
will fall into their own trap,[d]
but the blameless will receive a good inheritance.

11 The rich are wise in their own eyes;
one who is poor and discerning sees how deluded they are.

12 When the righteous triumph, there is great elation;[e]
but when the wicked rise to power, people go into hiding.[f]

13 Whoever conceals their sins[g] does not prosper,
but the one who confesses[h] and renounces them finds mercy.[i]

14 Blessed is the one who always trembles before God,
but whoever hardens their heart falls into trouble.

15 Like a roaring lion or a charging bear
is a wicked ruler over a helpless people.

16 A tyrannical ruler practices extortion,
but one who hates ill-gotten gain will enjoy a long reign.

17 Anyone tormented by the guilt of murder
will seek refuge[j] in the grave;
let no one hold them back.

18 The one whose walk is blameless is kept safe,[k]
but the one whose ways are perverse will fall[l] into the pit.[a]

28:10 [d] S Ps 57:6; S Pr 26:27 **28:12** [e] S 2Ki 11:20 [f] ver 28; Job 24:4; Pr 29:2 **28:13** [g] S 2Sa 12:13; S Job 31:33 [h] S Lev 5:5 [i] Ps 32:1-5; Da 4:27; 1Jn 1:9 **28:17** [j] 1Sa 30:17; 1Ki 20:20; Jer 41:15; 44:14 **28:18** [k] Jer 39:18 [l] S Est 6:13; Pr 10:9 **28:19** [m] Pr 12:11 **28:20** [n] ver 22 **28:21** [o] S Lev 19:15 [p] S Ps 94:21; S Pr 18:5 [q] Eze 13:19 **28:22** [r] ver 20 **28:23** [s] S Pr 27:5-6 **28:24** [t] Pr 19:26 [u] S Pr 18:9 **28:25** [v] S Pr 14:17 [w] Pr 29:25 **28:26** [x] S Ps 4:5; Pr 3:5 [y] 1Co 3:18 **28:27** [z] S Dt 24:19; S Pr 22:9 [a] S Ps 109:17 **28:28** [b] S ver 12; S Job 20:19

19 Those who work their land will have abundant food,
but those who chase fantasies will have their fill of poverty.[m]

20 A faithful person will be richly blessed,
but one eager to get rich will not go unpunished.[n]

21 To show partiality[o] is not good[p]—
yet a person will do wrong for a piece of bread.[q]

22 The stingy are eager to get rich
and are unaware that poverty awaits them.[r]

23 Whoever rebukes a person will in the end gain favor
rather than one who has a flattering tongue.[s]

24 Whoever robs their father or mother[t]
and says, "It's not wrong,"
is partner to one who destroys.[u]

25 The greedy stir up conflict,[v]
but those who trust in the LORD[w] will prosper.

26 Those who trust in themselves are fools,[x]
but those who walk in wisdom are kept safe.[y]

27 Those who give to the poor will lack nothing,[z]
but those who close their eyes to them receive many curses.[a]

28 When the wicked rise to power, people go into hiding;[b]

[a] 18 Syriac (see Septuagint); Hebrew *into one*

---

able. Like the sacrifice of the wicked in 15:8 (see note there; see 3:32 and note; see also Ps 66:18; Isa 1:15; 59:1–2; Jer 11:14).
28:10 *fall into their own trap.* See note on 26:27. *blameless.* See note on 2:7. *good inheritance.* See 3:35; Heb 6:12; 1Pe 3:9.
28:11 *The rich are wise in their own eyes.* Like the fool (26:5) or the sluggard (26:16).
28:12 *there is great elation.* See 11:10 and note. *people go into hiding.* See v. 28; Ps 55:6–8 and note.
28:13 *Whoever conceals their sins does not prosper.* See Ps 32:3–5 and note. *one who confesses and renounces them finds mercy.* Note the joy of forgiveness in Ps 32:5,10–11 (cf. 1Jn 1:9 and note).
28:14 *whoever hardens their heart.* Like the pharaoh (Ex 7:13), and like the Israelites who tested the Lord at Meribah and Massah (see Ps 95:8 and note; Ro 2:5).
28:15 *roaring lion.* Full of rage and murderous intent (cf. 19:12; Mt 2:16; 1Pe 5:8). *charging bear.* See 17:12 and note. *wicked ruler.* See v. 12.
28:16 *one who hates ill-gotten gain will enjoy a long reign.* Unlike those who love such gain (see 1:19 and note).
28:17 *will seek refuge in the grave.* Perhaps the sense is that the murderer is so tormented by a guilty conscience that he tries to commit suicide.
28:18 *blameless ... perverse.* Contrasted also in v. 6; 19:1. *will fall into the pit.* Cf. 11:5.
28:19 *chase fantasies.* See 12:11 and note.
28:20 *richly blessed.* With God's gifts and favors (see 3:13–18; 10:6; Ge 49:26; Dt 33:16). *one eager to get rich will not go unpunished.* Cf. similar warnings in 20:21; 23:4 (see notes there).
28:21 *To show partiality is not good.* See 18:5 and note; 24:23. *will do wrong for a piece of bread.* Perhaps a reference to a bribe, however small (cf. Eze 13:19 and note).
28:22 *stingy.* See 23:6. *eager to get rich.* A warning to him is given in v. 20; cf. similar warnings in 20:21; 23:4 (see note there). *poverty awaits them.* Because it is the generous who prosper (see note on 11:25).
28:23 *Whoever rebukes a person.* See Gal 2:14; cf. 15:31; 25:12. *who has a flattering tongue.* See 26:28; 29:5; cf. 16:13.
28:24 *Whoever robs their father or mother.* See note on 19:26; cf. Mt 15:4–6; Mk 7:10–12.
28:25 *stir up conflict.* See note on 6:14. *will prosper.* As does also the generous person (see 11:25 and note) and the one who is diligent (13:4, lit. "the desires of the diligent prosper").
28:26 *who walk in wisdom.* Equals "whoever trusts in the LORD" in 29:25; cf. 3:5–6.
28:27 *give to the poor.* See note on 14:21. *will lack nothing.* Generosity is the path to blessing (see 11:24; 14:21 and notes; 19:17). *close their eyes to them.* See 21:13.
28:28 *people go into hiding.* See v. 12 and note. *righteous thrive.* See 11:10; 29:2.

but when the wicked perish, the
righteous thrive.

29 Whoever remains stiff-necked[c]
after many rebukes
will suddenly be destroyed[d]—
without remedy.[e]

2 When the righteous thrive, the people
rejoice;[f]
when the wicked rule,[g] the people
groan.[h]

3 A man who loves wisdom brings joy to
his father,[i]
but a companion of prostitutes
squanders his wealth.[j]

4 By justice a king gives a country
stability,[k]
but those who are greedy for[a] bribes
tear it down.

5 Those who flatter their neighbors
are spreading nets for their feet.[l]

6 Evildoers are snared by their own sin,[m]
but the righteous shout for joy and
are glad.

7 The righteous care about justice for the
poor,[n]
but the wicked have no such
concern.

8 Mockers stir up a city,
but the wise turn away anger.[o]

9 If a wise person goes to court with a
fool,
the fool rages and scoffs, and there
is no peace.

10 The bloodthirsty hate a person of
integrity
and seek to kill the upright.[p]

29:1 [c] S Ex 32:9; S Dt 9:27 [d] Jer 19:15; 36:31; Hab 2:7 [e] S 2Ch 36:16; Pr 6:15
29:2 [f] S 2Ki 11:20 [g] Pr 30:22; Ecc 10:6 [h] S Pr 28:12
29:3 [i] S Pr 10:1; S 23:15-16 [j] Pr 5:8-10; Lk 15:11-32
29:4 [k] ver 14; S Pr 8:15-16
29:5 [l] S Job 32:21; S Pr 26:28
29:6 [m] S Job 5:13; S Pr 26:27; Ecc 9:12
29:7 [n] Pr 31:8-9
29:8 [o] Pr 11:11; S 16:14
29:10 [p] ver 27; 1Jn 3:12
29:11 [q] S Job 15:13 [r] Pr 12:16
29:12 [s] 2Ki 21:9 [t] S Job 34:30
29:13 [u] S Pr 22:2; Mt 5:45
29:14 [v] S ver 4; Ps 72:1-5; S Pr 16:12
29:15 [w] ver 17; S Pr 13:24
29:16 [x] S Ps 91:8; S 92:11
29:17 [y] S ver 15
29:18 [z] Ps 1:1-2; 19:11; 119:1-2
29:20 [a] Pr 19:2; 26:12

11 Fools give full vent to their rage,[q]
but the wise bring calm in the
end.[r]

12 If a ruler[s] listens to lies,
all his officials become wicked.[t]

13 The poor and the oppressor have this
in common:
The LORD gives sight to the eyes of
both.[u]

14 If a king judges the poor with fairness,
his throne will be established
forever.[v]

15 A rod and a reprimand impart wisdom,
but a child left undisciplined
disgraces its mother.[w]

16 When the wicked thrive, so does
sin,
but the righteous will see their
downfall.[x]

17 Discipline your children, and they will
give you peace;
they will bring you the delights you
desire.[y]

18 Where there is no revelation, people
cast off restraint;
but blessed is the one who heeds
wisdom's instruction.[z]

19 Servants cannot be corrected by mere
words;
though they understand, they will
not respond.

20 Do you see someone who speaks in
haste?
There is more hope for a fool than
for them.[a]

[a] 4 Or *who give*

29:1 *stiff-necked after many rebukes.* See note on Ex 32:9. Eli's sons died because of their stubbornness (see 1Sa 2:25 and note). *will suddenly be destroyed—without remedy.* Identical to 6:15. Cf. the fate of the mockers in 1:22–27.
29:2 *When the righteous thrive, the people rejoice.* See 11:10 and note. *when the wicked rule, the people groan.* See 28:12; Jdg 2:18 and notes.
29:3 *man who loves wisdom brings joy to his father.* See 10:1 and note. *companion of prostitutes squanders his wealth.* See 5:10; 6:26; Lk 15:13 and notes.
29:4 *By justice a king gives a country stability.* See 16:12 and note. *bribes.* See 17:8 and note.
29:5 *Those who flatter their neighbors.* See 28:23.
29:6 *snared by their own sin.* See 1:18 and note; 22:5.
29:7 *The righteous care about justice for the poor.* As Job did (see Job 29:11–17 and note on 29:12–13); see also Jer 22:16 and note; Jas 1:27; cf. Pr 19:17; 22:22; 29:14.
29:8 *Mockers stir up a city.* See notes on 6:14; 11:11; see also 26:21. *Mockers.* See 1:22 and note. *the wise turn away anger.* See Jas 3:17–18.
29:9 *the fool rages and scoffs.* Like an angry bear (17:12) or the tossing sea (Isa 57:20–21).
29:10 *The bloodthirsty hate a person of integrity.* Their schemes are described in 1:11–16; cf. Ps 5:6.
29:11 *give full vent to their rage.* See v. 9 and note; 14:16–17. *bring calm in the end.* See 16:32 and note.
29:12 *all his officials become wicked.* Cf. Isa 1:23.
29:13 *The LORD gives sight.* See Ex 4:11; Ps 94:9.
29:14 See Isa 9:7; cf. Pr 27:24.
29:15 *A rod and a reprimand.* See note on 13:24.
29:16 *When the wicked thrive.* See v. 2; 11:11 and note; 28:12,28. *righteous will see their downfall.* See 10:25 and note; 14:11; 21:12.
29:17 *Discipline your children.* Teach them and train them (see 13:24 and note; 22:6).
29:18 *revelation.* A message from God given through a prophet; a prophetic vision (see 1Sa 3:1; Isa 1:1; Ob 1). *people cast off restraint.* Possibly an allusion to the sinful actions of the Israelites while Moses was on Mount Sinai (see Ex 32:25 and note). *blessed is the one who heeds wisdom's instruction.* See 28:4 and note; see also 8:32.
29:19 *cannot be corrected by mere words.* Servants, like children (vv. 15,17), must be disciplined (see note on 22:6).
29:20 *who speaks in haste.* See 10:19; 17:27–28; Jas 1:19,26. *There is more hope … for them.* Identical to 26:12.

[21] A servant pampered from youth
will turn out to be insolent.

[22] An angry person stirs up conflict,
and a hot-tempered person commits many sins.[b]

[23] Pride brings a person low,[c]
but the lowly in spirit gain honor.[d]

[24] The accomplices of thieves are their own enemies;
they are put under oath and dare not testify.[e]

[25] Fear[f] of man will prove to be a snare,
but whoever trusts in the LORD[g] is kept safe.[h]

[26] Many seek an audience with a ruler,[i]
but it is from the LORD that one gets justice.[j]

[27] The righteous detest the dishonest;
the wicked detest the upright.[k]

Sayings of Agur

30 The sayings[l] of Agur son of Jakeh—
an inspired utterance.

This man's utterance to Ithiel:

"I am weary, God,
but I can prevail.[a]

[2] Surely I am only a brute, not a man;
I do not have human understanding.
[3] I have not learned wisdom,
nor have I attained to the knowledge of the Holy One.[m]
[4] Who has gone up[n] to heaven and come down?
Whose hands[o] have gathered up the wind?
Who has wrapped up the waters[p] in a cloak?[q]
Who has established all the ends of the earth?
What is his name,[r] and what is the name of his son?
Surely you know!

[5] "Every word of God is flawless;[s]
he is a shield[t] to those who take refuge in him.
[6] Do not add[u] to his words,
or he will rebuke you and prove you a liar.

[7] "Two things I ask of you, LORD;
do not refuse me before I die:
[8] Keep falsehood and lies far from me;
give me neither poverty nor riches,
but give me only my daily bread.[v]
[9] Otherwise, I may have too much and disown[w] you
and say, 'Who is the LORD?'[x]
Or I may become poor and steal,
and so dishonor the name of my God.[y]

[10] "Do not slander a servant to their master,
or they will curse you, and you will pay for it.

[11] "There are those who curse their fathers
and do not bless their mothers;[z]

[a] *1* With a different word division of the Hebrew; Masoretic Text *utterance to Ithiel, / to Ithiel and Ukal:*

29:22 [b] S Pr 14:17 **29:23** [c] S Est 5:12 [d] S Pr 11:2; S 15:33; S 16:18 **29:24** [e] S Lev 5:1 **29:25** [f] S 1Sa 15:24 [g] Pr 28:25 [h] S Pr 16:20 **29:26** [i] Pr 19:6 [j] S Pr 16:33 **29:27** [k] S ver 10 **30:1** [l] S Pr 22:17 **30:3** [m] S Pr 9:10 **30:4** [n] Dt 30:12; Ps 24:1-2; S Pr 8:22-31; Jn 3:13; Eph 4:7-10 [o] Isa 40:12 [p] Job 26:8 [q] S Ge 1:2 [r] Rev 19:12 **30:5** [s] S Ps 12:6; S 18:30 [t] S Ge 15:1 **30:6** [u] S Dt 4:2 **30:8** [v] Mt 6:11 **30:9** [w] Jos 24:27; Isa 1:4; 59:13 [x] Dt 6:12; 8:10-14; Hos 13:6 [y] S Dt 8:12 **30:11** [z] S Pr 20:20

29:21 *A servant pampered.* See v. 19 and note.
29:22 *angry person stirs up conflict.* See note on 6:14; see also 15:18.
29:23 See 15:33 and note; see also 18:12.
29:24 *they are put under oath.* They will be held responsible for failing to testify (cf. Lev 5:1).
29:25 *Fear of man.* Cf. 1Sa 15:24; Isa 51:12; Jn 12:42–43. *whoever trusts in the LORD is kept safe.* See 18:10; 28:26 and notes; cf. 3:5–6.
29:26 *Many seek an audience.* See 1Ki 10:24. *it is from the LORD that one gets justice.* God controls a king's actions (see note on 21:1) and defends the cause of the poor and the just (cf. Job 36:6).
29:27 The final proverb in this second Solomonic collection (chs. 25–29) highlights in the starkest terms the opposing perspectives that characterize the righteous and the wicked (cf. Ps 1:6 and note).
30:1–33 The first of two chapters that serve as an appendix to Proverbs.
30:1 *sayings.* See 22:17 and note; 24:23. Fourteen of Agur's sayings are recorded in this chapter. *Agur son of Jakeh.* Probably a non-Israelite wise man like Job and his friends. *inspired utterance.* Usually the message of a prophet (see note on Isa 13:1 ["prophecy"]).
30:2 *I am only a brute, not a man.* Similarly, Paul described himself as the "worst of sinners" (1Ti 1:16).
30:3 *knowledge of the Holy One.* See 9:10 and note.
30:4 The use of rhetorical questions to express God's greatness as Creator occurs also in Job 38:4—39:30; Isa 40:12–31 (see note there). *gathered up the wind.* Cf. Ps 135:7. *wrapped up the waters in a cloak.* See Job 26:8; 38:8–9. *What is ... the name of his son?* This question has been understood in several different ways, but its meaning remains obscure. *Surely you know!* God similarly challenged Job (see Job 38:4–5 and note).
30:5 Almost identical to Ps 18:30. *shield.* See notes on 2:7; Ps 3:3. *those who take refuge in him.* See 14:32; 18:10.
30:6 *Do not add to his words.* Cf. Moses' warning to the Israelites in Dt 4:2 (see note there); cf. also Rev 22:18–19 and note.
30:7 *Two things.* The use of lists characterizes Agur's sayings (see vv. 15,18,21,24,29).
30:8 *my daily bread.* Cf. Job 23:12 and the Lord's Prayer (see Mt 6:11 and note).
30:9 *I may have too much and disown you.* Moses predicted that the Israelites would forget God when their food was plentiful and their herds large (Dt 8:12–17; 31:20). *Who is the LORD?* Or, Why should I serve him (see Job 21:14–15)? *become poor and steal.* Cf. 6:30.
30:10 *you will pay for it.* Since the accusation is false, the servant's curse will be effective (cf. 26:2 and note)—so do not suppose you can take advantage of a servant's lowly position.
30:11 *curse their fathers.* Cf. v. 17; see 20:20 and note.

[12]those who are pure in their own eyes[a]
and yet are not cleansed of their filth;[b]
[13]those whose eyes are ever so haughty,[c]
whose glances are so disdainful;
[14]those whose teeth[d] are swords
and whose jaws are set with knives[e]
to devour[f] the poor[g] from the earth
and the needy from among mankind.[h]

[15]"The leech has two daughters.
'Give! Give!' they cry.

"There are three things that are never satisfied,[i]
four that never say, 'Enough!':
[16]the grave,[j] the barren womb,
land, which is never satisfied with water,
and fire, which never says, 'Enough!'

[17]"The eye that mocks[k] a father,
that scorns an aged mother,
will be pecked out by the ravens of the valley,
will be eaten by the vultures.[l]

[18]"There are three things that are too amazing for me,
four that I do not understand:
[19]the way of an eagle in the sky,
the way of a snake on a rock,
the way of a ship on the high seas,
and the way of a man with a young woman.

[20]"This is the way of an adulterous woman:
She eats and wipes her mouth
and says, 'I've done nothing wrong.'[m]

30:12 [a]S Pr 16:2 [b]Jer 2:23,35 **30:13** [c]S 2Sa 22:28; S Job 41:34 **30:14** [d]S Job 4:11; S Ps 3:7 [e]Ps 57:4 [f]S Job 24:9 [g]Am 8:4; Mic 2:2 [h]S Job 19:22 **30:15** [i]Pr 27:20 **30:16** [j]Isa 5:14; 14:9,11; Hab 2:5 **30:17** [k]Dt 21:18-21 [l]S Job 15:23 **30:20** [m]Pr 5:6
30:22 [n]S Pr 19:10; S 29:2 **30:25** [o]Pr 6:6-8 **30:26** [p]S Ps 104:18 **30:27** [q]S Ex 10:4 **30:32** [r]S Job 29:9

[21]"Under three things the earth trembles,
under four it cannot bear up:
[22]a servant who becomes king,[n]
a godless fool who gets plenty to eat,
[23]a contemptible woman who gets married,
and a servant who displaces her mistress.

[24]"Four things on earth are small,
yet they are extremely wise:
[25]Ants are creatures of little strength,
yet they store up their food in the summer;[o]
[26]hyraxes[p] are creatures of little power,
yet they make their home in the crags;
[27]locusts[q] have no king,
yet they advance together in ranks;
[28]a lizard can be caught with the hand,
yet it is found in kings' palaces.

[29]"There are three things that are stately in their stride,
four that move with stately bearing:
[30]a lion, mighty among beasts,
who retreats before nothing;
[31]a strutting rooster, a he-goat,
and a king secure against revolt.[a]

[32]"If you play the fool and exalt yourself,
or if you plan evil,
clap your hand over your mouth![r]
[33]For as churning cream produces butter,
and as twisting the nose produces blood,
so stirring up anger produces strife."

[a] *31* The meaning of the Hebrew for this phrase is uncertain.

30:12 *those who are pure in their own eyes.* Like the Pharisee in Lk 18:11 (cf. Isa 65:5 and note).
30:13 *whose eyes are ... haughty.* See note on 6:17; see also Isa 3:16.
30:14 *whose teeth are swords ... whose jaws are ... knives.* The wicked are like ravenous beasts that devour the prey (see Job 29:17). *to devour the poor ... the needy.* Cf. Ps 14:4; Mic 3:2–3 and notes.
30:15,18,21,29 *three ... four.* See note on 6:16.
30:15 *leech has two daughters.* The "two daughters" are the two suckers with which this parasite draws blood from its victims.
30:16 *grave.* Its appetite is never satisfied (Isa 5:14; Hab 2:5). *barren womb.* In ancient Israel, a wife without children was desolate, even desperate (cf. Ge 16:2 and note; 30:1; Ru 1:11–13,20–21; 1Sa 1:6,10–11; 2Ki 4:14 and note).
30:17 *The eye.* Haughty and disdainful (see v. 13). *mocks a father ... an aged mother.* See v. 11 and note; 15:20. *will be pecked out by the ravens ... the vultures.* The loss of an eye was a terrible curse (see the story of Samson in Jdg 16:21). Since vultures normally devoured the dead (see Jer 7:33 and note; Mt 24:28), the meaning may be that the body of a disgraceful son will lie unburied and exposed.
30:18–19 These four "ways" are difficult to understand because none of them leaves a track that can be readily followed.
30:19 *way of an eagle.* Soaring and swooping majestically (cf. Job 39:27; Jer 48:40; 49:22). *way of a man with a young woman.* Probably a reference to the mystery of courting and how it leads to consummation.
30:20 *adulterous woman.* See 2:16 and note. *She eats and wipes her mouth.* Eating food is used as a metaphor for making love also in 9:17 (see note there; see also 7:18 and note).
30:22 *servant who becomes king.* See 19:10.
30:23 *servant who displaces her mistress.* Perhaps because she was able to bear a child, whereas the wife was barren (cf. Hagar and Sarah in Ge 16:1–6).
30:25 *Ants.* See note on 6:6.
30:26 *in the crags.* Which provide a refuge for them (see Ps 104:18).
30:27 *locusts have no king.* Cf. the ant in 6:6–8. *advance together in ranks.* Locusts are portrayed as a mighty army in Joel 2:2–9 (see note on Joel 2:2).
30:28 *found in kings' palaces.* Lizards climb stone walls easily.
30:30 *lion, mighty among beasts.* See 2Sa 1:23; Mic 5:8.
30:31 *he-goat.* Goats were used to lead flocks of sheep (see Jer 50:8).
30:32 *exalt yourself.* Pride is condemned in 8:13; 11:2; 16:18. *plan evil.* Cf. 6:14; 16:27. *clap your hand over your mouth.* Stop your plotting immediately (cf. Job 21:5; 40:4).
30:33 *churning ... twisting ... stirring up.* See Introduction:

Sayings of King Lemuel

31 The sayings[s] of King Lemuel—
an inspired utterance his mother
taught him.

[2]Listen, my son! Listen, son of my
womb!
Listen, my son, the answer to my
prayers![t]
[3]Do not spend your strength[a] on
women,
your vigor on those who ruin
kings.[u]
[4]It is not for kings, Lemuel—
it is not for kings to drink wine,[v]
not for rulers to crave beer,
[5]lest they drink[w] and forget what has
been decreed,[x]
and deprive all the oppressed of
their rights.
[6]Let beer be for those who are
perishing,
wine[y] for those who are in anguish!
[7]Let them drink[z] and forget their
poverty
and remember their misery no
more.
[8]Speak[a] up for those who cannot speak
for themselves,
for the rights of all who are destitute.
[9]Speak up and judge fairly;
defend the rights of the poor and
needy.[b]

Epilogue: The Wife of Noble Character

[10] [b]A wife of noble character[c] who can
find?[d]
She is worth far more than rubies.
[11]Her husband[e] has full confidence in her
and lacks nothing of value.[f]
[12]She brings him good, not harm,
all the days of her life.
[13]She selects wool and flax
and works with eager hands.[g]
[14]She is like the merchant ships,
bringing her food from afar.
[15]She gets up while it is still night;
she provides food for her family
and portions for her female servants.
[16]She considers a field and buys it;
out of her earnings she plants a
vineyard.
[17]She sets about her work vigorously;
her arms are strong for her tasks.
[18]She sees that her trading is profitable,
and her lamp does not go out at night.
[19]In her hand she holds the distaff
and grasps the spindle with her
fingers.
[20]She opens her arms to the poor
and extends her hands to the needy.[h]
[21]When it snows, she has no fear for her
household;
for all of them are clothed in scarlet.

[a] 3 Or *wealth* [b] 10 Verses 10-31 are an acrostic poem, the verses of which begin with the successive letters of the Hebrew alphabet.

31:1 [s]S Pr 22:17 **31:2** [t]S Jdg 11:30 **31:3** [u]S Dt 17:17; S 1Ki 11:3; Pr 5:1-14 **31:4** [v]S Pr 20:1; Ecc 10:16-17; Isa 5:22 **31:5** [w]S 1Ki 16:9 [x]S Pr 16:12 **31:6** [y]S Ge 14:18 **31:7** [z]S Est 1:10 **31:8** [a]S 1Sa 19:4 **31:9** [b]S Pr 24:23; 29:7 **31:10** [c]S Ru 3:11; S Pr 18:22 [d]Pr 8:35 **31:11** [e]S Ge 2:18 [f]S Pr 12:4 **31:13** [g]1Ti 2:9-10 **31:20** [h]Dt 15:11

The Nature of a Proverb. *stirring up anger produces strife.* See notes on 6:14; 15:1; see also 29:22.

31:1–9 This brief section, consisting of three proverbs, is also of non-Israelite origin (see note on 30:1). King Lemuel is otherwise unknown. The threefold advice Lemuel's mother gives him highlights two major temptations of royalty (sexual promiscuity [vv. 2–3] and drunkenness [vv. 4–7]), as well as one of its primary obligations (defending the poor and needy [vv. 8–9; see Jer 22:15–16 and notes]).

31:1 *inspired utterance.* See note on 30:1. *his mother.* This entire chapter emphasizes the role and significance of wise women. In the ancient Near East, the queen mother was often an influential figure (see 1Ki 1:11–13 and note on 1:11).

31:2 *answer to my prayers.* Hannah also prayed for a son (see 1Sa 1:11 and note).

31:3 *your strength on women.* A warning against accumulating a large harem and engaging in sexual indulgence (see 5:9–11; 1Ki 11:1; Ne 13:26 and notes).

31:4 *It is not for kings ... to drink wine.* Woe to the land whose rulers are drunkards (Ecc 10:16–17; cf. Pr 20:1 and note; see Hos 7:5 and note).

31:5 *deprive all the oppressed of their rights.* See 30:14 and note; see also 17:15; Isa 5:23; 10:2.

31:6–7 Not a justification for overindulgence (see v. 4 and note), but an acknowledgment of the legitimacy of dulling pain and suffering with medicine (see 1Ti 5:23 and note; cf. Ps 104:15).

31:8–9 The king represents God as the defender of the poor and needy (see 16:10 and note; Ps 82:3; cf. Lev 19:15; Job 29:12–17; Isa 1:17 and note).

31:10–31 The epilogue: an acrostic poem (see NIV text note) praising the "wife of noble character" (v. 10). It corresponds to 1:1–7 as it describes a "woman who fears the LORD" (v. 30; see note on 1:7). Such a wife is almost a personification of wisdom. Like wisdom, she is "worth far more than rubies" (v. 10; see 3:15; 8:11), and those who find her "receive favor from the LORD" (8:35; 18:22). See Introduction: Literary Structure.

31:10 *wife of noble character.* Like Ruth (Ru 3:11). She is "her husband's crown" (12:4; see note there).

31:12 *She brings him good.* See 18:22; 19:14.

31:13 *flax.* Its fibers were made into linen and linen garments (see note on Ex 25:4; see also Pr 31:19,22,24; Isa 19:9).

31:14 *like the merchant ships.* She is an enterprising person (see v. 18). See photo, p. 1078.

31:15 *She gets up while it is still night.* She is the opposite of the sluggard (see 6:9–10; 26:14 and note). *portions for her female servants.* See 27:27; Lk 12:42.

31:16 *considers a field ... plants a vineyard.* She shows good judgment—unlike the sluggard, whose vineyard is overgrown with thorns and weeds (24:30–31).

31:17 *sets about her work vigorously.* See 10:4 and note.

31:18 *her trading is profitable.* Like wisdom, she is "worth far more than rubies" (v. 10; see note there). Wisdom "is more profitable than silver" (3:14; see note there).

31:19 *distaff ... spindle.* Spinning thread was women's work.

31:20 *opens her arms to the poor.* See note on 14:21; see also 22:9; Job 31:16–22.

31:21 *clothed in scarlet.* Of high quality, probably made of wool (cf. 2Sa 1:24; Rev 18:16).

[22] She makes coverings for her bed;
she is clothed in fine linen and purple.
[23] Her husband is respected at the city gate,
where he takes his seat among the elders[i] of the land.
[24] She makes linen garments and sells them,
and supplies the merchants with sashes.
[25] She is clothed with strength and dignity;
she can laugh at the days to come.
[26] She speaks with wisdom,
and faithful instruction is on her tongue.[j]
[27] She watches over the affairs of her household
and does not eat the bread of idleness.
[28] Her children arise and call her blessed;
her husband also, and he praises her:
[29] "Many women do noble things,
but you surpass them all."
[30] Charm is deceptive, and beauty is fleeting;
but a woman who fears the LORD is to be praised.
[31] Honor her for all that her hands have done,
and let her works bring her praise[k] at the city gate.

31:23 [i] S Ex 3:16 **31:26** [j] S Pr 10:31 **31:31** [k] Pr 11:16

31:22 *fine linen.* Associated with nobility (see notes on 7:16; Ex 25:4; see also Ge 41:42). *purple.* Linked with kings (Jdg 8:26; SS 3:10) or the rich (Lk 16:19; Rev 18:16).
31:23 *city gate.* The court (see note on 1:21).
31:24 *linen garments.* See Jdg 14:12 and note; Isa 3:23. *merchants.* Cf. v. 18.
31:25 *clothed with strength and dignity.* See Ps 109:29 and note; Isa 52:1; 1Ti 2:9–10. The opposite is to be "clothed with shame and disgrace" (Ps 35:26). *she can laugh at the days to come.* She is free of anxiety and worry (cf. Job 39:7).
31:26 *faithful instruction.* Given to her children and friends. She is a wise and loving counselor (see 1:8; 6:20).
31:28 *blessed.* That is, one who enjoys happy circumstances and from whom joy radiates to others. See Ge 30:13; Ps 72:17; SS 6:9; Mal 3:12; cf. Ru 4:14–15.
31:29 *do noble things.* The husband's reference to his wife's "noble" deeds climaxes the main body of the poem (vv. 10–29) that celebrates her "noble" character (v. 10). He further asserts that she surpasses all other women—she is, indeed, "worth far more than rubies" (v. 10). Cf. Isa 32:8.
31:30–31 A concluding reflection on the main body of the poem.
31:30 *Charm is deceptive.* Cf. 5:3 and note. *beauty is fleeting.* See 1Pe 3:3–5 and notes; cf. Job 14:2. *who fears the LORD.* See note on 1:7.
31:31 *Honor her for all that her hands have done.* See v. 16; 12:14 and notes. *bring her praise.* Honor comes through "humility" and "the fear of the LORD" (22:4). *city gate.* See v. 23 and note.

Roman merchant ship (Pompeii, first century AD). Proverbs 31:14 describes a wife of noble character as being "like the merchant ships, bringing her food from afar."

Z. Radovan/www.BibleLandPictures.com

ECCLESIASTES

INTRODUCTION

Author and Date

No time period or writer's name is mentioned in the book, but several passages suggest that King Solomon may be the author (1:1,12,16; 2:4–9; 7:26–29; 12:9; cf. 1Ki 2:9; 3:12; 4:29–34; 5:12; 10:1–8). On the other hand, the writer's title ("Teacher," Hebrew *qoheleth*; see note on 1:1), his unique style of Hebrew and his attitude toward rulers (suggesting that of a subject rather than a monarch — see, e.g., 4:1–2; 5:8–9; 8:2–4; 10:20) may point to another person and a later period (see note on 1:1).

Purpose and Teaching

The author of Ecclesiastes puts his powers of wisdom to work to examine the human experience and assess the human situation. His perspective is limited to what happens "under the sun" (as is that of all the wisdom teachers). He considers life as he has experienced and observed it between the horizons of birth and death — life within the boundaries of this visible world. His wisdom cannot penetrate beyond that last horizon; he can only observe the phenomenon of death and perceive the limits it places on human beings. Within the boundaries of human experience and observation, he is concerned to spell out what is good for people to do. And he represents a devout wisdom. Life in the world is under God — for all its enigmas. Hence what begins with "Meaningless! Meaningless!" (1:2) ends with "Remember your Creator" (12:1) and "Fear God and keep his commandments" (12:13).

With a wisdom matured by many years, he takes the measure of human beings, examining their limits and their lot. He has attempted to see what human wisdom can do (1:13,16–18; 7:24; 8:16), and he has discovered that human wisdom, even when it has its beginning in "the fear of the LORD" (Pr 1:7), has limits to its powers when it attempts to go it alone — limits that

a quick look

Author:
Unknown; possibly King Solomon

Audience:
The people of Israel

Date:
Unknown; possibly as early as the tenth century BC

Theme:
This wisdom teacher reveals what he has discovered about the meaninglessness of every human endeavor without God at the center of one's life.

> With a wisdom matured by many years, the author takes the measure of human beings, examining their limits and their lot. He has attempted to see what human wisdom can do and has discovered that its powers are limited.

circumscribe its perspectives and relativize its counsel. Most significantly, it cannot find out the larger purposes of God or the ultimate meaning of human existence. With respect to these, it can only pose questions.

Nevertheless, he does take a hard look at the human enterprise — an enterprise in which he himself has fully participated. He sees a busy human anthill in mad pursuit of many things, trying now this, now that, laboring away as if by dint of effort humans could master the world, lay bare its deepest secrets, change its fundamental structures, somehow burst through the bounds of human limitations, build for themselves enduring monuments, control their destiny, achieve a state of secure and lasting happiness — people laboring at life with an overblown conception of human powers and consequently pursuing unrealistic hopes and aspirations.

He takes a hard look and concludes that human life in this mode is "meaningless," its efforts all futile.

What, then, does wisdom teach him?

(1) Humans cannot by all their striving achieve anything of ultimate or enduring significance. Nothing appears to be going anywhere (1:5 – 11), and people cannot by all their efforts break out of this caged treadmill (1:2 – 4; 2:1 – 11); they cannot fundamentally change anything (1:12 – 15; 6:10; 7:13). Hence they often toil foolishly (4:4,7 – 8; 5:10 – 17; 6:7 – 9). All their striving "under the sun" (1:3) after unreal goals leads only to disillusionment.

(2) Wisdom is better than folly (2:13 – 14; 7:1 – 6,11 – 12,19; 8:1,5; 9:17 – 18; 10:1 – 3,12 – 15; 12:11) — it is God's gift to those who please him (2:26). But it is unwarranted to expect too much even from such wisdom — to expect that human wisdom is capable of solving all problems (1:16 – 18) or of securing for itself enduring rewards or advantages (2:12 – 17; 4:13 – 16; 9:13 – 16).

(3) Experience confronts humans with many apparent disharmonies and anomalies that wisdom cannot unravel. Of these the greatest of all is this: Human life comes to the same end as that of the animals — death (2:15; 3:16 – 17; 7:15; 8:14; 9:1 – 3; 10:5 – 7).

(4) Although God made humankind upright, people have gone in search of many schemes (for getting ahead by taking advantage of others; see 7:29; cf. Ps 10:2; 36:4; 140:2). So even humans are a disappointment (7:24 – 29).

(5) People cannot know or control what will come after them, or even what lies in the more immediate future; therefore all their efforts remain balanced on the razor's edge of uncertainty (2:18; 6:12; 7:14; 9:2).

(6) God keeps humans in their place (3:16 – 22).

(7) God has ordered all things (3:1 – 15; 5:19; 6:1 – 6; 9:1), and a human being cannot change God's appointments or fully understand them or anticipate them (3:1; 7; 11:1 – 6). But the world is not fundamentally chaotic or irrational. It is ordered by God, and it is for humans to accept matters as they are by God's appointments, including their own limitations. Everything has its "time" and is good in its time (ch. 3).

Therefore, wisdom counsels:

(1) Accept the human state as it is, shaped by God's appointments, and enjoy the life you have been given as fully as you can.

(2) Don't trouble yourself with unrealistic goals — know the measure of human capabilities.

(3) Be prudent in all your ways — follow wisdom's leading.

(4) "Fear God and keep his commandments" (12:13), beginning already in your youth before the fleeting days of life's enjoyments are gone and "the days of trouble" (12:1) come when the infirmities of advanced age vex you and hinder you from tasting, seeing and feeling the good things of life.

To sum up, Ecclesiastes provides instruction on how to live meaningfully, purposefully and joyfully under the reign of God — primarily by placing God at the center of one's life, work and activities, by contentedly accepting one's divinely appointed lot in life and by reverently trusting in and obeying the Creator-King. Note particularly 2:24 – 26; 3:11 – 14,22; 5:18 – 20; 8:15; 9:7 – 10; 11:7 — 12:1; 12:9 – 14 (see also any relevant notes on these passages).

Literary Features

The argument of Ecclesiastes does not flow smoothly. It meanders, with jumps and starts, through the general messiness of human experience, to which it is a response. There is also an intermingling of poetry and prose. Nevertheless, the following outline seeks to reflect, at least in a general

The Colossi of Memnon from the temple complex of Amunhotep III. The temple that once stood behind them was destroyed long ago, a poignant reminder of the ultimate meaninglessness of power and glory.

A Palestinian farmer plowing his field. "A time to plant and a time to uproot" (Ecc 3:2).
www.HolyLandPhotos.org

way, the structure of the book and its main discourses. The announced theme of "meaninglessness" (futility) provides a literary frame around the whole (1:2; 12:8). And the movement from the unrelieved disillusionment of chs. 1 – 2 to the more serene tone and sober instructions for life in chs. 11 – 12 marks a development in matured wisdom's coming to terms with the human situation.

A striking feature of the book is its frequent use of key words and phrases: e.g., "meaningless" (see notes on 1:2; 2:24 – 25), "work/labor/toil" (see note on 2:10), "good/better" (see note on 2:1), "gift/give" (see note on 5:19), "under the sun" (see note on 1:3), "chasing after the wind" (see note on 1:14). Also to be noted is the presence of passages interwoven throughout the book that serve as key indicators of the author's theme and purpose: 1:2 – 3,14,17; 2:10 – 11,17,24 – 26; 3:12 – 13,22; 4:4,6,16; 5:18 – 20; 6:9,12; 7:14,24; 8:7,15,17; 9:7,12; 10:14; 11:2,5 – 6,8 – 9; 12:1,8,13 – 14 (see notes on these passages where present). The enjoyment of life as God gives it is a key concept in the book (see 2:24 – 26 and note on 2:24 – 25; 3:12 – 13,22 and note on 3:12 – 13; 5:18 – 20; 7:14; 8:15 and note; 9:7 – 9; 11:8 – 9).

Outline

I. Author (1:1)
II. Theme: The Meaninglessness of Human Efforts on Earth Apart from God (1:2)

III. Introduction: The Profitlessness of Human Toil to Accumulate Things in Order to Achieve Happiness (1:3 – 11)
IV. Discourse, Part 1: In Spite of Life's Apparent Enigmas and Meaninglessness, It Is to Be Enjoyed as a Gift from God (1:12 — 11:6)
   A. Since Human Wisdom and Endeavors Are Meaningless, People Should Enjoy Their Life and Work and Its Fruits as Gifts from God (1:12 — 6:9)
      1. Introduction (1:12 – 18)
         a. Human endeavors are meaningless (1:12 – 15)
         b. Pursuing human wisdom is meaningless (1:16 – 18)
      2. Seeking pleasure is meaningless (2:1 – 11)
      3. Human wisdom is meaningless (2:12 – 17)
      4. Toiling to accumulate things is meaningless (2:18 — 6:9)
         a. Because people must leave the fruits of their labor to others (2:18 – 26)
         b. Because all human efforts remain under the government of God's sovereign appointments, which people cannot fully know and which all their toil cannot change (3:1 — 4:3)
         c. Because there are things better for people than the envy, greed and ambition that motivate such toil (4:4 – 16)
         d. Because the fruits of human labor can be lost, resulting in frustration (5:1 — 6:9)
   B. Since People Cannot Fully Know What Is Best to Do or What the Future Holds for Them, They Should Enjoy Now the Life and Work God Has Given Them (6:10 — 11:6)
      1. Introduction: What is predetermined by God is unalterable, and people cannot fully know what is best to do or what the future holds (6:10 – 12)
      2. People cannot fully know what is best to do (chs. 7 – 8)
      3. People cannot fully know what the future holds (9:1 — 11:6)
V. Discourse, Part 2: Since Old Age and Death Will Soon Come, People Should Enjoy Life in Their Youth, Remembering That God Will Judge (11:7 — 12:7)
   A. People Should Enjoy Their Life on Earth Because Their Future after Death Is Mysterious, and in That Sense Is Meaningless for Their Present Life (11:7 – 8)
   B. People Should Enjoy the Fleeting Joys of Youth but Remember That God Will Judge (11:9 – 10)
   C. People Should Remember Their Creator (and His Gifts) in Their Youth, before the Deteriorations of Old Age and the Dissolution of the Body Come (12:1 – 7)
VI. Theme Repeated (12:8)
VII. Conclusion: Reverently Trust in and Obey God (12:9 – 14)

Everything Is Meaningless

1 The words of the Teacher,[a][a] son of David, king in Jerusalem:[b]

2 "Meaningless! Meaningless!"
says the Teacher.
"Utterly meaningless!
Everything is meaningless."[c]

3 What do people gain from all their labors
at which they toil under the sun?[d]
4 Generations come and generations go,
but the earth remains forever.[e]
5 The sun rises and the sun sets,
and hurries back to where it rises.[f]
6 The wind blows to the south
and turns to the north;
round and round it goes,
ever returning on its course.
7 All streams flow into the sea,
yet the sea is never full.
To the place the streams come from,
there they return again.[g]
8 All things are wearisome,
more than one can say.
The eye never has enough of seeing,[h]
nor the ear its fill of hearing.
9 What has been will be again,
what has been done will be done again;[i]
there is nothing new under the sun.
10 Is there anything of which one can say,
"Look! This is something new"?
It was here already, long ago;
it was here before our time.
11 No one remembers the former generations,[j]
and even those yet to come
will not be remembered
by those who follow them.[k]

Wisdom Is Meaningless

12 I, the Teacher,[l] was king over Israel in
Jerusalem.[m] 13 I applied my mind to study
and to explore by wisdom all that is done
under the heavens.[n] What a heavy burden
God has laid on mankind![o] 14 I have seen
all the things that are done under the sun;
all of them are meaningless, a chasing after the wind.[p]

15 What is crooked cannot be straightened;[q]
what is lacking cannot be counted.

16 I said to myself, "Look, I have increased in wisdom more than anyone
who has ruled over Jerusalem before me;[r]
I have experienced much of wisdom and
knowledge." 17 Then I applied myself to
the understanding of wisdom,[s] and also of

1:1 [a] ver 12; Ecc 7:27; 12:10 [b] S Pr 1:1 **1:2** [c] Ps 39:5-6; 62:9; Ecc 12:8; Ro 8:20-21 **1:3** [d] Ecc 2:11, 22; 3:9; 5:15-16 **1:4** [e] S Job 8:19 **1:5** [f] Ps 19:5-6 **1:7** [g] Job 36:28 **1:8** [h] Pr 27:20 **1:9** [i] Ecc 2:12; 3:15 **1:11** [j] Ge 40:23; Ecc 9:15 [k] Ps 88:12; Ecc 2:16; 8:10; 9:5 **1:12** [l] S ver 1 [m] Ecc 2:9 **1:13** [n] S Job 28:3 [o] S Ge 3:17; Ecc 3:10 **1:14** [p] Ecc 2:11, 17; 4:4; 6:9 **1:15** [q] Ecc 7:13 **1:16** [r] S 1Ki 3:12 **1:17** [s] Ecc 7:23; 8:16

[a] 1 Or *the leader of the assembly*; also in verses 2 and 12

1:1 *Teacher.* The teacher of wisdom (12:9). The Hebrew term for "Teacher" (*qoheleth*) is related to that for "assembly" (see NIV text note; Ex 16:3; Nu 16:3). Perhaps the Teacher, whose work is described in 12:9–10, also held an office in the assembly. The Septuagint (the pre-Christian Greek translation of the OT) word for "Teacher" is *ekklesiastes*, from which most English titles of the book are taken, and from which such English words as "ecclesiastical" are derived. *son of David.* Suggests Solomon, though his name occurs nowhere in the book. The Hebrew word for "son" can refer to a descendant (even many generations removed) — or even to someone who follows in the footsteps of another (see Ge 4:21; see also Introduction: Author and Date).
1:2 Briefly states the author's theme (see 12:8 and note). *Meaningless!* This key term occurs 39 times in the book. The Hebrew for it originally meant "breath" (see Ps 39:5,11; 62:9; 144:4; cf. Ge 4:2 and note). The basic thrust of Ecclesiastes is that all of life is meaningless (useless, hollow, futile, vain) if it is not rightly related to God. Only when based on God and his word is life worthwhile. *Everything.* See v. 8; whatever human beings undertake apart from God.
1:3–11 The author elaborates his theme that human effort appears to be without benefit or purpose — and therefore without meaning.
1:3 Jesus expands on this question in Mk 8:36–38. *under the sun.* Another key expression (used 29 times), which refers to this present world and the limits of what it offers. "Under the heavens" and "on earth," though occurring less frequently (v. 13; 2:3; 3:1; 8:14,16), are used synonymously.
1:4–9 Toiling is profitless (v. 3) because humans live in a world of repetitiveness and sameness — one without apparent progress and meaning. This is seen in the endless succession and impermanence of human generations (v. 4) and in the behavior patterns of the sun (v. 5), the wind (v. 6) and the streams (v. 7). Hence the conclusion that "all things are wearisome" (v. 8) and "there is nothing new under the sun" (v. 9).
1:4 *earth remains forever.* By contrast, human life is fleeting.
1:8 *All things.* Everything mentioned in vv. 4–7 (see note on v. 2).
1:10 *something new.* Many things seem to be new simply because the past is easily and quickly forgotten. The old ways reappear in new guises.
1:12–18 Having set forth his theme that all human striving seems futile (see especially vv. 3,11, which frame that section), the Teacher now shows that both human endeavor (vv. 12–15; cf. 2:1–11) and the pursuit of human wisdom (vv. 16–18; cf. 2:12–17) are futile and meaningless.
1:12 *I.* The author shifts to the first person, returning to the third person only in the conclusion (12:9–14).
1:13 *under the heavens.* See note on v. 3. *God.* The only Hebrew word the writer uses for God is *Elohim* (used almost 30 times), which emphasizes his absolute sovereignty. He does not use the covenant name, *Yahweh* (translated "LORD"; see notes on Ge 2:4; Ex 3:14–15).
1:14 *chasing after the wind.* A graphic illustration of futility and meaninglessness (see Introduction: Purpose and Teaching). These words are used nine times in the first half of the discourse (here; v. 17; 2:11,17, 26; 4:4,6,16; 6:9; see also 5:16).
1:15 See 7:13 and note. Because of the unalterableness of events, human effort is meaningless and hopeless. We should therefore learn to happily accept things the way they are and to accept our divinely appointed lot in life, as the Teacher later counsels.
1:16 *increased in wisdom.* Cf. 1Ki 3:12; 4:29–34; 10:8,23–24. *anyone who has ruled over Jerusalem before me.* See 2:7,9. This does not necessarily exclude Solomon as the Teacher. The reference could include kings prior to David, such as Melchizedek (Ge 14:18), Adoni-Zedek (Jos

madness and folly,[t] but I learned that this,
too, is a chasing after the wind.

18 For with much wisdom comes much
sorrow;[u]
the more knowledge, the more grief.[v]

Pleasures Are Meaningless

2 I said to myself, "Come now, I will test
you with pleasure[w] to find out what is
good." But that also proved to be meaningless. 2 "Laughter,"[x] I said, "is madness.
And what does pleasure accomplish?" 3 I
tried cheering myself with wine,[y] and embracing folly[z]—my mind still guiding me
with wisdom. I wanted to see what was
good for people to do under the heavens
during the few days of their lives.
4 I undertook great projects: I built
houses for myself[a] and planted vineyards.[b]
5 I made gardens and parks and planted
all kinds of fruit trees in them. 6 I made
reservoirs to water groves of flourishing
trees. 7 I bought male and female slaves
and had other slaves[c] who were born in
my house. I also owned more herds and
flocks than anyone in Jerusalem before
me. 8 I amassed silver and gold[d] for myself,
and the treasure of kings and provinces.[e] I
acquired male and female singers,[f] and a
harem[a] as well—the delights of a man's
heart. 9 I became greater by far than anyone in Jerusalem[g] before me.[h] In all this
my wisdom stayed with me.

10 I denied myself nothing my eyes
desired;
I refused my heart no pleasure.
My heart took delight in all my
labor,
and this was the reward for all my
toil.
11 Yet when I surveyed all that my hands
had done
and what I had toiled to achieve,
everything was meaningless, a chasing
after the wind;[i]
nothing was gained under the sun.[j]

Wisdom and Folly Are Meaningless

12 Then I turned my thoughts to consider
wisdom,
and also madness and folly.[k]
What more can the king's successor do
than what has already been done?[l]
13 I saw that wisdom[m] is better than
folly,[n]
just as light is better than darkness.
14 The wise have eyes in their heads,
while the fool walks in the darkness;
but I came to realize
that the same fate overtakes them
both.[o]

15 Then I said to myself,

"The fate of the fool will overtake me
also.
What then do I gain by being wise?"[p]
I said to myself,
"This too is meaningless."
16 For the wise, like the fool, will not be
long remembered;[q]
the days have already come when
both have been forgotten.[r]
Like the fool, the wise too must die![s]

Toil Is Meaningless

17 So I hated life, because the work that
is done under the sun was grievous to me.
All of it is meaningless, a chasing after

1:17 [t] Ecc 2:3, 12; 7:25 **1:18** [u] Jer 45:3 [v] Ecc 2:23; 12:12 **2:1** [w] ver 24; Ecc 7:4; 8:15 **2:2** [x] S Pr 14:13 **2:3** [y] ver 24-25; S Jdg 9:13; Ru 3:3; Ecc 3:12-13; 5:18; 8:15 [z] S Ecc 1:17 **2:4** [a] 2Ch 2:1; 8:1-6 [b] SS 8:11 **2:7** [c] 2Ch 8:7-8 **2:8** [d] S 1Ki 9:28 [e] S Jdg 3:15 [f] S 2Sa 19:35 **2:9** [g] Ecc 1:12 [h] 1Ch 29:25

2:11 [i] S Ecc 1:14 [j] S Ecc 1:3 **2:12** [k] S Ecc 1:17 [l] S Ecc 1:9 **2:13** [m] Ecc 7:19; 9:18 [n] Ecc 7:11-12 **2:14** [o] Ps 49:10; Ecc 3:19; 6:6; 7:2; 9:3, 11-12 **2:15** [p] ver 19; Ecc 6:8 **2:16** [q] S Ps 112:6 [r] S Ecc 1:11 [s] Ps 49:10

[a] *8* The meaning of the Hebrew for this phrase is uncertain.

10:1) and Abdi-Khepa (mentioned in the Amarna letters from Egypt; see chart, p. xxii).

1:18 Wisdom without God leads to grief and sorrow (cf. 2:23; Jer 45:3).

2:1–11 The Teacher now shows that mere pleasure cannot give meaning or satisfaction (see 1:12–15; see also note on 1:12–18).

2:1–3 The pursuit of pleasure does not bring the fulfillment that human beings seek.

2:1 *I said to myself.* See v. 15; 1:16. *good.* A key term in the book ("good" and "better" occur about 40 times).

2:3 *my mind still guiding me with wisdom.* From first to last (v. 9) the author used wisdom to discover the good (v. 1) and the worthwhile (v. 3). *under the heavens.* See note on 1:3.

2:4–9 See 1Ki 4–11, which tells of Solomon's splendor and of his wives.

2:8 *provinces.* Probably the neighboring territories from which tribute was collected. *harem.* The Hebrew for this word occurs only here in Scripture (see NIV text note). The meaning seems to be indicated in an early Egyptian letter that uses a similar Canaanite term for concubines. It fits the situation of Solomon, who had 300 concubines in addition to 700 wives (1Ki 11:3).

2:9 See 1:16.

2:10 *labor … toil.* A key thought in Ecclesiastes is the meaninglessness (v. 11), apart from God, of "toil," "labor," "work"—words that occur almost 40 times.

2:12–17 The Teacher returns to the folly of trying to find satisfaction in merely human wisdom (see 1:16–18; see also note on 1:12–18).

2:12 *king's successor.* Either the Teacher himself (see 1:1) or one who would come after him (cf. 4:15–16).

2:13 *wisdom is better than folly.* Even secular wisdom is better than folly, but in the end it is of no value, since "the same fate overtakes them both" (i.e., overtakes both the wise believer and the foolish unbeliever, v. 14; see Ps 49:10). *better.* See note on 2:1.

2:14 *eyes.* Understanding.

2:16 People tend to soon forget even the greatest leaders and heroes (see 1:11).

2:17–23 To pursue human fulfillment through work done "under the sun" (vv. 17–20,22; see 1:3 and note) is grievous and meaningless and leads to despair; its fruits must be left to others, whose character one cannot predict.

the wind.[t] 18 I hated all the things I had
toiled for under the sun, because I must
leave them to the one who comes after
me.[u] 19 And who knows whether that person will be wise or foolish?[v] Yet they will
have control over all the fruit of my toil
into which I have poured my effort and
skill under the sun. This too is meaningless. 20 So my heart began to despair over
all my toilsome labor under the sun. 21 For
a person may labor with wisdom, knowledge and skill, and then they must leave
all they own to another who has not toiled
for it. This too is meaningless and a great
misfortune. 22 What do people get for all
the toil and anxious striving with which
they labor under the sun?[w] 23 All their days
their work is grief and pain;[x] even at night
their minds do not rest.[y] This too is meaningless.

24 A person can do nothing better than
to eat and drink[z] and find satisfaction in
their own toil.[a] This too, I see, is from
the hand of God,[b] 25 for without him, who
can eat or find enjoyment?[c] 26 To the person who pleases him, God gives wisdom,[d]
knowledge and happiness, but to the sinner he gives the task of gathering and storing up wealth[e] to hand it over to the one
who pleases God.[f] This too is meaningless,
a chasing after the wind.

A Time for Everything

3 There is a time[g] for everything,
and a season for every activity under
the heavens:

2 a time to be born and a time to die,
a time to plant and a time to
uproot,[h]
3 a time to kill[i] and a time to heal,
a time to tear down and a time to
build,
4 a time to weep and a time to laugh,
a time to mourn and a time to
dance,
5 a time to scatter stones and a time to
gather them,
a time to embrace and a time to
refrain from embracing,
6 a time to search and a time to give up,
a time to keep and a time to throw
away,
7 a time to tear and a time to mend,
a time to be silent[j] and a time to
speak,
8 a time to love and a time to hate,
a time for war and a time for peace.

9 What do workers gain from their toil?[k]
10 I have seen the burden God has laid on
the human race.[l] 11 He has made everything beautiful in its time.[m] He has also
set eternity in the human heart; yet[a] no
one can fathom[n] what God has done from
beginning to end.[o] 12 I know that there is
nothing better for people than to be happy and to do good while they live. 13 That
each of them may eat and drink,[p] and find
satisfaction[q] in all their toil—this is the
gift of God.[r] 14 I know that everything God
does will endure forever; nothing can be
added to it and nothing taken from it. God
does it so that people will fear him.[s]

15 Whatever is has already been,[t]
and what will be has been before;[u]
and God will call the past to
account.[b]

16 And I saw something else under the
sun:

In the place of judgment—wickedness
was there,
in the place of justice—wickedness
was there.

17 I said to myself,

"God will bring into judgment[v]
both the righteous and the wicked,

2:17 [t] S Ecc 1:14 **2:18** [u] Ps 39:6; 49:10 **2:19** [v] S ver 15 **2:22** [w] S Ecc 1:3 **2:23** [x] S Ecc 1:18 [y] S Ge 3:17; S Job 7:2 **2:24** [z] ver 3; 1Co 15:32 [a] S ver 1; Ecc 3:22 [b] S Job 2:10; Ecc 3:12-13; 5:17-19; 7:14; 9:7-10; 11:7-10 **2:25** [c] S Ps 127:2 **2:26** [d] S Job 9:4 [e] S Job 27:17 [f] S Pr 13:22 **3:1** [g] ver 11,17; Ecc 8:6 **3:2** [h] Isa 28:24 **3:3** [i] S Dt 5:17

3:7 [j] S Est 4:14 **3:9** [k] S Ecc 1:3 **3:10** [l] S Ecc 1:13 **3:11** [m] S ver 1 [n] S Job 11:7 [o] S Job 28:23; Ro 11:33 **3:13** [p] Ecc 2:3 [q] Ps 34:12 [r] S Dt 12:7,18; S Ecc 2:24 **3:14** [s] S Job 23:15; Ecc 5:7; 7:18; 8:12-13 **3:15** [t] Ecc 6:10 [u] S Ecc 1:9 **3:17** [v] S Job 19:29; Ecc 11:9; 12:14

[a] 11 Or *also placed ignorance in the human heart, so that*
[b] 15 Or *God calls back the past*

2:18 *leave them to the one who comes after me.* See v. 21; Ps 39:6; Lk 12:20.
2:19 *who knows . . . ?* For a more searching "Who knows . . . ?" for secular people, see 3:21.
2:24–25 The heart of Ecclesiastes, a theme repeated in 3:12–13,22; 5:18–20; 8:15; 9:7 and climaxed in 12:13. Only in God does life have meaning and true pleasure. Without him nothing satisfies, but with him we find satisfaction and enjoyment. True pleasure comes only when we acknowledge and revere God (12:13).
2:26 *but to the sinner.* For exceptions to this general principle, see 8:14; Ps 73:1–12.
3:1–22 Humans have little or no control over times and changes. The eternal God sovereignly determines all of life's activities (e.g., the 14 opposites of vv. 2–8).
3:1 Cf. 8:6. *under the heavens.* See note on 1:3.
3:2 *a time.* Divinely appointed (see Ps 31:15; Pr 16:1–9).
3:9 See note on 2:17–23.
3:11 The chapter summarized: God's beautiful but tantalizing world is too big for us, yet its satisfactions are too small. Since we were made for "eternity" (but cf. NIV text note), the things of time cannot fully and permanently satisfy.
3:12–13 A pointer to the book's conclusion. God's people find meaning in life when they cheerfully accept it from the hand of God.
3:14 *so that people will fear him.* Sums up the message of the book (cf. 12:13).
3:15 See 1:9.
3:17 *judgment.* God's true judgments are the answer to cynicism about human injustices. "The past" (v. 15) is not meaningless (as people dismiss it as being, 1:11), and God will override the perverse judgments (v. 16) of people (see 12:14). *the righteous and the wicked.* No one will escape divine judgment (cf. Ro 14:10; 2Co 5:10 and notes; cf. also Rev 20:12–13).

for there will be a time for every
activity,
a time to judge every deed."[w]

18 I also said to myself, "As for humans,
God tests them so that they may see that
they are like the animals.[x] 19 Surely the fate
of human beings[y] is like that of the animals;
the same fate awaits them both: As one
dies, so dies the other. All have the same
breath[a]; humans have no advantage over
animals. Everything is meaningless. 20 All
go to the same place; all come from dust,
and to dust all return.[z] 21 Who knows if the
human spirit rises upward[a] and if the spirit
of the animal goes down into the earth?"

22 So I saw that there is nothing better
for a person than to enjoy their work,[b] because that is their lot.[c] For who can bring
them to see what will happen after them?

Oppression, Toil, Friendlessness

4 Again I looked and saw all the oppression[d] that was taking place under the
sun:

I saw the tears of the oppressed—
and they have no comforter;
power was on the side of their
oppressors—
and they have no comforter.[e]
2 And I declared that the dead,[f]
who had already died,
are happier than the living,
who are still alive.[g]
3 But better than both
is the one who has never been
born,[h]
who has not seen the evil
that is done under the sun.[i]

4 And I saw that all toil and all achievement spring from one person's envy of another. This too is meaningless, a chasing
after the wind.[j]

5 Fools fold their hands[k]
and ruin themselves.
6 Better one handful with tranquillity
than two handfuls with toil[l]
and chasing after the wind.

7 Again I saw something meaningless
under the sun:

8 There was a man all alone;
he had neither son nor brother.
There was no end to his toil,
yet his eyes were not content[m] with
his wealth.
"For whom am I toiling," he asked,
"and why am I depriving myself of
enjoyment?"
This too is meaningless—
a miserable business!

9 Two are better than one,
because they have a good return for
their labor:
10 If either of them falls down,
one can help the other up.
But pity anyone who falls
and has no one to help them up.
11 Also, if two lie down together, they will
keep warm.
But how can one keep warm alone?
12 Though one may be overpowered,
two can defend themselves.
A cord of three strands is not quickly
broken.

Advancement Is Meaningless

13 Better a poor but wise youth than an
old but foolish king who no longer knows
how to heed a warning. 14 The youth may
have come from prison to the kingship, or
he may have been born in poverty within
his kingdom. 15 I saw that all who lived
and walked under the sun followed the

3:17 [w] ver 1
3:18 [x] S Ps 73:22
3:19 [y] S Ecc 2:14
3:20 [z] S Ge 2:7; S Job 34:15
3:21 [a] Ecc 12:7
3:22 [b] S Ecc 2:24 [c] S Job 31:2
4:1 [d] S Ps 12:5 [e] La 1:16
4:2 [f] Jer 20:17-18; 22:10 [g] S Job 3:17; S 10:18
4:3 [h] S Job 3:16 [i] S Job 3:22
4:4 [j] S Ecc 1:14
4:5 [k] S Pr 6:10
4:6 [l] Pr 15:16-17; S 16:8
4:8 [m] Pr 27:20

[a] 19 Or *spirit*

3:18 *like the animals.* Humans "under the sun" are as mortal as any animal; but, unlike animals, they must be made to see this condition and, through their dim awareness of eternity (v. 11), be distressed.
3:19 *same breath.* See Ps 104:29–30.
3:20 *to the same place.* Not heaven or hell but humankind's observable destination, which is a return to dust, just like the animals. Death is the great leveler of all living things (see Ge 3:19; Ps 103:14).
3:21 *Who knows ... ?* See 2:19 and note; cf. 12:7. On their own, human beings cannot know; they can only guess. The answer, revealed at first in glimpses (see e.g., Ps 16:9–11; 49:15; 73:23–26; Isa 26:19; Da 12:2 and note), was brought fully "to light through the gospel" (2Ti 1:10; see also Jn 5:24–29).
3:22 *nothing better.* As an end in itself, work too is meaningless (see 4:4; 9:9). Only receiving it as a gift from God (v. 13) gives it enduring worth (v. 14).
4:1 *oppression.* A theme already touched on (3:16) and another ingredient in the human tragedy. To find life meaningless is sad enough, but to taste its cruelty is bitter beyond words.
4:2 *happier than the living.* See Job 3; Jer 20:14–18. For faith that sees a bigger picture, see Ro 8:35–39.
4:4–6 Neither hard work (motivated by envy) nor idleness brings happiness, meaning or fulfillment.
4:4 *all toil and all achievement.* This too is meaningless unless done with God's blessing (see 3:13; cf. the selfless success of Joseph, Ge 39).
4:5 The ruin of the idle person is vividly pictured in 10:18; Pr 6:6–11; 24:30–34.
4:6 *tranquillity.* See Pr 30:7–9. Paul says the last word on this subject (Php 4:11–13).
4:7–12 Those who toil only for themselves—for whatever reason—lead meaningless and difficult lives.
4:12 *two ... three.* A climactic construction (see Job 5:19; Pr 6:16 and notes).
4:13–16 Advancement without God is another example of the meaninglessness of secularism.

youth, the king's successor. 16 There was
no end to all the people who were before
them. But those who came later were not
pleased with the successor. This too is
meaningless, a chasing after the wind.

Fulfill Your Vow to God

5 [a] Guard your steps when you go to the
house of God. Go near to listen rather
than to offer the sacrifice of fools, who do
not know that they do wrong.

2 Do not be quick with your mouth,
do not be hasty in your heart
to utter anything before God.[n]
God is in heaven
and you are on earth,
so let your words be few.[o]
3 A dream[p] comes when there are many
cares,
and many words mark the speech of
a fool.[q]

4 When you make a vow to God, do not
delay to fulfill it.[r] He has no pleasure in
fools; fulfill your vow.[s] 5 It is better not to
make a vow than to make one and not
fulfill it.[t] 6 Do not let your mouth lead you
into sin. And do not protest to the temple
messenger, "My vow was a mistake." Why
should God be angry at what you say and
destroy the work of your hands? 7 Much
dreaming and many words are meaningless. Therefore fear God.[u]

Riches Are Meaningless

8 If you see the poor oppressed[v] in a district, and justice and rights denied, do not
be surprised at such things; for one official
is eyed by a higher one, and over them
both are others higher still. 9 The increase
from the land is taken by all; the king himself profits from the fields.

10 Whoever loves money never has
enough;
whoever loves wealth is never
satisfied with their income.
This too is meaningless.

11 As goods increase,
so do those who consume them.
And what benefit are they to the
owners
except to feast their eyes on them?

12 The sleep of a laborer is sweet,
whether they eat little or much,
but as for the rich, their abundance
permits them no sleep.[w]

13 I have seen a grievous evil under the
sun:[x]

wealth hoarded to the harm of its
owners,
14 or wealth lost through some
misfortune,
so that when they have children
there is nothing left for them to
inherit.
15 Everyone comes naked from their
mother's womb,
and as everyone comes, so they
depart.[y]
They take nothing from their toil[z]
that they can carry in their hands.[a]

16 This too is a grievous evil:

As everyone comes, so they depart,
and what do they gain,
since they toil for the wind?[b]
17 All their days they eat in darkness,
with great frustration, affliction and
anger.

18 This is what I have observed to be
good: that it is appropriate for a person

5:2 [n] S Jdg 11:35 [o] S Job 6:24; S Pr 20:25 **5:3** [p] S Job 20:8 [q] Ecc 10:14 **5:4** [r] S Dt 23:21; S Jdg 11:35; Ps 119:60 [s] S Nu 30:2; Ps 66:13-14 **5:5** [t] Nu 30:2-4; Jnh 2:9 **5:7** [u] Ecc 3:14 **5:8** [v] S Ps 12:5 **5:12** [w] Job 20:20 **5:13** [x] Ecc 6:1-2 **5:15** [y] S Job 1:21 [z] Ps 49:17; 1Ti 6:7 [a] Ecc 1:3 **5:16** [b] S Ecc 1:3

[a] In Hebrew texts 5:1 is numbered 4:17, and 5:2-20 is numbered 5:1-19.

4:16 *were before them.* Stood before them and served them. *those who came later.* The next generation.

5:1 – 7 The theme of this section is the meaninglessness of superficial religion, as reflected in making rash vows.

5:1 *Guard your steps.* Think about what you ought to say and do. *house of God.* Here probably a reference to Solomon's temple. *listen.* Obey. 1Sa 15:22 uses the same Hebrew verb and makes the same contrast between real and superficial worship. *sacrifice.* Probably connected with the vow of vv. 4 – 6.

5:2 *quick with your mouth.* As in a rash vow (cf. Jdg 11:30 and note). *God … heaven … you … earth.* Highlights the contrast between God and humankind.

5:3 A proverb. In context it suggests that in the midst of cares one dreams of bliss (as a starving person dreams of a banquet), and in anticipation may offer rash vows ("many words") to God (see v. 7).

5:4 *vow.* See Dt 23:21 – 23; 1Sa 1:11, 24 – 28. *no pleasure in fools.* In Scripture the fool is not one who cannot learn but one who refuses to learn (see Pr 1:20 – 27; see also NIV text note on Pr 1:7).

5:6 *temple messenger.* Probably the priest (see Mal 2:7 and note). *Why should God be angry … ?* To break a vow is a serious matter (see Nu 30:2 and note on 30:1 – 16) and can have disastrous consequences (see Dt 23:21 – 23).

5:8 *do not be surprised.* For other frank appraisals of human society, see 4:1 – 3. This teacher, like Jesus, who "knew what was in" people (Jn 2:25), had no illusions or utopian schemes.

5:9 *king … profits from the fields.* See note on Am 7:1.

5:10 Greater wealth does not bring satisfaction (see 1Ti 6:6 – 8; see also Php 4:11 – 12 and notes).

5:11 – 12 Greater wealth brings greater anxiety (see vv. 13 – 14 and note on v. 13; Mt 13:22; 1Ti 6:9 – 10,17 – 19).

5:11 *those who consume them.* Human parasites.

5:13 *harm.* Including worry about one's possessions.

5:15 *They take nothing.* See Lk 12:13 – 21.

5:18 – 20 See note on 2:24 – 25.

to eat, to drink[c] and to find satisfaction in
their toilsome labor[d] under the sun during
the few days of life God has given them—
for this is their lot. 19 Moreover, when God
gives someone wealth and possessions,[e]
and the ability to enjoy them,[f] to accept
their lot[g] and be happy in their toil—this
is a gift of God.[h] 20 They seldom reflect on
the days of their life, because God keeps
them occupied with gladness of heart.[i]

6 I have seen another evil under the
sun, and it weighs heavily on mankind: 2 God gives some people wealth,
possessions and honor, so that they lack
nothing their hearts desire, but God does
not grant them the ability to enjoy them,[j]
and strangers enjoy them instead. This is
meaningless, a grievous evil.[k]
3 A man may have a hundred children
and live many years; yet no matter how
long he lives, if he cannot enjoy his prosperity and does not receive proper burial, I
say that a stillborn[l] child is better off than
he.[m] 4 It comes without meaning, it departs
in darkness, and in darkness its name is
shrouded. 5 Though it never saw the sun or
knew anything, it has more rest than does
that man— 6 even if he lives a thousand
years twice over but fails to enjoy his prosperity. Do not all go to the same place?[n]

7 Everyone's toil is for their mouth,
yet their appetite is never satisfied.[o]
8 What advantage have the wise over
fools?[p]
What do the poor gain
by knowing how to conduct
themselves before others?
9 Better what the eye sees
than the roving of the appetite.
This too is meaningless,
a chasing after the wind.[q]

10 Whatever exists has already been
named,[r]
and what humanity is has been
known;
no one can contend
with someone who is stronger.
11 The more the words,
the less the meaning,
and how does that profit anyone?

12 For who knows what is good for a person in life, during the few and meaningless days[s] they pass through like a shadow?[t] Who can tell them what will happen
under the sun after they are gone?

Wisdom

7 A good name is better than fine
perfume,[u]
and the day of death better than the
day of birth.[v]
2 It is better to go to a house of
mourning
than to go to a house of feasting,
for death[w] is the destiny[x] of everyone;
the living should take this to
heart.
3 Frustration is better than laughter,[y]
because a sad face is good for the
heart.
4 The heart of the wise is in the house of
mourning,
but the heart of fools is in the house
of pleasure.[z]
5 It is better to heed the rebuke[a] of a
wise person
than to listen to the song of fools.
6 Like the crackling of thorns[b] under the
pot,
so is the laughter[c] of fools.
This too is meaningless.

7 Extortion turns a wise person into a
fool,
and a bribe[d] corrupts the heart.

8 The end of a matter is better than its
beginning,
and patience[e] is better than pride.
9 Do not be quickly provoked[f] in your
spirit,
for anger resides in the lap of fools.[g]

5:18 [c] S Ecc 2:3 [d] Ecc 2:10,24
5:19 [e] S 1Ch 29:12 [f] Ecc 6:2 [g] S Job 31:2 [h] S Ecc 2:24
5:20 [i] S Dt 12:7, 18
6:2 [j] Ecc 5:19 [k] Ecc 5:13
6:3 [l] S Job 3:16 [m] S Job 3:3
6:6 [n] Ecc 2:14
6:7 [o] S Pr 27:20
6:8 [p] S Ecc 2:15
6:9 [q] S Ecc 1:14
6:10 [r] Ecc 3:15
6:12 [s] S Job 10:20; S 20:8 [t] S 1Ch 29:15; S Job 14:2; S Ps 39:6
7:1 [u] Pr 22:1; SS 1:3 [v] S Job 10:18
7:2 [w] S Pr 11:19 [x] S Ecc 2:14
7:3 [y] S Pr 14:13
7:4 [z] S Ecc 2:1; Jer 16:8
7:5 [a] S Pr 13:18; 15:31-32
7:6 [b] S Ps 58:9 [c] S Pr 14:13
7:7 [d] S Ex 18:21; S 23:8
7:8 [e] Pr 14:29
7:9 [f] S Mt 5:22 [g] S Pr 14:29

6:2–3,6 *enjoy.* Comparing v. 2 with 5:19 demonstrates that the ability to enjoy God's blessings is a bonus—a gift of God, not a right or guarantee. God calls the person who forgets this truth a "fool" (Lk 12:20).

6:2 *strangers enjoy them instead.* For example, when people are robbed of their wealth or die without heirs.

6:3 *does not receive proper burial.* Dies unlamented or dishonored, like King Jehoiakim (Jer 22:18–19). *stillborn child.* For the secularist, life is a pointless journey to extinction, to which being stillborn is the quickest and easiest route (cf. Job 3:16; Ps 58:8).

6:6 *to the same place.* Still talking in terms of what we can observe (that all people die), not of what lies beyond death and the grave (see v. 12; 3:20 and note).

6:7–12 In confronting complacency, the Teacher gives several causes for concern: the short-lived (v. 7), debatable (v. 8) and elusive (v. 9) rewards of life; the limits of our creativity, power and wisdom (vv. 10–11); and the unreliability of merely human values and predictions (v. 12).

6:9 It is better to be content with what one has than to nurture unrestrained desires (cf. Php 4:11–12 and note on 4:12; 1Ti 6:6,8).

6:10 *named.* Predetermined by God (see notes on 3:1–22; 3:2). *known.* Foreknown by God. *someone who is stronger.* God.

6:12 *like a shadow.* See Job 8:9 and note.

7:1 *day of death better.* The Christian has ample reason to say this (2Co 5:1–10; Php 1:21–23). But the Teacher's point is valid, as explained in vv. 2–6; namely, that happy times generally teach us less than hard times.

7:6 *crackling of thorns.* The "laughter of fools" is likened to a noisy, but short-lived, fire (see Ps 58:9 and note).

7:7 *bribe.* See Mt 28:11–15; Lk 22:4–6.

7:9 *anger.* See, e.g., Pr 16:32; 17:14; 1Co 13:4–5.

[10]Do not say, "Why were the old days[h]
better than these?"
For it is not wise to ask such
questions.

[11]Wisdom, like an inheritance, is a good
thing[i]
and benefits those who see the sun.[j]
[12]Wisdom is a shelter
as money is a shelter,
but the advantage of knowledge is this:
Wisdom preserves those who
have it.

[13]Consider what God has done:[k]

Who can straighten
what he has made crooked?[l]
[14]When times are good, be happy;
but when times are bad, consider
this:
God has made the one
as well as the other.[m]
Therefore, no one can discover
anything about their future.

[15]In this meaningless life[n] of mine I
have seen both of these:

the righteous perishing in their
righteousness,
and the wicked living long in their
wickedness.[o]
[16]Do not be overrighteous,
neither be overwise—
why destroy yourself?
[17]Do not be overwicked,
and do not be a fool—
why die before your time?[p]
[18]It is good to grasp the one
and not let go of the other.
Whoever fears God[q] will avoid all
extremes.[a]

[19]Wisdom[r] makes one wise person more
powerful[s]
than ten rulers in a city.

[20]Indeed, there is no one on earth who is
righteous,[t]
no one who does what is right and
never sins.[u]

[21]Do not pay attention to every word
people say,
or you[v] may hear your servant
cursing you—
[22]for you know in your heart
that many times you yourself have
cursed others.

[23]All this I tested by wisdom and I said,

"I am determined to be wise"[w]—
but this was beyond me.
[24]Whatever exists is far off and most
profound—
who can discover it?[x]
[25]So I turned my mind to understand,
to investigate and to search out
wisdom and the scheme of
things[y]
and to understand the stupidity of
wickedness
and the madness of folly.[z]

[26]I find more bitter than death
the woman who is a snare,[a]
whose heart is a trap
and whose hands are chains.
The man who pleases God will escape
her,
but the sinner she will ensnare.[b]

[27]"Look," says the Teacher,[b][c] "this is
what I have discovered:

"Adding one thing to another to
discover the scheme of
things—
[28]while I was still searching
but not finding—
I found one upright man among a
thousand,
but not one upright woman[d] among
them all.
[29]This only have I found:
God created mankind upright,

7:10 [h]S Ps 77:5 **7:11** [i]Ecc 2:13 [j]Ecc 11:7 **7:13** [k]Ecc 2:24 [l]Ecc 1:15 **7:14** [m]S Job 1:21; S Ecc 2:24 **7:15** [n]S Job 7:7 [o]S Job 21:7; Ecc 8:12-14; Jer 12:1 **7:17** [p]Job 15:32 **7:18** [q]S Ecc 3:14 **7:19** [r]S Ecc 2:13 [s]S Pr 8:14 **7:20** [t]S Ps 14:3 [u]S 2Ch 6:36; S Job 4:17; S Pr 20:9; Ro 3:12 **7:21** [v]Pr 30:10 **7:23** [w]S Ecc 1:17 **7:24** [x]S Job 28:12 **7:25** [y]S Job 28:3 [z]S Ecc 1:17 **7:26** [a]S Ex 10:7; S Jdg 14:15 [b]S Pr 2:16-19; 5:3-5; S 7:23; 22:14 **7:27** [c]S Ecc 1:1 **7:28** [d]1Ki 11:3

[a] 18 Or *will follow them both* [b] 27 Or *the leader of the assembly*

7:11 *see the sun.* Are alive.
7:12 *preserves those who have it.* Cf. Pr 3:13–18; 13:14.
7:13 *Who can straighten ... ?* Not fatalism, but a reminder that mere mortals cannot change what God determines (see note on 1:15; cf. also note on 3:1–22).
7:14 *God has made the one* [bad times] *as well as the other* [good times]. Cf. Ro 8:28–29.
7:15 *the righteous perishing.* Righteousness is no sure protection against hard times or an early death.
7:16 *not ... overrighteous ... overwise.* If true righteousness and wisdom do not necessarily prevent ruin, then extreme, legalistic righteousness and wisdom will surely not help.
7:17 *not ... overwicked.* Extreme wickedness is even more foolhardy.

7:18 *the one ... the other.* The God-fearing person will avoid both extremes (legalism and libertinism) and lead a balanced—truly righteous and wise—life (cf. Ro 6:14).

7:20 *no one on earth ... righteous.* A sober Biblical truth (see Ro 3:10–20,23).
7:24 See Job 28:12–28; 1Co 2:9–16.
7:26 See Pr 7:6–27.
7:27 *Teacher.* See note on 1:1. *Adding one thing to another to discover the scheme of things.* This inductive method can never be complete, nor can we reliably interpret all that we manage to observe (3:11b). Human wisdom and understanding must always yield to revealed truth.
7:28 *one upright man ... but not one upright woman.* According to the Teacher's experience. Scripture nowhere declares that women are morally inferior.
7:29 *God created mankind upright, but.* See Ge 3:1–6; Ro 5:12.

but they have gone in search of
many schemes."

8 Who is like the wise?
Who knows the explanation of
things?
A person's wisdom brightens their face
and changes its hard appearance.

Obey the King

2 Obey the king's command, I say, because you took an oath before God. 3 Do
not be in a hurry to leave the king's presence.[e] Do not stand up for a bad cause, for
he will do whatever he pleases. 4 Since a
king's word is supreme, who can say to
him, "What are you doing?[f]"

5 Whoever obeys his command will
come to no harm,
and the wise heart will know the
proper time and procedure.
6 For there is a proper time and
procedure for every matter,[g]
though a person may be weighed
down by misery.

7 Since no one knows the future,
who can tell someone else what is to
come?
8 As no one has power over the wind to
contain it,
so[a] no one has power over the time
of their death.
As no one is discharged in time of war,
so wickedness will not release those
who practice it.

9 All this I saw, as I applied my mind to
everything done under the sun. There is
a time when a man lords it over others to
his own[b] hurt. 10 Then too, I saw the wicked buried[h]—those who used to come and
go from the holy place and receive praise[c]
in the city where they did this. This too is
meaningless.

11 When the sentence for a crime is not
quickly carried out, people's hearts are
filled with schemes to do wrong. 12 Although a wicked person who commits a
hundred crimes may live a long time, I
know that it will go better[i] with those who
fear God,[j] who are reverent before him.[k]
13 Yet because the wicked do not fear God,[l]
it will not go well with them, and their
days[m] will not lengthen like a shadow.
14 There is something else meaningless
that occurs on earth: the righteous who
get what the wicked deserve, and the
wicked who get what the righteous deserve.[n] This too, I say, is meaningless.[o]
15 So I commend the enjoyment of life[p], because there is nothing better for a person
under the sun than to eat and drink[q] and
be glad.[r] Then joy will accompany them
in their toil all the days of the life God has
given them under the sun.
16 When I applied my mind to know
wisdom[s] and to observe the labor that is
done on earth[t]—people getting no sleep
day or night— 17 then I saw all that God
has done.[u] No one can comprehend what
goes on under the sun. Despite all their efforts to search it out, no one can discover
its meaning. Even if the wise claim they
know, they cannot really comprehend it.[v]

A Common Destiny for All

9 So I reflected on all this and concluded that the righteous and the wise and
what they do are in God's hands, but no
one knows whether love or hate awaits
them.[w] 2 All share a common destiny—the
righteous and the wicked, the good and
the bad,[d] the clean and the unclean, those
who offer sacrifices and those who do not.

8:3 [e] Ecc 10:4 **8:4** [f] Est 1:19 **8:6** [g] Ecc 3:1 **8:10** [h] S Ecc 1:11 **8:12** [i] S Dt 12:28 [j] S Ex 1:20 [k] Ecc 3:14 **8:13** [l] Ecc 3:14 [m] Dt 4:40; Job 5:26; Ps 34:12; Isa 65:20 **8:14** [n] S Job 21:7 [o] S Ecc 7:15 **8:15** [p] S Ps 42:8 [q] S Ex 32:6; S Ecc 2:3 [r] S Ecc 2:1 **8:16** [s] S Ecc 1:17 [t] Ecc 1:13 **8:17** [u] S Job 28:3 [v] S Job 28:23; Ro 11:33 **9:1** [w] Ecc 10:14

[a] 8 Or *over the human spirit to retain it, / and so* [b] 9 Or *to their* [c] 10 Some Hebrew manuscripts and Septuagint (Aquila); most Hebrew manuscripts *and are forgotten* [d] 2 Septuagint (Aquila), Vulgate and Syriac; Hebrew does not have *and the bad.*

8:2 *king's command.* Both principle (v. 2) and prudence (vv. 3–6) set limits on our freedom. *took an oath.* Of loyalty to the king (as seen, e.g., in 1Ch 29:24).
8:3 *Do not ... hurry to leave the king's presence.* To do so would show lack of respect—even disloyalty—to him.
8:4 *who can say ..., "What are you doing?"* Cf. Isa 45:9; Ro 9:20.
8:5 *Whoever obeys ... will come to no harm.* See Ro 13:3–5 and notes.
8:6 *though a person may be weighed down by misery.* People should put the king's command above their own misery.
8:7–8 *no one knows ... no one has power.* See Ps 31:15; Mt 6:34; 2Co 5:1–10; Jas 4:13–16.
8:8 *wickedness will not release.* Moral evil has great power to enslave (see Ro 7:15–24 and note on 7:17). But see Ro 7:25 and note.
8:10 *the wicked buried.* In this context implies undeserved respect (see note on 6:3; cf. Job 21:28–33; Lk 16:22).
8:11 Delayed punishment tends to induce more wrongdoing.
8:12 *I know.* Here the Teacher speaks from mature faith, not as one "still searching but not finding" (7:28). For similar declarations, see 3:17; 11:9; 12:14.
8:14 Job 21–24 enlarges on this; Ps 73 draws the sting of it; and Jn 5:28–29 gives the final explanation. *on earth.* See 1:3 and note.
8:15 *eat ... drink ... be glad.* Spoken gratefully (see 5:19; 9:7; Dt 8). For such words spoken arrogantly, see Lk 12:19–20; 1Co 15:32.
8:17 *No one can comprehend.* Dt 29:29 sums up what we are allowed and not allowed to know (cf. Ro 11:33).
9:1 *whether love or hate.* The future is under God's control, and no one knows whether that future will be good or bad.
9:2 *common destiny.* See v. 3 and note. Not only the wise and foolish (2:14) but also the good and the bad are seen leveled, in the sense noted at 3:20. For the Teacher's conviction (beyond mere observation) that God ultimately will see justice done, see note on 8:12.

As it is with the good,
so with the sinful;
as it is with those who take oaths,
so with those who are afraid to take
them.[x]

3 This is the evil in everything that happens under the sun: The same destiny
overtakes all.[y] The hearts of people, moreover, are full of evil and there is madness
in their hearts while they live,[z] and afterward they join the dead.[a] 4 Anyone who is
among the living has hope[a] — even a live
dog is better off than a dead lion!

5 For the living know that they will die,
but the dead know nothing;[b]
they have no further reward,
and even their name[c] is forgotten.[d]
6 Their love, their hate
and their jealousy have long since
vanished;
never again will they have a part
in anything that happens under the
sun.[e]

7 Go, eat your food with gladness, and
drink your wine[f] with a joyful heart,[g] for
God has already approved what you do.
8 Always be clothed in white,[h] and always
anoint your head with oil. 9 Enjoy life with
your wife,[i] whom you love, all the days of
this meaningless life that God has given
you under the sun — all your meaningless
days. For this is your lot[j] in life and in your
toilsome labor under the sun. 10 Whatever[k]
your hand finds to do, do it with all your
might,[l] for in the realm of the dead,[m] where
you are going, there is neither working nor
planning nor knowledge nor wisdom.[n]

11 I have seen something else under the
sun:

The race is not to the swift
or the battle to the strong,[o]
nor does food come to the wise[p]
or wealth to the brilliant
or favor to the learned;
but time and chance[q] happen to
them all.[r]

12 Moreover, no one knows when their
hour will come:

As fish are caught in a cruel net,
or birds are taken in a snare,
so people are trapped by evil times[s]
that fall unexpectedly upon them.[t]

Wisdom Better Than Folly

13 I also saw under the sun this example of wisdom[u] that greatly impressed me:
14 There was once a small city with only
a few people in it. And a powerful king
came against it, surrounded it and built
huge siege works against it. 15 Now there
lived in that city a man poor but wise, and
he saved the city by his wisdom. But nobody remembered that poor man.[v] 16 So
I said, "Wisdom is better than strength."
But the poor man's wisdom is despised,
and his words are no longer heeded.[w]

17 The quiet words of the wise are more
to be heeded
than the shouts of a ruler of fools.
18 Wisdom[x] is better than weapons of
war,
but one sinner destroys much good.

10 As dead flies give perfume a bad
smell,
so a little folly[y] outweighs wisdom
and honor.
2 The heart of the wise inclines to the
right,
but the heart of the fool to the left.
3 Even as fools walk along the road,
they lack sense
and show everyone[z] how stupid they
are.
4 If a ruler's anger rises against you,
do not leave your post;[a]
calmness can lay great offenses to
rest.[b]

5 There is an evil I have seen under the
sun,
the sort of error that arises from a
ruler:

[a] 4 Or *What then is to be chosen? With all who live, there is hope*

9:2 [x] Job 9:22; Ecc 2:14 **9:3** [y] S Job 9:22; S Ecc 2:14 [z] Jer 11:8; 13:10; 16:12; 17:9 [a] S Job 21:26 **9:5** [b] S Job 14:21 [c] S Ps 9:6 [d] S Ecc 1:11 **9:6** [e] S Job 21:21 **9:7** [f] S Nu 6:20 [g] S Ecc 2:24 **9:8** [h] S Rev 3:4 **9:9** [i] S Pr 5:18 [j] S Job 31:2 **9:10** [k] S 1Sa 10:7 [l] Ecc 11:6 [m] Nu 16:33; S Ps 6:5; Isa 38:18 [n] S Ecc 2:24 **9:11** [o] Am 2:14-15 [p] Job 32:13; Isa 47:10; Jer 9:23 [q] Ecc 2:14 [r] S Dt 8:18 **9:12** [s] S Pr 29:6 [t] S Ps 73:22; S Ecc 2:14 **9:13** [u] S 2Sa 20:22 **9:15** [v] S Ge 40:14; S Ecc 1:11 **9:16** [w] Est 6:3 **9:18** [x] S Ecc 2:13 **10:1** [y] Pr 13:16; 18:2 **10:3** [z] Pr 13:16 **10:4** [a] Ecc 8:3 [b] S Pr 16:14

9:3 *evil . . . evil.* The apparently common destiny (both the righteous and the wicked die) encourages some people to sin.
9:5 *no further reward.* The dead have lost all opportunity in this life for enjoyment and reward from labor (see v. 6).
9:7 – 9 The Babylonian Gilgamesh epic contains a section (10.3.6 – 14) remarkably similar to this passage, illustrating the international flavor of ancient wisdom literature (see chart, p. xxii, and essay, p. 786).
9:7 See note on 8:15.
9:8 *be clothed in white . . . anoint your head with oil.* Expressions of joy (cf. Ps 45:7 and note).
9:10 Cf. Col 3:23.

9:11 *time and chance.* Success is uncertain — more evidence that humans do not ultimately control events.
9:12 *hour.* Of disaster. *people are trapped.* Success is unpredictable, because people are not wise enough to know when misfortune may overtake them.
9:15 *But nobody remembered.* Further warning against placing too high hopes on one's wisdom. Its reputation fades, its good is soon undone (v. 18b) and it has no answer to death (2:15 – 16).
10:1 *a little folly outweighs.* 2Ki 20:12 – 19 presents a striking example.
10:2 *to the right . . . to the left.* These can stand for the greater good and the lesser good (cf. Ge 48:13 – 20); or perhaps here, as in some later Jewish writings, for good and evil (cf. Mt 25:33 – 34,41).
10:5 *error . . . from a ruler.* For the Teacher's observations on

Looking up at typical construction of a rural house roof in ancient times. "Through laziness, the rafters sag; because of idle hands, the house leaks" (Ecc 10:18).

Z. Radovan/www.BibleLandPictures.com

6 Fools are put in many high
  positions,[c]
 while the rich occupy the low
  ones.
7 I have seen slaves on horseback,
 while princes go on foot like
  slaves.[d]
8 Whoever digs a pit may fall
  into it;[e]
 whoever breaks through a wall
  may be bitten by a
  snake.[f]
9 Whoever quarries stones may
  be injured by them;
 whoever splits logs may be
  endangered by them.[g]
10 If the ax is dull
 and its edge unsharpened,
more strength is needed,
 but skill will bring success.
11 If a snake bites before it is
  charmed,
 the charmer receives no fee.[h]
12 Words from the mouth of the wise are
  gracious,[i]
 but fools are consumed by their own
  lips.[j]
13 At the beginning their words are folly;
 at the end they are wicked
  madness—
14 and fools multiply words.[k]

No one knows what is coming—
 who can tell someone else what will
  happen after them?[l]
15 The toil of fools wearies them;
 they do not know the way to town.
16 Woe to the land whose king was a
  servant[a][m]
 and whose princes feast in the
  morning.
17 Blessed is the land whose king is of
  noble birth
 and whose princes eat at a proper
  time—
 for strength and not for
  drunkenness.[n]

10:6 [c] S Pr 29:2 **10:7** [d] Pr 19:10 **10:8** [e] S Ps 57:6 [f] S Est 2:23; Ps 9:16; Am 5:19 **10:9** [g] S Pr 26:27 **10:11** [h] S Ps 58:5; S Isa 3:3 **10:12** [i] Pr 10:32 [j] S Pr 10:6; S 14:3; S 15:2; S 18:7 **10:14** [k] Ecc 5:3 [l] Ecc 9:1 **10:16** [m] Isa 3:4-5,12 **10:17** [n] S Dt 14:26; S 1Sa 25:36; S Pr 31:4 **10:18** [o] Pr 20:4; S 24:30-34 **10:19** [p] S Ge 14:18; S Jdg 9:13 **10:20** [q] S Ex 22:28 **11:1** [r] ver 6; Isa 32:20; Hos 10:12 [s] S Dt 24:19

18 Through laziness, the rafters sag;
 because of idle hands, the house
  leaks.[o]
19 A feast is made for laughter,
 wine[p] makes life merry,
 and money is the answer for
  everything.
20 Do not revile the king[q] even in your
  thoughts,
 or curse the rich in your bedroom,
because a bird in the sky may carry
  your words,
 and a bird on the wing may report
  what you say.

Invest in Many Ventures

11 Ship[r] your grain across the sea;
 after many days you may receive
  a return.[s]
2 Invest in seven ventures, yes, in eight;
 you do not know what disaster may
  come upon the land.
3 If clouds are full of water,
 they pour rain on the earth.

[a] 16 Or *king is a child*

human regimes, see vv. 4,6–7,16–17,20; 3:16; 4:1–3,13–16; 5:8–9; 8:2–6,10–11; 9:17.
10:6–7 See Pr 19:10 and note; 30:21–22.
10:12 *Words.* A favorite topic in wisdom literature (see, e.g., Pr 15; Jas 3:2–12).
10:15 *fools ... do not know the way to town.* Since in Scripture a fool is one who refuses God's teaching (see note on 5:4), this caustic saying (probably proverbial) refers to more than mere stupidity.
10:16 *whose king was a servant.* A small-minded upstart, not a "poor but wise youth" as in 4:13. See 2Ki 15:8–25; Hos 7:3–7, which portray some of the short-lived usurpers and vicious courtiers who hastened the downfall of Israel.
10:18 *laziness ... idle.* See note on 4:5. See photo above.
10:19 *money is the answer for everything.* Can be read at various levels—as a wry comment on human values, as sober advice to earn a good living rather than have a good time (see the first two lines) or as stating the great versatility of money (cf. Lk 16:9 and note).
11:1 Be adventurous, like those who accept the risks and reap the benefits of seaborne trade. Do not always play it safe (see Pr 11:24 and note).
11:2 Diversify your efforts because you never know which ventures may fail. "Don't put all your eggs in one basket." Diversify your undertakings and reduce the risks.
11:3–6 *clouds ... tree ... wind ... seed.* Do not toy with maybes

Whether a tree falls to the south or to the north,
in the place where it falls, there it will lie.
4 Whoever watches the wind will not plant;
whoever looks at the clouds will not reap.

5 As you do not know the path of the wind,[t]
or how the body is formed[a] in a mother's womb,[u]
so you cannot understand the work of God,
the Maker of all things.

6 Sow your seed in the morning,
and at evening let your hands not be idle,[v]
for you do not know which will succeed,
whether this or that,
or whether both will do equally well.

Remember Your Creator While Young

7 Light is sweet,
and it pleases the eyes to see the sun.[w]
8 However many years anyone may live,
let them enjoy them all.
But let them remember[x] the days of darkness,
for there will be many.
Everything to come is meaningless.

9 You who are young, be happy while you are young,
and let your heart give you joy in the days of your youth.
Follow the ways of your heart
and whatever your eyes see,
but know that for all these things
God will bring you into judgment.[y]
10 So then, banish anxiety[z] from your heart
and cast off the troubles of your body,
for youth and vigor are meaningless.[a]

12 Remember[b] your Creator
in the days of your youth,
before the days of trouble[c] come
and the years approach when you will say,
"I find no pleasure in them"—
2 before the sun and the light
and the moon and the stars grow dark,
and the clouds return after the rain;
3 when the keepers of the house tremble,
and the strong men stoop,
when the grinders cease because they are few,
and those looking through the windows grow dim;
4 when the doors to the street are closed
and the sound of grinding fades;
when people rise up at the sound of birds,
but all their songs grow faint;[d]
5 when people are afraid of heights
and of dangers in the streets;
when the almond tree blossoms
and the grasshopper drags itself along
and desire no longer is stirred.
Then people go to their eternal home[e]
and mourners[f] go about the streets.

6 Remember him—before the silver cord is severed,
and the golden bowl is broken;
before the pitcher is shattered at the spring,
and the wheel broken at the well,
7 and the dust returns[g] to the ground it came from,
and the spirit returns to God[h] who gave it.[i]

11:5 [t] Jn 3:8-10 [u] Ps 139:14-16 **11:6** [v] S Ecc 9:10 **11:7** [w] Ecc 7:11 **11:8** [x] Ecc 12:1 **11:9** [y] S Job 19:29; S Ecc 2:24; S 3:17 **11:10** [z] Ps 94:19 [a] S Ecc 2:24 **12:1** [b] Ecc 11:8 [c] S 2Sa 19:35 **12:4** [d] Jer 25:10 **12:5** [e] S Job 10:21 [f] Jer 9:17; Am 5:16 **12:7** [g] S Ge 2:7; S Ps 146:4 [h] Ecc 3:21 [i] S Job 20:8 **12:8** [j] Ecc 1:1 [k] S Ecc 1:2

[a] *5* Or *know how life* (or *the spirit*) / *enters the body being formed*

and might-have-beens. Start where you can, and recognize how limited your role (or knowledge) is.

11:5 *wind.* See NIV text note; cf. Jn 3:8 ("wind" and "spirit" translate the same word in the original in both verses).

11:7–10 Live life to the fullest (cf. Jn 10:10; Php 1:21 and notes).

11:8,10 *meaningless.* Warns against letting the wonderful gifts mentioned in vv. 7–10 dazzle and distract us. Verse 9 sets us on the true course.

11:9 *judgment.* See 12:14 and note. The prospect of divine praise or blame makes every detail of life significant rather than meaningless. To know this gives direction to our hearts and discrimination to our eyes. The stage is set for ch. 12.

12:1 *days of your youth.* Cf. La 3:27.

12:2–5 A graphic description of progressive deterioration; an allegory about aging.

12:3 *keepers of the house.* This and the other metaphors may refer to parts of the body (hands, legs, etc.). But the imagery should not be pressed to the extent that it destroys the poetry, which moves freely between figures such as darkness, storm, a house in decline and a deserted well, and such literal descriptions as in v. 5a.

12:5 *almond tree.* Its pale blossom possibly suggests the white hair of age. *grasshopper.* Normally agile, its slow movements on a cold morning (cf. Na 3:17) recall the stiffness of old age. *eternal home.* In context, probably points simply to the grave, not beyond it (see Job 10:21 and note; 17:13).

12:6 *silver cord … golden bowl.* A hanging lamp suspended by a silver chain. If only one link snaps, this light and beauty will perish, suggesting how fragile life is.

[8]"Meaningless! Meaningless!" says the
Teacher.[a][j]
"Everything is meaningless![k]"

The Conclusion of the Matter

[9]Not only was the Teacher wise, but he also imparted knowledge to the people. He pondered and searched out and set in order many proverbs.[l] [10]The Teacher[m] searched to find just the right words, and what he wrote was upright and true.[n]

[11]The words of the wise are like goads, their collected sayings like firmly embedded nails[o]—given by one shepherd.[b] [12]Be warned, my son, of anything in addition to them.

Of making many books there is no end,
and much study wearies the body.[p]

[13]Now all has been heard;
here is the conclusion of the matter:
Fear God[q] and keep his
commandments,[r]
for this is the duty of all mankind.[s]
[14]For God will bring every deed into
judgment,[t]
including every hidden thing,[u]
whether it is good or evil.

12:9 [l]1Ki 4:32 **12:10** [m]S Ecc 1:1 [n]Pr 22:20-21 **12:11** [o]S Ezr 9:8; S Job 6:25 **12:12** [p]S Ecc 1:18 **12:13** [q]S Ex 20:20; S 1Sa 12:24; S Job 23:15; S Ps 19:9 [r]S Dt 4:2 [s]S Dt 4:6; S Job 37:24 **12:14** [t]S Job 19:29; S Ecc 3:17 [u]S Job 34:21; S Ps 19:12; Jer 16:17; 23:24

[a] *8* Or *the leader of the assembly*; also in verses 9 and 10
[b] *11* Or *Shepherd*

12:8 *Meaningless!* See 1:2 and note; see also Introduction: Literary Features. Such is life "under the sun" (on earth, apart from God), ending in brokenness. But with a relationship to our Creator already demanded (v. 1), and with the fact of his judgment affirmed (11:9), meaninglessness is not the last word. *Teacher.* See note on 1:1.

12:9 *pondered and searched.* A rigorous process, with no pains spared in seeking truth and comprehension.

12:11 *given by one shepherd.* See NIV text note; the other side of the matter, recognizing that Scripture is in a class of its own, as v. 12 insists.

12:13 *Fear God.* Loving reverence is the foundation of wisdom (see Ps 111:10; Pr 1:7 and notes), as well as its content (Job 28:28) and its goal and conclusion. *the duty of all mankind.* Here is our fulfillment, our all—a far cry from meaninglessness.

12:14 *every deed into judgment.* Glimpses of this truth are given at intervals in the book: See 3:17; 8:12–13; 11:9 and note; see also Mt 12:36; 1Co 3:12–15 and notes; 2Co 5:9–10; Heb 4:12–13. *every hidden thing.* See Ro 2:16.

SONG OF SONGS

INTRODUCTION

Title

The title in the Hebrew text is "Solomon's Song of Songs," meaning a "song by, for or about Solomon." The phrase "Song of Songs" means "the greatest of songs" (cf. Dt 10:17, "God of gods and Lord of lords"; 1Ti 6:15, "King of kings").

Author and Date

Verse 1 appears to ascribe authorship to Solomon (see note on 1:1; but see also Title above). Solomon is referred to seven times (1:1,5; 3:7,9,11; 8:11 – 12), and several verses speak of the "king" (1:4,12; 7:5), but whether he was the author remains an open question.

To date the Song in the tenth century BC during Solomon's reign is not impossible. In fact, mention of Tirzah and Jerusalem in one breath (6:4; see note there) has been used to prove a date prior to King Omri (885 – 874 BC; see 1Ki 16:23 – 24), though the reason for Tirzah's mention is not clear. On the other hand, many have appealed to the language of the Song as proof of a much later date, but on present evidence the linguistic data are ambiguous.

Consistency of language, style, tone, perspective and recurring refrains seems to argue for a single author. However, many who have doubted that the Song came from one pen, or even from one time or place, explain this consistency by ascribing all the Song's parts to a single literary tradition, since Near Eastern traditions were very careful to maintain stylistic uniformity.

Author:
Unknown; possibly King Solomon

Audience:
The people of Israel

Date:
Unknown; possibly as early as the tenth century BC

Theme:
This wisdom writer celebrates the sexual union between a man and a woman as a joyful part of marital life in God's good creation.

Interpretation

To find the key for unlocking the Song, interpreters have looked to prophetic, wisdom and apocalyptic passages of Scripture, as well as to ancient Egyptian and Babylonian love songs, traditional Semitic wedding songs, and songs related to ancient Mesopotamian fertility religions. The closest parallels appear to be those found in Proverbs (see Pr 5:15 – 20; 6:24 – 29;

The Song of Songs belongs to Biblical wisdom literature, which speaks about both love and wisdom as gifts of God to be received with gratitude and celebration.

7:6 – 23). The description of love in 8:6 – 7 (cf. the descriptions of wisdom found in Pr 1 – 9 and Job 28) seems to confirm that the Song belongs to Biblical wisdom literature and that it is wisdom's description of an amorous relationship. The Bible speaks of both wisdom and love as gifts of God, to be received with gratitude and celebration.

This understanding of the Song contrasts with the long-held view that the Song is an allegory of the love relationship between God and Israel, or between Christ and the church, or between Christ and the soul (the NT nowhere quotes from or even alludes to the Song). It is also distinct from more modern interpretations of the Song, such as that which sees it as a poetic drama celebrating the triumph of a maiden's pure, spontaneous love for her rustic shepherd lover over the courtly blandishments of Solomon, who sought to win her for his royal harem. Rather, it views the Song as a linked chain of lyrics depicting love in all its spontaneity, beauty, power and exclusiveness — experienced in its varied moments of separation and intimacy, anguish and ecstasy, tension and contentment. The Song shares with the love poetry of many cultures its extensive use of highly sensuous and suggestive imagery drawn from nature.

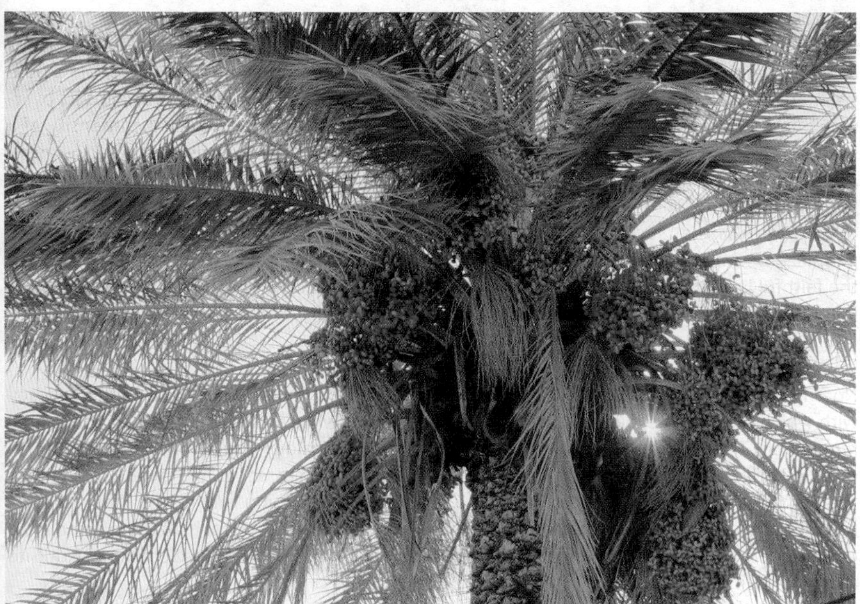

The date palm was a treasured tree in the ancient Near East. It was sometimes associated with fertility goddesses and is compared with the stature of a woman in Song of Songs 7:7.

www.HolyLandPhotos.org

Theme and Theology

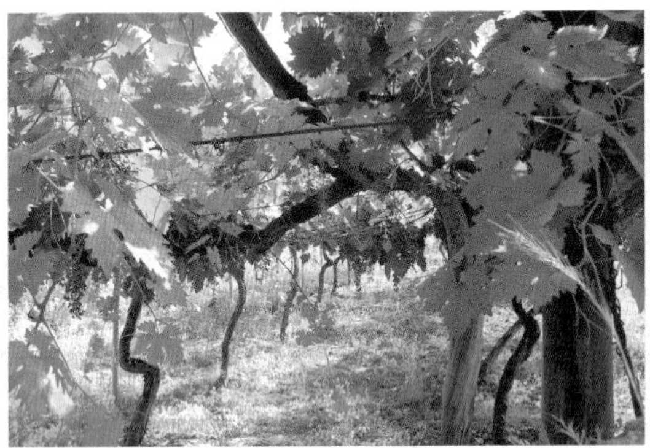

The beloved's darling took care of the vineyards (SS 1:6).

Kim Walton

In ancient Israel everything human came to expression in words: reverence, gratitude, anger, sorrow, suffering, trust, friendship, commitment, loyalty, hope, wisdom, moral outrage, repentance. In the Song, it is love that finds words — inspired words that disclose its exquisite charm and beauty as one of God's choicest gifts. The voice of love in the Song, like that of wisdom in Pr 8:1 — 9:12, is most often a woman's voice, suggesting that love and wisdom draw men powerfully with the subtlety and mystery of a woman's allurements.

This feminine voice speaks profoundly of love. She portrays its beauty and delights. She claims its exclusiveness ("My beloved is mine and I am his," 2:16) and insists on the necessity of its pure spontaneity ("Do not arouse or awaken love until it so desires," 2:7). She also proclaims its overwhelming power — it rivals that of the fearsome enemy, death; it burns with the intensity of a blazing fire; it is unquenchable even by the ocean depths (8:6 – 7a). She affirms its preciousness: All that one possesses cannot purchase it, nor (alternatively) should it be exchanged for it (8:7b). She hints, without saying so explicitly (see the second NIV text note on 8:6), that it is the Lord's gift.

God intends that such love — grossly distorted and abused by both ancient and modern people — be a normal part of marital life in his good creation (see Ge 1:26 – 31; 2:24). In the Song the faithful Israelite could ascertain how to live lovingly under the watchful reign of God. Such marital love is designed by the Creator to come to natural expression within his realm.

Literary Features

No one who reads the Song with care can question the artistry of the poet. The subtle delicacy with which the author evokes intense sensuous awareness while avoiding crude titillation is truly remarkable. This is accomplished largely by indirection, by analogy and by bringing to the foreground the sensuous in the world of nature (or in food, drink, cosmetics and jewelry). To liken a "beloved's" (1:13) enjoyment of his "darling" (1:9) to a gazelle browsing "among the lilies" (2:16), or her breasts to "twin fawns of a gazelle that browse among the lilies" (4:5), or his darling herself to a garden filled with choice fruits inviting the beloved to feast (4:12 – 16) — these combine exquisite artistry and fine sensitivity.

Whether the Song has the unity of a single dramatic line linking all the subunits into a continuing story is a matter of ongoing debate among interpreters. There do appear to be connected scenes in the love relationship (see Outline).

Virtually all agree that the literary climax of the Song is found in 8:5 – 7, where the unsurpassed power and value of love — the love that draws a man and a woman together — are finally expressly asserted. Literary relaxation follows the intenseness of that declaration. A final expression of mutual desire between the lovers brings the Song to an end, suggesting that love goes on. This last segment (8:8 – 14) is in some sense also a return to the beginning, as references to the darling's brothers, to her vineyard and to Solomon (the king) link 8:8 – 12 with 1:2 – 6. In this song of love the voice of the darling is dominant. It is her experience of love, both as the one who loves and as the one who is loved, that is most clearly expressed. The Song begins with her wish for the beloved's kiss and ends with her urgent invitation to him for love's intimacy.

Outline

I. Title (1:1)
II. The First Meeting (1:2 — 2:7)
III. The Second Meeting (2:8 — 3:5)
IV. The Third Meeting (3:6 — 5:1)
V. The Fourth Meeting (5:2 — 6:3)
VI. The Fifth Meeting (6:4 — 8:4)
VII. The Literary Climax (8:5 – 7)
VIII. The Conclusion (8:8 – 14)

1 Solomon's Song of Songs.[a]

She[a]

[2] Let him kiss me with the kisses of his mouth—
for your love[b] is more delightful than wine.[c]
[3] Pleasing is the fragrance of your perfumes;[d]
your name[e] is like perfume poured out.
No wonder the young women[f] love you!
[4] Take me away with you—let us hurry!
Let the king bring me into his chambers.[g]

Friends

We rejoice and delight[h] in you[b];
we will praise your love[i] more than wine.

She

How right they are to adore you!

[5] Dark am I, yet lovely,[j]
daughters of Jerusalem,[k]
dark like the tents of Kedar,[l]
like the tent curtains of Solomon.[c]
[6] Do not stare at me because I am dark,
because I am darkened by the sun.
My mother's sons were angry with me
and made me take care of the vineyards;[m]
my own vineyard I had to neglect.
[7] Tell me, you whom I love,
where you graze your flock
and where you rest your sheep[n] at midday.
Why should I be like a veiled[o] woman
beside the flocks of your friends?

Friends

[8] If you do not know, most beautiful of women,[p]
follow the tracks of the sheep
and graze your young goats
by the tents of the shepherds.

He

[9] I liken you, my darling, to a mare
among Pharaoh's chariot horses.[q]
[10] Your cheeks[r] are beautiful with earrings,
your neck with strings of jewels.[s]
[11] We will make you earrings of gold,
studded with silver.

She

[12] While the king was at his table,
my perfume spread its fragrance.[t]
[13] My beloved is to me a sachet of myrrh[u]
resting between my breasts.

1:1 [a] S 1Ki 4:32; Ps 45 Title **1:2** [b] ver 4; SS 4:10; 8:6 [c] S Ge 14:18; S Jdg 9:13 **1:3** [d] S Est 2:12; S Ps 45:8 [e] S Ecc 7:1 [f] Ps 45:14 **1:4** [g] Ps 45:15 [h] SS 2:3 [i] S ver 2 **1:5** [j] SS 2:14; 4:3 [k] SS 5:16 [l] S Ge 25:13 **1:6** [m] SS 2:15; 7:12; 8:12 **1:7** [n] Isa 13:20 [o] S Ge 24:65 **1:8** [p] SS 5:9; 6:1 **1:9** [q] 2Ch 1:17 **1:10** [r] SS 5:13 [s] Isa 61:10 **1:12** [t] SS 4:11-14 **1:13** [u] S Ge 37:25

[a] The main male and female speakers (identified primarily on the basis of the gender of the relevant Hebrew forms) are indicated by the captions *He* and *She* respectively. The words of others are marked *Friends*. In some instances the divisions and their captions are debatable. [b] *4* The Hebrew is masculine singular. [c] *5* Or *Salma*

1:1 *Solomon's.* See Introduction: Title; Author and Date. *Song of Songs.* Greatest of songs (see Introduction: Title). 1Ki 4:32 says that Solomon wrote 1,005 songs.

1:2–3 *kisses ... your love ... your perfumes.* Cf. 4:10–11, "your love ... your perfume ... Your lips."

1:2 See NIV text note on the heading *She. him ... his ... your.* These pronouns all refer to the same person, the beloved. *love.* Expressions of love—caresses, embraces and consummation (see v. 4; 4:10; 7:12; see also Pr 7:18; Eze 16:8; 23:17). *more delightful than wine.* See v. 4. In 4:10 the beloved speaks similarly of his darling's love.

1:3 *perfumes.* Aromatic spices and gums blended in cosmetic oil. *your name.* The very mention of the beloved's name fills the air as with a pleasant aroma. The Hebrew words for "name" and "perfume" sound alike. *young women.* Probably young women of the court or of the royal city (see 6:8–9).

1:4 *king.* Solomon. *his chambers.* The king's private quarters. *We.* Probably the young women of v. 3. *praise your love more than wine.* For the reason given in v. 2.

1:5 *Dark.* Deeply browned by the sun (see v. 6); not considered desirable. *daughters of Jerusalem.* Probably the young women of v. 3 and usually the "Friends" in the sectional headings. *tents ... tent curtains.* Handwoven from black goat hair. *Kedar.* See note on Isa 21:16.

1:6 *mother's.* Mothers are referred to seven times in the Song (here; 3:4,11; 6:9; 8:1,2,5); fathers are never mentioned. *my own vineyard.* Her body, as in 8:12 (see 2:15). Vineyard is an apt metaphor since it yields wine, and the excitements of love are compared with those produced by wine (see note on v. 2). The darling is also compared to a garden, yielding precious fruits for her beloved (see note on 4:12).

1:7 *whom I love.* See 3:1. *where you graze your flock.* The beloved is portrayed as a shepherd. In v. 8 his darling is depicted as a shepherd girl. *midday.* A time of rest in warm climates. *veiled woman.* Prostitute (see Ge 38:14–15). The darling does not wish to look for her beloved among the shepherds, appearing as though she were a prostitute.

1:8 *beautiful.* The darling; also in v. 15; 2:10,13; 4:1,7; 5:9; 6:1,4,10 ("fair"). The beloved is called "handsome" in v. 16 (in Hebrew the same word as that for "beautiful"). *your young goats.* The darling is pictured as a shepherd (see v. 7). *by the tents of the shepherds.* The darling is instructed to learn where her beloved is by joining the shepherds in the fields.

1:9 *my darling.* Used only of *She* (see v. 15; 2:2,10,13; 4:1,7; 5:2; 6:4; see also note on v. 13). *mare.* A flattering comparison, similar to Theocritus's praise of the beautiful Helen of Troy (*Idyl,* 18.30–31). *among Pharaoh's chariot horses.* Her beauty attracts attention the way a mare would among the Egyptian chariot stallions. According to 1Ki 10:28, Solomon imported horses from Egypt.

1:11 *We.* Perhaps the "daughters of Jerusalem" (v. 5).

1:12 *king.* Solomon. *at his table.* Reclining on his couch at the table. *my perfume.* Nard, an aromatic oil extracted from the roots of a perennial herb that grows in India (see 4:13–14; Mk 14:3; Jn 12:3).

1:13 *My beloved.* Used only of *He* (see v. 14,16; 2:3,8,9,10,16,17; 4:16; 5:2,4,5,6,8,9,10,16; 6:1,2,3; 7:9,10,11,13; 8:5,14; see also note on v. 9). *myrrh.* An aromatic gum exuding from the bark of a balsam tree that grows in Arabia, Ethiopia and India. It was commonly used as an alluring feminine perfume (Est 2:12; Pr 7:17). It was also used to perfume royal nuptial robes (Ps 45:8) and as an ingredient in the holy anointing oil (Ex

14 My beloved[v] is to me a cluster of henna[w] blossoms
from the vineyards of En Gedi.[x]

He

15 How beautiful[y] you are, my darling!
Oh, how beautiful!
Your eyes are doves.[z]

She

16 How handsome you are, my beloved![a]
Oh, how charming!
And our bed is verdant.

He

17 The beams of our house are cedars;[b]
our rafters are firs.

She[a]

2 I am a rose[bc] of Sharon,[d]
a lily[e] of the valleys.

He

2 Like a lily among thorns
is my darling among the young women.

She

3 Like an apple[c] tree among the trees of the forest
is my beloved[f] among the young men.
I delight[g] to sit in his shade,
and his fruit is sweet to my taste.[h]
4 Let him lead me to the banquet hall,[i]
and let his banner[j] over me be love.
5 Strengthen me with raisins,
refresh me with apples,[k]
for I am faint with love.[l]
6 His left arm is under my head,
and his right arm embraces me.[m]

1:14 [v] ver 16; SS 2:3,17; 5:8 [w] SS 4:13 [x] S 1Sa 23:29; S 2Ch 20:2 **1:15** [y] SS 4:7; 7:6 [z] Ps 74:19; SS 2:14; 4:1; 5:2,12; 6:9; Jer 48:28 **1:16** [a] S ver 14 **1:17** [b] 1Ki 6:9 **2:1** [c] Isa 35:1 [d] S 1Ch 27:29 [e] SS 5:13; Hos 14:5 **2:3** [f] S SS 1:14 [g] SS 1:4 [h] SS 4:16 **2:4** [i] Est 1:11 [j] S Nu 1:52 **2:5** [k] SS 7:8 [l] SS 5:8 **2:6** [m] SS 8:3

2:7 [n] SS 5:8 [o] SS 3:5; 8:4 **2:8** [p] ver 17; SS 8:14 **2:9** [q] S 2Sa 2:18 [r] ver 17; SS 8:14 **2:13** [s] Isa 28:4; Jer 24:2; Hos 9:10; Mic 7:1; Na 3:12 [t] SS 7:12 **2:14** [u] S Ge 8:8; S SS 1:15 [v] S SS 1:5

7 Daughters of Jerusalem, I charge you[n]
by the gazelles and by the does of the field:
Do not arouse or awaken love
until it so desires.[o]

8 Listen! My beloved!
Look! Here he comes,
leaping across the mountains,
bounding over the hills.[p]
9 My beloved is like a gazelle[q] or a young stag.[r]
Look! There he stands behind our wall,
gazing through the windows,
peering through the lattice.
10 My beloved spoke and said to me,
"Arise, my darling,
my beautiful one, come with me.
11 See! The winter is past;
the rains are over and gone.
12 Flowers appear on the earth;
the season of singing has come,
the cooing of doves
is heard in our land.
13 The fig tree forms its early fruit;[s]
the blossoming[t] vines spread their fragrance.
Arise, come, my darling;
my beautiful one, come with me."

He

14 My dove[u] in the clefts of the rock,
in the hiding places on the mountainside,
show me your face,
let me hear your voice;
for your voice is sweet,
and your face is lovely.[v]

[a] Or *He* [b] *1* Probably a member of the crocus family [c] *3* Or possibly *apricot*; here and elsewhere in Song of Songs

30:23). The Magi brought myrrh to the young Jesus as a gift fit for a king (Mt 2:2,11).
1:14 *henna.* A shrub (perhaps the cypress) with tightly clustered, aromatic blossoms. *En Gedi.* An oasis watered by a spring, located on the west side of the Dead Sea (see map, p. 451). David sought refuge there from King Saul (1Sa 24:1).
1:15 *How beautiful ... darling!* See 4:1; 6:4; cf. v. 16. *my darling.* See note on v. 9. *doves.* Probably refers to the shape and cosmetic highlighting of her eyes (see 4:1).
1:16 *handsome.* See note on v. 8 ("beautiful"). *verdant.* The lovers lie together in the field under the trees.
2:1 *rose.* See NIV text note and Isa 35:1–2. *Sharon.* The fertile coastal plain south of Mount Carmel (see map, pp. 2516–2517, at the end of this study Bible). *lily.* Probably either lotus or anemone.
2:2 *my darling.* See note on 1:9. *young women.* See note on 1:3.
2:3 *apple tree.* The precise nature of this fruit tree is uncertain (see NIV text note). *his fruit.* Probably a metaphor for the beloved's intimacies (see v. 5 and note).
2:4 *banner.* See 6:4; Nu 2:2; Ps 20:5. The king's love for her is displayed for all to see, like a large military banner.
2:5 *raisins ... apples.* Probably metaphors for love's caresses and embraces.
2:7 *Daughters of Jerusalem.* See note on 1:5. *charge.* Place under oath. *gazelles ... does.* Perhaps in the imaginative language of love the gazelles and does are portrayed as witnesses to the oath. This would be in harmony with the author's frequent reference to nature. *Do not arouse ... desires.* A recurring refrain in the Song (see 3:5; 8:4; cf. 5:8). It is always spoken by the darling and always in a context of physical intimacy with her beloved. *until it so desires.* Out of the darling's experience of love comes wise admonition that love is not to be artificially stimulated; utter spontaneity is essential to its genuine truth and beauty.
2:9 *gazelle.* Celebrated for its form and beauty. *young stag.* An apt simile for youthful vigor (cf. Isa 35:6). *gazing ... lattice.* The eager beloved tries to catch sight of his darling while she is still preparing herself for their meeting.
2:10 *Arise ... with me.* See v. 13; cf. 7:11–13. *my beautiful one.* See note on 1:8.
2:11–13 The first signs of spring appear (see 6:11; 7:12)—the time for love.
2:14 *dove ... on the mountainside.* Cf. Ps 55:6–8; Jer 48:28.

15 Catch for us the foxes,[w]
the little foxes
that ruin the vineyards,[x]
our vineyards that are in bloom.[y]

She

16 My beloved is mine and I am his;[z]
he browses among the lilies.[a]
17 Until the day breaks
and the shadows flee,[b]
turn, my beloved,[c]
and be like a gazelle
or like a young stag[d]
on the rugged hills.[a][e]

3

All night long on my bed
I looked[f] for the one my heart loves;
I looked for him but did not find
him.
2 I will get up now and go about the city,
through its streets and squares;
I will search for the one my heart
loves.
So I looked for him but did not find
him.
3 The watchmen found me
as they made their rounds in the
city.[g]
"Have you seen the one my heart
loves?"
4 Scarcely had I passed them
when I found the one my heart
loves.
I held him and would not let him go
till I had brought him to my
mother's house,[h]
to the room of the one who
conceived me.[i]
5 Daughters of Jerusalem, I charge you[j]
by the gazelles and by the does of
the field:
Do not arouse or awaken love
until it so desires.[k]

6 Who is this coming up from the
wilderness[l]
like a column of smoke,
perfumed with myrrh[m] and incense
made from all the spices[n] of the
merchant?
7 Look! It is Solomon's carriage,
escorted by sixty warriors,[o]
the noblest of Israel,
8 all of them wearing the sword,
all experienced in battle,
each with his sword at his side,
prepared for the terrors of the night.[p]
9 King Solomon made for himself the
carriage;
he made it of wood from Lebanon.
10 Its posts he made of silver,
its base of gold.
Its seat was upholstered with purple,
its interior inlaid with love.
Daughters of Jerusalem, 11 come out,
and look, you daughters of Zion.[q]
Look[b] on King Solomon wearing a
crown,
the crown with which his mother
crowned him
on the day of his wedding,
the day his heart rejoiced.[r]

He

4

How beautiful you are, my darling!
Oh, how beautiful!
Your eyes behind your veil[s] are
doves.[t]
Your hair is like a flock of goats
descending from the hills of Gilead.[u]

2:15 [w] Jdg 15:4 [x] S SS 1:6 [y] SS 7:12 **2:16** [z] SS 7:10 [a] SS 4:5; 6:3 **2:17** [b] SS 4:6 [c] S SS 1:14 [d] S ver 9 [e] S ver 8 **3:1** [f] SS 5:6 **3:3** [g] SS 5:7 **3:4** [h] SS 8:2 [i] SS 6:9; 8:5 **3:5** [j] S SS 2:7 [k] SS 8:4 **3:6** [l] SS 8:5 [m] SS 4:6, 14 [n] Ex 30:34 **3:7** [o] S 1Sa 8:11 **3:8** [p] S Job 15:22; Ps 91:5 **3:11** [q] Isa 3:16; 4:4; 32:9-13 [r] Isa 54:5; 62:5; Jer 3:14 **4:1** [s] S Ge 24:65 [t] S SS 1:15 [u] Ge 37:25; Nu 32:1; SS 6:5; Jer 22:6; Mic 7:14

[a] 17 Or *the hills of Bether* [b] 10,11 Or *interior lovingly inlaid / by the daughters of Jerusalem. / 11 Come out, you daughters of Zion, / and look*

2:15 Perhaps spoken by the darling. *vineyards.* As in 1:6 ("my own vineyard"), probably a metaphor for the lovers' physical beauty. Thus the desire is expressed that the lovers be kept safe from whatever ("foxes") might mar their mutual attractiveness. *in bloom.* Their attractiveness is in its prime.

2:16 *My beloved is mine and I am his.* See 6:3; 7:10. They belong to each other exclusively in a relationship that allows no intrusion. *browses among the lilies.* The beloved is compared to a gazelle (see v. 17). The browsing is a metaphor for the beloved's intimate enjoyment of her charms (see 6:2–3).

3:1 This verse begins a new moment in love's experience. *All night long.* Night, with its freedom from the distractions of the day, allows the heart to be filled with its own preoccupations.

3:3 *watchmen.* Were stationed at the city gates (see Ne 3:29; 11:19; 13:22) and on the walls (see 5:7; 2Sa 13:34; 18:24–27; 2Ki 9:17–20; Ps 127:1; Isa 52:8; 62:6). Apparently they also patrolled the streets at night (see 5:7).

3:4 *mother's.* See note on 1:6.

3:5 See note on 2:7. Once again the charge occurs at the moment of intimacy.

3:6–11 Perhaps spoken by the friends (see 8:5). If so, this section probably portrays the wedding procession of Solomon and his bride approaching the city.

3:6 This verse begins a new moment in the relationship. *Who … wilderness … ?* See 8:5, where the reference is to the darling. *wilderness.* Uncultivated seasonal grasslands. *smoke.* Incense (see note on Ex 30:34). *of the merchant.* Imported.

3:7 *carriage.* A richly adorned royal conveyance, a palanquin (see vv. 9–10).

3:8 *terrors of the night.* See Ps 91:5.

3:9 *wood from Lebanon.* See 5:15 and note.

3:10 *posts.* Supporting the canopy. *silver … gold.* Probably metals that overlay the Lebanon wood. *purple.* See notes on 7:5; Ex 25:4.

3:11 *daughters of Zion.* Elsewhere "daughters of Jerusalem" (see note on 1:5). *crown.* A wedding wreath (see Isa 61:10). *mother.* Bathsheba.

4:1–7 For other exuberant descriptions of the darling's beauty, see 6:4–9; 7:1–7.

4:1b–2 See 6:5b–6.

4:1 *How beautiful … darling!* See 1:15 and note. *eyes behind your veil.* With the rest of her face concealed, the beloved's attention is focused on his darling's eyes. *doves.* See 1:15 and note. *flock of goats.* The goats of Canaan were usually black

[2] Your teeth are like a flock of sheep just
shorn,
coming up from the washing.
Each has its twin;
not one of them is alone.[v]
[3] Your lips are like a scarlet ribbon;
your mouth[w] is lovely.[x]
Your temples behind your veil
are like the halves of a
pomegranate.[y]
[4] Your neck is like the tower[z] of David,
built with courses of stone[a];
on it hang a thousand shields,[a]
all of them shields of warriors.
[5] Your breasts[b] are like two fawns,
like twin fawns of a gazelle[c]
that browse among the lilies.[d]
[6] Until the day breaks
and the shadows flee,[e]
I will go to the mountain of myrrh[f]
and to the hill of incense.
[7] You are altogether beautiful,[g] my
darling;
there is no flaw[h] in you.

[8] Come with me from Lebanon, my
bride,[i]
come with me from Lebanon.
Descend from the crest of Amana,
from the top of Senir,[j] the summit of
Hermon,[k]
from the lions' dens
and the mountain haunts of
leopards.

[9] You have stolen my heart, my sister,
my bride;[l]
you have stolen my heart
with one glance of your eyes,
with one jewel of your necklace.[m]
[10] How delightful[n] is your love[o], my sister,
my bride!
How much more pleasing is your
love than wine,[p]
and the fragrance of your
perfume[q]
more than any spice!
[11] Your lips drop sweetness as the
honeycomb, my bride;
milk and honey are under your
tongue.[r]
The fragrance of your garments
is like the fragrance of Lebanon.[s]
[12] You are a garden[t] locked up, my sister,
my bride;[u]
you are a spring enclosed, a sealed
fountain.[v]
[13] Your plants are an orchard of
pomegranates[w]
with choice fruits,
with henna[x] and nard,
[14] nard and saffron,
calamus and cinnamon,[y]
with every kind of incense tree,
with myrrh[z] and aloes[a]
and all the finest spices.[b]

4:2 [v] SS 6:6
4:3 [w] SS 5:16 [x] S SS 1:5 [y] SS 6:7
4:4 [z] S Ps 144:12 [a] Eze 27:10
4:5 [b] SS 7:3 [c] S Pr 5:19 [d] S SS 2:16
4:6 [e] SS 2:17 [f] S SS 3:6
4:7 [g] S SS 1:15 [h] SS 5:2
4:8 [i] ver 9, 12; SS 5:1 [j] S Dt 3:9 [k] S 1Ch 5:23
4:9 [l] S ver 8 [m] S Ge 41:42; S Ps 73:6
4:10 [n] SS 7:6 [o] S SS 1:2 [p] S Jdg 9:13 [q] ver 16; S Ps 45:8; Isa 57:9
4:11 [r] S Ps 19:10; SS 5:1 [s] Hos 14:6
4:12 [t] ver 16; SS 5:1; 6:2; Isa 5:7 [u] S ver 8 [v] Pr 5:15-18
4:13 [w] SS 7:12 [x] SS 1:14
4:14 [y] S Ex 30:23 [z] S SS 3:6 [a] S Nu 24:6 [b] SS 1:12

[a] *4* The meaning of the Hebrew for this phrase is uncertain.

(see note on 1:5). The beloved's hair was also black (5:11). *descending from the hills of Gilead.* The darling's black tresses flowing from her head remind her beloved of a flock of sleek black goats streaming down one of the hills of Gilead (noted for its good pasturage).
4:2 *just shorn.* Clean and white. *coming up from the washing.* Still wet, like moistened teeth.
4:3 *Your lips … scarlet.* Perhaps the darling painted her lips, like Egyptian women. *temples behind … veil.* See note on v. 1. *halves of a pomegranate.* Round and blushed with red.
4:4 The darling's straight, bespangled neck is like a tower on the city wall adorned with warriors' shields (cf. 7:4).
4:5 See 7:3. *fawns.* Representing tender, delicate beauty, and promise rather than full growth (cf. 8:8). *gazelle.* See note on 2:9. Elsewhere the simile is used of the beloved. *browse among the lilies.* For a different use of this phrase, see 2:16 and note.
4:6 *Until … shadows flee.* See 2:17. *mountain of myrrh … hill of incense.* Metaphors for lovers' intimacy.
4:8 To the beloved, his darling seems to have withdrawn as if to a remote mountain. *Lebanon … Amana … Hermon.* Mountain peaks on the northern horizon. *Senir.* Name for Mount Hermon found in Assyrian sources (see Dt 3:9).
4:9 *my sister.* For lovers to address each other as "brother" and "sister" was common in the love poetry of the ancient Near East (see vv. 10,12; 5:1). *one glance of your eyes.* See 6:5 and note.
4:10 *more pleasing … than wine.* See note on 1:2. *fragrance of your perfume.* See 1:3. *spice.* See v. 14; 5:1,13; 6:2; 8:14. Spice was an imported luxury item (see 1Ki 10:2,10,25; Eze 27:22). Spices were used for fragrance in the holy anointing oil (Ex 25:6; 30:23 – 25; 35:8) and for fragrant incense (Ex 25:6; 35:8), as well as for perfume.
4:11 *Your lips drop sweetness.* The darling speaks to him of love (cf. Pr 5:3; 16:24). People in the ancient Near East associated sweetness with the delights of love. *milk and honey.* Perhaps reminiscent of the description of the promised land (see note on Ex 3:8). *under your tongue.* See Job 20:12; Ps 10:7.
4:12 *garden.* A place of sensual delights (see v. 16; 5:1; 6:2; see also note on 1:6). *locked up … enclosed … sealed.* Metaphors for the darling's virginity — or perhaps for the fact that she keeps herself exclusively for her husband. *spring … fountain.* Sources of refreshment; metaphors for the darling as a sexual partner, as in Pr 5:15 – 20 (see notes on Pr 5:15 – 16).
4:13 – 15 Verses 13 – 14 elaborate on the garden metaphor of v. 12a, and v. 15 elaborates on the fountain metaphor of v. 12b. The trees and spices in vv. 13 – 14 are mostly exotic, referring to the darling's charms.
4:13 *Your plants.* All the darling's features that delight the beloved. *orchard.* Hebrew *pardes* (from which the English word *paradise* comes), a loanword from Old Persian meaning "enclosure" or "park." In Ne 2:8 and Ecc 2:5 it refers to royal parks and forests. *henna.* See note on 1:14. *nard.* See note on 1:12.
4:14 *saffron.* A plant of the crocus family bearing purple or white flowers, parts of which, when dried, were used as a cooking spice. *calamus.* An imported (see Jer 6:20 and note), aromatic spice cane, used also in the holy anointing oil (Ex 30:23,25) and in incense (Isa 43:23 – 24). *cinnamon.* Used in the holy anointing oil (Ex 30:23,25). *myrrh.* See note on 1:13. *aloes.* Aromatic aloes, used to perfume royal nuptial robes (Ps 45:8). Pr 7:17 says the adulterous woman perfumed her bed "with myrrh, aloes and cinnamon."

15 You are[a] a garden[c] fountain,[d]
a well of flowing water
streaming down from Lebanon.

She

16 Awake, north wind,
and come, south wind!
Blow on my garden,[e]
that its fragrance[f] may spread
everywhere.
Let my beloved[g] come into his garden
and taste its choice fruits.[h]

He

5 I have come into my garden,[i] my
sister, my bride;[j]
I have gathered my myrrh with my
spice.
I have eaten my honeycomb and my
honey;
I have drunk my wine and my milk.[k]

Friends

Eat, friends, and drink;
drink your fill of love.

She

2 I slept but my heart was awake.
Listen! My beloved is knocking:
"Open to me, my sister, my darling,
my dove,[l] my flawless[m] one.[n]
My head is drenched with dew,
my hair with the dampness of the
night."
3 I have taken off my robe—
must I put it on again?
I have washed my feet—
must I soil them again?
4 My beloved thrust his hand through
the latch-opening;
my heart began to pound for him.
5 I arose to open for my beloved,
and my hands dripped with myrrh,[o]
my fingers with flowing myrrh,
on the handles of the bolt.
6 I opened for my beloved,[p]
but my beloved had left; he was
gone.[q]
My heart sank at his departure.[b]
I looked[r] for him but did not find him.
I called him but he did not answer.
7 The watchmen found me
as they made their rounds in the
city.[s]
They beat me, they bruised me;
they took away my cloak,
those watchmen of the walls!
8 Daughters of Jerusalem, I charge you[t]—
if you find my beloved,[u]
what will you tell him?
Tell him I am faint with love.[v]

Friends

9 How is your beloved better than
others,
most beautiful of women?[w]
How is your beloved better than
others,
that you so charge us?

She

10 My beloved is radiant and ruddy,
outstanding among ten thousand.[x]
11 His head is purest gold;
his hair is wavy
and black as a raven.
12 His eyes are like doves[y]
by the water streams,
washed in milk,[z]
mounted like jewels.
13 His cheeks[a] are like beds of spice[b]
yielding perfume.
His lips are like lilies[c]
dripping with myrrh.[d]
14 His arms are rods of gold
set with topaz.
His body is like polished ivory
decorated with lapis lazuli.[e]

4:15 [c] Isa 27:2; 58:11; Jer 31:12 [d] Pr 5:18 **4:16** [e] S ver 12 [f] S ver 10 [g] SS 7:13 [h] SS 2:3 **5:1** [i] S SS 4:12 [j] S SS 4:8 [k] S SS 4:11; Isa 55:1; Joel 3:18 **5:2** [l] S SS 1:15 [m] SS 4:7 [n] SS 6:9 **5:5** [o] ver 13 **5:6** [p] SS 6:1 [q] SS 6:2 [r] SS 3:1 **5:7** [s] SS 3:3 **5:8** [t] SS 2:7 [u] S SS 1:14 [v] SS 2:5 **5:9** [w] S SS 1:8 **5:10** [x] Ps 45:2 **5:12** [y] S SS 1:15 [z] Ge 49:12 **5:13** [a] SS 1:10 [b] SS 6:2 [c] S SS 2:1 [d] ver 5 **5:14** [e] S Job 28:6

[a] 15 Or *I am* (spoken by *She*) [b] 6 Or *heart had gone out to him when he spoke*

4:15 *flowing.* Fresh, not stagnant. *streaming ... from Lebanon.* Fresh, cool, sparkling water from the snowfields on the Lebanon mountains.
4:16 May the fragrance of my charms be wafted about to draw my beloved to me so that we may enjoy love's intimacies. *his garden.* She belongs to him and yields herself to her beloved (see 6:2).
5:1 The beloved claims his darling as his garden and enjoys all her delights. *my sister.* See note on 4:9. *Eat ... love.* The friends of the lovers applaud their enjoyment of love.
5:2–8 See 3:1–5 and note on 3:1.
5:2 *I slept ... was awake.* Love holds sway even in sleep—just as a new mother sleeps with an ear open to her baby's slightest whimper.
5:3 Instinctive reaction raises a foolish complaint before the language of love takes over.
5:5 *my hands ... flowing myrrh.* Love's eager imagination extravagantly lotioned the darling's hands with perfume.
5:9 The friends' question provides an opportunity for the darling to describe the beauty of her beloved—which she does only here.
5:10 *ruddy.* See 1Sa 16:12.
5:11 *black.* The darling's hair was also black (see note on 4:1).
5:12 *doves.* See note on 1:15. *by the water streams.* The beloved's eyes sparkle. *washed in milk.* Describing the white of the eye.
5:13 *spice ... lilies.* These similes probably compare sensuous effects rather than appearances, as do the following similes and metaphors, at least in part. *lilies.* See note on 2:1. *dripping with myrrh.* See v. 5 and note. Love's pleasant excitements are aroused by the beloved's lips.
5:14 *topaz.* See note on Eze 1:16. *lapis lazuli.* Hebrew *sappir* (from which the English word *sapphire* comes).

15 His legs are pillars of marble
set on bases of pure gold.
His appearance is like Lebanon,[f]
choice as its cedars.
16 His mouth[g] is sweetness itself;
he is altogether lovely.
This is my beloved,[h] this is my friend,
daughters of Jerusalem.[i]

Friends

6 Where has your beloved[j] gone,
most beautiful of women?[k]
Which way did your beloved turn,
that we may look for him with
you?

She

2 My beloved has gone[l] down to his
garden,[m]
to the beds of spices,[n]
to browse in the gardens
and to gather lilies.
3 I am my beloved's and my beloved is
mine;[o]
he browses among the lilies.[p]

He

4 You are as beautiful as Tirzah,[q] my
darling,
as lovely as Jerusalem,[r]
as majestic as troops with banners.[s]
5 Turn your eyes from me;
they overwhelm me.
Your hair is like a flock of goats
descending from Gilead.[t]
6 Your teeth are like a flock of sheep
coming up from the washing.
Each has its twin,
not one of them is missing.[u]

5:15 [f] 1Ki 4:33; SS 7:4 **5:16** [g] SS 4:3 [h] SS 7:9 [i] SS 1:5 **6:1** [j] SS 5:6 [k] S SS 1:8 **6:2** [l] SS 5:6 [m] S SS 4:12 [n] SS 5:13 **6:3** [o] SS 7:10 [p] S SS 2:16 **6:4** [q] S Jos 12:24; S 1Ki 15:33 [r] Ps 48:2; 50:2 [s] S Nu 1:52 **6:5** [t] S SS 4:1 **6:6** [u] SS 4:2

7 Your temples behind your veil[v]
are like the halves of a pomegranate.[w]
8 Sixty queens[x] there may be,
and eighty concubines,[y]
and virgins beyond number;
9 but my dove,[z] my perfect one,[a] is
unique,
the only daughter of her mother,
the favorite of the one who bore her.[b]
The young women saw her and called
her blessed;
the queens and concubines praised
her.

Friends

10 Who is this that appears like the dawn,
fair as the moon, bright as the sun,
majestic as the stars in procession?

He

11 I went down to the grove of nut trees
to look at the new growth in the
valley,
to see if the vines had budded
or the pomegranates were in bloom.[c]
12 Before I realized it,
my desire set me among the royal
chariots of my people.[a]

Friends

13 Come back, come back, O Shulammite;
come back, come back, that we may
gaze on you!

He

Why would you gaze on the
Shulammite
as on the dance[d] of Mahanaim?[b]

6:7 [v] S Ge 24:65 [w] SS 4:3 **6:8** [x] Ps 45:9 [y] S Ge 22:24; S Est 2:14 **6:9** [z] S SS 1:15 [a] SS 5:2 [b] S SS 3:4 **6:11** [c] SS 7:12 **6:13** [d] S Ex 15:20

[a] 12 Or *among the chariots of Amminadab;* or *among the chariots of the people of the prince* [b] 13 In Hebrew texts this verse (6:13) is numbered 7:1.

5:15 *appearance is like Lebanon.* Awesome and majestic. *choice as its cedars.* The cedars of Lebanon were renowned throughout the ancient Near East, and their wood was desired for adorning temples and palaces (see 3:9; 1Ki 5:6 and note).

5:16 *mouth.* The beloved's kisses and loving speech. *daughters of Jerusalem.* See note on 1:5.

6:1 The question asked by the friends forms a transition from the darling's description of her beloved to her delighted acknowledgment of his intimacy with her and the exclusiveness of their relationship.

6:2 *his garden.* His darling. *beds of spices.* Her sensuous attractions (cf. 5:13). *browse.* Enjoy (see note on 2:16). *gather lilies.* See note on 2:1. The beloved, enjoying intimacies with his darling, is compared to a graceful gazelle (see notes on 2:7,9) nibbling from lily to lily in undisturbed enjoyment of exotic delicacies.

6:3 *I ... mine.* See note on 2:16. Notice the reversal; here her yielding to her beloved is emphasized.

6:4 *Tirzah.* An old Canaanite city in the middle of the land (see Jos 12:24). It was chosen by Jeroboam I (930–909 BC) as the first royal city of the northern kingdom (see 1Ki 14:17; see also 1Ki 15:21; 16:23–24). Comparison of the darling's beauty to that of cities was perhaps not so unusual in the ancient Near East, since cities were regularly depicted as women (see note on 2Ki 19:21). *majestic.* See v. 10. *as troops with banners.* The darling's noble beauty evoked in her beloved emotions like those aroused by a troop marching under its banners.

6:5–7 See 4:1–3 and notes.

6:5 *your eyes ... overwhelm me.* The darling's eyes awaken in her beloved such intensity of love that he is held captive (see 4:9).

6:8 *queens ... concubines ... virgins.* The reference is either to Solomon's harem or to all the beautiful women of the realm.

6:9 *perfect one.* Cf. "flawless one" in 5:2. *only daughter.* Not literally, but the one uniquely loved (cf. Ge 22:2 and note; Jdg 11:34; Pr 4:3). *young women ... praised her.* All the other women praised her beauty (see 1:8; 5:9; 6:1).

6:10 See 5:9; 6:1.

6:11 *nut.* Perhaps walnut. *look ... in the valley.* For the first signs of spring (see note on 2:11–13).

6:12 The most obscure verse in the Song. See NIV text note for other possible translations. *chariots.* Solomon was famous for his chariots (1Ki 10:26).

6:13 *Shulammite.* The darling. It is either a variant of "Shunammite" (see 1Ki 1:3), i.e., a young woman from Shunem (see Jos 19:18), or a feminine form of the word "Solomon," meaning "Solomon's girl." In ancient Semitic languages the letters *l* and *n* were sometimes interchanged. *Mahanaim.* Perhaps the town in Gilead (see note on 2Sa 2:8).

7[a] How beautiful your sandaled feet,
O prince's[e] daughter!
Your graceful legs are like jewels,
the work of an artist's hands.
2 Your navel is a rounded goblet
that never lacks blended wine.
Your waist is a mound of wheat
encircled by lilies.
3 Your breasts[f] are like two fawns,
like twin fawns of a gazelle.
4 Your neck is like an ivory tower.[g]
Your eyes are the pools of Heshbon[h]
by the gate of Bath Rabbim.
Your nose is like the tower of Lebanon[i]
looking toward Damascus.
5 Your head crowns you like Mount
Carmel.[j]
Your hair is like royal tapestry;
the king is held captive by its
tresses.
6 How beautiful[k] you are and how
pleasing,
my love, with your delights![l]
7 Your stature is like that of the palm,
and your breasts[m] like clusters of
fruit.
8 I said, "I will climb the palm tree;
I will take hold of its fruit."
May your breasts be like clusters of
grapes on the vine,
the fragrance of your breath like
apples,[n]
9 and your mouth like the best wine.

She

May the wine go straight to my
beloved,[o]
flowing gently over lips and teeth.[b]
10 I belong to my beloved,
and his desire[p] is for me.[q]
11 Come, my beloved, let us go to the
countryside,
let us spend the night in the
villages.[c]
12 Let us go early to the vineyards[r]
to see if the vines have budded,[s]
if their blossoms[t] have opened,
and if the pomegranates[u] are in
bloom[v]—
there I will give you my love.
13 The mandrakes[w] send out their
fragrance,
and at our door is every delicacy,
both new and old,
that I have stored up for you, my
beloved.[x]

8 If only you were to me like a
brother,
who was nursed at my mother's
breasts!
Then, if I found you outside,
I would kiss you,
and no one would despise me.
2 I would lead you
and bring you to my mother's
house[y]—
she who has taught me.
I would give you spiced wine to
drink,
the nectar of my pomegranates.
3 His left arm is under my head
and his right arm embraces me.[z]
4 Daughters of Jerusalem, I charge
you:
Do not arouse or awaken love
until it so desires.[a]

7:1 [e]Ps 45:13 **7:3** [f]SS 4:5 **7:4** [g]S Ps 144:12 [h]Nu 21:26 [i]S SS 5:15 **7:5** [j]Isa 35:2 **7:6** [k]S SS 1:15 [l]SS 4:10 **7:7** [m]SS 4:5 **7:8** [n]SS 2:5 **7:9** [o]SS 5:16 **7:10** [p]Ps 45:11 [q]SS 2:16; 6:3 **7:12** [r]S SS 1:6 [s]SS 2:15 [t]SS 2:13 [u]S SS 4:13 [v]SS 6:11 **7:13** [w]S Ge 30:14 [x]SS 4:16 **8:2** [y]SS 3:4 **8:3** [z]SS 2:6 **8:4** [a]SS 2:7; S 3:5

[a] In Hebrew texts 7:1-13 is numbered 7:2-14. [b] 9 Septuagint, Aquila, Vulgate and Syriac; Hebrew *lips of sleepers* [c] 11 Or *the henna bushes*

7:1–7 Here the description moves up from the feet rather than down from the head (cf. 5:11–15).
7:1 Cf. v. 6. *prince's daughter.* Alludes to the nobility of her beauty (see Ps 45:13). *graceful.* The Hebrew for this word suggests "curvaceous."
7:2 *goblet.* A large, two-handled, ring-based bowl (see Ex 24:6; Isa 22:24; see also Am 6:6). *encircled by lilies.* The darling perhaps wore a loose garland of flowers around her waist.
7:3 See note on 4:5.
7:4 *ivory tower.* Mixed imagery, referring to shape as well as to color and texture. *pools.* The darling's eyes reflect like the surface of a pool; or the imagery may depict serenity and gentleness. *Heshbon.* Once the royal city of King Sihon (Nu 21:26), it was blessed with an abundant supply of spring water. *Bath Rabbim.* Means "daughter of many"; perhaps a popular name for Heshbon. *tower of Lebanon.* Perhaps a military tower on the northern frontier of Solomon's kingdom, but more likely the beautiful, towering Lebanon mountain range.
7:5 *Mount Carmel.* A promontory midway along the western coast of the kingdom, with a wooded top and known for its beauty. *royal tapestry.* A reference to purple, royal cloth, as in 3:10 (see note on Ex 25:4). *king.* Solomon. *tresses.* The Hebrew for this word suggests a similarity to flowing water (cf. 4:1; 6:5).
7:7 *palm.* The stately date palm. See photo, p. 1097.
7:8 *I said.* To myself. *I will climb.* The darling's beauty draws him irresistibly. *vine.* Grape. *apples.* Perhaps the fragrance of apple blossoms (but see note on 2:3).
7:9 *May the wine … to my beloved.* The darling offers the wine (see 5:1) of her love to her beloved.
7:10 *I belong.* See notes on 2:16; 6:3. *desire.* Cf. Ge 3:16.
7:11–12 In 2:10–13 the darling reports a similar invitation from her beloved.
7:12 *I will give you my love.* She offers herself completely to her beloved.
7:13 *mandrakes.* Short-stemmed herbs associated with fertility (see note on Ge 30:14). The odor of its blossom is pungent. *at our door.* Where the lovers meet. *every delicacy.* Metaphor for the delights the darling has for her beloved from her "garden" (cf. 4:13–14). *both new and old.* Those already shared and those still to be enjoyed.
8:1 *no one would despise me.* The darling could openly show affection without any public disgrace.
8:2 *I would give you.* She would offer her beloved the delights of her love. *nectar.* The Hebrew for this word refers to intoxicating juices.
8:4 See 2:7 and note.

Friends

[5]Who is this coming up from the
wilderness[b]
leaning on her beloved?

She

Under the apple tree I roused you;
there your mother conceived[c] you,
there she who was in labor gave you
birth.
[6]Place me like a seal over your heart,
like a seal on your arm;
for love[d] is as strong as death,
its jealousy[a][e] unyielding as the grave.
It burns like blazing fire,
like a mighty flame.[b]
[7]Many waters cannot quench love;
rivers cannot sweep it away.
If one were to give
all the wealth of one's house for
love,
it[c] would be utterly scorned.[f]

Friends

[8]We have a little sister,
and her breasts are not yet grown.
What shall we do for our sister
on the day she is spoken for?
[9]If she is a wall,
we will build towers of silver on her.
If she is a door,
we will enclose her with panels of
cedar.

She

[10]I am a wall,
and my breasts are like towers.
Thus I have become in his
eyes
like one bringing contentment.
[11]Solomon had a vineyard[g] in Baal
Hamon;
he let out his vineyard to
tenants.
Each was to bring for its fruit
a thousand shekels[d][h] of silver.
[12]But my own vineyard[i] is mine to
give;
the thousand shekels are for you,
Solomon,
and two hundred[e] are for those
who tend its fruit.

He

[13]You who dwell in the gardens
with friends in attendance,
let me hear your voice!

She

[14]Come away, my beloved,
and be like a gazelle[j]
or like a young stag[k]
on the spice-laden mountains.[l]

8:5 [b] SS 3:6 [c] S SS 3:4 **8:6** [d] S SS 1:2 [e] S Nu 5:14 **8:7** [f] S Pr 6:35 **8:11** [g] Ecc 2:4 [h] Isa 7:23 **8:12** [i] S SS 1:6 **8:14** [j] S Pr 5:19 [k] S SS 2:9 [l] S SS 2:8, 17

[a] *6* Or *ardor* [b] *6* Or *fire, / like the very flame of the* LORD [c] *7* Or *he* [d] *11* That is, about 25 pounds or about 12 kilograms; also in verse 12 [e] *12* That is, about 5 pounds or about 2.3 kilograms

8:5 *Who ... wilderness ... ?* See 3:6 and note. *Under the apple tree.* In the ancient world, sexual union and birth were often associated with fruit trees.

8:6–7 *love is ... grave. It burns ... flame. Many waters ... away.* These three wisdom statements (see essay, p. 786) characterize marital love as the strongest, most unyielding and invincible force in human experience. With these statements the Song reaches its literary climax and discloses its purpose.

8:6 *seal.* Seals were precious to their owners, as personal as their names (see note on Ge 38:18). *arm.* Perhaps a poetic synonym for "hand." *unyielding as the grave.* As the grave will not give up the dead, so love will not surrender the loved one. *mighty flame.* The Hebrew expression conveys the idea of a most intense flame, hinting that it has been kindled by the Lord (see NIV text note).

8:7 *Many waters.* Words that suggest not only the ocean depths (see Ps 107:23) but also the primeval waters that the people of the ancient Near East regarded as a permanent threat to the world (see note on Ps 32:6). The waters were also associated with the realm of the dead (see note on Ps 30:1). *If one ... scorned.* A fourth wisdom statement (see note on vv. 6–7), declaring love's unsurpassed worth.

8:8–14 In the closing lines of the Song, the words of the brothers (vv. 8–9), the darling's reference to her own vineyard (v. 12) and her final reference to Solomon (vv. 11–12) suggest a return to the beginning of the Song (see 1:2–7; see also Introduction: Literary Features). The lines may recall the darling's development into the age for love and marriage and the blossoming of her relationship with her beloved.

8:8 In the ancient Near East, brothers were often guardians of their sisters, especially in matters pertaining to marriage (see Ge 24:50–60; 34:13–27). *the day she is spoken for.* Marriage was often contracted at an early age.

8:9 This imaginative verse probably expresses the brothers' determination to defend their young sister (the darling) until her proper time for love and marriage has come. Or it may mean that the brothers are concerned to see that she is properly adorned for marriage before she is spoken for.

8:10 *I ... like towers.* In contrast to the time when she was watched over by her brothers, the darling rejoices in her maturity (cf. Eze 16:7–8). *his.* The beloved's.

8:11–12 *thousand shekels ... two hundred.* Whether these figures are to be taken literally (see Isa 7:23) is uncertain.

8:11 *Baal Hamon.* The Hebrew *hamon* sometimes means "wealth" or "abundance"; hence Baal (i.e., "lord") Hamon could mean "lord of abundance," bringing to mind Solomon's great wealth.

8:12 *my own vineyard.* Her body (see note on 1:6). *mine to give.* As Solomon is master of his vineyard, so the darling is mistress of her attractions to dispense as she will. She offers Solomon the owner's portion of her vineyard.

8:13 *in the gardens.* In 7:11–12 the darling invites her beloved to accompany her to the countryside and the vineyards. Here the imagery places her appropriately in a garden. *friends.* Male; perhaps the companions of the beloved (see 1:7). *let me hear your voice.* See 2:14.

8:14 *be like a gazelle or ... stag.* Display your virile strength and agility for my delight (see note on 2:9). *on the spice-laden mountains.* Cf. 2:17.

THE PROPHETS

Isaiah, Jeremiah, Ezekiel and the Twelve (the Minor Prophets are counted as one book in the Hebrew canon) are together known as the Latter Prophets (for the Former Prophets, see Introduction to Joshua: Title and Theological Theme) and are often further divided into two groups: (1) The Major Prophets are the books of Isaiah through Ezekiel (in the Hebrew Bible, Lamentations and Daniel are included among the Writings [see Lk 24:44 and note]) and are called "major" because of their relative length and the variety of topics addressed. (2) The remaining books (the Twelve) are called the Minor Prophets (see essay, p. 1439), because they are relatively short and usually address a particular context or deal with a more singular theme. While some prophetic messages included visions and dreams of the future, the primary task of all the prophets was to call the Israelites back to faithfulness to their covenant God and to obedience to the terms of their covenants with him.

ISAIAH

INTRODUCTION

Position in the Hebrew Bible

In the Hebrew Bible the book of Isaiah initiates a division called the Latter Prophets (for the Former Prophets, see Introduction to Joshua: Title and Theological Theme), including also Jeremiah, Ezekiel and the Twelve Minor Prophets (so called because of their small size by comparison with the major prophetic books of Isaiah, Jeremiah and Ezekiel, and not at all suggesting that they are of minor importance; see essay, p. 1439). Thus Isaiah occupies pride of place among the Latter Prophets. This is fitting since he is sometimes referred to as the prince of the prophets.

Author

Isaiah, son of Amoz, is often thought of as the greatest of the writing prophets. His name means "The LORD is salvation." He was a contemporary of Amos, Hosea and Micah, beginning his ministry in 740 BC, the year King Uzziah died (see note on 6:1). According to an unsubstantiated Jewish tradition (*The Ascension of Isaiah*), he was sawed in half during the reign of Manasseh (cf. Heb 11:37 and note). Isaiah was married and had at least two sons, Shear-Jashub (7:3) and Maher-Shalal-Hash-Baz (8:3). He probably spent most of his life in Jerusalem, enjoying his greatest influence under King Hezekiah (see 37:1 – 2). Isaiah is also credited with writing a history of the reign of King Uzziah (2Ch 26:22).

Many scholars today challenge the claim that Isaiah wrote both halves of the book (chs. 1 – 39 and chs. 40 – 66) that bears his name. Yet his is the only name attached to it (see 1:1; 2:1; 13:1). The strongest argument for the unity of Isaiah is the expression "the Holy One of Israel," a title for God that occurs 12 times in chs. 1 – 39 and 14 times in chs. 40 – 66. Outside Isaiah it appears in the OT only 6 times. There are other striking verbal parallels between the two halves. Compare the following verses:

1:2	66:24
1:5 – 6	53:4 – 5

a quick look

Author:
The prophet Isaiah

Audience:
The people of Judah and Jerusalem

Date:
Between 740 and 680 BC

Theme:
Isaiah predicts imminent judgment — but eventual restoration — for the people of Judah and Jerusalem.

5:27	40:30
6:1	52:13; 57:15
6:11 – 12	62:4
11:1	53:2
11:6 – 9	65:25
11:12	49:22
35:10	51:11

Altogether, there are at least 25 Hebrew words or forms found in Isaiah (i.e., in both major divisions of the book) that occur in no other prophetic writing.

Isaiah's use of fire as a figure of punishment (see 1:31; 10:17; 26:11; 33:11 – 14; 34:9 – 10; 66:24), his references to the "holy mountain" of Jerusalem (see note on 2:2 – 4) and his mention of the highway to Jerusalem (see note on 11:16) are themes that recur throughout the book.

The structure of Isaiah also argues for its unity. Chs. 36 – 39 constitute a historical interlude that concludes chs. 1 – 35 and introduces chs. 40 – 66 (see note on 36:1).

Several NT verses refer to the prophet Isaiah in connection with various parts of the book:

The great Isaiah Scroll from Qumran (1QIsa) is the oldest complete manuscript of the book of Isaiah (c. 150 – 125 BC). The complete scroll is 24 feet long.

God is the "Holy One of Israel," who must punish his rebellious people but will afterward redeem them.

Mt 12:17 – 21 (Isa 42:1 – 4); Mt 3:3 and Lk 3:4 (Isa 40:3); Ro 10:16,20 (Isa 53:1; 65:1); see especially Jn 12:38 – 41 (Isa 53:1; 6:10).

Date

Most of the events referred to in chs. 1 – 39 occurred during Isaiah's ministry (see 6:1; 14:28; 36:1), so these chapters may have been completed not long after 701 BC, the year the Assyrian army was destroyed (see note on 10:16). The prophet lived until at least 681 (see note on 37:38) and may have written chs. 40 – 66 during his later years. Assuming he wrote those chapters, his prophetic vision there looked forward to the Babylonian exile (see note on 40:1—66:24; cf. 39:6 – 7 and notes), and his message there was specifically intended for the Jews groaning in Babylonian captivity (cf. Ps 137). A parallel kind of situation might be Daniel's vision of the second-century BC conflicts between the Ptolemies and Seleucids (see Da 11 and notes; see also map and accompanying text, pp. 1436 – 1437).

Background

Isaiah lived during the stormy period marking the expansion of the Assyrian Empire and the decline of Israel. Under King Tiglath-Pileser III (745 – 727 BC) the Assyrians swept westward into Aram (Syria) and Canaan. In about 733 the kings of Aram and Israel tried to pressure Ahaz, king of Judah, into joining a coalition against Assyria. Ahaz chose instead to ask Tiglath-Pileser for help, a decision condemned by Isaiah (see note on 7:1). Assyria did assist Judah and conquered the northern kingdom in 722 – 721. This made Judah even more vulnerable, and in 701 King Sennacherib of Assyria threatened Jerusalem itself (see 36:1 and note). The godly King Hezekiah prayed earnestly, and Isaiah predicted that God would force the Assyrians to withdraw from the city (37:6 – 7).

Nevertheless, Isaiah warned Judah that her sin would bring captivity at the hands of Babylonia. The visit of the Babylonian king's envoys to Hezekiah set the stage for this prediction (see 39:1,6 and notes). Although the fall of Jerusalem would not take place until 586 BC, Isaiah assumes the destruction of Judah and proceeds to predict the restoration of the people from captivity (see 40:2 – 3 and notes). God would redeem his people from Babylonia, just as he had rescued them from Egypt (see notes on 35:9; 41:14). Isaiah predicts the rise of Cyrus the Persian, who would unite the Medes and Persians and conquer Babylon in 539 (see 41:2 and note). The decree of Cyrus would allow the Jews to return home in 538/537, a deliverance that prefigured the greater salvation from sin through Christ (see 52:7 and note).

Themes and Theology

Isaiah is a book that unveils the full dimensions of God's judgment and salvation. God is the "Holy One of Israel" (see 1:4; 6:1 and notes), who must punish his rebellious people (1:2) but will afterward redeem them (41:14,16). Israel is a nation blind and deaf (6:9 – 10; 42:7), a vineyard that will be trampled (5:1 – 7), a people devoid of justice or righteousness (5:7; 10:1 – 2). The awful judgment that will be unleashed upon Israel and all the nations that defy God is called "the day of the LORD." Although Israel has a foretaste of that day (5:30; 42:25), the nations bear its full power (see 2:11,17,20 and note). It is a day associated in the NT with Christ's second coming and the accompanying judgment (see 24:1,21; 34:1 – 2 and notes). Throughout the book God's judgment is referred to as "fire" (see 1:31; 30:33 and notes). He is the "Sovereign LORD" (see note on 25:8), far above all nations and rulers (40:15 – 24).

Yet God will have compassion on his people (14:1 – 2) and will rescue them from both political and spiritual oppression. Their restoration is like a new exodus (43:2,16 – 19; 52:10 – 12) as God redeems them (see 35:9; 41:14 and notes) and saves them (see 43:3; 49:8 and notes). Israel's mighty Creator (40:21 – 22; 48:13) will make streams spring up in the desert (32:2) as he graciously leads them home. The theme of a highway for the return of exiles is a prominent one (see 11:16; 40:3 and notes) in both major parts of the book. The Lord raises a banner to summon the nations to bring Israel home (see 5:26 and note).

Peace and safety mark this new time (11:6 – 9). A king (the Messiah) descended from David will reign in righteousness (9:7; 32:1), and all nations will stream to the holy mountain of Jerusalem (see 2:2 – 4 and note). God's people will no longer be oppressed by wicked rulers (11:14; 45:14), and Jerusalem will truly be the "City of the LORD" (60:14).

King Sargon II was one of the kings of Assyria during Isaiah's ministry. In 722–721 BC Samaria, the capital of the northern kingdom of Israel, was finally taken by Sargon II after a three-year siege started by Shalmaneser V.

Z. Radovan/www.BibleLandPictures.com

The Lord calls the Messianic King "my servant" in chs. 42 – 53, a term also applied to Israel as a nation (see 41:8 – 9; 42:1 and notes). It is through the suffering of the servant that salvation in its fullest sense is achieved. Cyrus was God's instrument to deliver Israel from Babylon (41:2), but the promised Messiah would deliver humankind from the prison of sin (52:13 — 53:12). He would become a "light for the Gentiles" (42:6), so that those nations that faced judgment (chs. 13 – 23) would also find salvation (55:4 – 5) and become "servants of the LORD" (see 54:17 and note).

The Lord's kingdom on earth, with its righteous Ruler and his righteous subjects, is the goal toward which the book of Isaiah steadily moves. The restored earth (a new creation: chs. 65 – 66) and the restored people will then conform to the divine ideal, and all will result in the praise and glory of the Holy One of Israel for what he has accomplished.

Literary Features

Isaiah contains both prose and poetry, with the main prose material found in chs. 3 – 9; 36 – 39 — the latter constituting the historical interlude that unites the two parts of the book (see Author). The beauty of Isaiah's poetry is unsurpassed in the OT; it is extremely rich in imagery and wordplay. And the work as a whole employs a larger Hebrew vocabulary than any other OT book.

One of Isaiah's favorite techniques is personification. The sun and moon are "ashamed" (24:23), while the desert and parched land "rejoice" (see 35:1 and note) and the mountains and forests "burst into song" (44:23). The trees "clap their hands" (55:12). A favorite basic metaphor often exploited is the vineyard. In 5:7, Israel is the vineyard God has cultivated. Elsewhere, treading the winepress is a picture of divine judgment (see 63:3 and note), and to drink God's "cup of … wrath" is to stagger under his punishment (see 51:17 and note). And legendary monsters, such as Leviathan and Rahab, represent nations (see 27:1; 30:7 and notes; 51:9).

The power of Isaiah's imagery is seen in 30:27 – 33, and he makes full use of sarcasm in his denunciation of idols in 44:9 – 20. A forceful example of wordplay appears in 5:7 (see note there), and alliteration and assonance appear in 24:16 – 17 (see note there). The "overwhelming scourge" of 28:15,18 is an illustration of mixed metaphor.

Isaiah often alludes to earlier events in Israel's history, especially the exodus from Egypt. The crossing of the "Red Sea" forms the background for 11:15 and 43:2,16 – 17, and other allusions occur in 4:5 – 6; 31:5; 37:36 (see notes on these verses). He also refers to the overthrow of Sodom and Gomorrah (1:9), and Gideon's victory over Midian is mentioned in 9:4; 10:26 (see also 28:21). Several times Isaiah draws upon the song of Moses in Dt 32 (compare 1:2 with Dt 32:1; 30:17 with Dt 32:30; and 43:11,13 with Dt 32:39). Isaiah, like Moses, called the nation to repentance and to faith in a holy, all-powerful God. See also note on 49:8.

The refrain in 48:22 and 57:21 divides the last 27 chapters into three sections of nine chapters each (40 – 48; 49 – 57; 58 – 66; see Outline, which also reveals the various literary forms employed in the book; see also notes on the various sections).

Outline

Part 1: The Book of Judgment (chs. 1 – 39)

- I. Messages of Rebuke and Promise (chs. 1 – 6)
  - A. Introduction: Indictment of Judah for Breaking the Covenant (ch. 1)
  - B. The Future Discipline and Glory of Judah and Jerusalem (chs. 2 – 4)
    1. Jerusalem's future blessings (2:1 – 5)
    2. The Lord's discipline of Judah (2:6 — 4:1)
    3. The restoration of Zion (4:2 – 6)
  - C. The Nation's Judgment and Exile (ch. 5)
  - D. Isaiah's Unique Commission (ch. 6)
- II. Prophecies Occasioned by the Aramean and Israelite Threat against Judah (chs. 7 – 12)
  - A. Ahaz Warned Not to Fear the Aramean and Israelite Alliance (ch. 7)
  - B. Isaiah's Son and David's Son (8:1 — 9:7)
  - C. Judgment against Israel (9:8 — 10:4)

- D. The Assyrian Empire and the Davidic Kingdom (10:5 — 12:6)
  1. The destruction of Assyria (10:5 – 34)
  2. The establishment of the Davidic king and his kingdom (ch. 11)
  3. Songs of praise for deliverance (ch. 12)
- III. Judgment against the Nations (chs. 13 – 23)
  - A. Against Babylonia and Assyria (13:1 — 14:27)
  - B. Against Philistia (14:28 – 32)
  - C. Against Moab (chs. 15 – 16)
  - D. Against Aram (ch. 17)
  - E. Against Cush (ch. 18)
  - F. Against Egypt and Cush (chs. 19 – 20)
  - G. Against Babylon (21:1 – 10)
  - H. Against Dumah (Edom) (21:11 – 12)
  - I. Against Arabia (21:13 – 17)
  - J. Against the Valley of Vision (Jerusalem) (ch. 22)
  - K. Against Tyre (ch. 23)
- IV. Judgment and Promise (the Lord's Kingdom) (chs. 24 – 27)
  - A. Universal Judgments for Universal Sin (ch. 24)
  - B. Deliverance and Blessing (ch. 25)
  - C. Praise for the Lord's Sovereign Care (ch. 26)
  - D. Israel's Enemies Punished but Israel's Remnant Restored (ch. 27)
- V. Six Woes: Five on the Unfaithful in Israel and One on Assyria (chs. 28 – 33)
  - A. Woe to Ephraim (Samaria) and also to Judah (ch. 28)
  - B. Woe to David's City (Jerusalem) (29:1 – 14)
  - C. Woe to Those Who Rely on Foreign Alliances (29:15 – 24)
  - D. Woe to the Obstinate Nation (ch. 30)
  - E. Woe to Those Who Rely on Egypt (chs. 31 – 32)
  - F. Woe to Assyria but Blessing for God's People (ch. 33)
- VI. More Prophecies of Judgment and Promise (chs. 34 – 35)
  - A. The Destruction of the Nations and the Avenging of God's People (ch. 34)
  - B. The Future Blessings of Restored Zion (ch. 35)
- VII. A Historical Transition from the Assyrian Threat to the Babylonian Exile (chs. 36 – 39)
  - A. Jerusalem Preserved from the Assyrian Threat (chs. 36 – 37)
    1. The siege of Jerusalem by Sennacherib and the Assyrian army (ch. 36)
    2. The Lord's deliverance of Jerusalem (ch. 37)
  - B. The Lord's Extension of Hezekiah's Life (ch. 38)
  - C. The Babylonian Exile Predicted (ch. 39)

Part 2: The Book of Comfort (chs. 40 – 66)

- VIII. The Deliverance and Restoration of Israel (chs. 40 – 48)
  - A. The Coming of the Victorious God (40:1 – 26)
  - B. Unfailing Strength for the Weary Exiles (40:27 – 31)

C. The Lord of History (41:1 — 42:9)
D. Praise and Exhortation (42:10 – 25)
E. The Regathering and Renewal of Israel (43:1 — 44:5)
F. The Only God (44:6 — 45:25)
G. The Lord's Superiority over Babylon's Gods (ch. 46)
H. The Fall of Babylon (ch. 47)
I. The Lord's Exhortations to His People (ch. 48)

IX. The Servant's Ministry and Israel's Restoration (chs. 49 – 57)
A. The Call and Mission of the Servant (49:1 – 13)
B. The Repopulation of Zion (49:14 – 26)
C. Israel's Sin and the Servant's Obedience (ch. 50)
D. The Remnant Comforted Because of Their Glorious Prospect (51:1 — 52:12)
E. The Sufferings and Glories of the Lord's Righteous Servant (52:13 — 53:12)
F. The Future Glory of Zion (ch. 54)
G. The Lord's Call to Salvation and Covenant Blessings (55:1 — 56:8)
H. The Condemnation of the Wicked in Israel (56:9 — 57:21)

X. Everlasting Deliverance and Everlasting Judgment (chs. 58 – 66)
A. False and True Worship (ch. 58)
B. Zion's Confession and Redemption (ch. 59)
C. Zion's Peace and Prosperity (ch. 60)
D. The Lord's Favor (ch. 61)
E. Zion's Restoration and Glory (62:1 — 63:6)
F. Prayer for Divine Deliverance (63:7 — 64:12)
G. The Lord's Answer: Mercy and Judgment (ch. 65)
H. Judgment for False Worshipers and Blessing for True Worshipers (ch. 66)

1 The vision[a] concerning Judah and Jerusalem[b] that Isaiah son of Amoz saw[c] during the reigns of Uzziah,[d] Jotham,[e] Ahaz[f] and Hezekiah,[g] kings of Judah.

A Rebellious Nation

2 Hear me, you heavens! Listen, earth![h]
For the LORD has spoken:[i]
"I reared children[j] and brought them up,
but they have rebelled[k] against me.
3 The ox knows[l] its master,
the donkey its owner's manger,[m]
but Israel does not know,[n]
my people do not understand.[o]"

4 Woe to the sinful nation,
a people whose guilt is great,[p]
a brood of evildoers,[q]
children given to corruption![r]
They have forsaken[s] the LORD;
they have spurned the Holy One[t] of Israel
and turned their backs[u] on him.

5 Why should you be beaten[v] anymore?
Why do you persist[w] in rebellion?[x]
Your whole head is injured,
your whole heart[y] afflicted.[z]
6 From the sole of your foot to the top of your head[a]
there is no soundness[b]—
only wounds and welts[c]
and open sores,
not cleansed or bandaged[d]
or soothed with olive oil.[e]
7 Your country is desolate,[f]
your cities burned with fire;[g]
your fields are being stripped by foreigners[h]
right before you,
laid waste as when overthrown by strangers.[i]
8 Daughter Zion[j] is left[k]
like a shelter in a vineyard,
like a hut[l] in a cucumber field,
like a city under siege.
9 Unless the LORD Almighty
had left us some survivors,[m]
we would have become like Sodom,
we would have been like Gomorrah.[n]

10 Hear the word of the LORD,[o]
you rulers of Sodom;[p]
listen to the instruction[q] of our God,
you people of Gomorrah![r]
11 "The multitude of your sacrifices—
what are they to me?" says the LORD.
"I have more than enough of burnt offerings,
of rams and the fat of fattened animals;[s]

1:1 [a] 1Sa 3:1; Isa 22:1,5; Ob 1:1; Na 1:1 [b] Isa 40:9; 44:26 [c] Isa 2:1; 13:1 [d] S 2Ki 14:21; S 2Ch 26:22 [e] S 1Ch 3:12 [f] S 2Ki 16:1 [g] S 1Ch 3:13 **1:2** [h] S Dt 4:26 [i] Jdg 11:10; Jer 42:5; Mic 1:2 [j] Isa 23:4; 63:16 [k] ver 4,23; Isa 24:5,20; 30:1,9; 46:8; 48:8; 57:4; 65:2; 66:24; Eze 24:3; Hag 1:12; Mal 1:6; 3:5 **1:3** [l] Job 12:9 [m] S Ge 42:27 [n] Jer 4:22; 5:4; 9:3,6; Hos 2:8; 4:1 [o] S Dt 32:28; Isa 42:25; 48:8; Hos 4:6; 7:9 **1:4** [p] Isa 5:18 [q] S ver 2; Isa 9:17; 14:20; 31:2; Jer 23:14 [r] Ps 14:3 [s] S Dt 32:15; S Ps 119:87 [t] S 2Ki 19:22; Isa 5:19,24; 31:1; 37:23; 41:14; 43:14; 45:11; 47:4; Eze 39:7 [u] S Pr 30:9; Isa 59:13 **1:5** [v] Pr 20:30 [w] Jer 2:30; 5:3; 8:5 [x] S ver 2; Isa 31:6; Jer 44:16-17; Heb 3:16 [y] La 2:11; 5:17 [z] Isa 30:26; 33:6, 24; 58:8; Jer 30:17 **1:6** [a] S Dt 28:35 [b] Ps 38:3 [c] Isa 53:5 [d] S Ps 147:3; Isa 30:26; Jer 8:22; 14:19; 30:17; La 2:13; Eze 34:4 [e] 2Sa 14:2; Ps 23:5; 45:7; 104:15; Isa 61:3; Lk 10:34 **1:7** [f] S Lev 26:34 [g] S Lev 26:31; S Dt 29:23 [h] Lev 26:16; Jdg 6:3-6; Isa 62:8; Jer 5:17 [i] S 2Ki 18:13; S Ps 109:11 **1:8** [j] S Ps 9:14; S Isa 10:32 [k] Isa 30:17; 49:21 [l] S Job 27:18 **1:9** [m] S Ge 45:7; S 2Ki 21:14; Isa 4:2; 6:13; 27:12; 28:5; 37:4,31-32; 45:25; 56:8; Jer 23:3; Joel 2:32 [n] S Ge 19:24; Ro 9:29* **1:10** [o] Isa 28:14 [p] S Ge 13:13; S 18:20; Eze 16:49; Ro 9:29; Rev 11:8 [q] Isa 5:24; 8:20; 30:9 [r] Isa 13:19 **1:11** [s] Ps 50:8; Am 6:4

1:1—6:13 The first section of Isaiah's prophecies, dominated by messages of judgment and climaxing in Isaiah's commission (ch. 6; cf. note on 7:1—12:6).

1:1-31 Compare the indictment of ch. 1 with that of ch. 5; the two enclose the first series of messages. Ch. 1 also serves as an introduction to the whole book.

1:1 The title of the book. Other headings occur in 2:1; 13:1; 14:28; 15:1; 17:1; 19:1; 21:1,11,13; 22:1; 23:1. *vision.* In the sense of "revelation" or "prophecy" (see Pr 29:18; Ob 1 and notes; see also 1Sa 3:1). *Amoz.* Not to be confused with the prophet Amos. *Uzziah, Jotham, Ahaz and Hezekiah.* These kings reigned from 792 to 686 BC. None of the kings of Israel is mentioned since Isaiah ministered primarily to the southern kingdom (Judah).

1:2 Isaiah begins and ends (66:24) with a condemnation of those who rebel against God. The prophet calls on the heavens and the earth to testify to the truth of God's accusation against Israel and the rightness of his judgment—since they were witnesses of his covenant (see Dt 30:19 and note; 31:28; 32:1; Ps 50:1 and note).

1:3 *manger.* Feeding trough. *does not know.* Refusal to know and understand God later resulted in Judah's exile from her land (5:13).

1:4 *Holy One of Israel.* Occurs 26 times in Isaiah (see especially 5:24) and only 6 times elsewhere in the OT (see Introduction: Author; see also note on 2Ki 19:22). *Holy One.* See Ex 3:5; Lev 11:44 and notes.

1:5-6 The pitiable moral and spiritual condition of Israel is transferred to the suffering servant in 53:4-5. The Hebrew words for "beaten," "injured" and "welts" correspond to those for "stricken," "pain" and "wounds."

1:6 The disease ravages the entire body, as with Job (2:7). *olive oil.* Commonly used for treating wounds (see Lk 10:34).

1:7-9 The desolation of the land of Judah is the result of foreign invasion: e.g., by Aram, the northern kingdom of Israel, Edom and Philistia (2Ch 28:5-18); later (701 BC) by King Sennacherib and the Assyrian army (36:1-2); still later (605-586) by King Nebuchadnezzar and the Neo-Babylonian army.

1:8 *Daughter Zion.* A personification of Jerusalem (see note on 2Ki 19:21). *shelter ... hut.* Temporary structures used by watchmen (Job 27:18), who were on the lookout for thieves and intruders. Thus Jerusalem was not very defensible.

1:9-10 *Sodom ... Gomorrah.* Classic examples of sinful cities that were completely destroyed (see 3:9; Ge 13:13; 18:20-21; 19:5,24-25). Just as Jesus addressed Peter as though he were Satan (Mt 16:23), so Isaiah addresses his fellow Israelites as though they were the "rulers of Sodom" and the "people of Gomorrah."

1:9 Quoted in Ro 9:29, where it is linked with Isa 10:22-23. Isaiah often refers to the remnant that will survive God's judgment on the nation and take possession of the land (see 4:3; 10:20-23; 11:11,16; 46:3).

1:11-15 The moral character and conduct of the worshipers, not the number of their religious activities, are most important (see 66:3; Jer 6:20; 7:22-23; Hos 6:6; Am 5:21-24; Mic 6:6-8 and notes).

1:11 *fattened animals.* Those kept in confinement for special feeding.

I have no pleasure[t]
in the blood of bulls[u] and lambs and
goats.[v]
12 When you come to appear before me,
who has asked this of you,[w]
this trampling of my courts?
13 Stop bringing meaningless offerings![x]
Your incense[y] is detestable[z] to me.
New Moons,[a] Sabbaths and
convocations[b]—
I cannot bear your worthless
assemblies.
14 Your New Moon[c] feasts and your
appointed festivals[d]
I hate with all my being.[e]
They have become a burden to me;[f]
I am weary[g] of bearing them.
15 When you spread out your hands[h] in
prayer,
I hide[i] my eyes from you;
even when you offer many prayers,
I am not listening.[j]

Your hands[k] are full of blood![l]

16 Wash[m] and make yourselves clean.
Take your evil deeds out of my sight;[n]
stop doing wrong.[o]
17 Learn to do right;[p] seek justice.[q]
Defend the oppressed.[a][r]
Take up the cause of the fatherless;[s]
plead the case of the widow.[t]

18 "Come now, let us settle the matter,"[u]
says the LORD.
"Though your sins are like scarlet,
they shall be as white as snow;[v]
though they are red as crimson,
they shall be like wool.[w]
19 If you are willing and obedient,[x]
you will eat the good things of the
land;[y]
20 but if you resist and rebel,[z]
you will be devoured by the sword."[a]
For the mouth of the LORD
has spoken.[b]

21 See how the faithful city
has become a prostitute![c]
She once was full of justice;
righteousness[d] used to dwell in
her—
but now murderers![e]
22 Your silver has become dross,[f]
your choice wine is diluted with
water.
23 Your rulers are rebels,[g]
partners with thieves;[h]
they all love bribes[i]
and chase after gifts.
They do not defend the cause of the
fatherless;
the widow's case does not come
before them.[j]

24 Therefore the Lord, the LORD Almighty,
the Mighty One[k] of Israel, declares:
"Ah! I will vent my wrath on my foes
and avenge[l] myself on my enemies.[m]
25 I will turn my hand against you;[b][n]
I will thoroughly purge[o] away your
dross[p]
and remove all your impurities.[q]
26 I will restore your leaders as in days of
old,[r]
your rulers as at the beginning.
Afterward you will be called[s]
the City of Righteousness,[t]
the Faithful City.[u]"

[a] *17* Or *justice. / Correct the oppressor* [b] *25* That is, against Jerusalem

1:11 [t]S Job 22:3 [u]Isa 66:3; Jer 6:20 [v]1Sa 15:22; S Ps 40:6; Mal 1:10; Heb 10:4 **1:12** [w]Ex 23:17; Dt 31:11 **1:13** [x]Pr 15:8; Isa 66:3; Hag 2:14 [y]Jer 7:9; 18:15; 44:8 [z]S 1Ki 14:24; Ps 115:8; Pr 28:9; Isa 41:24; Mal 2:11 [a]S Nu 10:10 [b]1Ch 23:31 **1:14** [c]S Ne 10:33 [d]Ex 12:16; Lev 23:1-44; Nu 28:11-29:39; Dt 16:1-17; Isa 5:12; 29:1; Hos 2:11 [e]S Ps 11:5 [f]S Job 7:12 [g]Ps 69:3; Isa 7:13; 43:22, 24; Jer 44:22; Mal 2:17; 3:14 **1:15** [h]S Ex 9:29 [i]S Dt 31:17; Isa 57:17; 59:2 [j]S Dt 1:45; S 1Sa 8:18; S Job 15:31; S Jn 9:31 [k]S Job 9:30 [l]Isa 4:4; 59:3; Jer 2:34; Eze 7:23; Hos 4:2; Joel 3:21 **1:16** [m]S Ru 3:3; Mt 27:24; Jas 4:8 [n]Nu 19:11, 16; Isa 52:11 [o]Isa 55:7; Jer 25:5 **1:17** [p]S Ps 34:14 [q]S Ps 72:1; Isa 11:4; 33:5; 56:1; 61:8; Am 5:14-15; Mic 6:8; Zep 2:3 [r]S Dt 14:29 [s]ver 23; Job 22:9; Ps 82:3; 94:6; Isa 10:2 [t]S Ex 22:22; Eze 18:31; 22:7; Lk 18:3; Jas 1:27 **1:18** [u]S 1Sa 2:25; Isa 41:1; 43:9, 26 [v]S Ps 51:7; Rev 7:14 [w]Isa 55:7 **1:19** [x]S Job 36:11; S Isa 50:10 [y]Dt 30:15-16; Ezr 9:12; Ps 34:10; Isa 30:23; 55:2; 58:14; 62:9; 65:13, 21-22 **1:20** [z]S 1Sa 12:15 [a]S Job 15:22; Isa 3:25; 27:1; 65:12; 66:16; Jer 17:27 [b]Nu 23:19; Isa 21:17; 34:16; 40:5; 58:14; Jer 49:13; Mic 4:4; Zec 1:6; Rev 1:16 **1:21** [c]Isa 57:3-9; Jer 2:20; 3:2, 9; 13:27; Eze 23:3; Hos 2:1-13 [d]Isa 5:7; 46:13; 59:14; Am 6:12 [e]S Pr 6:17 **1:22** [f]S Ps 119:119 **1:23** [g]S ver 2 [h]S Dt 19:14; Mic 2:1-2; 6:12 [i]S Ex 23:8; Am 5:12 [j]Isa 10:2; Jer 5:28; Eze 22:6-7; Mic 3:9; Hab 1:4 **1:24** [k]S Ge 49:24 [l]Isa 34:2, 8; 35:4; 47:3; 59:17; 61:2; 63:4; Jer 51:6; Eze 5:13 [m]S Dt 32:43; S Isa 10:3 **1:25** [n]Dt 28:63 [o]S Ps 78:38 [p]S Ps 119:119 [q]2Ch 29:15; Isa 48:10; Jer 6:29; 9:7; Eze 22:22; Mal 3:3 **1:26** [r]Jer 33:7, 11; Mic 4:8 [s]S Ge 32:28 [t]Isa 32:16; 33:5; 46:13; 48:18; 61:11; 62:1; Jer 31:23; Zec 8:3 [u]Isa 4:3; 48:2; 52:1; 60:14; 62:2; 64:10; Da 9:24

1:13 *meaningless offerings.* See 1Sa 15:22; Ps 51:16–17 and notes.
1:14 *New Moon feasts.* Celebrated on the first day of each Hebrew month. Special sacrifices and feasts were part of the observance (see Nu 28:11–15). *appointed festivals.* Included the annual festivals, such as Passover, Weeks (Pentecost) and Tabernacles (Ex 23:14–17; 34:18–25; Lev 23; Dt 16:1–17).
1:15 *hide my eyes.* In 8:17; 59:2 God hides his face from Israel (see also Mic 3:4 and note).
1:17 See Jer 22:16 and note; Jas 1:27. *fatherless ... widow.* Represented the weak and often oppressed part of society. Rulers were warned not to take advantage of them (see v. 23; 10:2; Ex 22:21–27 and note; Jer 22:3).
1:18 *scarlet ... crimson.* Refers to the blood that has stained the hands of murderers (see vv. 15,21). *white as snow.* A powerful figurative description of the result of forgiveness (see Ps 51:7 and note). This offer of forgiveness is conditioned on the reformation of life called for in v. 19.
1:19–20 *eat ... be devoured.* The vivid contrast is stressed by the use of the same Hebrew verb.
1:21 *become a prostitute.* Jerusalem (representing all Judah) has been unfaithful to the Lord. Here her unfaithfulness is specified as social abuse, exploitation of the powerless, and violence against one's neighbor—violating the Lord's moral order for the community of his people (see note on Ps 73:27; cf. note on Ex 34:15).
1:22 *Your silver has become dross.* See Ps 12:6 and note.
1:24 *The Lord, the LORD Almighty, the Mighty One of Israel.* Stressing God's sovereign authority as Judge (cf. Ps 50:1,6; cf. also Jos 22:22 and note). *the LORD Almighty.* See note on 1Sa 1:3.
1:25–26 *turn ... restore.* The use of the same Hebrew verb emphasizes the contrast (see note on vv. 19–20).
1:25 *purge away your dross.* Purifying fire is also mentioned in 4:4; 48:10.
1:26 *Faithful City.* See v. 21. Using a related Hebrew noun, Zec 8:3 also refers to the future Jerusalem as the "Faithful City."

27 Zion will be delivered with justice,
her penitent[v] ones with
righteousness.[w]
28 But rebels and sinners[x] will both be
broken,
and those who forsake[y] the LORD will
perish.[z]

29 "You will be ashamed[a] because of the
sacred oaks[b]
in which you have delighted;
you will be disgraced because of the
gardens[c]
that you have chosen.
30 You will be like an oak with fading
leaves,[d]
like a garden without water.
31 The mighty man will become tinder
and his work a spark;
both will burn together,
with no one to quench the fire.[e]"

The Mountain of the LORD

2:1-4pp — Mic 4:1-3

2 This is what Isaiah son of Amoz saw
concerning Judah and Jerusalem:[f]

2 In the last days[g]
the mountain[h] of the LORD's temple will
be established
as the highest of the mountains;[i]
it will be exalted[j] above the hills,
and all nations will stream to it.[k]

3 Many peoples[l] will come and say,

"Come, let us go[m] up to the mountain[n]
of the LORD,
to the temple of the God of Jacob.
He will teach us his ways,
so that we may walk in his paths."
The law[o] will go out from Zion,
the word of the LORD from Jerusalem.[p]
4 He will judge[q] between the nations
and will settle disputes[r] for many
peoples.
They will beat their swords into
plowshares
and their spears into pruning hooks.[s]
Nation will not take up sword against
nation,[t]
nor will they train for war anymore.

5 Come, descendants of Jacob,[u]
let us walk in the light[v] of the LORD.

The Day of the LORD

6 You, LORD, have abandoned[w] your people,
the descendants of Jacob.[x]
They are full of superstitions from the
East;
they practice divination[y] like the
Philistines[z]
and embrace[a] pagan customs.[b]
7 Their land is full of silver and gold;[c]
there is no end to their treasures.[d]
Their land is full of horses;[e]
there is no end to their chariots.[f]
8 Their land is full of idols;[g]
they bow down[h] to the work of their
hands,[i]
to what their fingers[j] have made.
9 So people will be brought low[k]
and everyone humbled[l] —
do not forgive them.[a][m]

10 Go into the rocks, hide[n] in the ground
from the fearful presence of the LORD
and the splendor of his majesty![o]

[a] 9 Or *not raise them up*

1:27 [v]Isa 30:15; 31:6; 59:20; Eze 18:30 [w]Isa 35:10; 41:14; 43:1; 52:3; 62:12; 63:4; Hos 2:19 **1:28** [x]Isa 33:14; 43:27; 48:8; 50:1; 59:2; Jer 4:18 [y]S Dt 32:15 [z]Ps 9:5; Isa 24:20; 66:24; Jer 16:4; 42:22; 44:12; 2Th 1:8-9 **1:29** [a]Ps 97:7; Isa 42:17; 44:9, 11; 45:16; Jer 10:14 [b]Isa 57:5; Eze 6:13; Hos 4:13 [c]Isa 65:3; 66:17 **1:30** [d]S Ps 1:3 **1:31** [e]Isa 4:4; 5:24; 9:18-19; 10:17; 24:6; 26:11; 30:27, 33; 33:14; 34:10; 66:15-16, 24; Jer 5:14; 7:20; 21:12; Ob 1:18; Mal 3:2; 4:1; S Mt 25:41 **2:1** [f]Isa 1:1 **2:2** [g]Ac 2:17; Heb 1:2 [h]Isa 11:9; 24:23; 25:6, 10; 27:13; 56:7; 57:13; 65:25; 66:20; Jer 31:23; Da 11:45; Joel 3:17; Mic 4:7 [i]Isa 65:9 [j]Zec 14:10 [k]S Ps 102:15; Jer 16:19 **2:3** [l]Isa 45:23; 49:1; 60:3-6, 14; 66:18; Jer 3:17; Joel 3:2; Zep 3:8; Zec 14:2 [m]Isa 45:14; 49:12, 23; 55:5 [n]S Dt 33:19; S Ps 137:5 [o]S Isa 1:10; 33:22; 51:4, 7 [p]Lk 24:47; S Jn 4:22

2:4 [q]Ps 7:6; S 9:19; 96:13; 98:9; Isa 1:27; 3:13; 9:7; 42:4; 51:4; Joel 3:14 [r]S Ge 49:10 [s]Joel 3:10 [t]Ps 46:9; Isa 9:5; 11:6-9; 32:18; 57:19; 65:25; Jer 30:10; Da 11:45; Hos 2:18; Mic 4:3; Zec 9:10 **2:5** [u]Isa 58:1 [v]Isa 60:1, 19-20; 1Jn 1:5, 7 **2:6** [w]S Dt 31:17 [x]Jer 12:7 [y]S Dt 18:10; S Isa 44:25 [z]S 2Ki 1:2; S 2Ch 26:6 [a]Pr 6:1 [b]S 2Ki 16:7; Mic 5:12 **2:7** [c]S Dt 17:17 [d]S Ps 17:14 [e]S Dt 17:16 [f]S Ge 41:43; Isa 31:1; Mic 5:10 **2:8** [g]Isa 10:9-11; Rev 9:20 [h]Isa 44:17 [i]S 2Ch 32:19; S Ps 135:15; Mic 5:13 [j]Isa 17:8 **2:9** [k]Ps 62:9 [l]ver 11, 17; Isa 5:15; 13:11 [m]S Ne 4:5 **2:10** [n]ver 19; Na 3:11 [o]S Ps 145:12; 2Th 1:9; Rev 6:15-16

1:27 – 28 This contrast between the redemption of Zion (Jerusalem) as a whole and the perishing of individuals who refuse to repent is developed in 65:8 – 16.

1:29 *sacred oaks ... gardens.* Pagan sacrifices were offered and sexual immorality occurred at such places (see 65:3; 66:17).

1:30 *garden without water.* Contrast Ps 1:3; Jer 17:8.

1:31 *fire.* A figure of punishment (see 33:11 – 14; 34:9 – 10; see also note on La 1:13).

2:1 A second heading, probably relating to chs. 2 – 4 or to chs. 2 – 12 (see 13:1; see also note on 1:1).

2:2 – 5 See note on 4:2 – 6.

2:2 – 4 Almost identical to Mic 4:1 – 3. The theme of the "mountain of the LORD" (Mount Zion) is common in Isaiah; it occurs in passages that depict the coming of both Jews and Gentiles to Jerusalem (Zion) in the last days (see 11:9; 27:13; 56:7; 57:13; 65:25; 66:20; see also 60:3 – 5; Zec 14:16 and note). Some believe that the peace described in this passage has been inaugurated through the coming of Christ and the preaching of the gospel and will be consummated at the return of Christ. Others maintain that it is solely a prophecy of conditions during a future reign of Christ on the earth.

2:2 *the last days.* Can refer to the future generally (see Ge 49:1), but usually it seems to have in view the Messianic era. In a real sense the last days began with the first coming of Christ (see Ac 2:17; Heb 1:1 – 2 and notes) and will be completely fulfilled at his second coming.

2:3 *The law will go out from Zion.* See Zec 14:16 and note.

2:4 *swords into plowshares.* The reverse process occurs in Joel 3:10. What is here called a plowshare was actually an iron point mounted on a wooden beam. Ancient plows did not have a plowshare proper.

2:6 *East.* Probably means Aram (Syria) and Mesopotamia. *divination like the Philistines.* See 1Sa 6:2 and note; for a description of such practices, see also Dt 18:10 – 11 and note on 18:9.

2:7 *silver and gold ... horses.* Accumulating large quantities of these was forbidden to the king (see Dt 17:16 – 17 and note). They usually led to a failure to trust in God (see 30:1 – 3,7; 31:1 – 3).

2:10,19,21 These verses contain a refrain that builds to a climax in v. 21.

2:10 *rocks ... ground.* During times of severe oppression the Israelites took refuge in caves and holes in the ground (see

11 The eyes of the arrogant[p] will be
humbled[q]
and human pride[r] brought low;[s]
the LORD alone will be exalted[t] in that
day.[u]

12 The LORD Almighty has a day[v] in store
for all the proud[w] and lofty,[x]
for all that is exalted[y]
(and they will be humbled),[z]
13 for all the cedars of Lebanon,[a] tall and
lofty,[b]
and all the oaks of Bashan,[c]
14 for all the towering mountains
and all the high hills,[d]
15 for every lofty tower[e]
and every fortified wall,[f]
16 for every trading ship[a][g]
and every stately vessel.
17 The arrogance of man will be brought
low[h]
and human pride humbled;[i]
the LORD alone will be exalted in that
day,[j]
18 and the idols[k] will totally
disappear.[l]

19 People will flee to caves[m] in the rocks
and to holes in the ground[n]
from the fearful presence[o] of the
LORD
and the splendor of his majesty,[p]
when he rises to shake the earth.[q]
20 In that day[r] people will throw away
to the moles and bats[s]
their idols of silver and idols of gold,[t]
which they made to worship.[u]
21 They will flee to caverns in the
rocks[v]
and to the overhanging crags
from the fearful presence of the
LORD
and the splendor of his majesty,[w]
when he rises[x] to shake the earth.[y]
22 Stop trusting in mere humans,[z]
who have but a breath[a] in their
nostrils.
Why hold them in esteem?[b]

Judgment on Jerusalem and Judah

3 See now, the Lord,
the LORD Almighty,
is about to take from Jerusalem and
Judah
both supply and support:[c]
all supplies of food[d] and all supplies of
water,[e]
2 the hero and the warrior,[f]
the judge and the prophet,
the diviner[g] and the elder,[h]
3 the captain of fifty[i] and the man of
rank,[j]
the counselor, skilled craftsman[k] and
clever enchanter.[l]

4 "I will make mere youths their
officials;
children will rule over them."[m]

5 People will oppress each other—
man against man, neighbor against
neighbor.[n]
The young will rise up against the old,
the nobody against the honored.

6 A man will seize one of his brothers
in his father's house, and say,
"You have a cloak, you be our
leader;
take charge of this heap of ruins!"

[a] 16 Hebrew *every ship of Tarshish*

2:11 [p] S Ne 9:29; Hab 2:5 [q] S ver 9 [r] Isa 5:15; 10:12; 37:23; Eze 31:10 [s] S Job 40:11 [t] S Ps 46:10 [u] ver 17,20; Isa 3:7,18; 4:1,2; 5:30; 7:18; 17:4,7; 24:21; 25:9; 26:1; 27:1 **2:12** [v] Isa 13:6,9; 22:5,8,12; 34:8; 61:2; Jer 30:7; La 1:12; Eze 7:7; 30:3; Joel 1:15; 2:11; Am 5:18; Zep 1:14 [w] S Ps 59:12 [x] S 2Sa 22:28 [y] Ps 76:12; Isa 24:4,21; 60:11; Mal 4:1 [z] S Job 40:11 **2:13** [a] S Jdg 9:15; Isa 10:34; 29:17; Eze 27:5 [b] Isa 10:33 [c] S Ps 22:12; Zec 11:2 **2:14** [d] Isa 30:25; 40:4 **2:15** [e] Isa 30:25; 32:14; 33:18 [f] Isa 25:2,12; Zep 1:16 **2:16** [g] *fn* S Ge 10:4; S 1Ki 9:26 **2:17** [h] S 2Sa 22:28; S Job 40:11 [i] S ver 9 [j] S ver 11 **2:18** [k] S 1Sa 5:2; Eze 36:25 [l] S Dt 9:21; Isa 21:9; Jer 10:11; Mic 5:13 **2:19** [m] S Jdg 6:2; Isa 7:19 [n] S Jdg 6:2; S Job 30:6; Lk 23:30; Rev 6:15 [o] S Dt 2:25 [p] S Ps 145:12 [q] ver 21; S Job 9:6; S Isa 14:16; Heb 12:26 **2:20** [r] S ver 11 [s] Lev 11:19 [t] S Job 22:24; Eze 36:25; Rev 9:20 [u] Eze 7:19-20; 14:6 **2:21** [v] S Ex 33:22 [w] S Ps 145:12 [x] Isa 33:10 [y] S ver 19 **2:22** [z] Ps 118:6,8; 146:3; Isa 51:12; Jer 17:5 [a] S Ge 2:7; S Ps 144:4 [b] S Job 12:19; Ps 8:4; 18:42; 144:3; Isa 17:13; 29:5; 40:15; S Jas 4:14 **3:1** [c] S Ps 18:18 [d] S Lev 26:26; Am 4:6 [e] Isa 5:13; 65:13; Eze 4:16 **3:2** [f] Eze 17:13 [g] Dt 18:10 [h] Isa 9:14-15 **3:3** [i] S 2Ki 1:9 [j] S Job 22:8 [k] 2Ki 24:14 [l] S Ecc 10:11; Jer 8:17 **3:4** [m] ver 12; Ecc 10:16 *fn* **3:5** [n] Ps 28:3; Isa 9:19; Jer 9:8; Mic 7:2,6

Jdg 6:1–2; 1Sa 13:6). *majesty.* The Hebrew for this word is translated "pride" when used of people. Pride is their attempt to be their own gods (see 14:13–14).

2:11,17,20 *in that day.* The phrase, which refers to the day of the Lord, occurs seven times in chs. 2–4 (see 3:7,18; 4:1–2) and in chs. 24–27 (see note on 24:21). The day of the Lord (see also v. 12) is a time of judgment and/or blessing, as God intervenes decisively in the affairs of the nations (see Joel 1:15; Am 5:18 and notes). Assyria and Babylonia would bring the terror of judgment upon Judah in Isaiah's day (5:30).

2:13 *cedars of Lebanon.* See SS 5:15 and note. Even inanimate things that people stand in awe of will be humbled so that "the LORD alone will be exalted" (v. 11). *Bashan.* A region east of the Jordan and north of Gilead. It was famous for its oaks (Eze 27:6) and its fat, sleek animals (see Eze 39:18 and note).

2:16 *trading ship.* These "ships of Tarshish" (see NIV text note) were large vessels such as those used by Solomon (1Ki 10:22) and the Phoenicians (Isa 23:1,14) to ply the sea in far-flung commercial ventures. For the location of Tarshish, see notes on 23:6; Eze 27:12; Jnh 1:3.

2:20 The futility of worshiping idols is repeatedly noted by Isaiah (see, e.g., 30:22; 31:7; 40:19–20; 44:9–20). See also note on 40:18–20.

2:22 *Stop trusting in.* Lit. "Cease from" or "Give up on." The verb is used to describe the rejection of the Messiah in 53:3. Ironically, people "rejected," "gave up on," the one Man who should have been trusted and "held ... in ... esteem" (equals "hold ... in esteem" here). He alone was worthy of the esteem wrongly given to frail leaders.

3:1–3 Leaders would be taken away by either death or deportation (see 2Ki 24:14; 25:18–21).

3:2–3 *diviner ... enchanter.* Occult practitioners and snake charmers (see Dt 18:10 and note on 18:9; Jer 8:17), whose activities were condemned. Both legitimate and illegitimate kinds of assistance would be removed or deported (see 2Ki 24:14–16; 25:12; Hos 3:4).

3:3 *captain of fifty.* A company of 50 was a common military unit (see 2Ki 1:9). It was also used for civil groupings (Ex 18:25).

3:6 Normally it was unnecessary to force anyone to be a lead-

Gold jewelry from Tel El-Ajjul, second millennium BC. Isaiah (3:18–23) predicts that the Lord will snatch away the "finery" of the women.

Z. Radovan/www.BibleLandPictures.com

7 But in that day[o] he will cry
out,
"I have no remedy.[p]
I have no food[q] or clothing in
my house;
do not make me the leader
of the people."[r]

8 Jerusalem staggers,
Judah is falling;[s]
their words[t] and deeds[u] are
against the LORD,
defying[v] his glorious
presence.
9 The look on their faces
testifies[w] against them;
they parade their sin like
Sodom;[x]
they do not hide it.
Woe to them!
They have brought disaster[y]
upon themselves.

10 Tell the righteous it will be well[z] with
them,
for they will enjoy the fruit of their
deeds.[a]
11 Woe to the wicked![b]
Disaster[c] is upon them!
They will be paid back[d]
for what their hands have done.[e]

12 Youths[f] oppress my people,
women rule over them.
My people, your guides lead you
astray;[g]
they turn you from the path.

13 The LORD takes his place in court;[h]
he rises to judge[i] the people.
14 The LORD enters into judgment[j]
against the elders and leaders of his
people:
"It is you who have ruined my
vineyard;
the plunder[k] from the poor[l] is in your
houses.
15 What do you mean by crushing my
people[m]
and grinding[n] the faces of the
poor?"[o]
declares the Lord,
the LORD Almighty.[p]

3:7 [o]S Isa 2:11 [p]Jer 30:12; Eze 34:4; Hos 5:13 [q]Joel 1:16 [r]Isa 24:2 **3:8** [s]Isa 1:7 [t]Isa 9:15, 17; 28:15; 30:9; 59:3, 13 [u]2Ch 33:6 [v]S Job 1:11; Ps 73:9, 11; Isa 65:7 **3:9** [w]Nu 32:23; Isa 59:12; Jer 14:7; Hos 5:5 [x]S Ge 13:13 [y]S 2Ch 34:24; S Pr 8:36; Ro 6:23 **3:10** [z]S Dt 5:33; S 12:28; 28:1-14; Ps 37:17; Jer 22:15 [a]S Ge 15:1; S Ps 128:2 **3:11** [b]S Job 9:13; Isa 57:20 [c]Dt 28:15-68 [d]S 2Ch 6:23 [e]Jer 21:14; La 5:16; Eze 24:14 **3:12** [f]S ver 4 [g]Isa 9:16; 19:14; 28:7; 29:9; Jer 23:13; 25:16; Mic 3:5 **3:13** [h]S Job 10:2

16 The LORD says,
"The women of Zion[q] are haughty,
walking along with outstretched
necks,[r]
flirting with their eyes,
strutting along with swaying hips,
with ornaments jingling on their
ankles.
17 Therefore the Lord will bring sores
on the heads of the women of
Zion;
the LORD will make their scalps
bald.[s]"

18 In that day[t] the Lord will snatch away
their finery: the bangles and headbands
and crescent necklaces,[u] 19 the earrings
and bracelets[v] and veils,[w] 20 the headdresses[x] and anklets and sashes, the perfume
bottles and charms, 21 the signet rings and
nose rings,[y] 22 the fine robes and the capes
and cloaks,[z] the purses 23 and mirrors,
and the linen garments[a] and tiaras[b] and
shawls.

[i]S Ps 82:1; S Isa 2:4 **3:14** [j]S 1Sa 12:7; S Job 22:4 [k]S Job 24:9; Jas 2:6 [l]Isa 11:4; 25:4 **3:15** [m]S Ps 94:5 [n]S Job 24:14 [o]Isa 10:6; 11:4; 26:6; 29:19; 32:6; 51:23 [p]Isa 5:7 **3:16** [q]S SS 3:11 [r]S Job 15:25 **3:17** [s]ver 24; Eze 27:31; Am 8:10 **3:18** [t]S Isa 2:11 [u]Ge 41:42; S Jdg 8:21 **3:19** [v]S Ge 24:47 [w]Eze 16:11-12 **3:20** [x]Ex 39:28; Eze 24:17, 23; 44:18 **3:21** [y]S Ge 24:22 **3:22** [z]Ru 3:15 **3:23** [a]Eze 16:10; 23:26 [b]S Ex 29:6; SS 3:11; Isa 61:3; 62:3

er. In 4:1 the same social upheaval is seen as seven women "take hold of" one man. *You have a cloak.* Perhaps the one brother was not as poor as the others. *heap of ruins.* Probably Jerusalem (v. 8).
3:7,18 *in that day.* See note on 2:11,17,20.
3:8 *Judah is falling.* Fulfilled almost 150 years later in 586 BC.
3:9 *Sodom.* See note on 1:9–10.
3:11 *paid back for what their hands have done.* Cf. Pr 26:27 and note; Gal 6:7–9 and note on 6:7.
3:12 In the Near East, neither the rule of the young nor that of women was looked on with favor.
3:14 *vineyard.* Represents Israel (see 5:1 and note).
3:15 The leaders were grinding the poor, as women grind grain between two millstones (see note on Jdg 9:53).
3:16–24 For NT warnings against overemphasis on outward adornment, see 1Ti 2:9–10; 1Pe 3:3–5 and notes.
3:17 *bald.* Baldness was associated with mourning over catastrophe (see v. 24; 15:2 and note).
3:18 *crescent necklaces.* Probably crescent-shaped; they implied veneration of the moon-god. See photo above.
3:20 *headdresses.* Perhaps a kind of turban (see Eze 24:17,23).
3:21 *signet rings.* Contained a seal and were a mark of authority (see Ge 41:42; Hag 2:23 and notes). *nose rings.* Made of gold and worn by brides (see Ge 24:22,53).

24 Instead of fragrance[c] there will be a
stench;[d]
instead of a sash,[e] a rope;
instead of well-dressed hair, baldness;[f]
instead of fine clothing, sackcloth;[g]
instead of beauty,[h] branding.[i]
25 Your men will fall by the sword,[j]
your warriors in battle.[k]
26 The gates[l] of Zion will lament and
mourn;[m]
destitute,[n] she will sit on the
ground.[o]

4 1 In that day[p] seven women
will take hold of one man[q]
and say, "We will eat our own food[r]
and provide our own clothes;
only let us be called by your name.
Take away our disgrace!"[s]

The Branch of the LORD

2 In that day[t] the Branch of the LORD[u]
will be beautiful[v] and glorious, and the
fruit[w] of the land will be the pride and
glory[x] of the survivors[y] in Israel. 3 Those
who are left in Zion,[z] who remain[a] in Jerusalem, will be called holy,[b] all who are
recorded[c] among the living in Jerusalem.
4 The Lord will wash away the filth[d] of
the women of Zion;[e] he will cleanse[f] the
bloodstains[g] from Jerusalem by a spirit[a]
of judgment[h] and a spirit[a] of fire.[i] 5 Then
the LORD will create[j] over all of Mount
Zion[k] and over those who assemble there
a cloud of smoke by day and a glow of
flaming fire by night;[l] over everything the
glory[bm] will be a canopy.[n] 6 It will be a shelter[o] and shade from the heat of the day,
and a refuge[p] and hiding place from the
storm[q] and rain.

3:24 [c] S Est 2:12 [d] Isa 4:4 [e] Pr 31:24 [f] S ver 17; S Lev 13:40; S Job 1:20 [g] S Ge 37:34; Job 16:15; Isa 20:2; Jer 4:8; La 2:10; Eze 27:30-31; Jnh 3:5-8 [h] 1Pe 3:3 [i] S 2Sa 10:4; Isa 20:4 **3:25** [j] S Isa 1:20 [k] Jer 15:8 **3:26** [l] Isa 14:31; 24:12; 45:2 [m] S Ps 137:1; Isa 24:4,7; 29:2; 33:9; Jer 4:28; 14:2 [n] S Lev 26:31 [o] S Job 2:13; La 4:5 **4:1** [p] S Isa 2:11 [q] Isa 13:12; 32:9 [r] 2Th 3:12 [s] S Ge 30:23 **4:2** [t] S Isa 2:11 [u] Isa 11:1-5; 52:13; 53:2; Jer 23:5-6; 33:15-16; Eze 17:22; Zec 3:8; 6:12 [v] Isa 33:17; 53:2 [w] S Ps 72:16; Eze 36:8 [x] Isa 60:15; Eze 34:29 [y] S Isa 1:9 **4:3** [z] S Isa 1:26 [a] Isa 1:9; Ro 11:5 [b] S Ex 19:6; Isa 26:2; 45:25; 52:1; 60:21; Joel 3:17; Ob 1:17; Zep 3:13 [c] S Ps 56:8; S 87:6; S Lk 10:20 **4:4** [d] Isa 3:24 [e] S SS 3:11 [f] S Ps 51:2

The Song of the Vineyard

5 I will sing for the one I love
a song about his vineyard:[r]
My loved one had a vineyard
on a fertile hillside.
2 He dug it up and cleared it of stones
and planted it with the choicest
vines.[s]
He built a watchtower[t] in it
and cut out a winepress[u] as well.
Then he looked for a crop of good
grapes,
but it yielded only bad fruit.[v]

3 "Now you dwellers in Jerusalem and
people of Judah,
judge between me and my
vineyard.[w]
4 What more could have been done for
my vineyard
than I have done for it?[x]
When I looked for good grapes,
why did it yield only bad?[y]
5 Now I will tell you
what I am going to do to my
vineyard:
I will take away its hedge,
and it will be destroyed;[z]
I will break down its wall,[a]
and it will be trampled.[b]

[a] 4 Or *the Spirit* [b] 5 Or *over all the glory there*

[g] S Isa 1:15 [h] Isa 28:6 [i] S Isa 1:31; S 30:30; S Zec 13:9; Mt 3:11; Lk 3:17 **4:5** [j] Isa 41:20; 65:18 [k] Rev 14:1 [l] S Ex 13:21 [m] Isa 35:2; 58:8; 60:1 [n] S Ps 18:11; Rev 7:15 **4:6** [o] Lev 23:34-43; Ps 27:5; Isa 8:14; 25:4; Eze 11:16 [p] Isa 14:32; 25:4; 30:2; 57:13 [q] S Ps 55:8 **5:1** [r] Ps 80:8-9; Isa 27:2; Jn 15:1 **5:2** [s] S Ex 15:17; Isa 16:8 [t] 1Sa 2:9; Isa 27:3; 31:5; 49:8; Mt 21:33 [u] S Job 24:11 [v] Mt 21:19; Mk 11:13; Lk 13:6 **5:3** [w] Mt 21:40 **5:4** [x] S 2Ch 36:15; Jer 2:5-7; Mic 6:3-4; Mt 23:37 [y] Jer 2:21; 24:2; 29:17 **5:5** [z] 2Ch 36:21; Isa 6:12; 27:10 [a] S Ps 80:12; S Isa 22:5 [b] Isa 10:6; 26:6; 28:3,18; 41:25; 63:3; Jer 12:10; 34:22; La 1:15; Hos 2:12; Mic 7:10; Mal 4:3; S Lk 21:24

3:24 *rope ... branding.* Captives were led away by ropes (see notes on 37:29; 2Ki 19:28; Am 4:2) and sometimes branded.

3:26 *gates of Zion.* The gates are personified, as in Ps 24:7,9. They will lament because the crowds that used to assemble there are gone.

4:1–2 *In that day.* See note on 2:11,17,20. After judgment comes salvation.

4:1 See note on 3:6. War will decimate the male population (3:25; see 13:12 and note), leaving many women with the double disgrace of being widows and childless. See 54:4.

4:2–6 A prophecy of redemption just before the long message of indictment and judgment in ch. 5. It balances that found in 2:2–5, which immediately follows the long message of indictment and judgment in ch. 1 (see note on 1:1–31). These two prophecies of redemption were intended to complement each other. Cf. also 28:5–8,15–17; 65:18.

4:2–3 *survivors ... are left.* See note on 1:9.

4:2 *Branch.* A Messianic title related to the "shoot" and "Branch" (11:1; 53:2) descended from David (see Jer 23:5 and note; 33:15; Zec 3:8; 6:12 and note)—but some believe that here "Branch" refers to Judah. *pride.* A legitimate pride in the fruitfulness of the land that will characterize the Messiah's reign (see Ps 72:3,6,16 and note on 72:3). Contrast the pride of 2:11,17. *glory.* Here the fruitfulness of the land will be Israel's glory; in 46:13 God's salvation will be her glory ("splendor"); in 60:19 God himself will be her glory.

4:3 *holy.* Means "set apart" to God. See 1:26; 6:13 and note; see also Lev 11:44; Zec 14:20–21 and notes.

4:4 *judgment ... fire.* Purifying fire is also mentioned in 1:25 (see also 48:10 and note).

4:5–6 *cloud ... fire ... shelter.* These words recall Israel's wilderness wanderings, when the pillar of cloud and fire guided and protected the people (see Ex 13:21 and note; 14:21–22). Isaiah often refers to the time of the exodus (see 11:15–16; 31:5; 51:10 and notes).

4:5 *the glory.* The manifestation of God's presence, represented by a glow of flaming fire (see Ex 16:10; 24:17; 40:34–35). *canopy.* The cloud of smoke.

4:6 God's presence in cloud and fire will protect and preserve redeemed Zion (cf. Ps 121:5–6).

5:1–30 See note on 1:1–31.

5:1 *loved one.* God. *vineyard.* Israel (see v. 7; 3:14; Ps 80:8–16). Jesus' parable of the tenants (Mt 21:33–44; Mk 12:1–11; Lk 20:9–18) is probably based on this song. See Jn 15:1–17.

5:2 *watchtower.* Contrast the more modest "shelter" of 1:8. God's vineyard had every advantage (see Mt 21:33 and note). *winepress.* Or "wine vat," a trough into which the grape juice flowed (see 16:10; Hag 2:16 and notes). *he looked for ... but.* The interpretation (v. 7) uses the same expression (cf. also 59:9,11).

6 I will make it a wasteland,[c]
neither pruned nor cultivated,
and briers and thorns[d] will grow there.
I will command the clouds
not to rain[e] on it."

7 The vineyard[f] of the LORD Almighty
is the nation of Israel,
and the people of Judah
are the vines he delighted in.
And he looked for justice,[g] but saw
bloodshed;
for righteousness,[h] but heard cries of
distress.[i]

Woes and Judgments

8 Woe[j] to you who add house to house
and join field to field[k]
till no space is left
and you live alone in the land.

9 The LORD Almighty[l] has declared in my
hearing:[m]

"Surely the great houses will become
desolate,[n]
the fine mansions left without
occupants.
10 A ten-acre vineyard will produce only a
bath[a] of wine;
a homer[b] of seed will yield only an
ephah[c] of grain."[o]

11 Woe[p] to those who rise early in the
morning
to run after their drinks,
who stay up late at night
till they are inflamed with wine.[q]
12 They have harps and lyres at their
banquets,
pipes[r] and timbrels[s] and wine,
but they have no regard[t] for the deeds
of the LORD,
no respect for the work of his hands.[u]
13 Therefore my people will go into exile[v]
for lack of understanding;[w]
those of high rank[x] will die of hunger
and the common people will be
parched with thirst.[y]
14 Therefore Death[z] expands its jaws,
opening wide its mouth;[a]
into it will descend their nobles and
masses
with all their brawlers and
revelers.[b]
15 So people will be brought low[c]
and everyone humbled,[d]
the eyes of the arrogant[e] humbled.
16 But the LORD Almighty will be exalted[f]
by his justice,[g]
and the holy God will be proved
holy[h] by his righteous acts.
17 Then sheep will graze as in their own
pasture;[i]
lambs will feed[d] among the ruins of
the rich.

18 Woe[j] to those who draw sin along with
cords[k] of deceit,
and wickedness[l] as with cart ropes,
19 to those who say, "Let God hurry;
let him hasten[m] his work
so we may see it.
The plan of the Holy One[n] of Israel—
let it approach, let it come into
view,
so we may know it."[o]

20 Woe[p] to those who call evil good[q]
and good evil,[r]
who put darkness for light
and light for darkness,[s]
who put bitter for sweet
and sweet for bitter.[t]

21 Woe to those who are wise in their
own eyes[u]
and clever in their own sight.

[a] *10* That is, about 6 gallons or about 22 liters
[b] *10* That is, probably about 360 pounds or about 160 kilograms
[c] *10* That is, probably about 36 pounds or about 16 kilograms
[d] *17* Septuagint; Hebrew / *strangers will eat*

5:6 [c]S Ge 6:13; S Lev 26:32; Isa 6:13; 49:17,19; 51:3; Joel 1:10 [d]ver 10,17; S 2Sa 23:6; Isa 7:23, 24; 32:13; 34:13; 55:13; Eze 28:24; Hos 2:12; Heb 6:8 [e]S Dt 28:24; S 2Sa 1:21; Am 4:7 **5:7** [f]Ps 80:8; Isa 17:10; 18:5; 37:30 [g]Isa 10:2; 29:21; 32:7; 59:15; 61:8; Eze 9:9; 22:29 [h]S Isa 1:21 [i]S Ps 12:5 **5:8** [j]ver 11,18, 20; Isa 6:5; 10:1; 24:16; Jer 22:13 [k]Job 20:19; Mic 2:2; Hab 2:9-12 **5:9** [l]Jer 44:11 [m]Isa 22:14 [n]Isa 6:11-12; Mt 23:38 **5:10** [o]S ver 6; Lev 26:26; S Dt 28:38; Zec 8:10 **5:11** [p]S ver 8 [q]S 1Sa 25:36; S Pr 23:29-30 **5:12** [r]S Job 21:12 [s]Ps 68:25; Isa 24:8 [t]S 1Sa 12:24 [u]Ps 28:5; Eze 26:13 **5:13** [v]Isa 49:21 [w]S Pr 10:21; S Isa 1:3; Hos 4:6 [x]S Job 22:8 [y]S Isa 3:1 **5:14** [z]S Pr 30:16 [a]S Nu 16:30 [b]Isa 22:2,13; 23:7; 24:8 **5:15** [c]Isa 10:33 [d]S Isa 2:9 [e]S Isa 2:11 **5:16** [f]Ps 97:9; Isa 33:10 [g]Isa 28:17; 30:18; 33:5; 61:8 [h]S Lev 10:3; Isa 29:23; Eze 36:23 **5:17** [i]Isa 7:25; 17:2; 32:14; Zep 2:6,14 **5:18** [j]S ver 8 [k]Hos 11:4 [l]Isa 59:4-8; Jer 23:14 **5:19** [m]Isa 60:22 [n]S Isa 1:4; 29:23; 30:11,12 [o]Jer 17:15; Eze 12:22; 2Pe 3:4 **5:20** [p]S ver 8 [q]S Ge 18:25; S 1Ki 22:8 [r]S Ps 94:21 [s]S Job 24:13; Mt 6:22-23; Lk 11:34-35 [t]Am 5:7 **5:21** [u]S Pr 3:7; Isa 47:10; Ro 12:16; 1Co 3:18-20

5:6 *briers and thorns.* This pair occurs five more times (7:23,24, 25; 9:18; 27:4). *not to rain.* The withholding of rain constituted a curse on the land. See Dt 28:23–24; 2Sa 1:21; 1Ki 17:1.

5:7 The song of the vineyard (vv. 1–6) is now interpreted. A powerful play on words makes the point: The words for "justice" and "bloodshed" (*mishpaṭ* and *miśpaḥ*) sound alike, as do those for "righteousness" (*ṣedaqah*) and "distress" (*ṣe'aqah*).

5:8–23 Six woes are pronounced on God's covenant-breaking people (vv. 8,11–12,18–19,20,21,22–23), followed by three judgment sections (vv. 9–10, 13–15,24–25).

5:8 *house to house … field to field.* Land in Israel could only be leased, never sold, because parcels had been permanently assigned to individual families (see Nu 27:7–11; 1Ki 21:1–3 and note on 21:3).

5:10 *ephah.* A tenth of a homer (see Eze 45:11). Meager crops often accompanied national sin (Dt 28:38–39; Hag 2:16–17). The amount of wine and grain is only a tiny fraction of what a "ten-acre vineyard" and a "homer of seed" would normally produce.

5:11–13 See Am 4:1–3; 6:4–7, where a lifestyle characterized by drunkenness and revelry is likewise condemned.

5:14 *Death.* Or "the grave" (see note on Ge 37:35). The grave has an insatiable appetite (see 25:8; Ps 49:14 and notes).

5:16 *be proved holy.* See Lev 10:3 and note.

5:18 *cords of deceit.* See Pr 5:22 and note.

5:19 The Hebrew for the words "hurry" and "hasten" corresponds to that of the first and third elements of the name Maher-Shalal-Hash-Baz (see 8:1 and NIV text note). When Isaiah named his son (8:3), he may have been responding to the sarcastic taunts of these sinners. God did bring swift judgment, according to 5:26. *Holy One of Israel.* See 1:4 and note.

22 Woe to those who are heroes at
drinking wine[v]
and champions at mixing drinks,[w]
23 who acquit the guilty for a bribe,[x]
but deny justice[y] to the
innocent.[z]
24 Therefore, as tongues of fire[a] lick up
straw[b]
and as dry grass sinks down in the
flames,
so their roots will decay[c]
and their flowers blow away like
dust;[d]
for they have rejected the law of the
LORD Almighty
and spurned the word[e] of the Holy
One[f] of Israel.
25 Therefore the LORD's anger[g] burns
against his people;
his hand is raised and he strikes
them down.
The mountains shake,[h]
and the dead bodies[i] are like refuse[j]
in the streets.[k]

Yet for all this, his anger is not turned
away,[l]
his hand is still upraised.[m]

26 He lifts up a banner[n] for the distant
nations,
he whistles[o] for those at the ends of
the earth.[p]
Here they come,
swiftly and speedily!
27 Not one of them grows tired[q] or
stumbles,
not one slumbers or sleeps;

5:22 [v] S 1Sa 25:36; S Pr 23:20; S Isa 22:13 [w] S Pr 31:4; Isa 65:11; Jer 7:18 **5:23** [x] S Ex 23:8; S Eze 22:12 [y] ver 7; S Isa 1:17; 10:2; 29:21; 59:4, 13-15 [z] S Ps 94:21; Am 5:12; Jas 5:6 **5:24** [a] S Isa 1:31 [b] Isa 47:14; Na 1:10 [c] S 2Ki 19:30; S Job 18:16 [d] S Job 24:24; Isa 40:8 [e] Ps 107:11; Isa 8:6; 30:9, 12 [f] Job 6:10; Isa 1:4; 10:20; 12:6 **5:25** [g] S 2Ki 22:13; S Job 40:11; Isa 10:17; 26:11; 31:9; 66:15; S Jer 6:12 [h] S Ex 19:18 [i] S Ps 110:6 [j] S 2Ki 9:37 [k] S 2Sa 22:43 [l] Jer 4:8; Da 9:16 [m] Isa 9:12, 17, 21; 10:4 **5:26** [n] S Ps 20:5 [o] Isa 7:18; Zec 10:8 [p] Dt 28:49; Isa 13:5; 18:3 **5:27** [q] Isa 14:31; 40:29-31 [r] Isa 22:21; Eze 23:15 [s] S Job 12:18

not a belt[r] is loosened at the waist,[s]
not a sandal strap is broken.[t]
28 Their arrows are sharp,[u]
all their bows[v] are strung;
their horses' hooves[w] seem like flint,
their chariot wheels like a
whirlwind.[x]
29 Their roar is like that of the lion,[y]
they roar like young lions;
they growl as they seize[z] their prey
and carry it off with no one to
rescue.[a]
30 In that day[b] they will roar over it
like the roaring of the sea.[c]
And if one looks at the land,
there is only darkness[d] and
distress;[e]
even the sun will be darkened[f] by
clouds.

Isaiah's Commission

6 In the year that King Uzziah[g] died,[h] I
saw the Lord,[i] high and exalted,[j] seated on a throne;[k] and the train of his robe[l]
filled the temple.
2 Above him were ser-
aphim,[m] each with six wings: With two
wings they covered their faces, with two
they covered their feet,[n] and with two they
were flying.
3 And they were calling to one
another:

[t] Joel 2:7-8 **5:28** [u] S Job 39:23; Ps 45:5 [v] S Ps 7:12 [w] Eze 26:11 [x] S 2Ki 2:1; S Job 1:19 **5:29** [y] S 2Ki 17:25; Jer 51:38; Zep 3:3; Zec 11:3 [z] Isa 10:6; 49:24-25 [a] Isa 42:22; Mic 5:8 **5:30** [b] S Isa 2:11 [c] S Ps 93:3; Jer 50:42; Lk 21:25 [d] S 1Sa 2:9; S Job 21:30; Ps 18:28; 44:19; S 82:5 [e] S Jdg 6:2; Isa 22:5; 33:2; Jer 4:23-28 [f] Isa 13:10; 50:3; Joel 2:10 **6:1** [g] S 2Ch 26:22, 23 [h] S 2Ki 15:7 [i] S Ex 24:10; S Nu 12:8; Jn 12:41 [j] Isa 52:13; 53:12 [k] S 1Ki 22:19; S Ps 9:4; S 123:1; S Rev 4:2 [l] Rev 1:13 **6:2** [m] Eze 1:5; 10:15; Rev 4:8 [n] Eze 1:11

5:22 *mixing drinks.* Spices were added to beer and wine (see Ps 75:8; Pr 23:30 and notes).
5:23 See 1:23; 10:1–2.
5:24 *spurned ... the Holy One of Israel.* See v. 19; see also 1:4 and note.
5:25 *The mountains shake.* When God takes action, even the mountains tremble (see 64:3; Ps 18:7; Jer 4:24–26; Mic 1:4; Na 1:15; Hab 3:6,10). *Yet ... upraised.* A refrain repeated in 9:12,17,21; 10:4.
5:26 *lifts up a banner.* A pole with a banner was often placed on a hill as a signal for gathering troops (13:2) or for summoning the nations to bring Israel back home (11:10,12; 49:22; 62:10). *distant nations.* Such as Assyria, whose armies struck Israel and Judah in 722 and 701 BC, and Babylonia, which began its invasions in 605. *those at the ends of the earth.* Nations like Egypt and Assyria.
5:27 *Not one ... grows tired or stumbles.* Cf. the use of these terms in 40:29–31.
5:30 *In that day.* See note on 2:11,17,20. *darkness and distress.* Similar words describe the horrors of war in 8:22.
6:1–13 Isaiah's commission, the climax of the first major section of his prophecies (see note on 1:1—6:13). In vv. 1–4 he sees the Lord in all his glory (v. 1); in vv. 5–7 he then sees himself in all his uncleanness (v. 5); in vv. 8–13 the prophet, now cleansed and forgiven (v. 7), sees the rebellious people to whom God is sending him to proclaim the divine message of judgment.

6:1 *the year that King Uzziah died.* 740 BC (cf. 14:28 and note). Isaiah's commission probably preceded his preaching ministry; the account was postponed to serve as a climax to the opening series of messages and to provide warrant for the shocking announcements of judgment they contain. The people had mocked the "Holy One of Israel" (5:19), and now he has commissioned Isaiah to call them to account. Uzziah reigned from 792 to 740 and was a godly and powerful king. When he insisted on burning incense in the temple, however, he was struck with "leprosy" and remained "leprous" until his death (see 2Ch 26:16–21 and NIV text note on 26:19). He was also called Azariah (2Ki 14:21; 2Ch 26:1). *I saw.* Probably in a vision of the temple throne room. *the Lord.* The true King (see v. 5). *high and exalted.* The same Hebrew words are applied to God also in 57:15, and similar terms are used of the suffering servant in 52:13. *train of his robe.* A long, flowing garment. Cf. the robe of the "son of man" in Rev 1:13. *temple.* Probably the heavenly temple, with which the earthly temple was closely associated. John's vision of God on his throne is similar (Rev 4:1–8).
6:2 *seraphim.* See v. 6; heavenly beings not mentioned elsewhere. Their actions correspond to those of the "living creatures" of Rev 4:6–9, each of whom also had six wings. *covered their faces.* Apparently they could not gaze directly at the glory of God.
6:3 *Holy, holy, holy.* See Lev 11:44; Rev 4:8 and notes. The triple repetition underscores God's infinite holiness. Note

"Holy, holy[o], holy is the LORD
Almighty;[p]
the whole earth[q] is full of his
glory."[r]

[4]At the sound of their voices the doorposts
and thresholds shook and the temple was
filled with smoke.[s]
[5]"Woe[t] to me!" I cried. "I am ruined![u]
For I am a man of unclean lips,[v] and I live
among a people of unclean lips,[w] and my
eyes have seen[x] the King,[y] the LORD Almighty."[z]
[6]Then one of the seraphim flew to me
with a live coal[a] in his hand, which he had
taken with tongs from the altar. [7]With it
he touched my mouth and said, "See, this
has touched your lips;[b] your guilt is taken
away and your sin atoned for.[c]"
[8]Then I heard the voice[d] of the Lord saying, "Whom shall I send?[e] And who will
go for us?[f]"

And I said, "Here am I.[g] Send me!"

[9]He said, "Go[h] and tell this people:

"'Be ever hearing, but never
understanding;
be ever seeing, but never
perceiving.'[i]
[10]Make the heart of this people
calloused;[j]
make their ears dull
and close their eyes.[a][k]
Otherwise they might see with their
eyes,
hear with their ears,[l]
understand with their hearts,
and turn and be healed."[m]

[11]Then I said, "For how long, Lord?"[n]
And he answered:

"Until the cities lie ruined[o]
and without inhabitant,
until the houses are left deserted[p]
and the fields ruined and ravaged,[q]
[12]until the LORD has sent everyone far
away[r]
and the land is utterly forsaken.[s]
[13]And though a tenth remains[t] in the
land,
it will again be laid waste.[u]
But as the terebinth and oak
leave stumps[v] when they are cut
down,
so the holy[w] seed will be the stump
in the land."[x]

The Sign of Immanuel

7 When Ahaz[y] son of Jotham, the son of
Uzziah, was king of Judah, King Rezin[z]
of Aram[a] and Pekah[b] son of Remaliah[c] king
of Israel marched up to fight against Jerusalem, but they could not overpower it.
[2]Now the house of David[d] was told,
"Aram has allied itself with[b] Ephraim[e]";

[a] 9,10 Hebrew; Septuagint *'You will be ever hearing, but never understanding; / you will be ever seeing, but never perceiving.' / [10]This people's heart has become calloused; / they hardly hear with their ears, / and they have closed their eyes* [b] 2 Or *has set up camp in*

6:3 [o]S Ex 15:11 [p]Ps 89:8 [q]Isa 11:9; 54:5; Mal 1:11 [r]S Ex 16:7; Nu 14:21; Ps 72:19; Rev 4:8 **6:4** [s]S Ex 19:18; S 40:34; Eze 43:5; 44:4; Rev 15:8 **6:5** [t]S Isa 5:8 [u]S Nu 17:12; S Dt 5:26 [v]Ex 6:12; Lk 5:8 [w]Isa 59:3; Jer 9:3-8 [x]S Ex 24:10 [y]Ps 45:3; Isa 24:23; 32:1; 33:17; Jer 51:57 [z]S Job 42:5 **6:6** [a]S Lev 10:1; Eze 10:2 **6:7** [b]Jer 1:9; Da 10:16 [c]S Lev 26:41; Isa 45:25; Da 12:3; 1Jn 1:7 **6:8** [d]S Job 40:9; Ac 9:4 [e]Jer 26:12, 15 [f]S Ge 1:26 [g]S Ge 22:1; S Ex 3:4 **6:9** [h]Eze 3:11; Am 7:15; Mt 28:19 [i]Jer 5:21; S Mt 13:15*; Lk 8:10* **6:10** [j]S Ex 4:21; Dt 32:15; Ps 119:70 [k]Isa 29:9; 42:18-20; 43:8; 44:18 [l]S Dt 29:4; Eze 12:2; Mk 8:18 [m]S Dt 32:39; Mt 13:13-15; Mk 4:12*; Jn 12:40* **6:11** [n]Ps 79:5 [o]S Lev 26:31; S Jer 4:13 [p]S Lev 26:43; Isa 24:10 [q]Ps 79:1; S 109:11; Jer 35:17 **6:12** [r]S Dt 28:64 [s]S Isa 5:5, 9; 60:15; 62:4; Jer 4:29; 30:17 **6:13** [t]S Isa 1:9; 10:22 [u]S Isa 5:6 [v]S Job 14:8 [w]S Lev 27:30; S Dt 14:2 [x]S Job 14:7 **7:1** [y]S 1Ch 3:13 [z]S ver 8; S 2Ki 15:37 [a]2Ch 28:5 [b]S 2Ki 15:25 [c]ver 5, 9; Isa 8:6 **7:2** [d]ver 13; S 2Sa 7:11; Isa 16:5; 22:22; Jer 21:12; Am 9:11 [e]Isa 9:9; Hos 5:3

the triple use of "the temple of the LORD" in Jer 7:4 to stress the people's confidence in the security of Jerusalem because of the presence of that sanctuary. *LORD Almighty.* See note on 1Sa 1:3. *full of his glory.* In Nu 14:21–22; Ps 72:18–19 the worldwide glory of God is linked with his miraculous signs (cf. note on Eze 1:1–28). Cf. also Jn 12:41 and note.

6:4 *doorposts ... shook ... filled with smoke.* Similarly, the power of God's voice terrified the Israelites at Mount Sinai, and the mountain was covered with smoke (see Ex 19:18–19; 20:18–19).

6:5 *eyes have seen the King.* Isaiah was dismayed because anyone who saw God expected to die immediately (see Ge 16:13; 32:30 and notes; Ex 33:20).

6:6 *live coal.* Coals of fire were taken inside the Most Holy Place on the Day of Atonement (Lev 16:12), when sacrifice was made to atone for sin. See note on 1:25.

6:7 *touched my mouth.* When God commissioned Jeremiah, his hand touched the prophet's mouth (Jer 1:9).

6:8–10 Isaiah's prophetic commission will have the ironic but justly deserved effect of hardening the callous hearts of rebellious Israel—and so rendering the warnings of judgment sure (see vv. 11–13). See also Jer 1:8,19; Eze 2:3–4.

6:8 *for us.* The heavenly King speaks in the divine council (see Ge 1:26; Ps 82:1 and notes). As a true prophet, Isaiah is made privy to that council, as were Micaiah (1Ki 22:19–20) and Jeremiah (23:18,22). Cf. Am 3:7. *Here am I.* See note on Ge 22:1.

6:9–10 Quoted by Jesus to explain why he taught in parables (Mt 13:14–15; Mk 4:12; Lk 8:10). See also Ro 11:7–10, 25 and notes. *this people.* In 1:3; 3:15; 5:13 the Lord refers to Israel as "my people." That their persistent and pervasive rebellion (1:1; 66:24) has begun to alienate them from him is indicated by numerous references to them as "this/these people" (e.g., 8:6,12; 29:13–14; cf. Ex 17:4 and note).

6:10 *heart ... ears ... eyes ... eyes ... ears ... hearts.* The *a-b-c/c-b-a* inversion is a common literary device in the OT. *ears dull ... close their eyes.* Israel's deafness and blindness are also mentioned in 29:9; 42:18; 43:8. One day, however, the nation will be able to see and hear (29:18; 35:5).

6:12 *far away.* See 5:13.

6:13 *a tenth.* A remnant—even it will be laid waste. *holy seed.* The few who are faithful in Israel (cf. 1Ki 19:18; see note on 1:9). *stump.* Out of which the nation will grow again. For a similar use of this imagery, see 11:1 and note.

7:1—12:6 The second section of Isaiah's prophecies (sometimes called "the book of Immanuel"), climaxing in the songs of praise found in ch. 12 (cf. note on 1:1—6:13).

7:1 The invasion by Rezin and Pekah (probably in 735/734 BC) is sometimes called the Syro-Ephraimite War. Aram (Syria) and Israel (Ephraim; see note on v. 2) were trying unsuccessfully to persuade Ahaz to join a coalition against Assyria, which had aggressive intentions against lands to the west. Isaiah was trying to keep Ahaz from forming a counter-alliance with Assyria (see 2Ki 16:5–18; 2Ch 28:16–21). *Pekah.* Ruled 752–732 BC (see 2Ki 15:27–31).

7:2 *house of David.* A reference to Ahaz, who belonged to David's dynasty (see 2Sa 7:8–11). *Ephraim.* Another name for

so the hearts of Ahaz and his people were
shaken,[f] as the trees of the forest are shak-
en by the wind.
3Then the LORD said to Isaiah, "Go out,
you and your son Shear-Jashub,[a][g] to meet
Ahaz at the end of the aqueduct of the
Upper Pool, on the road to the Launderer's
Field.[h] 4Say to him, 'Be careful, keep calm[i]
and don't be afraid.[j] Do not lose heart[k] because of these two smoldering stubs[l] of
firewood — because of the fierce anger[m] of
Rezin and Aram and of the son of Remaliah.[n] 5Aram, Ephraim and Remaliah's[o] son
have plotted[p] your ruin, saying, 6"Let us
invade Judah; let us tear it apart and divide it among ourselves, and make the son
of Tabeel king over it." 7Yet this is what
the Sovereign LORD says:[q]

" 'It will not take place,
it will not happen,[r]
8for the head of Aram is Damascus,[s]
and the head of Damascus is only
Rezin.[t]
Within sixty-five years
Ephraim will be too shattered[u] to be
a people.
9The head of Ephraim is Samaria,[v]
and the head of Samaria is only
Remaliah's son.
If you do not stand[w] firm in your faith,[x]
you will not stand at all.' "[y]

10Again the LORD spoke to Ahaz, 11"Ask
the LORD your God for a sign,[z] whether
in the deepest depths or in the highest
heights.[a]"
12But Ahaz said, "I will not ask; I will
not put the LORD to the test.[b]"
13Then Isaiah said, "Hear now, you
house of David![c] Is it not enough[d] to try
the patience of humans? Will you try the
patience[e] of my God[f] also? 14Therefore the
Lord himself will give you[b] a sign:[g] The
virgin[c][h] will conceive and give birth to a
son,[i] and[d] will call him Immanuel.[e][j] 15He
will be eating curds[k] and honey[l] when he
knows enough to reject the wrong and
choose the right, 16for before the boy
knows[m] enough to reject the wrong and
choose the right,[n] the land of the two
kings you dread will be laid waste.[o] 17The
LORD will bring on you and on your people and on the house of your father a time
unlike any since Ephraim broke away[p]
from Judah — he will bring the king of
Assyria.[q]"

7:2 [f] Isa 6:4; Da 5:6 **7:3** [g] Isa 10:21-22 [h] 2Ki 18:17; Isa 36:2 **7:4** [i] Isa 30:15; La 3:26 [j] S Ge 15:1; S Dt 3:2; Isa 8:12; 12:2; 35:4; 37:6; Mt 24:6 [k] S Dt 20:3; S Isa 21:4 [l] Am 4:11; Zec 3:2 [m] Isa 10:24; 51:13; 54:14 [n] S 2Ki 15:27 **7:5** [o] S ver 1 [p] ver 2 **7:7** [q] Isa 24:3; 25:8; 28:16 [r] Ps 2:1; Isa 8:10; 14:24; 28:18; 40:8; 46:10; Ac 4:25 **7:8** [s] S Ge 14:15 [t] ver 1; Isa 9:11 [u] 2Ki 17:24; Isa 8:4; 17:1-3 **7:9** [v] S 2Ki 15:29; Isa 9:9; 28:1,3 [w] S Ps 20:8; Isa 8:10; 40:8 [x] 2Ch 20:20 [y] Isa 8:6-8; 30:12-14 **7:11** [z] S Ex 7:9; S Dt 13:2 [a] Ps 139:8 **7:12** [b] Dt 4:34 **7:13** [c] S ver 2 [d] S Ge 30:15

[a] 3 *Shear-Jashub* means *a remnant will return.*
[b] 14 The Hebrew is plural. [c] 14 Or *young woman*
[d] 14 Masoretic Text; Dead Sea Scrolls *son, and he* or *son, and they* [e] 14 *Immanuel* means *God with us.*

[e] S Isa 1:14 [f] Ps 63:1; 118:28; Isa 25:1; 49:4; 61:10 **7:14** [g] S Ex 3:12; S Lk 2:12 [h] S Ge 24:43 [i] S Ge 3:15; Lk 1:31 [j] S Ge 21:22; Isa 8:8,10; Mt 1:23* **7:15** [k] S Ge 18:8 [l] ver 22 **7:16** [m] Isa 8:4 [n] Dt 1:39 [o] S Dt 13:16; Isa 17:3; Jer 7:15; Hos 5:9,13; Am 1:3-5 **7:17** [p] 1Ki 12:16 [q] S ver 20; S 2Ch 28:20

Israel, the northern kingdom. *hearts ... were shaken.* Ahaz had been defeated earlier by Aram and Israel (2Ch 28:5 – 8).

7:3 *Shear-Jashub.* See NIV text note; see also 10:20 – 22 and note. Isaiah gave each of his sons symbolic names (see 8:1,3,18). *aqueduct of the Upper Pool.* See 36:2 and note. Ahaz was probably inspecting the city's water supply. *Launderer's Field.* Clothes were cleaned by trampling on them in cold water and using a kind of soap or cleansing powder (see Mal 3:2 and note; Mk 9:3).

7:4 *two smoldering stubs.* Damascus (Aram's capital; see v. 8) was crushed by Tiglath-Pileser III in 732 BC, and Israel was soundly defeated the same year.

7:6 *Tabeel.* An Aramaic name sometimes associated with the "land of Tob" east of the Jordan River (see Jdg 11:3 and note).

7:8 *Within sixty-five years.* By c. 670 BC Esarhaddon (and, shortly after him, Ashurbanipal) king of Assyria settled foreign colonists in Israel. Their intermarriage with the few Israelites who had not been deported resulted in the "Samaritans" (see 2Ki 17:24 – 34 and note on 17:29) and marked the end of Ephraim as a separate nation.

7:9 *only Remaliah's son.* Pekah was a usurper and hardly worthy to challenge Ahaz, a son of David. Aram (v. 8) and Israel (v. 9) had human heads. Judah had a divine head; God was with her (v. 14; 8:8,10). *stand firm ... stand.* The use of the same Hebrew verb emphasizes the seriousness of the Lord's warning (see 1:19 – 20,25 – 26 and notes).

7:11 *sign.* God was willing to strengthen the faith of Ahaz through a sign (see Ex 3:12 and note).

7:13 *house of David.* See note on v. 2.

7:14 *sign.* A sign was normally fulfilled within a few years (see 20:3; 37:30; cf. 8:18). *The virgin.* May refer to a young woman betrothed to Isaiah (8:3), who was to become his second wife (his first wife presumably having died after Shear-Jashub was born). In Ge 24:43 the same Hebrew word *('almah)* refers to a woman about to be married (see also Pr 30:19). Matthew (1:23) understood the woman mentioned here to be a type (a foreshadowing) of the Virgin Mary. *Immanuel.* The name "God is with us" was meant to convince Ahaz that God could rescue him from his enemies. See Nu 14:9; 2Ch 13:12; Ps 46:7. The Hebrew for "Immanuel" is used again in 8:8,10, and it may be another name for Maher-Shalal-Hash-Baz (8:3). If so, the boys' names had complementary significance (see note on 8:3). Jesus was the final fulfillment of this prophecy, for he was "God with us" in the fullest sense (Mt 1:23; cf. Isa 9:6 – 7).

7:15 *curds and honey.* Curds (a kind of yogurt) and honey meant a return to the simple diet of those who lived off the land. The Assyrian invasions (732 – 722 BC) would devastate the countryside and make farming impossible. (See vv. 22 – 25 for the significance of the expression.) *when he knows ... wrong ... right.* Suggests the age of moral determination and responsibility under the law — most likely 12 or 13 years of age. Thus, "when" this boy is 12 or 13 (722/721 BC), he will be eating curds and honey instead of agricultural products — due to the devastation of Israel by Assyria. Some believe that this expression involves a shorter period of time, identical to that in v. 16 and 8:4.

7:16 *before the boy knows ... land ... laid waste.* See note on v. 4; cf. 8:4. "Before" the boy is 12 or 13 years old, Aram and Israel will be plundered. This happened in 732 BC, when the boy was about two years old.

7:17 *Ephraim broke away from Judah.* Almost two centuries earlier (930 BC; see 1Ki 12:19 – 20). *king of Assyria.* Ahaz's appeal to Assyria would bring temporary relief (2Ki 16:8 – 9), but eventually Assyria would attack Judah (see 8:7 – 8; 36:1 and notes).

Assyria, the LORD's Instrument

18 In that day[r] the LORD will whistle[s] for
flies from the Nile delta in Egypt and for
bees from the land of Assyria.[t] 19 They will
all come and settle in the steep ravines
and in the crevices[u] in the rocks, on all the
thornbushes[v] and at all the water holes.
20 In that day[w] the Lord will use[x] a razor
hired from beyond the Euphrates River[y]—the king of Assyria[z]—to shave your
head and private parts, and to cut off your
beard[a] also.[b] 21 In that day,[c] a person will
keep alive a young cow and two goats.[d]
22 And because of the abundance of the
milk they give, there will be curds to eat.
All who remain in the land will eat curds[e]
and honey.[f] 23 In that day,[g] in every place
where there were a thousand vines worth
a thousand silver shekels,[a][h] there will be
only briers and thorns.[i] 24 Hunters will go
there with bow and arrow, for the land
will be covered with briers[j] and thorns.
25 As for all the hills[k] once cultivated by
the hoe, you will no longer go there for
fear of the briers and thorns;[l] they will become places where cattle are turned loose
and where sheep run.[m]

Isaiah and His Children as Signs

8 The LORD said to me, "Take a large
scroll[n] and write on it with an ordinary pen: Maher-Shalal-Hash-Baz."[b][o] 2 So
I called in Uriah[p] the priest and Zechariah son of Jeberekiah as reliable witnesses[q]
for me. 3 Then I made love to the prophetess,[r] and she conceived and gave birth to
a son.[s] And the LORD said to me, "Name
him Maher-Shalal-Hash-Baz.[t] 4 For before
the boy knows[u] how to say 'My father' or
'My mother,' the wealth of Damascus[v] and
the plunder of Samaria will be carried off
by the king of Assyria.[w]"
5 The LORD spoke to me again:

6 "Because this people has rejected[x]
the gently flowing waters of
Shiloah[y]
and rejoices over Rezin
and the son of Remaliah,[z]
7 therefore the Lord is about to bring
against them
the mighty floodwaters[a] of the
Euphrates—
the king of Assyria[b] with all his
pomp.[c]
It will overflow all its channels,
run over all its banks[d]
8 and sweep on into Judah, swirling
over it,[e]
passing through it and reaching up
to the neck.
Its outspread wings[f] will cover the
breadth of your land,
Immanuel[c]!"[g]

9 Raise the war cry,[d][h] you nations, and
be shattered![i]
Listen, all you distant lands.
Prepare[j] for battle, and be shattered!
Prepare for battle, and be shattered!
10 Devise your strategy, but it will be
thwarted;[k]

[a] 23 That is, about 25 pounds or about 12 kilograms
[b] 1 *Maher-Shalal-Hash-Baz* means *quick to the plunder, swift to the spoil*; also in verse 3.
[c] 8 *Immanuel* means *God with us.*
[d] 9 Or *Do your worst*

7:18 [r] ver 20, 21; S Isa 2:11 [s] S Isa 5:26 [t] Isa 13:5 **7:19** [u] S Isa 2:19 [v] ver 25; Isa 17:9; 34:13; 55:13 **7:20** [w] S ver 18 [x] Isa 10:15; 29:16 [y] Isa 11:15; Jer 2:18 [z] ver 17; 2Ki 18:16; Isa 8:7; 10:5 [a] S 2Sa 10:4 [b] S Dt 28:49 **7:21** [c] ver 23; Isa 2:17 [d] Jer 39:10 **7:22** [e] S Ge 18:8 [f] ver 15; Isa 14:30 **7:23** [g] ver 21 [h] SS 8:11 [i] S Isa 5:6; Hos 2:12 **7:24** [j] S Isa 5:6 **7:25** [k] Hag 1:11 [l] S ver 19 [m] S Isa 5:17 **8:1** [n] S Dt 27:8; Job 19:23; Isa 30:8; Jer 51:60 [o] ver 3; Hab 2:2; Jer 20:3; Hos 1:4 **8:2** [p] S 2Ki 16:10 [q] ver 16; S Jos 24:22; S Ru 4:9; Jer 32:10, 12, 25, 44 **8:3** [r] S Ex 15:20 [s] S Ge 3:15 [t] S ver 1 **8:4** [u] Isa 7:16 [v] S Ge 14:15 [w] S Isa 7:8 **8:6** [x] S Isa 5:24 [y] S Ne 3:15; Jn 9:7 [z] S Isa 7:1 **8:7** [a] Isa 17:12-13; 28:2, 17; 30:28; 43:2; Da 11:40; Na 1:8 [b] S 2Ch 28:20; S Isa 7:20 [c] Isa 10:16 [d] S Jos 3:15 **8:8** [e] Isa 28:15 [f] Isa 18:6; 46:11; Jer 4:13; 48:40 [g] S Isa 7:14 **8:9** [h] S Jos 6:5; Isa 17:12-13 [i] S Job 34:24 [j] Jer 6:4; 46:3; 51:12, 27-28; Eze 38:7; Joel 3:9; Zec 14:2-3 **8:10** [k] S Job 5:12

7:18,20,23 *In that day.* Their difficulties will be a foretaste of the "day of the LORD." See note on 2:11,17,20.
7:18 *flies ... bees.* See Ex 23:28 and note.
7:19 *crevices in the rocks.* See note on 2:10. It will be impossible to escape from the invaders.
7:20 *shave ... head ... beard.* Such forcible shaving was considered a great insult (see 2Sa 10:4 and note).
7:23 *briers and thorns.* See note on 5:6. The destruction of the vineyards and the farmlands would fulfill 5:5–6.
8:1–2 *scroll ... witnesses.* The witnesses would attest to a legal transaction, either the marriage of Isaiah (see note on 7:14) or a symbolic deed connected with Maher-Shalal-Hash-Baz. The Hebrew word for "scroll" is related to the word for "unsealed copy" in Jer 32:11.
8:2 *Uriah the priest.* Served under King Ahaz (see 2Ki 16:10–11).
8:3–10 See 7:14–17 and notes.
8:3 *prophetess ... son.* Some interpret this as the initial fulfillment of 7:14. Note the repetition of "conceive," "give birth to," "son" and "call/name" from 7:14. The young woman may be called a prophetess here because she had become the wife of a prophet (Isaiah). *Maher-Shalal-Hash-Baz.* This symbolic name (see NIV text note on v. 1) meant that Ahaz's enemies would be plundered (see v. 4 and note on 7:4), but it also implied that Judah would suffer (see vv. 7–8).
8:4 *knows how to say.* At about age two. The time period is identical to that in 7:16 (see notes on 7:4,16). *plunder of Samaria will be carried off.* The first stage of the destruction of the northern kingdom (see note on 7:4), which was not completed until 722–721 BC (see note on 7:15).
8:6 *waters of Shiloah.* See NIV text note on Ne 3:15. The water in Jerusalem that flows from the Gihon spring (see 2Ch 32:30) to the Pool of Siloam (see Jn 9:7 and note) may be intended (see Ne 3:15 and note). Here it symbolizes the sustaining power of the Lord. *Rezin and the son of Remaliah.* Rezin and Pekah both died in 732 BC (see 2Ki 16:9; see note on Isa 7:1).
8:7–8 *floodwaters ... sweep on.* Mighty rivers were often used to symbolize a powerful invading army (see 17:12 and note; 28:17–19).
8:8 *up to the neck.* See 30:28 and note. Sennacherib's invasion in 701 BC overwhelmed all the cities of Judah except Jerusalem (see 1:7–9 and note), the head of Judah (cf. the initial references to Damascus and Samaria in 7:8–9). *outspread wings.* The figure changes to a powerful bird of prey. *Immanuel.* All seems lost, but "God is with us" (v. 10) and defeats the enemy (see note on 7:14).
8:9 *nations ... be shattered.* Just as Aram and Israel would be shattered (7:7–9), so Assyria and Babylonia would eventually fall.

8:10 *it will not stand.* Only God's plans and purposes will last. *God is with us.* See NIV text note; see also 2Ch 13:12.

propose your plan, but it will not
stand,[l]
for God is with us.[a][m]

[11]This is what the LORD says to me with
his strong hand upon me,[n] warning me not
to follow[o] the way of this people:

[12]"Do not call conspiracy[p]
everything this people calls a
conspiracy;
do not fear what they fear,[q]
and do not dread it.[r]
[13]The LORD Almighty is the one you are
to regard as holy,[s]
he is the one you are to fear,[t]
he is the one you are to dread.[u]
[14]He will be a holy place;[v]
for both Israel and Judah he will be
a stone[w] that causes people to
stumble[x]
and a rock that makes them fall.[y]
And for the people of Jerusalem he
will be
a trap and a snare.[z]
[15]Many of them will stumble;[a]
they will fall and be broken,
they will be snared and captured."

[16]Bind up this testimony of warning[b]
and seal[c] up God's instruction
among my disciples.
[17]I will wait[d] for the LORD,
who is hiding[e] his face from the
descendants of Jacob.
I will put my trust in him.[f]

[18]Here am I, and the children the LORD
has given me.[g] We are signs[h] and symbols[i]
in Israel from the LORD Almighty, who
dwells on Mount Zion.[j]

8:10 [l]S Pr 19:21; S 21:30; S Isa 7:7 [m]S Isa 7:14; Mt 1:23; Ro 8:31 **8:11** [n]Eze 1:3; 3:14 [o]Eze 2:8 **8:12** [p]Isa 7:2; 20:5; 30:1; 36:6 [q]S Isa 7:4; Mt 10:28 [r]1Pe 3:14* **8:13** [s]S Nu 20:12 [t]S Ex 20:20 [u]Isa 29:23 **8:14** [v]S Isa 4:6 [w]S Ps 118:22 [x]Jer 6:21; Eze 3:20; 14:3, 7; Lk 20:18 [y]S Lk 2:34; Ro 9:33*; 1Pe 2:8* [z]S Ps 119:110; Isa 24:17-18 **8:15** [a]Pr 4:19; Isa 28:13; 59:10; Ro 9:32 **8:16** [b]S Ru 4:7 [c]Isa 29:11-12; Jer 32:14; Da 8:26; 12:4 **8:17** [d]S Ps 27:14 [e]S Dt 31:17 [f]S Ps 22:5; Heb 2:13* **8:18** [g]S Ge 33:5; Heb 2:13* [h]S Ex 3:12; Eze 4:3; 12:6; 24:24; Lk 2:34 [i]S Dt 28:46; S Eze 12:11 [j]Ps 9:11 **8:19** [k]S 1Sa 28:8 [l]S Lev 19:31 [m]Isa 29:4 [n]S Nu 27:21 **8:20** [o]S Isa 1:10; Lk 16:29 [p]S Ru 4:7

The Darkness Turns to Light

[19]When someone tells you to consult[k]
mediums and spiritists,[l] who whisper and
mutter,[m] should not a people inquire[n] of
their God? Why consult the dead on behalf
of the living? [20]Consult God's instruction[o]
and the testimony of warning.[p] If anyone
does not speak according to this word, they
have no light[q] of dawn. [21]Distressed and
hungry,[r] they will roam through the land;[s]
when they are famished, they will become
enraged and, looking upward, will curse[t]
their king and their God. [22]Then they will
look toward the earth and see only distress
and darkness and fearful gloom,[u] and they
will be thrust into utter darkness.[v]

9[b] Nevertheless, there will be no more
gloom[w] for those who were in distress. In the past he humbled the land of
Zebulun and the land of Naphtali,[x] but in
the future he will honor Galilee of the nations, by the Way of the Sea, beyond the
Jordan—

[2]The people walking in darkness[y]
have seen a great light;[z]
on those living in the land of deep
darkness[a]
a light has dawned.[b]
[3]You have enlarged the nation[c]
and increased their joy;[d]
they rejoice before you
as people rejoice at the harvest,

[a] *10* Hebrew *Immanuel* [b] In Hebrew texts 9:1 is numbered 8:23, and 9:2-21 is numbered 9:1-20.

[q]ver 22; Isa 9:2; 59:9; 60:2; Mic 3:6 **8:21** [r]S Job 18:12 [s]Job 30:3 [t]S Ex 22:28; Rev 16:11 **8:22** [u]S Job 15:24 [v]S ver 20; S Job 3:13; S Isa 5:30; S Joel 2:2; Mt 25:30; Rev 16:10 **9:1** [w]S Job 15:24 [x]S 2Ki 15:29 **9:2** [y]S Ps 82:5; S 107:10, 14; S Isa 8:20 [z]S Ps 36:9; Isa 42:6; 49:6; 60:19; Mal 4:2; Eph 5:8 [a]S Lk 1:79 [b]Isa 58:8; Mt 4:15-16* **9:3** [c]S Job 12:23 [d]S Ps 4:7; S Isa 25:9

8:11 *his strong hand upon me.* See Eze 1:3 and note; 37:1; 40:1. The prophets were conscious of God's presence in and control over their lives.
8:12 The Lord warns the people not to rely on Assyria (see note on 7:1).
8:13 *the one you are to fear.* See 7:2; Pr 1:7 and note.
8:14 *holy place ... stone ... fall.* Either the Lord is the cornerstone of our lives (see 28:16) or he is a rock over which we fall. See Ro 9:33; 1Pe 2:6 and note for an application to Christ.
8:16 Perhaps a reference to the legal transaction connected with vv. 1–2 (see note there). *testimony of warning.* See v. 20. This term occurs elsewhere only in Ru 4:7 ("method of legalizing transactions"). *God's instruction.* See v. 20. The Hebrew for this phrase can also mean "law." The legal document containing Isaiah's teaching about Assyria's invasion was a scroll that was tied and sealed and then given to the prophet's followers, who were to preserve it until the time of its fulfillment, when God would authenticate it by the events of history (cf. Jer 32:12–14,44).
8:17–18 *I will put ... given me.* In Heb 2:13 these words are put on Jesus' lips.
8:17 *hiding his face.* See 1:15 and note; 59:2; Mic 3:4 and note.
8:18 *signs and symbols.* See notes on 7:3,14; cf. 20:3.
8:19 *mediums and spiritists.* See Dt 18:9–12 and note on 18:9. In the present crisis, people were turning to the spirits of the dead, as King Saul did when he went to a medium to contact the spirit of Samuel (1Sa 28:8–11) and learn about the future. See note on 3:2–3.
8:20 *God's instruction ... testimony of warning.* See v. 16 and note. Only by heeding the Lord's word through Isaiah—reinforced by the "signs and symbols" (v. 18) that Isaiah and his sons represented—would the light dawn for Israel.
8:21–22 The Assyrian invasion would bring deep distress on all Israel.
8:21 *curse ... king and ... God.* Because of their terrible suffering (cf. Pr 19:3)—but severe punishment awaited anyone who cursed God or a ruler (Ex 22:28; Lev 24:15–16).
9:1 *Naphtali.* This tribe in northern Israel suffered greatly when the Assyrian Tiglath-Pileser III attacked in 734 and 732 BC (2Ki 15:29). *will honor Galilee.* Fulfilled when Jesus ministered in Capernaum—near the major highway from Egypt to Damascus, called "the Way of the Sea" (Mt 4:13–16).
9:2 *great light.* Jesus and his salvation would be a "light for the Gentiles" (42:6; 49:6; cf. Mt 4:15–16 and note; Lk 2:32).

Boots worn by warriors during battle (Isa 9:5)
Kim Walton, courtesy of the British Museum

as warriors rejoice
when dividing the plunder.[e]
4 For as in the day of Midian's defeat,[f]
you have shattered[g]
the yoke[h] that burdens them,
the bar across their shoulders,[i]
the rod of their oppressor.[j]
5 Every warrior's boot used in battle
and every garment rolled in blood
will be destined for burning,[k]
will be fuel for the fire.
6 For to us a child is born,[l]
to us a son is given,[m]
and the government[n] will be on his
shoulders.[o]
And he will be called
Wonderful Counselor,[p] Mighty
God,[q]
Everlasting[r] Father,[s] Prince of
Peace.[t]
7 Of the greatness of his government[u]
and peace[v]
there will be no end.[w]
He will reign[x] on David's throne
and over his kingdom,
establishing and upholding it
with justice[y] and righteousness[z]
from that time on and forever.[a]
The zeal[b] of the LORD Almighty
will accomplish this.

The LORD's Anger Against Israel

8 The Lord has sent a message[c] against
Jacob;
it will fall on Israel.

9:3 [e] S Ex 15:9; S Jos 22:8; S Ps 119:162 **9:4** [f] S Jdg 7:25 [g] S Job 34:24; Isa 37:36-38 [h] Isa 14:25; 58:6, 9; Jer 2:20; 30:8; Eze 30:18; Na 1:13; Mt 11:30 [i] S Ps 81:6; S Isa 10:27 [j] Isa 14:4; 16:4; 29:5, 20; 49:26; 51:13; 54:14; 60:18 **9:5** [k] S Isa 2:4 **9:6** [l] S Ge 3:15; Isa 53:2; Lk 2:11 [m] Jn 3:16 [n] S Mt 28:18 [o] Isa 22:22 [p] S Job 15:8; Isa 28:29 [q] S Dt 7:21; Ps 24:8; Isa 10:21; 11:2; 42:13 [r] S Ps 90:2 [s] S Ex 4:22; Isa 64:8; Jn 14:9-10 [t] Isa 26:3, 12; 53:5; 66:12; Jer 33:6; Mic 5:5; S Lk 2:14 **9:7** [u] S Isa 2:4 [v] S Ps 85:8; 119:165; Isa 11:9; 26:3, 12; 32:17; 48:18 [w] Da 2:44; 4:3; S Lk 1:33; Jn 12:34 [x] Isa 1:26; 32:1; 60:17; 1Co 15:25 [y] Isa 11:4; 16:5; 32:1, 16; 33:5; 42:1; Jer 23:5; 33:14 [z] S Ps 72:2 [a] S 2Sa 7:13 [b] 2Ki 19:31; Isa 26:11; 37:32; 42:13; 59:17; 63:15 **9:8** [c] S Dt 32:2

9:4 *Midian's defeat.* Gideon defeated the hordes of Midian and broke their domination over Israel (Jdg 7:22–25). *yoke.* In 10:26–27 Isaiah predicts that God will destroy the Assyrian army and their oppressive yoke. This was fulfilled in 701 BC (see 37:36–38 and notes).

9:5 *boot…garment.* Military equipment will no longer be needed. See notes on 2:2–4; Mic 5:10–15. See also photo above.

9:6 *son.* A royal son, a son of David (see v. 7; see also 2Sa 7:14; Ps 2:7; Mt 1:1; 3:17; Lk 1:32; Jn 3:16 and notes). *Wonderful Counselor.* In Hebrew each of the four throne names of the Messiah consists of two elements. "Counselor" points to the Messiah as a king (see Mic 4:9) who determines upon and carries out a program of action (see 14:27, "purposed"; Ps 20:4, "plans"). As Wonderful Counselor, the coming Son of David will carry out a royal program that will cause all the world to marvel. What that program will be is spelled out in ch. 11, and more fully in chs. 24–27 (see 25:1—"wonderful things, things planned [counseled] long ago"). In 28:29 the same two Hebrew words underlying "Wonderful Counselor" describe the Lord "whose plan is wonderful" (see also Jdg 13:18 and note). *Mighty God.* See 10:21. His divine power as a warrior is stressed (cf. Ps 24:8). *Everlasting Father.* He will be an enduring, compassionate provider and protector (cf. 40:9–11). This does not mean that God the Father and God the Son are one and the same (a heresy called modalism; see Mt 28:19 and note). *Prince of Peace.* His rule will bring wholeness and well-being to individuals and to society (see 11:6–9).

9:7 *David's throne … righteousness … forever.* In spite of the sins of kings like Ahaz, Christ will be a descendant of David who will rule in righteousness forever (see 11:3–5; 2Sa 7:12–13,16; Jer 33:15, 20–22). *The zeal … this.* Repeated in 37:32. God is like a jealous lover who will not abandon his people.

9:8—10:4 Although Isaiah's prophetic message was primarily "concerning Judah and Jerusalem" (1:1), he also occasionally mediated Yahweh's word to "Ephraim and the inhabitants of Samaria" (9:9). This section is a message of divine judgment

9 All the people will know it—
Ephraim[d] and the inhabitants of
Samaria[e]—
who say with pride
and arrogance[f] of heart,
10 "The bricks have fallen down,
but we will rebuild with dressed
stone;[g]
the fig[h] trees have been felled,
but we will replace them with
cedars.[i]"
11 But the LORD has strengthened Rezin's[j]
foes against them
and has spurred their enemies on.
12 Arameans[k] from the east and
Philistines[l] from the west
have devoured[m] Israel with open
mouth.

Yet for all this, his anger[n] is not turned
away,
his hand is still upraised.[o]

13 But the people have not returned[p] to
him who struck[q] them,
nor have they sought[r] the LORD
Almighty.
14 So the LORD will cut off from Israel
both head and tail,
both palm branch and reed[s] in a
single day;[t]
15 the elders[u] and dignitaries[v] are the
head,
the prophets[w] who teach lies[x] are the
tail.
16 Those who guide[y] this people mislead
them,
and those who are guided are led
astray.[z]
17 Therefore the Lord will take no
pleasure in the young men,[a]
nor will he pity[b] the fatherless and
widows,
for everyone is ungodly[c] and wicked,[d]
every mouth speaks folly.[e]

Yet for all this, his anger is not turned
away,
his hand is still upraised.[f]

9:9 [d] S Isa 7:2 [e] S Isa 7:9 [f] Isa 46:12; 48:4; Eze 2:4; Zec 7:11 **9:10** [g] S Ge 11:3 [h] Am 7:14; Lk 19:4 [i] 1Ki 7:2-3 **9:11** [j] S Isa 7:8 **9:12** [k] 2Ki 16:6 [l] S 2Ch 28:18 [m] S Ps 79:7 [n] S Job 40:11 [o] S Isa 5:25 **9:13** [p] S 2Ch 28:22; Am 4:9; Zep 3:7; Hag 2:17 [q] Jer 5:3; Eze 7:9 [r] Isa 2:3; 17:7; 31:1; 55:6; Jer 50:4; Da 9:13; Hos 3:5; 7:7, 10; Am 4:6, 10; Zep 1:6 **9:14** [s] ver 14-15; Isa 19:15 [t] Rev 18:8 **9:15** [u] Isa 3:2-3 [v] S Isa 5:13 [w] Isa 28:7; Eze 13:2 [x] S Job 13:4; S Isa 3:8; 44:20; Eze 13:22; Mt 24:24 **9:16** [y] Mt 15:14; 23:16, 24 [z] S Isa 3:12 **9:17** [a] Jer 9:21; 11:22; 18:21; 48:15; 49:26; Am 4:10; 8:13 [b] S Job 5:4; Isa 27:11; Jer 13:14 [c] Isa 10:6; 32:6; Mic 7:2 [d] S Isa 1:4 [e] S Isa 3:8; Mt 12:34; Ro 3:13-14 [f] S Isa 5:25 **9:18** [g] S Dt 29:23; S Isa 1:31 [h] S Isa 5:6 [i] S Ps 83:14 **9:19** [j] S Job 40:11; Isa 13:9, 13 [k] Jer 17:27 [l] S Ps 97:3; S Isa 1:31 [m] S Isa 3:5

18 Surely wickedness burns like a fire;[g]
it consumes briers and thorns,[h]
it sets the forest thickets ablaze,[i]
so that it rolls upward in a column
of smoke.
19 By the wrath[j] of the LORD Almighty
the land will be scorched[k]
and the people will be fuel for the fire;[l]
they will not spare one another.[m]
20 On the right they will devour,
but still be hungry;[n]
on the left they will eat,[o]
but not be satisfied.
Each will feed on the flesh of their own
offspring[a]:
21 Manasseh will feed on Ephraim, and
Ephraim on Manasseh;[p]
together they will turn against
Judah.[q]

Yet for all this, his anger is not turned
away,
his hand is still upraised.[r]

10 Woe[s] to those who make unjust
laws,
to those who issue oppressive
decrees,[t]
2 to deprive[u] the poor of their rights
and withhold justice from the
oppressed of my people,[v]
making widows their prey
and robbing the fatherless.[w]
3 What will you do on the day of
reckoning,[x]
when disaster[y] comes from afar?
To whom will you run for help?[z]
Where will you leave your riches?
4 Nothing will remain but to cringe
among the captives[a]
or fall among the slain.[b]

[a] 20 Or *arm*

9:20 [n] S Lev 26:26; S Job 18:12 [o] Isa 49:26; Zec 11:9 **9:21** [p] S Jdg 7:22; S 12:4 [q] S 2Ch 28:6 [r] S Isa 5:25 **10:1** [s] S Isa 5:8 [t] S Ps 58:2 **10:2** [u] Isa 3:14 [v] S Isa 5:23 [w] S Dt 10:18; S Job 6:27; S Isa 1:17 **10:3** [x] S Job 31:14 [y] ver 25; Ps 59:5; Isa 1:24; 13:6; 14:23; 24:6; 26:14; 47:11; Jer 5:9; 9:9; 50:15; Lk 19:44 [z] S Ps 108:12; Isa 20:6; 30:7; 31:3 **10:4** [a] Isa 24:22; Zec 9:11 [b] Isa 22:2; 34:3; 66:16; Jer 39:6; Na 3:3

against the northern kingdom. It consists of four balanced stanzas (vv. 8–12,13–17,18–21; 10:1–4), each of which ends with the same refrain (see note on 9:12,17,21).

9:9 *Ephraim.* See note on 7:2.

9:10 *bricks have fallen down.* Bricks made of clay and dried by the sun crumbled easily. *dressed stone.* Amos denounces the stone mansions of the wicked (Am 5:11). *cedars.* The cedars of Lebanon provided the most valuable wood in the ancient Near East (see 1Ki 7:2–3).

9:11 *Rezin's foes.* The Assyrians (see note on 7:1).

9:12,17,21 *Yet ... upraised.* See 5:25. This refrain is repeated in 10:4, where the anger of the Lord reaches a climax in the captivity of his people.

9:14 *head and tail ... palm branch and reed.* The leaders of Israel (see also 3:1–3). These two pairs refer to Egyptian leaders in 19:15.

9:17 *fatherless and widows.* They often suffered at the hands of the powerful (see note on 1:17), but now even they are wicked, as the rest of the verse makes clear.

9:18 *briers and thorns.* See note on 5:6.

9:19 *fuel for the fire.* Contrast v. 5.

9:21 *Manasseh ... Ephraim.* These two prominent tribes in the northern kingdom were descended from the two sons of Joseph (see Ge 46:20; see also Ge 48:5–6 and notes). They had fought each other centuries earlier (Jdg 12:4).

10:1 *Woe.* Cf. the series of woes in 5:8–23.

10:2 *the poor.* See note on Ex 22:21–27; cf. Jer 22:15–16. *widows ... fatherless.* See notes on 1:17; 9:17.

10:4 *captives ... slain.* Jer 39:6–7 similarly describes the plight of Judah's rulers when Nebuchadnezzar captured Jerusalem in 586 BC. *Yet ... upraised.* See note on 9:12,17,21.

Yet for all this, his anger is not turned
away,[c]
his hand is still upraised.

God's Judgment on Assyria

5 "Woe[d] to the Assyrian,[e] the rod[f] of my
anger,
in whose hand is the club[g] of my
wrath![h]
6 I send him against a godless[i] nation,
I dispatch[j] him against a people who
anger me,[k]
to seize loot and snatch plunder,[l]
and to trample[m] them down like mud
in the streets.
7 But this is not what he intends,[n]
this is not what he has in mind;
his purpose is to destroy,
to put an end to many nations.
8 'Are not my commanders[o] all kings?' he
says.
9 'Has not Kalno[p] fared like
Carchemish?[q]
Is not Hamath[r] like Arpad,[s]
and Samaria[t] like Damascus?[u]
10 As my hand seized the kingdoms of
the idols,[v]
kingdoms whose images excelled
those of Jerusalem and
Samaria—
11 shall I not deal with Jerusalem and her
images
as I dealt with Samaria and her
idols?[w]' "

12 When the Lord has finished all his
work[x] against Mount Zion[y] and Jerusalem,
he will say, "I will punish the king of Assyria[z] for the willful pride[a] of his heart and
the haughty look[b] in his eyes. 13 For he says:

" 'By the strength of my hand[c] I have
done this,[d]
and by my wisdom, because I have
understanding.
I removed the boundaries of nations,
I plundered their treasures;[e]
like a mighty one I subdued[a] their
kings.[f]
14 As one reaches into a nest,[g]
so my hand reached for the wealth[h]
of the nations;
as people gather abandoned eggs,
so I gathered all the countries;[i]
not one flapped a wing,
or opened its mouth to chirp.[j]' "
15 Does the ax raise itself above the
person who swings it,
or the saw boast against the one
who uses it?[k]
As if a rod were to wield the person
who lifts it up,
or a club[l] brandish the one who is
not wood!
16 Therefore, the Lord, the LORD Almighty,
will send a wasting disease[m] upon
his sturdy warriors;[n]
under his pomp[o] a fire[p] will be kindled
like a blazing flame.
17 The Light of Israel will become a fire,[q]
their Holy One[r] a flame;
in a single day it will burn and
consume
his thorns[s] and his briers.[t]
18 The splendor of his forests[u] and fertile
fields
it will completely destroy,[v]
as when a sick person wastes away.
19 And the remaining trees of his forests[w]
will be so few[x]
that a child could write them down.

[a] 13 Or *treasures; / I subdued the mighty,*

10:4 [c]S Isa 5:25; 12:1; 63:10; 64:5; Jer 4:8; 30:24; La 1:12 **10:5** [d]S 2Ki 19:21; S Isa 28:1 [e]ver 12, 18; S Isa 7:20; 14:25; 31:8; 37:7; Zep 2:13 [f]Isa 14:5; 54:16 [g]ver 15, 24; Isa 30:31; 41:15; 45:1; Jer 50:23; 51:20 [h]Isa 9:4; 13:3, 5, 13; 26:20; 30:30; 34:2; 63:6; 66:14; Eze 30:24-25 **10:6** [i]S Isa 9:17 [j]Hab 1:12 [k]S 2Ch 28:9; Isa 9:19 [l]S Jdg 6:4; S Isa 5:29; 8:1 [m]S 2Sa 22:43; S Ps 7:5; S Isa 5:5; 37:26-27 **10:7** [n]S Ge 50:20; Ac 4:23-28 **10:8** [o]2Ki 18:24 **10:9** [p]S Ge 10:10 [q]S 2Ch 35:20 [r]Nu 34:8; 2Ch 8:4; Isa 11:11 [s]2Ki 18:34 [t]2Ki 17:6 [u]S Ge 14:15; 2Ki 16:9; Jer 49:24 **10:10** [v]2Ki 19:18 **10:11** [w]S 2Ki 19:13; S Isa 2:8; 36:18-20; 37:10-13 **10:12** [x]Isa 28:21-22; 65:7; 66:4; Jer 5:29 [y]2Ki 19:31 [z]S ver 5; S 2Ki 19:7; Isa 30:31-33; 37:36-38; Jer 50:18 [a]S Isa 2:11; S Eze 28:17 [b]Ps 18:27 **10:13** [c]S Dt 8:17 [d]S Dt 32:26-27; Isa 47:7; Da 4:30 [e]Eze 28:4 [f]Isa 14:13-14 **10:14** [g]Jer 49:16; Ob 1:4; Hab 2:6-11 [h]S Job 31:25 [i]Isa 14:6 [j]2Ki 19:22-24; Isa 37:24-25 **10:15** [k]S Isa 7:20; 45:9; Ro 9:20-21 [l]S ver 5 **10:16** [m]ver 18; S Nu 11:33; Isa 17:4 [n]Ps 78:31 [o]S Isa 8:7 [p]Jer 21:14 **10:17** [q]S Job 41:21; S Isa 1:31; 31:9; Zec 2:5 [r]Isa 37:23 [s]S Nu 11:1-3; S 2Sa 23:6 [t]S Isa 9:18 **10:18** [u]S 2Ki 19:23 [v]S ver 5 **10:19** [w]ver 33-34; Isa 32:19 [x]Isa 17:6; 21:17; 27:13; Jer 44:28

10:5 *Woe.* See v. 1 and note. *rod … club.* See 9:4 and note. Babylonia was another hammer or club used by God to punish other nations (Jer 50:23; 51:20; Hab 1:6).
10:6 *godless nation.* Judah (see v. 10). *loot … plunder.* The last part of the fulfillment symbolized by Maher-Shalal-Hash-Baz ("loot" here is the translation of Hebrew *shalal*, and "plunder" is the translation of *baz*). See 8:1–4 and note on 8:3.
10:9 *Kalno.* A region in northern Aram (Syria). See Kalneh in Am 6:2 (see also note there). *Carchemish.* The great fortress on the Euphrates River east of Kalno (see Jer 46:2 and note). *Hamath.* A city on the Orontes River that marked the northern extent of Solomon's rule (2Ch 8:4). See note on 2Ki 17:24. *Arpad.* A city near Hamath and just south of Kalno. All these areas submitted to Assyria by c. 717 BC (see 36:19).
10:10,14 *my hand seized … my hand reached.* The Hebrew verb is the same in both verses. The repetition of the phrase underscores the unquenchable greed of the Assyrian king.
10:10 *images … of Jerusalem and Samaria.* No Israelite was supposed to worship idols (see Ex 20:4 and note), but the land was full of them (2:8). Samaria fell to Shalmaneser V (2Ki 17:3–6) and Sargon II (see 20:1 and note) in 722–721 BC.
10:12 The Lord's instruments of judgment are not themselves exempt from his judgment. *pride.* Judgment against the proud was announced in 2:11,17.
10:13–14 *my … I.* The king of Assyria boastfully refers to himself nine times. Cf. 14:13–14; Eze 28:2–5.
10:15 *ax … saw … rod … club.* See v. 5; 9:4 and notes.
10:16 *the Lord, the LORD Almighty.* See 1:24 and note. *wasting disease.* When the angel put to death 185,000 soldiers of the Assyrian king Sennacherib in 701 BC, he may have used a rapidly spreading plague (see note on 37:36; see also 2Sa 24:15–16; 1Ch 21:22,27).
10:17,20 *Holy One.* See note on 1:4.
10:18–19 *forests.* A reference to the Assyrian army. See vv. 33–34 and note on v. 33.
10:19 Probably fulfilled between 612 BC (fall of Nineveh) and 605 (battle of Carchemish).

The Remnant of Israel

20 In that day[y] the remnant of Israel,
the survivors[z] of Jacob,
will no longer rely[a] on him
who struck them down[b]
but will truly rely[c] on the LORD,
the Holy One of Israel.[d]
21 A remnant[e] will return,[a][f] a remnant of Jacob
will return to the Mighty God.[g]
22 Though your people be like the sand[h]
by the sea, Israel,
only a remnant will return.[i]
Destruction has been decreed,[j]
overwhelming and righteous.
23 The Lord, the LORD Almighty, will carry out
the destruction decreed[k] upon the whole land.[l]

24 Therefore this is what the Lord, the LORD Almighty, says:

"My people who live in Zion,[m]
do not be afraid[n] of the Assyrians,
who beat[o] you with a rod[p]
and lift up a club against you, as Egypt did.
25 Very soon[q] my anger against you will end
and my wrath[r] will be directed to their destruction.[s]"

26 The LORD Almighty will lash[t] them
with a whip,
as when he struck down Midian[u] at the rock of Oreb;
and he will raise his staff[v] over the waters,[w]
as he did in Egypt.
27 In that day[x] their burden[y] will be lifted
from your shoulders,
their yoke[z] from your neck;[a]
the yoke[b] will be broken
because you have grown so fat.[b]
28 They enter Aiath;
they pass through Migron;[c]
they store supplies[d] at Mikmash.[e]
29 They go over the pass, and say,
"We will camp overnight at Geba.[f]"
Ramah[g] trembles;
Gibeah[h] of Saul flees.[i]
30 Cry out, Daughter Gallim![j]
Listen, Laishah!
Poor Anathoth![k]
31 Madmenah is in flight;
the people of Gebim take cover.
32 This day they will halt at Nob;[l]
they will shake their fist[m]
at the mount of Daughter Zion,[n]
at the hill of Jerusalem.

33 See, the Lord, the LORD Almighty,
will lop off[o] the boughs with great power.
The lofty trees will be felled,[p]
the tall[q] ones will be brought low.[r]
34 He will cut down[s] the forest thickets
with an ax;
Lebanon[t] will fall before the Mighty One.[u]

[a] 21 Hebrew *shear-jashub* (see 7:3 and note); also in verse 22 [b] 27 Hebrew; Septuagint *broken / from your shoulders*

10:20 [y]ver 27; Isa 11:10,11; 12:1,4; 19:18,19; 24:21; 28:5; 52:6; Zec 9:16 [z]S Isa 1:9; Eze 7:16 [a]S 2Ki 16:7 [b]2Ch 28:20 [c]2Ch 14:11; Isa 17:7; 48:2; 50:10; Jer 21:2; Hos 3:5; 6:1; Mic 3:11; 7:7 [d]S Isa 5:24 **10:21** [e]S Ge 45:7; Isa 6:13; Zep 3:13 [f]Isa 7:3 [g]S Isa 9:6 **10:22** [h]S Ge 12:2; Isa 48:19; Jer 33:22 [i]Ezr 1:4; Isa 11:11; 46:3 [j]ver 23; Isa 28:22; Jer 40:2; Da 9:27 **10:23** [k]S ver 22 [l]Isa 6:12; 28:22; Ro 9:27-28* **10:24** [m]Ps 87:5-6 [n]S Isa 7:4 [o]S Ex 5:14 [p]S ver 5 **10:25** [q]Isa 17:14; 29:17; Hag 2:6 [r]ver 5; Ps 30:5; Isa 13:5; 24:21; 26:20; 30:30; 34:2; 66:14; Da 8:19; 11:36 [s]S ver 3; Mic 5:6 **10:26** [t]Isa 37:36-38 [u]S Isa 9:4 [v]Isa 30:32 [w]S Ex 14:16 **10:27** [x]S ver 20 [y]S Ps 66:11 [z]S Lev 26:13; S Isa 9:4 [a]Isa 14:25; 47:6; 52:2 [b]Jer 30:8 **10:28** [c]S 1Sa 14:2 [d]S Jos 1:11 [e]1Sa 13:2 **10:29** [f]S Jos 18:24; S Ne 11:31 [g]S Jos 18:25 [h]S Jdg 19:14 [i]Isa 15:5 **10:30** [j]1Sa 25:44 [k]S Ne 11:32 **10:32** [l]S 1Sa 21:1 [m]S Job 15:25 [n]S Ps 9:14; Isa 16:1; Jer 6:23 **10:33** [o]Isa 18:5; 27:11; Eze 17:4 [p]S Ex 12:12 [q]Isa 2:13; Am 2:9 [r]Isa 5:15 **10:34** [s]Na 1:12; Zec 11:2 [t]S 2Ki 19:23 [u]S Ge 49:24; Ps 93:4; Isa 33:21

10:20,27 *In that day.* The day of victory and joy, the positive aspect of the "day of the LORD" (see notes on 2:11,17,20; 9:4). Israel is restored and the people praise God. Ch. 11 connects this "day" with the Messianic age (see 11:10–11 and notes; see also 12:1,4).
10:20–22 *remnant.* See note on 1:9. "A remnant will return" (v. 21) was the name of Isaiah's first son (see NIV text note on 7:3). A faithful remnant led by Hezekiah survived the Assyrian invasion of 701 BC (see 37:4 and note). Later, a remnant returned from Babylonian exile.
10:20 *him who struck them.* The king of Assyria (see note on 7:17).
10:21 *Mighty God.* See note on 9:6.
10:22 *the sand by the sea.* See notes on Ge 13:16; 22:17. *Destruction ... decreed.* Because of Israel's sin, God would punish the nation through foreign invaders.
10:23–24 *The Lord, the LORD Almighty.* See 1:24 and note.
10:24 *rod ... club.* See v. 5; 9:4 and notes.
10:26–27 *Midian ... burden ... yoke.* See note on 9:4.
10:26 *Oreb.* One of the Midianite leaders (Jdg 7:25). *the waters ... in Egypt.* When Moses stretched out his hand over the "Red Sea," the waters engulfed the chariots of the pharaoh (see Ex 14:26–28).
10:27 *fat.* Like a sturdy animal, Israel is able to break the yoke.
10:28–32 As if seeing a vision, Isaiah describes the approach of the Assyrian army to Jerusalem from about ten miles north of the city. Cf. Mic 1:8–16 and notes.
10:28 *Mikmash.* Located about seven miles north of Jerusalem.
10:29 *Ramah.* The home of Samuel. It was about five miles from Jerusalem (1Sa 7:17; see note on 1Sa 1:1). *Gibeah of Saul.* About three miles from Jerusalem. It had been the capital of Israel's first king (see 1Sa 10:26).
10:30 *Daughter Gallim.* A personification of a Benjamite town of Saulide association (see 1Sa 25:44; see also note on 2Ki 19:21). *Poor Anathoth.* Jeremiah's hometown (see Jer 1:1 and note). The Hebrew for "poor" is a wordplay on "Anathoth."
10:32 *Nob.* Perhaps on Mount Scopus, on the outskirts of Jerusalem (see 1Sa 21:1 and note). *Daughter Zion.* A personification of Jerusalem (see note on 2Ki 19:21).
10:33 *the Lord, the LORD Almighty.* See 1:24 and note. *boughs ... trees.* Sennacherib and his armies will fall (see vv. 16–19 and notes).
10:34 *Lebanon.* Refers to the famed cedars of Lebanon (see notes on 2:13; 9:10; 14:8).

The Branch From Jesse

11 A shoot[v] will come up from the
stump[w] of Jesse;[x]
from his roots a Branch[y] will bear fruit.[z]
2 The Spirit[a] of the LORD will rest on him—
the Spirit of wisdom[b] and of
understanding,
the Spirit of counsel and of might,[c]
the Spirit of the knowledge and fear
of the LORD—
3 and he will delight in the fear[d] of the
LORD.

He will not judge by what he sees with
his eyes,[e]
or decide by what he hears with his
ears;[f]
4 but with righteousness[g] he will judge
the needy,[h]
with justice[i] he will give decisions
for the poor[j] of the earth.
He will strike[k] the earth with the rod of
his mouth;[l]
with the breath[m] of his lips he will
slay the wicked.[n]
5 Righteousness will be his belt[o]
and faithfulness[p] the sash around his
waist.[q]
6 The wolf will live with the lamb,[r]
the leopard will lie down with the
goat,
the calf and the lion and the yearling[a]
together;
and a little child will lead them.
7 The cow will feed with the bear,
their young will lie down together,
and the lion will eat straw like the ox.[s]
8 The infant[t] will play near the cobra's
den,
and the young child will put its hand
into the viper's[u] nest.
9 They will neither harm nor destroy[v]
on all my holy mountain,[w]
for the earth[x] will be filled with the
knowledge[y] of the LORD
as the waters cover the sea.

10 In that day[z] the Root of Jesse[a] will
stand as a banner[b] for the peoples; the
nations[c] will rally to him,[d] and his resting
place[e] will be glorious.[f] 11 In that day[g] the
Lord will reach out his hand a second time
to reclaim the surviving remnant[h] of his
people from Assyria,[i] from Lower Egypt,
from Upper Egypt,[j] from Cush,[b][k] from
Elam,[l] from Babylonia,[c] from Hamath[m] and
from the islands[n] of the Mediterranean.[o]

12 He will raise a banner[p] for the nations
and gather[q] the exiles of Israel;[r]
he will assemble the scattered people[s]
of Judah
from the four quarters of the earth.[t]
13 Ephraim's jealousy will vanish,
and Judah's enemies[d] will be
destroyed;

[a] *6* Hebrew; Septuagint *lion will feed* [b] *11* That is, the upper Nile region [c] *11* Hebrew *Shinar*
[d] *13* Or *hostility*

11:1 [v] S 2Ki 19:26; S Job 14:7 [w] S Job 14:8 [x] ver 10; Isa 9:7; S Mt 1:1; S Rev 5:5 [y] S Isa 4:2 [z] S 2Ki 19:30; S Isa 27:6 **11:2** [a] S Jdg 3:10; Isa 32:15; 42:1; 44:3; 48:16; 59:21; 61:1; Eze 37:14; 39:29; Joel 2:28; Mt 3:16; Jn 1:32-33; 16:13 [b] S Ex 28:3; S Eph 1:17; S Col 2:3 [c] S Isa 9:6; 2Ti 1:7 **11:3** [d] Isa 33:6 [e] Jn 7:24 [f] Jn 2:25 **11:4** [g] S Ps 72:2 [h] S Ps 72:4; S Isa 14:30 [i] S Isa 9:7; Rev 19:11 [j] S Job 5:16; S Isa 3:14 [k] Isa 27:7; 30:31; Zec 14:12; Mal 4:6 [l] S Job 40:18; Ps 2:9; Rev 19:15 [m] S Job 4:9; Ps 18:8; Isa 30:28, 33; 40:24; 59:19; Eze 21:31; 2Th 2:8 [n] S Ps 139:19 **11:5** [o] Ex 12:11; 1Ki 18:46 [p] Isa 25:1 [q] Eph 6:14 **11:6** [r] Isa 65:25 **11:7** [s] S Job 40:15 **11:8** [t] Isa 65:20

[u] Isa 14:29; 30:6; 59:5 **11:9** [v] S Nu 25:12; S Isa 2:4; S 9:7 [w] S Ps 48:1; S Isa 2:2 [x] 1Sa 17:46; Ps 98:2-3; Isa 45:22; 48:20; 52:10 [y] Ex 7:5; Isa 19:21; 45:6, 14; 49:26; Jer 24:7; 31:34; Hab 2:14 **11:10** [z] S Isa 10:20 [a] S ver 1 [b] S Ps 20:5; Isa 18:3; Jer 4:6; Jn 12:32 [c] Isa 2:4; 14:1; 49:23; 56:3,6; 60:5, 10; Lk 2:32; Ac 11:18 [d] Ro 15:12* [e] S Ps 116:7; Isa 14:3; 28:12; 32:17-18; 40:2; Jer 6:16; 30:10; 46:27 [f] Hag 2:9; Zec 2:5 **11:11** [g] S Isa 10:20 [h] S Dt 30:4; S Isa 1:9 [i] Isa 19:24; Hos 11:11; Mic 7:12; Zec 10:10 [j] Jer 44:1, 15; Eze 29:14; 30:14 [k] S Ge 10:6; Ac 8:27 [l] S Ge 10:22 [m] S Isa 10:9 [n] Isa 24:15; 41:1, 5; 42:4, 10, 12; 49:1; 51:5; 59:18; 60:9; 66:19 [o] Isa 49:12; Jer 16:15; 46:27; Eze 38:8; Zec 8:7 **11:12** [p] S Ps 20:5 [q] Isa 14:2; 43:5; 49:22; 54:7; Jer 16:15; 31:10; 32:37 [r] S Ne 1:9; S Ps 106:47; Isa 14:1; 41:14; 49:5 [s] Eze 28:25; Zep 3:10 [t] S Ps 48:10; 67:7; Isa 41:5; Rev 7:1

11:1 *shoot ... stump.* The Assyrians all but destroyed Judah, but it was the Babylonian exile that brought the kingdom of Judah to an end in 586 BC. The Messiah will grow as a shoot from that stump of David's dynasty. See 6:13 and note. *Jesse.* David's father (see 1Sa 16:10–13). *Branch.* See notes on 4:2; Mt 2:23.

11:2 *The Spirit ... will rest on him.* The Messiah, like David (1Sa 16:13), will be empowered by the Holy Spirit (see 61:1 and note). *counsel ... might.* The Spirit will endow him with the wisdom to undertake wise purposes and with the power to carry them out (see note on 9:6). *fear of the LORD.* See Pr 1:7 and note.

11:3 *delight in the fear of the LORD.* See Jn 8:29.

11:4 *righteousness ... justice.* The rulers of Isaiah's day lacked these qualities (see 1:17; 5:7; see also note on 9:7). *rod of his mouth.* Assyria was God's rod in 10:5,24, but the Messiah will rule the nations with an iron scepter (see Ps 2:9; Rev 2:27 and notes; 19:15).

11:5 *belt.* When a man prepared for vigorous action, he tied up his loose, flowing garments with a belt (see 5:27).

11:6–9 The peace and safety of the Messianic age are reflected in the fact that little children will be unharmed as they play with formerly ferocious animals. Such conditions are a description of the future consummation of the Messianic kingdom. See 2:2–4; 35:9; 65:20–25 and notes; Eze 34:25–29.

11:9 *my holy mountain.* See 2:2–4 and note. *filled with the knowledge.* See 2:3, where the word of the Lord is taught in Jerusalem (see also Hab 2:14 and note).

11:10 *In that day.* See note on 10:20,27. *Root of Jesse.* A Messianic title closely connected with v. 1 (see also 53:2; Ro 15:12; Rev 5:5; 22:16 and notes). *banner.* See 5:26 and note.

11:11 *second time.* The first time was the exodus from Egypt (see v. 16). The second is probably the return from Assyrian and Babylonian exile, though some interpreters, who believe that the passage refers to the dispersion after the destruction of Jerusalem in AD 70, place the regathering at Christ's second coming. *remnant.* See notes on 1:9; 10:20–22. *Lower Egypt.* The delta region of the Nile, in the north. *Upper Egypt.* Southern Egypt, upstream from the delta. *Elam.* The land northeast of the lower Tigris River valley (see 21:2 and note; Jer 49:34–39; Da 8:2). *Hamath.* See note on 10:9. *islands of the Mediterranean.* The coastlands are probably also intended (see 41:1,5; 42:4; Ge 10:5).

11:12 *gather the exiles.* See 27:13; 49:22; 56:8; 62:10; 66:20. *four quarters.* Lit. "four wings." "Four quarters of the earth" is equivalent to "ends of the earth" (24:16; Job 37:3).

11:13 *Ephraim's jealousy.* See note on 7:2. Prior to the exile, Ephraim and Judah were frequently fighting each other (see 9:21 and note).

Ephraim will not be jealous of
Judah,
nor Judah hostile toward Ephraim.[u]
14 They will swoop down on the slopes of
Philistia[v] to the west;
together they will plunder the people
to the east.[w]
They will subdue Edom[x] and Moab,[y]
and the Ammonites[z] will be subject
to them.[a]
15 The LORD will dry up[b]
the gulf of the Egyptian sea;
with a scorching wind[c] he will sweep
his hand[d]
over the Euphrates River.[e]
He will break it up into seven
streams
so that anyone can cross over in
sandals.[f]
16 There will be a highway[g] for the
remnant[h] of his people
that is left from Assyria,[i]
as there was for Israel
when they came up from Egypt.[j]

Songs of Praise

12 In that day[k] you will say:

"I will praise[l] you, LORD.
Although you were angry with me,
your anger has turned away[m]
and you have comforted[n] me.
2 Surely God is my salvation;[o]
I will trust[p] and not be afraid.
The LORD, the LORD himself,[q] is my
strength[r] and my defense[a];
he has become my salvation.[s]"
3 With joy you will draw water[t]
from the wells[u] of salvation.

4 In that day[v] you will say:

"Give praise to the LORD, proclaim his
name;[w]
make known among the nations[x]
what he has done,
and proclaim that his name is
exalted.[y]
5 Sing[z] to the LORD, for he has done
glorious things;[a]
let this be known to all the world.
6 Shout aloud and sing for joy,[b] people of
Zion,
for great[c] is the Holy One of Israel[d]
among you.[e]"

A Prophecy Against Babylon

13 A prophecy[f] against Babylon[g] that
Isaiah son of Amoz[h] saw:[i]

11:13 [u]S 2Ch 28:6; Jer 3:18; Eze 37:16-17, 22; Hos 1:11 **11:14** [v]S 2Ch 26:6; S 28:18 [w]S Jdg 6:3 [x]S Nu 24:18; S Ps 137:7; Isa 34:5-6; 63:1; Jer 49:22; Eze 25:12; Da 11:41; Joel 3:19; Ob 1:1; Mal 1:4 [y]Isa 15:1; 16:14; 25:10; Jer 48:40; Zep 2:8-11 [z]Jdg 11:14-18 [a]Isa 25:3; 60:12 **11:15** [b]S Ex 14:22; S Dt 11:10; Isa 37:25; 42:15; Jer 50:38; 51:36 [c]S Ge 41:6 [d]Isa 19:16; 30:32 [e]S Isa 7:20 [f]S Ex 14:29 **11:16** [g]Isa 19:23; 35:8; 40:3; 49:11; 51:10; 57:14; 62:10; Jer 50:5 [h]S Ge 45:7 [i]S ver 11 [j]Ex 14:26-31 **12:1** [k]S Isa 10:20 [l]Ps 9:1; Isa 25:1 [m]S Job 13:16 [n]S Ps 71:21 **12:2** [o]Isa 17:10; 25:9; 33:6; 45:17; 51:5, 6; 54:8; 59:16; 61:10; 62:11

[a] 2 Or *song*

[p]S Job 13:15; S Ps 26:1; S 112:7; Isa 26:3; Da 6:23 [q]Isa 26:4; 38:11 [r]S Ps 18:1 [s]S Ex 15:2 **12:3** [t]S 2Ki 3:17; Ps 36:9; Jer 2:13; 17:13; Jn 4:10, 14 [u]Ex 15:25 **12:4** [v]S Isa 10:20 [w]Ex 3:15; Ps 80:18; 105:1; Isa 24:15; 25:1; 26:8, 13; Hos 12:5 [x]Isa 54:5; 60:3; Jer 10:7; Zep 2:11; Mal 1:11 [y]S Ps 113:2 **12:5** [z]S Ex 15:1 [a]S Ps 98:1 **12:6** [b]S Ge 21:6; S Ps 98:4; Isa 24:14; 48:20; 52:8; Jer 20:13; 31:7; Zec 2:10 [c]Ps 48:1 [d]S Ps 78:41; 99:2; Isa 1:24; 10:20; 17:7; 29:19; 37:23; 43:3, 14; 45:11; 49:26; 55:5; Eze 39:7 [e]S Ps 46:5; Zep 3:14-17 **13:1** [f]Isa 14:28; 15:1; 21:1; Na 1:1; Hab 1:1; Zec 9:1; 12:1; Mal 1:1 [g]ver 19; S Ge 10:10; Isa 14:4; 21:9; 46:1-2; 48:14; Jer 24:1; 25:12; Rev 14:8 [h]Isa 20:2; 37:2 [i]S Isa 1:1

11:14 *people to the east.* Perhaps the Midianites, who plundered Israel, along with other eastern peoples (see 9:4). *Edom ... Moab ... Ammonites.* After the exodus, Israel did not attack these nations (see Jdg 11:14–18). Israel's future political domination is also referred to in 14:2; 49:23; 60:12 (see also 25:10; 34:5).

11:15 *dry up ... the Egyptian sea.* An allusion to the drying up of the "Red Sea" during the exodus (see Ex 14:21–22). *gulf.* Lit. "tongue" (see "bay" in Jos 15:2,5). *Euphrates.* Rev 16:12 refers to the drying up of the Euphrates, perhaps symbolizing the removal of barriers preventing the coming of "the kings from the East."

11:16 *highway.* The removal of obstacles and the building of a highway leading to Jerusalem are also described in 57:14; 62:10 (cf. 35:8–10 and note on 35:8; 40:3–4 and note on 40:3).

12:1–6 Two short psalms of praise for deliverance (vv. 1–3,4–6) climax chs. 7–11 (see note on 7:1—12:6; see also note on 6:1).

12:1,4 *In that day.* See note on 10:20,27.

12:1 *I will praise you.* The "I" is probably the nation, praising the Lord for the deliverance he is sure to bring. *your anger has turned away.* See note on 9:12,17,21. After God punishes Israel, his anger will be directed against nations like Assyria and Babylonia.

12:2 *The LORD, the LORD.* See notes on Ex 3:15; 34:6–7; Dt 28:58. *the LORD ... salvation.* These lines echo Ex 15:2, a verse commemorating the defeat of the Egyptians at the "Red Sea." See also Ps 118:14 and note.

12:3 *wells.* Perhaps an allusion to God's abundant provision of water for Israel during the wilderness wanderings (cf. Ex 15:25,27). But here God's future saving act is itself the well from which Israel will draw life-giving water (see Ps 36:9; Jer 2:13; Jn 4:10 and notes).

12:6 *Shout aloud and sing for joy.* These two imperatives occur again in 54:1, where Zion rejoices over the restoration of her people. *Holy One of Israel.* See notes on 1:4; 6:1.

13:1—23:18 A series of prophecies against the nations (see also Jer 46–51; Eze 25–32; Am 1–2; Zep 2:4–15 and notes). They begin with Babylonia (13:1—14:23) and Assyria (14:24–27) before moving on to smaller nations. God's judgment on his people does not mean that the pagan nations will be spared (see Jer 25:29). In fact, God's judgments on the nations are often a part of his salvation of his people (see, e.g., 10:12).

13:1—14:27 Since in Isaiah's day Babylon was part of the Assyrian Empire, indeed one of its most important cities, it may be that the prophecy against Babylonia (13:1—14:23) is actually a prophecy also against the Assyrian Empire (see 14:24–27, which has no new "prophecy" heading). This is not to say that some elements of the prophecy against the city of Babylon did not reach beyond the period of the Assyrian Empire (e.g., see notes on 13:1,20).

13:1 See note on 1:1. *prophecy.* The Hebrew for this word is related to a Hebrew verb meaning "to lift up, carry" and is possibly to be understood as either lifting up one's voice or carrying a burden. Such a "prophecy" often contains a message of doom. *Babylon.* See 21:1–9; 46:1–2; 47:1–15; Jer 50–51 and notes. Its judgment is announced first because of the present Assyrian threat and because Babylonia would later bring about the downfall of Judah and Jerusalem between 605 and 586 BC. Babylon was conquered by Cyrus the

2 Raise a banner[j] on a bare hilltop,
shout to them;
beckon to them
to enter the gates[k] of the nobles.
3 I have commanded those I prepared for battle;
I have summoned my warriors[l] to carry out my wrath[m] —
those who rejoice[n] in my triumph.

4 Listen, a noise on the mountains,
like that of a great multitude![o]
Listen, an uproar[p] among the kingdoms,
like nations massing together!
The LORD Almighty[q] is mustering[r]
an army for war.
5 They come from faraway lands,
from the ends of the heavens[s] —
the LORD and the weapons[t] of his wrath[u] —
to destroy[v] the whole country.

6 Wail,[w] for the day[x] of the LORD is near;
it will come like destruction[y] from the Almighty.[a][z]
7 Because of this, all hands will go limp,[a]
every heart will melt with fear.[b]
8 Terror[c] will seize them,
pain and anguish will grip[d] them;
they will writhe like a woman in labor.[e]
They will look aghast at each other,
their faces aflame.[f]

9 See, the day[g] of the LORD is coming
— a cruel[h] day, with wrath[i] and fierce anger[j] —
to make the land desolate
and destroy the sinners within it.
10 The stars of heaven and their constellations
will not show their light.[k]
The rising sun[l] will be darkened[m]
and the moon will not give its light.[n]
11 I will punish[o] the world for its evil,
the wicked[p] for their sins.
I will put an end to the arrogance of the haughty[q]
and will humble[r] the pride of the ruthless.[s]
12 I will make people[t] scarcer than pure gold,
more rare than the gold of Ophir.[u]
13 Therefore I will make the heavens tremble;[v]
and the earth will shake[w] from its place
at the wrath[x] of the LORD Almighty,
in the day of his burning anger.[y]

14 Like a hunted[z] gazelle,
like sheep without a shepherd,[a]
they will all return to their own people,
they will flee[b] to their native land.[c]
15 Whoever is captured will be thrust through;
all who are caught will fall[d] by the sword.[e]
16 Their infants[f] will be dashed to pieces
before their eyes;
their houses will be looted and their wives violated.[g]

[a] 6 Hebrew *Shaddai*

13:2 [j]S Ps 20:5; Jer 50:2; 51:27 [k]Isa 24:12; 45:2; Jer 51:58 **13:3** [l]ver 17; Isa 21:2; Jer 51:11; Da 5:28,31; Joel 3:11 [m]S Job 40:11; S Isa 10:5 [n]S Ps 149:2 **13:4** [o]Joel 3:14 [p]S Ps 46:6 [q]Isa 47:4; 51:15 [r]Isa 42:13; Jer 50:41 **13:5** [s]S Isa 5:26 [t]Isa 45:1; 54:16; Jer 50:25 [u]S Isa 10:25 [v]S Jos 6:17; Isa 24:1; 30:25; 34:2 **13:6** [w]Isa 14:31; 15:2; 16:7; 23:1; Eze 30:2; Jas 5:1 [x]S Isa 2:12 [y]S Isa 10:3; S 14:15 [z]S Ge 17:1 **13:7** [a]S 2Ki 19:26; S Job 4:3; S Jer 47:3 [b]S Jos 2:11; Eze 21:7 **13:8** [c]S Ps 31:13; S 48:5; S Isa 21:4 [d]Ex 15:14 [e]S Ge 3:16; S Jn 16:21 [f]Joel 2:6; Na 2:10 **13:9** [g]S Isa 2:12; Jer 51:2 [h]Jer 6:23 [i]S Isa 9:19 [j]Isa 26:21; 66:16; Jer 25:31; Joel 3:2 **13:10** [k]S Job 9:7 [l]Isa 24:23; Zec 14:7 [m]S Ex 10:22; S Isa 5:30; Rev 8:12 [n]Eze 32:7; Am 5:20; 8:9; S Mt 24:29*; Mk 13:24* **13:11** [o]Isa 3:11; 11:4; 26:21; 65:6-7; 66:16 [p]S Ps 125:3 [q]S Ps 10:5; S Pr 16:18; Da 5:23 [r]S Isa 2:9; 23:9; Eze 28:2; Da 4:37 [s]Isa 25:3,5; 29:5,20; 49:25,26 **13:12** [t]S Isa 4:1 [u]S Ge 10:29 **13:13** [v]S Ps 102:26; Isa 34:4; 51:6 [w]S Job 9:6; S Isa 14:16; Mt 24:7; Mk 13:8 [x]S Isa 9:19 [y]S Job 9:5 **13:14** [z]Pr 6:5 [a]S 1Ki 22:17; S Mt 9:36; S Jn 10:11 [b]S Ge 11:9; Isa 17:13; 21:15; 22:3; 33:3; Jer 4:9 [c]Jer 46:16; 50:16; 51:9; Na 3:7 **13:15** [d]Jer 51:4 [e]Isa 14:19; Jer 50:25 **13:16** [f]ver 18; S Nu 16:27; S 2Ki 8:12 [g]S Ge 34:29; S Hos 13:16

Persian (see 45:1; 47:1) in 539. Subsequently it came to symbolize the world powers arrayed against God's kingdom (cf. 1Pe 5:13), and its final destruction is announced in Rev 14:8; 16:19; 17–18. Here, however, Babylon is still part of the Assyrian Empire (see 14:24–27; see also note on 13:1—14:27).
13:2 *Raise a banner.* See note on 5:26.
13:3 *those I prepared for battle.* Or "my consecrated ones," those set apart to carry out God's will. Here the reference is probably to the Persians under Cyrus the Great (see note on v. 1). Cf. 10:5, where the Lord calls Assyria "the rod of my anger"; see also 45:1 and note. *wrath.* God's anger is no longer turned against Israel (see 5:25; 9:12,17,21; 10:4) but against her enemies (see vv. 5,9,13; cf. 30:27). God must punish sin, particularly arrogance (see v. 11).
13:4 *The LORD Almighty is mustering an army.* See note on 1Sa 1:3. The Hebrew for "army" is the singular form of the word for "Almighty." God is the head of the armies of Israel (1Sa 17:45), of angelic powers (1Ki 22:19; Lk 2:13) and, here, of the armies that will destroy Babylon.
13:5 *weapons of his wrath.* Assyria was the club in God's hand during Isaiah's day, and Babylon itself would later serve as God's weapon (see 10:5 and note).
13:6,9 *day of the LORD.* See note on 2:11,17,20.
13:6 *destruction.* Hebrew *shod*, forming a wordplay on "Almighty" (Hebrew *Shaddai*)—as also in Joel 1:15. See note on 5:7. For *Shaddai*, see note on Ge 17:1.
13:7 *hands will go limp.* Courage will fail. See Jer 6:24.
13:8 *Terror.* The Lord's warfare in behalf of his people usually brings panic to the enemy (see Ex 15:14–16; Jdg 7:22 and note). *pain ... labor.* The prophets often compare the suffering of judgment and war with the pain and anguish that frequently accompany childbirth (see 26:17; Jer 4:31; 6:24).
13:10 *stars ... sun ... moon.* Cosmic darkness is associated with the day of the Lord also in Joel 2:10,31; Rev 6:12–13. Cf. Jdg 5:20.
13:11 *arrogance ... pride.* Cf. 2:9,11,17; 5:15.
13:12 *scarcer ... rare.* War will reduce the male population drastically (see 4:1 and note). *Ophir.* Solomon imported large quantities of gold from this place (see 1Ki 9:28; 10:11 and notes).
13:13 *heavens tremble ... earth ... shake.* Thunderstorms and earthquakes often accompany the powerful presence of the Lord (see notes on v. 10; 34:4; Ex 19:16). Hail may also be involved (cf. 30:30; Jos 10:11).
13:14 *flee.* From parts of the Assyrian Empire.
13:16 *infants ... dashed to pieces.* Invading armies often slaughtered infants and children; thus there would be no future warriors, nor would there be a remnant through which

17 See, I will stir up[h] against them the Medes,[i]
who do not care for silver
and have no delight in gold.[j]
18 Their bows[k] will strike down the young men;[l]
they will have no mercy[m] on infants,
nor will they look with compassion on children.[n]
19 Babylon,[o] the jewel of kingdoms,[p]
the pride and glory[q] of the Babylonians,[a]
will be overthrown[r] by God
like Sodom and Gomorrah.[s]
20 She will never be inhabited[t]
or lived in through all generations;
there no nomads[u] will pitch their tents,
there no shepherds will rest their flocks.
21 But desert creatures[v] will lie there,
jackals[w] will fill her houses;
there the owls[x] will dwell,
and there the wild goats[y] will leap about.
22 Hyenas[z] will inhabit her strongholds,[a]
jackals[b] her luxurious palaces.
Her time is at hand,[c]
and her days will not be prolonged.[d]

14 The LORD will have compassion[e] on Jacob;
once again he will choose[f] Israel
and will settle them in their own land.[g]
Foreigners[h] will join them
and unite with the descendants of Jacob.
2 Nations will take them
and bring[i] them to their own place.
And Israel will take possession of the nations[j]
and make them male and female servants in the LORD's land.
They will make captives[k] of their captors
and rule over their oppressors.[l]

3 On the day the LORD gives you relief[m]
from your suffering and turmoil[n] and from
the harsh labor forced on you,[o] 4 you will
take up this taunt[p] against the king of Babylon:[q]

How the oppressor[r] has come to an end!
How his fury[b] has ended!
5 The LORD has broken the rod[s] of the wicked,[t]
the scepter[u] of the rulers,
6 which in anger struck down peoples[v]
with unceasing blows,
and in fury subdued[w] nations
with relentless aggression.[x]
7 All the lands are at rest and at peace;[y]
they break into singing.[z]
8 Even the junipers[a] and the cedars of Lebanon
gloat over you and say,

[a] 19 Or *Chaldeans* [b] 4 Dead Sea Scrolls, Septuagint and Syriac; the meaning of the word in the Masoretic Text is uncertain.

13:17 [h] Jer 50:9, 41; 51:1 [i] S ver 3 [j] 2Ki 18:14-16; Pr 6:34-35 **13:18** [k] S Ps 7:12; Isa 41:2; Jer 50:9, 14, 29 [l] S Dt 32:25; Jer 49:26; 50:30; 51:4 [m] Isa 47:6; Jer 6:23; 50:42 [n] S ver 16; Isa 14:22; 47:9 **13:19** [o] S ver 1 [p] Isa 47:5; Da 2:37-38 [q] Da 4:30 [r] S Ps 137:8; S Rev 14:8 [s] S Ge 19:25; Isa 1:9-10; Ro 9:29 **13:20** [t] Isa 14:23; 34:10-15; Jer 51:29, 37-43, 62 [u] 2Ch 17:11 **13:21** [v] S Ps 74:14; Rev 18:2 [w] Jer 14:6 [x] S Lev 11:16-18; S Dt 14:15-17 [y] Lev 17:7; 2Ch 11:15 **13:22** [z] Isa 34:14 [a] Isa 25:2; 32:14 [b] Isa 34:13; 35:7; 43:20; Jer 9:11; 49:33; 51:37; Mal 1:3 [c] Dt 32:35; Jer 48:16; 51:33 [d] Jer 50:39 **14:1** [e] Ps 102:13; Isa 49:10, 13; 54:7-8, 10; Jer 33:26; Zec 10:6 [f] Ge 18:19; 2Ch 6:6; Isa 41:8; 42:1; 44:1; 45:4; 49:7; 65:9, 22; Zec 1:17; 2:12; 3:2 [g] Jer 3:18; 16:15; 23:8 [h] S Ex 12:43; S Isa 11:10; Eze 47:22; Zec 8:22-23; Eph 2:12-19 **14:2** [i] S Isa 11:12; 60:9 [j] S Ps 49:14; Isa 26:15; 43:14; 49:7, 23; 54:3 [k] Ps 149:8; Isa 45:14; 49:25; 60:12; Jer 40:1 [l] Isa 60:14; 61:5; Jer 30:16; 49:2; Eze 39:10; Zep 3:19; Zec 2:9 **14:3** [m] S Isa 11:10 [n] S Job 3:17 [o] S Ex 1:14 **14:4** [p] Mic 2:4; Hab 2:6 [q] S Isa 13:1 [r] S Isa 9:4 **14:5** [s] S Isa 10:15 [t] S Ps 125:3 [u] S Ps 110:2 **14:6** [v] Isa 10:14 [w] S Ps 47:3 [x] S 2Ki 15:29; Isa 47:6; Hab 1:17 **14:7** [y] S Nu 6:26; Jer 50:34; Zec 1:11 [z] Ps 98:1; 126:1-3; Isa 12:6 **14:8** [a] S 1Ch 16:33; S Ps 65:13; Eze 31:16

the city (or country or people) might be revived (see Ps 137:8–9; Hos 10:14 and notes; Na 3:10). *wives violated.* Women also suffered greatly in war. With their husbands killed, they were often used as prostitutes (see note on Am 7:17).

13:17 *Medes.* Inhabited what is today northwestern Iran. There was conflict between Assyria and Media during the eighth century BC. Some, however, relate the fulfillment of this verse to the period when the Medes joined the Babylonians in defeating Assyria in 612–609 but later united with Cyrus to conquer Babylon in 539. See notes on vv. 19–20; Ezr 6:2 and note; Jer 51:11,28; Da 5:31; 6:28.

13:19 *pride and glory.* Babylon with its temples and palaces became a very beautiful city (see Da 4:29–30 and note on 4:30). The hanging gardens of Nebuchadnezzar were one of the seven wonders of the ancient world. In 4:2 the Hebrew words for "glory" and "pride" were used to describe the "Branch of the LORD." *Babylonians.* The Neo-Babylonian Empire of 612–539 BC was led by the Chaldean people of southern Babylonia (see NIV text note). Nabopolassar welded the tribes together c. 626, and his son Nebuchadnezzar became their most powerful ruler (605–562). *Sodom and Gomorrah.* Previously Isaiah compared Judah to these cities (see 1:9–10 and note).

13:20–22 See the similar description of the desolation of Edom in 34:10–15. Cf. Rev 18:2.

13:20 *never be inhabited.* Babylon was almost totally destroyed for the last time by the Persian king Xerxes I in 478 BC. Then, after the time of Alexander the Great in 330, the city was basically deserted, fell into complete disrepair and ruin and has remained that way ever since.

13:21 *wild goats.* This term is connected with "goat idols" in Lev 17:7; 2Ch 11:15. In Rev 18:2 fallen Babylon is described as a home for demons and evil spirits.

14:1 *will have compassion ... will settle them.* Babylon's fall will be linked with Israel's restoration. God's compassion on his people is the theme of chs. 40–66 (see 40:1 and note). *in their own land.* See 2:2–4; 11:10–12 and notes. *Foreigners will join them.* See 11:10; 56:6–7; 60:3 and note.

14:2 *Nations ... place.* See note on 5:26. *will take possession of the nations.* See note on 11:14.

14:3–21 However exalted (and almost divine) the king of Babylon may have thought himself (see vv. 12–14), he will go the way of all world rulers—down to the grave.

14:3 *suffering ... harsh labor forced on you.* The Babylonian captivity was much like Israel's experience in Egypt (see Ex 1:14 and note).

14:4 *taunt.* Cf. the taunts against Babylon in Rev 18. *king of Babylon.* Another title used by the king of Assyria at this time.

14:5 *rod ... scepter.* See 10:5 and note; see also 10:24.

14:7 *break into singing.* See 12:6 and note.

14:8 *junipers ... cedars.* Isaiah often personified nature. The trees along with the mountains burst into song in 44:23 (cf.

"Now that you have been laid low,
no one comes to cut us down."[b]
9 The realm of the dead[c] below is all astir
to meet you at your coming;
it rouses the spirits of the departed[d] to greet you—
all those who were leaders[e] in the world;
it makes them rise from their thrones—
all those who were kings over the nations.[f]
10 They will all respond,
they will say to you,
"You also have become weak, as we are;
you have become like us."[g]
11 All your pomp has been brought down to the grave,[h]
along with the noise of your harps;[i]
maggots are spread out beneath you
and worms[j] cover you.[k]

12 How you have fallen[l] from heaven,
morning star,[m] son of the dawn!
You have been cast down to the earth,
you who once laid low the nations![n]
13 You said in your heart,
"I will ascend[o] to the heavens;
I will raise my throne[p]
above the stars of God;
I will sit enthroned on the mount of assembly,[q]
on the utmost heights[r] of Mount Zaphon.[a]
14 I will ascend above the tops of the clouds;[s]
I will make myself like the Most High."[t]

15 But you are brought down[u] to the realm of the dead,[v]
to the depths[w] of the pit.[x]
16 Those who see you stare at you,
they ponder your fate:[y]
"Is this the man who shook[z] the earth
and made kingdoms tremble,
17 the man who made the world a wilderness,[a]
who overthrew[b] its cities
and would not let his captives go home?"[c]

18 All the kings of the nations lie in state,
each in his own tomb.[d]
19 But you are cast out[e] of your tomb
like a rejected branch;
you are covered with the slain,[f]
with those pierced by the sword,[g]
those who descend to the stones of the pit.[h]
Like a corpse trampled underfoot,
20 you will not join them in burial,[i]
for you have destroyed your land
and killed your people.

Let the offspring[j] of the wicked[k]
never be mentioned[l] again.
21 Prepare a place to slaughter his children[m]
for the sins of their ancestors;[n]
they are not to rise to inherit the land
and cover the earth with their cities.

[a] 13 Or *of the north*; Zaphon was the most sacred mountain of the Canaanites.

14:8 [b] S 2Ki 19:23; Isa 37:24 **14:9** [c] S Pr 30:16; Eze 32:21 [d] S Job 26:5 [e] Zec 10:3 [f] S Job 3:14 **14:10** [g] Eze 26:20; 32:21 **14:11** [h] S Nu 16:30; S Pr 30:16 [i] Isa 5:12; Eze 26:13; Am 6:5 [j] S Job 7:5; 24:20; Isa 51:8; 66:24 [k] S Job 21:26 **14:12** [l] Lk 10:18 [m] 2Pe 1:19; Rev 2:28; 8:10; 9:1 [n] Eze 26:17 **14:13** [o] Da 5:23; 8:10; Ob 1:4; Mt 11:23 [p] Eze 28:2; 2Th 2:4 [q] Ps 82:1 [r] Isa 37:24 **14:14** [s] S Job 20:6 [t] S Ge 3:5; S Nu 24:16; Isa 10:13; 47:8; Jer 50:29; 51:53; Da 11:36; 2Th 2:4 **14:15** [u] Isa 13:6; 45:7; 47:11; Jer 51:8,43 [v] S Job 21:13 [w] Mt 11:23; Lk 10:15 [x] S Ps 55:23; Eze 31:16; 32:23 **14:16** [y] Jer 50:23; Rev 18:9 [z] S Isa 2:19; 13:13; Joel 3:16; Hag 2:6,21 **14:17** [a] Isa 15:6; Joel 2:3 [b] Ps 52:7 [c] Ex 7:14; S 2Ki 15:29; Jer 50:33; Rev 18:18 **14:18** [d] Job 21:32 **14:19** [e] Isa 22:16-18; Jer 8:1; 36:30 [f] Isa 34:3 [g] S Isa 13:15 [h] Jer 41:7-9 **14:20** [i] S 1Ki 21:19 [j] S Job 18:19 [k] S Isa 1:4 [l] S Dt 32:26 **14:21** [m] S Nu 16:27 [n] S Ge 9:25; S Lev 26:39

55:12). *cedars of Lebanon.* These highly prized timbers were hauled away by the kings of Assyria and Babylonia for centuries (see notes on 2:13; 9:10).

14:9 *leaders.* Lit. "goats"; a goat often led a flock of sheep (see Jer 50:8 and note). In Zec 10:3 the term is parallel to "shepherds." *rise from their thrones.* Conditions among the dead are described in terms of their roles on earth. *kings over the nations.* See v. 18. Even the greatest and most powerful must go down to the "realm of the dead below."

14:11 *pomp ... grave.* Cf. 5:14. *brought down to the grave.* See v. 15 ("brought down to the realm of the dead"; the Hebrew is virtually identical). *noise of your harps.* Music was sometimes a sign of luxury and pleasure (see Am 6:5–6).

14:12–15 Some believe that Isaiah is giving a description of the fall of Satan (cf. Lk 10:18—where, however, Jesus is referring to an event contemporary with himself). But the passage clearly applies to the king of Babylon, who is later used as a type (prefiguration) of the "beast" who will lead the Babylon of the last days (see Rev 13:4; 17:3). Cf. the description of the king of Tyre in Eze 28.

14:12 *morning star.* The Hebrew for this expression is translated *lucifer* (lit. "light-bearer") in the Latin Vulgate, the origin of "Lucifer" in early English translations of this verse. For the true Morning Star, see Rev 22:16 (see also 2Pe 1:19; cf. Nu 24:17 and note).

14:13 *utmost heights.* Babylonia's king is destined for the "depths" of the pit (v. 15; the Hebrew word for "utmost heights" and "depths" is the same)—though he aspires to be "like the Most High" (v. 14). *Mount Zaphon.* See NIV text note; also called Mount Casius, located in northern Syria. The Canaanites considered it the dwelling and meeting place of the gods, much like Mount Olympus for the Greeks (see Ps 48:2 and note). Cf. Ps 82:1.

14:16–20a These verses seem to take place on earth, not in the realm of the dead (Sheol)—probably also vv. 9–10.

14:17 *captives go home.* Babylon, like Assyria, deported large segments of defeated populations to subdue the rebellious among them (see 2Ki 24:14–16).

14:18 *kings of the nations.* See note on v. 9.

14:19 *cast out of your tomb.* A proper burial was considered important. To have one's body simply discarded was a terrible fate. *corpse trampled.* See 5:25.

14:21 *slaughter his children.* A man's children, as well as his tombstone, were his memorial (cf. 2Sa 18:18). The king of Babylon would have neither (cf. 47:9).

22 "I will rise up[o] against them,"
declares the LORD Almighty.
"I will wipe out Babylon's name[p] and
survivors,
her offspring and descendants,[q]"
declares the LORD.
23 "I will turn her into a place for owls[r]
and into swampland;
I will sweep her with the broom of
destruction,[s]"
declares the LORD Almighty.[t]

24 The LORD Almighty has sworn,[u]

"Surely, as I have planned,[v] so it will be,
and as I have purposed, so it will
happen.[w]
25 I will crush the Assyrian[x] in my land;
on my mountains I will trample him
down.
His yoke[y] will be taken from my people,
and his burden removed from their
shoulders.[z]"

26 This is the plan[a] determined for the
whole world;
this is the hand[b] stretched out over
all nations.
27 For the LORD Almighty has purposed,[c]
and who can thwart him?
His hand[d] is stretched out, and who
can turn it back?[e]

A Prophecy Against the Philistines

28 This prophecy[f] came in the year[g] King
Ahaz[h] died:

29 Do not rejoice, all you Philistines,[i]
that the rod that struck you is broken;
from the root of that snake will spring
up a viper,[j]
its fruit will be a darting, venomous
serpent.[k]
30 The poorest of the poor will find
pasture,
and the needy[l] will lie down in
safety.[m]
But your root I will destroy by
famine;[n]
it will slay[o] your survivors.[p]

31 Wail,[q] you gate![r] Howl, you city!
Melt away, all you Philistines![s]
A cloud of smoke comes from the
north,[t]
and there is not a straggler in its
ranks.[u]
32 What answer shall be given
to the envoys[v] of that nation?
"The LORD has established Zion,[w]
and in her his afflicted people will
find refuge.[x]"

A Prophecy Against Moab

16:6-12pp — Jer 48:29-36

15 A prophecy[y] against Moab:[z]

Ar[a] in Moab is ruined,[b]
destroyed in a night!
Kir[c] in Moab is ruined,
destroyed in a night!

14:22 [o] S Ps 94:16 [p] S Job 18:17; Ps 109:13; Na 1:14 [q] 2Sa 18:18; 1Ki 14:10; Job 18:19; S Ps 9:6; S Isa 13:18 **14:23** [r] S Lev 11:16-18; Isa 34:11-15; Zep 2:14 [s] S Isa 10:3; Jer 25:12 [t] Jer 50:3; 51:62 **14:24** [u] Isa 45:23; 49:18; 54:9; 62:8 [v] Isa 19:12, 17; 23:8-9; 25:1; Da 4:35 [w] S Job 9:3; S Isa 7:7; 46:10-11; Eze 12:25; Ac 4:28 **14:25** [x] S Isa 10:5, 12; 37:36-38 [y] S Isa 9:4 [z] S Isa 10:27 **14:26** [a] Isa 23:9 [b] Ex 15:12; S Job 30:21 **14:27** [c] Jer 49:20 [d] S Ex 14:21 [e] S 2Ch 20:6; Isa 43:13; Da 4:35 **14:28** [f] S Isa 13:1 [g] S 2Ki 15:7 [h] S 2Ki 16:1 **14:29** [i] S Jos 13:3; S 2Ki 1:2; S 2Ch 26:6 [j] S Isa 11:8 [k] S Dt 8:15 **14:30** [l] Isa 3:15; 25:4 [m] S Isa 7:21-22 [n] Isa 8:21; 9:20; 51:19 [o] Jer 25:16; Zec 9:5-6 [p] Eze 25:15-17; Zep 2:5 **14:31** [q] S Isa 13:6 [r] S Isa 3:26 [s] S Ge 10:14 [t] Isa 41:25; Jer 1:14; 4:6; 6:1, 22; 10:22; 13:20; 25:9; 46:20, 24; 47:2; 50:41; Eze 32:30 [u] S Isa 5:27 **14:32** [v] Isa 37:9 [w] S Ps 51:18; 87:2, 5; Isa 2:2; 26:1; 28:16; 31:5; 33:5, 20; 44:28; 51:21; 54:11 [x] S Isa 4:6; Jas 2:5 **15:1** [y] S Isa 13:1 [z] Nu 22:3-6; S Dt 23:6; S Isa 11:14 [a] S Nu 21:15 [b] S Nu 17:12; Isa 25:12; 26:5; Jer 48:24, 41; 51:58 [c] S 2Ki 3:25

14:22 – 23 The taunt is extended to include Babylon itself (see note on vv. 3 – 21); fulfilled, at least partially, through Sennacherib's destruction of Babylon in 689 BC — ultimately by the Medes and Persians after they took Babylon in 539 (see also note on 13:20).
14:22 *survivors.* A remnant; Israel will survive through a remnant (see 10:20 – 22 and note; 11:11,16), but Babylonia will not.
14:23 See 13:20 – 22 and notes. *swampland.* Southern Babylonia, where the Chaldean tribes (see note on Ezr 5:12) once lived, was a region of marshlands.
14:24 – 27 See Zep 2:13 – 15 and notes; see also note on Isa 13:1 — 14:27.
14:24 *it will happen.* See 8:10 and note. God's sovereign purposes regarding Assyria and Babylonia will be carried out.
14:25 *I will crush the Assyrian in my land.* In 701 BC "the angel of the LORD ... put to death" 185,000 Assyrian soldiers (37:36). *yoke ... burden.* See 9:4 and note.
14:26 – 27 *hand stretched out.* See 9:12; 12:1 and notes. God's hand was stretched out against Egypt at the "Red Sea" (see Ex 15:12).
14:28 – 32 See Jer 47; Eze 25:15 – 17; Am 1:6 – 8; Zep 2:4 – 7 and notes.
14:28 *prophecy.* See note on 13:1. *the year.* Perhaps 715 BC. *King Ahaz died.* Cf. 6:1 and note. The occasion appears to be the Philistine revolt against Assyria while King Sargon (see 20:1) was too preoccupied with serious revolts elsewhere to give much attention to Canaan.
14:29 *Philistines.* See note on Ge 10:14. Philistine territory was vulnerable to attack by the great empires (Egypt and Assyria) since it lay along the main route from Egypt to Mesopotamia. *the rod.* Probably Sargon II of Assyria (see 20:1 and note). *is broken.* If the rod was Sargon, reference is to the threats to his empire by a series of revolts in Babylonia and Asia Minor. *root ... fruit.* A figure of speech that refers to the whole (tree) by speaking of its two extremes. After Sargon will come other Assyrian kings: Sennacherib, Esarhaddon, Ashurbanipal (see chart, p. 511).
14:30 *poor ... needy.* Israelites (see v. 32).
14:31 *Wail.* Cf. the similar reaction in 13:6; 15:2; 16:7; 23:1. *cloud of smoke.* The dust raised by the marching feet and the chariots of the Assyrians — who always invaded Canaan from the north. *not a straggler.* A longer description is found in 5:26 – 29.
14:32 *has established Zion.* God will protect Jerusalem from the Assyrians (compare 31:4 – 5 with 2:2; see note on v. 25).
15:1 — 16:14 See Jer 48; Eze 25:8 – 11; Am 2:1 – 3; Zep 2:8 – 11 and notes.
15:1 *prophecy.* See note on 13:1. *Moab.* A country east of the Dead Sea that was a perpetual enemy of Israel (see 25:10 and note; 2Ki 13:20). *ruined.* The same word describes Isaiah's feelings about himself in 6:5. The destruction of Moab probably resulted from an invasion by Sargon of Assyria in 715/713 BC. Cf. Jer 48:1 – 17. *Kir.* Probably Kir Hareseth (see note on 2Ki 3:25). Kir means "city."

2 Dibon[d] goes up to its temple,
to its high places[e] to weep;
Moab wails[f] over Nebo[g] and Medeba.
Every head is shaved[h]
and every beard cut off.[i]
3 In the streets they wear sackcloth;[j]
on the roofs[k] and in the public
squares[l]
they all wail,[m]
prostrate with weeping.[n]

Israelites bowing during the Assyrian siege of Lachish. The typical hairstyle and beards can be seen. It was common for a person to shave their head and beard when they were in mourning (Isa 15:2).

Caryn Reeder, courtesy of the British Muesum

15:2 [d] S Nu 21:30 [e] 1Ki 11:7; Isa 16:12; Jer 48:35 [f] S Isa 13:6; 65:14 [g] S Nu 32:38 [h] S Lev 13:40; S Job 1:20 [i] S 2Sa 10:4 **15:3** [j] S Isa 3:24 [k] S Jos 2:8 [l] Jer 48:38 [m] Isa 14:31; Jer 47:2 [n] ver 5; Isa 16:9; 22:4; La 2:11; Eze 7:18; Mic 1:8
15:4 [o] S Nu 21:25; S Jos 13:26 [p] S Nu 32:3 [q] S Nu 21:23 **15:5** [r] S ver 3 [s] Isa 16:11; Jer 48:31 [t] S Nu 21:29 [u] S Ge 13:10 [v] Jer 48:3,34 [w] Jer 4:20; 48:5 **15:6** [x] Isa 19:5-7; Jer 48:34 [y] Ps 37:2; Isa 16:8; 24:4, 7,11; 33:9; 34:4; 37:27; 40:7; 51:6, 12; Hos 4:3; Joel 1:12 [z] S Isa 14:17 [a] Jer 14:5 **15:7** [b] Isa 30:6; Jer 48:36 **15:8** [c] S Nu 21:16 **15:9** [d] S 2Ki 17:25 [e] Eze 25:8-11 **16:1** [f] S 2Ki 3:4 [g] S 2Ch 32:23 [h] S Jdg 1:36; Ob 3 *fn* [i] S Isa 10:32 **16:2** [j] Pr 27:8

4 Heshbon[o] and Elealeh[p] cry out,
their voices are heard all the way to
Jahaz.[q]
Therefore the armed men of Moab cry
out,
and their hearts are faint.
5 My heart cries out[r] over Moab;[s]
her fugitives[t] flee as far as Zoar,[u]
as far as Eglath Shelishiyah.
They go up the hill to Luhith,
weeping as they go;
on the road to Horonaim[v]
they lament their destruction.[w]
6 The waters of Nimrim are dried up[x]
and the grass is withered;[y]
the vegetation is gone[z]
and nothing green is left.[a]
7 So the wealth they have acquired[b] and
stored up
they carry away over the Ravine of
the Poplars.
8 Their outcry echoes along the border
of Moab;
their wailing reaches as far as Eglaim,
their lamentation as far as Beer[c] Elim.
9 The waters of Dimon[a] are full of blood,
but I will bring still more upon
Dimon[a] —
a lion[d] upon the fugitives of Moab[e]
and upon those who remain in the
land.

16 Send lambs[f] as tribute[g]
to the ruler of the land,
from Sela,[h] across the desert,
to the mount of Daughter Zion.[i]
2 Like fluttering birds
pushed from the nest,[j]

[a] 9 *Dimon*, a wordplay on *Dibon* (see verse 2), sounds like the Hebrew for *blood.*

15:2 *Dibon.* Located four miles north of the Arnon River and given to the tribe of Gad at one time (see Nu 32:34). *high places.* Shrines originally built on hilltops and usually associated with pagan worship (see note on 1Ki 3:2). *Nebo.* North of the Arnon River, perhaps near Mount Nebo (Dt 34:1; cf. note on Ezr 10:43). *Medeba.* About six miles south of Heshbon (see v. 4) and once captured by Israel from Sihon (see Nu 21:26,30). *head is shaved ... beard cut off.* Characteristic of intense mourning (Jer 48:37). See photo above.
15:3 *sackcloth.* The coarse garb of mourners (see note on Rev 11:3). *roofs.* Perhaps chosen because incense was sometimes offered there (see Jer 19:13 and note). See photo, p. 1140.
15:4 *Heshbon.* Located about 18 miles east of the northern tip of the Dead Sea. See also Jer 48:34. It was King Sihon's capital before Israel captured it (see Nu 21:23–26). *Elealeh.* About a mile north of Heshbon and always mentioned with it. *Jahaz.* Just north of the Arnon River and about 20 miles from Heshbon (Nu 21:23; Jer 48:34).
15:5 *Zoar.* Probably located near the southern end of the Dead Sea. Lot fled there from Sodom (see Ge 14:2; 19:23,30).
15:6 *waters of Nimrim.* Perhaps to be identified with the Wadi en-Numeirah, ten miles from the southern end of the Dead Sea (cf. Jer 48:34).
15:7 *Ravine of the Poplars.* Probably at the border between Moab and Edom (see v. 8).
15:8 *Eglaim.* Perhaps near the northern border of Moab. *Beer Elim.* Hebrew *be'er* means "well" (cf. Nu 21:16). This site may have been close to the southern border.
15:9 *waters of Dimon ... blood.* The Hebrew for "blood" (*dam*) sounds like "Dimon." This is probably also a wordplay on the name "Dibon" (v. 2; see note there). Many Moabites will die in the conflict. *lion.* A reference to either the Assyrian army (cf. 5:29; Jer 50:17) or actual lions (cf. 13:21–22).
16:1 *lambs as tribute.* As King Mesha sent 100,000 lambs to King Ahab of Israel each year (see 2Ki 3:4 and note), so now proud Moab, which has often oppressed Israel, is advised in her crisis to submit to the king in Jerusalem. *Sela.* The naturally fortified capital of the Edomites, south of the Dead Sea, situated on a rocky plateau that towers 1,000 feet above the nearby Petra (cf. 42:11). The name means "cliff." The tribute would be sent around the southern end of the Dead Sea. *Daughter Zion.* A personification of Jerusalem (see note on 2Ki 19:21).
16:2 *fords of the Arnon.* The women were fleeing south (see note on Jos 12:1), away from the northern invader.

Sarcophagus depicting mourning women wearing sackcloth. "In the streets they wear sackcloth; on the roofs and in the public squares they all wail, prostrate with weeping" (Isa 15:3).

Library of Congress, LC-DIG-matpc-03493

so are the women of Moab[k]
at the fords[l] of the Arnon.[m]

3 "Make up your mind," Moab says.
"Render a decision.
Make your shadow like night —
at high noon.
Hide the fugitives,[n]
do not betray the refugees.
4 Let the Moabite fugitives stay with you;
be their shelter[o] from the destroyer."

The oppressor[p] will come to an end,
and destruction will cease;[q]
the aggressor will vanish from the land.
5 In love a throne[r] will be established;[s]
in faithfulness a man will sit on it —
one from the house[a] of David[t] —
one who in judging seeks justice[u]
and speeds the cause of righteousness.

6 We have heard of Moab's[v] pride[w] —
how great is her arrogance! —
of her conceit, her pride and her insolence;
but her boasts are empty.
7 Therefore the Moabites wail,[x]
they wail together for Moab.
Lament and grieve
for the raisin cakes[y] of Kir Hareseth.[z]
8 The fields of Heshbon[a] wither,[b]
the vines of Sibmah[c] also.
The rulers of the nations
have trampled down the choicest vines,[d]
which once reached Jazer[e]
and spread toward the desert.
Their shoots spread out[f]
and went as far as the sea.[b][g]
9 So I weep,[h] as Jazer weeps,
for the vines of Sibmah.
Heshbon and Elealeh,[i]
I drench you with tears![j]
The shouts of joy[k] over your ripened fruit
and over your harvests[l] have been stilled.
10 Joy and gladness are taken away from the orchards;[m]
no one sings or shouts[n] in the vineyards;
no one treads[o] out wine at the presses,[p]
for I have put an end to the shouting.
11 My heart laments for Moab[q] like a harp,[r]
my inmost being[s] for Kir Hareseth.
12 When Moab appears at her high place,[t]
she only wears herself out;
when she goes to her shrine[u] to pray,
it is to no avail.[v]

16:2 [k] Nu 21:29 [l] Jdg 12:5 [m] Nu 21:13-14; Jer 48:20
16:3 [n] S 1Ki 18:4
16:4 [o] Isa 58:7 [p] S Isa 9:4 [q] Isa 2:2-4
16:5 [r] S 1Sa 13:14; Da 7:14; Mic 4:7 [s] S Pr 20:28 [t] S Isa 7:2; Lk 1:32 [u] S Isa 9:7
16:6 [v] Jer 25:21; Eze 25:8; Am 2:1; Zep 2:8 [w] S Lev 26:19; S Job 20:6; Jer 49:16; Ob 1:3; Zep 2:10
16:7 [x] S Isa 13:6; Jer 48:20; 49:3 [y] S 1Ch 16:3 [z] S 2Ki 3:25
16:8 [a] S Nu 21:25 [b] S Isa 15:6 [c] S Nu 32:3 [d] S Isa 5:2 [e] S Nu 21:32 [f] S Job 8:16 [g] Ps 80:11
16:9 [h] S Isa 15:3; Eze 27:31 [i] S Nu 32:3 [j] S Job 7:3 [k] S Ezr 3:13 [l] Jer 40:12
16:10 [m] Isa 24:7-8 [n] Jer 25:30 [o] S Jdg 9:27 [p] S Job 24:11; S Isa 5:2
16:11 [q] S Isa 15:5 [r] S Job 30:31 [s] Isa 63:15; Hos 11:8; Php 2:1
16:12 [t] 1Ki 11:7 [u] S Isa 15:2 [v] S 1Ki 18:29; Ps 115:4-7; Isa 44:17-18; 1Co 8:4

[a] 5 Hebrew *tent* [b] 8 Probably the Dead Sea

16:3 *Hide the fugitives.* The Moabites are asking Judah for refuge (contrast Ru 1:1; 1Sa 22:3 – 4 and note on 22:3). See map, p. 1142.
16:4 *destroyer.* Probably Assyria (see notes on 15:1; 33:1). *oppressor.* Moab.
16:5 *house of David.* See 9:7; 2Sa 7:11 – 16; 1Ki 12:19; Am 9:11 and notes. "House" equals "dynasty" (see note on 7:2). *in judging seeks justice.* See 11:2 – 4 and notes. The Messiah is again in view.
16:6 *Moab's pride.* Though a small nation, Moab is proud and defiant like Assyria and Babylonia. Cf. 10:12; 14:13; 25:11; Jer 48:42.
16:7 *Kir Hareseth.* See note on 15:1. The four cities in vv. 7 – 8 appear in inverted (*a-b-c-d/d-c-b-a*) order in vv. 9 – 11.
16:8 *Heshbon.* See note on 15:4. *Sibmah.* Perhaps three miles west of Heshbon. See Jer 48:32. *choicest vines.* The poet shifts to a metaphor, comparing Moab to a vineyard (cf. 5:1 – 7 and notes). He returns to a literal description again in v. 10. *Jazer.* Possibly located about 15 miles north of the Dead Sea. *desert.* On the eastern edge of Moab. *shoots spread out.* This is figurative language, as in Ps 80:11, where Israel is the vine. *sea.* See NIV text note.
16:9 – 11 *I . . . I . . . I . . . My . . . my.* The Lord (and/or Isaiah) weeps and laments over the destruction brought on proud Moab to humble her.
16:9 *Elealeh.* See note on 15:4.
16:10 *treads out wine.* The grapes were trampled on, and the juice flowed into the wine vat (see note on 5:2; cf. Jer 48:33; Am 9:13; Hag 2:16 and note).
16:11 Cf. Jer 48:36.
16:12 *high place.* See 15:2 and note. *pray . . . to no avail.* Moab's god, Chemosh, was a mere idol (see 44:17 – 20 and notes; 1Ki 11:7).

13 This is the word the LORD has already
spoken concerning Moab. 14 But now the
LORD says: “Within three years,[w] as a servant bound by contract[x] would count
them,[y] Moab’s splendor and all her many
people will be despised,[z] and her survivors
will be very few and feeble.”[a]

A Prophecy Against Damascus

17 A prophecy[b] against Damascus:[c]

“See, Damascus will no longer be a city
but will become a heap of ruins.[d]
2 The cities of Aroer[e] will be deserted
and left to flocks,[f] which will lie down,[g]
with no one to make them afraid.[h]
3 The fortified[i] city will disappear from
Ephraim,
and royal power from Damascus;
the remnant of Aram will be
like the glory[j] of the Israelites,”[k]
declares the LORD Almighty.

4 “In that day[l] the glory[m] of Jacob will
fade;
the fat of his body will waste[n] away.
5 It will be as when reapers harvest the
standing grain,
gathering[o] the grain in their arms—
as when someone gleans heads of grain[p]
in the Valley of Rephaim.[q]
6 Yet some gleanings will remain,[r]
as when an olive tree is beaten,[s]
leaving two or three olives on the
topmost branches,
four or five on the fruitful boughs,”
declares the LORD, the God
of Israel.

7 In that day[t] people will look[u] to their
Maker[v]
and turn their eyes to the Holy One[w]
of Israel.
8 They will not look to the altars,[x]
the work of their hands,[y]
and they will have no regard for the
Asherah poles[a][z]
and the incense altars their fingers[a]
have made.

9 In that day their strong cities, which
they left because of the Israelites, will be
like places abandoned to thickets and undergrowth.[b] And all will be desolation.

10 You have forgotten[c] God your Savior;[d]
you have not remembered the Rock,[e]
your fortress.[f]
Therefore, though you set out the
finest plants
and plant imported vines,[g]
11 though on the day you set them out,
you make them grow,
and on the morning[h] when you plant
them, you bring them to bud,
yet the harvest[i] will be as nothing[j]
in the day of disease and incurable[k]
pain.[l]

12 Woe to the many nations that rage[m]—
they rage like the raging sea![n]

[a] *8* That is, wooden symbols of the goddess Asherah

16:14 [w] Isa 20:3; 37:30 [x] S Lev 25:50 [y] S Lev 19:13 [z] Isa 25:10; Jer 48:42 [a] Isa 21:17 **17:1** [b] Isa 13:1 [c] S Ge 14:15; Ac 9:2 [d] S Dt 13:16; S Isa 25:2 **17:2** [e] S 2Ki 10:33 [f] S Isa 5:17; 7:21; Eze 25:5 [g] Isa 27:10 [h] S Lev 26:6; Jer 7:33; Mic 4:4 **17:3** [i] Isa 25:2, 12; Hos 10:14 [j] ver 4; Isa 21:16; Hos 9:11 [k] Isa 7:8, 16; 8:4 **17:4** [l] S Isa 2:11 [m] S ver 3 [n] S Isa 10:16 **17:5** [o] ver 11; Isa 33:4; Jer 51:33; Joel 3:13; Mt 13:30 [p] Job 24:24 [q] S Jos 17:15; S 1Ch 11:15 **17:6** [r] S Dt 4:27; S Isa 10:19; S 24:13 [s] ver 11; Isa 27:12 **17:7** [t] S Isa 2:11 [u] S Isa 9:13; S 10:20 [v] S Ps 95:6 [w] S Isa 12:6 **17:8** [x] S Lev 26:30 [y] S 2Ch 32:19; Isa 2:18, 20; 30:22; 46:6; Rev 9:20 [z] S Jdg 3:7; S 2Ki 17:10 [a] Isa 2:8 **17:9** [b] S Isa 7:19 **17:10** [c] S Dt 6:12; 8:11; Ps 50:22; 106:21; Isa 51:13; 57:11; Jer 2:32; 3:21; 13:25; 18:15; Eze 22:12; 23:35; Hos 8:14; 13:6 [d] S Isa 12:2; S Lk 1:47 [e] S Ge 49:24 [f] S Ps 18:2 [g] S Isa 5:7 **17:11** [h] Ps 90:6 [i] S ver 5 [j] S Lev 26:20; Hos 8:7; Joel 1:11; Hag 1:6 [k] Jer 10:19; 30:12 [l] S Dt 28:39; S Job 4:8 **17:12** [m] ver 13; Isa 41:11 [n] S Ps 18:4; Lk 21:25

16:13–14 An epilogue to 15:1—16:12.
16:14 *Within three years.* Other signs that have a three-year limit are given in 20:3; 37:30; see also notes on 7:14,16. Moab’s three years were over by c. 715 BC (see note on 15:1). *servant bound by contract.* Cf. 21:16–17, where the prophecy against Kedar follows the pattern of this verse.
17:1–14 See Jer 49:23–27; Am 1:3–5 and notes.
17:1 *prophecy.* See note on 13:1. *Damascus.* The capital of Aram (Syria), located northeast of Mount Hermon on strategic trade routes between Mesopotamia, Egypt and Arabia. Since the time of David, the Arameans of Damascus were frequent enemies of Israel (see 2Sa 8:5; 1Ki 22:31). *will become a heap of ruins.* See notes on v. 3; 7:4.
17:2 *Aroer.* About 14 miles east of the Dead Sea on the Arnon River. It marked the southern boundary of Aram’s sphere of control (see 2Ki 10:32–33 and notes).
17:3 *Ephraim.* The northern kingdom (see note on 7:2) is mentioned here because of its alliance with Damascus against Assyria (see note on 7:1). *royal power.* In 732 BC Tiglath-Pileser III captured Damascus and made it an Assyrian province. Many of the cities of Israel were also captured (see note on 9:1). *remnant of Aram ... like the glory of the Israelites.* Like Israel, Aram will be reduced to a remnant.
17:4–11 The prophet shifts from Damascus to Israel (likely the northern kingdom)—a shift prepared for at the end of v. 3. This association of judgment on Damascus and Israel reflects the same linkage as that in ch. 7.
17:4,7,9 *In that day.* See notes on 2:11,17,20; 10:20,27.
17:5 *harvest the standing grain.* “Harvest” here signifies a time of judgment (see Joel 3:13 and note). *Valley of Rephaim.* A fertile area west and southwest of Jerusalem (Jos 15:8) and the scene of Philistine raids (1Ch 14:9).
17:7–8 Cf. 2:20; 10:20.
17:7 *Holy One of Israel.* See note on 1:4.
17:8 *altars.* Probably altars for Baal (cf. 1Ki 16:32). *Asherah poles.* See notes on Ex 34:13; Jdg 2:13; see also NIV text note here. *incense altars.* Associated with high places in Lev 26:30 and with altars for Baal in 2Ch 34:4.
17:9 *they.* Perhaps the Canaanites, whose religious practices are referred to in v. 8. *thickets and undergrowth.* Cf. 7:23–25.
17:10 *Rock.* See 26:4; 30:29; 44:8; Ge 49:24 and note; Dt 32:4,15,18; Ps 18:2 and note; 19:14. *vines.* Probably representing the people of Israel (see 5:7; 18:5; 37:30–31; see also notes on Ps 80:8–16 and 80:8–11).
17:11 *disease and incurable pain.* Brought by the Assyrian invasions.
17:12–14 The same sequence of a powerful invader that is quickly cut down occurs in 10:28–34. Both passages may refer to Sennacherib’s invasion of Judah in 701 BC (see 37:36–37 and notes). But it is more likely that the prophet here speaks more generally of Israel’s experience of the world of nations as a perpetual threat to her existence.
17:12 *raging sea.* Assyria is called “floodwaters” in 8:7 (see notes on 8:7–8).

Woe to the peoples who roar[o]—
they roar like the roaring of great
waters![p]
13 Although the peoples roar[q] like the roar
of surging waters,
when he rebukes[r] them they flee[s] far
away,
driven before the wind like chaff[t] on
the hills,
like tumbleweed before a gale.[u]
14 In the evening, sudden[v] terror![w]
Before the morning, they are gone![x]
This is the portion of those who loot us,
the lot of those who plunder us.

A Prophecy Against Cush

18 Woe[y] to the land of whirring
wings[a]
along the rivers of Cush,[b][z]
2 which sends envoys[a] by sea
in papyrus[b] boats over the water.
Go, swift messengers,
to a people tall and smooth-skinned,[c]
to a people feared far and wide,
an aggressive[d] nation of strange
speech,
whose land is divided by rivers.[e]

3 All you people of the world,[f]
you who live on the earth,
when a banner[g] is raised on the
mountains,
you will see it,
and when a trumpet[h] sounds,
you will hear it.
4 This is what the LORD says to me:
"I will remain quiet[i] and will look on
from my dwelling place,[j]

17:12 [o]S Ps 46:6; Isa 8:9 [p]Isa 8:7 **17:13** [q]S Ps 46:3 [r]S Dt 28:20; S Ps 9:5 [s]S Ps 68:1; S Isa 13:14 [t]S Job 13:25; S Isa 2:22; 41:2, 15-16; Da 2:35 [u]Job 21:18; S Ps 65:7 **17:14** [v]Isa 29:5; 30:13; 47:11; 48:3 [w]Isa 33:18; 54:14 [x]S 2Ki 19:35 **18:1** [y]Isa 5:8 [z]S Ge 10:6; S Ps 68:31; S Eze 29:10 **18:2** [a]Ob 1:1 [b]Ex 2:3; Job 9:26 [c]S Ge 41:14 [d]S Ge 10:8-9; S 2Ch 12:3 [e]ver 7 **18:3** [f]S Ps 33:8 [g]S Ps 60:4; Isa 5:26; 11:10; 13:2; 31:9; Jer 4:21 [h]S Jos 6:20; S Jdg 3:27 **18:4** [i]Isa 62:1; 64:12 [j]Isa 26:21; Hos 5:15; Mic 1:3

[a] *1* Or *of locusts* [b] *1* That is, the upper Nile region

17:13 *chaff ... tumbleweed.* Symbolic of the enemy also in 29:5; 41:15-16; Ps 83:13.
18:1-7 See Zep 2:12 and note.
18:1 *whirring wings.* Either a reference to insects (perhaps locusts) or a figurative description of the armies of Cush (see 7:18-19). *Cush.* Nubia or ancient Ethiopia (not to be confused with modern Ethiopia, which is located farther to the southeast), south of Egypt (see NIV text note). In 715 BC a Cushite named Shabako gained control of Egypt and founded the Twenty-Fifth Dynasty.
18:2 *sea.* Perhaps the Nile River (cf. 19:5; Na 3:8, where the same Hebrew word is translated "river"). *papyrus boats.* See note on Ex 2:3. *Go, swift messengers.* With the message contained in vv. 3-6. *people tall and smooth-skinned.* See v. 7; probably the peoples of Cush and Egypt. Unlike Semites, they were clean-shaven (see note on Ge 41:14). *rivers.* The Nile and its tributaries.
18:3 *All you people of the world.* All the nations arrayed against God's people Israel (see 17:12-14 and note). *banner.* See 5:26 and note. *trumpet.* Used to summon troops (see, e.g., Jdg 3:27; 6:34; 2Sa 2:28).
18:4 *remain quiet.* In the face of the hostility of the nations,

NATIONS AND CITIES MENTIONED IN ISAIAH

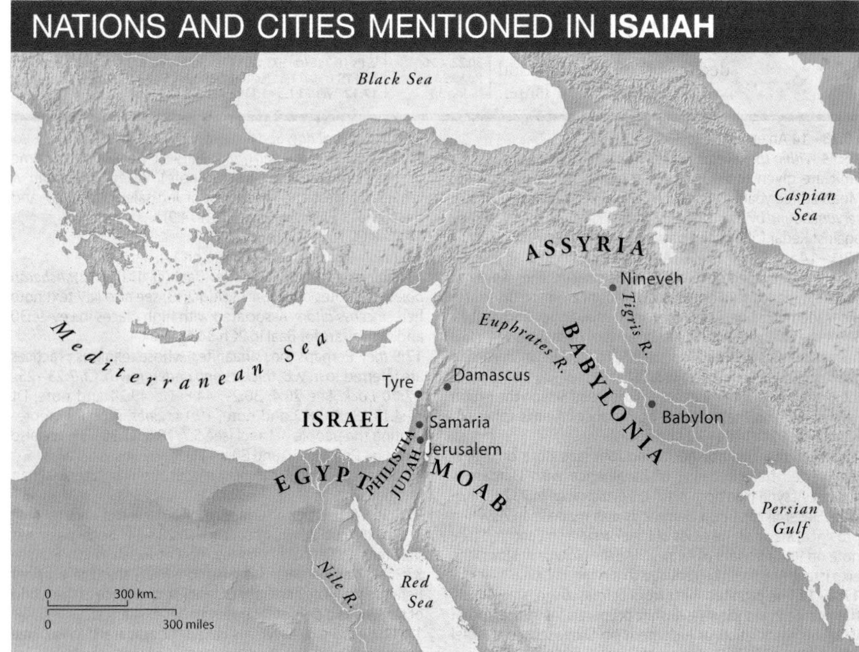

like shimmering heat in the sunshine,[k]
like a cloud of dew[l] in the heat of harvest."
5 For, before the harvest, when the blossom is gone
and the flower becomes a ripening grape,
he will cut off[m] the shoots with pruning knives,
and cut down and take away the spreading branches.[n]
6 They will all be left to the mountain birds of prey[o]
and to the wild animals;[p]
the birds will feed on them all summer,
the wild animals all winter.

7 At that time gifts[q] will be brought to
the LORD Almighty

from a people tall and smooth-skinned,[r]
from a people feared[s] far and wide,
an aggressive nation of strange speech,
whose land is divided by rivers[t]—

the gifts will be brought to Mount Zion,
the place of the Name of the LORD Almighty.[u]

A Prophecy Against Egypt

19 A prophecy[v] against Egypt:[w]

See, the LORD rides on a swift cloud[x]
and is coming to Egypt.
The idols of Egypt tremble before him,
and the hearts of the Egyptians melt[y] with fear.

2 "I will stir up Egyptian against Egyptian—
brother will fight against brother,[z]
neighbor against neighbor,
city against city,
kingdom against kingdom.[a]

18:4 [k]S Jdg 5:31; S Ps 18:12; Hab 3:4 [l]2Sa 1:21; S Ps 133:3; Isa 26:19; Hos 14:5 **18:5** [m]S Isa 10:33 [n]Isa 17:10-11; Eze 17:6 **18:6** [o]S Isa 8:8 [p]Isa 37:36; 56:9; Jer 7:33; Eze 32:4; 39:17 **18:7** [q]S 2Ch 9:24; S Isa 60:7 [r]S Ge 41:14 [s]Hab 1:7 [t]ver 2 [u]Ps 68:31 **19:1** [v]Isa 13:1 [w]S Ex 12:12; Isa 20:3; S Jer 44:3; Joel 3:19 [x]S Dt 10:14; S 2Sa 22:10; S Rev 1:7 [y]S Jos 2:11 **19:2** [z]S Jdg 7:22; S 12:4; Mt 10:21,36 [a]S 2Ch 15:6; 20:23; Mt 24:7; Mk 13:8; Lk 21:10

19:3 [b]Ps 18:45 [c]ver 11; S Job 5:12 [d]1Ch 10:13 [e]S Lev 19:31; Isa 47:13; Da 2:2, 10; 3:8; 5:7 **19:4** [f]Isa 20:4; Jer 46:26; Eze 29:19; 32:11 **19:5** [g]Isa 44:27; 50:2; Jer 50:38; 51:36 [h]S 2Sa 14:14 **19:6** [i]Ex 7:18 [j]Isa 37:25; Eze 30:12 [k]S Ge 41:2; S Job 8:11 [l]Isa 15:6 **19:7** [m]Nu 11:5 [n]Dt 29:23; Isa 23:3

3 The Egyptians will lose heart,[b]
and I will bring their plans[c] to nothing;[d]
they will consult the idols and the spirits of the dead,
the mediums and the spiritists.[e]
4 I will hand the Egyptians over
to the power of a cruel master,
and a fierce king[f] will rule over them,"
declares the Lord, the LORD Almighty.

5 The waters of the river will dry up,[g]
and the riverbed will be parched and dry.[h]
6 The canals will stink;[i]
the streams of Egypt will dwindle and dry up.[j]
The reeds[k] and rushes will wither,[l]
7 also the plants[m] along the Nile,
at the mouth of the river.
Every sown field[n] along the Nile
will become parched, will blow away and be no more.[o]
8 The fishermen[p] will groan and lament,
all who cast hooks[q] into the Nile;
those who throw nets on the water
will pine away.
9 Those who work with combed flax[r]
will despair,
the weavers of fine linen[s] will lose hope.
10 The workers in cloth will be dejected,
and all the wage earners will be sick at heart.

11 The officials of Zoan[t] are nothing but fools;
the wise counselors[u] of Pharaoh give senseless advice.[v]
How can you say to Pharaoh,
"I am one of the wise men,[w]
a disciple of the ancient kings"?

[o]Zec 10:11 **19:8** [p]Nu 11:5; Eze 47:10 [q]Am 4:2; Hab 1:15 **19:9** [r]S Jos 2:6 [s]Pr 7:16; Eze 16:10; 27:7 **19:11** [t]S Nu 13:22 [u]S Ge 41:37 [v]S ver 3 [w]S 1Ki 4:30; Ac 7:22

---

the Lord will not act immediately; but when they are in the full growth of summer (v. 5), he will cut them down.
18:6 *birds of prey ... wild animals.* Cf. 56:9; see Jer 7:33; Eze 32:4; 39:17–20; Rev 19:17 and notes.
18:7 See v. 2 and note. *gifts.* According to 2Ch 32:23 gifts were brought to Hezekiah after Sennacherib's death. The Moabites were asked to send tribute to Mount Zion in 16:1 (cf. 45:14; Zep 3:10). *place of the Name.* See Dt 12:5 and note.
19:1—20:6 See Jer 46; Eze 29–32 and notes.
19:1 *prophecy.* See note on 13:1. *rides on a swift cloud.* A metaphor used also in Ps 68:4 (see note there); 104:3; cf. Mt 26:64. *idols ... tremble.* See Jer 50:2 and note. God had also previously judged Egypt's false gods during the ten plagues (see Ex 12:12 and note). *hearts ... melt.* See 13:7.
19:2 *Egyptian against Egyptian.* Cf. 9:21. The Libyan dynasty clashed with the Cushites (see note on 18:1) and with the Saites of Dynasty 24.
19:3 *consult ... spiritists.* Israel also did so in desperate times (see 8:19 and note). See photo, p. 1144.
19:4 *cruel master.* The king of Assyria (see 20:4). Esarhaddon conquered Egypt in 670 BC.
19:5 *river will dry up.* The Nile was the lifeline of Egypt; its annual flooding provided essential water and produced the only fertile soil there.
19:6 *canals.* For irrigation.
19:7 *sown field.* Egypt's crops were normally abundant, and some were exported.
19:8 *The fishermen.* Fish were usually plentiful (see Nu 11:5 and note).
19:9 *work with ... flax.* Large amounts of water were needed to process flax. *fine linen.* A well-known Egyptian export (see Pr 7:16 and note).
19:11 *Zoan.* A city (possibly Tanis) in the northeastern part of the Nile delta, familiar to the Israelites during their years in Egypt (see Nu 13:22; Ps 78:12,43). It was the northern capital for the Twenty-Fifth Dynasty (see note on 18:1). *wise men.* See v. 12. Egypt was famous for its wise men (see 1Ki 4:30 and note).

[12]Where are your wise men[x] now?
Let them show you and make known
what the LORD Almighty
has planned[y] against Egypt.
[13]The officials of Zoan[z] have become
fools,
the leaders of Memphis[a] are
deceived;
the cornerstones[b] of her peoples
have led Egypt astray.
[14]The LORD has poured into them
a spirit of dizziness;[c]
they make Egypt stagger in all that she
does,
as a drunkard staggers[d] around in his
vomit.
[15]There is nothing Egypt can do —
head or tail, palm branch or reed.[e]

[16]In that day[f] the Egyptians will become
weaklings.[g] They will shudder with fear[h] at
the uplifted hand[i] that the LORD Almighty
raises against them. [17]And the land of Judah will bring terror to the Egyptians; everyone to whom Judah is mentioned will
be terrified,[j] because of what the LORD Almighty is planning[k] against them.
[18]In that day[l] five cities[m] in Egypt will
speak the language of Canaan and swear
allegiance[n] to the LORD Almighty. One of
them will be called the City of the Sun.[a][o]
[19]In that day[p] there will be an altar[q] to
the LORD in the heart of Egypt,[r] and a monument[s] to the LORD at its border. [20]It will be
a sign and witness[t] to the LORD Almighty
in the land of Egypt. When they cry out
to the LORD because of their oppressors,
he will send them a savior[u] and defender,
and he will rescue[v] them. [21]So the LORD
will make himself known to the Egyptians,
and in that day they will acknowledge[w] the
LORD. They will worship[x] with sacrifices

An ancient Egyptian temple wall at Thebes painted with a large depiction of the jackal-headed god Anubis — associated with mummification and the afterlife. Isaiah 19 prophesies against Egypt: "The idols of Egypt tremble before him" (v. 1), and "the Egyptians will lose heart, and I will bring their plans to nothing; they will consult the idols and the spirits of the dead" (v. 3).

19:12 [x]1Co 1:20 [y]S Isa 14:24; Ro 9:17
19:13 [z]S Nu 13:22 [a]Jer 2:16; 44:1; 46:14, 19; Eze 30:13, 16; Hos 9:6 [b]S Ps 118:22
19:14 [c]S Pr 12:8; Mt 17:17 [d]S Ps 107:27
19:15 [e]S Isa 9:14
19:16 [f]Isa 2:17; 11:10 [g]Jer 50:37; 51:30; Na 3:13 [h]S Dt 2:25; Heb 10:31 [i]S Isa 11:15
19:17 [j]S Ge 35:5 [k]S Isa 14:24
19:18 [l]S Isa 10:20 [m]Jer 44:1 [n]Ps 22:27; S 63:11; Isa 48:1; Jer 4:2; Zep 3:9 [o]Isa 17:1; 24:12; 32:19; *fn* Jer 43:13
19:19 [p]S Isa 10:20 [q]S Jos 22:10 [r]S Ps 68:31 [s]S Ge 28:18
19:20 [t]S Ge 21:30 [u]S Dt 28:29; S Jdg 2:18; S Isa 25:9 [v]Isa 49:24-26
19:21 [w]S Isa 11:9; S 43:10 [x]ver 19; S Ge 27:29; S Ps 86:9; Isa 56:7; 60:7; Mal 1:11

[a] *18* Some manuscripts of the Masoretic Text, Dead Sea Scrolls, Symmachus and Vulgate; most manuscripts of the Masoretic Text *City of Destruction*

19:13 *Memphis.* An important city 15 miles south of the delta that was the capital during the Old Kingdom (c. 2686 – 2160 BC). *cornerstones.* Prophets and priests, as well as political leaders (see 9:15 – 16 and note).
19:14 *a drunkard staggers.* Cf. Israel's leaders in 28:7 – 8.
19:15 *head or tail, palm branch or reed.* Egypt's leaders. The same two pairs are used of Israel's leaders in 9:14 – 15 (see note on 9:14).
19:16 – 25 A chain of four announcements of coming events associated with "that day": (1) An act of divine judgment will cause Egypt to "shudder with fear" (v. 16) and be in terror of Judah (vv. 16 – 17). (2) "Five cities" in Egypt will "swear allegiance" to the Lord (v. 18). (3) Because of a divine act of deliverance and healing in Egypt, an altar will be erected in Egypt where Egyptians will offer sacrifices to the Lord (vv. 19 – 22). (4) Egypt, Assyria and Israel will be linked into one people of the Lord (vv. 23 – 25). The prophet looks well beyond the present realities in which the world powers do not acknowledge the true God and proudly pursue their own destinies, running roughshod over the people of the Lord. He foresees a series of divine acts that will bring about the conversion of the nations.
19:16,18 – 19,23 – 24 *In that day.* The coming day of the Lord (see 10:20,27 and note; cf. 11:10 – 11).
19:16 *shudder with fear.* Like the people of Jericho (Jos 2:9,11). *hand … the LORD … raises.* See 14:26 – 27 and note.
19:17 *land of Judah.* The Egyptians will somehow recognize (perhaps through court contacts with Hezekiah) that it is the God of Judah who has brought judgment upon them.
19:18 *five.* Perhaps in the sense of "many." *speak the language of Canaan.* Either a symbolic reference to Egypt's allegiance to the Lord (see vv. 21 – 22,25) or a literal reference to Jews living in Egypt. After the fall of Jerusalem in 586 BC, many Jews fled to Egypt (see Jer 44:1 and note). *City of the Sun.* Heliopolis, city of the sun-god; it was destroyed by Nebuchadnezzar (see Jer 43:13 and note; see also NIV text note here).
19:19 *altar.* The reference appears to be to a conversion to the Lord of a significant number of Egyptians.
19:20 *sign and witness.* Cf. the purpose of the altar built near the Jordan River by the Transjordan tribes in Jos 22:26 – 27. *oppressors … savior.* The language of the book of Judges (see Jdg 2:18 and note). It is uncertain who this savior and defender is, but the prophet may well have in mind the promised Son of the house of David (see 11:1 – 10 and notes).
19:21 *make himself known.* Cf. Ex 7:5. *worship with sacrifices.* Offerings of foreigners are also mentioned in 56:7; 60:7 (cf. Zec 14:16 – 19 and note on 14:16).

and grain offerings; they will make vows
to the LORD and keep them.[y] 22 The LORD
will strike[z] Egypt with a plague;[a] he will
strike them and heal them. They will turn[b]
to the LORD, and he will respond to their
pleas and heal[c] them.
23 In that day[d] there will be a highway[e]
from Egypt to Assyria.[f] The Assyrians will
go to Egypt and the Egyptians to Assyria. The Egyptians and Assyrians will worship[g] together. 24 In that day[h] Israel will be
the third, along with Egypt and Assyria,[i]
a blessing[aj] on the earth. 25 The LORD Almighty will bless[k] them, saying, "Blessed
be Egypt my people,[l] Assyria my handiwork,[m] and Israel my inheritance.[n]"

A Prophecy Against Egypt and Cush

20 In the year that the supreme commander,[o] sent by Sargon king of Assyria, came to Ashdod[p] and attacked and
captured it— 2 at that time the LORD spoke
through Isaiah son of Amoz.[q] He said to
him, "Take off the sackcloth[r] from your
body and the sandals[s] from your feet."
And he did so, going around stripped[t] and
barefoot.[u]
3 Then the LORD said, "Just as my servant[v] Isaiah has gone stripped and barefoot for three years,[w] as a sign[x] and portent[y] against Egypt[z] and Cush,[ba] 4 so the
king[b] of Assyria will lead away stripped[c]
and barefoot the Egyptian captives[d] and
Cushite[e] exiles, young and old, with buttocks bared[f]—to Egypt's shame.[g] 5 Those
who trusted[h] in Cush[i] and boasted in
Egypt[j] will be dismayed and put to shame.[k]
6 In that day[l] the people who live on this
coast will say, 'See what has happened[m]
to those we relied on,[n] those we fled to for
help[o] and deliverance from the king of Assyria! How then can we escape?[p]' "

A Prophecy Against Babylon

21 A prophecy[q] against the Desert[r] by
the Sea:

Like whirlwinds[s] sweeping through the
southland,[t]
an invader comes from the desert,
from a land of terror.

2 A dire[u] vision has been shown to me:
The traitor betrays,[v] the looter takes
loot.
Elam,[w] attack! Media,[x] lay siege!
I will bring to an end all the
groaning she caused.

[a] *24* Or *Assyria, whose names will be used in blessings* (see Gen. 48:20); or *Assyria, who will be seen by others as blessed* [b] *3* That is, the upper Nile region; also in verse 5

19:21 [y]S Nu 30:2; S Dt 23:21 **19:22** [z]Ex 12:23; Heb 12:11 [a]Ex 11:10 [b]Isa 45:14; Eze 33:11; Hos 6:1; 10:12; 12:6; 14:1; Joel 2:13 [c]S Dt 32:39 **19:23** [d]S ver 16, 24; Isa 20:6 [e]S Isa 11:16 [f]Mic 7:12 [g]S Ge 27:29; Isa 2:3; 27:13; 66:23 **19:24** [h]S ver 23 [i]S Isa 11:11 [j]S Ge 12:2 **19:25** [k]S Ge 12:3; Eph 2:11-14 [l]Ps 87:4; S 100:3 [m]Isa 29:23; 43:7; 45:11; 60:21; 64:8; Eph 2:10 [n]S Ex 34:9; Jer 30:22; Hos 2:23 **20:1** [o]2Ki 18:17 [p]S Jos 11:22; S 13:3 **20:2** [q]S Isa 13:1 [r]2Ki 1:8; S Isa 3:24; Zec 13:4; Mt 3:4 [s]Eze 24:17,23 [t]S 1Sa 19:24 [u]Eze 4:1-12; Mic 1:8 **20:3** [v]Isa 22:20; 41:8-9; 42:1; 43:10; 49:3, 5-7; 50:10; 52:13; 53:11; Jer 7:25; Hag 2:23; Zec 4:14 [w]S Isa 16:14 [x]S Ex 3:12; S Isa 8:18; 37:30; 38:7; Ac 21:11 [y]S Dt 28:46 [z]S Isa 19:1 [a]ver 5; S Ge 10:6; Isa 37:9; 43:3 **20:4** [b]S Isa 19:4 [c]S Job 12:17 [d]Jer 46:19; Na 3:10 [e]Isa 18:1; Zep 2:12 [f]S Isa 3:24 [g]Isa 47:3; Jer 13:22,26; Na 3:5 **20:5** [h]S Isa 8:12 [i]S ver 3 [j]S 2Ki 18:21; S Isa 30:5 [k]Eze 29:16 **20:6** [l]Isa 2:11; S 19:23 [m]S 2Ki 18:21 [n]Jer 46:25 [o]S Isa 10:3 [p]Jer 30:15-17; 31:2; Mt 23:33; 1Th 5:3; Heb 2:3 **21:1** [q]S Isa 13:1 [r]Isa 13:21; Jer 50:12; 51:43 [s]S Job 1:19 [t]Da 11:40; Zec 9:14 **21:2** [u]Ps 60:3 [v]Isa 24:16; 33:1 [w]S Ge 10:22; Isa 22:6 [x]S Isa 13:3; Jer 25:25; 51:28

19:22 *strike Egypt with a plague.* Oppression (see v. 20) and plague were two common forms of divine affliction. Contrast the results of the plague on the firstborn in Ex 12:23. *turn ... heal.* Cf. 6:10; here parallel to sending Egypt a "savior and defender" (v. 20). Earlier a hardhearted pharaoh had not turned to the Lord (Ex 9:34–35).

19:23 *highway.* Cf. the highway to Jerusalem in 11:16; 35:8–10 (see notes there). For centuries Egyptians and Assyrians had fought each other (see 20:4), but in the future they would be linked in a bond of friendship sealed by their common allegiance to the Lord (cf. 25:3). *worship together.* This description of peace and of unity in worship is similar to 2:2–4 (see note there; see also note on 19:21).

19:25 *will bless them.* A fulfillment of Ge 12:3 (see note on Ge 12:2–3). *Egypt my people.* Such a universal vision seems possible for Isaiah only in the light of what has been said about the "shoot ... from the stump of Jesse" (11:1; see 11:1–10). Cf. 45:14; Eph 2:11–13.

20:1–6 An epilogue to chs. 18–19, as 16:13–14 is to 15:1—16:12.

20:1 *the year.* Probably 712 BC. *Sargon.* Sargon II, who reigned 721–705 BC (see chart, p. 511; see also photos, pp. 507, 1113). He is mentioned by name only here in the OT. *Ashdod.* One of the five Philistine cities (see map, p. 359), Ashdod was located near the Mediterranean Sea about 18 miles northeast of Gaza. The city rebelled against Assyria in 713 BC under King Azuri. In 1963 three fragments of at least one Assyrian monument commemorating Sargon's victory (in 711) were discovered at Ashdod.

20:2 *sackcloth.* Normally the garment of mourners (see note on Rev 11:3); sometimes the garb of prophets (see 2Ki 1:8; Zec 13:4–6 and notes). *stripped and barefoot.* See vv. 3–4; cf. 2Ch 28:15; Mic 1:8 and note.

20:3 *my servant.* See note on 41:8–9. *three years.* See 16:14 and note. *sign and portent.* See 8:18; see also 7:3,14 and notes. The prophet Ezekiel's behavior also had symbolic significance (Eze 24:24,27; cf. Zec 3:8). *Egypt and Cush.* See 18:1; 19:1 and notes.

20:5 *trusted in Cush ... Egypt.* After Assyria conquered the northern kingdom of Israel in 722–721 BC, King Hezekiah of Judah was under great pressure to make an alliance with Egypt. Isaiah urgently warned against such a policy (cf. 30:1–2; 31:1 and notes).

21:1 *prophecy.* See note on 13:1. *Desert.* The coming judgment would eventually turn Babylon (see v. 9) into a wasteland (cf. 13:20–22). *the Sea.* Refers either to the Persian Gulf, which was southeast of Babylon, or to the plain laid down by the Euphrates and Tigris Rivers and their tributaries. *whirlwinds ... desert.* The desert sometimes spawns powerful winds (see Hos 13:15). *an invader.* Lit. "it"; it is not clear whether "comes from the desert, from a land of terror" is ascribed to an invader or continues the description of the whirlwinds.

21:2 *Elam.* See note on 11:11; see also Jer 49:34–39. The Elamites were perpetual enemies of Assyria and Babylonia. Much later, they were part of the Persian army that conquered Babylon under Cyrus in 539 BC. *Media.* See note on 13:17. *she.* Babylon.

[3]At this my body is racked with
pain,[y]
pangs seize me, like those of
a woman in labor;[z]
I am staggered by what I hear,
I am bewildered[a] by what I
see.
[4]My heart[b] falters,
fear makes me tremble;[c]
the twilight I longed for
has become a horror[d] to me.

[5]They set the tables,
they spread the rugs,
they eat, they drink![e]
Get up, you officers,
oil the shields![f]

[6]This is what the Lord says to me:

"Go, post a lookout[g]
and have him report what he
sees.
[7]When he sees chariots[h]
with teams of horses,
riders on donkeys
or riders on camels,[i]
let him be alert,
fully alert."

[8]And the lookout[a][j] shouted,

"Day after day, my lord, I stand on the
watchtower;
every night I stay at my post.
[9]Look, here comes a man in a chariot[k]
with a team of horses.
And he gives back the answer:
'Babylon[l] has fallen,[m] has fallen!
All the images of its gods[n]
lie shattered[o] on the ground!' "

[10]My people who are crushed on the
threshing floor,[p]
I tell you what I have heard
from the LORD Almighty,
from the God of Israel.

Watchtower at Masada. Lookouts would be posted at the watchtower to warn a village of an enemy attack (Isa 21:6,8).

Todd Bolen/www.BiblePlaces.com

A Prophecy Against Edom

[11]A prophecy against Dumah[b]:[q]

Someone calls to me from Seir,[r]
"Watchman, what is left of the night?
Watchman, what is left of the night?"
[12]The watchman replies,
"Morning is coming, but also the
night.
If you would ask, then ask;
and come back yet again."

A Prophecy Against Arabia

[13]A prophecy[s] against Arabia:[t]

You caravans of Dedanites,[u]
who camp in the thickets of Arabia,

[a] 8 Dead Sea Scrolls and Syriac; Masoretic Text *A lion*
[b] 11 *Dumah*, a wordplay on *Edom*, means *silence* or *stillness*.

21:3 [y]S Job 14:22 [z]S Ge 3:16; Ps 48:6; Isa 26:17; 37:3; Jer 30:6; 48:41; 49:22; Jn 16:21 [a]Da 7:28; 8:27; 10:16 **21:4** [b]Isa 7:4; 35:4 [c]S Isa 13:8; Da 5:9 [d]S Ps 55:5 **21:5** [e]Isa 5:12; 22:2, 13; 23:7; 24:8; 32:13; Jer 25:16, 27; 51:39, 57; Da 5:2 [f]2Sa 1:21; 1Ki 10:16-17; Jer 46:3; 51:11 **21:6** [g]S 2Ki 9:17 **21:7** [h]ver 9 [i]S Jdg 6:5 **21:8** [j]Mic 7:7; Hab 2:1 **21:9** [k]ver 7 [l]S Isa 13:1; 47:1, 5; S Rev 14:8 [m]Isa 47:11; Jer 51:8; Da 5:30 [n]S Lev 26:30; Isa 46:1; Jer 50:2; 51:44 [o]S Isa 2:18 **21:10** [p]Isa 27:12; 28:27, 28; 41:15; Jer 51:33; Mic 4:13; Hab 3:12; Mt 3:12 **21:11** [q]S Ge 25:14; S Isa 34:11 [r]Ge 32:3 **21:13** [s]Isa 13:1 [t]S 2Ch 9:14 [u]S Ge 10:7; S 25:3

21:3 *racked with pain, pangs seize me.* See note on 16:9–11; see also Daniel's reaction to visions in Da 8:27; 10:16–17.
21:4 *twilight.* Perhaps the end of the Babylonian Empire (see note on v. 12). *a horror to me.* The devastation is beyond even what he had desired.
21:5 *eat ... drink.* With the kind of confident assurance reflected in Belshazzar's feast (see Da 5:1). *Get up ... !* Rhetorically the prophet, who has seen in a vision the coming attack on Babylon, calls on the officers of Babylon to prepare. *oil the shields.* See note on 2Sa 1:21.
21:6 *Go, post a lookout.* Probably on the walls of Jerusalem.
21:7 *chariots ... donkeys ... camels.* Bearing messengers from afar.
21:9 *Babylon ... has fallen!* See 13:19. Babylon fell in 689 BC and again in 539. These words were adapted by John in Rev 14:8; 18:2. *its gods lie shattered.* The fall of a kingdom meant the disgrace of its gods (cf. 46:1–2; 1Sa 5:3–7 and notes).
21:10 *crushed.* Judah would be punished by the Babylonians and taken into captivity (see 39:5–7 and notes). *on the threshing floor.* Threshing was a common metaphor for judgment or destruction from war (see Am 1:3 and note).
21:11–12 See Jer 49:7–22; Eze 25:12–14; Am 1:11–12; Obadiah and notes.
21:11 *prophecy.* See note on 13:1. *Dumah.* See NIV text note. *Seir.* A synonym for Edom (Ge 32:3), homeland of Esau's descendants, south of the Dead Sea. Edom is dealt with more extensively in 34:5–15 (see notes there; cf. 63:1 and note).
21:12 *Morning ... but also the night.* Perhaps meaning that the long night of Assyrian oppression is almost over, but only a short "morning" will precede Babylonian domination (see v. 4 and note).
21:13–17 See Jer 49:28–33 and notes.
21:13 *prophecy.* See note on 13:1. *Dedanites.* An Arabian tribe whose merchant activities are mentioned also in Eze 27:20; 38:13. *thickets.* The caravans had to hide from the invader (cf. Jdg 5:6). The Assyrians began to attack the Arabs in 732 BC,

14 bring water for the thirsty;
you who live in Tema,[v]
bring food for the fugitives.
15 They flee[w] from the sword,[x]
from the drawn sword,
from the bent bow
and from the heat of battle.

16 This is what the Lord says to me:
"Within one year, as a servant bound by
contract[y] would count it, all the splendor[z]
of Kedar[a] will come to an end. 17 The survivors of the archers, the warriors of Kedar,
will be few.[b]" The LORD, the God of Israel,
has spoken.[c]

A Prophecy About Jerusalem

22 A prophecy[d] against the Valley[e] of Vision:[f]

What troubles you now,
that you have all gone up on the roofs,[g]
2 you town so full of commotion,
you city of tumult[h] and revelry?[i]
Your slain[j] were not killed by the sword,[k]
nor did they die in battle.
3 All your leaders have fled[l] together;
they have been captured[m] without using the bow.
All you who were caught were taken prisoner together,
having fled while the enemy was still far away.
4 Therefore I said, "Turn away from me;
let me weep[n] bitterly.
Do not try to console me
over the destruction of my people."[o]

5 The Lord, the LORD Almighty, has a day[p]
of tumult and trampling[q] and terror[r]
in the Valley of Vision,[s]
a day of battering down walls[t]
and of crying out to the mountains.
6 Elam[u] takes up the quiver,[v]
with her charioteers and horses;
Kir[w] uncovers the shield.
7 Your choicest valleys[x] are full of chariots,
and horsemen are posted at the city gates;[y]
8 The Lord stripped away the defenses of Judah,
and you looked in that day[z]
to the weapons[a] in the Palace of the Forest.[b]
9 You saw that the walls of the City of David
were broken through[c] in many places;
you stored up water
in the Lower Pool.[d]
10 You counted the buildings in Jerusalem
and tore down houses[e] to strengthen the wall.[f]
11 You built a reservoir between the two walls[g]
for the water of the Old Pool,[h]
but you did not look to the One who made it,
or have regard[i] for the One who planned[j] it long ago.

21:14 [v]S Ge 25:15 **21:15** [w]S Isa 13:14 [x]Isa 31:8 **21:16** [y]S Lev 25:50 [z]S Isa 17:3 [a]S Ge 25:13 **21:17** [b]S Dt 4:27; S Isa 10:19 [c]S Isa 1:20; 16:14 **22:1** [d]Isa 13:1 [e]Ps 125:2; Jer 21:13; Joel 3:2,12, 14 [f]S Isa 1:1 [g]S Jos 2:8; Jer 48:38 **22:2** [h]Eze 22:5 [i]S Isa 5:14; S 21:5 [j]S Isa 10:4 [k]S 2Ki 25:3 **22:3** [l]S Isa 13:14 [m]S 2Ki 25:6 **22:4** [n]S Isa 15:3; S La 1:16; Eze 21:6; Lk 19:41 [o]Jer 9:1 **22:5** [p]S Isa 2:12 [q]S Job 40:12; S Ps 108:13 [r]S 2Sa 22:43; Isa 13:3; Jer 30:7; La 1:5; Eze 8:17-18; 9:9-10; Joel 2:31; Am 5:18-20; Zep 1:15 [s]S Isa 1:1 [t]Ne 6:15; S Ps 89:40; Isa 5:5; Jer 39:8; Eze 13:14 **22:6** [u]S Isa 21:2 [v]Ps 46:9; Jer 49:35; 51:56 [w]S 2Ki 16:9 **22:7** [x]Jos 15:8 [y]S 2Ch 32:1-2 **22:8** [z]S Isa 2:12 [a]S 2Ch 32:5 [b]S 1Ki 7:2 **22:9** [c]S Ne 1:3 [d]S 2Ki 18:17; S 2Ch 32:4 **22:10** [e]Jer 33:4 [f]S 2Ch 32:5 **22:11** [g]2Ki 25:4; 2Ch 32:5; Jer 39:4 [h]S 2Ch 32:4 [i]S 1Sa 12:24 [j]2Ki 19:25

and the Babylonians did the same under Nebuchadnezzar (see Jer 25:17,23–24).
21:14 *Tema.* An oasis in northern Arabia about 400 miles southwest of Babylon (cf. Job 6:19; Jer 25:23 and last notation on map, p. 1423).
21:15 *sword ... bow.* The simple bows of the Arabs were ineffective against the swords and composite bows of Assyria.
21:16 *servant bound by contract.* See 16:14 and note. *splendor.* See 14:11; 16:14. *Kedar.* The home of nomadic tribes in the Arabian Desert. Kedar was known for its flocks (60:7; Eze 27:21). Nebuchadnezzar defeated the people of Kedar (Jer 49:28–29; cf. Jer 2:10 and note).
21:17 *survivors ... will be few.* Cf. 10:19; 16:14; 17:6.
22:1–13 The notes on this prophecy assume that it refers primarily to the final Babylonian siege of Jerusalem in 588–586 BC. But it is also possible that the primary reference is to the siege by the Assyrian king Sennacherib in 701.
22:1 *prophecy.* See note on 13:1. *Valley of Vision.* A valley where God revealed himself in visions, probably one of the valleys near Jerusalem (see note on v. 7). See also v. 5. *roofs.* See 15:3 and note.
22:2 *tumult and revelry.* See v. 13; 5:11–13 and note; 32:13. Jerusalem is behaving just like Babylon (see 21:5 and note; cf. 23:7). *not killed by the sword.* Perhaps a reference to death from disease and famine when the Babylonians besieged Jerusalem in 586 BC.
22:3 *leaders have fled.* King Zedekiah and his army fled Jerusalem but were captured near Jericho (see 2Ki 25:4–6).
22:4 *my people.* Lit. "the daughter of my people" (see note on 2Ki 19:21).
22:5 *has a day.* See 2:12 and note on 2:11,17,20. Also cf. "in that day" in v. 8 and "on that day" in v. 12. *tumult.* A fulfillment of the curse of Dt 28:20.
22:6 *Elam.* See note on 11:11; see also Jer 49:34–39. Elamites probably fought in the Babylonian army. *takes up the quiver.* See Jer 49:35. *Kir.* Perhaps another name for Media (see 21:2; Am 1:5 and note).
22:7 *choicest valleys.* The Kidron Valley lay east of Jerusalem, the Hinnom Valley to the south and west (see map, p. 748).
22:8 *Palace of the Forest.* Built by King Solomon out of cedars from Lebanon (see 1Ki 7:2–6 and notes; 10:17,21).
22:9 *City of David.* See 2Sa 5:6–7,9 and notes; cf. Isa 29:1. *Lower Pool.* Probably the same as the "Old Pool" of v. 11. Hezekiah made a pool and a tunnel as a precaution against Sennacherib's invasion (see 2Ki 20:20 and note). The "Upper Pool" is mentioned in 7:3; 36:2.
22:10 *strengthen the wall.* Cf. Hezekiah's preparations in 2Ch 32:5.
22:11 *did not look to the One.* In 31:1 those who look to horses and chariots rather than to God are similarly condemned.

12 The Lord, the LORD Almighty,
called you on that day[k]
to weep[l] and to wail,
to tear out your hair[m] and put on
sackcloth.[n]
13 But see, there is joy and revelry,[o]
slaughtering of cattle and killing of
sheep,
eating of meat and drinking of wine![p]
"Let us eat and drink," you say,
"for tomorrow we die!"[q]

14 The LORD Almighty has revealed this
in my hearing:[r] "Till your dying day this
sin will not be atoned[s] for," says the Lord,
the LORD Almighty.

15 This is what the Lord, the LORD Almighty, says:

"Go, say to this steward,
to Shebna[t] the palace[u]
administrator:[v]
16 What are you doing here and who gave
you permission
to cut out a grave[w] for yourself[x] here,
hewing your grave on the height
and chiseling your resting place in
the rock?

17 "Beware, the LORD is about to take firm
hold of you
and hurl[y] you away, you mighty man.
18 He will roll you up tightly like a ball
and throw[z] you into a large country.
There you will die
and there the chariots[a] you were so
proud of
will become a disgrace to your
master's house.

19 I will depose you from your office,
and you will be ousted[b] from your
position.[c]

20 "In that day[d] I will summon my servant,[e] Eliakim[f] son of Hilkiah. 21 I will clothe
him with your robe and fasten your sash[g]
around him and hand your authority[h] over
to him. He will be a father to those who
live in Jerusalem and to the people of Judah. 22 I will place on his shoulder[i] the key[j]
to the house of David;[k] what he opens no
one can shut, and what he shuts no one
can open.[l] 23 I will drive him like a peg[m]
into a firm place;[n] he will become a seat[a] of
honor[o] for the house of his father. 24 All the
glory of his family will hang on him: its offspring and offshoots — all its lesser vessels,
from the bowls to all the jars.

25 "In that day,[p]" declares the LORD Almighty, "the peg[q] driven into the firm
place will give way; it will be sheared off
and will fall, and the load hanging on it
will be cut down." The LORD has spoken.[r]

A Prophecy Against Tyre

23 A prophecy against Tyre:[s]

Wail,[t] you ships[u] of Tarshish![v]
For Tyre is destroyed[w]
and left without house or harbor.
From the land of Cyprus
word has come to them.

22:12 [k] S Isa 2:12 [l] Joel 1:9; 2:17 [m] S Lev 13:40; Mic 1:16 [n] S Isa 3:24 **22:13** [o] S Isa 21:5 [p] S 1Sa 25:36; Ecc 8:15; Isa 5:22; 28:7-8; 56:12; Lk 17:26-29 [q] 1Co 15:32* **22:14** [r] Isa 5:9 [s] S 1Sa 2:25; Isa 13:11; 26:21; 30:13-14; Eze 24:13 **22:15** [t] S 2Ki 6:30; S 18:18 [u] S Ge 41:40 [v] ver 21 **22:16** [w] Mt 27:60 [x] S Ge 50:5; S Nu 32:42 **22:17** [y] Jer 10:18; 13:18; 22:26 **22:18** [z] S Job 18:11; Isa 14:19; 17:13 [a] S Ge 41:43 **22:19** [b] S 1Sa 2:7; S Ps 52:5 [c] Lk 16:3 **22:20** [d] ver 25 [e] S Isa 20:3 [f] S 2Ki 18:18; S Isa 36:3 **22:21** [g] S Isa 5:27 [h] ver 15 **22:22** [i] Isa 9:6 [j] 1Ch 9:27; Mt 16:19; Rev 3:7 [k] S Isa 7:2 [l] S Job 12:14 **22:23** [m] ver 25; Eze 15:3; Zec 10:4

[a] 23 Or *throne*

[n] S Ezr 9:8; S Job 6:25 [o] S 1Sa 2:7-8; S Job 36:7 **22:25** [p] ver 20 [q] S ver 23 [r] Isa 46:11; Mic 4:4 **23:1** [s] Jos 19:29; 1Ki 5:1; Jer 47:4; Joel 3:4-8; Am 1:9-10 [t] S Isa 13:6 [u] S 1Ki 10:22 [v] S Ge 10:4; Isa 2:16 *fn* [w] S Ge 1:2; Eze 26:4

22:12 *tear out your hair.* The hair was either torn out or shaved off (cf. Jer 16:6; Eze 27:31).
22:13 *joy and revelry.* The same Hebrew phrase is translated "gladness and joy" in 35:10; 51:11, passages depicting great hope in connection with restoration. But this was a time to mourn (Ecc 3:4). See note on v. 2. *Let us eat … we die.* Quoted by Paul in 1Co 15:32 to underscore the utter futility of life without a belief in resurrection from the dead. Cf. Lk 12:19; cf. also Ecc 8:15 and note.
22:15 *Shebna.* Apparently a foreigner, possibly Egyptian; a contemporary of King Hezekiah. *palace administrator.* A position second only to the king (see note on v. 21; cf. 36:3; 1Ki 4:6; 2Ki 15:5).
22:16 *cut out a grave.* One's place of burial was considered very important, and Shebna coveted a tomb worthy of a king (cf. 2Ch 16:14).
22:17 *hurl you away.* Cf. Jer 22:24 – 26 and notes.
22:18 *There you will die.* Apparently without an honorable burial (see note on 14:19). *chariots.* A sign of high office (see Ge 41:43).
22:20 *In that day.* When the Lord acts in judgment (see vv. 17 – 19). *my servant.* See note on 20:3. *Eliakim.* See 36:3,11,22; 37:2.
22:21 *hand your authority over to him.* By 701 BC (see 36:3) Eliakim had replaced Shebna, who was demoted to "secretary."
22:22 Quoted in part in Rev 3:7 (see note there). The mention of "father" (v. 21) and of the responsibility "on his shoulder" recalls the words about the Messiah in 9:6. *key to the house of David.* Cf. Rev 3:7 and note; the authority delegated to him by the king, who belongs to David's dynasty — perhaps controlling entrance into the royal palace. Cf. the "keys of the kingdom" given to Peter (Mt 16:19; see note there).
22:23 *peg.* Normally the Hebrew for this word refers to a tent peg, but here to a peg driven into wood (see Eze 15:3; Zec 10:4 and note). *seat of honor.* Cf. 1Sa 2:8.
22:25 *In that day.* Another (unspecified) day when the Lord will come in judgment. *peg … will give way.* Eliakim, like Shebna, will eventually fall from power.
23:1 – 18 See Eze 26:1 — 28:19; Am 1:9 – 10 and notes.
23:1 *prophecy.* See note on 13:1. *Tyre.* The main seaport along the Phoenician coast, about 35 miles north of Mount Carmel. Part of the city was built on two rocky islands about half a mile from the shore. King Hiram of Tyre supplied cedars and craftsmen for the temple (see 1Ki 5:8 – 9) and sailors for Solomon's commercial fleet (1Ki 9:27). *Wail, you ships.* See v. 14. *ships of Tarshish.* Trading ships (see note on 2:16). *destroyed.* Fulfilled through Assyria, Nebuchadnezzar and Alexander. Nebuchadnezzar captured the mainland city in 572 BC (see Eze 26:7 – 11), but the island fortress was not taken until Alexander the Great destroyed it in 332 (cf. Eze 26:3 – 5; see Zec 9:3 and note). *Cyprus.* An island in the eastern Mediterranean that had close ties with Tyre (see Eze 27:6 and note).

2 Be silent,[x] you people of the island
and you merchants[y] of Sidon,[z]
whom the seafarers have enriched.
3 On the great waters
came the grain of the Shihor;[a]
the harvest of the Nile[ab] was the
revenue of Tyre,[c]
and she became the marketplace of
the nations.

4 Be ashamed, Sidon,[d] and you fortress
of the sea,
for the sea has spoken:
"I have neither been in labor nor given
birth;[e]
I have neither reared sons nor
brought up daughters."
5 When word comes to Egypt,
they will be in anguish[f] at the report
from Tyre.[g]

6 Cross over to Tarshish;[h]
wail, you people of the island.
7 Is this your city of revelry,[i]
the old, old city,
whose feet have taken her
to settle in far-off lands?
8 Who planned this against Tyre,
the bestower of crowns,
whose merchants[j] are princes,
whose traders[k] are renowned in the
earth?
9 The LORD Almighty planned[l] it,
to bring down[m] her pride in all her
splendor
and to humble[n] all who are
renowned[o] on the earth.

10 Till[b] your land as they do along the Nile,
Daughter Tarshish,
for you no longer have a harbor.
11 The LORD has stretched out his hand[p]
over the sea
and made its kingdoms tremble.[q]

23:2 [x]S Job 2:13 [y]Eze 27:5-24 [z]Jdg 1:31 **23:3** [a]S Ge 41:5 [b]S Isa 19:7 [c]S Ps 83:7 **23:4** [d]S Ge 10:15, 19 [e]Isa 54:1 **23:5** [f]Eze 30:9 [g]Eze 26:17-18 **23:6** [h]S Ge 10:4 **23:7** [i]ver 12; S Isa 5:14; S 21:5; 32:13; Eze 26:13 **23:8** [j]Na 3:16 [k]Eze 28:5; Rev 18:23 **23:9** [l]S Isa 14:24 [m]S Job 40:11 [n]S Isa 13:11 [o]Isa 5:13; 9:15; Eze 27:3 **23:11** [p]S Ex 14:21 [q]S Ps 46:6 [r]ver 14; Isa 25:2; Eze 26:4; Zec 9:3-4 **23:12** [s]S ver 7; Rev 18:22 [t]Isa 37:22; 47:1; Jer 14:17; 46:11; La 2:13; Zep 3:14; Zec 2:10 [u]S Ge 10:4 **23:13** [v]Isa 43:14; Jer 51:12 [w]Isa 10:5 [x]S Ps 74:14; Isa 18:6 [y]S 2Ki 25:1 [z]Isa 10:7 **23:14** [a]S 1Ki 10:22 [b]S Ge 10:4; Isa 2:16 *fn* [c]S ver 11 **23:15** [d]Jer 25:22 [e]S Ps 90:10 **23:16** [f]Pr 7:10 **23:17** [g]S Ps 90:10

He has given an order concerning
Phoenicia
that her fortresses be destroyed.[r]
12 He said, "No more of your reveling,[s]
Virgin Daughter[t] Sidon, now
crushed!

"Up, cross over to Cyprus;[u]
even there you will find no rest."
13 Look at the land of the Babylonians,[cv]
this people that is now of no
account!
The Assyrians[w] have made it
a place for desert creatures;[x]
they raised up their siege towers,[y]
they stripped its fortresses bare
and turned it into a ruin.[z]

14 Wail, you ships[a] of Tarshish;[b]
your fortress is destroyed![c]

15 At that time Tyre[d] will be forgotten for
seventy years,[e] the span of a king's life.
But at the end of these seventy years, it
will happen to Tyre as in the song of the
prostitute:

16 "Take up a harp, walk through the city,
you forgotten prostitute;[f]
play the harp well, sing many a song,
so that you will be remembered."

17 At the end of seventy years,[g] the LORD
will deal with Tyre. She will return to her
lucrative prostitution[h] and will ply her
trade with all the kingdoms on the face of
the earth.[i] 18 Yet her profit and her earnings
will be set apart for the LORD;[j] they will not

[a] *2,3* Masoretic Text; Dead Sea Scrolls *Sidon, / who cross over the sea; / your envoys* [3]*are on the great waters. / The grain of the Shihor, / the harvest of the Nile,*
[b] *10* Dead Sea Scrolls and some Septuagint manuscripts; Masoretic Text *Go through* [c] *13* Or *Chaldeans*

[h]Dt 23:17-18; Eze 16:26; Na 3:4; Rev 17:1; 18:3,9 [i]Jer 25:26 **23:18** [j]Ex 28:36; S 39:30; Jos 6:17-19; Ps 72:10

23:2,4,12 *Sidon.* See Eze 28:20–26 and notes; the other prominent Phoenician city, about 25 miles north of Tyre.
23:2 *island.* Tyre (see v. 1 and note). *merchants … seafarers.* Tyre's commercial ventures affected the entire Mediterranean world (see vv. 3,8).
23:3 *Shihor.* Probably the easternmost branch of the Nile (see NIV text note on Jer 2:18). *harvest of the Nile.* See 19:7 and note.
23:4 *fortress of the sea.* Tyre (see note on v. 1). *labor … birth.* Contrast 54:1 (see note there).
23:6 *Tarshish.* Perhaps Tartessus in Spain (see note on Eze 27:12), an island in the western Mediterranean or a site on the coast of North Africa.
23:7 *revelry.* See note on 22:2. *old, old city.* Tyre was founded before 2000 BC. *settle in far-off lands.* Carthage in North Africa was a colony of Tyre. Tarshish may have been another.
23:8–9 *planned.* See 14:24,26–27; 25:1 and notes.
23:8 *bestower of crowns.* Tyre crowned kings in her colonies. *traders are renowned.* See Eze 28:4–5.
23:9 *her pride in all her splendor.* See Eze 27:3–4 and notes.
23:10 *Daughter Tarshish.* A personification of Tarshish (see note on 2Ki 19:21).
23:11 *stretched out his hand.* See note on 14:26–27. *Phoenicia.* Roughly the same as modern Lebanon.
23:12 *Virgin Daughter Sidon.* A personification of Sidon (see note on 2Ki 19:21). *now crushed.* Sidon was captured by Esarhaddon in the seventh century BC and later by Nebuchadnezzar c. 587 (cf. Jer 25:22,26 and notes).
23:13 *Assyrians.* Sennacherib destroyed the city of Babylon in 689 BC. Phoenicia would look like the Babylon of that time. *desert creatures.* Cf. 13:21. *siege towers.* See note on 2Ki 25:1.
23:14 See v. 1 and note.
23:15 *seventy years.* Also the length of the Babylonian captivity (see Jer 25:11–12; 29:10 and notes) and the length of time the Babylonian god Marduk (according to an inscription of King Esarhaddon) decreed that Babylon should remain devastated.
23:16 Cf. Pr 7:10–15.
23:17 *lucrative prostitution.* A "prostitute" nation was one that sought to make the highest profits, regardless of the means. Self-gratification was the key (cf. Rev 14:8; 17:5 and notes).
23:18 *set apart for the LORD.* The earnings of a prostitute could not be given to the Lord (Dt 23:18), but the silver and gold of

be stored up or hoarded. Her profits will go to those who live before the LORD,[k] for abundant food and fine clothes.[l]

The LORD's Devastation of the Earth

24 See, the LORD is going to lay waste
the earth[m]
and devastate[n] it;
he will ruin its face
and scatter[o] its inhabitants—
2 it will be the same
for priest as for people,[p]
for the master as for his servant,
for the mistress as for her servant,
for seller as for buyer,[q]
for borrower as for lender,
for debtor as for creditor.[r]
3 The earth will be completely laid
waste[s]
and totally plundered.[t]
The LORD has spoken[u]
this word.

4 The earth dries up[v] and withers,[w]
the world languishes and withers,
the heavens[x] languish with the earth.[y]
5 The earth is defiled[z] by its people;
they have disobeyed[a] the laws,
violated the statutes
and broken the everlasting
covenant.[b]
6 Therefore a curse[c] consumes the earth;
its people must bear their guilt.
Therefore earth's inhabitants are
burned up,[d]
and very few are left.
7 The new wine dries up[e] and the vine
withers;[f]
all the merrymakers groan.[g]
8 The joyful timbrels[h] are stilled,
the noise[i] of the revelers[j] has stopped,
the joyful harp[k] is silent.[l]
9 No longer do they drink wine[m] with a
song;
the beer is bitter[n] to its drinkers.
10 The ruined city[o] lies desolate;[p]
the entrance to every house is
barred.
11 In the streets they cry out[q] for wine;[r]
all joy turns to gloom,[s]
all joyful sounds are banished from
the earth.
12 The city is left in ruins,[t]
its gate[u] is battered to pieces.
13 So will it be on the earth
and among the nations,
as when an olive tree is beaten,[v]
or as when gleanings are left after
the grape harvest.[w]

14 They raise their voices, they shout for
joy;[x]
from the west[y] they acclaim the
LORD's majesty.
15 Therefore in the east[z] give glory[a] to the
LORD;
exalt[b] the name[c] of the LORD, the God
of Israel,
in the islands[d] of the sea.
16 From the ends of the earth[e] we hear
singing:[f]
"Glory[g] to the Righteous One."[h]

But I said, "I waste away, I waste
away![i]
Woe[j] to me!
The treacherous[k] betray!
With treachery the treacherous
betray![l]"

23:18 [k]Isa 18:7; 60:5-9; 61:6; Mic 4:13 [l]Am 1:9-10; Zec 14:1,14 **24:1** [m]ver 20; Isa 2:19-21; 33:9; Jer 25:29 [n]S Jos 6:17; S Isa 13:5 [o]S Ge 11:9 **24:2** [p]Hos 4:9 [q]Eze 7:12; 1Co 7:29-31 [r]S Lev 25:35-37; Dt 23:19-20; Isa 3:1-7 **24:3** [s]S Ge 6:13 [t]Isa 6:11-12; 10:6 [u]S Isa 7:7 **24:4** [v]Jer 12:11; 14:4; Joel 1:10 [w]S Isa 15:6 [x]S Isa 2:12 [y]S Isa 3:26 **24:5** [z]S Ge 3:17 [a]S Isa 1:2; 9:17; 10:6; 59:12; Jer 7:28 [b]S Ge 9:11; S Jer 11:10 **24:6** [c]S Jos 23:15 [d]S Isa 1:31 **24:7** [e]Jer 48:33; Joel 1:5 [f]Isa 7:23; S 15:6; 32:10 [g]S Isa 3:26; 16:8-10 **24:8** [h]S Ge 31:27; S Isa 5:12 [i]Jer 7:34; 16:9; 25:10; 33:11; Hos 2:11 [j]S Isa 5:14; S 21:5 [k]S Ps 137:2; Rev 18:22 [l]La 5:14; Eze 26:13 **24:9** [m]Isa 5:11, 22 [n]Isa 5:20 **24:10** [o]Isa 25:2; 26:5 [p]S Ge 1:2; S Isa 6:11 **24:11** [q]S Ps 144:14 [r]La 2:12 [s]S Isa 15:6; 16:10; 32:13; Jer 14:3 **24:12** [t]S Isa 19:18 [u]S Isa 3:26; S 13:2 **24:13** [v]S Dt 30:4; S Isa 17:6 [w]Ob 1:5; Mic 7:1 **24:14** [x]S Isa 12:6 [y]Isa 43:5; 49:12 **24:15** [z]S Ps 113:3 [a]Isa 42:12; 66:19; 2Th 1:12 [b]S Ex 15:2; Isa 25:3; 59:19; Mal 1:11 [c]S Isa 12:4 [d]S Isa 11:11 **24:16** [e]S Ps 48:10 [f]S Ps 65:8 [g]Isa 28:5; 60:1, 19 [h]S Ezr 9:15 [i]S Lev 26:39 [j]1Sa 4:8; S Isa 5:8; Jer 10:19; 45:3 [k]S Ps 25:3 [l]Isa 21:2; 33:1; Jer 3:6,20; 5:11; 9:2; Hos 5:7; 9:1

---

a city that is devoted to destruction (see note on Dt 2:34) were placed in the Lord's treasury (see Jos 6:17,19 and note on 6:17; cf. Mic 4:13). *to those.* Israel will one day receive the wealth of the nations (see note on 18:7; cf. 60:5–11 and notes; 61:6).

24:1—27:13 Chs. 24–27 deal with judgment and blessing in the last days, the time of God's final victory over the forces of evil. These chapters form a conclusion to chs. 13–23, just as chs. 34–35 form a conclusion to chs. 28–33.

24:1 *lay waste the earth.* Cf. 2:10,19,21; see also 13:13 and note. *scatter its inhabitants.* See Ge 11:8–9 and notes.

24:2 Social distinctions will provide no escape from the judgment (cf. 3:1–3 and notes).

24:4 *dries up and withers.* Words applied to Moab in 15:6; 16:8. Cf. 34:4.

24:5 *broken the everlasting covenant.* Reference is probably to the covenant of Ge 9:8–17 (see chart, p. 23; Ge 9:11 and note). See also v. 18 and note. Although everlasting from the divine viewpoint, God's covenants can be broken by sinful people (see Jer 31:32 and note).

24:6 *curse.* Because of the intensification of evil in the world, God's devastating curse will burn up the earth's inhabitants (cf. Ge 8:21–22; cf. also the covenant of Ge 9:8–17).

24:7 *vine withers.* See v. 4 and note.

24:8 *joyful timbrels are stilled.* Cf. v. 11; 22:2,13; 23:7.

24:9 *wine with a song.* Characteristic of Judah in 5:11–13 (see note there).

24:10 *ruined city.* The same idea appears in 25:2; 26:5; 27:10 (cf. 17:1; 19:18). It is probably a composite of all the cities opposed to God—such as Babylon, Tyre, Jerusalem and Rome.

24:13 Only a few olives and grapes will be left (see v. 6; 17:6,11).

24:14 *They.* The godly remnant that survives the judgment.

24:15 *islands.* See note on 11:11.

24:16 *ends of the earth.* See note on 11:12. *I.* Probably collective for the godly community that wastes away because of the villainy of the treacherous nations that seek to crush the people of God. *I waste away ... betray!* In the Hebrew text these last four lines of the verse (*Razi li, razi li! 'Oy li! Bogedim bagadu! Ubeged bogedim bagadu!*) contain powerful examples of alliteration and assonance (see 5:7 and note; see also Introduction: Literary Features). *Woe to me!* Isaiah had the same reaction in 6:5. *The treacherous.* The enemies of God's people.

17 Terror[m] and pit and snare[n] await you,
people of the earth.[o]
18 Whoever flees[p] at the sound of terror
will fall into a pit;[q]
whoever climbs out of the pit
will be caught in a snare.[r]

The floodgates of the heavens[s] are
opened,
the foundations of the earth shake.[t]
19 The earth is broken up,[u]
the earth is split asunder,[v]
the earth is violently shaken.
20 The earth reels like a drunkard,[w]
it sways like a hut[x] in the wind;
so heavy upon it is the guilt of its
rebellion[y]
that it falls[z] — never to rise again.[a]

21 In that day[b] the LORD will punish[c]
the powers[d] in the heavens above
and the kings[e] on the earth below.
22 They will be herded together
like prisoners[f] bound in a dungeon;[g]
they will be shut up in prison
and be punished[a] after many days.[h]
23 The moon will be dismayed,
the sun[i] ashamed;
for the LORD Almighty will reign[j]
on Mount Zion[k] and in Jerusalem,
and before its elders — with great
glory.[l]

Praise to the LORD

25 LORD, you are my God;[m]
I will exalt you and praise your
name,[n]
for in perfect faithfulness[o]
you have done wonderful things,[p]
things planned[q] long ago.

2 You have made the city a heap of
rubble,[r]
the fortified[s] town a ruin,[t]
the foreigners' stronghold[u] a city no
more;
it will never be rebuilt.[v]
3 Therefore strong peoples will honor
you;[w]
cities of ruthless[x] nations will revere
you.
4 You have been a refuge[y] for the poor,[z]
a refuge for the needy[a] in their
distress,
a shelter from the storm[b]
and a shade from the heat.
For the breath of the ruthless[c]
is like a storm driving against a wall
5 and like the heat of the desert.
You silence[d] the uproar of foreigners;[e]
as heat is reduced by the shadow of
a cloud,
so the song of the ruthless[f] is stilled.

6 On this mountain[g] the LORD Almighty
will prepare
a feast[h] of rich food for all peoples,
a banquet of aged wine —
the best of meats and the finest of
wines.[i]
7 On this mountain he will destroy
the shroud[j] that enfolds all peoples,[k]
the sheet that covers all nations;

[a] 22 Or *released*

24:17 [m] Dt 32:23-25 [n] Isa 8:14; Jer 48:43 [o] Lk 21:35 **24:18** [p] S Job 20:24 [q] Isa 42:22 [r] S Job 18:9; S Isa 8:14; La 3:47; Eze 12:13 [s] S Ge 7:11 [t] S Jdg 5:4; S Job 9:6; S Ps 11:3; S Eze 38:19 **24:19** [u] S Ps 46:2 [v] S Dt 11:6 **24:20** [w] S Job 12:25 [x] S Job 27:18 [y] S Isa 1:2, 28; 43:27; 58:1 [z] S Ps 46:2 [a] S Job 12:14 **24:21** [b] S Isa 2:11; S 10:20; Rev 16:14 [c] Isa 10:12; 13:11; Jer 25:29 [d] 1Co 6:3; Eph 6:11-12 [e] S Isa 2:12 **24:22** [f] S Isa 10:4 [g] Isa 42:7, 22; Lk 8:31; Rev 20:7-10 [h] Eze 38:8 **24:23** [i] S Isa 13:10 [j] S Ps 97:1; Rev 22:5 [k] S Isa 2:2; Heb 12:22 [l] Isa 28:5; 41:16; 45:25; 60:19; Eze 48:35; Zec 2:5; Rev 21:23 **25:1** [m] S Isa 7:13 [n] S Ps 145:2; S Isa 12:1, 4 [o] Isa 11:5 [p] Ps 40:5; 98:1; Joel 2:21, 26 [q] Nu 23:19; S Isa 14:24; 37:26; 46:11; Eph 1:11 **25:2** [r] Isa 17:1; 26:5; 37:26 [s] S Isa 17:3 [t] S Dt 13:16 [u] S Isa 13:22 [v] S Job 12:14 **25:3** [w] S Ex 6:2; S Ps 22:23; S Isa 11:14 [x] S Isa 13:11 **25:4** [y] S 2Sa 22:3; S Ps 118:8; S Isa 4:6; 17:10; 27:5; 33:16; Joel 3:16 [z] S Isa 3:14 [a] S Isa 14:30; 29:19 [b] S Ps 55:8 [c] Isa 29:5; 49:25 **25:5** [d] Jer 51:55 [e] S Ps 18:44 [f] S Isa 13:11 **25:6** [g] S Isa 2:2 [h] S Ge 29:22; 1Ki 1:25; Isa 1:19; 55:1-2; 66:11; Joel 3:18; Mt 8:11; 22:4; Rev 19:9 [i] S Ps 36:8; S Pr 9:2 **25:7** [j] 2Co 3:15-16; Eph 4:18 [k] S Job 4:9

24:17 – 18 Cf. Am 5:19 – 20 and note.
24:17 *Terror and pit and snare.* Another example (see note on v. 16) of alliteration and assonance (see note on Jer 48:43). The Hebrew words are *paḥad, paḥat* and *pah.*
24:18a God's judgment is inescapable (cf. Am 5:19 – 20; 9:2 – 4 and notes).
24:18b *floodgates of the heavens.* An echo of Noah's flood (Ge 7:11; 8:2). *foundations ... shake.* Earthquakes and thunder (see note on 13:13; cf. Joel 3:16).
24:20 *like a drunkard.* Cf. 19:14. *like a hut.* See 1:8 and note.
24:21 *In that day.* The phrase, which refers to the day of the Lord (see notes on 2:11,17,20; 10:20,27), occurs seven times in chs. 24 – 27 (see 25:9; 26:1; 27:1 – 2,12 – 13). *powers in the heavens ... kings.* All powers in the creation that exalt themselves against God (see 2:6 – 21; Eph 6:11 – 12).
24:22 *shut up in prison.* Cf. Rev 20:2. *punished after many days.* See NIV text note; cf. Rev 20:7 – 10.
24:23 *The moon ... dismayed, the sun ashamed.* The sun and moon do not shine during judgment (see note on 13:10) or when the Lord is the "everlasting light" (60:19 – 20; cf. Rev 21:23; 22:5). *reign on Mount Zion.* See 2:2 – 4 and note.
25:1 – 5 A song of praise celebrating the deliverance brought about by the judgments of ch. 24 (see 24:14 – 16; see also ch. 12).
25:1 *planned long ago.* See 14:24,26 – 27; 23:8 – 9.
25:2 *the city ... a ruin.* See 24:10 and note. *never be rebuilt.* Cf. 24:20.
25:3 *strong peoples ... ruthless nations.* Such as Egypt and Assyria (see 19:18 – 25 and notes). *honor you ... revere you.* See 24:15 – 16.
25:4 – 5 *refuge ... shelter ... shade ... cloud.* See 4:5 – 6 and note; cf. 32:2.
25:6 – 8 A description of the eschatological feast of God, the Messianic banquet (see 1Ch 12:38 – 40; Mt 8:11; Lk 14:15; 22:16 and notes).
25:6 – 7,10 *this mountain.* Mount Zion. See 2:2 – 4 and note; cf. 24:23.
25:6 *feast ... banquet.* Associated with a coronation (1Ki 1:25) or wedding (see Jdg 14:10 and note); cf. the "wedding supper of the Lamb" (Rev 19:9). *rich food.* Symbolic of great spiritual blessings (see 55:2 and note). *aged wine.* The best wine — aged while being left on its dregs (see Jer 48:11 and note; Zep 1:12).
25:7 – 8 Christ has brought about the ultimate destruction of death itself (see 2Ti 1:10; cf. Heb 2:14 – 15 and notes).
25:7 *shroud ... sheet.* Or "covering ... veil," with which faces were covered in mourning — in any event, the associations are with death.

[8] he will swallow up death[l] forever.
The Sovereign LORD will wipe away the tears[m]
from all faces;
he will remove his people's disgrace[n]
from all the earth.
The LORD has spoken.[o]

[9]In that day[p] they will say,

"Surely this is our God;[q]
we trusted[r] in him, and he saved[s] us.
This is the LORD, we trusted in him;
let us rejoice[t] and be glad in his salvation."[u]

[10]The hand of the LORD will rest on this mountain;[v]
but Moab[w] will be trampled in their land
as straw is trampled down in the manure.
[11]They will stretch out their hands in it,
as swimmers stretch out their hands to swim.
God will bring down[x] their pride[y]
despite the cleverness[a] of their hands.
[12]He will bring down your high fortified walls[z]
and lay them low;[a]
he will bring them down to the ground,
to the very dust.

A Song of Praise

26 In that day[b] this song will be sung[c] in the land of Judah:

We have a strong city;[d]
God makes salvation
its walls[e] and ramparts.[f]
[2]Open the gates[g]
that the righteous[h] nation may enter,
the nation that keeps faith.
[3]You will keep in perfect peace[i]
those whose minds are steadfast,
because they trust[j] in you.
[4]Trust[k] in the LORD forever,[l]
for the LORD, the LORD himself, is the Rock[m] eternal.
[5]He humbles those who dwell on high,
he lays the lofty city low;
he levels it to the ground[n]
and casts it down to the dust.[o]
[6]Feet trample[p] it down—
the feet of the oppressed,[q]
the footsteps of the poor.[r]

[7]The path of the righteous is level;[s]
you, the Upright One,[t] make the way of the righteous smooth.[u]
[8]Yes, LORD, walking in the way of your laws,[b][v]
we wait[w] for you;
your name[x] and renown
are the desire of our hearts.
[9]My soul yearns for you in the night;[y]
in the morning my spirit longs[z] for you.
When your judgments[a] come upon the earth,
the people of the world learn righteousness.[b]
[10]But when grace is shown to the wicked,[c]
they do not learn righteousness;
even in a land of uprightness they go on doing evil[d]
and do not regard[e] the majesty of the LORD.
[11]LORD, your hand is lifted high,[f]
but they do not see[g] it.

[a] *11* The meaning of the Hebrew for this word is uncertain. [b] *8* Or *judgments*

25:8 [l]Isa 26:19; Hos 13:14; 1Co 15:54-55* [m]Isa 15:3; 30:19; 35:10; 51:11; 65:19; Jer 31:16; Rev 7:17; 21:4 [n]S Ge 30:23; S Ps 119:39; Mt 5:11; 1Pe 4:14; Rev 7:14 [o]S Isa 7:7 **25:9** [p]S Isa 2:11; S 10:20 [q]Isa 40:9 [r]S Ps 22:5; S Isa 12:2 [s]Ps 145:19; Isa 19:20; 33:22; 35:4; 43:3,11; 45:15, 21; 49:25-26; 60:16; 63:8; Jer 14:8 [t]S Dt 32:43; S Ps 9:2; Isa 9:3; 35:2, 10; 41:16; 51:3; 61:7,10; 66:14 [u]S Ps 13:5; S Isa 12:2 **25:10** [v]S Isa 2:2 [w]S Ge 19:37; S Nu 21:29; S Dt 23:6; S Isa 11:14; Am 2:1-3 **25:11** [x]Isa 5:25; 14:26; 16:14 [y]S Lev 26:19; S Job 40:12 **25:12** [z]S Isa 2:15 [a]S Job 40:11; S Isa 15:1; S Jer 51:44 **26:1** [b]S Isa 10:20 [c]Isa 30:29 [d]S Isa 14:32 [e]Isa 32:18; 60:18; Zec 2:5; 9:8 [f]S Ps 48:13 **26:2** [g]S Ps 24:7 [h]Ps 24:3-4; 85:13; S Isa 1:26; S 4:3; 9:7; 50:8; 53:11; 54:14; 58:8; 62:2 **26:3** [i]S Job 22:21; S Isa 9:6,7; Php 4:7 [j]S 1Ch 5:20; S Ps 22:5; S 28:7; S Isa 12:2 **26:4** [k]S Isa 12:2; 50:10 [l]S Ps 62:8 [m]S Ge 49:24 **26:5** [n]S Isa 25:12; Eze 26:11 [o]S Isa 25:2 **26:6** [p]S Isa 5:5 [q]Isa 49:26 [r]S Isa 3:15; S 14:30 **26:7** [s]S Ps 26:12 [t]S Ps 25:8 [u]S Ex 14:19; Isa 40:4; 42:16 **26:8** [v]S Dt 18:18; Ps 1:2; Isa 56:1; 64:5 [w]S Ps 37:9; S 130:5 [x]S Ps 145:2; S Isa 12:4 **26:9** [y]S Ps 119:55 [z]Ps 42:1-3; 63:1; 78:34; Isa 55:6 [a]S 1Ch 16:14 [b]Mt 6:33 **26:10** [c]Mt 5:45 [d]Isa 32:6; 59:7,13 [e]S 1Sa 12:24; Isa 22:12-13; Jer 2:19; Hos 11:7; Jn 5:37-38; Ro 2:4 **26:11** [f]S Ps 10:12 [g]Isa 18:3; 44:9,18

25:8 Quoted in part in 1Co 15:54. *swallow up death.* Death, the great swallower (see Ps 49:14 and note), will be swallowed up by the Lord. *Sovereign LORD.* See 7:7; 28:16; 30:15; 40:10; 49:22; 52:4; 61:11; 65:13. *wipe away the tears.* See Rev 7:17; 21:4. *remove his people's disgrace.* See 54:4.
25:9 Another brief song of praise. *In that day.* See 12:1,4; 24:21; see also 10:20,27 and note. *we trusted … he saved.* Cf. Ps 22:4–5. *rejoice and be glad.* Cf. 35:10; 51:11; 66:10.
25:10–12 An elaboration on the theme of judgment.
25:10 *Moab.* Representative of all the enemies of God, like Edom in 34:5–17. See note on 15:1.
25:11 *pride.* See note on 16:6.
25:12 *high fortified walls.* See v. 2; 2:15; 2Ki 3:27; Jer 51:44,58 and note on 51:44.
26:1–15 Another song of praise for God's deliverance (see note on 25:1–5).
26:1 *In that day.* See 12:1,4; 24:21; 25:9; see also note on 10:20,27. *salvation its walls and ramparts.* God's saving acts are Zion's security and strength (cf. Ps 46; 48). *ramparts.* Sloping fortifications of earth or stone (cf. 2Sa 20:15).
26:3 See 30:15 and note. *minds are steadfast.* Cf. Ps 112:6–8 and notes. *trust.* Cf. 25:9.
26:4 *Rock.* See 17:10; Ps 18:2 and notes.
26:5 *lofty city.* See note on 24:10. *levels it … to the dust.* Cf. 25:2,12.
26:6 *feet of the oppressed.* The oppressors are humiliated also in 49:24–26; 51:22–23 (contrast 3:14–15).
26:7 *path … level … way … smooth.* A theme found also in 40:3–4; 42:16; 45:13 (see notes there; see also Pr 4:26 and note; contrast La 3:9).
26:8 A desire for God to reveal his power in their behalf (see Hos 12:5–6). *name and renown.* See v. 13; 24:15; 25:1.
26:9 *judgments.* Punishment (cf. 4:4).
26:10 *grace.* Such as the blessings of harvest and general prosperity (cf. Mt 5:45 and note).
26:11 *hand is lifted high.* A sign of power. See 9:12,17,21 and

Let them see your zeal[h] for your people
and be put to shame;[i]
let the fire[j] reserved for your enemies
consume them.

12 LORD, you establish peace[k] for us;
all that we have accomplished you
have done[l] for us.
13 LORD our God, other lords[m] besides you
have ruled over us,
but your name[n] alone do we honor.[o]
14 They are now dead,[p] they live no more;
their spirits[q] do not rise.
You punished them and brought them
to ruin;[r]
you wiped out all memory of them.[s]
15 You have enlarged the nation, LORD;
you have enlarged the nation.[t]
You have gained glory for yourself;
you have extended all the borders[u] of
the land.

16 LORD, they came to you in their
distress;[v]
when you disciplined[w] them,
they could barely whisper[x] a prayer.[a]
17 As a pregnant woman about to give
birth[y]
writhes and cries out in her pain,
so were we in your presence, LORD.
18 We were with child, we writhed in
labor,
but we gave birth[z] to wind.
We have not brought salvation[a] to the
earth,
and the people of the world have not
come to life.[b]
19 But your dead[c] will live, LORD;
their bodies will rise—
let those who dwell in the dust[d]
wake up and shout for joy—
your dew[e] is like the dew of the
morning;
the earth will give birth to her dead.[f]
20 Go, my people, enter your rooms
and shut the doors[g] behind you;
hide[h] yourselves for a little while
until his wrath[i] has passed by.[j]
21 See, the LORD is coming[k] out of his
dwelling[l]
to punish[m] the people of the earth
for their sins.
The earth will disclose the blood[n] shed
on it;
the earth will conceal its slain no
longer.

Deliverance of Israel

27 In that day,[o]
the LORD will punish with his
sword[p]—
his fierce, great and powerful
sword—
Leviathan[q] the gliding serpent,[r]
Leviathan the coiling serpent;
he will slay the monster[s] of the sea.

2 In that day[t]—

"Sing[u] about a fruitful vineyard:[v]
3 I, the LORD, watch over it;
I water[w] it continually.
I guard[x] it day and night
so that no one may harm[y] it.

[a] *16* The meaning of the Hebrew for this clause is uncertain.

26:11 [h]S Isa 9:7; Joel 2:18; Zec 1:14 [i]Mic 7:16 [j]S Isa 1:31; Heb 10:27 **26:12** [k]S Ps 119:165; S Isa 9:6 [l]S Ps 68:28 **26:13** [m]Isa 2:8; 10:5,11 [n]S Isa 12:4 [o]Isa 42:8; 63:7 **26:14** [p]S Dt 4:28 [q]S Job 26:5 [r]S Ps 9:5; S Isa 10:3 [s]S Ps 9:6 **26:15** [t]S Job 12:23; S Isa 14:2 [u]Isa 33:17 **26:16** [v]S Jdg 6:2; S Isa 5:30 [w]S Ps 39:11 [x]Isa 29:4 **26:17** [y]S Isa 21:3; S Jn 16:21; Rev 12:2 **26:18** [z]Isa 33:11; 59:4 [a]S Ge 49:10; Ps 17:14 [b]Isa 42:6; 49:6; 51:4; Jer 12:16 **26:19** [c]S Isa 25:8; Eph 5:14 [d]Ps 22:29 [e]S Ge 27:28; S Isa 18:4 [f]Isa 66:24; Eze 37:1-14; Da 12:2 **26:20** [g]Ex 12:23 [h]Ps 91:1,4 [i]S Isa 10:25; S 30:27 [j]S Job 14:13 **26:21** [k]Isa 29:6; Jude 1:14 [l]S Isa 18:4 [m]S Isa 13:9,11; 30:12-14 [n]S Job 16:18; Lk 11:50-51 **27:1** [o]ver 13; S Isa 2:11; 28:5 [p]S Ge 3:24; S Dt 32:41; Isa 31:8; 34:6; 65:12; 66:16; Eze 21:3; Na 3:15 [q]S Job 3:8 [r]Job 26:13 [s]S Ps 68:30; S 74:13; Rev 12:9 **27:2** [t]Isa 24:21 [u]S Isa 5:1 [v]Jer 2:21 **27:3** [w]Isa 58:11 [x]S Ps 91:4; S Isa 5:2 [y]S Jn 6:39

---

note; Ps 89:13. *zeal.* See 9:7 and note; cf. 37:32; 63:15. *fire.* See note on 1:31.
26:12 *peace.* See v. 3.
26:13 *other lords.* Foreign rulers, such as those of Egypt or Assyria.
26:14 *They are now dead ... their spirits do not rise.* Cf. the fate of the king of Babylon in 14:9–10—and contrast the resurrection scene in 26:19 (see note there).
26:15 *enlarged the nation.* Applied to the return from Babylonian exile in 54:2–3; cf. also 9:3; Zec 2:4 and note.
26:16–18 The prophet speaks to the Lord on behalf of God's people.
26:16 *distress.* Perhaps the Assyrian oppression, described in 5:30; 8:21–22 (see notes there). The period of the judges is also possible (see Jdg 6:2,6).
26:17–18 *give birth writhes ... in labor.* See 13:8 and note (cf. 37:3).
26:18 *salvation to the earth.* See 49:6.
26:19–21 The prophet speaks a word of reassurance to God's people.
26:19 *your dead will live ... bodies will rise.* A reference to the restoration of Israel (see Eze 37:11–12,14 and notes)—perhaps including the resurrection of the body (see Da 12:2 and note). Cf. 25:8; contrast 26:14. *dew.* A symbol of fruitfulness (see 2Sa 1:21; Hos 14:5 and note).
26:20–21 See 24:21–22 and note on 2:11,17,20.
26:20 *a little while ... wrath.* See 10:25; 54:7–8 and notes; cf. Ps 30:5 and note. Assyrian tyranny and Babylonian exile, as well as all other oppressions, will end.
26:21 *punish.* See 66:14–16 and notes. *will disclose ... will conceal ... no longer.* The blood and bodies of the innocent/righteous who have been slaughtered by the oppressive powers will no longer be hidden in the ground but will be brought forth to testify against their murderers, so that God may in judgment avenge their deaths (see Ge 4:10 and note).
27:1–2,12–13 *In that day.* See 10:20,27; 24:21 and notes; see also 12:1,4; 25:9; 26:1.
27:1 The climactic word of judgment in 24:1—27:13 (see note there). *his sword.* See Ps 7:12–13 and note. *Leviathan ... monster.* A symbol (drawn from Canaanite myths) of wicked nations, such as Egypt (see 30:7 ["Rahab"]; 51:9; Eze 29:3; 32:2 and notes). *gliding ... coiling serpent.* Cf. Job 3:8; 41:1; Ps 74:13–14.
27:2–6 A second vineyard song (see 5:1–7 and notes).
27:2 *vineyard.* Israel.

4 I am not angry.
If only there were briers and thorns
confronting me!
I would march against them in
battle;
I would set them all on fire.[z]
5 Or else let them come to me for
refuge;[a]
let them make peace[b] with me,
yes, let them make peace with me."

6 In days to come Jacob will take root,[c]
Israel will bud and blossom[d]
and fill all the world with fruit.[e]

7 Has the LORD struck her
as he struck[f] down those who struck
her?
Has she been killed
as those were killed who killed her?
8 By warfare[a] and exile[g] you contend
with her—
with his fierce blast he drives her out,
as on a day the east wind[h] blows.
9 By this, then, will Jacob's guilt be
atoned[i] for,
and this will be the full fruit of the
removal of his sin:[j]
When he makes all the altar stones[k]
to be like limestone crushed to
pieces,
no Asherah poles[b][l] or incense altars[m]
will be left standing.
10 The fortified city stands desolate,[n]
an abandoned settlement, forsaken[o]
like the wilderness;
there the calves graze,[p]
there they lie down;[q]
they strip its branches bare.
11 When its twigs are dry, they are broken
off[r]
and women come and make fires[s]
with them.
For this is a people without
understanding;[t]
so their Maker has no compassion
on them,
and their Creator[u] shows them no
favor.[v]

12 In that day the LORD will thresh[w] from
the flowing Euphrates to the Wadi of
Egypt,[x] and you, Israel, will be gathered[y]
up one by one. 13 And in that day[z] a great
trumpet[a] will sound. Those who were perishing in Assyria and those who were exiled[b] in Egypt[c] will come and worship[d] the
LORD on the holy mountain[e] in Jerusalem.

Woe to the Leaders of Ephraim and Judah

28 Woe[f] to that wreath, the pride of
Ephraim's[g] drunkards,
to the fading flower, his glorious
beauty,
set on the head of a fertile valley[h]—
to that city, the pride of those laid
low by wine![i]
2 See, the Lord has one who is powerful[j]
and strong.
Like a hailstorm[k] and a destructive
wind,[l]
like a driving rain and a flooding[m]
downpour,
he will throw it forcefully to the
ground.
3 That wreath, the pride of Ephraim's[n]
drunkards,
will be trampled[o] underfoot.

[a] *8* See Septuagint; the meaning of the Hebrew for this word is uncertain. [b] *9* That is, wooden symbols of the goddess Asherah

27:4 [z] S ver 11; S Isa 10:17; Mt 3:12; Heb 6:8 **27:5** [a] S Isa 25:4 [b] S Job 22:21; S Ps 119:165; Ro 5:1; 2Co 5:20 **27:6** [c] S 2Ki 19:30; Isa 11:10 [d] S Ge 40:10 [e] S Ps 72:16; Isa 11:1; 37:31; Eze 17:23; 36:8; Hos 14:8 **27:7** [f] Isa 10:26; S 11:4; 37:36-38 **27:8** [g] Isa 49:14; 50:1; 54:7 [h] S Ge 41:6 **27:9** [i] S Ps 78:38 [j] Ro 11:27* [k] S Ex 23:24 [l] S Ex 34:13 [m] S Lev 26:30; S 2Ch 14:5 **27:10** [n] S Ge 1:2; S Dt 13:16; Isa 5:6; 32:14; Jer 10:22; 26:6; La 1:4; 5:18 [o] S Isa 5:5 [p] S Isa 5:17 [q] Isa 17:2 **27:11** [r] S Isa 10:33 [s] S ver 4; Isa 33:12 [t] S Dt 32:28; S Isa 1:3 [u] Dt 32:18; Isa 41:8; 43:1,7, 15; 44:1-2,21, 24 [v] S Isa 9:17; Jer 11:16 **27:12** [w] S Isa 21:10; Mt 3:12 [x] S Ge 15:18 [y] S Dt 30:4; S Isa 1:9; S 11:12; S 17:6 **27:13** [z] S ver 1 [a] S Lev 25:9; S Jdg 3:27; S Mt 24:31 [b] S Ps 106:47 [c] S Isa 10:19; 19:21,25 [d] S Ge 27:29; S Ps 22:29; S 86:9 [e] S Isa 2:2 **28:1** [f] Isa 10:5; 29:1; 30:1; 31:1; 33:1 [g] ver 3; Isa 7:2; 9:9 [h] ver 4 [i] S Lev 10:9; Isa 5:11; Hos 7:5; Am 6:6 **28:2** [j] Isa 40:10 [k] S Jos 10:11 [l] Isa 29:6 [m] S Isa 8:7; S Da 9:26 **28:3** [n] S ver 1 [o] S Job 40:12; S Isa 5:5

27:4–5 A picture of Israel's lukewarmness toward the Lord—not "briers and thorns" (v. 4) like the other nations, but not fully trusting in the Lord either (see 29:13 and note).
27:4 *briers and thorns.* See 5:6 and note.
27:6 *take root.* See 11:1,10 and notes. *bud and blossom.* See 4:2 and note. The Messianic age is in view. *fill all the world.* Contrast 26:18.
27:7–11 What the Lord is going to do with Israel in the judgments that are about to overtake her in Isaiah's day.
27:7 *struck her.* Cf. 10:24–26.
27:8 *exile.* Probably the Babylonian captivity. *east wind.* A hot wind from the desert (see Jer 4:11 and note; Eze 19:12).
27:9 *atoned for.* Israel (Jacob) will have to atone for her guilt through the coming judgment. *altar ... Asherah poles ... incense altars.* See 17:8 and note. *crushed to pieces.* See Ex 34:13 and note.
27:10 *fortified city.* Jerusalem. *desolate ... forsaken.* Cf. 6:11–12. *calves graze.* Cf. 5:5; 7:25.
27:12–13 The redemption that lies beyond the coming judgment.
27:12 *will thresh.* Judgment on the nations among which Israel has been dispersed (see note on 21:10). The threshing will separate Israelites from Gentiles. *Wadi of Egypt.* Probably the Wadi el-Arish, the southern border of the promised land (see map, p. 677); the Euphrates is the northern border. See Ge 15:18; 1Ki 4:21; 8:65 and notes.
27:13 *great trumpet.* Used especially to summon troops (see 1Sa 13:3). *Assyria ... Egypt.* See 11:11–12 and notes. *holy mountain.* Mount Zion (see 2:2–4 and note; see also 11:6–9; 24:23; 25:6–7,10 and note; 65:25).
28:1—35:10 A series of six woes (28:1; 29:1; 29:15; 30:1; 31:1; 33:1), ending with an announcement of judgment on the nations (ch. 34) and a song celebrating the joy of the redeemed (ch. 35). Cf. the six woes in ch. 5 (see note on 5:8–23).
28:1 *wreath.* Samaria, the capital of the northern kingdom, was a beautiful city on a prominent hill (see note on 1Ki 16:24). *pride.* See v. 3 and note on 16:6. *Ephraim's.* See note on 7:2. *drunkards.* In the eighth century BC Samaria was a city of luxury and indulgence. See 5:11–13; Am 3:12 and notes; 6:4–7. *fertile valley.* Cf. 5:1.
28:2 *one who is powerful.* The king of Assyria. *hailstorm ... flooding downpour.* See v. 17; 8:7–8 and note; 17:12 and note. Cf. 30:30; 32:19.

4 That fading flower, his glorious beauty,
set on the head of a fertile valley,[p]
will be like figs[q] ripe before harvest—
as soon as people see them and take them in hand,
they swallow them.

5 In that day[r] the LORD Almighty
will be a glorious[s] crown,[t]
a beautiful wreath
for the remnant[u] of his people.
6 He will be a spirit of justice[v]
to the one who sits in judgment,[w]
a source of strength
to those who turn back the battle[x] at the gate.

7 And these also stagger[y] from wine[z]
and reel[a] from beer:
Priests[b] and prophets[c] stagger from beer
and are befuddled with wine;
they reel from beer,
they stagger when seeing visions,[d]
they stumble when rendering decisions.
8 All the tables are covered with vomit[e]
and there is not a spot without filth.
9 "Who is it he is trying to teach?[f]
To whom is he explaining his message?[g]
To children weaned[h] from their milk,[i]
to those just taken from the breast?
10 For it is:
Do this, do that,
a rule for this, a rule for that*[a]*;
a little here, a little there.[j]"
11 Very well then, with foreign lips and strange tongues[k]
God will speak to this people,[l]
12 to whom he said,
"This is the resting place, let the weary rest";[m]
and, "This is the place of repose"—
but they would not listen.
13 So then, the word of the LORD to them will become:
Do this, do that,
a rule for this, a rule for that;
a little here, a little there[n]—
so that as they go they will fall backward;
they will be injured[o] and snared and captured.[p]

14 Therefore hear the word of the LORD,[q]
you scoffers[r]
who rule this people in Jerusalem.
15 You boast, "We have entered into a covenant with death,[s]
with the realm of the dead we have made an agreement.
When an overwhelming scourge sweeps by,[t]
it cannot touch us,
for we have made a lie[u] our refuge
and falsehood*[b]* our hiding place.[v]"

16 So this is what the Sovereign LORD
says:

"See, I lay a stone in Zion,[w] a tested stone,[x]
a precious cornerstone for a sure foundation;[y]
the one who relies on it
will never be stricken with panic.[z]
17 I will make justice[a] the measuring line
and righteousness the plumb line;[b]
hail[c] will sweep away your refuge, the lie,
and water will overflow[d] your hiding place.

a 10 Hebrew / *sav lasav sav lasav / kav lakav kav lakav* (probably meaningless sounds mimicking the prophet's words); also in verse 13 *b* 15 Or *false gods*

28:4 [p] ver 1 [q] S SS 2:13; Hos 9:10; Na 3:12 **28:5** [r] S Isa 10:20; S 27:1; 29:18; 30:23 [s] S Isa 24:16, 23 [t] Isa 62:3; Jer 13:18; Eze 16:12; 21:26; Zec 9:16 [u] S Isa 1:9 **28:6** [v] S 2Sa 14:20; Isa 11:2-4; 32:1,16; 33:5 [w] Isa 4:4; Jn 5:30 [x] Jdg 9:44-45; S 2Ch 32:8 **28:7** [y] S Isa 3:12 [z] S Lev 10:9; S Isa 22:13; S Eph 5:18 [a] S Ps 107:27 [b] Isa 24:2 [c] S Isa 9:15 [d] S Isa 1:1; 29:11 **28:8** [e] Jer 48:26 **28:9** [f] ver 26; Ps 32:8; Isa 2:3; 30:20; 48:17; 50:4; 54:13; Jer 31:34; 32:33 [g] Isa 52:7; 53:1 [h] Ps 131:2 [i] Heb 5:12-13; 1Pe 2:2 **28:10** [j] ver 13 **28:11** [k] S Ge 11:7; Isa 33:19; Jer 5:15 [l] Eze 3:5; 1Co 14:21* **28:12** [m] S Ex 14:14; S Jos 1:13; S Job 11:18; S Isa 11:10; Mt 11:28-29 **28:13** [n] ver 10 [o] Mt 21:44 [p] S Isa 8:15 **28:14** [q] Isa 1:10 [r] 2Ch 36:16 **28:15** [s] S Job 5:23; Isa 8:19 [t] ver 2, 18; Isa 8:7-8; 10:26; 29:6; 30:28; Da 11:22 [u] S Isa 9:15 [v] S Jdg 9:35; Isa 29:15; Jer 23:24 **28:16** [w] S Isa 14:32 [x] Ps 118:22; Isa 8:14-15; Da 2:34-35,45; Zec 12:3; S Ac 4:11 [y] Jer 51:26; 1Co 3:11; 2Ti 2:19 [z] Isa 29:22; 45:17; 50:7; 54:4; Ro 9:33*; 10:11*; 1Pe 2:6* **28:17** [a] S Ps 11:7; S Isa 5:16 [b] S 2Ki 21:13 [c] S Jos 10:11 [d] S Isa 8:7

28:5 *In that day.* See 4:1–2; 10:20,27 and note; 12:1,4; 24:21; 25:9; 26:1; 27:1–2,12–13. *glorious … beautiful.* See 4:2 and note. *remnant.* See note on 1:9.
28:6 *spirit of justice.* See 11:2–4 and notes. *gate.* The most vulnerable part of a city.
28:7 *wine … beer.* The religious leaders should have been filled with the Spirit, not with wine. See Lev 10:9; see also Nu 11:29; Eph 5:18 and notes.
28:8 *vomit.* Cf. Jer 25:16,27.
28:9–10 The mocking response of Isaiah's hearers (see NIV text note on v. 10). Cf. the mocking tones of 5:19.
28:11–12 Quoted in part in 1Co 14:21 (see note on 1Co 14:21–22).
28:11 *foreign lips.* The language of the Assyrians.
28:12 *resting place.* The land given to them by the Lord, in whom they were to trust (see 26:3; 30:15; 40:31; Jos 1:13 and notes). *would not listen.* Cf. Jer 6:16 and note.
28:13 *will become.* They say the prophet is speaking nonsense (vv. 9–10), so the word of the Lord that he speaks will remain nonsense to them (see 6:9–10 and notes).
28:15,18 *covenant with death.* By using a vivid figure of speech, Isaiah mocks their sense of assurance against national calamity, placing on their lips a claim to have a covenant with death that it will not harm them (cf. Hos 2:18 and note). *overwhelming scourge.* A mixed metaphor referring to the armies of Assyria and Babylonia. "Overwhelming" pictures an army as a flooding river (see 8:7–8 and note); a "scourge" is a whip (10:26).
28:16 *stone.* The Lord (see 8:14; 17:10 and notes). *cornerstone.* Cf. Ps 118:22 (see note there). *sure foundation.* See 1Co 3:11; cf. 1Pe 2:4–8 and notes.
28:17 *measuring line … plumb line.* The standards and tests the Lord will apply are his "justice" and "righteousness" (cf. 34:11 and note). *hail.* See v. 2; 30:30; 32:19.

18 Your covenant with death will be annulled;
your agreement with the realm of the dead will not stand.[e]
When the overwhelming scourge sweeps by,[f]
you will be beaten down[g] by it.
19 As often as it comes it will carry you away;[h]
morning after morning,[i] by day and by night,
it will sweep through."

The understanding of this message will bring sheer terror.[j]
20 The bed is too short to stretch out on,
the blanket too narrow to wrap around you.[k]
21 The LORD will rise up as he did at Mount Perazim,[l]
he will rouse himself as in the Valley of Gibeon[m] —
to do his work,[n] his strange work,
and perform his task, his alien task.
22 Now stop your mocking,[o]
or your chains will become heavier;
the Lord, the LORD Almighty, has told me
of the destruction decreed[p] against the whole land.[q]

23 Listen[r] and hear my voice;
pay attention and hear what I say.
24 When a farmer plows for planting,[s]
does he plow continually?
Does he keep on breaking up and working the soil?
25 When he has leveled the surface,
does he not sow caraway and scatter cumin?[t]
Does he not plant wheat in its place,[a]
barley[u] in its plot,[a]
and spelt[v] in its field?
26 His God instructs him
and teaches[w] him the right way.
27 Caraway is not threshed[x] with a sledge,[y]
nor is the wheel of a cart rolled over cumin;
caraway is beaten out with a rod,[z]
and cumin with a stick.
28 Grain must be ground to make bread;
so one does not go on threshing it forever.
The wheels of a threshing cart[a] may be rolled over it,
but one does not use horses to grind grain.
29 All this also comes from the LORD Almighty,
whose plan is wonderful,[b]
whose wisdom is magnificent.[c]

Woe to David's City

29 Woe[d] to you, Ariel, Ariel,[e]
the city[f] where David settled!
Add year to year
and let your cycle of festivals[g] go on.
2 Yet I will besiege Ariel;[h]
she will mourn and lament,[i]
she will be to me like an altar hearth.[b][j]
3 I will encamp against you on all sides;
I will encircle[k] you with towers
and set up my siege works[l] against you.
4 Brought low, you will speak from the ground;
your speech will mumble[m] out of the dust.[n]
Your voice will come ghostlike[o] from the earth;
out of the dust your speech will whisper.[p]

5 But your many enemies will become like fine dust,[q]
the ruthless[r] hordes like blown chaff.[s]

[a] 25 The meaning of the Hebrew for this word is uncertain. [b] 2 The Hebrew for *altar hearth* sounds like the Hebrew for *Ariel.*

28:18 [e] S Isa 7:7 [f] S ver 15 [g] S Isa 5:5; 63:18; Da 8:13 **28:19** [h] 2Ki 24:2 [i] S Ps 5:3 [j] S Job 18:11 **28:20** [k] Isa 59:6 **28:21** [l] S Ge 38:29; S 1Ch 14:11 [m] S Jos 9:3 [n] Isa 10:12; 65:7; Lk 19:41-44 **28:22** [o] S 2Ch 36:16; Jer 29:18; La 2:15; Zep 2:15 [p] S Isa 10:22 [q] S Isa 10:23 **28:23** [r] Isa 32:9 **28:24** [s] Ecc 3:2 **28:25** [t] Mt 23:23 [u] S Ex 9:31 [v] Ex 9:32; Eze 4:9 **28:26** [w] S Ps 94:10 **28:27** [x] S Isa 21:10 [y] S Job 41:30 [z] Isa 10:5 **28:28** [a] S Isa 21:10 **28:29** [b] S Isa 9:6 [c] S Ps 92:5; Ro 11:33 **29:1** [d] Isa 22:12-13; S 28:1 [e] ver 2,7 [f] S 2Sa 5:7 [g] S Isa 1:14 **29:2** [h] S ver 1 [i] S Isa 3:26; La 2:5 [j] Eze 43:15 **29:3** [k] Lk 19:43-44 [l] S 2Ki 25:1 **29:4** [m] Isa 8:19 [n] Isa 47:1; 52:2 [o] S Lev 19:31 [p] Isa 26:16 **29:5** [q] S Dt 9:21; Ps 78:39; 103:15; S Isa 2:22; 37:27; 40:6; 51:12 [r] S Isa 13:11 [s] S Isa 17:13

28:20 *too short ... too narrow.* Israel was unprepared both militarily and spiritually.
28:21 *Mount Perazim.* Where God "broke out" against the Philistines (see 2Sa 5:20 and note). *Valley of Gibeon.* Where God sent hail to overwhelm the Amorites (see Jos 10:10 – 13 and notes). *strange work ... alien task.* This time God would fight against Israel.
28:22 *destruction decreed.* See 10:22 – 23 and note on 10:22.
28:23 – 29 A wisdom poem (a poetic parable) in two stanzas, each ending in a verse that praises the wisdom of God. In the context, and since "threshing" is emphasized (vv. 27 – 28), the point may be that though God must punish Israel, his actions will be as measured and as well-timed as a farmer's. See 27:12 and note.
28:25 *cumin.* An herb for seasoning (see Mt 23:23 and note). *spelt.* A kind of wheat (see note on Ex 9:32).
28:27 *rod.* See 10:5 and note.
28:29 *plan is wonderful.* See 9:6 and note.
29:1 – 2,7 *Ariel.* Jerusalem (Ariel may mean "City of God" or "Lion of God"). Fighting and bloodshed will turn the city into a virtual "altar hearth" (Hebrew *'ari'el;* see NIV text note on v. 2; see also note on Eze 43:15).
29:1 *Woe.* See note on 28:1. *city where David settled.* See 2Sa 5:6 – 9 and notes; cf. Isa 22:9. *cycle of festivals.* See 1:13 – 14 and note on 1:14.
29:3 *towers.* Pushed up to the city wall by attackers so they could fight the defenders on the same level.
29:4 *whisper.* Used of mediums and spiritists in 8:19. Judah speaks as from the realm of the dead ("ground ... dust ... earth") — so much for their covenant with death (see 28:15,18 and note).
29:5 – 8 In God's time, those nations that devastate Jerusalem will be devastated (see 10:5 – 19; 27:1; cf. Ge 12:2 – 3 and note). The sudden destruction of the enemy resembles that of Assyria's army in 701 BC (see 10:16 and note).
29:5 *chaff.* See 17:13; Ps 1:4 and notes.

Suddenly,[t] in an instant,
6 the LORD Almighty will come[u]
with thunder[v] and earthquake[w] and
great noise,
with windstorm and tempest[x] and
flames of a devouring fire.[y]
7 Then the hordes of all the nations[z] that
fight against Ariel,[a]
that attack her and her fortress and
besiege her,
will be as it is with a dream,[b]
with a vision in the night—
8 as when a hungry person dreams of
eating,
but awakens[c] hungry still;
as when a thirsty person dreams of
drinking,
but awakens faint and thirsty still.[d]
So will it be with the hordes of all the
nations
that fight against Mount Zion.[e]

9 Be stunned and amazed,[f]
blind yourselves and be sightless;[g]
be drunk,[h] but not from wine,[i]
stagger,[j] but not from beer.
10 The LORD has brought over you a deep
sleep:[k]
He has sealed your eyes[l] (the
prophets);[m]
he has covered your heads (the
seers).[n]

11 For you this whole vision[o] is nothing
but words sealed[p] in a scroll. And if you
give the scroll to someone who can read,
and say, "Read this, please," they will answer, "I can't; it is sealed." 12 Or if you give
the scroll to someone who cannot read,
and say, "Read this, please," they will answer, "I don't know how to read."

13 The Lord says:

"These people[q] come near to me with
their mouth
and honor me with their lips,[r]
but their hearts are far from me.[s]
Their worship of me
is based on merely human rules they
have been taught.[a][t]
14 Therefore once more I will astound
these people
with wonder upon wonder;[u]
the wisdom of the wise[v] will perish,
the intelligence of the intelligent will
vanish."[w]
15 Woe to those who go to great
depths
to hide[x] their plans from the LORD,
who do their work in darkness and
think,
"Who sees us?[y] Who will know?"[z]
16 You turn things upside down,
as if the potter were thought to be
like the clay![a]
Shall what is formed say to the one
who formed[b] it,
"You did not make me"?
Can the pot say to the potter,[c]
"You know nothing"?[d]
17 In a very short time,[e] will not Lebanon[f]
be turned into a fertile field[g]
and the fertile field seem like a
forest?[h]
18 In that day[i] the deaf[j] will hear the
words of the scroll,
and out of gloom and darkness[k]
the eyes of the blind will see.[l]
19 Once more the humble[m] will rejoice in
the LORD;

[a] 13 Hebrew; Septuagint *They worship me in vain; / their teachings are merely human rules*

29:5 [t]S Ps 55:15; S Isa 17:14; 1Th 5:3 **29:6** [u]S Isa 26:21; Zec 14:1-5 [v]S Ex 19:16 [w]Mt 24:7; Mk 13:8; Lk 21:11; S Rev 6:12; 11:19 [x]S Ps 50:3; S 55:8; S Isa 28:15 [y]S Lev 10:2; Ps 83:13-15 **29:7** [z]Mic 4:11-12; Zec 12:9 [a]S ver 1 [b]S Job 20:8 **29:8** [c]S Ps 73:20 [d]ver 5,7; Isa 41:11,15; Jer 30:16; Zec 12:3 [e]Isa 17:12-14; 54:17 **29:9** [f]ver 14; Jer 4:9; Hab 1:5 [g]S Isa 6:10 [h]Isa 51:17; 63:6; Jer 13:13; 25:27 [i]S Lev 10:9; Isa 28:1; 51:21-22 [j]S Ps 60:3; S Isa 3:12 **29:10** [k]S Jdg 4:21; Jnh 1:5 [l]Ps 69:23; S Isa 6:9-10; 44:18; Ro 11:8*; 2Th 2:9-11 [m]Mic 3:6 [n]S 1Sa 9:9 **29:11** [o]S Isa 28:7 [p]S Isa 8:16; Da 8:26; 12:9; Mt 13:11; Rev 5:1-2 **29:13** [q]Jer 14:11; Hag 1:2; 2:14 [r]S Ps 50:16 [s]S Ps 119:70; Isa 58:2; Jer 12:2; Eze 33:31 [t]Mt 15:8-9*; Mk 7:6-7*; Col 2:22 **29:14** [u]S Job 10:16 [v]S Job 5:13; Jer 8:9; 49:7 [w]Isa 6:9-10; 1Co 1:19* **29:15** [x]S Ge 3:8; S Isa 28:15 [y]S Job 8:3; Ps 10:11-13; 94:7; Isa 47:10; 57:12; Eze 8:12; 9:9 [z]S 2Ki 21:16; S Job 22:13 **29:16** [a]S Job 10:9; S Isa 10:15 [b]S Ge 2:7 [c]Isa 45:9; 64:8; Jer 18:6; Ro 9:20-21* [d]S Job 9:12 **29:17** [e]S Isa 10:25 [f]S Isa 2:13 [g]Ps 84:6; 107:33 [h]Isa 32:15 **29:18** [i]S Isa 28:5 [j]Mk 7:37 [k]S Ps 107:14 [l]S Ps 146:8; S Isa 32:3; Mt 11:5; Lk 7:22 **29:19** [m]Ps 25:9; 37:11; Isa 61:1; Mt 5:5; 11:29

29:6 *thunder and earthquake ... windstorm and tempest.* As in Jdg 5:4–5; Ps 18:7–15; Hab 3:3–7; see also 28:2; Ps 83:13–15 and notes.
29:9–14 Isaiah speaks again of Israel's spiritual state and warns of the Lord's impending judgment.
29:9 *blind yourselves ... be drunk.* Refers to spiritual stupor (see 6:10 and note; cf. 28:1,7 and note).
29:10 Quoted in part in Ro 11:8 (see note there). *seers.* See 1Sa 9:9 and note; 2Ki 17:13.
29:11–12 God's revelation to Isaiah here is a closed book ("sealed," v. 11) to all the people.
29:13 Quoted in part by Jesus to show the hypocrisy of the Pharisees (see Mk 7:6 and note). *These people.* Not "my people" (cf. 6:9; 8:6,11–12; cf. also Ex 17:4; Jer 14:10–11; Hag 1:2 and notes).
29:14 Quoted in part in 1Co 1:19 (see note there). *wonder upon wonder.* He who showed them wonders in the exodus (see Ex 15:11; Ps 78:12–16 and note) will now show them wonders in judgment. *wisdom ... will perish.* Cf. 44:25; Jer 8:9.
29:15 *Woe.* A new woe begins (see note on 28:1—35:10). *their plans.* Perhaps the alliance between Ahaz and Assyria or between Hezekiah and Egypt (see 30:1–2 and notes). *Who sees us?* See note on Ps 10:11.
29:16 See 45:9; 64:8; see also notes on Jer 18:1–6. This verse is quoted in part in Ro 9:20 (see notes on Ro 9:20–21). Cf. the creation of Adam in Ge 2:7 (see note there); cf. also Isa 10:15; Ps 139.
29:17–24 Another sudden shift to the theme of redemption, as in 28:5–8.
29:17 *Lebanon.* Perhaps symbolic of Assyria (see 10:34). The forests of Lebanon were unequaled (see 2:13 and note), so "fertile field" represents a lesser status (see 32:15 and note).
29:18 *In that day.* See notes on 10:20,27; 26:1. Beyond the day of Assyria's destruction lies the day of Israel's restoration. *deaf will hear ... blind will see.* The opposite of 6:9; linked with the Messianic age in 35:5.
29:19 *needy.* See 11:4. *Holy One of Israel.* See Introduction: Author; see also note on 1:4.

the needy[n] will rejoice in the Holy
One[o] of Israel.
20 The ruthless[p] will vanish,[q]
the mockers[r] will disappear,
and all who have an eye for evil[s] will
be cut down —
21 those who with a word make someone
out to be guilty,
who ensnare the defender in court[t]
and with false testimony[u] deprive
the innocent of justice.[v]

22 Therefore this is what the LORD, who
redeemed[w] Abraham,[x] says to the descendants of Jacob:

"No longer will Jacob be ashamed;[y]
no longer will their faces grow pale.[z]
23 When they see among them their
children,[a]
the work of my hands,[b]
they will keep my name holy;[c]
they will acknowledge the holiness
of the Holy One[d] of Jacob,
and will stand in awe of the God of
Israel.
24 Those who are wayward[e] in spirit will
gain understanding;[f]
those who complain will accept
instruction."[g]

Woe to the Obstinate Nation

30 "Woe[h] to the obstinate children,"[i]
declares the LORD,
"to those who carry out plans that are
not mine,
forming an alliance,[j] but not by my
Spirit,
heaping sin upon sin;
2 who go down to Egypt[k]
without consulting[l] me;
who look for help to Pharaoh's
protection,[m]
to Egypt's shade for refuge.[n]
3 But Pharaoh's protection will be to
your shame,
Egypt's shade[o] will bring you
disgrace.[p]
4 Though they have officials in Zoan[q]
and their envoys have arrived in
Hanes,
5 everyone will be put to shame
because of a people[r] useless[s] to them,
who bring neither help[t] nor advantage,
but only shame and disgrace.[u]"

6 A prophecy[v] concerning the animals of
the Negev:[w]

Through a land of hardship and
distress,[x]
of lions[y] and lionesses,
of adders and darting snakes,[z]
the envoys carry their riches on
donkeys'[a] backs,
their treasures[b] on the humps of
camels,
to that unprofitable nation,
7 to Egypt, whose help is utterly
useless.[c]
Therefore I call her
Rahab[d] the Do-Nothing.

8 Go now, write it on a tablet[e] for them,
inscribe it on a scroll,[f]
that for the days to come
it may be an everlasting witness.[g]
9 For these are rebellious[h] people,
deceitful[i] children,
children unwilling to listen to the
LORD's instruction.[j]

29:19 [n] S Ps 72:4; S Isa 3:15; S 14:30; Mt 11:5; Lk 7:22; Jas 1:9; 2:5 [o] ver 23; Isa 1:4; S 5:19; S 12:6; 30:11 **29:20** [p] S Isa 9:4; S 13:11 [q] Isa 34:12 [r] S 2Ch 36:16; Isa 28:22 [s] S Job 15:35; Ps 7:14; Isa 32:7; 33:11; 59:4; Eze 11:2; Mic 2:1; Na 1:11 **29:21** [t] Am 5:10, 15 [u] Pr 21:28 [v] S Isa 5:23; 32:7; Hab 1:4 **29:22** [w] S Ex 6:6 [x] Ge 17:16; Isa 41:8; 51:2; 63:16 [y] Ps 22:5; 25:3; S Isa 28:16; 49:23; 61:7; Joel 2:26; Zep 3:11 [z] Jer 30:6,10; Joel 2:6,21; Na 2:10 **29:23** [a] Isa 49:20-26; 53:10; 54:1-3 [b] S Ps 8:6; S Isa 19:25 [c] Mt 6:9 [d] S ver 19; S Isa 5:19 **29:24** [e] Ps 95:10; S Pr 12:8; Isa 28:7; Heb 5:2 [f] Isa 1:3; 32:4; 41:20; 60:16 [g] Isa 30:21; 42:16 **30:1** [h] S Isa 28:1 [i] S Dt 21:18; S Isa 1:2 [j] S 2Ki 17:4; S Isa 8:12 **30:2** [k] 2Ki 25:26; Isa 31:1; 36:6; Jer 2:18, 36; 42:14; Eze 17:15; 29:16 [l] S Ge 25:22; S Nu 27:21 [m] Isa 36:9 [n] S Isa 4:6 **30:3** [o] Jdg 9:8-15 [p] ver 5; S Ps 44:13; Isa 20:4-5; 36:6 **30:4** [q] S Nu 13:22 **30:5** [r] ver 7; Isa 20:5; 31:1; 36:6 [s] S 2Ki 18:21 [t] S Ps 108:12; Jer 37:3-5 [u] S ver 3; S 2Ki 18:21; Eze 17:15 **30:6** [v] Isa 13:1 [w] S Jdg 1:9 [x] S Ex 1:13; 5:10,21; Isa 5:30; 8:22; Jer 11:4 [y] S Isa 5:29; 35:9 [z] S Dt 8:15 [a] S Ge 42:26; S 1Sa 25:18 [b] S Isa 15:7 **30:7** [c] S 2Ki 18:21; S Jer 2:36 [d] S Job 9:13 **30:8** [e] S Dt 27:8 [f] S Ex 17:14; S Isa 8:1; Jer 25:13; 30:2; 36:28; Hab 2:2 [g] Jos 24:26-27 **30:9** [h] S Ps 78:8; S Isa 1:2; S Eze 2:6 [i] Isa 28:15; 59:3-4 [j] S Isa 1:10

29:20 *ruthless.* See v. 21. *mockers.* Cf. 28:14,22.
29:21 *deprive . . . of justice.* See 1:17; 9:17 and notes; see also 10:2; Am 5:10,12,24 and note.
29:22 *redeemed.* Normally used of the deliverance of Israel from Egypt (see Ex 6:6 and note; 15:13). Cf. 43:1,3,14. But Abraham also had an "exodus" out of a pagan world (see Ge 12:1; Jos 24:2 – 3,14 – 15 and notes). *be ashamed.* Cf. 45:17; 50:7; 54:4. *grow pale.* From fear of the enemy.
29:23 *see . . . their children.* Cf. 49:20 – 21; 54:1 – 2 and notes. Restoration from exile may be in view. See also 53:10 and note. *children, the work of my hands.* See 45:11 (cf. Eph 2:10 and note). *acknowledge the holiness . . . stand in awe.* See 8:13. Isaiah's contemporaries showed little respect for the Lord. *Holy One of Jacob.* Cf. v. 19; see note on 1:4.
29:24 *wayward in spirit.* See 19:14. *gain understanding.* Contrast 1:3 (see also note there).
30:1 *Woe.* See note on 28:1 — 35:10. *obstinate children.* See 1:2 and note. *plans . . . not mine.* See 29:15 and note. *alliance.* After Shabako became pharaoh in 715 BC, the smaller nations in Aram (Syria) and Canaan sought his help against Assyria. Judah apparently joined them (see 20:5 and note). *my Spirit.* Who spoke through his prophet.
30:2 Hezekiah did this (see 2Ki 18:21 and note). *shade.* A metaphor for a king as one who provides protection (see Jdg 9:15; La 4:20 and notes). The Lord should have been Israel's "shade" (cf. 49:2; 51:16; see Ps 91:1; 121:5 and notes).
30:4 *Zoan.* Ironically, where the Israelites once served as slaves; see 19:11 and note. *Hanes.* Possibly Heracleopolis Magna, about 50 miles south of Cairo, or perhaps a city in the Nile delta, close to Zoan.
30:6 *prophecy.* See 13:1 and note. *Negev.* The dry region in the southern part of the Holy Land (see Ge 12:9 and note; cf. Jdg 1:9). *hardship and distress.* Perhaps it was necessary to use back roads because the Assyrians had control of the main coastal road (see Dt 8:15; Jdg 5:6 and note). *darting snakes.* See 14:29.
30:7 *Rahab.* A mythical sea monster, here symbolic of Egypt. The name itself means "storm," and also "arrogance." See 27:1 ("Leviathan") and note.
30:8 *write it.* Probably the name "Rahab the Do-Nothing" (v. 7).
30:9 *rebellious people.* See v. 1; see also 1:2 and note.

10 They say to the seers,[k]
"See no more visions[l]!"
and to the prophets,
"Give us no more visions of
what is right!
Tell us pleasant things,[m]
prophesy illusions.[n]
11 Leave this way,[o]
get off this path,
and stop confronting[p] us
with the Holy One[q] of
Israel!"

12 Therefore this is what the
Holy One[r] of Israel says:

"Because you have rejected
this message,[s]
relied on oppression[t]
and depended on deceit,
13 this sin will become for you
like a high wall,[u] cracked
and bulging,
that collapses[v] suddenly,[w] in
an instant.
14 It will break in pieces like pottery,[x]
shattered so mercilessly
that among its pieces not a fragment
will be found
for taking coals from a hearth
or scooping water out of a cistern."

15 This is what the Sovereign[y] LORD, the
Holy One[z] of Israel, says:

"In repentance and rest[a] is your
salvation,
in quietness and trust[b] is your
strength,
but you would have none of it.[c]
16 You said, 'No, we will flee[d] on horses.'[e]
Therefore you will flee!
You said, 'We will ride off on swift
horses.'
Therefore your pursuers will be
swift!
17 A thousand will flee
at the threat of one;
at the threat of five[f]
you will all flee[g] away,

Clay tablets were used to record early writings: "Go now, write it on a tablet for them, inscribe it on a scroll" (Isa 30:8).

Z. Radovan/www.BibleLandPictures.com

30:10 [k]S 1Sa 9:9 [l]Jer 11:21; 32:3; Am 7:13 [m]S 1Ki 22:8; S Jer 4:10 [n]Jer 23:26; 25:9; 26:9; 36:29; Eze 13:7; Ro 16:18; 2Ti 4:3-4 **30:11** [o]ver 21; Pr 3:6; Isa 35:8-9; 48:17 [p]S Job 21:14 [q]S Isa 29:19 **30:12** [r]ver 15; S Isa 5:19; 31:1 [s]S Isa 5:24 [t]S Ps 10:7; S 12:5; S Isa 5:7 **30:13** [u]S Ne 2:17; Ps 62:3; S 80:12 [v]S 1Ki 20:30 [w]S Isa 17:14 **30:14** [x]S Ps 2:9 **30:15** [y]Jer 7:20; Eze 3:11 [z]S ver 12 [a]S Ex 14:14; S Jos 1:13 [b]S 2Ch 20:12; Isa 32:17 [c]Isa 8:6; 42:24; 57:17 **30:16** [d]Jer 46:6 [e]S Dt 17:16;

till you are left[h]
like a flagstaff on a mountaintop,
like a banner[i] on a hill."

18 Yet the LORD longs[j] to be gracious to
you;
therefore he will rise up to show you
compassion.[k]
For the LORD is a God of justice.[l]
Blessed are all who wait for him![m]

19 People of Zion, who live in Jerusalem,
you will weep no more.[n] How gracious he
will be when you cry for help![o] As soon as
he hears, he will answer[p] you. 20 Although
the Lord gives you the bread[q] of adversity and the water of affliction, your teachers[r] will be hidden[s] no more; with your
own eyes you will see them. 21 Whether
you turn to the right or to the left, your
ears will hear a voice[t] behind you, saying,

1Ki 10:28-29; S Ps 20:7; Isa 31:1,3; 36:8 **30:17** [f]S Lev 26:8 [g]Lev 26:36; Dt 28:25; S 2Ki 7:7 [h]S Isa 1:8 [i]S Ps 20:5 **30:18** [j]S Ge 43:31; Isa 42:14; 2Pe 3:9,15 [k]Ps 78:38; Isa 48:9; Jnh 3:10 [l]S Ps 11:7; S Isa 5:16 [m]S Ps 27:14; Isa 25:9; 33:2; 40:31; 64:4; La 3:25; Da 12:12 **30:19** [n]S Isa 25:8; 60:20; 61:3 [o]S Job 24:12 [p]Job 22:27; Ps 50:15; S 86:7; Isa 41:17; 58:9; 65:24; Zec 13:9; Mt 7:7-11 **30:20** [q]1Ki 22:27 [r]S Isa 28:9 [s]Ps 74:9; Am 8:11 **30:21** [t]S Isa 29:24

30:10 *seers.* See 1Sa 9:9 and note; 2Ki 17:13. *See no more visions.* Cf. Am 2:12; 7:13,16; Mic 2:6. *Tell us pleasant things.* As false prophets do (see 1Ki 22:13; Jer 6:14; 8:11; 23:16–17,26; Mic 2:11; 3:5,11 and notes; cf. 2Ti 4:3–4 and note on 4:3).
30:11–12,15 *Holy One of Israel.* See 1:4 and note.
30:12 *oppression.* Especially in their domestic policy (see 1:15–17,23; 5:7; 29:21; 58:3–4; 59:3,6–8,13). *deceit.* Especially in their foreign policy (see vv. 1–2; 29:15).
30:13 *like a high wall.* Oppression and deceit (v. 12) had been the "wall" they built to assure their safety and prosperity, but it will be shattered to pieces (v. 14).
30:15 See 26:3. *repentance and rest.* The true way to salvation and security.
30:16 *horses.* See Ps 20:7–8 and note; 33:17; Pr 21:31 and note.
30:17 *A thousand will flee.* A fulfillment of the curse of Dt 32:30. *flagstaff ... banner.* See 5:26 and note (see also 1:8 and note).
30:18 *longs to be gracious.* After punishing Israel, God will once again bless his people (cf. 40:2 and note).
30:19 *weep no more.* See 25:8 and note. God's response is similar to his zeal for the vineyard (Israel) in 27:2–6 (see notes there).
30:20 *bread of adversity ... water of affliction.* Prisoners' food (see 1Ki 22:27). *teachers.* Prophets, like Isaiah. Or the Hebrew for "teachers" can be rendered "Teacher" and be a reference to the Lord, who will instruct them, and this time they will respond with obedience (vv. 21–22); cf. Jer 31:31–34; Eze 11:19–20; 36:25–27.
30:21 *This is the way; walk in it.* See Dt 5:32–33. Contrast the attitude shown in v. 9 (cf. 29:24; Jer 6:16 and note).

"This is the way;[u] walk in it." 22 Then you
will desecrate your idols[v] overlaid with silver and your images covered with gold;[w]
you will throw them away like a menstrual[x] cloth and say to them, "Away with
you![y]"

23 He will also send you rain[z] for the
seed you sow in the ground, and the food
that comes from the land will be rich[a]
and plentiful.[b] In that day[c] your cattle will
graze in broad meadows.[d] 24 The oxen[e] and
donkeys that work the soil will eat fodder[f]
and mash, spread out with fork[g] and shovel. 25 In the day of great slaughter,[h] when
the towers[i] fall, streams of water will
flow[j] on every high mountain and every
lofty hill. 26 The moon will shine like the
sun,[k] and the sunlight will be seven times
brighter, like the light of seven full days,
when the LORD binds up the bruises of his
people and heals[l] the wounds he inflicted.

27 See, the Name[m] of the LORD comes
from afar,
with burning anger[n] and dense
clouds of smoke;
his lips are full of wrath,[o]
and his tongue is a consuming fire.[p]
28 His breath[q] is like a rushing torrent,[r]
rising up to the neck.[s]
He shakes the nations in the sieve[t] of
destruction;
he places in the jaws of the peoples
a bit[u] that leads them astray.
29 And you will sing
as on the night you celebrate a holy
festival;[v]
your hearts will rejoice[w]
as when people playing pipes[x] go up
to the mountain[y] of the LORD,
to the Rock[z] of Israel.
30 The LORD will cause people to hear his
majestic voice[a]
and will make them see his arm[b]
coming down
with raging anger[c] and consuming fire,[d]
with cloudburst, thunderstorm[e] and
hail.[f]
31 The voice of the LORD will shatter
Assyria;[g]
with his rod he will strike[h] them
down.
32 Every stroke the LORD lays on them
with his punishing club[i]
will be to the music of timbrels[j] and
harps,
as he fights them in battle with the
blows of his arm.[k]
33 Topheth[l] has long been prepared;
it has been made ready for the king.
Its fire pit has been made deep and
wide,
with an abundance of fire and
wood;
the breath[m] of the LORD,
like a stream of burning sulfur,[n]
sets it ablaze.[o]

Woe to Those Who Rely on Egypt

31 Woe[p] to those who go down to
Egypt[q] for help,
who rely on horses,[r]
who trust in the multitude of their
chariots[s]
and in the great strength of their
horsemen,

30:21 [u]S ver 11; S Job 33:11 **30:22** [v]S Ex 32:4; S Isa 17:8 [w]S Job 22:24; Isa 31:7 [x]Lev 15:19-23 [y]Eze 7:19-20 **30:23** [z]S Dt 28:12; Isa 65:21-22 [a]Isa 25:6; 55:2; Jer 31:14 [b]S Job 36:31; Isa 62:8 [c]S Isa 28:5 [d]S Ps 65:13 **30:24** [e]Isa 32:14, 20 [f]S Job 6:5 [g]Mt 3:12; Lk 3:17 **30:25** [h]S Isa 13:5; 34:6; 65:12; Jer 25:32; 50:27 [i]S Isa 2:15 [j]S Ex 17:6; Isa 32:2; 41:18; Joel 3:18; Zec 14:8 **30:26** [k]Isa 24:23; 60:19-20; Zec 14:7; Rev 21:23; 22:5 [l]S Dt 32:39; S 2Ch 7:14; Ps 107:20; S Isa 1:5; Jer 3:22; 17:14; Hos 14:4 **30:27** [m]1Ki 18:24; Ps 20:1; Isa 59:19; 64:2 [n]Isa 26:20; 66:14; Eze 22:31 [o]Isa 10:5; 13:5 [p]S ver 30; S Job 41:21 **30:28** [q]S Isa 11:4 [r]S Ps 50:3; S Isa 28:15 [s]S Isa 8:8

[t]Am 9:9 [u]2Ki 19:28 **30:29** [v]Isa 25:6 [w]Isa 12:1 [x]S 1Sa 10:5 [y]S Ps 42:4; Mt 26:30 [z]S Ge 49:24 **30:30** [a]S Ps 68:33 [b]Isa 9:12; 40:10; 51:9; 52:10; 53:1; 59:16; 62:8; 63:12 [c]S ver 27; S Isa 10:25 [d]S Isa 4:4; 47:14 [e]Ex 20:18; Ps 29:3 [f]S Ex 9:18 **30:31** [g]S Isa 10:5, 12 [h]S Isa 11:4 **30:32** [i]Isa 10:26 [j]S Ex 15:20 [k]S Isa 11:15; Eze 32:10 **30:33** [l]S 2Ki 23:10 [m]S Ex 15:10; S 2Sa 22:16 [n]S Ge 19:24; S Rev 9:17 [o]S Isa 1:31 **31:1** [p]S Isa 28:1 [q]S Dt 17:16; S Isa 30:2, 5; S Jer 37:5 [r]S Isa 30:16 [s]S Isa 2:7

30:22 *desecrate your idols.* In repentance, not in despair, as in 2:20 (see note there).
30:23 *rain … food … rich and plentiful.* Part of the covenant blessings promised in Dt 28:11–12. See 5:6 and note. *In that day.* Cf. 29:18; see notes on 10:20,27; 26:1. *cattle will graze.* Cf. 32:20 and note.
30:24 *mash.* Seasoned, tasty fodder.
30:25 *day of great slaughter.* Cf. 24:1; 34:2,6 and note. Assyria's fall (v. 31) is one illustration. *streams … on every high mountain.* Paradise-like conditions will return to the land (see 41:18; Ps 104:13–15 and notes).
30:26 *moon … brighter.* The darkness will be past: Night will be like the day, and day will be illumined with sevenfold light. *binds up the bruises … heals the wounds.* Israel was bruised politically because of the sins of the people (see 1:5–6; 61:1; Jer 33:6 and notes).
30:27 *the Name.* The revelation of God, especially his power and glory. *anger … clouds of smoke.* The language of theophany (a manifestation or appearance of God). God is portrayed as coming in a storm (see v. 30; see also 28:2; 29:6; Ps 18:7–15 and notes). *consuming fire.* Perhaps lightning.
30:28 *rising up to the neck.* The army of Assyria was similarly described in 8:8 (see note there). *bit.* Cf. 37:29.
30:29 *sing … holy festival.* Perhaps the Passover, alluded to in 31:5 (cf. Mt 26:30). *mountain of the LORD.* Zion, where the temple was (see 2:2–4 and note). *Rock.* God himself (see 17:10 and note).
30:30–31 *voice.* Associated with thunder in Ex 20:18–19; Ps 29:3–9 (see note there).
30:30 *arm coming down.* See 9:12,17,21; 51:9 and notes. *cloudburst … hail.* See 28:2.
30:31 *voice of the LORD will shatter.* Cf. 10:5; Ps 29:5–9.
30:32 *his punishing club.* See 11:4 and note. *music of timbrels.* After a great victory the women rejoiced with singing and dancing (see Ex 15:20–21 and notes; 1Sa 18:6).
30:33 *Topheth.* A region outside Jerusalem where children were sacrificed to Molek (see 2Ki 23:10; Jer 7:31–32; 19:6,11–14 and notes), the god of the Ammonites (see 1Ki 11:7). Thus it was a place of burning. *king.* Of Assyria (or perhaps a reference to Molek; see note on Jdg 10:6). *burning sulfur.* See 1:31; Ge 19:24 and notes.
31:1 See 30:1 and note. In shorter form, ch. 31 recapitulates the structure and content of ch. 30. *go down to Egypt.* See Ge 26:2. *horses … chariots.* Egypt had large numbers of horses and chariots (see 1Ki 10:28–29; Ps 20:7–8 and notes). *Holy One of Israel.* See 1:4 and note.

but do not look to the Holy One[t] of
Israel,
or seek help from the LORD.[u]
2 Yet he too is wise[v] and can bring
disaster;[w]
he does not take back his words.[x]
He will rise up against that wicked
nation,[y]
against those who help evildoers.
3 But the Egyptians[z] are mere mortals
and not God;[a]
their horses[b] are flesh and not spirit.
When the LORD stretches out his hand,[c]
those who help will stumble,
those who are helped[d] will fall;
all will perish together.[e]

4 This is what the LORD says to me:

"As a lion[f] growls,
a great lion over its prey—
and though a whole band of
shepherds[g]
is called together against it,
it is not frightened by their shouts
or disturbed by their clamor[h]—
so the LORD Almighty will come down[i]
to do battle on Mount Zion and on
its heights.
5 Like birds hovering[j] overhead,
the LORD Almighty will shield[k]
Jerusalem;
he will shield it and deliver[l] it,
he will 'pass over'[m] it and will
rescue it."

6 Return,[n] you Israelites, to the One you
have so greatly revolted[o] against. 7 For in
that day[p] every one of you will reject the
idols of silver and gold[q] your sinful hands
have made.[r]

8 "Assyria[s] will fall by no human sword;
a sword, not of mortals, will devour[t]
them.
They will flee before the sword
and their young men will be put to
forced labor.[u]
9 Their stronghold[v] will fall because of
terror;
at the sight of the battle standard[w]
their commanders will panic,[x]"
declares the LORD,
whose fire[y] is in Zion,
whose furnace[z] is in Jerusalem.

The Kingdom of Righteousness

32 See, a king[a] will reign in
righteousness
and rulers will rule with justice.[b]
2 Each one will be like a shelter[c] from
the wind
and a refuge from the storm,[d]
like streams of water[e] in the desert[f]
and the shadow of a great rock in a
thirsty land.

3 Then the eyes of those who see will no
longer be closed,[g]
and the ears[h] of those who hear will
listen.
4 The fearful heart will know and
understand,[i]
and the stammering tongue[j] will be
fluent and clear.
5 No longer will the fool[k] be called noble
nor the scoundrel be highly
respected.
6 For fools speak folly,[l]
their hearts are bent on evil:[m]
They practice ungodliness[n]
and spread error[o] concerning the
LORD;

31:1 [t]Job 6:10; S Isa 1:4; S 30:12 [u]S Dt 20:1; S Pr 21:31; S Isa 9:13; Jer 46:9; Eze 29:16 **31:2** [v]S Ps 92:5; Ro 16:27 [w]Isa 45:7; 47:11; Am 3:6 [x]Nu 23:19; S Pr 19:21 [y]S Isa 1:4; 29:15; 32:6 **31:3** [z]Isa 20:5; 36:9 [a]S Ps 9:20; Eze 28:9; 2Th 2:4 [b]S Isa 30:16 [c]Ne 1:10; S Job 30:21; Isa 9:17,21; Jer 51:25; Eze 20:34 [d]Isa 10:3; 30:5-7 [e]S Isa 20:6; Jer 17:5 **31:4** [f]Nu 24:9; S 1Sa 17:34; Hos 11:10; Am 3:8 [g]Jer 3:15; 23:4; Eze 34:23; Na 3:18 [h]Ps 74:23 [i]Isa 42:13 **31:5** [j]S Ge 1:2; S Mt 23:37 [k]S Ps 91:4; S Isa 5:2; S Zec 9:15 [l]S Ps 34:7; Isa 37:35; 38:6 [m]S Ex 12:23 **31:6** [n]S Job 22:23; S Isa 1:27 [o]S Isa 1:5 **31:7** [p]Isa 29:18 [q]S Isa 30:22 [r]S Ps 135:15 **31:8** [s]S Isa 10:12 [t]S Ex 12:12; Isa 10:12; 14:25; S 27:1; 33:1; 37:7; Jer 25:12; Hab 2:8 [u]S Ge 49:15; S Dt 20:11

31:9 [v]Dt 32:31,37 [w]S Isa 18:3; S Jer 4:6 [x]Jer 51:9; Na 3:7 [y]S Isa 10:17 [z]Ps 21:9; Mal 4:1 **32:1** [a]S Ps 149:2; S Isa 6:5; 55:4; Eze 37:24 [b]Ps 72:1-4; S Isa 9:7; S 28:6 **32:2** [c]S 1Ki 18:4 [d]S Ps 55:8 [e]S Ps 23:2; S Isa 30:25; 49:10; Jer 31:9 [f]S Ps 107:35; Isa 44:3 **32:3** [g]S Isa 29:18; 35:5; 42:7,16 [h]S Dt 29:4 **32:4** [i]Isa 6:10; S 29:24 [j]Isa 35:6 **32:5** [k]S 1Sa 25:25 **32:6** [l]S Pr 19:3 [m]S Pr 24:2; S Isa 26:10 [n]S Isa 9:17 [o]Isa 3:12; 9:16

31:2 *he too is wise.* People had questioned God's wisdom in 29:14–16 (see notes there).
31:3 *Egyptians are mere mortals and not God.* Cf. Hos 11:9. *God ... spirit.* See Jn 4:24 and note. *stretches out his hand.* Cf. the refrain in 5:25 (see note there); 9:12,17,21; 10:4. *those who help will stumble.* Cf. 30:3,5.
31:4 *lion.* A simile, but perhaps also an allusion to the Assyrian king (see notes on 15:9; Jer 2:15). *shepherds.* Perhaps an allusion to the rulers of the nations (see NIV text note on Na 3:18).
31:5 *birds ... will shield.* Cf. Dt 32:10–11. *pass over.* The technical word used of the destroying angel who "passed over" every house in Egypt that had blood on the doorposts (see Ex 12:13,23 and notes). Cf. Isa 37:35.
31:6 *greatly revolted.* See 1:2 and note.
31:7 *reject the idols.* See 2:20 and note.
31:8 *sword, not of mortals.* The angel of the Lord struck down 185,000 soldiers (see 37:36 and note; see also Ps 7:12–13 and note). *put to forced labor.* As prisoners of war.
31:9 *stronghold.* Nineveh was destroyed by the Medes and Babylonians in 612 BC (see Na 3:7). *commanders will panic.* Cf. Na 2:10 and note. *fire ... furnace.* The Lord's glory resides in Zion, and from that center of his people his fire of judgment breaks out upon the wicked (see 10:17; 30:33 and note; cf. Lev 10:2; cf. also Joel 3:16; Am 1:2 and notes).
32:1 *king ... in righteousness.* The Messianic age is again in view (see 9:7; 11:4; 16:5 and notes). Cf. vv. 16–17; 33:17 and note.
32:2 *Each one will be like.* The Lord's redeemed, as sources of protection and blessing, will reflect him (see the rest of this note; see also vv. 3–8). *shelter ... refuge ... shadow.* Similar terms are applied to the Lord in 25:4 (see 4:5–6 and note). *streams ... in the desert.* See 35:6–7; 41:18; 49:10 and notes.
32:3 *eyes ... no longer be closed ... ears ... listen.* See 35:5 and note (contrast 6:9–10; see notes there).
32:5–8 The redeemed will no longer be among the fools. The contrast between the fool and the wise or noble is characteristic of wisdom literature (compare Pr 9:1–6 with Pr 9:13–18).
32:6 A full explication of what the OT calls a "fool" (see Pr 1:7 and note; see also NIV text note there). *fools speak folly.* Cf. 9:16–17; Ps 14:1 and note; 53:1.

the hungry they leave empty[p]
and from the thirsty they withhold water.
7 Scoundrels use wicked methods,[q]
they make up evil schemes[r]
to destroy the poor with lies,
even when the plea of the needy[s] is just.[t]
8 But the noble make noble plans,
and by noble deeds[u] they stand.[v]

The Women of Jerusalem

9 You women[w] who are so complacent,
rise up and listen[x] to me;
you daughters who feel secure,[y]
hear what I have to say!
10 In little more than a year[z]
you who feel secure will tremble;
the grape harvest will fail,[a]
and the harvest of fruit will not come.
11 Tremble,[b] you complacent women;
shudder, you daughters who feel secure![c]
Strip off your fine clothes[d]
and wrap yourselves in rags.[e]
12 Beat your breasts[f] for the pleasant fields,
for the fruitful vines[g]
13 and for the land of my people,
a land overgrown with thorns and briers[h]—
yes, mourn[i] for all houses of merriment
and for this city of revelry.[j]
14 The fortress[k] will be abandoned,
the noisy city deserted;[l]
citadel and watchtower[m] will become a wasteland forever,
the delight of donkeys,[n] a pasture for flocks,[o]
15 till the Spirit[p] is poured on us from on high,
and the desert becomes a fertile field,[q]
and the fertile field seems like a forest.[r]
16 The LORD's justice[s] will dwell in the desert,[t]
his righteousness[u] live in the fertile field.
17 The fruit of that righteousness[v] will be peace;[w]
its effect will be quietness and confidence[x] forever.
18 My people will live in peaceful[y] dwelling places,
in secure homes,[z]
in undisturbed places of rest.[a]
19 Though hail[b] flattens the forest[c]
and the city is leveled[d] completely,
20 how blessed you will be,
sowing[e] your seed by every stream,[f]
and letting your cattle and donkeys range free.[g]

Distress and Help

33 Woe[h] to you, destroyer,
you who have not been destroyed!
Woe to you, betrayer,
you who have not been betrayed!
When you stop destroying,
you will be destroyed;[i]
when you stop betraying,
you will be betrayed.[j]

2 LORD, be gracious[k] to us;
we long for you.
Be our strength[l] every morning,
our salvation[m] in time of distress.[n]

32:6 [p]S Isa 3:15 **32:7** [q]Jer 5:26-28; Da 12:10 [r]S Isa 29:20; Mic 7:3 [s]S Ps 72:4; Isa 29:19; 61:1 [t]S Isa 29:21 **32:8** [u]1Ch 29:9; S Pr 11:25 [v]Isa 14:24 **32:9** [w]S Isa 4:1 [x]Isa 28:23 [y]ver 11; Isa 47:8; Da 4:4; Am 6:1; Zep 2:15 **32:10** [z]Isa 37:30 [a]Isa 5:5-6; S 24:7 **32:11** [b]Isa 33:14 [c]S ver 9 [d]Isa 47:2; Mic 1:8; Na 3:5 [e]S Isa 3:24 **32:12** [f]Na 2:7 [g]Isa 16:9 **32:13** [h]S Isa 5:6; Hos 10:8 [i]S Isa 24:11 [j]S Isa 23:7 **32:14** [k]S Isa 13:22 [l]S Isa 6:11; S 27:10 [m]S Isa 2:15; 34:13 [n]S Ps 104:11 [o]S Isa 5:17 **32:15** [p]S Isa 11:2; S Eze 37:9 [q]Ps 107:35; Isa 35:1-2 [r]Isa 29:17 **32:16** [s]S Isa 9:7; S 28:6 [t]Isa 35:1, 6; 42:11 [u]S Ps 48:1; S Isa 1:26 **32:17** [v]S Ps 85:10 [w]S Ps 119:165; S Isa 9:7; Ro 14:17; Heb 12:11; Jas 3:18 [x]S Isa 30:15 **32:18** [y]S Isa 2:4 [z]S Isa 26:1; 33:20; 37:33; 65:21; 66:14; Am 9:14 [a]S Jos 1:13; S Job 11:18; Hos 2:18-23 **32:19** [b]Isa 28:17 [c]S Isa 10:19; Zec 11:2 [d]S Job 40:11; S Isa 19:18; 24:10; 27:10 **32:20** [e]S Ecc 11:1 [f]S Dt 28:12 [g]Job 39:8; S Isa 30:24 **33:1** [h]S 2Ki 19:21; S Isa 28:1 [i]S Isa 31:8; S Mt 7:2 [j]S Isa 21:2; Jer 30:16; Eze 39:10 **33:2** [k]S Ge 43:29; S Ezr 9:8 [l]Isa 40:10; 51:9; 59:16; 63:5 [m]S Ps 13:5; S Isa 12:2 [n]S Isa 5:30

32:7 *plea of the needy.* See 1:17 and note.

32:8 *the noble ... noble deeds.* Conduct reveals character (cf. Mt 7:16–17; 12:33; Jas 3:11–12 and note). *plans ... stand.* See 8:10 and note.

32:9 *women.* Cf. 3:16—4:1 and notes. *complacent ... feel secure.* See v. 11; Am 6:1 and note. These words are used in a good sense in v. 18 (the Hebrew for "undisturbed" is the same as that for "complacent").

32:10 *a year.* Perhaps the invasion of Sennacherib (701 BC) is in view. *grape harvest will fail.* Cf. 37:30. The armies of Assyria would bring widespread destruction, ruining the summer fruit.

32:11 *Strip.* Cf. 47:2–3 and notes.

32:12 *Beat your breasts.* Like the slave girls of Nineveh (Na 2:7). *for the fruitful vines.* Cf. the Lord's weeping in 16:9.

32:13 *thorns and briers.* See 5:6; 7:23 and notes. *merriment ... revelry.* See 22:2 and note; cf. Jer 16:8–9.

32:14 *fortress ... noisy city.* Assyria's invasion is a warning that Jerusalem (see 24:10 and note) will one day be destroyed. *donkeys ... flocks.* Cf. 7:25; 13:21–22; 34:13.

32:15 *till the Spirit is poured on.* The outpouring of the Spirit is linked with abundance also in 44:3 (see note there; see also 11:2; Joel 2:28–32; Zec 12:10 and notes). *fertile field ... forest.* The forest probably stands for Lebanon (see 29:17 and note; cf. 35:1–2 and notes).

32:16 *justice ... righteousness.* See v. 1 and note.

32:17 *peace.* Cf. 9:7; 11:6–9 and note. *quietness and confidence.* Contrast 30:15 ("you would have none of it").

32:18 *secure ... undisturbed.* See note on v. 9. *places of rest.* See 28:12 and note.

32:19 *hail.* Cf. 28:2. *forest.* Probably Assyria. See 10:33–34 and notes. *city.* See 24:10 and note.

32:20 The abundance of the day of the Lord is described (see 30:23–24 and notes).

33:1 *Woe.* See note on 28:1—35:10. *destroyer ... betrayer.* Probably Assyria—depicted as treacherous (see 10:5–6; 16:4; 21:2; 24:16 and notes).

33:2–9 A prayer asking the Lord to bring about the promised destruction of Assyria.

33:2 *be gracious.* See 30:18 and note; cf. Nu 6:25. *strength ... salvation.* See 12:2 and note; cf. 59:16 and note. *every morning.* See Ps 88:13; 143:8 and note; see also introduction to Ps 57. *distress.* See 37:3.

3 At the uproar of your army,[o] the
peoples flee;[p]
when you rise up,[q] the nations
scatter.
4 Your plunder,[r] O nations, is harvested[s]
as by young locusts;[t]
like a swarm of locusts people
pounce on it.
5 The LORD is exalted,[u] for he dwells on
high;[v]
he will fill Zion with his justice[w] and
righteousness.[x]
6 He will be the sure foundation for your
times,
a rich store of salvation[y] and wisdom
and knowledge;
the fear[z] of the LORD is the key to this
treasure.[a][a]
7 Look, their brave men[b] cry aloud in the
streets;
the envoys[c] of peace weep bitterly.
8 The highways are deserted,
no travelers[d] are on the roads.[e]
The treaty is broken,[f]
its witnesses[b] are despised,
no one is respected.
9 The land dries up[g] and wastes away,
Lebanon[h] is ashamed and
withers;[i]
Sharon[j] is like the Arabah,
and Bashan[k] and Carmel[l] drop their
leaves.
10 "Now will I arise,[m]" says the LORD.
"Now will I be exalted;[n]
now will I be lifted up.
11 You conceive[o] chaff,
you give birth[p] to straw;
your breath is a fire[q] that consumes
you.
12 The peoples will be burned to ashes;[r]
like cut thornbushes[s] they will be set
ablaze.[t]"
13 You who are far away,[u] hear[v] what I
have done;
you who are near, acknowledge my
power!
14 The sinners[w] in Zion are terrified;
trembling[x] grips the godless:
"Who of us can dwell with the
consuming fire?[y]
Who of us can dwell with everlasting
burning?"
15 Those who walk righteously[z]
and speak what is right,[a]
who reject gain from extortion[b]
and keep their hands from accepting
bribes,[c]
who stop their ears against plots of
murder
and shut their eyes[d] against
contemplating evil—
16 they are the ones who will dwell on
the heights,[e]
whose refuge[f] will be the mountain
fortress.[g]
Their bread will be supplied,
and water will not fail[h] them.
17 Your eyes will see the king[i] in his beauty[j]
and view a land that stretches afar.[k]
18 In your thoughts you will ponder the
former terror:[l]
"Where is that chief officer?

33:3 [o] S Ps 46:6; S 68:33 [p] S Ps 68:1; S Isa 13:14 [q] ver 10; Nu 10:35; Ps 12:5; Isa 59:16-18 **33:4** [r] S Nu 14:3; S 2Ki 7:16 [s] S Isa 17:5; Joel 3:13 [t] Joel 1:4 **33:5** [u] S Isa 5:16 [v] S Job 16:19 [w] S Isa 9:7; S 28:6 [x] S Isa 1:26 **33:6** [y] S Isa 12:2; 26:1; 51:6; 60:18 [z] S Pr 1:7; Isa 11:2-3; Mt 6:33 [a] S Ge 39:3; S Job 22:25 **33:7** [b] Isa 10:34 [c] S 2Ki 18:37 **33:8** [d] Isa 60:15; Zec 7:14 [e] S Jdg 5:6; Isa 30:21; 35:8 [f] S 2Ki 18:14 **33:9** [g] S Isa 3:26 [h] S 2Ki 19:23; Isa 2:13; 35:2; 37:24; Jer 22:6 [i] S Isa 15:6 [j] S 1Ch 27:29 [k] Mic 7:14 [l] 1Ki 18:19; Isa 35:2; Na 1:4 **33:10** [m] S ver 3; Isa 2:21 [n] S Isa 5:16 **33:11** [o] Ps 7:14; Isa 59:4; Jas 1:15 [p] S Isa 26:18 [q] Isa 1:31 **33:12** [r] Am 2:1 [s] S Isa 5:6 [t] S Isa 10:17; S 27:11 **33:13** [u] Ps 48:10; 49:1 [v] Isa 34:1; 48:16; 49:1

[a] *6* Or *is a treasure from him* [b] *8* Dead Sea Scrolls; Masoretic Text / *the cities*

33:14 [w] S Isa 1:28 [x] S Isa 32:11 [y] S Isa 1:31; S 30:30; S Zec 13:9; Heb 12:29 **33:15** [z] Isa 58:8 [a] Ps 15:2; 24:4 [b] Eze 22:13; 33:31 [c] S Pr 15:27 [d] Ps 119:37 **33:16** [e] S Dt 32:13 [f] S Ps 46:1; S Isa 25:4 [g] Ps 18:1-2; Isa 26:1 [h] Isa 48:21; 49:10; 65:13 **33:17** [i] S Isa 6:5 [j] S Isa 4:2 [k] S Isa 26:15 **33:18** [l] S Isa 17:14

33:3 *rise up ... scatter.* An allusion to Nu 10:35–36 (see notes there); cf. Ps 68:1 and note.
33:5 *fill ... righteousness.* See 1:26; 32:1 and note.
33:6 *wisdom ... knowledge ... fear of the LORD.* Terms linked with the Messiah in 11:2 (see note there). See 9:6; Pr 1:7 and notes.
33:7 *their brave men.* The men of Judah, during Sennacherib's invasion of 701 BC (see 10:28–34 and notes). *envoys of peace.* Perhaps the three officials who conferred with the Assyrian field commander (see 36:3,22).
33:8 *highways are deserted.* Travel and trade were impossible, creating economic hardship (see Jdg 5:6 and note). *treaty.* Perhaps the agreement made when Hezekiah paid large sums to Sennacherib (see 2Ki 18:14 and note).
33:9 *land ... wastes away.* Farmland and pastures were ruined by the invaders. See 24:4 and note. *Lebanon.* Renowned for its cedars (2:13) and animals (40:16). *Sharon.* A plain along the Mediterranean coast north of Joppa, known for its beautiful foliage and superb grazing land (see 35:2 and note; 65:10; 1Ch 27:29). *Arabah.* Desert land associated with the Jordan River and the Dead Sea (see Dt 1:1; 2:8 and notes). *Bashan.* See 2:13 and note. *Carmel.* See note on 1Ki 18:19; means "fertile field" (as in 29:17; 32:15) or "orchards" (as in 16:10) and is also associated with lush pasturelands (see 35:2 and note; Mic 7:14 and NIV text note; Na 1:4 and note).
33:10 *be exalted.* Through the judgment he brings on his rebellious people (see v. 14 and note).
33:11 *conceive ... give birth.* Cf. 26:18. *breath is a fire.* They only produce what results in their destruction.
33:12 *to ashes.* The burning will be complete (see Am 2:1). *thornbushes.* They burn very quickly (see 27:4; 2Sa 23:6–7).
33:13 *hear ... acknowledge.* Cf. 34:1.
33:14 *sinners in Zion.* See 1:27–28 and note; 4:4. *consuming fire.* The presence of the God of judgment (see 29:6; 30:27,30; Ex 24:17; Dt 4:24; 9:3; 2Sa 22:9; Ps 18:8; Heb 12:29).
33:15 Similar requirements are found in Ps 15:2–5; 24:3–6 (see notes there). *bribes.* See 1:23.
33:16 *heights ... fortress.* Symbolic of the security found in God (cf. Ps 18:2 and note). *bread ... water.* Cf. 49:10.
33:17 *king.* See 32:1 and note; cf. 6:1,5 and notes. *in his beauty.* Reflecting on the splendor and majesty of a Davidic king; probably a foreshadowing of the Messianic kingdom (cf. 4:2; Ps 45:3–5 and notes; contrast Isa 53:2–3 [see notes there]). *land ... afar.* See 26:15 and note.
33:18 *former terror.* The Assyrian invasion (see 17:12–14 and note). *revenue.* Forced tribute (see note on v. 8). *towers.*

Where is the one who took the revenue?
Where is the officer in charge of the
towers?[m]"
19 You will see those arrogant people[n] no
more,
people whose speech is obscure,
whose language is strange and
incomprehensible.[o]

20 Look on Zion,[p] the city of our festivals;
your eyes will see Jerusalem,
a peaceful abode,[q] a tent[r] that will
not be moved;[s]
its stakes will never be pulled up,
nor any of its ropes broken.
21 There the LORD will be our Mighty[t] One.
It will be like a place of broad rivers
and streams.[u]
No galley with oars will ride them,
no mighty ship[v] will sail them.
22 For the LORD is our judge,[w]
the LORD is our lawgiver,[x]
the LORD is our king;[y]
it is he who will save[z] us.

23 Your rigging hangs loose:
The mast is not held secure,
the sail is not spread.
Then an abundance of spoils will be
divided
and even the lame[a] will carry off
plunder.[b]
24 No one living in Zion will say, "I am ill";[c]
and the sins of those who dwell
there will be forgiven.[d]

Judgment Against the Nations

34 Come near, you nations, and
listen;[e]
pay attention, you peoples![f]
Let the earth[g] hear, and all that is in it,
the world, and all that comes out
of it![h]
2 The LORD is angry with all nations;
his wrath[i] is on all their armies.
He will totally destroy[a][j] them,
he will give them over to slaughter.[k]
3 Their slain[l] will be thrown out,
their dead bodies[m] will stink;[n]
the mountains will be soaked with
their blood.[o]
4 All the stars in the sky will be
dissolved[p]
and the heavens rolled up[q] like a
scroll;
all the starry host will fall[r]
like withered[s] leaves from the vine,
like shriveled figs from the fig tree.

5 My sword[t] has drunk its fill in the
heavens;
see, it descends in judgment on
Edom,[u]
the people I have totally destroyed.[v]
6 The sword[w] of the LORD is bathed in
blood,
it is covered with fat—
the blood of lambs and goats,
fat from the kidneys of rams.
For the LORD has a sacrifice[x] in Bozrah[y]
and a great slaughter[z] in the land of
Edom.

33:18 [m]S Isa 2:15 **33:19** [n]S Ps 5:5 [o]S Ge 11:7; S Isa 28:11 **33:20** [p]S Ps 125:1 [q]S Isa 32:18 [r]S Ge 26:22 [s]ver 6; Ps 46:5 **33:21** [t]S Isa 10:34 [u]S Ex 17:6; S Ps 1:3; Isa 32:2; 41:18; 48:18; 49:10; 66:12; Na 3:8 [v]Isa 23:1 **33:22** [w]Isa 11:4 [x]S Isa 2:3; Jas 4:12 [y]S Ps 89:18 [z]S Isa 25:9 **33:23** [a]S 2Ki 7:8 [b]S 2Ki 7:16 **33:24** [c]S Isa 30:26 [d]S Nu 23:21; S 2Ch 6:21; Isa 43:1; 48:20; Jer 31:34; 33:8; 1Jn 1:7-9 **34:1** [e]S Isa 33:13 [f]Isa 41:1; 43:9 [g]S Dt 4:26; Ps 49:1 [h]Ps 24:1 **34:2** [i]S Isa 10:25 [j]S Isa 13:5; S Zec 5:3 [k]S Isa 30:25 **34:3** [l]S Isa 5:25; S 10:4 [m]S Ps 110:6; Eze 39:11 [n]Joel 2:20; Am 4:10 [o]ver 7; S 2Sa 1:22; Isa 63:6; Eze 5:17; 14:19; 32:6; 35:6; 38:22 **34:4** [p]S Job 9:7; S Isa 13:13; 2Pe 3:10 [q]Isa 38:12; Heb 1:12 [r]S Mt 24:29*; Mk 13:25* [s]S Job 8:12; S Isa 15:6; Mt 21:19 **34:5** [t]Dt 32:41-42; Jer 47:6; Eze 21:5; Zec 13:7 [u]S 2Sa 8:13-14; S 2Ch 28:17; Am 1:11-12 [v]S Dt 13:15; S Jos 6:17; Isa 24:6; Am 3:14-15; 6:11 **34:6** [w]S Dt 32:41; S Isa 27:1 [x]S Lev 3:9 [y]S Ge 36:33 [z]S Isa 30:25; S Jer 25:34; Rev 19:17

[a] *2* The Hebrew term refers to the irrevocable giving over of things or persons to the LORD, often by totally destroying them; also in verse 5.

Judah's fortifications were probably under strict Assyrian control (see 2:15).
33:19 *arrogant.* Cf. 10:12 and note. *speech is obscure.* The Assyrian language was related to Hebrew but was different enough to sound strange to Israelite ears. See 28:11; Dt 28:49.
33:20 *Look on Zion.* The redeemed city, in contrast to the city described in vv. 7–9. *festivals.* See 1:14 and note. *peaceful abode.* See 32:17–18 and notes. *tent … not … moved.* Her exile will be over. *stakes … ropes.* Cf. the similar description of Jerusalem in 54:2.
33:21 *Mighty One.* See 10:34 (cf. Ps 93:3–4 and notes). *broad rivers.* To prevent easy access to her borders—thus like Tyre (23:1) or Thebes (see Na 3:8 and note).
33:22 *our judge.* See 2:4; 11:4 and note. *our lawgiver.* See 2:3; 51:4 and note. *our king.* See v. 17; 32:1 and notes; see also Ps 46; 48. *save.* See Jdg 2:16–19 and note.
33:23 *rigging.* Jerusalem is pictured as a ship, unprepared to sail into battle against Assyria. *Then.* When God strikes down the Assyrian army (see 10:33–34; 37:36 and notes). *plunder.* See v. 4.
33:24 Looking beyond Isaiah's own day to the physically and spiritually whole Jerusalem of vv. 17,20–22.
34:1—35:10 Chs. 34–35 conclude chs. 28–33 and comprise an eschatological section corresponding to chs. 24–27, which conclude chs. 13–23 (see note on 24:1—27:13).
34:2 *angry … wrath.* In the day of the Lord (see 2:11,17,20; 26:20–21 and notes). See also 13:3,13 and notes. *totally destroy.* The kind of destruction the Canaanites had deserved. See NIV text note; see also v. 5; Jos 6:17 and note. *slaughter.* See 30:25 and note.
34:3 *thrown out.* Not to have a proper burial was considered a disgrace (see 14:19; Jer 22:19 and notes).
34:4 *stars … dissolved.* Disturbances in the heavens characterize the day of the Lord (see 13:10,13 and notes; cf. Eze 32:7–8). *sky … scroll … starry host will fall.* Referred to in Mk 13:25 (see note there); Rev 6:13–14 in connection with the "great distress" (Mt 24:21) and the second coming of Christ. *withered leaves.* Cf. 24:4; 40:7–8.
34:5–6 *My sword … The sword of the LORD.* See Ps 7:12–13 and note.
34:5 *drunk its fill.* Cf. Eze 39:18–20 and notes. *Edom.* Symbolic of all the enemies of God and his people, like Moab in 25:10–12 (see note on 25:10). See note on 21:11. The Edomites were driven from their homeland by the Nabatean Arabs, perhaps as early as 500 BC.
34:6 *fat.* Considered the best part of the meat, and therefore offered to the Lord in the sacrifices (see Lev 3:9–11,16 and note on 3:16). *lambs and goats.* Symbolizing the people. *sacrifice.* Battles are often compared to sacrifices (see Jer 46:10 and note; 50:27; Eze 39:17–19 and notes; cf. Rev 19:17–18). *Boz-*

7 And the wild oxen[a] will fall with
them,
the bull calves and the great bulls.[b]
Their land will be drenched with
blood,[c]
and the dust will be soaked with fat.

8 For the LORD has a day[d] of vengeance,[e]
a year of retribution,[f] to uphold
Zion's cause.
9 Edom's streams will be turned into
pitch,
her dust into burning sulfur;[g]
her land will become blazing
pitch!
10 It will not be quenched[h] night or day;
its smoke will rise forever.[i]
From generation to generation[j] it will
lie desolate;[k]
no one will ever pass through it
again.
11 The desert owl[a][l] and screech owl[a] will
possess it;
the great owl[a] and the raven[m] will
nest there.
God will stretch out over Edom[n]
the measuring line of chaos[o]
and the plumb line[p] of desolation.
12 Her nobles will have nothing there to
be called a kingdom,
all her princes[q] will vanish[r] away.
13 Thorns[s] will overrun her citadels,
nettles and brambles her
strongholds.[t]
She will become a haunt for jackals,[u]
a home for owls.[v]
14 Desert creatures[w] will meet with
hyenas,[x]
and wild goats will bleat to each
other;
there the night creatures[y] will also lie
down
and find for themselves places of
rest.
15 The owl will nest there and lay
eggs,
she will hatch them, and care for
her young
under the shadow of her wings;[z]
there also the falcons[a] will gather,
each with its mate.

16 Look in the scroll[b] of the LORD and
read:

None of these will be missing,[c]
not one will lack her mate.
For it is his mouth[d] that has given the
order,[e]
and his Spirit will gather them
together.
17 He allots their portions;[f]
his hand distributes them by
measure.
They will possess it forever
and dwell there from generation to
generation.[g]

Joy of the Redeemed

35 The desert[h] and the parched land
will be glad;
the wilderness will rejoice and
blossom.[i]
Like the crocus,[j] 2 it will burst into
bloom;
it will rejoice greatly and shout for
joy.[k]
The glory of Lebanon[l] will be given
to it,
the splendor of Carmel[m] and
Sharon;[n]
they will see the glory[o] of the LORD,
the splendor of our God.[p]

[a] *11* The precise identification of these birds is uncertain.

34:7 [a]S Nu 23:22 [b]S Ps 68:30 [c]S 2Sa 1:22 **34:8** [d]S Isa 2:12 [e]S Isa 1:24; 35:4; 47:3; 63:4 [f]Isa 59:18; Eze 25:12-17; Joel 3:4; Am 1:6-8, 9-10 **34:9** [g]S Ge 19:24 **34:10** [h]S Isa 1:31 [i]Rev 14:10-11; 19:3 [j]ver 17 [k]Isa 13:20; 24:1; Jer 49:18; Eze 29:12; 35:3; Mal 1:3 **34:11** [l]S Lev 11:16-18; S Dt 14:15-17; Rev 18:2 [m]S Ge 8:7 [n]Isa 21:11; Eze 35:15; Joel 3:19; Ob 1:1; Mal 1:4 [o]S Ge 1:2 [p]S 2Ki 21:13; Am 7:8 **34:12** [q]Job 12:21; Ps 107:40; Isa 40:23; Jer 21:7; 27:20; 39:6; Eze 24:5 [r]Isa 29:20; 41:11-12 **34:13** [s]S Isa 5:6; S 7:19 [t]S Isa 13:22 [u]Ps 44:19; S Isa 13:22; Jer 9:11; 10:22 [v]S Lev 11:16-18 **34:14** [w]S Ps 74:14 [x]Isa 13:22 [y]Rev 18:2 **34:15** [z]S Ps 17:8 [a]Dt 14:13 **34:16** [b]Isa 30:8 [c]Isa 40:26; 48:13 [d]Isa 1:20; 58:14 [e]S Isa 1:20 **34:17** [f]Isa 17:14; Jer 13:25 [g]ver 10 **35:1** [h]Isa 27:10; 32:15, 16; 41:18-19 [i]Isa 27:6; 51:3 [j]SS 2:1 **35:2** [k]S Ge 21:6; Ps 105:43; Isa 12:6; S 25:9; 44:23; 51:11; 52:9; 55:12 [l]S Ezr 3:7; S Isa 33:9 [m]SS 7:5 [n]S 1Ch 27:29; Isa 65:10 [o]S Ex 16:7; S Isa 4:5; S 59:19 [p]S Isa 25:9

rah. An important city of Edom and a sheepherding center, it was located about 25 miles southeast of the southern end of the Dead Sea. The name means "grape-gathering" (cf. 63:1–3).
34:7 *wild oxen … great bulls.* Symbolizing the troops and/or leaders of the nations. *drenched with blood.* See v. 3.
34:8 *day of vengeance.* See 35:4; 61:2. The Edomites opposed Israel at every opportunity (see 2Sa 8:13–14) and rejoiced when Jerusalem was destroyed (see La 4:21; see also Ps 137:7; Jer 49:8; Ob 12–14 and notes). But Edom's day would come (see 63:1–4 and notes).
34:9 *burning sulfur.* Edom's destruction is compared with the overthrow of Sodom and Gomorrah (see Jer 49:17–18 and notes). See also 1:31; Ge 19:24 and notes.
34:10 *smoke … forever.* Applied to Babylon in Rev 19:3 (see also Rev 14:10–11 and notes). *lie desolate.* See 13:20–22; Mal 1:3–4 and notes.
34:11 *desert owl … screech owl … great owl … raven.* "Unclean" birds (see Dt 14:14–17). Such birds would also live in the ruins of Babylon (13:21) and Nineveh (Zep 2:14). *measuring line … plumb line.* Cf. 28:17 and note. *chaos … desolation.* The Hebrew for these words is used in Ge 1:2 (see note there) to describe the earth in its "formless" and "empty" state (see also Jer 4:23 and note).
34:13 *Thorns … nettles.* Cf. 7:24–25.
34:14 *Desert creatures … hyenas.* See 13:20–22 and note. *wild goats.* Sometimes connected with demons (see note on 13:21).
34:15 *owl … falcons.* Ceremonially unclean (see v. 11 and note; Dt 14:13,15–17).
34:16 *scroll.* After the destruction of Edom, people will read this prophecy given by Isaiah. *these.* The creatures just listed.
34:17 *allots their portions.* God will give the creatures of vv. 11,13–15 clear title to the land of Edom.
35:1 *desert … will be glad.* The personification of nature is common in Isaiah (see 33:9; 44:23; 55:12). *wilderness.* The Arabah (see note on 33:9). *crocus.* See NIV text note on SS 2:1.
35:2 *rejoice … shout for joy.* See 54:1 and note. *Lebanon … Carmel … Sharon.* Fertile areas renowned for their beautiful trees and foliage (see note on 33:9). *glory of the LORD.* In the great transformation just announced. See 6:3 and note.

[3]Strengthen the feeble hands,
steady the knees[q] that give way;
[4]say[r] to those with fearful hearts,[s]
"Be strong, do not fear;[t]
your God will come,[u]
he will come with vengeance;[v]
with divine retribution
he will come to save[w] you."

[5]Then will the eyes of the blind be
opened[x]
and the ears of the deaf[y] unstopped.
[6]Then will the lame[z] leap like a deer,[a]
and the mute tongue[b] shout for joy.[c]
Water will gush forth in the wilderness
and streams[d] in the desert.
[7]The burning sand will become a pool,
the thirsty ground[e] bubbling
springs.[f]
In the haunts where jackals[g] once lay,
grass and reeds[h] and papyrus will
grow.

[8]And a highway[i] will be there;
it will be called the Way of
Holiness;[j]
it will be for those who walk on that
Way.
The unclean[k] will not journey on it;
wicked fools will not go about on it.
[9]No lion[l] will be there,
nor any ravenous beast;[m]
they will not be found there.
But only the redeemed[n] will walk
there,
10 and those the LORD has rescued[o] will
return.
They will enter Zion with singing;[p]
everlasting joy[q] will crown their
heads.
Gladness[r] and joy will overtake
them,
and sorrow and sighing will flee
away.[s]

35:3 [q]S Job 4:4; Heb 12:12 **35:4** [r]2Ch 32:6; Isa 40:2; Zec 1:13 [s]S Dt 20:3; S Isa 21:4 [t]S Jos 1:9; S Isa 7:4; Da 10:19 [u]Isa 40:9,10-11; 51:5; 62:11; Rev 22:12 [v]S Isa 1:24; S 34:8 [w]S Isa 25:9 **35:5** [x]S Ps 146:8; Jn 9:6-7; Ac 26:18 [y]Isa 29:18; 42:18; 50:4 **35:6** [z]Mt 15:30; Lk 7:22; Jn 5:8-9; Ac 3:8 [a]S 2Sa 22:34 [b]Isa 32:4; Mt 9:32-33; 12:22; Mk 7:35; Lk 11:14 [c]Ps 20:5 [d]S Ex 17:6; Jn 7:38 **35:7** [e]S Ps 68:6; Isa 41:17; 44:3; 55:1 [f]Ps 107:35; Isa 49:10; 58:11 [g]S Isa 13:22 [h]S Job 8:11; S 40:21 **35:8** [i]S Isa 11:16; S 33:8; S Jer 31:21; Mt 7:13-14 [j]Isa 4:3; 1Pe 1:15 [k]Isa 52:1 **35:9** [l]S Isa 30:6 [m]Isa 11:6; 13:22; 34:14 [n]S Ex 6:6; Lev 25:47-55; Isa 51:11; 62:12; 63:4 **35:10** [o]S Job 19:25; S Isa 1:27 [p]Isa 30:29 [q]S Ps 4:7; S 126:5; S Isa 25:9 [r]S Ps 51:8; S Isa 51:3 [s]S Isa 30:19; Rev 7:17; 21:4 **36:1** [t]S 2Ki 18:9 [u]S 2Ch 32:1 [v]S Ps 109:11 **36:2** [w]S Jos 10:3 [x]S Isa 7:3 **36:3** [y]Isa 22:20-21; 37:2 [z]S Ge 41:40 [a]S 2Ki 18:18 [b]S 2Sa 8:17 [c]ver 11 [d]S 2Sa 8:16

Sennacherib Threatens Jerusalem

36:1-22pp — 2Ki 18:13,17-37; 2Ch 32:9-19

36 In the fourteenth year of King Hezekiah's[t] reign, Sennacherib[u] king
of Assyria attacked all the fortified cities
of Judah and captured them.[v] [2]Then the
king of Assyria sent his field commander
with a large army from Lachish[w] to King
Hezekiah at Jerusalem. When the commander stopped at the aqueduct of the
Upper Pool, on the road to the Launderer's
Field,[x] [3]Eliakim[y] son of Hilkiah the palace
administrator,[z] Shebna[a] the secretary,[b] and
Joah[c] son of Asaph the recorder[d] went out
to him.
[4]The field commander said to them,
"Tell Hezekiah:

"'This is what the great king, the
king of Assyria, says: On what are
you basing this confidence of yours?
[5]You say you have counsel and might
for war — but you speak only empty
words. On whom are you depending,

35:3 See Heb 12:12.
35:4 *Be strong, do not fear.* Cf. God's words of encouragement to Joshua in Jos 1:6–7,9 (see note on Jos 1:18). *God will come.* Cf. 40:9–10. Similar language is used of the coming of the Messiah (see 62:11 and note; cf. Rev 22:12,20 and notes). *vengeance … retribution.* See note on 34:8.
35:5 *eyes … ears.* See 29:18; 32:3; 42:7 and notes. Spiritual and physical healing are also linked together in Christ's ministry (see Lk 7:22 and note).
35:6 *lame leap … mute tongue shout.* Signs of the Messianic age (see Mt 12:22; Ac 3:7–8). *Water … streams.* See 32:2 and note. Cf. God's provision of water in Ex 17:6; 2Ki 3:15–20 (see note on 2Ki 3:17).
35:7 *springs.* Cf. 41:18. *reeds and papyrus.* Plants that grow in marshes and lakes (cf. 19:6–7).
35:8 *highway.* A road built up to make travel easier (see 11:16; 40:3 and notes). *the Way of Holiness.* The way set apart for those who are holy; only the redeemed (v. 9) could use it. In ancient times, certain roads between temples were open only to those who were ceremonially pure.
35:9 *lion … beast.* Sometimes wild animals made travel dangerous (see Dt 8:15; Jdg 14:5 and note). *redeemed.* Those the Lord has delivered from bondage (cf. 1:27; 51:10; 62:12; Ex 6:6–8 and notes; Lev 25:47–48; Dt 7:8).
35:10 Repeated in 51:11. *enter Zion with singing.* As the Israelites did when they returned from Babylonian exile (see introduction to Ps 126). *overtake them.* They will be pursued, not by wild animals (v. 9), but by gladness and joy (cf. Ps 23:6 and note). *sorrow … will flee.* Cf. 25:8; 65:19.
36:1 — 39:8 Much of chs. 36–39 is paralleled, sometimes verbatim, in 2Ki 18:13 — 20:19 (see notes there). The compiler of 2 Kings may have used Isa 36–39 as one of his sources, or both may have drawn on a common source. Chs. 36–37 describe the fulfillment of many predictions about Assyria's collapse, while chs. 38–39 point toward the Babylonian context of chs. 40–66.
36:1 *fourteenth year of … Hezekiah's reign.* 701 BC, the 14th year of his sole reign. Hezekiah ruled as sole king from 715 to 686 but was a coregent from c. 729 (see note on 2Ki 18:1). *Sennacherib.* Reigned over Assyria from 705 to 681 (see chart, p. 511). *all the … cities.* In his annals Sennacherib lists 46 such cities (see note on 2Ki 18:13).
36:2 *large army.* Cf. 37:36 and note. *Lachish.* An important city about 30 miles southwest of Jerusalem that guarded the main approach to Judah's capital from that direction (see Jer 34:7 and note). *aqueduct … Field.* See 7:3 and note; see also note on 2Ki 18:17.
36:3 *Eliakim.* See 22:20–21 and notes. *palace administrator.* In charge of the palace (see 22:15 and note). *Shebna.* See 22:15 and note. *secretary.* Perhaps equivalent to secretary of state (see Jer 36:12; see also note on 2Sa 8:17). *recorder.* An official position also associated elsewhere with "secretary" (see 1Ki 4:3). See also note on 2Sa 8:16.
36:4,13 *great king.* See note on 2Ki 18:19.
36:5 *rebel.* By refusing to pay the expected tribute (see 2Ki 17:4; 18:7 and note).

that you rebel[e] against me? 6 Look, I
know you are depending[f] on Egypt,[g]
that splintered reed[h] of a staff, which
pierces the hand of anyone who leans
on it! Such is Pharaoh king of Egypt
to all who depend on him. 7 But if you
say to me, "We are depending[i] on the
LORD our God"—isn't he the one
whose high places and altars Hezekiah removed,[j] saying to Judah and
Jerusalem, "You must worship before
this altar"?[k]
8 " 'Come now, make a bargain with
my master, the king of Assyria: I will
give you two thousand horses[l]—if
you can put riders on them! 9 How
then can you repulse one officer of
the least of my master's officials, even
though you are depending on Egypt[m]
for chariots[n] and horsemen[a]?[o] 10 Furthermore, have I come to attack and
destroy this land without the LORD?
The LORD himself told[p] me to march
against this country and destroy it.' "

11 Then Eliakim, Shebna and Joah[q] said
to the field commander, "Please speak to
your servants in Aramaic,[r] since we understand it. Don't speak to us in Hebrew
in the hearing of the people on the wall."
12 But the commander replied, "Was it
only to your master and you that my master sent me to say these things, and not to
the people sitting on the wall—who, like
you, will have to eat their own excrement
and drink their own urine?[s]"
13 Then the commander stood and
called out in Hebrew,[t] "Hear the words
of the great king, the king of Assyria![u]
14 This is what the king says: Do not let
Hezekiah deceive[v] you. He cannot deliver
you! 15 Do not let Hezekiah persuade you
to trust in the LORD when he says, 'The
LORD will surely deliver[w] us; this city will
not be given into the hand of the king of
Assyria.'[x]
16 "Do not listen to Hezekiah. This is

36:5 [e] S 2Ki 18:7
36:6 [f] S 2Ki 17:4; S Isa 8:12 [g] S Isa 30:2,5; Eze 17:17 [h] Isa 42:3; 58:5; Eze 29:6-7
36:7 [i] Ps 22:8; Mt 27:43 [j] S 2Ki 18:4 [k] Dt 12:2-5; S 2Ch 31:1
36:8 [l] S Ps 20:7; S Isa 30:16
36:9 [m] S Isa 31:3 [n] Isa 37:24 [o] S Ps 20:7; Isa 30:2-5
36:10 [p] S 1Ki 13:18; Isa 10:5-7
36:11 [q] ver 3 [r] S Ezr 4:7
36:12 [s] 2Ki 6:25; Eze 4:12
36:13 [t] S 2Ch 32:18 [u] Isa 37:4
36:14 [v] S 2Ch 32:15
36:15 [w] S Ps 3:2,7 [x] Isa 37:10

Sennacherib's attack on Lachish. From Lachish, Sennacherib sent a messenger to King Hezekiah at Jerusalem to threaten him (Isa 36:2). However, Hezekiah is reassured by Isaiah: "He will not enter this city or shoot an arrow here. He will not come before it with shield or build a siege ramp against it" (Isa 37:33).

Caryn Reeder, courtesy of the British Muesum

what the king of Assyria says: Make peace
with me and come out to me. Then each
of you will eat fruit from your own vine
and fig tree[y] and drink water from your
own cistern,[z] 17 until I come and take you
to a land like your own[a]—a land of grain
and new wine,[b] a land of bread and vineyards.
18 "Do not let Hezekiah mislead you
when he says, 'The LORD will deliver us.'
Have the gods of any nations ever delivered their lands from the hand of the king

36:16 [y] S 1Ki 4:25 [z] Pr 5:15
36:17 [a] S 2Ki 15:29 [b] S Ge 27:28; S Dt 28:51

[a] 9 *Or charioteers*

36:6,9 *depending on Egypt.* Cf. 10:20.
36:6 *Egypt.* Hezekiah had been under pressure to make an alliance with Egypt since 715 BC or earlier (see 20:5; 30:1 and notes). *splintered reed.* Egypt is compared to a reed again in Eze 29:6–7 (see note on 29:6). *Such is Pharaoh.* Cf. 30:3,7.
36:7 *high places and altars.* Hezekiah had destroyed these popular shrines often dedicated to Baal worship (see note on 2Ki 18:4; see also 2Ch 31:1). *this altar.* In Solomon's temple.
36:8 *two thousand horses.* A sizable number for any army. Horses and chariots were highly prized (see note on 30:16). *if you can put riders on them!* See note on 2Ki 18:23. *riders.* Probably charioteers, since cavalry was not employed by these nations this early (see v. 9).
36:10 *The LORD … told me.* The Lord had used Assyria to punish Israel (see 10:5–6), but now it was Assyria's turn to be judged. Pharaoh Necho claimed God's approval on his mission according to 2Ch 35:21.
36:11 *Eliakim … Joah.* See v. 3 and note. *Aramaic.* The diplomatic language of that day (see note on 2Ki 18:26). *Don't speak … in Hebrew.* The officials feared that the commander's speech might damage the people's morale.
36:12 *eat … excrement … drink … urine.* A crude way of describing the horrors of famine if Jerusalem were to be besieged (cf. 2Ki 6:25 and note). Contrast v. 16 (see note there).
36:14 *deceive you.* Cf. 37:10 and note.
36:16 *own vine and fig tree.* Symbols of security and prosperity in the best of times (see 1Ki 4:25; Mic 4:4 and note; Zec 3:10 and note).
36:17 *come and take you.* The Assyrians deported rebellious peoples to reduce their will to revolt (see 2Ki 15:29; 17:6 and notes). *grain and new wine.* Two of the staples of Israel (cf. Dt 28:51; Hag 1:11 and note).
36:18–20 The commander's words echo the boasts of the proud Assyrians in 10:8–11. See note on 2Ki 18:33–35.

of Assyria? 19 Where are the gods of Hamath and Arpad?[c] Where are the gods of Sepharvaim?[d] Have they rescued Samaria[e] from my hand? 20 Who of all the gods[f] of these countries have been able to save their lands from me? How then can the LORD deliver Jerusalem from my hand?"[g]

21 But the people remained silent and said nothing in reply, because the king had commanded, "Do not answer him."[h]

22 Then Eliakim[i] son of Hilkiah the palace administrator, Shebna the secretary and Joah son of Asaph the recorder[j] went to Hezekiah, with their clothes torn,[k] and told him what the field commander had said.

Jerusalem's Deliverance Foretold

37:1-13pp — 2Ki 19:1-13

37 When King Hezekiah heard this, he tore his clothes[l] and put on sackcloth[m] and went into the temple[n] of the LORD. 2 He sent Eliakim[o] the palace administrator, Shebna[p] the secretary, and the leading priests, all wearing sackcloth, to the prophet Isaiah son of Amoz.[q] 3 They told him, "This is what Hezekiah says: This day is a day of distress[r] and rebuke and disgrace, as when children come to the moment of birth[s] and there is no strength to deliver them. 4 It may be that the LORD your God will hear the words of the field commander, whom his master, the king of Assyria, has sent to ridicule[t] the living God,[u] and that he will rebuke him for the words the LORD your God has heard.[v] Therefore pray[w] for the remnant[x] that still survives."

5 When King Hezekiah's officials came to Isaiah, 6 Isaiah said to them, "Tell your master, 'This is what the LORD says: Do not be afraid[y] of what you have heard — those words with which the underlings of the king of Assyria have blasphemed[z] me. 7 Listen! When he hears a certain report,[a] I will make him want[b] to return to his own country, and there I will have him cut down[c] with the sword.' "

8 When the field commander heard that the king of Assyria had left Lachish,[d] he withdrew and found the king fighting against Libnah.[e]

9 Now Sennacherib[f] received a report[g] that Tirhakah, the king of Cush,[a][h] was marching out to fight against him. When he heard it, he sent messengers to Hezekiah with this word: 10 "Say to Hezekiah king of Judah: Do not let the god you depend on deceive[i] you when he says, 'Jerusalem will not be given into the hands of the king of Assyria.'[j] 11 Surely you have heard what the kings of Assyria have done to all the countries, destroying them completely. And will you be delivered?[k] 12 Did the gods of the nations that were destroyed by my predecessors[l] deliver them — the gods of Gozan, Harran,[m] Rezeph and the people of Eden[n] who were in Tel Assar? 13 Where is the king of Hamath or the king of Arpad?[o] Where are the kings of Lair, Sepharvaim,[p] Hena and Ivvah?"[q]

Hezekiah's Prayer

37:14-20pp — 2Ki 19:14-19

14 Hezekiah received the letter[r] from the messengers and read it. Then he went up to the temple[s] of the LORD and spread it out before the LORD. 15 And Hezekiah prayed[t]

[a] 9 That is, the upper Nile region

36:19 [c] S 2Ki 18:34 [d] S 2Ki 17:24 [e] S 2Ki 15:29 **36:20** [f] S 1Ki 20:23 [g] Ex 5:2; 2Ch 25:15; Isa 10:8-11; 37:10-13, 18-20; 40:18; Da 3:15 **36:21** [h] Pr 9:7-8; S 26:4 **36:22** [i] S 2Ki 18:18 [j] S 2Sa 8:16 [k] S Ge 37:29; S 2Ch 34:19 **37:1** [l] S Ge 37:29; S 2Ch 34:19 [m] S Ge 37:34 [n] S ver 14; S 1Ki 8:33; Mt 21:13 **37:2** [o] S 2Ki 18:18; S Isa 36:3 [p] S 2Ki 18:18 [q] ver 21; Isa 1:1; S 13:1; 38:1 **37:3** [r] S Jdg 6:2; S Isa 5:30 [s] Isa 26:18; 66:9; Hos 13:13 **37:4** [t] ver 23-24; S 2Ch 32:17 [u] S Jos 3:10 [v] Isa 36:13, 18-20 [w] S 1Sa 7:8 [x] S Isa 1:9; Am 7:2 **37:6** [y] S Jos 1:9; S Isa 7:4 [z] S Nu 15:30 **37:7** [a] ver 9 [b] 1Ch 5:26 [c] S Isa 31:8 **37:8** [d] S Jos 10:3 [e] S Nu 33:20 **37:9** [f] S 2Ch 32:1 [g] ver 7 [h] S Isa 20:3

37:10 [i] 2Ch 32:11, 15 [j] Isa 36:15 **37:11** [k] Isa 36:18-20 **37:12** [l] 2Ki 18:11 [m] Ge 11:31; 12:1-4; Ac 7:2 [n] Eze 27:23; Am 1:5 **37:13** [o] Isa 10:9 [p] S 2Ki 17:24 [q] S Isa 36:20 **37:14** [r] 2Ch 32:17 [s] ver 1, 38; S 1Ki 8:33 **37:15** [t] S 2Ch 32:20

36:19 *Hamath and Arpad.* See 10:9 and note. *Sepharvaim.* Probably located in northern Aram (Syria) not far from Hamath. Residents of Sepharvaim were deported to Samaria, though they still worshiped the gods Adrammelek and Anammelek. See 2Ki 17:24,31 and note on 17:24. *Samaria.* The Assyrians assumed that each people had its own gods and so did not associate the God of Judah with that of Samaria.
36:21 *people remained silent.* The Assyrians had hoped that the masterful psychology of vv. 4 – 20 would produce panic.
36:22 See v. 3 and note. *clothes torn.* See note on 2Ki 18:37.
37:1 *clothes ... sackcloth.* See Ge 37:34 and note; see also note on 2Ki 18:37. *temple.* Designated as a place of prayer by Solomon (see 1Ki 8:33). The Assyrian references to Hezekiah's dependence on the Lord (36:7,15,18) were true (see note on 36:7).
37:2 *Eliakim ... Shebna.* See note on 36:3. *leading priests.* See note on 2Ki 19:2. *Isaiah son of Amoz.* See note on 1:1. Prophet, priests and king join in supplication.
37:3 *day of distress.* See 5:30; 26:16; 33:2 and notes. *moment of birth.* An even more vivid description than that of the pains of childbirth (see 13:8 and note).
37:4 *ridicule.* See vv. 17,23 – 24. *pray.* See note on 2Ki 19:4. *remnant.* Jerusalem was left almost alone (see 36:1 and notes on 1:9; 2Ki 19:4; see also 10:20 – 22 and note).
37:6 *Do not be afraid.* Cf. 7:4; see 35:4 and note.
37:7 *report.* See note on 2Ki 19:7. *return ... cut down with the sword.* See vv. 37 – 38 and note on v. 38.
37:8 *Lachish.* See note on 36:2. *Libnah.* See note on 2Ki 8:22; see also Jos 10:31.
37:9 *Tirhakah, the king of Cush.* In 701 BC he was actually a prince (the "lieutenant" of the new pharaoh Shebitku, who sent him with an army to help Hezekiah withstand the Assyrian invasion); he did not become king until 690. But this part of Isaiah was not written before 681 (see note on v. 38), so it was natural at that time to speak of Tirhakah as king. See 18:1 and note.
37:10 *god ... deceive.* See 36:14 – 15,18. The message of vv. 10 – 13 is similar to that of 36:18 – 20 (see note there).
37:12 *Gozan.* A city in northern Mesopotamia to which some of the Israelites had been deported by the Assyrians (see 2Ki 17:6 and note). *Harran.* A city west of Gozan where Abraham lived for a number of years (see Ge 11:31 and note). *Rezeph.* A city between Harran and the Euphrates River. *Eden.* The state of Bit Adini, located between the Euphrates and Balikh Rivers (see note on 2Ki 19:12).
37:13 *Hamath ... Arpad.* See 10:9 and note. *Sepharvaim.* See 36:19; 2Ki 17:24 and notes.
37:14 *temple.* See v. 1 and note. *spread it out.* Contrast the hypocritical spreading out of hands to pray in 1:15 (see note on 1:11 – 15).

to the LORD: 16 "LORD Almighty, the God of
Israel, enthroned[u] between the cherubim,[v]
you alone are God[w] over all the kingdoms[x]
of the earth. You have made heaven and
earth.[y] 17 Give ear, LORD, and hear;[z] open
your eyes, LORD, and see;[a] listen to all the
words Sennacherib[b] has sent to ridicule[c]
the living God.[d]
18 "It is true, LORD, that the Assyrian
kings have laid waste all these peoples
and their lands.[e] 19 They have thrown their
gods into the fire[f] and destroyed them,[g] for
they were not gods[h] but only wood and
stone, fashioned by human hands.[i] 20 Now,
LORD our God, deliver[j] us from his hand,
so that all the kingdoms of the earth[k] may
know that you, LORD, are the only God.[al]"

Sennacherib's Fall

37:21-38pp — 2Ki 19:20-37; 2Ch 32:20-21

21 Then Isaiah son of Amoz[m] sent a message to Hezekiah: "This is what the LORD,
the God of Israel, says: Because you have
prayed to me concerning Sennacherib king
of Assyria, 22 this is the word the LORD has
spoken against him:

"Virgin Daughter[n] Zion[o]
despises and mocks you.
Daughter Jerusalem
tosses her head[p] as you flee.
23 Who is it you have ridiculed and
blasphemed?[q]
Against whom have you raised your
voice[r]
and lifted your eyes in pride?[s]
Against the Holy One[t] of Israel!
24 By your messengers
you have ridiculed the Lord.
And you have said,
'With my many chariots[u]
I have ascended the heights of the
mountains,
the utmost heights[v] of Lebanon.[w]
I have cut down its tallest cedars,
the choicest of its junipers.[x]
I have reached its remotest heights,
the finest of its forests.
25 I have dug wells in foreign lands[b]
and drunk the water there.
With the soles of my feet
I have dried up[y] all the streams of
Egypt.[z]'

26 "Have you not heard?
Long ago I ordained[a] it.
In days of old I planned[b] it;
now I have brought it to pass,
that you have turned fortified cities
into piles of stone.[c]
27 Their people, drained of power,
are dismayed and put to shame.
They are like plants in the field,
like tender green shoots,
like grass[d] sprouting on the roof,[e]
scorched[c] before it grows up.

28 "But I know where you are
and when you come and go[f]
and how you rage[g] against me.
29 Because you rage against me
and because your insolence[h] has
reached my ears,
I will put my hook[i] in your nose[j]
and my bit in your mouth,
and I will make you return
by the way you came.[k]

30 "This will be the sign[l] for you, Hezekiah:

37:16 [u] S Ps 2:4 [v] S Ge 3:24 [w] Dt 10:17; S Ps 46:10; 86:10; 136:2-3 [x] Da 4:34 [y] S Ge 1:1; S Isa 11:12; 41:9; 43:6; Ac 4:24 **37:17** [z] S 1Ki 8:29; S 2Ch 6:40 [a] Jer 25:29; Da 9:18 [b] S 2Ch 32:1 [c] S 2Ch 32:17 [d] S Jos 3:10 **37:18** [e] S 2Ki 15:29; Na 2:11-12 **37:19** [f] S Jos 7:15 [g] Isa 26:14; 36:20 [h] 2Ch 13:9; Isa 40:17; 41:24, 29; Jer 2:11; 5:7; 16:20; Gal 4:8 [i] S 2Ch 32:19; S Ps 135:15; Isa 40:18-20; 44:9-11 **37:20** [j] S Ps 3:2, 7; S Pr 20:22 [k] S Jos 4:24 [l] S 1Sa 17:46; S Ps 46:10 **37:21** [m] S ver 2 **37:22** [n] S Isa 23:12 [o] S Isa 10:32 [p] S Job 16:4 **37:23** [q] ver 4; S Nu 15:30; Isa 52:5; Eze 36:20, 23; Da 7:25 [r] S Job 15:25 [s] S Isa 2:11 [t] S Isa 1:4; S 12:6 **37:24** [u] Isa 36:9 [v] Isa 14:13 [w] S 1Ki 7:2; S Isa 14:8; S 33:9 [x] 1Ki 5:8-10; Isa 41:19; 55:13; 60:13; Hos 14:8 **37:25** [y] S Isa 19:6; 44:27 [z] S Dt 11:10; S Isa 10:14; Da 4:30 **37:26** [a] Ac 2:23; 4:27-28; 1Pe 2:8 [b] Isa 10:6; S 25:1 [c] S Dt 13:16; S Isa 25:2 **37:27** [d] S Isa 15:6 [e] Ps 129:6 **37:28** [f] Ps 139:1-3 [g] Ps 2:1 **37:29** [h] Isa 10:12 [i] S 2Ch 33:11 [j] S Job 40:24 [k] ver 34 **37:30** [l] S Isa 20:3

[a] 20 Dead Sea Scrolls (see also 2 Kings 19:19); Masoretic Text *you alone are the LORD* [b] 25 Dead Sea Scrolls (see also 2 Kings 19:24); Masoretic Text does not have *in foreign lands.* [c] 27 Some manuscripts of the Masoretic Text, Dead Sea Scrolls and some Septuagint manuscripts (see also 2 Kings 19:26); most manuscripts of the Masoretic Text *roof / and terraced fields*

37:16 *LORD Almighty.* See 13:4 and note. *enthroned ... cherubim.* See notes on 1Sa 4:4; 2Sa 6:2. *all the kingdoms.* Cf. 40:17 and note. *made heaven and earth.* The role of God as Creator is emphasized also in 40:26,28; 42:5; 45:12 (see note on 40:21).
37:17 *Give ear ... open your eyes.* Cf. Solomon's prayer in 1Ki 8:52; 2Ch 6:40. *ridicule the living God.* See v. 4 and note.
37:19 *not gods.* See 36:19 and note. *wood and stone.* Cf. 2:8; 44:9–20 and notes.
37:20 *that all the kingdoms of the earth may know.* See note on 2Ki 19:19. *you ... are the only God.* Cf. v. 16; 43:11; 45:18,21–22; see note on Ex 20:3; see also note and NIV text note on Dt 6:4.
37:22 *Virgin Daughter Zion ... Daughter Jerusalem.* A personification of Jerusalem (see note on 2Ki 19:21). *tosses her head.* A gesture of mocking (see Ps 22:7; 44:14 and notes).
37:23 *lifted ... in pride.* Assyria's great pride had been condemned earlier (see 10:12 and note). *Holy One of Israel.* A designation of the God of Israel characteristic of Isaiah (see 1:4 and note).
37:24 *many chariots.* See 36:8 and note. *ascended the heights.* Cf. the words of the king of Babylon in 14:13–14. *Lebanon.* See 33:9; 35:2 and notes. *cut down ... cedars.* For many centuries the kings of Mesopotamia had used the cedars of Lebanon in their royal buildings (see notes on 2:13; 9:10; 14:8; cf. 1Ki 5:8–10).
37:25 *dug wells.* Desert lands could not stop him. *dried up all the streams.* The branches of the Nile were no obstacle, either. This boast was almost a claim to deity. See 11:15; 44:27 and notes.
37:26 *ordained ... planned ... brought it to pass.* See Ps 33:10–11. Cf. 40:21 and note. *cities into piles of stone.* Assyria had been God's tool of judgment against the nations (see 10:5–6 and note on 10:5).
37:27 See 40:6–8 and notes; Ps 37:1–2. *grass ... on the roof.* Roofs in the Near East were flat (cf. 2Sa 11:2 and note).
37:29 *hook in your nose.* The Assyrians often led away captives by tying ropes to rings placed in their noses (see note on 2Ki 19:28). *bit.* Cf. 30:28.
37:30 *sign.* See 7:11,14 and notes. *what grows by itself.* See note on 2Ki 19:29. *second ... third year.* See note on 2Ki 19:29.

"This year[m] you will eat what grows by itself,
and the second year what springs from that.
But in the third year[n] sow and reap,
plant vineyards[o] and eat their fruit.[p]
31 Once more a remnant of the kingdom of Judah
will take root[q] below and bear fruit[r] above.
32 For out of Jerusalem will come a remnant,[s]
and out of Mount Zion a band of survivors.[t]
The zeal[u] of the LORD Almighty
will accomplish this.

33 "Therefore this is what the LORD says
concerning the king of Assyria:

"He will not enter this city[v]
or shoot an arrow here.
He will not come before it with shield
or build a siege ramp[w] against it.
34 By the way that he came he will return;[x]
he will not enter this city,"
declares the LORD.
35 "I will defend[y] this city and save it,
for my sake[z] and for the sake of
David[a] my servant!"

36 Then the angel[b] of the LORD went
out and put to death[c] a hundred and
eighty-five thousand in the Assyrian[d]
camp. When the people got up the next
morning—there were all the dead bodies!
37 So Sennacherib[e] king of Assyria broke
camp and withdrew. He returned to Nineveh[f] and stayed there.
38 One day, while he was worshiping in
the temple[g] of his god Nisrok, his sons
Adrammelek and Sharezer killed him with
the sword, and they escaped to the land of
Ararat.[h] And Esarhaddon[i] his son succeeded him as king.[j]

37:30 [m] Isa 32:10 [n] S Isa 16:14 [o] S Lev 25:4 [p] Ps 107:37; Isa 30:23; 65:21; Jer 31:5 **37:31** [q] Isa 11:10 [r] S Isa 27:6 **37:32** [s] S Isa 11:11 [t] S Isa 1:9 [u] S Isa 9:7 **37:33** [v] S Isa 32:18 [w] S 2Sa 20:15 **37:34** [x] ver 29 **37:35** [y] S Isa 31:5 [z] Isa 43:25; 48:9, 11; Eze 36:21-22 [a] S 1Ch 17:19 **37:36** [b] S Ex 12:23 [c] S Ex 12:12 [d] S Isa 10:12 **37:37** [e] S 2Ch 32:1 [f] S Ge 10:11; S Na 1:1 **37:38** [g] S ver 14 [h] Ge 8:4; Jer 51:27 [i] S 2Ki 17:24 [j] S Isa 9:4; 10:26; S 14:25 **38:1** [k] S Isa 37:2 [l] 2Sa 17:23 [m] 2Ki 8:10 **38:3** [n] Ps 26:3 [o] S 1Ki 8:61; S 1Ch 29:19 [p] S Dt 6:18; S 10:20 [q] Ps 6:8 **38:4** [r] 1Sa 13:13; Isa 39:5 **38:5** [s] 2Ki 18:3 [t] Ps 6:6 [u] S 2Ki 18:2 **38:6** [v] S Isa 31:5 **38:7** [w] S Ge 24:14; S 2Ch 32:31; Isa 7:11, 14; S 20:3 **38:8** [x] Jos 10:13

Hezekiah's Illness

38:1-8pp — 2Ki 20:1-11; 2Ch 32:24-26

38 In those days Hezekiah became ill
and was at the point of death. The
prophet Isaiah son of Amoz[k] went to him
and said, "This is what the LORD says: Put
your house in order,[l] because you are going to die; you will not recover."[m]
2 Hezekiah turned his face to the wall
and prayed to the LORD, 3 "Remember,
LORD, how I have walked[n] before you faithfully and with wholehearted devotion[o] and
have done what is good in your eyes.[p]"
And Hezekiah wept[q] bitterly.
4 Then the word[r] of the LORD came to
Isaiah: 5 "Go and tell Hezekiah, 'This is
what the LORD, the God of your father David,[s] says: I have heard your prayer and
seen your tears;[t] I will add fifteen years[u] to
your life. 6 And I will deliver you and this
city from the hand of the king of Assyria.
I will defend[v] this city.
7 " 'This is the LORD's sign[w] to you that
the LORD will do what he has promised: 8 I
will make the shadow cast by the sun go
back the ten steps it has gone down on the
stairway of Ahaz.' " So the sunlight went
back the ten steps it had gone down.[x]

9 A writing of Hezekiah king of Judah
after his illness and recovery:

10 I said, "In the prime of my life[y]
must I go through the gates of death[z]
and be robbed of the rest of my years?[a]"

38:10 [y] Ps 102:24 [z] S Job 17:16; Ps 107:18; 2Co 1:9 [a] S Job 17:11

Probably the second year was to begin shortly, so the total time was less than 36 months. Another three-year sign was given in 20:3. *plant vineyards and eat.* The response to Assyria's proposal in 36:16 (see note there).
37:31 – 32 *remnant.* See notes on v. 4; 1:9; 2Ki 19:4,30 – 31.
37:31 *take root ... bear fruit.* See 4:2; 11:1,10; 27:6 and notes.
37:32 *The zeal ... this.* See 9:7 and note.
37:33 *siege ramp.* To help the invaders bring up battering rams and scale the walls (see 2Sa 20:15).
37:35 *sake of David.* God had promised David an enduring throne in Jerusalem (see 9:7; 55:3; 2Sa 7:16 and notes). *my servant.* See note on 41:8 – 9.
37:36 *angel of the LORD ... put to death.* The Lord often sent his angel as his agent to bring plagues. Cf. the striking down of the firstborn in Egypt (Ex 12:12 – 13) and the angel's sword poised against Jerusalem (see 2Sa 24:15 – 16 and note on 24:16; 1Ch 21:22, 27). The Greek historian Herodotus attributed this destruction to a bubonic plague. The death of these soldiers fulfills the prophecies of 10:33 – 34 (see notes there); 30:31; 31:8 (see note there).
37:37 *Nineveh.* The capital of Assyria (see Jnh 1:2 and note).
37:38 *in the temple.* Hezekiah had gone to the Lord's temple and gained strength (vv. 1,14). Twenty years later (681 BC) Sennacherib went to the temple of his god and was killed (see note on 2Ki 19:37). *Ararat.* Urartu, north of Assyria in Armenia (see note on Ge 8:4). *Esarhaddon.* Reigned 681 – 669 (see chart, p. 511; see also 2Ki 19:37 and note; Ezr 4:2).
38:1 *In those days.* Sometime before Sennacherib's invasion of 701 BC (see v. 6). *Isaiah.* He is prominent in this historical interlude (chs. 36 – 39). *Put your house in order.* See note on 2Ki 20:1. *you are going to die.* See note on 2Ki 20:1. Elisha similarly predicted the death of Ben-Hadad (see 2Ki 8:9 – 10 and notes). *you will not recover.* See v. 21 and note.
38:2 *wall.* Perhaps of the nearby temple. *prayed.* Cf. also Hezekiah's prayer of thanksgiving in vv. 10 – 20 (see note there).
38:3 *wholehearted devotion.* Like David (1Ki 11:4), Hezekiah was truly faithful (see 2Ki 18:3 – 5 and notes).
38:5 *fifteen years.* From c. 701 to c. 686 BC (see note on 2Ki 20:6).
38:6 *deliver ... this city.* See 31:5; 37:35 and notes.
38:7 *sign.* See 7:11,14 and notes.
38:8 *stairway of Ahaz.* See note on 2Ki 20:11. *sunlight went back.* Perhaps the miracle involved the refraction of light. See 2Ki 20:9 – 11 and notes; Jos 10:12 – 14 and note on 10:13.
38:10 – 20 A hymn of thanksgiving in two stanzas, similar to many of the psalms. Hezekiah was deeply interested in the psalms of David and Asaph (see 2Ch 29:30).
38:10 – 14 Hezekiah voices his complaint about his past affliction (v. 1).

11 I said, "I will not again see the LORD
himself[b]
in the land of the living;[c]
no longer will I look on my fellow man,
or be with those who now dwell in
this world.
12 Like a shepherd's tent[d] my house
has been pulled down[e] and taken
from me.
Like a weaver I have rolled[f] up my life,
and he has cut me off from the
loom;[g]
day and night[h] you made an end
of me.
13 I waited patiently[i] till dawn,
but like a lion he broke[j] all my
bones;[k]
day and night[l] you made an end
of me.
14 I cried like a swift or thrush,
I moaned like a mourning dove.[m]
My eyes grew weak[n] as I looked to the
heavens.
I am being threatened; Lord, come to
my aid!"[o]

15 But what can I say?[p]
He has spoken to me, and he himself
has done this.[q]
I will walk humbly[r] all my years
because of this anguish of my soul.[s]
16 Lord, by such things people live;
and my spirit finds life in them too.
You restored me to health
and let me live.[t]
17 Surely it was for my benefit[u]
that I suffered such anguish.[v]
In your love you kept me
from the pit[w] of destruction;
you have put all my sins[x]
behind your back.[y]

38:11 [b] S Isa 12:2 [c] S Job 28:13; S Ps 116:9 **38:12** [d] Isa 33:20; 2Co 5:1, 4; 2Pe 1:13-14 [e] S Job 4:21 [f] S Isa 34:4; Heb 1:12 [g] S Nu 11:15; S Job 7:6; S Ps 31:22 [h] ver 13; Ps 32:4; 73:14 **38:13** [i] S Ps 37:7 [j] S Job 9:17; Ps 51:8 [k] S Job 10:16; Jer 34:17; La 3:4; Da 6:24 [l] S ver 12 **38:14** [m] S Ge 8:8; S Isa 59:11 [n] S Ps 6:7 [o] S Ge 50:24; S Job 17:3 **38:15** [p] 2Sa 7:20 [q] S Ps 39:9 [r] 1Ki 21:27 [s] S Job 7:11 **38:16** [t] Ps 119:25; Heb 12:9 **38:17** [u] Ro 8:28; Heb 12:11 [v] S Job 7:11; Ps 119:71, 75 [w] S Job 17:16; S Ps 30:3 [x] Ps 103:3; Jer 31:34 [y] S Ps 103:12; Isa 43:25; Mic 7:19 **38:18** [z] S Nu 16:30; S Ecc 9:10 [a] Ps 6:5; 88:10-11; 115:17 [b] S Ps 30:9 **38:19** [c] Ps 118:17; 119:175

18 For the grave[z] cannot praise you,
death cannot sing your praise;[a]
those who go down to the pit[b]
cannot hope for your faithfulness.
19 The living, the living—they praise[c]
you,
as I am doing today;
parents tell their children[d]
about your faithfulness.

20 The LORD will save me,
and we will sing[e] with stringed
instruments[f]
all the days of our lives[g]
in the temple[h] of the LORD.

21 Isaiah had said, "Prepare a poultice of
figs and apply it to the boil, and he will
recover."
22 Hezekiah had asked, "What will be
the sign[i] that I will go up to the temple of
the LORD?"

Envoys From Babylon

39:1-8pp — 2Ki 20:12-19

39 At that time Marduk-Baladan son
of Baladan king of Babylon[j] sent
Hezekiah letters and a gift, because he had
heard of his illness and recovery. 2 Hezekiah received the envoys[k] gladly and showed
them what was in his storehouses—the
silver, the gold,[l] the spices, the fine olive
oil—his entire armory and everything
found among his treasures.[m] There was
nothing in his palace or in all his kingdom
that Hezekiah did not show them.
3 Then Isaiah the prophet went to King
Hezekiah and asked, "What did those men
say, and where did they come from?"

[d] S Dt 11:19 **38:20** [e] Ps 68:25 [f] S Ps 33:2; S 45:8 [g] Ps 23:6; S 63:4; 116:2 [h] Ps 116:17-19 **38:22** [i] S 2Ch 32:31 **39:1** [j] S 2Ch 32:31 **39:2** [k] 2Ch 32:31 [l] S 2Ki 18:15 [m] 2Ch 32:27-29

38:11 *the LORD himself.* See 26:4. *land of the living.* Cf. Ps 27:13 and note.
38:12 *rolled up my life.* Cf. the rolling up of the sky like a scroll in 34:4 (see also Heb 1:12).
38:13 *broke all my bones.* Physical or spiritual distress is often described in terms of aching or broken bones (see Ps 6:2; 32:3).
38:15–20 Hezekiah offers praise for God's healing (see v. 5).
38:15 *what can I say?* Hezekiah wonders how he can praise God (cf. 2Sa 7:20).
38:16 *by such things.* Perhaps referring to God's promises and gracious acts, though his gracious acts can include such experiences as sickness and peril.
38:17 *pit of destruction.* The grave (see Ps 55:23 and note). *all my sins.* Physical and spiritual healing are sometimes linked together (see 53:4–5 and notes). *sins behind your back.* God not only puts our sins out of sight; he also puts them out of reach (Ps 103:12; Mic 7:19), out of mind (Jer 31:34) and out of existence (Isa 43:25; 44:22; Ps 51:1,9; Jer 50:20; Ac 3:19).
38:18 *cannot hope.* Knowledge about the afterlife was limited in the OT period, but the gospel of Christ has "brought ... immortality to light" (2Ti 1:10).
38:20 *sing with stringed instruments.* Instrumental music and hymns of praise were closely linked in worship (cf. Ps 33:1–3; 150). *all ... our lives in the temple.* Hezekiah, like David (Ps 23:6), loved God's house.
38:21 *Prepare ... apply.* The verbs are plural (probably addressed to the court physicians). *poultice of figs.* Figs were also used for medicinal purposes in ancient Ugarit. *he will recover.* Contrast v. 1. God answered Hezekiah's prayer for healing (see v. 5).
38:22 *sign.* Perhaps the healing of the boil (see v. 21).
39:1 *At that time.* About 703 BC. *Marduk-Baladan.* Reigned 721–710 and again in 703 (see note on 2Ki 20:12). *Babylon.* See note on 13:1. *sent ... letters and a gift.* Marduk-Baladan probably wanted Hezekiah's support in a campaign against Assyria. During his career he organized several revolts against his hated neighbors. See note on 2Ki 20:12.
39:2 *silver ... gold ... treasures.* See 2Ch 32:27–29,31 and notes. Probably Hezekiah was seeking help from the Babylonians against the Assyrian threat (see note on 2Ki 20:13). But the information gained during this ill-advised tour escorted by Hezekiah would be valuable to Marduk-Baladan's powerful successors (vv. 5–7).
39:3 *Isaiah the prophet.* Earlier God had sent Isaiah to confront Ahaz (7:3); cf. also Nathan's rebuke of David (see 2Sa 12:1,7 and note on 12:1).

"From a distant land,[n]" Hezekiah replied. "They came to me from Babylon."
4 The prophet asked, "What did they see
in your palace?"
"They saw everything in my palace,"
Hezekiah said. "There is nothing among
my treasures that I did not show them."
5 Then Isaiah said to Hezekiah, "Hear
the word[o] of the LORD Almighty: 6 The time
will surely come when everything in your
palace, and all that your predecessors
have stored up until this day, will be carried off to Babylon.[p] Nothing will be left,
says the LORD. 7 And some of your descendants, your own flesh and blood who will
be born to you, will be taken away, and
they will become eunuchs in the palace of
the king of Babylon.[q]"
8 "The word of the LORD you have spoken is good,[r]" Hezekiah replied. For he
thought, "There will be peace and security in my lifetime.[s]"

Comfort for God's People

40 Comfort, comfort[t] my people,
says your God.
2 Speak tenderly[u] to Jerusalem,
and proclaim to her
that her hard service[v] has been
completed,[w]
that her sin has been paid for,[x]
that she has received from the LORD's
hand
double[y] for all her sins.
3 A voice of one calling:
"In the wilderness prepare
the way[z] for the LORD[a];
make straight[a] in the desert
a highway for our God.[b][b]
4 Every valley shall be raised up,[c]
every mountain and hill[d] made low;
the rough ground shall become level,[e]
the rugged places a plain.
5 And the glory[f] of the LORD will be
revealed,
and all people will see it together.[g]
For the mouth of the LORD
has spoken."[h]

6 A voice says, "Cry out."
And I said, "What shall I cry?"

"All people are like grass,[i]
and all their faithfulness is like the
flowers of the field.
7 The grass withers[j] and the flowers fall,
because the breath[k] of the LORD
blows[l] on them.
Surely the people are grass.
8 The grass withers and the flowers[m]
fall,
but the word[n] of our God endures[o]
forever.[p]"

[a] 3 Or *A voice of one calling in the wilderness: / "Prepare the way for the LORD* [b] 3 Hebrew; Septuagint *make straight the paths of our God*

39:3 [n] S Dt 28:49 **39:5** [o] S Isa 38:4 **39:6** [p] S Jdg 6:4; S 2Ki 24:13 **39:7** [q] S 2Ki 24:15; Da 1:1-7 **39:8** [r] S Jdg 10:15; Job 1:21; Ps 39:9 [s] S 2Ch 32:26 **40:1** [t] Isa 12:1; 49:13; 51:3, 12; 52:9; 57:18; 61:2; 66:13; Jer 31:13; Zep 3:14-17; Zec 1:17; 2Co 1:3 **40:2** [u] S Ge 34:3; S Isa 35:4 [v] S Job 7:1 [w] Isa 41:11-13; 49:25 [x] S Lev 26:41 [y] Isa 51:19; 61:7; Jer 16:18; 17:18; Zec 9:12; Rev 18:6 **40:3** [z] S Isa 11:16; 43:19; Mal 3:1 [a] S Pr 3:5-6 [b] Mt 3:3*; Mk 1:3*; Jn 1:23* **40:4** [c] Isa 49:11 [d] S Isa 2:14 [e] S Ps 26:12; S Isa 26:7; 45:2, 13; Jer 31:9 **40:5** [f] S Ex 16:7; S Nu 14:21; S Isa 59:19 [g] Isa 52:10; 62:2; Lk 2:30; 3:4-6* [h] S Isa 1:20; 58:14 **40:6** [i] S Ge 6:3; S Isa 29:5 **40:7** [j] S Job 8:12; S Isa 15:6 [k] S Ex 15:10; S Job 41:21 [l] S Ps 103:16; S Eze 22:21 **40:8** [m] S Isa 5:24; Jas 1:10 [n] Isa 55:11; 59:21 [o] S Pr 19:21; S Isa 7:7, 9; S Jer 39:16 [p] S Ps 119:89; S Mt 5:18; 1Pe 1:24-25*

39:5 *word of the LORD.* Contrast the word of hope in 38:4–6.
39:6 *carried off to Babylon.* Isaiah's first mention of Babylon as Jerusalem's conqueror, though 14:3–4 implied the Babylonian exile (see notes there). The wickedness of Hezekiah's son Manasseh was a major cause of the captivity (see 2Ki 21:11–15). See also notes on 2Ki 20:17; 21:15.
39:7 *your descendants.* Such as King Jehoiachin (see 2Ki 24:15 and note). *eunuchs.* Cf. Da 1:3–6, where the Hebrew for "court officials" (Da 1:3) can also be translated "eunuchs." *king of Babylon.* Nebuchadnezzar.
39:8 *word … is good.* See note on 2Ki 20:19. *peace … in my lifetime.* See 2Ki 22:20 and note. "Peace" recurs in a refrain in 48:22; 57:21, dividing the last 27 chapters into 3 sections of 9 chapters each (40–48; 49–57; 58–66).
40:1—66:24 In chs. 1–35 Isaiah prophesied against the backdrop of the Assyrian threat against Judah and Jerusalem, and in chs. 36–39 he recorded Assyria's failure and warned about the future rise of Babylonia; chs. 40–66 assume that the Babylonian exile of Judah is almost over (see Introduction: Author).
40:1 *Comfort, comfort.* That is, comfort greatly. The double imperative for emphasis is found also in 51:9,17; 52:1,11; 57:14; 62:10.
40:2 *Speak tenderly.* The Hebrew for this phrase is used also in 2Ch 32:6, where Hezekiah "encouraged" Judah to trust in God in spite of the Assyrian invasion. *hard service.* The exile in Babylon (cf. Ps 137:1–6; La 1:1–2,9,16–17,21). *sin … paid for.* By enduring the punishment of captivity (see Lev 26:41). *double.* Full (or enough) punishment. Cf. the "double calamities" of 51:19.
40:3–5 See 35:1–2 and note on 35:2.
40:3 *voice.* Three voices are mentioned (vv. 3,6,9), each showing how the comfort of v. 1 will come about. The NT links the voice of v. 3 with John the Baptist in Mt 3:3; Lk 3:4; Jn 1:23 (see notes there). *prepare the way.* Clear obstacles out of the road (cf. 57:14; 62:10). The language of vv. 3–4 has in view the ancient Near Eastern custom of sending representatives ahead to prepare the way for the visit of a monarch. The picture is that of preparing a processional highway for the Lord's coming to Jerusalem. In Mt 3:1–8 John declares that repentance is necessary to prepare the way for Christ. *make straight … a highway.* See 11:16; 35:8 and notes.
40:4 *rough ground … level.* See 26:7 and note.
40:5 *glory … revealed.* God (through Cyrus, king of Persia) would redeem Israel from Babylon (see 35:9–10; 44:23–24), and all the nations would see the deliverance (see 52:10 and note; cf. Lk 3:6 and note). Ultimately the glory of the redeeming God would be seen in Jesus Christ (see Jn 1:14; 11:4; 17:4; Heb 1:3 and notes), especially at his return (Mt 16:27; 24:30; 25:31; Rev 1:7)—but also in the redeemed (see 1Co 10:31; 2Co 3:18; Eph 3:21 and notes). See also Isa 6:3 and note.
40:6,8 Quoted in part in 1Pe 1:24–25.
40:6 The second voice (see note on v. 3). *like grass.* See 37:27 and note; 51:12. *all their faithfulness … field.* Even the power of Assyria and Babylonia would soon vanish.
40:8 *word of our God endures.* The plans and purposes of the nations will not prevail (see 8:10; Ps 119:89 and notes).

[9] You who bring good news[q] to Zion,
go up on a high mountain.
You who bring good news to
Jerusalem,[a][r]
lift up your voice with a shout,
lift it up, do not be afraid;
say to the towns of Judah,
"Here is your God!"[s]
[10] See, the Sovereign LORD comes[t] with
power,[u]
and he rules[v] with a mighty arm.[w]
See, his reward[x] is with him,
and his recompense accompanies
him.
[11] He tends his flock like a shepherd:[y]
He gathers the lambs in his arms[z]
and carries them close to his heart;[a]
he gently leads[b] those that have
young.[c]

[12] Who has measured the waters[d] in the
hollow of his hand,[e]
or with the breadth of his hand
marked off the heavens?[f]
Who has held the dust of the earth in a
basket,
or weighed the mountains on the
scales
and the hills in a balance?[g]
[13] Who can fathom the Spirit[b][h] of the
LORD,
or instruct the LORD as his
counselor?[i]
[14] Whom did the LORD consult to
enlighten him,
and who taught him the right way?
Who was it that taught him
knowledge,[j]
or showed him the path of
understanding?[k]

[15] Surely the nations are like a drop in a
bucket;
they are regarded as dust on the
scales;[l]
he weighs the islands as though they
were fine dust.[m]
[16] Lebanon[n] is not sufficient for altar
fires,
nor its animals[o] enough for burnt
offerings.
[17] Before him all the nations[p] are as
nothing;[q]
they are regarded by him as
worthless
and less than nothing.[r]

[18] With whom, then, will you compare
God?[s]
To what image[t] will you liken him?
[19] As for an idol,[u] a metalworker
casts it,
and a goldsmith[v] overlays it with
gold[w]
and fashions silver chains for it.
[20] A person too poor to present such an
offering
selects wood[x] that will not rot;
they look for a skilled worker
to set up an idol[y] that will not
topple.[z]

[21] Do you not know?
Have you not heard?[a]
Has it not been told[b] you from the
beginning?[c]
Have you not understood[d] since the
earth was founded?[e]

40:9 [q] Isa 41:27; 44:28; 52:7-10; 61:1; Na 1:15; S Ac 13:32; Ro 10:15; 1Co 15:1-4 [r] S Isa 1:1 [s] Isa 25:9 **40:10** [t] Isa 35:4; 59:20; Mt 21:5; Rev 22:7 [u] Isa 28:2 [v] Isa 9:6-7 [w] S Ps 44:3; S Isa 30:30; S 33:2 [x] S Isa 35:4; Rev 22:12 **40:11** [y] S Ge 48:15; S Ps 28:9; S Mic 5:4; S Jn 10:11 [z] S Nu 11:12 [a] S Dt 26:19 [b] Isa 49:10 [c] S Ge 33:13; S Dt 30:4 **40:12** [d] S Job 12:15; S 38:10 [e] Pr 30:4 [f] S Job 38:5; Heb 1:10-12 [g] S Job 38:18; Pr 16:11 **40:13** [h] Isa 11:2; 42:1 [i] S Job 15:8; Ro 11:34*; 1Co 2:16* **40:14** [j] Job 21:22; Col 2:3 [k] S Job 12:13; S 34:13; Isa 55:9 **40:15** [l] S Ps 62:9 [m] S Dt 9:21; Isa 2:22 **40:16** [n] Isa 33:9; 37:24 [o] Ps 50:9-11; Mic 6:7; Heb 10:5-9 **40:17** [p] Isa 30:28 [q] S Job 12:19; Isa 29:7 [r] S Isa 37:19; Da 4:35

[a] 9 *Or Zion, bringer of good news, / go up on a high mountain. / Jerusalem, bringer of good news*
[b] 13 *Or mind*

40:18 [s] S Ex 8:10; S 1Sa 2:2 [t] S Dt 4:15; Ac 17:29 **40:19** [u] S Ex 20:4; Ps 115:4; S Isa 37:19; 42:17; Jer 2:8,28; 10:8; 16:19; Hab 2:18; Zec 10:2 [v] Isa 41:7; 46:6; Jer 10:3 [w] Isa 2:20; 31:7 **40:20** [x] Isa 44:19 [y] S 1Sa 12:21 [z] S 1Sa 5:3 **40:21** [a] ver 28; 2Ki 19:25; Isa 41:22; 42:9; 44:8; 48:3,5 [b] Ps 19:1; 50:6; Ac 14:17 [c] S Ge 1:1 [d] Ro 1:19 [e] Isa 48:13; 51:13

40:9 The third voice (see notes on vv. 3,6). *good news.* The news that God is leading his people back to Judah (vv. 10–11). He cares for his people and will redeem them (see 52:7–10; 61:1 and notes). The NT expands this "good news" ("gospel") to refer to the salvation that Christ brings to all who receive him by faith (see 1Co 15:2–3; Gal 1:7; 2:16 and notes). See NIV text note for an alternative translation. *Here is your God!* The Lord is returning to Jerusalem (see v. 10). These words apply to the return from exile (see 52:7–9 and notes), the first coming of Christ (Mt 21:5) and the second coming of Christ (62:11; Rev 22:12). See 35:4 and note.
40:10 *rules with a mighty arm.* Cf. 51:9; 59:16 and notes. The Lord is characterized by both strength and gentleness (v. 11). *reward ... recompense.* His delivered people, the flock of v. 11 (see 62:11–12 and notes).
40:11 *tends his flock.* Cf. Jer 31:10; Eze 34:11–16 and notes.
40:12–31 Rhetorical questions are used to persuade the people to trust in the Lord, who has the ability to deliver, strengthen and restore his people.
40:12 *measured the waters.* See Job 28:25; 38:8. In Job 38–41 the Lord overwhelms Job with a description of his greatness. *marked off the heavens.* See 48:13 and note.
40:13 Quoted in Ro 11:34; 1Co 2:16. *counselor.* See 9:6 and note.
40:15 *nations ... a drop in a bucket.* See note on v. 6. *dust.* See 17:13 and note; 29:5.
40:16 *Lebanon.* The wood of its cedar trees. *its animals.* Cf. Ps 104:16–18 and note. Sacrifices, however numerous, could never do justice to the greatness of God.
40:17 *nothing ... worthless.* In spite of the temporary splendor they might possess (see 13:19 and note).
40:18–20 More than any other prophet, Isaiah shows the folly of worshiping idols. His sarcastic caricature, satire and denunciation of these false gods reach a peak in 44:9–20 (see notes there; see also 41:7,22–24; 42:17; 46:5–7; 48:5 and note).
40:18 *With whom ... compare God?* See v. 25 and note; 46:5.
40:19 *metalworker ... goldsmith.* See 41:7; 44:10–12. *gold ... silver.* See 2:20; Hab 2:18–19 and notes.
40:20 *wood.* See 44:14–16,19 and notes. *that will not topple.* See 41:7; 46:7.
40:21 *from the beginning.* God's work as Creator is emphasized in the rest of the chapter (cf. 37:26; 41:4,26).

22 He sits enthroned[f] above the circle of
the earth,
and its people are like grasshoppers.[g]
He stretches out the heavens[h] like a
canopy,[i]
and spreads them out like a tent[j] to
live in.[k]
23 He brings princes[l] to naught
and reduces the rulers of this world
to nothing.[m]
24 No sooner are they planted,
no sooner are they sown,
no sooner do they take root[n] in the
ground,
than he blows[o] on them and they
wither,[p]
and a whirlwind sweeps them away
like chaff.[q]

25 "To whom will you compare me?[r]
Or who is my equal?" says the Holy
One.[s]
26 Lift up your eyes and look to the
heavens:[t]
Who created[u] all these?
He who brings out the starry host[v] one
by one
and calls forth each of them by
name.
Because of his great power and mighty
strength,[w]
not one of them is missing.[x]

27 Why do you complain, Jacob?
Why do you say, Israel,
"My way is hidden from the LORD;
my cause is disregarded by my
God"?[y]
28 Do you not know?
Have you not heard?[z]
The LORD is the everlasting[a] God,
the Creator[b] of the ends of the
earth.[c]
He will not grow tired or weary,[d]
and his understanding no one can
fathom.[e]
29 He gives strength[f] to the weary[g]
and increases the power of the
weak.
30 Even youths grow tired and weary,
and young men[h] stumble and fall;[i]
31 but those who hope[j] in the LORD
will renew their strength.[k]
They will soar on wings like eagles;[l]
they will run and not grow weary,
they will walk and not be faint.[m]

The Helper of Israel

41 "Be silent[n] before me, you
islands![o]
Let the nations renew their
strength![p]
Let them come forward[q] and speak;
let us meet together[r] at the place of
judgment.

2 "Who has stirred[s] up one from the
east,[t]
calling him in righteousness[u] to his
service[a]?[v]
He hands nations over to him
and subdues kings before him.
He turns them to dust[w] with his
sword,
to windblown chaff[x] with his bow.[y]
3 He pursues them and moves on
unscathed,[z]
by a path his feet have not traveled
before.

[a] 2 Or *east, / whom victory meets at every step*

40:22 [f]S 2Ch 6:18; S Ps 2:4 [g]S Nu 13:33 [h]S Ge 1:1; S Isa 48:13 [i]S Ge 1:8; S Job 22:14 [j]S Job 36:29 [k]S Job 26:7 **40:23** [l]S Job 12:18; S Isa 34:12 [m]S Job 12:19; Am 2:3 **40:24** [n]S Job 5:3 [o]S 2Sa 22:16; S Isa 11:4; 41:16 [p]S Job 8:12; S 18:16 [q]S Job 24:24; S Isa 41:2 **40:25** [r]S 1Sa 2:2; S 1Ch 16:25 [s]Isa 1:4; 37:23 **40:26** [t]Isa 51:6 [u]ver 28; Ps 89:11-13; Isa 42:5; 66:2 [v]S 2Ki 17:16; S Ne 9:6; S Job 38:32 [w]S Job 9:4; S Isa 45:24; Eph 1:19 [x]S Isa 34:16 **40:27** [y]S Job 6:29; S 27:2; Lk 18:7-8 **40:28** [z]S ver 21 [a]S Dt 33:27; S Ps 90:2 [b]S ver 26 [c]S Isa 37:16 [d]Isa 44:12 [e]S Ps 147:5; Ro 11:33 **40:29** [f]S Ge 18:14; S Ps 68:35; S 119:28 [g]Isa 50:4; 57:19; Jer 31:25 **40:30** [h]Isa 9:17; Jer 6:11; 9:21 [i]S Ps 20:8; Isa 5:27 **40:31** [j]S Ps 37:9; 40:1; S Isa 30:18; Lk 18:1 [k]S 1Sa 2:4; S 2Ki 6:33; S 2Co 4:16 [l]S Ex 19:4 [m]2Co 4:1; Heb 12:1-3 **41:1** [n]Ps 37:7; Hab 2:20; Zep 1:7; Zec 2:13 [o]S Isa 11:11 [p]S 1Sa 2:4 [q]Isa 48:16; 57:3 [r]S Isa 1:18; 34:1; 50:8 **41:2** [s]S Ezr 1:2 [t]ver 25; Isa 13:4, 17; 44:28; 45:1, 13; 48:14; Jer 50:3; 51:11 [u]Isa 45:8, 13 [v]Isa 44:28; Jer 25:9 [w]S 2Sa 22:43 [x]Ps 1:4; Isa 40:24 [y]S Isa 13:18 **41:3** [z]Da 8:4

40:22 *sits enthroned.* Cf. 66:1; see 37:16 and note. *circle.* Or "horizon." See Job 22:14; Pr 8:27. *stretches out the heavens . . . like a tent.* See 42:5; 44:24; 51:13; Ps 104:2; see also note on Ps 19:4b–6.

40:23 *princes . . . rulers . . . to nothing.* See v. 17; 2:22 and notes; cf. Jer 25:17–26; Da 2:21.

40:24 *whirlwind . . . like chaff.* See 17:13 and note; 41:15–16.

40:25 See v. 18. Apparently some Israelite doubters were comparing their God with the gods of their captors, and they believed that the Lord was failing the test. *Holy One.* See 1:4 and note.

40:26 *created.* See vv. 21–22 and notes. *brings out.* The Hebrew for this expression is used for bringing forth the constellations in Job 38:32. *starry host.* Also worshiped by the people (see 47:13; Jer 19:13 and note). *by name.* See note on Ps 147:4–6. *not one . . . missing.* See 34:16 and note.

40:27–31 As in many psalms of praise, Isaiah now stresses the goodness of God after describing his majesty (vv. 12–26). Such a God is able to deliver and restore his distressed people if they will wait in faith for him to act. They are to trust in him and draw strength from him.

40:27 *way.* Condition. *hidden . . . disregarded.* Cf. 49:14; 54:8.

40:28 *everlasting God.* See 9:6. *Creator.* See vv. 21–22 and notes. *ends of the earth.* See 11:12 and note; cf. 5:26; 41:9; 43:6. *not grow tired.* Contrast 44:12.

40:30 *grow tired . . . stumble.* See note on 5:27.

40:31 *hope in.* Trust in or look expectantly to (see 5:2; 49:23). *renew.* Lit. "exchange"; see 41:1 and note. Their human weakness will be exchanged for God's strength (v. 29). *eagles.* Known for their vigor (see Ps 103:5 and note) and speed (Jer 4:13; 48:40).

41:1,5 *islands.* Or "coastlands" (see 11:11 and note).

41:1 *renew their strength.* See 40:31 and note. The nations and their gods are challenged to display the same power and wisdom as Israel's God (see vv. 21–24).

41:2 *one from the east.* Cyrus the Great, king of Persia (559–530 BC), who conquered Babylon in 539 (see 13:17 and note) and issued the decree allowing the Jews to return to Jerusalem (see Ezr 1:1–4; 6:3–5). Cyrus is referred to also in v. 25; 44:28—45:5,13; 46:11. *calling him in righteousness.* Like the servant of the Lord in 42:6, Cyrus was chosen to carry out God's righteous purposes. *subdues kings.* Such as Croesus, king of Lydia in Asia Minor. *windblown chaff.* See 17:13 and note. *his bow.* The Persians were renowned for their ability as archers.

4 Who has done this and carried it
through,
calling[a] forth the generations from
the beginning?[b]
I, the LORD — with the first of them
and with the last[c] — I am he.[d]"
5 The islands[e] have seen it and fear;
the ends of the earth[f] tremble.
They approach and come forward;
6 they help each other
and say to their companions, "Be
strong![g]"
7 The metalworker[h] encourages the
goldsmith,[i]
and the one who smooths with the
hammer
spurs on the one who strikes the anvil.
One says of the welding, "It is good."
The other nails down the idol so it
will not topple.[j]

8 "But you, Israel, my servant,[k]
Jacob, whom I have chosen,[l]
you descendants of Abraham[m] my
friend,[n]
9 I took you from the ends of the earth,[o]
from its farthest corners I called[p] you.
I said, 'You are my servant';[q]
I have chosen[r] you and have not
rejected you.
10 So do not fear,[s] for I am with you;[t]
do not be dismayed, for I am your
God.
I will strengthen[u] you and help[v] you;
I will uphold you[w] with my righteous
right hand.[x]

11 "All who rage[y] against you
will surely be ashamed and
disgraced;[z]
those who oppose[a] you
will be as nothing and perish.[b]
12 Though you search for your enemies,
you will not find them.[c]
Those who wage war against you
will be as nothing[d] at all.
13 For I am the LORD your God
who takes hold of your right hand[e]
and says to you, Do not fear;
I will help[f] you.
14 Do not be afraid,[g] you worm[h] Jacob,
little Israel, do not fear,
for I myself will help[i] you," declares
the LORD,
your Redeemer,[j] the Holy One[k] of
Israel.
15 "See, I will make you into a threshing
sledge,[l]
new and sharp, with many teeth.
You will thresh the mountains[m] and
crush them,
and reduce the hills to chaff.[n]
16 You will winnow[o] them, the wind will
pick them up,
and a gale[p] will blow them away.[q]
But you will rejoice[r] in the LORD
and glory[s] in the Holy One[t] of
Israel.

41:4 [a] ver 9; Isa 43:7 [b] ver 26; S Ge 1:1; Isa 46:10 [c] Isa 44:6; 48:12; Rev 1:8,17 [d] S Dt 32:39 **41:5** [e] S Isa 11:11; Eze 26:17-18 [f] S Dt 30:4; S Isa 11:12 **41:6** [g] S Jos 1:6 **41:7** [h] Isa 44:13; Jer 10:3-5 [i] S Isa 40:19 [j] S 1Sa 5:3; Isa 46:7 **41:8** [k] S Ps 136:22; S Isa 27:11 [l] S Isa 14:1 [m] S Isa 29:22; 51:2; 63:16 [n] 2Ch 20:7; Jas 2:23 **41:9** [o] Isa 11:12; S 37:16 [p] S ver 4 [q] S Isa 20:3 [r] S Dt 7:6 **41:10** [s] S Ge 15:1 [t] S Dt 3:22; Jos 1:9; Isa 43:2, 5; Jer 30:10; 46:27-28; Ro 8:31 [u] S Ps 68:35; S 119:28 [v] ver 13-14; Isa 44:2; 49:8; 50:7,9 [w] S Ps 18:35; S 119:117 [x] S Ex 3:20; S Job 40:14 **41:11** [y] S Isa 17:12 [z] Isa 29:22; 45:24; 54:17 [a] S Ex 23:22 [b] S Isa 29:8; S Jer 2:3 **41:12** [c] Ps 37:35-36; S Isa 34:12 [d] S Job 7:8; Isa 17:14; 29:20 **41:13** [e] Ps 73:23; Isa 42:6; 45:1; 51:18 [f] ver 10 **41:14** [g] S Ge 15:1 [h] S Job 4:19; S Ps 22:6 [i] S ver 10 [j] S Ex 15:13; S Job 19:25; S Isa 1:27 [k] ver 16, 20; S Isa 1:4 **41:15** [l] S Job 41:30; S Isa 10:5; S 21:10 [m] S Ex 19:18; S Ps 107:33; Jer 9:10; Eze 33:28 [n] S ver 2 **41:16** [o] Jer 15:7; 51:2 [p] Isa 40:24 [q] Da 2:35 [r] S Isa 25:9 [s] Isa 45:25; 60:19 [t] S ver 14; S Mk 1:24

41:4 *from the beginning.* See 40:21 and note. *with the first ... with the last.* Since the Lord was present with the first of the generations and will still be there with the last of them, he is the eternal Lord of history and nations (see Heb 13:8; Rev 1:8,17; 2:8; 21:6; 22:13).

41:5 – 7 By 546 BC Cyrus had fought his way victoriously to the west coast of Asia Minor, where his leading opponent was Croesus, king of Lydia. Sarcasm and satire are used in the description of the frantic efforts in vv. 6 – 7 — all of them futile (cf. 40:19 – 20).

41:5 *ends of the earth.* See 11:12 and note.

41:6 *Be strong!* See 35:4 and note.

41:7 *hammer.* Cf. 44:12. *so it will not topple.* See 40:18 – 20 and notes.

41:8 – 9 *my servant.* A significant term in chs. 41 – 53, referring sometimes to the nation of Israel and other times to an individual. In these passages the title refers to one who occupies a special position in God's royal administration of his kingdom, as in "my servant Moses" (Nu 12:7), "my servant David" (2Sa 3:18; 7:5,8), "my servants the prophets" (2Ki 17:13; Jer 7:25). See note on 42:1; see also 20:3; 22:20; 42:1,19; 43:10; 44:1 – 2,21; 45:4; 49:3,5 – 7; 50:10; 52:13; 53:11.

41:8 *But.* In contrast to the nations of vv. 5 – 7, Israel does not need to be afraid (v. 10). *my friend.* See Ge 18:17 and note; 2Ch 20:7; Jas 2:23 and note.

41:9 *ends of the earth.* See v. 5; probably a reference to Mesopotamia and Egypt (see Ge 11:31; 12:1; 15:7; Ps 114:1 – 2; Jer 31:32).

41:10 *do not fear ... be dismayed.* See vv. 13 – 14; 43:1,5; see also 35:4 and note. *strengthen ... help you.* As one called to God's service (see vv. 9,15 – 16). See also v. 14; 40:29; 44:2; 49:8. *right hand.* A hand of power and salvation (see Ex 15:6,12; Ps 20:6; 48:10; 89:13; 98:1).

41:11 *be ashamed and disgraced.* Cf. 45:17; 50:7; 54:4. *will be as nothing.* See vv. 15 – 16 and notes.

41:13 *takes hold ... right hand.* To strengthen them and keep them from stumbling. *Do not fear.* See v. 10 and note.

41:14 *worm.* A reference to their feeble and despised condition in exile (cf. Job 25:6; Ps 22:6). *Redeemer.* Deliverer from Babylonian exile (in a new exodus). The Hebrew for this word refers to an obligated family protector and thus portrays the Lord as the family protector of Israel. He is related to Israel as father (63:16; 64:8) and husband (54:5). As Guardian-Redeemer (or family protector), he redeems his people's property (for he regathers them to their land, 54:1 – 8), guarantees their freedom (35:9; 43:1 – 4; 48:20; 52:11 – 12), avenges them against their tormentors (47:3 – 4; 49:25 – 26; 64:4) and secures their posterity for the future (61:8 – 9). See note on Ru 2:20. *Holy One of Israel.* See vv. 16,20; see also 1:4 and note. The title occurs with "Redeemer" also in 43:14; 47:4; 48:17; 49:7; 54:5.

41:15 *threshing sledge.* Cf. 28:27; Am 1:3 and note; Mic 4:13; Hab 3:12. *mountains ... hills.* Probably represent the nations. See 2:14. *reduce ... to chaff.* See v. 2; 17:13 and note; 29:5 – 6.

41:16 *winnow.* A figure of judgment used also in Jer 51:2 (see note on Ru 1:22). *rejoice.* Cf. 25:9; 35:10; 51:11.

17 "The poor and needy search for water,[u]
but there is none;
their tongues are parched with thirst.[v]
But I the LORD will answer[w] them;
I, the God of Israel, will not forsake[x]
them.
18 I will make rivers flow[y] on barren
heights,
and springs within the valleys.
I will turn the desert[z] into pools of
water,[a]
and the parched ground into springs.[b]
19 I will put in the desert[c]
the cedar and the acacia,[d] the myrtle
and the olive.
I will set junipers[e] in the wasteland,
the fir and the cypress[f] together,[g]
20 so that people may see and know,[h]
may consider and understand,[i]
that the hand[j] of the LORD has done this,
that the Holy One[k] of Israel has
created[l] it.

21 "Present your case,[m]" says the LORD.
"Set forth your arguments," says
Jacob's King.[n]
22 "Tell us, you idols,
what is going to happen.[o]
Tell us what the former things[p] were,
so that we may consider them
and know their final outcome.
Or declare to us the things to come,[q]
23 tell us what the future holds,
so we may know[r] that you are gods.
Do something, whether good or bad,[s]
so that we will be dismayed[t] and
filled with fear.
24 But you are less than nothing[u]
and your works are utterly worthless;[v]
whoever chooses you is detestable.[w]

25 "I have stirred[x] up one from the north,[y]
and he comes—
one from the rising sun who calls on
my name.
He treads[z] on rulers as if they were
mortar,
as if he were a potter treading the clay.
26 Who told of this from the beginning,[a]
so we could know,
or beforehand, so we could say, 'He
was right'?
No one told of this,
no one foretold[b] it,
no one heard any words[c] from you.
27 I was the first to tell[d] Zion, 'Look, here
they are!'
I gave to Jerusalem a messenger of
good news.[e]
28 I look but there is no one[f]—
no one among the gods to give
counsel,[g]
no one to give answer[h] when I ask
them.
29 See, they are all false!
Their deeds amount to nothing;[i]
their images[j] are but wind[k] and
confusion.

The Servant of the LORD

42 "Here is my servant,[l] whom I
uphold,
my chosen one[m] in whom I delight;[n]
I will put my Spirit[o] on him,
and he will bring justice[p] to the
nations.[q]

41:17 [u] Isa 43:20 [v] S Isa 35:7 [w] S Isa 30:19 [x] S Dt 31:6; S Ps 27:9 **41:18** [y] S Isa 30:25 [z] Isa 43:19 [a] S 2Ki 3:17 [b] S Job 38:26; S Isa 35:7 **41:19** [c] S Isa 35:1; 51:3 [d] Ex 25:5, 10, 13 [e] S Isa 37:24 [f] Isa 44:14 [g] Isa 60:13 **41:20** [h] S Ex 6:7 [i] S Isa 29:24 [j] Ezr 7:6; 8:31; Isa 50:2; 51:9; 59:1; 66:14; Jer 32:17 [k] S ver 14; Isa 43:3, 14 [l] S Isa 4:5 **41:21** [m] S ver 1 [n] Isa 43:15; 44:6 **41:22** [o] ver 26; Isa 43:9; 44:7; 45:21; 48:14 [p] Isa 43:18, 26; 46:9; 48:3 [q] Isa 42:9; 43:19; 46:10; 48:6; 65:17; Jn 13:19 **41:23** [r] Isa 45:3 [s] Jer 10:5 [t] S 2Ki 19:26 **41:24** [u] S Isa 37:19; 1Co 8:4 [v] S 1Sa 12:21; Jer 8:19; 10:5, 8, 15 [w] S Ps 109:7; S Isa 1:13; S 48:8 **41:25** [x] S Ezr 1:2 [y] S ver 2; Jer 50:9, 41; 51:48 [z] S 2Sa 22:43; S Isa 5:5; Na 3:14 **41:26** [a] S ver 4 [b] S ver 22; Isa 52:6 [c] S 1Ki 18:26; Hab 2:18-19 **41:27** [d] Isa 48:3, 16 [e] S Isa 40:9 **41:28** [f] Ps 22:11; Isa 50:2; 59:16; 63:5; 64:7; Eze 22:30 [g] Isa 40:13-14 [h] S 1Ki 18:26; Isa 65:12; 66:4; Jer 25:4 **41:29** [i] S 1Sa 12:21 [j] S Isa 37:19 [k] Jer 5:13 **42:1** [l] S Isa 20:3; S Mt 20:28 [m] S Isa 14:1; Lk 9:35; 23:35; 1Pe 2:4, 6 [n] Mt 3:17 [o] S Isa 11:2; S 44:3; Mt 3:16-17; S Jn 3:34 [p] S Isa 9:7 [q] S Ge 49:10

41:17 *poor and needy.* Israel in exile or on the way home (cf. v. 14; 32:7). *will answer.* See 30:19 and note.
41:18 *rivers … on barren heights.* See 30:25 and note. *desert into pools … springs.* See 32:2; 35:6 – 7 and notes.
41:19 These trees will beautify the desert (cf. 35:1 – 2). Several are named in 60:13 in connection with adorning the place of God's sanctuary. Acacia wood was used for the tabernacle (see Ex 25:5,10,13 and note on 25:5). The juniper tree and myrtle replace thorns and briers in 55:13.
41:20 *created it.* These fruitful conditions are part of God's new creation in behalf of his people (see 48:7; 57:19; 65:17 – 18).
41:21 – 22 God takes the nations and their idols to court (see v. 1 and note).
41:22 *former things.* Earlier divine predictions or accomplishments (see 42:9; 43:9,18; 46:9; 48:3).
41:23 *Do something … good or bad.* See note on 40:18 – 20; see also Ps 115:2 – 11; Jer 10:2 – 16.
41:24 *less than nothing … your works are utterly worthless.* Like the nations that worship them. See 40:17; 44:9; Hos 9:10. *detestable.* Like those who marry idolaters (see Mal 2:11 and note).
41:25 *stirred up.* See v. 2 and note. *from the north.* Cyrus came from the east (v. 2) but conquered a number of kingdoms north of Babylon early in his reign. From the perspective of those living in Jerusalem, invasions came primarily from the north (see 14:31; Jer 1:14; 6:1,22; 10:22; 46:20; 50:3,9,41; 51:48). *calls on my name.* Cyrus used the Lord's name in his decree (Ezr 1:2) but did not acknowledge him (see 45:4 – 5 and note on 45:4). *treads on … mortar … clay.* Similar to Assyria in 10:6. Cf. Mic 7:10; Na 3:14.
41:26 *from the beginning.* Before these events began to unfold (cf. v. 4). *you.* Idols or their worshipers.
41:27 *here they are.* Words about the deliverance from Babylon. *messenger of good news.* Isaiah. See 40:9; 52:7 and notes.
41:28 *no one to give answer.* See 46:7.
41:29 *amount to nothing.* See v. 24.
42:1 – 4 Quoted in part in Mt 12:18 – 21 (see note there) with reference to Christ. There are four "servant songs" in which the servant is the Messiah: 42:1 – 4 (or 42:1 – 7 or 42:1 – 9); 49:1 – 6 (or 49:1 – 7 or 49:1 – 13); 50:4 – 9 (or 50:4 – 11); 52:13 — 53:12; cf. 61:1 – 2 and notes. He is "Israel" in its ideal form (49:3). The nation was to be a kingdom of priests (see Ex 19:6 and note), but the Messiah would be the high priest who would atone for the sins of the world (53:4 – 12). Cyrus was introduced in ch. 41 as a deliverer from Babylon, but the servant would deliver the world from its bondage to sin (see v. 7).
42:1 *my servant.* See 41:8 – 9; Zec 3:8 and notes. In the royal terminology of the ancient Near East "servant" meant some-

2 He will not shout or cry out,[r]
or raise his voice in the streets.
3 A bruised reed[s] he will not break,[t]
and a smoldering wick he will not
snuff out.[u]
In faithfulness he will bring forth
justice;[v]
4 he will not falter or be discouraged
till he establishes justice[w] on earth.
In his teaching[x] the islands[y] will put
their hope."[z]

5 This is what God the LORD says—
the Creator of the heavens,[a] who
stretches them out,
who spreads out the earth[b] with all
that springs from it,[c]
who gives breath[d] to its people,
and life to those who walk on it:
6 "I, the LORD, have called[e] you in
righteousness;[f]
I will take hold of your hand.[g]
I will keep[h] you and will make you
to be a covenant[i] for the people
and a light[j] for the Gentiles,[k]
7 to open eyes that are blind,[l]
to free[m] captives from prison[n]
and to release from the dungeon
those who sit in darkness.[o]

8 "I am the LORD;[p] that is my name![q]
I will not yield my glory to another[r]
or my praise to idols.[s]
9 See, the former things[t] have taken place,
and new things I declare;
before they spring into being
I announce[u] them to you."

Song of Praise to the LORD

10 Sing[v] to the LORD a new song,[w]
his praise[x] from the ends of the
earth,[y]
you who go down to the sea, and all
that is in it,[z]
you islands,[a] and all who live in
them.
11 Let the wilderness[b] and its towns raise
their voices;
let the settlements where Kedar[c]
lives rejoice.
Let the people of Sela[d] sing for joy;
let them shout from the
mountaintops.[e]
12 Let them give glory[f] to the LORD
and proclaim his praise[g] in the
islands.[h]
13 The LORD will march out like a
champion,[i]
like a warrior[j] he will stir up his zeal;[k]
with a shout[l] he will raise the battle
cry
and will triumph over his enemies.[m]

14 "For a long time I have kept silent,[n]
I have been quiet and held myself
back.[o]
But now, like a woman in childbirth,
I cry out, I gasp and pant.[p]
15 I will lay waste[q] the mountains[r] and hills
and dry up all their vegetation;
I will turn rivers into islands
and dry up[s] the pools.
16 I will lead[t] the blind[u] by ways they
have not known,
along unfamiliar paths I will guide
them;

42:2 [r] Pr 8:1-4 **42:3** [s] S Isa 36:6 [t] S Job 30:24 [u] S Job 13:25 [v] Ps 72:2; 96:13 **42:4** [w] S Isa 2:4 [x] ver 21; Ex 34:29; Isa 51:4 [y] S Isa 11:11 [z] S Ge 49:10; Mt 12:18-21* **42:5** [a] S Ge 1:6; Ps 102:25; Isa 48:13 [b] S Ge 1:1 [c] Ps 24:2; Ac 17:24 [d] S Ge 2:7; Ac 17:25 **42:6** [e] Ex 31:2; S Jdg 4:10; Isa 41:9-10; 43:1 [f] Isa 45:24; Jer 23:6; Da 9:7 [g] Isa 41:13; 45:1 [h] Isa 26:3; 27:3 [i] Isa 49:8; 54:10; 59:21; 61:8; Jer 31:31; 32:40; Mal 3:1; S Lk 22:20 [j] S Isa 9:2 [k] S Isa 26:18; S Lk 2:32 **42:7** [l] S Ps 146:8; S Isa 32:3; Mt 11:5 [m] Isa 49:9; 51:14; 52:2; Zec 2:7 [n] S Ps 66:11; S Isa 24:22; 48:20; Zec 9:11; S Lk 4:19; 2Ti 2:26; Heb 2:14-15 [o] S Ps 107:10, 14; Ac 26:18 **42:8** [p] Ps 81:10; Isa 43:3, 11, 15; 46:9; 49:23 [q] S Ex 3:15; S 6:3 [r] Isa 48:11 [s] S Ex 8:10; S 20:4 **42:9** [t] S Isa 41:22 [u] S Isa 40:21; Eze 2:4 **42:10** [v] S Ex 15:1 [w] S Ps 96:1 [x] 1Ki 10:9; Isa 60:6 [y] S Dt 30:4; S Ps 48:10; 65:5; Isa 49:6 [z] S 1Ch 16:32; Ps 96:11 [a] S Isa 11:11 **42:11** [b] S Isa 32:16 [c] S Ge 25:13; Isa 60:7 [d] S Jdg 1:36 [e] Isa 52:7; Na 1:15 **42:12** [f] S 1Ch 16:24; S Isa 24:15 [g] S Ps 26:7; S 66:2; 1Pe 2:9 [h] S Isa 11:11 **42:13** [i] S Isa 9:6 [j] S Ex 14:14 [k] S Isa 26:11 [l] S Jos 6:5; Jer 25:30; Hos 11:10; Joel 3:16; Am 1:2; 3:4, 8 [m] Isa 66:14 **42:14** [n] S Est 4:14; S Ps 50:21 [o] S Ge 43:31; Lk 18:7; 2Pe 3:9 [p] Jer 4:31 **42:15** [q] Eze 38:20 [r] S Ps 107:33 [s] S Isa 11:15; 50:2; Na 1:4-6 **42:16** [t] S Isa 29:24; 40:11; 57:18; 58:11; Jer 31:8-9; Lk 1:78-79 [u] S Isa 32:3

thing like "trusted envoy" or "confidential representative." *chosen one.* See 41:8–9 and note. *delight.* Cf. Lk 3:22. *my Spirit on him.* Like the "Branch" of 11:1–2 (see note on 11:2); cf. 61:1. *justice.* A righteous world order (see v. 4); see also 9:7; 11:4 and notes.

42:2 *not shout or cry out.* He will bring peace (see 9:6).

42:3 *bruised reed.* Someone who is weak (see Ps 72:2,4). The servant will mend broken lives.

42:4 *falter.* Cf. 40:28. *justice.* Perfect order (see v. 1 and note). *In his teaching … hope.* As do the nations in 2:2–4. The servant will be a new Moses (see Dt 18:15–18; Ac 3:21–23,26). *islands.* See note on 11:11.

42:5 *Creator of the heavens … stretches.* See 40:22 and note. *gives breath … life.* Cf. 57:15.

42:6 *called … righteousness.* Similar to the call of Cyrus (see 41:2 and note). *take hold of your hand.* See 41:13 and note. *covenant.* See 49:8. Through the Messiah as king, the Davidic covenant (see 2Sa 7:12–16; cf. Isa 55:3 and note) would be fulfilled (9:7), and he would institute the new covenant by his death (see Jer 31:31–34; Heb 8:6–13; 9:15 and notes). *people.* Probably the Israelites (see 49:8; Ac 26:17–18). *light for the Gentiles.* See note on 9:2. *light.* Parallel to "salvation" in 49:6 (cf. 51:4; Lk 2:32).

42:7 *open eyes.* See 29:18; 32:3; 35:5 and notes. *free … from prison.* From the prison of Babylon and also from spiritual and moral bondage (compare 61:1 with Lk 4:18).

42:8 *my glory.* See 40:5 and note.

42:9 *former things.* See 41:22 and note. *new things.* The restoration of Israel (43:19). Cf. 48:6.

42:10 *new song.* To celebrate the "new things" of v. 9. *ends of the earth.* See 11:12 and note; 41:5. *islands.* See v. 12; 11:11 and note.

42:11 *wilderness.* See 35:1 and note. *Kedar.* See note on 21:16. *Sela.* See note on 16:1.

42:12 *give glory … praise.* See 24:14–16.

42:13 *champion.* God will fight as he did at the "Red Sea" (Ex 15:3); see 9:6 and note. *zeal.* Cf. 9:7; 37:32; 59:17; 63:15. *raise the battle cry.* To cause panic among the enemy (see Jos 6:5 and note; 1Sa 4:5–8).

42:14 *For a long time.* During Israel's humiliation and exile. *held myself back.* See 63:15; 64:12. The Hebrew verb is also used of Joseph, who controlled his emotions while he tested his brothers (Ge 43:31; 45:1). See 30:18 and note.

42:15 *lay waste … dry up.* The opposite of 35:1–2; 41:18. *rivers into islands.* Perhaps to make travel easier. See 37:25; 44:27.

42:16 *blind.* Israel (vv. 19–20). *rough places smooth.* See note on 26:7. *not forsake.* Cf. 40:27; 49:14; 54:8.

I will turn the darkness into light[v]
before them
and make the rough places smooth.[w]
These are the things I will do;
I will not forsake[x] them.
17 But those who trust in idols,
who say to images, 'You are our
gods,'[y]
will be turned back in utter shame.[z]

Israel Blind and Deaf

18 "Hear, you deaf;[a]
look, you blind, and see!
19 Who is blind[b] but my servant,[c]
and deaf like the messenger[d] I send?
Who is blind like the one in covenant[e]
with me,
blind like the servant of the LORD?
20 You have seen many things, but you
pay no attention;
your ears are open, but you do not
listen."[f]
21 It pleased the LORD
for the sake[g] of his righteousness
to make his law[h] great and
glorious.
22 But this is a people plundered[i] and
looted,
all of them trapped in pits[j]
or hidden away in prisons.[k]
They have become plunder,
with no one to rescue them;[l]
they have been made loot,
with no one to say, "Send them
back."

23 Which of you will listen to this
or pay close attention[m] in time to
come?
24 Who handed Jacob over to become
loot,
and Israel to the plunderers?[n]
Was it not the LORD,[o]
against whom we have sinned?

42:16 [v] S Ps 18:28; Isa 58:8, 10; S Ac 26:18 [w] S Isa 26:7; Lk 3:5 [x] S Dt 4:31; Heb 13:5 **42:17** [y] S Ex 32:4 [z] S Ps 97:7; S Isa 1:29 **42:18** [a] S Isa 35:5 **42:19** [b] Isa 43:8; Eze 12:2 [c] Isa 41:8-9 [d] Isa 44:26; Hag 1:13 [e] Isa 26:3 **42:20** [f] Isa 6:9-10; 43:8; Jer 5:21; 6:10 **42:21** [g] Isa 43:25 [h] S ver 4; 2Co 3:7 **42:22** [i] S Jdg 6:4; S 2Ki 24:13 [j] S Isa 24:18 [k] S Ps 66:11; S Isa 24:22 [l] S Isa 5:29 **42:23** [m] Dt 32:29; Ps 81:13; Isa 47:7; 48:18; 57:11 **42:24** [n] S 2Ki 17:6; Isa 43:28; 47:6 [o] Isa 10:5-6 [p] S Isa 30:15 [q] S Jos 1:7; S Ps 119:136; Isa 5:24; Jer 44:10 **42:25** [r] S 2Ki 22:13; S Job 40:11; S Isa 51:17; S Eze 7:19 [s] 2Ki 25:9; Isa 66:15; Jer 4:4; 21:12; La 2:3; Na 1:6 [t] S Isa 1:3 [u] Isa 29:13; 47:7; 57:1, 11; Hos 7:9 **43:1** [v] S Isa 27:11

For they would not follow[p] his ways;
they did not obey his law.[q]
25 So he poured out on them his burning
anger,[r]
the violence of war.
It enveloped them in flames,[s] yet they
did not understand;[t]
it consumed them, but they did not
take it to heart.[u]

Israel's Only Savior

43 But now, this is what the LORD
says—
he who created[v] you, Jacob,
he who formed[w] you, Israel:[x]
"Do not fear, for I have redeemed[y]
you;
I have summoned you by name;[z] you
are mine.[a]
2 When you pass through the waters,[b]
I will be with you;[c]
and when you pass through the
rivers,
they will not sweep over you.
When you walk through the fire,[d]
you will not be burned;
the flames will not set you ablaze.[e]
3 For I am the LORD your God,[f]
the Holy One[g] of Israel, your
Savior;[h]
I give Egypt[i] for your ransom,
Cush[a][j] and Seba[k] in your stead.[l]
4 Since you are precious and honored[m] in
my sight,
and because I love[n] you,
I will give people in exchange for you,
nations in exchange for your life.

[a] *3* That is, the upper Nile region

[w] S ver 7; S Ge 2:7 [x] Ge 32:28; Isa 44:21 [y] S Ex 6:6; S Job 19:25 [z] S Isa 42:6; 45:3-4; 49:1 [a] S Dt 7:6; Mal 3:17 **43:2** [b] S Isa 8:7 [c] S Ge 26:3; S Ex 14:22 [d] Isa 29:6; 30:27 [e] Ps 66:12; Da 3:25-27 **43:3** [f] S Ex 20:2 [g] S Isa 41:20 [h] S Ex 14:30; S Jdg 2:18; S Ps 3:8; S Isa 25:9 [i] S Ps 68:31; Isa 19:1; Eze 29:20 [j] S Isa 20:3 [k] S Ge 10:7 [l] S Pr 21:18 **43:4** [m] Ex 19:5; Isa 49:5 [n] Isa 63:9; Rev 3:9

42:18 *deaf ... blind.* See 6:10 and note.
42:19 *my servant.* Israel. See note on 41:8–9. *messenger I send.* A term associated with prophets (see Hag 1:13; cf. Isa 44:26; Mal 3:1).
42:21 *law great and glorious.* Especially the law of Moses, given in the awesome setting of Mount Sinai (see Ex 34:29).
42:22 *plundered and looted.* By the Assyrians (see 10:6 and note) and the Babylonians (see 39:6). *trapped in pits ... prisons.* See v. 7 and note. Cf. Jdg 6:2–4.
42:24 *Who handed Jacob over ... ?* Babylonia conquered Israel, not because her gods were stronger than the Lord (see 40:17–18; 1Ki 20:23 and note), but because the Lord was punishing his people.
42:25 *poured out ... anger.* Israel had a foretaste of the day of the Lord (see 5:25; 9:12,17,21; 13:3; 34:2 and notes; cf. Jer 10:25).
43:1 *created ... formed.* God made the nation Israel as surely as he made the first man and woman (see Ge 1:27 and note; see also Isa 43:7,15,21; 44:2,24). *Do not fear.* See 41:10 and note. *redeemed you.* See notes on 35:9; 41:14. The verb is also used in 29:22; 44:22–23; 48:20 (cf. Ex 15:13). *summoned ... by name.* God chose Israel to serve him in a special way. See 45:3–4 (Cyrus). In Ex 31:2; 35:30 the Hebrew underlying this expression is translated "chosen."
43:2 *waters ... rivers.* Probably an allusion to crossing the "Red Sea" (Ex 14:21–22) and the Jordan River (Jos 3:14–17). Cf. Ps 66:6,12. *walk through the fire.* Fulfilled literally in the experience of Shadrach, Meshach and Abednego (Da 3:25–27). Contrast 42:25.
43:3 *Holy One of Israel.* See notes on 1:4; 41:14. *Savior.* Who delivers from the oppression of Egypt or Babylonia and from the spiritual oppression of sin (see 19:20; 25:9 and notes; 33:22; 35:4 and note; 43:11–12; 45:15,21–22; 49:25; 60:16; 63:8–9). The name "Isaiah" means "The LORD is salvation." *ransom.* The Persians conquered Egypt, Cush and Seba, and perhaps this was a reward or ransom for Persia's kindness to Israel (see note on 41:2; cf. Eze 29:19–20). *Cush.* See note on 18:1. *Seba.* A land near Cush (cf. 45:14) or Sheba (Ps 72:10). It was probably either in south Arabia (see Ge 10:7 and note; see also Eze 27:21–22) or in east Africa.

5 Do not be afraid,[o] for I am with you;[p]
I will bring your children[q] from the east
and gather[r] you from the west.[s]
6 I will say to the north, 'Give them up!'
and to the south,[t] 'Do not hold them back.'
Bring my sons from afar
and my daughters[u] from the ends of the earth[v] —
7 everyone who is called by my name,[w]
whom I created[x] for my glory,[y]
whom I formed and made.[z]"

8 Lead out those who have eyes but are blind,[a]
who have ears but are deaf.[b]
9 All the nations gather together[c]
and the peoples assemble.
Which of their gods foretold[d] this
and proclaimed to us the former things?
Let them bring in their witnesses to prove they were right,
so that others may hear and say, "It is true."
10 "You are my witnesses,[e]" declares the LORD,
"and my servant[f] whom I have chosen,
so that you may know[g] and believe me
and understand that I am he.
Before me no god[h] was formed,
nor will there be one after me.[i]
11 I, even I, am the LORD,[j]
and apart from me there is no savior.[k]
12 I have revealed and saved and proclaimed —
I, and not some foreign god[l] among you.
You are my witnesses,[m]" declares the LORD, "that I am God.

43:5 [o]S Ge 15:1; Isa 44:2 [p]S Ge 21:22; S Ex 14:22; Jer 30:10-11 [q]Isa 41:8; 54:3; 61:9; 66:22 [r]S Isa 11:12; S 49:18 [s]S Isa 24:14; Zec 8:7; S Mt 8:11 **43:6** [t]Ps 107:3 [u]Isa 60:4; Eze 16:61; 2Co 6:18 [v]S Dt 30:4; S Isa 11:12; Jer 23:8; Eze 36:24 **43:7** [w]Isa 48:1; 56:5; 62:2; 63:19; 65:1; Jer 15:16; Jas 2:7 [x]S Isa 27:11 [y]S Ps 86:9 [z]ver 1,21; Ps 100:3; S Isa 19:25 **43:8** [a]S Isa 6:9-10 [b]S Isa 42:20; Eze 12:2 **43:9** [c]S Isa 41:1; 45:20; 48:14 [d]S Isa 41:26 **43:10** [e]ver 12; S Jos 24:22 [f]S Isa 20:3; 41:8-9 [g]S Ex 6:7 [h]ver 11; S Ps 86:10; Isa 19:21; 44:6, 8; 45:5-6, 14 [i]S Dt 4:35; S 32:39; Jer 14:22 **43:11** [j]S Ex 6:2; S Isa 42:8 [k]S ver 10; S Ps 3:8; S 18:31; S Isa 25:9; 64:4 **43:12** [l]S Dt 32:12 [m]S ver 10 **43:13** [n]Ps 90:2 [o]S Dt 32:39; Isa 46:4;

13 Yes, and from ancient days[n] I am he.[o]
No one can deliver out of my hand.
When I act, who can reverse it?"[p]

God's Mercy and Israel's Unfaithfulness

14 This is what the LORD says —
your Redeemer,[q] the Holy One[r] of Israel:
"For your sake I will send to Babylon
and bring down as fugitives[s] all the Babylonians,[a][t]
in the ships in which they took pride.
15 I am the LORD,[u] your Holy One,
Israel's Creator,[v] your King.[w]"
16 This is what the LORD says —
he who made a way through the sea,
a path through the mighty waters,[x]
17 who drew out[y] the chariots and horses,[z]
the army and reinforcements together,[a]
and they lay[b] there, never to rise again,
extinguished, snuffed out like a wick:[c]
18 "Forget the former things;[d]
do not dwell on the past.
19 See, I am doing a new thing![e]
Now it springs up; do you not perceive it?
I am making a way in the wilderness[f]
and streams in the wasteland.[g]

[a] 14 Or *Chaldeans*

48:12 [p]S Nu 23:8; S Job 9:12 **43:14** [q]S Ex 15:13; S Job 19:25 [r]S Isa 1:4; S 41:20 [s]Isa 13:14-15 [t]S Isa 23:13 **43:15** [u]S Isa 42:8 [v]S Isa 27:11; 45:11 [w]S Isa 41:21 **43:16** [x]S Ex 14:29; S 15:8; S Isa 11:15 **43:17** [y]Ps 118:12; Isa 1:31 [z]S Ex 14:22 [a]S Ex 14:9 [b]Ps 76:5-6 [c]S Job 13:25; Jer 51:21; Eze 38:4 **43:18** [d]S Isa 41:22 **43:19** [e]S Isa 41:22; Jer 16:14-15; 23:7-8; 2Co 5:17; Rev 21:5 [f]S Isa 40:3 [g]S Ps 126:4; S Isa 33:21; S 35:7

43:5 *Do not be afraid.* See 41:10 and note. *east.* Especially Assyria and Babylonia. See 11:11–12 and notes; cf. Ps 107:3. *west.* For example, the "islands" of 11:11 (see also 24:14–15; 49:12).
43:6 *north.* For example, Hamath (see 10:9 and note; 11:11). *south.* Egypt. *ends of the earth.* See note on 11:12 (cf. 41:5; 42:10).
43:7 *called by my name.* People belonging to God. *created … formed.* See v. 1 and note.
43:8 *blind … deaf.* Probably referring to Israel (see 6:10 and note; 42:18–20).
43:9–13 A court scene; see also 41:21–22.
43:9 *nations … peoples assemble.* See 41:1 and note. *foretold.* See 41:26 and note. *former things.* See 41:22 and note. *witnesses.* To verify the accuracy of earlier predictions by idols or their worshipers (see 41:26).
43:10 *You are my witnesses.* See also v. 12; 44:8. God's work in behalf of Israel is proof of his saving power. *my servant.* See 41:8–9 and note.
43:11 The main thrust is repeated in 44:6,8; 45:5–6,18,21–22; 46:9 (see also Dt 32:39). *savior.* See v. 3 and note.
43:12 *foreign god.* Cf. Dt 32:12,16. Israel repeatedly worshiped other gods (see Jdg 2:12–13 and notes). *witnesses.* See v. 10 and note.
43:13 See v. 11. *No one can deliver … hand.* Identical to Dt 32:39.
43:14 *Redeemer.* See 41:14 and note. *Holy One of Israel.* See 1:4; 41:14 and notes. *Babylon.* See note on 13:1. *fugitives … in the ships.* The Babylonians used the Persian Gulf, as well as the Tigris and Euphrates Rivers, for trading purposes. But their splendid ships (cf. 2:16) would one day become their means of flight (cf. Jer 51:13).
43:15 *Creator.* See v. 1 and note. *King.* God was called "king over Jeshurun" (Israel) in Dt 33:5 (contrast 1Sa 8:7).
43:16–17 A reference to crossing the "Red Sea" (see v. 2 and note). The pharaoh's chariots and horsemen were destroyed as Israel's God fought against them (see 51:10; Ex 14:28; 15:1–5,10).
43:17 *snuffed out like a wick.* Contrast 42:3.
43:18–19 *former things … new thing.* See 41:22; 42:9 and notes.
43:19 *way in the wilderness.* See 35:8; 40:3 and notes. *streams in the wasteland.* See v. 20; 32:2 and note. Contrast 42:15 and note.

20 The wild animals[h] honor me,
the jackals[i] and the owls,
because I provide water[j] in
the wilderness
and streams in the
wasteland,
to give drink to my people,
my chosen,
21 the people I formed[k] for
myself[l]
that they may proclaim my
praise.[m]

22 "Yet you have not called on
me, Jacob,
you have not wearied[n]
yourselves for[a] me,
Israel.[o]
23 You have not brought me
sheep for burnt
offerings,[p]
nor honored[q] me with your
sacrifices.[r]
I have not burdened[s] you with grain
offerings
nor wearied you with demands[t] for
incense.[u]
24 You have not bought any fragrant
calamus[v] for me,
or lavished on me the fat[w] of your
sacrifices.
But you have burdened me with your
sins
and wearied[x] me with your
offenses.[y]

25 "I, even I, am he who blots out
your transgressions,[z] for my own
sake,[a]
and remembers your sins[b] no
more.[c]
26 Review the past for me,
let us argue the matter together;[d]
state the case[e] for your innocence.
27 Your first father[f] sinned;
those I sent to teach[g] you rebelled[h]
against me.

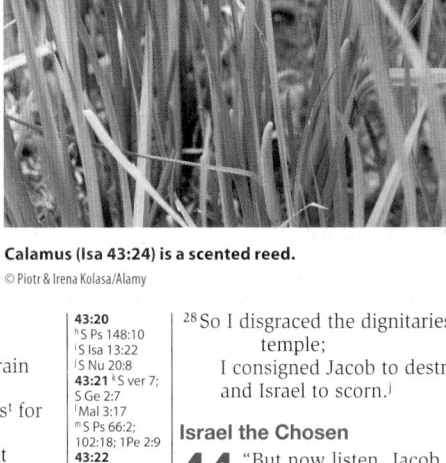

Calamus (Isa 43:24) is a scented reed.

43:20 [h] S Ps 148:10 [i] S Isa 13:22 [j] S Nu 20:8 **43:21** [k] S ver 7; S Ge 2:7 [l] Mal 3:17 [m] S Ps 66:2; 102:18; 1Pe 2:9 **43:22** [n] S Jos 22:5; S Isa 1:14 [o] Isa 30:11 **43:23** [p] S Ex 29:41 [q] Zec 7:5-6; Mal 1:6-8 [r] Am 5:25 [s] Mic 6:3; Mal 1:12-13 [t] Jer 7:22 [u] Ex 30:35; S Lev 2:1 **43:24** [v] S Ex 30:23 [w] Lev 3:9 [x] S Isa 1:14; S 7:13; S Jer 8:21 [y] Jer 44:22; Mal 2:17 **43:25** [z] S 2Sa 12:13; S 2Ch 6:21; Mk 2:7; Lk 5:21; Ac 3:19 [a] S Isa 37:35;

28 So I disgraced the dignitaries of your
temple;
I consigned Jacob to destruction[b][i]
and Israel to scorn.[j]

Israel the Chosen

44 "But now listen, Jacob, my
servant,[k]
Israel, whom I have chosen.[l]
2 This is what the LORD says—
he who made[m] you, who formed you
in the womb,[n]
and who will help[o] you:
Do not be afraid,[p] Jacob, my servant,[q]
Jeshurun,[c][r] whom I have chosen.

[a] 22 Or *Jacob; / surely you have grown weary of*
[b] 28 The Hebrew term refers to the irrevocable giving over of things or persons to the LORD, often by totally destroying them. [c] 2 *Jeshurun* means *the upright one,* that is, Israel.

S Eze 20:44 [b] Isa 64:9; Mic 7:18 [c] S Job 7:21; S Isa 38:17 **43:26** [d] S Isa 1:18 [e] S Isa 41:1; 49:25; 50:8 **43:27** [f] S Ge 12:18 [g] Isa 9:15; 28:7; Jer 5:31 [h] S Isa 24:20; S 48:8 **43:28** [i] S Nu 5:27; S Dt 13:15; S Isa 42:24; S Zec 5:3 [j] S Ps 39:8; Jer 24:9; Eze 5:15 **44:1** [k] ver 21 [l] S Ge 16:11; S Isa 14:1 **44:2** [m] ver 21; S Ps 149:2 [n] S Ge 2:7; S Ps 139:13; S Isa 27:11 [o] S Isa 41:10 [p] S Isa 43:5 [q] Jer 30:10; 46:27 [r] S Nu 23:21; S Dt 32:15

43:20 *jackals … owls.* Creatures of the desert (see 13:21–22; 34:13–15; 35:7).
43:21 *people … proclaim my praise.* Cf. 42:12.
43:22–24 The Israelites may have brought sacrifices (see 1:11–15 and note), but their hearts were not right with God.
43:22 *not called … not wearied.* Apparently their prayers were halfhearted (contrast Ps 69:3).
43:23 *not burdened … nor wearied.* God did not make excessive demands on his people.
43:24 *calamus.* Linked with incense (see v. 23) also in SS 4:14; Jer 6:20. *fat.* See note on 34:6. *burdened … wearied.* See 1:14.
43:25 *blots out … transgressions.* In spite of the punishment Israel must suffer (v. 28), God is eager to forgive and restore his people (see 1:18; 44:22–23; see also 40:2 and note).
43:26 *state the case.* The Lord takes Israel to court, as he did the nations in 41:21–22.
43:27 *first father.* Either (1) Adam (the ultimate father; see Ge 5:3 and note; see also note on Lk 3:23–38), (2) Abraham (the more immediate father; see 51:2) or (3) Jacob (the even more immediate father; cf. vv. 22,28). All were sinners, the main point for the present sinful generation. *those I sent to teach you.* Probably the priests and prophets.
43:28 *consigned … to destruction.* See NIV text note; see also note on 34:2. Any town of Israel that harbored idolatry was to suffer this fate (Dt 13:12–15). Jerusalem suffered destruction at the hands of the Babylonians (2Ki 25:8–9) because of idolatry (see Eze 7:15–22).
44:1–2 *my servant.* See 41:8–9 and note.
44:2 *formed you.* See 43:1 and note. *in the womb.* See v. 24. The tenderness of the Creator is shown (see also 49:5; Jer 1:5 and note). *Do not be afraid.* See v. 8; 41:10 and note. *Jeshurun.* Israel (see NIV text note and v. 1); found elsewhere only in Dt 32:15; 33:5,26.

3 For I will pour water[s] on the thirsty land,
and streams on the dry ground;[t]
I will pour out my Spirit[u] on your offspring,
and my blessing[v] on your descendants.[w]
4 They will spring up like grass[x] in a meadow,
like poplar trees[y] by flowing streams.[z]
5 Some will say, 'I belong[a] to the LORD';
others will call themselves by the name of Jacob;
still others will write on their hand,[b]
'The LORD's,'[c]
and will take the name Israel.

The LORD, Not Idols

6 "This is what the LORD says—
Israel's King[d] and Redeemer,[e] the LORD Almighty:
I am the first and I am the last;[f]
apart from me there is no God.[g]
7 Who then is like me?[h] Let him proclaim it.
Let him declare and lay out before me
what has happened since I established my ancient people,
and what is yet to come—
yes, let them foretell[i] what will come.
8 Do not tremble, do not be afraid.
Did I not proclaim[j] this and foretell it long ago?
You are my witnesses. Is there any God[k] besides me?
No, there is no other Rock;[l] I know not one."
9 All who make idols[m] are nothing,
and the things they treasure are worthless.[n]
Those who would speak up for them are blind;[o]
they are ignorant, to their own shame.[p]
10 Who shapes a god and casts an idol,[q]
which can profit nothing?[r]
11 People who do that will be put to shame;[s]
such craftsmen are only human beings.
Let them all come together and take their stand;
they will be brought down to terror and shame.[t]

12 The blacksmith[u] takes a tool
and works with it in the coals;
he shapes an idol with hammers,
he forges it with the might of his arm.[v]
He gets hungry and loses his strength;
he drinks no water and grows faint.[w]
13 The carpenter[x] measures with a line
and makes an outline with a marker;
he roughs it out with chisels
and marks it with compasses.
He shapes it in human form,[y]
human form in all its glory,
that it may dwell in a shrine.[z]
14 He cut down cedars,
or perhaps took a cypress or oak.
He let it grow among the trees of the forest,
or planted a pine,[a] and the rain made it grow.
15 It is used as fuel[b] for burning;
some of it he takes and warms himself,
he kindles a fire and bakes bread.
But he also fashions a god and worships[c] it;
he makes an idol and bows[d] down to it.
16 Half of the wood he burns in the fire;
over it he prepares his meal,
he roasts his meat and eats his fill.
He also warms himself and says,
"Ah! I am warm; I see the fire."[e]

44:3 [s] Joel 3:18; Jn 4:10 [t] S Pr 9:5; S Isa 32:2; S 35:7 [u] S Isa 11:2; Eze 36:27; S Mk 1:8; S Ac 2:17 [v] Mal 3:10 [w] Isa 61:9; 65:23 **44:4** [x] S Job 5:25; S Ps 72:16 [y] S Lev 23:40 [z] S Job 40:22 **44:5** [a] Ps 116:16; Isa 19:21; Jer 50:5 [b] Ex 13:9 [c] Isa 60:3; 66:23; Zec 8:20-22; 13:9; 14:16 **44:6** [d] S Isa 41:21 [e] S Job 19:25; Isa 43:1 [f] S Isa 41:4; Rev 1:8,17 [g] S Dt 6:4; S 1Ch 17:20; S Ps 18:31; S Isa 43:10 **44:7** [h] S Dt 32:39 [i] S Isa 41:22,26 **44:8** [j] S Isa 40:21; S 42:9 [k] S Isa 43:10 [l] S Ge 49:24 **44:9** [m] S Ex 20:4; S Lev 19:4; Isa 40:19 [n] S Isa 41:24 [o] S Isa 26:11 [p] S Isa 1:29; 65:13; 66:5; Jer 22:22 **44:10** [q] S Isa 40:19 [r] Isa 41:29; Jer 10:5; Ac 19:26 **44:11** [s] S ver 9; S Isa 1:29 [t] S 2Ki 19:18; S Isa 37:19 **44:12** [u] S Isa 40:19; 41:6-7; 54:16 [v] Ac 17:29 [w] Isa 40:28 **44:13** [x] S Isa 41:7 [y] Ps 115:4-7 [z] S Jdg 17:4-5 **44:14** [a] S Isa 41:19 **44:15** [b] ver 19 [c] S Ex 20:5; Rev 9:20 [d] S 2Ch 25:14 **44:16** [e] Isa 47:14

44:3 *pour water ... streams.* See 30:25; 32:2; 35:6–7 and notes; see also 41:18. *pour out my Spirit.* Associated with the Messianic age in 32:15; Joel 2:28 (see notes there; see also note on Zec 12:10).
44:4 *grass.* A symbol of luxuriant growth also in 35:7 (contrast 37:27; 40:6–8).
44:5 *call ... by the name.* A willingness to identify with Jacob, the Lord's people. See 43:7 and note. *write on their hand.* Perhaps a mark of ownership (cf. 49:16; Rev 13:16) or a reminder of one's allegiance (cf. Ex 13:9,16).
44:6 *King.* See 43:15 and note. *Redeemer.* See v. 24; 41:14 and note. *first ... last.* See 41:4 and note. *apart ... God.* See 43:11; Ex 20:3 and notes.
44:7 *foretell.* See 41:22,26 and notes.
44:8 *You are my witnesses.* See 43:10 and note. *Rock.* See 17:10 and note. As in v. 2; 43:11–13, Isaiah may be drawing on the song of Moses, which describes God as "the Rock" (Dt 32:4,15,30–31), but the metaphor is also common in the Psalms (see note on Ps 18:2).
44:9–20 A satire on the folly of idolatry (see 40:18–20 and note).
44:9 *nothing ... worthless.* Like the nations and their idols (see 40:17; 41:24 and notes). *shame.* Cf. v. 11; 42:17; 45:16.
44:11 *craftsmen.* See 40:19 and note.
44:12–13 *blacksmith ... carpenter.* See 48:5.
44:12 *loses his strength.* But God never gets tired (40:28).
44:13 *human form.* Human beings were made in the image of God (see Ge 1:26–27 and notes), but an idol is made in their image (see Dt 4:16; Ro 1:23 and note).
44:14 *cedars ... cypress ... oak.* The most valuable kinds of wood known at that time. See 2:13; 9:10; 14:8 and notes.
44:15 *worships ... bows down.* Repeated in vv. 17,19; see 2:8,20.
44:16 *roasts his meat ... warms himself.* Although wood serves common purposes, it is also made into an idol (see v. 19).

17 From the rest he makes a god, his idol;
he bows down to it and worships.[f]
He prays[g] to it and says,
"Save[h] me! You are my god!"
18 They know nothing, they understand[i] nothing;
their eyes[j] are plastered over so they cannot see,
and their minds closed so they cannot understand.
19 No one stops to think,
no one has the knowledge or understanding[k] to say,
"Half of it I used for fuel;[l]
I even baked bread over its coals,
I roasted meat and I ate.
Shall I make a detestable[m] thing from what is left?
Shall I bow down to a block of wood?"[n]
20 Such a person feeds on ashes;[o] a deluded[p] heart misleads him;
he cannot save himself, or say,
"Is not this thing in my right hand a lie?[q]"

21 "Remember[r] these things, Jacob,
for you, Israel, are my servant.[s]
I have made you, you are my servant;[t]
Israel, I will not forget you.[u]
22 I have swept away[v] your offenses like a cloud,
your sins like the morning mist.
Return[w] to me,
for I have redeemed[x] you."

23 Sing for joy,[y] you heavens, for the LORD has done this;
shout aloud, you earth[z] beneath.
Burst into song, you mountains,[a]
you forests and all your trees,[b]
for the LORD has redeemed[c] Jacob,
he displays his glory[d] in Israel.

Jerusalem to Be Inhabited

24 "This is what the LORD says—
your Redeemer,[e] who formed[f] you in the womb:[g]

I am the LORD,
the Maker of all things,
who stretches out the heavens,[h]
who spreads out the earth[i] by myself,
25 who foils[j] the signs of false prophets
and makes fools of diviners,[k]
who overthrows the learning of the wise[l]
and turns it into nonsense,[m]
26 who carries out the words[n] of his servants
and fulfills[o] the predictions of his messengers,

who says of Jerusalem,[p] 'It shall be inhabited,'
of the towns of Judah, 'They shall be rebuilt,'
and of their ruins,[q] 'I will restore them,'[r]
27 who says to the watery deep, 'Be dry,
and I will dry up[s] your streams,'
28 who says of Cyrus,[t] 'He is my shepherd
and will accomplish all that I please;

44:17 [f]S Ex 20:5; Isa 2:8; Jer 1:16 [g]S 1Ki 18:26 [h]S Jdg 10:14; Isa 45:20; 46:7; 47:15 **44:18** [i]Isa 1:3; S 16:12; Jer 4:22; 10:8, 14, 14-15 [j]S Isa 6:9-10; S 29:10 **44:19** [k]ver 18-19; Isa 5:13; 27:11; 45:20 [l]ver 15 [m]S Dt 27:15 [n]Isa 40:20 **44:20** [o]Ps 102:9 [p]S Job 15:31; Ro 1:21-23, 28; 2Th 2:11; 2Ti 3:13 [q]S Dt 4:28; Isa 59:3, 4, 13; Jer 9:3; 10:14; 51:17; Hos 10:5; 13:2; Ro 1:25 **44:21** [r]Isa 46:8; Zec 10:9 [s]S Isa 43:1 [t]S Ps 136:22; S Isa 27:11 [u]Ps 27:10; Isa 49:15; Jer 31:20 **44:22** [v]S 2Sa 12:13; S 2Ch 6:21; Ac 3:19 [w]S Job 22:23; Isa 45:22; 55:7; Jer 36:3; Mal 3:7 [x]S Isa 33:24; S Mt 20:28; 1Co 6:20 **44:23** [y]S Ps 98:4; S Isa 12:6 [z]S 1Ch 16:31; Ps 148:7 [a]S Ps 98:8 [b]S Ps 65:13 [c]S Ex 6:6; Isa 51:11; 62:12 [d]S Ex 16:7; S Lev 10:3; S Isa 4:2; 43:7; 46:13; 49:3; 52:1; 55:5; 60:9, 21; 61:3; Jer 30:19 **44:24** [e]S Job 19:25; Isa 43:14 [f]S Isa 27:11 [g]S Ps 139:13 [h]S Ge 2:1; S Isa 42:5 [i]S Ge 1:1 **44:25** [j]Ps 33:10 [k]Lev 19:26; 1Sa 6:2; Isa 2:6; 8:19; 47:13; Jer 27:9; Da 2:2, 10; 4:7; Mic 3:7; Zec 10:2 [l]S Job 5:13; 1Co 1:27 [m]2Sa 15:31; 1Co 1:19-20 **44:26** [n]Isa 59:21; Zec 1:6 [o]Isa 46:10; 55:11; Jer 23:20; 39:16; La 2:17; Da 9:12; S Mt 5:18 [p]S Isa 1:1 [q]S Ps 74:3; S Isa 51:3 [r]S Ezr 9:9; S Ps 51:18; Isa 49:8-21; S 61:4 **44:27** [s]S Isa 11:15; S 19:5; Rev 16:12 **44:28** [t]S 2Ch 36:22; S Isa 41:2

44:17 *Save me!* King Amaziah was condemned for worshiping the gods of Seir (Edom), a nation he had defeated in battle (see note on 2Ch 25:14–25). Isaiah denounces such idolatry as totally irrational (see 45:20). Whereas those who worshiped idols associated the god with the idol, for Isaiah there was no god for the idol to represent, so he depicts idolatry as worship of a mere "block of wood" (v. 19).

44:18 *eyes are plastered … minds closed.* Israel's condition in 6:9–10 (see note there). The description ironically characterizes both the idols and those who worship them. See also Ps 82:5 and note.

44:19 *detestable thing.* The Lord detests idols (see Dt 27:15). In 1Ki 11:5,7; 2Ki 23:13 Molek and Chemosh are called detestable gods. Those who worship idols are also called detestable (see 41:24 and note).

44:20 *feeds on ashes.* Even devoted worship does not benefit the idolater. Cf. Hos 12:1. *lie.* Or "fraud." See 2Th 2:11 and note.

44:21 *my servant.* See vv. 1–2; 41:8–9 and note.

44:22 *swept away your offenses.* As in 40:2 (see note there), the suffering of Israel has paved the way for forgiveness and the restoration of the nation (see 43:25 and note). *Return to me.* Cf. Jer 31:18; Zec 1:3 and note. *redeemed.* Cf. v. 23; see notes on 35:9; 41:14; 43:1.

44:23 *Sing for joy … shout aloud.* Nature is called on to join in praise (see also 35:1; 49:13). *Burst into song, you mountains.* See 49:13; 55:12. *displays his glory.* See 35:2; 40:5 and notes.

44:24 *Redeemer.* See 41:14 and note. *stretches out … spreads out.* See 40:22 and note; cf. 51:13.

44:25 *signs of false prophets.* See Dt 13:1–5 and notes. *diviners.* The Hebrew for this word is used of Balaam (see Jos 13:22 and note), the medium at Endor (1Sa 28:8), and false prophets (see Jer 27:9 and note). It is linked with enchanting and sorcery (see 3:2–3 and note; Dt 18:9–11 and note on 18:9). *overthrows … the wise.* See 29:14 and note.

44:26 *servants … messengers.* The true prophets (see 42:19; Jer 7:25 and notes). *inhabited … rebuilt.* See Jer 32:15; cf. Isa 58:12; 61:4. *ruins … restore.* Contrast 6:11.

44:27 *Be dry.* A reference to the crossing of the "Red Sea" (see 11:15; 37:25; 43:16–17 and notes; cf. 50:2; 51:10).

44:28 *Cyrus.* See 41:2 and note; see also chart, p. 511. *shepherd.* Often applied to rulers (see 2Sa 5:2; Jer 23:2). *Jerusalem … temple.* The decree of Cyrus (Ezr 1:2–4; 6:3–5) authorized the rebuilding of the temple, which would lead to a restored Jerusalem (see 45:13).

he will say of Jerusalem,[u] "Let it be
rebuilt,"
and of the temple,[v] "Let its
foundations[w] be laid." '

45

"This is what the LORD says to his
anointed,[x]
to Cyrus,[y] whose right hand I take
hold[z] of
to subdue nations[a] before him
and to strip kings of their armor,
to open doors before him
so that gates will not be shut:
2 I will go before you[b]
and will level[c] the mountains[a];
I will break down gates[d] of bronze
and cut through bars of iron.[e]
3 I will give you hidden treasures,[f]
riches stored in secret places,[g]
so that you may know[h] that I am the
LORD,
the God of Israel, who summons you
by name.[i]
4 For the sake of Jacob my servant,[j]
of Israel my chosen,
I summon you by name
and bestow on you a title of honor,
though you do not acknowledge[k] me.
5 I am the LORD, and there is no other;[l]
apart from me there is no God.[m]
I will strengthen you,[n]
though you have not acknowledged
me,
6 so that from the rising of the sun
to the place of its setting[o]
people may know[p] there is none
besides me.[q]
I am the LORD, and there is no other.
7 I form the light and create darkness,[r]
I bring prosperity and create
disaster;[s]
I, the LORD, do all these things.

44:28 [u]S Isa 14:32 [v]Ezr 1:2-4 [w]S Isa 28:16; 58:12 **45:1** [x]S Ps 45:7 [y]S 2Ch 36:22; S Isa 41:2 [z]Ps 73:23; Isa 41:13; 42:6 [a]Isa 48:14; Jer 50:35; 51:20,24; Mic 4:13 **45:2** [b]Ex 23:20 [c]S Isa 40:4 [d]S Isa 13:2 [e]Ps 107:16; 147:13; Jer 51:30; La 2:9; Na 3:13 **45:3** [f]S 2Ki 24:13; Jer 50:37; 51:13 [g]Jer 41:8 [h]Isa 41:23 [i]S Ex 33:12; S Isa 43:1 **45:4** [j]S Isa 14:1; 41:8-9 [k]Ac 17:23 **45:5** [l]S Isa 44:8 [m]S Dt 32:12; S Ps 18:31; S Isa 43:10 [n]S Ps 18:39; Eze 30:24-25 **45:6** [o]S Ps 113:3; Isa 43:5 [p]S Isa 11:9 [q]ver 5,18; Isa 14:13-14; 47:8,10; Zep 2:15 **45:7** [r]S Ge 1:4; S Ex 10:22 [s]S Isa 14:15; S 31:2; La 3:38 **45:8** [t]Ps 72:6; S 133:3; Joel 3:18 [u]ver 24; Ps 85:11; S Isa 41:2; 46:13; 48:18; 60:21; 61:10, 11; 62:1; Hos 10:12; Joel 2:23; Am 5:24; Mal 4:2 [v]S Ps 85:9; Isa 12:3 **45:9** [w]S Job 12:13; S 15:25; S 27:2; 1Co 10:22 [x]S Job 33:13 [y]Ps 22:15 [z]S Isa 29:16; Ro 9:20-21* [a]S Job 9:12; Da 4:35 [b]S Isa 10:15 **45:11** [c]S Isa 1:4 [d]S Ps 149:2; S Isa 51:13 [e]S Ps 8:6; S Isa 19:25 **45:12** [f]S Ge 1:1 [g]S Ge 2:1; S Isa 48:13 [h]S Ne 9:6; S Job 38:32 **45:13** [i]S 2Ch 36:22; S Isa 41:2 [j]S 1Ki 8:36; S Ps 26:12; S Isa 40:4

8 "You heavens above, rain[t] down my
righteousness;[u]
let the clouds shower it down.
Let the earth open wide,
let salvation[v] spring up,
let righteousness flourish with it;
I, the LORD, have created it.
9 "Woe to those who quarrel[w] with their
Maker,[x]
those who are nothing but potsherds[y]
among the potsherds on the ground.
Does the clay say to the potter,[z]
'What are you making?'[a]
Does your work say,
'The potter has no hands'?[b]
10 Woe to the one who says to a father,
'What have you begotten?'
or to a mother,
'What have you brought to birth?'
11 "This is what the LORD says—
the Holy One[c] of Israel, and its Maker:[d]
Concerning things to come,
do you question me about my children,
or give me orders about the work of
my hands?[e]
12 It is I who made the earth[f]
and created mankind on it.
My own hands stretched out the
heavens;[g]
I marshaled their starry hosts.[h]
13 I will raise up Cyrus[b][i] in my
righteousness:
I will make all his ways straight.[j]

[a] *2* Dead Sea Scrolls and Septuagint; the meaning of the word in the Masoretic Text is uncertain. [b] *13* Hebrew *him*

45:1 *anointed.* "Messiah" comes from the Hebrew for this word. Cyrus, a foreign emperor, is called "his anointed" just as he is called "my shepherd" (44:28), because God has appointed him to carry out a divine commission in his role as king. Nebuchadnezzar is similarly called "my servant" (see Jer 25:9 and note; 27:6; 43:10). The servant—Christ (see note on 42:1–4)—is called "the Anointed One" in Da 9:25–26 (see NIV text note on Mt 1:1). See also Ps 2:2 and note. *right hand I … hold.* See 41:13 and note.
45:2 *gates of bronze … bars of iron.* Normally the doors of city gates were made of wood, and the bars were metal (see Jdg 16:3 and note).
45:3 *that you may know.* God's actions reveal his power (cf. Eze 6:7; 7:27). *summons you by name.* To indicate God's control of Cyrus's activities. See v. 4; see also note on 43:1.
45:4 *my servant.* See 41:8–9 and note. *title of honor.* Perhaps "anointed" (v. 1). *though … not acknowledge me.* See v. 5. Cyrus worshiped the chief Babylonian deity, Marduk (whom he praised in his inscriptions), as well as other gods (see 41:25; 46:1; Est 2:5; Da 1:7; 4:8 and notes).
45:5 *I … there is no other.* See vv. 6,14,18,21–22; 43:11 and note.
45:6 *rising … to … setting.* The whole earth (see Mal 1:11 and note).
45:7 *darkness … disaster.* Such as the darkness that plagued the Egyptians (see Ex 10:21–23; Ps 105:28; cf. Isa 47:11; Am 3:6).
45:8 *rain down … shower.* A picture of abundance (see Hos 10:12 and note). *righteousness.* In v. 13; 41:2 Cyrus is mentioned in connection with God's righteousness. God is making things right through the Persian king. *salvation spring up.* God will deliver his people. *righteousness flourish.* Peace and justice will prevail (cf. 11:4).
45:9 *clay say to the potter.* See 29:16 and note; cf. 64:8; Jer 18:6; see also Ro 9:20–21 and notes.
45:11 *Holy One of Israel.* See 1:4 and note. *children … work of my hands.* See 29:23 and note.
45:12 *stretched … heavens.* See 40:22 and note. *marshaled … starry hosts.* See 40:26 and note.
45:13 *Cyrus in my righteousness.* See note on 41:2. *make … ways straight.* Enabling him to reach his goals (see v. 2; see also 40:3 and note; cf. Pr 3:6 and note). *rebuild my city.* See note on 44:28. *not for a price.* Since God had not received a payment when he sold them (see 52:3 and note; contrast note on 43:3).

He will rebuild my city[k]
and set my exiles free,
but not for a price or reward,[l]
says the LORD Almighty."

14 This is what the LORD says:

"The products[m] of Egypt and the
merchandise of Cush,[a]
and those tall Sabeans[n] —
they will come over to you[o]
and will be yours;
they will trudge behind you,[p]
coming over to you in chains.[q]
They will bow down before you
and plead[r] with you, saying,
'Surely God is with you,[s] and there is
no other;
there is no other god.[t]' "

15 Truly you are a God who has been
hiding[u] himself,
the God and Savior[v] of Israel.
16 All the makers of idols will be put to
shame and disgraced;[w]
they will go off into disgrace
together.
17 But Israel will be saved[x] by the LORD
with an everlasting salvation;[y]
you will never be put to shame or
disgraced,[z]
to ages everlasting.

18 For this is what the LORD says —
he who created the heavens,
he is God;
he who fashioned and made the earth,[a]
he founded it;
he did not create it to be empty,[b]
but formed it to be inhabited[c] —
he says:
"I am the LORD,
and there is no other.[d]
19 I have not spoken in secret,[e]
from somewhere in a land of
darkness;[f]
I have not said to Jacob's descendants,[g]
'Seek[h] me in vain.'
I, the LORD, speak the truth;
I declare what is right.[i]

20 "Gather together[j] and come;
assemble, you fugitives from the
nations.
Ignorant[k] are those who carry[l] about
idols of wood,
who pray to gods that cannot save.[m]
21 Declare what is to be, present it —
let them take counsel together.
Who foretold[n] this long ago,
who declared it from the distant
past?[o]
Was it not I, the LORD?
And there is no God apart from me,[p]
a righteous God[q] and a Savior;[r]
there is none but me.

22 "Turn[s] to me and be saved,[t]
all you ends of the earth;[u]
for I am God, and there is no other.[v]
23 By myself I have sworn,[w]
my mouth has uttered in all
integrity[x]
a word that will not be revoked:[y]
Before me every knee will bow;[z]
by me every tongue will swear.[a]
24 They will say of me, 'In the LORD
alone
are deliverance[b] and strength.[c]' "
All who have raged against him
will come to him and be put to
shame.[d]
25 But all the descendants[e] of Israel
will find deliverance[f] in the LORD
and will make their boast in him.[g]

[a] 14 That is, the upper Nile region

45:13 [k] S Ezr 1:2 [l] Isa 52:3 **45:14** [m] 2Sa 8:2; Isa 18:7; 60:5 [n] S Isa 2:3; 60:11; 62:2; Zec 8:20-22 [o] S Isa 2:3 [p] S Ge 27:29 [q] S 2Sa 3:34; S Isa 14:1-2 [r] Jer 16:19; Zec 8:20-23 [s] 1Co 14:25 [t] S Ps 18:31; S Isa 11:9; S 43:10 **45:15** [u] S Dt 31:17; Ps 44:24; S Isa 1:15 [v] S Isa 25:9 **45:16** [w] S Ps 35:4; S Isa 1:29 **45:17** [x] Jer 23:6; 33:16; Ro 11:26 [y] S Isa 12:2 [z] S Ge 30:23; S Isa 29:22; S 41:11 **45:18** [a] S Ge 1:1 [b] S Ge 1:2 [c] S Ge 1:26 [d] ver 5; Dt 4:35 **45:19** [e] Isa 48:16; 65:4 [f] Jer 2:31 [g] ver 25; Isa 41:8; 65:9; Jer 31:36 [h] S Dt 4:29; S 2Ch 15:2 [i] S Dt 30:11 **45:20** [j] S Isa 43:9 [k] S Isa 44:19 [l] Ps 115:7; Isa 46:1; Jer 10:5 [m] Dt 32:37; S Isa 44:17; Jer 1:16; 2:28 **45:21** [n] S Isa 41:22 [o] Isa 46:10 [p] ver 5; S Ps 46:10; Isa 46:9; Mk 12:32 [q] Ps 11:7 [r] S Ps 3:8; S Isa 25:9

45:22 [s] S Isa 44:22; Zec 12:10 [t] Nu 21:8-9; S 2Ch 20:12 [u] S Ge 49:10; S Isa 11:9,12; 49:6,12 [v] Hos 13:4 **45:23** [w] S Ge 22:16; S Isa 14:24 [x] S Dt 30:11; Heb 6:13 [y] Isa 55:11 [z] S ver 14 [a] S Ps 63:11; S Isa 19:18; Ro 14:11*; Php 2:10-11 **45:24** [b] S ver 8; Jer 33:16 [c] S Dt 33:29; S Ps 18:39; S Isa 40:26; 63:1 [d] S Isa 41:11 **45:25** [e] S ver 19 [f] S Isa 4:3; S 49:4 [g] S Isa 24:23; S 41:16

45:14 *products ... merchandise.* See 18:7 and note. *Egypt ... Cush ... Sabeans.* See notes on 18:1; 43:3. *coming over to you ... bow down.* See Ps 68:31. Israel's future domination over her former enemies has been mentioned in 11:14; 14:1–2 (see note on 14:1); it is also the theme of 49:23; 54:3; 60:11–14. *Surely God is with you.* One day the nations will acknowledge Israel's God (see v. 23; 19:23,25; Zec 8:20–23 and notes).
45:15 *hiding himself.* God's plans and actions are a mystery to humans (cf. 54:8; 55:8–9). *Savior.* See v. 21 and note on 43:3.
45:16 *put to shame.* See 42:17; 44:9.
45:17 *everlasting salvation.* Cf. the "everlasting kindness" of 54:8. *never be put to shame.* See 29:22 and note.
45:18 *created ... fashioned.* See 40:21–22 and notes. *empty.* Or "formless" or "chaotic" (see Ge 1:2 and note). *to be inhabited.* The Holy Land was now "empty" (see 6:11; Jer 4:23–26) and chaotic but would soon have inhabitants (see 44:26,28) and be orderly again.
45:19 *in secret ... darkness.* Probably an allusion to the clandestine ways of mediums and spiritists (see 8:19–20 and notes; 29:4). *Seek me in vain.* Cf. Jer 29:13–14.
45:20 *Ignorant ... save.* See 44:17–18 and notes. *idols of wood.* See 44:17,19 and notes.
45:21 *Declare ... present.* See 41:21–22 and note. *foretold ... distant past.* See 41:26 and note.
45:22 *Turn ... be saved.* See 49:6 and note; see also the invitation of 55:7. *ends of the earth.* See 11:12 and note; 42:10.
45:23 *By myself I have sworn.* Explained in Heb 6:13 (see note there). See also 62:8. *word ... not ... revoked.* See 55:10–11. *every knee ... every tongue.* See v. 14 and note. Paul quotes this portion of Isaiah in Ro 14:11 and Php 2:10–11 to describe Christ's exalted position.
45:24 *In the LORD alone ... strength.* See v. 5 and note. This is the climax of the refrain that runs through the chapter. *All ... put to shame.* Very similar to 41:11 except for "against you" (Israel).
45:25 *make their boast.* The Hebrew for this verb is translated "glory" in 41:16.

Gods of Babylon

46 Bel[h] bows down, Nebo stoops
low;
their idols[i] are borne by beasts of
burden.[a]
The images that are carried[j] about are
burdensome,
a burden for the weary.
2 They stoop and bow down together;
unable to rescue the burden,
they themselves go off into
captivity.[k]

3 "Listen[l] to me, you descendants of
Jacob,
all the remnant[m] of the people of
Israel,
you whom I have upheld since your
birth,[n]
and have carried[o] since you were
born.[p]
4 Even to your old age and gray hairs[q]
I am he,[r] I am he who will sustain
you.
I have made you and I will carry you;
I will sustain[s] you and I will rescue
you.

5 "With whom will you compare me or
count me equal?
To whom will you liken me that we
may be compared?[t]
6 Some pour out gold from their bags
and weigh out silver on the scales;
they hire a goldsmith[u] to make it into a
god,
and they bow down and worship it.[v]
7 They lift it to their shoulders and
carry[w] it;
they set it up in its place, and there
it stands.
From that spot it cannot move.[x]
Even though someone cries out to it, it
cannot answer;[y]
it cannot save[z] them from their
troubles.

46:1 [h] S Isa 21:9; Jer 50:2; 51:44 [i] S 1Sa 5:2 [j] ver 7; S Isa 45:20 **46:2** [k] S Jdg 18:17-18; S 2Sa 5:21; Jer 51:47 **46:3** [l] ver 12; Isa 48:12; 51:1 [m] S Isa 1:9 [n] S Ps 139:13; Isa 44:2 [o] S Dt 1:31; S Ps 28:9 [p] S Ps 22:10 **46:4** [q] Ps 71:18 [r] S Dt 32:39; S Isa 43:13 [s] S Ps 18:35; S 119:117 **46:5** [t] S Ex 15:11; Job 41:10; Isa 40:18, 25; Jer 49:19 **46:6** [u] S Isa 40:19 [v] S Ex 20:5; Isa 44:17; Hos 13:2 **46:7** [w] S ver 1 [x] S 1Sa 5:3; S Isa 41:7 [y] S 1Ki 18:26 [z] S Isa 44:17; S 47:13

46:8 [a] S Isa 44:21 [b] S Isa 1:2 **46:9** [c] S Isa 41:22 [d] S Dt 32:7 [e] S Ex 8:10; S Isa 45:5, 21; Mk 12:32 **46:10** [f] S Isa 41:4 [g] S Isa 45:21 [h] S Isa 41:22 [i] S Pr 19:21; S Isa 7:7, 9; S 44:26; Ac 5:39; Eph 1:11 **46:11** [j] S Jdg 4:10; S Ezr 1:2 [k] S Isa 8:8 [l] S Isa 25:1 [m] S Ge 41:25; Jer 44:28 **46:12** [n] S ver 3 [o] S Ex 32:9;

8 "Remember[a] this, keep it in mind,
take it to heart, you rebels.[b]
9 Remember the former things,[c] those of
long ago;[d]
I am God, and there is no other;
I am God, and there is none like me.[e]
10 I make known the end from the
beginning,[f]
from ancient times,[g] what is still to
come.[h]
I say, 'My purpose will stand,[i]
and I will do all that I please.'
11 From the east I summon[j] a bird of prey;[k]
from a far-off land, a man to fulfill
my purpose.
What I have said, that I will bring
about;
what I have planned,[l] that I will do.[m]
12 Listen[n] to me, you stubborn-hearted,[o]
you who are now far from my
righteousness.[p]
13 I am bringing my righteousness[q] near,
it is not far away;
and my salvation[r] will not be
delayed.
I will grant salvation to Zion,[s]
my splendor[t] to Israel.

The Fall of Babylon

47 "Go down, sit in the dust,[u]
Virgin Daughter[v] Babylon;
sit on the ground without a throne,
queen city of the Babylonians.[bw]
No more will you be called
tender or delicate.[x]
2 Take millstones[y] and grind[z] flour;
take off your veil.[a]
Lift up your skirts,[b] bare your legs,
and wade through the streams.

[a] *1* Or *are but beasts and cattle* [b] *1* Or *Chaldeans;* also in verse 5

S Isa 9:9 [p] Ps 119:150; Isa 48:1; Jer 2:5 **46:13** [q] S Isa 1:26; S 45:8; Ro 3:21 [r] S Ps 85:9 [s] S Ps 74:2; Joel 2:32 [t] S Isa 44:23 **47:1** [u] S Job 2:13; S Isa 29:4 [v] S Isa 21:9; S 23:12 [w] Ps 137:8; Jer 50:42; 51:33; Zec 2:7 [x] Dt 28:56 **47:2** [y] Ex 11:5; Mt 24:41 [z] S Jdg 16:21 [a] S Ge 24:65 [b] S Isa 32:11

46:1 *Bel.* Another name for Marduk, the chief deity of Babylon. The name "Bel" is equivalent to Canaanite "Baal" and means "lord." *bows down ... stoops.* In disgrace (see v. 2; 21:9 and note). *Nebo.* Nabu, the son of Marduk and the god of learning and writing (see note on Ezr 10:43).
46:2 *go off into captivity.* The idols join their worshipers in exile (see Jer 48:7 and note; 49:3; Hos 10:5; Am 1:15).
46:3 *remnant.* See 1:9 and note. *since ... birth ... since ... born.* See 44:2 and note.
46:4 *old age and gray hairs.* Cf. Ps 37:25. *sustain ... made ... rescue.* Unlike the helpless idols of vv. 1–2. See 41:10,13; 43:1–2 and notes.
46:5–7 See 40:18–20 and note.
46:6 *bow down and worship.* See 44:15,17,19.
46:7 *carry.* See v. 1. *cannot save.* See 44:17 and note.
46:8 *rebels.* Israel. See 1:2 and note; cf. 1:20,23,28; 30:1; 57:4.
46:9 *former things.* See 41:22 and note. *there is no other.* See 43:11 and note.
46:10–11 *My purpose.* Especially God's purposes and plans regarding Babylon and Israel (see 8:9–10; 14:24; 48:14 and notes). Cf. Ps 33:11.
46:10 *from the beginning.* See 41:26 and note.
46:11 *east ... bird of prey.* Cyrus, king of Persia (see 41:2 and note). The swiftness and power of a bird of prey are in view (see 8:8 and note; Jer 49:22; cf. Da 8:4).
46:12 *stubborn-hearted.* See v. 8; 48:4; Eze 2:4.
46:13 *righteousness.* Here equivalent to salvation. See 41:2; 45:8 and notes. *salvation.* See note on 43:3. *splendor.* See 35:2; 40:5 and notes; see also 44:23; 49:3.
47:1 *sit in the dust ... on the ground.* A sign of mourning (see 3:26). *Virgin Daughter Babylon.* A personification of Babylon (see note on 2Ki 19:21).
47:2 *millstones and grind.* A menial task performed by women (see Ex 11:5; Jdg 9:53 and notes; see also photo, p. 1186). *through the streams.* Probably on the way to exile.

Arab women working a millstone. Grain would be ground between the two stones in order to make flour: "Take millstones and grind flour" (Isa 47:2).

Library of Congress, LC-matpc-06017/www.LifeintheHolyLand.com

3 Your nakedness[c] will be exposed
and your shame[d] uncovered.
I will take vengeance;[e]
I will spare no one.[f]"

4 Our Redeemer[g]—the LORD Almighty[h] is his name[i]—
is the Holy One[j] of Israel.

5 "Sit in silence,[k] go into darkness,[l]
queen city of the Babylonians;[m]
no more will you be called
queen[n] of kingdoms.[o]
6 I was angry[p] with my people
and desecrated my inheritance;[q]
I gave them into your hand,[r]
and you showed them no mercy.[s]
Even on the aged
you laid a very heavy yoke.
7 You said, 'I am forever[t]—
the eternal queen!'[u]
But you did not consider these things
or reflect[v] on what might happen.[w]

8 "Now then, listen, you lover of pleasure,
lounging in your security[x]
and saying to yourself,
'I am, and there is none besides me.[y]
I will never be a widow[z]
or suffer the loss of children.'
9 Both of these will overtake you
in a moment,[a] on a single day:
loss of children[b] and widowhood.[c]
They will come upon you in full measure,
in spite of your many sorceries[d]
and all your potent spells.[e]
10 You have trusted[f] in your wickedness
and have said, 'No one sees me.'[g]
Your wisdom[h] and knowledge mislead[i] you
when you say to yourself,
'I am, and there is none besides me.'
11 Disaster[j] will come upon you,
and you will not know how to conjure it away.
A calamity will fall upon you
that you cannot ward off with a ransom;
a catastrophe you cannot foresee
will suddenly[k] come upon you.

12 "Keep on, then, with your magic spells
and with your many sorceries,[l]
which you have labored at since childhood.
Perhaps you will succeed,
perhaps you will cause terror.
13 All the counsel you have received has only worn you out![m]
Let your astrologers[n] come forward,

47:3 [c]S Ge 2:25; Eze 16:37; Na 3:5 [d]S Isa 20:4 [e]S Isa 1:24; S 34:8 [f]Isa 13:18-19 **47:4** [g]S Job 19:25 [h]S Isa 13:4 [i]Isa 48:2; Jer 50:34; Am 4:13 [j]S Isa 1:4; 48:17 **47:5** [k]S Job 2:13 [l]Isa 9:2; 13:10 [m]S Isa 21:9 [n]ver 7; La 1:1; Rev 18:7 [o]S Isa 13:19; Rev 17:18 **47:6** [p]S 2Ch 28:9 [q]S Dt 13:15; S Isa 42:24; Jer 2:7; 50:11 [r]Isa 10:13 [s]S Isa 14:6 **47:7** [t]S Isa 10:13; Da 4:30 [u]S ver 5; Rev 18:7 [v]S Isa 42:23, 25 [w]S Dt 32:29 **47:8** [x]S Isa 32:9 [y]S Isa 45:6 [z]Isa 49:21; 54:4; La 1:1; Rev 18:7 **47:9** [a]S Ps 55:15; 73:19; 1Th 5:3; Rev 18:8-10 [b]S Isa 13:18 [c]Isa 4:1; Jer 15:8; 18:21 [d]ver 12; Na 3:4; Mal 3:5 [e]Dt 18:10-11; Rev 9:21; 18:23 **47:10** [f]S Job 15:31; Ps 52:7; 62:10 [g]S 2Ki 21:16; S Isa 29:15 [h]S Isa 5:21 [i]Isa 44:20 **47:11** [j]S Isa 10:3; S 14:15; S 21:9; S 31:2; Lk 17:27 [k]S Ps 55:15; S Isa 17:14; 1Th 5:3 **47:12** [l]S ver 9; S Ex 7:11 **47:13** [m]Isa 57:10; Jer 51:58; Hab 2:13 [n]S Isa 19:3; S 44:25

47:3 *nakedness will be exposed.* See Eze 16:36. Babylon is no longer a queen (see vv. 5,7); she is reduced to a servant girl or a prostitute (see v. 8). *take vengeance.* See 34:8 and note. *spare no one.* See 13:18–20.
47:4 *Redeemer.* See note on 41:14. *LORD Almighty.* See 13:4 and note. *Holy One of Israel.* See 1:4; 41:14 and notes.
47:5 *queen city of the Babylonians.* See v. 1. *queen of kingdoms.* Babylon was a very beautiful city (see 13:19 and note) and the power center of the empire.
47:6 *angry … desecrated my inheritance.* See 10:5–6 (where Assyria is God's tool); 42:24 and note; 43:28 and note; La 2:2. *Even on the aged.* Their suffering fulfilled Moses' curse for covenant disobedience (Dt 28:49–50).
47:7 *I am forever.* Cf. the arrogant words of Nebuchadnezzar in Da 4:30.
47:8,10 *I am … none besides me.* Almost a claim of deity (cf. the Lord's words in 43:11; 45:5–6,18,22; cf. also Ex 3:14–15; 20:3; Dt 6:4 and notes; see also Isa 14:12–15 and note).
47:8 *lounging in your security.* Similar language is used of the complacent women of Jerusalem in 32:9,11. *widow.* Deserted and distressed. *loss of children.* See v. 9; 13:16,18; 14:22.
47:9,12 *sorceries … spells.* Magical practices to avoid danger and to inflict harm on the enemy (see 3:2–3 and note).
47:10 *No one sees me.* See 29:15 and note.
47:11 *with a ransom.* The Medes and Persians would not accept any settlement short of surrender (see 13:17).
47:13 *astrologers … stargazers.* Babylonia probably utilized their services more than any other nation (see Da 2:2,10).

those stargazers who make predictions
month by month,
let them save[o] you from what is
coming upon you.
14 Surely they are like stubble;[p]
the fire[q] will burn them up.
They cannot even save themselves
from the power of the flame.[r]
These are not coals for warmth;
this is not a fire to sit by.
15 That is all they are to you—
these you have dealt with
and labored[s] with since childhood.
All of them go on in their error;
there is not one that can save[t] you.

Stubborn Israel

48 "Listen to this, you descendants
of Jacob,
you who are called by the name of
Israel[u]
and come from the line of Judah,[v]
you who take oaths[w] in the name of
the LORD[x]
and invoke[y] the God of Israel—
but not in truth[z] or righteousness—
2 you who call yourselves citizens of the
holy city[a]
and claim to rely[b] on the God of
Israel—
the LORD Almighty is his name:[c]
3 I foretold the former things[d] long ago,
my mouth announced[e] them and I
made them known;
then suddenly[f] I acted, and they
came to pass.
4 For I knew how stubborn[g] you were;
your neck muscles[h] were iron,
your forehead[i] was bronze.
5 Therefore I told you these things long
ago;
before they happened I announced[j]
them to you

47:13 [o] ver 15; S Isa 5:29; 43:13; 46:7 **47:14** [p] S Isa 5:24 [q] S Isa 30:30 [r] Isa 10:17; Jer 51:30, 32,58 **47:15** [s] Rev 18:11 [t] S ver 13; S Isa 44:17 **48:1** [u] S Ge 17:5 [v] S Ge 29:35 [w] S Isa 19:18 [x] S 1Sa 20:42; S Isa 43:7 [y] Ex 23:13; 2Sa 14:11; Ps 50:16; Isa 58:2; Jer 7:9-10; 44:26 [z] Isa 59:14; Jer 4:2; 5:2; Da 8:12; Zec 8:3 **48:2** [a] S Ne 11:1; S Isa 1:26; S Mt 4:5 [b] S Isa 10:20; Ro 2:17 [c] S Isa 47:4 **48:3** [d] S Isa 41:22 [e] S Isa 40:21; 45:21 [f] S Isa 17:14; 30:13 **48:4** [g] S Isa 9:9 [h] S Ex 32:9; S Dt 9:27; Ac 7:51 [i] Eze 3:9 **48:5** [j] S Isa 40:21; S 42:9 [k] Jer 44:15-18 **48:6** [l] S Isa 41:22; S Ro 16:25 **48:7** [m] Isa 65:18 [n] Isa 45:21 [o] S Ex 6:7 **48:8** [p] S Isa 1:3 [q] S Dt 29:4 [r] Isa 41:24; Mal 2:11, 14 [s] Dt 9:7, 24; Ps 58:3; S Isa 1:2; 43:27; 58:1

so that you could not say,
'My images brought them about;[k]
my wooden image and metal god
ordained them.'
6 You have heard these things; look at
them all.
Will you not admit them?

"From now on I will tell you of new
things,[l]
of hidden things unknown to you.
7 They are created[m] now, and not long
ago;[n]
you have not heard of them before
today.
So you cannot say,
'Yes, I knew[o] of them.'
8 You have neither heard nor
understood;[p]
from of old your ears[q] have not been
open.
Well do I know how treacherous[r] you
are;
you were called a rebel[s] from
birth.
9 For my own name's sake[t] I delay my
wrath;[u]
for the sake of my praise I hold it
back from you,
so as not to destroy you
completely.[v]
10 See, I have refined[w] you, though not as
silver;
I have tested[x] you in the furnace[y] of
affliction.
11 For my own sake,[z] for my own sake,
I do this.
How can I let myself be defamed?[a]
I will not yield my glory to
another.[b]

48:9 [t] S 1Sa 12:22; S Isa 37:35 [u] S Job 9:13; S Isa 30:18 [v] S Ne 9:31 **48:10** [w] S Isa 1:25; Zec 13:9; Mal 3:3; 1Pe 1:7 [x] S Ex 15:25 [y] S Ex 1:13; S 1Ki 8:51 **48:11** [z] S 1Sa 12:22; S Isa 37:35 [a] S Lev 18:21; Dt 32:27; Jer 14:7,21; Eze 20:9,14,22,44 [b] Isa 42:8

47:14 *stubble.* This will be a rapid, powerful fire. See note on 1:31; cf. Mal 4:1 and note. *cannot … save themselves.* In contrast to the mighty Savior of Israel (see 43:3 and note), astrologers and sorcerers are as helpless as idols (see 44:17 and note). *not coals for warmth.* A subtle reference to firewood, a material from which pagans sometimes made idols (see 44:15).
48:1 *called by the name.* They belong to Israel (see 43:7 and note). *Israel.* See Ge 32:28 and note. *Judah.* The main tribe of the southern kingdom. See Ge 49:8 and note. *not in truth.* Contrast the oaths of 65:16 (see note there; cf. 1:11–15 and note).
48:2 *holy city.* Jerusalem, where the temple was located (see 2:2–4 and note; 52:1; 56:7; 57:13; 64:10–11; 65:11). See also 1:26; 4:3 and notes; Da 9:24. *rely on … God.* Superficially (see 10:20; contrast 31:1; 36:6,9; Eze 29:6–7). *LORD Almighty.* See 13:4 and note.
48:3 *former things.* See 41:22 and note. *they came to pass.* See 42:9.
48:4 *stubborn … bronze.* See Jer 6:28; cf. Eze 3:7.
48:5 *My images brought them about.* See Isaiah's harsh words about idolatry in 44:17–20 (see notes there). *wooden image and metal god.* See note on 44:12–13.
48:6 *new things.* For example, Israel's restoration by God through Cyrus (see 42:9 and note). The Messianic age and the new heavens and new earth may also be in view (cf. 65:17). *hidden things.* Cf. Ro 16:25–26 and notes.
48:7 *created now.* Now given substance in the prophetic announcement of their coming.
48:8 *neither heard nor understood.* See 1:3. *ears … not … open.* See 6:10 and note. *rebel.* See 1:2; 46:8 and notes.
48:9 *delay my wrath.* Cf. Ps 78:38. *my praise.* The praise God is worthy of.
48:10 *refined … tested.* Images of judgment (see Ps 12:6; Jer 9:7; Eze 22:18 and notes). Purifying fire is also mentioned in 1:25; 4:4. *furnace of affliction.* For Israel, Egypt had been an "iron-smelting furnace" (Dt 4:20 [see note there]; 1Ki 8:51; Jer 11:4). The fall of Jerusalem and the Babylonian exile were a similar furnace.
48:11 *For … defamed.* Jerusalem's fall and God's scattered people had brought dishonor to God's name (see Eze 36:20–23 and notes). *my glory.* See 40:5 and note.

Israel Freed

12 "Listen[c] to me, Jacob,
Israel, whom I have called:[d]
I am he;[e]
I am the first and I am the last.[f]
13 My own hand laid the foundations of the earth,[g]
and my right hand spread out the heavens;[h]
when I summon them,
they all stand up together.[i]

14 "Come together,[j] all of you, and listen:
Which of the idols has foretold[k] these things?
The LORD's chosen ally[l]
will carry out his purpose[m] against Babylon;[n]
his arm will be against the Babylonians.[a]
15 I, even I, have spoken;
yes, I have called[o] him.
I will bring him,
and he will succeed[p] in his mission.

16 "Come near[q] me and listen[r] to this:

"From the first announcement I have not spoken in secret;[s]
at the time it happens, I am there."

And now the Sovereign LORD[t] has sent[u] me,
endowed with his Spirit.[v]

17 This is what the LORD says—
your Redeemer,[w] the Holy One[x] of Israel:
"I am the LORD your God,
who teaches[y] you what is best for you,
who directs[z] you in the way[a] you should go.
18 If only you had paid attention[b] to my commands,
your peace[c] would have been like a river,[d]
your well-being[e] like the waves of the sea.
19 Your descendants[f] would have been like the sand,[g]
your children like its numberless grains;[h]
their name would never be blotted out[i]
nor destroyed from before me."

20 Leave Babylon,
flee[j] from the Babylonians!
Announce this with shouts of joy[k]
and proclaim it.
Send it out to the ends of the earth;[l]
say, "The LORD has redeemed[m] his servant Jacob."
21 They did not thirst[n] when he led them through the deserts;
he made water flow[o] for them from the rock;
he split the rock
and water gushed out.[p]

22 "There is no peace,"[q] says the LORD,
"for the wicked."[r]

The Servant of the LORD

49 Listen[s] to me, you islands;[t]
hear this, you distant nations:
Before I was born[u] the LORD called[v] me;
from my mother's womb he has spoken my name.[w]

[a] 14 Or *Chaldeans*; also in verse 20

48:12 [c]S Isa 46:3 [d]Isa 41:8; 42:6; 43:1 [e]S Isa 43:13 [f]S Isa 41:4; S Rev 1:17 **48:13** [g]Heb 1:10-12 [h]S Ge 2:1; Ex 20:11; Job 9:8; Isa 40:22; S 42:5; 45:18; 51:16; 65:17 [i]S Isa 34:16 **48:14** [j]S Isa 43:9 [k]S Isa 41:22 [l]S Isa 41:2 [m]Isa 46:10-11 [n]S Isa 21:9; S 45:1; Jer 50:45 **48:15** [o]S Jdg 4:10; Isa 45:1 [p]Isa 44:28-45:4 **48:16** [q]S Isa 41:1 [r]S Isa 33:13 [s]S Isa 45:19 [t]Isa 50:5,7,9 [u]Zec 2:9,11 [v]S Isa 11:2 **48:17** [w]S Job 19:25; Isa 49:7; 54:8 [x]S Isa 47:4 [y]S Isa 28:9; S Jer 7:13 [z]Isa 49:10; 57:18; 58:11 [a]S Isa 30:11 **48:18** [b]S Isa 42:23 [c]Ps 147:14; S Isa 9:7; 54:13; 66:12 [d]S Isa 33:21 [e]S Isa 1:26; S 45:8 **48:19** [f]Isa 43:5; 44:3; 61:9 [g]S Ge 12:2 [h]S Job 5:25 [i]Isa 56:5; 65:23; 66:22; Jer 35:19 **48:20** [j]Isa 52:11; Jer 48:6; 50:8; 51:6,45; Zec 2:6-7; Rev 18:4 [k]S Isa 12:6; 49:13; 51:11 [l]S Ge 49:10; S Dt 30:4; S Jer 25:22 [m]S Ex 6:6; S Isa 33:24; 52:9; 63:9; Mic 4:10 **48:21** [n]S Isa 33:16 [o]S Isa 30:25 [p]S Nu 20:11; S Isa 35:6 **48:22** [q]S Job 3:26 [r]S Isa 3:11; 57:21 **49:1** [s]S Isa 33:13 [t]S Isa 11:11 [u]Isa 44:24; 46:3; Mt 1:20 [v]Isa 7:14; 9:6; 44:2; Jer 1:5; Gal 1:15 [w]S Ex 33:12; S Isa 43:1

48:12 *called.* To be God's servant, his chosen people. See 42:6; see also 41:2; 43:1 and notes. *first and ... last.* See 41:4 and note.
48:13 *laid the foundations ... spread out the heavens.* Isaiah often refers to God as Creator (see 40:21–22; 42:5; 51:13 and notes). Cf. Ps 102:25. *when I summon ... all stand up.* All creation does God's bidding (see 40:26 and note; Ps 103:22).
48:14 *the idols ... foretold.* See 41:21–23,26; 43:9 and notes. *chosen ally.* Cyrus the Great (see 41:2 and note). *his purpose.* See 46:10–11 and note. *Babylon.* See 13:1 and note.
48:15 *called him.* Cyrus (see 41:2 and note). *will succeed.* See 44:28; 45:1–4 and notes.
48:16 *first announcement.* The prediction about Cyrus and his mission (see 41:25–27 and notes). *not spoken in secret.* See 45:19 and note. *has sent me.* A reference to either Isaiah or the servant of the Lord. *endowed with his Spirit.* The Spirit of the Lord comes upon the servant in 42:1 (see note there) and upon the Messianic prophet of 61:1 (see note there).
48:17 *Redeemer, the Holy One of Israel.* See 41:14 and note. *teaches you ... the way you should go.* Through the prophets or priests (see 30:20–21; Ps 32:8–10 and notes).
48:18 *peace ... like a river, your well-being like the waves.* Abundant and overflowing "peace" and "well-being"; see also 45:8; Am 5:24 and notes. Peace and "well-being" ("righteousness" in Hebrew) are also linked in 9:7; 32:17; 54:13–14; 60:17; Ps 85:10 (see note there); Heb 7:2; Jas 3:18.
48:19 *descendants ... like the sand.* See 10:22; see also Ge 13:16 and note; Ge 22:17; Jer 33:22 and note. *name ... never be blotted out.* Israel's name would not be completely obliterated (see v. 9; 54:3; Jer 31:36).
48:20 *Leave Babylon, flee.* Although the Jews did not have to flee (see 52:12), they were encouraged to depart quickly because of the judgment coming on Babylon (cf. Rev 18:4). This is the last mention of Babylon by name in Isaiah. *shouts of joy.* See 44:23; 49:13; 52:9 and notes. *ends of the earth.* See 11:12; 42:10 and notes. *redeemed.* See 43:1 and note. *his servant.* See 41:8–9 and note.
48:21 *did not thirst ... water ... from the rock.* A reference to God's provision after the exodus (see Ex 17:6 and note; Nu 20:11; see also Isa 32:2; 35:6; 43:19; 49:10 and notes). God's people would have water on the way home from Babylonian exile also.
48:22 Repeated almost verbatim in 57:21. *peace.* See 39:8 and note; see also Introduction: Literary Features. *wicked.* Those who rebel against the Lord (see note on 1:2).
49:1–6 (or **1–7** or **1–13**) The second of the four servant songs (see note on 42:1–4).
49:1 *islands.* Or "coastlands." In 42:4 the islands "put their

2 He made my mouth[x] like a sharpened
sword,[y]
in the shadow of his hand[z] he hid me;
he made me into a polished arrow[a]
and concealed me in his quiver.
3 He said to me, "You are my servant,[b]
Israel, in whom I will display my
splendor.[c]"
4 But I said, "I have labored in vain;[d]
I have spent my strength for nothing
at all.
Yet what is due me is in the LORD's
hand,[e]
and my reward[f] is with my God."[g]

5 And now the LORD says—
he who formed me in the womb[h] to
be his servant
to bring Jacob back to him
and gather Israel[i] to himself,
for I am[a] honored[j] in the eyes of the
LORD
and my God has been my
strength[k]—
6 he says:
"It is too small a thing for you to be
my servant[l]
to restore the tribes of Jacob
and bring back those of Israel I have
kept.[m]
I will also make you a light[n] for the
Gentiles,[o]
that my salvation may reach to the
ends of the earth."[p]

49:2 [x]S Job 40:18 [y]S Ps 64:3; Eph 6:17; S Rev 1:16 [z]S Ex 33:22; S Ps 91:1 [a]S Dt 32:23; Zec 9:13 **49:3** [b]S Isa 20:3; Zec 3:8 [c]S Lev 10:3; S Isa 44:23 **49:4** [d]S Lev 26:20; Isa 55:2; 65:23 [e]Isa 45:25; 50:8; 53:10; 54:17 [f]S Isa 35:4 [g]S Job 27:2 **49:5** [h]S Ps 139:13; Gal 1:15 [i]S Dt 30:4; S Isa 11:12 [j]S Isa 43:4 [k]S Ps 18:1 **49:6** [l]S ver 3 [m]Isa 1:9 [n]S Isa 9:2; Jn 1:9 [o]S Isa 26:18; 55:5; Zec 8:22; S Lk 2:32 [p]S Dt 30:4; S Ps 48:10; S Mt 28:19; Jn 11:52; Ac 13:47*

49:7 [q]S Isa 48:17 [r]S Ps 22:6; 69:7-9 [s]S Ezr 1:2; Isa 52:15 [t]S Ge 27:29; S Ps 22:29; S 86:9 [u]S Dt 7:9; S 1Co 1:9

7 This is what the LORD says—
the Redeemer and Holy One of
Israel[q]—
to him who was despised[r] and
abhorred by the nation,
to the servant of rulers:
"Kings[s] will see you and stand up,
princes will see and bow down,[t]
because of the LORD, who is faithful,[u]
the Holy One of Israel, who has
chosen[v] you."

Restoration of Israel

8 This is what the LORD says:

"In the time of my favor[w] I will answer
you,
and in the day of salvation I will
help you;[x]
I will keep[y] you and will make you
to be a covenant for the people,[z]
to restore the land[a]
and to reassign its desolate
inheritances,[b]
9 to say to the captives,[c] 'Come out,'
and to those in darkness,[d] 'Be free!'

"They will feed beside the roads
and find pasture on every barren hill.[e]

[a] 5 Or *him, / but Israel would not be gathered; / yet I will be*

[v]S Isa 14:1 **49:8** [w]Ps 69:13; Isa 60:10; 61:2 [x]S Isa 41:10; 2Co 6:2* [y]S Isa 5:2; 26:3 [z]S Isa 42:6 [a]Lev 25:10; S Ps 37:9; Isa 44:26; 58:12; 61:4; Eze 36:10, 33; Am 9:11, 14 [b]S Nu 34:13; S Isa 60:21 **49:9** [c]Isa 42:7; 61:1; S Lk 4:19 [d]S Ps 107:10 [e]Isa 41:18

hope" in the servant's teaching. *Before I was born … called me.* Cf. v. 5. The language is similar to that of the call of the prophet Jeremiah (see Jer 1:5 and note) and of the apostle Paul (Gal 1:15). Cf. 41:9. *spoken my name.* See 43:1 and note.

49:2 *my mouth … sharpened sword.* See Rev 1:16; 2:12,16; 19:15,21; cf. Isa 11:4; Eph 6:17; Heb 4:12. *shadow of his hand.* Descriptive of protection (see 30:2–3; 51:16). *polished arrow.* Arrows are used of God's judgment in Dt 32:23,42, of the deadly words of the wicked in Ps 64:3–4 and of Satan's schemes and temptations in Eph 6:11,16.

49:3 *my servant, Israel.* See notes on 41:8–9; 42:1–4; 42:1. "Servant" here cannot mean literally national Israel, since in v. 5 this servant has a mission to Israel. Rather, the Messianic servant is the ideal Israel, through whom the Lord will be glorified. He will succeed where national Israel failed. *display my splendor.* Through the redemption he will accomplish (see notes on 35:2; 40:5).

49:4 *labored in vain … for nothing at all.* Just as the nation Israel had toiled in vain (see 65:23), so Christ would encounter strong opposition during his ministry and would temporarily suffer apparent failure. The "suffering servant" theme is developed in the third and fourth of the four servant songs (50:4–9 or 50:4–11; 52:13—53:12). *what is due me … my reward.* Perhaps referring to the spiritual offspring of the servant (see 53:10)—Jews and Gentiles alike who believe in him (vv. 5–6); see 40:10 and note. In any case, he will be vindicated and rewarded (50:8; 53:10–12; 1Ti 3:16).

49:5 *formed me in the womb.* See v. 1; 44:2 and notes. *bring Jacob back … gather Israel.* A prophecy of release from captivity in Babylon (see vv. 9–12,22; 41:2 and note) and from the greater captivity of sin (see 42:7 and note). *my strength.* See 12:2.

49:6 Together with Ge 12:1–3; Ex 19:5–6, this verse is sometimes called the "great commission of the OT" and is quoted in part by Paul and Barnabas in Ac 13:47. *those … I have kept.* Probably referring to the remnant (see 1:9 and note). *light for the Gentiles.* See 9:2; 42:6 and notes; Ac 26:23. Christ is the light of the world (Lk 2:30–32; Jn 8:12; 9:5), and Christians are to reflect his light (Mt 5:14). *ends of the earth.* See 11:12 and note; see also 41:5; 42:10; 48:20.

49:7 *Redeemer and Holy One of Israel.* See 41:14 and note. *despised.* Applied twice to the suffering servant in 53:3. In 60:14 Zion is despised by her enemies. *nation.* Refers to either Israel (1:4) or Gentiles. *Kings will see … bow down.* See v. 23. This reaction to the servant is similar to that of 52:15. Former oppressors bow before a restored Jerusalem in 60:14 (cf. 45:14; 60:11–12; 66:23). *chosen you.* See 41:8–9; 42:1 and notes.

49:8 Quoted in part in 2Co 6:2. *time of my favor … day of salvation.* The background of this verse is probably the Year of Jubilee (see 61:1–2; Lev 25:10). The return from exile will bring the same restoration of land for the people as that year of liberty did. *keep you … to be a covenant.* See 42:6 and note. *reassign its desolate inheritances.* See 44:26. It was under Joshua that the land had been divided among individual tribes and families (Jos 14:1–5). The Messianic servant will be a new Joshua—as well as a new Moses (see vv. 9–10, which echo Israel's deliverance from Egypt and her wilderness experiences under Moses during the period of the exodus).

49:9 *captives.* The exiles. See 42:7 and note. *barren hill.* See 41:18 and note.

10 They will neither hunger nor thirst,[f]
nor will the desert heat or the sun
beat down on them.[g]
He who has compassion[h] on them will
guide[i] them
and lead them beside springs[j] of
water.
11 I will turn all my mountains into
roads,
and my highways[k] will be raised up.[l]
12 See, they will come from afar[m]—
some from the north, some from the
west,[n]
some from the region of Aswan.[a]"

13 Shout for joy,[o] you heavens;
rejoice, you earth;[p]
burst into song, you mountains![q]
For the LORD comforts[r] his people
and will have compassion[s] on his
afflicted ones.[t]

14 But Zion[u] said, "The LORD has
forsaken[v] me,
the Lord has forgotten me."

15 "Can a mother forget the baby at her
breast
and have no compassion on the
child[w] she has borne?
Though she may forget,
I will not forget you![x]
16 See, I have engraved[y] you on the palms
of my hands;
your walls[z] are ever before me.
17 Your children hasten back,
and those who laid you waste[a]
depart from you.
18 Lift up your eyes and look around;
all your children gather[b] and come to
you.
As surely as I live,[c]" declares the
LORD,
"you will wear[d] them all as
ornaments;
you will put them on, like a bride.
19 "Though you were ruined and made
desolate[e]
and your land laid waste,[f]
now you will be too small for your
people,[g]
and those who devoured[h] you will
be far away.
20 The children born during your
bereavement
will yet say in your hearing,
'This place is too small for us;
give us more space to live in.'[i]
21 Then you will say in your heart,
'Who bore me these?[j]
I was bereaved[k] and barren;
I was exiled and rejected.[l]
Who brought these[m] up?
I was left[n] all alone,[o]
but these—where have they come
from?' "

22 This is what the Sovereign LORD[p] says:

"See, I will beckon to the nations,
I will lift up my banner[q] to the
peoples;
they will bring[r] your sons in their arms
and carry your daughters on their
hips.[s]
23 Kings[t] will be your foster fathers,
and their queens your nursing
mothers.[u]
They will bow down[v] before you with
their faces to the ground;
they will lick the dust[w] at your feet.
Then you will know that I am the
LORD;[x]
those who hope[y] in me will not be
disappointed.[z]"

[a] 12 Dead Sea Scrolls; Masoretic Text *Sinim*

49:10 [f]S Isa 33:16 [g]Ps 121:6; Rev 7:16 [h]S Isa 14:1 [i]S Ps 48:14; S Isa 42:16; S 48:17 [j]S Isa 33:21; S 35:7 **49:11** [k]S Isa 11:16 [l]Isa 40:4; Jer 31:9 **49:12** [m]S Isa 2:3; S 11:11; 43:5-6 [n]Isa 59:19; S Mt 8:11 **49:13** [o]S Isa 48:20 [p]S Ps 96:11 [q]S Ps 65:12-13; 98:4; Isa 44:23 [r]S Ps 71:21; S Isa 40:1; S 2Co 1:4 [s]S Isa 14:1 [t]S Ps 9:12 **49:14** [u]Isa 40:9 [v]S Ps 9:10; S 71:11; S Isa 27:8 **49:15** [w]S 1Ki 3:26; Isa 66:13 [x]S Isa 44:21 **49:16** [y]S Ge 38:18; S Ex 28:9 [z]Ps 48:12-13; Isa 62:6 **49:17** [a]S Isa 5:6; 10:6; 37:18 **49:18** [b]S Isa 11:12; 14:1; 43:5; 51:3; 54:7 [c]S Nu 14:21; Isa 45:23; 54:9; 62:8; Ro 14:11* [d]Isa 52:1; 61:10; Jer 2:32 **49:19** [e]S Lev 26:33; Isa 54:1,3; 60:18; 62:4 [f]S Isa 5:6 [g]Eze 36:10-11; Zec 10:10 [h]S Isa 1:20 **49:20** [i]Isa 54:1-3; Zec 2:4; 10:10 **49:21** [j]Isa 29:23; 66:7-8 [k]S Isa 47:8; 54:1 [l]Isa 5:13; 54:6 [m]Isa 60:8 [n]S Isa 1:8 [o]S Ps 142:4; Isa 51:18; Jer 10:20 **49:22** [p]S Ge 15:2 [q]S Isa 11:10 [r]S Isa 11:12; S 14:2 [s]Lk 15:5 **49:23** [t]Isa 60:3,10-11 [u]S Nu 11:12; S Isa 60:16 [v]S Ge 27:29; Rev 3:9 [w]S Ge 3:14; Ps 72:9 [x]S Ex 6:2; S Ps 22:23; S Isa 42:8 [y]S Ps 37:9; S 130:5 [z]S Ps 22:5; S Isa 29:22; S 41:11

49:10 *neither hunger nor thirst.* See 48:21 and note. *has compassion.* See 14:1 and note. *will guide them.* As a shepherd (see 40:11 and note). This whole verse is also a picture of heaven according to Rev 7:16–17.
49:11 *mountains into roads.* See 26:7 and note. *highways … raised up.* See 11:16; 35:8; 40:3; 62:10 and notes.
49:12 *come from afar.* See 11:11 and note; 60:4. *north … west.* See 43:5–6 and notes. *Aswan.* See Eze 29:10 and note; 30:6; located in the most southern part of Egypt.
49:13 *Shout for joy … mountains.* Nature is personified often in Isaiah. See 44:23 and note. *comforts his people.* As he redeems and saves them. Cf. 2Co 1:3–4. *will have compassion.* See v. 10 and note; 54:7–10.
49:14 *forsaken … forgotten.* See 40:27; 54:7; La 5:20–22.
49:15 *Can a mother forget … ?* Cf. Ps 27:10.
49:16 *engraved you on … my hands.* As the names of the tribes of Israel were engraved on stones and fastened to the ephod of the high priest as a memorial before the Lord (Ex 28:9–12; cf. SS 8:6). *ever before me.* Cf. Ps 137:5–6.
49:17 *children.* Or "builders," following the reading of the Dead Sea Scrolls and some ancient versions (cf. note on 62:5). See photo, p. 1111.
49:18 *children gather.* See vv. 5,12 and notes. *ornaments.* Beautiful clothes and jewels symbolize strength and joy.
49:19–20 *too small.* The restoration of Israel will be astonishing and complete. The prophecy was partially fulfilled in the return from Babylon (see note on 11:11) and may include spiritual offspring among both Jews and Gentiles (see 54:17 and note).
49:19 *ruined … desolate.* Cf. v. 8; see 44:26 and note.
49:21 *bereaved and barren.* The concept of Israel as a barren woman is stressed in 54:1 (cf. Ps 113:9 and note).
49:22 *lift up my banner.* See 5:26 and note; 13:2. *bring your sons … daughters.* See 11:12 and note. The nations bring Israel back also in 14:2; 43:6; 60:9. *in their arms.* Cf. 60:4; see 40:11 and note.
49:23 *Kings … will bow down.* See v. 7; 11:14 and notes. *know that I am the LORD.* See v. 26; 60:16; Eze 12:20; 13:9; 36:38. *hope*

24 Can plunder be taken from warriors,[a]
or captives be rescued from the
fierce[a]?

25 But this is what the LORD says:

"Yes, captives[b] will be taken from
warriors,[c]
and plunder retrieved from the fierce;[d]
I will contend with those who contend
with you,[e]
and your children I will save.[f]
26 I will make your oppressors[g] eat[h] their
own flesh;
they will be drunk on their own
blood,[i] as with wine.
Then all mankind will know[j]
that I, the LORD, am your Savior,[k]
your Redeemer,[l] the Mighty One of
Jacob.[m]"

Israel's Sin and the Servant's Obedience

50 This is what the LORD says:

"Where is your mother's certificate of
divorce[n]
with which I sent her away?
Or to which of my creditors
did I sell[o] you?
Because of your sins[p] you were sold;[q]
because of your transgressions your
mother was sent away.
2 When I came, why was there no one?
When I called, why was there no
one to answer?[r]
Was my arm too short[s] to deliver you?
Do I lack the strength[t] to rescue you?
By a mere rebuke[u] I dry up the sea,[v]
I turn rivers into a desert;[w]
their fish rot for lack of water
and die of thirst.
3 I clothe the heavens with darkness[x]
and make sackcloth[y] its covering."

4 The Sovereign LORD[z] has given me a
well-instructed tongue,[a]
to know the word that sustains the
weary.[b]
He wakens me morning by morning,[c]
wakens my ear to listen like one
being instructed.[d]
5 The Sovereign LORD[e] has opened my
ears;[f]
I have not been rebellious,[g]
I have not turned away.
6 I offered my back to those who
beat[h] me,
my cheeks to those who pulled out
my beard;[i]
I did not hide my face
from mocking and spitting.[j]
7 Because the Sovereign LORD[k] helps[l] me,
I will not be disgraced.
Therefore have I set my face like
flint,[m]
and I know I will not be put to
shame.[n]

49:24 [a] Mt 12:29; Mk 3:27; Lk 11:21 **49:25** [b] S Isa 14:2 [c] Jer 50:33-34; Mk 3:27 [d] S Isa 13:11; S 25:4 [e] S 1Sa 24:15; Isa 25:5; S 43:26; 51:22; Jer 50:34 [f] Isa 25:9; 33:22; 35:4 **49:26** [g] S Isa 9:4; S 13:11 [h] S Isa 9:20 [i] Nu 23:24; Jer 25:27; Na 1:10; 3:11; Rev 16:6 [j] Ex 6:7; S Isa 11:9; Eze 39:7 [k] S Isa 25:9 [l] S Job 19:25; S Isa 48:17 [m] S Ge 49:24; S Ps 132:2 **50:1** [n] S Dt 24:1; Hos 2:2; Mt 19:7; Mk 10:4 [o] S Ne 5:5; S Mt 18:25 [p] S Isa 1:28 [q] S Dt 32:30; S Jdg 3:8 **50:2** [r] S 1Sa 8:19; S Isa 41:28 [s] Nu 11:23; Isa 59:1 [t] S Ge 18:14; S Ps 68:35; Jer 14:9 [u] S Ps 18:15 [v] S Ex 14:22 [w] S Ps 107:33 **50:3** [x] S Ex 10:22; S Isa 5:30 [y] Rev 6:12 **50:4** [z] ver 5; Isa 61:1 [a] S Ex 4:12 [b] S Isa 40:29; Mt 11:28 [c] Ps 5:3; 88:13; 119:147; 143:8 [d] S Isa 28:9 **50:5** [e] S Isa 48:16 [f] Isa 35:5 [g] Eze 2:8; 24:3; S Mt 26:39; Jn 8:29; 14:31; 15:10; Ac 26:19; Heb 5:8 **50:6** [h] Isa 53:5; Mt 27:30; Mk 14:65; 15:19; Lk 22:63; Jn 19:1 [i] S 2Sa 10:4 [j] S Nu 12:14; La 3:30; Mt 26:67; Mk 10:34 **50:7** [k] S Isa 48:16 [l] S Isa 41:10; 42:1 [m] Jer 1:18; 15:20; Eze 3:8-9 [n] S Isa 28:16; S 29:22

[a] *24* Dead Sea Scrolls, Vulgate and Syriac (see also Septuagint and verse 25); Masoretic Text *righteous*

in me. See 40:31 and note. *not be disappointed.* See 29:22 and note.

49:24 *warriors ... fierce.* The Babylonians (see 51:13).

49:25 *captives will be taken.* See Ezr 2:1,64–65; Jer 50:33–34; 52:27–30. *I will contend.* God takes up the case of his people. He will "defend their cause" (Jer 50:34). *I will save.* See 35:4 and note.

49:26 *oppressors.* See 14:4; 16:4; 51:13. *eat their own flesh.* During the siege of Jerusalem its people were reduced to cannibalism (La 4:10; cf. Zec 11:9 and note). *drunk on their own blood.* Cf. 51:22–23. *mankind will know.* See v. 23 and note. *Savior.* See 43:3 and note; 60:16. *Redeemer.* See 41:14 and note. *Mighty One of Jacob.* See 1:24 and note; 60:16.

50:1 *certificate of divorce.* A husband was required to give this to a wife he wished to divorce (see Dt 24:1–4; Mt 19:3; Mk 10:2,5–6 and notes). According to Jer 3:8 God gave the northern kingdom of Israel her certificate of divorce, and Isa 54:6–7 indicates that God had left Judah (see 62:4). Perhaps Isaiah's point is that God did not initiate the divorce; Judah broke her relationship with him. The exile, then, was actually a temporary period of separation (see 54:7) rather than a divorce. *my creditors.* If a man's debts were not paid, his children could be sold into slavery (see 2Ki 4:1 and note). But God has no creditors. *you were sold.* Cf. 45:13; 52:3.

50:2 *I came ... called.* Through his servants the prophets (see Jer 7:25 and note). *no one to answer.* Israel was deaf toward God (see 6:10 and note; 66:4). *arm too short.* The arm represented power (cf. 59:1). *dry up the sea.* A reference to crossing the "Red Sea" (see 43:16–17 and notes; Ps 106:9). *rivers into a desert.* See 42:15 and note. *fish rot.* Perhaps a reference to one of the plagues in Egypt (see 19:5–6,8; Ex 7:18).

50:3 *the heavens with darkness.* Perhaps an allusion to the plague of darkness (Ex 10:21); but see 13:10 and note.

50:4–9 (or **4–11**) The third of the four servant songs (see note on 42:1–4).

50:4–5,7,9 *Sovereign LORD.* The only uses of this title in the servant songs.

50:4 *word that sustains the weary.* In 42:3 the servant assisted the weak (contrast 49:2). Cf. Jer 31:25. *wakens my ear.* Unlike Israel (see v. 2), the servant was responsive to God.

50:5 *opened my ears.* A sign of obedience (see 1:19; Ps 40:6 and note). *not been rebellious.* Unlike Israel (see 1:2 and note; 1:20).

50:6 *my back to those who beat me.* Beatings were for criminals or fools (see Pr 10:13; 19:29; 26:3; Mt 27:26; Jn 19:1). *pulled out my beard.* A sign of disrespect and contempt (see 2Sa 10:4–5; Ne 13:25). *mocking and spitting.* To show hatred (Job 30:10) or to insult or disgrace (Dt 25:9; Job 17:6; Mt 27:30). This treatment of the servant anticipates his ultimate suffering in 52:13—53:12.

50:7 *helps me.* See v. 9; 49:8. *not be disgraced ... put to shame.* See 29:22 and note. Ultimately the servant will be honored (see 49:7; 52:13; 53:10–12). *my face like flint.* Like the prophets, the servant will endure with great determination. Cf. Lk 9:51, where Jesus "resolutely set out for Jerusalem" (lit. "resolutely set his face to go to Jerusalem").

[8]He who vindicates[o] me is near.[p]
Who then will bring charges
against me?[q]
Let us face each other![r]
Who is my accuser?
Let him confront me!
[9]It is the Sovereign LORD[s] who helps[t] me.
Who will condemn[u] me?
They will all wear out like a garment;
the moths[v] will eat them up.

[10]Who among you fears[w] the LORD
and obeys[x] the word of his servant?[y]
Let the one who walks in the dark,
who has no light,[z]
trust[a] in the name of the LORD
and rely on their God.
[11]But now, all you who light fires
and provide yourselves with flaming
torches,[b]
go, walk in the light of your fires[c]
and of the torches you have set
ablaze.
This is what you shall receive from my
hand:[d]
You will lie down in torment.[e]

Everlasting Salvation for Zion

51 "Listen[f] to me, you who pursue
righteousness[g]
and who seek[h] the LORD:
Look to the rock[i] from which you were
cut
and to the quarry from which you
were hewn;
[2]look to Abraham,[j] your father,
and to Sarah, who gave you birth.
When I called him he was only one
man,
and I blessed him and made him
many.[k]
[3]The LORD will surely comfort[l] Zion[m]
and will look with compassion on all
her ruins;[n]
he will make her deserts like Eden,[o]
her wastelands[p] like the garden of
the LORD.
Joy and gladness[q] will be found in her,
thanksgiving[r] and the sound of
singing.

[4]"Listen to me, my people;[s]
hear me,[t] my nation:
Instruction[u] will go out from me;
my justice[v] will become a light to the
nations.[w]
[5]My righteousness draws near speedily,
my salvation[x] is on the way,[y]
and my arm[z] will bring justice to the
nations.
The islands[a] will look to me
and wait in hope[b] for my arm.
[6]Lift up your eyes to the heavens,
look at the earth beneath;
the heavens will vanish like smoke,[c]
the earth will wear out like a
garment[d]
and its inhabitants die like flies.
But my salvation[e] will last forever,[f]
my righteousness will never fail.[g]

[7]"Hear me, you who know what is right,[h]
you people who have taken my
instruction to heart:[i]
Do not fear the reproach of mere
mortals
or be terrified by their insults.[j]

50:8 [o]S Isa 26:2; S 49:4 [p]S Ps 34:18 [q]S Job 13:19; S Isa 43:26; Ro 8:32-34 [r]S Isa 41:1 **50:9** [s]S Isa 48:16 [t]S Isa 41:10 [u]Ro 8:1,34 [v]S Job 13:28; S Isa 51:8 **50:10** [w]S Pr 1:7 [x]Isa 1:19; Hag 1:12 [y]S Isa 49:3 [z]S Ps 107:14; Ac 26:18 [a]S Isa 10:20; S 26:4 **50:11** [b]Pr 26:18 [c]Isa 1:31; Jas 3:6 [d]S Dt 21:22-23; S Pr 26:27 [e]S Job 15:20; Isa 65:13-15 **51:1** [f]S Isa 46:3 [g]ver 7; S Dt 7:13; 16:20; Ps 94:15; Isa 63:8; Ro 9:30-31 [h]Isa 55:6; 65:10 [i]Isa 17:10 **51:2** [j]S Ge 17:6; S Isa 29:22; Ro 4:16; Heb 11:11 [k]S Ge 12:2
51:3 [l]S Isa 40:1 [m]S Ps 51:18; S Isa 61:4 [n]Isa 44:26; 52:9; 61:4 [o]S Ge 2:8 [p]S Isa 5:6; S 41:19 [q]S Isa 25:9; 35:10; 65:18; 66:10; Jer 16:9 [r]Jer 17:26; 30:19; 33:11 **51:4** [s]Ex 6:7; Ps 50:7; Isa 3:15; 63:8; 64:9 [t]S Ps 78:1 [u]S Dt 18:18 [v]S Isa 2:4 [w]S Isa 26:18; S 49:6 **51:5** [x]S Ps 85:9; S Isa 12:2 [y]S Isa 35:4 [z]Ps 98:1; Isa 40:10; 50:2; 52:10; 59:16; 63:1,5 [a]S Isa 11:11 [b]S Ge 49:10; S Ps 37:9 **51:6** [c]S Ps 37:20; S 102:26; Mt 24:35; Lk 21:33; 2Pe 3:10 [d]Ps 102:25-26; Heb 1:10-12 [e]S Isa 12:2 [f]ver 8; S Ps 119:89 [g]Ps 89:33; Isa 54:10 **51:7** [h]S ver 1 [i]S Dt 6:6; Ps 119:11 [j]S Ps 119:39; Isa 50:7; 54:4; Mt 5:11; Lk 6:22; Ac 5:41

50:8 *vindicates me.* The Lord will find him righteous (see 45:25; for its ultimate fulfillment, see 1Ti 3:16). *bring charges.* See 49:25 and note. Because Christ was sinless, he also nullifies the charges brought against any who believe in him (see Ro 8:31 – 34 and notes). *my accuser.* Cf. 54:17.
50:9 *Who will condemn me?* Cf. the similar language Paul uses in Ro 8:34. *wear out like a garment; the moths.* Those who falsely accuse the righteous succumb to moths in 51:8 (i.e., they will be destroyed).
50:10 *fears the LORD.* See Ge 20:11; Pr 1:7 and notes. Cf. 25:3; 59:19. *in the dark.* Perhaps trouble or distress, similar to the experience of the servant (cf. 8:22). *trust ... rely.* The Lord encouraged such trust in 12:2; 31:1.
50:11 *light fires ... flaming torches.* Perhaps a reference to wicked practices that will ultimately destroy those who engage in them. Fire is a frequent figure of punishment (see 1:31 and note; cf. 9:18; 47:14; Ps 7:13). *torment.* Cf. 66:24.
51:1 *Listen to me.* See vv. 4,7. *who pursue righteousness.* Cf. v. 7; Dt 16:20; Pr 15:9. *rock.* Abraham (v. 2). Elsewhere God is called "the Rock" (see 17:10 and note).
51:2 *was only one man.* See Ge 12:1; Eze 33:24. *blessed him and made him many.* See Ge 12:2 – 3; 13:16; 15:5; 17:5 and note; 22:17.
51:3 *comfort ... compassion.* See 49:13 and note. *deserts like Eden.* See 35:1 – 2. The contrast between the lush splendor of Eden and the barrenness of the desert is found also in Joel 2:3 (see note there). Cf. Ge 2:8,10. *Joy and gladness.* See v. 11; 25:9 and note.
51:4 *Instruction ... my justice.* The rule of the servant would bring justice also (see 2:2 – 4; 42:4 and notes). *light to the nations.* The servant is the light in 42:6; 49:6.
51:5 *righteousness draws near.* In the deliverance from exile. Ultimately, salvation through Christ will come to all nations. See 46:13 and note. *arm.* Symbolizes power. *islands.* See 11:11 and note. *look to me ... hope.* See 40:31; 42:4 and notes.
51:6 *Lift ... to the heavens.* See 40:26. *heavens will vanish.* See 34:4 and note. *earth will wear out like a garment.* See 24:4; Heb 1:10 – 11; cf. Isa 50:9. *last forever.* See v. 8; 45:17. The word of God will also endure forever (see 40:8 and note; Mt 24:35; Lk 21:33).
51:7 *who know what is right.* See v. 1 and note. *who have taken my instruction to heart.* See Ps 37:31; Jer 31:33 and note. *reproach ... insults.* Such as those borne by the servant in 50:6 – 7.

8 For the moth will eat them up like a garment;[k]
the worm[l] will devour them like wool.
But my righteousness will last forever,[m]
my salvation through all generations."

9 Awake, awake,[n] arm[o] of the LORD,
clothe yourself with strength![p]
Awake, as in days gone by,
as in generations of old.[q]
Was it not you who cut Rahab[r] to pieces,
who pierced that monster[s] through?
10 Was it not you who dried up the sea,[t]
the waters of the great deep,[u]
who made a road in the depths of the sea[v]
so that the redeemed[w] might cross over?
11 Those the LORD has rescued[x] will return.
They will enter Zion with singing;[y]
everlasting joy will crown their heads.
Gladness and joy[z] will overtake them,
and sorrow and sighing will flee away.[a]

12 "I, even I, am he who comforts[b] you.
Who are you that you fear[c] mere mortals,[d]
human beings who are but grass,[e]
13 that you forget[f] the LORD your Maker,[g]
who stretches out the heavens[h]
and who lays the foundations of the earth,
that you live in constant terror[i] every day
because of the wrath of the oppressor,
who is bent on destruction?
For where is the wrath of the oppressor?[j]
14 The cowering prisoners will soon be set free;[k]
they will not die in their dungeon,
nor will they lack bread.[l]
15 For I am the LORD your God,
who stirs up the sea[m] so that its waves roar[n] —
the LORD Almighty[o] is his name.
16 I have put my words in your mouth[p]
and covered you with the shadow of my hand[q] —
I who set the heavens in place,
who laid the foundations of the earth,[r]
and who say to Zion, 'You are my people.[s]' "

The Cup of the LORD's Wrath

17 Awake, awake![t]
Rise up, Jerusalem,
you who have drunk from the hand of the LORD
the cup[u] of his wrath,[v]
you who have drained to its dregs[w]
the goblet that makes people stagger.[x]
18 Among all the children[y] she bore
there was none to guide her;[z]
among all the children she reared
there was none to take her by the hand.[a]
19 These double calamities[b] have come upon you —
who can comfort you?[c] —
ruin and destruction,[d] famine[e] and sword[f] —
who can[a] console you?
20 Your children have fainted;
they lie at every street corner,[g]
like antelope caught in a net.[h]

[a] 19 Dead Sea Scrolls, Septuagint, Vulgate and Syriac; Masoretic Text / *how can I*

51:8 [k]S Job 13:28; Jas 5:2 [l]S Isa 14:11 [m]S ver 6 **51:9** [n]S Jdg 5:12 [o]S Ps 98:1; S Isa 30:30; S 33:2 [p]S Ge 18:14; S Ps 65:6; Isa 40:31; 52:1 [q]Ex 6:6; Dt 4:34; S 32:7 [r]S Job 9:13 [s]S Ps 68:30; S 74:13 **51:10** [t]S Ex 14:22; Zec 10:11; Rev 16:12 [u]Ex 15:5,8 [v]S Job 36:30 [w]S Ex 15:13 **51:11** [x]S Isa 35:9; S 44:23 [y]S Ps 109:28; Isa 65:14; Jer 30:19; Zep 3:14 [z]S Isa 48:20; Jer 33:11 [a]S Isa 30:19; Jer 31:13; S Rev 7:17 **51:12** [b]S Isa 40:1; S 2Co 1:4 [c]S 2Ki 1:15 [d]S Isa 2:22 [e]S Isa 15:6; 40:6-7; 1Pe 1:24 **51:13** [f]S Job 8:13; S Isa 17:10 [g]S Job 4:17; Isa 17:7; 45:11; 54:5 [h]S Ge 1:1; S Isa 48:13 [i]S Isa 7:4 [j]S Isa 9:4 **51:14** [k]S Isa 42:7 [l]Isa 49:10 **51:15** [m]S Ex 14:21 [n]S Ps 93:3 [o]S Isa 13:4 **51:16** [p]S Ex 4:12,15 [q]S Ex 33:22 [r]S Isa 48:13 [s]Jer 7:23; 11:4; 24:7; Eze 14:11; Zec 8:8 **51:17** [t]S Jdg 5:12; Isa 52:1 [u]S ver 22; S Ps 16:5; S Mt 20:22 [v]ver 20; Job 21:20; Isa 42:25; 66:15; Rev 14:10; 16:19 [w]S Ps 75:8 [x]S ver 23; S Ps 60:3 **51:18** [y]Ps 88:18 [z]S Job 31:18; S Isa 49:21 [a]S Isa 41:13 **51:19** [b]S Isa 40:2; 47:9 [c]Isa 49:13; 54:11; Jer 15:5; Na 3:7 [d]Isa 60:18; 62:4; Jer 48:3; La 3:47 [e]S Isa 14:30 [f]Jer 14:12; 24:10 **51:20** [g]Isa 5:25; Jer 14:16; La 2:19 [h]S Job 18:10

51:8 *moth ... like a garment.* See 50:9 and note; cf. 51:6.
51:9,17; 52:1 *Awake, awake ... !* See 40:1 and note.
51:9 *arm of the LORD.* Symbol of God's power (cf. v. 5). See 30:30; 50:2 and notes; 52:10; 53:1; 63:12. *clothe ... with strength.* Cf. 50:2; see note on 40:31. *Rahab ... monster.* Egypt. See 27:1; 30:7 and notes.
51:10 *sea.* The "Red Sea" (see 50:2 and note). *the redeemed.* See 35:9 and note.
51:11 Identical to 35:10 (see note there).
51:12 *who comforts.* See v. 3; 49:13 and note. *grass.* See 37:27; 40:6 and notes.
51:13 *stretches out the heavens and ... earth.* See v. 16; 48:13 and note. *wrath of the oppressor.* See 49:26 and note. Babylon's wrath was insignificant beside the mighty wrath of God (cf. 13:3,5; 30:27).
51:14 *prisoners ... set free.* The exiles in Babylon (see 42:7 and note; 49:9). *in their dungeon.* Cf. 42:7; Jer 37:16.
51:15 *stirs up the sea.* Cf. Job 26:12; Ps 107:25; Jer 31:35. *LORD Almighty.* See 13:4 and note.
51:16 *my words.* See "my instruction" (v. 7). Like the servant of 49:2, the people are responding to God's word (cf. 59:21; Jos 1:8). *shadow of my hand.* See 49:2 and note. *set the heavens ... earth.* See v. 13 and note.
51:17 *cup of his wrath.* See vv. 20–22; 13:3 and note. Experiencing God's judgment is often compared to becoming drunk on strong wine. It is the fate of wicked nations in particular. See 29:9; 63:6; Ps 60:3 and note; 75:8; Jer 25:15–16 and notes; La 4:21; Eze 23:31 and note; Hab 2:16 and note; Zec 12:2; cf. Jn 18:11.
51:18 Children were expected to take care of parents who were sick or unsteady (cf. 1Ti 5:8 and note).
51:19 *who can comfort you?* A question also asked in Jer 15:5. Contrast v. 3.
51:20 *caught in a net.* Cf. Pr 7:22. *rebuke.* See 17:13; 54:9; 66:15.

They are filled with the wrath[i] of the LORD,
with the rebuke[j] of your God.

21 Therefore hear this, you afflicted[k] one,
made drunk,[l] but not with wine.
22 This is what your Sovereign LORD says,
your God, who defends[m] his people:
"See, I have taken out of your hand
the cup[n] that made you stagger;
from that cup, the goblet of my wrath,
you will never drink again.
23 I will put it into the hands of your tormentors,[o]
who said to you,
'Fall prostrate[p] that we may walk[q] on you.'
And you made your back like the ground,
like a street to be walked on."[r]

52 Awake, awake,[s] Zion,
clothe yourself with strength![t]
Put on your garments of splendor,[u]
Jerusalem, the holy city.[v]
The uncircumcised[w] and defiled[x]
will not enter you again.[y]
2 Shake off your dust;[z]
rise up,[a] sit enthroned, Jerusalem.
Free yourself from the chains on your neck,[b]
Daughter Zion,[c] now a captive.

3 For this is what the LORD says:

"You were sold for nothing,[d]
and without money[e] you will be redeemed.[f]"

4 For this is what the Sovereign LORD says:

"At first my people went down to Egypt[g] to live;
lately, Assyria[h] has oppressed them.

5 "And now what do I have here?" declares the LORD.

"For my people have been taken away for nothing,
and those who rule them mock,[a]"
declares the LORD.
"And all day long
my name is constantly blasphemed.[i]
6 Therefore my people will know[j] my name;[k]
therefore in that day[l] they will know
that it is I who foretold[m] it.
Yes, it is I."

7 How beautiful on the mountains[n]
are the feet of those who bring good news,[o]
who proclaim peace,[p]
who bring good tidings,
who proclaim salvation,
who say to Zion,
"Your God reigns!"[q]
8 Listen! Your watchmen[r] lift up their voices;[s]
together they shout for joy.[t]
When the LORD returns[u] to Zion,[v]
they will see it with their own eyes.
9 Burst into songs of joy[w] together,
you ruins[x] of Jerusalem,
for the LORD has comforted[y] his people,
he has redeemed Jerusalem.[z]
10 The LORD will lay bare his holy arm[a]
in the sight of all the nations,[b]

[a] 5 Dead Sea Scrolls and Vulgate; Masoretic Text *wail*

51:20 [i]S ver 17; S Job 40:11; Jer 44:6 [j]S Dt 28:20 **51:21** [k]S Isa 14:32 [l]ver 17; S Isa 29:9 **51:22** [m]S Isa 49:25 [n]S ver 17; Jer 25:15; 51:7; Hab 2:16; S Mt 20:22 **51:23** [o]Isa 14:4; 49:26; Jer 25:15-17, 26, 28; 49:12 [p]ver 17; Zec 12:2 [q]S Jos 10:24 [r]Ps 66:12; Mic 7:10 **52:1** [s]S Isa 51:17 [t]S 1Sa 2:4; S Isa 51:9 [u]Ex 28:2, 40; Est 6:8; Ps 110:3; Isa 49:18; 61:10; Zec 3:4 [v]S Ne 11:1; S Isa 1:26; Mt 4:5; S Rev 21:2 [w]S Ge 34:14 [x]S Isa 35:8 [y]Joel 3:17; Na 1:15; Zec 9:8; Rev 21:27 **52:2** [z]S Isa 29:4 [a]Isa 60:1 [b]S Ps 81:6; S Isa 10:27 [c]Ps 9:14 **52:3** [d]S Ps 44:12 [e]Isa 45:13 [f]S Isa 1:27; 1Pe 1:18 **52:4** [g]S Ge 46:6 [h]Isa 10:24 **52:5** [i]S Isa 37:23; Ro 2:24* **52:6** [j]S Isa 49:23 [k]S Ex 6:3 [l]S Isa 10:20 [m]S Isa 41:26 **52:7** [n]S Isa 42:11 [o]S 2Sa 18:26; S Isa 40:9; Ro 10:15* [p]Na 1:15; Lk 2:14; Eph 6:15 [q]S 1Ch 16:31; S Ps 97:1; 1Co 15:24-25 **52:8** [r]S 1Sa 14:16; Isa 56:10; 62:6; Jer 6:17; 31:6; Eze 3:17; 33:7 [s]Isa 40:9 [t]S Isa 12:6 [u]S Nu 10:36 [v]Isa 59:20; Zec 8:3 **52:9** [w]S Ps 98:4; S Isa 35:2 [x]S Ps 74:3; S Isa 51:3 [y]S Isa 40:1; Lk 2:25 [z]S Ezr 9:9; S Isa 48:20 **52:10** [a]S 2Ch 32:8; S Ps 44:3; S Isa 30:30 [b]Isa 66:18

51:21 *afflicted one.* Jerusalem (see 54:11). *made drunk.* On God's wrath (see v. 17 and note).
51:22 *defends his people.* See 49:25 and note. *cup ... of my wrath.* See v. 17 and note.
51:23 *your tormentors.* The Babylonians. See vv. 13–14; 14:4. *your back like the ground.* Perhaps figurative, but cf. Jos 10:24 and note.
52:1 *Awake, awake.* See 51:9,17. *garments of splendor.* Perhaps the robes of the priests, which belong to Jerusalem as "the holy city." See 49:18 and note. *holy city.* See 48:2 and note. *uncircumcised and defiled.* Foreign invaders. See 35:8; Jdg 14:3 and notes.
52:2 *Shake off your dust.* Contrast the fate of Babylon in 47:1 (see note there). *Free yourself.* See 42:7 and note; 49:9; 51:14. *Daughter Zion.* A personification of Jerusalem (see note on 2Ki 19:21).
52:3 *sold for nothing.* The enemy paid the Lord nothing for acquiring Jerusalem. See 45:13; 50:1 and notes. *without money ... redeemed.* See 41:14 and note; 43:1; 45:13.
52:4 *Assyria ... oppressed them.* See 9:4 and note.
52:5 Quoted in part in Ro 2:24. *for nothing.* See v. 3 and note. *my name is ... blasphemed.* The captivity brought disrespect to the God of helpless Jerusalem (see Eze 36:20–23 and notes). Cf. Assyria's blasphemy in 37:23–24.
52:6 *know my name.* See 49:26 and note. *in that day.* The day of deliverance from Babylon. See 10:20,27 and note. *foretold it.* The return from exile.
52:7 *feet of those who bring good news.* A reference to messengers who ran from the scene of a battle to bring news of the outcome to a waiting king and people (see 2Sa 18:26; Na 1:15 and note). Here the news refers to the return from exile (vv. 11–12; see 40:9 and note; 41:27), a deliverance that prefigures Christ's deliverance from sin. See Ro 10:15; Eph 6:15 and notes. *salvation.* See 49:8 and note. *Your God reigns!* See Ps 93:1 and note. The return of God's people to Jerusalem emphasizes his sovereign rule over the world (see 40:9 and note). God's kingdom will come more fully at the second coming of Christ (see Rev 19:6).
52:8 *watchmen.* Stationed on Jerusalem's walls (see 62:6–7; Ps 127:1 and note).
52:9 *Burst into songs.* See 44:23 and note. *comforted.* See 49:13 and note. *redeemed.* See v. 3 and note.
52:10 *holy arm.* See 51:9 and note. God's arm is often associated with redemption and salvation (see Ex 6:6). *all the ends*

and all the ends of the earth[c] will see
the salvation[d] of our God.

11 Depart,[e] depart, go out from there!
Touch no unclean thing![f]
Come out from it and be pure,[g]
you who carry the articles[h] of the
LORD's house.
12 But you will not leave in haste[i]
or go in flight;
for the LORD will go before you,[j]
the God of Israel will be your rear
guard.[k]

The Suffering and Glory of the Servant

13 See, my servant[l] will act wisely[a];
he will be raised and lifted up and
highly exalted.[m]
14 Just as there were many who were
appalled[n] at him[b]—
his appearance was so disfigured[o]
beyond that of any human
being
and his form marred beyond human
likeness[p]—
15 so he will sprinkle[q] many nations,[c]
and kings[r] will shut their mouths[s]
because of him.
For what they were not told, they will
see,
and what they have not heard, they
will understand.[t]

52:10 [c]S Jos 4:24; S Isa 11:9 [d]S Ps 67:2; Lk 2:30; 3:6 **52:11** [e]S Isa 48:20 [f]S Isa 1:16; 2Co 6:17* [g]S Nu 8:6; 2Ti 2:19 [h]S 2Ch 36:10 **52:12** [i]S Ex 12:11 [j]Mic 2:13; Jn 10:4 [k]S Ex 14:19 **52:13** [l]S Jos 1:8; S Isa 4:2; S 20:3 [m]S Isa 6:1; 57:15; Ac 3:13; S Php 2:9 **52:14** [n]S Lev 26:32; S Job 18:20 [o]S 2Sa 10:4 [p]S Job 2:12; S 16:16 **52:15** [q]S Lev 14:7; S 16:14-15 [r]S Isa 49:7 [s]S Jdg 18:19; Ps 107:42 [t]Ro 15:21*; Eph 3:4-5 **53:1** [u]S Isa 28:9; Ro 10:16* [v]S Ps 98:1; S Isa 30:30 [w]Jn 12:38* **53:2** [x]S 2Ki 19:26;

53 Who has believed our message[u]
and to whom has the arm[v] of the
LORD been revealed?[w]
2 He grew up before him like a tender
shoot,[x]
and like a root[y] out of dry
ground.
He had no beauty or majesty to attract
us to him,
nothing in his appearance[z] that we
should desire him.
3 He was despised and rejected by
mankind,
a man of suffering,[a] and familiar
with pain.[b]
Like one from whom people hide[c] their
faces
he was despised,[d] and we held him
in low esteem.

4 Surely he took up our pain
and bore our suffering,[e]
yet we considered him punished by
God,[f]
stricken by him, and afflicted.[g]

[a] 13 Or *will prosper* [b] 14 Hebrew *you* [c] 15 Or *so will many nations be amazed at him* (see also Septuagint)

S Job 14:7; S Isa 4:2 [y]S Isa 11:10 [z]Isa 52:14 **53:3** [a]Ps 69:29 [b]ver 4, 10; S Ex 1:10; S Mt 16:21; Lk 18:31-33; Heb 5:8 [c]S Dt 31:17; Isa 1:15 [d]S 1Sa 2:30; S Ps 22:6; Mt 27:29; Jn 1:10-11 **53:4** [e]Mt 8:17* [f]S Dt 5:24; S Job 4:5; Jer 23:5-6; 25:34; Eze 34:23-24; Mic 5:2-4; Zec 13:7; Jn 19:7 [g]S ver 3; S Ge 12:17; S Ru 1:21

of the earth. Equivalent to all humankind (see note on 40:5). Cf. 45:22.

52:11 Quoted in part in 2Co 6:17. *Depart, depart . . . !* See note on 40:1. *unclean thing.* Perhaps referring to pagan religious objects (cf. Ge 31:19; 35:2). *you who carry the articles.* Cyrus allowed the people to take back the articles of the temple seized by Nebuchadnezzar (Ezr 1:7 – 11). The priests and Levites were responsible for them (see Nu 3:6 – 8; 2Ch 5:4 – 7).

52:12 *not leave in haste.* See 48:20 and note. *go before you . . . be your rear guard.* As he did for the Israelites when they were freed from Egypt (see Ex 13:21; 14:19 – 20 and notes; cf. Isa 42:16; 49:10; 58:8).

52:13 — 53:12 The fourth and longest of the four servant songs (see note on 42:1 – 4). It constitutes the central and most important unit in chs. 40 – 66, as well as in chs. 49 – 57 (see note on 39:8). The song contains five stanzas of three numbered verses apiece, each stanza longer than the previous one. It is frequently quoted in the NT and is often referred to as the "gospel in the OT" or the "gospel of Isaiah."

52:13 *my servant.* See note on 42:1. The Aramaic Targum identifies the Lord's servant here as "the Messiah." *act wisely.* A mark of God's blessing (see 1Sa 18:14) and of obedience to God's word (see Jos 1:8). The Messianic King will "reign wisely" (Jer 23:5). Cf. 53:10. *raised and lifted up.* Words that describe the Lord in Isaiah's vision (see 6:1 and note; 57:15). Christ's exaltation is referred to in Ac 2:33; 3:13; Eph 1:20 – 23; Php 2:9 – 11 (see also 1Pe 1:10 – 11).

52:14 *appalled at him.* When they saw Christ's suffering on the cross. Cf. the reaction to the ruined city of Tyre (Eze 27:35). *disfigured.* A term used of a "blemished animal," which should not be offered to the Lord (Mal 1:14). Cf. the disgraceful treatment of the servant (see 50:6 and note). *beyond that of any human being.* Cf. Ps 22:6. His treatment was inhuman.

52:15 *sprinkle many nations.* With the sprinkling of cleansing (see Lev 14:7; Nu 8:7; 19:18 – 19) and/or of consecration (see Ex 29:21; Lev 8:11,30). But see NIV text note. *kings will shut their mouths.* In astonishment at the suffering and exaltation of the servant (see 49:6 – 7 and notes). Cf. Job 21:5. *For what . . . understand.* Quoted in Ro 15:21. Even though they have not heard the prophetic word, kings will understand the mission of the servant when they see his humiliation and exaltation (contrast 6:9 – 10).

53:1 Quoted in whole in Jn 12:38 and in part in Ro 10:16. *our message.* The good news about salvation, given by the prophets to Israel and the nations (see 52:7,10). *arm of the LORD.* See 51:9 and note.

53:2 *tender shoot.* The Messiah would grow from the "stump of Jesse" (11:1; see note there; cf. 4:2; Zec 3:8 and notes). His beginnings would be humble. *root.* See 11:10 and note. *beauty.* The Hebrew for this word is used of David in 1Sa 16:18, where it is translated "fine-looking." *majesty.* Christ had nothing of the bearing or trappings of royalty.

53:3 *despised.* See 49:7 and note; Ps 22:6. *rejected . . . held . . . in low esteem.* The Hebrew words used here occur together also in 2:22 (see note there). Cf. Jn 1:10 – 11. *suffering.* The Hebrew for this word is used of both physical and mental pain (see v. 4; Ex 3:7). *hide their faces.* See 1:15 and note; 8:17.

53:4 Quoted in part in Mt 8:17 with reference to Jesus' healing ministry. *pain.* Diseases often result from sinful living and are ultimately the consequences of original (Adamic) sin. See 1:5 – 6 and note. *punished by God.* With a terrible disease (see Ge 12:17; 2Ki 15:5). People (Israel in particular) thought the servant was suffering for his own sins. *afflicted.* Or "humbled" or "oppressed" (see v. 7; 58:10).

QUOTATIONS FROM AND REFERENCES TO **ISAIAH 53** IN THE NEW TESTAMENT

ISAIAH 53	NEW TESTAMENT
53:1–12	Lk 24:27,46; 1Pe 1:11
53:1	Jn 12:38; Ro 10:16
53:2	Mt 2:23
53:3	Mk 9:12
53:4	Mt 8:17; 1Pe 2:24
53:4–5	Ro 4:25
53:5	Mt 26:67; 1Pe 2:24
53:5–6	Ac 10:43
53:6	1Pe 2:25
53:6–7	Jn 1:29
53:7	Mt 26:63; 27:12,14; Mk 14:60–61; 15:4–5; 1Co 5:7; 1Pe 2:23; Rev 5:6,12; 13:8
53:7–8 LXX	Ac 8:32–33
53:8–9	1Co 15:3
53:9	Mt 26:24; 1Pe 2:22; 1Jn 3:5; Rev 14:5
53:11	Ro 5:19
53:12	Mt 27:38; Lk 22:37; 23:33–34; Heb 9:28; 1Pe 2:24

Taken from *The Zondervan Encyclopedia of the Bible*: Vol. 5 by MOISÉS SILVA.

5 But he was pierced[h] for our
transgressions,[i]
he was crushed[j] for our iniquities;
the punishment[k] that brought us peace[l]
was on him,
and by his wounds[m] we are healed.[n]
6 We all, like sheep, have gone astray,[o]
each of us has turned to our own
way;[p]
and the LORD has laid on him
the iniquity[q] of us all.

7 He was oppressed[r] and afflicted,
yet he did not open his mouth;[s]
he was led like a lamb[t] to the
slaughter,[u]
and as a sheep before its shearers is
silent,
so he did not open his mouth.
8 By oppression[a] and judgment[v] he was
taken away.
Yet who of his generation
protested?
For he was cut off from the land of the
living;[w]
for the transgression[x] of my people
he was punished.[b]
9 He was assigned a grave with the
wicked,[y]
and with the rich[z] in his death,
though he had done no violence,[a]
nor was any deceit in his mouth.[b]

10 Yet it was the LORD's will[c] to crush[d] him
and cause him to suffer,[e]

[a] 8 Or *From arrest* [b] 8 Or *generation considered / that he was cut off from the land of the living, / that he was punished for the transgression of my people?*

53:5 [h] S Ps 22:16 [i] S Ex 28:38; S Ps 39:8; S Jn 3:17; Ro 4:25; 1Co 15:3; Heb 9:28 [j] Ps 34:18 [k] S Isa 50:6 [l] S Isa 9:6; Ro 5:1 [m] Isa 1:6; Mt 27:26; Jn 19:1 [n] S Dt 32:39; S 2Ch 7:14; 1Pe 2:24-25 **53:6** [o] S Ps 95:10; 1Pe 2:24-25 [p] S 1Sa 8:3; Isa 56:11; 57:17; Mic 3:5 [q] ver 12; S Ex 28:38; Ro 4:25 **53:7** [r] Isa 49:26 [s] S Mk 14:61; 1Pe 2:23 [t] Mt 27:31; S Jn 1:29 [u] S Ps 44:22 **53:8** [v] Mk 14:49 [w] Ps 88:5; Da 9:26; Ac 8:32-33* [x] ver 12; S Ps 39:8 **53:9** [y] Mt 27:38; Mk 15:27; Lk 23:32; Jn 19:18 [z] Mt 27:57-60; Mk 15:43-46; Lk 23:50-53; Jn 19:38-41 [a] Isa 42:1-3 [b] S Job 16:17; 1Pe 2:22*; 1Jn 3:5; Rev 14:5 **53:10** [c] Isa 46:10; 55:11; Ac 2:23 [d] ver 5 [e] S ver 3; S Ge 12:17

53:5 The centering verse of 52:13—53:12, the last, longest and arguably the loveliest of the suffering servant songs in the book of Isaiah (see note on 42:1–4). This final song, in turn, is the middle chapter of the middle section (chs. 49–57) of Part 2 (chs. 40–66) of the book (see Introduction: Outline). "Peace" (Hebrew *shalom*) in this verse is the key word in the final verse of Part 1 (chs. 1–39) and recurs in a refrain in 48:22 and 57:21, the final verses of chs. 40–48 and 49–57 respectively (see 39:8 and note). "Peace," therefore, is a central theme in chs. 40–66 generally and 52:13—53:12 specifically. Such overarching and overwhelming *shalom* could be "brought" to God's people only by the atoning sacrifice of the One who was "pierced for our transgressions" and "crushed for our iniquities" (see v. 12 and note; cf. also Ro 4:25). *pierced.* See Ps 22:16; Zec 12:10; Jn 19:34 and notes. *crushed.* In spirit (see Ps 34:18; cf. Isa 57:15). The sins of the world weighed heavily upon him. *healed.* Here probably equivalent to "forgiven" (see 6:10; Jer 30:17; see also note on 1Pe 2:24).

53:6 *have gone astray.* Cf. Ps 119:176 and note; Jer 50:6; Eze 34:4–6,16; 1Pe 2:25 and note. *laid on him the iniquity of us all.* Just as the priest laid his hands on the scapegoat and symbolically put Israel's sins on it (see Lev 16:20–22 and note). See also 1Pe 2:24 and note.

53:7–8 Verses read by the Ethiopian eunuch in the presence of Philip (see Ac 8:34 and note).

53:7 *oppressed.* Like Israel. See 49:26 and note. The Hebrew for this word is translated "slave drivers" in Ex 5:6. *lamb to the slaughter.* Cf. Ps 44:22; Rev 5:6 and note. John the Baptist called Jesus "the Lamb of God" (Jn 1:29,36; see note on 1:29). *did not open his mouth.* Jesus remained silent before the chief priests and Pilate (Mt 27:12–14; Mk 14:60–61; 15:4–5; Jn 19:8–9) and before Herod (Lk 23:8–9).

53:8 *By oppression and judgment.* Jesus was given an unfair trial. See NIV text notes.

53:9 *the wicked.* The manner of his death would indicate that, as far as those who condemned him were concerned, he was to be buried with executed criminals. *the rich.* Not as a burial with honor. The parallelism (with its effective wordplay in Hebrew) makes clear that Isaiah here associates the rich with the wicked, as do many OT writers—because they acquired their wealth by wicked means and/or trusted in their wealth rather than in God (see, e.g., Ps 37:16,35; Pr 18:23; 28:6,20; Jer 5:26–27; Mic 6:10,12). According to the Gospels (Mt 27:57–60 and parallels), the wealthy Joseph of Arimathea gave Jesus an honorable burial by placing his body in his own tomb. But this was undoubtedly an act of love growing out of his awareness that he had been forgiven much (see Lk 7:47). Thus the fulfillment fitted but also transcended the prophecy. *he had done no violence, nor … deceit in his mouth.* Peter quotes these lines as he encourages believers to endure unjust suffering (1Pe 2:22).

53:10 *crush him.* See v. 5 and note. *an offering for sin.* Or "a guilt offering," an offering where restitution was usually

and though the LORD makes[a] his life
an offering for sin,[f]
he will see his offspring[g] and prolong
his days,
and the will of the LORD will prosper[h]
in his hand.
11 After he has suffered,[i]
he will see the light[j] of life[b] and be
satisfied[c];
by his knowledge[d] my righteous
servant[k] will justify[l] many,
and he will bear their iniquities.[m]
12 Therefore I will give him a portion
among the great,[e][n]
and he will divide the spoils[o] with
the strong,[f]
because he poured out his life unto
death,[p]
and was numbered with the
transgressors.[q]
For he bore[r] the sin of many,[s]
and made intercession[t] for the
transgressors.

The Future Glory of Zion

54 "Sing, barren woman,[u]
you who never bore a child;
burst into song, shout for joy,[v]
you who were never in labor;[w]
because more are the children[x] of the
desolate[y] woman
than of her who has a husband,[z]"
says the LORD.
2 "Enlarge the place of your tent,[a]
stretch your tent curtains wide,
do not hold back;
lengthen your cords,
strengthen your stakes.[b]
3 For you will spread out to the right and
to the left;
your descendants[c] will dispossess
nations[d]
and settle in their desolate[e] cities.
4 "Do not be afraid;[f] you will not be put
to shame.[g]
Do not fear disgrace;[h] you will not
be humiliated.
You will forget the shame of your youth[i]
and remember no more the reproach[j]
of your widowhood.[k]
5 For your Maker[l] is your husband[m]—
the LORD Almighty is his name—
the Holy One[n] of Israel is your
Redeemer;[o]
he is called the God of all the earth.[p]
6 The LORD will call you back[q]
as if you were a wife deserted[r] and
distressed in spirit—
a wife who married young,[s]
only to be rejected," says your God.
7 "For a brief moment[t] I abandoned[u] you,
but with deep compassion[v] I will
bring you back.[w]
8 In a surge of anger[x]
I hid[y] my face from you for a moment,

53:10 [f]S Lev 5:15; Jn 3:17 [g]S Ps 22:30 [h]S Jos 1:8; S Isa 49:4 **53:11** [i]Jn 10:14-18 [j]S Job 33:30 [k]S Isa 20:3; Ac 7:52 [l]S Isa 6:7; Jn 1:29; Ac 10:43; S Ro 4:25 [m]S Ex 28:38 **53:12** [n]S Isa 6:1; S Php 2:9 [o]S Ex 15:9; S Ps 119:162; Lk 11:22 [p]Mt 26:28, 38, 39, 42 [q]Mt 27:38; Mk 15:27*; Lk 22:37*; 23:32 [r]S ver 6; 1Pe 2:24 [s]Heb 9:28 [t]Isa 59:16; S Ro 8:34 **54:1** [u]S Ge 30:1 [v]S Ge 21:6; S Ps 98:4 [w]Isa 66:7 [x]Isa 49:20 [y]S Isa 49:19 [z]S 1Sa 2:5; Gal 4:27* **54:2** [a]S Ge 26:22; Isa 26:15; 49:19-20 [b]Ex 35:18; 39:40 **54:3** [c]S Ge 13:14; S Isa 48:19 [d]S Job 12:23; S Isa 14:2; 60:4-11 [e]S Isa 49:19 **54:4** [f]Jer 30:10; Joel 2:21 [g]S Isa 28:16; S 29:22 [h]S Ge 30:23; S Ps 119:39; S Isa 41:11 [i]S Ps 25:7; S Jer 2:2; S 22:21 [j]S Isa 51:7 [k]S Isa 47:8 **54:5** [l]S Ps 95:6; S 149:2; S Isa 51:13 [m]S SS 3:11; Jer 3:14; 31:32; Hos 2:7, 16 [n]S Isa 1:4; 49:7; 55:5; 60:9 [o]S Isa 48:17 [p]S Isa 6:3; S 12:4 **54:6** [q]Isa 49:14-21 [r]ver 6-7; Isa 1:4; 50:1-2; 60:15; 62:4, 12; Jer 44:2; Hos 1:10 [s]S Ex 20:14; Mal 2:15 **54:7** [t]S Job 14:13; Isa 26:20 [u]S Ps 71:11; S Isa 27:8 [v]S Ps 51:1 [w]S Isa 49:18 **54:8** [x]Isa 9:12; 26:20; 60:10 [y]S Isa 1:15

[a] 10 Hebrew *though you make* [b] 11 Dead Sea Scrolls (see also Septuagint); Masoretic Text does not have *the light of life.* [c] 11 Or (with Masoretic Text) [11]*He will see the fruit of his suffering / and will be satisfied* [d] 11 Or *by knowledge of him* [e] 12 Or *many* [f] 12 Or *numerous*

required and the offender sacrificed a ram (but see note on Lev 5:15). *his offspring.* Spiritual progeny. *prolong his days.* Christ would live forever (see 9:7 and note). *prosper.* See 52:13 and NIV text note there.

53:11 *light of life.* A reference to the resurrection of Christ; see 1Co 15:4 (but see also the first two NIV text notes here). For "of life," see Job 33:30 and note; Ps 49:19; 56:13 and note. *be satisfied.* In 1:11, where the same Hebrew word appears, God had "more than enough" of innumerable sacrifices that accomplished nothing. Here the one sacrifice of Christ brings perfect satisfaction. *his knowledge.* His true knowledge of the true God (see 1:3; 6:9; 43:10; 45:4–5; 52:6; 56:10). The Spirit of knowledge (11:2) rested on the Messiah (but see the third NIV text note here). Cf. 52:13. *my … servant.* See 41:8–9; 42:1 and notes. *justify.* Cause many to be declared righteous. See 5:23 ("acquit"); Ro 5:19 and note. *many.* See NIV text notes on v. 12; see also 52:15; Da 12:3.

53:12 *among the great … with the strong.* God will reward his servant as if he were a king sharing in the spoils of a great victory (see 52:15). *divide the spoils.* God's gift to his suffering servant (cf. 9:3). *poured out his life.* As a sacrifice (see v. 10). *unto death.* See Php 2:8 and note. *and was numbered with the transgressors.* Quoted in Lk 22:37 with reference to Jesus (see note there). *bore.* The Hebrew for this verb is translated "took up" in v. 4. *made intercession.* See Jer 7:16 ("pray"); 27:18 ("plead"). Cf. 59:16; Heb 7:25.

54:1 This verse is applied by Paul to Sarah and the covenant of promise, representing "the Jerusalem that is above" (Gal 4:26–27; see notes there). *Sing … burst into song.* See 12:6; 44:23; 52:9 and notes. *barren woman.* Jerusalem (representing Israel), especially during the exile (see 49:21). In the Near East, barrenness was considered a disgrace (see 4:1 and note). *more are the children of the desolate woman.* See 49:19–20 and note. Israel will be restored, both physically and spiritually (cf. 62:4). *husband.* See 50:1 and note.

54:2 See 26:15; 33:20 and notes. *your tent.* Jerusalem is viewed as a woman living in her own tent.

54:3 *spread out.* See 49:19–20 and note; cf. Ge 28:14. *dispossess nations.* See 11:14; 49:7 and notes.

54:4 *not be put to shame … disgrace.* See 29:22 and note; 45:17. *shame of your youth.* Probably the period of slavery in Egypt. Cf. Jer 31:19; Eze 16:60. *reproach of your widowhood.* Probably referring to the exile, when Israel was alone, like a widow (vv. 6–7).

54:5 *husband.* See 62:4–5. *Holy One of Israel … Redeemer.* See 1:4, 41:14 and notes.

54:6–7 *wife deserted … abandoned.* Israel's experience in exile (see 49:14; 50:1 and note; 62:4).

54:7–8,10 *compassion.* See 14:1; 49:10,13; 51:3.

54:7 *brief moment.* The Babylonian exile was relatively brief (see 26:20; 50:1 and notes).

54:8 *surge of anger.* See 9:12,17,21 and note; 60:10. *hid my*

but with everlasting kindness[z]
I will have compassion[a] on you,"
says the LORD your Redeemer.[b]

9 "To me this is like the days of Noah,
when I swore that the waters of
Noah would never again cover
the earth.[c]
So now I have sworn[d] not to be angry[e]
with you,
never to rebuke[f] you again.
10 Though the mountains be shaken[g]
and the hills be removed,
yet my unfailing love[h] for you will not
be shaken[i]
nor my covenant[j] of peace[k] be
removed,"
says the LORD, who has compassion[l]
on you.

11 "Afflicted[m] city, lashed by storms[n] and
not comforted,[o]
I will rebuild you with stones of
turquoise,[a][p]
your foundations[q] with lapis lazuli.[r]
12 I will make your battlements of rubies,
your gates[s] of sparkling jewels,
and all your walls of precious stones.
13 All your children will be taught by the
LORD,[t]
and great will be their peace.[u]
14 In righteousness[v] you will be
established:[w]
Tyranny[x] will be far from you;
you will have nothing to fear.[y]
Terror[z] will be far removed;
it will not come near you.
15 If anyone does attack you, it will not
be my doing;
whoever attacks you will surrender[a]
to you.

54:8 [z] ver 10; S Ps 25:6; 92:2; Isa 55:3; 63:7 [a] S Ps 102:13; S Isa 14:1; Hos 2:19 [b] S Isa 48:17 **54:9** [c] S Ge 8:21 [d] S Isa 14:24; S 49:18 [e] Ps 13:1; 103:9; Isa 12:1; 57:16; Jer 3:5, 12; Eze 39:29; Mic 7:18 [f] S Dt 28:20 **54:10** [g] S Ps 46:2; Rev 6:14 [h] S Ps 6:4 [i] S Isa 51:6; Heb 12:27 [j] S Ge 9:16; Ex 34:10; Ps 89:34; S Isa 42:6 [k] S Nu 25:12 [l] ver 8; S Isa 14:1; 55:7 **54:11** [m] S Isa 14:32 [n] Isa 28:2; 29:6 [o] S Isa 51:19 [p] 1Ch 29:2; Rev 21:18 [q] S Isa 28:16; Rev 21:19-20 [r] S Ex 24:10; S Job 28:6 **54:12** [s] Rev 21:21 **54:13** [t] S Isa 28:9; Mic 4:2; Jn 6:45*; Heb 8:11 [u] S Lev 26:6; S Isa 48:18 **54:14** [v] S Isa 26:2 [w] Jer 30:20 [x] S 2Sa 7:10; S Isa 9:4 [y] Zep 3:15; Zec 9:8 [z] S Isa 17:14 **54:15** [a] Isa 41:11-16

16 "See, it is I who created the
blacksmith[b]
who fans the coals into flame
and forges a weapon[c] fit for its
work.
And it is I who have created the
destroyer[d] to wreak havoc;
17 no weapon forged against you will
prevail,[e]
and you will refute[f] every tongue
that accuses you.
This is the heritage of the servants[g] of
the LORD,
and this is their vindication[h] from
me,"
declares the LORD.

Invitation to the Thirsty

55 "Come, all you who are thirsty,[i]
come to the waters;[j]
and you who have no money,
come, buy[k] and eat!
Come, buy wine and milk[l]
without money and without cost.[m]
2 Why spend money on what is not
bread,
and your labor on what does not
satisfy?[n]
Listen, listen to me, and eat what is
good,[o]
and you will delight in the richest[p] of
fare.

[a] *11* The meaning of the Hebrew for this word is uncertain.

54:16 [b] S Isa 44:12 [c] S Isa 10:5 [d] S Isa 13:5 **54:17** [e] S Isa 29:8 [f] S Isa 41:11 [g] Isa 56:6-8; 63:17; 65:8,9, 13-15; 66:14 [h] S Ps 17:2; Zec 1:20-21 **55:1** [i] S Pr 9:5; S Isa 35:7; Mt 5:6; Lk 6:21; Jn 4:14; 7:37 [j] Jer 2:13; Eze 47:1,12; Zec 14:8 [k] La 5:4; Mt 13:44; Rev 3:18 [l] S SS 5:1; 1Pe 2:2 [m] Hos 14:4; Mt 10:8; Rev 21:6; 22:17 **55:2** [n] Ps 22:26; Ecc 6:2; Isa 49:4; Jer 12:13; Hos 4:10; 8:7; Mic 6:14; Hag 1:6 [o] S Isa 1:19 [p] S Isa 30:23

---

face. See 1:15 and note. *everlasting kindness.* See v. 10; 55:3 and note. Cf. 45:17. *Redeemer.* See v. 5.

54:9 *never again cover the earth.* See Ge 9:11 and note. *not to be angry.* Cf. 12:1 and note. *never to rebuke you again.* As I did when I sent you into exile.

54:10 *mountains ... be removed.* Cf. 51:6; Ps 46:2; 102:26–27. *unfailing love ... covenant of peace.* A reference to God's covenantal commitments to Israel, embodied in the Abrahamic, Sinaitic, Davidic and new covenants (see chart, p. 23). Cf. Jer 33:20–21; for the language, see Nu 25:11–13.

54:11–12 A figurative description of restored Jerusalem, echoed in the description of the new Jerusalem in Rev 21:10,18–21.

54:11 *Afflicted city.* Jerusalem. See 51:21. *lashed by storms.* See 28:2 and note. *turquoise.* A bluish-green stone. It was used in Solomon's temple (1Ch 29:2). *lapis lazuli.* Cf. the "pavement made of lapis lazuli" (a blue stone) in Ex 24:10 (see also Eze 1:26; 10:1).

54:12 *battlements.* Parapets on the tops of walls. *walls.* Cf. 26:1.

54:13–14 *peace ... righteousness.* See 48:18 and note.

54:13 Quoted in part in Jn 6:45. *taught by the LORD.* Like the servant of the Lord in 50:4. Cf. Jer 31:34 and note.

54:14 *Tyranny ... Terror ... far removed.* Cf. 14:4; 33:18–19.

54:15 *surrender to you.* See v. 3.

54:16 *created the destroyer.* God raised up nations such as Assyria and Babylonia to punish Israel (see 10:5; 33:1 and notes).

54:17 *refute every tongue.* Just as no legitimate charges could be brought against the servant of 50:8–9. *servants of the LORD.* After ch. 53 the singular "servant" no longer occurs in Isaiah. The "servants" (see 63:17; 65:8–9,13–15; 66:14) are true believers—both Jew and Gentile (see 56:6–8)—who are faithful to the Lord. They are in a sense the "offspring" of the servant (53:10). See 49:19–20 and note.

55:1 The exiles are summoned to return and be restored. *thirsty.* Spiritual thirst is primarily in view (see 41:17; 44:3; Ps 42:1–2 and notes; 63:1). *waters.* Figurative for spiritual refreshment. Cf. Lady Wisdom's invitation in Pr 9:5 (see note there). Christ similarly invited people to drink the water of life (see Jn 4:14 and note; 7:37; cf. Rev 22:17). *no money.* In hard times even water had to be purchased (see La 5:4). *wine and milk.* Symbols of abundance, enjoyment and nourishment. *without money.* The death of the servant (53:5–9) paid for the free gift of life (see Ro 6:23 and note).

55:2 *what is not bread.* Perhaps the husks of pagan religious practices. Cf. Dt 8:3 and note. *richest of fare.* Great spiritual blessings are compared to a banquet (see 25:6 and note; Ps 22:26; 34:8; Jer 31:14).

3 Give ear and come to me;
listen,[q] that you may live.[r]
I will make an everlasting covenant[s]
with you,
my faithful love[t] promised to
David.[u]
4 See, I have made him a witness[v] to the
peoples,
a ruler and commander[w] of the
peoples.
5 Surely you will summon nations[x] you
know not,
and nations you do not know will
come running to you,[y]
because of the LORD your God,
the Holy One[z] of Israel,
for he has endowed you with
splendor."[a]
6 Seek[b] the LORD while he may be
found;[c]
call[d] on him while he is near.
7 Let the wicked forsake[e] their ways
and the unrighteous their thoughts.[f]
Let them turn[g] to the LORD, and he will
have mercy[h] on them,
and to our God, for he will freely
pardon.[i]
8 "For my thoughts[j] are not your
thoughts,
neither are your ways my ways,"[k]
declares the LORD.
9 "As the heavens are higher than the
earth,[l]
so are my ways higher than your
ways
and my thoughts than your
thoughts.[m]
10 As the rain[n] and the snow
come down from heaven,
and do not return to it
without watering the earth
and making it bud and flourish,[o]
so that it yields seed[p] for the sower
and bread for the eater,[q]
11 so is my word[r] that goes out from my
mouth:
It will not return to me empty,[s]
but will accomplish what I desire
and achieve the purpose[t] for which I
sent it.
12 You will go out in joy[u]
and be led forth in peace;[v]
the mountains and hills
will burst into song[w] before you,
and all the trees[x] of the field
will clap their hands.[y]
13 Instead of the thornbush will grow the
juniper,
and instead of briers[z] the myrtle[a] will
grow.
This will be for the LORD's renown,[b]
for an everlasting sign,
that will endure forever."

Salvation for Others

56 This is what the LORD says:

"Maintain justice[c]
and do what is right,[d]
for my salvation[e] is close at hand
and my righteousness[f] will soon be
revealed.
2 Blessed[g] is the one who does this—
the person who holds it fast,
who keeps the Sabbath[h] without
desecrating it,
and keeps their hands from doing
any evil."

55:3 [q] S Ps 78:1 [r] S Lev 18:5; S Jn 6:27; Ro 10:5 [s] S Ge 9:16; S Isa 54:10; S Heb 13:20 [t] S Isa 54:8 [u] Ac 13:34* **55:4** [v] Rev 1:5 [w] S 1Sa 13:14; S 2Ch 7:18; S Isa 32:1 **55:5** [x] S Isa 49:6 [y] S Isa 2:3 [z] S Isa 12:6; S 54:5 [a] S Isa 44:23 **55:6** [b] S Dt 4:29; S 2Ch 15:2; S Isa 9:13 [c] Ps 32:6; Isa 49:8; Ac 17:27; 2Co 6:1-2 [d] S Ps 50:15; Isa 65:24; Jer 29:12; 33:3 **55:7** [e] S 2Ch 7:14; S 30:9; Eze 18:27-28 [f] Isa 32:7; 59:7 [g] S Isa 44:22; S Jer 26:3; S Eze 18:32 [h] S Isa 54:10 [i] S 2Ch 6:21; Isa 1:18; 40:2 **55:8** [j] Php 2:5; 4:8 [k] Isa 53:6; Mic 4:12 **55:9** [l] S Job 11:8; Ps 103:11 [m] S Nu 23:19; S Isa 40:13-14 **55:10** [n] Isa 30:23 [o] S Lev 25:19; S Job 14:9; S Ps 67:6 [p] S Ge 47:23 [q] 2Co 9:10 **55:11** [r] S Dt 32:2; Jn 1:1 [s] Isa 40:8; 45:23; S Mt 5:18; Heb 4:12 [t] S Pr 19:21; S Isa 44:26; Eze 12:25 **55:12** [u] S Ps 98:4; S Isa 35:2 [v] Isa 54:10, 13 [w] S Ps 65:12-13; S 96:12-13 [x] S 1Ch 16:33 [y] Ps 98:8 **55:13** [z] S Nu 33:55; S Isa 5:6 [a] Isa 41:19 [b] S Ps 102:12; Isa 63:12; Jer 32:20; 33:9 **56:1** [c] S Ps 11:7; S Isa 1:17; S Jer 22:3 [d] S Isa 26:8 [e] S Ps 85:9 [f] Jer 23:6; Da 9:24 **56:2** [g] S Ps 119:2 [h] S Ex 20:8, 10

55:3 *everlasting covenant.* David had been promised an unending dynasty, one that would culminate in the Messiah (see 9:7; 54:10; 61:8; 2Sa 7:14–16 and notes). *faithful love.* Assuring the continuation of the nation. See 54:8 and note. Christ's resurrection was further proof of God's faithfulness to David (see Ac 13:34, which quotes from this verse).

55:4 *witness to the peoples.* A reference either to David, who exalted the Lord among the nations (see Ps 18:43,49–50 and notes), or to David's Son, the Messiah, who was (and is) a light to the nations (see 42:6; 49:6 and notes). *ruler ... of the peoples.* Similar titles are used of David (1Sa 13:14; 25:30) and the Messiah (Da 9:25).

55:5 *you will summon nations.* The attraction of nations to Zion and to the God of Israel is a major Biblical theme (see, e.g., 2:2–4; 45:14; Zec 8:22 and notes). *Holy One of Israel.* See 1:4; 41:14 and notes. *endowed ... with splendor.* See 4:2; 60:9. The nation will be restored physically and spiritually.

55:6 *Seek the LORD.* See Jer 29:13–14; Hos 3:5; Am 5:4,6,14 (contrast the hypocritical seeking of 58:2).

55:7 *wicked forsake.* See 1:16. *turn to the LORD ... freely pardon.* See 43:25; 44:22 and notes.

55:9 *my ways higher.* See Ps 145:3.

55:11 *my word.* Especially the promises of vv. 3,5,12. The word is viewed as a messenger also in 9:8; Ps 107:20 (see note there). Cf. Jn 1:1 and note. *achieve the purpose.* See 46:10–11 and note; cf. 40:8; Heb 4:12 and note.

55:12 *go out in joy.* The departure from Babylon provides the background (see 35:10; 52:9–12 and notes). *mountains ... will burst into song.* See 44:23 and note. *hands.* Branches. The language is figurative (cf. 1Ch 16:33; Ps 98:8 and note; 114:3–6).

55:13 *thornbush ... juniper ... briers ... myrtle.* The reverse of the desolation Isaiah had prophesied about earlier (5:6; 32:13). For the significance of trees, see 35:2; see also 41:19 and note. *LORD's renown.* Similar to God's fame in the exodus (see 63:12,14). *everlasting sign.* God's deliverance would never be forgotten. Cf. 19:20; 56:5.

56:1 *justice ... what is right.* See note on Ps 119:121. *salvation ... righteousness.* See 45:8; 46:13; 51:5 and notes.

56:2 *keeps the Sabbath.* See vv. 4,6. Just as the Sabbath had been instituted after the exodus from Egypt (see notes on Ex 20:8–10) as a sign of the Sinaitic covenant (see Ex 31:13–17 and notes), so God's new deliverance (55:12)

[3]Let no foreigner[i] who is bound to the
LORD say,
"The LORD will surely exclude me
from his people."[j]
And let no eunuch[k] complain,
"I am only a dry tree."

[4]For this is what the LORD says:

"To the eunuchs[l] who keep my
Sabbaths,
who choose what pleases me
and hold fast to my covenant[m]—
[5]to them I will give within my temple
and its walls[n]
a memorial[o] and a name
better than sons and daughters;
I will give them an everlasting name[p]
that will endure forever.[q]
[6]And foreigners[r] who bind themselves
to the LORD
to minister[s] to him,
to love the name[t] of the LORD,
and to be his servants,
all who keep the Sabbath[u] without
desecrating it
and who hold fast to my covenant—
[7]these I will bring to my holy
mountain[v]
and give them joy in my house of
prayer.
Their burnt offerings and sacrifices[w]
will be accepted on my altar;
for my house will be called
a house of prayer for all nations."[x][y]
[8]The Sovereign LORD declares—
he who gathers the exiles of Israel:
"I will gather[z] still others to them
besides those already gathered."

56:3 [i]S Ex 12:43; S 1Ki 8:41; S Isa 11:10; Zec 8:20-23 [j]Dt 23:3 [k]S Lev 21:20; Jer 38:7 *fn*; Ac 8:27 **56:4** [l]Jer 38:7 *fn* [m]S Ex 31:13 **56:5** [n]Isa 26:1; 60:18 [o]S Nu 32:42; 1Sa 15:12 [p]S Isa 43:7 [q]S Isa 48:19; 55:13 **56:6** [r]S Ex 12:43; S 1Ki 8:41 [s]S 1Ch 22:2; Isa 60:7, 10; 61:5 [t]Mal 1:11 [u]ver 2, 4 **56:7** [v]S Isa 2:2; Eze 20:40 [w]S Isa 19:21; Ro 12:1; Php 4:18; Heb 13:15 [x]Mt 21:13*; Lk 19:46* [y]Mk 11:17* **56:8** [z]S Dt 30:4; S Isa 1:9; S 11:12; 60:3-11; Eze 34:12; Jn 10:16 **56:9** [a]Isa 18:6; Jer 12:9; Eze 34:5, 8; 39:17-20 **56:10** [b]S Isa 52:8; 62:6; Jer 6:17; 31:6; Eze 3:17; 33:7 [c]Jer 2:8; 10:21; 14:13-14 [d]Na 3:18 **56:11** [e]Jer 23:1; Eze 34:2 [f]Isa 1:3 [g]S Isa 53:6; Hos 4:7-8 [h]Isa 57:17; Jer 6:13; 8:10;

God's Accusation Against the Wicked

[9]Come, all you beasts of the field,[a]
come and devour, all you beasts of
the forest!
[10]Israel's watchmen[b] are blind,
they all lack knowledge;[c]
they are all mute dogs,
they cannot bark;
they lie around and dream,
they love to sleep.[d]
[11]They are dogs with mighty appetites;
they never have enough.
They are shepherds[e] who lack
understanding;[f]
they all turn to their own way,[g]
they seek their own gain.[h]
[12]"Come," each one cries, "let me get wine![i]
Let us drink our fill of beer!
And tomorrow will be like today,
or even far better."[j]

57 The righteous perish,[k]
and no one takes it to heart;[l]
the devout are taken away,
and no one understands
that the righteous are taken away
to be spared from evil.[m]
[2]Those who walk uprightly[n]
enter into peace;
they find rest[o] as they lie in death.

[3]"But you—come here, you children of
a sorceress,[p]
you offspring of adulterers[q] and
prostitutes![r]

22:17; Eze 13:19; Mic 3:11 **56:12** [i]S Lev 10:9; S Pr 23:20; S Isa 22:13 [j]Ps 10:6; Lk 12:18-19 **57:1** [k]S Ps 12:1; Eze 21:3 [l]S Isa 42:25 [m]S 2Ki 22:20 **57:2** [n]Isa 26:7 [o]Da 12:13 **57:3** [p]S Ex 22:18; Mal 3:5 [q]ver 7-8; Mt 16:4; Jas 4:4 [r]Isa 1:21; Jer 2:20

afforded an opportunity to obey him fully, an obedience summed up in keeping the Sabbath (see 58:13; 66:23; Jer 17:21–27 and notes; Eze 20:20–21).

56:3 *foreigner.* See vv. 6–7. Members of certain nations who came to live among the Israelites had been excluded from worship, at least for several generations (see Ex 12:43; Dt 23:3,7–8). But the work of the servant of the Lord would change this (see 49:19–20; 54:17; 60:10 and notes). Cf. 14:1. *eunuch.* See v. 4; Mt 19:12 and note. Eunuchs were also excluded from the assembly of the Lord (see Dt 23:1 and note), but they could still be part of God's people (see Ac 8:27, 38–40).

56:4,6 *hold fast to my covenant.* Keeping the Sabbath was a sign of the Sinaitic covenant (see note on v. 2; see also Eze 20:12,20 and note on 20:12; cf. notes on Ge 9:12–13; 17:11).

56:5 *memorial.* Absalom built a "monument" (same Hebrew word) as a memorial since he had no surviving sons (2Sa 18:18). *name.* The Hebrew for this word is translated "renown" in 55:13. The Hebrew for "a memorial and a name" (*yad vashem*) was chosen from v. 5 as the name of the main Holocaust monument in Jerusalem in modern Israel. *that will endure forever.* An idiom sometimes referring to the preserving of a name through one's descendants.

56:6 *minister.* Cf. 60:7,10.

56:7 *my holy mountain.* See 2:2–4 and note. *offerings … accepted on my altar.* Cf. 60:7; contrast 1:11–13. *my house … for all nations.* Quoted by Jesus in Mk 11:17 and parallels. *house of prayer for all nations.* Solomon may have anticipated this in his prayer of dedication for the temple (see 1Ki 8:41–42 and notes).

56:8 *gathers the exiles.* See 11:11–12 and notes. *gather still others.* Including Gentiles (see v. 3 and note; cf. Jn 10:16 and note).

56:9—59:15 Many verses in these sections could apply to conditions before or during the Babylonian exile.

56:9 *beasts.* Foreign invaders (see 18:6 and note).

56:10 *watchmen.* The prophets (see note on Eze 3:17; cf. note on Isa 52:8). *blind … love to sleep.* Cf. 29:9–10. *mute dogs.* Watchdogs who guarded the sheep (cf. Job 30:1).

56:11 *mighty appetites.* They devour the sheep. See Eze 34:3. *shepherds.* Rulers may be included. See Eze 34:2–5 and notes. *all turn to their own way.* See 53:6.

56:12 *wine … beer.* Cf. the behavior of priests and prophets in 28:7. *tomorrow will be … far better.* Cf. the words of the rich fool in Lk 12:19.

57:1 *spared from evil.* Huldah explained that righteous King Josiah would die before disaster struck (2Ki 22:19–20).

57:2 *peace.* Contrast v. 21. *find rest.* Cf. Paul's words in Php 1:21,23.

57:3 *sorceress.* A woman who practices magic or consults evil spirits (see 3:2–3 and note; 47:12; Dt 18:10). *adulterers and prostitutes.* Spiritual adultery (idolatry) is in view (see vv. 5–8; see also Ex 34:15 and note).

4 Who are you mocking?
At whom do you sneer
and stick out your tongue?
Are you not a brood of rebels,[s]
the offspring of liars?
5 You burn with lust among the oaks[t]
and under every spreading tree;[u]
you sacrifice your children[v] in the ravines
and under the overhanging crags.
6 The idols[w] among the smooth stones of the ravines are your portion;
indeed, they are your lot.
Yes, to them you have poured out drink offerings[x]
and offered grain offerings.
In view of all this, should I relent?[y]
7 You have made your bed on a high and lofty hill;[z]
there you went up to offer your sacrifices.[a]
8 Behind your doors and your doorposts
you have put your pagan symbols.
Forsaking me, you uncovered your bed,
you climbed into it and opened it wide;
you made a pact with those whose beds you love,[b]
and you looked with lust on their naked bodies.[c]
9 You went to Molek[a][d] with olive oil
and increased your perfumes.[e]
You sent your ambassadors[b][f] far away;
you descended to the very realm of the dead![g]
10 You wearied[h] yourself by such going about,
but you would not say, 'It is hopeless.'[i]
You found renewal of your strength,[j]
and so you did not faint.

11 "Whom have you so dreaded and feared[k]
that you have not been true to me,
and have neither remembered[l] me
nor taken this to heart?[m]
Is it not because I have long been silent[n]
that you do not fear me?
12 I will expose your righteousness and your works,[o]
and they will not benefit you.
13 When you cry out[p] for help,
let your collection of idols save[q] you!
The wind will carry all of them off,
a mere breath will blow[r] them away.
But whoever takes refuge[s] in me
will inherit the land[t]
and possess my holy mountain."[u]

Comfort for the Contrite

14 And it will be said:

"Build up, build up, prepare the road![v]
Remove the obstacles out of the way of my people."[w]
15 For this is what the high and exalted[x] One says—
he who lives forever,[y] whose name is holy:
"I live in a high[z] and holy place,
but also with the one who is contrite[a] and lowly in spirit,[b]
to revive the spirit of the lowly
and to revive the heart of the contrite.[c]
16 I will not accuse[d] them forever,
nor will I always be angry,[e]
for then they would faint away because of me—
the very people[f] I have created.
17 I was enraged by their sinful greed;[g]
I punished them, and hid[h] my face in anger,
yet they kept on in their willful ways.[i]

[a] 9 Or *to the king* [b] 9 Or *idols*

57:4 [s] S Isa 1:2 **57:5** [t] S Isa 1:29 [u] S Dt 12:2; 2Ki 16:4 [v] S Lev 18:21; S Dt 18:10; Ps 106:37-38; Eze 16:20 **57:6** [w] S 2Ki 17:10; Jer 3:9; Hab 2:19 [x] Jer 7:18; 19:13; 44:18 [y] Jer 5:9, 29; 9:9 **57:7** [z] Jer 3:6; Eze 6:3; 16:16; 20:29 [a] Isa 65:7; Jer 13:27; Eze 6:13; 20:27-28 **57:8** [b] Eze 16:26; 23:7 [c] Eze 16:15, 36; 23:18 **57:9** [d] S Lev 18:21; S 1Ki 11:5 [e] S SS 4:10 [f] Eze 23:16,40 [g] S Isa 8:19 **57:10** [h] S Isa 47:13 [i] Jer 2:25; 18:12; Mal 3:14 [j] S 1Sa 2:4 **57:11** [k] S 2Ki 1:15; Pr 29:25; Isa 7:2 [l] S Isa 17:10; Jer 2:32; 3:21; 13:25; 18:15; Eze 22:12 [m] S Isa 42:23 [n] S Est 4:14; S Ps 50:21; S 83:1 **57:12** [o] Isa 29:15; 58:1; 59:6,12; 65:7; 66:18; Eze 16:2; Mic 3:2-4,8 **57:13** [p] Jer 22:20; 30:15 [q] S Jdg 10:14 [r] Isa 40:7,24 [s] S Ps 118:8 [t] S Ps 37:9 [u] Isa 2:2-3; 56:7; 65:9-11 **57:14** [v] S Isa 11:16 [w] Isa 62:10; Jer 18:15 **57:15** [x] S Isa 52:13 [y] S Dt 33:27; S Ps 90:2 [z] S Job 16:19 [a] Ps 147:3 [b] Ps 34:18; 51:17; Isa 66:2; Mic 6:8; Mt 5:3 [c] S 2Ki 22:19; S Job 5:18; S Mt 23:12 **57:16** [d] S Ps 50:21; Isa 3:13-14 [e] S Ps 103:9; S Isa 54:9 [f] S Ge 2:7; Zec 12:1 **57:17** [g] S Isa 56:11; Jer 8:10 [h] S Isa 1:15 [i] Isa 1:4; S 30:15; S 53:6; 66:3

57:4 *mocking … sneer.* The people mocked Isaiah in 28:9,14. *brood of rebels.* See 1:4; 46:8 and note.
57:5 *oaks.* Sacred trees (see 1:29 and note). *spreading tree.* Associated with high places of pagan worship in 1Ki 14:23. Cf. Jer 2:20 and note; 3:13. *sacrifice your children.* Often associated with the worship of Molek (cf. v. 9; see note on 30:33) or Baal (Jer 19:5; see notes on Jer 7:31–32). Ps 106:37–38 says that children were sacrificed to idols and demons.
57:6 *ravines.* Possibly the Hinnom Valley (see Jer 7:31 and note). *drink offerings.* These pagan libations were especially popular.
57:7 *high and lofty hill.* There were many such "high places" (see Eze 6:3 and note; 16:16) or "mountain shrines" (Eze 22:9) in Canaan.
57:8 *those … you love.* Pagan deities or idols.
57:9 *Molek.* The main god of the Ammonites (see v. 5; 1Ki 11:5 and notes). *olive oil.* Used as an ointment for perfume. See SS 4:10, where the Hebrew word for "oil" is translated "perfume." *to the … realm of the dead.* Cf. 8:19.
57:10 *It is hopeless.* Ironically, the people said that turning away from their own plans or from foreign gods was hopeless. *renewal of your strength.* Cf. 40:31 and note.
57:11 *so dreaded and feared.* They feared mere mortals (see 51:12). *neither remembered me.* See 51:13. *long been silent.* God had not acted in judgment (see 42:14 and note).
57:12 *righteousness.* See 58:2–3; 64:6.
57:13 *collection of idols save you.* See 44:17 and note. *wind will carry … breath will blow.* Idols are no stronger than their worshipers. *takes refuge in me.* See 25:4. *inherit the land.* See 49:8 and note. *my holy mountain.* See 2:2–4 and note.
57:14 *Build up, build up.* See note on 40:1. *prepare the road.* See 40:3 and note.
57:15 *high and exalted One.* See 6:1; 52:13 and notes; cf. 33:5. *contrite.* Or "crushed" (see 53:5).
57:16 *not accuse them forever.* He had taken Israel to court repeatedly (see 3:13–14). *nor … be angry.* See 54:9 and note; Jer 3:12.
57:17 *hid my face in anger.* See 54:8; see also 1:15 and note.

[18]I have seen their ways, but I will heal[j] them;
I will guide[k] them and restore comfort[l] to Israel's mourners,
[19] creating praise on their lips.[m]
Peace, peace,[n] to those far and near,"[o]
says the LORD. "And I will heal them."
[20]But the wicked[p] are like the tossing sea,[q]
which cannot rest,
whose waves cast up mire[r] and mud.
[21]"There is no peace,"[s] says my God, "for the wicked."[t]

True Fasting

58 "Shout it aloud,[u] do not hold back.
Raise your voice like a trumpet.[v]
Declare to my people their rebellion[w]
and to the descendants of Jacob their sins.[x]
[2]For day after day they seek[y] me out;
they seem eager to know my ways,
as if they were a nation that does what is right
and has not forsaken[z] the commands of its God.
They ask me for just decisions
and seem eager for God to come near[a] them.
[3]'Why have we fasted,'[b] they say,
'and you have not seen it?
Why have we humbled[c] ourselves,
and you have not noticed?'[d]

"Yet on the day of your fasting, you do as you please[e]
and exploit all your workers.
[4]Your fasting ends in quarreling and strife,[f]
and in striking each other with wicked fists.
You cannot fast as you do today
and expect your voice to be heard[g] on high.
[5]Is this the kind of fast[h] I have chosen,
only a day for people to humble[i] themselves?
Is it only for bowing one's head like a reed[j]
and for lying in sackcloth and ashes?[k]
Is that what you call a fast,
a day acceptable to the LORD?

[6]"Is not this the kind of fasting[l] I have chosen:
to loose the chains of injustice[m]
and untie the cords of the yoke,
to set the oppressed[n] free
and break every yoke?[o]
[7]Is it not to share your food with the hungry[p]
and to provide the poor wanderer with shelter[q]—
when you see the naked, to clothe[r] them,
and not to turn away from your own flesh and blood?[s]
[8]Then your light will break forth like the dawn,[t]
and your healing[u] will quickly appear;
then your righteousness[a][v] will go before you,
and the glory of the LORD will be your rear guard.[w]

57:18 [j]S Dt 32:39; S 2Ch 7:14; S Isa 30:26 [k]S Ps 48:14; S Isa 42:16; S 48:17 [l]Isa 49:13; 61:1-3 **57:19** [m]Isa 6:7; 51:16; 59:21; Heb 13:15 [n]S Isa 2:4; 26:3, 12; 32:17; S Lk 2:14 [o]Ac 2:39 **57:20** [p]Job 18:5-21 [q]S Ge 49:4; Eph 4:14; Jude 1:13 [r]Ps 69:14 **57:21** [s]S Isa 26:3; 59:8; Eze 13:16 [t]S Isa 48:22 **58:1** [u]Isa 40:6 [v]S Ex 20:18 [w]S Isa 24:20; S 48:8 [x]S Isa 57:12; Eze 3:17 **58:2** [y]S Isa 48:1; Titus 1:16; Jas 4:8 [z]S Dt 32:15; S Ps 119:87 [a]Isa 29:13 **58:3** [b]S Lev 16:29 [c]S Ex 10:3; S 2Ch 6:37; Jer 44:10 [d]Mal 3:14 [e]Isa 22:13; Zec 7:5-6 **58:4** [f]1Ki 21:9-13; Isa 59:6; Jer 6:7; Eze 7:11; Mal 2:16 [g]S 1Sa 8:18; Isa 59:2; La 3:44; Eze 8:18; Mic 3:4 **58:5** [h]Zec 7:5 [i]1Ki 21:27; Mt 6:16 [j]S Isa 36:6 [k]S Job 2:8 **58:6** [l]Joel 2:12-14 [m]Ne 5:10-11 [n]S Dt 14:29; Isa 61:1; Jer 34:9; Am 4:1; S Lk 4:19 [o]S Isa 9:4 **58:7** [p]S Job 22:7; Eze 18:16; Lk 3:11 [q]Isa 16:4; Heb 13:2 [r]Job 31:19-20; S Mt 25:36 [s]S Ge 29:14; Lk 10:31-32 **58:8** [t]S Job 11:17; S Isa 9:2 [u]S Isa 1:5; S 30:26 [v]S Isa 26:2 [w]S Ex 14:19

[a] 8 Or *your righteous One*

57:18 *heal them.* See v. 19; 6:10; 30:26; Jer 3:22. God will forgive and restore his people. *guide.* Cf. 40:11; 42:16; 49:10. *restore comfort.* See 49:13 and note. *mourners.* Those mourning the judgment on Jerusalem (see 66:10).
57:19 *Peace, peace.* Contrast Jer 6:13–14 (see note on 6:14). *those far.* Either Gentiles or exiled Jews. Paul probably had this verse in mind in Eph 2:17.
57:20 *like the tossing sea.* See Jer 49:23. *cannot rest.* Contrast v. 2.
57:21 Almost identical to 48:22 (see note there; see also 39:8 and note).
58:1 *voice like a trumpet.* God's powerful voice is compared to a trumpet blast at Mount Sinai (see Ex 19:19; 20:18–19). *rebellion.* See 1:2 and note. *sins.* See 1:4; 59:12–13.
58:2 *seek me out.* See 55:6 and note. Cf. the frequent sacrifices of 1:11. *eager for God to come near.* The same hypocrisy is mentioned in 29:13 (see note there).
58:3 *fasted ... fasting.* See v. 6; a time of self-denial, self-humbling and repentance for sin. After the fall of Jerusalem, the number of days for fasting increased (see Lev 16:29 and NIV text note; see also Zec 8:19 and note). *humbled ourselves.* Cf. 2Ch 7:14; 1Ki 21:29. *you have not noticed.* The same attitude is seen in Mal 3:14 (see note there; cf. Lk 18:12). *exploit all your workers.* See 3:14–15; 10:2.
58:4 *to be heard on high.* Such hypocritical religious activity is actually a hindrance to prayer (see 1:11–15; 59:2 and notes).
58:5 *fast ... humble themselves.* See Mt 6:16–18. *like a reed.* A sign of weakness and humility (see 42:3 and note). *sackcloth and ashes ... fast.* See notes on Ge 37:34; Ezr 8:23; 10:6; Joel 1:13–14; Jnh 3:5–6; Rev 11:3. *acceptable.* A term often applied to sacrifices (see 56:7; 60:7; Lev 1:3; cf. Ro 12:1).
58:6 *chains of injustice.* During the siege of Jerusalem, Hebrew slaves were rightly released—only to be reclaimed by their masters (see Jer 34:8–11 and notes). *yoke.* See v. 9; 9:4; 10:27, where the yoke imposed by Assyria is mentioned. *oppressed.* See 1:17.
58:7 *share your food ... provide ... shelter ... clothe.* The outward evidence of genuine righteousness. See Job 31:17–20; Eze 18:7,16 and Jesus' identification with the hungry and naked in Mt 25:34–40 (see notes there). *flesh and blood.* Probably refers to close relatives (Ge 37:27), but see 2Sa 5:1 and note.
58:8 *light.* The joy, prosperity and salvation brought by the Lord (see 9:2; 60:1–3; Ps 27:1 and note). *healing.* See 57:18 and note. *go before you ... be your rear guard.* See 52:12 and note. The Lord will protect them and guide them. *glory of the*

9 Then you will call,[x] and the LORD will answer;[y]
you will cry for help, and he will say: Here am I.

"If you do away with the yoke of oppression,
with the pointing finger[z] and malicious talk,[a]
10 and if you spend yourselves in behalf of the hungry
and satisfy the needs of the oppressed,[b]
then your light[c] will rise in the darkness,
and your night will become like the noonday.[d]
11 The LORD will guide[e] you always;
he will satisfy your needs[f] in a sun-scorched land[g]
and will strengthen[h] your frame.
You will be like a well-watered garden,[i]
like a spring[j] whose waters never fail.
12 Your people will rebuild the ancient ruins[k]
and will raise up the age-old foundations;[l]
you will be called Repairer of Broken Walls,[m]
Restorer of Streets with Dwellings.

13 "If you keep your feet from breaking the Sabbath[n]
and from doing as you please on my holy day,
if you call the Sabbath a delight[o]
and the LORD's holy day honorable,
and if you honor it by not going your own way
and not doing as you please or speaking idle words,[p]
14 then you will find your joy[q] in the LORD,
and I will cause you to ride in triumph on the heights[r] of the land
and to feast on the inheritance[s] of your father Jacob."
For the mouth of the LORD has spoken.[t]

58:9 [x]S Ps 50:15 [y]S Job 8:6; S Isa 30:19; Da 9:20; S Zec 10:6 [z]S Pr 6:13 [a]Ps 12:2; Isa 59:13 **58:10** [b]Dt 15:7-8 [c]S Isa 42:16 [d]S Job 11:17 **58:11** [e]S Ps 48:14; S Isa 42:16; S 48:17 [f]S Ps 104:28; S 107:9 [g]S Ps 68:6 [h]S Ps 72:16 [i]S SS 4:15 [j]S Isa 35:7; Jn 4:14 **58:12** [k]S Isa 49:8 [l]S Isa 44:28 [m]Ne 2:17 **58:13** [n]S Ex 20:8 [o]Ps 37:4; 42:4; 84:2,10 [p]Isa 59:3 **58:14** [q]S Job 22:26 [r]S Dt 32:13 [s]Ps 105:10-11 [t]S Isa 1:20 **59:1** [u]S Isa 41:20 [v]S Isa 50:2 [w]Isa 30:19; 58:9; 65:24 **59:2** [x]Jer 5:25; Eze 39:23 [y]S Ps 18:41; S Isa 58:4; S Jer 11:11; S Jn 9:31 **59:3** [z]S 2Ki 21:16; S Isa 1:15; S Eze 22:9 [a]Ps 7:3 [b]S Isa 3:8 **59:4** [c]S Isa 5:23 [d]S Job 15:31 [e]S Isa 44:20 [f]S Job 4:8; S Isa 29:20; Jas 1:15

Sin, Confession and Redemption

59 Surely the arm[u] of the LORD is not too short[v] to save,
nor his ear too dull to hear.[w]
2 But your iniquities have separated[x] you from your God;
your sins have hidden his face from you,
so that he will not hear.[y]
3 For your hands are stained with blood,[z]
your fingers with guilt.[a]
Your lips have spoken falsely,[b]
and your tongue mutters wicked things.
4 No one calls for justice;[c]
no one pleads a case with integrity.
They rely[d] on empty arguments, they utter lies;[e]
they conceive trouble and give birth to evil.[f]
5 They hatch the eggs of vipers[g]
and spin a spider's web.[h]
Whoever eats their eggs will die,
and when one is broken, an adder is hatched.
6 Their cobwebs are useless for clothing;
they cannot cover themselves with what they make.[i]
Their deeds are evil deeds,
and acts of violence[j] are in their hands.

59:5 [g]S Isa 11:8; Mt 3:7 [h]S Job 8:14 **59:6** [i]Isa 28:20 [j]S Ps 55:9; S Pr 4:17; S Isa 58:4

LORD. Probably a reference to the pillar of cloud and fire in the wilderness (see 4:5–6; Ex 13:21; 14:20 and notes).

58:9 *LORD will answer.* See 30:19 and note. *Here am I.* See 65:1. *pointing finger.* A gesture of either contempt or accusation (see note on Pr 6:12–14). *malicious talk.* See Pr 2:12; 6:12,17,19 and notes.

58:10 *hungry … oppressed.* See vv. 6–7 and notes. *light.* See v. 8 and note.

58:11 *guide you.* See 57:18 and note. *needs.* Both material and spiritual (see note on 32:2). *sun-scorched land.* See 35:7; 49:10. *well-watered garden.* In 1:30 Jerusalem was a garden without water. *spring … never fail.* Contrast Jer 15:18 (see note there). Cf. the "living water" Jesus gives in Jn 4:10,14 (see notes there).

58:12 *ancient ruins … age-old foundations.* See 44:26,28 and notes; 61:4; Eze 36:10; Am 9:11,13–15 and notes. *Repairer of Broken Walls.* Cf. note on Ezr 4:12; cf. also the work of Nehemiah in Ne 2:17 (see note there).

58:13 *Sabbath.* See 56:2 and note. *my holy day.* A day set apart to God (see Ex 3:5 and note). *delight.* They were also to delight themselves in the Lord (Ps 37:4) and in his law (see Ps 1:2 and note). *going your own way.* Perhaps to engage in business (see Am 8:5).

58:14 *joy in the LORD.* See 61:10. *ride in triumph on the heights.* Thus controlling the land. See 33:16 and note; see also Hab 3:19. *feast on the inheritance.* Enjoying plentiful food in the promised land (see Dt 32:13–14). *mouth … has spoken.* See 40:5 and note.

59:1 *arm … too short.* See 51:9 and note. *too dull to hear.* See 30:19 and note.

59:2 *hidden his face … he will not hear.* See 1:15 and note.

59:3–4 *spoken falsely … utter lies.* See v. 13; 28:15; Hos 4:2 and note.

59:3 *stained with blood.* See v. 7; 1:15,21; Eze 7:23; see also notes on Eze 18:4,21.

59:4 *calls for justice … pleads a case.* The poor and helpless could not receive fair trials (see v. 14; 1:17–23; 5:7,23). *they conceive … evil.* Identical to Job 15:35 (see note there). Cf. Isa 33:11; Ps 7:14.

59:5 *spider's web.* Verse 6 and Job 8:14–15 stress how fragile it is.

59:6 *acts of violence.* See v. 3; Jer 6:7; Eze 7:11.

7 Their feet rush into sin;
they are swift to shed innocent blood.[k]
They pursue evil schemes;[l]
acts of violence mark their ways.[m]
8 The way of peace they do not know;[n]
there is no justice in their paths.
They have turned them into crooked roads;[o]
no one who walks along them will know peace.[p]

9 So justice is far from us,
and righteousness does not reach us.
We look for light, but all is darkness;[q]
for brightness, but we walk in deep shadows.
10 Like the blind[r] we grope along the wall,
feeling our way like people without eyes.
At midday we stumble[s] as if it were twilight;
among the strong, we are like the dead.[t]
11 We all growl like bears;
we moan mournfully like doves.[u]
We look for justice, but find none;
for deliverance, but it is far away.

12 For our offenses[v] are many in your sight,
and our sins testify[w] against us.
Our offenses are ever with us,
and we acknowledge our iniquities:[x]
13 rebellion[y] and treachery against the LORD,
turning our backs[z] on our God,
inciting revolt and oppression,[a]
uttering lies[b] our hearts have conceived.
14 So justice[c] is driven back,
and righteousness[d] stands at a distance;
truth[e] has stumbled in the streets,
honesty cannot enter.
15 Truth[f] is nowhere to be found,
and whoever shuns evil becomes a prey.

The LORD looked and was displeased
that there was no justice.[g]
16 He saw that there was no one,[h]
he was appalled that there was no one to intervene;[i]
so his own arm achieved salvation[j] for him,
and his own righteousness[k] sustained him.
17 He put on righteousness as his breastplate,[l]
and the helmet[m] of salvation on his head;
he put on the garments[n] of vengeance[o]
and wrapped himself in zeal[p] as in a cloak.
18 According to what they have done,
so will he repay[q]
wrath to his enemies
and retribution to his foes;
he will repay the islands[r] their due.
19 From the west,[s] people will fear the name of the LORD,
and from the rising of the sun,[t] they will revere his glory.[u]

59:7 [k]S 2Ki 21:16; S Pr 6:17; S Mic 3:10 [l]S Pr 24:2; S Isa 26:10; Mk 7:21-22 [m]Ro 3:15-17* **59:8** [n]Ro 3:15-17* [o]S Jdg 5:6 [p]S Isa 57:21; Lk 1:79 **59:9** [q]S Job 19:8; S Ps 107:14; S Isa 5:30; S 8:20; S Lk 1:79 **59:10** [r]Dt 28:29; S Isa 6:9-10; 56:10; La 4:14; Zep 1:17 [s]S Job 3:23; S Isa 8:15; Jn 11:9-10 [t]La 3:6 **59:11** [u]S Ge 8:8; Ps 74:19; Isa 38:14; Jer 48:28; Eze 7:16; Na 2:7 **59:12** [v]S Ezr 9:6; S Isa 57:12 [w]S Ge 4:7; S Isa 3:9; S Jer 2:19 [x]Ps 51:3 **59:13** [y]Isa 46:8; 48:8 [z]S Nu 11:20; S Pr 30:9; Mt 10:33; Titus 1:16 [a]S Ps 12:5; S Isa 5:7 [b]S Isa 3:8; S 44:20; Mk 7:21-22 **59:14** [c]S Isa 29:21 [d]S Isa 1:21 [e]S Isa 48:1; S Jer 33:16 **59:15** [f]Jer 7:28; 9:5; Da 8:12 [g]S Isa 5:7 **59:16** [h]S Isa 41:28 [i]S Isa 53:12 [j]S Isa 51:5 [k]Isa 45:8, 13; 46:13 **59:17** [l]Eph 6:14; 1Th 5:8 [m]Eph 6:17; 1Th 5:8 [n]S Job 27:6; Isa 63:3 [o]S Isa 1:24 [p]S Isa 9:7; Eze 5:13 **59:18** [q]S Lev 26:28; S Nu 10:35; S Isa 34:8; S Mt 16:27 [r]Isa 11:11; 41:5 **59:19** [s]S Isa 49:12; S Mt 8:11 [t]S Ps 113:3 [u]Ps 97:6; S Isa 24:15; 35:2; 40:5; 52:10; 66:18

59:7–8 Quoted in part in Ro 3:15–17 by Paul to show the universality of sin.
59:7 *Their feet rush ... to shed innocent blood.* This sentence appears in Pr 1:16 (see note there). *evil schemes.* God's thoughts are different (see 55:7–9). *acts of violence.* Contrast 60:18.
59:8 *way of peace.* Cf. 26:3,12; 57:20–21; Lk 1:79. *crooked roads.* Unsafe (see Jdg 5:6 and note).
59:9 *justice ... righteousness.* Personified here and in v. 14. See v. 4 and note; 1:21. *us ... We.* The prophet includes himself with the people. *We look for ... but.* See v. 11; cf. note on 5:2. *darkness ... deep shadows.* Similar language describes conditions when Assyria invaded Israel (see 5:30; 8:21–22; 9:1–2). Contrast 58:8.
59:10 *Like the blind we grope ... At midday.* The fulfillment of the curse for disobedience in Dt 28:29. Cf. Job 5:14. *strong.* Perhaps enemies or oppressors.
59:11 *growl like bears.* Impatient and frustrated.
59:12 *offenses ... sins ... iniquities.* In Hebrew the three most common OT words for evil thoughts and deeds (see Ps 32:5 and note). *offenses are many.* See 58:1. *we acknowledge our iniquities.* Like Ezra (9:6–7), Isaiah confesses the sins of the nation.
59:13 *rebellion and treachery.* See 46:8; 48:8 and notes. *turning our backs.* See 1:4. *oppression.* See 30:12. *lies.* See vv. 3–4.
59:14 *justice ... truth.* Cf. the personification of wisdom in Pr 8:1—9:12 (see note on 8:1–36). *righteousness stands at a distance.* Cf. v. 9; contrast 46:13 (see note there).
59:15 *becomes a prey.* See 32:7.
59:16 *there was no one.* To help (see 63:5, a parallel to the whole verse). Cf. Eze 22:30 and note. *appalled.* Cf. the reaction to the servant in 52:14. *intervene.* Cf. the intercession of the servant in 53:12 (see note there). *his own arm achieved salvation.* See 51:9; 52:10. For the meaning of salvation, see 43:3; 49:8; 52:7 and notes. *righteousness.* For the relationship between righteousness and salvation, see 45:8; 46:13 and notes.
59:17 *put on ... wrapped himself in.* See note on Ps 109:29. *righteousness as his breastplate.* The Lord's armor is compared to the believer's armor in the battle against Satan in Eph 6:14 (see note there; see also photo, p. 1205). *garments of vengeance.* Cf. the blood-spattered garments of 63:1–3. God's vengeance is described also in 34:8 (see note there); 63:4. It is part of the day of the Lord (see 34:2 and note). *zeal.* God's jealous love (see 9:7 and note; 37:32; 42:13).
59:18 *enemies ... foes.* God will judge the nations, but he must also punish wicked Israelites (see 65:6–7; 66:6; Jer 25:29). Only the remnant will be blessed (see v. 20; see also 1:9 and note). *islands.* See note on 11:11.
59:19 *From the west ... rising of the sun.* All nations will see God's saving work in behalf of his people (see 40:5; 45:6;

For he will come like a pent-up flood
that the breath[v] of the LORD drives
along.[a]
20 "The Redeemer[w] will come to Zion,[x]
to those in Jacob who repent of their
sins,"[y]
declares the LORD.

21 "As for me, this is my covenant[z] with
them," says the LORD. "My Spirit,[a] who is
on you, will not depart from you,[b] and my
words that I have put in your mouth[c] will
always be on your lips, on the lips of your
children and on the lips of their descendants — from this time on and forever,"
says the LORD.

The Glory of Zion

60 "Arise,[d] shine, for your light[e] has
come,
and the glory[f] of the LORD rises upon
you.
2 See, darkness[g] covers the earth
and thick darkness[h] is over the
peoples,
but the LORD rises upon you
and his glory appears over you.
3 Nations[i] will come to your light,[j]
and kings[k] to the brightness of your
dawn.

4 "Lift up your eyes and look about you:
All assemble[l] and come to you;
your sons come from afar,[m]
and your daughters[n] are carried on
the hip.[o]
5 Then you will look and be radiant,[p]
your heart will throb and swell with
joy;[q]
the wealth[r] on the seas will be brought
to you,
to you the riches of the nations will
come.
6 Herds of camels[s] will cover your land,
young camels of Midian[t] and
Ephah.[u]
And all from Sheba[v] will come,
bearing gold and incense[w]
and proclaiming the praise[x] of the
LORD.

Assyrian soldier with scaled breastplate and helmet. "He put on righteousness as his breastplate, and the helmet of salvation on his head" (Isa 59:17).

Z. Radovan/www.BibleLandPictures.com

59:19 [v]S Isa 11:4 **59:20** [w]S Job 19:25; Isa 60:16; 63:16 [x]S Isa 52:8; S Joel 3:21 [y]S Job 22:23; S Isa 1:27; S Jer 35:15; Ac 2:38-39; Ro 11:26-27* **59:21** [z]S Ge 9:16; S Dt 29:14; S Isa 42:6 [a]S Isa 11:2; S 44:3 [b]S Jos 1:8 [c]S Ex 4:15 **60:1** [d]Isa 52:2 [e]S Ps 36:9; S 118:27; S Isa 9:2; Jn 8:12; Eph 5:14 [f]S Ex 16:7; S Isa 4:5; Rev 21:11 **60:2** [g]S 1Sa 2:9; S Ps 82:5; S 107:14; S Isa 8:20 [h]Jer 13:16; Col 1:13 **60:3** [i]S Isa 44:5; S 45:14; Mt 2:1-11; Rev 21:24 [j]S Isa 9:2; 42:6 [k]S Isa 49:23 **60:4** [l]S Isa 11:12 [m]S Isa 2:3; Jer 30:10 [n]S Isa 43:6 [o]Isa 49:20-22 **60:5** [p]S Ex 34:29 [q]Isa 35:2; 65:13; 66:14; Zec 10:7 [r]S Dt 33:19; S Jdg 3:15; Rev 21:26 **60:6** [s]S Jdg 6:5 [t]S Ge 25:2 [u]Ge 25:4 [v]S Ge 10:7, 28 [w]Isa 43:23; Jer 6:20; Mt 2:11 [x]S 1Ki 5:7; S Isa 42:10

[a] 19 Or *When enemies come in like a flood, / the Spirit of the LORD will put them to flight*

52:10 and notes). *name.* See 30:27 and note. *pent-up flood.* The coming of the Lord will be irresistible, like a "rushing torrent" (30:28) that overwhelms the enemy.

59:20 *Redeemer.* See 41:14 and note. *come to Zion.* In the return from exile, but more fully in the person of Christ (see Ro 11:26–27 and notes). See 35:4; 40:9; 52:7 and notes. Cf. Zec 8:3. *those ... who repent.* See 1:27–28 and note; 30:15; 31:6; see also Eze 18:30–32 and notes.

59:21 *covenant.* The description best fits the "new covenant" (see 42:6; Jer 31:31–34 and notes). *My Spirit.* See 11:2; 32:15; Eze 36:27; Jn 16:13 and notes. *you ... your ... your ... your.* In Hebrew the pronouns are singular but are probably intended in a collective sense — the citizens of Zion. *my words ... in your mouth.* Then Israel will truly be God's people (see 51:16; Jer 31:33 and notes). *always be on your lips.* See Jos 1:8.

60:1–2 *glory.* Probably an allusion to the pillar of cloud, but announcing a new manifestation of God's redeeming glory (see 58:8 and note). See also 35:2 and note.

60:1 *light.* See 58:8 and note. Here the Lord himself is viewed as the light (see vv. 19–20).

60:2 *darkness.* A symbol of gloom, oppression, sin and judgment (see 8:22; 9:2; 59:9).

60:3 *Nations will come.* See vv. 5,10–12 and notes. This theme was first mentioned in 2:2–4 (see note there). *light.* See 42:6; 49:6 and notes.

60:4 The first two lines are almost identical to the beginning of 49:18, the last two to the end of 49:22 (see note there). The setting there was the return from exile, but here much broader implications are involved. *afar.* See v. 9; 49:12 and note.

60:5 *wealth on the seas.* Jerusalem will be enriched by the nations (see v. 11; 61:6; 66:12; see also 18:7; 23:18; 45:14 and notes). The contribution of King Darius to Zerubbabel's temple may be a partial fulfillment (see Ezr 6:8–9 and notes). Some interpret this verse as referring to conditions during the future phase of the Messianic kingdom, while others apply it to the influx of Gentiles into the church (see note on 2:2–4). Still others believe that all three of these may be in view (progressive fulfillment). See Rev 21:26 (the new Jerusalem); see also Hag 2:7; Zec 14:14 and notes.

60:6 *camels will cover your land.* As caravans bringing goods. Ironically it was on camels that the Midianites once devastated Israel (see 9:4; Jdg 6:1–6 and notes). *Midian.* Abraham's son through Keturah (Ge 25:2). The Midianites roamed the deserts of Transjordan. *Ephah.* A son of Midian

7 All Kedar's[y] flocks will be gathered to
you,
the rams of Nebaioth will serve you;
they will be accepted as offerings[z] on
my altar,[a]
and I will adorn my glorious temple.[b]

8 "Who are these[c] that fly along like
clouds,[d]
like doves to their nests?
9 Surely the islands[e] look to me;
in the lead are the ships of Tarshish,[a][f]
bringing[g] your children from afar,
with their silver and gold,[h]
to the honor[i] of the LORD your God,
the Holy One[j] of Israel,
for he has endowed you with
splendor.[k]

10 "Foreigners[l] will rebuild your walls,
and their kings[m] will serve you.
Though in anger I struck you,
in favor[n] I will show you
compassion.[o]
11 Your gates[p] will always stand open,
they will never be shut, day or night,
so that people may bring you the
wealth of the nations[q]—
their kings[r] led in triumphal
procession.
12 For the nation or kingdom that will not
serve[s] you will perish;
it will be utterly ruined.[t]

13 "The glory of Lebanon[u] will come to
you,
the juniper, the fir and the cypress
together,[v]
to adorn my sanctuary;[w]
and I will glorify the place for my feet.[x]

60:7 [y] S Ge 25:13 [z] Isa 18:7; Eze 20:40; 43:27; Zep 3:10 [a] S Isa 19:21 [b] ver 13; Hag 2:3,7,9 **60:8** [c] Isa 49:21 [d] Isa 19:1 **60:9** [e] S Isa 11:11 [f] S Ge 10:4; Isa 2:16 *fn* [g] S Isa 14:2; S 43:6 [h] S 1Ki 10:22 [i] S Ps 22:23 [j] ver 14; Isa 1:4; S 54:5 [k] S Isa 44:23; 55:5; Jer 30:19 **60:10** [l] S Ex 1:11; S Isa 14:1-2; S 56:6 [m] S Ezr 1:2; Rev 21:24 [n] S Isa 49:8 [o] S Ps 102:13 **60:11** [p] ver 18; S Ps 24:7; Isa 62:10; Mic 2:13; Rev 21:25 [q] S ver 5; Isa 61:6; Rev 21:26 [r] Ps 149:8; S Isa 2:12 **60:12** [s] S Isa 11:14; S 14:2 [t] S Ge 27:29; S Ps 110:5; Da 2:34 **60:13** [u] S Ezr 3:7 [v] Isa 41:19 [w] S ver 7 [x] S 1Ch 28:2 **60:14** [y] S Isa 14:2 [z] S Ge 27:29; S Isa 2:3; Rev 3:9

14 The children of your oppressors[y] will
come bowing before you;
all who despise you will bow down[z]
at your feet
and will call you the City[a] of the LORD,
Zion[b] of the Holy One[c] of Israel.

15 "Although you have been forsaken[d]
and hated,
with no one traveling[e] through,
I will make you the everlasting pride[f]
and the joy[g] of all generations.
16 You will drink the milk of nations
and be nursed[h] at royal breasts.
Then you will know[i] that I, the LORD,
am your Savior,[j]
your Redeemer,[k] the Mighty One of
Jacob.[l]
17 Instead of bronze I will bring you
gold,[m]
and silver in place of iron.
Instead of wood I will bring you
bronze,
and iron in place of stones.
I will make peace[n] your governor
and well-being your ruler.[o]
18 No longer will violence[p] be heard in
your land,
nor ruin or destruction[q] within your
borders,
but you will call your walls Salvation[r]
and your gates Praise.[s]

[a] 9 Or *the trading ships*

[a] S Ge 32:28; S Isa 1:26 [b] Heb 12:22 [c] S ver 9 **60:15** [d] Isa 1:7-9; S 6:12; S 54:6 [e] S Isa 33:8 [f] S Isa 4:2 [g] S Ps 126:5; Isa 65:18 **60:16** [h] S Ex 6:2; Isa 49:23; 66:11,12 [i] S Ex 6:7 [j] S Ex 14:30; S Isa 25:9 [k] S Job 19:25; S Isa 59:20 [l] S Ge 49:24; S Ps 132:2 **60:17** [m] 1Ki 10:21 [n] S Ps 85:8; Isa 66:12; Hag 2:9 [o] S Isa 9:7 **60:18** [p] S Lev 26:6; S 2Sa 7:10; S Isa 9:4 [q] S Isa 49:19; S 51:19 [r] S Isa 33:6 [s] Isa 61:11; 62:7; Jer 33:9; Zep 3:20

(Ge 25:4). *Sheba.* A wealthy land in southern Arabia, perhaps roughly equal to modern Yemen (see Ge 25:3; 1Ki 10:1 and note). *gold and incense.* The queen of Sheba brought gold and spices to Solomon (1Ki 10:2). Jer 6:20 mentions the incense of Sheba. Cf. Ps 72:10; Mt 2:11. *proclaiming the praise.* Cf. the queen's words in 1Ki 10:9 (but see note there).
60:7 *Kedar's flocks.* See note on 21:16. *Nebaioth.* The firstborn son of Ishmael (Ge 25:13). The name is probably preserved in that of the later Nabatean kingdom. *serve.* See v. 10; 56:6. *accepted as offerings.* See 56:7; 58:5 and notes.
60:9 *islands look to me.* See 11:11 and note. *ships of Tarshish.* See note on 2:16. *bringing your children.* See 49:22 and note. *silver and gold.* Ships of Tarshish had brought these to Solomon every three years (1Ki 10:22). *Holy One of Israel.* See v. 14; 1:4 and note. *endowed ... with splendor.* See 55:5 and note.
60:10 *Foreigners ... kings.* See vv. 12,14; 49:7,23; 61:5. *will rebuild your walls.* In 444 BC King Artaxerxes issued the decree allowing Nehemiah to rebuild the walls of Jerusalem (Ne 2:8). Some interpreters also apply the rebuilt walls to the building up of the church through Gentile believers (Ac 15:14–16). *Though in anger ... compassion.* See 54:7–8 and notes.
60:11 *gates ... always ... open.* As are the gates of the new Jerusalem (Rev 21:25). *wealth.* See v. 5 and note.
60:12 *nation ... will perish.* Israel's future political domination is referred to also in 11:14; 14:2; 49:23 (cf. vv. 10,14).

60:13 *glory of Lebanon.* Its magnificent cedar trees, which were used in the construction of Solomon's temple, along with juniper trees (1Ki 5:10,18). See also 35:2. The glory of Solomon's era would return. *juniper ... fir ... cypress.* See 41:19 and note. Perhaps the trees would be ornamental rather than building material. *adorn ... sanctuary.* See v. 7. *place for my feet.* The temple, and especially the ark of the covenant, God's "footstool."
60:14 *oppressors ... bow down.* See 49:7,23 and notes. Cf. vv. 10,12. *City of the LORD.* Cf. the names for the future Jerusalem in 1:26; 62:4; Eze 48:35; Zec 8:3; Heb 12:22 (see notes there).
60:15 *forsaken and hated.* See 6:11–12; 62:4; Jer 30:17. *pride ... joy.* See 4:2 and note.
60:16 *nursed at royal breasts.* Jerusalem will receive the very best nourishment, the "riches of the nations" (v. 5). *Then ... Jacob.* For this sentence, see 49:26 and note.
60:17 *gold ... silver.* As in Solomon's day gold and silver were plentiful (1Ki 10:21,27), so the future Jerusalem will have the most valuable metals, as well as the strongest ("iron"). Cf. 9:10. *peace ... well-being.* Both are also present in the rule of the Messianic king in 9:7 (where the Hebrew for "well-being" is rendered "righteousness"). See note on 48:18.
60:18 *No longer ... violence.* Cf. 54:14. *ruin or destruction.* See 51:19 and note. *walls Salvation.* See 26:1.

19 The sun will no more be your light by
day,
nor will the brightness of the moon
shine on you,
for the LORD will be your everlasting
light,[t]
and your God will be your glory.[u]
20 Your sun[v] will never set again,
and your moon will wane no more;
the LORD will be your everlasting light,
and your days of sorrow[w] will end.
21 Then all your people will be righteous[x]
and they will possess[y] the land
forever.
They are the shoot I have planted,[z]
the work of my hands,[a]
for the display of my splendor.[b]
22 The least of you will become a
thousand,
the smallest a mighty nation.[c]
I am the LORD;
in its time I will do this swiftly."[d]

The Year of the LORD's Favor

61 The Spirit[e] of the Sovereign LORD[f]
is on me,
because the LORD has anointed[g] me
to proclaim good news[h] to the poor.[i]
He has sent me to bind up[j] the
brokenhearted,
to proclaim freedom[k] for the captives[l]
and release from darkness for the
prisoners,[a]
2 to proclaim the year of the LORD's
favor[m]
and the day of vengeance[n] of our God,
to comfort[o] all who mourn,[p]
3 and provide for those who grieve in
Zion—
to bestow on them a crown[q] of beauty
instead of ashes,[r]
the oil[s] of joy
instead of mourning,[t]
and a garment of praise
instead of a spirit of despair.
They will be called oaks of
righteousness,
a planting[u] of the LORD
for the display of his splendor.[v]

4 They will rebuild the ancient ruins[w]
and restore the places long
devastated;
they will renew the ruined cities
that have been devastated for
generations.
5 Strangers[x] will shepherd your flocks;
foreigners will work your fields and
vineyards.
6 And you will be called priests[y] of the
LORD,
you will be named ministers of our
God.
You will feed on the wealth[z] of
nations,
and in their riches you will boast.

60:19 [t] S Ps 36:9; S 118:27; Rev 22:5 [u] S Ps 85:9; S Isa 24:16,23; Rev 21:23 **60:20** [v] Isa 30:26 [w] S Isa 30:19; S 35:10; S Rev 7:17 **60:21** [x] S Isa 4:3; S 26:2; Rev 21:27 [y] Ps 37:11, 22; Isa 49:8; 57:13; 61:7; 65:9; Zec 8:12 [z] S Ex 15:17; Ps 44:2; 80:8-11; Jer 32:41; Am 9:15; Mt 15:13 [a] S Job 10:3; S Ps 8:6; S Isa 19:25; Eph 2:10 [b] S Lev 10:3; S Isa 44:23 **60:22** [c] S Ge 12:2; S Dt 1:10 [d] Isa 5:19 **61:1** [e] S Isa 11:2; 2Co 3:17 [f] S Isa 50:4 [g] S Ps 45:7; S Da 9:24-26; S Ac 4:26 [h] S 2Sa 18:26; S Isa 40:9 [i] S Job 5:16; S Mt 11:5; Lk 7:22 [j] S 2Ki 22:19; S Job 5:18 [k] S Lev 25:10 [l] S Ps 68:6; S Isa 49:9

[a] 1 Hebrew; Septuagint *the blind*

61:2 [m] S Isa 49:8; S Lk 4:18-19* [n] S Isa 1:24 [o] S Isa 40:1; Mt 5:4 [p] S Job 5:11; Lk 6:21 **61:3** [q] S Isa 3:23 [r] S Job 2:8 [s] S Ru 3:3; S Isa 1:6; Heb 1:9 [t] Jer 31:13; Mt 5:4 [u] Ps 1:3; 92:12-13; Mt 15:13; 1Co 3:9 [v] S Isa 44:23 **61:4** [w] S Isa 44:26; 51:3; 65:21; Eze 36:33; Am 9:14; Zec 1:16-17 **61:5** [x] S Isa 14:1-2; S 56:6 **61:6** [y] S Ex 19:6; 1Pe 2:5 [z] Dt 33:19; S Isa 60:11

60:19 *sun ... moon.* According to Rev 21:23; 22:5 their light will no longer be needed in the new Jerusalem, since God and the Lamb will be the "everlasting light." *glory.* See vv. 1–2 and note; Zec 2:5; cf. notes on Ex 40:34; Ps 26:8.

60:20 *sun will never set.* There will be no night there (cf. Rev 22:5) but only the light of joy and salvation (see 58:8 and note). *sorrow will end.* See 25:8; 35:10; 51:11; 65:19; Rev 21:4; 22:3–5.

60:21 *people will be righteous.* Only the redeemed will be there (see 4:3; 35:8; Rev 21:27). *possess the land forever.* Enter into full blessing (see 49:8 and note; see also 57:13; 61:7; Ps 37:11,22). *shoot I have planted.* Cf. the vineyard of 5:2,7 (see also 11:1). *work of my hands.* God made them as a potter forms clay (see 64:8; see also 29:23; 45:11). *display of my splendor.* They are the evidence of God's redemptive work. See 49:3; 61:3; see also notes on 35:2; 40:5.

60:22 *least ... will become a thousand.* See 51:2; 54:3 and notes. The blessing of Lev 26:8 is similar. *do this swiftly.* Cf. 5:19, where the same Hebrew verb is translated "hasten."

61:1–2 Jesus applied these verses to himself in the synagogue at Nazareth (see Lk 4:16–20 and notes; cf. Mt 11:5).

61:1 *Spirit ... is on me.* The statement may refer to Isaiah in a limited sense, but the Messianic servant is the main figure intended (cf. what is said of him in 42:1; see 11:2; 48:16 and notes). *Sovereign LORD.* See 50:4–5,7,9 and note. *anointed me.* See 45:1 and note. *good news.* See 40:9 and note. *poor.* Cf. 11:4; 29:19. *bind up the brokenhearted.* See 30:26 and note. *freedom for the captives.* Freedom is proclaimed in the Year of Jubilee in Lev 25:10 (see 49:8 and note; see also note on Lk 4:19).

61:2 *year of the LORD's favor.* Corresponds to the "day of salvation" in 49:8 (see note there) and the "year for me to redeem" in 63:4. Christ ended his quotation at this point (Lk 4:19–20), probably because the "day of vengeance" will not occur until his second coming. *day of vengeance.* See 34:2,8 and notes. *comfort all who mourn.* See 49:13; 57:19 and notes; 66:10; Jer 31:13; Mt 5:4.

61:3 *bestow on them ... a garment of praise.* See note on Ps 109:29. *crown of beauty.* A "turban" (as the Hebrew for this phrase is translated in Eze 24:17) or headdress. In 3:20 the women of Jerusalem were to lose their beautiful headdresses. *oil of joy.* Anointing with olive oil was common on joyous occasions (see Ps 23:5; 45:7 and notes; 104:15; 133:1–2; cf. 2Sa 14:2). See also 1:6 and note. *garment of praise.* Contrast the "garments of vengeance" in 59:17. *oaks of righteousness.* Contrast the oak of 1:30. *planting ... for the display.* See 60:21 and note.

61:4 *rebuild the ancient ruins ... ruined cities.* See 58:12 and note.

61:5 *Strangers ... foreigners.* See 14:1–2; 56:3; 60:10 and notes.

61:6 *priests of the LORD.* See 66:21. True Israel will be a "kingdom of priests" among the Gentiles (see Ex 19:6; Zec 3:1–10; 1Pe 2:9 and notes). *ministers.* Priests. See 1Ki 8:11, where the Hebrew word for "minister" is translated "perform their service." *wealth of nations.* See 60:5 and note.

7 Instead of your shame[a]
you will receive a double[b] portion,
and instead of disgrace
you will rejoice in your inheritance.
And so you will inherit[c] a double
portion in your land,
and everlasting joy[d] will be yours.

8 "For I, the LORD, love justice;[e]
I hate robbery and wrongdoing.
In my faithfulness I will reward my
people
and make an everlasting covenant[f]
with them.
9 Their descendants[g] will be known
among the nations
and their offspring among the
peoples.
All who see them will acknowledge
that they are a people the LORD has
blessed."[h]

10 I delight greatly in the LORD;
my soul rejoices[i] in my God.
For he has clothed me with garments
of salvation
and arrayed me in a robe of his
righteousness,[j]
as a bridegroom adorns his head[k] like a
priest,
and as a bride[l] adorns herself with
her jewels.
11 For as the soil makes the sprout come up
and a garden[m] causes seeds to grow,
so the Sovereign LORD will make
righteousness[n]
and praise spring up before all
nations.

Zion's New Name

62 For Zion's sake I will not keep
silent,[o]
for Jerusalem's sake I will not
remain quiet,
till her vindication[p] shines out like the
dawn,[q]
her salvation[r] like a blazing torch.
2 The nations[s] will see your
vindication,
and all kings your glory;
you will be called by a new name[t]
that the mouth of the LORD will
bestow.
3 You will be a crown[u] of splendor in the
LORD's hand,
a royal diadem in the hand of your
God.
4 No longer will they call you
Deserted,[v]
or name your land Desolate.[w]
But you will be called Hephzibah,[a][x]
and your land Beulah[b];
for the LORD will take delight[y] in you,
and your land will be married.[z]
5 As a young man marries a young
woman,
so will your Builder marry you;
as a bridegroom[a] rejoices over his
bride,
so will your God rejoice[b] over
you.

6 I have posted watchmen[c] on your
walls, Jerusalem;
they will never be silent day or
night.
You who call on the LORD,
give yourselves no rest,[d]
7 and give him no rest[e] till he establishes
Jerusalem
and makes her the praise[f] of the
earth.

[a] 4 *Hephzibah* means *my delight is in her.* [b] 4 *Beulah* means *married.*

61:7 [a] S Isa 29:22; S 41:11 [b] S Dt 21:17; S Isa 40:2 [c] S Isa 60:21 [d] S Ps 126:5; S Isa 25:9 **61:8** [e] S Ps 11:7; S Isa 1:17; S 5:16 [f] S Ge 9:16; S Isa 42:6; S Heb 13:20 **61:9** [g] S Isa 43:5; S 48:19 [h] S Ge 12:2; S Dt 28:3-12 **61:10** [i] S Ps 2:11; S Isa 7:13; S 25:9; Hab 3:18; S Lk 1:47 [j] S Job 27:6; S Ps 132:9; S Isa 52:1; Rev 19:8 [k] S Ex 39:28 [l] S Isa 49:18; Rev 21:2 **61:11** [m] S Ge 47:23; Isa 58:11 [n] S Isa 45:8 **62:1** [o] S Est 4:14; S Ps 50:21; S 83:1 [p] S Isa 1:26; S 45:8 [q] S Job 11:17 [r] S Ps 67:2 **62:2** [s] S Ps 67:2; S Isa 40:5; S 45:14; 52:10 [t] S Ge 32:28; S Isa 1:26; Rev 2:17; 3:12 **62:3** [u] S Isa 28:5; 1Th 2:19 **62:4** [v] S Lev 26:43; S Isa 6:12; S 54:6 [w] S Isa 49:19; S 51:19 [x] 2Ki 21:1 [y] Isa 65:19; Jer 32:41; Zep 3:17; Mal 3:12 [z] Isa 54:5; Jer 3:14; Hos 2:19 **62:5** [a] S SS 3:11 [b] S Dt 28:63; Isa 65:19; Jer 31:12; Zep 3:17 **62:6** [c] S Isa 52:8; Heb 13:17 [d] Ps 132:4 **62:7** [e] Mt 15:21-28; Lk 18:1-8 [f] S Dt 26:19; S Isa 60:18

61:7 *shame … disgrace.* See 45:17; 54:4. *double portion.* The firstborn son received a double share of the inheritance (see Dt 21:17; 2Ki 2:9; Zec 9:12 and notes). Contrast the "double" punishment Israel received (40:2). *everlasting joy.* See 35:10; 51:11; cf. Ps 16:11.
61:8 *love justice.* Cf. 30:18; 59:15. *robbery and wrongdoing.* Israel had been mistreated by her conquerors. Cf. 42:24; 59:18. *everlasting covenant.* Probably the new covenant (see 55:3; 59:21 and notes; cf. Jer 31:35 – 37; 32:40 and notes).
61:9 *people the LORD has blessed.* See 44:3; 65:23 and the promises to Abraham in Ge 12:1 – 3 (see also notes there).
61:10 Zion is probably the speaker. *clothed me with … arrayed me in.* See note on Ps 109:29. *garments of salvation.* See v. 3; 52:1 and note. *head like a priest.* Putting on a turban or headband (see note on v. 3). *bride … with her jewels.* See 49:18 and note.
61:11 *sprout … grow.* Cf. 55:10. *righteousness and praise spring up.* See 45:8 and note.
62:1 *not keep silent … quiet.* See v. 6; 42:14; 57:11 and note; 64:12; 65:6; see also Ps 28:1. *vindication … salvation.* See 46:13 and note (there the Hebrew for "vindication" is translated "righteousness"). *dawn.* Cf. 58:8.
62:2 *nations will see … glory.* See 52:10; see also 40:5; 60:3 and notes. *your.* Jerusalem's (see vv. 1,6). *new name.* To reflect a new status (see vv. 4,12; see also 1:26; 60:14; Ge 32:28 and notes).
62:3 *crown of splendor.* In 28:5 the Lord is a "glorious crown" for his people (cf. Zec 9:16).
62:4 *Deserted … Desolate.* See 54:6 – 7; 60:15 and note. *Hephzibah.* See NIV text note; also the name of Hezekiah's wife (2Ki 21:1). *Beulah.* See NIV text note. *married.* Israel's relationship with the Lord will be restored. See 50:1 and note.
62:5 *Builder marry you.* See note on 49:17.
62:6 *watchmen.* Probably those (the prophets especially; see note on 56:10) waiting for the messenger with good news (see 52:8 and note). *never be silent.* They will be praying that God will not be silent (see v. 1) but will restore Jerusalem. *give yourselves no rest.* Cf. David's intense prayer as he searched for a home for the ark (Ps 132:1 – 5).
62:7 *praise of the earth.* Cf. Jer 33:9; Zep 3:19 – 20; see 60:3 and note.

8 The LORD has sworn[g] by his right hand
and by his mighty arm:
"Never again will I give your grain[h]
as food for your enemies,
and never again will foreigners drink
the new wine
for which you have toiled;
9 but those who harvest it will eat[i] it
and praise the LORD,[j]
and those who gather the grapes will
drink it
in the courts of my sanctuary."[k]

10 Pass through, pass through the
gates![l]
Prepare the way for the people.
Build up, build up the highway![m]
Remove the stones.
Raise a banner[n] for the nations.

11 The LORD has made proclamation
to the ends of the earth:[o]
"Say to Daughter Zion,[p]
'See, your Savior comes![q]
See, his reward is with him,
and his recompense accompanies
him.' "[r]
12 They will be called[s] the Holy People,[t]
the Redeemed[u] of the LORD;
and you will be called Sought After,
the City No Longer Deserted.[v]

God's Day of Vengeance and Redemption

63 Who is this coming from Edom,[w]
from Bozrah,[x] with his garments
stained crimson?[y]
Who is this, robed in splendor,
striding forward in the greatness of
his strength?[z]

"It is I, proclaiming victory,
mighty to save."[a]

2 Why are your garments red,
like those of one treading the
winepress?[b]
3 "I have trodden the winepress[c] alone;
from the nations no one was with me.
I trampled[d] them in my anger
and trod them down in my wrath;[e]
their blood spattered my garments,[f]
and I stained all my clothing.
4 It was for me the day of vengeance;[g]
the year for me to redeem had come.
5 I looked, but there was no one[h] to
help,
I was appalled that no one gave
support;
so my own arm[i] achieved salvation
for me,
and my own wrath sustained me.[j]
6 I trampled[k] the nations in my anger;
in my wrath I made them drunk[l]
and poured their blood[m] on the
ground."

Praise and Prayer

7 I will tell of the kindnesses[n] of the LORD,
the deeds for which he is to be
praised,
according to all the LORD has done
for us—
yes, the many good things[o]
he has done for Israel,
according to his compassion[p] and
many kindnesses.

62:8 [g] S Ge 22:16; S Isa 14:24; S 49:18 [h] Dt 28:30-33; S Isa 1:7 **62:9** [i] S Isa 1:19; Am 9:14 [j] S Dt 12:7; Joel 2:26 [k] Lev 23:39 **62:10** [l] S Ps 24:7; S Isa 60:11 [m] S Isa 11:16; Isa 57:14 [n] S Isa 11:10 **62:11** [o] S Dt 30:4 [p] S Ps 9:14; Zec 9:9; Mt 21:5 [q] S Isa 35:4; Rev 22:12 [r] S Isa 40:10 **62:12** [s] S Ge 32:28 [t] S Ex 19:6; 1Pe 2:9 [u] S Ps 106:10; S Isa 35:9; S 44:23 [v] S Ps 27:9; Isa 42:16; S 54:6 **63:1** [w] S 2Ch 28:17; S Isa 11:14 [x] S Ge 36:33; Am 1:12 [y] Rev 19:13 [z] S Job 9:4; S Isa 45:24 [a] ver 5; Isa 46:13; S 51:5; Jer 42:11; Zep 3:17 **63:2** [b] S Ge 49:11 **63:3** [c] S Jdg 6:11; S Rev 14:20 [d] S Job 40:12; S Ps 108:13; S Isa 5:5 [e] S Isa 22:5 [f] Rev 19:13 **63:4** [g] S Isa 1:24; S Jer 50:15 **63:5** [h] S 2Ki 14:26; S Isa 41:28 [i] S Ps 44:3; S 98:1; S Isa 33:2 [j] Isa 59:16 **63:6** [k] S Job 40:12; S Ps 108:13 [l] S Isa 29:9; La 4:21 [m] S Isa 34:3 **63:7** [n] S Isa 54:8 [o] S Ex 18:9 [p] S Ps 51:1; Eph 2:4

62:8 *has sworn.* Cf. 45:23; 54:9. *mighty arm.* See 51:9 and note. *grain ... for your enemies ... foreigners drink the new wine.* Punishment Moses warned about in Lev 26:16; Dt 28:33. See also 52:1 and note; Jer 5:17.
62:9 *eat it ... drink it.* See 65:13,21–23. *in the courts of my sanctuary.* During a festival, or when they brought the tithe to the Lord (Lev 23:39–40; Dt 14:22–26).
62:10 *Pass through, pass through.* See note on 40:1. *gates.* Probably of Babylon (cf. 48:20; Mic 2:12–13). *Prepare the way ... build up the highway.* See 40:3; 49:11 and notes. *Remove the stones.* See 57:14. *banner.* See 5:26 and note.
62:11 *ends of the earth.* See 11:12; 49:6 and notes. *Daughter Zion.* A personification of Jerusalem (see note on 2Ki 19:21). *your Savior comes!* See 40:9; 43:3; Zec 9:9 and notes; Mt 21:5. *reward ... recompense.* See 40:10 and note; cf. Rev 22:12.
62:12 *Holy People.* See 4:3; Ex 19:6 and notes. *Redeemed.* See 35:9 and note. *Sought After ... No Longer Deserted.* See v. 4.
63:1 *Edom.* See 21:11; 34:5 and notes. Edom here symbolizes a world that hates God's people. *Bozrah.* See 34:6 and note. *stained crimson.* Cf. Christ's robe "dipped in blood" (Rev 19:13; see note there) as he wages war at his second coming. *proclaiming victory, mighty to save.* See 45:8; 59:16 and notes.
63:2 *Why ... ?* Isaiah responds with a question. *treading the winepress.* See 16:10 and note.
63:3 *trodden the winepress.* A figure of judgment (see notes on La 1:15; Joel 3:13; Rev 14:19; 19:15). *in my anger ... wrath.* On the day of the Lord. See v. 6; 13:3; 34:2 and notes.
63:4 *day of vengeance ... year for me to redeem.* See 61:2 and note. The day of judging the enemy meant at the same time redemption for God's people. See 35:9; 41:14 and notes.
63:5 See 59:16 (a parallel to the whole verse) and note. *wrath.* In 59:16 "righteousness" is used. God's righteousness and holiness resulted in his wrath.
63:6 *made them drunk.* They drank the "cup of his wrath" (see 51:17 and note). *poured their blood.* Here the battle is compared to a sacrifice, as in 34:6.
63:7—64:12 A prayer of Isaiah, asking the Lord to bring about the redemption he has promised—as one of the "watchmen" the Lord has posted on the walls of Jerusalem (see 62:6 and note). It is similar to a national lament (see, e.g., Ps 44).
63:7 *kindnesses.* Demonstrations of God's unfailing love as he stood true to his covenant with Israel (see note on Ps 6:4). *many good things.* Cf. Jos 21:45; 1Ki 8:66. *compassion.* See 54:7–8,10 and note.

[8]He said, "Surely they are my people,[q]
children who will be true to me";
and so he became their Savior.[r]
[9]In all their distress he too was
distressed,
and the angel[s] of his presence[t] saved
them.[a]
In his love and mercy he redeemed[u]
them;
he lifted them up and carried[v] them
all the days of old.[w]
[10]Yet they rebelled[x]
and grieved his Holy Spirit.[y]
So he turned and became their enemy[z]
and he himself fought[a] against them.

[11]Then his people recalled[b] the days of
old,
the days of Moses and his people—
where is he who brought them through
the sea,[b]
with the shepherd of his flock?[c]
Where is he who set
his Holy Spirit[d] among them,
[12]who sent his glorious arm[e] of power
to be at Moses' right hand,
who divided the waters[f] before them,
to gain for himself everlasting
renown,[g]
[13]who led[h] them through the depths?[i]
Like a horse in open country,
they did not stumble;[j]
[14]like cattle that go down to the plain,
they were given rest[k] by the Spirit of
the LORD.
This is how you guided your people
to make for yourself a glorious
name.

[15]Look down from heaven[l] and see,
from your lofty throne,[m] holy and
glorious.
Where are your zeal[n] and your
might?
Your tenderness and compassion[o]
are withheld[p] from us.
[16]But you are our Father,[q]
though Abraham does not know us
or Israel acknowledge[r] us;
you, LORD, are our Father,
our Redeemer[s] from of old is your
name.
[17]Why, LORD, do you make us wander[t]
from your ways
and harden our hearts[u] so we do not
revere[v] you?
Return[w] for the sake of your
servants,
the tribes that are your inheritance.[x]
[18]For a little while[y] your people
possessed your holy place,
but now our enemies have trampled[z]
down your sanctuary.[a]
[19]We are yours from of old;
but you have not ruled over them,
they have not been called[c] by your
name.[b]

64

[d] Oh, that you would rend the
heavens[c] and come down,[d]
that the mountains[e] would tremble
before you!
[2]As when fire sets twigs ablaze
and causes water to boil,

a 9 Or *Savior* [9]*in their distress. / It was no envoy or angel / but his own presence that saved them* *b* 11 Or *But may he recall* *c* 19 Or *We are like those you have never ruled, / like those never called* *d* In Hebrew texts 64:1 is numbered 63:19b, and 64:2-12 is numbered 64:1-11.

63:8 [q] S Ps 100:3; S Isa 51:4 [r] S Ex 14:30; S Isa 25:9 **63:9** [s] S Ex 14:19 [t] S Ex 33:14 [u] Dt 7:7-8; S Ezr 9:9; S Isa 48:20 [v] S Dt 1:31; S Ps 28:9 [w] S Dt 32:7; S Job 37:23 **63:10** [x] S Ps 78:17; Eze 20:8; Ac 7:39-42 [y] S Ps 51:11; Ac 7:51; Eph 4:30 [z] Ps 106:40; S Isa 10:4 [a] S Jos 10:14 **63:11** [b] S Ex 14:22, 30 [c] S Ps 77:20 [d] S Nu 11:17 **63:12** [e] S Ge 49:24; S Ex 3:20 [f] Ex 14:21-22; Isa 11:15 [g] S Ps 102:12; S Isa 55:13; S Jer 13:11 **63:13** [h] S Dt 32:12 [i] S Ex 14:22 [j] S Ps 119:11; Jer 31:9 **63:14** [k] S Ex 33:14; S Dt 12:9 **63:15** [l] S Dt 26:15; La 3:50 [m] S 1Ki 22:19; S Ps 123:1 [n] S Isa 9:7; S 26:11 [o] S 1Ki 3:26; S Ps 25:6 [p] S Ge 43:31; Isa 64:12 **63:16** [q] S Ex 4:22; S Jer 3:4; Jn 8:41 [r] S Job 14:21 [s] Isa 41:14; 44:6; S 59:20 **63:17** [t] S Ge 20:13; La 3:9 [u] S Ex 4:21 [v] Isa 29:13 [w] S Nu 10:36 [x] S Ex 34:9 **63:18** [y] Dt 4:26; 11:17 [z] S Isa 28:18; Da 8:13; S Lk 21:24 [a] S Lev 26:31; S 2Ki 25:9 **63:19** [b] S Isa 43:7; S Jer 14:9 **64:1** [c] Ps 18:9; 144:5 [d] ver 3; Mic 1:3 [e] S Ex 19:18

63:8 *my people, children who will be true to me.* But see 1:2–4. *Savior.* See 43:3 and note.

63:9 *In all their distress ... distressed.* The suffering in Egypt and during the period of the judges is probably in view (see Jdg 10:16). *angel of his presence.* See Ex 23:20–23; 33:14–15. *redeemed.* See 41:14; 43:1 and notes. *lifted ... carried.* Like a father (see Dt 1:31; 32:10–12).

63:10 *rebelled.* In the wilderness (see 1:2 and note; 30:1; Nu 20:10; Ps 78:40–55 and note). *grieved his Holy Spirit.* See Ps 51:11; 106:33 and note; cf. Isa 11:1–2; 42:1; Eph 4:30 and note. *became their enemy.* See 43:28 and note.

63:11 *sea.* The "Red Sea" (see 50:2 and note; 51:10). *shepherd.* Moses. *Holy Spirit.* See note on Ps 51:11. The Spirit rested on Moses and 70 elders (Nu 11:17,25). See also v. 14.

63:12 *arm of power.* See 51:9 and note; Ex 15:16. *divided the waters.* See Ex 14:21; cf. Isa 11:15; 51:10. *everlasting renown.* See 55:13 and note.

63:13 *depths.* Of the "Red Sea" (see Ex 15:5,8; Ps 106:9). But the crossing of the Jordan (Jos 3) may be intended as well (see v. 14 and note).

63:14 *to the plain.* To find pasture and water. *given rest.* They found a home in Canaan, the promised land (see Dt 12:9; Jos 1:13 and note; 21:44).

63:15 *lofty throne.* See 6:1. *zeal.* See 9:7; 42:13 and notes. *tenderness and compassion.* Cf. Hos 11:8. *withheld.* See 42:14 and note.

63:16 *Father.* See 64:8; Dt 32:6. *Abraham does not know.* Even if their human fathers abandon them, God will not (see 49:14–15 and notes). *Redeemer.* See 41:14 and note.

63:17 *make us wander.* When Israel went astray (see 53:6), God let his people wander. *harden our hearts.* Their hearts were hard (see 6:10; Ps 95:8), and the Lord confirmed that condition (see 6:10; Ex 4:21 and notes). *servants.* True believers (see 54:17 and note).

63:18 *enemies.* The Babylonians. *trampled down your sanctuary.* Graphically described in Ps 74:3–8 (see notes there); cf. Isa 64:11. Since it was God's sanctuary, his honor was at stake (cf. 48:11).

63:19 *called by your name.* See 43:7 and note.

64:1 *rend the heavens.* The sky is compared to a tent curtain. For this and the further description of the cosmic effects of God's coming in judgment and redemption, see Jdg 5:4–5; Ps 18:7–15; 144:5; Na 1:5; Hab 3:3–7 and notes.

64:2 *make your name known.* See 30:27 and note.

come down to make your name[f]
known to your enemies
and cause the nations to quake[g]
before you!
3 For when you did awesome[h] things
that we did not expect,
you came down, and the mountains
trembled[i] before you.
4 Since ancient times no one has
heard,
no ear has perceived,
no eye has seen any God besides you,[j]
who acts on behalf of those who
wait for him.[k]
5 You come to the help of those who
gladly do right,[l]
who remember your ways.
But when we continued to sin against
them,
you were angry.[m]
How then can we be saved?
6 All of us have become like one who is
unclean,[n]
and all our righteous[o] acts are like
filthy rags;
we all shrivel up like a leaf,[p]
and like the wind our sins sweep us
away.[q]
7 No one[r] calls on your name[s]
or strives to lay hold of you;
for you have hidden[t] your face from us
and have given us over[u] to[a] our sins.
8 Yet you, LORD, are our Father.[v]
We are the clay, you are the
potter;[w]
we are all the work of your hand.[x]
9 Do not be angry[y] beyond measure,
LORD;
do not remember our sins[z] forever.
Oh, look on us, we pray,
for we are all your people.[a]
10 Your sacred cities[b] have become a
wasteland;
even Zion is a wasteland, Jerusalem
a desolation.[c]
11 Our holy and glorious temple,[d] where
our ancestors praised you,
has been burned with fire,
and all that we treasured[e] lies in
ruins.
12 After all this, LORD, will you hold
yourself back?[f]
Will you keep silent[g] and punish us
beyond measure?

Judgment and Salvation

65 "I revealed myself to those who
did not ask for me;
I was found by those who did not
seek me.[h]
To a nation[i] that did not call on my
name,[j]
I said, 'Here am I, here am I.'
2 All day long I have held out my
hands
to an obstinate people,[k]
who walk in ways not good,
pursuing their own imaginations[l]—
3 a people who continually provoke me
to my very face,[m]
offering sacrifices in gardens[n]
and burning incense[o] on altars of
brick;

[a] 7 Septuagint, Syriac and Targum; Hebrew *have made us melt because of*

64:2 [f] S Isa 30:27 [g] Ps 99:1; 119:120; Jer 5:22; 33:9 **64:3** [h] S Ps 65:5 [i] S Ps 18:7 **64:4** [j] S Isa 43:10-11 [k] S Isa 30:18; 1Co 2:9* **64:5** [l] S Isa 26:8 [m] S Isa 10:4 **64:6** [n] S Lev 5:2; S 12:2 [o] Isa 46:12; 48:1 [p] S Ps 1:3; 90:5-6 [q] Ps 1:4; Jer 4:12 **64:7** [r] S Isa 41:28; 59:4; 63:5; Jer 8:6; Eze 22:30 [s] S Ps 14:4 [t] Dt 31:18; Isa 1:15; 54:8 [u] S Isa 9:18; Eze 22:18-22 **64:8** [v] S Ex 4:22; S Jer 3:4 [w] S Isa 29:16; Ro 9:20-21 [x] S Job 10:3; S Isa 19:25 **64:9** [y] Isa 54:8; 57:17; 60:10; La 5:22 [z] S Isa 43:25 [a] S Ps 100:3; S Isa 51:4 **64:10** [b] Ps 78:54; S Isa 1:26 [c] S Dt 29:23 **64:11** [d] S Lev 26:31; S 2Ki 25:9; Ps 74:3-7; La 2:7 [e] ver 10-11; La 1:7,10 **64:12** [f] S Ge 43:31; Ps 74:10-11 [g] S Est 4:14; S Ps 50:21; S 83:1

65:1 [h] Hos 1:10; Ro 9:24-26; 10:20* [i] Ro 9:30; Eph 2:12 [j] S Ps 14:4; S Isa 43:7 **65:2** [k] S Ps 78:8; S Isa 1:2,23; Ro 10:21* [l] Ps 81:11-12; S Pr 24:2; Isa 66:18 **65:3** [m] S Job 1:11 [n] S Isa 1:29 [o] S Lev 2:2; Jer 41:5; 44:17; Eze 23:41

64:3 *awesome things.* See Ps 66:3,5–7 and notes.
64:4 *no ... God besides you.* See 43:11 and note. *wait for him.* See 30:18; see also 40:31 and note.
64:5 *do right.* See 56:1. *you were angry.* See 9:12,17,21 and note. God's anger culminated in the exile. *saved.* Or "delivered" (see 43:3 and note).
64:6 *unclean.* Ceremonially unclean, like a person with a terrible disease (see 6:5; see also notes on Lev 4:12; 11:2; 13:45–46; cf. Introduction to Leviticus: Theological Themes). *righteous acts.* See 57:12 and note. *filthy rags.* The cloths a woman uses during her menstrual period, a time when she is "unclean" (see Ge 31:35 and note; Lev 15:19–24; Eze 36:17). *shrivel up like a leaf.* A figure used also in 1:30. *like the wind.* Which blows away the chaff (see 17:13; 40:24; Ps 1:4 and notes).
64:7 *No one calls on your name.* The Lord urges earnest prayer in times of distress (see, e.g., 2Ch 7:14). *hidden your face.* See 1:15 and note.
64:8 *Father.* See 63:16 and note. *clay ... potter.* See 29:16; Jer 18:6 and notes. *work of your hand.* See 60:21 and note.
64:9 *Do not be angry.* Cf. the promise to end that anger in 54:7–8 (see notes there). *do not remember our sins.* See 43:25 and note; Jer 31:34; Mic 7:18. *your people.* See 63:17–19; Ps 79:13.
64:10 *sacred cities.* Sacred because Israel was the "holy land" (Zec 2:12 [see note there]; cf. Ps 78:54). Jerusalem is often called the "holy city" (see 48:2 and note). *Zion is a wasteland ... desolation.* See 1:7–9 and note; 6:11; Jer 12:11.
64:11 *holy and glorious temple.* See 60:7; 63:15. *burned with fire.* Isaiah here reaches the climax of his lament. See 63:18 and note.
64:12 *hold yourself back ... keep silent.* See 42:14; 57:11; 62:1,6–7 and notes.
65:1—66:24 The grand conclusion to chs. 58–66, as well as to chs. 40–66 and to the whole book.
65:1–2 *I revealed ... people.* Paul makes use of these prophetic words in Ro 10:20–21. *a nation ... an obstinate people.* See v. 3; see also note on 6:9–10.
65:1 *did not ask ... did not seek.* The Lord now proceeds to answer Isaiah's prayer. Israel failed to stay close to the Lord, though the people sought him in a superficial way (see 55:6; 58:2 and notes). *did not call on my name.* See 64:7. *Here am I.* See 58:9; cf. also 40:1 and note.
65:2 *obstinate people.* See 1:2; 30:1,9 and notes. *imaginations.* See 59:7 and note.
65:3 *provoke me.* By worshiping idols (see Jdg 2:12–13 and notes). *to my very face.* Defiantly (cf. 3:8–9). *gardens.* See 1:29 and note. *burning incense.* As when worshiping the Queen of Heaven (see Jer 44:17–19 and notes).

[4]who sit among the graves[p]
and spend their nights keeping secret vigil;
who eat the flesh of pigs,[q]
and whose pots hold broth of impure meat;
[5]who say, 'Keep away; don't come near me,
for I am too sacred[r] for you!'
Such people are smoke[s] in my nostrils,
a fire that keeps burning all day.

[6]"See, it stands written before me:
I will not keep silent[t] but will pay back[u] in full;
I will pay it back into their laps[v]—
[7]both your sins[w] and the sins of your ancestors,"[x]
says the LORD.
"Because they burned sacrifices on the mountains
and defied me on the hills,[y]
I will measure into their laps
the full payment[z] for their former deeds."

[8]This is what the LORD says:

"As when juice is still found in a cluster of grapes[a]
and people say, 'Don't destroy it,
there is still a blessing in it,'
so will I do in behalf of my servants;[b]
I will not destroy them all.
[9]I will bring forth descendants[c] from Jacob,
and from Judah those who will possess[d] my mountains;
my chosen[e] people will inherit them,
and there will my servants live.[f]
[10]Sharon[g] will become a pasture for flocks,[h]
and the Valley of Achor[i] a resting place for herds,
for my people who seek[j] me.

[11]"But as for you who forsake[k] the LORD
and forget my holy mountain,[l]
who spread a table for Fortune
and fill bowls of mixed wine[m] for Destiny,
[12]I will destine you for the sword,[n]
and all of you will fall in the slaughter;[o]
for I called but you did not answer,[p]
I spoke but you did not listen.[q]
You did evil in my sight
and chose what displeases me."[r]

[13]Therefore this is what the Sovereign LORD says:

"My servants will eat,[s]
but you will go hungry;[t]
my servants will drink,[u]
but you will go thirsty;[v]
my servants will rejoice,[w]
but you will be put to shame.[x]
[14]My servants will sing[y]
out of the joy of their hearts,
but you will cry out[z]
from anguish of heart
and wail in brokenness of spirit.
[15]You will leave your name
for my chosen ones to use in their curses;[a]
the Sovereign LORD will put you to death,
but to his servants he will give another name.[b]

65:4 [p]S Lev 19:31; S Isa 8:19 [q]S Lev 11:7 **65:5** [r]S Ps 40:4; Mt 9:11; Lk 7:39; 18:9-12 [s]Pr 10:26 **65:6** [t]S Ps 50:3 [u]S 2Ch 6:23; Isa 59:18; Jer 16:18 [v]S Ps 79:12; Eze 9:10; Lk 6:38 **65:7** [w]S Isa 22:14 [x]Ex 20:5; Jer 32:18 [y]S Isa 57:7 [z]S Pr 10:24; S Isa 10:12 **65:8** [a]Isa 5:2 [b]S Isa 54:17 **65:9** [c]S Isa 45:19 [d]S Nu 34:13; S Isa 60:21; Jer 50:19; Am 9:11-15 [e]S Isa 14:1 [f]Isa 32:18 **65:10** [g]S 1Ch 27:29; S Isa 35:2; Ac 9:35 [h]Jer 31:12; 33:12; Eze 34:13-14 [i]S Jos 7:26 [j]S Isa 51:1 **65:11** [k]Dt 28:20; 29:24-25; S 32:15; Isa 1:28; Jer 2:13; 19:4 [l]S Dt 33:19; S Ps 137:5 [m]S Isa 5:22 **65:12** [n]S Isa 1:20; S 27:1 [o]S Isa 30:25 [p]S Pr 1:24-25; S Isa 41:28; 66:4; Jer 7:27 [q]2Ch 36:15-16; Jer 7:13; 13:11; 25:3; 26:5 [r]Ps 149:7; Isa 1:24; 66:4; Mic 5:15 **65:13** [s]S Isa 1:19 [t]S Job 18:12; Lk 6:25 [u]S Isa 33:16 [v]S Isa 3:1; 41:17 [w]S Isa 60:5; 61:7 [x]S Isa 44:9 **65:14** [y]S Ps 109:28; Zep 3:14-20; Jas 5:13 [z]S Isa 15:2; Mt 8:12; Lk 13:28 **65:15** [a]S Nu 5:27; S Ps 102:8 [b]S Ge 32:28; Rev 2:17

65:4 *sit among the graves.* Perhaps to consult the dead (see 8:19 and note; 57:9; Dt 18:11). *flesh of pigs.* Considered ceremonially unclean (see 66:3,17; Lev 11:7–8).
65:5 *I am too sacred for you.* Those who engage in pagan rituals often believe they are superior to others (cf. the attitude of the Pharisees in Mt 9:11; Lk 7:39; 18:9–12).
65:6 *not keep silent.* The answer to 64:12. *pay back.* See 59:18 and note.
65:7 *burned sacrifices on the mountains.* Offered to Baal on the high places (see 57:7; Hos 2:13 and note). *defied me.* See Eze 20:27–28.
65:8 *cluster of grapes.* Israel was a vineyard that had produced bad grapes (5:2,4,7). *my servants.* See vv. 9,13–14; 54:17 and note. Here the Lord's servants are equivalent to the remnant (see 1:9 and note).
65:9 *descendants.* See Jer 31:36 and note. *Jacob … Judah.* The northern and southern kingdoms, respectively. *possess my mountains.* See 49:8; 60:21 and notes. "Mountains" refers to the whole land, since so much of it was hilly (see Jdg 1:9; Eze 6:2–3). *chosen people.* See 41:8–9 and note. *inherit.* See 57:13 and note.
65:10 *Sharon.* See 33:9 and note. *Valley of Achor.* A valley near Jericho (see Jos 7:24,26; Hos 2:15 and notes). Since Sharon and Achor are on the western and eastern edges of the land, respectively, they probably represent the whole country. *seek me.* See v. 1; 51:1 and notes.
65:11 *forsake the LORD.* See 1:4. *holy mountain.* See 2:2–4 and note. *spread a table … mixed wine.* A meal and drink offering presented to deities. See note on 5:22; cf. v. 3; Jer 7:18 and note. *Fortune … Destiny.* The pagan gods of good fortune and fate. See Jos 11:17, where "Gad" may mean "Fortune."
65:12 *sword.* Designed for God's enemies, such as Edom (34:5–6), but the wicked of Israel would also suffer (see 1:20; 59:18 and note; 66:16). *called … not answer.* See 50:2; 2Ch 24:19 and notes. *chose what displeases me.* Contrast the faithfulness of the eunuchs in 56:4. The last four lines of v. 12 are almost identical to those of 66:4.
65:13 *eat … drink.* See 41:17–18; 49:10. *go hungry … thirsty.* See 5:13; 8:21. *rejoice.* See 61:7 and note; 66:14. *put to shame.* See 42:17; 44:9,11.
65:14 *sing out of … joy.* See 35:10; 54:1 and notes. *brokenness of spirit.* They had refused God's healing. See 61:1 and note.
65:15 *chosen ones.* See v. 9 and note. *use in their curses.* The rebellious Israelites will be used as an example when curses are uttered (see Jer 29:22). *another name.* Perhaps the "new name" of 62:2 (see note there).

16 Whoever invokes a blessing[c] in the
land
will do so by the one true God;[d]
whoever takes an oath in the land
will swear[e] by the one true God.
For the past troubles[f] will be forgotten
and hidden from my eyes.

New Heavens and a New Earth

17 "See, I will create
new heavens and a new earth.[g]
The former things will not be
remembered,[h]
nor will they come to mind.
18 But be glad and rejoice[i] forever
in what I will create,
for I will create Jerusalem[j] to be a
delight
and its people a joy.
19 I will rejoice[k] over Jerusalem
and take delight[l] in my people;
the sound of weeping and of crying[m]
will be heard in it no more.

20 "Never again will there be in it
an infant[n] who lives but a few days,
or an old man who does not live out
his years;[o]
the one who dies at a hundred
will be thought a mere child;
the one who fails to reach[a] a hundred
will be considered accursed.
21 They will build houses[p] and dwell in
them;
they will plant vineyards and eat
their fruit.[q]
22 No longer will they build houses and
others live in them,[r]
or plant and others eat.
For as the days of a tree,[s]
so will be the days[t] of my people;
my chosen[u] ones will long enjoy
the work of their hands.
23 They will not labor in vain,[v]
nor will they bear children doomed
to misfortune;[w]
for they will be a people blessed[x] by
the LORD,
they and their descendants[y] with
them.
24 Before they call[z] I will answer;[a]
while they are still speaking[b] I will
hear.
25 The wolf and the lamb[c] will feed
together,
and the lion will eat straw like the ox,[d]
and dust will be the serpent's[e] food.
They will neither harm nor destroy
on all my holy mountain,"[f]
says the LORD.

Judgment and Hope

66 This is what the LORD says:

"Heaven is my throne,[g]
and the earth is my footstool.[h]
Where is the house[i] you will build
for me?
Where will my resting place be?
2 Has not my hand made all these things,[j]
and so they came into being?"
declares the LORD.

"These are the ones I look on with favor:
those who are humble and contrite
in spirit,[k]
and who tremble at my word.[l]

[a] 20 Or *the sinner who reaches*

65:16 [c] S Dt 29:19 [d] Ps 31:5; Rev 3:14 [e] S Ps 63:11; S Isa 19:18 [f] S Job 11:16 **65:17** [g] S Isa 41:22; 66:22; 2Co 5:17; S 2Pe 3:13 [h] Isa 43:18; Jer 3:16; S Rev 7:17 **65:18** [i] S Dt 32:43; Ps 98:1-9; S Isa 25:9 [j] Rev 21:2 **65:19** [k] S Isa 35:10; S 62:5 [l] S Dt 30:9 [m] S Isa 25:8; Rev 7:17 **65:20** [n] Isa 11:8 [o] Ge 5:1-32; S 15:15; S Ecc 8:13; Zec 8:4 **65:21** [p] S Isa 32:18; S 61:4 [q] S 2Ki 19:29; S Isa 37:30; Eze 28:26; Am 9:14 **65:22** [r] S Dt 28:30 [s] Ps 1:3; 92:12-14 [t] Ps 21:4; 91:16 [u] S Isa 14:1 **65:23** [v] S Isa 49:4; 1Co 15:58 [w] Dt 28:32, 41; Jer 16:3-4 [x] S Ge 12:2; S Dt 28:3-12 [y] S Isa 44:3; Ac 2:39 **65:24** [z] S Isa 55:6; Mt 6:8 [a] S Job 8:6; S Isa 30:19; S Zec 10:6 [b] Da 9:20-23; 10:12 **65:25** [c] Isa 11:6 [d] S Job 40:15 [e] Ge 3:14; Mic 7:17 [f] S Job 5:23; S Isa 2:4 **66:1** [g] S 2Ch 6:18; S Ps 2:4; S 9:7; Mt 23:22 [h] S 1Ki 8:27; Mt 5:34-35 [i] S 2Sa 7:7; Jn 4:20-21; Ac 7:49*; 17:24 **66:2** [j] S Isa 40:26; Ac 7:50*; 17:24 [k] S Isa 57:15; Mt 5:3-4; Lk 18:13-14 [l] S Ezr 9:4

65:16 *invokes a blessing.* See 48:1; Dt 29:19. *one true God.* God is true to his promises. The Hebrew word for "true" here is *amen* (see Dt 27:15; Ro 1:25; 1Co 14:15 – 17; 2Co 1:20; Rev 3:14 and notes). *swear by.* See 45:23. Perhaps a contrast is intended with those who took oaths in the name of Baal (see Jer 12:16; cf. Dt 6:13 and note).
65:17 *new heavens and a new earth.* See 66:22; the climax of the "new things" Isaiah has been promising (see 42:9; 48:6; 2Pe 3:13 and notes). *former things.* The "old order of things" (Rev 21:4), including pain and sorrow.
65:18 *be glad and rejoice.* See 66:10; see also 51:3 and note. *create Jerusalem.* John links the notion of a new heaven and a new earth with the "new Jerusalem" (Rev 21:1 – 2). A restored Jerusalem after the exile and in the Messianic kingdom points toward this greater Jerusalem. See note on 54:11 – 12. Some interpreters, however, believe that the phrase "new heavens and a new earth" (v. 17) here refers to conditions during the Messiah's millennial reign (see Rev 20:1 – 6 and notes), described in vv. 18 – 25 (cf. 11:1 – 10 and note on 11:6 – 9; ch. 35).
65:19 *rejoice . . . take delight.* See 62:4 – 5 and notes. *weeping . . . crying.* See 25:8 and note; 35:10.
65:20 – 25 See 11:6 – 9 and note.
65:20 *hundred . . . mere child.* Comparable to the longevity of Adam and his early descendants. See the genealogy of Ge 5 (but see note on Ge 5:5).
65:21 – 22 Contrast Moses' curse for disobedience in Dt 28:30; cf. the same contrast in Am 5:11; 9:14; cf. also Mic 6:15.
65:21 *plant vineyards.* See 62:8 – 9.
65:22 *days of a tree.* Compared to the righteous also in Ps 1:3 (see note there); 92:12 – 14. *chosen ones.* See 41:8 – 9 and note. *long enjoy.* Cf. Ps 91:16.
65:23 *labor in vain.* See 49:4 and note. *misfortune.* Such as death or captivity. *people blessed by the LORD.* See 61:9 and note.
65:24 *Before they call I will answer.* See 30:19; 58:9; Ps 118:5 and note; Da 9:20 – 23; Mt 6:8.
65:25 *wolf . . . lamb . . . lion.* See 11:6 – 9 and notes. *dust . . . serpent's food.* See Ge 3:14 and note. The serpent will be harmless (see 11:8). *They . . . mountain.* Identical to the first two lines of 11:9.
66:1 *throne . . . footstool.* See 40:22 and note. *Where is the house . . . ?* Solomon realized that God could not be localized in a temple built by humans, magnificent though it may be (see 1Ki 8:27 and note).
66:2 *made all these things.* See 40:26 and note. *humble and contrite.* See 57:15 and note.

[3]But whoever sacrifices a bull[m]
is like one who kills a person,
and whoever offers a lamb
is like one who breaks a dog's neck;
whoever makes a grain offering
is like one who presents pig's[n]
blood,
and whoever burns memorial incense[o]
is like one who worships an idol.
They have chosen their own ways,[p]
and they delight in their
abominations;[q]
[4]so I also will choose harsh treatment
for them
and will bring on them what they
dread.[r]
For when I called, no one answered,[s]
when I spoke, no one listened.
They did evil[t] in my sight
and chose what displeases me."[u]

[5]Hear the word of the LORD,
you who tremble at his word:[v]
"Your own people who hate[w] you,
and exclude you because of my
name, have said,
'Let the LORD be glorified,
that we may see your joy!'
Yet they will be put to shame.[x]
[6]Hear that uproar from the city,
hear that noise from the temple!
It is the sound[y] of the LORD
repaying[z] his enemies all they
deserve.

[7]"Before she goes into labor,[a]
she gives birth;
before the pains come upon her,
she delivers a son.[b]
[8]Who has ever heard of such things?
Who has ever seen[c] things like this?
Can a country be born in a day[d]
or a nation be brought forth in a
moment?
Yet no sooner is Zion in labor
than she gives birth to her children.[e]
[9]Do I bring to the moment of birth[f]
and not give delivery?" says the
LORD.
"Do I close up the womb
when I bring to delivery?" says your
God.
[10]"Rejoice[g] with Jerusalem and be glad
for her,
all you who love[h] her;
rejoice greatly with her,
all you who mourn[i] over her.
[11]For you will nurse[j] and be satisfied
at her comforting breasts;[k]
you will drink deeply
and delight in her overflowing
abundance."[l]

[12]For this is what the LORD says:

"I will extend peace[m] to her like a
river,[n]
and the wealth[o] of nations like a
flooding stream;
you will nurse and be carried[p] on her
arm
and dandled on her knees.
[13]As a mother comforts her child,[q]
so will I comfort[r] you;
and you will be comforted over
Jerusalem."

[14]When you see this, your heart will
rejoice[s]
and you will flourish[t] like grass;
the hand[u] of the LORD will be made
known to his servants,[v]
but his fury[w] will be shown to his
foes.
[15]See, the LORD is coming with fire,[x]
and his chariots[y] are like a
whirlwind;[z]
he will bring down his anger with
fury,
and his rebuke[a] with flames of fire.

66:3 [m]S Isa 1:11 [n]S Lev 11:7 [o]S Lev 2:2 [p]S Isa 57:17 [q]ver 17; S Dt 27:15; Eze 8:9-13 **66:4** [r]S Pr 10:24; S Isa 10:12 [s]S 1Sa 8:19; S Isa 41:28 [t]2Ki 21:2,4,6; Isa 59:12 [u]S Isa 65:12 **66:5** [v]S Ezr 9:4 [w]Ps 38:20; Isa 60:15; Jn 15:21 [x]S Isa 44:9; Lk 13:17 **66:6** [y]S 1Sa 2:10; S Ps 68:33 [z]S Lev 26:28; Isa 65:6; Joel 3:7 **66:7** [a]S Isa 54:1 [b]Rev 12:5 **66:8** [c]Isa 64:4; Jer 18:13 [d]S Isa 49:20 [e]S Isa 49:21 **66:9** [f]S Isa 37:3 **66:10** [g]S Dt 32:43; S Isa 25:9; Ro 15:10 [h]S Ps 26:8 [i]Isa 57:19; 61:2 **66:11** [j]S Nu 11:12; S Isa 60:16 [k]Ge 49:25 [l]S Nu 25:1; S Isa 25:6 **66:12** [m]S Ps 119:165; S Isa 9:6 [n]S Isa 33:21 [o]Ps 72:3; Isa 60:5; 61:6 [p]S Nu 11:12; Isa 60:4 **66:13** [q]S Isa 49:15; 1Th 2:7 [r]S Isa 40:1; S 2Co 1:4 **66:14** [s]S Isa 25:9; S 60:5; S Joel 2:23 [t]S Ps 72:16 [u]S Ezr 5:5; S Isa 41:20 [v]S Isa 54:17 [w]S Isa 10:5; S 30:27 **66:15** [x]S Isa 1:31; S 42:25 [y]S 2Ki 2:11; S Ps 68:17 [z]S 2Ki 2:1 [a]S Dt 28:20; S Ps 9:5; S 39:11

66:3 Cf. Isaiah's harsh words in 1:11–14 about ineffective sacrifices. *breaks a dog's neck.* The dog was "unclean" and not used in offerings. Cf. the law in Ex 13:13 about breaking a donkey's neck. *pig's blood.* See 65:4 and note. The dog and pig are mentioned together also in Mt 7:6; 2Pe 2:22 (see note there). *worships an idol.* See 44:19 and note. *abominations.* Probably idols (see Jer 4:1).
66:4 *choose harsh treatment.* Cf. 65:7. *For when ... displeases me.* For these last four lines, see 65:12 and note.
66:5 *tremble.* See v. 2. *Your own people.* Lit. "Your brothers," i.e., your fellow Israelites (see Ac 11:1 and note). *Let ... joy.* Apparently spoken sarcastically, much like 5:19; Ps 22:8.
66:6 *city.* Probably Jerusalem. *repaying his enemies.* See 59:18 and note; 65:6–7.
66:7 *Before ... labor.* See 54:1 (and note), where Zion was barren.
66:8 *country ... born in a day.* See 49:19–20 and note.
66:9 *moment of birth.* See 37:3 and note.
66:10 *Rejoice ... be glad.* See 65:18 and note. *all ... who love her.* Cf. Ps 137:6. *who mourn.* See 57:19; 61:2 and notes.
66:11 *nurse and be satisfied.* In 60:16 (see note there) Jerusalem was drinking the milk of nations. Here she is the mother (cf. v. 12; 49:23).
66:12 *peace ... like a river.* See 48:18 and note. *wealth of nations.* See 60:5 and note. *flooding stream.* Contrast the destructive flood of 8:7–8 (see note there). *on her arm.* See 40:11.
66:13 *comforted over Jerusalem.* See 49:13 and note. Cf. 2Co 1:3–4.
66:14 *heart will rejoice.* See 60:5. *grass.* Usually a symbol of weakness. See 37:27 and note; 51:12; but contrast 44:4. *hand of the LORD.* Cf. Ezr 7:9; 8:31. *servants.* See 54:17 and note. *fury.* See v. 15; 13:3 and note.
66:15–16 *fire.* A figure of judgment (see 1:31 and note; 30:27).
66:15 *chariots ... like a whirlwind.* See 5:28; 2Ki 2:11 and note; 6:17; Ps 68:17 and note. *anger.* See 34:2; 42:25 and notes. *rebuke.* See 51:20 and note.

16For with fire[b] and with his sword[c]
the LORD will execute judgment[d] on
all people,
and many will be those slain[e] by the
LORD.

17"Those who consecrate and purify
themselves to go into the gardens,[f] following one who is among those who eat
the flesh of pigs,[g] rats[h] and other unclean
things — they will meet their end[i] together with the one they follow," declares the
LORD.
18"And I, because of what they have
planned and done,[j] am about to come[a]
and gather the people of all nations[k] and
languages, and they will come and see my
glory.[l]
19"I will set a sign[m] among them, and
I will send some of those who survive[n]
to the nations — to Tarshish,[o] to the Libyans[b] and Lydians[p] (famous as archers),
to Tubal[q] and Greece,[r] and to the distant
islands[s] that have not heard of my fame
or seen my glory.[t] They will proclaim my
glory among the nations.
20And they will
bring[u] all your people, from all the nations, to my holy mountain[v] in Jerusalem
as an offering to the LORD — on horses, in
chariots and wagons, and on mules and
camels,"[w] says the LORD. "They will bring
them, as the Israelites bring their grain offerings, to the temple of the LORD in ceremonially clean vessels.[x]
21And I will select
some of them also to be priests[y] and Levites," says the LORD.

22"As the new heavens and the new
earth[z] that I make will endure before me,"
declares the LORD, "so will your name and
descendants endure.[a]
23From one New
Moon to another and from one Sabbath[b] to
another, all mankind will come and bow
down[c] before me," says the LORD.
24"And
they will go out and look on the dead bodies[d] of those who rebelled[e] against me; the
worms[f] that eat them will not die, the fire
that burns them will not be quenched,[g]
and they will be loathsome to all mankind."

66:16 [b]Isa 30:30; Am 7:4; Mal 4:1 [c]S Isa 1:20; S 27:1; S Eze 14:21 [d]S Isa 13:9, 11; S Jer 2:35; S Eze 36:5 [e]S Isa 10:4 **66:17** [f]S Isa 1:29 [g]S Lev 11:7 [h]Lev 11:29 [i]Ps 37:20; Isa 1:28 **66:18** [j]S Pr 24:2; S Isa 65:2 [k]S Isa 2:3; S Zec 12:3 [l]S Ex 16:7; S Isa 59:19 **66:19** [m]Isa 11:10; 49:22; Mt 24:30 [n]S 2Ki 19:31 [o]S Isa 2:16 [p]Jer 46:9; Eze 27:10 [q]S Ge 10:2 [r]Jer 31:10; Da 11:18 [s]Isa 11:11 [t]S 1Ch 16:24; S Isa 24:15 **66:20** [u]S Isa 11:12; S Jer 25:22; Eze 34:13 [v]S Dt 33:19; S Isa 2:2; Jer 31:23 [w]S Ezr 2:66 [x]Isa 52:11 **66:21** [y]S Ex 19:6; 1Pe 2:5,9 **66:22** [z]S Isa 65:17; Heb 12:26-27; S 2Pe 3:13 [a]S Isa 48:19; Jn 10:27-29; 1Pe 1:4-5 **66:23** [b]Eze 46:1-3 [c]S Ps 22:29; S Isa 19:21; S 44:5; Rev 15:4 **66:24** [d]S Ps 110:6 [e]S Isa 1:2 [f]S Isa 14:11 [g]S Isa 1:31; S Mt 25:41; Mk 9:48*

[a] *18* The meaning of the Hebrew for this clause is uncertain. [b] *19* Some Septuagint manuscripts *Put* (Libyans); Hebrew *Pul*

66:16 *sword.* See 27:1; 31:8; 35:5 – 6 and note on Ps 7:12 – 13. *execute judgment.* The day of the Lord (see note on 2:11,17,20; cf. Eze 38:21 – 22).
66:17 *consecrate and purify themselves.* By special rituals required by their pagan religion. Cf. 2Ch 30:17. *gardens.* See 1:29 and note. *flesh of pigs.* See 65:4 and note.
66:18 *what they have planned and done.* Wicked Israelites may be the antecedent. *gather … all nations.* Cf. Joel 3:2 and note; Zep 3:8; Zec 12:3 and note. *see my glory.* Usually linked with God's deliverance of his people (see 35:2 – 4; 40:5 and notes).
66:19 *sign.* Possibly the banner of 11:10,12 (see note on 5:26; cf. Ps 74:4). Cf. the "sign of the Son of Man" (Mt 24:30) at his second coming. *those who survive.* After the judgment of v. 16. Cf. Zec 14:16. *Tarshish.* See 23:6 and note. *Libyans.* People who lived west of Egypt. See Na 3:9. *Lydians.* People probably from western Asia Minor (see Ge 10:13 and note). *archers.* See Jer 46:9. *Tubal.* Usually mentioned with Meshek (see Ge 10:2; Eze 27:13; 38:2 – 3; 39:1 and notes). It was probably a region southeast of the Black Sea. For the location of several of these nations, see map, p. 26. *islands.* See 11:11 and note. *proclaim my glory.* See 42:12; 1Ch 16:24.
66:20 *bring all your people.* Gentiles will bring back the remnant (see 11:11 – 12; 49:22; 60:4 and notes). *holy mountain.* See 2:2 – 4 and note. *as an offering … to the temple.* As the Israelites were to bring their tithes and offerings (see Dt 12:5 – 7).
66:21 *some of them.* A reference either to believing Jews (see 61:6 and note) or to Gentiles as part of the church or Messianic kingdom (see 1Pe 2:5,9 and notes).
66:22 *new heavens … new earth.* See 65:17 and note. *name and descendants endure.* See 48:19 and note.
66:23 *New Moon.* See 1:14 and note. *all mankind … bow down.* See 19:21; Zec 14:16 and notes.
66:24 Quoted in part in Mk 9:48 (see note there; see also Mk 9:47, where "hell" renders Greek *gehenna*). The Valley of Hinnom (Hebrew *ge' hinnom,* from which the word Gehenna comes) was located southwest of Jerusalem and became a picture of hell (see note on Mt 5:22). See Ne 11:30; Jer 7:31 and note. *dead bodies.* See 5:25; 34:3. *rebelled.* See 1:2 and note; 24:20. *worms that eat them will not die.* There will be everlasting torment. See 14:11; 48:22; 50:11; 57:21. *fire … not be quenched.* See 1:31 and note; Mt 3:12. *loathsome.* The Hebrew for this word is translated "contempt" in Da 12:2.

JEREMIAH

INTRODUCTION

Author and Date

The book preserves an account of the prophetic ministry of Jeremiah (1:1), whose personal life and struggles are shown to us in greater depth and detail than those of any other OT prophet. The meaning of his name is uncertain. Suggestions include "The LORD exalts" and "The LORD establishes," but a more likely proposal is "The LORD throws," either in the sense of "hurling" the prophet into a hostile world or of "throwing down" the nations in divine judgment for their sins. Jeremiah's prophetic ministry began in 626 BC and ended sometime after 586 (see notes on 1:2 – 3). His ministry was immediately preceded by that of Zephaniah. Habakkuk was a contemporary, and Obadiah may have been also. Since Ezekiel began his ministry in Babylon in 593, he too was a late contemporary of the great prophet in Jerusalem. How and when Jeremiah died is not known; Jewish tradition, however, asserts that while living in Egypt he was put to death by being stoned (cf. Heb 11:37).

Jeremiah was a member of the priestly household of Hilkiah. His hometown was Anathoth (1:1), so he may have been a descendant of Abiathar (1Ki 2:26), a priest during the days of King Solomon. The Lord commanded Jeremiah not to marry and raise children because the impending divine judgment on Judah would sweep away the next generation (see 16:1 – 4 and note on 16:2). Primarily a prophet of doom, he attracted only a few friends, among whom were Ahikam (26:24), Gedaliah (Ahikam's son, 39:14) and Ebed-Melek (38:7 – 13; cf. 39:15 – 18). Jeremiah's closest companion was his faithful secretary, Baruch, who wrote down Jeremiah's words as the prophet dictated them (36:4 – 32). He was advised by Jeremiah not to succumb to the temptations of ambition but to be content with his lot (ch. 45). He also received from Jeremiah and deposited for safekeeping a deed of purchase (32:11 – 16) and accompanied the prophet on the long road to exile in Egypt (43:6 – 7). It is possible that Baruch was also responsible for the final compilation of the book of Jeremiah itself, since no event recorded

a quick look

Author:
Jeremiah

Audience:
The people of Judah and Jerusalem during the reigns of their last five kings

Date:
Between 626 and 586 BC

Theme:
Jeremiah, the prophet of the new covenant, predicts Judah's Babylonian exile and ultimate restoration under the Davidic Messiah.

in chs. 1 – 51 occurred after 580 BC (ch. 52 is an appendix added by a later hand).

Given to self-analysis and self-criticism (10:24), Jeremiah has revealed a great deal about himself. Although timid by nature (1:6), he received the Lord's assurance that he would become strong and courageous (1:18; 6:27; 15:20). In his "confessions" (see 11:18 – 23; 12:1 – 4; 15:10 – 21; 17:12 – 18; 18:18 – 23; 20:7 – 18 and notes) he laid bare the deep struggles of his inmost being, sometimes making startling statements about his feelings toward God (12:1; 15:18). On occasion, he engaged in calling for redress against his personal enemies (12:1 – 3; 15:15; 17:18; 18:19 – 23; see note on Ps 5:10) — a practice that explains the origin of the English word *jeremiad*, referring to a denunciatory tirade or complaint. Jeremiah, so often expressing his anguish of spirit (4:19; 9:1; 10:19 – 20; 23:9), has justly been called the "weeping prophet." But it is also true that the memory of his divine call (1:17) and the Lord's frequent reaffirmations of his commissioning as a prophet (see, e.g., 3:12; 7:2,27 – 28; 11:2,6; 13:12 – 13; 17:19 – 20) made Jeremiah fearless and faithful in the service of his God (cf. 15:20).

Sistine Chapel painting of the prophet Jeremiah by Michelangelo
Wikimedia Commons

Background

Jeremiah began prophesying in Judah halfway through the reign of Josiah (640 – 609 BC) and continued throughout the reigns of Jehoahaz (609), Jehoiakim (609 – 598), Jehoiachin (598 – 597) and Zedekiah (597 – 586). It was a period of storm and stress, when the doom of entire nations — including Judah itself — was being sealed. The smaller states of western Asia were often pawns in the power plays of such imperial giants as Egypt, Assyria and Babylonia, and the time of Jeremiah's ministry was no exception. Ashurbanipal, last of the great Assyrian rulers, died in 627. His successors were no match for Nabopolassar, the founder of the Neo-Babylonian Empire, who began his rule in 626 (the year of Jeremiah's call to prophesy). Soon after Assyria's capital city, Nineveh, fell under the onslaught of a coalition of Babylonians and Medes in 612, Egypt (no friend of Babylonia) marched northward in an attempt to rescue Assyria, which would soon be destroyed. King Josiah of Judah made the mistake of trying to stop the Egyptian advance, and his untimely death near Megiddo in 609 at the hands of Pharaoh Necho II was the sad result (2Ch 35:20 – 24). Jeremiah, who had found

CHRONOLOGY OF JEREMIAH

DATE	EVENT
686	Manasseh assumes sole kingship
648	Birth of Josiah
642	Amon succeeds Manasseh as king
640	Josiah succeeds Amon
633	Josiah seeks after God (2Ch 34:3) Cyaxares becomes king of Media
628	Josiah begins reforms
626	Jeremiah called to be a prophet Nabopolassar becomes king of Babylonia
621	Book of the Law found in the temple
612	Nineveh destroyed
609	Josiah slain at Megiddo Jehoahaz rules three months Jehoiakim enthroned in Jerusalem
605	Babylonia defeats Egypt at Carchemish Hostages and vessels taken to Babylon Nebuchadnezzar becomes king of Babylonia
604	Nebuchadnezzar returns to Judah to receive tribute
601	Nebuchadnezzar defeated near Egypt
598	Jehoiakim's reign ends Jehoiachin rules Dec. 9, 598, to Mar. 16, 597
597	Jehoiachin deported Apr. 22 Zedekiah becomes king in Judah
588	Siege of Jerusalem begins Jan. 15
587	Jeremiah imprisoned (Jer 32:1–2)
586	July 18, Zedekiah flees (Jer 39:4) Aug. 14, destruction begins (2Ki 25:8–10) Oct. 7, Gedaliah slain; Jews migrate to Egypt.

Adapted from *The Zondervan Encyclopedia of the Bible*: Vol. 3 by MOISÉS SILVA.

a kindred spirit in the godly Josiah and perhaps had proclaimed the messages recorded in 11:1 – 8; 17:19 – 27 during the king's reformation movement, lamented Josiah's death (see 2Ch 35:25 and note).

Josiah's son Jehoahaz (see NIV text note on 22:11), also known as Shallum, is mentioned only briefly in the book of Jeremiah (22:10b – 12), and then in an unfavorable way. Necho put Jehoahaz in chains and made Eliakim, another of Josiah's sons, king in his place, renaming him Jehoiakim. Jehoahaz had ruled for a scant three months (2Ch 36:2), and his reign marks the turning point in the king's attitude toward Jeremiah. Once the friend and confidant of the king, the prophet now entered a dreary round of persecution and imprisonment, alternating with only brief periods of freedom (20:1 – 2; 26:8 – 9; 32:2 – 3; 33:1; 36:26; 37:12 – 21; 38:6 – 13,28).

Jehoiakim remained relentlessly hostile toward Jeremiah. On one occasion, when an early draft of the prophet's writings was being read to Jehoiakim (36:21), the king used a scribe's knife to cut the scroll apart, three or four columns at a time, and threw it piece by piece into the firepot in his winter apartment (vv. 22 – 23). At the Lord's command, however, Jeremiah simply dictated his prophecies to Baruch a second time, adding "many similar words" to them (v. 32).

Just prior to this episode in Jeremiah's life, an event of extraordinary importance took place that changed the course of history: In 605 BC the Egyptians were crushed at Carchemish on the Euphrates by Nebuchadnezzar (46:2), the gifted general who succeeded his father, Nabopolassar, as ruler of Babylonia that same year. Necho returned to Egypt after heavy losses, and Babylonia was given a virtually free hand in western Asia for the next 70 years. Nebuchadnezzar besieged Jerusalem in 605, humiliating Jehoiakim (Da 1:1 – 2) and carrying off Daniel and his three companions to Babylon (Da 1:3 – 6). Later, in 598 – 597, Nebuchadnezzar attacked Jerusalem again, and the rebellious Jehoiakim was heard of no more. His son Jehoiachin ruled Judah for only three months (2Ch 36:9). Jeremiah foretold the captivity of Jehoiachin and his followers (22:24 – 30), a prediction that was later fulfilled (24:1; 29:1 – 2).

Called to the unhappy task of announcing the destruction of the kingdom of Judah, Jeremiah is commissioned by God to lodge his indictment against his people and proclaim the end of an era.

Mattaniah, Jehoiachin's uncle and a son of Josiah, was renamed Zedekiah and placed on Judah's throne by Nebuchadnezzar in 597 BC (37:1; 2Ch 36:9 – 14). Zedekiah, a weak and vacillating ruler, sometimes befriended Jeremiah and sought his advice but at other times allowed the prophet's enemies to mistreat and imprison him. Near the end of Zedekiah's reign, Jeremiah entered into an agreement with him to reveal God's will to him in exchange for his own personal safety (38:14 – 27). Even then the prophet was under virtual house arrest until Jerusalem was captured in 586 (38:28).

While trying to flee the city, Zedekiah was overtaken by the pursuing Babylonians. In his presence his sons were executed, after which he himself was blinded by Nebuchadnezzar (39:1 – 7). Nebuzaradan, commander of the imperial guard, advised Jeremiah to live with Gedaliah, whom Nebuchadnezzar had made governor over Judah (40:1 – 6). After only three months in office, Gedaliah was murdered by his opponents (41:1 – 9). Others in Judah feared Babylonian reprisal and fled to Egypt, taking Jeremiah and Baruch with them (43:4 – 7). By that time the prophet was probably over 70 years old. His last recorded words are found in 44:24 – 30, the last verse of which is the only explicit reference in the Bible to Pharaoh Hophra, who ruled Egypt from 589 to 570 BC.

Theological Themes and Message

Referred to frequently as "Jeremiah the prophet" (or "the prophet Jeremiah") in the book that bears his name (20:2; 25:2; 28:5,10 – 12,15; 29:1,29; 32:2; 34:6; 36:8,26; 37:2,3,6; 38:9 – 10,14; 42:2,4; 43:6; 45:1; 46:1,13; 47:1; 49:34; 50:1) and elsewhere (2Ch 36:12; Da 9:2; Mt 2:17; 27:9; see Mt 16:14), Jeremiah was ever conscious of his call from the Lord (1:5; 15:19) to be a prophet. As such, he proclaimed words given him by God himself (19:2) and therefore certain of fulfillment (28:9; 32:24). Jeremiah had only contempt for false prophets (14:13 – 18; 23:13 – 40; 27:14 – 18) like Hananiah (ch. 28) and Shemaiah (29:24 – 32). Many of his own predictions were fulfilled in the short term (e.g., 16:15; 20:4; 25:11 – 14; 27:19 – 22; 29:10; 34:4 – 5; 43:10 – 11; 44:30; 46:13), and others were — or will yet be — fulfilled in the long term (e.g., 23:5 – 6; 30:8 – 9; 31:31 – 34; 33:15 – 16).

As hinted earlier, an aura of conflict surrounded Jeremiah almost from the beginning. He lashed out against the sins of his fellow citizens (44:23), criticizing them severely for their idolatry (16:10 – 13,20; 22:9; 32:29; 44:2 – 3,8,17 – 19,25) — which sometimes even involved sacrificing their children to foreign gods (see 7:30 – 34 and notes). But Jeremiah loved the people of Judah in spite of their sins, and he prayed for them (14:7,20) even when the Lord told him not to (7:16; 11:14; 14:11).

Judgment is one of the all-pervasive themes in Jeremiah's writings, though he was careful to point out that repentance, if sincere, would postpone the otherwise inevitable. His counsel of submission to Babylonia and his message of "life as usual" for the exiles of the early deportations branded him as a traitor in the eyes of many. Actually, of course, his advice not to rebel against Babylonia marked him as a true patriot, a man who loved his own people too much to stand by silently and watch them destroy themselves. By warning them to submit and not rebel, Jeremiah was revealing God's will to them — always the most sensible prospect under any circumstances.

For Jeremiah, God was ultimate. The prophet's theology conceived of the Lord as the Creator of all that exists (10:12 – 16; 51:15 – 19), as all-powerful (32:27; 48:15; 51:57) and everywhere present (23:24). Jeremiah ascribed the most elevated attributes to the God he served (32:17 – 25), viewing him as the Lord not only of Judah but also of the nations (5:15; 18:7 – 10; 25:17 – 28; chs. 46 – 51).

At the same time, God is very much concerned about individual people and their accountability to him. Jeremiah's emphasis in this regard (see, e.g., 31:29 – 30) is similar to that of Ezekiel (see Eze 18:2 – 4), and the two men have become known as the "prophets of individual responsibility." The undeniable relationship between sin and its consequences, so visible to Jeremiah as he watched his beloved Judah in her death throes, made him — in the pursuit of his divine vocation — a fiery preacher (5:14; 20:9; 23:29) of righteousness, and his messages have lost none of their power with the passing of the centuries.

Called to the unhappy task of announcing the destruction of the kingdom of Judah (thoroughly corrupted by the long and evil reign of Manasseh and only superficially affected by Josiah's efforts at reform), it was Jeremiah's commission to lodge God's indictment against his people and proclaim the end of an era. At long last, the Lord was about to inflict on the remnant of his people the ultimate covenant curse (see Lev 26:31 – 33; Dt 28:49 – 68). He would undo all that he had done for them since the day he brought them out of Egypt. It would then seem that the end had come, that Israel's stubborn and uncircumcised (unconsecrated) heart had sealed her final destiny, that God's chosen people had been cast off, that all the ancient promises and covenants had come to nothing.

A brick from the palace of Nebuchadnezzar, king of the Neo-Babylonian Empire (605 – 562 BC), who conquered Judah and Jerusalem and sent the Jews into exile in 586
Kim Walton, courtesy of the Oriental Institute Museum

But God's judgment of his people (and the nations), though terrible, was not to be the last word, the final work of God in history. Mercy and covenant faithfulness would triumph over wrath. Beyond the judgment would come restoration and renewal. Israel would be restored, the nations that crushed her would be crushed, and the old covenants (with Israel, David and the Levites) would be honored. God would make a new covenant with his people, in which he would write his law on their hearts (see 31:31 – 34 and notes; see also Heb 8:8 – 12 and note) and thus consecrate them to his service. The new covenant was cast in the form of ancient Near Eastern royal grant treaties and contained unconditional, gracious and profoundly spiritual, moral, ethical and relational promises (see chart, p. 23). The house of David would rule God's people in righteousness, and faithful priests would serve. God's commitment to Israel's redemption was as unfailing as the secure order of creation (31:35 – 37; ch. 33).

Jeremiah's message illumined the distant as well as the near horizon. It was false prophets who proclaimed peace to a rebellious nation, as though the God of Israel's peace were indifferent to her unfaithfulness. But the very God who compelled Jeremiah to denounce sin and pronounce judgment was the God who authorized him to announce that the divine wrath had its bounds, its 70 years. Afterward forgiveness and cleansing would come — and a new day, in which all the old expectations, aroused by God's past acts and his promises and covenants, would yet be fulfilled in a manner transcending all God's mercies of old.

Literary Features

Jeremiah is the longest book in the Bible, containing more Hebrew words than any other book. Although a number of chapters were written mainly in prose (chs. 7; 11; 16; 19; 21; 24–29; 32–45), including the appendix (ch. 52), most sections are predominantly poetic in form. Jeremiah's poetry is lofty and lyrical. A creator of beautiful phrases, he has given us an abundance of memorable passages (e.g., 2:13,26–28; 7:4,11,34; 8:20,22; 9:23–24; 10:6–7,10,12–13; 13:23; 15:20; 17:5–9; 20:13; 29:13; 30:7,22; 31:3,15,29–30,31–34; 33:3; 51:10).

Poetic repetition was used by Jeremiah with particular skill (see, e.g., 4:23–26; 51:20–23). He understood the effectiveness of repeating a striking phrase over and over. An example is "sword, famine and plague," found in 15 separate verses (14:12; 21:7,9; 24:10; 27:8,13; 29:17–18; 32:24,36; 34:17; 38:2; 42:17,22; 44:13). He made use of cryptograms (see NIV text notes on 25:26; 51:1,41) on appropriate occasions. Alliteration and assonance were also a part of his literary style, examples being *zarim wezeruha* ("foreigners ... to winnow her," 51:2) and *paḥad wapaḥat wapaḥ* ("Terror and pit and snare," 48:43; see note on Isa 24:17). Like Ezekiel, Jeremiah was often instructed to use symbolism to highlight his message: a ruined and useless belt (13:1–11), a smashed clay jar (19:1–12), a yoke of straps and crossbars (ch. 27), large stones in a brick pavement (43:8–13). Symbolic value is also seen in the Lord's commands to Jeremiah not to marry and raise children (16:1–4), not to enter a house where there was a funeral meal or where there was feasting (16:5–9), and to buy a field in his hometown, Anathoth (32:6–15). Similarly, the Lord used visual aids in conveying his message to Jeremiah: potter's clay (18:1–10) and two baskets of figs (ch. 24).

Outline

Unlike Ezekiel, the messages in Jeremiah are not arranged in chronological order. If they had been so arranged, the sequence of sections within the book would have been approximately as follows: 1:1—7:15; ch. 26; 7:16—20:18; ch. 25; chs. 46–51; 36:1–8; ch. 45; 36:9–32; ch. 35; chs. 21–24; chs. 27–31; 34:1–7; 37:1–10; 34:8–22; 37:11—38:13; 39:15–18; chs. 32–33; 38:14—39:14; 52:1–30; chs. 40–44; 52:31–34. The outline below represents an analysis of the book of Jeremiah in its present canonical order.

- I. Call of the Prophet (ch. 1)
- II. Warnings and Exhortations to Judah (chs. 2–35)
  - A. Earliest Discourses (chs. 2–6)
  - B. Temple Message (chs. 7–10)
  - C. Covenant and Conspiracy (chs. 11–13)
  - D. Messages concerning the Drought (chs. 14–15)
  - E. Disaster and Comfort (16:1—17:18)
  - F. Command to Keep the Sabbath Day Holy (17:19–27)
  - G. Lessons from the Potter (chs. 18–20)
  - H. Condemnation of Kings, Prophets and People (chs. 21–24)

- I. Foretelling the Babylonian Exile (chs. 25–29)
- J. Promises of Restoration (chs. 30–33)
- K. Historical Appendix (chs. 34–35)

III. Sufferings and Persecutions of the Prophet (chs. 36–38)
- A. Burning Jeremiah's Scroll (ch. 36)
- B. Imprisoning Jeremiah (chs. 37–38)

IV. The Fall of Jerusalem and Its Aftermath (chs. 39–45)
- A. The Fall Itself (ch. 39)
- B. Accession and Assassination of Gedaliah (40:1—41:15)
- C. Migration to Egypt (41:16—43:13)
- D. Prophecy against the Jewish Exiles in Egypt (ch. 44)
- E. Historical Appendix (ch. 45)

V. Judgment against the Nations (chs. 46–51)
- A. Against Egypt (ch. 46)
- B. Against Philistia (ch. 47)
- C. Against Moab (ch. 48)
- D. Against Ammon (49:1–6)
- E. Against Edom (49:7–22)
- F. Against Damascus (49:23–27)
- G. Against Kedar and Hazor (Arabia) (49:28–33)
- H. Against Elam (49:34–39)
- I. Against Babylonia (chs. 50–51)

VI. Historical Appendix (ch. 52)

1 The words of Jeremiah son of Hilkiah, one of the priests at Anathoth[a] in
the territory of Benjamin. 2 The word of the
LORD came[b] to him in the thirteenth year of
the reign of Josiah[c] son of Amon king of Judah, 3 and through the reign of Jehoiakim[d]
son of Josiah king of Judah, down to the
fifth month of the eleventh year of Zedekiah[e] son of Josiah king of Judah, when the
people of Jerusalem went into exile.[f]

The Call of Jeremiah

4 The word of the LORD came to me, saying,

5 "Before I formed you in the womb[g] I
knew[a][h] you,
before you were born[i] I set you apart;[j]
I appointed you as a prophet to the
nations.[k]"

6 "Alas, Sovereign LORD," I said, "I do not
know how to speak;[l] I am too young."[m]
7 But the LORD said to me, "Do not say, 'I
am too young.' You must go to everyone I
send you to and say whatever I command
you. 8 Do not be afraid[n] of them, for I am
with you[o] and will rescue[p] you," declares
the LORD.[q]
9 Then the LORD reached out his hand
and touched[r] my mouth and said to me,
"I have put my words in your mouth.[s]
10 See, today I appoint you over nations[t]
and kingdoms to uproot[u] and tear down,
to destroy and overthrow, to build and to
plant."[v]

[a] 5 Or *chose*

1:1 [a] S Jos 21:18 **1:2** [b] Eze 1:3; Hos 1:1; Joel 1:1 [c] S 2Ki 22:1 **1:3** [d] S 2Ki 23:34 [e] S 2Ki 24:17 [f] Ezr 5:12; Jer 52:15 **1:5** [g] S Ps 139:13 [h] Ps 139:16 [i] S Isa 49:1 [j] Jn 10:36 [k] ver 10; Jer 25:15-26 **1:6** [l] S Ex 3:11; S 6:12 [m] 1Ki 3:7 **1:8** [n] S Ge 15:1; S Jos 8:1 [o] S Ge 26:3; S Jos 1:5; Jer 15:20 [p] ver 19; Jer 15:21; 26:24; 36:26; 42:11 [q] Jer 20:11 **1:9** [r] S Isa 6:7 [s] S Ex 4:12 **1:10** [t] Jer 25:17; 46:1 [u] Jer 12:17 [v] Jer 18:7-10; 24:6; 31:4,28

1:1–3 The background and setting of Jeremiah's call are stated concisely but comprehensively.

1:1 *The words of.* See 36:10; see also Ne 1:1; Ecc 1:1; Am 1:1; cf. Dt 1:1. *Jeremiah.* For the meaning of his name, see Introduction: Author and Date. Eight other OT men had the same name (see 1Ch 5:24; 12:4,10,13; Ne 10:2; 12:1,12,34), two of whom were the prophet's contemporaries (Jer 35:3; 52:1). *Hilkiah.* Means "The LORD is my portion." For Hilkiah's possible relationship to a priestly house dating back to King Solomon, see Introduction: Author and Date. Two other men named Hilkiah (a common OT name) were also Jeremiah's contemporaries (see 29:3; Ezr 7:1 and note). *priests.* Like Ezekiel (Eze 1:3) and Zechariah (see Introduction to Zechariah: Author and Unity), Jeremiah was both a prophet and a member of a priestly family. *Anathoth.* See 11:21–23; 32:6–9. The Hebrew word is the plural form of the name of the Canaanite deity Anat(h), goddess of war. Anathoth had had priestly connections in Israel as early as the times of Joshua (Jos 21:18) and Solomon (1Ki 2:26), and its pagan origins had presumably been almost forgotten by Jeremiah's time. Present-day Anata, three miles northeast of Jerusalem, preserves the ancient name and may be the ancient site itself. *Benjamin.* Anathoth was one of the four Levitical towns in the tribal territory of Benjamin (Jos 21:17–18), and after the exile Benjamites settled there again (Ne 11:31–32).

1:2 *The word of the LORD came.* The most common way of introducing a divine prophecy at the beginning of a prophetic book (see Eze 1:3; Jnh 1:1 and note; Hag 1:1; Zec 1:1 and note; cf. Hos 1:1; Joel 1:1 and note; Mic 1:1; Zep 1:1). *to him.* Beginning in v. 4, Jeremiah speaks in the first person (see, e.g., vv. 11,13; 2:1). *thirteenth year.* 626 BC (see 25:3). *Josiah.* See 3:6; 36:2. He was the last good and godly king of Judah. Jeremiah sympathized with and supported his attempts at spiritual reformation and renewal (see 22:15b–16), which began in earnest in 621 (see 2Ki 22:3—23:25; 2Ch 34:8—35:19; cf. 2Ch 34:3–7).

1:3 *Jehoiakim.* His predecessor (Jehoahaz) and successor (Jehoiachin) are not mentioned, since they each reigned only three months. In contrast to his father, Josiah, Jehoiakim was a wicked ruler (see 2Ki 23:36–37; 2Ch 36:5)—as Jeremiah discovered almost immediately (see Introduction: Background; see also 22:13–15a,17–19; 26:20–23). *fifth month of the eleventh year.* Av (July-August), 586 BC (see 52:12). *Zedekiah.* The last king of Judah (see Introduction: Background), as wicked in his own way as Jehoiakim (see 52:1–2; 2Ch 36:11–14; see also Jer 24:8; 37:1–2). *exile.* The main captivity of Judah's people coincided with the destruction of Jerusalem and Solomon's temple by Nebuchadnezzar in 586 (see 2Ki 25:8–11).

1:4–19 The account of Jeremiah's call includes two prophetic visions (vv. 10–16) and some closing words of exhortation and encouragement (vv. 17–19).

1:4 See note on v. 2.

1:5 *I formed you.* See Isa 49:5. God's creative act (see Ge 2:7; Ps 119:73) is the basis of his sovereign right (see 18:4–6; Isa 43:21) to call Jeremiah into his service. *I knew you.* In the sense of making Jeremiah the object of his choice (see NIV text note). The Hebrew verb used here is translated "chosen" in Ge 18:19; Am 3:2. *I set you apart.* I consecrated you (cf. Jdg 13:5; Isa 49:1; Ro 1:1; Gal 1:15 and note). *I appointed you.* The Hebrew for this verb is not the same as that in v. 10, but both refer to the commissioning of the prophet. *prophet.* Lit. "one who has been called" to be God's spokesman (see Ex 7:1–2; 1Sa 9:9; Zec 1:1 and notes). *nations.* Although Judah's neighbors are probably the primary focus (see 25:8–38; chs. 46–51), Judah herself is not excluded.

1:6 *not know how to speak.* Like Moses (see Ex 4:10 and note), Jeremiah claimed inability to be a prophet; God nevertheless made him his "spokesman" (15:19). *too young.* See 1Ki 3:7. Jeremiah's objection is denied immediately by the Lord (v. 7).

1:7 Youth and inexperience do not disqualify when God calls (see 1Ti 4:12); he equips and sustains those he commissions.

1:8 *Do not be afraid.* See 10:5; 30:10; 40:9; 42:11; 46:27–28; 51:46; see also Isa 35:4 and note; 41:10,13–14; 43:1; Zep 3:11; Hag 2:5. *I am with you.* See v. 19; 15:20. God's promise of his continuing presence should calm the fears of the most reluctant of prophets (see Ge 26:3; Ex 3:12–15; Jos 1:5 and notes). *rescue.* See v. 19; 15:20; 39:17. The Lord does not promise that Jeremiah will not be persecuted or imprisoned but that no serious physical harm will come to him.

1:9 *touched my mouth.* Either in prophetic vision (see note on v. 11) or figuratively—or both (cf. Isa 6:7). *I have put my words in your mouth.* Continues the figure of speech begun earlier in the verse and provides a classic description of the relationship between the Lord and his prophet (see 5:14; Ex 4:15; Nu 22:38; 23:5,12,16; Dt 18:18; Isa 51:16; cf. 2Pe 1:21).

1:10 *appoint.* See note on v. 5. *uproot and tear down ... destroy and overthrow ... build and ... plant.* See 12:14–15,17; 18:7–10; 24:6; 31:28; 42:10; 45:4. The first two pairs of verbs are negative, stressing the fact that Jeremiah is to be primarily a prophet of doom, while the last pair is positive, indicating that he is also to be a prophet of restoration—even if only secondarily. The first verb ("uproot") is the opposite of the last ("plant"), and fully half of the verbs ("tear down," "destroy," "overthrow") are the opposite of "build."

11 The word of the LORD came to me: "What do you see, Jeremiah?"[w]

"I see the branch of an almond tree," I replied.

12 The LORD said to me, "You have seen correctly, for I am watching[a][x] to see that my word is fulfilled."

13 The word of the LORD came to me again: "What do you see?"[y]

"I see a pot that is boiling," I answered. "It is tilting toward us from the north."

14 The LORD said to me, "From the north[z] disaster will be poured out on all who live in the land. 15 I am about to summon all the peoples of the northern kingdoms," declares the LORD.

"Their kings will come and set up their
thrones
in the entrance of the gates of
Jerusalem;
they will come against all her
surrounding walls
and against all the towns of Judah.[a]
16 I will pronounce my judgments[b] on my
people
because of their wickedness[c] in
forsaking me,[d]
in burning incense to other gods[e]
and in worshiping[f] what their hands
have made.[g]

17 "Get yourself ready! Stand up and say[h] to them whatever I command you. Do not be terrified[i] by them, or I will terrify you before them. 18 Today I have made you[j] a fortified city, an iron pillar and a bronze wall to stand against the whole land—against the kings of Judah, its officials, its priests and the people of the land. 19 They will fight against you but will not overcome[k] you, for I am with you[l] and will rescue[m] you," declares the LORD.

1:11 [w] Jer 24:3; Am 7:8 1:12 [x] S Job 29:2; Jer 44:27 1:13 [y] Jer 24:3; Zec 4:2; 5:2 1:14 [z] S Isa 14:31 1:15 [a] Jer 4:16; 9:11; 10:22 1:16 [b] Jer 4:12 [c] S Ge 6:5; Jer 44:5 [d] Jer 2:13; 17:13 [e] S Ex 20:3; Jer 7:9; 19:4; 44:3 [f] S Nu 25:3 [g] Ps 115:4-8; S 135:15 1:17 [h] ver 7; Jer 7:27; 26:2, 15; 42:4 [i] S Dt 31:6; S 2Ki 1:15 1:18 [j] S Isa 50:7 1:19 [k] S Ps 129:2 [l] S Ge 26:3; Isa 43:2; Jer 20:11 [m] S ver 8; S Pr 20:22; Ac 26:17 2:1 [n] Isa 38:4; Eze 1:3; Mic 1:1 2:2 [o] Ps 71:17; Isa 54:4; Jer 3:4; Eze 16:8-14, 60; Hos 2:15; 11:1; Rev 2:4 [p] S Ex 13:21; S Dt 1:19 2:3 [q] S Dt 7:6

Israel Forsakes God

2 The word[n] of the LORD came to me: 2 "Go and proclaim in the hearing of Jerusalem:

"This is what the LORD says:

" 'I remember the devotion of your
youth,[o]
how as a bride you loved me
and followed me through the
wilderness,[p]
through a land not sown.
3 Israel was holy[q] to the LORD,[r]
the firstfruits[s] of his harvest;
all who devoured[t] her were held
guilty,[u]
and disaster overtook them,' "
declares the LORD.

[a] 12 The Hebrew for *watching* sounds like the Hebrew for *almond tree.*

[r] S Ex 19:6; S Dt 7:6 [s] Lev 23:9-14; Jas 1:18; Rev 14:4 [t] Isa 41:11; Jer 10:25; 30:16 [u] Jer 50:7

1:11 *What do you see ... ?* Often spoken by the Lord (or his representative) to introduce a prophetic vision (see v. 13; Am 7:8; 8:2; Zec 4:2; 5:2).

1:12 *watching.* See NIV text note. Just as the almond tree (v. 11) blooms first in the year (and therefore "wakes up" early—the Hebrew word for "watching" means to be wakeful), so the Lord is ever watchful to make sure his word is fulfilled (see Isa 55:10–11).

1:13 *pot.* The Hebrew for this word is translated "caldron" in Job 41:31 and stresses its large size (see Eze 24:3–5).

1:14 *From the north disaster.* See note on Isa 41:25. *will be poured out.* The Hebrew for this word has a sound similar to that for "boiling" in v. 13. *land.* Judah (see v. 15).

1:15 *northern kingdoms.* Since Assyria posed only a minimal threat to Judah after the death of Ashurbanipal in 627 BC, reference is most likely to Babylonia and her allies. *set up their thrones in ... the gates of Jerusalem.* For the fulfillment, see 39:3. Since the gateway of a city was the place where its ruling council sat (see notes on Ge 19:1; Ru 4:1), the Babylonians replaced Judah's royal authority with their own (cf. 43:10; 49:38).

1:16 *my judgments on my people.* God, sovereign over his own, judges them for their sins, using the Babylonians as his agents of judgment. *burning incense to other gods.* A common feature of pagan worship (e.g., 7:9; 11:12–13,17; 18:15; 19:13; 32:29; 44:17). *what their hands have made.* Idols (see 16:19–20; 25:6; 2Ki 22:17; 2Ch 33:22; Isa 46:6).

1:17 *Get yourself ready!* Lit. "Tighten your belt around your waist!" For related expressions, see Ex 12:11; 1Ki 18:46; 2Ki 4:29; 9:1; Job 38:3; 40:7.

1:18 *fortified city.* A symbol of security and impregnability (see 5:17; Pr 18:11,19). *iron pillar.* Unique in the OT, the expression signifies dignity and strength. *bronze wall.* See 15:20. Jeremiah would be able to withstand the abuse and persecution that his divine commission would evoke, even though his enemies themselves would be "bronze and iron" (6:28). *kings ... officials ... priests ... people.* The whole nation would defy the prophet and his God (see, e.g., 2:26; 23:8; 32:32).

1:19 See note on v. 8; see also 15:20.

2:1—6:30 It is generally agreed that these chapters are among Jeremiah's earliest discourses, delivered during the reign of Josiah (3:6). The basic theme is the virtually total apostasy of Judah (chs. 2–5), leading inevitably to divine retribution through foreign invasion (ch. 6).

2:1—3:5 The wickedness and backsliding of God's people are vividly portrayed in numerous colorful figures of speech.

2:1 See note on 1:2.

2:2 *devotion.* The Hebrew for this word refers to the most intimate degree of loyalty, love and faithfulness that can exist between two people or between an individual and the Lord. *youth ... as a bride.* Early in her history, Israel had enjoyed a close and cordial relationship with the Lord, who is often described figuratively as Israel's husband (3:14; 31:32; Isa 54:5; Hos 2:16). *you loved me.* But later God's people forsook him and loved "foreign gods" (v. 25), tragically abandoning their first love (cf. Rev 2:4). *followed me.* But later they followed "worthless idols" (vv. 5,8), "the Baals" (v. 23). *wilderness.* Sinai (see v. 6).

2:3 *holy to the LORD.* Set apart to him and his service (see notes on Ex 3:5; Lev 11:44; Dt 7:6). *firstfruits.* Just as the "best of the firstfruits" of Israel's crops were to be brought to the Lord (Ex 23:19; see Nu 18:12; 2Ch 31:5; Eze 44:30), so also the people themselves were his first and choicest treasure (cf. Jas 1:18; Rev 14:4 and note). *disaster overtook them.* See, e.g., Ex 17:8–16.

4 Hear the word of the LORD, you
descendants of Jacob,
all you clans of Israel.

5 This is what the LORD says:

"What fault did your ancestors
find in me,
that they strayed so far from me?
They followed worthless idols[v]
and became worthless[w]
themselves.
6 They did not ask, 'Where is the
LORD,
who brought us up out of
Egypt[x]
and led us through the barren
wilderness,
through a land of deserts[y] and
ravines,[z]
a land of drought and utter
darkness,
a land where no one travels[a]
and no one lives?'
7 I brought you into a fertile land
to eat its fruit and rich produce.[b]
But you came and defiled my land
and made my inheritance
detestable.[c]
8 The priests did not ask,
'Where is the LORD?'
Those who deal with the law did not
know me;[d]
the leaders[e] rebelled against me.
The prophets prophesied by Baal,[f]
following worthless idols.[g]

9 "Therefore I bring charges[h] against you
again,"
declares the LORD.
"And I will bring charges against
your children's children.
10 Cross over to the coasts of Cyprus[i] and
look,
send to Kedar[a][j] and observe closely;
see if there has ever been anything
like this:
11 Has a nation ever changed its gods?
(Yet they are not gods[k] at all.)
But my people have exchanged their
glorious[l] God
for worthless idols.

The throne/podium discovered at the city gate of Dan. "Their kings will come and set up their thrones in the entrance of the gates of Jerusalem" (Jer 1:15).

[a] *10* In the Syro-Arabian desert

2:5 [v] S Dt 32:21; S 1Sa 12:21; Ps 31:6 [w] 2Ki 17:15 **2:6** [x] S Ex 6:6; Hos 13:4 [y] S Dt 1:19 [z] S Dt 32:10 [a] Jer 51:43 **2:7** [b] S Nu 13:27; Dt 8:7-9; 11:10-12 [c] Ps 106:34-39; Jer 3:9; 7:30; 16:18; Eze 11:21; 36:17 **2:8** [d] S 1Sa 2:12; Jer 4:22 [e] Jer 3:15; 23:1; 25:34; 50:6 [f] S 1Ki 18:22 [g] ver 25; S Isa 40:19; S 56:10; Jer 5:19; 9:14; 16:19; 22:9 **2:9** [h] Jer 25:31; Hos 4:1; Mic 6:2 **2:10** [i] S Ge 10:4 [j] S Ge 25:13 **2:11** [k] S Isa 37:19; Jer 16:20; Gal 4:8 [l] S 1Sa 4:21; Ro 1:23

2:4 *Hear.* A common divine imperative in prophetic writings, summoning God's people—as well as the nations—into his courts to remind them of their legal obligations to him and, when necessary, to pass judgment on them (see, e.g., 7:2; 17:20; 19:3; 21:11; 22:2,29; 31:10; 42:15; 44:24,26; Isa 1:10; Eze 13:2; Hos 4:1; Am 7:16).

2:5 *This is what the LORD says.* The messenger formula, introducing God's word through the prophet. Though frequent in overall occurrence, its use in the prophetic books is restricted to Jeremiah, Isaiah (e.g., 7:7), Ezekiel (e.g., 2:4), Amos (e.g., 1:3), Obadiah (1), Micah (3:5), Nahum (1:12), Haggai (e.g., 1:2), Zechariah (e.g., 1:3) and Malachi (1:4). *strayed.* See 4:1; 23:13,32; 31:19; 50:6; Isa 53:6; Eze 34:4–6,16; 1Pe 2:25. *followed worthless idols.* See vv. 8,23; see also note on v. 2. "Worthless" is Jeremiah's favorite way of describing idols (8:19; 10:8,15; 14:22; 16:19; 51:18). *became worthless themselves.* See 2Ki 17:15. Idolaters are no better than the idols they worship (see Ps 115:8 and note).

2:6 *LORD … brought us up out of Egypt.* The Lord, Israel's Redeemer (see notes on Ge 2:4; Ex 3:15), freed his people from Egyptian bondage so that they might serve him alone (Ex 20:2–6). *led us.* As a shepherd leads his sheep (see v. 17; Dt 8:15; Ps 23:2–3). *land of deserts … land of … darkness.* The desert often symbolized darkness with its attendant dangers, including death (see v. 31 and note; 9:10; 12:12; 17:6; 23:10; Ps 44:19).

2:7 *fertile.* The Hebrew for this word is *karmel*, translated "orchards" in 48:33 and also used as the name of a place (see Isa 33:9 and note). Rendered "fruitful land" in 4:26, it is the opposite of a desert. *defiled my land.* Made it ceremonially unclean (see 3:1–2,9; 16:18; see also note on Lev 4:12). *inheritance.* The promised land, given by God to Israel as a legacy and often intimately associated with the people themselves (see especially 12:7–9,14–15). *detestable.* See note on Lev 7:21.

2:8 No one consulted the Lord (see v. 6). *priests … leaders … prophets.* See note on 1:18. *Those who deal with the law.* Priests (see Dt 31:11 and note). *leaders.* Lit. "shepherds," a term used elsewhere to denote rulers (23:1–4; 49:19; 50:44; see especially Eze 34:1–10,23–24). *by Baal.* In the name of Baal (cf. 11:21; 14:15; 23:25; 26:9; see note on Jdg 2:13). *following worthless idols.* See v. 23. *worthless.* Lit. "unprofitable" (see v. 11).

2:9 *bring charges against.* See note on v. 4; see also 25:31; Hos 4:1; 12:2; Mic 6:2.

2:10 *Cyprus.* See Nu 24:24; Eze 27:6 and notes. *Kedar.* Represents the eastern nations and regions (see NIV text note; see also 49:28; Isa 21:16 and note).

2:11 *Has … gods?* A rhetorical question, clearly expecting a negative answer and emphasizing how incredible is Judah's practice of substituting idolatry for the worship of the Lord. *their glorious God.* See Ps 106:20; Hos 4:7; see also 1Sa 15:29. *worthless.* See note on v. 8.

12 Be appalled at this, you heavens,
and shudder with great horror,"
declares the LORD.
13 "My people have committed two sins:
They have forsaken[m] me,
the spring of living water,[n]
and have dug their own cisterns,
broken cisterns that cannot hold water.
14 Is Israel a servant, a slave[o] by birth?
Why then has he become plunder?
15 Lions[p] have roared;
they have growled at him.
They have laid waste[q] his land;
his towns are burned[r] and deserted.[s]
16 Also, the men of Memphis[t] and Tahpanhes[u]
have cracked your skull.
17 Have you not brought this on yourselves[v]
by forsaking[w] the LORD your God
when he led you in the way?
18 Now why go to Egypt[x]
to drink water from the Nile[a]?[y]
And why go to Assyria[z]
to drink water from the Euphrates?[a]
19 Your wickedness will punish you;
your backsliding[b] will rebuke[c] you.
Consider then and realize
how evil and bitter[d] it is for you
when you forsake[e] the LORD your God
and have no awe[f] of me,"
declares the Lord,
the LORD Almighty.

2:13 [m] S Dt 31:16; S Isa 65:11 [n] S Isa 12:3; Jn 4:14 **2:14** [o] Ex 4:22; Jer 31:9 **2:15** [p] Jer 4:7; 50:17 [q] S Isa 1:7 [r] S 2Ki 25:9 [s] S Lev 26:43 **2:16** [t] S Isa 19:13 [u] Jer 43:7-9 **2:17** [v] Jer 4:18 [w] S Isa 1:28; Jer 17:13; 19:4 **2:18** [x] S Isa 30:2 [y] S Jos 13:3 [z] S 2Ki 16:7; Hos 5:13; 7:11; 8:9 [a] S Isa 7:20 **2:19** [b] Jer 3:11, 22; 7:24; 11:10; 14:7; Hos 14:4 [c] Isa 3:9; 59:12; Hos 5:5 [d] S Job 20:14; Am 8:10 [e] Jer 19:4 [f] S Ps 36:1 **2:20** [g] S Lev 26:13 [h] Ps 2:3; Jer 5:5 [i] S Job 21:14 [j] Isa 57:7; Jer 3:23; 17:2 [k] S Dt 12:2 [l] S Isa 1:21; Eze 16:15 **2:21** [m] S Ex 15:17 [n] S Ps 80:8 [o] S Isa 5:4 **2:22** [p] S Ps 51:2; La 1:8,17 [q] S Job 9:30

20 "Long ago you broke off your yoke[g]
and tore off your bonds;[h]
you said, 'I will not serve you!'[i]
Indeed, on every high hill[j]
and under every spreading tree[k]
you lay down as a prostitute.[l]
21 I had planted[m] you like a choice vine[n]
of sound and reliable stock.
How then did you turn against me
into a corrupt,[o] wild vine?
22 Although you wash[p] yourself with soap[q]
and use an abundance of cleansing powder,
the stain of your guilt is still before me,"
declares the Sovereign LORD.[r]
23 "How can you say, 'I am not defiled;[s]
I have not run after the Baals'?[t]
See how you behaved in the valley;[u]
consider what you have done.
You are a swift she-camel
running[v] here and there,
24 a wild donkey[w] accustomed to the desert,[x]
sniffing the wind in her craving—
in her heat who can restrain her?

[a] 18 Hebrew *Shihor;* that is, a branch of the Nile

[r] Jer 17:1 **2:23** [s] S Pr 30:12 [t] ver 25; Jer 9:14; 23:27 [u] S 2Ki 23:10; Jer 7:31; 19:2; 31:40 [v] ver 33; Jer 31:22 **2:24** [w] S Ge 16:12; Jer 14:6 [x] S Job 39:6

2:12 *Be appalled ... you heavens.* See note on Isa 1:2; see also Mic 6:1–2 and note. The Hebrew for these phrases offers a striking play on words: *shommu shamayim.*

2:13 See 1:16. *forsaken me.* See v. 19. *me, the spring of living water.* See 17:13. God himself provides life-giving power to his people (see Ps 36:9; see also note on Jn 4:10; Isa 55:1 and note; Rev 21:6). *broken cisterns.* Watertight plaster was used to keep cisterns from losing water. Idols, like broken cisterns, will always fail their worshipers; by contrast, God provides life abundant and unfailing (cf. Jn 10:10 and note).

2:14 *Is ... birth?* Another rhetorical question (see note on v. 11), again expecting a negative answer in the light of God's redemptive acts during the period of the exodus (see Ex 6:6; 20:2). *plunder.* To Assyria and Egypt (see vv. 15–16).

2:15 *Lions.* Probably symbolizing Assyria (see v. 18; 50:17; see also notes on 4:7; Isa 15:9). *roared ... growled.* See Am 3:4. *laid waste his land.* See 4:7; 18:16; 50:3. *towns are burned and deserted.* The Hebrew for this phrase is very similar to that in 4:7, rendered there "towns will lie in ruins without inhabitant" (cf. 22:6).

2:16 *Memphis.* See 44:1; 46:14,19; see also note on Isa 19:13. *Tahpanhes.* Probably the city later called Daphnai by the Greeks, located just south of Lake Menzaleh in the eastern delta region of Egypt and known today as Tell Defneh (see 43:7–9; 44:1; 46:14; Eze 30:18; see also map, p. 1311).

2:17 *he led you.* See note on v. 6. *the way.* See Ex 18:8; 23:20; Dt 1:33.

2:18 See v. 36. The tendency of Israel or Judah to seek help alternately from Egypt and Assyria was not restricted to Jeremiah's time (see, e.g., Hos 7:11; 12:2). *drink water.* Provided by enemies, whether national or spiritual, rather than by God (see v. 13; Isa 8:6–8 and notes).

2:19 *backsliding.* See 3:22; 5:6; 14:7. The word implies repeated apostasy. *LORD Almighty.* A title for God occurring about 75 times in Jeremiah—more than in any other OT book (see note on 1Sa 1:3).

2:20—3:6 The rebellion of Judah against God is vividly portrayed by Jeremiah with the use of numerous figures of speech.

2:20 Like a stubborn farm animal (see Hos 4:16), Judah refuses to obey the Lord's commands. *broke off your yoke and tore off your bonds.* See 5:5; see also 31:18; cf. Ps 2:3. Judah has broken God's law and violated his covenant. *on every high hill and under every spreading tree.* Locales of pagan worship (see 1Ki 14:23; 2Ki 17:10; Eze 6:13). *as a prostitute.* See v. 2; Ex 34:15 and notes.

2:21 See Isa 5:1–7; see also Ps 80:8–16; Eze 17:1–10; Hos 10:1–2; cf. Jn 15:1–8. *choice vine.* See Isa 5:2. The Hebrew for this word refers to a grape of exceptional quality. *wild.* Lit. "foreign." A vine symbolizing Israel should not be like a vine symbolizing Israel's enemies (see Dt 32:32).

2:22 *soap ... cleansing powder.* Vegetable alkali and mineral alkali, respectively. Sins can be removed and forgiven (see Ps 51:2,7; Isa 1:18), but only when the sinner repents and confesses (see Pr 28:13; cf. 1Jn 1:7,9).

2:23 *defiled.* Ceremonially unclean (see 19:13; see also note on Lev 4:12). *run after.* See note on v. 2; see also v. 25. *Baals.* See 9:14; see also notes on Jdg 2:11,13. *the valley.* Probably the Hinnom Valley (see note on Jos 15:5), known also as the Valley of Ben Hinnom (7:31–32; 19:2,6; 32:35). *running here and there.* Instead, the people of Judah should have been obeying the Lord, not turning aside either "to the right or to the left" (Dt 28:14).

2:24 *wild donkey.* Properly the wild ass, an unruly (see Ge 16:12) and intractable (see Job 39:5–8) animal. *accustomed*

Any males that pursue her need not
tire themselves;
at mating time they will find her.
25 Do not run until your feet are bare
and your throat is dry.
But you said, 'It's no use![y]
I love foreign gods,[z]
and I must go after them.'[a]

26 "As a thief is disgraced[b] when he is
caught,
so the people of Israel are disgraced—
they, their kings and their officials,
their priests[c] and their prophets.[d]
27 They say to wood,[e] 'You are my father,'
and to stone,[f] 'You gave me birth.'
They have turned their backs[g] to me
and not their faces;[h]
yet when they are in trouble,[i] they say,
'Come and save[j] us!'
28 Where then are the gods[k] you made for
yourselves?
Let them come if they can save you
when you are in trouble![l]
For you, Judah, have as many gods
as you have towns.[m]

29 "Why do you bring charges against me?
You have all[n] rebelled against me,"
declares the LORD.
30 "In vain I punished your people;
they did not respond to correction.[o]
Your sword has devoured your
prophets[p]
like a ravenous lion.

31 "You of this generation, consider the
word of the LORD:

"Have I been a desert to Israel
or a land of great darkness?[q]
Why do my people say, 'We are free to
roam;
we will come to you no more'?[r]
32 Does a young woman forget her
jewelry,
a bride her wedding ornaments?
Yet my people have forgotten[s] me,
days without number.
33 How skilled you are at pursuing[t] love!
Even the worst of women can learn
from your ways.
34 On your clothes is found
the lifeblood[u] of the innocent poor,
though you did not catch them
breaking in.[v]
Yet in spite of all this
35 you say, 'I am innocent;[w]
he is not angry with me.'
But I will pass judgment[x] on you
because you say, 'I have not
sinned.'[y]
36 Why do you go about so much,
changing[z] your ways?
You will be disappointed by Egypt[a]
as you were by Assyria.
37 You will also leave that place
with your hands on your head,[b]
for the LORD has rejected those you
trust;
you will not be helped[c] by them.

3 "If a man divorces[d] his wife
and she leaves him and marries
another man,
should he return to her again?
Would not the land be completely
defiled?[e]

2:25 [y] S Isa 57:10 [z] Dt 32:16; Jer 3:13; 14:10 [a] S ver 8, S 23 **2:26** [b] Jer 48:27; La 1:7; Eze 16:54; 36:4 [c] Eze 22:26 [d] Jer 32:32; 44:17,21 **2:27** [e] Jer 10:8 [f] Jer 3:9 [g] S 1Ki 14:9; S 2Ch 29:6; Ps 14:3; Eze 8:16 [h] Jer 18:17; 32:33; Eze 7:22 [i] Jdg 10:10; Isa 26:16 [j] Isa 37:20; Hos 5:15 **2:28** [k] S Isa 45:20 [l] S Dt 32:37; S Isa 40:19 [m] S 2Ki 17:29 **2:29** [n] Jer 5:1; 6:13; Da 9:11; Mic 3:11; 7:2 **2:30** [o] S Lev 26:23 [p] S Ne 9:26; S Jer 11:21; Ac 7:52; 1Th 2:15 **2:31** [q] Isa 45:19 [r] S Job 21:14 **2:32** [s] S Dt 32:18; S Isa 57:11 **2:33** [t] S ver 23 **2:34** [u] S 2Ki 21:16; S Pr 6:17 [v] S Ex 22:2 **2:35** [w] S Pr 30:12 [x] Isa 66:16; Jer 25:31; 39:7; 45:5; Eze 17:20; 20:35; Joel 3:2 [y] S 2Sa 12:13; 1Jn 1:8,10 **2:36** [z] Jer 31:22 [a] S Ps 108:12; S Isa 30:2,3,7; Jer 37:7 **2:37** [b] 2Sa 13:19 [c] Jer 37:7 **3:1** [d] Dt 24:1-4 [e] S Ge 3:17

to the desert. See 14:6; Job 24:5. *sniffing the wind.* The picture is one of active searching, not passive waiting (see Hos 2:7,13).

2:25 *your feet are bare.* You wear out your sandals. *It's no use!* See 18:12 and note. *I love foreign gods.* As opposed to the love Judah was expected to express toward God under the terms of their covenant relationship (see, e.g., Dt 6:5; 7:9; Hos 2:16; see also Ex 39:15 and note). *go after them.* See v. 23; see also note on v. 2.

2:26 *disgraced when he is caught.* See, e.g., Ex 22:3–4. The Hebrew word underlying "disgraced" means lit. "shame," a term often used as a pejorative synonym for the name of Baal, the chief god of Canaan (see 11:13 and note; Hos 9:10; see also note on Jdg 6:32). *kings ... officials ... priests ... prophets.* See note on 1:18.

2:27 See Isa 44:13–17; contrast Dt 32:6,18; Isa 64:8; Mal 2:10. *wood ... stone.* Materials used to make idols (see 3:9 and note). *Come ... save.* See v. 28.

2:28 *as many gods as ... towns.* See 11:13; cf. 1Co 8:5. Every ancient Near Eastern town of any importance had its own patron deity (cf. Ac 19:28,34–35), and many towns were named after deities (see, e.g., note on 1:1).

2:29 *bring charges against.* Cf. v. 9; see 12:1; Job 33:13.

2:30 *I punished your people.* Cf. Heb 12:6. *did not respond to correction.* See 5:3. *sword has devoured your prophets.* See, e.g., 26:20–23; 2Ki 21:16; 24:4; see also Ne 9:26.

2:31 *generation.* Often has negative connotations (see, e.g., Dt 1:35; 32:5; Mt 12:39; 16:4; 17:17; Ac 2:40; Php 2:15; Heb 3:10). *Have I been a desert ... a land of great darkness?* On the contrary, the Lord led his people through the desert and its darkness (v. 6). The phrase "great darkness" translates the Hebrew for "darkness of the LORD" (i.e., darkness sent by the Lord; cf. 1Sa 26:12), just as "mighty flame" in SS 8:6 translates "flame of the LORD" (see note and NIV text note there).

2:32 See Isa 49:15,18 and notes. *bride.* Cf. v. 2. *my people have forgotten me.* See 18:15; see also 3:21; 13:25; Isa 17:10; Eze 22:12; 23:35; Hos 8:14. Israel was always to "remember" the Lord and all that he had done for her (Dt 7:18; 8:18) and so trust and worship him alone, but she often "forgot" him—put him out of mind (see Jdg 2:10; Hos 2:13).

2:33 *love.* See v. 25 and note.

2:34 See Am 2:6–8; 4:1; 5:11–12. *catch them breaking in.* See Ex 22:2 and note.

2:36 *disappointed by Egypt ... by Assyria.* See vv. 15–18 and notes. The days of Ahaz (see 2Ch 28:21), and perhaps the days of Zedekiah (see 37:7), are in view here.

2:37 *with your hands on your head.* Ancient reliefs depict captives with wrists tied together above their heads. *those you trust.* Egypt and Assyria.

3:1 *If ... defiled?* Cf. Dt 24:1–4. Divorce and remarriage on a widespread scale defiles not only the participants

But you have lived as a prostitute with
many lovers[f]—
would you now return to me?"[g]
declares the LORD.
2 "Look up to the barren heights[h] and
see.
Is there any place where you have
not been ravished?
By the roadside[i] you sat waiting for
lovers,
sat like a nomad in the desert.
You have defiled the land[j]
with your prostitution[k] and
wickedness.
3 Therefore the showers have been
withheld,[l]
and no spring rains[m] have fallen.
Yet you have the brazen[n] look of a
prostitute;
you refuse to blush with shame.[o]
4 Have you not just called to me:
'My Father,[p] my friend from my
youth,[q]
5 will you always be angry?[r]
Will your wrath continue forever?'
This is how you talk,
but you do all the evil you can."

Unfaithful Israel

6 During the reign of King Josiah,[s] the
LORD said to me, "Have you seen what
faithless[t] Israel has done? She has gone up
on every high hill and under every spreading tree[u] and has committed adultery[v] there.
7 I thought that after she had done all this
she would return to me but she did not,
and her unfaithful sister[w] Judah saw it.[x]
8 I gave faithless Israel[y] her certificate of
divorce[z] and sent her away because of all
her adulteries. Yet I saw that her unfaithful sister Judah had no fear;[a] she also went
out and committed adultery. 9 Because Israel's immorality mattered so little to her, she
defiled the land[b] and committed adultery[c]
with stone[d] and wood.[e] 10 In spite of all this,
her unfaithful sister Judah did not return[f]
to me with all her heart, but only in pretense,[g]" declares the LORD.[h]
11 The LORD said to me, "Faithless Israel
is more righteous[i] than unfaithful[j] Judah.[k]
12 Go, proclaim this message toward the
north:[l]

" 'Return,[m] faithless[n] Israel,' declares
the LORD,
'I will frown on you no longer,
for I am faithful,'[o] declares the LORD,
'I will not be angry[p] forever.
13 Only acknowledge[q] your guilt—
you have rebelled against the LORD
your God,
you have scattered your favors to
foreign gods[r]
under every spreading tree,[s]
and have not obeyed[t] me,' "
declares the LORD.

14 "Return,[u] faithless people," declares
the LORD, "for I am your husband.[v] I will
choose you—one from a town and two

3:1 [f] S 2Ki 16:7; S Isa 1:21; Jer 2:20,25; 4:30; La 1:2; Eze 16:26,29; Hos 2:5,12; 3:1 [g] Hos 2:7 **3:2** [h] ver 21 [i] Ge 38:14; Eze 16:25 [j] ver 9 [k] S Nu 15:39; S Isa 1:21 **3:3** [l] Lev 26:19; Jer 5:25; Am 4:7 [m] S Dt 11:14; Jer 14:4; Joel 1:10 [n] Eze 3:7; 16:30 [o] Jer 6:15; 8:12; Zep 2:1; 3:5 **3:4** [p] ver 19; S Dt 32:6; S Ps 89:26; Isa 63:16; 64:8; Jer 31:9 [q] S Jer 2:2 **3:5** [r] S Ps 103:9; S Isa 54:9 **3:6** [s] S 1Ch 3:14 [t] ver 12,22; S Isa 24:16; Jer 31:22; 49:4 [u] S Dt 12:2; Jer 17:2; Eze 20:28; Hos 4:13 [v] S Lev 17:7; Jer 2:20 **3:7** [w] Eze 16:46; 23:2,11 [x] Am 4:8 **3:8** [y] Jer 11:10 [z] S Dt 4:27; S 24:1 [a] Eze 16:47; 23:11 **3:9** [b] ver 2 [c] S Lev 17:7; S Isa 1:21 [d] S Isa 57:6 [e] Jer 2:27 **3:10** [f] Isa 31:6; Am 4:9; Hag 2:17 [g] Jer 12:2; Eze 33:31 [h] S 2Ki 17:19 **3:11** [i] Eze 16:52; 23:11 [j] ver 7 [k] S Jer 2:19 **3:12** [l] 2Ki 17:3-6 [m] ver 14; S Dt 4:30; Jer 31:21,22; Eze 14:6; 33:11; Hos 14:1 [n] S ver 6 [o] S 1Ki 3:26; S Ps 6:2 [p] S Ps 103:9; S Isa 54:9 **3:13** [q] Dt 30:1-3; Jer 14:20; 1Jn 1:9 [r] S Jer 2:25 [s] S Dt 12:2 [t] ver 25; Jer 22:21 **3:14** [u] S ver 12; S Job 22:23; Jer 4:1 [v] S Isa 54:5

but also the land in which they live (cf. v. 2; Lev 18:25–28). *lived as a prostitute with many lovers.* A metaphor carried forward from ch. 2 and used throughout ch. 3 (see 2:20,25,33 and note on 2:25). *many.* See note on 2:28. *return to me.* Repent of your sins against me (see vv. 12–14,22; 4:1).

3:2 *barren heights.* Places where pagan gods were consulted and worshiped (see v. 21; 12:12; Nu 23:3). *ravished.* Cf. Dt 28:30. *By the roadside you sat.* See Ge 38:14 and note; Pr 7:10,12. *like a nomad in the desert.* Waiting in ambush to waylay a traveler (cf. Lk 10:30). *defiled the land.* See v. 9.

3:3 *showers have been withheld.* See 14:1–6; Am 4:7–8. This is the reverse of God's gracious response to his people in Hos 2:21; 6:3. *spring rains.* See notes on Dt 11:14; Jas 5:7. *brazen look.* See Pr 7:13.

3:4 *My Father.* See v. 19; contrast 2:27 and see note there. Compared to the NT, the title "Father" for God is relatively rare in the OT. However, it often occurs in personal names—compound names that begin with Abi- (e.g., Abinadab and Abiram) refer to God as "(my) Father." *my friend.* Claiming intimate association (see Ps 55:13; Pr 16:28; 17:9; Mic 7:5); perhaps even claiming to be the Lord's faithful wife (cf. Pr 2:17). *from my youth.* See note on 2:2.

3:5 *Will your wrath continue forever?* Not if God's people repent (vv. 12–13).

3:6—6:30 The unfaithfulness of Judah (3:6—5:31) will ultimately bring the Babylonians as God's instrument of judgment (ch. 6).

3:6 *King Josiah.* See Introduction: Background; see also note on 1:2. *faithless Israel.* The northern kingdom, destroyed in 722–721 BC (see vv. 8,11–12).

3:7 *her unfaithful sister Judah.* The southern kingdom (see vv. 8,10–11). Samaria (Israel's capital) and Jerusalem (Judah's capital) are similarly compared as adulterous sisters in Eze 23. *it.* Israel's adultery.

3:8 *certificate of divorce.* See v. 1 and note; see also Dt 24:1–4; Isa 50:1 and notes. *sent her away.* Into exile in 721 BC. *Judah had no fear.* She refused to learn from Israel's tragic experience.

3:9 *committed adultery with stone and wood.* Worshiped pagan deities (see notes on 2:27; Ex 34:15).

3:10 *in pretense.* Judah's response to Josiah's reform measures (see note on 1:2) was superficial and hypocritical.

3:11 *Israel is more righteous than … Judah.* See note on v. 8; see also Eze 16:51–52; 23:11.

3:12 *Go, proclaim.* See 2:2. *north.* Assyria's northern provinces, to which many Israelites had been exiled. *Return.* Repent (see v. 13). *faithful.* The Hebrew for this word is used of God elsewhere only in Ps 145:13,17. *not be angry forever.* See note on v. 5.

3:13 *scattered your favors.* See Eze 16:15,33–34 and note on 16:33. *foreign gods.* See note on 2:25. *under every spreading tree.* See note on 2:20.

3:14 *husband.* See 31:32; Hos 2:16–17. The Hebrew root underlying this word is *ba'al.* Instead of allowing God to be

from a clan—and bring you to Zion.
15 Then I will give you shepherds[w] after my
own heart,[x] who will lead you with knowledge and understanding. 16 In those days,
when your numbers have increased greatly
in the land," declares the LORD, "people will
no longer say, 'The ark[y] of the covenant of
the LORD.' It will never enter their minds or
be remembered;[z] it will not be missed, nor
will another one be made. 17 At that time
they will call Jerusalem The Throne[a] of the
LORD, and all nations[b] will gather in Jerusalem to honor[c] the name of the LORD. No
longer will they follow the stubbornness of
their evil hearts.[d] 18 In those days the people of Judah will join the people of Israel,[e]
and together[f] they will come from a northern[g] land to the land[h] I gave your ancestors
as an inheritance.
19 "I myself said,

" 'How gladly would I treat you like my
children
and give you a pleasant land,[i]
the most beautiful inheritance[j] of
any nation.'
I thought you would call me 'Father'[k]
and not turn away from following me.
20 But like a woman unfaithful to her
husband,
so you, Israel, have been unfaithful[l]
to me,"
declares the LORD.
21 A cry is heard on the barren heights,[m]
the weeping[n] and pleading of the
people of Israel,
because they have perverted their ways
and have forgotten[o] the LORD their
God.

3:15 [w]S Isa 31:4 [x]Ac 13:22 **3:16** [y]S Nu 3:31; S 1Ch 15:25 [z]S Isa 65:17 **3:17** [a]S Ps 47:8; Jer 17:12; 33:16; Eze 1:26; 43:7; 48:35 [b]S Isa 2:3; Mic 4:1 [c]S Ps 22:23; Jer 13:11; 33:9 [d]Ps 81:12; Jer 7:24; 9:14; 11:8; 13:10; 16:12; 18:12 **3:18** [e]Jer 30:3; Eze 37:19 [f]S Isa 11:13; Jer 50:4 [g]Jer 16:15; 31:8 [h]Dt 31:7; S Isa 14:1; Eze 11:17; 37:22; Am 9:15 **3:19** [i]S Dt 8:7 [j]Ps 106:24; Eze 20:6 [k]S ver 4; S Ex 4:22; S 2Sa 7:14 **3:20** [l]S Isa 24:16 **3:21** [m]ver 2 [n]Jer 31:18 [o]S Isa 57:11 **3:22** [p]S ver 12; S Job 22:23 [q]S Isa 30:26; 57:18; Jer 33:6; Hos 6:1 [r]S Jer 2:19 **3:23** [s]S Jer 2:20 [t]Ps 3:8; Jer 17:14 **3:24** [u]Jer 11:13; Hos 9:10 **3:25** [v]S Ezr 9:6; Jer 31:19; Da 9:7 [w]S Jdg 10:10; S 1Ki 8:47 [x]Jer 14:20 [y]S Ps 25:7; S Jer 22:21 [z]S ver 13; Eze 2:3 **4:1** [a]S Dt 4:30; S 2Ki 17:13; S Hos 12:6 [b]S 2Ki 21:4; Jer 16:18; 35:15; Eze 8:5 **4:2** [c]Dt 10:20; S Isa 19:18; 65:16 [d]S Nu 14:21; Jer 5:2; 12:16; 44:26; Hos 4:15 [e]S Ge 12:2; Gal 3:8 [f]Jer 9:24

22 "Return,[p] faithless people;
I will cure[q] you of backsliding."[r]

"Yes, we will come to you,
for you are the LORD our God.
23 Surely the idolatrous commotion on
the hills[s]
and mountains is a deception;
surely in the LORD our God
is the salvation[t] of Israel.
24 From our youth shameful[u] gods have
consumed
the fruits of our ancestors' labor—
their flocks and herds,
their sons and daughters.
25 Let us lie down in our shame,[v]
and let our disgrace cover us.
We have sinned[w] against the LORD our
God,
both we and our ancestors;[x]
from our youth[y] till this day
we have not obeyed[z] the LORD our
God."

4 "If you, Israel, will return,[a]
then return to me,"
declares the LORD.
"If you put your detestable idols[b] out
of my sight
and no longer go astray,
2 and if in a truthful, just and righteous
way
you swear,[c] 'As surely as the LORD
lives,'[d]
then the nations will invoke blessings[e]
by him
and in him they will boast.[f]"

Israel's husband, his people followed "the Baals" (2:23; see note on Jdg 2:11). *one ... two.* A remnant will return (see note on Isa 10:20–22). *Zion.* Jerusalem.

3:15 See 23:4. *shepherds.* Rulers (see note on 2:8). *after my own heart.* Like David (see 1Sa 13:14; see also Eze 34:23; Hos 3:5).

3:16 *In those days.* The Messianic age (see v. 18; 31:29). *numbers have increased.* See 23:3; Eze 36:11. For the fuller meaning of the Hebrew underlying this phrase, see note on Ge 1:28. *nor will another one be made.* The ark of the covenant, formerly symbolizing God's royal presence (see 1Sa 4:3 and note), will be irrelevant when the Messiah comes.

3:17 *Throne.* The Lord sat "enthroned between the cherubim" above the ark (see 1Sa 4:4 and note), but Jerusalem itself would someday be his throne. *all nations will gather.* See Zec 2:11; see also note on Isa 2:2–4. *they.* Israel. *follow the stubbornness of their evil hearts.* A stock phrase referring to Israel's disobedience and often involving the worship of pagan gods (see 9:14; 11:8; 13:10; 16:12; 18:12; 23:17).

3:18 *Judah will join ... Israel.* In the Messianic age God's divided people will again be united (see, e.g., 31:31; Isa 11:12; Eze 37:15–23; Hos 1:11; Zec 11:7 and note). *northern land.* Where they had been exiles (see note on v. 12; see also 31:8). *land I gave ... as an inheritance.* See note on 2:7.

3:19 *my children.* Israel was the Lord's firstborn (see Ex 4:22; cf. Hos 11:1). *pleasant land.* See Ps 106:24; Zec 7:14. *beautiful inheritance.* Judah, Jerusalem, the people themselves—ideally, all were beautiful in God's eyes (see 6:2; 11:16). *Father.* See note on v. 4.

3:20 A concise summary of the story told in Hos 1–3 (see note on Ex 34:15).

3:21 *barren heights.* See note on v. 2. *weeping and pleading.* A description of repentance, verbalized in vv. 22b–25. *forgotten.* See note on 2:32.

3:22 See v. 14. *Return, faithless ... backsliding.* Each of these three words is derived from the same Hebrew root, producing a striking series of puns. *I will cure you.* See 30:17; 33:6; Hos 6:1; 14:4. *Yes.* The people's repentance begins.

3:23 *commotion.* See, e.g., 1Ki 18:25–29. *in the LORD ... is ... salvation.* See Ge 49:18; Ps 3:8; Jnh 2:9 and note.

3:24 *our youth.* The period of the judges. *shameful gods.* See notes on 2:26; 11:13. *consumed the fruits.* False worship is costly, both financially and spiritually. *sons and daughters.* Often sacrificed to pagan gods (see note on 7:31).

3:25 *shame.* The Hebrew for this word is translated "shameful gods" in v. 24.

4:2 *truthful, just and righteous.* The piling up of qualifying words underscores the need for repentance that is sincere and not perfunctory. *As surely as the LORD lives.* See

3 This is what the LORD says to the people of Judah and to Jerusalem:

"Break up your unplowed ground[g]
and do not sow among thorns.[h]
4 Circumcise yourselves to the LORD,
circumcise your hearts,[i]
you people of Judah and inhabitants of Jerusalem,
or my wrath[j] will flare up and burn like fire[k]
because of the evil[l] you have done—
burn with no one to quench[m] it.

Disaster From the North

5 "Announce in Judah and proclaim[n] in Jerusalem and say:
'Sound the trumpet[o] throughout the land!'
Cry aloud and say:
'Gather together!
Let us flee to the fortified cities!'[p]
6 Raise the signal[q] to go to Zion!
Flee for safety without delay!
For I am bringing disaster[r] from the north,[s]
even terrible destruction."

7 A lion[t] has come out of his lair;[u]
a destroyer[v] of nations has set out.
He has left his place
to lay waste[w] your land.
Your towns will lie in ruins[x]
without inhabitant.
8 So put on sackcloth,[y]
lament[z] and wail,
for the fierce anger[a] of the LORD
has not turned away from us.

9 "In that day," declares the LORD,
"the king and the officials will lose heart,[b]
the priests will be horrified,
and the prophets will be appalled."[c]

10 Then I said, "Alas, Sovereign LORD!
How completely you have deceived[d] this
people and Jerusalem by saying, 'You will
have peace,'[e] when the sword is at our
throats!"
11 At that time this people and Jerusalem
will be told, "A scorching wind[f] from the
barren heights in the desert blows toward
my people, but not to winnow or cleanse;
12 a wind[g] too strong for that comes from
me. Now I pronounce my judgments[h]
against them."

13 Look! He advances like the clouds,[i]
his chariots[j] come like a whirlwind,[k]
his horses[l] are swifter than eagles.[m]
Woe to us! We are ruined![n]
14 Jerusalem, wash[o] the evil from your heart and be saved.[p]
How long[q] will you harbor wicked thoughts?
15 A voice is announcing from Dan,[r]
proclaiming disaster from the hills of Ephraim.[s]

4:3 [g] Hos 10:12 [h] Mk 4:18 **4:4** [i] S Lev 26:41 [j] Zep 1:18; 2:2 [k] S Job 41:21 [l] S Ex 32:22 [m] Isa 1:31; Am 5:6 **4:5** [n] Jer 5:20; 11:2,6 [o] S ver 21; S Nu 10:2,7; S Job 39:24 [p] S Jos 10:20 **4:6** [q] ver 21; Ps 74:4; S Isa 11:10; 31:9; Jer 50:2 [r] Jer 11:11; 18:11 [s] S Isa 14:31; Jer 50:3 **4:7** [t] S 2Ki 24:1; S Jer 2:15 [u] Jer 25:38; Hos 5:14; 13:7; Na 2:12 [v] Jer 6:26; 15:8; 22:7; 48:8; 51:1, 53; Eze 21:31; 25:7 [w] S Isa 1:7; Eze 12:20 [x] ver 29; S Lev 26:31; S Isa 6:11 **4:8** [y] 1Ki 21:27; S Isa 3:24; Jer 6:26; Eze 7:18; Joel 1:8 [z] Jer 7:29; 9:20; Am 5:1 [a] S Isa 10:4; S Jer 30:24 **4:9** [b] S 1Sa 17:32 [c] S Isa 29:9 **4:10** [d] S Ex 5:23; 2Th 2:11 [e] Isa 30:10; Jer 6:14; 8:11; 14:13; 23:17; Eze 13:10; Mic 3:5; 1Th 5:3 **4:11** [f] S Ge 41:6; S Lev 26:33; S Job 1:19 **4:12** [g] S Isa 64:6 [h] Jer 1:16 **4:13** [i] S 2Sa 22:10; Isa 19:1 [j] Isa 66:15; Eze 26:10; Na 2:4 [k] S 2Ki 2:1 [l] Hab 3:8 [m] S Dt 28:49; Hab 1:8 [n] ver 20,27; Isa 6:11; 24:3; Jer 7:34; 9:11,19; 12:11; 25:11; 44:6; Mic 2:4 **4:14** [o] S Ru 3:3; S Ps 51:2; Jas 4:8 [p] Isa 45:22 [q] S Ps 6:3 **4:15** [r] S Ge 30:6 [s] Jer 31:6

note on Ge 42:15. *nations will invoke blessings by him.* Reflects the language of the seventh of God's great promises to Abram (see Ge 12:2–3 and note). Israel's repentance is a necessary precondition for the ultimate blessing of the nations.

4:3 *Break up your unplowed ground.* Probably quoted from Hos 10:12. *do not sow among thorns.* See Mt 13:7,22. Openness to the Lord's overtures is necessary, as is total commitment to him (see Eze 18:31).

4:4 *circumcise your hearts.* Consecrate your hearts (see 6:10 and NIV text note; 9:26; see also Ge 17:10 and note; Dt 10:16; 30:6; cf. Ro 2:29 and note; 1Co 7:19; Col 2:11). *wrath will … burn with no one to quench.* See 21:12; see also Isa 1:31; Am 5:6 and note. *because of the evil you have done.* Probably quoted from Dt 28:20.

4:5–31 The invaders from the north will bring God's judgment against his unrepentant people (see ch. 6).

4:5 *Sound the trumpet.* To warn of impending doom (see 6:1; see also note on Joel 2:1). *flee to the fortified cities.* See v. 6. To avoid capture by hostile troops, people living in the countryside would take refuge in the nearest walled town (see 5:17; 8:14; 34:7; 48:18).

4:6 See 6:1. *Raise the signal.* See note on Isa 5:26. *disaster from the north.* See 1:14; 6:22; the Babylonians (see 25:9; Isa 41:25 and notes). *terrible destruction.* See 6:1; cf. 48:3; 50:22; 51:54.

4:7 *lion.* A symbol of Babylonia (see note on 2:15). *destroyer.* Usually refers to Babylonia (6:26; 15:8; 48:8,32), but in 51:1,56 it refers to Persia and her allies (see 51:48,53). *towns … without inhabitant.* See note on 2:15; see also v. 25; 46:19.

4:8 *sackcloth.* See notes on Ge 37:34; Rev 11:3. *anger … has not turned away.* Contrast 2:35.

4:9 *In that day.* See note on Isa 2:11,17,20. *king … officials … priests … prophets.* See note on 1:18.

4:10 *you have deceived.* Not directly, but through false prophets (see, e.g., 1Ki 22:20–23 and note on 22:23). *You will have peace.* Here the words of false prophets, not of God (see 14:13; 23:17; see also 6:13–14; 8:10–11). *throats.* The Hebrew for this word is usually translated "soul" or "life," but originally it had the meaning "throat, neck" (see, e.g., Ps 69:1).

4:11 *scorching wind.* The sirocco or khamsin, a hot, dry wind that brings sand and dust (see Ps 11:6; Isa 11:15; Jnh 4:8). *winnow.* See note on Ru 1:22.

4:12 *too strong for that.* Neither winnowing (separating grain from chaff) nor cleansing (blowing dust from the grain), God's judgments will sweep away good and bad alike.

4:13 *advances like the clouds.* Cf. Eze 38:16. *chariots … like a whirlwind.* See 2Ki 2:11; 6:17; Ps 68:17; Isa 66:15. *horses are swifter than eagles.* See Hab 1:8, where the Babylonians (Hab 1:6) use horses that are "swifter than leopards" and employ cavalry that "fly like an eagle" (see also Dt 28:49). *ruined.* See v. 20; 9:19; 48:1.

4:14 *Jerusalem.* As the royal city of Judah and the most important metropolis of the nation, Jerusalem is addressed as representative of the nation. *wash.* See 2:22 and note. *wicked thoughts.* Against other people (see Pr 6:18; Isa 59:7).

4:15 *Dan.* Far away, close to the northern border of Israel (see 8:16). *Ephraim.* A few miles north of Jerusalem. The enemy,

16 "Tell this to the nations,
proclaim concerning Jerusalem:
'A besieging army is coming from a
distant land,[t]
raising a war cry[u] against the cities
of Judah.[v]
17 They surround[w] her like men guarding
a field,
because she has rebelled[x] against
me,' "
declares the LORD.
18 "Your own conduct and actions[y]
have brought this on you.[z]
This is your punishment.
How bitter[a] it is!
How it pierces to the heart!"
19 Oh, my anguish, my anguish![b]
I writhe in pain.[c]
Oh, the agony of my heart!
My heart pounds[d] within me,
I cannot keep silent.[e]
For I have heard the sound of the
trumpet;[f]
I have heard the battle cry.[g]
20 Disaster follows disaster;[h]
the whole land lies in ruins.[i]
In an instant my tents[j] are destroyed,
my shelter in a moment.
21 How long must I see the battle
standard[k]
and hear the sound of the
trumpet?[l]
22 "My people are fools;[m]
they do not know me.[n]
They are senseless children;
they have no understanding.[o]
They are skilled in doing evil;[p]
they know not how to do good."[q]

23 I looked at the earth,
and it was formless and empty;[r]
and at the heavens,
and their light[s] was gone.
24 I looked at the mountains,
and they were quaking;[t]
all the hills were swaying.
25 I looked, and there were no people;
every bird in the sky had flown
away.[u]
26 I looked, and the fruitful land was a
desert;[v]
all its towns lay in ruins[w]
before the LORD, before his fierce
anger.[x]

27 This is what the LORD says:

"The whole land will be ruined,[y]
though I will not destroy[z] it
completely.
28 Therefore the earth will mourn[a]
and the heavens above grow dark,[b]
because I have spoken and will not
relent,[c]
I have decided and will not turn
back.[d]"

29 At the sound of horsemen and
archers[e]
every town takes to flight.[f]
Some go into the thickets;
some climb up among the rocks.[g]
All the towns are deserted;[h]
no one lives in them.

4:16 [t]S Dt 28:49 [u]ver 19; Eze 21:22 [v]S Jer 1:15 **4:17** [w]S 2Ki 25:1,4 [x]S 1Sa 12:15; Jer 5:23 **4:18** [y]Ps 107:17; S Isa 1:28; Jer 5:25 [z]Jer 2:17 [a]Jer 2:19 **4:19** [b]Isa 22:4; Jer 6:24; 9:10; La 1:20 [c]S Job 6:10; S 14:22; Jer 10:19 [d]S Job 37:1; Jer 23:9 [e]S Job 4:2; Jer 20:9 [f]S ver 21; S Nu 10:2; S Job 39:24 [g]S ver 16; Nu 10:9; Jer 49:2; Zep 1:16 **4:20** [h]S Dt 31:17 [i]S ver 13 [j]S Nu 24:5; Jer 10:20; La 2:4 **4:21** [k]S ver 6; S Nu 2:2; S Isa 18:3 [l]ver 5, 19; S Jos 6:20; Jer 6:1; Hos 5:8; Am 3:6; Zep 1:16 **4:22** [m]Jer 5:21; 10:8 [n]S Isa 1:3; 27:11; Jer 2:8; 8:7; Hos 5:4; 6:6 [o]S Ps 14:4; S 53:2 [p]Jer 13:23; S 1Co 14:20 [q]S Ps 36:3 **4:23** [r]S Ge 1:2 [s]ver 28; S Job 9:7; 30:26; S Isa 5:30; 59:9; La 3:2 **4:24** [t]S Ex 19:18; S Job 9:6 **4:25** [u]Jer 7:20; 9:10; 12:4; Hos 4:3; Zep 1:3 **4:26** [v]S Ge 13:10; Jer 12:4; 23:10 [w]S Isa 6:11 [x]Jer 12:13; 25:38 **4:27** [y]S ver 13 [z]S Lev 26:44; Jer 5:10, 18; 12:12; 30:11; 46:28; Eze 20:17; Am 9:8 **4:28** [a]Jer 12:4, 11; 14:2; Hos 4:3 [b]S ver 23 [c]S Nu 23:19 [d]ver 8; Jer 23:20; 30:24 **4:29** [e]S ver 13; Jer 6:23; 8:16 [f]2Ki 25:4 [g]S Ex 33:22; S 1Sa 26:20 [h]S ver 7; S Isa 6:12

---

in the mind's eye of the prophet, is making fearfully rapid progress toward the holy city. Cf. Mic 1:10–16.

4:16 *besieging army.* See Isa 1:8. *distant land.* Babylonia. *raising a war cry.* The Hebrew underlying this phrase is translated "growled" in 2:15.

4:17 *surround her.* See 1:15.

4:18 *Your own ... actions have brought this on you.* See Pr 26:27 and note.

4:19–26 A brief personal interlude, broken only by the divine complaint in v. 22. Jeremiah voices his agony at the approaching destruction of his beloved land and its people.

4:19 See 10:19–20. *anguish.* Often associated with labor pangs, as here (see 6:24; 49:24; 50:43). *heart pounds.* See Job 37:1; Ps 38:10; Hab 3:16. *sound of the trumpet.* See note on v. 5.

4:20 *lies in ruins.* See v. 13; 9:19; 48:1. *shelter.* Lit. "tent curtains" (as in Isa 54:2), usually made of goat hair (see Ex 26:7) and therefore strong enough to protect from cold and rain (see 10:20).

4:21 *battle standard ... sound of the trumpet.* See notes on vv. 5–6.

4:22 The Lord speaks. *fools.* See NIV text note on Pr 1:7. *do not know me.* See 2:8. Leaders and people alike had committed the ultimate sin (see Isa 1:2–3; Hos 4:1). *senseless.* See 5:21; 10:8,14,21; 51:17. *skilled in doing evil.* See Mic 7:3. *know not how to do good.* See Ps 14:1–3 and note on 14:1.

4:23–26 The striking repetition of "I looked" at the beginning of each verse ties this poem together and underscores its visionary character, as the prophet sees his beloved land in ruins after the Babylonian onslaught. Creation, as it were, has been reversed.

4:23 *formless and empty.* The phrase occurs elsewhere only in Ge 1:2 (see note there). In Jeremiah's vision, the primeval chaos has returned. *light was gone.* Contrast Ge 1:3.

4:24 See Na 1:5.

4:25 *there were no people.* The Hebrew underlying this phrase occurs elsewhere only in Ge 2:5, where it is translated "there was no one." Again, uncreation has replaced creation.

4:26 *fruitful land.* See note on 2:7. *fierce anger.* See v. 8; Isa 13:13; Na 1:6.

4:27 *not destroy it completely.* See 5:10,18; 30:11; 46:28. God's mercy tempers the total judgment envisioned by Jeremiah in vv. 23–26.

4:28 *will not relent.* Unless his people repent (see 18:7–10 and note).

4:29 *archers.* Babylonia's evil deeds against Judah will someday recoil on her (see 50:29). *Some go.* See Jdg 6:2; 1Sa 13:6; Isa 2:19,21. Even people living in fortified towns feel unsafe. *deserted.* Contrast Isa 62:4.

30 What are you doing,[i] you devastated one?
Why dress yourself in scarlet
and put on jewels[j] of gold?
Why highlight your eyes with makeup?[k]
You adorn yourself in vain.
Your lovers[l] despise you;
they want to kill you.[m]

31 I hear a cry as of a woman in labor,[n]
a groan as of one bearing her first child—
the cry of Daughter Zion[o] gasping for breath,[p]
stretching out her hands[q] and saying,
"Alas! I am fainting;
my life is given over to murderers."[r]

Not One Is Upright

5 "Go up and down[s] the streets of Jerusalem,
look around and consider,[t]
search through her squares.
If you can find but one person[u]
who deals honestly[v] and seeks the truth,
I will forgive[w] this city.
2 Although they say, 'As surely as the LORD lives,'[x]
still they are swearing falsely.[y]"

3 LORD, do not your eyes[z] look for truth?
You struck[a] them, but they felt no pain;
you crushed them, but they refused correction.[b]
They made their faces harder than stone[c]
and refused to repent.[d]
4 I thought, "These are only the poor;
they are foolish,[e]
for they do not know[f] the way of the LORD,
the requirements of their God.
5 So I will go to the leaders[g]
and speak to them;
surely they know the way of the LORD,
the requirements of their God."
But with one accord they too had broken off the yoke
and torn off the bonds.[h]
6 Therefore a lion from the forest[i] will attack them,
a wolf from the desert will ravage[j] them,
a leopard[k] will lie in wait near their towns
to tear to pieces any who venture out,
for their rebellion is great
and their backslidings many.[l]

7 "Why should I forgive you?
Your children have forsaken me
and sworn[m] by gods that are not gods.[n]
I supplied all their needs,
yet they committed adultery[o]
and thronged to the houses of prostitutes.[p]
8 They are well-fed, lusty stallions,
each neighing for another man's wife.[q]
9 Should I not punish them for this?"[r]
declares the LORD.
"Should I not avenge[s] myself
on such a nation as this?

10 "Go through her vineyards and ravage them,
but do not destroy them completely.[t]

4:30 [i] Isa 10:3-4 [j] Eze 16:11; 23:40 [k] S 2Ki 9:30 [l] Job 19:14; La 1:2; Eze 23:9, 22 [m] S Ps 35:4 **4:31** [n] S Ge 3:16; Jer 6:24; 13:21; 22:23; 30:6; Mic 4:10 [o] S Ps 9:14 [p] Isa 42:14 [q] Isa 1:15; La 1:17 [r] S Dt 32:25; La 2:21 **5:1** [s] 2Ch 16:9; Eze 22:30 [t] Ps 45:10 [u] Ge 18:32; S Jer 2:29 [v] ver 31; Jer 14:14; Eze 13:6 [w] S Ge 18:24 **5:2** [x] S Jer 4:2 [y] S Lev 19:12 **5:3** [z] 2Ch 16:9 [a] S Isa 9:13 [b] S Lev 26:23 [c] Jer 7:26; 19:15; Eze 3:8-9; 36:26; Zec 7:12 [d] S 2Ch 28:22; S Isa 1:5; Eze 2:4-5; Am 4:6; Zec 7:11 **5:4** [e] S ver 21; S Jer 4:22 [f] S Pr 10:21; S Isa 1:3 **5:5** [g] Mic 3:1,9 [h] S Jer 2:20 **5:6** [i] S Ps 17:12 [j] S Lev 26:22 [k] Hos 13:7 [l] Jer 14:7; 30:14 **5:7** [m] S Jos 23:7 [n] Dt 32:21; Jer 2:11; 16:20; Gal 4:8 [o] S Nu 25:1 [p] Jer 13:27 **5:8** [q] Jer 29:23; Eze 22:11; 33:26 **5:9** [r] ver 29; Jer 9:9 [s] S Isa 57:6 **5:10** [t] S Jer 4:27; Am 9:8

4:30 *you … yourself.* All the second person pronouns in this verse represent feminine pronouns or verbs in Hebrew, indicating that Jerusalem is being addressed (see v. 14 and note). She is here portrayed as an adulterous wife trying to allure her lovers. *makeup.* Antimony, a black powder used to enlarge the eyes and make them more attractive (see 2Ki 9:30; Eze 23:40). *lovers.* The Hebrew root underlying this word is found elsewhere only in Eze 23:5,7,9,12,16,20, where it is used of Samaria and Jerusalem, the adulterous sisters (see notes on Jer 2:25; 3:1,7) who "lusted" after foreign nations and their gods. *want to kill you.* They are intent only on murdering you (see v. 31).
4:31 *woman in labor.* See 6:24; 13:21; 22:23; 30:6; 31:8; 48:41; 49:22,24; 50:43; see also v. 19; Isa 13:8 and notes. *Daughter Zion.* A personification of Jerusalem (see note on 2Ki 19:21). *stretching out her hands.* In prayer for help (see Job 11:13).
5:1–31 Jeremiah resumes his vivid description of the wickedness of the people of Judah and Jerusalem.
5:1 See Zep 1:12. The Lord challenges anyone to find just one righteous person in Israel—a rhetorical way of charging that corruption pervaded the city (see Ps 14:1–3; Isa 64:6–7; Hos 4:1–2; Mic 7:2). *If you can find … I will forgive.* See Ge 18:26–32.
5:2 *As surely as the LORD lives.* See 4:2; see also Ge 42:15 and note. *they are swearing falsely.* In violation of Lev 19:12 (see note on Ex 20:7). The Hebrew underlying this phrase is translated "commit … perjury" in 7:9 (see NIV text note there).
5:3 *refused correction.* See 2:30. *made their faces harder than stone.* A striking portrayal of rebellion (see Eze 3:7–9).
5:4 *poor.* Concerned about basic physical needs (cf. 39:10; 40:7), they are uninformed of God's word and way. *foolish.* See 4:22; see also Nu 12:11 and NIV text note on Pr 1:7. *do not know … requirements of their God.* They are more ignorant than the birds of the heavens (see 8:7).
5:5 *leaders.* Lit. "great ones." Although possessing every advantage, they were no more righteous than the poorest of the common people. *broken … bonds.* See note on 2:20.
5:6 *lion … wolf … leopard.* See Lev 26:22; Eze 14:15; cf. 2Ki 17:25–26. *lie in wait.* The Hebrew for this phrase is translated "watching" in 1:12. *backslidings.* See 2:19; 3:22; 14:7. The word implies repeated apostasy.
5:7 *Why should I forgive you?* See v. 1. *Your children.* Jerusalem is depicted as the "mother" city of the nation. *gods that are not gods.* Idols (see 2:11). *I supplied … yet they.* See Dt 32:15–16; Hos 2:8. *committed adultery.* See 2:25 and note.
5:8 *lusty stallions.* See 13:27; 50:11; Eze 23:20.
5:9 *Should I not punish … such a nation as this?* Repeated in v. 29; 9:9.
5:10 *Go.* Addressed to Israel's enemies (see v. 15). *vineyards.* Vines and vineyards are often symbolic of Israel (see notes

Strip off her branches,
for these people do not belong to the LORD.
11 The people of Israel and the people of Judah
have been utterly unfaithful[u] to me,"
declares the LORD.
12 They have lied[v] about the LORD;
they said, "He will do nothing!
No harm will come to us;[w]
we will never see sword or famine.[x]
13 The prophets[y] are but wind[z]
and the word is not in them;
so let what they say be done to them."

14 Therefore this is what the LORD God
Almighty says:

"Because the people have spoken these words,
I will make my words in your mouth[a] a fire[b]
and these people the wood it consumes.[c]
15 People of Israel," declares the LORD,
"I am bringing a distant nation[d] against you—
an ancient and enduring nation,
a people whose language[e] you do not know,
whose speech you do not understand.
16 Their quivers[f] are like an open grave;
all of them are mighty warriors.
17 They will devour[g] your harvests and food,
devour[h] your sons and daughters;
they will devour[i] your flocks and herds,
devour your vines and fig trees.[j]
With the sword[k] they will destroy
the fortified cities[l] in which you trust.[m]

18 "Yet even in those days," declares the
LORD, "I will not destroy[n] you completely.
19 And when the people ask,[o] 'Why has the
LORD our God done all this to us?' you will
tell them, 'As you have forsaken me and
served foreign gods[p] in your own land, so
now you will serve foreigners[q] in a land
not your own.'

20 "Announce this to the descendants of Jacob
and proclaim[r] it in Judah:
21 Hear this, you foolish and senseless people,[s]
who have eyes[t] but do not see,
who have ears but do not hear:[u]
22 Should you not fear[v] me?" declares the LORD.
"Should you not tremble[w] in my presence?
I made the sand a boundary for the sea,[x]
an everlasting barrier it cannot cross.
The waves may roll, but they cannot prevail;
they may roar,[y] but they cannot cross it.
23 But these people have stubborn and rebellious[z] hearts;
they have turned aside[a] and gone away.
24 They do not say to themselves,
'Let us fear[b] the LORD our God,
who gives autumn and spring rains[c] in season,
who assures us of the regular weeks of harvest.'[d]
25 Your wrongdoings have kept these away;
your sins have deprived you of good.[e]
26 "Among my people are the wicked[f]
who lie in wait[g] like men who snare birds
and like those who set traps[h] to catch people.

5:11 [u] S 1Ki 19:10; S Ps 73:27; S Isa 24:16 **5:12** [v] Isa 28:15 [w] Jer 23:17 [x] Jer 14:13; 27:8 **5:13** [y] Jer 14:15 [z] S 2Ch 36:16; S Job 6:26 **5:14** [a] Hos 6:5 [b] S Ps 39:3; Jer 23:29 [c] S Isa 1:31 **5:15** [d] S Dt 28:49; S 2Ki 24:2 [e] S Ge 11:7; S Isa 28:11 **5:16** [f] S Job 39:23 **5:17** [g] Lev 26:16; S Isa 1:7; Jer 8:16; 30:16 [h] Dt 28:32; Jer 50:7,17 [i] Dt 28:31 [j] S Nu 16:14; Jer 8:13; Hos 2:12 [k] S Lev 26:25 [l] S Jos 10:20 [m] Dt 28:33 **5:18** [n] S Jer 4:27 **5:19** [o] S Dt 4:28; S 1Ki 9:9 [p] S Jer 2:8; 15:14; 16:13; 17:4 [q] Dt 28:48 **5:20** [r] S Jer 4:5 **5:21** [s] ver 4; S Dt 32:6; S Jer 4:22; Hab 2:18 [t] Isa 6:10; Eze 12:2 [u] S Dt 29:4; S Isa 42:20; S Mt 13:15; Mk 8:18 **5:22** [v] S Dt 28:58 [w] S Job 4:14; S Isa 64:2 [x] S Ge 1:9 [y] S Ps 46:3 **5:23** [z] S Dt 21:18 [a] Ps 14:3 **5:24** [b] Dt 6:24 [c] S Lev 26:4; S 2Sa 1:21; Jas 5:7 [d] S Ge 8:22; Ac 14:17 **5:25** [e] Ps 84:11 **5:26** [f] S Mt 7:15 [g] S Ps 10:8 [h] Ecc 9:12; Jer 9:8; Hos 5:1; Mic 7:2

on 2:21; Isa 5:1). *not destroy them completely.* See v. 18; see also note on 4:27. *Strip off her branches.* See Isa 18:5; Jn 15:2,6. *people do not belong to the LORD.* See Hos 1:9.

5:11 See note on 3:7.

5:12 *He will do nothing!* Either good or bad (see Zep 1:12). *sword or famine.* Jeremiah introduces us to the first two elements of his characteristic triad: "sword, famine and plague" (see note on 14:12).

5:13 *prophets are but wind.* Like images of false gods (see Isa 41:29). *let what they say be done to them.* See note on 4:29; see also Ps 7:16; 54:5.

5:14 *my words in your mouth a fire.* In contrast to the total lack of God's word in the mouths of false prophets (v. 13). See 20:9 and note. *consumes.* See note on Isa 1:31.

5:15 *distant nation.* See note on 4:16. *ancient and enduring nation.* Babylonia's history reached back 2,000 years and more. *whose language you do not know.* See Dt 28:49 and note.

5:16 *open grave.* Symbolizing insatiability, destruction and death (see Ps 5:9; Pr 30:15–16).

5:17 *devour your sons and daughters.* Either as sacrifices to pagan gods (see note on 3:24) or as casualties of war (see 10:25). *fortified cities in which you trust.* See note on 4:5; see also Dt 28:52.

5:18 See v. 10; see also note on 4:27.

5:21 *Hear this.* See note on 2:4. *foolish and senseless.* See 4:22; see also NIV text note on Pr 1:7. *who have eyes … do not hear.* See note on Isa 6:10; see also Dt 29:4; Ps 115:4–8; 135:15–18.

5:22 *fear me.* See note on Ge 20:11. *boundary for the sea.* See Job 38:8–11; Ps 104:6–9.

5:23 Though the sea never crosses its divinely appointed boundaries, God's people have violated the limits he has set for them.

5:24 *God, who gives.* See v. 7 and note. *autumn and spring rains.* See 3:3; see also note on Dt 11:14. *regular weeks of harvest.* Perhaps the seven weeks between Passover and the Festival of Weeks (see Lev 23:15–16).

5:26 *traps.* Lit. "destroyer" (see, e.g., Ex 12:23) or "destruction" (see, e.g., Eze 21:31). *people.* Innocent (see Isa 29:21), godly, upright people (see Mic 7:2).

[27]Like cages full of birds,
their houses are full of deceit;[i]
they have become rich[j] and powerful
28 and have grown fat[k] and sleek.
Their evil deeds have no limit;
they do not seek justice.
They do not promote the case of the fatherless;[l]
they do not defend the just cause of the poor.[m]
[29]Should I not punish them for this?"
declares the LORD.
"Should I not avenge[n] myself
on such a nation as this?

[30]"A horrible[o] and shocking thing
has happened in the land:
[31]The prophets prophesy lies,[p]
the priests[q] rule by their own authority,
and my people love it this way.
But what will you do in the end?[r]

Jerusalem Under Siege

6 "Flee for safety, people of Benjamin!
Flee from Jerusalem!
Sound the trumpet[s] in Tekoa![t]
Raise the signal over Beth Hakkerem![u]
For disaster looms out of the north,[v]
even terrible destruction.
[2]I will destroy Daughter Zion,[w]
so beautiful and delicate.[x]
[3]Shepherds[y] with their flocks will come against her;
they will pitch their tents around[z] her,
each tending his own portion."

[4]"Prepare for battle against her!
Arise, let us attack at noon![a]
But, alas, the daylight is fading,
and the shadows of evening grow long.
[5]So arise, let us attack at night
and destroy her fortresses!"

[6]This is what the LORD Almighty says:

"Cut down the trees[b]
and build siege ramps[c] against Jerusalem.
This city must be punished;
it is filled with oppression.[d]
[7]As a well pours out its water,
so she pours out her wickedness.
Violence[e] and destruction[f] resound in her;
her sickness and wounds are ever before me.
[8]Take warning, Jerusalem,
or I will turn away[g] from you
and make your land desolate
so no one can live in it."

[9]This is what the LORD Almighty says:

"Let them glean the remnant[h] of Israel
as thoroughly as a vine;
pass your hand over the branches again,
like one gathering grapes."

5:27 [i]Jer 8:5; 9:6 [j]Jer 12:1 **5:28** [k]S Dt 32:15 [l]Zec 7:10 [m]Ex 22:21-24; S Ps 82:3; S Isa 1:23; Jer 7:6; Eze 16:49; Am 5:12 **5:29** [n]S Isa 57:6 **5:30** [o]ver 30-31; Jer 18:13; 23:14; Hos 6:10 **5:31** [p]S ver 1; Mic 2:11 [q]La 4:13 [r]Hos 9:5 **6:1** [s]S Nu 10:7; S Jer 4:21 [t]2Ch 11:6; Am 1:1 [u]Ne 3:14 [v]S Jer 4:6 **6:2** [w]S Ps 9:14 [x]La 4:5 **6:3** [y]Jer 12:10 [z]S 2Ki 25:4; Lk 19:43 **6:4** [a]Jer 15:8; 22:7 **6:6** [b]Dt 20:19-20 [c]S 2Sa 20:15; Jer 32:24; 52:4; Eze 26:8 [d]S Dt 28:33; Jer 25:38; Zep 3:1 **6:7** [e]S Ps 55:9; S Isa 58:4 [f]Jer 20:8 **6:8** [g]Eze 23:18 **6:9** [h]S Ge 45:7

5:27 *cages.* Traps woven of wicker; the Hebrew for this word is translated "basket" in Am 8:1–2. *deceit.* Riches gained through extortion and deception (see Hab 2:6).
5:28 *grown fat and sleek.* Symbolic of prosperity (see Dt 32:15; Jas 5:5 and note). *evil deeds have no limit.* See Ps 73:7. *They do not promote the case.* What the wicked will not do, God must do (see Dt 10:18)—and so must those who truly know and serve him (see 22:16; Jas 1:27).
5:29 Repeated from v. 9; see also 9:9.
5:31 See 1:18 and note. *prophesy lies.* See 20:6 (often, and arrogantly, in God's name; see 23:25; 27:15; 29:9). *my people love it this way.* See note on Am 4:5.
6:1–30 The prophet envisions the future Babylonian attack on Jerusalem.
6:1 The Lord speaks in vv. 1–3. Verse 1 is strongly reminiscent of 4:6 (see note there). But whereas in 4:6 the command was to seek protection in Jerusalem, in 6:1 the people are to flee from Jerusalem, because no place—not even the holy city itself—will be safe from the invader. *Benjamin.* The tribal territory bordering Judah north of Jerusalem. Jeremiah himself was from Benjamite territory (see 1:1). *Sound … Tekoa.* In the Hebrew there is a play on these words. Tekoa was the hometown of Amos (see Introduction to Amos: Author). *Raise … signal.* In the Hebrew there is a play on words, made possible by using a different Hebrew word (found also in Lachish Letter 4:10) for "signal" (caused by the smoke of a fire; see Jdg 20:38,40) than the one used in 4:6. *Beth Hakkerem.* Mentioned elsewhere only in Ne 3:14 (see note there). *disaster … out of the north.* See 1:14 and note.
6:2 *Daughter Zion.* A personification of Jerusalem (see note on 2Ki 19:21). *delicate.* Used to describe the city of Babylon in Isa 47:1.
6:3 See 1:15. *Shepherds with their flocks.* Rulers (see note on 2:8) with their troops. *pitch.* The Hebrew for this verb continues the pun on "Tekoa" in v. 1 (see note on v. 8). *each … his own portion.* The Hebrew for this phrase is used similarly ("each … their own place") in Nu 2:17. *tending.* Grazing or depasturing, and thus destroying.
6:4 The invaders speak in vv. 4–5. *Prepare for.* Lit. "Consecrate" (also in Joel 3:9; Mic 3:5). Since ancient battles had religious connotations, soldiers had to prepare themselves ritually, as well as militarily (see Dt 20:2–4; 1Sa 21:4 and note). *at noon.* To take advantage of the element of surprise, since the usual time of attack was early in the morning (see, e.g., Jos 8:10,14).
6:5 *at night.* Since attacking soldiers normally retired for the night and resumed siege the following morning, the phrase underscores their eagerness and determination (see Jdg 7:19 and note).
6:6 The Lord addresses the Babylonian troops. *siege ramps.* To help them bring up battering rams and scale Jerusalem's walls (see 33:4). *oppression.* Against its own people (see note on Isa 30:12).
6:7 *sickness and wounds.* Jerusalem suffers from spiritual decay and disease (see v. 14) and is not aware of it.
6:8 *Take warning.* The better part of wisdom (see v. 10; Ps 2:10). *turn away.* In sorrow, but also in disgust. The Hebrew for this phrase continues the pun on "Tekoa" in v. 1 (see note on v. 3). *desolate so no one can live in it.* See 22:6.
6:9 *glean.* See notes on Ru 2:2; Isa 17:5. *remnant.* See 11:23; 23:3; 31:7; 40:11,15; 42:2,15,19; 43:5; 44:7,12,14,28; 50:20; see

10 To whom can I speak and give
warning?
Who will listen[i] to me?
Their ears are closed[a][j]
so they cannot hear.[k]
The word[l] of the LORD is offensive to
them;
they find no pleasure in it.
11 But I am full of the wrath[m] of the LORD,
and I cannot hold it in.[n]

"Pour it out on the children in the
street
and on the young men[o] gathered
together;
both husband and wife will be caught
in it,
and the old, those weighed down
with years.[p]
12 Their houses will be turned over to
others,[q]
together with their fields and their
wives,[r]
when I stretch out my hand[s]
against those who live in the land,"
declares the LORD.
13 "From the least to the greatest,
all[t] are greedy for gain;[u]
prophets and priests alike,
all practice deceit.[v]
14 They dress the wound of my people
as though it were not serious.
'Peace, peace,' they say,
when there is no peace.[w]
15 Are they ashamed of their detestable
conduct?
No, they have no shame at all;
they do not even know how to
blush.[x]
So they will fall among the fallen;
they will be brought down when I
punish[y] them,"
says the LORD.

16 This is what the LORD says:

"Stand at the crossroads and look;
ask for the ancient paths,[z]
ask where the good way[a] is, and walk
in it,
and you will find rest[b] for your souls.
But you said, 'We will not walk in it.'
17 I appointed watchmen[c] over you and
said,
'Listen to the sound of the trumpet!'[d]
But you said, 'We will not listen.'[e]
18 Therefore hear, you nations;
you who are witnesses,
observe what will happen to them.
19 Hear, you earth:[f]
I am bringing disaster[g] on this people,
the fruit of their schemes,[h]
because they have not listened to my
words[i]
and have rejected my law.[j]
20 What do I care about incense from
Sheba[k]
or sweet calamus[l] from a distant land?
Your burnt offerings are not
acceptable;[m]
your sacrifices[n] do not please me."[o]

21 Therefore this is what the LORD says:

"I will put obstacles before this people.
Parents and children alike will
stumble[p] over them;
neighbors and friends will perish."

22 This is what the LORD says:

"Look, an army is coming
from the land of the north;[q]
a great nation is being stirred up
from the ends of the earth.[r]

[a] *10* Hebrew *uncircumcised*

6:10 [i] Jer 7:13, 24; 35:15 [j] Jer 4:4; Ac 7:51 [k] S Isa 42:20 [l] Jer 15:10, 15; 20:8 **6:11** [m] Jer 7:20; 15:17 [n] Job 32:20; Jer 20:9 [o] S 2Ch 36:17; S Isa 40:30 [p] La 2:21 **6:12** [q] S Dt 28:30; Mic 2:4 [r] 1Ki 11:4; Jer 8:10; 29:23; 38:22; 43:6; 44:9, 15 [s] Isa 5:25; Jer 21:5; 32:21; Eze 6:14; 35:3; Zep 1:4 **6:13** [t] S Jer 2:29 [u] S Isa 56:11 [v] La 4:13 **6:14** [w] S Isa 30:10; S Jer 4:10 **6:15** [x] Jer 3:3; 8:10-12; Mic 3:7; Zec 13:4 [y] 2Ch 25:16; Jer 27:15 **6:16** [z] Jer 18:15 [a] S 1Ki 8:36; S Ps 119:3 [b] S Jos 1:13; S Isa 11:10; Mt 11:29 **6:17** [c] S Isa 52:8 [d] S Ex 20:18 [e] Jer 11:7-8; Eze 33:4; Zec 1:4 **6:19** [f] S Dt 4:26; Jer 22:29; Mic 1:2 [g] S Jos 23:15; Jer 11:11; 19:3 [h] Pr 1:31 [i] Jer 29:19 [j] Jer 8:9; Eze 20:13; Am 2:4 **6:20** [k] S Ge 10:7 [l] S Ex 30:23 [m] Am 5:22; Mal 1:9 [n] Ps 50:8-10; Jer 7:21; Mic 6:7-8 [o] S Isa 1:11; Jer 14:12; Hos 8:13; 9:4 **6:21** [p] S Lev 26:37; S Isa 8:14 **6:22** [q] S Jer 4:6 [r] S Dt 28:49

also note on Isa 10:20–22. *thoroughly.* Stopping just short of complete destruction (see 4:27; 5:10,18; 30:11; 46:28). *vine.* Symbolic of Israel (see 2:21 and note; 5:10).

6:10 Jeremiah speaks. *give warning.* See note on v. 8. *ears are closed.* See NIV text note; see also 4:4 and note. The imagery of uncircumcised ears is found elsewhere only in Ac 7:51 (see note there).

6:11 The prophet speaks, then the Lord resumes his speech (through v. 23). *full of the wrath.* See 25:15 and note. *children ... young men ... husband and wife ... old.* All will be judged, from youngest to oldest (see v. 13). *in the street.* Where children play (see 9:21; Zec 8:5).

6:12–15 Repeated almost verbatim in 8:10–12.

6:12 *houses ... fields ... wives.* Cf. Ex 20:17; Dt 5:21. *turned over to others.* As Dt 28:30 warned—one of the covenant curses. *stretch out my hand against.* To destroy (see 15:6).

6:13 See 1:18 and note.

6:14 *wound.* See note on v. 7. *Peace ... when there is no peace.* A common message of false and greedy prophets (see Eze 13:10; Mic 3:5). The wicked, in any case, cannot expect to enjoy peace (Isa 48:22; 57:21).

6:16 *ancient paths.* The tried and true ways of Judah's godly ancestors (see 18:15; Dt 32:7). *walk in it.* See Isa 30:21. *you will find rest for your souls.* Quoted by Jesus in Mt 11:29 (see Isa 28:12; cf. Ps 119:165).

6:17 *watchmen.* True prophets (see Eze 3:17 and note; Hab 2:1). *sound of the trumpet.* To warn of approaching danger (see v. 1; see also note on Joel 2:1).

6:18 *hear, you nations.* See Mic 1:2.

6:19 *rejected my law.* Disobeyed the law of Moses (see 8:8–9).

6:20 *Sheba.* Located in southwestern Arabia, it was the center of the spice trade (see Isa 60:6 and note). *calamus.* See Ex 25:6; SS 4:14; Isa 43:24 and notes. It probably came from India and was an ingredient in the sacred anointing oil (Ex 30:25). *burnt offerings are not acceptable.* The attitude of one's heart and the manner of one's life are far more important than the ritual of sacrifice (see note on Isa 1:11–15).

6:21 *obstacles.* The Babylonian invaders (see v. 22).

6:22–24 Repeated almost verbatim in 50:41–43.

6:22 *land of the north.* Babylonia (see 4:6; Isa 41:25 and notes). *from the ends of the earth.* See 25:32; 31:8.

23 They are armed with bow and spear;
they are cruel and show no mercy.[s]
They sound like the roaring sea[t]
as they ride on their horses;[u]
they come like men in battle formation
to attack you, Daughter Zion.[v]"

24 We have heard reports about them,
and our hands hang limp.[w]
Anguish[x] has gripped us,
pain like that of a woman in labor.[y]
25 Do not go out to the fields
or walk on the roads,
for the enemy has a sword,
and there is terror on every side.[z]
26 Put on sackcloth,[a] my people,
and roll in ashes;[b]
mourn with bitter wailing[c]
as for an only son,[d]
for suddenly the destroyer[e]
will come upon us.

27 "I have made you a tester[f] of metals
and my people the ore,
that you may observe
and test their ways.
28 They are all hardened rebels,[g]
going about to slander.[h]
They are bronze and iron;[i]
they all act corruptly.
29 The bellows blow fiercely
to burn away the lead with fire,
but the refining[j] goes on in vain;
the wicked are not purged out.
30 They are called rejected silver,[k]
because the LORD has rejected
them."[l]

False Religion Worthless

7 This is the word that came to Jeremiah
from the LORD: 2 "Stand[m] at the gate of
the LORD's house and there proclaim this
message:
"'Hear the word of the LORD, all you
people of Judah who come through these
gates to worship the LORD. 3 This is what
the LORD Almighty, the God of Israel, says:
Reform your ways[n] and your actions, and
I will let you live[o] in this place. 4 Do not
trust[p] in deceptive[q] words and say, "This
is the temple of the LORD, the temple of
the LORD, the temple of the LORD!" 5 If you
really change[r] your ways and your actions
and deal with each other justly,[s] 6 if you do
not oppress[t] the foreigner, the fatherless
or the widow and do not shed innocent

6:23 [s] S Isa 13:18 [t] S Ps 18:4; S 93:3 [u] S Jer 4:29 [v] S Isa 10:32 **6:24** [w] Isa 13:7 [x] S Jer 4:19 [y] S Jer 4:31; 50:41-43 **6:25** [z] S Job 15:21; S Ps 31:13; Jer 49:29 **6:26** [a] S Jer 4:8 [b] S Job 2:8; Jer 25:34; Eze 27:30; Jnh 3:6 [c] Jer 9:1; 18:22; 20:16; 25:36 [d] S Ge 21:16 [e] S Ex 12:23; S Jer 4:7 **6:27** [f] Jer 9:7; Zec 13:9 **6:28** [g] Jer 5:23 [h] S Lev 19:16 [i] Eze 22:18 **6:29** [j] Mal 3:3 **6:30** [k] Pr 17:3; Eze 22:18 [l] Ps 53:5; 119:119; Jer 7:29; La 5:22; Hos 9:17 **7:2** [m] Jer 17:19 **7:3** [n] Jer 18:11; 26:13; 35:15 [o] ver 7

7:4 [p] S Job 15:31 [q] ver 8; Jer 28:15; Mic 3:11 **7:5** [r] ver 3; Jer 18:11; 26:13; 35:15 [s] S Ex 22:22; S Lev 25:17; S Isa 1:17 **7:6** [t] S Jer 5:28; Eze 22:7

6:23 *spear.* The Hebrew for this word is translated "javelin" in 1Sa 17:6. Another possibility is "sword," as attested in *The War of the Sons of Light against the Sons of Darkness,* one of the Dead Sea Scrolls (see essay, pp. 1574–1576). *like the roaring sea.* See Isa 5:30; see also Isa 17:12 and note. *horses.* See note on 4:13; see also 8:16. *Daughter Zion.* See v. 2 and note.

6:24–26 The prophet speaks to, and on behalf of, the people of Judah.

6:24 *hands hang limp.* Courage fails (see 47:3; Isa 13:7 and notes). *Anguish.* See note on 4:19. *woman in labor.* See note on 4:31.

6:25 *terror on every side.* A favorite expression of Jeremiah (20:10; 46:5; 49:29; cf. La 2:22); it is used once as a proper name (20:3).

6:26 *Put on sackcloth.* See 4:8; see also note on Ge 37:34. *roll in ashes; mourn.* See Eze 27:30–31; cf. Mic 1:10. *only son.* A father's most precious possession (see Ge 22:12,16; Ex 11:5 and note; Am 8:10; Zec 12:10; Ro 8:32). *destroyer.* Babylonia (see note on 4:7).

6:27–30 The Lord speaks to Jeremiah and appoints him to test the people of Judah as a refiner tests metals (see 9:7; Ps 12:6 and note; Isa 1:25; Mal 3:2–3).

6:27 *tester of metals.* See Job 23:10.

6:28 *going about to slander.* Contrary to Lev 19:16. *bronze and iron.* Base metals when compared to gold and silver. *act corruptly.* See Dt 31:29; Isa 1:4.

6:29 In ancient times, lead was added to silver ore in the refining process. When the crucible was heated, the lead oxidized and acted as a flux to remove the alloys. Here the process fails because the ore is not pure enough (cf. Eze 24:11–13).

6:30 *They are ... rejected.* The "hardened rebels" (v. 28), the "wicked" (v. 29), have failed to pass the Lord's test. Nothing worthwhile can be made of them.

7:1—10:25 A series of temple messages delivered by Jeremiah, perhaps over a period of several years. Since 26:2–6,12–15 is very similar in content to ch. 7, it is possible that chs. 7–10 (or at least ch. 7) date to the reign of Jehoiakim (see 26:1). On the other hand, Jeremiah may have repeated various themes on several occasions during his lengthy ministry. In any event, nothing in chs. 7–10 is inappropriate to the time of King Josiah.

7:1—8:3 The straightforward narrative of this section asserts that Solomon's temple in Jerusalem will not escape the fate of the earlier sanctuary at Shiloh if the people of Judah persist in worshiping false gods.

7:1 *the word that came.* See 1:2 and note; 1:4,11,13; 2:1.

7:2 *gate.* In the wall between the inner and outer courts of the temple, perhaps the so-called New Gate (26:10; 36:10). *Hear.* See note on 2:4. *all you people ... who come ... to worship.* Perhaps during one of the three annual pilgrimage festivals (see Dt 16:16 and note). *gates.* Leading into the outer court.

7:3 *this place.* Used almost 30 times in Jeremiah to designate the land God had given them (see, e.g., v. 7; 14:13,15; 24:5–6).

7:4 *deceptive words.* Spoken by false prophets. The idea that God would not destroy Jerusalem simply because his dwelling, the temple, was located there was a delusion, fostered in part by the miraculous deliverance of the city during the reign of Hezekiah (see 2Ki 19:32–36; cf. 2Sa 7:11b–13; Ps 132:13–14). In the light of Judah's sinful rebellion against the Lord, such an idea was "worthless" (v. 8; see Mic 3:11). *This is.* Lit. "They are," referring to the buildings that constituted the entire temple complex. *temple ... temple ... temple.* Vain and repetitious babbling (cf. Mt 6:7). Often such a threefold repeating of a word or phrase is for emphasis (see 22:29; see also note on Isa 6:3).

7:6 Rulers and people alike needed to hear and act on these prophetic words (see 22:2–3). *foreigner ... fatherless ... widow.* See Dt 16:11,14; 24:19–21; 26:12–13; 27:19; cf. Jas 1:27. *innocent blood.* See 19:4; 22:17; 26:15; see also the frightening example of King Manasseh (2Ki 21:16).

blood[u] in this place, and if you do not follow other gods[v] to your own harm, 7 then I
will let you live in this place, in the land[w]
I gave your ancestors[x] for ever and ever.
8 But look, you are trusting[y] in deceptive[z]
words that are worthless.
9 " 'Will you steal[a] and murder,[b] commit adultery[c] and perjury,[a][d] burn incense
to Baal[e] and follow other gods[f] you have
not known, 10 and then come and stand[g]
before me in this house,[h] which bears my
Name, and say, "We are safe" — safe to
do all these detestable things?[i] 11 Has this
house,[j] which bears my Name, become a
den of robbers[k] to you? But I have been
watching![l] declares the LORD.
12 " 'Go now to the place in Shiloh[m]
where I first made a dwelling[n] for my
Name,[o] and see what I did[p] to it because
of the wickedness of my people Israel.
13 While you were doing all these things,
declares the LORD, I spoke[q] to you again

7:6 [u] S 2Ki 21:16; Jer 2:34; 19:4; 22:3 [v] S Ex 20:3; S Dt 8:19 **7:7** [w] S Dt 4:40 [x] S Jos 1:6 **7:8** [y] S Job 15:31 [z] S ver 4 **7:9** [a] Ex 20:15 [b] Ex 20:13 [c] Ex 20:14; S Nu 25:1 [d] Ex 20:16; S Lev 19:12; Zec 8:17; Mal 3:5 [e] S Isa 1:13; Jer 11:13, 17; 32:29 [f] S Ex 20:3; Hos 2:13 **7:10** [g] S Isa 48:1 [h] ver 30; 2Ki 21:4-5; Jer 23:11; 32:34; Eze 23:38-39 [i] Eze 33:25 **7:11** [j] Isa 56:7 [k] Mt 21:13*; Mk 11:17*; Lk 19:46* [l] Ge 31:50; Jdg 11:10; Jer 29:23; 42:5 **7:12** [m] S Jos 18:1; S 1Sa 2:32 [n] S Ex 40:2; S Jos 18:10 [o] Da 9:18 [p] S 1Sa 4:10-11, 22; Ps 78:60-64 **7:13** [q] Ps 71:17; Isa 48:17; Jer 32:33

[a] 9 Or *and swear by false gods*

7:7 *land . . . for ever and ever.* See Ge 17:8 and note.
7:8 *deceptive words.* See note on v. 4.
7:9 This one verse mentions the violation of fully half of the Ten Commandments (cf. Hos 4:2 and note). *burn incense to Baal.* See note on 1:16. *follow other gods you have not known.* See 19:4. Tragically, such sins would be the cause of their exile to lands they had not known (see 9:14,16; 16:11,13).
7:10 *house, which bears my Name.* See vv. 11,14,30; 25:29; 32:34; 34:15; Dt 12:5 and note; 1Ki 8:16 and note; 2Ch 6:33; 20:9; Da 9:18. The "Name" of God is equivalent to his gracious presence in such passages (see vv. 12,15; see also note on Ps 5:11). *We are safe.* See 12:12. *detestable.* See 2:7; see also note on Lev 7:21.
7:11 Together with the last half of Isa 56:7, part of this verse is quoted by Jesus in Mt 21:13; Mk 11:17; Lk 19:46. *den of robbers.* As thieves hide in caves and think they are safe, so the people of Judah falsely trust in the temple to protect them in spite of their sins.
7:12 See note on 7:1 — 8:3. *place in Shiloh . . . see what I did to it.* See v. 14; 26:6,9; Ps 78:60 – 61. The tabernacle had been set up in Shiloh after the conquest of Canaan (Jos 18:1) and was still there at the end of the period of the judges (see 1Sa 1:9). Modern Seilun, near a main highway about 18 miles north of Jerusalem, preserves the name of the ancient site. Archaeological excavations there indicate that it was destroyed by the Philistines c. 1050 BC. The tabernacle itself was not included in that destruction, since it was still in existence at Gibeon during David's reign (see 1Ch 21:29). One or more auxiliary buildings had apparently been erected at Shiloh near the tabernacle in connection with various aspects of public worship there (cf. the reference to the "doors of the house of the LORD" in 1Sa 3:15; see note on 1Sa 1:9). Such structures would have been destroyed with the city itself, perhaps sometime after the events of 1Sa 4. See photo below.
7:13 *again and again.* The Hebrew idiom underlying this phrase is found frequently in Jeremiah (v. 25; 11:7; 25:3 – 4;

Area of Shiloh — where God first made a dwelling for his Name (Jer 7:12)

Z. Radovan/www.BibleLandPictures.com

and again,[r] but you did not listen;[s] I called[t] you, but you did not answer.[u] 14 Therefore, what I did to Shiloh[v] I will now do to the house that bears my Name,[w] the temple[x] you trust in, the place I gave to you and your ancestors. 15 I will thrust you from my presence,[y] just as I did all your fellow Israelites, the people of Ephraim.'[z]

16 "So do not pray for this people nor offer any plea[a] or petition for them; do not plead with me, for I will not listen[b] to you. 17 Do you not see what they are doing in the towns of Judah and in the streets of Jerusalem? 18 The children gather wood, the fathers light the fire, and the women knead the dough and make cakes to offer to the Queen of Heaven.[c] They pour out drink offerings[d] to other gods to arouse[e] my anger. 19 But am I the one they are provoking?[f] declares the LORD. Are they not rather harming themselves, to their own shame?[g]

20 " 'Therefore this is what the Sovereign[h] LORD says: My anger[i] and my wrath will be poured[j] out on this place—on man and beast, on the trees of the field and on the crops of your land—and it will burn and not be quenched.[k]

21 " 'This is what the LORD Almighty, the God of Israel, says: Go ahead, add your burnt offerings to your other sacrifices[l] and eat[m] the meat yourselves! 22 For when I brought your ancestors out of Egypt and spoke to them, I did not just give them commands[n] about burnt offerings and sacrifices,[o] 23 but I gave them this command:[p] Obey[q] me, and I will be your God and you will be my people.[r] Walk in obedience to all[s] I command you, that it may go well[t] with you. 24 But they did not listen[u] or pay attention;[v] instead, they followed the stubborn inclinations of their evil hearts.[w] They went backward[x] and not forward. 25 From the time your ancestors left Egypt until now, day after day, again and again[y] I sent you my servants[z] the prophets.[a] 26 But they did not listen to me or pay attention.[b] They were stiff-necked[c] and did more evil than their ancestors.'[d]

27 "When you tell[e] them all this, they will not listen[f] to you; when you call to them, they will not answer.[g] 28 Therefore say to them, 'This is the nation that has not obeyed the LORD its God or responded to correction.[h] Truth[i] has perished; it has vanished from their lips.

29 " 'Cut off[j] your hair and throw it away; take up a lament[k] on the barren heights, for the LORD has rejected and abandoned[l] this generation that is under his wrath.

The Valley of Slaughter

30 " 'The people of Judah have done evil[m] in my eyes, declares the LORD. They have set up their detestable idols[n] in the

7:13 [r]S 2Ch 36:15 [s]S ver 26; S Isa 65:12 [t]S Pr 1:24 [u]Jer 35:17 **7:14** [v]S Jdg 18:31; S 1Sa 2:32 [w]S 1Ki 9:7 [x]ver 4; Eze 24:21 **7:15** [y]S Ge 4:14; S Ex 33:15; S 2Ki 17:20; Jer 23:39 [z]S Ps 78:67 **7:16** [a]S Ex 32:10; Dt 9:14; Jer 15:1 [b]S Nu 23:19 **7:18** [c]Jer 44:17-19 [d]S Isa 57:6 [e]S Dt 31:17; S 1Ki 14:9 **7:19** [f]Dt 32:21; Jer 44:3 [g]S Job 7:20; Jer 9:19; 20:11; 22:22 **7:20** [h]S Isa 30:15 [i]S Job 40:11; Jer 42:18; La 2:3-5 [j]Jer 6:11-12; La 4:11 [k]S Isa 1:31; Jer 11:16; 13:14; 15:6, 14; 17:4, 27; Eze 20:47-48 **7:21** [l]S Jer 6:20; Am 5:21-22 [m]S 1Sa 2:12-17; Hos 8:13 **7:22** [n]Isa 43:23 [o]S 1Sa 15:22 **7:23** [p]1Jn 3:23 [q]S Ex 19:5 [r]S Lev 26:12; S Isa 51:16 [s]S 1Ki 8:36; S Ps 119:3 [t]S Dt 5:33 **7:24** [u]S Jer 6:10 [v]Jer 11:8; 17:23; 34:14 [w]S Jer 3:17 [x]S Jer 2:19; Eze 37:23 **7:25** [y]S 2Ch 36:15 [z]S Isa 20:3 [a]S Nu 11:29; Jer 25:4; 35:15 **7:26** [b]ver 13, 24; S 2Ch 36:16; Ps 81:11; Jer 13:11; 22:21; 25:3; 35:15; Eze 20:8, 21 [c]S Ex 32:9; Ac 7:51 [d]Jer 16:12; Mal 3:7; Lk 11:47 **7:27** [e]Eze 2:7 [f]ver 13; Eze 3:7; Zec 7:13 [g]S Isa 65:12 **7:28** [h]S Lev 26:23; Zep 3:7 [i]S Ps 15:2; S Isa 59:15 **7:29** [j]S Lev 21:5; S Job 1:20 [k]S Jer 4:8; S Eze 19:1 [l]S Jer 6:30; 12:7; Hos 11:8; Mic 5:3 **7:30** [m]S ver 10; S Lev 18:21 [n]S Jer 2:7; S 4:1; Eze 7:20-22

26:5; 29:19; 32:33; 35:14–15; 44:4) but appears nowhere else in the OT.

7:15 *thrust you from my presence.* Into exile (see Dt 29:28). *just as I did all your fellow Israelites.* God sent Israel, the northern kingdom, into captivity in 721 BC (see 2Ki 17:20). *Ephraim.* Another name for Israel (see, e.g., 31:9)—and, ironically, the tribal territory in which Shiloh was located.

7:16 Perhaps the events of ch. 26 belong chronologically between vv. 15 and 16 (see Introduction: Outline). *do not pray for this people.* As a true prophet would (see 27:18; Ex 32:31–32; 1Sa 12:23). See 11:14; 14:11. There is virtually no hope for them (cf. Eze 14:14,20). On various occasions, however, Jeremiah prayed for his countrymen (see, e.g., 18:20). *this people.* See note on Ex 17:4.

7:18 *children ... fathers ... women.* Entire families participate in idolatrous worship. *cakes.* See 44:19. *Queen of Heaven.* A Babylonian title for Ishtar, an important goddess in the Babylonian pantheon (see 44:17–19,25). *drink offerings to other gods.* And sometimes to the Queen of Heaven herself (see 44:19,25). *arouse my anger.* See Dt 31:29.

7:19 *their own shame.* See 3:25.

7:20 All nature suffers when God judges sinners (see 5:17; Ro 8:20–22). *burn and not be quenched.* See 4:4; 21:12; see also Isa 1:31; Am 5:6.

7:21 Because of your sinful deeds your sacrifices are worthless, so you might as well eat them yourselves.

7:22–23 Sacrifices are valid only when accompanied by sincere repentance and joyful obedience (see 6:20; Isa 1:11–15 and notes).

7:23 *your God ... my people.* The most basic summary of the relationship between God and Israel implied in the covenant at Sinai (see 31:33; Ex 6:7; Lev 26:12; Zec 8:8 and notes; Dt 26:17–18).

7:24 *followed ... evil hearts.* See note on 3:17; see also Ge 6:5 and note.

7:25 *again and again.* See note on v. 13. *my servants the prophets.* See 25:4; 26:5; 29:19; 35:15; 44:4; see also Zec 1:6 and note. God had promised that Moses would be the first in a long line of prophets who would speak in the Lord's name and serve him faithfully (see Dt 18:15–22 and notes), a promise fulfilled in Christ (see Ac 3:22,26 and note).

7:26 *stiff-necked.* See 17:23; 19:15; Ex 32:9 and note.

7:28 *not ... responded to correction.* See 2:30; 5:3. *Truth ... has vanished from their lips.* No one seeks the truth (see 5:1 and note).

7:29 Addressed to Jerusalem. *Cut off your hair.* A sign of mourning (see Job 1:20; Mic 1:16). The Hebrew for the word "hair" is related to the word "Nazirite" (Nu 6:2; see note there) and referred originally to the diadem worn by the high priest (see Ex 29:6). The Nazirite's hair was the symbol of their separation or consecration (Nu 6:7). As the Nazirite was commanded to cut off their hair when they became ceremonially unclean (Nu 6:9), so also Jerusalem must cut off her hair because of her sins. *lament on the barren heights.* See 3:21; see also note on 3:2.

7:30 *set up their ... idols in the house.* Manasseh had put a carved Asherah pole (see NIV text note on 2Ki 13:6) in the temple (2Ki 21:7). Jeremiah's contemporary, the

house that bears my Name and have defiled[o] it. 31 They have built the high places of Topheth[p] in the Valley of Ben Hinnom[q] to burn their sons and daughters[r] in
the fire — something I did not command,
nor did it enter my mind.[s] 32 So beware,
the days are coming, declares the LORD,
when people will no longer call it Topheth
or the Valley of Ben Hinnom, but the Valley of Slaughter,[t] for they will bury[u] the
dead in Topheth until there is no more
room. 33 Then the carcasses[v] of this people
will become food[w] for the birds and the
wild animals, and there will be no one to
frighten them away.[x] 34 I will bring an end
to the sounds[y] of joy and gladness and to
the voices of bride and bridegroom[z] in the
towns of Judah and the streets of Jerusalem,[a] for the land will become desolate.[b]

8 " 'At that time, declares the LORD, the
bones of the kings and officials of Judah, the bones of the priests and prophets, and the bones[c] of the people of Jerusalem will be removed[d] from their graves.
2 They will be exposed to the sun and the
moon and all the stars of the heavens,
which they have loved and served[e] and
which they have followed and consulted
and worshiped.[f] They will not be gathered
up or buried,[g] but will be like dung lying on the ground.[h] 3 Wherever I banish
them,[i] all the survivors of this evil nation
will prefer death to life,[j] declares the LORD
Almighty.'

7:30 [o] S Lev 20:3; Jer 32:34 **7:31** [p] S 2Ki 23:10 [q] S Jos 15:8; 2Ch 33:6 [r] S Lev 18:21; Eze 16:20 [s] Jer 19:5; 32:35; Eze 20:31; Mic 6:7 **7:32** [t] Jer 19:6 [u] Jer 19:11 **7:33** [v] S Ge 15:11 [w] S Dt 28:26; Eze 29:5 [x] Jer 6:11; 14:16 **7:34** [y] S Isa 24:8 [z] Rev 18:23 [a] Isa 24:7-12; Jer 33:10 [b] S Lev 26:34; Zec 7:14; Mt 23:38 **8:1** [c] S Ps 53:5 [d] S Isa 14:19 **8:2** [e] S 2Ki 23:5; Jer 19:13; Zep 1:5; Ac 7:42 [f] S Job 31:27 [g] Jer 14:16; Eze 29:5; 37:1 [h] S 2Ki 9:37; Jer 31:40; 36:30 **8:3** [i] Dt 29:28 [j] S Job 3:22; Rev 9:6 **8:4** [k] Pr 24:16; Mic 7:8 [l] Ps 119:67; Jer 31:19 **8:5** [m] S Jer 5:27 [n] Zec 7:11 **8:6** [o] Mal 3:16 [p] Rev 9:20 [q] Ps 14:1-3 **8:7** [r] S Dt 32:28; S Jer 4:22

Sin and Punishment

4 "Say to them, 'This is what the LORD says:

" 'When people fall down, do they not
get up?[k]
When someone turns away,[l] do they
not return?
5 Why then have these people turned
away?
Why does Jerusalem always turn
away?
They cling to deceit;[m]
they refuse to return.[n]
6 I have listened[o] attentively,
but they do not say what is right.
None of them repent[p] of their wickedness,
saying, "What have I done?"
Each pursues their own course[q]
like a horse charging into battle.
7 Even the stork in the sky
knows her appointed seasons,
and the dove, the swift and the thrush
observe the time of their migration.
But my people do not know[r]
the requirements of the LORD.

good King Josiah, removed the pole and other accessories to idol worship (2Ki 23:4 – 7). But less than 20 years after Josiah's death, Ezekiel reported that there were numerous idols in the temple courts (see Eze 8:3,5 – 6,10,12). *defiled it.* See note on 2:7.

7:31 *high places.* Pagan shrines, usually (but not here) located on natural heights (see 1Sa 9:13 – 14; 10:5; 1Ki 11:7). *Topheth.* See v. 32; 19:6,11 – 14; see also note on Isa 30:33. The word is of Aramaic origin and means "fireplace," though in cultures outside Israel it was used as a common noun meaning "place of child sacrifice." Its vowel pattern was perhaps intentionally conformed to that of Hebrew *bosheth,* "shameful thing" (see note on Jdg 6:32), often used in connection with idol worship (see notes on 2:26; 3:25). The OT Topheth had a fire pit (see Isa 30:33), into which the hapless children were apparently thrown. *Valley of Ben Hinnom.* See v. 32; 19:2,6; 32:35; see also note on Jos 15:5. It was used as a trash dump and also as a place for sacrificing children to pagan gods. The abbreviated Hebrew name *ge' hinnom* ("Valley of Hinnom"; see Ne 11:30 and note) became "Gehenna" (Greek *geenna*), consistently translated in the NT as "hell," the place of eternal, fiery punishment (see Mt 5:22 and note; 18:9; Mk 9:47 – 48). *burn their sons and daughters in the fire.* A horrible ritual, prohibited in the law of Moses (see Lev 18:21 and note; Dt 18:10) but practiced by Ahaz (see 2Ki 16:2 – 3) and Manasseh (2Ki 21:1,6). *nor did it enter my mind.* Stresses how terribly evil such an act is to God (see 19:5; 32:35).

7:32 *So beware … Valley of Slaughter.* Repeated almost verbatim in 19:6. Their place of sacrifice would become their cemetery when the people of Judah were slaughtered by the Babylonian invaders.

7:33 The punishment announced here is one of the curses for covenant disobedience (see Dt 28:26). *food for the birds … wild animals.* See 16:4; 19:7; see also 34:20, where the same judgment is the result of violating God's covenant (34:18 – 19). To remain unburied was an unspeakable abomination in ancient times (cf. 22:19 and note).

7:34 See 16:9; 25:10; contrast 33:10 – 11. *land will become desolate.* Another covenant curse (Lev 26:31,33).

8:1 *bones … removed from their graves.* A gross indignity and sacrilege (see 2Ki 23:16,18; Am 2:1 and note). *kings … officials … priests … prophets.* See 2:26; see also note on 1:18.

8:2 *exposed to the sun … moon … stars.* To hasten their disintegration, and perhaps also to demonstrate that the heavenly bodies, which had been worshiped by some of Judah's kings (see 2Ki 21:3,5; 23:11), among others, were powerless to help. *loved and served and … followed and consulted and worshiped.* Acts of homage and adoration that should have been given to God alone. *They.* The bones. *not be gathered up or buried.* Contrast 2Sa 21:13 – 14. *dung.* See 9:22; 16:4; 25:33.

8:3 *survivors.* See note on 6:9.

8:4 — 9:26 In contrast to 7:1 — 8:3, this section is almost completely in poetic form. Jeremiah resumes his extended commentary on the inevitability of divine judgment against sinners.

8:4 *Say to them.* Connects this section with the previous (see 7:28). *turns away … return.* The Hebrew for these two verbs is identical, forming a play on words.

8:5 The general truths stated in v. 4 are routinely and perversely violated by the people of Jerusalem. *turned away … turn away … return.* Continuing the wordplay of v. 4.

8:6 *I.* The Lord. *pursues.* The Hebrew for this word continues the wordplay of vv. 4 – 5. *their own course.* And therefore evil (see 23:10).

8:7 See Isa 1:3. Although migratory birds obey their God-given instincts, God's rebellious people refuse to obey his laws. *swift.* Of similar build and habit as the swallow

8 " 'How can you say, "We are wise,
for we have the law[s] of the LORD,"
when actually the lying pen of the scribes
has handled it falsely?
9 The wise[t] will be put to shame;
they will be dismayed[u] and trapped.[v]
Since they have rejected the word[w] of the LORD,
what kind of wisdom[x] do they have?
10 Therefore I will give their wives to other men
and their fields to new owners.[y]
From the least to the greatest,
all are greedy for gain;[z]
prophets[a] and priests alike,
all practice deceit.[b]
11 They dress the wound of my people
as though it were not serious.
"Peace, peace," they say,
when there is no peace.[c]
12 Are they ashamed of their detestable conduct?
No, they have no shame[d] at all;
they do not even know how to blush.
So they will fall among the fallen;
they will be brought down when they are punished,[e]
says the LORD.[f]

13 " 'I will take away their harvest,
declares the LORD.
There will be no grapes on the vine.[g]
There will be no figs[h] on the tree,
and their leaves will wither.[i]
What I have given them
will be taken[j] from them.[a]' "

14 Why are we sitting here?
Gather together!
Let us flee to the fortified cities[k]
and perish there!
For the LORD our God has doomed us to perish
and given us poisoned water[l] to drink,
because we have sinned[m] against him.
15 We hoped for peace[n]
but no good has come,
for a time of healing
but there is only terror.[o]
16 The snorting of the enemy's horses[p]
is heard from Dan;[q]
at the neighing of their stallions
the whole land trembles.[r]
They have come to devour[s]
the land and everything in it,
the city and all who live there.

17 "See, I will send venomous snakes[t] among you,
vipers that cannot be charmed,[u]
and they will bite you,"
declares the LORD.

18 You who are my Comforter[b] in sorrow,
my heart is faint[v] within me.
19 Listen to the cry of my people
from a land far away:[w]
"Is the LORD not in Zion?
Is her King[x] no longer there?"

"Why have they aroused[y] my anger
with their images,
with their worthless[z] foreign idols?"[a]

8:8 [s]Ro 2:17
8:9 [t]S Isa 29:14 [u]S 2Ki 19:26 [v]S Job 5:13 [w]S Jer 6:19 [x]Pr 1:7; 1Co 1:20
8:10 [y]S Jer 6:12 [z]S Isa 56:11 [a]Jer 14:14; La 2:14 [b]Jer 23:11,15
8:11 [c]ver 15; S Jer 4:10; Eze 7:25
8:12 [d]S Jer 3:3 [e]Ps 52:5-7; Isa 3:9 [f]S Jer 6:15
8:13 [g]Hos 2:12; Joel 1:7 [h]Lk 13:6 [i]Mt 21:19 [j]S Jer 5:17
8:14 [k]S Jos 10:20; Jer 35:11 [l]S Dt 29:18; Jer 9:15; 23:15 [m]Jer 14:7,20; Da 9:5
8:15 [n]S ver 11 [o]S Job 19:8; Jer 14:19
8:16 [p]S Jer 4:29 [q]S Ge 30:6 [r]Jer 51:29 [s]S Jer 5:17
8:17 [t]Nu 21:6; S Dt 32:24 [u]S Ps 58:5; S Isa 3:3
8:18 [v]La 5:17
8:19 [w]Dt 28:64; Jer 9:16 [x]Mic 4:9 [y]Jer 44:3 [z]S Isa 41:24 [a]S Dt 32:21

[a] *13* The meaning of the Hebrew for this sentence is uncertain. [b] *18* The meaning of the Hebrew for this word is uncertain.

---

but not related to it (see 38:14, where it is also linked with the thrush). *do not know ... requirements of the LORD.* See note on 5:4.

8:8–9 *law of the LORD ... word of the LORD.* Misinterpreting and manipulating the first (the written law of Moses) leads to rejection of the second (God's truth as found in the law and proclaimed by his servants the prophets).

8:8 *lying pen.* Symbolizes mistreatment of the written law. *scribes.* The earliest mention of them as a recognizable group. They were apparently organized on the basis of families (see 1Ch 2:55; 2Ch 34:13; see also note on Ezr 7:6). *handled it falsely.* Contrast 2Ti 2:15.

8:9 *rejected ... wisdom.* Contrast Dt 4:5–6.

8:10–12 See 6:12–15 and notes.

8:11 *my people.* Lit. "the Daughter of my people" (also in v. 21; see Isa 22:4 and note).

8:13—9:24 This section is read aloud in synagogues every year on the ninth of Av (see chart, p. 113), the day the temple in Jerusalem was destroyed by the Babylonians in 586 BC and again by the Romans in AD 70.

8:13 *grapes ... figs.* Symbolic of individual people also in Mic 7:1; see ch. 24. *vine.* Israel (see 2:21 and note). *leaves will wither.* Contrast 17:8; Ps 1:3.

8:14–16 On behalf of the people the prophet speaks, envisioning the Babylonian invasion.

8:14 *Gather together!* See 4:5. The Hebrew for this phrase forms a wordplay with the Hebrew for "take away" and "harvest" in v. 13. *flee to the fortified cities.* See note on 4:5. *poisoned water.* The phrase is unique to the prophet Jeremiah (see 9:15; 23:15; cf. 25:15).

8:15 Repeated almost verbatim in 14:19. *peace.* Under the circumstances, a false hope (see notes on 4:10; 6:14). *healing.* See note on 6:7.

8:16 *the enemy's horses.* See note on 4:13. *Dan.* Close to the northern border of Israel. It would be the first to feel the effects of the Babylonian invasion. *stallions.* Lit. "mighty ones"; the Hebrew word is translated "stallions" again in 50:11, "steeds" in 47:3.

8:17 *vipers that cannot be charmed.* Such are the wicked always (see Ps 58:4–5).

8:18 The prophet speaks. *my heart is faint.* See La 1:22; 5:17.

8:19 The prophet speaks in the first part of the verse, the Lord in the last part. *my people from a land far away.* Judah in Babylonian exile (see Ps 137:1–4) as Jeremiah envisions the future. *Is the LORD not in Zion?* Cf. Mic 3:11. The people are perplexed at their fate, still wondering how God could have permitted the destruction of his land and temple (see note on 7:4). *King.* God (see Isa 33:22 and note). *aroused my anger.* See 7:18; Dt 31:29. *worthless ... idols.* See note on 2:5.

20 "The harvest is past,
the summer has ended,
and we are not saved."
21 Since my people are crushed,[b] I am
crushed;
I mourn,[c] and horror grips me.
22 Is there no balm in Gilead?[d]
Is there no physician[e] there?
Why then is there no healing[f]
for the wound of my people?

9 [a] 1 Oh, that my head were a spring of
water
and my eyes a fountain of tears![g]
I would weep[h] day and night
for the slain of my people.[i]
2 Oh, that I had in the desert[j]
a lodging place for travelers,
so that I might leave my people
and go away from them;
for they are all adulterers,[k]
a crowd of unfaithful[l] people.
3 "They make ready their tongue
like a bow, to shoot lies;[m]
it is not by truth
that they triumph[b] in the land.
They go from one sin to another;
they do not acknowledge[n] me,"
declares the LORD.
4 "Beware of your friends;[o]
do not trust anyone in your clan.[p]
For every one of them is a deceiver,[c][q]
and every friend a slanderer.[r]
5 Friend deceives friend,[s]
and no one speaks the truth.[t]
They have taught their tongues to lie;[u]
they weary themselves with sinning.
6 You[d] live in the midst of deception;[v]
in their deceit they refuse to
acknowledge me,"
declares the LORD.

8:21 [b] S Ps 94:5 [c] Ps 78:40; Isa 43:24; Jer 4:19; 10:19; 14:17; 30:14; La 2:13; Eze 6:9 **8:22** [d] S Ge 37:25 [e] Job 13:4 [f] S Isa 1:6; Jer 30:12 **9:1** [g] S Ps 119:136 [h] Jer 13:17; 14:17; La 2:11, 18; 3:48 [i] Isa 22:4 **9:2** [j] Ps 55:7 [k] S Nu 25:1; Jer 23:10; Hos 4:2; 7:4 [l] S 1Ki 19:10; S Isa 24:16 **9:3** [m] ver 8; S Ex 20:16; Ps 64:3; S Isa 44:20; Jer 18:18; Mic 6:12 [n] S Isa 1:3 **9:4** [o] S 2Sa 15:12 [p] Mic 7:5-6 [q] S Ge 27:35 [r] S Ex 20:16; S Lev 19:16 **9:5** [s] S Lev 6:2 [t] S Ps 15:2; S Isa 59:15 [u] S Ps 52:3 **9:6** [v] S Jer 5:27 **9:7** [w] S Job 28:1; S Isa 1:25 [x] S Jer 6:27 **9:8** [y] S ver 3; S Ps 35:20 [z] S Isa 3:5 [a] S Jer 5:26 [b] ver 4 **9:9** [c] S Dt 32:43; S Isa 10:3 **9:10** [d] Jer 23:10; Joel 1:19 [e] S Jer 4:25; 12:4; Hos 4:3; Joel 1:18 **9:11** [f] Jer 26:18 [g] S Job 30:29; S Isa 34:13 [h] S Jer 1:15

7 Therefore this is what the LORD Almighty says:

"See, I will refine[w] and test[x] them,
for what else can I do
because of the sin of my people?
8 Their tongue[y] is a deadly arrow;
it speaks deceitfully.
With their mouths they all speak
cordially to their neighbors,[z]
but in their hearts they set traps[a] for
them.[b]
9 Should I not punish them for this?"
declares the LORD.
"Should I not avenge[c] myself
on such a nation as this?"

10 I will weep and wail for the
mountains
and take up a lament concerning the
wilderness grasslands.[d]
They are desolate and untraveled,
and the lowing of cattle is not
heard.
The birds[e] have all fled
and the animals are gone.

11 "I will make Jerusalem a heap[f] of
ruins,
a haunt of jackals;[g]
and I will lay waste the towns of
Judah[h]
so no one can live there."[i]

12 Who is wise[j] enough to understand
this? Who has been instructed by the LORD
and can explain it? Why has the land been

[a] In Hebrew texts 9:1 is numbered 8:23, and 9:2-26 is numbered 9:1-25. [b] 3 *Or lies; / they are not valiant for truth* [c] 4 *Or a deceiving Jacob* [d] 6 That is, Jeremiah (the Hebrew is singular)

[i] S Lev 26:31; Isa 25:2; S Jer 4:13; 26:9; 33:10; 50:3, 13; 51:62; La 1:4 **9:12** [j] S Ps 107:43

8:20 The people speak from the hopelessness of their exile. *we are not saved.* We have been captured by the enemy.
8:21 Jeremiah identifies himself with his exiled countrymen. *grips me.* See 6:24.
8:22 *balm in Gilead.* See 46:11; cf. 51:8. The territory of Gilead was an important source of spices and medicinal herbs (see Ge 37:25 and note). *no healing for the wound.* Contrast 30:17.
9:1–2 The prophet's frustration is highlighted as he speaks of his countrymen with tender sympathy in v. 1 and with indignant disgust in v. 2.
9:1 Jeremiah is often called the "weeping prophet"—a well-deserved title (see v. 10; the book of Lamentations; cf. 2Sa 18:33; Lk 19:41; Ro 9:2–4; 10:1).
9:2 The prophet wants to get as far away from his wicked countrymen as possible (cf. Ps 55:6–8). *adulterers … unfaithful people.* See v. 14; see also Ex 34:15 and note. *crowd.* The Hebrew for this word is always used elsewhere in the OT in the sense of a solemn religious assembly (see, e.g., Dt 16:8), sometimes perverted by the worshipers and therefore falling under divine judgment (see Isa 1:13; Am 5:21).
9:3–9 The Lord speaks.
9:3 *tongue like a bow.* See vv. 5,8; see also Ps 64:3–4; cf. Jas 3:5–12. *do not acknowledge me.* See v. 6; Jdg 2:10; 1Sa 2:12; Job 18:21; Hos 4:1 and note; Ro 1:28; contrast Hos 6:3.
9:4 *deceiver.* See NIV text note; Ge 25:26 and note; NIV text note on Ge 27:36; Hos 12:2–3 and NIV text note on 12:2.
9:6 *refuse to acknowledge me.* The situation has deteriorated even further (v. 3 says simply "do not acknowledge me").
9:7 *refine and test.* See 6:27–30 and notes. The Lord will test his people "in the furnace of affliction" (Isa 48:10; see note there).
9:8 *tongue … speaks deceitfully.* See v. 3 and note. *With their mouths … but in their hearts.* See Ps 55:21. *cordially.* The Hebrew for this word is translated "peace" in 6:14 (see note there).
9:9 Repeated from 5:9,29.
9:10 The prophet speaks. See 4:23–26 and notes. *weep and wail.* See v. 18; see also note on v. 1. *wilderness grasslands.* Good for poor grazing at best (see 1Sa 17:28; cf. Ex 3:1). *desolate.* Lit. "burned" (as in 2:15); here parched by the blazing sun. *untraveled.* See v. 12; Eze 33:28.
9:11 The Lord speaks. *haunt of jackals.* See 10:22; 49:33; 51:37; Ps 44:19; Isa 13:21–22; La 5:18; Eze 13:4; Mal 1:3; contrast Isa 35:7. *no one can live there.* See 2:15; 4:7 and notes.
9:12 The prophet asks a series of questions. *Who is wise … ?* See Hos 14:9.

ruined and laid waste like a desert that no
one can cross?
13 The LORD said, "It is because they have
forsaken my law, which I set before them;
they have not obeyed me or followed my
law.[k] 14 Instead, they have followed[l] the
stubbornness of their hearts;[m] they have
followed the Baals, as their ancestors
taught them." 15 Therefore this is what the
LORD Almighty, the God of Israel, says:
"See, I will make this people eat bitter
food[n] and drink poisoned water.[o] 16 I will
scatter them among nations[p] that neither
they nor their ancestors have known,[q] and
I will pursue them with the sword[r] until I
have made an end of them."[s]

17 This is what the LORD Almighty says:

"Consider now! Call for the wailing
women[t] to come;
send for the most skillful of
them.
18 Let them come quickly
and wail over us
till our eyes overflow with tears
and water streams from our
eyelids.[u]
19 The sound of wailing is heard from
Zion:
'How ruined[v] we are!
How great is our shame!
We must leave our land
because our houses are in ruins.' "

20 Now, you women, hear the word of the
LORD;
open your ears to the words of his
mouth.[w]
Teach your daughters how to wail;
teach one another a lament.[x]
21 Death has climbed in through our
windows[y]
and has entered our fortresses;
it has removed the children from the
streets
and the young men[z] from the public
squares.

22 Say, "This is what the LORD declares:

" 'Dead bodies will lie
like dung[a] on the open field,
like cut grain behind the reaper,
with no one to gather them.' "

23 This is what the LORD says:

"Let not the wise boast of their
wisdom[b]
or the strong boast of their strength[c]
or the rich boast of their riches,[d]
24 but let the one who boasts boast[e]
about this:
that they have the understanding to
know[f] me,
that I am the LORD,[g] who exercises
kindness,[h]
justice and righteousness[i] on
earth,
for in these I delight,"
declares the LORD.

25 "The days are coming," declares the
LORD, "when I will punish all who are circumcised only in the flesh[j]— 26 Egypt, Judah, Edom, Ammon, Moab and all who
live in the wilderness in distant places.[a][k]
For all these nations are really uncircumcised,[l] and even the whole house of Israel
is uncircumcised in heart.[m]"

9:13 [k] S 2Ch 7:19; S Ps 89:30-32
9:14 [l] S Jer 2:8, 23; Am 2:4 [m] S Jer 3:17; S 7:24
9:15 [n] La 3:15 [o] S Jer 8:14
9:16 [p] S Lev 26:33 [q] S Dt 4:32; S Jer 8:19 [r] Jer 14:12; 24:10; Eze 5:2 [s] Jer 44:27; Eze 5:12
9:17 [t] S Ecc 12:5
9:18 [u] S Ps 119:136; La 3:48
9:19 [v] S Jer 4:13
9:20 [w] Jer 23:16 [x] Isa 32:9-13
9:21 [y] Joel 2:9 [z] S 2Ch 36:17; S Isa 40:30; S Jer 16:6
9:22 [a] S 2Ki 9:37
9:23 [b] S Job 4:12; S Ecc 9:11 [c] S 1Ki 20:11 [d] Ps 62:10; S Pr 11:28; Jer 48:7; 49:4; Eze 28:4-5
9:24 [e] S Ps 34:2; 1Co 1:31*; Gal 6:14 [f] S Ps 36:10 [g] 2Co 10:17* [h] Ps 51:1 [i] Ps 36:6
9:25 [j] S Lev 26:41; Ro 2:25
9:26 [k] Jer 25:23; 49:32 [l] S 1Sa 14:6; Eze 31:18 [m] Ac 7:51

[a] 26 Or *wilderness and who clip the hair by their foreheads*

9:13 The Lord answers the prophet and then continues to speak through v. 19. *law, which I set before them.* In the days of Moses (see Dt 4:8).
9:14 *stubbornness.* See note on 3:17. *Baals.* See 2:23 and note.
9:15 *eat bitter food and drink poisoned water.* Repeated in 23:15; see note on 8:14. Centuries earlier, Moses had warned the Israelites concerning just such a fate (see Dt 29:18).
9:16 *I will scatter them.* See 13:24; 18:17; 30:11; 46:28. This warning was given in Dt 28:64 as one of the curses for persistent covenant unfaithfulness. *pursue them with the sword.* See 42:16. *made an end of them.* But not to the last man (see note on 4:27; see especially 44:27–28).
9:17 *wailing women.* Professionals, paid to mourn at funerals and other sorrowful occasions (see 2Ch 35:25; Ecc 12:5; Am 5:16).
9:18 *wail.* See v. 10. *eyes overflow with tears.* See v. 1.
9:19 *How ruined we are!* See 4:13,20; cf. 48:1.
9:20–21 The prophet speaks.
9:20 The wailing women will have to teach their daughters how to lament, so great will be the need for their services.
9:21 *Death.* Personified here (as in Hab 2:5). Canaanite mythology included a deity named Mot (a word related to the Hebrew word for "death"), the god of infertility and the netherworld. *climbed in through our windows.* Said of an army of "locusts" in Joel 2:9 (see note there). *children … young men.* See 6:11.
9:22 *Dead bodies.* See 7:33 and note. *like dung.* See note on 8:2. *reaper.* The concept of death as the "grim reaper" comes largely from this verse.
9:23 *Let not … the rich boast of their riches.* An almost exact parallel occurs in the Aramaic *Words of Ahiqar,* written about a century after Jeremiah's time: "Let not the rich say, 'In my riches I am glorious.'"
9:24 1Co 1:31 summarizes: "Let the one who boasts boast in the Lord." *this … these.* Ultimately, only God and our knowledge of and love for him are worthwhile. *have the understanding to know me.* See 3:15; see also note on 4:22. *I am the LORD.* Ex 6:2–8, a key passage on the doctrine of redemption, begins and ends with this statement of divine self-disclosure. *kindness.* The Hebrew for this word is translated "devotion" in 2:2 (see note there). *in these I delight.* See Ps 11:7; 33:5; 99:4; 103:6; Mic 6:8; 7:18.
9:25–26 See Ro 2:25–29; see also note on Ge 17:10.
9:26 *who live … in distant places.* Arab tribes (see 25:23; 49:32), later to be attacked by the Babylonians under Nebuchadnezzar (see 49:28–33). With the NIV text note here, contrast Lev 19:27. *uncircumcised in heart.* See 4:4 and note.

God and Idols

10:12-16pp — Jer 51:15-19

10 Hear what the LORD says to you,
people of Israel. 2 This is what the
LORD says:

"Do not learn the ways of the nations[n]
or be terrified by signs[o] in the heavens,
though the nations are terrified by them.
3 For the practices of the peoples are worthless;
they cut a tree out of the forest,
and a craftsman[p] shapes it with his chisel.[q]
4 They adorn it with silver[r] and gold;
they fasten it with hammer and nails
so it will not totter.[s]
5 Like a scarecrow in a cucumber field,
their idols cannot speak;[t]
they must be carried
because they cannot walk.[u]
Do not fear them;
they can do no harm[v]
nor can they do any good."[w]

6 No one is like you,[x] LORD;
you are great,[y]
and your name is mighty in power.
7 Who should not fear[z] you,
King of the nations?[a]
This is your due.
Among all the wise leaders of the nations
and in all their kingdoms,
there is no one like you.
8 They are all senseless[b] and foolish;[c]
they are taught by worthless wooden idols.[d]

10:2 [n] S Ex 23:24; S Lev 20:23 [o] S Ge 1:14 **10:3** [p] S Isa 40:19 [q] Dt 9:21; S 1Ki 8:36; Jer 44:8; Eze 7:20 **10:4** [r] Ps 135:15; Hos 13:2; Hab 2:19 [s] S 1Sa 5:3; Isa 41:7 **10:5** [t] S 1Ki 18:26; 1Co 12:2 [u] S Isa 45:20 [v] Isa 41:23 [w] S Isa 41:24; 44:9-20; 46:7; Ac 19:26 **10:6** [x] S Ex 8:10 [y] S 2Sa 7:22; S Ps 48:1 **10:7** [z] Jer 5:22 [a] Ps 22:28; S Isa 12:4; Rev 15:4 **10:8** [b] S Isa 44:18 [c] S Isa 40:19; S Jer 4:22 [d] S Dt 32:21

10:9 [e] S Ge 10:4 [f] Ps 115:4; S Isa 40:19 **10:10** [g] S Jos 3:10; S Mt 16:16 [h] S Ge 21:33; Da 6:26

9 Hammered silver is brought from Tarshish[e]
and gold from Uphaz.
What the craftsman and goldsmith have made[f]
is then dressed in blue and purple—
all made by skilled workers.
10 But the LORD is the true God;
he is the living God,[g] the eternal King.[h]

Statue of the Canaanite god El. God states in Jeremiah 10:3–5 that all the time and effort spent on creating idols that "cannot speak" or "walk" are "worthless."

10:1–25 Jeremiah concludes his series of temple messages with a poetic section that focuses primarily on the vast difference between idols and the Lord (vv. 2–16). Idols and their worshipers are condemned in vv. 2–5,8–9,11,14–15, while the one true God is praised in the alternate passages (vv. 6–7,10,12–13,16). See Isa 40:18–20 and note; 41:7; 44:9–20; 46:5–7.
10:1 *Hear.* See note on 2:4.
10:2 *Do not … be terrified.* See 1:17. *ways.* The Hebrew for this word is singular and refers to the religious practices of the nations. The early Christians often called their distinctive beliefs and lifestyle the "Way" (see Ac 9:2; 19:9,23; 22:4; 24:14,22). *signs in the heavens.* The heavenly bodies were created by the Lord for purposes other than idolatrous worship (see Ge 1:14–18 and notes). *nations are terrified.* Not only by the heavenly bodies themselves but also by unusual phenomena associated with them (such as comets, meteors and eclipses).
10:3 *worthless.* See note on 2:5. *cut a tree.* See Isa 44:14–15. *craftsman.* The Hebrew for this word is often used of idolmakers who work usually—but not always (see Isa 40:19)—with wood (see Isa 41:7). *chisel.* Cf. Isa 44:13.
10:4 *silver and gold.* Wooden idols were plated with precious metals to beautify them (see Isa 30:22; 40:19). *fasten it … so it will not totter.* See Isa 40:20; 41:7; cf. 46:7; contrast 1Sa 5:2–4.
10:5 The impotence of idols is described in classic form in Ps 115:4–7; 135:15–18. *scarecrow.* Verse 70 in the Apocryphal *Letter of Jeremiah* uses the same imagery. *cucumber field.* See Isa 1:8. *must be carried.* Usually on the backs of animals. See Isa 46:1. *harm nor … good.* Idols can do nothing at all (see Isa 41:22–24).
10:6 *No one.* Among the gods (see Ps 86:8). *your name is mighty in power.* See 16:21.
10:7 *fear you, King of the nations.* See Ps 47:8–9 and notes; 96:10; Rev 15:3–4 and notes. Unlike the gods of the surrounding nations, limited to their own territories, the Lord is King over all (see Ge 28:15; 2Ki 5:17 and notes). *This.* Reverence ("fear"). *Among all the wise leaders … no one like you.* See Isa 19:12; 29:14; 1Co 1:20.
10:8 *senseless and foolish.* See vv. 14,21; 5:21; see also NIV text note on Pr 1:7. *taught by … idols.* Instead of by the Lord (see Dt 11:2; Job 5:17; Pr 3:11, where the Hebrew word for "taught by" is translated "discipline").
10:9 *silver … from Tarshish.* See Eze 27:12; see also note on Isa 23:6. *Uphaz.* Mentioned only here. *craftsman and goldsmith.* See Isa 40:19 and note. *dressed in blue and purple.* To make it look regal. *all.* The idols.
10:10 Everything that idols are not, the Lord is. *true.* See 1Th 1:9. *living God.* See 23:36; Dt 5:26; 2Ki 19:4 and

When he is angry,[i] the earth trembles;[j]
the nations cannot endure his
wrath.[k]

11 "Tell them this: 'These gods, who did
not make the heavens and the earth, will
perish[l] from the earth and from under the
heavens.' "[a]

12 But God made[m] the earth[n] by his
power;
he founded the world by his
wisdom[o]
and stretched out the heavens[p] by
his understanding.
13 When he thunders,[q] the waters in the
heavens roar;
he makes clouds rise from the ends
of the earth.
He sends lightning[r] with the rain[s]
and brings out the wind from his
storehouses.[t]

14 Everyone is senseless and without
knowledge;
every goldsmith is shamed[u] by his
idols.
The images he makes are a fraud;[v]
they have no breath in them.
15 They are worthless,[w] the objects of
mockery;
when their judgment comes, they
will perish.
16 He who is the Portion[x] of Jacob is not
like these,
for he is the Maker of all things,[y]
including Israel, the people of his
inheritance[z]—
the LORD Almighty is his name.[a]

Coming Destruction

17 Gather up your belongings[b] to leave
the land,
you who live under siege.

10:10 [i] S Ps 18:7 [j] S Jdg 5:4; S Job 9:6; Ps 29:8 [k] Ps 76:7; Jer 21:12; Na 1:6
10:11 [l] S Isa 2:18
10:12 [m] S 1Sa 2:8 [n] S ver 16 [o] S Ge 1:31 [p] S Ge 1:1,8
10:13 [q] S Job 36:29 [r] S Job 36:30 [s] S Ps 104:13; S 135:7 [t] S Dt 28:12
10:14 [u] S Ps 97:7; S Isa 1:29 [v] S Isa 44:20
10:15 [w] S Isa 41:24; S Jer 14:22
10:16 [x] S Dt 32:9; S Ps 119:57 [y] ver 12; Jer 32:17; 33:2 [z] S Ex 34:9; Ps 74:2 [a] Jer 31:35; 32:18
10:17 [b] Eze 12:3-12
10:18 [c] S 1Sa 25:29; S Isa 22:17 [d] S Dt 28:52
10:19 [e] Job 34:6; Jer 14:17; 15:18; 30:12, 15; La 2:13; Mic 1:9; Na 3:19 [f] Mic 7:9
10:20 [g] S Jer 4:20 [h] Jer 31:15; La 1:5
10:21 [i] Jer 22:22; 23:1; 25:34; 50:6 [j] ver 8 [k] S Isa 56:10 [l] Jer 22:30 [m] Jer 23:2; Eze 34:6
10:22 [n] Jer 6:22; 27:6; 49:28,30 [o] Eze 12:19 [p] S Isa 34:13
10:23 [q] S Job 33:29; S Pr 3:5-6; 20:24
10:24 [r] Ps 6:1; 38:1; S Jer 7:20; 18:23 [s] Jer 30:11; 46:28
10:25 [t] S Ps 69:24; Zep 2:2; 3:8

18 For this is what the LORD says:
"At this time I will hurl[c] out
those who live in this land;
I will bring distress[d] on them
so that they may be captured."

19 Woe to me because of my injury!
My wound[e] is incurable!
Yet I said to myself,
"This is my sickness, and I must
endure[f] it."
20 My tent[g] is destroyed;
all its ropes are snapped.
My children are gone from me and are
no more;[h]
no one is left now to pitch my tent
or to set up my shelter.
21 The shepherds[i] are senseless[j]
and do not inquire of the LORD;[k]
so they do not prosper[l]
and all their flock is scattered.[m]
22 Listen! The report is coming—
a great commotion from the land of
the north![n]
It will make the towns of Judah
desolate,[o]
a haunt of jackals.[p]

Jeremiah's Prayer

23 LORD, I know that people's lives are not
their own;
it is not for them to direct their
steps.[q]
24 Discipline me, LORD, but only in due
measure—
not in your anger,[r]
or you will reduce me to nothing.[s]
25 Pour out your wrath on the nations[t]
that do not acknowledge you,

[a] *11* The text of this verse is in Aramaic.

note. *eternal.* See Ex 15:18; Ps 10:16; 29:10. *When ... wrath.* See Ps 97:5; Na 1:5.
10:11 See NIV text note. The other major Aramaic passages in the OT are Ezr 4:8—6:18; 7:12–26; Da 2:4—7:28. *them.* Pagan idolaters, who would have been more likely to understand Aramaic (the language of diplomacy during this period) than Hebrew.
10:12–16 Repeated almost verbatim in 51:15–19.
10:12 *But God.* In contrast to the false gods of v. 11. *stretched out the heavens.* Like a tent or canopy (see Ps 104:2; Isa 40:22 and note).
10:13 *he makes clouds ... his storehouses.* Repeated in Ps 135:7, where the one true God is contrasted to false gods (see Ps 135:5,15–17); cf. Job 38:22.
10:14 *senseless.* See vv. 8,21; see also note on 4:22. *images.* Cast in metal; the Hebrew for this word is translated "metal god" in Isa 48:5 and "metal images" in Da 11:8. *no breath.* See Ps 135:17.
10:15 *worthless.* See note on v. 3.
10:16 *Portion of Jacob.* A title for God, used again only in 51:19 (see Ps 73:26 and note; 119:57; 142:5; La 3:24). *people of his inheritance.* See Isa 63:17. *the LORD Almighty is his name.* See 2:19 and note; Isa 54:5; Am 4:13.
10:17–22 Destruction and exile are imminent.
10:18 *hurl out.* As from a sling.
10:19–20 On behalf of his countrymen, the prophet bemoans their fate and his own (see 4:19–21).
10:20 *My children.* The people of Judah and Jerusalem (Jeremiah never married or had children; see 16:2). *shelter.* See note on 4:20.
10:21 *shepherds ... flock.* Rulers and people (see note on 2:8). *senseless.* See vv. 8,14; see also note on 4:22. *do not inquire of the LORD.* Instead, they consult the heavenly bodies (see 8:2). *scattered.* See note on 9:16.
10:22 *great commotion.* The sound of the invaders (see 6:23; 8:16). *land of the north.* Babylonia (see 1:15 and note; 4:6; 6:22; see also note on Isa 41:25). *haunt of jackals.* See 9:11 and note.
10:23–25 On the people's behalf, the prophet prays for divine justice.

10:23 Only the Lord can direct people's steps (see Ps 37:23; Pr 16:9 and note).
10:25 Repeated almost verbatim in Ps 79:6–7, where the context (see Ps 79:1–5) shows that the prayer is

on the peoples who do not call on
your name.[u]
For they have devoured[v] Jacob;
they have devoured him completely
and destroyed his homeland.[w]

The Covenant Is Broken

11 This is the word that came to Jeremiah from the LORD: 2 "Listen to the
terms of this covenant[x] and tell them to
the people of Judah and to those who live
in Jerusalem. 3 Tell them that this is what
the LORD, the God of Israel, says: 'Cursed[y]
is the one who does not obey the terms of
this covenant— 4 the terms I commanded
your ancestors when I brought them out of
Egypt,[z] out of the iron-smelting furnace.[a]' I
said, 'Obey[b] me and do everything I command you, and you will be my people,[c]
and I will be your God. 5 Then I will fulfill
the oath I swore[d] to your ancestors, to give
them a land flowing with milk and honey'[e]—the land you possess today."
I answered, "Amen,[f] LORD."
6 The LORD said to me, "Proclaim[g] all
these words in the towns of Judah and
in the streets of Jerusalem: 'Listen to the
terms of this covenant and follow[h] them.
7 From the time I brought your ancestors
up from Egypt until today, I warned them
again and again,[i] saying, "Obey me." 8 But
they did not listen or pay attention;[j] instead, they followed the stubbornness of
their evil hearts.[k] So I brought on them
all the curses[l] of the covenant I had commanded them to follow but that they did
not keep.[m]' "
9 Then the LORD said to me, "There is
a conspiracy[n] among the people of Judah
and those who live in Jerusalem. 10 They
have returned to the sins of their ancestors,[o] who refused to listen to my words.[p]
They have followed other gods[q] to serve
them.[r] Both Israel and Judah have broken
the covenant[s] I made with their ancestors.
11 Therefore this is what the LORD says: 'I
will bring on them a disaster[t] they cannot
escape.[u] Although they cry[v] out to me, I
will not listen[w] to them. 12 The towns of
Judah and the people of Jerusalem will go
and cry out to the gods to whom they burn
incense,[x] but they will not help them at all
when disaster[y] strikes. 13 You, Judah, have
as many gods[z] as you have towns;[a] and the
altars you have set up to burn incense[b] to
that shameful[c] god Baal are as many as the
streets of Jerusalem.'
14 "Do not pray[d] for this people or offer
any plea or petition for them, because I
will not listen[e] when they call to me in the
time of their distress.

15 "What is my beloved doing in my
temple
as she, with many others, works out
her evil schemes?
Can consecrated meat[f] avert your
punishment?[g]
When you engage in your wickedness,
then you rejoice.[a]"

16 The LORD called you a thriving olive
tree[h]
with fruit beautiful in form.

[a] 15 Or *Could consecrated meat avert your punishment? / Then you would rejoice*

10:25 [u]S Ps 14:4 [v]S Ps 79:7; S Jer 2:3 [w]Ps 79:6-7 **11:2** [x]S Dt 5:2 **11:3** [y]Dt 11:26-28; 27:26; 28:15-68; Gal 3:10 **11:4** [z]ver 7 [a]S 1Ki 8:51 [b]S Ex 24:8; Jer 7:23 [c]Jer 7:23; 31:33; Eze 11:20 **11:5** [d]S Ex 6:8; 13:5; Dt 7:12; Ps 105:8-11 [e]S Ex 3:8 [f]S Dt 27:26 **11:6** [g]S Jer 4:5 [h]S Ex 15:26; S Dt 15:5; Jas 1:22 **11:7** [i]S 2Ch 36:15 **11:8** [j]S Jer 7:26 [k]S Ecc 9:3; S Jer 3:17 [l]Lev 26:14-43; Dt 28:15-68; S Jos 23:15 [m]S 2Ch 7:19; Ps 78:10; Jer 26:4; 32:23; 44:10 **11:9** [n]Eze 22:25 **11:10** [o]Dt 9:7; S 2Ch 30:7 [p]Zec 7:11 [q]S Jdg 2:12-13; S 10:13 [r]Jer 16:11; Eze 20:8 [s]Isa 24:5; Jer 34:18; Hos 6:7; 8:1 **11:11** [t]S 2Ki 22:16; S Jer 4:6 [u]S Job 11:20; La 2:22 [v]S Job 27:9; Jer 14:12; Eze 8:18; Mal 2:13 [w]ver 14; S Ps 66:18; Pr 1:28; S Isa 1:15; 59:2; Eze 8:8; Zec 7:13 **11:12** [x]S Dt 32:38; S Jer 44:17 [y]S Dt 32:37; S Jdg 10:14 **11:13** [z]S Ex 20:3; Jer 19:4 [a]S 2Ki 17:29 [b]S Jer 7:9; 44:21 [c]S Jer 3:24 **11:14** [d]S Ex 32:10 [e]S ver 11 **11:15** [f]Hag 2:12 [g]S Jer 7:9-10 **11:16** [h]S Ps 1:3; Hos 14:6

not vengeful but is an appeal for God's justice (see note on Ps 5:10). The verse is recited annually by Jews during their Passover service.

11:1—13:27 Because of Judah's violations of its covenant obligations, the people will be exiled to Babylonia. The section is perhaps to be dated to the reign of Josiah (but see note on 13:18).

11:1-17 God's people have broken his covenant with them.

11:2 *Listen.* See note on 2:4. *terms.* Lit. "words," a technical term for covenant stipulations (see vv. 3-4,6; 34:18; see also note on Ex 20:1). *this covenant.* See vv. 3,6,8,10; Dt 29:9. Reference is to the covenant established by God with Israel through Moses at Mount Sinai (see v. 4; Ex 19-24). *tell them.* Periodic public reading of covenants was a common and necessary practice (see Dt 31:10-13; Jos 8:34-35).

11:3 *Cursed is the one.* "Cursed is anyone" appears at the beginning of every covenant curse in Dt 27:15-26, and the people respond to each of the curses with their "Amen." Blessings resulted from obedience to the covenant (see Dt 28:1-14); curses resulted from disobedience (see Dt 28:15-68; see also Dt 11:26-28; 29:20-21).

11:4 *out of Egypt ... the iron-smelting furnace.* See note on Dt 4:20. *Obey me.* See v. 7; 7:23; Ex 19:5. *my people ... your God.* See note on 7:23.

11:5 *fulfill the oath I swore.* See Ge 15:17-18 and notes; Dt 7:8. *land flowing with milk and honey.* See 32:22; see also note on Ex 3:8. *Amen.* See note on v. 3.

11:6 *Proclaim.* See 2:2; 3:12.

11:7 *again and again.* See note on 7:13.

11:8 See 7:24. *stubbornness of their evil hearts.* See note on 3:17. *So I brought on them.* See 2Ki 17:18-23. *curses of the covenant.* See note on v. 3.

11:9 *conspiracy.* Against the intended reforms of Josiah (see Introduction: Background; see also note on 1:2).

11:10 *refused.* Their sin was deliberate (see note on 9:6). *the covenant.* Lit. "my covenant," emphasizing its origin in God himself.

11:11 *I will bring on them.* Judah will be judged, just as Israel had been judged earlier (see v. 10; see also 2Ki 17:18-23).

11:12 *burn incense.* See vv. 13,17; see also note on 1:16.

11:13 *as many gods as ... towns.* See note on 2:28. *altars ... as many as the streets.* See 2Ch 28:24. *to that shameful god Baal.* See 3:24; see also notes on 2:26; Jdg 6:32.

11:14 *Do not pray for this people.* See note on 7:16; cf. 1Jn 5:16.

11:15 See 7:10-11,21-24. *my beloved.* Judah (see 12:7; cf. Dt 33:12, where Benjamin is called the "beloved of the LORD").

11:16 *called you ... olive tree.* See Ps 52:8; 128:3. *storm.* The Hebrew for this word appears elsewhere only in Eze 1:24,

But with the roar of a mighty storm
he will set it on fire,[i]
and its branches will be broken.[j]

17 The LORD Almighty, who planted[k] you,
has decreed disaster[l] for you, because the
people of both Israel and Judah have done
evil and aroused[m] my anger by burning incense to Baal.[n]

Censers: carved stone receptacles used for placing incense on an altar. God is disappointed in his people because they burn incense to other gods (Jer 11:11 – 13).

Z. Radovan/www.BibleLandPictures.com

Plot Against Jeremiah

18 Because the LORD revealed their plot to
me, I knew it, for at that time he showed
me what they were doing. 19 I had been
like a gentle lamb led to the slaughter;[o]
I did not realize that they had plotted[p]
against me, saying,

"Let us destroy the tree and its fruit;
let us cut him off from the land of
the living,[q]
that his name be remembered[r] no
more."
20 But you, LORD Almighty, who judge
righteously[s]
and test the heart[t] and mind,[u]
let me see your vengeance[v] on them,
for to you I have committed my cause.

21 Therefore this is what the LORD says
about the people of Anathoth[w] who are
threatening to kill you,[x] saying, "Do not
prophesy[y] in the name of the LORD or you
will die[z] by our hands"— 22 therefore this is
what the LORD Almighty says: "I will punish them. Their young men[a] will die by the
sword, their sons and daughters by famine.
23 Not even a remnant[b] will be left to them,
because I will bring disaster on the people of
Anathoth in the year of their punishment.[c]"

Jeremiah's Complaint

12 You are always righteous,[d] LORD,
when I bring a case[e] before you.
Yet I would speak with you about your
justice:[f]
Why does the way of the wicked
prosper?[g]
Why do all the faithless live at ease?
2 You have planted[h] them, and they have
taken root;
they grow and bear fruit.[i]

11:16 [i] S Jer 7:20; 21:14 [j] S Isa 27:11; Ro 11:17-24
11:17 [k] S Ex 15:17; Isa 5:2; Jer 12:2; 45:4 [l] ver 11 [m] Jer 7:18 [n] S Jer 7:9
11:19 [o] S Ps 44:22 [p] ver 21; S Ps 44:16; 54:3; 71:10; Jer 18:18; 20:10 [q] S Job 28:13; S Ps 116:9; Isa 53:8 [r] Ps 83:4
11:20 [s] Ps 7:11 [t] S 1Sa 2:3; S 1Ch 29:17 [u] S Ps 26:2 [v] S Ps 58:10; La 3:60
11:21 [w] S Jos 21:18 [x] S ver 19; Jer 12:6; 21:7; 34:20 [y] S Isa 30:10 [z] Jer 2:30; 18:23; 26:8,11; 38:4
11:22 [a] S Isa 9:17; Jer 18:21
11:23 [b] Jer 6:9 [c] Jer 23:12
12:1 [d] S Ezr 9:15; Job 8:3; Da 9:14 [e] S Job 5:8 [f] Eze 18:25 [g] S Job 21:7, 13; Ps 37:7; Jer 5:27-28
12:2 [h] S Jer 11:17 [i] S Job 5:3

---

where it is translated "tumult" in reference to the noise made by an army (see Isa 13:4). *branches will be broken.* See Eze 31:12.
11:17 Fulfilled when Judah was destroyed in 586 BC (see 44:2 – 3). *aroused my anger.* See 8:19; Dt 31:29.
11:18 – 23 The first of Jeremiah's six "confessions" (see Introduction: Author and Date).
11:18 *their ... they.* Jeremiah's personal enemies, the "people of Anathoth" (vv. 21,23), his hometown.
11:19 *lamb led to the slaughter.* See 51:40; see also Isa 53:7 and note. *destroy the tree and its fruit.* Contrast 12:2. *cut him off from the land of the living.* See Isa 53:8; contrast Ps 27:13. *name.* Since Jeremiah had no children (see 16:2), his name would die with him. *be remembered no more.* As though he were evil (see Job 24:20; Eze 21:32).
11:20 Repeated almost verbatim in 20:12; see also 17:10. *you ... who judge righteously.* See note on Ge 18:25.
11:21 *people of Anathoth who are threatening to kill you.* See 12:6. "A man's enemies are the members of his own household" (Mic 7:6, quoted by Jesus in Mt 10:36).
11:22 *sword ... famine.* See note on 5:12.
11:23 *remnant.* See 6:9; Isa 10:20 – 22 and notes. *them.* The conspirators in Anathoth, not its entire population, since 128 men of Anathoth returned to their hometown after the exile (see Ezr 2:23).
12:1 – 4 The second of Jeremiah's "confessions" (see Introduction: Author and Date), continuing and closely related to the first (11:18 – 23). Jeremiah speaks in vv. 1 – 4, and God responds in vv. 5 – 6.
12:1 *You are ... righteous.* See note on Ge 18:25; see also 11:20; Ps 51:4; Ro 3:4. Because God is righteous, he is a dependable arbiter and judge. *Yet.* He is nevertheless ready to listen to our questions and complaints. *Why does ... the wicked prosper?* The question is not unique to Jeremiah (see, e.g., Job 21:7 – 15; Mal 3:15). The Lord replies that ultimately the wicked in Judah will perish (vv. 7 – 13) and that the wicked invaders who destroy them will themselves be destroyed (vv. 14 – 17).
12:2 *You have planted them.* But a sovereign God can always reconsider his intentions if conditions warrant a change (see 18:9 – 10). *bear fruit.* The wicked flourish, while Jeremiah's fellow citizens plot to destroy his own "fruit" (see 11:19). *on their lips ... far from their hearts.* Quoted in part by Jesus in Mt 15:8 – 9.

You are always on their lips
but far from their hearts.[j]
3 Yet you know me, LORD;
you see me and test[k] my thoughts
about you.
Drag them off like sheep[l] to be
butchered!
Set them apart for the day of
slaughter![m]
4 How long will the land lie parched[n]
and the grass in every field be
withered?[o]
Because those who live in it are wicked,
the animals and birds have
perished.[p]
Moreover, the people are saying,
"He will not see what happens to us."

God's Answer

5 "If you have raced with men on foot
and they have worn you out,
how can you compete with horses?
If you stumble[a] in safe country,
how will you manage in the thickets[q]
by[b] the Jordan?
6 Your relatives, members of your own
family—
even they have betrayed you;
they have raised a loud cry against
you.[r]
Do not trust them,
though they speak well of you.[s]

7 "I will forsake[t] my house,
abandon[u] my inheritance;
I will give the one I love[v]
into the hands of her enemies.[w]
8 My inheritance has become to me
like a lion[x] in the forest.
She roars at me;
therefore I hate her.[y]
9 Has not my inheritance become to me
like a speckled bird of prey
that other birds of prey surround and
attack?
Go and gather all the wild beasts;
bring them to devour.[z]
10 Many shepherds[a] will ruin my vineyard
and trample down my field;
they will turn my pleasant field
into a desolate wasteland.[b]
11 It will be made a wasteland,[c]
parched and desolate before me;[d]
the whole land will be laid waste
because there is no one who cares.
12 Over all the barren heights in the
desert
destroyers will swarm,
for the sword[e] of the LORD[f] will devour[g]
from one end of the land to the
other;[h]
no one will be safe.[i]
13 They will sow wheat but reap thorns;
they will wear themselves out but
gain nothing.[j]
They will bear the shame of their harvest
because of the LORD's fierce anger."[k]

14 This is what the LORD says: "As for all
my wicked neighbors who seize the inheritance[l] I gave my people Israel, I will
uproot[m] them from their lands and I will
uproot[n] the people of Judah from among
them. 15 But after I uproot them, I will

[a] 5 Or *you feel secure only* [b] 5 Or *the flooding of*

12:2 [j] S Isa 29:13; S Jer 3:10; S Eze 22:27; Mt 15:8; Mk 7:6; Titus 1:16 **12:3** [k] Ps 7:9; 11:5; 139:1-4 [l] S Ps 44:11 [m] Jer 16:18; 17:18; 20:11 **12:4** [n] S Jer 4:28 [o] S ver 11; S Jer 4:26; Joel 1:10-12; Am 1:2 [p] Dt 28:15-18; S Jer 4:25; S 9:10 **12:5** [q] Jer 49:19; 50:44 **12:6** [r] S Pr 26:24-25; Jer 9:4 [s] Ps 12:2 **12:7** [t] S 2Ki 21:14 [u] S Jer 7:29 [v] Isa 5:1 [w] Jer 17:4 **12:8** [x] S Ps 17:12 [y] Ps 5:5; Hos 9:15; Am 6:8 **12:9** [z] S Dt 28:26; Isa 56:9; Jer 15:3; Eze 23:25; 39:17-20 **12:10** [a] Jer 23:1; 25:34; Eze 34:2-10 [b] Isa 5:1-7; Jer 9:10; 25:11 **12:11** [c] S Isa 5:6; S 24:4 [d] ver 4; Jer 9:12; 14:4; 23:10 **12:12** [e] Eze 21:3-4 [f] S Dt 32:41; Isa 31:8; Jer 46:10; 47:6; Eze 14:17; 21:28; 33:2 [g] S Dt 32:42 [h] Jer 3:2 [i] Jer 7:10 **12:13** [j] S Lev 26:20; S Dt 28:38 [k] S Ex 15:7; S Jer 4:26 **12:14** [l] S Dt 29:28; S 2Ch 7:20 [m] S Ps 9:6; Zec 2:7-9 [n] S Dt 28:63

12:3 *test my thoughts.* See 11:20. *like sheep to be butchered.* Jeremiah asks that his wicked countrymen receive the fate mentioned for himself in 11:19. His request arises not so much out of a desire for revenge as for the vindication of God's righteousness (see note on 10:25). *day of slaughter.* An expression found elsewhere only in Jas 5:5 (see note there).
12:4 *parched ... withered.* See 23:10; see also 3:3; 14:1 and note. Apparently there was a series of droughts in Judah during Jeremiah's ministry. *He will not see.* The prophet's enemies do not believe that his predictions will be fulfilled. Or they believe that if they are, Jeremiah will not live to see their fulfillment.
12:5 The Lord warns Jeremiah that in the future his troubles will increase (see, e.g., 38:4–6). *stumble.* The Hebrew for this word usually means "trust" (see NIV text note). *thickets.* Providing cover for lions (see 49:19; 50:44; Zec 11:3). If the Hebrew for this word means "flooding" (see NIV text note) here, an ancient example is described in Jos 3:15.
12:6 *family.* Lit. "house," linking this verse verbally with the following context (see v. 7). Apparently, members of Jeremiah's own family were included in the "people of Anathoth" (11:21,23) who wanted to kill him.
12:7–17 The Lord will judge Judah (vv. 7–13) as well as the wicked neighboring nations (vv. 14–17).
12:7 *house.* Judah (see, e.g., 11:17). *inheritance.* God's land and people (see vv. 8–9,14–15; see also Ex 15:17 and note; Dt 4:20; Isa 19:25; 47:6). *the one I love.* See note on 11:15.
12:8 *I hate her.* I will withdraw my love from her by giving her "into the hands of her enemies" (v. 7; see Mal 1:3 and note).
12:9 *other birds of prey ... wild beasts.* Judah's enemies (see Isa 56:9 and note).
12:10 *shepherds.* Rulers (see note on 2:8). *my vineyard.* Judah (see 2:21 and note). *pleasant field.* See 3:19 and note.
12:11 *parched.* See v. 4 and note. A total of seven *s*-sounds and seven *m*-sounds in the Hebrew of this brief verse punctuates its theme and provides a striking example of Jeremiah's literary gifts (see Introduction: Literary Features).
12:12 *barren heights.* Places of idolatrous worship (see 3:2; Nu 23:3). *destroyers.* The Babylonians (see note on 4:7). *sword of the LORD.* Symbolizing God's instruments of judgment (see 25:29; 47:6 and note on Ps 7:12–13). *from one end ... to the other.* See 25:33. *no one will be safe.* Lit. "there will be no peace/safety for anyone" (see 6:14 and note).
12:13 See 14:2–4.
12:14 *wicked neighbors.* See, e.g., 2Ki 24:2. *seize.* Lit. "touch," used in the context of attack and plunder in Zec 2:8. *uproot.* Carry off into exile (see, e.g., 1Ki 14:15).
12:15 The exiles from Judah, and those from the neighboring nations, will eventually be brought back to their respective lands (see v. 16; 32:37,44; 33:26; 48:47; 49:6).

again have compassion[o] and will bring[p]
each of them back to their own inheritance and their own country. 16 And if
they learn[q] well the ways of my people
and swear by my name, saying, 'As surely as the LORD lives'[r]—even as they once
taught my people to swear by Baal[s]—then
they will be established among my people.[t] 17 But if any nation does not listen,
I will completely uproot and destroy[u] it,"
declares the LORD.

A Linen Belt

13 This is what the LORD said to me:
"Go and buy a linen belt and put it
around your waist, but do not let it touch
water." 2 So I bought a belt, as the LORD directed, and put it around my waist.
3 Then the word of the LORD came to me
a second time:[v] 4 "Take the belt you bought
and are wearing around your waist, and
go now to Perath[a][w] and hide it there in a
crevice in the rocks." 5 So I went and hid it
at Perath, as the LORD told me.[x]
6 Many days later the LORD said to me,
"Go now to Perath and get the belt I told
you to hide there." 7 So I went to Perath
and dug up the belt and took it from the
place where I had hidden it, but now it
was ruined and completely useless.
8 Then the word of the LORD came to
me: 9 "This is what the LORD says: 'In
the same way I will ruin the pride of Judah and the great pride[y] of Jerusalem.
10 These wicked people, who refuse to
listen[z] to my words, who follow the stubbornness of their hearts[a] and go after other gods[b] to serve and worship them,[c] will
be like this belt—completely useless![d]
11 For as a belt is bound around the waist,
so I bound all the people of Israel and all
the people of Judah to me,' declares the
LORD, 'to be my people for my renown[e]
and praise and honor.[f] But they have not
listened.'[g]

Wineskins

12 "Say to them: 'This is what the LORD,
the God of Israel, says: Every wineskin
should be filled with wine.' And if they
say to you, 'Don't we know that every
wineskin should be filled with wine?'
13 then tell them, 'This is what the LORD
says: I am going to fill with drunkenness[h] all who live in this land, including
the kings who sit on David's throne, the
priests, the prophets and all those living
in Jerusalem. 14 I will smash them one
against the other, parents and children
alike, declares the LORD. I will allow no
pity[i] or mercy or compassion[j] to keep me
from destroying[k] them.' "

Threat of Captivity

15 Hear and pay attention,
do not be arrogant,
for the LORD has spoken.[l]
16 Give glory[m] to the LORD your God

12:15 [o] S Ps 6:2 [p] S Dt 30:3; Am 9:14-15 **12:16** [q] Jer 18:8 [r] S Jer 4:2 [s] S Jos 23:7 [t] S Isa 26:18; 49:6; Jer 3:17 **12:17** [u] S Ge 27:29 **13:3** [v] Jer 33:1 **13:4** [w] S Ge 2:14 **13:5** [x] Ex 40:16 **13:9** [y] S Lev 26:19; S Mt 23:12; S Lk 1:51 **13:10** [z] Jer 22:21 [a] S Ecc 9:3; S Jer 3:17 [b] S Dt 8:19; Jer 9:14 [c] S Jdg 10:13 [d] Eze 15:3 **13:11** [e] Isa 63:12; Jer 32:20 [f] Ex 19:5-6; Isa 43:21; S Jer 3:17 [g] S Isa 65:12; S Jer 7:26 **13:13** [h] Ps 60:3; 75:8; S Isa 29:9; Jer 25:18; 51:57 **13:14** [i] Eze 7:4; 8:18; 9:5, 10; 24:14; Zec 11:6 [j] S Isa 9:17; Jer 16:5 [k] Dt 29:20; Isa 9:19-21; S Jer 7:20; 49:32, 36; La 2:21; Eze 5:10 **13:15** [l] S Ex 23:21; Ps 95:7-8

[a] 4 Or possibly *to the Euphrates*; similarly in verses 5-7

12:16 To be fulfilled in the Messianic age (see Isa 56:6–7 and note on 56:7). *ways.* See note on 10:2. *Baal.* See note on Jdg 2:13. *be established.* The Hebrew for this phrase is translated "prosper" in Mal 3:15.

13:1–27 A series of five warnings, the first two (vv. 1–11,12–14) written in prose and the last three (vv. 15–17,18–19,20–27) in poetry.

13:1–11 The story of the ruined, useless belt is the first major example of the Lord's commanding Jeremiah to perform symbolic acts to illustrate his message (see Introduction: Literary Features).

13:1–2,4–7 *Go and buy ... So I bought ... Take the belt ... and hide it ... So I went and hid it ... Go now to Perath and get the belt ... So I went to Perath and dug up the belt.* Like his spiritual ancestor Abraham (see note on Ge 12:4), Jeremiah was characterized by prompt obedience.

13:1 *linen.* The material of which the priests' garments were made (see Eze 44:17–18), symbolic of Israel's holiness as a "kingdom of priests" (see Ex 19:6 and note). The linen belt is a symbol of the formerly intimate relationship between God and Judah (see v. 11). *do not let it touch water.* Do not wash it—symbolic of Judah's sinful pride (see v. 9).

13:3 *Then.* Some time later.

13:4 *Perath.* Perhaps the same as Parah (Jos 18:23), near the modern Wadi Farah, three miles northeast of Anathoth. Since in other contexts the Hebrew for Perath refers to the river Euphrates (see NIV text note), it serves as an appropriate symbol of the corrupting Assyrian and Babylonian influence on Judah that began during the reign of Ahaz (see 2Ki 16). *crevice in the rocks.* See note on 16:16.

13:6 *Many days later.* Perhaps a reference to the lengthy Babylonian exile.

13:7 *dug up.* The belt had either been buried by the prophet or silted over by the water of the wadi. *it was ruined.* As foreseen in Lev 26:39, God's people in exile would waste away because of their sins and the sins of their ancestors.

13:9 *pride ... great pride.* Contrast 9:23–24. Judah's vaunted pride would be a cause of her downfall and exile (see vv. 15,17), as foreshadowed in Lev 26:19.

13:10 *refuse to listen.* See note on 9:6. *stubbornness of their hearts.* See note on 3:17. *completely useless.* See 24:8.

13:11 *But they have not listened.* And therefore the promise of Dt 26:19 can no longer be fulfilled in them.

13:12–14 The Lord uses the imagery of filled wineskins to point toward the eventual destruction of Judah's leaders and people.

13:13 *drunkenness.* In a literal sense (see, e.g., Isa 28:7), but also symbolizing the effects of the wine of God's wrath (see 25:15–29; Ps 60:3; Isa 51:17–23; Eze 23:32–34). *kings ... priests ... prophets ... all those living in Jerusalem.* See 26:16; see also note on 1:18.

13:14 *smash them one against the other.* The various factions in Judah produced only confusion and chaos in the face of determined outside enemies. *no pity or mercy or compassion.* See 21:7; see also Eze 5:11.

13:15–17 Sinful pride carries the seeds of its own destruction, says the prophet.

13:15 *Hear.* See note on 2:4. *do not be arrogant.* See v. 17; see also note on v. 9.

before he brings the darkness,
before your feet stumble[n]
on the darkening hills.
You hope for light,
but he will turn it to utter darkness
and change it to deep gloom.[o]
17 If you do not listen,[p]
I will weep in secret
because of your pride;
my eyes will weep bitterly,
overflowing with tears,[q]
because the LORD's flock[r] will be
taken captive.[s]

18 Say to the king[t] and to the queen
mother,[u]
"Come down from your thrones,
for your glorious crowns[v]
will fall from your heads."
19 The cities in the Negev will be
shut up,
and there will be no one to open
them.
All Judah[w] will be carried into exile,
carried completely away.

20 Look up and see
those who are coming from the
north.[x]
Where is the flock[y] that was entrusted
to you,
the sheep of which you boasted?
21 What will you say when the LORD sets
over you
those you cultivated as your special
allies?[z]
Will not pain grip you
like that of a woman in labor?[a]
22 And if you ask yourself,
"Why has this happened to me?"[b] —
it is because of your many sins[c]
that your skirts have been torn
off[d]
and your body mistreated.[e]
23 Can an Ethiopian[a] change his skin
or a leopard its spots?
Neither can you do good
who are accustomed to doing
evil.[f]

24 "I will scatter you like chaff[g]
driven by the desert wind.[h]
25 This is your lot,
the portion[i] I have decreed for you,"
declares the LORD,
"because you have forgotten[j] me
and trusted in false gods.[k]
26 I will pull up your skirts over your
face
that your shame may be seen[l] —
27 your adulteries and lustful
neighings,
your shameless prostitution![m]
I have seen your detestable acts
on the hills and in the fields.[n]
Woe to you, Jerusalem!
How long will you be unclean?"[o]

Drought, Famine, Sword

14 This is the word of the LORD that came to Jeremiah concerning the drought:[p]

2 "Judah mourns,[q]
her cities languish;
they wail for the land,
and a cry goes up from Jerusalem.

[a] *23* Hebrew *Cushite* (probably a person from the upper Nile region)

13:16 [m]S Jos 7:19 [n]S Lev 26:37; S Job 3:23; Isa 51:17; Jer 23:12 [o]S 1Sa 2:9; S Job 3:5; S Ps 82:5 **13:17** [p]Mal 2:2 [q]S Jer 9:1 [r]Ps 80:1; Jer 23:1 [s]Jer 14:18; 29:1 **13:18** [t]Jer 21:11; 22:1 [u]S 1Ki 2:19; S 2Ki 24:8; S Isa 22:17 [v]S 2Sa 12:30; La 5:16; Eze 16:12; 21:26 **13:19** [w]Jer 20:4; 52:30; La 1:3 **13:20** [x]Jer 6:22; Hab 1:6 [y]Jer 23:2 **13:21** [z]S Ps 41:9; Jer 4:30; 20:10; 38:22; Ob 1:7 [a]S Jer 4:31 **13:22** [b]S 1Ki 9:9 [c]Jer 9:2-6; 16:10-12 [d]S Isa 20:4 [e]La 1:8; Eze 16:37; 23:26; Na 3:5-6 **13:23** [f]S 2Ch 6:36 **13:24** [g]S Ps 1:4 [h]S Lev 26:33; S Job 1:19; S 27:21 **13:25** [i]S Job 20:29; Mt 24:51 [j]S Isa 17:10 [k]S Dt 31:20; S Ps 4:2; 106:19-21 **13:26** [l]La 1:8; Eze 16:37; Na 3:5 **13:27** [m]Eze 23:29 [n]S Isa 57:7; Eze 6:13 [o]Hos 8:5 **14:1** [p]S Dt 28:22; S Isa 5:6 **14:2** [q]S Isa 3:26

13:16 *Give glory to ... God.* Confess your sins (cf. Jos 7:19; Jn 9:24). *You hope for light, but.* Cf. the description of the day of the Lord in Am 5:18 – 20; 8:9.
13:17 *I will weep.* See note on 9:1. *pride.* See v. 15; see also note on v. 9. *flock.* People (see v. 20; Zec 10:3; see also note on 10:21). *taken captive.* Into exile (see v. 19).
13:18 – 19 The prophet speaks: Exile is imminent.
13:18 *king and ... queen mother.* Probably Jehoiachin and Nehushta (2Ki 24:8). If so, the date is 597 BC, about 12 years after Josiah's death (see note on 11:1 — 13:27). *your ... crowns will fall.* See 22:24 – 26; 29:2; 2Ki 24:15; cf. Eze 21:25 – 27 and notes.
13:19 *Negev.* The dry southland (see note on Ge 12:9). *shut up.* Blocked by debris (see Isa 24:10). *All Judah.* The nation as a whole. *carried completely away.* Cf. Am 1:6,9 ("whole communities").
13:20 – 27 First the prophet speaks (vv. 20 – 23), then the Lord (vv. 24 – 27). Judah's willful rebellion has made exile inevitable.
13:20 *you ... you.* Jerusalem, personified as a woman (see vv. 21 – 22,26 – 27), is being addressed. *the north.* Babylonia (see 4:6; see also note on Isa 41:25). *flock ... sheep.* See note on v. 17.
13:21 *special allies.* Perhaps Egypt and Babylonia, who alternated in dominating Judah (see Introduction: Background). *like ... a woman in labor.* See note on 4:31.
13:22 *skirts ... torn off.* Disgraced publicly, like a common prostitute (see vv. 26 – 27; Isa 47:2 – 3; Hos 2:3,10).
13:23 *Can ... spots?* A rhetorical question, expecting a negative answer (see 17:9).
13:24 *like chaff driven.* The fate of the wicked (see, e.g., Ps 1:4). *desert wind.* See note on 4:11.
13:25 *forgotten me.* See 2:32 and note.
13:26 See v. 22 and note.
13:27 *adulteries and lustful neighings.* See note on 5:8. *shameless prostitution.* See Eze 16:26; see also Ex 34:15 and note. *How long ... ?* There is yet hope, however slender, to postpone the divine wrath (cf., e.g., 12:14 – 16).
14:1 — 15:21 Messages delivered by Jeremiah during an especially severe drought, the date of which is unknown.
14:1 — 15:9 After an initial vivid description of the drought (14:2 – 6), Jeremiah alternately prays (14:7 – 9, 13,19 – 22) and God responds (14:10 – 12, 14 – 18; 15:1 – 9).
14:1 *drought.* See 17:8. Unlike that in 3:3; 12:4, the suffering is increased because an enemy has invaded the land (see v. 18). Drought was one of the curses threatened (see 23:10) for disobedience to the covenant (see Lev 26:19 – 20; Dt 28:22 – 24).
14:2 *cities.* Lit. "gates" (see note on Ge 22:17); see 15:7.

3 The nobles send their servants for water;
they go to the cisterns
but find no water.[r]
They return with their jars unfilled;
dismayed and despairing,
they cover their heads.[s]
4 The ground is cracked
because there is no rain in the land;[t]
the farmers are dismayed
and cover their heads.
5 Even the doe in the field
deserts her newborn fawn
because there is no grass.[u]
6 Wild donkeys stand on the barren heights[v]
and pant like jackals;
their eyes fail
for lack of food."[w]

7 Although our sins testify[x] against us,
do something, LORD, for the sake of your name.[y]
For we have often rebelled;[z]
we have sinned[a] against you.
8 You who are the hope[b] of Israel,
its Savior[c] in times of distress,[d]
why are you like a stranger in the land,
like a traveler who stays only a night?
9 Why are you like a man taken by surprise,
like a warrior powerless to save?[e]
You are among[f] us, LORD,
and we bear your name;[g]
do not forsake[h] us!

10 This is what the LORD says about this people:

"They greatly love to wander;
they do not restrain their feet.[i]
So the LORD does not accept[j] them;
he will now remember[k] their wickedness
and punish them for their sins."[l]

11 Then the LORD said to me, "Do not
pray[m] for the well-being of this people.
12 Although they fast, I will not listen to
their cry;[n] though they offer burnt offerings[o] and grain offerings,[p] I will not accept[q] them. Instead, I will destroy them
with the sword,[r] famine[s] and plague."[t]
13 But I said, "Alas, Sovereign LORD! The
prophets[u] keep telling them, 'You will not
see the sword or suffer famine.[v] Indeed, I
will give you lasting peace[w] in this place.' "
14 Then the LORD said to me, "The prophets are prophesying lies[x] in my name. I
have not sent[y] them or appointed them or
spoken to them. They are prophesying to
you false visions,[z] divinations,[a] idolatries[a]
and the delusions of their own minds.
15 Therefore this is what the LORD says
about the prophets who are prophesying
in my name: I did not send them, yet they
are saying, 'No sword or famine will touch
this land.' Those same prophets will perish[b] by sword and famine.[c]
16 And the peo-
ple they are prophesying to will be thrown
out into the streets of Jerusalem because
of the famine and sword. There will be no
one to bury[d] them, their wives, their sons
and their daughters.[e] I will pour out on
them the calamity they deserve.[f]

17 "Speak this word to them:

" 'Let my eyes overflow with tears[g]
night and day without ceasing;

14:3 [r]S Dt 28:48; S 2Ki 18:31; Job 6:19-20 [s]S Est 6:12 **14:4** [t]S Jer 3:3; S 12:11; Am 4:8; Zec 14:17 **14:5** [u]Isa 15:6 **14:6** [v]S Job 39:5-6; S Ps 104:11; S Jer 2:24 [w]S Ge 47:4 **14:7** [x]S Isa 3:9; Hos 5:5 [y]S 1Sa 12:22; S Ps 79:9 [z]S Jer 2:19; 5:6 [a]S Jer 8:14 **14:8** [b]S Ps 9:18; Jer 17:13; 50:7 [c]Ps 18:46; S Isa 25:9 [d]Ps 46:1 **14:9** [e]S Isa 50:2 [f]S Ge 17:7; Jer 8:19 [g]Isa 63:19; Jer 15:16 [h]S Ps 27:9 **14:10** [i]Ps 119:101; Jer 2:25 [j]Jer 6:20; Am 5:22 [k]Hos 7:2; 9:9; Am 8:7 [l]Jer 44:21-23; Hos 8:13; Am 3:2 **14:11** [m]S Ex 32:10; S 1Sa 2:25 **14:12** [n]S Dt 1:45; S 1Sa 8:18; S Jer 11:11 [o]Lev 1:1-17; Jer 7:21 [p]S Lev 2:1-16 [q]Am 5:22 [r]S Isa 51:19; S Jer 9:16 [s]Jer 15:2; 16:4 [t]Jer 21:6; 27:8, 13; 32:24; 34:17; Eze 14:21 **14:13** [u]Dt 18:22; Jer 27:14; 37:19 [v]S Jer 5:12 [w]S Isa 30:10; S Jer 4:10 **14:14** [x]S Jer 5:1; 23:25; 27:14; Eze 13:2 [y]Jer 23:21,32; 29:31; Eze 13:6 [z]Jer 23:16; La 2:9 [a]Eze 12:24 **14:15** [b]Jer 20:6; Eze 14:9 [c]Jer 5:12-13; 16:4; La 1:19 **14:16** [d]Ps 79:3 [e]S Jer 7:33 [f]S Pr 1:31; S Jer 17:10 **14:17** [g]S Ps 119:136

[a] 14 Or *visions, worthless divinations*

14:3 *nobles.* A drought is no respecter of class distinctions. *cover their heads.* In mourning (see v. 4; 2Sa 15:30; cf. 2Sa 19:4).
14:4 *because there is no rain.* See 1Ki 17:7. Unlike Egypt, where the mighty Nile waters the ground, the Holy Land depends on adequate rainfall.
14:6 *pant.* The Hebrew underlying this word is translated "sniffing the wind" in 2:24. There a female wild donkey (Jerusalem) was in the heat of desire, while here the male wild donkeys are panting because of a drought brought on by Judah's sin. *eyes fail.* See Ps 6:7 and note.
14:7–9 The prophet prays on behalf of the people (see v. 11).
14:7 *for the sake of your name.* See v. 21; Jos 7:9; Isa 48:9–11. *rebelled.* See 2:19; 3:22; 5:6 (translated "backsliding" in these verses). The word implies apostasy.
14:8 *hope of Israel.* See v. 22; 17:13; 50:7; Ac 28:20.
14:9 *we bear your name.* We belong to you, our ever-present Savior (see note on 7:10).
14:10–12 The Lord responds.
14:10–11 *this people.* God does not acknowledge them as his own (see Isa 6:9–10; 8:6,11–12; see also note on Ex 17:4).
14:10 *wander.* After false gods (see 2:23,31). *the LORD does not ... their sins.* The Hebrew for these three lines is quoted verbatim from Hos 8:13 (cf. Hos 9:9).
14:11 *Do not pray.* See note on 7:16; cf. 1Sa 7:8; 12:19.
14:12 *not accept them.* See v. 10. Sacrifice is to no avail when unaccompanied by repentance (see note on 6:20). *sword, famine and plague.* Curses for violating God's covenant (see Lev 26:25–26); the first occurrence of this triad, which occurs 15 times in Jeremiah (see Introduction: Literary Features; see also Eze 5:16–17 and note).
14:13 Jeremiah reminds the Lord of what the false prophets are saying. *not ... sword or ... famine.* See 5:12. *lasting peace.* Jeremiah's elaboration of the false prophets' "Peace, peace" (see 6:14; 8:11).
14:14–18 The Lord responds.
14:14 *lies.* See 5:12. *in my name.* See Dt 18:20,22. *delusions of their own minds.* See 23:26.
14:15 *Those ... prophets will perish.* See 28:15–17; Dt 18:20.
14:16 *no one to bury them.* See note on 7:33. *wives ... sons ... daughters.* All would perish, because all had worshiped false gods (see note on 7:18).
14:17 *my eyes overflow with tears.* See 9:18; 13:17. *Virgin*

for the Virgin[h] Daughter, my people,
has suffered a grievous wound,
a crushing blow.[i]
18 If I go into the country,
I see those slain by the sword;
if I go into the city,
I see the ravages of famine.[j]
Both prophet and priest
have gone to a land they know
not.[k]' "
19 Have you rejected Judah completely?[l]
Do you despise Zion?
Why have you afflicted us
so that we cannot be healed?[m]
We hoped for peace
but no good has come,
for a time of healing
but there is only terror.[n]
20 We acknowledge[o] our wickedness,
LORD,
and the guilt of our ancestors;[p]
we have indeed sinned[q] against
you.
21 For the sake of your name[r] do not
despise us;
do not dishonor your glorious
throne.[s]
Remember your covenant[t] with us
and do not break it.
22 Do any of the worthless idols[u] of the
nations bring rain?[v]
Do the skies themselves send down
showers?
No, it is you, LORD our God.
Therefore our hope is in you,
for you are the one who does all
this.[w]

15 Then the LORD said to me: "Even if
Moses[x] and Samuel[y] were to stand
before me, my heart would not go out to
this people.[z] Send them away from my
presence![a] Let them go! 2 And if they ask
you, 'Where shall we go?' tell them, 'This
is what the LORD says:

" 'Those destined for death, to
death;
those for the sword, to the sword;[b]
those for starvation, to starvation;[c]
those for captivity, to captivity.'[d]

3 "I will send four kinds of destroyers[e]
against them," declares the LORD, "the
sword[f] to kill and the dogs[g] to drag away
and the birds[h] and the wild animals to devour and destroy.[i] 4 I will make them abhorrent[j] to all the kingdoms of the earth[k]
because of what Manasseh[l] son of Hezekiah king of Judah did in Jerusalem.

5 "Who will have pity[m] on you,
Jerusalem?
Who will mourn for you?
Who will stop to ask how you are?
6 You have rejected[n] me," declares the
LORD.
"You keep on backsliding.
So I will reach out[o] and destroy you;
I am tired of holding back.[p]
7 I will winnow[q] them with a winnowing
fork
at the city gates of the land.

14:17 [h]S 2Ki 19:21; S Isa 23:12 [i]S Jer 8:21 **14:18** [j]Eze 7:15 [k]S 2Ch 36:10; S Jer 13:17 **14:19** [l]Jer 7:29 [m]S Isa 1:6; Jer 30:12-13 [n]S Job 19:8; S Jer 8:15 **14:20** [o]S Jer 3:13 [p]S Lev 26:40; S 1Ki 8:47; S Ezr 9:6 [q]S Jdg 10:10; Da 9:7-8 **14:21** [r]ver 7; S Jos 7:9 [s]Isa 62:7; Jer 3:17 [t]S Ex 2:24 **14:22** [u]S Isa 41:24; S 44:10; Jer 10:15; 16:19; Hab 2:18 [v]S 1Ki 8:36; S Ps 135:7 [w]S Isa 43:10
15:1 [x]S Ex 32:11; Nu 14:13-20 [y]S 1Sa 1:20; S 7:8 [z]S 1Sa 2:25; S Jer 7:16 [a]S 2Ki 17:20; Jer 16:13 **15:2** [b]Jer 42:22; 43:11; 44:13 [c]S Dt 28:26; S Jer 14:12; La 4:9 [d]Eze 12:11; Rev 13:10 **15:3** [e]S Nu 33:4 [f]S Lev 26:25 [g]S 1Ki 21:19; S 2Ki 9:36 [h]S Dt 28:26 [i]S Lev 26:22; Eze 14:21; 33:27 **15:4** [j]Jer 24:9; 29:18; 34:17 [k]S Dt 28:25; S Job 17:6 [l]S 2Ki 21:2; 23:26-27 **15:5** [m]Isa 27:11; 51:19; S Jer 13:14; 16:13; 21:7; Na 3:7 **15:6** [n]S Dt 32:15; Jer 6:19 [o]Isa 31:3; Zep 1:4 [p]S Jer 7:20; Am 7:8 **15:7** [q]S Isa 41:16

Daughter, my people. Lit. "the virgin of the daughter of my people" (see 8:11; Isa 22:4 and note on 2Ki 19:21).

14:19 – 22 The prophet prays on behalf of the people.

14:20 *guilt of our ancestors.* See 2:5 – 6; 7:25 – 26. *we have ... sinned.* Repentance brings restoration (see Dt 30:2 – 3).

14:21 *For the sake of your name.* See Eze 20:9 and note. *your glorious throne.* The Jerusalem temple (see 17:12; 2Ki 19:14 – 15; Ps 99:1 – 2). *Remember your covenant ... do not break it.* Jeremiah pleads the ancient promise of God found in Lev 26:44 – 45.

14:22 See Hos 2:8,21 – 22. *worthless idols.* See note on 2:5. *it is you.* Only the Lord (not Baal) can send the showers to end the drought (see v. 1). *our hope is in you.* See note on v. 8.

15:1 – 9 The Lord responds, concluding this section (see note on 14:1 — 15:9).

15:1 *Moses and Samuel.* Very special agents of God's rule over Israel who were also famous for their intercessions for sinful Israel (see Ex 32:11 – 14,30 – 34; Nu 14:13 – 23; Dt 9:18 – 20,25 – 29; 1Sa 7:5 – 9; 12:19 – 25; Ps 99:6 – 8). *stand before me.* The posture of God's servants as they are about to pray to him (see Ge 18:22; 1Ch 17:16 and note; Mk 11:25). *Send them away.* The people are so wicked that God refuses to hear prayers offered on their behalf. They are beyond divine help (see notes on 7:16; 14:11 – 12).

15:2 See Eze 14:21; 33:27. *death.* Probably by plague; see 14:12 (and note), where "sword, famine and plague" are God's three agents of destruction, paralleling the first three here (the Hebrew word for "starvation" here is the same as that for "famine" in 14:12).

15:3 – 4 Foreseen in Dt 28:25 – 26.

15:3 *four kinds.* Not the same four as in v. 2, but an elaboration of three of the fates awaiting the corpses of those killed by the sword. The seventh-century BC vassal treaties of Esarhaddon present similar curses: "May Ninurta, leader of the gods, fell you with his fierce arrow, fill the plain with your corpses, and give your flesh to the eagles and vultures to feed on ... May dogs and pigs eat your flesh." *dogs.* See 1Ki 21:23. *wild animals.* See Rev 6:8.

15:4 *abhorrent.* The Hebrew for this word is translated "a thing of horror" in the parallel in Dt 28:25. *what Manasseh ... did in Jerusalem.* Manasseh, good King Josiah's grandfather, was the most wicked king in Judah's long history (see 2Ki 21:1 – 11,16). His sins were a primary cause of Judah's eventual destruction (see 2Ki 21:12 – 15; 23:26 – 27; 24:3 – 4).

15:5 – 9 A poem concerning the forthcoming destruction of Jerusalem in 586 BC (see La 1:1,12,21; 2:13,20).

15:5 Cf. Mt 23:37.

15:6 *You keep on backsliding.* Lit. "You go backward" (cf. 7:24; see note on 2:19).

15:7 *winnow.* See note on Ru 1:22. Winnowing as a figure of judgment is found also in 51:2; Pr 20:8,26; Isa 41:16. *city gates of the land.* Or, more simply, "gates of your land" (as in Na 3:13), i.e., the approaches to the land. *bereavement ... on*

I will bring bereavement[r] and
destruction on my people,[s]
for they have not changed their
ways.[t]
8 I will make their widows[u] more
numerous
than the sand of the sea.
At midday I will bring a destroyer[v]
against the mothers of their young
men;
suddenly I will bring down on them
anguish and terror.[w]
9 The mother of seven will grow faint[x]
and breathe her last.[y]
Her sun will set while it is still day;
she will be disgraced[z] and
humiliated.
I will put the survivors to the sword[a]
before their enemies,"[b]
declares the LORD.

10 Alas, my mother, that you gave me
birth,[c]
a man with whom the whole land
strives and contends![d]
I have neither lent[e] nor borrowed,
yet everyone curses[f] me.

11 The LORD said,

"Surely I will deliver you[g] for a good
purpose;
surely I will make your enemies
plead[h] with you
in times of disaster and times of
distress.

12 "Can a man break iron—
iron from the north[i]—or bronze?

15:7 [r] Isa 3:26 [s] Jer 18:21 [t] S 2Ch 28:22 **15:8** [u] S Isa 47:9 [v] S Jer 4:7; S 6:4 [w] S Job 18:11 **15:9** [x] 1Sa 2:5 [y] S Job 8:13 [z] Jer 7:19 [a] Jer 21:7; 25:31 [b] 2Ki 25:7; Jer 19:7 **15:10** [c] S Job 3:1; S 10:18-19 [d] Jer 1:19 [e] S Lev 25:36; Ne 5:1-12 [f] S Jer 6:10 **15:11** [g] ver 21; Jer 40:4 [h] Jer 21:1-2; 37:3; 42:1-3 **15:12** [i] S Dt 28:48; Jer 28:14; La 1:14; Hos 10:11 **15:13** [j] S 2Ki 25:15 [k] S 2Ki 24:13; Eze 38:12-13 [l] S Ps 44:12 [m] Jer 17:3 **15:14** [n] S Dt 28:36; S Jer 5:19 [o] S Ps 21:9 **15:15** [p] Jdg 16:28; S Ps 119:84 [q] S Ex 34:6 [r] Ps 44:22; 69:7-9; S Jer 6:10 **15:16** [s] Eze 2:8; 3:3; Rev 10:10 [t] S Job 15:11; Ps 119:72, 103 [u] S Isa 43:7; S Jer 14:9 **15:17** [v] Ru 3:3; Ps 1:1; 26:4-5; Jer 16:8 [w] S 2Ki 3:15 **15:18** [x] S Job 6:4; S Jer 10:19; 30:12; Mic 1:9 [y] S Job 6:15; S Ps 9:10

13 "Your wealth[j] and your treasures
I will give as plunder,[k] without
charge,[l]
because of all your sins
throughout your country.[m]
14 I will enslave you to your enemies
in[a] a land you do not know,[n]
for my anger will kindle a fire[o]
that will burn against you."

15 LORD, you understand;
remember me and care for me.
Avenge me on my persecutors.[p]
You are long-suffering[q]—do not take
me away;
think of how I suffer reproach for
your sake.[r]
16 When your words came, I ate[s] them;
they were my joy and my heart's
delight,[t]
for I bear your name,[u]
LORD God Almighty.
17 I never sat[v] in the company of revelers,
never made merry with them;
I sat alone because your hand[w] was on me
and you had filled me with
indignation.
18 Why is my pain unending
and my wound grievous and
incurable?[x]
You are to me like a deceptive brook,
like a spring that fails.[y]

[a] *14* Some Hebrew manuscripts, Septuagint and Syriac (see also 17:4); most Hebrew manuscripts *I will cause your enemies to bring you / into*

my people. The young men will fall in battle, and Judah and Jerusalem will be left childless (see Eze 5:17). *not changed.* Lit. "not repented of," reminiscent of the refrain in Am 4:6,8–11: "yet you have not returned to me," where the same Hebrew verb is used (see note on 3:1).
15:8 *widows more numerous than the sand of the sea.* A tragic reversal of the covenant promise of innumerable offspring (see Ge 22:17 and note). *At midday ... suddenly.* Military attacks at noon were unexpected (see note on 6:4). *destroyer.* Babylonia (see note on 4:7). *anguish.* See note on 4:19.
15:9 *seven.* The complete, ideal number of sons (see Ru 4:15 and note)—soon to be destroyed. *sun will set while it is still day.* See Am 8:9; cf. Mt 27:45 and note. *survivors.* Lit. "remnant" (see note on 6:9). Even they will be put to the sword (see Mic 6:14).
15:10–21 The third of Jeremiah's "confessions" (see Introduction: Author and Date), including in this case two responses by the Lord (vv. 11–14,19–21).
15:10 See 20:14–15 and notes; Job 3:3–10. *have neither lent nor borrowed.* Have not become involved in matters likely to evoke dispute or difference of opinion.
15:11–14 The Lord speaks, first to Jeremiah (v. 11), then to the people of Judah (vv. 12–14).
15:11 God encourages Jeremiah. *I will make your enemies plead with you.* Fulfilled, e.g., in 21:1–2; 37:3; 38:14–26; 42:1–3.
15:12 A rhetorical question assuming a negative answer. *iron.* Symbolic of great strength (see 28:13). *from the north.* From Babylonia (see note on Isa 41:25).
15:13–14 Repeated in large part in 17:3–4.
15:13 Fulfilled in 52:17–23. *without charge.* Cf. Isa 55:1. People and plunder alike would be free for the taking (see note on Isa 52:3).
15:14 *for my anger will kindle a fire.* Quoted verbatim from Dt 32:22, where the same Hebrew is translated "For a fire will be kindled by my wrath."
15:15 *you understand.* The Lord is aware of what Jeremiah has suffered (see v. 10). *remember.* Express concern for (see note on Ge 8:1).
15:16 *your words ... I ate them.* I digested them, I assimilated them, I made them a part of me (see Eze 2:8—3:3; Rev 10:9–10). *came.* Lit. "were found"—perhaps referring to the discovery of the Book of the Law in the temple during the reign of Josiah in 621 BC (see 2Ki 22:13; 23:2; see also note on 1:2). *they were ... my heart's delight.* See Ps 1:2. *I bear your name.* See 14:9; I belong to you (see note on 7:10).
15:17 *sat alone.* Jeremiah never married (see 16:2), and he attracted only a few friends (see Introduction: Author and Date). *your hand.* Divine constraint (see 2Ki 3:15; Isa 8:11 and note; Eze 1:3; 3:14,22; 37:1; 40:1). *indignation.* At the sins of Judah (see 6:11).
15:18 Two rhetorical questions used by Jeremiah to express his nagging doubts about himself, his mission and God's faithfulness. *pain unending ... wound grievous*

19 Therefore this is what the LORD says:

"If you repent, I will restore you
that you may serve[z] me;
if you utter worthy, not worthless,
words,
you will be my spokesman.[a]
Let this people turn to you,
but you must not turn to them.
20 I will make you a wall[b] to this people,
a fortified wall of bronze;
they will fight against you
but will not overcome[c] you,
for I am with you
to rescue and save you,"[d]
declares the LORD.
21 "I will save[e] you from the hands of the
wicked[f]
and deliver[g] you from the grasp of
the cruel."[h]

Day of Disaster

16 Then the word of the LORD came
to me: 2 "You must not marry[i] and
have sons or daughters in this place." 3 For
this is what the LORD says about the sons
and daughters born in this land and about
the women who are their mothers and the
men who are their fathers:[j] 4 "They will
die of deadly diseases. They will not be
mourned or buried[k] but will be like dung
lying on the ground.[l] They will perish by
sword and famine,[m] and their dead bodies will become food for the birds and the
wild animals."[n]
5 For this is what the LORD says: "Do
not enter a house where there is a funeral

15:19 [z] Zec 3:7 [a] S Ex 4:16 **15:20** [b] S Isa 50:7 [c] S Ps 129:2 [d] S Jer 1:8; 20:11; 42:11; Eze 3:8 **15:21** [e] S Jer 1:8 [f] S Ps 97:10 [g] Jer 50:34 [h] S Ge 48:16 **16:2** [i] Mt 19:12; 1Co 7:26-27 **16:3** [j] Jer 6:21 **16:4** [k] ver 6; Jer 25:33 [l] S Jer 9:22 [m] S Jer 14:15 [n] S Dt 28:26; Ps 79:1-3; S Jer 14:12; 19:7 **16:5** [o] S Jer 15:5 **16:6** [p] Jer 9:21; Eze 9:5-6 [q] S ver 4 [r] S Lev 19:28 [s] S Lev 21:5; S Job 1:20 **16:7** [t] S 2Sa 3:35 [u] Jer 22:10; Eze 24:17; Hos 9:4 [v] La 1:9, 16 **16:8** [w] S Ex 32:6; S Ecc 7:2-4; S Jer 15:17 **16:9** [x] S Isa 24:8; S 51:3; Eze 26:13; Am 6:4-7 [y] S Ps 78:63 [z] Isa 22:12-14; Rev 18:23 **16:10** [a] S Dt 29:24; Jer 5:19 **16:11** [b] S Job 31:27

meal; do not go to mourn or show sympathy, because I have withdrawn my blessing, my love and my pity[o] from this people," declares the LORD. 6 "Both high and
low will die in this land.[p] They will not be
buried or mourned,[q] and no one will cut[r]
themselves or shave[s] their head for the
dead. 7 No one will offer food[t] to comfort
those who mourn[u] for the dead—not even
for a father or a mother—nor will anyone
give them a drink to console[v] them.
8 "And do not enter a house where there
is feasting and sit down to eat and drink.[w]
9 For this is what the LORD Almighty, the
God of Israel, says: Before your eyes and in
your days I will bring an end to the sounds[x]
of joy and gladness and to the voices of
bride[y] and bridegroom in this place.[z]
10 "When you tell these people all this
and they ask you, 'Why has the LORD decreed such a great disaster against us?
What wrong have we done? What sin
have we committed against the LORD our
God?'[a] 11 then say to them, 'It is because
your ancestors forsook me,' declares the
LORD, 'and followed other gods and served
and worshiped[b] them. They forsook me
and did not keep my law.[c] 12 But you have
behaved more wickedly than your ancestors.[d] See how all of you are following the
stubbornness of your evil hearts[e] instead
of obeying me. 13 So I will throw you out of
this land[f] into a land neither you nor your

[c] Dt 29:25-26; S 1Ki 9:9; Ps 106:35-43 **16:12** [d] S Ex 32:8; S Jer 7:26; Eze 20:30; Am 2:4 [e] S Ecc 9:3; S Jer 3:17 **16:13** [f] S 2Ch 7:20

---

and incurable. Jerusalem is similarly described in 30:12–15, together with God's promise of healing in 30:17. *deceptive brook.* See Mic 1:14, where also "deceptive" probably refers to the kind of intermittent streams described in Job 6:15–20. Jeremiah here accuses God of being undependable, in contrast to the Lord's own earlier description of himself as a "spring of living water" (see 2:13 and note).

15:19–21 The Lord commands Jeremiah to repent, then encourages him and renews his call.

15:19 *repent ... restore ... turn ... turn.* The Hebrew root is the same for all four words (see notes on 3:1; Isa 1:25–26). *serve.* Lit. "stand before"—the appropriate posture for the obedient servant (see Nu 16:9; Dt 10:8). *spokesman.* Lit. "mouth" (see 1:9 and note; Ex 4:15–16; see also note on Ex 7:1–2).

15:20 See 1:8,18–19 and notes.

15:21 *save you from ... the wicked.* See, e.g., 36:26; 38:6–13.

16:1—17:18 Messages of disaster and comfort, with the note of disaster predominating (16:1–13,16–18; 16:21—17:6; 17:9–13,18). The first half of the section is prose (16:1–18), the second half poetry (16:19—17:18).

16:2 Jeremiah's ministry was such that he had to face life alone (see note on 15:17), without the comfort and support a family can provide. *You must not.* The Hebrew underlying this phrase is used for the most forceful of negative commands, as, e.g., in the Ten Commandments (see Ex 20:3–4,7,13–17). *this place.* Judah and Jerusalem, especially the latter (see, e.g., Zep 1:4).

16:4 *diseases.* The Hebrew for this word is translated "ravages" in 14:18. *not be mourned or buried.* See v. 6; 7:33 and note; 8:2; 14:16; 25:33. *dung.* See 8:2; 9:22; 25:33. *perish by sword and famine.* See 14:15–16; see also note on 5:12. *food for the birds and the wild animals.* See note on 7:33.

16:5 *do not go to mourn.* See the similar command of God in Eze 24:16–17,22–23.

16:6 *cut themselves ... shave their head.* Actions forbidden in the law (see Lev 19:28; 21:5 and note; Dt 14:1 and note), but sometimes practiced by Israelites as a sign of mourning (see 41:5; Eze 7:18; Mic 1:16).

16:7 Food was customarily offered to mourners (see 2Sa 3:35; 12:16–17; Eze 24:17,22; Hos 9:4). *drink to console them.* Lit. "cup of consolation," in later Judaism a special cup of wine for the chief mourner.

16:8 *do not enter a house where there is feasting.* The present crisis is a time for neither feasting nor mourning (see v. 5).

16:9 See 7:34; 25:10; contrast 33:10–11.

16:10–13 The same question but a more elaborate answer than in 5:19 (see 9:12–16; 22:8–9; Dt 29:24–28; 1Ki 9:8–9).

16:10 Cf. the similar questions in Mal 1:6–7; 2:17; 3:7–8,13.

16:11 See 11:10, where committing sins like those mentioned here is called breaking the Lord's covenant.

16:12 *behaved more wickedly than your ancestors.* See 1Ki 14:9. The coming judgment cannot be blamed on the sins of previous generations (see 31:29–30 and notes; Eze 18:2–4). *following the stubbornness of your evil hearts.* See note on 3:17; see also 7:24.

16:13 See Dt 28:36,64. *I will throw you out.* Into exile (see

ancestors have known,[g] and there you will
serve other gods[h] day and night, for I will
show you no favor.'[i]
14 "However, the days are coming,"[j] declares the LORD, "when it will no longer
be said, 'As surely as the LORD lives, who
brought the Israelites up out of Egypt,'[k]
15 but it will be said, 'As surely as the LORD
lives, who brought the Israelites up out of
the land of the north[l] and out of all the
countries where he had banished them.'[m]
For I will restore[n] them to the land I gave
their ancestors.[o]
16 "But now I will send for many fishermen," declares the LORD, "and they will
catch them.[p] After that I will send for many
hunters, and they will hunt[q] them down on
every mountain and hill and from the crevices of the rocks.[r] 17 My eyes are on all their
ways; they are not hidden[s] from me, nor is
their sin concealed from my eyes.[t] 18 I will
repay[u] them double[v] for their wickedness
and their sin, because they have defiled
my land[w] with the lifeless forms of their
vile images[x] and have filled my inheritance
with their detestable idols.[y]"[z]

19 LORD, my strength and my fortress,
my refuge[a] in time of distress,
to you the nations will come[b]
from the ends of the earth and say,
"Our ancestors possessed nothing but
false gods,[c]
worthless idols[d] that did them no
good.[e]

20 Do people make their own gods?
Yes, but they are not gods!"[f]

21 "Therefore I will teach them—
this time I will teach them
my power and might.
Then they will know
that my name[g] is the LORD.

17 "Judah's sin is engraved with an
iron tool,[h]
inscribed with a flint point,
on the tablets of their hearts[i]
and on the horns[j] of their altars.
2 Even their children remember
their altars and Asherah poles[a][k]
beside the spreading trees
and on the high hills.[l]
3 My mountain in the land
and your[b] wealth and all your
treasures
I will give away as plunder,[m]
together with your high places,[n]
because of sin throughout your
country.[o]
4 Through your own fault you will lose
the inheritance[p] I gave you.
I will enslave you to your enemies[q]
in a land[r] you do not know,

16:13 [g] S Dt 28:36; S Jer 5:19 [h] S Dt 4:28; S 1Ki 9:9 [i] S Jer 15:5 **16:14** [j] Jer 29:10; 30:3; 31:27,38 [k] S Dt 15:15 **16:15** [l] S Jer 3:18 [m] S Isa 11:11; Jer 23:8 [n] Ps 53:6; S Isa 11:12; Jer 30:3; 32:44; Eze 38:14; Joel 3:1 [o] S Dt 30:3; S Isa 14:1 **16:16** [p] Am 4:2; Hab 1:14-15 [q] Am 9:3; Mic 7:2 [r] S 1Sa 26:20 **16:17** [s] S Ge 3:8; S Ecc 12:14; S Mk 4:22; 1Co 4:5; S Heb 4:13 [t] S Ps 51:9; Pr 15:3; Zep 1:12 **16:18** [u] S Isa 65:6 [v] S Isa 40:2; S Jer 12:3; Rev 18:6 [w] Nu 35:34; Jer 2:7 [x] S Ps 101:3 [y] S 1Ki 14:24 [z] S Jer 2:7; S 4:1; Eze 5:11; 8:10 **16:19** [a] S 2Sa 22:3; S Ps 46:1 [b] S Isa 2:2; Jer 3:17 [c] S Ps 4:2 [d] S Dt 32:21; S 1Sa 12:21 [e] S Isa 40:19; S Jer 14:22 **16:20** [f] Ps 115:4-7; S Jer 2:11; Ro 1:23 **16:21** [g] S Ex 3:15 **17:1** [h] Job 19:24 [i] S Dt 6:6; S 2Co 3:3 [j] S Ex 27:2 **17:2** [k] S 2Ch 24:18 [l] S Jer 2:20 **17:3** [m] S 2Ki 24:13 [n] Jer 26:18; Mic 3:12 [o] Jer 15:13 **17:4** [p] La 5:2 [q] Dt 28:48; S Jer 12:7 [r] Jer 16:13; 22:28

[a] 2 That is, wooden symbols of the goddess Asherah
[b] 2,3 Or *hills / 3and the mountains of the land. / Your*

7:15; 22:26; Dt 29:28). *land neither you nor your ancestors have known.* Babylonia (see 9:16).

16:14–15 Repeated almost verbatim in 23:7–8, the passage outlines nearly 1,000 years of Israelite history: exodus (c. 1446 BC), exile (586), restoration (537). See Isa 43:16–21; 48:20–21; 51:9–11. *As surely as the LORD lives.* See note on Ge 42:15.

16:15 *land of the north.* Babylonia (see note on Isa 41:25).

16:16 *fishermen … hunters.* Symbolic of conquerors (see Eze 12:13; 29:4; Am 4:2 and note). *mountain and hill.* To which the people would flee in vain (see 4:29 and note). *crevices of the rocks.* The phrase occurs outside Jeremiah only in Isa 7:19. The Lord may be recalling here the episode of the ruined linen belt, hidden in a "crevice in the rocks" (13:4).

16:17 *My eyes are on all their ways.* See 32:19. *they are not hidden from me.* See 23:24 and note.

16:18 *repay them double.* See 17:18; Isa 40:2 and note. *defiled my land.* Made it ceremonially unclean (see 2:7; 3:1–2; see also note on Lev 4:12). *lifeless forms of their vile images.* See Lev 26:30. Idols have no life in them (see Ps 115:4–7; 135:15–17). *my inheritance.* God's land (see 17:4; see also note on 2:7). *detestable.* Abominable in the Lord's eyes (see 2:7; see also note on Lev 7:21).

16:19–20 The prophet interjects a few brief words of hope.

16:19 *strength … fortress … refuge in time of distress.* Such descriptions of God's dependability and protecting power are common in the Psalms (see, e.g., Ps 18:1–2; 28:7–8; 59:9,16–17). *to you the nations will come.* See 4:2 and note; see also Isa 2:2–4; 42:4; 45:14; 49:6; Zec 8:20–23; 14:16. *worthless idols.* See note on 2:5. *did them no good.* Were unprofitable to them (see note on 2:8).

16:20 *not gods.* See 5:7.

16:21—17:4 The Lord responds to Jeremiah and continues his solemn warnings that began in v. 1.

16:21 *teach … teach … know.* The same Hebrew root underlies each of these words. God would "cause them to know," and then they would surely "know." *them … they.* Probably includes Judah as well as the nations (see Eze 36:23; 37:14). *know that my name is the LORD.* "Name" often means "person" or "being" in the OT (see note on Ps 5:11). Ezekiel's equivalent of Jeremiah's phrase is "know that I am the LORD," found in his prophecy about 70 times (see Introduction to Ezekiel: Themes; see also notes on Eze 5:13; 6:7).

17:1 *engraved with an iron tool.* The method used to inscribe the most permanent of records (see Job 19:24). *flint.* An extremely hard stone from which tools and weapons were made (see notes on Ex 4:25; Jos 5:2; see also Eze 3:9; Zec 7:12). *tablets of their hearts.* For the same imagery, see Pr 3:3; 7:3. *horns of their altars.* The people of Judah have backslid so badly that their sins are engraved not only on their hearts but also on their altars—to be remembered by God rather than to be atoned for (see Lev 16:18).

17:2 *altars and Asherah poles.* See notes on Ex 34:13; Dt 7:5. *spreading trees … high hills.* See note on 2:20.

17:3–4 Repeated in large part from 15:13–14 (see notes there).

17:3 *My mountain.* Mount Zion, the location of the temple in Jerusalem (see Ps 24:3; Isa 2:3; Zec 8:3). *high places.* Locales of idolatrous worship (see note on 1Ki 3:2).

17:4 *inheritance.* The land of Canaan (see 16:18; see also note on 2:7).

for you have kindled my anger,
and it will burn[s] forever."
5 This is what the LORD says:

"Cursed is the one who trusts in man,[t]
who draws strength from mere flesh
and whose heart turns away from
the LORD.[u]
6 That person will be like a bush in the
wastelands;
they will not see prosperity when it
comes.
They will dwell in the parched places[v]
of the desert,
in a salt[w] land where no one lives.
7 "But blessed[x] is the one who trusts[y] in
the LORD,
whose confidence is in him.
8 They will be like a tree planted by the
water
that sends out its roots by the
stream.[z]
It does not fear when heat comes;
its leaves are always green.
It has no worries in a year of drought[a]
and never fails to bear fruit."[b]
9 The heart[c] is deceitful above all things
and beyond cure.
Who can understand it?
10 "I the LORD search the heart[d]
and examine the mind,[e]
to reward[f] each person according to
their conduct,
according to what their deeds
deserve."[g]

17:4 [s] S Jer 7:20
17:5 [t] S Ps 108:12; S Isa 2:22 [u] 2Co 1:9
17:6 [v] Job 30:3 [w] Dt 29:23; S Job 39:6; Ps 107:34; Jer 48:9
17:7 [x] S Ps 146:5 [y] S Ps 26:1; 34:8; 40:4; Pr 16:20; Jer 39:18
17:8 [z] S Job 14:9 [a] Jer 14:1-6 [b] Ps 1:3; 92:12-14; Eze 19:10; 47:12
17:9 [c] S Ecc 9:3; Mt 13:15; Mk 7:21-22
17:10 [d] S Jos 22:22; S 2Ch 6:30; S Rev 2:23 [e] Ps 17:3; 139:23; Jer 11:20; 20:12; Eze 11:5; 38:10 [f] S Lev 26:28; Ps 62:12; Jer 32:19; S Mt 16:27 [g] Jer 12:13; 14:16; 21:14; 32:19
17:11 [h] Lk 12:20
17:12 [i] S Jer 3:17
17:13 [j] Ps 71:5; Jer 14:8 [k] S Jer 2:17 [l] S Ps 69:28; 87:6; Eze 13:9; Da 12:1 [m] S Isa 12:3; Jn 4:10

11 Like a partridge that hatches eggs it did
not lay
are those who gain riches by unjust
means.
When their lives are half gone, their
riches will desert them,
and in the end they will prove to be
fools.[h]

12 A glorious throne,[i] exalted from the
beginning,
is the place of our sanctuary.
13 LORD, you are the hope[j] of Israel;
all who forsake[k] you will be put to
shame.
Those who turn away from you will be
written in the dust[l]
because they have forsaken the LORD,
the spring of living water.[m]

14 Heal me, LORD, and I will be healed;[n]
save[o] me and I will be saved,
for you are the one I praise.[p]
15 They keep saying to me,
"Where is the word of the LORD?
Let it now be fulfilled!"[q]
16 I have not run away from being your
shepherd;
you know I have not desired the day
of despair.
What passes my lips[r] is open before you.
17 Do not be a terror[s] to me;
you are my refuge[t] in the day of
disaster.[u]

17:14 [n] S Isa 30:26; Jer 15:18 [o] S Ps 119:94 [p] S Ex 15:2; S Ps 109:1 **17:15** [q] S Isa 5:19; 2Pe 3:4 **17:16** [r] Ps 139:4 **17:17** [s] Ps 88:15-16 [t] S Ps 46:1; Jer 16:19; Na 1:7 [u] S Ps 18:18

17:5–8 See Ps 1 and notes.
17:5 *Cursed.* See note on 11:3. *flesh.* The opposite of "spirit" (see Isa 31:3; cf. Job 10:4).
17:6 *bush.* The Hebrew for this word suggests destitution (see Ps 102:17, "destitute"). *prosperity.* Lit. "good." The Hebrew for this word is translated "bounty" in Dt 28:12, where it refers to rain. *salt land.* An evidence of God's curse also in Dt 29:23.
17:7 *trusts … confidence.* The same Hebrew root underlies both words.
17:8 *planted.* Or "transplanted." *stream.* See Isa 44:4, where the same Hebrew root is used again to illustrate the source of the righteous person's strength. *drought.* See note on 14:1. *bear fruit.* The Lord's answer to Jeremiah's complaint in 12:1–2 (see notes there).
17:9 The prophet makes an observation, then asks a rhetorical question. *heart.* Wickedness must not be allowed to take root in one's heart (see Ps 4:7 and note; Pr 4:23). *deceitful.* The Hebrew root for this word is the basis of the name Jacob (see NIV text note on Ge 27:36).
17:10 The Lord responds to Jeremiah's question. *search … examine.* See 11:20; 12:3. *mind.* Lit. "kidneys" (see 11:20). The Hebrew for this word is translated "hearts" in 12:2. *what their deeds deserve.* Lit. "the fruit of their deeds" (cf. 6:19).
17:11 The prophet uses a proverb to make his point (as in v. 9). *partridge.* Mentioned elsewhere in the OT only in 1Sa 26:20. *fools.* Morally and spiritually bankrupt (see note on Pr 1:7).
17:12–18 The fourth of Jeremiah's "confessions" (see Introduction: Author and Date).
17:12 *glorious throne.* See note on 14:21; see also Isa 6:1. The Lord is often represented as sitting on a throne between the cherubim on the ark of the covenant in the tabernacle and temple (see 1Sa 4:4 and note; Ps 80:1; 99:1). *exalted.* Mount Zion is the "high mountain of Israel" (Eze 20:40). *from the beginning.* From time immemorial, Zion had been chosen by God as the place of his sanctuary (see Ex 15:17).
17:13 *hope of Israel.* See note on 14:8. *dust.* Lit. "earth," sometimes referring to the netherworld (see note on Ps 61:2; see also note on Job 7:21), as also in Canaanite and Mesopotamian literature. "Written in the dust" would then mean "destined for death," the opposite of "written in the book" of life (Da 12:1; see Ex 32:32; see also Ps 69:28; Lk 10:20; Rev 3:5 and notes). *forsaken … spring of living water.* Contrast 15:18; see note on 2:13.
17:14 *Heal me.* See 15:18; Ps 6:2. *you are the one I praise.* See Ps 22:3 and note.
17:15 See 20:8. Jeremiah's enemies accuse him of being a false prophet (see Dt 18:21–22). The accusation must have been voiced before the first invasion of Judah by the Babylonians in 605 BC, after the battle of Carchemish (see 46:2; see also Introduction: Background).
17:16 *shepherd.* Symbolic of leadership and therefore of Jeremiah's role as a prophet (see notes on 2:8; Ps 23:1; Jn 10:1–30).
17:17 *my refuge.* See 16:19 and note. *day of disaster.* See v. 18; 15:11.

18 Let my persecutors be put to shame,
but keep me from shame;
let them be terrified,
but keep me from terror.
Bring on them the day of disaster;
destroy them with double
destruction.[v]

Keeping the Sabbath Day Holy

19 This is what the LORD said to me:
"Go and stand at the Gate of the People,[a]
through which the kings of Judah go in
and out; stand also at all the other gates
of Jerusalem.[w] 20 Say to them, 'Hear the
word of the LORD, you kings of Judah and
all people of Judah and everyone living in
Jerusalem[x] who come through these gates.[y]
21 This is what the LORD says: Be careful not
to carry a load on the Sabbath[z] day or bring
it through the gates of Jerusalem. 22 Do not
bring a load out of your houses or do any
work on the Sabbath, but keep the Sabbath
day holy, as I commanded your ancestors.[a]
23 Yet they did not listen or pay attention;[b]
they were stiff-necked[c] and would not listen or respond to discipline.[d] 24 But if you
are careful to obey me, declares the LORD,
and bring no load through the gates of
this city on the Sabbath, but keep the Sabbath day holy[e] by not doing any work on
it, 25 then kings who sit on David's throne[f]
will come through the gates of this city
with their officials. They and their officials
will come riding in chariots and on horses, accompanied by the men of Judah and
those living in Jerusalem, and this city will
be inhabited forever.[g] 26 People will come
from the towns of Judah and the villages around Jerusalem, from the territory of
Benjamin and the western foothills, from
the hill country and the Negev,[h] bringing
burnt offerings and sacrifices, grain offerings and incense, and bringing thank offerings to the house of the LORD. 27 But if
you do not obey[i] me to keep the Sabbath[j]
day holy by not carrying any load as you
come through the gates of Jerusalem on
the Sabbath day, then I will kindle an unquenchable fire[k] in the gates of Jerusalem
that will consume her fortresses.' "[l]

At the Potter's House

18 This is the word that came to Jeremiah from the LORD: 2 "Go down
to the potter's house, and there I will give
you my message." 3 So I went down to the
potter's house, and I saw him working at
the wheel. 4 But the pot he was shaping
from the clay was marred in his hands;
so the potter formed it into another pot,
shaping it as seemed best to him.
5 Then the word of the LORD came to me.
6 He said, "Can I not do with you, Israel, as

17:18 v Ps 35:1-8; S Isa 40:2; S Jer 12:3 **17:19** w Jer 7:2; 26:2 **17:20** x Jer 19:3 y Jer 22:2 **17:21** z Nu 15:32-36; S Dt 5:14; Ne 13:15-21; Jn 5:10 **17:22** a S Ge 2:3; S Ex 20:8; Isa 56:2-6 **17:23** b Jer 7:26 c Jer 19:15 d S 2Ch 28:22; S Jer 7:28; Zec 7:11 **17:24** e ver 22 **17:25** f S 2Sa 7:13; Isa 9:7; Jer 22:2, 4; Lk 1:32 g Jer 30:10; 33:16; Eze 28:26 **17:26** h Jer 32:44; 33:13; Zec 7:7 **17:27** i S 1Ki 9:6; Jer 22:5 j S Ne 10:31 k S Jer 7:20 l S 2Ki 25:9; Hos 8:14; Am 2:5

a *19* Or *Army*

17:18 *my persecutors.* See 15:15. *double.* See 16:18; Isa 40:2 and note.
17:19–27 An extended commentary on the Sabbath-day commandment (the covenant sign of God's relationship with Israel; see Ex 31:13–17; Eze 20:12), probably the version recorded in Dt 5:12–15 (see note on v. 22 below).
17:19 *People.* Lit. "Sons of the People." The Hebrew for this word is translated "common people" in 26:23; 2Ki 23:6 and "lay people" in 2Ch 35:5,7. The latter meaning seems intended here, and therefore the "Gate of the People" is likely the east gate of the temple, where the people assembled in large numbers and which the kings would be expected to use frequently.
17:20 *kings of Judah.* The current king and all subsequent ruling members of David's dynasty (see, e.g., v. 25; 1:18; 2:26; 13:13; 19:3).
17:21 *Be careful.* See Jos 23:11. The Hebrew underlying this phrase is translated "watch yourselves ... carefully" in Dt 4:15, and a similar expression is translated "be on your guard" in Mal 2:15, stressing the urgency and solemnity of the Lord's command.
17:22 *Do not.* See note on 16:2. The Hebrew for this negative expression is stronger than that in v. 21. *not ... do any work ... keep the Sabbath day holy.* Specific references to the Sabbath-day commandment of Ex 20:8,10; Dt 5:12,14. *as I commanded.* The Hebrew underlying this phrase is unique to the Ten Commandments as recorded in Deuteronomy (see Dt 5:12, 15–16; see note on vv. 19–27).
17:23 *did not listen ... were stiff-necked.* Repeated from 7:26 (see note there; see also 11:10). *not ... respond to discipline.* See 2:30; 5:3.
17:25 Repeated in part in 22:4. King David's dynasty will last forever (see 23:5–6; 30:9; 33:15; 2Sa 7:12–17), and Jerusalem will be inhabited for all time (31:38–40; Zec 2:2–12; 8:3; 14:11), if the people of Judah obey the Lord (see v. 27)—and they will ultimately, according to 31:33–34.
17:26 *territory of Benjamin.* Jeremiah's hometown was located there (see 1:1). *western foothills ... hill country.* See note on Dt 1:7. *Negev.* See note on Ge 12:9. *bringing thank offerings.* See 33:11.
17:27 Disobedience will bring disaster and will negate—at least temporarily—the promises of vv. 24–26. *gates of Jerusalem.* The symbols of Sabbath violation would be the first structures destroyed. *kindle ... fire ... consume her fortresses.* Common prophetic language for divine judgment against rebellious cities (see 49:27; 50:32; Am 1:4,7,10,12,14; 2:2,5; cf. Jer 21:14).
18:1—20:18 Three chapters focusing on lessons the Lord taught Jeremiah at the potter's workshop, probably before 605 BC (see note on 17:15).
18:1–17 As the potter controls what he does with the clay, so the Lord is sovereign over the people of Judah.
18:2 *Go down.* The potter's workshop was probably located on the slopes of the Valley of Ben Hinnom, near the Potsherd Gate (see 19:2 and note). See photo, p. 1257.
18:3 *wheel.* Lit. "two stones." Both wheels were attached to a single upright shaft, one end of which was sunk permanently in the ground. The potter would spin the lower wheel with his foot and would work the clay on the upper wheel; the process is described in the Apocryphal book of Ecclesiasticus (38:29–30). See photo, p. 805.
18:4 *marred.* The Hebrew for this word is translated "ruined" in 13:7 with respect to the linen belt that Jeremiah had hidden (see note there). *as seemed best to him.* The flaw was in the clay itself, not in the potter's skill.
18:6 *Like clay ... so are you.* Biblical imagery often pictures humankind as made of clay by a potter (see Job

this potter does?" declares the LORD. "Like
clay[m] in the hand of the potter, so are you
in my hand,[n] Israel. 7 If at any time I announce that a nation or kingdom is to be
uprooted,[o] torn down and destroyed, 8 and
if that nation I warned repents of its evil,
then I will relent[p] and not inflict on it the
disaster[q] I had planned. 9 And if at another time I announce that a nation
or kingdom is to be built[r] up and
planted, 10 and if it does evil[s] in
my sight and does not obey me,
then I will reconsider[t] the good I
had intended to do for it.[u]
11 "Now therefore say to the
people of Judah and those living
in Jerusalem, 'This is what the LORD
says: Look! I am preparing a disaster[v]
for you and devising a plan[w] against
you. So turn[x] from your evil ways,[y] each
one of you, and reform your ways and
your actions.'[z] 12 But they will reply, 'It's
no use.[a] We will continue with our own
plans; we will all follow the stubbornness
of our evil hearts.[b]' "

13 Therefore this is what the LORD says:

"Inquire among the nations:
Who has ever heard anything like
this?[c]
A most horrible[d] thing has been done
by Virgin[e] Israel.
14 Does the snow of Lebanon
ever vanish from its rocky slopes?
Do its cool waters from distant sources
ever stop flowing?[a]
15 Yet my people have forgotten[f] me;
they burn incense[g] to worthless
idols,[h]
which made them stumble[i] in their ways,
in the ancient paths.[j]
They made them walk in byways,
on roads not built up.[k]

Water decanters from Judah, c. sixth century BC—around the time of Jeremiah's ministry (see 19:1 and note)

Z. Radovan/www.BibleLandPictures.com

18:6 [m] S Isa 29:16; 45:9; Ro 9:20-21 [n] S Ge 2:7 **18:7** [o] Jer 1:10 **18:8** [p] S Ex 32:14; Ps 25:11; Jer 26:13; 36:3; Jnh 3:8-10 [q] Jer 31:28; 42:10; Da 9:14; Hos 11:8-9; Joel 2:13; Jnh 4:2 **18:9** [r] Jer 1:10; 31:28 **18:10** [s] Eze 33:18 [t] 1Sa 2:29-30; 13:13 [u] S Jer 1:10 **18:11** [v] S 2Ki 22:16; S Jer 4:6 [w] ver 18 [x] S Dt 4:30; S 2Ki 17:13; Isa 1:16-19 [y] S Jer 7:3 [z] S Job 16:17

16 Their land will be an object of horror[l]
and of lasting scorn;[m]
all who pass by will be appalled[n]
and will shake their heads.[o]
17 Like a wind[p] from the east,
I will scatter them before their
enemies;
I will show them my back and not my
face[q]
in the day of their disaster."

18 They said, "Come, let's make plans[r]
against Jeremiah; for the teaching of the
law by the priest[s] will not cease, nor will

[a] 14 The meaning of the Hebrew for this sentence is uncertain.

18:12 [a] S Isa 57:10 [b] S Jer 3:17 **18:13** [c] S Isa 66:8 [d] S Jer 5:30 [e] S 2Ki 19:21 **18:15** [f] S Isa 17:10 [g] S Isa 1:13; Jer 44:15,19 [h] Jer 10:15; 51:18; Hos 11:2 [i] Eze 44:12; Mal 2:8 [j] Jer 6:16 [k] S Isa 57:14; 62:10 **18:16** [l] S Dt 28:37; Jer 25:9; Eze 33:28-29 [m] Jer 19:8; 42:18 [n] S Lev 26:32 [o] S 2Ki 19:21; S Job 16:4; Ps 22:7; La 1:12 **18:17** [p] S Job 7:10; Jer 13:24 [q] S 2Ch 29:6; S Jer 2:27 **18:18** [r] ver 11; Jer 11:19 [s] Jer 2:8; Hag 2:11; Mal 2:7

4:19 and note; Ro 9:20–21). *potter.* The Hebrew for this word is translated "Maker" in 10:16 with reference to God.

18:7–10 *If … if … if … if.* God's promises and threats are conditioned on human actions. God, who himself does not change (see Nu 23:19; Mal 3:6; Jas 1:17), nevertheless does change his preannounced response to people, depending on what they do (see note on 4:28; see also Joel 2:13; Jnh 3:8—4:2 and note on 3:9; 4:11).

18:7 *uprooted, torn down and destroyed.* See 1:10 and note.

18:8 See 26:3. *evil … disaster.* The Hebrew is the same for both words (also in v. 11).

18:9 *built up and planted.* See 1:10 and note.

18:11 *devising a plan.* See Est 8:3; 9:25; Eze 38:10. *turn from.* The Hebrew underlying this phrase is translated "repents of" in v. 8.

18:12 *It's no use.* See 2:25; see also note on Isa 57:10. *follow the stubbornness of our evil hearts.* See note on 3:17.

18:13–17 See 2:10–13.

18:13 *horrible thing.* See 5:30; 23:14; Hos 6:10. *Virgin Israel.* See note on 2Ki 19:21.

18:14–15 Although nature is reliable (v. 14), Judah is fickle and unfaithful (v. 15).

18:14 *Lebanon.* One of the highest of the northern mountains (see 22:6), reaching an altitude of over 10,000 feet.

18:15 *my people have forgotten me.* Repeated from 2:32 (see note there). *burn incense.* See note on 1:16. *worthless idols.* Lit. "nothing" (Ps 31:6; see Jer 2:8 and note). *which made them stumble.* See 2Ch 28:23. *ancient paths.* See note on 6:16. *roads not built up.* See note on Isa 35:8.

18:16 *object of horror … appalled.* The same Hebrew root underlies both words. *lasting scorn.* See 19:8; 25:9,18; 29:18; 51:37. The phrase implies hissing or whistling to express shock, ridicule and contempt. *all … appalled.* See 19:8; 1Ki 9:8. *shake their heads.* See 48:27; Job 16:4 and note; see also Ps 44:14; 109:25.

18:17 *wind from the east.* See 4:11; Ps 48:7 and notes. *show them my back and not my face.* As the people themselves had done to God (see 2:27). His face symbolizes his gracious blessing and favor (see Nu 6:24–26 and note on 6:25).

18:18–23 The fifth of Jeremiah's "confessions" (see Introduction: Author and Date).

18:18 *They.* Jeremiah's enemies (see note on 17:15). *plans against Jeremiah.* See v. 12; 11:18–23; 12:6; 15:10–11,15–21.

counsel from the wise,[t] nor the word from
the prophets.[u] So come, let's attack him
with our tongues[v] and pay no attention to
anything he says."

[19]Listen to me, LORD;
hear what my accusers[w] are saying!
[20]Should good be repaid with evil?[x]
Yet they have dug a pit[y] for me.
Remember that I stood[z] before you
and spoke in their behalf[a]
to turn your wrath away from them.
[21]So give their children over to famine;[b]
hand them over to the power of the sword.[c]
Let their wives be made childless and widows;[d]
let their men be put to death,
their young men[e] slain by the sword in battle.
[22]Let a cry[f] be heard from their houses
when you suddenly bring invaders against them,
for they have dug a pit[g] to capture me
and have hidden snares[h] for my feet.
[23]But you, LORD, know
all their plots to kill[i] me.
Do not forgive[j] their crimes
or blot out their sins from your sight.
Let them be overthrown before you;
deal with them in the time of your anger.[k]

19

This is what the LORD says: "Go
and buy a clay jar from a potter.[l]
Take along some of the elders[m] of the people and of the priests [2]and go out to the
Valley of Ben Hinnom,[n] near the entrance
of the Potsherd Gate. There proclaim the
words I tell you, [3]and say, 'Hear the word
of the LORD, you kings[o] of Judah and people of Jerusalem. This is what the LORD
Almighty, the God of Israel, says: Listen! I
am going to bring a disaster[p] on this place
that will make the ears of everyone who
hears of it tingle.[q] [4]For they have forsak-
en[r] me and made this a place of foreign
gods[s]; they have burned incense[t] in it to
gods that neither they nor their ancestors
nor the kings of Judah ever knew, and
they have filled this place with the blood
of the innocent.[u] [5]They have built the high
places of Baal to burn their children[v] in
the fire as offerings to Baal—something
I did not command or mention, nor did it
enter my mind.[w] [6]So beware, the days are
coming, declares the LORD, when people
will no longer call this place Topheth[x] or
the Valley of Ben Hinnom,[y] but the Valley
of Slaughter.[z]

[7]" 'In this place I will ruin[a] the plans[a]
of Judah and Jerusalem. I will make them
fall by the sword before their enemies,[b] at
the hands of those who want to kill them,
and I will give their carcasses[c] as food[d] to
the birds and the wild animals. [8]I will dev-

[a] 7 The Hebrew for *ruin* sounds like the Hebrew for *jar* (see verses 1 and 10).

18:18 [t]S Job 5:13; Eze 7:26 [u]Jer 5:13 [v]Ps 52:2; 64:2-8; S Jer 9:3 **18:19** [w]Ps 71:13 **18:20** [x]S Ge 44:4 [y]Ps 35:7; 57:6; S 119:85 [z]Jer 15:1 [a]S Ge 20:7; S Dt 9:19; Ps 106:23; Jer 14:7-9 **18:21** [b]Jer 11:22; 14:16 [c]S Ps 63:10 [d]S 1Sa 15:33; Ps 109:9; S Isa 47:9; La 5:3 [e]S Isa 9:17 **18:22** [f]S Jer 6:26 [g]S Ps 119:85 [h]Ps 35:15; 140:5; Jer 5:26; 20:10 **18:23** [i]S Jer 11:21; 37:15 [j]S Ne 4:5 [k]Ps 59:5; S Jer 10:24 **19:1** [l]Jer 18:2 [m]S Nu 11:17; 1Ki 8:1 **19:2** [n]S Jos 15:8 **19:3** [o]Jer 17:20 [p]S Jer 6:19 [q]S 1Sa 3:11 **19:4** [r]S Dt 31:16; Dt 28:20; S Isa 65:11 [s]S Ex 20:3; S Jer 1:16 [t]S Lev 18:21 [u]S 2Ki 21:16 **19:5** [v]S Lev 18:21; S 2Ki 3:27; Ps 106:37-38 [w]S Jer 7:31; Eze 16:36 **19:6** [x]S 2Ki 23:10 [y]S Jos 15:8 [z]Jer 7:32 **19:7** [a]Ps 33:10-11 [b]S ver 9; S Lev 26:17; S Dt 28:25 [c]S Jer 16:4; 34:20 [d]S Dt 28:26

teaching of the law. Delegated to the priests (see note on Hos 4:4–9). *priest . . . wise . . . prophets.* Despite Jeremiah's prophecies to the contrary (see 6:13–15; cf. 23:9–40; Eze 7:26 and note), the people thought that the various sources for receiving guidance from the Lord would continue as usual. *attack him with our tongues.* See note on 9:3.

18:20 *good . . . repaid with evil.* See Ps 35:12. *dug a pit.* Symbolic of his enemies' plots against him (see v. 22; Ps 57:6 and note; Pr 22:14; 23:27). *stood before you.* See note on 15:1. *spoke in their behalf.* See 14:7–9,21.

18:21 *hand them over to the power of the sword.* The Hebrew underlying this phrase occurs also in Ps 63:10; Eze 35:5. *be put to death.* Lit. "be slain by death," probably referring to plague, as in 15:2 (see note there).

18:22–23 See Ps 141:8–10.

18:22 *hidden snares.* See Ps 140:5; 142:3.

18:23 *you, LORD, know.* See 12:3; 15:15. *Do not forgive their crimes . . . Let them be overthrown before you.* A prayer not for human vengeance but for divine vindication (see note on 10:25). *blot out their sins.* See Ps 51:1–2 and notes.

19:1–15 A jar deliberately broken by Jeremiah (vv. 1–10) symbolizes the forthcoming destruction of Judah and Jerusalem (vv. 11–15). In ch. 18 the potter's clay was still moist and pliable, making it possible to reshape and rework it (see 18:1–11). In ch. 19, however, the clay jar is hard and, if unsuitable for the owner's use, can only be destroyed (see v. 11).

19:1 *jar.* The Hebrew for this word implies a vessel with a narrow neck, perhaps the water decanter frequently found in excavations and ranging from 5 to 12 inches high. *elders.* See note on Ex 3:16. *of the people.* See 1Ki 8:1–3. *of the priests.* See 2Ki 19:2, "leading priests" (lit. "elders of the priests"). Elders in Israel were of two kinds, one performing primarily civil functions and the other primarily religious functions.

19:2 *Valley of Ben Hinnom.* See note on 7:31. *Potsherd Gate.* The Jerusalem Targum (an ancient Aramaic paraphrase) identifies the Potsherd Gate (so called because it overlooked the main dump for broken pottery) with the Dung Gate of Ne 2:13 (see note there); 3:13–14; 12:31.

19:3 *kings.* See note on 17:20. *disaster . . . make the ears . . . tingle.* Echoed from 2Ki 21:12 (see 1Sa 3:11). The phrase refers to the shock of hearing an announcement of threatened punishment.

19:4 *they.* All who tried to combine the worship of idols with the worship of the one true God. *this . . . place.* Jerusalem. *burned incense.* See note on 1:16. *filled this place with the blood of the innocent.* The blood of godly people (see 2:34; 7:6; 22:3,17; 26:15), specifically as shed by wicked King Manasseh (see 15:4 and note; see also 2Ki 21:16).

19:5–6 Repeated in large part from 7:31–32 (see notes there).

19:7 *ruin.* Lit. "pour out"; see NIV text note (see also note on v. 1). As Jeremiah was saying this, he may have been pouring water from the jar to the ground (cf. 2Sa 14:14). *fall by the sword before their enemies.* The Babylonians are the instruments of the divine threat (see 20:6). *carcasses as food . . . wild animals.* See 7:33 and note.

19:8 Echoes the language of 18:16 (see note there; see also Eze 27:35; Zep 2:15). *devastate . . . appalled.* The same Hebrew

astate this city and make it an object of horror and scorn;[e] all who pass by will be appalled[f] and will scoff because of all its wounds.[g] 9 I will make them eat[h] the flesh of their sons and daughters, and they will eat one another's flesh because their enemies[i] will press the siege so hard against them to destroy them.'

10 "Then break the jar[j] while those who go with you are watching, 11 and say to them, 'This is what the LORD Almighty says: I will smash[k] this nation and this city just as this potter's jar is smashed and cannot be repaired. They will bury[l] the dead in Topheth until there is no more room. 12 This is what I will do to this place and to those who live here, declares the LORD. I will make this city like Topheth. 13 The houses[m] in Jerusalem and those of the kings of Judah will be defiled[n] like this place, Topheth—all the houses where they burned incense on the roofs[o] to all the starry hosts[p] and poured out drink offerings[q] to other gods.' "

14 Jeremiah then returned from Topheth, where the LORD had sent him to prophesy, and stood in the court[r] of the LORD's temple and said to all the people, 15 "This is what the LORD Almighty, the God of Israel, says: 'Listen! I am going to bring on this city and all the villages around it every disaster[s] I pronounced against them, because they were stiff-necked[t] and would not listen[u] to my words.' "

Jeremiah and Pashhur

20 When the priest Pashhur son of Immer,[v] the official[w] in charge of the temple of the LORD, heard Jeremiah prophesying these things, 2 he had Jeremiah the prophet beaten[x] and put in the stocks[y] at the Upper Gate of Benjamin[z] at the LORD's temple. 3 The next day, when Pashhur released him from the stocks, Jeremiah said to him, "The LORD's name[a] for you is not Pashhur, but Terror on Every Side.[b] 4 For this is what the LORD says: 'I will make you a terror to yourself and to all your friends; with your own eyes[c] you will see them fall by the sword of their enemies. I will give[d] all Judah into the hands of the king of Babylon, who will carry[e] them away to Babylon or put them to the sword. 5 I will deliver all the wealth[f] of this city into the hands of their enemies—all its products, all its valuables and all the treasures of the kings of Judah. They will take it away[g] as plunder and carry it off

19:8 [e] S Dt 28:37; S Jer 18:16; 25:9 [f] S Lev 26:32; La 2:15-16 [g] S Dt 29:22 **19:9** [h] S Lev 26:29; Dt 28:49-57; La 4:10 [i] S ver 7; Jer 21:7; 34:20 **19:10** [j] ver 1; S Ps 2:9; Jer 13:14 **19:11** [k] Ps 2:9; Isa 30:14 [l] Jer 7:32 **19:13** [m] Jer 32:29; 52:13; Eze 16:41 [n] Ps 74:7 [o] S 2Ki 23:12 [p] Dt 4:19; S 2Ki 17:16; S Job 38:32; Jer 8:2; Ac 7:42 [q] S Isa 57:6; Eze 20:28 **19:14** [r] 2Ch 20:5; S Jer 7:2; 26:2 **19:15** [s] ver 3; Jer 11:11 [t] S Ne 9:16; Ac 7:51 [u] Jer 22:21 **20:1** [v] S 1Ch 24:14 [w] 2Ki 25:18; Lk 22:52 **20:2** [x] Dt 25:2-3; S Jer 1:19; 15:15; 37:15; 2Co 11:24 [y] S Job 13:27; Jer 29:26; Ac 16:24; Heb 11:36 [z] S Job 29:7; Jer 37:13; 38:7; Zec 14:10 **20:3** [a] Hos 1:4 [b] S ver 10; S Ps 31:13 **20:4** [c] Jer 29:21 [d] Jer 21:10; 25:9 [e] Jer 13:19; 39:9; 52:27 **20:5** [f] S 2Ki 25:15; Jer 17:3 [g] S 2Ki 20:17

---

root underlies both words—the devastation of the city will have a similar effect on those who see its ruins. *scorn ... scoff.* The same Hebrew root underlies both words.

19:9 One of the covenant curses (see Lev 26:29; Dt 28:53–57). *eat the flesh of their sons and daughters ... eat one another's flesh.* When Jerusalem's food supply ran out during the Babylonian siege in 586 BC, cannibalism resulted (see La 2:20; 4:10; Eze 5:10). Such shocking activity was not unprecedented in Israel (see 2Ki 6:28–29), and it would occur again in AD 70 during the Roman siege of Jerusalem (see Zec 11:9 and note): "A woman ... who ... had fled to Jerusalem ... killed her son, roasted him, and ate one half, concealing and saving the rest" (Josephus, *Wars*, 6.3.4).

19:11 *smash this nation ... as this potter's jar is smashed.* Egyptians of the Twelfth Dynasty (c. 1983–1795 BC) inscribed the names of their enemies on pottery bowls and then smashed them, hoping to break the power of their enemies by so doing. *cannot be repaired.* See note on vv. 1–15.

19:13 *will be defiled like ... Topheth.* King Josiah had earlier "desecrated Topheth" (2Ki 23:10). *burned incense.* See note on 1:16. *on the roofs.* See 32:29; see also note on Isa 15:3. The kings of Judah had built pagan altars on the roof of the palace in Jerusalem (see 2Ki 23:12). The Ugaritic Keret epic of the fourteenth century BC (see chart, p. xxiv) describes a similar practice: "Go to the top of a tower, bestride the top of the wall ... Honor Baal with your sacrifice ... Then descend ... from the housetops." *starry hosts.* Worship of the sun, moon and stars was common in Judah throughout much of the later history of the monarchy (see, e.g., 2Ki 17:16; 21:3,5; 23:4–5; Zep 1:5). *drink offerings to other gods.* See note on 7:18.

19:14 *all the people.* A much larger audience than the elders of v. 1.

19:15 *the villages around it.* The towns of Judah that were dependent on Jerusalem (see 1:15; 9:11). *were stiff-necked and would not listen.* Repeated from 7:26 (see note there; see also 11:10).

20:1–6 Pashhur's response to Jeremiah's symbolic act (vv. 1–2), and Jeremiah's rejoinder (vv. 3–6).

20:1 *Pashhur.* One or more different men with the same name appear in 21:1; 38:1. The name Pashhur occurs on an ostracon (see note on 34:7) found at Arad and dating to the time of Jeremiah. *Immer.* Perhaps a descendant of the head of the 16th division of priests in the Jerusalem temple (see 1Ch 24:14). *official in charge.* The priest in charge of punishing troublemakers, real or imagined, in the temple courts (see v. 2; 29:26). The position was second only to that of the chief priest himself (compare 29:25–26 with 52:24).

20:2 The first of many recorded acts of physical violence against Jeremiah. *the prophet.* The first time Jeremiah is so called in the book (see Introduction: Theological Themes and Message), here to stress the enormity of Pashhur's actions. *beaten.* Probably in accordance with the Mosaic law of Dt 25:2–3 (see note on Dt 25:3). *stocks.* Lit. "restraint, confinement." *Upper Gate of Benjamin.* Probably the same as the "north gate of the inner court" (Eze 8:3; see 2Ki 15:35; see also Eze 9:2). *at the LORD's temple.* This qualifying phrase distinguishes the temple's Gate of Benjamin from the "Benjamin Gate" in the city wall (37:13; 38:7). Both gates were in the northern part of the city, facing the territory of Benjamin.

20:3 *Terror on Every Side.* See note on 6:25.

20:4 Pashhur's new name symbolizes terror to all Judah, whose people will be exiled to Babylonia or put to death. *friends.* Associates and allies in the sense of covenant partners (see v. 6). *king of Babylon.* Nebuchadnezzar, who acceded to the Babylonian throne in 605 BC (see notes on 17:15; 18:1—20:18).

20:5 Fulfilled in 597 BC (see 2Ki 24:13) and in 586 (see 52:17–23; 2Ki 25:13–17).

to Babylon. 6 And you, Pashhur, and all
who live in your house will go into exile
to Babylon. There you will die and be buried, you and all your friends to whom you
have prophesied[h] lies.' "

Jeremiah's Complaint

7 You deceived[a][i] me, LORD, and I was
deceived[a];
you overpowered[j] me and prevailed.
I am ridiculed[k] all day long;
everyone mocks[l] me.
8 Whenever I speak, I cry out
proclaiming violence and
destruction.[m]
So the word of the LORD has
brought me
insult and reproach[n] all day long.
9 But if I say, "I will not mention his
word
or speak anymore in his name,"[o]
his word is in my heart like a fire,[p]
a fire shut up in my bones.
I am weary of holding it in;[q]
indeed, I cannot.
10 I hear many whispering,
"Terror[r] on every side!
Denounce[s] him! Let's denounce
him!"
All my friends[t]
are waiting for me to slip,[u] saying,
"Perhaps he will be deceived;
then we will prevail[v] over him
and take our revenge[w] on him."

20:6 [h] S Jer 14:15; La 2:14 **20:7** [i] S Ex 5:23; 22:16 [j] Isa 8:11; Am 3:8; 1Co 9:16 [k] Job 12:4 [l] S Job 17:2; S Ps 119:21 **20:8** [m] Jer 6:7; 28:8 [n] S 2Ch 36:16; S Jer 6:10 **20:9** [o] Jer 44:16 [p] S Ps 39:3; S Jer 4:19 [q] S Job 4:2; S Jer 6:11; Am 3:8; Ac 4:20 **20:10** [r] Jer 6:25 [s] Ne 6:6-13; Isa 29:21 [t] S Job 19:14; S Jer 13:21 [u] S Ps 57:4; S Jer 18:22; Lk 11:53-54 [v] S 1Ki 19:2 [w] S 1Sa 18:25; S Jer 11:19

20:11 [x] Jer 1:8; Ro 8:31 [y] Jer 15:15; 17:18 [z] S Ps 129:2 [a] S Jer 7:19; 23:40 **20:12** [b] S Ps 7:9; S Jer 17:10 [c] Dt 32:35; S Ro 12:19 [d] Ps 62:8; Jer 11:20 **20:13** [e] S Isa 12:6 [f] Ps 34:6; 35:10 [g] S Ps 97:10

11 But the LORD[x] is with me like a mighty
warrior;
so my persecutors[y] will stumble and
not prevail.[z]
They will fail and be thoroughly
disgraced;[a]
their dishonor will never be
forgotten.
12 LORD Almighty, you who examine the
righteous
and probe the heart and mind,[b]
let me see your vengeance[c] on them,
for to you I have committed[d] my
cause.

13 Sing[e] to the LORD!
Give praise to the LORD!
He rescues[f] the life of the needy
from the hands of the wicked.[g]

14 Cursed be the day I was born![h]
May the day my mother bore me not
be blessed!
15 Cursed be the man who brought my
father the news,
who made him very glad, saying,
"A child is born to you—a son!"
16 May that man be like the towns[i]
the LORD overthrew without pity.
May he hear wailing[j] in the morning,
a battle cry at noon.

[a] 7 Or *persuaded*

20:14 [h] S Job 3:8,16; Jer 15:10 **20:16** [i] S Ge 19:25 [j] S Jer 6:26

20:6 *you, Pashhur, ... will go into exile.* Probably in 597 BC, because shortly after that year (see 29:2) two other men in succession had replaced Pashhur as chief officer in the temple (see 29:25–26). *you have prophesied lies.* The priest Pashhur had pretended to be a prophet.

20:7–18 The sixth, last and longest of Jeremiah's "confessions" (see Introduction: Author and Date; see also note on 11:18–23). In some respects, it is the most daring and bitter of them all.

20:7 Cf. 15:18. *deceived.* Lit. "seduce[d]" (Ex 22:16) or "entice[d]" (1Ki 22:20–22); see v. 10. Jeremiah feels that when the Lord originally called him to be a prophet he had overly persuaded him (see NIV text note; see also 1:7–8,17–19; cf. Eze 14:9).

20:8 Jeremiah attributes his suffering to the Lord's demands on his life. *violence and destruction.* The prophet's message echoes the Lord's word (see 6:7). *reproach.* See Ps 44:13; 79:4.

20:9 A classic description of prophetic reluctance overcome by divine compulsion (see 1:6–8; Am 3:8; Ac 4:20; 1Co 9:16). *his word is ... like a fire.* See 5:14; 23:29. The figure is unique to the prophet Jeremiah (see also La 1:13).

20:10 The Hebrew of the first two lines is identical with that of the first two lines of Ps 31:13. *Terror on every side!* See note on 6:25. The phrase is here used to mock Jeremiah in the light of his doleful message. *friends.* Lit. "men of my peace/welfare" (cf. Ps 41:9 and note). *waiting for me to slip.* See Ps 35:15; 38:16. *deceived.* See v. 7 and note. *we will prevail over him.* Or so they think (see v. 11). *take our revenge on him.* His enemies will not give up, no matter what it takes (see 11:19; 12:6; 26:11; cf. Ps 56:5–6; 71:10).

20:11 *the LORD is with me.* See 1:8 and note. *mighty.* The Hebrew for this word is translated "cruel" in 15:21, where it describes Jeremiah's enemies. Here it has a different nuance and is applied to God, whose "might" overcomes all "cruelty." *warrior.* See notes on Ex 14:14; 15:3.

20:12 *vengeance.* See 11:20 and notes on Dt 32:35; Ps 5:10.

20:13 *Sing ... Give praise.* See 31:7; see also introduction to Ps 9. *rescues ... from the hands of the wicked.* See 15:21; 21:12. *needy.* See 22:16. By Jeremiah's time, "poor/needy" had become virtually synonymous with "righteous" (see Am 2:6; see also notes on Ps 9:18; 34:6).

20:14–18 See Job 3:3–19. From the heights of exultation (v. 13) Jeremiah now sinks to the depths of despair. The irreversibility of his divine call (v. 9), the betrayal of his friends (v. 10), the relentless pursuit of his enemies (vv. 7,11), the negative and condemnatory nature of his message (v. 8)—all have combined to bring to his lips a startling expression of despondency and hopelessness. The passage serves also as a transition to the next major section of the book. Judah and Jerusalem, Jeremiah will soon say, are now irrevocably doomed (see 21:1–10).

20:14 *Cursed be the day I was born!* See note on Job 3:3. The prophet questions the very basis of his divine commission (see 1:5).

20:15 News of the birth of a son, normally a blessing in ancient times (see, e.g., Ge 29:31–35), Jeremiah sees as a curse in his own case. *Cursed be the man.* A rhetorical curse, not directed against the man personally.

20:16 *towns the LORD overthrew.* Sodom and Gomorrah (see Ge 19:24–25,29). By Jeremiah's time their wickedness had long been proverbial (see 23:14; Dt 29:23; see also note on Isa 1:9–10). *battle cry.* See 4:19. *at noon.* See note on 6:4.

17 For he did not kill me in the womb,[k]
with my mother as my grave,
her womb enlarged forever.
18 Why did I ever come out of the
womb[l]
to see trouble[m] and sorrow
and to end my days in shame?[n]

God Rejects Zedekiah's Request

21 The word came to Jeremiah from
the LORD when King Zedekiah[o] sent
to him Pashhur[p] son of Malkijah and the
priest Zephaniah[q] son of Maaseiah. They
said: 2 "Inquire[r] now of the LORD for us because Nebuchadnezzar[a s] king of Babylon[t]
is attacking us. Perhaps the LORD will perform wonders[u] for us as in times past so
that he will withdraw from us."
3 But Jeremiah answered them, "Tell
Zedekiah, 4 'This is what the LORD, the
God of Israel, says: I am about to turn[v]
against you the weapons of war that are in
your hands, which you are using to fight
the king of Babylon and the Babylonians[b]
who are outside the wall besieging[w] you.
And I will gather them inside this city.
5 I myself will fight[x] against you with an
outstretched hand[y] and a mighty arm[z] in
furious anger and in great wrath. 6 I will
strike[a] down those who live in this city—
both man and beast—and they will die
of a terrible plague.[b] 7 After that, declares
the LORD, I will give Zedekiah[c] king of Judah, his officials and the people in this
city who survive the plague,[d] sword and
famine, into the hands of Nebuchadnezzar king of Babylon[e] and to their enemies[f]
who want to kill them.[g] He will put them
to the sword;[h] he will show them no mercy
or pity or compassion.'[i]
8 "Furthermore, tell the people, 'This is
what the LORD says: See, I am setting before you the way of life[j] and the way of
death. 9 Whoever stays in this city will die
by the sword, famine or plague.[k] But whoever goes out and surrenders[l] to the Babylonians who are besieging you will live;
they will escape with their lives.[m] 10 I have
determined to do this city harm[n] and not
good, declares the LORD. It will be given
into the hands[o] of the king of Babylon, and
he will destroy it with fire.'[p]
11 "Moreover, say to the royal house[q] of
Judah, 'Hear the word of the LORD. 12 This
is what the LORD says to you, house of
David:

20:17 [k]S Job 3:16; S 10:18-19 **20:18** [l]S Job 3:10-11; S Ecc 4:2 [m]S Ge 3:17; S Job 5:7 [n]S 1Ki 19:4; Ps 90:9; 102:3 **21:1** [o]2Ki 24:18; Jer 52:1 [p]S 1Ch 9:12 [q]S 2Ki 25:18 **21:2** [r]S Ge 25:22; S 2Ki 22:18 [s]S 2Ki 25:1 [t]S Ge 10:10 [u]Ps 44:1-4; Jer 32:17 **21:4** [v]Jer 32:5 [w]Jer 37:8-10 **21:5** [x]S Jos 10:14; Eze 5:8 [y]S 2Ki 22:13; S Jer 6:12 [z]S Ex 3:20 **21:6** [a]S Jer 7:20 [b]S Jer 14:12 **21:7** [c]S 2Ki 25:7; Jer 52:9; Eze 12:14 [d]Jer 14:12; 27:8 [e]S 2Ch 36:10; Jer 27:6; 32:4; 34:3; 37:17; 38:18; 39:5; Eze 29:19 [f]S Lev 26:17; S Jer 19:9 [g]S Jer 11:21 [h]S Jer 15:9 [i]S 2Ch 36:17; S Jer 15:5; Eze 7:9; Hab 1:6 **21:8** [j]S Dt 30:15 **21:9** [k]Jer 14:12; Eze 5:12 [l]Jer 27:11; 40:9 [m]Jer 27:12; 38:2,17; 39:18; 45:5 **21:10** [n]Jer 44:11,27; Am 9:4 [o]S Jer 20:4; 32:28; 38:2-3 [p]S 2Ki 25:9; S 2Ch 36:19 **21:11** [q]S Jer 13:18

[a] 2 Hebrew *Nebuchadrezzar,* of which *Nebuchadnezzar* is a variant; here and often in Jeremiah and Ezekiel
[b] 4 Or *Chaldeans*; also in verse 9

20:17 *enlarged.* Lit. "pregnant." In his anguish, Jeremiah wishes that his mother's womb, which gave him birth, had been instead his eternal tomb.

21:1—24:10 The prophet denounces Judah's rulers (21:1—23:7), false prophets (23:8–40) and sinful people (ch. 24). Although for the most part chs. 1–20 relate events in chronological order, chs. 21–52 are arranged on the basis of subject matter rather than chronology (see 24:1; 25:1; 26:1; 27:1; 29:2; 32:1; 35:1; 36:1; 37:1; 45:1; 49:34; 51:59; 52:4).

21:1—23:7 The rulers of Judah, who bear the primary responsibility for the nation's economic, social and spiritual ills, are the first to be denounced by Jeremiah.

21:1 *The word came.* The phrase does not appear again until 25:1, suggesting that chs. 21–24 constitute an integral section in the book. *Zedekiah.* Means "The LORD is my righteousness." See Introduction: Background. *Pashhur son of Malkijah.* Not the same as the Pashhur of 20:1–6 (see 38:1). *the priest Zephaniah son of Maaseiah.* Not the same as the prophet Zephaniah (see 29:25,29; 37:3; 52:24; see also Zep 1:1).

21:2 *Inquire ... of the LORD.* A request for knowledge or information (see Ge 25:22; 2Ki 22:13), not necessarily for help. *Nebuchadnezzar.* See NIV text note; see also chart, p. 511, and note on 2Ki 24:1. *is attacking.* About 588, because the brash Zedekiah had rebelled against Babylon (see 52:3). *us.* Jerusalem. *perform wonders ... as in times past.* For example, in the days of Hezekiah (see Isa 37:36). *he will withdraw.* See Isa 37:37.

21:4 *turn against you the weapons.* Your defense of Jerusalem will fail. *Babylonians.* See NIV text note; see also note on Job 1:17. *gather them inside this city.* Either (1) the weapons, meaning that Judah's troops would be totally unable to defend the approaches to the city, or (2) the Babylonians, meaning that Jerusalem's defeat is imminent and inevitable.

21:5 *I myself will fight against you.* The Lord, usually his people's defender, will now destroy them and seal their doom. *with an outstretched hand and a mighty arm.* See 27:5; 32:17. A similar phrase is used to describe God's powerful redemption of Israel at the exodus (see 32:21; Dt 4:34; 5:15; 7:19; 26:8), but here God turns his wrath against his own people. *in furious anger and in great wrath.* Probably quoted from Dt 29:28.

21:7 *I will give Zedekiah ... his officials and the people ... into the hands of Nebuchadnezzar.* Fulfilled in 52:8–11,24–27 (see Eze 12:13–14). *plague, sword and famine.* See v. 9. For this triad, see note on 14:12. *no mercy or pity or compassion.* For this triad, see 13:14; see also Eze 5:11. The three triads here heighten the literary effect of the passage.

21:8–10 See 27:12–13. Similar advice is offered in 38:2–3,17–18 (see Dt 30:15–20).

21:8 *See, I am setting before you.* See Dt 11:26. The people are offered a choice, but few of them will make the right decision. *the way of life and the way of death.* See Dt 30:15,19; see also Pr 6:23.

21:9 Repeated almost verbatim in 38:2. Jeremiah's counsel of surrender branded him as a traitor in the eyes of many (see 37:13), but he was in fact a true patriot who wanted to stay in Judah even after Jerusalem was destroyed (see 37:14; 40:6; 42:7–22). *whoever ... surrenders to the Babylonians ... will live.* Fulfilled in 39:9; 52:15. *they will escape with their lives.* Lit. "their lives will be their (only) plunder." The victorious in battle can expect to share plunder; the defeated are fortunate indeed if their lives are spared.

21:10 *determined.* Lit. "set my face" (see 44:11; Isa 50:7 and note). *harm and not good.* See Am 9:4; contrast 24:6. *It will be given ... destroy it with fire.* See 34:2.

21:12 *Administer justice.* See 5:28; 22:16; 1Ki 3:28; La 3:59. The king was obliged and expected to do so, as was the future

" 'Administer justice[r] every morning;
rescue from the hand of the oppressor[s]
the one who has been robbed,
or my wrath will break out and burn like fire[t]
because of the evil[u] you have done—
burn with no one to quench[v] it.
13 I am against[w] you, Jerusalem,
you who live above this valley[x]
on the rocky plateau, declares the LORD—
you who say, "Who can come against us?
Who can enter our refuge?"[y]
14 I will punish you as your deeds[z] deserve,
declares the LORD.
I will kindle a fire[a] in your forests[b]
that will consume everything around you.' "

Judgment Against Wicked Kings

22 This is what the LORD says: "Go
down to the palace of the king[c] of
Judah and proclaim this message there:
2 'Hear[d] the word of the LORD to you,
king of Judah, you who sit on David's
throne[e]—you, your officials and your people who come through these gates.[f] 3 This
is what the LORD says: Do what is just[g]
and right. Rescue from the hand of the oppressor[h] the one who has been robbed. Do
no wrong or violence to the foreigner, the
fatherless or the widow,[i] and do not shed
innocent blood[j] in this place. 4 For if you
are careful to carry out these commands,
then kings[k] who sit on David's throne will
come through the gates of this palace,
riding in chariots and on horses, accompanied by their officials and their people.
5 But if you do not obey[l] these commands,
declares the LORD, I swear[m] by myself that
this palace will become a ruin.' "
6 For this is what the LORD says about the
palace of the king of Judah:

"Though you are like Gilead[n] to me,
like the summit of Lebanon,[o]
I will surely make you like a wasteland,[p]
like towns not inhabited.
7 I will send destroyers[q] against you,
each man with his weapons,
and they will cut[r] up your fine cedar beams
and throw them into the fire.[s]

8 "People from many nations will pass
by this city and will ask one another,
'Why has the LORD done such a thing to
this great city?'[t] 9 And the answer will be:
'Because they have forsaken the covenant
of the LORD their God and have worshiped
and served other gods.[u]' "

10 Do not weep for the dead[v] king or
mourn[w] his loss;
rather, weep bitterly for him who is exiled,
because he will never return[x]
nor see his native land again.

21:12 [r] S Ex 22:22; S Lev 25:17 [s] S Ps 27:11 [t] S Isa 42:25; S Jer 10:10 [u] Jer 23:2 [v] S Isa 1:31 **21:13** [w] Jer 23:30; 50:31; 51:25; Eze 5:8; 13:8; 21:3; 29:10; 34:10; Na 2:13; 3:5 [x] Ps 125:2 [y] 2Sa 5:6-7; Jer 49:4; La 4:12; Ob 1:3-4 **21:14** [z] S Pr 1:31; S Isa 3:10-11; S Jer 17:10 [a] S 2Ch 36:19; La 2:3 [b] S 2Ki 19:23; Eze 20:47 **22:1** [c] S Jer 13:18; 34:2 **22:2** [d] Am 7:16 [e] S Jer 17:25; Lk 1:32 [f] Jer 17:20 **22:3** [g] S Lev 25:17; Isa 56:1; Jer 5:1; Eze 33:14; 45:9; Hos 12:6; Am 5:24; Mic 6:8; Zec 7:9 [h] Ps 72:4; Jer 21:12 [i] S Ex 22:22; S Isa 1:17; Jer 5:28 [j] S Jer 7:6 **22:4** [k] S Jer 17:25 **22:5** [l] S Jer 17:27 [m] S Ge 22:16; Heb 6:13

22:6 [n] S Ge 31:21; S SS 4:1 [o] S 1Ki 7:2; S Isa 33:9 [p] Mic 3:12 **22:7** [q] S Jer 4:7; S 6:4 [r] Ps 74:5; Isa 10:34 [s] S 2Ch 36:19; Zec 11:1 **22:8** [t] Dt 29:25-26; 1Ki 9:8-9; Jer 16:10-11 **22:9** [u] S 1Ki 9:9; Jer 16:11; Eze 39:23 **22:10** [v] S Ecc 4:2 [w] ver 18; Eze 24:16 [x] ver 27; Jer 24:9; 29:18; 42:18

Messiah (see 23:5; 33:15). *every morning.* When the mind is clear and the day is cool (see Ps 101:8 and note). *rescue … robbed.* Repeated in 22:3. *or my wrath … no one to quench it.* Repeated verbatim from 4:4 (see Am 5:6). *wrath will … burn.* See 15:14; 17:4,27.

21:13 *valley.* Jerusalem, surrounded on three sides by valleys (see note on Isa 22:7), is called the "Valley of Vision" in Isa 22:1,5. *rocky plateau.* Mount Zion. *you who say.* The pronouns are plural in the second half of the verse (referring to Jerusalem's inhabitants), singular in the first half (referring to Jerusalem personified). *Who can come against us?* The people think that no one can successfully lay siege to them (see notes on 7:4; 8:19).

21:14 *as your deeds deserve.* See note on 17:10. *kindle a fire … consume.* See note on 17:27. *forests.* The Hebrew for this word is singular and perhaps refers figuratively to Jerusalem's royal palace, called the "Palace of the Forest of Lebanon" (1Ki 7:2; 10:17,21; see Isa 22:8) because of the cedar (see 22:7,14,15,23) used in its construction. The palace (see 22:1) is compared to the "summit of Lebanon" in 22:6 (see 22:23 and NIV text note).

22:1 *Go down.* The palace was at a lower elevation than the temple (see 26:10; 36:10–12). *king of Judah.* Probably Zedekiah (see 21:3,7; compare v. 3 with 21:12), whose predecessors are mentioned in sequence later in the chapter (Josiah, vv. 10a,15b–16; Jehoahaz/Shallum, vv. 10b–12; Jehoiakim, vv. 13–15a,17–19; Jehoiachin/Koniah, vv. 24–30).

22:2 *David's throne.* Though all the kings of the Davidic dynasty failed to a greater or lesser degree, the victorious Messiah would someday appear as the culmination of David's royal line (see 23:5 and NIV text note; 33:15; Eze 34:23–24; Mt 1:1). *who come through these gates.* See 17:25 and note.

22:3 Contrast Isa 11:3–5 with Eze 22:6–7.

22:4 Repeated in part from 17:25.

22:5 See 17:27 and note. *swear by myself.* See notes on Ge 22:16; Isa 45:23; see also 49:13; 51:14; cf. 44:26. *become a ruin.* Fulfilled in 52:13 (see 27:17).

22:6 *Gilead … Lebanon.* Renowned for their forests. Lebanon in particular supplied cedar for the royal palace (see note on 21:14; see also 1Ki 5:6,8–10; 7:2–3; 10:27).

22:7 *send.* Lit. "consecrate" (see note on 6:4). *destroyers.* The Babylonians (see note on 4:7; see also 12:12). *each man with his weapons.* See Eze 9:2. *cut up your … cedar.* Cf. Isa 10:33–34; cf. especially the vivid description of the Babylonian troops smashing the carved paneling of the Jerusalem temple with their axes and hatchets (Ps 74:3–6).

22:8–9 Echoed in 1Ki 9:8–9; see Dt 29:24–26.

22:9 *forsaken the covenant … and served other gods.* A gross violation of the first and second stipulations of the Sinaitic covenant (see Ex 20:3–5 and notes).

22:10 *weep for the dead king.* Josiah, who was mourned long after his death (see 2Ch 35:24–25). *him who is exiled.* Jehoahaz/Shallum. In 609 BC the Egyptian pharaoh Necho "carried him off to Egypt, and there he died" (2Ki 23:34).

11 For this is what the LORD says about Shallum[a][y] son of Josiah, who succeeded his
father as king of Judah but has gone from
this place: "He will never return. 12 He will
die[z] in the place where they have led him
captive; he will not see this land again."

13 "Woe[a] to him who builds[b] his palace
by unrighteousness,
his upper rooms by injustice,
making his own people work for
nothing,
not paying[c] them for their labor.
14 He says, 'I will build myself a great
palace[d]
with spacious upper rooms.'
So he makes large windows in it,
panels it with cedar[e]
and decorates it in red.[f]

15 "Does it make you a king
to have more and more cedar?
Did not your father have food and drink?
He did what was right and just,[g]
so all went well[h] with him.
16 He defended the cause of the poor and
needy,[i]
and so all went well.
Is that not what it means to know[j] me?"
declares the LORD.
17 "But your eyes and your heart
are set only on dishonest gain,[k]
on shedding innocent blood[l]
and on oppression and extortion."[m]

18 Therefore this is what the LORD says about
Jehoiakim son of Josiah king of Judah:

"They will not mourn[n] for him:
'Alas, my brother! Alas, my sister!'
They will not mourn for him:
'Alas, my master! Alas, his
splendor!'
19 He will have the burial[o] of a donkey—
dragged away and thrown[p]
outside the gates of Jerusalem."

20 "Go up to Lebanon and cry out,[q]
let your voice be heard in Bashan,[r]
cry out from Abarim,[s]
for all your allies[t] are crushed.
21 I warned you when you felt secure,[u]
but you said, 'I will not listen!'
This has been your way from your
youth;[v]
you have not obeyed[w] me.
22 The wind[x] will drive all your
shepherds[y] away,
and your allies[z] will go into exile.
Then you will be ashamed and
disgraced[a]
because of all your wickedness.
23 You who live in 'Lebanon,[b][b]'
who are nestled in cedar buildings,

[a] 11 Also called *Jehoahaz* [b] 23 That is, the palace in Jerusalem (see 1 Kings 7:2)

22:11 [y] S 2Ki 23:31 **22:12** [z] 2Ki 23:34 **22:13** [a] S Isa 5:8 [b] Mic 3:10; Hab 2:9 [c] S Lev 19:13; Jas 5:4 **22:14** [d] Isa 5:8-9 [e] S 2Sa 7:2 [f] Eze 23:14 **22:15** [g] 2Ki 23:25 [h] Ps 128:2; S Isa 3:10 **22:16** [i] Ps 72:1-4, 12-13; S 82:3; S Pr 24:23 [j] S Ps 36:10 **22:17** [k] S Isa 56:11 [l] S 2Ki 24:4 [m] S Dt 28:33; Eze 18:12; Mic 2:2 **22:18** [n] S 2Sa 1:26 **22:19** [o] 2Ki 24:6 [p] Jer 8:2; 36:30 **22:20** [q] S Isa 57:13 [r] S Ps 68:15 [s] S Nu 27:12 [t] ver 22; Jer 30:14; La 1:19; Eze 16:33-34; Hos 8:9 **22:21** [u] Zec 7:7 [v] Dt 9:7; Ps 25:7; Isa 54:4; Jer 3:25; 31:19; 32:30 [w] S Jer 3:13; 7:23-28; Zep 3:2 **22:22** [x] S Dt 28:64; S Job 27:21 [y] S Jer 10:21 [z] S ver 20 [a] S Jer 7:19 **22:23** [b] S 1Ki 7:2; Eze 17:3

22:11 *Shallum.* See 1Ch 3:15. Shallum was his personal name, Jehoahaz his throne name (the latter means "The LORD seizes").
22:12 *the place where they have led him captive.* Egypt (see note on v. 10).
22:13–19 A scathing denunciation of King Jehoiakim, who is described in the third person (vv. 13–14), then rhetorically addressed in the second person (vv. 15,17) and identified by name (v. 18), meaning "The LORD raises up." Good King Josiah is referred to in vv. 15b–16 by way of contrast.
22:13 *Woe to him who builds.* See Hab 2:9,12. *by unrighteousness … by injustice.* Contrast v. 3; 21:12. *upper rooms.* See note on Jdg 3:20. *making his own people work for nothing.* Contrary to the law (see Lev 25:39; Dt 24:14–15). Jehoiakim's refusal to pay them may have been due partly to inability, since Judah was under heavy tribute to Egypt during the early part of his reign (see 2Ki 23:35).
22:14 *large windows.* The windows described here may well be the same as those found in the ruins of Beth Hakkerem (see 6:1; see also note on Ne 3:14) by archaeologists in the early 1960s. *panels.* Haggai similarly deplores the use of paneling as an extravagant and unneeded luxury in certain situations (see Hag 1:4).
22:15 *your father.* Josiah. *have food and drink.* Enjoy life (see Ecc 2:24–25; 3:12–13). *did what was right and just.* Like his ancestor David (see 2Sa 8:15); contrast v. 13 (see note there; see also note on Ps 119:121).
22:16 James defines a proper relationship to God in similar terms (Jas 1:27); contrast 5:28 (see note there). *poor and needy.* See note on 20:13. *to know me.* To love God fully, which results in living a pious life and serving those in need (see Dt 10:12–13; Hos 6:6; Mic 6:8).
22:17 *your.* Jehoiakim's (see v. 18). *dishonest gain.* See 6:13; 8:10. *shedding innocent blood.* See note on 19:4; for an illustration of Jehoiakim's cruelty in this regard, see 26:20–23. *oppression.* See v. 3; 6:6; 21:12.
22:18 Contrast 2Ch 35:24–25. *They will not mourn for him: 'Alas, my brother!'* Contrast 1Ki 13:30.
22:19 *burial of a donkey.* Tantamount to no burial at all (see 36:30); fulfilled in 2Ki 24:6, where no burial is described and where it says that Jehoiakim "rested with his ancestors," a euphemism for dying (see notes on Ge 25:8; 1Ki 1:21). *dragged away.* See 15:3.
22:20–23 The Lord speaks to Jerusalem, which is personified as a woman (see v. 23).
22:20 *Lebanon … Bashan … Abarim.* Mountainous regions (see v. 6; Nu 27:12; 33:47–48; Dt 32:49; Jdg 3:3; Ps 68:15), the first two in the north and the third in the south, suitable heights from which the whole land of Israel could be rhetorically addressed. *allies.* Lit. "lovers" (see 4:30 and note), here referring to nations joined together by treaty. Judah's one-time allies included Egypt, Assyria (see 2:36), Edom, Moab, Ammon and Phoenicia (see 27:3), all of whom had been—or soon would be—conquered by Babylonia (see 27:6–7; 28:14). *crushed.* See 14:17.
22:21 *not listen … not obeyed me.* See 7:22–26; 11:7–8. *your youth.* The days of Israel's early history in Egypt (see 2:2 and note; Hos 2:15).
22:22 *wind will drive … away.* See 13:24; Job 27:21; Isa 27:8. *shepherds.* See 2:8 and note; 10:21; 23:1–4. The initial fulfillment of this verse took place in 597 BC (see 2Ki 24:12–16).
22:23 *Lebanon … cedar.* See NIV text note; see also 21:14 and note; Eze 17:3–4,12. *pain like that of a woman in labor.* See 4:19,31 and notes.

how you will groan when pangs come
upon you,
pain[c] like that of a woman in labor!

24 "As surely as I live," declares the LORD,
"even if you, Jehoiachin[a][d] son of Jehoiakim king of Judah, were a signet ring[e]
on my right hand, I would still pull you
off. 25 I will deliver[f] you into the hands
of those who want to kill you, those you
fear — Nebuchadnezzar king of Babylon
and the Babylonians.[b] 26 I will hurl[g] you
and the mother[h] who gave you birth into
another country, where neither of you was
born, and there you both will die. 27 You
will never come back to the land you long
to return[i] to."

28 Is this man Jehoiachin[j] a despised,
broken pot,[k]
an object no one wants?
Why will he and his children be
hurled[l] out,
cast into a land[m] they do not know?
29 O land,[n] land, land,
hear the word of the LORD!
30 This is what the LORD says:
"Record this man as if childless,[o]
a man who will not prosper[p] in his
lifetime,
for none of his offspring[q] will prosper,
none will sit on the throne[r] of
David
or rule anymore in Judah."

22:23 [c]S Jer 4:31 **22:24** [d]S 2Ki 24:6, 8 [e]S Ge 38:18 **22:25** [f]S 2Ki 24:16; S 2Ch 36:10 **22:26** [g]S 1Sa 25:29; S 2Ki 24:8; 2Ch 36:10; S Isa 22:17; Eze 19:9-14 [h]S 1Ki 2:19 **22:27** [i]S ver 10 **22:28** [j]S 2Ki 24:6 [k]Ps 31:12; S Jer 19:10; 25:34; 48:38 [l]Jer 15:1 [m]S Jer 17:4 **22:29** [n]S Jer 6:19 **22:30** [o]1Ch 3:18; Jer 38:23; 52:10; Mt 1:12 [p]Jer 10:21 [q]S Job 18:19 [r]S Ps 94:20

23:1 [s]Jer 10:21; 12:10; 25:36; Eze 34:1-10; Zec 10:2; Zec 11:15-17 [t]S Isa 56:11 [u]Ps 100:3; S Jer 13:17; Eze 34:31 **23:2** [v]Jn 10:8 [w]S Jer 10:21; 13:20 [x]Jer 21:12; Eze 34:8-10 **23:3** [y]Isa 11:10-12; Jer 32:37; Eze 34:11-16 [z]S 1Ki 8:48 **23:4** [a]S Ge 48:15; S Isa 31:4; Jer 31:10 [b]Jer 30:10; 46:27-28 [c]S Jn 6:39 **23:5** [d]S 2Ki 19:26; S Isa 4:2; Eze 17:22 [e]S Mt 2:2 [f]Isa 9:7; S Mt 1:1 [g]S Ge 18:19

The Righteous Branch

23 "Woe to the shepherds[s] who are
destroying and scattering[t] the
sheep of my pasture!"[u] declares the LORD.
2 Therefore this is what the LORD, the God
of Israel, says to the shepherds[v] who tend
my people: "Because you have scattered
my flock[w] and driven them away and have
not bestowed care on them, I will bestow
punishment on you for the evil[x] you have
done," declares the LORD. 3 "I myself will
gather the remnant[y] of my flock out of all
the countries where I have driven them
and will bring them back to their pasture,[z]
where they will be fruitful and increase
in number. 4 I will place shepherds[a] over
them who will tend them, and they will no
longer be afraid[b] or terrified, nor will any
be missing,[c]" declares the LORD.

5 "The days are coming," declares the
LORD,
"when I will raise up for David[c] a
righteous Branch,[d]
a King[e] who will reign[f] wisely
and do what is just and right[g] in the
land.

[a] *24* Hebrew *Koniah,* a variant of *Jehoiachin;* also in verse 28 [b] *25* Or *Chaldeans* [c] *5* Or *up from David's line*

22:24–30 A prophecy against King Jehoiachin (fulfilled in 24:1; 29:2), who was also known as Koniah (see NIV text note on v. 24), a shortened form of Jeconiah (see NIV text note on 24:1); see Introduction: Background. All three forms of the name mean "The LORD establishes."
22:24 *As surely as I live.* See note on Ge 42:15. *even if you … were a signet ring.* The curse on Jehoiachin is apparently reversed in Hag 2:23 (see note there).
22:25 *deliver you into the hands of … those you fear.* Contrast 39:17.
22:26 Fulfilled in 597 BC (see 29:2; 2Ki 24:15). *hurl … into another country.* Send into exile in Babylonia (see 7:15; 16:13; Dt 29:28). *you and the mother who gave you birth.* Jehoiachin and Nehushta (see note on 13:18).
22:28 Two rhetorical questions, answered in v. 30. *broken pot … hurled out.* Jehoiachin and his descendants, like Judah itself (see 19:10–11), are under God's judgment. *he and his children.* Though Jehoiachin was only 18 years old at the time of his exile (see 2Ki 24:8), he already had more than one wife (see 2Ki 24:15) and therefore probably one or more children.
22:29 *land, land, land.* The repetition implies the strongest possible emphasis and intensity (see 7:4 and note; 23:30–32; Isa 6:3 and note; Eze 21:27).
22:30 *as if childless.* Not in the sense of Jehoiachin's having no children at all (he had at least seven; see 1Ch 3:17–18), but of having none to sit on the throne of David in Judah. Jehoiachin's grandson Zerubbabel (1Ch 3:17–19; Mt 1:12) became governor of Judah (see Hag 1:1), but not king. Zedekiah was a son of Josiah (see 37:1), not of Jehoiachin, and he and his sons died before the latter (see 52:10–11). Jehoiachin therefore was Judah's last surviving Davidic king — until Christ.

23:1–8 A summary statement (probably dating to Zedekiah's reign; see note on v. 6) that includes God's intention to judge the wicked rulers and leaders of Judah (vv. 1–2), to ultimately bring his people back from exile (vv. 3–4,7–8) and to raise up an ideal Davidic King (vv. 5–6).
23:1 See 10:21 and note. *sheep.* The people of Judah (see v. 2).
23:2 *bestowed care … bestow punishment.* The same Hebrew root underlies both phrases (see v. 4 and note). What Judah's rulers had failed to do is summarized in Eze 34:4.
23:3 *remnant.* See note on 6:9. *I have driven.* Although Judah's sins and the sins of her leaders had caused the people to be "driven … away" (v. 2) into exile, the Lord himself ultimately carried out the results of their repeated violations of their covenant commitments. *be fruitful and increase.* See note on Ge 1:28.
23:4 *be afraid … terrified.* The absence of a concerned shepherd invites attacks by wild animals (see Eze 34:8). *be missing.* See Nu 31:49. The Hebrew root underlying this phrase is the same as that for "bestowed care" and "bestow punishment" in v. 2 (see note there).
23:5–6 One of the most important Messianic passages in Jeremiah, echoed in 33:15–16.
23:5 *raise up.* See 2Sa 7:12; see also 30:9; Eze 34:23–24; 37:24. The Hebrew for this phrase is translated "place" in v. 4. *for David.* See NIV text note; see also Mt 1:1 and NIV text note. The Messiah, unlike any previous descendant of David, would be the ideal King. He would sum up in himself all the finest qualities of the best rulers, and infinitely more. *Branch.* A Messianic title (see notes on Isa 4:2; 11:1; Zec 3:8; 6:12). The Targum (ancient Aramaic paraphrase) reads "Messiah" here. *reign wisely.* See note on Isa 52:13. *do what is just*

[6] In his days Judah will be saved
and Israel will live in safety.[h]
This is the name[i] by which he will be called:
The LORD Our Righteous Savior.[j]

[7] "So then, the days are coming,"[k] declares
the LORD, "when people will no longer say,
'As surely as the LORD lives, who brought
the Israelites up out of Egypt,'[l] [8] but they
will say, 'As surely as the LORD lives, who
brought the descendants of Israel up out
of the land of the north and out of all the
countries where he had banished them.'
Then they will live in their own land."[m]

Lying Prophets

[9] Concerning the prophets:

My heart[n] is broken within me;
all my bones tremble.[o]
I am like a drunken man,
like a strong man overcome by wine,
because of the LORD
and his holy words.[p]
[10] The land is full of adulterers;[q]
because of the curse[a][r] the land lies parched
and the pastures[s] in the wilderness are withered.[t]
The prophets follow an evil course
and use their power unjustly.

[11] "Both prophet and priest are godless;[u]
even in my temple[v] I find their wickedness,"
declares the LORD.
[12] "Therefore their path will become slippery;[w]
they will be banished to darkness
and there they will fall.
I will bring disaster on them
in the year they are punished,[x]"
declares the LORD.

[13] "Among the prophets of Samaria
I saw this repulsive thing:
They prophesied by Baal[y]
and led my people Israel astray.[z]
[14] And among the prophets of Jerusalem
I have seen something horrible:[a]
They commit adultery and live a lie.[b]
They strengthen the hands of evildoers,[c]
so that not one of them turns from their wickedness.[d]
They are all like Sodom[e] to me;
the people of Jerusalem are like Gomorrah."[f]

[15] Therefore this is what the LORD Almighty says concerning the prophets:

"I will make them eat bitter food
and drink poisoned water,[g]
because from the prophets of Jerusalem
ungodliness[h] has spread throughout the land."

[16] This is what the LORD Almighty says:

"Do not listen[i] to what the prophets
are prophesying to you;
they fill you with false hopes.
They speak visions[j] from their own minds,
not from the mouth[k] of the LORD.
[17] They keep saying[l] to those who despise me,
'The LORD says: You will have peace.'[m]

[a] 10 Or *because of these things*

23:6 [h] S Lev 25:18; S Dt 32:8; Hos 2:18 [i] Ex 23:21; Jer 33:16; Mt 1:21-23 [j] S Ezr 9:15; S Isa 42:6; Ro 3:21-22; S 1Co 1:30 **23:7** [k] Jer 30:3 [l] S Dt 15:15 **23:8** [m] S Isa 14:1; S 43:5-6; Jer 30:10; Eze 20:42; 34:13; Am 9:14-15 **23:9** [n] S Jer 4:19 [o] S Job 4:14 [p] Jer 20:8-9 **23:10** [q] S Jer 9:2 [r] Dt 28:23-24 [s] Ps 107:34; S Jer 9:10 [t] S Jer 4:26; S 12:11 **23:11** [u] Jer 6:13; S 8:10; Zep 3:4 [v] S 2Ki 21:4; S Jer 7:10 **23:12** [w] S Dt 32:35; S Job 3:23; Jer 13:16 [x] Jer 11:23 **23:13** [y] S 1Ki 18:22 [z] ver 32; S Isa 3:12; Eze 13:10 **23:14** [a] S Jer 5:30; Hos 6:10 [b] Jer 29:23 [c] ver 22 [d] S Isa 5:18 [e] S Ge 18:20; Mt 11:24 [f] Jer 20:16; Am 4:11 **23:15** [g] S Jer 8:14; 9:15 [h] S Jer 8:10 **23:16** [i] Jer 27:9-10, 14; S Mt 7:15 [j] S Jer 14:14; Eze 13:3 [k] Jer 9:20 **23:17** [l] ver 31 [m] S 1Ki 22:8; S Jer 4:10

and right. See 22:3,15 and note on 22:15; said also of King David (see 2Sa 8:15).

23:6 *Judah ... and Israel.* God's reunited people will be restored (see 31:31 and note; Eze 37:15–22). *be saved ... live in safety.* The deliverance will be both spiritual and physical (see Dt 33:28–29). *The LORD Our Righteous Savior.* Although Zedekiah did not live up to the meaning of his name, "The LORD is my righteousness," the Messiah would bestow on his people the abundant blessings (see Eze 34:25–31) that come from the hands of a King who does "what is just and right" (v. 5).

23:7–8 Repeated almost verbatim from 16:14–15 (see notes there).

23:9–40 False prophets denounced (see 2:8; 4:9; 5:30–31; 6:13–15; 8:10–12; 14:13–15; 18:18–23; 26:8,11,16; 27–28; Isa 28:7–13; Eze 13; Mic 3:5–12).

23:9 *Concerning.* Introduces headings also in 46:2; 48:1; 49:1,7,23,28. *his holy words.* Contrast the unholy words of the false prophets (see vv. 16–18).

23:10 See Isa 24:4–6. *adulterers.* See 5:7–8; 9:2 and notes. *curse.* Brought on by violating the Lord's covenant (see 11:3 and note; 11:8). *parched ... withered.* See 12:4 and note. To worship other gods is to deny to the land the fertility that only the Lord can bring (see Hos 2:5–8,21–22; Am 4:4–9). *pastures in the wilderness.* See note on 9:10. *evil course.* Evil because it is their own and not God's (see 8:6).

23:11 *even in my temple ... wickedness.* For examples, see 32:34; 2Ki 16:10–14; 21:5; Eze 8:5,10,14,16.

23:12 *their path will become slippery ... banished to darkness.* See Ps 35:5–6; see also Ps 73:18.

23:13 *prophesied by Baal.* See 2:8 and note; see also 1Ki 18:19–40.

23:14 *They ... live a lie.* See 14:13 and note; cf. 1Jn 1:6. *strengthen the hands of.* The Hebrew underlying this phrase is translated "encouraged" in Eze 13:22. *not one of them turns from their wickedness.* See Eze 13:22. *like Sodom ... like Gomorrah.* See note on 20:16.

23:15 *I will make ... poisoned water.* Repeated almost verbatim from 9:15 (see note there). *ungodliness.* See v. 11.

23:16 *visions.* "Revelations" or "prophecies" (see 1Sa 3:1; Pr 29:18; Isa 1:1; Ob 1 and notes). *from their own minds.* See v. 26; 14:14. False prophets are like preachers of a "different gospel" (Gal 1:6–9).

23:17 *You will have peace.* The essential message of the false prophets (see 6:14 and note; 8:11; 14:13 and note; cf. 28:8–9). *stubbornness of their hearts.* See note on 3:17.

And to all who follow the
stubbornness[n] of their hearts
they say, 'No harm[o] will come to you.'
18 But which of them has stood in the
council[p] of the LORD
to see or to hear his word?
Who has listened and heard his
word?
19 See, the storm[q] of the LORD
will burst out in wrath,
a whirlwind[r] swirling down
on the heads of the wicked.
20 The anger[s] of the LORD will not turn
back[t]
until he fully accomplishes
the purposes of his heart.
In days to come
you will understand it clearly.
21 I did not send[u] these prophets,
yet they have run with their message;
I did not speak to them,
yet they have prophesied.
22 But if they had stood in my council,[v]
they would have proclaimed[w] my
words to my people
and would have turned[x] them from
their evil ways
and from their evil deeds.[y]

23 "Am I only a God nearby,[z]"
declares the LORD,
"and not a God far away?
24 Who can hide[a] in secret places
so that I cannot see them?"
declares the LORD.
"Do not I fill heaven and earth?"[b]
declares the LORD.

25 "I have heard what the prophets say
who prophesy lies[c] in my name. They say,
'I had a dream![d] I had a dream!' 26 How
long will this continue in the hearts of
these lying prophets, who prophesy the
delusions[e] of their own minds?[f] 27 They
think the dreams they tell one another will
make my people forget[g] my name, just as
their ancestors forgot[h] my name through
Baal worship.[i] 28 Let the prophet who has a
dream[j] recount the dream, but let the one
who has my word[k] speak it faithfully. For
what has straw to do with grain?" declares
the LORD. 29 "Is not my word like fire,"[l] declares the LORD, "and like a hammer[m] that
breaks a rock in pieces?
30 "Therefore," declares the LORD, "I
am against[n] the prophets[o] who steal from
one another words supposedly from me.
31 Yes," declares the LORD, "I am against
the prophets who wag their own tongues
and yet declare, 'The LORD declares.'[p] 32 Indeed, I am against those who prophesy
false dreams,[q]" declares the LORD. "They
tell them and lead my people astray[r] with
their reckless lies,[s] yet I did not send[t] or
appoint them. They do not benefit[u] these
people in the least," declares the LORD.

False Prophecy

33 "When these people, or a prophet or
a priest, ask you, 'What is the message[v]
from the LORD?' say to them, 'What message? I will forsake[w] you, declares the
LORD.' 34 If a prophet or a priest or anyone else claims, 'This is a message[x] from
the LORD,' I will punish[y] them and their
household. 35 This is what each of you

23:17 [n] S Jer 13:10 [o] Jer 5:12; Am 9:10; Mic 3:11 **23:18** [p] S 1Ki 22:19; S Ro 11:34 **23:19** [q] Isa 30:30; Jer 25:32; 30:23 [r] Zec 7:14 **23:20** [s] S 2Ki 23:26 [t] S Jer 4:28 **23:21** [u] S Jer 14:14; 27:15 **23:22** [v] S 1Ki 22:19 [w] S Dt 33:10 [x] S 2Ki 17:13; Jer 25:5; Zec 1:4 [y] ver 14; Am 3:7 **23:23** [z] Ps 139:1-10 **23:24** [a] S Ge 3:8; S Job 11:20; 22:12-14; S Ecc 12:14; S Isa 28:15; 1Co 4:5 [b] S 1Ki 8:27 **23:25** [c] ver 16; Jer 14:14; 27:10 [d] ver 28, 32; S Dt 13:1; Jer 27:9; 29:8 **23:26** [e] S Isa 30:10; 1Ti 4:1-2 [f] Jer 14:14; Eze 13:2 **23:27** [g] Dt 13:1-3; Jer 29:8 [h] S Jdg 3:7; S 8:33-34 [i] S Jer 2:23 **23:28** [j] S ver 25 [k] S 1Sa 3:17 **23:29** [l] S Ps 39:3; Jer 5:14; S 1Co 3:13

[m] Heb 4:12 **23:30** [n] S Ps 34:16 [o] ver 2; Dt 18:20; Jer 14:15; S 21:13 **23:31** [p] ver 17 **23:32** [q] S ver 25 [r] S ver 13; S Jer 50:6 [s] S Job 13:4; Eze 13:3; 22:28 [t] S Jer 14:14 [u] Jer 7:8; La 2:14 **23:33** [v] Mal 1:1 [w] S 2Ki 21:14 **23:34** [x] La 2:14 [y] Zec 13:3

23:18 *council of the LORD.* God's heavenly confidants (see v. 22; Job 15:7–10 and note; see also 1Ki 22:19–22; Job 1:6; 2:1; 29:4 and note; Ps 89:7). In Am 3:7 the Hebrew for "council" is translated "plan," the purposes that God has promised to reveal to his chosen servants (see v. 20).
23:19–20 Repeated almost verbatim in 30:23–24.
23:19 *storm ... whirlwind.* A vivid image of God's wrath.
23:20 *you will understand it clearly.* Unlike the false prophets, who continued to mislead their hearers even in Babylonia after the exile of 597 BC (see 29:20–23).
23:21 *I did not send.* See v. 32; 29:9; contrast 1:7; Isa 6:8; Eze 3:5. *did not speak to them.* See 29:23.
23:22 *my council.* See note on v. 18.
23:23 *God nearby ... God far away.* God is both immanent and transcendent; he lives "in a high and holy place, but also with the one who is ... lowly in spirit" (Isa 57:15).
23:24 *hide ... so that I cannot see them.* See Job 26:6; Ps 139:7–12; Am 9:2–4. *I fill heaven and earth.* See Isa 66:1.
23:25 *lies.* See 5:12. *in my name.* See Dt 18:20,22. *dream.* An infrequent mode of divine revelation to a true prophet (see 27:9; Dt 13:1–3; 1Sa 28:6; Zec 10:2; but cf. Nu 12:6; Joel 2:28).
23:26 *hearts ... minds.* The Hebrew is the same for both words (see note on Ps 4:7). *their own minds.* See note on v. 16.
23:27 *my name.* To forget the Lord's name is tantamount to forgetting him (see note on Ps 5:11). *forgot ... through Baal worship.* When Judah's ancestors forgot God, they began to serve Baal (see Jdg 3:7; 1Sa 12:9–10). *forgot.* See Ps 9:17 and note.
23:28–29 The true word of God is symbolized in three figures of speech (grain, fire, hammer).
23:28 *straw ... grain.* Of the two, only grain can feed and nourish (see note on 15:16).
23:29 *like fire.* See note on 20:9. The fire of the divine word ultimately tests "the quality of each person's work" (1Co 3:13; see note there). *like a hammer.* Similarly, the divine word works relentlessly, like a sword or hammer, to judge "the thoughts and attitudes of the heart" (Heb 4:12; see note there).
23:30–32 *I am against.* The threefold statement is for emphasis (see note on 22:29).
23:31 *prophets who ... declare.* False prophets are claiming that their own prophecies are the messages of God. The Hebrew for this verb is used only here with someone other than God as the subject. The phrase "declares the LORD" or its equivalent occurs hundreds of times in the OT, more frequently in Jeremiah (over 175 times) than in any other book.
23:32 *did not send.* See v. 21 and note.
23:33 *message.* The Hebrew for this word can also mean "burden," a term that may refer to a burdensome message from the Lord (see, e.g., Na 1:1).

A basket of bad figs and a basket of good figs, as in Jeremiah 24

Todd Bolen/www.BiblePlaces.com

keeps saying to your friends
and other Israelites: 'What is
the LORD's answer?'[z] or 'What
has the LORD spoken?' 36 But you
must not mention 'a message
from the LORD' again, because
each one's word becomes their
own message. So you distort[a]
the words of the living God,[b] the
LORD Almighty, our God. 37 This
is what you keep saying to a
prophet: 'What is the LORD's answer to you?' or 'What has the
LORD spoken?' 38 Although you
claim, 'This is a message from
the LORD,' this is what the LORD
says: You used the words, 'This
is a message from the LORD,'
even though I told you that you
must not claim, 'This is a message from the LORD.' 39 Therefore,
I will surely forget you and cast[c] you out
of my presence along with the city I gave
to you and your ancestors. 40 I will bring
on you everlasting disgrace[d]—everlasting
shame that will not be forgotten."

Two Baskets of Figs

24 After Jehoiachin[a][e] son of Jehoiakim
king of Judah and the officials, the
skilled workers and the artisans of Judah
were carried into exile from Jerusalem to
Babylon by Nebuchadnezzar king of Babylon, the LORD showed me two baskets of
figs[f] placed in front of the temple of the
LORD. 2 One basket had very good figs, like
those that ripen early;[g] the other basket
had very bad[h] figs, so bad they could not
be eaten.
3 Then the LORD asked me, "What do
you see,[i] Jeremiah?"
"Figs," I answered. "The good ones are
very good, but the bad ones are so bad
they cannot be eaten."
4 Then the word of the LORD came to me:
5 "This is what the LORD, the God of Israel, says: 'Like these good figs, I regard
as good the exiles from Judah, whom
I sent[j] away from this place to the land
of the Babylonians.[b] 6 My eyes will watch
over them for their good, and I will bring
them back[k] to this land. I will build[l] them
up and not tear them down; I will plant[m]
them and not uproot them. 7 I will give
them a heart to know[n] me, that I am the
LORD. They will be my people,[o] and I will
be their God, for they will return[p] to me
with all their heart.[q]
8 " 'But like the bad[r] figs, which are so

[a] *1* Hebrew *Jeconiah,* a variant of *Jehoiachin*
[b] *5* Or *Chaldeans*

23:35 [z] Jer 33:3; 42:4 **23:36** [a] Gal 1:7-8; 2Pe 3:16 [b] S Jos 3:10 **23:39** [c] S Jer 7:15 **23:40** [d] S Jer 20:11; Eze 5:14-15 **24:1** [e] S 2Ki 24:16; S 2Ch 36:9 [f] Ex 23:19; Dt 26:2; Am 8:1-2 **24:2** [g] S SS 2:13 [h] S Isa 5:4 **24:3** [i] Jer 1:11; Am 8:2 **24:5** [j] Jer 29:4,20 **24:6** [k] S Dt 30:3; Jer 27:22; 29:10; 30:3; Eze 11:17 [l] Jer 33:7; 42:10 [m] S Dt 30:9; S Jer 1:10; Am 9:14-15 **24:7** [n] S Isa 11:9 [o] S Lev 26:12; S Isa 51:16; S Zec 2:11; Heb 8:10 [p] Jer 32:40 [q] S 2Ch 6:37; Eze 11:19 **24:8** [r] Jer 29:17

23:36 The three divine titles at the end of the verse enhance the solemnity of what is being said. *living God.* See 10:10; Dt 5:26.
23:39 *forget.* The Hebrew for this word is a pun on the Hebrew for the word "message" in vv. 33–34,36,38—by which Jeremiah highlights his word of judgment. *the city.* Jerusalem.
23:40 Echoed from 20:11.
24:1–10 See Am 8:1–3. Having denounced Judah's leaders (21:1—23:8) and false prophets (23:9–40), Jeremiah now describes the division of Judah's people into good and bad (24:1–3) and summarizes the Lord's determination to restore the good (vv. 4–7) but destroy the bad (vv. 8–10).
24:1 *Jehoiachin … and the officials … were carried into exile.* In 597 BC. *skilled workers and the artisans.* See 29:2; 2Ki 24:14,16. Only the poorest and weakest people were left behind in Judah (see 2Ki 24:14; for the later period [586], cf. Jer 39:10). *the LORD showed me.* A common way of introducing prophetic visions (see Am 7:1,4,7). *figs.* See note on 8:13. *placed.* The Hebrew root underlying this word is translated "meet" in Ex 29:42–43. As the Lord desired to "meet" with the Israelites at the entrance to the tabernacle, so the figs (symbolizing the people of Judah) would be "met" by him in front of the Jerusalem temple.
24:2 *very good figs … that ripen early.* The first figs in June are especially juicy and delicious (see Isa 28:4; Hos 9:10; Mic 7:1; Na 3:12). See photo above.
24:3 *What do you see … ?* See note on 1:11.
24:5–6 Just as good figs should be protected and preserved by their owner, so also the exiles of 597 BC, who were the best of Judah's leaders and craftsmen (see 2Ki 24:14–16), would be watched over and cared for by the Lord (see 29:4–14). See photo, p. 1268.
24:6 *My eyes will watch over them for their good.* Contrast the word of judgment in Am 9:4. *bring them back.* In 538/537 BC. *build them up … tear them down … plant … uproot.* See 1:10 and note.
24:7 *a heart to know me.* For a more comprehensive prediction including the same promise, see 31:31–34. *my people … their God.* The classic statement of covenant relationship (see 31:33; 32:38; see also notes on 7:23; Ge 17:7; Zec 8:8). *with all their heart.* See 29:13.
24:8 *live in Egypt.* Perhaps those deported with Jehoahaz in 609 BC (see 22:10b–12 and notes; 2Ki 23:31–34) and/or

A wall painting from Beni Hasan (1920 – 1900 BC) showing men gathering figs

Z. Radovan/www.BibleLandPictures.com

bad they cannot be eaten,' says the LORD, 'so will I deal with Zedekiah[s] king of Judah, his officials[t] and the survivors[u] from Jerusalem, whether they remain in this land or live in Egypt.[v] 9 I will make them abhorrent[w] and an offense to all the kingdoms of the earth, a reproach and a byword,[x] a curse[ay] and an object of ridicule, wherever I banish[z] them. 10 I will send the sword,[a] famine[b] and plague[c] against them until they are destroyed from the land I gave to them and their ancestors.[d]' "

Seventy Years of Captivity

25 The word came to Jeremiah concerning all the people of Judah in the fourth year of Jehoiakim[e] son of Josiah king of Judah, which was the first year of Nebuchadnezzar[f] king of Babylon. 2 So Jeremiah the prophet said to all the people of Judah[g] and to all those living in Jerusalem: 3 For twenty-three years—from the thirteenth year of Josiah[h] son of Amon king of Judah until this very day—the word of the LORD has come to me and I have spoken to you again and again,[i] but you have not listened.[j]

4 And though the LORD has sent all his servants the prophets[k] to you again and again, you have not listened or paid any attention.[l] 5 They said, "Turn[m] now, each

24:8 [s] Jer 32:4-5; 38:18, 23; 39:5; 44:30 [t] Jer 39:6 [u] Jer 39:9 [v] Jer 44:1, 26; 46:14 **24:9** [w] S Jer 15:4; 25:18 [x] S Dt 28:25; S 1Ki 9:7 [y] S 2Ki 22:19; S Jer 29:18 [z] S Dt 28:37; Da 9:7 **24:10** [a] S Isa 51:19; S Jer 9:16; Rev 6:8 [b] Jer 15:2 [c] Jer 27:8 [d] S Dt 28:21 **25:1** [e] S 2Ki 24:2 [f] S 2Ki 24:1 **25:2** [g] Jer 18:11 **25:3** [h] S 1Ch 3:14 [i] Jer 11:7; 26:5 [j] S Isa 65:12; S Jer 7:26 **25:4** [k] Jer 6:17; S 7:25; 29:19 [l] S Jer 7:26; 34:14; 44:5 **25:5** [m] S Jdg 6:8; S 2Ch 7:14; S 30:9; S Jer 23:22

[a] 9 That is, their names will be used in cursing (see 29:22); or, others will see that they are cursed.

those who fled to Egypt after the Babylonians defeated the Egyptians in the battle of Carchemish in 605 (see 46:2).

24:9 *abhorrent … to all the kingdoms.* See 34:17. *reproach … object of ridicule.* See Dt 28:37. *byword.* See notes on 1Ki 9:7; Job 17:6.

24:10 *sword, famine and plague.* See note on 14:12. *destroyed from the land.* In 586 BC (see 52:4 – 27).

25:1 — 29:32 The dominant theme in chs. 25 – 29 is the forthcoming destruction of Jerusalem and exile to Babylonia in 586 BC (hinted at briefly in 24:10).

25:1 - 38 Divine judgment will descend not only on Judah but on "all the surrounding nations" (v. 9) as well (see notes on 46:1 — 51:64; Isa 13:1 — 23:18; Am 1:3 — 2:16; 5:18; Mic 1:2; Zep 2:4 — 3:8).

25:1 *fourth year of Jehoiakim … first year of Nebuchadnezzar.* The synchronism yields the date 605 BC (see note on Da 1:1).

25:3 *twenty-three years.* Nineteen under Josiah and four under Jehoiakim (see v. 1). *thirteenth year of Josiah.* 626 BC (or possibly as early as 627); see 1:2. *again and again.* See v. 4; see also note on 7:13. *you have not listened.* Jeremiah, now halfway through his prophetic ministry, had been warned at the time of his call that the people of Judah would oppose him (see 1:17 – 19).

25:4 Echoed from 7:25 – 26; see also 35:15. *his servants the prophets.* See note on 7:25.

25:5 *stay in the land the LORD gave … your ancestors for ever and ever.* Echoed from 7:7; see Ge 17:8 and note.

of you, from your evil ways and your evil
practices, and you can stay in the land[n] the
LORD gave to you and your ancestors for
ever and ever. 6Do not follow other gods[o]
to serve and worship them; do not arouse
my anger with what your hands have
made. Then I will not harm you."
7"But you did not listen to me," declares
the LORD, "and you have aroused[p] my anger with what your hands have made,[q] and
you have brought harm[r] to yourselves."
8Therefore the LORD Almighty says
this: "Because you have not listened to
my words, 9I will summon[s] all the peoples of the north[t] and my servant[u] Nebuchadnezzar[v] king of Babylon," declares
the LORD, "and I will bring them against
this land and its inhabitants and against
all the surrounding nations. I will completely destroy[aw] them and make them an
object of horror and scorn,[x] and an everlasting ruin.[y] 10I will banish from them the
sounds[z] of joy and gladness, the voices of
bride and bridegroom,[a] the sound of millstones[b] and the light of the lamp.[c] 11This
whole country will become a desolate
wasteland,[d] and these nations will serve[e]
the king of Babylon seventy years.[f]
12"But when the seventy years[g] are fulfilled, I will punish the king of Babylon[h]
and his nation, the land of the Babylonians,[b] for their guilt," declares the LORD,
"and will make it desolate[i] forever. 13I will
bring on that land all the things I have spoken against it, all that are written[j] in this
book and prophesied by Jeremiah against
all the nations. 14They themselves will
be enslaved[k] by many nations[l] and great
kings; I will repay[m] them according to their
deeds and the work of their hands."

The Cup of God's Wrath

15This is what the LORD, the God of
Israel, said to me: "Take from my hand
this cup[n] filled with the wine of my wrath
and make all the nations to whom I send[o]
you drink it. 16When they drink[p] it, they
will stagger[q] and go mad[r] because of the
sword[s] I will send among them."
17So I took the cup from the LORD's
hand and made all the nations to whom
he sent[t] me drink it: 18Jerusalem[u] and the
towns of Judah, its kings and officials, to
make them a ruin[v] and an object of horror
and scorn,[w] a curse[cx]—as they are today;[y]
19Pharaoh king[z] of Egypt,[a] his attendants,
his officials and all his people, 20and all
the foreign people there; all the kings of
Uz;[b] all the kings of the Philistines[c] (those
of Ashkelon,[d] Gaza,[e] Ekron, and the people

25:5 [n]S Ge 12:7; S Dt 4:40 **25:6** [o]S Ex 20:3; S Dt 8:19 **25:7** [p]Jer 30:14; 32:35; 44:5 [q]Dt 32:21 [r]2Ki 17:20; 21:15 **25:9** [s]Isa 13:3-5 [t]S Isa 14:31 [u]S Isa 41:2; Jer 27:6 [v]S 2Ch 36:6 [w]S Nu 21:2 [x]S 2Ch 29:8 [y]S Jer 19:8; S 20:4; Eze 12:20 **25:10** [z]S Isa 24:8; Eze 26:13 [a]Jer 7:34; 33:11 [b]Ecc 12:3-4 [c]S Job 18:5; La 5:15; Rev 18:22-23 **25:11** [d]S Lev 26:31, 32; Jer 4:26-27; 12:11-12 [e]Jer 28:14 [f]S 2Ch 36:21 **25:12** [g]Jer 27:7; 29:10 [h]S Ge 10:10; S Ps 137:8 [i]S Isa 13:19-22; 14:22-23 **25:13** [j]S Isa 30:8 **25:14** [k]Isa 14:6; Jer 27:7 [l]Jer 50:9; 51:27-28 [m]S Dt 32:41; S Job 21:19; S Jer 51:6 **25:15** [n]S Isa 51:17; Jer 49:12; La 4:21; Eze 23:31; Rev 14:10 [o]Jer 1:5 **25:16** [p]ver 26 [q]S Ps 60:3 [r]Jer 51:7 [s]ver 27-29 **25:17** [t]Jer 1:10; 27:3 **25:18** [u]S Jer 13:13 [v]S Job 12:19 [w]S 2Ch 29:8 [x]S Jer 24:9 [y]S Ge 19:13; Jer 44:22 **25:19** [z]S 2Ki 18:21 [a]Isa 19:1; 20:3; Jer 44:30; Eze 29:2 **25:20** [b]S Ge 10:23 [c]S Jos 13:3; S 2Ch 26:6; S 28:18; Zep 2:4-7 [d]Jer 47:5; Am 1:7-8 [e]S Ge 10:19

[a] *9* The Hebrew term refers to the irrevocable giving over of things or persons to the LORD, often by totally destroying them. [b] *12* Or *Chaldeans* [c] *18* That is, their names to be used in cursing (see 29:22); or, to be seen by others as cursed

25:6 *arouse my anger.* See 7:18; Dt 31:29. *what your hands have made.* Idols (see note on 1:16).

25:7 *brought harm to yourselves.* See 7:6.

25:9 *peoples of the north.* Babylonia and her allies (see 1:15 and note). *my servant Nebuchadnezzar.* See 27:6; 43:10. "Servant" is used here not in the sense of "worshiper" but of "vassal" or "agent of judgment," just as the pagan ruler Cyrus is called the Lord's "shepherd" in Isa 44:28 and his "anointed" in Isa 45:1. *this land.* Judah. *surrounding nations.* Named in vv. 19–26. *completely destroy.* See NIV text note; 50:21,26; 51:3; see also note on Dt 2:34. *object of horror and scorn.* See note on 18:16. *everlasting ruin.* See 49:13; Ps 74:3; Isa 58:12 and note.

25:11–12 *seventy years.* This round number (as in Ps 90:10; Isa 23:15) represents the period from 605 (see notes on v. 1; Da 1:1) to 538/537 BC, which marked the beginning of Judah's return from exile (see 2Ch 36:20–23; see also notes on Da 9:1–2). The 70 years of Zec 1:12 are not necessarily the same as those here and in 29:10. They probably represent the period from 586 (when Solomon's temple was destroyed) to 516 (when Zerubbabel's temple was completed). See note on Zec 7:5.

25:11 *This ... country ... and these nations.* Judah and the nations named in vv. 19–26.

25:12 *punish the king ... and his nation.* See 50:18. The city of Babylon was captured by the Medes and Persians in 539 BC (near the end of Jeremiah's 70 years; see note on vv. 11–12). *for their guilt.* See 50:11,31–32; 51:6,49,53,56; Isa 13:19. *make it desolate forever.* See 50:12–13; 51:26; see also note on Isa 13:20.

25:13 *book.* After this word, the Septuagint (the pre-Christian Greek translation of the OT) inserts the material found in chs. 46–51, though rearranged.

25:14 *many nations.* Media, Persia and their allies. *great kings.* Cyrus and his associates. *repay them according to their deeds.* See 50:29; 51:24; Pr 26:27 and note.

25:15 *cup filled with the wine of my wrath.* Symbolic of divine judgment, especially against wicked nations (see Isa 51:17 and note; see also Jer 51:7; Rev 18:6). *nations to whom I send you.* See 1:5 and note.

25:16 *stagger and go mad.* See 13:12–14 and notes; Rev 14:8. *because of the sword.* As the sting of wine causes people to stagger, so the stroke of the sword causes them to fall, never to rise again (see v. 27).

25:17 A symbolic description of Jeremiah's announcement of divine judgment against the nations.

25:18 *Jerusalem and ... Judah.* God's own people are to be judged first (see v. 29; see also Eze 9:6; 1Pe 4:17). *its kings.* See note on 17:20. *ruin ... horror ... scorn ... curse.* See vv. 9,11; 18:16; 19:8.

25:19–26 The roster of nations begins with Egypt and ends with Babylonia, as in chs. 46–51; but Damascus (see 49:23–27) is omitted, and a few other regions are added.

25:19 *Egypt.* See 46:2–28.

25:20 *foreign people.* See v. 24; Ne 13:3. *Uz.* See note on Job 1:1. *Philistines.* See ch. 47; see also note on Ge 10:14. *Ashkelon, Gaza, Ekron.* See note on Jdg 1:18; see also map, p. 359. *people left at Ashdod.* According to the Greek historian Herodotus (2.157), the Egyptian pharaoh Psammetichus I (664–610 BC) destroyed Ashdod after a long siege. By Nehemiah's time

left at Ashdod); 21 Edom,[f] Moab[g] and Ammon;[h] 22 all the kings of Tyre[i] and Sidon;[j]
the kings of the coastlands[k] across the sea;
23 Dedan,[l] Tema,[m] Buz[n] and all who are in
distant places[a];[o] 24 all the kings of Arabia[p]
and all the kings of the foreign people[q]
who live in the wilderness; 25 all the kings
of Zimri,[r] Elam[s] and Media;[t] 26 and all the
kings of the north,[u] near and far, one after the other—all the kingdoms[v] on the
face of the earth. And after all of them, the
king of Sheshak[b][w] will drink it too.
27 "Then tell them, 'This is what the LORD
Almighty, the God of Israel, says: Drink,
get drunk[x] and vomit, and fall to rise no
more because of the sword[y] I will send
among you.' 28 But if they refuse to take the
cup from your hand and drink[z], tell them,
'This is what the LORD Almighty says: You
must drink it! 29 See, I am beginning to
bring disaster[a] on the city that bears my
Name,[b] and will you indeed go unpunished?[c] You will not go unpunished, for I
am calling down a sword[d] on all[e] who live
on the earth,[f] declares the LORD Almighty.'
30 "Now prophesy all these words
against them and say to them:

" 'The LORD will roar[g] from on high;
he will thunder[h] from his holy
dwelling[i]
and roar mightily against his land.
He will shout like those who tread[j] the
grapes,
shout against all who live on the earth.
31 The tumult[k] will resound to the ends of
the earth,
for the LORD will bring charges[l]
against the nations;
he will bring judgment[m] on all[n]
mankind
and put the wicked to the sword,[o]' "
declares the LORD.

32 This is what the LORD Almighty says:

"Look! Disaster[p] is spreading
from nation to nation;[q]
a mighty storm[r] is rising
from the ends of the earth."[s]

33 At that time those slain[t] by the LORD will
be everywhere—from one end of the earth
to the other. They will not be mourned or
gathered[u] up or buried,[v] but will be like
dung lying on the ground.

34 Weep and wail, you shepherds;[w]
roll[x] in the dust, you leaders of the
flock.
For your time to be slaughtered[y] has
come;
you will fall like the best of the rams.[c][z]
35 The shepherds will have nowhere to flee,
the leaders of the flock no place to
escape.[a]
36 Hear the cry[b] of the shepherds,[c]
the wailing of the leaders of the flock,
for the LORD is destroying their
pasture.

[a] 23 Or *who clip the hair by their foreheads*
[b] 26 *Sheshak* is a cryptogram for Babylon.
[c] 34 Septuagint; Hebrew *fall and be shattered like fine pottery*

25:21 [f] S Ge 25:30 [g] S Ge 19:37; S Dt 23:6 [h] S Ge 19:38; Jer 27:3; 49:1 **25:22** [i] S Jos 19:29 [j] S Ge 10:15 [k] Isa 11:11; 48:20; 66:20; Jer 31:10; Eze 27:15; 39:6; Da 11:18 **25:23** [l] S Ge 25:3 [m] S Ge 25:15 [n] S Ge 22:21 [o] Jer 9:26; 49:32 **25:24** [p] S 2Ch 9:14 [q] ver 20 **25:25** [r] Ge 25:2 [s] S Ge 10:22 [t] S Isa 21:2 **25:26** [u] ver 9; Jer 50:3,9; 51:11,48 [v] Isa 23:17 [w] Jer 51:41 **25:27** [x] ver 16, 28; S Isa 29:9; S 49:26; Jer 51:57; Eze 23:32-34; Na 3:18; Hab 2:16 [y] S Jer 12:12; Eze 14:17; 21:4 **25:28** [z] S Isa 51:23 **25:29** [a] S 2Sa 5:7; Isa 10:12; Jer 13:12-14; 39:1 [b] S Dt 28:10; S Isa 37:17 [c] S Pr 11:31 [d] ver 27 [e] ver 30-31; Isa 34:2 [f] S Isa 24:1 **25:30** [g] Isa 16:10; S 42:13 [h] S Ps 46:6 [i] S Ps 68:5 [j] Isa 63:3; Joel 3:13; Rev 14:19-20 **25:31** [k] Jer 23:19 [l] S Jer 2:9 [m] S 1Sa 12:7; S Jer 2:35; S Eze 36:5 [n] S ver 29 [o] S Jer 15:9 **25:32** [p] S Isa 30:25 [q] Isa 34:2 [r] S Jer 23:19 [s] S Dt 28:49 **25:33** [t] Isa 66:16; Eze 39:17-20 [u] S Jer 8:2 [v] S Ps 79:3 **25:34** [w] S Jer 2:8; Zec 10:3 [x] S Jer 6:26 [y] S Ps 44:22; S Isa 34:6; Jer 50:27; 51:40; Zec 11:4,7 [z] S Jer 22:28 **25:35** [a] S Job 11:20 **25:36** [b] S Jer 6:26 [c] S Jer 23:1; Zec 11:3

it was inhabited again (see note on Ne 4:7). The fifth main Philistine city, Gath (see Jos 13:3), though important earlier (see, e.g., 1Sa 21:10–12), was destroyed and apparently not rebuilt (in later centuries it is not mentioned with the other four cities; see Am 1:6–8; Zep 2:4; Zec 9:5–6).

25:21–22 See 27:3–5.

25:21 *Edom.* See 49:7–22; see also note on Ge 36:1. *Moab and Ammon.* See 48:1—49:6; see also note on Ge 19:36–38.

25:22 *Tyre and Sidon.* See 47:4; see also notes on Isa 23:1–2,4,12. *coastlands across the sea.* Mediterranean islands and maritime regions, some of them Phoenician colonies (see Eze 27:15; Da 11:18 and notes).

25:23 *Dedan.* See 49:8; see also notes on Isa 21:13; Eze 25:13. *Tema.* See note on Isa 21:14. *Buz.* A desert region in the east. *who are in distant places.* See note on 9:26.

25:24 *Arabia.* See 49:28–33. *foreign people.* See v. 20; Ne 13:3. The same Hebrew root underlies "Arabia" and "foreign people."

25:25 *Zimri.* Not to be confused with the Israelite king of that name, Zimri is perhaps the same as Zimran, whom Keturah bore to Abraham (see Ge 25:1–2). The region known as Zimri would then have been named after him. *Elam.* See 49:34–39; see also note on Ge 10:22. *Media.* Later to join the Persians in conquering Babylon (see 51:11,28; see also note on Isa 13:17).

25:26 *Sheshak.* See NIV text note. The cryptogram is formed by substituting the first consonant of the Hebrew alphabet for the last, the second for the next-to-last, etc. Its purpose is not fully understood, though in some cases the cryptogram itself bears a suitable meaning (see note on 51:1). *will drink it too.* The Lord's agents of judgment are not themselves exempt from his judgment (see 51:48–49).

25:27 *fall ... because of the sword.* See note on v. 16.

25:29 *beginning.* See note on v. 18. *city that bears my Name.* Jerusalem (see note on 7:10). *sword.* See note on 12:12.

25:30 *The LORD will roar ... thunder.* An echo of Joel 3:16; Am 1:2 (see note there; see also Hos 11:10; Am 3:8). *his land.* Judah. *shout like those who tread the grapes.* See Isa 9:3; 16:9–10; 63:3 and note; see also Isa 16:10 and note.

25:31 *tumult.* The sounds of war (see Am 2:2). *bring charges ... bring judgment.* See note on 2:9; see also 2:35; 12:1.

25:32 *mighty storm ... from the ends of the earth.* The wrath of God (see 23:19), mediated through the coming Babylonian invasion (see note on Isa 41:25).

25:33 *not be mourned ... like dung lying on the ground.* Repeated from 8:2 (see note there); 16:4.

25:34–36 *shepherds ... leaders of the flock.* See 2:8 and note; 10:21; 22:22; Eze 34:2 and note.

25:34 *roll in the dust.* Or "roll in ashes" (as in 6:26). *your time ... has come.* See La 4:18. *fall like the best of the rams.* See NIV text note. For the reading given there, cf. the description of Jehoiachin in 22:28.

25:36 *their pasture.* The land of Judah.

37 The peaceful meadows will be laid
waste
because of the fierce anger of the
LORD.
38 Like a lion[d] he will leave his lair,
and their land will become desolate[e]
because of the sword[a] of the oppressor[f]
and because of the LORD's fierce
anger.[g]

Jeremiah Threatened With Death

26 Early in the reign of Jehoiakim[h] son
of Josiah king of Judah, this word
came from the LORD: 2 "This is what the
LORD says: Stand in the courtyard[i] of the
LORD's house and speak to all the people
of the towns of Judah who come to worship in the house of the LORD.[j] Tell[k] them
everything I command you; do not omit[l] a
word. 3 Perhaps they will listen and each
will turn[m] from their evil ways. Then I will
relent[n] and not inflict on them the disaster
I was planning because of the evil they
have done. 4 Say to them, 'This is what the
LORD says: If you do not listen[o] to me and
follow my law,[p] which I have set before
you, 5 and if you do not listen to the words
of my servants the prophets, whom I have
sent to you again and again (though you
have not listened[q]), 6 then I will make this
house like Shiloh[r] and this city a curse[b][s]
among all the nations of the earth.' "
7 The priests, the prophets and all the
people heard Jeremiah speak these words
in the house of the LORD. 8 But as soon as
Jeremiah finished telling all the people everything the LORD had commanded[t] him
to say, the priests, the prophets and all the
people seized[u] him and said, "You must
die![v] 9 Why do you prophesy in the LORD's
name that this house will be like Shiloh
and this city will be desolate and deserted?"[w] And all the people crowded[x] around
Jeremiah in the house of the LORD.
10 When the officials[y] of Judah heard
about these things, they went up from
the royal palace to the house of the LORD
and took their places at the entrance of
the New Gate[z] of the LORD's house. 11 Then
the priests and the prophets said to the
officials and all the people, "This man
should be sentenced to death[a] because he
has prophesied against this city. You have
heard it with your own ears!"[b]
12 Then Jeremiah said to all the officials[c]
and all the people: "The LORD sent me
to prophesy[d] against this house and this
city all the things you have heard.[e] 13 Now
reform[f] your ways and your actions and
obey[g] the LORD your God. Then the LORD
will relent[h] and not bring the disaster he
has pronounced against you. 14 As for me,
I am in your hands;[i] do with me whatever
you think is good and right. 15 Be assured,
however, that if you put me to death, you
will bring the guilt of innocent blood[j] on
yourselves and on this city and on those
who live in it, for in truth the LORD has
sent me to you to speak all these words[k] in
your hearing."
16 Then the officials[l] and all the people
said to the priests and the prophets, "This
man should not be sentenced to death![m]
He has spoken to us in the name of the
LORD our God."
17 Some of the elders of the land stepped
forward and said to the entire assembly

25:38 [d] S Job 10:16; S Jer 4:7 [e] Jer 44:22 [f] Jer 46:16; 50:16 [g] S Ex 15:7; S Jer 4:26 **26:1** [h] 2Ki 23:36 **26:2** [i] Jer 19:14 [j] S Jer 17:19 [k] S ver 12; S Jer 1:17; Mt 28:20; Ac 20:27 [l] Dt 4:2 **26:3** [m] Dt 30:2; 2Ch 33:12-13; Isa 55:7; Jer 35:15; 36:7 [n] S Jer 18:8 **26:4** [o] Lev 26:14; Jer 25:3 [p] Ex 20:1-23:33; S 1Ki 9:6; S Jer 11:8 **26:5** [q] S Pr 1:24; S Isa 65:12; Jer 25:4; 44:5 **26:6** [r] S Jos 18:1; S Jdg 18:31 [s] S Dt 28:25; S 2Ki 22:19 **26:8** [t] Jer 43:1 [u] Ac 6:12; 21:27 [v] Lev 24:15-16; S Ne 9:26; S Jer 11:21 **26:9** [w] S Lev 26:32; S Jer 9:11 [x] Ac 21:32 **26:10** [y] ver 16; Jer 34:19; Eze 22:27 [z] S Ge 23:10 **26:11** [a] Dt 18:20; S Jer 11:21; 18:23; Mt 26:66; Ac 6:11 [b] S Ps 44:1 **26:12** [c] Jer 1:18 [d] S Isa 6:8; Am 7:15; Ac 4:18-20; 5:29 [e] S ver 2, 15 **26:13** [f] S Jer 7:5; Joel 2:12-14 [g] Jer 11:4 [h] S Jer 18:8 **26:14** [i] Jos 9:25; Jer 38:5 **26:15** [j] S Dt 19:10 [k] S ver 12; S Jer 1:17 **26:16** [l] S ver 10; S Ac 23:9 [m] Ac 23:29

[a] 38 Some Hebrew manuscripts and Septuagint (see also 46:16 and 50:16); most Hebrew manuscripts *anger*
[b] 6 That is, its name will be used in cursing (see 29:22); or, others will see that it is cursed.

26:1–24 A summary (vv. 2–6)—and its results (vv. 7–24)—of one of Jeremiah's temple messages in ch. 7 (see note on 7:1—10:25).
26:1 *Early in the reign.* See 27:1. The Babylonian equivalent of the Hebrew for this phrase implies that the first year of King Jehoiakim (609–608 BC) is probably meant.
26:2 *courtyard of the LORD's house.* Perhaps near the New Gate (see v. 10; see also note on 7:2). *who come to worship.* See 7:2 and note. *do not omit a word.* See Dt 4:2 and note.
26:3 See 7:3,5–7. *relent.* See vv. 13,19; see also notes on 4:28; 18:7–10.
26:4 *If you do not listen.* See v. 5; 7:13. *my law.* See 7:6,9 and notes.
26:5 See 7:13,25–26. *my servants the prophets.* See note on 7:25. *again and again.* See note on 7:13.
26:6 *make this house like Shiloh.* See v. 9; see also note on 7:12. *this city.* Jerusalem. *curse.* See NIV text note and 24:9; 25:18; see also note on Zec 8:13.
26:8 *You must die!* A similar phrase describes the ultimate penalty for gross violations of the law of Moses (see, e.g., Ex 21:15–17; Lev 24:16–17,21; Dt 18:20; cf. 1Ki 21:13).
26:9 *crowded around.* With hostile intent (see Nu 16:3).
26:10 *officials of Judah.* Those responsible for making legal decisions concerning disputes taking place in the temple precincts. The priests and (false) prophets, who had a vested interest in Jerusalem and its temple, felt that Jeremiah should be sentenced to death because he was predicting the destruction of both the city and the Lord's house (see vv. 8–9,11). After hearing Jeremiah's defense (vv. 12–15), the officials decided in his favor (v. 16). The people, fickle and easily swayed, first opposed Jeremiah (vv. 8–9), then supported him (v. 16). *New Gate.* See 36:10; possibly the same as the "Upper Gate of Benjamin" (see 20:2 and note).
26:11 Jeremiah's enemies judge him before he has a chance to defend himself (cf. Dt 19:6; Jos 20:1–9 and note).
26:12 *The LORD sent me.* Contrast 23:21.
26:13 *reform your ways and your actions.* Repeated from 7:3 (see also 18:11; 35:15). *relent.* See vv. 3,19; see also notes on 4:28; 18:7–10.
26:15 *innocent blood.* See 7:6 and note; see also Mt 27:24–25; Ac 5:28.
26:16 Contrast v. 11; see note on v. 10.
26:17 *elders.* See 19:1 and note.

of people, 18 "Micah[n] of Moresheth prophesied in the days of Hezekiah king of Judah. He told all the people of Judah, 'This
is what the LORD Almighty says:

" 'Zion[o] will be plowed like a field,
Jerusalem will become a heap of
rubble,[p]
the temple hill[q] a mound overgrown
with thickets.'[a][r]

19 "Did Hezekiah king of Judah or anyone else in Judah put him to death? Did
not Hezekiah[s] fear the LORD and seek[t]
his favor? And did not the LORD relent,[u]
so that he did not bring the disaster[v] he
pronounced against them? We are about
to bring a terrible disaster[w] on ourselves!"
20 (Now Uriah son of Shemaiah from
Kiriath Jearim[x] was another man who
prophesied in the name of the LORD; he
prophesied the same things against this
city and this land as Jeremiah did. 21 When
King Jehoiakim[y] and all his officers and
officials[z] heard his words, the king was
determined to put him to death.[a] But Uriah heard of it and fled[b] in fear to Egypt.
22 King Jehoiakim, however, sent Elnathan[c]
son of Akbor to Egypt, along with some
other men. 23 They brought Uriah out of
Egypt and took him to King Jehoiakim,
who had him struck down with a sword[d]
and his body thrown into the burial place
of the common people.)[e]
24 Furthermore, Ahikam[f] son of Shaphan supported Jeremiah, and so he was
not handed over to the people to be put
to death.

26:18 [n] Mic 1:1 [o] Isa 2:3 [p] S 2Ki 25:9; S Ne 4:2; Jer 9:11 [q] Mic 4:1; Zec 8:3 [r] S Jer 17:3
26:19 [s] S 1Ch 3:13; 2Ch 32:24-26; Isa 37:14-20 [t] S 1Sa 13:12 [u] S Ex 32:14; S Jer 18:8 [v] Jer 44:7 [w] Hab 2:10
26:20 [x] S Jos 9:17
26:21 [y] S 1Ki 19:2 [z] ver 10 [a] Jer 2:30; Mt 23:37 [b] S Ge 31:21; Mt 10:23
26:22 [c] Jer 36:12,25
26:23 [d] Heb 11:37 [e] 2Ki 23:6
26:24 [f] S 2Ki 22:12
27:1 [g] S 2Ch 36:11
27:2 [h] S Lev 26:13; S 1Ki 22:11
27:3 [i] S Jer 25:17 [j] S Jer 25:21 [k] S Ge 10:15; S Jer 25:22

Judah to Serve Nebuchadnezzar

27 Early in the reign of Zedekiah[b][g] son
of Josiah king of Judah, this word
came to Jeremiah from the LORD: 2 This is
what the LORD said to me: "Make a yoke[h]
out of straps and crossbars and put it on
your neck. 3 Then send[i] word to the kings
of Edom, Moab, Ammon,[j] Tyre and Sidon[k]
through the envoys who have come to Jerusalem to Zedekiah king of Judah. 4 Give
them a message for their masters and say,
'This is what the LORD Almighty, the God
of Israel, says: "Tell this to your masters:

[a] 18 Micah 3:12 [b] 1 A few Hebrew manuscripts and Syriac (see also 27:3,12 and 28:1); most Hebrew manuscripts *Jehoiakim* (Most Septuagint manuscripts do not have this verse.)

26:18–19 The elders cite the precedent of Micah, who lived a century earlier and who (together with Isaiah) convinced King Hezekiah to pray for forgiveness on behalf of his people. The Lord answered the prayers of the king and the prophets, and in 701 BC Jerusalem and the temple were spared (see Isa 37:33–37).

26:18 *Micah of Moresheth.* See Introduction to Micah: Author. *Zion will be plowed ... overgrown with thickets.* Quoted verbatim from Mic 3:12 (see note there)—the only place in the OT where one prophet quotes another and identifies his source.

26:19 *seek his favor.* Lit. "stroke his face" (cf. Ps 119:58), "pat his cheek." See Ex 32:11; 1Sa 13:12; 2Ki 13:4. *relent.* See vv. 3,13; see also notes on 4:28; 18:7–10.

26:20–23 A parenthesis, cited as an example of the contrast between how a good king, Hezekiah, treated the Lord's prophets and how a wicked king, Jehoiakim, was known to have treated them.

26:20 *Uriah.* Not mentioned elsewhere in the OT, though it has been claimed (but not substantiated) that he appears in one of the Lachish ostraca (see note on 34:7; see also chart, p. xxiii).

26:21 *officers.* Lit. "strong men" (perhaps the royal bodyguard). *Uriah ... fled ... to Egypt.* A fatal mistake, for now he could be accused of treason and sedition.

26:22 *Elnathan son of Akbor.* One of King Jehoiakim's highest officials (see 36:12), he was impressed on another occasion by Jeremiah's prophecies (see 36:16), "urged the king not to burn" Jeremiah's scroll (36:25), and warned the prophet to hide (see 36:19). An Elnathan (perhaps the same man) was Jehoiakim's father-in-law (see 2Ki 24:6,8). An Akbor (perhaps the father of this Elnathan) was one of King Josiah's officials (see 2Ki 22:12,14; see also note on v. 24).

26:23 *brought Uriah out of Egypt.* Mutual rights of extradition were a part of the treaty imposed on Judah by Egypt when Jehoiakim became the vassal of the Egyptian pharaoh Necho II (see 2Ki 23:34–35). *Jehoiakim ... had him struck down.* Apart from divine intervention, Jeremiah probably would have fallen victim to the same fate (see 36:26) *burial place of the common people.* See note on 17:19. Commoners were buried in the Kidron Valley east of Jerusalem (see 2Ki 23:6).

26:24 *Ahikam son of Shaphan.* One of King Josiah's officials (see 2Ki 22:12,14), along with an Akbor who may have been the father of the Elnathan in v. 22 (see note there). Ahikam was also the father of Gedaliah, who would become governor of Judah after Jerusalem was destroyed in 586 BC (see 40:5) and who also befriended Jeremiah (see 39:14). *supported Jeremiah.* Ahikam's high position in Jehoiakim's court was doubtless instrumental in saving the prophet's life.

27:1—29:32 Further attempts by Jeremiah to counteract the teachings of false prophets, who were claiming that Babylon's doom was near and that rebellion against Nebuchadnezzar was therefore warranted and desirable.

27:1–22 Jeremiah tells the nations (vv. 3–11), King Zedekiah (vv. 12–15) and the priests and people of Judah (vv. 16–22) to submit to the Babylonian yoke.

27:1 *Early in the reign.* See note on 26:1. In this case, however, the phrase has been extended in meaning to include Zedekiah's fourth year (593 BC; see 28:1).

27:2 *yoke.* Of the kind worn by oxen (see note on Eze 34:27), it was a symbol of political submission (see vv. 8,11–12; Lev 26:13). That Jeremiah actually wore such a yoke for a time is clear from 28:10,12.

27:3 *send word.* In his role as a "prophet to the nations" (1:5). *Edom, Moab, Ammon.* Lands east and south of Judah (see 25:21 and note). *Tyre and Sidon.* Prominent cities in Phoenicia, north of Judah (see 25:22 and note). *envoys ... have come ... to Zedekiah.* Perhaps to discuss rebellion against Babylonia They may have counted on support from Egypt, where Psammetichus II had become pharaoh in 595 BC. Zedekiah went to Babylon in 593 (see 51:59), perhaps to be interrogated by Nebuchadnezzar. In any case, Zedekiah rebelled against him (see 52:3).

5 With my great power and outstretched arm[l] I made[m] the earth and its people and the animals[n] that are on it, and I give[o] it to anyone I please. 6 Now I will give all your countries into the hands of my servant[p] Nebuchadnezzar[q] king of Babylon; I will make even the wild animals subject to him.[r] 7 All nations will serve[s] him and his son and his grandson until the time[t] for his land comes; then many nations and great kings will subjugate[u] him.

8 " 'If, however, any nation or kingdom will not serve Nebuchadnezzar king of Babylon or bow its neck under his yoke, I will punish[v] that nation with the sword,[w] famine[x] and plague,[y] declares the LORD, until I destroy it by his hand. 9 So do not listen to your prophets,[z] your diviners,[a] your interpreters of dreams,[b] your mediums[c] or your sorcerers[d] who tell you, 'You will not serve[e] the king of Babylon.' 10 They prophesy lies[f] to you that will only serve to remove[g] you far from your lands; I will banish you and you will perish. 11 But if any nation will bow its neck under the yoke[h] of the king of Babylon and serve him, I will let that nation remain in its own land to till it and to live[i] there, declares the LORD.' "

12 I gave the same message to Zedekiah king of Judah. I said, "Bow your neck under the yoke[j] of the king of Babylon; serve him and his people, and you will live.[k] 13 Why will you and your people die[l] by the sword, famine and plague[m] with which the LORD has threatened any nation that will not serve the king of Babylon? 14 Do not listen[n] to the words of the prophets[o] who say to you, 'You will not serve the king of Babylon,' for they are prophesying lies[p] to you. 15 'I have not sent[q] them,' declares the LORD. 'They are prophesying lies in my name.[r] Therefore, I will banish you and you will perish,[s] both you and the prophets who prophesy to you.' "

16 Then I said to the priests and all these people, "This is what the LORD says: Do not listen to the prophets who say, 'Very soon now the articles[t] from the LORD's house will be brought back from Babylon.' They are prophesying lies to you. 17 Do not listen[u] to them. Serve the king of Babylon, and you will live.[v] Why should this city become a ruin? 18 If they are prophets and have the word of the LORD, let them plead[w] with the LORD Almighty that the articles remaining in the house of the LORD and in the palace of the king of Judah and in Jerusalem not be taken to Babylon. 19 For this is what the LORD Almighty says about the pillars, the bronze Sea,[x] the movable stands and the other articles[y] that are left in this city, 20 which Nebuchadnezzar king of Babylon did not take away when he carried[z] Jehoiachin[a][a] son of Jehoiakim king of Judah into exile from Jerusalem to Babylon, along with all the nobles of Judah and Jerusalem— 21 yes, this is what the LORD Almighty, the God of Israel, says about the things that are left in the house of the LORD and in the palace of the king of Judah and in Jerusalem: 22 'They will be taken[b] to Babylon and there they will remain until the day[c] I come for them,' declares the LORD. 'Then I will bring[d] them back and restore them to this place.' "

The False Prophet Hananiah

28 In the fifth month of that same year, the fourth year, early in the reign of Zedekiah[e] king of Judah, the

[a] 20 Hebrew *Jeconiah,* a variant of *Jehoiachin*

27:5 [l] S Dt 9:29 [m] S Ge 1:1 [n] S Ge 1:25 [o] Ps 115:16; Da 4:17 **27:6** [p] S Jer 25:9 [q] S Jer 21:7 [r] Jer 28:14; Da 2:37-38 **27:7** [s] S 2Ch 36:20; Da 5:18 [t] S Jer 25:12 [u] S Jer 25:14; 51:47; Da 5:28 **27:8** [v] Jer 9:16 [w] Jer 21:9 [x] S Jer 5:12 [y] S Jer 14:12 **27:9** [z] Eze 13:1-23 [a] S Ge 30:27; S Isa 44:25 [b] S Dt 13:1; S Jer 23:25 [c] S Dt 18:11 [d] S Ex 7:11 [e] Jer 6:14 **27:10** [f] S Jer 23:25; S Mk 13:5 [g] S 2Ki 23:27 **27:11** [h] S Jer 21:9 [i] Dt 6:2 **27:12** [j] Jer 17:4 [k] S Jer 21:9 **27:13** [l] Eze 18:31 [m] S Jer 14:12 **27:14** [n] S Jer 23:16 [o] S Jer 14:13 [p] S Jer 14:14; S Mt 7:15 **27:15** [q] S Jer 23:21 [r] Jer 29:9; 44:16 [s] S Jer 6:15; Mt 15:12-14 **27:16** [t] 1Ki 7:48-50; S 2Ki 24:13 **27:17** [u] Jer 23:16 [v] Jer 42:11 **27:18** [w] S Nu 21:7; S 1Sa 7:8 **27:19** [x] 1Ki 7:23-26 [y] S 1Ki 7:51; Jer 52:17-23 **27:20** [z] S Dt 28:36; S 2Ch 36:10 [a] Jer 22:24; Mt 1:11 **27:22** [b] S 2Ki 20:17; 25:13 [c] S 2Ch 36:21; S Jer 24:6 [d] S Ezr 7:19 **28:1** [e] S 2Ch 36:11

27:5 *great power and outstretched arm.* See note on 21:5.
27:6 *my servant Nebuchadnezzar.* See note on 25:9. *make … wild animals subject to him.* Nothing would be beyond the reach of Nebuchadnezzar's dominion (see 28:14; Da 2:38).
27:7 *him … his son … his grandson.* Three generations of rulers, not necessarily in direct father-son relationships (see note on Da 5:1; see also NIV text notes on Ge 10:2,8). *time for his land comes.* Babylonia will be judged (see note on 25:26). *many nations and great kings.* See note on 25:14.
27:8 *yoke.* See note on v. 2. *sword, famine and plague.* See note on 14:12. *until I destroy.* See 9:16; 24:10.
27:9 See 29:8. *your prophets.* False prophets. *diviners … mediums … sorcerers.* Forbidden in Israel (see Lev 19:26; Dt 18:10–11 and note on 18:9). *interpreters of dreams.* Including prophets and diviners (see 23:25–28; 29:8).
27:10 *prophesy lies.* See note on 5:31; cf. 2Ti 4:3–4.
27:11 *yoke.* See note on v. 2. *serve … till.* The Hebrew underlying both words is the same ("work" is the common denominator in serving and tilling).
27:12 *your neck … serve … live.* The Hebrew for all these words is plural, since Jeremiah is speaking to the people of Judah as well as to Zedekiah (see v. 13). *yoke.* See note on v. 2.
27:13 See v. 8. *sword, famine and plague.* See note on 14:12.
27:14 See vv. 9–10.
27:15 See 14:14; 23:21 and note.
27:16 *prophets who say, 'Very soon now …'* As the prophet Hananiah was saying (see 28:1–3). *articles from the LORD's house.* Some were carried off to Babylonia by Nebuchadnezzar in 605 BC (see Da 1:1–2), others in 597 (see 2Ki 24:13). Still others would be carried off in 586 (see vv. 21–22; 52:17–23).
27:18 *If they are prophets … let them plead.* If they are true prophets and in communion with the Lord, let them intercede for Judah, because the Lord has announced his intention to judge the nation.
27:19 *the pillars, the bronze Sea, the movable stands.* See 52:17; see also 1Ki 7:15–37 and notes.
27:22 *They will be taken to Babylon.* In 586 BC (see 52:17–23). *I will bring them back.* In 538/537 and shortly afterward (see Ezr 1:7–11).
28:1–17 The true prophet Jeremiah confronts the false prophet Hananiah.
28:1 *fourth year … of Zedekiah.* 593 BC. *early in the reign.* See notes on 26:1; 27:1. *prophet.* The word is used for all prophets, whether true (vv. 5,10–12,15) or false (vv. 1,5,10,12,15,17).

prophet Hananiah son of Azzur, who was
from Gibeon,[f] said to me in the house of
the LORD in the presence of the priests and
all the people: 2 "This is what the LORD
Almighty, the God of Israel, says: 'I will
break the yoke[g] of the king of Babylon.
3 Within two years I will bring back to this
place all the articles[h] of the LORD's house
that Nebuchadnezzar king of Babylon removed from here and took to Babylon. 4 I
will also bring back to this place Jehoiachin[a][i] son of Jehoiakim king of Judah and
all the other exiles from Judah who went
to Babylon,' declares the LORD, 'for I will
break the yoke of the king of Babylon.' "[j]
5 Then the prophet Jeremiah replied to
the prophet Hananiah before the priests
and all the people who were standing in
the house of the LORD. 6 He said, "Amen!
May the LORD do so! May the LORD fulfill
the words you have prophesied by bringing the articles of the LORD's house and all
the exiles back to this place from Babylon.[k]
7 Nevertheless, listen to what I have to say
in your hearing and in the hearing of all
the people: 8 From early times the prophets
who preceded you and me have prophesied war, disaster and plague[l] against many
countries and great kingdoms. 9 But the
prophet who prophesies peace will be recognized as one truly sent by the LORD only
if his prediction comes true.[m]"
10 Then the prophet Hananiah took the
yoke[n] off the neck of the prophet Jeremiah
and broke it, 11 and he said[o] before all the
people, "This is what the LORD says: 'In the
same way I will break the yoke of Nebuchadnezzar king of Babylon off the neck of
all the nations within two years.' " At this,
the prophet Jeremiah went on his way.
12 After the prophet Hananiah had broken the yoke off the neck of the prophet
Jeremiah, the word of the LORD came to
Jeremiah: 13 "Go and tell Hananiah, 'This
is what the LORD says: You have broken a
wooden yoke, but in its place you will get
a yoke of iron. 14 This is what the LORD Almighty, the God of Israel, says: I will put
an iron yoke[p] on the necks of all these nations to make them serve[q] Nebuchadnezzar[r] king of Babylon, and they will serve
him. I will even give him control over the
wild animals.[s]' "
15 Then the prophet Jeremiah said to
Hananiah the prophet, "Listen, Hananiah! The LORD has not sent[t] you, yet you
have persuaded this nation to trust in lies.[u]
16 Therefore this is what the LORD says: 'I
am about to remove you from the face of
the earth.[v] This very year you are going to
die,[w] because you have preached rebellion[x]
against the LORD.' "
17 In the seventh month of that same
year, Hananiah the prophet died.[y]

A Letter to the Exiles

29 This is the text of the letter[z] that
the prophet Jeremiah sent from Jerusalem to the surviving elders among the
exiles and to the priests, the prophets and
all the other people Nebuchadnezzar had
carried into exile from Jerusalem to Babylon.[a] 2 (This was after King Jehoiachin[a][b]
and the queen mother,[c] the court officials
and the leaders of Judah and Jerusalem,

28:1 [f] S Jos 9:3 **28:2** [g] Jer 27:12 **28:3** [h] S 2Ki 24:13 **28:4** [i] S 2Ki 25:30; Jer 22:24-27 [j] Hos 7:3 **28:6** [k] Zec 6:10 **28:8** [l] Lev 26:14-17; Isa 5:5-7; Na 1:14 **28:9** [m] S Dt 18:22; Eze 33:33 **28:10** [n] S Lev 26:13; S 1Ki 22:11 **28:11** [o] Jer 14:14; 27:10 **28:14** [p] S Dt 28:48; S Jer 15:12 [q] Jer 25:11 [r] Jer 39:1; Da 1:1; 5:18 [s] S Jer 27:6 **28:15** [t] Jer 29:31 [u] S Jer 7:4; 20:6; 29:21; La 2:14; Eze 13:6 **28:16** [v] S Ge 7:4 [w] Dt 18:20; Zec 13:3 [x] Dt 13:5; Jer 29:32 **28:17** [y] S 2Ki 1:17 **29:1** [z] ver 28 [a] S 2Ch 36:10; S Jer 13:17 **29:2** [b] S 2Ki 24:12 [c] S 2Ki 24:8

[a] 4,2 Hebrew *Jeconiah,* a variant of *Jehoiachin*

Hananiah. Means "The LORD is gracious," an appropriate name for a prophet who believed strongly (though mistakenly) that the Lord would soon bring back the exiles of Judah and the temple articles (see vv. 3–4,11). *Gibeon.* See 41:12,16; see also note on Jos 9:3.

28:2 *This is what the LORD ... says.* See v. 11. Though a false prophet, Hananiah claims to have the same authority as Jeremiah (see vv. 13–14,16; see also 23:31). *yoke.* See note on 27:2.

28:3 Hananiah's prediction directly contradicts the words of Jeremiah (see 27:16–22 and notes). *two years.* See v. 11. Contrast Jeremiah's 70 years (25:11–12; 29:10).

28:4 *bring back.* Contradicting Jeremiah's prophecy (see 22:24–27), which was fulfilled (see 52:34). *Jehoiachin ... went to Babylon.* In 597 BC. *yoke.* See note on 27:2.

28:6 See 1Ki 1:36. *Amen.* See 11:5 and note. *May the LORD fulfill.* One of the signs of true prophecy (see v. 9; see also Dt 18:21–22 and note). For another sign (or test), see Dt 13:1–5 and note.

28:7 *Nevertheless.* Though in sympathy with what Hananiah is predicting, Jeremiah reminds him that their true predecessors were basically prophets of doom (see v. 8).

28:8 *war, disaster and plague.* An appropriate modification of Jeremiah's usual triad (see note on 14:12).

28:9 *peace.* Ordinarily the message of false prophets (see 6:14 and note).

28:10 *yoke off the neck of the prophet.* See note on 27:2. *broke it.* Perhaps symbolically to break the power of Jeremiah's earlier prophecies (see 25:11–12; 27:7), which contradicted his own.

28:11 *two years.* See note on v. 3.

28:13 *yoke of iron.* The wooden yoke of submission (see note on 27:2) would be exchanged for the iron yoke of servitude (see v. 14; 38:17–23).

28:14 *all these nations ... will serve him.* See 27:7. *control over the wild animals.* See 27:6 and note.

28:15 *The LORD has not sent you.* A mark of the false prophet (see 23:21 and note).

28:16 *remove.* The Hebrew root underlying this word is the same as that underlying "sent" in v. 15. The Lord had not "sent" Hananiah to prophesy; therefore he would soon be "sent away" to his death. *preached rebellion.* Such activity on the part of false prophets was punishable by death (see Dt 13:5; see also Dt 18:20; cf. Eze 11:13; Ac 5:1–11).

28:17 *In the seventh month ... Hananiah ... died.* He who had falsely prophesied restoration "within two years" (vv. 3,11) himself died within two months (see v. 1).

29:1–32 Jeremiah's letter to the exiles of 597 BC (vv. 4–23) is followed by God's message of judgment against the false prophet Shemaiah (vv. 24–32).

29:2 *queen mother.* Nehushta (see note on 13:18). *skilled workers and the artisans.* See 24:1 and note.

the skilled workers and the artisans had gone into exile from Jerusalem.) 3 He entrusted the letter to Elasah son of Shaphan and to Gemariah son of Hilkiah, whom Zedekiah king of Judah sent to King Nebuchadnezzar in Babylon. It said:

4 This is what the LORD Almighty, the God of Israel, says to all those I carried[d] into exile from Jerusalem to Babylon: 5 "Build[e] houses and settle down; plant gardens and eat what they produce. 6 Marry and have sons and daughters; find wives for your sons and give your daughters in marriage, so that they too may have sons and daughters. Increase in number there; do not decrease.[f] 7 Also, seek[g] the peace and prosperity of the city to which I have carried you into exile. Pray[h] to the LORD for it, because if it prospers, you too will prosper." 8 Yes, this is what the LORD Almighty, the God of Israel, says: "Do not let the prophets[i] and diviners among you deceive[j] you. Do not listen to the dreams[k] you encourage them to have.[l] 9 They are prophesying lies[m] to you in my name. I have not sent[n] them," declares the LORD.

10 This is what the LORD says: "When seventy years[o] are completed for Babylon, I will come to you[p] and fulfill my good promise[q] to bring you back[r] to this place. 11 For I know the plans[s] I have for you," declares the LORD, "plans to prosper[t] you and not to harm you, plans to give you hope and a future.[u] 12 Then you will call[v] on me and come and pray[w] to me, and I will listen[x] to you. 13 You will seek[y] me and find me when you seek me with all your heart.[z] 14 I will be found by you," declares the LORD, "and will bring you back[a] from captivity.[a] I will gather you from all the nations and places where I have banished you," declares the LORD, "and will bring you back to the place from which I carried you into exile."[b]

15 You may say, "The LORD has raised up prophets for us in Babylon," 16 but this is what the LORD says about the king who sits on David's throne and all the people who remain in this city, your fellow citizens who did not go with you into exile— 17 yes, this is what the LORD Almighty says: "I will send the sword, famine and plague[c] against them and I will make them like figs[d] that are so bad they cannot be eaten. 18 I will pursue them with the sword, famine and plague and will make them abhorrent[e] to all the kingdoms of the earth, a curse[b][f] and an object of horror,[g] of scorn[h] and reproach, among all the nations where I drive them. 19 For they have not listened to my words,"[i] declares

29:4 [d]S Jer 24:5 **29:5** [e]ver 28 **29:6** [f]Jer 30:19 **29:7** [g]S Est 3:8 [h]1Ti 2:1-2 **29:8** [i]1Jn 4:1 [j]Jer 37:9 [k]S Dt 13:1; S Jer 23:25 [l]S Jer 23:27 **29:9** [m]S Jer 27:15; La 2:14; Eze 13:6 [n]Jer 23:21 **29:10** [o]S 2Ch 36:21; S Da 9:2 [p]S Ru 1:6 [q]1Ki 8:56; Jer 32:42; 33:14 [r]S Jer 16:14; S 24:6 **29:11** [s]Ps 40:5 [t]Isa 55:12 [u]S Job 8:7; Zec 8:15 **29:12** [v]Hos 2:23; Zep 3:12; Zec 13:9 [w]S 1Ki 8:30 [x]Ps 145:19; S Isa 55:6 **29:13** [y]Mt 7:7 [z]S Dt 4:29; S 2Ch 6:37 **29:14** [a]S Dt 30:3; Jer 30:3; Eze 39:25; Am 9:14; Zep 3:20 [b]Jer 23:3-4; 30:10; 46:27; Eze 37:21 **29:17** [c]Jer 27:8 [d]S Isa 5:4 **29:18** [e]S Jer 15:4 [f]S Nu 5:27; S Jer 18:16; S 22:10; 44:12 [g]S Dt 28:25 [h]S Dt 28:37; S Isa 28:22; S Mic 2:6 **29:19** [i]Jer 6:19

[a] 14 Or *will restore your fortunes* [b] 18 That is, their names will be used in cursing (see verse 22); or, others will see that they are cursed.

29:3 *entrusted the letter to.* Placed it in the ancient equivalent of the diplomatic pouch to ensure its safe arrival. *Shaphan.* Perhaps the father also of Ahikam (see 26:24 and note) and/or Gemariah (see 36:10), both of whom were sympathetic to Jeremiah and his mission. *Gemariah.* A common name in Jeremiah's time (see, e.g., 36:10), found on one of the Lachish ostraca (see note on 34:7), as well as in at least two of the Elephantine papyri (see note on 32:11) a century later. *Hilkiah.* Perhaps the Hilkiah who was high priest under Josiah (see 2Ki 22:12, where Hilkiah and one or more Shaphans are mentioned together). *Zedekiah … sent to King Nebuchadnezzar.* Possibly at or about the same time (593 BC) that Zedekiah himself went to Babylon for a brief period (see 51:59). The purpose of the journey(s) is unknown.
29:4 *I.* The Lord (see v. 7). Since it is God who has exiled his people, they are to submit to their captors and not rebel against them.
29:5 *Build … plant.* Reminiscent of Jeremiah's call (see 1:10), but here used in a literal sense. *settle down.* Ezekiel, e.g., lived in his own house in Babylonia (see Eze 8:1 and note).
29:6 *find wives.* But among the exiles themselves, not among the women of Babylonia (cf. Dt 7:3–4; Ezr 9:1–2).
29:7 An unprecedented and unique concept in the ancient world: working toward and praying for the prosperity of one's captors. *peace and prosperity … prospers … prosper.* The Hebrew word is *shalom* in all three cases. *city.* Every place in which the exiles settle down. *Pray … for it.* See Ezr 6:10 and note; Mt 5:44; in the Apocrypha, cf. 1 Maccabees 7:33.
29:8 *prophets and diviners … dreams.* See 27:9 and note. *among you.* The exiles in Babylonia had their share of false prophets (see vv. 21,31), who had doubtless accompanied them when they were deported in 597 BC.
29:9 See v. 31; see also notes on 23:16,21.
29:10 *seventy years.* See note on 25:11–12. *bring you back.* See note on 27:22.
29:11 *I know.* See v. 23. Appearances to the contrary notwithstanding, the Lord has not forgotten his people. *prosper.* See note on v. 7. *and not … harm.* God is the ultimate source of both prosperity and disaster (see Isa 45:7).
29:12–13 Echoed from Dt 4:29–30. The Lord's gracious gift of prosperity is contingent on his people's willingness to repent.
29:14 A summary of Dt 30:3–5. *bring you back from captivity.* See NIV text note; see also 30:3,18; 31:23; 32:44; 33:7,11,26; 48:47; 49:6,39 and note on Ps 126:4.
29:15 *prophets … in Babylon.* See note on v. 8.
29:16 *the king … on David's throne.* Zedekiah. *sits … remain.* The Hebrew for both words is identical. King and people alike are guilty.
29:17 *sword, famine and plague.* See v. 18; see also note on 14:12. *like figs … so bad they cannot be eaten.* See 24:8.
29:18 See 24:9 and note.
29:19 *again and again.* See note on 7:13. *my servants the prophets.* See note on 7:25. *you exiles have not listened.* See Eze 2:5,7; 3:7,11.

the LORD, "words that I sent to them again and again[j] by my servants the prophets.[k] And you exiles have not listened either," declares the LORD.

20 Therefore, hear the word of the LORD, all you exiles whom I have sent[l] away from Jerusalem to Babylon. 21 This is what the LORD Almighty, the God of Israel, says about Ahab son of Kolaiah and Zedekiah son of Maaseiah, who are prophesying lies[m] to you in my name: "I will deliver them into the hands of Nebuchadnezzar king of Babylon, and he will put them to death before your very eyes. 22 Because of them, all the exiles from Judah who are in Babylon will use this curse: 'May the LORD treat you like Zedekiah and Ahab, whom the king of Babylon burned[n] in the fire.' 23 For they have done outrageous things in Israel; they have committed adultery[o] with their neighbors' wives, and in my name they have uttered lies—which I did not authorize. I know[p] it and am a witness[q] to it," declares the LORD.

Message to Shemaiah

24 Tell Shemaiah the Nehelamite, 25 "This is what the LORD Almighty, the God of Israel, says: You sent letters in your own name to all the people in Jerusalem, to the priest Zephaniah[r] son of Maaseiah, and to all the other priests. You said to Zephaniah, 26 'The LORD has appointed you priest in place of Jehoiada to be in charge of the house of the LORD; you should put any maniac[s] who acts like a prophet into the stocks[t] and neck-irons. 27 So why have you not reprimanded Jeremiah from Anathoth, who poses as a prophet among you? 28 He has sent this message[u] to us in Babylon: It will be a long time.[v] Therefore build[w] houses and settle down; plant gardens and eat what they produce.' "

29 Zephaniah[x] the priest, however, read the letter to Jeremiah the prophet. 30 Then the word of the LORD came to Jeremiah: 31 "Send this message to all the exiles: 'This is what the LORD says about Shemaiah[y] the Nehelamite: Because Shemaiah has prophesied to you, even though I did not send[z] him, and has persuaded you to trust in lies, 32 this is what the LORD says: I will surely punish Shemaiah the Nehelamite and his descendants.[a] He will have no one left among this people, nor will he see the good[b] things I will do for my people, declares the LORD, because he has preached rebellion[c] against me.' "

Restoration of Israel

30 This is the word that came to Jeremiah from the LORD: 2 "This is what the LORD, the God of Israel, says: 'Write[d] in a book all the words I have spoken to you. 3 The days[e] are coming,' declares the LORD, 'when I will bring[f] my people Israel and Judah back from captivity[a] and restore[g]

[a] 3 Or *will restore the fortunes of my people Israel and Judah*

29:19 [j] Jer 7:25 [k] S Jer 25:4 **29:20** [l] S Jer 24:5 **29:21** [m] ver 9; Jer 14:14 **29:22** [n] Da 3:6 **29:23** [o] S Jer 23:14 [p] S Heb 4:13 [q] S Ge 31:48; S Jer 7:11 **29:25** [r] S 2Ki 25:18 **29:26** [s] S 1Sa 10:11; Hos 9:7; S Jn 10:20 [t] Jer 20:2 **29:28** [u] ver 1 [v] ver 10 [w] ver 5 **29:29** [x] Jer 21:1 **29:31** [y] ver 24 [z] S Jer 14:14 **29:32** [a] S 1Sa 2:30-33 [b] ver 10 [c] S Jer 28:16 **30:2** [d] S Isa 30:8; S Jer 36:2 **30:3** [e] S Jer 16:14; S 24:6 [f] S Jer 29:14 [g] S Jer 16:15

29:21 *Ahab ... and Zedekiah.* Not the well-known kings (of Israel and Judah respectively); rather, they were false prophets (see note on v. 8).

29:22 *fire.* Used in Babylonia as a method of execution (see Da 3:6,24; this is also evident in the Code of Hammurapi, sections 25; 110; 157).

29:23 *done outrageous things in Israel.* See Ge 34:7 and note. *committed adultery ... and ... uttered lies.* See note on 23:10. *I know.* See v. 11.

29:24 *Shemaiah.* A false prophet (see v. 31). *Nehelamite.* The Hebrew root underlying this word is the same as that for "dreams" in v. 8 (see 27:9 and note). Jeremiah is perhaps suggesting that Shemaiah is not a true prophet but a mere dreamer.

29:25 *Zephaniah.* Not the prophet of that name (see note on 21:1).

29:26 *Jehoiada.* Not the same as the priest during the days of King Joash (see 2Ki 12:7). *in charge of the house of the LORD.* See note on 20:1. *maniac.* Prophetic behavior sometimes appeared deranged to the casual observer (see 2Ki 9:11). *stocks.* See 20:2 and note.

29:27 *Anathoth.* See note on 1:1.

29:28 See v. 5 and note. *a long time.* Here 70 years (see 25:11–12 and note; see also 2Sa 3:1).

29:29 *Zephaniah ... however.* He was apparently sympathetic toward Jeremiah (see 21:1–2; 37:3).

29:31–32 The Lord's threat against Shemaiah is similar to that against Hananiah (see 28:15–16).

29:31 *persuaded you to trust in lies.* See 28:15.

29:32 *preached rebellion against.* See 28:16 and note.

30:1—33:26 Often called Jeremiah's "book of consolation," the section depicts the ultimate restoration of both Israel (the northern kingdom) and Judah (the southern kingdom) and is the longest sustained passage in Jeremiah concerned with the future hope of the people of God (for other and briefer passages on restoration, see 3:14–18; 16:14–15; 23:3–8; 24:4–7). The information in 32:1 may be used to date the entire section to 587 BC, the year before Jerusalem was destroyed by Nebuchadnezzar and its people exiled to Babylon.

30:1—31:40 Written almost entirely in poetry, these two chapters are filled with optimism as the prophet looks forward to the time when God would redeem his people.

30:1 The heading for chs. 30–31 (and perhaps chs. 32–33 as well).

30:2 *Write.* In order to preserve for future generations the predictions of restoration. *book.* In scroll form (see, e.g., 36:2,4; 45:1; see also Ex 17:14 and note). *all the words I have spoken to you.* Concerning the future redemption of God's people. The phrase is less comprehensive here than in 36:2.

30:3 *bring ... back from captivity.* See note on 29:14. *Israel and Judah.* The northern and southern kingdoms, the first of which was exiled in 721 BC and the second of which would be entering the final stage of its exile in about a year (see note on 30:1—33:26).

them to the land I gave their ancestors to
possess,' says the LORD."
4 These are the words the LORD spoke
concerning Israel and Judah: 5 "This is
what the LORD says:

"'Cries of fear[h] are heard—
terror, not peace.
6 Ask and see:
Can a man bear children?
Then why do I see every strong man
with his hands on his stomach like a woman in labor,[i]
every face turned deathly pale?[j]
7 How awful that day[k] will be!
No other will be like it.
It will be a time of trouble[l] for Jacob,
but he will be saved[m] out of it.

8 "'In that day,' declares the LORD Almighty,
'I will break the yoke[n] off their necks
and will tear off their bonds;[o]
no longer will foreigners enslave them.[p]
9 Instead, they will serve the LORD their God
and David[q] their king,[r]
whom I will raise up for them.

10 "'So do not be afraid,[s] Jacob my servant;[t]
do not be dismayed, Israel,'
declares the LORD.
'I will surely save[u] you out of a distant place,
your descendants from the land of their exile.
Jacob will again have peace and security,[v]
and no one will make him afraid.[w]
11 I am with you[x] and will save you,'
declares the LORD.
'Though I completely destroy all the nations
among which I scatter you,
I will not completely destroy[y] you.
I will discipline[z] you but only in due measure;
I will not let you go entirely unpunished.'[a]

12 "This is what the LORD says:

"'Your wound[b] is incurable,
your injury beyond healing.[c]
13 There is no one to plead your cause,[d]
no remedy for your sore,
no healing[e] for you.
14 All your allies[f] have forgotten you;
they care nothing for you.
I have struck you as an enemy[g] would
and punished you as would the cruel,[h]
because your guilt is so great
and your sins[i] so many.
15 Why do you cry out over your wound,
your pain that has no cure?[j]
Because of your great guilt and many sins
I have done these things to you.[k]

16 "'But all who devour[l] you will be devoured;
all your enemies will go into exile.[m]
Those who plunder[n] you will be plundered;
all who make spoil of you I will despoil.
17 But I will restore you to health
and heal[o] your wounds,'
declares the LORD,
'because you are called an outcast,[p]
Zion for whom no one cares.'[q]

30:5 [h]Jer 6:25 **30:6** [i]S Jer 4:31 [j]S Isa 29:22 **30:7** [k]S Isa 2:12 [l]S Isa 22:5; Zep 1:15 [m]ver 10; Jer 23:3 **30:8** [n]S Isa 9:4 [o]Ps 107:14 [p]Jer 25:14; 27:7; Eze 34:27 **30:9** [q]S Mt 1:1 [r]ver 21; S 1Sa 13:14; Jer 33:15; Eze 34:23-24; 37:24; Hos 1:11; 3:5 **30:10** [s]S Isa 41:10 [t]S Isa 44:2 [u]S ver 7; S Jer 29:14 [v]Isa 35:9; S Jer 17:25 [w]S Isa 29:22; S 54:4; S Jer 23:4; Eze 34:25-28 **30:11** [x]S Jos 1:5 [y]S Lev 26:44; S Jer 5:18; 46:28 [z]S Jer 10:24 [a]Hos 11:9; Am 9:8 **30:12** [b]S Job 6:4; S Jer 10:19 [c]S Jer 8:22 **30:13** [d]S Jdg 6:31 [e]S Jer 8:22; 14:19; 46:11; Na 3:19 **30:14** [f]S Jer 22:20; La 1:2 [g]S Job 13:24 [h]S Job 30:21 [i]S Jer 25:7 **30:15** [j]S Jer 10:19 [k]S Pr 1:31; La 1:5 **30:16** [l]S Isa 29:8; S 33:1; S Jer 2:3 [m]S Isa 14:2; Joel 3:4-8 [n]Jer 49:2; 50:10 **30:17** [o]S Isa 1:5; Hos 6:1 [p]S Isa 6:12; Jer 33:24 [q]Ps 142:4

30:5 *Cries of fear ... terror.* The sounds of battle and destruction.

30:6 *woman in labor.* A symbol of anguish and distress (see notes on 4:19,31).

30:7 A description of the day of the Lord (see notes on Isa 2:11,17,20; Am 5:18; 8:9). Jeremiah's immediate reference is to the foreseeable future (see vv. 8,18), but a more remote time in the Messianic age is also in view. *awful.* Lit. "great" (as in Joel 2:11; Zep 1:14; cf. Joel 1:15). *No other will be like it.* See Da 12:1; Joel 2:2; Mt 24:21. *time of trouble.* The Hebrew for this phrase is translated "time of distress" in Da 12:1 (see Mt 24:21 and note; Rev 16:18). *Jacob.* Israel (see v. 10).

30:8 *In that day.* See note on Isa 2:11,17,20. *yoke.* See note on 27:2. *tear off their bonds.* The Hebrew underlying this phrase is translated "break their chains" in Ps 2:3, where the nations plot to free themselves from the Lord and his anointed ruler. Here the Lord promises to free his people from enslavement to the nations. *foreigners.* Including, but not limited to, Babylonia.

30:9 *David their king.* The Messiah (see note on 23:5). The Targum (ancient Aramaic paraphrase) here reads "Messiah, the son of David, their king." *raise up.* See 23:5 and note.

30:10–11 Repeated almost verbatim in 46:27–28.

30:10 *Jacob my servant.* See Isa 41:8–9 and note; 44:1–2,21; 45:4; 48:20. *no one will make him afraid.* Contrast v. 5; see Lev 26:6; Job 11:19; Isa 17:2; Eze 34:28; 39:26; Mic 4:4 and note; Zep 3:13.

30:11 *I am with you and will save you.* Words spoken originally to Jeremiah alone (see 1:8,19; 15:20) are now spoken to all God's people. *scatter.* See 9:16 and note; 23:1–2. *not completely destroy.* See 4:27 and note. *not ... go ... unpunished.* See 25:29; 49:12.

30:12–13 See 8:22; Hos 5:13; 6:1; 7:1; 11:3.

30:12 *Your.* Judah's. *wound is incurable.* See 15:18 and note. *injury beyond healing.* See 14:17.

30:13 *plead your cause.* Against your enemies. *no remedy for your sore.* See Hos 5:13.

30:14 *allies.* See note on 22:20. Egypt, e.g., often supported Judah against the Babylonians (see 37:5–7). *because your guilt ... so many.* See 5:6; 13:22. The Hebrew for this clause is repeated verbatim in v. 15.

30:16 *all who devour you.* See 3:24; 5:17; 8:16; 10:25. *will be devoured.* See note on 25:26; see also 51:48–49. *will be plundered.* See Isa 17:14.

30:17 *restore you to health.* Contrast 8:22; see 33:6; Isa 58:8. *Zion.* See note on 2Sa 5:7.

18 "This is what the LORD says:

" 'I will restore the fortunes[r] of Jacob's
tents[s]
and have compassion[t] on his
dwellings;
the city will be rebuilt[u] on her ruins,
and the palace will stand in its
proper place.
19 From them will come songs[v] of
thanksgiving[w]
and the sound of rejoicing.[x]
I will add to their numbers,[y]
and they will not be decreased;
I will bring them honor,[z]
and they will not be disdained.
20 Their children[a] will be as in days of
old,
and their community will be
established[b] before me;
I will punish[c] all who oppress them.
21 Their leader[d] will be one of their own;
their ruler will arise from among
them.[e]
I will bring him near[f] and he will come
close to me—
for who is he who will devote
himself
to be close to me?'
declares the LORD.
22 " 'So you will be my people,[g]
and I will be your God.[h]' "

23 See, the storm[i] of the LORD
will burst out in wrath,
a driving wind swirling down
on the heads of the wicked.
24 The fierce anger[j] of the LORD will not
turn back[k]
until he fully accomplishes
the purposes of his heart.
In days to come
you will understand[l] this.

31 "At that time," declares the LORD, "I
will be the God[m] of all the families
of Israel, and they will be my people."
2 This is what the LORD says:

"The people who survive the sword
will find favor[n] in the wilderness;
I will come to give rest[o] to Israel."

3 The LORD appeared to us in the past,[a]
saying:

"I have loved[p] you with an everlasting
love;
I have drawn[q] you with unfailing
kindness.
4 I will build you up again,
and you, Virgin[r] Israel, will be
rebuilt.[s]
Again you will take up your
timbrels[t]
and go out to dance[u] with the
joyful.[v]

30:18 [r] ver 3; S Dt 30:3; Jer 31:23; 32:44 [s] S Nu 24:5 [t] Ps 102:13; Jer 33:26; Eze 39:25 [u] Jer 31:4, 24,38; 33:7; Eze 36:10,33; Am 9:14 **30:19** [v] S Ps 9:2; Isa 35:10; S 51:11 [w] S Isa 51:3 [x] Ps 126:1-2; Jer 31:4 [y] S Ge 15:5; 22:17; Jer 33:22; Eze 37:26; Zec 2:4 [z] S Isa 44:23; S 60:9 **30:20** [a] Isa 54:13; Jer 31:17; Zec 8:5 [b] Isa 54:14 [c] S Ex 23:22 **30:21** [d] S ver 9; Jer 23:5-6 [e] Dt 17:15 [f] Nu 16:5 **30:22** [g] S Isa 19:25; Hos 2:23 [h] S Lev 26:12 **30:23** [i] S Jer 23:19 **30:24** [j] Jer 4:8; La 1:12 [k] S Jer 4:28 [l] Jer 23:19-20 **31:1** [m] S Lev 26:12 **31:2** [n] Nu 14:20 [o] S Ex 33:14; S Dt 12:9

[a] 3 Or *LORD has appeared to us from afar*

31:3 [p] S Dt 4:37 [q] Hos 11:4; Jn 6:44 **31:4** [r] S 2Ki 19:21 [s] S Jer 1:10; S 30:18 [t] S Ge 31:27 [u] S Ex 15:20 [v] S Jer 30:19

30:18 *restore the fortunes.* See note on 29:14. *the city ... the palace.* Lit. "a city ... a palace," perhaps referring to Judah's cities and palaces in general (see Am 9:14). It is possible, however, that only Jerusalem and its palace are intended (see 31:38). *ruins.* The Hebrew for this word is *tel(l)*, referring to a mound of ruins resulting from the accumulation of the debris of many years or centuries of occupation and on which successive series of towns were often built (see, e.g., Jos 11:13 and note).
30:19 *songs of thanksgiving.* See 33:11. *rejoicing.* See 31:4 and note; contrast 15:17. *add ... not be decreased.* See 29:6; Eze 36:37–38. *honor ... not be disdained.* See Isa 9:1.
30:20 *days of old.* Probably the early days of the united kingdom, especially the reign of David. *community.* In 1Ki 12:20 the Hebrew for this word is translated "assembly," the political and religious governing body of the people. *will be established before me.* See Ps 102:28 and note.
30:21 *leader ... ruler.* Although the Targum renders "Messiah" here, the terms probably refer in the first place to the rulers of Judah immediately after the exile. But Jesus Christ ultimately fulfills the promise. *one of their own ... from among them.* Not foreigners (cf. Dt 18:15,18). *bring him near ... come close.* See Nu 16:5; contrast Ex 24:2. Unauthorized approaches into God's presence were punishable by death (see Ex 19:21; Nu 8:19).
30:22 See 31:1; see also note on 7:23.
30:23–24 Repeated almost verbatim from 23:19–20 (see notes there).
31:1–40 Continuing the theme of restoration begun in 30:1, Jeremiah records the words of the Lord to (1) all the people of God, v. 1 (prose); (2) the restored northern kingdom of Israel, vv. 2–22 (poetry); (3) the restored southern kingdom of Judah, vv. 23–26 (prose); and (4) Israel and Judah together, vv. 27–40 (prose prologue, vv. 27–30; poetic body, vv. 31–37; prose epilogue, vv. 38–40—each section beginning with the words "The days are coming"; see note on v. 31).
31:1 See 30:22; see also note on 7:23. *God of ... my people.* See note on Zec 8:8. *all the families of Israel.* All 12 tribes.
31:2 *people who survive the sword.* The righteous remnant (see v. 7; see also note on 6:9), who will return from captivity. *wilderness.* The Arabian Desert, the antitype of the Sinai Desert through which Israel's ancestors marched after the exodus. Return from exile is often pictured as or compared to release from Egyptian slavery at the time of the exodus (see 16:14–15; Isa 35:1–11 and notes; 40:3–4; 42:14–16; 43:18–21; 48:20–21; 51:9–11; cf. Hos 2:14–15). *rest.* See 6:16; contrast Dt 28:65. See notes on Dt 3:20; Jos 1:13. *Israel.* The northern kingdom (see also vv. 4,7,9–10,21). Other names for it are Samaria (v. 5), Ephraim (vv. 6,9,18,20), Jacob (vv. 7,11) and Rachel (v. 15).
31:3 *drawn ... with unfailing kindness.* The Hebrew underlying this phrase is translated "Continue ... love" in Ps 36:10 (see note on Ps 6:4).
31:4 *build.* See 1:10 and note. *Virgin Israel.* See note on 2Ki 19:21. *timbrels.* Used on joyful occasions (see Ps 68:25), especially following a military victory (see Ex 15:20 and note; Jdg 11:34)—in contrast to Judah's experience during the exile (see Ps 137:1–3). *dance.* See v. 13; often a religious activity in ancient times (see 2Sa 6:14; Ps 149:3; 150:4).

5 Again you will plant[w] vineyards
on the hills of Samaria;[x]
the farmers will plant them
and enjoy their fruit.[y]
6 There will be a day when watchmen[z]
cry out
on the hills of Ephraim,
'Come, let us go up to Zion,
to the LORD our God.' "[a]

7 This is what the LORD says:

"Sing[b] with joy for Jacob;
shout for the foremost[c] of the nations.
Make your praises heard, and say,
'LORD, save[d] your people,
the remnant[e] of Israel.'
8 See, I will bring them from the land of
the north[f]
and gather[g] them from the ends of
the earth.
Among them will be the blind[h] and the
lame,[i]
expectant mothers and women in
labor;
a great throng will return.
9 They will come with weeping;[j]
they will pray as I bring them back.
I will lead[k] them beside streams of
water[l]
on a level[m] path where they will not
stumble,
because I am Israel's father,[n]
and Ephraim is my firstborn son.

10 "Hear the word of the LORD, you
nations;
proclaim it in distant coastlands:[o]
'He who scattered[p] Israel will gather[q]
them
and will watch over his flock like a
shepherd.'[r]
11 For the LORD will deliver Jacob
and redeem[s] them from the hand of
those stronger[t] than they.
12 They will come and shout for joy[u] on
the heights[v] of Zion;
they will rejoice in the bounty[w] of
the LORD—
the grain, the new wine and the olive
oil,[x]
the young of the flocks[y] and herds.
They will be like a well-watered
garden,[z]
and they will sorrow[a] no more.
13 Then young women will dance and be
glad,
young men and old as well.
I will turn their mourning[b] into
gladness;
I will give them comfort[c] and joy[d]
instead of sorrow.
14 I will satisfy[e] the priests[f] with
abundance,
and my people will be filled with my
bounty,[g]"
declares the LORD.

15 This is what the LORD says:

"A voice is heard in Ramah,[h]
mourning and great weeping,

31:5 [w] S Dt 20:6 [x] Jer 33:13; 50:19; Ob 1:19 [y] S Isa 37:30; Am 9:14 **31:6** [z] S Isa 52:8; S 56:10 [a] ver 12; S Dt 33:19; Jer 50:4-5; Mic 4:2 **31:7** [b] S Isa 12:6 [c] Dt 28:13; Isa 61:9 [d] Ps 14:7; 28:9 [e] S Isa 37:31 **31:8** [f] S Jer 3:18 [g] S Ge 33:13; S Dt 30:4; S Ps 106:47; Eze 34:12-14 [h] Isa 42:16 [i] Eze 34:16; Mic 4:6 **31:9** [j] S Ezr 3:12; Ps 126:5 [k] Isa 63:13 [l] S Nu 20:8; S Ps 1:3; S Isa 32:2 [m] S Isa 40:4; S 49:11 [n] S Ex 4:22; S Jer 3:4 **31:10** [o] Isa 49:1; S 66:19; S Jer 25:22 [p] S Lev 26:33 [q] S Dt 30:4; S Isa 11:12; Jer 50:19 [r] Isa 40:11; Eze 34:12 **31:11** [s] S Ex 6:6; Zec 9:16 [t] Ps 142:6 **31:12** [u] S Ps 126:5 [v] Eze 17:23; 20:40; 40:2; Mic 4:1 [w] S Ps 36:8; Joel 3:18 [x] S Nu 18:12; Hos 2:21-22; Joel 2:19 [y] ver 24; S Isa 65:10 [z] S SS 4:15 [a] S Isa 30:19; S 62:5; Jn 16:22; S Rev 7:17 **31:13** [b] S Isa 61:3 [c] S Isa 40:1 [d] Ps 30:11; S Isa 51:11 **31:14** [e] ver 25 [f] Lev 7:35-36 [g] S Ps 36:8; S Isa 30:23 **31:15** [h] S Jos 18:25

31:5 *plant.* See 1:10 and note. *Samaria.* Conquered in 722–721 BC (see 2Ki 17:24), it would someday be resettled by God's people. *plant them and enjoy their fruit.* See Dt 28:30; Isa 62:8–9; 65:21–22. Since the law stipulated that the fruit of a tree could not be eaten until the fifth year after planting it (see Lev 19:23–25), a return to normalcy is envisioned here.
31:6 *watchmen ... on the hills.* Watchmen were stationed in appropriate locations to observe and give notice of the appearance of various phases of the moon to fix the times of the most important festivals (see Dt 16:16 and note). *Ephraim ... to Zion.* In the days of Jeroboam I the people of the northern kingdom had been required to worship at northern shrines (see 1Ki 12:26–30). In the future, however, they would worship the Lord only in Jerusalem (cf. Jn 4:20). *go up.* In ancient Israel one always "went up" to Jerusalem (see, e.g., Ezr 1:3; 7:7; Isa 2:3; Jn 2:13), not only because its elevation was above the surrounding countryside but also because it was the royal city and the main center of the nation's religious life.
31:7 *foremost of the nations.* See Dt 26:19; Am 6:1. Israel was the greatest nation, not because of intrinsic merit but because of divine grace and appointment (see Dt 7:6–8; 2Sa 7:23–24). *save.* The Hebrew for this word is the basis of "Hosanna," the cry of the people of Jerusalem on Palm Sunday (see Mt 21:9 and NIV text note; see also Ps 20:9; 28:9; 86:2; and especially 118:25). *remnant.* See note on 6:9.
31:8 *land of the north.* See 3:18; 4:6 and notes; 6:22; 16:15. *ends of the earth.* See 6:22; 25:32. *blind ... lame.* See Isa 35:5–6 and notes; 42:16. *women in labor.* See note on 4:31.
31:9 *with weeping.* Contrast Ps 126:5–6; Isa 55:12. *lead them.* See Isa 40:11; 48:21; contrast Isa 20:4. *beside streams of water.* See Ps 23:2 and note; Isa 49:10; cf. Isa 41:18. *level path.* See Isa 40:3–4 and notes; 43:16,19. *I am Israel's father.* See 3:4 and note; see also Dt 32:6; Isa 63:16; 64:8. *firstborn son.* Cf. v. 20; see Ex 4:22 and note; Hos 11:1–4.
31:10 *distant coastlands.* Remote areas to the west of Israel (see 2:10; 25:22 and note; 47:4; Ps 72:10; Isa 41:1,5; 42:10,12; 49:1). *scattered Israel ... watch over his flock like a shepherd.* See 23:1–3 and notes.
31:11 *redeem.* See note on Ru 2:20. As the Lord had redeemed his people from Egyptian slavery (see Ex 6:6 and note; 15:13; Dt 7:8; 9:26), so now he would redeem their descendants from Babylonian exile (see Isa 41:14; 43:1 and notes; 52:9). *from ... those stronger than they.* See Ps 35:10.
31:12 *heights of Zion.* See note on 17:12. *bounty of the LORD.* Primarily material blessings (see v. 14; Hos 3:5). *grain ... new wine ... olive oil.* See note on Dt 7:13; see also Hos 2:8. *like a well-watered garden.* See Isa 58:11 and note. *sorrow no more.* See Isa 25:8.
31:14 *abundance.* Either (1) a synonym for God's bounty (see Ps 36:8; 63:5; Isa 55:2) or (2) a reference to the special portions of the sacrificial animal reserved for the priests (see Lev 7:31–36).
31:15 Quoted in Mt 2:18, where Herod's orders to kill all the male infants "in Bethlehem and its vicinity" (Mt 2:16) are stated to be a fulfillment of this passage. *Ramah.* Located about five miles north of Jerusalem, it was one of the

Rachel weeping for her children
and refusing to be comforted,[i]
because they are no more."[j]

16 This is what the LORD says:

"Restrain your voice from weeping
and your eyes from tears,[k]
for your work will be rewarded,[l]"
declares the LORD.
"They will return[m] from the land of
the enemy.
17 So there is hope[n] for your
descendants,"
declares the LORD.
"Your children[o] will return to their
own land.

18 "I have surely heard Ephraim's
moaning:
'You disciplined[p] me like an unruly
calf,[q]
and I have been disciplined.
Restore[r] me, and I will return,
because you are the LORD my God.
19 After I strayed,[s]
I repented;
after I came to understand,
I beat[t] my breast.
I was ashamed[u] and humiliated
because I bore the disgrace of my
youth.'[v]
20 Is not Ephraim my dear son,
the child[w] in whom I delight?
Though I often speak against him,
I still remember[x] him.
Therefore my heart yearns for him;
I have great compassion[y] for him,"
declares the LORD.

31:15 [i] S Ge 37:35 [j] S Jer 10:20; Mt 2:17-18* **31:16** [k] S Ps 30:5; S Isa 25:8; 30:19 [l] S Ru 2:12; S 2Ch 15:7 [m] Jer 30:3; Eze 11:17 **31:17** [n] S Job 8:7; La 3:29 [o] S Jer 30:20 **31:18** [p] S Job 5:17 [q] Jer 50:11; Hos 4:16; 10:11 [r] S Ps 80:3 **31:19** [s] S Ps 95:10; S Jer 8:4; Eze 36:31 [t] Eze 21:12; Lk 18:13 [u] Ezr 9:6 [v] S Ps 25:7; S Jer 22:21 **31:20** [w] La 3:33 [x] S Isa 44:21 [y] S 1Ki 3:26; S Ps 6:2; Isa 55:7; Mic 7:18 **31:21** [z] Eze 21:19 [a] Isa 35:8; Jer 50:5 [b] Isa 52:11; S Jer 3:12 [c] ver 4 **31:22** [d] S Jer 2:23 [e] S Jer 3:6 [f] Isa 43:19 [g] S Dt 32:10 **31:23** [h] S Jer 30:18 [i] S Ge 28:3; S Nu 6:24 [j] S Isa 1:26 [k] S Ps 48:1; S Isa 2:2

21 "Set up road signs;
put up guideposts.[z]
Take note of the highway,[a]
the road that you take.
Return,[b] Virgin[c] Israel,
return to your towns.
22 How long will you wander,[d]
unfaithful[e] Daughter Israel?
The LORD will create a new thing[f] on
earth—
the woman will return to[a][g] the man."

23 This is what the LORD Almighty, the
God of Israel, says: "When I bring them
back from captivity,[b][h] the people in the
land of Judah and in its towns will once
again use these words: 'The LORD bless[i]
you, you prosperous city,[j] you sacred
mountain.'[k] 24 People will live[l] together
in Judah and all its towns—farmers and
those who move about with their flocks.[m]
25 I will refresh the weary[n] and satisfy the
faint."[o]
26 At this I awoke[p] and looked around.
My sleep had been pleasant to me.
27 "The days are coming,"[q] declares the
LORD, "when I will plant[r] the kingdoms of
Israel and Judah with the offspring of people and of animals. 28 Just as I watched[s]
over them to uproot[t] and tear down, and
to overthrow, destroy and bring disaster,[u]
so I will watch over them to build and to
plant,"[v] declares the LORD. 29 "In those days
people will no longer say,

[a] 22 Or *will protect* [b] 23 Or *I restore their fortunes*

31:24 [l] S Jer 30:18; Zec 8:4-8 [m] S ver 12 **31:25** [n] S Isa 40:29 [o] Jn 4:14 **31:26** [p] Zec 4:1 **31:27** [q] S Jer 16:14 [r] Hos 2:23 **31:28** [s] S Job 29:2 [t] S Dt 29:28 [u] S Jer 18:8 [v] S Dt 28:63; S 30:9; S Jer 1:10; Eze 36:10-11; Am 9:14

towns through which Jerusalem's people passed on their way to exile in Babylonia (see 40:1; cf. Isa 10:29; Hos 5:8). *Rachel.* Jacob's favorite wife (see Ge 29:30) and the grandmother of Ephraim and Manasseh (see Ge 30:22–24; 48:1–2), the two most powerful tribes in the northern kingdom. The name is used here to personify that kingdom (see note on v. 2).

31:16 *for your work will be rewarded.* Echoed in 2Ch 15:7. Here the work is the bearing and raising of children.

31:17 *hope for your descendants.* See 29:11. *children will return.* Cf. Hos 11:10–11.

31:18–19 *Restore … return … strayed.* The same Hebrew root underlies all three words (see 8:4–5 and notes).

31:18 *like an unruly calf.* See Hos 4:16 and note.

31:19 *beat my breast.* A gesture of mourning and grief (see Eze 21:12; Lk 23:48 and note). Similar expressions are found in other ancient literature, such as the Babylonian *Descent of Ishtar*, verse 21; Homer, *Iliad*, 15.397–398; 16.125; *Odyssey*, 13.198–199. *ashamed and humiliated.* See Isa 45:16. *youth.* Early history (see 2:2; 3:24–25; 22:21; 32:30; Isa 54:4; Eze 16:22).

31:20 *child in whom I delight.* Cf. Isa 5:7. *Though … I have great compassion for him.* See Hos 11:1–4,8–9. *my heart yearns.* See Isa 16:11.

31:21 The departing exiles are advised to set up markers along their path to exile so that in due time they will be able to find their way back to Judah (see notes on 30:1—33:26; 32:1). *road signs.* Tombstone-shaped markers (see 2Ki 23:17; Eze 39:15). *Virgin Israel.* See v. 4 and note.

31:22 *unfaithful Daughter.* A personification of the people of Judah (see note on 2Ki 19:21), who are apostate (see 3:14,22). *create a new thing.* See Isa 42:9 and note. *return to.* Judah would someday return to the Lord and love him as her husband without reservation (see v. 32 and note). The meaning of the NIV text note ("protect") may be that, instead of God protecting Israel, Israel will at last protect God's interests (cf. Zec 3:7 and note).

31:23 *bring … back from captivity.* See note on 29:14. *The LORD bless you.* See Ps 128:5; 134:3. *prosperous city.* Jerusalem (cf. Isa 1:21,26). *sacred mountain.* The temple hill (see Ps 2:6; 48:1–2; Isa 2:2–3; 11:9; 27:13; 66:20).

31:26 *I awoke.* Jeremiah had evidently received the previous divine revelation (beginning in 30:3) in a dream (for similar examples, see Da 10:9; Zec 4:1). *sleep … pleasant.* See Pr 3:24 and note.

31:27 *plant … offspring.* See Eze 36:8–11. The same Hebrew root underlies both words. *Israel and Judah.* North and south would again be united (see 3:18 and note.)

31:28 *watched … watch.* See note on 1:12. *uproot … tear down … overthrow, destroy … build … plant.* See note on 1:10.

31:29 *The parents … set on edge.* Repeated in Eze 18:2. This was apparently a popular proverb that originated in a misunderstanding of such passages as Ex 20:5 and Nu

'The parents[w] have eaten sour
grapes,
and the children's teeth are set on
edge.'[x]

30 Instead, everyone will die for their own
sin;[y] whoever eats sour grapes—their own
teeth will be set on edge.

31 "The days are coming," declares the
LORD,
"when I will make a new
covenant[z]
with the people of Israel
and with the people of Judah.
32 It will not be like the covenant[a]
I made with their ancestors[b]
when I took them by the hand
to lead them out of Egypt,[c]
because they broke my covenant,
though I was a husband[d] to[a] them,[b]"
declares the LORD.
33 "This is the covenant I will make with
the people of Israel
after that time," declares the LORD.
"I will put my law in their minds[e]
and write it on their hearts.[f]
I will be their God,
and they will be my people.[g]
34 No longer will they teach[h] their
neighbor,
or say to one another, 'Know the
LORD,'
because they will all know[i] me,
from the least of them to the
greatest,"
declares the LORD.
"For I will forgive[j] their wickedness
and will remember their sins[k] no
more."

35 This is what the LORD says,

he who appoints[l] the sun
to shine by day,
who decrees the moon and stars
to shine by night,[m]
who stirs up the sea[n]
so that its waves roar[o]—
the LORD Almighty is his name:[p]
36 "Only if these decrees[q] vanish from my
sight,"
declares the LORD,
"will Israel[r] ever cease
being a nation before me."

37 This is what the LORD says:

"Only if the heavens above can be
measured[s]
and the foundations of the earth
below be searched out

31:29 [w] S Ge 9:25; Dt 24:16; La 5:7 [x] Eze 18:2 **31:30** [y] S 2Ki 14:6; S Isa 3:11; Gal 6:7 **31:31** [z] S Dt 29:14; S Isa 42:6; S 54:10; S Lk 22:20; Heb 8:8-12*; 10:16-17 **31:32** [a] S Ex 24:8 [b] Dt 5:3 [c] Jer 11:4 [d] S Isa 54:5 **31:33** [e] S Ex 4:15 [f] S Dt 6:6; S 2Co 3:3 [g] S Jer 11:4; Heb 10:16 **31:34** [h] 1Jn 2:27 [i] S Isa 11:9; S Jn 6:45 [j] Ps 85:2; 130:4; Jer 33:8; 50:20 [k] S Job 7:21; S Isa 38:17; Mic 7:19; Heb 10:17* **31:35** [l] Ps 136:7-9 [m] S Ge 1:16 [n] S Ex 14:21 [o] S Ps 93:3 [p] S Jer 10:16 **31:36** [q] S Job 38:33; Jer 33:20-26 [r] Ps 89:36-37 **31:37** [s] S Job 38:5; Jer 33:22

[a] 32 Hebrew; Septuagint and Syriac / *and I turned away from* [b] 32 Or *was their master*

14:18, which teach that sins can have a negative effect on descendants. In the time of Jeremiah and Ezekiel, many people felt that God's hand of judgment against them was due not to their own sins but to the sins of their ancestors.

31:30 *everyone will die for their own sin.* See Dt 24:16; Eze 18:3,20; 33:7–18. Although group or collective responsibility is an important concept, Jeremiah and Ezekiel emphasize individual responsibility as both preparation and explanation for the imminent destruction of Jerusalem, which the people might have been tempted to blame on the sins of their ancestors.

31:31–34 The high point of Jeremiah's prophecies, this passage is the longest sequence of OT verses to be quoted in its entirety in the NT (see note on Heb 8:8–12; see also Heb 10:16–17). Verse 31 contains the only OT use of the phrase "new covenant," which (together with its NT echoes) has come down to us (via Latin) as "new testament," the name that would later be applied to the distinctively Christian part of the Biblical canon.

31:31 *The days are coming.* See vv. 27,38; a phrase that often refers to the Messianic era. *make.* Lit. "cut" (see notes on 34:18; Ge 15:18). *new covenant.* See note on vv. 31–34. As the old covenant was put into effect with the shedding of the blood of animals (Ex 24:4–8), so the new would be put into effect with the shedding of the blood of Christ (see Mt 26:28 and NIV text note; Mk 14:24; Lk 22:20 and notes; 1Co 11:25; 2Co 3:6; Heb 9:15; 12:24). *people of Israel ... people of Judah.* The reunited people of God (see 3:18 and note).

31:32 *covenant I made with their ancestors.* See 7:23; 11:1–8; Ex 19:5; 20:22—23:19 and notes. The covenant at Sinai eventually became known as the "old covenant" (2Co 3:14) or "first covenant" (Heb 8:7; 9:15,18). *took them by the hand.* See Hos 11:3–4. *they broke my covenant.* See 11:10. The people, not God, were responsible for violating his covenant (see note on Isa 24:5). *I was a husband.* See 3:14 and note.

31:33 *people of Israel.* Here includes both Israel and Judah (see v. 31 and note on 3:18). *put my law in their minds.* Internally (see Dt 6:6; 11:18; 30:14; Eze 11:19; 18:31; 36:26–27), in contrast to setting it before them externally (see 9:13; Dt 4:8; 11:32). *write it on their hearts.* So that it effectively governs their lives, in contrast to the ineffectiveness of merely presenting it in writing, though inscribed on durable stone (see Ex 24:4; 31:18; 32:15–16; 34:28–29; Dt 4:13; 5:22; 9:9,11; 10:4). *their God ... my people.* See note on 7:23. The "new" covenant fulfills the "old" and achieves its purpose (cf. Mt 5:17 and note).

31:34 *No longer ... teach their neighbor.* When the Lord has done his new work, there will no longer be among his people those who are ignorant of him and his will for human lives. True knowledge of the Lord will be shared by all—young and old, the peasant and the powerful (see 5:4–5 and notes; see also 32:38–40; Isa 54:13 and note; Eze 11:19–20; 36:25–27; Eph 3:12; Heb 4:16; 10:19–22). *Know.* In the experiential, not the academic, sense (see Ex 6:3 and note). *I will forgive ... their sins.* The glorious benefit of the new covenant (see Ro 11:27; Heb 10:16–18 and notes).

31:35 *appoints the sun ... moon ... stars.* See Ge 1:16–18 and notes. *who stirs up ... is his name.* The same line is found in Isa 51:15 (see Ps 46:3; Isa 17:12).

31:36 See 33:20–21,25–26. Just as God's creation order is established and secure, so also Israel will always have descendants.

31:37 *Only if ... will I reject all.* Israel will continue to exist as a remnant (cf. Lev 26:44; Ro 11:5 and notes), even though a terrible judgment is about to sweep the kingdom of Judah away.

will I reject[t] all the descendants of
Israel
because of all they have done,"
declares the LORD.

38 "The days are coming," declares the
LORD, "when this city will be rebuilt[u] for
me from the Tower of Hananel[v] to the
Corner Gate.[w] 39 The measuring line[x] will
stretch from there straight to the hill of Gareb and then turn to Goah. 40 The whole
valley[y] where dead bodies[z] and ashes are
thrown, and all the terraces out to the Kidron Valley[a] on the east as far as the corner of the Horse Gate,[b] will be holy[c] to the
LORD. The city will never again be uprooted or demolished."

Jeremiah Buys a Field

32 This is the word that came to Jeremiah from the LORD in the tenth[d]
year of Zedekiah king of Judah, which
was the eighteenth[e] year of Nebuchadnezzar. 2 The army of the king of Babylon was
then besieging[f] Jerusalem, and Jeremiah
the prophet was confined[g] in the courtyard
of the guard[h] in the royal palace of Judah.
3 Now Zedekiah king of Judah had imprisoned him there, saying, "Why do you
prophesy[i] as you do? You say, 'This is
what the LORD says: I am about to give
this city into the hands of the king of Babylon, and he will capture[j] it. 4 Zedekiah[k]
king of Judah will not escape[l] the Babylonians[a][m] but will certainly be given into
the hands of the king of Babylon, and will
speak with him face to face and see him
with his own eyes. 5 He will take[n] Zedekiah to Babylon, where he will remain until
I deal with him,[o] declares the LORD. If you
fight against the Babylonians, you will not
succeed.' "[p]
6 Jeremiah said, "The word of the LORD
came to me: 7 Hanamel son of Shallum
your uncle is going to come to you and
say, 'Buy my field at Anathoth,[q] because
as nearest relative it is your right and duty[r]
to buy it.'
8 "Then, just as the LORD had said, my
cousin Hanamel came to me in the courtyard of the guard and said, 'Buy my field[s]
at Anathoth in the territory of Benjamin.
Since it is your right to redeem it and possess it, buy it for yourself.'
"I knew that this was the word of the
LORD; 9 so I bought the field[t] at Anathoth
from my cousin Hanamel and weighed out
for him seventeen shekels[b] of silver.[u] 10 I
signed and sealed the deed,[v] had it witnessed,[w] and weighed out the silver on the
scales. 11 I took the deed of purchase—the
sealed copy containing the terms and conditions, as well as the unsealed copy—
12 and I gave this deed to Baruch[x] son of
Neriah,[y] the son of Mahseiah, in the presence of my cousin Hanamel and of the

[a] 4 Or *Chaldeans;* also in verses 5, 24, 25, 28, 29 and 43
[b] 9 That is, about 7 ounces or about 200 grams

31:37 [t] Jer 33:24-26; Ro 11:1-5 **31:38** [u] S Jer 30:18 [v] S Ne 3:1 [w] S 2Ki 14:13; S 2Ch 25:23 **31:39** [x] S 1Ki 7:23 **31:40** [y] S Jer 2:23; 7:31-32 [z] S Jer 8:2 [a] S 2Sa 15:23; Jn 18:1 [b] S 2Ki 11:16 [c] S Isa 4:3; Joel 3:17; Zec 14:21 **32:1** [d] 2Ki 25:1 [e] Jer 25:1 **32:2** [f] S 2Ki 25:1 [g] S Ps 88:8 [h] S Ne 3:25 **32:3** [i] Jer 26:8-9 [j] ver 28; Jer 21:4; 34:2-3 **32:4** [k] Jer 34:21; 44:30 [l] S Jer 21:7; 38:18,23; 39:5-7; 52:9 [m] ver 24 **32:5** [n] Jer 39:7; Eze 12:13 [o] S 2Ki 25:7 [p] Jer 21:4; La 1:14 **32:7** [q] S Jos 21:18 [r] Lev 25:24-25; S Ru 4:3-4; Mt 27:10* **32:8** [s] ver 25 **32:9** [t] Jer 37:12 [u] S Ge 23:16 **32:10** [v] Ge 23:20 [w] S Ru 4:9; S Isa 8:2 **32:12** [x] ver 16; Jer 36:4; 43:3,6; 45:1 [y] Jer 51:59

31:38–40 See Zec 14:10–11.
31:38 *this city.* Jerusalem. *Tower of Hananel ... Corner Gate.* The eastern and western ends of the northern wall (see note on Zec 14:10).
31:39 *measuring line.* Mentioned in connection with restored Jerusalem also in Eze 40:3; Zec 1:16; 2:1. *Gareb ... Goah.* Probably west of Jerusalem.
31:40 *valley.* Probably the Hinnom Valley (see 2:23 and note). *Horse Gate.* See note on Ne 3:28. *holy to the LORD.* See Zec 14:20 and note. *uprooted ... demolished.* See note on 1:10. Jerusalem, the city of God, will endure. For the ultimate fulfillment, cf. Gal 4:26 and note; Rev 21:1–5.
32:1–44 Though with some reluctance (see v. 25), Jeremiah obeys the Lord's command to buy a field in Anathoth from his cousin (see vv. 8–9) even as the Babylonians are laying siege to Jerusalem (see vv. 2,24).
32:1 *tenth year of Zedekiah ... eighteenth year of Nebuchadnezzar.* 587 BC, the year before Jerusalem was destroyed by the Babylonians (see 52:12–13). The siege began in 588 (see 39:1–2 and notes).
32:2 *confined in the courtyard of the guard.* See Ne 3:25 and note. Jeremiah was imprisoned by King Zedekiah (see 37:21) and remained in the courtyard of the guard until Jerusalem fell (see 38:13,28; 39:14).
32:3–5 See 21:3–7; 34:2–5; 37:17. The fulfillment is recorded in 52:7–14.
32:5 *until I deal with him.* After his capture by the Babylonians, Zedekiah was taken to Babylon, where he eventually died (see 52:11). *you will not succeed.* See note on 29:4.
32:7 *Anathoth.* Jeremiah's hometown (see note on 1:1). *as nearest relative ... duty to buy it.* In accordance with the ancient law of redemption (see Lev 25:23–25 and notes on 25:24–25; see also notes on Ru 2:20; 4:3).
32:8 *came to me in the courtyard.* Though imprisoned, Jeremiah was allowed to have visitors. *in the territory of Benjamin.* Some time earlier Jeremiah had been on his way home "to get his share of the property" in Benjamin (37:12), but he was arrested, falsely accused of treason and thrown into prison (see 37:13–16).
32:9 *so I bought.* In obedience to the Lord's command (see v. 7). *weighed out.* Coinage had not yet been invented. *seventeen shekels of silver.* See NIV text note. The size of the field is unknown, but the price was probably not exorbitant (contrast Ge 23:15; see note there).
32:10 *sealed.* Not to attest his signature (as, e.g., in Est 3:12; see note on Ge 38:18) but to guarantee the contents of the deed and keep it from being tampered with (see Isa 8:16; 29:11; Da 12:4,9; Rev 15:1–5).
32:11 *unsealed copy.* For ready reference, the authenticity of which would then be guaranteed by the sealed copy if the unsealed deed should be lost, damaged or changed (deliberately or otherwise). Examples of tied and sealed papyrus documents of the fifth and subsequent centuries BC have been found at Elephantine in southern Egypt, in the desert of Judah west of the Dead Sea, and elsewhere (see chart, p. xxii).
32:12 *Baruch.* Means "blessed (by the LORD)." He was Jeremiah's faithful secretary and friend (see Introduction: Author and Date).

witnesses who had signed the deed and
of all the Jews sitting in the courtyard of
the guard.
13 "In their presence I gave Baruch these
instructions: 14 'This is what the LORD Almighty, the God of Israel, says: Take these
documents, both the sealed[z] and unsealed
copies of the deed of purchase, and put
them in a clay jar so they will last a long
time. 15 For this is what the LORD Almighty,
the God of Israel, says: Houses, fields and
vineyards will again be bought in this land.'[a]
16 "After I had given the deed of purchase to Baruch[b] son of Neriah, I prayed
to the LORD:

17 "Ah, Sovereign LORD,[c] you have
made the heavens and the earth[d] by
your great power and outstretched
arm.[e] Nothing is too hard[f] for you.
18 You show love[g] to thousands but
bring the punishment for the parents'
sins into the laps[h] of their children[i]
after them. Great and mighty God,[j]
whose name is the LORD Almighty,[k]
19 great are your purposes and mighty
are your deeds.[l] Your eyes are open
to the ways of all mankind;[m] you reward each person according to their
conduct and as their deeds deserve.[n]
20 You performed signs and wonders[o]
in Egypt[p] and have continued them to
this day, in Israel and among all mankind, and have gained the renown[q]
that is still yours. 21 You brought your
people Israel out of Egypt with signs
and wonders, by a mighty hand[r] and
an outstretched arm[s] and with great
terror.[t] 22 You gave them this land you
had sworn to give their ancestors, a
land flowing with milk and honey.[u]
23 They came in and took possession[v]
of it, but they did not obey you or follow your law;[w] they did not do what
you commanded them to do. So you
brought all this disaster[x] on them.
24 "See how the siege ramps[y] are
built up to take the city. Because of
the sword, famine and plague,[z] the
city will be given into the hands of
the Babylonians who are attacking it.
What you said[a] has happened,[b] as you
now see. 25 And though the city will
be given into the hands of the Babylonians, you, Sovereign LORD, say
to me, 'Buy the field[c] with silver and
have the transaction witnessed.[d]' "

26 Then the word of the LORD came to
Jeremiah: 27 "I am the LORD, the God of all
mankind.[e] Is anything too hard for me?[f]
28 Therefore this is what the LORD says: I
am about to give this city into the hands of
the Babylonians and to Nebuchadnezzar[g]
king of Babylon, who will capture it.[h] 29 The
Babylonians who are attacking this city will
come in and set it on fire; they will burn it
down,[i] along with the houses[j] where the
people aroused my anger by burning incense on the roofs to Baal and by pouring
out drink offerings[k] to other gods.[l]
30 "The people of Israel and Judah have
done nothing but evil in my sight from
their youth;[m] indeed, the people of Israel have done nothing but arouse my anger[n] with what their hands have made,[o]
declares the LORD. 31 From the day it was

32:14 [z] S Isa 8:16 **32:15** [a] ver 43-44; Isa 44:26; Jer 30:18; Eze 28:26; Am 9:14-15 **32:16** [b] S ver 12 **32:17** [c] Jer 1:6 [d] S Ge 1:1; S Jer 10:16 [e] S Dt 9:29; 2Ki 19:15; Ps 102:25 [f] S 2Ki 3:18; Jer 51:15; S Mt 19:26 **32:18** [g] S Dt 5:10 [h] S Ps 79:12 [i] S Ex 20:5; S Ps 109:14 [j] Jer 10:6 [k] S Jer 10:16 **32:19** [l] S Job 12:13; Da 2:20 [m] S Job 14:16; S Pr 5:21; Jer 16:17 [n] S Job 34:11; S Mt 16:27 **32:20** [o] S Ex 3:20; S Job 9:10 [p] Ex 9:16 [q] S Isa 55:13; S Jer 13:11 **32:21** [r] S Ex 6:6; Da 9:15 [s] S Dt 5:15; S Jer 6:12 [t] S Dt 26:8 **32:22** [u] S Ex 3:8; Eze 20:6 **32:23** [v] S Ps 44:2; 78:54-55 [w] S Ex 16:28; S Jos 1:7; S 1Ki 9:6; S Jer 11:8 [x] S Dt 28:64; 31:29; Da 9:14 **32:24** [y] S 2Sa 20:15; S Jer 6:6 [z] S Jer 14:12 [a] Dt 4:25-26; Jos 23:15-16 [b] S Dt 28:2 **32:25** [c] S ver 8 [d] S Isa 8:2 **32:27** [e] S Nu 16:22 [f] S Ge 18:14; S 2Ki 3:18 **32:28** [g] S 2Ch 36:17 [h] S ver 3; S Jer 21:10 **32:29** [i] S 2Ch 36:19 [j] S Jer 19:13 [k] Jer 44:18 [l] S Jer 7:9 **32:30** [m] S Ps 25:7; S Jer 22:21 [n] Jer 8:19 [o] Jer 25:7

32:14 *put them in a clay jar so they will last a long time.* Documents found in clay jars at Elephantine (see note on v. 11) and Qumran (west of the Dead Sea) were preserved almost intact for more than 2,000 years (see essay, pp. 1574–1576).
32:15 Jeremiah's deed of purchase would enable him (or his heirs) to reclaim the field as soon as normal economic activity resumed after the exile.
32:17 See 27:5. *great power and outstretched arm.* See v. 21; see also note on 21:5. *Nothing is too hard for you.* See note on Ge 18:14. The Lord's reply to Jeremiah echoes these words (see v. 27).
32:18 *show love to thousands but ... punishment for the parents' sins.* See Ex 20:5–6; 34:7; see also note on Ex 20:6. *bring ... into the laps.* A symbol of retribution (see Ps 79:12; Isa 65:6–7; cf. Lk 6:38 and note). *Great and mighty God.* See Dt 10:17. *whose name is the LORD Almighty.* See 31:35; Isa 54:5; Am 4:13; see also note on 1Sa 1:3.
32:19 *great are your purposes and ... deeds.* See Ps 66:5; Isa 9:6; 28:29. *you reward each person ... as their deeds deserve.* Repeated verbatim from 17:10 (see note there; see also Ro 2:6 and note; 1Co 3:8; Eph 6:8).
32:20 *signs and wonders.* See v. 21; Ex 7:3; see also notes on Ex 3:12; 4:8.
32:21 Echoes Dt 26:8 (see also Dt 4:34). *mighty hand ... outstretched arm.* See v. 17 and note on 21:5. *great terror.* See Ex 15:14–16.
32:22 *land flowing with milk and honey.* See 11:5; see also note on Ex 3:8.
32:24 *siege ramps.* See 6:6; 33:4; see also note on Isa 37:33. *sword, famine and plague.* See note on 14:12.
32:25 Jeremiah expresses his doubts concerning what must seem to him to be an unwise investment. Nevertheless, he remains the obedient servant (see vv. 8–9).
32:27 *the LORD, the God of all mankind.* Echoes Nu 16:22; 27:16, emphasizing God's universal dominion. *Is anything too hard for me?* Responds to the description in Jeremiah's prayer (see v. 17 and note on Ge 18:14), stressing God's omnipotence. God is worthy of obedience because he is always faithful in fulfilling his promises.
32:29 *burn it down.* See 21:10; 34:2; 37:8. *aroused my anger.* See 7:18; Dt 31:29. *burning incense ... to Baal.* See 1:16 and note. *on the roofs.* See note on 19:13. *drink offerings to other gods.* See 7:18 and note; 19:13.
32:30 Echoes Dt 31:29. *youth.* See note on 31:19. *what their hands have made.* A reference to idols.
32:31 *remove it from my sight.* See 52:3; 2Ki 24:3.

built until now, this city[p] has so aroused my anger and wrath that I must remove[q] it from my sight. 32 The people of Israel and Judah have provoked[r] me by all the evil[s] they have done—they, their kings and officials,[t] their priests and prophets, the people of Judah and those living in Jerusalem. 33 They turned their backs[u] to me and not their faces; though I taught[v] them again and again, they would not listen or respond to discipline.[w] 34 They set up their vile images[x] in the house that bears my Name[y] and defiled[z] it. 35 They built high places for Baal in the Valley of Ben Hinnom[a] to sacrifice their sons and daughters to Molek,[b] though I never commanded—nor did it enter my mind[c]—that they should do such a detestable[d] thing and so make Judah sin.[e]

36 "You are saying about this city, 'By the sword, famine and plague[f] it will be given into the hands of the king of Babylon'; but this is what the LORD, the God of Israel, says: 37 I will surely gather[g] them from all the lands where I banish them in my furious anger[h] and great wrath; I will bring them back to this place and let them live in safety.[i] 38 They will be my people,[j] and I will be their God. 39 I will give them singleness[k] of heart and action, so that they will always fear[l] me and that all will then go well for them and for their children after them. 40 I will make an everlasting covenant[m] with them: I will never stop doing good to them, and I will inspire[n] them to fear me, so that they will never turn away from me.[o] 41 I will rejoice[p] in doing them good[q] and will assuredly plant[r] them in this land with all my heart and soul.[s]

42 "This is what the LORD says: As I have brought all this great calamity[t] on this people, so I will give them all the prosperity I have promised[u] them. 43 Once more fields will be bought[v] in this land of which you say, 'It is a desolate[w] waste, without people or animals, for it has been given into the hands of the Babylonians.' 44 Fields will be bought for silver, and deeds[x] will be signed, sealed and witnessed[y] in the territory of Benjamin, in the villages around Jerusalem, in the towns of Judah and in the towns of the hill country, of the western foothills and of the Negev,[z] because I will restore[a] their fortunes,[a] declares the LORD."

Promise of Restoration

33 While Jeremiah was still confined[b] in the courtyard[c] of the guard, the word of the LORD came to him a second time:[d] 2 "This is what the LORD says, he who made the earth,[e] the LORD who formed it and established it—the LORD is his name:[f] 3 'Call[g] to me and I will answer you and tell you great and unsearchable[h]

32:31 [p] 1Ki 11:7-8; 2Ki 21:4-5; Mt 23:37 [q] S 2Ki 23:27 **32:32** [r] S 1Ki 14:9 [s] Da 9:8 [t] S Jer 2:26; S 44:9 **32:33** [u] S 1Ki 14:9; S Ps 14:3; Jer 2:27; Eze 8:16; Zec 7:11 [v] S Dt 4:5; S Isa 28:9; S Jer 7:13 [w] S Jer 7:28 **32:34** [x] S 2Ki 21:4; Eze 8:3-16 [y] Jer 7:10; 34:15 [z] S Jer 7:30 **32:35** [a] Jer 19:2 [b] S Lev 18:21 [c] S Jer 19:5 [d] S 1Ki 14:24 [e] S Jer 25:7 **32:36** [f] ver 24 **32:37** [g] S Isa 11:12 [h] Jer 21:5 [i] S Lev 25:18; Eze 34:28; 39:26 **32:38** [j] Jer 24:7; 2Co 6:16* **32:39** [k] S 2Ch 30:12; S Ps 86:11; Jn 17:21; Ac 4:32 [l] S Dt 6:24; S 10:16 **32:40** [m] S Ge 9:16; S Isa 42:6 [n] S Dt 4:10 [o] S Jer 24:7

[a] 44 Or *will bring them back from captivity*

32:41 [p] S Dt 28:63; S Isa 62:4 [q] S Dt 28:3-12 [r] Jer 24:6; 31:28 [s] Mic 7:18 **32:42** [t] La 3:38 [u] S Jer 29:10 **32:43** [v] ver 15 [w] Jer 33:12 **32:44** [x] ver 10 [y] S Ru 4:9; S Isa 8:2 [z] S Jer 17:26 [a] S Ezr 9:9; Ps 14:7 **33:1** [b] S Ps 88:8 [c] Jer 37:21; 38:28 [d] Jer 13:3 **33:2** [e] S Ps 136:6; S Jer 10:16 [f] S Ex 3:15 **33:3** [g] S Isa 55:6 [h] S Job 28:11

32:32 *kings ... officials ... priests ... prophets.* See 1:18 and note.
32:33 *again and again.* See note on 7:13. *not ... respond to discipline.* See 2:30; 5:3; 7:28; 17:23.
32:34–35 Repeated from 7:30–31 (see notes there).
32:34 *house that bears my Name.* See 7:10 and note.
32:35 *Molek.* The god of the Ammonites (see 49:1,3; see also note on Lev 18:21). *nor did it enter my mind.* See 7:31 and note.
32:36 *You.* The people of Judah as a whole. *sword, famine and plague.* See note on 14:12. *but.* After judgment on the wicked comes restoration for the righteous.
32:37 See Dt 30:1–5. *furious anger and great wrath.* See note on 21:5. *bring them back ... let them live.* See Eze 36:11,33; Hos 11:11. The Hebrew underlying the first phrase sounds like that underlying the second.
32:38 See 31:33; see also note on 7:23.
32:39 *singleness of heart.* See 24:7; 31:32 and note; Eze 11:19. *their children after them.* See Dt 4:9–10.
32:40 *everlasting covenant.* See 31:37; 33:17–26; Isa 55:3 and notes; Eze 16:60; 37:26. *inspire them to fear me.* See Dt 6:24; see also note on Ge 20:11. *never turn away from me.* See 26:3; Isa 53:6.
32:41 *rejoice in doing them good.* See Dt 30:9; Isa 62:5; 65:19.
32:43–44 *fields will be bought.* The field purchased by Jeremiah (see v. 9) is symbolic of the many fields that will be purchased in Judah after the Babylonian exile, when economic conditions return to normal (see note on v. 15).
32:43 *you.* See note on v. 36. *desolate waste, without people or animals.* See 4:23–26 and notes.
32:44 *territory of Benjamin.* See 1:1. Here Benjamin is mentioned first because it was the region in which Jeremiah's hometown was located (see vv. 7–8 and notes). *hill country ... western foothills.* See note on Dt 1:7. *Negev.* See note on Ge 12:9. *restore their fortunes.* See NIV text note; see also note on 29:14.
33:1–26 Concluding Jeremiah's "book of consolation" (see note on 30:1—33:26), the section is divided into two roughly equal parts: (1) vv. 1–13, which continue and build on ch. 32, and (2) vv. 14–26, which summarize a wider range of earlier passages in Jeremiah and elsewhere. This section is not found in the Septuagint (the pre-Christian Greek translation of the OT).
33:1 *still confined.* In 587 BC (see note on 32:1). *courtyard of the guard.* See 32:2 and note. *a second time.* Ch. 32 comprises the first time.
33:2 See 10:12; 32:17; 51:15; see also 31:35 and note.
33:3 *Call ... and I will answer.* The prayers of God's people invite—and assure—God's response (see Ps 3:4; 4:3; 18:6; 27:7; 28:1–2; 30:8; 55:17; 118:5 and note; Mt 7:7; contrast 11:14). *great and unsearchable.* The Hebrew for this phrase usually refers to the formidable cities of Canaan and is translated "large, with walls up to the sky" (Dt 1:28; see Nu 13:28; Dt 9:1; Jos 14:12). *unsearchable things you do not know.* The Hebrew (with the change of one letter) for this phrase echoes Isa 48:6: "hidden things unknown to you." As the rest of ch. 33 demonstrates, the Lord will first judge his people (vv. 4–5) and then restore them in ways that will be nothing short of incredible (vv. 6–26).

things you do not know.' 4 For this is what the LORD, the God of Israel, says about the houses in this city and the royal palaces of Judah that have been torn down to be used against the siege[i] ramps[j] and the sword 5 in the fight with the Babylonians[a]: 'They will be filled with the dead bodies of the people I will slay in my anger and wrath.[k] I will hide my face[l] from this city because of all its wickedness.

6 " 'Nevertheless, I will bring health and healing to it; I will heal[m] my people and will let them enjoy abundant peace[n] and security. 7 I will bring Judah[o] and Israel back from captivity[b][p] and will rebuild[q] them as they were before.[r] 8 I will cleanse[s] them from all the sin they have committed against me and will forgive[t] all their sins of rebellion against me. 9 Then this city will bring me renown,[u] joy, praise[v] and honor[w] before all nations on earth that hear of all the good things I do for it; and they will be in awe and will tremble[x] at the abundant prosperity and peace I provide for it.'

10 "This is what the LORD says: 'You say about this place, "It is a desolate waste, without people or animals."[y] Yet in the towns of Judah and the streets of Jerusalem that are deserted,[z] inhabited by neither people nor animals, there will be heard once more 11 the sounds of joy and gladness,[a] the voices of bride and bridegroom, and the voices of those who bring thank offerings[b] to the house of the LORD, saying,

"Give thanks to the LORD Almighty,
for the LORD is good;[c]
his love endures forever."[d]

For I will restore the fortunes[e] of the land as they were before,[f]' says the LORD.

12 "This is what the LORD Almighty says: 'In this place, desolate[g] and without people or animals[h]—in all its towns there will again be pastures for shepherds to rest their flocks.[i] 13 In the towns of the hill[j] country, of the western foothills and of the Negev,[k] in the territory of Benjamin, in the villages around Jerusalem and in the towns of Judah, flocks will again pass under the hand[l] of the one who counts them,' says the LORD.

14 " 'The days are coming,' declares the LORD, 'when I will fulfill the good promise[m] I made to the people of Israel and Judah.

15 " 'In those days and at that time
I will make a righteous[n] Branch[o]
sprout from David's line;[p]
he will do what is just and right in
the land.
16 In those days Judah will be saved[q]
and Jerusalem will live in safety.[r]
This is the name by which it[c] will be
called:[s]
The LORD Our Righteous Savior.'[t]

17 For this is what the LORD says: 'David will never fail[u] to have a man to sit on the throne of Israel, 18 nor will the Levitical[v] priests[w] ever fail to have a man to stand before me continually to offer burnt

33:4 [i] S 2Ki 25:1; Eze 4:2 [j] Jer 32:24; Eze 26:8; Hab 1:10 **33:5** [k] Jer 21:4-7 [l] S Dt 31:17; S Isa 8:17 **33:6** [m] S Dt 32:39; S Isa 30:26 [n] S Isa 9:6 **33:7** [o] Jer 32:44 [p] Jer 30:3; Eze 39:25; Am 9:14 [q] S Jer 24:6 [r] S Isa 1:26 **33:8** [s] S Lev 16:30; Heb 9:13-14 [t] S 2Sa 24:14; S Jer 31:34 **33:9** [u] S Isa 55:13 [v] S Isa 60:18 [w] S Jer 3:17 [x] S Isa 64:2 **33:10** [y] Jer 32:43 [z] S Lev 26:32; S Jer 9:11 **33:11** [a] S Ps 51:8; S Isa 24:8; S 51:3 [b] S Lev 7:12 [c] S 2Ch 7:3; Ps 25:8; S 136:1; Na 1:7 [d] S 1Ch 16:34; 2Ch 5:13; Ps 100:4-5 [e] Ps 14:7 [f] S Isa 1:26 **33:12** [g] Jer 32:43 [h] ver 10 [i] S Isa 65:10; Eze 34:11-15 **33:13** [j] S Jer 31:5 [k] S Jer 17:26; Ob 1:20 [l] S Lev 27:32

[a] 5 Or *Chaldeans* [b] 7 Or *will restore the fortunes of Judah and Israel* [c] 16 Or *he*

33:14 [m] Dt 28:1-14; S Jos 23:15; S Jer 29:10 **33:15** [n] S Ps 72:2 [o] S Isa 4:2 [p] S 2Sa 7:12 **33:16** [q] S Isa 45:17 [r] S Jer 17:25; S 32:37 [s] Isa 59:14; Jer 3:17; Eze 48:35; Zep 3:13; Zec 8:3, 16 [t] S 1Co 1:30 **33:17** [u] S 2Sa 7:13; S 2Ch 7:18; Ps 89:29-37; S Lk 1:33 **33:18** [v] S Dt 18:1 [w] S Nu 25:11-13; Heb 7:17-22

33:4 Jerusalem's houses—including those of the king—were torn down so that their stones could be used to repair the city's battered walls (see Isa 22:10 and note). *siege ramps.* See 6:6 and note.
33:5 *fight with the Babylonians.* See 32:5. *dead bodies.* Of Jerusalem's defenders.
33:6–16 The glorious restoration of Jerusalem (see Isa 35:1–10 and notes).
33:6 *health and healing.* See 30:17; contrast 8:22.
33:7 *bring ... back from captivity.* See vv. 11,26; see also note on 29:14. *Judah and Israel.* See note on 3:18.
33:8 *forgive all their sins.* The basis of the institution of the new covenant (see 31:34 and note; see also 50:20; Eze 36:25–26).
33:9 *tremble at the abundant prosperity.* See Hos 3:5 and note.
33:10 See 32:43 and note.
33:11 *joy and gladness ... bride and bridegroom.* The glorious reversal of the judgment proclaimed in 7:34; 16:9; 25:10. *those who bring thank offerings.* See note on 17:26. *restore the fortunes.* See note on 29:14.
33:13 *hill country ... towns of Judah.* See 17:26 and note; 32:44. *flocks ... pass under the hand ... counts them.* See Eze 20:37 and note.
33:15–16 Repeated from 23:5–6 (see notes there).
33:15 *what is just and right.* See note on Ps 119:121.
33:16 *it will be called.* Because of Jerusalem's intimate relationship to the Messiah, it is given the same name by which he is called in 23:6 (for other examples, see Jdg 6:24; Eze 48:35). But see NIV text note.
33:17–26 In the face of the impending judgment in which the nation will be swept away and the promised land reduced to a desolate wasteland, all God's past covenants with his people appear to be rendered of no effect—his covenants with Israel, with David and with Phinehas (see chart, p. 23). This series of messages, however, gives reassurance that the ancient covenants are not being repudiated, that they are as secure as God's covenant concerning the creation order and that in the future restoration they will all yet be fulfilled.
33:17 See 2Sa 7:12–16; 1Ki 2:4; 8:25; 9:5; 2Ch 6:16; 7:18. This passage is fulfilled ultimately in Jesus (see Lk 1:32–33 and notes).
33:18 See Nu 25:13. The priestly covenant with the Levites, like the royal covenant with David, was not a private grant to the priestly family involving only that family and the Lord. It was rather an integral part of the Lord's dealings with his people, in which Israel was assured of the ministry of a priesthood that was acceptable to the Lord and through whose mediation God's people could enjoy communion with him. That ministry was and is being fulfilled by

offerings, to burn grain offerings and to present sacrifices.[x]' "

[19]The word of the LORD came to Jeremiah: [20]"This is what the LORD says: 'If you can break my covenant with the day[y] and my covenant with the night, so that day and night no longer come at their appointed time,[z] [21]then my covenant[a] with David my servant—and my covenant with the Levites[b] who are priests ministering before me—can be broken and David will no longer have a descendant to reign on his throne.[c] [22]I will make the descendants of David my servant and the Levites who minister before me as countless[d] as the stars in the sky and as measureless as the sand on the seashore.' "

[23]The word of the LORD came to Jeremiah: [24]"Have you not noticed that these people are saying, 'The LORD has rejected the two kingdoms[a][e] he chose'? So they despise[f] my people and no longer regard them as a nation.[g] [25]This is what the LORD says: 'If I have not made my covenant with day and night[h] and established the laws[i] of heaven and earth,[j] [26]then I will reject[k] the descendants of Jacob[l] and David my servant and will not choose one of his sons to rule over the descendants of Abraham, Isaac and Jacob. For I will restore their fortunes[b][m] and have compassion[n] on them.' "

33:18 [x]Heb 13:15
33:20 [y]Ps 89:36 [z]S Ge 1:14
33:21 [a]Ps 89:34 [b]S Dt 18:1 [c]S 2Sa 7:13; S 2Ch 7:18
33:22 [d]S Ge 12:2; S Jer 30:19; Hos 1:10
33:24 [e]Eze 37:22 [f]S Ne 4:4 [g]S Jer 30:17; Eze 36:20
33:25 [h]S Ge 1:18 [i]S Ps 148:6 [j]Ps 74:16-17
33:26 [k]S Lev 26:44 [l]S Isa 14:1 [m]ver 7; Ps 14:7 [n]S Jer 30:18
34:1 [o]Jer 27:7 [p]2Ki 25:1; Jer 39:1
34:2 [q]S 2Ch 36:11 [r]ver 22; Jer 32:29; 37:8
34:3 [s]S 2Ki 25:7; S Jer 21:7
34:4 [t]Jer 52:11
34:5 [u]S 2Ch 16:14 [v]Jer 22:18

Warning to Zedekiah

34 While Nebuchadnezzar king of Babylon and all his army and all the kingdoms and peoples[o] in the empire he ruled were fighting against Jerusalem[p] and all its surrounding towns, this word came to Jeremiah from the LORD: [2]"This is what the LORD, the God of Israel, says: Go to Zedekiah[q] king of Judah and tell him, 'This is what the LORD says: I am about to give this city into the hands of the king of Babylon, and he will burn it down.[r] [3]You will not escape from his grasp but will surely be captured and given into his hands.[s] You will see the king of Babylon with your own eyes, and he will speak with you face to face. And you will go to Babylon.

[4]" 'Yet hear the LORD's promise to you, Zedekiah king of Judah. This is what the LORD says concerning you: You will not die by the sword;[t] [5]you will die peacefully. As people made a funeral fire[u] in honor of your predecessors, the kings who ruled before you, so they will make a fire in your honor and lament, "Alas,[v] master!" I myself make this promise, declares the LORD.' "

[6]Then Jeremiah the prophet told all this to Zedekiah king of Judah, in Jerusalem, [7]while the army of the king of Babylon

[a] *24* Or *families* [b] *26* Or *will bring them back from captivity*

Jesus, who administers a higher and better priesthood (see Ps 110:4; Heb 5:6–10; 6:19–20; 7:11–25). *Levitical priests.* See Dt 17:9,18.

33:20 *covenant with the day and ... the night.* See v. 25; 31:35–36. Although reference may be to God's sovereign establishment of the creation order in the beginning, more likely the covenant of Ge 9:8–17 (see Ge 8:22) is in view.

33:21 *covenant with the Levites.* See Mal 2:4.

33:22 In words that echo the covenant promises to the patriarchs (Abraham, Ge 22:17; Isaac, Ge 26:4; Jacob, Ge 32:12), the Lord assures the flourishing of the two mediatorial (royal and priestly) families and thus the continuation of this ministry in the spiritual commonwealth he has established with his people. This promise of a numerous progeny to both the royal and priestly families is no doubt fulfilled in that great throng who (will) reign with Christ (see Ro 5:17; 8:17; 1Co 6:3; 2Ti 2:12; Rev 3:21; 5:10; 20:5–6; 22:5; see also Mt 19:28; Lk 22:30) and who in Christ have been consecrated to be priests (see 1Pe 2:5,9; Rev 1:6; 5:10; 20:6; see also Isa 66:21; Ro 6:13; 12:1; 15:16; Eph 5:2; Php 4:18; Heb 13:15–16).

33:24 *two kingdoms.* Israel and Judah. But since the Hebrew uses a word here that commonly refers to families (see NIV text note), the reference may be to the two mediatorial (royal and priestly) families, or to the families of Jacob and David (see v. 26). *he chose.* See Am 3:2 and note.

33:25–26 See v. 20 and note.

33:26 *restore their fortunes and have compassion.* Echoes Dt 30:3; see note on 29:14.

34:1—35:19 The first major division of the book (chs. 2–35) now comes to a close. Jeremiah's warnings and exhortations to Judah are concluded with a historical appendix (chs. 34–35), a technique used to conclude the third major division of the book (chs. 39–45) as well (see note on 45:1–5). Ch. 52, written by someone other than Jeremiah (see 51:64), serves as a fitting historical appendix to the entire book.

34:1–22 The chapter divides naturally into two parts (vv. 1–7 and 8–22), each of which dates to 588 BC (see notes on vv. 7,21–22).

34:1–7 Jeremiah's warning to King Zedekiah parallels the prophet's similar admonition in 21:1–10 (see notes there).

34:1 *kingdoms and peoples in the empire he ruled.* Nebuchadnezzar's empire was vast (see Eze 26:7; Da 3:2–4; 4:1; cf. the similar description of the Medes in 51:28). *fighting against Jerusalem.* Subject nations were expected to supply troops to fight alongside those of their overlord (see 2Ki 24:2). In a fourteenth-century BC treaty between the Hittite ruler Mursilis II and Duppi-Tessub, king of the Amorites, Mursilis says, "If you do not send your son or brother with your foot soldiers and charioteers to help the Hittite king, you act in disregard of the gods of the oath." *all its surrounding towns.* See 19:15 and note.

34:2–3 See 32:3–5 and note; see also 39:4–7; Eze 12:12–13; 17:11–20.

34:4 *not die by the sword.* See 32:5; 38:17,20; 52:11; Eze 17:16.

34:5 *funeral fire in honor of ... the kings who ruled before you.* Not cremation (see 2Ch 16:14; 21:19; see also note on Am 6:10). *Alas, master!* Words of mourning at the death of a king (see 22:18; cf. 1Ki 13:30).

34:7 *Lachish and Azekah.* Solomon's son Rehoboam had fortified them (see 2Ch 11:5,9), but Lachish was later besieged (701 BC) during Hezekiah's reign by the Assyrian king Sennacherib (see 2Ch 32:9). A contemporary relief depicting Sennacherib's conquest states that he "sat on a throne and passed in review the plunder taken from Lachish." In 1935, 18 ostraca (broken pottery fragments used as writing material) were discovered at Lachish (see chart, p. xxiii),

was fighting against Jerusalem and the
other cities of Judah that were still holding
out—Lachish[w] and Azekah.[x] These were
the only fortified cities left in Judah.

Freedom for Slaves

8 The word came to Jeremiah from the
LORD after King Zedekiah had made a covenant with all the people[y] in Jerusalem to
proclaim freedom[z] for the slaves. 9 Everyone was to free their Hebrew slaves, both

The Lachish letters (ostraca; see Jer 34:7 and note) were discovered in a guardroom below the gate tower inside the outer wall at Lachish. They are written in ancient Hebrew (597–587 BC) and give valuable insight into the political situation during the last days of the southern kingdom of Judah.

Kim Walton, courtesy of the British Museum

male and female; no one was to hold a
fellow Hebrew in bondage.[a] 10 So all the
officials and people who entered into this
covenant agreed that they would free their
male and female slaves and no longer hold
them in bondage. They agreed, and set
them free. 11 But afterward they changed
their minds[b] and took back the slaves they
had freed and enslaved them again.

12 Then the word of the LORD came to
Jeremiah: 13 "This is what the LORD, the
God of Israel, says: I made a covenant
with your ancestors[c] when I brought them
out of Egypt, out of the land of slavery.[d]
I said, 14 'Every seventh year each of you
must free any fellow Hebrews who have
sold themselves to you. After they have
served you six years, you must let them
go free.'[a][e] Your ancestors, however, did
not listen to me or pay attention[f] to me.
15 Recently you repented and did what is
right in my sight: Each of you proclaimed
freedom to your own people.[g] You even
made a covenant before me in the house
that bears my Name.[h] 16 But now you have
turned around[i] and profaned[j] my name;
each of you has taken back the male and
female slaves you had set free to go where
they wished. You have forced them to become your slaves again.

17 "Therefore this is what the LORD says:
You have not obeyed me; you have not
proclaimed freedom to your own people.
So I now proclaim 'freedom' for you,[k] declares the LORD—'freedom' to fall by the
sword, plague[l] and famine.[m] I will make
you abhorrent to all the kingdoms of the
earth.[n] 18 Those who have violated my covenant[o] and have not fulfilled the terms of
the covenant they made before me, I will

[a] *14* Deut. 15:12

34:7 [w] S Jos 10:3 [x] Jos 10:10; 2Ch 11:9
34:8 [y] S 2Ki 11:17 [z] S Ex 21:2; Lev 25:10,39-41; Ne 5:5-8
34:9 [a] Dt 15:12-18
34:11 [b] Ps 78:37
34:13 [c] S Ex 24:8 [d] S Dt 15:15
34:14 [e] S Ex 21:2 [f] 2Ki 17:14; S Jer 7:26
34:15 [g] ver 8 [h] S Jer 32:34
34:16 [i] Eze 3:20; 18:24 [j] S Lev 19:12
34:17 [k] S Mt 7:2; Gal 6:7 [l] Jer 21:7 [m] S Jer 14:12 [n] Jer 15:4; S 24:9; S 29:18
34:18 [o] S Jer 11:10

---

nearly all of them in the ruins of the latest occupation level (588 BC) of the Israelite gate-tower. Ostracon 4, written to the commander at Lachish shortly after the events described here, ends as follows: "We are watching for the fire-signals of Lachish … for we cannot see Azekah." See note on 6:1.

34:8–22 Contemporary with the events of 37:4–12 (see note on vv. 21–22).

34:8 *proclaim freedom.* See Lev 25:10 and note. *freedom for the slaves.* In accordance with the general provisions of the law of Moses (see Ex 21:2–11 and notes; Lev 25:39–55; Dt 15:12–18).

34:9 *Hebrew.* See Ex 21:2 and note. *no one … hold a fellow Hebrew in bondage.* See Lev 25:39,42.

34:10 *They … set them free.* To gain God's blessing, and/or in the hope that the freed slaves would be more willing to help defend Jerusalem.

34:11 *afterward.* When the Babylonian siege was temporarily lifted due to Egyptian intervention (see vv. 21–22; 37:5,11). *took back the slaves they had freed.* In violation of Dt 15:12. *enslaved them.* Cf. 2Ch 28:10.

34:13 *land of slavery.* Lit. "house of slaves" (see Ex 13:3,14; 20:2; Dt 5:6; 6:12; 8:14; 13:5; Jos 24:17; Jdg 6:8). The Israelites were to free their slaves because God had earlier freed the Israelites (see Dt 15:15).

34:14 *Every seventh year … let them go free.* A loose quotation of Dt 15:12.

34:15–16 *you repented … you have turned around.* The Hebrew for the two phrases is identical, providing an ironic play on words (see note on v. 18).

34:15 *house that bears my Name.* See 7:10 and note.

34:16 *you have … profaned my name.* By breaking the Lord's covenant. Zedekiah was a man whose word could not be trusted (see Eze 17:15,18). *go where they wished.* See Dt 21:14.

34:17 *sword, plague and famine.* See note on 14:12. *abhorrent to all the kingdoms of the earth.* See 15:4 and note.

34:18 *violated … walked.* The Hebrew root underlying both words is the same, again providing an ironic play on words (see note on vv. 15–16). *made … cut.* The Hebrew for the two words is identical. In ancient times, making a covenant involved a self-maledictory oath ("May thus and so be done to me if I do not keep this covenant"), which was often symbolized by cutting an animal in two and walking between the two halves (see Ge 15:18 and note). *between its pieces.* See note on Ge 15:17.

treat like the calf they cut in two and then
walked between its pieces.[p] 19The leaders of Judah and Jerusalem, the court officials,[q] the priests and all the people of
the land who walked between the pieces
of the calf, 20I will deliver[r] into the hands
of their enemies who want to kill them.[s]
Their dead bodies will become food for
the birds and the wild animals.[t]
21"I will deliver Zedekiah[u] king of Judah and his officials[v] into the hands of
their enemies[w] who want to kill them, to
the army of the king of Babylon,[x] which
has withdrawn[y] from you. 22I am going
to give the order, declares the LORD, and I
will bring them back to this city. They will
fight against it, take[z] it and burn[a] it down.
And I will lay waste[b] the towns of Judah
so no one can live there."

The Rekabites

35 This is the word that came to Jeremiah from the LORD during the
reign of Jehoiakim[c] son of Josiah king of
Judah: 2"Go to the Rekabite[d] family and
invite them to come to one of the side
rooms[e] of the house of the LORD and give
them wine to drink."
3So I went to get Jaazaniah son of Jeremiah, the son of Habazziniah, and his
brothers and all his sons—the whole family of the Rekabites. 4I brought them into
the house of the LORD, into the room of the
sons of Hanan son of Igdaliah the man of
God.[f] It was next to the room of the officials, which was over that of Maaseiah son
of Shallum[g] the doorkeeper.[h] 5Then I set
bowls full of wine and some cups before
the Rekabites and said to them, "Drink
some wine."
6But they replied, "We do not drink
wine, because our forefather Jehonadab[a][i]
son of Rekab gave us this command: 'Neither you nor your descendants must ever
drink wine.[j] 7Also you must never build
houses, sow seed or plant vineyards; you
must never have any of these things, but
must always live in tents.[k] Then you will
live a long time in the land[l] where you are
nomads.' 8We have obeyed everything our
forefather[m] Jehonadab son of Rekab commanded us. Neither we nor our wives nor
our sons and daughters have ever drunk
wine 9or built houses to live in or had
vineyards, fields or crops.[n] 10We have lived
in tents and have fully obeyed everything
our forefather Jehonadab commanded us.
11But when Nebuchadnezzar king of Babylon invaded[o] this land, we said, 'Come,
we must go to Jerusalem[p] to escape the
Babylonian[b] and Aramean armies.' So we
have remained in Jerusalem."
12Then the word of the LORD came to
Jeremiah, saying: 13"This is what the LORD
Almighty, the God of Israel, says: Go and
tell[q] the people of Judah and those living

[a] 6 Hebrew *Jonadab,* a variant of *Jehonadab;* here and often in this chapter [b] 11 Or *Chaldean*

34:18 [p]S Ge 15:10 **34:19** [q]S Jer 26:10; Zep 3:3-4 **34:20** [r]Jer 21:7; Eze 16:27; 23:28 [s]S Jer 11:21 [t]S Dt 28:26 **34:21** [u]S Jer 32:4 [v]2Ki 25:21; Jer 39:6; 52:24-27 [w]S Jer 21:7 [x]S 2Ch 36:10 [y]Jer 37:5 **34:22** [z]Jer 39:1-2 [a]S Ne 2:17; Jer 38:18; 39:8; Eze 23:47 [b]S Lev 26:32; S Isa 1:7 **35:1** [c]S 2Ch 36:5 **35:2** [d]S 2Ki 10:15 [e]S 1Ki 6:5 **35:4** [f]S Dt 33:1 [g]1Ch 9:19 [h]S 2Ki 12:9; S 23:4 **35:6** [i]S 2Ki 10:15 [j]S Lev 10:9; Nu 6:2-4; S Lk 1:15 **35:7** [k]Heb 11:9 [l]S Ex 20:12; Eph 6:2-3 **35:8** [m]Pr 1:8; Col 3:20 **35:9** [n]1Ti 6:6 **35:11** [o]2Ki 24:1 [p]S Jos 10:20; Jer 8:14 **35:13** [q]Jer 11:6

34:20 *food for the birds ... wild animals.* See 7:33 and note.
34:21–22 Because of the arrival of the Egyptians on the scene, the Babylonians in 588 BC temporarily lifted the siege of Jerusalem (see notes on v. 11; 37:3).
34:21 *withdrawn from you.* See the hope expressed in 21:2.
34:22 *I will bring them back.* See 37:8.
35:1–19 The family of the Rekabites, who obeyed their forefather's command, are an example and rebuke to the people of Judah, who have disobeyed the Lord (see v. 16). The mention of "Babylonian and Aramean armies" (v. 11) dates the chapter to no earlier than the eighth year of King Jehoiakim, who began his reign in 609 BC, whose capital city of Jerusalem was besieged in 605 (see Da 1:1 and note) by Nebuchadnezzar and who rebelled against Nebuchadnezzar three or four years later—an unwise act that led to raids on his territory by Babylonians, Arameans and others (see 2Ki 24:1–2). (The raids are perhaps reflected in 12:7–13.)
35:1 *during the reign of Jehoiakim.* Chs. 35–36 (see 36:1) are a flashback to the reign of Jehoiakim (609–598 BC; see Introduction: Outline).
35:2 *Rekabite family.* A nomadic tribal group related to the Kenites (see 1Ch 2:55), some of whom lived among or near the Israelites (see Jdg 1:16; 4:11; 1Sa 27:10) and were on friendly terms with them (see 1Sa 15:6; 30:26,29). *side rooms of the house of the LORD.* Used for storage and/or as living quarters (see 1Ki 6:5; 1Ch 28:12; 2Ch 31:11; Ne 13:4–5).
35:3 *Jaazaniah.* Means "The LORD hears." It was a common name in Jeremiah's time (see 40:8; Eze 8:11; 11:1) and appears on a stamp seal (discovered at Tell en-Nasbeh north of Jerusalem and dating c. 600 BC), as well as on one of the Lachish ostraca (see note on 34:7). *Jeremiah.* Not the prophet.
35:4 *sons.* Perhaps here in the sense of "disciples" (see Am 7:14 and note). *man of God.* A synonym for "prophet" (see 1Ki 12:22; see also note on 1Sa 9:9), emphasizing his relationship to the One who has called him. *Maaseiah.* Perhaps the man of the same name mentioned in 21:1; 29:25; 37:3. *doorkeeper.* One of three supervisors (see 52:24) over those who guarded the entrances to the temple (see 2Ki 12:9).
35:5 *bowls.* Large vessels, from which smaller cups would be filled.
35:6 *We do not drink wine.* A permanent vow taken by the Rekabites; cf. the Nazirites' temporary vow (see Nu 6:2–3,20; Jdg 13:4–7). Malkijah son of Rekab may have been a later renegade exception to the Rekabite vow, since he was "ruler of the district of Beth Hakkerem" (Ne 3:14), which means "house of the vineyard." *Jehonadab.* See 2Ki 10:15,23. Nearly 250 years before the days of Jeremiah, he helped King Jehu destroy Baal worship (at least temporarily) in the northern kingdom.
35:7 *must always live in tents.* Except during times of national emergency (see v. 11). *Then you will live a long time in the land.* An echo of Ex 20:12, where honoring one's parents is commanded.
35:8 *We have obeyed ... Jehonadab.* Contrast Judah's disobedience toward God (see v. 16).
35:11 See note on vv. 1–19.
35:13 *learn a lesson.* The Hebrew underlying this phrase is translated "respond(ed) to correction" in 2:30; 7:28 (see 5:3; 17:23 and note).

in Jerusalem, 'Will you not learn a lesson[r]
and obey my words?' declares the LORD.
14 'Jehonadab son of Rekab ordered his descendants not to drink wine and this command has been kept. To this day they do
not drink wine, because they obey their
forefather's command.[s] But I have spoken
to you again and again,[t] yet you have not
obeyed[u] me. 15 Again and again I sent all
my servants the prophets[v] to you. They
said, "Each of you must turn[w] from your
wicked ways and reform[x] your actions; do
not follow other gods[y] to serve them. Then
you will live in the land[z] I have given to
you and your ancestors." But you have not
paid attention or listened[a] to me. 16 The
descendants of Jehonadab son of Rekab
have carried out the command their forefather[b] gave them, but these people have
not obeyed me.'

17 "Therefore this is what the LORD God
Almighty, the God of Israel, says: 'Listen!
I am going to bring on Judah and on everyone living in Jerusalem every disaster[c]
I pronounced against them. I spoke to
them, but they did not listen;[d] I called to
them, but they did not answer.' "[e]

18 Then Jeremiah said to the family of
the Rekabites, "This is what the LORD Almighty, the God of Israel, says: 'You have
obeyed the command of your forefather[f]
Jehonadab and have followed all his instructions and have done everything he
ordered.' 19 Therefore this is what the LORD
Almighty, the God of Israel, says: 'Jehonadab son of Rekab will never fail[g] to have a
descendant to serve[h] me.' "

Jehoiakim Burns Jeremiah's Scroll

36 In the fourth year of Jehoiakim[i] son
of Josiah king of Judah, this word
came to Jeremiah from the LORD: 2 "Take a
scroll[j] and write on it all the words[k] I have
spoken to you concerning Israel, Judah
and all the other nations from the time I
began speaking to you in the reign of Josiah[l] till now. 3 Perhaps[m] when the people of
Judah hear[n] about every disaster I plan to
inflict on them, they will each turn[o] from
their wicked ways; then I will forgive[p]
their wickedness and their sin."

4 So Jeremiah called Baruch[q] son of Neriah,[r] and while Jeremiah dictated[s] all the
words the LORD had spoken to him, Baruch wrote them on the scroll.[t] 5 Then Jeremiah told Baruch, "I am restricted; I am
not allowed to go to the LORD's temple.
6 So you go to the house of the LORD on a
day of fasting[u] and read to the people from
the scroll the words of the LORD that you
wrote as I dictated.[v] Read them to all the
people of Judah[w] who come in from their
towns. 7 Perhaps they will bring their petition[x] before the LORD and will each turn[y]
from their wicked ways, for the anger[z] and
wrath pronounced against this people by
the LORD are great."

8 Baruch son of Neriah did everything
Jeremiah the prophet told him to do; at
the LORD's temple he read the words of the
LORD from the scroll. 9 In the ninth month[a]
of the fifth year of Jehoiakim son of Josiah king of Judah, a time of fasting[b] before
the LORD was proclaimed for all the people in Jerusalem and those who had come
from the towns of Judah. 10 From the room
of Gemariah[c] son of Shaphan[d] the secretary,[e] which was in the upper courtyard
at the entrance of the New Gate[f] of the
temple, Baruch read to all the people at
the LORD's temple the words of Jeremiah
from the scroll.

11 When Micaiah son of Gemariah, the
son of Shaphan, heard all the words of the

35:13 [r]Jer 6:10; 32:33 **35:14** [s]ver 6-10,16 [t]S Jer 7:13 [u]Isa 30:9 **35:15** [v]S Jer 7:25 [w]S 2Ki 17:13; S Jer 26:3 [x]S Isa 1:16-17; S 59:20; Jer 4:1; 18:11; Eze 14:6; 18:30 [y]S Ex 20:3 [z]S Dt 4:40; Jer 25:5 [a]S Jer 6:10; S 7:26; 44:4-5 **35:16** [b]S Lev 20:9; Mal 1:6 **35:17** [c]S Jos 23:15; S 1Ki 13:34; Jer 21:4-7 [d]S Pr 1:24; Ro 10:21 [e]Jer 7:13 **35:18** [f]S Ge 31:35 **35:19** [g]S Isa 48:19; Jer 33:17 [h]Jer 15:19 **36:1** [i]S 2Ch 36:5 **36:2** [j]S ver 4; S Ex 17:14; S Ps 40:7; Jer 30:2; Hab 2:2 [k]Eze 2:7 [l]Jer 1:2; 25:3 **36:3** [m]ver 7; Eze 12:3; Am 5:15 [n]Isa 6:9; Mk 4:12 [o]S 2Ki 17:13; S Isa 44:22; S Jer 26:3; Ac 3:19 [p]S Jer 18:8 **36:4** [q]S Jer 32:12 [r]Jer 51:59 [s]ver 18 [t]ver 2; Eze 2:9; Da 7:1; Zec 5:1 **36:6** [u]ver 9 [v]S Ex 4:16 [w]2Ch 20:4 **36:7** [x]Jer 37:20; 42:2 [y]S Jer 26:3 [z]S Dt 31:17 **36:9** [a]ver 22 [b]S 2Ch 20:3 **36:10** [c]ver 12,25; Jer 29:3 [d]Jer 26:24 [e]Jer 52:25 [f]S Ge 23:10

35:14 – 15 *again and again.* See note on 7:13.
35:15 See 25:4 – 5 and notes.
35:17 See 11:11.
35:19 *never fail to have a descendant to serve me.* See 33:18. Various traditions in the Jewish Mishnah (see note on Ne 10:34) claim that the Rekabites were later given special duties to perform in connection with the Jerusalem temple built after the return from Babylonian exile.
36:1 — 38:28 Three chapters united by the common theme of Jeremiah's suffering and persecution.
36:1 - 32 An account of King Jehoiakim's attempt to destroy Jeremiah's written prophecies.
36:1 *fourth year of Jehoiakim.* 605 BC — a critical year in Judah's history (see notes on 25:1; 46:2).
36:2 *scroll.* See notes on 30:2; Ex 17:14. *write on it.* To preserve Jeremiah's messages for future generations. *all the words I have spoken to you.* This earliest edition of Jeremiah's prophecies may have included all or most of chs. 1 – 26; 46 – 51. *began speaking to you in the reign of Josiah.* See note on 1:2.

36:3 *Perhaps ... then.* If the people repent, the Lord will relent (see 18:7 – 10 and note; 26:3; Jnh 3:9 and note).
36:4 *Baruch.* See note on 32:12.
36:5 *I am restricted.* Perhaps because of his unpopular temple message(s) (see 7:2 – 15; 26:2 – 6), or perhaps because of the events recorded in 19:1 — 20:6.
36:6 *day of fasting.* Proclaimed because of a national emergency (cf. Joel 2:15), perhaps in this case the Babylonian attack of 605 BC (see Da 1:1 and note).
36:7 See v. 3 and note.
36:8 If the book presented Jeremiah's prophecies in chronological order, ch. 45 would appear after this verse (see Introduction: Outline).
36:9 *ninth month of the fifth year.* December, 604 BC, during a time of cold weather (see v. 22).
36:10 Cf. 2Ki 23:2. *room.* See note on 35:2. *Gemariah son of Shaphan.* This official's name has been found in Jerusalem on a seal impression. *Shaphan.* Secretary of state under King Josiah (see 2Ki 22:3; see also notes on 26:24; 29:3). *entrance of the New Gate.* See 26:10 and note.

LORD from the scroll, 12 he went down to
the secretary's[g] room in the royal palace,
where all the officials were sitting: Elishama the secretary, Delaiah son of Shemaiah, Elnathan[h] son of Akbor, Gemariah son
of Shaphan, Zedekiah son of Hananiah,
and all the other officials.[i] 13 After Micaiah
told them everything he had heard Baruch
read to the people from the scroll, 14 all the
officials sent Jehudi[j] son of Nethaniah, the
son of Shelemiah, the son of Cushi, to say
to Baruch, "Bring the scroll[k] from which
you have read to the people and come." So
Baruch son of Neriah went to them with
the scroll in his hand. 15 They said to him,
"Sit down, please, and read it to us."
So Baruch read it to them. 16 When they
heard all these words, they looked at each
other in fear[l] and said to Baruch, "We
must report all these words to the king."
17 Then they asked Baruch, "Tell us, how
did you come to write[m] all this? Did Jeremiah dictate it?"
18 "Yes," Baruch replied, "he dictated[n] all
these words to me, and I wrote them in
ink on the scroll."
19 Then the officials[o] said to Baruch,
"You and Jeremiah, go and hide.[p] Don't
let anyone know where you are."
20 After they put the scroll in the room
of Elishama the secretary, they went to
the king in the courtyard and reported
everything to him. 21 The king sent Jehudi[q] to get the scroll, and Jehudi brought
it from the room of Elishama the secretary and read it to the king[r] and all the
officials standing beside him. 22 It was the
ninth month and the king was sitting in
the winter apartment,[s] with a fire burning
in the firepot in front of him. 23 Whenever Jehudi had read three or four columns
of the scroll,[t] the king cut them off with

36:12 [g] S 2Sa 8:17 [h] S Jer 26:22 [i] Jer 38:4 **36:14** [j] ver 21 [k] ver 4 **36:16** [l] S Ps 36:1 **36:17** [m] Jer 30:2 **36:18** [n] ver 4 **36:19** [o] Jer 26:16 [p] S 1Ki 17:3 **36:21** [q] ver 14 [r] 2Ki 22:10 **36:22** [s] Am 3:15 **36:23** [t] ver 2

a scribe's knife and threw them into the
firepot, until the entire scroll was burned
in the fire.[u] 24 The king and all his attendants who heard all these words showed
no fear,[v] nor did they tear their clothes.[w]
25 Even though Elnathan, Delaiah[x] and
Gemariah[y] urged the king not to burn the
scroll, he would not listen to them. 26 Instead, the king commanded Jerahmeel, a
son of the king, Seraiah son of Azriel and
Shelemiah son of Abdeel to arrest[z] Baruch
the scribe and Jeremiah the prophet. But
the LORD had hidden[a] them.
27 After the king burned the scroll containing the words that Baruch had written
at Jeremiah's dictation,[b] the word of the
LORD came to Jeremiah: 28 "Take another
scroll[c] and write on it all the words that
were on the first scroll, which Jehoiakim
king of Judah burned up. 29 Also tell Jehoiakim king of Judah, 'This is what the
LORD says: You burned that scroll and
said, "Why did you write on it that the
king of Babylon would certainly come
and destroy this land and wipe from it[d]
both man and beast?"[e] 30 Therefore this
is what the LORD says about Jehoiakim[f]
king of Judah: He will have no one to sit
on the throne of David; his body will be
thrown out[g] and exposed[h] to the heat by
day and the frost by night.[i] 31 I will punish
him and his children[j] and his attendants
for their wickedness; I will bring on them
and those living in Jerusalem and the people of Judah every disaster[k] I pronounced
against them, because they have not listened.[l]' "
32 So Jeremiah took another scroll and
gave it to the scribe Baruch son of Neriah,
and as Jeremiah dictated,[m] Baruch wrote[n]
on it all the words of the scroll that Jehoiakim king of Judah had burned[o] in the

[u] 1Ki 22:8 **36:24** [v] S Ps 36:1 [w] S Ge 37:29; S Nu 14:6 **36:25** [x] ver 12 [y] S ver 10 **36:26** [z] Mt 23:34 [a] S 1Ki 17:3; Ps 11:1; S Jer 1:8; 15:21 **36:27** [b] ver 4 **36:28** [c] ver 2 **36:29** [d] S Isa 30:10 [e] Jer 33:12 **36:30** [f] Jer 52:2 [g] S Isa 14:19 [h] S 2Ki 24:6 [i] S Jer 8:2 **36:31** [j] Ex 20:5 [k] S Pr 29:1 [l] S Pr 1:24 **36:32** [m] ver 4 [n] Ex 34:1; Jer 30:2 [o] ver 23

36:12 *Elnathan son of Akbor.* See note on 26:22.

36:18 *ink.* Mentioned only here in the OT (but see also 2Co 3:3; 2Jn 12; 3Jn 13). In ancient times, ink was made from soot or lampblack mixed with gum arabic, oil, or a metallic substance (as in the case of the Lachish ostraca; see note on 34:7).

36:19 The officials were understandably concerned about the safety of Jeremiah and Baruch (cf. 26:20–23).

36:20 *put.* For safekeeping (the Hebrew root for this word is translated "store" in Isa 10:28).

36:22 *ninth month.* See note on v. 9. *winter apartment.* Lit. "winter house" (as in Am 3:15), here probably a large room in the king's palace. *firepot.* A depression or container in the middle of the floor where coals were kept burning to warm the room.

36:23 Contrast King Josiah's desire to know the word of God and obey it (see 2Ki 22:11—23:3; 23:21–24). *columns.* Lit. "doors," so called because of their rectangular shape. *cut.* Lit. "tore." Instead of tearing his clothes in repentance (see note on v. 24), the king tore the prophet's scroll.

36:24 *attendants ... showed no fear.* See v. 31. Contrast the response of the "officials" (v. 12; see vv. 16,25). *nor did they tear their clothes.* Contrast the response of Jehoiakim's father, Josiah (see 2Ki 22:11; cf. 1Ki 21:27).

36:26 *Jerahmeel, a son of the king.* This official's name, along with his title, has been found on a seal impression discovered in a burnt archive near Jerusalem. *son of the king.* Since Jehoiakim was only about 30 years old (see 2Ki 23:36), the phrase probably is not to be understood literally but means "member of the royal court" (as also in 38:6; 1Ki 22:26; Zep 1:8).

36:30 *Jehoiakim ... will have no one to sit on the throne.* His son Jehoiachin (see 2Ki 24:6) ruled only 3 months (see 2Ki 24:8) and then was captured and carried off to exile in Babylonia (see 2Ki 24:15), where he eventually died (see 52:33–34). *his body will be thrown out.* As punishment for the fact that he "threw" (v. 23) the prophet's scroll into the fire (see 22:18–19 and notes).

36:31 See 11:11; 19:15; 35:17. *attendants.* See note on v. 24.

36:32 *another scroll.* Cf. similarly Ex 34:1. *the scribe Baruch son of Neriah.* This precise identification has been found on two seal impressions (made with the same seal) discovered in the same burnt archive mentioned in the note on v. 26.

fire. And many similar words were added
to them.

Jeremiah in Prison

37 Zedekiah[p] son of Josiah was made
king[q] of Judah by Nebuchadnezzar
king of Babylon; he reigned in place of Jehoiachin[a][r] son of Jehoiakim. 2Neither he
nor his attendants nor the people of the
land paid any attention[s] to the words the
LORD had spoken through Jeremiah the
prophet.

3King Zedekiah, however, sent[t] Jehukal[u]
son of Shelemiah with the priest Zephaniah[v] son of Maaseiah to Jeremiah the
prophet with this message: "Please pray[w]
to the LORD our God for us."

4Now Jeremiah was free to come and
go among the people, for he had not yet
been put in prison.[x] 5Pharaoh's army had
marched out of Egypt,[y] and when the Babylonians[b] who were besieging Jerusalem
heard the report about them, they withdrew[z] from Jerusalem.[a]

6Then the word of the LORD came to
Jeremiah the prophet: 7"This is what the
LORD, the God of Israel, says: Tell the king
of Judah, who sent you to inquire[b] of me,
'Pharaoh's army, which has marched[c] out
to support you, will go back to its own
land, to Egypt.[d] 8Then the Babylonians
will return and attack this city; they will
capture[e] it and burn[f] it down.'

9"This is what the LORD says: Do not deceive[g] yourselves, thinking, 'The Babylonians will surely leave us.' They will not!
10Even if you were to defeat the entire Babylonian[c] army that is attacking you and only
wounded men were left in their tents, they
would come out and burn[h] this city down."

37:1 [p] S 2Ki 24:17 [q] 1Sa 11:1; Eze 17:13 [r] S 2Ki 24:8, 12; Jer 22:24
37:2 [s] S 2Ki 24:19
37:3 [t] ver 17; Jer 38:14 [u] Jer 38:1 [v] S 2Ki 25:18; Jer 29:25; 52:24 [w] S Ex 8:28; S Nu 21:7; 1Sa 12:19; 1Ki 13:6; 2Ki 19:4; Jer 42:2
37:4 [x] ver 15; Jer 32:2
37:5 [y] S Ge 15:18; Isa 31:1; Eze 17:15 [z] Jer 34:21 [a] S Isa 30:5; Jer 34:11
37:7 [b] S Ge 25:22; S 2Ki 22:18 [c] ver 5 [d] S 2Ki 18:21; S Jer 2:36; La 1:7; 4:17
37:8 [e] Jer 38:3 [f] Jer 21:10; 38:18; 39:8
37:9 [g] Jer 29:8; S Mk 13:5
37:10 [h] Jer 21:10
37:11 [i] ver 5
37:12 [j] S Jer 32:9
37:13 [k] S Jer 20:2 [l] Jer 21:9
37:14 [m] Isa 58:6; Jer 40:4
37:15 [n] S Jer 20:2; Heb 11:36 [o] S 1Ki 22:27 [p] ver 20; Jer 38:26

11After the Babylonian army had withdrawn[i] from Jerusalem because of Pharaoh's army, 12Jeremiah started to leave the
city to go to the territory of Benjamin to get
his share of the property[j] among the people
there. 13But when he reached the Benjamin Gate,[k] the captain of the guard, whose
name was Irijah son of Shelemiah, the son
of Hananiah, arrested him and said, "You
are deserting to the Babylonians!"[l]

14"That's not true!" Jeremiah said. "I
am not deserting to the Babylonians." But
Irijah would not listen to him; instead, he
arrested[m] Jeremiah and brought him to the
officials. 15They were angry with Jeremiah and had him beaten[n] and imprisoned[o]
in the house[p] of Jonathan the secretary,
which they had made into a prison.

16Jeremiah was put into a vaulted cell
in a dungeon, where he remained a long
time. 17Then King Zedekiah sent[q] for him
and had him brought to the palace, where
he asked[r] him privately,[s] "Is there any
word from the LORD?"

"Yes," Jeremiah replied, "you will be delivered[t] into the hands of the king of Babylon."

18Then Jeremiah said to King Zedekiah,
"What crime[u] have I committed against
you or your attendants or this people, that
you have put me in prison? 19Where are
your prophets[v] who prophesied to you,
'The king of Babylon will not attack you
or this land'? 20But now, my lord the king,

[a] *1* Hebrew *Koniah,* a variant of *Jehoiachin*
[b] *5* Or *Chaldeans;* also in verses 8, 9, 13 and 14
[c] *10* Or *Chaldean;* also in verse 11

37:17 [q] S ver 3 [r] S Ge 25:22; Jer 15:11 [s] Jer 38:16 [t] S Jer 21:7
37:18 [u] S 1Sa 26:18; Jn 10:32; Ac 25:8 **37:19** [v] S Jer 14:13; Eze 13:2

37:1—38:28 During the last two years of Zedekiah's reign (588–586 BC) Jeremiah is imprisoned by the authorities (see 20:2 and note).

37:1 See 2Ki 24:15,17–18. *Zedekiah.* Means "The LORD is my righteousness." See Introduction: Background. *reigned in place of Jehoiachin.* In 597 BC. This fulfills the prophecy concerning Jehoiakim in 36:30.

37:3 *Zedekiah ... sent ... to Jeremiah.* See 21:1. *Jehukal son of Shelemiah.* This precise name was found on a seal impression dating to the time of Jeremiah. Jehukal later became Jeremiah's enemy (see 38:1,4). *the priest Zephaniah son of Maaseiah.* See 21:1 and note. *pray ... for us.* See 21:2 and note; perhaps to ask the Lord to make the temporary withdrawal of the Babylonians in 588 BC (see note on 34:21–22) permanent.

37:5 *Pharaoh's army.* The troops of Hophra (see 44:30). *marched out of Egypt.* Probably to help Zedekiah at his request; Lachish ostracon 3 (see note on 34:7) mentions a visit to Egypt made by the commander of Judah's army. All such ploys by Zedekiah would fail, however (see Eze 17:15,17). *Babylonians ... withdrew.* To deal with the Egyptian threat (see 34:21 and note).

37:7 *Pharaoh's army ... will go back ... to Egypt.* Hophra would soon be defeated by Nebuchadnezzar (see note on Eze 30:21).

37:10 *wounded.* Lit. "pierced through," "mortally wounded." Though seriously handicapped, the Babylonians would still destroy Jerusalem.

37:12 *territory of Benjamin.* Where Jeremiah's hometown, Anathoth, was located (see note on 1:1). *get his share of the property.* While there was a brief lull in the Babylonian invasion, Jeremiah wanted to settle matters of estate with the other members of his family.

37:13 *Benjamin Gate.* See 38:7; see also note on Zec 14:10. *You are deserting to the Babylonians.* Irijah's fear was understandable, since Jeremiah recommended surrendering to the Babylonians (see 21:9; 38:2) and since many Judahites in fact defected (see 38:19; 39:9; 52:15).

37:14 *That's not true!* Lit. "A lie" (see 2Ki 9:12).

37:15 *had him beaten.* See 20:2 and note. *house of Jonathan.* Jeremiah would later look back on this prison as a place of great danger for him (see v. 20; 38:26).

37:16 *dungeon.* Lit. "house of the cistern" (see Ex 12:29).

37:17 *Zedekiah ... asked him privately.* Not wanting to do so in the presence of his officials, whom he apparently feared (see note on 38:5). *you will be delivered into the hands of the king of Babylon.* See 32:4; 34:3.

37:19 *your prophets.* False prophets (see Dt 18:22 and note).

37:20 *bring my petition before you.* See 36:7.

please listen. Let me bring my petition
before you: Do not send me back to the
house of Jonathan the secretary, or I will
die there."[w]
21 King Zedekiah then gave orders for
Jeremiah to be placed in the courtyard of
the guard and given a loaf of bread from
the street of the bakers each day until all
the bread[x] in the city was gone.[y] So Jeremiah remained in the courtyard of the
guard.[z]

Jeremiah Thrown Into a Cistern

38 Shephatiah son of Mattan, Gedaliah son of Pashhur[a], Jehukal[ab] son
of Shelemiah, and Pashhur son of Malkijah heard what Jeremiah was telling all
the people when he said, 2 "This is what
the LORD says: 'Whoever stays in this city
will die by the sword, famine or plague,[c]
but whoever goes over to the Babylonians[b] will live. They will escape with their
lives; they will live.'[d] 3 And this is what the
LORD says: 'This city will certainly be giv-
en into the hands of the army of the king
of Babylon, who will capture it.' "[e]
4 Then the officials[f] said to the king,
"This man should be put to death.[g] He is
discouraging[h] the soldiers who are left in
this city, as well as all the people, by the
things he is saying to them. This man is
not seeking the good of these people but
their ruin."
5 "He is in your hands,"[i] King Zedekiah
answered. "The king can do nothing[j] to
oppose you."
6 So they took Jeremiah and put him into
the cistern of Malkijah, the king's son,
which was in the courtyard of the guard.[k]
They lowered Jeremiah by ropes[l] into the
cistern; it had no water in it,[m] only mud,
and Jeremiah sank down into the mud.[n]
7 But Ebed-Melek,[o] a Cushite,[c] an official[dp] in the royal palace, heard that they
had put Jeremiah into the cistern. While
the king was sitting in the Benjamin Gate,[q]
8 Ebed-Melek went out of the palace and
said to him, 9 "My lord the king, these
men have acted wickedly in all they have
done to Jeremiah the prophet. They have
thrown him into a cistern,[r] where he will
starve to death when there is no longer
any bread[s] in the city."
10 Then the king commanded Ebed-Melek the Cushite, "Take thirty men from
here with you and lift Jeremiah the prophet out of the cistern before he dies."
11 So Ebed-Melek took the men with
him and went to a room under the treasury in the palace. He took some old rags
and worn-out clothes from there and let
them down with ropes[t] to Jeremiah in the
cistern. 12 Ebed-Melek the Cushite said to
Jeremiah, "Put these old rags and worn-
out clothes under your arms to pad the
ropes." Jeremiah did so, 13 and they pulled
him up with the ropes and lifted him out
of the cistern. And Jeremiah remained in
the courtyard of the guard.[u]

Zedekiah Questions Jeremiah Again

14 Then King Zedekiah sent[v] for Jeremiah the prophet and had him brought to the
third entrance to the temple of the LORD. "I

37:20 [w] S ver 15
37:21 [x] S Lev 26:26; Isa 33:16; Jer 38:9; La 1:11 [y] S 2Ki 25:3 [z] Jer 32:2; 38:6, 13,28; 39:13-14
38:1 [a] S 1Ch 9:12 [b] Jer 37:3
38:2 [c] Jer 34:17 [d] ver 17; S Jer 21:9; 39:18; 45:5
38:3 [e] S Jer 21:4,10
38:4 [f] S Jer 36:12 [g] S Jer 11:21 [h] S 1Sa 17:32
38:5 [i] S Jer 26:14 [j] 1Sa 15:24
38:6 [k] S Jer 37:21 [l] S Jos 2:15 [m] S Ge 37:24 [n] S Job 30:19; La 3:53
38:7 [o] Jer 39:16 [p] *fn* Isa 56:3-5; Ac 8:27 [q] S Job 29:7
38:9 [r] S Ge 37:20 [s] S Jer 37:21
38:11 [t] S Jos 2:15
38:13 [u] S Jer 37:21
38:14 [v] S Jer 37:3

[a] *1* Hebrew *Jukal,* a variant of *Jehukal*
[b] *2* Or *Chaldeans;* also in verses 18, 19 and 23
[c] *7* Probably from the upper Nile region [d] *7* Or *a eunuch*

37:21 *courtyard of the guard.* A less objectionable prison than the dungeon of v. 16 (see note on 32:2). *street of the bakers.* Perhaps near the Tower of the Ovens (see note on Ne 3:11). *until all the bread ... was gone.* The Hebrew word for "bread" is translated "food" in 52:6.
38:1 *Pashhur.* See note on 20:1. *Jehukal son of Shelemiah.* See note on 37:3. *Pashhur son of Malkijah.* See note on 21:1. *Jeremiah was telling all the people.* Though he was confined in the courtyard of the guard (see 37:21), he was allowed to have visitors and to speak freely to them (see 32:8,12).
38:2 Echoes 21:9 (see note there).
38:3 Echoes 32:28 (see 34:2; 37:8).
38:4 *officials.* Those named in v. 1. *discouraging.* See Ezr 4:4; lit. "weakening the hands of," as in a similar situation in Lachish ostracon 6 (see note on 34:7): "The words of the officials are not good; they serve only to weaken our hands." Contrast Isa 35:3. *seeking the good.* The Hebrew underlying this phrase is translated "seek the peace and prosperity" in 29:7 (see note there). *good ... ruin.* The Hebrew for these words is translated "prosperity ... disaster" in Isa 45:7.
38:5 *The king can do nothing.* Not because of inability or lack of authority but through failure of nerve. He feared his own officials (see vv. 25–26; see also 37:17 and note).
38:6 *cistern.* A pit with a relatively small opening at the top (see 37:16 and note). *king's son.* See note on 36:26. *cistern ... had no water in it.* Zedekiah's officials wanted to kill Jeremiah (see v. 4), but not by taking his life with their own hands (cf. Ge 37:20–24).
38:7 *Ebed-Melek.* Means "king's servant." *king was sitting in the Benjamin Gate.* See 37:13; see also note on Zec 14:10. Since a city gateway was often used as a courtroom or town hall (see notes on Ge 19:1; Ru 4:1), Zedekiah may have been settling various legal complaints on this occasion (see 2Sa 15:2–4) and would therefore have been in a position to help Ebed-Melek.
38:9 *no longer any bread in the city.* See 37:21 and note.
38:10 *thirty men.* The large number was probably to keep the officials (see v. 4) and their friends from trying to prevent Jeremiah's rescue.
38:11 *room under the treasury.* Perhaps a wardrobe storeroom (see 2Ki 10:22).
38:12 *Put these old rags ... to pad the ropes.* Ebed-Melek's kindnesses to Jeremiah were evidence that he trusted in the Lord, and the Lord rewarded him (see 39:15–18).
38:13 *remained in the courtyard of the guard.* See note on 32:2.
38:14–26 Jeremiah's final interview with King Zedekiah.
38:14 *third entrance.* Mentioned only here; perhaps the king's private access to the temple. *something ... anything.* Lit. "a

am going to ask you something," the king said to Jeremiah. "Do not hide[w] anything from me."

15 Jeremiah said to Zedekiah, "If I give you an answer, will you not kill me? Even if I did give you counsel, you would not listen to me."

16 But King Zedekiah swore this oath secretly[x] to Jeremiah: "As surely as the LORD lives, who has given us breath,[y] I will neither kill you nor hand you over to those who want to kill you."[z]

17 Then Jeremiah said to Zedekiah, "This is what the LORD God Almighty, the God of Israel, says: 'If you surrender[a] to the officers of the king of Babylon, your life will be spared and this city will not be burned down; you and your family will live.[b] 18 But if you will not surrender to the officers of the king of Babylon, this city will be given into the hands[c] of the Babylonians and they will burn[d] it down; you yourself will not escape[e] from them.' "

19 King Zedekiah said to Jeremiah, "I am afraid[f] of the Jews who have gone over[g] to the Babylonians, for the Babylonians may hand me over to them and they will mistreat me."

20 "They will not hand you over," Jeremiah replied. "Obey[h] the LORD by doing what I tell you. Then it will go well[i] with you, and your life[j] will be spared. 21 But if you refuse to surrender, this is what the LORD has revealed to me: 22 All the women[k] left in the palace of the king of Judah will be brought out to the officials of the king of Babylon. Those women will say to you:

" 'They misled you and overcame
you —
those trusted friends[l] of yours.
Your feet are sunk in the mud;[m]
your friends have deserted you.'

23 "All your wives and children[n] will be brought out to the Babylonians. You yourself will not escape[o] from their hands but will be captured[p] by the king of Babylon; and this city will[a] be burned down."[q]

24 Then Zedekiah said to Jeremiah, "Do not let anyone know[r] about this conversation, or you may die. 25 If the officials hear that I talked with you, and they come to you and say, 'Tell us what you said to the king and what the king said to you; do not hide it from us or we will kill you,' 26 then tell[s] them, 'I was pleading with the king not to send me back to Jonathan's house[t] to die there.' "

27 All the officials did come to Jeremiah and question him, and he told them everything the king had ordered him to say. So they said no more to him, for no one had heard his conversation with the king.

28 And Jeremiah remained in the courtyard of the guard[u] until the day Jerusalem was captured.

The Fall of Jerusalem

39:1-10pp — 2Ki 25:1-12; Jer 52:4-16

39 This is how Jerusalem[v] was taken: 1 In the ninth year of Zedekiah[w] king of Judah, in the tenth month, Nebuchadnezzar[x] king of Babylon marched against Jerusalem with his whole army and laid siege[y] to it. 2 And on the ninth day of the fourth[z] month of Zedekiah's eleventh year, the city wall[a] was broken through.[b] 3 Then all the officials[c] of the king of Babylon came and took seats in the Middle Gate: Nergal-Sharezer of Samgar, Nebo-Sarsekim a

38:14 [w]S 1Sa 3:17 [x]Jer 37:17
38:16 [y]Isa 42:5; 57:16 [z]ver 4
38:17 [a]Jer 27:8 [b]S Jer 21:9
38:18 [c]ver 3 [d]S Jer 37:8 [e]S Jer 24:8; S 32:4
38:19 [f]Isa 51:12; Jn 12:42 [g]Jer 39:9; 52:15
38:20 [h]Jer 11:4 [i]S Dt 5:33; Jer 40:9 [j]Isa 55:3
38:22 [k]S Jer 6:12 [l]S Job 19:14; S Jer 13:21 [m]S Job 30:19; Ps 69:14
38:23 [n]S 2Ki 25:6 [o]S Jer 32:4; Eze 17:15 [p]S Jer 24:8 [q]Jer 21:10; 37:8
38:24 [r]Jer 37:17
38:26 [s]1Sa 16:2 [t]S Jer 37:15
38:28 [u]S Jer 37:21 [v]S Jer 25:29
39:1 [w]S 2Ch 36:11 [x]S 2Ki 24:1; S Jer 28:14 [y]S 2Ki 25:1; Jer 52:4; Eze 4:3; 24:2
39:2 [z]Zec 8:19 [a]S 2Ki 14:13 [b]Eze 33:21
39:3 [c]ver 13; Jer 21:4

[a] 23 Or *and you will cause this city to*

---

word ... a word," probably referring to a "word" from the Lord (see 37:17).

38:16 *As surely as the LORD lives.* See note on Ge 42:15. *those who want to kill you.* Zedekiah's officials (see v. 4 and note).

38:17 – 18 See vv. 2 – 3; 21:9 – 10; 32:3 – 4; 34:2 – 5. *surrender.* Lit. "come out" (see 2Ki 18:31; 24:12). *officers of the king of Babylon.* Those in charge of the siege of Jerusalem (see 39:3,13).

38:19 *I am afraid.* See v. 5 and note. If Zedekiah had trusted in the Lord, he would not have had to fear either officials or deserters (see Pr 29:25 and note). *gone over to the Babylonians.* See 37:13 and note. *mistreat me.* Do violence to me (see Jdg 19:25; 1Ch 10:4).

38:22 *women ... in the palace ... brought out to the officials.* Women in a conquered king's harem became the property of the conquerors (cf. 2Sa 16:21 – 22). *misled you and overcame you — those trusted friends of yours.* Repeated almost verbatim in Ob 7 (see 20:10 and note). Zedekiah's so-called friends were his officials (see v. 4) and false prophets (see 37:19). *feet are sunk in the mud.* Symbolic of great distress (see Ps 69:14).

38:26 See 37:20. *Jonathan's house.* See 37:15 and note.

38:27 *told them everything the king had ordered him to say.* Jeremiah was not obliged to give the officials the other information, which had been shared in confidence.

38:28 *remained in the courtyard of the guard.* See v. 13; see also note on 32:2.

39:1 — 45:5 The most detailed account in the OT of the Babylonian conquest of Jerusalem and its aftermath. The section concludes with a brief appendix (ch. 45).

39:1 - 10 A vivid summary of the siege and fall of Jerusalem and of the exile of its inhabitants (see 52:4 – 27).

39:1 - 2 Summarizes 52:4 – 7a.

39:1 *ninth year of Zedekiah ... tenth month.* The final Babylonian siege of Jerusalem began on the tenth day of the month (see 52:4; 2Ki 25:1; Eze 24:1 – 2), i.e., Jan. 15, 588 BC.

39:2 *ninth day ... fourth month ... eleventh year.* July 18, 586 BC (see 52:5 – 6; 2Ki 25:2 – 3). The siege lasted just over two and a half years.

39:3 *took seats in the Middle Gate.* In fulfillment of 1:15. The Middle Gate may have been located in the wall separating the citadel of Mount Zion from the lower city, therefore serving as a strategic vantage point for the invaders. *Nergal-Sharezer.* Means "Nergal [a god; see 2Ki 17:30], protect the king." One of the two men so named here (see v. 13) is probably Neriglissar, who later became a successor of Nebuchadnezzar as ruler of Babylonia (560 – 556 BC). *Nebo-Sarsekim a chief officer.* In 2007 this man's name, along with

chief officer, Nergal-Sharezer a high official and all the other officials of the king of
Babylon. 4When Zedekiah king of Judah
and all the soldiers saw them, they fled;
they left the city at night by way of the
king's garden, through the gate between
the two walls,[d] and headed toward the Arabah.[a][e]
5But the Babylonian[b] army pursued
them and overtook Zedekiah[f] in the plains
of Jericho. They captured[g] him and took
him to Nebuchadnezzar king of Babylon
at Riblah[h] in the land of Hamath, where
he pronounced sentence on him. 6There
at Riblah the king of Babylon slaughtered
the sons of Zedekiah before his eyes and
also killed all the nobles[i] of Judah. 7Then
he put out Zedekiah's eyes[j] and bound
him with bronze shackles to take him to
Babylon.[k]
8The Babylonians[c] set fire[l] to the royal palace and the houses of the people
and broke down the walls[m] of Jerusalem.
9Nebuzaradan commander of the imperial guard carried into exile to Babylon the
people who remained in the city, along
with those who had gone over to him,[n]
and the rest of the people.[o] 10But Nebuzaradan the commander of the guard left behind in the land of Judah some of the poor
people, who owned nothing; and at that
time he gave them vineyards and fields.
11Now Nebuchadnezzar king of Babylon
had given these orders about Jeremiah
through Nebuzaradan commander of the
imperial guard: 12"Take him and look after him; don't harm[p] him but do for him
whatever he asks." 13So Nebuzaradan the
commander of the guard, Nebushazban a
chief officer, Nergal-Sharezer a high official and all the other officers[q] of the king
of Babylon 14sent and had Jeremiah taken
out of the courtyard of the guard.[r] They
turned him over to Gedaliah[s] son of Ahikam,[t] the son of Shaphan,[u] to take him
back to his home. So he remained among
his own people.[v]
15While Jeremiah had been confined
in the courtyard of the guard, the word
of the LORD came to him: 16"Go and tell
Ebed-Melek[w] the Cushite, 'This is what the
LORD Almighty, the God of Israel, says: I
am about to fulfill my words[x] against this
city — words concerning disaster,[y] not
prosperity. At that time they will be fulfilled before your eyes. 17But I will rescue[z]
you on that day, declares the LORD; you
will not be given into the hands of those
you fear. 18I will save[a] you; you will not
fall by the sword[b] but will escape with
your life,[c] because you trust[d] in me, declares the LORD.' "

Jeremiah Freed

40 The word came to Jeremiah from
the LORD after Nebuzaradan commander of the imperial guard had released
him at Ramah.[e] He had found Jeremiah
bound in chains among all the captives[f]
from Jerusalem and Judah who were being carried into exile to Babylon. 2When
the commander[g] of the guard found Jeremiah, he said to him, "The LORD your
God decreed[h] this disaster[i] for this place.[j]

[a] 4 Or *the Jordan Valley* [b] 5 Or *Chaldean* [c] 8 Or *Chaldeans*

39:4 [d] S Isa 22:11 [e] Eze 12:12 **39:5** [f] S Jer 24:8; S 32:4 [g] S Jer 21:7 [h] S Nu 34:11 **39:6** [i] S Isa 34:12 **39:7** [j] S Nu 16:14; Eze 12:13 [k] S Jer 2:35 **39:8** [l] S Jer 34:22 [m] S Ne 1:3; S Ps 80:12; S Isa 22:5; La 2:8 **39:9** [n] Jer 21:9 [o] Jer 40:1; La 1:5 **39:12** [p] S Pr 16:7; Jer 15:20-21; 1Pe 3:13 **39:13** [q] S ver 3 **39:14** [r] S Ne 3:25; Jer 37:21 [s] S 2Ki 25:22 [t] S 2Ki 22:12 [u] S 2Ki 22:3 [v] Jer 40:5 **39:16** [w] Jer 38:7 [x] Ps 33:11; Isa 14:27; 40:8; Jer 44:28; La 2:17; S Mt 1:22 [y] S Jos 23:15; Jer 21:10 **39:17** [z] Ps 34:22; 41:1-2 **39:18** [a] S 1Sa 17:47; Ac 16:31 [b] S Job 5:20 [c] S Jer 21:9; S 38:2 [d] S Jer 17:7; Ro 10:11 **40:1** [e] S Jos 18:25; 1Sa 8:4; Mt 2:18 [f] S Dt 21:10; S 2Ki 24:1; S 2Ch 36:10; Na 3:10 **40:2** [g] Ro 13:4 [h] S Isa 10:22 [i] S 2Ch 34:24; S Ps 18:18; S Pr 8:36; Gal 6:7-8 [j] S Jos 23:15

his title, was found on a clay tablet in London's British Museum collection. The name means "Nabu [a god; see note on 2Ki 24:1] has preserved his kingship." The date on the tablet is Nebuchadnezzar's tenth year (595 BC, seven years before the siege of Jerusalem began; see v. 1 and note). *chief officer.* See v. 13; see also note on 2Ki 18:17. *high official.* See v. 13. The Hebrew for this phrase is cognate to Babylonian *rab mu(n)gi*, a high military official who sometimes served as an envoy to foreign rulers.

39:4 – 7 See 52:7 – 11; see also 2Ki 25:4 – 7 and notes.

39:4 *Arabah.* See note on Dt 1:1.

39:5 *plains.* The Hebrew for this word is the plural of the word for "Arabah" (v. 4).

39:8 – 10 See 52:12 – 16; see also 2Ki 25:8 – 12 and notes.

39:12 *look after him.* See note on 40:4.

39:14 *had Jeremiah taken out.* Either (1) a summary statement of Jeremiah's release from prison, the specific details of which are given in 40:1 – 6; or (2) a brief description of the first of two releases, the second of which (made necessary because Jeremiah had been arrested again by mistake in the confusion surrounding the capture and transporting of thousands of exiles) is detailed in 40:1 – 6. *courtyard of the guard.* See note on 32:2. *Gedaliah son of Ahikam, the son of Shaphan.* See note on 26:24. *his home.* The governor's residence. An early sixth-century seal impression found at Lachish reads: "Belonging to Gedaliah [probably the man named in this verse], who is over the house."

39:15 – 18 See note on 38:12.

39:16 *Go and tell.* Though confined in prison, Jeremiah was permitted to have visitors (see note on 38:1). *I am about to fulfill my words against this city.* See 19:15.

39:17 *those you fear.* The court officials (see 38:1), who, in Ebed-Melek's judgment, had "acted wickedly" (38:9).

39:18 *escape with your life.* See 21:9 and note; 45:5. *you trust in me.* Ebed-Melek had expressed his faith in God by securing Jeremiah's release from the cistern (see 38:7 – 13; see also note on 38:12).

40:1 — 44:30 A lively narrative of the aftermath of the fall of Jerusalem. Chronologically, the chapters are the latest in the book (although 52:31 – 34 is later, it is part of the appendix and not of the book proper; see 51:64 and note).

40:1 *The word came.* A heading introducing the prophecies of Jeremiah after the exile, just as "The word ... came" (1:2) introduces his prophecies from the time of his call up to the exile (see 1:3). *Nebuzaradan ... released him.* See note on 39:14. *Ramah.* See note on 31:15. *chains.* Manacles that were fastened to the wrists (see v. 4; see also Job 36:8; Isa 45:14).

40:2 – 3 Nebuzaradan doubtless knew the basic content of Jeremiah's prophetic message against Jerusalem, and he here repeats it to the prophet in summary fashion.

3 And now the LORD has brought it about;
he has done just as he said he would. All
this happened because you people sinned[k]
against the LORD and did not obey[l] him.
4 But today I am freeing[m] you from the
chains[n] on your wrists. Come with me to
Babylon, if you like, and I will look after
you; but if you do not want to, then don't
come. Look, the whole country lies before
you; go wherever you please."[o] 5 However,
before Jeremiah turned to go,[a] Nebuzaradan added, "Go back to Gedaliah[p] son
of Ahikam,[q] the son of Shaphan, whom
the king of Babylon has appointed[r] over
the towns[s] of Judah, and live with him
among the people, or go anywhere else
you please."[t]

Then the commander gave him provisions and a present[u] and let him go. 6 So
Jeremiah went to Gedaliah son of Ahikam
at Mizpah[v] and stayed with him among the
people who were left behind in the land.

Gedaliah Assassinated

40:7-9; 41:1-3pp — 2Ki 25:22-26

7 When all the army officers and their
men who were still in the open country
heard that the king of Babylon had appointed Gedaliah son of Ahikam as governor[w] over the land and had put him in
charge of the men, women and children
who were the poorest[x] in the land and who
had not been carried into exile to Babylon,
8 they came to Gedaliah at Mizpah[y] — Ishmael[z] son of Nethaniah, Johanan[a] and
Jonathan the sons of Kareah, Seraiah son
of Tanhumeth, the sons of Ephai the Netophathite,[b] and Jaazaniah[b] the son of the
Maakathite,[c] and their men. 9 Gedaliah son
of Ahikam, the son of Shaphan, took an
oath to reassure them and their men. "Do
not be afraid to serve[d] the Babylonians,[c e]"
he said. "Settle down in the land and serve
the king of Babylon, and it will go well
with you.[f] 10 I myself will stay at Mizpah[g]
to represent you before the Babylonians
who come to us, but you are to harvest the
wine,[h] summer fruit and olive oil, and put
them in your storage jars,[i] and live in the
towns you have taken over."[j]

11 When all the Jews in Moab,[k] Ammon,
Edom[l] and all the other countries[m] heard
that the king of Babylon had left a remnant in Judah and had appointed Gedaliah son of Ahikam, the son of Shaphan,
as governor over them, 12 they all came
back to the land of Judah, to Gedaliah at
Mizpah, from all the countries where they
had been scattered.[n] And they harvested
an abundance of wine and summer fruit.

13 Johanan[o] son of Kareah and all the
army officers still in the open country
came to Gedaliah at Mizpah[p] 14 and said to
him, "Don't you know that Baalis king of
the Ammonites[q] has sent Ishmael[r] son of
Nethaniah to take your life?" But Gedaliah
son of Ahikam did not believe them.

15 Then Johanan[s] son of Kareah said privately to Gedaliah in Mizpah, "Let me go
and kill[t] Ishmael son of Nethaniah, and
no one will know it. Why should he take
your life and cause all the Jews who are
gathered around you to be scattered[u] and
the remnant[v] of Judah to perish?"

16 But Gedaliah son of Ahikam said to
Johanan[w] son of Kareah, "Don't do such a
thing! What you are saying about Ishmael
is not true."

41 In the seventh month Ishmael[x] son
of Nethaniah, the son of Elishama,
who was of royal blood and had been one
of the king's officers, came with ten men
to Gedaliah son of Ahikam at Mizpah.
While they were eating together there,
2 Ishmael[y] son of Nethaniah and the ten
men who were with him got up and struck
down Gedaliah son of Ahikam, the son of
Shaphan, with the sword,[z] killing the one

[a] 5 Or *Jeremiah answered* [b] 8 Hebrew *Jezaniah*, a variant of *Jaazaniah* [c] 9 Or *Chaldeans*; also in verse 10

40:3 [k] S Pr 13:21; Ro 6:23; Jas 1:15 [l] S Lev 26:33; Dt 28:45-52; 29:24-28; 31:17-18; S 1Ki 9:9; Jer 22:8-9; Da 9:14; Ac 7:39; Ro 2:5-9 **40:4** [m] Ps 105:18-20; S Jer 37:14 [n] La 3:7 [o] S Ge 13:9 **40:5** [p] S 2Ki 25:22 [q] 2Ki 22:12-14 [r] Ne 5:14; Jer 41:2 [s] Jer 44:2; Zec 1:12 [t] Jer 39:14 [u] S Ge 32:20; S 1Sa 9:7 **40:6** [v] ver 10; Jdg 20:1; 1Sa 7:5-17 **40:7** [w] S Ge 41:41; S Ne 5:14 [x] S 2Ki 24:14; S Ac 24:17; Jas 2:5 **40:8** [y] ver 13 [z] ver 14; Jer 41:1,2 [a] ver 15; Jer 41:11 [b] S 2Sa 23:28 [c] S Dt 3:14 **40:9** [d] Jer 5:19; 27:11; Ro 13:1-2; Eph 6:5-8 [e] Eze 23:23 [f] S Jer 38:20; La 1:1 **40:10** [g] S ver 6 [h] S Ge 27:28; S Ex 23:16 [i] Ex 7:19; 2Co 4:7 [j] Dt 1:39 **40:11** [k] S Nu 21:11; 25:1 [l] S Ge 25:30 [m] Jer 12:14 **40:12** [n] Jer 43:5 **40:13** [o] Jer 42:1 [p] ver 8 **40:14** [q] S Ge 19:38; 2Sa 10:1-19; Jer 25:21; 41:10; 49:1 [r] S ver 8 **40:15** [s] S ver 8 [t] S Dt 5:17; Mt 5:21-22 [u] S Ge 11:4; S Lev 26:33; Mt 26:31; Jn 11:52; Jas 1:1 [v] S 2Ki 21:14; S Isa 1:9; Ro 11:5 **40:16** [w] Jer 43:2 **41:1** [x] S Jer 40:8 **41:2** [y] Ps 41:9; 109:5 [z] S Jos 11:10; Jer 40:15; Heb 11:37

40:4 *I will look after you.* Nebuzaradan promises to carry out Nebuchadnezzar's wishes concerning Jeremiah (see 39:12). *the whole country lies before you.* Cf. Abram's offer to Lot in Ge 13:9.

40:5 – 9 See 2Ki 25:22 – 24 and notes.

40:5 *Gedaliah son of Ahikam.* See note on 26:24. *provisions.* The Hebrew for this word is translated "allowance" in 52:34.

40:8 *Jaazaniah.* See note on 2Ki 25:23.

40:10 *harvest the wine, summer fruit and olive oil.* Nebuzaradan (see 39:9) had arrived in Jerusalem in August of 586 BC (see note on 2Ki 25:8). Grapes, figs and olives were harvested in the Holy Land during August and September.

40:14 *Baalis.* Three royal inscriptions have been found that may relate to this king: (1) "King Ba'lay," as his name is written on an early sixth-century BC bottle discovered in Jordan; (2) "Ba'al-Yasha," an Ammonite king whose name appears on a stamp seal found at Tall al-'Umayri in Jordan in 1984; (3) "Baalis king of [the Ammonites]," as his name reads on an Ammonite stamp seal that came to light in 1998. *Ammonites.* Ammon was among the nations that earlier had been allies against Babylonia (see 27:3 and note; see also Eze 21:18 – 32).

40:15 *privately.* See note on 38:16. *remnant.* See note on 6:9.

40:16 *not true.* Lit. "a lie" (see 37:14 and note). Gedaliah's naive faith in Ishmael's integrity would cost him his life (see 41:2).

41:1 – 3 See 2Ki 25:25 and note.

41:1 *one of the king's officers.* Ishmael's loyalty to Zedekiah might explain his assassination of Gedaliah, whom he considered to be a Babylonian puppet ruler. *they were eating together.* Ancient custom with respect to hospitality probably made Gedaliah assume that his guests would not harm him, much less kill him (see note on Jdg 4:21).

whom the king of Babylon had appointed[a]
as governor over the land.[b] 3Ishmael also
killed all the men of Judah who were with
Gedaliah at Mizpah, as well as the Babylonian[a] soldiers who were there.
4The day after Gedaliah's assassination,
before anyone knew about it, 5eighty men
who had shaved off their beards,[c] torn
their clothes[d] and cut[e] themselves came
from Shechem,[f] Shiloh[g] and Samaria,[h]
bringing grain offerings and incense[i] with
them to the house of the LORD.[j] 6Ishmael
son of Nethaniah went out from Mizpah
to meet them, weeping[k] as he went. When
he met them, he said, "Come to Gedaliah
son of Ahikam."[l] 7When they went into
the city, Ishmael son of Nethaniah and the
men who were with him slaughtered them
and threw them into a cistern.[m] 8But ten
of them said to Ishmael, "Don't kill us!
We have wheat and barley, olive oil and
honey, hidden in a field."[n] So he let them
alone and did not kill them with the others. 9Now the cistern where he threw all
the bodies of the men he had killed along
with Gedaliah was the one King Asa[o] had
made as part of his defense[p] against Baasha[q] king of Israel. Ishmael son of Nethaniah filled it with the dead.
10Ishmael made captives of all the rest
of the people[r] who were in Mizpah — the
king's daughters[s] along with all the others
who were left there, over whom Nebuzaradan commander of the imperial guard
had appointed Gedaliah son of Ahikam.
Ishmael son of Nethaniah took them captive and set out to cross over to the Ammonites.[t]
11When Johanan[u] son of Kareah and
all the army officers who were with him
heard about all the crimes Ishmael son of
Nethaniah had committed, 12they took all
their men and went to fight[v] Ishmael son
of Nethaniah. They caught up with him
near the great pool[w] in Gibeon. 13When all
the people[x] Ishmael had with him saw Johanan son of Kareah and the army officers
who were with him, they were glad. 14All
the people Ishmael had taken captive at
Mizpah[y] turned and went over to Johanan
son of Kareah. 15But Ishmael son of Nethaniah and eight of his men escaped[z] from
Johanan and fled to the Ammonites.

Flight to Egypt

16Then Johanan son of Kareah and all
the army officers[a] who were with him led
away all the people of Mizpah who had
survived,[b] whom Johanan had recovered
from Ishmael son of Nethaniah after Ishmael had assassinated Gedaliah son of
Ahikam — the soldiers, women, children
and court officials he had recovered from
Gibeon. 17And they went on, stopping at
Geruth Kimham[c] near Bethlehem[d] on their
way to Egypt[e] 18to escape the Babylonians.[b]
They were afraid[f] of them because Ishmael
son of Nethaniah had killed Gedaliah[g] son
of Ahikam, whom the king of Babylon had
appointed as governor over the land.

42 Then all the army officers, including Johanan[h] son of Kareah and
Jezaniah[c] son of Hoshaiah,[i] and all the
people from the least to the greatest[j] approached 2Jeremiah the prophet and said
to him, "Please hear our petition and pray[k]
to the LORD your God for this entire rem-

[a] *3* Or *Chaldean* [b] *18* Or *Chaldeans* [c] *1* Hebrew; Septuagint (see also 43:2) *Azariah*

41:2 [a] S Jer 40:5 [b] 2Sa 3:27; 20:9-10; S Jer 40:8 **41:5** [c] S Lev 19:27; Jer 47:5; 48:37 [d] S Ge 37:29; S Lev 10:6; S Mk 14:63 [e] S Lev 19:28 [f] Ge 12:6; 33:18; Jdg 9:1-57; 1Ki 12:1 [g] S Jos 18:1 [h] 1Ki 16:24 [i] S Nu 16:40; S Lk 1:9 [j] 1Ki 3:2; 6:38; 2Ki 25:9 **41:6** [k] 2Sa 3:16 [l] Ps 5:9; Hos 7:11; Rev 20:10 **41:7** [m] S Ge 37:24; 2Ki 10:14 **41:8** [n] Isa 45:3 **41:9** [o] S 1Ki 15:22; S 2Ch 16:6 [p] S Jdg 6:2 [q] S 2Ch 16:1 **41:10** [r] Jer 40:7, 12 [s] Jer 38:23 [t] S Jer 40:14 **41:11** [u] S Jer 40:8 **41:12** [v] S Ex 14:14; Jn 18:36 [w] S Jos 9:3; Jn 9:7 **41:13** [x] ver 10 **41:14** [y] Jer 40:6 **41:15** [z] Job 21:30; S Pr 28:17 **41:16** [a] Jer 42:1; 43:2 [b] Isa 1:9; Jer 43:4; Eze 7:16; 14:22; Zep 2:9 **41:17** [c] 2Sa 19:37 [d] Ge 35:19; Mic 5:2 [e] Jer 42:14 **41:18** [f] S Nu 14:9; Isa 51:12; Jer 42:16; Lk 12:4-5 [g] S 2Ki 25:22 **42:1** [h] S Jer 40:13 [i] S Jer 41:16 [j] Jer 6:13; 44:12 **42:2** [k] S Ge 20:7; S Jer 36:7; Ac 8:24; Jas 5:16

41:5 *had shaved off their beards, torn their clothes and cut themselves.* Signs of mourning (see 16:6 and note; see also note on Ezr 9:3), probably over the destruction of Jerusalem. *came.* In the "seventh month" (v. 1) to celebrate the Festival of Tabernacles (see note on Ex 23:16). *Shechem, Shiloh and Samaria.* Formerly worship centers in the north (see notes on 7:12; Ge 12:6; see also Jos 24:25 – 26). After the northern kingdom was destroyed in 722 – 721 BC, many Israelites made periodic pilgrimages to Jerusalem, especially during the reform movements of Hezekiah (see 2Ch 30:11) and Josiah (see 2Ch 34:9). *grain offerings and incense.* Bloodless offerings, since the altar of the Jerusalem temple had been destroyed. *house of the LORD.* Though the temple itself was in ruins, the site was still considered holy.

41:6 *weeping.* Pretending to share the sorrow of the mourners from the north.

41:7 *the city.* Mizpah. *cistern.* A favorite place to dispose of victims, whether living or dead (see 37:16 and note; 38:6).

41:8 *wheat and barley, olive oil and honey.* Supplies that Ishmael perhaps would have taken with him when he fled to Ammon (see v. 15).

41:9 *the cistern ... was the one King Asa had made.* Probably as part of the fortifications Asa had built at Mizpah (see 1Ki 15:22), since cisterns were essential for storing water during times of siege. Archaeologists have discovered numerous cisterns in the ruins of ancient Mizpah (modern Tell en-Nasbeh, seven and a half miles north of Jerusalem).

41:10 *king's daughters.* Women who had been members of King Zedekiah's court, not necessarily daughters of the king himself (see note on 36:26). *Ammonites.* See 40:14 and note.

41:12 *great pool in Gibeon.* Perhaps the same as the one mentioned in 2Sa 2:13 (see note there).

41:15 *eight of his men escaped.* Ishmael lost only two of his men (see v. 2) in the fight with Johanan.

41:17 *Geruth Kimham.* Perhaps means "lodging place of Kimham," a friend of David who returned with him to Jerusalem after Absalom's death (see 2Sa 19:37 – 40).

42:1 *Jezaniah son of Hoshaiah.* Possibly the same as "Jaazaniah the son of the Maakathite" (40:8; see NIV text note there). Apparently Jezaniah was also known as Azariah (see NIV text note; see also 43:2), as was King Uzziah (see NIV text notes on 2Ki 14:21; 2Ch 26:1).

42:2 *Jeremiah.* Had probably been among the "people of Mizpah who had survived" (41:16). *hear our petition.* See v. 9; 37:20. *remnant.* See vv. 15,19; see also note on 6:9.

nant.[l] For as you now see, though we were
once many, now only a few[m] are left. 3 Pray
that the LORD your God will tell us where
we should go and what we should do."[n]
4 "I have heard you," replied Jeremiah
the prophet. "I will certainly pray[o] to the
LORD your God as you have requested; I
will tell[p] you everything the LORD says and
will keep nothing back from you."[q]
5 Then they said to Jeremiah, "May
the LORD be a true[r] and faithful[s] witness[t]
against us if we do not act in accordance
with everything the LORD your God sends
you to tell us. 6 Whether it is favorable or
unfavorable, we will obey the LORD our
God, to whom we are sending you, so that
it will go well[u] with us, for we will obey[v]
the LORD our God."
7 Ten days later the word of the LORD
came to Jeremiah. 8 So he called together
Johanan son of Kareah and all the army
officers[w] who were with him and all the
people from the least to the greatest.[x] 9 He
said to them, "This is what the LORD, the
God of Israel, to whom you sent me to present your petition,[y] says:[z] 10 'If you stay in
this land,[a] I will build[b] you up and not tear
you down; I will plant[c] you and not uproot
you,[d] for I have relented concerning the
disaster I have inflicted on you.[e] 11 Do not
be afraid of the king of Babylon,[f] whom
you now fear.[g] Do not be afraid of him, declares the LORD, for I am with you and will
save[h] you and deliver you from his hands.[i]
12 I will show you compassion[j] so that he
will have compassion on you and restore
you to your land.'[k]
13 "However, if you say, 'We will not
stay in this land,' and so disobey[l] the LORD
your God, 14 and if you say, 'No, we will go
and live in Egypt,[m] where we will not see
war or hear the trumpet[n] or be hungry for
bread,'[o] 15 then hear the word of the LORD,[p]
you remnant of Judah. This is what the
LORD Almighty, the God of Israel, says: 'If
you are determined to go to Egypt and you
do go to settle there, 16 then the sword[q] you
fear[r] will overtake you there, and the famine[s] you dread will follow you into Egypt,
and there you will die.[t] 17 Indeed, all who
are determined to go to Egypt to settle
there will die by the sword, famine and
plague;[u] not one of them will survive or
escape the disaster I will bring on them.'
18 This is what the LORD Almighty, the God
of Israel, says: 'As my anger and wrath[v]
have been poured out on those who lived
in Jerusalem,[w] so will my wrath be poured
out on you when you go to Egypt. You will
be a curse[a][x] and an object of horror,[y] a
curse[a] and an object of reproach;[z] you will
never see this place again.'[a]
19 "Remnant[b] of Judah, the LORD has told
you, 'Do not go to Egypt.'[c] Be sure of this:
I warn you today 20 that you made a fatal mistake when you sent me to the LORD
your God and said, 'Pray to the LORD our
God for us; tell us everything he says and
we will do it.'[d] 21 I have told you today, but
you still have not obeyed the LORD your
God in all he sent me to tell you.[e] 22 So
now, be sure of this: You will die by the
sword, famine[f] and plague[g] in the place
where you want to go to settle."[h]

43 When Jeremiah had finished telling the people all the words of the
LORD their God—everything the LORD had
sent him to tell them[i]— 2 Azariah son of
Hoshaiah[j] and Johanan[k] son of Kareah
and all the arrogant[l] men said to Jeremiah, "You are lying![m] The LORD our God has
not sent you to say, 'You must not go to
Egypt to settle there.'[n] 3 But Baruch[o] son of
Neriah is inciting you against us to hand
us over to the Babylonians,[b] so they may
kill us or carry us into exile to Babylon."[p]
4 So Johanan son of Kareah and all

[a] *18* That is, your name will be used in cursing (see 29:22); or, others will see that you are cursed.
[b] *3* Or *Chaldeans*

42:2 [l] S Isa 1:9 [m] S Lev 26:22; La 1:1 **42:3** [n] ver 20; Ps 86:11; S Pr 3:6; S Jer 15:11 **42:4** [o] Ex 8:29; 1Sa 12:23 [p] S Jer 1:17 [q] S Nu 22:18; S 1Sa 3:17 **42:5** [r] 1Ki 22:16; Ps 119:160; Ro 3:4 [s] S Dt 7:9; Jn 8:26; S 1Co 1:9 [t] S Ge 31:48; S Dt 4:26; S Isa 1:2; S Ro 1:9; Rev 1:5 **42:6** [u] Dt 5:29; 6:3; Jer 7:23; 22:15 [v] S ver 19; S Ex 24:7; S Jos 24:24 **42:8** [w] ver 1 [x] Jer 41:16; S Mk 9:35; Lk 7:28; Heb 8:11 **42:9** [y] ver 2 [z] 2Ki 22:15 **42:10** [a] Jer 43:4 [b] S Jer 24:6 [c] S Dt 30:9 [d] S Dt 29:28; Ecc 3:2; Jer 45:4; Eze 36:36; Da 11:4 [e] S 2Ch 34:24; Isa 30:26; S Jer 18:8 **42:11** [f] Jer 27:11 [g] S Nu 14:9; S 1Sa 15:24; Ps 23:4; Mt 10:28; 2Ti 1:7 [h] Ps 18:27; 69:35; S 119:94; S Isa 63:1; Heb 7:25 [i] S Ps 3:7; S Pr 20:22; S Jer 1:8; Ro 8:31 **42:12** [j] S Ex 3:21; S 2Sa 24:14; 2Co 1:3 [k] S Ge 31:3; S Ne 1:9; Ps 106:44-46 **42:13** [l] S Dt 11:28 **42:14** [m] Nu 11:4-5; S Dt 17:16; S Isa 30:2 [n] S Jos 6:20; S Mt 24:31 [o] S Dt 8:3; 1Sa 2:5; Pr 10:3; Isa 65:13; Mt 4:2-4 **42:15** [p] Jer 44:24 **42:16** [q] S Lev 26:33; Eze 11:8; 14:17 [r] S Jer 41:18 [s] S Ge 41:55 [t] S Ge 2:17; 2Ch 25:4; S Job 21:20; Eze 3:19; 18:4 **42:17** [u] ver 22; S Jer 21:7; 44:13 **42:18** [v] Dt 29:18-20; S 2Ch 12:7 [w] S 2Ch 36:19; Jer 39:1-9 [x] S Nu 5:27; S Jer 25:18 [y] S Dt 28:25, 37 [z] S Ps 44:13 [a] S Jer 22:10 **42:19** [b] Jer 40:15 [c] S ver 6; Dt 17:16; Isa 30:7; Jer 43:2; 44:16 **42:20** [d] ver 2; Eze 14:7-8 **42:21** [e] S Ex 24:7; Jer 40:3; Eze 2:7; 12:2; Zec 7:11-12 **42:22** [f] S Isa 1:28 [g] S ver 17; Jer 24:10; Eze 6:11 [h] S Jer 15:2; Hos 9:6 **43:1** [i] Jer 26:8; 42:9-22 **43:2** [j] S Jer 41:16 [k] Jer 40:16 [l] S Ne 9:29; 1Co 4:18-21 [m] S Ge 19:14; S Dt 13:3; Ro 9:1; 2Co 11:31; 1Ti 2:7 [n] S Ex 24:7; 2Ki 25:24; Jer 18:19; S 42:19; Eze 37:14 **43:3** [o] S Jer 32:12 [p] Jer 38:4; 41:18; 52:30

42:3 The people may be asking the Lord to confirm what they sincerely believe to be their only option: flight to Egypt (see v. 17; 41:17).

42:6 *we will obey the LORD our God.* Though they twice declare here their desire to do God's will, they soon demonstrate that they have already decided to follow their own inclinations (see 43:2).

42:7 *Ten days later.* Jeremiah does not bring God's word to the people until he is sure of it himself (see 28:10–17).

42:10 *build you up … tear you down … plant … uproot.* See 1:10 and note; see also 31:4,28; 33:7.

42:12 *he will have compassion on you.* For similar examples, see Ge 43:14; 1Ki 8:50.

42:16 *the sword you fear will overtake you there.* See 43:11 and note.

42:17–18 See 44:11–14.

42:17 *sword, famine and plague.* See note on 14:12.

42:18 *my anger and wrath have been poured out.* See 7:20; 44:6. *curse … reproach.* See NIV text note; see also notes on 24:9; 25:18; cf. 29:18. *this place.* Jerusalem.

42:19 *I warn you.* See 11:7.

43:2 *Azariah.* See note on 42:1. *arrogant men.* They demonstrate themselves to be such by their words.

43:3 *Baruch.* See note on 32:12. Jeremiah's opponents decide to put the blame on someone they consider less spiritually formidable than the prophet himself.

the army officers and all the people[q] disobeyed the LORD's command[r] to stay in
the land of Judah.[s] 5 Instead, Johanan
son of Kareah and all the army officers
led away all the remnant of Judah who
had come back to live in the land of Judah from all the nations where they had
been scattered.[t] 6 They also led away all
those whom Nebuzaradan commander of
the imperial guard had left with Gedaliah
son of Ahikam, the son of Shaphan—the
men, the women,[u] the children and the
king's daughters. And they took Jeremiah the prophet and Baruch[v] son of Neriah
along with them. 7 So they entered Egypt[w]
in disobedience to the LORD and went as
far as Tahpanhes.[x]
8 In Tahpanhes[y] the word of the LORD
came to Jeremiah: 9 "While the Jews are
watching, take some large stones[z] with
you and bury them in clay in the brick[a]
pavement at the entrance to Pharaoh's
palace[b] in Tahpanhes. 10 Then say to them,
'This is what the LORD Almighty, the God
of Israel, says: I will send for my servant[c]
Nebuchadnezzar[d] king of Babylon, and
I will set his throne[e] over these stones I
have buried here; he will spread his royal
canopy[f] above them. 11 He will come and
attack Egypt,[g] bringing death[h] to those
destined[i] for death, captivity to those destined for captivity,[j] and the sword to those
destined for the sword.[k] 12 He will set fire[l]
to the temples[m] of the gods[n] of Egypt; he
will burn their temples and take their gods
captive.[o] As a shepherd picks[p] his garment
clean of lice, so he will pick Egypt clean
and depart. 13 There in the temple of the
sun[a][q] in Egypt he will demolish the sacred
pillars[r] and will burn down the temples of
the gods of Egypt.' "

43:4 [q]S Jer 41:16 [r]2Ch 25:16; Jer 42:5-6 [s]Jer 42:10 **43:5** [t]Jer 40:12 **43:6** [u]S Jer 6:12 [v]S Jer 32:12 **43:7** [w]S 2Ki 25:26 [x]Jer 2:16; 44:1; 46:14; Eze 30:18 **43:8** [y]Ps 139:7; Jer 2:16 **43:9** [z]Ge 31:45-53; Jos 4:1-7; 1Ki 18:31-32 [a]S Ge 11:3 [b]S Ge 47:14 **43:10** [c]Isa 44:28; 45:1; Jer 25:9; 27:6 [d]Jer 46:13 [e]Jer 49:38 [f]S Ps 18:11 **43:11** [g]Jer 46:13-26; Eze 29:19-20 [h]S Pr 11:19; Ro 6:23 [i]S Ps 49:14; Heb 9:27 [j]S Dt 28:64; Rev 13:10 [k]S Jer 15:2; Eze 32:11; Zec 11:9 **43:12** [l]S Jos 7:15 [m]S 1Ki 16:32 [n]ver 13; S Ex 12:12; S Isa 2:18; Jer 46:25; Eze 30:13; Zec 13:2 [o]Da 11:8 [p]S Ps 104:2; 109:18-19 **43:13** [q]S Ge 1:16; Isa 19:18 *fn*; S Dt 4:19 [r]Jer 52:17; Eze 26:11 **44:1** [s]S Dt 32:42;

Disaster Because of Idolatry

44 This word came to Jeremiah concerning all the Jews living in Lower
Egypt[s]—in Migdol,[t] Tahpanhes[u] and Memphis[v]—and in Upper Egypt:[w] 2 "This is
what the LORD Almighty, the God of Israel,
says: You saw the great disaster[x] I brought
on Jerusalem and on all the towns of Judah.[y] Today they lie deserted and in ruins[z] 3 because of the evil[a] they have done.
They aroused my anger[b] by burning incense[c] to and worshiping other gods[d] that
neither they nor you nor your ancestors[e]
ever knew. 4 Again and again[f] I sent my
servants the prophets,[g] who said, 'Do not
do this detestable[h] thing that I hate!' 5 But
they did not listen or pay attention;[i] they
did not turn from their wickedness[j] or stop
burning incense[k] to other gods.[l] 6 Therefore, my fierce anger was poured out;[m] it
raged against the towns of Judah and the
streets of Jerusalem and made them the
desolate ruins[n] they are today.
7 "Now this is what the LORD God Almighty, the God of Israel, says: Why
bring such great disaster[o] on yourselves
by cutting off from Judah the men and
women,[p] the children and infants, and
so leave yourselves without a remnant?[q]
8 Why arouse my anger with what your
hands have made,[r] burning incense[s] to

[a] *13* Or *in Heliopolis*

S Jer 24:8 [t]S Ex 14:2 [u]S Jer 43:7,8 [v]S Isa 19:13 [w]S Isa 11:11 **44:2** [x]S 2Ch 34:24 [y]S Jer 40:5 [z]S Lev 26:31; S Dt 29:23; S Isa 6:11 **44:3** [a]S Ex 32:22 [b]S Nu 11:33 [c]S Nu 16:40 [d]ver 8; S Nu 25:3; Dt 13:6-11; 29:26; Isa 19:1 [e]S Jdg 2:19 **44:4** [f]S Jer 7:13 [g]S Nu 11:29 [h]S Dt 18:9; S 1Ki 14:24; 1Pe 4:3 **44:5** [i]S Jer 25:4; Da 9:6 [j]S Ge 6:5; Ro 1:18; 2Ti 2:19 [k]ver 21; Jer 1:16; Eze 8:11; 16:18; 23:41 [l]Jer 11:8-10; S 25:7 **44:6** [m]Eze 8:18; 20:34 [n]S Lev 26:31,34; S Dt 29:23; La 1:13; Zec 7:14 **44:7** [o]Jer 26:19 [p]Jer 51:22 [q]S 2Ki 21:14 **44:8** [r]S Isa 40:18-20; S Jer 10:3; Ro 1:23 [s]ver 17-25; Jer 41:5

43:5 *remnant of Judah.* Jews who had fled from the Babylonians to neighboring countries (see 40:11–12).

43:6 *king's daughters.* See note on 41:10. *Jeremiah … and Baruch.* No doubt they went to Egypt unwillingly, in the light of 32:6–15; 40:1–6; 42:13–22.

43:7 *Tahpanhes.* See note on 2:16.

43:9 *Pharaoh's palace.* Not necessarily his main residence. One of the Elephantine papyri (see chart, p. xxii), e.g., mentions the "king's house," apparently a more modest dwelling for the pharaoh's use when he visited Elephantine in southern Egypt.

43:10 *my servant Nebuchadnezzar.* See note on 25:9. *his throne.* Symbolizing his authority.

43:11 See 15:2 and note. *He will … attack Egypt.* A fragmentary text now owned by the British Museum in London states that Nebuchadnezzar carried out a punitive expedition against Egypt in his 37th year (568–567 BC) during the reign of Pharaoh Amasis (see Eze 29:17–20 and notes).

43:12 *As a shepherd picks his garment clean … so he will pick Egypt clean.* Routinely and confidently.

43:13 *temple of the sun in Egypt.* Lit. "Beth Shemesh in Egypt," not to be confused with "Beth Shemesh in Judah" (2Ki 14:11). The Egyptian city is probably to be identified with Heliopolis (Greek for "city of the sun"; see NIV text note), called *On* in Hebrew (see note on Ge 41:45). *sacred pillars.* Obelisks, for which ancient Heliopolis was famous.

44:1–30 The last of Jeremiah's recorded prophecies (see note on 40:1—44:30).

44:1 *Jews living in … Egypt.* As a result of previous deportations (see, e.g., 2Ki 23:34) and/or the Jews mentioned in 43:5–7. In either case, some time must have elapsed between chs. 43 and 44 to bring about the gathering mentioned in v. 15. *Lower Egypt … Upper Egypt.* See note on Isa 11:11. *Migdol.* Probably in northern Egypt (see 46:14). The name means "watchtower." *Tahpanhes and Memphis.* See notes on 2:16; Isa 19:13.

44:3 See note on 1:16; see also 11:17; 19:4; 32:32.

44:4 See 7:25 and note. *Do not do this detestable thing.* See Jdg 19:24.

44:6 *my fierce anger was poured out.* See 7:20; 42:18.

44:7 *bring … disaster on yourselves.* See 26:19. *men and women, the children and infants.* A stock phrase meaning "everyone" (see 1Sa 15:3; 22:19).

44:8 *what your hands have made.* Idols (see 1:16 and note; see also note on Ex 34:15). *curse and … reproach.* See 42:18 and note; see also notes on 24:9; 25:18.

other gods in Egypt,[t] where you have come to live?[u] You will destroy yourselves and make yourselves a curse[a] and an object of reproach[v] among all the nations on earth. 9 Have you forgotten the wickedness committed by your ancestors[w] and by the kings[x] and queens[y] of Judah and the wickedness committed by you and your wives[z] in the land of Judah and the streets of Jerusalem?[a] 10 To this day they have not humbled[b] themselves or shown reverence,[c] nor have they followed my law[d] and the decrees[e] I set before you and your ancestors.[f]

11 "Therefore this is what the LORD Almighty,[g] the God of Israel, says: I am determined to bring disaster[h] on you and to destroy all Judah. 12 I will take away the remnant[i] of Judah who were determined to go to Egypt to settle there. They will all perish in Egypt; they will fall by the sword or die from famine. From the least to the greatest,[j] they will die by sword or famine.[k] They will become a curse and an object of horror, a curse and an object of reproach.[l] 13 I will punish[m] those who live in Egypt with the sword,[n] famine and plague,[o] as I punished Jerusalem. 14 None of the remnant of Judah who have gone to live in Egypt will escape or survive to return to the land of Judah, to which they long to return and live; none will return except a few fugitives."[p]

15 Then all the men who knew that their wives[q] were burning incense[r] to other gods, along with all the women[s] who were present — a large assembly — and all the people living in Lower and Upper Egypt,[t] said to Jeremiah, 16 "We will not listen[u] to the message you have spoken to us in the name of the LORD![v] 17 We will certainly do everything we said we would:[w] We will burn incense[x] to the Queen of Heaven[y] and will pour out drink offerings to her just as we and our ancestors, our kings and our officials[z] did in the towns of Judah and in the streets of Jerusalem.[a] At that time we had plenty of food[b] and were well off and suffered no harm.[c] 18 But ever since we stopped burning incense to the Queen of Heaven and pouring out drink offerings[d] to her, we have had nothing and have been perishing by sword and famine.[e]"

19 The women added, "When we burned incense[f] to the Queen of Heaven[g] and poured out drink offerings to her, did not our husbands[h] know that we were making cakes[i] impressed with her image[j] and pouring out drink offerings to her?"

20 Then Jeremiah said to all the people, both men and women, who were answering him, 21 "Did not the LORD remember[k] and call to mind the incense[l] burned in the towns of Judah and the streets of Jerusalem[m] by you and your ancestors,[n] your kings and your officials and the people of the land?[o] 22 When the LORD could no longer endure[p] your wicked actions and the detestable things you did, your land became a curse[q] and a desolate waste[r] without inhabitants, as it is today.[s] 23 Because you have burned incense and have sinned against the LORD and have not obeyed him or followed[t] his law or his decrees[u] or his stipulations, this disaster[v] has come upon you, as you now see."[w]

24 Then Jeremiah said to all the people, including the women,[x] "Hear the word of the LORD, all you people of Judah in Egypt.[y] 25 This is what the LORD Almighty, the God of Israel, says: You and your wives[z] have done what you said you would do when you promised, 'We will certainly carry out the vows we made to burn incense and pour out drink offerings to the Queen of Heaven.'[a]

"Go ahead then, do what you promised!

a 8 That is, your name will be used in cursing (see 29:22); or, others will see that you are cursed; also in verse 12; similarly in verse 22.

44:8 [t] S ver 3; S Ex 12:12 [u] S 1Co 10:22 [v] S Ps 44:13 **44:9** [w] S Jdg 2:19 [x] S 2Ki 23:11 [y] 1Ki 21:25 [z] S Pr 31:10; S Jer 6:12 [a] ver 17,21; Jer 11:12; 32:32 **44:10** [b] S Dt 8:3; S Mt 23:12; Php 2:8 [c] S Dt 6:13; S Ps 5:7 [d] S Jos 1:7; S Jer 11:8; Mt 5:17-20; Gal 3:19; 1Jn 3:4 [e] S Lev 18:4 [f] 1Ki 9:6-9; 2Ki 17:17 **44:11** [g] Rev 4:8 [h] S 2Ch 34:24; Am 9:4 **44:12** [i] ver 7; Jer 40:15 [j] S Jer 42:1 [k] S Isa 1:28 [l] S Dt 28:25; S Jer 29:18 **44:13** [m] S Ex 32:34; Lev 26:14-17 [n] S Jer 15:2 [o] S Jer 42:17 **44:14** [p] Jer 22:24-27; 49:5; La 4:15; Eze 6:8; S Ro 9:27 **44:15** [q] S Pr 31:10; S Jer 6:12 [r] S Jer 18:15 [s] S Ge 3:6; 1Ti 2:14 [t] S Isa 11:11 **44:16** [u] S 1Sa 8:19; Job 15:25-26; Jer 11:8-10 [v] S Jer 42:19 **44:17** [w] ver 28; Dt 23:23; Zec 1:6 [x] S Isa 65:3 [y] ver 25; Jer 11:12 [z] Ne 9:34 [a] S ver 9; S Jer 2:26 [b] S Ex 16:3; Nu 11:4-6 [c] S Job 21:15; Isa 3:9; Hos 2:5-13; 9:1

44:18 [d] Lev 23:18 [e] Jer 42:16; Mal 3:13-15 **44:19** [f] S Jer 18:15 [g] Jer 7:18 [h] S Ge 3:6; Eph 5:22 [i] Lev 7:12 [j] S Lev 26:1; Ac 17:29 **44:21** [k] Isa 64:9; S Jer 14:10; Hos 8:13 [l] S Jer 11:13 [m] ver 9 [n] S Ps 79:8 [o] S Jer 2:26 **44:22** [p] S Isa 1:14 [q] S Jer 25:18 [r] S Lev 26:31,32 [s] S Ge 19:13; Ps 107:33-34; Eze 33:28-29 **44:23** [t] S 1Ki 9:6 [u] S Lev 18:4 [v] Jer 40:2 [w] S Lev 26:33; S 1Ki 9:9; Jer 7:13-15; Eze 39:23; Da 9:11-12 **44:24** [x] S Ge 3:6 [y] Jer 43:7 **44:25** [z] S Pr 31:10 [a] S ver 17; S Dt 32:38

44:9 *wickedness committed by … queens … and your wives.* The women joined their husbands in worshiping the "Queen of Heaven" (v. 19; see v. 15).

44:10 *nor … followed my law.* See 9:13; 26:4; see also 7:9 and note.

44:11 – 14 See 42:17 – 18 and notes.

44:11 *am determined.* Lit. "set my face" (see 21:10 and note).

44:15 *wives … women.* See v. 19; see also note on v. 9. *Lower and Upper Egypt.* See v. 1; see also note on Isa 11:11.

44:17 *Queen of Heaven.* See note on 7:18. *At that time we … were well off.* Judah had been relatively prosperous during King Manasseh's lengthy reign.

44:18 *ever since we stopped.* As a result of King Josiah's reform movement, which began in 621 BC. *we have had nothing.* Beginning with Josiah's death in 609, a series of disasters, including invasion and exile, had struck Judah. The people understandably (though mistakenly) attributed their misfortune to their failure to worship the Queen of Heaven.

44:19 *women.* Since Ishtar (the "Queen of Heaven") was a Babylonian goddess of fertility, women played a major role in her worship. *did not our husbands know … ?* To have validity, a religious vow made by a married woman (see v. 25) had to be confirmed by her husband (see Nu 30:10 – 15). *we were making cakes impressed with her image.* See 7:18.

44:22 *curse.* See v. 12. *desolate waste.* See v. 6.

44:23 *stipulations.* Of the Lord's covenant with his people (see Dt 4:45; 6:17,20).

44:25 *Go ahead then.* Spoken in irony (see 7:21 and note).

Keep your vows![b] 26 But hear the word of
the LORD, all you Jews living in Egypt:[c] 'I
swear[d] by my great name,' says the LORD,
'that no one from Judah living anywhere
in Egypt will ever again invoke my name
or swear, "As surely as the Sovereign[e] LORD
lives."[f] 27 For I am watching[g] over them for
harm,[h] not for good; the Jews in Egypt
will perish[i] by sword and famine[j] until
they are all destroyed.[k] 28 Those who escape the sword[l] and return to the land of
Judah from Egypt will be very few.[m] Then
the whole remnant[n] of Judah who came to
live in Egypt will know whose word will
stand[o] — mine or theirs.[p]
29 " 'This will be the sign[q] to you that
I will punish[r] you in this place,' declares
the LORD, 'so that you will know that my
threats of harm against you will surely
stand.'[s] 30 This is what the LORD says: 'I am
going to deliver Pharaoh[t] Hophra king of
Egypt into the hands of his enemies who
want to kill him, just as I gave Zedekiah[u]
king of Judah into the hands of Nebuchadnezzar king of Babylon, the enemy who
wanted to kill him.' "[v]

A Message to Baruch

45 When Baruch[w] son of Neriah[x] wrote
on a scroll[y] the words Jeremiah the
prophet dictated in the fourth year of Jehoiakim[z] son of Josiah king of Judah, Jeremiah said this to Baruch: 2 "This is what
the LORD, the God of Israel, says to you,
Baruch: 3 You said, 'Woe[a] to me! The LORD
has added sorrow[b] to my pain;[c] I am worn
out with groaning[d] and find no rest.'[e] 4 But
the LORD has told me to say to you, 'This is
what the LORD says: I will overthrow what I
have built and uproot[f] what I have planted,[g]
throughout the earth.[h] 5 Should you then
seek great[i] things for yourself? Do not seek
them.[j] For I will bring disaster[k] on all people,[l] declares the LORD, but wherever you go
I will let you escape[m] with your life.' "[n]

A Message About Egypt

46 This is the word of the LORD that
came to Jeremiah the prophet concerning the nations:[o]

2 Concerning Egypt:[p]

This is the message against the army of
Pharaoh Necho[q] king of Egypt, which was
defeated at Carchemish[r] on the Euphrates[s]
River by Nebuchadnezzar king of Babylon
in the fourth year of Jehoiakim[t] son of Josiah king of Judah:

3 "Prepare your shields,[u] both large and
small,
and march out for battle!
4 Harness the horses,
mount the steeds!
Take your positions
with helmets on!
Polish[v] your spears,
put on your armor![w]

44:25 [b] S Pr 20:25; Eze 20:39; Jas 1:13-15 **44:26** [c] S Jer 24:8 [d] S Ge 22:16; S Isa 48:1; Ac 19:13; Heb 6:13-17 [e] S Ge 15:2 [f] Dt 32:40; Ps 50:16; S Jer 4:2 **44:27** [g] S Jer 1:12 [h] S Jer 21:10 [i] S Lev 26:38; S Job 15:22; 2Pe 3:9 [j] S Ge 41:55 [k] S Jer 9:16; Da 9:14; Am 9:8 **44:28** [l] Jer 45:5; Eze 6:8 [m] ver 13-14; S Isa 10:19 [n] S 2Ki 21:14 [o] S Isa 7:9; S Jer 39:16; 42:15-18 [p] S ver 17, 25-26 **44:29** [q] S Ge 24:14; S Ex 3:12; S Nu 16:38; S Mt 12:38; 24:3 [r] S Ex 32:34 [s] S Pr 19:21 **44:30** [t] S Jer 25:19; 46:26; Eze 30:21; 32:32 [u] 2Ki 25:1-7; S Jer 24:8 [v] Jer 43:9-13 **45:1** [w] S Jer 32:12 [x] Jer 51:59 [y] S Ex 17:14; S Ps 40:7 [z] S 2Ch 36:5

45:3 [a] S Isa 24:16; 1Co 9:16 [b] S Ps 119:28; Mk 14:34; Ro 9:2 [c] S Job 6:10 [d] S Job 23:2; Ps 69:3 [e] S Jos 1:13; Mt 11:28; Heb 4:3 **45:4** [f] S Jer 42:10 [g] S Jer 11:17 [h] S Dt 28:63; S 30:9; Isa 5:5-7; Jer 18:7-10 **45:5** [i] Ps 131:1 [j] Mt 6:25-27,33 [k] Jer 11:11; 40:2 [l] S Jer 2:35 [m] S Ps 68:20; S Jer 44:28 [n] S Jer 21:9 **46:1** [o] S Jer 1:10 **46:2** [p] S Ex 1:8 [q] S 2Ki 23:29 [r] S 2Ch 35:20 [s] S Ge 2:14 [t] Jer 1:3; 25:1; 35:1; 36:1; 45:1; Da 1:1 **46:3** [u] S Isa 21:5 **46:4** [v] Eze 21:9-11 [w] 1Sa 17:5,38; 2Ch 26:14; Ne 4:16

44:26 *I swear by my great name.* See note on 22:5. *As surely as the Sovereign LORD lives.* See note on Ge 42:15.
44:27 *watching.* See note on 1:12; see also 31:28.
44:28 *very few.* See v. 14.
44:30 *Hophra.* Ruled Egypt 589–570 BC (see 37:5 and note). *his enemies who want to kill him.* Hophra was killed by his Egyptian rivals during a power struggle. *I gave Zedekiah … into the hands of Nebuchadnezzar.* See 39:5–7.
45:1–5 A brief message of encouragement to Baruch, Jeremiah's faithful secretary (see note on 32:12). Though out of chronological order, the section provides a suitable historical appendix to chs. 39–44, as well as a smooth transition to chs. 46–51 (see notes on v. 1; 46:2).
45:1 *wrote on a scroll.* See 36:4; see also 36:2 and note. *fourth year of Jehoiakim.* 605 BC. Ch. 45 fits chronologically between 36:8 and 36:9 (see note on 36:8).
45:3 To some extent Baruch shared Jeremiah's anguish, the result of Jeremiah's prophetic call and ministry (see, e.g., 8:18—9:2; 20:7–18). *worn out with groaning.* See Ps 6:6. *find no rest.* See La 5:5.
45:4 *overthrow … built … uproot … planted.* See note on 1:10; see also 2:21; 31:4–5,28,40; 32:41; 33:7. *earth.* See "all people" in v. 5; see also 25:15,31; 46–51.
45:5 *great things … Do not seek them.* See Ps 131:1. Baruch's brother Seraiah would occupy an important position under King Zedekiah (see 32:12; 51:59), but Baruch himself was not to be ambitious or self-seeking. *escape with your life.* See note on 21:9.
46:1 — 51:64 See notes on 25:1–38; 25:13; 25:19–26. Chs. 46–51 consist of a series of prophecies against the nations (see Isa 13–23; Eze 25–32; Am 1–2; Zep 2:4–15). They begin with Egypt (ch. 46) and end with Babylonia (chs. 50–51), the two powers that vied for control of Judah during Jeremiah's ministry. The arrangement of the prophecies is in a generally west-to-east direction.
46:1 *This is the word of the LORD … concerning.* See 14:1; 47:1; 49:34; 50:1. *nations.* To whom Jeremiah was called to prophesy (see 1:5 and note).
46:2 *Concerning Egypt.* See Isa 19–20; Eze 29–32. *Necho.* Ruled Egypt 610–595 BC. *Carchemish.* See 2Ch 35:20; Isa 10:9 and note. The name means "fortress of Chemosh" (chief god of Moab; see 2Ki 23:13), as clarified by the Ebla tablets (see Introduction to Genesis: Background; see also chart, p. xxii). *Euphrates River.* See note on Ge 15:18. *by Nebuchadnezzar.* Egypt's defeat by Babylonia at Carchemish was one of the most decisive battles in the ancient world, ending Egypt's agelong claims and pretensions to power in Syro-Palestine. *fourth year of Jehoiakim.* 605 BC, the first year of Nebuchadnezzar's reign (see 25:1).
46:3 *Prepare.* Spoken to the Egyptians in sarcasm (see, e.g. Na 2:1; 3:14 and notes).
46:4 *horses.* Egypt was a prime source for the finest horses (see 1Ki 10:28). *put on your armor.* See 51:3.

5 What do I see?
They are terrified,
they are retreating,
their warriors are defeated.
They flee[x] in haste
without looking back,
and there is terror[y] on every side,"
declares the LORD.
6 "The swift cannot flee[z]
nor the strong escape.
In the north by the River Euphrates[a]
they stumble and fall.[b]

7 "Who is this that rises like the Nile,
like rivers of surging waters?[c]
8 Egypt rises like the Nile,[d]
like rivers of surging waters.
She says, 'I will rise and cover the earth;
I will destroy cities and their people.'[e]
9 Charge, you horses!
Drive furiously, you charioteers![f]
March on, you warriors—men of Cush[a][g] and Put who carry shields,
men of Lydia[h] who draw the bow.
10 But that day[i] belongs to the Lord, the LORD Almighty—
a day of vengeance[j], for vengeance on his foes.
The sword will devour[k] till it is satisfied,
till it has quenched its thirst with blood.[l]
For the Lord, the LORD Almighty, will offer sacrifice[m]
in the land of the north by the River Euphrates.[n]

11 "Go up to Gilead and get balm,[o]
Virgin[p] Daughter Egypt.
But you try many medicines in vain;
there is no healing[q] for you.
12 The nations will hear of your shame;
your cries will fill the earth.
One warrior will stumble over another;
both will fall[r] down together."

13 This is the message the LORD spoke to
Jeremiah the prophet about the coming of
Nebuchadnezzar king of Babylon[s] to at-
tack Egypt:[t]

14 "Announce this in Egypt, and proclaim it in Migdol;
proclaim it also in Memphis[u] and Tahpanhes:[v]
'Take your positions and get ready,
for the sword devours[w] those around you.'
15 Why will your warriors be laid low?
They cannot stand, for the LORD will push them down.[x]
16 They will stumble[y] repeatedly;
they will fall[z] over each other.
They will say, 'Get up, let us go back
to our own people[a] and our native lands,
away from the sword of the oppressor.'[b]
17 There they will exclaim,
'Pharaoh king of Egypt is only a loud noise;[c]
he has missed his opportunity.[d]'

[a] 9 That is, the upper Nile region

46:5 [x] ver 21; Jer 48:44 [y] S Ps 31:13; S 48:5 **46:6** [z] Isa 30:16 [a] Ge 2:14; 15:18 [b] ver 12,16; S Ps 20:8 **46:7** [c] Jer 47:2 **46:8** [d] Eze 29:3, 9; 30:12; Am 8:8 [e] Da 11:10 **46:9** [f] Jer 47:3; Eze 26:10; Na 3:2 [g] S Ge 10:6 [h] S Isa 66:19 **46:10** [i] Eze 32:10; Joel 1:15; Ob 1:15 [j] S Nu 31:3; S Dt 32:41; 2Ki 23:29-30 [k] S Dt 32:42; S 2Sa 2:26; Zep 2:12 [l] S Dt 32:42 [m] S Lev 3:9; Zep 1:7 [n] Ge 2:14; 15:18 **46:11** [o] S Ge 37:25 [p] S 2Ki 19:21 [q] S Jer 30:13; S Mic 1:9 **46:12** [r] S ver 6; Isa 19:4; Na 3:8-10 **46:13** [s] ver 26; Eze 32:11 [t] Isa 19:1; Jer 27:7 **46:14** [u] S Isa 19:13 [v] S Jer 43:8 [w] S Dt 32:42; S 2Sa 2:26; S Jer 24:8 **46:15** [x] S Jos 23:5; Isa 66:15-16 **46:16** [y] S Lev 26:37 [z] S ver 6 [a] S Isa 13:14 [b] S Jer 25:38 **46:17** [c] 1Ki 20:10-11 [d] Isa 19:11-16

46:5 *terror on every side.* The phrase is used in 6:25 (see note there) with reference to the Babylonian army (see 6:22 and note).
46:7–8 *rivers of surging waters.* In the northern Egyptian delta, where the Nile branches out into numerous streams.
46:8 *rise and cover the earth.* The same metaphor is used of Assyria in Isa 8:7–8 (see note there). *cities.* The Hebrew for this word is in the singular but is used as a generic plural ("city" is generic also in 8:16).
46:9 *Charge.* See note on v. 3; see also 8:6; Na 3:3. *Drive furiously, you charioteers!* See Na 2:4. *Put.* See note on Ge 10:6. *Lydia.* See note on Isa 66:19. Men from Cush, Put and Lydia were mercenaries in the Egyptian army.
46:10 *day of vengeance.* See Isa 34:8 and note. The Lord will avenge Egypt's cruelties toward Judah (see, e.g., 2Ki 23:29,33–35). *sword will devour.* See v. 14. *quenched its thirst with blood … offer sacrifice.* Slaughter in battle is often compared with sacrifices (see Isa 34:5–7 and notes; Zep 1:7–8).
46:11 *Gilead … balm.* See 8:22 and note. *Virgin Daughter Egypt.* A personification of Egypt (see note on 2Ki 19:21). *medicines in vain … no healing for you.* The statement is ironic in the light of Egypt's reputation for expertise in the healing arts.
46:12 *stumble … fall.* See vv. 6,16.
46:13 *Nebuchadnezzar … to attack Egypt.* In 568–567 BC (see note on 43:11), long after the battle of Carchemish (see note on v. 2).
46:14 *Migdol.* See note on 44:1. *Memphis and Tahpanhes.* See 44:1; see also notes on 2:16; Isa 19:13. *Take your positions.* See v. 4. *sword devours.* See v. 10. See also photo, p. 1302.
46:15 *warriors.* The Hebrew for this word is not the same as that for "warrior[s]" in vv. 5,9,12. It is lit. "strong ones," often referring to powerful animals ("stallions" in 8:16; 50:11; "steeds" in 47:3; Jdg 5:22). In Ps 22:12; 50:13; 68:30; Isa 34:7 the Hebrew word is translated "bulls" (see note on Ps 68:30). *be laid low.* The Hebrew for this phrase is translated "Apis has fled" in the Septuagint (the pre-Christian Greek translation of the OT). Apis was a bull-god worshiped in Egypt, especially at Memphis (see v. 14). An alternative translation of v. 15 would then read as follows: "Why did Apis flee? Why did your bull [many manuscripts have the singular form] not stand? Because the LORD pushed him down."
46:16 *They will stumble repeatedly.* See vv. 6,12; lit. "He will make many stumble." *They will say, '… let us go.'* The mercenaries in the pharaoh's army (see v. 9 and note) will decide to return to their homelands. *sword of the oppressor.* See 25:38; 50:16.
46:17 *only a loud noise.* In Isa 30:7, Egypt is called "the Do-Nothing." *missed his opportunity.* After the battle of Carchemish (see v. 2), Nebuchadnezzar returned to Babylonia on learning of his father's death. Egypt failed to press its advantage at that time.

Excavations at Memphis. The Lord warns of Nebuchadnezzar's impending attack on Egypt (Jer 46:14).

Todd Bolen/www.BiblePlaces.com

18 "As surely as I live," declares the
King,[e]
whose name is the LORD Almighty,
"one will come who is like Tabor[f]
among the mountains,
like Carmel[g] by the sea.
19 Pack your belongings for exile,[h]
you who live in Egypt,
for Memphis[i] will be laid waste[j]
and lie in ruins without inhabitant.

20 "Egypt is a beautiful heifer,
but a gadfly is coming
against her from the north.[k]
21 The mercenaries[l] in her ranks
are like fattened calves.[m]
They too will turn and flee[n] together,
they will not stand their ground,
for the day[o] of disaster is coming upon
them,
the time[p] for them to be punished.

46:18 [e] Jer 48:15 [f] S Jos 19:22 [g] 1Ki 18:42 **46:19** [h] S Isa 20:4 [i] S Isa 19:13 [j] Eze 29:10,12; 35:7 **46:20** [k] ver 24; S Isa 14:31; Jer 47:2 **46:21** [l] S 2Ki 7:6 [m] Lk 15:27 [n] S ver 5; S Job 20:24 [o] Ps 18:18; 37:13; Jer 18:17 [p] S Job 18:20 **46:22** [q] Ps 74:5 **46:23** [r] S Dt 28:42; S Jdg 7:12 **46:24** [s] S 2Ki 24:7 **46:25** [t] Eze 30:14; Na 3:8

22 Egypt will hiss like a fleeing serpent
as the enemy advances in force;
they will come against her with axes,
like men who cut down trees.[q]
23 They will chop down her forest,"
declares the LORD,
"dense though it be.
They are more numerous than locusts,[r]
they cannot be counted.
24 Daughter Egypt will be put to shame,
given into the hands of the people of
the north.[s]"

25 The LORD Almighty, the God of Israel, says: "I am about to bring punishment
on Amon god of Thebes,[t] on Pharaoh,[u] on
Egypt and her gods[v] and her kings, and on
those who rely[w] on Pharaoh. 26 I will give
them into the hands[x] of those who want

[u] 2Ki 24:7; Eze 30:22 [v] S Jer 43:12 [w] Isa 20:6 **46:26** [x] S Jer 44:30

46:18 *As surely as I live.* See notes on Ge 22:16; 42:15. *King.* God is called "King" also in 8:19; 10:7,10; 48:15; 51:57. *one.* Nebuchadnezzar. *Tabor ... Carmel.* Two prominent mountains in Israel (see notes on Jdg 4:6; SS 7:5; Isa 33:9).
46:19 *Pack your belongings for exile.* Echoed in Eze 12:3. *Egypt.* Lit. "Daughter (of) Egypt" (see v. 11 and note). *laid waste.* Judah is so described in 2:15; 9:12.
46:20 *heifer.* Perhaps an ironic reference to Egyptian bull-worship (see note on v. 15). *gadfly.* Nebuchadnezzar. Insects are often used to symbolize an attacking enemy (see note on Ex 23:28).
46:21 *mercenaries.* See note on v. 9. *calves.* See note on v. 20. *day of disaster.* See 18:17. *time for them to be punished.* See 11:23; 23:12; 50:27.
46:22 *serpent.* Often used by Egyptian pharaohs as a symbol of their sovereignty (see note on Ex 4:3). *the enemy ... like men who cut down trees.* See 21:14; see also Isa 10:18–19,33–34 and notes.
46:23 *more numerous than locusts.* Here an invading army is compared to locusts. In Joel 2:11,25 locusts are compared to an invading army (see also 51:14).
46:24 *Daughter Egypt.* See v. 11 and note.
46:25 *Amon.* The chief god of Egypt during much of its history. Wicked King Manasseh may have named his son after the Egyptian deity (see 2Ki 21:18; 2Ch 33:22). *Thebes.* The capital of Upper (southern) Egypt (see Eze 30:14–16).
46:26 *Egypt will be inhabited as in times past.* Cf. 48:47; 49:6,39. Egypt would be restored in the Messianic age (see Isa 19:23–25 and notes).

to kill them — Nebuchadnezzar king[y] of
Babylon and his officers. Later, however,
Egypt will be inhabited[z] as in times past,"
declares the LORD.

27 "Do not be afraid,[a] Jacob[b] my servant;[c]
do not be dismayed, Israel.
I will surely save you out of a distant
place,
your descendants from the land of
their exile.[d]
Jacob will again have peace and
security,
and no one will make him afraid.
28 Do not be afraid, Jacob my servant,
for I am with you,"[e] declares the
LORD.
"Though I completely destroy[f] all the
nations
among which I scatter you,
I will not completely destroy you.
I will discipline you but only in due
measure;
I will not let you go entirely
unpunished."

A Message About the Philistines

47 This is the word of the LORD that
came to Jeremiah the prophet concerning the Philistines[g] before Pharaoh attacked Gaza:[h]

2 This is what the LORD says:

"See how the waters are rising in the
north;[i]
they will become an overflowing
torrent.
They will overflow the land and
everything in it,
the towns and those who live in
them.
The people will cry out;
all who dwell in the land will wail[j]
3 at the sound of the hooves of galloping
steeds,
at the noise of enemy chariots[k]
and the rumble of their wheels.
Parents will not turn to help their
children;
their hands will hang limp.[l]
4 For the day has come
to destroy all the Philistines
and to remove all survivors
who could help Tyre[m] and Sidon.[n]
The LORD is about to destroy the
Philistines,[o]
the remnant from the coasts of
Caphtor.[a][p]
5 Gaza will shave[q] her head in
mourning;
Ashkelon[r] will be silenced.
You remnant on the plain,
how long will you cut[s] yourselves?

6 " 'Alas, sword[t] of the LORD,
how long till you rest?
Return to your sheath;
cease and be still.'[u]
7 But how can it rest
when the LORD has commanded it,
when he has ordered it
to attack Ashkelon and the coast?"[v]

A Message About Moab

48:29-36pp — Isa 16:6-12

48 Concerning Moab:[w]

This is what the LORD Almighty, the God
of Israel, says:

"Woe to Nebo,[x] for it will be ruined.
Kiriathaim[y] will be disgraced and
captured;
the stronghold[b] will be disgraced
and shattered.

46:26 [y]S ver 13; S Isa 19:4 [z]Eze 29:11-16 **46:27** [a]Isa 43:5; Jer 51:46 [b]Isa 41:8; 44:1; Mal 1:2 [c]S Isa 44:2 [d]S Isa 11:11; S Jer 29:14; 50:19 **46:28** [e]S Ex 14:22; S Nu 14:9; Isa 8:9-10 [f]S Jer 4:27 **47:1** [g]S Ge 10:14; S Jdg 3:31 [h]S Ge 10:19; Zec 9:5-7 **47:2** [i]S Isa 14:31 [j]S Isa 15:3 **47:3** [k]S Jer 46:9; S Eze 23:24 [l]Isa 13:7; Jer 50:43; Eze 7:17; 21:7 **47:4** [m]S Isa 23:1; Am 1:9-10; Zec 9:2-4 [n]S Ge 10:15; S Jer 25:22 [o]S Ge 10:14; Joel 3:4 [p]S Dt 2:23 **47:5** [q]S Jer 41:5 [r]S Jer 25:20 [s]S Lev 19:28 **47:6** [t]S Isa 34:5; Jer 12:12; 48:10; 50:35 [u]Eze 21:30 **47:7** [v]Eze 25:15-17 **48:1** [w]S Ge 19:37; S Dt 23:6 [x]S Nu 32:38 [y]S Nu 32:37; S Jos 13:19

[a] *4* That is, Crete [b] *1* Or *captured; / Misgab*

46:27 – 28 Repeated almost verbatim from 30:10 – 11 (see notes there).
47:1 *concerning the Philistines.* See Isa 14:28 – 32; Eze 25:15 – 17; Am 1:6 – 8; Zep 2:4 – 7. *Pharaoh.* It is uncertain whether Necho II (see 46:2; see also note on 2Ki 23:29) or Hophra (see notes on 37:5; 44:30) is intended. *Gaza.* See v. 5; 25:20; see also note on Jdg 1:18.
47:2 *waters are rising.* See notes on 46:7 – 8. *the north.* Babylonia, as in 1:13 – 14; 46:20. *the land … live in them.* The Hebrew for this phrase is repeated verbatim from 8:16. *land.* Phoenicia and Philistia. *towns.* See note on 46:8; includes Tyre and Sidon (see v. 4) as well as Gaza, Ashkelon (see v. 5) and other Philistine cities.
47:3 *steeds.* Lit. "strong ones" (see note on 46:15). *hands will hang limp.* Paralyzed by terror (see 6:24; Isa 13:7 and notes).
47:4 *Tyre and Sidon.* See notes on v. 2; 25:22; 27:3. *remnant.* See v. 5; see also 2Ki 19:30 – 31; Isa 1:9; 10:20 – 22 and notes. *Caphtor.* Crete (see NIV text note; the Kerethites of Zep 2:5 and elsewhere were probably Cretans), one of many islands in the Mediterranean believed to be the original homeland of the Philistines (see Ge 10:14 and note; see also Dt 2:23).
47:5 *Gaza.* See v. 1; 25:20; see also note on Jdg 1:18. *shave her head in mourning.* See note on 16:6; see also 48:37 and notes on Isa 3:17; 7:20. *Ashkelon.* See v. 7; 25:20; see also note on Jdg 1:18. *be silenced.* A sign of mourning (see La 2:10). *plain.* Roughly equivalent to the modern Gaza Strip, it lay west of the foothills that separated Philistia from Judah. *cut yourselves.* See note on 16:6; see also 48:37.
47:6 *sword.* See 12:12 and note.
47:7 *attack Ashkelon.* The immediate fulfillment took place under Nebuchadnezzar in 604 BC. *coast.* See Eze 25:16; the Philistine plain (see note on v. 5).
48:1 *Concerning Moab.* See Isa 15 – 16; Eze 25:8 – 11; Am 2:1 – 3; Zep 2:8 – 11. Josephus (*Antiquities*, 10.9.7) implies that Jeremiah's prophecy concerning the future destruction of Moab was fulfilled in the "twenty-third year of Nebuchadnezzar's reign" (582 BC). *Nebo.* See v. 22; a town originally allotted to the tribe of Reuben (see Nu 32:3,37 – 38; see also Isa 15:2 and note). *Kiriathaim.* See v. 23. An ancient town (see Ge 14:5), it too was allotted to Reuben (see Jos 13:19 and note). Nebo, Kiriathaim and several other towns referred to in this chapter are mentioned also in an important

2 Moab will be praised[z] no more;
in Heshbon[a][a] people will plot her downfall:
'Come, let us put an end to that nation.'[b]
You, the people of Madmen,[b] will also be silenced;
the sword will pursue you.
3 Cries of anguish arise from Horonaim,[c]
cries of great havoc and destruction.
4 Moab will be broken;
her little ones will cry out.[c]
5 They go up the hill to Luhith,[d]
weeping bitterly as they go;
on the road down to Horonaim[e]
anguished cries over the destruction are heard.
6 Flee![f] Run for your lives;
become like a bush[d] in the desert.[g]
7 Since you trust in your deeds and riches,[h]
you too will be taken captive,
and Chemosh[i] will go into exile,[j]
together with his priests and officials.[k]
8 The destroyer[l] will come against every town,
and not a town will escape.
The valley will be ruined
and the plateau[m] destroyed,
because the LORD has spoken.
9 Put salt[n] on Moab,
for she will be laid waste[e];[o]
her towns will become desolate,
with no one to live in them.

10 "A curse on anyone who is lax in doing the LORD's work!
A curse on anyone who keeps their sword[p] from bloodshed![q]

11 "Moab has been at rest[r] from youth,
like wine left on its dregs,[s]
not poured from one jar to another—
she has not gone into exile.
So she tastes as she did,
and her aroma is unchanged.
12 But days are coming,"
declares the LORD,
"when I will send men who pour from pitchers,
and they will pour her out;
they will empty her pitchers
and smash her jars.
13 Then Moab will be ashamed[t] of Chemosh,[u]
as Israel was ashamed
when they trusted in Bethel.[v]

14 "How can you say, 'We are warriors,[w]
men valiant in battle'?
15 Moab will be destroyed and her towns invaded;
her finest young men[x] will go down in the slaughter,[y]"
declares the King,[z] whose name is the LORD Almighty.[a]
16 "The fall of Moab is at hand;[b]
her calamity will come quickly.
17 Mourn for her, all who live around her,
all who know her fame;[c]
say, 'How broken is the mighty scepter,[d]
how broken the glorious staff!'

48:2 [z]Isa 16:14 [a]S Nu 21:25; S Jos 13:26 [b]ver 42 **48:3** [c]S Isa 15:5 **48:5** [d]Isa 15:5 [e]ver 3 **48:6** [f]S Ge 19:17 [g]Jer 17:6 **48:7** [h]S Ps 49:6; S Pr 11:28 [i]S Nu 21:29 [j]Isa 46:1-2; Jer 49:3 [k]Am 2:3 **48:8** [l]S Ex 12:23; S Jer 4:7 [m]S Jos 13:9 **48:9** [n]Jdg 9:45 [o]Jer 51:29 **48:10** [p]S Jer 47:6 [q]S 1Sa 15:11; 1Ki 20:42; 2Ki 13:15-19 **48:11** [r]Zec 1:15 [s]Zep 1:12 **48:13** [t]Hos 10:6 [u]ver 7 [v]S Jos 7:2 **48:14** [w]Ps 33:16 **48:15** [x]S Isa 9:17 [y]Jer 51:40 [z]S Jer 46:18 [a]Jer 51:57 **48:16** [b]Isa 13:22 **48:17** [c]2Ki 3:4-5 [d]S Ps 110:2

[a] 2 The Hebrew for *Heshbon* sounds like the Hebrew for *plot.* [b] 2 The name of the Moabite town Madmen sounds like the Hebrew for *be silenced.* [c] 4 Hebrew; Septuagint / *proclaim it to Zoar* [d] 6 Or *like Aroer* [e] 9 Or *Give wings to Moab, / for she will fly away*

Moabite inscription written by Mesha, king of Moab (see 2Ki 3:4), and discovered in 1868 (see chart, p. xxiii).
48:2 *Heshbon.* See vv. 34,45; 49:3; Nu 21:25. Originally allotted to Reuben (see Nu 32:37; Jos 13:17), it was later reassigned to Gad as a Levitical town (see Jos 21:39). *Madmen.* Perhaps a longer spelling of "Dimon" (Isa 15:9—but see note there). In Isa 25:10 the feminine form of the Hebrew word *madmen* is translated "manure." *sword will pursue you.* See 9:16; 42:16.
48:4 *broken.* Like a clay jar (see 19:11).
48:6 *Flee! Run for your lives.* See 51:6. *like a bush.* See note on 17:6.
48:7 *Chemosh.* See vv. 13,46; the national god of Moab (see 1Ki 11:7,33; 2Ki 23:13). The Hebrew text here implies the alternate spelling Chemish, as in "Carchemish" (see note on 46:2). *will go into exile . . . and officials.* A stock phrase (see 49:3; Am 1:15). Images of pagan deities were often carried about from place to place (see 43:12; Am 5:26).
48:8 *destroyer.* See v. 32; probably Nebuchadnezzar. *valley . . . plateau.* Much of western Moab overlooks the Jordan River.
48:9 See 17:6. *Put salt on Moab.* To make its farmland unproductive and barren (see note on Jdg 9:45).
48:10 *lax.* Or "lazy" (as in Pr 10:4; 12:24). Those whom the Lord designates to destroy Moab are urged on in their appointed task.
48:11 A copy of the Hebrew text of this verse has been found inscribed on a large clay seal, dating to the early Christian era and apparently used for stamping the bitumen with which the mouths of wine jars were sealed. *from youth.* From her early history. *like wine.* An apt figure, since Moab was noted for her vineyards (see vv. 32–33; Isa 16:8–10). *left on its dregs.* In order to improve with age (see Isa 25:6). *she has not gone into exile.* Unlike Israel.
48:12 *days are coming.* Moab will be destroyed (see note on v. 1). *pour from pitchers.* Ordinarily in order to leave the unwanted sediment in the bottom, but these people will be the agents of divine judgment and will "smash" Moab (see v. 4 and note).
48:13 *Israel.* The northern kingdom, destroyed and exiled in 722–721 BC. *Bethel.* Either (1) the well-known town where one of Jeroboam's golden calves was placed (see 1Ki 12:28–30) or, (2) in parallelism with Chemosh, the West Semitic deity known from contemporary Babylonian inscriptions, as well as from the Elephantine papyri a century later (see chart, p. xxii).
48:14 *How can you say . . . ?* See 2:23; 8:8.
48:15 *go down in the slaughter.* See 50:27; for war depicted as the slaughter of sacrificial animals, see Isa 34:6 and note. *King.* See note on 46:18. The true King is the Lord, not Chemosh.
48:16 See Dt 32:35.
48:17 *who live around her . . . who know her fame.* Nations near and far, respectively. *mighty.* At one time Moab had

18 "Come down from your glory
and sit on the parched ground,[e]
you inhabitants of Daughter Dibon,[f]
for the one who destroys Moab
will come up against you
and ruin your fortified cities.[g]
19 Stand by the road and watch,
you who live in Aroer.[h]
Ask the man fleeing and the woman
escaping,
ask them, 'What has happened?'
20 Moab is disgraced, for she is shattered.
Wail[i] and cry out!
Announce by the Arnon[j]
that Moab is destroyed.
21 Judgment has come to the plateau[k]—
to Holon,[l] Jahzah[m] and Mephaath,[n]
22 to Dibon,[o] Nebo[p] and Beth
Diblathaim,
23 to Kiriathaim,[q] Beth Gamul and Beth
Meon,[r]
24 to Kerioth[s] and Bozrah[t]—
to all the towns[u] of Moab, far and
near.
25 Moab's horn[a][v] is cut off;
her arm[w] is broken,"
declares the LORD.

26 "Make her drunk,[x]
for she has defied[y] the LORD.
Let Moab wallow in her vomit;[z]
let her be an object of ridicule.[a]
27 Was not Israel the object of your
ridicule?[b]
Was she caught among thieves,[c]
that you shake your head[d] in scorn[e]
whenever you speak of her?
28 Abandon your towns and dwell among
the rocks,
you who live in Moab.
Be like a dove[f] that makes its nest
at the mouth of a cave.[g]
29 "We have heard of Moab's pride[h]—
how great is her arrogance!—
of her insolence, her pride, her conceit
and the haughtiness[i] of her heart.
30 I know her insolence but it is futile,"
declares the LORD,
"and her boasts[j] accomplish nothing.
31 Therefore I wail[k] over Moab,
for all Moab I cry out,
I moan for the people of Kir Hareseth.[l]
32 I weep for you, as Jazer[m] weeps,
you vines of Sibmah.[n]
Your branches spread as far as the sea[b];
they reached as far as[c] Jazer.
The destroyer has fallen
on your ripened fruit and grapes.
33 Joy and gladness are gone
from the orchards and fields of Moab.
I have stopped the flow of wine[o] from
the presses;
no one treads them with shouts of
joy.[p]
Although there are shouts,
they are not shouts of joy.

34 "The sound of their cry rises
from Heshbon[q] to Elealeh[r] and
Jahaz,[s]
from Zoar[t] as far as Horonaim[u] and
Eglath Shelishiyah,
for even the waters of Nimrim are
dried up.[v]

[a] *25 Horn* here symbolizes strength. [b] *32* Probably the Dead Sea [c] *32* Two Hebrew manuscripts and Septuagint; most Hebrew manuscripts *as far as the Sea of*

48:18 [e]Isa 47:1 [f]S Nu 21:30; S Jos 13:9 [g]ver 8 **48:19** [h]S Nu 32:34 **48:20** [i]S Isa 16:7 [j]S Nu 21:13 **48:21** [k]S Jos 13:9,21 [l]S Jos 15:51 [m]S Nu 21:23; S Isa 15:4 [n]S Jos 13:18 **48:22** [o]S Nu 21:30; S Jos 13:9,17 [p]S Nu 32:38 **48:23** [q]S Nu 32:37; S Jos 13:19 [r]S Jos 13:17 **48:24** [s]Am 2:2 [t]Jer 49:13 [u]S Isa 15:1 **48:25** [v]Ps 75:10 [w]Ps 10:15; 37:17; Eze 30:21 **48:26** [x]Jer 25:16,27; 51:39 [y]ver 42; 1Sa 17:26 [z]S Isa 28:8 [a]ver 39 **48:27** [b]S Jer 2:26 [c]2Ki 17:3-6 [d]S Job 16:4; Ps 44:14; Jer 18:16 [e]S Dt 28:37; Mic 7:8-10; Zep 2:8,10 **48:28** [f]S Ge 8:8; S SS 1:15 [g]S Jdg 6:2 **48:29** [h]S Lev 26:19; S Job 40:12 [i]S Ps 10:5; S Pr 16:18 **48:30** [j]S Ps 10:3 **48:31** [k]ver 36; Isa 15:5-8 [l]S 2Ki 3:25 **48:32** [m]S Jos 13:25 [n]S Nu 32:3 **48:33** [o]S Isa 24:7 [p]Joel 1:12; Am 5:17 **48:34** [q]S Nu 21:25; S Jos 13:26 [r]S Nu 32:3 [s]S Nu 21:23; S Isa 15:4 [t]S Ge 13:10 [u]S Isa 15:5 [v]S Isa 15:6

been powerful and feared (see 27:3; 2Ki 1:1; 3:5; 24:2). *scepter ... staff.* Symbols of authority and dominion (see Ge 49:10; Nu 24:17 and note; Ps 2:9; Eze 19:11,14; 21:10,13 and notes).

48:18 *Come down ... sit.* See Isa 47:1 and note. *Daughter Dibon.* A personification of the important (apparently at one time royal) Moabite city of Dibon (see note on 2Ki 19:21), where the famous Mesha Stele (Moabite Stone) of King Mesha was discovered (see chart, p. xxiii; see also Introduction to 1 Kings: Theme: Kingship and Covenant). *Dibon.* See v. 22; Nu 21:30; see also note on Isa 15:2.

48:19 *Aroer.* See NIV text note on v. 6; see also Nu 32:34; Dt 2:36.

48:20 *Arnon.* Moab's most important river.

48:21 *plateau.* See note on v. 8. *Holon.* Not the same as the town mentioned in Jos 15:51; 21:15. *Jahzah.* See 1Ch 6:78; elsewhere called Jahaz (see v. 34; see also Isa 15:4 and note).

48:22 *Dibon.* See v. 18. *Nebo.* See note on v. 1. *Beth Diblathaim.* Perhaps the same as, or near, Almon Diblathaim (see Nu 33:46).

48:23 *Kiriathaim.* See note on v. 1. *Beth Gamul.* Modern Khirbet Jumeil, five miles east of Aroer. *Beth Meon.* The same as Baal Meon (see Nu 32:38) and Beth Baal Meon (see Jos 13:17).

48:24 *Kerioth.* See note on Am 2:2. *Bozrah.* Not the same as Bozrah in Edom (see 49:13,22), but another name for Bezer in Moab (see note on Dt 4:43).

48:26 The Lord speaks to the Babylonian invaders. *Make her drunk.* By drinking down the cup of God's wrath (see 13:13; 25:15–17,28). *wallow in her vomit.* See 25:27; Isa 19:14. *let her be an object of ridicule.* As she had once ridiculed others (see v. 27; Zep 2:8,10).

48:27 *shake your head in scorn.* See 18:16 and note; see also Ps 64:8.

48:28 *like a dove ... mouth of a cave.* See Ps 55:6–8; SS 2:14.

48:29–30 An expanded version of the description of Moab found in Isa 16:6.

48:29 *Moab's pride.* It had long since become proverbial (see Isa 25:10–11; Zep 2:8–10).

48:31–33 See Isa 16:7–10.

48:31–32 *I.* The prophet (as in Isa 16:9; cf. Isa 15:5).

48:31 *moan.* Like a mourning dove (see Isa 38:14; 59:11). *Kir Hareseth.* See Isa 16:7,11; see also note on Isa 15:1.

48:32 *as Jazer.* Or "more than Jazer" (so also in Isa 16:9). *Jazer ... Sibmah ... sea.* See note on Isa 16:8. *vines.* See note on v. 11. *destroyer.* See v. 8; probably Nebuchadnezzar.

48:33 *orchards.* See note on 2:7. *treads.* See note on Isa 16:10. *not shouts of joy.* Instead, shouts of judgment (see 25:30; 51:14).

48:34 See Isa 15:4–6 and notes.

35 In Moab I will put an end
to those who make offerings on the high places[w]
and burn incense[x] to their gods,"
declares the LORD.
36 "So my heart laments[y] for Moab like the music of a pipe;
it laments like a pipe for the people of Kir Hareseth.[z]
The wealth they acquired[a] is gone.
37 Every head is shaved[b]
and every beard[c] cut off;
every hand is slashed
and every waist is covered with sackcloth.[d]
38 On all the roofs in Moab
and in the public squares[e]
there is nothing but mourning,
for I have broken Moab
like a jar[f] that no one wants,"
declares the LORD.
39 "How shattered[g] she is! How they wail!
How Moab turns her back in shame!
Moab has become an object of ridicule,[h]
an object of horror to all those around her."

40 This is what the LORD says:

"Look! An eagle is swooping[i] down,
spreading its wings[j] over Moab.
41 Kerioth[a][k] will be captured
and the strongholds taken.
In that day the hearts of Moab's warriors[l]
will be like the heart of a woman in labor.[m]
42 Moab will be destroyed[n] as a nation[o]
because she defied[p] the LORD.
43 Terror[q] and pit and snare[r] await you,
you people of Moab,"
declares the LORD.

48:35 [w] S Isa 15:2 [x] Jer 11:13 **48:36** [y] S ver 31 [z] S 2Ki 3:25 [a] S Isa 15:7 **48:37** [b] Isa 15:2; S Jer 41:5; Eze 27:31; 29:18 [c] S Lev 19:27; S 2Sa 10:4 [d] S Ge 37:34; S Isa 3:24; Jer 16:6; Am 8:10 **48:38** [e] S Isa 15:3 [f] S Jer 22:28 **48:39** [g] Jer 50:23 [h] ver 26 **48:40** [i] S Dt 28:49; Hab 1:8 [j] S Isa 8:8 **48:41** [k] S Isa 15:1 [l] Am 2:16 [m] S Isa 21:3 **48:42** [n] S Isa 16:14 [o] ver 2 [p] S ver 26 **48:43** [q] Jer 49:5 [r] S Isa 24:17 **48:44** [s] 1Ki 19:17; S Job 20:24; Isa 24:18; S Jer 46:5 [t] Jer 11:23; 23:12 **48:45** [u] S Nu 21:21, 26-28; S Jos 12:2 [v] Nu 24:17 **48:46** [w] S Nu 21:29 **48:47** [x] Ps 14:7; Isa 11:11; Jer 12:15; 49:6, 39; Eze 16:53; Da 11:41 **49:1** [y] S Ge 19:38; S 1Sa 11:1-11; 2Sa 10:1-19 [z] S Lev 18:21 [a] Ge 30:11 **49:2** [b] S Jer 4:19 [c] S Dt 3:11

44 "Whoever flees[s] from the terror
will fall into a pit,
whoever climbs out of the pit
will be caught in a snare;
for I will bring on Moab
the year[t] of her punishment,"
declares the LORD.

45 "In the shadow of Heshbon
the fugitives stand helpless,
for a fire has gone out from Heshbon,
a blaze from the midst of Sihon;[u]
it burns the foreheads of Moab,
the skulls[v] of the noisy boasters.
46 Woe to you, Moab![w]
The people of Chemosh are destroyed;
your sons are taken into exile
and your daughters into captivity.

47 "Yet I will restore[x] the fortunes of Moab
in days to come,"
declares the LORD.

Here ends the judgment on Moab.

A Message About Ammon

49 Concerning the Ammonites:[y]

This is what the LORD says:

"Has Israel no sons?
Has Israel no heir?
Why then has Molek[b][z] taken possession of Gad?[a]
Why do his people live in its towns?
2 But the days are coming,"
declares the LORD,
"when I will sound the battle cry[b]
against Rabbah[c] of the Ammonites;

[a] 41 Or *The cities* [b] 1 Or *their king*; also in verse 3

48:36 See Isa 16:11. *pipe.* Played by mourners at funerals (see Mt 9:23–24 and note on 9:23).
48:37 Signs of mourning (see Isa 15:2–3 and notes). *is slashed.* See note on 16:6.
48:38 *broken ... like a jar that no one wants.* See v. 4 and note on v. 12; cf. the description of King Jehoiachin in 22:28 (see note there).
48:39 *object of ridicule.* See v. 26 and note.
48:40–41 Echoed in 49:22 with respect to Edom.
48:40 *eagle.* Nebuchadnezzar (as in Eze 17:3); see Dt 28:49 and note.
48:41 *woman in labor.* See note on 4:31.
48:43 *Terror and pit and snare.* The Hebrew original illustrates Jeremiah's fondness for the well-turned phrase (see Introduction: Literary Features)—though in this case Jeremiah was not its creator (see Isa 24:17–18 and note on 24:17).
48:44 *Whoever flees ... will fall ... whoever climbs ... will be caught.* Divine judgment, once determined, is unavoidable (see Am 5:19).
48:45–46 Echoed from Nu 21:28–29; 24:17. Balaam's messages against Moab are about to be fulfilled.
48:45 *Heshbon.* See note on v. 2. Apparently at this time it was controlled by the Ammonites (see 49:3). *Sihon.* Refers to the associates of Sihon, king of the Amorites, whose chief city was Heshbon (see Nu 21:27) during the time of the exodus. *boasters.* See note on v. 29.
48:46 *Chemosh.* See note on v. 7.
48:47 See 46:26. *restore the fortunes.* See note on 29:14. *in days to come.* During the Messianic era. *Here ends.* A note by the final compiler of the book of Jeremiah (see 51:64).
49:1 *Concerning the Ammonites.* See Eze 25:1–7; Am 1:13–15; Zep 2:8–11. Ammon was east of the Jordan and north of Moab (see note on Ge 19:36–38). *Has Israel no ... heir?* Rhetorical questions to underscore how the Ammonites have humiliated Israel. *Molek.* The chief god of the Ammonites (see 1Ki 11:5,7,33), also known as Milkom (see note on 1Ki 11:5). Both titles are related to the West Semitic word for "king" (see NIV text note here). *taken possession of Gad.* Probably refers to the aftermath of Tiglath-Pileser III's conquest of Transjordan in 734–732 BC. The Ammonites later apparently recovered from their defeat and overran some of the territory owned by the Israelite tribe of Gad. *his.* Molek's.
49:2 *battle cry.* See Am 1:14. *Rabbah of the Ammonites.* See note on Dt 3:11. *mound of ruins.* See 30:18 and note.

it will become a mound of ruins,[d]
and its surrounding villages will be set on fire.
Then Israel will drive out
those who drove her out,[e]"
says the LORD.
3 "Wail, Heshbon,[f] for Ai[g] is destroyed!
Cry out, you inhabitants of Rabbah!
Put on sackcloth[h] and mourn;
rush here and there inside the walls,
for Molek[i] will go into exile,[j]
together with his priests and officials.
4 Why do you boast of your valleys,
boast of your valleys so fruitful?
Unfaithful Daughter Ammon,[k]
you trust in your riches[l] and say,
'Who will attack me?'[m]
5 I will bring terror on you
from all those around you,"
declares the Lord,
the LORD Almighty.
"Every one of you will be driven away,
and no one will gather the fugitives.[n]
6 "Yet afterward, I will restore[o] the fortunes of the Ammonites,"
declares the LORD.

A Message About Edom

49:9-10pp — Ob 5-6
49:14-16pp — Ob 1-4

7 Concerning Edom:[p]
This is what the LORD Almighty says:

"Is there no longer wisdom in Teman?[q]
Has counsel perished from the prudent?
Has their wisdom decayed?
8 Turn and flee, hide in deep caves,[r]
you who live in Dedan,[s]
for I will bring disaster on Esau
at the time when I punish him.
9 If grape pickers came to you,
would they not leave a few grapes?
If thieves came during the night,
would they not steal only as much as they wanted?
10 But I will strip Esau bare;
I will uncover his hiding places,[t]
so that he cannot conceal himself.
His armed men are destroyed,
also his allies and neighbors,
so there is no one[u] to say,
11 'Leave your fatherless children;[v] I will keep them alive.
Your widows[w] too can depend on me.'"

12 This is what the LORD says: "If those
who do not deserve to drink the cup[x] must
drink it, why should you go unpunished?[y]
You will not go unpunished, but must
drink it. 13 I swear[z] by myself," declares
the LORD, "that Bozrah[a] will become a ruin
and a curse,[a] an object of horror[b] and reproach;[c] and all its towns will be in ruins
forever."[d]

14 I have heard a message from the LORD;
an envoy was sent to the nations to say,
"Assemble yourselves to attack it!
Rise up for battle!"
15 "Now I will make you small among the nations,
despised by mankind.

49:2 [d] S Dt 13:16 [e] S Isa 14:2; S Jer 30:16; Eze 21:28-32; 25:2-11 **49:3** [f] S Jos 13:26 [g] S Ge 12:8; S Jos 8:28 [h] S Ge 37:34 [i] Zep 1:5 [j] S Jer 48:7 **49:4** [k] S Jer 3:6 [l] S Jer 9:23; 1Ti 6:17 [m] S Jer 21:13 **49:5** [n] S Jer 44:14 **49:6** [o] Jer 12:14-17; S 48:47 **49:7** [p] S Ge 25:30; S Ps 83:6 [q] S Ge 36:11, 15, 34 **49:8** [r] S Jdg 6:2 [s] S Ge 10:7; S 25:3 **49:10** [t] S Ge 3:8 [u] Isa 34:10-12; S Jer 11:23; Eze 35:4; Ob 1:18; Mal 1:2-5 **49:11** [v] Hos 14:3 [w] S Dt 10:18; Jas 1:27 **49:12** [x] S Isa 51:23; S Jer 25:15; Mt 20:22 [y] S Pr 11:31 **49:13** [z] S Ge 22:16 [a] S Ge 36:33 [b] ver 17 [c] Jer 42:18 [d] S Jer 19:8; Eze 35:9

[a] 13 That is, its name will be used in cursing (see 29:22); or, others will see that it is cursed.

49:3 *Heshbon.* See note on 48:45; see also Jdg 11:26–27. *Ai.* Not the Ai of Jos 8. *walls.* The Hebrew for this word refers not to city walls but to walls separating vineyards from each other (see Nu 22:24; Isa 5:5). *Molek.* See note on v. 1. *will go into exile … and officials.* See note on 48:7.
49:4 *Unfaithful Daughter.* A personification of the Ammonites (see note on 2Ki 19:21); the same language is used of the people of Judah in 31:22. *you trust in your riches.* Spoken to Moab in 48:7. *Who will attack me?* According to Josephus (*Antiquities*, 10.9.7) Nebuchadnezzar destroyed Ammon in the 23rd year of his reign (582 BC).
49:7–22 Shares many memorable phrases and concepts with the book of Obadiah (see Introduction to Obadiah: Unity and Theme).
49:7 *Concerning Edom.* See Isa 21:11–12; Eze 25:12–14; Am 1:11–12; Ob 1–16. *wisdom.* For which Edom was justly famed (see notes on Job 1:1; 2:11). *Teman.* An important Edomite town located south of the Dead Sea (see note on Job 2:11). In v. 20 it is used in parallelism with Edom itself.
49:8 *Turn and flee.* See v. 24; 46:21. *Dedan.* See 25:23; see also notes on Isa 21:13; Eze 25:13. *Esau.* The patriarch Jacob's brother, and another name for Edom (see Ge 25:29–30; 36:1), just as Israel was another name for Jacob (see Ge 32:28). The fact that Esau was Jacob's brother made Edom's enmity toward Israel all the more reprehensible (see Am 1:11; Ob 10 and notes).
49:9–10 Paralleled in Ob 5–6 (see notes there).
49:9 *grape pickers.* See note on v. 13. *leave a few grapes.* For the poor to glean (see note on Ru 2:2).
49:10 *strip … bare.* See note on 13:22. *destroyed.* See 31:15; Isa 19:7.
49:11 When the men of Edom go off to war and die, the Lord will protect their widows and orphans.
49:12 Echoed from 25:28–29. *those who do not deserve … must drink it.* Though they are God's chosen ones, the people of Judah will be punished because of their sin (see 25:28; Am 3:2 and notes).
49:13 *swear by myself.* See notes on Ge 22:16; Isa 45:23; see also 22:5; 51:14. *Bozrah.* Not the Bozrah of 48:24 (see note there); the Edomite Bozrah was probably the capital of Edom in the days of Jeremiah (see v. 22; Ge 36:33; see also notes on Isa 34:6; Am 1:12). The Hebrew root underlying Bozrah is the same as that for "grape pickers" in v. 9. *ruin … reproach.* See 25:18. *towns.* Surrounding villages. *in ruins forever.* See 25:9; Ps 74:3; Isa 58:12 and note.
49:14–16 Paralleled in Ob 1–4.

16 The terror you inspire
and the pride[e] of your heart have deceived you,
you who live in the clefts of the rocks,[f]
who occupy the heights of the hill.
Though you build your nest[g] as high as the eagle's,
from there I will bring you down,"
declares the LORD.
17 "Edom will become an object of horror;[h]
all who pass by will be appalled and will scoff
because of all its wounds.[i]
18 As Sodom[j] and Gomorrah[k] were overthrown,
along with their neighboring towns,"
says the LORD,
"so no one will live there;
no people will dwell[l] in it.

19 "Like a lion[m] coming up from Jordan's thickets[n]
to a rich pastureland,
I will chase Edom from its land in an instant.
Who is the chosen one I will appoint for this?
Who is like[o] me and who can challenge me?[p]
And what shepherd[q] can stand against me?"

20 Therefore, hear what the LORD has planned against Edom,[r]
what he has purposed[s] against those who live in Teman:[t]
The young of the flock[u] will be dragged away;
their pasture will be appalled at their fate.[v]
21 At the sound of their fall the earth will tremble;[w]
their cry[x] will resound to the Red Sea.[a]
22 Look! An eagle will soar and swoop[y] down,
spreading its wings over Bozrah.[z]
In that day the hearts of Edom's warriors[a]
will be like the heart of a woman in labor.[b]

A Message About Damascus

23 Concerning Damascus:[c]

"Hamath[d] and Arpad[e] are dismayed,
for they have heard bad news.
They are disheartened,
troubled like[b] the restless sea.[f]
24 Damascus has become feeble,
she has turned to flee
and panic has gripped her;
anguish and pain have seized her,
pain like that of a woman in labor.[g]
25 Why has the city of renown not been abandoned,
the town in which I delight?
26 Surely, her young men[h] will fall in the streets;
all her soldiers will be silenced[i] in that day,"
declares the LORD Almighty.
27 "I will set fire[j] to the walls of Damascus;[k]
it will consume[l] the fortresses of Ben-Hadad.[m]"

A Message About Kedar and Hazor

28 Concerning Kedar[n] and the kingdoms of Hazor,[o] which Nebuchadnezzar[p] king of Babylon attacked:

This is what the LORD says:

"Arise, and attack Kedar
and destroy the people of the East.[q]

[a] *21* Or *the Sea of Reeds* [b] *23* Hebrew *on* or *by*

49:16 [e] Eze 35:13; Ob 1:12 [f] S Job 39:28 [g] S Job 39:27 **49:17** [h] ver 13 [i] S Dt 29:22; Eze 35:7 **49:18** [j] Jer 23:14 [k] S Ge 19:24 [l] ver 33; S Isa 34:10 **49:19** [m] S 1Sa 17:34 [n] S Jer 12:5 [o] S Ex 8:10; S 2Ch 20:6; S Isa 46:5 [p] S Job 9:19; Jer 50:44 [q] 1Sa 17:35 **49:20** [r] Isa 34:5 [s] Isa 14:27 [t] ver 7; S Ge 36:11 [u] Jer 50:45 [v] Jer 50:45 **49:21** [w] Ps 114:7; Eze 26:15; 27:28; 31:16 [x] Jer 50:46; 51:29; Eze 26:18 **49:22** [y] S Dt 28:49; Hos 8:1; Hab 1:8 [z] S Ge 36:33 [a] Jer 50:36; Na 3:13 [b] Isa 13:8 **49:23** [c] S Ge 14:15; 2Ki 14:28; 2Ch 16:2; Ac 9:2 [d] 1Ki 8:65; Isa 10:9; Eze 47:16; Am 6:2; Zec 9:2 [e] S 2Ki 18:34; S 19:13 [f] S Ge 49:4 **49:24** [g] Jer 13:21 **49:26** [h] S Isa 9:17; S 13:18 [i] Isa 17:12-14 **49:27** [j] Jer 21:14; 43:12; 50:32; Eze 30:8; 39:6; Am 1:4 [k] S Ge 14:15 [l] Isa 17:1 [m] S 1Ki 15:18 **49:28** [n] S Ge 25:13 [o] S Jos 11:1 [p] S Jer 10:22 [q] S Jdg 6:3

49:16 *pride.* Edom's besetting sin (see v. 4; Ob 11–13; cf. 48:29–30). *heights of the hill.* Edom was noted for its mountain strongholds (cf. notes on Isa 16:1; Ob 3).
49:17 Echoed from 19:8.
49:18 Repeated almost verbatim in 50:40, and echoed in part in v. 33. *Sodom and Gomorrah were overthrown.* See Ge 19:24–25. Later calamities were often compared with the one that befell Sodom and Gomorrah (see note on Am 4:11). *their neighboring towns.* Primarily Admah and Zeboyim (see Ge 14:2,8; Dt 29:23; Hos 11:8 and note).
49:19–21 Repeated almost verbatim in the message against Babylon (see 50:44–46).
49:19 *Jordan's thickets.* See 12:5 and note. *shepherd.* Ruler (see note on 2:8).
49:20 *Teman.* See note on v. 7. *flock.* The people of Edom.
49:22 Echoed from 48:40–41. *eagle.* Represents Nebuchadnezzar in 48:40 (see note there), and probably here also. A more complete subjugation of the Edomites, however, was accomplished by Nabatean Arabs (perhaps the "desert jackals" of Mal 1:3) beginning c. 550 BC. *Bozrah.* See note on v. 13. *woman in labor.* See note on 4:31.
49:23 *Concerning Damascus.* See Isa 17; Am 1:3–5 (see also note on Isa 17:1). *Hamath.* An important city in the kingdom of Aram (see Isa 10:9; Zec 9:2 and notes). *Arpad.* See note on Isa 10:9. *bad news.* The threat of Babylonian invasion. *troubled like the restless sea.* See Isa 57:20.
49:24 *anguish.* See note on 4:19.
49:26 Repeated almost verbatim in 50:30.
49:27 A conventional word of judgment (see note on Am 1:4).
49:28 *Concerning Kedar.* See Isa 21:13–17; see also 2:10 and note. *kingdoms of Hazor.* See vv. 30,33; not the Hazor north of the Sea of Galilee (see Jos 11:1). These kingdoms may have included Dedan, Tema, Buz and other Arab regions (see 25:23–24 and notes), since the Hebrew root of the proper name Hazor often serves as a common noun meaning "settlement" (see especially Isa 42:11; see also Ge 25:16). *Nebu-*

29 Their tents and their flocks[r] will be taken;
their shelters will be carried off
with all their goods and camels.
People will shout to them,
'Terror[s] on every side!'

30 "Flee quickly away!
Stay in deep caves,[t] you who live in Hazor,[u]"
declares the LORD.
"Nebuchadnezzar[v] king of Babylon has plotted against you;
he has devised a plan against you.

31 "Arise and attack a nation at ease,
which lives in confidence,"
declares the LORD,
"a nation that has neither gates nor bars;[w]
its people live far from danger.
32 Their camels[x] will become plunder,
and their large herds[y] will be spoils of war.
I will scatter to the winds[z] those who are in distant places[aa]
and will bring disaster on them from every side,"
declares the LORD.
33 "Hazor[b] will become a haunt of jackals,[c]
a desolate[d] place forever.
No one will live there;
no people will dwell[e] in it."

A Message About Elam

34 This is the word of the LORD that came
to Jeremiah the prophet concerning Elam,[f]
early in the reign of Zedekiah[g] king of Judah:

35 This is what the LORD Almighty says:

"See, I will break the bow[h] of Elam,
the mainstay of their might.

49:29 [r] ver 32 [s] S Jer 6:25 **49:30** [t] S Jdg 6:2 [u] Jos 11:1 [v] S Jer 10:22 **49:31** [w] Eze 38:11 **49:32** [x] S Jdg 6:5 [y] ver 29 [z] ver 36; Jer 13:24 [a] S Jer 9:26 **49:33** [b] S Jos 11:1 [c] S Isa 13:22 [d] Jer 48:9 [e] S ver 18; Jer 51:37 **49:34** [f] S Ge 10:22 [g] 2Ki 24:18 **49:35** [h] S Ps 37:15; S Isa 22:6
49:36 [i] S ver 32 [j] Da 11:4 **49:37** [k] Jer 30:24 [l] Jer 9:16; Eze 32:24 **49:39** [m] S Jer 48:47 **50:1** [n] S Ge 10:10; S Ps 137:8 **50:2** [o] S Dt 30:4; Jer 4:16 [p] S Ps 20:5; S Isa 13:2 [q] ver 9; Jer 51:31 [r] S Isa 21:9; S 46:1 [s] Ps 97:7; Jer 51:52 [t] ver 38; Isa 46:6; Jer 51:47 [u] S Lev 26:30 **50:3** [v] S ver 26; S Isa 41:25; S Jer 25:26

36 I will bring against Elam the four winds[i]
from the four quarters of heaven;[j]
I will scatter them to the four winds,
and there will not be a nation
where Elam's exiles do not go.
37 I will shatter Elam before their foes,
before those who want to kill them;
I will bring disaster on them,
even my fierce anger,"[k]
declares the LORD.
"I will pursue them with the sword[l]
until I have made an end of them.
38 I will set my throne in Elam
and destroy her king and officials,"
declares the LORD.

39 "Yet I will restore[m] the fortunes of Elam
in days to come,"
declares the LORD.

A Message About Babylon

51:15-19pp — Jer 10:12-16

50 This is the word the LORD spoke through Jeremiah the prophet concerning Babylon[n] and the land of the Babylonians[b]:

2 "Announce and proclaim[o] among the nations,
lift up a banner[p] and proclaim it;
keep nothing back, but say,
'Babylon will be captured;[q]
Bel[r] will be put to shame,[s]
Marduk[t] filled with terror.
Her images will be put to shame
and her idols[u] filled with terror.'
3 A nation from the north[v] will attack her
and lay waste her land.

[a] 32 Or *who clip the hair by their foreheads*
[b] 1 Or *Chaldeans*; also in verses 8, 25, 35 and 45

chadnezzar... attacked. In 599–598 BC. *people of the East.* See Jdg 6:3 and note; Job 1:3; Eze 25:4.
49:29 *Terror on every side.* See note on 6:25.
49:30 *Stay in deep caves.* See v. 8.
49:31 *at ease.* Completely secure (see Job 21:23). *in confidence.* In safety, unsuspecting (see Jdg 18:7 and note; Eze 38:11). *has neither gates nor bars.* Lives in unwalled villages (see Dt 3:5; cf. 1Sa 23:7).
49:32 *scatter to the winds.* See Eze 5:12; 12:4. *who are in distant places.* See note on 9:26. *disaster... from every side.* Contrast the description of Solomon's realm in 1Ki 5:4.
49:33 *haunt of jackals.* See note on 9:11. *no people... dwell in it.* Echoes v. 18.
49:34 *This is the word of the LORD... concerning.* See note on 46:1. *Elam.* See note on Isa 11:11.
49:35 *bow.* The Elamites were skilled archers (see Isa 22:6).
49:36 Contrast Isa 11:12. *to the four winds.* In every direction (see Eze 37:9; Da 7:2; 8:8).
49:37 *I will pursue... made an end of them.* Echoes 9:16.
49:38 *set my throne in.* See 1:15 and note.
50:1—51:64 See Isa 13:1—14:23; 21:1–9. Jeremiah's prophecy concerning Babylonia is by far the longest of his messages against foreign nations (chs. 46–51) and expands on his earlier and briefer statements (see 25:12–14,26). Its date, in whole or in part, is 593 BC (see 51:59 and note). The two chapters divide into three main sections (50:2–28; 50:29—51:26; 51:27–58), each of which begins with a summons concerning war against Babylonia, Judah's mortal enemy (see 50:2–3; 50:29–32; 51:27–32).
50:1 *word.* Or "message" (as in 46:13), comprising chs. 50–51. *through.* See 37:2. The message would eventually be sent by the prophet to Babylon itself (see 51:59–61).
50:2 *Announce and proclaim.* See 4:5; 46:14. *lift up a banner.* See note on Isa 5:26. The Hebrew for this phrase is translated "raise the signal" in 4:6. *Babylon will be captured.* Fulfilled in 539 BC. *Bel.* See 51:44; Isa 46:1 and note. *put to shame... filled with terror.* The repetition of each of these phrases emphasizes that the chief god of Babylon and his images and idols are alike doomed. *Her... her.* Babylon's. *idols.* See note on Lev 26:30. Derogatory references concerning idols and idolatry are common in the OT (see, e.g., Isa 44:9–20).
50:3 *nation from the north.* In Jeremiah, the foe from the north is almost always Babylonia (see, e.g., 1:14–15). Here, however, the reference is probably to Persia. Babylon's

No one will live[w] in it;
both people and animals[x] will flee away.

4 "In those days, at that time,"
declares the LORD,
"the people of Israel and the people of Judah together[y]
will go in tears[z] to seek[a] the LORD their God.
5 They will ask the way[b] to Zion
and turn their faces toward it.
They will come[c] and bind themselves to the LORD
in an everlasting covenant[d]
that will not be forgotten.

6 "My people have been lost sheep;[e]
their shepherds[f] have led them astray[g]
and caused them to roam on the mountains.
They wandered over mountain and hill[h]
and forgot their own resting place.[i]
7 Whoever found them devoured[j] them;
their enemies said, 'We are not guilty,[k]
for they sinned against the LORD, their verdant pasture,
the LORD, the hope[l] of their ancestors.'

8 "Flee[m] out of Babylon;[n]
leave the land of the Babylonians,
and be like the goats that lead the flock.
9 For I will stir[o] up and bring against Babylon
an alliance of great nations[p] from the land of the north.[q]
They will take up their positions against her,
and from the north she will be captured.[r]
Their arrows[s] will be like skilled warriors
who do not return empty-handed.
10 So Babylonia[a] will be plundered;[t]
all who plunder her will have their fill,"
declares the LORD.

11 "Because you rejoice and are glad,
you who pillage my inheritance,[u]
because you frolic like a heifer[v] threshing grain
and neigh like stallions,
12 your mother will be greatly ashamed;
she who gave you birth will be disgraced.[w]
She will be the least of the nations—
a wilderness, a dry land, a desert.[x]
13 Because of the LORD's anger she will not be inhabited
but will be completely desolate.[y]
All who pass Babylon will be appalled;[z]
they will scoff[a] because of all her wounds.[b]

14 "Take up your positions around Babylon,
all you who draw the bow.[c]
Shoot at her! Spare no arrows,[d]
for she has sinned against the LORD.
15 Shout[e] against her on every side!
She surrenders, her towers fall,
her walls[f] are torn down.
Since this is the vengeance[g] of the LORD,
take vengeance on her;
do to her[h] as she has done to others.[i]
16 Cut off from Babylon the sower,
and the reaper with his sickle at harvest.

[a] 10 Or *Chaldea*

50:3 [w] S ver 13; S Isa 14:22-23; S Jer 9:11 [x] Zep 1:3 **50:4** [y] S Jer 3:18; Eze 37:22 [z] S Ezr 3:12 [a] S Isa 9:13; Eze 37:17; Hos 3:5 **50:5** [b] S Isa 11:16; S Jer 31:21 [c] S 1Sa 29:1; Jer 33:7 [d] S Dt 29:14; Isa 55:3; Jer 32:40; Heb 8:6-10 **50:6** [e] S Ps 119:176; Mt 9:36; 10:6 [f] S Jer 2:8; S 10:21 [g] S Ps 95:10; Jer 23:32; Eze 13:10 [h] Jer 3:6; Eze 34:6 [i] ver 19 **50:7** [j] S Jer 5:17; 10:25; Eze 35:12 [k] Jer 2:3 [l] S Jer 14:8 **50:8** [m] S Isa 48:20 [n] ver 28 **50:9** [o] S Isa 13:17 [p] S Jer 25:14 [q] S Isa 41:25; S Jer 25:26 [r] S ver 2 [s] S Isa 13:18 **50:10** [t] Isa 47:11; S Jer 30:16 **50:11** [u] S Isa 47:6 [v] S Jer 31:18 **50:12** [w] Jer 51:47 [x] ver 13; S Isa 21:1; Jer 25:12; 51:26 **50:13** [y] ver 3, S 12; S Jer 9:11; 48:9; 51:62 [z] Jer 51:41 [a] S Jer 18:16; 51:37; Eze 27:36; Hab 2:6 [b] S Dt 29:22 **50:14** [c] ver 29,42 [d] S Isa 13:18 **50:15** [e] Jer 51:14 [f] S 2Ki 25:4; S Jer 51:44,58 [g] ver 28; S Isa 10:3; 63:4; Jer 51:6 [h] ver 29; Ps 137:8; Rev 18:6 [i] Jer 51:24; Hab 2:7-8

---

nemesis is expanded to "an alliance of great nations" in v. 9, specified by name in 51:27–28. *people and animals will flee.* Babylon will suffer the same fate as Jerusalem (see 33:12).
50:4 *Israel and ... Judah together.* See note on 3:18. *tears.* Of repentance (see 3:21–22; 31:9).
50:5 *everlasting covenant.* See 32:40 and note; see also 31:31–34; 33:20–21.
50:6 *lost sheep.* See Jesus' parable in Lk 15:3–7. *shepherds.* Rulers (see note on 2:8). *mountain and hill.* Places where pagan gods were worshiped (see note on 2:20). *their own resting place.* The Lord (see v. 7).
50:7 *hope of their ancestors.* A phrase found only here (see 14:8,22; cf. Ac 28:20).
50:8 *like the goats that lead the flock.* Judah would be among the first of the captive peoples to be released from exile in Babylon.
50:9 *alliance of great nations.* See Isa 13:4. They are named in 51:27–28 (see note on v. 3).
50:11 *you.* Babylonia. *my inheritance.* God's land and people (see 2:7; 12:7 and notes). *frolic like a heifer.* See Mal 4:2. *stallions.* See note on 8:16.
50:12 *mother.* Either (1) the city or, more likely, (2) the land (see Isa 50:1; Hos 2:5). *least.* Lit. "last." As Amalek, "first among the nations" (Nu 24:20) to attack Israel, was destroyed, so Babylonia, the last to attack Israel (up to Jeremiah's time), would be destroyed.
50:13 *not be inhabited.* See Isa 13:20 and note. *All who pass ... because of all her wounds.* Said of Jerusalem in 19:8 and of Edom in 49:17.
50:14 *you who draw the bow.* Including the Medes (see Isa 13:17–18).
50:15 *Shout.* Give the battle cry (see Jos 6:16). *vengeance of the LORD.* See v. 28; 51:11. Though originating in his sovereign holiness, it was often carried out by his people (see Nu 31:3). *do to her ... to others.* See v. 29; Pr 26:27 and note; cf. Gal 6:7–8.
50:16 *sword of the oppressor.* See 46:16. *let everyone ... to their own land.* The Hebrew for this passage has a parallel in

Because of the sword[j] of the oppressor
let everyone return to their own
people,[k]
let everyone flee to their own
land.[l]

17 "Israel is a scattered flock[m]
that lions[n] have chased away.
The first to devour[o] them
was the king[p] of Assyria;
the last to crush their bones[q]
was Nebuchadnezzar[r] king[s] of
Babylon."

18 Therefore this is what the LORD Almighty, the God of Israel, says:

"I will punish the king of Babylon and
his land
as I punished the king[t] of Assyria.[u]
19 But I will bring[v] Israel back to their
own pasture,
and they will graze on Carmel and
Bashan;
their appetite will be satisfied[w]
on the hills[x] of Ephraim and Gilead.[y]
20 In those days, at that time,"
declares the LORD,
"search will be made for Israel's guilt,
but there will be none,[z]
and for the sins[a] of Judah,
but none will be found,
for I will forgive[b] the remnant[c] I
spare.

21 "Attack the land of Merathaim
and those who live in Pekod.[d]
Pursue, kill and completely destroy[a]
them,"
declares the LORD.
"Do everything I have commanded
you.

[a] *21* The Hebrew term refers to the irrevocable giving over of things or persons to the LORD, often by totally destroying them; also in verse 26.

50:16 [j] S Jer 25:38 [k] S Isa 13:14 [l] Jer 51:9 **50:17** [m] S Lev 26:33; S Ps 119:176 [n] S 2Ki 24:1; S Jer 2:15 [o] S Jer 5:17 [p] S Dt 4:27; S 2Ki 15:29 [q] S Nu 24:8; La 3:4 [r] Jer 51:34 [s] S 2Ki 24:17; S 25:7 **50:18** [t] S Isa 10:12 [u] Eze 31:3; Zep 2:13 **50:19** [v] S Jer 31:10; Eze 34:13 [w] Jer 31:14 [x] S Jer 31:5 [y] Mic 7:14; Zec 10:10 **50:20** [z] S Ps 17:3 [a] Ps 103:12; S Isa 38:17; Eze 33:16; Mic 7:18,19; Zec 3:4,9 [b] S Isa 33:24 [c] S Ge 45:7; Isa 1:9; 10:20-22; S Ro 9:27 **50:21** [d] Eze 23:23

Isa 13:14. The captive peoples are warned to flee Babylon in order to avoid being cut down by her invaders.
50:17 *scattered flock.* See Joel 3:2. *lions.* Symbolic of Assyria and Babylonia (see 4:7; Isa 15:9 and notes). *The first ... was the king of Assyria.* The Assyrians destroyed Israel (the northern kingdom) in 722–721 BC. *the last ... was Nebuchadnezzar.* The Babylonians destroyed Judah (the southern kingdom) in 586 BC.
50:18 *I punished the king of Assyria.* Nineveh, the proud Assyrian capital, fell in 612 BC, and Assyria herself was conquered by a coalition of Medes and Babylonians in 609.
50:19 *Carmel.* See Isa 33:9 and note. *Bashan.* See note on Isa 2:13. *hills of Ephraim.* The lush mountains of central Israel (see Eze 34:13–14). *Gilead.* See note on Ge 31:21; see also Nu 32:1; Mic 7:14.
50:20 See 33:8 and note; see also 36:3; Mic 7:18–19.
50:21 *Merathaim.* Means "double rebellion [against the Lord]," perhaps referring to vv. 24,29 (see Jdg 3:8; Isa 40:2 and notes). It is probably a pun on the Babylonian word *marratu,* which sometimes referred to a region in southern Babylonia that was characterized by briny waters. *Pekod.* See Eze 23:23; means "punishment [from the Lord]," a pun on *Puqudu,* the Babylonian name for an Aramean tribe living on the eastern

NATIONS AND CITIES UNDER JUDGMENT IN JEREMIAH

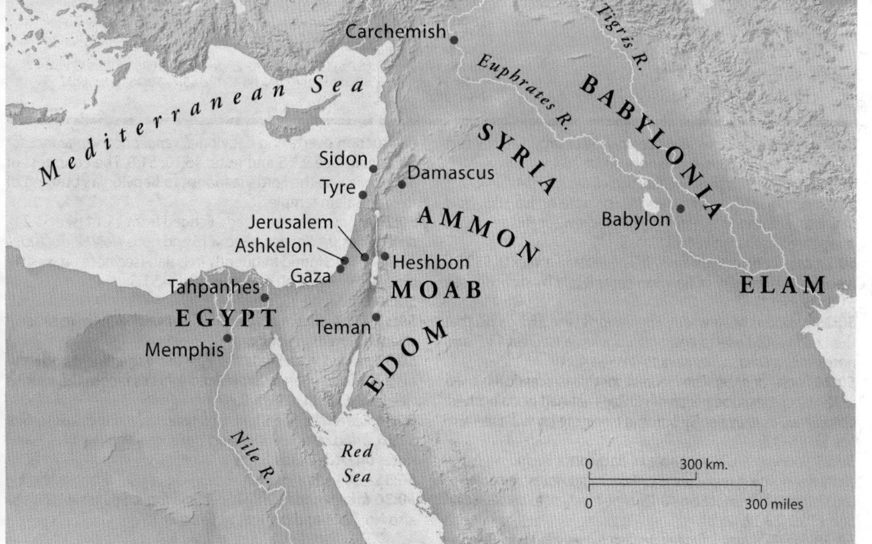

[22]The noise[e] of battle is in the land,
the noise of great destruction!
[23]How broken and shattered
is the hammer[f] of the whole
earth![g]
How desolate[h] is Babylon
among the nations!
[24]I set a trap[i] for you, Babylon,
and you were caught before you
knew it;
you were found and captured[j]
because you opposed[k] the LORD.
[25]The LORD has opened his arsenal
and brought out the weapons[l] of his
wrath,
for the Sovereign LORD Almighty has
work to do
in the land of the Babylonians.[m]
[26]Come against her from afar.[n]
Break open her granaries;
pile her up like heaps of grain.[o]
Completely destroy[p] her
and leave her no remnant.
[27]Kill all her young bulls;[q]
let them go down to the slaughter![r]
Woe to them! For their day[s] has
come,
the time[t] for them to be punished.
[28]Listen to the fugitives[u] and refugees
from Babylon
declaring in Zion[v]
how the LORD our God has taken
vengeance,[w]
vengeance for his temple.[x]

[29]"Summon archers against Babylon,
all those who draw the bow.[y]
Encamp all around her;
let no one escape.[z]
Repay[a] her for her deeds;[b]
do to her as she has done.
For she has defied[c] the LORD,
the Holy One[d] of Israel.
[30]Therefore, her young men[e] will fall in
the streets;
all her soldiers will be silenced in
that day,"
declares the LORD.
[31]"See, I am against[f] you, you arrogant
one,"
declares the Lord, the LORD
Almighty,
"for your day[g] has come,
the time for you to be punished.
[32]The arrogant[h] one will stumble and fall[i]
and no one will help her up;[j]
I will kindle a fire[k] in her towns
that will consume all who are
around her."

[33]This is what the LORD Almighty says:

"The people of Israel are oppressed,[l]
and the people of Judah as well.
All their captors hold them fast,
refusing to let them go.[m]
[34]Yet their Redeemer[n] is strong;
the LORD Almighty[o] is his name.
He will vigorously defend their
cause[p]
so that he may bring rest[q] to their
land,
but unrest to those who live in
Babylon.

[35]"A sword[r] against the Babylonians!"[s]
declares the LORD—
"against those who live in Babylon
and against her officials and wise[t]
men!
[36]A sword against her false prophets!
They will become fools.
A sword against her warriors![u]
They will be filled with terror.[v]

50:22 [e]Jer 4:19-21; 51:54 **50:23** [f]S Isa 10:5 [g]Jer 51:25 [h]S Isa 14:16 **50:24** [i]Jer 51:12 [j]Jer 51:31 [k]Job 9:4 **50:25** [l]S Isa 13:5 [m]Jer 51:25,55 **50:26** [n]ver 3, 41; Jer 51:11 [o]S Ru 3:7 [p]S Isa 14:22-23 **50:27** [q]S Ps 68:30; Jer 48:15 [r]S Isa 30:25; S Jer 25:34 [s]S Job 18:20 [t]Jer 51:6 **50:28** [u]ver 8 [v]Isa 48:20; Jer 51:10 [w]S ver 15 [x]2Ki 24:13; Jer 51:11; 52:13 **50:29** [y]S ver 14 [z]S Isa 13:18; Jer 51:3 [a]S Dt 32:41; S Job 21:19; S Jer 51:6; Rev 18:6 [b]Eze 35:11; Ob 1:15 [c]S Isa 14:13-14; 47:10; Da 5:23 [d]Ps 78:41; Isa 41:20; Jer 51:5 **50:30** [e]S Isa 13:18 **50:31** [f]S Jer 21:13 [g]S Job 18:20; Rev 18:7-8 **50:32** [h]S Ps 119:21 [i]S Ps 20:8 [j]Am 5:2 [k]S Jer 49:27 **50:33** [l]Isa 58:6 [m]S Isa 14:17 **50:34** [n]S Ex 6:6; S Job 19:25 [o]Jer 31:35; 51:19 [p]S Ps 119:154; S Isa 49:25; Jer 15:21; 51:36; La 3:58 [q]S Isa 14:7 **50:35** [r]S Jer 47:6 [s]S Isa 45:1 [t]Da 5:7 **50:36** [u]S Jer 49:22 [v]Jer 51:30,32

bank of the lower Tigris River. *completely destroy.* See NIV text note; v. 26; 25:9; 51:3; see also note on Dt 2:34.
50:22 *great destruction.* See 4:6; 6:1; cf. 48:3; 51:54.
50:23 *hammer of the whole earth.* See note on Isa 10:5. *How desolate ... among the nations!* The Hebrew for this sentence is repeated verbatim in 51:41.
50:24 *caught before you knew it.* The Persian attack in 539 BC would catch the city of Babylon completely by surprise (see 51:8; Isa 47:11).
50:25 *weapons of his wrath.* The nations (see 51:27–28) that the Lord would use to conquer Babylonia (see Isa 13:5 and note). *the ... LORD ... has work to do.* See 48:10.
50:26 *heaps of grain.* The Hebrew for this expression is used in Ne 4:2 to describe heaps of rubble that had been burned. *Completely destroy her.* By burning (see note on v. 21; see also Jos 11:11–13).
50:27 *young bulls.* The people of Babylonia, including especially her fighting men (see Isa 34:6–7 and notes). *go down to the slaughter.* See note on 48:15. *time for them to be punished.* See 11:23; 23:12; 46:21.
50:28 *fugitives and refugees.* Jewish exiles who had fled the destruction overtaking Babylonia. *vengeance, vengeance for his temple.* See v. 15 and note; 46:10; 51:6. The conquest of Babylonia was the Lord's response to Babylonia's burning of the Jerusalem temple.
50:29 *Repay her for her deeds.* Echoed from 25:14 (see 51:24). *do to her as she has done.* See v. 15 and note. *Holy One of Israel.* A title of God found frequently in Isaiah (see note on Isa 1:4), it occurs in Jeremiah only here and in 51:5.
50:30 Echoes 49:26.
50:31–32 A distant echo of 21:13–14, spoken there to Jerusalem but here to Babylon.
50:33 *their captors.* See Isa 14:2. *refusing to let them go.* Reminiscent of the pharaoh's repeated refusals before the exodus (see, e.g., Ex 7:14; 8:2,32; 9:2,7).
50:34 *Redeemer.* See 31:11 and note. *defend their cause.* See 51:36. *bring rest.* See 31:2 and note; see also Isa 14:3,7 and notes on Dt 3:20; Jos 1:13.
50:35–38 Cf. Eze 21.
50:36 *false prophets ... will become fools.* See Isa 44:25; see also Nu 12:11 and NIV text note on Pr 1:7.

37 A sword against her horses and
chariots[w]
and all the foreigners in her ranks!
They will become weaklings.[x]
A sword against her treasures![y]
They will be plundered.
38 A drought on[a] her waters![z]
They will dry[a] up.
For it is a land of idols,[b]
idols that will go mad with terror.

39 "So desert creatures[c] and hyenas will
live there,
and there the owl will dwell.
It will never again be inhabited
or lived in from generation to
generation.[d]
40 As I overthrew Sodom and
Gomorrah[e]
along with their neighboring
towns,"
declares the LORD,
"so no one will live there;
no people will dwell in it.[f]
41 "Look! An army is coming from the
north;[g]
a great nation and many kings
are being stirred[h] up from the ends
of the earth.[i]
42 They are armed with bows[j] and
spears;
they are cruel[k] and without mercy.[l]
They sound like the roaring sea[m]
as they ride on their horses;
they come like men in battle
formation
to attack you, Daughter Babylon.[n]
43 The king of Babylon has heard reports
about them,
and his hands hang limp.[o]
Anguish has gripped him,
pain like that of a woman in
labor.[p]
44 Like a lion coming up from Jordan's
thickets[q]
to a rich pastureland,
I will chase Babylon from its land in an
instant.
Who is the chosen[r] one I will
appoint for this?
Who is like me and who can challenge
me?[s]
And what shepherd can stand
against me?"
45 Therefore, hear what the LORD has
planned against Babylon,
what he has purposed[t] against the
land of the Babylonians:[u]
The young of the flock will be dragged
away;
their pasture will be appalled at their
fate.
46 At the sound of Babylon's capture the
earth will tremble;[v]
its cry[w] will resound among the
nations.

51 This is what the LORD says:

"See, I will stir[x] up the spirit of a
destroyer
against Babylon[y] and the people of
Leb Kamai.[b]
2 I will send foreigners[z] to Babylon
to winnow[a] her and to devastate her
land;
they will oppose her on every side
in the day[b] of her disaster.
3 Let not the archer string his bow,[c]
nor let him put on his armor.[d]
Do not spare her young men;
completely destroy[c] her army.
4 They will fall[e] down slain in
Babylon,[d]
fatally wounded in her streets.[f]
5 For Israel and Judah have not been
forsaken[g]
by their God, the LORD
Almighty,
though their land[e] is full of guilt[h]
before the Holy One of Israel.

50:37 [w] S 2Ki 19:23; Jer 51:21 [x] S Isa 19:16 [y] S Isa 45:3 **50:38** [z] Ps 137:1; Jer 51:13 [a] S Isa 11:15; Jer 51:36 [b] S ver 2 **50:39** [c] S Ps 74:14 [d] Isa 13:19-22; 34:13-15; Jer 51:37; Rev 18:2 **50:40** [e] S Ge 19:24; S Mt 10:15 [f] Jer 51:62 **50:41** [g] S ver 26; S Isa 41:25 [h] S Isa 13:17 [i] S Isa 13:4; Jer 51:22-28 **50:42** [j] S ver 14 [k] S Job 30:21 [l] S Isa 13:18 [m] S Isa 5:30 [n] S Isa 47:1 **50:43** [o] S Jer 47:3 [p] Jer 6:22-24 **50:44** [q] S Jer 12:5 [r] S Nu 16:5 [s] S Job 41:10; Isa 46:9; S Jer 49:19 **50:45** [t] Ps 33:11; Jer 51:11 [u] S Isa 48:14 **50:46** [v] S Jdg 5:4; S Jer 49:21 [w] S Job 24:12; Rev 18:9-10 **51:1** [x] S Isa 13:17 [y] Jer 25:12 **51:2** [z] Isa 13:5 [a] S Isa 41:16; Mt 3:12 [b] S Isa 13:9 **51:3** [c] S Jer 50:29 [d] Jer 46:4 **51:4** [e] Isa 13:15 [f] S Isa 13:18 **51:5** [g] S Lev 26:44; Isa 54:6-8 [h] Hos 4:1

[a] 38 Or *A sword against* [b] 1 *Leb Kamai* is a cryptogram for Chaldea, that is, Babylonia. [c] 3 The Hebrew term refers to the irrevocable giving over of things or persons to the LORD, often by totally destroying them. [d] 4 Or *Chaldea* [e] 5 Or *Almighty, / and the land of the Babylonians*

50:37 *against her horses and chariots.* See Isa 43:17; see also Ps 20:7. *foreigners.* See 25:20,24; Ne 13:3. *will become weaklings.* See Na 3:13 and note.
50:38 *idols.* See 51:52; see also note on Isa 21:9. *go mad.* See 25:16 and note.
50:39 See Isa 13:20–22 and notes.
50:40 Echoes 49:18 (see note there).
50:41–43 Echoes 6:22–24 (see notes there). The earlier message, referring to Jerusalem, is here applied to Babylon.
50:42 *Daughter Babylon.* A personification of the city of Babylon (see note on 2Ki 19:21).
50:43 *woman in labor.* See note on 4:31.
50:44–46 Echoes 49:19–21 (see notes there). The message against Edom is here applied to Babylon.
51:1 *stir up the spirit.* See 1Ch 5:26; Hag 1:14. The Hebrew underlying this phrase is translated "aroused ... the hostility of" in 2Ch 21:16. *destroyer.* See note on 4:7; here including the "kings of the Medes" (v. 11). *Leb Kamai.* Lit. "the heart of my attackers" (cf. Rev 17:5, where Babylon is called "the mother of prostitutes and of the abominations of the earth"). See NIV text note; see also note on 25:26.
51:2 *foreigners ... to winnow her.* The Hebrew for this phrase is an excellent example of alliteration and assonance (see Introduction: Literary Features).
51:3 *completely destroy.* See NIV text note; 25:9; 50:21,26; see also note on Dt 2:34.
51:4 *fall ... in her streets.* See 49:26; 50:30.
51:5 *forsaken.* Lit. "widowed"; contrast Isa 54:4,6–7 and notes. *Holy One of Israel.* See note on 50:29.

6 "Flee[i] from Babylon!
Run for your lives!
Do not be destroyed because of her
sins.[j]
It is time[k] for the LORD's vengeance;[l]
he will repay[m] her what she
deserves.
7 Babylon was a gold cup[n] in the LORD's
hand;
she made the whole earth drunk.
The nations drank her wine;
therefore they have now gone mad.
8 Babylon will suddenly fall[o] and be
broken.
Wail over her!
Get balm[p] for her pain;
perhaps she can be healed.

9 " 'We would have healed Babylon,
but she cannot be healed;
let us leave[q] her and each go to our
own land,
for her judgment[r] reaches to the
skies,
it rises as high as the heavens.'

10 " 'The LORD has vindicated[s] us;
come, let us tell in Zion
what the LORD our God has done.'[t]

11 "Sharpen the arrows,[u]
take up the shields![v]
The LORD has stirred up the kings[w] of
the Medes,[x]
because his purpose[y] is to destroy
Babylon.
The LORD will take vengeance,[z]
vengeance for his temple.[a]
12 Lift up a banner[b] against the walls of
Babylon!
Reinforce the guard,
station the watchmen,[c]
prepare an ambush![d]
The LORD will carry out his purpose,[e]
his decree against the people of
Babylon.

51:6 [i] S Isa 48:20 [j] Nu 16:26; Rev 18:4 [k] Jer 50:27 [l] S Isa 1:24; S Jer 50:15 [m] ver 24,56; Dt 32:35; S Job 21:19; Jer 25:14; 50:29; La 3:64 **51:7** [n] S Isa 51:22; Jer 25:15-16; 49:12; Rev 14:8-10 **51:8** [o] S Isa 14:15; S 21:9; S Rev 14:8 [p] Jer 8:22; 46:11 **51:9** [q] S Isa 13:14; S 31:9; Jer 50:16 [r] Rev 18:4-5 **51:10** [s] Mic 7:9 [t] Ps 64:9; S Jer 50:28 **51:11** [u] Jer 50:9 [v] S Isa 21:5 [w] S Isa 41:2 [x] ver 28; S Isa 13:3; S 41:25 [y] S Jer 50:45 [z] S Lev 26:25 [a] S Jer 50:28 **51:12** [b] ver 27; S Ps 20:5 [c] 2Sa 18:24; Eze 33:2 [d] Jer 50:24 [e] S Ps 33:11

51:13 [f] S Jer 50:38 [g] S Isa 45:3; Eze 22:27; Hab 2:9 [h] Jer 50:3 **51:14** [i] S Ge 22:16; Am 6:8 [j] ver 27; Am 7:1; Na 3:15 [k] Jer 50:15 **51:15** [l] Ps 104:24 [m] S Ge 1:1; S Ps 104:2 [n] S Ps 136:5 **51:16** [o] Ps 18:11-13 [p] S Job 28:26

13 You who live by many waters[f]
and are rich in treasures,[g]
your end has come,
the time for you to be destroyed.[h]
14 The LORD Almighty has sworn by
himself:[i]
I will surely fill you with troops, as
with a swarm of locusts,[j]
and they will shout[k] in triumph over
you.

15 "He made the earth by his power;
he founded the world by his
wisdom[l]
and stretched[m] out the heavens by
his understanding.[n]
16 When he thunders,[o] the waters in the
heavens roar;
he makes clouds rise from the ends
of the earth.
He sends lightning with the rain[p]
and brings out the wind from his
storehouses.[q]

17 "Everyone is senseless and without
knowledge;
every goldsmith is shamed by his
idols.
The images he makes are a fraud;[r]
they have no breath in them.
18 They are worthless,[s] the objects of
mockery;
when their judgment comes, they
will perish.
19 He who is the Portion[t] of Jacob is not
like these,
for he is the Maker of all things,
including the people of his
inheritance[u]—
the LORD Almighty is his name.

20 "You are my war club,[v]
my weapon for battle—

[q] S Dt 28:12; S Ps 135:7; Jnh 1:4 **51:17** [r] S Isa 44:20; Hab 2:18-19 **51:18** [s] S Jer 18:15 **51:19** [t] S Ps 119:57 [u] S Ex 34:9 **51:20** [v] S Isa 10:5; Zec 9:13

51:6 *Flee . . . ! Run for your lives!* See v. 45; 48:6. This was spoken to the people of Judah (as in 50:8). *the LORD's vengeance.* See note on 50:15. *repay her what she deserves.* See Isa 59:18; 66:6.
51:7 See 25:15–16 and notes. *Babylon was . . . gold.* See note on Da 2:32–43.
51:8 *Babylon will . . . fall.* See Isa 21:9 and note. *balm.* See note on 8:22.
51:9 The speakers are the nations conquered by Babylonia. *each go to our own land.* See 50:16 and note. *her judgment.* Her sin, deserving of judgment. *reaches to the skies . . . high as the heavens.* Poetic exaggeration (see Dt 1:28; Ps 57:10; 108:4).
51:10 Judah speaks (see 50:28). *The LORD has vindicated us.* See Ps 37:6.
51:11 *stirred up.* Lit. "stirred up the spirit of" (see note on v. 1). *Medes.* See v. 28; Isa 13:17 and note; 21:2; Da 5:28,31; 6:8,12,15; 8:20. *vengeance, vengeance for his temple.* See note on 50:28.
51:12 *prepare an ambush.* To keep defenders from retreating to the safety of their fortifications (see Jos 8:14–22; Jdg 20:29–39).
51:13 *many waters.* The "rivers of Babylon" (Ps 137:1), including the mighty Euphrates, along with a magnificent system of irrigation canals, were proverbial. *destroyed.* Like a thread from the loom (see Isa 38:12).
51:14 *sworn by himself.* See note on Ge 22:16. *as with . . . locusts.* See 46:23. *shout in triumph.* See note on 48:33.
51:15–19 Echoes 10:12–16 (see notes there).
51:20–23 Illustrates Jeremiah's fondness for the effective use of repetition (see 4:23–26; see also Introduction: Literary Features).
51:20 *You are my war club.* Cf. Pr 25:18; either (1) Cyrus of Persia, soon to conquer Babylon, or, more likely, (2) Babylonia, destroyer of nations (see 50:23; see also note on Isa 10:5). *shatter.* See vv. 21–23. The Hebrew root for this verb is the same as that for "war club." See also Ex 15:6. The Hebrew verb is translated "dash (to pieces)" in Ps 2:9; 137:9; Hos 10:14; 13:16.

with you I shatter[w] nations,[x]
with you I destroy kingdoms,
21 with you I shatter horse and rider,[y]
with you I shatter chariot[z] and driver,
22 with you I shatter man and woman,
with you I shatter old man and youth,
with you I shatter young man and young woman,[a]
23 with you I shatter shepherd and flock,
with you I shatter farmer and oxen,
with you I shatter governors and officials.[b]

24 "Before your eyes I will repay[c] Babylon[d] and all who live in Babylonia[a] for
all the wrong they have done in Zion," declares the LORD.

25 "I am against[e] you, you destroying mountain,
you who destroy the whole earth,"[f]
declares the LORD.
"I will stretch out my hand[g] against you,
roll you off the cliffs,
and make you a burned-out mountain.[h]
26 No rock will be taken from you for a cornerstone,
nor any stone for a foundation,
for you will be desolate[i] forever,"
declares the LORD.

27 "Lift up a banner[j] in the land!
Blow the trumpet among the nations!
Prepare the nations for battle against her;
summon against her these kingdoms:[k]
Ararat,[l] Minni and Ashkenaz.[m]
Appoint a commander against her;
send up horses like a swarm of locusts.[n]
28 Prepare the nations for battle against her—
the kings of the Medes,[o]
their governors and all their officials,
and all the countries they rule.[p]
29 The land trembles[q] and writhes,
for the LORD's purposes[r] against Babylon stand—
to lay waste[s] the land of Babylon
so that no one will live there.[t]
30 Babylon's warriors[u] have stopped fighting;
they remain in their strongholds.
Their strength is exhausted;
they have become weaklings.[v]
Her dwellings are set on fire;[w]
the bars[x] of her gates are broken.
31 One courier[y] follows another
and messenger follows messenger
to announce to the king of Babylon
that his entire city is captured,[z]
32 the river crossings seized,
the marshes set on fire,[a]
and the soldiers terrified.[b]"

33 This is what the LORD Almighty, the
God of Israel, says:

"Daughter Babylon[c] is like a threshing floor[d]
at the time it is trampled;
the time to harvest[e] her will soon come.[f]"

34 "Nebuchadnezzar[g] king of Babylon has devoured[h] us,[i]
he has thrown us into confusion,
he has made us an empty jar.
Like a serpent he has swallowed us
and filled his stomach with our delicacies,
and then has spewed[j] us out.

51:20 [w] S Job 34:24; Mic 4:13 [x] S Isa 45:1 **51:21** [y] S Ex 15:1 [z] S Isa 43:17; S Jer 50:37 **51:22** [a] S 2Ch 36:17; Isa 13:17-18 **51:23** [b] ver 57 **51:24** [c] S ver 6, 35; S Dt 32:41; S Jer 50:15; La 3:64 [d] S Isa 45:1 **51:25** [e] S Jer 21:13 [f] Jer 50:23 [g] S Ex 3:20 [h] Zec 4:7 **51:26** [i] ver 29; S Isa 13:19-22; S Jer 50:12 **51:27** [j] S Ps 20:5; S Isa 13:2 [k] S Jer 25:14 [l] S Ge 8:4 [m] Ge 10:3 [n] S ver 14 **51:28** [o] S ver 11 [p] ver 48 **51:29** [q] S Jdg 5:4; S Jer 49:21 [r] S Ps 33:11 [s] Jer 48:9 [t] ver 43; S Isa 13:20 **51:30** [u] S Jer 50:36 [v] S Isa 19:16 [w] S Isa 47:14 [x] S Isa 45:2 **51:31** [y] 2Sa 18:19-31 [z] S Jer 50:2; Da 5:30 **51:32** [a] S Isa 47:14 [b] S Jer 50:36 **51:33** [c] S Isa 47:1 [d] S Isa 21:10 [e] S Isa 17:5 [f] S Isa 13:22 **51:34** [g] S Jer 50:17 [h] Na 2:12 [i] Hos 8:8 [j] ver 44; S Lev 18:25

[a] 24 Or *Chaldea;* also in verse 35

51:24 *your.* Judah's. *repay … for all the wrong they have done.* See v. 6; 50:15,29 and notes.
51:25 *destroying mountain.* Symbolizes a powerful kingdom (see Da 2:35,44–45), here Babylonia. *burned-out mountain.* After being judged by the Lord, Babylonia will be like an extinct volcano.
51:26 *desolate forever.* See 25:12; 50:12–13; see also note on Isa 13:20.
51:27 See 50:29. *Lift up a banner … ! Blow the trumpet … !* See 4:5–6; 6:1 and notes. *Prepare … for battle.* Lit. "Consecrate" (see note on 6:4). *these kingdoms.* Allies of the Medes (see v. 11 and note). *Ararat.* See note on Ge 8:4. *Minni.* A region mentioned in Assyrian inscriptions, it was located somewhere in Armenia. *Ashkenaz.* See note on Ge 10:3. *commander.* The Hebrew for this word appears again in the OT only in Na 3:17 ("officials"). It is a Babylonian loanword meaning lit. "scribe." *like … locusts.* See note on 46:23.
51:28 *Medes.* See note on v. 11. *all the countries they rule.* See note on 34:1; see also 1Ki 9:19.
51:29 *land trembles and writhes.* At the fearful prospect of war.
51:30 *exhausted … weaklings.* In the Hebrew there is a play on words. *become weaklings.* See 50:37; Na 3:13 and note.
51:31 *One courier follows another.* They run to the palace from all parts of the city.
51:32 *river crossings.* Fords and ferries (and perhaps bridges). *marshes set on fire.* To destroy the reeds and prevent fugitives from hiding among them.
51:33 *Daughter Babylon.* A personification of the city of Babylon (see note on 2Ki 19:21). *threshing floor.* The destruction of a city or nation is often depicted as a harvest (see Isa 27:12; Joel 3:13 and notes; Mic 4:12–13; cf. Rev 14:14–20 and note on 14:15).
51:34 *serpent.* The Hebrew for this word is translated "monster" in Isa 51:9, where it symbolizes Egypt (see Ge 1:21 and note). *delicacies.* See Ge 49:20.

35 May the violence[k] done to our flesh[a] be
on Babylon,"
say the inhabitants of Zion.
"May our blood be on those who live
in Babylonia,"
says Jerusalem.[l]

36 Therefore this is what the LORD says:

"See, I will defend your cause[m]
and avenge[n] you;
I will dry up[o] her sea
and make her springs dry.
37 Babylon will be a heap of ruins,
a haunt[p] of jackals,
an object of horror and scorn,[q]
a place where no one lives.[r]
38 Her people all roar like young lions,[s]
they growl like lion cubs.
39 But while they are aroused,
I will set out a feast for them
and make them drunk,[t]
so that they shout with laughter—
then sleep forever[u] and not awake,"
declares the LORD.[v]
40 "I will bring them down
like lambs to the slaughter,
like rams and goats.[w]

41 "How Sheshak[b][x] will be captured,[y]
the boast of the whole earth
seized!
How desolate[z] Babylon will be
among the nations!
42 The sea will rise over Babylon;
its roaring waves[a] will cover her.
43 Her towns will be desolate,
a dry and desert[b] land,
a land where no one lives,
through which no one travels.[c]
44 I will punish Bel[d] in Babylon
and make him spew out[e] what he
has swallowed.
The nations will no longer stream to
him.
And the wall[f] of Babylon will fall.

45 "Come out[g] of her, my people!
Run[h] for your lives!
Run from the fierce anger[i] of the
LORD.
46 Do not lose heart[j] or be afraid[k]
when rumors[l] are heard in the land;
one rumor comes this year, another the
next,
rumors of violence in the land
and of ruler against ruler.
47 For the time will surely come
when I will punish the idols[m] of
Babylon;
her whole land will be disgraced[n]
and her slain will all lie fallen within
her.[o]
48 Then heaven and earth and all that is
in them
will shout[p] for joy over Babylon,
for out of the north[q]
destroyers[r] will attack her,"
declares the LORD.

49 "Babylon must fall because of Israel's
slain,
just as the slain in all the earth
have fallen because of Babylon.[s]
50 You who have escaped the sword,
leave[t] and do not linger!
Remember[u] the LORD in a distant land,[v]
and call to mind Jerusalem."

51 "We are disgraced,[w]
for we have been insulted
and shame covers our faces,
because foreigners have entered
the holy places of the LORD's house."[x]

52 "But days are coming," declares the
LORD,
"when I will punish her idols,[y]

[a] *35* Or *done to us and to our children* [b] *41* *Sheshak* is a cryptogram for Babylon.

51:35 [k]Joel 3:19; Hab 2:17 [l]S ver 24; Ps 137:8 **51:36** [m]Ps 140:12; Jer 50:34; La 3:58 [n]ver 6; Jer 20:12; S Ro 12:19 [o]S Isa 11:15; S 19:5; Hos 13:15 **51:37** [p]S Isa 13:22; Rev 18:2 [q]Na 3:6; Mal 2:9 [r]S Jer 50:13, 39 **51:38** [s]S Isa 5:29 **51:39** [t]S Isa 21:5 [u]S Ps 13:3 [v]ver 57; S Jer 50:24 **51:40** [w]Eze 39:18 **51:41** [x]S Jer 25:26 [y]Isa 13:19 [z]Jer 50:13 **51:42** [a]S Ps 18:4; Isa 8:7 **51:43** [b]S Isa 21:1 [c]S ver 29, 62; S Isa 13:20; Jer 2:6 **51:44** [d]S Isa 21:9; S 46:1 [e]S ver 34 [f]ver 58; S 2Ki 25:4; Isa 25:12; Jer 50:15 **51:45** [g]ver 50 [h]S Isa 48:20 [i]Ps 76:10; 79:6 **51:46** [j]Ps 18:45 [k]S Jer 46:27 [l]S 2Ki 19:7 **51:47** [m]S Isa 46:1-2; S Jer 50:2 [n]Jer 50:12 [o]S Jer 27:7 **51:48** [p]S Job 3:7; S Ps 149:2; Rev 18:20 [q]ver 11; S Isa 41:25; S Jer 25:26 [r]ver 53, 56 **51:49** [s]Ps 137:8; S Jer 50:29 **51:50** [t]ver 45 [u]S Ps 137:6 [v]Jer 23:23 **51:51** [w]Ps 44:13-16; 79:4 [x]La 1:10 **51:52** [y]ver 47

51:35 *flesh.* See Mic 3:2–3.
51:36 *avenge you.* See vv. 6,11; see also note on 50:15. *sea ... springs.* See note on v. 13. Babylonia is called the "Desert by the Sea" in Isa 21:1 (see note there).
51:37 See 9:11; 18:16 and notes.
51:38 *roar like young lions.* See 2:15 and note.
51:39 *aroused.* Lit. "heated"; for a similar image, see Hos 7:4–7. *drunk.* See v. 57; see also notes on 25:15–16,26.
51:40 *lambs ... rams and goats.* Symbolic of the people (see Isa 34:6; Eze 39:18) of Babylon. *slaughter.* See Isa 53:7 and note.
51:41 *Sheshak.* See NIV text note; see also note on 25:26.
51:42 *sea ... its roaring waves.* See Isa 17:12 and note; here and in v. 55, Babylon's enemies (see 46:7 and note).
51:43 See 48:9; 49:18,33; 50:12–13.
51:44 *Bel.* See 50:2; Isa 46:1 and note. *what he has swallowed.* Captive peoples (including Judah) and plundered goods (including vessels from the temple in Jerusalem; see Da 5:2–3). *wall of Babylon.* A wall of double construction, the outer wall (12 feet thick) being separated from the inner wall (21 feet thick) by a dry moat 23 feet wide.
51:45 *Run for your lives!* See note on v. 6. *fierce anger.* See 4:8,26; Isa 13:13; Na 1:6.
51:46 *Do not ... be afraid when rumors are heard.* While giving his Olivet discourse, Jesus may have had this passage in mind (see Mt 24:6; Mk 13:7; Lk 21:9).
51:47 *punish the idols of Babylon.* See v. 52; see also note on 50:2.
51:48 *heaven and earth ... will shout for joy.* See Isa 44:23; Rev 18:20; 19:1–3. *out of the north.* See note on 50:3.
51:49 See note on 25:26.
51:50 *leave.* See note on v. 6.
51:51 *foreigners have entered the holy places.* Refers to Nebuchadnezzar's defiling the Jerusalem temple in 586 BC. The same sacrilege would occur under Antiochus Epiphanes in 168 BC and under the Romans in AD 70.

and throughout her land
the wounded will groan.[z]
53 Even if Babylon ascends to the heavens[a]
and fortifies her lofty stronghold,
I will send destroyers[b] against her,"
declares the LORD.

54 "The sound of a cry[c] comes from Babylon,
the sound of great destruction[d]
from the land of the Babylonians.[a]
55 The LORD will destroy Babylon;
he will silence[e] her noisy din.
Waves[f] of enemies will rage like great waters;
the roar of their voices will resound.
56 A destroyer[g] will come against Babylon;
her warriors will be captured,
and their bows will be broken.[h]
For the LORD is a God of retribution;
he will repay[i] in full.
57 I will make her officials[j] and wise[k] men drunk,[l]
her governors, officers and warriors as well;
they will sleep[m] forever and not awake,"
declares the King,[n] whose name is the LORD Almighty.

58 This is what the LORD Almighty says:

"Babylon's thick wall[o] will be leveled
and her high gates[p] set on fire;
the peoples[q] exhaust[r] themselves for nothing,
the nations' labor is only fuel for the flames."[s]

51:52 [z] S Job 24:12
51:53 [a] S Ge 11:4; S Isa 14:13-14 [b] S ver 48; S Job 15:21
51:54 [c] S Job 24:12 [d] S Jer 50:22
51:55 [e] Isa 25:5 [f] S Ps 18:4
51:56 [g] S ver 48; S Job 15:21 [h] Ps 46:9 [i] S ver 6; S Ge 4:24; S Dt 32:41; Ps 94:1-2; Hab 2:8
51:57 [j] S ver 23 [k] S Job 5:13 [l] S Isa 21:5 [m] S ver 39; Ps 76:5; S Jer 25:27 [n] S Isa 6:5
51:58 [o] S ver 44; S 2Ki 25:4; S Isa 15:1 [p] S Isa 13:2 [q] ver 64 [r] S Isa 47:13 [s] S Isa 47:14

59 This is the message Jeremiah the
prophet gave to the staff officer Seraiah
son of Neriah,[t] the son of Mahseiah, when
he went to Babylon with Zedekiah[u] king
of Judah in the fourth[v] year of his reign.
60 Jeremiah had written on a scroll[w] about
all the disasters that would come upon
Babylon—all that had been recorded concerning Babylon. 61 He said to Seraiah,
"When you get to Babylon, see that you
read all these words aloud. 62 Then say,
'LORD, you have said you will destroy this
place, so that neither people nor animals
will live in it; it will be desolate[x] forever.'
63 When you finish reading this scroll, tie
a stone to it and throw it into the Euphrates.[y] 64 Then say, 'So will Babylon sink to
rise no more[z] because of the disaster I will
bring on her. And her people[a] will fall.'"[b]

The words of Jeremiah end[c] here.

The Fall of Jerusalem

52:1-3pp — 2Ki 24:18-20; 2Ch 36:11-16
52:4-16pp — Jer 39:1-10
52:4-21pp — 2Ki 25:1-21; 2Ch 36:17-20

52 Zedekiah[d] was twenty-one years
old when he became king, and
he reigned in Jerusalem eleven years. His
mother's name was Hamutal daughter
of Jeremiah; she was from Libnah.[e] 2 He
did evil in the eyes of the LORD, just as
Jehoiakim[f] had done. 3 It was because of
the LORD's anger that all this happened to
Jerusalem and Judah,[g] and in the end he
thrust them from his presence.[h]
Now Zedekiah rebelled[i] against the king
of Babylon.
4 So in the ninth year of Zedekiah's

[a] 54 Or *Chaldeans*

51:59 [t] Jer 36:4 [u] Jer 52:1 [v] Jer 28:1
51:60 [w] S Ex 17:14; Jer 30:2; 36:2
51:62 [x] S Isa 13:20; S Jer 9:11; S 50:13,39
51:63 [y] S Ge 2:14
51:64 [z] Eze 26:21; 28:19 [a] S ver 58 [b] Rev 18:21 [c] S Job 31:40
52:1 [d] S 2Ki 24:17 [e] S Nu 33:20; Jos 10:29; 2Ki 8:22
52:2 [f] S Jer 36:30
52:3 [g] Isa 3:1 [h] S Ge 4:14; S Ex 33:15 [i] Eze 17:12-16

51:53 *ascends to the heavens.* See Ge 11:4 and note; Isa 14:13–15. *destroyers.* See vv. 48,56.
51:54 See 50:46. *great destruction.* See note on 4:6.
51:55 *Waves.* See note on v. 42. *like great waters.* See note on Ps 32:6.
51:56 *God of retribution.* See note on v. 24.
51:57 *officials and wise men.* See 50:35. *drunk.* See v. 39; see also notes on 25:15–16,26. *King.* See note on 46:18. The true King is the Lord, not Bel/Marduk (see 50:2 and note).
51:58 *thick wall.* See note on v. 44. *high gates.* The famous Ishtar Gate was almost 40 feet high. *the peoples ... fuel for the flames.* Very similar to Hab 2:13.
51:59–64 A prose conclusion to the book in general and to the message against Babylon in particular.
51:59 *staff officer.* Lit. "resting-place officer" (see Nu 10:33), the official responsible for determining when and where his men on the march should stay overnight. *Seraiah son of Neriah.* An ancient seal has been found that bears the inscription "Belonging to Seraiah son of Neriah," and it no doubt refers to the man mentioned here. He was a brother of Jeremiah's secretary, Baruch (see 32:12). *he.* Seraiah. *Zedekiah ... fourth year.* 593 BC. Zedekiah may have been summoned to Babylon by Nebuchadnezzar to be interrogated by him (see note on 27:3).
51:60 *scroll.* See note on Ex 17:14. *all that had been recorded concerning Babylon.* Probably the message of 50:2—51:58 (see note on 50:1).
51:62 *you have said.* See v. 26.
51:64 *The words of Jeremiah end here.* A note by the final compiler of the book of Jeremiah (see 48:47).
52:1–27,31–34 Paralleled almost verbatim in 2Ki 24:18—25:21,27–30 (see notes there). (52:4–27 is summarized in 39:1–10; see notes there.) The writer(s) of Kings and the writer of the appendix to Jeremiah (perhaps Baruch) doubtless had access to the same sources. It is unlikely that either of the two accounts copied from the other, since each has peculiarities characteristic of the larger work that it concludes. In a few passages, Jeremiah is fuller than Kings (compare especially vv. 10–11 with 2Ki 25:7; v. 15 with 2Ki 25:11; vv. 19–23 with 2Ki 25:15–17; v. 31 with 2Ki 25:27; v. 34 with 2Ki 25:30).
52:1 *Jeremiah.* Not the prophet. *Libnah.* See note on 2Ki 8:22.

reign, on the tenth[j] day of the tenth month, Nebuchadnezzar king of Babylon marched against Jerusalem[k] with his whole army. They encamped outside the city and built siege works[l] all around it.[m] 5 The city was kept under siege until the eleventh year of King Zedekiah.

6 By the ninth day of the fourth month the famine in the city had become so severe that there was no food for the people to eat.[n] 7 Then the city wall was broken through, and the whole army fled.[o] They left the city at night through the gate between the two walls near the king's garden, though the Babylonians[a] were surrounding the city. They fled toward the Arabah,[b] 8 but the Babylonian[c] army pursued King Zedekiah and overtook him in the plains of Jericho. All his soldiers were separated from him and scattered, 9 and he was captured.[p]

He was taken to the king of Babylon at Riblah[q] in the land of Hamath,[r] where he pronounced sentence on him. 10 There at Riblah the king of Babylon killed the sons[s] of Zedekiah before his eyes; he also killed all the officials of Judah. 11 Then he put out Zedekiah's eyes, bound him with bronze shackles and took him to Babylon, where he put him in prison till the day of his death.[t]

12 On the tenth day of the fifth[u] month, in the nineteenth year of Nebuchadnezzar king of Babylon, Nebuzaradan[v] commander of the imperial guard, who served the king of Babylon, came to Jerusalem. 13 He set fire[w] to the temple[x] of the LORD, the royal palace and all the houses[y] of Jerusalem. Every important building he burned down. 14 The whole Babylonian army, under the commander of the imperial guard, broke down all the walls[z] around Jerusalem. 15 Nebuzaradan the commander of the guard carried into exile[a] some of the poorest people and those who remained in the city, along with the rest of the craftsmen[d] and those who had deserted[b] to the king of Babylon. 16 But Nebuzaradan left behind[c] the rest of the poorest people of the land to work the vineyards and fields.

17 The Babylonians broke up the bronze pillars,[d] the movable stands[e] and the bronze Sea[f] that were at the temple of the LORD and they carried all the bronze to Babylon.[g] 18 They also took away the pots, shovels, wick trimmers, sprinkling bowls,[h] dishes and all the bronze articles used in the temple service.[i] 19 The commander of the imperial guard took away the basins, censers,[j] sprinkling bowls, pots, lampstands,[k] dishes[l] and bowls used for drink offerings[m]—all that were made of pure gold or silver.[n]

20 The bronze from the two pillars, the Sea and the twelve bronze bulls[o] under it, and the movable stands, which King Solomon had made for the temple of the LORD, was more than could be weighed.[p] 21 Each pillar was eighteen cubits high and twelve cubits in circumference[e]; each was four fingers thick, and hollow.[q] 22 The bronze capital[r] on top of one pillar was five cubits[f] high and was decorated with a network and pomegranates[s] of bronze all around. The other pillar, with its pomegranates, was similar. 23 There were ninety-six pomegranates on the sides; the total number of pomegranates[t] above the surrounding network was a hundred.[u]

24 The commander of the guard took as prisoners Seraiah[v] the chief priest, Zephaniah[w] the priest next in rank and the three doorkeepers.[x] 25 Of those still in the city, he took the officer in charge of the fighting men, and seven royal advisers. He also took the secretary[y] who was chief officer in charge of conscripting the people of the land, sixty of whom were found in the city. 26 Nebuzaradan[z] the commander took them all and brought them to the king of Babylon at Riblah. 27 There at Riblah,[a] in the land of Hamath, the king had them executed.

So Judah went into captivity, away[b] from her land. 28 This is the number of the people Nebuchadnezzar carried into exile:[c]

in the seventh year, 3,023 Jews;
29 in Nebuchadnezzar's eighteenth year,
832 people from Jerusalem;

52:4 [j] Zec 8:19 [k] Jer 34:1 [l] S Jer 6:6 [m] Eze 24:1-2 **52:6** [n] S Lev 26:26; S Isa 3:1; La 1:11 **52:7** [o] La 4:19 **52:9** [p] S Jer 21:7; S 32:4 [q] S Nu 34:11 [r] S Nu 13:21 **52:10** [s] S Jer 22:30 **52:11** [t] Jer 34:4; Eze 12:13; 17:16 **52:12** [u] Zec 7:5; 8:19 [v] ver 26 **52:13** [w] S 2Ch 36:19; S Ps 74:8; La 2:6 [x] S Dt 29:24; Ps 79:1; Mic 3:12 [y] S Dt 13:16; S Jer 19:13 **52:14** [z] S Ne 1:3; La 2:8 **52:15** [a] S 2Ki 24:1; S Jer 1:3 [b] S Jer 38:19 **52:16** [c] Jer 40:6 **52:17** [d] S 1Ki 7:15 [e] 1Ki 7:27-37 [f] S 1Ki 7:23 [g] Jer 27:19-22 **52:18** [h] S Nu 4:14 [i] S Ex 27:3; 1Ki 7:45 **52:19** [j] S Lev 10:1; S 1Ki 7:50 [k] S Nu 3:31 [l] Ex 25:29 [m] S Nu 4:7 [n] S Ezr 1:7; Da 5:2 **52:20** [o] 1Ki 7:25 [p] S 1Ki 7:47 **52:21** [q] S 1Ki 7:15 **52:22** [r] S 1Ki 7:16 [s] S Ex 28:33 **52:23** [t] 1Ki 7:20 [u] S ver 17; S Jer 27:19 **52:24** [v] S 2Ki 25:18 [w] S 2Ki 25:18; S Jer 37:3 [x] S 2Ki 12:9 **52:25** [y] Jer 36:10 **52:26** [z] S ver 12 **52:27** [a] S Nu 34:11 [b] S Jer 20:4 **52:28** [c] S Dt 28:36; S 2Ch 36:20; S Ne 1:2

[a] 7 Or *Chaldeans*; also in verse 17 [b] 7 Or *the Jordan Valley* [c] 8 Or *Chaldean*; also in verse 14 [d] 15 Or *the populace* [e] 21 That is, about 27 feet high and 18 feet in circumference or about 8.1 meters high and 5.4 meters in circumference [f] 22 That is, about 7 1/2 feet or about 2.3 meters

52:12 *tenth day.* The parallel in 2Ki 25:8 reads "seventh day"; one of the numbers is a copyist's error, but we cannot tell which (see vv. 22,25,31 and notes).
52:18–19 See notes on 1Ki 7:40,45,50.
52:20 *twelve bronze bulls.* See note on 2Ch 4:4.
52:21–23 See notes on 1Ki 7:15–23.
52:22 *five.* The parallel in 2Ki 25:17 reads "three" (see NIV text note there), probably a copyist's error (see also note on 2Ki 25:17).
52:25 *seven.* The parallel in 2Ki 25:19 reads "five"; see note on v. 12.
52:28 *seventh year.* Of Nebuchadnezzar's reign (see vv. 29–30), which was 597 BC. *3,023.* Probably includes only adult males, since the corresponding figure(s) in 2Ki 24:14,16 are significantly higher.
52:29 *eighteenth year.* 586 BC. In v. 12 the same year is called the "nineteenth year"; the difference is due to alternate ways of computing regnal years (for a similar case, see note on Da 1:1).

30 in his twenty-third year,
745 Jews taken into exile[d] by Nebuzaradan the commander of the imperial guard.
There were 4,600 people in all.[e]

Jehoiachin Released

52:31-34pp — 2Ki 25:27-30

31 In the thirty-seventh year of the exile
of Jehoiachin[f] king of Judah, in the year
Awel-Marduk became king of Babylon, on
the twenty-fifth day of the twelfth month,
he released Jehoiachin king of Judah and
freed him from prison. 32 He spoke kindly
to him and gave him a seat of honor higher than those of the other kings who were
with him in Babylon. 33 So Jehoiachin put
aside his prison clothes and for the rest of
his life ate regularly at the king's table.[g]
34 Day by day the king of Babylon gave Jehoiachin a regular allowance[h] as long as
he lived, till the day of his death.

52:30 [d] S Jer 43:3 [e] S Jer 13:19
52:31 [f] S 2Ch 36:9
52:33 [g] S 2Sa 9:7
52:34 [h] 2Sa 9:10

52:30 *twenty-third year.* 581 BC. *taken into exile by Nebuzaradan.* Either (1) to quell further rebellion (see v. 3) or (2) in belated reprisal for Gedaliah's assassination (see 41:1–3).
52:31–34 Paralleled almost verbatim in 2Ki 25:27–30 (see notes there). Jeremiah and Kings thus conclude with the same happy ending.
52:31 *twenty-fifth.* The parallel in 2Ki 25:27 reads "twenty-seventh"; see note on v. 12.
52:32 See 2Ki 25:28 and note.
52:34 *till the day of his death.* See v. 11. Since the phrase does not appear in the parallel verses in 2 Kings in either case, its intention is probably to highlight the contrast between Zedekiah, who remained in prison till the day he died (see v. 11), and Jehoiachin, who was released from prison and treated well by the Babylonian kings till the day he died (see notes on 2Ki 25:27–28).

LAMENTATIONS

INTRODUCTION

Title

The Hebrew title of the book is *'ekah* ("How . . . !"), the first word not only in 1:1 but also in 2:1; 4:1. Because of its subject matter, the book is also referred to in Jewish tradition as *qinot*, "Lamentations," a title taken over by the Septuagint (the pre-Christian Greek translation of the OT) and by the fourth-century Latin Vulgate, as well as by English versions.

Author and Date

Lamentations is anonymous, although ancient Jewish and early Christian traditions ascribe it to Jeremiah. These traditions are based in part on 2Ch 35:25 (though the "laments" referred to there are not to be identified with the OT book of Lamentations); in part on such texts as Jer 7:29; 8:21; 9:1,10,20; and in part on the similarity of vocabulary and style between Lamentations and the prophecies of Jeremiah. Moreover, such an ascription gains a measure of plausibility from the fact that Jeremiah was an eyewitness to the divine judgment on Jerusalem in 586 BC, which is so vividly portrayed here. Nevertheless, we cannot be certain who authored these carefully crafted poems or who is responsible for putting them together into a single scroll. Lamentations poignantly expresses the people's overwhelming sense of loss that accompanied the destruction of Jerusalem and the temple, as well as the exile of Judah's inhabitants from the land Yahweh had covenanted to give Israel as a perpetual national homeland.

The earliest possible date for the book is 586 BC, and the latest is 516 (when the rebuilt Jerusalem temple was dedicated). The graphic immediacy of Lamentations argues for an earlier date, probably before 575.

a quick look

Author:
Probably Jeremiah

Audience:
Jews in Babylonian exile who are lamenting the destruction of Jerusalem

Date:
Shortly after the fall of Jerusalem in 586 BC

Theme:
The prophet and his fellow Jews lament the devastation of their beloved city at the hands of the Babylonians.

Literary Features

The entire book is poetic. The first, second, fourth and fifth laments all contain 22 verses, reflecting the number of letters in the Hebrew alphabet. In the first and second laments each

Jews still pray and weep over their holy city at the "Wailing Wall" in Jerusalem. The "Wailing Wall," or Western Wall, is a remnant of the ancient wall that surrounded the Jewish temple's courtyard, dating back to the Second Temple period.

Left: © Elisei Shafer/www.BigStockPhoto.com
Right: © Kobby Dagan/www.BigStockPhoto.com

verse contains three poetic lines; in the fourth each verse contains two lines; and in the fifth each verse contains only one line. The first four laments are alphabetic acrostics (see NIV text notes on 1:1; 2:1; 3:1; 4:1). In the first, second and fourth, each numbered verse begins with the letter of the Hebrew alphabet dictated by the traditional order of that alphabet. The third (middle) lament is distinctive in that while it too is made up of 22 three-line units (like laments 1 and 2), in it the three lines of each unit all begin with the sequenced order of the letters of the alphabet (thus three *aleph* lines followed by three *beth* lines, etc.) — after the manner of Ps 119 (see diagram, p. 1330). The fifth lament continues to reflect the alphabetic pattern in its 22-line structure, but the initial letters of these lines do not follow the alphabetic sequence (see note on 5:1 – 22). Use of the alphabet as a formal structuring element indicates that, however passionate these laments, they were composed with studied care.

Themes and Theology

Lamentations is not the only OT book that contains individual or community laments. (A large number of the psalms are lament poems, and every prophetic book except Haggai includes one or more examples of the lament genre.) Lamentations is the only book, however, that consists solely of laments.

As a series of laments over the destruction of Jerusalem (the royal city of the Lord's kingdom) in 586 BC, the book stands in a tradition with such ancient non-Biblical writings as the Sumerian "Lamentation over the Destruction of Ur," "Lamentation over the Destruction of Sumer and Ur," and "Lamentation over the Destruction of Nippur." Orthodox Jews customarily read it aloud in its entirety on the ninth day of Av, the traditional date of the destruction of Solomon's temple in 586, as well as the date of the destruction of Herod's temple in AD 70. Many also read it each week at the Western Wall (the "Wailing Wall") in the Old City of Jerusalem. In addition, the book is important in traditional Roman Catholic liturgy, where it is customarily read during the last three days of Holy Week.

Stele with funeral dance, from the tomb of Pharaoh Horemheb (c. 1319 – 1291 BC) in Saqqara, Egypt. The Jews similarly lamented over the impending destruction of Jerusalem.

Scala/Art Resource, NY

This Christian practice reminds us that the book of Lamentations not only bemoans Jerusalem's destruction but also contains profound theological insights. The horrors accompanying the Babylonian destruction of Judah are recited in some detail:

(1) Wholesale devastation and slaughter engulfed kings (2:6,9; 4:20), princes (1:6; 2:2,9; 4:7 – 8; 5:12), elders (1:19; 2:10; 4:16; 5:12), priests (1:4,19; 2:6,20; 4:16), prophets (2:9,20) and commoners (2:10 – 12; 3:48; 4:6) alike.

(2) Starving mothers were reduced to cannibalism (2:20; 4:10).

(3) The flower of Judah's inhabitants was dragged off into humiliating exile (1:3,18).

(4) An elaborate system of ceremony and worship came to an end (1:4,10).

The author of these laments understands clearly that the Babylonians were merely the human agents of divine judgment.

But this recital is integrally woven into the fabric of a poetic wrestling with the ways of God, who as the Lord of history was dealing with his wayward people.

The author of these laments understands clearly that the Babylonians were merely the human agents of divine judgment. It was God himself who had destroyed the city and temple (1:12–15; 2:1–8,17,22; 4:11). This was not a merely arbitrary act on the Lord's part; blatant, God-defying sin and covenant-breaking rebellion were at the root of his people's woes (1:5,8–9; 4:13; 5:7,16). Although weeping (1:16; 2:11,18; 3:48–51) is to be expected and cries for redress against the enemy (1:22; 3:59–66) are understandable (see note on Ps 5:10), the proper response to judgment is acknowledgment of sin (1:5,8,14,22; 2:14; 3:39; 4:13; 5:7,16) and heartfelt contrition (3:40–42). Trust in God's mercies and faithfulness must not falter. The book that begins with lament (1:1–2) rightly ends with an appeal to the Lord for restoration (5:21–22).

In the middle of the book, the theology of Lamentations reaches its apex as it focuses on the goodness of God. He is the Lord of hope (3:21,24–25), of love (3:22), of faithfulness (3:23), of salvation and restoration (3:26). In spite of all evidence to the contrary, "his compassions never fail. / They are new every morning; / great is your faithfulness" (3:22–23).

Near the end of the book, faith rises from Jerusalem's lamentable condition to acknowledge Yahweh's eternal reign: "You, LORD, reign forever; / your throne endures from generation to generation" (5:19; see introductions to Ps 47; 93; see also note on Ps 102:12).

Outline

I. Jerusalem's Misery and Desolation (ch. 1)
II. The Lord's Anger against His People (ch. 2)
III. Judah's Complaint — and Basis for Consolation (ch. 3)
IV. The Contrast between Zion's Past and Present (ch. 4)
V. Judah's Appeal to the Lord for Forgiveness and Restoration (ch. 5)

1 [a] How deserted[a] lies the city,
once so full of people![b]
How like a widow[c] is she,
who once was great[d] among the nations!
She who was queen among the provinces
has now become a slave.[e]

2 Bitterly she weeps[f] at night,
tears are on her cheeks.
Among all her lovers[g]
there is no one to comfort her.
All her friends have betrayed[h] her;
they have become her enemies.[i]

3 After affliction and harsh labor,
Judah has gone into exile.[j]
She dwells among the nations;
she finds no resting place.[k]
All who pursue her have overtaken her[l]
in the midst of her distress.

4 The roads to Zion mourn,[m]
for no one comes to her appointed festivals.
All her gateways are desolate,[n]
her priests groan,
her young women grieve,
and she is in bitter anguish.[o]

5 Her foes have become her masters;
her enemies are at ease.
The LORD has brought her grief[p]
because of her many sins.[q]
Her children have gone into exile,[r]
captive before the foe.[s]

6 All the splendor has departed
from Daughter Zion.[t]
Her princes are like deer
that find no pasture;
in weakness they have fled[u]
before the pursuer.

7 In the days of her affliction and wandering
Jerusalem remembers all the treasures
that were hers in days of old.
When her people fell into enemy hands,
there was no one to help her.[v]
Her enemies looked at her
and laughed[w] at her destruction.

8 Jerusalem has sinned[x] greatly
and so has become unclean.[y]
All who honored her despise her,
for they have all seen her naked;[z]
she herself groans[a]
and turns away.

9 Her filthiness clung to her skirts;
she did not consider her future.[b]
Her fall[c] was astounding;
there was none to comfort[d] her.
"Look, LORD, on my affliction,[e]
for the enemy has triumphed."

10 The enemy laid hands
on all her treasures;[f]
she saw pagan nations
enter her sanctuary[g] —
those you had forbidden[h]
to enter your assembly.

[a] This chapter is an acrostic poem, the verses of which begin with the successive letters of the Hebrew alphabet.

1:1 [a] S Lev 26:43 [b] S Jer 42:2 [c] S Isa 47:8 [d] S 1Ki 4:21 [e] Isa 3:26; S Jer 40:9; Eze 5:5 **1:2** [f] Ps 6:6 [g] S Jer 3:1 [h] S Jer 4:30; Mic 7:5 [i] ver 16; S Jer 30:14 **1:3** [j] S Jer 13:19 [k] Dt 28:65 [l] S Ex 15:9 **1:4** [m] S Ps 137:1 [n] S Isa 27:10; S Jer 9:11 [o] ver 21; Joel 1:8-13 **1:5** [p] S Isa 22:5; S Jer 30:15 [q] S Ps 5:10 [r] S Jer 10:20; S 39:9; 52:28-30 [s] S Ps 137:3; La 2:17 **1:6** [t] S Ps 9:14; Jer 13:18 [u] S Lev 26:36 **1:7** [v] S 2Ki 14:26; S Jer 37:7; La 4:17 [w] S Jer 2:26 **1:8** [x] ver 20; Isa 59:2-13 [y] S Jer 2:22 [z] S Jer 13:22, 26 [a] ver 21,22; S Ps 6:6; S 38:8 **1:9** [b] Dt 32:28-29; Eze 24:13 [c] Jer 13:18 [d] S Ecc 4:1; S Jer 16:7 [e] Ps 25:18 **1:10** [f] S Isa 64:11 [g] Ps 74:7-8; 79:1; Jer 51:51 [h] Dt 23:3

1:1–22 As is widely done in OT prophecy and psalmody, Jerusalem is here presented as a woman — and represents the nation of which she is the political head and symbolic heart.
1:1–11 In the first half of this first lament, Jerusalem's condition is described by one who speaks of her in the third person — yet as one who bemoans the city's desperate situation. For the transition to Jerusalem's own voice, see the quoted words at the end of v. 11.
1:1 *How ... !* Expresses a mixture of shock and deep dismay (see 2:1; 4:1–2; 2Sa 1:25,27; Jer 9:19; 48:17,39; Eze 26:17). *deserted lies.* Due to the Babylonian exile (v. 3). The Hebrew underlying this phrase is translated "sat alone" in Jer 15:17. There the prophet sat alone; here his beloved city does the same. *city.* Jerusalem. *once so full of people.* Cf. Isa 1:21. *great among the nations.* Cf. Jer 49:15. *slave.* The Hebrew for this word is translated "forced labor" in Ex 1:11; 1Ki 4:6.
1:2 *Bitterly she weeps.* As did Jeremiah, and for much the same reason (Jer 13:17). *at night.* See 2:18–19. *lovers ... friends.* International allies to whom the people of Jerusalem and Judah looked for security rather than to the Lord (see Jer 2:36–37; 27:3; Eze 16:26,28–29; 23:11–21; see also Ex 34:15 and note). *no one to comfort her.* See vv. 9,16–17,21. *All ... have betrayed her.* See v. 19; like Edom (4:21–22; Ps 137:7) and Ammon (Jer 40:14; Eze 25:2–3,6). *become her enemies.* See v. 17.
1:3 *gone into exile.* To Babylonia (see Jer 20:4–5 and thereafter in Jeremiah). *among the nations ... finds no resting place.* As Moses warned in Dt 28:65.
1:4 *mourn.* Are deserted and desolate (see Jdg 5:6; Isa 33:8 and notes). *appointed festivals.* See Ex 23:14–17 and notes; Lev 23:2. *young women grieve.* A sign of utter defeat (see Jer 9:20; contrast Ex 15:20 and note; 1Sa 18:6; Ps 68:25; Jer 31:13).
1:5 *masters.* Lit. "head" — in accordance with Dt 28:44 (contrast Dt 28:13).
1:6 *Daughter Zion.* A personification of Jerusalem (see note on 2Ki 19:21). *Her princes ... have fled before the pursuer.* See Jer 52:7–8. *like deer that find no pasture.* Hence are weakened and become easy prey for predators.
1:7 *affliction and wandering.* See 3:19. *treasures.* See vv. 10–11. *days of old.* For example, the days of David and Solomon. *fell into enemy hands.* See 2Sa 24:14. *destruction.* Lit. "cessation" (see notes on Ge 2:2–3). The Hebrew root for this word is the same as that for "Sabbath" — and may be intended as an ironic pun (see Lev 26:34–35).
1:8 *unclean.* See v. 17 and note. It refers to the ceremonial uncleanness of a woman during her monthly period (see Lev 12:2,5; 15:19). *her naked.* See Isa 47:3; Eze 16:37 and notes.
1:9 *filthiness.* Ceremonial uncleanness (see note on Lev 4:12), here caused by willful sin. *did not consider her future.* Just as Babylon did not (Isa 47:7). *Look, LORD.* Jerusalem's desolation is further depicted by quoting the cry that bursts from her lips (see v. 11 and note). *enemy has triumphed.* See v. 16.
1:10 *forbidden to enter your assembly.* See Eze 44:7,9 and notes.

11 All her people groan[i]
as they search for bread;[j]
they barter their treasures for food
to keep themselves alive.
"Look, LORD, and consider,
for I am despised."

12 "Is it nothing to you, all you who
pass by?[k]
Look around and see.
Is any suffering like my suffering[l]
that was inflicted on me,
that the LORD brought on me
in the day of his fierce anger?[m]

13 "From on high he sent fire,
sent it down into my bones.[n]
He spread a net[o] for my feet
and turned me back.
He made me desolate,[p]
faint[q] all the day long.

14 "My sins have been bound into a
yoke[a],[r]
by his hands they were woven
together.
They have been hung on my neck,
and the Lord has sapped my
strength.
He has given me into the hands[s]
of those I cannot withstand.

15 "The Lord has rejected
all the warriors in my midst;[t]
he has summoned an army[u] against me
to[b] crush my young men.[v]
In his winepress[w] the Lord has
trampled[x]
Virgin Daughter[y] Judah.

16 "This is why I weep
and my eyes overflow with tears.[z]
No one is near to comfort[a] me,
no one to restore my spirit.
My children are destitute
because the enemy has prevailed."[b]

17 Zion stretches out her hands,[c]
but there is no one to comfort her.
The LORD has decreed for Jacob
that his neighbors become his foes;[d]
Jerusalem has become
an unclean[e] thing[f] among them.

18 "The LORD is righteous,[g]
yet I rebelled[h] against his command.
Listen, all you peoples;
look on my suffering.[i]
My young men and young women
have gone into exile.[j]

19 "I called to my allies[k]
but they betrayed me.
My priests and my elders
perished[l] in the city
while they searched for food
to keep themselves alive.

20 "See, LORD, how distressed[m] I am!
I am in torment[n] within,
and in my heart I am disturbed,[o]
for I have been most rebellious.[p]
Outside, the sword bereaves;
inside, there is only death.[q]

21 "People have heard my groaning,[r]
but there is no one to comfort me.[s]
All my enemies have heard of my
distress;
they rejoice[t] at what you have done.
May you bring the day[u] you have
announced
so they may become like me.

1:11 [i]S Ps 6:6; S 38:8 [j]S Jer 37:21; S 52:6 **1:12** [k]S Jer 18:16 [l]ver 18 [m]S Isa 10:4; 13:13; S Jer 30:24 **1:13** [n]S Job 30:30; Ps 102:3 [o]S Job 18:8 [p]S Jer 44:6 [q]Hab 3:16 **1:14** [r]S Dt 28:48; S Isa 47:6; S Jer 15:12 [s]S Jer 32:5 **1:15** [t]Jer 37:10 [u]Isa 41:2 [v]Isa 28:18; S Jer 18:21 [w]S Jdg 6:11 [x]S Isa 5:5 [y]Jer 14:17 **1:16** [z]S Job 7:3; S Ps 119:136; S Isa 22:4; La 2:11, 18; 3:48-49 [a]S Ps 69:20; Ecc 4:1; S Jer 16:7 [b]S ver 2; Jer 13:17; 14:17 **1:17** [c]S Jer 4:31 [d]S Ex 23:21 [e]Jer 2:22 [f]S Lev 18:25-28 **1:18** [g]S Ex 9:27; S Ezr 9:15 [h]S 1Sa 12:14 [i]ver 12 [j]Dt 28:32,41 **1:19** [k]S Jer 22:20 [l]S Jer 14:15; La 2:20 **1:20** [m]S Jer 4:19 [n]La 2:11 [o]S Job 20:2 [p]S ver 8 [q]S Dt 32:25; Eze 7:15 **1:21** [r]S ver 8; S Ps 6:6; S 38:8 [s]ver 4 [t]La 2:15 [u]Isa 47:11; Jer 30:16

[a] 14 Most Hebrew manuscripts; many Hebrew manuscripts and Septuagint *He kept watch over my sins*
[b] 15 Or *has set a time for me / when he will*

1:11 *search for bread.* Food shortages were an ever-present problem during and after the siege of Jerusalem. *keep themselves alive.* See v. 19; 2Ki 6:24–29. *Look, LORD.* Again, Jerusalem's desperate cry to the Lord is suddenly introduced. From here to the end of this lament, personified Jerusalem speaks.
1:12 *who pass by.* See Jer 18:16 and note. *Look … like my suffering.* In his magisterial *The Messiah*, Handel borrowed these lines (as they appeared in the KJV: "Behold, and see if there be any sorrow like unto my sorrow") and placed them on the lips of the Messiah—perhaps associating them with Isa 53:4 ("Surely he hath borne our griefs, and carried our sorrows …"); cf. also Isa 53:3 ("a man of sorrows"). *fierce anger.* See 2:3,6; 4:11. The expression is common in Jeremiah (see Jer 4:8,26; 12:13; 25:37–38; 44:6; 49:37; 51:45).
1:13 *From on high he sent fire.* The fire of his judgment (see 2:3–4; Lev 10:2; Nu 11:1–3; 16:35; 2Ki 1:10,12; Isa 29:6; 30:30; 66:15–16; Jer 4:4; 21:14; 49:27; 50:32; Am 7:4). *my bones.* The bones of Jerusalem (personified as a woman; see note on v. 8). In a strikingly similar image, the word of the Lord was like fire in the bones of the prophet (see Jer 20:9 and note). *spread a net for my feet.* See Ps 57:6; Pr 29:5. *desolate.* Like Absalom's sister Tamar (see 2Sa 13:20).
1:15 *In his winepress … trampled.* A common metaphor of divine judgment (see Isa 63:2–3; Joel 3:13; Rev 14:19–20; 19:15). *Virgin Daughter Judah.* A personification of Judah (see note on 2Ki 19:21).
1:16 *eyes overflow with tears.* See 2:11; 3:48; Jer 9:1,18 and note on 9:1; 13:17; 14:17. *enemy has prevailed.* See v. 9.
1:17 *become his foes.* See v. 2. *unclean thing.* See note on v. 8; for the same imagery elsewhere, see Ezr 9:11; Isa 30:22; 64:6; Eze 7:19–20; 36:17.
1:18 *is righteous.* Has dealt rightly with me. *yet I rebelled.* Better "for I have rebelled." *Listen … look.* The nations are called to take note of the Lord's righteous acts of judgment, as well as of his righteous acts of deliverance.
1:19 *allies … betrayed me.* See v. 2 and note. *keep themselves alive.* See note on v. 11.
1:20 *I am in torment within.* Repeated in 2:11. *Outside … inside.* See Jer 14:18. The Sumerian "Lamentation over the Destruction of Ur" contains a striking parallel: "Inside it we die of famine, outside we are killed by weapons" (lines 403–404).
1:21 *day you have announced.* Day of God's judgment on the nations (see 4:21–22; Jer 25:15–38 and notes).

22 "Let all their wickedness come before you;
deal with them
as you have dealt with me
because of all my sins.[v]
My groans[w] are many
and my heart is faint."

2 [a] How the Lord has covered Daughter Zion
with the cloud of his anger[b]![x]
He has hurled down the splendor of Israel
from heaven to earth;
he has not remembered his footstool[y]
in the day of his anger.[z]

2 Without pity[a] the Lord has swallowed[b] up
all the dwellings of Jacob;
in his wrath he has torn down
the strongholds[c] of Daughter Judah.
He has brought her kingdom and its princes
down to the ground[d] in dishonor.

3 In fierce anger he has cut off
every horn[c,d][e] of Israel.
He has withdrawn his right hand[f]
at the approach of the enemy.
He has burned in Jacob like a flaming fire
that consumes everything around it.[g]

4 Like an enemy he has strung his bow;[h]
his right hand is ready.
Like a foe he has slain
all who were pleasing to the eye;[i]
he has poured out his wrath[j] like fire[k]
on the tent[l] of Daughter Zion.

5 The Lord is like an enemy;[m]
he has swallowed up Israel.
He has swallowed up all her palaces
and destroyed her strongholds.[n]
He has multiplied mourning and lamentation[o]
for Daughter Judah.[p]

6 He has laid waste his dwelling like a garden;
he has destroyed[q] his place of meeting.[r]
The LORD has made Zion forget
her appointed festivals and her Sabbaths;[s]
in his fierce anger he has spurned
both king and priest.[t]

7 The Lord has rejected his altar
and abandoned his sanctuary.[u]
He has given the walls of her palaces[v]
into the hands of the enemy;
they have raised a shout in the house of the LORD
as on the day of an appointed festival.[w]

8 The LORD determined to tear down
the wall around Daughter Zion.[x]
He stretched out a measuring line[y]
and did not withhold his hand from destroying.
He made ramparts[z] and walls lament;
together they wasted away.[a]

9 Her gates[b] have sunk into the ground;
their bars[c] he has broken and destroyed.

1:22 [v] Ne 4:5 [w] S ver 8; S Ps 6:6 **2:1** [x] La 3:44 [y] Ps 99:5; 132:7 [z] S Jer 12:7 **2:2** [a] ver 17; La 3:43 [b] Ps 21:9 [c] Ps 89:39-40; Mic 5:11 [d] S Isa 25:12 **2:3** [e] Ps 75:5, 10 [f] Ps 74:11 [g] S Isa 42:25; Jer 21:4-5, 14 **2:4** [h] S Job 3:23; 16:13; La 3:12-13 [i] S Ps 48:2; Eze 24:16, 25 [j] S 2Ch 34:21; Eze 20:34 [k] Isa 42:25; S Jer 7:20 [l] S Jer 4:20 **2:5** [m] S Job 13:24 [n] ver 2 [o] S Isa 29:2 [p] S Jer 7:20; 9:17-20 **2:6** [q] 2Ch 36:19 [r] S Jer 52:13 [s] Zep 3:18 [t] Isa 43:28; S Jer 7:14; La 4:16; 5:12 **2:7** [u] S Lev 26:31; S Eze 7:24 [v] Ps 74:7-8; S Isa 64:11; Jer 33:4-5; Eze 7:21-22 [w] Jer 21:4; 52:13 **2:8** [x] ver 18 [y] S 2Ki 21:13 [z] S Ps 48:13 [a] Isa 3:26; S Jer 39:8; S 52:14 **2:9** [b] S Ne 1:3 [c] S Isa 45:2; Hos 11:6

[a] This chapter is an acrostic poem, the verses of which begin with the successive letters of the Hebrew alphabet. [b] *1* Or *How the Lord in his anger / has treated Daughter Zion with contempt* [c] *3* Or *off / all the strength*; or *every king* [d] *3* *Horn* here symbolizes strength.

1:22 *wickedness … before you.* See Ps 109:14–15. *my heart is faint.* The same expression is found in Jer 8:18; see La 5:17; Isa 1:5.

2:1–22 Jerusalem is again personified as a woman—and represents the nation (see note on 1:1–22). In vv. 1–10 Jerusalem's experience of God's wrath is described by a voice that speaks of her in the third person. In vv. 12–19 Jerusalem is directly addressed (second-person pronouns abound). At the center (vv. 11–12) the author begins to speak in the first person (see note on 1:1–11). The first-person voice of vv. 20–22 is that of Jerusalem.

2:1 *How … !* See note on 1:1. *Daughter Zion.* A personification of Jerusalem (see the same or similar idiom in vv. 2,4–5, 8,10,13,15,18; see also note on 2Ki 19:21). *hurled down the splendor of Israel.* The imagery is that of a falling star (as in Isa 14:12). *footstool.* Either (1) the ark of the covenant (see 1Ch 28:2) or, more likely, (2) Mount Zion (see Ps 99:5 and note).

2:2 *swallowed up all the dwellings.* See v. 5. *Daughter Judah.* See note on v. 1.

2:3 *cut off every horn.* See NIV text note. *flaming fire that consumes.* See 1:13 and note.

2:4 *strung his bow.* See 3:12; Dt 32:42; Ps 7:12–13; Hab 3:9. *poured out.* Widely used imagery in the OT for the display of God's wrath (see Ps 69:24; 79:6; Jer 6:11; 7:20; 10:25; 42:18; 44:6; Hos 5:10; Zep 3:8). *Daughter Zion.* See note on v. 1.

2:5 *palaces … strongholds.* See Hos 8:14. *multiplied mourning and lamentation.* The Sumerian "Lamentation over the Destruction of Sumer and Ur" offers this parallel: "In the desolate city there was uttered nothing but laments and dirges" (lines 361–362, 486–487). *Daughter Judah.* See note on v. 1. See photos, p. 1321.

2:6 *his dwelling … his place of meeting.* The temple in Jerusalem (see 1Ki 8:29; 9:3; 2Ch 6:2; 7:1–3; Ps 27:7–10 and note; 132:8,13–14). *like a garden.* Cf. Isa 5:5–6; Jer 5:10; 12:10.

2:7 *rejected … abandoned.* These two verbs are found in Ps 89:38–39 ("rejected … renounced") in connection with the Lord's forsaking of the king from the dynasty of David. *raised a shout in the house of the LORD.* See Ps 74:4. *as on the day of an appointed festival.* See Ps 42:4; 47:5; 81:1–4. But there is bitter irony in the fact that the triumphant shouts of the enemy have silenced the joyful shouts of those who had worshiped at the temple.

2:8 *determined to tear down.* See Jer 1:15; 32:31. *Daughter Zion.* See note on v. 1. *stretched out a measuring line.* To destroy with the same standards of precision used in building (see Isa 28:17; Am 7:7–8 and notes). *ramparts … walls.* Cf. Isa 26:1. The ramparts were the outer fortifications (see 2Sa 20:15).

2:9 *the law is no more.* There are no longer any priests (see v. 20) to teach and interpret the covenant law (see Jer 18:18; Hos 4:4–9 and notes). *prophets no longer find*

Her king and her princes are exiled[d]
    among the nations,
  the law[e] is no more,
and her prophets[f] no longer find
  visions[g] from the LORD.

10 The elders of Daughter Zion
  sit on the ground in silence;[h]
they have sprinkled dust[i] on their heads[j]
  and put on sackcloth.[k]
The young women of Jerusalem
  have bowed their heads to the
    ground.[l]

11 My eyes fail from weeping,[m]
  I am in torment within[n];
my heart[o] is poured out[p] on the ground
  because my people are destroyed,[q]
because children and infants faint[r]
  in the streets of the city.

12 They say to their mothers,
  "Where is bread and wine?"[s]
as they faint like the wounded
  in the streets of the city,
as their lives ebb away[t]
  in their mothers' arms.[u]

13 What can I say for you?[v]
  With what can I compare you,
  Daughter[w] Jerusalem?
To what can I liken you,
  that I may comfort you,
  Virgin Daughter Zion?[x]
Your wound is as deep as the sea.[y]
  Who can heal you?

14 The visions of your prophets
  were false[z] and worthless;
they did not expose your sin
  to ward off your captivity.[a]
The prophecies they gave you
  were false and misleading.[b]

15 All who pass your way
  clap their hands at you;[c]
they scoff[d] and shake their heads[e]
  at Daughter Jerusalem:[f]
"Is this the city that was called
  the perfection of beauty,[g]
  the joy of the whole earth?"[h]

16 All your enemies open their mouths
  wide against you;[i]
they scoff and gnash their teeth[j]
  and say, "We have swallowed her up.[k]
This is the day we have waited for;
  we have lived to see it."[l]

17 The LORD has done what he planned;
  he has fulfilled[m] his word,
  which he decreed long ago.[n]
He has overthrown you without pity,[o]
  he has let the enemy gloat over you,[p]
  he has exalted the horn[a] of your foes.[q]

18 The hearts of the people
  cry out to the Lord.[r]
You walls of Daughter Zion,[s]
  let your tears[t] flow like a river
  day and night;[u]
give yourself no relief,
  your eyes no rest.[v]

19 Arise, cry out in the night,
  as the watches of the night begin;
pour out your heart[w] like water
  in the presence of the Lord.[x]
Lift up your hands[y] to him
  for the lives of your children,
who faint[z] from hunger
  at every street corner.

[a] *17 Horn* here symbolizes strength.

2:9 [d] Dt 28:36; S 2Ki 24:15; Jer 16:13; Hos 3:4 [e] S 2Ch 15:3 [f] S 1Sa 3:1 [g] S Jer 14:14 **2:10** [h] La 3:28 [i] S Jos 7:6 [j] Job 2:12 [k] S Isa 3:24 [l] S Job 2:13; S Isa 3:26; Eze 27:30-31 **2:11** [m] S Ps 119:82; S Isa 15:3; S La 1:16; 3:48-51 [n] S Job 30:27; La 1:20 [o] S Isa 1:5 [p] ver 19; Ps 22:14 [q] S Jer 9:1 [r] La 4:4 **2:12** [s] Isa 24:11 [t] S Job 3:24 [u] La 4:4 **2:13** [v] S Isa 1:6 [w] S 2Ki 19:21 [x] Isa 37:22 [y] Jer 14:17; 30:12-15; La 1:12 **2:14** [z] S Jer 28:15 [a] Jer 8:11 [b] Jer 2:8; S 20:6; 23:25-32, 33-40; S 29:9; Eze 13:3; 22:28 **2:15** [c] S Nu 24:10; Eze 25:6 [d] S Dt 28:37; S Isa 28:22; Jer 19:8; S Na 3:19 [e] S Job 16:4 [f] S La 1:21 [g] Ps 45:11; S 48:2; 50:2; Eze 16:14 [h] Ps 48:2 **2:16** [i] Ps 22:13; La 3:46 [j] S Job 16:9 [k] S Ps 35:25 [l] Eze 36:3; Mic 4:11 **2:17** [m] S Jer 39:16 [n] Dt 28:15-45 [o] S ver 2; Eze 5:11; 7:9; 8:18 [p] S Ps 22:17 [q] Ps 89:42; S Isa 44:26; S La 1:5; Zec 1:6 **2:18** [r] S Ps 119:145 [s] ver 8 [t] S La 1:16 [u] S Jer 9:1 [v] La 3:49 **2:19** [w] 1Sa 1:15 [x] S ver 11; Isa 26:9 [y] S Ps 28:2 [z] S Isa 51:20

visions. The Lord was no longer communicating to his people through prophets (see Ps 74:9; Am 8:11 and note; Mic 3:7).
2:10 *elders.* See note on Ex 3:16. *Daughter Zion.* See note on v. 1. *sit on the ground in silence … sprinkled dust on their heads and put on sackcloth … bowed their heads.* Signs of mourning (see Job 2:12–13; Ps 35:13–14). *young women of Jerusalem.* See 1:4 and note.
2:11 *My … I … my … my.* See note on vv. 1–22. Presumably the speaker is the same as that heard in vv. 1–10 and in 1:1–11 (see note there). He begins at this point with an expression of deep personal grief over Jerusalem's condition, especially that of her little ones (vv. 11–12), and then addresses Jerusalem directly (vv. 13–19). *weeping.* See note on 1:16. *I am in torment within.* Repeated from 1:20. *my people.* Lit. "the daughter of my people" (see note on v. 1). This particular phrase occurs also in 3:48; 4:3,6,10; Isa 22:4; Jer 8:11,21; cf. Jer 14:17.
2:13 *What can I say for you?* The author has no words that can bring comfort to suffering Jerusalem. *Daughter Jerusalem … Virgin Daughter Zion.* See note on v. 1.
2:14 *prophets … false.* Jeremiah often denounced the false prophets (see Jer 5:12–13; 6:13–14; 8:10–11; 14:13–15; 23:9–40; 27:9—28:17; cf. Jer 26:7–11,16; Eze 22:26, 28). *worthless.* Or "mere whitewash"; for an explanation of this image, see Eze 13:10–16; 22:28. *misleading.* The unusual Hebrew word underlying this word comes from the same root as that underlying "banish" in Jer 27:10,15: The lies of false prophets "mislead" the people and thus lead to "banishment" by the Lord—so they are "banishing" in their effect.
2:15 *who pass your way.* See 1:12. *clap their hands.* See Job 27:23; 34:37. *scoff.* See v. 16; see also note on Jer 19:8. *shake their heads.* See Job 16:4 and note; Ps 44:14; 64:8; 109:25; Jer 18:16. *Daughter Jerusalem.* See note on v. 1. *was called the perfection of beauty.* As in Ps 50:2 (see note there). *was called … the joy of the whole earth.* As in Ps 48:2 (see note there; cf. Jer 51:41).
2:16 *open their mouths wide.* To taunt or to devour (see Nu 16:30; Ps 22:13; Isa 5:14; 9:12). *swallowed her up.* See vv. 2,5; Jer 51:34.
2:17 *fulfilled his word.* See Isa 55:11 and note. *long ago.* The days of Moses (see, e.g., the threats of Lev 26:23–39; Dt 28:15–68). *exalted the horn.* Increased the strength (see NIV text note; see also 1Sa 2:1; Ps 75:4).
2:18 See Jer 14:17. *You walls.* A city gate is similarly addressed in Isa 14:31. *Daughter Zion.* See note on v. 1.
2:19 *watches of the night begin.* See note on Jdg 7:19; see also Ps 63:6. *pour out your heart.* In earnest prayer (see Ps 62:8).

20 "Look, LORD, and consider:
Whom have you ever treated like this?
Should women eat their offspring,[a]
the children they have cared for?[b]
Should priest and prophet be killed[c]
in the sanctuary of the Lord?[d]

21 "Young and old lie together
in the dust of the streets;
my young men and young women
have fallen by the sword.[e]
You have slain them in the day of your anger;
you have slaughtered them without pity.[f]

22 "As you summon to a feast day,
so you summoned against me
terrors[g] on every side.
In the day of the LORD's anger
no one escaped[h] or survived;
those I cared for and reared[i]
my enemy has destroyed."

3 [a] I am the man who has seen affliction[j]
by the rod of the LORD's wrath.[k]
2 He has driven me away and made me walk
in darkness[l] rather than light;
3 indeed, he has turned his hand against me[m]
again and again, all day long.

4 He has made my skin and my flesh grow old[n]
and has broken my bones.[o]
5 He has besieged me and surrounded me
with bitterness[p] and hardship.[q]
6 He has made me dwell in darkness
like those long dead.[r]

7 He has walled me in so I cannot escape;[s]
he has weighed me down with chains.[t]
8 Even when I call out or cry for help,[u]
he shuts out my prayer.[v]
9 He has barred[w] my way with blocks of stone;
he has made my paths crooked.[x]

10 Like a bear lying in wait,
like a lion[y] in hiding,[z]
11 he dragged me from the path and mangled[a] me
and left me without help.
12 He drew his bow[b]
and made me the target[c] for his arrows.[d]

13 He pierced[e] my heart
with arrows from his quiver.[f]
14 I became the laughingstock[g] of all my people;[h]
they mock me in song[i] all day long.

2:20 [a] S Dt 28:53; Jer 19:9; Eze 5:10 [b] La 4:10 [c] Ps 78:64; S Jer 14:15; 23:11-12 [d] S La 1:19 **2:21** [e] S Dt 32:25; S 2Ch 36:17; Ps 78:62-63; Jer 6:11 [f] S Jer 13:14; La 3:43; Zec 11:6 **2:22** [g] S Ps 31:13; S Jer 20:10 [h] S Jer 11:11 [i] Job 27:14; Hos 9:13 **3:1** [j] Jer 15:17-18 [k] S Job 19:21; Ps 88:7 **3:2** [l] S Job 19:8; S Ps 82:5; S Jer 4:23 **3:3** [m] Ps 38:2; Isa 5:25 **3:4** [n] S Job 30:30; La 4:8 [o] Ps 51:8; S Isa 38:13; S Jer 50:17 **3:5** [p] ver 19 [q] Jer 23:15 **3:6** [r] Ps 88:5-6; 143:3; Isa 59:10 **3:7** [s] S Job 3:23 [t] Jer 40:4 **3:8** [u] Ps 5:2 [v] ver 44; S Dt 1:45; S Job 30:20; Ps 22:2 **3:9** [w] S Job 19:8 [x] S Job 9:24; S Isa 63:17; Hos 2:6

[a] This chapter is an acrostic poem; the verses of each stanza begin with the successive letters of the Hebrew alphabet, and the verses within each stanza begin with the same letter.

3:10 [y] S Job 10:16 [z] Hos 13:8; Am 5:18-19 **3:11** [a] Hos 6:1 **3:12** [b] S La 2:4 [c] Job 7:20 [d] S Job 16:12; Ps 7:12-13; 38:2 **3:13** [e] S Job 16:13 [f] Job 6:4 **3:14** [g] S Ge 38:23; Ps 22:6-7; Jer 20:7 [h] S Job 17:2 [i] S Job 30:9

like water. A common simile with "pour out" (see Dt 12:16,24; 15:23; Ps 79:3; Hos 5:10). *Lift up your hands.* In prayer (see Ps 28:2 and note; 1Ti 2:8). *children, who faint from hunger.* See vv. 11–12.
2:20–22 Jerusalem's heartbroken prayer in response to v. 19.
2:20 *women eat their offspring.* See 4:10; Jer 19:9 and note.
2:21 See Jer 6:11 and note.
2:22 *summon to a feast day.* The same Lord who had called Israel to come to him in worship and to celebrate his saving acts in her history (see, e.g., Ps 81; 95; 114) now issues a quite different summons. *summoned against me.* See 1:15. *terrors on every side.* See note on Jer 6:25. *day of the LORD's anger.* The lament ends as it began (see v. 1). *no one escaped or survived.* See Jer 42:17; 44:14. *those I cared for.* Jerusalem's inhabitants.
3:1–66 This lament at the center of the book stands apart in significant ways. As to form: Like chs. 1 and 2, it is an alphabetic acrostic and is made up of 22 three-line units, but here each line of each unit begins with the same letter (see Introduction: Literary Features; see also diagram, p. 1330). That probably accounts for why in this lament each poetic line, rather than each stanza, has traditionally been set off as a grammatical unit and assigned a separate verse number. As to content: It begins (vv. 1–39) like the prayers of individuals found in the Psalter (which it extensively echoes) without any clear reference to the destruction of Jerusalem and the exile of the nation. This extended introduction may have been intended to put the communal lament that follows (vv. 40–66; see note on vv. 48–66) in a context that models how the community should react to its present distress.
3:1 The exact center of the book. The speaker identifies himself as one who exemplifies those who have suffered much under the rod of God's wrath. *affliction.* See v. 19. *rod of the LORD's wrath.* See Job 9:34; 21:9; cf. Isa 10:5 and note.
3:2 *darkness rather than light.* See Job 12:25; Ps 143:3; Isa 50:10; 59:9; cf. Am 5:18 and note.
3:4 *grow old.* See Ps 32:3 ("wasted away"); Ps 49:14 ("decay"). *broken my bones.* See Ps 51:8; Isa 38:13 and note.
3:5 *surrounded me.* See Job 19:6. *bitterness.* Lit. "poison" (see Jer 8:14 and note). *hardship.* See Ex 18:8; Nu 20:14; Ne 9:32.
3:6 See Ps 143:3 and note.
3:7 *walled.* The Hebrew for this word is the same as that for "barred" in v. 9 (see Job 19:8; Hos 2:6). *cannot escape.* See Ps 88:8.
3:8 *shuts out my prayer.* See v. 44; Job 30:20; Ps 18:41; 22:2; Pr 1:28; Jer 7:16 and note.
3:9 *blocks of stone.* Of enormous size, like those used in the foundation of Solomon's temple (see 1Ki 5:17). *made … crooked.* Rather than level (see Isa 26:7; 45:2; Jer 31:9 and note) or straight (see Ps 5:8; Pr 3:6 and notes; 11:5; Isa 45:13).
3:10 *Like a bear … like a lion.* See Jer 4:7; 5:6; 49:19; 50:44; Am 1:2 and note; 5:19; cf. Ps 7:2 and note.
3:11 See 1:2.
3:12 *drew his bow.* See note on 2:4. *made me the target.* See note on Job 6:4.
3:13 *heart.* Lit. "kidneys" (as in Job 16:13). *with arrows.* See Ps 38:2 and note.
3:14 See Jeremiah's complaint in Jer 20:7. *mock me in song.* See v. 63; Ps 69:12; see also Ps 22:6–7; cf. Isa 28:9–10 and note.

15 He has filled me with bitter herbs
and given me gall to drink.[j]
16 He has broken my teeth with
gravel;[k]
he has trampled me in the dust.[l]
17 I have been deprived of peace;
I have forgotten what prosperity is.
18 So I say, "My splendor is gone
and all that I had hoped from the
LORD."[m]

19 I remember my affliction and my
wandering,
the bitterness[n] and the gall.[o]
20 I well remember them,
and my soul is downcast[p] within
me.[q]
21 Yet this I call to mind
and therefore I have hope:

22 Because of the LORD's great love[r] we
are not consumed,[s]
for his compassions never fail.[t]
23 They are new every morning;
great is your faithfulness.[u]
24 I say to myself, "The LORD is my
portion;[v]
therefore I will wait for him."

25 The LORD is good to those whose hope
is in him,
to the one who seeks him;[w]
26 it is good to wait quietly[x]
for the salvation of the LORD.[y]
27 It is good for a man to bear the yoke
while he is young.

28 Let him sit alone in silence,[z]
for the LORD has laid it on him.
29 Let him bury his face in the dust[a] —
there may yet be hope.[b]
30 Let him offer his cheek to one who
would strike him,[c]
and let him be filled with disgrace.[d]

31 For no one is cast off
by the Lord forever.[e]
32 Though he brings grief, he will show
compassion,
so great is his unfailing love.[f]
33 For he does not willingly bring
affliction
or grief to anyone.[g]

34 To crush underfoot
all prisoners in the land,
35 to deny people their rights
before the Most High,[h]
36 to deprive them of justice —
would not the Lord see such things?[i]

37 Who can speak and have it happen
if the Lord has not decreed it?[j]

3:15 [j] ver 19; Jer 9:15 **3:16** [k] S Pr 20:17 [l] S Ps 7:5 **3:18** [m] S ver 54; S Job 17:15 **3:19** [n] ver 5 [o] S ver 15 **3:20** [p] S Ps 42:5 [q] Ps 42:11; 43:5 **3:22** [r] S Ps 103:11 [s] S Job 34:15; S Hos 11:9 [t] Ps 78:38; 130:7 **3:23** [u] S Ex 34:6; Zep 3:5 **3:24** [v] S Ps 119:57 **3:25** [w] S Ps 33:18; Isa 25:9; S 30:18 **3:26** [x] S Isa 7:4 [y] Ps 37:7; 40:1 **3:28** [z] Jer 15:17; La 2:10 **3:29** [a] S Job 2:8 [b] S Jer 31:17 **3:30** [c] S Job 16:10; S Isa 50:6 [d] Mic 5:1 **3:31** [e] Ps 94:14; Isa 54:7 **3:32** [f] Ps 78:38; 106:43-45; Hos 11:8; Na 1:12 **3:33** [g] S Job 37:23; S Jer 31:20; Eze 18:23; 33:11 **3:35** [h] Ge 14:18,19,20,22 **3:36** [i] Ps 140:12; S Pr 17:15; S Jer 22:3; Hab 1:13 **3:37** [j] Ps 33:9-11; S Pr 19:21; S 21:30

3:15 *filled me with bitter herbs.* The Hebrew underlying this phrase is translated "overwhelm me with misery" in Job 9:18 (see note on Jer 9:15). For the significance of the bitter herbs eaten during the Passover meal, see note on Ex 12:8.
3:16 *broken my teeth with gravel.* Cf. Ps 72:9; Mic 7:17. *trampled me in the dust.* See Ps 7:5.
3:18 *all that I had hoped from the LORD.* See Ps 39:7; the first explicit mention of God in ch. 3.
3:19–20 The author again recalls all his troubles but now in preparation for his words of hope and encouragement in vv. 21–39.
3:19 *affliction and … wandering.* See 1:7. *the bitterness and the gall.* See vv. 5,15; cf. Jer 9:15.
3:21–26 The theological — and spiritual — high point of the book of Lamentations (see Introduction: Themes and Theology).
3:22 *great love.* See v. 32. The Hebrew for this phrase is plural (as also in Ps 107:43) and denotes the Lord's loving faithfulness to his covenant promises (see Ps 89:1). See note on Ps 6:4; see also Isa 63:7 ("kindnesses") and note. *we.* The Lord's people.
3:23 *They.* The "great love" and "compassions" (v. 22) of the Lord. *new every morning.* See Ps 30:5 and note; Isa 33:2. *great is your faithfulness.* It is beyond measure (see note on v. 32; see also Ps 36:5 and note).
3:24 *The LORD is my portion.* See Ps 73:26; 142:5 and notes. He was the inheritance share of the priests and Levites (see Nu 18:20; see also note on Ge 15:1). *therefore I will wait.* See Ps 27:14; 71:14 and notes. The Hebrew for this phrase is the same as that for "therefore I have hope" in v. 21 and serves as a refrain.
3:25 *The LORD is good.* See Ps 34:8 and note on 34:8–14; 86:5. *whose hope is in him.* See Ps 25:3; 33:18; 37:9 and note.
3:26 See Ps 40:1; Isa 26:3; 30:15.
3:27 *It is good.* See Pr 3:11–12 and note. *a man to bear the yoke.* Echoes the thought of v. 1: "the man who has seen affliction." *while … young.* Cf. Ecc 12:1.
3:28 *sit alone.* Patiently suffering the mockery of his enemies (see v. 30). *in silence.* See v. 39; Ps 39:9. *it.* The yoke (see v. 27).
3:29 *bury his face in the dust.* Showing humble submission to God. *there may yet be hope.* See 2Sa 12:22; Job 2:14; Am 5:15; Jnh 3:9.
3:30 *offer his cheek.* See Mt 5:39. *filled with disgrace.* See Ps 123:3–4.
3:31 *no one is cast off … forever.* See Isa 49:14–16; cf. note on Jer 3:5; cf. also Ro 11:11–32 and notes.
3:32 The same God who judges also restores (see Ps 30:5; Isa 54:7–8). *great is his unfailing love.* See note on v. 22; see also "great is your faithfulness" (v. 23) — faithfulness and unfailing love are often used together to sum up God's covenant mercies toward his people (see Ps 25:10; 26:3 and notes).
3:33 *does not willingly bring affliction.* See Eze 18:23,32; Hos 11:8; 2Pe 3:9.
3:34 *crush underfoot.* As the Babylonians had done in 586 BC.
3:35 *deny … rights.* As the leaders of Judah had done, in direct violation of the law (see Ex 23:6). *before the Most High.* In the presence of those whom the Most High designates to dispense justice (see Ex 22:8–9 and NIV text notes; see also introduction to Ps 82). *Most High.* See note on Ge 14:19.
3:36 *deprive … of justice.* People might, but God never does (see Job 8:3; 34:12). *the Lord see such things.* Contrary to what the wicked think (see Ps 10:11 and note), the Lord does see and will call to account (see Psalm 10:13–15).
3:37 *speak and have it happen.* No one is equal to God (see Ge 1:3 and note; Ps 33:9–11 and note on 33:4–11); so no one can override the Lord's governing authority (cf. Job 1:12; 2:6 and notes).

38 Is it not from the mouth of the Most
High
that both calamities and good things
come?[k]
39 Why should the living complain
when punished for their sins?[l]

40 Let us examine our ways and test
them,[m]
and let us return to the LORD.[n]
41 Let us lift up our hearts and our hands
to God in heaven,[o] and say:
42 "We have sinned and rebelled[p]
and you have not forgiven.[q]

43 "You have covered yourself with anger
and pursued[r] us;
you have slain without pity.[s]
44 You have covered yourself with a
cloud[t]
so that no prayer[u] can get through.[v]
45 You have made us scum[w] and refuse
among the nations.

46 "All our enemies have opened their
mouths
wide[x] against us.[y]
47 We have suffered terror and pitfalls,[z]
ruin and destruction.[a]"
48 Streams of tears[b] flow from my eyes[c]
because my people are destroyed.[d]

49 My eyes will flow unceasingly,
without relief,[e]
50 until the LORD looks down
from heaven and sees.[f]
51 What I see brings grief to my soul
because of all the women of my
city.

52 Those who were my enemies without
cause
hunted me like a bird.[g]
53 They tried to end my life in a pit[h]
and threw stones at me;
54 the waters closed over my head,[i]
and I thought I was about to perish.[j]

55 I called on your name, LORD,
from the depths[k] of the pit.[l]
56 You heard my plea:[m] "Do not close
your ears
to my cry for relief."

3:38 [k] S Job 2:10; S Isa 45:7; Jer 32:42 **3:39** [l] S Jer 30:15; Mic 7:9 **3:40** [m] 2Co 13:5 [n] Ps 119:59; 139:23-24 **3:41** [o] S Ps 25:1; S 28:2 **3:42** [p] Jer 14:20; Da 9:5 [q] S 2Ki 24:4; Jer 5:7-9 **3:43** [r] ver 66; Ps 35:6 [s] S La 2:2, 17, 21 **3:44** [t] Ps 97:2; La 2:1 [u] S ver 8; Zec 7:13 [v] S Isa 58:4 **3:45** [w] 1Co 4:13 **3:46** [x] Ps 22:13 [y] La 2:16 **3:47** [z] Jer 48:43 [a] S Isa 24:17-18; S 51:19 **3:48** [b] S Ps 119:136 [c] S Jer 9:1, 18; La 1:16 [d] La 2:11 **3:49** [e] Jer 14:17; S La 2:18 **3:50** [f] S Ps 14:2; 80:14; S Isa 63:15 **3:52** [g] Ps 35:7 **3:53** [h] Jer 37:16; S 38:6 **3:54** [i] Ps 69:2; Jnh 2:3-5 [j] ver 18; Ps 88:5; Eze 37:11 **3:55** [k] S Ps 88:6 [l] Ps 130:1; Jnh 2:2 **3:56** [m] S Ps 55:1; 116:1-2

LAMENTATIONS AND ACROSTICS

Lamentations 1 – 4 is a series of alphabetic acrostics. Each verse in chapters 1, 2 and 4 begins with the next letter of the 22-letter Hebrew alphabet. In Lamentations 3 each of the three lines of the first stanza begins with the first letter of the alphabet, and so on for 22 stanzas, thus comprised of 66 verses. Note, e.g., this attempt to put Lamentations 3:1 – 9 into English:

Ah, what straits have I not known, under
the avenging rod!
Asked I for light, into deeper shadow the
Lord's guidance led me;
Always upon me, none other, falls
endlessly the blow.
Broken this frame, under the wrinkled
skin, the sunk flesh.
Bitterness of despair fills my prospect,
walled in on every side.
Buried in darkness, and, like the dead,
interminably.
Closely he fenced me in, beyond hope of
rescue; loads me with fetters.
Cry out for mercy as I will, prayer of mine
wins no audience;
Climb these smooth walls I may not;
every way of escape he has undone.

Adapted from *Zondervan Illustrated Bible Backgrounds Commentary: OT: Vol. 4* by JOHN H. WALTON. Lamentations — Copyright © 2009 by Paul W. Ferris Jr., p. 377. Used by permission of Zondervan.

3:38 See Job 2:10; Pr 3:11 – 12; Isa 45:7; Am 3:3 – 6 and notes; see also Jer 32:42.
3:39 *complain.* See v. 28 and note.
3:40 – 41 Here the voice of the community breaks in, responding to the model set before them in vv. 1 – 39 (see note on v. 1). Appropriately, the community begins with a confession of sin (see 1:8 and note; see also Ps 32:3 – 5; 39:7 – 10; 40:11 – 12; 41:4).
3:40 *let us return to the LORD.* See Hos 6:1; cf. Jer 3:1; 4:1; Hos 14:1; Joel 2:12 – 13; Zec 1:3.
3:41 *lift up . . . hands.* See note on 2:19. *heaven.* Where God is enthroned (see Ps 2:4; Isa 63:15; 66:1).
3:42 *We have sinned and rebelled.* For similar confessions, see Ps 106:6; Da 9:5.
3:43 *covered yourself with anger.* Cf. Isa 59:17 – 18. *pursued us . . . slain without pity.* See v. 66; 2:21; Jer 29:18.
3:46 See 2:16 and note.
3:48 – 66 The voice returns to first-person singular. It could be the same voice as that heard in vv. 1 – 39, but more likely the community now speaks in first-person singular (see, e.g., Ps 44:1,4 and note on 44:4). To its prayer the community adds expressions of assurance of being heard and a call for redress against the enemies who have attacked them "without cause" (v. 52) — both of which are common elements in the prayers of individuals in the Psalter (cf. Ps 5:10; Ps 54 and notes).
3:48 *tears flow from my eyes.* See note on 1:16. *my people.* Lit. "the daughter of my people" (see note on 2:11).
3:50 *looks down . . . sees.* See 5:1; Ps 80:14; Isa 63:15.
3:51 *women of my city.* See 1:4,18; 2:20 – 21; 5:11.
3:52 *enemies without cause.* See note on Ps 35:19. *like a bird.* See Ps 124:7.
3:53 *end my life in a pit.* See Ps 35:7. *threw stones at.* See 2Sa 16:6; 1Ki 12:18.
3:54 *waters closed over my head.* See Ps 32:6; 42:7; 69:1 – 2 and notes; Jnh 2:5. *perish.* Cf. Ps 18:4 – 5; 30:3 and notes; Isa 53:8; Jnh 2:2 and note.
3:55 *from the depths of the pit.* See Ps 30:1 and note.
3:56 *cry for relief.* See Job 32:20; Ps 118:5.

57 You came near[n] when I called you,
and you said, "Do not fear."[o]
58 You, Lord, took up my case;[p]
you redeemed my life.[q]
59 LORD, you have seen the wrong done
to me.[r]
Uphold my cause![s]
60 You have seen the depth of their
vengeance,
all their plots against me.[t]

61 LORD, you have heard their insults,[u]
all their plots against me—
62 what my enemies whisper and
mutter
against me all day long.[v]
63 Look at them! Sitting or standing,
they mock me in their songs.[w]

64 Pay them back what they deserve,
LORD,
for what their hands have done.[x]
65 Put a veil over their hearts,[y]
and may your curse be on them!
66 Pursue[z] them in anger and destroy
them
from under the heavens of the LORD.

4 [a] How the gold has lost its luster,
the fine gold become dull!
The sacred gems are scattered
at every street corner.[a]

2 How the precious children of Zion,[b]
once worth their weight in gold,
are now considered as pots of clay,
the work of a potter's hands!

3 Even jackals offer their breasts
to nurse their young,
but my people have become heartless
like ostriches in the desert.[c]

4 Because of thirst[d] the infant's tongue
sticks to the roof of its mouth;[e]
the children beg for bread,
but no one gives it to them.[f]

5 Those who once ate delicacies
are destitute in the streets.
Those brought up in royal purple[g]
now lie on ash heaps.[h]

6 The punishment of my people
is greater than that of Sodom,[i]
which was overthrown in a moment
without a hand turned to help her.

7 Their princes were brighter than snow
and whiter than milk,
their bodies more ruddy than rubies,
their appearance like lapis lazuli.

8 But now they are blacker[j] than soot;
they are not recognized in the
streets.
Their skin has shriveled on their
bones;[k]
it has become as dry as a stick.

9 Those killed by the sword are better off
than those who die of famine;[l]
racked with hunger, they waste away
for lack of food from the field.[m]

10 With their own hands compassionate
women
have cooked their own children,[n]
who became their food
when my people were destroyed.

[a] This chapter is an acrostic poem, the verses of which begin with the successive letters of the Hebrew alphabet.

3:57 [n]S Ps 46:1 [o]Isa 41:10
3:58 [p]S Jer 51:36 [q]Ps 34:22; S Jer 50:34
3:59 [r]Jer 18:19-20 [s]Ps 35:23; 43:1
3:60 [t]S Jer 11:20; 18:18
3:61 [u]Ps 89:50; Zep 2:8
3:62 [v]Eze 36:3
3:63 [w]S Job 30:9
3:64 [x]S Ps 28:4; S Jer 51:6
3:65 [y]Ex 14:8; Dt 2:30; Isa 6:10
3:66 [z]S ver 43
4:1 [a]Eze 7:19
4:2 [b]Isa 51:18
4:3 [c]S Job 39:16
4:4 [d]S Dt 28:48; S 2Ki 18:31 [e]S Ps 22:15 [f]La 2:11,12
4:5 [g]Jer 6:2 [h]S Isa 3:26; Am 6:3-7
4:6 [i]S Ge 19:25
4:8 [j]S Job 30:28 [k]Ps 102:3-5; S La 3:4
4:9 [l]S 2Ki 25:3 [m]S Jer 15:2; S 16:4; La 5:10
4:10 [n]S Lev 26:29; Dt 28:53-57; Jer 19:9; La 2:20; Eze 5:10

3:57 *near when I called.* See Ps 145:18. *Do not fear.* A frequent reassuring word from God (see Jer 1:8 and note).
3:58 *redeemed my life.* See Ps 25:22; 103:4 and notes.
3:59 *you have seen.* See Ps 10:14; 35:22. *Uphold my cause!* See Ps 35:23; 43:1; 119:154.
3:61 *you have heard.* The Lord has heard, as well as seen (vv. 59–60), what the enemies are doing.
3:62 *whisper … mutter.* See Ps 5:9 and note.
3:63 *Sitting or standing.* Engaging in any kind of activity (see Dt 6:7; 11:19; Ps 139:2; Isa 37:28). *mock me in their songs.* See note on v. 14.
3:64 Paralleled in Ps 28:4; see Ps 5:10 and note.
3:65 *Put a veil over their hearts.* So they cannot see the error of their ways or foresee the consequences. *may your curse be on them!* See Ps 109:16–20 and note.
3:66 *Pursue them.* Just as you have pursued us without pity because of our sins (v. 43), so now pursue them without pity for what they have done to us.
4:1–22 Another lamentation over the conquest of Jerusalem by the Babylonians—apparently by someone who had experienced the long siege of the city and the subsequent dispersion of its people. Verses 1–10 describe the terrible conditions of the siege, vv. 11–19 speak of the taking of the city and the fate of the refugees, v. 20 expresses the people's shock and dismay at the crushing of the Davidic king, and vv. 21–22 close the lament with words about the contrasting futures of exultant Edom and desolate Zion.
4:1 *How … !* See note on 1:1. *gold … gems.* Metaphors for God's chosen people (see v. 2). For similar imagery, see SS 5:11–12,14–15; Zec 9:16; cf. "The Babylonian Theodicy": "O … my precious brother, … jewel of gold" (lines 56–57; see chart, p. xxii). *at every street corner.* See 2:19; Isa 51:20.
4:3 *my people.* Lit. "the daughter of my people" (see note on 2:11). *become heartless.* See v. 10 and note. *like ostriches.* See Job 39:14–16.
4:5 *delicacies … purple.* See Ge 49:20. Purple was the color of royalty (see, e.g., Jdg 8:26; see also note on SS 7:5); cf. the expressions "born to the purple" and "royal blue." *lie on ash heaps.* See Job 2:8 and note; cf. Jer 6:26 and note.
4:6 *my people.* Lit. "the daughter of my people" (see note on 2:11). *Sodom.* See note on Jer 20:16. *overthrown in a moment.* And therefore spared the suffering of a lengthy siege (like that of Jerusalem).
4:7 *whiter … ruddy.* The Hebrew underlying these two words is translated "radiant … ruddy" in SS 5:10. *than rubies.* See Job 28:18. *lapis lazuli.* See SS 5:14; Isa 54:11 and notes.
4:8 *skin has shriveled on their bones.* See Job 19:20.
4:10 See 2:20; Jer 19:9 and note. *my people.* Lit. "the daughter of my people" (see note on 2:11).

11 The LORD has given full vent to his
wrath;[o]
he has poured out[p] his fierce anger.[q]
He kindled a fire[r] in Zion
that consumed her foundations.[s]

12 The kings of the earth did not believe,
nor did any of the peoples of the
world,
that enemies and foes could enter
the gates of Jerusalem.[t]

13 But it happened because of the sins of
her prophets
and the iniquities of her priests,[u]
who shed within her
the blood[v] of the righteous.

14 Now they grope through the streets
as if they were blind.[w]
They are so defiled with blood[x]
that no one dares to touch their
garments.

15 "Go away! You are unclean!" people
cry to them.
"Away! Away! Don't touch us!"
When they flee and wander[y] about,
people among the nations say,
"They can stay here no longer."[z]

16 The LORD himself has scattered them;
he no longer watches over them.[a]
The priests are shown no honor,
the elders[b] no favor.[c]

17 Moreover, our eyes failed,
looking in vain[d] for help;[e]
from our towers we watched
for a nation[f] that could not save us.

18 People stalked us at every step,
so we could not walk in our streets.
Our end was near, our days were
numbered,
for our end had come.[g]

19 Our pursuers were swifter
than eagles[h] in the sky;
they chased us[i] over the mountains
and lay in wait for us in the desert.[j]

20 The LORD's anointed,[k] our very life
breath,
was caught in their traps.[l]
We thought that under his shadow[m]
we would live among the nations.

21 Rejoice and be glad, Daughter Edom,
you who live in the land of Uz.[n]
But to you also the cup[o] will be passed;
you will be drunk and stripped
naked.[p]

22 Your punishment will end, Daughter
Zion;[q]
he will not prolong your exile.
But he will punish your sin, Daughter
Edom,
and expose your wickedness.[r]

5 Remember, LORD, what has happened
to us;
look, and see our disgrace.[s]
2 Our inheritance[t] has been turned over
to strangers,[u]
our homes[v] to foreigners.[w]

4:11 [o] S Job 20:23 [p] S 2Ch 34:21 [q] Na 1:6; Zep 2:2; 3:8 [r] Jer 17:27 [s] S Dt 32:22; S Jer 7:20; Eze 22:31 **4:12** [t] S 1Ki 9:9; S Jer 21:13 **4:13** [u] Jer 5:31; 6:13; Eze 22:28; Mic 3:11 [v] S 2Ki 21:16 **4:14** [w] S Isa 59:10 [x] Jer 19:4 **4:15** [y] S Jer 44:14 [z] Lev 13:46; Mic 2:10 **4:16** [a] Isa 9:14-16 [b] La 5:12 [c] S La 2:6 **4:17** [d] S Ge 15:18; S Isa 20:5; Eze 29:16 [e] S La 1:7 [f] Jer 37:7 **4:18** [g] Eze 7:2-12; Am 8:2 **4:19** [h] S Dt 28:49 [i] S Lev 26:36; Isa 5:26-28 [j] Jer 52:7 **4:20** [k] S 1Sa 26:9; 2Sa 19:21 [l] Jer 39:5; Eze 12:12-13; 19:4,8 [m] S Ps 91:1 **4:21** [n] S Ge 10:23 [o] S Ps 16:5; S Jer 25:15 [p] Isa 34:6-10; S 63:6; Eze 35:15; Am 1:11-12; Ob 1:16; Hab 2:16 **4:22** [q] Isa 40:2; Jer 33:8 [r] S Ps 137:7; Eze 25:12-14; Mal 1:4 **5:1** [s] Ps 44:13-16; 89:50 **5:2** [t] Ps 79:1 [u] S Ps 109:11 [v] Zep 1:13 [w] Jer 17:4

4:11 *fierce anger.* See 1:12 and note. *kindled a fire … consumed.* See Jer 17:27 and note.
4:12 *peoples.* Or "rulers" (parallel to "kings"); the Hebrew form underlying this word is translated "king" in Am 1:5,8.
4:13 See 2:14 and note; see also Eze 22:26,28.
4:14 *grope … as if they were blind.* See Dt 28:28 – 29; Isa 29:9 and note; 59:10 and note; Zep 1:17. *defiled with blood.* See Isa 59:3.
4:15 *unclean!* The cry of the person with a much dreaded skin disease (see Lev 13:45). *people … no longer.* Threatened in Dt 28:65 – 66.
4:16 As threatened in Dt 28:49 – 50.
4:17 *our eyes failed.* See Dt 28:28; Ps 69:3. *nation that could not save us.* For example, Egypt (see Eze 29:16).
4:19 *eagles.* See Jer 4:13; 48:40 and notes.
4:20 *The LORD's anointed.* King Zedekiah of the dynasty of David — under which the people of Judah felt secure because of God's covenant with David (see 2Sa 7; Ps 89; 132; Isa 55:3 and note). *our very life breath.* Lit. "the breath of our nostrils" (a title used also of Pharaoh Rameses II in an inscription found at Abydos in Egypt). *was caught.* See Jer 39:4 – 7; 52:7 – 11. *shadow.* Protection (see Jdg 9:15; Ps 17:8 and notes). This verse beautifully expresses the hope that came to be focused in the promised Messiah — the "Anointed One" from the house of David.
4:21 *Rejoice and be glad.* Irony — exult for the little time you have left before God's judgment sweeps over you (see v. 22). *Daughter Edom.* A personification of Edom (see note on 2Ki 19:21). *Edom.* Because of its close relationship with Israel from earliest times and its persistent hostility (see note on Ge 25:26), Edom often served OT writers as representative of all Israel's enemies (see Ps 137:7 and note; Isa 13:1 – 6 and note on 13:1; 34:5 and note; Jer 49:7 – 22 and note on 49:8; Am 9:12 and note; Introduction to Obadiah: Unity and Theme; Ob 8 and note). *land of Uz.* See Jer 25:20; see also note on Job 1:1. *cup.* See note on Jer 25:15. *stripped naked.* See 1:8; see also Jer 49:10; Na 3:5.
4:22 *Daughter Zion.* A personification of Jerusalem (see note on 2Ki 19:21). *will not prolong your exile.* See Jer 31 – 33. *expose your wickedness.* Contrast Ps 32:1; 85:2.
5:1 – 22 Although not an explicitly alphabetic acrostic like chs. 1 – 4, this lament is still controlled by the alphabet in that it is composed of just 22 poetic lines (see introduction to Ps 33). The first-person plural language identifies it as the voice of the community (like Ps 44; 60; 74; 80). The circumstances described suggest the time immediately after the fall of Jerusalem, when all was chaotic in the land (see v. 18; see also Jer 40:7 — 41:45). Some interpreters have suggested that the diminution of formal structure in this final lament may have been chosen to reflect the social disintegration brought on by the Babylonian destruction of the state of Judah.
5:1 *Remember … see.* Initial appeal to the Lord to give his full attention to the plight of his people (see Ps 44:13; 79:4).
5:2 *Our inheritance.* The land of Judah (see Jer 2:7 and note; 3:18).

3 We have become fatherless,
our mothers are widows.[x]
4 We must buy the water we drink;[y]
our wood can be had only at a price.[z]
5 Those who pursue us are at our heels;
we are weary[a] and find no rest.[b]
6 We submitted to Egypt and Assyria[c]
to get enough bread.
7 Our ancestors[d] sinned and are no more,
and we bear their punishment.[e]
8 Slaves[f] rule over us,
and there is no one to free us from
their hands.[g]
9 We get our bread at the risk of our lives
because of the sword in the desert.
10 Our skin is hot as an oven,
feverish from hunger.[h]
11 Women have been violated[i] in Zion,
and virgins in the towns of Judah.
12 Princes have been hung up by their
hands;
elders[j] are shown no respect.[k]
13 Young men toil at the millstones;
boys stagger under loads of wood.
14 The elders are gone from the city gate;
the young men have stopped their
music.[l]
15 Joy is gone from our hearts;
our dancing has turned to
mourning.[m]
16 The crown[n] has fallen from our
head.[o]
Woe to us, for we have sinned![p]
17 Because of this our hearts[q] are faint,[r]
because of these things our eyes[s]
grow dim[t]
18 for Mount Zion,[u] which lies desolate,[v]
with jackals prowling over it.

19 You, LORD, reign forever;[w]
your throne endures[x] from
generation to generation.
20 Why do you always forget us?[y]
Why do you forsake[z] us so long?
21 Restore[a] us to yourself, LORD, that we
may return;
renew our days as of old
22 unless you have utterly rejected us[b]
and are angry with us beyond
measure.[c]

5:3 [x]S Ex 22:24; Jer 15:8; S 18:21 **5:4** [y]S Isa 55:1; Eze 4:16-17 [z]Isa 3:1 **5:5** [a]S Ne 9:37; Isa 47:6 [b]S Jos 1:13 **5:6** [c]Jer 2:36; Hos 5:13; 7:11; 9:3 **5:7** [d]S Jer 31:29 [e]Jer 14:20; 16:12 **5:8** [f]Ne 5:15 [g]Zec 11:6 **5:10** [h]S Job 30:30; S La 4:8-9 **5:11** [i]S Ge 34:29; Zec 14:2 **5:12** [j]S Lev 19:32 [k]S La 2:6; 4:16 **5:14** [l]S Isa 24:8; Jer 7:34 **5:15** [m]S Jer 25:10; Am 8:10 **5:16** [n]Ps 89:39; S Jer 13:18 [o]S Job 19:9 [p]S Isa 3:11; Jer 14:20 **5:17** [q]S Isa 1:5 [r]S Jer 8:18 [s]S Ps 6:7 [t]S Job 16:8 **5:18** [u]Ps 74:2-3 [v]S Isa 27:10; Mic 3:12 **5:19** [w]S 1Ch 16:31 [x]S Ps 45:6; 102:12,24-27 **5:20** [y]S Ps 13:1; 44:24 [z]S Ps 71:11 **5:21** [a]S Ps 80:3; Isa 60:20-22 **5:22** [b]S Ps 53:5; 60:1-2; S Jer 6:30 [c]S Isa 64:9

5:3 *have become fatherless ... widows.* Are as helpless as these (see notes on Ex 22:21–27; Isa 1:17).
5:4 *We must buy the water ... wood.* Contrast Dt 29:11; Jos 9:21,23,27. *wood.* Firewood.
5:5 *find no rest.* The promised "rest" has been taken from them (see Dt 3:20 and note).
5:6 *submitted.* See 1Ch 29:24; 2Ch 30:8; Jer 50:15; lit. "gave the hand" (as in 2Ki 10:15; Ezr 10:19; Eze 17:18). *Egypt ... Assyria.* By this time a conventional way of referring to the great world powers to which the Israelites had often turned for protective alliances (see Isa 7:18; 11:16; 19:23–25; 52:4; Jer 2:18,36; see also Hos 7:11; 9:3; 11:5,11; 12:1 and notes; cf. Mic 7:12; Zec 10:10 and note).
5:7 Fathers and sons alike are responsible for the calamity that has befallen Jerusalem (see v. 16; Jer 3:25; 16:11–12; 31:29–30; Eze 18:2–4; cf. Isa 65:7).
5:8 *Slaves.* An ironic reference to the Babylonian officials who now rule over Jerusalem (formerly "queen among the provinces," 1:1); see Pr 30:21–22.
5:9 *sword in the desert.* Marauding bandits.
5:12 *hung.* An added indignity following execution (see notes on Dt 21:22–23).
5:13 *toil at the millstones.* Humiliating work (see note on Jdg 9:53; see also Isa 47:2).
5:14 *city gate.* The municipal court (see Jos 20:4), but also a gathering place for conversation and entertainment (cf. 1:4).
5:15 See Jer 7:34; 16:9; 25:10; contrast Ps 30:11; Jer 31:13.
5:16 *crown.* Symbolizes the glory and honor embodied in the city of Jerusalem (see 1:1; 2:15; cf. Isa 28:1,3).
5:17 *hearts are faint.* See note on 1:22. *eyes grow dim.* See 2:11; see also note on Ps 6:7.
5:18 *jackals.* The Hebrew for this word, different from that used in 4:3, can also mean "foxes" (see note on Jdg 15:4). For similar imagery of desolation, see Isa 13:21–22; 34:11–15; Zep 2:13–15.
5:19 Paralleled in Ps 102:12 (see note there). Elsewhere also prayer begins with praise (see Ps 44:1–8; 74:12–14; 80:1–2; 89:1–18; cf. Ac 24:23 and note). See Introduction: Themes and Theology (last paragraph).
5:20 *Why ... ? Why ... ?* See note on Ps 6:3.
5:21 *Restore us to yourself.* This language suggests a prayer for renewed commitment to the Lord (see 1Ki 8:33,48; Ne 1:9; Jer 3:7,10; Hos 7:10). *we may return.* See Jer 31:18 and note on 31:18–19. *renew.* See Ps 104:30.
5:22 See Jer 14:19. *unless.* Or "but." A similarly somber ending characterizes not only other laments (e.g., Ps 88) but also other OT books (e.g., Isaiah and Malachi).

EZEKIEL

INTRODUCTION

Background

Ezekiel lived during a time of international upheaval. The Assyrian Empire that had once conquered the Syro-Palestinian area and destroyed the northern kingdom of Israel (which fell to the Assyrians in 722 – 721 BC) began to crumble under the blows of a resurgent Babylonia. In 612 the great Assyrian city of Nineveh fell to a combined force of Babylonians and Medes. Three years later, Pharaoh Necho II of Egypt marched north to assist the Assyrians and to try to reassert Egypt's age-old influence over Canaan and Aram (Syria). At Megiddo, King Josiah of Judah, who may have been an ally of Babylonia as King Hezekiah had been, attempted to intercept the Egyptian forces but was crushed, losing his life in the battle (see 2Ki 23:29 – 30 and note on 23:29; 2Ch 35:20 – 24).

Jehoahaz, a son of Josiah, ruled Judah for only three months, after which Necho installed Jehoiakim, another son of Josiah, as his royal vassal in Jerusalem (609 BC). In 605 the Babylonians overwhelmed the Egyptian army at Carchemish (see Jer 46:2), then pressed south as far as the Philistine plain. In the same year, Nebuchadnezzar was elevated to the Babylonian throne and Jehoiakim shifted allegiance to him. When a few years later the Egyptian and Babylonian forces met in a standoff battle, Jehoiakim rebelled against his new overlord.

Nebuchadnezzar soon responded by sending a force against Jerusalem, subduing it in 597 BC. Jehoiakim's son Jehoiachin and about 10,000 Jews (see 2Ki 24:14), including Ezekiel, were exiled to Babylonia, where they joined those who had been exiled in Jehoiakim's "third year" (see Da 1:1 and note). Nebuchadnezzar placed Jehoiachin's uncle, Zedekiah, on the throne in Jerusalem, but within five or six years he too rebelled. The Babylonians laid siege to Jerusalem in 588, and in July, 586, the walls were breached and the city plundered. On Aug. 14, 586, the city and temple were burned.

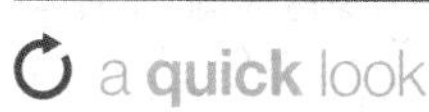

a **quick** look

Author:
Ezekiel

Audience:
Jews who were taken captive to Babylonia in 597 BC

Date:
Between 593 and 571 BC

Theme:
Ezekiel the priest assures his fellow Jews that God will one day return them to Jerusalem and restore the temple.

Under Nebuchadnezzar and his successors, Babylonia dominated the international scene until t was crushed by Cyrus the Persian in 539 BC. The reign of the house of David came to an end; the kingdom of Judah ceased to be an independent nation; Jerusalem and the Lord's temple lay n ruins.

Author

What is known of Ezekiel is derived solely from the book that bears his name. He was among the Jews exiled to Babylonia by Nebuchadnezzar in 597 BC, and there among the exiles he received his call to become a prophet (see 1:1 – 3). He was married (see 24:15 – 18), lived in a house of his own (see 3:24; 8:1) and along with his fellow exiles, though confined to Babylonia, had a relatively free existence there.

He was a member of a priestly family (see note on 1:3) and therefore was eligible to serve as a priest. As a priest-prophet called to minister to the exiles (separated from the temple of the Lord with its symbolism, sacrifices, priestly ministrations and worship rituals), his message had much to do with the temple (see especially chs. 8 – 11; 40 – 48) and its ceremonies.

Ezekiel was obviously a man of broad knowledge, not only of his own national traditions but also of international affairs and history. His acquaintance with general matters of culture, from ship-building to literature, is equally amazing. He was gifted with a powerful intellect and was capable of grasping large issues and of dealing with them in grand and compelling images. His style is often detached, but in places it is passionate and earthy (see chs. 16; 23).

More than any other prophet (more even than Hosea and Jeremiah) he was directed to involve himself personally in the divine word by acting it out in prophetic symbolism.

Occasion, Purpose and Summary of Contents

Though Ezekiel lived with his fellow exiles in Babylonia, his divine call forced him to suppress any natural expectations he may have had of an early return to an undamaged Jerusalem. For the first seven years of his ministry (593 – 586 BC) he faithfully relayed to his fellow Jews the stern, heart-rending, hope-crushing word of divine judgment: Because of all her sins, Jerusalem would fall (see chs. 1 – 24). The fact that Israel was God's covenant people and that Jerusalem was the city of his temple would not bring early release from exile or prevent Jerusalem from being destroyed (see Jer 29 – 30). The only hope the prophet was authorized to extend to his hearers was that of living at peace with themselves and with God during their exile.

After being informed by the Lord that Jerusalem was under siege and would surely fall (24:1 – 14), Ezekiel was told that his beloved wife would soon die. The delight of his eyes would be taken from him, just as the temple, the delight of Israel's eyes, would be taken from her. He was not to mourn openly for his wife, as a sign to his people not to mourn openly for Jerusalem (24:15 – 27). He was then directed to pronounce a series of judgments on Ammon, Moab, Edom, Philistia, Tyre, Sidon and Egypt (chs. 25 – 32). The day of God's wrath was soon to come, but not on Israel alone.

Once news was received that Jerusalem had fallen, Ezekiel's message turned to the Lord's consoling word of hope for his people — they would experience revival, restoration and a glorious future as the redeemed and perfected kingdom of God in the world (chs. 33 – 48).

Date

Since the book of Ezekiel contains more dates (see chart below) than any other OT prophetic book, its prophecies can be dated with considerable precision. In addition, modern scholarship, using archaeology (Babylonian annals on cuneiform tablets) and astronomy (accurate dating of eclipses referred to in ancient archives), provides precise modern calendar equivalents.

Twelve of the thirteen dates specify times when Ezekiel received a divine message. The other is the date of the arrival of the messenger who reported the fall of Jerusalem (33:21).

Having received his call in July, 593 BC, Ezekiel was active for 22 years, his last dated message being received in April, 571 (see 29:17). Since the "thirtieth year" of 1:1 (see note there) refers to Ezekiel's age at the time of his call, his prophetic career exceeded a normal priestly term of service by two years (see Nu 4:3). His period of activity coincides with Jerusalem's darkest hour, preceding the 586 destruction by 7 years and following it by 14.

DATES IN **EZEKIEL**

REFERENCE	YEAR	MONTH	DAY	MODERN RECKONING	EVENT
1. 1:1	30	4	5	July 31, 593 BC	Inaugural vision
1:2	5	—	5		
3:16	"At the end of seven days"				
2. 8:1	6	6	5	Sept. 17, 592	Transport to Jerusalem
3. 20:1–2	7	5	10	Aug. 14, 591	Negative view of Israel's history
4. 24:1	9	10	10	Jan. 15, 588	Beginning of siege (see also 2Ki 25:1)
5. 26:1	11	—	1	Apr. 23, 587 to Apr. 13, 586	Prophecy against Tyre (see note on 26:1)
6. 29:1	10	10	12	Jan. 7, 587	Prophecy against Egypt
7. 29:17	27	1	1	Apr. 26, 571	Egypt in exchange for Tyre
8. 30:20	11	1	7	Apr. 29, 587	Prophecy against Pharaoh
9. 31:1	11	3	1	June 21, 587	Prophecy against Pharaoh
10. 32:1	12	12	1	Mar. 3, 585	Lament over Pharaoh
11. 32:17	12	—	15	Apr. 13, 586 to Apr. 1, 585	Egypt dead
12. 33:21	12	10	5	Jan. 8, 585	Arrival of first fugitive
13. 40:1	25	1	10	Apr. 28, 573	Vision of the future
40:1	"fourteenth year after the fall of the city"				

Themes

The OT in general and the prophets in particular presuppose and teach God's sovereignty over all creation, over people and nations and the course of history. And nowhere in the Bible are God's initiative and control expressed more clearly and pervasively than in the book of Ezekiel. From the first chapter, which graphically describes the overwhelming invasion of the divine presence into

Ezekiel powerfully depicts the grandeur and glory of God's sovereign rule and his holiness, which he jealously safeguards.

Ezekiel's world, to the last phrase of Ezekiel's vision ("THE LORD IS THERE"), the book sounds and echoes God's sovereignty.

This sovereign God resolved that he would be known and acknowledged. Approximately 65 occurrences of the clause (or variations on) "Then they will know that I am the LORD" testify to that divine desire and intention (see note on 6:7). Overall, chs. 1 – 24 teach that God will be revealed in the fall of Jerusalem and the destruction of the temple; chs. 25 – 32 teach that the nations likewise will know God through his judgments; and chs. 33 – 48 promise that God will be known through the restoration and spiritual renewal of Israel.

God's total sovereignty is also evident in his mobility. He is not limited to the temple in Jerusalem. He can respond to his people's sin by leaving his sanctuary in Israel, and he can graciously condescend to visit his exiled children in Babylonia.

God is free to judge, and he is equally free to be gracious. His stern judgments on Israel ultimately reflect his grace. He allows the total dismemberment of Israel's political and religious life so that her renewed life and his presence with her will be clearly seen as a gift from the Lord of the universe.

Furthermore, as God's spokesman, Ezekiel's "son of man" status (see note on 2:1) testifies to the sovereign God he was commissioned to serve.

See also Theological Significance below.

Literary Features

The three Major Prophets (Isaiah, Jeremiah, Ezekiel) and Zephaniah all have the same basic sequence of messages: (1) messages against Israel, (2) messages against the nations, (3) consolation for Israel. In no other book is this pattern clearer than in Ezekiel (see Outline).

Besides clarity of structure, the book of Ezekiel reveals symmetry. The vision of the desecrated temple fit for destruction (chs. 8 – 11) is balanced by the vision of the restored and purified temple (chs. 40 – 48). The God presented in agitated wrath (ch. 1) is also shown to be a God of comfort ("THE LORD IS THERE," 48:35). Ezekiel's call to be a watchman announcing divine judgment (ch. 3) is balanced by his call to be a watchman announcing the new age to follow (ch. 33). In one place (ch. 6) the mountains of Israel receive a prophetic rebuke, but in another (ch. 36) they are consoled.

Prophetic books are usually largely poetic, the prophets apparently having spoken in imaginative and rhythmic styles. Most of Ezekiel, however, is prose, perhaps due to his priestly background. His repetitions have an unforgettable hammering effect, and his priestly orientation is also reflected in a case-law type of sentence (compare 3:19, "If you do warn the wicked ...," with Ex 21:2, "If you buy a Hebrew servant ...").

The book contains four major visions (chs. 1 – 3; 8 – 11; 37:1 – 14; 40 – 48) and 12 symbolic acts (3:22 – 26; 4:1 – 3; 4:4 – 8; 4:9 – 11; 4:12 – 14; 5:1 – 3; 12:1 – 16; 12:17 – 20; 21:6 – 7; 21:18 – 24; 24:15 – 24; 37:15 – 28). Five messages are in the form of parables (chs. 15; 16; 17; 19; 23).

Theological Significance

Other prophets deal largely with Israel's idolatry, with her moral corruption in public and private affairs and with her international intrigues and alliances, upon which she relied instead of on the Lord. They announce God's impending judgment on his rebellious nation but speak also of a future

Luxor temple at Thebes, Egypt. Ezekiel 30:14 predicts the destruction of Thebes by Nebuchadnezzar.

redemption: a new exodus, a new covenant, a restored Jerusalem, a revived Davidic dynasty, a worldwide recognition of the Lord and his Messiah and a paradise-like peace.

The contours and sweep of Ezekiel's message are similar, but he focuses uniquely on Israel as the holy people of the holy temple, the holy city and the holy land. By defiling her worship, Israel had rendered herself unclean and had defiled temple, city and land. From such defilement God could only withdraw and judge his people with national destruction.

But God's faithfulness to his covenant and his desire to save were so great that he would revive his people once more, shepherd them with compassion, cleanse them of all their defilement, reconstitute them as a perfect expression of his kingdom under the hand of "David" (34:23 – 24), overwhelm all the forces and powers arrayed against them, display his glory among the nations and restore the glory of his presence to the holy city.

Ezekiel powerfully depicts the grandeur and glory of God's sovereign rule (see Themes) and his holiness, which he jealously safeguards. The book's theological center is the unfolding of God's saving purposes in the history of the world — from the time in which he must withdraw from the defilement of his covenant people to the culmination of his grand design of redemption. The message of Ezekiel, which is ultimately eschatological, anticipates — even demands — God's future works in history proclaimed by the NT.

Outline

- I. Messages of Judgment against Israel (chs. 1–24)
  - A. Ezekiel's Inaugural Vision (chs. 1–3)
    1. Overwhelming display of the glory of the Lord (ch. 1)
    2. Ezekiel's call to be a prophet (2:1—3:15)
    3. Ezekiel's call as watchman (3:16–21)
    4. Restraints on Ezekiel's prophetic ministry (3:22–27)
  - B. Symbolic Acts Portraying the Siege of Jerusalem (chs. 4–5)
    1. Ezekiel's symbolic siege of Jerusalem (ch. 4)
    2. God's razor of judgment at work (ch. 5)
  - C. Messages of Divine Judgment (chs. 6–7)
    1. Doom for the mountains of Israel (ch. 6)
    2. The end has come on the land (ch. 7)
  - D. Corruption of the Temple and Its Consequences (chs. 8–11)
    1. Idolatry in the temple (ch. 8)
    2. Judgment on the idolaters (ch. 9)
    3. God's glory departs from the temple (ch. 10)
    4. God's sure judgment on Jerusalem (11:1–14)
    5. Those in exile to be restored (11:15–21)
    6. Conclusion (11:22–25)
  - E. Ezekiel Symbolizes the Exile of Jerusalem (ch. 12)
    1. An exile's baggage (12:1–16)
    2. Anxious eating (12:17–20)
    3. The imminence of judgment (12:21–28)
  - F. Messages concerning God's Judgment on Judah (13:1—24:14)
    1. Condemnation of the false prophets (ch. 13)
    2. Condemnation of the idolaters (14:1–11)
    3. No mediators can turn back God's judgment (14:12–23)
    4. Jerusalem compared to a piece of burnt vine (ch. 15)
    5. Jerusalem allegorized as an adulterous wife (ch. 16)
    6. Allegory of two eagles and a vine (ch. 17)
    7. The one who sins will die (ch. 18)
    8. Lament over the fall of Jerusalem's kings (ch. 19)
    9. Apostate Israel purged and renewed through judgment (20:1–44)
    10. Babylonia, God's sword of judgment (20:45—21:32)
    11. The sins for which Jerusalem is judged (ch. 22)
    12. Jerusalem and Samaria allegorized as adulterous sisters (ch. 23)
    13. Jerusalem cooked over the fire (24:1–14)
  - G. The Death of Ezekiel's Wife Symbolizes Jerusalem's Fall (24:15–27)
- II. Messages of Judgment against the Nations (chs. 25–32)
  - A. A Prophecy against Ammon (25:1–7)
  - B. A Prophecy against Moab (25:8–11)

- C. A Prophecy against Edom (25:12 – 14)
- D. A Prophecy against Philistia (25:15 – 17)
- E. A Prophecy against Tyre (26:1 — 28:19)
  1. Tyre's destruction announced (ch. 26)
  2. A lament over Tyre (ch. 27)
  3. A prophecy against the king of Tyre (28:1 – 19)
- F. A Prophecy against Sidon (28:20 – 24)
  (For Israel, a restoration, 28:25 – 26)
- G. A Prophecy against Egypt (chs. 29 – 32)
  1. Egypt a doomed monster (29:1 – 16)
  2. Egypt a payment to Nebuchadnezzar (29:17 – 21)
  3. Laments over Egypt (30:1 – 19)
  4. The pharaoh's arms are broken (30:20 – 26)
  5. The pharaoh a felled Lebanon cedar (ch. 31)
  6. Lament over the pharaoh (32:1 – 16)
  7. The pharaoh consigned to the realm of the dead (32:17 – 32)

III. Messages of Consolation for Israel (chs. 33 – 48)
- A. Renewal of Ezekiel's Call as Watchman (33:1 – 20)
- B. Jerusalem's Fall Reported and Its Remnant Condemned (33:21 – 33)
- C. The Lord to Be Israel's Shepherd (ch. 34)
- D. A Prophecy against Edom (ch. 35)
- E. Israel's Complete Restoration Announced (ch. 36)
- F. Israel's Dry Bones Revived and Unity Restored (ch. 37)
  1. Israel's dry bones restored to life (37:1 – 14)
  2. Again one nation under one King (37:15 – 28)
- G. The Great Battle of the Ages (chs. 38 – 39)
- H. The New Order for Purified Israel (chs. 40 – 48)
  1. The temple area restored (40:1 – 47)
  2. The new temple (40:48 — 42:20)
  3. God's glory returns to the temple (43:1 – 12)
  4. Restoration of the altar of burnt offering (43:13 – 27)
  5. Restoration of the priesthood (ch. 44)
  6. Restoration of the theocratic order (chs. 45 – 46)
  7. The river of life from the temple (47:1 – 12)
  8. The boundaries of the land (47:13 – 23)
  9. The distribution of the land (48:1 – 29)
  10. The twelve gates of the new city (48:30 – 35)

Ezekiel's Inaugural Vision

1 In my thirtieth year, in the fourth
month on the fifth day, while I was
among the exiles[a] by the Kebar River,[b] the
heavens were opened[c] and I saw visions[d]
of God.
2 On the fifth of the month—it was the
fifth year of the exile of King Jehoiachin[e]—
3 the word of the LORD came to Ezekiel[f] the
priest, the son of Buzi, by the Kebar River
in the land of the Babylonians.[a] There the
hand of the LORD was on him.[g]
4 I looked, and I saw a windstorm[h] coming out of the north[i]—an immense cloud
with flashing lightning and surrounded by
brilliant light. The center of the fire looked
like glowing metal,[j] 5 and in the fire was
what looked like four living creatures.[k] In
appearance their form was human,[l] 6 but
each of them had four faces[m] and four
wings. 7 Their legs were straight; their feet
were like those of a calf and gleamed like
burnished bronze.[n] 8 Under their wings on
their four sides they had human hands.[o]
All four of them had faces and wings, 9 and
the wings of one touched the wings of another. Each one went straight ahead; they
did not turn as they moved.[p]
10 Their faces looked like this: Each of
the four had the face of a human being,
and on the right side each had the face of
a lion, and on the left the face of an ox;
each also had the face of an eagle.[q] 11 Such
were their faces. They each had two wings[r]
spreading out upward, each wing touching that of the creature on either side;
and each had two other wings covering
its body. 12 Each one went straight ahead.
Wherever the spirit would go, they would
go, without turning as they went.[s] 13 The
appearance of the living creatures was like
burning coals[t] of fire or like torches. Fire
moved back and forth among the creatures; it was bright, and lightning[u] flashed
out of it. 14 The creatures sped back and
forth like flashes of lightning.[v]
15 As I looked at the living creatures,[w] I
saw a wheel[x] on the ground beside each
creature with its four faces. 16 This was the
appearance and structure of the wheels:
They sparkled like topaz,[y] and all four
looked alike. Each appeared to be made
like a wheel intersecting a wheel. 17 As
they moved, they would go in any one of
the four directions the creatures faced; the

1:1 [a]S Dt 21:10; Eze 11:24-25 [b]S Ps 137:1 [c]S Mt 3:16 [d]S Ex 24:10
1:2 [e]S 2Ki 24:15
1:3 [f]Eze 24:24 [g]S 2Ki 3:15; Isa 8:11; Eze 3:14, 22; 8:1; 33:22; 37:1; 40:1
1:4 [h]S Job 38:1 [i]Jer 1:14 [j]Eze 8:2
1:5 [k]S Isa 6:2; Rev 4:6 [l]ver 26; Da 7:13
1:6 [m]Eze 10:14
1:7 [n]Eze 40:3; Da 10:6; S Rev 1:15
1:8 [o]Eze 10:8
1:9 [p]Eze 10:22
1:10 [q]Eze 10:14; Rev 4:7
1:11 [r]Isa 6:2
1:12 [s]Eze 10:16-19
1:13 [t]S 2Sa 22:9 [u]Rev 4:5
1:14 [v]S Ps 29:7
1:15 [w]Eze 3:13 [x]Eze 10:2; Da 7:9
1:16 [y]S Ex 28:20

[a] 3 Or *Chaldeans*

1:1–28 Forced into Babylonian exile far from the Lord's temple with its symbolic evocations of God's glory (see notes on Ex 26:1; 40:34; Ps 24:2; see also Ps 24:8–10; 26:8; 29:9; 96:6 and notes), Ezekiel is inaugurated into his prophetic mission (see 1:1 and note) with an overwhelming vision of God's glory (see note on 1:28)—much as Isaiah was granted an awesome vision of God enthroned on high and attended by winged "seraphim" (see Isa 6:1–2 and notes) at the inauguration of his prophetic ministry (cf. 1Ki 22:19 and note).

1:1 *my thirtieth year.* Ezekiel's age. According to Nu 4:3, a person entered active priestly ministry in his 30th year. Denied the ministry of the priesthood, Ezekiel received another commission—that of prophet. *Kebar River.* A canal of the Euphrates near the city of Nippur, south of Babylon, and possibly a place of prayer for the exiles (see Ps 137:1; cf. Ac 16:13). *visions of God.* A special term, always in the plural and always with the word "God" (not with the more personal "LORD"). The expression precedes this and the two other major visions of the prophet (8:3; 40:2).

1:2 *fifth year of the exile.* Verses 2–3, written in the third person (the only third-person narrative in the book), clarify the date in v. 1. *King Jehoiachin.* Was forced to accompany an early group of exiles to Babylon in 597 BC (see Introduction: Background). Ezekiel was among them and received his prophetic call in 593 (see chart, p. 1336).

1:3 *Ezekiel.* The prophet's name occurs elsewhere in the book only in 24:24 (see note there) and thus frames the first major literary unit in his message. His name means "God is strong" (cf. 3:14), "God strengthens" (cf. 30:25; 34:16) or "God makes hard" (cf. 3:8). *priest.* Member of a priestly family. *hand of the LORD.* A phrase occurring seven times in the book (see also 3:14,22; 8:1; 33:22; 37:1; 40:1), indicating an overpowering experience of divine revelation.

1:4 *I looked.* Introduces the first part of the vision: storm and living creatures (vv. 4–14). The "I looked" of v. 15 introduces the second part: wheels and the glory of the Lord. *a windstorm.* A storm cloud—accompanied by wind, lightning and thunder—often served as a symbol of God's powerful and active presence (see Ex 19:16–18; Ps 18:7–15; 77:16–19 and notes; cf. Job 38:1).

1:5 *four living creatures.* "Four," which stands for completeness (cf. the four directions in Ge 13:14 and the four quarters of the earth in Isa 11:12), is used often in this chapter—and over 40 times in the book. The living creatures, called "cherubim" in ch. 10, are throne attendants (see Ex 25:18 and note). Here (see v. 10 and note) they contribute to the whole complex scenario that symbolically represents God's creation. These four creatures (cf. the "seraphim" of Isa 6:2–4) appear again in Rev 4:7. They were often depicted in the paintings and sculptures of the Middle Ages, but in this later use they represent the four Gospels. *their form ... human.* God's noblest creature on earth (see v. 10 and note).

1:6 *four faces.* See v. 10 and note. *four wings.* Signifying their mobility as throne attendants of the heavenly King, who is ever on the move through history.

1:7 *like those of a calf.* Perhaps indicates agility (cf. Ps 29:6; Mal 4:2).

1:10 *face of a human being.* God's appointed ruler on earth (see Ge 1:26–28; Ps 8:3–8 and notes). *a lion.* The most ferocious of wild animals known in Israel and Mesopotamia, and reputedly the strongest of such beasts (see Jdg 14:18). *an ox.* The most powerful of domesticated animals. *an eagle.* The mightiest of the birds. Cf. Rev 4:7 and note.

1:12 *straight ahead ... without turning.* In their mobility they were multidirectional (see v. 14). *the spirit.* The directing presence in the cherubim (see v. 20).

1:13 *like burning coals.* Cf. Ps 18:8. *like torches.* Cf. Ge 15:17.

1:15 *wheel.* Also symbolic of mobility (see note on v. 12).

1:16 *topaz.* The precise identification of this stone is uncertain. See Ex 28:20 (and NIV text note), where the stone appears in the priestly breastplate. *a wheel intersecting a wheel.* Probably two wheels intersecting at right angles in order to move in all four directions (see v. 17). The imagery symbolizes the omnipresence of God.

wheels did not change direction[z] as the creatures went. 18 Their rims were high and awesome, and all four rims were full of eyes[a] all around.

19 When the living creatures moved, the wheels beside them moved; and when the living creatures rose from the ground, the wheels also rose. 20 Wherever the spirit would go, they would go,[b] and the wheels would rise along with them, because the spirit of the living creatures was in the wheels. 21 When the creatures moved, they also moved; when the creatures stood still, they also stood still; and when the creatures rose from the ground, the wheels rose along with them, because the spirit of the living creatures was in the wheels.[c]

22 Spread out above the heads of the living creatures was what looked something like a vault,[d] sparkling like crystal, and awesome. 23 Under the vault their wings were stretched out one toward the other, and each had two wings covering its body. 24 When the creatures moved, I heard the sound of their wings, like the roar of rushing[e] waters, like the voice[f] of the Almighty,[a] like the tumult of an army.[g] When they stood still, they lowered their wings.

25 Then there came a voice from above the vault over their heads as they stood with lowered wings. 26 Above the vault over their heads was what looked like a throne[h] of lapis lazuli,[i] and high above on the throne was a figure like that of a man.[j] 27 I saw that from what appeared to be his waist up he looked like glowing metal, as if full of fire, and that from there down he looked like fire; and brilliant light surrounded him.[k] 28 Like the appearance of a rainbow[l] in the clouds on a rainy day, so was the radiance around him.[m]

This was the appearance of the likeness of the glory[n] of the LORD. When I saw it, I fell facedown,[o] and I heard the voice of one speaking.

Ezekiel's Call to Be a Prophet

2 He said to me, "Son of man,[b][p] stand[q] up on your feet and I will speak to you.[r]" 2 As he spoke, the Spirit came into me and raised me[s] to my feet, and I heard him speaking to me.

3 He said: "Son of man, I am sending you to the Israelites, to a rebellious nation that has rebelled against me; they and their ancestors have been in revolt against me to this very day.[t] 4 The people to whom I am sending you are obstinate and stubborn.[u] Say to them, 'This is what the Sovereign LORD says.'[v] 5 And whether they listen or fail to listen[w]—for they are a rebellious people[x]—they will know that a prophet has been among them.[y] 6 And you, son of man, do not be afraid[z] of them or their words. Do not be afraid, though briers and thorns[a] are all around you and you live among scorpions. Do not be afraid of what they say or be terrified by them, though they are a rebellious people.[b] 7 You must speak[c] my words to them, whether they listen or fail to listen, for they are rebellious.[d] 8 But you, son of man, listen to what I say to you. Do not rebel[e] like that

[a] 24 Hebrew *Shaddai* [b] 1 The Hebrew phrase *ben adam* means *human being.* The phrase *son of man* is retained as a form of address here and throughout Ezekiel because of its possible association with "Son of Man" in the New Testament.

1:17 [z] ver 9 **1:18** [a] Rev 4:6 **1:20** [b] ver 12 **1:21** [c] Eze 10:9-12 **1:22** [d] Eze 10:1 **1:24** [e] S Ps 46:3; Eze 3:13 [f] Eze 10:5; 43:2; Da 10:6; Rev 1:15; 14:2; 19:6 [g] S 2Ki 7:6 **1:26** [h] S 1Ki 22:19; Isa 6:1; S Jer 3:17 [i] S Ex 24:10 [j] S ver 5; S Eze 2:1; S Rev 1:13 **1:27** [k] Eze 8:2 **1:28** [l] S Ge 9:13; Rev 10:1 [m] S Rev 4:2 [n] S Ex 16:7; S 24:16; Lk 2:9 [o] S Ge 17:3; S Nu 14:5 **2:1** [p] S Job 25:6; Ps 8:4; S Eze 1:26; Da 7:13; 8:15 [q] Da 10:11; Ac 14:10; 26:16 [r] Ac 9:6 **2:2** [s] Eze 3:24; Da 8:18 **2:3** [t] S Jer 3:25; Eze 5:6; 20:8-24; 24:3 **2:4** [u] S Ex 32:9; S Isa 9:9; Eze 3:7 [v] Am 7:15 **2:5** [w] Eze 3:11 [x] Eze 3:27 [y] S Jer 5:3; Eze 33:33; Jn 15:22 **2:6** [z] S Dt 31:6; S 2Ki 1:15 [a] S Nu 33:55; Isa 9:18; Mic 7:4 [b] S Isa 1:2; 30:9; Eze 24:3; 44:6 **2:7** [c] Jer 7:27 [d] Jer 1:7; S 42:21; Eze 3:10-11 **2:8** [e] Nu 20:10-13; Isa 8:11

1:18 *full of eyes.* Symbolizes God's all-seeing nature (cf. notes on Zec 3:9; 4:10).
1:22 *vault.* The same word occurs in Ge 1:6–8, where its function is to separate the waters above from the waters below. Here it separates the creatures from the glory of the Lord. *like crystal ... awesome.* Cf. Rev 4:6 and note; 15:2.
1:25 *stood with lowered wings.* Awaiting a word from the throne.
1:26 *Above the vault ... on the throne.* Cf. Ex 24:10. *a figure like that of a man.* Ezekiel is reporting his vision of God, but he carefully avoids saying he saw God directly (see Ge 16:13; Ex 3:6; Jdg 13:22).
1:28 *appearance of the likeness.* See note on v. 26. *glory of the LORD.* See note on 1:1–28. When God's glory was symbolically revealed, it took the form of brilliant light (see Ex 40:34 and note; Isa 6:3). What is remarkable about Ezekiel's experience is that God's glory had for centuries been associated with the temple in Jerusalem (see 1Ki 8:11; Ps 26:8; 63:2; 96:6; 102:16). Now God had left his temple and was appearing to his exiled people in Babylonia—a major theme in the first half of Ezekiel's message (see 10:4; 11:23). In his vision of the restored Jerusalem the prophet saw the glory of the Lord returning (43:2). *I fell facedown.* See Ge 17:3; Ex 3:6; cf. Isa 6:5.
2:1—3:15 God does not abandon his covenant people even though he banishes them from the promised land because of their long history of rebellion against him. He commissions Ezekiel to bring his word to those in exile, still calling them by their covenant name, "Israel" (see 2:3; 3:4–5,7; cf. Am 8:11 and note). Ezekiel's mission to the exiles overlapped that of Jeremiah, another member of a priestly family called to the prophetic office, whose mission was to the Israelites still living in and around Jerusalem.
2:1 *Son of man.* See NIV text note; a term used 93 times in Ezekiel, emphasizing the prophet's humanity as he was addressed by the transcendent God (see note on Ps 8:4). Da 7:13 and 8:17 are the only other places where the phrase is used as a title in the OT. Jesus' frequent use of the phrase in referring to himself showed that he was the eschatological figure spoken of in Da 7:13 (see, e.g., Mk 8:31 and note).
2:2 *the Spirit came into me and raised me to my feet.* The Spirit of God governs and empowers the prophet's entire ministry (see 11:5; 36:27; 37:14; 39:29; see also 3:12 and note).
2:3 *to a rebellious nation.* A theme that became a keynote of Ezekiel's preaching.
2:6 *briers and thorns ... scorpions.* Vivid images of those who would make life difficult for the prophet.

rebellious people;[f] open your mouth and
eat[g] what I give you."
9 Then I looked, and I saw a hand[h]
stretched out to me. In it was a scroll,[i]
10 which he unrolled before me. On both
sides of it were written words of lament
and mourning and woe.[j]
3 And he said to me, "Son of man, eat
what is before you, eat this scroll;
then go and speak to the people of Israel."
2 So I opened my mouth, and he gave me
the scroll to eat.
3 Then he said to me, "Son of man, eat
this scroll I am giving you and fill your
stomach with it." So I ate[k] it, and it tasted
as sweet as honey[l] in my mouth.
4 He then said to me: "Son of man, go
now to the people of Israel and speak my
words to them.[m] 5 You are not being sent
to a people of obscure speech and strange
language,[n] but to the people of Israel—
6 not to many peoples of obscure speech
and strange language, whose words you
cannot understand. Surely if I had sent
you to them, they would have listened to
you.[o] 7 But the people of Israel are not willing to listen[p] to you because they are not
willing to listen to me, for all the Israelites
are hardened and obstinate.[q] 8 But I will
make you as unyielding and hardened as
they are.[r] 9 I will make your forehead[s] like
the hardest stone, harder than flint.[t] Do
not be afraid of them or terrified by them,
though they are a rebellious people.[u]"
10 And he said to me, "Son of man, listen
carefully and take to heart[v] all the words
I speak to you. 11 Go[w] now to your people
in exile and speak to them. Say to them,
'This is what the Sovereign LORD says,'[x]
whether they listen or fail to listen.[y]"
12 Then the Spirit lifted me up,[z] and I
heard behind me a loud rumbling sound
as the glory of the LORD rose from the
place where it was standing.[a] 13 It was the
sound of the wings of the living creatures[a]
brushing against each other and the sound
of the wheels beside them, a loud rumbling sound.[b] 14 The Spirit[c] then lifted me
up[d] and took me away, and I went in bitterness and in the anger of my spirit, with
the strong hand of the LORD[e] on me. 15 I
came to the exiles who lived at Tel Aviv
near the Kebar River.[f] And there, where
they were living, I sat among them for sev-
en days[g]—deeply distressed.

Ezekiel's Task as Watchman

16 At the end of seven days the word of
the LORD came to me:[h] 17 "Son of man, I
have made you a watchman[i] for the people of Israel; so hear the word I speak and
give them warning from me.[j] 18 When I say
to a wicked person, 'You will surely die,[k]'
and you do not warn them or speak out
to dissuade them from their evil ways in
order to save their life, that wicked person
will die for[b] their sin, and I will hold you
accountable for their blood.[l] 19 But if you

a 12 Probable reading of the original Hebrew text; Masoretic Text *sound—may the glory of the LORD be praised from his place* *b* 18 Or *in;* also in verses 19 and 20

2:8 [f]S Isa 50:5 [g]Ps 81:10; S Jer 15:16; Rev 10:9 **2:9** [h]Eze 8:3 [i]S Ps 40:7; S Jer 36:4; Rev 5:1-5; 10:8-10 **2:10** [j]Isa 3:11; Rev 8:13 **3:3** [k]S Jer 15:16 [l]S Ps 19:10; Rev 10:9-10 **3:4** [m]Eze 11:4, 25 **3:5** [n]S Isa 28:11; Jnh 1:2 **3:6** [o]Jnh 3:5-10; Mt 11:21-23; Ac 13:46-48 **3:7** [p]S Jer 7:27 [q]Isa 48:4; Jer 3:3; S Eze 2:4; Jn 15:20-23 **3:8** [r]Jer 1:18; S 15:20 **3:9** [s]S Isa 48:4 [t]S Jer 5:3 [u]Isa 50:7; Eze 2:6; 44:6; Mic 3:8 **3:10** [v]S Job 22:22 **3:11** [w]S Isa 6:9 [x]ver 27 [y]Eze 2:4-5,7; 11:24-25 **3:12** [z]ver 14; Eze 8:3; 43:5 **3:13** [a]Eze 1:15 [b]Eze 1:24; 10:5, 16-17 **3:14** [c]S 1Ki 18:12 [d]S ver 12 [e]ver 22; S Isa 8:11; Eze 37:1 **3:15** [f]S Ps 137:1 [g]S Ge 50:10 **3:16** [h]Jer 42:7 **3:17** [i]S Isa 52:8 [j]S Isa 58:1; Jer 1:17; Eze 11:4; Hab 2:1 **3:18** [k]S Ge 2:17; Jn 8:21,24 [l]ver 20

2:10 *On both sides.* Normally, ancient scrolls were written on one side only. See Ex 32:15 and note. *lament and mourning and woe.* Although Ezekiel was later commanded to preach hope (see note on 33:1—48:35), his initial commission (until the fall of Jerusalem) was to declare God's displeasure and the certainty of his judgment on Jerusalem and all of Judah.
3:1 *eat this scroll.* Ezekiel must ingest the Lord's message that he is commissioned to bring to the exiles, so that it becomes, as it were, a very part of his being (cf. Jer 15:16 and note).
3:3 *sweet as honey in my mouth.* What Jeremiah experienced emotionally (Jer 15:16) was experienced by Ezekiel in a more sensory way: Words from God are sweet to the taste (see Ps 19:10; 119:103)—even when their content is bitter (see Rev 10:9–10).
3:6 *Surely if I had sent you to them, they would have listened.* For the greater readiness of other peoples to hear and heed the word of God, see Jnh 3:5; Mal 1:10–11; Mt 11:20–24; Ro 10:20–21.
3:9 *I will make your forehead like the hardest stone.* Strength and courage were necessary equipment for a prophet, especially when preaching judgment. Jeremiah was similarly equipped (see Jer 1:18; cf. Isa 50:7).
3:10 *listen carefully and take to heart.* The prophet is to stand in marked contrast to the people, who do not listen.
3:11 *Go now to your people in exile.* Ezekiel's ministry was to the exilic community, most of whom refused to believe that God would abandon Jerusalem and the temple. After the fall of Jerusalem, therefore, they were strongly inclined to despair.
3:12–15 The dramatic conclusion to Ezekiel's call experience, with echoes of his initial vision.
3:12 *the Spirit lifted me up.* See v. 14; 8:3; 11:1,24; 37:1; 43:5; cf. 2:2 and note.
3:14 *in bitterness and in the anger of my spirit.* The prophet, knowing the righteousness of God's anger, personally identified with the divine emotions. *strong hand of the LORD on me.* See note on 1:3.
3:15 *Tel Aviv.* The only mention of the specific place where the exiles lived. In Babylonian the name meant "mound of the deluge" and was used to refer to ancient cities that had been reduced to mere mounds (*tells*). When used of the modern Israeli city of Tel Aviv, this name is understood to mean "hill of new growth" (cf. Ex 12:2 and note). *seven days.* The traditional period of mourning (see Ge 50:10; 1Sa 31:13). *deeply distressed.* Because of his horror over Judah's impending doom (cf. Ezr 9:3–4; Job 2:13 and note; Da 8:27).
3:16–21 Ezekiel's appointment to serve as a "watchman" for Israel—a metaphor drawn from urban life. His special task as watchman is spelled out here; its urgency is more fully elaborated in ch. 18.
3:17 *I have made you a watchman.* In ancient Israel, watchmen were stationed on city walls to serve as the eyes of the city (see 2Sa 18:24–27; 2Ki 9:17–20; SS 3:3; 5:7;

do warn the wicked person and they do
not turn[m] from their wickedness[n] or from
their evil ways, they will die[o] for their sin;
but you will have saved yourself.[p]
20 "Again, when a righteous person
turns[q] from their righteousness and does
evil, and I put a stumbling block[r] before
them, they will die. Since you did not
warn them, they will die for their sin. The
righteous things that person did will not
be remembered, and I will hold you accountable for their blood.[s] 21 But if you
do warn the righteous person not to sin
and they do not sin, they will surely live
because they took warning, and you will
have saved yourself.[t]"
22 The hand of the LORD[u] was on me
there, and he said to me, "Get up and go[v]
out to the plain,[w] and there I will speak
to you." 23 So I got up and went out to
the plain. And the glory of the LORD was
standing there, like the glory I had seen
by the Kebar River,[x] and I fell facedown.[y]
24 Then the Spirit came into me and
raised me[z] to my feet. He spoke to me
and said: "Go, shut yourself inside your
house.[a] 25 And you, son of man, they will
tie with ropes; you will be bound so that
you cannot go out among the people.[b] 26 I
will make your tongue stick to the roof[c]
of your mouth so that you will be silent
and unable to rebuke them, for they are a
rebellious people.[d] 27 But when I speak to
you, I will open your mouth and you shall
say to them, 'This is what the Sovereign
LORD says.'[e] Whoever will listen let them
listen, and whoever will refuse let them
refuse; for they are a rebellious people.[f]

3:19 [m] S Ps 7:12 [n] S Ge 6:5 [o] S Jer 42:16 [p] S 2Ki 17:13; Eze 14:14, 20; Ac 18:6; 20:26; 1Ti 4:14-16
3:20 [q] S Jer 34:16 [r] S Lev 26:37; S Isa 8:14; S Eze 7:19 [s] ver 18; Ps 125:5; Eze 18:24; 33:12, 18
3:21 [t] Ac 20:31
3:22 [u] S ver 14; S Eze 1:3 [v] Ac 9:6 [w] Eze 8:4
3:23 [x] Eze 1:1 [y] S Ge 17:3
3:24 [z] S Eze 2:2 [a] Jer 15:17
3:25 [b] Eze 4:8
3:26 [c] S Ps 22:15 [d] Eze 2:5; 24:27; 33:22; Hos 4:4
3:27 [e] ver 11 [f] Eze 2:5; 12:3; 24:27; 29:21; 33:22; Rev 22:11
4:2 [g] S Jer 6:6; Eze 17:17; Da 11:15 [h] S Jer 33:4; Eze 21:22
4:3 [i] S Lev 2:5 [j] ver 7; Eze 20:46; 21:2 [k] S Isa 8:18; S 20:3; Jer 13:1-7; 18:1-4; 19:1-2; Eze 5:1-4; 12:3-6

Siege of Jerusalem Symbolized

4 "Now, son of man, take a block of
clay, put it in front of you and draw
the city of Jerusalem on it. 2 Then lay siege
to it: Erect siege works against it, build a
ramp[g] up to it, set up camps against it and
put battering rams around it.[h] 3 Then take
an iron pan,[i] place it as an iron wall between you and the city and turn your face
toward[j] it. It will be under siege, and you
shall besiege it. This will be a sign[k] to the
people of Israel.[l]
4 "Then lie on your left side and put the
sin of the people of Israel upon yourself.[a]
You are to bear their sin for the number of
days you lie on your side. 5 I have assigned
you the same number of days as the years
of their sin. So for 390 days you will bear
the sin of the people of Israel.
6 "After you have finished this, lie down
again, this time on your right side, and
bear the sin[m] of the people of Judah. I
have assigned you 40 days, a day for each
year.[n] 7 Turn your face[o] toward the siege of
Jerusalem and with bared arm prophesy

[a] 4 Or *upon your side*

[l] S Jer 39:1 **4:6** [m] S Ex 28:38 [n] Nu 14:34; Da 9:24-26; 12:11-12
4:7 [o] S ver 3; Eze 6:2; S 13:17

Isa 52:8; 62:6), especially to warn of approaching danger (see 33:2–3,6; Ps 127:1; Isa 21:6; 56:10; Jer 6:17; Hos 9:8).
3:20 *I put a stumbling block before them.* Those who have abandoned righteousness and embraced what is evil will be put to the test by the Lord himself (see 14:9; cf. Dt 13:3; 2Sa 24:1 and note; 2Ch 32:31; Ps 66:10 and note; see also Mt 6:13).
3:22–27 God places severe limitations on Ezekiel's freedom to carry out his mission, very likely to signify that the Lord knows that the exiles will not be responsive to his warnings.
3:22 *hand of the LORD.* See note on 1:3.
3:25 *you ... they will tie with ropes.* Perhaps better: "you ... will be tied with ropes" (metaphorically) — the Hebrew construction sometimes is equivalent to a passive. Reference is to the restraints that God will place on Ezekiel's movements (cf. 4:8).
3:26 *you will be silent.* Verses 26–27 indicate that the prophet would be unable to speak except when he had a direct word from the Lord. His enforced silence underscored Israel's stubborn refusal to take God's word seriously — and was itself a part of God's judgment on his rebellious people (see 7:26 and note; 20:3,31). This condition was relieved only after the fall of Jerusalem (24:27; 33:22). From that time on Ezekiel was given messages of hope, which he continually shared with his fellow exiles.
4:1—5:17 By means of a series of symbolic acts, Ezekiel is to portray the siege of Jerusalem and its outcome. In 4:1–3 the siege itself is portrayed; in 4:4–8 Ezekiel symbolically bears the punishment of the people of Israel and Judah; in 4:9–17 Ezekiel's assigned food symbolizes both the limitations of food that those under siege will suffer and the fact that they and the exiles will be forced to eat food the law specified to be "unclean" and therefore prohibited; in 5:1–4 Ezekiel is instructed to shave off his hair and use it to symbolize that only a small remnant of Israel will be left from God's unfolding judgment; in 5:5–17 these symbolic acts are explained.
4:1 *take a block of clay.* The first of several symbolic acts to be performed by the prophet. After inscribing a likeness of the city of Jerusalem on a moist clay block, Ezekiel was to place around it models of siege works to represent the city under attack (v. 2). He was then to place an iron pan (perhaps a baking griddle) between himself and the symbolized city (v. 3) to indicate the unbreakable strength of the siege.
4:3 *you shall besiege it.* Ezekiel's own presence in the scene signified that the siege would actually be laid by the Lord himself. *sign.* For Ezekiel as a "sign," see also 12:6,11; 24:24,27. These references to "sign" mark off significant literary transitions in the book (see notes on 12:1–28; 24:15–27).
4:4 *You are to bear their sin.* A representative rather than a substitutionary bearing of sin. The prophet's action symbolized the punishment Israel would suffer for her sins; it did not remove the sins.
4:5 *for 390 days.* The 390 years (see v. 6) may represent the period from the time of Solomon's unfaithfulness to the fall of Jerusalem. Correspondingly, the 40 years of v. 6 may represent the long reign of wicked Manasseh before his repentance (see 2Ki 21:11–15; 23:26–27; 24:3–4; 2Ch 33:12–13).
4:6 *on your right side.* Lying on his left side (v. 4) while facing Jerusalem (v. 7) probably placed Ezekiel to the north of the symbolic city (v. 1); lying on his right side would then have placed him to the south — signifying the northern and southern kingdoms, respectively.
4:7 *prophesy against her.* By means of his symbolic actions.

against her. 8 I will tie you up with ropes
so that you cannot turn from one side to
the other until you have finished the days
of your siege.[p]
9 "Take wheat and barley, beans and lentils, millet and spelt;[q] put them in a storage
jar and use them to make bread for yourself. You are to eat it during the 390 days
you lie on your side. 10 Weigh out twenty shekels[a][r] of food to eat each day and
eat it at set times. 11 Also measure out a
sixth of a hin[b] of water and drink it at set
times.[s] 12 Eat the food as you would a loaf
of barley bread; bake it in the sight of the
people, using human excrement[t] for fuel."
13 The LORD said, "In this way the people
of Israel will eat defiled food among the
nations where I will drive them."[u]
14 Then I said, "Not so, Sovereign LORD![v]
I have never defiled myself. From my
youth until now I have never eaten anything found dead[w] or torn by wild animals. No impure meat has ever entered
my mouth.[x]"
15 "Very well," he said, "I will let you
bake your bread over cow dung instead of
human excrement."
16 He then said to me: "Son of man, I
am about to cut off[y] the food supply in
Jerusalem. The people will eat rationed
food in anxiety and drink rationed water
in despair,[z] 17 for food and water will be
scarce.[a] They will be appalled at the sight
of each other and will waste away because
of[c] their sin.[b]

God's Razor of Judgment

5 "Now, son of man, take a sharp sword
and use it as a barber's razor[c] to
shave[d] your head and your beard.[e] Then
take a set of scales and divide up the hair.

4:8 [p] Eze 3:25 **4:9** [q] S Isa 28:25 **4:10** [r] S Ex 30:13 **4:11** [s] ver 16 **4:12** [t] S Isa 36:12 **4:13** [u] Hos 9:3; Am 7:17 **4:14** [v] Jer 1:6; Eze 9:8; 20:49 [w] S Lev 11:39 [x] S Ex 22:31; Dt 14:3; 32:37-38; Da 1:8; Hos 9:3-4 **4:16** [y] S Ps 105:16 [z] ver 10-11; S Lev 26:26; Isa 3:1; Eze 12:19 **4:17** [a] La 5:4; Eze 5:16; 12:18-19; Am 4:8 [b] S Lev 26:39; Eze 24:23; 33:10 **5:1** [c] S Nu 6:5 [d] Eze 44:20 [e] S Lev 21:5; S 2Sa 10:4

[a] *10* That is, about 8 ounces or about 230 grams
[b] *11* That is, about 2/3 quart or about 0.6 liter
[c] *17* Or *away in*

4:9 *Take wheat and barley, beans and lentils, millet and spelt.* A scant, vegetarian diet representing the meager provisions of a besieged city.
4:15 *cow dung.* When thoroughly dried, it was commonly used in the Near East as a fuel for baking and is still sometimes so used even today. Ezekiel again showed his sensitivity to things ceremonially unclean (see note on 1:3), and God graciously responded to the prophet's objection by allowing this substitute for human excrement.
5:1 – 17 The fate of the people of Jerusalem in the judgment that is about to overtake them — only the merest remnant will be left (cf. notes on 2Ki 19:30 – 31; Isa 1:9; 10:20 – 22).
5:1 *take a sharp sword.* What Isaiah had expressed in a metaphor (Isa 7:20) Ezekiel acted out in prophetic symbolism.

Masada with a siege ramp along the right side of the photo. Enemies would build a ramp up to the top of a city wall to make it easier to attack the city. In Ezekiel 4:1 – 2, God instructs Ezekiel, "Take a block of clay, put it in front of you and draw the city of Jerusalem on it. Then lay siege to it: Erect siege works against it, build a ramp up to it, set up camps against it and put battering rams around it."

Assyrian soldiers destroying the walls of a city with a battering ram (Nimrud, c. 865 BC)

Z. Radovan/www.BibleLandPictures.com

[2]When the days of your siege come to an end, burn[f] a third[g] of the hair inside the city. Take a third and strike it with the sword all around the city. And scatter a third to the wind.[h] For I will pursue them with drawn sword.[i] [3]But take a few hairs and tuck them away in the folds of your garment.[j] [4]Again, take a few of these and throw them into the fire[k] and burn them up. A fire will spread from there to all Israel.

[5]"This is what the Sovereign LORD says: This is Jerusalem, which I have set in the center of the nations, with countries all around her.[l] [6]Yet in her wickedness she has rebelled against my laws and decrees more than the nations and countries around her. She has rejected my laws and has not followed my decrees.[m]

[7]"Therefore this is what the Sovereign LORD says: You have been more unruly than the nations around you and have not followed my decrees or kept my laws. You have not even[a] conformed to the standards of the nations around you.[n]

[8]"Therefore this is what the Sovereign LORD says: I myself am against you, Jerusalem, and I will inflict punishment on you in the sight of the nations.[o] [9]Because of all your detestable idols, I will do to you what I have never done before and will never do again.[p] [10]Therefore in your midst parents will eat their children, and children will eat their parents.[q] I will inflict punishment on you and will scatter all your survivors to the winds.[r] [11]Therefore as surely as I live,[s] declares the Sovereign[t] LORD, because you have defiled my sanctuary[u] with all your vile images[v] and

[a] 7 Most Hebrew manuscripts; some Hebrew manuscripts and Syriac *You have*

5:2 [f]Jer 21:10; Eze 15:7 [g]Zec 13:8 [h]ver 10; Jer 13:24 [i]ver 12; S Lev 26:33; S Jer 9:16; S 39:1-2 **5:3** [j]2Ki 25:12; S Ps 74:11; Jer 39:10 **5:4** [k]Eze 10:7; 15:7 **5:5** [l]S Dt 4:6; S La 1:1; Eze 16:14 **5:6** [m]S 2Ki 17:15; Ne 9:17; Jer 11:10; S Eze 2:3; 16:47-51; Zec 7:11 **5:7** [n]S 2Ki 21:9; S 2Ch 33:9; Jer 2:10-11; Eze 16:47 **5:8** [o]S Jer 21:5, 13; 24:9; Eze 11:9; 15:7; Zec 14:2 **5:9** [p]Da 9:12; S Mt 24:21 **5:10** [q]S Lev 26:29; S La 2:20 [r]S Lev 26:33; S Ps 44:11; S Jer 13:14; Eze 12:14 **5:11** [s]S Nu 14:21 [t]S Ge 15:2 [u]S Lev 15:31 [v]Eze 7:20; 11:18

5:2 *with drawn sword.* See 12:14; 21:3–5; 30:25; 32:10; Ps 7:12–13 and note.

5:5 *This is Jerusalem.* After wordlessly acting out the symbols (beginning in 4:1), Ezekiel received and probably related the divine explanations. *center of the nations.* God had chosen for his people Israel and for his earthly temple a place at the crossroads of the continents of Africa, Asia and Europe so that Israel and what he does for them might be a strong witness to the nations that he is the one and only God with whom all peoples have to do and from whom alone come life and blessing. This made Israel's responsibility and judgment all the more severe (see also 38:12 and note).

5:6 *more than the nations … around her.* See v. 7; 16:47–48; 2Ki 21:9; Am 3:9 and note.

5:8 *I myself am against you.* A short and effective phrase of judgment used often by Ezekiel (see 13:8; 21:3; 26:3; 28:22; 29:3,10; 30:22; 34:10; 35:3; 38:3; 39:1; see also Jer 23:30–32; 50:31; 51:25; Na 2:13; 3:5). *inflict punishment on you in the sight of the nations.* Just as he had acted to bring about Israel's freedom and privileged position as his people (see Lev 26:45; Jos 2:11; 5:1; cf. Isa 52:10).

5:10 *parents will eat their children.* Cannibalism, the most gruesome extremity of life under siege (see 2Ki 6:28), was threatened as a consequence of breaking the covenant (Dt 28:53; see Jer 19:9 and note; La 2:20; Zec 11:9 and note).

5:11 *as surely as I live.* A divine oath, revealing God's unalterable intention. It is used often in Ezekiel (see 14:16,18,20; 16:48; 17:16,19; 18:3; 20:3,31,33; 33:11, 27; 34:8; 35:6,11; see also Heb 6:13 and note). *you have defiled my sanctuary.* See ch. 8.

detestable practices,[w] I myself will shave
you; I will not look on you with pity or
spare you.[x] 12 A third of your people will
die of the plague or perish by famine inside you; a third will fall by the sword
outside your walls; and a third I will scatter to the winds[y] and pursue with drawn
sword.[z]
13 "Then my anger will cease and my
wrath[a] against them will subside, and I
will be avenged.[b] And when I have spent
my wrath on them, they will know that I
the LORD have spoken in my zeal.[c]
14 "I will make you a ruin and a reproach
among the nations around you, in the
sight of all who pass by.[d] 15 You will be a
reproach[e] and a taunt, a warning[f] and an
object of horror to the nations around you
when I inflict punishment on you in anger
and in wrath and with stinging rebuke.[g]
I the LORD have spoken.[h] 16 When I shoot
at you with my deadly and destructive arrows of famine, I will shoot to destroy you.
I will bring more and more famine upon
you and cut off your supply of food.[i] 17 I
will send famine and wild beasts[j] against
you, and they will leave you childless.
Plague and bloodshed[k] will sweep through
you, and I will bring the sword against
you. I the LORD have spoken.[l]"

Doom for the Mountains of Israel

6 The word of the LORD came to me:
2 "Son of man, set your face[m] against
the mountains[n] of Israel; prophesy against
them[o] 3 and say: 'You mountains of Israel, hear the word of the Sovereign LORD.
This is what the Sovereign LORD says to
the mountains and hills, to the ravines
and valleys:[p] I am about to bring a sword
against you, and I will destroy your high
places.[q] 4 Your altars will be demolished
and your incense altars[r] will be smashed;
and I will slay your people in front of your
idols.[s] 5 I will lay the dead bodies of the
Israelites in front of their idols, and I will
scatter your bones[t] around your altars.[u]
6 Wherever you live,[v] the towns will be laid
waste and the high places[w] demolished, so
that your altars will be laid waste and devastated, your idols[x] smashed and ruined,
your incense altars[y] broken down, and
what you have made wiped out.[z] 7 Your
people will fall slain[a] among you, and you
will know that I am the LORD.[b]
8 " 'But I will spare some, for some of
you will escape[c] the sword when you are
scattered among the lands and nations.[d]
9 Then in the nations where they have
been carried captive, those who escape
will remember[e] me — how I have been
grieved[f] by their adulterous hearts, which
have turned away from me, and by their
eyes, which have lusted after their idols.[g]
They will loathe themselves for the evil[h]
they have done and for all their detestable practices.[i] 10 And they will know that
I am the LORD;[j] I did not threaten in vain to
bring this calamity on them.[k]
11 " 'This is what the Sovereign LORD
says: Strike your hands together and
stamp your feet and cry out "Alas!" because of all the wicked and detestable
practices of the people of Israel, for they
will fall by the sword, famine and plague.[l]

5:11 [w] 2Ch 36:14; Eze 8:6 [x] S Job 27:22; S Jer 16:18; S La 2:17; Eze 7:4,9; 8:18; 9:5 **5:12** [y] ver 10; Jer 13:24 [z] S ver 2,17; S Ps 107:39; S Jer 15:2; S 21:9; Eze 6:11-12; 7:15; 12:14; Am 9:4; Zec 13:8; Rev 6:8 **5:13** [a] S 2Ch 12:7; S Job 20:23; Eze 21:17; 24:13 [b] S Isa 1:24 [c] S Isa 59:17; Eze 16:42; 38:19; Hos 10:10; Zec 6:8 **5:14** [d] S Lev 26:32; Ne 2:17; Ps 74:3-10; 79:1-4; Isa 64:11; Eze 6:6; 22:4; Da 9:16; Mic 3:12 **5:15** [e] S Isa 43:28 [f] S Dt 28:46 [g] S Dt 28:20; S 1Ki 9:7; S Jer 22:8-9; 24:9; Eze 14:8 [h] S Jer 23:40 **5:16** [i] S Lev 26:26; S Dt 32:24 **5:17** [j] Eze 14:15 [k] Eze 38:22 [l] S ver 12; S Lev 26:25; Eze 14:21; 28:23 **6:2** [m] S Eze 4:7 [n] Eze 18:6; Mic 6:1 [o] ver 13 **6:3** [p] Eze 36:4

[q] S Lev 26:30 **6:4** [r] S 2Ch 14:5 [s] Eze 9:6; 14:3; 20:16 **6:5** [t] S Nu 19:16; S Ps 53:5; Jer 8:1-2 [u] ver 13; S Lev 26:30 **6:6** [v] S Ex 12:20 [w] Hos 10:8 [x] Eze 30:13; Mic 1:7; Zec 13:2 [y] S Lev 26:30 [z] S 1Sa 5:4; Isa 6:11; S Eze 5:14 **6:7** [a] Eze 9:7 [b] ver 10,13,14; Eze 11:10-12 **6:8** [c] S Ps 68:20; S Jer 44:28 [d] S Ge 11:4; S Ps 44:11; Isa 6:13; S Jer 44:14; Eze 7:16; 12:16; 14:22 **6:9** [e] S Ps 137:6; Zec 10:9 [f] S Isa 7:13; S Jer 8:21 [g] S Ex 22:20; Eze 20:7,24; Mic 5:13 [h] S Ex 32:22 [i] S Job 42:6; Eze 20:43; 23:14-16; 36:31 **6:10** [j] S ver 7 [k] S Dt 28:52; Jer 40:2 **6:11** [l] S Jer 42:22; Eze 21:14,17; 22:13; 25:6

5:13 *spent my wrath on.* An expression frequently used by the Lord in this book (see 6:12; 7:8; 13:15; 20:8,21). *they will know that I the LORD have spoken.* See 17:21; 36:36; 37:14; see also 6:7 and note.
5:15 *a reproach and a taunt, a warning and an object of horror.* A fourfold list (see note on 1:5).
5:16–17 These verses contain echoes of the threatened forces of judgment for covenant unfaithfulness found in Dt 32:22–25. Note especially that God's "arrows" of judgment are the four main causes of death among the peoples of the ancient Near East: famine, disease, sword (violent death at human hands) and wild beasts (see 14:12–21; see also 6:11–12; 7:15; 12:16; cf. 34:25–31; see also Jer 14:12 and note; cf. Rev 6:8).
5:16 *my ... arrows.* A widely used metaphor for God's judgments (see note on Ge 9:13).
6:1–14 After announcing judgment on Jerusalem (chs. 4–5), Ezekiel is instructed to pronounce judgment on the whole land; the "mountains of Israel" were the heavily cultivated central highlands (see Ps 104:13–15 and note), which also provided the principal sites for the pagan sanctuaries set up to worship the Baals. The judgment Ezekiel is to pronounce echoes Lev 26:27–39.
6:3 *high places.* Open-air sanctuaries of Canaanite origin, condemned throughout the OT. The high places, together with the "altars," "incense altars" and "idols" (v. 4), make up a list of four objects (see note on 1:5).
6:4 *incense altars.* Made of baked clay, about two feet high, usually inscribed with animal figures and idols of Canaanite gods. *idols.* The Hebrew word is a derisive term (see note on Lev 26:30) used especially by Ezekiel (38 times, as opposed to only 9 times elsewhere in the OT).
6:7 *you will know that I am the LORD.* See 36:11 and note. This assertion that God's mighty acts in history (his dealings with Israel and the nations in judgment and redemption) will result in his being known and acknowledged by Israel and the nations echoes throughout chs. 6–39 (see Introduction: Themes; see also 5:13 and note).
6:9 *those who escape will remember me.* The corrective outcome God intends from the severe judgment to come (see v. 10). *their adulterous hearts ... lusted after their idols.* See Ex 34:15 and note.
6:11 *Strike your hands together and stamp your feet.* A command to Ezekiel to punctuate his words of judgment with symbolic acts (see 21:14,17)—acts of quite different intent from those of Israel's enemies in 25:6. *sword, famine and plague.* See 5:16–17 and note.

12 One who is far away will die of the
plague, and one who is near will fall by
the sword, and anyone who survives and
is spared will die of famine. So will I pour
out my wrath[m] on them.[n] 13 And they will
know that I am the LORD, when their people lie slain among their idols[o] around
their altars, on every high hill and on all
the mountaintops, under every spreading
tree and every leafy oak[p] — places where
they offered fragrant incense to all their
idols.[q] 14 And I will stretch out my hand[r]
against them and make the land a desolate
waste from the desert to Diblah[a] — wherever they live. Then they will know that I
am the LORD.[s]' "

The End Has Come

7 The word of the LORD came to me:
2 "Son of man, this is what the Sovereign LORD says to the land of Israel:

" 'The end![t] The end has come
upon the four corners[u] of the land!
3 The end is now upon you,
and I will unleash my anger against
you.
I will judge you according to your
conduct[v]
and repay you for all your detestable
practices.[w]
4 I will not look on you with pity;[x]
I will not spare you.
I will surely repay you for your
conduct
and for the detestable practices
among you.

" 'Then you will know that I am the LORD.'[y]

5 "This is what the Sovereign LORD says:

" 'Disaster![z] Unheard-of[b] disaster!
See, it comes!
6 The end[a] has come!
The end has come!
It has roused itself against you.
See, it comes!
7 Doom has come upon you,
upon you who dwell in the land.
The time has come! The day[b] is
near![c]
There is panic, not joy, on the
mountains.

8 I am about to pour out my wrath[d] on
you
and spend my anger against you.
I will judge you according to your
conduct
and repay you for all your detestable
practices.[e]
9 I will not look on you with pity;
I will not spare you.[f]
I will repay you for your conduct
and for the detestable practices
among you.[g]

" 'Then you will know that it is I the LORD
who strikes you.[h]

10 " 'See, the day!
See, it comes!
Doom has burst forth,
the rod[i] has budded,
arrogance has blossomed!
11 Violence[j] has arisen,[c]
a rod to punish the wicked.
None of the people will be left,
none of that crowd —
none of their wealth,
nothing of value.[k]
12 The time has come!
The day has arrived!
Let not the buyer[l] rejoice
nor the seller grieve,
for my wrath is on the whole
crowd.[m]
13 The seller will not recover
the property that was sold —
as long as both buyer and seller live.
For the vision concerning the whole
crowd
will not be reversed.
Because of their sins, not one of them
will preserve their life.[n]

14 " 'They have blown the trumpet,[o]
they have made all things ready,
but no one will go into battle,
for my wrath[p] is on the whole crowd.
15 Outside is the sword;
inside are plague and famine.
Those in the country
will die by the sword;

6:12 [m] S Job 20:23 [n] S Eze 5:12; 7:15 **6:13** [o] S Lev 26:30 [p] S Isa 1:29 [q] S 1Ki 14:23; S Jer 2:20; Eze 18:6; 20:28; Hos 4:13 **6:14** [r] S Ex 7:5; S Job 30:21; S Jer 6:12; 51:25; Eze 20:34 [s] Eze 12:19; 14:13 **7:2** [t] Am 8:2, 10 [u] Rev 7:1; 20:8 **7:3** [v] Eze 18:30 [w] S Ge 6:13 **7:4** [x] S Jer 13:14; S Eze 5:11 [y] S Eze 5:11; 23:49 **7:5** [z] S 2Ki 21:12 **7:6** [a] Eze 39:8 **7:7** [b] S Job 18:20; S Isa 2:12; Am 5:18-20 [c] Eze 12:23; 30:3; Zep 1:14; Mal 3:2

7:8 [d] Isa 42:25; Eze 9:8; 14:19; 22:22; Hos 5:10; Na 1:6 [e] Eze 20:8, 21; 36:19 **7:9** [f] S Jer 21:7; S Eze 5:11 [g] Eze 22:31 [h] Dt 32:35; S Ps 39:10; S Isa 9:13 **7:10** [i] Ps 89:32; Isa 10:5 **7:11** [j] S Ps 55:9; S Isa 58:4 [k] Jer 16:6; Zep 1:18 **7:12** [l] S Isa 24:2 [m] ver 7; Isa 5:13-14; Eze 30:3 **7:13** [n] Lev 25:24-28 **7:14** [o] S Job 39:24 [p] Jer 25:38

a 14 Most Hebrew manuscripts; a few Hebrew manuscripts *Riblah* *b* 5 Most Hebrew manuscripts; some Hebrew manuscripts and Syriac *Disaster after* *c* 11 Or *The violent one has become*

6:14 *I will stretch out my hand against.* A common expression in Ezekiel (see 14:9,13; 16:27; 25:7; 35:3). *Diblah.* Perhaps the Beth Diblathaim of Jer 48:22, a city in Moab; or Riblah, a city north of Damascus on the Orontes River (see NIV text note).
7:1 – 27 God's word of judgment on the "mountains of Israel" (6:2; see ch. 6 and note on 6:1 – 14) is elaborated in the fateful declaration that God's patience with Israel's stubborn rebelliousness has run out: "The end! The end has come" (v. 2; see vv. 3,6,24; see also Jer 51:13; La 4:18; cf. Am 7:8; 8:2).
7:7 *The day.* The "day of the LORD's wrath" (v. 19), i.e., the day of reckoning when God brings down his righteous judgments on the wickedness of his people (see also vv. 10,12). Ezekiel's language may be a deliberate echo of the "day of the LORD" of which many of the prophets spoke (see Am 5:18 and note). *panic, not joy.* Cf. Am 5:20 ("darkness, not light").
7:8 *pour out my wrath.* A common expression in Ezekiel (see 9:8; 14:19; 20:8,13,21; 22:31; 30:15; 36:18).
7:12 *Let not the buyer rejoice.* Advice similar to that of Jesus (see Mt 24:17 – 18).
7:15 *sword . . . plague and famine.* See 5:16 – 17 and note.

those in the city
will be devoured by famine and plague.[q]
16 The fugitives[r] who escape
will flee to the mountains.
Like doves[s] of the valleys,
they will all moan,
each for their own sins.[t]
17 Every hand will go limp;[u]
every leg will be wet with urine.[v]
18 They will put on sackcloth[w]
and be clothed with terror.[x]
Every face will be covered with shame,
and every head will be shaved.[y]
19 " 'They will throw their silver into the streets,[z]
and their gold will be treated as a thing unclean.
Their silver and gold
will not be able to deliver them
in the day of the LORD's wrath.[a]
It will not satisfy[b] their hunger
or fill their stomachs,
for it has caused them to stumble[c] into sin.[d]
20 They took pride in their beautiful jewelry
and used it to make[e] their detestable idols.
They made it into vile images;[f]
therefore I will make it a thing unclean for them.[g]
21 I will give their wealth as plunder[h] to foreigners
and as loot to the wicked of the earth,
who will defile it.[i]
22 I will turn my face[j] away from the people,
and robbers will desecrate the place I treasure.

7:15 [q]S Dt 32:25; Jer 14:18; S La 1:20; S Eze 5:12; 33:27
7:16 [r]S Isa 10:20; S Jer 41:16; 42:17 [s]S Ge 8:8; S Isa 59:11 [t]S Ezr 9:15; Jer 9:19; S Eze 6:8
7:17 [u]S 2Ki 19:26; S Jer 47:3; Eze 21:7; 22:14 [v]Da 5:6
7:18 [w]S Jer 4:8; 48:37; 49:3 [x]S Ps 55:5 [y]S Isa 15:2-3; Eze 27:31; Am 8:10
7:19 [z]S La 4:1 [a]Isa 42:25; Eze 13:5; 30:3; Joel 1:15; 2:1; Zep 1:7,18; 2:2 [b]Isa 55:2 [c]Eze 3:20; 14:3; Hos 4:5 [d]S Pr 11:4
7:20 [e]S Jer 10:3 [f]S Eze 5:11 [g]S Isa 2:20; 30:22; Eze 16:17
7:21 [h]S Nu 14:3 [i]S 2Ki 24:13
7:22 [j]S Jer 2:27; Eze 39:23-24
[k]Ps 74:7-8; Jer 19:13; S La 2:7
7:23 [l]S 2Ki 21:16; S Isa 1:15; S Eze 22:9 [m]S Ge 6:11; Eze 11:6
7:24 [n]La 2:7; Eze 24:21 [o]2Ch 7:20; Eze 28:7
7:25 [p]Jer 6:14; S 8:11; Eze 13:10,16

They will enter it
and will defile it.[k]
23 " 'Prepare chains!
For the land is full of bloodshed,[l]
and the city is full of violence.[m]
24 I will bring the most wicked of nations
to take possession of their houses.
I will put an end to the pride of the mighty,
and their sanctuaries[n] will be desecrated.[o]
25 When terror comes,
they will seek peace in vain.[p]
26 Calamity upon calamity[q] will come,
and rumor upon rumor.
They will go searching for a vision from the prophet,[r]
priestly instruction in the law will cease,
the counsel of the elders will come to an end.[s]
27 The king will mourn,
the prince will be clothed with despair,[t]
and the hands of the people of the land will tremble.
I will deal with them according to their conduct,[u]
and by their own standards I will judge them.

" 'Then they will know that I am the LORD.[v]' "

Idolatry in the Temple

8 In the sixth year, in the sixth month on the fifth day, while I was sitting in my house and the elders[w] of Judah were sitting

7:26 [q]S Dt 29:21; S 31:17 [r]S 1Sa 3:1 [s]Isa 47:11; S Jer 18:18; Eze 20:1-3; Am 8:11; Mic 3:6 **7:27** [t]S Ps 109:19; Eze 26:16 [u]S Isa 3:11; Eze 18:20 [v]S ver 4 **8:1** [w]S 2Ki 6:32; Eze 14:1

7:17 *Every hand will go limp.* See 21:7; 30:25; Isa 13:7 and note; Jer 6:24; 47:3 and note; 50:43; Zep 3:16 and note.
7:18 *They will put on sackcloth . . . every head will be shaved.* As signs of intense mourning (see Ge 37:34; Job 1:20; Isa 15:2; Rev 11:3 and notes).
7:19 *They will throw their silver.* See Isa 2:20.
7:20 *beautiful jewelry.* See Ex 32:2–4.
7:22 *the place I treasure.* The Jerusalem temple.
7:23 *full of bloodshed . . . violence.* See 9:9; 11:6; 12:19; see also 2Ki 21:16; 24:4; Jer 19:4; 22:17; La 4:13; Mic 3:10; Hab 1:2–4; cf. Hab 2:8,12,17.
7:24 *pride of the mighty.* The Jerusalem temple, described by the word "pride" (as in 24:21; 33:28).
7:26 *prophet . . . priestly . . . elders.* There would be no guidance from God and no direction from the elders (see 1Sa 28:6; Am 8:11–12 and note on 8:11; Mic 3:6–7; see also Jer 18:18 and note).
7:27 *king . . . prince.* Here both nouns probably refer to the same person, namely, King Jehoiachin. *clothed with.* See note on Ps 109:29. *people of the land.* The full citizens of Judah (those holding inherited family property and subject to military service; see 12:19; 45:16,22; 46:3).

8:1 — 11:25 The vision has six movements: (1) God shows Ezekiel the idolatry practiced in the temple in Jerusalem (ch. 8); (2) God pronounces his judgment on the idolaters there (ch. 9); (3) Ezekiel is shown God's glory departing from the temple (ch. 10); (4) God declares that the complacent Jerusalemites will not escape his judgment (11:1–13); (5) God promises that the exiles, whom those still in Jerusalem have written off, will be restored (11:14–21); and (6) the conclusion of the vision (11:22–25).
8:1–8 Ezekiel is shown four examples of idolatrous worship being carried on in the very temple of the Lord: (1) "idol of jealousy" (v. 5), (2) "crawling things and unclean animals" (v. 10), (3) "mourning the god Tammuz" (v. 14), and (4) "bowing down to the sun" (v. 16).
8:1 *In the sixth year, in the sixth month on the fifth day.* Sept. 17, 592 BC—the second of 13 dates in Ezekiel (see chart, p. 1336). This one, like those in 1:2 and 40:1, introduces a vision. *sitting in my house.* The exiles were free to build houses (see Jer 29:5). *elders of Judah were sitting before me.* They also had freedom of movement, assembly and worship (see 14:1; 20:1). A year and two months after his inaugural vision and preaching, the prophet commanded a hearing. Some have

before[x] me, the hand of the Sovereign LORD
came on me there.[y] 2 I looked, and I saw a
figure like that of a man.[a] From what appeared to be his waist down he was like
fire, and from there up his appearance was
as bright as glowing metal.[z] 3 He stretched
out what looked like a hand[a] and took me
by the hair of my head. The Spirit lifted
me up[b] between earth and heaven and in
visions[c] of God he took me to Jerusalem,
to the entrance of the north gate of the inner court,[d] where the idol that provokes to
jealousy[e] stood. 4 And there before me was
the glory[f] of the God of Israel, as in the
vision I had seen in the plain.[g]
5 Then he said to me, "Son of man, look
toward the north." So I looked, and in the
entrance north of the gate of the altar I
saw this idol[h] of jealousy.
6 And he said to me, "Son of man, do
you see what they are doing—the utterly
detestable[i] things the Israelites are doing
here, things that will drive me far from my
sanctuary?[j] But you will see things that are
even more detestable."
7 Then he brought me to the entrance to
the court. I looked, and I saw a hole in the
wall. 8 He said to me, "Son of man, now
dig into the wall." So I dug into the wall
and saw a doorway there.
9 And he said to me, "Go in and see the
wicked and detestable things they are doing here." 10 So I went in and looked, and I
saw portrayed all over the walls[k] all kinds
of crawling things and unclean[l] animals
and all the idols of Israel.[m] 11 In front of
them stood seventy elders[n] of Israel, and
Jaazaniah son of Shaphan was standing
among them. Each had a censer[o] in his
hand, and a fragrant cloud of incense[p] was
rising.[q]

8:1 [x] Eze 33:31 [y] Eze 1:1-3; 24:1; 40:1 **8:2** [z] Eze 1:4, 26-27 **8:3** [a] S Eze 2:9 [b] S Eze 3:12; 11:1 [c] S Ex 24:10 [d] ver 16 [e] ver 5; Ex 20:5; Dt 32:16 **8:4** [f] S Ex 24:16 [g] Eze 3:22 **8:5** [h] Ps 78:58; S Jer 4:1; 32:34 **8:6** [i] Ps 78:60; S Eze 5:11 [j] Hos 5:6 **8:10** [k] S Jdg 17:4-5; Eze 23:14 [l] Jer 44:4 [m] Ex 20:4; Dt 4:15-18; S Jer 16:18; Eze 11:12 **8:11** [n] S Ex 3:16 [o] S Lev 10:1; Nu 16:17 [p] Nu 16:35; S Jer 44:5 [q] Eze 11:1-2 **8:12** [r] S Job 22:13 [s] S 2Ki 21:16; Ps 10:11; S Isa 29:15; Eze 9:9; Zep 1:12 **8:14** [t] Eze 11:12 **8:16** [u] ver 3 [v] Joel 2:17 [w] S Ge 1:16 [x] Dt 4:19; S 17:3; S Job 31:28; S Jer 2:27; Eze 9:6; 11:1, 12; 40:6; 43:1 **8:17** [y] Eze 16:2 [z] S Ge 6:11 [a] S Nu 11:33; S 1Ki 14:9; Eze 16:26 **8:18** [b] S Jer 44:6 [c] S Jer 13:14; S Eze 5:11; 9:10; 24:14 [d] S 1Sa 8:18; S Isa 58:4; S Jer 11:11

12 He said to me, "Son of man, have you
seen what the elders of Israel are doing
in the darkness,[r] each at the shrine of his
own idol? They say, 'The LORD does not
see[s] us; the LORD has forsaken the land.' "
13 Again, he said, "You will see them doing
things that are even more detestable."
14 Then he brought me to the entrance of
the north gate of the house of the LORD, and
I saw women sitting there, mourning the
god Tammuz.[t] 15 He said to me, "Do you see
this, son of man? You will see things that
are even more detestable than this."
16 He then brought me into the inner
court[u] of the house of the LORD, and there
at the entrance to the temple, between the
portico and the altar,[v] were about twenty-five men. With their backs toward the
temple of the LORD and their faces toward
the east, they were bowing down to the
sun[w] in the east.[x]
17 He said to me, "Have you seen this,
son of man? Is it a trivial matter for the
people of Judah to do the detestable
things[y] they are doing here? Must they
also fill the land with violence[z] and continually arouse my anger?[a] Look at them
putting the branch to their nose! 18 Therefore I will deal with them in anger;[b] I will
not look on them with pity[c] or spare them.
Although they shout in my ears, I will not
listen[d] to them."

Judgment on the Idolaters

9 Then I heard him call out in a loud
voice, "Bring near those who are appointed to execute judgment on the city,
each with a weapon in his hand." 2 And I
saw six men coming from the direction of

[a] 2 Or *saw a fiery figure*

seen in such meetings the beginnings of the synagogue form of worship. *hand of the Sovereign LORD.* See note on 1:3.
8:2 *figure like that of a man.* An angel, similar in appearance to the vision of God in 1:26–27. *like fire ... as bright as glowing metal.* A way of describing the blinding brightness of the divine messenger (see Mt 28:3; cf. Ac 9:3).
8:3 *The Spirit lifted me up.* See 3:12 and note. *took me to Jerusalem.* Ezekiel had been directed to prophesy stern judgments on Jerusalem (chs. 1–7). Now he was transported to Jerusalem in visions of God (see 11:24) and shown the reason for the judgments. *idol that provokes to jealousy.* Any idol in the temple provoked the Lord to jealousy (see Ex 20:5 and note), but this one seems to be a statue of Asherah, the Canaanite goddess of fertility, which Josiah had removed some 30 years previously (see 2Ki 23:6).
8:5 *idol of jealousy.* See note on v. 3.
8:10 *all kinds of crawling things and unclean animals.* Probably reflecting Egyptian influence (cf. 2Ki 23:31–35).
8:11 *Jaazaniah.* Not the same person as in 11:1. Ironically, the name means "The LORD hears," and the irony is sharpened by the quotation in v. 12.
8:14 *Tammuz.* The only Biblical reference to this Babylonian fertility god. The women of Jerusalem were bewailing his dying (which supposedly happened seasonally at the height of the summer heat), which they thought caused the annual summer die-off of the vegetation. According to some interpreters, he is alluded to in Da 11:37 ("the one desired by women"; see note there).
8:16 *twenty-five men.* A representative number (see 11:1). *With their backs toward the temple.* Almost all ancient temples were oriented toward the east. Worshiping the sun as it rose required people to turn their backs to the temple. *bowing down to the sun.* For other references to sun worship, see Dt 4:19; 17:3; 2Ki 23:5,11; cf. 2Ki 17:16; 21:3,5; Jer 43:13.
8:17 *fill the land with violence.* See 7:23 and note. *putting the branch to their nose.* A ceremonial gesture in pagan worship, not documented elsewhere in the Bible.
9:1–11 See note on 8:1—11:25.
9:1 *loud voice.* The thunderous voice of God (see Ex 19:19 and NIV text note; see also Ps 29).
9:2 *six men coming from the direction of the upper gate.* These six guardian angels of the city, plus the seventh clothed in linen, came from the place where the idol that provoked to jealousy stood (see 8:3 and note).

the upper gate, which faces north, each
with a deadly weapon in his hand. With
them was a man clothed in linen[e] who had
a writing kit at his side. They came in and
stood beside the bronze altar.
3 Now the glory[f] of the God of Israel
went up from above the cherubim,[g] where
it had been, and moved to the threshold
of the temple. Then the LORD called to the
man clothed in linen who had the writing kit at his side 4 and said to him, "Go
throughout the city of Jerusalem[h] and put
a mark[i] on the foreheads of those who
grieve and lament[j] over all the detestable
things that are done in it.[k]"
5 As I listened, he said to the others, "Follow him through the city and kill, without
showing pity[l] or compassion.[m] 6 Slaughter[n]
the old men, the young men and wom-
en, the mothers and children,[o] but do not
touch anyone who has the mark.[p] Begin
at my sanctuary." So they began with the
old men[q] who were in front of the temple.[r]
7 Then he said to them, "Defile the
temple and fill the courts with the slain.[s]
Go!" So they went out and began killing
throughout the city. 8 While they were killing and I was left alone, I fell facedown,[t]
crying out, "Alas, Sovereign LORD![u] Are
you going to destroy the entire remnant of
Israel in this outpouring of your wrath[v] on
Jerusalem?[w]"
9 He answered me, "The sin of the people of Israel and Judah is exceedingly
great; the land is full of bloodshed and
the city is full of injustice.[x] They say, 'The
LORD has forsaken the land; the LORD does
not see.'[y] 10 So I will not look on them
with pity[z] or spare them, but I will bring
down on their own heads what they have
done.[a]"
11 Then the man in linen with the writing kit at his side brought back word, saying, "I have done as you commanded."

9:2 [e] S Lev 16:4; Eze 10:2; Da 10:5; 12:6; Rev 15:6 **9:3** [f] S 1Sa 4:21; Eze 10:4 [g] Eze 11:22 **9:4** [h] Jer 25:29 [i] S Ge 4:15; Ex 12:7; 2Co 1:22; S Rev 7:3 [j] Ps 119:136; Jer 7:29; 13:17; Eze 21:6; Am 6:6 [k] Ps 119:53 **9:5** [l] S Jer 13:14; S Eze 5:11 [m] S Ex 32:27; Isa 13:18 **9:6** [n] Jer 7:32 [o] S Jer 16:6 [p] S Ge 4:15; S Ex 12:7 [q] Eze 8:11-13, 16 [r] S 2Ch 36:17; Jer 25:29; S Eze 6:4; 1Pe 4:17 **9:7** [s] Eze 6:7 **9:8** [t] S Jos 7:6 [u] S Eze 4:14 [v] S Eze 7:8 [w] Eze 11:13; Am 7:1-6 **9:9** [x] S Ps 58:2; Jer 12:1; Eze 22:29; Hab 1:4 [y] S Job 22:13; S Eze 8:12; 14:23 **9:10** [z] S Jer 13:14; S Eze 8:18 [a] S Isa 22:5; S 65:6; Eze 11:21; 23:49

10:1 [b] S Rev 4:2 [c] S Ex 24:10 [d] Eze 1:22 [e] S Ge 3:24 **10:2** [f] S Eze 9:2 [g] S Eze 1:15 [h] Rev 8:5 [i] S 2Sa 22:9 **10:4** [j] S Ex 24:16; Eze 9:3; 44:4 **10:5** [k] S Job 40:9 [l] S Eze 3:13

God's Glory Departs From the Temple

10 I looked, and I saw the likeness of
a throne[b] of lapis lazuli[c] above the
vault[d] that was over the heads of the cherubim.[e] 2 The LORD said to the man clothed
in linen,[f] "Go in among the wheels[g] beneath the cherubim. Fill[h] your hands with
burning coals[i] from among the cherubim
and scatter them over the city." And as I
watched, he went in.
3 Now the cherubim were standing on
the south side of the temple when the man
went in, and a cloud filled the inner court.
4 Then the glory of the LORD[j] rose from above
the cherubim and moved to the threshold
of the temple. The cloud filled the temple,
and the court was full of the radiance of the
glory of the LORD. 5 The sound of the wings
of the cherubim could be heard as far away
as the outer court, like the voice[k] of God
Almighty[a] when he speaks.[l]
6 When the LORD commanded the man in
linen, "Take fire from among the wheels,[m]
from among the cherubim," the man went
in and stood beside a wheel. 7 Then one
of the cherubim reached out his hand to
the fire[n] that was among them. He took up
some of it and put it into the hands of the
man in linen, who took it and went out.
8 (Under the wings of the cherubim could
be seen what looked like human hands.)[o]
9 I looked, and I saw beside the cherubim four wheels, one beside each of the
cherubim; the wheels sparkled like topaz.[p] 10 As for their appearance, the four of
them looked alike; each was like a wheel
intersecting a wheel. 11 As they moved,
they would go in any one of the four directions the cherubim faced; the wheels
did not turn about[b] as the cherubim went.

[a] 5 Hebrew *El-Shaddai* [b] 11 Or *aside*

10:6 [m] Da 7:9 **10:7** [n] S Eze 5:4 **10:8** [o] Eze 1:8 **10:9** [p] S Ex 28:20; Rev 21:20

9:3 *the glory ... went up.* God began to vacate the temple, his glory moving to the door (see note on 8:1—11:25).
9:4 *mark.* A *taw*, the last letter of the Hebrew alphabet, which originally looked like an "x" (see Rev 7:2-4 and note on 7:2; cf. Rev 13:16 and note). *those who grieve and lament.* The remnant (see 1Ki 19:18).
9:5 *kill, without showing pity.* See La 2:21.
9:6 *Begin at my sanctuary.* Because that was a primary source of the evil that pervaded Jerusalem (see ch. 8). Cf. an echo in 1Pe 4:17.
9:8 *crying out.* See 11:13. As those who served as intermediaries between God and his people, the prophets frequently interceded on behalf of the people when God's judgments threatened (see Ex 32:31; Nu 14:13-19; 1Sa 12:23; Jer 14:19-21; 15:1; Am 7:2,5).
9:9 *land is full of bloodshed.* See 7:23 and note.
9:10 *bring down on their own heads what they have done.* See 16:43; Jer 50:15; Pr 26:27 and note.
10:1-22 See note on 8:1—11:25.
10:1 *I looked.* Ch. 10 echoes ch. 1, underscoring the identity of what Ezekiel saw at the Kebar River with what he now sees in his vision (see 8:4). The creatures in ch. 1 are here called cherubim (see note on 1:5).
10:2 *burning coals.* While in 1:13 the living creatures looked like burning coals, here there are real coals. *scatter them over the city.* A judgment by fire (see Ge 19:24; Am 7:4).
10:3 *cloud.* The cloud that enclosed the "glory of the LORD" (v. 4), which otherwise would have blinded those who saw it (see 1:4; Ex 16:10; 24:15-17; 40:34-35,38; Nu 9:15-16; 16:42; Dt 5:23; 1Ki 8:10-12; Hag 2:7 and note; cf. Mt 13:5; 24:30; 26:64; Mk 9:7; 13:26; 14:62; Lk 9:34-35; 21:27; Ac 1:9; Rev 1:7; 14:14-16).
10:7 *one of the cherubim reached out his hand.* Though the "man clothed in linen" was initially commanded to get the coals himself (v. 2), he received them from the hand of one of the creatures (see 1:8). *who took it and went out.* No further report is given, but the destructive spreading of the coals over Jerusalem is assumed.

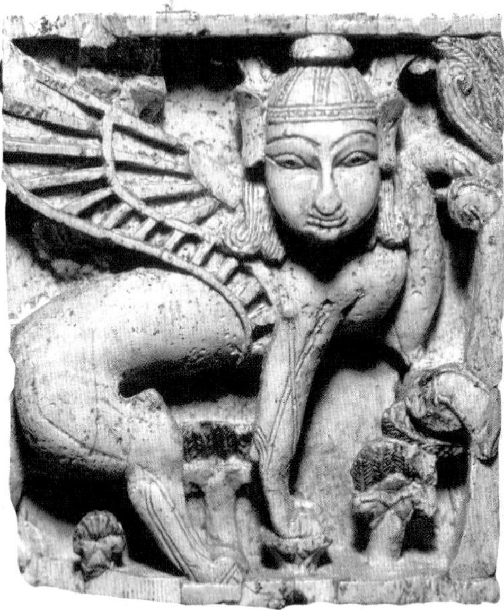

Phoenician ivory of a winged creature (c. ninth century BC). Ezekiel 10:1 – 5 mentions the cherubim in God's temple.

Z. Radovan/www.BibleLandPictures.com

The cherubim went in whatever direction
the head faced, without turning as they
went. 12 Their entire bodies, including their
backs, their hands and their wings, were
completely full of eyes,[q] as were their four
wheels.[r] 13 I heard the wheels being called
"the whirling wheels." 14 Each of the cherubim[s] had four faces:[t] One face was that of
a cherub, the second the face of a human
being, the third the face of a lion,[u] and the
fourth the face of an eagle.[v]
15 Then the cherubim rose upward.
These were the living creatures[w] I had
seen by the Kebar River.[x] 16 When the
cherubim moved, the wheels beside them
moved; and when the cherubim spread
their wings to rise from the ground, the
wheels did not leave their side. 17 When
the cherubim stood still, they also stood
still; and when the cherubim rose, they
rose with them, because the spirit of the
living creatures was in them.[y]
18 Then the glory[z] of the LORD departed
from over the threshold of the temple and
stopped above the cherubim.[a] 19 While I
watched, the cherubim spread their wings
and rose from the ground, and as they
went, the wheels went with them.[b] They
stopped at the entrance of the east gate of
the LORD's house, and the glory[c] of the God
of Israel was above them.
20 These were the living creatures I had
seen beneath the God of Israel by the Kebar River,[d] and I realized that they were
cherubim. 21 Each had four faces[e] and four
wings,[f] and under their wings was what
looked like human hands. 22 Their faces
had the same appearance as those I had
seen by the Kebar River.[g] Each one went
straight ahead.

God's Sure Judgment on Jerusalem

11 Then the Spirit lifted me up and
brought me to the gate of the house
of the LORD that faces east. There at the entrance of the gate were twenty-five men,
and I saw among them Jaazaniah son of
Azzur and Pelatiah[h] son of Benaiah, leaders[i]
of the people.[j] 2 The LORD said to me, "Son
of man, these are the men who are plotting evil[k] and giving wicked advice in this
city.[l] 3 They say, 'Haven't our houses been
recently rebuilt? This city is a pot,[m] and we
are the meat in it.'[n] 4 Therefore prophesy[o]
against them; prophesy, son of man."
5 Then the Spirit of the LORD came on
me, and he told me to say: "This is what
the LORD says: That is what you are saying, you leaders in Israel, but I know what
is going through your mind.[p] 6 You have
killed many people in this city and filled
its streets with the dead.[q]
7 "Therefore this is what the Sovereign
LORD says: The bodies you have thrown

10:12 [q] Rev 4:6-8 [r] Eze 1:15-21 **10:14** [s] 1Ki 7:36 [t] Eze 1:6 [u] 1Ki 7:29 [v] Eze 1:10; 41:19; Rev 4:7 **10:15** [w] S Isa 6:2 [x] S Ps 137:1 **10:17** [y] S Eze 3:13 **10:18** [z] S 1Sa 4:21 [a] S Ps 18:10 **10:19** [b] Eze 11:1, 22 [c] Eze 43:4 **10:20** [d] Eze 1:1 **10:21** [e] Eze 41:18 [f] Eze 1:6 **10:22** [g] Eze 1:1 **11:1** [h] ver 13 [i] Jer 5:5 [j] S Eze 8:16; S 10:19; 43:4-5 **11:2** [k] S Isa 29:20; Na 1:11 [l] Eze 8:11 **11:3** [m] Jer 1:13; Eze 24:3 [n] ver 7, 11; Eze 12:22, 27; Mic 3:3 **11:4** [o] S Eze 3:4, 17 **11:5** [p] S Ps 26:2; S Jer 17:10 **11:6** [q] S Eze 7:23; 22:6

10:14 *One face was that of a cherub.* While the faces of the human being, lion and eagle are identical with those in 1:10 (see note on 1:5), the ox is here called a cherub (see note on Ge 3:24).
10:15 *Kebar River.* See 1:1 and note.
10:19 *east gate ... and the glory of the God of Israel was above them.* A second movement of the glory, again in an easterly direction (see 9:3; 10:4; see also note on 8:1 — 11:25). See ch. 43 for the return of the glory of the Lord to the temple by way of the east gate (see note on 43:1 – 12).
11:1 – 13 See note on 8:1 — 11:25.
11:1 *the Spirit lifted me up.* See 3:12 and note. *twenty-five men.* See 8:16 and note. *Jaazaniah.* See note on 8:11. *Pelatiah.* Means "The LORD delivers."
11:3 *Haven't our houses been recently rebuilt?* The residents of Jerusalem who were not exiled by the Babylonians in 597 BC felt smugly secure, thinking they had no further Babylonian threat to fear. *pot.* As in ch. 24, Jerusalem is compared to a cooking pot. Those left behind boasted that they were the "meat," the choice portions — the inference being that the exiles in Babylon were the discarded bones (see v. 15).
11:5 *the Spirit of the LORD came on me.* See 2:2 and note.
11:6 *killed many ... filled its streets with the dead.* See 7:23 and note.
11:7 *The bodies you have thrown there are the meat.* The meat, redefined by the prophet, is not those in power in Jerusalem (who will be driven out) but the innocent people they killed.

there are the meat and this city is the pot,[r]
but I will drive you out of it.[s] 8You fear the
sword,[t] and the sword is what I will bring
against you, declares the Sovereign LORD.[u]
9I will drive you out of the city and deliver you into the hands[v] of foreigners and
inflict punishment on you.[w] 10You will fall
by the sword, and I will execute judgment
on you at the borders of Israel.[x] Then you
will know that I am the LORD. 11This city
will not be a pot[y] for you, nor will you be
the meat in it; I will execute judgment on
you at the borders of Israel. 12And you will
know that I am the LORD,[z] for you have
not followed my decrees[a] or kept my laws
but have conformed to the standards of
the nations around you.[b]"

13Now as I was prophesying, Pelatiah[c]
son of Benaiah died. Then I fell facedown
and cried out in a loud voice, "Alas, Sovereign LORD! Will you completely destroy
the remnant of Israel?[d]"

The Promise of Israel's Return

14The word of the LORD came to me:
15"Son of man, the people of Jerusalem
have said of your fellow exiles and all the
other Israelites, 'They are far away from
the LORD; this land was given to us as our
possession.'[e]

16"Therefore say: 'This is what the Sovereign LORD says: Although I sent them
far away among the nations and scattered
them among the countries, yet for a little
while I have been a sanctuary[f] for them in
the countries where they have gone.'

17"Therefore say: 'This is what the Sovereign LORD says: I will gather you from the
nations and bring you back from the countries where you have been scattered, and I
will give you back the land of Israel again.'[g]

18"They will return to it and remove all
its vile images[h] and detestable idols.[i] 19I
will give them an undivided heart[j] and put
a new spirit in them; I will remove from
them their heart of stone[k] and give them a
heart of flesh.[l] 20Then they will follow my
decrees and be careful to keep my laws.[m]
They will be my people,[n] and I will be
their God.[o] 21But as for those whose hearts
are devoted to their vile images and detestable idols,[p] I will bring down on their
own heads what they have done, declares
the Sovereign LORD.[q]"

22Then the cherubim, with the wheels
beside them, spread their wings, and
the glory[r] of the God of Israel was above
them.[s] 23The glory[t] of the LORD went up
from within the city and stopped above
the mountain[u] east of it. 24The Spirit[v] lifted me up and brought me to the exiles
in Babylonia[a] in the vision[w] given by the
Spirit of God.

Then the vision I had seen went up
from me, 25and I told the exiles everything
the LORD had shown me.[x]

The Exile Symbolized

12 The word of the LORD came to
me: 2"Son of man, you are living
among a rebellious people.[y] They have
eyes to see but do not see and ears to hear
but do not hear, for they are a rebellious
people.[z]

3"Therefore, son of man, pack your belongings for exile and in the daytime, as
they watch, set out and go from where you
are to another place. Perhaps[a] they will
understand,[b] though they are a rebellious
people.[c] 4During the daytime, while they
watch, bring out your belongings packed

[a] 24 Or *Chaldea*

11:7 [r]Jer 1:13 [s]ver 3; Eze 24:3-13; Mic 3:2-3 **11:8** [t]S Lev 26:25; S Jer 42:16 [u]S Pr 10:24; Isa 66:4 **11:9** [v]Ps 106:41 [w]Dt 28:36; S Eze 5:8 **11:10** [x]2Ki 14:25 **11:11** [y]ver 3; Eze 24:6 **11:12** [z]S Eze 6:7 [a]S Lev 18:4; Eze 18:9 [b]Eze 8:10 **11:13** [c]ver 1 [d]S Eze 9:8; Am 7:2 **11:15** [e]Eze 33:24 **11:16** [f]Ps 31:20; 90:1; 91:9; S Isa 4:6 **11:17** [g]S Ne 1:9; S Jer 3:18; 24:5-6; S 31:16; Eze 20:41; 28:25; 34:13; 36:28 **11:18** [h]S Eze 5:11 [i]Eze 37:23 **11:19** [j]S 2Ch 30:12; S Ps 86:11 [k]Zec 7:12; Ro 2:5 [l]Eze 18:31; S 2Co 3:3 **11:20** [m]S Ps 1:2 [n]S Jer 11:4; 32:38 [o]S Ex 6:7; Eze 14:11; 34:30; 36:26-28; Hos 1:9; Zec 8:8; Heb 8:10 **11:21** [p]Jer 16:18 [q]Jer 16:11; S Eze 9:10; 16:43 **11:22** [r]S Ex 24:16 [s]Eze 9:3; S 10:19

11:23 [t]Eze 1:28; S 10:4 [u]Zec 14:4 **11:24** [v]Eze 37:1; 43:5 [w]2Co 12:2-4 **11:25** [x]S Eze 3:4,11 **12:2** [y]Ps 78:40; S Jer 42:21 [z]S Isa 6:10; S Mt 13:15; Mk 4:12; 8:18 **12:3** [a]S Jer 36:3 [b]Jer 26:3 [c]ver 11; S Eze 3:27; 2Ti 2:25-26

11:11 *at the borders of Israel.* At Riblah (see 2Ki 25:20–21).
11:13 *cried out.* See note on 9:8.
11:14–21 See note on 8:1—11:25.
11:16 *I have been a sanctuary for them.* A key verse in Ezekiel. Although the exiles had been driven from Jerusalem and its sanctuary (the symbol of God's presence among his people), God himself became their sanctuary, i.e., he was present among them to preserve and bless them.
11:19 *undivided heart ... new spirit.* Inner spiritual and moral transformation that results in single-minded commitment to the Lord and to his will (see 36:26). *remove ... heart of stone ... give ... heart of flesh.* Give Israel a new heart, responsive to God's will (see 2Co 3:3 and note).
11:20 *my people ... their God.* The heart of God's covenant promise (see Ex 6:7; Jer 7:23; Zec 8:8 and notes).
11:21 *bring down on their own heads what they have done.* See note on 9:10.
11:22–25 See note on 8:1—11:25.
11:23 *The glory of the LORD went up.* The final eastward movement of the glory (as the Lord left his temple), which stopped above the Mount of Olives (see 9:3; 10:4,19; see also note on 8:1—11:25). God's glory returns in ch. 43.
11:24 See note on 8:3.
12:1–28 The first series of messages concludes with Ezekiel being called upon to symbolize by personal actions the coming exile of Jerusalem—just as the second series of messages culuminates (24:15–27) in Ezekiel suffering the death of his wife as a symbolic representation of the fall of Jerusalem. Verses 1–2 and v. 28 frame the chapter; two symbolic acts (vv. 3–16,17–20) are followed by the refutation of two sayings with which the Jerusalemites vainly try to reassure themselves (vv. 21–25,26–27).
12:2 *eyes to see but do not see.* The hardening about which the Lord had spoken to Isaiah (see Isa 6:8–10 and notes). The Israelites in Jerusalem refuse to recognize that the end has come for them (see v. 28; 7:2–6).
12:3 *pack your belongings.* Another symbolic act, which, like those in chs. 4–5, follows a vision. *Perhaps they will understand.* Some hope remained that they would change.

for exile. Then in the evening, while they
are watching, go out like those who go
into exile.[d] 5 While they watch, dig through
the wall[e] and take your belongings out
through it. 6 Put them on your shoulder as
they are watching and carry them out at
dusk. Cover your face so that you cannot
see the land, for I have made you a sign[f]
to the Israelites."
7 So I did as I was commanded.[g] During
the day I brought out my things packed for
exile. Then in the evening I dug through
the wall with my hands. I took my belongings out at dusk, carrying them on my
shoulders while they watched.
8 In the morning the word of the LORD
came to me: 9 "Son of man, did not the
Israelites, that rebellious people, ask you,
'What are you doing?'[h]
10 "Say to them, 'This is what the Sovereign LORD says: This prophecy concerns
the prince in Jerusalem and all the Israelites who are there.' 11 Say to them, 'I am a
sign[i] to you.'
"As I have done, so it will be done to
them. They will go into exile as captives.[j]
12 "The prince among them will put his
things on his shoulder at dusk[k] and leave,
and a hole will be dug in the wall for him
to go through. He will cover his face so
that he cannot see the land.[l] 13 I will spread
my net[m] for him, and he will be caught in
my snare;[n] I will bring him to Babylonia,
the land of the Chaldeans,[o] but he will not
see[p] it, and there he will die.[q] 14 I will scatter to the winds all those around him—his
staff and all his troops—and I will pursue
them with drawn sword.[r]
15 "They will know that I am the LORD,
when I disperse them among the nations[s]
and scatter them through the countries.
16 But I will spare a few of them from the
sword, famine and plague, so that in the
nations where they go they may acknowledge all their detestable practices. Then
they will know that I am the LORD.[t]"
17 The word of the LORD came to me:
18 "Son of man, tremble as you eat your
food,[u] and shudder in fear as you drink
your water. 19 Say to the people of the land:
'This is what the Sovereign LORD says
about those living in Jerusalem and in the
land of Israel: They will eat their food in
anxiety and drink their water in despair,
for their land will be stripped of everything[v] in it because of the violence of all
who live there.[w] 20 The inhabited towns will
be laid waste and the land will be desolate.
Then you will know that I am the LORD.[x]' "

There Will Be No Delay

21 The word of the LORD came to me:
22 "Son of man, what is this proverb[y] you
have in the land of Israel: 'The days go
by and every vision comes to nothing'?[z]
23 Say to them, 'This is what the Sovereign
LORD says: I am going to put an end to this
proverb, and they will no longer quote it
in Israel.' Say to them, 'The days are near[a]
when every vision will be fulfilled.[b] 24 For
there will be no more false visions or flattering divinations[c] among the people of
Israel. 25 But I the LORD will speak what
I will, and it shall be fulfilled without delay.[d] For in your days, you rebellious people, I will fulfill[e] whatever I say, declares
the Sovereign LORD.[f]' "
26 The word of the LORD came to me:
27 "Son of man, the Israelites are saying,
'The vision he sees is for many years from
now, and he prophesies about the distant
future.'[g]

12:4 [d] ver 12; 2Ki 25:4; S Jer 39:4 **12:5** [e] Jer 52:7; Am 4:3 **12:6** [f] ver 12; S Isa 8:18; S 20:3 **12:7** [g] Eze 24:18; 37:10 **12:9** [h] Eze 17:12; 20:49; 24:19 **12:11** [i] Isa 8:18; Zec 3:8 [j] S 2Ki 25:7; S Jer 15:2; 52:15 **12:12** [k] S Jer 39:4 [l] Jer 52:7 **12:13** [m] Eze 17:20; 19:8; 32:3; Hos 7:12 [n] S Isa 24:17-18 [o] Eze 1:3 [p] S Jer 39:7 [q] S Jer 24:8; S 52:11; S La 4:20; Eze 17:16 **12:14** [r] S 2Ki 25:5; S Jer 21:7; S Eze 5:10, 12; 17:21 **12:15** [s] S Lev 26:33 **12:16** [t] S Jer 22:8-9; Eze 6:8-10; 14:22; 36:20 **12:18** [u] La 5:9 **12:19** [v] Jer 10:22; S Eze 6:6-14; Mic 7:13; Zec 7:14 [w] S Eze 4:16; 23:33 **12:20** [x] Isa 7:23-24; S Jer 4:7; S 25:9 **12:22** [y] S Ps 49:4 [z] S Isa 5:19; Eze 11:3; Am 6:3; 2Pe 3:4

12:23 [a] S Eze 7:7 [b] S Ps 37:13; Eze 18:3; Joel 2:1; Zep 1:14 **12:24** [c] Jer 14:14; Eze 13:23; Mic 3:6; Zec 13:2-4 **12:25** [d] Hab 2:3 [e] S Nu 11:23; Eze 13:6 [f] Nu 14:28-34; S Isa 14:24; S 55:11; Jer 16:9; Hab 1:5 **12:27** [g] S Eze 11:3; Da 10:14; Mt 24:48-50; 2Pe 3:4

12:5 *dig through the wall.* Not the city wall, which was made of stone and was many feet thick, but the sun-dried brick wall of his house.

12:6 *sign.* Prophets were often instructed to perform symbolic acts (see, e.g., v. 11; 24:24,27; cf. 1Ki 11:29–31; 13:23–32; 20:35–43; Isa 8:18; Jer 13:1–11; 16:1–9; 19:1–15; 27:2—28:14; 32:6–15).

12:8 *In the morning.* After Ezekiel "did as ... commanded" (v. 7). Again the divine explanation follows the prophet's unquestioning obedience (see note on 8:3).

12:9 *What are you doing?* The book's first indication of the people's response to the prophet's symbolic acts.

12:10 *prince in Jerusalem.* Zedekiah.

12:13 *Chaldeans.* See notes on 23:23; Ezr 5:12; Job 1:17. *he will not see it.* Nebuchadnezzar's men would put out Zedekiah's eyes (see 2Ki 25:7).

12:14 *with drawn sword.* See 5:2 and note.

12:15 *know that I am the LORD.* See vv. 16,20; see also note on 6:7.

12:16 *sword, famine and plague.* See 5:16–17 and note.

12:18 *tremble as you eat.* Another prophetic symbol. Ezekiel's trembling must have been particularly violent, because the Hebrew word for "tremble" is used elsewhere to describe an earthquake (see 1Ki 19:11; Am 1:1).

12:19 *people of the land.* See note on 7:27. *because of the violence.* See 7:23 and note.

12:22 For more than 30 years Jeremiah had been prophesying Jerusalem's fall, but the city still stood. So among its inhabitants, whose ears were deaf to Jeremiah's warnings (v. 2), a mocking proverb was making the rounds, reinforced by the false prophets (see ch. 13; Jer 23:9–40; 28), which said in effect: "The days go by" and none of the visions of coming disaster have come true, so forget them.

12:23 The Lord refutes the first saying (v. 22) of the Israelites that dismisses his prophet's announcements of impending judgment.

12:24 *no more false visions ... divinations.* Events will silence the false prophets, whose "visions are false and their divinations a lie" (13:6).

12:27 Another saying (see note on v. 23) is being passed around among the Israelites, this one apparently among those in exile. It pertains to Ezekiel's "visions" and dismisses

28 "Therefore say to them, 'This is what the Sovereign LORD says: None of my words will be delayed any longer; whatever I say will be fulfilled, declares the Sovereign LORD.' "

False Prophets Condemned

13 The word of the LORD came to me: 2 "Son of man, prophesy against the prophets[h] of Israel who are now prophesying. Say to those who prophesy out of their own imagination:[i] 'Hear the word of the LORD![j] 3 This is what the Sovereign LORD says: Woe to the foolish[a] prophets[k] who follow their own spirit and have seen nothing![l] 4 Your prophets, Israel, are like jackals among ruins. 5 You have not gone up to the breaches in the wall to repair[m] it for the people of Israel so that it will stand firm in the battle on the day of the LORD.[n] 6 Their visions are false[o] and their divinations a lie. Even though the LORD has not sent[p] them, they say, "The LORD declares," and expect him to fulfill their words.[q] 7 Have you not seen false visions[r] and uttered lying divinations when you say, "The LORD declares," though I have not spoken?

8 " 'Therefore this is what the Sovereign LORD says: Because of your false words and lying visions, I am against you,[s] declares the Sovereign LORD. 9 My hand will be against the prophets who see false visions and utter lying[t] divinations. They will not belong to the council of my people or be listed in the records[u] of Israel, nor will they enter the land of Israel. Then you will know that I am the Sovereign LORD.[v]

10 " 'Because they lead my people astray,[w] saying, "Peace,"[x] when there is no peace, and because, when a flimsy wall is built, they cover it with whitewash,[y] 11 therefore tell those who cover it with whitewash that it is going to fall. Rain will come in torrents, and I will send hailstones[z] hurtling down,[a] and violent winds will burst forth.[b] 12 When the wall collapses, will people not ask you, "Where is the whitewash you covered it with?"

13 " 'Therefore this is what the Sovereign LORD says: In my wrath I will unleash a violent wind, and in my anger hailstones[c] and torrents of rain[d] will fall with destructive fury.[e] 14 I will tear down the wall[f] you have covered with whitewash and will level it to the ground so that its foundation[g] will be laid bare. When it[b] falls,[h] you will be destroyed in it; and you will know that I am the LORD. 15 So I will pour out my wrath against the wall and against those who covered it with whitewash. I will say to you, "The wall is gone and so are those who whitewashed it, 16 those prophets of Israel who prophesied to Jerusalem and saw visions of peace for her when there was no peace, declares the Sovereign LORD.[i]" '

17 "Now, son of man, set your face[j] against the daughters[k] of your people who prophesy out of their own imagination. Prophesy against them[l] 18 and say, 'This is what the Sovereign LORD says: Woe to the women who sew magic charms on all their wrists and make veils of various lengths for their heads in order to ensnare people. Will you ensnare the lives of my

[a] 3 Or *wicked* [b] 14 Or *the city*

13:2 [h] S Isa 9:15 [i] Jer 28:15 [j] ver 17; S Jer 23:16; S 37:19; Eze 22:28 **13:3** [k] S La 2:14; Hos 9:7 [l] S Jer 23:25-32 **13:5** [m] Isa 58:12; Eze 22:30 [n] S Eze 7:19; 30:3 **13:6** [o] S Jer 5:1; 23:16 [p] S Jer 14:14 [q] S Jer 28:15; S 29:9; Eze 12:24-25; 22:28 **13:7** [r] S Isa 30:10 **13:8** [s] S Jer 21:13 **13:9** [t] S Dt 13:3 [u] S Ex 32:32; S Jer 17:13 [v] S Ex 6:2; Jer 20:3-6; Eze 20:38 **13:10** [w] S Jer 23:13; S 50:6 [x] S Jer 4:10 [y] S Eze 7:25; 22:28 **13:11** [z] S Jos 10:11 [a] S Job 38:23 [b] Ps 11:6; Eze 38:22 **13:13** [c] S Jos 10:11; Rev 11:19; 16:21 [d] Job 14:19 [e] S Ex 9:25; S Job 38:23; Isa 30:30 **13:14** [f] S Isa 22:5 [g] Mic 1:6 [h] Jer 6:15 **13:16** [i] S Isa 57:21; Jer 6:14; S Eze 7:25 **13:17** [j] S Eze 4:7; 25:2; 28:21 [k] S Ex 15:20; Rev 2:20 [l] S ver 2

them as having to do only with far-off events that need not concern the present generation.

12:28 *None of my words will be delayed any longer.* The Lord also refutes this saying (v. 27) circulating among his "rebellious people" (v. 2; see note on 12:1–28).

13:1–23 The Lord's condemnation of the false prophets, both men and women—as through Jeremiah in Jerusalem (Jer 23:9–40; 28), so through Ezekiel in Babylonia. This begins a series of messages concerning God's judgment on Judah that concludes with a parable in which Jerusalem is likened to a pot cooking on a fire (24:1–14).

13:2 *out of their own imagination.* Cf. Jer 23:16, 26–32.

13:3 *have seen nothing.* No revelation from God was received (cf. Jer 23:18,22 and note on 23:18).

13:4 *jackals.* Animals that travel in packs and feed on dead flesh—a powerfully negative image (see Ps 63:10; La 5:18).

13:5 *to repair it for the people of Israel.* The function of true prophets is described (cf. 22:30; Ps 106:23). *day of the LORD.* See note on 7:7.

13:6 *Their visions are false.* Whether the false prophets had actual visions is unknown, but they claimed to have received revelations from God when in reality their messages only proclaimed what their hearers wanted to hear (see 12:24 and note; Isa 30:10; Jer 23:9–17; 2Ti 4:3).

13:8 *I am against you.* See 5:8 and note.

13:9 *They will not belong ... land of Israel.* A threefold punishment, resulting in total exclusion from the community. *council of my people.* See Ps 111:1 and note. *records of Israel.* See Ezr 2:62; cf. Da 12:1; see also Ps 69:28 and note.

13:10 *saying, "Peace."* Very likely in echo of the priestly benediction (see Nu 6:24–26 and note on 6:26), ignoring the fact that God's promise of "peace" to his people was conditional on their faithfulness to him. *when there is no peace.* See v. 16; Jer 6:14 and note; 8:11. *whitewash.* See vv. 11,14–15; 22:28; an uncommon word used only by Ezekiel, perhaps chosen by him to evoke the like-sounding word rendered "repulsive thing" in Jer 23:13 and "worthless" in La 2:14, both pertaining to the proclamations of the false prophets.

13:11 *Rain will come in torrents.* The violent thunderstorm of God's judgment (imagery frequently used in the OT) was about to sweep them away (see, e.g., Ps 18:7–15; 77:17–18; 83:15; Isa 28:17; 30:30; Jer 23:19; 30:23).

13:18 *magic charms.* Exactly what the women were doing is not known, but that it was some kind of black magic or voodoo is clear. The Bible consistently avoids explicit description of occult practices.

people but preserve your own? 19 You have profaned[m] me among my people for a few handfuls of barley and scraps of bread.[n] By lying to my people, who listen to lies, you have killed those who should not have died and have spared those who should not live.[o]

20 " 'Therefore this is what the Sovereign LORD says: I am against your magic charms with which you ensnare people like birds and I will tear them from your arms; I will set free the people that you ensnare like birds.[p] 21 I will tear off your veils and save my people from your hands, and they will no longer fall prey to your power. Then you will know that I am the LORD.[q] 22 Because you disheartened the righteous with your lies,[r] when I had brought them no grief, and because you encouraged the wicked not to turn from their evil ways and so save their lives,[s] 23 therefore you will no longer see false visions[t] or practice divination.[u] I will save[v] my people from your hands. And then you will know that I am the LORD.[w]' "

Idolaters Condemned

14 Some of the elders of Israel came to me and sat down in front of me.[x] 2 Then the word of the LORD came to me: 3 "Son of man, these men have set up idols in their hearts[y] and put wicked stumbling blocks[z] before their faces. Should I let them inquire of me at all?[a] 4 Therefore speak to them and tell them, 'This is what the Sovereign LORD says: When any of the Israelites set up idols in their hearts and put a wicked stumbling block before their faces and then go to a prophet, I the LORD will answer them myself in keeping with their great idolatry. 5 I will do this to recapture the hearts of the people of Israel, who have all deserted[b] me for their idols.'[c]

6 "Therefore say to the people of Israel, 'This is what the Sovereign LORD says: Repent![d] Turn from your idols and renounce all your detestable practices![e]

7 " 'When any of the Israelites or any foreigner[f] residing in Israel separate themselves from me and set up idols in their hearts and put a wicked stumbling block[g] before their faces and then go to a prophet to inquire[h] of me, I the LORD will answer them myself. 8 I will set my face against[i] them and make them an example[j] and a byword.[k] I will remove them from my people. Then you will know that I am the LORD.[l]

9 " 'And if the prophet[m] is enticed[n] to utter a prophecy, I the LORD have enticed that prophet, and I will stretch out my hand against him and destroy him from among my people Israel.[o] 10 They will bear their guilt—the prophet will be as guilty as the one who consults him. 11 Then the people of Israel will no longer stray[p] from me, nor will they defile themselves anymore with all their sins. They will be my people,[q] and I will be their God, declares the Sovereign LORD.[r]' "

Jerusalem's Judgment Inescapable

12 The word of the LORD came to me: 13 "Son of man, if a country sins[s] against me by being unfaithful and I stretch out my hand against it to cut off its food supply[t] and send famine upon it and kill its people and their animals,[u] 14 even if these three men—Noah,[v] Daniel[a][w] and Job[x]—were in it, they could save only themselves by their righteousness,[y] declares the Sovereign LORD.

[a] 14 Or *Danel,* a man of renown in ancient literature; also in verse 20

13:19 [m] Jer 44:26; Eze 20:39; 22:26; 36:20; 39:7 [n] S Isa 56:11 [o] Pr 28:21; Mic 3:11 **13:20** [p] Ps 124:7 **13:21** [q] Ps 91:3 **13:22** [r] S Isa 9:15 [s] Jer 23:14; Eze 18:21; 33:14-16 **13:23** [t] Ne 6:12 [u] S Eze 12:24 [v] S Ps 72:14 [w] Mic 3:6 **14:1** [x] S Eze 8:1; 20:1 **14:3** [y] S Eze 6:4 [z] S ver 7; S Eze 7:19 [a] Isa 1:15; Eze 20:31 **14:5** [b] S Dt 32:15; Eze 16:45; Hos 5:7; Zec 11:8 [c] Jer 2:11 **14:6** [d] Ne 1:9; S Jer 3:12; S 35:15 [e] S Isa 2:20; S 30:22 **14:7** [f] Ex 12:48; 20:10 [g] ver 3; S Isa 8:14; Hos 4:5; 5:5 [h] S Ge 25:22 **14:8** [i] Eze 15:7 [j] S Nu 16:38 [k] S Ps 102:8; S Eze 5:15 [l] S Jer 42:20 **14:9** [m] S Jer 14:15 [n] Isa 63:17; Jer 4:10 [o] 1Ki 22:23; S 2Ch 18:22; Zec 13:3 **14:11** [p] Eze 48:11 [q] S Isa 51:16 [r] S Eze 11:19-20; 37:23 **14:13** [s] S Pr 13:21 [t] S Lev 26:26 [u] S Eze 5:16; 6:14; 15:8 **14:14** [v] Ge 6:8 [w] ver 20; Eze 28:3; Da 1:6; 6:13 [x] S Job 1:1 [y] S Ge 6:9; S Job 42:9; Jer 15:1; S Eze 3:19; 18:20

13:19 *profaned me.* See note on Lev 18:21. *for a few handfuls of barley.* Involvement in religious matters of any kind for mere gain is consistently condemned in the Bible (see, e.g., Jer 6:13; 8:10; Mic 3:5,11; Ac 8:9–24; 2Co 2:17; Titus 1:11). For the proper attitude and motivation, see 2Co 11:7; 2Th 3:8; 1Ti 3:3. *you have killed.* The women had used their evil powers for unjust ends, involving even matters of life and death.

14:1–11 The idolatry among the Israelites that God here condemns took the form of worshiping the gods of neighboring peoples (see notes on Ge 20:9; Ex 34:15) along with the worship of Yahweh—the people thought they should take all the gods seriously—an apostasy that struck at the very heart of Israel's covenant relationship with Yahweh (see Ex 20:3–5 and notes). And this idolatry was not limited to those still living in Jerusalem; Ezekiel had to confront it also among the exiles.

14:1 *elders of Israel.* Apparently interchangeable with "elders of Judah" (see note on 8:1).

14:3 *idols.* See note on 6:4. *wicked stumbling blocks.* The physical representations of the idols. *inquire.* A technical term for seeking a message from a prophet (see 2Ki 1:16; 3:11; 8:8).

14:4 *I the LORD will answer them myself.* Not through a prophet but by direct action. The punishment for idolatry was death (Dt 13:6–18).

14:6 *Repent!* First of three calls for repentance from Ezekiel, who elsewhere proclaims inescapable judgment (see 18:30; 33:11).

14:9 *enticed.* Related to God's testing of his people's loyalty (see 3:20 and note; cf. 1Ki 22:19–23).

14:11 The harsh judgment about to fall on idolatrous Israel has a redemptive purpose: to restore Israel to covenant faithfulness (see 20:32–44; cf. 33:11). *my people … their God.* Covenant terminology (see note on 11:20).

14:12–23 Israel must know that once God's judgments have been sent upon an unfaithful nation, no one can persuade him to call them back—and that will be even more true of Jerusalem (cf. Jer 15:1 and note). The judgments in view here include the four often mentioned in Ezekiel: famine (v. 13), wild beasts (v. 15), sword (v. 17) and plague (v. 19; see also v. 21 and note on 5:16–17).

14:14,20 *Noah, Daniel and Job.* Three ancient men of renown, selected because of their proverbial righ-

15 "Or if I send wild beasts[z] through that country and they leave it childless and it becomes desolate so that no one can pass through it because of the beasts,[a] 16 as surely as I live, declares the Sovereign LORD, even if these three men were in it, they could not save their own sons or daughters. They alone would be saved, but the land would be desolate.[b]

17 "Or if I bring a sword[c] against that country and say, 'Let the sword pass throughout the land,' and I kill its people and their animals,[d] 18 as surely as I live, declares the Sovereign LORD, even if these three men were in it, they could not save their own sons or daughters. They alone would be saved.

19 "Or if I send a plague into that land and pour out my wrath[e] on it through bloodshed,[f] killing its people and their animals,[g] 20 as surely as I live, declares the Sovereign LORD, even if Noah, Daniel and Job were in it, they could save neither son nor daughter. They would save only themselves by their righteousness.[h]

21 "For this is what the Sovereign LORD says: How much worse will it be when I send against Jerusalem my four dreadful judgments[i] — sword[j] and famine[k] and wild beasts and plague[l] — to kill its men and their animals![m] 22 Yet there will be some survivors[n] — sons and daughters who will be brought out of it.[o] They will come to you, and when you see their conduct[p] and their actions, you will be consoled[q] regarding the disaster I have brought on Jerusalem — every disaster I have brought on it. 23 You will be consoled when you see their conduct and their actions, for you will know that I have done nothing in it without cause, declares the Sovereign LORD.[r]"

14:15 [z] Eze 5:17 [a] S Lev 26:22 **14:16** [b] S Ge 19:29; Eze 18:20 **14:17** [c] S Lev 26:25; S Jer 25:27; S 42:16 [d] Eze 25:13; Zep 1:3 **14:19** [e] S Eze 7:8 [f] S Isa 34:3 [g] Jer 14:12; Eze 38:22 **14:20** [h] S ver 14 **14:21** [i] S Nu 33:4 [j] Isa 31:8; 34:6; 66:16; Eze 21:3, 19 [k] S 2Sa 24:13 [l] S Jer 14:12; 27:8 [m] S Jer 15:3; S Eze 5:17; 33:27; Am 4:6-10; Rev 6:8 **14:22** [n] S Jer 41:16 [o] S Eze 12:16 [p] Eze 20:43 [q] Eze 31:16; 32:31 **14:23** [r] S Jer 22:8-9; Eze 8:6-18; S 9:9 **15:2** [s] Ps 80:8-16; Isa 5:1-7; 27:2-6; Jer 2:21; Hos 10:1; S Jn 15:2 **15:3** [t] Jer 13:10 [u] S Isa 22:23 **15:4** [v] Eze 17:3-10; 19:14; Jn 15:6 **15:7** [w] S Lev 26:17; Ps 34:16; Eze 14:8 [x] S Eze 5:2; S Eze 5:4 [y] Isa 24:18; Am 9:1-4 **15:8** [z] S Eze 14:13

Jerusalem as a Useless Vine

15 The word of the LORD came to me: 2 "Son of man, how is the wood of a vine[s] different from that of a branch from any of the trees in the forest? 3 Is wood ever taken from it to make anything useful?[t] Do they make pegs[u] from it to hang things on? 4 And after it is thrown on the fire as fuel and the fire burns both ends and chars the middle, is it then useful for anything?[v] 5 If it was not useful for anything when it was whole, how much less can it be made into something useful when the fire has burned it and it is charred?

6 "Therefore this is what the Sovereign LORD says: As I have given the wood of the vine among the trees of the forest as fuel for the fire, so will I treat the people living in Jerusalem. 7 I will set my face against[w] them. Although they have come out of the fire[x], the fire will yet consume them. And when I set my face against them, you will know that I am the LORD.[y] 8 I will make the land desolate[z] because they have been unfaithful,[a] declares the Sovereign LORD."

Jerusalem as an Adulterous Wife

16 The word of the LORD came to me: 2 "Son of man, confront[b] Jerusalem with her detestable practices[c] 3 and say, 'This is what the Sovereign LORD says to Jerusalem: Your ancestry[d] and birth were in the land of the Canaanites; your father[e] was an Amorite[f] and your mother a

[a] Eze 17:20; 18:24 **16:2** [b] S Isa 57:12; Eze 23:36 [c] Eze 8:17; 20:4; 22:2 **16:3** [d] Ge 11:25-29; Eze 21:30 [e] S Ge 12:18 [f] S Ge 15:16

---

teousness. As the NIV text note indicates, another Daniel may be referred to (Ugaritic literature speaks of an honored "Danel"; see chart, p. xxiv), since the Biblical Daniel's righteousness probably had not become proverbial so soon (Daniel and Ezekiel were contemporaries; see Da 1:1).

14:20 *neither son nor daughter.* When God comes in judgment against a nation or people, they cannot count on another's righteousness — not even that of their parents — to deliver them.

14:23 *You.* Plural; i.e., the exiles in Babylonia. *will be consoled.* When the exiles see the wickedness of those brought to Babylonia from Jerusalem, they will know that God's judgment on the city was just.

15:1 – 8 God compares Jerusalem to a vine (cf. Ps 80:8 – 16 and note) that yields no grapes and is therefore good for nothing but to be used as fuel.

15:3 *Do they make pegs from it to hang things on?* See Isa 22:23 – 25.

15:4 *is it then useful for anything?* Whereas Isaiah (5:1 – 7) and Jeremiah (2:21) express divine disappointment over Israel's failure to produce good fruit, Ezekiel typically laments her total uselessness.

15:7 *Although they have come out of the fire.* A reference to the siege of Jerusalem in 597 BC, which resulted in the exile of which Ezekiel was a part (see 1:2; 2Ki 24:10 – 16). *fire will yet consume them.* Prophecy threatening another and more devastating siege — Ezekiel's main message before 586 (see 5:2,4; 10:2,7).

16:1 – 63 The whole history of God's dealings with Jerusalem is graphically portrayed in an allegory that highlights the Lord's great goodness to the city on the one hand and the depth of the city's unfaithfulness to him on the other. Here Jerusalem as a royal city among the other cities of the world is in focus and serves as an analogue and representative of Israel. She is the city God had chosen to be the site of his temple (see 1Ki 9:3; 2Ch 7:1 – 3; Ps 68:16; 78:68 – 69; 132:13 – 16), and he had elevated her as "the city of the Great King" (Ps 48:2), to be the earthly center of his kingly rule in human affairs (see 5:5 and note). He had married her (see v. 8 and note) and provided for her richly. But she turned to the false gods to supply her needs and allied herself with the great empires around her (Egypt [v. 26], Assyria [v. 28] and Babylonia [v. 29]) to provide her security. So God accuses her of unfaithfulness to him, like that of an adulterous wife (see Ex 34:15 and note).

16:3 *Your ancestry and birth.* Jerusalem had a centuries-old, pre-Israelite history (see notes on Ge 14:18; Ecc 1:16), and the city had long resisted Israelite conquest (Jos 15:63). It became fully Israelite only after David's conquest (2Sa 5:6 – 9). *father ... mother.* A reference to Jerusalem's non-Israelite

Hittite.[g] [4]On the day you were born[h] your cord was not cut, nor were you washed with water to make you clean, nor were you rubbed with salt or wrapped in cloths. [5]No one looked on you with pity or had compassion enough to do any of these things for you. Rather, you were thrown out into the open field, for on the day you were born you were despised.

[6]" 'Then I passed by and saw you kicking about in your blood, and as you lay there in your blood I said to you, "Live!"[a][i] [7]I made you grow[j] like a plant of the field. You grew and developed and entered puberty. Your breasts had formed and your hair had grown, yet you were stark naked.[k]

[8]" 'Later I passed by, and when I looked at you and saw that you were old enough for love, I spread the corner of my garment[l] over you and covered your naked body. I gave you my solemn oath and entered into a covenant[m] with you, declares the Sovereign LORD, and you became mine.[n]

[9]" 'I bathed you with water and washed[o] the blood from you and put ointments on you. [10]I clothed you with an embroidered[p] dress and put sandals of fine leather on you. I dressed you in fine linen[q] and covered you with costly garments.[r] [11]I adorned you with jewelry:[s] I put bracelets[t] on your arms and a necklace[u] around your neck, [12]and I put a ring on your nose,[v] earrings[w] on your ears and a beautiful crown[x] on your head.[y] [13]So you were adorned with gold and silver; your clothes[z] were of fine linen and costly fabric and embroidered cloth. Your food was honey, olive oil[a] and the finest flour. You became very beautiful and rose to be a queen.[b] [14]And your fame[c] spread among the nations on account of your beauty,[d] because the splendor I had given you made your beauty perfect, declares the Sovereign LORD.[e]

[15]" 'But you trusted in your beauty and used your fame to become a prostitute. You lavished your favors on anyone who passed by[f] and your beauty became his.[g] [16]You took some of your garments to make gaudy high places,[h] where you carried on your prostitution.[i] You went to him, and he possessed your beauty.[b] [17]You also took the fine jewelry I gave you, the jewelry made of my gold and silver, and you made for yourself male idols and engaged in prostitution with them.[j] [18]And you took your embroidered clothes to put on them, and you offered my oil and incense[k] before them. [19]Also the food I provided for you—the flour, olive oil and honey I gave you to eat—you offered as fragrant incense before them. That is what happened, declares the Sovereign LORD.[l]

[20]" 'And you took your sons and daughters[m] whom you bore to me[n] and sacrificed them as food to the idols. Was your prostitution not enough?[o] [21]You slaughtered my children and sacrificed them to the idols.[p] [22]In all your detestable practices and your prostitution you did not remember the days of your youth,[q] when you were naked and bare,[r] kicking about in your blood.[s]

[a] 6 A few Hebrew manuscripts, Septuagint and Syriac; most Hebrew manuscripts repeat *and as you lay there in your blood I said to you, "Live!"* [b] 16 The meaning of the Hebrew for this sentence is uncertain.

16:3 [g]ver 45; S Ge 10:15; S Dt 7:1; Jos 24:14-15 **16:4** [h]Hos 2:3 **16:6** [i]ver 22; S Ex 19:4; Eze 18:23,32 **16:7** [j]S Dt 1:10 [k]S Ex 1:7 **16:8** [l]Ru 3:9 [m]ver 59; S Jer 11:10; Mal 2:14 [n]Jer 2:2; Hos 2:7,19-20 **16:9** [o]S Ru 3:3 **16:10** [p]S Ex 26:36; S Isa 19:9 [q]Eze 27:16 [r]ver 18; S Isa 3:23 **16:11** [s]S Jer 4:30; Eze 23:40 [t]Isa 3:19; Eze 23:42 [u]S Ge 41:42; S Ps 73:6 **16:12** [v]Isa 3:21 [w]S Ge 35:4 [x]S Isa 28:5; S Jer 13:18 [y]Pr 1:9; S Isa 3:19 **16:13** [z]Est 5:1 [a]1Sa 10:1 [b]Dt 32:13-14; S 1Ki 4:21; S Est 2:9,17 **16:14** [c]1Ki 10:24 [d]S Est 1:11; S Ps 48:2; S La 2:15 [e]S Eze 5:5 **16:15** [f]ver 25 [g]S Isa 57:8; S Jer 2:20; Eze 23:3; 27:3 **16:16** [h]S Isa 57:7 [i]S 2Ki 23:7 **16:17** [j]S Eze 7:20; Hos 2:13 **16:18** [k]S Jer 44:5 **16:19** [l]Hos 2:8 **16:20** [m]S Jer 7:31 [n]Ex 13:2 [o]Ps 106:37-38; S Isa 57:5; Eze 23:37 **16:21** [p]S 2Ki 17:17; S Jer 19:5 **16:22** [q]S Ps 25:7; S 88:15; Jer 2:2; Hos 2:15; 11:1 [r]Hos 2:3 [s]ver 6

origin generally, not to any specific individuals. *Amorite.* Cf. v. 45. Like the Canaanites, the Amorites were pre-Israelite, Semitic inhabitants of Canaan (see Ge 10:16 and note; 48:22; Jos 5:1 and note; 10:5; Jdg 1:34–36). *Hittite.* The Hittites were non-Semitic residents of Canaan, who had flourished in Asia Minor during the second millennium BC (see Ge 10:15 and note; 23:10–20; 26:34; 1Sa 26:6; 2Sa 11:2–27; 1Ki 11:1).

16:4 *rubbed with salt.* This practice has been observed among Arab peasants as late as AD 1918. *wrapped in cloths.* Cf. Lk 2:7.

16:5 *thrown out into the open field.* Abandoned to die. Exposure of infants, common in ancient pagan societies, was abhorrent to Israel.

16:6 *blood.* Of childbirth. *Live!* God's basic desire for all people, summed up in one word (see 18:23,32; 1Ti 2:4; 2Pe 3:9).

16:7 *hair.* Pubic hair.

16:8 *spread the corner of my garment.* Symbolic of entering a marriage relationship (see notes on Dt 22:30; Ru 3:9). *covenant.* Since the young woman symbolizes Jerusalem, this does not refer to the Sinaitic covenant but to marriage as a covenant (see Mal 2:14).

16:9 *blood.* Menstrual blood, indicating sexual maturity.

16:10 *embroidered dress ... sandals of fine leather ... fine linen.* Representative of the very best garments. *embroidered dress.* See 27:16,24; colored, variegated material fit for a queen (see Ps 45:14). *sandals of fine leather.* The same kind of leather was used to cover the tabernacle (see Ex 25:5; 26:14).

16:11 *bracelets on your arms.* See Ge 24:22.

16:12 *ring.* Not piercing the nose but worn on the outer part of the nose (see Ge 24:47). *earrings.* Circular ear ornaments, worn by men (Nu 31:50). The Hebrew for this word is not the same as that used in Ge 35:4; Ex 32:2–3. *crown.* The wedding crown (see SS 3:11, where the groom wears it).

16:13 *gold and silver.* Cf. Hos 2:8. *olive oil.* Cf. Hos 2:8. For the combination of honey and oil, see Dt 32:13. *finest flour.* Used in offerings and therefore of high quality (see v. 19; 46:14). *You became very beautiful.* Cf. Eph 5:27.

16:14 *your fame spread.* Especially in the time of David and Solomon.

16:15 *favors.* Sexual favors. Verb and noun forms of the Hebrew for this word occur 23 times in this chapter. *anyone who passed by.* Cf. Ge 38:14–16.

16:16 *garments.* All of the Lord's previous gifts were used by Jerusalem in prostituting herself. Cloths of some kind were needed in the Asherah worship practices (see 2Ki 23:7). They may have been used as curtains or as bedding (see Am 2:7–8).

16:20 *sons and daughters ... sacrificed.* See 20:26,31 and note; 23:37; 2Ki 21:6; 23:10; Jer 7:31 and note; 19:5; 32:35. For laws against child sacrifice, see Lev 18:21; Dt 18:10; cf. Lev 20:2–5; Dt 12:31.

23 " 'Woe![t] Woe to you, declares the Sovereign LORD. In addition to all your other
wickedness, 24 you built a mound for yourself and made a lofty shrine[u] in every public square.[v] 25 At every street corner[w] you
built your lofty shrines and degraded your
beauty, spreading your legs with increasing promiscuity to anyone who passed by.[x]
26 You engaged in prostitution[y] with the
Egyptians,[z] your neighbors with large genitals, and aroused my anger[a] with your increasing promiscuity.[b] 27 So I stretched out
my hand[c] against you and reduced your
territory; I gave you over[d] to the greed of
your enemies, the daughters of the Philistines,[e] who were shocked by your lewd
conduct. 28 You engaged in prostitution
with the Assyrians[f] too, because you were
insatiable; and even after that, you still
were not satisfied.[g] 29 Then you increased
your promiscuity to include Babylonia,[a][h] a
land of merchants, but even with this you
were not satisfied.[i]
30 " 'I am filled with fury against you,[b]
declares the Sovereign LORD, when you do
all these things, acting like a brazen prostitute![j] 31 When you built your mounds at
every street corner and made your lofty
shrines[k] in every public square, you were
unlike a prostitute, because you scorned
payment.
32 " 'You adulterous wife! You prefer
strangers to your own husband! 33 All prostitutes receive gifts,[l] but you give gifts[m] to
all your lovers, bribing them to come to
you from everywhere for your illicit favors.[n] 34 So in your prostitution you are the
opposite of others; no one runs after you
for your favors. You are the very opposite,
for you give payment and none is given
to you.
35 " 'Therefore, you prostitute, hear the
word of the LORD! 36 This is what the Sovereign LORD says: Because you poured out
your lust and exposed your naked body
in your promiscuity with your lovers, and
because of all your detestable idols, and
because you gave them your children's
blood,[o] 37 therefore I am going to gather all
your lovers, with whom you found pleasure, those you loved as well as those you
hated. I will gather them against you from
all around and will strip[p] you in front of
them, and they will see you stark naked.[q]
38 I will sentence you to the punishment
of women who commit adultery and who
shed blood;[r] I will bring on you the blood
vengeance of my wrath and jealous anger.[s]
39 Then I will deliver you into the hands[t] of
your lovers, and they will tear down your
mounds and destroy your lofty shrines.
They will strip you of your clothes and
take your fine jewelry and leave you stark
naked.[u] 40 They will bring a mob against
you, who will stone[v] you and hack you to
pieces with their swords. 41 They will burn
down[w] your houses and inflict punishment
on you in the sight of many women.[x] I will
put a stop[y] to your prostitution, and you
will no longer pay your lovers. 42 Then my
wrath against you will subside and my
jealous anger will turn away from you; I
will be calm and no longer angry.[z]
43 " 'Because you did not remember[a]
the days of your youth but enraged me
with all these things, I will surely bring
down[b] on your head what you have done,
declares the Sovereign LORD. Did you not
add lewdness to all your other detestable
practices?[c]
44 " 'Everyone who quotes proverbs[d] will
quote this proverb about you: "Like mother, like daughter." 45 You are a true daughter of your mother, who despised[e] her
husband[f] and her children; and you are
a true sister of your sisters, who despised

[a] *29* Or *Chaldea* [b] *30* Or *How feverish is your heart,*

16:23 [t]Eze 24:6 **16:24** [u]ver 31; Isa 57:7 [v]Ps 78:58; S Jer 2:20; 3:2; S 44:21; Eze 20:28 **16:25** [w]S Jer 3:2 [x]ver 15; S Pr 9:14 **16:26** [y]S Isa 23:17 [z]S Jer 3:1 [a]S 1Ki 14:9; S Eze 8:17 [b]S Isa 57:8; Jer 11:15; Eze 20:8; 23:19-21 **16:27** [c]Eze 20:33; 25:13 [d]S Jer 34:20 [e]S 2Ch 28:18 **16:28** [f]S 2Ki 16:7 [g]Isa 57:8 **16:29** [h]S Jer 3:1; Eze 23:14-17 [i]Na 3:4 **16:30** [j]S Jer 3:3 **16:31** [k]S ver 24 **16:33** [l]S Ge 30:15 [m]Isa 30:6; 57:9 [n]Hos 8:9-10 **16:36** [o]S Jer 19:5; Eze 23:10 **16:37** [p]Hos 2:3 [q]S Isa 47:3; S Jer 13:22; Eze 23:22; Hos 2:10; 8:10; Rev 17:16 **16:38** [r]S Ge 38:24 [s]S Lev 20:10; Ps 79:3,5; Eze 23:25; Zep 1:17 **16:39** [t]S 2Ki 18:11 [u]Eze 21:31; Hos 2:3 **16:40** [v]Jn 8:5,7 **16:41** [w]S Dt 13:16; S Jer 19:13 [x]Eze 23:10 [y]Eze 22:15; 23:27,48

16:42 [z]2Sa 24:25; Isa 40:1-2; 54:9; S Eze 5:13; 39:29 **16:43** [a]S Ex 15:24; Ps 78:42 [b]Eze 22:31 [c]Eze 11:21 **16:44** [d]S Ps 49:4 **16:45** [e]S Eze 14:5 [f]Jer 44:19

16:24 *mound ... lofty shrine.* Centers of idol worship were built not only in the countryside but also in Jerusalem itself.
16:26–29 *Egyptians ... Philistines ... Assyrians ... Babylonia.* The historical sequence of Jerusalem's political alliances with these four powers.
16:26 *neighbors.* Nowhere else in the OT are the Egyptians called "neighbors." *large genitals.* See 23:20. The language reflects both God's and Ezekiel's disgust with Jerusalem's apostasy.
16:27 *reduced your territory.* After the 701 BC siege of Jerusalem, the Assyrian king, Sennacherib, gave some of Jerusalem's territory to the Philistines. *shocked by your lewd conduct.* Cf. Am 3:9,13 and notes.
16:29 *Babylonia, a land of merchants.* See note on Rev 14:8; see also Rev 18:11–19,23.
16:32 *your own husband.* The Lord himself (see v. 8 and note; see also Jer 3:14; 31:32; Hos 2:16–17 and notes; cf. Ex 34:15 and note).
16:33 *you give gifts to all your lovers.* Jerusalem's perversity is here pictured as worse than adultery and ordinary prostitution (see also v. 34).
16:37 *strip you.* A reversal of the marriage covering (v. 8) and a return to the state described in v. 7.
16:38 *sentence you.* The punishment prescribed in the law was death (see Lev 20:10; Dt 22:22) by stoning (Dt 22:21–24; Jn 8:5–7). *jealous anger.* See v. 42; see also notes on Ex 20:5; Zec 1:14.
16:39 *your mounds ... your lofty shrines.* See vv. 24–25.
16:40 See 23:46–47.
16:43 *bring down on your head what you have done.* See note on 9:10.
16:44 *Like mother, like daughter.* Referring to Jerusalem's continual and seemingly hereditary tendency toward evil (cf. vv. 3,45).
16:45 *Hittite ... Amorite.* See note on v. 3.

their husbands and their children. Your
mother was a Hittite and your father an
Amorite.[g] 46 Your older sister[h] was Samaria, who lived to the north of you with her
daughters; and your younger sister, who
lived to the south of you with her daughters, was Sodom.[i] 47 You not only followed
their ways and copied their detestable
practices, but in all your ways you soon
became more depraved than they.[j] 48 As
surely as I live, declares the Sovereign[k]
LORD, your sister Sodom[l] and her daughters never did what you and your daughters have done.[m]
49 " 'Now this was the sin of your sister
Sodom:[n] She and her daughters were arrogant,[o] overfed and unconcerned;[p] they did
not help the poor and needy.[q] 50 They were
haughty[r] and did detestable things before
me. Therefore I did away with them as you
have seen.[s] 51 Samaria did not commit half
the sins you did. You have done more detestable things than they, and have made
your sisters seem righteous by all these
things you have done.[t] 52 Bear your disgrace, for you have furnished some justification for your sisters. Because your
sins were more vile than theirs, they appear more righteous[u] than you. So then, be
ashamed and bear[v] your disgrace, for you
have made your sisters appear righteous.
53 " 'However, I will restore[w] the fortunes
of Sodom and her daughters and of Samaria and her daughters, and your fortunes
along with them,[x] 54 so that you may bear
your disgrace[y] and be ashamed of all you
have done in giving them comfort. 55 And
your sisters, Sodom with her daughters
and Samaria with her daughters, will return to what they were before; and you
and your daughters will return to what
you were before.[z] 56 You would not even
mention your sister Sodom in the day of
your pride, 57 before your wickedness was
uncovered. Even so, you are now scorned[a]
by the daughters of Edom[a][b] and all her
neighbors and the daughters of the Philistines—all those around you who despise
you. 58 You will bear the consequences of
your lewdness and your detestable practices, declares the LORD.[c]
59 " 'This is what the Sovereign LORD
says: I will deal with you as you deserve,
because you have despised my oath by
breaking the covenant.[d] 60 Yet I will remember the covenant[e] I made with you
in the days of your youth,[f] and I will establish an everlasting covenant[g] with you.
61 Then you will remember your ways and
be ashamed[h] when you receive your sisters, both those who are older than you
and those who are younger. I will give
them to you as daughters,[i] but not on the
basis of my covenant with you. 62 So I will
establish my covenant[j] with you, and you
will know that I am the LORD.[k] 63 Then,
when I make atonement[l] for you for all
you have done, you will remember and
be ashamed[m] and never again open your
mouth[n] because of your humiliation, declares the Sovereign LORD.[o]' "

Two Eagles and a Vine

17 The word of the LORD came to me:
2 "Son of man, set forth an allegory
and tell it to the Israelites as a parable.[p]
3 Say to them, 'This is what the Sovereign
LORD says: A great eagle[q] with powerful
wings, long feathers and full plumage of
varied colors came to Lebanon.[r] Taking

16:45 [g] ver 3; Eze 23:2 **16:46** [h] S Jer 3:7 [i] Ge 13:10-13; S 18:20; Jer 3:8-11; Eze 23:4; Rev 11:8 **16:47** [j] S Eze 5:7 **16:48** [k] S Ge 15:2 [l] S Ge 19:25 [m] Mt 10:15; 11:23-24 **16:49** [n] S Isa 1:10 [o] Ps 138:6; Eze 28:2 [p] Isa 22:13 [q] S Ge 13:13; 19:9; S Jer 5:28; Eze 18:7, 12, 16; Am 6:4-6; Lk 12:16-20; 16:19; Jas 5:5 **16:50** [r] Ps 18:27 [s] Ge 18:20-21; S 19:5 **16:51** [t] Jer 3:8-11; Eze 5:6-7; 23:11 **16:52** [u] S Jer 3:11 [v] Eze 23:35 **16:53** [w] S Dt 30:3; Isa 19:24-25; S Jer 48:47 [x] Eze 39:25 **16:54** [y] S Jer 2:26 **16:55** [z] Eze 36:11; Mal 3:4 **16:57** [a] S Ps 137:3 [b] 2Ki 16:6 **16:58** [c] Eze 23:49 **16:59** [d] S ver 8; Eze 17:19 **16:60** [e] S Ge 6:18; S 9:15 [f] S Ps 25:7; S Jer 2:2 [g] S Ge 9:16; Eze 37:26 **16:61** [h] ver 63; Eze 20:43; 43:10; 44:13 [i] S Isa 43:6 **16:62** [j] S Dt 29:14 [k] S Jer 24:7; Eze 20:37, 43-44; 34:25; 37:26; Hos 2:19-20 **16:63** [l] Ps 65:3; 78:38; 79:9 [m] Eze 36:31-32 [n] Ro 3:19 [o] Ps 39:9; Da 9:7-8 **17:2** [p] S Jdg 14:12; S Eze 20:49 **17:3** [q] S Dt 28:49; Jer 49:22; Da 7:4; Hos 8:1 [r] S Jer 22:23

[a] 57 Many Hebrew manuscripts and Syriac; most Hebrew manuscripts, Septuagint and Vulgate *Aram*

16:46 *Your older sister was Samaria.* Historically, Samaria was not founded as a royal city until after 880 BC (see note on 1Ki 16:24), so "older" in this allegory apparently alludes to the fact that Samaria ruled over a significantly larger kingdom than Jerusalem did. *daughters.* Suburbs or satellite cities.

16:47 *more depraved than they.* The Bible frequently compares a city or people to Sodom (see v. 46) as the epitome of evil and degradation (see Ge 13:10 and note; Dt 29:23; 32:32; Isa 1:9–10 and note; 3:9; Jer 23:14; La 4:6; Mt 10:15; 11:23–24; Jude 7).

16:49 *sin of your sister Sodom.* Here social injustice rather than sexual perversion (Ge 19) is highlighted.

16:51–52 *righteous.* Relatively innocent.

16:56 *day of your pride.* Referring to a time long before Ezekiel, when Jerusalem (as an Israelite city) was still relatively uncorrupted—as in the days of David and the early years of Solomon.

16:57 *scorned by the daughters of Edom.* The OT frequently condemns Edom for this (see 25:12–14; 35:5 and note; Isa 63:1; Introduction to Obadiah: Unity and Theme; Ob 10–14 and notes).

16:59–63 In God's concluding word concerning Jerusalem's future reformation and restoration, the city's role as representative of Israel in the allegory is foregrounded (see note on vv. 1–63), so that his words about remembering the covenant and establishing an everlasting covenant (see v. 60; cf. v. 62) parallel what is elsewhere said of Israel itself (see 37:26; Isa 55:3; Jer 32:40 and notes).

16:59 *covenant.* See v. 8 and note.

16:60 *I will remember the covenant.* Though Jerusalem did not (v. 43).

16:61 *will remember ... be ashamed.* See v. 63. Jerusalem (Israel) will remember—to her everlasting shame.

16:63 *when I make atonement for you.* God himself will do for faithless Jerusalem what she cannot do for herself (cf. Ro 3:23; 1Jn 2:2 and notes).

17:1–24 An allegory/parable symbolizing King Zedekiah's vacillating royal policy that led to his downfall. The allegory is presented in vv. 1–10; its explanation follows in vv. 11–21; and vv. 22–24 append a promise of better times to come, utilizing the imagery of the allegory.

17:3 *great eagle.* Nebuchadnezzar (see v. 12). *Lebanon.* Jerusalem (see v. 12). *cedar.* David's dynasty; his royal family.

hold of the top of a cedar, 4 he broke off[s]
its topmost shoot and carried it away to a
land of merchants, where he planted it in
a city of traders.
5 " 'He took one of the seedlings of the
land and put it in fertile soil. He planted
it like a willow by abundant water,[t] 6 and
it sprouted and became a low, spreading
vine. Its branches[u] turned toward him, but
its roots remained under it. So it became a
vine and produced branches and put out
leafy boughs.[v]
7 " 'But there was another great eagle
with powerful wings and full plumage.
The vine now sent out its roots toward
him from the plot where it was planted
and stretched out its branches to him for
water.[w] 8 It had been planted in good soil
by abundant water so that it would produce branches,[x] bear fruit and become a
splendid vine.'
9 "Say to them, 'This is what the Sovereign LORD says: Will it thrive? Will it not
be uprooted and stripped of its fruit so that
it withers? All its new growth will wither.
It will not take a strong arm or many people to pull it up by the roots.[y] 10 It has been
planted,[z] but will it thrive? Will it not wither
completely when the east wind strikes it—
wither away in the plot where it grew?[a]' "
11 Then the word of the LORD came to
me: 12 "Say to this rebellious people, 'Do
you not know what these things mean?[b]'
Say to them: 'The king of Babylon went
to Jerusalem and carried off her king and
her nobles,[c] bringing them back with him
to Babylon.[d] 13 Then he took a member of
the royal family and made a treaty[e] with
him, putting him under oath.[f] He also carried away the leading men[g] of the land,
14 so that the kingdom would be brought
low,[h] unable to rise again, surviving only
by keeping his treaty. 15 But the king rebelled[i] against him by sending his envoys
to Egypt[j] to get horses and a large army.[k]
Will he succeed? Will he who does such
things escape? Will he break the treaty
and yet escape?[l]
16 " 'As surely as I live, declares the Sovereign LORD, he shall die[m] in Babylon,
in the land of the king who put him on
the throne, whose oath he despised and
whose treaty he broke.[n] 17 Pharaoh[o] with
his mighty army and great horde will be
of no help to him in war, when ramps[p]
are built and siege works erected to destroy many lives.[q] 18 He despised the oath
by breaking the covenant. Because he had
given his hand in pledge[r] and yet did all
these things, he shall not escape.
19 " 'Therefore this is what the Sovereign
LORD says: As surely as I live, I will repay
him for despising my oath and breaking
my covenant.[s] 20 I will spread my net[t] for
him, and he will be caught in my snare.
I will bring him to Babylon and execute
judgment[u] on him there because he was
unfaithful[v] to me. 21 All his choice troops
will fall by the sword,[w] and the survivors[x]
will be scattered to the winds.[y] Then you
will know that I the LORD have spoken.[z]
22 " 'This is what the Sovereign LORD
says: I myself will take a shoot[a] from the
very top of a cedar and plant it; I will break
off a tender sprig from its topmost shoots
and plant it on a high and lofty mountain.[b]
23 On the mountain heights[c] of Israel I will
plant it; it will produce branches and bear
fruit[d] and become a splendid cedar. Birds
of every kind will nest in it; they will find
shelter in the shade of its branches.[e] 24 All
the trees of the forest[f] will know that I the

17:4 [s] S Isa 10:33 **17:5** [t] Dt 8:7-9; Ps 1:3; Isa 44:4; Eze 31:5 **17:6** [u] S Isa 18:5 [v] S Job 5:3 **17:7** [w] Eze 31:4 **17:8** [x] Job 18:19; Mal 4:1 **17:9** [y] Jer 42:10; Am 2:9 **17:10** [z] S Job 1:19; Hos 12:1; 13:15 [a] S Eze 15:4 **17:12** [b] S Eze 12:9 [c] S 2Ki 24:15 [d] S Dt 21:10; S 2Ch 36:10; Eze 24:19 **17:13** [e] S Ex 23:32; S Jer 37:1 [f] 2Ch 36:13 [g] Isa 3:2 **17:14** [h] Eze 29:14 **17:15** [i] Jer 52:3 [j] S Isa 30:2; S Jer 37:5 [k] S Dt 17:16 [l] S Ps 56:7; S Isa 30:5; Jer 34:3; 38:18; Eze 29:16 **17:16** [m] S Jer 52:11; Eze 12:13 [n] S 2Ki 24:17 **17:17** [o] Jer 37:7 [p] S Eze 4:2 [q] S Isa 36:6; Jer 37:5; Eze 29:6-7 **17:18** [r] S 2Ki 10:15; 1Ch 29:24 **17:19** [s] Jer 7:9; S Eze 16:59; 21:23; Hos 10:4 **17:20** [t] S Eze 12:13; 32:3 [u] S Jer 2:35 [v] S Eze 15:8 **17:21** [w] S Eze 12:14 [x] 2Ki 25:11 [y] S Lev 26:33; S 2Ki 25:5; Zec 2:6 [z] S Jer 27:8 **17:22** [a] S 2Ki 19:30; S Isa 4:2 [b] ver 23; Isa 2:2; S Jer 23:5; Eze 20:40; 36:1,36; 37:22; 40:2; 43:12 **17:23** [c] S ver 22; S Jer 31:12 [d] S Isa 27:6 [e] Ps 92:12; S Isa 2:2; Eze 31:6; Da 4:12; Hos 14:5-7; S Mt 13:32 **17:24** [f] S Ps 96:12; Isa 2:13

17:4 *topmost shoot.* Jehoiachin. *land of merchants.* The country of Babylonia (see v. 12; 16:29 and note). *city of traders.* Babylon.
17:5 *one of the seedlings.* Zedekiah, son of Josiah; he was the brother of Jehoahaz and Jehoiakim and uncle of Jehoiachin (see 2Ki 23–24). *planted it.* Made him king (2Ki 24:17).
17:6 *low, spreading vine.* No longer a tall cedar, because thousands of Judah's leading citizens had been deported (see 2Ki 24:15–16; see also Jer 52:28). But see note on 15:1–8.
17:7 *another great eagle.* An Egyptian pharaoh, either Psammetichus II (595–589 BC) or Hophra (589–570). Hophra, mentioned in Jer 44:30, is probably the pharaoh who offered help to Jerusalem in 586 (see Jer 37:5). If the fact that ch. 17 is located between ch. 8 (dated 592) and ch. 20 (dated 591) is chronologically meaningful, Psammetichus is meant. *sent out its roots toward him.* Zedekiah appealed to Egypt for military aid (v. 15), an act of rebellion against Nebuchadnezzar (see 2Ki 24:20).
17:10 *east wind.* The hot, dry wind known today as the khamsin, which withers vegetation (see 19:12). Here it stands for Nebuchadnezzar and his Babylonian forces.
17:12 *this rebellious people.* See 2:3 and note.
17:15 *Will he break the treaty and yet escape?* The point of the chapter (see vv. 16,18).
17:16 *he shall die in Babylon.* See 2Ki 25:7.
17:19 *my oath ... my covenant.* The king of Judah would have sworn faithfulness to the treaty in the name of the Lord. His oath would have taken some such form as "May the Lord slay me if I do not remain true to this treaty" (a self-maledictory oath; see notes on Ge 9:13; 15:17; 17:10). To swear such an oath and then violate it was to treat the Lord as if he were powerless.
17:22 *I myself.* A beautiful Messianic promise follows, using the previous imagery in a totally new and unexpected way. *shoot.* A member of David's family (cf. Isa 11:1; Zec 3:8; 6:12 and notes). *cedar.* See note on v. 3. *plant it.* Make him king (see v. 5). *high and lofty mountain.* Jerusalem (see Isa 2:2–4 and note).
17:23 *Birds ... will nest in it.* For similar imagery applied to a mighty king, see Da 4:10–12,20–22; cf. Mk 4:32.
17:24 *trees of the forest.* Kings and rulers of the world. *bring down the tall tree ... make the dry tree flourish.* See 1Sa 2:4–8 and notes; cf. Isa 2:12–18.

LORD bring down[g] the tall tree and make
the low tree grow tall. I dry up the green
tree and make the dry tree flourish.[h]
"'I the LORD have spoken, and I will
do it.[i]'"

The One Who Sins Will Die

18 The word of the LORD came to me:
2"What do you people mean by
quoting this proverb about the land of Israel:

"'The parents eat sour grapes,
and the children's teeth are set on
edge'?[j]

3"As surely as I live, declares the Sovereign LORD, you will no longer quote this
proverb[k] in Israel. 4For everyone belongs
to me, the parent as well as the child—
both alike belong to me. The one who sins[l]
is the one who will die.[m]

5"Suppose there is a righteous man
who does what is just and right.
6He does not eat at the mountain[n]
shrines
or look to the idols[o] of Israel.
He does not defile his neighbor's
wife
or have sexual relations with a
woman during her period.[p]
7He does not oppress[q] anyone,
but returns what he took in pledge[r]
for a loan.
He does not commit robbery[s]
but gives his food to the hungry[t]
and provides clothing for the naked.[u]
8He does not lend to them at interest
or take a profit from them.[v]
He withholds his hand from doing wrong
and judges fairly[w] between two parties.
9He follows my decrees[x]
and faithfully keeps my laws.
That man is righteous;[y]
he will surely live,[z]
declares the Sovereign LORD.

10"Suppose he has a violent son, who
sheds blood[a] or does any of these other
things[a] 11(though the father has done none
of them):

"He eats at the mountain shrines.[b]
He defiles his neighbor's wife.
12He oppresses the poor[c] and needy.
He commits robbery.
He does not return what he took in
pledge.[d]
He looks to the idols.
He does detestable things.[e]
13He lends at interest and takes a profit.[f]

Will such a man live? He will not! Because
he has done all these detestable things, he

[a] 10 Or *things to a brother*

17:24 [g]S Ps 52:5 [h]S Nu 17:8; Da 5:21 [i]S 1Sa 2:7-8; Eze 19:12; 21:26; 22:14; 37:13; Am 9:11 **18:2** [j]S Job 21:19; Isa 3:15; Jer 31:29 **18:3** [k]S Ps 49:4 **18:4** [l]S 2Ki 14:6; S Pr 13:21 [m]ver 20; S Ge 18:23; S Ex 17:14; S Job 21:20; Isa 42:5; Eze 33:8; S Ro 6:23 **18:6** [n]S Eze 6:2 [o]Dt 4:19; S Eze 6:13; 20:24; Am 5:26 [p]S Lev 12:2; S 15:24 **18:7** [q]Ex 22:21; Mal 3:5; Jas 5:4 [r]S Ex 22:26 [s]S Ex 20:15 [t]S Job 22:7 [u]Dt 15:11; S Eze 16:49; S Mt 25:36; Lk 3:11 **18:8** [v]S Ex 18:21; 22:25; S Lev 25:35-37; Dt 23:19-20 [w]S Jer 22:3; Zec 8:16 **18:9** [x]S Lev 19:37 [y]Hab 2:4 [z]S Lev 18:5; S Eze 11:12; 20:11; Am 5:4 **18:10** [a]Ex 21:12; Eze 22:6 **18:11** [b]Eze 22:9 **18:12** [c]S Ex 22:22; S Job 24:9; Am 4:1 [d]S Ex 22:27 [e]2Ki 21:11; Isa 59:6-7; S Jer 22:17; S Eze 16:49; Hab 2:6 **18:13** [f]Ex 22:25

18:1–32 A word to silence those who complained that they were being made to suffer for the sins of their ancestors rather than for their own sins. That sin and guilt are not always purely individual but often have a communal and thus also a cumulative dimension is the pervasive testimony of the OT (see, e.g., Ex 20:5; Jdg 7:24; 1Ki 14:14–16 and notes; see also Ex 34:7; 1Ki 22:16–20; 23:26–27; 24:1–4; 2Ki 21:10–15; Isa 5:1–7; Jer 1:15–16; 5:1–17; 17:1–4; Am 2:4–16; 5:12). But when the Jerusalemites charged God with injustice, as if they themselves were not guilty, that called for a sharp corrective word—they had not turned away from the sinful ways of their ancestors after the manner specified in vv. 14–17, 27–28. This justification of God's way with Israel stands at the center of the series of messages found in 13:1—24:14 (see note on 13:1–23).

18:2 *this proverb.* Jer 31:29 indicates that the proverb arose first in Jerusalem. Jeremiah predicted the cessation of the proverb, and Ezekiel said that its end had come. *about the land of Israel.* And about the fate of those who have suffered loss. *The parents ... on edge.* The proverb expresses self-pity and mocks the justice of God. *set on edge.* The Hebrew for this phrase perhaps means "blunted" or "worn" (cf. Ecc 10:10), but it may refer to the sensation in the mouth when eating something bitter or sour.

18:3 *As surely as I live.* See note on 5:11.

18:4 *The one who sins is the one who will die.* Or "Only the one ..." Ezekiel spoke out against a false use the people were making of a doctrine of inherited guilt (perhaps based on a false understanding of Ex 20:5; 34:7). What follows is his description of three men, standing for three generations, who break the three/four-generation pattern.

18:5 *righteous man.* The first generation that keeps the law. The following 15 commandments are partly ceremonial but are mostly moral injunctions. See the Ten Commandments in Ex 20 and Dt 5; cf. Ps 15:2–5; 24:3–6; Isa 33:15; cf. also notes on Ps 1:5; 119:121. *just and right.* Emphasized by Ezekiel in chs. 18 (see vv. 19,21,27) and 33 (see vv. 14,16,19; see also note on Ps 119:121).

18:6 *eat at the mountain shrines.* Eating meat sacrificed to idols on the high places (see 6:3; Hos 4:13). *look to.* Seek help from (see 23:27; 33:25; Ps 121:1). *idols.* See note on 6:4. *defile.* Adultery (condemned in Ex 20:14; Dt 22:22; Lev 18:20; 20:10) is here associated with a menstrual prohibition (see Lev 15:19–24; 18:19; 20:18), which is absent from the two listings that follow (cf. vv. 11,15).

18:7 *oppress.* The rich taking advantage of the poor. *returns what he took in pledge.* See Ex 22:26; Dt 24:12–13; Am 2:8. *robbery.* See the commandment against stealing in Ex 20:15; Dt 5:19. This is violent (armed) robbery rather than secret theft or burglary (see Lev 19:13). *food to the hungry.* See Dt 15:7–11; Mt 25:31–46.

18:8 *lend ... at interest.* See 22:12; see also Ex 22:25–27 and note.

18:9 *That man is righteous; he will surely live.* After the checklist of commandments has been gone over, the verdict is rendered (cf. Ps 15:5; 24:5). *live.* See note on 16:6. This is life as more than mere existence; it includes communion with God (see Ps 63:3; 73:27–28).

18:10 *violent son.* Evil, second generation. About half (eight) of the previous commandments follow, but in a different order.

18:13 *his blood will be on his own head.* He is held responsible for his own sin (see Lev 20:9,11–12,16,27).

is to be put to death; his blood will be on
his own head.[g]
14 “But suppose this son has a son who
sees all the sins his father commits, and
though he sees them, he does not do such
things:[h]

15 “He does not eat at the mountain
shrines[i]
or look to the idols[j] of Israel.
He does not defile his neighbor’s
wife.
16 He does not oppress anyone
or require a pledge for a loan.
He does not commit robbery
but gives his food to the hungry[k]
and provides clothing for the
naked.[l]
17 He withholds his hand from
mistreating the poor
and takes no interest or profit from
them.
He keeps my laws[m] and follows my
decrees.

He will not die for his father’s sin; he will
surely live. 18 But his father will die for
his own sin, because he practiced extortion, robbed his brother and did what was
wrong among his people.
19 “Yet you ask, ‘Why does the son not
share the guilt of his father?’ Since the son
has done what is just and right and has
been careful to keep all my decrees, he
will surely live.[n] 20 The one who sins is the
one who will die.[o] The child will not share
the guilt of the parent, nor will the parent
share the guilt of the child. The righteousness of the righteous will be credited to
them, and the wickedness of the wicked
will be charged against them.[p]
21 “But if[q] a wicked person turns away
from all the sins they have committed and
keeps all my decrees[r] and does what is
just and right, that person will surely live;
they will not die.[s] 22 None of the offenses
they have committed will be remembered

18:13 [g] S Lev 20:9; Eze 33:4-5; Hos 12:14 **18:14** [h] 2Ch 34:21; S Pr 23:24 **18:15** [i] Eze 22:9 [j] S Ps 24:4 **18:16** [k] Isa 58:7 [l] S Ex 22:27; Ps 41:1; Isa 58:10; S Eze 16:49 **18:17** [m] S Ps 1:2 **18:19** [n] Ex 20:5; Dt 5:9; Jer 15:4; Zec 1:3-6 **18:20** [o] S Nu 15:31 [p] Dt 24:16; S 1Ki 8:32; 2Ki 14:6; Isa 3:11; S Eze 7:27; S 14:14; S Mt 16:27; Jn 9:2 **18:21** [q] Jer 18:8 [r] S Ge 26:5 [s] S Eze 13:22; 36:27 **18:22** [t] Ps 18:20-24; S Isa 43:25; Da 4:27; Mic 7:19 **18:23** [u] Ps 147:11 [v] S Job 37:23; S La 3:33; S Eze 16:6; Mic 7:18; S 1Ti 2:4 **18:24** [w] S Jer 34:16 [x] S Eze 15:8 [y] S 1Sa 15:11; 2Ch 24:17-20; S Job 35:8; Pr 21:16; S Eze 3:20; 20:27; 2Pe 2:20-22 **18:25** [z] Jer 2:29 [a] S Ge 18:25; Jer 12:1; Eze 33:17; Zep 3:5; Mal 2:17; 3:13-15 **18:27** [b] S Isa 1:18; S Eze 13:22 **18:28** [c] S Isa 55:7

against them. Because of the righteous
things they have done, they will live.[t]
23 Do I take any pleasure in the death of
the wicked? declares the Sovereign LORD.
Rather, am I not pleased[u] when they turn
from their ways and live?[v]
24 “But if a righteous person turns[w] from
their righteousness and commits sin and
does the same detestable things the wicked person does, will they live? None of the
righteous things that person has done will
be remembered. Because of the unfaithfulness[x] they are guilty of and because of
the sins they have committed, they will
die.[y]
25 “Yet you say, ‘The way of the Lord is
not just.’[z] Hear, you Israelites: Is my way
unjust?[a] Is it not your ways that are unjust? 26 If a righteous person turns from
their righteousness and commits sin, they
will die for it; because of the sin they have
committed they will die. 27 But if a wicked person turns away from the wickedness they have committed and does what
is just and right, they will save their life.[b]
28 Because they consider all the offenses
they have committed and turn away from
them, that person will surely live; they
will not die.[c] 29 Yet the Israelites say, ‘The
way of the Lord is not just.’ Are my ways
unjust, people of Israel? Is it not your ways
that are unjust?
30 “Therefore, you Israelites, I will judge
each of you according to your own ways,
declares the Sovereign LORD. Repent![d] Turn
away from all your offenses; then sin will
not be your downfall.[e] 31 Rid[f] yourselves of
all the offenses you have committed, and
get a new heart[g] and a new spirit. Why[h]
will you die, people of Israel?[i] 32 For I take
no pleasure in the death of anyone, declares the Sovereign LORD. Repent[j] and
live![k]

18:30 [d] S Isa 1:27; S Jer 35:15; Mt 3:2 [e] Eze 7:3; 24:14; 33:20; Hos 12:6; 1Pe 1:17 **18:31** [f] S Jdg 6:8 [g] Ps 51:10 [h] Jer 27:13 [i] S Isa 1:16-17; S Eze 11:19; 36:26 **18:32** [j] S Job 22:23; Isa 55:7; Mal 3:7 [k] S 2Ch 7:14; S Job 37:23; S Eze 16:6; 33:11

18:14 *a son.* Righteous, third generation. Twelve commandments follow.

18:20 *righteousness … credited to them.* See Ps 106:31 and note.

18:21 *But if a wicked person turns … and keeps … that person will surely live.* Verses 1 – 20 indicate that the chain of inherited guilt can be broken, and vv. 21 – 29 teach that the power of guilt accumulated within a person’s life can be overcome.

18:23 *Do I take any pleasure in the death of the wicked?* In addition to the answer in this verse and in v. 32, see 33:11; Jnh 4:11 and notes; cf. 2Pe 3:9 and note.

18:24 *But if a righteous person turns.* See Heb 2:3; 2Pe 2:20 – 22 for warnings against those who knowingly and willfully turn from righteousness.

18:25 *Is my way unjust?* See 33:17; cf. Ge 18:25 and note; Dt 32:4; Jer 12:1 and note.

18:26 *If a righteous person.* Verses 26 – 29 repeat the argument developed in vv. 21 – 25.

18:30 *Therefore.* Concluding summary message. Compare the language of this conclusion with the closing words of the last (the 14th) message in this series (24:14). *each of you.* While the house of Israel as a whole was guilty, God’s judgment would be just and individual. *Repent!* Second call to repentance (see 14:6 and note).

18:31 *get a new heart.* What had been promised unconditionally (11:19; 36:26) is here portrayed as attainable but not inevitable (cf. the same tension between Php 2:12 and 2:13).

18:32 *I take no pleasure.* Verse 23 is echoed in this final, grand summary, called by some the most important message in the whole book of Ezekiel (see note on 16:6).

A Lament Over Israel's Princes

19 "Take up a lament[l] concerning the princes[m] of Israel 2and say:

"'What a lioness[n] was your mother
among the lions!
She lay down among them
and reared her cubs.[o]
3She brought up one of her cubs,
and he became a strong lion.
He learned to tear the prey
and he became a man-eater.
4The nations heard about him,
and he was trapped in their pit.
They led him with hooks[p]
to the land of Egypt.[q]

5"'When she saw her hope unfulfilled,
her expectation gone,
she took another of her cubs[r]
and made him a strong lion.[s]
6He prowled among the lions,
for he was now a strong lion.
He learned to tear the prey
and he became a man-eater.[t]
7He broke down[a] their strongholds
and devastated[u] their towns.
The land and all who were in it
were terrified by his roaring.
8Then the nations[v] came against him,
those from regions round about.
They spread their net[w] for him,
and he was trapped in their pit.[x]
9With hooks[y] they pulled him into a cage
and brought him to the king of
Babylon.[z]
They put him in prison,
so his roar[a] was heard no longer
on the mountains of Israel.[b]

10"'Your mother was like a vine in your
vineyard[b][c]
planted by the water;[d]
it was fruitful and full of branches
because of abundant water.[e]
11Its branches were strong,
fit for a ruler's scepter.
It towered high
above the thick foliage,
conspicuous for its height
and for its many branches.[f]
12But it was uprooted[g] in fury
and thrown to the ground.
The east wind[h] made it shrivel,
it was stripped of its fruit;
its strong branches withered
and fire consumed them.[i]
13Now it is planted in the desert,[j]
in a dry and thirsty land.[k]
14Fire spread from one of its main[c] branches
and consumed[l] its fruit.
No strong branch is left on it
fit for a ruler's scepter.'[m]

"This is a lament[n] and is to be used as a lament."

Rebellious Israel Purged

20 In the seventh year, in the fifth
month on the tenth day, some of
the elders of Israel came to inquire[o] of the
LORD, and they sat down in front of me.[p]
2Then the word of the LORD came to me:
3"Son of man, speak to the elders[q] of Israel
and say to them, 'This is what the Sovereign
LORD says: Have you come to inquire[r] of me?
As surely as I live, I will not let you inquire
of me, declares the Sovereign LORD.[s]'
4"Will you judge them? Will you judge
them, son of man? Then confront them

[a] 7 Targum (see Septuagint); Hebrew *He knew*
[b] 10 Two Hebrew manuscripts; most Hebrew manuscripts *your blood*
[c] 14 Or *from under its*

19:1 [l]ver 14; Jer 7:29; 9:10, 20; Eze 26:17; 27:2,32; 28:12; 32:2,16; Am 5:1 [m]S 2Ki 24:6 **19:2** [n]S Nu 23:24 [o]S Ge 49:9 **19:4** [p]S Job 41:2 [q]2Ki 23:33-34; 2Ch 36:4; S La 4:20 **19:5** [r]S Ge 49:9 [s]2Ki 23:34 **19:6** [t]2Ki 24:9; 2Ch 36:9 **19:7** [u]Eze 29:10; 30:12 **19:8** [v]2Ki 24:2 [w]S Eze 12:13 [x]2Ki 24:11; S La 4:20 **19:9** [y]S 2Ki 19:28 [z]S 2Ki 25:7; S 2Ch 36:6 [a]Zec 11:3 [b]S 2Ki 24:15 **19:10** [c]S Ge 49:22 [d]S Jer 17:8 [e]Ps 80:8-11 **19:11** [f]Eze 31:3; Da 4:11 **19:12** [g]S Dt 29:28 [h]S Ge 41:6 [i]S Isa 27:11; S Eze 17:24; 28:17; Hos 13:15 **19:13** [j]Eze 20:35; Hos 2:14 [k]Hos 2:3 **19:14** [l]Eze 20:47 [m]S Eze 15:4 [n]S ver 1 **20:1** [o]S Ge 25:22 [p]Eze 1:1-2; S 8:1; 21:1 **20:3** [q]S Eze 7:26 [r]S Ge 25:22; Eze 14:3 [s]S 1Sa 28:6; Isa 1:15; Am 8:12; Mic 3:7

19:1 – 14 A twofold dirge lamenting the fall of the royal family of Judah, one part employing the imagery of a lioness and her brood of whelps (vv. 1 – 9), the other utilizing the imagery of a once flourishing vine (vv. 10 – 14).
19:1 *lament.* A chant usually composed for funerals of fallen leaders (as in 2Sa 1:17 – 27), but often used sarcastically by the OT prophets to lament or to ironically predict the death of a nation (see Isa 14:4 – 21; Am 5:1 – 3 and note on 5:1). See also 2:10. *princes.* Kings.
19:2 An allegorical reference to the people of Israel or the nation of Judah.
19:3 *one of her cubs.* Jehoahaz (see 2Ki 23:31 – 34; Jer 22:10 – 12), who reigned only three months. *became a man-eater.* A reference to his oppressive policies.
19:5 *another of her cubs.* Perhaps Jehoiachin (who also reigned only three months, 2Ki 24:8), but probably Zedekiah (of whom v. 7 appears a more likely description). Both were taken to Babylon (v. 9). If the reference is to Jehoiachin (2Ki 24:15), this was a true lament; if to Zedekiah, it was a prediction (2Ki 25:7).
19:10 *Your mother was like a vine.* The one previously pictured as a lioness (v. 2) is here a vine (for other uses of the vine imagery, see 15:1 – 8; 17:7 and notes).
19:12 *east wind.* Nebuchadnezzar and his army (see note on 17:10).
19:13 *desert.* Babylonia — which to Israel seemed like a desert (see 20:35; Isa 21:1 and note).
19:14 *Fire.* Rebellion (see 2Ki 24:20). *one of its main branches.* Zedekiah. *to be used as a lament.* Indicates repeated use (see Ps 137:1).
20:1 – 44 This word (to be addressed to the elders of Israel) came to Ezekiel on Aug. 14, 591 BC, some 11 months after the preceding dated vision (see 8:1 and note on 8:1 — 11:25; see also chart, p. 1336). It begins with an overview of Israel's long history of apostasy (vv. 1 – 29), which leads into an announcement of the Lord's purpose to purge and renew his apostate people through the judgment now overtaking them (vv. 30 – 44).
20:1 *seventh year ... fifth month ... tenth day.* The third date (see previous note) supplied in the book of Ezekiel (see 1:2; 8:1). *elders of Israel.* See notes on 8:1; 14:1. *inquire.* See v. 3 and note on 14:3.
20:3 *As surely as I live.* See note on 5:11. *I will not let you inquire of me.* See v. 31; see also 3:26; 7:26 and notes.
20:4 *Will you judge them? ... Then confront them.* As the one sent to pronounce God's judgment on Israel, Ezekiel is

with the detestable practices of their ancestors[t] 5 and say to them: 'This is what
the Sovereign LORD says: On the day I
chose[u] Israel, I swore with uplifted hand[v]
to the descendants of Jacob and revealed
myself to them in Egypt. With uplifted
hand I said to them, "I am the LORD your
God.[w]" 6 On that day I swore[x] to them that
I would bring them out of Egypt into a
land I had searched out for them, a land
flowing with milk and honey,[y] the most
beautiful of all lands.[z] 7 And I said to them,
"Each of you, get rid of the vile images[a]
you have set your eyes on, and do not defile yourselves with the idols[b] of Egypt. I
am the LORD your God.[c]"
8 " 'But they rebelled against me and
would not listen to me;[d] they did not get
rid of the vile images they had set their
eyes on, nor did they forsake the idols
of Egypt.[e] So I said I would pour out
my wrath on them and spend my anger
against them in Egypt.[f] 9 But for the sake
of my name, I brought them out of Egypt.[g]
I did it to keep my name from being profaned[h] in the eyes of the nations among
whom they lived and in whose sight I had
revealed myself to the Israelites. 10 Therefore I led them out of Egypt and brought
them into the wilderness.[i] 11 I gave them
my decrees and made known to them
my laws, by which the person who obeys
them will live.[j] 12 Also I gave them my
Sabbaths[k] as a sign[l] between us,[m] so they
would know that I the LORD made them
holy.[n]
13 " 'Yet the people of Israel rebelled[o]
against me in the wilderness. They did not
follow my decrees but rejected my laws[p]—
by which the person who obeys them will
live—and they utterly desecrated my
Sabbaths.[q] So I said I would pour out my
wrath[r] on them and destroy[s] them in the
wilderness.[t] 14 But for the sake of my name
I did what would keep it from being profaned[u] in the eyes of the nations in whose
sight I had brought them out.[v] 15 Also with
uplifted hand I swore[w] to them in the wilderness that I would not bring them into
the land I had given them—a land flowing
with milk and honey, the most beautiful
of all lands[x]— 16 because they rejected my
laws[y] and did not follow my decrees and
desecrated my Sabbaths. For their hearts[z]
were devoted to their idols.[a] 17 Yet I looked
on them with pity and did not destroy[b]
them or put an end to them in the wilderness. 18 I said to their children in the
wilderness, "Do not follow the statutes of
your parents[c] or keep their laws or defile
yourselves[d] with their idols. 19 I am the
LORD your God;[e] follow my decrees and be
careful to keep my laws.[f] 20 Keep my Sabbaths[g] holy, that they may be a sign[h] between us. Then you will know that I am
the LORD your God.[i]"
21 " 'But the children rebelled against
me: They did not follow my decrees,
they were not careful to keep my laws,[j]
of which I said, "The person who obeys
them will live by them," and they desecrated my Sabbaths. So I said I would pour
out my wrath on them and spend my anger[k] against them in the wilderness.[l] 22 But
I withheld[m] my hand, and for the sake of
my name[n] I did what would keep it from
being profaned in the eyes of the nations
in whose sight I had brought them out.
23 Also with uplifted hand I swore to them
in the wilderness that I would disperse

20:4 [t] S Eze 16:2; 22:2; Mt 23:32 **20:5** [u] S Dt 7:6 [v] S Ge 14:22; S Nu 14:30 [w] S Lev 11:44 **20:6** [x] S Ex 6:8 [y] S Ex 3:8 [z] S Dt 8:7; Da 8:9; 11:41; Mal 3:12 **20:7** [a] Ex 20:4 [b] S Eze 6:9 [c] S Ex 20:2; Lev 18:3; Dt 29:18 **20:8** [d] S Jer 7:26 [e] S Jer 11:10; S Eze 7:8; S 16:26 [f] S Ex 32:7; Dt 9:7; S Isa 63:10 **20:9** [g] Eze 36:22; 39:7 [h] S Isa 48:11 **20:10** [i] S Ex 13:18; 19:1 **20:11** [j] Ex 20:1-23; Lev 18:5; Dt 4:7-8; S Eze 18:9; S Ro 10:5 **20:12** [k] S Ex 20:10 [l] S Ex 31:13 [m] Jer 17:22 [n] S Lev 20:8 **20:13** [o] Ps 78:40 [p] S Jer 6:19; 11:8 [q] ver 24 [r] S Dt 9:8 [s] S Ex 32:10 [t] Lev 26:15,43; S Nu 14:29; Ps 95:8-10; Isa 56:6 **20:14** [u] S Isa 48:11 [v] Eze 36:23 **20:15** [w] S Dt 1:34 [x] Nu 14:22-23; Ps 95:11; 106:26; Heb 3:11 **20:16** [y] Jer 11:8; Am 2:4 [z] S Nu 15:39 [a] ver 24; S Eze 6:4; Am 5:26 **20:17** [b] S Jer 4:27 **20:18** [c] S 2Ch 30:7; Zec 1:4 [d] S Ps 106:39 **20:19** [e] S Ex 20:2 [f] Dt 5:32-33; 6:1-2; S 8:1; 11:1; S 12:1 **20:20** [g] S Ex 20:10 [h] S Ex 31:13 [i] Jer 17:22 **20:21** [j] S Jer 7:26 [k] Nu 25:3 [l] S Eze 7:8 **20:22** [m] Ps 78:38 [n] S Isa 48:11

---

instructed to spell out the "detestable practices" for which that judgment comes on them (see also 22:2; 23:36).

20:5–26 These verses present Israel's history of apostasy in three acts (Act 1: vv. 5–9, Egypt; Act 2: vv. 10–17, Wilderness, Part 1; Act 3: vv. 18–26, Wilderness, Part 2). Each act has four scenes: (1) revelation, (2) rebellion, (3) wrath, (4) reconsideration. But see also note on v. 28.

20:5 *With uplifted hand.* A symbolic act accompanying the swearing of an oath (see vv. 15,23,42; Ge 14:22 and note; Ex 6:8). *I am the LORD your God.* See Ex 3:6,14–15 and notes.

20:6 *land flowing with milk and honey.* See note on Ex 3:8. *most beautiful of all lands.* Cf. Dt 8:7–10; Jer 3:19 for the land's natural beauty. Its real beauty lay in being selected as God's dwelling place (Dt 12:5,11).

20:7 *idols.* See note on 6:4.

20:8 *But they rebelled.* See vv. 13,21; see also Jos 24:14. *So I said I would pour out my wrath on them.* An internal refrain (see vv. 13,21); see also note on 7:8. *spend my anger against.* See note on 5:13.

20:9 *for the sake of my name.* See vv. 14,22,44. Name and person are closely connected in the Bible. God's name is his identity and reputation—that by which he is known (see note on Ps 5:11). The phrase used here is equivalent to "for my own sake" (cf. Isa 37:35; 43:25). God's acts of deliverance—past and future—identify him, revealing his true nature (see 36:22; Ps 23:3 and notes; Isa 48:9). *profaned.* Made light of—as through ridicule (see Nu 14:15–16).

20:10 *wilderness.* Act 2 (see note on vv. 5–26).

20:11 *will live.* See vv. 13,21; contrast v. 25. See notes on 16:6; 18:9; see also Lev 18:5 and note.

20:12 *Sabbaths as a sign.* Israel's observance of the Sabbath was to serve as a sign that they were the Lord's holy people (see Ex 31:16–17 and note). Ezekiel highlights the Sabbath (see 22:8,26; 23:38; 44:24; 45:17; 46:3), as did Isaiah (see Isa 56:1–8 and notes) and Jeremiah (Jer 17:19–27; cf. Ne 13:17–18). Jewish legalism later corrupted the Sabbath law (see Mt 12:1–14).

20:13 *desecrated.* By not observing the Sabbath-rest (see Jer 17:21–23) or by not observing it in the manner and spirit God intended (see Am 8:5).

20:15 *land flowing with milk and honey.* See note on Ex 3:8.

20:18 *I said to their children.* Act 3 (see note on vv. 5–26). God began anew with the second generation in the wilderness (see Nu 14:26–35).

them among the nations and scatter[o] them through the countries, 24 because they had not obeyed my laws but had rejected my decrees[p] and desecrated my Sabbaths,[q] and their eyes lusted after[r] their parents' idols.[s] 25 So I gave[t] them other statutes that were not good and laws through which they could not live;[u] 26 I defiled them through their gifts — the sacrifice[v] of every firstborn — that I might fill them with horror so they would know that I am the LORD.[w]'

27 "Therefore, son of man, speak to the people of Israel and say to them, 'This is what the Sovereign LORD says: In this also your ancestors[x] blasphemed[y] me by being unfaithful to me:[z] 28 When I brought them into the land[a] I had sworn to give them and they saw any high hill or any leafy tree, there they offered their sacrifices, made offerings that aroused my anger, presented their fragrant incense and poured out their drink offerings.[b] 29 Then I said to them: What is this high place[c] you go to?' " (It is called Bamah[a] to this day.)

Rebellious Israel Renewed

30 "Therefore say to the Israelites: 'This is what the Sovereign LORD says: Will you defile yourselves[d] the way your ancestors did and lust after their vile images?[e] 31 When you offer your gifts — the sacrifice of your children[f] in the fire — you continue to defile yourselves with all your idols to this day. Am I to let you inquire of me, you Israelites? As surely as I live, declares the Sovereign LORD, I will not let you inquire of me.[g]

32 " 'You say, "We want to be like the nations, like the peoples of the world, who serve wood and stone." But what you have in mind will never happen. 33 As surely as I live, declares the Sovereign LORD, I will reign over you with a mighty hand and an outstretched arm[h] and with outpoured wrath.[i] 34 I will bring you from the nations[j] and gather[k] you from the countries where you have been scattered — with a mighty hand[l] and an outstretched arm and with outpoured wrath.[m] 35 I will bring you into the wilderness[n] of the nations and there, face to face, I will execute judgment[o] upon you. 36 As I judged your ancestors in the wilderness of the land of Egypt, so I will judge you, declares the Sovereign LORD.[p] 37 I will take note of you as you pass under my rod,[q] and I will bring you into the bond of the covenant.[r] 38 I will purge[s] you of those who revolt and rebel against me. Although I will bring them out of the land where they are living, yet they will not enter the land of Israel. Then you will know that I am the LORD.[t]

39 " 'As for you, people of Israel, this is what the Sovereign LORD says: Go and serve your idols,[u] every one of you! But afterward you will surely listen to me and no longer profane my holy name[v] with your gifts and idols.[w] 40 For on my holy

[a] 29 *Bamah* means *high place.*

20:23 [o] S Lev 26:33; S Ps 9:11 **20:24** [p] Am 2:4 [q] ver 13 [r] S Eze 6:9 [s] S ver 16; S Eze 2:3; S 18:6 **20:25** [t] S Ps 81:12; Ro 1:28 [u] Isa 66:4; 2Th 2:11 **20:26** [v] S Lev 18:21 [w] Lev 20:2-5; 2Ki 17:17 **20:27** [x] S Ps 78:57 [y] S Nu 15:30; Ro 2:24 [z] S Eze 18:24 **20:28** [a] Ne 9:23; Ps 78:55,58 [b] S Jer 2:7; S 3:6; S 19:13; S Eze 6:13 **20:29** [c] Eze 16:16; 43:7 **20:30** [d] ver 43 [e] S Jdg 2:16-19; S Jer 16:12 **20:31** [f] S Eze 16:20 [g] Ps 106:37-39; S Jer 7:31; S Eze 14:3; Am 8:12; Zec 7:13 **20:33** [h] S Eze 16:27 [i] Jer 21:5; Eze 25:16 **20:34** [j] 2Co 6:17* [k] S Dt 30:4; S Ps 106:47 [l] S Isa 31:3 [m] Isa 27:12-13; S Jer 44:6; S La 2:4; S Eze 6:14 **20:35** [n] S Eze 19:13 [o] S 1Sa 12:7; S Job 22:4; S Jer 2:35 **20:36** [p] Nu 11:1-35; 14:28-30; 1Co 10:5-10 **20:37** [q] S Lev 27:32 [r] S Eze 16:62 **20:38** [s] Eze 34:17-22; Am 9:9-10 [t] Ps 95:11; Jer 44:14; S Eze 13:9; 23:49; Hos 2:14; Zec 13:8-9; Mal 3:3; 4:1-3; Heb 4:3 **20:39** [u] S Jer 44:25 [v] S Ex 20:7; S Eze 13:19 [w] Eze 43:7; Am 4:4

20:25 *So I gave them ... laws through which they could not live.* Just as God's judgments undo the creation order (see note on Ge 6:9 — 9:29) and undo human history (see note on Ge 11:1 - 9), so as an act of judgment he turns the laws he gave as the way to life (see vv. 12 - 13,21 and note on v. 11) into laws that produced death. This is a hard saying, but it most likely refers to God's requirement that Israel dedicate to him every firstborn male (Ex 13:2; 22:29) — which kings Ahaz and Manasseh, under the influence of the pagan religions of Israel's neighbors, radicalized into a law calling for actual sacrifice of the firstborn (v. 26; cf. Ro 1:24 - 32 and notes).

20:26 *sacrifice of every firstborn.* See v. 31 and note on 16:20. *so they would know that I am the LORD.* God will go to any lengths to get his people to acknowledge him (see note on 6:7).

20:28 *When I brought them into the land.* Apparently Act 4 in Ezekiel's history (see note on vv. 5 - 26), but it is not carried through with the same schematic consistency.

20:30 - 44 See note on vv. 1 - 44.

20:30 *Will you defile yourselves the way your ancestors did ...?* See note on vv. 5 - 26.

20:31 *inquire.* See v. 3 and note.

20:32 *like the nations.* The temptation to lose its uniqueness was always present for Israel (see 1Sa 8:5 and note). *will never happen.* As happened to those who were exiled to Egypt (see Jer 44:15 - 19). God will not abandon them to their idolatrous ways but will firmly turn them back to the way of covenant faithfulness to him.

20:33 *mighty hand ... outstretched arm.* Terminology of the exodus (cf. Dt 4:34; 5:15; 7:19; 11:2; 26:8).

20:35 *wilderness of the nations.* Exile among the nations would be for Israel like a return to the wilderness through which she journeyed on the way to the promised land (see Hos 2:14 and note).

20:37 *pass under my rod.* The way a shepherd counts or separates his flock (see Lev 27:32; Jer 33:13; cf. Mt 25:32 - 33). *I will bring you into the bond of the covenant.* As he had in the Sinai Desert (see note on 16:59 - 63).

20:38 *purge.* As in the first wilderness experience, many were not allowed to enter the land (see Nu 14:26 - 35 and notes).

20:39 *Go and serve your idols.* Irony, as in Am 4:4. *profane my holy name.* See Lev 18:21 and note.

20:40 *my holy mountain.* Mentioned only here in Ezekiel, it refers to Jerusalem or Zion (see Ps 2:6; Isa 2:2 - 4 and notes; 65; Ob 16; Zep 3:11). *all the people of Israel.* Includes a remnant of the northern kingdom, which fell in 722 - 721 BC (see 11:15; 36:10 and note). *offerings.* Possibly refers to a prescribed contribution. The other 19 occurrences in Ezekiel of the Hebrew for this word are confined to chs. 44 - 48, where the reference is to the land set aside for the temple and priests (see 45:1; 48:8 - 10, "portion") or to the special gifts for the priests (see 44:30). *choice gifts.* Voluntary contributions (but see NIV text note).

mountain, the high mountain of Israel,[x]
declares the Sovereign LORD, there in the
land all the people of Israel will serve me,
and there I will accept them. There I will
require your offerings[y] and your choice
gifts,[a] along with all your holy sacrifices.[z] 41 I will accept you as fragrant incense[a]
when I bring you out from the nations and
gather[b] you from the countries where you
have been scattered, and I will be proved
holy[c] through you in the sight of the nations.[d] 42 Then you will know that I am the
LORD,[e] when I bring you into the land of
Israel,[f] the land I had sworn with uplifted
hand to give to your ancestors.[g] 43 There
you will remember your conduct[h] and all
the actions by which you have defiled
yourselves, and you will loathe yourselves[i]
for all the evil you have done.[j] 44 You will
know that I am the LORD, when I deal with
you for my name's sake[k] and not according to your evil ways and your corrupt
practices, you people of Israel, declares
the Sovereign LORD.[l] "

Prophecy Against the South

45 The word of the LORD came to me:
46 "Son of man, set your face toward[m] the
south; preach against the south and prophesy against[n] the forest of the southland.[o]
47 Say to the southern forest:[p] 'Hear the
word of the LORD. This is what the Sovereign LORD says: I am about to set fire to
you, and it will consume[q] all your trees,
both green and dry. The blazing flame
will not be quenched, and every face from
south to north[r] will be scorched by it.[s] 48 Everyone will see that I the LORD have kindled
it; it will not be quenched.[t] "
49 Then I said, "Sovereign LORD,[u] they
are saying of me, 'Isn't he just telling parables?[v] ' "[b]

Babylon as God's Sword of Judgment

21 [c] The word of the LORD came to
me:[w] 2 "Son of man, set your face
against[x] Jerusalem and preach against the
sanctuary.[y] Prophesy against[z] the land of
Israel 3 and say to her: 'This is what the
LORD says: I am against you.[a] I will draw
my sword[b] from its sheath and cut off from
you both the righteous and the wicked.[c]
4 Because I am going to cut off the righteous and the wicked, my sword[d] will be
unsheathed against everyone from south
to north.[e] 5 Then all people will know that
I the LORD have drawn my sword[f] from its
sheath; it will not return[g] again.'[h]
6 "Therefore groan, son of man! Groan
before them with broken heart and bitter
grief.[i] 7 And when they ask you, 'Why are
you groaning?[j]' you shall say, 'Because of
the news that is coming. Every heart will
melt with fear[k] and every hand go limp;[l]
every spirit will become faint[m] and every
leg will be wet with urine.'[n] It is coming!
It will surely take place, declares the Sovereign LORD."
8 The word of the LORD came to me:
9 "Son of man, prophesy and say, 'This is
what the Lord says:

[a] 40 Or *and the gifts of your firstfruits* [b] 49 In Hebrew texts 20:45-49 is numbered 21:1-5. [c] In Hebrew texts 21:1-32 is numbered 21:6-37.

20:40 [x] S Eze 17:22; 34:14 [y] S Isa 60:7 [z] S Isa 56:7; Mal 3:4 **20:41** [a] S 2Co 2:14 [b] S Dt 30:4 [c] Eze 28:25; 36:23 [d] S Isa 5:16; S Eze 11:17; 2Co 6:17 **20:42** [e] Eze 38:23 [f] S Jer 23:8; Eze 34:13; 36:24 [g] Jer 30:3; Eze 34:27; 37:21 **20:43** [h] Eze 14:22 [i] S Lev 26:41 [j] S Eze 6:9; S 16:61; Hos 5:15 **20:44** [k] Ps 109:21; Isa 43:25; Eze 36:22 [l] S Eze 16:62; 36:32 **20:46** [m] S Eze 4:3; S 13:17 [n] Eze 21:2; Am 7:16 [o] Isa 30:6; Jer 13:19 **20:47** [p] S 2Ki 19:23 [q] Eze 19:14 [r] Eze 21:4 [s] Isa 9:18-19; S 13:8 **20:48** [t] S Jer 7:20; Eze 21:5,32; 23:25 **20:49** [u] S Eze 4:14 [v] S Jdg 14:12; S Ps 78:2; S Eze 12:9; Mt 13:13; S Jn 16:25 **21:1** [w] S Eze 20:1

21:2 [x] S Eze 13:17 [y] Eze 9:6 [z] Jer 26:11-12; S Eze 20:46 **21:3** [a] S Jer 21:13 [b] S Isa 27:1; S Eze 14:21 [c] ver 9-11; S Job 9:22; S Isa 57:1; Jer 47:6-7 **21:4** [d] S Lev 26:25; S Jer 25:27 [e] Eze 20:47 **21:5** [f] S Isa 34:5 [g] ver 30 [h] S Eze 20:47-48; Na 1:9 **21:6** [i] ver 12; S Isa 22:4; Jer 30:6; S Eze 9:4 **21:7** [j] S Job 23:2 [k] S Jos 7:5 [l] S Jer 47:3; Eze 22:14 [m] S Ps 6:2 [n] S Lev 26:36; S Job 11:16

20:41 *as fragrant incense.* In a metaphorical sense (as in Eph 5:2). *bring you out.* Cf. v. 34. *I will be proved holy.* See Lev 10:3 and note.

20:43 *you will remember … and … loathe yourselves.* A thorough repentance (see 6:9 and note; 16:63; 36:31; Lk 15:17–19).

20:44 *for my name's sake.* Summarizes and concludes the message (see note on v. 9).

20:45—21:32 Babylon will be God's sword to bring a ruinous destruction as total as that of a forest fire—primarily on Judah and Jerusalem (20:45—21:27), but also on the Ammonites (21:28–29)—and then Babylon, too, will feel God's wrath (21:30–32).

20:46 *set your face.* A posture required eight times of Ezekiel (here; 13:17; 21:2; 25:2; 28:21; 29:2; 35:2; 38:2). *toward the south.* Toward Judah and Jerusalem. Any Babylonian invasion would traverse Israel from north to south (see 26:7 and note).

20:47 *set fire.* Common figurative language for God's devastating judgments (see Isa 10:16–19), which often took the form of invasion by some world power (see Am 1:4 and note). *both green and dry.* All trees (cf. 17:24; Lk 23:31). *from south to north.* Expresses totality, not direction; equivalent to saying, "from the border on the right to that on the left."

20:49 *parables.* See note on 17:1–24; for other ridiculing of the prophet, see 12:21–28; 33:32.

21:2 *set your face.* See note on 20:46. *against the sanctuary.* See 9:6 and note.

21:3–5 *my sword … my sword … my sword.* See 5:2 and note. The threefold repetition is for emphasis (see note on Jer 7:4).

21:3 *I am against you.* See note on 5:8. *my sword.* This is the first of five sword messages (see vv. 8–17, 18–24,25–27,28–32). Here the sword refers to Babylonia and Nebuchadnezzar (v. 19). *both the righteous and the wicked.* Indicates the completeness of the judgment that is about to come on Israel. No one will escape its devastating effects, not even the righteous in the land. Contrast God's deliverance of Noah (Ge 6:7–8) and Lot (Ge 18:23; 19:12–13).

21:4 *from south to north.* See note on 20:47.

21:6 *groan … with broken heart and bitter grief.* Ezekiel's display of intense grief is to serve as another prophetic sign and as an occasion for a new message of impending judgment. This is Ezekiel's seventh symbolic act (see Introduction: Literary Features).

21:7 *every leg will be wet with urine.* See 7:17.

21:9 *A sword, a sword.* A sword song (see vv. 3–5 and note; see also note on v. 3), possibly accompanied by dancing or symbolic actions. Such songs may have been sung by warriors about to go into battle (see note on 2Sa 1:18).

" 'A sword, a sword,
sharpened and polished —
10 sharpened for the slaughter,[o]
polished to flash like lightning!

" 'Shall we rejoice in the scepter of my
royal son? The sword despises every such
stick.[p]

11 " 'The sword is appointed to be
polished,[q]
to be grasped with the hand;
it is sharpened and polished,
made ready for the hand of the
slayer.
12 Cry out and wail, son of man,
for it is against my people;
it is against all the princes of Israel.
They are thrown to the sword
along with my people.
Therefore beat your breast.[r]

13 " 'Testing will surely come. And what
if even the scepter, which the sword despises, does not continue? declares the
Sovereign LORD.'

14 "So then, son of man, prophesy
and strike your hands[s] together.
Let the sword strike twice,
even three times.
It is a sword for slaughter —
a sword for great slaughter,
closing in on them from every
side.[t]
15 So that hearts may melt with fear[u]
and the fallen be many,
I have stationed the sword for
slaughter[a]
at all their gates.
Look! It is forged to strike like
lightning,
it is grasped for slaughter.[v]
16 Slash to the right, you sword,
then to the left,
wherever your blade is turned.
17 I too will strike my hands[w] together,
and my wrath[x] will subside.
I the LORD have spoken.[y]"

18 The word of the LORD came to me:
19 "Son of man, mark out two roads for the
sword[z] of the king of Babylon to take, both
starting from the same country. Make a
signpost[a] where the road branches off to
the city. 20 Mark out one road for the sword
to come against Rabbah of the Ammonites[b]
and another against Judah and fortified
Jerusalem. 21 For the king of Babylon will
stop at the fork in the road, at the junction of the two roads, to seek an omen:
He will cast lots[c] with arrows, he will consult his idols,[d] he will examine the liver.[e]
22 Into his right hand will come the lot for
Jerusalem, where he is to set up battering
rams, to give the command to slaughter, to
sound the battle cry,[f] to set battering rams
against the gates, to build a ramp[g] and to
erect siege works.[h] 23 It will seem like a
false omen to those who have sworn allegiance to him, but he will remind[i] them of
their guilt[j] and take them captive.

24 "Therefore this is what the Sovereign LORD says: 'Because you people have
brought to mind your guilt by your open
rebellion, revealing your sins in all that
you do — because you have done this, you
will be taken captive.

25 " 'You profane and wicked prince of Israel, whose day has come,[k] whose time of
punishment has reached its climax,[l] 26 this
is what the Sovereign LORD says: Take off

21:10 [o] Ps 110:5-6; Isa 34:5-6 [p] Dt 32:41 **21:11** [q] Jer 46:4 **21:12** [r] Jer 31:19 **21:14** [s] ver 17; S Nu 24:10 [t] S Eze 6:11; 30:24 **21:15** [u] S 2Sa 17:10 [v] Ps 22:14 **21:17** [w] ver 14; Eze 22:13 [x] S Eze 5:13 [y] S Eze 6:11; S 16:42 **21:19** [z] S Eze 14:21; 32:11 [a] Jer 31:21 **21:20** [b] S Dt 3:11 **21:21** [c] S Pr 16:33 [d] Zec 10:2 [e] Nu 22:7; S 23:23 **21:22** [f] S Jer 4:16 [g] Jer 32:24 [h] S 2Ki 25:1; S Eze 4:2; 26:9 **21:23** [i] S Nu 5:15 [j] S Eze 17:19 **21:25** [k] Eze 22:4 [l] Eze 35:5

[a] *15* Septuagint; the meaning of the Hebrew for this word is uncertain.

21:10 *Shall we rejoice ... every such stick.* To think that the Babylonians would conquer every other country except Judah was a false hope. *scepter.* Represents rule, government or kingdom. *my royal son.* Referring to the reigning king of the house of David (see vv. 25–27; Ps 2:7 and notes). *sword.* Babylonia and Nebuchadnezzar (v. 19).
21:11 *slayer.* Nebuchadnezzar (v. 19).
21:12 *Cry out and wail ... beat your breast.* Eighth symbolic act (see Introduction: Literary Features).
21:13 *come.* On Judah. *what if even the scepter ... does not continue?* See note on v. 10. The question anticipates the final interruption of Davidic kingship, which came in 586 BC (see vv. 25–27).
21:14 *strike your hands.* See 6:11 and note. *Let the sword strike twice.* Cf. 2Ki 13:18–19.
21:17 *strike my hands.* As Ezekiel was commanded to do in v. 14.
21:19 *king of Babylon.* Nebuchadnezzar. *same country.* Babylonia, or possibly Aram (Syria) — Nebuchadnezzar headquartered at Riblah in northern Aram (see 2Ki 25:6).
21:20 *Rabbah.* Capital of Ammon (Jer 49:2); modern Amman (capital of Jordan).
21:21 *cast lots with arrows.* Divination with arrows, for the purpose of seeking good omens for the coming campaign — a practice not elsewhere mentioned in the Bible. Apparently arrows were labeled (e.g., "Rabbah," "Jerusalem"), placed into a quiver and drawn out, one with each hand. Right-hand selection was seen as a good omen (see v. 22). *idols.* The Hebrew for this word is translated "household gods" in Ge 31:19 (see note there). Consulting them is referred to in Hos 3:4; Zec 10:2. The household gods of Ge 31:19–35 were small enough to hide in a saddle, but others were life-size (1Sa 19:13–16). *examine the liver.* Looking at the color and configurations of sheep livers to foretell the future was common in ancient Babylonia and Rome, but the practice is not mentioned elsewhere in the Bible.
21:23 *false omen.* The leaders of Jerusalem, once submissive to Nebuchadnezzar but now in rebellion (2Ki 24:20), hoped that the result of the omen-seeking (vv. 21–22) was misleading.
21:25,29 *whose day ... has reached its climax.* The same fate that awaits the Ammonites also awaits Judah's king.
21:25 *prince of Israel.* Zedekiah (see note on 7:27).
21:26 *turban.* Only here is it mentioned as royal headwear. Elsewhere it is worn by priests (Ex 28:4,37,39; 29:6; 39:28,31; Lev 8:9; 16:4) as a setting for the crown (Ex 28:36–37; 29:6; 39:31; Lev 8:9). It was made of fine linen (Ex 28:39; 39:28). *lowly ... exalted ... exalted ... brought low.* A common Biblical

the turban, remove the crown.[m] It will not
be as it was: The lowly will be exalted and
the exalted will be brought low.[n] 27 A ruin!
A ruin! I will make it a ruin! The crown
will not be restored until he to whom it
rightfully belongs shall come;[o] to him I
will give it.'[p]
28 "And you, son of man, prophesy and
say, 'This is what the Sovereign LORD says
about the Ammonites[q] and their insults:

" 'A sword,[r] a sword,
drawn for the slaughter,
polished to consume
and to flash like lightning!
29 Despite false visions concerning you
and lying divinations[s] about you,
it will be laid on the necks
of the wicked who are to be slain,
whose day has come,
whose time of punishment has
reached its climax.[t]

30 " 'Let the sword return to its
sheath.[u]
In the place where you were
created,
in the land of your ancestry,[v]
I will judge you.
31 I will pour out my wrath on you
and breathe[w] out my fiery anger[x]
against you;
I will deliver you into the hands of
brutal men,
men skilled in destruction.[y]
32 You will be fuel for the fire,[z]
your blood will be shed in your land,
you will be remembered[a] no more;
for I the LORD have spoken.' "

21:26 [m]S Isa 28:5; S Jer 13:18 [n]S Ps 75:7; Isa 40:4; S Eze 17:24; S Mt 23:12 **21:27** [o]Ge 49:10 [p]Ps 2:6; Jer 23:5-6; Eze 37:24; Hag 2:21-22 **21:28** [q]S Ge 19:38; Zep 2:8 [r]S Jer 12:12 **21:29** [s]Jer 27:9 [t]ver 25; Eze 22:28; 35:5 **21:30** [u]ver 5; Jer 47:6 [v]S Eze 16:3 **21:31** [w]Ps 18:15; S Isa 11:4 [x]Ps 79:6; Eze 22:20-21 [y]S Jer 4:7; 51:20-23; S Eze 16:39 **21:32** [z]S Eze 20:47-48; Mal 4:1 [a]Eze 25:10

22:2 [b]Eze 24:6, 9; Hos 4:2; Na 3:1; Hab 2:12 [c]S Eze 16:2; 23:36 **22:3** [d]ver 6, 13, 27; Eze 23:37, 45; 24:6 **22:4** [e]S 2Ki 21:16 [f]Eze 21:25 [g]S Ps 137:3 [h]Ps 44:13-14; S Eze 5:14 **22:5** [i]S Isa 22:2 **22:6** [j]S Eze 11:6; 18:10; 33:25 **22:7** [k]S Dt 5:16; Mic 7:6 [l]S Ex 23:9

Judgment on Jerusalem's Sins

22 The word of the LORD came to me:
2 "Son of man, will you judge her? Will
you judge this city of bloodshed?[b] Then
confront her with all her detestable practices[c] 3 and say: 'This is what the Sovereign LORD says: You city that brings on
herself doom by shedding blood[d] in her
midst and defiles herself by making idols,
4 you have become guilty because of the
blood you have shed[e] and have become
defiled by the idols you have made. You
have brought your days to a close, and
the end of your years has come.[f] Therefore I will make you an object of scorn[g] to
the nations and a laughingstock to all the
countries.[h] 5 Those who are near and those
who are far away will mock you, you infamous city, full of turmoil.[i]
6 " 'See how each of the princes of Israel who are in you uses his power to shed
blood.[j] 7 In you they have treated father
and mother with contempt;[k] in you they
have oppressed the foreigner[l] and mistreated the fatherless and the widow.[m]
8 You have despised my holy things and
desecrated my Sabbaths.[n] 9 In you are slanderers[o] who are bent on shedding blood;[p]
in you are those who eat at the mountain
shrines[q] and commit lewd acts.[r] 10 In you
are those who dishonor their father's bed;[s]
in you are those who violate women during their period,[t] when they are ceremonially unclean.[u] 11 In you one man commits

[m]S Ex 22:21-22 **22:8** [n]S Ex 20:8; Eze 23:38-39 **22:9** [o]S Lev 19:16 [p]Isa 59:3; S Eze 11:6; Hos 4:2; 6:9 [q]Eze 18:11 [r]Eze 23:29; Hos 4:10, 14 **22:10** [s]Lev 18:7 [t]S Lev 12:2 [u]S Lev 18:8, 19

expression for the reversal of human conditions because of the intervention of the Lord (see 17:24 and note; 1Sa 2:7–8; Pr 26:27 and note; Lk 1:52–53).

21:27 *A ruin! A ruin! ... a ruin!* Threefold repetition for emphasis (see Isa 6:3; Jer 7:4 and notes). *The crown.* Representing dominion (the kingdom of Judah). *until he to whom it rightfully belongs shall come.* The Messiah; probably an allusion to Ge 49:10 (see note there).

21:28 *Ammonites.* See v. 20. After judgment on Jerusalem, they too will be dealt with (see 25:1–7; see also Jer 9:26; 49:1–6; Am 1:13–15; Zep 2:8–11). *their insults.* See 25:3,6; cf. 36:15. *A sword, a sword.* Nebuchadnezzar's (see vv. 9,19 and notes).

21:29 *false visions ... lying divinations.* Apparently Ammon also had false prophets of peace (see v. 10 and note; 13:10; Jer 6:14; 8:11–12). *it.* The sword.

21:30–32 When the Lord has accomplished his purpose through the Babylonians, they too will come under his judgment for all their evil ways (see Jer 50:15,27,29,31; 51:6,49; Hab 2:4–20; cf. Isa 10:5–19 and note on 10:12).

21:30 *Let the sword return.* Addressing Nebuchadnezzar.

21:31 *brutal men.* The people of the East, as in 25:4.

21:32 *fuel for the fire.* See 20:47 and note.

22:1–31 Ezekiel is instructed to confront Jerusalem (vv. 1–12) and the land of Judah (vv. 23–29) with all the sins they are guilty of and for which they were about to feel the fiery wrath of Yahweh (vv. 13–22,30–31). Under Manasseh, Amon and Jehoiakim, Jerusalem had become a city of idolatry and pervasive moral corruption (see 2Ki 21:2–26; Jer 22:13–17). In the land of Judah all who held power cruelly exploited the weak.

22:2 *will you judge her?* Cf. 20:4 and note. *this city.* Jerusalem, the usual focal point of Ezekiel's prophecy (see 5:5 and note).

22:3 *shedding blood ... making idols.* Two categories of sins are developed: social injustices and idol worship. *idols.* See note on 6:4.

22:6 *princes of Israel.* Leaders generally, not kings; contrast 21:12 with 19:1.

22:7 *treated father and mother with contempt.* See Mic 7:6 and note. Both passages are the opposite of what God commands in Ex 20:12 (see note there). *foreigner ... fatherless ... widow.* See Ex 22:21–27 and notes; Dt 10:18; 16:11,14; 24:17; 27:19; Ps 68:5–6 and note; 82:3; Isa 1:17 and note; 23; Jer 7:6; 22:3; Jas 1:27.

22:8 *Sabbaths.* A major concern in Ezekiel (see note on 20:12).

22:9 *eat at the mountain shrines.* See 18:6 and note. *commit lewd acts.* In their pagan worship practices (see Hos 4:14 and note).

22:10 *violate women.* Cf. 18:6 and note.

22:11 *detestable offense.* All the sins mentioned in this verse were specifically forbidden in the law (Lev 18:7–20; 20:10–21; Dt 22:22–23,30; 27:22).

a detestable offense with his neighbor's
wife,[v] another shamefully defiles his
daughter-in-law,[w] and another violates
his sister,[x] his own father's daughter.[y] 12 In
you are people who accept bribes[z] to shed
blood; you take interest[a] and make a profit
from the poor. You extort unjust gain from
your neighbors.[b] And you have forgotten[c]
me, declares the Sovereign LORD.[d]
13 " 'I will surely strike my hands[e] together at the unjust gain[f] you have made
and at the blood[g] you have shed in your
midst.[h] 14 Will your courage endure[i] or
your hands[j] be strong in the day I deal
with you? I the LORD have spoken,[k] and
I will do it.[l] 15 I will disperse you among
the nations and scatter[m] you through the
countries; and I will put an end to[n] your
uncleanness.[o] 16 When you have been defiled[a] in the eyes of the nations, you will
know that I am the LORD.' "
17 Then the word of the LORD came to
me: 18 "Son of man, the people of Israel
have become dross[p] to me; all of them are
the copper, tin, iron and lead left inside
a furnace.[q] They are but the dross of silver.[r] 19 Therefore this is what the Sovereign
LORD says: 'Because you have all become
dross,[s] I will gather you into Jerusalem.
20 As silver, copper, iron, lead and tin are
gathered into a furnace to be melted with
a fiery blast, so will I gather you in my anger and my wrath and put you inside the
city and melt you.[t] 21 I will gather you and
I will blow[u] on you with my fiery wrath,
and you will be melted inside her.[v] 22 As
silver is melted[w] in a furnace, so you will
be melted inside her, and you will know
that I the LORD have poured out my wrath[x]
on you.' "[y]
23 Again the word of the LORD came to
me: 24 "Son of man, say to the land, 'You
are a land that has not been cleansed or
rained on in the day of wrath.'[z] 25 There is a
conspiracy[a] of her princes[b] within her like
a roaring lion[b] tearing its prey; they devour people,[c] take treasures and precious
things and make many widows[d] within
her. 26 Her priests do violence to my law[e]
and profane my holy things; they do not
distinguish between the holy and the common;[f] they teach that there is no difference
between the unclean and the clean;[g] and
they shut their eyes to the keeping of my
Sabbaths, so that I am profaned[h] among
them.[i] 27 Her officials[j] within her are like
wolves[k] tearing their prey; they shed blood
and kill people[l] to make unjust gain.[m]
28 Her prophets whitewash[n] these deeds
for them by false visions and lying divinations.[o] They say, 'This is what the Sovereign LORD says'—when the LORD has not
spoken.[p] 29 The people of the land practice
extortion and commit robbery;[q] they oppress the poor and needy and mistreat the
foreigner,[r] denying them justice.[s]
30 "I looked for someone among them
who would build up the wall[t] and stand
before me in the gap on behalf of the land
so I would not have to destroy it, but I
found no one.[u] 31 So I will pour out my
wrath on them and consume them with
my fiery anger,[v] bringing down[w] on their
own heads all they have done, declares the
Sovereign LORD.[x]"

Two Adulterous Sisters

23 The word of the LORD came to
me: 2 "Son of man, there were two
women, daughters of the same mother.[y]
3 They became prostitutes in Egypt,[z] engaging in prostitution[a] from their youth.[b]
In that land their breasts were fondled and
their virgin bosoms caressed.[c] 4 The older
was named Oholah, and her sister was

[a] 16 Or *When I have allotted you your inheritance*
[b] 25 Septuagint; Hebrew *prophets*

22:11 [v]S Jer 5:8 [w]S Ge 11:31; Lev 18:15 [x]S Lev 18:9; S 2Sa 13:14 [y]Eze 18:6 **22:12** [z]S Ex 18:21; Dt 27:25; Ps 26:10; Isa 5:23; Am 5:12; Mic 7:3 [a]S Eze 18:8 [b]Lev 19:13 [c]Ps 106:21; S Isa 17:10; S 57:11 [d]S Eze 11:6 **22:13** [e]S Nu 24:10; S Eze 21:17 [f]S ver 27; S Isa 33:15 [g]S ver 3 [h]S Eze 6:11 **22:14** [i]Ps 76:7; Joel 2:11; Na 1:6; Mal 3:2 [j]S Eze 7:17 [k]Eze 24:14 [l]S Eze 17:24 **22:15** [m]S Lev 26:33; Dt 4:27; Zec 7:14 [n]S Eze 16:41 [o]Eze 24:11 **22:18** [p]S Ps 119:119 [q]Isa 48:10 [r]Jer 6:28-30 **22:19** [s]S Ps 119:119 **22:20** [t]Hos 8:10; Mal 3:2 **22:21** [u]Isa 40:7; Hag 1:9 [v]Ps 68:2; Eze 21:31 **22:22** [w]S Isa 1:25 [x]S Eze 7:8 [y]S Isa 64:7 **22:24** [z]Eze 24:13 **22:25** [a]Jer 11:9 [b]S Ps 22:13 [c]Hos 6:9 [d]Jer 15:8; 18:21 **22:26** [e]Hos 9:7-8; Zep 3:4; Mal 2:7-8 [f]Eze 42:20; 44:23 [g]S Lev 20:25 [h]S Lev 18:21; S Eze 13:19 [i]ver 8; S 1Sa 2:12-17; Jer 2:8,26; Hag 2:11-14 **22:27** [j]S Jer 26:10; Zep 3:3 [k]Mt 7:15 [l]S ver 3; S Eze 11:6; 33:25; 34:2-3; Mic 3:2,10 [m]ver 13; S Ge 37:24; S Isa 1:23; S Jer 12:2; S 51:13; Eze 33:31 **22:28** [n]S Eze 13:10 [o]S La 2:14; S 4:13; S Eze 21:29 [p]S Eze 13:2,6-7 **22:29** [q]S Ps 62:10 [r]S Ex 22:21 [s]S Isa 5:7 **22:30** [t]S Eze 13:5 [u]Ps 106:23; S Isa 64:7; Jer 5:1 **22:31** [v]Ex 32:10; S Isa 30:27; S La 4:11 [w]Eze 16:43 [x]Eze 7:8-9; Ro 2:8 **23:2** [y]S Jer 3:7; S Eze 16:45 **23:3** [z]Jos 24:14 [a]S Lev 17:7; S Isa 1:21 [b]S Ps 25:7 [c]S Eze 16:15

22:12 *you take interest and make a profit from the poor.* See 18:8 and note.
22:13 *strike my hands.* In anger (see 21:14,17).
22:17–22 Jerusalem will become God's "furnace" in which he melts down all those remaining in and around the city in order to cleanse away the "dross" (see Ps 12:6 and note).
22:25 *princes.* Ezekiel begins to speak plainly concerning the "dross" of vv. 18–22. All of Jerusalem's leaders and people were included: princes (here), priests (v. 26), officials (v. 27), prophets (v. 28), people (v. 29). *like a roaring lion.* Cf. v. 27; 13:4; Zep 3:3.
22:26 *distinguish between the holy and the common.* One of the main duties of the priests (see 44:23 and note; see also Lev 10:10 and note). *Sabbaths.* See note on v. 8. *I am profaned.* See Lev 18:21 and note.
22:28 *whitewash.* See 13:10 and note.
22:29 *people of the land.* See 7:27 and note.
22:30 *I looked for someone.* Cf. Isa 59:16; 63:5 and notes. *stand before me in the gap.* See 13:5 and note. Some interpret the task here as prophetic intercession with God in behalf of the people (see Ge 20:7; 1Sa 12:23; Jer 37:3; 42:2). Others interpret it as teaching, particularly calling the people to repentance. Cf. the task of the prophetic "watchman" (3:17–21; 33:1–6).
22:31 *bringing down on their own heads all they have done.* See note on Pr 26:27.
23:1–49 This extended allegory depicting in lurid colors the sins of Israel (similar to that found in ch. 16) climaxes the series of messages of judgment on Jerusalem and Judah begun in ch. 13 (see notes on 13:1–23; 18:1–32).
23:4 *The older.* See 16:46 and note. *Oholah.* Means "her tent," probably referring to the fact that Samaria had its own un-

Oholibah. They were mine and gave birth
to sons and daughters. Oholah is Samaria,
and Oholibah is Jerusalem.[d]
5 "Oholah engaged in prostitution while
she was still mine; and she lusted after her
lovers, the Assyrians[e] — warriors[f] 6 clothed
in blue, governors and commanders, all of
them handsome young men, and mounted
horsemen. 7 She gave herself as a prostitute to all the elite of the Assyrians and
defiled herself with all the idols of everyone she lusted after.[g] 8 She did not give up
the prostitution she began in Egypt,[h] when
during her youth men slept with her, caressed her virgin bosom and poured out
their lust on her.[i]
9 "Therefore I delivered her into the
hands[j] of her lovers,[k] the Assyrians, for
whom she lusted.[l] 10 They stripped[m] her
naked, took away her sons and daughters
and killed her with the sword. She became
a byword among women,[n] and punishment was inflicted[o] on her.[p]
11 "Her sister Oholibah saw this,[q] yet in
her lust and prostitution she was more depraved than her sister.[r] 12 She too lusted
after the Assyrians — governors and commanders, warriors in full dress, mounted
horsemen, all handsome young men.[s] 13 I
saw that she too defiled herself; both of
them went the same way.[t]
14 "But she carried her prostitution
still further. She saw men portrayed on
a wall,[u] figures of Chaldeans[a] portrayed
in red,[v] 15 with belts[w] around their waists
and flowing turbans on their heads; all of
them looked like Babylonian chariot officers, natives of Chaldea.[b] 16 As soon as she
saw them, she lusted after them and sent
messengers[x] to them in Chaldea.[y] 17 Then
the Babylonians[z] came to her, to the bed
of love, and in their lust they defiled
her. After she had been defiled by them,
she turned away from them in disgust.[a]
18 When she carried on her prostitution
openly and exposed her naked body,[b] I
turned away[c] from her in disgust, just as I
had turned away from her sister.[d] 19 Yet she

23:4 [d]S Eze 16:46 **23:5** [e]S 2Ki 16:7; Hos 5:13 [f]Hos 8:9 **23:7** [g]Isa 57:8; Hos 5:3; 6:10 **23:8** [h]Ex 32:4 [i]S Eze 16:15 **23:9** [j]S 2Ki 18:11 [k]S Jer 4:30 [l]Hos 11:5 **23:10** [m]Hos 2:10 [n]Eze 16:41 [o]Jer 42:10 [p]Eze 16:36 **23:11** [q]S Jer 3:7 [r]Jer 3:8-11; S Eze 16:51 **23:12** [s]2Ki 16:7-15; S 2Ch 28:16; S Eze 16:15,28 **23:13** [t]S 2Ki 17:19; Hos 12:2 **23:14** [u]S Eze 8:10 [v]Jer 22:14; Na 2:3 **23:15** [w]S Isa 5:27 **23:16** [x]S Isa 57:9 [y]S Eze 6:9 **23:17** [z]Jer 40:9 [a]S Eze 16:29 **23:18** [b]S Isa 57:8 [c]Ps 78:59; 106:40; Jer 6:8 [d]Jer 12:8; Am 5:21 **23:21** [e]S Eze 16:26 **23:22** [f]S Jer 4:30 [g]S Eze 16:37 **23:23** [h]2Ki 20:14-18; S Jer 40:9 [i]S Ge 11:28 [j]Jer 50:21 [k]S 2Ki 24:2 **23:24** [l]Jer 47:3; Eze 26:7, 10; Na 2:4 [m]Jer 39:5-6 **23:25** [n]S Dt 29:20 [o]ver 47; Eze 24:21 [p]S Jer 12:9; S Eze 16:38; S 20:47-48

became more and more promiscuous as
she recalled the days of her youth, when
she was a prostitute in Egypt. 20 There
she lusted after her lovers, whose genitals were like those of donkeys and whose
emission was like that of horses. 21 So you
longed for the lewdness of your youth,
when in Egypt your bosom was caressed
and your young breasts fondled.[c][e]
22 "Therefore, Oholibah, this is what the
Sovereign LORD says: I will stir up your
lovers[f] against you, those you turned away
from in disgust, and I will bring them
against you from every side[g] — 23 the Babylonians[h] and all the Chaldeans,[i] the men
of Pekod[j] and Shoa and Koa, and all the
Assyrians with them, handsome young
men, all of them governors and commanders, chariot officers and men of high rank,
all mounted on horses.[k] 24 They will come
against you with weapons,[d] chariots and
wagons[l] and with a throng of people; they
will take up positions against you on every side with large and small shields and
with helmets. I will turn you over to them
for punishment,[m] and they will punish you
according to their standards. 25 I will direct
my jealous anger[n] against you, and they
will deal with you in fury. They will cut
off your noses and your ears, and those
of you who are left will fall by the sword.
They will take away your sons and daughters,[o] and those of you who are left will be
consumed by fire.[p] 26 They will also strip[q]
you of your clothes and take your fine jewelry.[r] 27 So I will put a stop[s] to the lewdness
and prostitution you began in Egypt. You
will not look on these things with longing
or remember Egypt anymore.
28 "For this is what the Sovereign LORD
says: I am about to deliver you into the

[a] *14* Or *Babylonians* [b] *15* Or *Babylonia*; also in verse 16 [c] *21* Syriac (see also verse 3); Hebrew *caressed because of your young breasts* [d] *24* The meaning of the Hebrew for this word is uncertain.

23:26 [q]S Jer 13:22 [r]S Isa 3:18-23; S Eze 16:39 **23:27** [s]S Eze 16:41

---

authorized sanctuary. *Oholibah.* Means "My tent is in her," probably referring to the Lord's sanctuary in Jerusalem. Cf. the two sisters of Jer 3:6–12 and note on 3:7.

23:5 *prostitution.* Here represents political alliances with pagan powers — not idolatry as in ch. 16 (see Ex 34:15 and note). The graphic language of the chapter underscores God's and Ezekiel's disgust with Israel for playing the worldly game of international politics rather than relying on the Lord for her security — as clear a case of religious prostitution as idolatry. *Assyrians.* See 2Ki 15:19 and note.

23:8 *in Egypt.* Cf. 20:5–8. Israel's entire history was marked by unfaithfulness. For her attachment to Egypt, see Ex 17:3; Nu 11:5,18,20; 14:2–4; 21:5.

23:10 *stripped her naked.* A reference to the fall of Samaria to the Assyrians in 722–721 BC.

23:14 *portrayed in red.* Jeremiah, too, noted red interior decorations with disfavor (Jer 22:14).

23:15 *belts.* Cf. Isa 5:27 for similar Assyrian military equipment.

23:20 *genitals.* See note on 16:26.

23:23 *Babylonians ... Chaldeans.* Often identified with one another (see 1:3 and NIV text note there; 12:13), here distinguished (as in v. 15), probably because the Chaldeans were relative newcomers. *Pekod.* Aramaic people located east of Babylon. *Shoa and Koa.* Babylonian allies of uncertain origin and location.

23:24 *their standards.* Which were cruel and gruesome (see v. 25).

23:25 *jealous anger.* See 16:38 and note. *fire.* See notes on 15:7; 20:47.

23:27 *in Egypt.* See note on v. 8.

hands[t] of those you hate, to those you
turned away from in disgust. 29 They will
deal with you in hatred and take away everything you have worked for. They will
leave you stark naked,[u] and the shame of
your prostitution will be exposed.[v] Your
lewdness[w] and promiscuity[x] 30 have brought
this on you, because you lusted after the
nations and defiled yourself with their
idols.[y] 31 You have gone the way of your sister; so I will put her cup[z] into your hand.[a]
32 "This is what the Sovereign LORD says:

"You will drink your sister's cup,
a cup large and deep;
it will bring scorn and derision,[b]
for it holds so much.[c]
33 You will be filled with drunkenness
and sorrow,
the cup of ruin and desolation,
the cup of your sister Samaria.[d]
34 You will drink it[e] and drain it dry
and chew on its pieces —
and you will tear your breasts.

I have spoken, declares the Sovereign LORD.[f]

35 "Therefore this is what the Sovereign
LORD says: Since you have forgotten[g] me
and turned your back on me,[h] you must
bear[i] the consequences of your lewdness
and prostitution."
36 The LORD said to me: "Son of man,
will you judge Oholah and Oholibah?
Then confront[j] them with their detestable practices,[k] 37 for they have committed
adultery and blood is on their hands. They
committed adultery with their idols; they
even sacrificed their children, whom they
bore to me, as food for them.[l] 38 They have
also done this to me: At that same time
they defiled my sanctuary[m] and desecrated my Sabbaths.[n] 39 On the very day they
sacrificed their children to their idols, they
entered my sanctuary and desecrated[o] it.
That is what they did in my house.[p]
40 "They even sent messengers for men
who came from far away,[q] and when they
arrived you bathed yourself for them, applied eye makeup[r] and put on your jewelry.[s] 41 You sat on an elegant couch,[t] with a
table[u] spread before it on which you had
placed the incense[v] and olive oil that belonged to me.[w]
42 "The noise of a carefree[x] crowd was
around her; drunkards[y] were brought from
the desert along with men from the rabble, and they put bracelets[z] on the wrists
of the woman and her sister and beautiful
crowns on their heads.[a] 43 Then I said about
the one worn out by adultery, 'Now let
them use her as a prostitute,[b] for that is all
she is.' 44 And they slept with her. As men
sleep with a prostitute, so they slept with
those lewd women, Oholah and Oholibah.
45 But righteous judges will sentence them
to the punishment of women who commit
adultery and shed blood,[c] because they are
adulterous and blood is on their hands.[d]
46 "This is what the Sovereign LORD says:
Bring a mob[e] against them and give them
over to terror and plunder.[f] 47 The mob
will stone them and cut them down with
their swords; they will kill their sons and
daughters[g] and burn[h] down their houses.[i]
48 "So I will put an end[j] to lewdness in
the land, that all women may take warning and not imitate you.[k] 49 You will suffer
the penalty for your lewdness and bear
the consequences of your sins of idolatry.[l]
Then you will know that I am the Sovereign LORD.[m]"

Jerusalem as a Cooking Pot

24 In the ninth year, in the tenth
month on the tenth day, the word
of the LORD came to me:[n] 2 "Son of man,
record[o] this date, this very date, because
the king of Babylon has laid siege to Jerusalem this very day.[p] 3 Tell this rebellious
people[q] a parable[r] and say to them: 'This
is what the Sovereign LORD says:

23:28 [t]S Jer 34:20 **23:29** [u]Mic 1:11 [v]S Jer 13:27 [w]S Eze 22:9 [x]Dt 28:48; S Eze 16:36 **23:30** [y]Ps 106:37-38; Zep 3:1 **23:31** [z]S Jer 25:15 [a]2Ki 21:13 **23:32** [b]Ps 44:13; Hos 7:16 [c]Ps 60:3; Isa 51:17; Jer 25:15 **23:33** [d]Jer 25:15-16; S Eze 12:19 **23:34** [e]S Ps 16:5 [f]S Jer 25:27 **23:35** [g]S Dt 32:18; S Isa 17:10 [h]S 1Ki 14:9; S 2Ch 29:6 [i]Eze 16:52 **23:36** [j]S Eze 16:2 [k]Isa 58:1; S Eze 22:2; Mic 3:8 **23:37** [l]S Eze 16:36 **23:38** [m]S Lev 15:31 [n]S Ne 10:31 **23:39** [o]S 2Ki 21:4 [p]S Jer 7:10; Eze 22:8 **23:40** [q]S Isa 57:9 [r]2Ki 9:30 [s]S Jer 4:30; Eze 16:13-19; Hos 2:13 **23:41** [t]S Est 1:6; S Pr 7:17 [u]Isa 65:11; Eze 41:22; 44:16; Mal 1:7, 12 [v]Isa 57:9; S 65:3; S Jer 44:5 [w]S Nu 18:12 **23:42** [x]S Ps 73:5 [y]S 2Ch 9:1 [z]S Ge 24:30 [a]S Eze 16:11-12 **23:43** [b]ver 3 **23:45** [c]S Eze 22:3 [d]S Lev 20:10; S Eze 16:38; Hos 2:2; 6:5 **23:46** [e]Eze 16:40 [f]S Dt 28:25; S Jer 25:9 **23:47** [g]S ver 25 [h]2Ch 36:19; S Jer 34:22 [i]S 2Ch 36:17 **23:48** [j]Eze 16:41 [k]2Pe 2:6 **23:49** [l]Eze 24:13 [m]S Eze 7:4; S 9:10; 16:58; S 20:38 **24:1** [n]S Eze 8:1; 26:1; 29:17 **24:2** [o]Isa 30:8; Hab 2:2 [p]2Ki 25:1; S Jer 39:1 **24:3** [q]S Isa 1:2; S Eze 2:3,6 [r]S Eze 20:49

23:31 *cup.* Filled with the anger of the Lord. To drink it was to die. For a development of the imagery, see Ps 16:5 and note; 75:8; Isa 51:17,22; Jer 25:15 and note; 49:12; La 4:21; Ob 16 and note; Hab 2:16; Mt 20:22; 26:39; Rev 14:10 and note.
23:34 *tear your breasts.* Beating the breasts — a sign of mourning (see 21:12; see also Jer 31:19; Lk 23:48 and notes) — is here poetically intensified to the point of tearing them in a frantic attempt to find relief from intolerable suffering.
23:35 *you have forgotten me.* See 22:12; Jer 2:32 and note.
23:37 *sacrificed their children.* See note on 16:20.
23:38 *defiled my sanctuary.* See ch. 8. *Sabbaths.* See note on 22:8.
23:40 *They even sent messengers for men.* Possibly a reference to the Jerusalem summit meeting in Zedekiah's time (Jer 27). *you.* Jerusalem. *applied eye makeup.* By daubing the eyelids with kohl, a soot-like compound, to draw attention to the eyes.
23:41 *couch, with a table spread before it.* Ready for a banquet (see Isa 21:5; also Pr 9:2).
23:42 *drunkards.* Drunkenness is consistently condemned in Scripture (see notes on Pr 20:1; Isa 5:11 – 13).
24:1 – 14 The series of messages beginning with ch. 13 (see note on 13:1 – 23) ends with a depiction of Jerusalem as a pot cooking over an open fire, concluding with words that echo the final words of the seventh message in this series (see 18:30; 24:14 and notes).
24:1 *ninth year ... tenth month ... tenth day.* Of King Zedekiah's reign (2Ki 25:1); Jan. 15, 588 BC, some two and a half years after the preceding dated message (see 20:1 and chart, p. 1336); Ezekiel's fourth date (see 1:2; 8:1; 20:1).
24:2 *record this date ... because.* God revealed to Ezekiel what was happening in Jerusalem.
24:3 *rebellious people.* The last occurrence of this condemn-

“ ‘Put on the cooking pot;[s] put it on
and pour water into it.
4 Put into it the pieces of meat,
all the choice pieces — the leg and
the shoulder.
Fill it with the best of these bones;[t]
5 take the pick of the flock.[u]
Pile wood beneath it for the bones;
bring it to a boil
and cook the bones in it.[v]

6 “ ‘For this is what the Sovereign LORD says:

“ ‘Woe[w] to the city of bloodshed,[x]
to the pot now encrusted,
whose deposit will not go away!
Take the meat out piece by piece
in whatever order[y] it comes.[z]

7 “ ‘For the blood she shed is in her midst:
She poured it on the bare rock;
she did not pour it on the ground,
where the dust would cover it.[a]
8 To stir up wrath and take revenge
I put her blood on the bare rock,
so that it would not be covered.

9 “ ‘Therefore this is what the Sovereign
LORD says:

“ ‘Woe to the city of bloodshed!
I, too, will pile the wood high.
10 So heap on the wood
and kindle the fire.
Cook the meat well,
mixing in the spices;
and let the bones be charred.
11 Then set the empty pot on the coals
till it becomes hot and its copper glows,
so that its impurities may be melted
and its deposit burned away.[b]
12 It has frustrated all efforts;
its heavy deposit has not been
removed,
not even by fire.

13 “ ‘Now your impurity is lewdness. Because I tried to cleanse you but you would
not be cleansed[c] from your impurity, you
will not be clean again until my wrath
against you has subsided.[d]

14 “ ‘I the LORD have spoken.[e] The time
has come for me to act.[f] I will not hold
back; I will not have pity,[g] nor will I relent.[h] You will be judged according to your
conduct and your actions,[i] declares the
Sovereign LORD.[j] ’ ”

Ezekiel’s Wife Dies

15 The word of the LORD came to me:
16 “Son of man, with one blow[k] I am about
to take away from you the delight of your
eyes.[l] Yet do not lament or weep or shed
any tears.[m] 17 Groan quietly;[n] do not mourn
for the dead. Keep your turban[o] fastened
and your sandals[p] on your feet; do not
cover your mustache and beard[q] or eat the
customary food of mourners.[r]”

18 So I spoke to the people in the morning,
and in the evening my wife died. The next
morning I did as I had been commanded.[s]

19 Then the people asked me, “Won’t
you tell us what these things have to do
with us?[t] Why are you acting like this?”

24:3 [s] S Eze 11:3 **24:4** [t] S Eze 11:7 **24:5** [u] S Isa 34:12; Jer 52:10 [v] Jer 52:24-27; Mic 3:2-3 **24:6** [w] S Eze 16:23 [x] S Eze 22:2 [y] S Job 6:27; Joel 3:3; Ob 1:11; Na 3:10 [z] S Eze 11:11 **24:7** [a] S Lev 17:13 **24:11** [b] Jer 21:10 **24:13** [c] S Isa 22:14 [d] Jer 6:28-30; La 1:9; S Eze 16:42; 22:24; 23:36-49; Hos 7:1; Zec 6:8 **24:14** [e] Eze 22:14 [f] S Nu 11:23 [g] S Eze 8:18 [h] S Job 27:22 [i] Eze 36:19; Zec 8:14 [j] S Isa 3:11; S Eze 18:30 **24:16** [k] S Ps 39:10 [l] ver 21; Ps 84:1; S La 2:4 [m] Jer 13:17; 16:5; S 22:10 **24:17** [n] Ps 39:9 [o] S Ex 28:39; S Isa 3:20 [p] S Isa 20:2 [q] S Lev 13:45 [r] ver 22; S Jer 16:7 **24:18** [s] S Eze 12:7 **24:19** [t] Eze 12:9; 37:18

ing phrase in Ezekiel (see 2:5,6,8; 3:9,26 – 27; 12:2 – 3,9,25; 17:12). Jerusalem’s rebellion would soon be crushed. *parable.* Cf. 17:2. *cooking pot.* A reuse of the imagery found in 11:3 – 12. The cooking pot is Jerusalem (cf. 11:3 and note). In what follows, the imagery shifts from cooking the meat and bones in the pot (vv. 4 – 5) to burning away the impurities that adhere to the pot (vv. 6 – 8) and then repeats the cycle (vv. 9 – 10, cooking the meat and bones; vv. 11 – 12, burning off the encrusted impurities).

24:4 *choice pieces.* The people of Jerusalem who thought they were spared the exile in 597 BC because of their goodness (see 11:3 and note).

24:5 *wood.* Nebuchadnezzar’s siege equipment.

24:6 *city of bloodshed.* Cf. v. 9; 22:2 – 3. *encrusted.* Representing Jerusalem’s irredeemable situation. *in whatever order it comes.* After the siege of Jerusalem in 597, perhaps the Babylonians had cast lots to see whom they would take away into exile. Now everyone would go.

24:7 *blood . . . on the bare rock.* Jerusalem had brazenly left on display the blood she unjustly shed (cf. Isa 3:9). For uncovered blood, see Ge 4:10; Job 16:18 and notes; cf. Lev 17:13 – 14.

24:8 *wrath.* God’s wrath. What Jerusalem had done would be done to her (see 16:43 and note; see also 1Ki 8:32; Isa 3:1; cf. Ex 4:21; 21:23 – 25; Lev 24:17 – 22; Dt 19:21 and notes).

24:11 *empty pot.* Jerusalem, emptied of inhabitants, would be set to the torch in a vain, final effort at purification.

24:13 *lewdness.* See 16:1 – 63; 23:1 – 49 and notes.

24:14 *The time has come.* See 7:2 – 3 and note on 7:1 – 27. *judged according to your conduct and your actions.* See notes on Ro 2:1 – 16; 2:6 – 8; Rev 20:12.

24:15 – 27 Following the series of messages concerning God’s judgment on Judah (13:1 — 24:14), Ezekiel’s action upon the death of his wife serves to symbolize how the exiles would react to the fall of Jerusalem, just as his earlier symbolic actions symbolized the exile of the people of Jerusalem (see 12:1 – 28 and note). These two symbolic acts thus serve as a literary frame around this second series of messages in Ezekiel.

24:16 *blow.* Some swiftly fatal disease, one that often reached plague proportions (see Ex 9:14; Nu 14:37). *delight of your eyes.* The object of loving attention (see vv. 21,25) — apparently a conventional way of referring to a man’s wife (cf. Jdg 14:3, “She’s the right one for me” [lit. “She is right in my eyes”]; see also SS 8:10).

24:17 *Keep your turban fastened.* Mourners normally removed turbans and put dust on their heads (see Jos 7:6; 1Sa 4:12 and notes). *sandals on your feet.* To remove them showed grief (see 2Sa 15:30 and note). *cover . . . mustache and beard.* A gesture of shame (Mic 3:7). *food of mourners.* The funeral meal (see Jer 16:7 and note).

24:18 *in the evening my wife died.* She died the same day the temple was burned (Aug. 14, 586 BC; see vv. 25 – 27; 2Ki 25:8 and note; see also Introduction: Occasion, Purpose and Summary of Contents).

24:19 *Then the people asked me.* The third time the people responded to Ezekiel’s behavior (see 12:9; 21:7 and notes).

20 So I said to them, "The word of the LORD came to me: 21 Say to the people of Israel, 'This is what the Sovereign LORD says: I am about to desecrate my sanctuary[u]—the stronghold in which you take pride,[v] the delight of your eyes,[w] the object of your affection. The sons and daughters[x] you left behind will fall by the sword.[y] 22 And you will do as I have done. You will not cover your mustache and beard[z] or eat the customary food of mourners.[a] 23 You will keep your turbans[b] on your heads and your sandals[c] on your feet. You will not mourn[d] or weep but will waste away[e] because of[a] your sins and groan among yourselves.[f] 24 Ezekiel[g] will be a sign[h] to you; you will do just as he has done. When this happens, you will know that I am the Sovereign LORD.'

25 "And you, son of man, on the day I take away their stronghold, their joy and glory, the delight of their eyes,[i] their heart's desire,[j] and their sons and daughters[k] as well— 26 on that day a fugitive will come to tell you[l] the news. 27 At that time your mouth will be opened; you will speak with him and will no longer be silent.[m] So you will be a sign to them, and they will know that I am the LORD.[n]"

A Prophecy Against Ammon

25 The word of the LORD came to me: 2 "Son of man, set your face against[o] the Ammonites[p] and prophesy against them.[q] 3 Say to them, 'Hear the word of the Sovereign LORD. This is what the Sovereign LORD says: Because you said "Aha![r]" over my sanctuary when it was desecrated[s] and over the land of Israel when it was laid waste and over the people of Judah when they went into exile,[t] 4 therefore I am going to give you to the people of the East[u] as a possession. They will set up their camps[v] and pitch their tents among you; they will eat your fruit and drink your milk.[w] 5 I will turn Rabbah[x] into a pasture for camels and Ammon into a resting place for sheep.[y] Then you will know that I am the LORD. 6 For this is what the Sovereign LORD says: Because you have clapped your hands[z] and stamped your feet, rejoicing with all the malice of your heart against the land of Israel,[a] 7 therefore I will stretch out my hand[b] against you and give you as plunder[c] to the nations. I will wipe you out from among the nations and exterminate you from the countries. I will destroy[d] you, and you will know that I am the LORD.[e]' "

A Prophecy Against Moab

8 "This is what the Sovereign LORD says: 'Because Moab[f] and Seir[g] said, "Look, Judah has become like all the other nations," 9 therefore I will expose the flank of Moab, beginning at its frontier towns—Beth Jeshimoth[h], Baal Meon[i] and Kiriathaim[j]—

[a] 23 Or *away in*

24:21 [u] S Lev 26:31; S Eze 7:24 [v] S Lev 26:19 [w] S ver 16; Ps 27:4 [x] S Eze 23:25 [y] Jer 7:14, 15; Hos 9:12, 16; Mal 2:12 **24:22** [z] S Lev 13:45 [a] Jer 16:7 **24:23** [b] S Ex 28:39; S Isa 3:20 [c] S Isa 20:2 [d] Ex 33:4 [e] S Lev 26:16 [f] Ps 78:64 **24:24** [g] Eze 1:3 [h] S Isa 20:3; Eze 12:11 **24:25** [i] S La 2:4 [j] S Ps 20:4 [k] Dt 28:32; Jer 11:22 **24:26** [l] S 1Sa 4:12; Job 1:15-19 **24:27** [m] Da 10:15 [n] S Eze 3:26; 33:22 **25:2** [o] S Eze 13:17; 29:2 [p] S Eze 21:28 [q] Jer 49:1-6 **25:3** [r] S Ps 35:21; Eze 26:2; 36:2 [s] Zep 2:8 [t] S Pr 17:5 **25:4** [u] S Ge 25:6; S Jdg 6:3 [v] S Nu 31:10 [w] Dt 28:33, 51; S Jdg 6:33 **25:5** [x] S Dt 3:11 [y] S S Isa 17:2

25:6 [z] S Nu 24:10 [a] S Eze 6:11; Ob 1:12; Zep 2:8 **25:7** [b] Zep 1:4 [c] S Nu 14:3 [d] Eze 21:31 [e] ver 13-14, 17; Am 1:14-15 **25:8** [f] S Ge 19:37; S Dt 23:6; S Isa 16:6 [g] S Ge 14:6 **25:9** [h] S Nu 33:49 [i] S Nu 32:3; S Jos 13:17 [j] S Nu 32:37; S Jos 13:19

24:21 *desecrate.* By letting Nebuchadnezzar burn it down.
24:24 *Ezekiel.* The Lord speaks of Ezekiel in the third person. Elsewhere the prophet's name occurs only in 1:3 (see note there). *sign.* See v. 27 and note on 12:6.
24:26 *fugitive.* The first of the exiles of 586 BC. *news.* About the siege—its beginning (verifying the accuracy of vv. 1–2) and its ending (see note on 33:21).
24:27 *At that time.* When the fugitive arrived from Jerusalem (see 33:21 and note). *no longer be silent.* The muteness that had been imposed on him at the beginning of his ministry was now lifted (see 3:26 and note).
25:1—32:32 Messages against the nations. Frequently in the Prophets, God's word of judgment on Israel is accompanied by messages of judgment on the nations (see note on Jer 46:1—51:64). These make clear that, while judgment begins "with God's household" (1Pe 4:17), the pagan nations would not escape God's wrath. Often these judgments are implicit messages of salvation for Israel (see 28:25–26 and notes) since the Lord's victories over hostile powers remove enemies of his people or punish them for their cruel attacks on his people. In the case of Ezekiel, there are seven prophecies (the seventh of which has seven parts, each introduced by the phrase "The word of the LORD came to me"; see Introduction: Outline). The structure of these prophecies follows the pattern "Because [introducing the evil committed] ..., therefore [introducing the judgment] ... know that I am the LORD" (e.g., 25:3–7).
25:2 *set your face.* See note on 20:46. *Ammonites.* Ammon (part of modern Jordan) was immediately east of Israel (see 21:20 and note; see also Jer 9:26; 49:1–6; Am 1:13–15; Zep 2:8–11). For hostile Ammonite action during this time and later, see 2Ki 24:2; Ne 4:7.
25:3 *Aha!* A cry of malicious joy (cf. 26:2; 36:2; Ps 35:21–25).
25:4 *people of the East.* Probably nomadic tribes of the desert east of Ammon, though this could be a reference to Nebuchadnezzar and his army (see 21:31).
25:5 *Rabbah.* See note on 21:20. *pasture ... resting place.* A common OT description of destroyed cities (see Isa 34:13–15; Zep 2:13–15). The sites were returned to the conditions they were in before the cities were built, representing the undoing of human efforts.
25:6 *clapped your hands.* See 6:11 and note.
25:7 *I will stretch out my hand against.* See note on 6:14. *plunder to the nations.* Cf. 26:5; 34:28. *wipe you out.* Cf. v. 16.
25:8 *Moab.* Immediately to the south of Ammon, east of the Dead Sea (see Ge 19:36–38 and note; Isa 15–16; Jer 48; Am 2:1–3; Zep 2:8–11). *Seir.* Edom, a country south of Moab and south of the Dead Sea (see ch. 35, especially v. 15; 36:5; Isa 34:5–17; 63:1–6; Jer 49:7–11; Am 1:11–12). *like all the other nations.* Israel wanted to be like the nations (see 20:32 and note), but when the nations saw Judah in her apparent vulnerability and lost their awe of her, they failed to take her God seriously (cf. La 4:12).
25:9 *flank of Moab.* Lower hills rising from the Dead Sea, visible from Jerusalem. *Beth Jeshimoth.* A town in the plains of Moab. *Baal Meon.* A major Moabite town mentioned in an inscribed monument of Mesha, king of Moab (see chart, p. xxiii). *Kiriathaim.* A city also mentioned in the Mesha inscription (cf. 2Ki 3:4–5 and note on 2Ki 1:1).

the glory of that land. 10 I will give Moab
along with the Ammonites to the people of
the East as a possession, so that the Ammonites will not be remembered[k] among
the nations; 11 and I will inflict punishment
on Moab. Then they will know that I am
the LORD.' "[l]

A Prophecy Against Edom

12 "This is what the Sovereign LORD
says: 'Because Edom[m] took revenge on Judah and became very guilty by doing so,
13 therefore this is what the Sovereign LORD
says: I will stretch out my hand[n] against
Edom and kill both man and beast.[o] I will
lay it waste, and from Teman[p] to Dedan[q]
they will fall by the sword.[r] 14 I will take
vengeance on Edom by the hand of my
people Israel, and they will deal with
Edom in accordance with my anger[s] and
my wrath; they will know my vengeance,
declares the Sovereign LORD.' "[t]

A Prophecy Against Philistia

15 "This is what the Sovereign LORD
says: 'Because the Philistines[u] acted in
vengeance and took revenge with malice[v]
in their hearts, and with ancient hostility
sought to destroy Judah, 16 therefore this is
what the Sovereign LORD says: I am about
to stretch out my hand against the Philistines,[w] and I will wipe out the Kerethites[x]
and destroy those remaining along the
coast.[y] 17 I will carry out great vengeance[z]
on them and punish[a] them in my wrath.
Then they will know that I am the LORD,[b]
when I take vengeance on them.[c] "

A Prophecy Against Tyre

26 In the eleventh month of the
twelfth[a] year, on the first day of the
month, the word of the LORD came to me:[d]
2 "Son of man, because Tyre[e] has said of
Jerusalem, 'Aha![f] The gate to the nations
is broken, and its doors have swung open
to me; now that she lies in ruins I will
prosper,' 3 therefore this is what the Sovereign LORD says: I am against you, Tyre, and
I will bring many nations against you, like
the sea[g] casting up its waves. 4 They will
destroy[h] the walls of Tyre[i] and pull down
her towers; I will scrape away her rubble
and make her a bare rock. 5 Out in the sea[j]
she will become a place to spread fishnets,[k] for I have spoken, declares the Sovereign LORD. She will become plunder[l] for
the nations,[m] 6 and her settlements on the
mainland will be ravaged by the sword.
Then they will know that I am the LORD.

25:10 [k]Eze 21:32 **25:11** [l]Isa 15:9; 16:1-14; Jer 48:1; Am 2:1-3 **25:12** [m]S 2Sa 8:13-14; S 2Ch 28:17; S Isa 11:14 **25:13** [n]S Ex 7:5; S Eze 16:27 [o]Eze 29:8 [p]S Ge 36:11, 15, 34 [q]Jer 25:23 [r]S Jer 49:10; S Eze 14:17 **25:14** [s]Eze 35:11 [t]S Ps 137:7; Eze 32:29; 35:2-3; 36:5; Am 1:11; Ob 1:1, 10-16; Mal 1:4 **25:15** [u]S Jos 13:3; S 2Ch 28:18 [v]S Ps 73:8 **25:16** [w]S 2Ch 26:6; Am 1:8 [x]S 1Sa 30:14 [y]S Eze 20:33 **25:17** [z]S Nu 31:3 [a]Jer 44:13 [b]S Ex 6:2; S 8:22 [c]S Isa 11:14; S Isa 14:30; Jer 47:7; Joel 3:4 **26:1** [d]S Eze 24:1; 29:1; 30:20

[a] *1* Probable reading of the original Hebrew text; Masoretic Text does not have *month of the twelfth.*

26:2 [e]S Jos 19:29; 2Sa 5:11 [f]S Eze 25:3 **26:3** [g]ver 19; Isa 5:30; Jer 50:42; 51:42 **26:4** [h]S Isa 23:1, 11 [i]Am 1:10 **26:5** [j]Eze 27:32 [k]Eze 47:10 [l]S Nu 14:3; Eze 29:19 [m]Zec 9:2-4

25:12 *Edom.* See note on v. 8 ("Seir"). *took revenge.* By not harboring Judah's refugees after 586 BC (see Ob 11 – 14 and notes).
25:13 *Teman.* A district near Petra in central Edom (see Jer 49:7,20; Am 1:12; Ob 9; Hab 3:3 and notes). *Dedan.* A tribe and territory in southern Edom (see 27:20; 38:13; Isa 21:13 and note; Jer 49:8).
25:15 *Philistines.* Inhabitants of the coastal plain along the Mediterranean west of Judah (1Sa 6:17; see note on Ge 10:14) who strove for control of Canaan until subdued by David. Their hostility to Israel continued, however (see Isa 14:29 – 31; Jer 47; Am 1:6 – 8; Zep 2:4 – 7), until Nebuchadnezzar deported them.
25:16 *Kerethites.* Related to, if not identical with, the Philistines (see 1Sa 30:14 and note; 2Sa 8:18; 15:18; 20:7). *coast.* Of the Mediterranean.
26:1 — 28:19 A series of prophecies against Tyre, the chief seaport of Phoenicia (present-day Lebanon). Tyre was an island fortress that had an additional harbor on the mainland. After Nebuchadnezzar's victory at Carchemish in 605 BC, Tyre acknowledged the hegemony of the Babylonian king, but in 594 BC it joined a coalition of states to throw off the Babylonian yoke (Jer 27:3). Ancient historians relate that Nebuchadnezzar laid siege to Tyre for 15 years (cf. 29:18 and note) and may have succeeded in once more establishing some kind of authority over it, but he did not succeed in destroying the city. The island fortress was not overrun until Alexander the Great conquered it after a seven-month siege in 332 BC (see notes on Isa 23:1; Zec 9:3).
26:1 *eleventh month of the twelfth year ... first day of the month.* The fifth date in the book (see 1:2; 8:1; 20:1; 24:1). As the NIV text note indicates, the Masoretic Text (the traditional Hebrew text) does not have "month of the twelfth." Thus it reads "eleventh year," which dates from Apr. 23, 587, to Apr. 13, 586 BC. If this is the correct text, the prophecy must date from the end of that year, in the 11th (Feb. 13, 586) or the 12th month (Mar. 15, 586). But there is a problem with these dates: This prophecy describes Tyre's gloating over the destruction of Jerusalem (v. 2), yet Jerusalem did not fall until July 18, 586 (see note on 2Ki 25:2 – 3), and was not burned until Aug. 14, 586 (see note on 2Ki 25:8) — several months after the date given here for Tyre's celebration of the fact that Jerusalem "now ... lies in ruins" (v. 2). To solve the problem, many interpreters believe that the probable reading of the original Hebrew text was "In the eleventh month of the twelfth year, on the first day of the month" and that the words "month of the twelfth" must have been inadvertently omitted by a copyist (hence the NIV reading). The restored reading would yield the date Feb. 3, 585, which would nicely fit the chronology in 33:21 (see note there). If, on the other hand, the Hebrew text that has come down to us is correct, then the Lord (through Ezekiel) is prophesying what Tyre's response to Jerusalem's fall will be and how the Lord, in turn, will judge Tyre.
26:2 *Tyre.* For other prophecies against Tyre, see Isa 23; Jer 25:22; 47:4; Joel 3:4 – 5; Am 1:9 – 10; Zec 9:2 – 4. *Aha!* See note on 25:3. *gate to the nations.* Because of its geographic location, its political importance and the central role it played in international trade. The anti-Babylonian summit meeting was held there (see Jer 27).
26:3 *I am against you.* See note on 5:8. *like the sea casting up its waves.* For invading armies likened to waves of the sea, cf. Isa 17:12 – 13. Since Tyre was mainly a fortified island, the metaphor is especially appropriate here.
26:5 *plunder for the nations.* Cf. 25:7; 34:28.
26:6 *know that I am the LORD.* See Introduction: Themes.

[7]"For this is what the Sovereign LORD
says: From the north I am going to bring
against Tyre Nebuchadnezzar[a][n] king of
Babylon, king of kings,[o] with horses and
chariots,[p] with horsemen and a great
army. 8 He will ravage your settlements on
the mainland with the sword; he will set
up siege works[q] against you, build a ramp[r]
up to your walls and raise his shields
against you. 9 He will direct the blows of
his battering rams against your walls and
demolish your towers with his weapons.[s]
10 His horses will be so many that they will
cover you with dust. Your walls will tremble at the noise of the warhorses, wagons
and chariots[t] when he enters your gates
as men enter a city whose walls have
been broken through. 11 The hooves[u] of
his horses will trample all your streets; he
will kill your people with the sword, and
your strong pillars[v] will fall to the ground.[w]
12 They will plunder your wealth and loot
your merchandise; they will break down
your walls and demolish your fine houses
and throw your stones, timber and rubble
into the sea.[x] 13 I will put an end[y] to your

26:7 [n] Jer 27:6; 39:1 [o] S Ezr 7:12 [p] S Eze 23:24; Na 2:3-4 **26:8** [q] S Jer 6:6 [r] S Jer 33:4 **26:9** [s] S Eze 21:22 **26:10** [t] S Jer 4:13; S 46:9; S Eze 23:24 **26:11** [u] Isa 5:28 [v] S Jer 43:13 [w] S Isa 26:5 **26:12** [x] Isa 23:8; S Jer 4:7; Eze 27:3-27; 28:8; Hab 1:8 **26:13** [y] S Jer 7:34

[a] 7 Hebrew *Nebuchadrezzar,* of which *Nebuchadnezzar* is a variant; here and often in Ezekiel and Jeremiah

26:7 *north.* The direction from which Nebuchadnezzar would descend on Tyre after first marching his army up the Euphrates River valley rather than across the Arabian Desert (cf. Jer 1:13). *I am going to bring.* A clear indication of God's sovereignty over the nations (cf. 28:7; 29:8). *Nebuchadnezzar.* The first of four references to him in Ezekiel (see 29:18 – 19; 30:10). He ruled from 605 to 562 BC, and his name means "O (god) Nabu, protect my son" or "O (god) Nabu, protect my boundary." Jeremiah and Ezekiel both proclaimed that this pagan king would be used by God to do his work (see Jer 25:9 and note; 27:6).
26:8 *siege.* See note on 26:1 — 28:19.

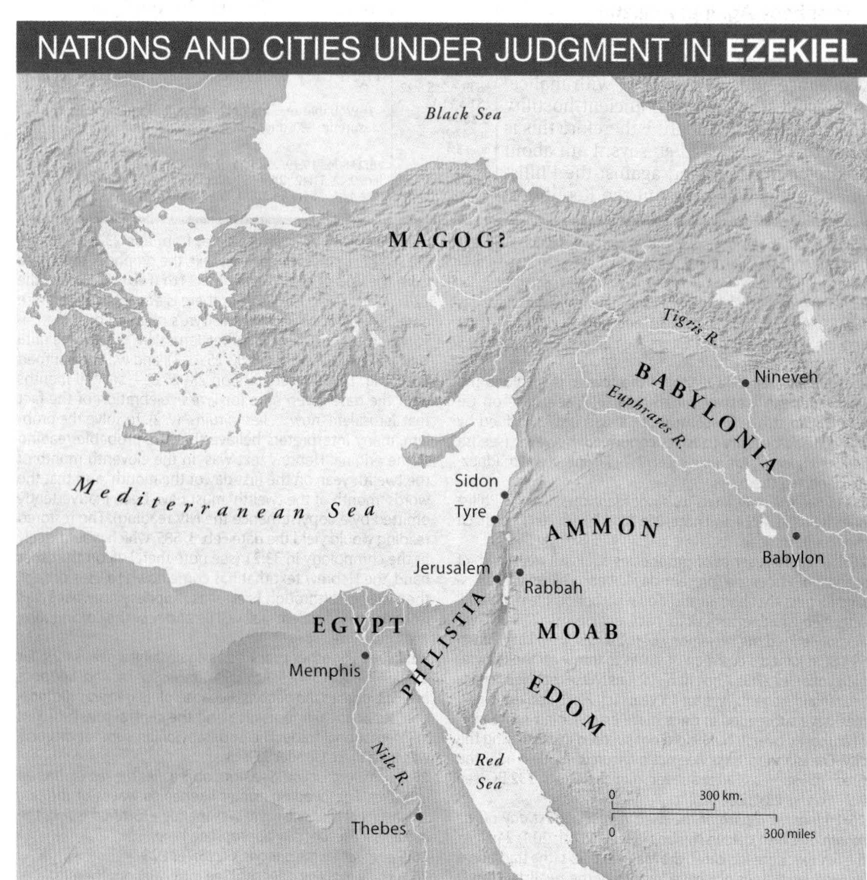

noisy songs,[z] and the music of your harps[a]
will be heard no more.[b] 14 I will make you a
bare rock, and you will become a place to
spread fishnets. You will never be rebuilt,[c]
for I the LORD have spoken, declares the
Sovereign LORD.

15 "This is what the Sovereign LORD says
to Tyre: Will not the coastlands[d] tremble[e] at the sound of your fall, when the
wounded groan[f] and the slaughter takes
place in you? 16 Then all the princes of the
coast will step down from their thrones
and lay aside their robes and take off their
embroidered[g] garments. Clothed[h] with terror, they will sit on the ground,[i] trembling[j]
every moment, appalled[k] at you. 17 Then
they will take up a lament[l] concerning you
and say to you:

" 'How you are destroyed, city of renown,
peopled by men of the sea!
You were a power on the seas,
you and your citizens;
you put your terror
on all who lived there.[m]
18 Now the coastlands tremble[n]
on the day of your fall;
the islands in the sea
are terrified at your collapse.'[o]

19 "This is what the Sovereign LORD says:
When I make you a desolate city, like cities no longer inhabited, and when I bring
the ocean depths[p] over you and its vast
waters cover you,[q] 20 then I will bring you
down with those who go down to the pit,[r]
to the people of long ago. I will make you
dwell in the earth below, as in ancient
ruins, with those who go down to the
pit, and you will not return or take your
place[a] in the land of the living.[s] 21 I will
bring you to a horrible end and you will be
no more.[t] You will be sought, but you will
never again be found, declares the Sovereign LORD."[u]

26:13 [z]S Isa 23:7 [a]S Ps 137:2; S Isa 14:11 [b]S Job 30:31; S Jer 16:9; S 25:10; Rev 18:22 **26:14** [c]S Job 12:14; Mal 1:4 **26:15** [d]Isa 41:5; Eze 27:35 [e]S Jer 49:21 [f]S Job 24:12 **26:16** [g]S Ex 26:36 [h]S Job 8:22 [i]S Job 2:8, 13 [j]Hos 11:10 [k]S Lev 26:32; Eze 32:10 **26:17** [l]S Eze 19:1 [m]Isa 14:12 **26:18** [n]S Ps 46:6; S Jer 49:21 [o]Isa 23:5; S 41:5; Eze 27:35 **26:19** [p]S Ge 7:11 [q]S ver 3; Isa 8:7-8 **26:20** [r]Nu 16:30; Ps 28:1; 88:6; Eze 31:14; 32:18; Am 9:2; Jnh 2:2, 6 [s]S Job 28:13; S Isa 14:9-10; Eze 32:24, 30 **26:21** [t]S Jer 51:64; Da 11:19 [u]Jer 20:4; Eze 27:36; 28:19; Rev 18:21

27:2 [v]S Eze 19:1 **27:3** [w]S Ps 83:7 [x]ver 33; Hos 9:13 [y]S Isa 23:9; S Eze 16:15 **27:4** [z]Eze 28:12 **27:5** [a]S Dt 3:9 [b]S Isa 2:13 **27:6** [c]Nu 21:33; S Ps 29:9; Jer 22:20; Zec 11:2 [d]S Ge 10:4; Isa 23:12 **27:7** [e]S Ex 26:36; S Isa 19:9 [f]Ex 25:4; Jer 10:9 [g]Ge 10:4 **27:8** [h]Ge 10:18 [i]1Ki 9:27 **27:9** [j]S Jos 13:5 [k]S Ps 104:26

A Lament Over Tyre

27 The word of the LORD came to me:
2 "Son of man, take up a lament[v]
concerning Tyre. 3 Say to Tyre,[w] situated
at the gateway to the sea,[x] merchant of
peoples on many coasts, 'This is what the
Sovereign LORD says:

" 'You say, Tyre,
"I am perfect in beauty.[y]"
4 Your domain was on the high seas;
your builders brought your beauty to
perfection.[z]
5 They made all your timbers
of juniper from Senir[b];[a]
they took a cedar from Lebanon[b]
to make a mast for you.
6 Of oaks[c] from Bashan
they made your oars;
of cypress wood[c] from the coasts of
Cyprus[d]
they made your deck, adorned with
ivory.
7 Fine embroidered linen[e] from Egypt
was your sail
and served as your banner;
your awnings were of blue and purple[f]
from the coasts of Elishah.[g]
8 Men of Sidon and Arvad[h] were your
oarsmen;
your skilled men, Tyre, were aboard
as your sailors.[i]
9 Veteran craftsmen of Byblos[j] were on
board
as shipwrights to caulk your seams.
All the ships of the sea[k] and their
sailors
came alongside to trade for your
wares.

[a] 20 Septuagint; Hebrew *return, and I will give glory* [b] 5 That is, Mount Hermon [c] 6 Targum; the Masoretic Text has a different division of the consonants.

26:14 *never be rebuilt.* Eventually fulfilled by Alexander's devastating siege in 332 BC (see 26:1—28:19; Isa 23:1 and notes).
26:16 *princes of the coast.* Called kings in 27:35, they were probably trading partners with Tyre. *lay aside their robes.* Usually mourners tore their clothes (Job 2:12) and put on sackcloth, but cf. the king of Nineveh (Jnh 3:6). *Clothed with terror.* Because of political shock waves from the fall of such a powerful city (cf. 7:27; Ps 35:26; 109:29 and note).
26:17 *lament.* See note on 19:1.
26:19 *ocean depths.* The primeval, chaotic mass—the "deep" of Ge 1:2. Tyre's collapse into the sea is described in almost cosmic terms.
26:20 *pit.* The grave, "the earth below" (see note on Ps 30:1). *people of long ago.* Those long dead (Ps 143:3; La 3:6). *not return or take your place in the land of the living.* As Israel would (see 37:1–14).
26:21 See 27:36; 28:19.
27:2 *lament.* See note on 19:1.
27:3 *I am perfect in beauty.* See 28:12 and note; cf. 28:2 for a similar prideful statement. Since Tyre is described as a stately ship in the following verses, some translate, "You are a ship, perfect in beauty."
27:4 *brought your beauty to perfection.* See v. 11.
27:5 *Senir.* Amorite name for Hermon, the Anti-Lebanon mountain (or range) famed for cedar.
27:6 *Bashan.* See note on 39:18. *Cyprus.* Translates Hebrew *Kittim*, originally the name of a town in southern Cyprus colonized by Phoenicia.
27:7 *Elishah.* A city on the east side of Cyprus; also the oldest name for Cyprus (but see note on Ge 10:4).
27:8 *Sidon.* A harbor city 25 miles north of Tyre, which sometimes rivaled her in political and commercial importance (see note on 28:21). *Arvad.* Another Phoenician island-city, off the Mediterranean coast and north of Sidon.
27:9 *Byblos.* An important ancient city on the coast between Sidon and Arvad (see 1Ki 5:18; see also map, p. 2520, at the end of this study Bible).

10 " 'Men of Persia,[l] Lydia[m] and Put[n]
served as soldiers in your army.
They hung their shields[o] and helmets
on your walls,
bringing you splendor.
11 Men of Arvad and Helek
guarded your walls on every side;
men of Gammad
were in your towers.
They hung their shields around your
walls;
they brought your beauty to
perfection.[p]

12 " 'Tarshish[q] did business with you because of your great wealth of goods;[r] they
exchanged silver, iron, tin and lead for
your merchandise.
13 " 'Greece,[s] Tubal and Meshek[t] did
business with you; they traded human beings[u] and articles of bronze for your wares.
14 " 'Men of Beth Togarmah[v] exchanged
chariot horses, cavalry horses and mules
for your merchandise.
15 " 'The men of Rhodes[a][w] traded with
you, and many coastlands[x] were your customers; they paid you with ivory[y] tusks
and ebony.
16 " 'Aram[b][z] did business with you because of your many products; they exchanged turquoise,[a] purple fabric, embroidered work, fine linen,[b] coral[c] and rubies
for your merchandise.
17 " 'Judah and Israel traded with you;
they exchanged wheat[d] from Minnith[e] and
confections,[c] honey, olive oil and balm[f] for
your wares.[g]
18 " 'Damascus[h] did business with you
because of your many products and great
wealth of goods.[i] They offered wine from
Helbon, wool from Zahar 19 and casks
of wine from Izal[j] in exchange for your
wares: wrought iron, cassia[k] and calamus.
20 " 'Dedan[l] traded in saddle blankets
with you.
21 " 'Arabia[m] and all the princes of Kedar[n]
were your customers; they did business
with you in lambs, rams and goats.
22 " 'The merchants of Sheba[o] and Raamah traded with you; for your merchandise they exchanged the finest of all kinds
of spices[p] and precious stones, and gold.[q]
23 " 'Harran,[r] Kanneh and Eden[s] and
merchants of Sheba, Ashur[t] and Kilmad
traded with you. 24 In your marketplace
they traded with you beautiful garments,
blue fabric, embroidered work and multi-
colored rugs with cords twisted and tightly
knotted.

25 " 'The ships of Tarshish[u] serve
as carriers for your wares.

27:10 [l] 2Ch 36:20; Ezr 1:1; Eze 38:5; Da 8:20 [m] S Isa 66:19 [n] S Ge 10:6; Eze 30:5; Na 3:9 [o] SS 4:4 **27:11** [p] ver 27 **27:12** [q] S Ge 10:4 [r] ver 18,33 **27:13** [s] Joel 3:6 [t] Ge 10:2; Isa 66:19; Eze 32:26; 38:2; 39:1 [u] Rev 18:13 **27:14** [v] S Ge 10:3 **27:15** [w] S Ge 10:7 [x] S Jer 25:22 [y] 1Ki 10:22; Rev 18:12 **27:16** [z] Jdg 10:6; Isa 7:1-8 [a] Ex 28:18; 39:11; Eze 28:13 [b] S Eze 16:10 [c] Job 28:18 **27:17** [d] S 1Ki 5:9 [e] Jdg 11:33 [f] S Ge 43:11 [g] Ac 12:20 **27:18** [h] S Ge 14:15; Eze 47:16-18 [i] S ver 12 **27:19** [j] Ge 10:27 [k] S Ex 30:24 **27:20** [l] S Ge 10:7

[a] *15* Septuagint; Hebrew *Dedan* [b] *16* Most Hebrew manuscripts; some Hebrew manuscripts and Syriac *Edom* [c] *17* The meaning of the Hebrew for this word is uncertain.

27:21 [m] S 2Ch 9:14 [n] S Ge 25:13; Isa 21:17 **27:22** [o] S Ge 10:7, 28 [p] S Ge 43:11 [q] Rev 18:12 **27:23** [r] S Ge 11:26 [s] S Isa 37:12 [t] S Ge 10:22; S Nu 24:24 **27:25** [u] S Ge 10:4; Isa 2:16 *fn*

27:10 *Persia.* Or "Paras" (identification uncertain). *Lydia.* In Asia Minor; the Lydians are known to have served as mercenaries for the Egyptians. *Put.* Libya, in North Africa, west of Egypt. *soldiers.* The ship image is abandoned, and Tyre is now described literally—as a city (note references to walls and towers here and in v. 11), complete with a mercenary army gathered from many peoples.
27:11 *Arvad.* See note on v. 8. *Helek.* Cilicia, the mountainous region in southeast Asia Minor. *Gammad.* Either (1) northern Asia Minor or (2) a coastal town near Arvad.
27:12 *Tarshish.* Traditionally located on the coast of southern Spain, but the island of Sardinia has also been suggested. Passages such as 1Ki 10:22; Jnh 1:3 imply that it was a long distance from the Canaanite coast. The list of places in vv. 12–23 generally follows a west-to-east direction.
27:13 *Tubal and Meshek.* Both in Asia Minor.
27:14 *Beth Togarmah.* In eastern Asia Minor, present-day Armenia (see 38:6). *chariot horses.* Asia Minor was known for its horses (see 1Ki 10:28 and NIV text note there on "Kue").
27:15 *Rhodes.* A large island off the southwest coast of Asia Minor that served as gateway to the Aegean islands. It was an early major trading center (see Ac 21:1).
27:16 *Aram.* Modern Syria. Since Damascus, the capital of Aram, is mentioned in v. 18, perhaps Edom is meant here (see NIV text note; see also 25:12 and note).
27:17 *Israel traded with you.* In the past. Since 722–721 BC Israel had ceased to exist as a political state. *Minnith.* An Ammonite town, apparently famous for its wheat; "wheat from Minnith" possibly denoted a superior quality of wheat. *balm.* Gum or oil from one of several plants; a product of Gilead (see Ge 37:25 and note; Jer 8:22; 46:11).
27:18 *Damascus.* Capital of Aram (see note on v. 16; see also Isa 7:8). *Helbon.* A town north of Damascus, still in existence and still a wine-making center. The name occurs only here in the Bible. *Zahar.* Modern Ṣaḥra, an area northwest of Damascus, where grazing is still common today.
27:19 *Izal.* Perhaps the area between Harran and the Tigris. *cassia.* Similar to the cinnamon tree. The only other Biblical mention of it is in Ex 30:24, where it appears in a list of aromatic plants. *calamus.* An aromatic reed.
27:20 *Dedan.* See note on 25:13.
27:21 *Arabia and … Kedar.* A general expression for the nomadic tribes from Aram to the Arabian Desert. For Kedar, see Isa 21:16 and note; 42:11; 60:7; Jer 49:28.
27:22 *Sheba.* See note on 23:42. *Raamah.* A city in southern Arabia.
27:23 *Harran.* A city east of Carchemish, in present-day eastern Turkey. It was well-known in ancient times as a center both for trade and for the worship of the moon-god, Sin. From here Abram moved to Canaan (see Ge 11:31 and note; 12:4). *Kanneh.* Of uncertain location, presumably in Mesopotamia. It is often identified with Kalno or Kalneh (Isa 10:9; Am 6:2). *Eden.* A district south of Harran, mentioned in connection with Harran in 2Ki 19:12 (see note there). Cf. Beth Eden in Am 1:5 (but see note there). *Sheba.* See note on 23:42. *Ashur.* Can mean the city, the country (Assyria) or the people (Assyrians). Here it is probably the city south of Nineveh that gave its name to the country. *Kilmad.* If a town, it is yet unidentified; presumably in Mesopotamia. Some read "all Media."
27:25 *Tarshish.* See note on v. 12. The ship image is resumed (see notes on vv. 3,10).

You are filled with heavy cargo
as you sail the sea.[v]
26 Your oarsmen take you
out to the high seas.
But the east wind[w] will break
you to pieces
far out at sea.
27 Your wealth,[x] merchandise and
wares,
your mariners, sailors and
shipwrights,
your merchants and all your
soldiers,
and everyone else on board
will sink into the heart of the
sea[y]
on the day of your shipwreck.
28 The shorelands will quake[z]
when your sailors cry out.
29 All who handle the oars
will abandon their ships;
the mariners and all the sailors
will stand on the shore.
30 They will raise their voice
and cry bitterly over you;
they will sprinkle dust[a] on their
heads
and roll[b] in ashes.[c]
31 They will shave their heads[d]
because of you
and will put on sackcloth.
They will weep[e] over you with
anguish of soul
and with bitter mourning.[f]
32 As they wail and mourn over you,
they will take up a lament[g]
concerning you:
"Who was ever silenced like Tyre,
surrounded by the sea?[h]"
33 When your merchandise went out on
the seas,[i]
you satisfied many nations;
with your great wealth[j] and your
wares
you enriched the kings of the earth.
34 Now you are shattered by the sea
in the depths of the waters;
your wares and all your company
have gone down with you.[k]
35 All who live in the coastlands[l]
are appalled[m] at you;
their kings shudder with horror
and their faces are distorted with
fear.[n]

Colonnaded street in Tyre from the Roman period. Ezekiel 27 announces God's judgment on Tyre.

Z. Radovan/www.BibleLandPictures.com

27:25 [v]Rev 18:3 **27:26** [w]S Ge 41:6; Jer 18:17 **27:27** [x]Pr 11:4 [y]Eze 28:8 **27:28** [z]S Jer 49:21 **27:30** [a]S Jos 7:6; S 2Sa 1:2 [b]S Jer 6:26 [c]Rev 18:18-19 **27:31** [d]S Lev 13:40; S Job 1:20; S Isa 3:17; S Jer 48:37 [e]S Isa 16:9; Rev 18:15 [f]S Est 4:1; Job 3:20; Isa 22:12; Jer 6:26; S La 2:10; S Eze 7:18 **27:32** [g]S Eze 19:1 [h]Isa 23:1-6;

36 The merchants among the nations scoff
at you;[o]
you have come to a horrible end
and will be no more.[p]' "

A Prophecy Against the King of Tyre

28 The word of the LORD came to me: 2 "Son of man[q], say to the ruler of Tyre, 'This is what the Sovereign LORD says:

" 'In the pride of your heart
you say, "I am a god;
I sit on the throne[r] of a god
in the heart of the seas."[s]
But you are a mere mortal and not a god,
though you think you are as wise as
a god.[t]

Eze 26:5 **27:33** [i]S ver 3 [j]S ver 12; Eze 28:4-5 **27:34** [k]Zec 9:4 **27:35** [l]S Eze 26:15 [m]S Lev 26:32; S Job 18:20 [n]S Eze 26:17-18; 32:10 **27:36** [o]Jer 19:8; S 49:17; S 50:13; Zep 2:15 [p]S Ps 37:10, 36; S Eze 26:21 **28:2** [q]S Isa 13:11 [r]S Isa 14:13 [s]Zep 2:15 [t]S Ge 3:5; S Ps 9:20; 82:6-7; S Eze 16:49; 2Th 2:4

27:26 *east wind.* Disastrous at sea (Ps 48:7) as well as on land (Jer 18:17). It perhaps symbolizes Nebuchadnezzar (as in 17:10; 19:12).
27:30 *dust on their heads.* See 26:16 for a similar scene. *roll in ashes.* Cf. Mic 1:10 and note.
27:31 *shave their heads.* Cf. 7:18; Isa 15:2 and note; 22:12. *sackcloth.* See notes on Ge 37:34; Rev 11:3.
27:36 *horrible end ... be no more.* See 26:21; 28:19; see also note on Isa 23:1.
28:2,8 *in the heart of the seas.* Emphasizes Tyre's location as an island fortress and as a dominant force in maritime commerce.
28:2 *ruler of Tyre.* May refer to the city of Tyre as ruler, or to Ethbaal II, Tyre's king (see v. 12), not to be confused with

[3] Are you wiser than Daniel[a]?[u]
Is no secret hidden from you?
[4] By your wisdom and understanding
you have gained wealth for yourself
and amassed gold and silver
in your treasuries.[v]
[5] By your great skill in trading[w]
you have increased your wealth,[x]
and because of your wealth
your heart has grown proud.[y]

[6] " 'Therefore this is what the Sovereign
LORD says:

" 'Because you think you are wise,
as wise as a god,
[7] I am going to bring foreigners against
you,
the most ruthless of nations;[z]
they will draw their swords against
your beauty and wisdom[a]
and pierce your shining splendor.[b]
[8] They will bring you down to the pit,[c]
and you will die a violent death[d]
in the heart of the seas.[e]
[9] Will you then say, "I am a god,"
in the presence of those who kill
you?
You will be but a mortal, not a god,[f]
in the hands of those who slay you.[g]
[10] You will die the death of the
uncircumcised[h]
at the hands of foreigners.

I have spoken, declares the Sovereign
LORD.' "

[11] The word of the LORD came to me:
[12] "Son of man, take up a lament[i] concerning the king of Tyre and say to him: 'This
is what the Sovereign LORD says:

" 'You were the seal of perfection,
full of wisdom and perfect in
beauty.[j]
[13] You were in Eden,[k]
the garden of God;[l]
every precious stone[m] adorned you:
carnelian, chrysolite and emerald,
topaz, onyx and jasper,
lapis lazuli, turquoise[n] and beryl.[b]
Your settings and mountings[c] were
made of gold;
on the day you were created they
were prepared.[o]
[14] You were anointed[p] as a guardian
cherub,[q]
for so I ordained you.
You were on the holy mount of God;
you walked among the fiery stones.
[15] You were blameless in your ways
from the day you were created
till wickedness was found in you.
[16] Through your widespread trade
you were filled with violence,[r]
and you sinned.
So I drove you in disgrace from the
mount of God,
and I expelled you, guardian
cherub,[s]
from among the fiery stones.
[17] Your heart became proud[t]
on account of your beauty,
and you corrupted your wisdom
because of your splendor.
So I threw you to the earth;
I made a spectacle of you before
kings.[u]
[18] By your many sins and dishonest
trade
you have desecrated your
sanctuaries.
So I made a fire[v] come out from you,
and it consumed you,
and I reduced you to ashes[w] on the
ground
in the sight of all who were
watching.[x]

28:3 [u] S Eze 14:14; Da 1:20; 2:20-23,28; 5:11-12 **28:4** [v] Isa 10:13; Zec 9:3 **28:5** [w] S Isa 23:8 [x] S Jer 9:23; S Eze 27:33 [y] S Job 31:25; Ps 52:7; 62:10; Hos 12:8; 13:6 **28:7** [z] Eze 30:11; 31:12; 32:12; Hab 1:6 [a] Jer 9:23 [b] S Eze 7:24 **28:8** [c] S Ps 55:23; Eze 32:30 [d] Rev 18:7 [e] S Eze 26:12; 27:27 **28:9** [f] S Isa 31:3 [g] S Eze 16:49 **28:10** [h] S 1Sa 14:6; S Jer 9:26; Eze 32:19,24 **28:12** [i] S Eze 19:1 [j] Eze 27:2-4 **28:13** [k] S Ge 2:8 [l] Eze 31:8-9 [m] Rev 17:4 [n] S Eze 27:16 [o] Isa 14:11; Rev 21:20 **28:14** [p] Ex 30:26; 40:9 [q] Ex 25:17-20 **28:16** [r] S Ge 6:11; Hab 2:17 [s] S Ge 3:24 **28:17** [t] Isa 10:12; Eze 16:49; 31:10 [u] S Eze 19:12 **28:18** [v] Ob 1:18 [w] Mal 4:3 [x] Zec 9:2-4

[a] *3* Or *Danel*, a man of renown in ancient literature
[b] *13* The precise identification of some of these precious stones is uncertain.
[c] *13* The meaning of the Hebrew for this phrase is uncertain.

Ethbaal I (see 1Ki 16:31). *pride.* Cf. 27:3; Pr 11:2 and note; 16:18; Ac 12:21–23. *I am a god.* Cf. the proud boasts of the king of Babylon in Isa 14:12–15 (see note there).
28:3 *Daniel.* See note on 14:14.
28:7 *foreigners.* The Babylonians; see next phrase.
28:8 *pit.* Cf. Job 33:22,24; see note on 26:20.
28:10 *uncircumcised.* Used here in the sense of barbarian or uncouth. The Phoenicians, like the Israelites and the Egyptians, practiced circumcision (see 31:18; 32:19).
28:12 *lament.* See note on 19:1. *king of Tyre.* Cf. v. 2, but see note on Isa 14:12–15. *seal of perfection.* For "seal," see Hag 2:23, where Zerubbabel is called God's "signet ring" (see note there). With cutting irony Ezekiel depicts the proud king of Tyre as the first man created, radiant with wisdom and beauty. *perfect in beauty.* See 27:3 and note.
28:13 *You were in Eden.* Like Adam (Ge 2:15). Ezekiel continues to use imagery of the creation and the fall to picture the career of the king of Tyre (see 31:9,16,18). *every precious stone.* Unlike Adam, who was naked (Ge 2:25), the king is pictured as a fully clothed priest, ordained (v. 14) to guard God's holy place. The 9 stones are among the 12 worn by the priest (Ex 28:17–20). (The Septuagint, the pre-Christian Greek translation of the OT, lists all 12.) *settings and mountings.* For the precious stones. *on the day you were created.* Cf v. 15; Ge 5:2.
28:14 *as a guardian cherub.* Cf. v. 16. The Genesis account has cherubim (plural) stationed at the border of the garden after the expulsion of Adam and Eve (see Ge 3:24 and note). Some read "with" instead of "as." *holy mount of God.* Cf. v. 16. This does not reflect the Genesis story. See Isa 14:13 for the figure of God dwelling on a mountain. *fiery stones.* The precious stones (v. 13; cf. Rev 4:1–6; 21:15–21).
28:15 *You were blameless ... till.* The parallel to Ge 2–3 is clear (see Ge 6:9 and note; 17:1).
28:16 *widespread trade ... filled with violence.* Tyre's major crime.
28:17 *threw you to the earth.* Expulsion from the heavenly garden.

19 All the nations who knew you
are appalled[y] at you;
you have come to a horrible end
and will be no more.[z]' "

A Prophecy Against Sidon

20 The word of the LORD came to me:
21 "Son of man, set your face against[a] Sidon;[b] prophesy against her 22 and say:
'This is what the Sovereign LORD says:

" 'I am against you, Sidon,
and among you I will display my
glory.[c]
You will know that I am the LORD,
when I inflict punishment[d] on you
and within you am proved to be
holy.[e]
23 I will send a plague upon you
and make blood flow in your
streets.
The slain will fall within you,
with the sword against you on every
side.
Then you will know that I am the
LORD.[f]

24 " 'No longer will the people of Israel
have malicious neighbors who are painful
briers and sharp thorns.[g] Then they will
know that I am the Sovereign LORD.
25 " 'This is what the Sovereign LORD
says: When I gather[h] the people of Israel from the nations where they have been
scattered,[i] I will be proved holy[j] through
them in the sight of the nations. Then they
will live in their own land, which I gave to
my servant Jacob.[k] 26 They will live there
in safety[l] and will build houses and plant[m]
vineyards; they will live in safety when I
inflict punishment[n] on all their neighbors
who maligned them. Then they will know
that I am the LORD their God.[o]' "

28:19 [y]S Lev 26:32 [z]S Jer 51:64; S Eze 26:21 **28:21** [a]S Eze 13:17 [b]S Ge 10:15; S Jer 25:22 **28:22** [c]Eze 39:13 [d]Eze 30:19 [e]S Lev 10:3 **28:23** [f]S Eze 5:17; 38:22 **28:24** [g]S Isa 5:6; S Eze 2:6 **28:25** [h]Ps 106:47; Jer 32:37 [i]S Isa 11:12 [j]S Eze 20:41 [k]Jer 12:15; 23:8; S Eze 11:17; 34:27; 37:25 **28:26** [l]S Lev 25:18; S 1Ki 4:25; S Jer 17:25 [m]S Dt 20:6 [n]S Ps 149:9 [o]S Isa 65:21; S Jer 32:15; Eze 38:8; 39:26-27; Hos 2:15; 11:11; Am 9:14-15

29:1 [p]ver 17; S Eze 26:1 **29:2** [q]S Eze 25:2 [r]S Jer 25:19 [s]Isa 19:1-17; Jer 46:2; Eze 30:1-26; 31:1-18; 32:1-32 **29:3** [t]Jer 44:30 [u]S Ps 68:30; S 74:13; Eze 32:2 [v]S Jer 46:8 **29:4** [w]S 2Ki 19:28; S Job 41:2 [x]Eze 38:4 **29:5** [y]S Jer 8:2 [z]S Jer 7:33; 34:20; Eze 31:13; 32:4-6; 39:4 **29:6** [a]S 2Ki 18:21

A Prophecy Against Egypt

Judgment on Pharaoh

29 In the tenth year, in the tenth
month on the twelfth day, the word
of the LORD came to me:[p] 2 "Son of man, set
your face against[q] Pharaoh king of Egypt[r]
and prophesy against him and against all
Egypt.[s] 3 Speak to him and say: 'This is
what the Sovereign LORD says:

" 'I am against you, Pharaoh[t] king of
Egypt,
you great monster[u] lying among your
streams.
You say, "The Nile[v] belongs to me;
I made it for myself."
4 But I will put hooks[w] in your jaws
and make the fish of your streams
stick to your scales.
I will pull you out from among your
streams,
with all the fish sticking to your scales.[x]
5 I will leave you in the desert,
you and all the fish of your streams.
You will fall on the open field
and not be gathered[y] or picked up.
I will give you as food
to the beasts of the earth and the
birds of the sky.[z]

6 Then all who live in Egypt will know that
I am the LORD.

" 'You have been a staff of reed[a] for
the people of Israel. 7 When they grasped
you with their hands, you splintered[b] and
you tore open their shoulders; when they
leaned on you, you broke and their backs
were wrenched.[a][c]

[a] 7 Syriac (see also Septuagint and Vulgate); Hebrew *and you caused their backs to stand*

29:7 [b]2Ki 18:21; Isa 36:6 [c]Jer 17:5; Eze 17:15-17

28:19 *horrible end … be no more.* See note on 27:36.
28:21 *set your face.* See note on 20:46. *Sidon.* See 27:8 and note. This is the only time in the OT that Sidon is mentioned apart from Tyre (cf. Isa 23:1–4; Jer 47:4; Joel 3:4; Zec 9:2).
28:22 *I am against you.* Possibly because of Sidon's involvement in the Jerusalem summit conference (Jer 27:3; see note on 5:8). *among you I will display my glory.* The Lord's glory would be recognized in Sidon's punishment. *am proved to be holy.* See v. 25; Lev 10:3 and note.
28:24 *painful briers.* For references to Israel's enemies as briers, see Nu 33:55; Jos 23:13.
28:25 *When I gather … Israel.* A frequent promise in Ezekiel and later (see 11:17; 20:34,41–42; 29:13; 34:13; 36:24; 37:21; 38:8; 39:27; Ne 1:9; Zec 10:8,10). *my servant Jacob.* Cf. 37:25. For the promise, see Ge 28:13; 35:12; Ps 105:10–11.
28:26 *live there in safety.* A perennial ideal that had become an especially meaningful promise (cf. 34:28; 38:8,11,14; 39:26; Lev 25:18–19; Jer 23:6; 32:37; 33:16)—closely related to God's promised "rest" (see Dt 3:20 and note). *houses … vineyards.* Basic necessities of the good life (cf. Isa 65:21; Jer 29:5,28; Am 9:14).
29:1—32:32 A series of seven prophecies against Egypt (for their dates, see notes below), most of which came during Jerusalem's last years when the Egyptian pharaoh was offering encouragement to King Zedekiah to rebel against Nebuchadnezzar (see 17:15; Jer 37:5–8).
29:1 *tenth year … tenth month … twelfth day.* Jan. 7, 587 BC; the sixth date in Ezekiel (see 1:2; 8:1; 20:1; 24:1; 26:1). All the prophecies against Egypt are dated except one (30:1).
29:2 *set your face.* See note on 20:46. *Pharaoh.* Hophra, 589–570 BC (see Jer 44:30).
29:3 *I am against you.* See note on 5:8. *great monster.* Or "crocodile"; pictured as being in the Nile. See notes on Job 41:1; Ps 74:13–14; Isa 27:1. *your streams.* Nile delta and canals (cf. Isa 7:18; 19:6; 37:25). *You say.* Boasts inscribed on Egyptian monuments had become proverbial.
29:4 *hooks.* Cf. 19:4. *fish of your streams.* Egypt's conquered territories or mercenaries.
29:5 *food to the beasts.* Particularly frustrating to the pharaoh's great hopes for an afterlife, as symbolized by the pyramids and expressed in the Egyptian "Book of the Dead."
29:6 *You have been a staff of reed.* A comparison made earlier (see Isa 36:6 and note). Pharaoh Hophra briefly but unsuccessfully diverted the Babylonians from laying siege to Jerusalem (see Jer 37:1–10).

The Babylonian Chronicles describe Nebuchadnezzar's battles from 605 to 595 BC, which include battles against Carchemish and Egyptian forces and the capture of Jerusalem. Ezekiel predicts Nebuchadnezzar's victory over Egypt (Eze 29:19 – 20).

Todd Bolen/www.BiblePlaces.com

8“ ‘Therefore this is what the Sovereign
LORD says: I will bring a sword against you
and kill both man and beast.[d] 9Egypt will
become a desolate wasteland. Then they
will know that I am the LORD.
“ ‘Because you said, “The Nile[e] is mine;
I made it,[f]” 10therefore I am against you[g]
and against your streams, and I will make
the land of Egypt[h] a ruin and a desolate
waste[i] from Migdol[j] to Aswan,[k] as far as
the border of Cush.[a][l] 11The foot of neither
man nor beast will pass through it; no
one will live there for forty years.[m] 12I will
make the land of Egypt desolate[n] among
devastated lands, and her cities will lie
desolate forty years among ruined cities.
And I will disperse the Egyptians among
the nations and scatter them through the
countries.[o]
13“ ‘Yet this is what the Sovereign LORD
says: At the end of forty years I will gather
the Egyptians from the nations where they
were scattered. 14I will bring them back
from captivity and return them to Upper
Egypt,[p] the land of their ancestry. There
they will be a lowly[q] kingdom.[r] 15It will be
the lowliest of kingdoms and will never
again exalt itself above the other nations.[s] I
will make it so weak that it will never again
rule over the nations. 16Egypt will no longer be a source of confidence[t] for the people of Israel but will be a reminder[u] of their
sin in turning to her for help.[v] Then they
will know that I am the Sovereign LORD.[w]’ ”

Nebuchadnezzar's Reward

17In the twenty-seventh year, in the first
month on the first day, the word of the
LORD came to me:[x] 18“Son of man, Nebuchadnezzar[y] king of Babylon drove his
army in a hard campaign against Tyre;
every head was rubbed bare[z] and every
shoulder made raw.[a] Yet he and his army
got no reward from the campaign he led
against Tyre. 19Therefore this is what the
Sovereign LORD says: I am going to give
Egypt to Nebuchadnezzar king[b] of Babylon, and he will carry off its wealth. He
will loot and plunder[c] the land as pay for
his army.[d] 20I have given him Egypt[e] as a
reward for his efforts because he and his
army did it for me, declares the Sovereign
LORD.[f]
21“On that day I will make a horn[b][g]
grow for the Israelites, and I will open
your mouth[h] among them. Then they will
know that I am the LORD.[i]”

29:8 [d] Eze 25:13; 32:11-13 **29:9** [e] S Jer 46:8 [f] Eze 30:7-8, 13-19 **29:10** [g] S Jer 21:13 [h] S Ex 3:22 [i] S Jer 46:19 [j] S Ex 14:2 [k] Eze 30:6 [l] Isa 18:1; Eze 30:4 **29:11** [m] Eze 32:13 **29:12** [n] S Isa 34:10 [o] S Jer 46:19; Eze 30:7,23,26

[a] *10* That is, the upper Nile region [b] *21 Horn* here symbolizes strength.

29:14 [p] S Isa 11:11; Eze 30:14 [q] Eze 17:14 [r] S Isa 19:22; Jer 46:26 **29:15** [s] Zec 10:11 **29:16** [t] 2Ch 32:10 [u] S Nu 5:15 [v] S La 4:17 [w] Isa 20:5; S 30:2; Hos 8:13 **29:17** [x] S ver 1; S Eze 24:1; 30:20; 40:1 **29:18** [y] Jer 27:6; 39:1 [z] S Lev 13:40; S Job 1:20; S Jer 48:37 [a] Ge 49:15 **29:19** [b] S Isa 19:4 [c] S Eze 26:5 [d] Jer 43:10-13; Eze 30:4, 10, 24-25; 32:11 **29:20** [e] S Isa 43:3 [f] Isa 10:6-7; 45:1; S Jer 25:9 **29:21** [g] S Ps 132:17; S Lk 1:69 [h] Eze 33:22 [i] S Eze 3:27

29:8 *sword.* Nebuchadnezzar's (see 5:2 and note).
29:10 *Migdol.* Probably in northern Egypt (see Jer 44:1 and note). *Aswan.* A town in southern Egypt. "From Migdol to Aswan" (30:6) probably indicated all Egypt, just as "from Dan to Beersheba" meant all Israel (see, e.g., Jdg 20:1; 1Sa 3:20 and notes).
29:11 *forty years.* Sometimes used to signify a long and difficult period (cf. 4:6).
29:14 *Upper Egypt.* Southern Egypt (see 30:14; Isa 11:11 and note; Jer 44:1,15).
29:17 The second prophecy against Egypt (see note on v. 1). *twenty-seventh year … first month … first day.* Apr. 26, 571 BC; the seventh date in Ezekiel (see v. 1; 1:2; 8:1; 20:1; 24:1; 26:1). This is the latest date in Ezekiel; accordingly, this prophecy intrudes in the series of dated prophecies against Egypt, all the rest of which come within the years 587 – 585.
29:18 *hard campaign.* Nebuchadnezzar besieged Tyre for 15 years, from 586 to 571 BC (see 26:7 – 14). *every head was rubbed bare.* Probably from the leather helmets.
29:19 *I am going to give.* God's sovereignty over the nations is again proclaimed.
29:21 *make a horn grow for.* Revive the strength of (see NIV text note). The passage is not a Messianic prophecy. *open your mouth.* Ezekiel's muteness (3:26; 24:27) would be removed, which anticipates 33:22.

A Lament Over Egypt

30 The word of the LORD came to me:
[2]"Son of man, prophesy and say:
'This is what the Sovereign LORD says:

" 'Wail[j] and say,
"Alas for that day!"
[3]For the day is near,[k]
the day of the LORD[l] is near—
a day of clouds,
a time of doom for the nations.
[4]A sword will come against Egypt,[m]
and anguish will come upon Cush.[a][n]
When the slain fall in Egypt,
her wealth will be carried away
and her foundations torn down.[o]

[5]Cush and Libya,[p] Lydia and all Arabia,[q]
Kub and the people[r] of the covenant land
will fall by the sword along with Egypt.[s]
[6]" 'This is what the LORD says:

" 'The allies of Egypt will fall
and her proud strength will fail.
From Migdol to Aswan[t]
they will fall by the sword within her,
declares the Sovereign LORD.
[7]" 'They will be desolate
among desolate lands,
and their cities will lie
among ruined cities.[u]
[8]Then they will know that I am the LORD,
when I set fire[v] to Egypt
and all her helpers are crushed.[w]

[9]" 'On that day messengers will go out
from me in ships to frighten Cush[x] out of
her complacency. Anguish[y] will take hold
of them on the day of Egypt's doom, for it
is sure to come.[z]

[10]" 'This is what the Sovereign LORD says:

" 'I will put an end to the hordes of Egypt
by the hand of Nebuchadnezzar[a]
king of Babylon.[b]
[11]He and his army—the most ruthless of
nations[c]—
will be brought in to destroy the land.
They will draw their swords against
Egypt
and fill the land with the slain.[d]
[12]I will dry up[e] the waters of the Nile[f]
and sell the land to an evil nation;
by the hand of foreigners
I will lay waste[g] the land and
everything in it.

I the LORD have spoken.

[13]" 'This is what the Sovereign LORD
says:

" 'I will destroy the idols[h]
and put an end to the images in
Memphis.[i]
No longer will there be a prince in
Egypt,[j]
and I will spread fear throughout the
land.
[14]I will lay[k] waste Upper Egypt,
set fire to Zoan[l]
and inflict punishment on Thebes.[m]
[15]I will pour out my wrath on Pelusium,
the stronghold of Egypt,
and wipe out the hordes of Thebes.
[16]I will set fire[n] to Egypt;
Pelusium will writhe in agony.
Thebes will be taken by storm;
Memphis[o] will be in constant
distress.
[17]The young men of Heliopolis[p] and
Bubastis
will fall by the sword,
and the cities themselves will go into
captivity.
[18]Dark will be the day at Tahpanhes[q]
when I break the yoke of Egypt;[r]
there her proud strength will come
to an end.

30:2 [j]S Isa 13:6; Jas 5:1 **30:3** [k]S Eze 7:7; Joel 1:15; 2:1, 11; Ob 1:15 [l]ver 18; S Eze 7:12, 19; 32:7; 34:12 **30:4** [m]Jer 25:19; Da 11:43 [n]S Ge 10:6; S Eze 29:10 [o]S Eze 29:19 **30:5** [p]S Eze 27:10 [q]S 2Ch 9:14 [r]Jer 25:20 [s]Na 3:9 **30:6** [t]Eze 29:10 **30:7** [u]S Eze 29:12 **30:8** [v]S Jer 49:27; Eze 39:6; Am 1:4, 7, 10; Na 1:6 [w]S Eze 29:9 **30:9** [x]S Ge 10:6 [y]Isa 23:5 [z]Eze 32:9-10; Zep 2:12 **30:10** [a]Jer 39:1 [b]S Eze 29:19 **30:11** [c]S Eze 28:7 [d]ver 24-25 **30:12** [e]S Isa 19:6 [f]S Jer 46:8; Eze 29:9 [g]S Eze 19:7 **30:13** [h]S Jer 43:12; S Eze 6:6 [i]S Isa 19:13 [j]Zec 10:11 **30:14** [k]S Eze 29:14 [l]S Nu 13:22 [m]S Jer 46:25 **30:16** [n]S Jos 7:15 [o]S Isa 19:13 **30:17** [p]Ge 41:45 **30:18** [q]S Jer 43:7 [r]S Lev 26:13; S Isa 9:4

[a] 4 That is, the upper Nile region; also in verses 5 and 9

30:1 The third prophecy against Egypt (see note on 29:1). No date is given, but it was probably between January and April of 587 BC. Compare 29:1 with 30:20. Jerusalem was under siege at this time.
30:2–3 *that day ... the day of the LORD.* The day of God's coming in judgment (see 7:7 and note). Egypt's judgment is announced.
30:3 *the day is near.* See 7:2–3,6 and note on 7:1–27; cf. Isa 13:6. *day of clouds.* Cf. Joel 2:2; Zep 1:15.
30:4 *sword.* Nebuchadnezzar's (see 29:8 and note).
30:5 *Libya.* In North Africa (see note on 27:10). *Lydia.* See 27:10 and note. *Kub.* Probably best understood as an unidentified place. *people of the covenant land.* Apparently Jews living in Egypt (see Jer 44 and note on 44:1).
30:6 *From Migdol to Aswan.* See note on 29:10.
30:8 *set fire to.* See note on 20:47.
30:9 *messengers ... in ships.* See Isa 18 for a similar prophecy against Cush, involving ships on the Nile.
30:11 *most ruthless of nations.* A common phrase for the Babylonians, who were known for their cruelty (see 2Ki 25:7).
30:13 *idols.* See note on 6:4. *Memphis.* Located 15 miles south of Cairo, Memphis was a former capital of Egypt and one of her largest cities. The following list of towns shows no discernible geographic pattern but is a literary device used to underscore the scope of the destruction (cf. Isa 10:9–11,27–32; Mic 1:10–15; Zep 2:4). *prince.* King.
30:14 *Upper Egypt.* See 29:14 and note. *Zoan.* A city in northeast Egypt in the delta region; also called Tanis (see Isa 19:11; 30:4 and notes). *Thebes.* Capital of Upper Egypt; present-day Luxor and Karnak. See photos, pp. 1338; 1384.
30:15 *Pelusium.* A fortress in the eastern delta region of the Nile.
30:17 *Heliopolis.* Greek name (meaning "city of the sun") for Hebrew *On*, located six miles northeast of Cairo. *Bubastis.* At one time the capital of Lower (northern) Egypt; located 40 miles northeast of Cairo.
30:18 *Dark.* A common Biblical metaphor describing ruin, destruction or death. *Tahpanhes.* In extreme northeast Egypt. Johanan, son of Kareah, and his men fled there after the murder of Gedaliah (see Jer 43:4–7). *covered with clouds.* See v. 3 and note; 32:7.

She will be covered with clouds,
and her villages will go into
captivity.[s]
19 So I will inflict punishment[t] on Egypt,
and they will know that I am the
LORD.' "

Pharaoh's Arms Are Broken

20 In the eleventh year, in the first month
on the seventh day, the word of the LORD
came to me:[u] 21 "Son of man, I have broken the arm[v] of Pharaoh[w] king of Egypt.
It has not been bound up to be healed[x]
or put in a splint so that it may become
strong enough to hold a sword. 22 Therefore this is what the Sovereign LORD says:
I am against Pharaoh king of Egypt.[y] I will
break both his arms, the good arm as well
as the broken one, and make the sword fall
from his hand.[z] 23 I will disperse the Egyptians among the nations and scatter them
through the countries.[a] 24 I will strengthen[b]
the arms of the king of Babylon and put
my sword[c] in his hand, but I will break
the arms of Pharaoh, and he will groan[d]
before him like a mortally wounded man.
25 I will strengthen the arms of the king of
Babylon, but the arms of Pharaoh will fall
limp. Then they will know that I am the
LORD, when I put my sword[e] into the hand
of the king of Babylon and he brandish-
es it against Egypt.[f] 26 I will disperse the
Egyptians among the nations and scatter
them through the countries. Then they
will know that I am the LORD.[g]"

Pharaoh as a Felled Cedar of Lebanon

31 In the eleventh year,[h] in the third
month on the first day, the word
of the LORD came to me:[i] 2 "Son of man,
say to Pharaoh king of Egypt and to his
hordes:

" 'Who can be compared with you in
majesty?
3 Consider Assyria,[j] once a cedar in
Lebanon,[k]
with beautiful branches
overshadowing the forest;

30:18 [s] S ver 3 **30:19** [t] Eze 28:22 **30:20** [u] S Eze 26:1; S 29:17; 31:1; 32:1 **30:21** [v] S Jer 48:25 [w] S Jer 44:30 [x] Jer 30:13; 46:11 **30:22** [y] S Ge 15:18; S Jer 46:25 [z] Ps 37:17; Zec 11:17 **30:23** [a] S Eze 29:12 **30:24** [b] Zec 10:6, 12; 12:5 [c] S Eze 21:14; Zep 2:12 [d] Jer 51:52 **30:25** [e] 1Ch 21:12 [f] S Isa 10:5; 45:1,5; S Eze 29:19 **30:26** [g] S Eze 29:12 **31:1** [h] Jer 52:5 [i] S Eze 30:20; 32:17

31:3 [j] S Jer 50:18 [k] S 2Ki 19:23; Hab 2:17; Zec 11:1

30:20 The fourth prophecy against Egypt (see note on 29:1). *eleventh year ... first month ... seventh day.* Apr. 29, 587 BC; the eighth date in Ezekiel (see 1:2; 8:1; 20:1; 24:1; 26:1; 29:1,17).
30:21 *broken the arm.* Refers to Pharaoh Hophra's defeat by Nebuchadnezzar the previous year (see notes on 29:6; Jer 37:10).
30:24 *put my sword in his hand.* See note on 21:3.
30:25 *my sword.* See 5:2 and note.
31:1 The fifth prophecy against Egypt (see note on 29:1). *eleventh year ... third month ... first day.* June 21, 587 BC; the ninth date in Ezekiel (see 1:2; 8:1; 20:1; 24:1; 26:1; 29:1,17; 30:20).
31:3 *Consider Assyria.* A great nation that had fallen. In 609 BC Pharaoh Necho and his army marched north to help the

The monumental entrance to the Luxor temple at Thebes. This temple, built by Pharaohs Amunhotep III (1387 – 1350 BC) and Rameses II (1279 – 1212 BC), was later besieged by Nebuchadnezzar.

Z. Radovan/www.BibleLandPictures.com

it towered on high,
its top above the thick foliage.[l]
4 The waters[m] nourished it,
deep springs made it grow tall;
their streams flowed
all around its base
and sent their channels
to all the trees of the field.[n]
5 So it towered higher[o]
than all the trees of the field;
its boughs increased
and its branches grew long,
spreading because of abundant waters.[p]
6 All the birds of the sky
nested in its boughs,
all the animals of the wild
gave birth[q] under its branches;
all the great nations
lived in its shade.[r]
7 It was majestic in beauty,
with its spreading boughs,
for its roots went down
to abundant waters.[s]
8 The cedars[t] in the garden of God
could not rival it,
nor could the junipers
equal its boughs,
nor could the plane trees[u]
compare with its branches—
no tree in the garden of God
could match its beauty.[v]
9 I made it beautiful
with abundant branches,
the envy of all the trees of Eden[w]
in the garden of God.[x]

10 " 'Therefore this is what the Sovereign
LORD says: Because the great cedar towered over the thick foliage, and because it
was proud[y] of its height, 11 I gave it into the
hands of the ruler of the nations, for him
to deal with according to its wickedness.
I cast it aside,[z] 12 and the most ruthless of
foreign nations[a] cut it down and left it. Its
boughs fell on the mountains and in all
the valleys;[b] its branches lay broken in all
the ravines of the land. All the nations of
the earth came out from under its shade
and left it.[c] 13 All the birds settled on the
fallen tree, and all the wild animals lived
among its branches.[d] 14 Therefore no other trees by the waters are ever to tower
proudly on high, lifting their tops above
the thick foliage. No other trees so well-
watered are ever to reach such a height;
they are all destined[e] for death,[f] for the
earth below, among mortals who go down
to the realm of the dead.[g]

15 " 'This is what the Sovereign LORD
says: On the day it was brought down to
the realm of the dead I covered the deep
springs with mourning for it; I held back
its streams, and its abundant waters were
restrained. Because of it I clothed Lebanon
with gloom, and all the trees of the field
withered away.[h] 16 I made the nations tremble[i] at the sound of its fall when I brought
it down to the realm of the dead to be with
those who go down to the pit. Then all
the trees[j] of Eden,[k] the choicest and best
of Lebanon, the well-watered trees, were
consoled[l] in the earth below.[m] 17 They too,
like the great cedar, had gone down to the
realm of the dead, to those killed by the
sword,[n] along with the armed men who
lived in its shade among the nations.

18 " 'Which of the trees of Eden can be
compared with you in splendor and majesty? Yet you, too, will be brought down
with the trees of Eden to the earth below;
you will lie among the uncircumcised,[o]
with those killed by the sword.

" 'This is Pharaoh and all his hordes, declares the Sovereign LORD.' "

A Lament Over Pharaoh

32 In the twelfth year, in the twelfth
month on the first day, the word of
the LORD came to me:[p] 2 "Son of man, take
up a lament[q] concerning Pharaoh king of
Egypt and say to him:

31:3 [l] Isa 10:34; S Eze 19:11 **31:4** [m] Eze 17:7 [n] Da 4:10 **31:5** [o] ver 10 [p] S Nu 24:6; S Eze 17:5 **31:6** [q] S Ge 31:7-9 [r] S Eze 17:23; S Mt 13:32 **31:7** [s] S Job 14:9 **31:8** [t] Ps 80:10 [u] S Ge 30:37 [v] Ge 2:8-9 **31:9** [w] S Ge 2:8 [x] S Ge 13:10; Eze 28:13 **31:10** [y] S Isa 2:11; S 14:13-14; S Eze 28:17 **31:11** [z] Da 5:20 **31:12** [a] S Eze 28:7 [b] Eze 32:5; 35:8 [c] Eze 32:11-12; Da 4:14 **31:13** [d] S Isa 18:6; S Eze 29:5; 32:4 **31:14** [e] S Ps 49:14 [f] S Ps 82:7 [g] S Nu 14:11; Ps 63:9; S Eze 26:20; 32:24 **31:15** [h] S 2Sa 1:21 **31:16** [i] S Jer 49:21 [j] S Isa 14:8 [k] S Ge 2:8 [l] S Eze 14:22 [m] S Isa 14:15; Eze 32:18 **31:17** [n] Ps 9:17 **31:18** [o] S Jer 9:26 **32:1** [p] S Eze 31:1; 33:21 **32:2** [q] 2Sa 1:17; 3:33; 2Ch 35:25; S Eze 19:1

Assyrians, who were reeling from Babylonian attacks. The effort ultimately failed, and Assyria passed from history. *once a cedar.* The beginning of another allegory (see Ezekiel's allegorical use of the cedar in ch. 17). *Lebanon.* Known for its cedars (see vv. 15–18; Jdg 9:15; 1Ki 4:33; 5:6; 2Ki 14:9; Ezr 3:7; Ps 29:5; 92:12; 104:16).

31:4 *waters.* The Tigris and Euphrates. *deep springs.* Or "the deep" (see note on 26:19).

31:6 *birds of the sky.* See 17:23 and note.

31:8 *garden of God.* Cf. 28:13.

31:11 *ruler of the nations.* Probably Nabopolassar, or possibly Nebuchadnezzar. *its wickedness.* Pride (see v. 10; Ge 11:1–8).

31:12 *most ruthless.* Babylonia (see note on 30:11).

31:14 *the earth below … the realm of the dead.* See note on Ps 30:1.

31:15 *deep springs.* See v. 4 and note. *clothed … with gloom.* See note on Ps 109:29.

31:16 *nations tremble.* As at Tyre's fall (see 27:35; 28:19). *were consoled.* Because the mightiest of trees had joined them in the "realm of the dead" (Sheol). See note on Ps 30:1.

31:17 *those killed by the sword.* Those who met a premature death.

31:18 *you.* The Egyptian pharaoh. *you, too.* What had happened to Assyria would also happen to the pharaoh. *uncircumcised.* See note on 28:10.

32:1 The sixth prophecy against Egypt (see note on 29:1). *twelfth year … twelfth month … first day.* Mar. 3, 585 BC; the tenth date in Ezekiel (see 1:2; 8:1; 20:1; 24:1; 26:1; 29:1,17; 30:20; 31:1). If the Septuagint (the pre-Christian Greek translation of the OT) is followed ("eleventh year"), then the chronological order of the Egypt prophecies is preserved (and the date would be Mar. 13, 586). Cf. 29:1; 30:20; 31:1; see v. 17 and note.

32:2 *lament.* See note on 19:1. *lion among the nations.* A figure for royalty and grandeur (see 19:1–9). *monster.* See 29:3 and note. *seas … streams.* Canals of the Nile (see note on 29:3).

"'You are like a lion[r] among the
nations;
you are like a monster[s] in the seas[t]
thrashing about in your streams,
churning the water with your feet
and muddying the streams.[u]

[3]"'This is what the Sovereign LORD says:

"'With a great throng of people
I will cast my net over you,
and they will haul you up in my net.[v]
[4]I will throw you on the land
and hurl you on the open field.
I will let all the birds of the sky settle
on you
and all the animals of the wild gorge
themselves on you.[w]
[5]I will spread your flesh on the
mountains
and fill the valleys[x] with your
remains.
[6]I will drench the land with your
flowing blood[y]
all the way to the mountains,
and the ravines will be filled with
your flesh.[z]
[7]When I snuff you out, I will cover the
heavens
and darken their stars;
I will cover the sun with a cloud,
and the moon will not give its light.[a]
[8]All the shining lights in the heavens
I will darken[b] over you;
I will bring darkness over your land,[c]
declares the Sovereign LORD.
[9]I will trouble the hearts of many
peoples
when I bring about your destruction
among the nations,
among[a] lands you have not known.
[10]I will cause many peoples to be
appalled at you,
and their kings will shudder with
horror because of you
when I brandish my sword[d] before
them.
On the day[e] of your downfall
each of them will tremble
every moment for his life.[f]

32:2 [r]S 2Ki 24:1; Na 2:11-13 [s]S Job 3:8; S Ps 74:13 [t]S Ge 1:21 [u]ver 13; Job 41:31; S Eze 29:3; 34:18 **32:3** [v]S Eze 12:13; Hab 1:15 **32:4** [w]S Isa 18:6; Eze 31:12-13; 39:4-5,17 **32:5** [x]S Eze 31:12 **32:6** [y]S Isa 34:3 [z]S Eze 29:5 **32:7** [a]S Isa 13:10; 34:4; S Eze 30:3; Joel 2:2, 31; 3:15; S Mt 24:29; Rev 8:12 **32:8** [b]S Ps 102:26 [c]S Job 9:7; S Jer 4:23; Joel 2:10 **32:10** [d]S Isa 30:32 [e]S Jer 46:10 [f]S Eze 26:16; S 27:35; 30:9; Rev 18:9-10

32:11 [g]S Eze 21:19 [h]S Isa 19:4; S Jer 46:13 [i]S Eze 29:19 **32:12** [j]S Eze 28:7 [k]Eze 31:11-12 **32:13** [l]S ver 2; S Eze 29:8,11 **32:15** [m]Ex 7:5; S 14:4,18; Ps 107:33-34 **32:16** [n]S Ge 50:10; S Eze 19:1 **32:17** [o]S ver 1 **32:18** [p]Jer 1:10 [q]Eze 26:20; S 31:14,16; Mic 1:8 **32:19** [r]ver 29-30; S Eze 28:10 **32:20** [s]Ps 28:3 [t]Eze 31:17-18 **32:21** [u]S Isa 14:9

[11]"'For this is what the Sovereign LORD says:

"'The sword[g] of the king of Babylon[h]
will come against you.[i]
[12]I will cause your hordes to fall
by the swords of mighty men—
the most ruthless of all nations.[j]
They will shatter the pride of
Egypt,
and all her hordes will be
overthrown.[k]
[13]I will destroy all her cattle
from beside abundant waters
no longer to be stirred by the foot of
man
or muddied by the hooves of
cattle.[l]
[14]Then I will let her waters settle
and make her streams flow like oil,
declares the Sovereign LORD.
[15]When I make Egypt desolate
and strip the land of everything
in it,
when I strike down all who live there,
then they will know that I am the
LORD.[m]'

[16]"This is the lament[n] they will chant
for her. The daughters of the nations will
chant it; for Egypt and all her hordes they
will chant it, declares the Sovereign LORD."

Egypt's Descent Into the Realm of the Dead

[17]In the twelfth year, on the fifteenth
day of the month, the word of the LORD
came to me:[o] [18]"Son of man, wail for
the hordes of Egypt and consign[p] to the
earth below both her and the daughters
of mighty nations, along with those who
go down to the pit.[q] [19]Say to them, 'Are
you more favored than others? Go down
and be laid among the uncircumcised.'[r]
[20]They will fall among those killed by the
sword. The sword is drawn; let her be
dragged[s] off with all her hordes.[t] [21]From
within the realm of the dead[u] the mighty
leaders will say of Egypt and her allies,

[a] 9 Hebrew; Septuagint *bring you into captivity among the nations, / to*

32:3 *cast my net.* Earlier it was Zedekiah over whom God's net was thrown (see 12:13; 17:20; 19:8).
32:4 *I will throw.* God's actions here are very similar to those described in 29:3–5.
32:7–8 A piling up of language that evokes the darkness associated with the day of the Lord (see Joel 2:2,10,31 and note on 2:2; 3:15; Am 5:18 and note; Zep 1:15).
32:9 *trouble the hearts.* This and the next verse reflect the fear brought about whenever great world powers fall, reminding lesser nations that they are even more vulnerable. Cf. similar feelings aroused by Tyre's fall (26:16–18; 27:35; 28:19).
32:10 *my sword.* See 5:2 and note.
32:11 *king of Babylon.* Nebuchadnezzar (cf. 21:19).
32:12 *most ruthless of all nations.* Babylonia (see note on 30:11). *pride of Egypt.* The army in which she took pride ("her hordes"; cf. Am 6:8).
32:14 *streams flow like oil.* Their surface undisturbed by any form of life.
32:16 *daughters of the nations.* A world chorus of professional wailers (see Jer 9:17–18 and notes).
32:17 The seventh and last prophecy against Egypt (see note on 29:1). *twelfth year … fifteenth day.* No month is given (as in 26:1; 40:1). The whole year dates from Apr. 13, 586, to Apr. 1, 585 BC. The Septuagint suggests the first month, the 15th day of which would be Apr. 27, 586.
32:18 *earth below.* Same as "realm of the dead" (Sheol) in 31:15. *daughters of mighty nations.* See note on v. 16.
32:19 *uncircumcised.* See note on 28:10.

‘They have come down and they lie with
the uncircumcised,[v] with those killed by
the sword.’
22 “Assyria is there with her whole army;
she is surrounded by the graves of all her
slain, all who have fallen by the sword.
23 Their graves are in the depths of the pit[w]
and her army lies around her grave.[x] All
who had spread terror in the land of the
living are slain, fallen by the sword.
24 “Elam[y] is there, with all her hordes
around her grave. All of them are slain,
fallen by the sword.[z] All who had spread
terror in the land of the living[a] went down
uncircumcised to the earth below. They
bear their shame with those who go down
to the pit.[b] 25 A bed is made for her among
the slain, with all her hordes around her
grave. All of them are uncircumcised,[c]
killed by the sword. Because their terror
had spread in the land of the living, they
bear their shame with those who go down
to the pit; they are laid among the slain.
26 “Meshek and Tubal[d] are there, with
all their hordes around their graves. All
of them are uncircumcised, killed by the
sword because they spread their terror in
the land of the living. 27 But they do not lie
with the fallen warriors of old,[a][e] who went
down to the realm of the dead with their
weapons of war—their swords placed under their heads and their shields[b] resting
on their bones—though these warriors
also had terrorized the land of the living.
28 “You too, Pharaoh, will be broken and
will lie among the uncircumcised, with
those killed by the sword.
29 “Edom[f] is there, her kings and all her
princes; despite their power, they are laid
with those killed by the sword. They lie
with the uncircumcised, with those who
go down to the pit.[g]
30 “All the princes of the north[h] and all
the Sidonians[i] are there; they went down
with the slain in disgrace despite the terror
caused by their power. They lie uncircumcised[j] with those killed by the sword and
bear their shame with those who go down
to the pit.[k]
31 “Pharaoh—he and all his army—will
see them and he will be consoled[l] for all
his hordes that were killed by the sword,
declares the Sovereign LORD. 32 Although I
had him spread terror in the land of the
living, Pharaoh[m] and all his hordes will be
laid among the uncircumcised, with those
killed by the sword, declares the Sovereign
LORD.”[n]

Renewal of Ezekiel’s Call as Watchman

33 The word of the LORD came to me:
2 “Son of man, speak to your people
and say to them: ‘When I bring the sword[o]
against a land, and the people of the land
choose one of their men and make him
their watchman,[p] 3 and he sees the sword
coming against the land and blows the
trumpet[q] to warn the people, 4 then if anyone hears the trumpet but does not heed
the warning[r] and the sword comes and
takes their life, their blood will be on their
own head.[s] 5 Since they heard the sound of
the trumpet but did not heed the warning,
their blood will be on their own head.[t] If
they had heeded the warning, they would
have saved themselves.[u] 6 But if the watchman sees the sword coming and does not
blow the trumpet to warn the people and
the sword comes and takes someone’s life,
that person’s life will be taken because of
their sin, but I will hold the watchman accountable for their blood.’[v]
7 “Son of man, I have made you a watchman[w] for the people of Israel; so hear the
word I speak and give them warning from
me.[x] 8 When I say to the wicked, ‘You
wicked person, you will surely die,[y]’ and
you do not speak out to dissuade them
from their ways, that wicked person will
die for[c] their sin, and I will hold you accountable for their blood.[z] 9 But if you do
warn the wicked person to turn from their
ways and they do not do so,[a] they will die
for their sin, though you yourself will be
saved.[b]

32:21 [v] Eze 28:10 **32:23** [w] S Isa 14:15 [x] Na 1:14 **32:24** [y] S Ge 10:22 [z] S Jer 49:37 [a] S Job 28:13 [b] S Eze 26:20 **32:25** [c] Eze 28:10 **32:26** [d] S Eze 27:13 **32:27** [e] Eze 28:10 **32:29** [f] S Ps 137:7; Isa 34:5-15; Jer 49:7; Eze 35:15; Ob 1:1 [g] Eze 25:12-14 **32:30** [h] S Isa 14:31; Jer 25:26; Eze 38:6; 39:2 [i] S Ge 10:15; S Jer 25:22 [j] Eze 28:10 [k] S Eze 26:20; S 28:8 **32:31** [l] S Eze 14:22 **32:32** [m] S Jer 44:30 [n] S Job 3:14 **33:2** [o] S Lev 26:25; S Jer 12:12 [p] S 1Sa 14:16; Isa 21:6-9; S Jer 51:12 **33:3** [q] S Ex 20:18; S Nu 10:7; Hos 5:8; 8:1 **33:4** [r] 2Ch 25:16 [s] S Lev 20:9; S Jer 6:17; Zec 1:4; Ac 18:6 **33:5** [t] S Lev 20:9 [u] S Ex 9:21 **33:6** [v] Isa 56:10-11; S Eze 3:18 **33:7** [w] S Isa 52:8 [x] Jer 1:17; 26:2 **33:8** [y] ver 14 [z] S Isa 3:11; S Eze 18:4 **33:9** [a] S Ps 7:12 [b] Eze 3:17-19

[a] 27 Septuagint; Hebrew *warriors who were uncircumcised* [b] 27 Probable reading of the original Hebrew text; Masoretic Text *punishment* [c] 8 Or *in*; also in verse 9

32:24 *Elam.* A country east of Assyria, in present-day Iran (see note on Isa 11:11).
32:26 *Meshek and Tubal.* Peoples and territories in Asia Minor (see 38:2 and note).
32:29 *Edom.* See note on Ge 36:1,8; see also Isa 34:5; Am 1:11–12; Introduction to Obadiah: Unity and Theme; map, p. 1376.
32:30 *Sidonians.* See note on 28:21.
33:1—48:35 A section depicting consolation for Israel (see Introduction: Outline).
33:1—37:28 Sermons and messages of comfort following the fall of Jerusalem. Interspersed are words of warning and judgment (e.g., 33:23–33; 34:1–19; 35).
33:1–20 At this juncture, when his message takes on a radically different theme, Ezekiel’s call to be a “watchman” for Israel is renewed (see 3:16–19 and note on 3:17).
33:2 *your people.* Fellow Israelites in exile with Ezekiel. *sword.* The invading army (cf. 5:2 and note). *people of the land.* See note on 7:27.
33:3 *trumpet.* An instrument made from a ram’s horn (see notes on Jos 6:4–5), used to warn of approaching danger (Ne 4:18–20; Jer 4:19; Am 3:6).
33:4 *their blood will be on their own head.* See note on 18:13.
33:6 *their blood.* Their life, blood being the life principle (see Ge 9:5; 42:22; Lev 17:11 and note).
33:7–9 Cf. 3:17–19.

[10]"Son of man, say to the Israelites, 'This is what you are saying: "Our offenses and sins weigh us down, and we are wasting away[c] because of[a] them. How then can we live?[d]"' [11]Say to them, 'As surely as I live, declares the Sovereign LORD, I take no pleasure in the death of the wicked, but rather that they turn from their ways and live.[e] Turn![f] Turn from your evil ways! Why will you die, people of Israel?'[g]

[12]"Therefore, son of man, say to your people,[h] 'If someone who is righteous disobeys, that person's former righteousness will count for nothing. And if someone who is wicked repents, that person's former wickedness will not bring condemnation. The righteous person who sins will not be allowed to live even though they were formerly righteous.'[i] [13]If I tell a righteous person that they will surely live, but then they trust in their righteousness and do evil, none of the righteous things that person has done will be remembered; they will die for the evil they have done.[j] [14]And if I say to a wicked person, 'You will surely die,' but they then turn away from their sin and do what is just[k] and right— [15]if they give back what they took in pledge[l] for a loan, return what they have stolen,[m] follow the decrees that give life, and do no evil—that person will surely live; they will not die.[n] [16]None of the sins[o] that person has committed will be remembered against them. They have done what is just and right; they will surely live.[p]

[17]"Yet your people say, 'The way of the Lord is not just.' But it is their way that is not just. [18]If a righteous person turns from their righteousness and does evil,[q] they will die for it.[r] [19]And if a wicked person turns away from their wickedness and does what is just and right, they will live by doing so.[s] [20]Yet you Israelites say, 'The way of the Lord is not just.' But I will judge each of you according to your own ways."[t]

Jerusalem's Fall Explained

[21]In the twelfth year of our exile, in the tenth month on the fifth day, a man who had escaped[u] from Jerusalem came to me and said, "The city has fallen!"[v] [22]Now the evening before the man arrived, the hand of the LORD was on me,[w] and he opened my mouth[x] before the man came to me in the morning. So my mouth was opened and I was no longer silent.[y]

[23]Then the word of the LORD came to me: [24]"Son of man, the people living in those ruins[z] in the land of Israel are saying, 'Abraham was only one man, yet he possessed the land. But we are many;[a] surely the land has been given to us as our possession.'[b] [25]Therefore say to them, 'This is what the Sovereign LORD says: Since you eat[c] meat with the blood[d] still in it and look to your idols and shed blood, should you then possess the land?[e] [26]You rely on your sword, you do detestable things,[f] and each of you defiles his neighbor's wife.[g] Should you then possess the land?'

[27]"Say this to them: 'This is what the Sovereign LORD says: As surely as I live, those who are left in the ruins will fall by the sword, those out in the country I will give to the wild animals to be devoured, and those in strongholds and caves will die of a plague.[h] [28]I will make the land a desolate waste, and her proud strength will come to an end, and the mountains[i] of Israel will become desolate so that no one

[a] *10* Or *away in*

33:10 [c]S Lev 26:16 [d]S Lev 26:39; S Eze 4:17 **33:11** [e]S La 3:33 [f]S 2Ch 30:9; S Isa 19:22; S Jer 3:12 [g]Jer 44:7-8; S Eze 18:23; Hos 11:8; Joel 2:12; S 1Ti 2:4 **33:12** [h]ver 2 [i]2Ch 7:14; S Eze 3:20; S 18:21 **33:13** [j]Heb 10:38; 2Pe 2:20-21 **33:14** [k]S Jer 22:3 **33:15** [l]S Ex 22:26 [m]Ex 22:1-4; S Lev 6:2-5 [n]Isa 55:7; Jer 18:7-8; S Lk 19:8 **33:16** [o]S Jer 50:20 [p]S Isa 43:25 **33:18** [q]Jer 18:10 [r]S Eze 3:20 **33:19** [s]S ver 14-15 **33:20** [t]S Job 34:11 **33:21** [u]Eze 24:26 [v]S 2Ki 25:4, 10; Jer 39:1-2; 52:4-7; S Eze 32:1 **33:22** [w]S Eze 1:3 [x]Eze 29:21; Lk 1:64 [y]Eze 3:26-27; S 24:27 **33:24** [z]Eze 36:4 [a]S Dt 1:10 [b]Isa 51:2; Jer 40:7; Eze 11:15; Lk 3:8; Ac 7:5 **33:25** [c]Jer 7:21 [d]S Ge 9:4 [e]Jer 7:9-10; S Eze 22:6, 27 **33:26** [f]Jer 41:7 [g]Eze 22:11 **33:27** [h]1Sa 13:6; Isa 2:19; S Jer 42:22; S Eze 7:15; S 14:21; 39:4 **33:28** [i]S Isa 41:15

33:10 *Our offenses and sins.* The first time the exiles expressed consciousness of sin. Previously they had blamed their fathers (18:2) and even God (18:19,25).

33:11 *As surely as I live.* See note on 5:11. *I take no pleasure.* The question of 18:23 (see note there) is now a statement. God's basic intention for his creation is life, not death (see note on 16:6). *Turn!* The third call for repentance (see 14:6; 18:30).

33:12–20 Cf. 18:21–29 (see notes there).

33:14 *what is just and right.* See notes on 18:5; Ps 119:121.

33:15 *give back what they took in pledge … return what they have stolen.* See note on 18:7. *decrees that give life.* The purpose of God's law was to foster and protect life (see note on 20:11). *that person will surely live.* The entire section is Ezekiel's answer to the despairing question of v. 10.

33:17 *The way of the Lord is not just.* See note on 18:25.

33:21–33 When news of Jerusalem's fall reaches Ezekiel, he must still reinforce his earlier word that "the end" (7:2) had truly come on the city (see note on 7:1–27); even the remnant eking out an existence in the ruins of the city will be destroyed.

33:21 *twelfth year … tenth month … fifth day.* Jan. 8, 585 BC, five months after the Jerusalem temple was burned. See date in 2Ki 25:8, which in modern reckoning is Aug. 14, 586. The journey between Jerusalem and Babylon could be made in four months (Ezr 7:9). *man who had escaped.* The first of the exiles of 586 (see 24:26, "fugitive"; see also note there). He had "escaped" alive from the disaster at Jerusalem. *The city has fallen!* With this statement all of Ezekiel's previous prophecies were fulfilled and vindicated. He was then sent with a new mission: pastoral comfort.

33:22 *no longer silent.* See 24:27 and note.

33:24 *people living in those ruins.* The residents of Jerusalem not exiled in 586 BC. *Abraham was only one man … But we are many.* A boast by the unrepentant, similar to that of 11:15 (cf. Lk 3:8).

33:25 *eat meat with the blood.* Forbidden in Ge 9:4 (see note there; see also note on Lev 17:11). *look to your idols.* See note on 18:6.

33:27 *As surely as I live.* See note on 5:11. *sword … wild animals … plague.* Cf. the threefold threat in 5:12; 7:15; 12:16 and the fourfold threat in 14:12–21 (see note on 5:16–17).

will cross them.[j] 29 Then they will know
that I am the LORD, when I have made the
land a desolate[k] waste because of all the
detestable things they have done.'[l]
30 "As for you, son of man, your people
are talking together about you by the walls
and at the doors of the houses, saying to
each other, 'Come and hear the message
that has come from the LORD.' 31 My people come to you, as they usually do, and
sit before[m] you to hear your words, but
they do not put them into practice. Their
mouths speak of love, but their hearts are
greedy[n] for unjust gain.[o] 32 Indeed, to them
you are nothing more than one who sings
love songs[p] with a beautiful voice and
plays an instrument well, for they hear
your words but do not put them into practice.[q]
33 "When all this comes true—and it
surely will—then they will know that a
prophet has been among them.[r]"

The LORD Will Be Israel's Shepherd

34 The word of the LORD came to me:
2 "Son of man, prophesy against
the shepherds of Israel; prophesy and say
to them: 'This is what the Sovereign LORD
says: Woe to you shepherds of Israel who
only take care of yourselves! Should not
shepherds take care of the flock?[s] 3 You eat
the curds, clothe yourselves with the wool
and slaughter the choice animals, but you
do not take care of the flock.[t] 4 You have
not strengthened the weak or healed[u] the
sick or bound up[v] the injured. You have
not brought back the strays or searched
for the lost. You have ruled them harshly
and brutally.[w] 5 So they were scattered because there was no shepherd,[x] and when
they were scattered they became food for
all the wild animals.[y] 6 My sheep wandered
over all the mountains and on every high
hill.[z] They were scattered[a] over the whole
earth, and no one searched or looked for
them.[b]
7 " 'Therefore, you shepherds, hear the
word of the LORD: 8 As surely as I live, declares the Sovereign LORD, because my
flock lacks a shepherd and so has been
plundered[c] and has become food for all
the wild animals,[d] and because my shepherds did not search for my flock but cared
for themselves rather than for my flock,[e]
9 therefore, you shepherds, hear the word
of the LORD: 10 This is what the Sovereign
LORD says: I am against[f] the shepherds and
will hold them accountable for my flock.
I will remove them from tending the flock
so that the shepherds can no longer feed
themselves. I will rescue[g] my flock from
their mouths, and it will no longer be food
for them.[h]
11 " 'For this is what the Sovereign LORD
says: I myself will search for my sheep[i]
and look after them. 12 As a shepherd[j]
looks after his scattered flock when he is
with them, so will I look after my sheep. I
will rescue them from all the places where
they were scattered on a day of clouds
and darkness.[k] 13 I will bring them out
from the nations and gather[l] them from

33:28 [j] S Ge 6:7; Jer 9:10 **33:29** [k] S Lev 26:34 [l] S Jer 18:16; S 44:22; Eze 36:4; Mic 7:13 **33:31** [m] S Eze 8:1 [n] Ps 119:36 [o] Ps 78:36-37; S Isa 29:13; S 33:15; S Jer 3:10; S 6:17; S Eze 22:27; Mt 13:22; 1Jn 3:18 **33:32** [p] S 1Ki 4:32 [q] Mk 6:20 **33:33** [r] S 1Sa 3:20; S Jer 28:9; S Eze 2:5 **34:2** [s] Ps 78:70-72; Isa 40:11; Jer 3:15; S 23:1; Mic 3:11; Jn 10:11; 21:15-17; Jude 1:12 **34:3** [t] Isa 56:11; S Eze 22:27; Am 6:4; Zec 11:5 **34:4** [u] S Isa 3:7 [v] S Isa 1:6 [w] ver 16; S Lev 25:43; Mic 3:3; Zec 11:15-17 **34:5** [x] S Nu 27:17 [y] ver 28; S Isa 56:9; Ac 20:29 **34:6** [z] S Jer 50:6 [a] S Lev 26:33; S Ps 95:10; S Jer 10:21 [b] 2Ch 18:16; Ps 142:4; Hos 7:13; S Mt 9:36; 18:12-13; Lk 15:5; 1Pe 2:25 **34:8** [c] S Jdg 2:14 [d] S Isa 56:9 [e] Jude 1:12 **34:10** [f] S Jer 21:13 [g] S Ps 72:14 [h] 1Sa 2:29-30; S Jer 23:2; Zec 10:3 **34:11** [i] S Ps 119:176 **34:12** [j] Isa 40:11; S Jer 31:10; Zec 10:3; Lk 19:10 [k] S Eze 32:7 **34:13** [l] S Ge 48:21; S Dt 30:4

33:29 *know that I am the LORD.* See Introduction: Themes.

33:30–33 Words addressed to Ezekiel, but included here as a rebuke and admonition to the remnant from Jerusalem living in exile.

33:31 *sit before you.* As the elders had (8:1; 14:1). *greedy.* The people were waiting for Ezekiel to tell them how they could personally profit from the situation. They were not interested in God's designs for them (cf. Mt 20:20–28).

33:32 *one who sings.* May indicate that Ezekiel chanted his prophecies (see 2Ki 3:15; Isa 5:1), but more likely the Lord was using a metaphor. *they hear … but do not … practice.* See Isa 29:13 and note; Mt 21:28–32; cf. Jas 1:22–25.

34:1–31 The Lord gives the Israelites in exile the reassuring word that in the future he will himself be their Shepherd. In vv. 1–10 he denounces Israel's worthless "shepherds"; in vv. 11–16 he promises to seek out his scattered flock; in vv. 17–22 he declares that he will judge the strong sheep who have oppressed the weak; in vv. 23–24 he promises to set over his flock his servant "David"; in vv. 25–31 he speaks climactically of his "covenant of peace" that will secure Israel's blessed state.

34:2 *shepherds of Israel.* Those responsible for providing leadership, especially the kings and their officials (see 2Sa 7:7 and note; Jer 25:18–19), but also the prophets and priests (see Isa 56:11; Jer 23:9–11). Ezekiel had earlier singled out the princes, priests and prophets for special rebuke (ch. 22). To call a king a shepherd was common throughout the ancient Near East (see note on Ps 23:1). For David's rise from shepherd to shepherd-king, see Ps 78:70–71. For condemnation of the shepherds, cf. Jer 23:1–4.

34:3 *eat … clothe … slaughter.* Legitimate rewards for shepherds. Their crime was that they did not care for the flock.

34:4 *searched for the lost.* Cf. Jer 50:6; Zec 11:15–17; Mt 18:12–14; Lk 15:4; 19:10.

34:5 *scattered.* Often used by Ezekiel to describe Israel's exile and dispersion (11:16–17; 12:15; 20:23,34,41; 22:15; 28:25). *no shepherd.* That is, no true shepherd (cf. Mk 6:34).

34:8 *wild animals.* Hostile foreign nations; but see v. 28, where they are contrasted.

34:10 *I am against the shepherds.* See note on 5:8.

34:11 *I myself will search for my sheep.* Having dealt with the faithless shepherds (vv. 1–10), the Lord committed himself to shepherd his flock (see Jer 23:3–4).

34:12 *from all the places.* Babylonia was not the only place where the Israelites had gone (see Jer 43:1–7). *day of clouds and darkness.* The day of the Lord that had come upon Israel when Jerusalem fell in the summer of 586 BC (see 7:7; 32:7 and notes).

34:13 *I will bring them out.* The promises of restoration—begun in 11:17 and repeated in 20:34,41–42; 28:25—find

the countries, and I will bring them into
their own land.[m] I will pasture them on
the mountains of Israel, in the ravines
and in all the settlements in the land.[n] 14 I
will tend them in a good pasture, and the
mountain heights of Israel[o] will be their
grazing land. There they will lie down in
good grazing land, and there they will feed
in a rich pasture[p] on the mountains of Israel.[q] 15 I myself will tend my sheep and
have them lie down,[r] declares the Sovereign LORD.[s] 16 I will search for the lost and
bring back the strays. I will bind up[t] the
injured and strengthen the weak,[u] but the
sleek and the strong I will destroy.[v] I will
shepherd the flock with justice.[w]
17 " 'As for you, my flock, this is what
the Sovereign LORD says: I will judge between one sheep and another, and between rams and goats.[x] 18 Is it not enough[y]
for you to feed on the good pasture? Must
you also trample the rest of your pasture
with your feet?[z] Is it not enough for you
to drink clear water? Must you also muddy the rest with your feet? 19 Must my
flock feed on what you have trampled
and drink what you have muddied with
your feet?
20 " 'Therefore this is what the Sovereign
LORD says to them: See, I myself will judge
between the fat sheep and the lean sheep.[a]
21 Because you shove with flank and shoulder, butting all the weak sheep with your
horns[b] until you have driven them away,
22 I will save my flock, and they will no
longer be plundered. I will judge between
one sheep and another.[c] 23 I will place over
them one shepherd, my servant David,
and he will tend[d] them; he will tend them
and be their shepherd.[e] 24 I the LORD will
be their God,[f] and my servant David[g] will
be prince among them.[h] I the LORD have
spoken.[i]
25 " 'I will make a covenant[j] of peace[k]
with them and rid the land of savage
beasts[l] so that they may live in the wilderness and sleep in the forests in safety.[m] 26 I will make them and the places
surrounding my hill a blessing.[a][n] I will
send down showers in season;[o] there
will be showers of blessing.[p] 27 The trees
will yield their fruit[q] and the ground will
yield its crops;[r] the people will be secure[s]
in their land. They will know that I am
the LORD, when I break the bars of their
yoke[t] and rescue them from the hands of
those who enslaved them.[u] 28 They will no
longer be plundered by the nations, nor
will wild animals devour them. They will
live in safety,[v] and no one will make them
afraid.[w] 29 I will provide for them a land
renowned[x] for its crops, and they will no
longer be victims of famine[y] in the land
or bear the scorn[z] of the nations.[a] 30 Then
they will know that I, the LORD their God,
am with them and that they, the Israelites, are my people, declares the Sovereign
LORD.[b] 31 You are my sheep,[c] the sheep of
my pasture,[d] and I am your God, declares
the Sovereign LORD.' "

[a] 26 Or *I will cause them and the places surrounding my hill to be named in blessings* (see Gen. 48:20); or *I will cause them and the places surrounding my hill to be seen as blessed*

34:13 [m] S Isa 66:20; S Jer 23:8; S Eze 11:17; Mic 4:6 [n] Jer 23:3; S Jer 50:19; S Eze 28:25; 36:24 **34:14** [o] S Eze 20:40 [p] Ps 23:2; S 37:3 [q] S Isa 65:10; Eze 36:29-30; 37:22; Am 9:14; Mic 7:14 **34:15** [r] Zep 3:13 [s] Ps 23:1-2; S Jer 33:12; Mic 5:4 **34:16** [t] S Ps 147:3 [u] Mic 4:6; Zep 3:19 [v] Lk 19:10 [w] Isa 10:16; S Jer 31:8; Lk 5:32 **34:17** [x] Mt 25:32-33 **34:18** [y] S Ge 30:15 [z] S Eze 32:2 **34:20** [a] Mt 25:32 **34:21** [b] S Dt 33:17 **34:22** [c] Ps 72:12-14; Jer 23:2-3; Eze 20:37-38 **34:23** [d] Isa 40:11 [e] S Isa 31:4; Mic 5:4 **34:24** [f] Eze 36:28 [g] Ps 89:49 [h] S Isa 53:4; Zec 13:7 [i] Jer 23:4-5; S 30:9; S 33:14; Jn 10:16; Rev 7:17 **34:25** [j] S Eze 16:62 [k] S Nu 25:12 [l] Lev 26:6 [m] S Lev 25:18; Isa 11:6-9; Hos 2:18 **34:26** [n] S Ge 12:2 [o] Ps 68:9; Joel 2:23 [p] Dt 11:13-15; S 28:12; Isa 44:3 **34:27** [q] S Ps 72:16 [r] S Job 14:9; S Ps 67:6 [s] S Nu 24:21 [t] S Lev 26:13 [u] S Jer 30:8; S Eze 20:42; S 28:25 **34:28** [v] S Jer 32:37 [w] S Jer 30:10; S Eze 28:26; 39:26; Hos 11:11; Am 9:15; Zep 3:13; Zec 14:11 **34:29** [x] S Isa 4:2 [y] Eze 36:29 [z] S Ps 137:3; Eze 36:6; Joel 2:19 [a] Eze 36:15 **34:30** [b] S Eze 14:11; 37:27 **34:31** [c] S Ps 28:9 [d] S Jer 23:1

special emphasis in this part (chs. 33–39) of Ezekiel (see 36:24–32 and notes; 37:21; 38:8 and note; 39:27). *mountains of Israel.* Compare the tone of 6:3–7 with judgment now past (see v. 12). The mountains perhaps represented the scene of salvation.

34:14 *I will tend them.* See Isa 40:11; Jn 10:11.

34:16 *the sleek and the strong.* Those with power who had fattened themselves by oppressing the other "sheep" (see vv. 17–22).

34:17 *rams and goats.* People of power and influence who were oppressing poorer Israelites. This prophetic word shows the same concern for social justice found elsewhere in the Prophets (see Isa 3:13–15; 5:8; Am 5:12; 6:1–7; see also Mic 2:1–5 and notes). Cf. the treatment of slaves Jeremiah observed (Jer 34:8–11).

34:23–24 *my servant David.* A ruler like David and from his line (see Ps 89:4,20,29; see also Jer 23:5–6 and notes).

34:24 *prince.* The Lord announced a kingdom where he would be King and the earthly king a "prince" (cf. 37:25; 44:3; 45:7,16–17,22; 46:2–18; 48:21–22).

34:25 *covenant of peace.* Cf. 37:26. All of God's covenants aim at peace (see Ge 26:28–31; Nu 25:12; Isa 54:10; Mal 2:5). This covenant (the "new covenant" spoken of by Jeremiah, 31:31–34) looks to the final peace, initiated by Christ (Php 4:7) and still awaiting final fulfillment. The "peace" (Hebrew *shalom*) envisioned here is that of a restored relationship with God and the secure enjoyment of a life made full and rich through his blessings. None of the threats to life experienced under God's judgments will mar this "peace" (compare vv. 25–29 with 5:16–17 and note). *sleep in the forests.* Often dangerous (see Ps 104:20–21; Jer 5:6).

34:26 *showers in season.* Autumn rains, which signal the beginning of the rainy season, and spring rains, which come at the end (cf. Jer 5:24). *showers of blessing.* Blessing, the power of life promised to God's people through Abraham (Ge 12:1–3), is beautifully symbolized in the life-giving effects of rain.

34:27 *bars of their yoke.* The bars were wooden pegs inserted down through holes in the yoke and tied below the animal's neck with cords (Isa 58:6) to form a collar (cf. 30:18; Lev 26:13; Jer 27:2; 28:10–13). The entire picture represents foreign domination.

34:29 *scorn of the nations.* See 22:4.

34:30 *their God ... my people.* Covenant language (see 11:20; Ex 6:7; Hos 1:9; Zec 8:8 and notes).

A Prophecy Against Edom

35 The word of the LORD came to me:
2 "Son of man, set your face against
Mount Seir;[e] prophesy against it 3 and say:
'This is what the Sovereign LORD says: I am
against you, Mount Seir, and I will stretch
out my hand[f] against you and make you
a desolate waste.[g] 4 I will turn your towns
into ruins[h] and you will be desolate. Then
you will know that I am the LORD.[i]
5 " 'Because you harbored an ancient
hostility and delivered the Israelites over
to the sword[j] at the time of their calamity,[k]
the time their punishment reached its climax,[l] 6 therefore as surely as I live, declares
the Sovereign LORD, I will give you over to
bloodshed[m] and it will pursue you.[n] Since
you did not hate bloodshed, bloodshed
will pursue you. 7 I will make Mount Seir a
desolate waste[o] and cut off from it all who
come and go.[p] 8 I will fill your mountains
with the slain; those killed by the sword
will fall on your hills and in your valleys
and in all your ravines.[q] 9 I will make you
desolate forever;[r] your towns will not be
inhabited. Then you will know that I am
the LORD.[s]
10 " 'Because you have said, "These two
nations and countries will be ours and
we will take possession[t] of them," even
though I the LORD was there, 11 therefore
as surely as I live, declares the Sovereign
LORD, I will treat you in accordance with
the anger[u] and jealousy you showed in
your hatred of them and I will make myself
known among them when I judge you.[v]
12 Then you will know that I the LORD have
heard all the contemptible things you have
said against the mountains of Israel. You
said, "They have been laid waste and have
been given over to us to devour.[w]" 13 You
boasted[x] against me and spoke against me
without restraint, and I heard it.[y] 14 This is
what the Sovereign LORD says: While the
whole earth rejoices, I will make you desolate.[z] 15 Because you rejoiced[a] when the
inheritance of Israel became desolate, that
is how I will treat you. You will be desolate, Mount Seir,[b] you and all of Edom.[c]
Then they will know that I am the LORD.' "

35:2 [e] S Ge 14:6 **35:3** [f] S Jer 6:12 [g] S Isa 34:10; Eze 25:12-14 **35:4** [h] Jer 44:2 [i] ver 9; S Jer 49:10 **35:5** [j] S Ps 63:10 [k] Ob 1:13 [l] Ps 137:7; S Eze 21:29 **35:6** [m] S Isa 34:3 [n] Isa 63:2-6 **35:7** [o] S Jer 46:19 [p] S Jer 49:17 **35:8** [q] S Eze 31:12 **35:9** [r] Ob 1:10 [s] S Isa 34:5-6; S Jer 49:13 **35:10** [t] S Ps 83:12; Eze 36:2,5 **35:11** [u] Eze 25:14 [v] S Ps 9:16; Ob 1:15; S Mt 7:2 **35:12** [w] S Jer 50:7 **35:13** [x] S Jer 49:16 [y] Da 11:36 **35:14** [z] Jer 51:48 **35:15** [a] Eze 36:5; Ob 1:12 [b] ver 3 [c] S Isa 34:5-6, 11; Jer 50:11-13; S La 4:21; S Eze 32:29 **36:1** [d] S Eze 17:22 **36:2** [e] Eze 6:2-3 [f] S Eze 25:3 [g] S Dt 32:13 [h] S Eze 35:10 **36:3** [i] Ob 1:13 [j] Ps 44:13-14; S La 2:16; 3:62 **36:4** [k] Eze 6:3 [l] Eze 33:24

Hope for the Mountains of Israel

36 "Son of man, prophesy to the
mountains of Israel[d] and say,
'Mountains of Israel, hear the word of the
LORD. 2 This is what the Sovereign LORD
says:[e] The enemy said of you, "Aha![f] The
ancient heights[g] have become our possession.[h]" ' 3 Therefore prophesy and say,
'This is what the Sovereign LORD says: Because they ravaged[i] and crushed you from
every side so that you became the possession of the rest of the nations and the object of people's malicious talk and slander,[j]
4 therefore, mountains of Israel, hear the
word of the Sovereign LORD: This is what
the Sovereign LORD says to the mountains
and hills, to the ravines and valleys,[k] to
the desolate ruins[l] and the deserted[m]
towns that have been plundered and ridiculed[n] by the rest of the nations around
you[o]— 5 this is what the Sovereign LORD
says: In my burning[p] zeal I have spoken
against the rest of the nations, and against

[m] S Lev 26:43 [n] S Jer 2:26 [o] Dt 11:11; S Ps 79:4; S Eze 33:28-29 **36:5** [p] S Dt 29:20

35:1–15 The counterpart of Israel's restoration as the Lord's people is the desolation of her enemies—of which Edom serves here as representative (see 36:5). Given the historic relationship between Israel and Edom (see notes on vv. 2,5), the spiteful treatment of Judah by the Edomites at the time of Jerusalem's fall was especially reprehensible (see Isa 63:1–6 and notes; Introduction to Obadiah: Unity and Theme; see also notes on Am 9:12; Ob 8).
35:2 *set your face against.* See note on 20:46. *Mount Seir.* Edom (v. 15), Israel's relative (Jacob and Esau being twins, Ge 25:21–30) and constant enemy, from whom brotherhood was sought but seldom found (cf. Am 1:11). Edom had to be dealt with before Israel could find peace (cf. Ge 32–33). See 25:12 and note.
35:3 *I am against you.* See note on 5:8.
35:5 *ancient hostility.* Beginning with Jacob's deception of Isaac for Esau's blessing (Ge 27; see especially v. 41) and continuing later (Nu 20:14–21; 2Sa 8:13–14; 1Ki 9:26–28). *time of their calamity.* Edom looted Jerusalem in 586 BC (see Ob 11–14 and notes).
35:6 *as surely as I live.* See note on 5:11. *bloodshed … will pursue you.* Retributive justice, in accordance with Ge 9:6 (see note there).
35:9 *desolate forever.* To experience no restoration like Egypt's (see 29:13–16). *know that I am the LORD.* See Introduction: Themes.
35:10 *These two nations.* Israel and Judah. *I the LORD was there.* See 48:35 and note.
35:13 *You boasted against me.* Cf. Ob 12; Zep 2:8,10; also Ps 35:26; Jer 48:26,42.
36:1–38 How God, whose name has been profaned among the nations, will display his holiness in the restoration of his people: Verses 1–15 set forth God's promise to cause the now desolate land ("mountains") of Israel to prosper once more so that it is a place of blessing for Israel, thereby removing its disgrace; vv. 16–38 spell out God's promise to cleanse and restore his now defiled and scattered people, thereby removing the disgrace that Israel has brought on his name and once again showing to all nations his holiness.
36:1–15 The comforting counterpart to ch. 6. Verses 1–7 announce God's coming judgment on the nations for the scorn they heaped on the land of Israel; vv. 8–15 announce God's future renewal of the prosperity of the land.
36:2 *The enemy said of you.* See 25:3; 26:2. *Aha!* See note on 25:3. *ancient heights.* The promised land, of which the elevated region between the Jordan River and the Mediterranean coast was the central core.
36:3 *rest of the nations.* All nations that in the past had conquered parts of Israel—until finally they took full possession.
36:4 *mountains … hills … ravines … valleys.* See 6:3 and note on 1:5.

36:5 *my burning zeal.* The Lord was personally offended by the ridicule of the nations because it was

all Edom, for with glee and with malice in their hearts they made my land their own possession so that they might plunder its pastureland.'[q] 6 Therefore prophesy concerning the land of Israel and say to the mountains and hills, to the ravines and valleys: 'This is what the Sovereign LORD says: I speak in my jealous wrath because you have suffered the scorn of the nations.[r] 7 Therefore this is what the Sovereign LORD says: I swear with uplifted hand[s] that the nations around you will also suffer scorn.[t]

8 " 'But you, mountains of Israel, will produce branches and fruit[u] for my people Israel, for they will soon come home. 9 I am concerned for you and will look on you with favor; you will be plowed and sown,[v] 10 and I will cause many people to live on you—yes, all of Israel. The towns will be inhabited and the ruins[w] rebuilt.[x] 11 I will increase the number of people and animals living on you, and they will be fruitful[y] and become numerous. I will settle people[z] on you as in the past[a] and will make you prosper more than before.[b] Then you will know that I am the LORD. 12 I will cause people, my people Israel, to live on you. They will possess you, and you will be their inheritance;[c] you will never again deprive them of their children.

13 " 'This is what the Sovereign LORD says: Because some say to you, "You devour people[d] and deprive your nation of its children," 14 therefore you will no longer devour people or make your nation childless, declares the Sovereign LORD. 15 No longer will I make you hear the taunts of the nations, and no longer will you suffer the scorn of the peoples or cause your nation to fall, declares the Sovereign LORD.[e]' "

Israel's Restoration Assured

16 Again the word of the LORD came to me: 17 "Son of man, when the people of Israel were living in their own land, they defiled it by their conduct and their actions. Their conduct was like a woman's monthly uncleanness[f] in my sight.[g] 18 So I poured out[h] my wrath on them because they had shed blood in the land and because they had defiled it with their idols. 19 I dispersed them among the nations, and they were scattered[i] through the countries; I judged them according to their conduct and their actions.[j] 20 And wherever they went among the nations they profaned[k] my holy name, for it was said of them, 'These are the LORD's people, and yet they had to leave his land.'[l] 21 I had concern for my holy name, which the people of Israel profaned among the nations where they had gone.[m]

22 "Therefore say to the Israelites, 'This is what the Sovereign LORD says: It is not for your sake, people of Israel, that I am going to do these things, but for the sake of my holy name,[n] which you have profaned[o] among the nations where you have gone.[p] 23 I will show the holiness of my great name,[q] which has been profaned[r] among the nations, the name you have profaned among them. Then the nations will know that I am the LORD,[s] declares the

36:5 [q] Isa 66:16; Jer 25:31; 50:11; Eze 25:12-14; S 35:10,15; 38:22; Joel 3:2,14 **36:6** [r] Ps 123:3-4; Eze 34:29 **36:7** [s] S Nu 14:30 [t] S Jer 25:9 **36:8** [u] S Isa 4:2; S 27:6; Eze 47:12 **36:9** [v] ver 34-36; Jer 31:27 **36:10** [w] S Isa 49:8 [x] Isa 49:17-23; S Jer 30:18 **36:11** [y] S Ge 1:22 [z] S Isa 49:19 [a] Mic 7:14 [b] Lev 26:9; Job 42:13; S Jer 31:28; S Eze 16:55; Zec 10:8 **36:12** [c] Eze 47:14,22 **36:13** [d] S Nu 13:32 **36:15** [e] Ps 89:50-51; Isa 54:4; S Eze 34:29 **36:17** [f] S Lev 5:2; S 12:2 [g] Ps 106:37-38; S Jer 2:7 **36:18** [h] S 2Ch 34:21 **36:19** [i] Dt 28:64 [j] Lev 18:24-28; S Eze 7:8; S 24:14; 39:24 **36:20** [k] S Lev 18:21; S Eze 13:19; Ro 2:24 [l] Isa 52:5; S Jer 33:24; S Eze 12:16 **36:21** [m] Ps 74:18; Isa 48:9 **36:22** [n] S Isa 37:35; S Eze 20:44 [o] Ro 2:24* [p] Dt 9:5-6; Ps 106:8; S Eze 20:9 **36:23** [q] S Nu 6:27 [r] S Isa 37:23 [s] S Ps 46:10

---

his special land they were mocking and plundering (see "my land" later in the verse). *Edom.* Singled out because of its long-standing hostility to Israel (see ch. 35, especially vv. 2,5 and notes).

36:6 *jealous wrath.* See 16:38 and note.

36:7 *with uplifted hand.* See 20:5 and note.

36:8 *branches and fruit.* Signs of productivity (see 17:8,23) and the Lord's restored favor (see Lev 26:3–5); to be contrasted with Edom's desolation in 35:3,7,15. *soon.* Even as judgment fell, a speedy return of the exiles was announced.

36:9 *I ... will look on you with favor.* Cf. Lev 26:9 for the identical clause in a similar context.

36:10 *yes, all of Israel.* In this chapter (as in 37:15–23) Ezekiel is speaking of the restoration of all Israel.

36:11 *be fruitful and become numerous.* Identical terminology to the divine blessing at creation (Ge 1:22,28; see Ge 8:17; 9:1,7) and the subsequent covenant blessing (see Ge 17:6; 35:11; 48:3–4; Ex 1:7). *know that I am the LORD.* See note on 6:7. These words of recognition, used throughout the book to express God's revelation through judgment, here point to God's self-disclosure in salvation (see 35:9 and note).

36:12 *live on you.* The mountains of Israel are still being addressed. *deprive them of their children.* The mountains are poetically pictured as having contributed to the depopulation brought by the exile. This may refer to the fact that the promised land had contained the Canaanites and their religious centers ("high places") that had led Israel astray and so brought God's wrath down on his people (see 6:3 and note).

36:16–38 God's restoration of his defiled and scattered people. Verses 16–23 remind Israel that the nation was exiled from her land because of her uncleanness and that her restoration is for the sake of God's holy name; vv. 24–27 announce God's renewal of defiled Israel and its effects on Israel (vv. 28–32) and on the nations (vv. 33–36); vv. 37–38 provide a concluding summary.

36:18 *shed blood ... defiled it with their idols.* A summary reference to Israel's social injustices and idolatrous religious practices (see 22:3 and note). *idols.* See note on 6:4.

36:20 *they profaned my holy name.* Because Israel had been removed from her land, it seemed to the nations that her God was unable to protect and preserve his people (see 20:9 and note; cf. Nu 14:15–16; 2Ki 18:32–35; 19:10–12).

36:22 *It is not for your sake.* Not because God did not care for Israel, but because his people did not deserve what he was about to do (cf. Dt 9:4–6). Statements like these make Ezekiel a preacher of pure grace. *for the sake of my holy name.* The reason given in ch. 20 for the withholding of divine punishment (see 20:9,14,22) is here given as a reason for divine restoration.

36:23 *Then the nations will know that I am the LORD.* The ultimate purpose of God's plans with Israel is that the

Sovereign LORD, when I am proved holy[t]
through you before their eyes.[u]
24“ ‘For I will take you out of the nations;
I will gather you from all the countries and
bring you back into your own land.[v] 25I
will sprinkle[w] clean water on you, and you
will be clean; I will cleanse[x] you from all
your impurities[y] and from all your idols.[z]
26I will give you a new heart[a] and put a
new spirit in you; I will remove from you
your heart of stone[b] and give you a heart
of flesh.[c] 27And I will put my Spirit[d] in you
and move you to follow my decrees[e] and
be careful to keep my laws.[f] 28Then you
will live in the land I gave your ancestors; you will be my people,[g] and I will be
your God.[h] 29I will save you from all your
uncleanness. I will call for the grain and
make it plentiful and will not bring famine[i] upon you. 30I will increase the fruit of
the trees and the crops of the field, so that
you will no longer suffer disgrace among
the nations because of famine.[j] 31Then you
will remember your evil ways and wicked deeds, and you will loathe yourselves
for your sins and detestable practices.[k] 32I
want you to know that I am not doing this
for your sake, declares the Sovereign LORD.
Be ashamed[l] and disgraced for your conduct, people of Israel![m]
33“ ‘This is what the Sovereign LORD
says: On the day I cleanse[n] you from all
your sins, I will resettle your towns, and

36:23 [t]S Eze 20:41 [u]Ps 126:2; S Isa 5:16; Eze 20:14; 38:23; 39:7, 27-28
36:24 [v]S Isa 43:5-6; S Eze 34:13; 37:21
36:25 [w]S Lev 14:7; S 16:14-15; Heb 9:13 [x]S Ps 51:2,7 [y]S Ezr 6:21 [z]Isa 2:18; Joel 3:21; Zec 3:4; 13:2; S Ac 22:16
36:26 [a]Jer 24:7 [b]S Jer 5:3 [c]S Ps 51:10; S Eze 18:31; S 2Co 3:3
36:27 [d]S Isa 44:3; Joel 2:29; Jn 3:5 [e]S Eze 18:21 [f]Jer 50:20; 1Th 4:8
36:28 [g]Jer 30:22; 31:33 [h]S Eze 11:17; S 14:11; 34:24; 37:14,27; Zec 8:8
36:29 [i]Eze 34:29
36:30 [j]Lev 26:4-5; S Eze 34:13-14; Hos 2:21-22
36:31 [k]Isa 6:5; S Jer 31:19; S Eze 6:9

the ruins[o] will be rebuilt.[p] 34The desolate land will be cultivated instead of lying desolate in the sight of all who pass
through it. 35They will say, “This land that
was laid waste has become like the garden
of Eden;[q] the cities that were lying in ruins, desolate and destroyed, are now fortified and inhabited.[r]” 36Then the nations
around you that remain will know that I
the LORD have rebuilt what was destroyed
and have replanted what was desolate. I
the LORD have spoken, and I will do it.’[s]
37“This is what the Sovereign LORD says:
Once again I will yield to Israel’s plea[t] and
do this for them: I will make their people
as numerous as sheep,[u] 38as numerous as
the flocks for offerings[v] at Jerusalem during her appointed festivals. So will the ruined cities be filled with flocks of people.
Then they will know that I am the LORD.[w]”

The Valley of Dry Bones

37 The hand of the LORD was on me,[x]
and he brought me out by the Spir-
it[y] of the LORD and set me in the middle of
a valley;[z] it was full of bones.[a] 2He led me
back and forth among them, and I saw a
great many bones on the floor of the valley,

36:32 [l]Eze 16:63 [m]Dt 9:5 **36:33** [n]S Lev 16:30 [o]S Lev 26:31 [p]S Isa 49:8 **36:35** [q]S Ge 2:8 [r]Am 9:14 **36:36** [s]S Jer 42:10; S Eze 17:22; 37:14; 39:27-28 **36:37** [t]Zec 10:6; 13:9 [u]Ps 102:17; Jer 29:12-14 **36:38** [v]1Ki 8:63; 2Ch 35:7-9 [w]S Ex 6:2
37:1 [x]S Eze 1:3 [y]S Eze 11:24; Lk 4:1; Ac 8:39 [z]Jer 7:32 [a]S Jer 8:2; Eze 40:1

whole world may know the true God (see v. 11 and note). *I am proved holy.* See Lev 10:3 and note.

36:24–27 The four elements in the promised restoration: (1) return of the exiles (v. 24), (2) cleansing from sin (v. 25), (3) renewal of heart (v. 26) and (4) enablement by God’s Spirit to live God’s way (v. 27).

36:25 *I will sprinkle clean water.* For sprinkling with water as a ritual act of cleansing, see Ex 30:19–20; Lev 14:51; Nu 19:18; cf. Zec 13:1; Heb 10:22. *I will cleanse.* See v. 33; 37:23; Jer 33:8. *idols.* See note on 6:4.

36:26–27 Contains “new covenant” terminology (see Jer 31:33–34 and notes).

36:26 *new heart.* See notes on 11:19; 18:31. *put a new spirit in you.* Transform your mind and heart. Here and in 11:19 God declared that he would bring about the change. In 18:31 (see note there) he called on his people to effect the change. What he requires of his people he always provides. *heart of flesh.* “Flesh” in the OT is often a symbol for weakness and frailty (Isa 31:3); in the NT it often stands for our propensity toward sin that opposes God (as in Ro 8:5–8). Here it stands (in opposition to stone) for a pliable, teachable heart.

36:27 *my Spirit.* God bestows his Spirit to enable the human spirit to do his will (see 37:14 and note on 2:2). Verses 25–27 are closely paralleled in Ps 51:7–11 (see notes there).

36:28–32 The results of Israel’s renewal: restoration to prosperity (vv. 28–30) and a deep sense of shame for all her sins (vv. 31–32).

36:28 *my people ... your God.* Covenant language (see 11:20 and note).

36:29 *from all your uncleanness.* From idol worship and moral defilement (see v. 25; 37:23).

36:30 *disgrace.* As in v. 15.

36:31 *Then you will remember.* God’s undeserved grace leads to recollection and repentance (cf. 6:9; 16:63; 20:43; Ps 130:4).

36:32 *not ... for your sake.* See note on v. 22.

36:33–36 The impact of Israel’s restoration on the nations.

36:33 *On the day.* Connects the promise of cleansing (vv. 24–32) and the promise of repopulation (vv. 33–36).

36:35 *garden of Eden.* Cf. 28:13; 31:9. *fortified.* In contrast to 38:11.

36:36 *nations ... will know.* See note on v. 23.

36:37–38 In summary, Israel’s full standing with God will be restored.

36:37 *yield to Israel’s plea.* Allowing petitions to come to him again, God reversed his earlier refusals to hear (cf. 14:3; 20:3,31).

36:38 *as numerous as the flocks for offerings.* See 1Ki 8:63; 1Ch 29:21; 2Ch 35:7 for the appropriateness of the comparison.

37:1–28 Although one of Ezekiel’s major visions, it surprisingly bears no date (see chart, p. 1336). However, it must have come to Ezekiel sometime after 586 BC. The symbolic vision given to Ezekiel (vv. 1–15) is immediately followed by a symbolic act that Ezekiel is instructed to perform (vv. 16–28). Both speak of the restoration of Israel, the central theme of chs. 34–36.

37:1 *hand of the LORD.* See note on 1:3. *brought me out by the Spirit.* See 3:12 and note. *valley.* The Hebrew for this word is the same as that translated “plain” in 3:22–23; 8:4. Ezekiel now received a message of hope, whereas previously he had heard God’s word of judgment. *bones.* Verse 11 interprets them as symbolizing Israel’s apparently hopeless condition in exile.

37:2 *a great many bones.* Symbolizing the whole community of exiles. *very dry.* Long dead, far beyond the reach of resuscitation (1Ki 17:17–24; 2Ki 4:18–37; but see 2Ki 13:21).

bones that were very dry. 3He asked me,
"Son of man, can these bones live?"
I said, "Sovereign LORD, you alone
know.[b]"
4Then he said to me, "Prophesy to these
bones and say to them, 'Dry bones, hear
the word of the LORD![c] 5This is what the
Sovereign LORD says to these bones: I will
make breath[a] enter you, and you will
come to life.[d] 6I will attach tendons to you
and make flesh come upon you and cover
you with skin; I will put breath in you,
and you will come to life. Then you will
know that I am the LORD.[e]' "
7So I prophesied as I was commanded. And as I was prophesying, there was
a noise, a rattling sound, and the bones
came together, bone to bone. 8I looked,
and tendons and flesh appeared on them
and skin covered them, but there was no
breath in them.
9Then he said to me, "Prophesy to the
breath;[f] prophesy, son of man, and say to
it, 'This is what the Sovereign LORD says:
Come, breath, from the four winds[g] and
breathe into these slain, that they may
live.' " 10So I prophesied as he commanded[h] me, and breath entered them; they
came to life and stood up on their feet — a
vast army.[i]
11Then he said to me: "Son of man,
these bones are the people of Israel. They
say, 'Our bones are dried up and our hope
is gone; we are cut off.'[j] 12Therefore prophesy and say to them: 'This is what the Sovereign LORD says: My people, I am going to
open your graves and bring you up from
them; I will bring you back to the land of
Israel.[k] 13Then you, my people, will know
that I am the LORD,[l] when I open your
graves and bring you up from them.[m] 14I
will put my Spirit[n] in you and you will live,
and I will settle[o] you in your own land.
Then you will know that I the LORD have
spoken, and I have done it, declares the
LORD.[p]' "

One Nation Under One King

15The word of the LORD came to me:
16"Son of man, take a stick of wood and
write on it, 'Belonging to Judah and the
Israelites[q] associated with him.[r]' Then take
another stick of wood, and write on it,
'Belonging to Joseph (that is, to Ephraim)
and all the Israelites associated with him.'
17Join them together into one stick so that
they will become one in your hand.[s]
18"When your people ask you, 'Won't
you tell us what you mean by this?'[t] 19say
to them, 'This is what the Sovereign LORD
says: I am going to take the stick of Joseph — which is in Ephraim's hand — and
of the Israelite tribes associated with him,
and join it to Judah's stick. I will make
them into a single stick of wood, and they
will become one in my hand.'[u] 20Hold before their eyes the sticks you have written
on 21and say to them, 'This is what the
Sovereign LORD says: I will take the Israelites out of the nations where they have
gone. I will gather them from all around
and bring them back into their own land.[v]
22I will make them one nation in the land,
on the mountains of Israel.[w] There will be
one king over all of them and they will
never again be two nations or be divided
into two kingdoms.[x] 23They will no longer defile[y] themselves with their idols and
vile images or with any of their offenses,
for I will save them from all their sinful
backsliding,[b][z] and I will cleanse them.
They will be my people, and I will be their
God.[a]

[a] 5 The Hebrew for this word can also mean *wind* or *spirit* (see verses 6-14). [b] 23 Many Hebrew manuscripts (see also Septuagint); most Hebrew manuscripts *all their dwelling places where they sinned*

37:3 [b]Dt 32:39; S 1Sa 2:6; Isa 26:19; 1Co 15:35 **37:4** [c]Jer 22:29 **37:5** [d]S Ge 2:7; Ps 104:29-30; Rev 11:11 **37:6** [e]S Ex 6:2; Eze 38:23 **37:9** [f]ver 14; Ps 104:30; Isa 32:15; Eze 39:29; Zec 12:10 [g]Jer 49:36; Da 7:2; 8:8; 11:4; Zec 2:6; 6:5; Rev 7:1 **37:10** [h]S Eze 12:7 [i]Rev 11:11 **37:11** [j]S Job 17:15; S La 3:54 **37:12** [k]ver 21; Dt 32:39; 1Sa 2:6; Isa 26:19; Jer 29:14; Hos 13:14; Am 9:14-15; Zep 3:20; Zec 8:8 **37:13** [l]S Ex 6:2 [m]S Eze 17:24; Hos 13:14 **37:14** [n]S ver 9; S Isa 11:2; Joel 2:28-29 [o]S Jer 43:2 [p]Eze 36:27-28, 36; Rev 11:11 **37:16** [q]S 1Ki 12:20; 2Ch 10:17-19 [r]Nu 17:2-3; 2Ch 15:9 **37:17** [s]ver 24; Isa 11:13; S Jer 50:4; Hos 1:11 **37:18** [t]S Eze 24:19 **37:19** [u]Zec 10:6 **37:21** [v]S ver 12; S Isa 43:5-6; S Eze 20:42; 39:27; Mic 4:6 **37:22** [w]S Eze 17:22; S 34:13-14 [x]Isa 11:13; Jer 33:24; S 50:4; Hos 1:11 **37:23** [y]Eze 43:7 [z]S Jer 7:24 [a]Eze 11:18; S 36:28; Na 2:2

37:4 *Prophesy to these bones.* Ezekiel had previously prophesied to inanimate objects (mountains, 6:2; 36:1; forests, 20:47); now he prophesies to lifeless bones and "the breath" (v. 9). Cf. Jn 5:25 and note.
37:6 *tendons ... flesh ... skin ... breath.* Lists of four items are common in Ezekiel (see note on 1:5).
37:8 *but there was no breath.* This visionary re-creation of God's people recalls the two-step creation of Adam in Ge 2:7.
37:9 *breath.* See NIV text note on v. 5. *four.* See note on 1:5. *slain.* What Ezekiel saw was a battlefield strewn with the bones of the fallen (see v. 10).
37:11 *Our bones ... cut off.* A sense of utter despair, to which the vision offers hope.
37:12 *graves.* The imagery shifts from a scattering of bones on a battlefield (see note on v. 9) to a cemetery with sealed graves.
37:14 *I will put my Spirit in you.* See 36:27 and note. *I will settle you in your own land.* These words make it clear that the Lord is not speaking here of a resurrection from the dead but of the national restoration of Israel.
37:16 *take a stick.* Ezekiel's last symbolic act involving a material object (cf. 4:1,3,9; 5:1). *write on it.* Zec 11:7 seems to be based on this passage in Ezekiel.
37:18 *Won't you tell us ... ?* The symbolic act successfully aroused the people's curiosity (see 12:9; 21:7; 24:19).
37:19 *they will become one in my hand.* God would duplicate Ezekiel's symbolic act by uniting the two kingdoms separated since Solomon's death (see 1Ki 12). For similar prophecies of the reunion of Israel, see 33:23,29; Jer 3:18; 23:5 – 6; Hos 1:11; Am 9:11.
37:22 *mountains of Israel.* See 6:2 – 3; 34:13; 36:1. *one king.* Only here and in v. 24 is the word "king" used of the future ruler. Usually "prince" is used (see note on 34:24), as in v. 25. See 7:27 and note; see also 44:3; 45:7 – 9 and frequently in chs. 45 – 48, where the ruler in the ideal age is always referred to as "prince."
37:23 *idols.* The old and basic offense (see note on 6:4). *backsliding.* Cf. Jer 2:19; 3:22. *cleanse.* Cf. 36:25 for the same notion. *my people ... their God.* See 11:20 and note.

24 “ ‘My servant David[b] will be king[c] over
them, and they will all have one shepherd.[d] They will follow my laws and be
careful to keep my decrees.[e] 25 They will
live in the land I gave to my servant Jacob, the land where your ancestors lived.[f]
They and their children and their children’s children will live there forever,[g]
and David my servant will be their prince
forever.[h] 26 I will make a covenant of peace[i]
with them; it will be an everlasting covenant.[j] I will establish them and increase
their numbers,[k] and I will put my sanctuary among them[l] forever.[m] 27 My dwelling
place[n] will be with them; I will be their
God, and they will be my people.[o] 28 Then
the nations will know that I the LORD make
Israel holy,[p] when my sanctuary is among
them forever.[q]’ ”

The LORD’s Great Victory Over the Nations

38 The word of the LORD came to
me: 2 “Son of man, set your face
against Gog,[r] of the land of Magog,[s] the
chief prince of[a] Meshek and Tubal;[t] prophesy against him 3 and say: ‘This is what
the Sovereign LORD says: I am against you,
Gog, chief prince of[b] Meshek and Tubal.[u]
4 I will turn you around, put hooks[v] in your
jaws and bring you out with your whole
army — your horses, your horsemen fully
armed, and a great horde with large and
small shields, all of them brandishing their
swords.[w] 5 Persia, Cush[c][x] and Put[y] will be
with them, all with shields and helmets,
6 also Gomer[z] with all its troops, and Beth
Togarmah[a] from the far north[b] with all its
troops — the many nations with you.
7 “ ‘Get ready; be prepared,[c] you and all
the hordes gathered about you, and take
command of them. 8 After many days[d] you
will be called to arms. In future years you
will invade a land that has recovered from
war, whose people were gathered from
many nations[e] to the mountains of Israel,

37:24 [b] Isa 55:4; Hos 3:5 [c] S 1Sa 13:14; S Isa 32:1 [d] Zec 13:7 [e] Ps 78:70-71; S Jer 30:21; S Eze 21:27 **37:25** [f] S Eze 28:25 [g] S Ezr 9:12; Am 9:15 [h] S Ps 89:3-4; Isa 11:1; S Eze 34:23-24 **37:26** [i] S Nu 25:12 [j] S Ge 9:16; S Dt 29:14; S Heb 13:20 [k] S Jer 30:19 [l] Lev 26:11 [m] S Eze 16:62 **37:27** [n] S Lev 26:11 [o] S Eze 34:30; S 36:28; S 2Co 6:16* **37:28** [p] S Ex 31:13 [q] Eze 43:9; Hos 1:10-11; Zep 3:15 **38:2** [r] ver 14; Eze 39:11 [s] S Ge 10:2 [t] S Eze 27:13 **38:3** [u] Eze 39:1

[a] 2 Or *the prince of Rosh,* [b] 3 Or *Gog, prince of Rosh,* [c] 5 That is, the upper Nile region

38:4 [v] S 2Ki 19:28 [w] S Isa 43:17; Eze 29:4; 39:2; Da 11:40 **38:5** [x] S Ge 10:6 [y] S Ge 10:6; S Eze 27:10 **38:6** [z] S Ge 10:2 [a] S Ge 10:3 [b] S Eze 32:30 **38:7** [c] S Isa 8:9 **38:8** [d] Isa 24:22 [e] S Isa 11:11

37:24–26 These verses appear to recall the Davidic covenant (v. 24a), the Sinaitic covenant (v. 24b) and the Abrahamic covenant (v. 25) — all of which will be fulfilled in the “covenant of peace” (v. 26).

37:24 *My servant David.* As in 34:23 (see note there) the coming Messianic ruler is called David because he would be a descendant of David and would achieve for Israel what David had — except more fully. *king.* See note on v. 22. *shepherd.* As in 34:23 the coming ruler is likened to a shepherd who cares for his flock (cf. Jn 10, especially v. 16).

37:25 *my servant Jacob.* See 28:25 and note.

37:26 *covenant of peace.* See vv. 24–26; 34:25 and notes. *everlasting covenant.* See note on 16:59–63. The phrase occurs 16 times in the OT, referring at times to the Noahic covenant (Ge 9:16), the Abrahamic (Ge 17:7,13,19), the Davidic (2Sa 23:5) and the “new” (Jer 32:40). Cf. the covenant with Phinehas (Nu 25:12–13). *put my sanctuary among them.* As he had done before. This word is further developed in Ezekiel’s vision of the future age, in which the rebuilt sanctuary would have central position (chs. 40–48). See vv. 27–28 and map, p. 1410.

37:27 *their God ... my people.* See note on Zec 8:8.

38:1—39:29 The great battle of the ages, when the future restoration of Israel under the reign of the house of David (ch. 37) evokes a massive coalition of world powers to destroy God’s kingdom. The vast host that comes against Jerusalem will end up as dead bodies strewn over the fields of the promised land, which will become the cemetery of all the enemy hordes that invade it (cf. ch. 39). Three prophecies against Gog (38:1–13,14–23; 39:1–16) are followed by the depiction of a great feast in which the enemy warriors are described in terms of sacrificial animals (39:17–20). Two final words put this great battle in the context of God’s ways with Israel in exile and restoration: (1) The nations will then know that Israel was carried into exile not because her God was incapable of protecting his own but because he had punished her for being unfaithful to him (39:21–24), and (2) Israel’s restoration following her punishment will show the nations that her God is truly the Holy One (39:25–29).

38:1 This statement, repeated often for receiving God’s word, stands as an introduction to chs. 38–39, which are a unit.

38:2 *Son of man.* See note on 2:1. *set your face.* See note on 20:46. *Gog.* Apparently a leader or king whose name appears only in chs. 38–39; Rev 20:8. Several identifications have been attempted, notably Gyges, king of Lydia (c. 660 BC). Possibly the name is purposely vague, standing for a mysterious, as yet undisclosed, enemy of God’s people. *of the land of Magog.* In Ge 10:2; 1Ch 1:5 Magog is one of the sons of Japheth, thus the name of a people. In Eze 39:6 it appears to refer to a people. But since the prefix *ma-* can mean “place of,” Magog may here simply mean “land of Gog.” Israel had long experienced the hostility of the Hamites and other Semitic peoples; the future coalition here envisioned will include — and in fact be led by — peoples descended from Japheth (cf. Ge 10). *chief prince.* Military commander-in-chief. The NIV text note gives the possible translation “prince of Rosh,” and if it is correct, Rosh is probably the name of an unknown people or place. Identification with Russia is unlikely and in any case cannot be proven. *Meshek and Tubal.* These sons of Japheth (see Ge 10:2 and note; 1Ch 1:5) are probably located in eastern Asia Minor (cf. 27:13; 32:26). They are peoples and territories to the north of Israel (cf. vv. 6,15; 39:2). As in the days of the Assyrians and Babylonians, the major attack will come from the north.

38:3 *I am against you.* See note on 5:8.

38:4 *I will turn you around.* Emphasis is on the fact that God is in complete control of all that is to follow. *put hooks in your jaws.* As with the pharaoh in 29:4, Gog is likened to a beast led around by God.

38:5 *Cush.* See NIV text note. The invading forces from the north (see v. 2 and note) are joined by armies from the south. *Put.* Libya.

38:6 *Gomer.* Another of Gog’s northern allies (see note on v. 2), mentioned in Ge 10:3 and 1Ch 1:6 as one of the sons of Japheth. According to non-Biblical sources, these peoples originated north of the Black Sea. *Beth Togarmah.* See note on 27:14. According to Ge 10:3 and 1Ch 1:6, Togarmah is one of the children of Gomer.

38:8 *After many days ... In future years.* After all the events of Israel’s restoration described in chs. 34–37 are completed.

which had long been desolate. They had been brought out from the nations, and now all of them live in safety.[f] 9You and all your troops and the many nations with you will go up, advancing like a storm;[g] you will be like a cloud[h] covering the land.[i]

10"'This is what the Sovereign LORD says: On that day thoughts will come into your mind[j] and you will devise an evil scheme.[k] 11You will say, "I will invade a land of unwalled villages; I will attack a peaceful and unsuspecting people[l]—all of them living without walls and without gates and bars.[m] 12I will plunder and loot and turn my hand against the resettled ruins and the people gathered from the nations, rich in livestock and goods, living at the center of the land.[a]" 13Sheba[n] and Dedan[o] and the merchants of Tarshish[p] and all her villages[b] will say to you, "Have you come to plunder? Have you gathered your hordes to loot, to carry off silver and gold, to take away livestock and goods and to seize much plunder?[q]"'

14"Therefore, son of man, prophesy and say to Gog: 'This is what the Sovereign LORD says: In that day, when my people Israel are living in safety,[r] will you not take notice of it? 15You will come from your place in the far north,[s] you and many nations with you, all of them riding on horses, a great horde, a mighty army.[t] 16You will advance against my people Israel like a cloud[u] that covers the land.[v] In days to come, Gog, I will bring you against my land, so that the nations may know me when I am proved holy[w] through you before their eyes.[x]

17"'This is what the Sovereign LORD says: You are the one I spoke of in former days by my servants the prophets of Israel. At that time they prophesied for years that I would bring you against them. 18This is what will happen in that day: When Gog attacks the land of Israel, my hot anger will be aroused, declares the Sovereign LORD. 19In my zeal and fiery wrath I declare that at that time there shall be a great earthquake[y] in the land of Israel.[z] 20The fish in the sea, the birds in the sky, the beasts of the field, every creature that moves along the ground, and all the people on the face of the earth will tremble[a] at my presence. The mountains will be overturned,[b] the cliffs will crumble[c] and every wall will fall to the ground.[d] 21I will summon a sword[e] against Gog on all my mountains, declares the Sovereign LORD. Every man's sword will be against his brother.[f] 22I will execute judgment[g] on him with plague and bloodshed;[h] I will pour down torrents of rain, hailstones[i] and burning sulfur[j] on him and on his troops and on the many nations with him.[k] 23And so I will show my greatness and my holiness, and I will make myself known in the sight of many nations. Then they will know that I am the LORD.[l]'

39 "Son of man, prophesy against Gog[m] and say: 'This is what the Sovereign LORD says: I am against you, Gog, chief prince of[c] Meshek[n] and Tubal.[o] 2I will turn you around and drag you along. I will bring you from the far north[p] and send you against the mountains of Israel.[q] 3Then I will strike your bow[r] from your left hand and make your arrows[s]

38:8 [f]ver 14; Jer 23:6; S Eze 28:26; Joel 3:1 **38:9** [g]Isa 25:4; 28:2 [h]ver 16; Jer 4:13; Joel 2:2 [i]Rev 20:8 **38:10** [j]S Jer 17:10 [k]Ps 36:4; Mic 2:1 **38:11** [l]S Ge 34:25 [m]Jer 49:31; Zec 2:4 **38:13** [n]S Ge 10:7 [o]S Ge 25:3 [p]S Ge 10:4 [q]Isa 10:6; 33:23; S Jer 15:13 **38:14** [r]S ver 8; S Lev 25:18; S Jer 16:15; Zec 2:5 **38:15** [s]Eze 32:30 [t]Eze 39:2; Rev 20:8 **38:16** [u]S ver 9 [v]Joel 3:11 [w]S Lev 10:3 [x]Isa 29:23; Eze 39:21 **38:19** [y]Isa 24:18; Joel 2:10; 3:16; S Rev 6:12 [z]Ps 18:7; S Eze 5:13; Hag 2:6,21 **38:20** [a]S Ex 15:14 [b]Isa 42:15 [c]Job 14:18 [d]S Ps 76:8; Hos 4:3; Na 1:5 **38:21** [e]Isa 66:16; Jer 25:29 [f]S 1Sa 14:20; S 2Ch 20:23; Hag 2:22 **38:22** [g]Isa 66:16; Jer 25:31; S Eze 36:5 [h]S Eze 14:19; S 28:23 [i]S Ex 9:18; Ps 18:12; Rev 16:21 [j]S Ge 19:24; S Rev 9:17 [k]S Eze 13:11 **38:23** [l]Eze 20:42; S 36:23; S 37:6 **39:1** [m]Rev 20:8 [n]S Ge 10:2 [o]S Eze 27:13; S 38:2,3 **39:2** [p]S Eze 32:30 [q]S Eze 38:4, 15 **39:3** [r]Hos 1:5; Am 2:15 [s]Ps 76:3

[a] 12 The Hebrew for this phrase means *the navel of the earth.* [b] 13 Or *her strong lions* [c] 1 Or *Gog, prince of Rosh,*

38:9 *like a cloud.* In Jer 4:13 Jeremiah similarly describes an invasion from the north.

38:10 *On that day.* A phrase also common to other prophetic writings; here it refers to the day of Gog's invasion of Israel. *thoughts will come into your mind.* The divine initiative (v. 4) is paralleled, as it often is in Scripture, by human action (cf. Dt 31:3; Isa 10:6–7). *evil scheme.* A raiding expedition (see v. 12).

38:11 *land of unwalled villages.* Speaks of a blissfully peaceful, ideal future time when walls will no longer be needed. See Zec 2:4–5 (and notes), which assumes, as does this passage, that the Lord alone is sufficient protection (cf. 36:35–36).

38:12 *center of the land.* The Hebrew for "center" also means "navel," a graphic image for the belief that Israel was the vital link between God and the world (the idea occurs also in 5:5). Since the Hebrew for "land" can also mean "earth," theologically Jerusalem is both the center of the land of Israel and the center of the world.

38:13 *Sheba.* Southwest corner of the Arabian peninsula (modern Yemen), known for trading (Job 6:19; see 23:42; 27:22; Ge 10:28 and note). *Dedan.* See note on 25:13. *Tarshish.* See note on 27:12.

38:16 *I am proved holy.* See Lev 10:3 and note.

38:17 *You are the one I spoke of.* Probably a general reference to earlier messages of divine judgment on the nations arrayed against God and his people (see note on v. 2, "Gog").

38:19 *earthquake.* Signaling the mighty presence of God, who comes to overwhelm the great army invading his land.

38:20 The fourfold listing of the animal world indicates the totality of nature (see note on 1:5; cf. Ge 9:2; 1Ki 4:33; Job 12:7–8 for similar listings).

38:21 *I will summon a sword.* God's sword of judgment (see 5:2 and note). *Every man's sword will be against his brother.* The coalition of Israel's enemies will turn on itself, as did the armies that attacked Judah in the time of Jehoshaphat (2Ch 20:22–23).

38:22 The list of divine weapons suggests that God will intervene directly, without the benefit of an earthly army.

39:1–16 The same basic events as those of ch. 38 are described, though some new details are added.

39:1 *Gog, chief prince of Meshek.* See note on 38:2.

39:2 *from the far north.* As in 38:6,15.

39:3 *bow.* Cf. Jer 6:23. The Lord will disarm Israel's enemies before they can shoot an arrow.

drop from your right hand. 4 On the mountains of Israel you will fall, you and all
your troops and the nations with you. I
will give you as food to all kinds of carrion birds[t] and to the wild animals.[u] 5 You
will fall in the open field, for I have spoken, declares the Sovereign LORD.[v] 6 I will
send fire[w] on Magog[x] and on those who
live in safety in the coastlands,[y] and they
will know[z] that I am the LORD.
7 " 'I will make known my holy name
among my people Israel. I will no longer
let my holy name be profaned,[a] and the
nations will know[b] that I the LORD am the
Holy One in Israel.[c] 8 It is coming! It will
surely take place, declares the Sovereign
LORD. This is the day[d] I have spoken of.
9 " 'Then those who live in the towns of
Israel will go out and use the weapons for
fuel and burn them up—the small and
large shields, the bows and arrows,[e] the
war clubs and spears. For seven years they
will use them for fuel.[f] 10 They will not need
to gather wood from the fields or cut it from
the forests, because they will use the weapons for fuel. And they will plunder[g] those
who plundered them and loot those who
looted them, declares the Sovereign LORD.[h]
11 " 'On that day I will give Gog a burial place in Israel, in the valley of those
who travel east of the Sea. It will block the
way of travelers, because Gog and all his
hordes will be buried[i] there. So it will be
called the Valley of Hamon Gog.[a][j]
12 " 'For seven months the Israelites will
be burying them in order to cleanse the
land.[k] 13 All the people of the land will
bury them, and the day I display my glory[l] will be a memorable day for them, declares the Sovereign LORD. 14 People will
be continually employed in cleansing the
land. They will spread out across the land
and, along with others, they will bury any
bodies that are lying on the ground.
" 'After the seven months they will carry
out a more detailed search. 15 As they go
through the land, anyone who sees a human bone will leave a marker beside it until the gravediggers bury it in the Valley of
Hamon Gog, 16 near a town called Hamonah.[b] And so they will cleanse the land.'
17 "Son of man, this is what the Sovereign LORD says: Call out to every kind of
bird[m] and all the wild animals: 'Assemble
and come together from all around to the
sacrifice I am preparing for you, the great
sacrifice on the mountains of Israel. There
you will eat flesh and drink blood.[n] 18 You
will eat the flesh of mighty men and drink
the blood of the princes of the earth as
if they were rams and lambs, goats and
bulls—all of them fattened animals from
Bashan.[o] 19 At the sacrifice[p] I am preparing for you, you will eat fat till you are
glutted and drink blood till you are drunk.
20 At my table you will eat your fill of horses and riders, mighty men and soldiers of
every kind,' declares the Sovereign LORD.[q]
21 "I will display my glory among the
nations, and all the nations will see the
punishment I inflict and the hand I lay on
them.[r] 22 From that day forward the people
of Israel will know that I am the LORD their
God. 23 And the nations will know that the

39:4 [t] S Ge 40:19 [u] ver 17-20; S Jer 25:33; S Eze 29:5; S 33:27 **39:5** [v] S Eze 32:4 **39:6** [w] S Eze 30:8; Rev 20:9 [x] S Ge 10:2 [y] S Jer 25:22 [z] S Ex 6:7 **39:7** [a] S Ex 20:7; S Eze 13:19 [b] S Isa 49:26 [c] S Isa 12:6; S 54:5; S Eze 20:9; S 36:16, 23 **39:8** [d] Eze 7:6 **39:9** [e] Ps 76:3 [f] S Ps 46:9 **39:10** [g] S Ex 3:22 [h] S Isa 14:2; S 33:1; Hab 2:8 **39:11** [i] S Isa 34:3 [j] S Eze 38:2 **39:12** [k] Dt 21:23 **39:13** [l] Eze 28:22 **39:17** [m] S Job 15:23 [n] S Eze 32:4 **39:18** [o] S Ps 22:12; Jer 51:40 **39:19** [p] S Lev 3:9 **39:20** [q] S Isa 56:9; S Jer 12:9; Rev 19:17-18 **39:21** [r] Ex 9:16; Isa 37:20; S Eze 38:16

[a] *11 Hamon Gog* means *hordes of Gog.* [b] *16 Hamonah* means *horde.*

39:4 *food to all kinds of carrion birds.* A theme expanded in vv. 17–20.
39:6 *I will send fire.* See 20:47 and note.
39:7 *no longer let my holy name be profaned.* See Lev 18:21 and note. *the Holy One.* See Lev 11:44 and note.
39:9 *seven.* A symbolic number stressing the size of the invading armies and the finality of this great battle against God's people, though some understand "seven years" literally.
39:11 *valley.* Probably that of Jezreel/Megiddo, which runs from the Mediterranean in the west to the Jordan River in the east. *the Sea.* Probably the Mediterranean. *Hamon Gog.* See NIV text note.
39:12 *seven.* Cf. v. 9 and note. *cleanse the land.* Ritual purity is a basic element in Ezekiel's theology (see 22:26; 24:13; 36:25,33; 37:23). Corpses were especially unclean (see Lev 5:2; 21:1,11; 22:4; Nu 5:2; 6:6–12; 19:16; 31:19).
39:13 *people of the land.* See 7:27 and note, though here a special class may not be implied.
39:14 *People will be continually employed.* After the seven-month burial period observed by all the people, special squads will be hired full-time to ensure total cleansing of the land—by marking for burial any human bones that may have been missed. Total ritual purity is the aim.
39:17–20 These verses involve a restating of vv. 9–16, employing a different figure of speech (see Isa 34:6 and note; Jer 46:10; Zep 1:7). The metaphor of sacrifice suggests a consecration to the Lord in judgment, as with Jericho (see Jos 6:17 and NIV text note there).
39:18 *You will eat the flesh of mighty men.* A gory description of what birds of prey commonly do (see previous note and Rev 19:17–21). *as if they were.* The bodies of the victims are compared to animals commonly used for sacrifices. *Bashan.* Rich pastureland east of the Sea of Galilee, known for its sleek cattle (Dt 32:14; Ps 22:12; Am 4:1) and its oak trees (27:6; Isa 2:13).
39:19 *eat fat … drink blood.* Further indication that this is the Lord's sacrificial feast, in that fat and blood were normally reserved for God (see 44:15; see also Lev 3:16; 1Sa 2:15 ; Isa 34:6 and notes).
39:20 *my table.* Sacrificial altar. See 40:38–43 and 41:22 for description of the tables in the new temple.
39:21 *my glory.* God's visible presence in the world (see note on 1:28). Here that visibility is due to divine intervention in history.
39:22–23 *the people of Israel will know … And the nations will know.* As God had made himself known to Israel and the nations through his saving acts in Israel's behalf (see Ex 6:7; 7:5,17; 10:2; 14:18; 16:6–7,12; Jos 3:10; 4:24; cf. Jos 2:9–11; 5:1), so now Israel and the nations see him at work as he judges his people for their sin (see v. 27; 6:7 and note).
39:23 *I hid my face.* Expression of divine displeasure (see Ps 13:1 and note; 30:7; Isa 54:8; 57:17).

people of Israel went into exile for their
sin, because they were unfaithful to me.
So I hid my face from them and handed
them over to their enemies, and they all
fell by the sword.[s] 24 I dealt with them according to their uncleanness and their offenses, and I hid my face from them.[t]
25 "Therefore this is what the Sovereign
LORD says: I will now restore the fortunes
of Jacob[a][u] and will have compassion[v] on
all the people of Israel, and I will be zealous for my holy name.[w] 26 They will forget
their shame and all the unfaithfulness they
showed toward me when they lived in
safety[x] in their land with no one to make
them afraid.[y] 27 When I have brought them
back from the nations and have gathered
them from the countries of their enemies,
I will be proved holy through them in the
sight of many nations.[z] 28 Then they will
know that I am the LORD their God, for
though I sent them into exile among the
nations, I will gather them[a] to their own
land, not leaving any behind.[b] 29 I will no
longer hide my face[c] from them, for I will
pour out my Spirit[d] on the people of Israel,
declares the Sovereign LORD.[e]"

The Temple Area Restored

40 In the twenty-fifth year of our exile,
at the beginning of the year, on the
tenth of the month, in the fourteenth year
after the fall of the city[f]—on that very day
the hand of the LORD was on me[g] and he
took me there. 2 In visions[h] of God he took
me to the land of Israel and set me on a
very high mountain,[i] on whose south side
were some buildings that looked like a
city. 3 He took me there, and I saw a man
whose appearance was like bronze;[j] he
was standing in the gateway with a lin-
en cord and a measuring rod[k] in his hand.
4 The man said to me, "Son of man, look
carefully and listen closely and pay attention to everything I am going to show you,[l]
for that is why you have been brought
here. Tell[m] the people of Israel everything
you see.[n]"

The East Gate to the Outer Court

5 I saw a wall completely surrounding
the temple area. The length of the measuring rod in the man's hand was six long
cubits,[b] each of which was a cubit and a
handbreadth. He measured[o] the wall; it
was one measuring rod thick and one rod
high.
6 Then he went to the east gate.[p] He
climbed its steps and measured the threshold of the gate; it was one rod deep. 7 The
alcoves[q] for the guards were one rod long

39:23 [s] Isa 1:15; 59:2; S Jer 22:8-9; S 44:23 **39:24** [t] 2Ki 17:23; Jer 2:17, 19; 4:18; S Eze 7:22; Da 9:7 **39:25** [u] S Jer 33:7 [v] S Jer 30:18 [w] Isa 27:12-13; S Eze 16:53 **39:26** [x] S 1Ki 4:25; S Jer 32:37; S Eze 38:8 [y] Isa 17:2; Eze 34:28; Mic 4:4 **39:27** [z] S Eze 37:21 **39:28** [a] Ps 147:2 [b] S Eze 36:23, 36 **39:29** [c] S Dt 31:17 [d] S Isa 11:2; S Eze 37:9; S Ac 2:17 [e] S Eze 16:42 **40:1** [f] S 2Ki 25:7; Jer 39:1-10; 52:4-11 [g] S Eze 1:3; S 29:17 **40:2** [h] S Ex 24:10; Da 7:1, 7 [i] S Jer 31:12; S Eze 17:22; Rev 21:10 **40:3** [j] S Eze 1:7; Rev 1:15 [k] Eze 47:3; Zec 2:1-2; Rev 11:1; 21:15 **40:4** [l] S Dt 6:6 [m] Jer 26:2 [n] Eze 44:5 **40:5** [o] Eze 42:20 **40:6** [p] S Eze 8:16 **40:7** [q] ver 36

[a] 25 Or *now bring Jacob back from captivity* [b] 5 That is, about 11 feet or about 3.2 meters; also in verse 12. The long cubit of about 21 inches or about 53 centimeters is the basic unit of measurement of length throughout chapters 40–48.

39:24 *their uncleanness and their offenses.* Spelled out especially in ch. 22, but also throughout chs. 6–24.

39:25 *Jacob.* The nation of Israel, as in 20:5. *my holy name.* See 20:9 and note.

39:26 *They will forget their shame.* The remembrance of shame previously called for (6:9; 20:43; 36:31) is here erased.

39:27 *I will be proved holy through them.* God will reveal himself anew in a restored, holy people (see Lev 10:3 and note).

39:28 *know that I am the LORD.* See note on vv. 22–23.

39:29 *I will pour out my Spirit.* The gift of God's enabling Spirit (see 36:27; 37:14; see also notes on 2:2; Joel 2:28).

40:1—48:35 The restoration of Israel as a purified people calls for a purified land and a new order in the commonwealth of the people of God. This is the subject of Ezekiel's last vision, which presents an idealized picture of the new order to be put in place. For the basic outline of the vision's various topics, see Introduction: Outline under "The New Order for Purified Israel," as well as the summary (overview) notes below.

40:1–47 Restoration of the temple area.

40:1 *twenty-fifth year ... beginning ... tenth.* Apr. 28, 573 BC. *of our exile.* All the dates in the book of Ezekiel (see chart, p. 1336) are reckoned from the 597 exile, but only here and in 33:21 is the exile specifically mentioned (see 1:2). *the beginning of the year.* Hebrew *Rosh Hashanah,* the well-known Jewish New Year festival. It had long occurred in the fall (in either September or October), but since throughout the book Ezekiel uses a different and older religious calendar, the spring date as given above is correct (see note on Lev 23:24). *hand of the LORD was on me.* See note on 1:3.

40:2 *visions of God.* Introduces all three of Ezekiel's major visions (see 1:1; 8:3). *very high mountain.* Mount Zion, also seen as extraordinarily high in other prophetic visions (17:22; Isa 2:2; Mic 4:1; Zec 14:10). Height here signifies importance, as the earthly seat of God's reign. *on whose south side.* With the city located on its southern slopes, the mountain is to the north (cf. Ps 48; see Ps 48:2 and note).

40:3 *like bronze.* Indicates that the man was other than human. *in the gateway.* Presumably of the outer court (see vv. 17–19). *linen cord.* Used for longer measurements, such as those in 47:3. *measuring rod.* Used for shorter measurements—about ten feet and four inches long.

40:5 *wall completely surrounding the temple area.* Separating the sacred from the secular. *six long cubits.* In using the long cubit (seven handbreadths, or about 21 inches), which was older than the shorter cubit (six handbreadths, or about 18 inches), Ezekiel was returning to more ancient standards for the new community (see 2Ch 3:3).

40:6 *east gate.* The gate of the outer court. The three gates (east, north, south) of the outer court were similar to the three in the inner court (v. 32), having six alcoves for the guards (three on each side) and a portico (vv. 8–9). Comparable gate plans have been discovered at Megiddo, Gezer and Hazor, all dating from the time of Solomon (see 1Ki 9:15 and note). The guards kept out anyone who might profane the temple area (see Ezr 2:62). *climbed its steps.* The first of three sets of stairs leading to the temple. This one had seven steps (v. 22); the next one (inner court), eight (v. 31); the last (temple), ten (v. 49; see NIV text note there)—possibly indicating increasing degrees of "holiness" (sacredness).

and one rod wide, and the projecting
walls between the alcoves were five cubits[a] thick. And the threshold of the gate
next to the portico facing the temple was
one rod deep.
8 Then he measured the portico of the
gateway; 9 it[b] was eight cubits[c] deep and
its jambs were two cubits[d] thick. The portico of the gateway faced the temple.
10 Inside the east gate were three alcoves
on each side; the three had the same measurements, and the faces of the projecting
walls on each side had the same measurements. 11 Then he measured the width of
the entrance of the gateway; it was ten
cubits and its length was thirteen cubits.[e]
12 In front of each alcove was a wall one

[a] *7* That is, about 8 3/4 feet or about 2.7 meters; also in verse 48 [b] *8,9* Many Hebrew manuscripts, Septuagint, Vulgate and Syriac; most Hebrew manuscripts *gateway facing the temple; it was one rod deep. 9Then he measured the portico of the gateway; it* [c] *9* That is, about 14 feet or about 4.2 meters [d] *9* That is, about 3 1/2 feet or about 1 meter [e] *11* That is, about 18 feet wide and 23 feet long or about 5.3 meters wide and 6.9 meters long

40:9 *portico of the gateway faced the temple.* The reverse position of the porticoes of the inner court gates, which faced away from the temple (v. 34).

40:10 *three alcoves.* The alcoves for the guards, mentioned in v. 7.

EZEKIEL'S TEMPLE

Ezekiel uses a long or "royal" cubit, about 21 inches or 53 centimeters ("cubit and a handbreadth," Eze 40:5) as opposed to the standard Hebrew cubit of about 18 inches or 46 centimeters.

Scripture describes a floor plan but provides few height dimensions. This artwork shows an upward projection of the temple over the floor plan. This temple existed only in a vision of Ezekiel (Eze 40:2) and was never actually built as were the temples of Solomon, Zerubbabel and Herod, but some premillennial interpreters believe that it will be built in the future.

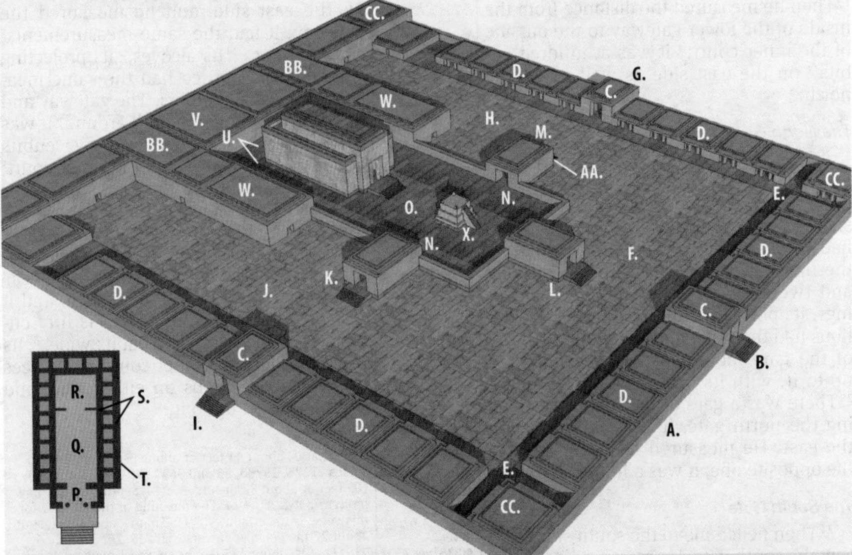

A. Wall (40:5,16–20)
B. East gate (40:6–14,16)
C. Portico (40:8)
D. Outer court (40:17)
E. Pavement (40:17)
F. East inner court (40:19)
G. North gate (40:20–22)
H. North inner court (40:23)
I. South gate (40:24–26)
J. South inner court (40:27)
K. Gateway (40:28–31)
L. Gateway (40:32–34)
M. Gateway (40:35–38)
N. Priests' rooms (40:44–45)
O. Court (40:47)
P. Temple portico (40:48–49)
Q. Outer sanctuary (41:1–2)
R. Most Holy Place (41:3–4)
S. Temple walls (41:5–7,9,11)
T. Base (41:8)
U. Open area (41:10)
V. West building (41:12)
W. Priests' rooms (42:1–10)
X. Altar (43:13–17)
AA. Rooms for preparing sacrifices (40:39–43)
BB. Ovens (46:19–20)
CC. Kitchens (46:21–24)

cubit high, and the alcoves were six cubits square. 13 Then he measured the gateway from the top of the rear wall of one alcove to the top of the opposite one; the distance was twenty-five cubits[a] from one parapet opening to the opposite one. 14 He measured along the faces of the projecting walls all around the inside of the gateway—sixty cubits.[b] The measurement was up to the portico[c] facing the courtyard.[d][r] 15 The distance from the entrance of the gateway to the far end of its portico was fifty cubits.[e] 16 The alcoves and the projecting walls inside the gateway were surmounted by narrow parapet openings all around, as was the portico; the openings all around faced inward. The faces of the projecting walls were decorated with palm trees.[s]

The Outer Court

17 Then he brought me into the outer court.[t] There I saw some rooms and a pavement that had been constructed all around the court; there were thirty rooms[u] along the pavement.[v] 18 It abutted the sides of the gateways and was as wide as they were long; this was the lower pavement. 19 Then he measured the distance from the inside of the lower gateway to the outside of the inner court;[w] it was a hundred cubits[f][x] on the east side as well as on the north.

The North Gate

20 Then he measured the length and width of the north gate, leading into the outer court. 21 Its alcoves[y]—three on each side—its projecting walls and its portico[z] had the same measurements as those of the first gateway. It was fifty cubits long and twenty-five cubits wide. 22 Its openings, its portico[a] and its palm tree decorations had the same measurements as those of the gate facing east. Seven steps led up to it, with its portico opposite them.[b] 23 There was a gate to the inner court facing the north gate, just as there was on the east. He measured from one gate to the opposite one; it was a hundred cubits.[c]

The South Gate

24 Then he led me to the south side and I saw the south gate. He measured its jambs and its portico, and they had the same measurements[d] as the others. 25 The gateway and its portico had narrow openings all around, like the openings of the others. It was fifty cubits long and twenty-five cubits wide.[e] 26 Seven steps led up to it, with its portico opposite them; it had palm tree decorations on the faces of the projecting walls on each side.[f] 27 The inner court[g] also had a gate facing south, and he measured from this gate to the outer gate on the south side; it was a hundred cubits.[h]

The Gates to the Inner Court

28 Then he brought me into the inner court through the south gate, and he measured the south gate; it had the same measurements[i] as the others. 29 Its alcoves,[j] its projecting walls and its portico had the same measurements as the others. The gateway and its portico had openings all around. It was fifty cubits long and twenty-five cubits wide.[k] 30 (The porticoes[l] of the gateways around the inner court were twenty-five cubits wide and five cubits deep.) 31 Its portico[m] faced the outer court; palm trees decorated its jambs, and eight steps led up to it.[n]

32 Then he brought me to the inner court on the east side, and he measured the gateway; it had the same measurements[o] as the others. 33 Its alcoves,[p] its projecting walls and its portico had the same measurements as the others. The gateway and its portico had openings all around. It was fifty cubits long and twenty-five cubits wide. 34 Its portico[q] faced the outer court; palm trees decorated the jambs on either side, and eight steps led up to it.

35 Then he brought me to the north gate[r] and measured it. It had the same measurements[s] as the others, 36 as did its alcoves,[t] its projecting walls and its portico, and it had openings all around. It was fifty cubits long and twenty-five cubits wide. 37 Its portico[g][u] faced the outer court; palm trees decorated the jambs on either side, and eight steps led up to it.[v]

40:14 [r] S Ex 27:9 **40:16** [s] ver 21-22; 2Ch 3:5; Eze 41:26 **40:17** [t] Rev 11:2 [u] Eze 41:6 [v] Eze 42:1 **40:19** [w] Eze 46:1 [x] ver 23,27 **40:21** [y] ver 7 [z] ver 30 **40:22** [a] ver 49 [b] S ver 16,26 **40:23** [c] S ver 19 **40:24** [d] ver 32, 35 **40:25** [e] ver 33 **40:26** [f] S ver 22 **40:27** [g] ver 32 [h] S ver 19 **40:28** [i] ver 35 **40:29** [j] ver 7 [k] ver 25 **40:30** [l] ver 21 **40:31** [m] ver 22 [n] ver 34,37 **40:32** [o] S ver 24 **40:33** [p] ver 7 **40:34** [q] ver 22 **40:35** [r] Eze 44:4; 47:2 [s] S ver 24 **40:36** [t] ver 7 **40:37** [u] ver 22 [v] ver 34

[a] *13* That is, about 44 feet or about 13 meters; also in verses 21, 25, 29, 30, 33 and 36 [b] *14* That is, about 105 feet or about 32 meters [c] *14* Septuagint; Hebrew *projecting wall* [d] *14* The meaning of the Hebrew for this verse is uncertain. [e] *15* That is, about 88 feet or about 27 meters; also in verses 21, 25, 29, 33 and 36 [f] *19* That is, about 175 feet or about 53 meters; also in verses 23, 27 and 47 [g] *37* Septuagint (see also verses 31 and 34); Hebrew *jambs*

40:16 *palm trees.* As in Solomon's temple (see 1Ki 6:29,32,35 and note on 6:29).
40:17 *thirty rooms.* The exact location of these rooms is not given. They were probably intended for the people's use (see Jer 35:2,4 and note on 35:2).
40:19 *hundred cubits.* Over 170 feet (see note on v. 5) separated the outer wall from the inner wall and was the width of the outer court.
40:20 *north gate.* Both it and the south gate (v. 24) were identical to the east gate (see note on v. 6).
40:22 *Seven steps.* See note on v. 6.
40:28 *south gate.* Of the inner wall, which is not described but must be assumed. *it had the same measurements as the others.* In both the outer walls (see note on v. 6).
40:34 *eight steps.* See note on v. 6.

The Rooms for Preparing Sacrifices

38 A room with a doorway was by the
portico in each of the inner gateways,
where the burnt offerings[w] were washed.
39 In the portico of the gateway were two
tables on each side, on which the burnt offerings,[x] sin offerings[a][y] and guilt offerings[z]
were slaughtered.[a] 40 By the outside wall of
the portico of the gateway, near the steps at
the entrance of the north gateway were two
tables, and on the other side of the steps
were two tables. 41 So there were four tables
on one side of the gateway and four on the
other—eight tables in all—on which the
sacrifices were slaughtered. 42 There were
also four tables of dressed stone[b] for the
burnt offerings, each a cubit and a half
long, a cubit and a half wide and a cubit
high.[b] On them were placed the utensils
for slaughtering the burnt offerings and
the other sacrifices.[c] 43 And double-pronged
hooks, each a handbreadth[c] long, were attached to the wall all around. The tables
were for the flesh of the offerings.

The Rooms for the Priests

44 Outside the inner gate, within the inner court, were two rooms, one[d] at the
side of the north gate and facing south,
and another at the side of the south[e] gate
and facing north. 45 He said to me, "The
room facing south is for the priests who
guard the temple,[d] 46 and the room facing
north[e] is for the priests who guard the altar.[f] These are the sons of Zadok,[g] who are
the only Levites who may draw near to the
LORD to minister before him.[h]"
47 Then he measured the court: It was
square—a hundred cubits long and a
hundred cubits wide. And the altar was in
front of the temple.[i]

The New Temple

48 He brought me to the portico of the
temple[j] and measured the jambs of the
portico; they were five cubits wide on either side. The width of the entrance was
fourteen cubits[f] and its projecting walls
were[g] three cubits[h] wide on either side.
49 The portico[k] was twenty cubits[i] wide,
and twelve[j] cubits[k] from front to back.
It was reached by a flight of stairs,[l] and
there were pillars[l] on each side of the
jambs.

41 Then the man brought me to the
main hall[m] and measured the
jambs; the width of the jambs was six cubits[m] on each side.[n] 2 The entrance was ten
cubits[o] wide, and the projecting walls on
each side of it were five cubits[p] wide. He
also measured the main hall; it was forty
cubits long and twenty cubits wide.[q][n]
3 Then he went into the inner sanctuary
and measured the jambs of the entrance;
each was two cubits[r] wide. The entrance
was six cubits wide, and the projecting
walls on each side of it were seven cubits[s]
wide. 4 And he measured the length of the
inner sanctuary; it was twenty cubits, and
its width was twenty cubits across the end
of the main hall.[o] He said to me, "This is
the Most Holy Place.[p]"
5 Then he measured the wall of the temple; it was six cubits thick, and each side
room around the temple was four cubits[t]

40:38 [w] S 2Ch 4:6; Eze 42:13 **40:39** [x] Eze 46:2 [y] Lev 4:3,28 [z] S Lev 7:1 [a] ver 42 **40:42** [b] Ex 20:25 [c] ver 39 **40:45** [d] 1Ch 9:23 **40:46** [e] Eze 42:13 [f] Nu 18:5 [g] S 2Sa 8:17; S Ezr 7:2 [h] Nu 16:5; Eze 43:19; 44:15; 45:4; 48:11 **40:47** [i] Eze 41:13-14 **40:48** [j] 1Ki 6:2 **40:49** [k] ver 22; 1Ki 6:3 [l] S 1Ki 7:15 **41:1** [m] ver 23 **41:2** [n] 2Ch 3:3 **41:4** [o] 1Ki 6:20 [p] S Ex 26:33; Heb 9:3-8

[a] 39 Or *purification offerings* [b] 42 That is, about 2 2/3 feet long and wide and 21 inches high or about 80 centimeters long and wide and 53 centimeters high [c] 43 That is, about 3 1/2 inches or about 9 centimeters [d] 44 Septuagint; Hebrew *were rooms for singers, which were* [e] 44 Septuagint; Hebrew *east* [f] 48 That is, about 25 feet or about 7.4 meters [g] 48 Septuagint; Hebrew *entrance was* [h] 48 That is, about 5 1/4 feet or about 1.6 meters [i] 49 That is, about 35 feet or about 11 meters [j] 49 Septuagint; Hebrew *eleven* [k] 49 That is, about 21 feet or about 6.4 meters [l] 49 Hebrew; Septuagint *Ten steps led up to it* [m] 1 That is, about 11 feet or about 3.2 meters; also in verses 3, 5 and 8 [n] 1 One Hebrew manuscript and Septuagint; most Hebrew manuscripts *side, the width of the tent* [o] 2 That is, about 18 feet or about 5.3 meters [p] 2 That is, about 8 3/4 feet or about 2.7 meters; also in verses 9, 11 and 12 [q] 2 That is, about 70 feet long and 35 feet wide or about 21 meters long and 11 meters wide [r] 3 That is, about 3 1/2 feet or about 1.1 meters; also in verse 22 [s] 3 That is, about 12 feet or about 3.7 meters [t] 5 That is, about 7 feet or about 2.1 meters

40:38 *portico in each of the inner gateways.* The porticoes of the inner gateways were on the side of the outer court, facing away from the temple. *washed.* The inner parts and the legs were washed (Lev 1:9).

40:39 *burnt offerings.* Probably one of the oldest kinds of sacrifice. The entire animal was burned in consecration to God (see note on Lev 1:3). *sin offerings and guilt offerings.* Discussed in Lev 4–7 (see notes there). The fellowship offerings, which were more festive, are notable by their absence from this listing (see 43:27; 45:17; 46:2,12; see also chart, p. 164).

40:46 *sons of Zadok.* For the distinction between the sons of Zadok and the Levites, see the fuller discussion in the notes on 44:15–31.

40:47 *altar.* Described in 43:13–17 (see notes there).

40:48—42:20 Description of the new temple (see diagram, p. 1399).

40:48 *portico.* Similar to the portico in Solomon's temple but slightly larger (see 1Ki 6:3).

40:49 *pillars.* Called Jakin and Boaz in Solomon's temple (see 1Ki 7:21 and NIV text notes).

41:1 *main hall.* Or nave, the largest of the three rooms comprising the temple (see 1Ki 6:3–5). This main hall was identical in size to Solomon's (see 1Ki 6:17).

41:3 *he went into the inner sanctuary.* Only the angel, not Ezekiel, entered the Most Holy Place. Lev 16 forbids any but the high priest to enter it, and then only once a year (see Heb 9:7 and note). *six cubits wide.* Note the progressive narrowing of the door openings as one approaches the inner sanctuary (40:48, 14 cubits; 41:2, 10 cubits; here, 6 cubits).

41:4 *Most Holy Place.* See notes on Ex 26:31–35; 27:12–13; 1Ki 6:2,23; 2Ch 3:8; Ezr 6:15; Ps 28:2; Mt 27:51; Heb 8:2; 10:19–20.

wide. 6 The side rooms were on three levels, one above another, thirty[q] on each level. There were ledges all around the wall of the temple to serve as supports for the side rooms, so that the supports were not inserted into the wall of the temple.[r] 7 The side rooms all around the temple were wider at each successive level. The structure surrounding the temple was built in ascending stages, so that the rooms widened as one went upward. A stairway[s] went up from the lowest floor to the top floor through the middle floor.

8 I saw that the temple had a raised base all around it, forming the foundation of the side rooms. It was the length of the rod, six long cubits. 9 The outer wall of the side rooms was five cubits thick. The open area between the side rooms of the temple 10 and the priests' rooms was twenty cubits wide all around the temple. 11 There were entrances to the side rooms from the open area, one on the north and another on the south; and the base adjoining the open area was five cubits wide all around.

12 The building facing the temple courtyard on the west side was seventy cubits[a] wide. The wall of the building was five cubits thick all around, and its length was ninety cubits.[b]

13 Then he measured the temple; it was a hundred cubits[c] long, and the temple courtyard and the building with its walls were also a hundred cubits long. 14 The width of the temple courtyard on the east, including the front of the temple, was a hundred cubits.[t]

15 Then he measured the length of the building facing the courtyard at the rear of the temple, including its galleries[u] on each side; it was a hundred cubits.

The main hall, the inner sanctuary and the portico facing the court, 16 as well as the thresholds and the narrow windows[v] and galleries around the three of them—everything beyond and including the threshold was covered with wood. The floor, the wall up to the windows, and the windows were covered.[w] 17 In the space above the outside of the entrance to the inner sanctuary and on the walls at regular intervals all around the inner and outer sanctuary 18 were carved[x] cherubim[y] and palm trees.[z] Palm trees alternated with cherubim. Each cherub had two faces:[a] 19 the face of a human being toward the palm tree on one side and the face of a lion toward the palm tree on the other. They were carved all around the whole temple.[b] 20 From the floor to the area above the entrance, cherubim and palm trees were carved on the wall of the main hall.

21 The main hall[c] had a rectangular doorframe, and the one at the front of the Most Holy Place was similar. 22 There was a wooden altar[d] three cubits[d] high and two cubits square[e]; its corners, its base[f] and its sides were of wood. The man said to me, "This is the table[e] that is before the LORD." 23 Both the main hall[f] and the Most Holy Place had double doors.[g] 24 Each door had two leaves—two hinged leaves[h] for each door. 25 And on the doors of the main hall were carved cherubim and palm trees like those carved on the walls, and there was a wooden overhang on the front of the portico. 26 On the sidewalls of the portico were narrow windows with palm trees carved on each side. The side rooms of the temple also had overhangs.[i]

The Rooms for the Priests

42 Then the man led me northward into the outer court and brought me to the rooms[j] opposite the temple courtyard[k] and opposite the outer wall on the north side.[l] 2 The building whose door faced north was a hundred cubits long and fifty cubits wide.[g] 3 Both in the section twenty cubits[h] from the inner court and in the section opposite the pavement of the outer court, gallery[m] faced gallery at the three levels.[n] 4 In front of the rooms was an inner passageway ten cubits wide and

41:6 [q] Eze 40:17 [r] S 1Ki 6:5 **41:7** [s] 1Ki 6:8 **41:14** [t] Eze 40:47 **41:15** [u] Eze 42:3 **41:16** [v] 1Ki 6:4 [w] ver 25-26; 1Ki 6:15; Eze 42:3
41:18 [x] S 1Ki 6:18 [y] Ex 37:7; S 2Ch 3:7 [z] S 1Ki 6:29; 7:36 [a] Eze 10:21 **41:19** [b] S Eze 10:14 **41:21** [c] ver 1 **41:22** [d] S Ex 30:1 [e] S Ex 25:23; S Eze 23:41 **41:23** [f] ver 1 [g] 1Ki 6:32 **41:24** [h] 1Ki 6:34 **41:26** [i] ver 15-16; Eze 40:16 **42:1** [j] ver 13 [k] S Ex 27:9; Eze 41:12-14 [l] Eze 40:17 **42:3** [m] Eze 41:15 [n] Eze 41:16

[a] *12* That is, about 123 feet or about 37 meters
[b] *12* That is, about 158 feet or about 48 meters
[c] *13* That is, about 175 feet or about 53 meters; also in verses 14 and 15
[d] *22* That is, about 5 1/4 feet or about 1.5 meters
[e] *22* Septuagint; Hebrew *long*
[f] *22* Septuagint; Hebrew *length*
[g] *2* That is, about 175 feet long and 88 feet wide or about 53 meters long and 27 meters wide
[h] *3* That is, about 35 feet or about 11 meters

41:6 *thirty on each level.* These 90 side rooms were probably storerooms for the priests, possibly for the tithes (see Mal 3:10 and note).
41:13 *hundred.* The 100-cubit symmetry stood for perfection.
41:16 *everything ... was covered with wood.* As in Solomon's temple (1Ki 6:15).
41:18 *cherubim.* Who served as guards (cf. Ge 3:24 and note). These, as opposed to those mentioned in ch. 10 (see note on 1:5), have only two faces—a man's and a lion's (see 1Ki 6:29,32,35).
41:22 *wooden altar.* As the altar of burnt offering stood outside the temple proper (43:13–17), so a smaller altar (3'5" square by 5' high) stood outside the Most Holy Place. It served as a table, no doubt to hold the bread of the Presence (see Ex 25:30; Lev 24:5–9; 1Ki 7:48 and notes). Ezekiel makes no mention of an altar of incense or of lampstands, such as were found in Solomon's temple and in the tabernacle before it. Also not included are the "Sea" (1Ki 7:23) and the ark of the covenant (see notes on Ezr 6:15; Jer 3:16).
41:23 *double doors.* Folding doors, so that the entry could be made still narrower.
42:1 *rooms opposite the temple courtyard.* Their function is described in vv. 13–14. They have no parallel in Solomon's temple as described in 1Ki 6.

a hundred cubits[a] long.[b] Their doors were
on the north.[o] 5Now the upper rooms were
narrower, for the galleries took more space
from them than from the rooms on the
lower and middle floors of the building.
6The rooms on the top floor had no pillars, as the courts had; so they were smaller in floor space than those on the lower
and middle floors. 7There was an outer
wall parallel to the rooms and the outer
court; it extended in front of the rooms for
fifty cubits. 8While the row of rooms on
the side next to the outer court was fifty
cubits long, the row on the side nearest
the sanctuary was a hundred cubits long.
9The lower rooms had an entrance[p] on the
east side as one enters them from the outer court.
10On the south side[c] along the length of
the wall of the outer court, adjoining the
temple courtyard[q] and opposite the outer
wall, were rooms[r] 11with a passageway in
front of them. These were like the rooms
on the north; they had the same length
and width, with similar exits and dimensions. Similar to the doorways on the
north 12were the doorways of the rooms
on the south. There was a doorway at the
beginning of the passageway that was parallel to the corresponding wall extending
eastward, by which one enters the rooms.
13Then he said to me, "The north[s] and
south rooms[t] facing the temple courtyard[u]
are the priests' rooms, where the priests
who approach the LORD will eat the most
holy offerings. There they will put the
most holy offerings—the grain offerings,[v]
the sin offerings[d][w] and the guilt offerings[x]—for the place is holy.[y] 14Once the
priests enter the holy precincts, they are
not to go into the outer court until they
leave behind the garments[z] in which they
minister, for these are holy. They are to
put on other clothes before they go near
the places that are for the people.[a]"

15When he had finished measuring
what was inside the temple area, he led
me out by the east gate[b] and measured
the area all around: 16He measured the
east side with the measuring rod; it was
five hundred cubits.[e,f] 17He measured the
north side; it was five hundred cubits[g] by
the measuring rod. 18He measured the
south side; it was five hundred cubits by
the measuring rod. 19Then he turned to
the west side and measured; it was five
hundred cubits by the measuring rod. 20So
he measured[c] the area[d] on all four sides. It
had a wall around it,[e] five hundred cubits
long and five hundred cubits wide,[f] to separate the holy from the common.[g]

God's Glory Returns to the Temple

43 Then the man brought me to the gate
facing east,[h] 2and I saw the glory
of the God of Israel coming from the east.
His voice was like the roar of rushing waters,[i] and the land was radiant with his
glory.[j] 3The vision I saw was like the vision I had seen when he[h] came to destroy
the city and like the visions I had seen
by the Kebar River, and I fell facedown.
4The glory[k] of the LORD entered the temple
through the gate facing east.[l] 5Then the
Spirit[m] lifted me up[n] and brought me into
the inner court, and the glory[o] of the LORD
filled the temple.[p]
6While the man was standing beside
me, I heard someone speaking to me
from inside the temple. 7He said: "Son of
man, this is the place of my throne[q] and
the place for the soles of my feet. This is

42:4 [o]Eze 46:19 **42:9** [p]Eze 44:5; 46:19 **42:10** [q]Eze 41:12-14 [r]ver 1 **42:13** [s]Eze 40:46 [t]ver 1 [u]Eze 41:12-14 [v]Jer 41:5 [w]S Lev 10:17 [x]Lev 14:13 [y]S Ex 29:31; S Lev 6:29; 7:6; 10:12-13; Nu 18:9-10 **42:14** [z]Lev 16:23; Eze 44:19 [a]Ex 29:9; S Lev 8:7-9

42:15 [b]Eze 43:1 **42:20** [c]Eze 40:5 [d]Eze 43:12 [e]Zec 2:5 [f]Eze 45:2; Rev 21:16 [g]S Eze 22:26 **43:1** [h]S 1Ch 9:18; S Eze 8:16; 42:15; 44:1 **43:2** [i]S Ps 18:4; S Rev 1:15 [j]Isa 6:3; Rev 18:1; 21:11 **43:4** [k]Eze 1:28 [l]Eze 10:19; 44:2 **43:5** [m]S Eze 11:24 [n]S Eze 3:12 [o]S Ex 16:7 [p]S Isa 6:4 **43:7** [q]S Jer 3:17

[a] 4 Septuagint and Syriac; Hebrew *and one cubit* [b] 4 That is, about 18 feet wide and 175 feet long or about 5.3 meters wide and 53 meters long [c] 10 Septuagint; Hebrew *Eastward* [d] 13 Or *purification offerings* [e] 16 See Septuagint of verse 17; Hebrew *rods*; also in verses 18 and 19. [f] 16 Five hundred cubits equal about 875 feet or about 265 meters; also in verses 17, 18 and 19. [g] 17 Septuagint; Hebrew *rods* [h] 3 Some Hebrew manuscripts and Vulgate; most Hebrew manuscripts *I*

42:13 *priests who approach the LORD.* The sons of Zadok (see 40:6 and note on 44:15). *eat the most holy offerings.* The priests normally received partial maintenance by being allowed to eat certain sacrifices (see Lev 2:3; 5:13; 6:16,26,29; 7:6,10). *the place is holy.* See note on Lev 11:44; see also Introduction to Leviticus: Theological Themes.

42:20 *five hundred cubits long and five hundred cubits wide.* Perfect symmetry in the ideal temple's total area.

43:1–12 God's glory returns to the new temple.

43:2 *I saw the glory.* The high point of chs. 40–48 (see notes on 1:1–28; 1:28). The temple had been prepared for this moment, and all that follows flows from this appearance. *coming from the east.* The direction from which Ezekiel had seen God leave (see 11:23 and note). In the book of Ezekiel God's glory is always active (see vv. 4–5; 3:23; 9:3; 10:4,18; 44:4). *like the roar of rushing waters.* Ezekiel experienced an audition as well as a vision. For the comparison, see 1:24; Rev 1:15; 14:2; 19:6. *the land was radiant with his glory.* God's visible glory is frequently described as being very bright (see 10:4; Lk 2:9; Rev 21:11,23).

43:3 *like the vision I had seen.* But somewhat different, for no creatures or wheels are mentioned here. *when he came to destroy the city.* See ch. 9. *Kebar River.* See 1:1 and note. *I fell facedown.* See 1:28; 3:23; 9:8; 11:13; 44:4.

43:4 *through the gate facing east.* See note on v. 2.

43:5 *Then the Spirit lifted me up.* With God being nearer, the function of the guiding angel was taken over by the Spirit of God. Ezekiel was transported into the inner court but not into the temple (cf. 3:12 and note). *filled the temple.* As at the consecration of Solomon's temple (1Ki 8:10–11; see notes on Ex 40:34; 1Ki 8:10; cf. Isa 6:4).

43:6 *someone.* God, but out of reverence not named here, preserving an air of awe and mystery.

43:7 *place of my throne.* See 1Sa 4:4; Ps 47:8 and notes. *place for the soles of my feet.* See 1Ch 28:2; Ps 99:5 and note; 132:7; Isa 60:13 and note; La 2:1. *I will live among the Israelites forever.*

where I will live among the Israelites forever. The people of Israel will never again
defile[r] my holy name—neither they nor
their kings—by their prostitution and the
funeral offerings[a] for their kings at their
death.[b][s] 8 When they placed their threshold
next to my threshold and their doorposts
beside my doorposts, with only a wall between me and them, they defiled my holy
name by their detestable practices. So I destroyed them in my anger. 9 Now let them
put away from me their prostitution and
the funeral offerings for their kings, and I
will live among them forever.[t]
10 "Son of man, describe the temple
to the people of Israel, that they may be
ashamed[u] of their sins. Let them consider
its perfection, 11 and if they are ashamed of
all they have done, make known to them
the design of the temple—its arrangement, its exits and entrances—its whole
design and all its regulations[c] and laws.
Write these down before them so that they
may be faithful to its design and follow all
its regulations.[v]
12 "This is the law of the temple: All the
surrounding area[w] on top of the mountain
will be most holy.[x] Such is the law of the
temple.

The Great Altar Restored

13 "These are the measurements of the
altar[y] in long cubits,[d] that cubit being a
cubit and a handbreadth: Its gutter is a
cubit deep and a cubit wide, with a rim
of one span[e] around the edge. And this is
the height of the altar: 14 From the gutter
on the ground up to the lower ledge that
goes around the altar it is two cubits high,
and the ledge is a cubit wide.[f] From this
lower ledge to the upper ledge that goes
around the altar it is four cubits high, and
that ledge is also a cubit wide.[g] 15 Above
that, the altar hearth[z] is four cubits high,
and four horns[a] project upward from
the hearth. 16 The altar hearth is square,
twelve cubits[h] long and twelve cubits
wide.[b] 17 The upper ledge[c] also is square,
fourteen cubits[i] long and fourteen cubits
wide. All around the altar is a gutter of
one cubit with a rim of half a cubit.[e] The
steps[d] of the altar face east.[e]"
18 Then he said to me, "Son of man, this
is what the Sovereign LORD says: These
will be the regulations for sacrificing burnt
offerings[f] and splashing blood[g] against the
altar when it is built: 19 You are to give a
young bull[h] as a sin offering[j] to the Levitical priests of the family of Zadok,[i] who
come near[j] to minister before me, declares
the Sovereign LORD. 20 You are to take some
of its blood and put it on the four horns
of the altar[k] and on the four corners of the
upper ledge[l] and all around the rim, and
so purify the altar[m] and make atonement
for it. 21 You are to take the bull for the sin
offering and burn it in the designated part
of the temple area outside the sanctuary.[n]
22 "On the second day you are to offer a
male goat without defect for a sin offering,

43:7 [r]S Eze 37:23 [s]S Lev 26:30; S Eze 20:29,39 **43:9** [t]Eze 37:26-28 **43:10** [u]S Eze 16:61 **43:11** [v]Eze 44:5 **43:12** [w]Eze 42:20 [x]S Eze 17:22 **43:13** [y]S Ex 20:24; 2Ch 4:1 **43:15** [z]Isa 29:2 [a]S Ex 27:2 **43:16** [b]Rev 21:16 **43:17** [c]ver 20; Eze 45:19 [d]Ex 20:26 [e]S Ex 27:1 **43:18** [f]Ex 40:29 [g]Lev 1:5,11; Heb 9:21-22 **43:19** [h]S Lev 4:3 [i]S 2Sa 8:17; S Ezr 7:2 [j]Nu 16:40; S Eze 40:46 **43:20** [k]S Lev 4:7 [l]S ver 17 [m]Lev 16:19 **43:21** [n]Ex 29:14; Heb 13:11

[a] 7 Or *the memorial monuments*; also in verse 9
[b] 7 Or *their high places*
[c] 11 Some Hebrew manuscripts and Septuagint; most Hebrew manuscripts *regulations and its whole design*
[d] 13 That is, about 21 inches or about 53 centimeters; also in verses 14 and 17. The long cubit is the basic unit for linear measurement throughout Ezekiel 40–48.
[e] 13,17 That is, about 11 inches or about 27 centimeters
[f] 14 That is, about 3 1/2 feet high and 1 3/4 feet wide or about 105 centimeters high and 53 centimeters wide
[g] 14 That is, about 7 feet high and 1 3/4 feet wide or about 2.1 meters high and 53 centimeters wide
[h] 16 That is, about 21 feet or about 6.4 meters
[i] 17 That is, about 25 feet or about 7.4 meters
[j] 19 Or *purification offering*; also in verses 21, 22 and 25

Renewing the promise of 37:26–28 (see v. 9; 1Ki 6:13; Zec 2:11). *defile my holy name.* See Lev 18:21 and note. *prostitution.* See note on Ex 34:15. *funeral offerings.* As the NIV text note indicates, the reference is either to funeral offerings or to memorial monuments for past kings. Fourteen kings of Judah were buried in Jerusalem, possibly near (too near for Ezekiel) the temple area (see 2Ki 21:18,26; 23:30).

43:8 *their threshold next to my threshold.* Solomon's temple was surrounded by many of his own private structures (see 1Ki 7:1–12). The distinction between God's holy temple and the rest of the world is a central idea in the book of Ezekiel (see v. 12; 44:23). *So I destroyed them.* As elsewhere in Ezekiel, the unstable practices of the people and their kings brought about their destruction (see 5:11; 18:10–12; and especially 22:1–15).

43:12 *This is the law.* Refers to the contents of chs. 40–42.

43:13–27 Restoration of the altar of burnt offering.

43:13 *altar.* Alluded to in 40:47 and here described in detail. Although the material is not mentioned, dressed stones were probably to be used. Ex 20:24–26 allowed an altar to be made of earth, but use of dressed stones for those altars was strictly forbidden (see notes on Ex 20:24–25). Solomon's altar was bronze (1Ki 8:64). Ezekiel's altar, much larger than Solomon's, was over 20 feet tall (including the horns, v. 15), made up of three slabs of decreasing size, like an Egyptian pyramid or Babylonian ziggurat: the "lower ledge" (v. 14) two cubits high; the "upper ledge" (v. 14) four cubits high; and the "altar hearth" (v. 15) four cubits high.

43:15 *altar hearth.* The Hebrew for this term appears only here in the OT and may also mean "mountain of God" or "lion of God"; it is a variant of a form that appears in Isa 29:1–2,7 (see note there). *four horns.* Stone projections from each of the four corners of the altar hearth. On earlier altars they afforded a refuge of last resort for an accused person (see Ex 21:12–14; 1Ki 1:50–51; 2:28–29).

43:17 *steps of the altar.* Forbidden in Ex 20:26 but here required because of the size (see note on v. 13).

43:18 *burnt offerings.* See note on 40:39. *splashing blood.* See Ex 29:16; Lev 4:6; 5:9.

43:19 *sin offering.* To cleanse the altar from the pollution of human sin (see note on 40:39). *of the family of Zadok.* See note on 44:15.

43:21 *outside the sanctuary.* As prescribed in Ex 29:14; Lev 4:12,21; 8:17; 9:11; 16:27. This action foreshadows one aspect of Christ's sacrifice (see Heb 13:11–13 and notes).

43:22 *purified.* By the sprinkling of the blood (see v. 20).

and the altar is to be purified as it was purified with the bull. 23 When you have finished purifying it, you are to offer a young bull and a ram from the flock, both without defect.[o] 24 You are to offer them before the LORD, and the priests are to sprinkle salt[p] on them and sacrifice them as a burnt offering to the LORD.

25 "For seven days[q] you are to provide a male goat daily for a sin offering; you are also to provide a young bull and a ram from the flock, both without defect.[r] 26 For seven days they are to make atonement for the altar and cleanse it; thus they will dedicate it. 27 At the end of these days, from the eighth day[s] on, the priests are to present your burnt offerings[t] and fellowship offerings[u] on the altar. Then I will accept you, declares the Sovereign LORD."

The Priesthood Restored

44 Then the man brought me back to the outer gate of the sanctuary, the one facing east,[v] and it was shut. 2 The LORD said to me, "This gate is to remain shut. It must not be opened; no one may enter through it.[w] It is to remain shut because the LORD, the God of Israel, has entered through it. 3 The prince himself is the only one who may sit inside the gateway to eat in the presence[x] of the LORD. He is to enter by way of the portico of the gateway and go out the same way.[y]"

4 Then the man brought me by way of the north gate[z] to the front of the temple. I looked and saw the glory of the LORD filling the temple[a] of the LORD, and I fell facedown.[b]

5 The LORD said to me, "Son of man, look carefully, listen closely and give attention to everything I tell you concerning all the regulations and instructions regarding the temple of the LORD. Give attention to the entrance[c] to the temple and all the exits of the sanctuary.[d] 6 Say to rebellious Israel,[e] 'This is what the Sovereign LORD says: Enough of your detestable practices, people of Israel! 7 In addition to all your other detestable practices, you brought foreigners uncircumcised in heart[f] and flesh into my sanctuary, desecrating my temple while you offered me food, fat and blood, and you broke my covenant.[g] 8 Instead of carrying out your duty in regard to my holy things, you put others in charge of my sanctuary.[h] 9 This is what the Sovereign LORD says: No foreigner uncircumcised in heart and flesh is to enter my sanctuary, not even the foreigners who live among the Israelites.[i]

10 " 'The Levites who went far from me when Israel went astray[j] and who wandered from me after their idols must bear the consequences of their sin.[k] 11 They may serve in my sanctuary, having charge of the gates of the temple and serving in it; they may slaughter the burnt offerings[l] and sacrifices for the people and stand before the people and serve them.[m] 12 But because they served them in the presence of their idols and made the people of Israel fall[n] into sin, therefore I have sworn with uplifted hand[o] that they must bear the consequences of their sin, declares the Sovereign LORD.[p] 13 They are not to come near to serve me as priests or come near any of my holy things or my most holy offerings; they must bear the shame[q] of their detestable practices.[r] 14 And I will appoint them to guard the temple for all the work that is to be done in it.[s]

15 " 'But the Levitical priests, who are descendants of Zadok[t] and who guarded my sanctuary when the Israelites went astray from me, are to come near to minister before me; they are to stand before

43:23 [o] Ex 29:1; S Lev 22:20
43:24 [p] S Lev 2:13; Mk 9:49-50
43:25 [q] S Lev 8:33 [r] S Ex 29:37
43:27 [s] Lev 9:1 [t] S Isa 60:7 [u] S Ex 32:6; S Lev 17:5
44:1 [v] S Eze 43:1
44:2 [w] Eze 43:4-5
44:3 [x] S Ex 24:9-11 [y] Eze 46:2,8
44:4 [z] S Eze 40:35 [a] S Isa 6:4; S Eze 10:4; Rev 15:8 [b] Da 8:17
44:5 [c] S Eze 42:9 [d] Eze 40:4; 43:10-11
44:6 [e] S Eze 3:9
44:7 [f] S Lev 26:41 [g] Ge 17:14; Ex 12:48; Lev 22:25
44:8 [h] Lev 22:2; Nu 18:7
44:9 [i] Joel 3:17; Zec 14:21
44:10 [j] Ps 95:10 [k] Nu 18:23
44:11 [l] 2Ch 29:34 [m] Nu 3:5-37; S 16:9; S 1Ch 26:12-19
44:12 [n] S Jer 18:15 [o] Ps 106:26 [p] 2Ki 16:10-16; Jer 14:10
44:13 [q] S Eze 16:61 [r] Nu 18:3; Hos 5:1
44:14 [s] 1Sa 2:36; 2Ki 23:9; S 1Ch 23:28-32
44:15 [t] S 2Sa 8:17; S Ezr 7:2

43:27 *fellowship offerings.* After the seven-day consecration by burnt offerings and sin offerings, the altar was ready for the celebration of the more festive fellowship offerings, where the people partook of some of the meat (see note on Lev 3:1).
44:1 – 31 Restoration of the priesthood.
44:2 *It is to remain shut because.* The reason given here is that God entered through the east gate (43:1 – 2), thus making it holy. Related reasons may be that God would never again leave as before (10:19; 11:23) and that sun worship would be made impossible (see 8:16). Today the east gate (called the Golden Gate) of the sacred Moslem area (*Haram esh-Sharif*) in Jerusalem is likewise sealed shut as a result of a later but possibly related tradition.
44:3 *prince.* The first mention of the prince in chs. 40 – 48 (see 34:24 and note). *to eat.* Probably his part of the fellowship offering (see Lev 7:15; Dt 12:7; see also Eze 43:27 and note). While this honor is accorded the prince, it is significant that he is given no other part in the ceremonial functions, reserved now solely for the priests (see 2Ch 26:16 – 20). *by way of the portico.* From the inside of the outer court.
44:7 *uncircumcised in heart.* Spiritually unfit.
44:9 *No foreigner uncircumcised … is to enter my sanctuary.* Nehemiah enforced this restriction when he dismissed Tobiah (Ne 13:8), an Ammonite (Ne 2:10; see Dt 23:3). Foreigners could, however, be a part of Israel (see 47:22).
44:10 *Levites.* Some members of the tribe of Levi served as priests (see Dt 33:8 – 11; Jdg 17:13). *when Israel went astray.* The reference is mainly to the period of the monarchy, especially to the last years, during which Ezekiel so often criticized the people's idolatry (see 6:3 – 6; 14:3 – 11; 16:18 – 21; 23:36 – 49; 36:17 – 18; 37:23).
44:11 *stand before the people.* Cf. standing before the Lord (see v. 15); the Levites still had an honorable position.
44:12 *with uplifted hand.* See 20:5 and note.
44:15 *Zadok.* Traced his Levitical lineage to Aaron through Aaron's son Eleazar (1Ch 6:50 – 53). He served as priest under David, along with Abiathar (see 2Sa 8:17 and note; 15:24 – 29; 20:25). He supported Solomon (as opposed to Abiathar, who pledged himself to Adonijah) and thus secured for himself and his descendants the privilege of serving in the Jerusalem temple (see 1Ki 1). Later the Zadokites were removed from office, but the Qumran (Dead Sea

me to offer sacrifices of fat[u] and blood, declares the Sovereign LORD.[v] 16 They alone are to enter my sanctuary; they alone are to come near my table[w] to minister before me and serve me as guards.[x]

17 “ ‘When they enter the gates of the inner court, they are to wear linen clothes;[y] they must not wear any woolen garment while ministering at the gates of the inner court or inside the temple. 18 They are to wear linen turbans[z] on their heads and linen undergarments[a] around their waists. They must not wear anything that makes them perspire.[b] 19 When they go out into the outer court where the people are, they are to take off the clothes they have been ministering in and are to leave them in the sacred rooms, and put on other clothes, so that the people are not consecrated[c] through contact with their garments.[d]

20 “ ‘They must not shave[e] their heads or let their hair grow long, but they are to keep the hair of their heads trimmed.[f] 21 No priest is to drink wine when he enters the inner court.[g] 22 They must not marry widows or divorced women; they may marry only virgins of Israelite descent or widows of priests.[h] 23 They are to teach my people the difference between the holy and the common[i] and show them how to distinguish between the unclean and the clean.[j]

24 “ ‘In any dispute, the priests are to serve as judges[k] and decide it according to my ordinances. They are to keep my laws and my decrees for all my appointed festivals,[l] and they are to keep my Sabbaths holy.[m]

25 “ ‘A priest must not defile himself by going near a dead person; however, if the dead person was his father or mother, son or daughter, brother or unmarried sister, then he may defile himself.[n] 26 After he is cleansed, he must wait seven days.[o] 27 On the day he goes into the inner court of the sanctuary[p] to minister in the sanctuary, he is to offer a sin offering[a][q] for himself, declares the Sovereign LORD.

28 “ ‘I am to be the only inheritance[r] the priests have. You are to give them no possession in Israel; I will be their possession. 29 They will eat[s] the grain offerings, the sin offerings and the guilt offerings; and everything in Israel devoted[b] to the LORD[t] will belong to them.[u] 30 The best of all the firstfruits[v] and of all your special gifts will belong to the priests. You are to give them the first portion of your ground meal[w] so that a blessing[x] may rest on your household.[y] 31 The priests must not eat anything, whether bird or animal, found dead[z] or torn by wild animals.[a]

Israel Fully Restored

45 “ ‘When you allot the land as an inheritance,[b] you are to present to the LORD a portion of the land as a sacred district, 25,000 cubits[c] long and 20,000[d] cubits[e] wide; the entire area will be holy.[c] 2 Of this, a section 500 cubits[f] square[d] is

44:15 [u] S Ex 29:13 [v] S Jer 33:18; S Eze 40:46; Zec 3:7 **44:16** [w] S Eze 41:22 [x] Lev 3:16-17; 17:5-6; Nu 18:5; S 1Sa 2:35; Zec 3:7 **44:17** [y] Rev 19:8 **44:18** [z] S Ex 28:39; S Isa 3:20 [a] S Ex 28:42 [b] S Lev 16:4 **44:19** [c] S Lev 6:27 [d] Ex 39:27-29; Lev 6:10-11; S Eze 42:14 **44:20** [e] Eze 5:1 [f] S Lev 21:5; Nu 6:5 **44:21** [g] S Lev 10:9 **44:22** [h] Lev 21:7 **44:23** [i] S Eze 22:26 [j] S Ge 7:2; Lev 13:50; 15:31; Jer 15:19; Hag 2:11-13 **44:24** [k] Dt 17:8-9; 19:17; 21:5; S 1Ch 23:4 [l] S Lev 23:2 [m] 2Ch 19:8 **44:25** [n] Lev 21:1-4 **44:26** [o] Nu 19:14 **44:27** [p] S Nu 3:28 [q] S Lev 4:28; Nu 6:11 **44:28** [r] S Nu 18:20; Dt 18:1-2; S Jos 13:33 **44:29** [s] Lev 6:16 [t] S Lev 27:21 [u] Nu 18:9, 14; S Jos 13:14 **44:30** [v] Nu 18:12-13; S 2Ch 31:5 [w] S Nu 15:18-21 [x] S Lev 25:21 [y] S 2Ch 31:10; Ne 10:35-37 **44:31** [z] S Lev 11:39 [a] S Ex 22:31; S Lev 11:40 **45:1** [b] S Nu 34:13 [c] Eze 48:8-9, 29 **45:2** [d] Eze 42:20

[a] 27 Or *purification offering*; also in verse 29 [b] 29 The Hebrew term refers to the irrevocable giving over of things or persons to the LORD. [c] 1 That is, about 8 miles or about 13 kilometers; also in verses 3, 5 and 6 [d] 1 Septuagint (see also verses 3 and 5 and 48:9); Hebrew *10,000* [e] 1 That is, about 6 1/2 miles or about 11 kilometers [f] 2 That is, about 875 feet or about 265 meters

Scrolls) community remained loyal to them. *who guarded my sanctuary.* Contrast 22:26 and the thrust of all of ch. 8. In chs. 40–48 the Zadokites received special consideration because of their faithfulness (cf. Zec 3:7 and note). *fat and blood.* See 39:19 and note.

44:16 *They alone are to enter.* This elevation of the Zadokite priests and demotion of the Levites were part of the concern for ritual purity, a major theme of chs. 40–48. Only the fittest were to serve. *my table.* Either the table that held the bread (see 41:22 and note) or the large altar on which the Lord's food was presented (v. 7).

44:17 *linen.* Cooler than wool (see v. 18).

44:18 *turbans.* Ezekiel wore one (24:17).

44:19 *take off the clothes.* In the interest of ritual purity.

44:20 *must not shave their heads.* Because it was a mourning ritual (7:18) that rendered the mourner unclean (see Lev 21:1–5). *or let their hair grow long.* Because it implied the taking of a vow that might prevent the priest from serving (see Nu 6:5; Ac 21:23–26).

44:23 *difference between the holy and the common.* One of Ezekiel's central concerns. The important task of declaring God's will on matters of clean and unclean food, the fitness of sacrificial animals and ritual purity either had been done for pay (see Mic 3:11) or had been neglected altogether (see Jer 2:8; Eze 22:26 and note). See Hag 2:10–13 for a positive example. *distinguish between the unclean and the clean.* See Lev 11; Dt 14:3–21 and notes.

44:24 *priests are to serve as judges.* One of their functions from earliest days (see NIV text note on 1Sa 4:18; see also 2Ch 19:8–11).

44:25 *dead person.* Contact with the dead made a person ceremonially unclean (Lev 21:1–3; Hag 2:13).

44:28 *no possession.* The statement that priests were not to own land agrees with Nu 18:20,23–24; Dt 10:9; Jos 13:14,33; 18:7.

44:31 *found dead.* This restriction applied to all Israel according to Lev 7:24.

45:1—46:24 An idealized depiction of the restoration of Israel's theocratic order.

45:1 *When you allot the land.* Envisioned a new acquisition and redistribution of the land. *present to the LORD.* The entire square area in the center of the land was to be set aside for the Lord. *20,000 cubits.* With the 5,000-cubit city area (v. 6) it was a perfect square. *entire area will be holy.* Set apart for the Lord and owned by no tribe.

45:2 *section 500 cubits square.* The temple area discussed in 42:16–20. *open land.* An unoccupied strip of land that served as a buffer between the more holy and the less holy, though the whole area was holy (see 42:20).

to be for the sanctuary, with 50 cubits[a] around it for open land. 3In the sacred district, measure off a section 25,000 cubits long and 10,000 cubits[b] wide. In it will be the sanctuary, the Most Holy Place. 4It will be the sacred portion of the land for the priests,[e] who minister in the sanctuary and who draw near to minister before the LORD. It will be a place for their houses as well as a holy place for the sanctuary.[f] 5An area 25,000 cubits long and 10,000 cubits wide will belong to the Levites, who serve in the temple, as their possession for towns to live in.[c][g]

6" 'You are to give the city as its property an area 5,000 cubits[d] wide and 25,000 cubits long, adjoining the sacred portion; it will belong to all Israel.[h]

7" 'The prince will have the land bordering each side of the area formed by the sacred district and the property of the city. It will extend westward from the west side and eastward from the east side, running lengthwise from the western to the eastern border parallel to one of the tribal portions.[i] 8This land will be his possession in Israel. And my princes will no longer oppress my people but will allow the people of Israel to possess the land according to their tribes.[j]

9" 'This is what the Sovereign LORD says: You have gone far enough, princes of Israel! Give up your violence and oppression[k] and do what is just and right.[l] Stop dispossessing my people, declares the Sovereign LORD. 10You are to use accurate scales,[m] an accurate ephah[e][n] and an accurate bath.[f] 11The ephah[o] and the bath are to be the same size, the bath containing a tenth of a homer and the ephah a tenth of a homer; the homer is to be the standard measure for both. 12The shekel[g] is to consist of twenty gerahs.[p] Twenty shekels plus twenty-five shekels plus fifteen shekels equal one mina.[h]

13" 'This is the special gift you are to offer: a sixth of an ephah[i] from each homer of wheat and a sixth of an ephah[j] from each homer of barley. 14The prescribed portion of olive oil, measured by the bath, is a tenth of a bath[k] from each cor (which consists of ten baths or one homer, for ten baths are equivalent to a homer). 15Also one sheep is to be taken from every flock of two hundred from the well-watered pastures of Israel. These will be used for the grain offerings, burnt offerings[q] and fellowship offerings to make atonement[r] for the people, declares the Sovereign LORD. 16All the people of the land will be required to give this special offering to the prince in Israel. 17It will be the duty of the prince to provide the burnt offerings, grain offerings and drink offerings at the festivals, the New Moons[s] and the Sabbaths[t]—at all the appointed festivals of Israel. He will provide the sin offerings,[l] grain offerings, burnt offerings and fellowship offerings to make atonement for the Israelites.[u]

18" 'This is what the Sovereign LORD says: In the first month[v] on the first day you are to take a young bull without defect[w] and

45:4 [e]S Eze 40:46 [f]Eze 48:10-11 **45:5** [g]Eze 48:13 **45:6** [h]Eze 48:15-18 **45:7** [i]Eze 48:21 **45:8** [j]S Nu 26:53; Eze 46:18 **45:9** [k]Ps 12:5 [l]S Jer 22:3; Zec 7:9-10; 8:16 **45:10** [m]Dt 25:15; S Pr 11:1; Am 8:4-6; Mic 6:10-11 [n]S Lev 19:36 **45:11** [o]Isa 5:10 **45:12** [p]Ex 30:13; Lev 27:25; Nu 3:47 **45:15** [q]S Lev 1:4 [r]Lev 6:30 **45:17** [s]S Nu 10:10 [t]S Lev 23:38; Isa 66:23 [u]S 1Ki 8:62; S 2Ch 31:3; Eze 46:4-12 **45:18** [v]Ex 12:2 [w]S Lev 22:20; Heb 9:14

[a] *2* That is, about 88 feet or about 27 meters [b] *3* That is, about 3 1/3 miles or about 5.3 kilometers; also in verse 5 [c] *5* Septuagint; Hebrew *temple; they will have as their possession 20 rooms* [d] *6* That is, about 1 2/3 miles or about 2.7 kilometers [e] *10* An ephah was a dry measure having the capacity of about 3/5 bushel or about 22 liters. [f] *10* A bath was a liquid measure equaling about 6 gallons or about 22 liters. [g] *12* A shekel weighed about 2/5 ounce or about 12 grams. [h] *12* That is, 60 shekels; the common mina was 50 shekels. Sixty shekels were about 1 1/2 pounds or about 690 grams. [i] *13* That is, probably about 6 pounds or about 2.7 kilograms [j] *13* That is, probably about 5 pounds or about 2.3 kilograms [k] *14* That is, about 2 1/2 quarts or about 2.2 liters [l] *17* Or *purification offerings;* also in verses 19, 22, 23 and 25

45:3 *measure off a section.* The middle strip of the holy square was specifically for the temple (see map, p. 1410).
45:4 *land for the priests.* Not to own (see 44:28) but to live on.
45:5 *area ... to the Levites.* A section of equal size just to the north was for the Levites to dwell in, even though it was in the holy area. The Levites, as opposed to the Zadokite priests, could hold land as a possession.
45:6 *city.* The former Jerusalem contained the temple area. The new holy city would not, but would be adjacent to the temple. *5,000 cubits wide.* The southernmost section of the city completed the perfectly square area. *it will belong to all Israel.* Not to any one tribe or person, as in former days.
45:7 *The prince will have the land.* A considerable portion of territory. In view of the next verse (cf. 46:18), the generous allotment should have kept the prince from greed like that of Ahab (see 1Ki 21). The prince was also responsible for sizable offerings (v. 17).
45:9 *princes of Israel!* The language of this verse is reminiscent of the preaching Ezekiel did before 586 BC (see 22:6). *what is just and right.* See note on 33:14.
45:10 *You are to use accurate scales.* Israel was not to repeat the economic injustices of the past. The OT often warns against cheating in weights and measures (see Lev 19:35 and note; Dt 25:13–16; Mic 6:10–12).
45:11 *same size.* A little more than half a bushel. *homer.* About six bushels.
45:13 *special gift.* Given to the prince, as distinct from the gifts given to the priests (44:30). The prince is to use these gifts in part for the offerings to the Lord (see v. 16).
45:15 *make atonement.* See notes on Ex 25:17; Lev 16:20–22; 17:11; Ro 3:25.
45:16 *people of the land.* See v. 22; 7:27 and note.
45:17 *drink offerings.* Usually wine is meant (see Nu 15:5; Hos 9:4), although olive oil, not wine, is mentioned here (vv. 14,24).
45:18—46:24 This entire section involves so many variations from Pentateuchal law that the rabbis spent a great deal of effort trying to reconcile them. For example, the provision in 45:18 for an annual purification of the temple does not seem to take into consideration the Day of Atonement ritual of Lev 16.

purify the sanctuary.[x] 19 The priest is to
take some of the blood of the sin offering
and put it on the doorposts of the temple, on the four corners of the upper ledge[y]
of the altar[z] and on the gateposts of the
inner court. 20 You are to do the same on
the seventh day of the month for anyone
who sins unintentionally[a] or through ignorance; so you are to make atonement for
the temple.

21 "'In the first month on the fourteenth
day you are to observe the Passover,[b] a
festival lasting seven days, during which
you shall eat bread made without yeast.
22 On that day the prince is to provide a
bull as a sin offering for himself and for
all the people of the land.[c] 23 Every day
during the seven days of the festival he
is to provide seven bulls and seven rams[d]
without defect as a burnt offering to the
LORD, and a male goat for a sin offering.[e]
24 He is to provide as a grain offering[f] an
ephah for each bull and an ephah for each
ram, along with a hin[a] of olive oil for each
ephah.[g]

25 "'During the seven days of the festival,[h] which begins in the seventh month
on the fifteenth day, he is to make the
same provision for sin offerings, burnt offerings, grain offerings and oil.[i]

46 "'This is what the Sovereign LORD
says: The gate of the inner court[j]
facing east[k] is to be shut on the six working days, but on the Sabbath day and
on the day of the New Moon[l] it is to be
opened. 2 The prince is to enter from the
outside through the portico[m] of the gateway and stand by the gatepost. The priests
are to sacrifice his burnt offering[n] and his
fellowship offerings. He is to bow down
in worship at the threshold of the gateway
and then go out, but the gate will not be
shut until evening.[o] 3 On the Sabbaths[p] and
New Moons the people of the land are to
worship in the presence of the LORD at the
entrance of that gateway.[q] 4 The burnt offering the prince brings to the LORD on the
Sabbath day is to be six male lambs and a
ram, all without defect. 5 The grain offering given with the ram is to be an ephah,[b]
and the grain offering with the lambs is
to be as much as he pleases, along with
a hin[c] of olive oil for each ephah.[r] 6 On
the day of the New Moon[s] he is to offer a
young bull, six lambs and a ram, all without defect.[t] 7 He is to provide as a grain offering one ephah with the bull, one ephah
with the ram, and with the lambs as much
as he wants to give, along with a hin of oil
for each ephah.[u] 8 When the prince enters,
he is to go in through the portico[v] of the
gateway, and he is to come out the same
way.[w]

9 "'When the people of the land come
before the LORD at the appointed festivals,[x]
whoever enters by the north gate to worship is to go out the south gate; and whoever enters by the south gate is to go out
the north gate. No one is to return through
the gate by which they entered, but each
is to go out the opposite gate. 10 The prince
is to be among them, going in when they
go in and going out when they go out.[y]
11 At the feasts and the appointed festivals,
the grain offering is to be an ephah with
a bull, an ephah with a ram, and with the
lambs as much as he pleases, along with a
hin of oil for each ephah.[z]

12 "'When the prince provides[a] a freewill
offering[b] to the LORD—whether a burnt
offering or fellowship offerings—the gate
facing east is to be opened for him. He
shall offer his burnt offering or his fellowship offerings as he does on the Sabbath
day. Then he shall go out, and after he has
gone out, the gate will be shut.[c]

13 "'Every day you are to provide a year-
old lamb without defect for a burnt offering to the LORD; morning by morning[d] you

45:18 [x]S Lev 16:16, 33 **45:19** [y]S Eze 43:17 [z]Lev 16:18-19 **45:20** [a]Lev 4:27 **45:21** [b]S Ex 12:11 **45:22** [c]Lev 4:14 **45:23** [d]S Nu 22:40; S Job 42:8 [e]Nu 28:16-25 **45:24** [f]Nu 28:12-13 [g]Eze 46:5-7 **45:25** [h]Dt 16:13 [i]Lev 23:34-43; Nu 29:12-38 **46:1** [j]S Eze 40:19 [k]S 1Ch 9:18 [l]ver 6; Isa 66:23 **46:2** [m]ver 8 [n]Eze 40:39 [o]ver 12; S Eze 44:3 **46:3** [p]S Isa 66:23 [q]Lk 1:10

46:5 [r]ver 11 **46:6** [s]ver 1; S Nu 10:10 [t]S Lev 22:20 **46:7** [u]Eze 45:24 **46:8** [v]ver 2 [w]Eze 44:3 **46:9** [x]S Ex 23:14; S 34:20 **46:10** [y]2Sa 6:14-15; Ps 42:4 **46:11** [z]ver 5 **46:12** [a]S Eze 45:17 [b]S Lev 7:16 [c]ver 2 **46:13** [d]S Ps 5:3

a 24 That is, about 1 gallon or about 3.8 liters
b 5 That is, probably about 35 pounds or about 16 kilograms; also in verses 7 and 11
c 5 That is, about 1 gallon or about 3.8 liters; also in verses 7 and 11

45:19 *priest.* High priest.
45:20 *sins unintentionally or through ignorance.* See Nu 15:22–30 and notes.
45:22 *sin offering.* See note on 40:39.
45:25 *the festival, which begins in the seventh month.* In some respects the most important of the festivals—called the Festival of Ingathering (Ex 23:16; 34:22) and the Festival of Tabernacles (Dt 16:16; see note on Zec 14:16).
46:1 *gate of the inner court.* While the east gate of the outer court was permanently closed (44:2), the east gate of the inner court could be opened on festival days.
46:2 *through the portico of the gateway.* The portico of the gate of the inner court faced the outer court. *stand by the gatepost.* Which had been ritually cleansed (45:19). From there the prince could observe the sacrifices being performed on the altar of burnt offering in the inner court, but he was not allowed into the inner court itself.
46:3 *people of the land.* See note on 7:27. *at the entrance of that gateway.* But in the outer court.
46:4 *six male lambs and a ram.* Another example of a difference from Pentateuchal laws (see note on 45:18—46:24). Nu 28:9 calls for two lambs and no ram on the Sabbath.
46:5 *ephah.* Contrast Nu 28:9.
46:6 *day of the New Moon.* The first day of the month. Contrast the requirement of Nu 28:11.
46:7 *as a grain offering one ephah.* Contrast Nu 28:12.
46:9 *whoever enters by the north gate.* These appear to be crowd control measures. If so, the new era would see masses of people thronging the sanctuary on the festival day.
46:12 *freewill offering.* Above and beyond what was required of the prince.
46:13 *morning by morning.* Contrast Nu 28:3–8, where the daily sacrifice consists of one lamb in the morning and one in the evening (see 1Ch 16:40; 2Ch 13:11; 31:3). A different

shall provide it.[e] 14 You are also to provide with it morning by morning a grain offering, consisting of a sixth of an ephah[a] with a third of a hin[b] of oil[f] to moisten the flour. The presenting of this grain offering to the LORD is a lasting ordinance.[g] 15 So the lamb and the grain offering and the oil shall be provided morning by morning for a regular[h] burnt offering.[i]

16 " 'This is what the Sovereign LORD says: If the prince makes a gift from his inheritance to one of his sons, it will also belong to his descendants; it is to be their property by inheritance.[j] 17 If, however, he makes a gift from his inheritance to one of his servants, the servant may keep it until the year of freedom;[k] then it will revert to the prince. His inheritance belongs to his sons only; it is theirs. 18 The prince must not take[l] any of the inheritance[m] of the people, driving them off their property. He is to give his sons their inheritance out of his own property, so that not one of my people will be separated from their property.' "

19 Then the man brought me through the entrance[n] at the side of the gate to the sacred rooms facing north,[o] which belonged to the priests, and showed me a place at the western end. 20 He said to me, "This is the place where the priests are to cook the guilt offering and the sin offering[c] and bake the grain offering, to avoid bringing them into the outer court and consecrating[p] the people."[q]

21 He then brought me to the outer court and led me around to its four corners, and I saw in each corner another court. 22 In the four corners of the outer court were enclosed[d] courts, forty cubits long and thirty cubits wide;[e] each of the courts in the four corners was the same size. 23 Around the inside of each of the four courts was a ledge of stone, with places for fire built all around under the ledge. 24 He said to me, "These are the kitchens where those who minister at the temple are to cook the sacrifices of the people."

The River From the Temple

47 The man brought me back to the entrance to the temple, and I saw water[r] coming out from under the threshold of the temple toward the east (for the temple faced east). The water was coming down from under the south side of the temple, south of the altar.[s] 2 He then brought me out through the north gate[t] and led me around the outside to the outer gate facing east, and the water was trickling from the south side.

3 As the man went eastward with a measuring line[u] in his hand, he measured off a thousand cubits[f] and then led me through water that was ankle-deep. 4 He measured off another thousand cubits and led me through water that was knee-deep. He measured off another thousand and led me through water that was up to the waist. 5 He measured off another thousand, but now it was a river[v] that I could not cross, because the water had risen and was deep enough to swim in—a river that no one could cross.[w] 6 He asked me, "Son of man, do you see this?"

Then he led me back to the bank of the river. 7 When I arrived there, I saw a great number of trees on each side of the river.[x] 8 He said to me, "This water flows toward the eastern region and goes down into the Arabah,[g][y] where it enters the Dead Sea. When it empties into the sea, the salty water there becomes fresh.[z] 9 Swarms of

46:13 [e] Ex 29:38; S Nu 28:3
46:14 [f] Nu 15:6 [g] Da 8:11
46:15 [h] S Ex 29:42 [i] S Ex 29:38; Nu 28:5-6
46:16 [j] 2Ch 21:3
46:17 [k] S Lev 25:10
46:18 [l] 1Sa 8:14 [m] S Lev 25:23; Eze 45:8; Mic 2:1-2
46:19 [n] S Eze 42:9 [o] Eze 42:4
46:20 [p] S Lev 6:27 [q] ver 24; Zec 14:20
47:1 [r] S Isa 55:1 [s] Ps 46:4; Joel 3:18; Rev 22:1
47:2 [t] S Eze 40:35
47:3 [u] S Eze 40:3
47:5 [v] S Ge 2:10 [w] Isa 11:9; Hab 2:14
47:7 [x] ver 12; Rev 22:2
47:8 [y] S Dt 1:1; S 3:17 [z] Isa 41:18

[a] 14 That is, probably about 6 pounds or about 2.7 kilograms [b] 14 That is, about 1 1/2 quarts or about 1.3 liters [c] 20 Or *purification offering*
[d] 22 The meaning of the Hebrew for this word is uncertain. [e] 22 That is, about 70 feet long and 53 feet wide or about 21 meters long and 16 meters wide
[f] 3 That is, about 1,700 feet or about 530 meters
[g] 8 Or *the Jordan Valley*

custom appears in 2Ki 16:15, where a burnt offering was offered in the mornings, a grain offering in the evenings.
46:14 *sixth of an ephah ... third of a hin.* Contrast Nu 28:5.
46:16 *his descendants.* Ezekiel pictured a hereditary rulership.
46:17 *until the year of freedom.* The Year of Jubilee—held, theoretically, every 50th year (see Lev 25:8–15, especially v. 13).
46:18 *The prince must not take.* See note on 45:7.
46:19–24 Fits well after 42:13–14, where other rooms for priests are described. The provisions here are a fitting conclusion to the sacrifice laws. The priests' area (vv. 19–20) was to be kept separate from the cooking areas of the Levites (vv. 21–24).
47:1–12 The river of life flowing from the temple.
47:1 *man.* The angelic guide (40:3), who here appears for the last time, concluded Ezekiel's visionary tour of the new temple. *entrance to the temple.* Ezekiel was standing in the inner court. *water.* The rest of this section (vv. 1–12) makes it clear that healing, life-nurturing water is meant (see Ps 36:8; 46:4 and notes; see also Joel 3:18; Zec 13:1; 14:8; Rev 22:1–2). In the larger background was the river flowing from the Garden of Eden (Ge 2:10).
47:2 *brought me out through the north gate.* Because the east gate was closed (44:2).
47:5 *measured off another thousand.* For a total of four measurings (see note on 1:5). *river that no one could cross.* Amazing, in that a stream fed by no tributaries does not increase as it flows.
47:7 *great number of trees.* Reminiscent of Eden (Ge 2:9).
47:8 *toward the eastern region.* Contrast Zec 14:8. *Arabah.* Here the waterless region between Jerusalem and the Dead Sea (see NIV text note). *becomes fresh.* The Hebrew says, figuratively, "becomes healed." That this lowest (1,300 feet below sea level) and saltiest (25 percent) body of water in the world should sustain such an abundance of life indicates the wonderful renewing power of this "river of the water of life" (Rev 22:1).
47:9 *Swarms of living creatures.* Overtones of Ge 1:20–21 point to a new creation.

BOUNDARIES OF THE LAND IN EZEKIEL'S VISION

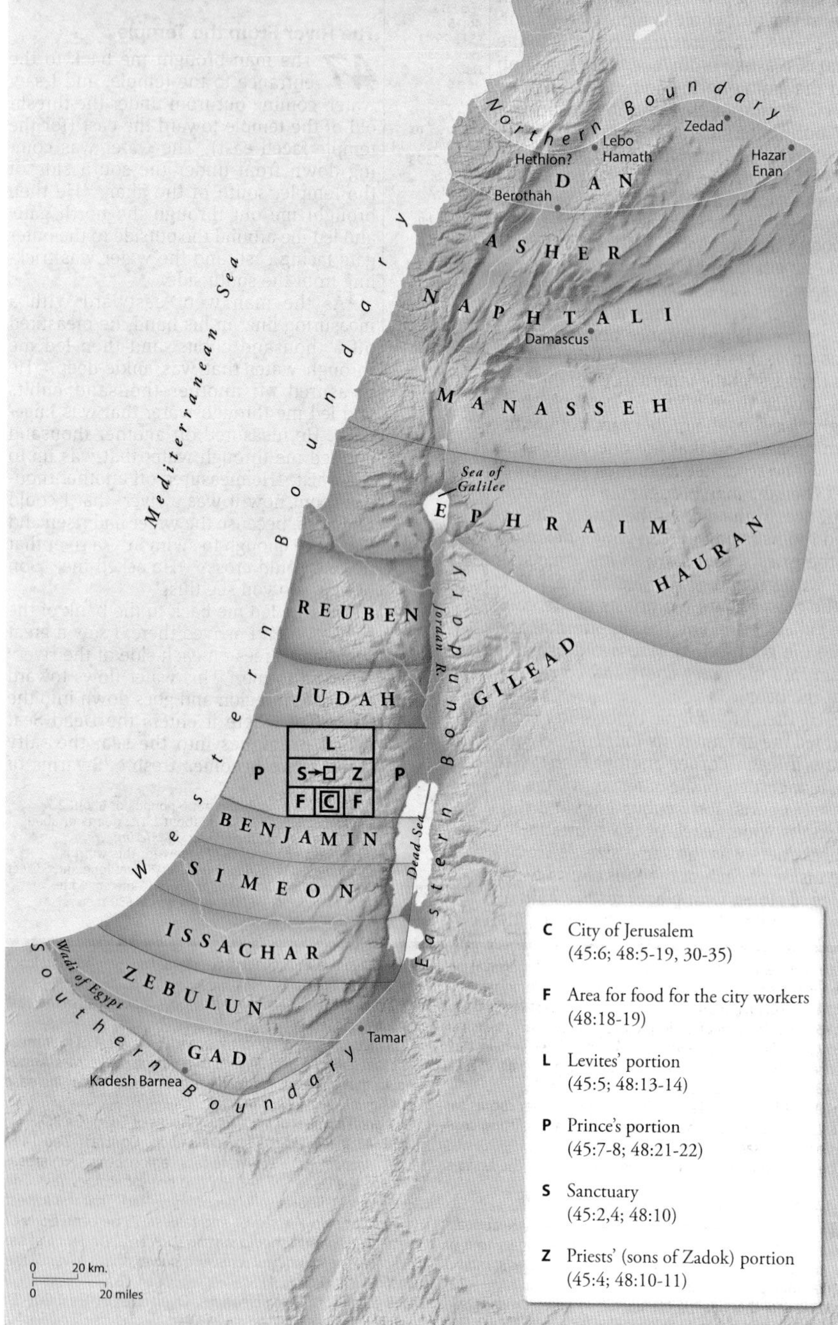

living creatures will live wherever the river flows. There will be large numbers of
fish, because this water flows there and
makes the salt water fresh; so where the
river flows everything will live.[a] 10 Fishermen[b] will stand along the shore; from En
Gedi[c] to En Eglaim there will be places for
spreading nets.[d] The fish will be of many
kinds[e]—like the fish of the Mediterranean Sea.[f] 11 But the swamps and marshes
will not become fresh; they will be left for
salt.[g] 12 Fruit trees of all kinds will grow on
both banks of the river.[h] Their leaves will
not wither, nor will their fruit[i] fail. Every
month they will bear fruit, because the
water from the sanctuary[j] flows to them.
Their fruit will serve for food and their
leaves for healing.[k]”

The Boundaries of the Land

13 This is what the Sovereign LORD says:
“These are the boundaries[l] of the land that
you will divide among the twelve tribes
of Israel as their inheritance, with two
portions for Joseph.[m] 14 You are to divide
it equally among them. Because I swore
with uplifted hand to give it to your ancestors, this land will become your inheritance.[n]

15 “This is to be the boundary of the
land:[o]

“On the north side it will run from the
Mediterranean Sea[p] by the Hethlon
road[q] past Lebo Hamath to Zedad,
16 Berothah[a][r] and Sibraim (which lies
on the border between Damascus and
Hamath),[s] as far as Hazer Hattikon,
which is on the border of Hauran.
17 The boundary will extend from the
sea to Hazar Enan,[b] along the northern border of Damascus, with the
border of Hamath to the north. This
will be the northern boundary.[t]

18 “On the east side the boundary will
run between Hauran and Damascus,
along the Jordan between Gilead and
the land of Israel, to the Dead Sea and
as far as Tamar.[c] This will be the eastern boundary.[u]

19 “On the south side it will run from
Tamar as far as the waters of Meribah Kadesh,[v] then along the Wadi
of Egypt[w] to the Mediterranean Sea.[x]
This will be the southern boundary.

20 “On the west side, the Mediterranean
Sea will be the boundary to a point
opposite Lebo Hamath.[y] This will be
the western boundary.[z]

21 “You are to distribute this land among
yourselves according to the tribes of Israel. 22 You are to allot it as an inheritance[a]
for yourselves and for the foreigners[b] residing among you and who have children.
You are to consider them as native-born
Israelites; along with you they are to be

47:9 [a] Isa 12:3; 55:1; Jn 4:14; 7:37-38
47:10 [b] S Isa 19:8; Mt 4:19 [c] S Jos 15:62 [d] Eze 26:5 [e] S Ps 104:25; Mt 13:47 [f] S Nu 34:6
47:11 [g] S Dt 29:23
47:12 [h] ver 7; Rev 22:2 [i] S Ps 1:3 [j] S Isa 55:1 [k] S Ge 2:9; S Jer 17:8; Eze 36:8
47:13 [l] Nu 34:2-12 [m] S Ge 48:16; S 49:26
47:14 [n] S Ge 12:7; S Dt 1:8; S Eze 36:12
47:15 [o] Nu 34:2 [p] ver 19; S Nu 34:6 [q] Eze 48:1
47:16 [r] 2Sa 8:8 [s] Nu 13:21; S Jer 49:23; Eze 48:1
47:17 [t] Eze 48:1
47:18 [u] S Eze 27:18
47:19 [v] Dt 32:51 [w] S Ge 15:18; Isa 27:12 [x] S ver 15; Eze 48:28
47:20 [y] S Nu 13:21; Eze 48:1 [z] Nu 34:6
47:22 [a] S Eze 36:12 [b] S Dt 24:19; S Isa 14:1; Mal 3:5

[a] 15,16 See Septuagint and 48:1; Hebrew *road to go into Zedad, 16Hamath, Berothah.* [b] 17 Hebrew *Enon,* a variant of *Enan* [c] 18 See Syriac; Hebrew *Israel. You will measure to the Dead Sea.*

47:10 *En Gedi.* Means “spring of the goat”; a strong spring midway along the western side of the Dead Sea (see note on SS 1:14). *En Eglaim.* Means “spring of the two calves.” It is possibly Ain Feshkha, at the northwestern corner of the Dead Sea, though some suggest a location on the east bank.
47:11 *they will be left for salt.* Perhaps to provide the salt needed in the sacrifices (43:24).
47:12 *Every month they will bear.* A marvelous extension of the promises in 34:27; 36:30 (see Am 9:13; cf. Rev 22:2).
47:13–23 The boundaries of the land in the new order (see map, p. 1410).
47:13 *two portions for Joseph.* Since the tribe of Levi received none (44:28), Ephraim and Manasseh, Joseph’s two sons adopted by Jacob (Ge 48:5,17–20), each received an allotment (see 48:4–5).
47:14 *Because I swore.* A reference to the covenant made with Abram (see Ge 15:9–21 and notes; Eze 20:5; 36:28). *with uplifted hand.* See 20:5 and note.
47:15 *This is to be the boundary.* Approximates Israel’s borders at the time of David and Solomon, except that Transjordan is not included (see v. 18)—which, in any event, was never within the boundaries of the promised land proper. The following specified boundaries closely resemble those in Nu 34:1–12. *Hethlon road.* Probably situated on the Mediterranean coast, somewhere in present-day Lebanon. *Lebo Hamath.* Lebo is now identified with modern Lebweh, about 15 miles northeast of Baalbek. At one time Lebo must have served as a fortress guarding the southern route to Hamath. Perhaps the phrase should be translated “Lebo of Hamath.” It is often referred to in Scripture as the northern limit of Israel (see v. 20; 48:1; Nu 13:21; 34:8; Jos 13:5; 1Ki 8:65; 2Ki 14:25; Am 6:14). *Lebo.* Traditionally rendered “to the entrance of.” *Zedad.* Mentioned in Nu 34:8 but otherwise unknown.
47:16 *Berothah.* Probably to be identified with the Berothai of 2Sa 8:8, but otherwise unknown. *Sibraim.* Probably the Sepharvaim of 2Ki 17:24; 18:34. *Damascus.* Capital of Aram (Syria); according to v. 17 it was included in Israel. *Hamath.* A city about 120 miles north of Damascus on the Orontes River. *Hazer Hattikon.* Means “the middle enclosure.” It is possibly the same as Hazar Enan in v. 17.
47:18 *Dead Sea.* See Joel 2:20; Zec 14:8. *Tamar.* Means “(place of) palms” (see v. 19; 48:28); mentioned in Ge 14:7 (Hazezon Tamar) and 1Ki 9:18 (see NIV text note there).
47:19 *Meribah Kadesh.* About 50 miles south of Beersheba, identified with Kadesh Barnea in Nu 34:4. *Wadi of Egypt.* The Wadi el-Arish, a deeply cut riverbed with seasonal flow that runs from the Sinai north-northwest until it enters the Mediterranean, 50 miles southwest of Gaza. It marked the southernmost extremity of Solomon’s kingdom (1Ki 8:65). See maps, pp. 677, 1410.
47:22 *You are to consider them as native-born Israelites.* A gracious inclusiveness that went beyond the provision of 14:7. It reflects the same universalism that is found in such prophecies as Isa 56:3–8 (see notes there).

allotted an inheritance among the tribes
of Israel.[c] 23In whatever tribe a foreigner
resides, there you are to give them their
inheritance," declares the Sovereign LORD.[d]

The Division of the Land

48 "These are the tribes, listed by
name: At the northern frontier,
Dan[e] will have one portion; it will follow
the Hethlon road[f] to Lebo Hamath;[g] Hazar Enan and the northern border of Damascus next to Hamath will be part of its
border from the east side to the west side.
2"Asher[h] will have one portion; it will
border the territory of Dan from east to
west.
3"Naphtali[i] will have one portion; it will
border the territory of Asher from east to
west.
4"Manasseh[j] will have one portion; it
will border the territory of Naphtali from
east to west.
5"Ephraim[k] will have one portion; it will
border the territory of Manasseh[l] from east
to west.[m]
6"Reuben[n] will have one portion; it will
border the territory of Ephraim from east
to west.
7"Judah[o] will have one portion; it will
border the territory of Reuben from east
to west.
8"Bordering the territory of Judah from
east to west will be the portion you are to
present as a special gift. It will be 25,000
cubits[a] wide, and its length from east to
west will equal one of the tribal portions;
the sanctuary will be in the center of it.[p]
9"The special portion you are to offer
to the LORD will be 25,000 cubits long
and 10,000 cubits[b] wide.[q] 10This will be
the sacred portion for the priests. It will
be 25,000 cubits long on the north side,
10,000 cubits wide on the west side,
10,000 cubits wide on the east side and
25,000 cubits long on the south side. In
the center of it will be the sanctuary of the
LORD.[r] 11This will be for the consecrated
priests, the Zadokites,[s] who were faithful
in serving me[t] and did not go astray as
the Levites did when the Israelites went
astray.[u] 12It will be a special gift to them
from the sacred portion of the land, a most
holy portion, bordering the territory of the
Levites.
13"Alongside the territory of the priests,
the Levites will have an allotment 25,000
cubits long and 10,000 cubits wide. Its
total length will be 25,000 cubits and its
width 10,000 cubits.[v] 14They must not
sell or exchange any of it. This is the best
of the land and must not pass into other
hands, because it is holy to the LORD.[w]
15"The remaining area, 5,000 cubits[c]
wide and 25,000 cubits long, will be for the
common use of the city, for houses and for
pastureland. The city will be in the center
of it 16and will have these measurements:
the north side 4,500 cubits,[d] the south side
4,500 cubits, the east side 4,500 cubits, and
the west side 4,500 cubits.[x] 17The pastureland for the city will be 250 cubits[e] on the
north, 250 cubits on the south, 250 cubits
on the east, and 250 cubits on the west.
18What remains of the area, bordering on
the sacred portion and running the length
of it, will be 10,000 cubits on the east side
and 10,000 cubits on the west side. Its produce will supply food for the workers of
the city.[y] 19The workers from the city who
farm it will come from all the tribes of Israel. 20The entire portion will be a square,
25,000 cubits on each side. As a special gift
you will set aside the sacred portion, along
with the property of the city.
21"What remains on both sides of the
area formed by the sacred portion and
the property of the city will belong to the
prince. It will extend eastward from the

47:22 [c] S Lev 24:22; Nu 15:29; 26:55-56; Isa 56:6-7; Ro 10:12; Eph 2:12-16; 3:6; Col 3:11 **47:23** [d] S Dt 10:19 **48:1** [e] S Ge 30:6 [f] Eze 47:15-17 [g] S Eze 47:20 **48:2** [h] Jos 19:24-31 **48:3** [i] Jos 19:32-39 **48:4** [j] Jos 17:1-11 **48:5** [k] Jos 16:5-9 [l] Jos 17:7-10 [m] Jos 17:17 **48:6** [n] Jos 13:15-21 **48:7** [o] Jos 15:1-63 **48:8** [p] ver 21 **48:9** [q] S Eze 45:1 **48:10** [r] ver 21; S Eze 45:3-4 **48:11** [s] S 2Sa 8:17 [t] S Lev 8:35 [u] Eze 14:11; S 44:15 **48:13** [v] Eze 45:5 **48:14** [w] S Lev 25:34; 27:10,28 **48:16** [x] Rev 21:16 **48:18** [y] Eze 45:6

[a] *8* That is, about 8 miles or about 13 kilometers; also in verses 9, 10, 13, 15, 20 and 21 [b] *9* That is, about 3 1/3 miles or about 5.3 kilometers; also in verses 10, 13 and 18 [c] *15* That is, about 1 2/3 miles or about 2.7 kilometers [d] *16* That is, about 1 1/2 miles or about 2.4 kilometers; also in verses 30, 32, 33 and 34 [e] *17* That is, about 440 feet or about 135 meters

48:1 – 29 The distribution of the land in the new order (see map, p. 1410).
48:1 *Dan.* Occupies its historical location as the northernmost tribe (see the phrase "from Dan to Beersheba," giving northern and southern boundaries — e.g., in Jdg 20:1; 1Sa 3:20). Dan was born to Rachel's maidservant Bilhah (Ge 35:25). *Hethlon … Lebo Hamath.* See note on 47:15. *Hazar Enan.* See note on 47:16.
48:2 *Asher.* Born to Leah's maidservant Zilpah (Ge 35:26). The tribes descended from maidservants were placed farthest from the sanctuary (see Dan, v. 1; Naphtali, v. 3; Gad, v. 27).
48:3 *Naphtali.* Born to Rachel's maidservant Bilhah (see note on v. 2).
48:4 *Manasseh.* See note on 47:13.
48:5 *Ephraim.* See note on 47:13.
48:6 *Reuben.* Leah's firstborn (Ge 29:31).
48:7 *Judah.* Son of Leah (Ge 35:23). He had the most prestigious place, bordering the central holy portion (v. 8), because his tribe was given the Messianic promise (see Ge 49:8 – 12 and note on 49:10).
48:8 – 22 An expansion of 45:1 – 8 (see notes there).
48:9 *10,000 cubits wide.* The width of the entire sacred district was 20,000 cubits (see 45:1). The present verse must refer to the width of either the priests' or the Levites' area. The Septuagint (the pre-Christian Greek translation of the OT), however, reads "20,000" here.
48:11 *Zadokites, who were faithful.* See note on 44:15.
48:14 *not sell or exchange.* Since it was the Lord's, it was not to be an object of commerce.
48:19 *from all the tribes of Israel.* The sacred district was national property, not the prince's private domain.

25,000 cubits of the sacred portion to the eastern border, and westward from the 25,000 cubits to the western border. Both these areas running the length of the tribal portions will belong to the prince, and the sacred portion with the temple sanctuary will be in the center of them.[z] 22 So the property of the Levites and the property of the city will lie in the center of the area that belongs to the prince. The area belonging to the prince will lie between the border of Judah and the border of Benjamin.

23 "As for the rest of the tribes: Benjamin[a] will have one portion; it will extend from the east side to the west side.

24 "Simeon[b] will have one portion; it will border the territory of Benjamin from east to west.

25 "Issachar[c] will have one portion; it will border the territory of Simeon from east to west.

26 "Zebulun[d] will have one portion; it will border the territory of Issachar from east to west.

27 "Gad[e] will have one portion; it will border the territory of Zebulun from east to west.

28 "The southern boundary of Gad will run south from Tamar[f] to the waters of Meribah Kadesh, then along the Wadi of Egypt to the Mediterranean Sea.[g]

29 "This is the land you are to allot as an inheritance to the tribes of Israel, and these will be their portions," declares the Sovereign LORD.[h]

The Gates of the New City

30 "These will be the exits of the city: Beginning on the north side, which is 4,500 cubits long, 31 the gates of the city will be named after the tribes of Israel. The three gates on the north side will be the gate of Reuben, the gate of Judah and the gate of Levi.

32 "On the east side, which is 4,500 cubits long, will be three gates: the gate of Joseph, the gate of Benjamin and the gate of Dan.

33 "On the south side, which measures 4,500 cubits, will be three gates: the gate of Simeon, the gate of Issachar and the gate of Zebulun.

34 "On the west side, which is 4,500 cubits long, will be three gates: the gate of Gad, the gate of Asher and the gate of Naphtali.[i]

35 "The distance all around will be 18,000 cubits.[a]

"And the name of the city from that time on will be:

THE LORD IS THERE.[j]"

48:21 [z] ver 8, 10; Eze 45:7
48:23 [a] Jos 18:11-28
48:24 [b] S Ge 29:33; Jos 19:1-9
48:25 [c] Jos 19:17-23
48:26 [d] Jos 19:10-16
48:27 [e] Jos 13:24-28
48:28 [f] S Ge 14:7 [g] S Nu 34:6; Eze 47:19
48:29 [h] S Eze 45:1
48:34 [i] S 2Ch 4:4; Rev 21:12-13
48:35 [j] S Isa 12:6; S 24:23; S Jer 3:17; 14:9; Joel 3:21; Rev 3:12; S 21:3

[a] 35 That is, about 6 miles or about 9.5 kilometers

48:23 *Benjamin.* Rachel's son (Ge 35:24).
48:24 *Simeon.* Leah's son (Ge 35:23).
48:25 *Issachar.* Leah's son (Ge 35:23).
48:26 *Zebulun.* Leah's son (Ge 35:23).
48:27 *Gad.* Son of Zilpah, Leah's maid (see note on v. 2).
48:28 *Tamar.* See note on 47:18. *Meribah Kadesh.* See note on 47:19. *Wadi of Egypt.* See note on 47:19.
48:30–35 The 12 gates of the new city of Jerusalem.
48:31 *Reuben . . . Judah . . . Levi.* Reuben (representing the firstborn), Judah (the Messianic tribe) and Levi (the tribe of the priesthood) had gates together on the north side. Since Levi was included in this list, Joseph (v. 32) represented Ephraim and Manasseh (see note on 47:13) in order to keep the number at 12. For the gates, cf. Rev 21:12–14.
48:35 *THE LORD IS THERE.* The great decisive word concerning the holy city. The Hebrew for this clause is *Yahweh Shammah*, which may be a wordplay on *Yerushalayim*, the Hebrew pronunciation of Jerusalem. For other names of Jerusalem, see 23:4; Isa 1:26; 29:1; 60:14; 62:2–4,12; Jer 3:17; 33:16; Zec 8:3. The book of Joel has a similar ending (see note on Joel 3:21).

DANIEL

INTRODUCTION

Author, Date and Authenticity

The book implies in several passages, such as 9:2; 10:2, that Daniel was its author. That Jesus concurred is clear from his reference to "'the abomination that causes desolation,' spoken of through the prophet Daniel" (Mt 24:15; see note there), quoting 9:27 (see note there); 11:31 (see note there); 12:11. The book was probably completed c. 530 BC, shortly after Cyrus the Great, king of Persia, captured the city of Babylon in 539 (see 10:1 and note).

The widely held view that the book of Daniel is largely fictional rests mainly on the modern philosophical assumption that long-range predictive prophecy is impossible. Therefore all fulfilled predictions in Daniel, it is claimed, had to have been composed no earlier than the Maccabean period (second century BC), after the fulfillments had taken place. But objective evidence excludes this hypothesis on several counts:

(1) To avoid fulfillment of long-range predictive prophecy in the book, the adherents of the late-date view usually maintain that the four empires of chs. 2 and 7 are Babylonia, Media, Persia and Greece. But in the mind of the author, "the Medes and Persians" (5:28; see note there) together constituted the second in the series of four kingdoms (2:32–43; see note there). Thus it becomes clear that the four empires are the Babylonian, Medo-Persian, Greek and Roman. See chart, p. 1429.

(2) The language itself argues for a date earlier than the second century. Linguistic evidence from the Dead Sea Scrolls (which furnish authentic samples of Hebrew and Aramaic writing from the third and second centuries BC; see essay, pp. 1574–1576) demonstrates that the Hebrew and Aramaic chapters of Daniel must have been composed centuries earlier. Furthermore, as recently demonstrated, the Persian and Greek words in Daniel do not require a late date. Some of the technical terms appearing in ch. 3 were already so obsolete by the second century BC that translators of the Septuagint (the pre-Christian Greek translation of the OT) translated them incorrectly.

(3) Several of the fulfillments of prophecies in Daniel could

a quick look

Author:
Daniel

Audience:
The Jewish exiles in Babylonia

Date:
About 530 BC

Theme:
The Most High God is sovereign over all human kingdoms.

Daniel's historical narratives and apocalyptic visions always show God as triumphant.

not have taken place by the second century anyway, so the prophetic element cannot be dismissed. The symbolism connected with the fourth kingdom makes it unmistakably predictive of the Roman Empire (see 2:33; 7:7,19), which did not take control of Syro-Palestine until 63 BC. Also, a plausible interpretation of the prophecy concerning the coming of "the Anointed One, the ruler," approximately 483 years after the word went out "to restore and rebuild Jerusalem" (9:25; see note on 9:25 – 27), works out to the time of Jesus' ministry.

Objective evidence, therefore, appears to exclude the late-date hypothesis and indicates that there is insufficient reason to deny Daniel's authorship.

Theological Theme

The theological theme of the book is summarized in 4:17; 5:21: "The Most High (God) is sovereign over all kingdoms on earth." Daniel's visions always show God as triumphant (7:11,26 – 27; 8:25; 9:27). The climax of his sovereign rule is described in Revelation: "The kingdom of the world has become the kingdom of our Lord and of his Messiah ['Anointed One'], and he will reign for ever and ever" (Rev 11:15; see Da 2:44; 7:27; 9:25 – 27 and notes).

Literary Forms

The book is made up primarily of historical narrative (found mainly in chs. 1 – 6) and apocalyptic ("revelatory") material (found mainly in chs. 7 – 12). The latter may be defined as symbolic, visionary, prophetic literature, usually composed during oppressive conditions and being chiefly eschatological in theological content. Apocalyptic literature is primarily a literature of encouragement to the people of God (see Introduction to Zechariah: Literary Forms and Themes; see also Introduction to Revelation: Literary Form). For the symbolic use of numbers in apocalyptic literature, see Introduction to Revelation: Distinctive Feature.

Cup with Daniel surrounded by lions with angels protecting him (sixth century BC)

Kim Walton, courtesy of the British Museum

Outline

- I. Prologue: The Setting (ch. 1; in Hebrew)
  - A. Historical Introduction (1:1 – 2)
  - B. Daniel and His Friends Are Taken Captive (1:3 – 7)
  - C. The Young Men Are Faithful (1:8 – 16)
  - D. The Young Men Are Elevated to High Positions (1:17 – 21)
- II. The Destinies of the Nations of the World (chs. 2 – 7; in Aramaic, beginning at 2:4b)
  - A. Nebuchadnezzar's Dream of a Large Statue (ch. 2)
  - B. Nebuchadnezzar's Making of a Gold Image and His Decree That It Be Worshiped (ch. 3)
  - C. Nebuchadnezzar's Dream of an Enormous Tree (ch. 4)

   D. Belshazzar's and Babylon's Downfall (ch. 5)
   E. Daniel's Deliverance from the Lions' Den (ch. 6)
   F. Daniel's Dream of Four Beasts (ch. 7)
III. The Destiny of the Nation of Israel (chs. 8 – 12; in Hebrew)
   A. Daniel's Vision of a Ram and a Goat (ch. 8)
   B. Daniel's Prayer and His Vision of the 70 "Sevens" (ch. 9)
   C. Daniel's Vision of Israel's Future (chs. 10 – 12)
      1. Revelation of things to come (10:1 – 3)
      2. Revelation from the angelic messenger (10:4 — 11:1)
      3. Prophecies concerning Persia and Greece (11:2 – 4)
      4. Prophecies concerning Egypt and Syria (11:5 – 35)
      5. Prophecies concerning the antichrist (11:36 – 45)
      6. Distress and deliverance (12:1)
      7. Two resurrections (12:2 – 3)
      8. Instruction to Daniel (12:4)
      9. Conclusion (12:5 – 13)

Daniel's Training in Babylon

1 In the third year of the reign of Jehoiakim[a] king of Judah, Nebuchadnezzar[b] king of Babylon[c] came to Jerusalem
and besieged it.[d] 2 And the Lord delivered
Jehoiakim king of Judah into his hand,
along with some of the articles from the
temple of God. These he carried[e] off to the
temple of his god in Babylonia[a] and put in
the treasure house of his god.[f]
3 Then the king ordered Ashpenaz,
chief of his court officials, to bring into
the king's service some of the Israelites
from the royal family and the nobility[g]—
4 young men without any physical defect,
handsome,[h] showing aptitude for every
kind of learning,[i] well informed, quick
to understand, and qualified to serve in
the king's palace. He was to teach them
the language[j] and literature of the Babylonians.[b] 5 The king assigned them a daily
amount of food and wine[k] from the king's
table.[l] They were to be trained for three
years,[m] and after that they were to enter
the king's service.[n]
6 Among those who were chosen were
some from Judah: Daniel,[o] Hananiah,
Mishael and Azariah.[p] 7 The chief official gave them new names: to Daniel, the
name Belteshazzar;[q] to Hananiah, Shadrach; to Mishael, Meshach; and to Azariah, Abednego.[r]
8 But Daniel resolved not to defile[s] himself with the royal food and wine, and
he asked the chief official for permission
not to defile himself this way. 9 Now God
had caused the official to show favor[t] and
compassion[u] to Daniel, 10 but the official
told Daniel, "I am afraid of my lord the
king, who has assigned your[c] food and
drink.[v] Why should he see you looking
worse than the other young men your age?
The king would then have my head because of you."
11 Daniel then said to the guard whom
the chief official had appointed over
Daniel, Hananiah, Mishael and Azariah,
12 "Please test[w] your servants for ten days:
Give us nothing but vegetables to eat and
water to drink. 13 Then compare our appearance with that of the young men who
eat the royal food, and treat your servants
in accordance with what you see."[x] 14 So
he agreed to this and tested[y] them for ten
days.
15 At the end of the ten days they looked
healthier and better nourished than any
of the young men who ate the royal food.[z]
16 So the guard took away their choice food
and the wine they were to drink and gave
them vegetables instead.[a]
17 To these four young men God gave
knowledge and understanding[b] of all kinds
of literature and learning.[c] And Daniel
could understand visions and dreams of
all kinds.[d]
18 At the end of the time[e] set by the king
to bring them into his service, the chief official presented them to Nebuchadnezzar.
19 The king talked with them, and he found

1:1 [a] S Jer 46:2 [b] S 2Ki 24:1; S Jer 28:14 [c] Jer 50:1 [d] 2Ki 24:1; S 2Ch 36:6; Jer 35:11 **1:2** [e] S 2Ki 24:13 [f] S 2Ch 36:7; Jer 27:19-20; Zec 5:5-11 **1:3** [g] S 2Ki 20:18; S 24:15; Isa 39:7 **1:4** [h] S Ge 39:6 [i] ver 17 [j] S Ezr 4:7 **1:5** [k] ver 8, 10 [l] S Est 2:9 [m] ver 18 [n] ver 19; S Est 2:5-6 **1:6** [o] S Eze 14:14 [p] Da 2:17,25 **1:7** [q] Da 2:26; 4:8; 5:12; 10:1 [r] S Isa 39:7; Da 2:49; 3:12 **1:8** [s] S Eze 4:13-14 **1:9** [t] S Ge 39:21; S Pr 16:7 [u] S 1Ki 8:50 **1:10** [v] ver 5 **1:12** [w] Rev 2:10 **1:13** [x] ver 16 **1:14** [y] Rev 2:10 **1:15** [z] Ex 23:25 **1:16** [a] ver 12-13 **1:17** [b] S Job 12:13 [c] Da 2:23; Col 1:9; Jas 1:5 [d] Da 2:19,30; 5:11; 7:1; 8:1 **1:18** [e] ver 5

[a] *2* Hebrew *Shinar* [b] *4* Or *Chaldeans*
[c] *10* The Hebrew for *your* and *you* in this verse is plural.

1:1 *third year.* According to the Babylonian system of computing the years of a king's reign, the third year of Jehoiakim would have been 605 BC, since his first full year of kingship began on New Year's Day after his accession in 608. But according to the system in Judah, which counted the year of accession as the first year of reign, this was "the fourth year of Jehoiakim" (Jer 25:1; 46:2; see notes there). *Jehoiakim king of Judah.* Reigned 609–598 BC. See 2Ki 23:34; 2Ch 36:5–8 and notes. *Nebuchadnezzar king of Babylon.* 605 BC was also the first year of his reign (see Jer 25:1; 2Ki 24:1 and note; see also chart, p. 511).

1:2 *carried off.* Judah was exiled to Babylonia because she disobeyed God's word regarding covenant-keeping, the sabbath years and idolatry (see Lev 25:4 and note; 26:27–35; Dt 28:15–68; 2Ki 25:1 and note; 2Ch 36:20–21 and note). The first deportation (605 BC) included Daniel, and the second (597) included Ezekiel. A third deportation took place in 586, when the Babylonians destroyed the city of Jerusalem and Solomon's temple. *his god.* Marduk (see note on Isa 45:4).

1:4 *language and literature of the Babylonians.* Including the classical literature in Sumerian and Akkadian cuneiform, a complicated syllabic writing system. But the language of normal communication in multiracial Babylon was Aramaic, written in an easily learned alphabetic script (see 2:4 and note).

1:6 *Daniel.* Means "God is (my) Judge." *Hananiah.* Means "The LORD shows grace." *Mishael.* Means "Who is what God is?" *Azariah.* Means "The LORD helps."

1:7 *gave them new names.* Indicating that they were now subject to Nebuchadnezzar's authority (see Ge 17:5; 41:45; 2Ki 23:34; 24:17 and notes). *Belteshazzar.* Probably means, in Babylonian, "Bel (i.e., Marduk), protect his life!" *Shadrach.* Probably means "command of Aku (Sumerian moon-god)." *Meshach.* Probably means "Who is what Aku is?" *Abednego.* Means "servant of Nego/Nebo (i.e., Nabu)."

1:8 *royal food and wine.* Israelites perhaps considered food from Nebuchadnezzar's table to be contaminated because the first portion of it was offered to idols. Likewise, a portion of the wine was poured out on a pagan altar. Ceremonially unclean animals were used and were neither slaughtered nor prepared according to the regulations of the law. *he asked … not to defile himself.* He demonstrated the courage of his convictions.

1:9 *God had caused the official to show favor … to Daniel.* The careers of Joseph and Daniel were similar in many respects (see Ge 39–41).

1:12 *test your servants.* Daniel used good judgment by offering an alternative instead of rebelling. *ten.* Often symbolized completeness.

1:17 With God's help, Daniel and his friends mastered the essential Babylonian literature on astrology and divination by dreams. But in the crucial tests of interpretation and prediction (see 2:2–11; 4:6–7), all the pagan literature proved worthless. Only by God's special revelation (2:17–28) was Daniel able to interpret correctly.

none equal to Daniel, Hananiah, Mishael and Azariah; so they entered the king's service.[f] 20 In every matter of wisdom and understanding about which the king questioned them, he found them ten times better than all the magicians[g] and enchanters in his whole kingdom.[h]

21 And Daniel remained there until the first year of King Cyrus.[i]

Nebuchadnezzar's Dream

2 In the second year of his reign, Nebuchadnezzar had dreams;[j] his mind was troubled[k] and he could not sleep.[l] 2 So the king summoned the magicians,[m] enchanters, sorcerers[n] and astrologers[a][o] to tell him what he had dreamed.[p] When they came in and stood before the king, 3 he said to them, "I have had a dream that troubles[q] me and I want to know what it means.[b]"

4 Then the astrologers answered the king,[c][r] "May the king live forever![s] Tell your servants the dream, and we will interpret it."

5 The king replied to the astrologers, "This is what I have firmly decided:[t] If you do not tell me what my dream was and interpret it, I will have you cut into pieces[u] and your houses turned into piles of rubble.[v] 6 But if you tell me the dream and explain it, you will receive from me gifts and rewards and great honor.[w] So tell me the dream and interpret it for me."

7 Once more they replied, "Let the king tell his servants the dream, and we will interpret it."

8 Then the king answered, "I am certain that you are trying to gain time, because you realize that this is what I have firmly decided: 9 If you do not tell me the dream, there is only one penalty[x] for you. You have conspired to tell me misleading and wicked things, hoping the situation will change. So then, tell me the dream, and I will know that you can interpret it for me."[y]

10 The astrologers[z] answered the king, "There is no one on earth who can do what the king asks! No king, however great and mighty, has ever asked such a thing of any magician or enchanter or astrologer.[a] 11 What the king asks is too difficult. No one can reveal it to the king except the gods,[b] and they do not live among humans."

12 This made the king so angry and furious[c] that he ordered the execution[d] of all the wise men of Babylon. 13 So the decree was issued to put the wise men to death, and men were sent to look for Daniel and his friends to put them to death.[e]

14 When Arioch, the commander of the king's guard, had gone out to put to death the wise men of Babylon, Daniel spoke to him with wisdom and tact. 15 He asked the king's officer, "Why did the king issue such a harsh decree?" Arioch then explained the matter to Daniel. 16 At this, Daniel went in to the king and asked for time, so that he might interpret the dream for him.

17 Then Daniel returned to his house and explained the matter to his friends Hananiah, Mishael and Azariah.[f] 18 He urged them to plead for mercy[g] from the God of heaven[h] concerning this mystery,[i] so that he and his friends might not be executed with the rest of the wise men of Babylon. 19 During the night the mystery[j] was revealed to Daniel in a vision.[k] Then Daniel praised the God of heaven[l] 20 and said:

"Praise be to the name of God for ever
and ever;[m]
wisdom and power[n] are his.
21 He changes times and seasons;[o]
he deposes[p] kings and raises up
others.[q]
He gives wisdom[r] to the wise
and knowledge to the discerning.[s]

1:19 f S Ge 41:46 **1:20** g S Ge 41:8 h S 1Ki 4:30; Est 2:15; S Eze 28:3; Da 2:13,28; 4:18; 6:3 **1:21** i S 2Ch 36:22; Da 6:28; 10:1 **2:1** j ver 3; S Ge 20:3; S Job 33:15,18; Da 4:5 k Ge 41:8 l S Est 6:1 **2:2** m S Ge 41:8 n Ex 7:11; Jer 27:9 o S ver 10; S Isa 19:3; S 44:25 p Da 4:6 **2:3** q Da 4:5 **2:4** r S Ezr 4:7 s S Ne 2:3 **2:5** t Ge 41:32 u ver 12 v Ezr 6:11; Da 3:29 **2:6** w ver 48; Da 5:7,16 **2:9** x Est 4:11 y Isa 41:22-24 **2:10** z ver 2; Da 3:8; 4:7 a ver 27; Da 5:8 **2:11** b S Ge 41:38 **2:12** c Da 3:13,19 d ver 5 **2:13** e S Da 1:20; 5:19 **2:17** f S Da 1:6 **2:18** g S Isa 37:4 h Ezr 1:2; Ne 1:4; Jnh 1:9; Rev 11:13 i ver 23; Jer 33:3 **2:19** j ver 28 k S Job 33:15; S Da 1:17 l S Jos 22:33 **2:20** m S Ps 113:2; 145:1-2 n S Job 9:4; S Jer 32:19 **2:21** o Da 7:25 p S Job 12:19; Ps 75:6-7; Ro 13:1 q Da 4:17 r S Ps 119:34; Jas 1:5 s S 2Sa 14:17

a 2 Or *Chaldeans*; also in verses 4, 5 and 10
b 3 Or *was*
c 4 At this point the Hebrew text has *in Aramaic*, indicating that the text from here through the end of chapter 7 is in Aramaic.

1:20 *ten.* See note on v. 12. *magicians.* See note on Ge 41:8.
1:21 *there.* In Babylonia. *first year of King Cyrus.* Over Babylon (539 BC; see chart, p. 511). Daniel spent about 70 years in Babylonia and was still living in the year 537 (10:1), so he saw the exiles return to Judah from Babylonian captivity.
2:1 *second year of ... Nebuchadnezzar.* 604 BC (see 1:1 and note). *he could not sleep.* See 6:18; Est 6:1 and note.
2:2 *magicians, enchanters, sorcerers.* See Dt 18:9–14 and note on 18:9.
2:4 See NIV text note. Since the astrologers were of various ethnic and cultural backgrounds, they communicated in Aramaic, the language everyone understood. From here to the end of ch. 7 the entire narrative is in Aramaic. These six chapters deal with matters of importance to the Gentile nations of the Near East and were written in a language understandable to all. But the last five chapters (8–12) revert to Hebrew, since they deal with special concerns of the chosen people. *your servants.* Us.
2:5 See 3:29.
2:10 *no one on earth who can do what the king asks.* But "God in heaven" can (through Daniel; see vv. 27–28).
2:11 *do not live among humans.* Are not readily accessible.
2:14 *Arioch.* Also the name of a Mesopotamian king who lived centuries earlier (Ge 14:1,9). *wisdom and tact.* See 1:12,20 and note on 1:12.
2:18 *God of heaven.* In this chapter this Persian title for a high god (see note on Ezr 1:2) is used to refer to Yahweh, the God of Israel. *mystery.* A key word in Daniel (vv. 19,27–30,47; 4:9). It also appears often in the writings (Dead Sea Scrolls) of the Qumran sect (see essay, pp. 1574–1576). The Greek equivalent is used in the NT to refer to the secret purposes of God that he reveals only to his chosen prophets and apostles (see notes on Ro 11:25; Rev 10:7).
2:21 *He gives wisdom ... to the discerning.* See Pr 1:2–5 and note on 1:2.

22 He reveals deep and hidden
things;[t]
he knows what lies in
darkness,[u]
and light[v] dwells with him.
23 I thank and praise you, God of
my ancestors:[w]
You have given me wisdom[x]
and power,
you have made known to me
what we asked of you,
you have made known to us
the dream of the king.[y]"

Reconstructed Ishtar Gate at the site of ancient Babylon in modern Iraq

The Ishtar Gate, Babylonian, c.580 BC/Iraq Museum, Baghdad/The Bridgeman Art Library

Daniel Interprets the Dream

24 Then Daniel went to Arioch,[z]
whom the king had appointed to
execute the wise men of Babylon,
and said to him, "Do not execute
the wise men of Babylon. Take
me to the king, and I will interpret his dream for him."
25 Arioch took Daniel to the
king at once and said, "I have
found a man among the exiles[a]
from Judah[b] who can tell the king
what his dream means."
26 The king asked Daniel (also
called Belteshazzar),[c] "Are you
able to tell me what I saw in my dream
and interpret it?"
27 Daniel replied, "No wise man, enchanter, magician or diviner can explain to
the king the mystery he has asked about,[d]
28 but there is a God in heaven who reveals
mysteries.[e] He has shown King Nebuchadnezzar what will happen in days to come.[f]
Your dream and the visions that passed
through your mind[g] as you were lying in
bed[h] are these:[i]
29 "As Your Majesty was lying there, your
mind turned to things to come, and the
revealer of mysteries showed you what is
going to happen.[j]
30 As for me, this mys-
tery has been revealed[k] to me, not because
I have greater wisdom than anyone else
alive, but so that Your Majesty may know
the interpretation and that you may understand what went through your mind.
31 "Your Majesty looked, and there before you stood a large statue—an enormous, dazzling statue,[l] awesome[m] in appearance.
32 The head of the statue was
made of pure gold, its chest and arms of
silver, its belly and thighs of bronze,
33 its
legs of iron, its feet partly of iron and partly of baked clay.
34 While you were watch-
ing, a rock was cut out, but not by human
hands.[n] It struck the statue on its feet of
iron and clay and smashed[o] them.[p]
35 Then
the iron, the clay, the bronze, the silver
and the gold were all broken to pieces and
became like chaff on a threshing floor in
the summer. The wind swept them away[q]
without leaving a trace. But the rock that
struck the statue became a huge mountain[r] and filled the whole earth.[s]

2:22 [t]S Ge 40:8; S Job 12:22; Da 5:11; 1Co 2:10 [u]Job 12:22; Ps 139:11-12; Jer 23:24; S Heb 4:13 [v]Isa 45:7; Jas 1:17 **2:23** [w]S Ge 31:5; S Ex 3:15 [x]S Da 1:17 [y]S Eze 28:3 **2:24** [z]ver 14 **2:25** [a]S Dt 21:10 [b]S Da 1:6; 5:13; 6:13 **2:26** [c]S Da 1:7 **2:27** [d]S ver 10; S Ge 41:8 **2:28** [e]S Ge 40:8; Jer 10:7; Am 4:13 [f]S Ge 49:1; Da 10:14; Mt 24:6; Rev 1:1; 22:6 [g]Da 4:5 [h]S Ps 4:4 [i]S Eze 28:3; S Da 1:20 **2:29** [j]S Ge 41:25 **2:30** [k]Isa 45:3; S Da 1:17; Am 4:13 **2:31** [l]Hab 1:7 [m]Isa 25:3-5 **2:34** [n]S Job 12:19; Zec 4:6 [o]S Job 34:24 [p]ver 44-45; Ps 2:9; S Isa 60:12; Da 8:25 **2:35** [q]Ps 1:4; 37:10; S Isa 17:13; 41:15-16 [r]Isa 2:3; Mic 4:1 [s]Zec 12:3

2:22 *light dwells with him.* See Ps 36:9 and note; cf. 1Jn 1:5 and note.
2:29 *the revealer of mysteries.* God (see v. 47).
2:32–43 See maps, pp. 2523, 2530, at the end of this study Bible; see also chart, p. 1429. The gold head represents the Neo-Babylonian Empire (v. 38; see Jer 51:7 and note; see also map, p. 1423); the silver chest and arms the Medo-Persian Empire established by Cyrus in 539 BC (the date of the fall of Babylon); the bronze belly and thighs the Greek Empire established by Alexander the Great c. 330; the iron legs and feet the Roman Empire (in the Apocrypha, cf. 2 Esdras 12:11). The toes (v. 41) are understood by some to represent a later confederation of states occupying the territory formerly controlled by the Roman Empire. The diminishing value of the metals from gold to silver to bronze to iron represents the decreasing power and grandeur (v. 39) of the rulers of the successive empires, from the absolute despotism of Nebuchadnezzar to the democratic system of checks and balances that characterized the Roman senates and assemblies. The metals also symbolize a growing degree of toughness and endurance, with each successive empire lasting longer than the preceding one.
2:33 *partly of iron and partly of baked clay.* "Partly strong and partly brittle" (v. 42).
2:35 *broken to pieces.* See Lk 20:18 and note.

36 "This was the dream, and now we will interpret it to the king.[t] 37 Your Majesty, you are the king of kings.[u] The God of heaven has given you dominion[v] and power and might and glory; 38 in your hands he has placed all mankind and the beasts of the field and the birds in the sky. Wherever they live, he has made you ruler over them all.[w] You are that head of gold.

39 "After you, another kingdom will arise, inferior to yours. Next, a third kingdom, one of bronze, will rule over the whole earth.[x] 40 Finally, there will be a fourth kingdom, strong as iron—for iron breaks and smashes everything—and as iron breaks things to pieces, so it will crush and break all the others.[y] 41 Just as you saw that the feet and toes were partly of baked clay and partly of iron, so this will be a divided kingdom; yet it will have some of the strength of iron in it, even as you saw iron mixed with clay. 42 As the toes were partly iron and partly clay, so this kingdom will be partly strong and partly brittle. 43 And just as you saw the iron mixed with baked clay, so the people will be a mixture and will not remain united, any more than iron mixes with clay.

44 "In the time of those kings, the God of heaven will set up a kingdom that will never be destroyed, nor will it be left to another people. It will crush[z] all those kingdoms[a] and bring them to an end, but it will itself endure forever.[b] 45 This is the meaning of the vision of the rock[c] cut out of a mountain, but not by human hands[d]—a rock that broke the iron, the bronze, the clay, the silver and the gold to pieces.

"The great God has shown the king what will take place in the future.[e] The dream is true[f] and its interpretation is trustworthy."

46 Then King Nebuchadnezzar fell prostrate[g] before Daniel and paid him honor and ordered that an offering[h] and incense be presented to him. 47 The king said to Daniel, "Surely your God is the God of gods[i] and the Lord of kings[j] and a revealer of mysteries,[k] for you were able to reveal this mystery.[l]"

48 Then the king placed Daniel in a high[m] position and lavished many gifts on him. He made him ruler over the entire province of Babylon and placed him in charge of all its wise men.[n] 49 Moreover, at Daniel's request the king appointed Shadrach, Meshach and Abednego administrators over the province of Babylon,[o] while Daniel himself remained at the royal court.[p]

The Image of Gold and the Blazing Furnace

3 King Nebuchadnezzar made an image[q] of gold, sixty cubits high and six cubits wide,[a] and set it up on the plain of Dura in the province of Babylon. 2 He then summoned the satraps,[r] prefects, governors, advisers, treasurers, judges, magistrates and all the other provincial officials[s] to come to the dedication of the image he had set up. 3 So the satraps, prefects, governors, advisers, treasurers, judges, magistrates and all the other provincial officials assembled for the dedication of the image that King Nebuchadnezzar had set up, and they stood before it.

4 Then the herald loudly proclaimed, "Nations and peoples of every language,[t] this is what you are commanded to do: 5 As soon as you hear the sound of the horn, flute, zither, lyre, harp,[u] pipe and all kinds of music, you must fall down and worship the image[v] of gold that King Nebuchadnezzar has set up.[w] 6 Whoever does not fall down and worship will immediately be thrown into a blazing furnace."[x]

7 Therefore, as soon as they heard the sound of the horn, flute, zither, lyre, harp and all kinds of music, all the nations and peoples of every language fell down and worshiped the image of gold that King Nebuchadnezzar had set up.[y]

[a] *1* That is, about 90 feet high and 9 feet wide or about 27 meters high and 2.7 meters wide

2:36 [t] S Ge 40:12 **2:37** [u] S Ezr 7:12 [v] S Jer 27:7; Da 4:26 **2:38** [w] S Jer 27:6; Da 4:21-22; 5:18 **2:39** [x] Da 7:5 **2:40** [y] Da 7:7, 23 **2:44** [z] S Ge 27:29; Ps 2:9; S 110:5; Mt 21:43-44; 1Co 15:24 [a] S 1Sa 9:20; Hag 2:22 [b] Ps 145:13; S Isa 9:7; Da 4:34; 6:26; 7:14, 27; Ob 1:21; Mic 4:7, 13; S Lk 1:33; Rev 11:15 **2:45** [c] S Isa 28:16 [d] Da 8:25 [e] S Ge 41:25 [f] Rev 22:6 **2:46** [g] Da 8:17; Ac 10:25 [h] Ac 14:13 **2:47** [i] S Dt 10:17; Da 11:36 [j] Da 4:25; 1Ti 6:15 [k] S ver 22, 28 [l] Da 4:9; 1Co 14:25 **2:48** [m] S 2Ki 25:28 [n] S ver 6; S Est 8:2; S Da 1:20; 4:9; 5:11; 8:27 **2:49** [o] S Da 1:7; 3:30 [p] Da 6:2 **3:1** [q] ver 14; S Isa 46:6; Jer 16:20; Hab 2:19 **3:2** [r] S Est 1:1 [s] ver 27; Da 6:7 **3:4** [t] Da 4:1; 6:25; Rev 10:11 **3:5** [u] S Ge 4:21 [v] Rev 13:12 [w] ver 10, 15 **3:6** [x] ver 11, 15, 21; Jer 29:22; Da 5:19; 6:7; Mt 13:42, 50; Rev 13:15 **3:7** [y] S ver 5

2:37 *king of kings.* That is, the greatest king (cf. v. 47; Ezr 7:12 and note; 1Ti 6:15; Rev 17:14 and note; 19:16).

2:44 The fifth kingdom is the eternal kingdom of God (see Rev 11:15), built on the ruins of the sinful empires of the world. Its authority will extend over "the whole earth" (v. 35) and ultimately over "a new heaven and a new earth" (Rev 21:1).

2:46 *offering ... be presented to him.* As to a god (cf. Ac 14:12 and note).

2:48 Cf. the story of Joseph (Ge 41:41–43).

2:49 Daniel requests that his administrative authority be shared with his three Jewish friends.

3:1 *image of gold.* Large statues of this kind were not made of solid gold but were plated with gold. *sixty cubits high.* Including the lofty pedestal on which it no doubt stood (see NIV text note; cf. Est 5:14 and note). *Dura.* Either the name of a place now marked by a series of mounds (located a few miles south of Babylon) or a common noun meaning "walled enclosure."

3:2 The seven classifications of government officials were to pledge full allegiance to the newly established empire as they stood before the image. The image perhaps represented the god Nabu, whose name formed the first element in Nebuchadnezzar's name (see note on 2Ki 24:1).

3:4 *every language.* Nebuchadnezzar's Babylon had become a cosmopolitan city whose population included people of many national and ethnic origins (see v. 7).

3:5 The words for "zither," "harp" and "pipe" (or perhaps "small drum") are Greek loanwords in Daniel. Greek musicians and instruments are mentioned in Assyrian inscriptions written before the time of Nebuchadnezzar. *fall down and worship the image.* See Ex 20:4–5 and note on 20:4.

8 At this time some astrologers[a][z] came forward and denounced the Jews. 9 They said
to King Nebuchadnezzar, "May the king
live forever![a] 10 Your Majesty has issued a
decree[b] that everyone who hears the sound
of the horn, flute, zither, lyre, harp, pipe
and all kinds of music must fall down and
worship the image of gold,[c] 11 and that whoever does not fall down and worship will be
thrown into a blazing furnace. 12 But there
are some Jews whom you have set over the
affairs of the province of Babylon—Shadrach, Meshach and Abednego[d]—who pay
no attention[e] to you, Your Majesty. They
neither serve your gods nor worship the
image of gold you have set up."[f]

13 Furious[g] with rage, Nebuchadnezzar
summoned Shadrach, Meshach and Abednego. So these men were brought before
the king, 14 and Nebuchadnezzar said to
them, "Is it true, Shadrach, Meshach and
Abednego, that you do not serve my gods[h]
or worship the image[i] of gold I have set
up? 15 Now when you hear the sound of
the horn, flute, zither, lyre, harp, pipe and
all kinds of music, if you are ready to fall
down and worship the image I made, very
good. But if you do not worship it, you
will be thrown immediately into a blazing
furnace. Then what god[j] will be able to
rescue[k] you from my hand?"

16 Shadrach, Meshach and Abednego[l] replied to him, "King Nebuchadnezzar, we
do not need to defend ourselves before
you in this matter. 17 If we are thrown into
the blazing furnace, the God we serve is
able to deliver[m] us from it, and he will deliver[n] us[b] from Your Majesty's hand. 18 But
even if he does not, we want you to know,
Your Majesty, that we will not serve your
gods or worship the image of gold you
have set up.[o]"

19 Then Nebuchadnezzar was furious
with Shadrach, Meshach and Abednego,
and his attitude toward them changed. He
ordered the furnace heated seven[p] times
hotter than usual 20 and commanded some
of the strongest soldiers in his army to
tie up Shadrach, Meshach and Abednego[q] and throw them into the blazing furnace. 21 So these men, wearing their robes,
trousers, turbans and other clothes, were
bound and thrown into the blazing furnace. 22 The king's command was so urgent and the furnace so hot that the flames
of the fire killed the soldiers who took up
Shadrach, Meshach and Abednego,[r] 23 and
these three men, firmly tied, fell into the
blazing furnace.

24 Then King Nebuchadnezzar leaped to
his feet in amazement and asked his advisers, "Weren't there three men that we
tied up and threw into the fire?"

They replied, "Certainly, Your Majesty."

25 He said, "Look! I see four men walking around in the fire, unbound and unharmed, and the fourth looks like a son
of the gods."

26 Nebuchadnezzar then approached the
opening of the blazing furnace and shouted, "Shadrach, Meshach and Abednego,
servants of the Most High God,[s] come out!
Come here!"

So Shadrach, Meshach and Abednego
came out of the fire, 27 and the satraps, prefects, governors and royal advisers[t] crowded around them.[u] They saw that the fire[v]
had not harmed their bodies, nor was a
hair of their heads singed; their robes were
not scorched, and there was no smell of
fire on them.

28 Then Nebuchadnezzar said, "Praise
be to the God of Shadrach, Meshach and
Abednego, who has sent his angel[w] and
rescued[x] his servants! They trusted[y] in
him and defied the king's command and
were willing to give up their lives rather than serve or worship any god except
their own God.[z] 29 Therefore I decree[a] that
the people of any nation or language who
say anything against the God of Shadrach,
Meshach and Abednego be cut into pieces and their houses be turned into piles
of rubble,[b] for no other god can save[c] in
this way."

[a] 8 Or *Chaldeans* [b] 17 Or *If the God we serve is able to deliver us, then he will deliver us from the blazing furnace and*

3:8 [z]S Isa 19:3; S Da 2:10 **3:9** [a]S Ne 2:3; Da 5:10; 6:6 **3:10** [b]Da 6:12 [c]ver 4-6 **3:12** [d]S Da 2:49 [e]Da 6:13 [f]S Est 3:3 **3:13** [g]S Da 2:12 **3:14** [h]Isa 46:1; Jer 50:2 [i]S ver 1 **3:15** [j]S Isa 36:18-20 [k]S 2Ch 32:15 **3:16** [l]S Da 1:7 **3:17** [m]S Ge 48:16; S Ps 18:48; 27:1-2 [n]S Job 5:19; Jer 1:8; Da 6:20 **3:18** [o]ver 28; S Ex 1:17; S Jos 24:15 **3:19** [p]Lev 26:18-28 **3:20** [q]S Da 1:7 **3:22** [r]S Da 1:7 **3:26** [s]Da 4:2, 34 **3:27** [t]ver 2; Da 6:7 [u]Ps 91:3-11; S Isa 43:2; Heb 11:32-34 [v]Da 6:23 **3:28** [w]S Ps 34:7; Da 6:22; Ac 5:19 [x]S Ps 97:10; Ac 12:11 [y]S Dt 31:20; S Job 13:15; S Ps 26:1; 84:12 [z]S ver 18 **3:29** [a]Da 6:26 [b]S Ezr 6:11 [c]Da 6:27

3:8 *Jews.* A shortened form of "Judahites" (see Zec 8:23 and note).

3:12 *They neither serve your gods nor worship the image.* They obeyed the word of God (Ex 20:3–5) above the word of the king.

3:15 *what god will be able to rescue you from my hand?* Such boastful taunts were characteristic of proud Mesopotamian rulers (see Isa 36:18–20 and note).

3:17 See vv. 26–27; Heb 11:34 and note. *the God we serve is able to deliver us.* For what God is "able" to do, see, e.g., 4:37; 6:19–22 (cf. Ro 11:23; 2Co 9:8; Heb 7:25; Jude 24–25 and notes).

3:18 *if he does not.* Whether God decides to rescue them (v. 17) or not, their faith is fully resigned to his will.

3:19 *seven times hotter than usual.* Probably figurative for "as hot as possible" (seven signifies completeness).

3:25 See Ps 91:9–12. *son of the gods.* Nebuchadnezzar was speaking as a pagan polytheist and was content to conceive of the fourth figure as a lesser heavenly being ("angel," v. 28) sent by the all-powerful God of the Jews (see also 6:22).

3:26 *Most High God.* Nebuchadnezzar had earlier acknowledged that Daniel's God is "the God of gods and the Lord of kings" (2:47).

3:28 *They trusted in him.* See 6:23 and note; Ps 11; 16; 23; 31; 52; Pr 3:5 and note.

3:29 See 2:5. *no other god can save.* See Isa 40:18–20; 41:24; 44:17 and notes (cf. Jn 14:6 and note).

30 Then the king promoted Shadrach, Meshach and Abednego in the province of Babylon.[d]

Nebuchadnezzar's Dream of a Tree

4 [a] King Nebuchadnezzar,

To the nations and peoples of every language,[e] who live in all the earth:

May you prosper greatly![f]

2 It is my pleasure to tell you about the miraculous signs[g] and wonders that the Most High God[h] has performed for me.

3 How great are his signs,
how mighty his wonders![i]
His kingdom is an eternal kingdom;
his dominion endures[j] from
generation to generation.

4 I, Nebuchadnezzar, was at home in my palace, contented[k] and prosperous. 5 I had a dream[l] that made me afraid. As I was lying in bed,[m] the images and visions that passed through my mind[n] terrified me.[o] 6 So I commanded that all the wise men of Babylon be brought before me to interpret[p] the dream for me. 7 When the magicians,[q] enchanters, astrologers[b] and diviners[r] came, I told them the dream, but they could not interpret it for me.[s] 8 Finally, Daniel came into my presence and I told him the dream. (He is called Belteshazzar,[t] after the name of my god, and the spirit of the holy gods[u] is in him.)

9 I said, "Belteshazzar, chief[v] of the magicians, I know that the spirit of the holy gods[w] is in you, and no mystery is too difficult for you. Here is my dream; interpret it for me. 10 These are the visions I saw while lying in bed:[x] I looked, and there before me stood a tree in the middle of the land. Its height was enormous.[y] 11 The tree grew large and strong and its top touched the sky; it was visible to the ends of the earth.[z] 12 Its leaves were beautiful, its fruit abundant, and on it was food for all. Under it the wild animals found shelter, and the birds lived in its branches;[a] from it every creature was fed.

13 "In the visions I saw while lying in bed,[b] I looked, and there before me was a holy one,[c] a messenger,[c] coming down from heaven. 14 He called in a loud voice: 'Cut down the tree[d] and trim off its branches; strip off its leaves and scatter its fruit. Let the animals flee from under it and the birds from its branches.[e] 15 But let the stump and its roots, bound with iron and bronze, remain in the ground, in the grass of the field.

" 'Let him be drenched with the dew of heaven, and let him live with the animals among the plants of the earth. 16 Let his mind be changed from that of a man and let him be given the mind of an animal, till seven times[d] pass by for him.[f]

17 " 'The decision is announced by messengers, the holy ones declare the verdict, so that the living may know that the Most High[g] is sovereign[h] over all kingdoms on earth and gives them to anyone he wishes and sets over them the lowliest[i] of people.'

18 "This is the dream that I, King Nebuchadnezzar, had. Now, Belteshazzar, tell me what it means, for none of the wise men in my kingdom can interpret it for me.[j] But you can,[k] because the spirit of the holy gods[l] is in you."[m]

Daniel Interprets the Dream

19 Then Daniel (also called Belteshazzar) was greatly perplexed for

3:30 [d] S Da 2:49
4:1 [e] S Da 3:4 [f] Da 6:25
4:2 [g] Ps 74:9 [h] S Da 3:26
4:3 [i] S Ps 105:27; Da 6:27 [j] Da 2:44
4:4 [k] Ps 30:6; S Isa 32:9
4:5 [l] S Da 2:1 [m] Ps 4:4 [n] Da 2:28 [o] ver 19; S Ge 41:8; S Job 3:26; Da 2:3; 5:6
4:6 [p] Da 2:2
4:7 [q] S Ge 41:8 [r] S Isa 44:25; S Da 2:2 [s] S Da 2:10
4:8 [t] S Da 1:7 [u] S Ge 41:38
4:9 [v] Da 2:48 [w] Da 5:11-12
4:10 [x] S ver 5; Ps 4:4 [y] Eze 31:3-4
4:11 [z] S Eze 19:11; 31:5
4:12 [a] S Eze 17:23; S Mt 13:32
4:13 [b] ver 10; Da 7:1 [c] S ver 23; S Dt 33:2
4:14 [d] S Job 24:20 [e] S Eze 31:12; S Mt 3:10
4:16 [f] ver 23,32
4:17 [g] ver 2, 25; Ps 83:18 [h] S Ps 103:19; Jer 27:5-7; Da 2:21; 5:18-21; Ro 13:1 [i] Da 11:21; Mt 23:12
4:18 [j] S Ge 41:8; Da 5:8,15 [k] S Ge 41:15 [l] S Ge 41:38 [m] ver 7-9; S Da 1:20

[a] In Aramaic texts 4:1-3 is numbered 3:31-33, and 4:4-37 is numbered 4:1-34. [b] *7* Or *Chaldeans* [c] *13* Or *watchman*; also in verses 17 and 23 [d] *16* Or *years*; also in verses 23, 25 and 32

4:1 – 3 Nebuchadnezzar reached this conclusion after the experiences of vv. 4 – 33. The language of his confession may reflect Daniel's influence.
4:3 *His kingdom ... from generation to generation.* See v. 34 and note.
4:7 *magicians ... diviners.* Condemned in Dt 18:9 – 13 (see note on 18:9).
4:8 *after the name of my god.* See note on 1:7. Bel ("lord") was a title for Marduk, chief god of the Babylonian pantheon and Nebuchadnezzar's personal god and so his favorite god.
4:9 *chief of the magicians.* See 2:48.
4:10 *tree.* Interpreted in v. 22.
4:11 *grew large and strong.* In one of Nebuchadnezzar's building inscriptions, Babylon is compared to a spreading tree (cf. v. 22). *its top touched the sky.* Hyperbole; a phrase often used of Mesopotamian temple-towers (see Ge 11:4 and note).
4:13 *messenger.* Angel (but see NIV text note).
4:15 *let the stump ... remain.* Implies that the tree will be revived later (see v. 26). *him.* The tree is here personified and later identified (v. 22).
4:16 *seven.* Signifies completeness (i.e., a full measure). *times.* See NIV text note; see also 7:25 and NIV text note). Alternatively, "times" can refer to indefinite periods.
4:17 *messengers.* The agents of God, who is the ultimate source of the "decision" (see v. 24). *the Most High is sovereign.* See Introduction: Theological Theme.
4:19 *Daniel ... was greatly perplexed.* Possibly over how to state the interpretation in an appropriate way. *My lord, if only ... adversaries!* Daniel prepared the king to fear the worst.

a time, and his thoughts terrified[n]
him. So the king said, "Belteshazzar,
do not let the dream or its meaning
alarm you."[o]
Belteshazzar answered, "My lord,
if only the dream applied to your enemies and its meaning to your adversaries! 20 The tree you saw, which
grew large and strong, with its top
touching the sky, visible to the whole
earth, 21 with beautiful leaves and
abundant fruit, providing food for
all, giving shelter to the wild animals, and having nesting places in
its branches for the birds[p]— 22 Your
Majesty, you are that tree![q] You have
become great and strong; your greatness has grown until it reaches the

4:19 [n]S ver 5; S Ge 41:8; Da 7:15,28; 8:27; 10:16-17 [o]S Ge 40:12
4:21 [p]S Eze 31:6
4:22 [q]S 2Sa 12:7

4:22 *Your Majesty, you are that tree!* Cf. 2:37–38. *your dominion extends … the earth.* Nebuchadnezzar's empire was the largest and most powerful in that part of the world up to that time (see map below).

THE NEO-BABYLONIAN EMPIRE 626–539 BC

The Babylonians, while continuing the militaristic tradition of Assyria, created an astonishing renaissance of Sumero-Akkadian civilization. Led by Nebuchadnezzar (605–562 BC), the Neo-Babylonian Empire carried out a building program of canals and monuments that was ambitious in the extreme.

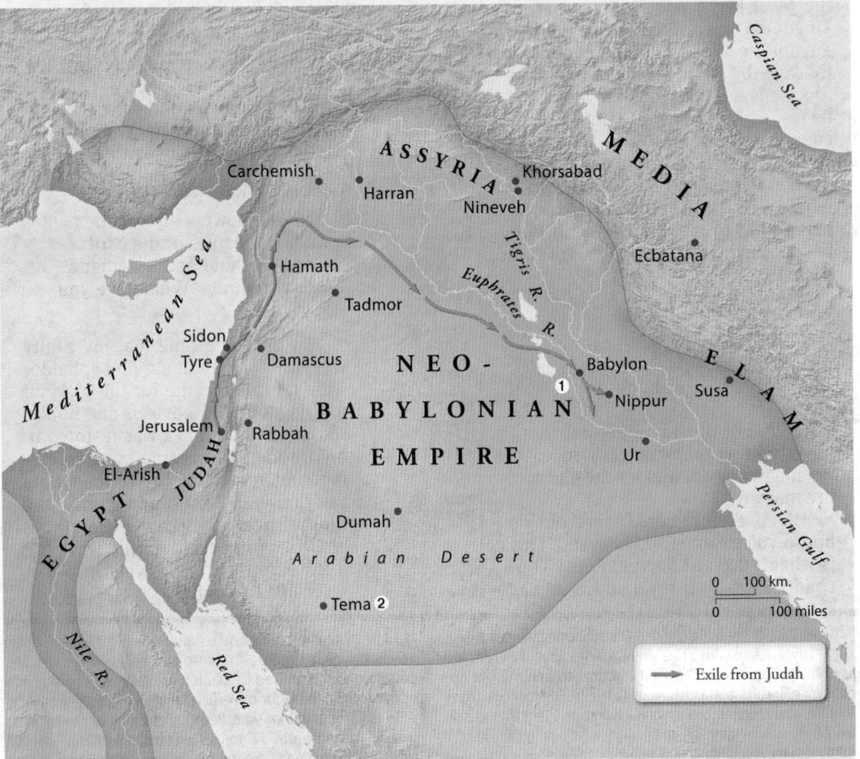

1

Early Greek and Roman authors rhapsodized about the capital city astride the Euphrates. A four-horse chariot could turn atop the high hundred-gated walls. Babylon also boasted one of the world's seven wonders, the famed hanging gardens, as well as a stepped temple-tower 295 feet high and, according to Herodotus, several colossal gold statues weighing many tons.

2

Discoveries of inscriptions in clay have shown that the last king of Babylonia, Nabonidus, absented himself at Tema in Arabia while Belshazzar acted as regent in the capital (see ch. 5).

sky, and your dominion extends to
distant parts of the earth.[r]
23 “Your Majesty saw a holy one,[s] a
messenger, coming down from heav-
en and saying, ‘Cut down the tree and
destroy it, but leave the stump, bound
with iron and bronze, in the grass of
the field, while its roots remain in the
ground. Let him be drenched with the
dew of heaven; let him live with the
wild animals, until seven times pass
by for him.’[t]
24 “This is the interpretation, Your
Majesty, and this is the decree[u] the
Most High has issued against my lord
the king: 25 You will be driven away
from people and will live with the
wild animals; you will eat grass like
the ox and be drenched[v] with the dew
of heaven. Seven times will pass by
for you until you acknowledge that
the Most High[w] is sovereign over all
kingdoms on earth and gives them to
anyone he wishes.[x] 26 The command
to leave the stump of the tree with its
roots[y] means that your kingdom will
be restored to you when you acknowledge that Heaven rules.[z] 27 Therefore,
Your Majesty, be pleased to accept my
advice: Renounce your sins by doing
what is right, and your wickedness by
being kind to the oppressed.[a] It may
be that then your prosperity[b] will continue.[c]”

The Dream Is Fulfilled

28 All this happened[d] to King Nebuchadnezzar. 29 Twelve months later,
as the king was walking on the roof
of the royal palace of Babylon, 30 he
said, “Is not this the great Babylon I
have built as the royal residence, by
my mighty power and for the glory[e] of
my majesty?”[f]
31 Even as the words were on his
lips, a voice came from heaven, “This
is what is decreed for you, King Nebuchadnezzar: Your royal authority has
been taken from you.[g] 32 You will be
driven away from people and will live
with the wild animals; you will eat
grass like the ox. Seven times will
pass by for you until you acknowledge that the Most High is sovereign
over all kingdoms on earth and gives
them to anyone he wishes.”[h]
33 Immediately what had been said
about Nebuchadnezzar was fulfilled.
He was driven away from people and
ate grass like the ox. His body was
drenched[i] with the dew of heaven until his hair grew like the feathers of
an eagle and his nails like the claws
of a bird.[j]

34 At the end of that time, I, Nebuchadnezzar, raised my eyes toward
heaven, and my sanity[k] was restored.
Then I praised the Most High; I honored and glorified him who lives forever.[l]

His dominion is an eternal
dominion;
his kingdom[m] endures from
generation to generation.[n]
35 All the peoples of the earth
are regarded as nothing.[o]
He does as he pleases[p]
with the powers of heaven
and the peoples of the earth.
No one can hold back[q] his hand[r]
or say to him: “What have you
done?”[s]

36 At the same time that my sanity
was restored, my honor and splendor
were returned to me for the glory of
my kingdom.[t] My advisers and nobles
sought me out, and I was restored to
my throne and became even greater
than before. 37 Now I, Nebuchadnezzar, praise and exalt[u] and glorify[v] the
King of heaven, because everything
he does is right and all his ways are
just.[w] And those who walk in pride[x]
he is able to humble.[y]

4:22 [r] Jer 27:7; Da 5:18-19 **4:23** [s] ver 13; Da 8:13 [t] S Eze 31:3-4; Da 5:21 **4:24** [u] Job 40:12; Ps 107:40; Jer 40:2 **4:25** [v] S Job 24:8 [w] S ver 17 [x] Jer 27:5; S Da 2:47; 5:21 **4:26** [y] ver 15 [z] S Da 2:37 **4:27** [a] Isa 55:6-7 [b] Jer 29:7 [c] S Dt 24:13; 1Ki 21:29; S Ps 41:3; S Pr 28:13; S Eze 18:22 **4:28** [d] Nu 23:19 **4:30** [e] Isa 13:19 [f] S Isa 10:13; S 37:24-25; Da 5:20; Hab 1:11; 2:4 **4:31** [g] S 2Sa 22:28; Da 5:20 **4:32** [h] S Job 9:12 **4:33** [i] S Job 24:8 [j] Da 5:20-21 **4:34** [k] S Job 12:20 [l] Da 12:7 [m] Isa 37:16 [n] Ps 145:13; S Da 2:44; 5:21; 6:26; Lk 1:33 **4:35** [o] S Isa 40:17 [p] Dt 21:8; Ps 115:3; S 135:6; Jnh 1:14 [q] S Isa 14:27 [r] S Dt 32:39 [s] S Job 9:4; S Isa 14:24; S 45:9; Da 5:21; Ro 9:20 **4:36** [t] S Pr 22:4; Da 5:18 **4:37** [u] S Ex 15:2 [v] S Ps 34:3 [w] Dt 32:4; Ps 33:4-5 [x] Ps 18:27; S 119:21 [y] S Job 31:4; 40:11-12; S Isa 13:11; Da 5:20, 23; Mt 23:12

4:25 *eat grass like the ox.* Nebuchadnezzar was possibly stricken with a rare mental illness (see v. 34) known as boanthropy, which causes its victims to assume the appearance, habits and posture of cattle (v. 33). *acknowledge that the Most High is sovereign.* He will soon learn that lesson (compare v. 30 with v. 37).

4:26 *Heaven.* A Jewish way of referring to God, later reflected in the NT expression "kingdom of heaven" (compare, e.g., Mt 5:3 with Lk 6:20).

4:28 *All this happened.* But only because Nebuchadnezzar did not follow Daniel's "advice" (v. 27).

4:30 *great Babylon.* Illustrated, e.g., in the city's ramparts, temples and hanging gardens (see note on Isa 13:19; see also map, p. 1423, and photo, p. 1419).

4:31 *as the words were on his lips.* See Lk 12:19 – 20.

4:33 *what had been said ... was fulfilled.* See Pr 11:2 and note; 16:18. *driven away.* Possibly into the palace gardens. His counselors, perhaps led by Daniel (see 2:48 – 49), could have administered the kingdom efficiently.

4:34 *At the end of that time.* Perhaps as much as seven years (see v. 16 and note). *I honored and glorified him.* Contrast v. 30. *His dominion ... from generation to generation.* Nebuchadnezzar returns to the grand theme with which he began (see v. 3; see also 6:26; 7:14).

4:35 See Ps 115:3 and note.

4:36 Cf. Job 42:10,12.

4:37 *everything he does is right and ... just.* See notes on Ps 119:121; Eze 18:25. *those who walk in pride he is able to humble.* See Pr 3:34; Jas 4:6,10; 1Pe 5:5 – 6.

The Writing on the Wall

5 King Belshazzar[z] gave a great banquet[a] for a thousand of his nobles[b]
and drank wine with them. 2 While Belshazzar was drinking[c] his wine, he gave
orders to bring in the gold and silver goblets[d] that Nebuchadnezzar his father[a] had
taken from the temple in Jerusalem, so
that the king and his nobles, his wives and
his concubines[e] might drink from them.[f]
3 So they brought in the gold goblets that
had been taken from the temple of God
in Jerusalem, and the king and his nobles, his wives and his concubines drank
from them. 4 As they drank the wine, they
praised the gods[g] of gold and silver, of
bronze, iron, wood and stone.[h]
5 Suddenly the fingers of a human hand
appeared and wrote on the plaster of the
wall, near the lampstand in the royal
palace. The king watched the hand as it
wrote. 6 His face turned pale[i] and he was
so frightened[j] that his legs became weak[k]
and his knees were knocking.[l]
7 The king summoned the enchanters,[m]
astrologers[b][n] and diviners.[o] Then he said
to these wise[p] men of Babylon, "Whoever reads this writing and tells me what it
means will be clothed in purple and have
a gold chain placed around his neck,[q] and
he will be made the third[r] highest ruler in
the kingdom."[s]
8 Then all the king's wise men[t] came
in, but they could not read the writing or
tell the king what it meant.[u] 9 So King Belshazzar became even more terrified[v] and
his face grew more pale. His nobles were
baffled.
10 The queen,[c] hearing the voices of the
king and his nobles, came into the banquet hall. "May the king live forever!"[w]
she said. "Don't be alarmed! Don't look
so pale! 11 There is a man in your kingdom who has the spirit of the holy gods[x]
in him. In the time of your father he was
found to have insight and intelligence and
wisdom[y] like that of the gods.[z] Your father,
King Nebuchadnezzar, appointed him
chief of the magicians, enchanters, astrologers and diviners.[a] 12 He did this because
Daniel, whom the king called Belteshazzar,[b] was found to have a keen mind and
knowledge and understanding, and also
the ability to interpret dreams, explain
riddles[c] and solve difficult problems.[d] Call
for Daniel, and he will tell you what the
writing means.[e]"
13 So Daniel was brought before the
king, and the king said to him, "Are you
Daniel, one of the exiles my father the
king brought from Judah?[f] 14 I have heard
that the spirit of the gods[g] is in you and
that you have insight, intelligence and
outstanding wisdom.[h] 15 The wise men
and enchanters were brought before me
to read this writing and tell me what it
means, but they could not explain it.[i]
16 Now I have heard that you are able to
give interpretations and to solve difficult
problems.[j] If you can read this writing and
tell me what it means, you will be clothed
in purple and have a gold chain placed
around your neck,[k] and you will be made
the third highest ruler in the kingdom."[l]
17 Then Daniel answered the king, "You
may keep your gifts for yourself and give
your rewards to someone else.[m] Nevertheless, I will read the writing for the king
and tell him what it means.
18 "Your Majesty, the Most High God
gave your father Nebuchadnezzar[n] sovereignty and greatness and glory and splendor.[o] 19 Because of the high position he
gave him, all the nations and peoples of
every language dreaded and feared him.
Those the king wanted to put to death, he
put to death;[p] those he wanted to spare,
he spared; those he wanted to promote, he
promoted; and those he wanted to humble, he humbled.[q] 20 But when his heart became arrogant and hardened with pride,[r]
he was deposed from his royal throne[s] and
stripped[t] of his glory.[u] 21 He was driven
away from people and given the mind of

a 2 Or *ancestor*; or *predecessor*; also in verses 11, 13 and 18 *b* 7 Or *Chaldeans*; also in verse 11
c 10 Or *queen mother*

5:1 [z] ver 30; Da 7:1; 8:1 [a] S 1Ki 3:15 [b] Jer 50:35 **5:2** [c] S Isa 21:5 [d] S 2Ki 24:13; S 2Ch 36:10; S Jer 52:19 [e] S Est 2:14 [f] S Est 1:7; Da 1:2 **5:4** [g] Jdg 16:24 [h] S Est 1:10; Ps 135:15-18; Hab 2:19; Rev 9:20 **5:6** [i] S Job 4:15 [j] S Da 4:5 [k] S Ps 22:14; Eze 7:17 [l] S Isa 7:2 **5:7** [m] S Ge 41:8 [n] S Isa 19:3 [o] Isa 44:25 [p] Jer 50:35; Da 4:6-7 [q] S Ge 41:42 [r] Est 10:3 [s] Da 2:5-6, 48 **5:8** [t] S Ex 8:18 [u] S Da 2:10, 27; S 4:18 **5:9** [v] S Ps 48:5; S Isa 21:4 **5:10** [w] S Ne 2:3; S Da 3:9 **5:11** [x] S Ge 41:38 [y] ver 14; S Da 1:17 [z] S Da 2:22 [a] Da 2:47-48 **5:12** [b] S Da 1:7 [c] S Nu 12:8 [d] ver 14-16; Da 6:3 [e] S Eze 28:3 **5:13** [f] S Est 2:5-6; Da 6:13 **5:14** [g] S Ge 41:38 [h] S Da 2:22 **5:15** [i] S Da 4:18 **5:16** [j] S Ge 41:15 [k] S Ge 41:42 [l] S Est 5:3; S Da 2:6 **5:17** [m] S 2Ki 5:16 **5:18** [n] S Jer 28:14 [o] S Jer 27:7; S Da 2:37-38; S 4:36 **5:19** [p] Da 2:12-13; S 3:6 [q] S Da 4:22 **5:20** [r] Da 4:30 [s] Jer 43:10 [t] Jer 13:18; S Da 4:31 [u] S Job 40:12; Isa 14:13-15; Eze 31:10-11; Da 8:8

5:1–4 The orgy of revelry and blasphemy on such occasions is mentioned also by the ancient Greek historians Herodotus and Xenophon.

5:1 *King.* Belshazzar (meaning "Bel, protect the king!") was the son and viceroy of Nabonidus (see chart, p. 511). He is called the "son" of Nebuchadnezzar (v. 22), but the Aramaic term could also mean "grandson" or "descendant" or even "successor" (see NIV text note on v. 22). See also note on v. 10 and NIV text note on v. 2.

5:2 *gold … that Nebuchadnezzar … had taken from the temple.* In the eighth year of his reign (597 BC; see 2Ki 24:12–13 and note on 24:12).

5:5 *Suddenly.* See 4:31; see also Pr 29:1; 1Th 5:3 and notes; cf. Lk 12:19–20.

5:7 *third highest ruler in the kingdom.* Nabonidus was first, Belshazzar second (see last notation on map, p. 1423).

5:10 *queen.* See NIV text note. She could have been (1) the wife of Nebuchadnezzar, (2) the daughter of Nebuchadnezzar and wife of Nabonidus or (3) the wife of Nabonidus but not the daughter of Nebuchadnezzar.

5:11 *the time of your father.* Nebuchadnezzar had died in 562 BC; the year is now 539.

5:16 *third highest ruler.* See v. 7 and note.

5:17 *keep your gifts for yourself.* See Ge 14:23; 2Ki 5:16 and notes.

5:21 *He was … given the mind of an animal.* See 4:25 and note. *until he acknowledged.* See note on 4:25. *the Most High God is sovereign over all kingdoms on earth.* See Introduction: Theological Theme.

an animal; he lived with the wild donkeys
and ate grass like the ox; and his body was
drenched with the dew of heaven, until he
acknowledged that the Most High God is
sovereign[v] over all kingdoms on earth and
sets over them anyone he wishes.[w]
22 "But you, Belshazzar, his son,[a] have
not humbled[x] yourself, though you knew
all this. 23 Instead, you have set yourself up
against[y] the Lord of heaven. You had the
goblets from his temple brought to you,
and you and your nobles, your wives[z] and
your concubines drank wine from them.
You praised the gods of silver and gold,
of bronze, iron, wood and stone, which
cannot see or hear or understand.[a] But
you did not honor the God who holds
in his hand your life[b] and all your ways.[c]
24 Therefore he sent the hand that wrote
the inscription.
25 "This is the inscription that was written:

MENE, MENE, TEKEL, PARSIN

26 "Here is what these words mean:

Mene[b]: God has numbered the
days[d] of your reign and
brought it to an end.[e]
27 *Tekel*[c]: You have been weighed
on the scales[f] and found
wanting.[g]
28 *Peres*[d]: Your kingdom is divided
and given to the Medes[h] and
Persians."[i]

29 Then at Belshazzar's command, Daniel was clothed in purple, a gold chain
was placed around his neck,[j] and he was
proclaimed the third highest ruler in the
kingdom.[k]
30 That very night Belshazzar,[l] king[m] of
the Babylonians,[e] was slain,[n] 31 and Darius[o]
the Mede[p] took over the kingdom, at the
age of sixty-two.[f]

5:21 [v] S Eze 17:24 [w] Da 4:16-17,35 **5:22** [x] S Ex 10:3 **5:23** [y] S Isa 14:13; S Jer 50:29 [z] Jer 44:9 [a] Ps 115:4-8; Hab 2:19; Rev 9:20 [b] Job 12:10; Ac 17:28 [c] S Job 31:4; S Isa 13:11; Jer 10:23; S 48:26 **5:26** [d] Jer 27:7 [e] Isa 13:6 **5:27** [f] S Job 6:2 [g] Ps 62:9 **5:28** [h] Isa 13:17 [i] S Jer 27:7; 50:41-43; Da 6:28 **5:29** [j] S Ge 41:42 [k] S Da 2:6 **5:30** [l] S ver 1 [m] Jer 50:35 [n] S Isa 21:9; S Jer 51:31 **5:31** [o] Jer 50:41; Da 6:1; 9:1; 11:1 [p] S Isa 13:3

6:1 [q] S Da 5:31 [r] S Est 1:1 **6:2** [s] Da 2:48-49 [t] Ezr 4:22 **6:3** [u] S Ge 41:41; S Est 10:3; S Da 1:20; 5:12-14 **6:4** [v] Jer 20:10 **6:5** [w] Ac 24:13-16 **6:6** [x] S Ne 2:3 **6:7** [y] S Da 3:2 [z] Ps 59:3; 64:2-6; S Da 3:6 **6:8** [a] S Est 1:19

Daniel in the Den of Lions

6[g] It pleased Darius[q] to appoint 120 satraps[r] to rule throughout the kingdom, 2 with three administrators over
them, one of whom was Daniel.[s] The
satraps were made accountable[t] to them
so that the king might not suffer loss.
3 Now Daniel so distinguished himself
among the administrators and the satraps
by his exceptional qualities that the king
planned to set him over the whole kingdom.[u] 4 At this, the administrators and the
satraps tried to find grounds for charges[v]
against Daniel in his conduct of government affairs, but they were unable to do
so. They could find no corruption in him,
because he was trustworthy and neither
corrupt nor negligent. 5 Finally these men
said, "We will never find any basis for
charges against this man Daniel unless it
has something to do with the law of his
God."[w]
6 So these administrators and satraps
went as a group to the king and said:
"May King Darius live forever![x] 7 The royal
administrators, prefects, satraps, advisers
and governors[y] have all agreed that the
king should issue an edict and enforce
the decree that anyone who prays to any
god or human being during the next thirty
days, except to you, Your Majesty, shall be
thrown into the lions' den.[z] 8 Now, Your
Majesty, issue the decree and put it in
writing so that it cannot be altered — in
accordance with the law of the Medes and
Persians, which cannot be repealed."[a] 9 So
King Darius put the decree in writing.

[a] 22 Or *descendant*; or *successor* [b] 26 *Mene* can mean *numbered* or *mina* (a unit of money). [c] 27 *Tekel* can mean *weighed* or *shekel*. [d] 28 *Peres* (the singular of *Parsin*) can mean *divided* or *Persia* or *a half mina* or *a half shekel*. [e] 30 Or *Chaldeans* [f] 31 In Aramaic texts this verse (5:31) is numbered 6:1. [g] In Aramaic texts 6:1-28 is numbered 6:2-29.

5:22 – 23 Three charges were brought against Belshazzar: (1) He sinned through disobedience and pride, not through ignorance (v. 22); (2) he defied God by desecrating the sacred vessels (v. 23a); and (3) he praised idols and so did not honor God (v. 23b).
5:23 The stark contrast between the false gods of the nations and the one true God is a pervasive theme in the Prophets (see, e.g., 3:29 and note; Isa 41:5 – 10; 44:6 – 23; Jer 10:1 – 16; Eze 8 – 9; Hos 13:1 – 8; Hab 2:18 – 20; see also Ps 115:2 – 8; 135:15 – 18).
5:24 *he sent the hand.* Daniel waits until the last moment before informing the king that God himself is the source of the inscription.
5:26 – 28 See NIV text notes. Three weights (mina, shekel and half mina/shekel) may be intended, symbolizing three rulers, (respectively): (1) Nebuchadnezzar, (2) either Awel-Marduk (see 2Ki 25:27 and note) or Nabonidus, and (3) Belshazzar.
5:27 *weighed on the scales.* Measured in the light of God's standards (see Job 31:6 and note; Ps 62:9).
5:28 *divided ... Persians.* Daniel employs a telling wordplay (see NIV text note). *Medes and Persians.* The second kingdom of the series of four predicted in ch. 2 (see Introduction: Author, Date and Authenticity; see also chart, p. 1429).
5:29 *gold chain was placed around his neck.* As a symbol of authority (see Ge 41:42 and note).
5:30 *That very night.* See v. 5; Pr 6:15 and notes; Lk 12:20.
5:31 *Darius the Mede.* Perhaps another name for Gubaru, referred to in Babylonian inscriptions as the governor that Cyrus put in charge of the newly conquered Babylonian territories. Or "Darius the Mede" may have been Cyrus's throne name in Babylon (see NIV text note on 6:28; see also 1Ch 5:26 and note). *took over the kingdom.* In 539 BC. The "head of gold" (2:38) is now no more, as predicted in 2:39.
6:7 The conspirators lied in stating that "all" the royal administrators supported the proposed decree since they knew that Daniel (totally unaware of the proposal) was the foremost of the three administrators. *lions' den.* A pit with a relatively small opening at the top (see v. 17), making it impossible for a prisoner to escape.
6:8,12 *law of the Medes and Persians, which cannot be repealed.* See v. 15; see also notes on Est 1:19; 8:8.

10Now when Daniel learned that the decree had been published, he went home
to his upstairs room where the windows
opened toward[b] Jerusalem. Three times a
day he got down on his knees[c] and prayed,
giving thanks to his God, just as he had
done before.[d] 11Then these men went as a
group and found Daniel praying and asking God for help.[e] 12So they went to the
king and spoke to him about his royal decree: "Did you not publish a decree that
during the next thirty days anyone who
prays to any god or human being except to
you, Your Majesty, would be thrown into
the lions' den?"
The king answered, "The decree
stands—in accordance with the law of
the Medes and Persians, which cannot be
repealed."[f]
13Then they said to the king, "Daniel,
who is one of the exiles from Judah,[g] pays
no attention[h] to you, Your Majesty, or to
the decree you put in writing. He still prays
three times a day." 14When the king heard
this, he was greatly distressed;[i] he was determined to rescue Daniel and made every
effort until sundown to save him.
15Then the men went as a group to King
Darius and said to him, "Remember, Your
Majesty, that according to the law of the
Medes and Persians no decree or edict that
the king issues can be changed."[j]
16So the king gave the order, and they
brought Daniel and threw him into the lions' den.[k] The king said to Daniel, "May
your God, whom you serve continually,
rescue[l] you!"
17A stone was brought and placed over
the mouth of the den, and the king sealed[m]
it with his own signet ring and with the
rings of his nobles, so that Daniel's situation might not be changed. 18Then the
king returned to his palace and spent the
night without eating[n] and without any entertainment being brought to him. And he
could not sleep.[o]
19At the first light of dawn, the king got
up and hurried to the lions' den. 20When
he came near the den, he called to Daniel
in an anguished voice, "Daniel, servant of
the living God, has your God, whom you
serve continually, been able to rescue you
from the lions?"[p]
21Daniel answered, "May the king live
forever![q] 22My God sent his angel,[r] and he
shut the mouths of the lions.[s] They have
not hurt me, because I was found innocent in his sight.[t] Nor have I ever done any
wrong before you, Your Majesty."
23The king was overjoyed and gave
orders to lift Daniel out of the den. And
when Daniel was lifted from the den, no
wound[u] was found on him, because he
had trusted[v] in his God.
24At the king's command, the men who
had falsely accused Daniel were brought
in and thrown into the lions' den,[w] along
with their wives and children.[x] And before
they reached the floor of the den, the lions
overpowered them and crushed all their
bones.[y]
25Then King Darius wrote to all the nations and peoples of every language[z] in all
the earth:

"May you prosper greatly![a]

26"I issue a decree that in every
part of my kingdom people must fear
and reverence[b] the God of Daniel.[c]

"For he is the living God[d]
and he endures forever;[e]
his kingdom will not be destroyed,
his dominion will never end.[f]
27He rescues and he saves;[g]
he performs signs and wonders[h]
in the heavens and on the earth.
He has rescued Daniel
from the power of the lions."[i]

28So Daniel prospered during the reign
of Darius and the reign of Cyrus[a][j] the Persian.[k]

Daniel's Dream of Four Beasts

7 In the first year of Belshazzar[l] king
of Babylon, Daniel had a dream, and
visions[m] passed through his mind[n] as he
was lying in bed.[o] He wrote[p] down the
substance of his dream.
2Daniel said: "In my vision at night I
looked, and there before me were the four

[a] 28 Or *Darius, that is, the reign of Cyrus*

6:10 [b] S 1Ki 8:29 [c] Ps 95:6 [d] Mt 6:6; Ac 5:29 **6:11** [e] 1Ki 8:48-50; Ps 55:17; 1Th 5:17-18 **6:12** [f] S Est 1:19; Da 3:8-12 **6:13** [g] S Eze 14:14; Da 2:25 [h] S Est 3:8 **6:14** [i] Mk 6:26 **6:15** [j] S Est 8:8 **6:16** [k] S ver 7 [l] S Job 5:19; Ps 37:39-40; S 97:10 **6:17** [m] Mt 27:66 **6:18** [n] S 2Sa 12:17; Da 10:3 [o] S Est 6:1 **6:20** [p] S Da 3:17 **6:21** [q] S Ne 2:3; Da 3:9 **6:22** [r] S Ge 32:1; S Da 3:28 [s] ver 27; Ps 91:11-13; Heb 11:33 [t] Ac 12:11; 2Ti 4:17 **6:23** [u] Da 3:27 [v] S 1Ch 5:20; S Isa 12:2 **6:24** [w] Dt 19:18-19; Est 7:9-10; Ps 54:5 [x] Dt 24:16; 2Ki 14:6 [y] S Isa 38:13 **6:25** [z] S Da 3:4 [a] Da 4:1 **6:26** [b] S Ps 5:7 [c] S Est 8:17; Ps 99:1-3; Da 3:29 [d] S Jos 2:11; S 3:10 [e] S Jer 10:10; Da 12:7; Rev 1:18 [f] S Da 2:44 **6:27** [g] Da 3:29 [h] S Da 4:3 [i] S ver 22 **6:28** [j] S 2Ch 36:22; S Da 1:21 [k] S Da 5:28 **7:1** [l] S Da 5:1 [m] S Eze 40:2 [n] S Da 1:17 [o] Ps 4:4; S Da 4:13 [p] S Jer 36:4

6:10 *toward Jerusalem.* See 2Ch 6:38–39. *Three times a day.* Cf. Ps 55:17. *prayed ... just as he had done before.* Not even the threat of death could keep Daniel from honoring his customary times of prayer to "his God."
6:13 *pays no attention to you.* But see vv. 22,24.
6:16 *serve continually.* See 1Co 15:58 and note.
6:18 *he could not sleep.* See 2:1; Est 6:1 and note.
6:20 *has your God ... been able to rescue you ... ?* See 3:17 and note.

6:23 *no wound was found on him.* See 3:27. *he ... trusted in his God.* That the lions were ravenously hungry (v. 24) was no obstacle to the Lord's rewarding Daniel's faith by saving his life (see 3:28 and note). See photo, p. 1415.
6:24 *along with their wives and children.* In accordance with Persian custom (cf. Jos 7:24 and note).
6:28 See NIV text note.
7:1 *first year of Belshazzar.* Probably 553 BC. The events of ch. 7 preceded those of ch. 5.
7:2 *the great sea.* The world of nations and peoples (see also vv. 3,17).

winds of heaven[q] churning up the great
sea. 3 Four great beasts,[r] each different
from the others, came up out of the sea.
4 "The first was like a lion,[s] and it had
the wings of an eagle.[t] I watched until its
wings were torn off and it was lifted from
the ground so that it stood on two feet like
a human being, and the mind of a human
was given to it.
5 "And there before me was a second
beast, which looked like a bear. It was
raised up on one of its sides, and it had
three ribs in its mouth between its teeth. It
was told, 'Get up and eat your fill of flesh!'[u]
6 "After that, I looked, and there before
me was another beast, one that looked
like a leopard.[v] And on its back it had four
wings like those of a bird. This beast had
four heads, and it was given authority to
rule.
7 "After that, in my vision[w] at night I
looked, and there before me was a fourth
beast—terrifying and frightening and
very powerful. It had large iron[x] teeth;
it crushed and devoured its victims and
trampled[y] underfoot whatever was left.[z] It
was different from all the former beasts,
and it had ten horns.[a]
8 "While I was thinking about the horns,
there before me was another horn, a little[b] one, which came up among them; and
three of the first horns were uprooted before it. This horn had eyes like the eyes of
a human being[c] and a mouth that spoke
boastfully.[d]
9 "As I looked,

"thrones were set in place,
  and the Ancient of Days[e] took his
    seat.[f]
His clothing was as white as snow;[g]
  the hair of his head was white like
    wool.[h]
His throne was flaming with fire,
  and its wheels[i] were all ablaze.
10 A river of fire[j] was flowing,
  coming out from before him.[k]
Thousands upon thousands attended
    him;
  ten thousand times ten thousand
    stood before him.
The court was seated,
  and the books[l] were opened.

11 "Then I continued to watch because
of the boastful words the horn was speaking.[m] I kept looking until the beast was
slain and its body destroyed and thrown
into the blazing fire.[n] 12 (The other beasts
had been stripped of their authority, but
were allowed to live for a period of time.)
13 "In my vision at night I looked, and
there before me was one like a son of
man,[a][o] coming[p] with the clouds of heav-
en.[q] He approached the Ancient of Days
and was led into his presence. 14 He was
given authority,[r] glory and sovereign power; all nations and peoples of every language worshiped him.[s] His dominion is
an everlasting dominion that will not pass
away, and his kingdom[t] is one that will
never be destroyed.[u]

The Interpretation of the Dream

15 "I, Daniel, was troubled in spirit, and
the visions that passed through my mind
disturbed me.[v] 16 I approached one of those
standing there and asked him the meaning
of all this.
"So he told me and gave me the interpretation[w] of these things: 17 'The four
great beasts are four kings that will rise

7:2 [q] S Eze 37:9; Da 8:8; 11:4; Rev 7:1 **7:3** [r] Rev 13:1 **7:4** [s] S 2Ki 24:1; Ps 7:2; Jer 4:7; Rev 13:2 [t] S Eze 17:3 **7:5** [u] Da 2:39 **7:6** [v] Rev 13:2 **7:7** [w] S Eze 40:2 [x] S Da 2:40 [y] Da 8:10 [z] Da 8:7 [a] S Rev 12:3 **7:8** [b] Da 8:9 [c] Rev 9:7 [d] S Ps 12:3; Rev 13:5-6 **7:9** [e] ver 22 [f] S 1Ki 22:19; 2Ch 18:18; Mt 19:28; Rev 4:2; 20:4 [g] S Mt 28:3 [h] Rev 1:14 [i] S Eze 1:15; 10:6 **7:10** [j] Ps 50:3; 97:3; Isa 30:27 [k] S Dt 33:2; Ps 68:17; Jude 1:14; Rev 5:11 [l] S Ex 32:32; S Ps 56:8; Rev 20:11-15 **7:11** [m] Rev 13:5-6 [n] Rev 19:20 **7:13** [o] S Eze 1:5; S 2:1; Mt 8:20*; Rev 1:13*; 14:14* [p] Isa 13:6; Zep 1:14; Mal 3:2; 4:1 [q] S Dt 33:26; S Rev 1:7 **7:14** [r] S Mt 28:18 [s] Ps 72:11; 102:22 [t] S Isa 16:5 [u] S Da 2:44; Heb 12:28; Rev 11:15 **7:15** [v] S Job 4:15; S Da 4:19 **7:16** [w] Da 8:16; 9:22; Zec 1:9

[a] 13 The Aramaic phrase *bar enash* means *human being.* The phrase *son of man* is retained here because of its use in the New Testament as a title of Jesus, probably based largely on this verse.

7:4–7 The lion with an eagle's wings is a cherub symbolizing the Neo-Babylonian Empire (see Ge 3:24 and note). The rest of v. 4 perhaps reflects the humbling of Nebuchadnezzar, as recorded in ch. 4. The bear (v. 5), "raised up on one of its sides," refers to the superior status of the Persians in the Medo-Persian alliance. The three ribs may represent its three principal conquests: Lydia (546 BC), Babylon (539) and Egypt (525). The leopard with four wings (v. 6) represents the speedy conquests of Alexander the Great (334–330), and the four heads correspond to the four main divisions into which his empire fell after his untimely death in 323 (see 8:22): Macedon and Greece (under Antipater and Cassander), Thrace and Asia Minor (under Lysimachus), Syria (under Seleucus I), and the Holy Land and Egypt (under Ptolemy I; see chart, p. 1436). The fourth beast (v. 7), with its irresistible power surpassing all its predecessors, points to the Roman Empire (cf. 11:30 and note; in the Apocrypha, see 2 Esdras 12:11). Its ten horns correspond to the ten toes of 2:41–42 (see note on 2:32–43). **7:7** *iron.* See 2:40–43 and note on 2:32–43. *ten horns.* Indicative of the comprehensiveness of the beast's sphere of authority (see note on 1:12).

7:8 *another horn, a little one.* The antichrist, or a world power sharing in the characteristics of the antichrist. *mouth that spoke boastfully.* See 11:36; 2Th 2:4 and notes; Rev 13:5–6.
7:9 *Ancient of Days.* God. *hair of his head was white like wool.* See Rev 1:14 and note. *throne … wheels.* See Eze 1:15–21,26–27.
7:10 *Thousands … ten thousand.* See 1Sa 18:7 and note. *court was seated … books were opened.* John echoes the language of this judgment scene in Rev 20:12.
7:13 *like a son of man.* See Mk 8:31 and note; Rev 1:13. This is the first reference to the Messiah as the Son of Man, a title that Jesus applied to himself. He will be enthroned as ruler over the whole earth (previously misruled by the four kingdoms that oppose God's kingdom), and his kingdom "will never be destroyed" (v. 14), whether on earth or in heaven (see v. 27 and note). *coming with the clouds of heaven.* See Mk 14:62 and note; Rev 1:7.
7:16 *one of those standing there.* An angel.
7:17 *four kings.* See 2:38–40 and note on 2:32–43. *the earth.* The world of nations and peoples—referred to as "the (great) sea" in vv. 2–3.

VISIONS IN DANIEL

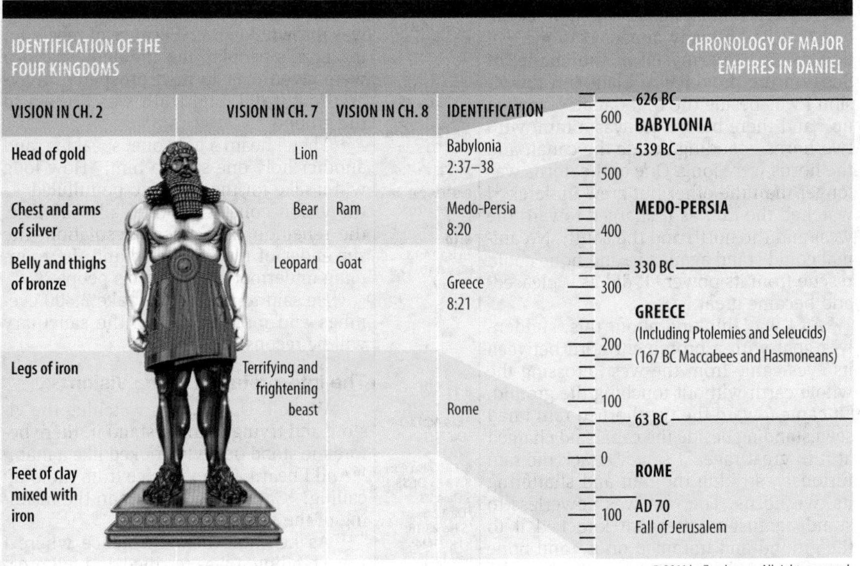

from the earth. 18But the holy people[x] of
the Most High will receive the kingdom[y]
and will possess it forever—yes, for ever
and ever.'[z]
19"Then I wanted to know the meaning
of the fourth beast, which was different
from all the others and most terrifying,
with its iron teeth and bronze claws—the
beast that crushed and devoured its victims and trampled underfoot whatever
was left. 20I also wanted to know about
the ten horns[a] on its head and about the
other horn that came up, before which
three of them fell—the horn that looked
more imposing than the others and that
had eyes and a mouth that spoke boastfully.[b] 21As I watched, this horn was waging
war against the holy people and defeating
them,[c] 22until the Ancient of Days came
and pronounced judgment in favor of the
holy people of the Most High, and the time
came when they possessed the kingdom.[d]
23"He gave me this explanation: 'The
fourth beast is a fourth kingdom that will
appear on earth. It will be different from
all the other kingdoms and will devour the
whole earth, trampling it down and crushing it.[e] 24The ten horns[f] are ten kings who
will come from this kingdom. After them
another king will arise, different from the
earlier ones; he will subdue three kings.
25He will speak against the Most High[g] and
oppress his holy people[h] and try to change
the set times[i] and the laws. The holy people will be delivered into his hands for a
time, times and half a time.[a][j]
26" 'But the court will sit, and his power will be taken away and completely destroyed[k] forever. 27Then the sovereignty,
power and greatness of all the kingdoms[l]
under heaven will be handed over to the
holy people[m] of the Most High.[n] His kingdom will be an everlasting[o] kingdom, and
all rulers will worship[p] and obey him.'
28"This is the end of the matter. I, Daniel, was deeply troubled[q] by my thoughts,[r]
and my face turned pale,[s] but I kept the
matter to myself."

7:18 [x]S Ps 16:3 [y]S Ps 49:14 [z]Isa 60:12-14; Lk 12:32; Heb 12:28; Rev 2:26; 20:4 **7:20** [a]Rev 17:12 [b]Rev 13:5-6 **7:21** [c]Rev 13:7 **7:22** [d]Mk 8:35 **7:23** [e]S Da 2:40 **7:24** [f]Rev 17:12 **7:25** [g]S Isa 37:23; Da 11:36 [h]Rev 16:6 [i]Da 2:21; Mk 1:15; Lk 21:8; Ac 1:6-7 [j]Da 8:24; 12:7; S Rev 11:2 **7:26** [k]Rev 19:20 **7:27** [l]S Isa 14:2 [m]1Co 6:2 [n]Ge 14:18 [o]S 2Sa 7:13; Ps 145:13; S Da 2:44; S 4:34; S Lk 1:33; Rev 11:15; 22:5 [p]S Ps 22:27; 72:11; 86:9

[a] *25* Or *for a year, two years and half a year*

7:28 [q]S Isa 21:3; S Da 4:19 [r]S Ps 13:2 [s]S Job 4:15

7:18 *holy people.* Exalted privileges will be enjoyed by Christ's followers in the Messianic kingdom (see Mt 19:28–29; see also Lk 22:29–30; Rev 1:6; 20:2–6 and notes). *will receive the kingdom.* See vv. 22,27 and note on v. 27.

7:24 *ten kings.* All the political powers (see note on 1:12; see also Rev 17:12–14) that will arise out of the fourth kingdom—not necessarily simultaneously (but see 2:44 ["In the time of those kings"] and note). *three kings.* Some of the ten. Three often signified a small, indefinite number (see Ex 3:18 and note).

7:25 *He.* See v. 8 and note. *a time, times and half a time.* See NIV text note.

7:27 *handed over to the holy people.* For their benefit. God and the Messiah will rule, as the last sentence in the verse makes clear (see v. 14 and note on v. 13; see also Rev 19–22).

Daniel's Vision of a Ram and a Goat

8 In the third year of King Belshazzar's[t]
reign, I, Daniel, had a vision,[u] after the
one that had already appeared to me. 2 In
my vision I saw myself in the citadel of
Susa[v] in the province of Elam;[w] in the vision I was beside the Ulai Canal. 3 I looked
up,[x] and there before me was a ram[y] with
two horns, standing beside the canal, and
the horns were long. One of the horns was
longer than the other but grew up later. 4 I
watched the ram as it charged toward the
west and the north and the south. No animal could stand against it, and none could
rescue from its power.[z] It did as it pleased[a]
and became great.
5 As I was thinking about this, suddenly a goat with a prominent horn between
its eyes came from the west, crossing the
whole earth without touching the ground.
6 It came toward the two-horned ram I had
seen standing beside the canal and charged
at it in great rage. 7 I saw it attack the ram
furiously, striking the ram and shattering
its two horns. The ram was powerless to
stand against it; the goat knocked it to
the ground and trampled on it,[b] and none
could rescue the ram from its power.[c] 8 The
goat became very great, but at the height
of its power the large horn was broken off,[d]
and in its place four prominent horns grew
up toward the four winds of heaven.[e]
9 Out of one of them came another horn,
which started small[f] but grew in power to
the south and to the east and toward the
Beautiful Land.[g] 10 It grew until it reached[h]
the host of the heavens, and it threw some
of the starry host down to the earth[i] and
trampled[j] on them. 11 It set itself up to be
as great as the commander[k] of the army
of the LORD;[l] it took away the daily sacrifice[m] from the LORD, and his sanctuary
was thrown down.[n] 12 Because of rebellion,
the LORD's people[a] and the daily sacrifice
were given over to it. It prospered in everything it did, and truth was thrown to
the ground.[o]
13 Then I heard a holy one[p] speaking, and
another holy one said to him, "How long
will it take for the vision to be fulfilled[q]—
the vision concerning the daily sacrifice,
the rebellion that causes desolation, the
surrender of the sanctuary and the trampling underfoot[r] of the LORD's people?"
14 He said to me, "It will take 2,300 evenings and mornings; then the sanctuary
will be reconsecrated."[s]

The Interpretation of the Vision

15 While I, Daniel, was watching the vision[t] and trying to understand it, there before me stood one who looked like a man.[u]
16 And I heard a man's voice from the Ulai[v]
calling, "Gabriel,[w] tell this man the meaning of the vision."[x]
17 As he came near the place where I
was standing, I was terrified and fell prostrate.[y] "Son of man,"[b] he said to me, "understand that the vision concerns the time
of the end."[z]
18 While he was speaking to me, I was in
a deep sleep, with my face to the ground.[a]
Then he touched me and raised me to my
feet.[b]

8:1 [t] S Da 5:1 [u] S Da 1:17 **8:2** [v] S Ezr 4:9; S Est 2:8 [w] S Ge 10:22 **8:3** [x] Da 10:5 [y] Rev 13:11 **8:4** [z] Isa 41:3 [a] Da 11:3, 16 **8:7** [b] S Da 7:7 [c] Da 11:11, 16 **8:8** [d] 2Ch 26:16-21; S Da 5:20 [e] S Da 7:2; Rev 7:1 **8:9** [f] Da 7:8 [g] S Eze 20:6; Da 11:16 **8:10** [h] S Isa 14:13 [i] Rev 8:10; 12:4 [j] S Da 7:7 **8:11** [k] ver 25 [l] Da 11:36-37 [m] Eze 46:13-14 [n] Da 11:31; 12:11 **8:12** [o] S Isa 48:1 **8:13** [p] S Dt 33:2; S Da 4:23 [q] Da 12:6 [r] S Isa 28:18; S Lk 21:24; Rev 11:2 **8:14** [s] Da 12:11-12 **8:15** [t] ver 1 [u] S Eze 2:1; Da 10:16-18 **8:16** [v] ver 2 [w] Da 9:21; S Lk 1:19 [x] S Da 7:16 **8:17** [y] Eze 1:28; 44:4; S Da 2:46; Rev 1:17 [z] ver 19; Hab 2:3 **8:18** [a] Da 10:9 [b] S Eze 2:2; Da 10:16-18; Zec 4:1

[a] 12 Or *rebellion, the armies* [b] 17 The Hebrew phrase *ben adam* means *human being*. The phrase *son of man* is retained as a form of address here because of its possible association with "Son of Man" in the New Testament.

8:1—12:13 These chapters are written in Hebrew (see note on 2:4).
8:1 *third year.* About 551 BC. The events of ch. 8 preceded those of ch. 5. *after the one that had already appeared to me.* Two years earlier (see 7:1 and note).
8:2 *citadel of Susa … Elam.* See notes on Ezr 4:9; Est 1:2; see also map, p. 1423.
8:3 The ram represents the Medo-Persian Empire (v. 20). The longer of his two horns reflects the predominant position of Persia (see 7:5 and note on 7:4–7).
8:5 The rapidly charging goat is Greece, and the "prominent horn" is Alexander the Great, "the first king" (v. 21; see chart, p. 1429).
8:7 *shattering its two horns.* Greece crushes Medo-Persia.
8:8 *large horn was broken off.* The death of Alexander the Great at the height of his power (323 BC). *four prominent horns.* Equivalent to the "four heads" of 7:6 (see note on 7:4–7).
8:9–12 "Another horn" (v. 9) emerges not from the ten horns belonging to the fourth kingdom (as in 7:8) but rather from one of the four horns belonging to the third kingdom. The horn that "started small" is Antiochus IV Epiphanes, who during the last few years of his reign (168–164 BC) made a determined effort to destroy the Jewish faith. He in turn served as a type of the even more ruthless beast of the last days (the antichrist), who is also referred to in 7:8 as a "little" horn. Antiochus was to extend his power over Israel, "the Beautiful Land" (v. 9; see Jer 3:19 and note), and defeat the godly believers there (referred to as "the host of the heavens," v. 10; see also v. 12), many of whom died for their faith. Then he set himself up to be the equal of "the commander of the army of the LORD" (v. 11) and ordered the daily sacrifices to end. Eventually the army of Judas Maccabeus recaptured Jerusalem and rededicated the temple (v. 14) to the Lord (December, 165)—the origin of the Festival of Hanukkah (see Jn 10:22 and note), still celebrated by Jews today (in the Apocrypha, see 1 Maccabees 1–4; see also bottom of chart, pp. 188–189).
8:13 *a holy one.* An angel.
8:14 There were two daily sacrifices for the continual burnt offering (see 9:21; Ex 29:38–39 and note), representing the atonement required for Israel as a whole. The "2,300 evenings and mornings" probably refer to the number of sacrifices consecutively offered on 1,150 days, the interval between the desecration of the Lord's altar by Antiochus Epiphanes and its reconsecration by Judas Maccabeus on Kislev 25, 165 BC.
8:16 *Gabriel.* An angel (see Lk 1:19 and note).
8:17 *Son of man.* Not to be confused with the "one like a son of man" in 7:13 (see note there; see also note on Eze 2:1).

19 He said: "I am going to tell you what
will happen later in the time of wrath,[c] because the vision concerns the appointed
time[d] of the end.[a][e] 20 The two-horned ram
that you saw represents the kings of Media
and Persia.[f] 21 The shaggy goat is the king
of Greece,[g] and the large horn between its
eyes is the first king.[h] 22 The four horns
that replaced the one that was broken off
represent four kingdoms that will emerge
from his nation but will not have the same
power.
23 "In the latter part of their reign, when
rebels have become completely wicked, a
fierce-looking king, a master of intrigue,
will arise. 24 He will become very strong,
but not by his own power. He will cause
astounding devastation and will succeed
in whatever he does. He will destroy those
who are mighty, the holy people.[i] 25 He will
cause deceit[j] to prosper, and he will consider himself superior. When they feel secure,
he will destroy many and take his stand
against the Prince of princes.[k] Yet he will be
destroyed, but not by human power.[l]
26 "The vision of the evenings and mornings that has been given you is true,[m] but
seal[n] up the vision, for it concerns the distant future."[o]
27 I, Daniel, was worn out. I lay exhausted[p] for several days. Then I got up and
went about the king's business.[q] I was appalled[r] by the vision; it was beyond understanding.

Daniel's Prayer

9 In the first year of Darius[s] son of Xerxes[b][t] (a Mede by descent), who was
made ruler over the Babylonian[c] kingdom— 2 in the first year of his reign, I,
Daniel, understood from the Scriptures,
according to the word of the LORD given to
Jeremiah the prophet, that the desolation
of Jerusalem would last seventy[u] years.
3 So I turned to the Lord God and pleaded
with him in prayer and petition, in fasting,[v] and in sackcloth and ashes.[w]
4 I prayed to the LORD my God and confessed:[x]

"Lord, the great and awesome God,[y]
who keeps his covenant of love[z] with

8:19 [c]S Isa 10:25 [d]S Ps 102:13 [e]Hab 2:3 **8:20** [f]S Eze 27:10 **8:21** [g]Da 10:20 [h]Da 11:3 **8:24** [i]S Da 7:25; 11:36 **8:25** [j]Da 11:23 [k]Da 11:36 [l]S Da 2:34; 11:21 **8:26** [m]Da 10:1 [n]S Isa 8:16; S 29:11; Rev 10:4; 22:10 [o]Da 10:14 **8:27** [p]Da 10:8 [q]S Da 2:48 [r]S Isa 21:3; S Da 4:19 **9:1** [s]S Da 5:31 [t]S Ezr 4:6 **9:2** [u]S 2Ch 36:21; Jer 29:10; Zec 1:12; 7:5 **9:3** [v]S 2Ch 20:3 [w]S 2Sa 13:19; S Ne 1:4; Jer 29:12; Da 10:12; Jnh 3:6 **9:4** [x]S 1Ki 8:30 [y]S Dt 7:21 [z]Dt 7:9; S 1Ki 8:23

[a] 19 Or *because the end will be at the appointed time* [b] 1 Hebrew *Ahasuerus* [c] 1 Or *Chaldean*

8:21 See v. 5 and note.
8:22 See v. 8 and note.
8:23–25 A description of Antiochus IV and his rise to power by intrigue and deceit (he was not the rightful successor to the Seleucid throne).
8:25 *consider himself superior.* Antiochus IV called himself Epiphanes ("God manifest"). Others, however, referred to him as Epimanes ("madman") because of his erratic behavior (Polybius, *Histories*, 26.1–14). *Prince of princes.* God. *destroyed, but not by human power.* Antiochus died in 164 BC at Tabae in Persia through illness or accident; God "destroyed" him.
8:26 *vision of the evenings and mornings.* See v. 14 and note.
9:1 *first year.* 539–538 BC. *Darius ... a Mede.* See 5:31 and note. *Xerxes.* See NIV text note; not the later Xerxes of the book of Esther.
9:2 *Jeremiah ... seventy years.* See note on Jer 25:11–12.
9:3–19 Daniel's prayer contains expressions of humility (v. 3), worship (v. 4), confession (vv. 5–15) and petition (vv. 16–19). See similar prayers in Ezr 9:5–15; Ne 9:5–37 (see note there).
9:3 *sackcloth and ashes.* See notes on Ge 37:34; Rev 11:3.
9:4 *who keeps his covenant of love.* See Dt 7:9,12 and note. *who love him and keep his commandments.* See Ne 1:5; cf. Ex 20:6 and note.

ALEXANDER'S EMPIRE

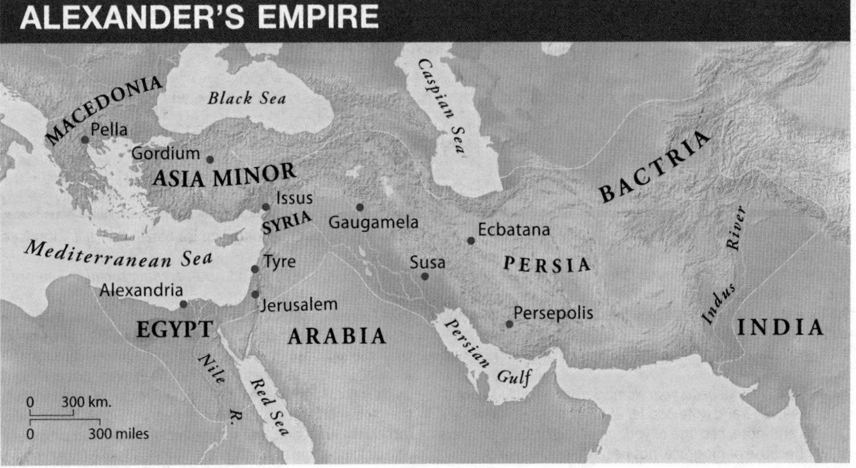

those who love him and keep his commandments, 5we have sinned[a] and done wrong.[b] We have been wicked and have rebelled; we have turned away[c] from your commands and laws.[d] 6We have not listened[e] to your servants the prophets,[f] who spoke in your name to our kings, our princes and our ancestors,[g] and to all the people of the land.

7"Lord, you are righteous,[h] but this day we are covered with shame[i]—the people of Judah and the inhabitants of Jerusalem and all Israel, both near and far, in all the countries where you have scattered[j] us because of our unfaithfulness[k] to you.[l] 8We and our kings, our princes and our ancestors are covered with shame, LORD, because we have sinned against you.[m] 9The Lord our God is merciful and forgiving,[n] even though we have rebelled against him;[o] 10we have not obeyed the LORD our God or kept the laws he gave us through his servants the prophets.[p] 11All Israel has transgressed[q] your law[r] and turned away, refusing to obey you.

"Therefore the curses[s] and sworn judgments[t] written in the Law of Moses, the servant of God, have been poured out on us, because we have sinned[u] against you. 12You have fulfilled[v] the words spoken against us and against our rulers by bringing on us great disaster.[w] Under the whole heaven nothing has ever been done like[x] what has been done to Jerusalem.[y] 13Just as it is written in the Law of Moses, all this disaster has come on us, yet we have not sought the favor of the LORD[z] our God by turning from our sins and giving attention to your truth.[a] 14The LORD did not hesitate to bring the disaster[b] on us, for the LORD our God is righteous in everything he does;[c] yet we have not obeyed him.[d]

15"Now, Lord our God, who brought your people out of Egypt with a mighty hand[e] and who made for yourself a name[f] that endures to this day, we have sinned, we have done wrong. 16Lord, in keeping with all your righteous acts,[g] turn away[h] your anger and your wrath[i] from Jerusalem,[j] your city, your holy hill.[k] Our sins and the iniquities of our ancestors have made Jerusalem and your people an object of scorn[l] to all those around us.

17"Now, our God, hear the prayers and petitions of your servant. For your sake, Lord, look with favor[m] on your desolate sanctuary. 18Give ear,[n] our God, and hear;[o] open your eyes and see[p] the desolation of the city that bears your Name.[q] We do not make requests of you because we are righteous, but because of your great mercy.[r] 19Lord, listen! Lord, forgive![s] Lord, hear and act! For your sake,[t] my God, do not delay, because your city and your people bear your Name."

The Seventy "Sevens"

20While I was speaking and praying, confessing[u] my sin and the sin of my people Israel and making my request to the LORD my God for his holy hill[v]— 21while I was still in prayer, Gabriel,[w] the man I had seen in the earlier vision, came to me in swift flight about the time of the evening sacrifice.[x] 22He instructed me and said to me, "Daniel, I have now come to give you insight and understanding.[y] 23As soon as you began to pray,[z] a word went out, which I have come to tell you, for you are highly esteemed.[a] Therefore, consider the word and understand the vision:[b]

24"Seventy 'sevens'[a] are decreed for your people and your holy city[c] to finish[b] transgression, to put an end to sin, to atone[d] for wickedness, to bring in ever-

[a] 24 Or *'weeks'*; also in verses 25 and 26 [b] 24 Or *restrain*

9:5 [a]S Jer 8:14 [b]Ps 106:6 [c]Isa 53:6 [d]ver 11; La 1:20; S 3:42 **9:6** [e]S 2Ki 18:12 [f]S 2Ch 36:16; S Jer 44:5; Jas 5:10; Rev 10:7 [g]S 2Ch 29:6 **9:7** [h]S Ezr 9:15; S Isa 42:6 [i]Ezr 9:7; Ps 44:15 [j]Dt 4:27; Am 9:9 [k]S Dt 7:3 [l]S Jer 3:25; S 24:9; S Eze 39:23-24 **9:8** [m]S Ne 9:33; S Jer 14:20; S Eze 16:63 **9:9** [n]S Ex 34:7; S 2Sa 24:14; Jer 42:12 [o]S Ne 9:17; Jer 14:7 **9:10** [p]2Ki 17:13-15; S 18:12; Rev 10:7 **9:11** [q]S Jer 2:29 [r]2Ki 22:16 [s]S Dt 11:26; S 13:15; S 28:15 [t]2Ki 17:23 [u]Isa 1:4-6; Jer 8:5-10 **9:12** [v]S Isa 44:26; Zec 1:6 [w]S Jer 44:23 [x]Jer 30:7 [y]Jer 44:2-6; Eze 5:9; Da 12:1; Joel 2:2; Zec 7:12 **9:13** [z]S Dt 4:29; S Isa 31:1 [a]S Isa 9:13; Jer 2:30 **9:14** [b]S Jer 18:8; S 44:27 [c]S Ge 18:25; S 2Ch 12:6; S Jer 12:1 [d]S Ne 9:33; S Jer 32:23; S 40:3 **9:15** [e]S Ex 3:20; S Jer 32:21 [f]S Ne 9:10 **9:16** [g]S Jdg 5:11; Ps 31:1 [h]S Isa 5:25 [i]S Ps 85:3 [j]Jer 32:32 [k]S Ex 15:17; S Ps 48:1 [l]S Ps 39:8; S Eze 5:14 **9:17** [m]Nu 6:24-26; Ps 80:19 **9:18** [n]S Ps 5:1 [o]Ps 116:1 [p]Ps 80:14 [q]S Dt 28:10; S Isa 37:17; Jer 7:10-12; 25:29 [r]Lk 18:13 **9:19** [s]Ps 44:23 [t]S 1Sa 12:22 **9:20** [u]S Ezr 10:1 [v]S ver 3; Ps 145:18; S Isa 58:9 **9:21** [w]S Da 8:16; S Lk 1:19 [x]S Ex 29:39 **9:22** [y]S Da 7:16; 10:14; Am 3:7 **9:23** [z]S Isa 65:24 [a]Da 10:19; Lk 1:28 [b]Da 10:11-12; Mt 24:15 **9:24** [c]S Isa 1:26 [d]S Isa 53:10

9:6 *your servants the prophets.* See v. 10; see also Jer 7:25; Zec 1:6 and notes.

9:7 *scattered us because of our unfaithfulness.* See 2Ki 17:7–23 and note; 2Ch 36:15–20.

9:11 *curses … written in the Law.* See Lev 26:33; Dt 28:64 and note.

9:14 *the LORD our God is righteous.* See Ps 4:1; Jer 12:1 and notes.

9:18 *city that bears your Name.* Jerusalem (1Ki 11:36; cf. Ps 132:13 and note; see Jer 25:29 and note). *Name.* See Dt 12:5 and note. *because of your great mercy.* God answers prayer because of his grace, not because of our works.

9:20 *While I was speaking.* See Isa 65:24. *holy hill.* Zion (see Ps 2:6 and note).

9:21 *Gabriel.* See 8:16 and note. *evening sacrifice.* See note on Ps 141:2.

9:24 *"sevens."* Probably seven-year periods of time, making a total of 490 years, but some take the numbers as symbolic. Of the six purposes mentioned (all to be fulfilled through the Messiah), some believe that the last three were not achieved by the crucifixion and resurrection of Christ but await his further action: the establishment of everlasting righteousness (on earth), the complete fulfillment of vision and prophecy and the anointing of the "Most Holy Place" (see NIV text note).

lasting righteousness,[e] to seal up vision
and prophecy and to anoint the Most Holy
Place.[a]
25 “Know and understand this: From
the time the word goes out to restore and
rebuild[f] Jerusalem until the Anointed
One,[bg] the ruler,[h] comes, there will be sev-
en ‘sevens,’ and sixty-two ‘sevens.’ It will
be rebuilt with streets and a trench, but
in times of trouble.[i] 26 After the sixty-two
‘sevens,’ the Anointed One will be put to
death[j] and will have nothing.[c] The people
of the ruler who will come will destroy the
city and the sanctuary. The end will come
like a flood:[k] War will continue until the
end, and desolations[l] have been decreed.[m]
27 He will confirm a covenant with many
for one ‘seven.’[d] In the middle of the ‘sev-
en’[d] he will put an end to sacrifice and
offering. And at the temple[e] he will set up
an abomination that causes desolation,
until the end that is decreed[n] is poured
out on him.[f]”[g]

Daniel’s Vision of a Man

10 In the third year of Cyrus[o] king of
Persia, a revelation was given to
Daniel (who was called Belteshazzar).[p]
Its message was true[q] and it concerned a
great war.[h] The understanding of the message came to him in a vision.
2 At that time I, Daniel, mourned[r] for
three weeks. 3 I ate no choice food; no meat
or wine touched my lips;[s] and I used no lotions at all until the three weeks were over.
4 On the twenty-fourth day of the first
month, as I was standing on the bank[t] of
the great river, the Tigris,[u] 5 I looked up[v]
and there before me was a man dressed
in linen,[w] with a belt of fine gold[x] from
Uphaz around his waist. 6 His body was
like topaz,[y] his face like lightning,[z] his eyes
like flaming torches,[a] his arms and legs
like the gleam of burnished bronze,[b] and
his voice[c] like the sound of a multitude.
7 I, Daniel, was the only one who saw
the vision; those who were with me did
not see it,[d] but such terror overwhelmed
them that they fled and hid themselves.
8 So I was left alone,[e] gazing at this great
vision; I had no strength left,[f] my face
turned deathly pale[g] and I was helpless.[h]
9 Then I heard him speaking, and as I listened to him, I fell into a deep sleep, my
face to the ground.[i]
10 A hand touched me[j] and set me trembling on my hands and knees.[k] 11 He said,
“Daniel, you who are highly esteemed,[l]
consider carefully the words I am about
to speak to you, and stand up,[m] for I have
now been sent to you.” And when he said
this to me, I stood up trembling.
12 Then he continued, “Do not be afraid,[n]
Daniel. Since the first day that you set your
mind to gain understanding and to humble[o] yourself before your God, your words[p]
were heard, and I have come in response
to them.[q] 13 But the prince[r] of the Persian
kingdom resisted me twenty-one days.
Then Michael,[s] one of the chief princes,
came to help me, because I was detained
there with the king of Persia. 14 Now I have
come to explain[t] to you what will happen
to your people in the future,[u] for the vision
concerns a time yet to come.[v]”

9:24 [e]S Isa 56:1; Heb 9:12 **9:25** [f]S Ezr 4:24; S 6:15 [g]Mt 1:17; Jn 4:25 [h]S 1Sa 13:14 [i]S Ezr 3:3 **9:26** [j]S Isa 53:8; Mt 16:21 [k]Isa 28:2; Da 11:10; Na 1:8 [l]S Ps 46:8 [m]Isa 61:1; S Eze 4:5-6; Hag 2:23; Zec 4:14 **9:27** [n]S Isa 10:22 **10:1** [o]S Da 1:21 [p]S Da 1:7 [q]Da 8:26 **10:2** [r]S Ezr 9:4 **10:3** [s]S Da 6:18 **10:4** [t]Da 12:5 [u]S Ge 2:14 **10:5** [v]Da 8:3 [w]S Eze 9:2; Rev 15:6 [x]Jer 10:9 **10:6** [y]S Ex 28:20 [z]Mt 17:2; S 28:3 [a]Job 41:19; Rev 19:12 [b]S Eze 1:7; S Rev 1:15 [c]S Eze 1:24 **10:7** [d]2Ki 6:17-20; Ac 9:7 **10:8** [e]Ge 32:24 [f]S Job 4:14; Da 8:27 [g]S Job 4:15 [h]Hab 3:16 **10:9** [i]Da 8:18; Mt 17:6 **10:10** [j]Jer 1:9 [k]Rev 1:17 **10:11** [l]S Ge 6:9; Da 9:23 [m]S Eze 2:1 **10:12** [n]S Mt 14:27 [o]S Lev 16:31; S Da 9:3 [p]S Isa 65:24 [q]Da 9:20

[a] 24 Or *the most holy One* [b] 25 Or *an anointed one*; also in verse 26 [c] 26 Or *death and will have no one*; or *death, but not for himself* [d] 27 Or *‘week’* [e] 27 Septuagint and Theodotion; Hebrew *wing* [f] 27 Or *it* [g] 27 Or *And one who causes desolation will come upon the wing of the abominable temple, until the end that is decreed is poured out on the desolated city* [h] 1 Or *true and burdensome*

10:13 [r]Isa 24:21 [s]ver 21; Da 12:1; S Jude 1:9 **10:14** [t]S Da 9:22 [u]S Eze 12:27 [v]S Da 2:28; 8:26; Hab 2:3

9:25–27 The time between the decree authorizing the rebuilding of Jerusalem (v. 25) and the coming of the Messiah (“the Anointed One”) was to be 69 (7 plus 62) “sevens,” or 483 years (see note on Ezr 7:11). The “seven ‘sevens’” may refer to the period of the complete restoration of Jerusalem (partially narrated in Ezra and Nehemiah), and the “sixty-two ‘sevens’” may refer to the period between that restoration and the Messiah’s coming to Israel. The final (70th) “seven” is not mentioned specifically until v. 27, following the prophecy of the destruction of Jerusalem by “the people of the ruler who will come” (Titus in AD 70). Therefore, while many hold that the 70th “seven” was fulfilled during Christ’s earthly ministry and the years immediately following, others conclude that there is an indeterminate interval between the 69th and the 70th “seven”—a period of “war” and “desolations” (v. 26). According to this latter opinion, in the 70th “seven” the little horn or beast (the antichrist) of the last days (referred to here as the one who sets up an “abomination that causes desolation” and who is the antitype of the Roman Titus; see Rev 13:1–8 and notes) will establish a covenant for seven years with the Jews (the “many”) but will violate the covenant halfway through that period (but see also note on v. 27). The death of the Anointed One (v. 26) refers to the crucifixion of Christ.

9:27 *He will confirm a covenant … will put an end to sacrifice.* According to some, a reference to the Messiah’s (“the Anointed One,” v. 26) instituting the new covenant and putting “an end” to the OT sacrificial system; according to others, a reference to the antichrist’s (“the [ultimate] ruler who will come,” v. 26) making a treaty with the Jews in the future and then disrupting their system of worship. *abomination that causes desolation.* See note on 11:31.

10:1 *third year of Cyrus.* 537 BC. This is the third year after his conquest of Babylon in 539 (see note on 1:1).

10:3 See 1:8–16 and note on 1:8.

10:5–6 See 7:9; Rev 1:12–16 and notes.

10:7 Cf. Ac 9:7.

10:13 *prince of the Persian kingdom.* Apparently a demon exercising influence over the Persian realm (see also v. 20 and note). His resistance was finally overcome by the archangel Michael, “the great prince who protects” the people of God (12:1).

10:14 *what will happen to your people in the future.* See chs. 11–12.

15 While he was saying this to me, I bowed with my face toward the ground and was speechless.[w] 16 Then one who looked like a man[a] touched my lips, and I opened my mouth and began to speak.[x] I said to the one standing before me, "I am overcome with anguish[y] because of the vision, my lord, and I feel very weak. 17 How can I, your servant, talk with you, my lord? My strength is gone and I can hardly breathe."[z]

18 Again the one who looked like a man touched[a] me and gave me strength.[b] 19 "Do not be afraid, you who are highly esteemed,"[c] he said. "Peace![d] Be strong now; be strong."[e]

When he spoke to me, I was strengthened and said, "Speak, my lord, since you have given me strength."[f]

20 So he said, "Do you know why I have come to you? Soon I will return to fight against the prince of Persia, and when I go, the prince of Greece[g] will come; 21 but first I will tell you what is written in the Book of Truth.[h] (No one supports me against them except Michael,[i] your prince.

11 1 And in the first year of Darius[j] the Mede, I took my stand to support and protect him.)

The Kings of the South and the North

2 "Now then, I tell you the truth:[k] Three more kings will arise in Persia, and then a fourth, who will be far richer than all the others. When he has gained power by his wealth, he will stir up everyone against the kingdom of Greece.[l] 3 Then a mighty king will arise, who will rule with great power and do as he pleases.[m] 4 After he has arisen, his empire will be broken up and parceled out toward the four winds of heaven.[n] It will not go to his descendants, nor will it have the power he exercised, because his empire will be uprooted[o] and given to others.

5 "The king of the South will become strong, but one of his commanders will become even stronger than he and will rule his own kingdom with great power. 6 After some years, they will become allies. The daughter of the king of the South will go to the king of the North to make an alliance, but she will not retain her power, and he and his power[b] will not last. In those days she will be betrayed, together with her royal escort and her father[c] and the one who supported her.

7 "One from her family line will arise to take her place. He will attack the forces of the king of the North[p] and enter his fortress; he will fight against them and be victorious. 8 He will also seize their gods,[q] their metal images and their valuable articles of silver and gold and carry them off to Egypt.[r] For some years he will leave the king of the North alone. 9 Then the king of the North will invade the realm of the king of the South but will retreat to his own country. 10 His sons will prepare for war and assemble a great army, which will sweep on like an irresistible flood[s] and carry the battle as far as his fortress.

11 "Then the king of the South will march out in a rage and fight against the king of the North, who will raise a large army, but it will be defeated.[t] 12 When the army is carried off, the king of the South will be filled with pride and will slaughter

10:15 [w] Eze 24:27; Lk 1:20
10:16 [x] S Isa 6:7; Jer 1:9; Da 8:15-18 [y] S Isa 21:3
10:17 [z] S Da 4:19
10:18 [a] ver 16 [b] S Da 8:18
10:19 [c] S Da 9:23 [d] Jdg 6:23; S Isa 35:4 [e] Jos 1:9 [f] Isa 6:1-8
10:20 [g] Da 8:21; 11:2
10:21 [h] Da 11:2 [i] S ver 13; S Jude 1:9
11:1 [j] S Da 5:31
11:2 [k] Da 10:21 [l] S Da 10:20
11:3 [m] S Da 8:4, 21
11:4 [n] S Da 7:2; 8:22 [o] S Jer 42:10
11:7 [p] ver 6
11:8 [q] Isa 37:19; S 46:1-2 [r] Jer 43:12
11:10 [s] Isa 8:8; Jer 46:8; S Da 9:26
11:11 [t] Da 8:7-8

[a] 16 Most manuscripts of the Masoretic Text; one manuscript of the Masoretic Text, Dead Sea Scrolls and Septuagint *Then something that looked like a human hand* [b] 6 Or *offspring* [c] 6 Or *child* (see Vulgate and Syriac)

10:16 *touched my lips, and I ... began to speak.* See Isa 6:7; Jer 1:9 and notes.
10:20 *prince of Greece.* See note on v. 13. This spiritual power will also have to be opposed.
10:21 *Book of Truth.* See 12:1; perhaps a reference to God's book of the destinies of all human beings (see Ex 32:32; Ps 69:28 and notes).
11:1 *Darius the Mede.* See note on 5:31.
11:2 *Three more kings.* Cambyses (530 – 522 BC), Pseudo-Smerdis or Gaumata (522) and Darius I (522 – 486). *fourth.* Xerxes I (486 – 465; see note on Est 1:1), who attempted to conquer Greece in 480.
11:3 *mighty king.* Alexander the Great (336 – 323).
11:4 *four winds.* See 7:2 – 3 and note on 7:4 – 7 (four heads).
11:5 *king of the South.* Ptolemy I Soter (323 – 285 BC) of Egypt (see chart and map, pp. 1436 – 1437). *one of his commanders.* Seleucus I Nicator (311 – 280). *his own kingdom.* Initially Babylonia, to which he then added extensive territories both east and west.
11:6 *daughter of the king of the South.* Berenice, daughter of Ptolemy II Philadelphus (285 – 246 BC) of Egypt. *king of the North.* Antiochus II Theos (261 – 246) of Syria. *alliance.* A treaty cemented by the marriage of Berenice to Antiochus. *she will not retain her power, and he ... will not last.* Antiochus's former wife, Laodice, conspired to have Berenice and Antiochus put to death. *her father.* Berenice's father, Ptolemy, died at about the same time.
11:7 *One from her family line.* Berenice's brother, Ptolemy III Euergetes (246 – 221 BC) of Egypt, who did away with Laodice. *king of the North.* Seleucus II Callinicus (246 – 226) of Syria. *his fortress.* Either (1) Seleucia (see Ac 13:4 and note), which was the port of Antioch, or (2) Antioch itself.
11:8 *their gods.* Images of Syrian deities, and also of Egyptian gods that the Persian Cambyses had carried off after conquering Egypt in 525 BC.
11:10 *His sons.* Seleucus III Ceraunus (226 – 223 BC) and Antiochus III (the Great) (223 – 187), sons of Seleucus II. *his fortress.* Ptolemy's fortress at Raphia (southwest of Gaza).
11:11 *king of the South.* Ptolemy IV Philopator (221 – 203 BC) of Egypt. *king of the North.* Antiochus III. *defeated.* At Raphia in 217.
11:12 *slaughter many thousands.* The Greek historian Polybius records that Antiochus lost nearly 10,000 infantrymen at Raphia.

many thousands, yet he will not remain triumphant. 13 For the king of the North will muster another army, larger than the first; and after several years, he will advance with a huge army fully equipped.

14 "In those times many will rise against the king of the South. Those who are violent among your own people will rebel in fulfillment of the vision, but without success. 15 Then the king of the North will come and build up siege ramps[u] and will capture a fortified city. The forces of the South will be powerless to resist; even their best troops will not have the strength to stand. 16 The invader will do as he pleases;[v] no one will be able to stand against him.[w] He will establish himself in the Beautiful Land and will have the power to destroy it.[x] 17 He will determine to come with the might of his entire kingdom and will make an alliance with the king of the South. And he will give him a daughter in marriage in order to overthrow the kingdom, but his plans[a] will not succeed[y] or help him. 18 Then he will turn his attention to the coastlands[z] and will take many of them, but a commander will put an end to his insolence and will turn his insolence back on him.[a] 19 After this, he will turn back toward the fortresses of his own country but will stumble and fall,[b] to be seen no more.[c]

20 "His successor will send out a tax collector to maintain the royal splendor.[d] In a few years, however, he will be destroyed, yet not in anger or in battle.

21 "He will be succeeded by a contemptible[e] person who has not been given the honor of royalty.[f] He will invade the kingdom when its people feel secure, and he will seize it through intrigue. 22 Then an overwhelming army will be swept away[g] before him; both it and a prince of the covenant will be destroyed.[h] 23 After coming to an agreement with him, he will act deceitfully,[i] and with only a few people he will rise to power. 24 When the richest provinces feel secure, he will invade them and will achieve what neither his fathers nor his forefathers did. He will distribute plunder, loot and wealth among his followers.[j] He will plot the overthrow of fortresses — but only for a time.

25 "With a large army he will stir up his strength and courage against the king of the South. The king of the South will wage war with a large and very powerful army, but he will not be able to stand because of the plots devised against him. 26 Those who eat from the king's provisions will try to destroy him; his army will be swept away, and many will fall in battle. 27 The two kings, with their hearts bent on evil,[k] will sit at the same table and lie[l] to each other, but to no avail, because an end will still come at the appointed time.[m] 28 The king of the North will return to his own country with great wealth, but his heart will be set against the holy covenant. He will take action against it and then return to his own country.

29 "At the appointed time he will invade the South again, but this time the outcome will be different from what it was before. 30 Ships of the western coastlands[n] will oppose him, and he will lose heart.[o] Then he will turn back and vent his fury[p] against the holy covenant. He will return and show favor to those who forsake the holy covenant.

31 "His armed forces will rise up to

11:15 [u]S Eze 4:2
11:16 [v]S Da 8:4 [w]S Jos 1:5; S Da 8:7 [x]S Da 8:9
11:17 [y]S Ps 20:4
11:18 [z]S Isa 66:19; S Jer 25:22 [a]Hos 12:14
11:19 [b]S Ps 27:2; S 46:2 [c]S Ps 37:36; S Eze 26:21
11:20 [d]Isa 60:17
11:21 [e]Da 4:17 [f]S Da 8:25
11:22 [g]S Isa 28:15 [h]Da 8:10-11
11:23 [i]Da 8:25
11:24 [j]Ne 9:25
11:27 [k]Ps 64:6 [l]Ps 12:2; Jer 9:5 [m]Hab 2:3
11:30 [n]S Ge 10:4 [o]S 1Sa 17:32 [p]S Job 15:13

[a] 17 Or *but she*

11:14 *king of the South.* Ptolemy V Epiphanes (203 – 181 BC) of Egypt. *Those who are violent among your own people.* Jews who joined the forces of Antiochus. *without success.* The Ptolemaic general Scopas crushed the rebellion in 200.
11:15 *fortified city.* The Mediterranean port of Sidon.
11:16 *The invader.* Antiochus, who was in control of the Holy Land by 197 BC. *Beautiful Land.* See note on 8:9 – 12.
11:17 *he will give him a daughter in marriage.* Antiochus gave his daughter Cleopatra I in marriage to Ptolemy V in 194 BC.
11:18 *he.* Antiochus. *coastlands.* Asia Minor and perhaps also mainland Greece. *commander.* The Roman consul Lucius Cornelius Scipio Asiaticus, who defeated Antiochus at Magnesia in Asia Minor in 190 BC.
11:19 *stumble and fall.* Antiochus died in 187 BC while attempting to plunder a temple in the province of Elymais.
11:20 *His successor.* Seleucus IV Philopator (187 – 175 BC), son and successor of Antiochus the Great. *tax collector.* Seleucus's finance minister, Heliodorus. *he will be destroyed.* Seleucus was the victim of a conspiracy engineered by Heliodorus.
11:21 *contemptible person.* Seleucus's younger brother, Antiochus IV Epiphanes (175 – 164 BC). *not been given the honor of royalty.* Antiochus seized power while the rightful heir to the throne, the son of Seleucus (later to become Demetrius I), was still very young. *kingdom.* Syro-Palestine.
11:22 *prince of the covenant.* Either the high priest Onias III, who was murdered in 170 BC, or, if the Hebrew for this phrase is translated "confederate prince," Ptolemy VI Philometor (181 – 146) of Egypt.
11:23 *he.* Antiochus.
11:24 *richest provinces.* Either of the Holy Land or of Egypt. *fortresses.* In Egypt.
11:25 *king of the South.* Ptolemy VI.
11:26 *his army.* Ptolemy's.
11:27 *two kings.* Antiochus and Ptolemy, who was living in Antiochus's custody.
11:28 *against the holy covenant.* In 169 BC Antiochus plundered the temple in Jerusalem, set up a garrison there and massacred many Jews in the city.
11:30 *Ships of the western coastlands.* Roman vessels under the command of Popilius Laenas. *those who forsake the holy covenant.* Apostate Jews (see also v. 32).
11:31 *abomination that causes desolation.* See 9:27; 12:11; the altar to the pagan god Zeus Olympius, set up in 168 BC by Antiochus Epiphanes and prefiguring a similar abomination that Jesus predicted would be erected in the future (see Mt 24:15; Lk 21:20 and notes).

desecrate the temple fortress and will
abolish the daily sacrifice.[q] Then they will
set up the abomination that causes desolation.[r] 32 With flattery he will corrupt those
who have violated the covenant, but the
people who know their God will firmly resist[s] him.
33 "Those who are wise will instruct[t]
many, though for a time they will fall by
the sword or be burned or captured or
plundered.[u] 34 When they fall, they will
receive a little help, and many who are
not sincere[v] will join them. 35 Some of the
wise will stumble, so that they may be
refined,[w] purified and made spotless until
the time of the end, for it will still come
at the appointed time.

The King Who Exalts Himself

36 "The king will do as he pleases. He will
exalt and magnify himself[x] above every god
and will say unheard-of things[y] against the
God of gods.[z] He will be successful until
the time of wrath[a] is completed, for what
has been determined must take place.[b]

11:31 [q] Hos 3:4 [r] S Jer 19:4; Da 8:11-13; S 9:27; Mt 24:15*; Mk 13:14* **11:32** [s] Mic 5:7-9 **11:33** [t] Da 12:3; Mal 2:7 [u] Mt 24:9; Jn 16:2; Heb 11:32-38 **11:34** [v] Mt 7:15; Ro 16:18 **11:35** [w] S Job 28:1; S Ps 78:38; S Isa 48:10; Da 12:10; Zec 13:9; Jn 15:2 **11:36** [x] Jude 1:16 [y] Rev 13:5-6 [z] S Dt 10:17; S Isa 14:13-14; S Da 7:25; 8:11-12,25; 2Th 2:4 [a] S Isa 10:25; 26:20 [b] Eze 35:13; S Da 8:24

11:33 *Those who are wise.* The godly leaders of the Jewish resistance movement, also called the Hasidim. *fall by the sword or be burned or captured or plundered.* See Heb 11:36–38.
11:34 *a little help.* The early successes of the guerrilla uprising (168 BC) that originated in Modein, 17 miles northwest of Jerusalem, under the leadership of Mattathias and his son Judas Maccabeus. In December, 165, the altar of the temple was rededicated.
11:35 *time of the end.* See v. 40; 12:4,9. Daniel concludes his predictions about Antiochus Epiphanes and begins to prophesy concerning the more distant future.
11:36 From here to the end of ch. 11 the antichrist (see notes on 7:8; 9:27) is in view. The details of this section do not fit what is known of Antiochus Epiphanes. See 2Th 2:3–4 and notes; cf. Rev 13:5–8.

PTOLEMIES AND SELEUCIDS

Soon after the death of Alexander the Great in 323 BC, his generals divided his empire into four parts, two of which—Egypt and Syria—were under the rule of the Ptolemies and Seleucids respectively. The Holy Land was controlled from Egypt by the Ptolemaic dynasty from 323 to 198, and was subsequently governed by the Seleucids of Syria from 198 to 142.

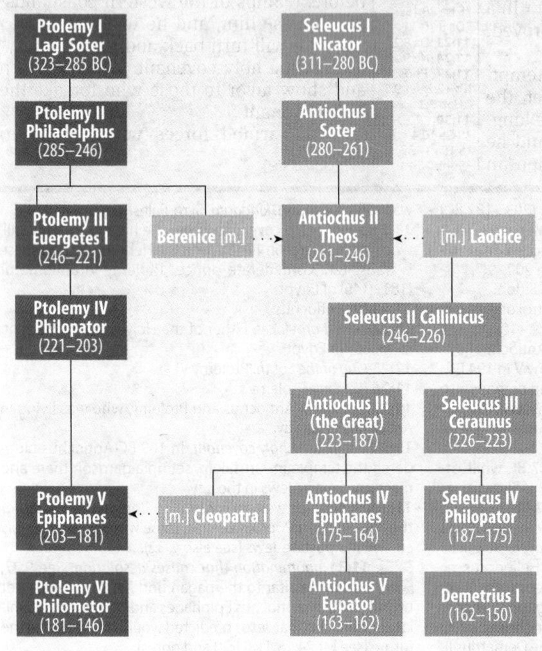

The Diadochi, as the successors of Alexander were called, struggled bitterly for power over his domain. At first Ptolemy I seized his own satrapy, Egypt and North Africa, which had splendid resources and natural defense capabilities. Seleucus gained Syria and Mesopotamia, and by 301 Lysimachus held Thrace and Asia Minor while Cassander ruled Macedon. The situation changed again by 277, when only three major Hellenistic kingdoms stabilized in Egypt, in Syria, and in Macedonia under the Antigonids (277–168). Each continued until the eventual triumph of Rome.

Daniel 11 treats the "king of the South" and the "king of the North," describing their conflicts, wars and alliances. Their hostility toward the people of God culminated in the "abomination that causes desolation" (11:31), identified historically with the reign of Antiochus IV Epiphanes (175–164). The Maccabean revolt followed, leading eventually to the founding of the Hasmonean dynasty.

Continued political rivalries in Judea brought the intervention of the Roman general Pompey in 63 BC. This event signaled the end of Jewish political independence, except for periods of brief autonomy during the ill-fated revolts of the first and second Christian centuries.

[37]He will show no regard for the gods of
his ancestors or for the one desired by
women, nor will he regard any god, but
will exalt himself above them all. [38]Instead
of them, he will honor a god of fortresses;
a god unknown to his ancestors he will
honor with gold and silver, with precious
stones and costly gifts. [39]He will attack the
mightiest fortresses with the help of a foreign god and will greatly honor those who
acknowledge him. He will make them rulers over many people and will distribute
the land at a price.[a]

[40]"At the time of the end the king of the
South[c] will engage him in battle, and the
king of the North will storm[d] out against
him with chariots and cavalry and a great
fleet of ships. He will invade many countries and sweep through them like a flood.[e]
[41]He will also invade the Beautiful Land.[f]
Many countries will fall, but Edom,[g] Moab[h]
and the leaders of Ammon will be delivered
from his hand. [42]He will extend his power
over many countries; Egypt will not escape.
[43]He will gain control of the treasures of
gold and silver and all the riches of Egypt,[i]
with the Libyans[j] and Cushites[b] in submission. [44]But reports from the east and the
north will alarm him, and he will set out in
a great rage to destroy and annihilate many.
[45]He will pitch his royal tents between the
seas at[c] the beautiful holy mountain.[k] Yet

11:40 [c]S Isa 21:1 [d]Isa 5:28 [e]S Isa 8:7; S Eze 38:4 **11:41** [f]S Eze 20:6; Mal 3:12 [g]S Isa 11:14 [h]S Jer 48:47 **11:43** [i]S Eze 30:4 [j]2Ch 12:3; Na 3:9 **11:45** [k]S Isa 2:2,4; Da 8:9

[a] 39 Or *land for a reward* [b] 43 That is, people from the upper Nile region [c] 45 Or *the sea and*

11:37 *the one desired by women.* Usually interpreted as either Tammuz (see Eze 8:14 and note) or the Messiah (see Hag 2:7 and note).

11:40–45 Many feel that these verses speak of conflicts to be waged between the antichrist and his political enemies. He will meet his end "at the beautiful holy mountain" (v. 45), Jerusalem's temple mount, perhaps in connection with the battle of Armageddon (cf. note on v. 36; cf. also 9:27b; Rev 16:13–16).

11:41 *Beautiful Land.* See note on 8:9–12.

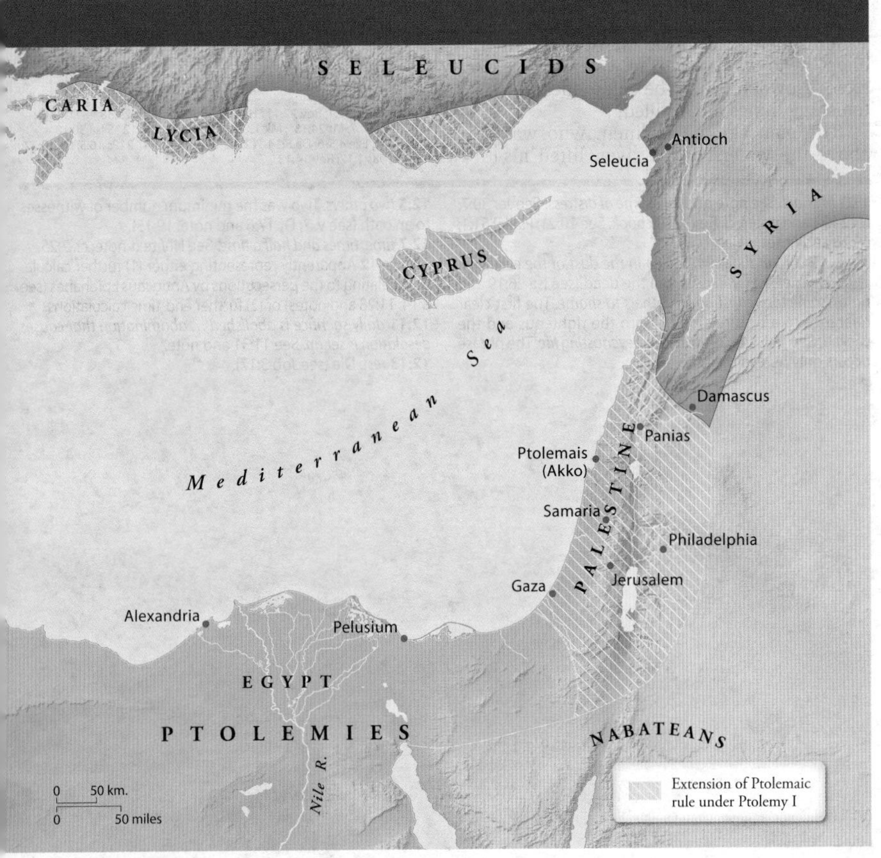

he will come to his end, and no one will
help him.

The End Times

12 "At that time Michael,[l] the great
prince who protects your people,
will arise. There will be a time of distress[m]
such as has not happened from the beginning of nations until then. But at that time
your people — everyone whose name is
found written in the book[n] — will be delivered.[o] 2 Multitudes who sleep in the dust
of the earth will awake:[p] some to everlasting life, others to shame and everlasting
contempt.[q] 3 Those who are wise[a][r] will
shine[s] like the brightness of the heavens,
and those who lead many to righteous-
ness,[t] like the stars for ever and ever.[u] 4 But
you, Daniel, roll up and seal[v] the words
of the scroll until the time of the end.[w]
Many will go here and there[x] to increase
knowledge."

5 Then I, Daniel, looked, and there before me stood two others, one on this bank
of the river and one on the opposite bank.[y]
6 One of them said to the man clothed in
linen,[z] who was above the waters of the
river, "How long will it be before these astonishing things are fulfilled?"[a]
7 The man clothed in linen, who was
above the waters of the river, lifted his
right hand[b] and his left hand toward heav-
en, and I heard him swear by him who
lives forever,[c] saying, "It will be for a time,
times and half a time.[b][d] When the power
of the holy people[e] has been finally broken, all these things will be completed.[f]"
8 I heard, but I did not understand. So I
asked, "My lord, what will the outcome of
all this be?"
9 He replied, "Go your way, Daniel, because the words are rolled up and sealed[g]
until the time of the end.[h] 10 Many will be
purified, made spotless and refined,[i] but
the wicked will continue to be wicked.[j]
None of the wicked will understand, but
those who are wise will understand.[k]
11 "From the time that the daily sacrifice[l] is abolished and the abomination
that causes desolation[m] is set up, there
will be 1,290 days.[n] 12 Blessed is the one
who waits[o] for and reaches the end of the
1,335 days.[p]
13 "As for you, go your way till the end.[q]
You will rest,[r] and then at the end of the
days you will rise to receive your allotted
inheritance.[s]"

[a] 3 Or *who impart wisdom* [b] 7 Or *a year, two years and half a year*

12:1 [l] S Da 10:13; Jude 1:9 [m] S Da 9:12; S Mt 24:21; Mk 13:19; Rev 16:18 [n] S Ex 32:32; S Ps 56:8; S Jer 17:13; S Lk 10:20 [o] Jer 30:7 **12:2** [p] Jn 11:24 [q] S Isa 26:19; Mt 25:46 **12:3** [r] S Da 11:33 [s] Mt 13:43; Jn 5:35; Php 2:15 [t] S Isa 6:7 [u] S Pr 4:18; 1Co 15:42 **12:4** [v] S Isa 8:16 [w] ver 9, 13; Rev 22:10 [x] Jer 5:1 **12:5** [y] Da 10:4 **12:6** [z] S Eze 9:2 [a] Da 8:13 **12:7** [b] S Ge 14:22 [c] S Da 6:26; Rev 10:5-6 [d] S Da 7:25; S Rev 11:2 [e] S Da 8:24 [f] Lk 21:24; Rev 10:7 **12:9** [g] S Isa 29:11 [h] S ver 4 **12:10** [i] S Isa 1:25; S Da 11:35 [j] S Isa 32:7; Rev 22:11 [k] Hos 14:9 **12:11** [l] S Ex 29:38 [m] S Da 8:11; S 9:27; Mt 24:15*; Mk 13:14* [n] Rev 11:2 **12:12** [o] S Isa 30:18 [p] S Eze 4:5-6; Da 8:14 **12:13** [q] S ver 4 [r] Isa 57:2 [s] Ps 16:5; Mt 10:22; Jas 1:12; Rev 14:13

12:1 *Michael.* See note on 10:13. *time of distress.* See Jer 30:7; Mt 24:21 and notes; cf. Rev 16:18. *book.* See 10:21; Ps 9:5; 51:1; 69:28 and notes.

12:2 *Multitudes who sleep in the dust of the earth will awake.* They will rise from the dead (see Isa 26:19 and note). *some to everlasting life, others to shame.* The first clear reference to a resurrection of both the righteous and the wicked. See Jn 5:24–29 and notes. *everlasting life.* The phrase occurs only here in the OT.

12:5 *two others.* Two was the minimum number of witnesses to an oath (see v. 7; Dt 17:6 and note; 19:15).

12:7 *time, times and half a time.* See NIV text note; cf. 7:25.

12:11–12 Apparently representing either (1) further calculations relating to the persecutions by Antiochus Epiphanes (see 8:14; 11:28 and notes) or (2) further end-time calculations.

12:11 *daily sacrifice is abolished … abomination that causes desolation is set up.* See 11:31 and note.

12:13 *rest.* Die (see Job 3:17).

THE BOOK OF THE TWELVE, OR THE MINOR PROPHETS

In Ecclesiasticus (an Apocryphal book written c. 190 BC), Jesus ben Sira spoke of "the twelve prophets" (Ecclesiasticus 49:10) as a unit parallel to Isaiah, Jeremiah and Ezekiel. He thus indicated that these 12 prophecies were at that time thought of as a unit and were probably already written together on one scroll, as is the case in the Dead Sea Scrolls. Josephus (*Against Apion,* 1.8) also was aware of this grouping. Augustine (*The City of God,* 18.25) called them the "Minor Prophets," referring to the small size of these books by comparison with the major prophetic books and not at all suggesting that they are of minor importance.

In the traditional Jewish canon these works are arranged in what was thought to be their chronological order: (1) the books that came from the period of Assyrian power (Hosea, Joel, Amos, Obadiah, Jonah, Micah), (2) those written about the time of the decline of Assyria (Nahum, Habakkuk, Zephaniah) and (3) those dating from the postexilic era (Haggai, Zechariah, Malachi). On the other hand, their order in the Septuagint (the pre-Christian Greek translation of the OT) is: Hosea, Amos, Micah, Joel, Obadiah, Jonah, Nahum, Habakkuk, Zephaniah, Haggai, Zechariah, Malachi (the order of the first six was probably determined by length, except for Jonah, which is placed last among them because of its different character).

In any event, it appears that within a century after the composition of Malachi the Jews had brought together the 12 shorter prophecies to form a book (scroll) of prophetic writing, which was received as canonical and paralleled the three major prophetic books of Isaiah, Jeremiah and Ezekiel. The great Greek manuscripts Alexandrinus and Vaticanus place the Twelve before the Major Prophets, but in the traditional Jewish canon and in all modern versions they appear after them.

The Habakkuk Commentary (1QpHab). Dead Sea Scroll containing the text and accompanying commentary on Habakkuk 1 and 2. The scroll was found in Cave 1 at Qumran.

Habakkuk Commentary, columns 5–8, Qumran Cave 1, first century BC/Israel Museum, Jerusalem, Israel/The Bridgeman Art Library

JERUSALEM DURING THE TIME OF THE PROPHETS

c. 750–586 BC

Refugees arrived in Jerusalem about the time of the fall of the northern kingdom (722 BC). Settlement spread to the western hill, and a new wall was added for protection. King Hezekiah's engineers carved an underground aqueduct out of solid rock to bring an ample water supply inside the city walls, enabling Jerusalem to survive the siege of Sennacherib in 701.

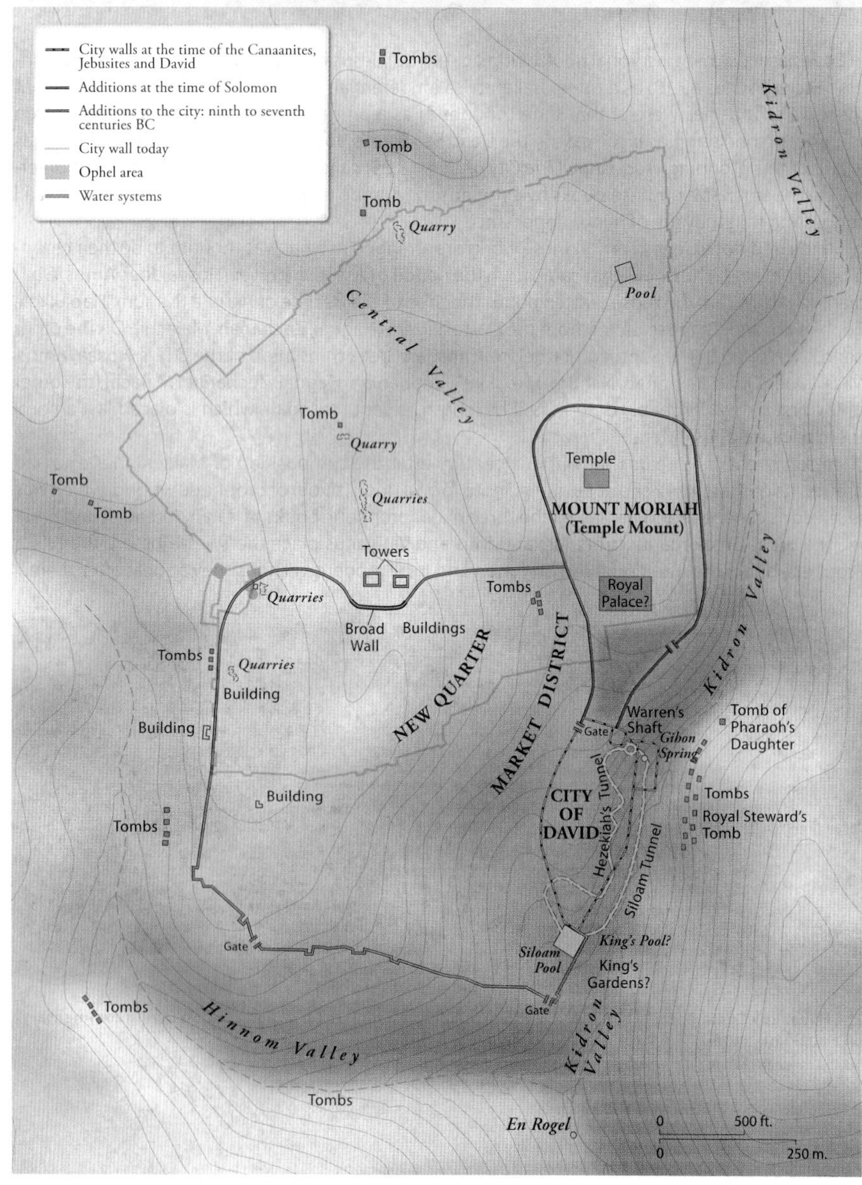

HOSEA

INTRODUCTION

Author and Date

Hosea, son of Beeri, prophesied about the middle of the eighth century BC, his ministry beginning during or shortly after that of Amos. Amos threatened God's judgment on Israel at the hands of an unnamed enemy; Hosea identifies that enemy as Assyria (7:11; 8:9; 10:6; 11:11). Judging from the kings mentioned in 1:1, Hosea must have prophesied for at least 38 years, though almost nothing is known about him from sources outside his book. He was the only one of the writing prophets to come from the northern kingdom (Israel), and his prophecy is primarily directed to that kingdom. But since his prophetic activity is dated by reference to kings of Judah, the book was probably written in Judah after the fall of the northern capital, Samaria (722 – 721 BC) — an idea suggested by references to Judah throughout the book (1:7,11; 4:15; 5:5,10,12 – 13; 6:4,11; 10:11; 11:12; 12:2). Whether Hosea himself authored the book that preserves his prophecies is not known. The book of Hosea stands first in the division of the Bible called the Book of the Twelve (in the Apocrypha, cf. Ecclesiasticus 49:10; see essay, p. 1439) or the Minor Prophets (a name referring to the brevity of these books as compared to Isaiah, Jeremiah and Ezekiel).

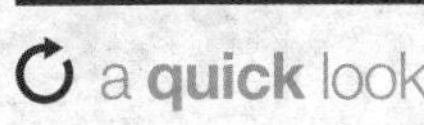

a quick look

Author:
Hosea

Audience:
Primarily the northern kingdom of Israel

Date:
Probably after the fall of the northern capital, Samaria (722 – 721 BC)

Theme:
Hosea proclaims God's compassion and covenant love that cannot let Israel go.

Background

Hosea lived in the tragic final days of the northern kingdom, during which six kings (following Jeroboam II) reigned within 25 years (2Ki 15:8 — 17:6). Four (Zechariah, Shallum, Pekahiah, Pekah) were murdered by their successors while in office, and one (Hoshea) was captured in battle; only one (Menahem) was succeeded on the throne by his son. These kings, given to Israel by God "in my anger" and taken away "in my wrath" (13:11), floated away "like a twig on the surface of the waters" (10:7). "Bloodshed" followed "bloodshed" (4:2). Assyria was expanding westward, and Menahem accepted that world power as overlord and paid tribute (2Ki 15:19 – 20). But shortly afterward, in 733 BC, Israel was dismembered by Assyria because of the intrigue of Pekah (who had gained Israel's throne by killing

Pekahiah, Menahem's son and successor). Only the territories of Ephraim and western Manasseh were left to the king of Israel. Then, because of the disloyalty of Hoshea (Pekah's successor), Samaria was captured and its people exiled in 722–721, bringing the northern kingdom to an end.

Theological Theme and Message

The first part of the book (chs. 1–3) narrates the family life of Hosea as a symbol (similar to the symbolism in the lives of Isaiah, Jeremiah and Ezekiel) to convey the message the prophet had from the Lord for his people. God ordered Hosea to marry a promiscuous woman, Gomer, and their three children were each given a symbolic name representing part of the ominous message. Ch. 2 alternates between Hosea's relation to Gomer and its symbolic representation of God's relation to Israel. The children are told to drive the unfaithful mother out of the house, but it was her reform, not her riddance, that was sought. The prophet was ordered to continue loving her, and he took her back and kept her in isolation for a while (ch. 3). The affair graphically represents the Lord's relation to the Israelites (cf. 2:4,9,18), who had been disloyal to him by worshiping Canaanite deities as the source of their abundance. Israel was to go through a period of exile (cf. 7:16; 9:3,6,17; 11:5). Just as Hosea took back his wife, Gomer, so the Lord loves his covenant people and longs to take them back. This return is described with imagery recalling the exodus from Egypt and settlement in Canaan (cf. 1:11; 2:14–23; 3:5; 11:10–11; 14:4–7). Hosea saw Israel's past experiences with the Lord as the fundamental pattern, or type, of God's future dealings with his people.

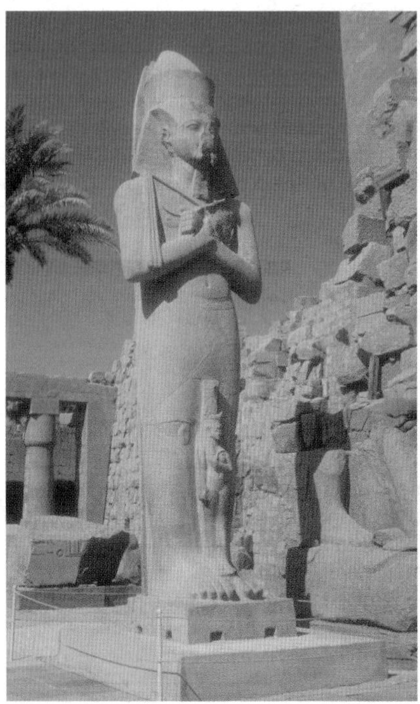

The subordinate status of a wife in the ancient Near East is depicted here in a statue of Rameses II and a miniature version of his wife.

The second part of the book (chs. 4–14) gives the details of Israel's involvement in Canaanite religion, but a systematic outline of the material is difficult. Like other prophetic books, Hosea issued a call to repentance. Israel's alternative to destruction was to forsake her idols and return to the Lord (chs. 6; 14). Information gleaned from materials discovered at Ugarit (dating from the fifteenth century BC; see chart, p. xxiv) enables us to know more clearly the religious practices against which Hosea protested.

Hosea saw the failure to acknowledge God (4:1,6; 8:2–3; 13:4) as Israel's basic problem. God's relation to Israel was that of love (2:19; 4:1; 6:6; 10:12; 12:6). The intimacy of the covenant rela-

Just as Hosea took back his wife, Gomer, so the Lord loves his covenant people and longs to take them back.

tionship between God and Israel, illustrated in the first part of the book by the husband-wife relationship, is later amplified by the father-child relationship (11:1 – 4). Disloyalty to God was spiritual adultery (4:13 – 14; 5:4; 9:1; cf. Jer 3; see note on Ex 34:15). Israel had turned to Baal worship and had sacrificed at the pagan high places, which included associating with the sacred prostitutes at the sanctuaries (4:14) and worshiping the calf images at Samaria (8:5; 10:5 – 6; 13:2). There were also international intrigue (5:13; 7:8 – 11) and materialism. Yet despite God's condemnation and the harshness of language with which the unavoidable judgment was announced, the major purpose of the book is to proclaim God's compassion and covenant love that cannot — finally — let Israel go.

Special Problems

The book of Hosea has at least two perplexing problems. The first concerns the nature of the story told in chs. 1 – 3 and the character of Gomer. While some interpreters have thought the story to be merely an allegory of the relation between God and Israel, others claim, more plausibly, that it is to be taken literally. Among the latter, some insist that Gomer was faithful at first and later became unfaithful, others that she was unfaithful even before the marriage.

The second problem of the book is the relation of ch. 3 to ch. 1. Despite the fact that no children are mentioned in ch. 3, some interpreters claim that the two chapters are different accounts of the same episode. The traditional interpretation, however, is more likely, namely, that ch. 3 is a sequel to ch. 1 — i.e., after Gomer proved unfaithful, Hosea was instructed to take her back.

Outline

- I. Superscription (1:1)
- II. The Unfaithful Wife and the Faithful Husband (1:2 — 3:5)
  - A. The Children as Signs (1:2 — 2:1)
  - B. The Unfaithful Wife (2:2 – 23)
    1. The Lord's judgment on Israel (2:2 – 13)
    2. The Lord's restoration of Israel (2:14 – 23)
  - C. The Faithful Husband (ch. 3)
- III. The Unfaithful Nation and the Faithful God (chs. 4 – 14)
  - A. Israel's Unfaithfulness (4:1 — 6:3)
    1. The general indictment (4:1 – 3)
    2. The cause declared and the results described (4:4 – 19)
    3. A special message to the people and leaders (ch. 5)
    4. The people's sorrowful plea (6:1 – 3)
  - B. Israel's Punishment (6:4 — 10:15)
    1. The case stated (6:4 — 7:16)
    2. The judgment pronounced (chs. 8 – 9)
    3. Summary and appeal (ch. 10)
  - C. The Lord's Faithful Love (chs. 11 – 14)
    1. The Lord's fatherly love (11:1 – 11)
    2. Israel's punishment for unfaithfulness (11:12 — 13:16)
    3. Israel's restoration after repentance (ch. 14)

1 The word of the LORD that came[a] to
Hosea son of Beeri during the reigns
of Uzziah,[b] Jotham,[c] Ahaz[d] and Hezekiah,[e]
kings of Judah,[f] and during the reign of
Jeroboam[g] son of Jehoash[a] king of Israel:[h]

Hosea's Wife and Children

2When the LORD began to speak through
Hosea, the LORD said to him, "Go, marry a promiscuous[i] woman and have children with her, for like an adulterous wife
this land is guilty of unfaithfulness[j] to the
LORD." 3So he married Gomer[k] daughter of
Diblaim, and she conceived and bore him
a son.
4Then the LORD said to Hosea, "Call him
Jezreel,[l] because I will soon punish the
house of Jehu for the massacre at Jezreel,
and I will put an end to the kingdom of Israel. 5In that day I will break Israel's bow
in the Valley of Jezreel.[m]"
6Gomer[n] conceived again and gave birth
to a daughter. Then the LORD said to Hosea, "Call her Lo-Ruhamah (which means
"not loved"),[o] for I will no longer show
love to Israel,[p] that I should at all forgive
them. 7Yet I will show love to Judah; and
I will save them—not by bow,[q] sword or
battle, or by horses and horsemen, but I,
the LORD their God,[r] will save them."
8After she had weaned Lo-Ruhamah,[s]
Gomer had another son. 9Then the LORD
said, "Call him Lo-Ammi (which means
"not my people"), for you are not my people, and I am not your God.[b][t]
10"Yet the Israelites will be like the sand
on the seashore, which cannot be measured or counted.[u] In the place where it
was said to them, 'You are not my people,'
they will be called 'children of the living
God.'[v] 11The people of Judah and the people of Israel will come together;[w] they will
appoint one leader[x] and will come up out
of the land,[y] for great will be the day of
Jezreel.[c][z]

2[d] "Say of your brothers, 'My people,'
and of your sisters, 'My loved one.'[a]

Israel Punished and Restored

2"Rebuke your mother,[b] rebuke her,
for she is not my wife,
and I am not her husband.
Let her remove the adulterous[c] look
from her face
and the unfaithfulness from between
her breasts.
3Otherwise I will strip[d] her naked
and make her as bare as on the day
she was born;[e]

[a] *1* Hebrew *Joash,* a variant of *Jehoash* [b] *9* Or *your I AM* [c] *11* In Hebrew texts 1:10,11 is numbered 2:1,2. [d] In Hebrew texts 2:1-23 is numbered 2:3-25.

1:1 [a]S Jer 1:2 [b]S 2Ki 14:21 [c]S 1Ch 3:12 [d]S 1Ch 3:13 [e]S 1Ch 3:13 [f]Isa 1:1; Mic 1:1 [g]S 2Ki 13:13 [h]Am 1:1 **1:2** [i]S Jer 3:1; Hos 2:2,5; 3:1 [j]Dt 31:16; Jer 3:14; Eze 23:3-21; Hos 5:3 **1:3** [k]ver 6 **1:4** [l]ver 11; S 1Sa 29:1; 1Ki 18:45; 2Ki 10:1-14; Hos 2:22 **1:5** [m]S Jos 15:56; S 1Sa 29:1; 2Ki 15:29 **1:6** [n]ver 3 [o]ver 8; Hos 2:23 [p]Hos 2:4 **1:7** [q]S Ps 44:6 [r]Zec 4:6 **1:8** [s]S ver 6 **1:9** [t]ver 10; S Eze 11:19-20; 1Pe 2:10 **1:10** [u]S Ge 22:17; S Jer 33:22 [v]S Jos 3:10; S ver 9; Hos 2:23; Ro 9:26* **1:11** [w]S Isa 11:12,13 [x]Jer 23:5-8; 30:9 [y]S Eze 37:15-28 [z]S ver 4 **2:1** [a]ver 23; 1Pe 2:10 **2:2** [b]ver 5; S Isa 50:1; S Hos 1:2; 4:5 [c]S Isa 1:21; S Eze 23:45 **2:3** [d]S Eze 16:37 [e]Eze 16:4,22

1:1 *word of the LORD.* A claim of authority paralleling that of Jeremiah (1:2,4), Ezekiel (1:3), Joel (1:1), Jonah (1:1; 3:1), Micah (1:1), Zephaniah (1:1), Haggai (1:1,3; 2:1,10,20), Zechariah (1:1,7; 9:1; 12:1) and Malachi (1:1). *Hosea.* Means "salvation." *Uzziah.* Reigned 792–740 BC; also known as Azariah (see 2Ki 14:21 and NIV text note). *Jotham.* 750–732. *Ahaz.* 735–715. *Hezekiah.* 729–686. Some of the reigns overlapped, the coregency of Ahaz and Hezekiah being the longest (see note on Isa 36:1). *Jeroboam.* Jeroboam II, 793–753. Hosea was a contemporary of Isaiah, Amos and Micah (see the similar first verse in their prophecies).

1:2 *marry a promiscuous woman.* See Introduction: Special Problems. *unfaithfulness.* The one great sin of which the Lord (through Hosea) accuses Israel (see Ex 34:15 and note).

1:3 *Gomer.* Not mentioned outside this book. *him.* The omission of this word in vv. 6,9 may indicate that Hosea was not the father of Gomer's next two children.

1:4 *Jezreel.* Means "God scatters," here used to reinforce the announcement of judgment on the reigning dynasty (see notes on v. 11; 2:22). Jeroboam II was of the dynasty of Jehu (841–814 BC), which was established at Jezreel by the overthrow of Ahab's son Joram (see 2Ki 9:14–29; see also 1Ki 19:16–17 and notes). Jehu's dynasty ended with the murder of King Zechariah in 753 (2Ki 15:8–10).

1:5 *Israel's bow.* Israel's military power, broken in 725 BC, though Samaria held out under siege for three years longer (see 2Ki 17:5–6 and notes). *Valley of Jezreel.* Located east of Megiddo, it provides the only major pass through the mountain range that traverses Israel from north to south and was therefore a major battleground in ancient times.

1:6 *Lo-Ruhamah.* The naming represents a reversal of the love (compassion) that God had earlier shown to Israel (see Ex 33:19; Dt 7:6–8 and note on 7:8) but that later was promised again (see 2:23 and NIV text note).

1:7 *Yet.* See v. 10 and note. *Judah ... I will save.* God's people were saved from Assyria by the Lord in 722–721 BC and again in 701 (see 2Ki 19:32–36).

1:9 *Lo-Ammi.* The naming represents a break in the covenant relationship between the Lord and Israel (see Ex 6:7; Jer 7:23 and note), which later, however, would be restored (v. 10; 2:1,23; see notes there). The warnings became more severe in moving from the first to the third child.

1:10 Cited in Ro 9:26; 1Pe 2:10 (see note there) and applied to the mission to the Gentiles. *Yet.* The threatened punishment (vv. 4–6,9) would be for only a limited time, and a period of blessing would follow. *sand on the seashore.* See the promise to Abraham and Jacob (Ge 22:17; 32:12; cf. Jer 33:22 and note; Heb 11:12). *children of the living God.* Contrasts with "children of adultery" (2:4; cf. 1:2). *living God.* Contrasts with idols—"which are not God" (Dt 32:17).

1:11 *come together.* Israel and Judah would become one nation again. *out of the land.* Possibly the land of exile (cf. Ex 1:10). Another interpretation is that they would spring up from the ground as plants do. *Jezreel.* Here "God scatters" (see note on v. 4) refers to sowing or planting, indicating a reversal of the meaning of the first child's name (see 2:21–23 and notes).

2:1 *My people ... My loved one.* The negatives [Lo = "not"] associated with the names of Hosea's children (see notes on 1:6,9) are dropped.

2:2 The Lord speaks to Hosea's children, continuing the analogy between Gomer and Israel. *not my wife.* The marriage was broken by unfaithfulness, but reconciliation, not divorce, was sought (cf. vv. 7–15).

2:3 *strip her.* The husband supplied the wife's clothing (see Ex 21:10; Eze 16:10), and here her unfaithfulness was exposed

I will make her like a desert,[f]
turn her into a parched land,
and slay her with thirst.
4 I will not show my love to her
children,[g]
because they are the children of
adultery.[h]
5 Their mother has been unfaithful
and has conceived them in
disgrace.
She said, 'I will go after my lovers,[i]
who give me my food and my water,
my wool and my linen, my olive oil
and my drink.'[j]
6 Therefore I will block her path with
thornbushes;
I will wall her in so that she cannot
find her way.[k]
7 She will chase after her lovers but not
catch them;
she will look for them but not find
them.[l]
Then she will say,
'I will go back to my husband[m] as at
first,[n]
for then I was better off[o] than now.'
8 She has not acknowledged[p] that I was
the one
who gave her the grain, the new
wine and oil,[q]
who lavished on her the silver and
gold[r]—
which they used for Baal.[s]

9 "Therefore I will take away my grain[t]
when it ripens,
and my new wine[u] when it is ready.
I will take back my wool and my linen,
intended to cover her naked body.
10 So now I will expose[v] her lewdness
before the eyes of her lovers;[w]
no one will take her out of my
hands.[x]
11 I will stop[y] all her celebrations:[z]
her yearly festivals, her New Moons,
her Sabbath days—all her appointed
festivals.[a]
12 I will ruin her vines[b] and her fig trees,[c]
which she said were her pay from
her lovers;[d]
I will make them a thicket,[e]
and wild animals will devour them.[f]
13 I will punish her for the days
she burned incense[g] to the Baals;[h]
she decked herself with rings and
jewelry,[i]
and went after her lovers,[j]
but me she forgot,[k]"
declares the LORD.[l]

14 "Therefore I am now going to allure
her;
I will lead her into the wilderness[m]
and speak tenderly to her.
15 There I will give her back her
vineyards,
and will make the Valley of Achor[a][n]
a door of hope.
There she will respond[b][o] as in the days
of her youth,[p]
as in the day she came up out of
Egypt.[q]

2:3 [f] Isa 32:13-14 **2:4** [g] S Eze 8:18; Hos 1:6 [h] Hos 5:7 **2:5** [i] S Jer 3:6; S Hos 1:2 [j] Jer 44:17-18 **2:6** [k] S Job 3:23; S 19:8; S La 3:9 **2:7** [l] Hos 5:13 [m] S Isa 54:5 [n] Jer 2:2; S 3:1 [o] S Eze 16:8 **2:8** [p] S Isa 1:3 [q] S Nu 18:12 [r] S Dt 8:18 [s] ver 13; Eze 16:15-19; Hos 8:4 **2:9** [t] Hos 8:7 [u] Hos 9:2 **2:10** [v] Eze 23:10 [w] Jer 13:26 [x] S Eze 16:37 **2:11** [y] Jer 7:34 [z] S Isa 24:8 [a] S Isa 1:14; Jer 16:9; Hos 3:4; 9:5; Am 5:21; 8:10 **2:12** [b] S Isa 7:23; S Jer 8:13 [c] S Jer 5:17 [d] S Jer 3:1 [e] S Isa 5:6 [f] Hos 5:7; 13:8 **2:13** [g] Isa 65:7 [h] ver 8; S Jer 7:9; Hos 11:2 [i] S Eze 16:17; S 23:40 [j] Hos 4:13 [k] Hos 4:6; 8:14; 13:6 [l] S Jer 44:17; Hos 13:1 **2:14** [m] S Eze 19:13 **2:15** [n] S Jos 7:24, 26 [o] Ex 15:1-18 [p] S Jer 2:2; S Eze 16:22 [q] S Eze 28:26; Hos 12:9

[a] *15* *Achor* means *trouble.* [b] *15* Or *sing*

(see Jer 13:26; Eze 16:39). *bare.* As Israel was when the Lord found her in Egypt—in slavery and with nothing (cf. Eze 16:4–8; Na 3:5).

2:4 *children of adultery.* See 1:2 and note. This contrasts with being "children of the living God" (1:10; cf. 11:1).

2:5 *go after.* The wife was chasing other men (see v. 13; Jer 3:2; Eze 16:33–34). *lovers.* See vv. 7,10. The reference is to Canaanite deities (such as Baal), whose worshipers hoped to gain agricultural fertility (see note on Ex 34:15). *who give me my food ... my drink.* Ugaritic texts attribute crops to rain given by Baal. *wool ... linen ... olive oil ... drink.* The agricultural staples of the Holy Land. Israel does not know the true source of her blessings.

2:6 *block her path ... wall her in.* Rather than punish Israel with death (cf. Dt 22:21; Eze 16:39–40; 23:47; Na 3:5–7), the Lord would isolate her.

2:7 *look for.* See 5:6,15 ("seek"). *not find.* See 5:6 and note. *go back.* The Hebrew for this expression often means "repent." *my husband.* The Lord.

2:8 *She has not acknowledged.* Along with the Canaanites, the Israelites attributed to Baal "the grain, the new wine and oil" (see Dt 7:13; Joel 1:10; Hag 1:11 and notes). *silver and gold.* Used for making idols (see 8:4; 13:2). *Baal.* The Canaanite god who was believed to control the weather and the fertility of crops, animals and people (see note on Jdg 2:13).

2:9 *take away.* By withholding the fruits of field and flock, the Lord made known the true source of those blessings.

2:10 *expose her lewdness.* The unfaithful wife was exposed to public shame (see La 1:8; Eze 16:37; 23:29). *no one will take her.* Baal had no power.

2:11 *stop ... celebrations.* In exile these joyous seasons would be only a memory. *yearly festivals.* See Ex 23:14–17; Dt 16:16 and notes. See also chart, pp. 188–189. *New Moons.* See 2Ki 4:23; Isa 1:14; Am 8:5 and notes. *Sabbath.* See Ex 20:8–11.

2:12 *pay from her lovers.* The prostitute's pay (see v. 5; 9:1; Dt 23:18; Eze 16:33; Mic 1:7). Israel attributed her agricultural products to the false gods she worshiped rather than to the Lord (see Dt 11:13–14).

2:13 *days.* Festival days. *Baals.* See v. 17; 11:2. Hosea used the plural here, suggesting the idols at the many local shrines (see Jdg 2:11–13 and notes; Jer 2:23,28 and note; 9:14). *went after.* See note on v. 5. *forgot.* The opposite of "acknowledge" (see note on v. 20) in Hosea (see 13:4–6 and note on 13:6; see also note on 1Sa 12:9).

2:14 *into the wilderness.* For a second betrothal (see vv. 19–20). It refers back to the days of Israel's wilderness wandering, before she was tempted by the Baals in Canaan. *speak tenderly to.* Reassure, encourage, comfort (cf. Ge 34:3; Ru 2:13; Isa 40:2). God continually shows love in the midst of judgment.

2:15 *Valley of Achor.* Near Jericho (see Jos 7:24,26; Isa 65:10). As the prophet reversed the meaning of the names of his children, so also the meaning of Achor (see NIV text note)—where God first judged his people in the promised land—became a symbol of new opportunity.

16 "In that day," declares the LORD,
"you will call me 'my husband';[r]
you will no longer call me 'my
master.[a]'
17 I will remove the names of the Baals
from her lips;[s]
no longer will their names be
invoked.[t]
18 In that day I will make a covenant for
them
with the beasts of the field, the birds
in the sky
and the creatures that move along
the ground.[u]
Bow and sword and battle
I will abolish[v] from the land,
so that all may lie down in safety.[w]
19 I will betroth[x] you to me forever;
I will betroth you in[b] righteousness
and justice,[y]
in[b] love and compassion.[z]
20 I will betroth you in[b] faithfulness,
and you will acknowledge[a] the
LORD.[b]

21 "In that day I will respond,"
declares the LORD—
"I will respond[c] to the skies,
and they will respond to the earth;
22 and the earth will respond to the
grain,
the new wine and the olive oil,[d]
and they will respond to Jezreel.[ce]
23 I will plant[f] her for myself in the land;
I will show my love to the one I
called 'Not my loved one.[dg]'
I will say to those called 'Not my
people,[e]' 'You are my people';[h]
and they will say, 'You are my God.[i]' "

Hosea's Reconciliation With His Wife

3 The LORD said to me, "Go, show your
love to your wife again, though she is
loved by another man and is an adulteress.[j] Love her as the LORD loves the Israelites, though they turn to other gods and
love the sacred raisin cakes.[k]"
2 So I bought her for fifteen shekels[f] of silver and about a homer and a lethek[g] of barley. 3 Then I told her, "You are to live with
me many days; you must not be a prostitute or be intimate with any man, and I will
behave the same way toward you."
4 For the Israelites will live many days
without king or prince,[l] without sacrifice[m] or sacred stones,[n] without ephod[o]
or household gods.[p] 5 Afterward the Israelites will return and seek[q] the LORD their

[a] *16* Hebrew *baal* [b] *19,20* Or *with* [c] *22* *Jezreel* means *God plants.* [d] *23* Hebrew *Lo-Ruhamah* (see 1:6) [e] *23* Hebrew *Lo-Ammi* (see 1:9) [f] *2* That is, about 6 ounces or about 170 grams [g] *2* A homer and a lethek possibly weighed about 430 pounds or about 195 kilograms.

2:16 [r] S Isa 54:5 **2:17** [s] Ex 23:13; Ps 16:4 [t] S Jos 23:7; Zec 13:2 **2:18** [u] S Job 5:22 [v] S Ps 46:9; S Isa 2:4; Zec 9:10 [w] S Job 5:23; S Jer 23:6; Eze 34:25 **2:19** [x] S Isa 62:4; 2Co 11:2 [y] S Isa 1:27 [z] S Isa 54:8 **2:20** [a] Jer 31:34; Hos 4:1; 6:6; 13:4 [b] S Eze 16:8 **2:21** [c] Isa 55:10; Zec 8:12; Mal 3:10-11 **2:22** [d] S Jer 31:12; Hos 14:7; Joel 2:19 [e] S Eze 36:29-30; S Hos 1:4 **2:23** [f] S Jer 31:27 [g] S Hos 1:6 [h] S ver 1; S Isa 19:25; S Hos 1:10 [i] S Jer 29:12; Ro 9:25*; 1Pe 2:10 **3:1** [j] S Hos 1:2 [k] S 2Sa 6:19 **3:4** [l] Hos 13:11 [m] Da 11:31; S Hos 2:11 [n] Hos 10:1 [o] S Ex 25:7 [p] Jdg 17:5-6; 18:14-17; S La 2:9; Zec 10:2 **3:5** [q] S Dt 4:29; S Isa 9:13; S 10:20; Hos 5:15; Mic 4:1-2

2:16–17 *husband ... master ... Baals.* A play on words. Of the two Hebrew words for husband, one (master) is identical to the name of the god Baal (see NIV text note on v. 16). There will be such a vigorous reaction against Baal worship that this Hebrew word for "master" will no longer be used of the Lord.
2:18 *make a covenant.* See 6:7; 8:1. Animals, the instruments of destruction in v. 12, as well as birds and insects, would no longer threaten life. Nature and history combine in a picture of peace (see Isa 11:6–9 and note; 65:25). *Bow and sword and battle.* See 1:5,7. War is terminated. *land.* Israel (see 1:2; 4:1,3; 9:3 and note; 10:1). *lie down in safety.* See Jer 33:16; Eze 34:24–28.
2:19–20 Rather than money, these five traits necessary to the covenant relationship make up the bride-price (see Ex 22:16; 1Sa 18:25 and notes).
2:19 *righteousness.* See 10:12; Ps 4:1; Jer 23:6 and notes. *justice.* See Am 5:24 and note. *love.* See 4:1; 6:4; 10:12 and note; 12:6. *compassion.* A reversal of God's threatened withdrawal of compassion (see 1:6 and note). "Lo-Ruhamah" means lit. "not shown compassion" (cf. Ps 51:1; 103:3–14).
2:20 *faithfulness.* Dependability (see Dt 32:4; Ps 88:11). *acknowledge.* The Hebrew for this word can refer to intimate sexual relations (Ge 19:8; Nu 31:17–18, 35 ["slept with"]), but it also refers to active acknowledgment of a covenant partner (see 6:3 and note; 8:2; 13:4).
2:21 *respond.* The woman (Israel) responded to the Lord's overtures (see v. 15); now God responded to her new behavior. The land also responded by becoming productive (vv. 21–22).
2:22 *Jezreel.* Here used in the sense "God plants" (see NIV text note and v. 23; see also 1:4,11 and notes). The threats represented by the names of the children are turned into blessings (see 1:10 and note). The basic statement describing the covenant relationship was "I will be your God and you will be my people" (Jer 7:23; see notes on Ex 6:7; Zec 8:8).
2:23 *my people ... my God.* See note on v. 22. *You are my God.* The people respond to God's graciousness. This verse is quoted in part in Ro 9:25–26 (see note there); 1Pe 2:10 and applied to Gentiles coming into the church.
3:1 *said to me.* Ch. 3 is narrated in the first person, ch. 1 in the third person. *Go ... love ... your wife.* Hosea's love for unfaithful Gomer illustrated God's love for unfaithful Israel. God's love for Israel (see 11:1 and note; 14:4) is the basic theme of the book. *other gods.* See Ex 20:3; Dt 31:20. *raisin cakes.* Offered to Baal in thanksgiving for harvest.
3:2 Gomer had evidently become a slave, and Hosea bought her back. *fifteen shekels.* Half the usual price of a slave (see Ex 21:32 and note) or of the redemption value of a woman's vow (Lev 27:4). *lethek.* See NIV text note. It appears that half her price was paid in money (silver) and half in produce (barley)—for a total value of 30 shekels.
3:3–5 A picture of exile and return.
3:3 *live with.* Suggests a period of isolation (see 2:6 and note), comparable to Israel's exile. *many days.* Not forever. There would be an "afterward" (v. 5), a future (see Jer 29:11).
3:4 *king.* See 1:4; 5:1; 8:4,10; 10:15; 13:10–11. *prince.* See 7:3,5; 8:4; 13:10. *without sacrifice.* See 6:6; 8:11,13. *sacred stones.* See 10:1–2; 1Ki 14:23 and note; 2Ki 17:10; Mic 5:13. *ephod.* Here an image associated with idols (see Jdg 8:27; 17:5 and notes). *household gods.* See Ge 31:19,30,34 and note on 31:19.
3:5 *return.* A basic word in Hosea's vocabulary (see 2:7 ["go back"]; 5:4; 6:1; 7:10; 11:5; 12:6; 14:1–2). *seek.* Israel's repentance is envisioned (see 5:15 and note)—the reverse of her present stubborn rebellion (7:10). *LORD their*

God and David their king.[r] They will come
trembling[s] to the LORD and to his blessings
in the last days.[t]

The Charge Against Israel

4 Hear the word of the LORD, you
Israelites,
because the LORD has a charge[u] to
bring
against you who live in the land:[v]
"There is no faithfulness,[w] no love,
no acknowledgment[x] of God in the
land.[y]
2 There is only cursing,[a] lying[z] and
murder,[a]
stealing[b] and adultery;[c]
they break all bounds,
and bloodshed follows bloodshed.[d]
3 Because of this the land dries up,[e]
and all who live in it waste away;[f]
the beasts of the field, the birds in the
sky
and the fish in the sea are swept away.[g]
4 "But let no one bring a charge,
let no one accuse another,
for your people are like those
who bring charges against a priest.[h]
5 You stumble[i] day and night,
and the prophets stumble with you.
So I will destroy your mother[j] —
6 my people are destroyed from lack of
knowledge.[k]

"Because you have rejected
knowledge,
I also reject you as my priests;
because you have ignored the law[l] of
your God,
I also will ignore your children.
7 The more priests there were,
the more they sinned against me;
they exchanged their glorious God[b][m]
for something disgraceful.[n]
8 They feed on the sins of my people
and relish their wickedness.[o]
9 And it will be: Like people, like
priests.[p]
I will punish both of them for their
ways
and repay them for their deeds.[q]
10 "They will eat but not have enough;[r]
they will engage in prostitution[s] but
not flourish,
because they have deserted[t] the LORD
to give themselves 11 to prostitution;[u]
old wine[v] and new wine
take away their understanding.[w]
12 My people consult a wooden idol,[x]
and a diviner's rod speaks to them.[y]

[a] *2* That is, to pronounce a curse on [b] *7* Syriac (see also an ancient Hebrew scribal tradition); Masoretic Text *me; / I will exchange their glory*

3:5 [r] S 1Sa 13:14 [s] S Ps 18:45 [t] S Dt 4:30; S Jer 50:4-5; Hos 11:10 **4:1** [u] S Job 10:2; S Jer 2:9 [v] Joel 1:2, 14 [w] S Pr 24:2 [x] S Pr 10:21; S Isa 1:3; Jer 7:28; S Hos 2:20 [y] S Jer 51:5 **4:2** [z] Isa 59:3; Hos 7:3; 10:4; 11:12 [a] Hos 5:2; 6:9 [b] Hos 7:1 [c] S Jer 9:2 [d] S 2Ki 21:16; S Isa 1:15; S Eze 22:2, 9; Hos 5:2; 10:13 **4:3** [e] S Jer 4:28 [f] S Isa 15:6; S 33:9 [g] S Jer 4:25; S 9:10; S Eze 38:20; Zep 1:3 **4:4** [h] Dt 17:12; S Eze 3:26 **4:5** [i] S Eze 7:19; S 14:7 [j] S Hos 2:2 **4:6** [k] S Pr 10:21; S Isa 1:3; S Hos 2:13; Mal 2:7-8 [l] Hos 8:1, 12 **4:7** [m] Hab 2:16 [n] Hos 9:11; 10:1, 6; 13:6 **4:8** [o] S Isa 56:11; Hos 14:1; Mic 3:11 **4:9** [p] S Isa 24:2 [q] Jer 5:31; Hos 8:13; 9:9, 15; 10:10; 12:2 **4:10** [r] S Lev 26:26; S Isa 55:2; Mic 6:14 [s] S Eze 22:9 [t] Hos 7:14; 9:17 **4:11** [u] ver 14; Hos 5:4 [v] S Lev 10:9; S 1Sa 25:36 [w] S Pr 20:1 **4:12** [x] Jer 2:27 [y] Hab 2:19

God. See 12:9; 13:4; Jer 50:4. *David their king.* The Messianic king from the dynasty of David (see Jer 30:9; Eze 34:24 and note). After the death of Solomon, Israel (the northern kingdom) had abandoned the Davidic kings. *his blessings.* The vineyards and olive groves that had been taken away (see 2:12) and all of God's gifts (cf. Jer 31:12–14). *last days.* The Hebrew for this phrase occurs 13 times in the OT, sometimes simply meaning the future ("days to come," Ge 49:1), but most of the time, as no doubt here, referring to the Messianic age ("afterward," Joel 2:28; cf. Ac 2:17; Heb 1:2).

4:1—14:9 Deals with Israel's involvement in Canaanite religion, her moral sins and her international intrigues.

4:1 *Hear the word.* See Jer 2:4 and note. *charge.* As the Lord's spokesman, Hosea brought charges against unfaithful, covenant-breaking Israel (cf. v. 4; 12:2; Isa 3:13; Jer 2:9; Mic 6:2). *faithfulness.* Loyalty (see 2:20 and note) to the covenant Lord (Jos 24:14) and right dealing with others (cf. Pr 3:3). *love.* See 2:19; 10:12. *acknowledgment of God.* See 2:20; 6:3 and notes.

4:2 *cursing ... adultery.* The sins detailed (paralleled in Jer 7:9) transgress several of the Ten Commandments (see Ex 20:13–16 and notes on 20:1–2). *bloodshed.* Includes (1) murder (see 6:8–9); (2) the assassinations following the death of Jeroboam II, when three kings reigned in one year (2Ki 15:10–14); and (3) human sacrifice (Ps 106:38; Eze 16:20–21; 23:37). Where God is not acknowledged (v. 1), moral uprightness disappears.

4:3 *land dries up.* God's judgment on human sin affects all living things in the world (see, e.g., Isa 24:3–6; Jer 4:23–28). *waste away.* See Isa 19:8; Jer 14:2; 15:9; Joel 1:10.

4:4–9 An indictment against the priests, whose duty it was to be guardians of God's law and to furnish religious instruction (see Lev 10:11; Dt 31:9–13; 33:10; 2Ch 17:8–9; Ezr 7:6,10; Jer 18:18; Eze 7:26 and note; Zep 3:4; Hag 2:11; Mal 2:7–9). Hosea warned the priests not to lodge charges against the people for bringing God's judgment down on the nation, for they themselves were guilty, and the people could also bring charges against them—as Hosea proceeded to do (see v. 9; cf. Isa 28:7; Jer 2:26; 4:9; 23:11).

4:5 *stumble.* Experience calamity (see 5:5). *prophets.* See Mic 2:6,11; 3:5–7. *your mother.* The nation (see 2:2,5; Isa 50:1).

4:6 *my people.* Israel (see vv. 8,12; 2:1,23; 6:11; 11:7; Mic 6:3,5). *destroyed from lack of knowledge.* Partly because the priests had failed to teach God's word to the people. *rejected knowledge ... reject you.* Punishment in kind. *law of your God.* Israel's source of life (see Dt 30:20 and note), which the priests should have been faithfully promoting.

4:7 *their glorious God.* See Ps 106:20 and note.

4:8 *feed on the sins.* Priests devoured the sacrifices (see 1Sa 2:13–17 and notes), profiting from the continuation of the sin rather than helping to cure it (see 8:13 and note).

4:9 *Like people, like priests.* Without exception, all would be punished for their sins.

4:10 *eat but not have enough.* The punishment (a futility curse; see note on Hag 1:6) fit the sin. *prostitution.* See vv. 12,18; 2:4; 6:10; 9:1; Jdg 2:17 and note; Ps 106:39. Instead of giving themselves to the Lord, they gave themselves to prostitution (vv. 11–15; see notes on Ge 20:9; Ex 34:15; Ps 73:27).

4:11 *old wine.* See 7:5. *new.* See 2:8–9,22; 7:14; 9:2.

4:12 *wooden idol.* An image of a god (see Jer 2:27; 10:8; Hab 2:19). *spirit of prostitution.* See 5:4. Hebrew idioms often speak of inner tendencies in terms of "spirit."

A spirit of prostitution[z] leads them
astray;[a]
they are unfaithful[b] to their God.
13 They sacrifice on the mountaintops
and burn offerings on the hills,
under oak,[c] poplar and terebinth,
where the shade is pleasant.[d]
Therefore your daughters turn to
prostitution[e]
and your daughters-in-law to adultery.[f]

14 "I will not punish your daughters
when they turn to prostitution,
nor your daughters-in-law
when they commit adultery,
because the men themselves consort
with harlots[g]
and sacrifice with shrine
prostitutes[h]—
a people without understanding[i] will
come to ruin![j]

15 "Though you, Israel, commit adultery,
do not let Judah become guilty.

"Do not go to Gilgal;[k]
do not go up to Beth Aven.[a][l]
And do not swear, 'As surely as the
LORD lives!'[m]
16 The Israelites are stubborn,[n]
like a stubborn heifer.[o]
How then can the LORD pasture them
like lambs[p] in a meadow?

4:12 [z] S Nu 15:39 [a] S Isa 44:20 [b] S Ps 73:27 **4:13** [c] S Isa 1:29 [d] S Jer 3:6; Hos 10:8; 11:2 [e] Jer 2:20; Am 7:17 [f] Hos 2:13 **4:14** [g] S ver 11 [h] S Ge 38:21; Hos 9:10 [i] S Pr 10:21 [j] ver 19 **4:15** [k] Hos 9:15; 12:11; Am 4:4; 5:5 [l] S Jos 7:2; S Hos 5:8 [m] S Jer 4:2 **4:16** [n] S Ex 32:9 [o] S Jer 31:18 [p] Isa 5:17; 7:25 **4:19** [q] Hos 12:1; 13:15 [r] ver 13-14; Isa 1:29 **5:1** [s] S Job 10:2 [t] Hos 6:9; 9:8 [u] S Jer 5:26 **5:2** [v] S Hos 4:2 [w] Hos 9:15 **5:3** [x] Am 5:12 [y] S Eze 23:7; S Hos 1:2; 6:10 **5:4** [z] Hos 7:10 [a] S Hos 4:11 [b] S Jer 4:22; S Hos 4:6

17 Ephraim is joined to idols;
leave him alone!
18 Even when their drinks are gone,
they continue their prostitution;
their rulers dearly love shameful
ways.
19 A whirlwind[q] will sweep them away,
and their sacrifices will bring them
shame.[r]

Judgment Against Israel

5 "Hear this, you priests!
Pay attention, you Israelites!
Listen, royal house!
This judgment[s] is against you:
You have been a snare[t] at Mizpah,
a net[u] spread out on Tabor.
2 The rebels are knee-deep in slaughter.[v]
I will discipline all of them.[w]
3 I know all about Ephraim;
Israel is not hidden[x] from me.
Ephraim, you have now turned to
prostitution;
Israel is corrupt.[y]

4 "Their deeds do not permit them
to return[z] to their God.
A spirit of prostitution[a] is in their
heart;
they do not acknowledge[b] the LORD.

[a] *15 Beth Aven* means *house of wickedness* (a derogatory name for Bethel, which means *house of God*).

4:13 *mountaintops.* Places commonly chosen for pagan altars (see 10:8; Dt 12:2; 1Ki 3:2 and note; Jer 2:20; 3:6). Clay tablets from Ugarit (see chart, p. xxiv) tell of fertility rites carried out by the Canaanites at the high places. *oak ... terebinth.* Trees noted for their shade. *turn to prostitution.* Canaanite fertility rites involved sexual activity (v. 14) that led to general erosion of morals (see, e.g., Nu 25:1–18 and notes).

4:14 *not punish.* The men would punish their women for immorality, but God would have no part in their hypocrisy. *harlots.* Common prostitutes (see Ge 34:31; Lev 21:14; Eze 16:31). *shrine prostitutes.* Women of the sanctuaries who served as partners for men in sexual activity that was part of their religious ritual (cf. Ge 38:21 and note; Dt 23:18). *without understanding.* Contrast 14:9.

4:15 *commit adultery.* See notes on Ge 20:9; Ex 34:15. *Judah.* An aside warning (see Introduction: Author and Date). *guilty.* See 10:2; 13:1. *Do not go.* The nation as a whole was addressed. *Gilgal.* A site near Jericho (see 9:15; 12:11; Jos 4:19; 1Sa 11:14 and notes) where the Israelites had established a religious shrine. *Beth Aven.* A sarcastic substitute name for Bethel (see NIV text note; see also 5:8), site of one of the two major worship centers established by Jeroboam I (see 1Ki 12:29 and note). *As surely as the LORD lives.* A form of solemn oath (see Ge 42:15 and note; Jdg 8:19; Ru 3:13; 1Sa 14:39; 26:10,16; Jer 4:2; 38:16). Though proper in itself—since it invoked the true God (Dt 6:13; 10:20; cf. Jos 23:7)—it was here forbidden because it was being used deceitfully, as though the Israelites were truly honoring the Lord (see Jer 5:2 and note).

4:16 *stubborn.* See Ne 9:29; Zec 7:11. *stubborn heifer.* See Jer 2:20; 31:18 and notes; an apt figure for unruly Israel (Hos 10:11; cf. 11:4).

4:17 *Ephraim.* Israel's largest tribe (see notes on 9:11; 13:1), whose name came to be used of the northern kingdom as a whole. *idols.* The golden calf (see 8:5 and note) and the Baals (see 2:8,13 and notes). *leave him alone.* Nothing could be done to help (see 2Sa 16:11; 2Ki 23:18).

4:19 *A whirlwind will sweep them away.* Lit. "The wind will catch them up with its wings," probably a metaphor from the threshing floor (see 13:3; Ru 1:22; Ps 1:4 and notes) for the sudden violence that would bring the exile. Since the Hebrew for the words "wind" and "spirit" is the same, there is a possible wordplay with the "spirit of prostitution" (see v. 12 and note). *shame.* By means of their sacrifices they hoped to flourish, but God's punishment for their idolatry would bring them into disgrace among the nations (see 10:6).

5:1 *priests ... Israelites ... royal house.* The three groups addressed were all responsible for maintaining justice, but it miscarried at their hands. *snare ... net.* Devices for catching animals and birds, here used as metaphors for those who by economic and legal schemes took cruel advantage of innocent people (see Job 18:8–10; Ps 140:5; Pr 29:5–6; La 1:13). *Mizpah.* Either (1) Mizpah in Gilead east of the Jordan (Ge 31:43–49) or (2) Mizpah in Benjamin (see 1Sa 7:5 and note). *Tabor.* A mountain at the southeastern edge of the Jezreel Valley. Reference must have been to well-known events that illustrated Israel's corruption.

5:2 *discipline.* A significant word in the Prophets for God's corrective action against his people (see Isa 26:16; Jer 2:30; 5:3; 7:28).

5:3 *Ephraim.* See note on 4:17. *prostitution.* See note on 4:10.

5:4 *Their deeds.* See 4:9; 7:2; 9:15; 12:2. Persistent sin can make repentance impossible (see Jer 13:23; Jn 8:34; Ro 6:6,16). *spirit of prostitution.* See 4:12 and note. *not acknowledge the LORD.* See 4:6; Isa 1:3 and note.

5 Israel's arrogance testifies[c] against
them;
the Israelites, even Ephraim,
stumble[d] in their sin;
Judah also stumbles with them.[e]
6 When they go with their flocks and
herds
to seek the LORD,[f]
they will not find him;
he has withdrawn[g] himself from
them.
7 They are unfaithful[h] to the LORD;
they give birth to illegitimate[i]
children.
When they celebrate their New Moon
feasts,[j]
he will devour[a][k] their fields.

8 "Sound the trumpet[l] in Gibeah,[m]
the horn in Ramah.[n]
Raise the battle cry in Beth Aven[b];[o]
lead on, Benjamin.
9 Ephraim will be laid waste[p]
on the day of reckoning.[q]
Among the tribes of Israel
I proclaim what is certain.[r]
10 Judah's leaders are like those
who move boundary stones.[s]
I will pour out my wrath[t] on them
like a flood of water.
11 Ephraim is oppressed,
trampled in judgment,
intent on pursuing idols.[c][u]
12 I am like a moth[v] to Ephraim,
like rot[w] to the people of Judah.

13 "When Ephraim[x] saw his sickness,
and Judah his sores,
then Ephraim turned to Assyria,[y]
and sent to the great king for help.[z]
But he is not able to cure[a] you,
not able to heal your sores.[b]
14 For I will be like a lion[c] to Ephraim,
like a great lion to Judah.
I will tear them to pieces[d] and go away;
I will carry them off, with no one to
rescue them.[e]
15 Then I will return to my lair[f]
until they have borne their guilt[g]
and seek my face[h] —
in their misery[i]
they will earnestly seek me.[j]"

5:5 [c] S Isa 3:9; S Jer 2:19; Hos 7:10 [d] S Eze 14:7 [e] Hos 14:1 **5:6** [f] Mic 6:6-7 [g] S Pr 1:28; Isa 1:15; Eze 8:6; Mal 1:10 **5:7** [h] S Isa 24:16; Hos 6:7 [i] Hos 2:4 [j] Isa 1:14 [k] S Hos 2:11-12 **5:8** [l] S Nu 10:2; S Jer 4:21; S Eze 33:3 [m] Jdg 19:12; Hos 9:9; 10:9 [n] S Isa 10:29 [o] S Jos 7:2; Hos 4:15; 10:5 **5:9** [p] S Isa 7:16 [q] Isa 37:3; Hos 9:11-17 [r] Isa 46:10; Zec 1:6 **5:10** [s] S Dt 19:14 [t] S Eze 7:8 **5:11** [u] Hos 9:16; Mic 6:16 **5:12** [v] S Job 13:28; S Isa 51:8 [w] S Job 18:16 **5:13** [x] S Isa 7:16 [y] S Eze 23:5; Hos 7:11; 8:9; 12:1 [z] S La 5:6; Hos 7:8; 10:6 [a] S Isa 3:7; Hos 14:3 [b] Hos 2:7 **5:14** [c] S Job 10:16; S Jer 4:7; Am 3:4 [d] Hos 6:1 [e] S Dt 32:39; Mic 5:8

Israel Unrepentant

6 "Come, let us return[k] to the LORD.
He has torn us to pieces[l]
but he will heal us;[m]
he has injured us
but he will bind up our wounds.[n]
2 After two days he will revive us;[o]
on the third day[p] he will restore[q] us,
that we may live in his presence.
3 Let us acknowledge the LORD;
let us press on to acknowledge
him.
As surely as the sun rises,
he will appear;

[a] *7* Or *Now their New Moon feasts / will devour them and* [b] *8* *Beth Aven* means *house of wickedness* (a derogatory name for Bethel, which means *house of God*). [c] *11* The meaning of the Hebrew for this word is uncertain.

5:15 [f] S Isa 18:4 [g] S Lev 26:40 [h] S Nu 21:7; S Ps 24:6; S Hos 3:5 [i] Ps 50:15; S Jer 2:27 [j] Isa 64:9; S Eze 20:43 **6:1** [k] S Isa 10:20; S 19:22 [l] S Job 16:9; La 3:11; Hos 5:14 [m] S Nu 12:13; S Jer 3:22 [n] S Dt 32:39; S Job 5:18; S Jer 30:17; Hos 14:4 **6:2** [o] Ps 30:5; S 80:18 [p] S Mt 16:21 [q] S Ps 71:20

5:5 *arrogance.* Stubborn rebellion against the Lord (see Dt 1:43; 1Sa 15:23; Ne 9:16; Job 35:12; Ps 10:2; Eze 16:56–57). *testifies.* In the case God presented against his people (see 4:1 and note). *stumble.* See 4:5 and note. *Judah.* See Introduction: Author and Date.

5:6 *seek the LORD.* Go to him with prayer and sacrifices (see 3:5 and note; Am 5:4–5). *not find him.* Offering sacrifices in their situation was useless (see 2:7; cf. Isa 1:10–15; Am 5:21–24; Mic 6:6–8). The Lord would be "found" by Israel only when she turned to him with integrity of heart (see v. 15; 3:5; Dt 4:29–31; Jer 29:13).

5:7 *unfaithful.* See 1:2 and note. *New Moon.* Usually a festive occasion (see, e.g., 2:11; 1Sa 20:5 and note; Am 8:5; Col 2:16), but now a time of judgment. Or the meaning may be that one month would be sufficient to accomplish their punishment.

5:8 Some interpreters suggest that the Aramean (Syrian)-Ephraimite (Israelite) war (see 2Ki 16:5–9; Isa 7:1–9 and notes) forms the background of the message in chs. 4–5. *trumpet.* Made of a ram's horn, which here sounds the alarm that an army is approaching (see 8:1; Joel 2:1 and note; Am 3:6). *Gibeah.* Two miles north of Jerusalem. *Ramah.* North of Gibeah. *Beth Aven.* See note on 4:15. *lead on, Benjamin.* Perhaps a Benjamite war cry.

5:9 *laid waste.* See Jer 25:11,38.

5:10 *move boundary stones.* Judah had seized Israelite territory (1Ki 15:16–22; see Dt 19:14 and note; 27:17; Pr 15:25 and note; 23:10; Isa 5:8; Mic 2:2). *my wrath.* See 13:11.

5:12 *moth ... rot.* Both consume (see Job 13:28).

5:13 *sickness ... sores.* Metaphors for the national wounds that Israel and Judah had suffered at the hands of their enemies (see Isa 1:5–6; 17:11; Jer 15:18; 30:12–15). *turned to Assyria.* Assyrian records tell of the tribute paid to Tiglath-Pileser III by the Israelite kings Menahem and Hoshea (cf. 2Ki 15:19–20; 17:3). *not able to cure.* The alliances were worthless.

5:14 *lion.* See 13:7; Am 1:2 and note; 3:8. The Lord might use human agents (see Isa 10:5 and note), but he would be responsible for Israel's punishment, from which there would be no escape (see Isa 5:29; 42:22; Am 9:1–4).

5:15 *return to my lair.* God threatened to withdraw from Israel until, out of desperation, she truly repented. This idea sets the stage for the prophet's next theme. *lair.* See v. 14.

6:1 *let us return.* A shallow (see v. 4) proposal of repentance (using phrases from 5:13–15), in which Israel acknowledged that God, not Assyria (cf. 5:13), was the true physician (cf. 7:1).

6:2 *two days ... third day.* A brief time. Israel supposed that God's wrath would only be temporary.

6:3 *acknowledge the LORD.* A key concept in Hosea (see v. 6; 2:20 and note; 4:1,6; 5:4). *like the winter rains ... spring rains.* Israel believed that, as surely as seasonal rains fell, reviving the earth, God's favor would return and restore her.

he will come to us like the winter rains,[r]
like the spring rains that water the
earth.[s]"

4 "What can I do with you, Ephraim?[t]
What can I do with you, Judah?
Your love is like the morning mist,
like the early dew that disappears.[u]
5 Therefore I cut you in pieces with my
prophets,
I killed you with the words of my
mouth[v] —
then my judgments go forth like the
sun.[a][w]
6 For I desire mercy, not sacrifice,[x]
and acknowledgment[y] of God rather
than burnt offerings.[z]
7 As at Adam,[b] they have broken the
covenant;[a]
they were unfaithful[b] to me there.
8 Gilead is a city of evildoers,[c]
stained with footprints of blood.
9 As marauders lie in ambush for a
victim,[d]
so do bands of priests;
they murder[e] on the road to Shechem,
carrying out their wicked schemes.[f]
10 I have seen a horrible[g] thing in Israel:
There Ephraim is given to prostitution,
Israel is defiled.[h]

11 "Also for you, Judah,
a harvest[i] is appointed.

"Whenever I would restore the
fortunes[j] of my people,

6:3 [r] S Job 4:3; Joel 2:23 [s] Ps 72:6; Hos 11:10; 12:6 **6:4** [t] Hos 11:8 [u] Hos 7:1; 13:3 **6:5** [v] Jer 1:9-10; 5:14; 23:29 [w] Heb 4:12 **6:6** [x] S 1Sa 15:22; S Isa 1:11; Mt 9:13*; 12:7*; Mk 12:33 [y] S Jer 4:22; S Hos 2:20 [z] S Ps 40:6; Mic 6:8 **6:7** [a] S Ge 9:11; S Jer 11:10; Hos 8:1 [b] S Hos 5:7 **6:8** [c] Hos 12:11 **6:9** [d] Ps 10:8 [e] S Hos 4:2 [f] Jer 5:30-31; 7:9-10; S Eze 22:9; S Hos 5:1; 7:1 **6:10** [g] S Jer 5:30 [h] S Jer 23:14; S Eze 23:7; S Hos 5:3 **6:11** [i] Jer 51:33; Joel 3:13 [j] S Ps 126:1; Zep 2:7

7:1 [k] S Eze 24:13; S Hos 6:4 [l] ver 13 [m] S Ex 22:2; Hos 4:2 [n] S Hos 6:9; 12:1 **7:2** [o] S Jer 14:10; S 44:21; S Hos 8:13

7 1 whenever I would heal Israel,
the sins of Ephraim are exposed
and the crimes of Samaria revealed.[k]
They practice deceit,[l]
thieves break into houses,[m]
bandits rob in the streets;[n]
2 but they do not realize
that I remember[o] all their evil
deeds.[p]
Their sins engulf them;[q]
they are always before me.

3 "They delight the king with their
wickedness,
the princes with their lies.[r]
4 They are all adulterers,[s]
burning like an oven
whose fire the baker need not stir
from the kneading of the dough till it
rises.
5 On the day of the festival of our king
the princes become inflamed with
wine,[t]
and he joins hands with the
mockers.[u]
6 Their hearts are like an oven;[v]
they approach him with intrigue.
Their passion smolders all night;
in the morning it blazes like a
flaming fire.

[a] 5 The meaning of the Hebrew for this line is uncertain.
[b] 7 Or *Like Adam*; or *Like human beings*

[p] S Job 35:15; Hos 9:15 [q] Jer 2:19; 4:18 **7:3** [r] Jer 28:1-4; S Hos 4:2; 10:13; Mic 7:3 **7:4** [s] S Jer 9:2 **7:5** [t] S Isa 28:1,7 [u] S Ps 1:1 **7:6** [v] Ps 21:9

6:4 *What can I do ... ?* See Isa 5:4. God saw through Israel's superficial repentance. *Ephraim.* See note on 4:17. *Judah.* See Introduction: Author and Date. *love.* See 2:19; see also note on v. 6. *morning mist ... dew.* Figurative for that which is temporary.

6:5 *my prophets.* God's spokesmen had denounced the people's sin. *words of my mouth.* The judgments spoken by the Lord's faithful prophets (see Jer 1:9; 15:19 and notes).

6:6 *mercy.* Hebrew *hesed*, a word that can refer to right conduct toward one's neighbor or loyalty to the Lord or both — the sum of what God requires of his servants. Here it perhaps refers to both. The same Hebrew word is translated "love" in v. 4 (see note on Ps 6:4). *not sacrifice.* Sacrifice apart from faithfulness to the Lord's will is wholly unacceptable to him (see 1Sa 15:22 – 23; Isa 1:11 – 15; Jer 7:21 – 23; Am 5:21 – 24; Mic 6:6 – 8; Mt 9:13; 12:7). *acknowledgment of God.* See v. 3; 2:20 and notes.

6:7 *As at Adam.* Adam is probably Tell ed-Damiyeh at the Jordan (see Jos 3:16 and notes on 3:13,15), as suggested by the reference to "there" at the end of the sentence. The allusion in "Like Adam" (see NIV text note) is uncertain since Scripture records no covenant with Adam. A third interpretation ("Like human beings"; see NIV text note) takes Hebrew *'adam* to mean "humankind." *broken the covenant.* See 8:1; Jos 7:11.

6:8 *Gilead.* See 12:11; Jdg 10:17; 12:7. *footprints of blood.* The allusion is unclear, but Hosea may have been referring to a more recent event than the bloodbath of Jdg 12:1 – 6 — such as Pekah's rebellion against Pekahiah (see 2Ki 15:25).

6:9 *they murder.* The specific event is unknown. *Shechem.* See Ge 33:18 and note.

6:10 *prostitution.* See note on 4:10.

6:11 *harvest.* Figurative for God's judgments (see 8:7; 10:12 – 13; Jer 51:33; Mt 13:30,39 – 42; Rev 14:15). *restore the fortunes.* Paralleling "heal" (7:1), the phrase refers to the restoration of the wounded national body (see Joel 3:1; Zep 3:20).

7:1 *heal.* See 5:13; 6:1; 11:3; 14:4; Jer 51:8 – 9. *sins.* See 4:8; 5:5; 8:13. *Ephraim.* See note on 4:17. *exposed ... revealed.* God sees them. *crimes.* See v. 3. *Samaria.* Another name for the northern kingdom, of which Samaria was the royal city, selected by Omri to be capital of Israel (see 1Ki 16:24 and note). *deceit.* See Jer 6:13; 8:10; probably refers to both feigned repentance and treacherous foreign alliances. *thieves.* See 4:2. *bandits.* See 6:9; Ge 49:19; Jer 18:22.

7:2 See Ps 90:8 and note. *I remember.* Everything is open before the Lord, but the wicked believe that God does not see (see Ps 10:6,11 and notes).

7:3 *delight the king.* Perhaps in conjunction with one of the palace revolts (see 2Ki 15:8 – 30). They were entertaining and flattering the king and princes while engaging in the "wickedness" of preparing to stab them in the back (vv. 6 – 7; see note on v. 7). *lies.* See 11:12; Ps 10:7 and note; Na 3:1.

7:4 *adulterers.* See note on 4:15. *fire.* A metaphor for political intrigue (see vv. 6 – 7). The fire was banked until ready to use; then it broke out. *baker.* Perhaps the leader of the conspiracy.

7:5 *festival of our king.* Probably a coronation or birthday that became a drunken orgy. King Elah died in drunkenness (see 1Ki 16:9 and note). *mockers.* See Pr 1:22 and note. Isaiah (28:1 – 8,14) condemned Israel's drunkenness and her scoffers.

7:6 The intrigue was kept secret until a suitable time.

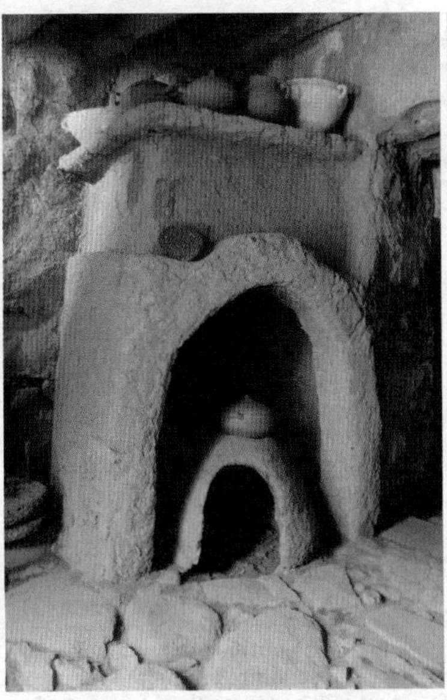

Reconstruction of a fourth-century AD house in northern Israel. In the center is a clay oven used to bake bread. "They are all adulterers, burning like an oven whose fire the baker need not stir from the kneading of the dough till it rises" (Hos 7:4).

Z. Radovan/www.BibleLandPictures.com

7 All of them are hot as an oven;
they devour their rulers.
All their kings fall,[w]
and none of them calls[x] on me.

8 "Ephraim mixes[y] with the nations;
Ephraim is a flat loaf not turned
over.

9 Foreigners sap his strength,[z]
but he does not realize it.
His hair is sprinkled with gray,
but he does not notice.

10 Israel's arrogance testifies against
him,[a]
but despite all this
he does not return[b] to the LORD
his God
or search[c] for him.

11 "Ephraim is like a dove,[d]
easily deceived and senseless—
now calling to Egypt,[e]
now turning to Assyria.[f]

12 When they go, I will throw my net[g]
over them;
I will pull them down like the birds
in the sky.
When I hear them flocking together,
I will catch them.

13 Woe[h] to them,
because they have strayed[i] from me!
Destruction to them,
because they have rebelled
against me!
I long to redeem them
but they speak about me[j] falsely.[k]

14 They do not cry out to me from their
hearts[l]
but wail on their beds.
They slash themselves,[a] appealing to
their gods
for grain and new wine,[m]
but they turn away from me.[n]

15 I trained[o] them and strengthened their
arms,
but they plot evil[p] against me.

16 They do not turn to the Most High;[q]
they are like a faulty bow.[r]
Their leaders will fall by the sword
because of their insolent[s] words.
For this they will be ridiculed[t]
in the land of Egypt.[u]

7:7 [w]Hos 13:10 [x]ver 16; S Ps 14:4; S Isa 9:13; Zep 1:6 **7:8** [y]ver 11; Ps 106:35; S Hos 5:13 **7:9** [z]Isa 1:7; Hos 8:7 **7:10** [a]Hos 5:5 [b]Hos 5:4 [c]ver 14; S Isa 9:13 **7:11** [d]S Ge 8:8 [e]ver 16; Hos 9:6 [f]S ver 8; S Jer 2:18; S La 5:6; Hos 9:3; 12:1 **7:12** [g]S Eze 12:13; S 32:3 **7:13** [h]Hos 9:12 [i]Jer 14:10; S Eze 34:4-6; Hos 9:17 [j]ver 1; Jer 51:9; Mt 23:37 [k]S Ps 116:11 **7:14** [l]Jer 3:10 [m]Am 2:8 [n]S ver 10; S Hos 4:10; 9:1; 13:16 **7:15** [o]Hos 11:3 [p]Ps 2:1; S 140:2; Na 1:9,11 **7:16** [q]S ver 7 [r]S Ps 78:9,57 [s]Mal 3:14 [t]S Eze 23:32 [u]S ver 11; Hos 9:3; 11:5

[a] *14* Some Hebrew manuscripts and Septuagint; most Hebrew manuscripts *They gather together*

7:7 *rulers ... kings.* Four kings were assassinated in 20 years, Zechariah and Shallum in a seven-month period (2Ki 15:10–14). *none of them calls on me.* The reason for the shameful situation.
7:8 *mixes with the nations.* See v. 11 and note. *flat loaf.* A metaphor describing unwise policies. Baked on hot stones (cf. 1Ki 19:6), the loaf was burned on the bottom and undone on the top.
7:9 *Foreigners sap his strength.* Tribute to Assyria (2Ki 15:19–20) and to Egypt (v. 11) had weakened the country economically. *hair ... gray.* He was old before his time but ignored the danger signals.
7:10 *return.* See 3:5; 5:4; Am 4:6–11. *search.* See 3:5; 5:6,15 and notes.
7:11 *dove.* See 11:11 and note, where a different image is intended. See also note on Ps 68:13. *senseless.* See Jer 5:21. Menahem turned to Assyria (2Ki 15:19–20); Hoshea alternated in allegiance to Assyria and Egypt (2Ki 17:3–4).
7:12 *my net.* The Lord himself was the hunter—not the nations—and Israel was certain to be caught.
7:13 *Woe.* Often used in conjunction with threats of judgment (see 9:12). *Destruction.* See 9:6; Isa 13:6. *redeem.* See 13:14; also used for deliverance from Egypt (see, e.g., Ex 6:6–8 and notes; Mic 6:4). *speak about me falsely.* Possibly by ascribing prosperity and destiny to gods other than the Lord.
7:14 *wail.* See Joel 1:13. *They slash themselves.* See Lev 19:28; 21:5 and notes. *grain and new wine.* See 2:8,22; 9:1–2.
7:15 *I trained them.* As children (see 11:3 and note) or, perhaps, as troops. *strengthened their arms.* See Eze 30:24–25.
7:16 *Most High.* See 11:7; Dt 32:8 and note. *faulty bow.* See Ps 78:57. The arrow missed the mark; Israel missed her purpose for being. *ridiculed.* Egypt would fail to assist Israel and then would belittle God's power (see Dt 9:28). *Egypt.* See 8:13; 11:5 and notes. There is no record of a forced exile of large numbers to Egypt. Some captives were taken there (2Ki 23:34; Jer 22:11–14), and some fugitives voluntarily went there (2Ki 25:26; Jer 42–44). A return from Egypt is envisioned in 11:11; Isa 11:11; 27:13; Zec 10:10.

Israel to Reap the Whirlwind

8 "Put the trumpet[v] to your lips!
An eagle[w] is over the house of the LORD
because the people have broken my
covenant[x]
and rebelled against my law.[y]
2 Israel cries out to me,
'Our God, we acknowledge you!'
3 But Israel has rejected what is good;
an enemy will pursue him.[z]
4 They set up kings without my consent;
they choose princes without my
approval.[a]
With their silver and gold
they make idols[b] for themselves
to their own destruction.
5 Samaria, throw out your calf-idol![c]
My anger burns against them.
How long will they be incapable of
purity?[d]
6 They are from Israel!
This calf—a metalworker has made it;
it is not God.[e]
It will be broken in pieces,
that calf[f] of Samaria.[g]

7 "They sow the wind
and reap the whirlwind.[h]
The stalk has no head;
it will produce no flour.[i]
Were it to yield grain,
foreigners would swallow it up.[j]
8 Israel is swallowed up;[k]
now she is among the nations
like something no one wants.[l]
9 For they have gone up to Assyria[m]
like a wild donkey[n] wandering alone.
Ephraim has sold herself to lovers.[o]
10 Although they have sold themselves
among the nations,
I will now gather them together.[p]
They will begin to waste away[q]
under the oppression of the mighty
king.

11 "Though Ephraim built many altars for
sin offerings,
these have become altars for sinning.[r]
12 I wrote for them the many things of
my law,
but they regarded them as something
foreign.[s]
13 Though they offer sacrifices as gifts
to me,
and though they eat[t] the meat,
the LORD is not pleased with them.[u]
Now he will remember[v] their
wickedness
and punish their sins:[w]
They will return to Egypt.[x]
14 Israel has forgotten[y] their Maker[z]
and built palaces;
Judah has fortified many towns.
But I will send fire on their cities
that will consume their fortresses."[a]

Punishment for Israel

9 Do not rejoice, Israel;
do not be jubilant[b] like the other
nations.
For you have been unfaithful[c] to your
God;
you love the wages of a prostitute[d]
at every threshing floor.

8:1 [v]S Nu 10:2; S Eze 33:3 [w]S Dt 28:49; Jer 4:13 [x]S Jer 11:10 [y]S Hos 4:6; S 6:7 **8:3** [z]S Mt 7:23; Titus 1:16 **8:4** [a]Hos 13:10 [b]S Hos 2:8; 13:1-2 **8:5** [c]ver 6; Hos 10:5 [d]Jer 13:27 **8:6** [e]S Jer 16:20; Hos 14:3 [f]S Ex 32:4 [g]S ver 5 **8:7** [h]S Job 4:8; Pr 22:8; Isa 66:15; Hos 10:12-13; Na 1:3; Gal 6:8 [i]S Dt 28:38; S Isa 17:11; Hos 9:16 [j]Hos 2:9; S 7:9 **8:8** [k]Jer 51:34 [l]Jer 22:28 **8:9** [m]S Jer 2:18 [n]S Ge 16:12 [o]S Jer 22:20; Eze 23:5; S Hos 5:13 **8:10** [p]S Eze 16:37; S 22:20 [q]Jer 42:2 **8:11** [r]Hos 10:1; 12:11 **8:12** [s]S ver 1 **8:13** [t]S Jer 7:21 [u]S Jer 6:20; Hos 9:4 [v]Hos 7:2; 9:9; Am 8:7 [w]S Hos 4:9 [x]Hos 9:3,6 **8:14** [y]S Dt 32:18; S Isa 17:10; S Hos 2:13 [z]S Ps 95:6 [a]Jer 5:17; S 17:27; Am 2:5 **9:1** [b]Isa 22:12-13 [c]S Ps 73:27; S Isa 24:16; S Hos 7:14; 10:5 [d]S Ge 30:15

8:1 *trumpet.* See 5:8 and note. *your.* Hosea's. *eagle.* Or "vulture," referring to Assyria. *house of the LORD.* The land of Israel, not just the temple (see 9:15 and note; cf. Ex 15:17).
8:2 *we acknowledge you.* See 2:20; 6:3 and notes; but their worship of the Lord was thoroughly corrupted by pagan notions and practices, as vv. 3–6 indicate (see Am 2:4,7–8; 3:14; 5:26).
8:3 *an enemy.* The Assyrians.
8:4 *set up kings.* After Jeroboam II, five kings ruled over Israel in 13 years (2Ki 15:8–30), three of whom seized the throne by violence (see 7:7 and note).
8:5 *Samaria.* See note on 7:1. *calf-idol.* See 10:5; 13:2. Jeroboam I (930–909 BC) had set up golden calves in Bethel and Dan, saying, "Here are your gods" (see 1Ki 12:28–33 and note on 12:28).
8:6 *a metalworker has made it.* For prophetic satire on idolatry, see Isa 40:20; 41:22–24; 44:9–20; see also Ps 115:4–8 and notes. Israel's leaders (Ex 32:4) and Jeroboam I had said "These are your gods," but Hosea said "It is not God."
8:7 *They sow … whirlwind.* A familiar proverb about the results of doing evil (see 10:13; Job 4:8; Ps 126:5–6; Pr 11:18; 22:8; 2Co 9:6; Gal 6:7). Israel sowed the wind of idolatry and reaped the whirlwind of Assyria. *stalk … flour.* The prophet played on the similar sound of the Hebrew words. *foreigners.* Assyria.
8:8 Israel was chosen to be God's own people (see Ex 19:5; Am 3:2 and notes), but since she had conformed to the other nations she lost her special identity and so became to God "like something no one wants."
8:9 *wild donkey wandering alone.* See Jer 2:24 and note. *Ephraim.* See note on 4:17. *sold herself to lovers.* For the prostitute's fees (see 9:1 and note) of Assyrian protection. Menahem (2Ki 15:19) and Hoshea (2Ki 17:3), kings of Israel, paid tribute to Assyria.
8:10 Even though Israel paid tribute to Assyria, that would not buy her security, for God would send judgment by the king of Assyria. Israel's real enemy was the Lord himself (see 2:8–13; 7:12 and note).
8:13 *offer sacrifices.* See v. 2 and note. *eat the meat.* Some of the sacrifices were partly eaten by the offerer and priests (see Lev 7:11–18,28–36; Dt 12:7; Jer 7:21). *not pleased with them.* See 6:6 and note. *Egypt.* Israel, who had trusted in Egypt and Assyria, was to go back to "Egypt," i.e., into bondage in a foreign land, primarily Assyria (see 9:3). But see note on 7:16.
8:14 *Israel has forgotten.* The cause of all her problems (see 2:13 and note; cf. Jdg 2:10). *built palaces … fortified many towns.* Israel's trust was not in her Maker but in what she herself had accomplished. *Judah.* See Introduction: Author and Date. *fire … that will consume.* See Am 1:4 and note.
9:1 This verse begins a section that was probably spoken at a harvest festival, such as the Festival of Tabernacles (Lev 23:33–43; Dt 16:13–15). *unfaithful.* See 1:2; 2:2–5 and notes. *wages of a prostitute.* See 2:12 and note; not to be taken literally, but in the sense of spiritual adultery (see 2:12; Ex 34:15

2 Threshing floors and winepresses will
not feed the people;
the new wine[e] will fail them.
3 They will not remain[f] in the LORD's
land;
Ephraim will return to Egypt[g]
and eat unclean food in Assyria.[h]
4 They will not pour out wine offerings[i]
to the LORD,
nor will their sacrifices please[j] him.
Such sacrifices will be to them like the
bread of mourners;[k]
all who eat them will be unclean.[l]
This food will be for themselves;
it will not come into the temple of
the LORD.[m]

5 What will you do[n] on the day of your
appointed festivals,[o]
on the feast days of the LORD?
6 Even if they escape from destruction,
Egypt will gather them,[p]
and Memphis[q] will bury them.[r]
Their treasures of silver[s] will be taken
over by briers,
and thorns[t] will overrun their
tents.
7 The days of punishment[u] are coming,
the days of reckoning[v] are at hand.
Let Israel know this.
Because your sins[w] are so many
and your hostility so great,
the prophet is considered a fool,[x]
the inspired person a maniac.[y]
8 The prophet, along with my God,
is the watchman over Ephraim,[a]

9:2 [e]Isa 24:7; Hos 2:9; Joel 1:10 **9:3** [f]Lev 25:23 [g]S Hos 7:16; S 8:13 [h]Eze 4:13; S Hos 7:11; 10:5; Am 7:17 **9:4** [i]Joel 1:9, 13; 2:14 [j]S Hos 8:13 [k]S Jer 16:7 [l]S Dt 26:14; Hag 2:13-14 [m]S Eze 4:13-14 **9:5** [n]Isa 10:3; Jer 5:31 [o]S Hos 2:11 **9:6** [p]S Hos 7:11; S 8:13 [q]S Isa 19:13 [r]S Jer 42:22 [s]Zep 1:11 [t]Isa 5:6; Hos 10:8 **9:7** [u]Isa 34:8; Jer 10:15; Mic 7:4; Lk 21:22 [v]S Job 31:14 [w]Jer 16:18 [x]S 1Sa 10:11; Isa 44:25; S La 2:14; Eze 14:9-10 [y]S Jer 29:26; Hos 14:1 **9:8** [z]S Hos 5:1 [a]S Eze 22:26 **9:9** [b]Zep 3:7 [c]Jdg 19:16-30; S Hos 5:8 [d]S Hos 8:13 [e]S Hos 4:9 **9:10** [f]S SS 2:13 [g]S Isa 28:4 [h]Nu 25:1-5; Ps 106:28-29 [i]Jer 11:13; S Hos 4:14 **9:11** [j]S Isa 17:3 [k]S Hos 4:7; 10:5 [l]ver 14 **9:12** [m]ver 16; S Eze 24:21 [n]Hos 7:13 [o]S Dt 31:17 **9:13** [p]S Ps 78:67 [q]S Eze 27:3 [r]S Job 15:22; S La 2:22

yet snares[z] await him on all his paths,
and hostility in the house of his
God.[a]
9 They have sunk deep into corruption,[b]
as in the days of Gibeah.[c]
God will remember[d] their wickedness
and punish them for their sins.[e]

10 "When I found Israel,
it was like finding grapes in the
desert;
when I saw your ancestors,
it was like seeing the early fruit[f] on
the fig[g] tree.
But when they came to Baal Peor,[h]
they consecrated themselves to that
shameful idol[i]
and became as vile as the thing they
loved.
11 Ephraim's glory[j] will fly away like a
bird[k]—
no birth, no pregnancy, no
conception.[l]
12 Even if they rear children,
I will bereave[m] them of every one.
Woe[n] to them
when I turn away from them![o]
13 I have seen Ephraim,[p] like Tyre,
planted in a pleasant place.[q]
But Ephraim will bring out
their children to the slayer."[r]

[a] 8 Or *The prophet is the watchman over Ephraim, / the people of my God*

and notes). *at every threshing floor.* Since the threshing floor at threshing time was a man's world—the threshers feasted there at the end of the day's labors and stayed all night to protect the grain (see Ru 3:2–3 and notes)—prostitutes were not uncommon visitors.

9:3 *LORD's land.* The promised land, which the Lord claimed as his own (see Lev 25:23; Jos 22:19 and note; Jer 2:7; Eze 38:16; Joel 1:6). *Ephraim.* See note on 4:17. *Egypt … Assyria.* Israel was threatened with exile to the lands it depended on—where the temple sacrifice could not be offered (see v. 4; 7:16; 8:13 and notes). *unclean.* A foreign country was ceremonially unclean (see Am 7:17 and note). What grew there was likewise unclean, because it was the product of fertility credited to pagan gods (see 2:5 and note; Eze 4:13).

9:4 *bread of mourners.* Unclean, like bread in a house where there had been a death (see Nu 19:14 and note; Dt 26:14; Jer 16:7). All who touched it became ceremonially unclean. *not come into the temple of the LORD.* In exile Israel would have no place (not even those places established by Jeroboam I; 1Ki 12:28–33) where she could bring sacrifices to the Lord or celebrate her religious festivals (v. 5).

9:5 *appointed festivals … feast days.* See 2:11 and note.

9:6 *Egypt.* See 7:16; 8:13; 11:5 and notes. *Memphis.* The capital of Lower (northern) Egypt. *briers, and thorns.* Cf. a similar threat against Edom (Isa 34:13).

9:7 *inspired.* See Mic 3:8 and note. *maniac.* See 2Ki 9:11; Jer 29:26 and notes; cf. 1Sa 21:15.

9:8 *watchman.* See Eze 3:17; Hab 2:1 and notes. *snares … hostility.* Israel showed only hostility toward the watchmen (the true prophets) whom God sent to warn his people of the great dangers that threatened (see Jer 1:19; 11:19; 15:10; Am 7:10–13).

9:9 *corruption.* The word used of the Israelites who worshiped the golden calf (see Ex 32:7 and note; Dt 9:12). *days of Gibeah.* A reference to the corrupt behavior of the Benjamites so graphically described in Jdg 19–21. *God will remember.* Sins unrepented of are remembered, as well as the accumulated sins of generations (see 13:12).

9:10 *I found Israel … I saw your ancestors.* The covenant relation is traced back to "the desert" (see 2:14–15 and note on 2:14; 13:5; Dt 32:10). *grapes … fig.* Refreshing delicacies (see SS 2:13; Isa 28:4; Mic 7:1). The images used here (grapes in the desert, early fruit of the fig tree) beautifully convey God's delight in Israel when she, out of all the nations, committed herself to him in covenant at Sinai. *Baal Peor.* Peor was a mountain (Nu 23:28). "Baal Peor" refers to the god of Peor (Nu 25:1–3) and is here used to refer to Beth Peor, "the sanctuary of Peor" (see Dt 3:29 and note; 4:3,46; Jos 13:20). Hosea refers here to the incident in Nu 25. *that shameful idol.* See Jdg 6:32; Jer 2:26 and notes. *became … vile.* See Isa 5:2,4,7.

9:11 *Ephraim's glory.* Her large population and prosperity. The punishment fit the sin. Prostitution produces no increase (see 4:10; Jdg 2:17 and notes). *fly away like a bird.* Never to return (see Pr 23:5).

9:12 *Woe.* See 7:13 and note.

9:13 *Tyre.* Noted for its wealth, pleasant environment and security (see Eze 27:3–25).

14 Give them, LORD—
what will you give them?
Give them wombs that miscarry
and breasts that are dry.[s]

15 "Because of all their wickedness in Gilgal,[t]
I hated them there.
Because of their sinful deeds,[u]
I will drive them out of my house.
I will no longer love them;[v]
all their leaders are rebellious.[w]
16 Ephraim[x] is blighted,
their root is withered,
they yield no fruit.[y]
Even if they bear children,
I will slay[z] their cherished offspring."

17 My God will reject[a] them
because they have not obeyed[b] him;
they will be wanderers among the
nations.[c]

10 Israel was a spreading vine;[d]
he brought forth fruit for himself.
As his fruit increased,
he built more altars;[e]
as his land prospered,[f]
he adorned his sacred stones.[g]
2 Their heart is deceitful,[h]
and now they must bear their guilt.[i]
The LORD will demolish their altars[j]
and destroy their sacred stones.[k]

3 Then they will say, "We have no king
because we did not revere the LORD.
But even if we had a king,
what could he do for us?"
4 They make many promises,
take false oaths[l]
and make agreements;[m]
therefore lawsuits spring up
like poisonous weeds[n] in a plowed
field.
5 The people who live in Samaria fear
for the calf-idol[o] of Beth Aven.[a][p]
Its people will mourn over it,
and so will its idolatrous priests,[q]
those who had rejoiced over its
splendor,
because it is taken from them into
exile.[r]
6 It will be carried to Assyria[s]
as tribute[t] for the great king.[u]
Ephraim will be disgraced;[v]
Israel will be ashamed[w] of its foreign
alliances.
7 Samaria's king will be destroyed,[x]
swept away like a twig on the
surface of the waters.
8 The high places[y] of wickedness[b][z] will
be destroyed—
it is the sin of Israel.
Thorns[a] and thistles will grow up
and cover their altars.[b]
Then they will say to the mountains,
"Cover us!"[c]
and to the hills, "Fall on us!"[d]

9 "Since the days of Gibeah,[e] you have
sinned,[f] Israel,
and there you have remained.[c]
Will not war again overtake
the evildoers in Gibeah?
10 When I please, I will punish[g] them;
nations will be gathered against
them
to put them in bonds for their
double sin.
11 Ephraim is a trained heifer
that loves to thresh;
so I will put a yoke[h]
on her fair neck.

9:14 [s]ver 11; Lk 23:29 **9:15** [t]S Hos 4:15 [u]S Hos 7:2 [v]S Jer 12:8 [w]S Isa 1:23; S Hos 4:9; 5:2 **9:16** [x]S Hos 5:11 [y]S Job 15:32; S Hos 8:7 [z]S ver 12 **9:17** [a]S Jer 6:30 [b]S Hos 4:10 [c]S Dt 28:65; S Hos 7:13 **10:1** [d]S Eze 15:2 [e]S 1Ki 14:23 [f]Hos 13:15 [g]Hos 3:4; S 4:7; S 8:11; 12:11 **10:2** [h]1Ki 18:21 [i]Hos 13:16 [j]ver 8 [k]Mic 5:13 **10:4** [l]S Hos 4:2 [m]S Eze 17:19; Am 5:7 [n]Am 6:12 **10:5** [o]S Ex 32:4; S Isa 44:17-20 [p]ver 8; S Hos 5:8 [q]S 2Ki 23:5; Zep 1:4 [r]S Jdg 18:17-18; S Hos 8:5; S 9:1,3,11 **10:6** [s]S 2Ki 16:7; Hos 11:5 [t]S Jdg 3:15 [u]S Hos 5:13 [v]Isa 30:3; S Hos 4:7 [w]Jer 48:13 **10:7** [x]ver 15; Hos 13:11 **10:8** [y]S Eze 6:6 [z]S ver 5; 1Ki 12:28-30; S Hos 4:13 [a]S Hos 9:6 [b]ver 2; S Isa 32:13 [c]S Job 30:6; Am 3:14-15 [d]Am 7:9; Lk 23:30*; Rev 6:16 **10:9** [e]S Hos 5:8 [f]S Jos 7:11

[a] 5 *Beth Aven* means *house of wickedness* (a derogatory name for Bethel, which means *house of God*). [b] 8 Hebrew *aven,* a reference to Beth Aven (a derogatory name for Bethel); see verse 5. [c] 9 Or *there a stand was taken*

10:10 [g]S Eze 5:13; S Hos 4:9 **10:11** [h]S Jer 15:12; S 31:18

9:14 Hosea did not pray out of hateful vengeance against Israel but because he shared God's holy wrath against her sins.

9:15 *Gilgal.* See note on 4:15. *drive them out of my house.* As the unfaithful wife was driven from her husband's house, so Israel was driven from God's "house"—i.e., his land (see 8:1 and note). *no longer love them.* Because of their sins. But when they repent and ask the Lord to forgive them (see 14:1–2 and notes), he will "love them freely" (14:4).

9:17 *My God.* Hosea's words alone, for God was no longer Israel's God. *reject.* See 4:6; 2Ki 17:20. *wanderers.* Like Cain (Ge 4:12–16).

10:1 *Israel.* The nation personified and called by the name of its ancestor. *vine.* A frequent metaphor for Israel (see Ps 80:8–16 and note). *prospered.* The prosperity during the period of Jeroboam II (793–753 BC) is probably in view. *sacred stones.* See 3:4 and note.

10:2 *Their heart is deceitful.* See Jer 17:9 and note. Israel formally cried out to God, but the people dishonored him by pagan worship (see 8:2 and note).

10:3 *We have no king.* Such would soon be their condition when Assyria destroyed the nation.

10:4 *They make many promises.* The last kings of Israel were notoriously corrupt and deceitful.

10:5 *Samaria.* The royal city of Israel (see note on 7:1). *calf-idol of Beth Aven.* The idol that Jeroboam I had set up at Bethel (see NIV text note; see also 8:5 and note).

10:6 *tribute for the great king.* See 5:13 and note. *Ephraim.* See note on 4:17.

10:8 *high places.* See 4:13–14 and note on 4:13. *wickedness.* See NIV text note. *Cover us!… Fall on us!* Cries of utter despair; quoted by Jesus (see Lk 23:30 and note) and alluded to in Rev 6:16.

10:9 *Gibeah.* See 9:9 and note. As war came on Gibeah, so war and captivity would come on Israel.

10:11 *trained heifer.* Up to now Ephraim (Israel) had been as contented as a young cow that ate while threshing grain. But now God would cause Israel (here called both Ephraim and Jacob) and Judah to do the heavy work of plowing and harrowing under a yoke—a picture of going into the Assyrian and Babylonian captivities. *Judah.* See Introduction: Author and Date.

I will drive Ephraim,
Judah must plow,
and Jacob must break up the ground.
12 Sow[i] righteousness[j] for yourselves,
reap the fruit of unfailing love,
and break up your unplowed ground;[k]
for it is time to seek[l] the LORD,
until he comes
and showers his righteousness[m] on you.
13 But you have planted wickedness,
you have reaped evil,[n]
you have eaten the fruit of deception.[o]
Because you have depended on your own strength
and on your many warriors,[p]
14 the roar of battle will rise against your people,
so that all your fortresses will be devastated[q]—
as Shalman[r] devastated Beth Arbel on the day of battle,
when mothers were dashed to the ground with their children.[s]
15 So will it happen to you, Bethel,
because your wickedness is great.
When that day dawns,
the king of Israel will be completely destroyed.[t]

God's Love for Israel

11 "When Israel was a child,[u] I loved[v] him,
and out of Egypt I called my son.[w]
2 But the more they were called,
the more they went away from me.[a][x]
They sacrificed to the Baals[y]
and they burned incense to images.[z]
3 It was I who taught Ephraim to walk,
taking them by the arms;[a]
but they did not realize
it was I who healed[b] them.
4 I led them with cords of human kindness,
with ties of love.[c]
To them I was like one who lifts
a little child to the cheek,
and I bent down to feed[d] them.[e]

5 "Will they not return to Egypt[f]
and will not Assyria[g] rule over them
because they refuse to repent?[h]
6 A sword[i] will flash in their cities;
it will devour[j] their false prophets
and put an end to their plans.
7 My people are determined to turn[k] from me.[l]
Even though they call me God Most High,
I will by no means exalt them.

8 "How can I give you up,[m] Ephraim?[n]
How can I hand you over, Israel?
How can I treat you like Admah?
How can I make you like Zeboyim?[o]
My heart is changed within me;
all my compassion[p] is aroused.[q]
9 I will not carry out my fierce anger,[r]
nor will I devastate[s] Ephraim again.
For I am God, and not a man[t]—
the Holy One[u] among you.
I will not come against their cities.

[a] 2 Septuagint; Hebrew *them*

10:12 [i] S Ecc 11:1 [j] S Pr 11:18; Jas 3:18 [k] Jer 4:3 [l] S Isa 19:22; Hos 12:6 [m] S Isa 45:8 **10:13** [n] S Job 4:8; S Hos 7:3; 11:12; Gal 6:7-8 [o] S Pr 11:18; S Hos 8:7 [p] Ps 33:16 **10:14** [q] S Isa 17:3; Mic 5:11 [r] S 2Ki 17:3 [s] S Isa 13:16; Hos 13:16 **10:15** [t] S ver 7 **11:1** [u] S Jer 2:2; S Eze 16:22 [v] S Dt 4:37 [w] S Ex 4:22; Hos 12:9, 13; 13:4; Mt 2:15* **11:2** [x] ver 7 [y] S Hos 2:13 [z] S 2Ki 17:15; Isa 65:7; S Jer 18:15; S Hos 4:13; 13:1 **11:3** [a] S Dt 1:31; S 32:11; Hos 7:15 [b] S Ex 15:26; Jer 30:17 **11:4** [c] Jer 31:2-3 [d] Ex 16:32; Ps 78:25 [e] Jer 31:20 **11:5** [f] S Hos 7:16 [g] S Hos 10:6 [h] S Ex 13:17 **11:6** [i] Hos 13:16 [j] S La 2:9 **11:7** [k] S Isa 26:10 [l] ver 2; Jer 3:6-7; 8:5 **11:8** [m] S Jer 7:29 [n] Hos 6:4 [o] S Ge 14:8; S La 3:32 [p] S 1Ki 3:26; S Ps 25:6 [q] S Eze 33:11; Am 7:3 **11:9** [r] Dt 13:17; S Jer 18:8; S 30:11 [s] La 3:22; Mal 3:6 [t] S Nu 23:19 [u] S 2Ki 19:22; S Isa 31:1

10:12 *reap the fruit of unfailing love.* If Israel would only do what was right ("unfailing love" translates the Hebrew word *hesed;* see note on 6:6), God would bless her. *break up your unplowed ground.* Be no longer unproductive, but repentant, making a radical new beginning and becoming productive and fruitful. *righteousness.* God's covenant blessings that in righteousness he would shower on his people if they in righteousness were loyal to him, their covenant Lord.

10:13 *deception.* Israel had been living a lie—and by lies (see v. 4; 7:3; 11:12; 12:1; cf. 1Jn 1:6).

10:14 *Shalman devastated Beth Arbel.* The event is otherwise unknown, as are the names mentioned—though Shalman may be an abbreviated form of Shalmaneser V, the Assyrian king who laid siege to Samaria in 725 BC (see 2Ki 17:3–5). In any event, atrocities against civilians were common in ancient warfare (see 9:13; 13:16; see also Ps 137:9 and note).

10:15 *Bethel.* See v. 8 and NIV text note; 12:4 and note.

11:1 A third appeal to history (see 9:10; 10:9) traces God's choice of Israel back to Egypt, the exodus from that country (cf. 12:9; 13:4) having given birth to the nation. Israel's response to the Lord is now illustrated by the wayward son rather than by the unfaithful wife (chs. 1–3). Israel is also referred to as God's "son/child" elsewhere (see Ex 4:22–23 and notes; Isa 1:2,4). For God as Israel's "Father," see Dt 32:6; Isa 63:16; 64:8. Hosea saw God's love as the basis (see 3:1 and note) for the election of Israel. Matthew saw in Jesus' return from Egypt a typological fulfillment of Israel's deliverance from Egypt (see Mt 2:15 and note).

11:2 *Baals.* See 2:13 and note. *images.* See Dt 7:25.

11:3 *Ephraim.* See note on 4:17. *walk.* This picture of a father teaching his child to walk is one of the most tender in the OT. *did not realize.* See 2:5–8 and note on 2:8. *healed.* See 5:13; 6:1 and note; 7:1.

11:4 The imagery is unclear, but the figure seems to change to a farmer tending his work animals. Another interpretation sees a continuation of the son image, with the father lifting the son to his cheek. *feed them.* God supplied miraculous food in the wilderness (see Ex 16; Dt 8:16).

11:5 *Egypt . . . Assyria.* See 8:13; 9:3 and notes. The tender tone (vv. 1–4) changes to threat of exile to the two countries between which Israel has vacillated. It is ironic that the people rescued from Egypt should be returned there because of their disloyalty to the one who had rescued them.

11:7 *Most High.* See 7:16 and note.

11:8 The stubborn son was subject to stoning (Dt 21:18–21), but the Lord's compassion overcame his wrath and he refused to destroy Ephraim (Israel). *Admah . . . Zeboyim.* Cities of the plain (see Ge 10:19 and note; 14:2,8), overthrown when Sodom was destroyed (Ge 19:24–25; Dt 29:23; Jer 49:18) and symbolizing total destruction (see Am 4:11 and note).

11:9 *God, and not a man.* God will not be untrue to the love he has shown toward Israel (see vv. 1–4; 1Sa 15:29; Mal 3:6). Israel was to be punished, but not destroyed.

[10] They will follow the LORD;
he will roar[v] like a lion.[w]
When he roars,
his children will come trembling[x]
from the west.[y]
[11] They will come from Egypt,
trembling like sparrows,
from Assyria,[z] fluttering like
doves.[a]
I will settle them in their homes,"[b]
declares the LORD.

Israel's Sin

[12] Ephraim has surrounded me with
lies,[c]
Israel with deceit.
And Judah is unruly against God,
even against the faithful[d] Holy One.[a][e]

12[b] [1] Ephraim[f] feeds on the wind;[g]
he pursues the east wind all day
and multiplies lies and violence.[h]
He makes a treaty with Assyria[i]
and sends olive oil to Egypt.[j]
[2] The LORD has a charge[k] to bring against
Judah;[l]
he will punish[m] Jacob[c] according to
his ways
and repay him according to his
deeds.[n]
[3] In the womb he grasped his brother's
heel;[o]
as a man he struggled[p] with God.
[4] He struggled with the angel and
overcame him;
he wept and begged for his favor.
He found him at Bethel[q]
and talked with him there—
[5] the LORD God Almighty,
the LORD is his name![r]
[6] But you must return[s] to your God;
maintain love and justice,[t]
and wait for your God always.[u]

[7] The merchant uses dishonest scales[v]
and loves to defraud.
[8] Ephraim boasts,[w]
"I am very rich; I have become
wealthy.[x]
With all my wealth they will not find
in me
any iniquity or sin."

[9] "I have been the LORD your God
ever since you came out of
Egypt;[y]
I will make you live in tents[z] again,
as in the days of your appointed
festivals.
[10] I spoke to the prophets,
gave them many visions
and told parables[a] through them."[b]

[11] Is Gilead wicked?[c]
Its people are worthless!

11:10 [v] S Isa 42:13 [w] S Isa 31:4 [x] S Ps 18:45 [y] S Hos 3:5; S 6:1-3 **11:11** [z] S Isa 11:11 [a] S Ge 8:8 [b] S Eze 28:26; S 34:25-28 **11:12** [c] S Hos 4:2 [d] S Dt 7:9 [e] S Hos 10:13 **12:1** [f] S Ps 78:67 [g] S Ge 41:6; S Eze 17:10 [h] S Hos 4:19; S 7:1 [i] Hos 5:13; S 7:11 [j] S 2Ki 17:4 **12:2** [k] S Job 10:2; Mic 6:2 [l] Am 2:4 [m] S Ex 32:34 [n] S Hos 4:9; S 9:15 **12:3** [o] Ge 25:26 [p] Ge 32:24-29 **12:4** [q] S Ge 12:8; S 35:15 **12:5** [r] S Ex 3:15 **12:6** [s] S Isa 19:22; Jer 4:1; Joel 2:12 [t] S Ps 106:3; S Jer 22:3 [u] S Eze 18:30; Hos 6:1-3; 10:12; Mic 7:7 **12:7** [v] S Lev 19:36; Am 8:5 **12:8** [w] S Eze 28:5 [x] Ps 62:10; Rev 3:17 **12:9** [y] Lev 23:43; S Hos 2:15; S 11:1 [z] S Ne 8:17 **12:10** [a] S Jdg 14:12; S Eze 20:49 [b] 2Ki 17:13; Jer 7:25 **12:11** [c] S Hos 6:8

[a] *12* In Hebrew texts this verse (11:12) is numbered 12:1.
[b] In Hebrew texts 12:1-14 is numbered 12:2-15.
[c] *2* Jacob means *he grasps the heel,* a Hebrew idiom for *he takes advantage of* or *he deceives.*

---

the Holy One among you. God's holiness is alluded to in Hosea both here and in v. 12 (see notes on Ex 3:5; Lev 11:44).
11:10 The return from exile. *roar like a lion.* Rather than threatening destruction (cf. 5:14; 13:7), God's roar was now a clear signal to return from exile. *the west.* The islands and coastlands of the Mediterranean Sea.
11:11 *from Egypt … Assyria.* See 7:16 and note; 9:3. *like sparrows … like doves.* Suggests swiftness of return (cf. Isa 60:8) and is not derogatory, as was the earlier comparison to a silly dove (7:11).
11:12 *lies … deceit.* See 10:13 and note. *Judah.* See Introduction: Author and Date. *unruly against God.* See Jer 2:31. *Holy One.* See v. 9 and note.
12:1 *Ephraim.* See note on 4:17. *wind.* See 8:7; Ecc 1:14. *east wind.* See 13:15; Job 15:2; Jer 18:17. Pursuing the wind symbolized Israel's futile foreign policy, which vacillated between Egypt (2Ki 17:4; Isa 30:6–7) and Assyria (see 5:13; 7:11; 8:9 and notes; 2Ki 17:3).
12:2 *charge.* See 4:1 and note. *Judah.* See Introduction: Author and Date. *Jacob.* Israel (see 10:11). The Lord indicted both kingdoms—all the descendants of Father Jacob. In their deceitfulness Israel and Judah were living up to the name of their forefather (see NIV text note).
12:3 *In the womb.* See Ge 25:26; 27:36 and notes. *grasped his brother's heel.* See NIV text note on v. 2. God's covenant people here relived the experiences of Father Jacob and now had to return to God, just as Jacob was called back to Bethel (Ge 35:1–15).
12:4 *struggled with the angel.* See Ge 32:22–28 and NIV text note on 32:28. *Bethel.* See Ge 28:12–19 and NIV text note on 28:19; 35:1–15. In Hosea's time, Bethel was the most important royal sanctuary in the northern kingdom (cf. Am 7:13).
12:6 *love.* Hebrew *hesed;* see 6:6 ("mercy") and note. *justice.* See Am 5:24; Mic 6:8 and notes.
12:7 *merchant.* As Hosea had played on the meaning of Jacob in v. 2, he here uses a wordplay on Canaan (the Hebrew for "merchant" sounds like Canaan) to charge that Israel was no better than a Canaanite (see note on Zec 14:21). *dishonest scales.* See Lev 19:35; Pr 11:1 and notes.
12:8 *I am very rich.* Riches brought a sense of self-sufficiency (cf. 10:13; Dt 32:15–18; Lk 12:19; Rev 3:17). *not find in me any iniquity.* Like a dishonest merchant, Ephraim (Israel) was confident that her deceitfulness (see 10:13 and note) would not come to light.
12:9 *I have been the LORD your God ever since.* See 13:4; Ex 20:2 and note. *tents.* Recalling the wilderness journey of long ago (cf. 2:14–15). *appointed festivals.* Probably the Festival of Tabernacles (see Lev 23:33–43 and note on 23:42), which commemorated the wilderness journey.
12:10 *spoke to the prophets.* See 6:5; Am 2:11 and notes; Heb 1:1. There had been ample warning. *visions.* Revelations (see Nu 12:6–8 and note; Am 1:1). *parables.* Containing messages of warning from God (see 2Sa 12:1–4; Ps 78:2; Isa 5:1–7; Eze 17:2; 24:3).
12:11 *Gilead wicked.* See 6:8–9 and notes. Gilead was overrun by Assyria in 734–732 BC (2Ki 15:29). *Gilgal.* See 4:15 and note. The Hebrew contains a wordplay between "Gilgal" and "piles" (Hebrew *gallim*). Rather than assuring safety, the altars themselves would be destroyed. *on a plowed field.* Israelite farmers gathered into piles the stones turned up by their plows.

Do they sacrifice bulls in Gilgal?[d]
Their altars will be like piles of stones
on a plowed field.[e]
12 Jacob fled to the country of Aram[a];[f]
Israel served to get a wife,
and to pay for her he tended sheep.[g]
13 The LORD used a prophet to bring Israel
up from Egypt,[h]
by a prophet he cared for him.[i]
14 But Ephraim has aroused his bitter
anger;
his Lord will leave on him the guilt
of his bloodshed[j]
and will repay him for his
contempt.[k]

The LORD's Anger Against Israel

13 When Ephraim spoke, people
trembled;[l]
he was exalted[m] in Israel.
But he became guilty of Baal
worship[n] and died.
2 Now they sin more and more;
they make[o] idols for themselves from
their silver,[p]
cleverly fashioned images,
all of them the work of craftsmen.[q]
It is said of these people,
"They offer human sacrifices!
They kiss[b][r] calf-idols![s]"
3 Therefore they will be like the morning
mist,
like the early dew that disappears,[t]
like chaff[u] swirling from a threshing
floor,[v]
like smoke[w] escaping through a
window.

4 "But I have been the LORD your God
ever since you came out of
Egypt.[x]
You shall acknowledge[y] no God but
me,[z]
no Savior[a] except me.
5 I cared for you in the wilderness,[b]
in the land of burning heat.
6 When I fed them, they were satisfied;
when they were satisfied, they
became proud;[c]
then they forgot[d] me.[e]
7 So I will be like a lion[f] to them,
like a leopard I will lurk by the
path.
8 Like a bear robbed of her cubs,[g]
I will attack them and rip them
open;
like a lion[h] I will devour them—
a wild animal will tear them
apart.[i]
9 "You are destroyed, Israel,
because you are against me,[j] against
your helper.[k]
10 Where is your king,[l] that he may save
you?
Where are your rulers in all your
towns,
of whom you said,
'Give me a king and princes'?[m]
11 So in my anger I gave you a king,[n]
and in my wrath I took him away.[o]

[a] *12* That is, Northwest Mesopotamia [b] *2* Or *"Men who sacrifice / kiss*

12:11 [d] S Hos 4:15 [e] S Hos 8:11 **12:12** [f] Ge 28:5 [g] S Ge 29:18 **12:13** [h] S Hos 11:1 [i] Ex 13:3; 14:19-22; Isa 63:11-14 **12:14** [j] S Eze 18:13 [k] Da 11:18 **13:1** [l] Jdg 12:1 [m] S Jdg 8:1 [n] S Hos 11:2 **13:2** [o] Jer 44:8 [p] S Isa 46:6; S Jer 10:4 [q] Hos 14:3 [r] 1Ki 19:18 [s] S Isa 44:17-20; S Hos 8:4 **13:3** [t] S Hos 6:4 [u] S Job 13:25; Ps 1:4; S Isa 17:13 [v] Da 2:35 [w] Ps 68:2 **13:4** [x] S Jer 2:6; S Hos 12:9 [y] S Hos 2:20 [z] S Ex 20:3 [a] S Dt 28:29; Ps 18:46; Isa 43:11; 45:21-22 **13:5** [b] S Dt 1:19 **13:6** [c] S Eze 28:5 [d] S Dt 32:18; S Isa 17:10 [e] Dt 32:12-15; S Pr 30:7-9; S Jer 5:7; S Hos 2:13; S 4:7 **13:7** [f] S Job 10:16; S Jer 4:7 **13:8** [g] 2Sa 17:8 [h] S 1Sa 17:34; Ps 17:12 [i] Ps 50:22; S La 3:10; S Hos 2:12 **13:9** [j] Jer 2:17-19 [k] S Dt 33:29 **13:10** [l] 2Ki 17:4; Hos 7:7 [m] 1Sa 8:6; Hos 8:4 **13:11** [n] S Nu 11:20 [o] S Jos 24:20; S 1Sa 13:14; S 1Ki 14:10; Hos 3:4; S 10:7

12:12 Jacob fled from Esau to Paddan Aram (Ge 28:2,5), serving Laban seven years for each wife (Ge 29:20–28), and then continued six more years as Laban's herdsman (Ge 30:31; 31:41).
12:13 *prophet.* Moses (cf. Nu 12:6–8; Dt 18:15; 34:10). *cared for him.* As Jacob had cared for Laban's flocks, so the Lord cared for Israel during her wilderness wandering. Earlier leadership by the prophet Moses stands in contrast to Israel's present disregard for prophets (cf. 4:5; 6:5; 9:7).
12:14 *Ephraim ... aroused his bitter anger.* Despite warnings. *bloodshed.* Cf. 1:4; 4:2; 5:2; 6:8. This refers to violence committed against others, including human sacrifice (see 13:2 and note). In legal passages such as Lev 20:11–27, "their blood will be on their own heads" describes guilt. The prophet drew a contrast between past divine preservation and present divine anger that would bring punishment. *repay.* See Isa 65:7.
13:1 *When Ephraim spoke.* In accordance with Jacob's blessing (Ge 48:10–20), Ephraim became a powerful tribe (Jdg 8:1–3; 12:1–6; 1Sa 1:1–4), from which came such prominent leaders as Joshua (Nu 13:8,16; Jos 24:29–30) and Jeroboam I (1Ki 11:26; 12:20). *Ephraim.* See note on 4:17. *Israel.* The 12 tribes. *died.* The wages of sin was death (cf. Ro 6:23), and the end of the nation was at hand.
13:2 *idols.* See 4:12; 8:5–6 and notes; 11:2. *human sacrifices.* See Lev 18:21; 2Ki 16:13; 17:17; 23:10; Jer 7:31 and notes; Eze 20:26; Mic 6:7. For the sense of the NIV text note, see 1Ki 12:26–33. *kiss.* Show homage to (see Ps 2:12 and note). *calf-idols.* See 8:5 and note; 10:5.
13:3 "Mist" and "dew" (see 6:4), "chaff" (see Ps 1:4 and note; 35:5; Isa 17:13; 29:5; Zep 2:2) and "smoke" (see Ps 37:20; 68:2; Isa 51:6) are all figurative for Ephraim, which was soon to vanish as a nation.
13:4 *I have been the LORD your God ever since.* See 12:9; Ex 20:2 and note. The contrast is with Jeroboam's declaration, "Here are your gods" (1Ki 12:28). *acknowledge ... God.* See 2:20; 6:3 and notes.
13:5 *wilderness.* See 2:14; 9:10 and notes.
13:6 *satisfied.* See Dt 6:11–12; 8:10–14; 11:15. *forgot me.* See 2:13; Dt 6:10–12 and notes; 8:11,14,19; 32:18.
13:7–8 The Lord, previously pictured as a shepherd (4:16), would attack like the wild beasts that often ravaged the flocks.
13:7 *lion.* See 5:14 and note. *leopard.* See Jer 5:6; Rev 13:2.
13:8 *bear robbed of her cubs.* See 2Sa 17:8; Pr 17:12 and note.
13:9 *helper.* See Ps 10:14; 30:10; 54:4.
13:10 *Where is your king ... ?* Help comes only from the Lord (Ps 121:2), not from kings. The prophet likely alludes to the royal assassinations of his day (see 7:7; 8:4 and notes). *Give me a king.* Though all Israel asked for a king in the days of Samuel (see 1Sa 8:5 and note), the reference here is only to the northern monarchy. Israel selected Jeroboam I (1Ki 12:20) in preference to the Davidic kings.
13:11 Reference is to the kings of the northern kingdom of Israel.

12 The guilt of Ephraim is stored up,
his sins are kept on record.[p]
13 Pains as of a woman in childbirth[q]
come to him,
but he is a child without wisdom;
when the time[r] arrives,
he doesn't have the sense to come
out of the womb.[s]

14 "I will deliver this people from the
power of the grave;[t]
I will redeem them from death.[u]
Where, O death, are your plagues?
Where, O grave, is your
destruction?[v]

"I will have no compassion,
15 even though he thrives[w] among his
brothers.
An east wind[x] from the LORD will
come,
blowing in from the desert;
his spring will fail
and his well dry up.[y]
His storehouse will be plundered[z]
of all its treasures.
16 The people of Samaria[a] must bear their
guilt,[b]
because they have rebelled[c] against
their God.
They will fall by the sword;[d]
their little ones will be dashed[e] to
the ground,
their pregnant women[f] ripped
open."[a]

Repentance to Bring Blessing

14 [b] Return,[g] Israel, to the LORD your
God.
Your sins[h] have been your downfall![i]
2 Take words with you
and return to the LORD.
Say to him:
"Forgive[j] all our sins
and receive us graciously,[k]
that we may offer the fruit of our
lips.[c][l]
3 Assyria cannot save us;[m]
we will not mount warhorses.[n]
We will never again say 'Our gods'[o]
to what our own hands have
made,[p]
for in you the fatherless[q] find
compassion."

4 "I will heal[r] their waywardness[s]
and love them freely,[t]
for my anger has turned away[u] from
them.
5 I will be like the dew[v] to Israel;
he will blossom like a lily.[w]
Like a cedar of Lebanon[x]
he will send down his roots;[y]
6 his young shoots will grow.
His splendor will be like an olive
tree,[z]
his fragrance like a cedar of
Lebanon.[a]
7 People will dwell again in his
shade;[b]
they will flourish like the grain,
they will blossom[c] like the vine—
Israel's fame will be like the wine[d] of
Lebanon.[e]

13:12 [p] S Dt 32:34
13:13 [q] Isa 13:8; Mic 4:9-10 [r] 2Ki 19:3 [s] Isa 66:9
13:14 [t] S Ps 16:10; 49:15; S Eze 37:12-13 [u] S Isa 25:8 [v] 1Co 15:55*
13:15 [w] S Hos 10:1 [x] S Job 1:19; S Eze 19:12; S Hos 4:19 [y] S Jer 51:36 [z] Jer 20:5
13:16 [a] 2Ki 17:5 [b] Hos 10:2 [c] S Hos 7:14 [d] Hos 11:6 [e] S 2Ki 8:12; S Hos 10:14 [f] 2Ki 15:16; Isa 13:16; Am 1:13
14:1 [g] S Isa 19:22; S Jer 3:12 [h] S Hos 4:8 [i] S Hos 5:5; S 9:7
14:2 [j] S Ex 34:9 [k] Ps 51:16-17; Mic 7:18-19 [l] Heb 13:15
14:3 [m] S Hos 5:13 [n] Ps 33:17; S Isa 31:1; Mic 5:10 [o] Hos 8:6 [p] ver 8; Hos 13:2 [q] Ps 10:14; 68:5; Jer 49:11
14:4 [r] S Isa 30:26; S Hos 6:1 [s] S Jer 2:19 [t] S Isa 55:1; Jer 31:20; Zep 3:17 [u] S Job 13:16

[a] 16 In Hebrew texts this verse (13:16) is numbered 14:1. [b] In Hebrew texts 14:1-9 is numbered 14:2-10. [c] 2 Or *offer our lips as sacrifices of bulls*

14:5 [v] S Ge 27:28; S Isa 18:4 [w] S SS 2:1 [x] Isa 35:2 [y] Job 29:19
14:6 [z] Ps 52:8; S Jer 11:16 [a] S Ps 92:12; S SS 4:11 **14:7** [b] Ps 91:1-4 [c] S Ge 40:10 [d] S Hos 2:22 [e] S Eze 17:23

13:12 See 9:9 and note; Job 14:17. *sins ... on record.* See 7:2 and note; Dt 32:34.

13:13 *Pains as of ... childbirth.* Their helpless situation was comparable to that of a woman in childbirth (see Isa 13:8 and note; 21:3; Jer 13:21; Mic 4:9–10; Mt 24:8) who cannot deliver the child (see 2Ki 19:3) and consequently dies.

13:14 *I will deliver.* A promise of rescue from death. *Where, O death ... ?* The personified reference is to the death of the nation (see note on v. 1). Paul applies this passage to resurrection (1Co 15:55). *grave.* For a description of "the grave" (Hebrew *Sheol*), see Job 3:13–19; Isa 14:9–10; see also note on Ge 37:35.

13:15 *thrives.* In Hebrew a wordplay on Ephraim (meaning "fruitful"). *east wind.* The drought-bringing east wind (see 12:1; Ge 41:7 and note; Job 1:19; Isa 27:8; Jer 4:11; 13:24; 18:17) is here a figure for Assyria, an instrument of the Lord (see Isa 10:5 and note). Assyria invaded the northern kingdom in 734 BC, then crushed it and exiled its people in 722–721. *all its treasures.* See Na 2:9.

13:16 *Samaria.* See 7:1 and note; 8:5–6; 10:5,7; here, the northern kingdom. *rebelled against.* See Ps 5:10; Isa 1:2 and note; Eze 20:8,13,21. *little ones ... women.* For atrocities against women and children, see 10:14; Ps 137:9 and notes.

14:1 *Return.* Another appeal for repentance (see 10:12; 12:6). Unlike that of ch. 6, this repentance would have to be sincere in order for the people to receive the gracious response from the Lord promised in vv. 4–8 (cf. Ps 130:7–8; Isa 55:6–7).

14:2 *Take words.* None could appear before the Lord empty-handed (Ex 23:15; 34:20), but animal sacrifices would not be enough. Only words of true repentance would be sufficient. *fruit of our lips.* As thank offerings to the Lord (see Heb 13:15).

14:3 *what our own hands have made.* Idols (see v. 8; 13:2 and note). *fatherless.* Penitent Israel (see Ps 10:14; 68:5; La 5:3). *find compassion.* Cf. the name of the child Lo-Ruhamah (see 1:6 and note; see also 2:1,23).

14:4 *heal.* See 11:3 and note. *waywardness.* See 11:7. *love them freely.* That is, love them out of my own free choice (cf. 9:15 and note). *love.* See 3:1; 11:1 and notes. *anger ... turned away.* Contrasts with the burning anger that brought destruction (see 8:5).

14:5 *dew.* Here not a symbol of transitoriness (cf. 6:4; 13:3) but of God's blessing (see Dt 33:13; Mic 5:7 and note). *cedar of Lebanon.* See notes on Jdg 9:15; 1Ki 5:6; Isa 9:10. *cedar.* See Ps 80:8–11. *Lebanon.* See Ps 104:16–18 and note.

14:7 *shade.* Protection (see Jdg 9:15 and note; SS 2:3; Eze 31:6). *vine.* See 10:1; Ps 80:8–16 and note.

[8] Ephraim, what more have I[a] to do with
idols?[f]
I will answer him and care for him.
I am like a flourishing juniper;[g]
your fruitfulness comes from me."

[9] Who is wise?[h] Let them realize these
things.
Who is discerning? Let them
understand.[i]
The ways of the LORD are right;[j]
the righteous walk[k] in them,
but the rebellious stumble in
them.

14:8 [f] S ver 3 [g] S Isa 37:24 **14:9** [h] S Ps 107:43 [i] S Pr 10:29; S Isa 1:28; Da 12:10 [j] Ps 111:7-8; Zep 3:5; Ac 13:10 [k] Isa 26:7

[a] 8 Or Hebrew; Septuagint *What more has Ephraim*

14:8 *Ephraim.* See note on 4:17. *flourishing juniper.* Only here in the OT is God compared to a tree. For the point of the imagery, see Eze 31:3–7; Da 4:12. *fruitfulness.* Ephraim ("fruitful"; see Ge 41:52 and note) received his fruitfulness from the Lord (cf. 2:8).

14:9 *ways of the LORD.* See Ps 18:21; 25:4 and note. The prophet concludes by offering each reader the alternatives of walking or stumbling (cf. 4:5; 5:5)—of obedience or rebellion. *right.* See note on Ps 119:121.

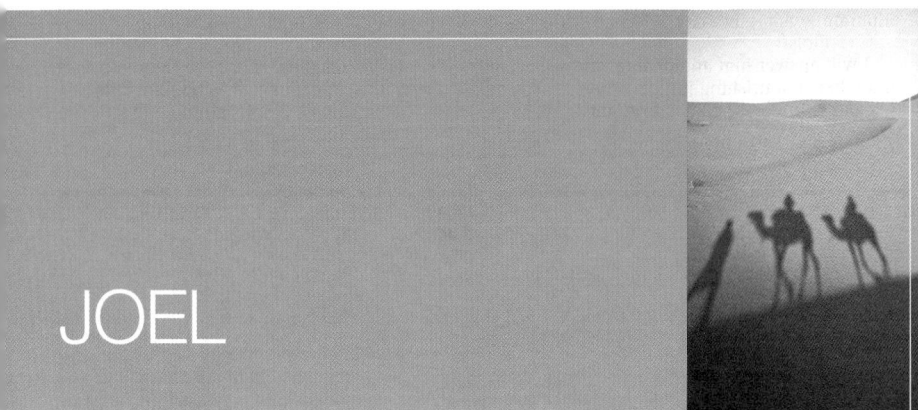

JOEL

INTRODUCTION

Author

The prophet Joel cannot be identified with any of the 12 other figures in the OT who have the same name. He is not mentioned outside the books of Joel and Acts (Ac 2:16). The non-Biblical legends about him are unconvincing. His father, Pethuel (1:1), is also unknown. Judging from his concern with Judah and Jerusalem (see 2:32; 3:1,6,8,16 – 20), it seems likely that Joel lived in that area. See note on 1:1.

Date

The book contains no references to datable historical events. Many interpreters date it somewhere between the late seventh and early fifth centuries BC. In any case, its message is not significantly affected by its dating.

The book of Joel has striking linguistic parallels to the language of Amos, Micah, Zephaniah, Jeremiah and Ezekiel. Some scholars maintain that the prophets borrowed phrases from one another; others hold that they drew more or less from the religious literary traditions that they and their readers shared in common — liturgical and otherwise.

Theological Message

Joel sees the massive locust plague and severe drought devastating Judah as a harbinger of the "great and dreadful day of the LORD" (2:31). (The locusts he mentions in 1:4; 2:25 are best understood as real insects, not as allegorical representations of the Babylonians, Medo-Persians, Greeks and Romans, as held by some interpreters.) Confronted with this crisis, he calls on everyone to repent: old and young (1:2 – 3), drunkards (1:5), farmers (1:11) and priests (1:13). He describes the locusts as the Lord's army and sees in their coming a reminder that the day of the Lord is near. He does not voice the popular notion that the day will be one of judgment on the nations but deliverance and blessing for Israel. Instead — with Isaiah (2:10 – 21), Jeremiah

Author:
Joel

Audience:
The people of Judah

Date:
Probably between the late seventh and early fifth centuries BC

Theme:
Restoration and blessing will come to the people of Judah only after judgment and repentance.

Joel sees the massive locust plague and severe drought devastating Judah as a harbinger of the "great and dreadful day of the LORD" and calls on everyone to repent.

(4:5 – 9), Amos (5:18 – 20) and Zephaniah (1:7 – 18)—he describes the day as one of punishment of unfaithful Israel as well. Restoration and blessing will come only after judgment and repentance.

Outline

I. Title (1:1)
II. Judah Experiences a Foretaste of the Day of the Lord (1:2—2:17)
  A. A Call to Mourning and Prayer (1:2 – 14)
  B. The Announcement of the Day of the Lord (1:15—2:11)
  C. A Call to Repentance and Prayer (2:12 – 17)
III. Judah Is Assured of Salvation in the Day of the Lord (2:18—3:21)
  A. The Lord's Restoration of Judah (2:18 – 27)
  B. The Lord's Renewal of His People (2:28 – 32)
  C. The Coming of the Day of the Lord (ch. 3)
    1. The nations judged (3:1 – 16)
    2. God's people blessed (3:17 – 21)

Joel tells of an invasion of locusts (1:4) and calls the people to repentance. Swarms of locusts were a significant agricultural threat in the ancient Near East, and remain so today. A desert locust swarm can be 460 square miles (1,200 square kilometers) in size and pack between 40 and 80 million locusts into less than half a square mile (one square kilometer). Each locust can eat its weight in plants each day, so a swarm of such size would eat 423 million pounds (192 million kilograms) of plants every day (see "Locust," ***National Geographic*****, http://animals.nationalgeographic.com/animals/bugs/locust/).**

1 The word of the LORD that came[a] to Joel[b] son of Pethuel.

An Invasion of Locusts

[2] Hear this,[c] you elders;[d]
listen, all who live in the land.[e]
Has anything like this ever happened
in your days
or in the days of your ancestors?[f]
[3] Tell it to your children,[g]
and let your children tell it to their
children,
and their children to the next
generation.[h]
[4] What the locust[i] swarm has left
the great locusts have eaten;
what the great locusts have left
the young locusts have eaten;
what the young locusts have left[j]
other locusts[a] have eaten.[k]

[5] Wake up, you drunkards, and
weep!
Wail, all you drinkers of wine;[l]
wail because of the new wine,
for it has been snatched[m] from your
lips.
[6] A nation has invaded my land,
a mighty army without number;[n]
it has the teeth[o] of a lion,
the fangs of a lioness.
[7] It has laid waste[p] my vines
and ruined my fig trees.[q]
It has stripped off their bark
and thrown it away,
leaving their branches white.

[8] Mourn like a virgin in sackcloth[r]
grieving for the betrothed of her
youth.

1:1 [a] S Jer 1:2 [b] Ac 2:16 **1:2** [c] Hos 5:1 [d] Joel 2:16 [e] S Hos 4:1 [f] Joel 2:2 **1:3** [g] S Ex 10:2 [h] S Ps 71:18 **1:4** [i] S Ex 10:14 [j] S Ex 10:5 [k] S Ex 10:15; S Dt 28:39; Am 7:1; Na 3:15 **1:5** [l] Joel 3:3 [m] S Isa 24:7 **1:6** [n] Ps 105:34; Joel 2:2,11,25 [o] Rev 9:8 **1:7** [p] Isa 5:6 [q] Am 4:9 **1:8** [r] ver 13; Isa 22:12; Am 8:10

1:9 [s] S Hos 9:4 [t] S Isa 22:12 **1:10** [u] S Isa 5:6; S 24:4; S Jer 3:3 [v] S Hos 9:2 [w] S Nu 18:12 **1:11** [x] S Job 6:20; Am 5:16 [y] S Ex 9:31 [z] S Isa 17:11 **1:12** [a] S Isa 15:6 [b] S Ex 28:33 [c] S Isa 16:8; Hag 2:19 **1:13** [d] S Ge 37:34; S Jer 4:8 [e] Joel 2:17 [f] ver 9; S Hos 9:4; Joel 2:14 **1:14** [g] S 2Ch 20:3

[9] Grain offerings and drink offerings[s]
are cut off from the house of the LORD.
The priests are in mourning,[t]
those who minister before the LORD.
[10] The fields are ruined,
the ground is dried up;[u]
the grain is destroyed,
the new wine[v] is dried up,
the olive oil fails.[w]

[11] Despair, you farmers,[x]
wail, you vine growers;
grieve for the wheat and the barley,[y]
because the harvest of the field is
destroyed.[z]
[12] The vine is dried up
and the fig tree is withered;[a]
the pomegranate,[b] the palm and the
apple[b] tree—
all the trees of the field—are dried
up.[c]
Surely the people's joy
is withered away.

A Call to Lamentation

[13] Put on sackcloth,[d] you priests, and
mourn;
wail, you who minister[e] before the
altar.
Come, spend the night in sackcloth,
you who minister before my God;
for the grain offerings and drink
offerings[f]
are withheld from the house of your
God.
[14] Declare a holy fast;[g]
call a sacred assembly.

[a] 4 The precise meaning of the four Hebrew words used here for locusts is uncertain. [b] 12 Or possibly *apricot*

1:1 *word of the LORD.* See Hos 1:1 and note. *Joel.* Means "The LORD is God"; cf. Elijah's name, which means "(My) God is the LORD."
1:2 *elders.* Either the older men of the community or the recognized officials (see v. 14; 2:16,28; see also note on Ex 3:16).
1:4 *locust swarm ... great locusts ... young locusts ... other locusts.* Either (1) various species of locusts or (2) locusts in various stages of their life cycle. See 2:25; Ex 10:4 and note.
1:5 *drunkards.* Although Joel calls for repentance, drunkenness is the only specific sin mentioned in the book (see notes on Pr 20:1; Eze 23:42). It suggests a self-indulgent lifestyle (cf. Isa 28:7–8; Am 4:1) pursued by those who value material things more than spiritual. *weep.* Various segments of the community (drunkards, here; general population, v. 8; farmers, v. 11; priests, v. 13) are called upon to mourn. The destruction of the vines by the locusts leaves the drunkards without a source of wine.
1:6 The locusts are compared here to a nation; cf. the ants and hyraxes in Pr 30:25–26, where the Hebrew word for "creatures" means lit. "(a) people." Elsewhere the locusts are called the Lord's "army" (2:11,25). The reverse comparison—that of armies to locusts in regard to numbers—is as old as Ugaritic literature (fifteenth century BC; see chart, p. xxiv) and is common in the OT (see Jdg 6:5 and note; Jer 46:23; 51:14,27; Na 3:15). *without number.* A phrase used to describe the locusts in the plague in Egypt (see Ps 105:34; see also Ex 10:4–6,12–15). *teeth.* Joel's comparison of the locusts' teeth to lions' teeth is reflected in Rev 9:8.
1:7 *my.* The personal pronouns here and elsewhere in Joel (vv. 6,13–14; 2:1,13–14,17–18,23,26–27; 3:2–5,17) offer a hint of hope, since they indicate that the people belong to the Lord (cf. Jos 22:19).
1:8 *virgin.* The community is addressed. In Israel, when a woman was pledged to be married to a man, he was called her husband and she his wife, though she was still a virgin (see Dt 22:23–24; cf. note on Mt 1:18). This verse refers to such a husband who died before the marriage was consummated. *sackcloth.* See v. 13; Ge 37:34; Rev 11:3 and notes.
1:9 *offerings.* See v. 13; 2:14. The locusts have left nothing that can be offered as sacrifice. The grain offering (Lev 2:1–2) and the drink offering, which was a libation of wine (Lev 23:13), were part of the daily offering (Ex 29:40; Nu 28:5–8).
1:10 *dried up.* The destruction caused by the locusts was intensified by drought. *grain ... new wine ... olive oil.* An important OT triad, related to the agriculture of that day (see 2:19).
1:13 *my God ... your God.* See note on v. 7. *grain offerings and drink offerings.* See note on v. 9.
1:14 *fast ... assembly.* See 2:15. Fasting, required on the Day of Atonement (see note and NIV text note on Lev 16:29) and also practiced in times of calamity (see Jdg 20:26;

Summon the elders
  and all who live in the land[h]
to the house of the LORD your God,
  and cry out[i] to the LORD.[j]

15 Alas for that[k] day!
  For the day of the LORD[l] is near;
  it will come like destruction from the
    Almighty.[a][m]

16 Has not the food been cut off[n]
  before our very eyes —
joy and gladness[o]
  from the house of our God?[p]
17 The seeds are shriveled
  beneath the clods.[b][q]
The storehouses are in ruins,
  the granaries have been broken down,
  for the grain has dried up.
18 How the cattle moan!
  The herds mill about
because they have no pasture;[r]
  even the flocks of sheep are
    suffering.[s]

19 To you, LORD, I call,[t]
  for fire[u] has devoured the pastures[v]
    in the wilderness
  and flames have burned up all the
    trees of the field.
20 Even the wild animals pant for you;[w]
  the streams of water have dried up[x]
  and fire has devoured the pastures[y]
    in the wilderness.

1:14 [h]S Hos 4:1 [i]Jnh 3:8 [j]2Ch 20:4 **1:15** [k]S Isa 2:12; Jer 30:7; S 46:10; S Eze 30:3; Mal 4:5 [l]Joel 2:1,11,31; 3:14; Am 5:18; Zep 1:14; Zec 14:1 [m]S Ge 17:1 **1:16** [n]Isa 3:7 [o]S Ps 51:8 [p]Dt 12:7 **1:17** [q]S Isa 17:10-11 **1:18** [r]S Ge 47:4 [s]S Jer 9:10 **1:19** [t]Ps 50:15 [u]S Ps 97:3; Am 7:4 [v]S Jer 9:10 **1:20** [w]S Ps 42:1; S 104:21 [x]1Ki 17:7 [y]Joel 2:22

2:1 [z]S Nu 10:2, 7 [a]ver 15 [b]S Ex 15:17 [c]S Joel 1:15; Zep 1:14-16 [d]S Eze 12:23; S 30:3; Ob 1:15 **2:2** [e]ver 10, 31; S Job 9:7; S Isa 8:22; S 13:10; Am 5:18 [f]S Eze 34:12; S Da 9:12; S Mt 24:21 [g]S Eze 38:9 [h]Zep 1:15; Rev 9:2

An Army of Locusts

2 Blow the trumpet[z] in Zion;[a]
  sound the alarm on my holy hill.[b]

Let all who live in the land
    tremble,
  for the day of the LORD[c] is
    coming.
It is close at hand[d] —
2   a day of darkness[e] and gloom,[f]
  a day of clouds[g] and blackness.[h]
Like dawn spreading across the
    mountains
  a large and mighty army[i] comes,
such as never was in ancient times[j]
  nor ever will be in ages to come.

3 Before them fire[k] devours,
  behind them a flame blazes.
Before them the land is like the garden
    of Eden,[l]
  behind them, a desert waste[m] —
  nothing escapes them.
4 They have the appearance of
    horses;[n]
  they gallop along like cavalry.
5 With a noise like that of chariots[o]
  they leap over the mountaintops,

[a] *15* Hebrew *Shaddai* [b] *17* The meaning of the Hebrew for this word is uncertain.

[i]S Joel 1:6 [j]Joel 1:2 **2:3** [k]S Ps 97:3; S Isa 1:31 [l]S Ge 2:8 [m]Ex 10:12-15; Ps 105:34-35; S Isa 14:17 **2:4** [n]Rev 9:7 **2:5** [o]Rev 9:9

2Sa 12:16; Est 4:3,16; Jer 14:12; Jnh 3:4 – 5; Zec 7:3), was a sign of penitence and humility. The Bible speaks against outward signs that do not reflect a corresponding inward belief or attitude (see Mt 6:1 – 8,16 – 18; 23:1 – 36). *elders.* See notes on v. 2; Ex 3:16; 2Sa 3:17.

1:15 *day of the LORD.* See notes on Isa 2:11,17,20; 10:20,27; Am 5:18. This phrase occurs five times in Joel and is its dominant theme (here; 2:1,11,31; 3:14). Six other prophets also use it: Isaiah (13:6,9), Ezekiel (13:5; 30:3), Amos (5:18,20), Obadiah (15), Zephaniah (1:7,14) and Malachi (4:5); and an equivalent expression occurs in Zec 14:1. Sometimes abbreviated as "that day," the term often refers to the decisive intervention of God in history, such as through the invasion of locusts in Joel or at the battle of Carchemish, 605 BC (see Jer 46:2,10). It can also refer to Christ's coming to consummate history (see Mal 4:5; 1Co 5:5; 2Co 1:14; 1Th 5:2 and note; 2Pe 3:10). When the term is not used for divine judgments in the midst of history, it refers to the final day of the Lord, which generally has two aspects: (1) God's triumph over and punishment of his enemies and (2) his granting of rest (security) and blessing to his people. *destruction ... Almighty.* See Isa 13:6 and note.

1:18 Cf. the description of a drought in Jer 14:5 – 6. *moan.* The Hebrew for this word is used for the groaning of Israel in Egypt (Ex 2:23) and of others in distress (Pr 29:2; Isa 24:7; La 1:4,8,11,21; Eze 9:4; 21:12). *mill about.* The Hebrew for this verb is used to describe Israel's confused movements in the wilderness (Ex 14:3). *even ... sheep.* Sheep are the last to suffer, because they can even grub the grass roots out of the soil.

1:19 – 20 *fire.* Although the destruction caused by the locusts is elsewhere compared to that of a fire (see 2:3), here the prophet may be describing the effects of a drought. In both cases he evokes the fire of God's judgment (see, e.g., Jer 4:4; 15:14; 17:27 and note; Eze 5:4; 15:6 – 7 and note on 15:7; 20:47; 21:32; Hos 8:14; Am 1:4 and note).

2:1 *trumpet.* See v. 15. Made of a ram's or bull's horn, it was used to signal approaching danger (see Jer 4:5; Eze 33:3 and notes). Its sound brought trembling (from fear) to the people (see Am 3:6). *Zion.* See v. 15; 3:17,21. Here it refers to Jerusalem as the capital of the nation. *day of the LORD.* See 1:15; Isa 2:11,17,20 and notes.

2:2 *day of darkness.* Darkness is a common prophetic figure used of the day of the Lord (see Am 5:18 and note; Zep 1:15) and is generally a metaphor for distress and suffering (see Isa 50:3; 59:9; Jer 2:6; 13:16; La 3:6; Eze 34:12 and notes). *dawn.* Usually suggests relief from sorrow or gloom, the end of darkness (cf. Isa 8:20; 58:8). Here, however, it is used as bitter irony, describing the locust infestation that fans out across the land like the light of dawn, which first lights up the eastern horizon and then spreads across the whole countryside.

2:3 – 11 The staccato character of the poetry is appropriate for the imagery of war (see Na 3:1 – 3).

2:3 *Before them.* Joel creates a special impact by using this phrase three times (twice in v. 3 and once in v. 10), "behind them" twice (v. 3) and "at the sight of them" once (v. 6). *fire.* See note on 1:19 – 20. *Eden.* See Ge 2:8,15 (the garden before the fall); Ge 13:10 (the valley of the Jordan before the destruction of Sodom); and Isa 51:3; Eze 31:8 – 9,16,18; 36:35 (all of which describe a desert that has become like Eden).

2:4 *horses.* Whereas the book of Job compares the horse to a locust (Job 39:19 – 20), Joel does the opposite.

2:5 *leap over the mountaintops.* Mountains, though barriers to ordinary horses and chariots, are no deterrent to locusts.

like a crackling fire[p] consuming
stubble,
like a mighty army drawn up for
battle.

6 At the sight of them, nations are in
anguish;[q]
every face turns pale.[r]
7 They charge like warriors;[s]
they scale walls like soldiers.
They all march in line,[t]
not swerving[u] from their course.
8 They do not jostle each other;
each marches straight ahead.
They plunge through defenses
without breaking ranks.
9 They rush upon the city;
they run along the wall.
They climb into the houses;[v]
like thieves they enter through the
windows.[w]

10 Before them the earth shakes,[x]
the heavens tremble,[y]
the sun and moon are darkened,[z]
and the stars no longer shine.[a]
11 The LORD[b] thunders[c]
at the head of his army;[d]
his forces are beyond number,
and mighty is the army that obeys
his command.
The day of the LORD is great;[e]
it is dreadful.
Who can endure it?[f]

Rend Your Heart

12 "Even now," declares the LORD,
"return[g] to me with all your
heart,[h]
with fasting and weeping and
mourning."

13 Rend your heart[i]
and not your garments.[j]
Return[k] to the LORD your God,
for he is gracious and
compassionate,[l]
slow to anger and abounding in
love,[m]
and he relents from sending
calamity.[n]
14 Who knows? He may turn[o] and
relent[p]
and leave behind a blessing[q] —
grain offerings and drink offerings[r]
for the LORD your God.

15 Blow the trumpet[s] in Zion,[t]
declare a holy fast,[u]
call a sacred assembly.[v]
16 Gather the people,
consecrate[w] the assembly;
bring together the elders,[x]
gather the children,
those nursing at the breast.
Let the bridegroom[y] leave his room
and the bride her chamber.
17 Let the priests, who minister[z] before
the LORD,
weep[a] between the portico and the
altar.[b]
Let them say, "Spare your people,
LORD.
Do not make your inheritance an
object of scorn,[c]
a byword[d] among the nations.
Why should they say among the
peoples,
'Where is their God?[e]' "

2:5 [p] Isa 5:24; 30:30 **2:6** [q] S Isa 13:8 [r] S Isa 29:22 **2:7** [s] S Job 16:14 [t] Pr 30:27 [u] Isa 5:27 **2:9** [v] Ex 10:6 [w] Jer 9:21 **2:10** [x] Ps 18:7; Na 1:5 [y] S Eze 38:19 [z] S ver 2; S Isa 5:30; S Mt 24:29; Mk 13:24; Rev 9:2 [a] S Job 9:7; S Ps 102:26; Isa 13:10; S Eze 32:8 **2:11** [b] S Isa 2:12; S Eze 30:3; S Joel 1:15; Ob 1:15 [c] S Ps 29:3 [d] S ver 2,25 [e] Zep 1:14 [f] S Eze 22:14; Zep 2:11; Rev 6:17 **2:12** [g] S Dt 4:30; S Eze 33:11; S Hos 12:6 [h] S 1Sa 7:3 **2:13** [i] Ps 51:17; Isa 57:15 [j] S Ge 37:29; S Nu 14:6; Job 1:20 [k] S Isa 19:22 [l] S Dt 4:31 [m] Ex 34:6; S Ps 86:5,15 [n] S Jer 18:8; Jnh 4:2 **2:14** [o] Jer 26:3; Jnh 3:9 [p] Am 5:15; Jnh 1:6 [q] Jer 31:14; Hag 2:19; Zec 8:13; Mal 3:10 [r] S Joel 1:13

2:15 [s] S Nu 10:2 [t] ver 1 [u] S 2Ch 20:3; Jer 36:9 [v] S Ex 32:5; Nu 10:3 **2:16** [w] S Ex 19:10,22 [x] Joel 1:2 [y] Ps 19:5 **2:17** [z] Joel 1:13 [a] S Isa 22:12 [b] Eze 8:16; Mt 23:35 [c] Dt 9:26-29; Ps 44:13 [d] S 1Ki 9:7; S Job 17:6 [e] S Ps 42:3

2:6 *At the sight of them.* Parallels "before them" (vv. 3,10). *in anguish.* Because of the famine that the locusts will cause.
2:9 *climb into the houses.* As in the Egyptian plague of locusts (Ex 10:6). Latticed windows with no glass would not stop them.
2:10 *earth shakes.* See Ps 68:8; 77:18; Isa 24:18–20; Jer 4:24; Am 8:8; Na 1:5. *heavens tremble.* See 2Sa 22:8; Isa 13:13; Hag 2:6,21; Heb 12:26–28. *darkened.* Joel links God's judgment through the locusts to the cosmic phenomena of the day of the Lord.
2:11 Just as Isaiah saw the Assyrians (see Isa 10:5 and note) and Jeremiah the Babylonians (Jer 25:9; 43:10) as the Lord's weapons, so Joel sees the locusts as the Lord's army (cf. Jos 5:14; Ps 68:17; Hab 3:8–9)—the army of the Lord with which he will come against his enemies in the day of the Lord (see 3:9–11 and note). This passage parallels Zep 1:14 (cf. v. 31; 3:14; Mal 4:1,5). *thunders.* See 3:16 and note. *great … dreadful.* Two ideas often associated in the OT, though sometimes the Hebrew word underlying "dreadful" means "awesome" (see Dt 7:21; 10:21; Ps 106:21–22). The terms are frequently used to describe the day of the Lord (see v. 31; Mal 4:5). *Who can endure it?* See Na 1:6 and note; Mal 3:2; Rev 6:17. There is no escape except in turning to God.
2:12–17 The first half of the book ends with a call to repentance ("return," vv. 12–13; see Hos 14:1 and note) and prayer (v. 17), balancing the call to mourning and prayer with which the section begins (1:2–14).
2:13 *Rend your heart.* See Ps 51:17 and note. *gracious … abounding in love.* Recalls the great self-characterization of God in Ex 34:6–7, which runs like a golden thread through the OT (see note on Ex 34:6–7; see also Dt 4:31; Mic 7:18).
2:14 *grain offerings and drink offerings.* See note on 1:9.
2:15 *trumpet.* Not an alarm as in v. 1, but a call to religious assembly (see Lev 23:24; 25:9; Nu 10:10; Jos 6:4–5; 2Ch 15:14; Ps 98:6 and note). *fast … assembly.* See note on 1:14.
2:16 As with the call to mourning in ch. 1, no segment of the community was exempt. *assembly.* The Hebrew for this word refers to the religious community (see Nu 16:3; 2Ch 30:2,4,23–25; Mic 2:5). *elders.* See note on 1:2. *chamber.* The place where the marriage was consummated.
2:17 *your inheritance.* Israel is God's special possession (see Ex 34:9; Jer 3:19 and note). Judah is to plead, not her innocence, but that God's honor is at stake before the world (see Ex 32:12; see also Nu 14:13; Jos 7:9 and notes). *byword.* See note on 1Ki 9:7. *Where is their God?* A rhetorical question with sarcastic intent (see Ps 3:2; 10:11; 115:2 and notes).

The LORD's Answer

18 Then the LORD was jealous[f] for his land
and took pity[g] on his people.

19 The LORD replied[a] to them:

"I am sending you grain, new wine[h]
and olive oil,[i]
enough to satisfy you fully;[j]
never again will I make you
an object of scorn[k] to the nations.

20 "I will drive the northern horde[l] far
from you,
pushing it into a parched and barren
land;
its eastern ranks will drown in the
Dead Sea
and its western ranks in the
Mediterranean Sea.
And its stench[m] will go up;
its smell will rise."

Surely he has done great things!
21 Do not be afraid,[n] land of Judah;
be glad and rejoice.[o]
Surely the LORD has done great
things![p]
22 Do not be afraid, you wild animals,
for the pastures in the wilderness are
becoming green.[q]
The trees are bearing their fruit;
the fig tree[r] and the vine[s] yield their
riches.[t]
23 Be glad, people of Zion,
rejoice[u] in the LORD your God,
for he has given you the autumn
rains
because he is faithful.[v]
He sends you abundant showers,[w]
both autumn[x] and spring rains,[y] as
before.

24 The threshing floors will be filled with
grain;
the vats will overflow[z] with new
wine[a] and oil.

25 "I will repay you for the years the
locusts[b] have eaten[c]—
the great locust and the young
locust,
the other locusts and the locust
swarm[b]—
my great army[d] that I sent among
you.
26 You will have plenty to eat, until you
are full,[e]
and you will praise[f] the name of the
LORD your God,
who has worked wonders[g] for you;
never again will my people be
shamed.[h]
27 Then you will know[i] that I am in
Israel,
that I am the LORD[j] your God,
and that there is no other;
never again will my people be
shamed.[k]

The Day of the LORD

28 "And afterward,
I will pour out my Spirit[l] on all
people.[m]
Your sons and daughters will
prophesy,[n]
your old men will dream dreams,[o]
your young men will see visions.

[a] 18,19 *Or LORD will be jealous . . . / and take pity . . . / 19The LORD will reply* [b] 25 The precise meaning of the four Hebrew words used here for locusts is uncertain.

2:18 [f]S Isa 26:11; Zec 1:14; 8:2 [g]S Ps 72:13 **2:19** [h]Ps 4:7 [i]S Jer 31:12 [j]S Lev 26:5 [k]S Eze 34:29 **2:20** [l]Jer 1:14-15 [m]S Isa 34:3 **2:21** [n]S Isa 29:22; S 54:4; Zep 3:16-17 [o]S Ps 9:2 [p]S Ps 126:3; S Isa 25:1 **2:22** [q]S Ps 65:12 [r]S 1Ki 4:25 [s]S Nu 16:14 [t]Joel 1:18-20; Zec 8:12 **2:23** [u]Ps 33:21; 97:12; 149:2; Isa 12:6; 41:16; 66:14; Hab 3:18; Zec 10:7 [v]S Isa 45:8 [w]S Job 36:28; S Eze 34:26 [x]Ps 84:6 [y]S Lev 26:4; S Ps 135:7; Jas 5:7 **2:24** [z]Lev 26:10; Mal 3:10 [a]S Pr 3:10; Joel 3:18; Am 9:13 **2:25** [b]S Ex 10:14; Am 4:9 [c]S Dt 28:39 [d]S Joel 1:6 **2:26** [e]S Lev 26:5 [f]S Lev 23:40; S Isa 62:9 [g]S Ps 126:3; S Isa 25:1 [h]S Isa 29:22 **2:27** [i]S Ex 6:7 [j]S Ex 6:2; S Isa 44:8; Joel 3:17 [k]Isa 45:17; 54:4; Zep 3:11 **2:28** [l]S Isa 11:2; S 44:3 [m]S Nu 11:17; S Mk 1:8; Gal 3:14 [n]S 1Sa 19:20 [o]Jer 23:25

2:18 Joel begins a new section by turning from the destruction caused by the locusts to the blessings God gave (or will give; see NIV text note on vv. 18,19) to a repentant people. *jealous.* See note on Ex 20:5. The Lord responded (or will respond) to the prayer of v. 17 and aroused (or will arouse) himself to defend his honor and have pity on his people.

2:19 *grain, new wine and olive oil.* See note on 1:10.

2:20 *northern horde.* Since enemies in ancient times did not invade from the sea or across the desert, Canaan's geographic location made her vulnerable only from the south (Egypt) and from the north (Assyria and Babylonia). The hordes of locusts are pictured here as a vast army of Israel's most feared enemies. *stench.* Because the locusts are now dead.

2:21–23 As there was a multiple call to grief (1:5,8,11,13), so there is a multiple call to joy: The land (v. 21), the wild animals (v. 22) and the people (v. 23) are called on to rejoice in the Lord's bounty.

2:22 The wild animals now find green, open pastures (cf. 1:19–20). The same land, with its trees that the locusts and drought had devastated (see 1:7,12,19), is now productive.

2:23 *autumn and spring rains.* See notes on Dt 11:14; Jas 5:7.

2:24 *threshing floors.* See note on Ru 1:22. *vats.* See note on Hag 2:16.

2:25 See 1:4 and note.

2:26 *wonders.* God performed wonders for the people when they were in Egypt (see Ex 3:20 and note; 7:3), and now he will work wonders in restoring the devastated land.

2:27 *Israel.* Probably refers to all God's people, with no distinction between the northern and southern kingdoms, as also in 3:2,16. *I am the LORD your God.* This clause recalls the covenant at Sinai (see Ex 20:2 and note). *there is no other.* See note on Dt 4:35.

2:28–32 Quoted by Peter on the day of Pentecost (Ac 2:16–21), but with a few variations from both the Hebrew text and the Septuagint (the pre-Christian Greek translation of the OT).

2:28 *afterward.* In the Messianic period, beyond the restoration just spoken of. *pour out my Spirit.* See v. 29; Isa 32:15; 44:3; Eze 39:29 and note; Zec 12:10—13:1. *all people.* All will participate without regard to gender, age or rank; and then Moses' wish (see Nu 11:29 and note) will be realized (cf. Gal 3:28). Peter extends the "all" of this verse and the "everyone" of v. 32 to the Gentiles ("all who are far off," Ac 2:39; see also note on Ac 2:17), who will not be excluded from the Spirit's outpouring or deliverance (cf. Ro 11:11–24). *prophesy . . . dream dreams . . . see visions.* See Nu 12:6.

29 Even on my servants,[p] both men and
women,
I will pour out my Spirit in those days.[q]
30 I will show wonders in the heavens[r]
and on the earth,[s]
blood and fire and billows of smoke.
31 The sun will be turned to darkness[t]
and the moon to blood
before the coming of the great and
dreadful day of the LORD.[u]
32 And everyone who calls
on the name of the LORD[v] will be
saved;[w]
for on Mount Zion[x] and in Jerusalem
there will be deliverance,[y]
as the LORD has said,
even among the survivors[z]
whom the LORD calls.[a][a]

The Nations Judged

3 [b] "In those days and at that time,
when I restore the fortunes[b] of
Judah[c] and Jerusalem,
2 I will gather[d] all nations
and bring them down to the Valley
of Jehoshaphat.[c][e]
There I will put them on trial[f]
for what they did to my inheritance,
my people Israel,
because they scattered[g] my people
among the nations
and divided up my land.
3 They cast lots[h] for my people
and traded boys for prostitutes;
they sold girls for wine[i] to drink.

2:29 [p] 1Co 12:13; Gal 3:28 [q] S Eze 36:27 **2:30** [r] Lk 21:11 [s] Mk 13:24-25 **2:31** [t] S ver 2; S Isa 22:5; S Jer 4:23; S Mt 24:29 [u] S Joel 1:15; Ob 1:15; Mal 3:2; 4:1,5 **2:32** [v] S Ge 4:26; S Ps 105:1 [w] S Ps 106:8; Ac 2:17-21*; Ro 10:13* [x] S Isa 46:13 [y] Ob 1:17 [z] S Isa 1:9; 11:11; Mic 4:7; 7:18; S Ro 9:27 [a] Ac 2:39 **3:1** [b] S Dt 30:3; S Jer 16:15; S Eze 38:8; Zep 3:20 [c] Jer 40:5 **3:2** [d] Zep 3:8 [e] ver 12; S Isa 22:1 [f] S Isa 13:9; S Jer 2:35; S Eze 36:5 [g] S Ge 11:4; S Lev 26:33 **3:3** [h] S Job 6:27; S Eze 24:6 [i] Joel 1:5; Am 2:6 **3:4** [j] S Ge 10:15; S Mt 11:21 [k] S Ps 87:4; Isa 14:29-31; Jer 47:1-7 [l] S Lev 26:28;

4 "Now what have you against me, Tyre
and Sidon[j] and all you regions of Philistia?[k] Are you repaying me for something
I have done? If you are paying me back,
I will swiftly and speedily return on your
own heads what you have done.[l] 5 For you
took my silver and my gold and carried
off my finest treasures to your temples.[d][m]
6 You sold the people of Judah and Jerusalem to the Greeks,[n] that you might send
them far from their homeland.
7 "See, I am going to rouse them out of
the places to which you sold them,[o] and
I will return[p] on your own heads what
you have done. 8 I will sell your sons[q] and
daughters to the people of Judah,[r] and
they will sell them to the Sabeans,[s] a nation far away." The LORD has spoken.[t]

9 Proclaim this among the nations:
Prepare for war![u]
Rouse the warriors![v]
Let all the fighting men draw near
and attack.
10 Beat your plowshares into swords
and your pruning hooks[w] into
spears.[x]

[a] *32* In Hebrew texts 2:28-32 is numbered 3:1-5. [b] In Hebrew texts 3:1-21 is numbered 4:1-21.
[c] *2* *Jehoshaphat* means *the LORD judges*; also in verse 12.
[d] *5* Or *palaces*

S Isa 34:8; S Eze 25:15-17; Zec 9:5-7 **3:5** [m] S 1Ki 15:18; S 2Ch 21:16-17 **3:6** [n] Eze 27:13; Zec 9:13 **3:7** [o] S Isa 43:5-6; Jer 23:8 [p] S Isa 66:6 **3:8** [q] Isa 60:14 [r] Isa 14:2 [s] S Ge 10:7; S 2Ch 9:1 [t] S Isa 23:1; S Jer 30:16 **3:9** [u] S Isa 8:9 [v] Jer 46:4 **3:10** [w] Isa 2:4 [x] S Nu 25:7

2:30–31 These cosmic events are often associated with the day of the Lord (see Isa 13:9–10,13; 34:4; Mt 24:29; Rev 6:12–13; 8:8–9; 9:1–19; 14:14–20; 16:4, 8–9).

2:30 *blood ... fire ... smoke.* From war; fire and smoke can also be signs of God's presence (see Ge 15:17 and note).

2:31 *darkness.* See v. 2 and note. *blood.* The moon will become blood-red. *great and dreadful day of the LORD.* See v. 11; 1:15 and notes.

2:32 *calls on the name of the LORD.* Worships God and prays to him (see Ge 4:26; 12:8; Ps 116:4). *saved.* Delivered from the wrath of God's judgment (see Mt 24:13). *as the LORD has said.* Perhaps Joel is recalling the Lord's covenant with David (see 2Sa 7; Ps 132:11–18). *survivors.* See Zec 13:8–9 and notes; 14:2.

3:1 *In those days.* At the time of Israel's final redemption (see v. 18 and note). *restore the fortunes of.* Or "bring back from captivity" (see vv. 6–7; see also note on Jer 29:14 and NIV text note there).

3:2 *Valley of Jehoshaphat.* See v. 12. Called the "valley of decision" in v. 14, it seems to be a symbolic name for a valley near Jerusalem that is here depicted as the place of God's ultimate judgment on the nations gathered against Jerusalem (see NIV text note; cf. Zec 6:1 and note). There King Jehoshaphat had witnessed one of the Lord's historic victories over the nations (see 2Ch 20:1–30). *my inheritance.* See note on 2:17. Eight times in three verses (vv. 2–3,5) God uses "my," emphasizing his covenant relationship with Israel. *Israel.* See note on 2:27.

3:3 *cast lots for my people.* This happened to Judah at the time of the captivity (586 BC) and is mentioned in Ob 11. The Israelites were treated by their enemies as mere chattel, to be traded off for the pleasures of prostitution and wine.

3:4–8 A parenthetical interlude. In vv. 1–3,9–16 God announces judgment against the nations hostile to Israel, but here he addresses the nations directly.

3:4 *me.* The Lord. *Tyre ... Sidon ... Philistia.* Tyre and Philistia had sold Israelites as slaves (see Am 1:6,9 and notes), and Philistia had often plundered Israel (see Jdg 13:1; 1Sa 5:1; 2Ch 21:16–17; Eze 25:15–17 and note on 25:15). God punished these nations by allowing Sidon to be destroyed and many of its people enslaved by Artaxerxes III c. 345 BC and by allowing Tyre to be captured by the Greeks (under Alexander the Great) in 332. *return on your own heads what you have done.* See v. 7; Pr 26:27 and note.

3:6 The Greeks were trading with the Phoenicians as early as 800 BC.

3:8 *Sabeans.* See Job 1:15 and note; from Sheba, whose queen visited Solomon (see 1Ki 10:1–13 and note on 10:1). *far away.* It was located in the southern part of the Arabian peninsula (present-day Yemen).

3:9–21 In vv. 9–11 Joel is the speaker; in vv. 12–13 God speaks; in vv. 14–16, Joel; and in vv. 17–21, God. When Joel speaks, he does so as the spokesman of the Lord, who has commissioned him to be his prophet.

3:9–11 Joel commands that the nations be told to prepare for battle, for the Lord would come against them with his invincible heavenly army and bring them into judgment (cf. Eze 38–39; Rev 19).

3:10 The first part of this verse is the reverse of Isa 2:4 (see note there) and Mic 4:3, where the peaceful effect of God's

Let the weakling[y] say,
"I am strong!"[z]
11 Come quickly, all you nations from every side,
and assemble[a] there.

Bring down your warriors,[b] LORD!

12 "Let the nations be roused;
let them advance into the Valley of Jehoshaphat,[c]
for there I will sit
to judge[d] all the nations on every side.
13 Swing the sickle,[e]
for the harvest[f] is ripe.
Come, trample the grapes,[g]
for the winepress[h] is full
and the vats overflow—
so great is their wickedness!"
14 Multitudes,[i] multitudes
in the valley[j] of decision!
For the day of the LORD[k] is near
in the valley of decision.[l]
15 The sun and moon will be darkened,
and the stars no longer shine.[m]
16 The LORD will roar[n] from Zion
and thunder from Jerusalem;[o]
the earth and the heavens will tremble.[p]
But the LORD will be a refuge[q] for his people,
a stronghold[r] for the people of Israel.

Blessings for God's People

17 "Then you will know[s] that I, the LORD your God,[t]
dwell in Zion,[u] my holy hill.[v]
Jerusalem will be holy;[w]
never again will foreigners invade her.[x]

18 "In that day the mountains will drip new wine,[y]
and the hills will flow with milk;[z]
all the ravines of Judah will run with water.[a]

3:10 [y]Zec 12:8 [z]S Jos 1:6 **3:11** [a]Eze 38:15-16; Zep 3:8 [b]S Isa 13:3 **3:12** [c]S ver 2 [d]S Ps 82:1; S Isa 2:4 **3:13** [e]Mk 4:29 [f]S Isa 17:5; S Hos 6:11; Mt 13:39; Rev 14:15-19 [g]S Jer 25:30 [h]S Jdg 6:11; S Rev 14:20 **3:14** [i]Isa 13:4 [j]S Isa 22:1 [k]Isa 34:2-8; S Joel 1:15; S Zep 1:7 [l]S Isa 2:4; S Eze 36:5 **3:15** [m]S Job 9:7; S Eze 32:7 **3:16** [n]S Isa 42:13 [o]Am 1:2 [p]S Jdg 5:4; S Isa 14:16; S Eze 38:19 [q]S Ps 46:1; S Isa 25:4; Zec 12:8 [r]S 2Sa 22:3; Jer 16:19; Zec 9:12 **3:17** [s]S Ex 6:7 [t]S Joel 2:27 [u]S Ps 74:2; S Isa 4:3 [v]Ps 2:6; S Isa 2:2; S Eze 17:22 [w]S Jer 31:40 [x]S Isa 52:1; S Eze 44:9; Zec 9:8 **3:18** [y]S Joel 2:24 [z]Ex 3:8; S SS 5:1 [a]S Isa 30:25; 35:6; S 44:3

Statue of a deity holding a vase with water flowing out (Iraq, 721–705 BC). In the ancient Near East, this type of statue was common and represented the life-giving quality of fresh water. Joel 3:18 describes the Lord's house as flowing with water.

Kim Walton, courtesy of the Oriental Institute Museum

reign is portrayed. Here God's enemies are summoned to their last great confrontation with him. *plowshares.* See note on Isa 2:4.

3:11 *assemble there.* In the Valley of Jehoshaphat for judgment (see vv. 2,12,14 and notes on vv. 2,14).

3:13 As a result of the Lord's great army of locusts that had marched against Judah (see 2:3–11 and note on 2:11), there had been no harvest (2:3). But that harvest was to be restored (2:19,22,24,26). In the final great day of the Lord, there will also be a harvest—the harvest of God's judgment on the nations. Rev 14:14–20 draws heavily on this picture of judgment (see notes on Rev 14:15,18–20). *vats.* See 2:24 and note.

3:14 *valley of decision.* The Valley of Jehoshaphat (judgment) of vv. 2,12. "Jehoshaphat" speaks of God's role as Judge (see note on v. 2). Here "decision" (from a different Hebrew word) refers to the heavenly Judge's decision or judicial decree. The valley is now viewed as the place where that decree will be executed. *day of the LORD.* See 1:15 and note.

3:15 See 2:10 and note.

3:16 *roar.* Like a lion, God will destroy the nations. The first two lines occur also in Am 1:2 (see note there; see also Jer 25:30). *from Zion.* See note on Am 1:2. *thunder.* As God at the head of his army had thundered against Jerusalem (2:11), so he will then thunder against Jerusalem's enemies, and he will do so from his royal city, from which he rules his inheritance (see v. 17; Am 1:2). *the earth and the heavens will tremble.* See 2:10 and note. *Israel.* See note on 2:27.

3:17–21 God blesses his people in a dual way: negatively, by destroying their enemies; and positively, by giving them good things.

3:17 *dwell in Zion.* The Lord himself will dwell with them (see v. 21). The same picture is found in 2:27; Ps 46:4 (cf. Rev 21:3). The final, blessed state of the now unholy and vulnerable city will be God's abiding presence in her (see v. 21 and note; Rev 21). Then she will be holy and impregnable (see Zec 14:21 and note). *Zion.* See 2:1 and note.

3:18 *In that day.* The same as "in those days" of v. 1. The Edenic lushness pictured in this verse is in great contrast to the drought in 1:10 (see Am 9:13). *mountains ... hills.* See Ps 104:13–15; Hag 1:11 and notes. *A fountain will flow out of the LORD's house.* Flowing from God's presence, streams of

A fountain will flow out of the LORD's
house[b]
and will water the valley of
acacias.[a][c]
19 But Egypt[d] will be desolate,
Edom[e] a desert waste,
because of violence[f] done to the people
of Judah,
in whose land they shed innocent
blood.
20 Judah will be inhabited forever[g]
and Jerusalem through all generations.
21 Shall I leave their innocent blood
unavenged?[h]
No, I will not.[i]"

The LORD dwells in Zion![j]

3:18 [b] Rev 22:1-2 [c] S Nu 25:1; S Isa 25:6; S Jer 31:12; S Eze 47:1; Am 9:13 **3:19** [d] S Isa 19:1 [e] S Isa 11:14; S 34:11 [f] S Jer 51:35; Ob 1:10 **3:20** [g] S Ezr 9:12; Am 9:15 **3:21** [h] S Isa 1:15 [i] S Eze 36:25 [j] S Ps 74:2; Isa 59:20; S Eze 48:35; Zec 8:3

[a] *18* Or *Valley of Shittim*

blessing will refresh his people and make their place endlessly fruitful (see Ps 36:8; 46:4 and notes; 87:7; Eze 47:1 – 12; Rev 22:1 – 2). *acacias.* See Ex 25:5 and note. Since acacias flourish in dry soil, the picture is that of a well-watered desert.

3:19 *Egypt ... Edom.* As old enemies of Israel, they here represent all the nations hostile to God's people (see notes on Eze 35:1 – 15; Zec 10:10). *desolate ... desert waste.* Figures for the removal of all life-sustaining blessings, thus setting in sharp focus the contrasting destinies of God's people and the enemies of God's kingdom. This picture of desolation also recalls the earlier description of Judah's condition (2:3).

3:20 *will be inhabited forever.* When God's judgment and redemption are consummated, his kingdom will endure and flourish eternally.

3:21 This book of judgment ends on a promising and encouraging note: "The LORD dwells in Zion," and therefore all is right with those who trust in God and live with him. The book of Ezekiel has a similar ending (see note on Eze 48:35).

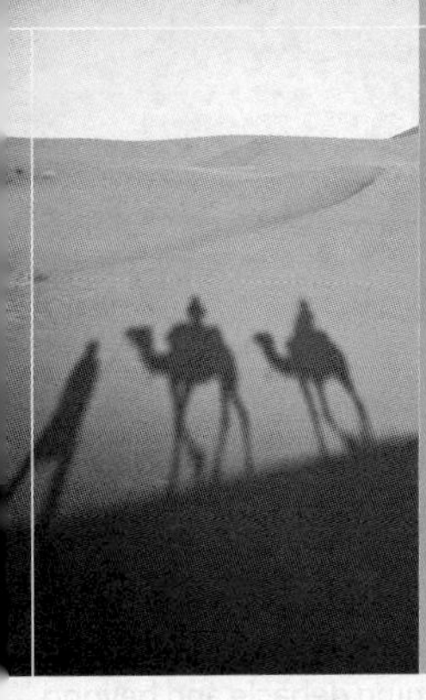

AMOS

INTRODUCTION

Author

Amos was from Tekoa (1:1), a small town in Judah about 6 miles south of Bethlehem and 11 miles from Jerusalem. He was not a man of the court like Isaiah, or a member of a priestly family like Jeremiah and Ezekiel. He earned his living from the flock and the sycamore-fig grove (1:1; 7:14–15). Whether he owned the flocks and groves or only worked as a hired hand is not known. His skill with words and the strikingly broad range of his general knowledge of history and the world preclude his being an ignorant peasant. Though his home was in Judah, he was sent to announce God's judgment on the northern kingdom (Israel). He probably ministered for the most part at Bethel (7:10–13; see 1Ki 12:28–30 and notes), Israel's main religious sanctuary, where the upper echelons of the northern kingdom worshiped.

The book brings his prophecies together in a carefully organized form intended to be read as a unit. It offers few, if any, clues as to the chronological order of his spoken messages—he may have repeated them on many occasions to reach everyone who came to worship. The book is ultimately addressed to all Israel (hence the references to Judah and Jerusalem).

Date and Historical Situation

According to the first verse, Amos prophesied during the reigns of Uzziah over Judah (792–740 BC) and Jeroboam II over Israel (793–753). The main part of his ministry was probably carried out c. 760–750. Both kingdoms were enjoying great prosperity and had reached new political and military heights (cf. 2Ki 14:23—15:7; 2Ch 26). It was also a time of idolatry, extravagant indulgence in luxurious living, immorality, corruption of judicial procedures and oppression of the poor. As a consequence, God would soon bring about the Assyrian captivity of the northern kingdom (722–721).

Israel at the time was politically secure and spiritually smug. About 40 years earlier, at the end of his ministry, Elisha had prophesied the resurgence of Israel's power (2Ki 13:17–19),

a quick look

Author:
Amos

Audience:
Primarily the idolatrous and indulgent people of the northern kingdom

Date:
About 760–750 BC

Theme:
The prophet Amos calls for social justice as the indispensable expression of true piety.

Amos was a vigorous spokesman for God's justice and righteousness, whereas Hosea emphasized God's love, grace, mercy and forgiveness.

and more recently Jonah had prophesied her restoration to a glory not known since the days of Solomon (2Ki 14:25). The nation felt sure, therefore, that she was in God's good graces. But prosperity increased Israel's religious and moral corruption. God's past punishments for unfaithfulness were forgotten, and his patience was at an end — which he sent Amos to announce.

With Amos, the messages of the prophets began to be preserved in permanent form, being brought together in books that would accompany Israel through the coming debacle and beyond. (Since Amos was a contemporary of Hosea and Jonah, see Introductions to those books.)

Theological Theme and Message

The dominant theme is clearly stated in 5:24, which calls for social justice as the indispensable expression of true piety. Amos was a vigorous spokesman for God's justice and righteousness, whereas Hosea emphasized God's love, grace, mercy and forgiveness. Amos declared that God was going to judge his unfaithful, disobedient, covenant-breaking people. Despite the Lord's special choice of Israel and his kindnesses to her during the exodus and conquest and in the days of David and Solomon, his people continually failed to honor and obey him. The worship centers that King Jeroboam I had set up in Bethel, Dan and elsewhere (1Ki 12:28 – 33) became thoroughly paganized. The Israelites came to believe that the observance of religious rites at the sacred places was all that God was interested in and that outside their worship activities they could do whatever

A view of Tekoa, located ten miles south of Jerusalem. Amos was a shepherd from Tekoa (1:1).
Kim Walton

they pleased — an essentially pagan notion. Without commitment to God's law, they had no basis for standards of conduct. Amos condemns all who make themselves powerful or rich at the expense of others. Those who had acquired great wealth at the expense of the poor and powerless through fraud in the marketplace and corruption of the courts would lose everything.

Jasper seal bearing the inscription "Amos the Scribe" (eighth – seventh century BC)

Z. Radovan/www.BibleLandPictures.com

God's imminent judgment on Israel would not be a mere punitive blow to warn (as often before; see 4:6 – 11 and note), but an almost total destruction. The unthinkable was about to happen: Because they had not faithfully consecrated themselves to his lordship, God would uproot his chosen people by the hands of a pagan nation. Even so, if they would repent, there was hope that "the LORD God Almighty [would] have mercy on the remnant" (5:15; see 5:4 – 6,14). In fact, the Lord had a glorious future for his people, beyond the impending judgment. The house of David would again rule over Israel — even extend its rule over many nations — and Israel would once more be secure in the promised land, feasting on wine and fruit (9:11 – 15). The God of Israel, the Lord of history, would not abandon his chosen people or his chosen program of redemption.

The God for whom Amos speaks is Lord over more than Israel. He is the Great King who rules the whole universe (4:13; 5:8; 9:5 – 6; see Introduction to Psalms: Theology: Major Themes). Because he is all-sovereign, the God of Israel holds the history and destiny of all peoples and of the world in his hands. Israel must know not only that he is the Lord of her future, but also that he is Lord over all, and that he has purposes and concerns that reach far beyond her borders. Israel had a unique, but not an exclusive, claim on God. She needed to remember not only his covenant commitments to her but also her covenant obligations to him. (See further the prophecy of Jonah.)

Outline

- I. Superscription (1:1)
- II. Introduction to Amos's Message (1:2)
- III. Prophecies against the Nations, including Judah and Israel (1:3 — 2:16)
  - A. Judgment on Aram (1:3 – 5)
  - B. Judgment on Philistia (1:6 – 8)
  - C. Judgment on Phoenicia (1:9 – 10)
  - D. Judgment on Edom (1:11 – 12)
  - E. Judgment on Ammon (1:13 – 15)
  - F. Judgment on Moab (2:1 – 3)
  - G. Judgment on Judah (2:4 – 5)
  - H. Judgment on Israel (2:6 – 16)
    - 1. Ruthless oppression of the poor (2:6 – 7a)

2. Unbridled profanation of religion (2:7b – 8)
3. Contrasted position of the Israelites (2:9 – 12)
4. The oppressive system will perish (2:13 – 16)

IV. Prophecies against Israel (3:1 — 5:17)
  A. Judgment on the Chosen People (ch. 3)
    1. God's punishment announced (3:1 – 2)
    2. The announcement vindicated (3:3 – 8)
    3. The punishment vindicated (3:9 – 15)
  B. Judgment on an Unrepentant People (ch. 4)
    1. Judgment on the socialites (4:1 – 3)
    2. Perversion of religious life (4:4 – 5)
    3. Past calamities brought no repentance (4:6 – 11)
    4. No hope for a hardened people (4:12 – 13)
  C. Judgment on an Unjust People (5:1 – 17)
    1. The death dirge (5:1 – 3)
    2. Exhortation to life (5:4 – 6)
    3. Indictment of injustices (5:7 – 13)
    4. Exhortation to life (5:14 – 15)
    5. Prosperity will turn to grief (5:16 – 17)

V. Announcements of Exile (5:18 — 6:14)
  A. A Message of Woe against Israel's Perverted Religion (5:18 – 27)
  B. A Message of Woe against Israel's Complacent Pride (6:1 – 7)
  C. A Sworn Judgment on the Proud and Unjust Nation (6:8 – 14)

VI. Visions of Divine Retribution (7:1 — 9:10)
  A. Judgment Relented (7:1 – 6)
    1. A swarm of locusts (7:1 – 3)
    2. A consuming fire (7:4 – 6)
  B. Judgment Unrelented (7:7 — 9:10)
    1. The plumb line (7:7 – 17)
      a. The vision (7:7 – 9)
      b. Amos challenged and vindicated (7:10 – 17)
    2. The basket of ripe fruit (ch. 8)
      a. The vision (8:1 – 3)
      b. The exposition (8:4 – 14)
    3. The Lord by the altar (9:1 – 10)
      a. The vision (9:1 – 4)
      b. The exposition (9:5 – 10)

VII. Restored Israel's Blessed Future (9:11 – 15)
  A. Revival of the House of David (9:11 – 12)
  B. Restoration of Israel to an Edenic Promised Land (9:13 – 15)

1 The words of Amos, one of the shepherds of Tekoa[a] — the vision he saw
concerning Israel two years before the
earthquake,[b] when Uzziah[c] was king of Judah and Jeroboam[d] son of Jehoash[a] was
king of Israel.[e]
2 He said:

"The LORD roars[f] from Zion
and thunders[g] from Jerusalem;[h]
the pastures of the shepherds dry up,
and the top of Carmel[i] withers."[j]

Judgment on Israel's Neighbors

3 This is what the LORD says:

"For three sins of Damascus,[k]
even for four, I will not relent.[l]
Because she threshed Gilead
with sledges having iron teeth,
4 I will send fire[m] on the house of Hazael[n]
that will consume the fortresses[o] of
Ben-Hadad.[p]
5 I will break down the gate[q] of
Damascus;
I will destroy the king who is in[b] the
Valley of Aven[c]

1:1 [a] S 2Sa 14:2 [b] Zec 14:5 [c] S 2Ki 14:21; S 2Ch 26:23 [d] S 2Ki 14:23 [e] S Hos 1:1 **1:2** [f] S Isa 42:13 [g] S Ps 29:3 [h] Joel 3:16 [i] Am 9:3 [j] S Jer 12:4 **1:3** [k] Isa 7:8; 8:4; 17:1-3 [l] ver 6, 9, 11, 13; Am 2:6 **1:4** [m] S Jer 49:27; S Eze 30:8 [n] S 1Ki 19:17; 2Ki 8:7-15 [o] Jer 17:27 [p] 1Ki 20:1; 2Ki 6:24; Jer 49:23-27 **1:5** [q] Jer 51:30 [r] S Isa 37:12 [s] S 2Ki 16:9; S Isa 22:6; Zec 9:1 [t] S Isa 7:16; Jer 49:27 **1:6** [u] S Ge 10:19; 1Sa 6:17; Zep 2:4 [v] S ver 3 [w] S Ge 14:6; Ob 1:11

and the one who holds the scepter in
Beth Eden.[r]
The people of Aram will go into exile
to Kir,[s]"
says the LORD.[t]

6 This is what the LORD says:

"For three sins of Gaza,[u]
even for four, I will not relent.[v]
Because she took captive whole
communities
and sold them to Edom,[w]
7 I will send fire on the walls of Gaza
that will consume her fortresses.
8 I will destroy the king[d] of Ashdod[x]
and the one who holds the scepter in
Ashkelon.
I will turn my hand[y] against Ekron,
till the last of the Philistines[z] are dead,"[a]
says the Sovereign LORD.[b]

[a] *1* Hebrew *Joash,* a variant of *Jehoash* [b] *5* Or *the inhabitants of* [c] *5* *Aven* means *wickedness.* [d] *8* Or *inhabitants*

1:8 [x] S 2Ch 26:6 [y] Ps 81:14 [z] S Eze 25:16 [a] S Isa 34:8 [b] Isa 14:28-32; Zep 2:4-7

1:1 *Amos.* Apparently a shortened form of a name like Amasiah (2Ch 17:16), meaning "The LORD carries" or "The LORD upholds." *shepherds.* The Hebrew for this word occurs elsewhere in the OT only in reference to the king of Moab (2Ki 3:4, where it is translated "raised sheep"). Cf. 7:14, where a different Hebrew word is used. Amos was not a professional prophet who earned his living from his ministry; he stood outside religious institutions. *Tekoa.* See Introduction: Author; see also photo, p. 1470. *saw.* Received by divine revelation. *earthquake.* Evidently a major shock, long remembered, and probably the one mentioned in Zec 14:5. Recent geological studies have detected a mammoth seismic event in this area dating to c. 750 BC. Reference to the earthquake suggests that the author viewed it as a kind of divine reinforcement of the words of judgment. *Uzziah.* See Introduction: Date and Historical Situation; see also note on Isa 6:1. *Jeroboam.* See Introduction: Date and Historical Situation.

1:2 A thematic verse, ominously announcing the main thrust of Amos's message. *roars.* Amos, a shepherd, was sent to Israel to warn her that he had heard a lion roar and that the lion is none other than the Lord himself, who has only wanted to be Israel's shepherd. For the use of this imagery in other contexts, see Jer 25:30; Joel 3:16. *from Zion.* The Lord established his earthly throne in Jerusalem, among his special people, and from there he announces his judgments on them, as well as on the other nations. *pastures … top of Carmel.* See 9:3. From the lowest and driest portions of the land to the highest and greenest, the Lord's judgment will be felt like a severe drought that devastates the whole land.

1:3 — 2:16 A series of prophecies against the nations; for parallel sections, see Isa 13:1 — 23:18 and note. After pronouncing judgment on Israel's neighbors for various atrocities — judgment that Israel would naturally applaud — Amos announces God's condemnation of his own two kingdoms for despising God's laws. His listing of Israel's sins under the same form of indictment used against the other nations shockingly pictures Israel's sins alongside those of her pagan neighbors.

1:3 *This is what the LORD says.* See vv. 6,9,11,13; 2:1,4,6. Amos, the Lord's spokesman, uses the messenger formula that identifies the true source of his prophecies. *For three sins … four.* For their many sins, especially the one named; see also vv. 6,9,11,13; 2:1,4,6. For similar numerical expressions, see Job 5:19; Pr 6:16; Mic 5:5 and notes. *Damascus.* Capital of the Aramean state directly north of Israel (see note on Isa 17:1) and a constant enemy in that day. Her crime was brutality against the conquered people of Gilead, Israel's territory east of Galilee. *not relent.* See vv. 6,9,11,13; 2:1,4,6; cf. Isa 9:12,17,21 and note; Jer 23:20. *threshed … sledges.* Heads of grain were threshed by driving a wooden sledge fitted with sharp teeth over the cut grain (cf. Job 41:30; Isa 28:27; 41:15; Hab 3:12; see 2Ki 13:7 and note on Ru 1:22).

1:4 *fire … that will consume.* See vv. 7,10,12,14; 2:2,5; a common description of the threat of divine judgment, usually carried out by a devastating war that resulted in the burning of major cities and fortresses (see Jer 17:27 and note; Hos 8:14). *Hazael.* King of Damascus (c. 843 – 796 BC) and founder of a new line of kings (see 2Ki 8:7 – 15 and note on 8:15). *fortresses.* See vv. 7,10,12,14; 2:2,5; perhaps referring not only to citadels but also to the fortress-like palatial dwellings of the rich and powerful. *Ben-Hadad.* Ben-Hadad III (c. 796 – 770 BC), son of Hazael (see 2Ki 13:3 and note; cf. 2Ki 8:14 – 15).

1:5 *king.* See v. 8; lit. "one who sits [enthroned]." *Valley of Aven.* Possibly the Beqaa Valley between the Lebanon and Anti-Lebanon mountains, but may refer to the river valley in which Damascus is located (see note on 2Ki 5:12), calling it the "valley of wickedness" (see NIV text note). *Beth Eden.* Probably Damascus, the garden spot of that region. *Aram.* See note on Dt 26:5. *Kir.* An unidentified place, possibly in the vicinity of Elam (see 2Ki 16:9 and note), from which the Arameans are said to have come (9:7).

1:6 *Gaza.* One of the five major Philistine cities (see map, p. 359); it guarded the entry to Canaan from Egypt. *whole communities.* See v. 9; not just warriors captured in battle. The reference may be to villages in south Judah on the trade route from Edom to Gaza. *to Edom.* See v. 9; trading the people like cattle to another country.

1:8 *Ashdod … Ashkelon … Ekron.* Three more cities of the Philistine group (see note on v. 6). Gath, the fifth (cf. 6:2), may already have been subdued by Uzziah (see 2Ch 26:6). *the last.*

9 This is what the LORD says:

"For three sins of Tyre,[c]
even for four, I will not relent.[d]
Because she sold whole communities
of captives to Edom,
disregarding a treaty of
brotherhood,[e]
10 I will send fire on the walls of
Tyre
that will consume her fortresses.[f]"

11 This is what the LORD says:

"For three sins of Edom,[g]
even for four, I will not relent.
Because he pursued his brother with a
sword[h]
and slaughtered the women of the
land,
because his anger raged continually
and his fury flamed unchecked,[i]
12 I will send fire on Teman[j]
that will consume the fortresses of
Bozrah.[k]"

13 This is what the LORD says:

"For three sins of Ammon,[l]
even for four, I will not relent.
Because he ripped open the pregnant
women[m] of Gilead
in order to extend his borders,
14 I will set fire to the walls of Rabbah[n]
that will consume[o] her fortresses
amid war cries[p] on the day of
battle,
amid violent winds[q] on a stormy
day.
15 Her king[a] will go into exile,
he and his officials together,[r]"
says the LORD.[s]

1:9 [c] 1Ki 5:1; 9:11-14; Jer 25:22; Joel 3:4; S Mt 11:21 [d] ver 3 [e] S 1Ki 5:12 **1:10** [f] Isa 23:1-18; S 34:8; S Jer 47:4; Eze 26:2-4; Zec 9:1-4 **1:11** [g] Nu 20:14-21; S 2Ch 28:17; S Ps 83:6 [h] S Ps 63:10 [i] S Eze 25:12-14; Zec 1:15 **1:12** [j] S Ge 36:11, 15 [k] S Isa 34:5; 63:1-6; Jer 25:21; Eze 25:12-14; 35:1-15; Ob 1:1; Mal 1:2-5 **1:13** [l] S Ge 19:38; S Eze 21:28 [m] S Ge 34:29; S 2Ki 8:12; S Hos 13:16 **1:14** [n] S Dt 3:11 [o] Isa 30:30 [p] S Job 39:25 [q] Jer 23:19 **1:15** [r] S Jer 25:21 [s] 1Ch 20:1; S Jer 49:1; Eze 21:28-32; 25:2-7

2:1 [t] S Isa 16:6 [u] Isa 33:12 **2:2** [v] Jer 48:24 [w] S Job 39:25 [x] S Jos 6:20 **2:3** [y] S Ps 2:10 [z] S Isa 40:23 [a] Isa 15:1-9; 16:1-14; S 25:10; Jer 48:1; S Eze 25:8-11; Zep 2:8-9

2

This is what the LORD says:

"For three sins of Moab,[t]
even for four, I will not relent.
Because he burned to ashes[u]
the bones of Edom's king,
2 I will send fire on Moab
that will consume the fortresses of
Kerioth.[b][v]
Moab will go down in great tumult
amid war cries[w] and the blast of the
trumpet.[x]
3 I will destroy her ruler[y]
and kill all her officials with him,"[z]
says the LORD.[a]

4 This is what the LORD says:

"For three sins of Judah,[b]
even for four, I will not relent.
Because they have rejected the law[c] of
the LORD
and have not kept his decrees,[d]
because they have been led astray[e] by
false gods,[c][f]
the gods[d] their ancestors followed,[g]
5 I will send fire[h] on Judah
that will consume the fortresses[i] of
Jerusalem.[j]"

Judgment on Israel

6 This is what the LORD says:

"For three sins of Israel,
even for four, I will not relent.[k]

[a] 15 Or / *Molek* [b] 2 Or *of her cities* [c] 4 Or *by lies* [d] 4 Or *lies*

2:4 [b] 2Ki 17:19; Hos 12:2 [c] S Jer 6:19 [d] S Eze 20:24 [e] Isa 9:16 [f] S Ex 34:15; S Dt 31:20; S Ps 4:2 [g] S 2Ki 22:13; S Jer 9:14; S 16:12 **2:5** [h] S 2Ki 25:9; S 2Ch 36:19 [i] Am 3:11 [j] S Jer 17:27; S Hos 8:14 **2:6** [k] S Am 1:3

There would be no remnant. Philistia was finally destroyed by Nebuchadnezzar.

1:9 *Tyre.* The dominant Phoenician merchant city, allied to Israel by a "treaty of brotherhood" in the days of David (1Ki 5:1), later in the time of Solomon (1Ki 5:12) and later still during the reign of Ahab, whose father-in-law ruled Tyre and Sidon (1Ki 16:30–31). *she sold.* Her crime was like Philistia's (v. 6).

1:10 *walls.* Tyre was an almost impregnable island, boastful of her security (cf. Eze 26:1—28:19).

1:11 *Edom.* The nation descended from Esau (Ge 36; see Ge 25:23–30; 27:39–40). *brother.* Israel (see Ob 8–10 and note on Ob 10). Reference may be to a treaty "brother" (see note on v. 9). Edom's crime was in violating this relationship by persistent hostility.

1:12 *Teman ... Bozrah.* Major cities of Edom, the former thought to be near Petra (see note on Ob 9), the latter now identified with Buseirah, 37 miles to the north. With their destruction, Edom would lose its capacity for continual warfare.

1:13 *Ammon.* Judgment centered on Rabbah (v. 14; see note on Dt 3:11), modern Amman. Greed for land bred a brutal genocide that would be punished by a tumult of men and nature, leaving the state without leaders to continue such practices (see 1Ki 8:12 and note).

1:14 Fulfilled through the Assyrians.

1:15 *Her king.* See NIV text note; see also Jer 49:3 and note on 49:1.

2:1 *Moab.* Located east of the Dead Sea (see note on Isa 15:1). *burned ... the bones of Edom's king.* Thus depriving the king's spirit of the rest that was widely believed to result from decent burial.

2:2 *Kerioth.* Perhaps a plural noun meaning "cities" (see NIV text note) or the name of a major town (see Jer 48:24) and shrine of Chemosh, the national god of Moab (see 1Ki 11:7,33).

2:4 *rejected the law of the LORD.* Judah's sins differed in kind from those of the other nations. Those nations violated the generally recognized laws of humanity, but Judah disobeyed the revealed law of God. These sins may be included in the indictment against Israel that follows.

2:5 *fire ... consume the fortresses.* See 1:4 and note. Judah's punishment is the same as Aram's (1:4), Philistia's (1:7), Phoenicia's (1:10), Edom's (1:12), Ammon's (1:14) and Moab's (2:2)—loss of the defenses and wealth in which they trusted.

2:6 Israel's sins revealed the general moral deterioration of the nation. *the innocent.* Probably those who were not in debt and whom there was no lawful reason to sell (cf. Lev 25:39–43). Alternatively, the "innocent" here may refer to "the poor" (v. 7; cf. 5:12; 8:6), in contrast to the sinfully wicked behavior of the wealthy and powerful (see 4:1–5; 6:1–7). *the needy.* God had commanded that they be helped (see Dt

They sell the innocent for silver,
and the needy for a pair of sandals.[l]
7 They trample on the heads of the poor
as on the dust of the ground
and deny justice to the oppressed.
Father and son use the same girl
and so profane my holy name.[m]
8 They lie down beside every altar
on garments taken in pledge.[n]
In the house of their god
they drink wine[o] taken as fines.[p]

9 "Yet I destroyed the Amorites[q] before them,
though they were tall[r] as the cedars
and strong as the oaks.[s]
I destroyed their fruit above
and their roots[t] below.
10 I brought you up out of Egypt[u]
and led[v] you forty years in the wilderness[w]
to give you the land of the Amorites.[x]

11 "I also raised up prophets[y] from among your children
and Nazirites[z] from among your youths.
Is this not true, people of Israel?"
declares the LORD.
12 "But you made the Nazirites drink wine
and commanded the prophets not to prophesy.[a]

13 "Now then, I will crush you
as a cart crushes when loaded with grain.[b]
14 The swift will not escape,[c]
the strong[d] will not muster their strength,
and the warrior will not save his life.[e]
15 The archer[f] will not stand his ground,
the fleet-footed soldier will not get away,
and the horseman[g] will not save his life.[h]
16 Even the bravest warriors[i]
will flee naked on that day,"
declares the LORD.

Witnesses Summoned Against Israel

3 Hear this word, people of Israel, the
word the LORD has spoken against
you[j]—against the whole family I brought
up out of Egypt:[k]

2 "You only have I chosen[l]
of all the families of the earth;
therefore I will punish[m] you
for all your sins.[n]"

3 Do two walk together
unless they have agreed to do so?

2:6 [l] S Joel 3:3; Am 8:6 **2:7** [m] S Lev 18:21; Am 5:11-12; 8:4 **2:8** [n] S Ex 22:26; Dt 24:12-13 [o] Hos 7:14; Am 4:1; 6:6 [p] Hab 2:6 **2:9** [q] Nu 21:23-26; Jos 10:12 [r] S Isa 10:33 [s] S Ps 29:9 [t] S 2Ki 19:30; S Job 18:16; S Eze 17:9 **2:10** [u] S Ex 6:6; 20:2; Am 3:1 [v] S Dt 8:2 [w] S Dt 2:7 [x] S Ex 3:8; S Nu 21:25; S Jos 13:4; Am 9:7 **2:11** [y] Dt 18:18; Jer 7:25 [z] S Jdg 13:5 **2:12** [a] Isa 30:10; Jer 11:21; Am 7:12-13; Mic 2:6 **2:13** [b] Am 7:16-17 **2:14** [c] S Job 11:20 [d] S 1Ki 20:11 [e] Ps 33:16; Isa 30:16-17 **2:15** [f] S Eze 39:3 [g] S Ex 15:21; Zec 10:5 [h] Ecc 9:11 **2:16** [i] Jer 48:41 **3:1** [j] Zep 2:5 [k] S Am 2:10

3:2 [l] S Ex 19:6; Dt 7:6; Lk 12:47 [m] ver 14 [n] S Jer 14:10; Mic 2:3; 1Pe 4:17

15:7–11 and note on 15:11), but they were instead sold for failure to repay a (perhaps paltry) debt, for which a "pair of sandals" had been given in pledge (see 8:6).

2:7 *trample.* See 5:11; 8:4. *poor ... oppressed.* To care for them and to protect them from injustice were clearly commanded by Israel's law (Ex 23:6–8); also, throughout the ancient Near East, kings were supposed to defend such people. *Father and son use the same girl.* Whether the girl in question was a household servant (in which case father and son used her as a family prostitute) is not clear. In any case, the law required that if there were sexual relations with a girl, marriage was obligatory (Ex 22:16; Dt 22:28–29). For a father and son to have sexual relations with the same girl or woman was strictly forbidden (Lev 18:7–8,15; 20:11–12). *profane my holy name.* Cf. Lev 18:21 and note; 19:12; 20:3; 21:6; 22:2,32; see Jer 34:16; Eze 20:9 and notes; 36:20–23; 39:7.

2:8 *beside every altar ... In the house of their god.* Israelites who broke the laws protecting the powerless brazenly used their wrongly gotten gains even in places supposed to be holy. *garments taken in pledge.* The law prohibited keeping a man's cloak overnight as security for a debt (see Ex 22:26–27 and note; Dt 24:12–13), or taking a widow's cloak at all (Dt 24:17). *fines.* Claimed as restitution for damages suffered. Exorbitant claims or even false charges of damage seem to be suggested.

2:9 *I destroyed.* Israel not only had known God's law but had been specially favored by his powerful help. *Amorites.* Here used for all the inhabitants of Canaan (see notes on Ge 10:16; 15:16; Jdg 6:10). *tall ... strong.* Neither the size of Canaan's people nor their military power (see Nu 13:27–33) was able to prevent God's victory over them (see Jos 10:5,12–13). *their fruit above and their roots below.* That is, totally.

2:10 *I brought you up.* See 3:1; see also Ex 20:2 and note. God's great blessings to Israel in the past added to her guilt, and now they are recalled as a part of the Lord's indictment against his people.

2:11 *I also raised up prophets ... and Nazirites.* Prophets, as God's faithful spokesmen (see Dt 18:15–20 and note on 18:15), and Nazirites, as those uniquely dedicated to him (see Nu 6:1–21 and note on 6:2; Jdg 13:5 and note), are singled out as special gifts to his people. These persons who were outside the priesthood were used by God through word and example to call his people to faithfulness.

2:12 *But you.* Israel showed utter disdain for God's faithful servants and thus demonstrated her callous insensitivity to God's working among them (cf. 7:16).

2:13 A loaded cart crushes anything that falls beneath its wheels.

2:14–16 None who might be expected to stand their ground or escape would be able to save themselves.

2:16 *that day.* The day God comes in judgment (see 5:18; Joel 1:15 and notes)—as he did through the Assyrian invasion that swept the northern kingdom away.

3:1—5:17 Prophecies that underscore the certainty of God's judgment on Israel.

3:1 *Hear this word.* See 4:1; 5:1. The Lord calls his people to account because of their sins.

3:2 *You only.* Israel's present strength and prosperity gave rise to complacency about her privileged status as the Lord's chosen people. She is shockingly reminded of the long-forgotten responsibilities her privileges entailed.

3:3–6 With these rhetorical questions (involving comparisons) Amos builds up to the statements of vv. 7–8, to explain why he is speaking such terrifying words. Each

4 Does a lion roar[o] in the thicket
when it has no prey?[p]
Does it growl in its den
when it has caught nothing?
5 Does a bird swoop down to a trap on the ground
when no bait[q] is there?
Does a trap spring up from the ground
if it has not caught anything?
6 When a trumpet[r] sounds in a city,
do not the people tremble?
When disaster[s] comes to a city,
has not the LORD caused it?[t]

7 Surely the Sovereign LORD does nothing
without revealing his plan[u]
to his servants the prophets.[v]

8 The lion[w] has roared[x]—
who will not fear?
The Sovereign LORD has spoken—
who can but prophesy?[y]

9 Proclaim to the fortresses of Ashdod[z]
and to the fortresses of Egypt:
"Assemble yourselves on the mountains of Samaria;[a]
see the great unrest within her
and the oppression among her people."

10 "They do not know how to do right,[b]"
declares the LORD,
"who store up in their fortresses[c]
what they have plundered[d] and looted."

11 Therefore this is what the Sovereign LORD says:

"An enemy will overrun your land,
pull down your strongholds
and plunder your fortresses.[e]"

12 This is what the LORD says:

"As a shepherd rescues from the lion's[f] mouth
only two leg bones or a piece of an ear,

NATIONS AND CITIES MENTIONED IN AMOS

3:4 [o] S Isa 42:13 [p] Ps 104:21; S Hos 5:14 **3:5** [q] S Ps 119:110 **3:6** [r] S Nu 10:2; S Job 39:24; S Jer 4:21 [s] S Isa 31:2 [t] Isa 14:24-27 **3:7** [u] Ge 18:17; S 1Sa 3:7; S Da 9:22; Jn 15:15; Rev 10:7 [v] S Jer 23:22 **3:8** [w] S Isa 31:4 [x] S Isa 42:13 [y] S Jer 20:9; Jnh 1:1-3; 3:1-3; Ac 4:20 **3:9** [z] S Jos 13:3; S 2Ch 26:6 [a] Am 4:1; 6:1 **3:10** [b] Am 5:7; 6:12 [c] S Ps 36:3; Mic 6:10; Zep 1:9 [d] Hab 2:8 **3:11** [e] Am 2:5; 6:14 **3:12** [f] S 1Sa 17:34

picture is of cause and effect, using figures drawn from daily life—and culminating in divine action (v. 6).

3:7 *his servants the prophets.* See Jer 7:25; Zec 1:6 and notes.

3:8 *lion has roared.* Echoes 1:2 (see note there). *who can but prophesy?* Amos must speak because God has spoken.

3:9 The rich and powerful of Philistia and Egypt are summoned to witness the Lord's indictment against those who store up ill-gotten riches in the fortresses of Samaria (see v. 15). *fortresses.* See note on 1:4. *great unrest.* The result of a violent, selfish power structure that was heedless of the justice called for in God's law.

3:10 *who store up.* Cf. 2:6–8. The prosperity of Israel's wealthy depended on oppression and robbery. The following verses announce God's judgment on such greed (cf. Hab 2:6–11).

3:11 *enemy.* Assyria. *plunder your fortresses.* Those that Samaria's wealthy had greedily filled with plunder.

3:12 *As a shepherd rescues … only two leg bones.* To prove to the owner that the sheep had been eaten by a wild animal, not stolen by the shepherd (see Ex 22:13). *be rescued.* Only some mutilated pieces would be "rescued." The nation as such would be more than wounded—it would be de-

so will the Israelites living in Samaria
be rescued,
with only the head of a bed
and a piece of fabric[a] from a couch.[bg]”

13 “Hear this and testify[h] against the descendants of Jacob,” declares the Lord, the
LORD God Almighty.

14 “On the day I punish[i] Israel for her sins,
I will destroy the altars of Bethel;[j]
the horns[k] of the altar will be cut off
and fall to the ground.
15 I will tear down the winter house[l]
along with the summer house;[m]
the houses adorned with ivory[n] will be
destroyed
and the mansions[o] will be
demolished,[p]”
declares the LORD.[q]

Israel Has Not Returned to God

4 Hear this word, you cows of Bashan[r]
on Mount Samaria,[s]
you women who oppress the poor[t]
and crush the needy[u]
and say to your husbands,[v] “Bring us
some drinks![w]”
2 The Sovereign LORD has sworn by his
holiness:
“The time[x] will surely come
when you will be taken away[y] with
hooks,[z]
the last of you with fishhooks.[c]
3 You will each go straight out
through breaches in the wall,[a]
and you will be cast out toward
Harmon,[d]”
declares the LORD.

4 “Go to Bethel[b] and sin;
go to Gilgal[c] and sin yet more.
Bring your sacrifices every morning,[d]
your tithes[e] every three years.[ef]
5 Burn leavened bread[g] as a thank
offering
and brag about your freewill
offerings[h]—
boast about them, you Israelites,
for this is what you love to do,”
declares the Sovereign LORD.

6 “I gave you empty stomachs in every
city
and lack of bread in every town,
yet you have not returned to me,”
declares the LORD.[i]

3:12 [g]S Est 1:6; Am 6:4 **3:13** [h]Eze 2:7 **3:14** [i]S ver 2; S Lev 26:18 [j]S Ge 12:8; Am 5:5-6 [k]S Ex 27:2 **3:15** [l]Jer 36:22 [m]Jdg 3:20 [n]S 1Ki 22:39 [o]Am 5:11; 6:11 [p]S Isa 34:5 [q]Hos 10:5-8, 14-15 **4:1** [r]S Ps 22:12 [s]S Am 3:9 [t]S Isa 58:6; S Eze 18:12 [u]S Dt 24:14 [v]Jer 44:19 [w]S Am 2:8; 5:11; 8:6 **4:2** [x]Jer 31:31 [y]Am 6:8 [z]S 2Ki 19:28; S 2Ch 33:11; S Isa 19:8 **4:3** [a]S Eze 12:5 **4:4** [b]S Jos 7:2 [c]S Hos 4:15 [d]S Nu 28:3 [e]Dt 14:28 [f]S Eze 20:39; Am 5:21-22 **4:5** [g]S Lev 7:13 [h]S Lev 22:18-21 **4:6** [i]S Isa 3:1; S 9:13; S Jer 5:3; Hag 2:17

[a] 12 The meaning of the Hebrew for this phrase is uncertain. [b] 12 Or *Israelites be rescued, / those who sit in Samaria / on the edge of their beds / and in Damascus on their couches.* [c] 2 Or *away in baskets, / the last of you in fish baskets* [d] 3 Masoretic Text; with a different word division of the Hebrew (see Septuagint) *out, you mountain of oppression* [e] 4 Or *days*

stroyed. If the NIV text note represents the correct reading of the Hebrew, reference would be to "those who sit" in idle luxury (see 6:4) "in Samaria on the edge of their beds and in Damascus on their couches." Since at this time Israel had extended its influence over Damascus, the rich merchants of Samaria may have maintained luxurious houses also in Damascus, along with market privileges in that city (see 1Ki 20:34 and note).

3:13 *Hear . . . testify.* Addressed to those summoned in v. 9. The rich and powerful of Philistia and Egypt are called upon to hear the Lord's indictment of the rich and powerful in Samaria and to testify that his indictment is true and that his judgment is warranted. Even these pagans will agree with God's judgment.

3:14 *altars of Bethel.* Israel's sins were rooted in the false shrine built by Jeroboam I at Bethel (1Ki 12:26–33). *horns of the altar.* Even the last refuge for a condemned person (cf. 1Ki 1:50–53) will afford Israel no protection.

3:15 *winter house . . . summer house.* Cf. 6:11; further signs of opulence that would not benefit their owners on the day of God's judgment—nor would expensive imported decorations, carvings and inlays of ivory (cf. 6:4). Many examples of such carvings have been found in ruined palaces in Samaria and other cities (see 1Ki 22:39 and note).

4:1 *Hear this word.* See note on 3:1. *cows of Bashan.* Upper-class women, directly addressed, are compared with the best breed of cattle in ancient Canaan, which were raised (and pampered) in the pastures of northern Transjordan (see Ps 22:12; Eze 39:18 and notes). Whether the metaphor was intended as an insult or as ironic flattery is uncertain. *Mount Samaria.* See 6:1 and note.

4:2 *The Sovereign LORD has sworn.* Stresses the solemnity of the situation and the certainty of the events. *by his holiness.* Contrasts with Israel's sin, reminding God's people of what they could have been (see Ex 19:6 and note) if they had faithfully kept their side of the covenant—as God had his. *hooks.* According to Assyrian reliefs (pictures engraved on stone), prisoners of war were led away with a rope fastened to a hook that pierced the nose or lower lip (see 2Ki 19:28 and note; 2Ch 33:11; Eze 19:4,9; Hab 1:15). The Hebrew word here may, in fact, refer to ropes.

4:3 *breaches in the wall.* Cf. 2Ki 17:5; Eze 13:5. *Harmon.* Appears to be a place-name, though it is not otherwise known (see NIV text note).

4:4–5 Spoken in irony.

4:4 *Bethel . . . Gilgal.* These towns had historical importance as places where God's help was commemorated (Ge 35:1–15; Jos 4:20–24), and both were popular places of worship in Amos's day (5:5; see Hos 4:15; 12:4 and notes). *sacrifices every morning.* See Ex 29:38–41. *tithes.* Apparently the special tithe that was to be brought "every three years" (Dt 14:28; 26:12). *years.* See NIV text note. The Hebrew word for "days" sometimes stands for years.

4:5 *leavened bread.* The burning of leavened bread in the sacrifices was strictly forbidden (see Lev 2:11; 6:17). Either Amos rebukes the Israelites for willful transgression of the law, or he speaks of burning in a general way for offering inappropriate gifts to the Lord. Leavened bread could accompany a fellowship offering (see Lev 7:13). *what you love to do.* They loved the forms and rituals of religion but did not love what God loves—goodness, mercy, kindness, justice (see 5:15; Isa 5:7; 61:8; Hos 6:6 and note; Mic 6:8).

4:6–11 In the past, God had used natural disasters to discipline and warn his people, but those lessons were soon forgotten (cf. the covenant curses in Dt 28:22–24,39–40,42,48,56–57).

4:6 *I.* These were not simply natural disasters; they were direct acts of God (3:6). *yet you have not returned to me.* A recurring accusation that runs like a refrain through vv. 8–11.

7 "I also withheld[j] rain from you
when the harvest was still three
months away.
I sent rain on one town,
but withheld it from another.[k]
One field had rain;
another had none and dried up.
8 People staggered from town to town
for water[l]
but did not get enough[m] to drink,
yet you have not returned[n] to me,"
declares the LORD.[o]

9 "Many times I struck your gardens and
vineyards,
destroying them with blight and
mildew.[p]
Locusts[q] devoured your fig and olive
trees,[r]
yet you have not returned[s] to me,"
declares the LORD.

10 "I sent plagues[t] among you
as I did to Egypt.[u]
I killed your young men[v] with the
sword,
along with your captured horses.
I filled your nostrils with the stench[w]
of your camps,
yet you have not returned to me,"[x]
declares the LORD.[y]

11 "I overthrew some of you
as I overthrew Sodom and
Gomorrah.[z]
You were like a burning stick[a] snatched
from the fire,
yet you have not returned to me,"
declares the LORD.[b]

12 "Therefore this is what I will do to
you, Israel,
and because I will do this to you,
Israel,
prepare to meet your God."

13 He who forms the mountains,[c]
who creates the wind,[d]
and who reveals his thoughts[e] to
mankind,
who turns dawn to darkness,
and treads on the heights of the
earth[f]—
the LORD God Almighty is his
name.[g]

A Lament and Call to Repentance

5 Hear this word, Israel, this lament[h] I
take up concerning you:

2 "Fallen is Virgin[i] Israel,
never to rise again,
deserted in her own land,
with no one to lift her up.[j]"

3 This is what the Sovereign LORD says
to Israel:

"Your city that marches out a thousand
strong
will have only a hundred left;
your town that marches out a hundred
strong
will have only ten left.[k]"

4 This is what the LORD says to Israel:

"Seek[l] me and live;[m]
5 do not seek Bethel,
do not go to Gilgal,[n]
do not journey to Beersheba.[o]
For Gilgal will surely go into exile,
and Bethel will be reduced to
nothing.[a][p]"
6 Seek[q] the LORD and live,[r]
or he will sweep through the tribes
of Joseph like a fire;[s]
it will devour them,
and Bethel[t] will have no one to
quench it.[u]

[a] 5 Hebrew *aven,* a reference to Beth Aven (a derogatory name for Bethel); see Hosea 4:15.

4:7 [j] S Jer 3:3; Zec 14:17 [k] Ex 9:4, 26; Dt 11:17; S 2Ch 7:13; S Isa 5:6 **4:8** [l] S Eze 4:16-17 [m] Hag 1:6 [n] S Jer 3:7 [o] S Job 36:31; S Jer 14:4 **4:9** [p] S Dt 28:22 [q] S Ex 10:13; S Joel 2:25 [r] Joel 1:7 [s] S Isa 9:13; S Jer 3:10 **4:10** [t] S Ex 9:3 [u] Ex 11:5 [v] S Isa 9:17 [w] S Isa 34:3 [x] S Dt 28:21 [y] S Isa 9:13 **4:11** [z] S Ge 19:24; S Jer 23:14 [a] S Isa 7:4; Jude 1:23 [b] S Job 36:13 **4:13** [c] Ps 65:6 [d] Ps 135:7 [e] S Da 2:28 [f] Mic 1:3 [g] S Isa 47:4; Am 5:8, 27; 9:6 **5:1** [h] S Jer 4:8; S Eze 19:1 **5:2** [i] S 2Ki 19:21; Jer 14:17 [j] Jer 50:32; Am 8:14 **5:3** [k] Isa 6:13; Am 6:9 **5:4** [l] S Dt 4:29 [m] Dt 32:46-47; Isa 55:3; Jer 29:13; S Eze 18:9 **5:5** [n] 1Sa 11:14; S Hos 4:15 [o] Ge 21:31; Am 8:14 [p] S 1Sa 7:16; S 8:2 **5:6** [q] Ps 22:26; 105:4; S Isa 31:1; 55:6; Zep 2:3 [r] ver 14; S Lev 18:5 [s] Dt 4:24 [t] S Am 3:14 [u] S Jer 4:4

4:7–8 Lack of rain three months before harvest would prevent full development of the grain.
4:9 *blight and mildew.* See Hag 2:17 and note. *Locusts.* See Ex 10:14 and note.
4:10 *plagues . . . as . . . Egypt.* See Ex 7:14—12:30.
4:11 *Sodom and Gomorrah.* Exemplified total destruction, God's judgment on those cities (see Ge 19:24–25) eventually becoming proverbial (see Dt 29:23; Isa 1:9; 13:19; see also Jer 49:18; Zep 2:9 and notes). *burning stick snatched from the fire.* Saved only by God's grace (see Zec 3:2 and note).
4:12 *prepare to meet your God.* Devastated Israel, brought to her knees by the Assyrians, would meet the God she had covenanted with at Sinai and had now so grievously offended.
4:13 See note on 5:8–9. The God of such power and majesty is easily able to execute the judgment announced in v. 12.
5:1 *Hear this word.* See note on 3:1. *this lament.* Amos sorrowfully fashioned a lament as if Israel were already dead.
5:2 *Virgin Israel.* A personification of Israel (see note on 2Ki 19:21). *deserted.* Left like a dead body on the open field (see Jer 8:2; 9:22).
5:3 *city . . . town.* The Hebrew expression denotes communities of varying size, all of which would suffer.
5:4 *Seek me and live.* This gracious invitation is expanded in v. 6, and yet again in v. 14, to heighten the rhetorical effect. If the people of Israel would seek the Lord, they (or at least a "remnant," v. 15) could yet escape the violent death anticipated in Amos's lament (see Zep 2:3 and note).
5:5 *Bethel . . . Gilgal.* See note on 4:4. *Beersheba.* Located in the south of Judah, it also had evidently become a place of pilgrimage and idolatry (see 8:14). All shrines where the worship of God was abused would be destroyed.
5:6 The places of idolatry were doomed; yet if Israel turned to God, there was hope for her as a nation. Otherwise her people, too, would be destroyed. *Seek . . . live.* See v. 4 and note. *tribes of Joseph.* The northern kingdom of Israel, dominated by the tribe of Ephraim, descendants of Joseph (see v. 15; 6:6; Hos 4:7 and note). *Bethel.* The main religious center of the northern kingdom (see 3:14; 4:4; 7:13; Hos 12:4 and notes). The god the Israelites worshiped there would be powerless to save the place when the true God brought his judgment.

7 There are those who turn justice into
bitterness[v]
and cast righteousness[w] to the
ground.[x]

8 He who made the Pleiades and
Orion,[y]
who turns midnight into dawn[z]
and darkens day into night,[a]
who calls for the waters of the sea
and pours them out over the face of
the land—
the LORD is his name.[b]
9 With a blinding flash he destroys the
stronghold
and brings the fortified city to ruin.[c]

10 There are those who hate the one who
upholds justice in court[d]
and detest the one who tells the
truth.[e]

11 You levy a straw tax on the poor[f]
and impose a tax on their grain.
Therefore, though you have built stone
mansions,[g]
you will not live in them;[h]
though you have planted lush
vineyards,
you will not drink their wine.[i]
12 For I know how many are your
offenses
and how great your sins.[j]

There are those who oppress the
innocent and take bribes[k]
and deprive the poor[l] of justice in
the courts.[m]

13 Therefore the prudent keep quiet[n] in
such times,
for the times are evil.[o]
14 Seek good, not evil,
that you may live.[p]
Then the LORD God Almighty will be
with you,
just as you say he is.
15 Hate evil,[q] love good;[r]
maintain justice in the courts.[s]
Perhaps[t] the LORD God Almighty will
have mercy[u]
on the remnant[v] of Joseph.

16 Therefore this is what the Lord, the
LORD God Almighty, says:

"There will be wailing[w] in all the
streets[x]
and cries of anguish in every public
square.
The farmers[y] will be summoned to weep
and the mourners to wail.
17 There will be wailing[z] in all the
vineyards,
for I will pass through[a] your midst,"
says the LORD.[b]

The Day of the LORD

18 Woe to you who long
for the day of the LORD![c]
Why do you long for the day of the
LORD?[d]
That day will be darkness,[e] not light.[f]

5:7 [v] Isa 5:20; Am 6:12 [w] S Am 3:10 [x] S Hos 10:4 **5:8** [y] S Ge 1:16; S Job 38:31 [z] S Job 38:12; Isa 42:16 [a] S Ps 104:20; Am 8:9 [b] Ps 104:6-9; Jer 16:21; S Am 4:13 **5:9** [c] Mic 5:11 **5:10** [d] S Isa 29:21 [e] 1Ki 22:8; Gal 4:16 **5:11** [f] Am 8:6 [g] S Am 3:15 [h] S Dt 28:30; Mic 1:6 [i] S Jdg 9:27; S Am 4:1; 9:14; Mic 6:15; Zep 1:13 **5:12** [j] Hos 5:3 [k] S Job 36:18; S Isa 1:23; S Eze 22:12 [l] S Jer 5:28 [m] S Job 5:4; S Isa 5:23; S Am 2:6-7 **5:13** [n] S Est 4:14 [o] Mic 2:3 **5:14** [p] S ver 6 **5:15** [q] S Ps 52:3; S 97:10; Ro 12:9 [r] S Ge 18:25 [s] S Isa 1:17; S 29:21; Zec 8:16 [t] S Jer 36:3 [u] S Joel 2:14 [v] Mic 5:7,8; 7:18 **5:16** [w] Jer 9:17; Am 8:3; Zep 1:10 [x] Jer 7:34 [y] S Joel 1:11

5:17 [z] S Ex 11:6 [a] Ex 12:12 [b] Isa 16:10; S Jer 48:33 **5:18** [c] S Isa 2:12; S Joel 1:15 [d] S Jer 30:5 [e] S 1Sa 2:9; S Joel 2:2 [f] S Job 20:28; Isa 5:19, 30; Jer 30:7

5:7 *those who turn justice into bitterness.* They corrupted the procedures and institutions of justice (the courts), making them instruments of injustice ("bitterness"). Turning God's order upside down is inevitable in a society that ignores his law and despises true religion (see 6:12 and note).
5:8–9 As in 4:13, a brief hymn is inserted (see 9:5–6 and notes). Here Amos highlights the contrast between "those who turn" good into bad (v. 7) and the One "who turns" night into day and governs the order of the universe—and whose power can smash the walls his people hide behind.
5:8 *Pleiades.* A group of seven stars (part of the constellation Taurus); always mentioned in connection with Orion (see note on Job 9:9). *midnight into dawn … day into night.* The orderly sequence of day and night (see Ge 8:22; Jer 31:35). *waters of the sea.* The waters above the atmosphere (see 9:6; Ge 1:7; see also notes on Ge 1:6; Ps 36:8; 42:7; 104:3); alternatively, waters evaporated from the sea and condensed as rain. *the LORD is his name.* The middle of three occurrences of this refrain (see 4:13, where the refrain is expanded; 9:6).
5:10 Continues the sentence begun in v. 7. This poetic paragraph is continued and completed in vv. 12b–13, which (in the Hebrew) use the third person, while the preceding passage (vv. 11–12a) uses the second person. The indictment of vv. 7,10,12b–13 is therefore more objective and descriptive, while that of vv. 11–12a is more direct and pointed.
5:11 *levy a straw tax on the poor.* Echoes the initial indictment against Israel (2:7). *though you have built.* God would take away their prized possessions acquired through wrongful gain. Their prosperity would be turned to grief (see the covenant curses in Dt 28:30, 38–40).
5:13 *the prudent.* They know they cannot change the state of affairs, and therefore only await judgment.
5:14 *Seek good.* Cf. "Seek me" (v. 4; see note there; see also Isa 1:16–17 and note on 1:17). *that you may live.* The purpose is more definitely expressed than in vv. 4,6, and the way to change is explicit. *with you.* As your security and source of blessing.
5:15 *Perhaps.* Emphasizes the danger of presuming on God's grace. Even a widespread change of attitude would need the test of time to prove its genuineness. *remnant.* Implies that a change now would benefit the individual survivors of the disaster, though the nation as a whole would perish. *Joseph.* See note on v. 6.
5:16–17 A return to the theme of lament with which this section began (vv. 1–2). *streets … square … farmers … vineyards.* All will be affected by God's punishment. Even farmers, usually too busy for such things, would join the professional mourners in lament, and mourning would overflow from the cities to the vineyards (see Joel 1:5 and note). When the holy God "will pass through" (as he did in Egypt, Ex 12:12), punishment for the unholy and unjust will be inescapable (cf. Isa 6:5).
5:18 *day of the LORD.* The time when God will show himself the victor over the world, vindicating his claims to be the Lord over all the earth (see notes on 8:9; Isa 2:11,17,20; Joel

19 It will be as though a man fled from a lion
only to meet a bear,[g]
as though he entered his house
and rested his hand on the wall
only to have a snake bite him.[h]
20 Will not the day of the LORD be darkness,[i] not light —
pitch-dark, without a ray of brightness?[j]

21 "I hate,[k] I despise your religious festivals;[l]
your assemblies[m] are a stench to me.
22 Even though you bring me burnt offerings[n] and grain offerings,
I will not accept them.[o]
Though you bring choice fellowship offerings,
I will have no regard for them.[p]
23 Away with the noise of your songs!
I will not listen to the music of your harps.[q]
24 But let justice[r] roll on like a river,
righteousness[s] like a never-failing stream![t]

25 "Did you bring me sacrifices[u] and offerings
forty years[v] in the wilderness, people of Israel?
26 You have lifted up the shrine of your king,
the pedestal of your idols,[w]
the star of your god[a] —
which you made for yourselves.
27 Therefore I will send you into exile[x] beyond Damascus,"
says the LORD, whose name is God Almighty.[y]

Woe to the Complacent

6 Woe to you[z] who are complacent[a] in Zion,
and to you who feel secure[b] on Mount Samaria,[c]
you notable men of the foremost nation,
to whom the people of Israel come![d]
2 Go to Kalneh[e] and look at it;
go from there to great Hamath,[f]
and then go down to Gath[g] in Philistia.
Are they better off than[h] your two kingdoms?
Is their land larger than yours?
3 You put off the day of disaster
and bring near a reign of terror.[i]
4 You lie on beds adorned with ivory
and lounge on your couches.[j]
You dine on choice lambs
and fattened calves.[k]
5 You strum away on your harps[l] like David
and improvise on musical instruments.[m]

5:19 [g] S La 3:10 [h] S Dt 32:24; Job 20:24; S Ecc 10:8; Isa 24:17-18; Jer 15:2-3; 48:44 **5:20** [i] S 1Sa 2:9 [j] S Isa 13:10; S Eze 7:7; Ob 1:15; Zep 1:15 **5:21** [k] Jer 44:4 [l] S Lev 26:31; S Hos 2:11 [m] S Eze 23:18 **5:22** [n] Lev 26:31 [o] S Ps 40:6; S Jer 7:21 [p] Isa 1:11-16; S Isa 66:3; Jer 14:12; S Am 4:4; Mic 6:6-7 **5:23** [q] Am 6:5 **5:24** [r] S Jer 22:3 [s] S Isa 45:8 [t] Mic 6:8 **5:25** [u] S Isa 43:23 [v] S Ex 16:35 **5:26** [w] S Eze 18:6; S 20:16 **5:27** [x] Am 6:7; 7:11,17; Mic 1:16 [y] Dt 32:17-19; Jer 38:17; S Am 4:13; Ac 7:42-43* **6:1** [z] Lk 6:24 [a] Zep 1:12 [b] S Job 24:23 [c] S Am 3:9 [d] Isa 32:9-11 **6:2** [e] S Ge 10:10 [f] S 2Ki 17:24; S Jer 49:23 [g] S Jos 11:22; 2Ch 26:6 [h] Na 3:8 **6:3** [i] S Isa 56:12; S Eze 12:22; Am 9:10 **6:4** [j] S Est 1:6; S Pr 7:17 [k] S Isa 1:11; S Eze 34:2-3; S Am 3:12 **6:5** [l] S Ps 137:2; S Isa 14:11; Am 5:23 [m] S 1Ch 15:16

[a] 26 Or *lifted up Sakkuth your king / and Kaiwan your idols, / your star-gods*; Septuagint *lifted up the shrine of Molek / and the star of your god Rephan, / their idols*

1:15). Israel expected to be exalted as his people and longed for that day to come. Amos warned that the day would come, but not as Israel expected — it would be a day of "darkness, not light" (v. 20; see 8:9 and note) for her, because she had not been faithful to God. (Cf. "the day of our Lord Jesus Christ" and variations in 1Co 1:8; 3:12 – 15; 5:5; 2Co 1:14; Php 1:6,10; 2:16.) Amos speaks primarily of an imminent and decisive judgment on Israel, not exclusively of the last day.

5:19 – 20 The two pictures (v. 19) emphasize vividly the inescapability of God's coming judgment.

5:21 – 27 Again God directly addresses Israel with the charge of unfaithfulness.

5:21 – 23 These three verses summarize and reject the current practice of religion in Israel. The institutions were not wrong in themselves; it was the worshipers and the ways they worshiped that were wrong. The people had no basis on which to come to God, because their conduct reflected disobedience to his law (see Isa 1:11 – 15 and note).

5:21 *are a stench to me.* Lit. "I do not inhale with delight."

5:24 *justice ... righteousness.* Prerequisites for acceptance by God (see Mic 6:8 and note); but these are what Israel had rejected and scorned (cf. vv. 7,10,12b). *river ... never-failing stream.* In contrast to stream beds that are dry much of the year (see Jer 15:18 and note). The simile is especially apt: As plant and animal life flourishes where there is water, so human life flourishes where there is justice and righteousness.

5:25 Israel's right relationship with the Lord was never established primarily by sacrifices. It was above all based on obedience (see 1Sa 15:22 and note; cf. Ro 1:5). *forty years in the wilderness.* See Nu 14:32 – 35 and note on 14:34.

5:26 The obscure language of this verse speaks of Israelite idolatry, but whether it was in the wilderness long ago or more recently in the promised land, or both, is not clear. The NIV text note takes two nouns as proper names derived from Akkadian. The Septuagint (the pre-Christian Greek translation of the OT) represents a somewhat different text, which is followed by Ac 7:43.

5:27 This punishment is the final one — exile from the God-given land to remote foreign places.

6:1 *in Zion ... on Mount Samaria.* Although Amos spoke primarily to Israel, Judah and Jerusalem (Zion) also deserved his rebuke (cf. 2:4 – 5), for Israel properly comprised all 12 tribes. *Mount Samaria.* See 4:1; Israel's capital city, founded by King Omri. It was located on an easily defended, lofty hill (see 1Ki 16:24 and note). *foremost nation.* In Israel's self-complacent eyes in this time of her newly recovered power and prosperity (see Introduction: Date and Historical Situation).

6:2 Perhaps Kalneh and Hamath had fallen in Jeroboam II's campaign (see 2Ki 14:25,28 and notes), and the wall of Gath had been broken down by Uzziah (2Ch 26:6). These words may have been spoken by the "people of Israel" (v. 1) who, when they came before their notables, flattered their vanity and thus reinforced their arrogant complacency.

6:3 *day of disaster.* See note on 5:18.

6:4 *lie ... lounge on your couches.* See 3:12 and note. *ivory.* See 3:15 and note.

6:5 *like David.* See 1Sa 16:15 – 23; 2Sa 23:1.

6 You drink wine[n] by the bowlful
and use the finest lotions,
but you do not grieve[o] over the ruin
of Joseph.[p]
7 Therefore you will be among the first
to go into exile;[q]
your feasting and lounging will end.[r]

The LORD Abhors the Pride of Israel

8 The Sovereign LORD has sworn by himself[s]—the LORD God Almighty declares:

"I abhor[t] the pride of Jacob[u]
and detest his fortresses;[v]
I will deliver up[w] the city
and everything in it.[x]"

9 If ten[y] people are left in one house,
they too will die. 10 And if the relative who
comes to carry the bodies out of the house
to burn them[a][z] asks anyone who might be
hiding there, "Is anyone else with you?"
and he says, "No," then he will go on to
say, "Hush![a] We must not mention the
name of the LORD."

11 For the LORD has given the command,
and he will smash[b] the great house[c]
into pieces
and the small house into bits.[d]

12 Do horses run on the rocky crags?
Does one plow the sea[b] with oxen?
But you have turned justice into poison[e]
and the fruit of righteousness[f] into
bitterness[g]—
13 you who rejoice in the conquest of Lo
Debar[c]
and say, "Did we not take Karnaim[d]
by our own strength?[h]"

6:6 [n]S Isa 28:1; S Am 2:8 [o]S Eze 9:4 [p]S Eze 16:49
6:7 [q]S Am 5:27 [r]S Jer 16:9; S La 4:5
6:8 [s]S Ge 22:16; Heb 6:13 [t]S Lev 26:30 [u]S Ps 47:4 [v]S Jer 12:8 [w]Am 4:2 [x]S Lev 26:19; Dt 32:19
6:9 [y]S Am 5:3
6:10 [z]S 1Sa 31:12 [a]Am 8:3
6:11 [b]S Isa 34:5 [c]S Am 3:15 [d]Isa 55:11
6:12 [e]Hos 10:4 [f]S Am 3:10 [g]S Isa 1:21; S Am 5:7
6:13 [h]S Job 8:15; Isa 28:14-15
6:14 [i]Jer 5:15 [j]S Nu 13:21 [k]S Am 3:11
7:1 [l]ver 7; Am 8:1 [m]Ps 78:46; S Jer 51:14; S Joel 1:4
7:2 [n]S Ex 10:15 [o]S Isa 37:4 [p]S Eze 11:13; S Am 4:9
7:3 [q]S Ex 32:14; Dt 32:36; S Jer 18:8; 26:19 [r]S Hos 11:8
7:4 [s]S Isa 66:16; S Joel 1:19 [t]Dt 32:22
7:5 [u]S ver 1-2; Joel 2:17
7:6 [v]S Ex 32:14; S Jer 18:8; Jnh 3:10 [w]Jer 42:10; S Eze 9:8

14 For the LORD God Almighty
declares,
"I will stir up a nation[i] against you,
Israel,
that will oppress you all the way
from Lebo Hamath[j] to the valley of
the Arabah.[k]"

Locusts, Fire and a Plumb Line

7 This is what the Sovereign LORD
showed me:[l] He was preparing swarms
of locusts[m] after the king's share had been
harvested and just as the late crops were
coming up. 2 When they had stripped the
land clean,[n] I cried out, "Sovereign LORD,
forgive! How can Jacob survive?[o] He is so
small![p]"
3 So the LORD relented.[q]
"This will not happen," the LORD said.[r]
4 This is what the Sovereign LORD
showed me: The Sovereign LORD was calling for judgment by fire;[s] it dried up the
great deep and devoured[t] the land. 5 Then
I cried out, "Sovereign LORD, I beg you,
stop! How can Jacob survive? He is so
small![u]"
6 So the LORD relented.[v]
"This will not happen either," the Sovereign LORD said.[w]

7 This is what he showed me: The Lord
was standing by a wall that had been built
true to plumb,[e] with a plumb line[f] in his

[a] 10 Or *to make a funeral fire in honor of the dead* [b] 12 With a different word division of the Hebrew; Masoretic Text *plow there* [c] 13 *Lo Debar* means *nothing.* [d] 13 *Karnaim* means *horns; horn* here symbolizes strength. [e] 7 The meaning of the Hebrew for this phrase is uncertain. [f] 7 The meaning of the Hebrew for this phrase is uncertain; also in verse 8.

6:6 *by the bowlful.* To extravagant and intemperate excess. *Joseph.* See note on 5:6.
6:8 *sworn by himself.* See notes on Ge 22:16; Heb 6:13. By this oath God declares that the verdict is final. *the pride of Jacob.* The strongholds in which the people took pride ("his fortresses"; cf. Eze 32:12 and note). *fortresses.* See note on 1:4.
6:10–11 A fearful scene: Apparently a survivor is cowering inside the house, the relative forbidding him even to pray because God's wrath had fallen on the city.
6:10 *carry the bodies out ... to burn them.* Reference may be to burning a memorial fire in honor of the dead (see Jer 34:5 and note). Cremation was not generally practiced, being reserved primarily for serious offenders (see Ge 38:24; Lev 20:14; 21:9; Jos 7:15,25; 1Sa 31:12 and note).
6:11 *great house ... small house.* Cf. perhaps the "summer house" and "winter house" of 3:15.
6:12 *plow the sea with oxen.* See NIV text note. Israel's perversion of justice flies in the face of even common human wisdom about the right order of things. See 5:7 and note.
6:13 *Lo Debar ... Karnaim.* See NIV text notes for Amos's ironic play on the meanings of these place-names. The towns may have been regained from Hazael by Jehoash (2Ki 10:32–33; 13:25) or by Jeroboam II (see 2Ki 14:25 and note), then taken by the Assyrians soon after Amos's day (2Ki 15:29)—beginning the sequence of events that would lead to the loss of all territory conquered by Jeroboam II.
6:14 *nation.* Assyria. *from Lebo Hamath to the valley of the Arabah.* From the Orontes River in north Lebanon to the Dead Sea—thus the whole land (see 2Ki 14:25).
7:1 *showed me.* Introduces reports of visions that convey God's message through things seen, as well as heard (see vv. 4,7; 8:1; Jer 1:11 and note; cf. Am 9:1). *locusts.* See 4:9; Ex 10:4 and note. *king's share.* Apparently the earlier crop, from which the royal taxes were taken. *late crops.* The growth that came up in the fields after the grains and early hay were harvested. On these the flocks and herds pastured until the summer dry season stopped all growth.
7:2 See v. 5. *How ... survive?* Mass starvation would afflict all the people. *Jacob.* Israel. *so small.* Powerless to withstand the calamity. Amos makes no appeal to the Lord's covenant with Israel—perhaps because Israel's unfaithfulness had removed all right to such an appeal.
7:3 See v. 6. *the LORD relented.* In response to the prophetic intercession (see Ge 20:7)—but forgiveness is not offered.
7:4 *great deep.* Probably the Mediterranean Sea. *land.* Lit. "portion," probably referring to the promised land or, more precisely, to everything growing on the land (cf. Joel 1:19).
7:5 See note on v. 2.
7:6 See note on v. 3.
7:7 Israel is compared to a wall built "true to plumb"—what she should have been, after all the Lord had done for her.

hand. 8 And the LORD asked me, "What do
you see,[x] Amos?[y]"
"A plumb line,[z]" I replied.
Then the Lord said, "Look, I am setting
a plumb line among my people Israel; I
will spare them no longer.[a]

9 "The high places[b] of Isaac will be
destroyed
and the sanctuaries[c] of Israel will be
ruined;
with my sword I will rise against the
house of Jeroboam.[d]"

Amos and Amaziah

10 Then Amaziah the priest of Bethel[e]
sent a message to Jeroboam[f] king of Israel:
"Amos is raising a conspiracy[g] against you
in the very heart of Israel. The land cannot bear all his words.[h] 11 For this is what
Amos is saying:

"'Jeroboam will die by the sword,
and Israel will surely go into exile,[i]
away from their native land.'"[j]

12 Then Amaziah said to Amos, "Get out,
you seer![k] Go back to the land of Judah.
Earn your bread there and do your prophesying there.[l] 13 Don't prophesy anymore
at Bethel,[m] because this is the king's sanctuary and the temple[n] of the kingdom.[o]"
14 Amos answered Amaziah, "I was neither a prophet[p] nor the son of a prophet,
but I was a shepherd, and I also took care
of sycamore-fig trees.[q] 15 But the LORD took
me from tending the flock[r] and said to
me, 'Go,[s] prophesy[t] to my people Israel.'[u]
16 Now then, hear[v] the word of the LORD.
You say,

"'Do not prophesy against[w] Israel,
and stop preaching against the
descendants of Isaac.'

17 "Therefore this is what the LORD says:

"'Your wife will become a prostitute[x]
in the city,
and your sons and daughters will fall
by the sword.
Your land will be measured and
divided up,
and you yourself will die in a pagan[a]
country.
And Israel will surely go into exile,[y]
away from their native land.[z]'"

A Basket of Ripe Fruit

8 This is what the Sovereign LORD
showed me:[a] a basket of ripe fruit.
2 "What do you see,[b] Amos?[c]" he asked.
"A basket[d] of ripe fruit," I answered.
Then the LORD said to me, "The time is

7:8 [x] Jer 1:11, 13 [y] Am 8:2 [z] S 2Ki 21:13 [a] S Jer 15:6; Eze 7:2-9 **7:9** [b] S Lev 26:30 [c] S Lev 26:31 [d] S 1Ki 13:34; 2Ki 15:9; Isa 63:18; S Hos 10:8 **7:10** [e] S Jos 7:2 [f] S 2Ki 14:23 [g] Jer 38:4 [h] 2Ki 14:24; Jer 26:8-11 **7:11** [i] S Am 5:27 [j] Jer 36:16 **7:12** [k] S 1Sa 9:9 [l] Mt 8:34 **7:13** [m] S Jos 7:2; S 1Ki 12:29 [n] Jer 36:5 [o] S Jer 20:2; S Am 2:12; Ac 4:18 **7:14** [p] S 1Sa 10:5; 2Ki 2:5; 4:38; Zec 13:5 [q] S 1Ki 10:27; S Isa 9:10 **7:15** [r] S Ge 37:2; S 2Sa 7:8 [s] S Isa 6:9 [t] S Jer 26:12 [u] Jer 7:1-2; S Eze 2:3-4 **7:16** [v] Jer 22:2 [w] S Eze 20:46; Mic 2:6 **7:17** [x] S Hos 4:13 [y] S Am 5:27 [z] S 2Ki 17:6; S Eze 4:13; S Hos 9:3; Am 2:12-13 **8:1** [a] S Am 7:1 **8:2** [b] Jer 1:13; 24:3 [c] Am 7:8 [d] S Ge 40:16

[a] 17 Hebrew *an unclean*

7:8–9 In vv. 1–6 God proposed wholesale punishments amounting to total destruction, but relented at Amos's prayer—though without promise of forgiveness. Now the Lord is no longer open to such intercession (see Jer 7:16; 15:1 and notes).

7:8 *What do you see . . . ?* See note on Jer 1:11. *plumb line.* God's people had been "built" (v. 7) according to God's standards. They were expected to be true to those standards, but were completely out of plumb when tested (see 2Ki 21:13 and note). *my people.* Here, for the first time in the book of Amos, the Lord calls Israel "my people" (see v. 15; 8:2; 9:10,14; see also note on Ex 17:4). *spare them no longer.* See 8:2; cf. 9:1–4.

7:9 *high places . . . sanctuaries . . . house.* The centers of religious and political pretension and of self-righteous pride would be wiped out. *Isaac.* Israel's (Jacob's) father, a way of referring to Israel found only in Amos (see v. 16). *Jeroboam.* The prophecies of chs. 1–6 were spoken to the leading people of Israel and Samaria as a whole; here Amos names one man, King Jeroboam II.

7:11 Amaziah's words summarize Amos's message (see note on v. 17). *Jeroboam.* That is, his "house" (v. 9), the king's name also representing his dynasty. *will die.* Jeroboam died naturally (2Ki 14:29), but his son and successor Zechariah (2Ki 15:8) was assassinated (2Ki 15:10).

7:12 *seer.* Amaziah dismissed Amos as a prophet for hire whom he need not take seriously. *Go back to . . . Judah . . . and do your prophesying there.* Return to your homeland (see Introduction: Author). You have no business or standing among us.

7:13 *king's sanctuary.* Amaziah served the king in Samaria, not Israel's heavenly King; hence he would not allow a prophetic word to be spoken against Jeroboam or his realm at the royal chapel.

7:14 *neither a prophet nor the son of a prophet.* Amos denied any previous connection with the prophets or their disciples (see note on 1Ki 20:35). No one had hired him to come and announce judgment on Jeroboam and Israel. *shepherd.* See note on 1:1, but the Hebrew uses a different word here—one not found elsewhere in the OT. The Hebrew for this word is, however, related to a word for "cattle," suggesting that Amos may also have tended cattle. *sycamore-fig trees.* They yield fig-like fruit, though smaller than figs and of inferior quality. To ensure good fruit, the gardener had to slit the top of each fig—which may be the procedure referred to by the obscure Hebrew word here rendered "took care of."

7:15 *tending.* Or "following," the Hebrew for which stresses the location of the shepherd rather than his activity. *Go.* Amos was in Bethel because God had sent him to prophesy there.

7:16 *Do not prophesy.* Cf. 2:12.

7:17 Amos turned to condemn the priest personally. *prostitute.* With the exile of Amaziah, the death of his children and the loss of the family estate, Amaziah's wife would be reduced to prostitution to survive. *Your land.* Amaziah's private estate would be "divided up" and given to others. *pagan country.* Where his ceremonial purity as a priest would be defiled (see NIV text note). *And Israel . . . native land.* Amos repeats—verbatim in the Hebrew—the last two lines of Amaziah's earlier summary of Amos's message (v. 11).

8:1 *showed me.* See note on 7:1.

8:2 *What do you see . . . ?* See 7:8 and note. *ripe fruit . . . time is ripe.* A wordplay in Hebrew; Israel was ready to be plucked. *my people.* See 7:8 and note. *spare them no longer.* See 7:8.

ripe for my people Israel; I will spare them
no longer.[e]
3 "In that day," declares the Sovereign
LORD, "the songs in the temple will turn to
wailing.[a][f] Many, many bodies—flung everywhere! Silence![g]"

4 Hear this, you who trample the
needy
and do away with the poor[h] of the
land,[i]

5 saying,

"When will the New Moon[j] be over
that we may sell grain,
and the Sabbath be ended
that we may market[k] wheat?"[l]—
skimping on the measure,
boosting the price
and cheating[m] with dishonest
scales,[n]
6 buying the poor[o] with silver
and the needy for a pair of
sandals,
selling even the sweepings with the
wheat.[p]

7 The LORD has sworn by himself, the
Pride of Jacob:[q] "I will never forget[r] anything they have done.[s]

8 "Will not the land tremble[t] for this,
and all who live in it mourn?
The whole land will rise like the
Nile;
it will be stirred up and then sink
like the river of Egypt.[u]

9 "In that day," declares the Sovereign
LORD,

"I will make the sun go down at noon
and darken the earth in broad
daylight.[v]
10 I will turn your religious festivals[w] into
mourning
and all your singing into
weeping.[x]
I will make all of you wear
sackcloth[y]
and shave[z] your heads.
I will make that time like mourning for
an only son[a]
and the end of it like a bitter day.[b]

11 "The days are coming," declares the
Sovereign LORD,
"when I will send a famine through
the land—
not a famine of food or a thirst for
water,
but a famine[d] of hearing the words
of the LORD.[e]
12 People will stagger from sea to sea
and wander from north to east,
searching for the word of the LORD,
but they will not find it.[f]

13 "In that day

"the lovely young women and strong
young men[g]
will faint because of thirst.[h]
14 Those who swear by the sin of
Samaria[i]—
who say, 'As surely as your god
lives, Dan,'[j]

[a] 3 Or "the temple singers will wail

8:2 [e] S La 4:18; Eze 7:2-9 **8:3** [f] S Am 5:16 [g] Am 6:10 **8:4** [h] S Pr 30:14 [i] S Job 20:19; S Ps 14:4; S Am 2:7 **8:5** [j] S Nu 10:10 [k] Isa 58:13 [l] S Ne 10:31 [m] S Ge 31:7 [n] Dt 25:15; 2Ki 4:23; Ne 13:15-16; Eze 45:10-12; S Hos 12:7; Mic 6:10-11; Zec 5:6 **8:6** [o] Am 5:11 [p] S Am 2:6; S 4:1 **8:7** [q] S Ps 47:4 [r] S Hos 8:13 [s] S Job 35:15 **8:8** [t] S Job 9:6; Jer 51:29 [u] Ps 18:7; S Jer 46:8; Am 9:5 **8:9** [v] S Job 5:14; Isa 59:9-10; Jer 13:16; 15:9; S Eze 32:7; S Am 5:8; Mic 3:6; Mt 27:45; Mk 15:33; Lk 23:44-45 **8:10** [w] S Lev 26:31 [x] S La 5:15; S Hos 2:11 [y] S Joel 1:8 [z] S Lev 13:40; S Isa 3:17 [a] S Ge 21:16 [b] S Jer 2:19; S Eze 7:18 **8:11** [c] Jer 30:3; 31:27 [d] S Isa 30:20 [e] S 1Sa 3:1; S 28:6; S 2Ch 15:3 **8:12** [f] S Eze 20:3,31 **8:13** [g] S Isa 9:17 [h] Isa 41:17; Hos 2:3 **8:14** [i] Mic 1:5 [j] S 1Ki 12:29

8:3 *that day.* See 5:18 and note. *wailing ... Silence!* There would be no thanksgiving songs for this harvest (contrast Lev 23:39–41)—only silence in the face of divine judgment (see note on Hab 2:20).
8:4 *Hear this.* See 3:1 and note. *trample.* See 5:11 and note.
8:5 *New Moon ... Sabbath.* The official religious festivals, when commerce ceased (see Nu 28:9–15; 2Ki 4:23 and note). *skimping on the measure, boosting the price ... dishonest scales.* See Lev 19:35; Pr 11:1 and notes; Hos 12:7.
8:6 See note on 2:6.
8:7 *The LORD has sworn by himself, the Pride of Jacob.* In ironic fashion, Amos echoes the phrase "pride of Jacob" in 6:8, where it refers not to God (as here) but to the fortresses of Israel.
8:8 See 9:5. *rise like the Nile.* Because of the heavy seasonal rains in Ethiopia, the Nile in Egypt annually rose by as much as 25 feet, flooding the whole valley except for the towns and villages standing above it. Its waters carried a large amount of rich soil, which was deposited on the land—perhaps referred to by the words "stirred up."
8:9 *that day.* See 5:18 and note. *darken the earth.* As elsewhere, the "day of the LORD" is described as one in which the cosmic (world) order is disrupted and light is turned to darkness (see 5:18,20; Isa 13:10; 24:23; 34:4; 50:3; Eze 32:7–8; Joel 2:2,10,31 and note on 2:2; Mic 3:6; Zep 1:15; Rev 6:12), as if creation is being undone (see Jer 4:23 and note).
8:10 *mourning.* Illustrated by King David (2Sa 18:33). *wear sackcloth ... shave your heads.* Signs of mourning (see Ge 37:34; Isa 15:2–3 and notes). *only son.* On whose life the future of the family depended (cf. 2Sa 18:18; Zec 12:10). *bitter day.* The opposite of the "day of celebration" (Est 9:22).
8:11 *days.* When God's judgment begins to take effect. *famine of hearing the words of the LORD.* In times of great distress Israel turned to the Lord for a prophetic word of hope or guidance (see, e.g., 2Ki 19:1–4,14–15; 22:13–14; Jer 21:1–2; Eze 14:7), but in the coming judgment the Lord will answer all such appeals with silence—the awful silence of God (see Eze 7:26 and note; 20:1–3; Mic 3:4,7).
8:12 *sea to sea ... north to east.* Throughout the land of Israel, from the Mediterranean to the Dead Sea, even to the Transjordan.
8:13 *thirst.* Both physical and spiritual. Their strength sapped, even the "lovely young women and strong young men" of the nation would faint and fall useless.
8:14 *Those who swear.* By the gods of their various religious centers—the false gods in which they trusted rather than in the Lord. *Samaria.* See note on 6:1. *Dan ... Beersheba.* Cities that not only marked the northern and southern limits of Israel (see note on Jdg 20:1) but also were noted as sites where pagan shrines had been built (see 5:5; 1Ki 12:29 and notes).

or, 'As surely as the god[a] of
Beersheba[k] lives' —
they will fall,[l] never to rise again.[m]"

Israel to Be Destroyed

9 I saw the Lord standing by the altar,
and he said:

"Strike the tops of the pillars
so that the thresholds shake.
Bring them down on the heads[n] of all
the people;
those who are left I will kill with the
sword.
Not one will get away,
none will escape.[o]
2 Though they dig down to the depths
below,[p]
from there my hand will take them.
Though they climb up to the heavens
above,[q]
from there I will bring them down.[r]
3 Though they hide themselves on the
top of Carmel,[s]
there I will hunt them down and
seize them.[t]
Though they hide from my eyes at the
bottom of the sea,[u]
there I will command the serpent[v] to
bite them.[w]
4 Though they are driven into exile by
their enemies,
there I will command the sword[x] to
slay them.

"I will keep my eye on them
for harm[y] and not for good.[z]"[a]

5 The Lord, the LORD Almighty —
he touches the earth and it melts,[b]
and all who live in it mourn;
the whole land rises like the Nile,
then sinks like the river of Egypt;[c]
6 he builds his lofty palace[b][d] in the
heavens
and sets its foundation[c] on the
earth;
he calls for the waters of the sea
and pours them out over the face of
the land —
the LORD is his name.[e]

7 "Are not you Israelites
the same to me as the Cushites[d]?"[f]
declares the LORD.
"Did I not bring Israel up from
Egypt,
the Philistines[g] from Caphtor[e][h]
and the Arameans from Kir?[i]

8 "Surely the eyes of the Sovereign LORD
are on the sinful kingdom.
I will destroy[j] it
from the face of the earth.
Yet I will not totally destroy
the descendants of Jacob,"
declares the LORD.[k]
9 "For I will give the command,
and I will shake the people of Israel
among all the nations
as grain[l] is shaken in a sieve,[m]
and not a pebble will reach the
ground.[n]
10 All the sinners among my people
will die by the sword,[o]
all those who say,
'Disaster will not overtake or meet
us.'[p]

8:14 [k]S Am 5:5 [l]S Ps 46:2 [m]S Am 5:2 **9:1** [n]Ps 68:21 [o]Jer 11:11 **9:2** [p]S Job 7:9; S Eze 26:20 [q]Jer 51:53 [r]Ob 1:4 **9:3** [s]Am 1:2 [t]Ps 139:8-10 [u]Ps 68:22 [v]Isa 27:1 [w]S Ge 49:17; S Job 11:20; Jer 16:16-17 **9:4** [x]S Lev 26:33; S Eze 5:12 [y]S Jer 21:10 [z]Jer 39:16; S Eze 15:7 [a]S Jer 44:11 **9:5** [b]S Ps 46:2 [c]S Am 8:8 **9:6** [d]Jer 43:9 [e]Ps 104:1-3,5-6,13; S Am 5:8 **9:7** [f]S 2Ch 12:3; Isa 20:4; 43:3 [g]S Ge 10:14 [h]S Dt 2:23 [i]S 2Ki 16:9; S Isa 22:6; S Am 2:10 **9:8** [j]S Jer 4:27 [k]S Jer 44:27 **9:9** [l]Lk 22:31 [m]Isa 30:28 [n]S Jer 31:36; S Da 9:7 **9:10** [o]Jer 49:37 [p]Jer 5:12; S 23:17; S Eze 20:38; S Am 6:3

[a] *14* Hebrew *the way* [b] *6* The meaning of the Hebrew for this phrase is uncertain. [c] *6* The meaning of the Hebrew for this word is uncertain. [d] *7* That is, people from the upper Nile region [e] *7* That is, Crete

9:1 *I saw the Lord.* See note on 7:1. God is now poised on earth. *by the altar.* God is about to initiate the destruction from the very place from which the people expect to hear a word of peace and blessing. *tops of the pillars.* God will shatter the temple completely, from the decorated capitals down to the heavy stone "thresholds." The next lines depict the destruction. *Not one ... will escape.* See note on 7:8.
9:2–4 See note on 7:8. These verses emphasize the impossibility of escape from God's impending judgment. The imaginary extremes to which a person might go may be compared with those in Ps 139:7–12 (see note there). God's domain includes every place, even the realm of the grave (v. 2).
9:3 *top of Carmel.* See note on 1:2. *serpent.* In pagan mythology, the fierce monster of the sea (see Ps 74:13–14 and note). If some of "the people" (v. 1) should seek to escape by hiding in the depths, they could still not evade God, for even there all are subject to him.
9:4 *driven ... by their enemies ... I will command.* Even those dispersed among the nations will not escape God's judgment. *I will keep my eye ... for harm.* Contrast Ps 33:18–19; 34:15.
9:5 *The Lord ... he touches.* Introduces a hymnic reminder that Israel's God is the Creator and Sustainer of the universe, thus underlining the pronouncements of the previous verses (see 4:13; 5:8–9 and notes). *earth ... melts.* See note on Ps 46:6. *rises like the Nile.* See 8:8 and note.
9:6 *his lofty palace.* Contrasts the scale of God with the scale of human beings, whose structures fall at the movement of the earth (v. 5). See Ps 104:3 and note. *waters of the sea.* See 5:8 and note.
9:7 *Cushites.* A dark-skinned people who lived south of Egypt (see Jer 13:23 and NIV text note there). *Did I not bring Israel up ... ?* See note on Ex 20:2. Israel could not rely on God's past blessings as an assurance of his future benevolence. Her stubborn rebelliousness robbed the exodus of all special meaning for her; her journey from Egypt is reduced to no more significance than the movements of other peoples. *Philistines from Caphtor.* See note on Jer 47:4. *Kir.* See note on 1:5.
9:8 *sinful kingdom.* Israel, the chosen, whose disobedience was far worse than the sins of other nations (see 1:3—2:16; 3:1–2 and note on 3:2). *Yet I will not totally destroy.* See note on v. 11.
9:9 *sieve.* Separates the wheat from small stones and other refuse gathered with it when scooped up from the ground. *not a pebble will reach.* Only the grain drops through, the refuse being screened out to be discarded.
9:10 *All the sinners ... will die.* For their persistent rebellion. *my people.* See 7:8 and note.

Israel's Restoration

11 "In that day

"I will restore David's[q] fallen
shelter[r] —
I will repair its broken walls
and restore its ruins[s] —
and will rebuild it as it used to be,[t]
12 so that they may possess the remnant
of Edom[u]
and all the nations that bear my
name,[av]"
declares the LORD,
who will do these things.[w]

13 "The days are coming,"[x] declares the
LORD,

"when the reaper[y] will be overtaken by
the plowman[z]
and the planter by the one treading[a]
grapes.
New wine[b] will drip from the mountains
and flow from all the hills,[c]
14 and I will bring[d] my people Israel
back from exile.[be]

"They will rebuild the ruined cities[f]
and live in them.
They will plant vineyards[g] and drink
their wine;
they will make gardens and eat their
fruit.[h]
15 I will plant[i] Israel in their own land,[j]
never again to be uprooted[k]
from the land I have given them,"[l]

says the LORD your God.[m]

[a] 12 Hebrew; Septuagint *so that the remnant of people / and all the nations that bear my name may seek me*
[b] 14 Or *will restore the fortunes of my people Israel*

9:11 [q] S Isa 7:2 [r] S Ge 26:22 [s] Ps 53:6; S Isa 49:8 [t] Ps 80:12; S Eze 17:24; Mic 7:8,11; Zec 12:7; 14:10 **9:12** [u] S Nu 24:18 [v] Isa 43:7; Jer 25:29 [w] Ac 15:16-17* **9:13** [x] Jer 31:38; 33:14 [y] S Ru 2:3 [z] Lev 26:5 [a] S Jdg 9:27 [b] S Joel 2:24 [c] S Joel 3:18 **9:14** [d] S Jer 29:14 [e] S Jer 33:7 [f] S Isa 32:18; S 49:8; S 61:4 [g] S 2Ki 19:29 [h] S Isa 62:9; S Jer 30:18; S 31:28; Eze 28:25-26; S 34:13-14; S Am 5:11 **9:15** [i] S Ex 15:17; S Isa 60:21 [j] S Jer 23:8 [k] S Joel 3:20 [l] S Isa 65:9; S Jer 3:18; Ob 1:17 [m] S Jer 18:9; S 24:6; S 32:15; S Eze 28:26; S 34:25-28; S 37:12,25

9:11–12 Quoted in Ac 15:16–17 (see note on Ac 15:16).

9:11 The verse is also regarded as Messianic in the Jewish Talmud. *I will restore.* Raises a hope underlying Amos's words—one that runs through the whole OT from Ge 3:15 on: God will bring blessing after judgment and will not ultimately reject Israel. *shelter.* See Isa 1:8; 4:6. While unfaithful Israel sometimes looked to Egypt for protection (see Isa 30:2 and note), faithful Israel always looked to the Lord for shelter (see Ps 91:1; cf. Ps 17:8 and note). They also looked to the Lord's anointed king from the house of David to provide the shade (protection) in which they would live safely among the nations (see La 4:20 and note). That protective "shelter" had now "fallen," but it would be restored. *as it used to be.* In the days of David and Solomon.

9:12 *remnant of Edom.* Whatever is left of Israel's bitter enemy (see note on 1:11) after her punishment. *all the nations that bear my name.* Refers to the extent of the rule of the Lord's anointed future King, recalling that David had reigned over many nations surrounding Israel. It represents the fulfillment of the Abrahamic and Davidic covenants. The Messiah will reign even over former enemies, of whom Edom is symbolic (see notes on Isa 34:5; Joel 3:19; Ob 8). *will do these things.* God does what he says.

9:13–15 After all the forecasts of destruction, dearth and death (see, e.g., 5:9,11,27), Amos's final words picture a glorious Edenic prosperity, when the seasons will run together so that sowing and reaping are without interval, and there will be a continuous supply of fresh produce—a reversal of the conditions portrayed in 4:6–11 (see notes there).

9:13 See Joel 3:18 and note.

9:14–15 *I will bring … They will rebuild … They will plant … I will plant.* In the promised land God will make his people productive, fruitful and secure.

9:14 *my people.* See note on 7:8; contrast Hos 1:9, but see Hos 2:23. *rebuild the ruined cities.* See Isa 58:12 and note.

9:15 *never again.* When Israel is finally and fully restored, she will never again be destroyed. *your God.* Contrast Hos 1:9, but see Hos 2:23.

OBADIAH

INTRODUCTION

Author

The author's name is Obadiah, which means "servant (or worshiper) of the LORD." His was a common name (see 1Ki 18:3 – 16; 1Ch 3:21; 7:3; 8:38; 9:16; 12:9; 27:19; 2Ch 17:7; 34:12; Ezr 8:9; Ne 10:5; 12:25). Neither his father's name nor the place of his birth is given.

Date and Place of Writing

The date and place of composition are disputed. Dating the prophecy is mainly a matter of relating vv. 11 – 14 to one of two specific events in Israel's history:

(1) The rebellion of Edom against Judah during the reign of Jehoram (853 – 841 BC); see 2Ki 8:20 – 22; 2Ch 21:8 – 15. In this case, Obadiah would be a contemporary of Elisha.

(2) The Babylonian attacks on Jerusalem (605 – 586). Obadiah would then be a contemporary of Jeremiah. This alternative seems more likely.

The striking parallels between Ob 1 – 6 and Jer 49:9 – 10, 14 – 16 have caused many to suggest some kind of interdependence between Obadiah and Jeremiah, but it may be that both prophets were drawing on a common source not otherwise known to us.

Unity and Theme

There is no compelling reason to doubt the unity of this brief prophecy, the shortest book in the OT. Its theme is that Edom, proud over her own security, has gloated over Israel's devastation by foreign powers. However, Edom's participation in that disaster will bring on God's wrath. She herself will be destroyed, but Mount Zion and Israel will be delivered and God's kingdom will triumph.

Edom's hostile activities have spanned the centuries of Israel's existence. The following Biblical references are helpful in understanding the relation of Israel and Edom: Ge 27:41 – 45;

a **quick** look

Author:
Obadiah

Audience:
The people of Judah suffering the treachery of the Edomites, descendants of Esau

Date:
Probably the time of the Babylonian attacks on Jerusalem (605 – 586 BC)

Theme:
Obadiah prophesies judgment against the proud Edomites, who are gloating over Jerusalem's devastation by foreign powers.

Edom will be destroyed, but Israel and Mount Zion will be delivered and God's kingdom will triumph.

32:1 – 21; 33; 36; Ex 15:15; Nu 20:14 – 21; Dt 2:1 – 6; 23:7 – 8; 1Sa 22 with Ps 52; 2Sa 8:13 – 14; 2Ki 8:20 – 22; 14:7; Ps 83; Eze 35; Joel 3:18 – 19; Am 1:11 – 12; 9:11 – 12.

Since the Edomites are related to the Israelites (v. 10), their hostility is all the more reprehensible. Edom is fully responsible for her failure to assist Israel and for her open aggression. The fact that God rejected Esau (Ge 25:23; Mal 1:3; Ro 9:13) in no way exonerates the Edomites. Edom, smug in its mountain strongholds, will be dislodged and sacked. But Israel will prosper because God is with her.

View of the mountains of Edom, southeast of the Dead Sea. Obadiah prophesied the coming destruction of Edom.

Todd Bolen/www.BiblePlaces.com

Outline

I. Title and Introduction (1)
II. Judgment on Edom (2 – 14)
  A. Edom's Destruction Announced (2 – 7)
    1. The humbling of her pride (2 – 4)
    2. The completeness of her destruction (5 – 7)
  B. Edom's Destruction Reaffirmed (8 – 14)
    1. Her shame and destruction (8 – 10)
    2. Her crimes against Israel (11 – 14)
III. The Day of the Lord (15 – 21)
  A. Judgment on the Nations but Deliverance for Zion (15 – 18)
  B. The Lord's Kingdom Established (19 – 21)

Obadiah's Vision

1-4pp — Jer 49:14-16
5-6pp — Jer 49:9-10

1 The vision[a] of Obadiah.

This is what the Sovereign LORD says about Edom[b] —

We have heard a message from the LORD:
An envoy[c] was sent to the nations to say,
"Rise, let us go against her for battle"[d] —

2 "See, I will make you small[e] among the nations;
you will be utterly despised.
3 The pride[f] of your heart has deceived you,
you who live in the clefts of the rocks[a][g]
and make your home on the heights,
you who say to yourself,
'Who can bring me down to the ground?'[h]
4 Though you soar like the eagle
and make your nest[i] among the stars,
from there I will bring you down,"[j]
declares the LORD.[k]
5 "If thieves came to you,
if robbers in the night —
oh, what a disaster awaits you! —
would they not steal only as much as they wanted?
If grape pickers came to you,
would they not leave a few grapes?[l]
6 But how Esau will be ransacked,
his hidden treasures pillaged!
7 All your allies[m] will force you to the border;
your friends will deceive and overpower you;
those who eat your bread[n] will set a trap for you,[b]
but you will not detect it.

8 "In that day," declares the LORD,
"will I not destroy[o] the wise men of Edom,
those of understanding in the mountains of Esau?
9 Your warriors, Teman,[p] will be terrified,
and everyone in Esau's mountains
will be cut down in the slaughter.
10 Because of the violence[q] against your brother Jacob,[r]
you will be covered with shame;
you will be destroyed forever.[s]
11 On the day you stood aloof
while strangers carried off his wealth
and foreigners entered his gates
and cast lots[t] for Jerusalem,
you were like one of them.[u]
12 You should not gloat[v] over your brother
in the day of his misfortune,[w]
nor rejoice[x] over the people of Judah
in the day of their destruction,[y]

[a] 3 Or *of Sela* [b] 7 The meaning of the Hebrew for this clause is uncertain.

1 [a]S Isa 1:1 [b]S Ge 25:14; S Isa 11:14; S 34:11; 63:1-6; Jer 49:7-22; S Eze 25:12-14; S 32:29; S Am 1:11-12 [c]Isa 18:2 [d]Jer 6:4-5 **2** [e]Nu 24:18 **3** [f]S Isa 16:6 [g]*fn* Isa 16:1 [h]S 2Ch 25:11-12 **4** [i]S Isa 10:14 [j]S Isa 14:13 [k]S Job 20:6 **5** [l]S Dt 4:27; 24:21; S Isa 24:13 **7** [m]Jer 30:14 [n]S Ps 41:9 **8** [o]Job 5:12; Isa 29:14 **9** [p]S Ge 36:11, 34 **10** [q]S Joel 3:19 [r]Ps 137:7; Am 1:11-12 [s]S Ps 137:7; S Eze 25:12-14; 35:9 **11** [t]S Job 6:27; S Eze 24:6 [u]S Am 1:6 **12** [v]Pr 24:17 [w]S Job 31:29 [x]S Eze 35:15 [y]S Pr 17:5

1–4 Paralleled in Jer 49:14–16.
1 *vision.* Commonly used in the OT to designate a revelation from God (see Pr 29:18; Isa 1:1 and notes). *Obadiah.* See Introduction: Author. *We.* Either (1) the editorial "we," (2) the prophet's association of Israel with himself or (3) other prophets' pronouncements against Edom. In any case, the rest of the verse sets the stage for Obadiah's prophetic message, which begins with v. 2. *message.* Or "report." An envoy had been sent to the nations, calling them to battle against Edom. Perhaps a conspiracy was under way among some of Edom's allies (v. 7). Although Edom feels secure (trusting in her mountain fortresses and her wise men, vv. 2–4,8–9), Obadiah announces God's judgment on her for her hostility to Israel.
2 *I will make you small.* Cf. the colloquial expression "cut one down to size."
3 *pride.* See v. 12; Jer 49:16 and note. *rocks.* See NIV text note. Sela was the capital of Edom. Perhaps the later Petra (both Sela and Petra mean "rock" or "cliff"), this rugged site is located some 50 miles south of the southern end of the Dead Sea (see note on Isa 16:1).
4 *eagle.* A proud and regal bird, noted for strength, keenness of vision and power of flight (see Dt 28:49; Isa 40:31; Jer 4:13; 49:22; Eze 17:3). *stars.* Hyperbole for high, inaccessible places in the mountains. See photo, p. 1487.
5–6 Paralleled in Jer 49:9–10.
5 *leave a few grapes.* See Jer 49:9 and note.
6 *hidden treasures.* The ancient Greek historian Diodorus Siculus indicates that the Edomites put their wealth — accumulated from trade — in vaults in the rocks.
7 *eat your bread.* See Ps 41:9 and note. *set a trap for you.* However the Hebrew for this expression is understood (see NIV text note), it must indicate some act of treachery on the part of previously trusted close friends.
8 *In that day.* The day of Edom's destruction; but the words also have an eschatological ring (see v. 15 and note). Since in OT prophecy Edom was often emblematic of all the world powers hostile to God and his kingdom, her judgment anticipates God's complete removal of all such opposition in that day (see note on Am 9:12). *wise men.* In whom Edom put so much confidence for her security (see Jer 49:7 and note). Eliphaz, one of Job's three friends, was a Temanite (see note on v. 9). *Esau.* Another name for Edom (see Ge 36:1 and note).
9 *Teman.* A reference to all Edom, as in Jer 49:7,20 (see notes on Jer 49:7; Am 1:12). Teman means "south," and the name probably refers to Edom as the southland. Some, however, identify Teman with Tawilan, a site about three miles east of Petra.
10 *your brother Jacob.* Edom's violent crimes are all the more reprehensible because they were committed against the brother nation. *covered with shame.* A striking expression, since shame is usually associated with nakedness.
11 See Introduction: Date and Place of Writing. *strangers ... foreigners.* These terms put in relief the sin of Edom: He did not act like a brother (v. 12) but was like one of the strangers. *cast lots for Jerusalem.* See Eze 24:6 and note.
12–14 A rebuke of Edom's hostile actions. The eight rebukes in this section proceed from the general to the particular. See Ps 137:7; Eze 35:13 for examples of Edom's reactions to Judah's misfortunes (see also note on Ps 137:7).
12 *boast.* See v. 3; Jer 49:16 and note.

nor boast[z] so much
in the day of their trouble.[a]
13 You should not march through the gates of my people
in the day of their disaster,
nor gloat over them in their calamity[b]
in the day of their disaster,
nor seize their wealth
in the day of their disaster.
14 You should not wait at the crossroads
to cut down their fugitives,[c]
nor hand over their survivors
in the day of their trouble.

15 "The day of the LORD is near[d]
for all nations.
As you have done, it will be done to you;
your deeds[e] will return upon your own head.
16 Just as you drank[f] on my holy hill,[g]
so all the nations will drink[h] continually;
they will drink and drink
and be as if they had never been.[i]
17 But on Mount Zion will be deliverance;[j]
it will be holy,[k]
and Jacob will possess his inheritance.[l]
18 Jacob will be a fire
and Joseph a flame;
Esau will be stubble,
and they will set him on fire[m] and destroy[n] him.
There will be no survivors[o]
from Esau."
The LORD has spoken.

19 People from the Negev will occupy
the mountains of Esau,
and people from the foothills will possess
the land of the Philistines.[p]
They will occupy the fields of Ephraim
and Samaria,[q]
and Benjamin[r] will possess Gilead.
20 This company of Israelite exiles who are in Canaan
will possess the land as far as Zarephath;[s]
the exiles from Jerusalem who are in Sepharad
will possess the towns of the Negev.[t]
21 Deliverers[u] will go up on[a] Mount Zion
to govern the mountains of Esau.
And the kingdom will be the LORD's.[v]

12 [z] Ps 137:7 [a] S Eze 25:6; Mic 4:11; 7:8 **13** [b] S Eze 35:5 **14** [c] S 1Ki 18:4 **15** [d] S Jer 46:10; S Eze 30:3; S Joel 2:31; S Am 5:18 [e] S Jer 50:29; Hab 2:8 **16** [f] Isa 51:17 [g] S Ex 15:17 [h] Jer 25:15; 49:12; S La 4:21-22 [i] S La 4:21; S Eze 25:12-14 **17** [j] S Ps 69:35; S Isa 14:1-2; Joel 2:32; S Am 9:11-15 [k] S Ps 74:2; S Isa 4:3 [l] Zec 8:12
18 [m] S Isa 1:31 [n] Zec 12:6 [o] S Jer 49:10 **19** [p] Isa 11:14 [q] S Jer 31:5 [r] S Nu 1:36 **20** [s] 1Ki 17:9-10; Lk 4:26 [t] S Jer 33:13 **21** [u] S Dt 28:29; S Jdg 3:9 [v] S Ps 22:28; 47:9; 66:4; S Da 2:44; Zec 14:9, 16; Mal 1:14; Rev 11:15

[a] 21 Or *from*

15 *The day of the LORD is near for all nations.* If there was an eschatological glimmering in "In that day" (v. 8), it here becomes a strong ray. The day of the Lord brings judgment for the nations (including, but not limited to, Edom) and salvation for the house of Jacob (see v. 17; Joel 1:15; Am 5:18 and notes). *return upon your own head.* The situation will be reversed in retribution for Edom's hostility against God's people, detailed in vv. 11–14. Ezekiel's denunciation of Edom (ch. 35) reflects a similar punishment-fits-the-crime principle (see also Pr 26:27; Eze 16:43).

16 *Just as you drank.* As the Edomites profaned the holy mountain by carousing, so the nations "will drink and drink." Their drinking, however, is that of the bitter potion of God's judgment—which they will be compelled to keep on drinking. For drinking as punishment, see Jer 25:15–16; 49:12 and notes.

17 *But on Mount Zion will be deliverance.* Beginning with this verse the blessings on the house of Jacob are mentioned. Eschatological references are twofold: judgment on God's enemies, blessing on God's people. *inheritance.* The land that God had promised them (see Jer 3:19; 12:7 and notes).

18 *Jacob ... Joseph.* Previously it was stated that the Lord would destroy Edom, using other nations (v. 7); now it is to be done by God's people. *no survivors.* The final word to Esau is that his house (or nation) will be totally destroyed; there will be no Edomite survivors. Yet compare Am 9:12 with Ac 15:17, and see note and NIV text note on Am 9:12.

19 *People ... will occupy.* With Edom annihilated, others will occupy Edomite territory. Although not expressly identified, these are most likely the remnant of Israel referred to in the lines immediately following. *Negev.* See note on Ge 12:9. *foothills.* See note on Mic 1:10–15. *Philistines.* See note on Ge 10:14. *Gilead.* See notes on Ge 31:21; SS 4:1.

20 *Zarephath.* See note on 1Ki 17:9. *Sepharad.* Usually taken to refer to Sardis in Asia Minor (present-day Turkey), though some think that Sparta (the city in Greece) might be meant.

21 *Deliverers.* Having developed the theme of possessing lands around Zion, the prophet now turns to the center. The "deliverers" come from Mount Zion and rule over the mountains of Esau. Mount Zion is exalted over the mountains of Esau. The Messiah, the Deliverer par excellence, may ultimately be in view. *the kingdom will be the LORD's.* The conclusion of the prophecy—and the final outcome of history. The last book of the Bible echoes this theme (Rev 11:15).

JONAH

INTRODUCTION

Title

The book is named after its principal character, whose name means "dove"; see the simile used of Ephraim in Hos 7:11 to portray the northern kingdom as "easily deceived and senseless." See also Ps 68:13; 74:19 and notes.

Authorship and Date

Though the book does not identify its author, tradition has ascribed it to the prophet himself, Jonah, son of Amittai (1:1), from Gath Hepher (2Ki 14:25; see note there) in Zebulun (Jos 19:10,13). In view of its many similarities with the narratives about Elijah and Elisha, however, it may come from the same prophetic circles that originally composed the accounts about those prophets, perhaps in the eighth century BC (see Introduction to 1 Kings: Author, Sources and Date).

For a number of reasons, including the preaching to Gentiles, the book is often assigned a postexilic date. At least, it is said, the book must have been written after the destruction of Nineveh in 612 BC. But these considerations are not decisive. The similarity of this narrative to the Elijah-Elisha accounts has already been noted. One may also question whether mention of the repentance of Nineveh and the consequent averted destruction of the city would have had so much significance to the author after Nineveh's overthrow. And to suppose that proclaiming God's word to Gentiles had no relevance in the eighth century is to overlook the fact that already in the previous century Elijah and Elisha had extended their ministries to foreign lands (1Ki 17:7–24; 2Ki 8:7–15). Moreover, the prophet Amos (c. 760–750) set God's redemptive work in behalf of Israel in the context of his dealings with the nations (Am 1:3—2:16; 9:7,12). Perhaps the third quarter of the eighth century is the

Author:
Unknown

Audience:
The northern kingdom of Israel

Date:
Jonah prophesied during the reign of Jeroboam II (793–753 BC); the date of the writing of the book was perhaps between 750 and 725.

Theme:
In this story of God's loving concern for all people, the stubbornly reluctant Jonah represents Israel's jealousy of her favored relationship with God and her unwillingness to share the Lord's compassion with the nations.

most likely date for the book, after the public ministries of Amos and Hosea and before the fall of Samaria to Assyria in 722–721.

Background

In the half century during which the prophet Jonah ministered (800–750 BC), a significant event affected the northern kingdom of Israel: King Jeroboam II (793–753) restored her traditional borders, ending almost a century of sporadic, seesaw conflict between Israel and Damascus.

Jeroboam, in God's good providence (2Ki 14:26–27), capitalized on Assyria's defeat of Damascus (in the latter half of the ninth century), which temporarily crushed that center of Aramean power. Prior to that time, not only had Israel been considerably reduced in size but the king of Damascus had even been able to control internal affairs in the northern kingdom (2Ki 13:7). However, after the Assyrian campaign against Damascus in 797, Jehoash, king of Israel, had been able to recover the territory lost to the king of Damascus (2Ki 13:25). Internal troubles in Assyria subsequently allowed Jeroboam to complete the restoration of Israel's northern borders. Nevertheless, Assyria remained the real threat from the north at this time.

Marble sarcophagus (c. AD 300) with scenes from the life of Jonah
Kim Walton, courtesy of the British Museum

The prophets of the Lord were speaking to Israel regarding these events. About 797 BC Elisha spoke to the king of Israel concerning future victories over Damascus (2Ki 13:14–19). A few years later Jonah prophesied the restoration that Jeroboam accomplished (2Ki 14:25). But soon after Israel had triumphed, she began to gloat over her newfound power. Because she was relieved of foreign pressures — relief that had come in accordance with encouraging words from Elisha and Jonah — she felt jealously complacent about her favored status with God (Am 6:1). She focused her religion on expectations of the "day of the LORD" (Am 5:18–20), when God's darkness would engulf the other nations, leaving Israel to bask in his light.

It was in such a time that the Lord sent Amos and Hosea to announce to his people Israel that he would "spare them no longer" (Am 7:8; 8:2) but would send them into exile "beyond Damascus" (Am 5:27), i.e., to Assyria (Hos 9:3; 10:6; 11:5). During this time the Lord also sent Jonah to Nineveh to warn it of the imminent danger of divine judgment.

Interpretation

Many have questioned whether the book of Jonah is historical. The supposed legendary character of some of the events (e.g., the episode involving the great fish) has caused them to suggest alternatives to the traditional view that the book is historical, biographical narrative. Although their specific suggestions range from fictional short story to allegory to parable, they share the common assumption that the account sprang essentially from the author's imagination, despite its serious and gracious message.

Such interpretations, often based in part on doubt about the miraculous as such, too quickly dismiss (1) the similarities between the narrative of Jonah and other parts of the OT and (2) the pervasive concern of the OT writers, especially the prophets, for history. They also fail to realize that OT narrators had a keen ear for recognizing how certain past events in Israel's pilgrimage with God illumine (by way of analogy) later events. (For example, the events surrounding the birth of Moses illumine the exodus, those surrounding Samuel's birth illumine the series of events narrated in the books of Samuel, and the ministries of Moses and Joshua illumine those of Elijah and Elisha.) Similarly, the prophets recognized that the future events they announced could be illumined by reference to analogous events of the past. Overlooking these features in OT narrative and prophecy, many have supposed that a story that too neatly fits the author's purpose must therefore be fictional.

On the other hand, it must be acknowledged that Biblical narrators were more than historians. They interpretatively recounted the past with the unswerving purpose of bringing it to bear on the present and the future. In the portrayal of past events, they used their materials to achieve this purpose effectively. Nonetheless, the integrity with which they treated the past ought not to be questioned. The book of Jonah recounts real events in the life and ministry of the prophet himself.

Model of a Philistine ship — similar to what Jonah may have boarded in Joppa

Z. Radovan/www.BibleLandPictures.com

> The book depicts the larger scope of God's purpose for Israel: that she might rediscover the truth of his concern for the whole creation and that she might better understand her own role in carrying out that concern.

Literary Characteristics

Unlike most other prophetic parts of the OT, this book is a narrative account of a single prophetic mission. Its treatment of that mission is thus similar to the accounts of the ministries of Elijah and Elisha found in 1,2 Kings and to certain narrative sections of Isaiah, Jeremiah and Ezekiel.

As is often the case in Biblical narratives, the author has compressed much into a small space; 40 verses tell the entire story (eight additional verses of poetry are devoted to Jonah's prayer of thanksgiving). In its scope (a single extended episode), compactness, vividness and character delineation, it is much like the book of Ruth.

Also as in Ruth, the author uses structural symmetry effectively. The story is developed in two parallel cycles that call attention to a series of comparisons and contrasts (see Outline). The story's climax is Jonah's grand prayer of confession, "Salvation comes from the LORD"—the middle confession of three from his lips (1:9; 2:9; 4:2). The last sentence emphasizes that the Lord's word is final and decisive, while Jonah is left sitting in the hot, open country outside Nineveh.

The author uses the art of representative roles in a straightforward manner. In this story of God's loving concern for all people, Nineveh, the great menace to Israel, is representative of the Gentiles. Correspondingly, stubbornly reluctant Jonah represents Israel's jealousy of her favored relationship with God and her unwillingness to share the Lord's compassion with the nations.

The book depicts the larger scope of God's purpose for Israel: that she might rediscover the truth of his concern for the whole creation and better understand her own role in carrying out that concern.

Outline

- I. Jonah Flees His Mission (chs. 1–2)
  - A. Jonah's Commission and Flight (1:1–3)
  - B. The Endangered Sailors' Cry to Their Gods (1:4–6)
  - C. Jonah's Disobedience Exposed (1:7–10)
  - D. Jonah's Punishment and Deliverance (1:11—2:1; 2:10)
  - E. Jonah's Prayer of Thanksgiving (2:2–9)
- II. Jonah Reluctantly Fulfills His Mission (chs. 3–4)
  - A. Jonah's Renewed Commission and Obedience (3:1–4)
  - B. The Endangered Ninevites' Repentant Appeal to the Lord (3:5–9)
  - C. The Ninevites' Repentance Acknowledged (3:10—4:4)
  - D. Jonah's Deliverance and Rebuke (4:5–11)

Jonah Flees From the LORD

1 The word of the LORD came to Jonah[a]
son of Amittai:[b] 2"Go to the great city
of Nineveh[c] and preach against it, because
its wickedness has come up before me."
3But Jonah ran[d] away from the LORD and
headed for Tarshish[e]. He went down to Joppa,[f] where he found a ship bound for that
port. After paying the fare, he went aboard
and sailed for Tarshish to flee from the LORD.[g]
4Then the LORD sent a great wind on the
sea, and such a violent storm arose that
the ship threatened to break up.[h] 5All the
sailors were afraid and each cried out to
his own god. And they threw the cargo
into the sea to lighten the ship.[i]
But Jonah had gone below deck, where
he lay down and fell into a deep sleep.
6The captain went to him and said, "How
can you sleep? Get up and call[j] on your
god! Maybe he will take notice of us so
that we will not perish."[k]

1:1 [a] Mt 12:39-41; 16:4; Lk 11:29-32 [b] 2Ki 14:25 **1:2** [c] S Ge 10:11; S Na 1:1 **1:3** [d] Ps 139:7 [e] S Ge 10:4 [f] S Jos 19:46; Ac 9:36,43 [g] Ex 4:13; S Jer 20:9; S Am 3:8 **1:4** [h] Ps 107:23-26 **1:5** [i] Ac 27:18-19 **1:6** [j] Jnh 3:8 [k] S Ps 107:28 **1:7** [l] Nu 32:23; Jos 7:10-18; S 1Sa 14:42 [m] S Pr 16:33 **1:9** [n] S Ps 96:9 [o] S Da 2:18; Ac 17:24 [p] S Ne 9:6 [q] S Ge 1:9

7Then the sailors said to each other,
"Come, let us cast lots to find out who is
responsible for this calamity."[l] They cast
lots and the lot fell on Jonah.[m] 8So they
asked him, "Tell us, who is responsible for
making all this trouble for us? What kind
of work do you do? Where do you come
from? What is your country? From what
people are you?"
9He answered, "I am a Hebrew and I
worship the LORD,[n] the God of heaven,[o]
who made the sea[p] and the dry land.[q]"
10This terrified them and they asked,
"What have you done?" (They knew he
was running away from the LORD, because
he had already told them so.)
11The sea was getting rougher and
rougher. So they asked him, "What should
we do to you to make the sea calm down
for us?"
12"Pick me up and throw me into the
sea," he replied, "and it will become calm.

1:1 *word of the LORD.* See 3:1; Hos 1:1 and note. *Jonah.* See Introduction: Title; Authorship and Date. In his account of Jonah's mission to Nineveh written for Israel's instruction, the author probably presents Jonah as a cameo representation of Israel, the people called out from the nations by God to be the channel of his redemptive purposes for the peoples of the world. In this narrative, the people of Israel are to see themselves as in a mirror: their unique position of privilege as the people to whom God had revealed himself in a special way, their particular vocation as God's chosen kingdom people, their stubborn resistance to fulfilling that vocation and the reason Israel must die as a nation (the judgment the prophets were announcing) and be raised up again, refined and renewed (the more distant future the prophets were envisioning). Cf. note on Jdg 13:1 — 16:31.

1:2 *great city.* See 3:2; 4:11; see also note on 3:3. According to Ge 10:11, Nineveh was first built by Nimrod and was traditionally known as the "great city" (see Ge 10:12 and note). About 700 BC Sennacherib made it the capital of Assyria, which it remained until its fall in 612 (see Introduction to Nahum: Background). Nineveh is over 500 miles from Gath Hepher, Jonah's hometown (see 2Ki 14:25 and note). Nineveh is also over 500 miles from Joppa (see v. 3 and note; see also chart, p. 336). *its wickedness has come up.* Cf. Sodom and Gomorrah (see Ge 18:20 – 21 and note on 18:20). Except for the "violence" (3:8) of Nineveh, her "evil ways" (3:8,10) are not described in Jonah. Nahum later states that Nineveh's sins included plotting evil against the Lord, cruelty and plundering in war, prostitution, witchcraft and commercial exploitation (see Na 1:11; 2:12 – 13; 3:1,4,16,19 and notes on 3:3,10).

1:3 *ran away.* Jonah gives his reason in 4:2. The futility of trying to run away from the Lord is acknowledged in Ps 139:7 – 12 (see note there). *Tarshish.* Perhaps the city of Tartessus in southern Spain, a Phoenician mining colony near Gibraltar. By heading in the opposite direction from Nineveh (see map, p. 1495) to what seemed like the end of the world, Jonah intended to escape his divinely appointed task. *Joppa.* See note on Ac 9:36.

1:4 – 16 Probably this account of the storm at sea is intended to be a graphic depiction, in exquisite miniature, of the pagan world of many nations (represented by the sailors) threatened by the judgments of God (represented by the storm), with Israel in their midst (represented by Jonah). If Jonah (Israel) does not fulfill his mission, the sailors (nations) will die calling on their gods. And because he is rebelling against his mission, he must "die" to save them. See note on 1:1; cf. note on Ac 27:13 – 44.

1:4 – 5 Although Jonah's mission was to bring God's warning of impending judgment to the pagan world, his refusal to go to Nineveh brings these pagan sailors into peril.

1:4 *the LORD sent a great wind.* God's sovereign working in Jonah's mission is evident at several other points also: the fish (v. 17), the release of Jonah (2:10), the leafy plant (4:6), the worm (4:7) and the "scorching east wind" (4:8).

1:5 *his own god.* Apparently the sailors, who may have come from various ports, worshiped several different pagan gods (see note on Ge 28:15).

1:6 *The captain went to him.* The pagan captain's concern for everyone on board contrasts with the believing prophet's refusal to carry God's warning to Nineveh.

1:7 *let us cast lots.* The casting of lots was a custom widely practiced in the ancient Near East. The precise method is unclear, though it appears that, for the most part, sticks or marked pebbles were drawn from a receptacle into which they had been "cast" (see notes on Ex 28:30; Ne 11:1; Pr 16:33 Eze 21:21; Ac 1:26). *lot fell on Jonah.* By the lot of judgment the Lord exposed the guilty one (see Jos 7:14 – 26 and note on 7:14; 1Sa 14:37 – 44 and note on 14:37).

1:9 *Hebrew.* See note on Ge 14:13. *I worship . . . the God of heaven, who made the sea and the dry land.* See note on Ezr 1:2. The sailors would have understood Jonah's words as being descriptive of the highest deity. Their present experiences confirmed this truth, since, in the religions of the ancient Near East generally, the supreme god was master of the seas (see note on Jos 3:10). This is Jonah's first confessional statement, and, like those that follow (2:9c; 4:2), it is thoroughly orthodox. Though orthodox in his beliefs, Jonah refuses to fulfill his divine mission to Nineveh.

1:10 *What have you done?* This rhetorical question is really an accusation.

1:12 *throw me into the sea.* Jonah's readiness to die to save the terrified sailors contrasts with his later callous departure from Nineveh to watch from a safe distance while the city perishes — at least he still hoped it would perish (see 4:5 and note).

THE BOOK OF JONAH

Nineveh and Tarshish represented opposite ends of the Mediterranean commercial sphere in ancient times. The story of Jonah extends to the boundaries of OT geographic knowledge and provides a rare glimpse of seafaring life in the Iron Age. Inscriptions and pottery from Spain demonstrate that Phoenician trade linked the far distant ends of the Mediterranean, perhaps as early as the twelfth century BC.

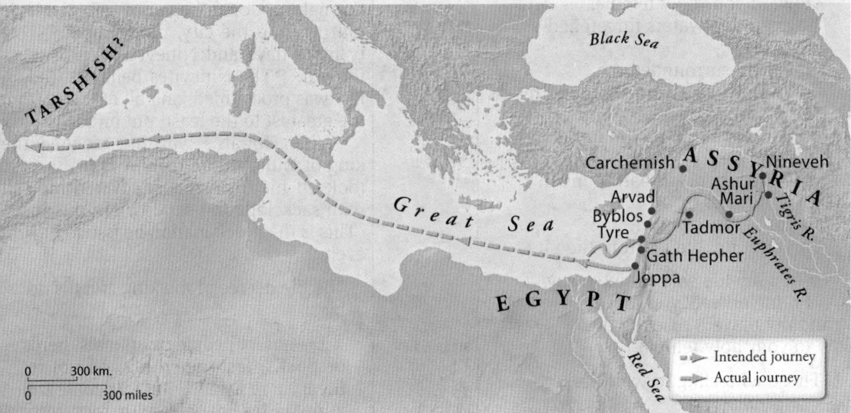

I know that it is my fault that this great
storm has come upon you."[r]
13 Instead, the men did their best to row
back to land. But they could not, for the
sea grew even wilder than before.[s] 14 Then
they cried out to the LORD, "Please, LORD,
do not let us die for taking this man's life.
Do not hold us accountable for killing an
innocent man,[t] for you, LORD, have done
as you pleased."[u] 15 Then they took Jonah
and threw him overboard, and the raging
sea grew calm.[v] 16 At this the men greatly
feared[w] the LORD, and they offered a sacrifice to the LORD and made vows[x] to him.

1:12 [r] 2Sa 24:17; 1Ch 21:17 **1:13** [s] S Pr 21:30 **1:14** [t] Dt 21:8 [u] S Da 4:35 **1:15** [v] S Ps 107:29; Lk 8:24 **1:16** [w] Mk 4:41 [x] S Nu 30:2; Ps 66:13-14 **1:17** [y] Jnh 4:6,7 [z] Mt 12:40; 16:4; Lk 11:30 **2:2** [a] La 3:55 [b] Ps 18:6; 120:1 [c] Ps 86:13

Jonah's Prayer

17 Now the LORD provided[y] a huge fish to
swallow Jonah,[z] and Jonah was in the belly of the fish three days and three nights.
2[a] 1 From inside the fish Jonah prayed to
the LORD his God. 2 He said:

"In my distress I called[a] to the LORD,[b]
and he answered me.
From deep in the realm of the dead[c] I
called for help,
and you listened to my cry.

[a] In Hebrew texts 2:1 is numbered 1:17, and 2:1-10 is numbered 2:2-11.

1:13 *did their best to row.* The Hebrew uses the picturesque word meaning "to dig" (with oars) to indicate strenuous effort. The ship could be driven by sails, oars, or both. The reluctance of the sailors to throw Jonah into the sea stands in sharp contrast to Jonah's reluctance to warn Nineveh of impending judgment.
1:14 *cried out to the LORD.* Earlier the sailors had cried out to their own gods (see v. 5 and note), but now in their desperation they plead for help from Jonah's God.
1:16 *greatly feared the LORD.* There is no evidence that the sailors renounced all other gods (contrast Naaman; see 2Ki 5:15 and note). Ancient pagans were ready to recognize the existence and power of many gods. At the least, however, the sailors acknowledged that the God of Israel was in control of the present events, that he was the one who both stirred up and calmed the storm and that at this moment he was the one to be recognized and worshiped.
1:17 *the LORD provided.* This characteristic phrase occurs also in 4:6–8. *huge fish.* The Hebrew here and the Greek of Mt 12:40 are both general terms for a large fish, not necessarily a whale. This great fish is carefully distinguished from the sinister "serpent" of the sea (Am 9:3)—otherwise called "Leviathan" (Isa 27:1), the "monster of the deep" (Job 7:12; see Ps 74:13; Eze 32:2). *three days and three nights.* The phrase used here may, as in Mt 12:40, refer to a period of time including one full day and parts of two others (see notes on Mt 12:40; 1Co 15:4). In any case, the NT clearly uses Jonah's experience as a type (foreshadowing) of the burial and resurrection of Jesus, who was entombed for "three days and three nights" (Mt 12:40; see Mt 16:4; Lk 11:29–30 and note on 11:30).
2:1 *prayed.* A prayer of thanksgiving for deliverance from drowning in the Mediterranean Sea (see note on vv. 2–9). For this use of "prayed" elsewhere, see 1Sa 2:1 and note.
2:2–9 A psalm of thanksgiving for deliverance from death in the Mediterranean Sea. Jonah recalls his prayer for help as he was sinking into the depths. His gratitude is heightened by his knowledge that he deserved death but that God had shown him extraordinary mercy. The language of this song indicates that Jonah was familiar with the praise literature of the Psalms.
2:2 *I called … he answered.* See note on Ps 118:5. *realm of the dead.* Figurative for Jonah's near-death experience in the sea (see Ps 30:3 and note). See also note on Ge 37:35.

3 You hurled me into the depths,[d]
into the very heart of the seas,
and the currents swirled about me;
all your waves[e] and breakers
swept over me.[f]
4 I said, 'I have been banished
from your sight;[g]
yet I will look again
toward your holy temple.'[h]
5 The engulfing waters threatened
me,[a]
the deep surrounded me;
seaweed was wrapped around my
head.[i]
6 To the roots of the mountains[j] I sank
down;
the earth beneath barred me in
forever.
But you, LORD my God,
brought my life up from the pit.[k]

7 "When my life was ebbing away,
I remembered[l] you, LORD,
and my prayer[m] rose to you,
to your holy temple.[n]

8 "Those who cling to worthless
idols[o]
turn away from God's love for
them.
9 But I, with shouts of grateful praise,[p]
will sacrifice[q] to you.
What I have vowed[r] I will make
good.
I will say, 'Salvation[s] comes from the
LORD.' "

10 And the LORD commanded the fish,
and it vomited Jonah onto dry land.

2:3 [d] S Ps 88:6 [e] S 2Sa 22:5 [f] S Ps 42:7 **2:4** [g] Ps 31:22; Jer 7:15 [h] S 1Ki 8:48 **2:5** [i] Ps 69:1-2 **2:6** [j] Job 28:9 [k] S Job 17:16; S 33:18; S Ps 30:3 **2:7** [l] Ps 77:11-12 [m] 2Ch 30:27 [n] S Ps 11:4; 18:6 **2:8** [o] S Dt 32:21; S 1Sa 12:21 **2:9** [p] S Ps 42:4 [q] Ps 50:14,23; Heb 13:15 [r] S Nu 30:2; Ps 116:14; S Ecc 5:4-5 [s] S Ex 15:2; S Ps 3:8

3:1 [t] Jnh 1:1 **3:4** [u] S Jer 18:7-10 **3:5** [v] Da 9:3; Mt 11:21; 12:41; Lk 11:32 **3:6** [w] Est 4:1-3; S Job 2:8,13; S Eze 27:30-31 **3:7** [x] S 2Ch 20:3; S Ezr 10:6 **3:8** [y] Ps 130:1; Jnh 1:6 [z] Jer 25:5 [a] Jer 7:3 [b] S Job 16:17 **3:9** [c] 2Sa 12:22 [d] S Jer 18:8 [e] S Joel 2:14 [f] S Ps 85:3

Jonah Goes to Nineveh

3 Then the word of the LORD came to Jonah[t] a second time: 2 "Go to the great
city of Nineveh and proclaim to it the message I give you."
3 Jonah obeyed the word of the LORD
and went to Nineveh. Now Nineveh was
a very large city; it took three days to go
through it. 4 Jonah began by going a day's
journey into the city, proclaiming,[u] "Forty more days and Nineveh will be overthrown." 5 The Ninevites believed God. A
fast was proclaimed, and all of them, from
the greatest to the least, put on sackcloth.[v]
6 When Jonah's warning reached the
king of Nineveh, he rose from his throne,
took off his royal robes, covered himself
with sackcloth and sat down in the dust.[w]
7 This is the proclamation he issued in Nineveh:

"By the decree of the king and his nobles:

Do not let people or animals, herds
or flocks, taste anything; do not let
them eat or drink.[x] 8 But let people and
animals be covered with sackcloth.
Let everyone call[y] urgently on God.
Let them give up[z] their evil ways[a] and
their violence.[b] 9 Who knows?[c] God
may yet relent[d] and with compassion
turn[e] from his fierce anger[f] so that we
will not perish."

10 When God saw what they did and
how they turned from their evil ways, he

[a] 5 Or *waters were at my throat*

2:3 *You hurled me … your waves.* Jonah recognizes that the sailors (1:15) were agents of God's judgment.
2:4 *yet I will look again toward your holy temple.* The same note of hopeful expectation found in the prayers of the Psalms (e.g., Ps 5:7; 27:4–6). "Temple" here probably refers to the temple in Jerusalem, while "temple" in v. 7 refers to God's heavenly temple. The Israelites held these two residences of God in inseparable association (see 1Ki 8:38–39).
2:6 *pit.* The grave (see note on v. 2; see also Ps 28:1; 30:1–3 and note on 30:1).
2:7 *holy temple.* See v. 4 and note.
2:9 *sacrifice … vowed.* Cf. the "sacrifice" and "vows" of the sailors (1:16). *What I have vowed.* In the book of Psalms prayers were commonly accompanied by vows, usually involving thank offerings (see, e.g., Ps 50:14 and note; 56:12; 61:8; 65:1; 66:13–15; 116:12–19). *make good.* See Ps 76:11; Ecc 5:1–7. *Salvation comes from the LORD.* The climax of Jonah's thanksgiving prayer and his second confessional statement (see note on 1:9). It stands aptly at the literary midpoint since it is the theological foundation of the whole book.
3:1 *word of the LORD.* See 1:1 and note.
3:2 *great city.* See 1:2 and note. *proclaim to it the message I give you.* A prophet was the bearer of a message from God, not primarily a foreteller of coming events.
3:3 *obeyed.* But reluctantly, still wanting the Ninevites to be destroyed (see 4:1–5 and notes). *very large city.* See 4:11, which says the city had more than 120,000 inhabitants. Archaeological excavations indicate that the later imperial city of Nineveh was about eight miles around. The fact however, that "it took three days to go through it" may suggest a larger area, such as the four-city complex of Nineveh Rehoboth Ir, Calah and Resen mentioned in Ge 10:11–12. Greater Nineveh covered an area of some 60 miles in circumference. On the other hand, "three days" may have been a conventional way of describing a medium-length distance (see Ge 30:36; Ex 3:18 and note; Jos 9:16–17).
3:5–6 *fast … sackcloth … dust.* Customary signs of humbling oneself in repentance (see 1Ki 21:27; Ne 9:1 and note).
3:5 *believed God.* This may mean that the Ninevites genuinely turned to the Lord (cf. Mt 12:41). On the other hand their belief in God may have gone no deeper than had the sailors' fear of God (see note on 1:16). At least they took the prophet's warning seriously and acted accordingly—something Israel was not doing.
3:6 *king of Nineveh.* King of Assyria.
3:8 *animals.* Inclusion of the domestic animals (see 4:11) was unusual and expressed the urgency with which the Ninevites sought mercy.
3:9 God often responds in mercy to human repentance by canceling threatened punishment (v. 10). See note on Jer 18:7–10.
3:10 *did not bring on them the destruction … threatened.* See 1Ki 21:28–29 and note on 21:29; see also Introduction to Nahum: Background; Na 3:19 and note.

relented[g] and did not bring on them the
destruction[h] he had threatened.[i]

Jonah's Anger at the LORD's Compassion

4 But to Jonah this seemed very wrong,
and he became angry.[j] 2He prayed to
the LORD, "Isn't this what I said, LORD,
when I was still at home? That is what
I tried to forestall by fleeing to Tarshish.
I knew[k] that you are a gracious[l] and
compassionate God, slow to anger and
abounding in love,[m] a God who relents[n]
from sending calamity.[o] 3Now, LORD, take
away my life,[p] for it is better for me to die[q]
than to live."[r]
4But the LORD replied, "Is it right for you
to be angry?"[s]
5Jonah had gone out and sat down at a
place east of the city. There he made himself a shelter, sat in its shade and waited to
see what would happen to the city. 6Then
the LORD God provided[t] a leafy plant[a] and
made it grow up over Jonah to give shade
for his head to ease his discomfort, and
Jonah was very happy about the plant.
7But at dawn the next day God provided a
worm, which chewed the plant so that it
withered.[u] 8When the sun rose, God provided a scorching east wind, and the sun
blazed on Jonah's head so that he grew
faint. He wanted to die,[v] and said, "It
would be better for me to die than to live."
9But God said to Jonah, "Is it right for
you to be angry about the plant?"[w]
"It is," he said. "And I'm so angry I wish
I were dead."
10But the LORD said, "You have been
concerned about this plant, though you
did not tend it or make it grow. It sprang
up overnight and died overnight. 11And
should I not have concern[x] for the great
city of Nineveh,[y] in which there are more
than a hundred and twenty thousand people who cannot tell their right hand from
their left—and also many animals?"

3:10 [g] S Am 7:6 [h] S Jer 18:8 [i] S Ex 32:14 **4:1** [j] ver 4; Mt 20:11; Lk 15:28 **4:2** [k] Jer 20:7-8 [l] S Dt 4:31; Ps 103:8 [m] S Ex 22:27; Ps 86:5,15 [n] S Nu 14:18 [o] S Joel 2:13 **4:3** [p] S Nu 11:15 [q] S Job 7:15 [r] Jer 8:3 **4:4** [s] Ge 4:6; Mt 20:11-15 **4:6** [t] S Jnh 1:17 **4:7** [u] Joel 1:12 **4:8** [v] S 1Ki 19:4 **4:9** [w] ver 4 **4:11** [x] Jnh 3:10 [y] Jnh 1:2; 3:2

[a] 6 The precise identification of this plant is uncertain; also in verses 7, 9 and 10.

4:1 *angry.* Jonah was angry that God would have compassion on an enemy of Israel. He wanted God's goodness to be shown only to Israelites, not to Gentiles.

4:2 *prayed to the LORD.* Now in anger, not in distress (see 2:1–2 and note on 2:2). *That is what I tried to forestall by fleeing to Tarshish.* See 1:3 and note. *gracious … love.* See Ex 34:6–7 and note. This is the third and last of Jonah's confessional statements (see notes on 1:9; 2:9). *slow to anger.* In contrast, Jonah became angry quickly (vv. 1,9).

4:3 *take away my life.* See 1Ki 19:4 and note (Elijah). To Jonah, God's mercy to the Ninevites meant an end to Israel's favored standing with him. Jonah shortly before had rejoiced in his deliverance from death (2:2–9), but now that Nineveh lives, he prefers to die.

4:5 *shelter.* Apparently this shelter did not provide enough shade since the next verse indicates that God provided a "leafy plant" (v. 6) to give more shade. *waited to see.* Jonah still hoped that Nineveh would be destroyed.

4:6 *the LORD God provided.* This characteristic phrase occurs also in vv. 7–8; 1:17. *leafy plant.* See NIV text note. It may have been a castor oil plant, a shrub growing over 12 feet high with large, shady leaves. God graciously increased the comfort of his stubbornly defiant prophet.

4:8 *better for me to die.* See note on v. 3.

4:10 *sprang up overnight and died overnight.* Indicative of fleeting value.

4:11 *should I not have concern … ?* According to v. 2, the answer is yes. God had the first word (1:1–2), and he also has the last. The commission he gave Jonah displayed his mercy and compassion to the Ninevites, and his last word to Jonah emphatically proclaimed that concern for every creature, both people and animals. Not only does the Lord "preserve both people and animals" (Ps 36:6; see Ne 9:6; Ps 145:16), but he takes "no pleasure in the death of the wicked, but [desires] rather that they turn from their ways and live" (Eze 33:11; see Eze 16:6; 18:23; 33:11 and notes; cf. 2Pe 3:9 and note). Jonah and his fellow Israelites traditionally rejoiced in God's special mercies to Israel but wished only his wrath on their enemies. God here rebukes such hardness and proclaims his own gracious benevolence. *great city.* See 1:2 and note. The book begins and ends by referring to Nineveh, the unlikely and unexpected scene of a remarkable display of divine compassion. *cannot tell their right hand from their left.* Like small children (see Dt 1:39 and note), the Ninevites needed God's fatherly compassion. *also many animals.* God's concern extended even to domestic animals (cf. 3:8 and chart, p. 287 [item 16]).

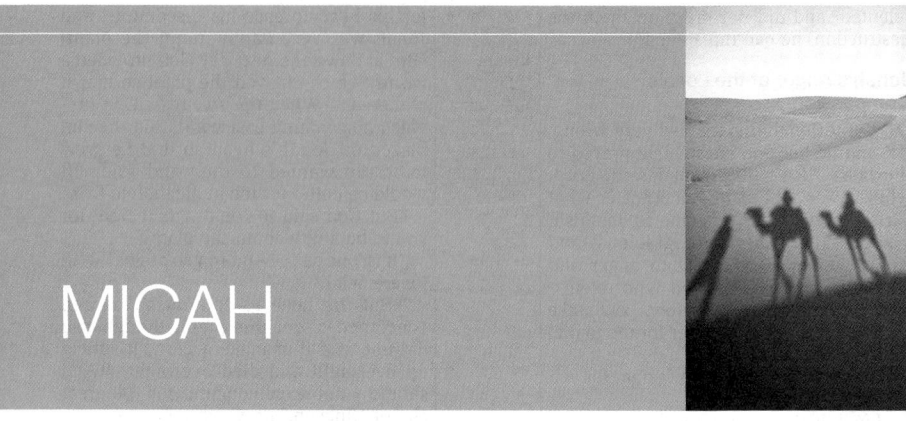

MICAH

INTRODUCTION

Author

Little is known about the prophet Micah beyond what can be learned from the book itself and from Jer 26:18. Micah was from the town of Moresheth (1:1), probably Moresheth Gath (1:14) in southern Judah. The prophecy attests to Micah's deep sensitivity to the social ills of his day, especially as they affected the small towns and villages of his homeland.

Date

Micah prophesied sometime between 750 and 686 BC during the reigns of Jotham, Ahaz and Hezekiah, kings of Judah (1:1; Jer 26:18). He was therefore a contemporary of Isaiah (see Isa 1:1) and Hosea (see Hos 1:1). Micah predicted the fall of Samaria (1:6), which took place in 722 – 721. This would place his early ministry in the overlapping reigns of Jotham (750 – 732) and Ahaz (735 – 715). Micah's message reflects social conditions prior to the religious reforms under Hezekiah (715 – 686). Micah's ministry most likely fell within the period 735 – 700.

If Micah himself wrote out his messages, the date for the earliest written form of his work would be c. 700. If one of his disciples arranged his messages in their present form, the date would be the early seventh century BC. If a later editor collected and arranged his messages, the date would still need to be early enough in the seventh century to allow time for his prophecy of Jerusalem's fall (3:12) to become familiar enough to be quoted in Jer 26:18 c. 608.

a **quick** look

Author:
Micah

Audience:
The people of Israel and Judah, especially the oppressive land-grabbers who supported Israel's corrupt political and religious leaders

Date:
Probably between 700 and 650 BC

Theme:
Micah's message alternates between prophecies of doom and prophecies of hope; the theme is divine judgment and deliverance.

Historical Background

The background of the book is the same as that found in the earlier portions of Isaiah, though Micah does not exhibit the same knowledge of Jerusalem's political life as Isaiah does. Perhaps this is because he, like Amos, was from a village in Judah.

The relevant Biblical texts covering this period (see Date above) are 2Ki 15:32 — 20:21; 2Ch 27 – 32; Isa 7; 20; 36 – 39.

Israel was in an apostate condition. Micah predicted the fall of her capital, Samaria (1:5 – 7), and also foretold the inevitable desolation of Judah (1:9 – 16).

Several significant historical events occurred during this period:

(1) In 734 – 732 BC Tiglath-Pileser III of Assyria led a military campaign against Aram (Syria), Philistia and parts of Israel and Judah. Ashkelon and Gaza were defeated. Judah, Ammon, Edom and Moab paid tribute to the Assyrian king, but Israel did not fare as well. According to 2Ki 15:29 the northern kingdom lost most of its territory, including all of Gilead and much of Galilee. Damascus fell in 732 and was annexed to the Assyrian Empire.

(2) In 722 – 721 Samaria fell, and the northern kingdom of Israel was conquered by Assyria.

(3) In 711 King Sargon II of Assyria captured Ashdod (see Isa 20:1 and note).

(4) In 701 Judah joined a revolt against Assyria and was overrun by King Sennacherib and his army, though Jerusalem was spared.

Aerial view of Bethlehem. The cross-shaped building in the center of the photo is the Church of the Nativity, built on the traditional location of the birth of Christ. Micah prophesied that the Messiah would come from Bethlehem (5:2).

Aerial view of Moresheth Gath, Micah's hometown (Mic 1:1,14)
Todd Bolen/www.BiblePlaces.com

Literary Analysis

(1) *Structure.* The book's collection of short prophetic messages is organized in a pattern of three cycles of judgment and salvation/deliverance messages (see Outline below).

(2) *Forms.* The book contains at least seven different literary forms (divine covenant lawsuit, lament, disputation, deliverance message, indictment/judgment message, judgment and salvation message, and prophetic liturgy). These are identified in the notes on the 20 individual units (see Outline below).

(3) *Style.* Micah's style is similar to that of Isaiah. Both prophets use vigorous language and many figures of speech (see, e.g., Mic 1:4–5,7; 2:4,6,11; 3:2–3; 4:3–4,12–13; 5:1); both show great tenderness in threatening punishment and in promising justice. Micah makes frequent use of plays on words, 1:10–15 (see NIV text notes there) being the classic example.

Theme and Message

As the Outline shows, Micah's message alternates between prophecies of doom and prophecies of hope — in terms of Ro 11:22, between God's "sternness" and his "kindness." The theme is divine

Micah stresses that God hates idolatry, injustice, rebellion and empty ritualism but delights in pardoning the penitent.

judgment and deliverance. Micah also stresses that God hates idolatry, injustice, rebellion and empty ritualism (see 3:8 and note) but delights in pardoning the penitent (see 7:18 – 19 and notes). Finally, the prophet declares that Zion will have greater glory in the future than ever before (see, e.g., 4:1 – 2 and note on 4:1 – 5). The Davidic kingdom, though it will seem to come to an end, will reach greater heights through the coming Messianic deliverer (see note on 5:1 – 4). Key passages include 1:2; 3:8 – 12; 5:1 – 4; 6:2,6 – 8; 7:18 – 20.

Outline

- I. Title (1:1)
- II. First Cycle: God's Judgment and Restoration of Israel and Judah (1:2 — 2:13)
  - A. Judgment on Israel and Judah (1:2 — 2:11)
    1. The predicted destruction (1:2 – 7)
    2. Lamentation over the destruction (1:8 – 16)
    3. Woe to oppressive land-grabbers (2:1 – 5)
    4. Condemnation of the wealthy wicked and their false prophets (2:6 – 11)
  - B. Restoration of a Remnant (2:12 – 13)
- III. Second Cycle: God's Indictment of Judah's Leaders, but Future Hope for God's People (chs. 3 – 5)
  - A. Indictment of Judah's Leaders (ch. 3)
    1. Guilty civil leaders (3:1 – 4)
    2. False prophets of peace and Micah's response (3:5 – 8)
    3. Corrupt leaders and Zion's fall (3:9 – 12)
  - B. Future Hope for God's People (chs. 4 – 5)
    1. The coming kingdom (4:1 – 5)
    2. Restoration of a remnant and Zion (4:6 – 8)
    3. From distress to deliverance (4:9 – 10)
    4. From siege to victory (4:11 – 13)
    5. From helpless ruler to ideal king (5:1 – 4)
    6. The ideal king delivers his people (5:5 – 6)
    7. The remnant among the nations (5:7 – 9)
    8. Obliteration of military might and pagan worship (5:10 – 15)
- IV. Third Cycle: God's Indictment of His People and the Ultimate Triumph of His Kingdom (chs. 6 – 7)
  - A. God's Indictment of His People (6:1 — 7:7)
    1. A divine covenant lawsuit (6:1 – 8)
    2. Further indictments and the sentence (6:9 – 16)
    3. A lament over a decadent society (7:1 – 7)
  - B. The Ultimate Triumph of God's Kingdom (7:8 – 20)
    1. An expression of trust (7:8 – 10)
    2. A promise of restoration (7:11 – 13)
    3. A prayer, the Lord's answer and the response (7:14 – 17)
    4. A hymn of praise to God (7:18 – 20)

1 The word of the LORD that came to Micah of Moresheth[a] during the reigns
of Jotham,[b] Ahaz[c] and Hezekiah,[d] kings
of Judah[e]—the vision[f] he saw concerning
Samaria and Jerusalem.

2 Hear,[g] you peoples, all of you,[h]
listen, earth[i] and all who live in it,
that the Sovereign LORD may bear
witness[j] against you,
the Lord from his holy temple.[k]

Judgment Against Samaria and Jerusalem

3 Look! The LORD is coming from his
dwelling[l] place;
he comes down[m] and treads on the
heights of the earth.[n]
4 The mountains melt[o] beneath him[p]
and the valleys split apart,[q]
like wax before the fire,
like water rushing down a slope.
5 All this is because of Jacob's
transgression,
because of the sins of the people of
Israel.
What is Jacob's transgression?
Is it not Samaria?[r]
What is Judah's high place?
Is it not Jerusalem?

6 "Therefore I will make Samaria a heap
of rubble,
a place for planting vineyards.[s]
I will pour her stones[t] into the valley
and lay bare her foundations.[u]
7 All her idols[v] will be broken to pieces;[w]
all her temple gifts will be burned
with fire;
I will destroy all her images.[x]
Since she gathered her gifts from the
wages of prostitutes,[y]
as the wages of prostitutes they will
again be used."

Weeping and Mourning

8 Because of this I will weep[z] and wail;
I will go about barefoot[a] and naked.
I will howl like a jackal
and moan like an owl.
9 For Samaria's plague[b] is incurable;[c]
it has spread to Judah.[d]
It has reached the very gate[e] of my
people,
even to Jerusalem itself.
10 Tell it not in Gath[a];
weep not at all.
In Beth Ophrah[b]
roll in the dust.

1:1 [a] ver 14; Jer 26:18 [b] S 1Ch 3:12 [c] S 1Ch 3:13 [d] S 1Ch 3:13 [e] Hos 1:1 [f] Isa 1:1 **1:2** [g] S Dt 32:1 [h] Ps 50:7 [i] S Jer 6:19 [j] S Ge 31:50; S Dt 4:26; S Isa 1:2 [k] S Ps 11:4 **1:3** [l] S Isa 18:4 [m] S Isa 64:1 [n] S Am 4:13 **1:4** [o] S Ps 46:2, 6 [p] S Job 9:5 [q] S Nu 16:31; Na 1:5 **1:5** [r] Am 8:14 **1:6** [s] S Dt 20:6 [t] S Am 5:11 [u] Eze 13:14 **1:7** [v] S Eze 6:6 [w] S Ex 32:20 [x] S Dt 9:21 [y] Dt 23:17-18 **1:8** [z] S Isa 15:3 [a] S Isa 20:2 **1:9** [b] Jer 46:11 [c] S Jer 10:19 [d] S 2Ki 18:13 [e] Isa 3:26

[a] 10 *Gath* sounds like the Hebrew for *tell.* [b] 10 *Beth Ophrah* means *house of dust.*

1:1 *word of the LORD.* See Hos 1:1 and note. *Micah.* Means "Who is like the LORD?" (cf. 7:18 and note). *Moresheth.* See Introduction: Author. *Jotham, Ahaz and Hezekiah.* See Introduction: Date. For background on these kings and the book of Micah, see Introduction: Historical Background. Isaiah, Hosea and Micah prophesied at roughly the same time (see Isa 1:1; Hos 1:1). *vision.* See Pr 29:18; Isa 1:1 and notes. *Samaria and Jerusalem.* The capitals of Israel and Judah, respectively. The judgment predicted by Micah involved these nations and not just their capital cities.
1:2—2:13 The first cycle of judgment (1:2—2:11) and salvation/restoration (2:12–13; see Introduction: Outline).
1:2–7 A divine covenant lawsuit, including a theophany (appearance of God, vv. 3–4). The Divine Warrior comes to judge Samaria and Israel (through Assyria).
1:2 *Hear.* The Hebrew for this word introduces prophetic addresses also in 3:1 and 6:1, where it is translated "Listen" (see also 3:9; 6:2). *peoples ... earth.* All nations—an announcement that the day of the Lord is at hand (see Am 5:18 and note), when God will call the nations to account. In view of that day Micah speaks in his prophecy of the impending judgments on Israel and Judah. *holy temple.* Heaven (see v. 3), as in Ps 11:4; Jnh 2:7; Hab 2:20.
1:3 *The LORD is coming.* An OT expression describing the Lord's intervention in history (see Ps 18:9; 96:13 and note; 144:5; Isa 26:21; 31:4; 64:1–3). *heights of the earth.* May refer to mountains as well as to pagan shrines, since both are cited here (vv. 4–5). Cf. Am 4:13; see Dt 33:29.
1:4 *mountains melt ... like wax.* See Ps 18:6–7; 97:5; Na 1:5; Hab 3:3 and note.
1:5 *All this.* The Lord's coming in judgment (vv. 3–4). *Jacob's.* Jacob was an alternate name for Israel (see Ge 32:28 and note; 35:10). *Israel.* Here (and in v. 13) specifically the northern kingdom, but Micah uses the name also for the southern kingdom (see 3:1,8–9; 5:1,3; 6:2) and for the whole covenant people (see vv. 14–15; 2:12; 5:2). *high place.* Pagan center of idolatry (see note on 1Ki 3:2).
1:6–7 God is the speaker. This prophecy was fulfilled during Micah's lifetime when Assyria destroyed Samaria in 722–721 BC (see 2Ki 17:6 and note).
1:6 *into the valley.* Samaria was built on a hill (see 1Ki 16:24 and note).
1:7 *prostitutes.* Prostitution is often an OT symbol for idolatry or spiritual unfaithfulness (see Ex 34:15 and note; Jdg 2:17; Eze 23:29–30). *wages.* The wealth that Samaria had gained from her idolatry will be taken by the Assyrians and placed in their own temples, to be used again in the worship of idols.
1:8–16 Micah laments not only the imminent destruction of Samaria but also the coming invasion of Judah, fulfilled by Sennacherib of Assyria in 701 BC.
1:8 *this.* The coming destruction of Samaria. *barefoot.* A sign of mourning (see 2Sa 15:30 and note). It is possible that Micah actually walked stripped and barefoot through Jerusalem (cf. Isa 20:2). The concept of mourning frames this section (see v. 16). *naked.* Perhaps clothed only in a loincloth.
1:9 *plague.* The judgment about to overtake Samaria. *incurable.* See Isa 1:6; see also Isa 17:11; Jer 30:12 and notes. *gate.* The Assyrian destruction of the northern kingdom will spread like a malignant disease to "the gate of Jerusalem" (v. 12; see note on vv. 8–16). The gate was where the process of town government was carried on (see Ge 19:1 and note; Ru 4:1–4 and note on 4:1).
1:10–15 Several plays on words are explained in the NIV text notes. The towns mentioned lie in the Shephelah, i.e., the foothills (500–1,500 feet high) between the Mediterranean coastal plain and the mountains of Judah.
1:10 *Tell it not in Gath.* These words introduce a funeral lament over Judah. Micah did not want the pagan people in Gath to gloat over the downfall of God's people (see 2Sa 1:20

[11] Pass by naked[f] and in shame,
you who live in Shaphir.[a]
Those who live in Zaanan[b]
will not come out.
Beth Ezel is in mourning;
it no longer protects you.
[12] Those who live in Maroth[c] writhe in
pain,
waiting for relief,[g]
because disaster[h] has come from the
LORD,
even to the gate of Jerusalem.
[13] You who live in Lachish,[i]
harness fast horses to the chariot.
You are where the sin of Daughter
Zion[j] began,
for the transgressions of Israel were
found in you.
[14] Therefore you will give parting gifts[k]
to Moresheth[l] Gath.
The town of Akzib[dm] will prove
deceptive[n]
to the kings of Israel.
[15] I will bring a conqueror against you
who live in Mareshah.[eo]
The nobles of Israel
will flee to Adullam.[p]
[16] Shave[q] your head in mourning
for the children in whom you
delight;
make yourself as bald as the vulture,
for they will go from you into exile.[r]

Human Plans and God's Plans

2 Woe to those who plan iniquity,
to those who plot evil[s] on their
beds![t]
At morning's light they carry it out
because it is in their power to do it.
[2] They covet fields[u] and seize them,[v]
and houses, and take them.
They defraud[w] people of their
homes,
they rob them of their inheritance.[x]

[3] Therefore, the LORD says:

"I am planning disaster[y] against this
people,
from which you cannot save
yourselves.
You will no longer walk proudly,[z]
for it will be a time of calamity.
[4] In that day people will ridicule you;
they will taunt you with this
mournful song:
'We are utterly ruined;[a]
my people's possession is divided
up.[b]
He takes it from me!
He assigns our fields to traitors.' "
[5] Therefore you will have no one in the
assembly of the LORD
to divide the land[c] by lot.[d]

False Prophets

[6] "Do not prophesy," their prophets say.
"Do not prophesy about these
things;
disgrace[e] will not overtake us.[f]"

1:11 [f] Eze 23:29 1:12 [g] Jer 14:19 [h] Jer 40:2 1:13 [i] S Jos 10:3 [j] S Ps 9:14 1:14 [k] 2Ki 16:8 [l] S ver 1 [m] S Jos 15:44 [n] Jer 15:18 1:15 [o] Jos 15:44 [p] S Jos 12:15 1:16 [q] S Lev 13:40; S Job 1:20 [r] S Dt 4:27; S Am 5:27 2:1 [s] S Isa 29:20 [t] Ps 36:4 2:2 [u] Isa 5:8 [v] S Pr 30:14 [w] S Jer 22:17 [x] S 1Sa 8:14; S Isa 1:23; S Eze 46:18 2:3 [y] Jer 18:11; S Am 3:1-2 [z] Isa 2:12 2:4 [a] S Lev 26:31; S Jer 4:13 [b] S Jer 6:12 2:5 [c] Dt 32:13; Jos 18:4 [d] S Nu 34:13 2:6 [e] Ps 44:13; Jer 18:16; 19:8; 25:18; 29:18; Mic 6:16 [f] S Am 2:12

[a] 11 *Shaphir* means *pleasant.* [b] 11 *Zaanan* sounds like the Hebrew for *come out.* [c] 12 *Maroth* sounds like the Hebrew for *bitter.* [d] 14 *Akzib* means *deception.* [e] 15 *Mareshah* sounds like the Hebrew for *conqueror.*

and note). *roll in the dust.* As a sign of grief over the coming catastrophe. See Isa 47:1 and note.

1:11 *naked and in shame.* A reference to their future humiliation as prisoners (see Isa 20:4). *will not come out.* Because of the invasion, the people will not dare to go outside their houses.

1:12 *has come.* Micah foresees the future so clearly that to him it seems as though it has already come (see v. 3 and note).

1:13 *Lachish.* One of the largest towns in Judah (see Isa 36:2 and note). Later, Sennacherib was so proud of capturing it that he decorated his palace at Nineveh with reliefs picturing his exploits. *harness fast horses.* In order to escape. *Daughter Zion.* A personification of Jerusalem (see note on 2Ki 19:21). *Israel.* See note on v. 5.

1:14 *parting gifts.* The Hebrew for these words is translated "wedding gift" in 1Ki 9:16. Jerusalem must give up Moresheth Gath to Assyria, as a father gives a "wedding gift" to his daughter when she marries. *Akzib.* See NIV text note. The word "deceptive" is used in Jer 15:18 (see note there) to describe a brook that has dried up in summer. Like such a brook, the city of Akzib will cease to exist. *Israel.* See note on v. 5.

1:15 Micah again represents God as speaking, as in vv. 6–7. *nobles of Israel.* "Nobles" is lit. "glory," referring to Israel's leaders (see Isa 5:13, "those of high rank," lit. "glory").

1:16 *Shave your head in mourning.* See note on Jer 16:6. *exile.* Israel was taken into exile by the Assyrians in 722–721 BC and Judah by the Babylonians in 586.

2:1–5 A judgment woe is pronounced on wealthy and oppressive land-grabbers. Their slogan is "Might makes right."

2:1 *plot evil.* Cf. Pr 6:14,18; Zec 7:10. *power to do it.* The rich, oppressing classes continued to get rich at the expense of the poor because they controlled the power structures of their society.

2:2 *They covet.* In violation of the tenth commandment (see Ex 20:17 and note; Dt 5:21). *inheritance.* Land that was to be the permanent possession of a particular family. See notes on Lev 25:13 (Year of Jubilee); Nu 27:1–11; 36:1–12 (Zelophehad's daughters); 1Ki 21:3 (Naboth's vineyard).

2:3 *Therefore.* Because of the sins of Israel's influential classes, calamity will strike. *disaster.* The impending exile.

2:4 *We... me.* The rich landowners, on whom God's judgment will fall. *He.* God. *traitors.* The treacherous Assyrians (see Isa 33:1 and note), who will capture the land.

2:5 *you.* The oppressing classes—the rich landowners. *no one ... to divide the land.* They will be cut off from all the promises of the covenant people.

2:6–11 A disputation: Micah and his God versus the wealthy wicked and their false prophets. The unit is framed by "prophesy" (vv. 6,11).

2:6 *their prophets.* The false prophets whose words were addressed to Micah.

7 You descendants of Jacob, should it be said,
"Does the LORD become[a] impatient?
Does he do such things?"

"Do not my words do good[g]
to the one whose ways are upright?[h]
8 Lately my people have risen up
like an enemy.
You strip off the rich robe
from those who pass by without a care,
like men returning from battle.
9 You drive the women of my people
from their pleasant homes.[i]
You take away my blessing
from their children forever.
10 Get up, go away!
For this is not your resting place,[j]
because it is defiled,[k]
it is ruined, beyond all remedy.
11 If a liar and deceiver[l] comes and says,
'I will prophesy for you plenty of wine and beer,'[m]
that would be just the prophet for this people![n]

Deliverance Promised

12 "I will surely gather all of you, Jacob;
I will surely bring together the remnant[o] of Israel.
I will bring them together like sheep in a pen,
like a flock in its pasture;
the place will throng with people.[p]
13 The One who breaks open the way will go up before[q] them;
they will break through the gate[r] and go out.
Their King will pass through before them,
the LORD at their head."

Leaders and Prophets Rebuked

3 Then I said,

"Listen, you leaders[s] of Jacob,
you rulers of Israel.
Should you not embrace justice,
2 you who hate good and love evil;
who tear the skin from my people
and the flesh from their bones;[t]
3 who eat my people's flesh,[u]
strip off their skin
and break their bones in pieces;[v]
who chop[w] them up like meat for the pan,
like flesh for the pot?[x]"

4 Then they will cry out to the LORD,
but he will not answer them.[y]
At that time he will hide his face[z] from them
because of the evil they have done.[a]

5 This is what the LORD says:

"As for the prophets
who lead my people astray,[b]
they proclaim 'peace'[c]
if they have something to eat,
but prepare to wage war against anyone
who refuses to feed them.
6 Therefore night will come over you, without visions,
and darkness, without divination.[d]
The sun will set for the prophets,[e]
and the day will go dark for them.[f]
7 The seers will be ashamed[g]
and the diviners disgraced.[h]
They will all cover[i] their faces[j]
because there is no answer from God.[k]"
8 But as for me, I am filled with power,
with the Spirit of the LORD,
and with justice and might,

2:7 [g] S Ps 119:65 [h] Ps 15:2; 84:11 **2:9** [i] Jer 10:20 **2:10** [j] S Dt 12:9 [k] Lev 18:25-29; Ps 106:38-39; S La 4:15 **2:11** [l] S 2Ch 36:16; Jer 5:31 [m] S Lev 10:9 [n] Isa 30:10 **2:12** [o] Mic 4:7; 5:7; 7:18 [p] S Ne 1:9 **2:13** [q] S Isa 52:12 [r] S Isa 60:11
3:1 [s] S Jer 5:5 **3:2** [t] Ps 53:4; S Eze 22:27 **3:3** [u] S Ps 14:4 [v] S Eze 34:4; Zep 3:3 [w] S Job 24:14 [x] S Eze 11:7; S 24:4-5 **3:4** [y] S Dt 1:45; S 1Sa 8:18; S Isa 58:4; S Jer 11:11 [z] S Dt 31:17 [a] S Job 15:31; S Eze 8:18 **3:5** [b] S Isa 3:12; S 9:16; S 53:6 [c] S Jer 4:10 **3:6** [d] Isa 8:19-22; S Eze 12:24 [e] Isa 29:10 [f] S Eze 7:26; S Am 8:11 **3:7** [g] S Jer 6:15; Mic 7:16 [h] S Isa 44:25 [i] S Est 6:12 [j] S Lev 13:45 [k] S Eze 20:3

[a] 7 Or *Is the Spirit of the LORD*

2:7 Verses 6–7a are spoken by Micah; vv. 7b–13 are spoken by God.
2:10 *resting place.* A place that could be regarded as one's own possession, where a people could settle in security (see Dt 3:20 and note; Jos 21:43–44; 22:4).
2:11 Anyone who promised greater affluence would gain a hearing.
2:12–13 A salvation message of deliverance. Although Israel will be carried into exile, a remnant will return (see note on Isa 1:9).
2:12 *Jacob ... Israel.* Here perhaps the entire nation, north and south. Contrast 1:5 (see note there).
2:13 *One who breaks open ... Their King ... the LORD.* Rabbinic interpretation refers all three to the Messiah.
3:1—5:15 The second cycle of judgment (ch. 3) and salvation/restoration (chs. 4–5; see Introduction: Outline).
3:1–12 Verses 1–4 deal with the sins of the leaders of Israel, vv. 5–7 with the false prophets and vv. 9–12 with the leaders, priests and prophets.
3:1–4 Probably another divine covenant lawsuit (see 1:2–7), in which God charges the civil leaders with acting like cannibals.
3:1 *Listen.* See note on 1:2; see also 6:1. *Jacob ... Israel.* Both names refer here to Judah (see vv. 9–10; 1:5 and note).
3:2–3 *tear the skin ... like flesh for the pot.* A series of figures of speech describing the cruel way the leaders treat the people.
3:2 *hate good and love evil.* Contrast Am 5:15; Ro 12:9.
3:4 *they.* The leaders. *he will not answer.* See v. 7. *hide his face.* See Dt 31:17; Isa 1:15 and note. Disobedience leads to separation from God.
3:5–8 Another disputation (see note on 2:6–11): Micah and the false prophets of peace.
3:5 *proclaim 'peace.'* The false prophets predicted peace for Judah, while Micah predicted destruction and captivity (see v. 12; 4:10). See also Jer 6:13–14 and note on 6:14; 8:10–11.
3:6–7 *without visions ... no answer from God.* See Jer 18:18 and note; Am 8:11–12 and note on 8:11.
3:7 *seers.* An older term for "prophets" (see note on 1Sa 9:9). *cover their faces.* In shame and humiliation.
3:8 *filled ... with the Spirit.* The prophets were Spirit-filled messengers (see Isa 48:16; 61:1 and note). *to declare ... his sin.* One of the chief purposes of Micah was to declare to Israel its sin.

to declare to Jacob his transgression,
to Israel his sin.[l]

9 Hear this, you leaders of Jacob,
you rulers of Israel,
who despise justice
and distort all that is right;[m]
10 who build[n] Zion with bloodshed,[o]
and Jerusalem with wickedness.[p]
11 Her leaders judge for a bribe,[q]
her priests teach for a price,[r]
and her prophets tell fortunes for
money.[s]
Yet they look[t] for the LORD's support
and say,
"Is not the LORD among us?
No disaster will come upon us."[u]
12 Therefore because of you,
Zion will be plowed like a field,
Jerusalem will become a heap of
rubble,[v]
the temple[w] hill a mound overgrown
with thickets.[x]

The Mountain of the LORD

4:1-3pp — Isa 2:1-4

4 In the last days

the mountain[y] of the LORD's temple will
be established
as the highest of the mountains;
it will be exalted above the hills,[z]
and peoples will stream to it.[a]

2 Many nations will come and say,

"Come, let us go up to the mountain of
the LORD,[b]
to the temple of the God of Jacob.[c]
He will teach us[d] his ways,[e]
so that we may walk in his paths."
The law[f] will go out from Zion,
the word of the LORD from
Jerusalem.

3:8 [l] S Isa 57:12; 61:2 **3:9** [m] Ps 58:1-2; S Isa 1:23 **3:10** [n] S Jer 22:13 [o] Isa 59:7; Mic 7:2; Na 3:1; Hab 2:12 [p] Jer 22:17; S Eze 22:27 **3:11** [q] S Ex 23:8; S Lev 19:15; Mal 2:9 [r] S Eze 13:19 [s] Isa 1:23; S 56:11; Jer 6:13; S La 4:13; S Hos 4:8, 18 [t] S Isa 10:20 [u] Jer 7:4; S Eze 34:2 **3:12** [v] S 2Ki 25:9; S Isa 6:11 [w] S Jer 52:13 [x] S Lev 26:31; S Jer 17:3; S 22:6; S La 5:18; S Eze 5:14 **4:1** [y] S Ps 48:1; Zec 8:3 [z] S Eze 17:22 [a] S Ps 22:27; 86:9; S Jer 3:17; S 31:12; S Da 2:35 **4:2** [b] S Jer 31:6; S Eze 20:40 [c] Zec 2:11; 14:16 [d] S Ps 119:171 [e] Ps 25:8-9; S Isa 54:13 [f] S Dt 18:18 **4:3** [g] S Isa 11:4 [h] Joel 3:10; Zec 9:10 [i] S Ps 46:9 [j] Zec 8:20-22 **4:4** [k] S 1Ki 4:25 [l] S Lev 26:6; S Eze 39:26 [m] S Isa 1:20 **4:5** [n] 2Ki 17:29; Ac 14:16 [o] Jos 24:14-15; Isa 26:8; Zec 10:12 **4:6** [p] S Jer 31:8

3 He will judge between many peoples
and will settle disputes for strong
nations far and wide.[g]
They will beat their swords into
plowshares
and their spears into pruning hooks.[h]
Nation will not take up sword against
nation,
nor will they train for war[i] anymore.[j]
4 Everyone will sit under their own vine
and under their own fig tree,[k]
and no one will make them afraid,[l]
for the LORD Almighty has spoken.[m]
5 All the nations may walk
in the name of their gods,[n]
but we will walk in the name of the
LORD
our God for ever and ever.[o]

The LORD's Plan

6 "In that day," declares the LORD,

"I will gather the lame;[p]
I will assemble the exiles[q]
and those I have brought to grief.[r]
7 I will make the lame my remnant,[s]
those driven away a strong nation.[t]
The LORD will rule over them in Mount
Zion[u]
from that day and forever.[v]
8 As for you, watchtower of the flock,
stronghold[a] of Daughter Zion,
the former dominion will be restored[w]
to you;
kingship will come to Daughter
Jerusalem.[x]"

9 Why do you now cry aloud —
have you no king[b][y]?

[a] 8 Or *hill* [b] 9 Or *King*

[q] S Ps 106:47 [r] S Eze 34:13, 16; S 37:21; Zep 3:19 **4:7** [s] S Joel 2:32; S Mic 2:12 [t] S Ge 12:2 [u] S Isa 2:2 [v] S Da 2:44; S 7:14; S Lk 1:33; Rev 11:15 **4:8** [w] S Isa 1:26 [x] Zec 9:9 **4:9** [y] Jer 8:19

3:9 – 12 A message of indictment and of judgment on corrupt leaders, resulting in Zion's fall.
3:9 *Hear.* See note on 1:2. *Jacob … Israel.* See v. 1 and note.
3:10 *who build Zion with bloodshed.* See Eze 7:23 and note.
3:11 *for a bribe.* See 1Sa 8:3 and note; Isa 1:23; 5:23.
3:12 The destruction of Jerusalem occurred in 586 BC. This verse was quoted a century later in Jer 26:18 (see note there). Jer 26:19 indicates that Micah's preaching may have been instrumental in the reformation under King Hezekiah (see 2Ki 18:1 – 6; 2Ch 29 – 31). *Jerusalem … heap of rubble.* Just like Samaria (see 1:6).
4:1 – 5 An eschatological ("In the last days," v. 1) salvation message: Zion's future exaltation. Although the temple will be destroyed (3:12), in the Zion of the future it will be restored in even grander style to become the worship and learning center for all nations.
4:1 – 3 See notes on Isa 2:2 – 4, a passage that is almost the same as these verses.
4:3 *plowshares.* See note on Isa 2:4.
4:4 *vine and … fig tree.* A reference to the peaceful security of the kingdom of God. See 1Ki 4:25; 2Ki 18:31; Zec 3:10. *no one will make them afraid.* Quoted in Zep 3:13. Fear will be a thing of the past.
4:5 *walk in the name of the LORD.* Confess, love, obey and rely on the Lord. Cf. Zec 10:12.
4:6 – 8 Another eschatological ("In that day," v. 6) salvation message: restoration of a remnant and Zion.
4:6 *In that day.* The Messianic period (see v. 1; see also notes on Isa 2:11,17,20; Joel 1:15).
4:7 *remnant.* The people of God (see 2:12; see also note on Isa 1:9).
4:8 *watchtower of the flock.* Jerusalem, the capital city of David, the shepherd-king. *Daughter Zion … Daughter Jerusalem.* See vv. 10,13; a personification of Jerusalem (see note on 2Ki 19:21). *former dominion.* The kingdom of David will be restored under the Messiah.
4:9 – 13 In vv. 9 – 10 Micah foresees the collapse of the monarchy and the impending exile in 586 BC, as well as the restoration beginning in 538. Verses 11 – 13 are a prophecy of judgment against the gloating enemies of Jerusalem.
4:9 – 10 A prophecy of judgment and salvation. The next three units (vv. 9 – 10,11 – 13; 5:1 – 4) all begin

Has your ruler[a] perished,
that pain seizes you like that of a
woman in labor?[z]
10 Writhe in agony, Daughter Zion,
like a woman in labor,
for now you must leave the city
to camp in the open field.
You will go to Babylon;[a]
there you will be rescued.
There the LORD will redeem[b] you
out of the hand of your enemies.

11 But now many nations
are gathered against you.
They say, "Let her be defiled,
let our eyes gloat[c] over Zion!"
12 But they do not know
the thoughts of the LORD;
they do not understand his plan,[d]
that he has gathered them like
sheaves to the threshing floor.
13 "Rise and thresh,[e] Daughter Zion,
for I will give you horns of iron;
I will give you hooves of bronze,
and you will break to pieces many
nations."[f]
You will devote their ill-gotten gains to
the LORD,[g]
their wealth to the Lord of all the
earth.

A Promised Ruler From Bethlehem

5 [b] Marshal your troops now, city of
troops,
for a siege is laid against us.
They will strike Israel's ruler
on the cheek[h] with a rod.

2 "But you, Bethlehem[i] Ephrathah,[j]
though you are small among the
clans[c] of Judah,
out of you will come for me
one who will be ruler[k] over Israel,
whose origins are from of old,[l]
from ancient times."[m]

3 Therefore Israel will be abandoned[n]
until the time when she who is in
labor bears a son,
and the rest of his brothers return
to join the Israelites.

4 He will stand and shepherd his flock[o]
in the strength of the LORD,
in the majesty of the name of the
LORD his God.
And they will live securely, for then his
greatness[p]
will reach to the ends of the earth.

5 And he will be our peace[q]
when the Assyrians invade[r] our land
and march through our fortresses.
We will raise against them seven
shepherds,
even eight commanders,[s]
6 who will rule[d] the land of Assyria with
the sword,
the land of Nimrod[t] with drawn
sword.[e][u]
He will deliver us from the Assyrians
when they invade our land
and march across our borders.[v]

7 The remnant[w] of Jacob will be
in the midst of many peoples
like dew[x] from the LORD,
like showers on the grass,[y]
which do not wait for anyone
or depend on man.

4:9 [z] S Ge 3:16; Jer 30:6; 48:41 **4:10** [a] S Dt 21:10; 2Ki 20:18; Isa 43:14 [b] S Isa 48:20 **4:11** [c] S La 2:16; S Ob 1:12; Mic 7:8 **4:12** [d] S Ge 50:20; S Isa 55:8; Ro 11:33-34 **4:13** [e] S Isa 21:10 [f] S Isa 45:1; S Da 2:44 [g] S Isa 23:18 **5:1** [h] La 3:30 **5:2** [i] S Jn 7:42 [j] S Ge 35:16; S 48:7 [k] S Nu 24:19; S 1Sa 13:14; S 2Sa 6:21; S 2Ch 7:18 [l] Ps 102:25 [m] Mt 2:6* **5:3** [n] S Jer 7:29 **5:4** [o] Isa 40:11; 49:9; S Eze 34:11-15, 23; Mic 7:14 [p] Isa 52:13; Lk 1:32 **5:5** [q] S Isa 9:6; S Lk 2:14; Col 1:19-20 [r] Isa 8:7 [s] Isa 10:24-27 **5:6** [t] Ge 10:8 [u] Zep 2:13 [v] Na 2:11-13 **5:7** [w] S Am 5:15; S Mic 2:12 [x] S Ps 133:3 [y] Isa 44:4

[a] 9 Or *Ruler* [b] In Hebrew texts 5:1 is numbered 4:14, and 5:2-15 is numbered 5:1-14. [c] 2 Or *rulers* [d] 6 Or *crush* [e] 6 Or *Nimrod in its gates*

with the Hebrew word for "now" and end with an assertion that the present or anticipated bad situation will be changed for the better (here: from distress to deliverance).
4:11–13 A prophecy of judgment and salvation: from siege to victory (see note on vv. 9–10).
5:1–4 A prophecy of judgment and salvation: from helpless ruler to ideal King (see note on 4:9–10), who will be born in Bethlehem and whose "greatness will reach to the ends of the earth" (v. 4).
5:1 Jerusalem will be besieged, and her kings will be seized and taken to Babylon (the last king, Zedekiah, was blinded; see 2Ki 25:7 and note).
5:2 Quoted in part in Mt 2:6. In contrast to the dire prediction of v. 1, Micah shifts to a positive note. *Ephrathah.* The region in which Bethlehem was located (see Ru 1:2 and note). *ruler.* Ultimately Christ, who will rule (see note on 4:8) for God the Father. *origins … from of old.* His beginnings were much earlier than his human birth (see Jn 8:58). A Hebrew expression equivalent to "from of old" here occurs in 7:20 ("in days long ago"). *from ancient times.* Within history (see 2Sa 7:12–16; Isa 9:6–7 and notes; Am 9:11)—and even from eternity (see Jn 1:1,14,18; 8:58; 17:5; Php 2:5–11; Col 1:15–20; Heb 1:1–3 and notes). An almost identical Hebrew expression occurs in 7:14 ("as in days long ago") and in Am 9:11 ("as it used to be") of the time of David. So these time phrases are anchored in history.
5:3 *Israel will be abandoned.* Until the Messiah is born and begins his rule. *Israel.* See note on 1:5.
5:4 The Messiah will shepherd and rule in the "strength" and "majesty" of God the Father.
5:5–6 A salvation message of deliverance: The ideal King will "deliver" (v. 6) his people. Note the *a–b–b/a–b–b* scansion pattern at the beginning and end of this unit. Or one could analyze the structure of the entire unit as consisting of an *a–b–c–d/d–a–b–c* pattern (a "chiasmus"), with each *d* representing two lines.
5:5 *our peace.* Jesus is "our peace" (Eph 2:14). In addition to freedom from war, the Hebrew word for "peace" also connotes prosperity in the OT. See notes on Isa 9:6 ("Prince of Peace"); Lk 2:14. *Assyrians.* Symbolic of all the enemies of God's people in every age. See Isa 11:11; Zec 10:10 and notes. *We.* The people of God. *seven … eight.* A figurative way of saying "many" (see note on Job 5:19).
5:6 *land of Nimrod.* Assyria. See Ge 10:8–12. *He.* The ruler of v. 2.
5:7–9 A salvation message of deliverance: the remnant among the nations.
5:7–8 *remnant.* See note on 4:7.
5:7 *like dew from the LORD.* See Isa 26:19; Hos 14:5 and notes.

8 The remnant of Jacob will be
among the nations,
in the midst of many
peoples,
like a lion among the beasts of
the forest,[z]
like a young lion among
flocks of sheep,
which mauls and mangles[a] as
it goes,
and no one can rescue.[b]
9 Your hand will be lifted up[c]
in triumph over your
enemies,
and all your foes will be
destroyed.

10 "In that day," declares the
LORD,
"I will destroy your horses
from among you
and demolish your chariots.[d]
11 I will destroy the cities[e] of your
land
and tear down all your
strongholds.[f]
12 I will destroy your witchcraft
and you will no longer cast
spells.[g]
13 I will destroy your idols[h]
and your sacred stones from
among you;
you will no longer bow down
to the work of your hands.[i]
14 I will uproot from among you
your Asherah poles[a][k]
when I demolish your cities.
15 I will take vengeance[l] in anger and
wrath
on the nations that have not obeyed
me."

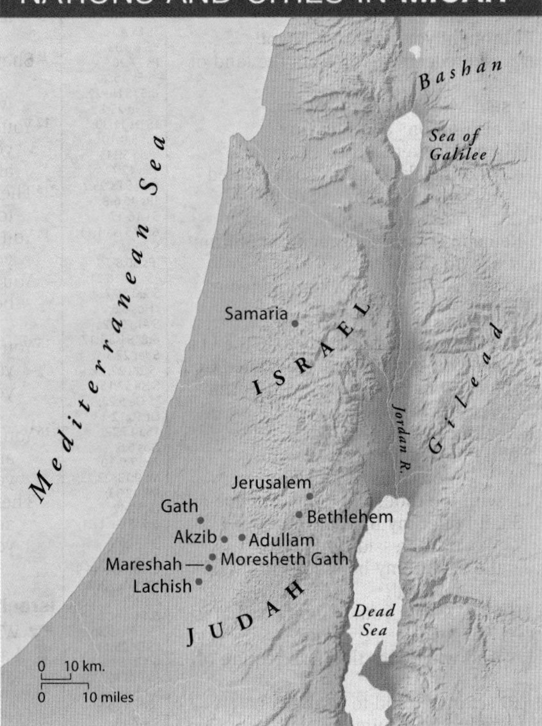

The LORD's Case Against Israel

6 Listen to what the LORD says:
"Stand up, plead my case before the
mountains;[m]
let the hills hear what you have to say.
2 "Hear,[n] you mountains, the LORD's
accusation;[o]
listen, you everlasting foundations of
the earth.
For the LORD has a case[p] against his
people;
he is lodging a charge[q] against Israel.

[a] 14 That is, wooden symbols of the goddess Asherah

5:8 [z] S Ge 49:9 [a] Mic 4:13; Zec 10:5 [b] S Ps 50:22; S Isa 5:29; S Hos 5:14 **5:9** [c] S Ps 10:12 **5:10** [d] Ex 15:4, 19; S Hos 14:3; Hag 2:22; Zec 9:10 **5:11** [e] S Dt 29:23; Isa 6:11 [f] S La 2:2; S Hos 10:14; Am 5:9 **5:12** [g] Dt 18:10-12; Isa 2:6; 8:19 **5:13** [h] Na 1:14 [i] Hos 10:2 [j] S Isa 2:18; S Eze 6:9; Zec 13:2 **5:14** [k] S Ex 34:13; S Jdg 3:7; S 2Ki 17:10 **5:15** [l] S Isa 65:12 **6:1** [m] S Ps 50:1; S Eze 6:2 **6:2** [n] Dt 32:1 [o] S Hos 12:2 [p] S Isa 3:13 [q] Ps 50:7; S Jer 2:9

5:8 *lion.* Like the previous simile (v. 7), this pictures the inevitable progress of the people of God toward triumph over their enemies (v. 9). God's kingdom will be victorious.
5:9 *Your.* The remnant's (vv. 7–8).
5:10–15 An eschatological ("In that day," v. 10) salvation message: obliteration of military power and pagan worship. In the Messianic era the people of God will not depend on weapons of war or pagan idols (cf. 4:3 and note on Isa 2:4). The successes of his people are always achieved by dependence on him.
5:10 *In that day.* See note on 4:6.
5:14 *Asherah poles.* See Ex 34:13 and note.
6:1—7:20 The third cycle of judgment (6:1—7:7) and salvation/restoration (7:8–20; see Introduction: Literary Analysis; Outline).
6:1–16 This chapter depicts a courtroom scene in which the Lord lodges a legal complaint against Israel.
6:1–8 A divine covenant lawsuit. In v. 1 the Lord instructs his prophet to present his (i.e., the Lord's; see v. 2) case; in v. 2 he summons the mountains to listen as witnesses to his accusation. Then the Lord speaks to his people in vv. 3–5, poignantly reminding them of his gracious acts in their behalf. In vv. 6–7 Israel speaks, and in v. 8 Micah responds directly to the nation, answering the questions of vv. 6–7.
6:1–2 *mountains ... foundations of the earth.* Inanimate objects were called on as third-party witnesses because of their enduring nature and because they were witnesses to the Lord's covenant (see Dt 32:1; Jos 24:27; Isa 1:2 and note).
6:1 *Listen.* See note on 1:2; see also 3:1.
6:2 *Israel.* Primarily Judah here (see note on 1:5).

3 "My people, what have I done to you?
How have I burdened[r] you?[s] Answer
me.
4 I brought you up out of Egypt[t]
and redeemed you from the land of
slavery.[u]
I sent Moses[v] to lead you,
also Aaron[w] and Miriam.[x]
5 My people, remember
what Balak[y] king of Moab plotted
and what Balaam son of Beor
answered.
Remember your journey from Shittim[z]
to Gilgal,[a]
that you may know the righteous
acts[b] of the LORD."

6 With what shall I come before[c] the LORD
and bow down before the exalted God?
Shall I come before him with burnt
offerings,
with calves a year old?[d]
7 Will the LORD be pleased with
thousands of rams,[e]
with ten thousand rivers of olive oil?[f]
Shall I offer my firstborn[g] for my
transgression,
the fruit of my body for the sin of
my soul?[h]
8 He has shown you, O mortal, what is
good.
And what does the LORD require of
you?
To act justly[i] and to love mercy
and to walk humbly[a][j] with your God.[k]

Israel's Guilt and Punishment

9 Listen! The LORD is calling to the city —
and to fear your name is wisdom —
"Heed the rod[l] and the One who
appointed it.[b]

6:3 [r] Jer 2:5 [s] Jer 2:5 **6:4** [t] S Ex 3:10; S 6:6 [u] Dt 7:8 [v] S Ex 4:16 [w] S Nu 33:1; Ps 77:20 [x] S Ex 15:20 **6:5** [y] S Nu 22:2 [z] S Nu 25:1 [a] S Dt 11:30; Jos 5:9-10 [b] Jdg 5:11; 1Sa 12:7 **6:6** [c] S Ps 95:2 [d] Ps 40:6-8; 51:16-17 **6:7** [e] S Isa 1:11; S 40:16 [f] Ps 50:8-10 [g] S Lev 18:21; S 2Ki 3:27 [h] Hos 5:6; S Am 5:22 **6:8** [i] S Isa 1:17; S Jer 22:3 [j] S 2Ki 22:19; S Isa 57:15 [k] S Ge 5:22; Dt 10:12-13; 1Sa 15:22; Hos 6:6; Zec 7:9-10; Mt 9:13; 23:23; Mk 12:33; Lk 11:42 **6:9** [l] S Ge 17:1; Isa 11:4

6:10 [m] Eze 45:9-10; S Am 3:10; 8:4-6 **6:11** [n] S Lev 19:36 [o] S Dt 25:13 **6:12** [p] S Isa 1:23 [q] S Ps 116:11; Isa 3:8 [r] S Ps 35:20; S Jer 9:3 **6:13** [s] Isa 1:7; 6:11 **6:14** [t] S Isa 9:20; S Hos 4:10 [u] Isa 30:6 **6:15** [v] S Dt 28:38; Jer 12:13 [w] Job 24:11; S Am 5:11; Zep 1:13 **6:16** [x] S 1Ki 16:25 [y] 1Ki 16:29-33 [z] Jer 7:24 [a] S Jer 25:9 [b] S Dt 28:37; S Jer 51:51; S Mic 2:6

10 Am I still to forget your ill-gotten
treasures, you wicked house,
and the short ephah,[c] which is
accursed?[m]
11 Shall I acquit someone with dishonest
scales,[n]
with a bag of false weights?[o]
12 Your rich people are violent;[p]
your inhabitants are liars[q]
and their tongues speak deceitfully.[r]
13 Therefore, I have begun to destroy[s] you,
to ruin[d] you because of your sins.
14 You will eat but not be satisfied;[t]
your stomach will still be empty.[e]
You will store up but save nothing,[u]
because what you save[f] I will give to
the sword.
15 You will plant but not harvest;[v]
you will press olives but not use the oil,
you will crush grapes but not drink
the wine.[w]
16 You have observed the statutes of Omri[x]
and all the practices of Ahab's[y] house;
you have followed their traditions.[z]
Therefore I will give you over to ruin[a]
and your people to derision;
you will bear the scorn[b] of the
nations.[g]"

Israel's Misery

7 What misery is mine!
I am like one who gathers summer fruit
at the gleaning of the vineyard;

[a] 8 Or *prudently* [b] 9 The meaning of the Hebrew for this line is uncertain. [c] 10 An ephah was a dry measure. [d] 13 Or *Therefore, I will make you ill and destroy you; / I will ruin* [e] 14 The meaning of the Hebrew for this word is uncertain. [f] 14 Or *You will press toward birth but not give birth, / and what you bring to birth* [g] 16 Septuagint; Hebrew *scorn due my people*

6:3,5 *My people.* Covenant language (see note on v. 8).
6:4 *brought you up out of Egypt.* See Ex 20:2 and note. *Moses ... Aaron and Miriam.* See Nu 12:1–2 and note on 12:2.
6:5 *Balak ... Balaam.* See Nu 22–24 and note on 22:8. *Shittim to Gilgal.* See Nu 25:1; Jos 2:1; 3:1—4:25; 4:19 and notes. *righteous acts of the LORD.* See 1Sa 12:7 and note.
6:6 The same thought is expressed in 1Sa 15:22; Ps 51:17; Isa 1:11–15; Hos 6:6 (see notes on these verses). Micah does not deny the desirability of sacrifices but shows that it does no good to offer them without obedience.
6:7 These rhetorical questions, charged with hyperbole, demand a resoundingly negative answer.
6:8 The most memorable statement in the OT defining a proper relationship to God (see Jer 22:16; Hos 6:6 and notes; cf. Jas 1:27). Micah here summarizes major themes found in the prophecies of his near contemporaries: Amos ("act justly"; cf. Am 5:24), Hosea ("love mercy"; cf. Hos 6:6) and Isaiah ("walk humbly with your God"; cf. Isa 29:19). Cf. also Mt 23:23. *O mortal.* Micah is speaking to all Israel as a corporate solidarity (see also Dt 10:12–13). *act justly ... love mercy.* The kind of obedience God expects from his covenant people. *act justly.* See note on Zec 8:16. *humbly.* Or "prudently" (see NIV text note), "carefully" or "wisely." *your God.* Covenant language in accordance with "My people" in vv. 3,5 (see note on Zec 8:8).
6:9–16 A divine covenant lawsuit containing further indictments and the sentence (a life of futility, frustration, scorn and destruction, vv. 13–15). Its outline: (1) opening statement (v. 9), (2) a list of commercial and social sins (vv. 10–12), (3) announcement of divine punishment (vv. 13–15) and (4) summary statement (v. 16).
6:9 *city.* Jerusalem.
6:10 *ephah.* About half a bushel.
6:11 See Lev 19:35; Pr 11:1 and notes; Hos 12:7; Am 8:5.
6:12 *Your.* Jerusalem's.
6:13 *Therefore.* See note on 2:3.
6:14–15 See Hag 1:6 and note.
6:16 *Omri ... Ahab's.* 1Ki 16:25,30 says that they did more evil than all the kings who preceded them. *ruin.* Disobedience brings disaster.
7:1–20 The speakers in this chapter are Micah (vv. 1–7), Zion (vv. 8–10), Micah (vv. 11–13), either Micah or Zion (v. 14), God (v. 15) and Micah (vv. 16–20). The chapter begins on a note of gloom but ends with a statement of hope.
7:1–7 Micah's lament over a decadent society.
7:1–2 Looking for the godly is like looking for summer

there is no cluster of grapes to eat,
  none of the early figs[c] that I crave.
2 The faithful have been swept from the
    land;[d]
  not one[e] upright person remains.
Everyone lies in wait[f] to shed blood;[g]
  they hunt each other[h] with nets.[i]
3 Both hands are skilled in doing
    evil;[j]
  the ruler demands gifts,
the judge accepts bribes,[k]
  the powerful dictate what they
    desire—
  they all conspire together.
4 The best of them is like a brier,[l]
  the most upright worse than a
    thorn[m] hedge.
The day God visits you has come,
  the day your watchmen sound the
    alarm.
  Now is the time of your confusion.[n]
5 Do not trust a neighbor;
  put no confidence in a friend.[o]
Even with the woman who lies in your
    embrace
  guard the words of your lips.
6 For a son dishonors his father,
  a daughter rises up against her
    mother,[p]
a daughter-in-law against her mother-
    in-law—
  a man's enemies are the members of
    his own household.[q]

7 But as for me, I watch[r] in hope[s] for the
    LORD,
  I wait for God my Savior;
  my God will hear[t] me.

Israel Will Rise

8 Do not gloat over me,[u] my enemy!
  Though I have fallen, I will rise.[v]
Though I sit in darkness,
  the LORD will be my light.[w]
9 Because I have sinned against him,
  I will bear the LORD's wrath,[x]
until he pleads my case[y]
  and upholds my cause.
He will bring me out into the light;[z]
  I will see his righteousness.[a]
10 Then my enemy will see it
  and will be covered with shame,[b]
she who said to me,
  "Where is the LORD your God?"[c]
My eyes will see her downfall;[d]
  even now she will be trampled[e]
    underfoot
  like mire in the streets.

11 The day for building your walls[f] will
    come,
  the day for extending your
    boundaries.
12 In that day people will come to you
  from Assyria[g] and the cities of
    Egypt,
even from Egypt to the Euphrates
  and from sea to sea
  and from mountain to mountain.[h]
13 The earth will become desolate
    because of its inhabitants,
  as the result of their deeds.[i]

Prayer and Praise

14 Shepherd[j] your people with your
    staff,[k]
  the flock of your inheritance,
which lives by itself in a forest,
  in fertile pasturelands.[a][l]
Let them feed in Bashan[m] and Gilead[n]
  as in days long ago.[o]

15 "As in the days when you came out of
    Egypt,
  I will show them my wonders.[p]"

16 Nations will see and be ashamed,[q]
  deprived of all their power.
They will put their hands over their
    mouths[r]
  and their ears will become deaf.

7:1 [c] S SS 2:13
7:2 [d] S Ps 12:1 [e] S Jer 2:29; 8:6 [f] Ps 10:8 [g] S Pr 6:17; S Mic 3:10 [h] S Isa 3:5 [i] S Jer 5:26
7:3 [j] S Pr 4:16 [k] S Ex 23:8; S Eze 22:12
7:4 [l] S Nu 33:55; S Eze 2:6 [m] S 2Sa 23:6 [n] S Job 31:14; Isa 22:5; S Hos 9:7
7:5 [o] Jer 9:4
7:6 [p] S Eze 22:7 [q] Mt 10:35-36*; S Mk 13:12
7:7 [r] S Isa 21:8 [s] Ps 130:5; Isa 25:9 [t] S Ps 4:3
7:8 [u] S Ps 22:17; S Pr 24:17; S Mic 4:11 [v] Ps 20:8; 37:24; S Am 9:11 [w] S 2Sa 22:29; Isa 9:2
7:9 [x] La 3:39-40 [y] S Ps 119:154 [z] S Ps 107:10 [a] Isa 46:13
7:10 [b] S Ps 35:26 [c] S Ps 42:3 [d] S Isa 51:23 [e] S 2Sa 22:43; S Job 40:12; S Isa 5:5; Zec 10:5
7:11 [f] Isa 54:11; S Am 9:11
7:12 [g] S Isa 11:11 [h] Isa 19:23-25; 60:4
7:13 [i] Isa 3:10-11; S Eze 12:19; S 33:28-29
7:14 [j] S Ps 28:9; S Mic 5:4 [k] Ps 23:4 [l] Ps 95:7 [m] S Isa 33:9 [n] S SS 4:1; S Jer 50:19 [o] Eze 36:11
7:15 [p] S Ex 3:20; Ps 78:12
7:16 [q] Isa 26:11 [r] S Jdg 18:19

[a] 14 Or *in the middle of Carmel*

fruit when the harvest has ended (see also Jer 5:1; 8:20 and notes).

7:3 Power often corrupts. *accepts bribes.* See 1Sa 8:3 and note; 12:3.

7:4 *the day your watchmen sound the alarm.* The day of judgment that the prophets warned about (see Eze 3:17–21 and note on 3:17). *visits you.* For punishment.

7:6 The family unit was disintegrating (cf. Mt 10:21,34–36).

7:7 Micah's complaint (vv. 1–6) is followed by his expression of confidence. Such a hopeful element is actually quite common in laments (see, e.g., Ps 55:16–17).

7:8–20 This completes the final salvation section in the three cycles of judgment and salvation. The unit is a prophetic liturgy made up of four subunits: (1) an expression of trust (vv. 8–10); (2) a promise of restoration (vv. 11–13); (3) a prayer, the Lord's answer and the response (vv. 14–17); and (4) a hymn of praise (vv. 18–20).

7:8 *me.* Zion. *my enemy.* Other nations (see v. 10). *Though I have fallen.* Micah foresees the destruction of Jerusalem in 586 BC.

7:10 *Where is the LORD ... ?* See notes on Ps 3:2; 10:11; 115:2; Joel 2:17; see also Ps 42:3,10; 79:10.

7:12 *In that day.* See Isa 2:11,17,20; 10:20,27; Joel 1:15 and notes. *people will come.* See 4:2.

7:14–17 It is possible that these verses constitute a prayer that God will show his wonders again as in the exodus, that the nations will see and be ashamed and that they will turn to the Lord in fear.

7:14 *Shepherd.* Rule over (see 5:4; Ps 23:1; Jer 2:8; Eze 34:2 and notes). *inheritance.* The land and people of Israel (see v. 18; Ps 94:14; see also Ps 127:3; Jer 2:7 and notes). *Bashan and Gilead.* Fertile areas with rich pasturelands (see Ge 31:21; Ps 22:12; Eze 39:18; Am 4:1 and notes).

7:16 When the nations see the awesome display of God's power (v. 15), they will be amazed.

[17]They will lick dust[s] like a snake,
like creatures that crawl on the ground.
They will come trembling[t] out of their dens;
they will turn in fear[u] to the LORD our God
and will be afraid of you.
[18]Who is a God[v] like you,
who pardons sin[w] and forgives[x] the transgression
of the remnant[y] of his inheritance?[z]
You do not stay angry[a] forever
but delight to show mercy.[b]
[19]You will again have compassion on us;
you will tread our sins underfoot
and hurl all our iniquities[c] into the depths of the sea.[d]
[20]You will be faithful to Jacob,
and show love to Abraham,[e]
as you pledged on oath to our ancestors[f]
in days long ago.[g]

7:17 [s]S Ge 3:14 [t]2Sa 22:46 [u]Isa 25:3; 59:19 **7:18** [v]S Ex 8:10; S 1Sa 2:2 [w]S Isa 43:25; S Jer 50:20; Zec 3:4 [x]S 2Ch 6:21; Ps 103:8-13 [y]S Joel 2:32; S Am 5:15; S Mic 2:12 [z]S Ex 34:9 [a]S Ps 103:9; S Isa 54:9 [b]S 2Ch 30:9; S Jer 31:20; 32:41; S Eze 18:23 **7:19** [c]S Isa 43:25 [d]S Jer 31:34 **7:20** [e]Gal 3:16 [f]Dt 7:8; Lk 1:72 [g]Ps 108:4

7:17 *lick dust like a snake.* A picture of defeat and death (see Ge 3:14 and note).

7:18–20 The conclusion to the whole book, not just to ch. 7.

7:18–19a See Ex 34:6–7a.

7:18 *Who is a God like you . . . ?* Perhaps a pun on Micah's name (see note on 1:1). See Ex 15:11 and note.

7:19 *tread . . . underfoot.* Or "subdue." When God takes away sin's guilt so that it does not condemn us (v. 18), he also takes away its power so that it does not rule over us (see Ps 19:13; cf. Ro 6:14). *iniquities into the depths of the sea.* See note on Isa 38:17; see also Jer 50:2.

7:20 *Jacob . . . Abraham.* God had sworn to Abraham (see Ge 13:16; 15:5; 22:17 and notes) and Jacob (Ge 28:14) that their descendants would be as numerous as the stars in the sky, the dust of the earth and the sand on the seashore, and he had promised Abraham that he would be the father of many nations (Ge 17:5; cf. Lk 1:54–55). All believers are ultimately included in this promise (Ro 4; Gal 3:6–29; Heb 11:12).

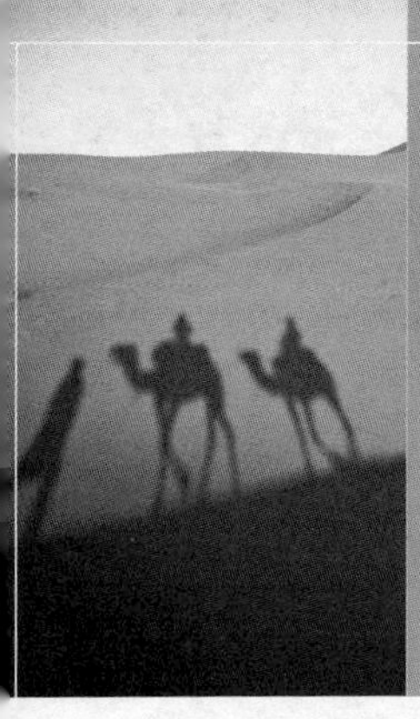

NAHUM

INTRODUCTION

Author

The book contains the "vision of Nahum" (1:1), whose name means "comfort" and is related to the name Nehemiah, meaning "The LORD comforts" or "comfort of the LORD." (Nineveh's fall, which is Nahum's theme, would bring comfort to Judah.) Nothing is known about him except his hometown (Elkosh), and even its general location is uncertain.

Date

In 3:8 – 10 the author speaks of the fall of Thebes, which happened in 663 BC, as already past. In all three chapters Nahum prophesied Nineveh's fall, which was fulfilled in 612. Nahum therefore uttered this message between 663 and 612, perhaps near the end of this period since he represents the fall of Nineveh as imminent (2:1; 3:14,19). This would place him during the reign of Josiah and make him a contemporary of Zephaniah and the young Jeremiah.

Background

Assyria (represented by Nineveh, 1:1) had already destroyed Samaria (722 – 721 BC), resulting in the captivity of the northern kingdom of Israel, and posed a present threat to Judah. The Assyrians were brutally cruel, their kings often being depicted as gloating over the gruesome punishments inflicted on conquered peoples. They conducted their wars with shocking ferocity, uprooted whole populations as state policy and deported them to other parts of their empire. The leaders of conquered cities were tortured and horribly mutilated before being executed (see note on 3:3). No wonder the dread of Assyria fell on all her neighbors!

About 700 BC King Sennacherib made Nineveh the capital of the Assyrian Empire, and it remained the capital until it was destroyed in 612. Jonah had announced its destruction earlier (Jnh 3:4), but the people put on at least a show of repentance, and the destruction was temporarily averted (see Jnh 3:10 and note). Not long after that, however, Nineveh reverted

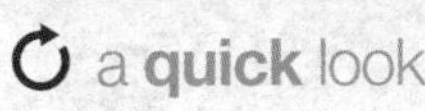

a quick look

Author:
Nahum

Audience:
The people of Judah

Date:
Shortly before 612 BC

Theme:
Nahum predicts the Lord's judgment on Nineveh for her oppression, cruelty, idolatry and wickedness.

to its extreme wickedness, cruelty and pride. The brutality reached its peak under Ashurbanipal (669 – 627), the last great ruler of the Assyrian Empire. After his death Assyria's influence and power waned rapidly until 612, when Nineveh was overthrown (see notes on 1:14; 2:1). (Further historical information is given in notes throughout the book.)

Recipients

Some words are addressed to Judah (see 1:12 – 13,15), but most are addressed to Nineveh (see 1:11,14; 2:1,13; 3:5 – 17,19) or its king (3:18). The book, however, was meant for Israelite readers living in Judah.

Literary Style

The contents are primarily made up of judgment prophecies, with appropriate descriptions and vocabulary, expressing intense moods, sights and sounds. The language is poetic, with frequent use of metaphors and similes, vivid word pictures, repetition and many short — often staccato — phrases (see, e.g., 3:1 – 3). Rhetorical questions punctuate the flow of thought, which has a marked stress on moral indignation toward injustice (cf. note on Zec 8:16).

Theological Themes

The focal point of the entire book is the Lord's judgment on Nineveh for her oppression, cruelty, idolatry and wickedness. The book ends with the destruction of the city.

According to Ro 11:22, God is not only kind but also stern. In Nahum, God is not only "slow to anger" (1:3) and "a refuge ... for those who trust in him" (1:7) but also one who "will not leave the guilty unpunished" (1:3). God's righteous and just kingdom will ultimately triumph, for kingdoms built on wickedness and tyranny must eventually fall, as Assyria did.

In addition, Nahum declares the universal sovereignty of God. God is Lord of history and of all nations; as such, he controls their destinies.

The Babylonian Chronicles describe the years 615–609 BC, including the destruction of Nineveh in 612 BC. Nahum predicts the destruction of Nineveh in great detail.

Kim Walton, courtesy of the British Museum

God's righteous and just kingdom will ultimately triumph, for kingdoms built on wickedness and tyranny must eventually fall, as Assyria did.

Outline

- I. Title (1:1)
- II. Nineveh's Judge (1:2–15)
  - A. The Lord's Kindness and Sternness (1:2–8)
  - B. Nineveh's Overthrow and Judah's Joy (1:9–15)
- III. Nineveh's Judgment (ch. 2)
  - A. Nineveh Besieged (2:1–10)
  - B. Nineveh's Desolation Contrasted with Her Former Glory (2:11–13)
- IV. Nineveh's Total Destruction (ch. 3)
  - A. Nineveh's Sins (3:1–4)
  - B. Nineveh's Doom (3:5–19)

1 A prophecy[a] concerning Nineveh.[b] The book of the vision[c] of Nahum the Elkoshite.

The Lord's Anger Against Nineveh

2 The LORD is a jealous[d] and avenging God;
the LORD takes vengeance[e] and is filled with wrath.
The LORD takes vengeance on his foes
and vents his wrath against his enemies.[f]
3 The LORD is slow to anger[g] but great in power;
the LORD will not leave the guilty unpunished.[h]
His way is in the whirlwind[i] and the storm,[j]
and clouds[k] are the dust of his feet.
4 He rebukes[l] the sea and dries it up;[m]
he makes all the rivers run dry.
Bashan and Carmel[n] wither
and the blossoms of Lebanon fade.
5 The mountains quake[o] before him
and the hills melt away.[p]
The earth trembles[q] at his presence,
the world and all who live in it.[r]
6 Who can withstand[s] his indignation?
Who can endure[t] his fierce anger?[u]
His wrath is poured out like fire;[v]
the rocks are shattered[w] before him.

7 The LORD is good,[x]
a refuge in times of trouble.[y]
He cares for[z] those who trust in him,[a]
8 but with an overwhelming flood[b]
he will make an end of Nineveh;
he will pursue his foes into the realm of darkness.

9 Whatever they plot[c] against the LORD
he will bring[a] to an end;
trouble will not come a second time.
10 They will be entangled among thorns[d]
and drunk[e] from their wine;
they will be consumed like dry stubble.[b][f]
11 From you, Nineveh, has one come forth
who plots evil against the LORD
and devises wicked plans.

12 This is what the LORD says:

"Although they have allies and are numerous,
they will be destroyed[g] and pass away.
Although I have afflicted you, Judah,
I will afflict you no more.[h]
13 Now I will break their yoke[i] from your neck
and tear your shackles away."[j]

14 The LORD has given a command concerning you, Nineveh:
"You will have no descendants to bear your name.[k]

[a] 9 Or *What do you foes plot against the LORD? / He will bring it* [b] 10 The meaning of the Hebrew for this verse is uncertain.

1:1 [a] S Isa 13:1; 19:1; Jer 23:33-34 [b] S Ge 10:11; S Jer 50:18; Na 2:8; 3:7 [c] S Isa 1:1 **1:2** [d] S Ex 20:5 [e] S Ge 4:24; S Dt 32:41; Ps 94:1 [f] S Dt 7:10 **1:3** [g] S Ne 9:17 [h] S Ex 34:7 [i] S Ex 14:21; S 2Ki 2:1 [j] S Ps 50:3 [k] S 2Sa 22:10; S Ps 104:3 **1:4** [l] S 2Sa 22:16 [m] S Ex 14:22 [n] S Isa 33:9 **1:5** [o] S Ex 19:18; S Job 9:6 [p] S Mic 1:4 [q] S Joel 2:10 [r] S Eze 38:20 **1:6** [s] S Ps 130:3 [t] S Eze 22:14 [u] S Ps 76:7 [v] S Isa 5:24-25; S 42:25; S Jer 10:10 [w] 1Ki 19:11 **1:7** [x] S Jer 33:11 [y] S Jer 17:17 [z] S Ps 1:6 [a] S Ps 22:9 **1:8** [b] S Isa 8:7; S Da 9:26 **1:9** [c] S Hos 7:15 **1:10** [d] S 2Sa 23:6 [e] S Isa 49:26 [f] S Isa 5:24; Mal 4:1 **1:12** [g] S Isa 10:34 [h] Isa 54:6-8; S La 3:31-32 **1:13** [i] S Isa 9:4 [j] S Job 12:18; S Ps 107:14 **1:14** [k] S Isa 14:22

1:1 The title of the book. *prophecy.* See Isa 13:1; Hab 1:1 and notes. *Nineveh.* See Introduction: Background; see also notes on Jnh 1:2; 3:3. Here the capital city stands for the entire Assyrian Empire. *vision.* See Pr 29:18; Isa 1:1; Ob 1 and notes. *Nahum the Elkoshite.* See Introduction: Author.

1:2–3 The covenant name Yahweh ("the LORD") is emphasized here (see notes on Ge 2:4; Ex 3:14–15; 6:6; Dt 28:58).

1:2 *jealous.* See note on Ex 20:5. *avenging … vengeance … vengeance.* God acts justly in judgment toward all who oppose him and his kingdom. The repetition is for emphasis (see note on Jer 7:4). "It is mine to avenge; I will repay" (Dt 32:35; see note there), says the Lord. *wrath.* See notes on Ps 2:5; Ro 1:18.

1:3 *slow to anger … not leave the guilty unpunished.* See Ex 34:6–7 and note. *the guilty.* Such as Nineveh. *whirlwind … storm … clouds.* Awesome natural phenomena that display God's majesty and power. See notes on Job 38:1; Ps 18:7–15; 68:4; 77:16–19; 104:3–4.

1:4 *rebukes the sea and dries it up.* As at the crossing of the "Red Sea" (see Ex 14:1—15:12; see also Ps 18:15 and note). *makes all the rivers run dry.* As at the crossing of the Jordan (see Jos 3:1—4:24 and note). *Bashan … Carmel … Lebanon.* See notes on Ps 22:12; SS 7:5; Isa 2:13; 33:9; 35:2; Eze 39:18; Am 4:1. These three places were noted for their fertility, vineyards and trees, but at the Lord's word they wither.

1:5 *mountains … hills … earth … world.* Emblems of stability and permanence.

1:6 *Who can withstand … ? Who can endure … ?* Rhetorical questions. If mountains quake before the Lord (v. 5), what human beings can think that they are not vulnerable? Cf. Ro 2:3–5; Rev 6:17.

1:7 *those who trust in him.* Such as Judah.

1:8 *overwhelming flood.* Symbolic of an invading army (see Isa 8:7–8; 28:17–19). *end … darkness.* In 612 BC that end came for Nineveh, and the darkness enveloped her.

1:9 *they plot.* See note on v. 11. *trouble will not come a second time.* God never permitted the Assyrians a second victory over his people; the first was the fall of Samaria (722–721 BC) and the northern kingdom of Israel (Sennacherib's invasion of Judah and Jerusalem in 701 was not a complete victory; see 2Ki 18:13—19:36).

1:10 *drunk from their wine.* See 3:11 and note; but perhaps the line here should read: "and drenched as with their wine,/ yet they …" (see NIV text note).

1:11 *one … who plots evil.* Possibly the Assyrian king Ashurbanipal (669–627 BC), the last great Assyrian king, whose western expeditions succeeded in subduing Egypt and to whom King Manasseh had to submit as a vassal (see 2Ch 33:11–13 and notes on 33:11; Ezr 4:9–10). *plots evil against the LORD.* All such schemes end in futility and destruction (Ps 2:1–4).

1:12 *they.* The Assyrians. *I have afflicted you.* God had used Assyria as the rod of his anger against his covenant-breaking people in the days of Ahaz (Isa 10:5) and again in the time of Manasseh.

1:13 See Jer 27:2 and note. *I will break their yoke.* Judah was Assyria's vassal; that yoke would be broken.

1:14 *I will prepare your grave.* God used the Babylonians and Medes to dig Nineveh's grave in 612 BC. For the fulfillment of this prophecy, see Eze 32:22–23.

I will destroy the images[l] and idols
that are in the temple of your gods.
I will prepare your grave,[m]
for you are vile."

15 Look, there on the mountains,
the feet of one who brings good news,[n]
who proclaims peace![o]
Celebrate your festivals,[p] Judah,
and fulfill your vows.
No more will the wicked invade you;[q]
they will be completely destroyed.[a]

Nineveh to Fall

2 [b] An attacker[r] advances against you,
Nineveh.
Guard the fortress,
watch the road,
brace yourselves,
marshal all your strength!

2 The LORD will restore[s] the splendor[t] of
Jacob
like the splendor of Israel,
though destroyers have laid them waste
and have ruined their vines.

3 The shields of the soldiers are red;
the warriors are clad in scarlet.[u]
The metal on the chariots flashes
on the day they are made ready;
the spears of juniper are
brandished.[c]

4 The chariots[v] storm through the streets,
rushing back and forth through the
squares.
They look like flaming torches;
they dart about like lightning.

5 Nineveh summons her picked troops,
yet they stumble[w] on their way.
They dash to the city wall;
the protective shield is put in place.

6 The river gates[x] are thrown open
and the palace collapses.

7 It is decreed[d] that Nineveh
be exiled and carried away.
Her female slaves moan[y] like doves
and beat on their breasts.[z]

8 Nineveh is like a pool
whose water is draining away.
"Stop! Stop!" they cry,
but no one turns back.

9 Plunder the silver!
Plunder the gold!
The supply is endless,
the wealth from all its treasures!

10 She is pillaged, plundered, stripped!
Hearts melt,[a] knees give way,
bodies tremble, every face grows
pale.[b]

11 Where now is the lions' den,[c]
the place where they fed their
young,
where the lion and lioness went,
and the cubs, with nothing to fear?

1:14 [l] Mic 5:13 [m] S Jer 28:8; Eze 32:22-23 **1:15** [n] Isa 40:9; Ro 10:15 [o] S Isa 52:7; Ac 10:36 [p] Lev 23:2-4 [q] S Isa 52:1 **2:1** [r] Jer 51:20 **2:2** [s] S Eze 37:23 [t] Isa 60:15 **2:3** [u] S Eze 23:14-15 **2:4** [v] S Jer 4:13; S Eze 23:24 **2:5** [w] Jer 46:12 **2:6** [x] Isa 45:1; Na 3:13 **2:7** [y] S Ge 8:8; S Isa 59:11 [z] Isa 32:12 **2:10** [a] S Jos 2:11; S 7:5 [b] S Isa 29:22 **2:11** [c] Isa 5:29

[a] *15* In Hebrew texts this verse (1:15) is numbered 2:1. [b] In Hebrew texts 2:1-13 is numbered 2:2-14. [c] *3* Hebrew; Septuagint and Syriac *ready; / the horsemen rush to and fro.* [d] *7* The meaning of the Hebrew for this word is uncertain.

1:15 *mountains.* Of Judah. *feet of one who brings good news.* This verse sets forth a principle that is applicable in several contexts of deliverance. Here the reference is to the good news of deliverance from the Assyrian threat; in Isa 52:7, deliverance from Babylonian exile; in Ro 10:15, deliverance from sin through the gospel ("good news") of Christ. *Celebrate your festivals.* In the joy of your deliverance. *fulfill your vows.* Those you uttered in the time of distress (see notes on Ps 7:17; 50:14; Jnh 2:9). *No more will the wicked invade you.* The Assyrian invasion in the days of Manasseh was the last (see v. 12 and note). *wicked.* See note on Dt 13:13. *completely destroyed.* Fulfilled in 612 when Nineveh fell (see note on v. 14).

2:1 *attacker.* Refers to the alliance of the Medes under Cyaxares and the Babylonians under Nabopolassar. *Guard the fortress ... marshal all your strength!* Probably irony, touched with sarcasm. *road.* By which the enemies will come.

2:2 *restore the splendor of Jacob ... Israel.* The nation will be restored to its previous greatness.

2:3 *the soldiers.* Those of the attacker (v. 1), or perhaps those of Nineveh itself. *red.* Either (1) the color of the shields, (2) a reference to blood on them or (3) the result of the reflection of the sun shining on them. *brandished.* Ready to use.

2:4 *chariots ... rushing.* Refers to either (1) the Assyrian war chariots, as the Assyrians take frantic but vain steps to defend themselves, or (2) the chariots of Nineveh's invaders.

2:5 *Nineveh.* That is, the king of Assyria. *city wall.* A moat 150 feet wide had to be filled in before reaching Nineveh's wall, which was almost 8 miles long with 15 gates. Then battering rams were moved up. *protective shield.* A large defensive framework covered with hides to deflect stones and arrows.

2:6 *river gates.* Perhaps the dams on the Khoser River, which ran through the city to the Tigris River. They were either already in place or quickly built to back up the river water, then suddenly released so the flood would damage the walls. *palace collapses.* One ancient historian (the author of the *Babylonian Chronicles*) speaks of a flood that washed away some of the wall, making it easier for the invaders to enter the city.

2:7 *female slaves.* Even the lowest in the social order will not escape the judgment.

2:8 *like a pool ... water is draining away.* Some think that this refers to the Tigris and the smaller rivers encircling and running through parts of the city, as well as to a system of dams to make the city more impenetrable. Others take the language less literally as a reference to Nineveh's people fleeing, like water draining from a pool.

2:9 The cry of the invaders.

2:10 *pillaged, plundered, stripped!* The Babylonian Chronicles confirm the fact that a great quantity of plunder was carried off by the invaders. *Hearts melt.* The powerful, insolent Ninevites become helpless with fear.

2:11–13 Nahum ironically contrasts the devastated and desolate city of Nineveh with its former glory and power, expressed in figurative terms.

2:11 *lion and lioness.* See Isa 5:29; Jer 4:7. The lion is an appropriate image to apply to Assyria because of the rapacious ways of the Assyrian monarchs and because Nineveh contained numerous lion sculptures.

[12]The lion killed[d] enough for his cubs
and strangled the prey for his mate,
filling his lairs[e] with the kill
and his dens with the prey.[f]

[13]"I am against[g] you,"
declares the LORD Almighty.
"I will burn up your chariots in smoke,[h]
and the sword[i] will devour your young lions.
I will leave you no prey on the earth.
The voices of your messengers
will no longer be heard."[j]

Woe to Nineveh

3 Woe to the city of blood,[k]
full of lies,[l]
full of plunder,
never without victims!
[2]The crack of whips,
the clatter of wheels,
galloping horses
and jolting chariots!
[3]Charging cavalry,
flashing swords
and glittering spears!
Many casualties,
piles of dead,
bodies without number,
people stumbling over the corpses[m]—
[4]all because of the wanton lust of a prostitute,
alluring, the mistress of sorceries,[n]
who enslaved nations by her prostitution[o]
and peoples by her witchcraft.

[5]"I am against[p] you," declares the LORD Almighty.
"I will lift your skirts[q] over your face.
I will show the nations your nakedness[r]
and the kingdoms your shame.
[6]I will pelt you with filth,[s]
I will treat you with contempt[t]
and make you a spectacle.[u]
[7]All who see you will flee[v] from you and say,
'Nineveh[w] is in ruins[x]—who will mourn for her?'[y]
Where can I find anyone to comfort[z] you?"

[8]Are you better than[a] Thebes,[b]
situated on the Nile,[c]
with water around her?
The river was her defense,
the waters her wall.
[9]Cush[a][d] and Egypt were her boundless strength;
Put[e] and Libya[f] were among her allies.
[10]Yet she was taken captive[g]
and went into exile.
Her infants were dashed[h] to pieces
at every street corner.
Lots[i] were cast for her nobles,
and all her great men were put in chains.[j]
[11]You too will become drunk;[k]
you will go into hiding[l]
and seek refuge from the enemy.

[12]All your fortresses are like fig trees
with their first ripe fruit;[m]
when they are shaken,
the figs[n] fall into the mouth of the eater.
[13]Look at your troops—
they are all weaklings.[o]

2:12 [d]S Jer 51:34 [e]S Jer 4:7 [f]S Isa 37:18 **2:13** [g]Isa 10:5-13; S Jer 21:13; Na 3:5 [h]Ps 46:9 [i]S 2Sa 2:26 [j]S Mic 5:6 **3:1** [k]S Eze 22:2; S Mic 3:10 [l]Ps 12:2 **3:3** [m]2Ki 19:35; Isa 34:3; Jer 47:3 **3:4** [n]S Isa 47:9 [o]S Isa 23:17; Eze 16:25-29 **3:5** [p]S Na 2:13 [q]S Isa 20:4; Jer 13:22 [r]S Isa 47:3 **3:6** [s]S Ex 29:14; S Job 9:31 [t]S 1Sa 2:30; S Jer 51:37 [u]Isa 14:16 **3:7** [v]S Isa 13:14; S 31:9 [w]S Na 1:1 [x]S Job 3:14 [y]S Jer 15:5 [z]S Isa 51:19 **3:8** [a]Am 6:2 [b]S Jer 46:25 [c]Isa 19:6-9 **3:9** [d]S Ge 10:6; S 2Ch 12:3 [e]S Eze 27:10 [f]Eze 30:5 **3:10** [g]S Isa 20:4 [h]S 2Ki 8:12; S Isa 13:16; Hos 13:16 [i]S Job 6:27; S Eze 24:6 [j]S Jer 40:1 **3:11** [k]S Isa 49:26 [l]S Isa 2:10 **3:12** [m]S SS 2:13 [n]S Isa 28:4 **3:13** [o]S Isa 19:16

[a] 9 That is, the upper Nile region

2:12 *filling his lairs . . . with the prey.* Nineveh was filled with the spoils of war from many conquered nations.
2:13 *I will burn up.* Nineveh's fall will be an act of divine judgment. Nineveh had been put on trial, found guilty and sentenced to destruction. *voices . . . no longer be heard.* History has confirmed this prediction.
3:1–3 See note on Joel 2:3–11.
3:1 *city of blood.* Nineveh's bloody massacres of her conquered rivals were well known. *never without victims.* The Assyrians were noted for their ruthlessness, brutality and terrible atrocities. Many of their victims were beheaded, impaled or burned.
3:3 *piles of dead.* The Assyrian king Shalmaneser III boasted of erecting a pyramid of chopped-off heads in front of an enemy's city. Other Assyrian kings stacked corpses like cordwood by the gates of defeated cities. Nahum's description of the cruel Assyrians is apropos.
3:4 *prostitute . . . prostitution.* The lure of luxury and wealth brought multitudes to Nineveh, but like the allurements of a prostitute it did not yield life's true pleasures. *sorceries . . . witchcraft.* Pagan practices (see Dt 18:10 and note on 18:9).
3:5 *lift your skirts over your face.* A common punishment of prostitutes and adulterous women (see notes on Isa 47:3; Jer 13:22; Hos 2:3,10).
3:7 *who . . . ? Where . . . ?* Rhetorical questions. Nineveh will receive no sympathy.
3:8 *Thebes.* Hebrew *No Amon,* which means "city of (the god) Amun." Thebes was the great capital of Upper (southern) Egypt. Its site is occupied today by the towns of Luxor and Karnak. It was destroyed by the Assyrians in 663 BC. See photos, pp. 1338, 1384.
3:9 *Put and Libya.* Perhaps better "Put (i.e., Libya)"; see notes on Ge 10:6; Eze 27:10; 30:5.
3:10 *Her infants were dashed to pieces.* See Ps 137:9; Isa 13:16; Hos 13:16 and notes. *her great men were put in chains.* Assyrian kings often did this; e.g., King Ashurbanipal gave this description of his treatment of a captured leader: "I . . . put a dog chain on him and made him occupy a kennel at the eastern gate of Nineveh."
3:11 *will become drunk.* Probably from the cup of God's wrath (see Isa 51:17; Jer 25:15; Eze 23:31 and notes).
3:12 *like fig trees with their first ripe fruit.* A simile for the eagerness with which the victors gather the rich loot of Nineveh. *figs fall into the mouth of the eater.* Nineveh's fortresses will finally fall just as easily.
3:13 *your troops . . . are all weaklings.* They are unable to stand against the invading armies.

The gates[p] of your land
are wide open to your enemies;
fire has consumed the bars of your
gates.[q]
14 Draw water for the siege,[r]
strengthen your defenses![s]
Work the clay,
tread the mortar,
repair the brickwork!
15 There the fire[t] will consume you;
the sword[u] will cut you down—
they will devour you like a swarm of
locusts.
Multiply like grasshoppers,
multiply like locusts![v]
16 You have increased the number of your
merchants
till they are more numerous than the
stars in the sky,
but like locusts[w] they strip the land
and then fly away.
17 Your guards are like locusts,[x]
your officials like swarms of locusts
that settle in the walls on a cold
day—
but when the sun appears they fly
away,
and no one knows where.
18 King of Assyria, your shepherds[a]
slumber;[y]
your nobles lie down to rest.[z]
Your people are scattered[a] on the
mountains
with no one to gather them.
19 Nothing can heal you;[b]
your wound is fatal.
All who hear the news about you
clap their hands[c] at your fall,
for who has not felt
your endless cruelty?[d]

3:13 [p] S Na 2:6 [q] S Isa 45:2 **3:14** [r] S 2Ch 32:4 [s] Na 2:1 **3:15** [t] S Isa 27:1 [u] S 2Sa 2:26 [v] S Jer 51:14; S Joel 1:4 **3:16** [w] S Ex 10:13 **3:17** [x] Jer 51:27 **3:18** [y] Ps 76:5-6; S Jer 25:27 [z] Isa 56:10 [a] S 1Ki 22:17 **3:19** [b] S Jer 30:13; S Mic 1:9 [c] S Job 27:23; S La 2:15; Zep 2:15 [d] Isa 37:18

[a] *18* That is, rulers

3:14 *Draw water.* A normal preparation for siege. *strengthen your defenses!* Irony, the point being that it will do no good (see 2:1 and note).

3:15 *There.* Inside your strong fortifications. *fire will consume you.* Confirmed by history and archaeology. Assyria's king died in the flames of his palace.

3:16 *your merchants … are more numerous than the stars.* Speaks of Assyria's vast trading and commercial enterprises.

3:17 *locusts.* Feared by the farmers of the ancient Near East, because they came in huge swarms and devoured everything in their path. Their activity provided an apt simile for the exploitative actions of Nineveh's officials during her destruction. *no one knows where.* Thus will Nineveh's officials disappear, without a trace. Interestingly, for centuries no one knew where Nineveh itself lay buried; in 1845 it was finally uncovered by archaeologists (see note on Zep 2:13).

3:18 *King.* The reigning king at the time of Nineveh's fall was Sin-Shar-Ishkun, so these words are prophetically addressed to him. *shepherds.* Leaders (see Jer 2:8 and note). *lie down to rest.* Die. *people are scattered.* The age-old scene of refugees fleeing a place of destruction is repeated at Nineveh.

3:19 *your wound is fatal.* Nineveh was so totally destroyed that it was never rebuilt, and within a few centuries it was covered with windblown sand. So that "great city" (Jnh 1:2; 3:2; 4:11; see note on Jnh 3:3) fell in 612 BC, never to rise again—all in fulfillment of God's word through his prophet Nahum. *your endless cruelty.* But now you lie in endless ruin.

HABAKKUK

INTRODUCTION

Author

Little is known about Habakkuk except that he was a contemporary of Jeremiah and a man of vigorous faith rooted deeply in the religious traditions of Israel. The account of his ministering to the needs of Daniel in the lions' den in the Apocryphal book Bel and the Dragon is legendary rather than historical.

Date

The prediction of the coming Babylonian invasion (1:6) indicates that Habakkuk lived in Judah toward the end of Josiah's reign (640 – 609 BC) or at the beginning of Jehoiakim's (609 – 598). The prophecy is generally dated a little before or after the battle of Carchemish (605), when Egyptian forces, which had earlier gone to the aid of the last Assyrian king, were routed by the Babylonians under Nabopolassar and Nebuchadnezzar and were pursued as far as the Egyptian border (Jer 46). Habakkuk, like Jeremiah, probably lived to see the initial fulfillment of his prophecy when Jerusalem was attacked by the Babylonians in 597.

a quick look

Author:
Habakkuk

Audience:
The people of Judah, struggling to comprehend the ways of God

Date:
About 605 BC

Theme:
The prophet Habakkuk argues with God over God's ways, which appear to him unfathomable, if not unjust; after receiving replies from God, Habakkuk responds with a beautiful confession of faith.

Theological Message

Among the prophetic writings, Habakkuk is somewhat unique in that it includes no messages addressed to Israel. It contains, rather, a dialogue between the prophet and God (see Outline). (The book of Jonah, while narrative, presents an account of conflict between the Lord and one of his prophets.) In the first two chapters, Habakkuk argues with God over God's ways, which appear to him unfathomable, if not unjust. Having received replies, he responds with a beautiful confession of faith (ch. 3).

This account of wrestling with God is, however, not just a fragment from a private journal that has somehow entered the public domain. It was composed for Israel. No doubt it represented the

Habakkuk expresses his perplexity that wickedness, strife and oppression are rampant in Judah and yet God seemingly does nothing.

Assyrian officials recording the loot taken from a conquered city. Habakkuk warns the Babylonian armies, which have plundered goods from the people of Judah, that the tables will soon turn (2:6–8).

Z. Radovan/www.BibleLandPictures.com

voice of the godly in Judah, struggling to comprehend the ways of God. God's answers therefore spoke to all who shared Habakkuk's troubled doubts. And Habakkuk's confession became a public expression—as indicated by its liturgical notations (see note on 3:1).

Habakkuk was perplexed that wickedness, strife and oppression were rampant in Judah but that God seemingly did nothing. When told that the Lord was preparing to do something about it through the "ruthless" Babylonians (1:6), his perplexity only intensified: How could God, who is "too pure to look on evil" (1:13), appoint such a nation "to execute judgment" (1:12) on a people "more righteous than themselves" (1:13)?

God makes it clear, however, that eventually the corrupt destroyer will itself be destroyed. In the end, Habakkuk learns to rest in God's sovereign appointments and await his working in a spirit of worship. He learns to wait patiently in faith (2:3–4) for God's kingdom to be expressed universally (2:14). See note on 3:18–19.

Literary Features

The author wrote clearly and with great feeling, and he penned many memorable phrases (2:2,4,14,20; 3:2,17–19). The book was popular during the intertestamental period;

a complete commentary on its first two chapters has been found among the Dead Sea Scrolls (see essay, pp. 1574–1576).

Outline

I. Title (1:1)
II. Habakkuk's First Complaint: Why Does the Evil in Judah Go Unpunished? (1:2–4)
III. God's Answer: The Babylonians Will Punish Judah (1:5–11)
IV. Habakkuk's Second Complaint: How Can a Just God Use the Wicked Babylonians to Punish a People More Righteous Than Themselves? (1:12—2:1)
V. God's Answer: Babylonia Will Also Be Punished, and Faith Will Be Rewarded (2:2–20)
VI. Habakkuk's Prayer: After Asking for Manifestations of God's Wrath and Mercy (as He Has Seen in the Past), He Closes with a Confession of Trust and Joy in God (ch. 3)

1 The prophecy[a] that Habakkuk the prophet received.

Habakkuk's Complaint

2 How long,[b] LORD, must I call for help,
but you do not listen?[c]
Or cry out to you, "Violence!"
but you do not save?[d]
3 Why do you make me look at injustice?
Why do you tolerate[e] wrongdoing?[f]
Destruction and violence[g] are before
me;
there is strife,[h] and conflict abounds.
4 Therefore the law[i] is paralyzed,
and justice never prevails.
The wicked hem in the righteous,
so that justice[j] is perverted.[k]

The LORD's Answer

5 "Look at the nations and watch —
and be utterly amazed.[l]
For I am going to do something in your
days
that you would not believe,
even if you were told.[m]
6 I am raising up the Babylonians,[a][n]
that ruthless and impetuous people,
who sweep across the whole earth[o]
to seize dwellings not their own.[p]
7 They are a feared and dreaded
people;[q]
they are a law to themselves
and promote their own honor.
8 Their horses are swifter[r] than leopards,
fiercer than wolves[s] at dusk.
Their cavalry gallops headlong;
their horsemen come from afar.
They fly like an eagle swooping to
devour;
9 they all come intent on violence.
Their hordes[b] advance like a desert
wind
and gather prisoners[t] like sand.
10 They mock kings
and scoff at rulers.[u]
They laugh at all fortified cities;
by building earthen ramps[v] they
capture them.
11 Then they sweep past like the wind[w]
and go on —
guilty people, whose own strength is
their god."[x]

Habakkuk's Second Complaint

12 LORD, are you not from everlasting?[y]
My God, my Holy One,[z] you[c] will
never die.[a]
You, LORD, have appointed[b] them to
execute judgment;
you, my Rock,[c] have ordained them
to punish.
13 Your eyes are too pure[d] to look on evil;
you cannot tolerate wrongdoing.[e]

1:1 [a] S Na 1:1 1:2 [b] S Ps 6:3 [c] Ps 13:1-2; 22:1-2 [d] Jer 14:9; Zec 1:12 1:3 [e] ver 13 [f] S Job 9:23 [g] Jer 20:8 [h] S Ps 55:9 1:4 [i] Ps 119:126 [j] S Isa 29:21 [k] S Job 19:7; S Isa 1:23; 5:20; S Eze 9:9 1:5 [l] S Isa 29:9 [m] Ac 13:41* 1:6 [n] S Dt 28:49; S 2Ki 24:2 [o] Rev 20:9 [p] S Jer 13:20; S 21:7 1:7 [q] Isa 18:7; Jer 39:5-9 1:8 [r] S Jer 4:13 [s] S Ge 49:27 1:9 [t] Hab 2:5 1:10 [u] S 2Ch 36:6 [v] S Jer 33:4 1:11 [w] Jer 4:11-12 [x] S Da 4:30 1:12 [y] S Ge 21:33 [z] Isa 31:1; 37:23 [a] Ps 118:17 [b] Isa 10:6 [c] S Ge 49:24; S Ex 33:22 1:13 [d] Ps 18:26 [e] S La 3:34-36

[a] 6 Or *Chaldeans* [b] 9 The meaning of the Hebrew for this word is uncertain. [c] 12 An ancient Hebrew scribal tradition; Masoretic Text *we*

1:1 *prophecy.* Such as the two found here (vv. 5–11; 2:2–20). Prophecies were frequently received in visions. The Hebrew word for "prophecy" (possibly meaning "burden," but perhaps only "pronouncement") often refers to revelations containing warnings of impending doom (see Isa 13:1 and note; 15:1; 19:1; 22:1), but in Zec 9:1; 12:1; Mal 1:1 it refers to messages that also contain hope. *Habakkuk.* The name is probably Babylonian and refers to a kind of garden plant. *prophet.* Habakkuk is called a prophet also in 3:1, tying ch. 3 closely to chs. 1–2. See notes on Ex 3:4; 7:1–2; 1Ki 22:19; Jnh 3:2; Zec 1:1.

1:2—2:20 A dialogue between the prophet and God. The basic themes are age-old: Why does evil seem to go unpunished? Why does God not respond to prayer?

1:2 *How long ... ?* See Ps 6:3 and note; 13:1–2; 22:1–2. *Violence!* At this time Judah was probably under King Jehoiakim, who was ambitious, cruel and corrupt. Habakkuk describes the social corruption and spiritual apostasy of Judah in the late seventh century BC.

1:3 *you tolerate.* See v. 13. The prophet was amazed that God seemed to condone cruelty and violence. *Destruction and violence are before me.* Jeremiah complains to the Lord in a similar vein (Jer 20:8).

1:4 *law is paralyzed ... justice is perverted.* Because wealthy landowners controlled the courts through bribery (see Mic 3:11; 7:3).

1:5 Paul concludes his sermon in Pisidian Antioch by quoting these words (Ac 13:41). *your ... you ... you.* Judah as a whole is addressed (the pronouns are plural). *would not believe.* To the people of Judah it was incredible that God would give them over to the arrogant Babylonians.

1:6 *I am raising up the Babylonians.* See Isa 10:5–6 and note on 10:5. The apostate nation of Judah is to be punished by an invasion of the Babylonians, a powerful people who regained their independence from Assyria in 626 BC, destroyed Assyrian power completely in 612–605 and flourished until 539. In this context, the Chaldeans (see NIV text note) are synonymous with the newly resurgent Babylonians. *seize dwellings.* See 2:6–8.

1:7 *promote their own honor.* A mark of arrogance.

1:8 The speed with which Babylonia conquered her enemies had become proverbial. *eagle.* See Dt 28:49–50 and note on 28:49.

1:9 *violence.* The rapacious cruelty of the Babylonians was more than a match for that of the people of Judah (see v. 2 and note; see also v. 3). *gather prisoners like sand.* Like their Assyrian predecessors, the Babylonians deported conquered peoples as a matter of deliberate national policy (see 2:5).

1:10 *building earthen ramps.* A siege method.

1:11 *whose own strength is their god.* The Babylonians were so proud and confident of their military might that it had virtually become their god (see v. 16).

1:12 Habakkuk cannot see the justice in Judah's being punished by an even more wicked nation, and he thinks that the Babylonians surely would not be allowed to conquer Judah completely. *from everlasting.* See Ps 90:2. *You, LORD, have appointed them.* The prophet recognizes Babylonia as God's agent of judgment (cf. Isa 7:18–20; 44:28—45:1). *Rock.* See 1Sa 2:2 and note.

1:13 A classic statement of the problem of evil within the context of Israel's faith: Why does evil appear to flourish unchecked by a just and holy God? See Ps 37; 73 and notes. *you tolerate.* See v. 3 and note. *treacherous ... wicked.* The Babylonians. *those more righteous.* Judah.

Why then do you tolerate[f] the
treacherous?[g]
Why are you silent while the wicked
swallow up those more righteous
than themselves?[h]
14 You have made people like the fish in
the sea,
like the sea creatures that have no
ruler.
15 The wicked[i] foe pulls all of them up
with hooks,[j]
he catches them in his net,[k]
he gathers them up in his dragnet;
and so he rejoices and is glad.
16 Therefore he sacrifices to his net
and burns incense[l] to his dragnet,
for by his net he lives in luxury
and enjoys the choicest food.
17 Is he to keep on emptying his net,
destroying nations without mercy?[m]

2 I will stand at my watch[n]
and station myself on the ramparts;[o]
I will look to see what he will say[p] to me,
and what answer I am to give to this
complaint.[a][q]

The Lord's Answer

2 Then the Lord replied:

"Write[r] down the revelation
and make it plain on tablets
so that a herald[b] may run with it.
3 For the revelation awaits an appointed
time;[s]
it speaks of the end[t]
and will not prove false.
Though it linger, wait[u] for it;
it[c] will certainly come
and will not delay.[v]

4 "See, the enemy is puffed up;
his desires are not upright—
but the righteous person[w] will live by
his faithfulness[d][x]—
5 indeed, wine[y] betrays him;
he is arrogant[z] and never at rest.
Because he is as greedy as the grave
and like death is never satisfied,[a]
he gathers to himself all the nations
and takes captive[b] all the peoples.

6 "Will not all of them taunt[c] him with
ridicule and scorn, saying,

" 'Woe to him who piles up stolen
goods
and makes himself wealthy by
extortion![d]
How long must this go on?'
7 Will not your creditors suddenly arise?
Will they not wake up and make you
tremble?
Then you will become their prey.[e]
8 Because you have plundered many
nations,
the peoples who are left will plunder
you.[f]
For you have shed human blood;[g]
you have destroyed lands and cities
and everyone in them.[h]

1:13 [f] ver 3 [g] S Ps 25:3 [h] S Job 21:7 **1:15** [i] Jer 5:26 [j] S Isa 19:8 [k] S Job 18:8; Jer 16:16 **1:16** [l] Jer 44:8 **1:17** [m] S Isa 14:6; 19:8 **2:1** [n] S Isa 21:8 [o] S Ps 48:13 [p] Ps 85:8 [q] S Ps 5:3; S Eze 3:17 **2:2** [r] S Isa 30:8; S Jer 36:2; S Eze 24:2; S Ro 4:24; Rev 1:19 **2:3** [s] Da 11:27 [t] Da 8:17 [u] S Ps 27:14 [v] S Eze 12:25 **2:4** [w] S Eze 18:9 [x] Ro 1:17*; Gal 3:11*; Heb 10:37-38* **2:5** [y] S Pr 20:1 [z] S Isa 2:11 [a] S Pr 27:20; S 30:15-16 [b] Hab 1:9 **2:6** [c] S Isa 14:4 [d] Am 2:8 **2:7** [e] S Pr 29:1 **2:8** [f] Isa 33:1; Jer 50:17-18; S Ob 1:15; Zec 2:8-9 [g] ver 17 [h] S Eze 39:10

[a] 1 Or *and what to answer when I am rebuked* [b] 2 Or *so that whoever reads it* [c] 3 Or *Though he linger, wait for him; / he* [d] 4 Or *faith*

1:15 *hooks.* See note on Am 4:2. *catches them in his net.* Babylonia's victims are as powerless as fish swimming into a net. Mesopotamian reliefs symbolically portray conquerors capturing their enemies in fishnets.
1:16 See note on v. 11.
2:1 See Eze 3:17 and note. *I will stand at my watch.* The figure of a guard looking out from a tower and expecting a response to his challenge. Any rebuke (see NIV text note) would be for questioning God's justice. *ramparts.* The walls of Jerusalem. *he.* God.
2:2–3 *revelation.* See 1Ch 17:15; Pr 29:18 and note. The Hebrew for this word refers specifically to a prophet's vision (see, e.g., Isa 1:1 and note).
2:2 *Write down.* See Isa 30:8; Jer 36:2 and note. *so that a herald may run with it.* Lit. "so that he who reads it may run," i.e., so that a messenger may run to deliver the message and read it to those to whom he has been sent.
2:3 *the end.* Of the Babylonians, though some refer it to the end times, when God's redemptive purposes would be completed. *wait for it.* The following message deals with the fall of Babylon in 539 BC, about 66 years after Habakkuk's prophecy. The Lord tells Habakkuk (and Judah) that fulfillment of the prophecy may "linger" but that he and the people are to expect it (see 3:16).
2:4 *the enemy.* Collective for the Babylonians, but with special reference to their king. *but.* In contrast to the Babylonians, whose "desires are not upright." *the righteous person will live by his faithfulness.* See NIV text note; Eze 18:9; see also Isa 26, especially vv. 1–6. In light of God's revelation about how (and when) he is working, his people are to wait patiently and live by faith—trusting in their sovereign God. The clause is quoted frequently in the NT to support the teaching that people are saved by grace through faith (Ro 1:17; Gal 3:11; cf. Eph 2:8 and note) and should live by faith (Heb 10:38–39; 11:7). Together with Ge 15:6 (see note there; see also Ro 4:3,9, 22–23; Gal 3:6; Jas 2:23 and note on 2:21), it became the rallying cry of the Protestant Reformation in the sixteenth century. The same principle that was applicable in the realm of national deliverance is applicable in the area of spiritual deliverance (salvation).
2:5 *greedy as the grave.* "The grave ... never says, 'Enough!'" (Pr 30:16; see note there; see also notes on Ps 49:14; Isa 5:14).
2:6–20 This taunt, an extended commentary on v. 4a (see note on 3:1), falls into two halves of ten (Hebrew) lines each (vv. 6–14 and vv. 15–20), each half concluding with a significant theological statement (vv. 14,20). Together these two statements set the five "woes" pronounced against Babylon (vv. 6,9,12,15,19; cf. Isa 5:8–23; Mt 23:13–32; Lk 6:24–26; Rev 9:12; 11:14) in a larger frame of reference. In addition, the first and fourth "woes" echo each other (see vv. 8,17).
2:6 *all of them taunt him.* The threatened victims of the Babylonian onslaught, especially Judah, will taunt ruthless Babylon (see Isa 14:4). *Woe.* The Babylonians' greed for conquest is condemned.
2:8 *you have shed human blood.* See v. 17. Therefore Babylon's blood would be shed (see Ge 9:6 and note).

[9] "Woe to him who builds[i] his house by
unjust gain,[j]
setting his nest[k] on high
to escape the clutches of ruin!
[10] You have plotted the ruin[l] of many
peoples,
shaming[m] your own house and
forfeiting your life.
[11] The stones[n] of the wall will cry out,
and the beams of the woodwork will
echo it.

[12] "Woe to him who builds a city with
bloodshed[o]
and establishes a town by injustice!
[13] Has not the LORD Almighty determined
that the people's labor is only fuel
for the fire,[p]
that the nations exhaust themselves
for nothing?[q]
[14] For the earth will be filled with the
knowledge of the glory[r] of
the LORD
as the waters cover the sea.[s]
[15] "Woe to him who gives drink[t] to his
neighbors,
pouring it from the wineskin till they
are drunk,
so that he can gaze on their naked
bodies!
[16] You will be filled with shame[u] instead
of glory.[v]
Now it is your turn! Drink[w] and let
your nakedness be exposed[a]![x]
The cup[y] from the LORD's right hand is
coming around to you,
and disgrace will cover your glory.
[17] The violence[z] you have done to
Lebanon will overwhelm you,
and your destruction of animals will
terrify you.[a]
For you have shed human blood;[b]
you have destroyed lands and cities
and everyone in them.

[18] "Of what value[c] is an idol[d] carved by a
craftsman?
Or an image[e] that teaches lies?
For the one who makes it trusts in his
own creation;
he makes idols that cannot speak.[f]
[19] Woe to him who says to wood, 'Come
to life!'
Or to lifeless stone, 'Wake up!'[g]
Can it give guidance?
It is covered with gold and silver;[h]
there is no breath in it."[i]
[20] The LORD is in his holy temple;[j]
let all the earth be silent[k] before him.

Habakkuk's Prayer

3 A prayer of Habakkuk the prophet. On *shigionoth.*[b][l]

[2] LORD, I have heard[m] of your fame;
I stand in awe[n] of your deeds, LORD.[o]

2:9 [i] S Jer 22:13 [j] S Jer 51:13 [k] S Job 39:27; S Isa 10:14 **2:10** [l] Jer 26:19 [m] ver 16; S Na 3:6 **2:11** [n] S Jos 24:27; Zec 5:4; Lk 19:40 **2:12** [o] S Eze 22:2; S Mic 3:10 **2:13** [p] Isa 50:11 [q] S Isa 47:13 **2:14** [r] S Ex 16:7; S Nu 14:21 [s] S Isa 11:9 **2:15** [t] S Pr 23:20 **2:16** [u] S ver 10 [v] S Eze 23:32-34; Hos 4:7 [w] S Lev 10:9 [x] S La 4:21 [y] S Ps 16:5; S Isa 51:22 **2:17** [z] S Jer 51:35 [a] S Jer 50:15 [b] ver 8 **2:18** [c] S 1Sa 12:21 [d] S Jdg 10:14; S Isa 40:19; S Jer 5:21; S 14:22 [e] S Lev 26:1 [f] Ps 115:4-5; Jer 10:14; 1Co 12:2 **2:19** [g] 1Ki 18:27 [h] S Jer 10:4 [i] S Da 5:4,23; S Hos 4:12 **2:20** [j] S Ps 11:4 [k] S Isa 41:1 **3:1** [l] Ps 7 Title **3:2** [m] S Job 26:14; Ps 44:1 [n] S Ps 119:120 [o] S Ps 90:16

[a] *16* Masoretic Text; Dead Sea Scrolls, Aquila, Vulgate and Syriac (see also Septuagint) *and stagger*
[b] *1* Probably a literary or musical term

2:9 *Woe.* The Babylonians' pride in building is condemned (see v. 12; cf. Jer 22:13). *nest on high.* Like the eagle building an inaccessible nest, the Babylonians thought their empire to be unconquerable (see Isa 14:4,13–15; cf. Ob 3–4).
2:11 *The stones … will cry out, and the beams.* The stones and beams in Babylonian houses were purchased with plunder and thus testified against the occupants. Cf. Lk 19:40.
2:12 *Woe.* Babylonian injustice is condemned. Cf. Mic 3:10; Zec 8:16 and note.
2:13 *fuel for the fire.* The cities built by the labor of the Babylonians (v. 12) will be burned (see Jer 51:58 and note).
2:14 Habakkuk quotes Isa 11:9 and expands its language. The Lord's future destruction of proud Babylonia and all her worldly glory will cause his greater glory to be known throughout the world (cf. Ex 14:4,17–18; Rev 17:1—19:4).
2:15 Cf. Ge 9:20–22. *Woe.* Babylonian violence is condemned. Her rapacious treatment of her neighbors, which stripped them of all their wealth (cf. what she later did to Jerusalem, 2Ki 25:8–21), is compared to one who makes his neighbors drunk so he can take lewd pleasure from their nakedness.
2:16 *be filled with shame … be exposed.* The Lord will do to Babylonia what she has done to others (see note on Ob 15). *cup from the LORD's right hand.* A symbol of divine retribution (see Ps 16:5 and note; Isa 51:17,21–22; Jer 25:15–17; La 4:21; Rev 14:10 and note; 16:19; see also note on Na 3:11).
2:17 *violence you have done to Lebanon.* The Babylonians apparently had ravaged the cedar forests of Lebanon to adorn their temples and palaces (see Isa 14:8 and note). *destruction of animals.* Assyrian inscriptions record hunting expeditions in the Lebanon range, and such sport may have been indulged in by the invading Babylonians as well. Babylonian violence was destructive of all forms of life, not only of lands and cities. *you have shed human blood.* See v. 8 and note.
2:18 *idols.* The Hebrew for this word means "godlets" or "nonentities" (cf. Isa 41:29; 44:9; Jer 10:15 and the condemnation of idolatry in Ex 20:4–5; see Ps 115:4–7 and note).
2:19 *Woe.* Babylonian idolatry is condemned. *Wake up!* Cf. Elijah's taunt of Baal's prophets on Mount Carmel (1Ki 18:27).
2:20 *The LORD is in his holy temple.* From his heavenly temple (cf. Jnh 2:7) he judges all people in accordance with his righteousness (see Ps 11:4–7 and note; Mic 1:2). *be silent before him.* The stone and wooden idols of the nations (v. 19) are to be silent in unprotecting submission to the awesome divine judgment (see Zep 1:7; Zec 2:13; cf. Am 6:10; 8:3 and note).
3:1 *prayer.* In the strict sense, petition is found in this prayer only in v. 2 but, as with many of the psalms, it is set in a larger context of recollection (vv. 3–15) and expression of confidence and trust (vv. 16–19). In fact, Habakkuk's prayer, an extended commentary on 2:4b (see note on 2:6–20), appears to have been used as a psalm; note the psalm-like heading (v. 1) and the musical and/or literary notations (vv. 1,3 [see NIV text note on this verse],9,13,19). *prophet.* See 1:1 and note. *shigionoth.* See Ps 7 title and note.
3:2 *heard of your fame.* See Ps 44:1; 78:3. In vv. 3–15 Habakkuk recites a poetic celebration of God's mighty,

Repeat[p] them in our day,
in our time make them known;
in wrath remember mercy.[q]

[3] God came from Teman,[r]
the Holy One[s] from Mount Paran.[a][t]
His glory covered the heavens[u]
and his praise filled the earth.[v]
[4] His splendor was like the sunrise;[w]
rays flashed from his hand,
where his power[x] was hidden.
[5] Plague[y] went before him;
pestilence followed his steps.
[6] He stood, and shook the earth;
he looked, and made the nations
tremble.
The ancient mountains crumbled[z]
and the age-old hills[a] collapsed[b]—
but he marches on forever.[c]
[7] I saw the tents of Cushan in distress,
the dwellings of Midian[d] in
anguish.[e]

[8] Were you angry with the rivers,[f] LORD?
Was your wrath against the streams?
Did you rage against the sea[g]
when you rode your horses
and your chariots to victory?[h]
[9] You uncovered your bow,
you called for many arrows.[i]
You split the earth with rivers;
[10] the mountains saw you and
writhed.[j]
Torrents of water swept by;
the deep roared[k]
and lifted its waves[l] on high.

3:2 [p]Ps 85:6 [q]Isa 54:8
3:3 [r]S Ge 36:11, 15 [s]Isa 31:1 [t]S Nu 10:12 [u]S Ps 8:1 [v]Ps 48:10
3:4 [w]S Isa 18:4 [x]S Job 9:6
3:5 [y]S Lev 26:25
3:6 [z]S Ps 46:2 [a]Ge 49:26 [b]S Ex 19:18; Ps 18:7; 114:1-6 [c]S Ge 21:33
3:7 [d]S Ge 25:2; S Nu 25:15; Jdg 7:24-25 [e]Ex 15:14
3:8 [f]S Ex 7:20 [g]S Ps 77:16 [h]S 2Ki 2:11; S Ps 68:17
3:9 [i]S Dt 32:23; Ps 7:12-13
3:10 [j]S Ps 77:16 [k]Ps 98:7 [l]S Ps 93:3
3:11 [m]Jos 10:13 [n]Ps 18:14 [o]S Ps 144:6; Zec 9:14
3:12 [p]S Isa 41:15
3:13 [q]S Ex 13:21 [r]S Ps 20:6; S 28:8 [s]S 2Sa 23:1 [t]Ps 68:21; 110:6
3:14 [u]Jdg 7:22 [v]Ps 64:2-5
3:15 [w]S Job 9:8 [x]Ex 15:8
3:16 [y]S Job 4:14 [z]S Ps 37:7

[11] Sun and moon stood still[m] in the
heavens
at the glint of your flying arrows,[n]
at the lightning[o] of your flashing
spear.
[12] In wrath you strode through the earth
and in anger you threshed[p] the
nations.
[13] You came out[q] to deliver[r] your people,
to save your anointed[s] one.
You crushed[t] the leader of the land of
wickedness,
you stripped him from head to foot.
[14] With his own spear you pierced his
head
when his warriors stormed out to
scatter us,[u]
gloating as though about to devour
the wretched[v] who were in hiding.
[15] You trampled the sea[w] with your
horses,
churning the great waters.[x]

[16] I heard and my heart pounded,
my lips quivered at the sound;
decay crept into my bones,
and my legs trembled.[y]
Yet I will wait patiently[z] for the day of
calamity
to come on the nation invading us.
[17] Though the fig tree does not bud
and there are no grapes on the
vines,

[a] *3* The Hebrew has *Selah* (a word of uncertain meaning) here and at the middle of verse 9 and at the end of verse 13.

saving acts of old—perhaps one he had heard at the temple (see v. 16).
3:3 *God came.* When celebrating the exodus, the OT poets (and poet-prophets) combined recollections of the mighty acts of God with conventional images of a fearsome manifestation of the Lord. He came down with his heavenly host and rode on the mighty thunderstorm as his chariot, with his arrows (lightning bolts; see note on Ps 18:14) flying in all directions, a cloudburst of rain descending on the earth and the mountains quaking before him (see Jdg 5:4–5; Ps 18:7–15; 68:7–10; 77:16–19; Mic 1:3 and notes). Such figures characterize many of the references in the following verses. *Teman.* Means "southland." God is pictured during the exodus as coming from the area south of Judah. *Mount Paran.* See Dt 33:2 and note; probably northwest of the Gulf of Aqaba and south of Kadesh Barnea, between Edom and Sinai. For *Selah,* see NIV text note and Introduction to Psalms: Authorship and Titles (or Superscriptions), last paragraph. *filled the earth.* See note on 2:14.
3:5 *Plague … pestilence.* Means of divine punishment (cf. Ex 7:14—12:30; Lev 26:25; Ps 91:3,6).
3:6 God's presence was frequently marked by earthquakes (see Ex 19:18; Ps 18:7; Jer 4:24; 10:10; Na 1:5). Landslides may also be alluded to here.
3:7 *Cushan … Midian.* Arab tribes living near Edom. *distress … anguish.* When Israel was delivered from Egypt under Moses, neighboring peoples were filled with fear (see Ex 15:14–16; Jos 2:9–10).
3:8 Poetic allusions to the plague on the Nile (Ex 7:20–24) and/or the stopping of the Jordan (Jos 3:15–17), as well as to the parting of the "Red Sea" (Ex 14:15–31).
3:9 *arrows.* Probably lightning bolts unleashed by the heavenly archer (see Ps 18:14 and note; 144:6). *rivers.* Caused by the accompanying thunderstorms.
3:11 *Sun and moon stood still.* Probably an allusion to the victory at Gibeon (see Jos 10:12–13 and note on 10:13), indicating that God's triumph over his enemies would be just as complete as on that occasion.
3:12 *threshed.* See note on Am 1:3.
3:13 *deliver your people.* God fought against the nations of Canaan (v. 12) but delivered his people. *save.* By giving victory to. *anointed one.* The covenant nation ("your people"; see Ps 28:9), the "kingdom of priests" (Ex 19:6; see note there), which God came to deliver. He destroyed the enemy and in this great act of wrath (v. 12) remembered mercy (v. 2). *leader of the land of wickedness.* The pharaoh (see Ex 14:5–9).
3:14–15 Another reference to the destruction of the Egyptians in the "Red Sea." God will likewise vanquish present foes.
3:15 *horses.* See v. 8 and note.
3:16 The hymnic recollection of God's mighty deeds of old in Israel's behalf (vv. 3–15) fills the prophet with an awe so profound that he feels physically weak. Alternatively, it is possible that the message from the Lord that Babylonia would be sent against Judah (1:5–11) had so devastated him that he felt ill—until he heard the Lord's further word. *wait patiently.* See 2:3 and note; Ps 37:7. *nation invading us.* Babylonia.
3:17 Probably anticipates the awful results of the imminent Babylonian invasion and devastation.

though the olive crop fails
and the fields produce no food,[a]
though there are no sheep in the pen
and no cattle in the stalls,[b]
18 yet I will rejoice in the LORD,[c]
I will be joyful in God my
Savior.[d]

19 The Sovereign LORD is my strength;[e]
he makes my feet like the feet of a deer,
he enables me to tread on the heights.[f]

For the director of music. On my stringed instruments.

3:17 [a]Joel 1:10-12, 18 [b]Jer 5:17 **3:18** [c]Ps 97:12; S Isa 61:10; Php 4:4 [d]S Ex 15:2; S Lk 1:47 **3:19** [e]S Dt 33:29; Ps 46:1-5 [f]S Dt 32:13; Ps 18:33

3:18–19 Habakkuk has learned the lesson of faith (2:4)—to trust in God's providence regardless of circumstances. He declares that even if God should send suffering and loss, he would still rejoice in God his Savior—one of the strongest affirmations of faith in all Scripture.
3:18 *rejoice in the LORD.* See Ps 32:11; Php 3:1; 4:4. *be joyful in God my Savior.* See Lk 1:47.

3:19 *makes my feet like the feet of a deer.* Gives me sure-footed confidence (see Ps 18:33). *director.* Probably the conductor of the temple musicians. This chapter may have formed part of the temple prayers that were chanted with the accompaniment of instruments (see 1Ch 16:4–7). *stringed instruments.* Including harp and lyre (Ps 33:2; 92:3; 144:9).

ZEPHANIAH

INTRODUCTION

Author

The prophet Zephaniah was evidently a person of considerable social standing in Judah and was probably related to the royal line. The prophecy opens with a statement of the author's ancestry (1:1), which in itself is an unusual feature of the Hebrew prophetic tradition. Zephaniah was a fourth-generation descendant of Hezekiah, a notable king of Judah from 715 to 686 BC. Apart from this statement, nothing more is said about his background. Whereas the prophet Micah dealt carefully and sympathetically with the problems of the common people of Judah, Zephaniah's utterances show a much greater familiarity with court circles and current political issues. Zephaniah was probably familiar with the writings of such prominent eighth-century prophets as Isaiah and Amos, whose utterances he reflects, and he may also have been aware of the ministry of the young Jeremiah.

Date

According to 1:1, Zephaniah prophesied during the reign of King Josiah (640–609 BC), making him a contemporary of Jeremiah, Nahum and perhaps Habakkuk. His prophecy is probably to be dated relatively early in Josiah's reign, before that king's attempt at reform (and while conditions brought about by the reigns of Manasseh and Amon still prevailed) and before the Assyrian king Ashurbanipal's death in 627 (while Assyria was still powerful, though threatened).

Background

See Introductions to Jeremiah and Nahum: Background; see also 2Ki 22:1—23:30; 2Ch 34:1—36:1 and notes.

Purpose and Theological Theme

The intent of the author was to announce to Judah God's approaching judgment. A Scythian incursion into Canaan may have provided the immediate occasion. This fierce people originated in what is now southern Russia, but by the seventh

a **quick** look

Author:
Zephaniah

Audience:
The people of Judah

Date:
Between 640 and 627 BC

Theme:
The prophet Zephaniah predicts the coming of the day of the Lord, when God will severely punish the nations, including apostate Judah, but will yet be merciful to his people.

Like many other prophets, Zephaniah ends his pronouncements of doom on the positive note of Judah's restoration by Yahweh, the King of Israel.

century BC they had migrated across the Caucasus and settled in and along the northern territories of the Assyrian Empire. Alternately the enemies and allies of Assyria, they seem to have thrust south along the Mediterranean sometime in the 620s, destroying Ashkelon and Ashdod and halting at the Egyptian border only because of a payoff by Pharaoh Psamtik (Psammetichus). Ultimately, however, the destruction prophesied by Zephaniah came at the hands of the Babylonians after they had overpowered Assyria and brought that ancient power to its end.

Zephaniah's main theme is the coming of the day of the Lord (see notes on Isa 2:11,17,20; Joel 1:15; 2:2; Am 5:18; 8:9), when God will severely punish the nations, including apostate Judah. Zephaniah portrays the stark horror of that ordeal with the same graphic imagery found elsewhere in the Prophets. But he also makes it clear that God will yet be merciful toward his people; like many other prophets, he ends his pronouncements of doom on the positive note of Judah's restoration by Yahweh, "King of Israel" (3:15; see note there).

Ashkelon tell. A tell is a hill formed by the accumulated debris of many ancient settlements one above the other. Ashkelon is one of the towns that Zephaniah predicted would be destroyed (2:4).

Outline

- I. Introduction (1:1–3)
  - A. Title: The Prophet Identified (1:1)
  - B. Prologue: Double Announcement of Total Judgment (1:2–3)
- II. The Day of the Lord Coming on Judah and the Nations (1:4–18)
  - A. Judgment on the Idolaters in Judah (1:4–9)
  - B. Wailing throughout Jerusalem (1:10–13)
  - C. The Inescapable Day of the Lord's Wrath (1:14–18)
- III. God's Judgment on the Nations (2:1—3:8)
  - A. Call to Judah to Repent (2:1–3)
  - B. Judgment on Philistia (2:4–7)
  - C. Judgment on Moab and Ammon (2:8–11)
  - D. Judgment on Cush (2:12)
  - E. Judgment on Assyria (2:13–15)
  - F. Judgment on Jerusalem (3:1–5)
  - G. Jerusalem's Refusal to Repent (3:6–8)
- IV. Redemption of the Remnant (3:9–20)
  - A. The Nations Purified, the Remnant Restored, Jerusalem Purged (3:9–13)
  - B. Rejoicing in the City (3:14–17)
  - C. The Nation Restored (3:18–20)

1 The word of the LORD that came to
Zephaniah son of Cushi, the son of
Gedaliah, the son of Amariah, the son of
Hezekiah, during the reign of Josiah[a] son
of Amon[b] king of Judah:

Judgment on the Whole Earth in the Day of the LORD

2 "I will sweep away everything
from the face of the earth,"[c]
declares the LORD.
3 "I will sweep away both man and
beast;[d]
I will sweep away the birds in the
sky[e]
and the fish in the sea—
and the idols that cause the wicked
to stumble."[a]

"When I destroy all mankind
on the face of the earth,"[f]
declares the LORD,[g]
4 "I will stretch out my hand[h] against
Judah
and against all who live in
Jerusalem.
I will destroy every remnant of Baal
worship in this place,[i]
the very names of the idolatrous
priests[j]—
5 those who bow down on the roofs
to worship the starry host,[k]
those who bow down and swear by the
LORD
and who also swear by Molek,[b][l]
6 those who turn back from following[m]
the LORD
and neither seek[n] the LORD nor
inquire[o] of him."

7 Be silent[p] before the Sovereign LORD,
for the day of the LORD[q] is near.
The LORD has prepared a sacrifice;[r]
he has consecrated those he has
invited.

8 "On the day of the LORD's sacrifice
I will punish[s] the officials
and the king's sons[t]
and all those clad
in foreign clothes.
9 On that day I will punish
all who avoid stepping on the
threshold,[c][u]
who fill the temple of their gods
with violence and deceit.[v]

10 "On that day,[w]"
declares the LORD,
"a cry will go up from the Fish Gate,[x]
wailing[y] from the New Quarter,
and a loud crash from the hills.
11 Wail,[z] you who live in the market
district[d];
all your merchants will be wiped
out,
all who trade with[e] silver will be
destroyed.[a]

1:1 [a]2Ki 22:1; 2Ch 34:1-35:25 [b]S 1Ch 3:14 **1:2** [c]S Ge 6:7 **1:3** [d]Jer 50:3 [e]S Jer 4:25 [f]ver 18; S Hos 4:3 [g]S Eze 14:17 **1:4** [h]S Jer 6:12 [i]Mic 5:13; Zep 2:11 [j]S Jer 15:6; S Hos 10:5 **1:5** [k]S Jer 8:2 [l]S Lev 18:21; Jer 5:7 **1:6** [m]Isa 1:4; Jer 2:13 [n]S Isa 9:13 [o]S Hos 7:7 **1:7** [p]S Isa 41:1 [q]ver 14; Isa 13:6; S Eze 7:19; S Joel 3:14; S Am 5:18-20 [r]S Lev 3:9; S Jer 46:10 **1:8** [s]Isa 24:21 [t]Jer 39:6 **1:9** [u]1Sa 5:5 [v]S Am 3:10 **1:10** [w]Isa 22:5 [x]S 2Ch 33:14 [y]S Am 5:16 **1:11** [z]Jas 5:1 [a]Hos 9:6

[a] 3 The meaning of the Hebrew for this line is uncertain. [b] 5 Hebrew *Malkam* [c] 9 See 1 Samuel 5:5. [d] 11 Or *the Mortar* [e] 11 Or *in*

1:1 *word of the LORD.* A common introductory phrase in the Prophets (see Jer 1:2; Hos 1:1 and notes). *Zephaniah.* Means "The LORD hides" or "The LORD protects," perhaps implying a prayer for God's protection of the child Zephaniah during the infamous reign of Manasseh. *son of ... Hezekiah.* Judging from the author's pedigree, it is likely that he was in his early 20s when he began to prophesy. He is more closely identified with the ruling class than was Isaiah, although Isaiah also moved regularly in court circles and was perhaps of noble birth.
1:2–3 *sweep away.* Zephaniah speaks of the coming catastrophe in language reminiscent of God's utterances prior to the flood (Ge 6:7). But this time it will be by God's fire (v. 18; 3:8).
1:3 *idols that cause the wicked to stumble.* See NIV text note; see also Ps 115:4–8; Isa 44:9–20; Hos 8:4–8; 9:10 and notes.
1:4–6 Seems to indicate that Zephaniah's main ministry took place before 621 BC, since the practices condemned here were abolished in Josiah's reforms (see 2Ki 23:4–16 and notes). Perhaps Zephaniah's message was partly instrumental in motivating King Josiah to undertake his reforms (cf. 2Ch 34:1–7).
1:4 Judah is censured for its unrepentant participation in the gross idolatry of Baal worship. *Baal.* See note on Jdg 2:13. *this place.* Jerusalem, where Zephaniah probably lived.
1:5 *on the roofs.* See 2Ki 23:12; Jer 19:13 and notes. *worship the starry host.* See Dt 4:19; 2Ki 17:16 and note; 21:3; Isa 47:13. *swear by the LORD ... also swear by Molek.* Syncretism (worship of one's own god along with other gods). *Molek.* Worshiped by the Ammonites, his rituals sometimes involved child sacrifice. Molek worship was forbidden to the Israelites (see Lev 18:21 and note; 20:1–5). Despite this, Solomon set up an altar to Molek on the Mount of Olives (1Ki 11:7). Manasseh established the rituals in the Valley of Ben Hinnom (see 2Ch 33:6; Jer 7:31 and note; 32:35).
1:7 *Be silent before the Sovereign LORD.* See Hab 2:20 and note. *day of the LORD.* Zephaniah's main theme (see Introduction: Purpose and Theological Theme); not of deliverance for Judah but of divine vengeance on the idolatrous covenant nation. See notes on Isa 2:11,17,20; 10:20,27; Joel 1:15; Am 5:18. *sacrifice.* The victim is Judah. *consecrated.* Since the coming slaughter of judgment is called a sacrifice, God's preparation of his guests is called his consecration of them—in preparation for their feasting on the plunder. *those ... invited.* The pagan conquerors (mainly Babylonia).
1:8 *foreign clothes.* Dress that indicated conformity to Babylonian, Egyptian or Assyrian ways.
1:9 *avoid stepping on the threshold.* Perhaps referring to a pagan custom that began in the time of Samuel (see 1Sa 5:5 and note).
1:10–13 Wailing throughout the city (contrast 3:14–17).
1:10 Merchants who had grown rich through corrupt business practices would be destroyed. *Fish Gate.* In the north wall of the city (see note on Ne 3:3). Jerusalem was most vulnerable to attacks from the north. *New Quarter.* See note on 2Ki 22:14; see also map, p. 2525, at the end of this study Bible.
1:11 *market district.* See map, p. 1440.

12 At that time I will search Jerusalem
with lamps
and punish those who are
complacent,[b]
who are like wine left on its dregs,[c]
who think, 'The LORD will do nothing,[d]
either good or bad.'[e]
13 Their wealth will be plundered,[f]
their houses demolished.
Though they build houses,
they will not live in them;
though they plant vineyards,
they will not drink the wine."[g]

14 The great day of the LORD[h] is near[i]—
near and coming quickly.
The cry on the day of the LORD is bitter;
the Mighty Warrior shouts his battle
cry.
15 That day will be a day of wrath—
a day of distress and anguish,
a day of trouble and ruin,
a day of darkness[j] and gloom,
a day of clouds and blackness[k]—
16 a day of trumpet and battle cry[l]
against the fortified cities
and against the corner towers.[m]

17 "I will bring such distress[n] on all
people
that they will grope about like those
who are blind,[o]
because they have sinned against the
LORD.
Their blood will be poured out[p] like dust
and their entrails like dung.[q]
18 Neither their silver nor their gold
will be able to save them
on the day of the LORD's wrath."[r]

In the fire of his jealousy[s]
the whole earth will be consumed,[t]
for he will make a sudden end
of all who live on the earth.[u]

1:12 [b] Am 6:1 [c] Jer 48:11 [d] S 2Ki 21:16; S Eze 8:12 [e] S Job 22:13 **1:13** [f] S 2Ki 24:13; Jer 15:13 [g] Dt 28:30, 39; La 5:2; S Am 5:11 **1:14** [h] S ver 7; S Joel 1:15 [i] S Eze 7:7; S Da 7:13 **1:15** [j] S 1Sa 2:9 [k] S Isa 22:5; Joel 2:2; Mk 13:24-25 **1:16** [l] S Jer 4:19 [m] S Dt 28:52; S Isa 2:15; S Joel 2:1 **1:17** [n] S Dt 28:52 [o] S Isa 59:10 [p] Ps 79:3 [q] S Ps 83:10 **1:18** [r] S Job 20:20; S 40:11; S Jer 4:4; S Eze 7:19 [s] S Dt 29:20 [t] S ver 2-3; Zep 3:8 [u] S Ge 6:7; S Eze 7:11

2:1 [v] 2Ch 20:4; Joel 1:14 [w] S Jer 3:3; 6:15 **2:2** [x] Isa 17:13; Hos 13:3 [y] S Jer 10:25; S La 4:11 [z] S Jer 4:4; S Eze 7:19 **2:3** [a] S Am 5:6 [b] S Isa 1:17 [c] Ps 45:4 [d] Ps 57:1 **2:4** [e] S Ge 10:19; S Am 1:6, 7-8; Zec 9:5-7 [f] Jer 47:5 **2:5** [g] S 1Sa 30:14 [h] S Lev 26:31; Am 3:1 [i] S Isa 14:30

Judah and Jerusalem Judged Along With the Nations

Judah Summoned to Repent

2 Gather together,[v] gather yourselves
together,
you shameful[w] nation,
2 before the decree takes effect
and that day passes like windblown
chaff,[x]
before the LORD's fierce anger[y]
comes upon you,
before the day of the LORD's wrath[z]
comes upon you.
3 Seek[a] the LORD, all you humble of the
land,
you who do what he commands.
Seek righteousness,[b] seek humility;[c]
perhaps you will be sheltered[d]
on the day of the LORD's anger.

Philistia

4 Gaza[e] will be abandoned
and Ashkelon[f] left in ruins.
At midday Ashdod will be emptied
and Ekron uprooted.
5 Woe to you who live by the sea,
you Kerethite[g] people;
the word of the LORD is against you,[h]
Canaan, land of the Philistines.
He says, "I will destroy you,
and none will be left."[i]
6 The land by the sea will become
pastures
having wells for shepherds
and pens for flocks.[j]
7 That land will belong
to the remnant[k] of the people of
Judah;
there they will find pasture.
In the evening they will lie down
in the houses of Ashkelon.

2:6 [j] S Isa 5:17 **2:7** [k] S Ge 45:7

1:12 *search Jerusalem with lamps.* The Babylonians later dragged people from houses, streets, sewers and tombs, where they had hidden. *like wine left on its dregs.* See Isa 25:6 and note. *The LORD will do nothing.* A typical depiction of the arrogance of the wicked (see note on Ps 10:11).

1:13 The assets of those who have become wealthy through dishonesty will be exposed and plundered (see Dt 28:30).

1:14–18 In a dramatic passage of great lyrical power, the Lord describes the destruction that will sweep the earth in the day of God's wrath.

1:15 *That day will be a day of wrath.* The inspiration for Thomas of Celano's great medieval hymn, *Dies Irae Dies Illa* (c. AD 1250). *darkness … blackness.* See Am 5:18–20.

1:17 *like those who are blind.* See Dt 28:28–29.

1:18 *Neither … silver nor … gold will … save them.* In the day of God's judgment, material wealth cannot buy deliverance from punishment. *fire of his jealousy.* See vv. 2–3 and note; 3:8.

2:1–3 The prophet's exhortation to Judah to repent. This call to repentance and the later indictment of Jerusalem for refusal to repent (see 3:6–8 and note) frame the series of judgments that illustratively detail God's acts in the coming day of the Lord (2:4—3:5).

2:2 *like windblown chaff.* See Ps 1:4 and note; 35:5; Isa 17:13; 29:5; Hos 13:3.

2:3 *Seek the LORD.* Even though destruction is imminent, there is still time to be sheltered from the calamity if only the nation will repent (see Am 5:4 and note). *humble.* Those who abandon the arrogance of their idolatry and wickedness and "seek humility."

2:4—3:8 God's coming judgment on the nations—including Jerusalem (see Am 1:3—2:16 and note).

2:4 *Gaza … Ashkelon … Ashdod … Ekron.* Philistine cities located west of Judah "by the sea" (vv. 5–6; see notes on Am 1:6,8; see also map, p. 359).

2:5 *Kerethite.* See note on 1Sa 30:14. *Canaan.* See note on Ge 10:6. *I … left.* The Lord's announced purpose.

2:6 The once-populous Philistine cities will revert to pastureland.

2:7 The faithful remnant of Judah will occupy this land and graze their flocks on it. *restore their fortunes.* See NIV text

The LORD their God will care for them;
he will restore their fortunes.[a l]

Moab and Ammon

8 "I have heard the insults[m] of Moab[n]
and the taunts of the Ammonites,[o]
who insulted[p] my people
and made threats against their land.[q]
9 Therefore, as surely as I live,"
declares the LORD Almighty,
the God of Israel,
"surely Moab[r] will become like Sodom,[s]
the Ammonites[t] like Gomorrah —
a place of weeds and salt pits,
a wasteland forever.
The remnant of my people will
plunder[u] them;
the survivors[v] of my nation will
inherit their land.[w]"
10 This is what they will get in return for
their pride,[x]
for insulting[y] and mocking
the people of the LORD Almighty.[z]
11 The LORD will be awesome[a] to them
when he destroys all the gods[b] of the
earth.[c]
Distant nations will bow down to him,[d]
all of them in their own lands.

Cush

12 "You Cushites,[b e] too,
will be slain by my sword.[f]"

Assyria

13 He will stretch out his hand against the
north
and destroy Assyria,[g]
leaving Nineveh[h] utterly desolate
and dry as the desert.[i]
14 Flocks and herds[j] will lie down there,
creatures of every kind.
The desert owl[k] and the screech owl[l]
will roost on her columns.
Their hooting will echo through the
windows,
rubble will fill the doorways,
the beams of cedar will be exposed.
15 This is the city of revelry[m]
that lived in safety.[n]
She said to herself,
"I am the one! And there is none
besides me."[o]
What a ruin she has become,
a lair for wild beasts![p]
All who pass by her scoff[q]
and shake their fists.[r]

Jerusalem

3 Woe to the city of oppressors,[s]
rebellious[t] and defiled![u]
2 She obeys[v] no one,
she accepts no correction.[w]
She does not trust[x] in the LORD,
she does not draw near[y] to her God.
3 Her officials within her
are roaring lions;[z]
her rulers are evening wolves,[a]
who leave nothing for the
morning.[b]
4 Her prophets are unprincipled;
they are treacherous people.[c]
Her priests profane the sanctuary
and do violence to the law.[d]

2:7 [l] S Dt 30:3; Ps 126:4; Jer 32:44; S Hos 6:11; S Joel 3:1; Am 1:6-8 **2:8** [m] S Jer 48:27 [n] S Ge 19:37; S Isa 16:6 [o] S Eze 21:28 [p] Eze 25:3 [q] S La 3:61 **2:9** [r] S Dt 23:6; Isa 15:1-16:14; Jer 48:1-47; Eze 25:8-11 [s] Dt 29:23; Isa 13:19; Jer 49:18 [t] Jer 49:1-6; Eze 25:1-7 [u] S Isa 11:14 [v] S 2Ki 19:31 [w] S Am 2:1-3 **2:10** [x] S Job 40:12; S Isa 16:6 [y] S Jer 48:27 [z] S Ps 9:6 **2:11** [a] S Joel 2:11 [b] S Zep 1:4 [c] S 1Ch 19:1; Eze 25:6-7 [d] Ps 86:9; S Isa 12:4; Zep 3:9 **2:12** [e] S Ge 10:6; S Isa 20:4 [f] S Jer 46:10 **2:13** [g] S Isa 10:5 [h] S Ge 10:11; S Na 1:1 [i] S Mic 5:6; Zec 10:11 **2:14** [j] S Isa 5:17 [k] S Isa 14:23 [l] S Ps 102:6; Rev 18:2 **2:15** [m] S Isa 32:9 [n] Isa 47:8 [o] Eze 28:2 [p] Jer 49:33 [q] S Isa 28:22; S Na 3:19 [r] S Eze 27:36 **3:1** [s] S Jer 6:6 [t] S Dt 21:18 [u] S Eze 23:30 **3:2** [v] S Jer 22:21 [w] S Lev 26:23; S Jer 7:28 [x] S Dt 1:32 [y] S Ps 73:28 **3:3** [z] S Ps 22:13 [a] S Ge 49:27 [b] S Mic 3:3 **3:4** [c] S Ps 25:3; S Isa 48:8; Jer 3:20; 9:4; Mal 2:10 [d] S Jer 23:11; S Eze 22:26

[a] *7* Or *will bring back their captives* [b] *12* That is, people from the upper Nile region

note. Here and in vv. 9,11 the prophet anticipates the ultimate outcome of the day of the Lord, which he spells out more fully in 3:9–20.

2:8 *Moab ... Ammonites.* Peoples living east of Judah (see notes on Ge 19:36–38; Am 1:13; 2:3). For the hostility of Ammon and Moab toward Israel, see Am 1:13; 2:3. They had often threatened to occupy Israelite territory (see Jdg 11:13 and note; Eze 25:2–7).

2:9 *Sodom ... Gomorrah.* See Ge 19. They were used in the OT to typify complete destruction at the hands of God (see Am 4:11 and note), and their mention added ominous overtones to the prophet's description of the day of the Lord. *weeds.* A symbol of depopulation (cf. Isa 7:23–25). *remnant ... will inherit their land.* See note on v. 7.

2:10 *in return for their pride, for insulting and mocking.* In reprisal, the faithful remnant will occupy Ammonite and Moabite territory.

2:11 *nations will bow down to him.* See 3:9 and note.

2:12 *You ... too.* Without elaboration, the prophet simply announces God's purpose against Egypt, located southwest of Judah (see vv. 5,8 and notes). *Cushites.* See NIV text note. Egypt was ruled from 715 to 663 BC by a Cushite dynasty. *my sword.* Probably Babylonia (see Eze 21:9–13,19; see also notes on Ps 7:12–13; Isa 10:5).

2:13 *north.* Although Nineveh was east of Judah, Assyrian armies normally invaded Canaan from the north (see notes on v. 12; 1:10), having first marched west along the Euphrates instead of through the Arabian Desert. *Nineveh.* See the books of Jonah and Nahum. Since Nineveh was destroyed in 612 BC, Zephaniah's ministry had to be before that date. *utterly desolate.* Even the site of Nineveh was later forgotten — until discovered through modern excavations (see Na 3:17 and note).

2:15 *I am ... none besides me.* See Isa 47:10. Assyria's boast belongs properly to God alone (see Isa 47:8,10 and note). *has become.* Anticipating Nineveh's impending destruction.

3:1 *city.* Apostate Jerusalem is condemned for its sins. *oppressors.* See Jer 22:3.

3:3–4 *officials ... rulers ... prophets ... priests.* All classes of Judah's leaders are castigated for indulging in conduct completely opposed to their vocations and responsibilities (see Jer 1:18 and note).

3:3 *roaring lions ... evening wolves.* Those in power are rapacious.

3:4 *unprincipled ... treacherous people.* Claiming to be prophets of the Lord, they proclaimed only lies (see Jer 5:31 and note; 14:14; 23:16,32). *priests ... do violence to the law.* When they should have been teachers of the law (see Dt 31:9–13; 2Ch 17:8–9; 19:8; Ezr 7:6; Jer 2:8; 18:18; Mal 2:7).

5 The LORD within her is righteous;[e]
he does no wrong.[f]
Morning by morning[g] he dispenses his justice,
and every new day he does not fail,[h]
yet the unrighteous know no shame.[i]

Jerusalem Remains Unrepentant

6 "I have destroyed nations;
their strongholds are demolished.
I have left their streets deserted,
with no one passing through.
Their cities are laid waste;[j]
they are deserted and empty.
7 Of Jerusalem I thought,
'Surely you will fear me
and accept correction!'[k]
Then her place of refuge[a] would not be destroyed,
nor all my punishments come upon[b] her.
But they were still eager
to act corruptly[l] in all they did.
8 Therefore wait[m] for me,"
declares the LORD,
"for the day I will stand up to testify.[c]
I have decided to assemble[n] the nations,[o]
to gather the kingdoms
and to pour out my wrath[p] on them —
all my fierce anger.[q]
The whole world will be consumed[r]
by the fire of my jealous anger.

Restoration of Israel's Remnant

9 "Then I will purify the lips of the peoples,
that all of them may call[s] on the name of the LORD[t]
and serve[u] him shoulder to shoulder.
10 From beyond the rivers of Cush[d][v]
my worshipers, my scattered people,
will bring me offerings.[w]
11 On that day you, Jerusalem, will not be put to shame[x]
for all the wrongs you have done to me,[y]
because I will remove from you
your arrogant boasters.[z]
Never again will you be haughty
on my holy hill.[a]
12 But I will leave within you
the meek[b] and humble.
The remnant of Israel
will trust[c] in the name of the LORD.
13 They[d] will do no wrong;[e]
they will tell no lies.[f]
A deceitful tongue
will not be found in their mouths.[g]
They will eat and lie down[h]
and no one will make them afraid.[i]"

14 Sing, Daughter Zion;[j]
shout aloud,[k] Israel!
Be glad and rejoice[l] with all your heart,
Daughter Jerusalem!
15 The LORD has taken away your punishment,
he has turned back your enemy.
The LORD, the King of Israel, is with you;[m]
never again will you fear[n] any harm.[o]

3:5 [e] S Ezr 9:15 [f] Dt 32:4 [g] S Ps 5:3 [h] S La 3:23 [i] S Jer 3:3; S Eze 18:25 **3:6** [j] S Lev 26:31 **3:7** [k] S Jer 7:28 [l] S Hos 9:9 **3:8** [m] S Ps 27:14 [n] S Joel 3:11 [o] S Isa 2:3 [p] Ps 79:6; Rev 16:1 [q] S Jer 10:25; S La 4:11 [r] S Zep 1:18
3:9 [s] S Zep 2:11 [t] S Ge 4:26 [u] S Isa 19:18 **3:10** [v] S Ge 10:6; S Ps 68:31 [w] S 2Ch 32:23; S Isa 60:7 **3:11** [x] S Isa 29:22; S Joel 2:26-27 [y] S Ge 50:15 [z] S Ps 59:12 [a] S Ex 15:17; S Lev 26:19 **3:12** [b] Isa 14:32 [c] S Jer 29:12; Na 1:7 **3:13** [d] S Isa 10:21 [e] Ps 119:3; S Isa 4:3 [f] S Jer 33:16; Rev 14:5 [g] S Job 16:17 [h] Eze 34:15; Zep 2:7 [i] S Lev 26:6; S Eze 34:25-28 **3:14** [j] S Ps 9:14; Zec 2:10 [k] S Ps 95:1; Isa 12:6; Zec 2:10 [l] S Ps 9:2; S Isa 51:11 **3:15** [m] Eze 37:26-28 [n] S Isa 54:14 [o] Zec 9:9

[a] 7 Or *her sanctuary* [b] 7 Or *all those I appointed over* [c] 8 Septuagint and Syriac; Hebrew *will rise up to plunder* [d] 10 That is, the upper Nile region

3:5 *Morning by morning ... he does not fail.* Cf. La 3:22–23 and notes.
3:6–8 Jerusalem's refusal to repent (see 2:1–3 and note).
3:6 *I have destroyed nations.* The destruction of other nations was meant to serve as a warning to wanton Judah, but to no avail (see v. 7).
3:7 *eager to act corruptly.* See, e.g., Jer 7:13,25–26.
3:8 *wait.* A sarcastic statement to Judah to wait for the threatened catastrophe. *to testify.* To lodge accusations (see Ps 50:7) — and then proceed to execute judgments. *I have decided.* Or "For I have decided." The Lord concludes his announcement of judgment with a general declaration of his intent. *consumed by the fire of my jealous anger.* See 1:2–3 and note; 1:18; La 1:13 and note.
3:9–20 A three-stanza prophecy (vv. 9–13,14–17, 18–20) announcing redemption that will follow God's judgment.
3:9–13 The Lord gives assurance that the nations will be purified, the scattered remnant restored and Jerusalem purged.
3:9 God's fearful judgment of the nations will effect (or be followed by) their purification, so that they will call on his name and serve him. Israel's God will be acknowledged by the nations, and God's people will be held in honor by them (cf. vv. 19–20).
3:10 *Cush.* See NIV text note; the most distant area imaginable (see 2:12; Isa 18:1 and notes). The most widely dispersed will be restored. *bring me offerings.* Rather than to Baal and Molek (cf. 1:4–5).
3:11 *me, / because.* In the Hebrew, this new line begins the same as the first line of v. 9. Hence it may be better to read: "me. / Then." Thus vv. 9–11a constitute a three-line unit (in Hebrew) and vv. 11b,c–12 a three-line unit. The latter speaks of a purified Jerusalem. Verse 13 is a summary conclusion. *my holy hill.* Mount Zion (see Ps 2:6 and note).
3:12 *remnant.* See 2:7; Isa 1:9 and notes.
3:13 *no one will make them afraid.* Quoted verbatim from Mic 4:4 (see note there).
3:14–17 Joy in the restored city (in two parts: vv. 14–15 and vv. 16–17) — the prophet's reassurance (contrast 1:10–13).
3:14 *Daughter Zion ... Daughter Jerusalem.* A personification of Jerusalem (see note on 2Ki 19:21).
3:15 *your enemy.* All those arrayed against Israel. *The LORD, the King of Israel.* See Isa 44:6; see also Introduction to Psalms: Theology: Major Themes.

16 On that day
they will say to Jerusalem,
"Do not fear, Zion;
do not let your hands hang limp.[p]
17 The LORD your God is with you,
the Mighty Warrior who saves.[q]
He will take great delight[r] in you;
in his love he will no longer rebuke you,[s]
but will rejoice over you with singing."[t]

18 "I will remove from you
all who mourn over the loss of your appointed festivals,
which is a burden and reproach for you.

3:16 [p] S 2Ki 19:26; S Job 4:3; Isa 35:3-4; Heb 12:12 **3:17** [q] S Isa 63:1; S Joel 2:21 [r] S Dt 28:63; S Isa 62:4 [s] S Hos 14:4 [t] S Isa 40:1

3:19 [u] S Isa 14:2 [v] S Eze 34:16; S Mic 4:6 [w] Isa 60:18 **3:20** [x] S Jer 29:14; S Eze 37:12 [y] Isa 56:5; 66:22 [z] S Dt 26:19; S Isa 60:18 [a] S Joel 3:1

19 At that time I will deal
with all who oppressed[u] you.
I will rescue the lame;
I will gather the exiles.[v]
I will give them praise[w] and honor
in every land where they have suffered shame.
20 At that time I will gather you;
at that time I will bring[x] you home.
I will give you honor[y] and praise[z]
among all the peoples of the earth
when I restore your fortunes[a][a]
before your very eyes,"
says the LORD.

[a] 20 Or *I bring back your captives*

3:16 *do not let your hands hang limp.* Do not be discouraged (see Jer 47:3 and note).
3:18–20 Summary announcement of restoration — the Lord's final assurance.
3:18 *mourn.* Israel's sorrow at not being able to celebrate its great religious festivals. *appointed festivals.* See Lev 23 and chart, pp. 188–189.
3:19–20 *gather the exiles … give them … gather you … give you.* The level of intimacy increases as the Lord concludes his words of assurance.
3:20 *give you honor and praise.* See v. 19; see also Ge 12:2–3 and note.

HAGGAI

INTRODUCTION

Author

Haggai (1:1) was a prophet who, along with Zechariah, encouraged the returned exiles to rebuild the temple (see Ezr 5:1 – 2; 6:14). Haggai means "festal," which may indicate that the prophet was born during one of the three pilgrimage festivals (Unleavened Bread, Pentecost or Weeks, and Tabernacles; cf. Dt 16:16). Based on 2:3 (see note there) Haggai may have witnessed the destruction of Solomon's temple. If so, he must have been in his 70s during his ministry.

Background

In 538 BC the conqueror of Babylon, Cyrus king of Persia, issued a decree allowing the Jews to return to Jerusalem and rebuild the temple (see Ezr 1:2 – 4; 6:3 – 5). Led by Zerubbabel (but see note on Ezr 1:8, "Sheshbazzar"), about 50,000 Jews journeyed home and began work on the temple. About two years later (536) they completed the foundation amid great rejoicing (Ezr 3:8 – 11). Their success aroused the Samaritans and other neighbors who feared the political and religious implications of a rebuilt temple in a thriving Jewish state. They therefore opposed the project vigorously and managed to halt work until 520, after Darius the Great became king of Persia in 522 (Ezr 4:1 – 5,24).

Darius was interested in the religions of his empire, and Haggai and Zechariah began to preach in his second year, 520 BC (see 1:1; Zec 1:1). The Jews were more to blame for their inactivity than their opponents, and Haggai tried to arouse them from their lethargy. When the governor of Trans-Euphrates and other officials tried to interfere with the rebuilding efforts, Darius fully supported the Jews (Ezr 5:3 – 6; 6:6 – 12). In 516 the temple was finished and dedicated (Ezr 6:15 – 18).

Author:
Haggai

Audience:
The postexilic Jews living in Judah

Date:
520 BC

Theme:
The prophet Haggai calls the complacent people of Judah to resume the rebuilding of the temple and in that way give glory to God.

Date

Haggai's messages are the most carefully and precisely dated in the entire OT. They were given during a four-month period in 520 BC, the second year of King Darius. The first message was

God gives great encouragement to those laboring under difficult conditions to rebuild his temple by assuring them that the future glory of the modest temple they build will be greater than the temple Solomon had built.

delivered on the first day of the sixth month (Aug. 29), the last on the 24th day of the ninth month (Dec. 18). See notes on 1:1; 2:1,10; see also Introduction to Zechariah: Dates.

Themes and Theological Teaching

Apart from Obadiah, Haggai is the shortest book in the OT, but its teachings are nonetheless significant. Haggai clearly shows the consequences of disobedience (1:6,11; 2:16 – 17) and obedience (2:7 – 9,19). When the people give priority to God and his house, they are blessed rather than cursed (cf. Lk 12:31 and note). Obedience brings the encouragement and strength of the Spirit of God (2:4 – 5).

Ancient manuscript showing Christ with the 12 minor prophets

Ms 132 fol.2r Christ with the 12 minor prophets, from 'Explanatio in Prophetas et Ecclesiasten' by St. Jerome, from Citeaux Abbey, French School, (twelfth century)/Bibliotheque Municipale, Dijon, France/Giraudon/The Bridgeman Art Library

In ch. 2 God gives great encouragement to those laboring under difficult conditions to rebuild his temple by assuring them that the future glory of the modest temple they build will be greater than that of the temple Solomon had built in the time of Israel's greatest wealth and power. The Jews in Judah may now be a much reduced community and under the hegemony of a powerful world empire, but the Lord will shake up the present world order and assert his claim to all the world's wealth, so that the glory of his future temple will be without rival. "What is desired by all nations will come, and I will fill this house with glory" (see 2:6 – 7; Eze 1:28; 43:2 and notes).

Literary Features

Like Malachi, Haggai uses a number of questions to highlight key issues (see 1:4,9; 2:3,19). He also makes effective use of repetition: "Give careful thought" occurs in 1:5,7; 2:15,18, and "I am with you" in 1:13; 2:4. "Shake the heavens and the earth" is found in 2:6,21. The major sections of the book are marked off by the precise date on which the word of the Lord came "through" (or "to") Haggai (1:1; 2:1,10,20).

Several times the prophet appears to reflect other passages of Scripture (compare 1:6 with Dt 28:38 – 39 and 2:17 with Dt 28:22). The threefold use of "be strong" in 2:4 (see note there) echoes the encouragement given in Jos 1:6 – 7,9,18. (For chiasm, see Outline.)

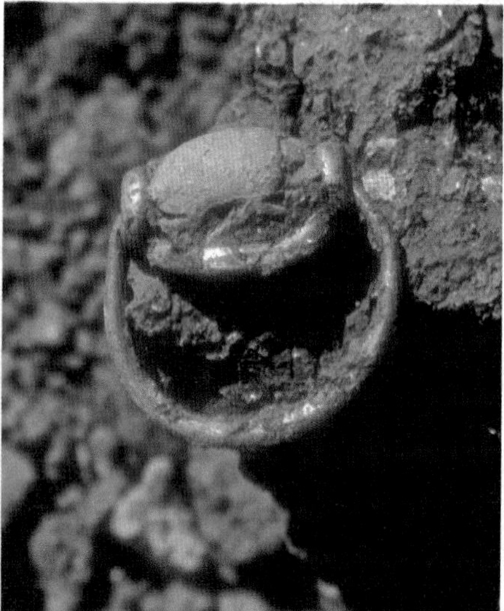

Gold scarab ring found at Ekron. Signet rings were used in the ancient Near East to sign one's name. The impression of the ring would be pressed into wax or clay to sign legal documents. In Haggai 2:23, the Lord tells Zerubbabel, "I will make you like my signet ring, for I have chosen you."

Outline

- I. First Message: The Call to Rebuild the Temple (1:1 – 11)
  - A. The People's Lame Excuse (1:1 – 4)
  - B. The Poverty of the People (1:5 – 6)
  - C. The Reason God Has Cursed Them (1:7 – 11)
- II. The Response of Zerubbabel and the People (1:12 – 15)
  - A. The Leaders and Remnant Obey (1:12)
  - B. The Lord Strengthens the Workers (1:13 – 15)
- III. Second Message: The Temple to Be Filled with Glory (2:1 – 9)
  - A. The People Encouraged (2:1 – 5)
  - B. The Promise of Glory and Peace (2:6 – 9)
- IV. Third Message: A Defiled People Purified and Blessed (2:10 – 19)
  - A. The Rapid Spread of Sin (2:10 – 14)
  - B. Poor Harvests because of Disobedience (2:15 – 17)
  - C. Blessing to Come as the Temple Is Rebuilt (2:18 – 19)
- V. Fourth Message: The Promise to Zerubbabel (2:20 – 23)
  - A. The Judgment of the Nations (2:20 – 22)
  - B. The Significance of Zerubbabel (2:23)

It is also possible to outline the book in a chiastic *a-b / b′-a′* pattern:

- *a* Negative effects of the unbuilt temple (1:1 – 11)
  - *b* The Lord's presence energizes the present work (1:12 – 15)
  - *b′* The Lord's presence guarantees future glory (2:1 – 9)
- *a′* Positive effects of the rebuilt temple (2:10 – 23)

Similar chiastic patterns exist in the subunits within these larger units.

A Call to Build the House of the LORD

1 In the second year of King Darius,[a] on the first day of the sixth month, the word of the LORD came through the prophet Haggai[b] to Zerubbabel[c] son of Shealtiel, governor[d] of Judah, and to Joshua[e] son of Jozadak,[a][f] the high priest:[g]

2 This is what the LORD Almighty[h] says: "These people[i] say, 'The time has not yet come to rebuild the LORD's house.[j]' "

3 Then the word of the LORD came through the prophet Haggai:[k] 4 "Is it a time for you yourselves to be living in your paneled houses,[l] while this house remains a ruin?[m]"

5 Now this is what the LORD Almighty says: "Give careful thought[n] to your ways. 6 You have planted much, but harvested little.[o] You eat, but never have enough.[p] You drink, but never have your fill.[q] You put on clothes, but are not warm. You earn wages,[r] only to put them in a purse with holes in it."

7 This is what the LORD Almighty says: "Give careful thought[s] to your ways. 8 Go up into the mountains and bring down timber[t] and build my house, so that I may take pleasure[u] in it and be honored,[v]" says the LORD. 9 "You expected much, but see, it turned out to be little.[w] What you brought home, I blew[x] away. Why?" declares the LORD Almighty. "Because of my house, which remains a ruin,[y] while each of you is busy with your own house. 10 Therefore, because of you the heavens have withheld[z] their dew[a] and the earth its crops.[b] 11 I called for a drought[c] on the fields and the mountains,[d] on the grain, the new wine,[e] the olive oil[f] and everything else the ground produces, on people and livestock, and on all the labor of your hands.[g]"

12 Then Zerubbabel[h] son of Shealtiel, Joshua son of Jozadak, the high priest, and the whole remnant[i] of the people obeyed[j] the voice of the LORD their God and the message of the prophet Haggai, because the LORD their God had sent him. And the people feared[k] the LORD.

13 Then Haggai,[l] the LORD's messenger,[m] gave this message of the LORD to the people: "I am with[n] you," declares the LORD. 14 So the LORD stirred up[o] the spirit of Zerubbabel[p] son of Shealtiel, governor of Judah, and the spirit of Joshua son of Jozadak,[q] the high priest, and the spirit of the whole remnant[r] of the people. They came and began to work on the house of the LORD Almighty, their God, 15 on the twenty-fourth day of the sixth month.[s]

1:1 [a] S Ezr 4:24 [b] S Ezr 5:1 [c] S 1Ch 3:19; Mt 1:12-13 [d] Ezr 5:3; S Ne 5:14 [e] S Ezr 2:2 [f] S 1Ch 6:15; S Ezr 3:2 [g] Zec 3:8 **1:2** [h] Isa 13:4 [i] S Isa 29:13 [j] Ezr 1:2 **1:3** [k] S Ezr 5:1 **1:4** [l] S 2Sa 7:2 [m] ver 9; Jer 33:12 **1:5** [n] ver 7; La 3:40; Hag 2:15, 18 **1:6** [o] S Lev 26:20; S Isa 5:10 [p] S Isa 9:20; S 55:2 [q] Am 4:8 [r] Hag 2:16; Zec 8:10 **1:7** [s] S ver 5 **1:8** [t] S 1Ch 14:1 [u] S Job 22:3; Ps 132:13-14 [v] S Ex 29:43; Jer 13:11 **1:9** [w] S Dt 28:38; S Isa 5:10 [x] S Ps 103:16; S Eze 22:21 [y] S ver 4; S Ne 13:11 **1:10** [z] S Dt 28:24 [a] S Ge 27:28; 1Ki 17:1 [b] Lev 26:19; Dt 28:23 **1:11** [c] S Dt 11:26; S 28:22; S Ru 1:1; S 1Ki 17:1; S Isa 5:6 [d] Isa 7:25 [e] S Dt 28:51; Ps 4:7 [f] S Nu 18:12 [g] Hag 2:17 **1:12** [h] ver 1 [i] ver 14; Isa 1:9; Hag 2:2 [j] S Job 36:11; S Isa 50:10; Mt 28:20 [k] S Dt 31:12; S Isa 1:2 **1:13** [l] ver 1 [m] S Nu 27:21; S 2Ch 36:15 [n] S Ge 26:3; S Nu 14:9; S Mt 28:20; Ro 8:31 **1:14** [o] S Ezr 1:5 [p] S Ezr 5:2 [q] S 1Ch 6:15 [r] S ver 12 **1:15** [s] ver 1; Hag 2:10, 20

[a] *1* Hebrew *Jehozadak*, a variant of *Jozadak*; also in verses 12 and 14

1:1 *second year ... first day ... sixth month.* Aug. 29, 520 BC. *King Darius.* Darius Hystaspes ruled Persia from 522 to 486 BC (see chart, p. 511). It was he who prepared the trilingual inscription on the Behistun cliff wall (located in modern Iran), through which cuneiform inscriptions were deciphered and the culture and history of ancient Mesopotamia were brought to light. *first day.* The New Moon was the day on which prophets were sometimes consulted (see 2Ki 4:22–23 and note on 4:23; see also note on Isa 1:14). *word of the LORD.* See v. 3; 2:2; Hos 1:1 and note. *Zerubbabel.* See note on Ezr 1:8 ("Sheshbazzar"). *son of Shealtiel.* See 1Ch 3:17–19 and note on 3:19. *governor ... high priest.* The civil and religious leaders of the restored Jewish community. *Joshua.* See note on Ezr 2:2; mentioned with Zerubbabel also in vv. 12,14; 2:2,4. *Jozadak.* Had been taken captive by Nebuchadnezzar (1Ch 6:15).

1:2 *LORD Almighty.* Used more than 90 times in Haggai, Zechariah and Malachi. See notes on 1Sa 1:3; Isa 13:4. *These people.* See 2:14. Because of their sin, the nation is not called "my people" (see Isa 6:9–10; 8:6,11–12; Jer 14:10–11; see also notes on Ex 17:4; Hos 1:9). *time has not yet come.* After the foundation of the temple had been laid in 536 BC (see Ezr 3:8–10), the people became discouraged and halted the work until 520 (see Ezr 4:1–5,24).

1:4 *paneled houses.* Usually connected with royal dwellings, which had cedar paneling (see 1Ki 7:3,7; Jer 22:14–15 and note on 22:14).

1:5 *Give careful thought.* Repeated in v. 7; 2:15,18.

1:6 *planted much ... harvested little.* A curse for disobedience (see Dt 28:38–39). Lev 26:20 also describes the unfruitfulness of a land judged by God. *drink ... fill.* Cf. Isa 55:1–2. The people experience futility in all their activities, legitimate or illegitimate (cf. Hos 4:10–11; Mic 6:13–15). *purse with holes.* Famine causes prices to rise sharply.

1:8 *mountains ... timber.* Perhaps wood from nearby hills was to supplement the cedar wood already purchased from Lebanon (see Ezr 3:7). *take pleasure in it.* And in the sacrifices offered there (contrast Isa 1:11). *be honored.* An obedient nation would bring praise and honor to God (see Jer 13:11).

1:9 *busy with.* Lit. "running to."

1:10 *dew.* Normally abundant in the growing season, and often as valuable as rain (see 2Sa 1:21; 1Ki 17:1).

1:11 *mountains.* The hills were cultivated, especially through terracing (see Ps 104:13–15; Isa 7:25; Joel 3:18). *the grain, the new wine, the olive oil.* The three basic crops of the land, often mentioned in a context of blessing or cursing (see Dt 7:13; Joel 1:10 and notes). Olive oil was used as food, ointment and medicine. *people and livestock.* The drought affected people and cattle and so could be said to be "on" them too.

1:12 *remnant.* See note on Isa 1:9. *feared the LORD.* Showing reverence, respect and obedience (see Ge 20:11 and note; Dt 31:12–13; Mal 1:6; 3:5,16).

1:13 *messenger.* A title for prophets (see 2Ch 36:15–16; Isa 42:19 and note) or priests (see Mal 2:7 and note). *I am with you.* A sure indication of success (see 2:4; Ge 26:3; Nu 14:9 and notes).

1:14 *stirred up the spirit.* The Hebrew for this expression is translated "(whose) heart (God) had moved" in Ezr 1:5, where God stirred up many of these same people to return home and rebuild the temple.

1:15 *twenty-fourth day of the sixth month.* Sept. 21, 520 BC.

The Promised Glory of the New House

2 In the second year of King Darius,[t]
1 on the twenty-first day of the seventh month,[u] the word of the LORD came
through the prophet Haggai:[v] 2 “Speak to
Zerubbabel[w] son of Shealtiel, governor of
Judah, to Joshua son of Jozadak,[a][x] the
high priest, and to the remnant[y] of the
people. Ask them, 3 ‘Who of you is left
who saw this house[z] in its former glory?
How does it look to you now? Does it not
seem to you like nothing?[a] 4 But now be
strong, Zerubbabel,’ declares the LORD.
‘Be strong,[b] Joshua son of Jozadak,[c] the
high priest. Be strong, all you people of
the land,’ declares the LORD, ‘and work.
For I am with[d] you,’ declares the LORD Almighty. 5 ‘This is what I covenanted[e] with
you when you came out of Egypt.[f] And
my Spirit[g] remains among you. Do not
fear.’[h]

6 “This is what the LORD Almighty says:
‘In a little while[i] I will once more shake
the heavens and the earth,[j] the sea and
the dry land. 7 I will shake all nations,
and what is desired[k] by all nations will
come, and I will fill this house[l] with glory,[m]’ says the LORD Almighty. 8 ‘The silver
is mine and the gold[n] is mine,’ declares the
LORD Almighty. 9 ‘The glory[o] of this present
house[p] will be greater than the glory of
the former house,’ says the LORD Almighty.
‘And in this place I will grant peace,[q]’ declares the LORD Almighty.”

Blessings for a Defiled People

10 On the twenty-fourth day of the ninth
month,[r] in the second year of Darius, the
word of the LORD came to the prophet
Haggai: 11 “This is what the LORD Almighty
says: ‘Ask the priests[s] what the law says:
12 If someone carries consecrated meat[t] in
the fold of their garment, and that fold
touches some bread or stew, some wine,
olive oil or other food, does it become consecrated?[u]’ ”

The priests answered, “No.”

13 Then Haggai said, “If a person defiled
by contact with a dead body touches one
of these things, does it become defiled?”

“Yes,” the priests replied, “it becomes
defiled.[v]”

14 Then Haggai said, “ ‘So it is with
this people[w] and this nation in my sight,’

[a] *2* Hebrew *Jehozadak*, a variant of *Jozadak*; also in verse 4

1:15 [t] S Ezr 4:24 **2:1** [u] ver 10,20; S Lev 23:34; Jn 7:37 [v] S Ezr 5:1 **2:2** [w] Hag 1:1 [x] S 1Ch 6:15 [y] S Hag 1:12 **2:3** [z] S Ezr 3:12; S Isa 60:7 [a] Zec 4:10 **2:4** [b] S 1Ch 28:20; Zec 8:9; S Eph 6:10 [c] S 1Ch 6:15 [d] S Ex 33:14; S Nu 14:9; S 2Sa 5:10; Ac 7:9 **2:5** [e] S Ge 6:18 [f] S Ex 29:46 [g] S Ne 9:20 [h] S Ge 15:1; 1Ch 28:20; S Ezr 5:2; Zec 8:13 **2:6** [i] S Isa 10:25 [j] S Ex 19:18; S Job 9:6; S Isa 14:16; S Eze 38:19; Heb 12:26* **2:7** [k] S 1Sa 9:20 [l] S Isa 60:7 [m] S Ex 16:7; S 29:43; Lk 2:32 **2:8** [n] S 1Ch 29:2 **2:9** [o] S Ps 85:9; S Isa 11:10 [p] S Ezr 3:12; S Isa 60:7 [q] S Lev 26:6; S Isa 60:17

2:10 [r] S ver 1; S Hag 1:15 **2:11** [s] S Lev 10:10-11; Dt 17:8-11; 33:8; S Jer 18:18 **2:12** [t] Jer 11:15 [u] S Ge 7:2; S Lev 6:27; Mt 23:19 **2:13** [v] Lev 22:4-6; Nu 19:13 **2:14** [w] S Isa 29:13

2:1 *twenty-first day of the seventh month.* Oct. 17, 520 BC, the last day of the Festival of Tabernacles. It was a time to celebrate the summer harvest (see Lev 23:34–43), though the crops were meager (see 1:11; cf. Jn 7:37). Solomon had dedicated his temple during this festival (see 1Ki 8:2 and note).
2:3 *is left.* Some of the older exiles (perhaps including Haggai himself) had seen Solomon's magnificent temple, destroyed by the Babylonians 66 years earlier. *this house in its former glory.* See vv. 7,9. Zerubbabel's temple was considered a continuation of Solomon's. *seem … like nothing.* Cf. the reaction when the foundation of the temple was finished (Ezr 3:12).
2:4 *be strong … work.* David used these words in 1Ch 28:20 when he encouraged Solomon to build the temple. The Lord had exhorted Joshua, son of Nun, with similar words (Jos 1:6–7,9,18). *be strong … Be strong.… Be strong.* See note on Jer 7:4. *I am with you.* See 1:13 and note; 1Ch 28:20. The same God who helped Solomon will empower Zerubbabel and the people.
2:5 *my Spirit.* The Holy Spirit had rested on Moses and the 70 elders as they had led the people out of Egypt and through the wilderness (see Nu 11:16–17,25; Isa 63:11). See also Ps 51:11; Zec 4:6 and notes. *Do not fear.* See notes on v. 4; Jos 1:18; Isa 41:10.
2:6 An announcement of the coming day of God's judgment on the nations—which the fall of Persia to Alexander the Great (333–330 BC) would foreshadow. Heb 12:26–27 relates this verse to the judgment of the nations at the second coming of Christ. The background for the shaking of the nations here and in vv. 21–22 is the judgment on Egypt at the "Red Sea." Cf. also Isa 14:16–17.
2:7 *desired … will come.* "Desired" can refer to individuals, as in Da 9:23 (where the same Hebrew verb is translated "highly esteemed"); cf. 1Sa 9:20. Thus it may have Messianic significance (see Da 11:37 and note; Mal 3:1). The same Hebrew word can also refer to articles of value, however (see 2Ch 20:25; 32:27)—such as the contribution of King Darius to the temple (Ezr 6:8). If that is the intent here, the bringing of the "riches of the nations" to Zion in Isa 60:5 is a close parallel (see note there). *fill … with glory.* "Glory" can refer to material splendor (see Isa 60:7,13 and notes) or to the presence of God (Ex 40:34–35; 1Ki 8:10–11; Eze 10:4). The latter references connect the glory of the Lord with the cloud that filled the sanctuary. When Christ came to the earthly temple in Jerusalem, God's presence was evident as never before (see Lk 2:27,32). Cf. notes on Eze 1:28; 43:2.
2:8 *silver … gold.* Provided for Solomon's temple (1Ch 29:2,7) and for Zerubbabel's (Ezr 6:5).
2:9 *glory … greater.* Ultimately because the Messiah would be present there (see v. 7 and note). *former house.* Solomon's temple. *this place.* Perhaps Jerusalem (see Zep 1:4 and note). *I will grant peace.* Perhaps an allusion to the priestly benediction (see Nu 6:26 and note).
2:10 *twenty-fourth day … ninth month.* Dec. 18, 520 BC—when winter crops were planted.
2:11 *priests.* They were consulted about the precise meaning of the law (see Dt 31:11; Jer 18:18; Mal 2:7–9 and notes).
2:12 *consecrated meat.* Meat from an animal set apart for a sacrifice. *does it become consecrated?* A question about transmitting holiness. Consecrated meat made the garment "holy" because it was in direct contact with that garment (see Lev 6:27), but the garment could not pass on that holiness to a third object.
2:13 *does it become defiled?* Ceremonial uncleanness is transmitted much more easily than holiness. Anything touched by an unclean person becomes unclean (see Nu 19:11–13,22).
2:14 *this people.* See 1:2 and note. *Whatever they do … is defiled.* Even though the people were back in the holy land, that holiness did not make them pure. They needed to obey the Lord, particularly with regard to rebuilding the temple. See notes on vv. 12–13.

declares the LORD. 'Whatever they do and
whatever they offer[x] there is defiled.
15 " 'Now give careful thought[y] to this
from this day on[a]—consider how things
were before one stone was laid[z] on another in the LORD's temple.[a] 16 When anyone came to a heap[b] of twenty measures,
there were only ten. When anyone went to
a wine vat[c] to draw fifty measures, there
were only twenty.[d] 17 I struck all the work
of your hands[e] with blight,[f] mildew and
hail,[g] yet you did not return[h] to me,' declares the LORD.[i] 18 'From this day on, from
this twenty-fourth day of the ninth month,
give careful thought[j] to the day when the
foundation[k] of the LORD's temple was laid.
Give careful thought: 19 Is there yet any
seed left in the barn? Until now, the vine
and the fig tree, the pomegranate[l] and the
olive tree have not borne fruit.[m]
" 'From this day on I will bless[n] you.' "

2:14 [x] S Ps 51:17; S Isa 1:13
2:15 [y] S Hag 1:5 [z] S Ezr 3:10 [a] Ezr 4:24
2:16 [b] S Ru 3:7 [c] S Job 24:11; S Isa 5:2 [d] S Dt 28:38; S Isa 5:10; S Hag 1:6
2:17 [e] Hag 1:11 [f] S Dt 28:22 [g] S Ex 9:18; Ps 78:48 [h] S Isa 9:13; S Jer 3:10 [i] S Am 4:6
2:18 [j] S Hag 1:5 [k] S Ezr 3:11
2:19 [l] S Ex 28:33 [m] S Joel 1:12 [n] S Ge 12:2; S Lev 25:21; Ps 128:1-6; S Joel 2:14
2:20 [o] S Ezr 5:1 [p] S ver 1; S Hag 1:15

Zerubbabel the LORD's Signet Ring

20 The word of the LORD came to Haggai[o]
a second time on the twenty-fourth day of
the month:[p] 21 "Tell Zerubbabel[q] governor of
Judah that I am going to shake[r] the heavens and the earth. 22 I will overturn[s] royal
thrones and shatter the power of the foreign kingdoms.[t] I will overthrow chariots[u]
and their drivers; horses and their riders[v]
will fall, each by the sword of his brother.[w]
23 " 'On that day,[x]' declares the LORD Almighty, 'I will take you, my servant[y] Zerubbabel[z] son of Shealtiel,' declares the
LORD, 'and I will make you like my signet
ring,[a] for I have chosen you,' declares the
LORD Almighty."

[a] 15 Or *to the days past*

2:21 [q] S Ezr 5:2 [r] S Isa 14:16; Eze 38:19-20 **2:22** [s] S Ge 19:25; S Job 2:13 [t] S Da 2:44 [u] S Mic 5:10 [v] S Ex 15:21 [w] S Jdg 7:22; S Eze 38:21 **2:23** [x] Isa 2:11; 10:20; Zec 4:10 [y] S Isa 20:3; S Da 9:24-26 [z] Mt 1:12 [a] S Ge 38:18; S Ex 28:9; 2Co 1:22

2:15 *before one stone was laid.* Before the 24th day of the sixth month (1:14–15).

2:16 *heap.* Probably of grain (see Jer 50:26). *only ten ... only twenty.* The poor harvests were related to the sin of the people (see 1:11; Isa 5:10 and note). *wine vat.* Usually a shallow pit cut into solid rock, into which grape juice flowed when the grapes were trodden and where it was retained until fermentation had begun. The juice was later transferred to jars or skins for further fermentation and storage. See photos, pp. 820, 2168.

2:17 *blight, mildew.* Mentioned as a curse for disobedience in Dt 28:22 (see also 1Ki 8:37; Am 4:9). The blight was probably caused by a scorching east wind (see Ge 41:6 and note). *hail.* Sent to destroy the fields and livestock of Egypt (see Ex 9:25; Ps 78:47–48). *you did not return.* See Am 4:6,8–11.

2:18 *when the foundation ... was laid.* The same potential for blessing had existed at the time when the foundation of the temple was laid in 536 BC (Ezr 3:11). This is a warning not to fail again.

2:19 *vine ... fig tree ... pomegranate ... olive tree.* Grapes, figs and pomegranates ripened in August and September, and olives from September to November. These harvests, like the earlier grain crops, had produced little (see 1:11 and note). *I will bless you.* Because of their response to Haggai's message, future abundance is assured. Cf. Mal 3:10.

2:20 See note on v. 10.

2:21 *shake ... the earth.* See v. 6 and note.

2:22 *overturn ... overthrow.* The Hebrew for these words is used with reference to Sodom and Gomorrah (see Ge 19:25; Am 4:11). *chariots ... horses ... riders.* Cf. the destruction of the pharaoh's army at the "Red Sea" (Ex 15:1,4,19,21). *each by ... his brother.* The plight of the armies of Midian (see Jdg 7:22 and note), Gog (see Eze 38:21 and note) and the nations fighting against Jerusalem in the last days (Zec 14:13).

2:23 *On that day.* The day of the Lord (see Isa 2:11,17,20; 10:20,27; Joel 1:15; Zec 2:11 and notes). *my servant.* A term applied to prophets (see Isa 20:3 and note), political leaders (Isa 22:20) and the Messiah (see Isa 41:8–9; 42:1 and notes). *signet ring.* A kind of seal that functioned as a signature (see Est 8:8) and was worn on one's finger (Est 3:10). Like other seals (see Ge 38:18 and note), it could be used as a pledge or guarantee of full payment. Its mention here apparently reverses the curse placed on King Jehoiachin in Jer 22:24 (see also Jdg 17:2 and note). Zerubbabel would then be a guarantee that indeed the future glory of the temple will be realized (see vv. 6–7,9; Zec 4:6–7 and notes). *chosen you.* See Isa 41:8–9; 42:1 and notes.

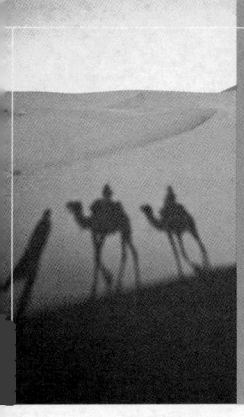

ZECHARIAH

INTRODUCTION

Background

Zechariah's prophetic ministry took place in the postexilic period, the time of the Jewish restoration from Babylonian captivity. For historical details, see Introduction to Haggai: Background.

Author and Unity

Like Jeremiah (1:1) and Ezekiel (1:3), Zechariah was not only a prophet (1:1) but also a member of a priestly family. He was born in Babylonia and was among those who returned to Judah in 538/537 BC under the leadership of Zerubbabel and Joshua (his grandfather Iddo is named among the returnees in Ne 12:4). At a later time, when Joiakim was high priest (see note on Ne 12:12–21), Zechariah apparently succeeded Iddo (1:1,7) as head of that priestly family (Ne 12:10–16). Since the grandson succeeded the grandfather, it has been suggested that the father (Berekiah, 1:1,7) died at an early age.

Zechariah was a contemporary of Haggai (Ezr 5:1; 6:14) but continued his ministry long after him (compare 1:1 and 7:1 with Hag 1:1; see also Ne 12:1–16). His young age (see 2:4 and note) in the early period of his ministry makes it possible that he ministered even into the reign of Artaxerxes I (465–424 BC).

Most likely Zechariah wrote the entire book that bears his name. Some have questioned his authorship of chs. 9–14, citing differences in style and other compositional features and giving historical and chronological references that allegedly require a different date and author from those of chs. 1–8. All these objections, however, can be explained in other satisfactory ways, so there is no compelling reason to question the unity of the book.

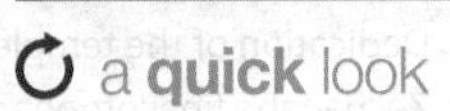

a quick look

Author:
Zechariah

Audience:
The postexilic Jews living in Judah

Date:
520 to about 480 BC

Theme:
The prophet Zechariah rebukes and encourages the discouraged exiles who have returned to Jerusalem from Babylonia to complete the rebuilding of the temple.

Dates

The dates of Zechariah's recorded messages are best correlated with those of Haggai and with other historical events as follows:

The dominant emphasis of the book is encouragement because of the glorious future that awaits the people of God.

(1)	Haggai's first message (Hag 1:1 – 11; Ezr 5:1)	Aug. 29, 520 BC
(2)	Resumption of the building of the temple (Hag 1:12 – 15; Ezr 5:2) (The rebuilding seems to have been hindered from 536 to c. 530 [Ezr 4:1 – 5], and the work ceased altogether from c. 530 to 520 [Ezr 4:24].)	Sept. 21, 520
(3)	Haggai's second message (Hag 2:1 – 9)	Oct. 17, 520
(4)	Beginning of Zechariah's preaching (1:1 – 6)	Oct./Nov., 520
(5)	Haggai's third message (Hag 2:10 – 19)	Dec. 18, 520
(6)	Haggai's fourth message (Hag 2:20 – 23)	Dec. 18, 520
(7)	Tattenai's letter to Darius concerning the rebuilding of the temple (Ezr 5:3 — 6:14) (There must have been a lapse of time between the resumption of the building and Tattenai's appearance.)	519 – 518
(8)	Zechariah's eight night visions (1:7 — 6:8)	Feb. 15, 519
(9)	Joshua crowned (6:9 – 15)	Feb. 16 (?), 519
(10)	Repentance urged, blessings promised (chs. 7 – 8)	Dec. 7, 518
(11)	Dedication of the temple (Ezr 6:15 – 18)	Mar. 12, 516
(12)	Zechariah's final prophecies (chs. 9 – 14)	After 480 (?)

Occasion and Purpose

The occasion is the same as that of the book of Haggai (see Background and Dates). The chief purpose of Zechariah (and Haggai) was to rebuke the people of Judah and to encourage and motivate them to complete the rebuilding of the temple (Zec 4:8 – 10; Hag 1 – 2), though both prophets were clearly interested in spiritual renewal as well. In addition, the purpose of the eight night visions (1:7 — 6:8) is explained in 1:3,5 – 6: The Lord said that if the people of Judah would return to him, he would return to them. Furthermore, his word would continue to be fulfilled.

Theological Teaching

The theology of Zechariah's prophecy matches his name, which means "The LORD (Yahweh) remembers." "The LORD" is the personal, covenant name of God and is a perpetual testimony to his faithfulness to his promises (see notes on Ge 2:4; Ex 3:14 – 15; 6:6; Dt 28:58). He "remembers" his covenant promises and takes action to fulfill them. In the book of Zechariah God's promised deliverance from Babylonian exile, including a restored kingdom community and a functioning temple, the location of the earthly throne of the divine King (see Introduction to Psalms: Theology: Major Themes), leads into even grander pictures of the salvation and restoration to come through the Messiah (see notes on 3:8 – 9; 4:3,14; 6:9 – 15; 9:9 – 10; 10:2,4; 11:4 – 14; 12:10 — 13:1; 13:7; 14:4 – 9).

The book as a whole also teaches the sovereignty of God in history, over people and nations — past, present and future (see, e.g., 1:10 – 11; 2:13; 4:10,14 and note; 6:5,7; 8:20 – 23; 9:10,13 – 14; 10:11; 12:1 – 5; 14:9,16 – 19). See also Literary Forms and Themes.

Twelfth-century fresco of Christ's entry into Jerusalem. Zechariah 9:9 prophesies that the Messianic King would ride into Jerusalem on a donkey (see Mt 21:5; Jn 12:15).

Literary Forms and Themes

The book is primarily a mixture of exhortation (call to repentance, 1:2–6); prophetic visions (1:7—6:8); a prophetic message of instruction or exhortation involving a symbolic coronation scene (6:9–15); hortatory messages (mainly of rebuke and hope), prompted by a question about fasting (chs. 7–8); and judgment and salvation messages (chs. 9–14). The prophetic visions of 1:7—6:8 are called apocalyptic (revelatory) literature, which is essentially a literature of encouragement to God's people. When the apocalyptic section is read along with the salvation (or deliverance) messages in chs. 9–14, it becomes obvious that the dominant emphasis of the book is encouragement because of the glorious future that awaits the people of God.

In fact, encouragement is the book's central theme—primarily encouragement to complete the rebuilding of the temple. Various means are used to accomplish this end, and these function as subthemes. For example, great stress is laid on the coming of the Messiah and the overthrow of all anti-kingdom forces by him so that God's rule can be finally and fully established on earth. The then-current local scene thus becomes the basis for contemplating the universal, eschatological picture.

Several interpreters have arranged the eight visions of 1:7—6:8 in a chiastic (or concentric) pattern of *a—b—b—c / c′—b′—b′—a′*:

a The Lord controls the events of history (1:7 – 17)
b Nations that devastated Israel will in turn be devastated (1:18 – 21)
b Israel will be fully restored (ch. 2)
c Israel will be restored as a priestly nation (ch. 3)
c′ Israel will be restored under royal and priestly leadership (ch. 4)
b′ Lawbreakers will be purged from Israel (5:1 – 4)
b′ The whole sinful system will be removed from the land (5:5 – 11)
a′ The Lord controls the events of history (6:1 – 8)

Outline

Part I (chs. 1 – 8)

- I. Introduction (1:1 – 6)
  - A. The Date and the Author's Name (1:1)
  - B. A Call to Repentance (1:2 – 6)
- II. A Series of Eight Visions in One Night (1:7 — 6:8)
  - A. The Horseman among the Myrtle Trees (1:7 – 17)
  - B. The Four Horns and the Four Craftsmen (1:18 – 21)
  - C. A Man with a Measuring Line (ch. 2)
  - D. Clean Garments for the High Priest (ch. 3)
  - E. The Gold Lampstand and the Two Olive Trees (ch. 4)
  - F. The Flying Scroll (5:1 – 4)
  - G. The Woman in a Basket (5:5 – 11)
  - H. The Four Chariots (6:1 – 8)
- III. The Symbolic Crowning of Joshua, the High Priest (6:9 – 15)
- IV. The Problem of Fasting and the Promise of the Future (chs. 7 – 8)
  - A. The Question by the Delegation from Bethel (7:1 – 3)
  - B. The Rebuke by the Lord (7:4 – 7)
  - C. The Command to Repent (7:8 – 14)
  - D. The Restoration of Israel to God's Favor (8:1 – 17)
  - E. Kingdom Joy and Jewish Favor (8:18 – 23)

Part II (chs. 9 – 14)

- V. Two Prophetic Messages: The Great Messianic Future and the Full Realization of God's Kingdom (chs. 9 – 14)
  - A. The First Message: The Coming and Rejection of the Messiah (chs. 9 – 11)
    - 1. The coming of the Messianic King (chs. 9 – 10)
      - a. The destruction of surrounding nations but the preservation of Zion (9:1 – 8)
      - b. The coming of Zion's King (9:9 – 10)
      - c. The deliverance and blessing of Zion's people (9:11 — 10:1)
      - d. The leaders warned and the people encouraged (10:2 – 4)
      - e. Israel's victory and restoration (10:5 – 12)

2. The rejection of the Messianic Shepherd-King (ch. 11)
   a. The prologue (11:1 – 3)
   b. The rejection of the Good Shepherd (11:4 – 14)
   c. The rise and fall of the worthless shepherd (11:15 – 17)

B. The Second Message: The Coming and Reception of the Messiah (chs. 12 – 14)

1. The deliverance and conversion of Israel (chs. 12 – 13)
   a. The siege of Jerusalem (12:1 – 3)
   b. The divine deliverance (12:4 – 9)
   c. Israel completely delivered from sin (12:10—13:9)
2. The Messiah's coming and his kingdom (ch. 14)
   a. The siege of Jerusalem (14:1 – 2)
   b. The Messiah's return and its effects (14:3 – 8)
   c. The establishment of the Messianic kingdom (14:9 – 11)
   d. The punishment of Israel's enemies (14:12 – 15)
   e. The universal worship of the holy King (14:16 – 21)

A Call to Return to the LORD

1 In the eighth month of the second year of Darius,[a] the word of the LORD came to the prophet Zechariah[b] son of Berekiah,[c] the son of Iddo:[d]

2 "The LORD was very angry[e] with your ancestors. 3 Therefore tell the people: This is what the LORD Almighty says: 'Return[f] to me,' declares the LORD Almighty, 'and I will return to you,'[g] says the LORD Almighty. 4 Do not be like your ancestors,[h] to whom the earlier prophets[i] proclaimed: This is what the LORD Almighty says: 'Turn from your evil ways[j] and your evil practices.' But they would not listen or pay attention to me,[k] declares the LORD.[l] 5 Where are your ancestors now? And the prophets, do they live forever? 6 But did not my words[m] and my decrees, which I commanded my servants the prophets, overtake your ancestors?[n]

"Then they repented and said, 'The LORD Almighty has done to us what our ways and practices deserve,[o] just as he determined to do.' "[p]

The Man Among the Myrtle Trees

7 On the twenty-fourth day of the eleventh month, the month of Shebat, in the second year of Darius, the word of the LORD came to the prophet Zechariah son of Berekiah, the son of Iddo.[q]

8 During the night I had a vision, and there before me was a man mounted on a red[r] horse. He was standing among the myrtle trees in a ravine. Behind him were red, brown and white horses.[s]

9 I asked, "What are these, my lord?"

The angel[t] who was talking with me answered, "I will show you what they are."[u]

10 Then the man standing among the myrtle trees explained, "They are the ones the LORD has sent to go throughout the earth."[v]

11 And they reported to the angel of the LORD[w] who was standing among the myrtle trees, "We have gone throughout the earth and found the whole world at rest and in peace."[x]

12 Then the angel of the LORD said, "LORD Almighty, how long[y] will you withhold mercy[z] from Jerusalem and from the towns of Judah,[a] which you have been angry with these seventy[b] years?" 13 So the LORD spoke[c] kind and comforting words[d] to the angel who talked with me.[e]

14 Then the angel who was speaking to me said, "Proclaim this word: This is what the LORD Almighty says: 'I am very jealous[f] for Jerusalem and Zion, 15 and I am very angry with the nations that feel secure.[g] I was only a little angry,[h] but they went too far with the punishment.'[i]

1:1 [a] S Ezr 4:24; S 6:15 [b] S Ezr 5:1 [c] Mt 23:35; Lk 11:51 [d] ver 7; S Ne 12:4 **1:2** [e] S 2Ch 36:16 **1:3** [f] S Job 22:23 [g] Mal 3:7; Jas 4:8 **1:4** [h] S 2Ch 36:15 [i] Zec 7:7 [j] S 2Ki 17:13; S 2Ch 7:14; Ps 106:6; S Jer 23:22 [k] S 2Ch 24:19; Ps 78:8; S Jer 6:17; 17:23 [l] S Eze 20:18; S 33:4 **1:6** [m] S Isa 44:26 [n] S Dt 28:2; S Da 9:12; S Hos 5:9 [o] Jer 12:14-17; La 2:17 [p] Jer 23:20; 39:16; S 44:17 **1:7** [q] S ver 1 **1:8** [r] Rev 6:4 [s] Zec 6:2-7 **1:9** [t] Zec 4:1, 4-5; 5:5 [u] S Da 7:16 **1:10** [v] Zec 6:5-8 **1:11** [w] Ge 16:7 [x] S Isa 14:7 **1:12** [y] S Ps 6:3 [z] Ps 40:11 [a] S Jer 40:5 [b] S 2Ch 36:21; S Da 9:2 **1:13** [c] S Isa 35:4 [d] S Job 15:11 [e] Zec 4:1 **1:14** [f] S Isa 26:11; S Joel 2:18 **1:15** [g] Jer 48:11 [h] S 2Ch 28:9 [i] S Ps 69:26; 123:3-4; S Am 1:11

1:1 *eighth month of the second year.* October-November, 520 BC. Haggai also began his prophetic ministry in Darius's second year (see Introduction: Dates), on the first day of the sixth month, i.e., on Aug. 29, 520 (Hag 1:1). *word of the LORD.* A technical phrase for the prophetic word of revelation (see v. 7; 9:1; 12:1; see also 4:8; Hos 1:1 and notes). *prophet.* One called by God to speak his word on his behalf (see note on Ex 7:1–2). *Iddo.* See v. 7; Ezr 5:1; 6:14; Ne 12:4,16; see also Introduction: Author and Unity.

1:2 *very angry with your ancestors.* The Lord was angry because of the covenant-breaking sins of the Jews' preexilic ancestors, resulting in the destruction of Jerusalem and the temple in 586 BC, followed by exile to Babylonia (2Ch 36:15–21).

1:3 *the LORD Almighty.* See note on 1Sa 1:3. *Return to me... and I will return to you.* Cf. 7:13; 8:3; Mal 3:7. If the people of Zechariah's day would change their course and go in the opposite direction from that of their ancestors (v. 4), the Lord would return to them with blessing instead of with a curse (see v. 16; see also Jer 18:7–10 and note).

1:4 *earlier prophets.* Such as Isaiah (see Isa 45:22 and note), Jeremiah (see Jer 18:11 and note) and Ezekiel (see Eze 33:11 and note). See also 7:7,12; Jer 25:4–5; 35:15.

1:5 *do they live forever?* No, but God's words through them live on to be fulfilled (see v. 6).

1:6 *did not my words ... overtake your ancestors?* Cf. Isa 40:6–8; 55:10–11. For the imagery of "overtake," see Dt 28:2 ("accompany" is lit. "overtake"),15,45. *my servants the prophets.* See 2Ki 9:7; 17:13,23; 21:10; 24:2; Ezr 9:11; Jer 7:25 and note; 25:4; Eze 38:17; Da 9:6,10; Am 3:7. *they repented.* Apparently a reference to what happened to some of the preexilic ancestors and/or their offspring during the exile and immediately afterward (cf. Ezr 9:1—10:17; Da 9:3–19).

1:7—6:8 See Introduction: Literary Forms and Themes.

1:7–17 The first vision. Although God's covenant people are troubled while the oppressing nations are more at ease, God is jealous (see note on Ex 20:5) for his people and will restore them and their towns and the temple. The imagery of the first vision is reflected in that of the eighth and final vision (6:1–8).

1:7 *twenty-fourth day of ... Shebat.* Feb. 15, 519 BC, about three months after the date of v. 1.

1:8 *During the night.* Zechariah had all eight visions (1:7—6:8) in one night. *vision.* Not a dream (see 4:1; see also Pr 29:18; Isa 1:1; Ob 1 and notes). The visions were given to Zechariah while he was fully awake. *man mounted on.* Later identified as the angel of the Lord (v. 11). He must not be confused with the interpreting angel, who is mentioned in vv. 9,13–14,19; 2:3; 4:1,4–5; 5:5,10; 6:4–5.

1:9 *angel.* See note on v. 8.

1:11 *angel of the LORD.* See 3:1; see also note on Ge 16:7. *at rest.* Cf. 6:8. While the Persian Empire as a whole was secure and at ease by this time (v. 15), the Jews in Judah were oppressed and still under foreign domination (v. 12).

1:12 *mercy.* Tender compassion (also in v. 16). *seventy years.* See 7:5; Ezr 1:1; Jer 25:11–12 and notes.

1:13 *comforting words.* Those of vv. 14–17.

1:14 *jealous.* See 8:2. Through the use of such language the Lord's love for Judah is shown (see note on Ex 20:5; cf. Jas 4:4). The key idea is that of God avenging Judah for the violations against her (v. 15; see Dt 32:35,41; Jer 50:15; 51:6,11).

1:15 *nations that feel secure.* A security that will be completely undone (see Isa 32:9–13; Hag 2:6–7 and notes). *went too far with the punishment.* God was angry with Israel and used the Assyrians (see Isa 10:5 and note) and Babylonians (see Isa

16 "Therefore this is what the LORD says: 'I will return[j] to Jerusalem with mercy, and there my house will be rebuilt. And the measuring line[k] will be stretched out over Jerusalem,' declares the LORD Almighty.[l]

17 "Proclaim further: This is what the LORD Almighty says: 'My towns will again overflow with prosperity, and the LORD will again comfort[m] Zion and choose[n] Jerusalem.' "[o]

Four Horns and Four Craftsmen

18 Then I looked up, and there before me were four horns. 19 I asked the angel who was speaking to me, "What are these?"

He answered me, "These are the horns[p] that scattered Judah, Israel and Jerusalem."

20 Then the LORD showed me four craftsmen. 21 I asked, "What are these coming to do?"

He answered, "These are the horns that scattered Judah so that no one could raise their head, but the craftsmen have come to terrify them and throw down these horns of the nations who lifted up their horns[q] against the land of Judah to scatter its people."[a][r]

A Man With a Measuring Line

2 [b] Then I looked up, and there before me was a man with a measuring line in his hand. 2 I asked, "Where are you going?"

He answered me, "To measure Jerusalem, to find out how wide and how long it is."[s]

3 While the angel who was speaking to me was leaving, another angel came to meet him 4 and said to him: "Run, tell that young man, 'Jerusalem will be a city without walls[t] because of the great number[u] of people and animals in it.[v] 5 And I myself will be a wall[w] of fire[x] around it,' declares the LORD, 'and I will be its glory[y] within.'[z]

6 "Come! Come! Flee from the land of the north," declares the LORD, "for I have scattered[a] you to the four winds of heaven,"[b] declares the LORD.[c]

7 "Come, Zion! Escape,[d] you who live in Daughter Babylon!"[e] 8 For this is what the LORD Almighty says: "After the Glorious One has sent me against the nations that have plundered you—for whoever touches you touches the apple of his eye[f]— 9 I will surely raise my hand against them so that their slaves will plunder them.[c][g] Then you will know that the LORD Almighty has sent me.[h]

10 "Shout[i] and be glad, Daughter Zion.[j] For I am coming,[k] and I will live among you,"[l] declares the LORD.[m] 11 "Many nations will be joined with the LORD in that day and will become my people.[n] I will live among you and you will know that the LORD Almighty has sent me to you.[o] 12 The LORD will inherit[p] Judah[q] as his portion in the holy land and will again choose[r] Jerusalem. 13 Be still[s] before the LORD, all mankind, because he has roused himself from his holy dwelling."[t]

1:16 [j] Zec 8:3 [k] S Job 38:5; Zec 2:1-2 [l] S Ezr 1:1
1:17 [m] S Isa 40:1 [n] S Isa 14:1 [o] S Ezr 9:9; S Ps 51:18; Isa 54:8-10; S 61:4
1:19 [p] Am 6:13
1:21 [q] S 1Ki 22:11; Ps 75:4 [r] S Ps 75:10; S Isa 54:16-17; Zec 12:9
2:2 [s] S Eze 40:3; S Zec 1:16; Rev 21:15
2:4 [t] S Eze 38:11 [u] S Isa 49:20; S Jer 30:19; S 33:22 [v] Zec 14:11
2:5 [w] S Isa 26:1; Eze 42:20 [x] S Isa 10:17 [y] S Ps 85:9; S Isa 11:10; S 24:23; Rev 21:23 [z] S Ps 46:5; S Ps 125:2; S Eze 38:14
2:6 [a] S Ps 44:11 [b] S Eze 17:21; S 37:9 [c] Mt 24:31; Mk 13:27
2:7 [d] S Isa 42:7 [e] S Isa 48:20; Jer 3:18
2:8 [f] S Dt 32:10
2:9 [g] S Isa 14:2; S Jer 12:14; S Hab 2:8 [h] S Isa 48:16; Zec 4:9; 6:15
2:10 [i] S Zep 3:14 [j] S Isa 23:12; S Zep 3:14 [k] Zec 9:9 [l] S Ex 25:8; Lev 26:12; S Nu 23:21; Zec 8:3 [m] S Rev 21:3
2:11 [n] S Jer 24:7; S Mic 4:2; Zec 8:8, 20-22 [o] Zec 4:9; 6:15
2:12 [p] S Ex 34:9; Ps 33:12; Jer 10:16 [q] Jer 40:5 [r] S Dt 12:5; S Isa 14:1
2:13 [s] S Ex 14:14; S Isa 41:1 [t] S Dt 26:15

[a] *21* In Hebrew texts 1:18-21 is numbered 2:1-4. [b] In Hebrew texts 2:1-13 is numbered 2:5-17. [c] *8,9* Or *says after . . . eye: 9"I . . . plunder them."*

47:6; Jer 25:9 and notes) to punish her, but they went too far by trying to destroy Israel as a people (cf. 2Ki 10:11 and note).
1:16 *I will return.* See note on v. 3. *mercy.* See v. 12 and note. *my house will be rebuilt.* See Ezr 6:14–16; Hag 1:8; see also Introduction to Haggai: Background. *measuring line.* A symbol of restoration (see Jer 31:38–40 and note on 31:39).
1:17 *comfort.* See v. 13 and note. *choose Jerusalem.* See 2:12; 3:2.
1:18–21 The second vision. The nations that devastated Israel (v. 19) will in turn be destroyed by other nations.
1:18 *four.* If the number is to be taken literally, the reference is probably to Assyria, Egypt, Babylonia and Persia. *horns.* Probably metallic, either bronze or iron; symbolic of strength in general (Ps 18:2) or of the strength of a country, i.e., its king (Ps 89:17; Da 7:7–8; 8:20–21; Rev 17:12) or, as here (see v. 21), the power of a nation in general.
1:20 *four.* If the number is to be understood literally, perhaps the reference is to Egypt, Babylonia, Persia and Greece. What is clear is that all Israel's enemies will ultimately be defeated (v. 21). *craftsmen.* Probably metalsmiths (see 1Ki 22:11).
1:21 *terrify them.* Contrast vv. 11 ("at rest and in peace") and 15 ("feel secure"; see note there).
2:1–13 The third vision. There will be full restoration and blessing for the covenant people, temple and city.
2:1 *measuring line.* See note on 1:16.
2:4 *young man.* Evidently Zechariah. *without walls.* The city's population will overflow to the point that it will be as though it had no walls (see 10:8,10; see also note on Isa 49:19–20).
2:5 *wall of fire.* Here symbolic of divine protection (see 9:8; see also Ex 13:21; Isa 4:5–6 and notes). *glory.* See Ex 40:34; Eze 1:28; 43:2; Hag 2:9 and notes.
2:6 *land of the north.* Babylonia (v. 7) invaded Judah from the north (see Isa 41:25 and note; Jer 1:14; 4:6; 6:1,22; 10:22). *to the four winds.* In all directions. The exiles would return from north, south, east and west (Isa 43:5–6; 49:12).
2:7 *Zion.* Jerusalem's exiles in Babylon. *Escape . . . Babylon.* Cf. Rev 18:2–4. *Daughter Babylon.* A personification of Babylon (see note on 2Ki 19:21).
2:8 *me.* See also v. 9; probably the angel of the Lord (see 1:8 and note). *apple of his eye.* See note on Dt 32:10.
2:10 See 9:9 and note. *Daughter Zion.* A personification of Jerusalem (see v. 7 and note). *I will live among you.* See v. 11; 8:3; Lev 26:11–12; Eze 37:27; Jn 1:14; 2Co 6:16; Rev 21:3.
2:11 *Many nations.* In fulfillment of the promise to Abraham (Ge 12:3; cf. Zec 8:20–23; 14:16; Ge 18:18; 22:18; Isa 2:2–4 and note; 19:24–25). *that day.* The day of the Lord (see 3:10; see also 12:3; Isa 2:11,17,20; Joel 1:15; Am 5:18 and notes).
2:12 *holy land.* See Ps 78:54. The land was rendered holy chiefly because it was the site of the earthly throne and sanctuary of the holy King, who dwelt there among his covenant people (see note on Ex 3:5). *choose Jerusalem.* See 1:17; 3:2.
2:13 *Be still before the LORD.* See Hab 2:20 and note. *roused himself.* To judge (cf. v. 9).

Clean Garments for the High Priest

3 Then he showed me Joshua[u] the high
priest standing before the angel of the
LORD, and Satan[a][v] standing at his right side
to accuse him. 2 The LORD said to Satan,
"The LORD rebuke you,[w] Satan! The LORD,
who has chosen[x] Jerusalem, rebuke you!
Is not this man a burning stick[y] snatched
from the fire?"[z]
3 Now Joshua was dressed in filthy
clothes as he stood before the angel. 4 The
angel said to those who were standing before him, "Take off his filthy clothes."
Then he said to Joshua, "See, I have
taken away your sin,[a] and I will put fine
garments[b] on you."
5 Then I said, "Put a clean turban[c] on his
head." So they put a clean turban on his
head and clothed him, while the angel of
the LORD stood by.
6 The angel of the LORD gave this charge
to Joshua: 7 "This is what the LORD Almighty says: 'If you will walk in obedience to me and keep my requirements,[d]
then you will govern my house[e] and have
charge[f] of my courts, and I will give you a
place among these standing here.[g]

3:1 [u] S Ezr 2:2; Zec 6:11 [v] S 2Sa 24:1; S 2Ch 18:21; S Ps 109:6; S Mt 4:10 **3:2** [w] Jude 1:9 [x] S Isa 14:1 [y] S Isa 7:4 [z] Jude 1:23 **3:4** [a] S 2Sa 12:13; S Eze 36:25; S Mic 7:18 [b] S Ge 41:42; S Ps 132:9; S Isa 52:1; Rev 19:8 **3:5** [c] S Ex 29:6 **3:7** [d] S Lev 8:35 [e] Dt 17:8-11; S Eze 44:15-16 [f] 2Ch 23:6 [g] Jer 15:19; Zec 6:15 **3:8** [h] Hag 1:1 [i] S Dt 28:46; S Eze 12:11 [j] S Isa 4:2; S 49:3; S Eze 17:22 **3:9** [k] S Ezr 2:2 [l] S 2Ch 16:9 [m] Isa 28:16 [n] S 2Sa 12:13; S Jer 50:20 **3:10** [o] S Job 11:18 [p] S Nu 16:14;

8 " 'Listen, High Priest[h] Joshua, you and
your associates seated before you, who
are men symbolic[i] of things to come: I am
going to bring my servant, the Branch.[j]
9 See, the stone I have set in front of Joshua![k] There are seven eyes[b][l] on that one
stone,[m] and I will engrave an inscription
on it,' says the LORD Almighty, 'and I will
remove the sin[n] of this land in a single
day.
10 " 'In that day each of you will invite
your neighbor to sit[o] under your vine and
fig tree,[p]' declares the LORD Almighty."

The Gold Lampstand and the Two Olive Trees

4 Then the angel who talked with me
returned and woke[q] me up, like someone awakened from sleep.[r] 2 He asked me,
"What do you see?"[s]
I answered, "I see a solid gold lampstand[t] with a bowl at the top and seven

[a] *1* Hebrew *satan* means *adversary*. [b] *9* Or *facets*

S 1Ki 4:25; Mic 4:4 **4:1** [q] S Da 8:18 [r] Jer 31:26 **4:2** [s] S Jer 1:13 [t] S Ex 25:31; Rev 1:12

3:1–10 The fourth vision. Israel will be cleansed and restored as a priestly nation (see Ex 19:6 and note).

3:1 *Joshua.* See note on Hag 1:1. Here he represents the sinful nation of Israel (see vv. 8–9). The name Joshua was common in ancient times. The Greek equivalent is spelled "Jesus" in English, and both forms of the name mean "The LORD saves" (see NIV text note on Mt 1:21). *standing before.* Ministering before—as priest (see Dt 10:8; 2Ch 29:11; Eze 44:15). *angel of the LORD.* See 1:11; see also note on Ge 16:7. *Satan.* See NIV text note; Job 1:6–12 and note on 1:6; 2:1–7; Rev 12:10 and note. *right side.* See Ps 109:6. *accuse.* The Hebrew for this word has the same root as the Hebrew for "Satan."

3:2 *rebuke … rebuke.* Repeated for emphasis (see 4:7; see also note on Isa 40:1). *chosen Jerusalem.* See 1:17; 2:12. *burning stick snatched from the fire.* The Jews were retrieved from the fire of Babylonian exile to carry out God's future purpose for them (see Am 4:11 and note; see also Zec 13:8–9; Dt 4:20 and note; 7:7–8; Jer 30:7; Rev 12:13–16; cf. 1Co 3:15; Jude 23 and notes).

3:4 *those who were standing before him.* Probably angels (see also v. 7). *Take off his filthy clothes.* Thus depriving him of his priestly office. The act is here symbolic also of the removal of sin (see note on v. 9; cf. Isa 64:6).

3:5 *Put a clean turban on his head.* Thus reinstating him into his high-priestly function so that Israel once again has a divinely authorized priestly mediator. On the front of the turban were the words "HOLY TO THE LORD" (Ex 28:36–37; 39:30–31; see Zec 14:20 and note).

3:7 If Joshua and his priestly associates are faithful, they will be co-workers with the angels in carrying out God's purposes for Zion and Israel (cf. Jer 31:22 and note). *these standing here.* See note on v. 4.

3:8 *associates.* Fellow priests. *my servant.* See notes on Ex 14:31; Ps 18 title; Isa 41:8–9; 42:1–4; 42:1; Ro 1:1. *Branch.* A Messianic title (see 6:12; Isa 4:2 and notes; 11:1; Jer 23:5 and note; 33:15).

3:9 *stone.* Probably another figure of the Messiah (see Ps 118:22; Isa 8:14; 28:16 and notes; Da 2:35,45). *seven eyes.* Perhaps symbolic of infinite intelligence (omniscience). See note on 4:10. *I will remove the sin of this land.* The symbolic act of v. 4 is now explained. "Land" stands for the people of Israel. For the cleansing spoken of here, see also 12:10—13:1; cf. Ro 11:26–27 and notes. *in a single day.* Ultimately Good Friday, though some believe that the reference also includes Christ's second coming.

3:10 *that day.* See 2:11 and note. *sit under your vine and fig tree.* A proverbial picture of peace, security and contentment (see Mic 4:4 and note; cf. 2Ki 18:31).

4:1–14 The fifth vision. The Jews are encouraged to rebuild the temple by being reminded of their divine resources. The light from the lampstand in the tabernacle/temple represents the reflection of God's glory in the consecration and holy service of God's people (see note on Ex 25:37)—made possible only by the power of God's Spirit (see v. 6; symbolized by the oil, v. 12). This enabling power will equip and sustain Zerubbabel in the rebuilding of the temple (vv. 6–10). And in the performance of their offices, Zerubbabel and Joshua (as representatives of the royal and priestly mediatorial offices) will channel the Spirit's enablement to God's people (vv. 11–14).

4:1 *woke me up.* On the same night (see note on 1:8).

4:2 *What do you see?* See 5:2; see also Jer 1:11 and note. The vision here was probably of seven lamps arranged around a large bowl that served as a bountiful reservoir of oil. The "seven channels to the lamps" conveyed the oil from the bowl to the lamps. But the text is also open to a different interpretation, namely, that the "channels" are "lips" or "spouts" that held the wicks of these oil lamps and that each of these lamps had seven of them (thus a total of 49 flames; see note on Ex 25:37). In any event, the bowl represents an abundant supply of oil, symbolizing the fullness of God's power through his Spirit (v. 6), and the "seven … seven" represents the abundant light shining from the lamps (seven being the number of fullness). Cf. Rev 1:4 and note.

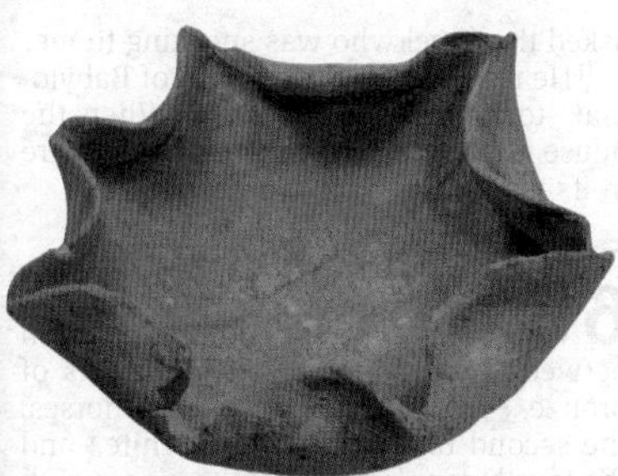

Seven-spouted bowl lamp from Dothan (see Zec 4:2 and note)

Kim Walton, courtesy of the Joseph P. Free Collection and Wheaton College

lamps[u] on it, with seven channels to the
lamps. 3Also there are two olive trees[v] by
it, one on the right of the bowl and the
other on its left."
4I asked the angel who talked with me,
"What are these, my lord?"
5He answered, "Do you not know what
these are?"
"No, my lord," I replied.[w]
6So he said to me, "This is the word of
the LORD to Zerubbabel:[x] 'Not[y] by might
nor by power,[z] but by my Spirit,'[a] says the
LORD Almighty.
7"What are you, mighty mountain?
Before Zerubbabel you will become level ground.[b] Then he will bring out the
capstone[c] to shouts[d] of 'God bless it! God
bless it!'"
8Then the word of the LORD came to me:
9"The hands of Zerubbabel have laid the
foundation[e] of this temple; his hands will
also complete it.[f] Then you will know that
the LORD Almighty has sent me[g] to you.
10"Who dares despise the day[h] of small
things,[i] since the seven eyes[j] of the LORD
that range throughout the earth will rejoice when they see the chosen capstone[a]
in the hand of Zerubbabel?"[k]
11Then I asked the angel, "What are
these two olive trees[l] on the right and the
left of the lampstand?"
12Again I asked him, "What are these
two olive branches beside the two gold
pipes that pour out golden oil?"
13He replied, "Do you not know what
these are?"
"No, my lord," I said.
14So he said, "These are the two who
are anointed[m] to[b] serve the Lord of all the
earth."

The Flying Scroll

5 I looked again, and there before me
was a flying scroll.[n]
2He asked me, "What do you see?"[o]
I answered, "I see a flying scroll, twenty
cubits long and ten cubits wide.[c]"

4:2 [u] Rev 4:5
4:3 [v] ver 11; S Ps 1:3; S Rev 11:4
4:5 [w] S Zec 1:9
4:6 [x] S 1Ch 3:19; S Ezr 5:2 [y] S 1Sa 13:22; S 1Ki 19:12 [z] S 1Sa 2:9 [a] S Ne 9:20; Isa 11:2-4; S Da 2:34; Hos 1:7
4:7 [b] S Ps 26:12; Jer 51:25 [c] S Ps 118:22 [d] S 1Ch 15:28
4:9 [e] S Ezr 3:11 [f] Ezr 3:8; S 6:15; Zec 6:12 [g] S Zec 2:9
4:10 [h] S Hag 2:23 [i] Hag 2:3 [j] S 2Ch 16:9; Rev 5:6 [k] S Ezr 5:1; S Ne 12:1; S Job 38:5
4:11 [l] S ver 3; S Rev 11:4
4:14 [m] Ex 29:7; 40:15; S Ps 45:7; S Isa 20:3; S Da 9:24-26
5:1 [n] S Ps 40:7; S Jer 36:4; Rev 5:1
5:2 [o] S Jer 1:13

[a] 10 Or *the plumb line* [b] 14 Or *two who bring oil and* [c] 2 That is, about 30 feet long and 15 feet wide or about 9 meters long and 4.5 meters wide

4:3 *two olive trees.* Cf. Rev 11:4 and note. The two olive trees stand for the priestly and royal offices and symbolize a continuing supply of oil. The two olive branches (v. 12) stand for Joshua the priest (ch. 3) and Zerubbabel from the royal house of David (ch. 4; cf. v. 14). These two leaders were to do God's work (e.g., on the temple and in the lives of the people) in the power of his Spirit (v. 6). The community that produced the Dead Sea Scrolls (see essay, pp. 1574–1576) looked forward to the coming of two Messiahs (the "Messiah of Aaron" and the "Messiah of Israel" [i.e., of the house of David]). But the embodiment of the priestly and royal lines and their functions in one individual points ultimately to the Messianic King-Priest and his offices and functions (see 6:13 and note).

4:4 *these.* The two olive trees of v. 3, as v. 11 makes clear. The answer to the question is postponed until v. 14.

4:6 *Not by might nor by power.* Zerubbabel does not possess the royal might and power that David and Solomon had enjoyed, and in any event such worldly power is inadequate for the purpose of rebuilding the Lord's temple. *by my Spirit.* Interprets the symbolism of the oil (v. 12). The angel encouraged Zerubbabel to complete the rebuilding of the temple (vv. 7–10) and assured him of the Spirit's enablement (see Hag 2:5 and note).

4:7 *mountain … level ground.* Faith in the power of God's Spirit (v. 6) can overcome mountainous obstacles. The figurative mountain probably included opposition (Ezr 4:1–5,24) and the people's unwillingness to persevere (cf. Hag 1:14; 2:1–5). Cf. the same or similar imagery in Isa 40:4; 41:15; 49:11; Mt 17:20; 21:21; 1Co 13:2; 2Co 10:4. *capstone.* The final stone to be put in place (see Ps 118:22 and note), marking the completion of the restoration temple by Zerubbabel (see v. 9). *God bless it! God bless it!* Repeated for emphasis (see 3:2; see also note on Isa 40:1).

4:8 Introduces a prophetic message (see 6:9; 7:4,8; 8:1,18; see also note on Hos 1:1).

4:9 *laid the foundation.* In 536 BC (Ezr 3:8–11; 5:16). *complete it.* In 516 (see Ezr 6:15 and note).

4:10 *day of small things.* Some thought the work on the temple was insignificant (see Ezr 3:12; Hag 2:3 and note), but God was in the rebuilding program and, by his Spirit (v. 6), would enable Zerubbabel to finish it. *seven eyes.* See note on 3:9. God oversees the whole earth and is therefore in control of the situation in Judah (cf. 2Ch 16:9). *chosen capstone.* See NIV text note ("plumb line"), but the main NIV text is preferable contextually (v. 7).

4:14 The meaning of the vision is now explained. *two … anointed.* Zerubbabel, from the royal line of David, and Joshua, the priest. The oil (v. 12) used in anointing symbolizes the Holy Spirit (v. 6). The combination of ruler and priest points ultimately to the Messianic King-Priest (cf. 6:13; Ps 110; Heb 7). *Lord of all the earth.* See 6:5; the master of the circumstances in which Zerubbabel and the people found themselves.

5:1–4 The sixth vision. Lawbreakers are condemned by the law they have broken; sinners will be purged from the land.

5:1 *flying.* Unrolled and waving like a banner, for all to read. *scroll.* See note on Ex 17:14.

5:2 *He.* The interpreting angel (v. 5; 4:11). *What do you see?* See 4:2 and note. *twenty … ten.* Unusually large (especially in its width), for all to see (see NIV text note). Such a bold, clear message of judgment against sin should spur the people on to repentance and righteousness.

3 And he said to me, "This is the curse[p]
that is going out over the whole land; for
according to what it says on one side, every thief[q] will be banished, and according to what it says on the other, everyone
who swears falsely[r] will be banished. 4 The
LORD Almighty declares, 'I will send it out,
and it will enter the house of the thief and
the house of anyone who swears falsely[s]
by my name. It will remain in that house
and destroy it completely, both its timbers
and its stones.[t]' "

The Woman in a Basket

5 Then the angel who was speaking to
me came forward and said to me, "Look
up and see what is appearing."
6 I asked, "What is it?"
He replied, "It is a basket.[u]" And he
added, "This is the iniquity[a] of the people
throughout the land."
7 Then the cover of lead was raised, and
there in the basket sat a woman! 8 He said,
"This is wickedness," and he pushed her
back into the basket and pushed its lead
cover down on it.[v]
9 Then I looked up—and there before
me were two women, with the wind in
their wings! They had wings like those of
a stork,[w] and they lifted up the basket between heaven and earth.
10 "Where are they taking the basket?" I
asked the angel who was speaking to me.
11 He replied, "To the country of Babylonia[b][x] to build a house[y] for it. When the
house is ready, the basket will be set there
in its place."[z]

Four Chariots

6 I looked up again, and there before me
were four chariots[a] coming out from
between two mountains—mountains of
bronze. 2 The first chariot had red horses,
the second black,[b] 3 the third white,[c] and
the fourth dappled—all of them powerful.
4 I asked the angel who was speaking to
me, "What are these, my lord?"
5 The angel answered me, "These are
the four spirits[c][d] of heaven, going out from
standing in the presence of the Lord of the
whole world.[e] 6 The one with the black
horses is going toward the north country,
the one with the white horses toward the
west,[d] and the one with the dappled horses toward the south."
7 When the powerful horses went out,
they were straining to go throughout the
earth.[f] And he said, "Go throughout the
earth!" So they went throughout the earth.
8 Then he called to me, "Look, those going toward the north country have given
my Spirit[e] rest[g] in the land of the north."[h]

5:3 [p] Isa 24:6; 34:2; 43:28; Mal 3:9; 4:6 [q] Ex 20:15; Mal 3:8 [r] Ex 20:7; Isa 48:1 **5:4** [s] Zec 8:17 [t] Lev 14:34-45; S Pr 3:33; S Hab 2:9-11; Mal 3:5 **5:6** [u] Mic 6:10 **5:8** [v] Mic 6:11 **5:9** [w] Lev 11:19 **5:11** [x] S Ge 10:10 [y] Jer 29:5, 28 [z] S Da 1:2 **6:1** [a] ver 5; S 2Ki 2:11 **6:2** [b] Rev 6:5 **6:3** [c] Rev 6:2 **6:5** [d] S Eze 37:9; Mt 24:31; Rev 7:1 [e] S Jos 3:11 **6:7** [f] Isa 43:6; Zec 1:8 **6:8** [g] S Eze 5:13; S 24:13 [h] S Zec 1:10

[a] 6 Or *appearance* [b] 11 Hebrew *Shinar* [c] 5 Or *winds* [d] 6 Or *horses after them* [e] 8 Or *spirit*

5:3 *curse.* See Dt 27:26 and note. *on one side ... on the other.* Like the two tablets of the law (see Ex 32:15 and note), the scroll is inscribed on both sides (see Eze 2:10 and note). *thief.* One who breaks the eighth commandment (Ex 20:15). *everyone who swears falsely.* See 8:17. Such a person violates the third commandment (compare v. 4 with Ex 20:7). Although theft and perjury may have been the most common forms of lawbreaking at the time, they are probably intended as representative sins. The people of Judah had been guilty of infractions against the whole law (see Jas 2:10 and note).

5:4 *The LORD Almighty.* See note on 1Sa 1:3. *it will enter ... and destroy.* "It" refers to the curse (v. 3). God's word, whether promise (ch. 4) or warning (as here), always accomplishes its purpose (cf. Ps 147:15; Isa 55:10–11; see Heb 4:12–13 and notes).

5:5–11 The seventh vision. Not only must flagrant, persistent sinners be removed from the land (vv. 1–4), but the whole sinful system will be removed—apparently to a more fitting place (Babylonia; see v. 11).

5:6 *basket.* Hebrew "ephah." A normal ephah-sized container would not be large enough to hold a person. This one was undoubtedly enlarged (like the flying scroll of vv. 1–2) for the purpose of the vision. *iniquity.* See v. 8 ("wickedness").

5:7 *woman.* Perhaps the reason the people's wickedness was personified as a woman (cf. Rev 17:1–6) is that the Hebrew word for "wickedness" (v. 8) is feminine in gender.

5:8 *wickedness.* A general word denoting moral, religious and civil evil—frequently used as an antonym of righteousness (e.g., Pr 13:6; Eze 33:12). The whole evil system was to be destroyed (cf. 2Th 2:6–8).

5:9 *two women.* Divinely chosen agents. *wind.* Also an instrument of God (see Ps 104:3–4 and note). The removal of wickedness would be the work of God alone.

5:11 *Babylonia.* See Ge 10:10 and NIV text note; 11:2 and NIV text note; Rev 17–18. Babylonia, a land of idolatry, was an appropriate locale for wickedness—but not Israel, where God chose to dwell with his people. Only after being purged of its evil would the promised land truly be the "holy land" (2:12).

6:1–8 The eighth and last vision. It corresponds to the first (1:7–17), though there are differences in details, such as in the order and colors of the horses. As in the first vision, the Lord is depicted as the one who controls the events of history (see Introduction: Literary Forms and Themes). He will conquer the nations that oppress Israel.

6:1 *four chariots.* Angelic spirits as agents of divine judgment (v. 5). *two mountains.* Possibly Mount Zion and the Mount of Olives, with the Kidron Valley between them (cf. Joel 3:2 and note), or perhaps reference is to the creation of two mountains through the splitting of the Mount of Olives in 14:4. *bronze.* Perhaps symbolic of judgment (cf. Nu 21:9).

6:2–3 *red ... black ... white ... dappled.* The horses may signify various divine judgments on the earth (see note on v. 8; see also Rev 6:1–8 and note on 6:2).

6:4 *these.* The chariots, with the horses harnessed to them.

6:5 *four spirits.* See note on v. 1. *Lord of the whole world.* See note on 4:14.

6:8 *north country.* Primarily Babylonia, but also the direction from which most of Israel's foes invaded them (see note on 2:6). *my Spirit.* If the alternative translation in the NIV text note ("spirit") is taken, the meaning is that the angelic beings dispatched to the north have triumphed and thus have pacified or appeased God's spirit (i.e., his anger; cf. Ecc 10:4, where the same Hebrew word is translated "anger"). See 1:15, where God's displeasure was aroused against oppressive nations. In either case, since conquest

A Crown for Joshua

9 The word of the LORD came to me:
10 "Take silver and gold from the exiles
Heldai, Tobijah and Jedaiah, who have
arrived from Babylon.[i] Go the same day
to the house of Josiah son of Zephaniah. 11 Take the silver and gold and make a
crown,[j] and set it on the head of the high
priest, Joshua[k] son of Jozadak.[a][l] 12 Tell him
this is what the LORD Almighty says: 'Here
is the man whose name is the Branch,[m]
and he will branch out from his place and
build the temple of the LORD.[n] 13 It is he
who will build the temple of the LORD, and
he will be clothed with majesty and will
sit and rule on his throne. And he[b] will be
a priest[o] on his throne. And there will be
harmony between the two.' 14 The crown
will be given to Heldai,[c] Tobijah, Jedaiah
and Hen[d] son of Zephaniah as a memorial[p] in the temple of the LORD. 15 Those
who are far away will come and help to
build the temple of the LORD,[q] and you will
know that the LORD Almighty has sent me
to you.[r] This will happen if you diligently
obey[s] the LORD your God."

Justice and Mercy, Not Fasting

7 In the fourth year of King Darius, the
word of the LORD came to Zechariah[t]
on the fourth day of the ninth month, the
month of Kislev.[u] 2 The people of Bethel had sent Sharezer and Regem-Melek,
together with their men, to entreat[v] the
LORD[w] 3 by asking the priests of the house
of the LORD Almighty and the prophets,
"Should I mourn[x] and fast in the fifth[y]
month, as I have done for so many years?"
4 Then the word of the LORD Almighty
came to me: 5 "Ask all the people of the
land and the priests, 'When you fasted[z]
and mourned in the fifth and seventh[a]
months for the past seventy years,[b] was it
really for me that you fasted? 6 And when
you were eating and drinking, were you
not just feasting for yourselves?[c] 7 Are
these not the words the LORD proclaimed
through the earlier prophets[d] when Jerusalem and its surrounding towns were at
rest[e] and prosperous, and the Negev and
the western foothills[f] were settled?' "[g]
8 And the word of the LORD came again
to Zechariah: 9 "This is what the LORD Almighty said: 'Administer true justice;[h]
show mercy and compassion to one another.[i] 10 Do not oppress the widow[j] or the
fatherless, the foreigner[k] or the poor.[l] Do
not plot evil against each other.'[m]

6:10 [i] Ezr 7:14-16; Jer 28:6 **6:11** [j] Ps 21:3 [k] S Ezr 2:2; S Zec 3:1 [l] S 1Ch 6:15; S Ezr 3:2 **6:12** [m] S Isa 4:2; S Eze 17:22 [n] Ezr 3:8-10; Zec 4:6-9 **6:13** [o] S Ps 110:4 **6:14** [p] S Ex 28:12 **6:15** [q] Isa 60:10 [r] Zec 2:9-11 [s] Isa 58:12; Jer 7:23; S Zec 3:7 **7:1** [t] S Ezr 5:1 [u] Ne 1:1 **7:2** [v] Jer 26:19; Zec 8:21 [w] Hag 2:10-14 **7:3** [x] Zec 12:12-14 [y] 2Ki 25:9; Jer 52:12-14 **7:5** [z] Isa 58:5 [a] 2Ki 25:25 [b] S Da 9:2 **7:6** [c] S Isa 43:23 **7:7** [d] Isa 1:11-20; Zec 1:4 [e] Jer 22:21 [f] S Jer 17:26 [g] Jer 44:4-5 **7:9** [h] S Jer 22:3; 42:5; Zec 8:16 [i] S Dt 22:1 **7:10** [j] Jer 49:11 [k] S Ex 22:21 [l] S Lev 25:17; Isa 1:23 [m] S Ex 22:22; S Job 35:8; S Isa 1:17; S Eze 45:9; S Mic 6:8

[a] *11* Hebrew *Jehozadak,* a variant of *Jozadak*
[b] *13* Or *there*
[c] *14* Syriac; Hebrew *Helem*
[d] *14* Or *and the gracious one, the*

was announced in the north, victory was assured over all enemies.

6:9–15 The two central visions (the fourth and fifth) were concerned with the high priest and the civil governor (in the Davidic line); see Introduction: Literary Forms and Themes. Zechariah now relates the message of those two visions to the Messianic King-Priest.

6:9 See note on 4:8.

6:10 *silver and gold.* Gifts for the temple (cf. Ezr 6:5; Hag 2:8).

6:11 *crown.* The Hebrew for this word is not the same as that used for the high priest's turban but refers to an ornate crown (cf. Rev 19:12). The royal crowning of the high priest foreshadows the goal and consummation of prophecy—the crowning and reign of the Messianic King-Priest (see vv. 12–13; cf. Ps 110:4; Heb 7:1–3).

6:12 *Here is the man.* Cf. Pilate's introduction of Jesus in Jn 19:5. *Branch.* See note on 3:8. According to the Aramaic Targum (a paraphrase), the Jerusalem Talmud (a collection of religious instruction) and the Midrash (practical exposition), Jews early regarded this verse as Messianic. *branch out.* The NIV here reflects the wordplay in the Hebrew text. *temple.* Cf. Isa 2:2–3; Eze 40–43; Hag 2:6–9.

6:13 *clothed with.* See note on Ps 109:29. *his throne.* See 2Sa 7:11,16; Isa 9:7; Lk 1:32 and notes. *priest on his throne.* The coming Davidic King will also be a priest. *two.* Probably the royal and priestly offices. Such a combination was not normally possible in Israel. For this reason, the sect of Qumran (see essay, p. 1576) expected two Messianic figures—a high-priestly Messiah and a Davidic one (see note on 4:3). But the two offices and functions would in fact be united in the one person of the Messiah (cf. Ps 110; Heb 7).

6:14 *Hen.* Means "gracious one" (see NIV text note), perhaps another name for Josiah—to honor him for his hospitality (v. 10).

6:15 *Those who are far away will … help.* Cf. Isa 60:4–7.

7:1—8:23 See Introduction: Literary Forms and Themes.

7:1 *fourth year … fourth day … ninth month.* Dec. 7, 518 BC—not quite two years after the eight night visions (see note on 1:7).

7:3 *prophets.* Including Zechariah. *I.* The people of Bethel collectively. *fast in the fifth month.* See note on 8:19. *so many years.* "The past seventy years" (v. 5).

7:4–7 A rebuke for selfish and insincere fasting on the part of the people and the priests.

7:4,8 See note on 4:8.

7:5 *fasted … fifth and seventh.* See note on 8:19. *seventy years.* See 1:12 and note. Since these fasts commemorated events related to the destruction of Jerusalem and the temple (see note on 8:19), the 70 years here are to be reckoned from 586 BC. Strictly speaking, 68 years had transpired; 70 is thus a round number.

7:6 *for yourselves.* Cf. Isa 1:11–17; 58:1–7,13–14.

7:7,12 *earlier prophets.* See note on 1:4.

7:7 *Negev.* See note on Ge 12:9. *western foothills.* Sloping toward the Mediterranean Sea.

7:9–10 Four tests of faithful covenant living, consisting of a series of social, moral and ethical commands.

7:9 *justice.* The proper ordering of all society (see 8:16–17 and note on 8:16; Isa 42:1,4; Mic 6:8 and notes). *mercy.* Or "faithful love" (see Hos 10:12; 12:6 and notes). *compassion.* See note on 1:12.

7:10 *oppress.* Oppression is denounced frequently in the OT (see, e.g., Am 2:6–8 and notes; 4:1; 5:11–12,21–24; 8:4–6). *widow … fatherless … foreigner … poor.* For the Biblical concern for such people, see, e.g., Dt 10:18; Isa 1:17 and note; Jer 5:28; Jas 1:27; 1Jn 3:16–18. In the ancient Near East, the ideal king was expected to protect the oppressed and needy members of society. *plot evil against each other.* See 8:17; cf. Mic 2:1–2 and note on 2:1.

11 “But they refused to pay attention;
stubbornly[n] they turned their backs[o] and
covered their ears.[p] 12 They made their
hearts as hard as flint[q] and would not
listen to the law or to the words that
the LORD Almighty had sent by his Spirit
through the earlier prophets.[r] So the LORD
Almighty was very angry.[s]
13 “ ‘When I called, they did not listen;[t]
so when they called, I would not listen,’[u]
says the LORD Almighty.[v] 14 ‘I scattered[w]
them with a whirlwind[x] among all the nations, where they were strangers. The land
they left behind them was so desolate that
no one traveled through it.[y] This is how
they made the pleasant land desolate.[z]’ ”

The LORD Promises to Bless Jerusalem

8 The word of the LORD Almighty came
to me.
2 This is what the LORD Almighty says:
“I am very jealous[a] for Zion; I am burning
with jealousy for her.”
3 This is what the LORD says: “I will return[b] to Zion[c] and dwell in Jerusalem.[d]
Then Jerusalem will be called the Faithful City,[e] and the mountain[f] of the LORD
Almighty will be called the Holy Mountain.[g]”
4 This is what the LORD Almighty says:
“Once again men and women of ripe old
age will sit in the streets of Jerusalem,[h]
each of them with cane in hand because
of their age. 5 The city streets will be filled
with boys and girls playing there.[i]”
6 This is what the LORD Almighty says:
“It may seem marvelous to the remnant of
this people at that time,[j] but will it seem
marvelous to me?[k]” declares the LORD Almighty.
7 This is what the LORD Almighty says: “I
will save my people from the countries of
the east and the west.[l] 8 I will bring them
back[m] to live[n] in Jerusalem; they will be
my people,[o] and I will be faithful and righteous to them as their God.[p]”
9 This is what the LORD Almighty says:
“Now hear these words, ‘Let your hands
be strong[q] so that the temple may be built.’
This is also what the prophets[r] said who
were present when the foundation[s] was
laid for the house of the LORD Almighty.
10 Before that time there were no wages[t] for
people or hire for animals. No one could
go about their business safely[u] because of
their enemies, since I had turned everyone
against their neighbor. 11 But now I will not
deal with the remnant of this people as
I did in the past,”[v] declares the LORD Almighty.
12 “The seed will grow well, the vine will
yield its fruit,[w] the ground will produce its
crops,[x] and the heavens will drop their
dew.[y] I will give all these things as an inheritance[z] to the remnant of this people.[a]
13 Just as you, Judah and Israel, have been
a curse[a][b] among the nations, so I will save[c]

7:11 [n] S Isa 9:9 [o] S Jer 32:33 [p] S Jer 5:3; 8:5; 11:10; S 17:23; S Eze 5:6 **7:12** [q] S Jer 5:3; 17:1; S Eze 11:19 [r] S Ne 9:29 [s] S Jer 42:21; S Da 9:12 **7:13** [t] S Jer 7:27 [u] Isa 1:15; S Jer 11:11; 14:12; S Mic 3:4 [v] S Pr 1:28; S La 3:44; S Eze 20:31 **7:14** [w] S Lev 26:33; Dt 4:27; 28:64-67; S Ps 44:11 [x] Jer 23:19 [y] S Isa 33:8 [z] S Jer 7:34; S 44:6; S Eze 12:19 **8:2** [a] S Joel 2:18 **8:3** [b] Zec 1:16 [c] S Isa 52:8; S Joel 3:21 [d] S Zec 2:10 [e] S Ps 15:2; S Isa 1:26; S 48:1; S Jer 33:16 [f] S Jer 26:18 [g] S Isa 1:26; S Mic 4:1 **8:4** [h] S Isa 65:20 **8:5** [i] S Jer 30:20; 31:13 **8:6** [j] Ps 118:23; 126:1-3 [k] Jer 32:17,27 **8:7** [l] Ps 107:3; S Isa 11:11; S 43:5 **8:8** [m] S Eze 37:12; Zec 10:10 [n] S Jer 31:24 [o] S Isa 51:16; S Eze 11:19-20; S 36:28; S Zec 2:11; Heb 8:10 [p] Jer 11:4; Zec 10:6 **8:9** [q] S Hag 2:4 [r] S Ezr 5:1 [s] S Ezr 3:11 **8:10** [t] S Isa 5:10; S Hag 1:6 [u] S 2Ch 15:5 **8:11** [v] Isa 12:1 **8:12** [w] S Ps 85:12; S Joel 2:22 [x] S Ps 67:6 [y] S Ge 27:28 [z] S Ps 65:13; S Isa 60:21; Ob 1:17 [a] S Hos 2:21 **8:13** [b] S Nu 5:27; S Dt 13:15; S Ps 102:8; Jer 42:18 [c] S Ps 48:8

[a] *13* That is, your name has been used in cursing (see Jer. 29:22); or, you have been regarded as under a curse.

7:11 *they.* The preexilic ancestors, as the reference to the "earlier prophets" in v. 12 shows. *stubbornly they turned their backs.* See Dt 9:6,13,27. *covered their ears.* See Ps 58:4; Isa 6:10 and notes; cf. Isa 33:15.

7:12 *hard as flint.* See Eze 3:8–9. *words ... sent by his Spirit.* The words of the prophets were inspired by God's Spirit (see Ne 9:30; Mic 3:8; 2Pe 1:21 and note). *very angry.* See 1:2,15.

7:13 See note on 1:3.

7:14 *scattered them.* One of the curses for covenant disobedience (see Dt 28:36–37,64–68 and note on 28:64). *whirlwind.* See Pr 1:27 and note; Isa 40:24; Hos 4:19. *land ... desolate.* See Dt 28:41–42,45–52. *This is how.* By their sins. *pleasant land.* See Ps 106:24 and note.

8:1–23 Ten promises of blessing, each beginning with "This is what the LORD (Almighty) says" (vv. 2,3,4,6,7,9,14,19,20,23).

8:1,18 See note on 4:8.

8:2 *jealous.* See 1:14 and note.

8:3 *I will return.* See 1:3 and note; 1:16. *dwell.* See note on 2:10. *the Faithful City.* See Isa 1:26 and note. *the Holy Mountain.* Cf. 14:20–21.

8:4–5 See Isa 11:6–9 and note; 65:20–25.

8:6,11–12 *remnant.* See notes on Isa 1:9; 10:20–22.

8:6 *will it seem marvelous to me?* See Jer 32:27 and note.

8:7 *save my people.* Deliver them from exile, bondage and dispersion (cf. Isa 11:11–12; 43:5–7; Jer 30:7–11; 31:7–8). *from the countries of the east and the west.* Lit. "from the land of the sunrise and from the land of the going in of the sun," i.e., from everywhere—wherever the people are (cf. Ps 50:1; 113:3; Mal 1:11).

8:8 *they will be my people, and I will be ... their God.* Covenant terminology, pertaining to intimate fellowship in the covenant relationship between God and his people (see 13:9; Ge 17:7 and note; Ex 6:7; 29:45–46; Lev 11:45; 22:33; 25:38; 26:12,45; Nu 15:41; Dt 29:13; Jer 7:23 and note; 24:7 and note; Eze 34:30–31; 36:28; 37:27; Hos 1:9–10; 11:20; 2Co 6:16; Heb 8:10; Rev 21:3). *faithful and righteous.* Judah's restoration to covenant favor and blessing rests on the faithfulness (dependability) and righteousness of God.

8:9 *hands be strong.* See v. 13. The Hebrew for this expression is translated "be encouraged" in Jdg 7:11. *prophets.* Including Haggai (1:1) and Zechariah (1:1; see Ezr 5:1–2).

8:10 *Before that time.* Before the temple foundation was laid (see v. 9). *no wages.* See Hag 1:6–11; 2:15–19. *their enemies.* For example, the Samaritans (Ezr 4:1–5).

8:11 *But now.* The reasons for discouragement have passed; God will now provide the grounds for encouragement.

8:12 Contrast with Hag 1:10–11. In Hag 2:19 God had predicted just such a reversal as is depicted here. Fertility and bounty are part of the covenant blessings for obedience promised in Lev 26:3–10; Dt 28:11–12; cf. Eze 34:25–27; Hos 1:21–24.

8:13 *Judah and Israel.* The whole nation will experience this deliverance and blessing (cf. Jer 31:1–31; Eze 37:15–28).

you, and you will be a blessing.[a][d] Do not be afraid,[e] but let your hands be strong.[f]"

[14]This is what the LORD Almighty says: "Just as I had determined to bring disaster[g] on you and showed no pity when your ancestors angered me," says the LORD Almighty, [15]"so now I have determined to do good[h] again to Jerusalem and Judah.[i] Do not be afraid. [16]These are the things you are to do: Speak the truth[j] to each other, and render true and sound judgment[k] in your courts;[l] [17]do not plot evil[m] against each other, and do not love to swear falsely.[n] I hate all this," declares the LORD.

[18]The word of the LORD Almighty came to me.

[19]This is what the LORD Almighty says: "The fasts of the fourth,[o] fifth,[p] seventh[q] and tenth[r] months will become joyful[s] and glad occasions and happy festivals for Judah. Therefore love truth[t] and peace."

[20]This is what the LORD Almighty says: "Many peoples and the inhabitants of many cities will yet come, [21]and the inhabitants of one city will go to another and say, 'Let us go at once to entreat[u] the LORD and seek[v] the LORD Almighty. I myself am going.' [22]And many peoples and powerful nations will come to Jerusalem to seek the LORD Almighty and to entreat him."[w]

[23]This is what the LORD Almighty says: "In those days ten people from all languages and nations will take firm hold of one Jew by the hem of his robe and say, 'Let us go with you, because we have heard that God is with you.'"[x]

Judgment on Israel's Enemies

9 A prophecy:[y]

The word of the LORD is against the
land of Hadrak
and will come to rest on
Damascus[z]—
for the eyes of all people and all the
tribes of Israel
are on the LORD—[b]
[2]and on Hamath[a] too, which borders
on it,
and on Tyre[b] and Sidon,[c] though they
are very skillful.
[3]Tyre has built herself a stronghold;
she has heaped up silver like dust,
and gold like the dirt of the streets.[d]

8:13 [d] S Ge 12:2; S Joel 2:14 [e] S Hag 2:5 [f] ver 9 **8:14** [g] S Eze 24:14 **8:15** [h] ver 13; S Jer 29:11; Mic 7:18-20 [i] Jer 31:28; 32:42 **8:16** [j] S Ps 15:2; S Jer 33:16; S Eph 4:25 [k] S Eze 18:8 [l] S Eze 45:9; S Am 5:15; S Zec 7:9 **8:17** [m] Pr 3:29 [n] S Pr 6:16-19; S Jer 7:9; Zec 5:4 **8:19** [o] S 2Ki 25:7; Jer 39:2 [p] S Jer 52:12 [q] 2Ki 25:25 [r] Jer 52:4 [s] Ps 30:11 [t] ver 16 **8:21** [u] S Zec 7:2 [v] Jer 26:19 **8:22** [w] S Ps 86:9; 117:1; Isa 2:2-3; S 44:5; S 45:14; 49:6; S Zec 2:11 **8:23** [x] S Ps 102:22; S Isa 14:1; S 45:14; S 56:3; 1Co 14:25 **9:1** [y] S Isa 13:1; Jer 23:33 [z] Isa 17:1; S Am 1:5 **9:2** [a] S Jer 49:23 [b] Eze 28:1-19 [c] S Ge 10:15 **9:3** [d] Job 27:16; S Eze 28:4

[a] *13* Or *and your name will be used in blessings* (see Gen. 48:20); or *and you will be seen as blessed*
[b] *1* Or *Damascus. / For the eye of the LORD is on all people, / as well as on the tribes of Israel,*

curse among the nations. Part of the covenant curses for disobedience threatened in Dt 28:15–68 (see Dt 28:37; Jer 24:9; 25:18). *blessing.* See vv. 20–23; cf. Ge 12:2. *hands be strong.* See note on v. 9.

8:14–17 Verses 14–15 specify God's part in the people's restoration to favor and blessing; vv. 16–17 delineate their part.

8:14 *your ancestors angered me.* See note on 1:2.

8:15 *do good.* See vv. 12–13.

8:16–17 See 7:9–10. Such moral and ethical behavior sums up the character of those who are in covenant relationship with the Lord.

8:16 *Speak the truth to each other.* See Eph 4:25 and note. *render true and sound judgment.* Because God requires justice (see 7:9; Dt 24:17–18; Ps 33:5; 89:14; 99:4; Am 2:7; 5:24 and notes; see also Introduction to Amos: Theological Theme and Message) and hates injustice (see v. 17; 5:3; 2Ch 19:7; Ne 5:6; Pr 6:16–19; Hab 1:4 and notes). *courts.* Lit. "gates" (see Ge 19:1 and note; 2Sa 18:24).

8:17 *swear falsely.* Perjure oneself (see note on 5:3). *I hate all this.* Pr 6:16–19 lists seven things the Lord hates, three of which relate directly to vv. 16–17 here: "a lying tongue," "a heart that devises wicked schemes" and "a false witness who pours out lies."

8:19 See 7:2–6. *fourth.* The fast that lamented the breaching of the walls of Jerusalem by Nebuchadnezzar (2Ki 25:3–4; Jer 39:2). *fifth.* Commemorated the burning of the temple and the other important buildings (2Ki 25:8–10). *seventh.* Marked the anniversary of Gedaliah's assassination (2Ki 25:22–25; Jer 41:1–3). *tenth.* Mourned the beginning of Nebuchadnezzar's siege of Jerusalem (2Ki 25:1; Jer 39:1; Eze 24:1–2). *happy festivals.* Cf. Isa 65:18–19; Jer 31:10–14.

8:20–23 For similar predictions about Gentiles seeking the Lord, see 2:11 and note; Mic 4:1–5.

8:22 *powerful.* Or "numerous" (as in Ex 1:9; see also NIV text note on Isa 53:12); anticipates a fulfillment of the promise of Gentile blessing in the Abrahamic covenant (Ge 12:3; Gal 3:8,26–29; see also Isa 55:5; 56:6–7; Mk 11:17 and note).

8:23 *ten.* One way of indicating a large or complete number in Hebrew (see Ge 31:7 and note; Lev 26:26; Nu 14:22 and note; 1Sa 1:8; Ne 4:12). *Jew.* A shortened form of "Judahite" (an inhabitant of the kingdom of Judah, where a remnant of Israelites was still living). Strictly speaking, the term "Jew" is properly applied only to the OT people of God and their descendants from the time of the Babylonian exile on. *we have heard that God is with you.* True godliness attracts others to the Lord (see Ge 21:22; 26:28; 30:27; see also notes on Ge 39:2–6; 1Co 14:24).

9:1–8 Probably a prophetic description of the Lord's march south to Jerusalem, destroying—as Divine Warrior—the traditional enemies of Israel. As history shows, the agent of his judgment was Alexander the Great (333–332 BC; see essay, p. 1571).

9:1 *A prophecy: The word of the LORD.* The Hebrew for this phrase occurs only two other times in the OT (12:1; Mal 1:1), making it likely that Zec 9–14 and Malachi were written during the same general period. *prophecy.* See note on Hab 1:1. *word of the LORD.* See 1:1; 12:1; Hos 1:1 and note. *Hadrak.* Hatarikka, north of Hamath on the Orontes River (see v. 2). *Damascus.* The leading city-state of the Arameans (see notes on Dt 26:5; Isa 17:1). *eyes … on the LORD.* The thought may be that the eyes of people, especially all the tribes of Israel, are turned toward the Lord (for deliverance). But see NIV text note.

9:2 *on Hamath too.* Judgment will rest on Hamath, just as on Hadrak and Damascus. Hamath is modern Hama (see Isa 10:9 and note). *it.* Damascus. *Tyre and Sidon.* Phoenician (modern Lebanese) coastal cities (see notes on Isa 23:1; 23:2,4,12). Their judgment (vv. 3–4) is also foretold in Isa 23; Eze 26:3–14; 28:20–24; Am 1:9–10.

9:3 *stronghold.* The Hebrew for this word is a pun on the Hebrew for "Tyre" (meaning "rock"). The stronghold was Tyre's

4 But the Lord will take away her
possessions
and destroy[e] her power on the sea,
and she will be consumed by fire.[f]
5 Ashkelon[g] will see it and fear;
Gaza will writhe in agony,
and Ekron too, for her hope will
wither.
Gaza will lose her king
and Ashkelon will be deserted.
6 A mongrel people will occupy Ashdod,
and I will put an end[h] to the pride of
the Philistines.
7 I will take the blood from their mouths,
the forbidden food from between
their teeth.
Those who are left will belong to our
God[i]
and become a clan in Judah,
and Ekron will be like the Jebusites.[j]
8 But I will encamp[k] at my temple
to guard it against marauding forces.[l]
Never again will an oppressor overrun
my people,
for now I am keeping watch.[m]

The Coming of Zion's King

9 Rejoice greatly, Daughter Zion![n]
Shout,[o] Daughter Jerusalem!
See, your king comes to you,[p]
righteous and victorious,[q]
lowly and riding on a donkey,[r]
on a colt, the foal of a donkey.[s]
10 I will take away the chariots from
Ephraim
and the warhorses from Jerusalem,
and the battle bow will be broken.[t]
He will proclaim peace[u] to the nations.
His rule will extend from sea to sea
and from the River[a] to the ends of
the earth.[v]
11 As for you, because of the blood of my
covenant[w] with you,
I will free your prisoners[x] from the
waterless pit.[y]
12 Return to your fortress,[z] you prisoners
of hope;
even now I announce that I will
restore twice[a] as much to you.
13 I will bend Judah as I bend my bow[b]
and fill it with Ephraim.[c]
I will rouse your sons, Zion,
against your sons, Greece,[d]
and make you like a warrior's sword.[e]

9:4 [e] S Isa 23:11 [f] S Isa 23:1; Jer 25:22; Eze 26:3-5; 27:32-36; 28:18 **9:5** [g] Jer 47:5 **9:6** [h] S Isa 14:30 **9:7** [i] S Job 25:2 [j] S Jer 47:1; S Joel 3:4; S Zep 2:4 **9:8** [k] S Isa 26:1 [l] Zec 14:21 [m] S Isa 52:1; S 54:14; S Joel 3:17 **9:9** [n] S Isa 62:11 [o] S 1Ki 1:39 [p] S Ps 24:7; S 149:2; Mic 4:8 [q] Isa 9:6-7; 43:3-11; Jer 23:5-6; Zep 3:14-15; Zec 2:10 [r] S Ge 49:11; S 1Ki 1:33 [s] Mt 21:5*; Jn 12:15* **9:10** [t] Hos 1:7; 2:18; Mic 4:3; 5:10; Zec 10:4 [u] S Isa 2:4 [v] Ps 72:8 **9:11** [w] S Ex 24:8; S Mt 26:28; S Lk 22:20 [x] S Isa 10:4; S 42:7 [y] Jer 38:6 **9:12** [z] S Joel 3:16

[a] *10* That is, the Euphrates

[a] S Dt 21:17; S Isa 40:2 **9:13** [b] S 2Sa 22:35 [c] S Isa 49:2 [d] S Joel 3:6 [e] S Jer 51:20

island fortress (Isa 23:4; Eze 26:5). It fell (v. 4) to Alexander in July, 332 BC, after a siege of seven months (see note on Eze 26:1—28:19). *silver like dust ... gold like the dirt.* Cf. 1Ki 10:21,27. Tyre was a center of trade and commerce, and her wealth was proverbial (see Isa 23:2–3,8,18; Eze 26:12; 27:3–27,33; 28:4–5,7,12–14,16–18).

9:4 *her power on the sea.* Tyre's exploitation of commercial sea lanes in the Mediterranean was the source of much of her wealth.

9:5–7 The Philistine cities were greatly alarmed at Alexander's steady advance.

9:5 *Ashkelon ... Gaza ... Ekron.* Three of the five major Philistine cities (see map, p. 359). *her hope will wither.* As the northernmost city of Philistia, Ekron would be the first to suffer. Her hope that Tyre would stem the tide would meet with disappointment.

9:6 *mongrel people.* People of mixed nationality; they characterized the postexilic period (Ne 13:23–24). *Ashdod.* The fourth remaining city in the Philistine group (see notes on v. 5; Am 1:8). *I.* God. *Philistines.* See note on Ge 10:14. At one time their control of Canaan was so extensive that the land was eventually named after them ("Palestine").

9:7 *blood.* Of idolatrous sacrifices. *forbidden food.* Ceremonially unclean food. *Jebusites.* These ancient inhabitants of Jerusalem (see notes on Ge 10:16; 2Sa 5:6) were absorbed into Judah (e.g., Araunah in 2Sa 24:16–24). So would it be with a remnant of the Philistines.

9:8 *encamp at my temple to guard it against marauding forces.* See 2:5. Alexander spared the temple and the city of Jerusalem (see Josephus, *Antiquities*, 11.8.4–5). *oppressor.* The Hebrew for this word is translated "slave driver" in Ex 3:7; 5:6,10 and elsewhere; thus it echoes the Egyptian bondage motif. *keeping watch.* See Ex 3:7; Ps 32:8; 121.

9:9 Quoted in the NT as Messianic and as referring ultimately to Jesus' entry into Jerusalem as King (Mt 21:5; Jn 12:15). *Daughter Zion ... Daughter Jerusalem.* A personification of Jerusalem (see note on 2Ki 19:21). *your king.* The Davidic ("your") Messianic King. *righteous.* Conforming to the divine standard of morality and ethics, particularly as revealed in the Mosaic legislation; a characteristic of the ideal king (see 2Sa 23:3–4 and note on 23:3; Ps 4:1 and note; 72:1–3; Isa 9:7 and note; 53:11; Jer 23:6 and note). *lowly.* Or "humble" (cf. Isa 53:2–3,7; Mt 11:29). *riding on a donkey.* A suitable choice, since the donkey was a lowly animal of peace (contrast the warhorse of v. 10), as well as a princely mount (Jdg 10:4; 12:14; 2Sa 16:2) before the horse came into common use. The royal mount used by David and his sons was the mule (see 2Sa 13:29 and note).

9:10 *take away the chariots ... warhorses ... battle bow.* A similar era of disarmament is foreseen in Isa 2:4; 9:5–7; 11:1–10; Mic 5:10–11. *Ephraim.* See note on v. 13. *peace to the nations.* In sharp contrast to Alexander's empire, which was founded on bloodshed, the Messianic King will establish a universal kingdom of peace as the ultimate fulfillment of the Abrahamic covenant (cf. 14:16; see Ge 12:2–3 and note, but cf. Rev 19:11 and note). *from sea to sea.* Variously explained as "from the Nile to the Euphrates," "from the Mediterranean to the 'Red Sea'" and "from the Mediterranean to the Dead Sea." The question is not important because the phrase is used to indicate totality or universality, as is true also of "from the River to the ends of the earth." The point is that the Davidic Messiah's rule will be universal (see Ps 22:27–28 and notes; 72:8–11 and note on 72:8; Isa 45:22; 52:10; 66:18).

9:11 *blood of my covenant with you.* Probably the Sinaitic covenant (Ex 24:3–8). *prisoners.* Perhaps those still in Babylonia, the land of exile. *waterless pit.* Cf. Ge 37:24; Jer 38:6.

9:12 *fortress.* Either (1) Jerusalem (Zion) and environs or (2) God himself (cf. 2:5). *hope.* In the future delivering King (vv. 9–10). *twice as much.* Full or complete restoration (Isa 61:7).

9:13 See note on 10:4. The Lord compares himself to a warrior who uses Judah as his bow and Ephraim (the northern

The Lord Will Appear

[14]Then the Lord will appear over them;[f]
his arrow will flash like lightning.[g]
The Sovereign Lord will sound the trumpet;[h]
he will march in the storms[i] of the south,
[15] and the Lord Almighty will shield[j] them.
They will destroy
and overcome with slingstones.[k]
They will drink and roar as with wine;[l]
they will be full like a bowl[m]
used for sprinkling[a] the corners[n] of the altar.
[16]The Lord their God will save his people on that day[o]
as a shepherd saves his flock.
They will sparkle in his land
like jewels in a crown.[p]
[17]How attractive and beautiful they will be!
Grain will make the young men thrive,
and new wine the young women.

The Lord Will Care for Judah

10 Ask the Lord for rain in the springtime;
it is the Lord who sends the thunderstorms.
He gives showers of rain[q] to all people,
and plants of the field[r] to everyone.
[2]The idols[s] speak deceitfully,
diviners[t] see visions that lie;
they tell dreams[u] that are false,
they give comfort in vain.[v]
Therefore the people wander like sheep
oppressed for lack of a shepherd.[w]
[3]"My anger burns against the shepherds,
and I will punish the leaders;[x]
for the Lord Almighty will care
for his flock, the people of Judah,
and make them like a proud horse in battle.[y]
[4]From Judah will come the cornerstone,[z]
from him the tent peg,[a]
from him the battle bow,[b]
from him every ruler.
[5]Together they[b] will be like warriors in battle
trampling their enemy into the mud of the streets.[c]
They will fight because the Lord is with them,
and they will put the enemy horsemen to shame.[d]

[6]"I will strengthen[e] Judah
and save the tribes of Joseph.
I will restore them
because I have compassion[f] on them.[g]
They will be as though
I had not rejected them,
for I am the Lord their God
and I will answer[h] them.

[a] *15* Or *bowl, / like* [b] *4,5* Or *ruler, all of them together. / [5]They*

9:14 [f] Isa 31:5 [g] Ps 18:14; S Hab 3:11 [h] S Lev 25:9; S Mt 24:31 [i] Isa 21:1; 66:15 **9:15** [j] Isa 31:5; 37:35; Zec 12:8 [k] Zec 14:3 [l] Zec 10:7 [m] Zec 14:20 [n] S Ex 27:2 **9:16** [o] S Isa 10:20 [p] S Jer 31:11 **10:1** [q] S Lev 26:4; S 1Ki 8:36; S Ps 104:13; S 135:7 [r] S Job 14:9 **10:2** [s] Eze 21:21 [t] S Isa 44:25 [u] Jer 23:16 [v] S Isa 40:19 [w] S Nu 27:17; S Jer 23:1; S Hos 3:4; S Mt 9:36 **10:3** [x] Isa 14:9; S Jer 25:34 [y] S Eze 34:8-10 **10:4** [z] S Ps 118:22; S Ac 4:11 [a] S Isa 22:23 [b] S Zec 9:10 **10:5** [c] S 2Sa 22:43; S Mic 7:10 [d] S Am 2:15; S Mic 5:8; Hag 2:22; Zec 12:4 **10:6** [e] S Eze 30:24 [f] S Ps 102:13; S Isa 14:1 [g] S Eze 36:37; 37:19; S Zec 8:7-8 [h] Ps 34:17; Isa 58:9; 65:24; Zec 13:9

kingdom) as his arrow. *your sons, Zion.* The Maccabees (see note on Da 11:34; see also essay, pp. 1573–1574). *your sons, Greece.* The Seleucids of Syria (after the breakup of Alexander's empire).

9:14 See Hab 3:3–15 and note on 3:3. *trumpet.* Probably a reference to thunder (see Ex 19:16–19 and note on 19:16). *south.* In the region of Mount Sinai, where the Sinaitic covenant was given (see v. 11 and note) and where the Lord's dwelling was (see Jdg 5:4–5; Ps 68:8; Hab 3:3 and note).

9:15 The Apocryphal book 1 Maccabees (3:16–24; 4:6–16; 7:40–50) records a partial fulfillment of this verse. *slingstones.* Hurled at defenders on the city wall and onto the inhabitants inside. *bowl used for sprinkling.* See Ex 27:1–3 and note on 27:3; Lev 4:6–7.

9:16 *that day.* See note on 2:11.

10:1 *it is the Lord who ... gives showers ... plants.* The Lord, not the Canaanite god Baal, is the one who controls the weather and the rain, giving life and fertility to the land (see Jer 14:22; Hos 2:8 and note; 6:3; Joel 2:21–27; Am 5:8; Mt 5:45). Therefore God's people are to pray to and trust in him.

10:2 *idols.* Household gods (see Ge 31:19 and note). They were used for divination during the period of the judges (see Jdg 17:5 and note; 18:14–20). *diviners.* Included among false prophets, they were the occult counterpart to true prophets. See Jer 27:9–10 and note on 27:9. Resorting to such sources for information and guidance is expressly forbidden in Dt 18:9–14 because God provided true prophets (and ultimately the Messianic Prophet) for that purpose (see Dt 13:1–5 and notes; 18:15–22 and note on 18:15; Isa 8:19–20 and notes; Jn 4:25; 6:14 and note; Ac 3:22–26 and note; see also note on Ge 30:27). *they give comfort in vain.* For example, when they wrongly promise rain, fruitful seasons, fertility, prosperity, peace and blessing. *people wander like sheep.* See Isa 53:6 and note. *lack of a shepherd.* Spiritual leadership is missing (cf. Mk 6:34). "Shepherd" is primarily a royal motif, whether referring to human kings (see Isa 44:28; Jer 2:8 and notes), to God as King (see Ps 23:1 and note) or to the Messianic, Davidic King (Eze 34:23–24; Jn 10:11–16; Heb 13:20; 1Pe 5:4; Rev 7:17).

10:3 *I will punish the leaders.* Cf. Eze 34:1–10. *like a proud horse.* Triumphant.

10:4 Probably Messianic (indicated by the Aramaic Targum). *From Judah.* See Ge 49:10; Jer 30:21 and note; Mic 5:2. *cornerstone.* See 3:9; Eph 2:20 and notes. *tent peg.* The ruler as the support of the state (see note on Isa 22:23; see also Isa 22:24). *battle bow.* Part of the Divine Warrior terminology (cf. 9:13; Ps 7:12; 45:5; La 2:4; 3:12; Hab 3:9).

10:5 *they.* Judah (v. 4), i.e., its people. *the Lord is with them.* See Jos 1:5; Jer 1:8 and note. *put the enemy horsemen to shame.* Partly fulfilled in the Maccabean victories (during the period between the OT and the NT; see essay, pp. 1573–1574).

10:6 *Judah ... Joseph.* The people of the southern and northern kingdoms will be reunited (see note on 8:13).

7The Ephraimites will become like
warriors,
and their hearts will be glad as with
wine.[i]
Their children will see it and be joyful;
their hearts will rejoice[j] in the LORD.
8I will signal[k] for them
and gather them in.
Surely I will redeem them;
they will be as numerous[l] as before.
9Though I scatter them among the
peoples,
yet in distant lands they will
remember me.[m]
They and their children will survive,
and they will return.
10I will bring them back from Egypt
and gather them from Assyria.[n]
I will bring them to Gilead[o] and Lebanon,
and there will not be room[p] enough
for them.
11They will pass through the sea of
trouble;
the surging sea will be subdued
and all the depths of the Nile will
dry up.[q]
Assyria's pride[r] will be brought down
and Egypt's scepter[s] will pass away.[t]
12I will strengthen[u] them in the LORD
and in his name they will live
securely,[v]"
declares the LORD.

10:7 [i]Zec 9:15 [j]S 1Sa 2:1; S Isa 60:5; S Joel 2:23 **10:8** [k]Isa 5:26 [l]S Jer 33:22; S Eze 36:11 **10:9** [m]S Isa 44:21; S Eze 6:9 **10:10** [n]S Isa 11:11; S Zec 8:8 [o]S Jer 50:19 [p]S Isa 49:19 **10:11** [q]Isa 19:5-7; S 51:10 [r]Zep 2:13 [s]Eze 30:13 [t]Eze 29:15 **10:12** [u]S Eze 30:24 [v]S Mic 4:5

11:1 [w]S Eze 31:3 [x]S 2Ch 36:19; Zec 12:6 **11:2** [y]S Isa 2:13 [z]Isa 32:19 [a]S Isa 10:34 **11:3** [b]S Isa 5:29 [c]Jer 2:15; 50:44; Eze 19:9 **11:4** [d]S Jer 25:34 **11:5** [e]Jer 50:7; S Eze 34:2-3 **11:6** [f]Zec 14:13 [g]Isa 9:19-21; S Jer 13:14; S La 2:21; 5:8; S Mic 5:8; 7:2-6 **11:7** [h]S Jer 25:34

11 Open your doors, Lebanon,[w]
so that fire[x] may devour your
cedars!
2Wail, you juniper, for the cedar has
fallen;
the stately trees are ruined!
Wail, oaks[y] of Bashan;
the dense forest[z] has been cut
down![a]
3Listen to the wail of the shepherds;
their rich pastures are destroyed!
Listen to the roar of the lions;[b]
the lush thicket of the Jordan is
ruined![c]

Two Shepherds

4This is what the LORD my God says:
"Shepherd the flock marked for slaughter.[d] 5Their buyers slaughter them and go
unpunished. Those who sell them say,
'Praise the LORD, I am rich!' Their own
shepherds do not spare them.[e] 6For I will
no longer have pity on the people of the
land," declares the LORD. "I will give everyone into the hands of their neighbors[f] and
their king. They will devastate the land,
and I will not rescue anyone from their
hands."[g]
7So I shepherded the flock marked for
slaughter,[h] particularly the oppressed
of the flock. Then I took two staffs and
called one Favor and the other Union, and

10:7 *Ephraimites.* See note on 9:13. *glad as with wine.* See Ps 104:15.
10:8 *signal.* Lit. "whistle," a continuation of the shepherd metaphor (vv. 2–3; see Jdg 5:16). *redeem.* The Hebrew for this word is often used of ransoming from slavery or captivity (see Isa 35:10; Mic 6:4; cf. 1Pe 1:18–19). *as numerous as before.* See Ex 1:6–20 and note on 1:7.
10:9 *they will remember me.* According to the meaning of Zechariah's name, "the LORD remembers" (his covenant people and promises). Now they will remember him.
10:10 *Egypt ... Assyria.* See v. 11; Hos 7:16 and note. Probably representing all the countries where the Israelites are dispersed, these two evoke memories of slavery and exile. *gather them.* See Isa 11:11–16; Eze 39:27–29. *Gilead.* See Ge 31:21 and note; SS 6:5; Jer 50:19; Mic 7:14 and note. *Lebanon.* See 2Ki 19:23; see also Isa 33:9; 35:2; Jer 22:6 and notes. *not be room enough.* See v. 8; 2:4 and note; see also note on Isa 49:19–20.
10:11 *pass through the sea of trouble.* As at the "Red Sea" (see Ex 14:22 and note).
11:1–3 Some interpret this brief poem as a taunt song related to the lament that will be sung over the destruction of the nations' power and arrogance (ch. 10), represented by the cedar, the pine and the oak (vv. 1–2). Their kings are represented by the shepherds and the lions (v. 3). Understood in this way, vv. 1–3 would provide the conclusion to the preceding section. Other interpreters, however, without denying the presence of figurative language, see the piece more literally as a description of the devastation of Syro-Palestine due to the rejection of the Messianic Good Shepherd (vv. 4–14). Verses 1–3 would then furnish the introduction to the next section. The geography of the text—Lebanon, Bashan and Jordan—would seem to favor this interpretation. Part of the fulfillment would be the destruction and further subjugation of the area by the Romans, including the fall of Jerusalem in AD 70 and of Masada in 73. Understood in this way, the passage is in sharp contrast with ch. 10 and its prediction of Israel's full deliverance and restoration to the covenant land. Now the scene is one of desolation for the land (vv. 1–3), followed by the threat of judgment and disaster for both land and people (vv. 4–6).
11:1 *Lebanon.* See 10:10 and note.
11:2 *Bashan.* See note on Isa 2:13. The Israelites took this region from the Amorite king Og at the time of the conquest of Canaan (Nu 21:33–35). It was allotted to the half-tribe of Manasseh (Jos 13:29–30; 17:5). *dense forest.* Of Lebanon.
11:3 If the language is figurative, the shepherds and lions represent the rulers or leaders of the Jews (see v. 5; 10:3; cf. Jer 25:34–36). *lush thicket of the Jordan.* Where the lions had their lairs.
11:4–14 The reason for the judgment on Israel in vv. 1–3 is now given, namely, the people's rejection of the Messianic Shepherd-King. Just as the Servant in the "servant songs" (see note on Isa 42:1–4) is rejected, so here the Good Shepherd (a royal figure) is rejected. The same Messianic King is in view in both instances.
11:4 *says.* To Zechariah. *flock.* Israel.
11:5 *buyers.* The sheep (the Jews) are bought as slaves by outsiders. Part of the fulfillment came in AD 70 and the following years. *Those who sell them.* "Their own shepherds (rulers or leaders)."
11:6 *land.* Israel. *king.* Perhaps the Roman emperor (cf. Jn 19:15). *They.* Includes the Romans prophetically.
11:7 *I.* Zechariah, as a type (foreshadowing) of the Messianic Shepherd-King. *called one Favor.* To ensure divine favor on the flock. *Union.* See Eze 37:15–28 and note on 37:16. Such unity would be the result of the gracious leadership of the

I shepherded the flock. 8 In one month I
got rid of the three shepherds.
The flock detested[i] me, and I grew weary of them 9 and said, "I will not be your
shepherd. Let the dying die, and the perishing perish.[j] Let those who are left eat[k]
one another's flesh."
10 Then I took my staff called Favor[l] and
broke it, revoking[m] the covenant I had
made with all the nations. 11 It was revoked
on that day, and so the oppressed of the
flock who were watching me knew it was
the word of the LORD.
12 I told them, "If you think it best, give
me my pay; but if not, keep it." So they
paid me thirty pieces of silver.[n]
13 And the LORD said to me, "Throw it to
the potter"—the handsome price at which
they valued me! So I took the thirty pieces
of silver[o] and threw them to the potter at
the house of the LORD.[p]
14 Then I broke my second staff called
Union, breaking the family bond between
Judah and Israel.
15 Then the LORD said to me, "Take again
the equipment of a foolish shepherd. 16 For
I am going to raise up a shepherd over the
land who will not care for the lost, or seek

11:8 [i] S Eze 14:5 **11:9** [j] S Jer 43:11 [k] S Isa 9:20 **11:10** [l] ver 7 [m] S Ps 89:39; Jer 14:21 **11:12** [n] S Ge 23:16; Mt 26:15 **11:13** [o] S Ex 21:32 [p] Mt 27:9-10*; Ac 1:18-19 **11:17** [q] Jer 23:1 [r] S Eze 30:21-22 [s] S Jer 23:1 **12:1** [t] S Isa 13:1 [u] S Ge 1:8; S Ps 104:2; S Jer 51:15 [v] Ps 102:25; Heb 1:10 [w] S Isa 57:16 **12:2** [x] S Ps 75:8 [y] S Ps 60:3; S Isa 51:23 [z] Zec 14:14 **12:3** [a] Isa 66:18; Zec 14:2 [b] S Isa 28:16; Da 2:34-35 [c] S Isa 29:8

the young, or heal the injured, or feed the
healthy, but will eat the meat of the choice
sheep, tearing off their hooves.

17 "Woe to the worthless shepherd,[q]
who deserts the flock!
May the sword strike his arm[r] and his
right eye!
May his arm be completely withered,
his right eye totally blinded!"[s]

Jerusalem's Enemies to Be Destroyed

12 A prophecy:[t] The word of the LORD
concerning Israel.

The LORD, who stretches out the heavens,[u] who lays the foundation of the
earth,[v] and who forms the human spirit
within a person,[w] declares: 2 "I am going
to make Jerusalem a cup[x] that sends all
the surrounding peoples reeling.[y] Judah[z]
will be besieged as well as Jerusalem. 3 On
that day, when all the nations[a] of the earth
are gathered against her, I will make Jerusalem an immovable rock[b] for all the
nations. All who try to move it will injure[c] themselves. 4 On that day I will strike
every horse with panic and its rider with
madness," declares the LORD. "I will keep

Good Shepherd. (For the significance of the subsequent breaking of the two staffs, see vv. 10,14 and notes.)

11:8 *got rid of the three shepherds.* Although the three cannot be specifically identified, the Good Shepherd will dispose of all such unfit leaders. *I grew weary of them.* Cf. Isa 1:13–14.

11:9 *Let the dying die.* The Good Shepherd terminates his providential care of the sheep. *eat one another's flesh.* According to Josephus, this actually happened during the Roman siege of Jerusalem in AD 70 (see Jer 19:9 and note).

11:10 *covenant.* Apparently a covenant of security and restraint, by which the Shepherd had been keeping the nations from attacking his people (cf. Eze 34:25; Hos 2:18). Now, however, the nations (e.g., the Romans) will be permitted to overrun them.

11:11 *the oppressed of the flock.* Probably the faithful few, who recognize the authoritative word of the Lord (see also v. 7). *it was the word of the LORD.* The faithful discern that what happens (e.g., the judgment on Jerusalem and the temple in AD 70) is a fulfillment of God's prophetic word—as a result of such actions as those denounced in Mt 23, which led to the rejection of the Good Shepherd.

11:12 *give me my pay.* Refers to the severance of the relationship. *keep it.* A more emphatic way of ending the relationship. *thirty pieces of silver.* The price of a slave among the Israelites in ancient times (see notes on Ex 21:32; Mt 26:15).

11:13 *handsome price.* Irony and sarcasm. *threw them to the potter at the house of the LORD.* For the NT use of vv. 12–13, see Mt 26:14–15; 27:3–10 and note on 27:9.

11:14 *broke my second staff called Union.* Signifying the dissolution of the covenant nation, particularly of the unity between the south and the north. The breaking up of the nation into parties hostile to each other was characteristic of later Jewish history; it greatly hindered the popular cause in the war against Rome (cf. Jn 11:48).

11:15 *again.* See v. 7. *foolish shepherd.* With the Shepherd of the Lord's choice removed from the scene, a foolish and worthless (v. 17) shepherd replaces him. A selfish, greedy, corrupt leader will arise and afflict the flock (the people of Israel).

11:16 *seek the young.* Cf. Ge 33:13; Isa 40:11. *tearing off their hooves.* Apparently in a greedy search for the last edible piece.

11:17 *worthless shepherd.* See note on v. 15. This counterfeit shepherd may have found a partial historical fulfillment in such leaders as Simeon bar Kosiba or Kokhba (who led the Jewish revolt against the Romans in AD 132–135 and who was hailed as the Messiah by Rabbi Akiba). But it would seem that the final stage of the progressive fulfillment of this prophecy awaits the rise of the final antichrist (cf. Eze 34:2–4; Da 11:36–39; Jn 5:43; 2Th 2:3–10; Rev 13:1–8). *deserts the flock.* Contrast the Good Shepherd of Jn 10:11–16. *May his arm be completely withered.* May his power be paralyzed. *his right eye totally blinded.* May his intelligence be nullified. Thus this leader will be powerless to fight.

12:1—14:21 This second prophetic message in Part II of the book revolves around two scenes: the final siege of Jerusalem and the Messiah's return to defeat Israel's enemies and establish his kingdom.

12:1 *A prophecy: The word of the LORD.* See note on 9:1. *Israel.* The whole nation, not just the northern kingdom. Judah and Jerusalem, however, are the main focus of attention (see v. 2). *The LORD, who stretches ... lays ... forms.* This description of the Lord's creative power shows that he is able to perform what he predicts; it also strengthens the royal and sovereign authority of the message.

12:2 *cup that sends all ... reeling.* See notes on Ps 16:5; Isa 51:17; Jer 25:15; Ob 16; Hab 2:16.

12:3 *that day.* See note on 2:11. The phrase is used often in chs. 12–14 (12:4,6,8–9,11; 13:1–2,4; 14:4,6, 8–9,13,20–21). *all the nations ... gathered against her.* See 14:2,12; Joel 3:9–16; cf. Rev 16:16–21.

12:4 *panic ... madness ... blind.* Listed in Dt 28:28 among Israel's curses for disobeying the stipulations of the covenant. Now these curses are turned against Israel's enemies. *watchful eye.* See Ps 32:8; 33:18; 121.

a watchful eye over Judah, but I will blind
all the horses of the nations.[d] 5 Then the
clans of Judah will say in their hearts,
'The people of Jerusalem are strong,[e] because the LORD Almighty is their God.'
6 "On that day I will make the clans of
Judah like a firepot[f] in a woodpile, like a
flaming torch among sheaves. They will
consume[g] all the surrounding peoples
right and left, but Jerusalem will remain
intact[h] in her place.
7 "The LORD will save the dwellings of
Judah first, so that the honor of the house
of David and of Jerusalem's inhabitants
may not be greater than that of Judah.[i]
8 On that day the LORD will shield[j] those
who live in Jerusalem, so that the feeblest[k]
among them will be like David, and the
house of David will be like God,[l] like the
angel of the LORD going before[m] them. 9 On
that day I will set out to destroy all the nations[n] that attack Jerusalem.[o]

Mourning for the One They Pierced

10 "And I will pour out on the house
of David and the inhabitants of Jerusalem a spirit[a][p] of grace and supplication.[q]
They will look on[b] me, the one they have
pierced,[r] and they will mourn for him as
one mourns for an only child,[s] and grieve
bitterly for him as one grieves for a firstborn son.[t] 11 On that day the weeping[u] in
Jerusalem will be as great as the weeping
of Hadad Rimmon in the plain of Megiddo.[v] 12 The land will mourn,[w] each clan by
itself, with their wives by themselves: the
clan of the house of David and their wives,
the clan of the house of Nathan and their
wives, 13 the clan of the house of Levi and
their wives, the clan of Shimei and their
wives, 14 and all the rest of the clans and
their wives.[x]

Cleansing From Sin

13 "On that day a fountain[y] will be
opened to the house of David and
the inhabitants of Jerusalem, to cleanse[z]
them from sin and impurity.
2 "On that day, I will banish the names
of the idols[a] from the land, and they will
be remembered no more,"[b] declares the
LORD Almighty. "I will remove both the
prophets[c] and the spirit of impurity from
the land. 3 And if anyone still prophesies,
their father and mother, to whom they
were born, will say to them, 'You must
die, because you have told lies[d] in the
LORD's name.' Then their own parents will
stab the one who prophesies.[e]
4 "On that day every prophet will be
ashamed[f] of their prophetic vision. They
will not put on a prophet's garment[g] of
hair[h] in order to deceive.[i] 5 Each will say, 'I
am not a prophet. I am a farmer; the land
has been my livelihood since my youth.[c]'[j]
6 If someone asks, 'What are these wounds

[a] 10 Or *the Spirit* [b] 10 Or *to* [c] 5 Or *farmer; a man sold me in my youth*

12:4 [d] Ps 76:6; S Zec 10:5 **12:5** [e] S Eze 30:24 **12:6** [f] Isa 10:17-18; S Zec 11:1 [g] Ob 1:18 [h] Zec 14:10 **12:7** [i] Jer 30:18; S Am 9:11 **12:8** [j] S Ps 91:4; S Joel 3:16; S Zec 9:15 [k] Joel 3:10 [l] Ps 82:6 [m] Mic 7:8 **12:9** [n] S Isa 29:7 [o] S Zec 1:21; 14:2-3 **12:10** [p] S Eze 37:9 [q] Isa 44:3; S Eze 39:29; Joel 2:28-29 [r] S Ps 22:16; Jn 19:34,37* [s] Jdg 11:34 [t] S Ge 21:16; Jer 31:19 **12:11** [u] Jer 50:4 [v] 2Ki 23:29 **12:12** [w] Mt 24:30; Rev 1:7 **12:14** [x] Zec 7:3 **13:1** [y] Jer 17:13 [z] S Lev 16:30; S Ps 51:2; Heb 9:14 **13:2** [a] S Jer 43:12; S Eze 6:6; S 36:25; S Hos 2:17 [b] S Mic 5:13 [c] 1Ki 22:22; Jer 23:14-15 **13:3** [d] S Jer 28:16 [e] Dt 13:6-11; 18:20; S Ne 6:14; Jer 23:34; S Eze 14:9 **13:4** [f] S Jer 6:15 [g] Mt 3:4 [h] S 1Ki 18:7; S Isa 20:2 [i] S Eze 12:24 **13:5** [j] S Am 7:14

12:5 *the LORD Almighty.* See note on 1Sa 1:3.

12:6 Like a fire destroying wood and sheaves of grain, Judah's discerning leaders (see v. 5) will consume their enemies (cf. Jdg 15:3–5; Mic 5:5–6; see note on Isa 1:31).

12:8 *like David.* Like a great warrior. *like God.* Cf. Ex 4:16; 7:1. *like the angel of the LORD.* See Ge 48:16 and note; Ex 14:19; 23:20; 32:34; 33:2; Hos 12:3–4; see also Ge 16:7 and note.

12:10 *a spirit.* See NIV text note; Isa 32:15; Eze 36:26–27 and notes; see also Isa 44:3; 59:20–21; Eze 39:29; Joel 2:28–29. *look on.* See NIV text note. The emphasis seems to be on looking "to" the Messiah in faith (cf. Nu 21:9; Isa 45:22; Jn 3:14–15). *me ... him ... him.* Same person. *pierced.* See Ps 22:16 and note; Jn 19:37. *mourns for an only child.* See Jer 6:26 and note. *grieves for a firstborn son.* Cf. Ex 11:5; Jer 6:26 and notes.

12:11 *Hadad Rimmon.* The name of either (1) a place near Megiddo, where the people mourned the death of King Josiah (2Ch 35:20–27; see v. 22 there for the plain of Megiddo and vv. 24–25 for the mourning); or (2) a Semitic storm god (see 2Ki 5:18 and note), whose name means "Hadad the thunderer" in Babylonian (as in the Gilgamesh Epic, 11:98; see chart, p. xxii; see also Eze 8:14 for an example of the practice of weeping for a Babylonian deity).

12:12 *Nathan.* David's son (2Sa 5:14; Lk 3:31).

12:13 *Shimei.* Son of Gershon, the son of Levi (Nu 3:17–18,21). The repentance and mourning are led, then, by the civil (royal) and religious leaders.

13:1 *cleanse them from sin.* See 3:4–9 and note on 3:9; one of the provisions of the new covenant (Jer 31:34; Eze 36:25).

13:2 *names of the idols.* The influence and fame, and even the very existence, of the idols. *prophets.* False prophecy was still a problem in the postexilic period (see Ne 6:12–14) and would again be a problem in the future (see Mt 24:4–5,11,23–24; 2Th 2:2–4).

13:3 *lies.* False prophecies. *parents will stab the one who prophesies.* See Dt 13:3,6–10. The Hebrew for "stab" is the same as the verb for "pierced" in 12:10, perhaps indicating that the feelings and actions exhibited in piercing the Messiah will now be directed toward the false prophets.

13:4–6 Because of the stern measures just mentioned, a false prophet will be reluctant to identify himself as such and will be evasive in his responses to interrogation. To help conceal his true identity, he will not wear a "prophet's garment of hair" (v. 4), such as Elijah wore (see 2Ki 1:8 and note). Instead, to avoid the death penalty (v. 3), he will deny being a prophet and will claim to have been a farmer since his youth (v. 5). And if a suspicious person notices marks on his body and inquires about them (v. 6), he will claim to have received them in a scuffle with friends (or perhaps as discipline from his parents during childhood). Apparently the accuser suspects that the false prophet's wounds were self-inflicted to arouse his prophetic ecstasy in idolatrous rites (as in 1Ki 18:28; see Jer 16:6 and note; 48:37).

13:5 *the land ... my youth.* If the alternative translation in the NIV text note is taken, the meaning is that someone sold him as a slave while he was still young.

13:6 Some take this verse as Messianic, but the interpretation given above seems preferable in this context (e.g., v. 5).

on your body[a]?' they will answer, 'The
wounds I was given at the house of my
friends.'

The Shepherd Struck, the Sheep Scattered

7 "Awake, sword,[k] against my shepherd,[l]
against the man who is close to me!"
declares the LORD Almighty.
"Strike the shepherd,
and the sheep will be scattered,[m]
and I will turn my hand against the
little ones.
8 In the whole land," declares the LORD,
"two-thirds will be struck down and
perish;
yet one-third will be left in it.[n]
9 This third I will put into the fire;[o]
I will refine them like silver[p]
and test them like gold.[q]
They will call[r] on my name[s]
and I will answer[t] them;
I will say, 'They are my people,'[u]
and they will say, 'The LORD is our
God.[v]' "

The LORD Comes and Reigns

14 A day of the LORD[w] is coming, Jerusalem, when your possessions[x] will
be plundered and divided up within your
very walls.
2 I will gather all the nations[y] to Jerusalem to fight against it;[z] the city will be
captured, the houses ransacked, and the
women raped.[a] Half of the city will go into
exile, but the rest of the people will not be
taken from the city.[b] 3 Then the LORD will
go out and fight[c] against those nations,
as he fights on a day of battle.[d] 4 On that
day his feet will stand on the Mount of
Olives,[e] east of Jerusalem, and the Mount
of Olives will be split[f] in two from east to
west, forming a great valley, with half of
the mountain moving north and half moving south. 5 You will flee by my mountain
valley, for it will extend to Azel. You will
flee as you fled from the earthquake[b][g] in
the days of Uzziah king of Judah. Then
the LORD my God will come,[h] and all the
holy ones with him.[i]
6 On that day there will be neither sunlight[j] nor cold, frosty darkness. 7 It will be
a unique[k] day—a day known only to the
LORD—with no distinction between day
and night.[l] When evening comes, there
will be light.[m]
8 On that day living water[n] will flow[o] out
from Jerusalem, half of it east[p] to the Dead
Sea and half of it west to the Mediterranean Sea, in summer and in winter.[q]
9 The LORD will be king[r] over the whole
earth.[s] On that day there will be one LORD,
and his name the only name.[t]
10 The whole land, from Geba[u] to Rimmon,[v] south of Jerusalem, will become

13:7 [k]S Isa 34:5; Jer 47:6 [l]Isa 40:11; S 53:4; Eze 37:24 [m]S 2Sa 17:2; Mt 26:31*; Mk 14:27* **13:8** [n]S Eze 5:2-4,12; Zec 14:2 **13:9** [o]S Isa 4:4; 33:14; Mal 3:2 [p]S Ps 12:6; S Da 11:35; 1Pe 1:6-7 [q]S Job 6:29; S Jer 6:27 [r]S Ps 50:15 [s]Ps 105:1 [t]S Ps 86:7; S Isa 30:19; S Zec 10:6 [u]S Lev 26:12; S Jer 30:22 [v]S Isa 44:5; S Jer 29:12; S Eze 20:38 **14:1** [w]Isa 13:6; S Joel 1:15; Mal 4:1 [x]S Isa 23:18 **14:2** [y]S Isa 2:3; S Zec 12:3 [z]S Eze 5:8 [a]S Ge 34:29; S La 5:11 [b]Isa 13:6; S Zec 13:8 **14:3** [c]Zec 9:14-15 [d]S Isa 8:9; S Zec 12:9 **14:4** [e]Eze 11:23 [f]S Nu 16:31 **14:5** [g]Am 1:1 [h]Isa 29:6; 66:15-16 [i]S Dt 33:2; Mt 16:27; 25:31; Jude 14 **14:6** [j]S Isa 13:10; S Jer 4:23 **14:7** [k]Jer 30:7 [l]Rev 21:23-25; 22:5 [m]S Isa 13:10; S 30:26 **14:8** [n]Eze 47:1-12; Jn 7:38; Rev 22:1-2 [o]S Isa 30:25 [p]Joel 2:20 [q]S Ge 8:22 **14:9** [r]S Ps 22:28; S Ob 1:21 [s]S Dt 6:4; Ps 47:7; Isa 45:24; Rev 11:15 [t]Hab 2:14; Eph 4:5-6 **14:10** [u]1Ki 15:22 [v]S Jos 15:32

[a] 6 Or *wounds between your hands* [b] 5 Or [5]*My mountain valley will be blocked and will extend to Azel. It will be blocked as it was blocked because of the earthquake*

13:7 *my shepherd.* The royal (Messianic) Good Shepherd (cf. the true Shepherd of 11:4–14; contrast the foolish and worthless shepherd of 11:15–17). *Strike the shepherd.* In 11:17 it was the worthless shepherd who was to be struck; now it is the Good Shepherd (cf. also 12:10). *sheep will be scattered.* In partial fulfillment of the curses for covenant disobedience (see Dt 28:64 and note; 29:24–25). These two clauses are quoted by Jesus not long before his arrest (Mt 26:31; Mk 14:27) and applied to the scattering of the apostles (Mt 26:56; Mk 14:49–50), who in turn are probably typological of the dispersion of the Jews in AD 70 and subsequent years.

13:8–9 These verses depict a refining process for Israel (see note on Isa 48:10).

13:8 *one-third.* A remnant, thus revealing God's mercy in the midst of judgment.

13:9 *I will refine them.* See Ps 12:6 and note. *my people ... our God.* See note on 8:8. They will be restored to proper covenant relationship with the Lord (see also Eze 20:30–44).

14:1 *A day of the LORD.* Cf. Isa 2:12; Eze 30:3; Joel 1:15 and note. *your ... your.* Jerusalem (v. 2) is the object of the plunder.

14:2 *all the nations ... fight against it.* See v. 12; see also note on 12:3.

14:3 *day of battle.* Any occasion when the Lord supernaturally intervenes to deliver his people, such as at the "Red Sea" (see Ex 14:14 and note).

14:4 *Mount of Olives.* Called by this name elsewhere in the OT only in 2Sa 15:30. It faced the temple mount and, being about 2,700 feet high, rose about 200 feet above it. Cf. Eze 11:23. This prophecy is probably referred to in Ac 1:11–12.

14:5 *Azel.* The name of a place east of Jerusalem, marking the eastern end of the newly formed valley. *earthquake in the days of Uzziah.* Amos dates his prophecy by referring to it (see Am 1:1 and note). *holy ones.* May include both believers and angels. They will accompany our Lord when he comes (cf. Mt 25:31; 1Th 3:13; Jude 14; Rev 19:14).

14:7 *unique day.* Due to the topographical, cosmic and cataclysmic changes. See also Isa 60:19–20 and notes.

14:8 *living water will flow.* Perhaps both literal and symbolic (see Isa 8:6; Joel 3:18 and note; Jn 7:38).

14:9 *The LORD will be king over the whole earth.* A pervasive theological theme in Scripture (see Introduction to Psalms: Theology: Major Themes). *one LORD.* See Dt 6:4; Isa 43:11 and notes.

14:10 *Geba.* About six miles north-northeast of Jerusalem at the northern boundary of Judah (see 2Ki 23:8 and note). *Rimmon.* Also called En Rimmon (see Ne 11:29 and note), it was about 35 miles south-southwest of Jerusalem, where the hill country of Judah slopes away into the Negev. *Arabah.* See note on Dt 1:1. All the land around Jerusalem is to be leveled. *Jerusalem will be raised up.* See Isa 2:2–4 and note. The elevation may be both physical and in prominence. *Benjamin Gate ... First Gate ... Tower of Hananel.* All were probably at the northeastern part of the city wall (cf. Jer 31:38; 37:12–13; 38:7). *Corner Gate.* At the northwest corner (cf. Jer 31:38).

like the Arabah. But Jerusalem will be
raised up[w] high from the Benjamin Gate[x]
to the site of the First Gate, to the Corner Gate,[y] and from the Tower of Hananel[z]
to the royal winepresses, and will remain
in its place.[a] 11 It will be inhabited;[b] never
again will it be destroyed. Jerusalem will
be secure.[c]

12 This is the plague with which the
LORD will strike[d] all the nations that fought
against Jerusalem: Their flesh will rot
while they are still standing on their feet,
their eyes will rot in their sockets, and
their tongues will rot in their mouths.[e]
13 On that day people will be stricken by
the LORD with great panic.[f] They will seize
each other by the hand and attack one
another.[g] 14 Judah[h] too will fight at Jerusalem. The wealth of all the surrounding nations will be collected[i]—great quantities
of gold and silver and clothing. 15 A similar
plague[j] will strike the horses and mules,
the camels and donkeys, and all the animals in those camps.

16 Then the survivors[k] from all the nations that have attacked Jerusalem will go
up year after year to worship[l] the King,[m]
the LORD Almighty, and to celebrate the
Festival of Tabernacles.[n] 17 If any of the
peoples of the earth do not go up to Jerusalem to worship[o] the King, the LORD Almighty, they will have no rain.[p] 18 If the
Egyptian people do not go up and take
part, they will have no rain. The LORD[a] will
bring on them the plague[q] he inflicts on
the nations that do not go up to celebrate
the Festival of Tabernacles.[r] 19 This will be
the punishment of Egypt and the punishment of all the nations that do not go up to
celebrate the Festival of Tabernacles.[s]

20 On that day HOLY TO THE LORD[t] will be
inscribed on the bells of the horses, and
the cooking pots[u] in the LORD's house will
be like the sacred bowls[v] in front of the
altar. 21 Every pot in Jerusalem and Judah
will be holy[w] to the LORD Almighty, and
all who come to sacrifice will take some
of the pots and cook in them. And on that
day[x] there will no longer be a Canaanite[b][y]
in the house[z] of the LORD Almighty.[a]

[a] *18* Or *part, then the LORD* [b] *21* Or *merchant*

14:10 [w] Isa 2:2; Jer 30:18; S Am 9:11 [x] S Jer 20:2 [y] S 2Ki 14:13 [z] S Ne 3:1 [a] Zec 12:6 **14:11** [b] Zec 2:4 [c] S Ps 48:8; S Eze 34:25-28 **14:12** [d] S Isa 11:4 [e] ver 18; S Lev 26:16; S Dt 28:22; Job 18:13 **14:13** [f] S Ge 35:5 [g] S Jdg 7:22; S Zec 11:6 **14:14** [h] Zec 12:2 [i] S Isa 23:18 **14:15** [j] ver 12 **14:16** [k] S 2Ki 19:31 [l] S Ps 22:29; S 86:9; S Isa 19:21 [m] S Ob 1:21 [n] S Ex 23:16; Isa 60:6-9; S Mic 4:2 **14:17** [o] S 2Ch 32:23 [p] S Jer 14:4; S Am 4:7 **14:18** [q] S Ge 27:29 [r] S ver 12 **14:19** [s] S Ezr 3:4 **14:20** [t] S Ex 39:30 [u] S Eze 46:20 [v] Zec 9:15 **14:21** [w] S Jer 31:40; Ro 14:6-7; 1Co 10:31 [x] Ne 8:10 [y] Zec 9:8 [z] S Ne 11:1 [a] S Eze 44:9

royal winepresses. Just south of the city. Thus the whole city is included.

14:11 *inhabited.* See 2:4 and note. *never again ... destroyed.* As at the time of the exile to Babylonia (see Isa 43:28 and note). *Jerusalem will be secure.* See Jer 31:40.

14:12 *plague.* See Isa 37:36 and note. *nations that fought against Jerusalem.* See v. 2; see also note on 12:3.

14:13 *great panic ... attack one another.* See Jdg 7:22 and note.

14:14 *gold and silver and clothing.* The plunder of battle, thus reversing the situation in v. 1.

14:15 A similar plague will strike the beasts of burden, preventing the people from using them to escape.

14:16 See Isa 2:2–4 and note. *Festival of Tabernacles.* See notes on Ex 23:16; Ps 81:3. Of the three great pilgrimage festivals (see Ex 23:14–17), perhaps Tabernacles was selected as the one for representatives of the various Gentile nations because it was the last and greatest festival of the Hebrew calendar, gathering up into itself the year's worship (see note on Eze 45:25). It was to be a time of grateful rejoicing (see Lev 23:40; Dt 16:13–15; Ne 8:17 and note). Beginning with the period of Ezra and Nehemiah, the reading and teaching of "the Book of the Law of God" became an integral part of the festivities (Ne 8:18; cf. Isa 2:3). The festival seems to speak of the final, joyful regathering and restoration of Israel, as well as of the ingathering of the nations. See chart, pp. 188–189.

14:17 *no rain.* One of the curses for covenant disobedience (Dt 28:22–24; cf. Zec 9:11—10:1).

14:18 *Egyptian people ... will have no rain.* See NIV text note. With either reading, the withholding of rain may still be included, for drought (v. 17) in the upper reaches of the Nile would cause the annual flooding of the Nile to fail.

14:20 *HOLY TO THE LORD.* Engraved on the gold plate worn on the high priest's turban (Ex 28:36–38) as a reminder of his consecration to the Lord's service (see note on 3:5). God's original purpose for Israel (see Ex 19:6 and note) will be realized.

14:21 *Every pot in Jerusalem ... holy.* See Joel 3:17 and note. Even common things become holy when they are used for God's service. *cook.* Portions from the sacrifices. *Canaanite.* Represents anyone who is morally or spiritually unclean—anyone who is not included among the chosen people of God (cf. Isa 35:8; Eze 43:7; 44:9; Rev 21:27).

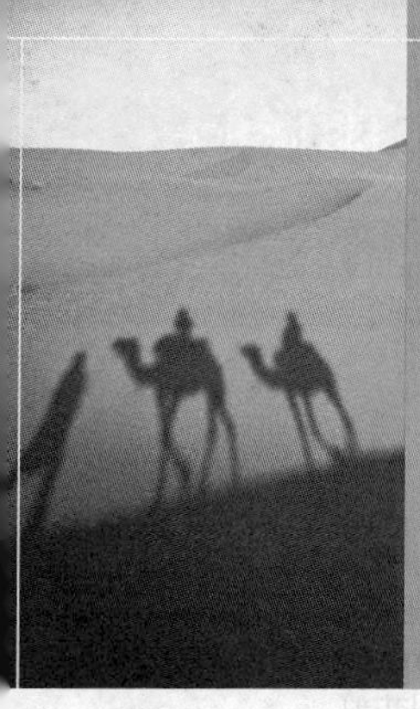

MALACHI

INTRODUCTION

Author

The book is ascribed to Malachi, whose name means "my messenger." Since the term occurs in 3:1, and since both prophets and priests were called messengers of the Lord (see 2:7; Hag 1:13), some have thought "Malachi" to be only a title that tradition has given the author. The view has been supported by appeal to the pre-Christian Greek translation of the OT (the Septuagint), which translates the term in 1:1 "his messenger" rather than as a proper noun. The matter, however, remains uncertain, and it is still very likely that Malachi was in fact the author's name.

Background

Spurred on by the prophetic activity of Haggai and Zechariah, the returned exiles under the leadership of their governor, Zerubbabel, finished the temple in 516 BC. In 458 the community was strengthened by the coming of the priest Ezra and several thousand more Jews. Artaxerxes, king of Persia, encouraged Ezra to reconstitute the temple worship (Ezr 7:17) and to make sure the law of Moses was being obeyed (Ezr 7:25 – 26).

Fourteen years later (444) the same Persian king permitted his cupbearer Nehemiah to return to Jerusalem and rebuild its walls (Ne 6:15). As newly appointed governor, Nehemiah also spearheaded reforms to help the poor (Ne 5:2 – 13) and convinced the people to shun mixed marriages (Ne 10:30), to keep the Sabbath (Ne 10:31) and to bring their tithes and offerings faithfully (Ne 10:37 – 39).

In 433 BC Nehemiah returned to the service of the Persian king, and during his absence the Jews fell into sin once more. Later, however, Nehemiah came back to Jerusalem to discover that the tithes were ignored, the Sabbath was broken, the people had intermarried with foreigners, and the priests had become corrupt (Ne 13:7 – 31). Several of these same sins are condemned by Malachi (see 1:6 – 14; 2:14 – 16; 3:8 – 11).

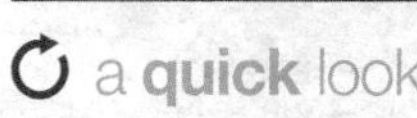

Author:
Malachi

Audience:
The postexilic Jews living in Judah

Date:
About 430 BC

Theme:
The prophet Malachi assures the postexilic Jewish community that the Messianic King will come not only to judge his people but also to bless and restore them.

Doubting God's covenant love and no longer trusting his justice, the Jews of the restored community begin to lose hope.

Date

The similarity between the sins denounced in Nehemiah and those denounced in Malachi suggests that the two leaders were contemporaries. Malachi may have been written after Nehemiah returned to Persia in 433 BC or during his second period as governor. Since the governor mentioned in 1:8 (see note there) was probably not Nehemiah, the first alternative may be more likely. Malachi was most likely the last prophet of the OT era (though some place Joel later).

Themes and Theology

The theological message of the book can be summed up in one sentence: The Great King (1:14) will come not only to judge his people (3:1 – 5; 4:1) but also to bless and restore them (3:6 – 12; 4:2).

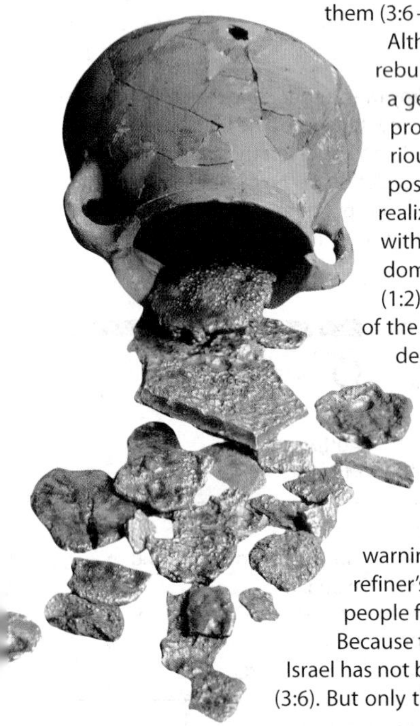

Although the Jews had been allowed to return from exile and rebuild the temple, several discouraging factors brought about a general religious malaise: (1) Their land remained but a small province in the backwaters of the Persian Empire, (2) the glorious future announced by the prophets (including the other postexilic prophets, Haggai and Zechariah) had not (yet) been realized and (3) their God had not (yet) come to his temple (3:1) with majesty and power (as celebrated in Ps 68) to exalt his kingdom in the sight of the nations. Doubting God's covenant love (1:2) and no longer trusting his justice (2:17; 3:14 – 15), the Jews of the restored community began to lose hope. So their worship degenerated into a listless perpetuation of mere forms, and they no longer took the law seriously.

Malachi rebukes their doubt of God's love (1:2 – 5) and the faithlessness of both priests (1:6 — 2:9) and people (2:10 – 16). To their charge that God is unjust (2:17) because he has failed to come in judgment to exalt his people, Malachi answers with an announcement and a warning. The Lord they seek will come — but he will come "like a refiner's fire" (3:1 – 4). He will come to judge — but he will judge his people first (3:5).

Because the Lord does not change in his commitments and purpose, Israel has not been completely destroyed for her persistent unfaithfulness (3:6). But only through repentance and reformation will she again experience God's blessing (3:6 – 12). Those who honor the Lord will be spared when he comes to judge (3:16 – 18).

Silver ingots found in a clay jar at En Gedi (ninth – eighth century BC). Malachi 3:2 – 3 uses the metaphor of the Lord putting his people through the refiner's fire so that they may be pure and refined like gold and silver.

Z. Radovan/www.BibleLandPictures.com

In conclusion, Malachi once more reassures and warns his readers that "the day ['that great and dreadful day of the LORD,' 4:5] is coming" and that "it will burn like a furnace" (4:1). In that day the righteous will rejoice, and "you will trample on the wicked" (4:2 – 3). So "remember the law of my servant Moses" (4:4). To prepare his people for that day the Lord will send "the prophet Elijah" to call them back to the godly ways of their forefathers (4:5–6).

Literary Features

Malachi is called a "prophecy" (1:1) and is written in what might be called lofty prose. The text features a series of questions asked by both God and the people. Frequently the Lord's statements are followed by sarcastic questions introduced by "(But) you ask" (1:2,6–7; 2:14,17; 3:7–8,13; cf. 1:13). In each case the Lord's response is given.

Repetition is a key element in the book. The name "LORD Almighty" occurs 20 times (see note on 1Sa 1:3). The book begins with a description of the wasteland of Edom (1:3–4) and ends with a warning of Israel's destruction (4:6).

Several vivid figures are employed within the book of Malachi. The priests sniff contemptuously at the altar of the Lord (1:13), and the Lord spreads on their faces the dung from their sacrifices (see 2:3 and note). As Judge, "he will be like a refiner's fire or a launderer's soap" (3:2), but for the righteous "the sun of righteousness will rise with healing in its rays. And you will go out and frolic like well-fed calves" (4:2).

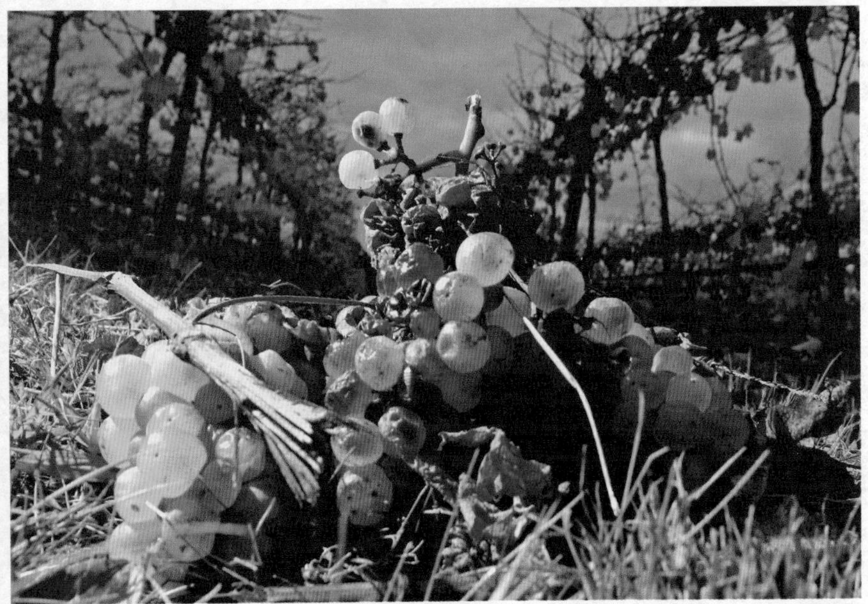

In Malachi 3, God challenges the people, promising them that if they bring the whole tithe into the storehouse, he will prevent their vines from dropping their fruit.

Mark Dadswell/Getty Images

Outline

I. Title (1:1)
II. Introduction: God's Faithful Covenant Love for Israel Affirmed (1:2 – 5)
III. Israel's Unfaithfulness Rebuked (1:6 — 2:16)
  A. The Unfaithfulness of the Priests (1:6 — 2:9)
    1. They dishonor God in their sacrifices (1:6 – 14)
    2. They do not faithfully teach the law (2:1 – 9)
  B. The Unfaithfulness of the People (2:10 – 16)
IV. The Lord's Coming Announced (2:17 — 4:6)
  A. The Lord Will Come to Purify the Priests and Judge the People (2:17 — 3:5)
  B. A Call to Repentance in View of the Lord's Coming (3:6 – 18)
    1. An exhortation to faithful giving (3:6 – 12)
    2. An exhortation to faithful service (3:13 – 18)
  C. The Day of the Lord Announced (ch. 4)

1 A prophecy:[a] The word[b] of the LORD to
Israel through Malachi.[a]

Israel Doubts God's Love

2 "I have loved[c] you," says the LORD.
"But you ask,[d] 'How have you loved us?'
"Was not Esau Jacob's brother?" declares the LORD. "Yet I have loved Jacob,[e]
3 but Esau I have hated,[f] and I have turned
his hill country into a wasteland[g] and left
his inheritance to the desert jackals.[h]"
4 Edom[i] may say, "Though we have been
crushed, we will rebuild[j] the ruins."
But this is what the LORD Almighty
says: "They may build, but I will demolish.[k] They will be called the Wicked Land,
a people always under the wrath of the
LORD.[l] 5 You will see it with your own eyes
and say, 'Great[m] is the LORD—even beyond
the borders of Israel!'[n]

Breaking Covenant Through Blemished Sacrifices

6 "A son honors his father,[o] and a slave
his master.[p] If I am a father, where is the
honor due me? If I am a master, where is
the respect[q] due me?" says the LORD Almighty.[r]
"It is you priests who show contempt
for my name.
"But you ask,[s] 'How have we shown
contempt for your name?'
7 "By offering defiled food[t] on my altar.
"But you ask,[u] 'How have we defiled
you?'
"By saying that the LORD's table[v] is contemptible. 8 When you offer blind animals
for sacrifice, is that not wrong? When you
sacrifice lame or diseased animals,[w] is that
not wrong? Try offering them to your governor! Would he be pleased[x] with you?
Would he accept you?" says the LORD Almighty.[y]
9 "Now plead with God to be gracious to
us. With such offerings[z] from your hands,
will he accept[a] you?"—says the LORD Almighty.
10 "Oh, that one of you would shut the
temple doors,[b] so that you would not light
useless fires on my altar! I am not pleased[c]
with you," says the LORD Almighty, "and I
will accept[d] no offering[e] from your hands.
11 My name will be great[f] among the nations,[g] from where the sun rises to where
it sets.[h] In every place incense[i] and pure
offerings[j] will be brought to me, because
my name will be great among the nations," says the LORD Almighty.
12 "But you profane it by saying, 'The
Lord's table[k] is defiled,' and, 'Its food[l] is
contemptible.' 13 And you say, 'What a burden!'[m] and you sniff at it contemptuously,[n]" says the LORD Almighty.
"When you bring injured, lame or
diseased animals and offer them as

[a] 1 *Malachi* means *my messenger.*

1:1 [a] S Na 1:1 [b] Ac 7:38; Ro 3:1-2; 1Pe 4:11 **1:2** [c] S Dt 4:37 [d] ver 6,7; Mal 2:14, 17; 3:7,13 [e] S Jer 46:27; Ro 9:13* **1:3** [f] Lk 14:26 [g] S Isa 34:10 [h] S Isa 13:22 **1:4** [i] S Isa 11:14; S 34:11 [j] Isa 9:10 [k] S Isa 34:5 [l] S La 4:22; S Eze 25:12-14; S 26:14 **1:5** [m] Ps 35:27; 48:1; Mic 5:4 [n] Isa 45:22; 52:10; S Am 1:11-12 **1:6** [o] S Lev 20:9; Mt 15:4; 23:9 [p] Lk 6:46 [q] S Dt 31:12; S Isa 1:2 [r] Job 5:17 [s] S ver 2 **1:7** [t] ver 12; Lev 21:6 [u] S ver 2 [v] S Eze 23:41 **1:8** [w] S Lev 1:3; S Dt 15:21 [x] S Ge 32:20 [y] S Isa 43:23 **1:9** [z] Lev 23:33-44; Ps 51:17; Mic 6:6-8; Ro 12:1; Heb 13:16 [a] S Jer 6:20 **1:10** [b] 2Ch 28:24 [c] S Hos 5:6 [d] Lev 22:20 [e] ver 13; Isa 1:11-14; Jer 14:12; Mal 2:12 **1:11** [f] S Isa 24:15; 56:6 [g] S Isa 6:3; S 12:4 [h] S Ps 113:3; S Mt 8:11 [i] Isa 60:6-7; Rev 5:8; 8:3 [j] S Isa 19:21; Heb 13:15 **1:12** [k] S Eze 41:22 [l] S ver 7 **1:13** [m] Isa 43:22-24 [n] S Nu 14:11

1:1 *A prophecy: The word of the LORD.* See Zec 9:1 and note; 12:1; see also Hab 1:1 and note. *word of the LORD.* See Hos 1:1 and note.
1:2 *loved you.* The Lord's reassuring word to his disheartened people.
1:3 *Esau I have hated.* If God's people doubt his covenant love, they should consider the contrast between God's ways with them and his ways with Jacob's (Israel's) brother, Esau (Edom). Paul explains God's love for Jacob and hatred for Esau on the basis of election (see Ro 9:10–13 and note on 9:13). God chose Jacob, not Esau. For the intended sense of "loved" and "hated" here, see Ge 29:31–33; Lk 14:26 and note. *wasteland.* Malachi's words about Edom echo those of the earlier prophets (see Am 1:11–12; Isa 34:5–15; Jer 49:7–22; Eze 25:12–14; 35:1–15; Obadiah). Between c. 550 and 400 BC the Nabatean Arabs gradually forced the Edomites from their homeland.
1:4 *Edom may say.* Her proud self-reliance has not assured her security and will not secure her future (cf. Jer 49:16).
1:5 *Great … Israel.* When she sees the ultimate fate of Edom, doubting Israel will acknowledge that the Lord is the great Ruler over all the nations (see Ps 47:2; 96:10; 97:1,9; see also 99:1–3 and notes).
1:6—2:9 The Lord rebukes the priests for unacceptable worship.
1:6 *son honors his father.* Cf. Isa 1:2–3. *priests who show contempt for my name.* Contrast 2:5; cf. Isa 1:4.
1:7 *food.* The animal offerings (see v. 12; Lev 21:8,21). *defiled you.* By offering defiled sacrifices they defile the Lord himself. *the LORD's table.* The altar (see v. 12; see also v. 8; Eze 44:16 and notes). Since the priests ate from the sacrifices, the altar was also the table from which they got their food. *contemptible.* As the priests considered the Lord's altar and its sacrifices (v. 12) contemptible, so the Lord would cause the priests to be considered contemptible by the people (see 2:9 and note).
1:8 *blind … lame.* Animals with defects or serious flaws were unacceptable as sacrifices (see Lev 1:3 and note; Dt 15:21). God desires the best. *governor.* Probably the Persian governor.
1:10 *shut the temple doors.* Better no sacrifices at all than sacrifices offered with contempt (see Isa 1:11–15 and note).
1:11 *great among the nations.* Cf. v. 14. God's judgment on Edom (v. 5) and other nations demonstrates his superiority over their gods, and it ultimately will evoke their recognition of him (see Zep 2:11; 3:9 and note). *incense and pure offerings.* Cf. the acceptable offerings presented by foreigners in Isa 56:6–7; 60:7. Some interpreters understand "incense" to mean "prayer" (cf. Rev 5:8) and "offerings" to mean "praise" (cf. Heb 13:15 and note).
1:12 *defiled … contemptible.* See v. 7 and note.
1:13 *sniff at it contemptuously.* Cf. the behavior of Eli's sons in 1Sa 2:15–17. *injured … diseased.* See v. 8 and note.

sacrifices,[o] should I accept them from your hands?"[p] says the LORD. 14 "Cursed is the cheat who has an acceptable male in his flock and vows to give it, but then sacrifices a blemished animal[q] to the Lord. For I am a great king,[r]" says the LORD Almighty,[s] "and my name is to be feared[t] among the nations.[u]

Additional Warning to the Priests

2 "And now, you priests, this warning is for you.[v] 2 If you do not listen,[w] and if you do not resolve to honor[x] my name," says the LORD Almighty, "I will send a curse[y] on you, and I will curse your blessings.[z] Yes, I have already cursed them, because you have not resolved to honor me.

3 "Because of you I will rebuke your descendants[a]; I will smear on your faces the dung[a] from your festival sacrifices, and you will be carried off with it.[b] 4 And you will know that I have sent you this warning so that my covenant with Levi[c] may continue," says the LORD Almighty. 5 "My covenant was with him, a covenant[d] of life and peace,[e] and I gave them to him; this called for reverence[f] and he revered me and stood in awe of my name. 6 True instruction[g] was in his mouth and nothing false was found on his lips. He walked[h] with me in peace[i] and uprightness,[j] and turned many from sin.[k]

7 "For the lips of a priest[l] ought to preserve knowledge, because he is the messenger[m] of the LORD Almighty and people seek instruction from his mouth.[n] 8 But you have turned from the way[o] and by your teaching have caused many to stumble;[p] you have violated the covenant[q] with Levi,"[r] says the LORD Almighty. 9 "So I have caused you to be despised[s] and humiliated[t] before all the people, because you have not followed my ways but have shown partiality[u] in matters of the law."[v]

Breaking Covenant Through Divorce

10 Do we not all have one Father[b]?[w] Did not one God create us?[x] Why do we profane the covenant[y] of our ancestors by being unfaithful[z] to one another?

11 Judah has been unfaithful. A detestable[a] thing has been committed in Israel and in Jerusalem: Judah has desecrated the sanctuary the LORD loves[b] by marrying[c] women who worship a foreign god.[d] 12 As for the man who does this, whoever he may be, may the LORD remove[e] him from the tents of Jacob[c][f]—even though he brings an offering[g] to the LORD Almighty.

[a] 3 Or *will blight your grain* [b] 10 Or *father*
[c] 12 Or *12 May the LORD remove from the tents of Jacob anyone who gives testimony in behalf of the man who does this*

1:13 [o] S ver 10 [p] S Dt 15:21 **1:14** [q] Ex 12:5; S Lev 22:18-21 [r] Ps 95:3; S Ob 1:21; 1Ti 6:15 [s] Jer 46:18 [t] S Dt 28:58 [u] Ps 72:8-11 **2:1** [v] ver 7 **2:2** [w] Jer 13:17 [x] Mt 15:7-9; Jn 5:23; 1Ti 6:16; Rev 5:12-13 [y] S Dt 11:26; S 28:20 [z] Nu 6:23-27 **2:3** [a] S Ex 29:14; S Lev 4:11; S Job 9:31 [b] 1Ki 14:10 **2:4** [c] S Nu 3:12 **2:5** [d] Dt 33:9; Ps 25:10; 103:18; S Mt 26:28; S Lk 22:20; Heb 7:22 [e] S Nu 25:12 [f] S Dt 14:23; S 28:58; Ps 119:161; Heb 12:28 **2:6** [g] S Dt 33:10 [h] S Ge 5:22 [i] Lk 2:14; S Jn 14:27; Gal 5:22 [j] S Ps 25:21 [k] S Ro 11:14; Jas 5:19-20 **2:7** [l] S Jer 18:18 [m] S Nu 27:21; S 2Ch 36:15; Mt 11:10; Mk 1:2 [n] S Lev 10:11; S 2Ch 17:7 **2:8** [o] S Ex 32:8; Jer 2:8 [p] S Jer 18:15 [q] Jer 33:21; S Eze 22:26 [r] S Hos 4:6 **2:9** [s] S 1Sa 2:30; S Ps 22:6; S Jer 51:37 [t] S Ps 35:4; Jer 3:25; Ac 8:32-33 [u] S Ex 18:16; S Lev 19:15; Ac 10:34; Ro 2:11 [v] S 1Sa 2:17 **2:10** [w] S Ex 4:22; Mt 5:16; 6:4, 18; Lk 11:2; 1Co 8:6 [x] S Job 4:17; Isa 43:1 [y] Ex 19:5; S 2Ki 17:15; Jer 31:32 [z] S Zep 3:3-4 **2:11** [a] S Isa 1:13; S 48:8 [b] S Dt 4:37 [c] S Ne 13:23 [d] S Ex 34:16; Jer 3:7-9 **2:12** [e] S 1Sa 2:30-33; S Eze 24:21 [f] S Nu 24:5; 2Sa 20:1 [g] S Mal 1:10

1:14 *vows ... a blemished animal.* An animal sacrificed in fulfillment of a vow had to be a male without defect or blemish (see Lev 22:18–23). *great king.* See Zec 14:9 and note. *my name ... feared.* More than the governor of v. 8 (see v. 11 and note).

2:2 *curse your blessings.* It was the function of the priests to pronounce God's blessing on the people (see Nu 6:23–27), but their blessings will become curses so that their uniquely priestly function will be worse than useless.

2:3 *Because of you.* Because of what you have done. *smear on your faces.* To disgrace you (see Na 3:6).

2:4 *Levi.* The priests were chosen from the tribe of Levi (see Dt 21:5 and note).

2:5 *covenant of life and peace.* An allusion to the covenant with Phinehas, Aaron's grandson, in Nu 25:10–13 (see note on Nu 25:11). Phinehas defended God's honor by killing two offenders involved in the idolatry and immorality connected with the Baal of Peor (Nu 25:1–7). *he revered me.* Phinehas showed this by his zeal for God (see Nu 25:13).

2:6–7 *instruction.* Priests were responsible to teach the law of Moses (see Lev 10:11; see also notes on Zep 3:4; Hag 2:11).

2:6 *peace and uprightness.* Linked together also in Ps 37:37, but here "walked with me in peace and uprightness" probably refers to covenant loyalty.

2:7 *messenger.* As teacher of the law and as one through whom people could inquire of God (see notes on 3:1; Hag 1:13).

2:8 *violated the covenant.* By unfaithful teaching, but also, it seems, by intermarriage with pagan foreigners (see Ezr 9:1 and note; 10:18–22; Ne 13:27–29). *with Levi.* See v. 4 and note on v. 5.

2:9 *despised.* In Hebrew the same word that is translated "contemptible" in 1:7,12 (see note on 1:7). *shown partiality.* Forbidden in Lev 19:15. The priests were to be like God in this respect (see Dt 10:17).

2:10–16 Malachi rebukes the people—in a passage framed by references to being "unfaithful." Two examples of their unfaithfulness are specifically mentioned: marrying pagan women and divorce.

2:10 *one Father.* See Isa 63:16. *create us.* As his special people (see Isa 43:1 and note). *covenant of our ancestors.* The covenant God had made with their ancestors at Mount Sinai. *being unfaithful.* The people could not even trust their own fellow Israelites or the national leaders—like the priests (see v. 16).

2:11 *women who worship a foreign god.* Pagan women. Such marriages were strictly forbidden in the covenant law, not for ethnic or cultural reasons but because they would lead to apostasy (see Ex 34:15–16; Dt 7:2–5 and notes; Jos 23:12–13 and note on 23:12). Ezra and Nehemiah both wrestled with this problem (see note on v. 8).

2:12 The alternative given in the NIV text note (particularly "gives testimony") is supported, e.g., by the use of the same Hebrew verb in Ge 30:33; Dt 5:20; 1Sa 12:3; 2Sa 1:16; Isa 3:9; Jer 14:7. On this reading, the one to be cut off is the one who speaks in defense of the wrongdoer. *tents of Jacob.* A figurative expression for the community (see Jer 30:18).

13 Another thing you do: You flood the
LORD's altar with tears.[h] You weep and
wail[i] because he no longer looks with
favor[j] on your offerings or accepts them
with pleasure from your hands.[k] 14 You
ask,[l] "Why?" It is because the LORD is the
witness[m] between you and the wife of
your youth.[n] You have been unfaithful to
her, though she is your partner, the wife of
your marriage covenant.[o]
15 Has not the one God made you?[p]
You belong to him in body and spirit.
And what does the one God seek? Godly offspring.[a][q] So be on your guard,[r] and
do not be unfaithful[s] to the wife of your
youth.
16 "The man who hates and divorces his
wife,[t]" says the LORD, the God of Israel,
"does violence to the one he should protect,"[b][u] says the LORD Almighty.
So be on your guard,[v] and do not be unfaithful.

Breaking Covenant Through Injustice

17 You have wearied[w] the LORD with your
words.
"How have we wearied him?" you ask.[x]
By saying, "All who do evil are good in
the eyes of the LORD, and he is pleased[y]
with them" or "Where is the God of justice?[z]"

3 "I will send my messenger,[a] who will
prepare the way before me.[b] Then
suddenly the Lord[c] you are seeking will
come to his temple; the messenger of the
covenant,[d] whom you desire,[e] will come,"
says the LORD Almighty.
2 But who can endure[f] the day of his
coming?[g] Who can stand[h] when he appears? For he will be like a refiner's fire[i]
or a launderer's soap.[j] 3 He will sit as a refiner and purifier of silver;[k] he will purify[l]
the Levites and refine them like gold and
silver.[m] Then the LORD will have men who
will bring offerings in righteousness,[n] 4 and
the offerings[o] of Judah and Jerusalem will
be acceptable to the LORD, as in days gone
by, as in former years.[p]
5 "So I will come to put you on trial. I
will be quick to testify against sorcerers,[q]
adulterers[r] and perjurers,[s] against those
who defraud laborers of their wages,[t] who
oppress the widows[u] and the fatherless,
and deprive the foreigners[v] among you of
justice, but do not fear[w] me," says the LORD
Almighty.

Breaking Covenant by Withholding Tithes

6 "I the LORD do not change.[x] So you, the
descendants of Jacob, are not destroyed.[y]

[a] *15* The meaning of the Hebrew for the first part of this verse is uncertain. [b] *16* Or *"I hate divorce," says the LORD, the God of Israel, "because the man who divorces his wife covers his garment with violence,"*

2:13 [h] S Jer 11:11 [i] Ps 39:12 [j] Ps 66:18; Jer 14:12 [k] Isa 58:2 **2:14** [l] S Mal 1:2 [m] S Ge 21:30; S Jos 24:22 [n] S Pr 5:18 [o] S Eze 16:8; Heb 13:4 **2:15** [p] S Ge 2:24; Mt 19:4-6 [q] S Dt 14:2; 1Co 7:14 [r] S Dt 4:15 [s] S Isa 54:6; 1Co 7:10; Heb 13:4 **2:16** [t] S Dt 24:1; Mt 5:31-32; 19:4-9; Mk 10:4-5 [u] S Ge 6:11; 34:25; S Pr 4:17; S Isa 58:4 [v] Ps 51:10 **2:17** [w] S Isa 1:14 [x] S Mal 1:2 [y] Ps 5:4 [z] S Ge 18:25; S Job 8:3; S Eze 18:25 **3:1** [a] S Nu 27:21; S 2Ch 36:15 [b] S Isa 40:3; S Mt 3:3; 11:10*; Mk 1:2*; Lk 7:27* [c] Mic 5:2 [d] S Isa 42:6 [e] S 1Sa 9:20 **3:2** [f] S Eze 22:14; Rev 6:17 [g] S Eze 7:7; S Da 7:13; S Joel 2:31; S Mt 16:27; Jas 5:8; 2Pe 3:4; S Rev 1:7 [h] S 1Sa 6:20 [i] S Isa 1:31; S 30:30; S Zec 13:9; Mt 3:10-12 [j] S Job 9:30 **3:3** [k] S Da 12:10; S 1Co 3:13 [l] S 1Ch 23:28; S Isa 1:25 [m] S Job 28:1; S Ps 12:6; 1Pe 1:7; Rev 3:18 [n] S Ps 132:9 **3:4** [o] 2Ch 7:12; Ps 51:19; Mal 1:11 [p] S 2Ch 7:3; S Eze 20:40 **3:5** [q] S Ex 7:11; S Isa 47:9 [r] Ex 20:14; Jas 2:11; 2Pe 2:12-14 [s] Lev 19:11-12; S Jer 7:9 [t] S Lev 19:13; Jas 5:4 [u] S Ex 22:22 [v] S Ex 22:21; S Dt 24:19; S Eze 22:7 [w] S Dt 31:12; S Isa 1:2 **3:6** [x] S Nu 23:19; S Heb 7:21; Jas 1:17 [y] S Job 34:15; S Hos 11:9

2:13 *weep and wail.* Because the Lord does not respond to their sacrifices with blessing, they add wailing to their prayers.

2:14 *witness … marriage covenant.* Marriage was a covenant (see Pr 2:17; Eze 16:8 and notes), and covenants were affirmed before witnesses (see notes on Dt 30:19; 1Sa 20:23; Isa 8:1–2).

2:15 *one God.* See Ex 20:3; Dt 4:35; 6:4 and notes. *Godly offspring.* Marriage "sanctifies" the children (see 1Co 7:14 and note). But see NIV text note.

2:16 *do not be unfaithful.* See note on vv. 10–16; see also v. 10 and note.

2:17—4:6 The second half of Malachi's prophecy speaks of God's coming to his people. They had given up on God (2:17) and had grown religiously cynical and morally corrupt. So God's coming will mean judgment and purification, as well as redemption.

2:17 *wearied the LORD with your words.* In Isa 43:24 Israel's sins had wearied God. *All who do evil are good.* Such was the depth of their cynicism. *Where is … justice?* Cf. the sarcastic taunts of Isa 5:19.

3:1 *my messenger.* The Hebrew for these words is *mal'aki* (see NIV text note on 1:1); it is normally used of a priest or prophet (see Hag 1:13 and note). These words are fulfilled in John the Baptist (see Mt 11:7–10; Mk 1:2–4; Lk 1:76). *who will prepare the way.* When the Lord comes, it will be to purify (v. 3) and judge (v. 5), but he will mercifully send one before him to prepare his people (see 4:5–6; Isa 40:3 and notes). *the Lord you are seeking … whom you desire, will come.* See Hag 2:7 and note. *messenger of the covenant.* The Messiah, who as the Lord's representative will confirm and establish the covenant (see note on Isa 42:6).

3:2 *day of his coming.* The day of the Lord (see 4:1; see also Isa 2:11,17,20; Joel 1:15 and notes). Malachi announces the Lord's coming to complete God's work in history, especially the work he outlines in the rest of his book. His word is fulfilled in the accomplishments of the Messiah. *Who can stand … ?* Those who desire the Lord's coming must know that clean hands and a pure heart are required (see Ps 24:3–4 and note on 24:4; Isa 33:14–15). *refiner's fire.* See Isa 1:25; Zec 13:8–9 and notes. *launderer's soap.* See Isa 7:3 and note. White clothes signified purity (cf. Mk 9:3; Rev 3:5).

3:3 *sit as a refiner and purifier.* See Ps 12:6 and note. *purify the Levites.* Those who are supposed to be "messengers" of the Lord and who serve at the altar will be purged of their sins and unfaithfulness—such as those the Lord has rebuked in 1:6—2:9.

3:4 *be acceptable.* See 1:8 and note. *days gone by.* Probably the time of Moses and Phinehas (see note on 2:5).

3:5 When he comes, the Lord will both purify the Levites (vv. 3–4) and judge the people. *sorcerers.* Common in the ancient Near East (see Ex 7:11; Dt 18:10 and note on 18:9).

3:6 *do not change.* See Jas 1:17. Contrary to what many in Malachi's day were thinking, God remains faithful to his covenant. *not destroyed.* In contrast to Edom (1:3–5) and in spite of Israel's history of unfaithfulness.

7 Ever since the time of your ancestors you
have turned away[z] from my decrees and
have not kept them. Return[a] to me, and I
will return to you,"[b] says the LORD Almighty.
"But you ask,[c] 'How are we to return?'
8 "Will a mere mortal rob[d] God? Yet you
rob me.
"But you ask, 'How are we robbing you?'
"In tithes[e] and offerings. 9 You are under
a curse[f]—your whole nation—because
you are robbing me. 10 Bring the whole
tithe[g] into the storehouse,[h] that there may
be food in my house. Test me in this," says
the LORD Almighty, "and see if I will not
throw open the floodgates[i] of heaven and
pour out[j] so much blessing[k] that there will
not be room enough to store it.[l] 11 I will
prevent pests from devouring[m] your crops,
and the vines in your fields will not drop
their fruit before it is ripe,[n]" says the LORD
Almighty. 12 "Then all the nations will call
you blessed,[o] for yours will be a delightful
land,"[p] says the LORD Almighty.[q]

Israel Speaks Arrogantly Against God

13 "You have spoken arrogantly[r] against
me," says the LORD.
"Yet you ask,[s] 'What have we said
against you?'
14 "You have said, 'It is futile[t] to serve[u]
God. What do we gain by carrying out his
requirements[v] and going about like mourners[w] before the LORD Almighty? 15 But now
we call the arrogant[x] blessed. Certainly evildoers[y] prosper,[z] and even when they put
God to the test, they get away with it.' "

3:7 [z] S Ex 32:8; S Jer 7:26; Ac 7:51 [a] S Isa 44:22; S Eze 18:32 [b] S Zec 1:3; Jas 4:8 [c] S Mal 1:2 **3:8** [d] S Zec 5:3 [e] S Lev 27:30; Nu 18:21; S Ne 13:10-12; Lk 18:12 **3:9** [f] S Dt 11:26; 28:15-68; S Zec 5:3 **3:10** [g] S Ex 22:29 [h] S Ne 13:12 [i] S 2Ki 7:2 [j] Isa 44:3 [k] S Lev 25:21; S Joel 2:14; 2Co 9:8-11 [l] S Joel 2:24 **3:11** [m] S Ex 10:15; S Dt 28:39 [n] S Ex 23:26 **3:12** [o] S Dt 28:3-12; Isa 61:9 [p] S Isa 62:4; S Eze 20:6 [q] S 2Ch 31:10 **3:13** [r] Mal 2:17 [s] S Mal 1:2 **3:14** [t] Ps 73:13; S Isa 57:10 [u] Ps 100:2; Jn 12:26; Ro 12:11 [v] S Jos 22:5; S Isa 1:14 [w] Isa 58:3 **3:15** [x] S Ps 119:21 [y] Ps 14:1; 36:1-2; Jer 7:10 [z] S Job 21:7 **3:16** [a] S Ps 34:15

The Faithful Remnant

16 Then those who feared the LORD
talked with each other, and the LORD listened and heard.[a] A scroll[b] of remembrance was written in his presence concerning those who feared[c] the LORD and
honored his name.
17 "On the day when I act," says the LORD
Almighty, "they will be my[d] treasured possession.[e] I will spare[f] them, just as a father has compassion and spares his son[g]
who serves him. 18 And you will again see
the distinction between the righteous[h] and
the wicked, between those who serve God
and those who do not.[i]

Judgment and Covenant Renewal

4 [a] "Surely the day is coming;[j] it will
burn like a furnace.[k] All the arrogant[l] and every evildoer will be stubble,[m]
and the day that is coming will set them
on fire,[n]" says the LORD Almighty. "Not a
root or a branch[o] will be left to them. 2 But
for you who revere my name,[p] the sun of
righteousness[q] will rise with healing[r] in its
rays. And you will go out and frolic[s] like
well-fed calves. 3 Then you will trample[t]

[a] In Hebrew texts 4:1-6 is numbered 3:19-24.

[b] S Ex 32:32; S Ps 56:8; S 87:6; S Lk 10:20 [c] S Dt 28:58; S 31:12; Ps 33:18; S Pr 1:7; Rev 11:18 **3:17** [d] Isa 43:21 [e] S Ex 8:22; S Dt 7:6; S Ro 8:14; S Titus 2:14 [f] Ne 13:22; Ps 103:13; Isa 26:20; Lk 15:1-32 [g] Ro 8:32 **3:18** [h] S Ge 18:25 [i] Dt 32:4; Mt 25:32-33, 41 **4:1** [j] S Da 7:13; S Joel 2:31; Mt 11:14; Ac 2:20 [k] S Isa 31:9 [l] S Isa 2:12 [m] S Isa 5:24; S Na 1:10 [n] S Isa 1:31 [o] S 2Ki 10:11; S Eze 17:8; S Mt 3:10 **4:2** [p] S Dt 28:58; Ps 61:5; 111:9; Rev 14:1 [q] S Ps 118:27; S Isa 9:2; S 45:8; Lk 1:78; Eph 5:14 [r] S 2Ch 7:14; S Isa 30:26; S Mt 4:23; Rev 22:2 [s] S Isa 35:6 **4:3** [t] S Job 40:12; Ps 18:40-42

3:7 *Return ... and I will return.* If the Lord is to come for Israel's redemption, she must repent (see Zec 1:3 and note).

3:9–10 *curse ... blessing.* See Dt 11:26–28.

3:10 *storehouse.* The treasury rooms of the sanctuary (see 1Ki 7:51; 2Ch 31:11–12; Ne 13:12). *floodgates of heaven.* Elsewhere the idiom refers to abundant provision of food (see 2Ki 7:2,19; Ps 78:23–24 and note on 78:23). *pour out ... blessing.* The promised covenant blessing (see Dt 28:12; cf. Isa 44:3).

3:11 *pests ... drop their fruit.* Examples of the threatened covenant curses (see Dt 28:39–40).

3:12 *call you blessed.* In fulfillment of the promise to Abraham (see Ge 12:2–3; Isa 61:9 and notes).

3:14 *It is futile to serve God.* Because the redemption they longed for had not yet been realized. *like mourners.* In sackcloth and ashes.

3:15 *arrogant.* Evildoers—those who challenge God (see note on Ps 10:11). *blessed.* In their unbelief, the Jews call blessed those whom the godly know to be cursed (see Ps 119:21 and note)—but it is they who will be called blessed if they repent (v. 12). *evildoers prosper ... get away with it.* The psalmist struggled with the prosperity of the wicked in Ps 73:3,9–12 (see also Hab 1:2–4 and notes).

3:16 *those who feared the LORD.* Those who had not given way to doubts and cynicism. *talked with each other.* In the face of the widespread complaining against God (vv. 14–15), they sought mutual encouragement in fellowship. *scroll of remembrance.* Analogous to the records of notable deeds kept by earthly rulers (see Est 6:1–3; Isa 4:3; Da 7:10; 12:1). *honored his name.* Contrast the priests (1:12) and many among the people (vv. 14–15; 2:17).

3:17 *my treasured possession.* See note on Ex 19:5. *spare them.* In the day of judgment (see 4:1–2). *who serves him.* Cf. 1:6.

3:18 *you will again see.* As they apparently do not now see—hence their cynicism. *the righteous and the wicked.* See 2:17 and note.

4:1 *the day.* The day of the Lord (see v. 5; 3:2 and note). *burn like a furnace.* See 3:2–3; Isa 1:31; 66:15–16 and notes. *arrogant.* See 3:15 and note. *stubble ... fire.* See Isa 47:14 and note; see also John the Baptist's prophecy about the work of Christ in Mt 3:12. *Not a root or a branch.* Nothing of them will be left (see Eze 17:8–9).

4:2 *you who revere my name.* Or "you who fear my name," i.e., you who reverently trust in the Lord and are committed to his will as revealed in his word (see notes on Ge 20:11; Ps 34:8–14; Pr 1:7). *sun of righteousness.* God and his glory are compared with the sun in Isa 60:19 (see note there). Christ is the "rising sun" from heaven (see Lk 1:78–79 and note on 1:78; see also Isa 9:2 and note). *righteousness ... healing.* Salvation and renewal are intended (see Isa 45:8; 46:13; 53:5; Jer 30:17 and notes). *its rays.* Cf. Ps 139:9. *like well-fed calves.* Frisky young calves often frolic about when released from confinement.

4:3 *trample ... the wicked.* As one treads the winepress (see Isa 63:2–3 and notes).

on the wicked; they will be ashes[u] under
the soles of your feet on the day when I
act," says the LORD Almighty.
4 "Remember the law[v] of my servant Moses, the decrees and laws I gave him at
Horeb[w] for all Israel.[x]
5 "See, I will send the prophet Elijah[y] to
you before that great and dreadful day of
the LORD comes.[z] 6 He will turn the hearts
of the parents to their children,[a] and the
hearts of the children to their parents; or
else I will come and strike[b] the land with
total destruction."[c]

4:3 [u]Eze 28:18 **4:4** [v]S Dt 28:61; S Ps 147:19; Mt 5:17; 7:12; Ro 2:13; 4:15; Gal 3:24 [w]S Ex 3:1 [x]S Ex 20:1 **4:5** [y]S 1Ki 17:1; S Mt 11:14; 16:14 [z]S Joel 2:31 **4:6** [a]Lk 1:17 [b]S Isa 11:4; Rev 19:15 [c]S Dt 11:26; S 13:15; S Jos 6:17; S 23:15; S Zec 5:3

4:4 *Remember the law.* A final exhortation to those who impatiently wait for the Lord's coming. *my servant Moses.* See Ex 14:31; Dt 34:5 and notes. *Horeb.* Mount Sinai (see Ex 3:1 and note).

4:5 See 3:1 and note. *Elijah.* As Elijah came before Elisha (whose ministry was one of judgment and redemption), so "Elijah" will be sent to prepare God's people for the Lord's coming. John the Baptist ministered "in the spirit and power of Elijah" (see Lk 1:17 and note; see also Mt 11:13 – 14; 17:12 – 13; Mk 9:11 – 13 and note on 9:13). And some feel that Elijah may also be one of the two witnesses in Rev 11:3 (see note there). *great and dreadful day.* See v. 1; see also 3:2; Joel 2:11 and note.

4:6 *turn the hearts.* Cf. Ge 18:19. According to Lk 1:17 John the Baptist sought to accomplish this. *total destruction.* If Israel does not repent, she will be dealt with as God had dealt with Edom (see 1:3 – 4; Isa 34:5).

FROM MALACHI TO CHRIST

The Persian Period
450–330 BC

For about 200 years after Nehemiah's time the Persians controlled Judah, but the Jews were allowed to carry on their religious observances and were not interfered with. During this time Judah was ruled by high priests, who answered to the Persian authorities.

The Hellenistic Period
330–166 BC

In the late fourth century BC, Alexander the Great defeated the Persians repeatedly in battle and quickly conquered the eastern Mediterranean region, including Syria, Egypt, Persia and Babylonia. Alexander believed in the superiority of Greek culture and was convinced that it was the one force that could unify the world. Alexander permitted the Jews to observe their laws and even granted them exemption from tribute or tax during their sabbath years. When he built Alexandria in Egypt, he encouraged Jews to live there. The Greek conquest prepared the way for the translation of the Hebrew Old Testament into Greek (Septuagint version), beginning c. 250 BC.

The Hasmonean Period
166–63 BC

When this historical period began, the Jews were being greatly oppressed. The Ptolemies of Egypt had been tolerant of the Jews and their religious practices, but the Seleucid rulers of Syria were determined to force Hellenism on them. Copies of the Scriptures were ordered destroyed, and laws were enforced banning circumcision and other Jewish practices. The oppressed Jews revolted, led by Judas Maccabeus.

The Roman Period
Begins in 63 BC

In the year 63 BC, Pompey, the Roman general, captured Jerusalem, and the provinces in the Holy Land became subject to Rome. The Romans ruled at times through local vassal kings and at other times through Roman governors who were appointed by the emperors. Herod the Great was ruler of that whole region at the time of Jesus' birth.

Rule of Alexander the Great

Rule of the Ptolemies of Egypt

Rule of the Seleucids of Syria

Hasmonean Dynasty

Herod the Great rules as king; subject to Rome

410, **400 BC**, 390, 380, 370, 360, 350, 340, 330, 320, 310, **300**, 290, 280, 270, 260, 250, 240, 230, 220, 210, **200**, 190, 180, 170, 160, 150, 140, 130, 120, 110, **100**, 90, 80, 70, 60, 50, 40, 30, 20, 10, 10, 20, AD 30

Malachi c. 430 BC

334–323 Alexander the Great conquers the East

330–328 Alexander's years of power

320 Ptolemy (I) Soter conquers Jerusalem

311 Seleucus conquers Babylon; Seleucid dynasty begins

226 Antiochus (III) of Syria conquers the Holy Land

223–187 Antiochus becomes Seleucid ruler of Syria

198 Antiochus defeats Egypt and gains control of the Holy Land

175–164 Antiochus (IV) Epiphanes rules Syria; Judaism is prohibited

167 Mattathias and his sons rebel against Antiochus; Maccabean revolt begins

166–160 Judas Maccabeus's leadership

160–143 Jonathan is high priest

142–134 Simon becomes high priest; establishes Hasmonean dynasty (see map and essay, pp. 1572 – 1574)

134–104 John Hyrcanus enlarges the independent Jewish state

103 Aristobulus's rule

102–76 Alexander Janneus's rule

75–67 Rule of Salome Alexandra with Hyrcanus II as high priest

66–63 Battle between Aristobulus II and Hyrcanus II

63 Pompey invades the Holy Land; Roman rule begins

63–40 Hyrcanus II governs but is subject to Rome

40–37 Parthians conquer Jerusalem

37 Herod becomes ruler of the Holy Land

19 Herod's temple begun

4 Herod dies; Archelaus succeeds him

THE TIME BETWEEN THE TESTAMENTS

The time between the Testaments was one of ferment and change — a time of the realignment of traditional power blocs and the passing of a Near Eastern cultural tradition that had been dominant for almost 3,000 years.

In Biblical history, the approximately 400 years that separate the time of Nehemiah from the birth of Christ are known as the intertestamental period (c. 433 – 5 BC). Sometimes called the "silent" years because of the absence of prophetic revelation, they were anything but silent in terms of historical significance and cultural change. The events, literature and social forces of these years would shape the world of the NT.

FOREIGN DOMINATION OF ISRAEL (722 BC–AD 135)

OLD TESTAMENT PERIOD	**The Assyrian Empire** (722 – 605 BC)
	The Babylonian Empire (605 – 539 BC)
	The Persian Empire (539 – 334 BC)
INTERTESTAMENTAL PERIOD	**The Macedonian-Greek Empire** (334 – 166 BC) • Alexander the Great (334 – 323 BC) • Ptolemaic Domination (323 – 198 BC) • Seleucid Domination (198 – 166 BC)
	Jewish Independence (166 – 63 BC) • The Maccabees • The Hasmonean Dynasty
NEW TESTAMENT PERIOD	**The Roman Empire** (63 BC – AD 135) • The Herodian Dynasty • Roman Governors • Destruction of Jerusalem (AD 70) • Second Revolt Ends the Jewish State (AD 135)

History

With the Babylonian exile, Israel ceased to be an independent nation and became a minor territory in a succession of larger empires. Very little is known about the latter years of Persian domination because the Jewish historian Josephus (c. AD 37 – 100), our primary source for the intertestamental period, all but ignores them.

With Alexander the Great's acquisition of the Holy Land (332 BC), a new and more insidious threat to Israel emerged. Alexander was committed to the creation of a world united by Greek language and culture, a policy followed by his successors. This policy, called Hellenization, had a dramatic impact on the Jews.

At Alexander's death (323 BC) the empire he won was divided among his generals. Two of them founded dynasties — the Ptolemies of Egypt and the Seleucids in Syria and Mesopotamia — that would contend for control of the Holy Land for over a century.

The rule of the Ptolemies was considerate of Jewish religious sensitivities, but in 198 BC the Seleucids took control and paved the way for one of the most heroic periods in Jewish history.

The early Seleucid years were largely a continuation of the tolerant rule of the Ptolemies, but Antiochus IV Epiphanes (whose title means "God made manifest" and who ruled 175 – 164 BC) changed that when he attempted to consolidate his fading empire through a policy of radical Hellenization. While a segment of the Jewish aristocracy had already adopted Greek ways, many Jews were outraged.

PALESTINE OF THE **MACCABEES AND HASMONEAN DYNASTY**

- Judea at the beginning of the revolt
- Additions of Jonathan, 160–142 BC
- Additions of Simon, 142–134 BC
- Additions of Hyrcanus I, 134–104 BC
- Additions of Aristobulus I, 104–103 BC
- Additions of Alexander Jannaeus, 103–76 BC
- Kingdom of Alexander Jannaeus

COELE-SYRIA
Sidon
Damascus
PHOENICIA
Tyre
Dan (Antiochia)
Paneas
Cadasa
Seleucia
Hazor
Bascama
Ptolemais
Bethsaida
Gamala
Gennesaret
Taricheae
Dathema
Sea of Galilee
Arbela
Hippus
Mt. Carmel
GALILEE
Philoteria
Sepphoris
Jezreel Valley
Dora
Mediterranean Sea
Strato's Tower
GALAADITIS
Scythopolis
Pella
SAMARIA
Gerasa
Jordan R.
Samaria
Ammathus
Shechem
Apollonia
Mt. Gerizim
Acrabeta
PEREA
Joppa
Alexandrium
Gadora
Arimathea
Apherema
Philadelphia
Lydda
Docus
Jamnia
Gazara
JUDEA
Jericho
Esbus
Azotus
Accaron
Samaga
Jerusalem
Hyrcania
Ascalon
PHILISTIA
Medeba
Herodium
Beth Zur
Machaerus
Marisa
Anthedon
Hebron
Adora
Gaza
En Gedi
Dead Sea
MOABITIS
Gerar
Orda
IDUMEA
Masada
Raphia
Beersheba
Malatha
Rhinocorura
NABATEANS
Wadi of Egypt
Petra

0 10 km.
0 10 miles

Antiochus's atrocities were aimed at the eradication of Jewish religion. He prohibited some of the central elements of Jewish practice, attempted to destroy all copies of the Torah (the Pentateuch) and required offerings to the Greek god Zeus. His crowning outrage was the erection of a statue of Zeus and the sacrificing of a pig in the Jerusalem temple itself.

Opposition to Antiochus was led by Mattathias, an elderly villager from a priestly family, and his five sons: Judas (called "Maccabeus"—probably meaning "hammerer"), Jonathan, Simon, John and Eleazar. Mattathias destroyed a Greek altar established in his village, Modein, and killed Antiochus's emissary. This triggered the Maccabean revolt, a 24-year war (166–142 BC) that resulted in the independence of Judah until the Romans took control in 63 BC.

The victory of Mattathias's family was a hollow one, however. With the death of his last son, Simon, the Hasmonean dynasty they founded soon evolved into an aristocratic, Hellenistic regime sometimes hard to distinguish from that of the Seleucids. During the reign of Simon's son, John Hyrcanus, the orthodox Jews who had supported the Maccabees fell out of favor. With only a few exceptions, the rest of the Hasmoneans supported the Jewish Hellenizers. The Pharisees were actually persecuted by Alexander Jannaeus (103–76 BC).

THE MACCABEAN-HASMONEAN PERIOD

SELEUCID KINGS		JEWISH LEADERS		PTOLEMAIC KINGS	
Seleucus I (Nicator)	321–281			Ptolemy I (Soter)	323–285
Antiochus I (Soter)	281–261				
Antiochus II (Theos)	261–246			Ptolemy II (Philadelphus)	285–246
Seleucus II (Callinicus)	246–225			Ptolemy III (Euergetes)	246–222
Seleucus III (Soter)	225–223			Ptolemy IV (Philopator)	221–205
Antiochus III (the Great)	223–187			Ptolemy V (Epiphanes)	204–180
Seleucus IV (Philopator)	187–175			Ptolemy VI (Philometor)	180–145
Antiochus IV (Epiphanes)	175–163	Mattathias Judas	166 166–160		
Antiochus V (Eupator)	163–162				
Demetrius I (Soter)	162–150	Jonathan	160–143		
Alexander Balas	150–145			Ptolemy VII (Neos Philopator)	145
Demetrius II (Nicator)	145–139	Simon	143–135	Ptolemy VII (Neos Philopator)	145
(Antiochus VI [Epiphanes Dionysus])	145–142			Ptolemy VIII (Euergetes II or Physcon)	145–116
Antiochus VII (Sidetes)	139–129	John Hyrcanus I	135–104		
Demetrius II (Nicator)	129–125				
Antiochus VIII (Grypus)	125/4–113			Ptolemy IX (Soter II or Lathyrus)	116–110
Antiochus IX (Philopator Cyzicenus)	113–111				
Antiochus VIII (Grypus)	111–95	Aristobulus	104–103	Ptolemy X (Alexander)	110–109 108–88
Seleucus VI	95–54	Alexander Jannaeus	103–76		
Antiochus X (Eusebes)	94–83			Ptolemy IX (Soter II or Lathyrus)	88–80
Tigranes, King of Armenia	83–69	Salome Alexandra	76–67	Ptolemy XI (Alexander II)	80 (20 days)
				Ptolemy XII (Philopator Philadelphus Neos Dionysus or Auletes)	80–51
Antiochus XIII (Asiaticus)	69–65	Hyrcanus II Aristobulus	67 (3 months) 67–63	Cleopatra VII	51–30

The Hasmonean dynasty ended when, in 63 BC, an expanding Roman empire intervened in a dynastic clash between the two sons of Jannaeus, Aristobulus II and Hyrcanus II. Pompey, the general who subdued the East for Rome, took Jerusalem after a three-month siege of the temple area, massacring priests in the performance of their duties and entering the Most Holy Place. This sacrilege began Roman rule in a way that Jews could neither forgive nor forget.

Literature

During these unhappy years of oppression and internal strife, the Jewish people produced a sizable body of literature that both recorded and addressed their era. Three of the more significant literary collections are the Septuagint, the Apocrypha and the Dead Sea Scrolls.

Septuagint. Jewish tradition says that 72 scholars, under the sponsorship of Ptolemy Philadelphus (c. 250 BC), were brought together on the island of Pharos, near Alexandria, where they produced a Greek translation of the OT in 72 days. From this tradition the Latin word for 70, "Septuagint," became the name attached to the translation. The Roman numeral for 70, LXX, is used as an abbreviation for it.

Behind that tradition lies the probability that at least the Torah (the five books of Moses) was translated into Greek c. 250 BC for the use of the Greek-speaking Jews of Alexandria. The rest of the OT and some noncanonical books were also included in the LXX before the dawning of the Christian era.

The Septuagint quickly became the Bible of the Jews outside the Holy Land who, like the Alexandrians, no longer spoke Hebrew. It would be difficult to overestimate its influence. It made the Scriptures available both to the Jews who no longer spoke their ancestral language and to the entire Greek-speaking world. It later became the Bible of the early church. Also, its widespread popularity and use contributed to the retention of the Apocrypha by some branches of Christendom.

Apocrypha. Derived from a Greek word that means "hidden," Apocrypha has acquired the meaning "false," but in a technical sense it describes a specific body of writings. This collection consists of a variety of books and additions to canonical books that, with the exception of 2 Esdras (c. AD 90), were written during the intertestamental period. Their recognition as authoritative in Roman and Eastern Christianity is the result of a complex historical process.

The limits of the Hebrew canon of the OT, also accepted by most Protestants today, were very likely established by the dawn of the second century AD. In spite of disagreements among some of the church fathers as to which books were canonical and which were not, the Apocryphal books (which were included in the Septuagint) continued in common use by most Christians until the Reformation. During this period most Protestants decided to follow the original Hebrew canon, while Rome, at the Council of Trent (1546), and more recently at the First Vatican Council (1869–70), affirmed the larger "Alexandrian" canon that includes the Apocrypha.

The Apocryphal books have retained their place primarily through the weight of ecclesiastical authority, without which they would not commend themselves as canonical literature. There is no evidence that Jesus or the apostles ever quoted any Apocryphal works as inspired Scripture. The Jewish community that produced them repudiated them, and the historical surveys in the apostolic sermons recorded in Acts completely ignore the period they cover. Even the sober, historical account of 1 Maccabees is tarnished by errors and anachronisms.

There is nothing of theological value in the Apocryphal books that cannot be duplicated in canonical Scripture. Nonetheless, this body of literature does provide a valuable source of information for the study of the intertestamental period.

Dead Sea Scrolls. In the spring of 1947 Arab shepherds chanced upon a cave in the hills overlooking the southwestern shore of the Dead Sea that contained what has been called the greatest manuscript discovery of modern times. The documents and fragments of documents found in a group of such caves, dubbed the "Dead Sea Scrolls," included OT books, a few books of the Apocrypha, apocalyptic works, pseudepigrapha (books that purport to be the work of ancient heroes of the faith) and a number of books peculiar to the sect that produced them.

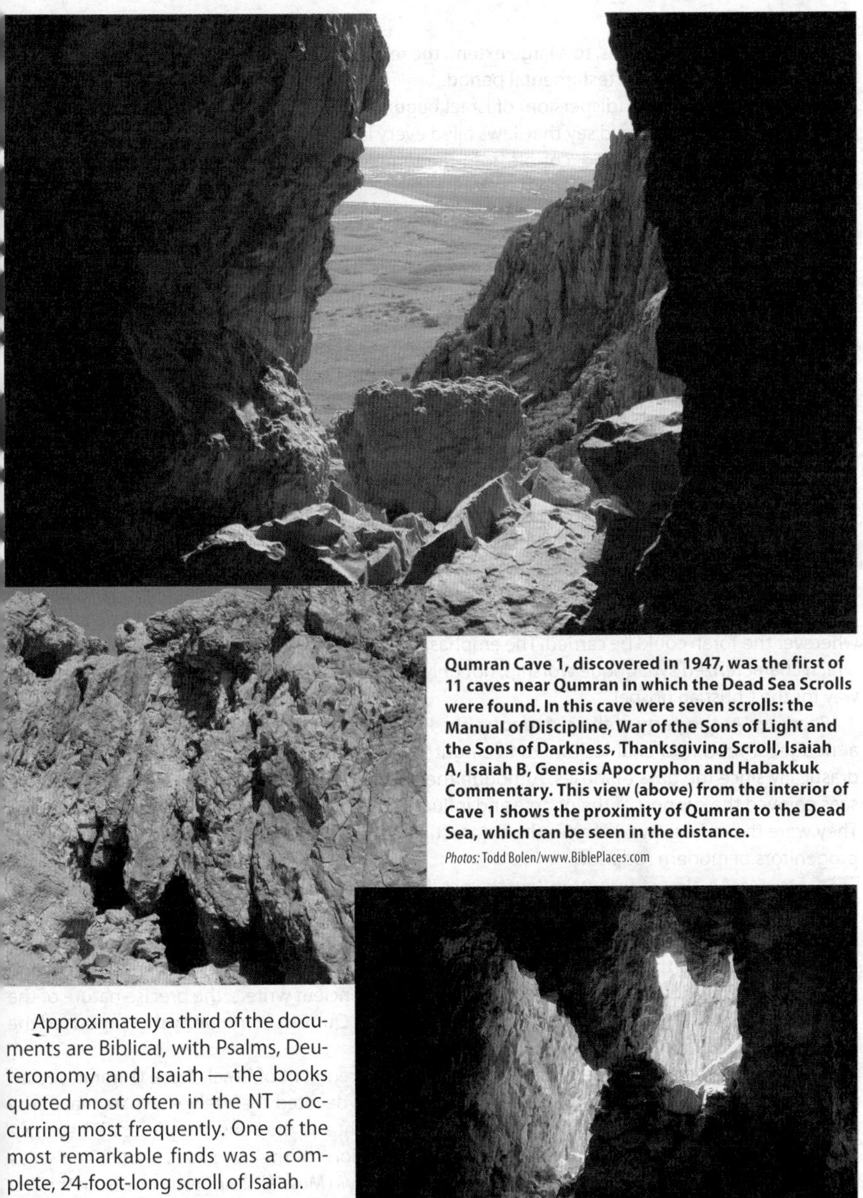

Qumran Cave 1, discovered in 1947, was the first of 11 caves near Qumran in which the Dead Sea Scrolls were found. In this cave were seven scrolls: the Manual of Discipline, War of the Sons of Light and the Sons of Darkness, Thanksgiving Scroll, Isaiah A, Isaiah B, Genesis Apocryphon and Habakkuk Commentary. This view (above) from the interior of Cave 1 shows the proximity of Qumran to the Dead Sea, which can be seen in the distance.

Photos: Todd Bolen/www.BiblePlaces.com

Approximately a third of the documents are Biblical, with Psalms, Deuteronomy and Isaiah — the books quoted most often in the NT — occurring most frequently. One of the most remarkable finds was a complete, 24-foot-long scroll of Isaiah.

The Scrolls have made a significant contribution to the quest for a form of the OT texts most accurately reflecting the original manuscripts; they provide copies more than 1,000 years closer to the time of originals than were previously known. The understanding of Biblical Hebrew and Aramaic and knowledge of the development of Judaism between the Testaments have been increased significantly. Of great importance to readers of the Bible is the demonstration of the care with which OT texts were copied, thus providing objective evidence for the extraordinary reliability of those texts.

Social Developments

The Judaism of Jesus' day was, to a large extent, the result of changes that came about in response to the pressures of the intertestamental period.

Diaspora. The Diaspora (dispersion) of Israel begun in the exile accelerated during these years until a writer of the day could say that Jews filled every land and sea.

Jews outside the Holy Land, cut off from the temple, concentrated their religious life in the study of the Torah and the life of the synagogue (see below). The missionaries of the early church began their Gentile ministries among the Diaspora, using the Greek translation of the OT (the Septuagint).

Sadducees. In the Holy Land, the Greek world made its greatest impact through the party of the Sadducees. Made up of aristocrats, it became the temple party. Because of their position, the Sadducees had a vested interest in the status quo.

Relatively few in number, they wielded disproportionate political power and controlled the high priesthood. They rejected all religious writings except the Torah, as well as any doctrine (such as resurrection from the dead) not found in those five books.

Synagogue. During the Babylonian exile, Israel was cut off from the temple, divested of nationhood and surrounded by pagan religious practices. The nation's faith was threatened. Under these circumstances, the exiles turned their religious focus from what they had lost to what they retained — the Torah and the belief that they were God's people. They concentrated on the law rather than nationhood, on personal piety rather than sacramental rectitude and on prayer as an acceptable replacement for the sacrifices denied to them.

When they returned from the exile, they brought with them this new form of religious expression, as well as the synagogue (its center), and Judaism became a faith that could be practiced wherever the Torah could be carried. The emphases on personal piety and a relationship with God, which characterized synagogue worship, not only helped preserve Judaism but also prepared the way for the Christian gospel.

Pharisees. As the party of the synagogue, the Pharisees strove to reinterpret the law. They built a "hedge" around it to enable Jews to live righteously before God in a world that had changed drastically since the days of Moses. Although they were comparatively few in number, the Pharisees enjoyed the support of the people and influenced popular opinion as well as national policy. They were the only party to survive the destruction of the temple in AD 70 and were the spiritual progenitors of modern Judaism.

Essenes. An almost forgotten Jewish sect (but referred to by Philo and Josephus) until the discovery of the Dead Sea Scrolls, the Essenes were a small, separatist group that grew out of the conflicts of the Maccabean age. Like the Pharisees, they stressed strict legal observance, but they considered the temple priesthood corrupt and rejected much of the temple ritual and sacrificial system. Though they are mentioned by several ancient writers, the precise nature of the Essenes is still not certain, though it is widely held that the Qumran community that produced the Dead Sea Scrolls was probably an Essene group.

Because they were convinced that they were the true remnant of Israel, these Qumran sectarians had separated themselves from Judaism at large and devoted themselves to personal purity and preparation for the final war between the "Sons of Light and the Sons of Darkness." They practiced an apocalyptic faith, looking back to the contributions of their previous leader, known as "Teacher of Righteousness," and forward to the coming of two Messiahs: a priestly one from the line of Aaron and a royal one from the line of David. In the Jewish War of AD 66 – 73, the community at Qumran was destroyed, and the Essenes dropped from history.

Attempts have been made to equate aspects of the beliefs of the Qumran community with the origins of Christianity. Some have seen a prototype of Jesus in their "Teacher of Righteousness," and John the Baptist's apocalyptic message and desert lifestyle have parallels with those at Qumran. Most of these parallels, however, are superficial, and there is no hard evidence of direct contact between either Jesus or John and the Qumran community.

NEW TESTAMENT CHRONOLOGY

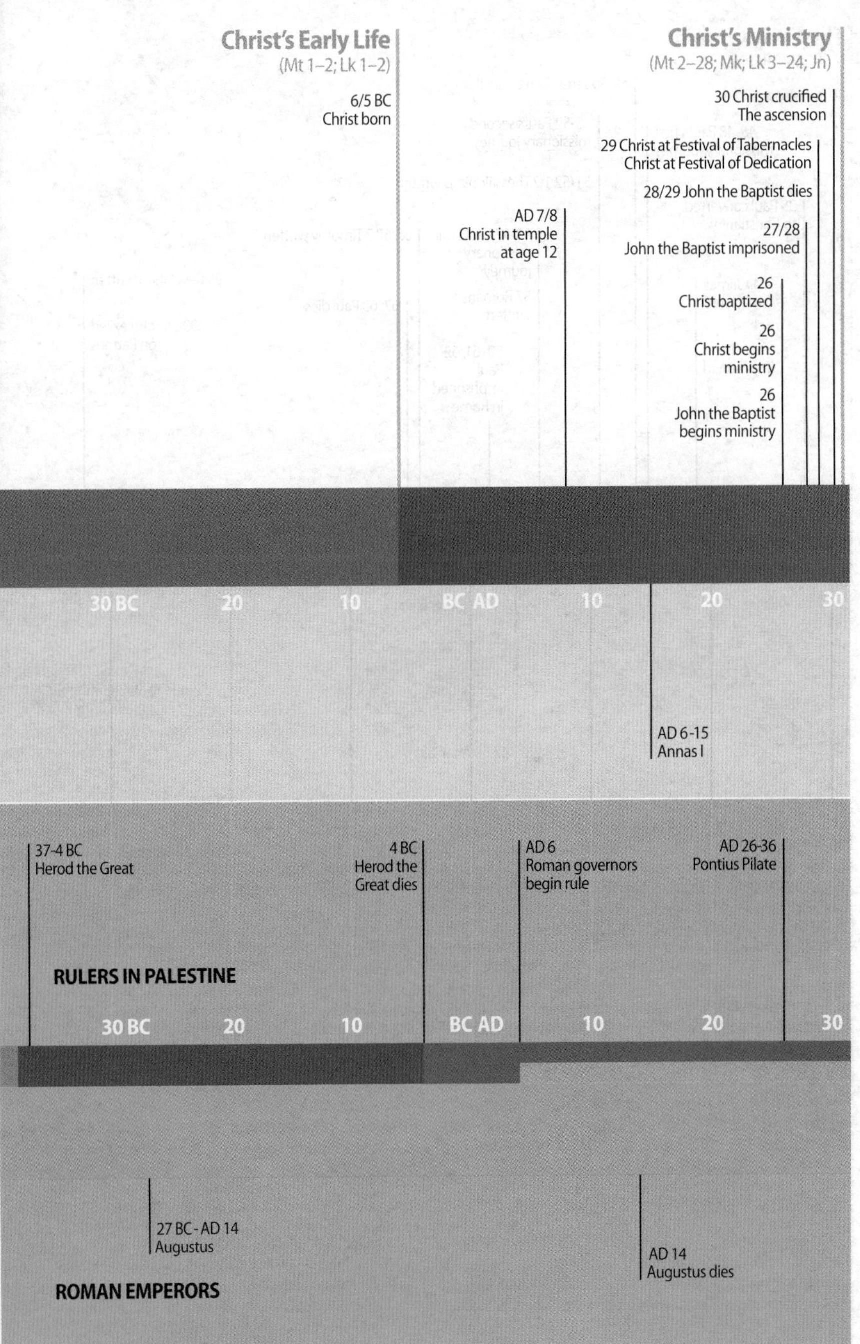

Christ's Early Life
(Mt 1–2; Lk 1–2)
6/5 BC
Christ born
Christ's Ministry
(Mt 2–28; Mk; Lk 3–24; Jn)
30 Christ crucified
The ascension
29 Christ at Festival of Tabernacles
Christ at Festival of Dedication
28/29 John the Baptist dies
AD 7/8
Christ in temple
at age 12
27/28
John the Baptist imprisoned
26
Christ baptized
26
Christ begins
ministry
26
John the Baptist
begins ministry
30 BC
20
10
BC AD
10
20
30
AD 6-15
Annas I
37-4 BC
Herod the Great
4 BC
Herod the
Great dies
AD 6
Roman governors
begin rule
AD 26-36
Pontius Pilate
RULERS IN PALESTINE
30 BC
20
10
BC AD
10
20
30
27 BC - AD 14
Augustus
AD 14
Augustus dies
ROMAN EMPERORS

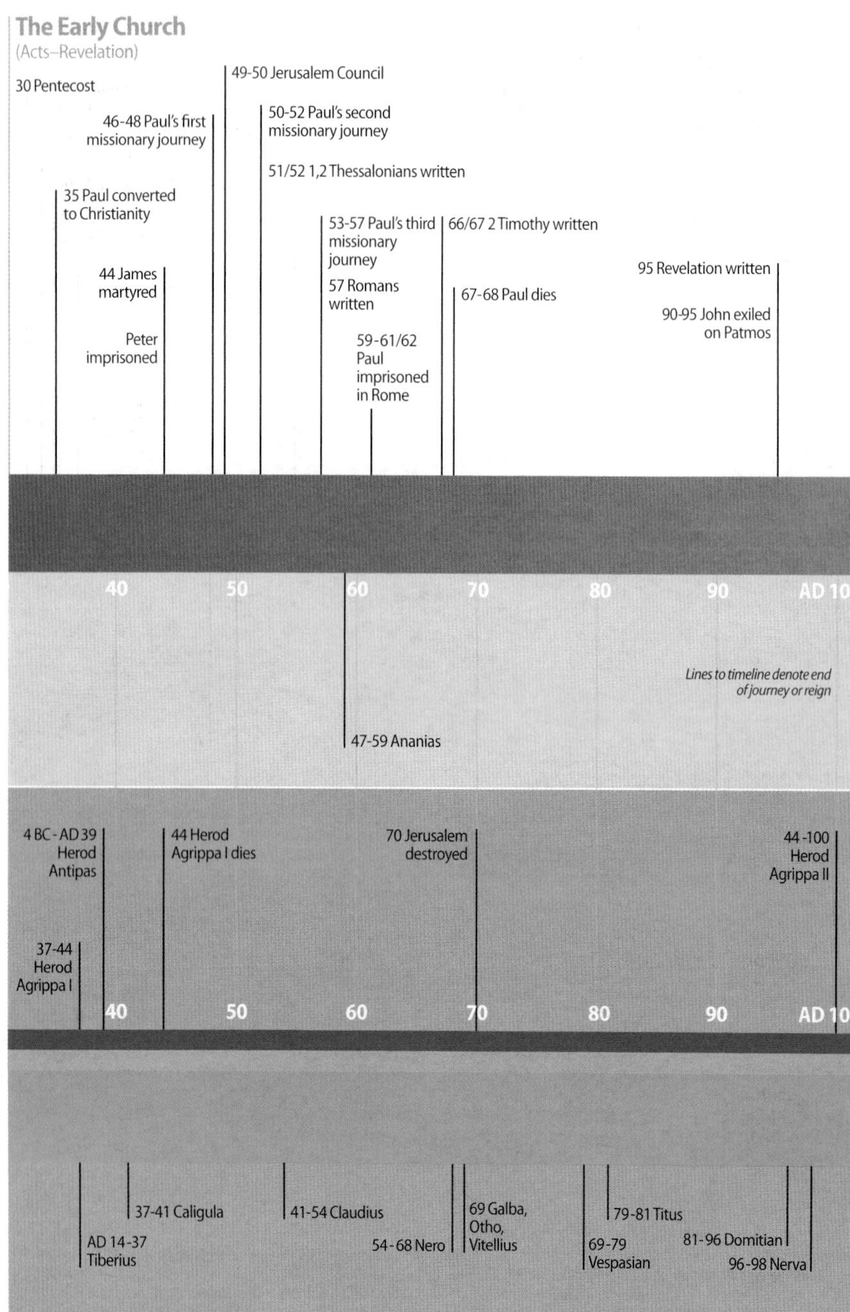
The Early Church
(Acts–Revelation)
30 Pentecost
35 Paul converted to Christianity
44 James martyred
Peter imprisoned
46-48 Paul's first missionary journey
49-50 Jerusalem Council
50-52 Paul's second missionary journey
51/52 1,2 Thessalonians written
53-57 Paul's third missionary journey
57 Romans written
59-61/62 Paul imprisoned in Rome
66/67 2 Timothy written
67-68 Paul dies
95 Revelation written
90-95 John exiled on Patmos
40
50
60
70
80
90
AD 100
Lines to timeline denote end of journey or reign
47-59 Ananias
4 BC - AD 39 Herod Antipas
37-44 Herod Agrippa I
44 Herod Agrippa I dies
70 Jerusalem destroyed
44 -100 Herod Agrippa II
AD 14-37 Tiberius
37-41 Caligula
41-54 Claudius
54 - 68 Nero
69 Galba, Otho, Vitellius
69-79 Vespasian
79-81 Titus
81-96 Domitian
96-98 Nerva

THE NEW TESTAMENT

THE GOSPELS AND THE EARLY CHURCH

The first four books of the NT are known as the Gospels, from the Greek word for "good news." The good news is that God's plan of salvation has come to fulfillment in the life, death and resurrection of Jesus Christ (see note on Lk 24:44). Matthew, Mark and Luke are often called the Synoptic Gospels because they are written from a similar viewpoint (see essay, pp. 1582–1583). These texts are historical narratives relating the story of the life and ministry of Christ. The Gospel of John differs in emphasis from the Synoptics. With a more theological tone, John is concerned with the meaning of Jesus' words, works and identity. The book of Acts is a companion piece written by Luke, picking up where the Gospel narrative ends and telling the story of the early church and the work of the Holy Spirit through the apostles, especially Peter and Paul.

THE SYNOPTIC GOSPELS

FOUR PORTRAITS OF THE ONE JESUS

MATTHEW	MARK	LUKE	JOHN
The Gospel of the Messiah	The Gospel of the suffering Son of God	The Gospel of the Savior for all people	The Gospel of the divine Son who reveals the Father
Most structured	**Most dramatic**	**Most thematic**	**Most theological**

Photo Credits (l to r): The Supper at Emmaus, Champaigne, Philippe de/Musee des Beaux-Arts, Angers, France/Giraudon/The Bridgeman Art Library; Scala/Art Resource, NY; Scala/Art Resource, NY; Erich Lessing/Art Resource, NY

A comparison of the four Gospels reveals that Matthew, Mark and Luke are noticeably similar, while John is quite different. The first three Gospels agree extensively in language, in the material they include, and in the order in which events and sayings from the life of Christ are recorded. (Chronological order does not appear to have been rigidly followed in any of the Gospels, however.) Because of this agreement, these three books are called the Synoptic Gospels (*syn*, "together with"; *optic*, "seeing"; thus "seeing together"). For an example of agreement in content, see Mt 9:2 – 8; Mk 2:3 – 12; Lk 5:18 – 26. An instance of verbatim agreement is found in Mt 10:22a; Mk 13:13a; Lk 21:17. A mathematical comparison shows that 91 percent of Mark's Gospel is contained in Matthew, while 53 percent of Mark is found in Luke. Such agreement raises questions as to the origin of the Synoptic Gospels. Did the authors rely on a common source? Were they interdependent? Questions such

THE SYNOPTICS AND JOHN

SYNOPTIC GOSPELS (MATTHEW, MARK, LUKE)	GOSPEL OF JOHN
1. Emphasize the Galilean setting of the first part of Jesus' ministry	1. Considerable movement between Galilee and Judea
2. Little information given to determine the length of Jesus' ministry; material could fit into a single year	2. Mentions at least three different Passover festivals (2:13; 6:4; 13:1), and so a ministry of 2½ to 3½ years
3. Jesus teaches mostly in parables, short sayings and epigrams	3. Relates long speeches by Jesus, dialogues with his opponents and interviews with individuals
4. Teaching focuses on the kingdom of God; healings and exorcisms demonstrate the power of the kingdom and the dawn of eschatological salvation	4. Teaching focuses on Jesus himself and the Son's revelation of the Father; signs or miracles reveal Jesus' identity and glorify the Father; no exorcisms

as these constitute what is known as the Synoptic Problem. Many solutions have been proposed, of which these are the most important:

(1) *Complete independence.* Some hold that the Synoptic writers worked independently of each other, perhaps using various written or oral sources. According to this view, the similar — sometimes even verbatim — choice and order of words and events are best explained by the infallible guidance of the Holy Spirit on the authors.

(2) *The use of an early Gospel.* Some have postulated that the Synoptic authors all had access to an earlier Gospel, now lost.

(3) *The use of two major sources.* The most common view currently is that the Gospel of Mark and a hypothetical document, called *Quelle* (German for "source") or *Q*, were used by Matthew and Luke as sources for most of the materials included in their Gospels.

(4) *The priority and use of Matthew.* Another view suggests that the other two Synoptics drew from Matthew as their main source.

(5) *A combination of the above.* This theory assumes that the authors of the Synoptic Gospels made use of oral tradition, written fragments, mutual dependence on other Synoptic writers or their Gospels, and the testimony of eyewitnesses.

TWO-SOURCE THEORY

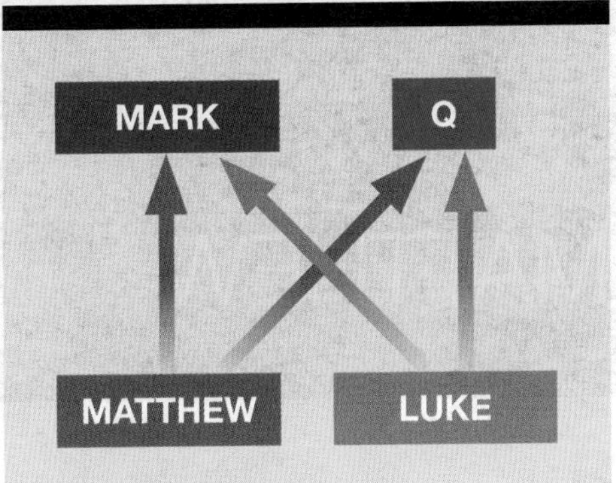

MATTHEAN PRIORITY

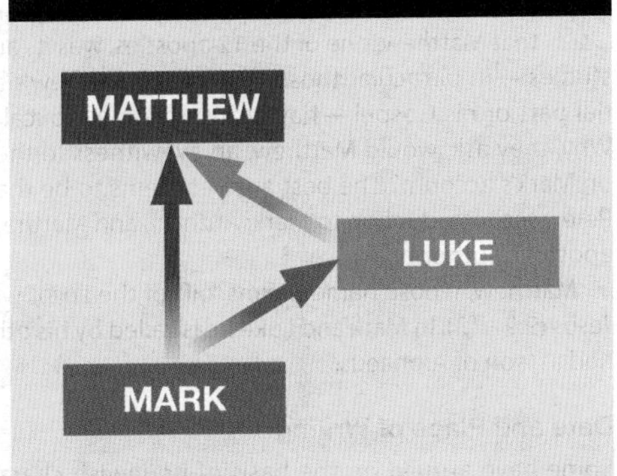

DATING THE **SYNOPTIC GOSPELS**

MARK → MATTHEW, LUKE		MATTHEW	MARK	LUKE
ASSUMPTION A— Matthew and Luke used Mark as a major source		**ASSUMPTION B**— Matthew and Luke did not use Mark as a source; any of the three could have been written from the 50s onward (see Introductions to Matthew, Mark and Luke)		
View No. 1	Mark written in the AD 50s or early 60s (1) Matthew written in late 50s or the 60s (2) Luke written 59–63			
View No. 2	Mark written 65–70 (1) Matthew written in the 70s or later (2) Luke written in the 70s or later			

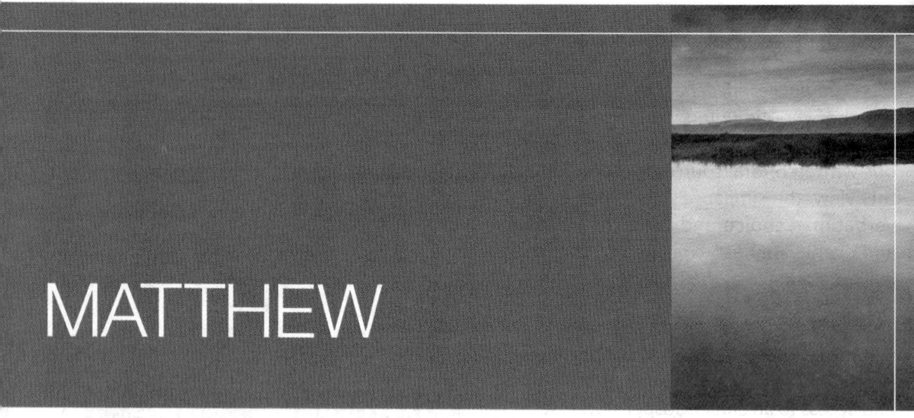

MATTHEW

INTRODUCTION

Author

Although the first Gospel is anonymous, the early church fathers were unanimous in holding that Matthew, one of the 12 apostles, was its author. However, the results of modern critical studies — in particular those that stress Matthew's alleged dependence on Mark for a substantial part of his Gospel — have caused some Biblical scholars to abandon Matthean authorship. Why, they ask, would Matthew, an eyewitness to the events of our Lord's life, depend so heavily on Mark's account? The best answer seems to be that Mark's Gospel represents the testimony of Peter (see Introduction to Mark: Author), and Matthew would certainly be willing to follow Peter's apostolic authority.

Matthew, whose name means "gift of the LORD," was a tax collector who left his work to follow Jesus (9:9 – 13). In Mark and Luke he is called by his other name, Levi; in Mk 2:14 he is further identified as "son of Alphaeus."

Date and Place of Writing

Some have argued on the basis of its Jewish characteristics that Matthew's Gospel was written in the early church period, possibly the early AD 50s, when the church was largely Jewish and the gospel was preached to Jews only (Ac 11:19). However, those who have concluded that both Matthew and Luke drew extensively from Mark's Gospel date it later — after the Gospel of Mark had been in circulation for a period of time. See essay and chart, pp. 1582 – 1583. Accordingly, some feel that Matthew would have been written in the late 50s or in the 60s. Others, who assume that Mark was written between 65 and 70, place Matthew in the 70s or even later. However, there is insufficient evidence to be dogmatic about either view.

The Jewish nature of Matthew's Gospel may suggest that it was written in the Holy Land, though many think it may have originated in Syrian Antioch. The church in Antioch had a large Greek-speaking Jewish population and was at the forefront of the mission to the Gentiles, a theme Matthew emphasizes (e.g., 28:18 – 20).

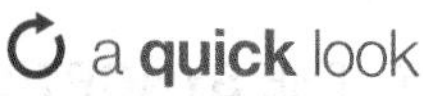

a **quick** look

Author:
Matthew, also called Levi

Audience:
Greek-speaking Jewish Christians

Date:
Between AD 50 and 70

Theme:
Matthew presents Jesus as the Jewish Messiah sent by God to fulfill OT prophecy.

Recipients

Many elements in Matthew's Gospel point to a Jewish or Jewish-Christian readership: Matthew's concern with fulfillment of the OT (he has more quotations from and allusions to the OT than any other NT author); his tracing of Jesus' descent from Abraham (1:1 – 17); his lack of explanation of Jewish customs (especially in contrast to Mark); his use of Jewish terminology (e.g., "kingdom of heaven," where "heaven" reveals the Jewish reverential reluctance to use the name of God; see note on 3:2); and his emphasis on Jesus' role as "Son of David" (1:1; 9:27; 12:23; 15:22; 20:30 – 31; 21:9,15; 22:41 – 45). This does not mean, however, that Matthew restricts his Gospel to Jews. He records the coming of the Magi (non-Jews) to worship the infant Jesus (2:1 – 12), as well as Jesus' statement that the "field is the world" (13:38). He also gives a full statement of the Great Commission (28:18 – 20). These passages show that, although Matthew's Gospel is Jewish, it has a universal outlook.

Purpose

Matthew's main purpose is to confirm for his Jewish-Christian readers that Jesus is their Messiah. He does this primarily by showing how Jesus in his life and ministry fulfilled the OT Scriptures. Although all the Gospel writers quote the OT, Matthew includes many proof texts unique to his

Aerial view of Capernaum, along the northern shore of the Sea of Galilee. Matthew was a tax collector in Capernaum and was met there and called by Jesus (Mt 9:9).

> Matthew includes many proof texts to drive home his basic theme: Jesus is the fulfillment of the Old Testament predictions of the Messiah.

Gospel (e.g., 1:22 – 23; 2:15; 2:17 – 18; 2:23; 4:14 – 16; 8:17; 12:17 – 21; 13:35; 27:9 – 10) to drive home his basic theme: Jesus is the fulfillment of the OT predictions of the Messiah. Matthew even finds the history of God's people in the OT recapitulated in some aspects of Jesus' life (see, e.g., his quotation of Hos 11:1 in 2:15). To accomplish his purpose Matthew also emphasizes Jesus' Davidic lineage (see Recipients; see also note on 1:1).

Structure

The way the material is arranged reveals an artistic touch. The whole Gospel is woven around five great discourses: (1) chs. 5 – 7; (2) ch. 10; (3) ch. 13; (4) ch. 18; (5) chs. 24 – 25. That this is deliberate is clear from the refrain that concludes each discourse: "When Jesus had finished saying these things," or similar words (7:28; 11:1; 13:53; 19:1; 26:1). The narrative sections, in each case, appropriately lead up to the discourses. The Gospel has a fitting prologue (chs. 1 – 2) and a challenging epilogue (28:16 – 20).

The fivefold division may suggest that Matthew has modeled his book on the structure of the Pentateuch (the first five books of the OT). He may also be presenting the gospel as a new Torah and Jesus as a new and greater Moses.

Aerial view of the Sea of Galilee, looking north

Baker Photo Archive

Matthew uses other structural features as well. Some, e.g., think the phrase "From that time on" marks three main sections of the book (4:17 [see note there]; 16:21; 26:16). The outline below follows a geographic structure interspersed with the five main discourses.

THE FIVE MAJOR DISCOURSES OF MATTHEW'S GOSPEL

1.	Sermon on the Mount (chs. 5–7)
2.	Commissioning of the Twelve (ch. 10)
3.	Parables of the Kingdom (ch. 13)
4.	Church Life and Discipline (ch. 18)
5.	Olivet Discourse (chs. 24–25)

Outline

I. The Birth and Early Years of Jesus (chs. 1 – 2)
  - A. His Genealogy (1:1 – 17)
  - B. His Birth (1:18 — 2:12)
  - C. His Stay in Egypt (2:13 – 23)

II. The Beginnings of Jesus' Ministry (3:1 — 4:11)
  - A. His Forerunner (3:1 – 12)
  - B. His Baptism (3:13 – 17)
  - C. His Temptation (4:1 – 11)

III. Jesus' Ministry in Galilee (4:12 — 14:12)
  - A. The Beginning of the Galilean Campaign (4:12 – 25)
  - B. **Discourse One:** The Sermon on the Mount (chs. 5 – 7)
  - C. A Collection of Miracles (chs. 8 – 9)
  - D. **Discourse Two:** The Commissioning of the 12 Apostles (ch. 10)
  - E. Ministry throughout Galilee (chs. 11 – 12)
  - F. **Discourse Three:** The Parables of the Kingdom (ch. 13)
  - G. Herod's Reaction to Jesus' Ministry (14:1 – 12)

IV. Jesus' Withdrawals from Galilee (14:13 — 17:20)
  - A. To the Eastern Shore of the Sea of Galilee (14:13 — 15:20)
  - B. To Phoenicia (15:21 – 28)
  - C. To the Decapolis (15:29 — 16:12)
  - D. To Caesarea Philippi (16:13 — 17:20)

V. Jesus' Last Ministry in Galilee (17:22 — 18:35)
  - A. Prediction of Jesus' Death (17:22 – 23)
  - B. Temple Tax (17:24 – 27)
  - C. **Discourse Four:** Discourse on Life in the Kingdom (ch. 18)

VI. Jesus' Ministry in Judea and Perea (chs. 19 – 20)
  - A. Teaching concerning Divorce (19:1 – 12)
  - B. Teaching concerning Little Children (19:13 – 15)
  - C. The Rich Young Man (19:16 – 30)
  - D. The Parable of the Workers in the Vineyard (20:1 – 16)
  - E. Prediction of Jesus' Death (20:17 – 19)
  - F. A Mother's Request (20:20 – 28)
  - G. Restoration of Sight at Jericho (20:29 – 34)

VII. Passion Week (chs. 21 – 27)
   A. The Entry of Jesus into Jerusalem as King (21:1 – 11)
   B. The Clearing of the Temple (21:12 – 17)
   C. The Last Controversies with the Jewish Leaders (21:18 — 23:39)
   D. **Discourse Five:** The Olivet Discourse (chs. 24 – 25)
   E. The Anointing of Jesus' Feet (26:1 – 13)
   F. The Arrest, Trials and Death of Jesus (26:14 — 27:66)

VIII. The Resurrection (ch. 28)
   A. The Earthquake and the Angel's Announcement (28:1 – 7)
   B. Jesus' Encounter with the Women (28:8 – 10)
   C. The Guards' Report and the Jewish Elders' Bribe (28:11 – 15)
   D. The Great Commission (28:16 – 20)

The Genealogy of Jesus the Messiah

1:1-17pp — Lk 3:23-38
1:3-6pp — Ru 4:18-22
1:7-11pp — 1Ch 3:10-17

1 This is the genealogy[a] of Jesus the Messiah[b] the son of David,[a] the son of Abraham:[b]

2 Abraham was the father of Isaac,[c]
Isaac the father of Jacob,[d]
Jacob the father of Judah and his brothers,[e]
3 Judah the father of Perez and Zerah, whose mother was Tamar,[f]
Perez the father of Hezron,
Hezron the father of Ram,
4 Ram the father of Amminadab,
Amminadab the father of Nahshon,
Nahshon the father of Salmon,
5 Salmon the father of Boaz, whose mother was Rahab,[g]
Boaz the father of Obed, whose mother was Ruth,
Obed the father of Jesse,
6 and Jesse the father of King David.[h]

David was the father of Solomon, whose mother had been Uriah's wife,[i]
7 Solomon the father of Rehoboam,
Rehoboam the father of Abijah,
Abijah the father of Asa,
8 Asa the father of Jehoshaphat,
Jehoshaphat the father of Jehoram,
Jehoram the father of Uzziah,
9 Uzziah the father of Jotham,
Jotham the father of Ahaz,
Ahaz the father of Hezekiah,
10 Hezekiah the father of Manasseh,[j]
Manasseh the father of Amon,
Amon the father of Josiah,
11 and Josiah the father of Jeconiah[c] and his brothers at the time of the exile to Babylon.[k]

12 After the exile to Babylon:
Jeconiah was the father of Shealtiel,[l]
Shealtiel the father of Zerubbabel,[m]
13 Zerubbabel the father of Abihud,
Abihud the father of Eliakim,
Eliakim the father of Azor,
14 Azor the father of Zadok,
Zadok the father of Akim,
Akim the father of Elihud,
15 Elihud the father of Eleazar,
Eleazar the father of Matthan,
Matthan the father of Jacob,
16 and Jacob the father of Joseph, the husband of Mary,[n] and Mary was the mother of Jesus who is called the Messiah.[o]

17 Thus there were fourteen generations in all from Abraham to David, fourteen from David to the exile to Babylon, and fourteen from the exile to the Messiah.

1:1 [a] 2Sa 7:12-16; Isa 9:6,7; 11:1; Jer 23:5,6; S Mt 9:27; Lk 1:32,69; Rev 22:16 [b] Ge 22:18; S Gal 3:16 **1:2** [c] Ge 21:3, 12 [d] Ge 25:26 [e] Ge 29:35; 49:10 **1:3** [f] Ge 38:27-30 **1:5** [g] S Heb 11:31 **1:6** [h] 1Sa 16:1; 17:12 [i] 2Sa 12:24 **1:10** [j] 2Ki 20:21 **1:11** [k] 2Ki 24:14-16; Jer 27:20; 40:1; Da 1:1,2 **1:12** [l] 1Ch 3:17 [m] 1Ch 3:19; Ezr 3:2 **1:16** [n] Lk 1:27 [o] Mt 27:17

[a] *1* Or *is an account of the origin* [b] *1* Or *Jesus Christ. Messiah* (Hebrew) and *Christ* (Greek) both mean *Anointed One*; also in verse 18. [c] *11* That is, Jehoiachin; also in verse 12

1:1–16 For a comparison of Matthew's genealogy with Luke's, see note on Lk 3:23–38. The types of people mentioned in this genealogy reveal the broad scope of those who make up the people of God as well as the genealogy of Jesus.
1:1 *son of David.* A Messianic title (see Introduction: Recipients; Purpose; see also note on 9:27) found several times in this Gospel (in 1:20 it is not a Messianic title). Jesus fulfills the Davidic covenant (see 2Sa 7:5–16 and note on 7:11). *son of Abraham.* Because Matthew was writing to Jews, it was important to identify Jesus in this way. Jesus fulfills the Abrahamic covenant (see Ge 12:2–3; 15:9–21; 17; Zec 9:10 and note).
1:3 *Tamar.* In Matthew's genealogy five women are named: Tamar (here), Rahab (v. 5), Ruth (v. 5), Bathsheba (not by name but by description—"Solomon, whose mother had been Uriah's wife," v. 6) and, of course, Mary (v. 16). All these women were in some sense outsiders. At least three of them were Gentiles (Tamar, Rahab and Ruth). Bathsheba was probably an Israelite (1Ch 3:5) but was closely associated with the Hittites because of Uriah, her Hittite husband. By including these women (contrary to custom) in his genealogy, Matthew may be indicating at the very outset of his Gospel that God's grace is not limited to men or to the people of Israel.
1:4 *Amminadab.* Father-in-law of Aaron (Ex 6:23).
1:5 *Rahab.* See notes on v. 3; Heb 11:31; Jas 2:25; see also Jos 2. Since quite a long time had elapsed between Rahab and David and because of Matthew's desire for systematic organization (see note on v. 17), many of the generations between these two ancestors were assumed, but not listed, by Matthew. *Ruth.* See note on v. 3.
1:6 *Solomon, whose mother.* His mother was Bathsheba (see note on v. 3).
1:8 *Jehoram the father.* Matthew calls Jehoram the father of Uzziah, but from 2Ch 21:4—26:23 it is clear that, again, several generations were assumed (Ahaziah, Joash and Amaziah) and that "father" is used in the sense of "forefather" or "ancestor" (see NIV text notes on 1Ch 1:5,10).
1:11 *Josiah the father.* Similarly (see note on v. 8), Josiah is called the father of Jeconiah (i.e., Jehoiachin; see NIV text note), whereas he was actually the father of Jehoiakim and the grandfather of Jehoiachin (2Ch 36:1–9).
1:12 *Shealtiel the father.* See note on 1Ch 3:19.
1:16 *husband of Mary.* Matthew does not say that Joseph was the father of Jesus but only that he was the husband of Mary and that Jesus was born of her. In this genealogy Matthew shows that, although Jesus is not the physical son of Joseph, he is the legal son and therefore a descendant of David (see Lk 2:33; Jn 1:45 and notes). *Mary … mother of Jesus.* See note on v. 3.
1:17 *fourteen generations … fourteen … fourteen.* These divisions reflect two characteristics of Matthew's Gospel: (1) an apparent fondness for numbers and (2) concern for systematic arrangement. The number 14 may have been chosen because it is twice seven (the number of completeness) and/or because it is the numerical value of the name David (see notes on Pr 10:1; Rev 13:17). For the practice of telescoping genealogies to achieve the desired number of names, see Introduction to 1 Chronicles: Genealogies.

Joseph Accepts Jesus as His Son

18 This is how the birth of Jesus the Messiah came about[a]: His mother Mary was
pledged to be married to Joseph, but before they came together, she was found to
be pregnant through the Holy Spirit.[p] 19 Because Joseph her husband was faithful to
the law, and yet[b] did not want to expose
her to public disgrace, he had in mind to
divorce[q] her quietly.
20 But after he had considered this, an
angel[r] of the Lord appeared to him in a
dream[s] and said, "Joseph son of David, do
not be afraid to take Mary home as your
wife, because what is conceived in her is
from the Holy Spirit. 21 She will give birth
to a son, and you are to give him the name
Jesus,[c][t] because he will save his people
from their sins."[u]
22 All this took place to fulfill[v] what the
Lord had said through the prophet: 23 "The
virgin will conceive and give birth to a
son, and they will call him Immanuel"[d][w]
(which means "God with us").

24 When Joseph woke up, he did what
the angel[x] of the Lord had commanded him and took Mary home as his wife.
25 But he did not consummate their marriage until she gave birth to a son. And he
gave him the name Jesus.[y]

The Magi Visit the Messiah

2 After Jesus was born in Bethlehem in
Judea,[z] during the time of King Herod,[a] Magi[e] from the east came to Jerusalem 2 and asked, "Where is the one who
has been born king of the Jews?[b] We saw
his star[c] when it rose and have come to
worship him."
3 When King Herod heard this he was disturbed, and all Jerusalem with him. 4 When
he had called together all the people's chief
priests and teachers of the law, he asked
them where the Messiah was to be born.

1:18 [p] Lk 1:35 **1:19** [q] Dt 24:1 **1:20** [r] S Ac 5:19 [s] S Mt 27:19 **1:21** [t] S Lk 1:31 [u] Ps 130:8; S Lk 2:11; S Jn 3:17; Ac 5:31; S Ro 11:14; Titus 2:14 **1:22** [v] Mt 2:15, 17,23; 4:14; 8:17; 12:17; 21:4; 26:54,56; 27:9; Lk 4:21; 21:22; 24:44; Jn 13:18; 19:24, 28,36 **1:23** [w] Isa 7:14; 8:8,10 **1:24** [x] S Ac 5:19 **1:25** [y] ver 21; S Lk 1:31 **2:1** [z] Lk 2:4-7 [a] Lk 1:5 **2:2** [b] Jer 23:5; Mt 27:11; Mk 15:2; Lk 23:38; Jn 1:49; 18:33-37 [c] Nu 24:17

[a] 18 Or *The origin of Jesus the Messiah was like this* [b] 19 Or *was a righteous man and* [c] 21 *Jesus* is the Greek form of *Joshua,* which means *the* LORD *saves.* [d] 23 Isaiah 7:14 [e] 1 Traditionally *wise men*

1:18 *pledged to be married.* There were no sexual relations during a Jewish betrothal period, but it was a much more binding relationship than a modern engagement and could be broken only by divorce (see v. 19). In Dt 22:24 a betrothed woman is called a "wife," though the preceding verse speaks of her as being "pledged to be married." Matthew uses the terms "husband" (v. 19) and "wife" (v. 24) of Joseph and Mary before their marriage was consummated (see note on Joel 1:8). *the Holy Spirit.* The common NT way of referring to the divine Spirit, who in the OT was almost always called "the Spirit of God" or "the Spirit of the LORD." See Ps 51:11 and note. Christian reflection on the Biblical word about him (see 3:16–17; 28:19; 2Co 13:14 and notes) led to the understanding that he is one of the three persons of the Trinity.
1:19 *divorce her quietly.* He would sign the necessary legal papers but not have her judged publicly and stoned (see Dt 22:23–24).
1:20 *in a dream.* The phrase occurs five times in the first two chapters of Matthew (here; 2:12,13,19,22) and indicates the means the Lord used for speaking to Joseph. *Joseph son of David.* See notes on 1:1,16; perhaps a hint that the message of the angel related to the expected Messiah. *take Mary home as your wife.* They were legally bound to each other but not yet living together as husband and wife. *what is conceived in her is from the Holy Spirit.* This agrees perfectly with the announcement to Mary (Lk 1:35), except that the latter is more specific (see note on Lk 1:26–35).
1:21 *the name Jesus.* See NIV text note; the meaning is more specifically explained in the rest of the verse. *save.* See Lk 2:11 and note.
1:22 *fulfill.* Twelve times (here; 2:15,23; 3:15; 4:14; 5:17; 8:17; 12:17; 13:14,35; 21:4; 27:9) Matthew speaks of the OT being fulfilled in the events of Jesus' life. Some of these are uniquely fulfilled by Jesus, while others are typological, where Jesus is the ultimate fulfillment of an OT type (see note on 2:15).
1:23 See note on Isa 7:14. This is the first of about 50 quotations, many of them Messianic in some sense, that Matthew takes from the OT (see NIV text notes throughout Matthew).
1:24 *angel of the Lord.* See Lk 2:9 and note.
1:25 *he did not consummate their marriage until she gave birth.* Both Matthew and Luke (1:26–35) make it clear that Jesus was born of a virgin. Although this doctrine is often ridiculed, it is an important part of the evangelical faith.
2:1 *Bethlehem in Judea.* A village about five miles south of Jerusalem. Matthew says nothing of the events in Nazareth (cf. Lk 1:26–56). Possibly wanting to emphasize Jesus' Davidic background, he begins with the events that happened in David's hometown. It is called "Bethlehem in Judea," not only to distinguish it from the town of the same name about seven miles northwest of Nazareth, but also to emphasize that Jesus came from the tribe (Judah) and territory that produced the line of Davidic kings. That Jews expected the Messiah to be born in Bethlehem and to be from David's family is clear from Jn 7:42. *King Herod.* Herod the Great (37–4 BC), to be distinguished from the other Herods in the Bible (see chart, pp. 1592–1593). Herod was a non-Jew, an Idumean, who was appointed king of Judea by the Roman Senate in 40 BC and gained control in 37. He was a ruthless ruler, murdering his wife, three of his sons, his mother-in-law, his brother-in-law, his uncle and many others he suspected of treachery—not to mention the male babies in Bethlehem (v. 16). His reign was also noted for splendor, as seen in the many theaters, amphitheaters, monuments, pagan altars, fortresses and other buildings he erected or refurbished—including the greatest work of all, the rebuilding of the temple in Jerusalem, begun in 19 or 20 BC and finished 68 years after his death (see note on Jn 2:20). *Magi.* Probably astrologers, perhaps from Persia or southern Arabia or Mesopotamia, all of which are east of the Holy Land. *Jerusalem.* Since they were looking for the "king of the Jews" (v. 2), they naturally came to the Jewish capital city (see map, p. 2525, at the end of this study Bible).
2:2 *born king.* The Magi realized that Jesus was born a king, not that he would become one later on. *king of the Jews.* Indicates the Magi were Gentiles. Matthew wants to show that people of all nations acknowledged Jesus as "king of the Jews" and came to worship him as Lord. *star.* Probably not an ordinary star, planet or comet, though some interpreters have identified it with the conjunction of Jupiter and Saturn or with other astronomical phenomena (cf. Nu 24:17 and note).
2:4 *chief priests.* See note on Mk 8:31. These were the ruling priests in charge of worship at the temple in Jerusalem.

5 "In Bethlehem[d] in Judea," they replied,
"for this is what the prophet has written:

6 " 'But you, Bethlehem, in the land of Judah,
are by no means least among the rulers of Judah;
for out of you will come a ruler
who will shepherd my people Israel.'[a]"[e]

7 Then Herod called the Magi secretly
and found out from them the exact time
the star had appeared. 8 He sent them to
Bethlehem and said, "Go and search carefully for the child. As soon as you find
him, report to me, so that I too may go
and worship him."
9 After they had heard the king, they
went on their way, and the star they had
seen when it rose went ahead of them until
it stopped over the place where the child
was. 10 When they saw the star, they were
overjoyed. 11 On coming to the house, they
saw the child with his mother Mary, and
they bowed down and worshiped him.[f]
Then they opened their treasures and presented him with gifts[g] of gold, frankincense
and myrrh. 12 And having been warned[h] in
a dream[i] not to go back to Herod, they returned to their country by another route.

The Escape to Egypt

13 When they had gone, an angel[j] of the
Lord appeared to Joseph in a dream.[k] "Get
up," he said, "take the child and his mother and escape to Egypt. Stay there until I
tell you, for Herod is going to search for
the child to kill him."[l]
14 So he got up, took the child and his
mother during the night and left for Egypt,
15 where he stayed until the death of Herod. And so was fulfilled[m] what the Lord
had said through the prophet: "Out of
Egypt I called my son."[b][n]
16 When Herod realized that he had been
outwitted by the Magi, he was furious,
and he gave orders to kill all the boys in
Bethlehem and its vicinity who were two
years old and under, in accordance with
the time he had learned from the Magi.
17 Then what was said through the prophet
Jeremiah was fulfilled:[o]

18 "A voice is heard in Ramah,
weeping and great mourning,
Rachel[p] weeping for her children
and refusing to be comforted,
because they are no more."[c][q]

The Return to Nazareth

19 After Herod died, an angel[r] of the Lord
appeared in a dream[s] to Joseph in Egypt
20 and said, "Get up, take the child and his
mother and go to the land of Israel, for
those who were trying to take the child's
life are dead."[t]
21 So he got up, took the child and his
mother and went to the land of Israel.
22 But when he heard that Archelaus was
reigning in Judea in place of his father
Herod, he was afraid to go there. Having
been warned in a dream,[u] he withdrew to
the district of Galilee,[v] 23 and he went and
lived in a town called Nazareth.[w] So was
fulfilled[x] what was said through the prophets, that he would be called a Nazarene.[y]

2:5 [d] Jn 7:42 **2:6** [e] 2Sa 5:2; Mic 5:2 **2:11** [f] Isa 60:3 [g] Ps 72:10 **2:12** [h] Heb 11:7 [i] ver 13, 19, 22; S Mt 27:19 **2:13** [j] S Ac 5:19 [k] ver 12, 19, 22; S Mt 27:19 [l] Rev 12:4 **2:15** [m] ver 17, 23; S Mt 1:22 [n] Ex 4:22, 23; Hos 11:1 **2:17** [o] ver 15, 23; S Mt 1:22 **2:18** [p] Ge 35:19 [q] Jer 31:15 **2:19** [r] S Ac 5:19 [s] ver 12, 13, 22; S Mt 27:19 **2:20** [t] Ex 4:19 **2:22** [u] ver 12, 13, 19; S Mt 27:19 [v] Lk 2:39 **2:23** [w] Mk 1:9; 6:1; S 1:24; Lk 1:26; 2:39, 51; 4:16, 23; Jn 1:45, 46 [x] ver 15, 17; S Mt 1:22 [y] S Mk 1:24

[a] *6* Micah 5:2,4 [b] *15* Hosea 11:1 [c] *18* Jer. 31:15

---

teachers of the law. The Jewish scholars of the day, professionally trained in the teaching and application of OT law (see notes on Mk 2:16; Lk 5:17).
2:6 See Mic 5:2 and note.
2:11 *house.* Contrary to tradition, the Magi did not visit Jesus at the manger on the night of his birth as did the shepherds. They came some months later and visited him as a "child" in his "house." *the child with his mother Mary.* Every time the child Jesus and his mother are mentioned together, he is mentioned first (vv. 11,13–14,20–21). *gold ... frankincense ... myrrh.* The three gifts perhaps gave rise to the legend that there were three "wise men." But the Bible does not indicate the number of the Magi, and they were almost certainly not kings. *myrrh.* See note on Ge 37:25.
2:13 *angel of the Lord.* See note on Lk 2:9.
2:15 *the death of Herod.* In 4 BC. *Out of Egypt I called my son.* This quotation from Hos 11:1 originally referred to God's calling the nation of Israel out of Egypt in the time of Moses. But Matthew, under the inspiration of the Spirit, applies it also to Jesus. He sees the history of Israel (God's "son") recapitulated in the life of Jesus (God's unique Son). Just as Israel as an infant nation went down into Egypt, so the child Jesus went there. And as Israel was led by God out of Egypt, so also was Jesus.
2:16 *kill all the boys ... two years old and under.* The number killed has often been exaggerated as being in the thousands. In so small a village as Bethlehem, however (even with the surrounding area included), the number was probably not large—though the act, of course, was no less brutal.
2:18 See note on Jer 31:15.
2:22 *Archelaus.* This son of Herod the Great ruled over Judea and Samaria for only ten years (4 BC–AD 6). He was unusually cruel and tyrannical and so was deposed. Judea then became a Roman province, administered by governors appointed by the emperor (see chart, p. 1592). *Galilee.* The northern part of the Holy Land in Jesus' day (see map, p. 2527, at the end of this study Bible; see also map, p. 1594).
2:23 *Nazareth.* A rather obscure town, nowhere mentioned in the OT. It was Jesus' hometown (21:11; 26:71; see Lk 2:39; 4:16–24; Jn 1:45–46). *be called a Nazarene.* These exact words are not found in the OT and probably refer to several OT prefigurations and/or predictions (note the plural "prophets") that the Messiah would be despised (e.g., Ps 22:6; Isa 53:3), for in Jesus' day "Nazarene" was virtually a synonym for "despised" (see Jn 1:45–46). Some hold that in speaking of Jesus as a "Nazarene," Matthew may be alluding to the "Branch" (Hebrew *neṣer*) of Isa 11:1, since the word also appears in the Targums (see note on Ne 8:8), rabbinic literature, and the Dead Sea Scrolls (see essay, pp. 1574–1576) as a Messianic title. However, Nazarene most likely means "of/from Nazareth" (cf. 26:71).

HOUSE OF HEROD

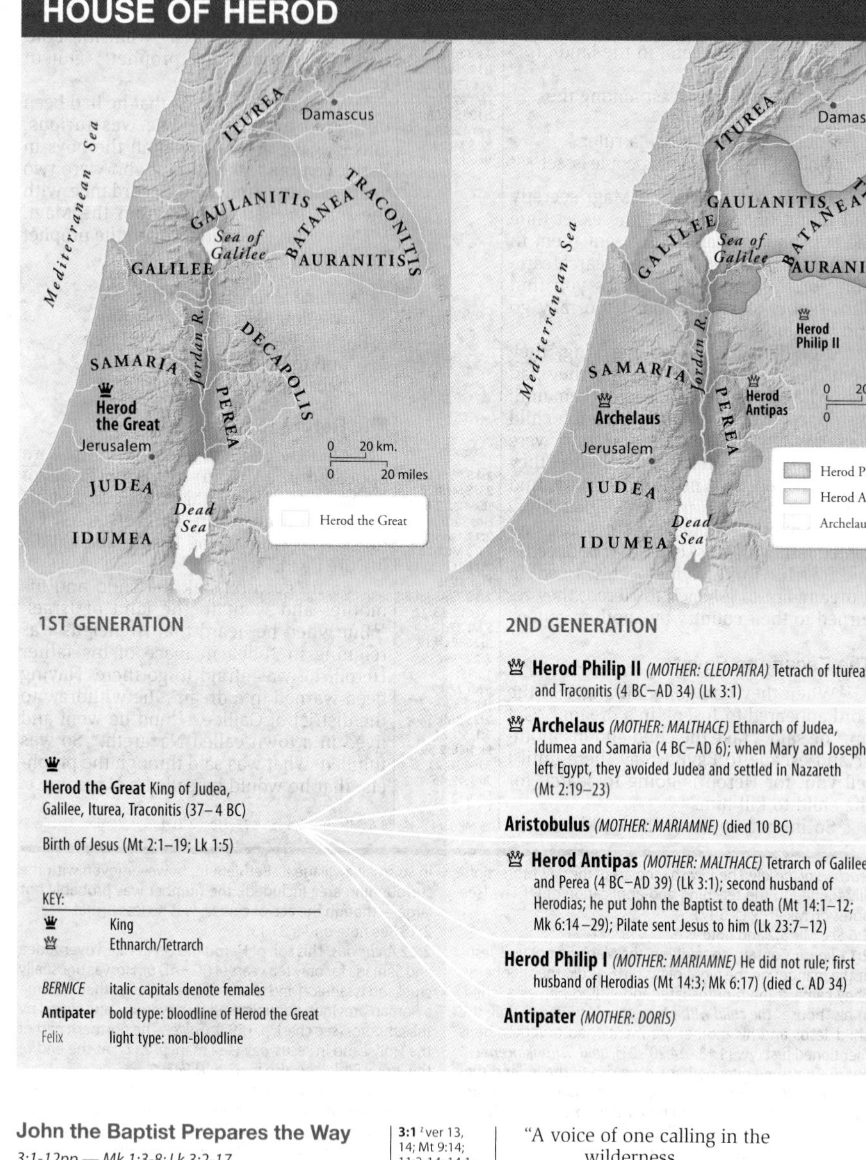

John the Baptist Prepares the Way

3:1-12pp — Mk 1:3-8; Lk 3:2-17

3 In those days John the Baptist[z] came,
preaching in the wilderness of Judea
2 and saying, "Repent, for the kingdom of
heaven[a] has come near." 3 This is he who
was spoken of through the prophet Isaiah:

"A voice of one calling in the
wilderness,
'Prepare the way for the Lord,
make straight paths for him.' "[a b]

3:1 [z] ver 13, 14; Mt 9:14; 11:2-14; 14:1-12; Lk 1:13, 57-66; 3:2-19; Ac 19:3,4 **3:2** [a] Da 7:14; Mt 4:17; 6:10; 7:21; S 25:34; Lk 11:20; 17:20, 21; 19:11; 21:31; Jn 3:3,5; Ac 1:3,6 **3:3** [b] Isa 40:3; Mal 3:1; Lk 1:76; Jn 1:23

[a] *3* Isaiah 40:3

3:1 *John the Baptist.* The forerunner of Jesus, born c. 7 BC to Zechariah, a priest, and his wife Elizabeth (see Lk 1:5–80). *wilderness of Judea.* An area that stretched some 20 miles from the Jerusalem-Bethlehem plateau down to the Jordan River and the Dead Sea, perhaps the same region where John lived (cf. Lk 1:80). The people of Qumran (often

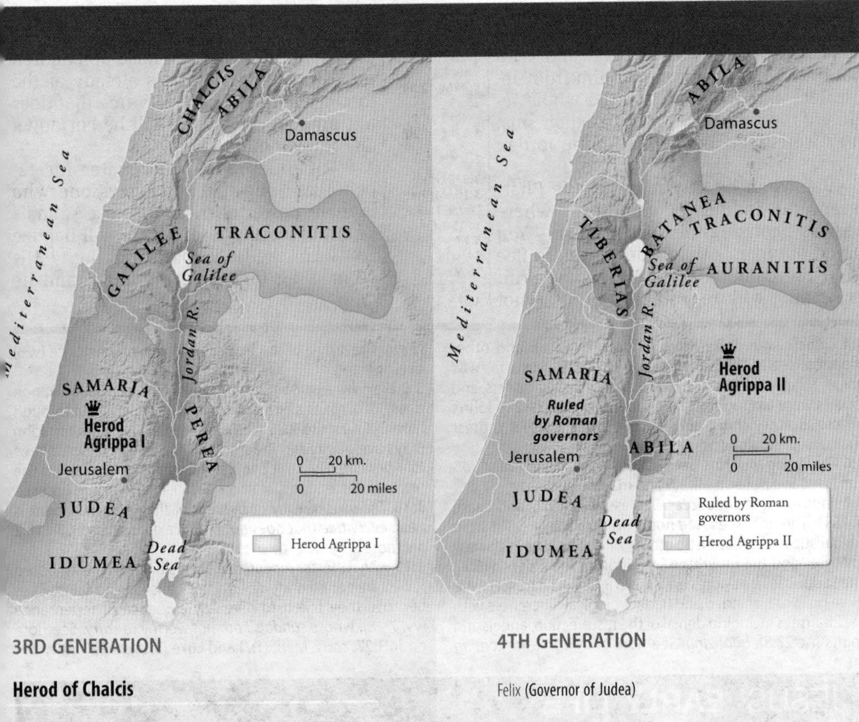

3RD GENERATION

Herod of Chalcis

♛ **Herod Agrippa I** King of Judea (AD 37–44); killed James; put Peter into prison; struck down by an angel (Ac 12:1–24)

HERODIAS Married her uncle Herod Philip I, and then a second uncle, Herod Antipas (Mt 14:3; Mk 6:17)

Denotes Herodias's marriage to Herod Antipas

Denotes Herodias's marriage to Herod Philip I and daughter of that marriage

4TH GENERATION

Felix (Governor of Judea)

DRUSILLA
Married Felix, governor of Judea (AD 52–59); Felix tried Paul (Ac 24:24)

♛ **Herod Agrippa II**

King of Judea; Paul makes a legal defense before him (Ac 25:13—26:32)

BERNICE
With her brother at the time of Paul's defense (Ac 25:13)

SALOME
Daughter of Herodias and Herod Philip I; danced in exchange for the head of John the Baptist (Mt 14:1–12; Mk 6:14–29)

---

associated with the Dead Sea Scrolls) lived in this area too (see essay, pp. 1574–1576).

3:2 *Repent.* Repentance is not merely a change of mind but a radical change in one's life as a whole that especially involves forsaking sin and turning or returning to God. *kingdom of heaven.* A phrase found only in Matthew, where it occurs 33 times. See Introduction: Recipients. Mark and Luke refer to "the kingdom of God," a term Matthew uses only four times (see note on Mk 11:30). The "kingdom of heaven/God" in the preaching of Jesus as recounted in the Gospels is the reign of God that he brings about through Jesus Christ—i.e., the establishment of God's rule in the hearts and lives of his people, the overcoming of all the forces of evil, the removal from the world of all the consequences of sin—including death and all that diminishes life—and the creation of a new order of righteousness and peace. The idea of God's kingdom is central to Jesus' teaching and is mentioned 50 times in Matthew alone. *has come near.* See note on Mk 1:15.

3:3 All three Synoptic Gospels quote Isa 40:3 (Luke quotes two additional verses) and apply it to John the Baptist. *make straight paths for him.* Equivalent to "Prepare the way for the Lord" (see note on Lk 3:4). The preparation was to be moral and spiritual.

[4]John's[c] clothes were made of camel's
hair, and he had a leather belt around his
waist.[d] His food was locusts[e] and wild
honey. [5]People went out to him from Jerusalem and all Judea and the whole region of the Jordan. [6]Confessing their sins,
they were baptized[f] by him in the Jordan
River.

[7]But when he saw many of the Pharisees and Sadducees coming to where
he was baptizing, he said to them: "You
brood of vipers![g] Who warned you to flee
from the coming wrath?[h] [8]Produce fruit
in keeping with repentance.[i] [9]And do not
think you can say to yourselves, 'We have
Abraham as our father.'[j] I tell you that out
of these stones God can raise up children
for Abraham. [10]The ax is already at the
root of the trees, and every tree that does
not produce good fruit will be cut down
and thrown into the fire.[k]

[11]"I baptize you with[a] water for repentance.[l] But after me comes one who
is more powerful than I, whose sandals
I am not worthy to carry. He will baptize
you with[a] the Holy Spirit[m] and fire.[n] [12]His
winnowing fork is in his hand, and he

3:4 [c]S Mt 3:1 [d]2Ki 1:8 [e]Lev 11:22 **3:6** [f]ver 11; S Mk 1:4 **3:7** [g]Mt 12:34; 23:33 [h]S Ro 1:18 **3:8** [i]Ac 26:20 **3:9** [j]S Lk 3:8 **3:10** [k]Mt 7:19; Lk 3:9; 13:6-9; Jn 15:2,6 **3:11** [l]ver 6; S Mk 1:4 [m]S Mk 1:8 [n]Isa 4:4; Ac 2:3,4

[a] *11* Or *in*

3:4 *camel's hair … leather belt.* Worn by Elijah and other prophets (see 2Ki 1:8; Zec 13:4–6 and notes). *locusts and wild honey.* People living in the wilderness often ate insects, and locusts were among the clean foods (Lev 11:21–22). John's simple food, clothing and lifestyle were a visual protest against self-indulgence.
3:6 *Confessing their sins.* See Pr 28:13; 1Jn 1:9 and notes. *Jordan River.* See note on Mk 1:5 and map below.
3:7 *Pharisees and Sadducees.* See essay, p. 1576, and chart, p. 1631. The Pharisees (see notes on Mk 2:16; Lk 5:17) were a legalistic and separatistic group who strictly kept the law of Moses and the unwritten "tradition of the elders" (15:2). The Sadducees (see notes on Mk 12:18; Lk 20:27; Ac 4:1) were more politically minded and had theological differences with the Pharisees including denial of the resurrection, angels and spirits (Ac 23:8). *baptizing.* See note on Mk 1:4. *the coming wrath.* The arrival of the Messiah will bring repentance (v. 8) or judgment.
3:9 *We have Abraham as our father.* See Jn 8:39. Salvation does not come as a birthright (even for the Jews) but through faith in Christ (Ro 2:28–29; Gal 3:7,9,29). *these stones.* John may have pointed to the stones in the Jordan River. *children for Abraham.* The true people of God are not limited to the physical descendants of Abraham (cf. Ro 9:6–8 and notes).
3:10 *The ax is already at the root of the trees.* Judgment is near. *every tree that does not produce good fruit.* Cf. Jn 15:2 and note.
3:11 *with water for repentance.* John's baptism presupposed repentance; he condemned the Pharisees and Sadducees because they failed to give any evidence of repentance (vv. 7–8). *whose sandals I am not worthy to carry.* See note on Jn 1:27. *carry.* Mark (1:7) and Luke (3:16) have "untie," but

JESUS' EARLY LIFE

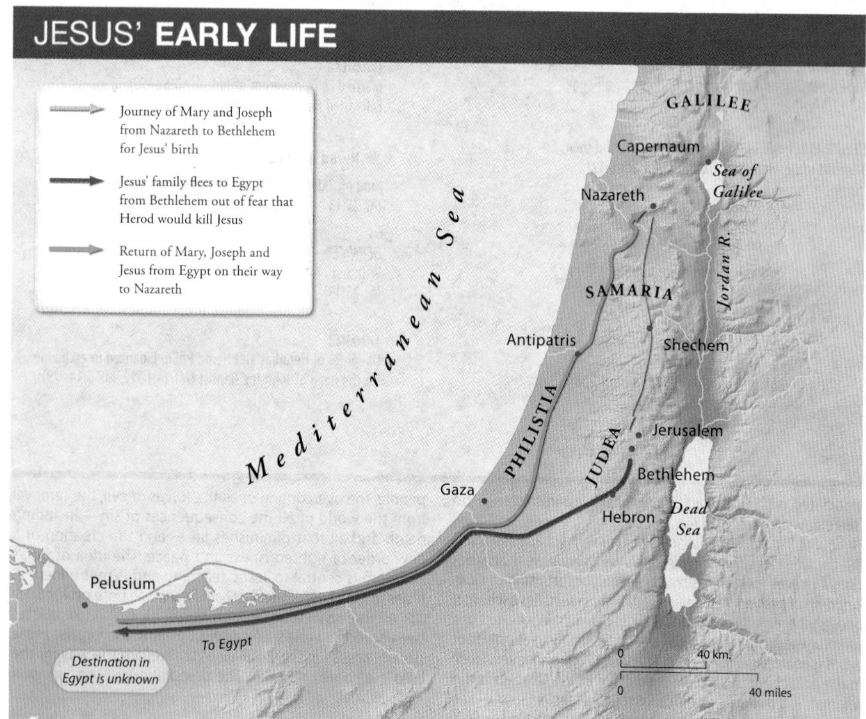

will clear his threshing floor, gathering his wheat into the barn and burning up the chaff with unquenchable fire."[o]

The Baptism of Jesus

3:13-17pp — Mk 1:9-11; Lk 3:21,22; Jn 1:31-34

13Then Jesus came from Galilee to the
Jordan to be baptized by John.[p] 14But John
tried to deter him, saying, "I need to be
baptized by you, and do you come to me?"
15Jesus replied, "Let it be so now; it is
proper for us to do this to fulfill all righteousness." Then John consented.
16As soon as Jesus was baptized, he
went up out of the water. At that moment heaven was opened,[q] and he saw the Spirit of God[r] descending like a dove and alighting on him. 17And a voice from heaven[s]
said, "This is my Son,[t] whom I love; with him I am well pleased."[u]

Jesus Is Tested in the Wilderness

4:1-11pp — Mk 1:12,13; Lk 4:1-13

4 Then Jesus was led by the Spirit into the wilderness to be tempted[a][v] by the
devil.[w] 2After fasting forty days and forty nights,[x] he was hungry. 3The tempter[y] came to him and said, "If you are the Son of God,[z] tell these stones to become bread."

[a] 1 The Greek for *tempted* can also mean *tested.*

3:12 [o] Mt 13:30; S 25:41 **3:13** [p] S Mt 3:1; S Mk 1:4 **3:16** [q] Eze 1:1; Jn 1:51; Ac 7:56; 10:11; Rev 4:1; 19:11 [r] Isa 11:2; 42:1 **3:17** [s] Dt 4:12; Mt 17:5; Jn 12:28 [t] Ps 2:7; Ac 13:33; Heb 1:1-5; 5:5; 2Pe 1:17, 18 [u] Isa 42:1; Mt 12:18; 17:5; Mk 1:11; 9:7; Lk 3:22; 9:35; 2Pe 1:17 **4:1** [v] Heb 4:15 [w] Ge 3:1-7 **4:2** [x] Ex 34:28; 1Ki 19:8

4:3 [y] 1Th 3:5 [z] S Mt 3:17; 14:33; 16:16; 27:54; Mk 3:11; Lk 1:35; 22:70; Jn 1:34,49; 5:25; 11:27; 20:31; Ac 9:20; Ro 1:4; 1Jn 5:10-13, 20; Rev 2:18

---

the Greek for "carry" can also mean "remove." *baptize you with the Holy Spirit.* See Jn 1:33 and note. *with the Holy Spirit and fire.* Demonstrated in a dramatic way at Pentecost (Ac 1:5,8; 2:1 – 13; 11:16), though here "fire" may refer to judgment to come (see v. 12). The outpouring of the Holy Spirit on all God's people was promised in Joel 2:28 – 29 and at least partially fulfilled in Ac 2:16 – 21.

3:12 *His winnowing fork.* For the process of winnowing, see note on Ru 1:22. Here it is figurative for the separation of the righteous ("wheat") from the wicked ("chaff"). *unquenchable fire.* Eschatological judgment (see 25:41 and note; cf. La 1:13 and note). The OT prophets and NT writers sometimes compress the first and second comings of Christ so that they seem to be one event (see, e.g., Isa 61:2 and note).

3:13 *Jesus . . . baptized by John.* See map and accompanying text, p. 1597.

3:15 Jesus' baptism marked the beginning of his Messianic ministry. There were several reasons for his baptism: (1) The first, mentioned here, was "to fulfill all righteousness." His baptism indicated that he was consecrated to God and officially approved by him, as especially shown in the descent of the Holy Spirit (v. 16) and the words of the Father (v. 17; cf. Ps 2:7; Isa 42:1). All God's righteous requirements for the Messiah were fully met in Jesus. (2) At Jesus' baptism John publicly announced the arrival of the Messiah and the inception of his ministry (Jn 1:31 – 34). (3) By his baptism Jesus completely identified himself with humanity's sin and failure (though he himself needed no repentance or cleansing from sin), becoming our substitute (2Co 5:21). (4) His baptism was an example to his followers.

3:16 – 17 All three persons of the Trinity are clearly seen here (see 28:19 and note).

3:16 *Spirit of God.* The Holy Spirit came upon Jesus not to overcome sin (for he was sinless) but to equip him (see note on Jdg 3:10) for his work as the divine-human Messiah. *like a dove.* Either in the form of a dove or in a descent like a dove. See also note on Mk 1:10.

3:17 *voice from heaven.* The voice (1) authenticated Jesus' Messianic sonship, echoing Ps 2:7 ("This is my Son"), (2) identified Jesus with the suffering servant of Isa 42:1 ("with him I am well pleased"), and perhaps (3) identified Jesus with Abraham's willingness to offer Isaac as a sacrifice, echoing Ge 22:2 ("whom I love"). This word from the Father must have greatly encouraged Jesus at the very outset of his earthly ministry. *my Son.* See notes on 14:33; Jn 3:16.

4:1 – 11 The significance of Jesus' temptations, especially because they occurred at the outset of his public ministry, seems best understood in terms of the kind of Messiah he was to be. He would not accomplish his mission by using his supernatural power for his own needs (first temptation), by using his power to win a large following by miracles or magic (second temptation) or by compromising with Satan (third temptation). Jesus' temptation was real, not merely symbolic. He was "tempted in every way, just as we are — yet he did not sin" (see Heb 4:15 and note; see also 2Co 5:21; Heb 7:26; 1Pe 2:22 and note; 1Jn 3:5). Although Jesus was the Son of God, he defeated Satan by using a weapon that everyone has at their disposal: "the sword of the Spirit, which is the word of God" (Eph 6:17). He met all three temptations with Scriptural truth (vv. 4,7,10) from Deuteronomy.

4:1 *Jesus . . . tempted by the devil.* See map and accompanying text, p. 1597. *led by the Spirit . . . to be tempted.* This testing of Jesus (the Greek verb translated "tempted" can also be rendered "tested"), which was divinely intended, has as its primary background Dt 8:1 – 5, from which Jesus also quotes in his first reply to the devil (see v. 4 and NIV text note). There Moses recalls how the Lord led the Israelites in the wilderness 40 years "to humble and test you in order to know what was in your heart, whether or not you would keep his commands" (Dt 8:2). Here at the beginning of his ministry Jesus is subjected to a similar test and shows himself to be the true Israelite who lives "on every word that comes from the mouth of the LORD" (Dt 8:3). And whereas Adam failed the great test and plunged the whole race into sin (Ge 3), Jesus was faithful and thus demonstrated his qualification to become the Savior of all who receive him. It was, moreover, important that Jesus be tested/tempted as Israel and we are, so that he could become our "merciful and faithful high priest" (Heb 2:17; see note there) and thus be "able to help those who are being tempted" (Heb 2:18; see Heb 4:15 – 16). Finally, as the one who remained faithful in temptation he became the model for all believers when they are tempted. *by the devil.* God surely tests his people, but it is the devil who tempts to evil (see notes on Ge 22:1; Jas 1:13; see also 1Jn 3:8; Rev 2:9 – 10 and notes; Rev 12:9 – 10). Like the Hebrew for "Satan," the Greek for "devil" means "accuser" or "slanderer." The devil is a personal being, not a mere force or influence. He is the great archenemy of God and the leader of the hosts of darkness.

4:2 *forty days and forty nights.* The number recalls the experiences of Moses (Ex 24:18; 34:28) and Elijah (1Ki 19:8), as well as the 40 years of Israel's temptation (testing) in the wilderness (see note on v. 1).

4:3 *If you are the Son of God.* Meaning "Since you are." The devil is not casting doubt on Jesus' divine sonship but is tempting him to use his supernatural powers as the Son of God for his own ends. *Son of God.* See notes on Ps 2:7; 45:6; Jn 3:16. *tell these stones to become bread.* See note on Lk 4:3.

HEROD'S TEMPLE

20 BC–AD 70

Begun in 20 BC, Herod's new structure towered 15 stories high, following the floor dimensions of the former temples in the Holy Place and the Most Holy Place. The high sanctuary shown here was built on the site of the former temples of Solomon and Zerubbabel.

The outer courts surrounding the temple mount were not completed until AD 64. The entire structure was demolished by the Romans in AD 70.

Dimensions of rooms, steps, doorways, cornices and exterior measurements are mentioned in history (Josephus and the Mishnah) but are subject to interpretation.

4 Jesus answered, "It is written: 'Man shall not live on bread alone, but on every word that comes from the mouth of God.'[a]"[a]

5 Then the devil took him to the holy city[b] and had him stand on the highest point of the temple. 6 "If you are the Son of God,"[c] he said, "throw yourself down. For it is written:

"'He will command his angels
concerning you,
and they will lift you up in their hands,
so that you will not strike your foot
against a stone.'[b]"[d]

7 Jesus answered him, "It is also written: 'Do not put the Lord your God to the test.'[c]"[e]

8 Again, the devil took him to a very high mountain and showed him all the kingdoms of the world and their splendor. 9 "All this I will give you," he said, "if you will bow down and worship me."

10 Jesus said to him, "Away from me, Satan![f] For it is written: 'Worship the Lord your God, and serve him only.'[d]"[g]

11 Then the devil left him,[h] and angels came and attended him.[i]

Jesus Begins to Preach

12 When Jesus heard that John had been put in prison,[j] he withdrew to Galilee.[k]

[a] 4 Deut. 8:3 [b] 6 Psalm 91:11,12 [c] 7 Deut. 6:16
[d] 10 Deut. 6:13

4:4 [a]Dt 8:3; Jn 4:34 **4:5** [b]Ne 11:1; Da 9:24; Mt 27:53 **4:6** [c]S ver 3 [d]Ps 91:11,12 **4:7** [e]Dt 6:16

4:10 [f]1Ch 21:1; Job 1:6-9; Mt 16:23; Mk 4:15; Lk 10:18; 13:16; 22:3, 31; Ro 16:20; 2Co 2:11; 11:14; 2Th 2:9; Rev 12:9 [g]Dt 6:13 **4:11** [h]Jas 4:7 [i]Mt 26:53; Lk 22:43; Heb 1:14

4:12 [j]Mt 14:3 [k]Mk 1:14

4:4 Just as God gave the Israelites manna in a supernatural way (see Dt 8:3 and note), so also people today must rely on God for spiritual nourishment. Jesus relied on his Father, not his own miracle power, for provision of food (cf. Jn 4:34 and note; 6:27).
4:5 See note on Lk 4:2. *highest point of the temple.* See note on Lk 4:9. *temple.* The temple, including the entire temple area, had been rebuilt by Herod the Great (see notes on 2:1; Jn 2:20; see also model, p. 1596).
4:6 *throw yourself down.* See note on Lk 4:9. *it is written.* See note on Lk 4:10.
4:9 *worship me.* See note on Lk 4:7.
4:10 *Satan.* See note on v. 1.
4:11 *the devil left him.* See note on Lk 4:13.
4:12 See map, p. 2526, at the end of this study Bible. *John had been put in prison.* See Mk 1:14 and note on Lk 3:20. The reason for John's imprisonment is given in 14:3–4.

JESUS' BAPTISM AND TEMPTATION

Events surrounding Jesus' baptism reveal the intense religious excitement and social ferment of the early days of John the Baptist's ministry. Herod had been cruel and rapacious; Roman military occupation was harsh. Some agitation centered around the change of governors from Gratus to Pilate in AD 26. Most of the people hoped for a religious solution to their intolerable political situation, and when they heard of a new prophet, they flocked out into the desert to hear him. The religious sect (Essenes) from Qumran professed similar doctrines of repentance and baptism. Jesus was baptized at Bethany on the other side of the Jordan (see Jn 1:28). John also baptized at "Aenon near Salim" (Jn 3:23).

For Jesus' temptation, see notes on Mt 4:1–11; Lk 4:1–13.

Many interpreters place John's baptismal ministry at a point on the middle reaches of the Jordan River, where trade routes converge at a natural ford not far from the modern site of Tel Shalem.

13 Leaving Nazareth, he went and lived
in Capernaum,[l] which was by the lake in
the area of Zebulun and Naphtali— 14 to
fulfill[m] what was said through the prophet
Isaiah:

15 "Land of Zebulun and land of
Naphtali,
the Way of the Sea, beyond the
Jordan,
Galilee of the Gentiles—
16 the people living in darkness
have seen a great light;
on those living in the land of the
shadow of death
a light has dawned."[a n]

17 From that time on Jesus began to
preach, "Repent, for the kingdom of heav-
en[o] has come near."

Jesus Calls His First Disciples

4:18-22pp — Mk 1:16-20; Lk 5:2-11; Jn 1:35-42

18 As Jesus was walking beside the Sea
of Galilee,[p] he saw two brothers, Simon
called Peter[q] and his brother Andrew. They
were casting a net into the lake, for they
were fishermen. 19 "Come, follow me,"[r]
Jesus said, "and I will send you out to fish
for people." 20 At once they left their nets
and followed him.[s]
21 Going on from there, he saw two other brothers, James son of Zebedee and his
brother John.[t] They were in a boat with
their father Zebedee, preparing their nets.
Jesus called them, 22 and immediately they
left the boat and their father and followed
him.[u]

Jesus Heals the Sick

23 Jesus went throughout Galilee,[v] teaching in their synagogues,[w] proclaiming the
good news[x] of the kingdom,[y] and healing
every disease and sickness among the
people.[z] 24 News about him spread all over
Syria,[a] and people brought to him all who
were ill with various diseases, those suffering severe pain, the demon-possessed,[b]
those having seizures,[c] and the paralyzed;[d]
and he healed them. 25 Large crowds from
Galilee, the Decapolis,[b] Jerusalem, Judea
and the region across the Jordan followed
him.[e]

Introduction to the Sermon on the Mount

5 Now when Jesus saw the crowds, he
went up on a mountainside and sat
down. His disciples came to him, 2 and he
began to teach them.

[a] 16 Isaiah 9:1,2 [b] 25 That is, the Ten Cities

4:13 [l] Mk 1:21; 9:33; Lk 4:23, 31; Jn 2:12; 4:46,47 **4:14** [m] S Mt 1:22 **4:16** [n] Isa 9:1,2; Lk 2:32; Jn 1:4, 5,9 **4:17** [o] S Mt 3:2 **4:18** [p] Mt 15:29; Mk 7:31; Jn 6:1 [q] Mt 16:17,18 **4:19** [r] ver 20, 22; Mt 8:22; Mk 10:21,28, 52; Lk 5:28; Jn 1:43; 21:19, 22 **4:20** [s] S ver 19 **4:21** [t] Mt 17:1; 20:20; 26:37; Mk 3:17; 13:3; Lk 8:51; Jn 21:2 **4:22** [u] S ver 19 **4:23** [v] Mk 1:39; Lk 4:15,44 [w] Mt 9:35; 13:54; Mk 1:21; Lk 4:15; Jn 6:59; 18:20 [x] Mk 1:14 [y] S Mt 3:2; Ac 20:25; 28:23, 31 [z] Mt 8:16; 14:14; 15:30; Mk 3:10; Lk 7:22; Ac 10:38 **4:24** [a] S Lk 2:2 [b] Mt 8:16,28; 9:32; 12:22; 15:22; Mk 1:32; 5:15,16,18 [c] Mt 17:15 [d] Mt 8:6; 9:2; Mk 2:3 **4:25** [e] Mk 3:7,8; Lk 6:17

4:13 *Capernaum.* Although not mentioned in the OT, it was evidently a sizable town in Jesus' day. Peter's house there became Jesus' base of operations during his extended ministry in Galilee (see Mk 2:1; 9:33). The ruins of a fifth-century basilica now stand over the possible site of Peter's house, and a fourth-century synagogue is located a short distance from it (see model, p. 1710).

4:15 – 16 Another Messianic prophecy from Isaiah (9:1 – 2). Jesus spent most of his public ministry "in the area of Zebulun and Naphtali" (v. 13), which is north and west of the Sea of Galilee.

4:15 *Galilee of the Gentiles.* A region that, from the Jewish perspective in Jesus' day, was "in darkness" and "the land of the shadow of death" (v. 16), probably because it was far removed from the religious influences of Jerusalem and because large numbers of Gentiles lived there. Matthew may have chosen this text (Isa 9:1 – 2) because of his interest in the universal appeal of the gospel (see 2:1 – 12; 13:38; 28:19; see also Introduction: Recipients).

4:17 *From that time on.* These words indicate an important turning point in the life of Jesus and occur three times in Matthew's Gospel (see also 16:21; 26:16, "from then on"). Some think these words mark the three main sections of the book. *Repent.* See note on Mk 1:4. Jesus began his public ministry with the same message as that of John the Baptist (see 3:2 and note). The people must repent because God's reign was drawing near in the person and ministry of Jesus Christ. *kingdom of heaven.* See note on 3:2. *has come near.* See note on Mk 1:15.

4:18 *Sea of Galilee.* See note on Mk 1:16. *net.* A circular casting net used either from a boat or while standing in shallow water.

4:19 *send you out to fish for people.* Evangelism was at the heart of Jesus' call to his disciples.

4:20 See note on Mk 1:17.

4:21 *boat.* In 1986 the remains of a 2,000-year-old typical fisherman's boat were found off the northwest shore of the Sea of Galilee. Its discoverers named it the Jesus Boat, and it is now on display in a museum near Magdala (see map, p. 2526, at the end of this study Bible). The boat is about 27 feet long, 7.5 feet wide and 4.3 feet high. *preparing their nets.* Washing, mending and hanging the nets up to dry in preparation for the next day's work.

4:23 *teaching ... proclaiming ... healing.* Jesus' threefold ministry. The synagogues (see note on Mk 1:21) provided a place for him to teach on the Sabbath. During the week he preached to larger crowds in the open air. *good news.* See note on Mk 1:1.

4:24 *Syria.* The area north of Galilee and between Damascus and the Mediterranean Sea. *those having seizures.* The Greek word for this expression originally meant "moonstruck" and reflects the ancient superstition that seizures were caused by changes of the moon.

4:25 *Large crowds.* Jesus' influence spread quickly over a large geographic area. *the Decapolis.* A league of free cities (see NIV text note and map, p. 1663) characterized by high Greek culture. All but one, Scythopolis (Beth Shan), were east of the Sea of Galilee and the Jordan River. The league stretched from a point northeast of the Sea of Galilee southward to Philadelphia (modern Amman). *followed him.* Not all who followed were true disciples; many were curious onlookers, as subsequent events revealed only too clearly.

5:1 — 7:29 The Sermon on the Mount is in effect King Jesus' inaugural address, explaining what he expects of members of his kingdom. It is the first of five great discourses in Matthew (chs. 5 – 7; 10; 13; 18; 24 – 25; see Introduction: Structure). It contains three types of material: (1) beatitudes, i.e., declarations of blessedness (5:1 – 12), (2) ethical admoni-

The Beatitudes

5:3-12pp — Lk 6:20-23

He said:

3 "Blessed are the poor in spirit,
for theirs is the kingdom of
heaven.[f]
4 Blessed are those who mourn,
for they will be comforted.[g]
5 Blessed are the meek,
for they will inherit the earth.[h]
6 Blessed are those who hunger and
thirst for righteousness,
for they will be filled.[i]
7 Blessed are the merciful,
for they will be shown mercy.[j]
8 Blessed are the pure in heart,[k]
for they will see God.[l]
9 Blessed are the peacemakers,[m]
for they will be called children of
God.[n]
10 Blessed are those who are
persecuted because of
righteousness,[o]
for theirs is the kingdom of
heaven.[p]

5:3 [f] ver 10,19; S Mt 25:34
5:4 [g] Isa 61:2,3; Rev 7:17
5:5 [h] Ps 37:11; Ro 4:13
5:6 [i] Isa 55:1,2
5:7 [j] S Jas 2:13
5:8 [k] Ps 24:3,4; 73:1 [l] Ps 17:15; 42:2; Heb 12:14; Rev 22:4
5:9 [m] Jas 3:18; S Ro 14:19 [n] ver 44,45; S Ro 8:14
5:10 [o] S 1Pe 3:14 [p] ver 3,19; S Mt 25:34
5:11 [q] Isa 51:7 [r] S Jn 15:21
5:12 [s] Ps 9:2; Ac 5:41; S 2Co 6:10; 12:10; Col 1:24; Jas 1:2; 1Pe 1:6; 4:13, 16 [t] 2Ch 36:16; Mt 23:31, 37; Ac 7:52; 1Th 2:15; Heb 11:32-38
5:13 [u] Mk 9:50; Lk 14:34,35

11 "Blessed are you when people insult
you,[q] persecute you and falsely say all
kinds of evil against you because of me.[r]
12 Rejoice and be glad,[s] because great is
your reward in heaven, for in the same
way they persecuted the prophets who
were before you.[t]

Salt and Light

13 "You are the salt of the earth. But if
the salt loses its saltiness, how can it be
made salty again? It is no longer good for
anything, except to be thrown out and
trampled underfoot.[u]
14 "You are the light of the world.[v] A
town built on a hill cannot be hidden.
15 Neither do people light a lamp and put
it under a bowl. Instead they put it on its
stand, and it gives light to everyone in the
house.[w] 16 In the same way, let your light
shine before others,[x] that they may see
your good deeds[y] and glorify[z] your Father
in heaven.

5:14 [v] Jn 8:12 **5:15** [w] Mk 4:21; Lk 8:16; 11:33 **5:16** [x] 1Co 10:31; Php 1:11 [y] S Titus 2:14 [z] S Mt 9:8

---

tions (5:13–20; 6:1—7:23) and (3) contrasts between Jesus' ethical teaching and Jewish legalistic traditions (5:21–48). The Sermon ends with a short parable stressing the importance of practicing what has just been taught (7:24–27) and an expression of amazement by the crowds at the authority with which Jesus spoke (7:28–29).

Opinion differs as to whether the Sermon is a summary of what Jesus taught on one occasion or a compilation of teachings presented on numerous occasions. Matthew possibly took a single sermon and expanded it with other relevant teachings of Jesus. While much of Matthew's Sermon appears in the parallel sermon in Lk 6:17–49, 34 of the verses occur in other contexts in Luke.

The moral and ethical standard called for in the Sermon on the Mount is so high that some have dismissed the Sermon as being completely unrealistic or have projected its fulfillment to the future kingdom. There is no doubt, however, that Jesus (and Matthew) gave the Sermon as a standard for all Christians, realizing that its demands cannot be met in our own power. It is also true that Jesus occasionally used hyperbole to make his point (see, e.g., note on 5:29–30).

5:1 *mountainside.* Perhaps the gently sloping hillside at the northwest corner of the Sea of Galilee, not far from Capernaum (see note on Lk 6:20–49). The new law, like the old (Ex 19:3), was given from a mountain. *sat down.* It was the custom for Jewish rabbis to be seated while teaching (see Mk 4:1 and note; 9:35; Lk 4:20 and note; 5:3; Jn 8:2). *disciples.* Or "learners" or "followers." Since at the end of the Sermon the "crowds" expressed amazement at Jesus' teaching (7:28), "disciples" may here be used in a broader sense than the Twelve. Or perhaps the Sermon is addressed to the Twelve with the crowds also listening.

5:3 *Blessed.* The word means more than "happy," because happiness is an emotion often dependent on outward circumstances. "Blessed" here refers to the ultimate well-being and distinctive spiritual joy of those who share in the salvation of the kingdom of God. See notes on Ps 1:1; Rev 1:3. *poor in spirit.* In contrast to the spiritually proud and self-sufficient. *theirs is the kingdom of heaven.* The kingdom is not something earned. It is more a gift than a reward.

5:4 *those who mourn.* Over both personal and corporate sins (see Ezr 9:4; Ps 119:36).

5:5 *meek.* This beatitude is taken from Ps 37:11 (see note there) and refers not so much to an attitude toward people as to a disposition before God, namely, humility. *the earth.* The new promised land (see Rev 21:1; cf. note on Ps 37:9).

5:6 *hunger and thirst for righteousness.* Have a deep longing for both personal righteousness and justice for the oppressed.

5:8 *heart.* The center of one's being, including mind, will and emotions (see note on Ps 4:7).

5:9 *peacemakers.* Those who promote peace, as far as it depends on them (Ro 12:18). In so doing, they reflect the character of their heavenly Father and so are called "children of God" (see Jas 3:17–18).

5:10 *Blessed ... persecuted.* Because persecution provides an opportunity for believers to prove their fitness for the kingdom (see Heb 12:4–11 and notes). *persecuted.* Righteous living is often offensive to unbelievers (cf. v. 11). *theirs is the kingdom of heaven.* For the blessings of God's kingdom, see 3:2 and note.

5:13 *salt.* Used for flavoring and preserving (cf. Mk 9:50 and note). *loses its saltiness.* Most of the salt used in Israel came from the Dead Sea and was full of impurities. This caused it to lose some of its flavor.

5:14 *light of the world.* Although Jesus himself fulfilled the mission of the Lord's servant to be "a light for the Gentiles" (Isa 42:6; see also Lk 2:32 and notes on Isa 49:6; Lk 2:31), he expected his followers to carry on the work (see vv. 15–16; cf. Jn 8:12; Php 2:15 and notes).

5:15 *lamp.* In Jesus' day people used small clay lamps that burned olive oil drawn up by a wick (see note on Ex 25:37). *bowl.* A bowl that held about eight quarts of ground meal or flour.

5:16 *glorify your Father.* Good deeds are not to be done in a public way for one's own honor ("in front of others, to be seen by them," 6:1) but for the glory of God (see 1Co 10:31; Php 1:11; 1Pe 2:12 and notes). *Father in heaven.* Matthew uses the phrase "Father in heaven" or "heavenly Father" 17 times, Mark and Luke only once each, and John not at all.

The Fulfillment of the Law

17 "Do not think that I have come to
abolish the Law or the Prophets; I have
not come to abolish them but to fulfill
them.[a] 18 For truly I tell you, until heaven
and earth disappear, not the smallest letter, not the least stroke of a pen, will by
any means disappear from the Law until
everything is accomplished.[b] 19 Therefore
anyone who sets aside one of the least of
these commands[c] and teaches others accordingly will be called least in the kingdom of heaven, but whoever practices and
teaches these commands will be called
great in the kingdom of heaven. 20 For I
tell you that unless your righteousness
surpasses that of the Pharisees and the
teachers of the law, you will certainly not
enter the kingdom of heaven.[d]

Murder

5:25,26pp — Lk 12:58,59

21 "You have heard that it was said to
the people long ago, 'You shall not murder,[a][e] and anyone who murders will be
subject to judgment.' 22 But I tell you that
anyone who is angry[f] with a brother or sister[b,c] will be subject to judgment.[g] Again,
anyone who says to a brother or sister,
'Raca,'[d] is answerable to the court.[h] And
anyone who says, 'You fool!' will be in
danger of the fire of hell.[i]

23 "Therefore, if you are offering your gift
at the altar and there remember that your
brother or sister has something against
you, 24 leave your gift there in front of the
altar. First go and be reconciled to them;
then come and offer your gift.

25 "Settle matters quickly with your adversary who is taking you to court. Do it
while you are still together on the way, or
your adversary may hand you over to the
judge, and the judge may hand you over
to the officer, and you may be thrown
into prison. 26 Truly I tell you, you will
not get out until you have paid the last
penny.

Adultery

27 "You have heard that it was said, 'You
shall not commit adultery.'[e][j] 28 But I tell
you that anyone who looks at a woman
lustfully has already committed adultery
with her in his heart.[k] 29 If your right eye
causes you to stumble,[l] gouge it out and
throw it away. It is better for you to lose
one part of your body than for your whole
body to be thrown into hell. 30 And if your
right hand causes you to stumble,[m] cut it
off and throw it away. It is better for you

5:17 [a] Jn 10:34, 35; Ro 3:31
5:18 [b] Ps 119:89; Isa 40:8; 55:11; Mt 24:35; Mk 13:31; Lk 16:17; 21:33
5:19 [c] Jas 2:10
5:20 [d] Isa 26:2; Mt 18:3; Jn 3:5
5:21 [e] Ex 20:13; 21:12; Dt 5:17
5:22 [f] Ecc 7:9; 1Co 13:5; Eph 4:26; Jas 1:19,20 [g] 1Jn 3:15 [h] Mt 26:59; Jn 11:47; Ac 5:21,27, 34,41; 6:12 [i] Mt 18:9; Mk 9:43,48; Lk 16:24; Jas 3:6
5:27 [j] Ex 20:14; Dt 5:18
5:28 [k] Pr 6:25; 2Pe 2:14
5:29 [l] ver 30; Mt 18:6,8,9; Mk 9:42-47; Lk 17:2; Ro 14:21; 1Co 8:13; S 2Co 6:3; 11:29
5:30 [m] S ver 29

[a] *21* Exodus 20:13 [b] *22* The Greek word for *brother or sister* (*adelphos*) refers here to a fellow disciple, whether man or woman; also in verse 23. [c] *22* Some manuscripts *brother or sister without cause* [d] *22* An Aramaic term of contempt [e] *27* Exodus 20:14

5:17 *the Law.* The first five books of the OT. *the Prophets.* Not only the Latter Prophets — Isaiah, Jeremiah and Ezekiel, which we call Major Prophets, and the 12 Minor Prophets (lumped together by the Jews as "the Book of the Twelve") — but also the Former Prophets (Joshua, Judges, Samuel and Kings). Taken together, "the Law" and "the Prophets" designated the entire OT, including the Writings, the third section of the Hebrew Bible. See 13:35, where Matthew introduces a quotation from the Writings (Ps 78:2) with "what was spoken through the prophet." *fulfill.* Jesus fulfilled the Law in the sense that he gave it its full meaning. He emphasized its deep, underlying principles and total commitment to it rather than mere external acknowledgment and obedience.

5:18 – 20 Jesus is not speaking against observing all the requirements of the Law but against hypocritical, Pharisaical legalism. Such legalism was not the keeping of all details of the Law but the hollow sham of keeping laws externally to gain merit before God while breaking them inwardly. It was following the letter of the Law while ignoring its spirit. Jesus repudiates the Pharisees' interpretation of the Law and their view of righteousness by works. He preaches a righteousness that comes only through faith in him and his work. In the rest of the chapter, he gives six examples of Pharisaical externalism. He thus explains what he means in vv. 21 – 48.

5:18 *smallest letter.* The Greek text has *iota*, the smallest letter of the Greek alphabet. It is the nearest equivalent to and cognate of Hebrew *yodh*, the smallest letter of the Hebrew alphabet (see Ps 119:73 title). *least stroke of a pen.* The Greek word for this phrase means "horn" and was used to designate the slight extension of certain letters of the Hebrew alphabet (somewhat like the bottom of a *j*).

5:20 *Pharisees.* See note on 3:7. *teachers of the law.* See note on 2:4. *kingdom of heaven.* See note on 3:2.

5:21 – 22 *it was said ... But I tell you.* See vv. 27 – 28, 31 – 32,33 – 34,38 – 39,43 – 44. Jesus calls for moving beyond merely external obedience to the letter of the Law to keeping the true spirit of the Law. *murder.* Several Hebrew and Greek verbs mean "kill." The ones used here and in Ex 20:13 mean specifically "murder."

5:22 *Raca.* May be related to the Aramaic word for "empty" and mean "Empty-head!" *court.* Lit. "Sanhedrin" (see note on Mk 14:55). *hell.* The Greek word is *ge(h)enna,* which derives its name from a deep ravine south of Jerusalem, the "Valley of (the Sons of) Hinnom" (Hebrew *ge' hinnom*). During the reigns of the wicked Ahaz and Manasseh, human sacrifices to the Ammonite god Molek were offered there. Josiah desecrated the valley because of the pagan worship there (2Ki 23:10; see Jer 7:31 – 32; 19:6). It was perhaps because of this desecration that the term came to be used for the place of final punishment (see notes on Isa 66:24; Jer 7:31).

5:23 – 26 Two illustrations of dealing with anger by means of reconciliation.

5:25 Cf. Lk 12:57 – 59.

5:26 *penny.* The smallest Roman copper coin (see note on Lk 12:59).

5:28 *looks at a woman lustfully.* Not a passing glance but a willful, calculated stare that arouses sexual desire. According to Jesus this is a form of adultery even if it is only "in his heart" (see Job 31:1; 2Pe 2:14 and notes).

5:29 – 30 Jesus is not teaching self-mutilation, for even a blind man can lust. What he is saying is that we should deal as drastically as necessary with sin, a point Jesus repeated on at least one other occasion (see 18:8 – 9; Mk 9:43 – 48).

to lose one part of your body than for your
whole body to go into hell.

Divorce

31 "It has been said, 'Anyone who divorces his wife must give her a certificate
of divorce.'[a][n] 32 But I tell you that anyone
who divorces his wife, except for sexual
immorality, makes her the victim of adultery, and anyone who marries a divorced
woman commits adultery.[o]

Oaths

33 "Again, you have heard that it was
said to the people long ago, 'Do not break
your oath,[p] but fulfill to the Lord the vows
you have made.'[q] 34 But I tell you, do not
swear an oath at all:[r] either by heaven,
for it is God's throne;[s] 35 or by the earth,
for it is his footstool; or by Jerusalem, for
it is the city of the Great King.[t] 36 And do
not swear by your head, for you cannot
make even one hair white or black. 37 All
you need to say is simply 'Yes' or 'No';[u]
anything beyond this comes from the evil
one.[b][v]

Eye for Eye

38 "You have heard that it was said, 'Eye
for eye, and tooth for tooth.'[c][w] 39 But I tell
you, do not resist an evil person. If anyone slaps you on the right cheek, turn to
them the other cheek also.[x] 40 And if anyone wants to sue you and take your shirt,
hand over your coat as well. 41 If anyone
forces you to go one mile, go with them
two miles. 42 Give to the one who asks
you, and do not turn away from the one
who wants to borrow from you.[y]

Love for Enemies

43 "You have heard that it was said,
'Love your neighbor[d][z] and hate your enemy.'[a] 44 But I tell you, love your enemies
and pray for those who persecute you,[b]
45 that you may be children[c] of your Father in heaven. He causes his sun to rise
on the evil and the good, and sends rain
on the righteous and the unrighteous.[d]
46 If you love those who love you, what
reward will you get?[e] Are not even the tax
collectors doing that? 47 And if you greet
only your own people, what are you doing
more than others? Do not even pagans do
that? 48 Be perfect, therefore, as your heavenly Father is perfect.[f]

Giving to the Needy

6 "Be careful not to practice your righteousness in front of others to be seen
by them.[g] If you do, you will have no reward from your Father in heaven.
2 "So when you give to the needy, do not
announce it with trumpets, as the hypocrites do in the synagogues and on the
streets, to be honored by others. Truly I
tell you, they have received their reward
in full. 3 But when you give to the needy,

5:31 [n] Dt 24:1-4
5:32 [o] S Lk 16:18
5:33 [p] Lev 19:12 [q] Nu 30:2; Dt 23:21; Mt 23:16-22
5:34 [r] Jas 5:12 [s] Isa 66:1; Mt 23:22
5:35 [t] Ps 48:2
5:37 [u] Jas 5:12 [v] Mt 6:13; 13:19, 38; Jn 17:15; Eph 6:16; 2Th 3:3; 1Jn 2:13, 14; 3:12; 5:18, 19
5:38 [w] Ex 21:24; Lev 24:20; Dt 19:21
5:39 [x] Lk 6:29; Ro 12:17, 19; 1Pe 3:9
5:42 [y] Dt 15:8; Lk 6:30
5:43 [z] Lev 19:18; Mt 19:19; 22:39; Mk 12:31; Lk 10:27; Ro 13:9; Gal 5:14; Jas 2:8 [a] Dt 23:6; Ps 139:21, 22
5:44 [b] Lk 6:27, 28; 23:34; Jn 15:20; Ac 7:60; Ro 8:35; 12:14; 1Co 4:12; 1Pe 2:23
5:45 [c] ver 9; Lk 6:35; S Ro 8:14 [d] Job 25:3
5:46 [e] Lk 6:32
5:48 [f] Lev 19:2; 1Pe 1:16
6:1 [g] Mt 5:16; 23:5

[a] 31 Deut. 24:1 [b] 37 Or *from evil* [c] 38 Exodus 21:24; Lev. 24:20; Deut. 19:21 [d] 43 Lev. 19:18

5:30 *hell.* See note on v. 22.
5:32 *except for sexual immorality.* See note on 19:3. Neither Mk 10:11 – 12 nor Lk 16:18 mentions this exception.
5:33 – 37 The OT recognized the useful role of swearing oaths in certain situations (even God swore oaths: see, e.g., Ge 22:16; Jos 5:6; Ps 89:3 – 4,35; Isa 45:22; Jer 22:5; Eze 26:7; see also notes on Ge 9:13; 15:17; Dt 6:13; Jer 22:5; Heb 6:13) — common profanity is not in view. Jesus urged such honesty and integrity in all human speech that swearing oaths in support of assertions or commitments would not be necessary.
5:39 *resist.* Here it probably means in a court of law. *slaps.* The Greek verb used here means "slaps you with the back of the hand." It was more an insult (cf. 26:67) than an act of violence. The point is that it is better to be insulted even twice than to take the matter to court. Ancient Near Eastern society had become very litigious.
5:40 *shirt … coat.* The first was an undergarment, the second a loose outer one. Since the outer garment was used to keep a person warm at night, OT law prohibited anyone from taking it even as collateral overnight (see Ex 22:26 – 27; Dt 24:12 – 13).
5:42 Probably not a general requirement to give to everyone who asks but a reference to the poor (cf. Dt 15:7 – 11; Ps 112:5,9).
5:43 *hate your enemy.* Words not found anywhere in the OT. However, hatred for one's enemies was an accepted part of the Jewish ethic at that time in some circles (cf., e.g., the Dead Sea Scrolls work *The Rule of the Community,* 1.4,10). See note on Lev 19:18.
5:44 *love your enemies.* See note on Ex 23:4 – 5. *pray.* Prayer is one of the practical ways love expresses itself (cf. Job 42:10; Ps 35:13 – 14 and notes).
5:45 *be children of your Father in heaven.* That is, be truly like him by loving "your enemies" and praying for "those who persecute you" (v. 44; see v. 48 and note). *the evil and the good.* God shows his love to people without distinction.
5:46 *tax collectors.* Traditionally known as "publicans," these were local men employed by Roman tax contractors to collect taxes for them. Because they worked for Rome and often demanded unreasonable payments, the tax collectors gained a bad reputation and were generally hated and considered traitors (see notes on Mk 2:14 – 15; Lk 3:12).
5:48 *Be perfect.* Christ sets up the high ideal of perfect love (see vv. 43 – 47) — not that we can fully attain it in this life. That, however, is God's high standard for us.
6:1 *practice … righteousness.* This verse introduces the discussion of three acts of righteousness: (1) giving (vv. 2 – 4), (2) praying (vv. 5 – 15) and (3) fasting (vv. 16 – 18). Jesus' concern here is with the motives behind such acts. *reward from your Father.* Spiritual growth and maturity or perhaps a heavenly reward of some kind — or both.
6:2 *when you give.* Not "if you give." Jesus presupposes the disciples' giving to the poor. *announce it with trumpets.* Perhaps a reference to the noise made by coins as they were thrown into the trumpet-shaped treasury receptacles (see note on Mk 12:41). Or the phrase may be used figuratively to mean "make a big show of it." *hypocrites.* The Greek word means "play-actor." Here it refers to those who fake being

do not let your left hand know what your
right hand is doing, 4so that your giving
may be in secret. Then your Father, who
sees what is done in secret, will reward
you.[h]

Prayer

6:9-13pp — Lk 11:2-4

5"And when you pray, do not be like the
hypocrites, for they love to pray standing[i]
in the synagogues and on the street corners
to be seen by others. Truly I tell you, they
have received their reward in full. 6But
when you pray, go into your room, close
the door and pray to your Father,[j] who is
unseen. Then your Father, who sees what
is done in secret, will reward you. 7And
when you pray, do not keep on babbling[k]
like pagans, for they think they will be
heard because of their many words.[l] 8Do
not be like them, for your Father knows
what you need[m] before you ask him.
9"This, then, is how you should pray:

"'Our Father[n] in heaven,
hallowed be your name,
10your kingdom[o] come,
your will be done,[p]
on earth as it is in heaven.
11Give us today our daily bread.[q]
12And forgive us our debts,
as we also have forgiven our
debtors.[r]
13And lead us not into temptation,[a][s]
but deliver us from the evil one.[b]'[t]

14For if you forgive other people when
they sin against you, your heavenly Father
will also forgive you.[u] 15But if you do not
forgive others their sins, your Father will
not forgive your sins.[v]

Fasting

16"When you fast,[w] do not look somber[x]
as the hypocrites do, for they disfigure
their faces to show others they are fasting.
Truly I tell you, they have received their
reward in full. 17But when you fast, put
oil on your head and wash your face, 18so
that it will not be obvious to others that
you are fasting, but only to your Father,
who is unseen; and your Father, who sees
what is done in secret, will reward you.[y]

Treasures in Heaven

6:22,23pp — Lk 11:34-36

19"Do not store up for yourselves trea-

6:4 [h] ver 6,18; Col 3:23,24 **6:5** [i] Mk 11:25; Lk 18:10-14 **6:6** [j] 2Ki 4:33 **6:7** [k] Ecc 5:2 [l] 1Ki 18:26-29 **6:8** [m] ver 32 **6:9** [n] Jer 3:19; Mal 2:10; 1Pe 1:17 **6:10** [o] S Mt 3:2 [p] S Mt 26:39 **6:11** [q] Pr 30:8 **6:12** [r] Mt 18:21-35 **6:13** [s] Jas 1:13 [t] S Mt 5:37 **6:14** [u] Mt 18:21-35; Mk 11:25,26; Eph 4:32; Col 3:13 **6:15** [v] Mt 18:35 **6:16** [w] Lev 16:29,31; 23:27-32; Nu 29:7 [x] Isa 58:5; Zec 7:5; 8:19 **6:18** [y] ver 4,6

[a] 13 The Greek for *temptation* can also mean *testing.*
[b] 13 Or *from evil;* some late manuscripts *one, / for yours is the kingdom and the power and the glory forever. Amen.*

---

pious. *their reward in full.* The honor they receive from people is all the reward they get.

6:3 *do not let your left hand know what your right hand is doing.* Not to be taken literally but as a way of emphasizing that one should not call attention to one's giving. Self-glorification is always a present danger.

6:6 Jesus' followers are not to make a show of their praying, in contrast to "the hypocrites" (v. 5). This does not mean that all prayer should be private, as the plurals "our" and "us" in vv. 9–13 indicate. *room.* The Greek word here probably means "storeroom," because unlike most of the rooms in the house, it had a door that could be shut.

6:7 *babbling like pagans.* They used long lists of the names of their gods in their prayers, hoping that by constantly repeating them they would call on the name of the god that could help them. Jesus is not necessarily condemning all long prayers, but meaningless verbiage in praying.

6:9–13 Commonly known as "The Lord's Prayer," it is really "The Disciples' Prayer," since it was meant as a model for them (the true "Lord's Prayer" is found in Jn 17). The prayer nestles at the literary center of the Sermon on the Mount, and the surrounding texts in the Sermon echo the prayer's concerns. It contains six petitions, three relating more directly to God (vv. 9–10) and three to us (vv. 11–13). The order of these petitions is significant and intentional. A similar prayer in Lk 11:2–4 occurs in a different historical setting.

6:9 *hallowed.* God is already holy (see Lev 11:44 and note; 1Pe 1:15), so the prayer is not that God be made holy but that he be regarded as holy. By his saving and judging acts in history he proves himself holy (see Lev 10:3; Eze 36:23 and notes). This petition is that he so achieve his saving purposes in the world that his holiness is displayed before the eyes of the world's people and acknowledged by them—which will happen only as his kingdom comes. *name.* See notes on Ps 5:11; Eze 20:9.

6:10 *your kingdom come.* Not in the sense of to "come" into existence—after all, it is already here (see 3:2; Lk 17:21 and notes)—but to "come" more and more completely until its full and final consummation. *your will be done.* Logically follows "your kingdom come." The NIV scansion and punctuation suggest that "on earth as it is in heaven" be read with each of the three preceding petitions.

6:11 That is, meet our needs "each day" (Lk 11:3; see Ex 16:4 and note).

6:12 *debts.* Moral debts, i.e., sins (see note on Lk 11:4).

6:13 *lead us not into temptation.* That is, do not lead us through trials so deep that they would tempt us to be unfaithful to you. God does not tempt (in the sense of enticing to sin; see Jas 1:13 and note; see also 1Co 10:13 and note). *the evil one.* Satan (see 13:19 and note). Others think the reference is to "evil," i.e., evil circumstances (see the first part of the second NIV text note). For the second part of the NIV text note, cf. 1Ch 29:10–11.

6:15 *forgive . . . forgive.* See Eph 4:32 and note.

6:16 *fast.* See notes on Mk 2:18; Lk 18:12. Jesus does not condemn fasting as such but ostentation in fasting. *hypocrites.* See note on v. 2. *their reward in full.* See note on v. 2.

6:17 *put oil on your head and wash your face.* That is, maintain your regular appearance. Jews put ashes on their heads when fasting.

6:19–21 The dangers of riches are often mentioned in the NT (e.g., v. 24; 13:22; 19:22; Mk 10:17–30; Lk 12:16–21; 1Ti 6:9–10,17–19; Heb 13:5; Jas 5:2–3), but nowhere are riches condemned in and of themselves. What Jesus condemns here is greed and the hoarding of money.

6:19 *Do not store up.* Or "Stop storing up." They may have already started to do it. *moths and vermin.* Representative of all agents and processes that destroy worldly possessions. *break in and steal.* Houses in the Holy Land had walls made of mud bricks and could be broken into easily.

sures on earth,[z] where moths and vermin
destroy,[a] and where thieves break in and
steal. 20 But store up for yourselves treasures in heaven,[b] where moths and vermin
do not destroy, and where thieves do not
break in and steal.[c] 21 For where your treasure is, there your heart will be also.[d]

22 "The eye is the lamp of the body. If
your eyes are healthy,[a] your whole body
will be full of light. 23 But if your eyes are
unhealthy,[b] your whole body will be full
of darkness. If then the light within you is
darkness, how great is that darkness!

24 "No one can serve two masters. Either
you will hate the one and love the other,
or you will be devoted to the one and despise the other. You cannot serve both God
and money.[e]

Do Not Worry

6:25-33pp — Lk 12:22-31

25 "Therefore I tell you, do not worry[f]
about your life, what you will eat or drink;
or about your body, what you will wear.
Is not life more than food, and the body
more than clothes? 26 Look at the birds of
the air; they do not sow or reap or store
away in barns, and yet your heavenly Father feeds them.[g] Are you not much more
valuable than they?[h] 27 Can any one of you
by worrying add a single hour to your
life[c]?[i]

28 "And why do you worry about clothes?
See how the flowers of the field grow. They
do not labor or spin. 29 Yet I tell you that
not even Solomon in all his splendor[j] was
dressed like one of these. 30 If that is how
God clothes the grass of the field, which
is here today and tomorrow is thrown into
the fire, will he not much more clothe
you — you of little faith?[k] 31 So do not worry, saying, 'What shall we eat?' or 'What
shall we drink?' or 'What shall we wear?'
32 For the pagans run after all these things,
and your heavenly Father knows that you
need them.[l] 33 But seek first his kingdom[m]
and his righteousness, and all these things
will be given to you as well.[n] 34 Therefore
do not worry about tomorrow, for tomorrow will worry about itself. Each day has
enough trouble of its own.

Judging Others

7:3-5pp — Lk 6:41,42

7 "Do not judge, or you too will be
judged.[o] 2 For in the same way you
judge others, you will be judged, and with
the measure you use, it will be measured
to you.[p]

3 "Why do you look at the speck of sawdust in your brother's eye and pay no
attention to the plank in your own eye?
4 How can you say to your brother, 'Let
me take the speck out of your eye,' when
all the time there is a plank in your own
eye? 5 You hypocrite, first take the plank
out of your own eye, and then you will
see clearly to remove the speck from your
brother's eye.

6 "Do not give dogs what is sacred; do
not throw your pearls to pigs. If you do,
they may trample them under their feet,
and turn and tear you to pieces.

Ask, Seek, Knock

7:7-11pp — Lk 11:9-13

7 "Ask and it will be given to you;[q] seek

6:19 [z] Pr 23:4; Lk 12:16-21; Heb 13:5 [a] S Jas 5:2,3 **6:20** [b] Mt 19:21; Lk 12:33; 16:9; 18:22; 1Ti 6:19 [c] Lk 12:33 **6:21** [d] Lk 12:34 **6:24** [e] Lk 16:13 **6:25** [f] ver 27, 28, 31, 34; Lk 10:41; 12:11, 22 **6:26** [g] Job 38:41; Ps 104:21; 136:25; 145:15; 147:9 [h] Mt 10:29-31 **6:27** [i] Ps 39:5 **6:29** [j] 1Ki 10:4-7 **6:30** [k] Mt 8:26; 14:31; 16:8; Lk 12:28 **6:32** [l] ver 8 **6:33** [m] S Mt 3:2 [n] Ps 37:4; Mt 19:29 **7:1** [o] Lk 6:37; Ro 14:4, 10, 13; 1Co 4:5; 5:12; Jas 4:11, 12 **7:2** [p] Eze 35:11; Mk 4:24; Lk 6:38; Ro 2:1 **7:7** [q] 1Ki 3:5; Mt 18:19; 21:22; Jn 14:13, 14; 15:7, 16; 16:23, 24; Jas 1:5-8; 4:2, 3; 5:16; 1Jn 3:22; 5:14, 15

[a] 22 The Greek for *healthy* here implies *generous.*
[b] 23 The Greek for *unhealthy* here implies *stingy.*
[c] 27 Or *single cubit to your height*

6:20 *treasures in heaven.* Anything done in this life that has eternal value will be rewarded. Cf. "rich toward God" (Lk 12:21).
6:21 See Lk 12:34. *heart.* See note on 5:8.
6:22 *The eye is the lamp of the body.* It lets light in to illumine the body. *your eyes are healthy.* You recognize the folly of storing up wealth (v. 19) — but see NIV text note. *whole body.* Entire person.
6:23 *your eyes are unhealthy.* They are blind to the deceitfulness of wealth — but see NIV text note.
6:24 See Lk 16:13; Jas 4:4.
6:25 *do not worry.* See Php 4:6 and note. *worry.* Undue anxiety, not a legitimate concern to provide for one's daily needs (cf. Lk 10:41 – 42; 2Th 3:6 – 12).
6:27 *add a single hour.* See NIV text note. The phrase could also mean "add a single step (cubit) to life's journey."
6:30 *thrown into the fire.* Grass was commonly used to heat clay ovens in the Holy Land. *you of little faith.* See 8:26; 14:31; 16:8; 17:20; Lk 12:28.
6:33 The heart of the matter. *kingdom.* See note on 3:2. *his righteousness.* The righteous life that God requires, as the content of the Sermon emphasizes (see, e.g., 5:6,10,20; 6:1).
7:1 The Christian is not to judge hypocritically or self-righteously, as can be seen from the context (v. 5). The same thought is expressed in 23:13 – 39 (cf. Ro 2:1). To obey Christ's commands in this chapter, we must first evaluate a person's character — whether one is a "dog" (v. 6) or a false prophet (v. 15), or whether one's life shows fruit (v. 16). Scripture repeatedly exhorts believers to evaluate carefully (see Jn 7:24) and choose between good and bad people and things (sexually immoral, 1Co 5:9; those who masquerade as angels of light, 2Co 11:14; dogs, Php 3:2; false prophets, 1Jn 4:1). The Christian is to "test them all" (1Th 5:21).
7:3 – 5 Jesus rebukes hypocritical judging.
7:3 *speck of sawdust . . . plank.* An example of hyperbole in the teachings of Jesus (cf. 19:24). Its purpose is to drive home a point (see Lk 6:41 and note).
7:5 *hypocrite.* See note on 6:2.
7:6 Teaching about the kingdom should be given in accordance with the spiritual capacity of the learners. *dogs.* The unclean dogs of the street were held in low esteem.
7:7 – 11 See note on Lk 11:5 – 13.
7:7 *Ask . . . seek . . . knock.* Greek present imperatives are used here, indicating continual asking, seeking and knocking. Persistent prayer is being emphasized (cf. Jas 4:2 – 3; cf. also Ge 32:26 and note).

and you will find; knock and the door will be opened to you. 8 For everyone who asks receives; the one who seeks finds;[r] and to the one who knocks, the door will be opened.

9 "Which of you, if your son asks for bread, will give him a stone? 10 Or if he asks for a fish, will give him a snake? 11 If you, then, though you are evil, know how to give good gifts to your children, how much more will your Father in heaven give good gifts[s] to those who ask him! 12 So in everything, do to others what you would have them do to you,[t] for this sums up the Law and the Prophets.[u]

The Narrow and Wide Gates

13 "Enter through the narrow gate.[v] For wide is the gate and broad is the road that leads to destruction, and many enter through it. 14 But small is the gate and narrow the road that leads to life, and only a few find it.

True and False Prophets

15 "Watch out for false prophets.[w] They come to you in sheep's clothing, but inwardly they are ferocious wolves.[x] 16 By their fruit you will recognize them.[y] Do people pick grapes from thornbushes, or figs from thistles?[z] 17 Likewise, every good tree bears good fruit, but a bad tree bears bad fruit. 18 A good tree cannot bear bad fruit, and a bad tree cannot bear good fruit.[a] 19 Every tree that does not bear good fruit is cut down and thrown into the fire.[b] 20 Thus, by their fruit you will recognize them.

True and False Disciples

21 "Not everyone who says to me, 'Lord, Lord,'[c] will enter the kingdom of heaven,[d] but only the one who does the will of my Father who is in heaven.[e] 22 Many will say to me on that day,[f] 'Lord, Lord, did we not prophesy in your name and in your name drive out demons and in your name perform many miracles?'[g] 23 Then I will tell them plainly, 'I never knew you. Away from me, you evildoers!'[h]

The Wise and Foolish Builders

7:24-27pp — Lk 6:47-49

24 "Therefore everyone who hears these words of mine and puts them into practice[i] is like a wise man who built his house on the rock. 25 The rain came down, the streams rose, and the winds blew and beat against that house; yet it did not fall, because it had its foundation on the rock. 26 But everyone who hears these words of mine and does not put them into practice is like a foolish man who built his house on sand. 27 The rain came down, the streams rose, and the winds blew and beat against that house, and it fell with a great crash."

28 When Jesus had finished saying these things,[j] the crowds were amazed at his teaching,[k] 29 because he taught as one who had authority, and not as their teachers of the law.

Jesus Heals a Man With Leprosy

8:2-4pp — Mk 1:40-44; Lk 5:12-14

8 When Jesus came down from the mountainside, large crowds followed him. 2 A man with leprosy[a][l] came and knelt before him[m] and said, "Lord, if you are willing, you can make me clean."

3 Jesus reached out his hand and touched

7:8 [r] Pr 8:17; Jer 29:12,13 **7:11** [s] Jas 1:17 **7:12** [t] Lk 6:31 [u] Ro 13:8-10; Gal 5:14 **7:13** [v] Lk 13:24; Jn 10:7,9 **7:15** [w] Jer 23:16; Mt 24:24; Lk 6:26; 2Pe 2:1; 1Jn 4:1; Rev 16:13 [x] Eze 22:27; Ac 20:29 **7:16** [y] Mt 12:33; Lk 6:44 [z] Jas 3:12 **7:18** [a] Lk 6:43 **7:19** [b] S Mt 3:10 **7:21** [c] Hos 8:2; Mt 25:11; S Jn 13:13; 1Co 12:3 [d] S Mt 3:2 [e] Mt 12:50; Ro 2:13; Jas 1:22; 1Jn 3:18 **7:22** [f] S Mt 10:15 [g] Lk 10:20; Ac 19:13; 1Co 13:1-3 **7:23** [h] Ps 6:8; Mt 25:12,41; Lk 13:25-27 **7:24** [i] ver 21; Jas 1:22-25 **7:28** [j] Mt 11:1; 13:53; 19:1; 26:1 [k] Mt 13:54; 22:33; Mk 1:22; 6:2; 11:18; Lk 4:32; Jn 7:46 **8:2** [l] Lev 13:45; Mt 10:8; 11:5; 26:6; Lk 5:12; 17:12 [m] Mt 9:18; 15:25; 18:26; 20:20

[a] 2 The Greek word traditionally translated *leprosy* was used for various diseases affecting the skin.

7:11 *good gifts.* See Lk 11:13 and note.
7:12 The so-called Golden Rule is found in negative form in rabbinic Judaism and also in Hinduism, Buddhism and Confucianism. It occurred in various forms in Greek and Roman ethical teaching. Jesus stated it in positive form. *in everything.* Probably refers to the teaching of the entire Sermon up to this point. *sums up.* Cf. 22:36–40; Ro 13:8–10 and relevant notes. *the Law and the Prophets.* See note on 5:17.
7:13–27 These verses present two ways (vv. 13–14), two trees and two fruits (vv. 15–23), and two foundations (vv. 24–27).
7:13 *narrow gate.* The gate that leads into the kingdom of heaven is synonymous with "life" (v. 14). *destruction.* Separation from God in hell.
7:15 *false prophets.* People who have not been sent by God but who claim that they have (see 24:24; Jer 23:16 and note).
7:19 See Jn 15:6 and note; cf. Mt 3:10.
7:20 Cf. Jn 15:7 and note.
7:21 *Lord.* Here seems to mean more than merely "sir" or "master" since Jesus is the one who makes the final decision about a person's eternal destiny. *kingdom of heaven.* See note on 3:2. *does the will of my Father.* The deciding factor as to who enters the kingdom (see Mk 3:35 and note).
7:22 *that day.* The day of judgment (cf. Mal 3:17–18). *prophesy.* In the Bible this verb primarily means to give a message from God, not necessarily to predict. *demons.* See note on Mk 1:23.
7:24–27 This parable ends the Sermon on the Mount and also the parallel sermon in Luke (6:47–49).
7:24 *rock.* The Bible often speaks metaphorically of God or Christ as a "rock" (see Ge 49:24; Ps 18:2; 1Co 10:4 and notes).
7:25 *rain came down.* The Holy Land is known for its torrential rains that often cause disastrous floods.
7:28 *were amazed.* A common reaction by Jesus' listeners to his teaching—both its presentation and its authority (see note on Mk 1:22).
7:29 *authority.* The teachers of the law quoted other rabbis to support their own teaching (see note on 2:4), but Jesus spoke with divine authority (see 9:6,8; cf. Jn 7:46).
8:1 *mountainside.* See 5:1 and note.
8:2 *leprosy.* See NIV text note; see also note on Lev 13:2. *Lord.* See note on 7:21. *make me clean.* Leprosy made a person ceremonially unclean (see Lev 13:3,8,11,20) and socially an outcast (see Lev 13:45–46).

MATTHEW'S **FULFILLMENT QUOTATIONS**

TEN FULFILLMENT STATEMENTS		OTHER FULFILLMENT CITATIONS	
1:22–23	Jesus' virgin birth fulfills Isaiah 7:14.	2:5–6	Jesus' Bethlehem birth fulfills Micah 5:2.
2:15	The escape to and return from Egypt fulfills Hosea 11:1.	3:3	John the Baptist fulfills Isaiah 40:3.
2:17–18	The murder of the male infants of Bethlehem fulfills Jeremiah 31:15.	5:17	Jesus fulfills the Law and the Prophets.
		10:34–35	The division of families fulfills Micah 7:6.
2:23	Jesus' childhood in Nazareth fulfills an unknown prophecy.*	11:2–6	Jesus performs Messianic signs, fulfilling Isaiah 35:5; 61:1, etc.
4:14–16	Jesus establishes his ministry in Galilee, fulfilling Isaiah 9:2.	11:10	John the Baptist fulfills Malachi 3:1.
8:17	Jesus heals disease, fulfilling Isaiah 53:4.	13:14–15	Parables conceal the truth from the hard-hearted (Isa 6:9).
12:17–21	Jesus fulfills the role of the Servant of Isaiah 42:2.	15:7–9	Israel's disobedience fulfills Isaiah 29:13.
13:35	Jesus speaks in parables, fulfilling Psalm 78:2; 2 Chronicles 29:30.	21:13	The temple is a den of robbers (Isa 56:7; Jer 7:11).
		21:16	Praise from the lips of children is predicted in Psalm 8:2.
21:4–5	Jesus enters Jerusalem as the humble king of Zechariah 9:9.	21:42	The rejected stone becomes the cornerstone (Ps 118:22).
27:9–10	Jesus is betrayed for 30 pieces of silver, fulfilling Zechariah 11:12–13.	26:31	The shepherd is struck down and the sheep scattered (Zec 13:7).

*"He would be called a Nazarene" may be a reference to the "Branch" (*neṣer*) of Isaiah 11:1, or a general statement of the humble origins of the Messiah.

the man. "I am willing," he said. "Be
clean!" Immediately he was cleansed of
his leprosy. 4 Then Jesus said to him, "See
that you don't tell anyone.[n] But go, show
yourself to the priest[o] and offer the gift Moses commanded,[p] as a testimony to them."

The Faith of the Centurion

8:5-13pp — Lk 7:1-10

5 When Jesus had entered Capernaum,
a centurion came to him, asking for help.
6 "Lord," he said, "my servant lies at home
paralyzed,[q] suffering terribly."
7 Jesus said to him, "Shall I come and
heal him?"
8 The centurion replied, "Lord, I do not
deserve to have you come under my roof.
But just say the word, and my servant will
be healed.[r] 9 For I myself am a man under
authority, with soldiers under me. I tell
this one, 'Go,' and he goes; and that one,
'Come,' and he comes. I say to my servant,
'Do this,' and he does it."
10 When Jesus heard this, he was
amazed and said to those following him,
"Truly I tell you, I have not found anyone in Israel with such great faith.[s] 11 I say
to you that many will come from the east
and the west,[t] and will take their places at
the feast with Abraham, Isaac and Jacob
in the kingdom of heaven.[u] 12 But the subjects of the kingdom[v] will be thrown outside, into the darkness, where there will
be weeping and gnashing of teeth."[w]

8:4 [n] Mt 9:30; 12:16; Mk 5:43; 7:36; S 8:30; Lk 4:41 [o] Lk 17:14 [p] Lev 14:2-32 **8:6** [q] S Mt 4:24
8:8 [r] Ps 107:20 **8:10** [s] Mt 15:28 **8:11** [t] Ps 107:3; Isa 49:12; 59:19; Mal 1:11 [u] Lk 13:29 **8:12** [v] Mt 13:38 [w] Mt 13:42, 50; 22:13; 24:51; 25:30; Lk 13:28

8:3 *touched the man.* See note on Mk 1:41.
8:4 *don't tell anyone.* Jesus did not wish to stir up the popular, but mistaken, expectations that a wonder-working Messiah would soon arise as king of the Jews and deliver them from the Roman yoke. For similar instructions, see 9:30; 12:16; 16:20 and note; 17:9. See also Introduction to Mark: Emphases (item 4). *show yourself to the priest.* See note on Lk 5:14. *a testimony to them.* See note on Mk 1:44. *them.* The priests and the people.
8:5–13 Although the incident in Jn 4:46–54 is similar, it probably is a separate episode in the life of Jesus.
8:5 *Capernaum.* See note on 4:13. *centurion.* A Roman military officer in charge of 100 soldiers. In Luke's account (Lk 7:1–5) Jewish elders and friends of the centurion came to Jesus on his behalf, but Matthew does not mention these intermediaries.
8:8 *I do not deserve to have you come under my roof.* In Greek the words "I do not deserve" are the same as those used by John the Baptist in 3:11 ("I am not worthy"). The entire statement reveals how highly the centurion regarded Jesus. Or perhaps his response reflects his own sense of moral guilt in the presence of Jesus.
8:10 *he was amazed.* See note on Lk 7:9. In his incarnate state Jesus experienced every human emotion. *such great faith.* See note on Lk 7:9.
8:11 The universality of the gospel is one of Matthew's themes (see Introduction: Recipients). *feast … in the kingdom of heaven.* The eschatological Messianic banquet that symbolizes the blessings of an intimate relationship with God (see Isa 25:6; Lk 14:15; Rev 19:9 and notes).
8:12 *subjects of the kingdom.* Jews who thought their Judaism was an inherited passport for entrance into the kingdom (see 3:9–10 and note on 3:9). *outside, into the darkness.* Hell. *weeping and gnashing of teeth.* A phrase used only in Matthew's Gospel (here; 13:42,50; 22:13; 24:51; 25:30) — though an almost identical phrase occurs in Lk 13:28 — to describe the horrible suffering experienced in hell.

13 Then Jesus said to the centurion, "Go! Let it be done just as you believed it would."[x] And his servant was healed at that moment.

Jesus Heals Many

8:14-16pp — Mk 1:29-34; Lk 4:38-41

14 When Jesus came into Peter's house, he saw Peter's mother-in-law lying in bed with a fever. 15 He touched her hand and the fever left her, and she got up and began to wait on him.

16 When evening came, many who were demon-possessed were brought to him, and he drove out the spirits with a word and healed all the sick.[y] 17 This was to fulfill[z] what was spoken through the prophet Isaiah:

> "He took up our infirmities
> and bore our diseases."[a][a]

The Cost of Following Jesus

8:19-22pp — Lk 9:57-60

18 When Jesus saw the crowd around him, he gave orders to cross to the other side of the lake.[b] 19 Then a teacher of the law came to him and said, "Teacher, I will follow you wherever you go."

20 Jesus replied, "Foxes have dens and birds have nests, but the Son of Man[c] has no place to lay his head."

21 Another disciple said to him, "Lord, first let me go and bury my father."

22 But Jesus told him, "Follow me,[d] and let the dead bury their own dead."

Jesus Calms the Storm

8:23-27pp — Mk 4:36-41; Lk 8:22-25
8:23-27Ref — Mt 14:22-33

23 Then he got into the boat and his disciples followed him. 24 Suddenly a furious storm came up on the lake, so that the waves swept over the boat. But Jesus was sleeping. 25 The disciples went and woke him, saying, "Lord, save us! We're going to drown!"

26 He replied, "You of little faith,[e] why are you so afraid?" Then he got up and rebuked the winds and the waves, and it was completely calm.[f]

27 The men were amazed and asked, "What kind of man is this? Even the winds and the waves obey him!"

Jesus Restores Two Demon-Possessed Men

8:28-34pp — Mk 5:1-17; Lk 8:26-37

28 When he arrived at the other side in the region of the Gadarenes,[b] two demon-possessed[g] men coming from the tombs met him. They were so violent that no one could pass that way. 29 "What do you want with us,[h] Son of God?" they shouted. "Have you come here to torture us before the appointed time?"[i]

30 Some distance from them a large herd of pigs was feeding. 31 The demons begged Jesus, "If you drive us out, send us into the herd of pigs."

32 He said to them, "Go!" So they came out and went into the pigs, and the whole herd rushed down the steep bank into the lake and died in the water. 33 Those tending the pigs ran off, went into the town and reported all this, including what had happened to the demon-possessed men. 34 Then the whole town went out to meet Jesus. And when they saw him, they pleaded with him to leave their region.[j]

8:13 [x] S Mt 9:22 **8:16** [y] S Mt 4:23, 24 **8:17** [z] S Mt 1:22 [a] Isa 53:4 **8:18** [b] Mk 4:35 **8:20** [c] Da 7:13; Mt 12:8, 32, 40; 16:13, 27, 28; 17:9; 19:28; Mk 2:10; 8:31 **8:22** [d] S Mt 4:19 **8:26** [e] S Mt 6:30 [f] Ps 65:7; 89:9; 107:29 **8:28** [g] S Mt 4:24 **8:29** [h] Jdg 11:12; 2Sa 16:10; 1Ki 17:18; Mk 1:24; Lk 4:34; Jn 2:4 [i] 2Pe 2:4 **8:34** [j] Lk 5:8; Ac 16:39

[a] 17 Isaiah 53:4 (see Septuagint) [b] 28 Some manuscripts *Gergesenes*; other manuscripts *Gerasenes*

8:14 *Peter's mother-in-law.* See notes on Mk 1:30; Lk 4:38.
8:15 *him.* Jesus. Mk 1:31 and Lk 4:39 have "them." She began to serve not only Jesus but also her guests, probably by preparing a meal for them.
8:16 *evening.* See Lk 4:40 and note. *demon-possessed.* See notes on Mk 1:23; Lk 4:33.
8:17 *bore.* Bore the burden of. The diseases were not transferred to Jesus in the sense of making him ill.
8:18 *the other side.* The east side.
8:19 *teacher of the law.* See note on 2:4.
8:20 *Son of Man.* See note on Mk 8:31.
8:21 *bury my father.* See note on Lk 9:59.
8:22 *let the dead bury their own dead.* Let the spiritually dead bury the physically dead. The time of Jesus' ministry was short and demanded full attention and commitment. This statement stresses the radical demands of Jesus' discipleship, since Jews placed great importance on the duty of children to bury their parents.
8:23–27 See note on Mk 4:35–41.
8:24 *furious storm.* See note on Mk 4:37. *But Jesus was sleeping.* See note on Mk 4:38.
8:26 *little faith.* See 6:30 and note.
8:27 *What kind of man is this?* See note on Mk 4:41.
8:28 *region of the Gadarenes.* The region around the city of Gadara, six miles southeast of the Sea of Galilee. Mark and Luke identify the region by the capital city Gerasa, located about 35 miles southeast of the Sea (see note on Lk 8:26). *two.* Mk 5:2 and Lk 8:27 (see note there) mention only one demon-possessed man. *demon-possessed.* See note on v. 16.
8:29 *Son of God.* See note on Lk 8:28. *appointed time.* The time of their judgment (see notes on Mk 5:10; Lk 8:31).
8:30 *herd of pigs.* Large numbers of Gentiles lived in Galilee. Normally Jews did not raise pigs, since they were considered the most ceremonially unclean of all animals.
8:32 Though Jesus seemingly consented to the demons' request, the pigs carried the demons into the depths of the sea — perhaps symbolic of the Abyss (see Lk 8:31 and note).
8:34 *pleaded with him to leave.* They were probably more concerned about their financial loss than about the deliverance of the miserable demon-possessed men (see note on Mk 5:17).

Jesus Forgives and Heals a Paralyzed Man

9:2-8pp — Mk 2:3-12; Lk 5:18-26

9 Jesus stepped into a boat, crossed over and came to his own town.[k] 2 Some men brought to him a paralyzed man,[l] lying on a mat. When Jesus saw their faith,[m] he said to the man, "Take heart,[n] son; your sins are forgiven."[o]

3 At this, some of the teachers of the law said to themselves, "This fellow is blaspheming!"[p]

4 Knowing their thoughts,[q] Jesus said, "Why do you entertain evil thoughts in your hearts? 5 Which is easier: to say, 'Your sins are forgiven,' or to say, 'Get up and walk'? 6 But I want you to know that the Son of Man[r] has authority on earth to forgive sins." So he said to the paralyzed man, "Get up, take your mat and go home." 7 Then the man got up and went home. 8 When the crowd saw this, they were filled with awe; and they praised God,[s] who had given such authority to man.

The Calling of Matthew

9:9-13pp — Mk 2:14-17; Lk 5:27-32

9 As Jesus went on from there, he saw a man named Matthew sitting at the tax collector's booth. "Follow me,"[t] he told him, and Matthew got up and followed him.

10 While Jesus was having dinner at Matthew's house, many tax collectors and sinners came and ate with him and his disciples. 11 When the Pharisees saw this, they asked his disciples, "Why does your teacher eat with tax collectors and sinners?"[u]

12 On hearing this, Jesus said, "It is not the healthy who need a doctor, but the sick. 13 But go and learn what this means: 'I desire mercy, not sacrifice.'[a][v] For I have not come to call the righteous, but sinners."[w]

Jesus Questioned About Fasting

9:14-17pp — Mk 2:18-22; Lk 5:33-39

14 Then John's[x] disciples came and asked him, "How is it that we and the Pharisees fast often,[y] but your disciples do not fast?"

15 Jesus answered, "How can the guests of the bridegroom mourn while he is with them?[z] The time will come when the bridegroom will be taken from them; then they will fast.[a]

16 "No one sews a patch of unshrunk cloth on an old garment, for the patch will pull away from the garment, making the tear worse. 17 Neither do people pour new wine into old wineskins. If they do, the skins will burst; the wine will run out and the wineskins will be ruined. No, they pour new wine into new wineskins, and both are preserved."

Jesus Raises a Dead Girl and Heals a Sick Woman

9:18-26pp — Mk 5:22-43; Lk 8:41-56

18 While he was saying this, a synagogue leader came and knelt before him[b] and said, "My daughter has just died. But come and put your hand on her,[c] and she will live." 19 Jesus got up and went with him, and so did his disciples.

20 Just then a woman who had been subject to bleeding for twelve years came up behind him and touched the edge of his cloak.[d] 21 She said to herself, "If I only touch his cloak, I will be healed."

22 Jesus turned and saw her. "Take heart,[e] daughter," he said, "your faith has healed you."[f] And the woman was healed at that moment.[g]

[a] 13 Hosea 6:6

9:1 [k] Mt 4:13
9:2 [l] S Mt 4:24 [m] S ver 22 [n] Jn 16:33 [o] Lk 7:48
9:3 [p] Mt 26:65; Jn 10:33
9:4 [q] Ps 94:11; Mt 12:25; Lk 6:8; 9:47; 11:17; Jn 2:25
9:6 [r] S Mt 8:20
9:8 [s] Mt 5:16; 15:31; Lk 7:16; 13:13; 17:15; 23:47; Jn 15:8; Ac 4:21; 11:18; 21:20
9:9 [t] S Mt 4:19
9:11 [u] Mt 11:19; Lk 5:30; 15:2; 19:7; Gal 2:15
9:13 [v] Hos 6:6; Mic 6:6-8; Mt 12:7
[w] Lk 19:10; 1Ti 1:15
9:14 [x] S Mt 3:1 [y] Mt 11:18, 19; Lk 18:12
9:15 [z] Jn 3:29 [a] Ac 13:2, 3; 14:23
9:18 [b] S Mt 8:2 [c] S Mk 5:23
9:20 [d] Mt 14:36; Mk 3:10; 6:56; Lk 6:19
9:22 [e] ver 2; Jn 16:33 [f] ver 29; Mt 8:13; Mk 10:52; Lk 7:50; 17:19; 18:42 [g] Mt 15:28

9:1 *crossed over.* The northern end of the Sea of Galilee. *his own town.* Capernaum (see note on 4:13).
9:2 *their faith.* The faith of the men who carried him as well as the faith of the paralyzed man. *your sins are forgiven.* See note on Mk 2:5. In this case, perhaps there was a relationship between the man's sin and his paralysis (cf. Jn 9:1–3).
9:3 *blaspheming.* Here the term includes usurping God's prerogative to forgive sins (see notes on Mk 2:7; Lk 5:21).
9:5–6 See notes on Mk 2:9–10; 14:64.
9:6 *Son of Man.* See note on Mk 8:31.
9:9 *Matthew.* Mark and Luke call this disciple Levi in the parallel accounts (but see also Mk 3:18; Lk 6:15; Ac 1:13). *tax collector's booth.* See note on Mk 2:14. *got up and followed him.* See note on Lk 5:28.
9:10 *tax collectors.* See notes on 5:46; Mk 2:16. *sinners.* See note on Mk 2:15.
9:11 *Pharisees.* See note on Mk 2:16.
9:12 *not the healthy who need a doctor, but the sick.* See note on Lk 5:31.
9:13 *I have not come to call the righteous, but sinners.* See note on Mk 2:17.
9:14 See notes on Mk 2:18; Lk 5:33.
9:15 See notes on Mk 2:19–20.
9:17 *new wineskins.* In ancient times goatskins were used to hold wine. As the fresh grape juice fermented, the wine would expand, and the new wineskin would stretch. But a used skin, already stretched, would break (see note on Job 32:19). Jesus brings a newness that cannot be confined within the old forms.
9:18 *synagogue leader.* His name was Jairus (see notes on Mk 5:22; Lk 8:41). *has just died.* Mk 5:23 has "is dying," but Matthew omits reference to the later messengers (Mk 5:35) and condenses (see notes on 21:12–17; 21:18–22) by presenting at the outset what was actually true before Jesus reached the house.
9:20 *subject to bleeding for twelve years.* Probably a menstrual disorder (see notes on Mk 5:25; Lk 8:43).
9:21 See notes on Mk 5:28; Lk 8:45.
9:22 *daughter.* See note on Lk 8:48. *healed.* See note on Mk 5:34.

23 When Jesus entered the synagogue
leader's house and saw the noisy crowd
and people playing pipes,[h] 24 he said, "Go
away. The girl is not dead[i] but asleep."[j]
But they laughed at him. 25 After the crowd
had been put outside, he went in and took
the girl by the hand, and she got up.[k]
26 News of this spread through all that region.[l]

Jesus Heals the Blind and the Mute

27 As Jesus went on from there, two
blind men followed him, calling out,
"Have mercy on us, Son of David!"[m]
28 When he had gone indoors, the blind
men came to him, and he asked them, "Do
you believe that I am able to do this?"
"Yes, Lord," they replied.[n]
29 Then he touched their eyes and said,
"According to your faith let it be done
to you";[o] 30 and their sight was restored.
Jesus warned them sternly, "See that no
one knows about this."[p] 31 But they went
out and spread the news about him all
over that region.[q]
32 While they were going out, a man
who was demon-possessed[r] and could not
talk[s] was brought to Jesus. 33 And when
the demon was driven out, the man who
had been mute spoke. The crowd was
amazed and said, "Nothing like this has
ever been seen in Israel."[t]
34 But the Pharisees said, "It is by the
prince of demons that he drives out demons."[u]

The Workers Are Few

35 Jesus went through all the towns and
villages, teaching in their synagogues, proclaiming the good news of the kingdom
and healing every disease and sickness.[v]
36 When he saw the crowds, he had compassion on them,[w] because they were harassed and helpless, like sheep without a
shepherd.[x] 37 Then he said to his disciples,
"The harvest[y] is plentiful but the workers
are few.[z] 38 Ask the Lord of the harvest,
therefore, to send out workers into his harvest field."

Jesus Sends Out the Twelve

10:2-4pp — Mk 3:16-19; Lk 6:14-16; Ac 1:13
10:9-15pp — Mk 6:8-11; Lk 9:3-5; 10:4-12
10:19-22pp — Mk 13:11-13; Lk 21:12-17
10:26-33pp — Lk 12:2-9
10:34,35pp — Lk 12:51-53

10 Jesus called his twelve disciples
to him and gave them authority to
drive out impure spirits[a] and to heal every
disease and sickness.[b]
2 These are the names of the twelve
apostles: first, Simon (who is called Peter) and his brother Andrew; James son of
Zebedee, and his brother John; 3 Philip and
Bartholomew; Thomas and Matthew the
tax collector; James son of Alphaeus, and
Thaddaeus; 4 Simon the Zealot and Judas
Iscariot, who betrayed him.[c]
5 These twelve Jesus sent out with the
following instructions: "Do not go among
the Gentiles or enter any town of the Samaritans.[d] 6 Go rather to the lost sheep of
Israel.[e] 7 As you go, proclaim this message:
'The kingdom of heaven[f] has come near.'
8 Heal the sick, raise the dead, cleanse
those who have leprosy,[a] drive out de-

[a] 8 The Greek word traditionally translated *leprosy* was used for various diseases affecting the skin.

9:23 [h] 2Ch 35:25; Jer 9:17,18 **9:24** [i] Ac 20:10 [j] Da 12:2; Ps 76:5; Jn 11:11-14; Ac 7:60; 13:36; 1Co 11:30; 15:6,18,20; 1Th 4:13-16 **9:25** [k] S Lk 7:14 **9:26** [l] ver 31; Mt 4:24; 14:1; Mk 1:28,45; Lk 4:14,37; 5:15; 7:17 **9:27** [m] S Mt 1:1; 12:23; 15:22; 20:30,31; 21:9,15; 22:42; Mk 10:47 **9:28** [n] Ac 14:9 **9:29** [o] S ver 22 **9:30** [p] S Mt 8:4 **9:31** [q] S ver 26; Mk 7:36 **9:32** [r] S Mt 4:24 [s] Mt 12:22-24 **9:33** [t] Mk 2:12 **9:34** [u] Mt 12:24 **9:35** [v] S Mt 4:23 **9:36** [w] Mt 14:14; 15:32; Mk 8:2 [x] Nu 27:17; 1Ki 22:17; Eze 34:5,6; Zec 10:2 **9:37** [y] Jn 4:35 [z] Lk 10:2 **10:1** [a] Mk 3:13-15; 6:7; Lk 4:36; 9:1 [b] S Mt 4:23 **10:4** [c] Mt 26:14-16,25,47; 27:3; Mk 14:10; Jn 6:71; 12:4; 13:2,26,27; Ac 1:16 **10:5** [d] 1Ki 16:24; 2Ki 17:24; Lk 9:52; 10:33; 17:16; Jn 4:4-26,39,40; 8:48; Ac 8:5,25 **10:6** [e] Jer 50:6; Mt 15:24 **10:7** [f] S Mt 3:2

9:23 *noisy crowd.* Mourners hired to wail and lament (see Jer 9:20; Mk 5:38 and notes). *people playing pipes.* Musicians hired to play in mourning ceremonies.
9:24 *not dead but asleep.* See note on Lk 8:52.
9:25 *took the girl by the hand.* Touching a dead body ordinarily resulted in ceremonial uncleanness (see Lev 11:31; 21:1,11 and note on 21:1; 22:4; Nu 19:14 and note), but Jesus' action brought life, not defilement.
9:27 *blind men.* Isaiah predicted the healing of the blind in the Messianic age (Isa 35:5). *Son of David.* A popular Jewish title for the coming Messiah (e.g., 12:23; 20:30; 21:9; 22:41–45; see note on 1:1).
9:29 *According to your faith.* That is, "Because you have faith," not "In proportion to your faith." Jesus did not provide healing according to the amount of faith the blind men had (see 17:20 and note). Cf. 8:13; Mk 9:23 and note; 11:23; Jn 11:40.
9:30 See notes on 8:4; 16:20.
9:32 *could not talk.* Isaiah also (see note on v. 27) predicted that the mute would talk in the Messianic age (Isa 35:6).
9:33 *amazed.* See 8:27; 13:54; 15:31; 21:20; 22:22; cf. Mk 1:22 and note.
9:34 *prince of demons.* See note on 10:25.
9:35 *synagogues.* See note on Mk 1:21. *good news.* See note on Mk 1:1.
9:36 *compassion.* Jesus' compassion for people is often noted in the Gospels (see 14:14; 15:22; 20:34; Mk 1:41; 6:34; 8:2). *like sheep without a shepherd.* See Eze 34:5; Zec 10:2; 13:7 and notes; Mk 6:34.
10:2–4 See notes on Lk 6:14–16.
10:2 *apostles.* The only occurrence of this word in Matthew's Gospel. See note on Mk 6:30.
10:3 *Thaddaeus.* Also called Judas (not Iscariot [Jn 14:22]); see Mk 3:18; Lk 6:16; Ac 1:13 and note.
10:4 *the Zealot.* Either a description of Simon's religious zeal or a reference to his membership in the party of the Zealots, a Jewish revolutionary group violently opposed to Roman rule over the Holy Land (see chart, p. 1631).
10:5 *Do not go.* The good news about the kingdom was to be proclaimed first to Jews only. After his death and resurrection, Jesus commanded the message to be taken to all nations (28:19; cf. 21:43). *Samaritans.* A mixed-blood race resulting from the intermarriage of Israelites left behind when the people of the northern kingdom were exiled and Gentiles who were brought into the land by the Assyrians (2Ki 17:24). Bitter hostility existed between Jews and Samaritans in Jesus' day (see Jn 4:9 and note).
10:7 *kingdom of heaven.* See note on 3:2.
10:8 *leprosy.* See NIV text note and note on Lev 13:2.

mons. Freely you have received; freely
give.
9 “Do not get any gold or silver or copper
to take with you in your belts[g]— 10 no bag
for the journey or extra shirt or sandals or
a staff, for the worker is worth his keep.[h]
11 Whatever town or village you enter,
search there for some worthy person and
stay at their house until you leave. 12 As
you enter the home, give it your greeting.[i]
13 If the home is deserving, let your peace
rest on it; if it is not, let your peace return
to you. 14 If anyone will not welcome you
or listen to your words, leave that home
or town and shake the dust off your feet.[j]
15 Truly I tell you, it will be more bearable
for Sodom and Gomorrah[k] on the day of
judgment[l] than for that town.[m]
16 “I am sending you out like sheep
among wolves.[n] Therefore be as shrewd
as snakes and as innocent as doves.[o] 17 Be
on your guard; you will be handed over to
the local councils[p] and be flogged in the
synagogues.[q] 18 On my account you will
be brought before governors and kings[r]
as witnesses to them and to the Gentiles.
19 But when they arrest you, do not worry
about what to say or how to say it.[s] At that
time you will be given what to say, 20 for it
will not be you speaking, but the Spirit of
your Father[t] speaking through you.
21 “Brother will betray brother to death,
and a father his child; children will rebel
against their parents[u] and have them put
to death.[v] 22 You will be hated by everyone
because of me,[w] but the one who stands
firm to the end will be saved.[x] 23 When you
are persecuted in one place, flee to another. Truly I tell you, you will not finish going through the towns of Israel before the
Son of Man comes.[y]
24 “The student is not above the teacher, nor a servant above his master.[z] 25 It is
enough for students to be like their teachers, and servants like their masters. If the
head of the house has been called Beelzebul,[a] how much more the members of his
household!
26 “So do not be afraid of them, for there
is nothing concealed that will not be disclosed, or hidden that will not be made
known.[b] 27 What I tell you in the dark,
speak in the daylight; what is whispered
in your ear, proclaim from the roofs. 28 Do
not be afraid of those who kill the body
but cannot kill the soul. Rather, be afraid
of the One[c] who can destroy both soul and
body in hell. 29 Are not two sparrows sold
for a penny? Yet not one of them will fall
to the ground outside your Father's care.[a]
30 And even the very hairs of your head are
all numbered.[d] 31 So don't be afraid; you
are worth more than many sparrows.[e]
32 “Whoever acknowledges me before
others,[f] I will also acknowledge before my

a 29 Or *will*; or *knowledge*

10:9 [g] Lk 22:35 **10:10** [h] S 1Ti 5:18 **10:12** [i] 1Sa 25:6 **10:14** [j] Ne 5:13; Mk 6:11; Lk 9:5; 10:11; Ac 13:51; 18:6 **10:15** [k] Ge 18:20; 19:24; 2Pe 2:6; Jude 7 [l] Mt 12:36; Ac 17:31; 2Pe 2:9; 3:7; 1Jn 4:17; Jude 6 [m] Mt 11:22,24 **10:16** [n] Lk 10:3; Ac 20:29 [o] S 1Co 14:20 **10:17** [p] S Mt 5:22 [q] Mt 23:34; Mk 13:9; Ac 5:40; 22:19; 26:11 **10:18** [r] Ac 25:24-26 **10:19** [s] Ex 4:12 **10:20** [t] Lk 12:11, 12; Ac 4:8 **10:21** [u] ver 35, 36; Mic 7:6 [v] Mk 13:12 **10:22** [w] S Jn 15:21 [x] Mt 24:13; Mk 13:13; Lk 21:19; Rev 2:10 **10:23** [y] S Lk 17:30 **10:24** [z] S Jn 13:16 **10:25** [a] S Mk 3:22 **10:26** [b] Mk 4:22; Lk 8:17 **10:28** [c] Isa 8:12, 13; Heb 10:31 **10:30** [d] 1Sa 14:45; 2Sa 14:11; 1Ki 1:52; Lk 21:18; Ac 27:34 **10:31** [e] Mt 6:26; 12:12 **10:32** [f] Ro 10:9

10:9 – 10 See notes on Mk 6:8 – 9.
10:10 *worker is worth his keep.* Cf. 1Co 9:4 – 14; 1Ti 5:17 – 18 and note on 5:18.
10:11 *stay at their house.* See note on Lk 9:4.
10:12 *your greeting.* The Jews' greeting was *shalom,* "peace" (see Lk 10:5).
10:13 *If the home is deserving.* That is, "If the head of the house loves peace" (Lk 10:6). *let your peace return to you.* Either (1) retract your blessing or (2) leave the house.
10:14 *shake the dust off your feet.* A symbolic act practiced by the Pharisees when they left a ceremonially unclean Gentile area. Here it represented an act of solemn warning to those who rejected God's message (see notes on Lk 9:5; Ac 13:51; cf. Ac 18:6).
10:15 *Truly I tell you.* See note on Mk 3:28. *Sodom and Gomorrah.* See Ge 19:23 – 29; Lk 10:12 and note.
10:16 Cf. 7:15; cf. also Paul's statement in Ro 16:19: "I want you to be wise about what is good, and innocent about what is evil."
10:17 *local councils.* The lower courts, connected with local synagogues, that tried less serious cases and flogged those found guilty. *synagogues.* See notes on Mk 1:21; Lk 21:12.
10:18 Anticipates the mission to the Gentiles. Matthew's Gospel emphasizes the universality of the gospel (see note on 8:11; see also Introduction: Recipients).
10:19 *do not worry about what to say.* Namely, to defend yourselves (Lk 21:14 – 15). *you will be given what to say.* "Words and wisdom" that cannot be resisted (Lk 21:15; see note there).
10:20 *the Spirit of your Father speaking.* See Mk 13:11; Lk 12:11 – 12; cf. Lk 21:14 – 15.
10:21 The allusion is to Mic 7:6, which is quoted in vv. 35 – 36.
10:22 *everyone.* Hyperbole. *the one who stands firm to the end will be saved.* See note on Mk 13:13.
10:23 Some take Jesus' saying here as a reference to his second coming at the end of the age (see 24:30), but it is hard to reconcile this with the failure of the disciples to "finish going through" (evangelize) the cities of Israel before this happens. It is therefore probably best understood as referring to his coming in judgment on the Jews when Jerusalem and the temple were destroyed in AD 70.
10:25 *Beelzebul.* The prince of demons (12:24); the Greek form of the Hebrew name Baal-Zebul ("Exalted Baal" or "Baal the Prince"). Baal-Zebub ("lord of flies") is a parody on and mockery of the actual epithet, Baal-Zebul (see note on Jdg 10:6). The name came to be used of Satan.
10:26 – 33 See Lk 12:2 – 9 and notes.
10:26 *them.* The persecutors (vv. 21 – 25).
10:28 *cannot kill the soul.* See Lk 12:4 and note. *soul.* The true self (see note on Ps 6:3). Body and soul are closely related in this life but are separated at death and then reunited at the resurrection (cf. 2Co 5:1 – 10 and notes; Php 1:23 – 24). *the One.* God. He alone determines the final destiny of us all. *destroy both soul and body in hell.* See Lk 12:5 and note. *hell.* See note on 5:22.
10:29 *two sparrows sold for a penny.* Cf. Lk 12:6 and note.
10:31 *worth more than many sparrows.* See 6:26.
10:32 – 33 See Lk 12:8 – 9 and notes.

Father in heaven. 33 But whoever disowns me before others, I will disown before my Father in heaven.[g]

34 "Do not suppose that I have come to bring peace to the earth. I did not come to bring peace, but a sword. 35 For I have come to turn

"'a man against his father,
a daughter against her mother,
a daughter-in-law against her mother-in-law[h]—
36 a man's enemies will be the members of his own household.'[a][i]

37 "Anyone who loves their father or mother more than me is not worthy of me; anyone who loves their son or daughter more than me is not worthy of me.[j] 38 Whoever does not take up their cross and follow me is not worthy of me.[k] 39 Whoever finds their life will lose it, and whoever loses their life for my sake will find it.[l]

40 "Anyone who welcomes you welcomes me,[m] and anyone who welcomes me welcomes the one who sent me.[n] 41 Whoever welcomes a prophet as a prophet will receive a prophet's reward, and whoever welcomes a righteous person as a righteous person will receive a righteous person's reward. 42 And if anyone gives even a cup of cold water to one of these little ones who is my disciple, truly I tell you, that person will certainly not lose their reward."[o]

Jesus and John the Baptist

11:2-19pp — Lk 7:18-35

11 After Jesus had finished instructing his twelve disciples,[p] he went on from there to teach and preach in the towns of Galilee.[b]

2 When John,[q] who was in prison,[r] heard about the deeds of the Messiah, he sent his disciples 3 to ask him, "Are you the one who is to come,[s] or should we expect someone else?"

4 Jesus replied, "Go back and report to John what you hear and see: 5 The blind receive sight, the lame walk, those who have leprosy[c] are cleansed, the deaf hear, the dead are raised, and the good news is proclaimed to the poor.[t] 6 Blessed is anyone who does not stumble on account of me."[u]

7 As John's[v] disciples were leaving, Jesus began to speak to the crowd about John: "What did you go out into the wilderness[w] to see? A reed swayed by the wind? 8 If not, what did you go out to see? A man dressed in fine clothes? No, those who wear fine clothes are in kings' palaces. 9 Then what did you go out to see? A prophet?[x] Yes, I tell you, and more than a prophet. 10 This is the one about whom it is written:

"'I will send my messenger ahead of you,[y]
who will prepare your way before you.'[d][z]

11 Truly I tell you, among those born of women there has not risen anyone greater than John the Baptist; yet whoever is least in the kingdom of heaven is greater than he. 12 From the days of John the Baptist until now, the kingdom of heaven has been subjected to violence,[e] and violent people have been raiding it. 13 For all the Prophets and the Law prophesied until John.[a] 14 And if you are willing to accept it, he is the

10:33 [g] Mk 8:38; 2Ti 2:12 **10:35** [h] ver 21 **10:36** [i] Mic 7:6 **10:37** [j] Lk 14:26 **10:38** [k] Mt 16:24; Lk 14:27 **10:39** [l] S Jn 12:25 **10:40** [m] Ex 16:8; Mt 18:5; Gal 4:14 [n] Lk 9:48; 10:16; Jn 12:44; 13:20 **10:42** [o] Pr 14:31; 19:17; Mt 25:40; Mk 9:41; Ac 10:4; Heb 6:10 **11:1** [p] S Mt 7:28 **11:2** [q] S Mt 3:1 [r] Mt 14:3 **11:3** [s] Ps 118:26; Jn 11:27; Heb 10:37 **11:5** [t] Isa 35:4-6; 61:1; Mt 15:31; Lk 4:18,19 **11:6** [u] Mt 13:21; 26:31 **11:7** [v] S Mt 3:1 [w] Mt 3:1 **11:9** [x] Mt 14:5; 21:26; Lk 1:76; 7:26 **11:10** [y] Jn 3:28 [z] Mal 3:1; Mk 1:2; Lk 7:27 **11:13** [a] Lk 16:16

[a] *36* Micah 7:6 [b] *1* Greek *in their towns* [c] *5* The Greek word traditionally translated *leprosy* was used for various diseases affecting the skin. [d] *10* Mal. 3:1 [e] *12* Or *been forcefully advancing*

10:34 At first glance this saying sounds like a contradiction of Isa 9:6 ("Prince of Peace"), Lk 2:14 ("on earth peace to those on whom his favor rests") and Jn 14:27 ("Peace I leave with you"). It is true that Christ came to bring peace—peace between the believer and God, and peace among humans. Yet the inevitable result of Christ's coming is conflict—between Christ and the antichrist, between light and darkness, between Christ's followers and the devil's followers. This conflict can occur even between members of the same family (vv. 35–36; Mk 10:29–30).
10:37 See Lk 14:26 and note.
10:38 *take up their cross.* The first mention of the cross in Matthew's Gospel. The cross was an instrument of death and here symbolizes the necessity of total commitment—even to the point of death—on the part of Jesus' disciples (see note on Mk 8:34).
10:39 See note on Lk 9:24.
10:40–42 During times of persecution, hospitality was especially important and could be dangerous. So Jesus indicates that those who provide it and show kindness to God's people will receive a reward.
10:42 *cup of cold water.* See note on Mk 9:41.
11:1 While the 12 apostles were carrying out their first mission, Jesus continued his ministry in Galilee. *Galilee.* See note on 2:2.
11:2 *John.* The Baptist (see note on 3:1). *in prison.* See note on Lk 7:19.
11:3 *the one who is to come.* The Messiah. *expect someone else.* See note on Lk 7:19.
11:4 *report to John what you hear and see.* See note on Lk 7:22.
11:5 *leprosy.* See NIV text note; see also note on Lev 13:2. *the good news is proclaimed to the poor.* See note on Lk 7:22.
11:6 *anyone who does not stumble.* See note on Lk 7:23.
11:7–10 See Lk 7:24–28 and notes.
11:10 See Mal 3:1 and note.
11:11 *greater than he.* John belonged to the age of the old covenant, which was preparatory to Christ. The least NT believer has a higher privilege in Christ as a part of his bride the church (Eph 5:25–27,32) than John the Baptist, who was only a friend of the bridegroom (Jn 3:29). Another view, however, stresses the expression "whoever is least," holding that the key to its meaning is found in 18:4—"whoever takes the lowly position of this child." Such a person, though "least," is regarded by God as even greater than John the Baptist.
11:12 *From the days of John the Baptist.* From the beginning of Jesus' ministry. *kingdom of heaven.* See note on 3:2. *sub-*

Elijah who was to come.[b] 15 Whoever has
ears, let them hear.[c]
16 "To what can I compare this generation? They are like children sitting in the
marketplaces and calling out to others:

17 " 'We played the pipe for you,
and you did not dance;
we sang a dirge,
and you did not mourn.'

18 For John came neither eating[d] nor drinking,[e] and they say, 'He has a demon.' 19 The
Son of Man came eating and drinking, and
they say, 'Here is a glutton and a drunkard, a friend of tax collectors and sinners.'[f]
But wisdom is proved right by her deeds."

Woe on Unrepentant Towns

11:21-23pp — Lk 10:13-15

20 Then Jesus began to denounce the
towns in which most of his miracles had
been performed, because they did not repent. 21 "Woe to you, Chorazin! Woe to
you, Bethsaida![g] For if the miracles that
were performed in you had been performed in Tyre and Sidon,[h] they would
have repented long ago in sackcloth and
ashes.[i] 22 But I tell you, it will be more
bearable for Tyre and Sidon on the day of
judgment than for you.[j] 23 And you, Capernaum,[k] will you be lifted to the heavens?
No, you will go down to Hades.[a][l] For if the
miracles that were performed in you had
been performed in Sodom, it would have
remained to this day. 24 But I tell you that
it will be more bearable for Sodom on the
day of judgment than for you."[m]

The Father Revealed in the Son

11:25-27pp — Lk 10:21,22

25 At that time Jesus said, "I praise you,
Father,[n] Lord of heaven and earth, because you have hidden these things from
the wise and learned, and revealed them
to little children.[o] 26 Yes, Father, for this is
what you were pleased to do.
27 "All things have been committed to
me[p] by my Father.[q] No one knows the Son
except the Father, and no one knows the
Father except the Son and those to whom
the Son chooses to reveal him.[r]
28 "Come to me,[s] all you who are weary
and burdened, and I will give you rest.[t]
29 Take my yoke upon you and learn from
me,[u] for I am gentle and humble in heart,
and you will find rest for your souls.[v] 30 For
my yoke is easy and my burden is light."[w]

Jesus Is Lord of the Sabbath

12:1-8pp — Mk 2:23-28; Lk 6:1-5
12:9-14pp — Mk 3:1-6; Lk 6:6-11

12 At that time Jesus went through
the grainfields on the Sabbath. His

[a] 23 That is, the realm of the dead

11:14 [b] Mal 4:5; Mt 17:10-13; Mk 9:11-13; Lk 1:17; Jn 1:21 **11:15** [c] Mt 13:9, 43; Mk 4:23; Lk 14:35; S Rev 2:7 **11:18** [d] Mt 3:4 [e] S Lk 1:15 **11:19** [f] S Mt 9:11 **11:21** [g] Mk 6:45; 8:22; Lk 9:10; Jn 1:44; 12:21 [h] Joel 3:4; Am 1:9; Mt 15:21; Mk 3:8; Lk 6:17; Ac 12:20 [i] Jnh 3:5-9 **11:22** [j] ver 24; Mt 10:15 **11:23** [k] S Mt 4:13 [l] Isa 14:13-15 **11:24** [m] S Mt 10:15 **11:25** [n] Mt 16:17; Lk 22:42; 23:34; Jn 11:41; 12:27, 28 [o] S Mt 13:11; 1Co 1:26-29 **11:27** [p] S Mt 28:18 [q] S Jn 3:35 [r] Jn 10:15; 17:25,26 **11:28** [s] Jn 7:37 [t] Ex 33:14 **11:29** [u] Jn 13:15; Php 2:5; 1Pe 2:21; 1Jn 2:6 [v] Ps 116:7; Jer 6:16 **11:30** [w] 1Jn 5:3

jected to violence. The ongoing persecution of the people of the kingdom. (But see NIV text note. The main NIV text, however, is probably to be preferred.)

11:13 *the Prophets and the Law.* The entire OT prophesied the coming of the kingdom. John represented the end of the old covenant era.

11:14 *he is the Elijah who was to come.* A reference to Mal 4:5 (see note there), which prophesied the reappearance of Elijah before the day of the Lord. Some of the people remembered the prophecy and asked John the Baptist, "Are you Elijah?" He answered, "I am not" (Jn 1:21). John was not literally the reincarnation of Elijah, but he did fulfill the function and role of the prophet (see Mt 17:10 – 13 and note on Lk 1:17).

11:16 *like children sitting in the marketplaces.* See note on Lk 7:32.

11:17 *played the pipe.* As at a wedding. *sang a dirge.* As at a funeral. The latter symbolized the ministry of John, the former that of Jesus. The people of Jesus' "generation" (v. 16) were like children who refused to respond on either occasion.

11:19 *Son of Man.* See note on Mk 8:31. *friend of tax collectors and sinners.* See note on Lk 7:34. *wisdom is proved right by her deeds.* Apparently means that God (wisdom) had sent both John and Jesus in specific roles, and that this would be vindicated by the lasting works of both Jesus and John (see note on Lk 7:35).

11:20 *repent.* See note on 3:2.

11:21 *Chorazin.* Mentioned in the Bible only twice (here and in Lk 10:13), it was near the Sea of Galilee, probably about two miles north of Capernaum. *Bethsaida.* On the northeast shore of the Sea of Galilee. Philip the tetrarch rebuilt Bethsaida and named it "Julias," after Julia, daughter of Caesar Augustus. *Tyre and Sidon.* Cities on the Phoenician coast north of the Holy Land (see note on Mk 7:31). *sackcloth.* Here a sign of repentance (see note on Ge 37:34). Cf. Rev 6:12. *ashes.* Also a sign of repentance.

11:23 *Capernaum.* See note on Lk 10:15. *Sodom.* See notes on 10:15; Ge 13:10; Lk 10:12.

11:25 *Lord of heaven and earth.* A title for God emphasizing his sovereignty and found only three times in the Bible (here; Lk 10:21; Ac 17:24). *these things.* Either the significance of Jesus' miracles (see vv. 20 – 24) or of his entire mission. *wise.* According to the standards of this age (see 1Co 1:26 – 29; cf. 1Co 3:18 and note). *little children.* The disciples or, more generally, the humble followers of Jesus.

11:26 *what you were pleased to do.* Since God is "Lord of heaven and earth" (v. 25), he sovereignly reveals and conceals.

11:27 *All things.* The full revelation of God (see v. 25). *No one knows the Son.* Total knowledge of the Son belongs only to the Father. Believers can "know" the Son for salvation (1Jn 5:20) and in a deep and satisfying way, but not completely (see Jn 10:14 and note; cf. Php 3:7 – 11 and notes). *except ... those to whom the Son chooses to reveal him.* Christ sovereignly chooses those to whom he reveals a saving knowledge of God (see Jn 14:6 and note).

11:28 *weary and burdened.* Probably a reference to the "heavy ... loads" the Pharisees placed "on other people's shoulders" by insisting on a legalistic interpretation of the law (23:4).

11:29 *yoke.* Cf. v. 30 and note; see note on Eze 34:27. *find rest for your souls.* See Jer 6:16 and note.

11:30 *my burden is light.* Cf. Ps 55:22; 1Jn 5:3 and notes.

12:1 *grainfields.* Of wheat or barley, the latter eaten by poorer people. *pick some heads of grain.* See note on Mk 2:23.

disciples were hungry and began to pick some heads of grain[x] and eat them. 2 When the Pharisees saw this, they said to him, "Look! Your disciples are doing what is unlawful on the Sabbath."[y]

3 He answered, "Haven't you read what David did when he and his companions were hungry?[z] 4 He entered the house of God, and he and his companions ate the consecrated bread — which was not lawful for them to do, but only for the priests.[a] 5 Or haven't you read in the Law that the priests on Sabbath duty in the temple desecrate the Sabbath[b] and yet are innocent? 6 I tell you that something greater than the temple is here.[c] 7 If you had known what these words mean, 'I desire mercy, not sacrifice,'[a][d] you would not have condemned the innocent. 8 For the Son of Man[e] is Lord of the Sabbath."

9 Going on from that place, he went into their synagogue, 10 and a man with a shriveled hand was there. Looking for a reason to bring charges against Jesus,[f] they asked him, "Is it lawful to heal on the Sabbath?"[g]

11 He said to them, "If any of you has a sheep and it falls into a pit on the Sabbath, will you not take hold of it and lift it out?[h] 12 How much more valuable is a person than a sheep![i] Therefore it is lawful to do good on the Sabbath."

13 Then he said to the man, "Stretch out your hand." So he stretched it out and it was completely restored, just as sound as the other. 14 But the Pharisees went out and plotted how they might kill Jesus.[j]

God's Chosen Servant

15 Aware of this, Jesus withdrew from that place. A large crowd followed him, and he healed all who were ill.[k] 16 He warned them not to tell others about him.[l] 17 This was to fulfill[m] what was spoken through the prophet Isaiah:

18 "Here is my servant whom I have chosen,
the one I love, in whom I delight;[n]
I will put my Spirit on him,[o]
and he will proclaim justice to the nations.
19 He will not quarrel or cry out;
no one will hear his voice in the streets.
20 A bruised reed he will not break,
and a smoldering wick he will not snuff out,
till he has brought justice through to victory.
21 In his name the nations will put their hope."[b][p]

Jesus and Beelzebul

12:25-29pp — Mk 3:23-27; Lk 11:17-22

22 Then they brought him a demon-possessed man who was blind and mute, and Jesus healed him, so that he could both talk and see.[q] 23 All the people were astonished and said, "Could this be the Son of David?"[r]

24 But when the Pharisees heard this, they said, "It is only by Beelzebul,[s] the prince of demons, that this fellow drives out demons."[t]

25 Jesus knew their thoughts[u] and said to them, "Every kingdom divided against itself will be ruined, and every city or household divided against itself will not stand. 26 If Satan[v] drives out Satan, he is divided against himself. How then can his kingdom stand? 27 And if I drive out demons by Beelzebul,[w] by whom do your people[x] drive them out? So then, they will be your judges. 28 But if it is by the Spirit

12:1 [x] Dt 23:25 **12:2** [y] ver 10; Ex 20:10; 23:12; Dt 5:14; Lk 13:14; 14:3; Jn 5:10; 7:23; 9:16 **12:3** [z] 1Sa 21:6 **12:4** [a] Lev 24:5,9 **12:5** [b] Nu 28:9, 10; Jn 7:22,23 **12:6** [c] ver 41,42 **12:7** [d] Hos 6:6; Mic 6:6-8; Mt 9:13 **12:8** [e] S Mt 8:20 **12:10** [f] Mk 3:2; 12:13; Lk 11:54; 14:1; 20:20 [g] S ver 2 **12:11** [h] Lk 14:5 **12:12** [i] Mt 6:26; 10:31 **12:14** [j] Ge 37:18; Ps 71:10; Mt 26:4; 27:1; Mk 3:6; Lk 6:11; Jn 5:18; 7:1,19; 11:53 **12:15** [k] S Mt 4:23 **12:16** [l] S Mt 8:4 **12:17** [m] S Mt 1:22 **12:18** [n] S Mt 3:17 [o] S Jn 3:34 **12:21** [p] Isa 42:1-4 **12:22** [q] S Mt 4:24 **12:23** [r] S Mt 9:27 **12:24** [s] S Mk 3:22 [t] Mt 9:34 **12:25** [u] S Mt 9:4 **12:26** [v] S Mt 4:10 **12:27** [w] ver 24 [x] Ac 19:13

[a] *7* Hosea 6:6 [b] *21* Isaiah 42:1-4

12:2 *Pharisees.* See note on 3:7. *what is unlawful on the Sabbath.* See note on Mk 2:24.
12:3 *what David did.* See note on Mk 2:25.
12:4 *consecrated bread.* Each Sabbath, 12 fresh loaves of bread were to be set on a table in the Holy Place (Ex 25:30; Lev 24:5 – 9). The old loaves were eaten by the priests.
12:5 *desecrate the Sabbath.* By doing required work associated with the sacrifices (see Nu 28:9; cf. Jn 7:22 – 23 and note on 7:22).
12:8 *the Son of Man is Lord of the Sabbath.* See note on Lk 6:5.
12:9 *synagogue.* See note on Mk 1:21.
12:10 *heal on the Sabbath.* The rabbis prohibited healing on the Sabbath, unless it was feared the victim would die before the next day. Obviously the man with the shriveled hand was in no danger of this.
12:11 – 12 Jesus contrasts the worth of an animal with that of a human being (cf. Lk 13:15 – 16; 14:5 and notes).
12:12 *lawful to do good on the Sabbath.* See Mk 3:4; Lk 6:9 and notes.
12:13 *"Stretch out your hand." So he stretched it out.* The fact that the man stretched out his shriveled hand shows there is a connection between faith and Jesus' healing power.
12:14 See notes on Mk 3:6; Lk 6:11.
12:16 *not to tell others about him.* See note on 8:4.
12:18 – 21 Another fulfillment passage (see note on 1:22). This one is from Isaiah's first servant song (see Isa 42:1 – 4 and note) and is the longest OT quotation in Matthew's Gospel. It summarizes the quiet ministry of the Lord's servant, who will bring justice and hope to the nations.
12:18 *my servant.* Jesus is called God's servant only here and in Ac 3:13,26 (see note on 3:13); 4:27,30. *chosen.* See Lk 9:35 and note. *the one I love, in whom I delight.* See note on 3:17. *put my Spirit on him.* See Isa 11:2; 61:1 and notes.
12:20 Jesus mends broken lives (see v. 15; Jn 4:4 – 42; 8:3 – 11).
12:22 *demon-possessed.* See notes on Mk 1:23; Lk 4:33.
12:23 *Son of David.* See note on 9:27.
12:24 *Beelzebul . . . prince of demons.* See 10:25; Lk 11:19 and notes.
12:25 *kingdom divided against itself.* See note on Lk 11:17.

of God that I drive out demons, then the
kingdom of God[y] has come upon you.
29 "Or again, how can anyone enter a
strong man's house and carry off his possessions unless he first ties up the strong
man? Then he can plunder his house.
30 "Whoever is not with me is against
me, and whoever does not gather with me
scatters.[z] 31 And so I tell you, every kind
of sin and slander can be forgiven, but
blasphemy against the Spirit will not be
forgiven.[a] 32 Anyone who speaks a word
against the Son of Man will be forgiven,
but anyone who speaks against the Holy
Spirit will not be forgiven, either in this
age[b] or in the age to come.[c]
33 "Make a tree good and its fruit will be
good, or make a tree bad and its fruit will
be bad, for a tree is recognized by its fruit.[d]
34 You brood of vipers,[e] how can you who
are evil say anything good? For the mouth
speaks[f] what the heart is full of. 35 A good
man brings good things out of the good
stored up in him, and an evil man brings
evil things out of the evil stored up in him.
36 But I tell you that everyone will have to
give account on the day of judgment for
every empty word they have spoken. 37 For
by your words you will be acquitted, and
by your words you will be condemned."[g]

The Sign of Jonah

12:39-42pp — Lk 11:29-32
12:43-45pp — Lk 11:24-26

38 Then some of the Pharisees and teachers of the law said to him, "Teacher, we
want to see a sign[h] from you."[i]
39 He answered, "A wicked and adulterous generation asks for a sign! But none
will be given it except the sign of the
prophet Jonah.[j] 40 For as Jonah was three
days and three nights in the belly of a
huge fish,[k] so the Son of Man[l] will be three
days and three nights in the heart of the
earth.[m] 41 The men of Nineveh[n] will stand
up at the judgment with this generation
and condemn it; for they repented at the
preaching of Jonah,[o] and now something
greater than Jonah is here. 42 The Queen
of the South will rise at the judgment with
this generation and condemn it; for she
came[p] from the ends of the earth to listen
to Solomon's wisdom, and now something
greater than Solomon is here.
43 "When an impure spirit comes out of a
person, it goes through arid places seeking
rest and does not find it. 44 Then it says, 'I
will return to the house I left.' When it arrives, it finds the house unoccupied, swept
clean and put in order. 45 Then it goes and
takes with it seven other spirits more
wicked than itself, and they go in and live
there. And the final condition of that person is worse than the first.[q] That is how it
will be with this wicked generation."

Jesus' Mother and Brothers

12:46-50pp — Mk 3:31-35; Lk 8:19-21

46 While Jesus was still talking to the
crowd, his mother[r] and brothers[s] stood outside, wanting to speak to him. 47 Someone
told him, "Your mother and brothers are
standing outside, wanting to speak to you."
48 He replied to him, "Who is my mother, and who are my brothers?" 49 Pointing
to his disciples, he said, "Here are my
mother and my brothers. 50 For whoever
does the will of my Father in heaven[t] is
my brother and sister and mother."

The Parable of the Sower

13:1-15pp — Mk 4:1-12; Lk 8:4-10
13:16,17pp — Lk 10:23,24
13:18-23pp — Mk 4:13-20; Lk 8:11-15

13 That same day Jesus went out of
the house[u] and sat by the lake.

12:28 [y] S Mt 3:2 **12:30** [z] Mk 9:40; Lk 11:23 **12:31** [a] Mk 3:28,29; Lk 12:10 **12:32** [b] Titus 2:12 [c] Mk 10:30; Lk 20:34,35; Eph 1:21; Heb 6:5 **12:33** [d] Mt 7:16, 17; Lk 6:43,44 **12:34** [e] Mt 3:7; 23:33 [f] Mt 15:18; Lk 6:45 **12:37** [g] Job 15:6; Pr 10:14; 18:21; Jas 3:2 **12:38** [h] S Jn 2:11; S 4:48 [i] Mt 16:1; Mk 8:11,12; Lk 11:16; Jn 2:18; 6:30; 1Co 1:22 **12:39** [j] Mt 16:4; Lk 11:29 **12:40** [k] Jnh 1:17 [l] S Mt 8:20 [m] S Mt 16:21 **12:41** [n] Jnh 1:2 [o] Jnh 3:5 **12:42** [p] 1Ki 10:1; 2Ch 9:1 **12:45** [q] 2Pe 2:20 **12:46** [r] Mt 1:18; 2:11,13,14, 20; Lk 1:43; 2:33,34,48,51; Jn 2:1,5; 19:25, 26 [s] Mt 13:55; Jn 2:12; 7:3,5; Ac 1:14; 1Co 9:5; Gal 1:19 **12:50** [t] Mt 6:10; Jn 15:14 **13:1** [u] ver 36; Mt 9:28

12:28 *kingdom of God.* See note on 3:2. *has come upon you.* See note on Mk 1:15.
12:30 There can be no double-mindedness in our relationship to Jesus (see note on Lk 11:23; cf. Ps 119:113; Mk 9:40; Lk 9:50 and note; Jas 1:8; 4:8).
12:31 *blasphemy against the Spirit will not be forgiven.* The context (vv. 24,28,32) suggests that the unpardonable sin was attributing to Satan Christ's authenticating miracles done in the power of the Holy Spirit (see note on Mk 3:29).
12:32 *Son of Man.* See note on Mk 8:31. *this age ... the age to come.* See Eph 1:21 and note.
12:33 See 3:16; cf. Jas 3:11–12.
12:34 *brood of vipers.* In the NT an expression used only by John the Baptist (3:7; Lk 3:7) and Jesus (here; 23:33). In this context it refers to the Pharisees (v. 24). *the mouth speaks what the heart is full of.* See 15:18–19; Pr 4:23 and note. *heart.* See note on Ps 4:7.
12:36 *day of judgment.* At Christ's second coming; sometimes referred to as "that day" (7:22; 2Ti 1:12,18), "the day of slaughter" (Jas 5:5; see note there).
12:38 *sign.* The Pharisees wanted to see a spectacular miracle, preferably in the sky (see Lk 11:16), as the sign that Jesus was the Messiah. Instead, he cites them a "sign" from history. See note on Lk 11:29.
12:39 *adulterous.* Referring to spiritual, not physical, adultery, in the sense that their generation had become unfaithful to its spiritual husband (God; see note on Ex 34:15). *sign of the prophet Jonah.* See note on Lk 11:30.
12:40 *three days and three nights.* Including at least part of the first day and part of the third day, a common Jewish reckoning of time. See note on Lk 24:46. *huge fish.* The Greek word does not mean "whale" but rather "sea creature," i.e., a huge fish (see note on Jnh 1:17). *Son of Man.* See note on Mk 8:31.
12:41–42 *something greater than Jonah ... something greater than Solomon.* See note on Lk 11:31–32.
12:42 *Queen of the South.* In 1Ki 10:1 she is called the queen of Sheba, a country in southwest Arabia now called Yemen.
12:43–45 See notes on Lk 11:24–25.
12:46 *mother and brothers.* See note on Lk 8:19.
12:50 *whoever does the will of my Father.* See notes on Mk 3:35; Lk 8:21.
13:1 *went out of the house.* See "went into the house" (v. 36).

2 Such large crowds gathered around
him that he got into a boat[v] and sat in it,
while all the people stood on the shore.
3 Then he told them many things in parables, saying: "A farmer went out to sow
his seed. 4 As he was scattering the seed,
some fell along the path, and the birds
came and ate it up. 5 Some fell on rocky
places, where it did not have much soil.
It sprang up quickly, because the soil was
shallow. 6 But when the sun came up, the
plants were scorched, and they withered
because they had no root. 7 Other seed
fell among thorns, which grew up and
choked the plants. 8 Still other seed fell on
good soil, where it produced a crop — a
hundred,[w] sixty or thirty times what was
sown. 9 Whoever has ears, let them hear."[x]
10 The disciples came to him and asked,
"Why do you speak to the people in parables?"
11 He replied, "Because the knowledge
of the secrets of the kingdom of heaven[y]
has been given to you,[z] but not to them.
12 Whoever has will be given more, and
they will have an abundance. Whoever
does not have, even what they have will
be taken from them.[a] 13 This is why I speak
to them in parables:

"Though seeing, they do not see;
though hearing, they do not hear or
understand.[b]

14 In them is fulfilled[c] the prophecy of Isaiah:

" 'You will be ever hearing but never
understanding;
you will be ever seeing but never
perceiving.
15 For this people's heart has become
calloused;
they hardly hear with their ears,
and they have closed their eyes.
Otherwise they might see with their
eyes,
hear with their ears,
understand with their hearts
and turn, and I would heal them.'[a][d]

16 But blessed are your eyes because they
see, and your ears because they hear.[e]
17 For truly I tell you, many prophets and
righteous people longed to see what you
see[f] but did not see it, and to hear what
you hear but did not hear it.
18 "Listen then to what the parable of
the sower means: 19 When anyone hears
the message about the kingdom[g] and does
not understand it, the evil one[h] comes and
snatches away what was sown in their
heart. This is the seed sown along the
path. 20 The seed falling on rocky ground
refers to someone who hears the word and
at once receives it with joy. 21 But since
they have no root, they last only a short
time. When trouble or persecution comes
because of the word, they quickly fall
away.[i] 22 The seed falling among the thorns
refers to someone who hears the word, but
the worries of this life and the deceitfulness of wealth[j] choke the word, making it
unfruitful. 23 But the seed falling on good
soil refers to someone who hears the word
and understands it. This is the one who
produces a crop, yielding a hundred, sixty
or thirty times what was sown."[k]

The Parable of the Weeds

24 Jesus told them another parable: "The
kingdom of heaven is like[l] a man who
sowed good seed in his field. 25 But while
everyone was sleeping, his enemy came

[a] 15 Isaiah 6:9,10 (see Septuagint)

13:2 [v] Lk 5:3 **13:8** [w] Ge 26:12 **13:9** [x] S Mt 11:15 **13:11** [y] S Mt 3:2 [z] Mt 11:25; 16:17; 19:11; Jn 6:65; 1Co 2:10, 14; Col 1:27; 1Jn 2:20,27 **13:12** [a] S Mt 25:29 **13:13** [b] Dt 29:4; Jer 5:21; Eze 12:2 **13:14** [c] ver 35; S Mt 1:22 **13:15** [d] Isa 6:9, 10; Jn 12:40; Ac 28:26,27; Ro 11:8 **13:16** [e] Mt 16:17 **13:17** [f] Jn 8:56; Heb 11:13; 1Pe 1:10-12 **13:19** [g] Mt 4:23 [h] S Mt 5:37 **13:21** [i] Mt 11:6; 26:31 **13:22** [j] Mt 19:23; 1Ti 6:9,10,17 **13:23** [k] ver 8 **13:24** [l] ver 31, 33,45,47; Mt 18:23; 20:1; 22:2; 25:1; Mk 4:26,30

These two phrases determine the setting of Jesus' teaching in vv. 1–35.
13:2 *sat in it.* See note on Mk 4:1.
13:3–9 See vv. 18–23 for the interpretation of this first parable.
13:3 *parables.* Our word "parable" comes from the Greek *parabole,* which means "a placing beside"— and thus a comparison or an illustration. Its most common use in the NT is for the illustrative stories that Jesus drew from nature and human life. The Synoptic Gospels contain about 30 of these stories. John's Gospel contains no parables but uses other figures of speech (see notes on Mk 4:2; Lk 8:4; see also chart, p. 1736). *to sow his seed.* See note on Lk 8:5. According to Mk 4:14; Lk 8:11 (see notes there), the seed is the word of God.
13:4–6 See note on Mk 4:3–8.
13:4 *birds.* Satan, "the evil one" (v. 19).
13:5 *rocky places.* Not ground covered with small stones, but shallow soil on top of solid rock. See note on Lk 8:6.
13:8 *a hundred.* See notes on Mk 4:8; Lk 8:8.
13:9 *let them hear.* See note on Lk 8:8.
13:10 See note on Lk 8:9.
13:11 *secrets of the kingdom of heaven.* See notes on Mk 4:11; Lk 8:10.
13:13–14 Jesus speaks in parables because of the spiritual dullness of the people (see note on Lk 8:4).
13:13 *Though seeing, they do not see.* See notes on Mk 4:12; Lk 8:10.
13:14–15 See Isa 6:9–10 and notes.
13:18 *what the parable of the sower means.* Jesus seldom interpreted his parables, but here he does.
13:19 *message.* Cf. Luke's "word of God" (8:11). *evil one.* Satan (the devil; see Mk 4:15; Lk 8:12 and note).
13:21 Cf. 24:10–12; see note on Lk 8:13.
13:22 *the worries of this life and the deceitfulness of wealth.* Lk 8:14 adds life's "pleasures" to these two phrases. *deceitfulness of wealth.* See note on Mk 4:19.
13:23 *understands.* Cf. the Isaiah quotation in vv. 14–15. Matthew uses this word six times in this chapter (here and in vv. 13,14,15,19,51). *hundred ... times.* See note on Lk 8:8.
13:24–30 See vv. 36–43 for the interpretation.
13:24 *The kingdom of heaven is like.* This phrase introduces six of the seven parables in this chapter (all but the parable of the sower).

and sowed weeds among the wheat, and
went away. 26 When the wheat sprouted
and formed heads, then the weeds also
appeared.
27 "The owner's servants came to him
and said, 'Sir, didn't you sow good seed
in your field? Where then did the weeds
come from?'
28 " 'An enemy did this,' he replied.
"The servants asked him, 'Do you want
us to go and pull them up?'
29 " 'No,' he answered, 'because while
you are pulling the weeds, you may uproot
the wheat with them. 30 Let both grow together until the harvest. At that time I will
tell the harvesters: First collect the weeds
and tie them in bundles to be burned;
then gather the wheat and bring it into my
barn.' "[m]

The Parables of the Mustard Seed and the Yeast

13:31,32pp — Mk 4:30-32
13:31-33pp — Lk 13:18-21

31 He told them another parable: "The
kingdom of heaven is like[n] a mustard
seed,[o] which a man took and planted in
his field. 32 Though it is the smallest of all
seeds, yet when it grows, it is the largest of
garden plants and becomes a tree, so that
the birds come and perch in its branches."[p]
33 He told them still another parable:
"The kingdom of heaven is like[q] yeast
that a woman took and mixed into about
sixty pounds[a] of flour[r] until it worked all
through the dough."[s]
34 Jesus spoke all these things to the
crowd in parables; he did not say anything
to them without using a parable.[t] 35 So was
fulfilled[u] what was spoken through the
prophet:

"I will open my mouth in parables,
I will utter things hidden since the
creation of the world."[b][v]

The Parable of the Weeds Explained

36 Then he left the crowd and went into
the house. His disciples came to him and
said, "Explain to us the parable[w] of the
weeds in the field."
37 He answered, "The one who sowed
the good seed is the Son of Man.[x] 38 The
field is the world, and the good seed
stands for the people of the kingdom.
The weeds are the people of the evil one,[y]
39 and the enemy who sows them is the
devil. The harvest[z] is the end of the age,[a]
and the harvesters are angels.[b]
40 "As the weeds are pulled up and
burned in the fire, so it will be at the end
of the age. 41 The Son of Man[c] will send out
his angels,[d] and they will weed out of his
kingdom everything that causes sin and
all who do evil. 42 They will throw them
into the blazing furnace, where there will
be weeping and gnashing of teeth.[e] 43 Then
the righteous will shine like the sun[f] in
the kingdom of their Father. Whoever has
ears, let them hear.[g]

The Parables of the Hidden Treasure and the Pearl

44 "The kingdom of heaven is like[h] treasure hidden in a field. When a man found
it, he hid it again, and then in his joy
went and sold all he had and bought that
field.[i]
45 "Again, the kingdom of heaven is like[j]
a merchant looking for fine pearls. 46 When
he found one of great value, he went away
and sold everything he had and bought it.

13:30 [m] Mt 3:12 **13:31** [n] S ver 24 [o] Mt 17:20; Lk 17:6 **13:32** [p] Ps 104:12; Eze 17:23; 31:6; Da 4:12 **13:33** [q] S ver 24 [r] Ge 18:6 [s] Gal 5:9 **13:34** [t] S Jn 16:25 **13:35** [u] ver 14; S Mt 1:22 [v] Ps 78:2; Ro 16:25, 26; 1Co 2:7; Eph 3:9; Col 1:26 **13:36** [w] Mt 15:15 **13:37** [x] S Mt 8:20 **13:38** [y] Jn 8:44, 45; 1Jn 3:10 **13:39** [z] Joel 3:13 [a] Mt 24:3; 28:20 [b] Rev 14:15 **13:41** [c] S Mt 8:20 [d] Mt 24:31 **13:42** [e] S Mt 8:12 **13:43** [f] Da 12:3 [g] S Mt 11:15 **13:44** [h] S ver 24 [i] Isa 55:1; Mt 19:21; Php 3:7,8 **13:45** [j] S ver 24

[a] 33 Or about 27 kilograms [b] 35 Psalm 78:2

13:25 *weeds.* Probably darnel, which looks very much like wheat while it is young, but can later be distinguished. This parable does not refer to unbelievers in the professing church. The field is the world (v. 38). Thus in this world the people of the kingdom live side by side with the people of the evil one.

13:30 *harvest.* The final judgment (see notes on Joel 3:13; Mk 4:29; Rev 14:15).

13:31 – 32 Although the kingdom will seem to have an insignificant beginning, it will eventually spread throughout the world (see note on Mk 4:30 – 34).

13:32 *the smallest ... the largest.* The mustard seed is not the smallest seed known today, but it was the smallest seed used by farmers and gardeners there and at that time, and under favorable conditions the plant could reach about ten feet in height. *a tree ... its branches.* Likely an allusion to Da 4:21, suggesting that the kingdom of heaven will expand to world dominion and that people from all nations will find rest in it (cf. Da 2:35,44 – 45; 7:27; Rev 11:15).

13:33 In the Bible, yeast usually symbolizes that which is evil or unclean (see note on Mk 8:15). Here, however, it is a symbol of growth. As yeast permeates a batch of dough, so the kingdom of heaven spreads through a person's life. Or it may signify the growth of the kingdom by the inner working of the Holy Spirit (using God's word). See note on Lk 13:21.

13:35 *spoken through the prophet.* The quotation is from Ps 78 (see note on 78:2), a psalm ascribed to Asaph, who according to 2Ch 29:30 was a "seer" (prophet).

13:37,41 *Son of Man.* See note on Mk 8:31.

13:42 *blazing furnace.* Often mentioned in connection with the final judgment in apocalyptic literature (see Rev 19:20; 20:14). *weeping and gnashing of teeth.* Occurs six times in Matthew's Gospel (here; v. 50; 8:12; 22:13; 24:51; 25:30) and nowhere else in the NT (but see note on 8:12).

13:43 *the righteous will shine like the sun.* See Da 12:3. *let them hear.* See note on Lk 8:8.

13:44 – 46 These two parables teach the same truth: The kingdom is of such great value that one should be willing to give up all one has in order to gain it. Jesus did not imply that one can purchase the kingdom with money or good deeds.

13:44 *treasure hidden in a field.* In ancient times it was common to hide treasure in the ground since there were no banks — though there were "bankers" (25:27; see note there).

The Parable of the Net

47 “Once again, the kingdom of heaven is like[k] a net that was let down into the lake and caught all kinds[l] of fish. 48 When it was full, the fishermen pulled it up on the shore. Then they sat down and collected the good fish in baskets, but threw the bad away. 49 This is how it will be at the end of the age. The angels will come and separate the wicked from the righteous[m] 50 and throw them into the blazing furnace, where there will be weeping and gnashing of teeth.[n]

51 “Have you understood all these things?” Jesus asked.

“Yes,” they replied.

52 He said to them, “Therefore every teacher of the law who has become a disciple in the kingdom of heaven is like the owner of a house who brings out of his storeroom new treasures as well as old.”

A Prophet Without Honor

13:54-58pp — Mk 6:1-6

53 When Jesus had finished these parables,[o] he moved on from there. 54 Coming to his hometown, he began teaching the people in their synagogue,[p] and they were amazed.[q] “Where did this man get this wisdom and these miraculous powers?” they asked. 55 “Isn’t this the carpenter’s son?[r] Isn’t his mother’s[s] name Mary, and aren’t his brothers[t] James, Joseph, Simon and Judas? 56 Aren’t all his sisters with us? Where then did this man get all these things?” 57 And they took offense[u] at him.

But Jesus said to them, “A prophet is not without honor except in his own town and in his own home.”[v]

58 And he did not do many miracles there because of their lack of faith.

John the Baptist Beheaded

14:1-12pp — Mk 6:14-29

14 At that time Herod[w] the tetrarch heard the reports about Jesus,[x] 2 and he said to his attendants, “This is John the Baptist;[y] he has risen from the dead! That is why miraculous powers are at work in him.”

3 Now Herod had arrested John and bound him and put him in prison[z] because of Herodias, his brother Philip’s wife,[a] 4 for John had been saying to him: “It is not lawful for you to have her.”[b] 5 Herod wanted to kill John, but he was afraid of the people, because they considered John a prophet.[c]

6 On Herod’s birthday the daughter of Herodias danced for the guests and pleased Herod so much 7 that he promised with an oath to give her whatever she asked. 8 Prompted by her mother, she said, “Give me here on a platter the head of John the Baptist.” 9 The king was distressed, but because of his oaths and his dinner guests, he ordered that her request be granted 10 and had John beheaded[d] in the prison. 11 His head was brought in on a platter and given to the girl, who carried it to her mother. 12 John’s disciples came and took his body and buried it.[e] Then they went and told Jesus.

13:47 [k] S ver 24 [l] Mt 22:10 **13:49** [m] Mt 25:32 **13:50** [n] S Mt 8:12 **13:53** [o] S Mt 7:28 **13:54** [p] S Mt 4:23 [q] S Mt 7:28 **13:55** [r] Lk 3:23; Jn 6:42 [s] S Mt 12:46 [t] S Mt 12:46 **13:57** [u] Jn 6:61 [v] Lk 4:24; Jn 4:44 **14:1** [w] Mk 8:15; Lk 3:1,19; 13:31; 23:7,8; Ac 4:27; 12:1 [x] Lk 9:7-9 **14:2** [y] S Mt 3:1 **14:3** [z] Mt 4:12; 11:2 [a] Lk 3:19, 20 **14:4** [b] Lev 18:16; 20:21 **14:5** [c] S Mt 11:9 **14:10** [d] Mt 17:12 **14:12** [e] Ac 8:2

13:47-51 The parable of the net teaches the same general lesson as the parable of the weeds: There will be a final separation of the righteous and the wicked. The parable of the weeds also emphasizes that we are not to try to make such a separation now. That is entirely the Lord’s business (vv. 28-30,41-42).
13:50 See note on v. 42.
13:51 *Yes.* Probably an overstatement by the disciples, especially in view of Jesus’ words in 15:16.
13:53 Concludes a teaching section and introduces a narrative section (cf. 7:28-29).
13:54 *his hometown.* Nazareth (see note on 2:23). *teaching the people in their synagogue.* See note on Mk 1:21. *synagogue.* See note on Mk 1:21. *amazed.* See note on 7:28.
13:55 *carpenter’s son.* See note on Mk 6:3. Apparently Joseph was not living at the time of this incident. *brothers.* Sons born to Joseph and Mary after the virgin birth of Jesus (see note on Lk 8:19). *James.* See Introduction to James: Author. *Judas.* See Introduction to Jude: Author.
13:58 *lack of faith.* The close relationship between faith and miracles is stressed in Matthew’s Gospel (cf. 8:10,13; 9:2,22,28-29).
14:1 *tetrarch.* The ruler of a fourth part of a region. “Herod the tetrarch” (Herod Antipas) was one of several sons of Herod the Great. When Herod the Great died, his kingdom was divided among three of his sons (see chart, p. 1592; see also map, p. 1707). Herod Antipas ruled over Galilee and Perea (4 BC-AD 39). Matthew correctly refers to him as tetrarch here, as Luke regularly does (Lk 3:19; 9:7; Ac 13:1). But in v. 9 Matthew calls him “king”—as Mk 6:14 also does—because that was his popular title among the Galileans, as well as in Rome.
14:2 *John … risen from the dead.* See note on Mk 6:16.
14:3 *Herod had arrested John.* See note on Mk 6:17. *Herodias.* A granddaughter of Herod the Great (see chart, p. 1593). First she married her uncle, Herod Philip (Herod the Great also had another son named Philip), who lived in Rome. While a guest in their home, Herod Antipas persuaded Herodias to leave her husband for him. Marriage to one’s brother’s wife while the brother was still living was forbidden by the Mosaic law (Lev 18:16). *Philip’s.* The son of Herod the Great and Mariamne, the daughter of Simon the high priest, and thus a half brother of Herod Antipas, born to Malthace (see chart, p. 1592).
14:6 *daughter of Herodias.* Salome, according to Josephus. She later married her granduncle, the other Philip (son of Herod the Great), who ruled the northern territories (Lk 3:1). At this time Salome was a young woman of marriageable age. Her dance was doubtless sensual, and the performance pleased both Herod and his guests.
14:7 *whatever she asked.* See Mk 6:22 and note.
14:8 *platter.* A flat wooden dish on which meat was served.
14:10 The Jewish historian Josephus also refers to Herod’s arrest and execution of John the Baptist (*Antiquities,* 18.5.2).

Jesus Feeds the Five Thousand

14:13-21pp — Mk 6:32-44; Lk 9:10-17; Jn 6:1-13
14:13-21Ref — Mt 15:32-38

13 When Jesus heard what had happened, he withdrew by boat privately to a
solitary place. Hearing of this, the crowds
followed him on foot from the towns.
14 When Jesus landed and saw a large
crowd, he had compassion on them[f] and
healed their sick.[g]
15 As evening approached, the disciples
came to him and said, "This is a remote
place, and it's already getting late. Send
the crowds away, so they can go to the
villages and buy themselves some food."
16 Jesus replied, "They do not need to
go away. You give them something to eat."
17 "We have here only five loaves[h] of
bread and two fish," they answered.
18 "Bring them here to me," he said.
19 And he directed the people to sit down
on the grass. Taking the five loaves and
the two fish and looking up to heaven, he
gave thanks and broke the loaves.[i] Then
he gave them to the disciples, and the disciples gave them to the people. 20 They all
ate and were satisfied, and the disciples
picked up twelve basketfuls of broken
pieces that were left over. 21 The number
of those who ate was about five thousand
men, besides women and children.

Jesus Walks on the Water

14:22-33pp — Mk 6:45-51; Jn 6:16-21
14:34-36pp — Mk 6:53-56

22 Immediately Jesus made the disciples
get into the boat and go on ahead of him
to the other side, while he dismissed the
crowd. 23 After he had dismissed them, he
went up on a mountainside by himself to
pray.[j] Later that night, he was there alone,
24 and the boat was already a considerable
distance from land, buffeted by the waves
because the wind was against it.
25 Shortly before dawn Jesus went out
to them, walking on the lake. 26 When the
disciples saw him walking on the lake,
they were terrified. "It's a ghost,"[k] they
said, and cried out in fear.
27 But Jesus immediately said to them:
"Take courage![l] It is I. Don't be afraid."[m]
28 "Lord, if it's you," Peter replied, "tell
me to come to you on the water."
29 "Come," he said.
Then Peter got down out of the boat,
walked on the water and came toward
Jesus. 30 But when he saw the wind, he
was afraid and, beginning to sink, cried
out, "Lord, save me!"
31 Immediately Jesus reached out his
hand and caught him. "You of little faith,"[n]
he said, "why did you doubt?"
32 And when they climbed into the boat,
the wind died down. 33 Then those who
were in the boat worshiped him, saying,
"Truly you are the Son of God."[o]
34 When they had crossed over, they
landed at Gennesaret. 35 And when the men
of that place recognized Jesus, they sent
word to all the surrounding country. People
brought all their sick to him 36 and begged
him to let the sick just touch the edge of his
cloak,[p] and all who touched it were healed.

That Which Defiles

15:1-20pp — Mk 7:1-23

15 Then some Pharisees and teachers of the law came to Jesus from

14:14 [f] S Mt 9:36 [g] S Mt 4:23 **14:17** [h] Mt 16:9 **14:19** [i] 1Sa 9:13; Mt 26:26; Mk 8:6; Lk 9:16; 24:30; Ac 2:42; 20:7, 11; 27:35; 1Co 10:16; 1Ti 4:4
14:23 [j] S Lk 3:21 **14:26** [k] Lk 24:37 **14:27** [l] Mt 9:2; Ac 23:11 [m] Da 10:12; Mt 17:7; 28:10; Lk 1:13, 30; 2:10; Ac 18:9; 23:11; Rev 1:17 **14:31** [n] S Mt 6:30 **14:33** [o] Ps 2:7; S Mt 4:3 **14:36** [p] S Mt 9:20

14:13–21 See 15:37; Mk 6:32–44; Lk 9:10–17; Jn 6:1–13 and notes.
14:13 *what had happened.* Probably refers to vv. 1–2, namely, Herod's response to reports about Jesus. *withdrew ... to a solitary place.* To avoid the threat of Herod and the pressing of the crowds. Jesus' time had not yet come (see Jn 2:4 and note; cf. Jn 6:15).
14:14 *compassion.* See note on 9:36.
14:20 *twelve basketfuls.* See note on Jn 6:13.
14:21 *besides women and children.* Matthew alone notes this. He was writing to the Jews, who did not permit women and children to eat with men in public. So they were in a place by themselves.
14:22 *made.* The Greek word used here means "to compel" and suggests a crisis. John records that after the miracle of the loaves and fish the crowds "intended to ... make him [Jesus] king by force" (6:15). This involved a complete misunderstanding of the mission of Jesus. The disciples may have been caught up in the enthusiasm and needed to be removed from the area quickly.
14:23 *pray.* Matthew speaks of Jesus praying only here and in Gethsemane (cf. 26:36–46).
14:24 *considerable distance from land.* See Jn 6:19 and note.
14:25 *Shortly before dawn.* Lit. "During the fourth watch of the night," 3:00–6:00 a.m. According to Roman reckoning the night was divided into four watches: (1) 6:00–9:00 p.m., (2) 9:00–midnight, (3) midnight–3:00 a.m. and (4) 3:00–6:00 a.m. (see note on Mk 13:35). The Jews had only three watches during the night: (1) sunset–10:00 p.m., (2) 10:00 p.m.–2:00 a.m. and (3) 2:00 a.m.–sunrise (see Jdg 7:19 and note; 1Sa 11:11). *walking on the lake.* See note on Mk 6:48. *lake.* The Sea of Galilee (see note on Mk 1:16).
14:26 *ghost.* See note on Mk 6:49.
14:27 *It is I.* Lit. "I am" (cf. Ex 3:14; Isa 43:10; 51:12; Jn 8:58 and note).
14:28 *if it's you.* A condition assumed to be true. Peter knew it was Jesus, and that is why he stepped out of the boat onto the water in the first place.
14:31 *You of little faith.* See note on 6:30. *why did you doubt?* See Jas 1:5–8.
14:33 *Son of God.* This is the first time the disciples use the full title in addressing Jesus (cf. 3:17, where God called him "my Son"; see also Jn 3:16 and note).
14:34 *Gennesaret.* Either the narrow plain (about four miles long and less than two miles wide) on the west side of the Sea of Galilee near the north end (north of Magdala), or a town in the plain. The plain was considered a garden spot, fertile and well watered.
14:36 *just touch the edge of his cloak.* See note on Mk 5:28.

Jerusalem and asked, 2“Why do your disciples break the tradition of the elders?
They don’t wash their hands before they
eat!”[q]
3Jesus replied, “And why do you break
the command of God for the sake of your
tradition? 4For God said, ‘Honor your father and mother’[a][r] and ‘Anyone who curses their father or mother is to be put to
death.’[b][s] 5But you say that if anyone declares that what might have been used to
help their father or mother is ‘devoted to
God,’ 6they are not to ‘honor their father
or mother’ with it. Thus you nullify the
word of God for the sake of your tradition.
7You hypocrites! Isaiah was right when he
prophesied about you:

8“ ‘These people honor me with their
lips,
but their hearts are far from me.
9They worship me in vain;
their teachings are merely human
rules.’[t][c][u]”

10Jesus called the crowd to him and
said, “Listen and understand. 11What
goes into someone’s mouth does not defile
them,[v] but what comes out of their mouth,
that is what defiles them.”[w]
12Then the disciples came to him and
asked, “Do you know that the Pharisees
were offended when they heard this?”
13He replied, “Every plant that my heavenly Father has not planted[x] will be pulled
up by the roots. 14Leave them; they are
blind guides.[d][y] If the blind lead the blind,
both will fall into a pit.”[z]
15Peter said, “Explain the parable
to us.”[a]
16“Are you still so dull?”[b] Jesus asked
them. 17“Don’t you see that whatever enters the mouth goes into the stomach and
then out of the body? 18But the things that
come out of a person’s mouth come from
the heart,[c] and these defile them. 19For out
of the heart come evil thoughts—murder,
adultery, sexual immorality, theft, false
testimony, slander.[d] 20These are what defile a person;[e] but eating with unwashed
hands does not defile them.”

15:2 [q]Lk 11:38 **15:4** [r]Ex 20:12; Dt 5:16; Eph 6:2 [s]Ex 21:17; Lev 20:9 **15:9** [t]Col 2:20-22 [u]Isa 29:13; Mal 2:2 **15:11** [v]S Ac 10:14,15 [w]ver 18 **15:13** [x]Isa 60:21; 61:3 **15:14** [y]Mt 23:16, 24; Ro 2:19 [z]Lk 6:39 **15:15** [a]Mt 13:36 **15:16** [b]Mt 16:9 **15:18** [c]Mt 12:34; Lk 6:45; Jas 3:6 **15:19** [d]Gal 5:19-21 **15:20** [e]Ro 14:14 **15:21** [f]S Mt 11:21 **15:22** [g]S Mt 9:27 [h]S Mt 4:24 **15:24** [i]Mt 10:6, 23; Ro 15:8 **15:25** [j]S Mt 8:2 **15:28** [k]S Mt 9:22

The Faith of a Canaanite Woman

15:21-28pp — Mk 7:24-30

21Leaving that place, Jesus withdrew to
the region of Tyre and Sidon.[f] 22A Canaanite woman from that vicinity came to him,
crying out, “Lord, Son of David,[g] have
mercy on me! My daughter is demon-possessed and suffering terribly.”[h]
23Jesus did not answer a word. So his
disciples came to him and urged him,
“Send her away, for she keeps crying out
after us.”
24He answered, “I was sent only to the
lost sheep of Israel.”[i]
25The woman came and knelt before
him.[j] “Lord, help me!” she said.
26He replied, “It is not right to take the
children’s bread and toss it to the dogs.”
27“Yes it is, Lord,” she said. “Even the
dogs eat the crumbs that fall from their
master’s table.”
28Then Jesus said to her, “Woman, you
have great faith![k] Your request is granted.”
And her daughter was healed at that moment.

Jesus Feeds the Four Thousand

15:29-31pp — Mk 7:31-37
15:32-39pp — Mk 8:1-10
15:32-39Ref — Mt 14:13-21

29Jesus left there and went along the Sea
of Galilee. Then he went up on a mountainside and sat down. 30Great crowds

[a] 4 Exodus 20:12; Deut. 5:16 [b] 4 Exodus 21:17; Lev. 20:9 [c] 9 Isaiah 29:13 [d] 14 Some manuscripts *blind guides of the blind*

15:2 *tradition of the elders.* After the Babylonian exile, the Jewish rabbis began to make meticulous rules and regulations governing the daily life of the people. These were interpretations and applications of the law of Moses, handed down from generation to generation. In Jesus' day this "tradition of the elders" was in oral form. It was not until c. AD 200 that it was put into writing in the Mishnah (see note on Ne 10:34). *wash.* See note on Mk 7:3.
15:5-6 See notes on Mk 7:11,13.
15:7-20 See Mk 7:6-23 and notes.
15:7 *hypocrites.* See note on 6:2.
15:8-9 See Isa 29:13 and note.
15:13 *Every plant that my heavenly Father has not planted.* Probably refers to the Pharisees and teachers of the law who were in Jesus' audience (vv. 1,12).
15:15 *parable.* See note on 13:3. The parable Peter refers to is found in v. 11.
15:18 See Mk 7:20 and note.
15:21 *Tyre.* See note on Mk 7:24. *Sidon.* About 25 miles north of Tyre.
15:22 *Canaanite.* A term found many times in the OT but only here in the NT. In NT times there was no country known as Canaan. Some think this was the Semitic manner of referring to the people of Phoenicia at this time. Mark says the woman was "a Greek, born in Syrian Phoenicia" (7:26; see note there). *Son of David.* See note on 9:27; shows that this pagan woman had some recognition of Jesus' Messianic claims. *demon-possessed.* See Mk 1:23; Lk 4:33 and notes.
15:26 *children's.* "The lost sheep of Israel" (v. 24). *bread.* God's covenanted blessings. *dogs.* Gentiles. Jesus' point was that the gospel was to be given first to Jews. The woman understood Jesus' implication and was willing to settle for "crumbs" (v. 27). Jesus rewarded her "great faith" (v. 28).
15:28 Jesus was pleased with the woman's reply (v. 27). It revealed not only her wit but also her faith and humility. *Woman.* See NIV text note on Jn 2:4.
15:29 *there.* The "region of Tyre and Sidon" (v. 21; see note on Mk 7:31).

came to him, bringing the lame, the blind,
the crippled, the mute and many others,
and laid them at his feet; and he healed
them.[l] 31 The people were amazed when
they saw the mute speaking, the crippled
made well, the lame walking and the blind
seeing. And they praised the God of Israel.[m]
32 Jesus called his disciples to him and
said, "I have compassion for these people;[n] they have already been with me three
days and have nothing to eat. I do not
want to send them away hungry, or they
may collapse on the way."
33 His disciples answered, "Where could
we get enough bread in this remote place
to feed such a crowd?"
34 "How many loaves do you have?"
Jesus asked.
"Seven," they replied, "and a few small
fish."
35 He told the crowd to sit down on the
ground. 36 Then he took the seven loaves
and the fish, and when he had given
thanks, he broke them[o] and gave them
to the disciples, and they in turn to the
people. 37 They all ate and were satisfied.
Afterward the disciples picked up seven
basketfuls of broken pieces that were left
over.[p] 38 The number of those who ate was
four thousand men, besides women and
children. 39 After Jesus had sent the crowd
away, he got into the boat and went to the
vicinity of Magadan.

15:30 [l]S Mt 4:23
15:31 [m]S Mt 9:8
15:32 [n]S Mt 9:36
15:36 [o]S Mt 14:19
15:37 [p]Mt 16:10
16:1 [q]S Ac 4:1 [r]S Mt 12:38

The Demand for a Sign

16:1-12pp — Mk 8:11-21

16 The Pharisees and Sadducees[q]
came to Jesus and tested him by
asking him to show them a sign from
heaven.[r]
2 He replied, "When evening comes, you
say, 'It will be fair weather, for the sky is
red,' 3 and in the morning, 'Today it will
be stormy, for the sky is red and overcast.'
You know how to interpret the appearance
of the sky, but you cannot interpret the
signs of the times.[a][s] 4 A wicked and adulterous generation looks for a sign, but
none will be given it except the sign of Jonah."[t] Jesus then left them and went away.

The Yeast of the Pharisees and Sadducees

5 When they went across the lake, the
disciples forgot to take bread. 6 "Be careful," Jesus said to them. "Be on your guard
against the yeast of the Pharisees and Sadducees."[u]
7 They discussed this among themselves
and said, "It is because we didn't bring
any bread."
8 Aware of their discussion, Jesus asked,
"You of little faith,[v] why are you talking
among yourselves about having no bread?
9 Do you still not understand? Don't you
remember the five loaves for the five thousand, and how many basketfuls you gathered?[w] 10 Or the seven loaves for the four
thousand, and how many basketfuls you
gathered?[x] 11 How is it you don't understand that I was not talking to you about
bread? But be on your guard against the
yeast of the Pharisees and Sadducees."
12 Then they understood that he was not
telling them to guard against the yeast
used in bread, but against the teaching of
the Pharisees and Sadducees.[y]

Peter Declares That Jesus Is the Messiah

16:13-16pp — Mk 8:27-29; Lk 9:18-20

13 When Jesus came to the region of
Caesarea Philippi, he asked his disciples,
"Who do people say the Son of Man is?"

16:3 [s]Lk 12:54-56
16:4 [t]Mt 12:39
16:6 [u]Lk 12:1
16:8 [v]S Mt 6:30
16:9 [w]Mt 14:17-21
16:10 [x]Mt 15:34-38
16:12 [y]S Ac 4:1

[a] 2,3 Some early manuscripts do not have *When evening comes . . . of the times.*

15:31 *amazed.* Cf. Mk 1:22 and note.
15:32–39 See notes on Mk 8:1–10.
15:32 *compassion.* See note on 9:36.
15:36 *when he had given thanks.* The Jewish practice at meals (see 1Ti 4:3–5).
15:37 The feeding of the 5,000 is recorded in all four Gospels, but the feeding of the 4,000 is only in Matthew and Mark. The 12 baskets mentioned in the accounts of the feeding of the 5,000 were possibly the lunch baskets of the 12 apostles. The 12 baskets of leftovers may also suggest a sufficient abundance to feed all 12 tribes of Israel (cf. note on Ex 25:30). The seven baskets mentioned here were probably larger.
15:39 *Magadan.* Also called Magdala, the home of Mary Magdalene. In 2009 the remains of a 2,000-year-old synagogue were discovered in Magdala. Mk 8:10 has "Dalmanutha" (see note there; see also map, p. 1776).
16:1 *Pharisees and Sadducees.* See note on 3:7. Normally these two groups were opponents, but they had a common enemy in Jesus. *sign from heaven.* See note on Mk 8:11.
16:4 *sign of Jonah.* See 12:39–40 and note on Lk 11:30.
16:6 *yeast of the Pharisees and Sadducees.* See v. 12; see also note on Mk 8:15.
16:7 *because we didn't bring any bread.* Apparently the disciples took Jesus' statement about "yeast" (v. 6) to somehow relate to their being short of bread. Perhaps they thought they would be required to bake bread when they arrived at the other side of the lake and were being warned by Jesus not to use any yeast provided by the spiritually contaminated religious leaders.
16:8 *little faith.* See 14:31 and note on 6:30.
16:12 Matthew often explains the meaning of Jesus' words (cf. 17:13).
16:13 *Caesarea Philippi.* To be distinguished from the magnificent city of Caesarea, which Herod the Great had built on the Mediterranean coast. Caesarea Philippi, rebuilt by Herod's son Philip (who named it after Tiberius Caesar and himself), was north of the Sea of Galilee near one of the three sources of the Jordan River. Originally it was called Paneas (the ancient name survives today as Banias) in honor of the Greek god Pan, whose shrine was located there. The

14 They replied, "Some say John the
Baptist;[z] others say Elijah; and still others,
Jeremiah or one of the prophets."[a]
15 "But what about you?" he asked.
"Who do you say I am?"
16 Simon Peter answered, "You are the
Messiah, the Son of the living God."[b]
17 Jesus replied, "Blessed are you, Simon
son of Jonah, for this was not revealed to
you by flesh and blood,[c] but by my Father in heaven.[d] 18 And I tell you that you
are Peter,[a][e] and on this rock I will build
my church,[f] and the gates of Hades[b] will
not overcome it. 19 I will give you the keys[g]
of the kingdom of heaven; whatever you
bind on earth will be[c] bound in heaven,
and whatever you loose on earth will be[c]
loosed in heaven."[h] 20 Then he ordered his
disciples not to tell anyone[i] that he was
the Messiah.

Jesus Predicts His Death

16:21-28pp — Mk 8:31 – 9:1; Lk 9:22-27

21 From that time on Jesus began to explain to his disciples that he must go to
Jerusalem[j] and suffer many things[k] at the
hands of the elders, the chief priests and
the teachers of the law,[l] and that he must
be killed[m] and on the third day[n] be raised
to life.[o]
22 Peter took him aside and began to rebuke him. "Never, Lord!" he said. "This
shall never happen to you!"
23 Jesus turned and said to Peter, "Get
behind me, Satan![p] You are a stumbling
block to me; you do not have in mind the
concerns of God, but merely human concerns."
24 Then Jesus said to his disciples,
"Whoever wants to be my disciple must
deny themselves and take up their cross
and follow me.[q] 25 For whoever wants to
save their life[d] will lose it, but whoever
loses their life for me will find it.[r] 26 What
good will it be for someone to gain the
whole world, yet forfeit their soul? Or

16:14 [z] S Mt 3:1 [a] Mk 6:15; Jn 1:21 **16:16** [b] S Mt 4:3; Ps 42:2; Jer 10:10; Ac 14:15; 2Co 6:16; 1Th 1:9; 1Ti 3:15; Heb 10:31; 12:22 **16:17** [c] 1Co 15:50; Eph 6:12; Heb 2:14 [d] S Mt 13:11 **16:18** [e] Jn 1:42 [f] S Eph 2:20 **16:19** [g] Isa 22:22; Rev 3:7 [h] Mt 18:18; Jn 20:23 **16:20** [i] S Mk 8:30 **16:21** [j] S Lk 9:51 [k] Ps 22:6; Isa 53:3; Mt 26:67,68; Mk 10:34; Lk 17:25; Jn 18:22,23; 19:3 [l] Mt 27:1,2 [m] Ac 2:23; 3:13 [n] Hos 6:2; Mt 12:40; Lk 24:21,46; Jn 2:19; 1Co 15:3,4 [o] Mt 17:22,23; 27:63; Mk 9:31; Lk 9:22; 18:31-33; 24:6,7 **16:23** [p] S Mt 4:10 **16:24** [q] Mt 10:38; Lk 14:27 **16:25** [r] S Jn 12:25

[a] *18* The Greek word for *Peter* means *rock.* [b] *18* That is, the realm of the dead [c] *19* Or *will have been* [d] *25* The Greek word means either *life* or *soul*; also in verse 26.

region was especially pagan. *Who do people say the Son of Man is?* See note on Lk 9:18. *Son of Man.* See note on Mk 8:31.

16:14 *John the Baptist.* See Mk 6:16 and note. *Elijah.* See Mk 6:15 and note.

16:16 *Peter answered.* See note on Lk 9:20. *Messiah.* See second NIV text note on 1:1; see also note on Jn 1:25. The Hebrew word for *Messiah* ("anointed one") can be used of anyone who was anointed with the holy oil, such as the priests and kings of Israel (e.g., Ex 29:7,21; 1Sa 10:1,6; 16:13; 2Sa 1:14,16). The word carries the idea of being chosen by God, consecrated to his service, and endowed with his power to accomplish the assigned task. Toward the end of the OT period the word assumed a special meaning. It denoted the ideal king anointed and empowered by God to rescue his people from their enemies and establish his righteous kingdom (Da 9:25 – 26). The ideas that clustered around the title *Messiah* tended to be political and national in nature. Probably for that reason Jesus seldom used the term. When he did accept it as applied to himself, he did so with reservations (cf. Mk 8:27 – 30; 14:61 – 63).

16:17 *Simon son of Jonah.* In Jn 1:42 Jesus identifies Peter as "Simon son of John." Probably Simon Peter was the son of Johanan (the Hebrew form of the name), and Jonah is an Aramaic abbreviation of Johanan, while John is from the Greek form of the name. *flesh and blood.* See notes on 1Co 15:50; Gal 1:16.

16:18 *Peter … rock … church.* In the Greek "Peter" is *petros* ("detached stone"), and "rock" is *petra* ("bedrock"). Several interpretations have been given to these words: The bedrock on which the church is built is (1) Christ; (2) Peter's confession of faith in Jesus as the Messiah (v. 16); (3) Christ's teachings — one of the great emphases of Matthew's Gospel; (4) Peter himself, understood in terms of his role on the day of Pentecost (Ac 2), the Cornelius incident (Ac 10) and his leadership among the apostles. Eph 2:20 indicates that the church is "built on the foundation of the apostles and prophets" (see note on Jn 1:42). *church.* In the Gospels this word is used only by Matthew (here and twice in 18:17). In the Septuagint (the pre-Christian Greek translation of the OT) it is used for the congregation of Israel. In Greek circles of Jesus' day it indicated the assembly of free, voting citizens in a city (cf. Ac 19:32,39,41). *Hades.* The place of departed spirits, generally equivalent to the Hebrew *Sheol* (see note on Ge 37:35). The "gates of Hades" (see note on Job 17:16) here may refer to the powers of death, i.e., all forces opposed to Christ and his kingdom.

16:19 *keys.* Perhaps Peter used these keys on the day of Pentecost (Ac 2) when he announced that the door of the kingdom was unlocked to Jews and converts to Judaism and later when he acknowledged that it was also opened to Gentiles (Ac 10; cf. Isa 22:22; Rev 3:7 and notes). *bind … loose.* Not authority to determine, but to announce, guilt or innocence (see 18:18 and context; cf. Jn 20:23 and note; Ac 5:3,9).

16:20 *not to tell.* Because of the false concepts of the Jews, who looked for an exclusively national and political Messiah, Jesus didn't want to precipitate a revolution against Rome (see notes on 8:4; Lk 9:21).

16:21 *began.* The beginning of a new emphasis in Jesus' ministry. Instead of teaching the crowds in parables, he concentrated on preparing the disciples for his coming suffering and death. *must go … suffer … be killed … be raised.* See 17:12,22 – 23; 20:17 – 19 and parallels in the other Gospels. This assertion by Jesus was contrary to all Jewish expectations (see Jn 12:34 and note). It was, nevertheless, in accordance with the OT (see 26:24,31,54; Mk 14:21,27,49; Lk 18:31 – 33; 22:37; 24:25 – 27,44 – 46 and note on 24:44).

16:22 *Peter … began to rebuke him.* See note on Mk 8:32.

16:23 *Satan.* A loanword from Hebrew, meaning "adversary" or "accuser" (see NIV text note on Job 1:6; see also notes on Mk 8:33; Rev 2:9).

16:24 See note on Mk 8:34. *take up their cross.* See note on 10:38 (Lk 9:23 adds "daily"; see also note there).

16:25 *save their life.* See note on Mk 8:35. *whoever loses their life.* See note on Lk 9:24.

16:26 *whole world.* See note on Mk 8:36. *soul.* See note on 10:28.

what can anyone give in exchange for
their soul? 27 For the Son of Man[s] is going
to come[t] in his Father's glory with his angels, and then he will reward each person
according to what they have done.[u]
28 "Truly I tell you, some who are standing here will not taste death before they see
the Son of Man coming in his kingdom."

The Transfiguration

17:1-8pp — Lk 9:28-36
17:1-13pp — Mk 9:2-13

17 After six days Jesus took with him
Peter, James and John[v] the brother
of James, and led them up a high mountain by themselves. 2 There he was transfigured before them. His face shone like
the sun, and his clothes became as white
as the light. 3 Just then there appeared before them Moses and Elijah, talking with
Jesus.
4 Peter said to Jesus, "Lord, it is good
for us to be here. If you wish, I will put up
three shelters — one for you, one for Moses and one for Elijah."
5 While he was still speaking, a bright
cloud covered them, and a voice from the
cloud said, "This is my Son, whom I love;
with him I am well pleased.[w] Listen to
him!"[x]
6 When the disciples heard this, they fell
facedown to the ground, terrified. 7 But
Jesus came and touched them. "Get up,"
he said. "Don't be afraid."[y] 8 When they
looked up, they saw no one except Jesus.
9 As they were coming down the mountain, Jesus instructed them, "Don't tell
anyone[z] what you have seen, until the Son
of Man[a] has been raised from the dead."[b]
10 The disciples asked him, "Why then
do the teachers of the law say that Elijah
must come first?"
11 Jesus replied, "To be sure, Elijah
comes and will restore all things.[c] 12 But
I tell you, Elijah has already come,[d] and
they did not recognize him, but have done
to him everything they wished.[e] In the
same way the Son of Man is going to suffer[f] at their hands." 13 Then the disciples
understood that he was talking to them
about John the Baptist.[g]

Jesus Heals a Demon-Possessed Boy

17:14-19pp — Mk 9:14-28; Lk 9:37-42

14 When they came to the crowd, a man
approached Jesus and knelt before him.
15 "Lord, have mercy on my son," he said.
"He has seizures[h] and is suffering greatly.
He often falls into the fire or into the water. 16 I brought him to your disciples, but
they could not heal him."
17 "You unbelieving and perverse generation," Jesus replied, "how long shall I stay
with you? How long shall I put up with
you? Bring the boy here to me." 18 Jesus
rebuked the demon, and it came out of the
boy, and he was healed at that moment.
19 Then the disciples came to Jesus in
private and asked, "Why couldn't we
drive it out?"
20 He replied, "Because you have so little

16:27 [s] S Mt 8:20 [t] S Lk 17:30; Jn 14:3; Ac 1:11; S 1Co 1:7; S 1Th 2:19; 4:16; S Rev 1:7; 22:7, 12, 20 [u] 2Ch 6:23; Job 34:11; Ps 62:12; Jer 17:10; Eze 18:20; 1Co 3:12-15; 2Co 5:10; Rev 22:12 **17:1** [v] S Mt 4:21 **17:5** [w] S Mt 3:17 [x] Ac 3:22, 23 **17:7** [y] S Mt 14:27 **17:9** [z] S Mk 8:30 [a] S Mt 8:20 [b] S Mt 16:21 **17:11** [c] Mal 4:6; Lk 1:16, 17 **17:12** [d] S Mt 11:14 [e] Mt 14:3, 10 [f] S Mt 16:21 **17:13** [g] S Mt 3:1 **17:15** [h] Mt 4:24

16:27 *Son of Man.* See note on Mk 8:31. *is going to come.* The second coming of Christ. *in his Father's glory.* See note on Mk 8:38; cf. Jn 17:1 – 5. *according to what they have done.* See Ps 62:12 and note; see also notes on Ro 2:1 – 16; 2:6 – 8.
16:28 There are two main interpretations of this verse: (1) It is a prediction of the transfiguration, which happened a week later (17:1) and which demonstrated that Jesus will return "in his Father's glory" (16:27). (2) It refers to the Son of Man's authority and kingly reign in his postresurrection church. Some of his disciples will witness — even participate in — this as described in the book of Acts. The context seems to favor the first view. See note on 2Pe 1:16.
17:1 – 9 The transfiguration was: (1) a revelation of the glory of the Son of God, a glory hidden now but to be fully revealed when he returns (see 2Th 1:10); (2) a confirmation of the difficult teaching given to the disciples at Caesarea Philippi (16:13 – 20); and (3) a beneficial experience for the disciples, who were discouraged after having been reminded so recently of Jesus' impending suffering and death (16:21). See notes on Mk 9:2 – 7; Lk 9:28 – 35.
17:1 *six days.* Mark also says "six days" (Mk 9:2), counting just the days between Peter's confession and the transfiguration, whereas Luke, counting all the days involved, says, "About eight days" (Lk 9:28). *Peter, James and John.* See 26:37; Mk 5:37 and note. *high mountain.* See note on Lk 9:28. *by themselves.* Luke adds "to pray" (Lk 9:28).
17:2 *he was transfigured.* His appearance changed. The three disciples saw Jesus in his glorified state (see Jn 17:5; 2Pe 1:17).
17:3 *Moses and Elijah.* Moses the lawgiver appears as the representative of the old covenant and the promise of salvation, which was soon to be fulfilled in the death of Jesus. Elijah the prophet appears as the appointed restorer of all things (Mal 4:5 – 6; Mk 9:11 – 13). Lk 9:31 says that they talked about Christ's death. See note on Lk 9:30.
17:4 *three shelters.* See notes on Mk 9:5; Lk 9:33.
17:5 *bright cloud.* Signifying the presence of God (see Ex 13:21; 19:16 and notes; 24:15 – 16; 34:5; 40:34 – 38; see also note on Mk 9:7). *them.* Jesus, Moses and Elijah. *This is my Son, whom I love; with him I am well pleased.* The same words spoken from heaven at Jesus' baptism (see 3:17 and note). No mere man, but the very Son of God, was transfigured. *Listen to him!* See note on Mk 9:7.
17:6 *terrified.* Primarily with a sense of awe at the presence and majesty of God.
17:9 *Don't tell anyone.* See note on Mk 9:9; cf. Lk 9:36.
17:10 Traditional Jewish eschatology, based on Mal 4:5 – 6, held that Elijah must appear before the coming of the Messiah. The disciples reasoned that if Jesus really was the Messiah, as the transfiguration proved him to be, why had not Elijah appeared?
17:12 *In the same way.* As John the Baptist was not recognized and was killed (see 14:1 – 12), so Jesus would be rejected and killed (see vv. 22 – 23 and note).
17:13 See note on 16:12.
17:15 *seizures.* See note on 4:24.
17:17 *unbelieving.* See v. 20 and note.
17:18 Not all seizures were the result of demon possession, but these were.

faith. Truly I tell you, if you have faith[i] as
small as a mustard seed,[j] you can say to
this mountain, 'Move from here to there,'
and it will move.[k] Nothing will be impossible for you." [21][a]

Jesus Predicts His Death a Second Time

22 When they came together in Galilee,
he said to them, "The Son of Man[l] is going to be delivered into the hands of men.
23 They will kill him,[m] and on the third day[n]
he will be raised to life."[o] And the disciples
were filled with grief.

The Temple Tax

24 After Jesus and his disciples arrived
in Capernaum, the collectors of the two-
drachma temple tax[p] came to Peter and
asked, "Doesn't your teacher pay the temple tax?"
25 "Yes, he does," he replied.
When Peter came into the house, Jesus
was the first to speak. "What do you think,
Simon?" he asked. "From whom do the
kings of the earth collect duty and taxes[q]—
from their own children or from others?"
26 "From others," Peter answered.
"Then the children are exempt," Jesus
said to him. 27 "But so that we may not
cause offense,[r] go to the lake and throw
out your line. Take the first fish you catch;
open its mouth and you will find a four-
drachma coin. Take it and give it to them
for my tax and yours."

The Greatest in the Kingdom of Heaven

18:1-5pp — Mk 9:33-37; Lk 9:46-48

18 At that time the disciples came to
Jesus and asked, "Who, then, is
the greatest in the kingdom of heaven?"

2 He called a little child to him, and
placed the child among them. 3 And he
said: "Truly I tell you, unless you change
and become like little children,[s] you will
never enter the kingdom of heaven.[t]
4 Therefore, whoever takes the lowly position of this child is the greatest in the kingdom of heaven.[u] 5 And whoever welcomes
one such child in my name welcomes me.[v]

Causing to Stumble

6 "If anyone causes one of these little ones — those who believe in me — to
stumble, it would be better for them to
have a large millstone hung around their
neck and to be drowned in the depths of
the sea.[w] 7 Woe to the world because of the
things that cause people to stumble! Such
things must come, but woe to the person
through whom they come![x] 8 If your hand
or your foot causes you to stumble,[y] cut it
off and throw it away. It is better for you to
enter life maimed or crippled than to have
two hands or two feet and be thrown into
eternal fire. 9 And if your eye causes you to
stumble,[z] gouge it out and throw it away.
It is better for you to enter life with one
eye than to have two eyes and be thrown
into the fire of hell.[a]

The Parable of the Wandering Sheep

18:12-14pp — Lk 15:4-7

10 "See that you do not despise one of
these little ones. For I tell you that their
angels[b] in heaven always see the face of
my Father in heaven. [11][b]
12 "What do you think? If a man owns a
hundred sheep, and one of them wanders
away, will he not leave the ninety-nine on
the hills and go to look for the one that

17:20 [i] S Mt 21:21 [j] Mt 13:31; Lk 17:6 [k] 1Co 13:2 **17:22** [l] S Mt 8:20 **17:23** [m] Ac 2:23; 3:13 [n] S Mt 16:21 [o] S Mt 16:21 **17:24** [p] Ex 30:13 **17:25** [q] Mt 22:17-21; Ro 13:7 **17:27** [r] Jn 6:61

18:3 [s] Mt 19:14; 1Pe 2:2 [t] S Mt 3:2 **18:4** [u] S Mk 9:35 **18:5** [v] Mt 10:40 **18:6** [w] Mk 9:42; Lk 17:2 **18:7** [x] Lk 17:1 **18:8** [y] S Mt 5:29 **18:9** [z] S Mt 5:29 [a] S Mt 5:22 **18:10** [b] Ge 48:16; Ps 34:7; Ac 12:11,15; Heb 1:14

[a] *21* Some manuscripts include here words similar to Mark 9:29. [b] *11* Some manuscripts include here the words of Luke 19:10.

17:20 *little faith.* Not so much the quantity of their faith as its quality — a faith that is bathed in prayer (see Mk 9:29). *mustard seed.* See 13:31 – 32 and notes. *say to this mountain, 'Move from here to there.'* A proverbial statement meaning to remove great difficulties (cf. Isa 54:10; Zec 4:7 and note; 1Co 13:2). In this context it probably refers to removing the problems associated with the work of the kingdom.
17:22 – 23 The second prediction of Christ's death, the first being in 16:21 (see note there).
17:22 *Galilee.* See note on Mk 9:30. *Son of Man.* See note on Mk 8:31.
17:24 *Capernaum.* See note on Mk 4:13. *two-drachma temple tax.* The annual temple tax required of every male 20 years of age and older (Ex 30:13; 2Ch 24:9; Ne 10:32). It was worth half a shekel (approximately two days' wages) and was used for the upkeep of the temple.
17:25 *What do you think . . . ?* Jesus frequently asks this question in Matthew's Gospel (18:12; 21:28; 22:17,42).
17:26 *the children are exempt.* The implication is that Peter and the rest of the disciples belonged to God's royal household, but unbelieving Jews did not (see 21:43).
17:27 *not cause offense.* The Son of God, who controls the entire universe (see Heb 1:2 – 3 and note), is careful not to offend (cf. 11:28 – 30; 12:20).
18:1 *Who . . . is the greatest . . . ?* See v. 4 and note on Lk 9:46.
18:3 *like little children.* Trusting and unpretentious.
18:4 *greatest.* See note on Lk 9:48.
18:6,10,14 *little ones.* All believers, regardless of age (see Mk 9:42 and note; Lk 17:2).
18:6 *large millstone.* Lit. "millstone of a donkey," i.e., a millstone turned by a donkey — far larger and heavier than the small millstones (24:41) used by women each morning.
18:8 – 9 Hyperbole: Deal as drastically as necessary with sin in order to remove it from your life. This calls for self-discipline. See note on 5:29 – 30.
18:8 *thrown into eternal fire.* See Rev 19:20 and note; 20:15.
18:9 *hell.* See note on 5:22.
18:10 *their angels.* Guardian angels not exclusively for children, but for God's people in general (Ps 34:7; 91:11; Heb 1:14). *always see the face of.* Have constant access to.
18:12 – 14 The parable of the lost/wandering (see vv. 12 – 13) sheep is also found in Lk 15:3 – 7. There it applies to unbeliev-

wandered off? 13 And if he finds it, truly
I tell you, he is happier about that one
sheep than about the ninety-nine that did
not wander off. 14 In the same way your
Father in heaven is not willing that any of
these little ones should perish.

Dealing With Sin in the Church

15 "If your brother or sister[a] sins,[b] go
and point out their fault,[c] just between the
two of you. If they listen to you, you have
won them over. 16 But if they will not listen, take one or two others along, so that
'every matter may be established by the
testimony of two or three witnesses.'[c][d]
17 If they still refuse to listen, tell it to the
church;[e] and if they refuse to listen even
to the church, treat them as you would a
pagan or a tax collector.[f]
18 "Truly I tell you, whatever you bind
on earth will be[d] bound in heaven, and
whatever you loose on earth will be[d]
loosed in heaven.[g]
19 "Again, truly I tell you that if two of
you on earth agree about anything they
ask for, it will be done for them[h] by my
Father in heaven. 20 For where two or three
gather in my name, there am I with them."[i]

The Parable of the Unmerciful Servant

21 Then Peter came to Jesus and asked,
"Lord, how many times shall I forgive my
brother or sister who sins against me?[j] Up
to seven times?"[k]
22 Jesus answered, "I tell you, not seven
times, but seventy-seven times.[e][l]
23 "Therefore, the kingdom of heaven
is like[m] a king who wanted to settle accounts[n] with his servants. 24 As he began
the settlement, a man who owed him ten
thousand bags of gold[f] was brought to
him. 25 Since he was not able to pay,[o] the
master ordered that he and his wife and
his children and all that he had be sold[p] to
repay the debt.

18:15 [c]Lev 19:17; Lk 17:3; Gal 6:1; Jas 5:19,20
18:16 [d]Nu 35:30; Dt 17:6; 19:15; Jn 8:17; 2Co 13:1; 1Ti 5:19; Heb 10:28
18:17 [e]1Co 6:1-6 [f]S Ro 16:17
18:18 [g]Mt 16:19; Jn 20:23
18:19 [h]S Mt 7:7
18:20 [i]S Mt 28:20
18:21 [j]S Mt 6:14 [k]Lk 17:4
18:22 [l]Ge 4:24
18:23 [m]S Mt 13:24 [n]Mt 25:19
18:25 [o]Lk 7:42 [p]Lev 25:39; 2Ki 4:1; Ne 5:5,8
18:26 [q]S Mt 8:2
18:35 [r]S Mt 6:14; S Jas 2:13
19:1 [s]S Mt 7:28
19:2 [t]S Mt 4:23

26 "At this the servant fell on his knees
before him.[q] 'Be patient with me,' he
begged, 'and I will pay back everything.'
27 The servant's master took pity on him,
canceled the debt and let him go.
28 "But when that servant went out, he
found one of his fellow servants who owed
him a hundred silver coins.[g] He grabbed
him and began to choke him. 'Pay back
what you owe me!' he demanded.
29 "His fellow servant fell to his knees
and begged him, 'Be patient with me, and
I will pay it back.'
30 "But he refused. Instead, he went off
and had the man thrown into prison until
he could pay the debt. 31 When the other servants saw what had happened, they
were outraged and went and told their
master everything that had happened.
32 "Then the master called the servant
in. 'You wicked servant,' he said, 'I canceled all that debt of yours because you
begged me to. 33 Shouldn't you have had
mercy on your fellow servant just as I had
on you?' 34 In anger his master handed him
over to the jailers to be tortured, until he
should pay back all he owed.
35 "This is how my heavenly Father will
treat each of you unless you forgive your
brother or sister from your heart."[r]

Divorce

19:1-9pp — Mk 10:1-12

19 When Jesus had finished saying
these things,[s] he left Galilee and
went into the region of Judea to the other
side of the Jordan. 2 Large crowds followed
him, and he healed them[t] there.

[a] *15* The Greek word for *brother or sister* (*adelphos*) refers here to a fellow disciple, whether man or woman; also in verses 21 and 35. [b] *15* Some manuscripts *sins against you* [c] *16* Deut. 19:15 [d] *18* Or *will have been* [e] *22* Or *seventy times seven* [f] *24* Greek *ten thousand talents*; a talent was worth about 20 years of a day laborer's wages. [g] *28* Greek *a hundred denarii*; a denarius was the usual daily wage of a day laborer (see 20:2).

ers, here to believers. Jesus used the same parable to teach different truths in different situations.
18:12 *sheep.* See note on Lk 15:4.
18:13 Cf. the "father" in the parable of the lost son (Lk 15:31–32).
18:14 *not willing that any … should perish.* See 1Ti 2:4; 2Pe 3:9 and notes.
18:15 *brother or sister.* Fellow believer. *just between the two of you.* To protect the brother from the harm caused by gossip.
18:17 *church.* Local congregation. Here and 16:18 (see note there) are the only two places where the Gospels use the word "church." *pagan.* For the Jews this meant any Gentile. *tax collector.* See note on 5:46. This verse establishes one basis for excommunication (when people refuse to respond to church discipline; see 2Th 3:14 and note; cf. Ro 16:17).
18:18 See note on 16:19.
18:19 *anything.* Probably not a reference to prayer generally but to disciplinary decisions, especially in the context of vv. 15–18.
18:20 Christ promises his presence with those involved in the proper disciplinary function of the church.
18:22 *seventy-seven times.* Times without number (see NIV text note).
18:23 *kingdom of heaven.* See note on 3:2.
18:24 *ten thousand bags of gold.* See NIV text note.
18:25 For this practice of selling into slavery, see Ex 21:2; Lev 25:39; 2Ki 4:1; Ne 5:5; Isa 50:1.
18:28 *hundred silver coins.* See NIV text note.
18:35 God is very forgiving, but he also judges those who refuse to forgive (v. 34; cf. 6:12,14–15).
19:1 *Judea.* See note on Mk 10:1. *other side of the Jordan.* The east side, known later as Transjordan or Perea and today simply as Jordan. Jesus now began ministering there (see note on Lk 13:22). *Jordan.* See note on Mk 1:5.

3Some Pharisees came to him to test
him. They asked, "Is it lawful for a man
to divorce his wife[u] for any and every reason?"
4"Haven't you read," he replied, "that
at the beginning the Creator 'made them
male and female,'[a][v] 5and said, 'For this
reason a man will leave his father and
mother and be united to his wife, and the
two will become one flesh'[b]?[w] 6So they
are no longer two, but one flesh. Therefore what God has joined together, let no
one separate."
7"Why then," they asked, "did Moses
command that a man give his wife a certificate of divorce and send her away?"[x]
8Jesus replied, "Moses permitted you to
divorce your wives because your hearts
were hard. But it was not this way from
the beginning. 9I tell you that anyone who
divorces his wife, except for sexual immorality, and marries another woman commits adultery."[y]
10The disciples said to him, "If this is
the situation between a husband and wife,
it is better not to marry."
11Jesus replied, "Not everyone can accept this word, but only those to whom it
has been given.[z] 12For there are eunuchs
who were born that way, and there are eunuchs who have been made eunuchs by
others—and there are those who choose
to live like eunuchs for the sake of the
kingdom of heaven. The one who can accept this should accept it."

19:3 [u] Mt 5:31
19:4 [v] Ge 1:27; 5:2
19:5 [w] Ge 2:24; 1Co 6:16; Eph 5:31
19:7 [x] Dt 24:1-4; Mt 5:31
19:9 [y] S Lk 16:18
19:11 [z] S Mt 13:11; 1Co 7:7-9, 17
19:13 [a] S Mk 5:23
19:14 [b] S Mt 25:34 [c] Mt 18:3; 1Pe 2:2
19:16 [d] S Mt 25:46 [e] Lk 10:25
19:17 [f] Lev 18:5
19:18 [g] Jas 2:11
19:19 [h] Ex 20:12-16; Dt 5:16-20 [i] Lev 19:18; S Mt 5:43
19:21 [j] Mt 5:48

The Little Children and Jesus

19:13-15pp — Mk 10:13-16; Lk 18:15-17

13Then people brought little children to
Jesus for him to place his hands on them[a]
and pray for them. But the disciples rebuked them.
14Jesus said, "Let the little children
come to me, and do not hinder them, for
the kingdom of heaven belongs[b] to such as
these."[c] 15When he had placed his hands
on them, he went on from there.

The Rich and the Kingdom of God

19:16-29pp — Mk 10:17-30; Lk 18:18-30

16Just then a man came up to Jesus and
asked, "Teacher, what good thing must I
do to get eternal life[d]?"[e]
17"Why do you ask me about what is
good?" Jesus replied. "There is only One
who is good. If you want to enter life, keep
the commandments."[f]
18"Which ones?" he inquired.
Jesus replied, "'You shall not murder,
you shall not commit adultery,[g] you shall
not steal, you shall not give false testimony, 19honor your father and mother,'[c][h] and
'love your neighbor as yourself.'[d]"[i]
20"All these I have kept," the young man
said. "What do I still lack?"
21Jesus answered, "If you want to be
perfect,[j] go, sell your possessions and give

[a] 4 Gen. 1:27 [b] 5 Gen. 2:24 [c] 19 Exodus 20:12-16; Deut. 5:16-20 [d] 19 Lev. 19:18

19:3 *Pharisees.* See note on Mk 2:16. *for any and every reason.* This last part of the question is not in the parallel passage in Mark (10:2). Matthew possibly included it because he was writing to Jews, who were aware of the dispute between the schools of Shammai and Hillel over the interpretation of Dt 24:1–4. Shammai held that "something indecent" (Dt 24:1) meant "sexual immorality" (Mt 19:9)—the only allowable cause for divorce. Hillel emphasized the preceding clause, "who becomes displeasing to him" (Dt 24:1). He would allow a man to divorce his wife if she did anything he disliked—even if she burned his food while cooking it. Jesus clearly took the side of Shammai (see v. 9), but only after first pointing back to God's original ideal for marriage in Ge 1:27; 2:24.
19:10–12 See 1Co 7:7–8,26,32–35.
19:11 *this word.* The disciples' conclusion in v. 10: "it is better not to marry." This teaching is not meant for everyone. In v. 12 Jesus gives three examples of persons for whom it is meant.
19:12 *born that way.* Impotent. *made eunuchs.* By castration. *choose to live like eunuchs for the sake of the kingdom of heaven.* Those who have voluntarily adopted a celibate lifestyle in order to give themselves more completely to God's work. Under certain circumstances celibacy is recommended in Scripture (cf. 1Co 7:25–38), but it is never presented as superior to marriage.
19:14 *kingdom of heaven.* See note on 3:2. *belongs to such as these.* See note on Mk 10:14.
19:15 *placed his hands on them.* Mk 10:16 adds "and blessed them."
19:16 *a man.* See note on Mk 10:17. *what good thing must I do . . . ?* The rich man was thinking in terms of righteousness by works. Jesus had to correct this misunderstanding first before answering the question more fully. *eternal life.* The first use of this term in Matthew's Gospel (see v. 29; 25:46). In John it occurs much more frequently, often taking the place of the term "kingdom of God (or heaven)" used in the Synoptics, which treat the following three expressions as synonymous: (1) eternal life (v. 16; Mk 10:17; Lk 18:18), (2) entering the kingdom of heaven (v. 23; cf. Mk 10:24; Lk 18:24) and (3) being saved (vv. 25–26; Mk 10:26–27; Lk 18:26–27).
19:17 *Why do you ask me about what is good?* Jesus wanted the man to think seriously about what is good, especially since Jesus' concept of it differed widely from that of the religious leaders (cf. Mk 10:18). *There is only One who is good.* The good is not something to be done as meritorious in itself. God alone is good, and all other goodness derives from him—even the keeping of the commandments, which Jesus proceeded to enumerate (vv. 18–20). *If you want to enter life, keep the commandments.* "To enter life" is the same as "to get eternal life" (v. 16). The requirement to "keep the commandments" is not to establish one's merit before God but is to be an expression of true faith. The Bible always teaches that salvation is a gift of God's grace received through faith (see Eph 2:8–9 and notes).
19:19 *love your neighbor as yourself.* See Lev 19:18 and note.
19:20 *All these I have kept.* See note on Mk 10:20.
19:21 *perfect.* The Greek word means "goal, end" (cf. note on Ro 10:4). His goal was eternal life, but wealth and lack of commitment stood in his way. *go, sell your possessions.* In his listing of the commandments (vv. 18–19), Jesus omitted "you shall not covet." This was the rich man's main

to the poor,[k] and you will have treasure in heaven.[l] Then come, follow me."

22 When the young man heard this, he went away sad, because he had great wealth.

23 Then Jesus said to his disciples, "Truly I tell you, it is hard for someone who is rich[m] to enter the kingdom of heaven. 24 Again I tell you, it is easier for a camel to go through the eye of a needle than for someone who is rich to enter the kingdom of God."

25 When the disciples heard this, they were greatly astonished and asked, "Who then can be saved?"

26 Jesus looked at them and said, "With man this is impossible, but with God all things are possible."[n]

27 Peter answered him, "We have left everything to follow you![o] What then will there be for us?"

28 Jesus said to them, "Truly I tell you, at the renewal of all things, when the Son of Man sits on his glorious throne,[p] you who have followed me will also sit on twelve thrones, judging the twelve tribes of Israel.[q] 29 And everyone who has left houses or brothers or sisters or father or mother or wife[a] or children or fields for my sake will receive a hundred times as much and will inherit eternal life.[r] 30 But many who are first will be last, and many who are last will be first.[s]

The Parable of the Workers in the Vineyard

20 "For the kingdom of heaven is like[t] a landowner who went out early in the morning to hire workers for his vineyard.[u] 2 He agreed to pay them a denarius[b] for the day and sent them into his vineyard.

3 "About nine in the morning he went out and saw others standing in the marketplace doing nothing. 4 He told them, 'You also go and work in my vineyard, and I will pay you whatever is right.' 5 So they went.

"He went out again about noon and about three in the afternoon and did the same thing. 6 About five in the afternoon he went out and found still others standing around. He asked them, 'Why have you been standing here all day long doing nothing?'

7 " 'Because no one has hired us,' they answered.

"He said to them, 'You also go and work in my vineyard.'

8 "When evening came,[v] the owner of the vineyard said to his foreman, 'Call the workers and pay them their wages, beginning with the last ones hired and going on to the first.'

9 "The workers who were hired about five in the afternoon came and each received a denarius. 10 So when those who came who were hired first, they expected to receive more. But each one of them also received a denarius. 11 When they received it, they began to grumble[w] against the landowner. 12 'These who were hired last worked only one hour,' they said, 'and you have made them equal to us who have borne the burden of the work and the heat[x] of the day.'

13 "But he answered one of them, 'I am not being unfair to you, friend.[y] Didn't you agree to work for a denarius? 14 Take your pay and go. I want to give the one who was hired last the same as I gave you. 15 Don't I have the right to do what I want with my own money? Or are you envious because I am generous?'[z]

16 "So the last will be first, and the first will be last."[a]

19:21 [k] S Ac 2:45 [l] S Mt 6:20
19:23 [m] Mt 13:22; 1Ti 6:9, 10
19:26 [n] Ge 18:14; Job 42:2; Jer 32:17; Lk 1:37; 18:27; Ro 4:21
19:27 [o] S Mt 4:19
19:28 [p] Mt 20:21; 25:31 [q] Lk 22:28-30; Rev 3:21; 4:4; 20:4
19:29 [r] Mt 6:33; S 25:46
19:30 [s] Mt 20:16; Mk 10:31; Lk 13:30
20:1 [t] S Mt 13:24 [u] Mt 21:28, 33
20:8 [v] Lev 19:13; Dt 24:15
20:11 [w] Jnh 4:1
20:12 [x] Jnh 4:8; Lk 12:55; Jas 1:11
20:13 [y] Mt 22:12; 26:50
20:15 [z] Dt 15:9; Mk 7:22
20:16 [a] S Mt 19:30

[a] *29* Some manuscripts do not have *or wife.* [b] *2* A denarius was the usual daily wage of a day laborer.

problem and was preventing him from entering life (see note on Mk 10:21).
19:22 *went away sad.* See note on Mk 10:22.
19:23 *kingdom of heaven.* See note on 3:2.
19:24 *camel to go through the eye of a needle.* See note on Mk 10:25.
19:26 See note on Mk 10:27.
19:28 *Truly I tell you.* See note on Mk 3:28. *Son of Man.* See note on Mk 8:31. *judging.* Governing or ruling (cf. OT "judge"; see Introduction to Judges: Title).
19:29 *receive a hundred times as much.* Mark adds, "along with persecutions" (see note on Mk 10:30). *inherit eternal life.* Eternal life is not earned; it is a gift. The word "inherit" often occurs in eschatological contexts in the NT (see 5:5; Mk 10:17; 1Co 6:9–10; 15:50; Gal 5:21; Heb 1:14; 6:12; Rev 21:7).
19:30 This saying of Jesus also appears in other contexts (see 20:16; Mk 10:31 and note; Lk 13:30). In the kingdom of heaven there are many reversals, and the day of judgment will bring many surprises.
20:1–16 This parable occurs only in Matthew's Gospel. In its original setting, its main point seems to be the sovereign graciousness and generosity of God extended to latecomers (the poor and the outcasts of society) into God's kingdom. It is addressed to the grumblers (v. 11) who just cannot handle this amazing expression of God's grace. They almost certainly represent the religious leaders who opposed Jesus.
20:2 *denarius.* The usual daily wage. A Roman soldier also received one denarius a day.
20:8 *When evening came.* Because farm workers were poor, the law of Moses required that they be paid at the end of each day (cf. Lev 19:13; Dt 24:14–15).
20:13 *friend.* A term of mild rebuke (see 22:12; 26:50).
20:15 *are you envious . . . ?* Lit. "is your eye evil . . . ?" Apparently the evil eye was associated with jealousy and envy (cf. 1Sa 18:9). *because I am generous.* It was not a matter of justice but of generosity.
20:16 See note on 19:30.

Jesus Predicts His Death a Third Time

20:17-19pp — Mk 10:32-34; Lk 18:31-33

17 Now Jesus was going up to Jerusalem. On the way, he took the Twelve aside
and said to them, 18 "We are going up to
Jerusalem,[b] and the Son of Man[c] will be
delivered over to the chief priests and the
teachers of the law.[d] They will condemn
him to death 19 and will hand him over to
the Gentiles to be mocked and flogged[e]
and crucified.[f] On the third day[g] he will be
raised to life!"[h]

A Mother's Request

20:20-28pp — Mk 10:35-45

20 Then the mother of Zebedee's sons[i]
came to Jesus with her sons and, kneeling
down,[j] asked a favor of him.

21 "What is it you want?" he asked.

She said, "Grant that one of these two
sons of mine may sit at your right and the
other at your left in your kingdom."[k]

22 "You don't know what you are asking," Jesus said to them. "Can you drink
the cup[l] I am going to drink?"

"We can," they answered.

23 Jesus said to them, "You will indeed
drink from my cup,[m] but to sit at my right
or left is not for me to grant. These places
belong to those for whom they have been
prepared by my Father."

24 When the ten heard about this, they
were indignant[n] with the two brothers.
25 Jesus called them together and said,
"You know that the rulers of the Gentiles lord it over them, and their high officials exercise authority over them. 26 Not
so with you. Instead, whoever wants to
become great among you must be your
servant,[o] 27 and whoever wants to be first
must be your slave— 28 just as the Son of
Man[p] did not come to be served, but to
serve,[q] and to give his life as a ransom[r]
for many."

20:18 [b] S Lk 9:51 [c] S Mt 8:20 [d] Mt 27:1,2 **20:19** [e] S Mt 16:21 [f] S Ac 2:23 [g] S Mt 16:21 [h] S Mt 16:21 **20:20** [i] S Mt 4:21 [j] S Mt 8:2 **20:21** [k] Mt 19:28 **20:22** [l] Isa 51:17, 22; Jer 49:12; Mt 26:39,42; Mk 14:36; Lk 22:42; Jn 18:11 **20:23** [m] Ac 12:2; Rev 1:9 **20:24** [n] Lk 22:24,25 **20:26** [o] S Mk 9:35 **20:28** [p] S Mt 8:20 [q] Isa 42:1; Lk 12:37; 22:27; Jn 13:13-16; 2Co 8:9; Php 2:7 [r] Ex 30:12; Isa 44:22; 53:10; Mt 26:28; 1Ti 2:6; Titus 2:14; Heb 9:28; 1Pe 1:18,19 **20:30** [s] S Mt 9:27 **21:1** [t] Mt 24:3; 26:30; Mk 14:26; Lk 19:37; 21:37; 22:39; Jn 8:1; Ac 1:12 **21:4** [u] S Mt 1:22

Two Blind Men Receive Sight

20:29-34pp — Mk 10:46-52; Lk 18:35-43

29 As Jesus and his disciples were leaving Jericho, a large crowd followed him.
30 Two blind men were sitting by the roadside, and when they heard that Jesus was
going by, they shouted, "Lord, Son of David,[s] have mercy on us!"

31 The crowd rebuked them and told
them to be quiet, but they shouted all the
louder, "Lord, Son of David, have mercy
on us!"

32 Jesus stopped and called them. "What
do you want me to do for you?" he asked.

33 "Lord," they answered, "we want our
sight."

34 Jesus had compassion on them and
touched their eyes. Immediately they received their sight and followed him.

Jesus Comes to Jerusalem as King

21:1-9pp — Mk 11:1-10; Lk 19:29-38
21:4-9pp — Jn 12:12-15

21 As they approached Jerusalem and
came to Bethphage on the Mount
of Olives,[t] Jesus sent two disciples, 2 saying to them, "Go to the village ahead of
you, and at once you will find a donkey
tied there, with her colt by her. Untie them
and bring them to me. 3 If anyone says
anything to you, say that the Lord needs
them, and he will send them right away."
4 This took place to fulfill[u] what was
spoken through the prophet:

20:17–19 See 16:21 and note; see also Mk 10:32–34; Lk 18:31–33 and notes.

20:19 *will hand him over to the Gentiles to be mocked and flogged and crucified.* An additional statement in this third prediction of the passion. Jesus would not be killed by the Jews, which would have been by stoning, but would be crucified by the Romans. All three predictions include his resurrection on the third day (16:21; 17:23).

20:20 *mother of Zebedee's sons.* Mark has "James and John, the sons of Zebedee," asking the question (Mk 10:35–37), yet there is no contradiction. The three joined in making the petition.

20:21 *want.* See note on Mk 10:35–36. *sit at your right and the other at your left.* See note on Mk 10:37.

20:22 *drink the cup.* A figure of speech meaning to "undergo" or "experience." Here the reference is to suffering (cf. 26:39). The same figure of speech is used in Jer 25:15; Eze 23:31–32; Hab 2:16; Rev 14:10; 16:19; 18:6 for divine wrath or judgment. See note on Mk 10:38.

20:23 *drink from my cup.* James was martyred (see Ac 12:2 and note); John was exiled (see Rev 1:9 and note). *is not for me to grant.* See note on Mk 10:40; see also Mt 11:27; 24:36; Jn 14:28.

20:24 See note on Mk 10:41.

20:26 *Not so with you.* See note on Mk 10:43.

20:28 *Son of Man.* See note on Mk 8:31. *ransom.* The Greek word was used most commonly for the price paid to redeem a slave. Similarly, Christ paid the ransom price of his own life to free us from the slavery of sin. *for.* Emphasizes the substitutionary nature of Christ's death. *many.* Christ "gave himself as a ransom for all people" (1Ti 2:6). Salvation is offered to "all," but only the "many" (i.e., the elect) receive it. See note on Mk 10:45.

20:29 *Jericho.* See note on Mk 10:46.

20:30 *Two blind men.* The other Synoptics mention only one (see note on Lk 18:35). *Son of David.* A Messianic title (see note on 9:27).

20:34 *compassion.* See note on 9:36.

21:1 *Jerusalem.* See map, p. 2525, at the end of this study Bible. *Bethphage.* Means "house of figs." It is mentioned in the Bible only in connection with the "Triumphal" Entry. See map, p. 1687. *Mount of Olives.* See note on Mk 11:1.

21:2 *donkey.* An animal symbolic of humility, peace and Davidic royalty (see notes on Zec 9:9; Lk 19:30). See also note on Mk 11:2. *colt.* See notes on Mk 11:2; Lk 19:30.

21:3 *Lord.* See note on Lk 19:31.

5 "Say to Daughter Zion,
'See, your king comes to you,
gentle and riding on a donkey,
and on a colt, the foal of a donkey.' "[a][v]

6 The disciples went and did as Jesus
had instructed them. 7 They brought the
donkey and the colt and placed their
cloaks on them for Jesus to sit on. 8 A very
large crowd spread their cloaks[w] on the
road, while others cut branches from the
trees and spread them on the road. 9 The
crowds that went ahead of him and those
that followed shouted,

"Hosanna[b] to the Son of David!"[x]

"Blessed is he who comes in the name
of the Lord!"[c][y]

"Hosanna[b] in the highest heaven!"[z]

10 When Jesus entered Jerusalem, the
whole city was stirred and asked, "Who
is this?"
11 The crowds answered, "This is Jesus,
the prophet[a] from Nazareth in Galilee."

Jesus at the Temple

21:12-16pp — Mk 11:15-18; Lk 19:45-47

12 Jesus entered the temple courts and
drove out all who were buying[b] and selling there. He overturned the tables of the
money changers[c] and the benches of those
selling doves.[d] 13 "It is written," he said to
them, " 'My house will be called a house
of prayer,'[d][e] but you are making it 'a den
of robbers.'[e]"[f]

14 The blind and the lame came to him
at the temple, and he healed them.[g] 15 But
when the chief priests and the teachers of
the law saw the wonderful things he did
and the children shouting in the temple
courts, "Hosanna to the Son of David,"[h]
they were indignant.[i]
16 "Do you hear what these children are
saying?" they asked him.
"Yes," replied Jesus, "have you never
read,

" 'From the lips of children and infants
you, Lord, have called forth your
praise'[f]?"[j]

17 And he left them and went out of the
city to Bethany,[k] where he spent the night.

Jesus Curses a Fig Tree

21:18-22pp — Mk 11:12-14,20-24

18 Early in the morning, as Jesus was on
his way back to the city, he was hungry.
19 Seeing a fig tree by the road, he went up
to it but found nothing on it except leaves.
Then he said to it, "May you never bear
fruit again!" Immediately the tree withered.[l]
20 When the disciples saw this, they
were amazed. "How did the fig tree wither
so quickly?" they asked.
21 Jesus replied, "Truly I tell you, if you
have faith and do not doubt,[m] not only can

21:5 [v]Isa 62:11; Zec 9:9 **21:8** [w]2Ki 9:13 **21:9** [x]ver 15; S Mt 9:27 [y]Ps 118:26; Mt 23:39 [z]Lk 2:14 **21:11** [a]Dt 18:15; Lk 7:16,39; 24:19; Jn 1:21, 25; 6:14; 7:40 **21:12** [b]Dt 14:26 [c]Ex 30:13 [d]Lev 1:14 **21:13** [e]Isa 56:7 [f]Jer 7:11 **21:14** [g]S Mt 4:23 **21:15** [h]ver 9; S Mt 9:27 [i]Lk 19:39 **21:16** [j]Ps 8:2 **21:17** [k]Mt 26:6; Mk 11:1; Lk 24:50; Jn 11:1,18; 12:1 **21:19** [l]Isa 34:4; Jer 8:13 **21:21** [m]Mt 17:20; Lk 17:6; 1Co 13:2; Jas 1:6

[a] *5* Zech. 9:9 [b] *9* A Hebrew expression meaning "Save!" which became an exclamation of praise; also in verse 15 [c] *9* Psalm 118:25,26 [d] *13* Isaiah 56:7 [e] *13* Jer. 7:11 [f] *16* Psalm 8:2 (see Septuagint)

21:5 See note on Zec 9:9.
21:7 *cloaks ... for Jesus to sit on.* We know from Mark (11:2) and Luke (19:30) that he rode the colt. Typically, a mother donkey followed her offspring closely. Matthew mentions two animals, while the other Gospels have only one (see note on Lk 19:30).
21:8 *spread their cloaks on the road.* An act of royal homage (see 2Ki 9:13). *branches.* See note on Mk 11:8.
21:9 These are three separate quotations, not necessarily spoken at the same time. *Hosanna.* See notes on Ps 118:25–26; Jer 31:7; expresses both prayer and praise (see NIV text note). *Son of David.* See note on 9:27. *in the highest heaven.* That is, may those in heaven sing "Hosanna" (see Ps 148:1–2; Lk 2:14). See Ps 118:25–26 and notes.
21:10 *Who is this?* Because of Jesus' dramatic entry into the city, the people were wondering who he really was.
21:11 *the prophet.* Refers either to a prophet in general (see 13:57) or to the prophet predicted in Dt 18:15–18 (see note on 18:15; see also Dt 34:10–12 and note on 34:12).
21:12–17 In the Synoptics the clearing of the temple occurs during the last week of Jesus' ministry; in John it takes place during the first few months (Jn 2:12–16). Two explanations are possible: (1) There were two clearings, one at the beginning and the other at the end of Jesus' public ministry. (2) There was only one clearing, which took place during Passion Week but which John placed at the beginning of his account for theological reasons — to show that God's judgment was operative through the Messiah from the outset of Jesus' ministry. However, different details are present in the two accounts (the selling of cattle and sheep in Jn 2:14, the whip in Jn 2:15, and the statements of Jesus in Mt 21:13; Jn 2:16). From Matthew's and Luke's accounts we might assume that the clearing of the temple took place on Sunday, following the so-called "Triumphal" Entry (21:1–11). But Mark (11:15–19) clearly indicates that it was on Monday. Matthew often compressed narratives.
21:12 *temple courts.* The "buying and selling" took place in the large outer court of the Gentiles, which covered several acres (see notes on Mk 11:15; Lk 19:45; Jn 2:14).
21:13 *house of prayer.* Mark adds "for all nations" (11:17; see note there). *den of robbers.* See Jer 7:11 and note.
21:16 See Ps 8:1b–2 and note.
21:17 *Bethany.* See note on Mk 11:1; a village on the eastern slope of the Mount of Olives, about two miles from Jerusalem and the final station on the road from Jericho to Jerusalem. It was the home of Mary, Martha and Lazarus (Jn 12:1–3).
21:18–22 See note on vv. 12–17; another example of compressing narratives. Mark (11:12–14,20–25) places the cursing of the fig tree on Monday morning and the disciples' finding it withered on Tuesday morning. In Matthew's account the tree withered as soon as Jesus cursed it, emphasizing the immediacy of judgment. For the theological meaning of this event, see note on Mk 11:14.
21:18 *city.* Jerusalem.
21:21 *have faith and do not doubt.* See 17:20 and note; Jas 1:5–8. *Go, throw yourself into the sea.* A proverbial hyperbolic statement (cf. 17:20 and note).

you do what was done to the fig tree, but
also you can say to this mountain, 'Go,
throw yourself into the sea,' and it will
be done. 22 If you believe, you will receive
whatever you ask for[n] in prayer."

The Authority of Jesus Questioned

21:23-27pp — Mk 11:27-33; Lk 20:1-8

23 Jesus entered the temple courts, and,
while he was teaching, the chief priests
and the elders of the people came to him.
"By what authority[o] are you doing these
things?" they asked. "And who gave you
this authority?"
24 Jesus replied, "I will also ask you one
question. If you answer me, I will tell you
by what authority I am doing these things.
25 John's baptism — where did it come
from? Was it from heaven, or of human
origin?"
They discussed it among themselves
and said, "If we say, 'From heaven,' he
will ask, 'Then why didn't you believe
him?' 26 But if we say, 'Of human origin' —
we are afraid of the people, for they all
hold that John was a prophet."[p]
27 So they answered Jesus, "We don't
know."
Then he said, "Neither will I tell you by
what authority I am doing these things.

The Parable of the Two Sons

28 "What do you think? There was a man
who had two sons. He went to the first
and said, 'Son, go and work today in the
vineyard.'[q]
29 " 'I will not,' he answered, but later he
changed his mind and went.
30 "Then the father went to the other son
and said the same thing. He answered, 'I
will, sir,' but he did not go.
31 "Which of the two did what his father
wanted?"
"The first," they answered.
Jesus said to them, "Truly I tell you, the
tax collectors[r] and the prostitutes[s] are entering the kingdom of God ahead of you.
32 For John came to you to show you the
way of righteousness,[t] and you did not believe him, but the tax collectors[u] and the
prostitutes[v] did. And even after you saw
this, you did not repent[w] and believe him.

The Parable of the Tenants

21:33-46pp — Mk 12:1-12; Lk 20:9-19

33 "Listen to another parable: There was
a landowner who planted[x] a vineyard. He
put a wall around it, dug a winepress in it
and built a watchtower.[y] Then he rented
the vineyard to some farmers and moved
to another place.[z] 34 When the harvest time
approached, he sent his servants[a] to the
tenants to collect his fruit.
35 "The tenants seized his servants; they
beat one, killed another, and stoned a
third.[b] 36 Then he sent other servants[c] to
them, more than the first time, and the
tenants treated them the same way. 37 Last
of all, he sent his son to them. 'They will
respect my son,' he said.
38 "But when the tenants saw the son,
they said to each other, 'This is the heir.[d]
Come, let's kill him[e] and take his inheritance.'[f] 39 So they took him and threw him
out of the vineyard and killed him.
40 "Therefore, when the owner of the
vineyard comes, what will he do to those
tenants?"
41 "He will bring those wretches to a
wretched end,"[g] they replied, "and he will
rent the vineyard to other tenants,[h] who
will give him his share of the crop at harvest time."
42 Jesus said to them, "Have you never
read in the Scriptures:

" 'The stone the builders rejected
has become the cornerstone;
the Lord has done this,
and it is marvelous in our eyes'[a]?[i]

43 "Therefore I tell you that the kingdom of God will be taken away from you[j]
and given to a people who will produce
its fruit. 44 Anyone who falls on this stone
will be broken to pieces; anyone on whom
it falls will be crushed."[b][k]

21:22 [n]S Mt 7:7 **21:23** [o]Ac 4:7; 7:27 **21:26** [p]S Mt 11:9 **21:28** [q]ver 33; Mt 20:1 **21:31** [r]Lk 7:29 [s]Lk 7:50 **21:32** [t]Mt 3:1-12 [u]Lk 3:12,13; 7:29 [v]Lk 7:36-50 [w]Lk 7:30 **21:33** [x]Ps 80:8 [y]Isa 5:1-7 [z]Mt 25:14,15 **21:34** [a]Mt 22:3 **21:35** [b]2Ch 24:21; Mt 23:34,37; Heb 11:36,37 **21:36** [c]Mt 22:4 **21:38** [d]Heb 1:2 [e]S Mt 12:14 [f]Ps 2:8 **21:41** [g]Mt 8:11,12 [h]S Ac 13:46 **21:42** [i]Ps 118:22,23; S Ac 4:11 **21:43** [j]Mt 8:12 **21:44** [k]S Lk 2:34

[a] *42* Psalm 118:22,23 [b] *44* Some manuscripts do not have verse 44.

21:22 See 1Jn 5:14 – 15 and note on 5:14.
21:23 *temple courts.* See note on Mk 11:27. *chief priests and the elders.* See notes on 2:4; Mk 8:31; Lk 19:47. *By what authority . . . ?* See notes on Mk 11:28; Lk 20:2.
21:25 *from heaven, or of human origin?* See notes on Mk 11:30; Lk 20:4.
21:31 *tax collectors.* See note on 5:46. *kingdom of God.* See notes on 3:2; Lk 4:43; 1Co 4:20.
21:32 *way of righteousness.* Doing what is right and obeying God's will, which included believing what Jesus was teaching about how one is to enter the kingdom of God.
21:33 – 46 See notes on Mk 12:1 – 12; Lk 20:9 – 19.
21:33 *winepress.* See notes on Isa 5:2; Rev 14:19. *watchtower.* For guarding the vineyard, especially when the grapes ripened, and for shelter (see Isa 5:2 and note).
21:35 – 37 The tenants represent the Jewish leaders. The servants represent the OT prophets, many of whom were killed. The son represents Christ, who was condemned to death by the religious leaders.
21:41 *other tenants.* Gentiles, to whom Paul turned when Jews, for the most part, rejected the gospel (Ac 13:46; 18:6). By the second century the church was composed almost entirely of Gentiles.
21:42 See note on Ps 118:22. *Have you never read . . . ?* See v. 16; 12:3; 19:4; Mk 12:10.
21:44 *will be broken to pieces.* See note on Lk 20:18.

45When the chief priests and the Pharisees heard Jesus' parables, they knew he
was talking about them. 46They looked for
a way to arrest him, but they were afraid
of the crowd because the people held that
he was a prophet.[l]

The Parable of the Wedding Banquet

22:2-14Ref — Lk 14:16-24

22 Jesus spoke to them again in parables, saying: 2"The kingdom of
heaven is like[m] a king who prepared a
wedding banquet for his son. 3He sent his
servants[n] to those who had been invited to
the banquet to tell them to come, but they
refused to come.
4"Then he sent some more servants[o]
and said, 'Tell those who have been invited that I have prepared my dinner: My
oxen and fattened cattle have been butchered, and everything is ready. Come to the
wedding banquet.'
5"But they paid no attention and went
off — one to his field, another to his business. 6The rest seized his servants, mistreated them and killed them. 7The king was
enraged. He sent his army and destroyed
those murderers[p] and burned their city.
8"Then he said to his servants, 'The
wedding banquet is ready, but those I invited did not deserve to come. 9So go to
the street corners[q] and invite to the banquet anyone you find.' 10So the servants
went out into the streets and gathered all
the people they could find, the bad as well
as the good,[r] and the wedding hall was
filled with guests.
11"But when the king came in to see the
guests, he noticed a man there who was
not wearing wedding clothes. 12He asked,
'How did you get in here without wedding
clothes, friend[s]?' The man was speechless.
13"Then the king told the attendants,
'Tie him hand and foot, and throw him
outside, into the darkness, where there
will be weeping and gnashing of teeth.'[t]
14"For many are invited, but few are
chosen."[u]

Paying the Imperial Tax to Caesar

22:15-22pp — Mk 12:13-17; Lk 20:20-26

15Then the Pharisees went out and laid
plans to trap him in his words. 16They sent
their disciples to him along with the Herodians.[v] "Teacher," they said, "we know
that you are a man of integrity and that
you teach the way of God in accordance
with the truth. You aren't swayed by others, because you pay no attention to who
they are. 17Tell us then, what is your opinion? Is it right to pay the imperial tax[a][w] to
Caesar or not?"
18But Jesus, knowing their evil intent,
said, "You hypocrites, why are you trying
to trap me? 19Show me the coin used for
paying the tax." They brought him a denarius, 20and he asked them, "Whose image is this? And whose inscription?"
21"Caesar's," they replied.
Then he said to them, "So give back to
Caesar what is Caesar's,[x] and to God what
is God's."
22When they heard this, they were
amazed. So they left him and went away.[y]

21:46 [l] S ver 11,26 **22:2** [m] S Mt 13:24 **22:3** [n] Mt 21:34 **22:4** [o] Mt 21:36 **22:7** [p] Lk 19:27 **22:9** [q] Eze 21:21 **22:10** [r] Mt 13:47,48 **22:12** [s] Mt 20:13; 26:50 **22:13** [t] S Mt 8:12 **22:14** [u] Rev 17:14 **22:16** [v] Mk 3:6 **22:17** [w] Mt 17:25 **22:21** [x] Ro 13:7 **22:22** [y] Mk 12:12

[a] *17* A special tax levied on subject peoples, not on Roman citizens

21:45 *chief priests.* See notes on 2:4; Mk 8:31; Lk 19:47. *Pharisees.* See notes on 3:7; Mk 2:16; Lk 5:17. *parables.* See notes on 13:3; Mk 4:2; Lk 8:4.
21:46 *afraid ... because the people held that he was a prophet.* Cf. v. 26.
22:1 – 14 In Luke's Gospel this parable is spoken by Jesus at a banquet in response to a remark made by one of the guests about "the feast in the kingdom of God" (Lk 14:15; see note there).
22:7 *burned their city.* A common military practice; here possibly an allusion to the coming destruction of Jerusalem in AD 70.
22:11 *not wearing wedding clothes.* It may have been the custom for a host to provide guests with wedding garments. This would have been necessary for the guests at this banquet in particular, for they were brought in directly from the streets (vv. 9 – 10). The failure of the man in question to avail himself of a wedding garment was therefore an insult to the host, who had made the garments available.
22:12 *friend.* See note on 20:13.
22:13 *gnashing of teeth.* See note on 13:42.
22:14 A proverb-like summary of the meaning of the parable. God invites "many" (perhaps "all" in view of the Semitic usage of "many"; cf. 20:28; 26:28; Ro 5:15,19) to be part of his kingdom, but only a comparative "few" are chosen by him. This does not mean that God chooses arbitrarily. The invitation must be accepted, followed by appropriate conduct. Proper behavior is evidence of being chosen.
22:15 – 17 The Pharisees were ardent nationalists, opposed to Roman rule, while the hated Herodians, as their name indicates, supported the Roman rule of the Herods. Now, however, the Pharisees enlisted the help of the Herodians to trap Jesus in his words (cf. note on Mk 3:6). After trying to put him off guard with flattery, they sprang their question: "Is it right to pay the imperial tax to Caesar or not?" (v. 17). If he said "No," the Herodians would report him to the Roman governor and he would be executed for treason. If he said "Yes," the Pharisees would denounce him to the people as disloyal to his nation.
22:17 *imperial tax to Caesar.* See note on Mk 12:14.
22:18 *hypocrites.* See note on 6:2.
22:19 *denarius.* The common Roman coin of that day (see note on 20:2). On one side was the portrait of Emperor Tiberius and on the other the inscription in Latin: "Tiberius Caesar Augustus, son of the divine Augustus." The coin was issued by Tiberius and was used for paying taxes to him.
22:21 *to God what is God's.* In distinguishing clearly between Caesar and God, Jesus also protested against the false and idolatrous claims made on the coins (see previous note; see also note on Mk 12:17).
22:22 *amazed.* See Mk 1:22 and note.

Marriage at the Resurrection

22:23-33pp — Mk 12:18-27; Lk 20:27-40

23 That same day the Sadducees,[z] who say there is no resurrection,[a] came to him with a question. 24 "Teacher," they said, "Moses told us that if a man dies without having children, his brother must marry the widow and raise up offspring for him.[b] 25 Now there were seven brothers among us. The first one married and died, and since he had no children, he left his wife to his brother. 26 The same thing happened to the second and third brother, right on down to the seventh. 27 Finally, the woman died. 28 Now then, at the resurrection, whose wife will she be of the seven, since all of them were married to her?"

29 Jesus replied, "You are in error because you do not know the Scriptures[c] or the power of God. 30 At the resurrection people will neither marry nor be given in marriage;[d] they will be like the angels in heaven. 31 But about the resurrection of the dead—have you not read what God said to you, 32 'I am the God of Abraham, the God of Isaac, and the God of Jacob'[a]?[e] He is not the God of the dead but of the living."

33 When the crowds heard this, they were astonished at his teaching.[f]

The Greatest Commandment

22:34-40pp — Mk 12:28-31

34 Hearing that Jesus had silenced the Sadducees,[g] the Pharisees got together. 35 One of them, an expert in the law,[h] tested him with this question: 36 "Teacher, which is the greatest commandment in the Law?"

37 Jesus replied: " 'Love the Lord your God with all your heart and with all your soul and with all your mind.'[b][i] 38 This is the first and greatest commandment. 39 And the second is like it: 'Love your neighbor as yourself.'[c][j] 40 All the Law and the Prophets hang on these two commandments."[k]

Whose Son Is the Messiah?

22:41-46pp — Mk 12:35-37; Lk 20:41-44

41 While the Pharisees were gathered together, Jesus asked them, 42 "What do you think about the Messiah? Whose son is he?"

"The son of David,"[l] they replied.

43 He said to them, "How is it then that David, speaking by the Spirit, calls him 'Lord'? For he says,

44 " 'The Lord said to my Lord:
"Sit at my right hand
until I put your enemies
under your feet." '[d][m]

45 If then David calls him 'Lord,' how can he be his son?" 46 No one could say a word in reply, and from that day on no one dared to ask him any more questions.[n]

A Warning Against Hypocrisy

23:1-7pp — Mk 12:38,39; Lk 20:45,46
23:37-39pp — Lk 13:34,35

23 Then Jesus said to the crowds and to his disciples: 2 "The teachers of the law[o] and the Pharisees sit in Moses' seat. 3 So you must be careful to do everything they tell you. But do not do what they do, for they do not practice what they preach. 4 They tie up heavy, cumbersome loads and put them on other people's shoulders, but they themselves are not willing to lift a finger to move them.[p]

5 "Everything they do is done for people to see:[q] They make their phylacteries[e][r] wide and the tassels on their garments[s] long; 6 they love the place of honor at banquets and the most important seats in the synagogues;[t] 7 they love to be greeted

22:23 [z] S Ac 4:1 [a] Ac 23:8; 1Co 15:12 **22:24** [b] Dt 25:5,6 **22:29** [c] Jn 20:9 **22:30** [d] Mt 24:38 **22:32** [e] Ex 3:6; Ac 7:32 **22:33** [f] S Mt 7:28 **22:34** [g] S Ac 4:1 **22:35** [h] Lk 7:30; 10:25; 11:45; 14:3 **22:37** [i] Dt 6:5 **22:39** [j] Lev 19:18; S Mt 5:43 **22:40** [k] Mt 7:12; Lk 10:25-28 **22:42** [l] S Mt 9:27 **22:44** [m] Ps 110:1; 1Ki 5:3; Ac 2:34, 35; 1Co 15:25; Heb 1:13; 10:13 **22:46** [n] Mk 12:34; Lk 20:40 **23:2** [o] Ezr 7:6, 25 **23:4** [p] Lk 11:46; Ac 15:10; Gal 6:13 **23:5** [q] Mt 6:1, 2,5,16 [r] Ex 13:9; Dt 6:8 [s] Nu 15:38; Dt 22:12 **23:6** [t] Lk 11:43; 14:7; 20:46

[a] *32* Exodus 3:6 [b] *37* Deut. 6:5 [c] *39* Lev. 19:18 [d] *44* Psalm 110:1 [e] *5* That is, boxes containing Scripture verses, worn on forehead and arm

22:23 *Sadducees.* See notes on 3:7; Ezr 7:2; Mk 12:18; Lk 20:27; Ac 4:1; see also chart, p. 1631, and essay, p. 1576.
22:23–40 See Mk 12:18–31; Lk 20:27–40 and notes.
22:24 *Moses told us.* Jesus quoted from the Pentateuch when arguing with the Sadducees, since those books had special authority for them (see note on Mk 12:18). The reference (Dt 25:5–10) is to the levirate law (from Latin *levir,* "brother-in-law"), which was given to protect the widow and guarantee continuance of the family line.
22:37 *with all your heart … soul … mind.* With your whole being. The Hebrew of Dt 6:5 (see note there) has "heart … soul … strength," but some manuscripts of the Septuagint (the pre-Christian Greek translation of the OT) add "mind." Jesus combined all four terms in Mk 12:30. *soul.* See note on 10:28.
22:39 See note on Lev 19:18.
22:40 *the Law and the Prophets.* The entire OT (see note on 5:17).
22:41–46 See notes on Mk 12:35–40; Lk 20:44–47.
22:44 See note on Ps 110:1. Jesus bases his argument on Ps 110, the most frequently quoted OT chapter in the NT (see introduction to Ps 110). He assumes the Davidic authorship of the psalm, which is essential to his argument. For the nature of the argument, see note on Lk 20:44.
23:2 *teachers of the law.* See note on 2:4. *Pharisees.* See notes on 3:7; Lk 5:17. *sit in Moses' seat.* A position of authority. They considered themselves to be the authorized successors of Moses as teachers of the law.
23:3 *not practice what they preach.* See Jas 1:22–25.
23:4 *tie up heavy, cumbersome loads and put them on other people's shoulders.* Cf. Jesus' words in 11:28–30 and see note on 11:28; see also note on Lk 11:46.
23:5 *phylacteries.* These boxes (see NIV text note) contained four Scripture passages (Ex 13:1–10; 13:11–16; Dt 6:4–9; 11:13–21). *tassels.* See note on Nu 15:38.
23:6 *most important seats in the synagogues.* See note on Mk 12:39.

JEWISH SECTS

PHARISEES	
Their roots can be traced to the Hasidim of the second century BC (see note on Mk 2:16).	(1) Along with the Torah, they accepted as equally inspired and authoritative all the commands set forth in the oral traditions preserved by the rabbis.
	(2) On free will and determination, they held to a mediating view that did not allow either human free will or the sovereignty of God to cancel out the other.
	(3) They accepted a rather developed hierarchy of angels and demons.
	(4) They believed in the immortality of the soul and in reward and retribution after death.
	(5) They believed in the resurrection of the dead.
	(6) The main emphasis of their teaching was ethical rather than theological.
SADDUCEES	
They probably had their beginning during the Hasmonean period (166–63 BC). Their demise occurred c. AD 70 with the fall of Jerusalem and the destruction of the temple.	(1) They considered only the books of Moses to be canonical Scripture, denying that the oral law was authoritative and binding.
	(2) They were very exacting in Levitical purity.
	(3) They attributed everything to free will.
	(4) They argued that there is neither resurrection of the dead nor a future life.
	(5) They rejected the idea of a spiritual world, including belief in angels and demons.
ESSENES	
They probably originated among the Hasidim, along with the Pharisees, from whom they later separated (1 Maccabees 2:42; 7:13). The Hasidim were a group of zealous Jews who took part with the Maccabeans in a revolt against the Syrians c. 165 – 155 BC. A group of Essenes probably moved to Qumran c. 150 BC, where they copied scrolls and deposited them in nearby caves (see essay, pp. 1574 – 1576).	(1) They strictly observed the purity laws of the Torah.
	(2) They practiced communal ownership of property.
	(3) They had a strong sense of mutual responsibility.
	(4) Daily worship was an important feature along with daily study of their sacred scriptures.
	(5) Solemn oaths of piety and obedience had to be taken.
	(6) Sacrifices were offered on holy days and during their sacred seasons, but not at the temple, which they considered to be corrupt.
	(7) Marriage was avoided by some but was not condemned in principle.
	(8) They attributed to fate everything that happened.
ZEALOTS	
They originated during the reign of Herod the Great c. 6 BC. A group of Zealots were among the last defenders against the Romans at Masada in AD 73.	(1) They opposed payment of taxes to a pagan emperor because they believed that allegiance was due to God alone.
	(2) They were fiercely loyal to Jewish tradition.
	(3) They endorsed the use of violence as long as it accomplished a good end.
	(4) They were opposed to the influence of Greek pagan culture in the Holy Land.

with respect in the marketplaces and to be
called 'Rabbi' by others.[u]
8 "But you are not to be called 'Rabbi,'
for you have one Teacher, and you are all
brothers. 9 And do not call anyone on earth
'father,' for you have one Father,[v] and he
is in heaven. 10 Nor are you to be called
instructors, for you have one Instructor,
the Messiah. 11 The greatest among you
will be your servant.[w] 12 For those who exalt themselves will be humbled, and those
who humble themselves will be exalted.[x]

Seven Woes on the Teachers of the Law and the Pharisees

13 "Woe to you, teachers of the law and
Pharisees, you hypocrites![y] You shut the
door of the kingdom of heaven in people's
faces. You yourselves do not enter, nor will
you let those enter who are trying to.[z] [14][a]
15 "Woe to you, teachers of the law and
Pharisees, you hypocrites! You travel over
land and sea to win a single convert,[a]
and when you have succeeded, you make
them twice as much a child of hell[b] as you
are.
16 "Woe to you, blind guides![c] You say,
'If anyone swears by the temple, it means
nothing; but anyone who swears by the
gold of the temple is bound by that oath.'[d]
17 You blind fools! Which is greater: the
gold, or the temple that makes the gold
sacred?[e] 18 You also say, 'If anyone swears
by the altar, it means nothing; but anyone who swears by the gift on the altar
is bound by that oath.' 19 You blind men!
Which is greater: the gift, or the altar that
makes the gift sacred?[f] 20 Therefore, anyone
who swears by the altar swears by it and
by everything on it. 21 And anyone who
swears by the temple swears by it and by
the one who dwells[g] in it. 22 And anyone
who swears by heaven swears by God's
throne and by the one who sits on it.[h]
23 "Woe to you, teachers of the law and
Pharisees, you hypocrites! You give a
tenth[i] of your spices—mint, dill and cumin. But you have neglected the more important matters of the law—justice, mercy
and faithfulness.[j] You should have practiced the latter, without neglecting the former. 24 You blind guides![k] You strain out a
gnat but swallow a camel.
25 "Woe to you, teachers of the law and
Pharisees, you hypocrites! You clean the
outside of the cup and dish,[l] but inside
they are full of greed and self-indulgence.[m]
26 Blind Pharisee! First clean the inside of
the cup and dish, and then the outside
also will be clean.
27 "Woe to you, teachers of the law and
Pharisees, you hypocrites! You are like
whitewashed tombs,[n] which look beautiful on the outside but on the inside are
full of the bones of the dead and everything unclean. 28 In the same way, on the
outside you appear to people as righteous
but on the inside you are full of hypocrisy
and wickedness.
29 "Woe to you, teachers of the law
and Pharisees, you hypocrites! You build
tombs for the prophets[o] and decorate the
graves of the righteous. 30 And you say, 'If
we had lived in the days of our ancestors,
we would not have taken part with them
in shedding the blood of the prophets.' 31 So
you testify against yourselves that you are
the descendants of those who murdered

23:7 [u] ver 8; Mt 26:25,49; Mk 9:5; 10:51; Jn 1:38,49; 3:2, 26; 20:16 **23:9** [v] Mal 1:6; Mt 6:9; 7:11 **23:11** [w] S Mk 9:35 **23:12** [x] 1Sa 2:8; Ps 18:27; Pr 3:34; Isa 57:15; Eze 21:26; Lk 1:52; 14:11 **23:13** [y] ver 15, 23,25,27,29 [z] Lk 11:52 **23:15** [a] Ac 2:11; 6:5; 13:43 [b] S Mt 5:22 **23:16** [c] ver 24; Isa 9:16; Mt 15:14 [d] Mt 5:33-35 **23:17** [e] Ex 30:29 **23:19** [f] Ex 29:37 **23:21** [g] 1Ki 8:13; Ps 26:8 **23:22** [h] Ps 11:4; Mt 5:34 **23:23** [i] Lev 27:30 [j] Mic 6:8; Lk 11:42 **23:24** [k] ver 16 **23:25** [l] Mk 7:4 [m] Lk 11:39 **23:27** [n] Lk 11:44; Ac 23:3 **23:29** [o] Lk 11:47,48

[a] *14* Some manuscripts include here words similar to Mark 12:40 and Luke 20:47.

23:7 *Rabbi.* A Hebrew word meaning "(my) teacher."
23:8–10 The warning is against seeking titles of honor to foster pride. We should avoid unreasonable literalism in applying such commands.
23:13–32 Seven woes pronounced by Jesus on the religious leaders (see the six woes in Lk 11:42–44,46–52; cf. the six woes in Isa 5:8–25 and in Isa 28:1—35:10 [see note there] and the five woes in Hab 2:6–20).
23:13 *hypocrites.* See vv. 15,23,25,27,29; see also note on 6:2. *shut the door of the kingdom ... in people's faces.* See Lk 11:52 and note.
23:15 Jesus does not criticize the Pharisees for their evangelistic zeal. He objects to its results. The converts became even more the children of hell (i.e., bound for hell) than their teachers. *convert.* The Greek for this word is found in the NT only here and in Ac 2:11 (see note there); 6:5 (see note there); 13:43. *hell.* See notes on 5:22; Lk 12:5.
23:16–26 *blind guides ... blind fools ... blind men ... Blind Pharisee!* Although the Pharisees were supposed to be Israel's teachers, they themselves were spiritually blind.
23:16–22 *If anyone swears.* When the teachers of the law and the Pharisees took an oath, they differentiated between what was binding and what was not. This allowed for evasive oath-taking. Jesus rejected all such subtleties by showing how foolish they were and by insisting that people simply tell the truth (see 5:33–37, where Jesus abolished all oaths).
23:23 Jesus does not criticize the observance of the minutiae of the law (he says, "without neglecting" them—including the tithe), but he does criticize the hypocrisy often involved (see notes on 5:18–20; Lk 11:42). *cumin.* A spice indigenous to western Asia and resembling caraway in taste and appearance. *justice, mercy and faithfulness.* See Mic 6:6,8 and notes.
23:24 *strain out.* The strict Pharisee would carefully strain his drinking water through a cloth to be sure he did not swallow a gnat, the smallest of ceremonially unclean animals. But, figuratively, he would swallow a camel—one of the largest. *swallow a camel.* Hyperbole (see 7:3 and note; 19:24; Mk 10:25 and note).
23:26 *clean the inside.* A total moral renewal that will manifest itself in righteous living (see v. 23).
23:27 *whitewashed tombs.* A person who stepped on a grave became ceremonially unclean (see Nu 19:16), so graves were whitewashed to make them easily visible, especially at night. They appeared clean and beautiful on the outside, but they were dirty and rotten on the inside.
23:29 *tombs for the prophets.* See note on Lk 11:47.
23:31 *descendants.* In the sense that they imitate the actions of their murderous ancestors.

the prophets.[p] 32 Go ahead, then, and complete[q] what your ancestors started![r]

33 "You snakes! You brood of vipers![s] How will you escape being condemned to hell?[t] 34 Therefore I am sending you prophets and sages and teachers. Some of them you will kill and crucify;[u] others you will flog in your synagogues[v] and pursue from town to town.[w] 35 And so upon you will come all the righteous blood that has been shed on earth, from the blood of righteous Abel[x] to the blood of Zechariah son of Berekiah,[y] whom you murdered between the temple and the altar.[z] 36 Truly I tell you, all this will come on this generation.[a]

37 "Jerusalem, Jerusalem, you who kill the prophets and stone those sent to you,[b] how often I have longed to gather your children together, as a hen gathers her chicks under her wings,[c] and you were not willing. 38 Look, your house is left to you desolate.[d] 39 For I tell you, you will not see me again until you say, 'Blessed is he who comes in the name of the Lord.'[a]"[e]

The Destruction of the Temple and Signs of the End Times

24:1-51pp — Mk 13:1-37; Lk 21:5-36

24 Jesus left the temple and was walking away when his disciples came up to him to call his attention to its buildings. 2 "Do you see all these things?" he asked. "Truly I tell you, not one stone here will be left on another;[f] every one will be thrown down."

3 As Jesus was sitting on the Mount of Olives,[g] the disciples came to him privately. "Tell us," they said, "when will this happen, and what will be the sign of your coming[h] and of the end of the age?"[i]

4 Jesus answered: "Watch out that no one deceives you.[j] 5 For many will come in my name, claiming, 'I am the Messiah,' and will deceive many.[k] 6 You will hear of wars and rumors of wars, but see to it that you are not alarmed. Such things must happen, but the end is still to come. 7 Nation will rise against nation, and kingdom against kingdom.[l] There will be famines[m] and earthquakes in various places. 8 All these are the beginning of birth pains.

9 "Then you will be handed over to be persecuted[n] and put to death,[o] and you will be hated by all nations because of me.[p] 10 At that time many will turn away from the faith and will betray and hate each other, 11 and many false prophets[q] will appear and deceive many people.[r] 12 Because of the increase of wickedness, the love of most will grow cold, 13 but the one who stands firm to the end will be saved.[s] 14 And this gospel of the kingdom[t] will be preached in the whole world[u] as a

a 39 Psalm 118:26

23:31 [p] S Mt 5:12 **23:32** [q] 1Th 2:16 [r] Eze 20:4 **23:33** [s] Mt 3:7; 12:34 [t] S Mt 5:22 **23:34** [u] 2Ch 36:15, 16; Lk 11:49 [v] S Mt 10:17 [w] Mt 10:23 **23:35** [x] Ge 4:8; Heb 11:4 [y] Zec 1:1 [z] 2Ch 24:21 **23:36** [a] Mt 10:23; 24:34; Lk 11:50, 51 **23:37** [b] 2Ch 24:21; S Mt 5:12 [c] Ps 57:1; 61:4; Isa 31:5 **23:38** [d] 1Ki 9:7, 8; Jer 22:5 **23:39** [e] Ps 118:26; Mt 21:9

24:2 [f] Lk 19:44 **24:3** [g] S Mt 21:1 [h] S Lk 17:30 [i] Mt 13:39; 28:20 **24:4** [j] S Mk 13:5 **24:5** [k] ver 11, 23, 24; 1Jn 2:18 **24:7** [l] Isa 19:2 [m] Ac 11:28 **24:9** [n] Mt 10:17 [o] Jn 16:2 [p] S Jn 15:21 **24:11** [q] S Mt 7:15 [r] S Mk 13:5 **24:13** [s] S Mt 10:22 **24:14** [t] S Mt 4:23 [u] Lk 2:1; 4:5; Ac 11:28; 17:6; S Ro 10:18

23:32 Cf. Ge 15:16; 1Th 2:14–16; spoken ironically. They would bring the sin of their ancestors to completion with the crucifixion of the Son of God (cf. 21:38–39 and note on 21:35–37).
23:33 *hell.* See notes on 5:22; Lk 12:5.
23:34 *prophets and sages and teachers.* Cf. Jer 18:18; Eze 7:26 and notes. *synagogues.* See note on Mk 1:21.
23:35 *Abel to … Zechariah.* Jesus was summing up the history of martyrdom in the OT. The murder of Abel is recorded in Ge 4:8 and that of Zechariah son (perhaps grandson, since he is here called "son of Berekiah"; see NIV text note on 1Ch 1:5; see also note on Da 5:1) of Jehoiada in 2Ch 24:20–22 (Chronicles comes at the close of the OT according to most Hebrew manuscripts). The expression was somewhat like our "from Genesis to Revelation." *between the temple and the altar.* Jesus' reference is more specific than the Chronicler's on the location of Zechariah's murder, perhaps referring to "the altar" as a place of sacrifice.
23:36 *all this.* All the righteous blood of the martyrs (see v. 30). *will come on this generation.* Jesus' contemporaries; a prophecy fulfilled, at least in part, in the destruction of Jerusalem and the temple in AD 70 (see vv. 37–38).
23:37–39 See notes on Lk 13:34–35.
24:1—25:46 The Olivet discourse, the fifth and last of the great discourses in Matthew's Gospel (see notes on 5:1—7:29; Mk 13:1–37; Lk 21:5–37; see also Introduction: Structure).
24:2 *not one stone … left.* Fulfilled literally in AD 70, when the Romans under Titus completely destroyed Jerusalem and the temple buildings. Stones were even pried apart to collect the gold leaf that melted from the roof when the temple was set on fire. *stone.* See note on Mk 13:1. *thrown down.* Excavations in 1968 uncovered large numbers of these stones, toppled from the walls by the invaders.
24:3 *Mount of Olives.* A ridge a little more than a mile long, beyond the Kidron Valley east of Jerusalem and rising about 200 feet above the city (see map, pp. 1686–1687). *when will this happen, and what will be the sign of your coming and of the end of the age?* Jesus deals with these questions but does not distinguish them sharply. However, it appears that the description of the last days (which begin with Jesus' incarnation and end with his second coming) is presented in vv. 4–14, the destruction of Jerusalem in vv. 15–22 (see Lk 21:20) and Christ's coming in vv. 23–31. The rest of the discourse is largely taken up with warnings and exhortations to live responsibly and courageously despite trials, persecutions and uncertainty about the exact time of his coming (24:32—25:46). This last section contains several eschatological parables (25:1–13,14–30,31–46).
24:4 *Watch out.* See note on Mk 13:5.
24:5–14 See Lk 21:8–18 and note on 21:9.
24:5 *in my name.* Claiming to be the Messiah (see Mk 13:6 and note). *Messiah.* See second NIV text note on 1:1. *will deceive many.* See 1Jn 2:18 and note.
24:8 *birth pains.* The rabbis spoke of "birth pains," i.e., sufferings, that would precede the coming of the Messiah (see Isa 13:8 and note).
24:13 See note on Mk 13:13; cf. 2Ti 2:10–13; Heb 10:36; 11:27; Jas 1:12; 5:11.
24:14 *preached in the whole world.* Despite his Jewish interests, Matthew has a universal outlook (see Introduction: Recipients). *testimony to all nations.* This missionary mandate

testimony to all nations, and then the end
will come.
15 “So when you see standing in the
holy place[v] ‘the abomination that causes desolation,’[a][w] spoken of through the
prophet Daniel—let the reader understand— 16 then let those who are in Judea
flee to the mountains. 17 Let no one on the
housetop[x] go down to take anything out
of the house. 18 Let no one in the field go
back to get their cloak. 19 How dreadful it
will be in those days for pregnant wom-
en and nursing mothers![y] 20 Pray that your
flight will not take place in winter or on
the Sabbath. 21 For then there will be great
distress, unequaled from the beginning
of the world until now—and never to be
equaled again.[z]
22 “If those days had not been cut short,
no one would survive, but for the sake
of the elect[a] those days will be shortened. 23 At that time if anyone says to you,
‘Look, here is the Messiah!’ or, ‘There he
is!’ do not believe it.[b] 24 For false messiahs
and false prophets will appear and perform great signs and wonders[c] to deceive,
if possible, even the elect. 25 See, I have
told you ahead of time.
26 “So if anyone tells you, ‘There he is,
out in the wilderness,’ do not go out; or,
‘Here he is, in the inner rooms,’ do not
believe it. 27 For as lightning[d] that comes
from the east is visible even in the west,
so will be the coming[e] of the Son of Man.[f]
28 Wherever there is a carcass, there the
vultures will gather.[g]
29 “Immediately after the distress of
those days

“ ‘the sun will be darkened,
and the moon will not give its
light;
the stars will fall from the sky,
and the heavenly bodies will be
shaken.’[b][h]

30 “Then will appear the sign of the Son
of Man in heaven. And then all the peoples of the earth[c] will mourn[i] when they
see the Son of Man coming on the clouds
of heaven,[j] with power and great glory.[d]
31 And he will send his angels[k] with a loud
trumpet call,[l] and they will gather his elect
from the four winds, from one end of the
heavens to the other.
32 “Now learn this lesson from the fig
tree: As soon as its twigs get tender and its
leaves come out, you know that summer
is near. 33 Even so, when you see all these
things, you know that it[e] is near, right at
the door.[m] 34 Truly I tell you, this generation will certainly not pass away until all

24:15 [v]S Ac 6:13 [w]Da 9:27; 11:31; 12:11 **24:17** [x]1Sa 9:25; Mt 10:27; Lk 12:3; Ac 10:9 **24:19** [y]Lk 23:29 **24:21** [z]Eze 5:9; Da 12:1; Joel 2:2 **24:22** [a]ver 24, 31 **24:23** [b]Lk 17:23; 21:8 **24:24** [c]Ex 7:11, 22; 2Th 2:9-11; Rev 13:13; 16:14; 19:20 **24:27** [d]Lk 17:24 [e]S Lk 17:30 [f]S Mt 8:20 **24:28** [g]Lk 17:37 **24:29** [h]Isa 13:10; 34:4; Eze 32:7; Joel 2:10, 31; Zep 1:15; Rev 6:12, 13; 8:12 **24:30** [i]Rev 1:7 [j]S Rev 1:7 **24:31** [k]Mt 13:41 [l]Isa 27:13; Zec 9:14; 1Co 15:52; 1Th 4:16; Rev 8:2; 10:7; 11:15 **24:33** [m]Jas 5:9

[a] *15* Daniel 9:27; 11:31; 12:11 [b] *29* Isaiah 13:10; 34:4 [c] *30* Or *the tribes of the land* [d] *30* See Daniel 7:13-14. [e] *33* Or *he*

(see 28:18–20 and notes) must be fulfilled before the end comes.

24:15 *the abomination that causes desolation.* The detestable thing causing the desolation of the holy place. The primary reference in Daniel (see NIV text note for references) was to 168 BC, when Antiochus Epiphanes erected a pagan altar to Zeus on the sacred altar in the temple of Jerusalem. According to some, there were still two more stages in the progressive fulfillment of the predictions in Daniel and Matthew: (1) the Roman destruction of the temple in AD 70, and (2) a still future setting up of an image of the antichrist in Jerusalem (see 2Th 2:4; Rev 13:14–15; see also notes on Da 9:25–27; 11:31). *let the reader understand.* These are possibly Jesus' words, not Matthew's, exhorting the readers of Daniel's prophecy to understand what they read (but see note on Mk 13:14).

24:16 *mountains.* The Transjordan mountains, where Pella was located. Christians in Jerusalem fled to that area during the Roman siege shortly before AD 70. Some believe a similar fleeing will occur in a future tribulation period (identified with the 70th "seven" in Da 9:27).

24:17 *housetop.* See notes on Mk 2:4; Lk 17:31.

24:19 See note on Mk 13:17.

24:20 *in winter.* See note on Mk 13:18. *or on the Sabbath.* Matthew alone includes this phrase because he was writing to Jews, who were forbidden to travel more than about three quarters of a mile on the Sabbath ("a Sabbath day's walk," Ac 1:12; see note there).

24:21 *great distress, unequaled.* Josephus, the Jewish historian who was there, describes the destruction of Jerusalem in almost identical language (*Wars*, 5.10.3–5; 6.3.3–5). Some believe the reference is also to a future period of great distress (see note on v. 16; see also Da 12:1 and note; cf. Rev 6–18).

24:22 *days . . . cut short.* Some hold that this statement means that the distress will be of such intensity that, if allowed to continue, it would destroy everyone. Others believe that Christ is referring to the cutting short of a previously determined time period (such as the 70th "seven" of Da 9:27 or the 42 months of Rev 11:2; 13:5). *the elect.* The chosen people of God (see also vv. 24,31).

24:24 *false messiahs.* See 1Jn 2:18 and note.

24:26 *inner rooms.* See Lk 12:3 and note.

24:27 Christ's second coming will not be in secret, witnessed by only a favored few; it will be visible to all (see v. 30). *as lightning.* See note on Lk 17:24.

24:28 *there the vultures will gather.* The gathering of vultures obviously indicates the presence of carrion; the coming of Christ will likewise be obvious. See note on Lk 17:37, where the saying is used in a slightly different sense.

24:29 See note on Mk 13:25.

24:30 *sign.* Here probably means "banner" or "standard" (see Isa 11:12; 18:3; 49:22; Jer 4:21; 51:27). *all the peoples . . . will mourn.* Because they now face judgment (see Rev 1:7; cf. Zec 12:10–12). *the Son of Man coming on the clouds.* Alludes to Da 7:13 and refers to Christ's second coming (see 2Th 1:7–10; Rev 19:11–16). *Son of Man.* See note on Mk 8:31. *on the clouds.* After the manner in which God came down on Mount Sinai (see 17:5 and note). *with power and great glory.* Cf. 1Ch 29:11; Ps 63:2; 66:2–3; Hab 3:3–4.

24:31 *gather his elect.* See note on Mk 13:27.

24:33 *it.* The kingdom of God (see Lk 21:31 and note on 21:29).

24:34 *Truly I tell you.* See note on Mk 3:28. *this generation.* See note on Lk 21:32.

these things have happened.[n] 35 Heaven and earth will pass away, but my words will never pass away.[o]

The Day and Hour Unknown

24:37-39pp — Lk 17:26,27
24:45-51pp — Lk 12:42-46

36 "But about that day or hour no one knows, not even the angels in heaven, nor the Son,[a] but only the Father.[p] 37 As it was in the days of Noah,[q] so it will be at the coming of the Son of Man. 38 For in the days before the flood, people were eating and drinking, marrying and giving in marriage,[r] up to the day Noah entered the ark; 39 and they knew nothing about what would happen until the flood came and took them all away. That is how it will be at the coming of the Son of Man.[s] 40 Two men will be in the field; one will be taken and the other left.[t] 41 Two women will be grinding with a hand mill; one will be taken and the other left.[u]

42 "Therefore keep watch, because you do not know on what day your Lord will come.[v] 43 But understand this: If the owner of the house had known at what time of night the thief was coming,[w] he would have kept watch and would not have let his house be broken into. 44 So you also must be ready,[x] because the Son of Man will come at an hour when you do not expect him.

45 "Who then is the faithful and wise servant,[y] whom the master has put in charge of the servants in his household to give them their food at the proper time? 46 It will be good for that servant whose master finds him doing so when he returns.[z] 47 Truly I tell you, he will put him in charge of all his possessions.[a] 48 But suppose that servant is wicked and says to himself, 'My master is staying away a long time,' 49 and he then begins to beat his fellow servants and to eat and drink with drunkards.[b] 50 The master of that servant will come on a day when he does not expect him and at an hour he is not aware of. 51 He will cut him to pieces and assign him a place with the hypocrites, where there will be weeping and gnashing of teeth.[c]

The Parable of the Ten Virgins

25 "At that time the kingdom of heaven will be like[d] ten virgins who took their lamps[e] and went out to meet the bridegroom.[f] 2 Five of them were foolish and five were wise.[g] 3 The foolish ones took their lamps but did not take any oil with them. 4 The wise ones, however, took oil in jars along with their lamps. 5 The bridegroom was a long time in coming, and they all became drowsy and fell asleep.[h]

6 "At midnight the cry rang out: 'Here's the bridegroom! Come out to meet him!'

7 "Then all the virgins woke up and trimmed their lamps. 8 The foolish ones said to the wise, 'Give us some of your oil; our lamps are going out.'[i]

9 " 'No,' they replied, 'there may not be enough for both us and you. Instead, go to those who sell oil and buy some for yourselves.'

10 "But while they were on their way to buy the oil, the bridegroom arrived. The virgins who were ready went in with him to the wedding banquet.[j] And the door was shut.

11 "Later the others also came. 'Lord, Lord,' they said, 'open the door for us!'

12 "But he replied, 'Truly I tell you, I don't know you.'[k]

13 "Therefore keep watch, because you do not know the day or the hour.[l]

The Parable of the Bags of Gold

25:14-30Ref — Lk 19:12-27

14 "Again, it will be like a man going on a journey,[m] who called his servants and entrusted his wealth to them. 15 To one he gave five bags of gold, to another two bags, and to another one bag,[b] each

[a] *36* Some manuscripts do not have *nor the Son.*
[b] *15* Greek *five talents . . . two talents . . . one talent*; also throughout this parable; a talent was worth about 20 years of a day laborer's wage.

24:34 [n] Mt 16:28; S 23:36 **24:35** [o] S Mt 5:18 **24:36** [p] Ac 1:7 **24:37** [q] Ge 6:5; 7:6-23 **24:38** [r] Mt 22:30 **24:39** [s] S Lk 17:30 **24:40** [t] Lk 17:34 **24:41** [u] Lk 17:35 **24:42** [v] Mt 25:13; Lk 12:40 **24:43** [w] S Lk 12:39 **24:44** [x] 1Th 5:6 **24:45** [y] Mt 25:21,23 **24:46** [z] Rev 16:15 **24:47** [a] Mt 25:21,23 **24:49** [b] Lk 21:34 **24:51** [c] S Mt 8:12 **25:1** [d] S Mt 13:24 [e] Lk 12:35-38; Ac 20:8; Rev 4:5 [f] Rev 19:7; 21:2 **25:2** [g] Mt 24:45 **25:5** [h] 1Th 5:6 **25:8** [i] Lk 12:35 **25:10** [j] Rev 19:9 **25:12** [k] ver 41; S Mt 7:23 **25:13** [l] Mt 24:42, 44; Mk 13:35; Lk 12:40 **25:14** [m] Mt 21:33; Lk 19:12

24:35 Jesus' words are more certain than the existence of the universe.
24:36 *that day.* See note on Lk 21:34. *nor the Son.* See note on Mk 13:32.
24:40–41 *taken.* See note on Lk 17:35.
24:42 *keep watch.* Vigilance is the order of the day, because the time of Christ's coming is unknown (see notes on Mk 13:32,37).
24:44 *be ready.* See 25:10,29; 1Th 5:6 and notes; cf. 1Jn 2:28.
24:51 *weeping and gnashing of teeth.* See note on 13:42.
25:1–12 The parable emphasizes the need for watchfulness in the event of an unexpectedly long delay in Christ's coming (see v. 13 and note).
25:1 *At that time.* The time of Christ's coming. *kingdom of heaven.* See note on 3:2. *ten virgins.* Perhaps the bridesmaids, who were responsible for preparing the bride to meet the bridegroom. *lamps.* Probably torches that consisted of a long pole with oil-drenched rags at the top.
25:3 *oil.* Olive oil.
25:7 *trimmed.* The charred ends of the rags were cut off and oil was added.
25:9 *No.* When Christ returns, preparedness cannot be shared or transferred. Personal responsibility is emphasized (see v. 12). *there may not be enough.* Torches required large amounts of oil in order to keep burning, and the oil had to be replenished about every 15 minutes.
25:13 *keep watch.* The main point of the parable. *the day or the hour.* Of the coming of Christ.
25:14–30 For a similar parable, see Lk 19:12–27.
25:15 *bag.* See NIV text note. The term *talent* was first used

THE LIFE OF CHRIST

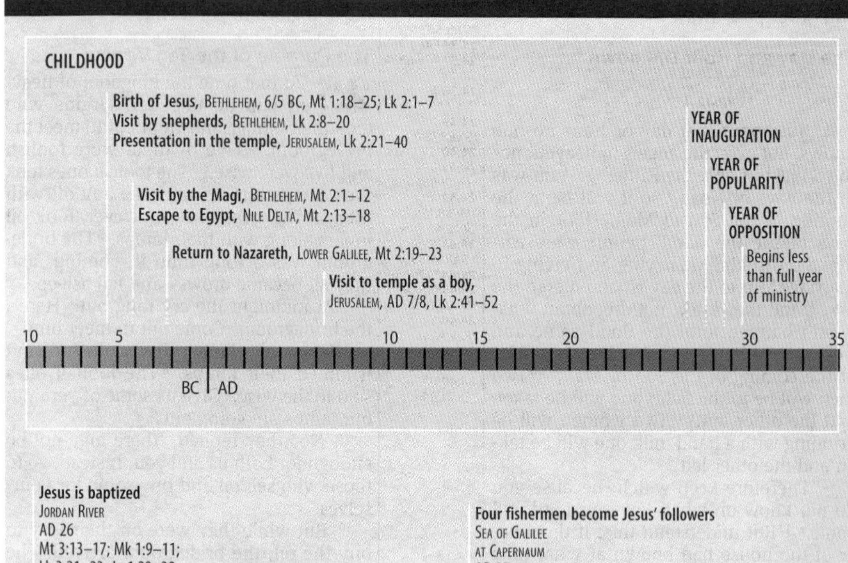

Jesus is baptized
JORDAN RIVER
AD 26
Mt 3:13–17; Mk 1:9–11;
Lk 3:21–23; Jn 1:29–39

Jesus is tempted by Satan
DESERT OF JUDEA
Mt 4:1–11; Mk 1:12–13; Lk 4:1–13

Jesus' first miracle
CANA
Jn 2:1–11

Four fishermen become Jesus' followers
SEA OF GALILEE
AT CAPERNAUM
AD 27
Mt 4:18–22; Mk 1:16–20;
Lk 5:1–11

Jesus heals Peter's mother-in-law
CAPERNAUM
Mt 8:14–17; Mk 1:29–34;
Lk 4:38–41

YEAR OF INAUGURATION — **YEAR OF POPULARITY**

AD 27 — 28

FALL | WINTER | SPRING | SUMMER | FALL | WINTER

Jesus clears the temple
AD 27
Jn 2:14–22

Jesus and Nicodemus
JERUSALEM
AD 27
Jn 3:1–21

Jesus talks to the Samaritan woman
SAMARIA
Jn 4:5–42

Jesus heals a royal official's son
CANA
Jn 4:46–54

The people of Jesus' hometown try to kill him
NAZARETH
Lk 4:16–31

Jesus begins his first preaching trip through Galilee
Mt 4:23–25; Mk 1:35–39;
Lk 4:42–44

Matthew decides to follow Jesus
CAPERNAUM
Mt 9:9–13; Mk 2:13–17; Lk 5:27–32

Jesus chooses the 12 disciples
AD 28
Mk 3:13–19; Lk 6:12–15

Jesus preaches the Sermon on the Mount
Mt 5:1—7:29; Lk 6:20–49

Dotted lines leading to the timeline are meant to define sequence of events only. All dates are approximate.

THE LIFE OF CHRIST (CONT.)

A sinful woman anoints Jesus
CAPERNAUM
Lk 7:36–50

Jesus ministers again in Galilee
Lk 8:1–3

Jesus tells parables about the kingdom
Mt 13:1–52; Mk 4:1–34; Lk 8:4–18

Jesus calms the storm
SEA OF GALILEE
Mt 8:23–27; Mk 4:35–41; Lk 8:22–25

Jesus feeds the 5,000
NEAR BETHSAIDA
Spring, AD 29
Mt 14:13–21; Mk 6:30–44; Lk 9:10–17; Jn 6:1–14

Jesus walks on water
Mt 14:22–33; Mk 6:45–52; Jn 6:16–21

Jesus withdraws to Tyre and Sidon
Mt 15:21–28; Mk 7:24–30

Jesus feeds the 4,000
Mt 15:32–39; Mk 8:1–9

Peter says that Jesus is the Son of God
Mt 16:13–20; Mk 8:27–30; Lk 9:18–21

Jesus tells his disciples he is going to die soon
CAESAREA PHILIPPI
Mt 16:21–26; Mk 8:31–37; Lk 9:22–25

Jesus is transfigured
Mt 17:1–13; Mk 9:2–13; Lk 9:28–36

Jesus pays his temple tax
CAPERNAUM
Later in that year
Mt 17:24–27

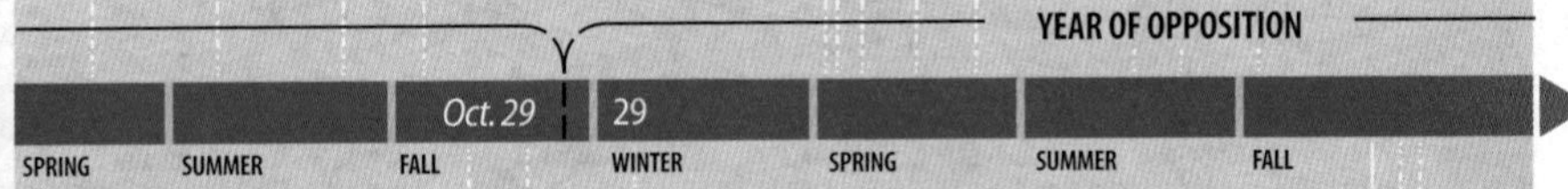

Jairus's daughter is brought back to life by Jesus
CAPERNAUM
Mt 9:18–26; Mk 5:21–43; Lk 8:40–56

Jesus sends the Twelve out to preach and heal
Mt 9:35—11:1; Mk 6:6–13; Lk 9:1–6

John the Baptist is killed by Herod
MACHAERUS
AD 28
Mt 14:1–12; Mk 6:14–29; Lk 9:7–9

Jesus attends the Festival of Tabernacles
JERUSALEM
October, AD 29
Jn 7:11–52

Jesus heals a man who was born blind
JERUSALEM
Jn 9:1–41

Jesus visits Mary and Martha
BETHANY
Lk 10:38–42

The most likely dates for Jesus' public ministry are AD 27–30; the next most likely option, however, is 30–33.

THE LIFE OF CHRIST (CONT.)

Jesus begins his last trip to Jerusalem
AD 30
Lk 17:11

Jesus blesses the little children
Across the Jordan
Mt 19:13–15; Mk 10:13–16; Lk 18:15–17

Jesus talks to the rich young man
Across the Jordan
Mt 19:16–30; Mk 10:17–31; Lk 18:18–30

Jesus again predicts his death and resurrection
Near the Jordan
Mt 20:17–19; Mk 10:32–34; Lk 18:31–34

Jesus heals blind Bartimaeus
Jericho
Mt 20:29–34; Mk 10:46–52; Lk 18:35–43

Jesus talks to Zacchaeus
Jericho
Lk 19:1–10

Jesus returns to Bethany to visit Mary and Martha
Bethany
Jn 11:55—12:1

THE LAST WEEK

The "Triumphal" Entry, Jerusalem, Sunday
Mt 21:1–11; Mk 11:1–10; Lk 19:29–44; Jn 12:12–19

Jesus curses the fig tree, Monday
Mt 21:18–19; Mk 11:12–14

Jesus clears the temple, Monday
Mt 21:12–13; Mk 11:15–18

The authority of Jesus questioned, Tuesday
Mt 21:23–27; Mk 11:27–33; Lk 20:1–8

Jesus teaches in the temple, Tuesday
Mt 21:28—23:39; Mk 12:1–44; Lk 20:9—21:4

Jesus anointed, Bethany, Tuesday
Mt 26:6–13; Mk 14:3–9; Jn 12:2–11

The plot against Jesus, Wednesday
Mt 26:14–16; Mk 14:10–11; Lk 22:3–6

The Last Supper, Thursday
Mt 26:17–29; Mk 14:12–25; Lk 22:7–20; Jn 13:1–38

Jesus comforts the disciples, Thursday
Jn 14:1—16:33

Gethsemane, Thursday
Mt 26:36–46; Mk 14:32–42; Lk 22:40–46

Jesus' arrest and trial, Thursday night and Friday
Mt 26:47—27:26; Mk 14:43—15:15; Lk 22:47—23:25; Jn 18:2—19:16

Jesus' crucifixion and death, Golgotha, Friday
Mt 27:27–56; Mk 15:16–41; Lk 23:26–49; Jn 19:17–30

The burial of Jesus, Joseph's Tomb, Friday
Mt 27:57–66; Mk 15:42–47; Lk 23:50–56; Jn 19:31–42

30 WINTER | SPRING | SUMMER | FALL | 31 WINTER | SPRING | SUMMER

Jesus raises Lazarus from the dead
Bethany
Winter, AD 30
Jn 11:1–44

AFTER THE RESURRECTION

The empty tomb, Jerusalem, Sunday
Mt 28:1–10; Mk 16:1–8; Lk 24:1–12; Jn 20:1–10

Mary Magdalene sees Jesus in the garden
Jerusalem, Sunday
Mt 16:9–11; Jn 20:11–18

Jesus appears to the two going to Emmaus
Sunday
Mk 16:12–13; Lk 24:13–35

Jesus appears to 10 disciples
Jerusalem, Sunday
Mk 16:14; Lk 24:36–43; Jn 20:19–25

Jesus appears to the 11 disciples
Jerusalem, One week later
Jn 20:26–31

Jesus talks with some of his disciples
Sea of Galilee, One week later
Jn 21:1–25

Jesus ascends to his Father in heaven
Mount of Olives, 40 days later
Mt 28:16–20; Mk 16:19–20; Lk 24:44–53

according to his ability.[n] Then he went on his journey. 16The man who had received five bags of gold went at once and put his money to work and gained five bags more. 17So also, the one with two bags of gold gained two more. 18But the man who had received one bag went off, dug a hole in the ground and hid his master's money.

19"After a long time the master of those servants returned and settled accounts with them.[o] 20The man who had received five bags of gold brought the other five. 'Master,' he said, 'you entrusted me with five bags of gold. See, I have gained five more.'

21"His master replied, 'Well done, good and faithful servant! You have been faithful with a few things; I will put you in charge of many things.[p] Come and share your master's happiness!'

22"The man with two bags of gold also came. 'Master,' he said, 'you entrusted me with two bags of gold; see, I have gained two more.'

23"His master replied, 'Well done, good and faithful servant! You have been faithful with a few things; I will put you in charge of many things.[q] Come and share your master's happiness!'

24"Then the man who had received one bag of gold came. 'Master,' he said, 'I knew that you are a hard man, harvesting where you have not sown and gathering where you have not scattered seed. 25So I was afraid and went out and hid your gold in the ground. See, here is what belongs to you.'

26"His master replied, 'You wicked, lazy servant! So you knew that I harvest where I have not sown and gather where I have not scattered seed? 27Well then, you should have put my money on deposit with the bankers, so that when I returned I would have received it back with interest.

28" 'So take the bag of gold from him and give it to the one who has ten bags. 29For whoever has will be given more, and they will have an abundance. Whoever does not have, even what they have will be taken from them.[r] 30And throw that worthless servant outside, into the darkness, where there will be weeping and gnashing of teeth.'[s]

The Sheep and the Goats

31"When the Son of Man comes[t] in his glory, and all the angels with him, he will sit on his glorious throne.[u] 32All the nations will be gathered before him, and he will separate[v] the people one from another as a shepherd separates the sheep from the goats.[w] 33He will put the sheep on his right and the goats on his left.

34"Then the King will say to those on his right, 'Come, you who are blessed by my Father; take your inheritance, the kingdom[x] prepared for you since the creation of the world.[y] 35For I was hungry and you gave me something to eat, I was thirsty and you gave me something to drink, I was a stranger and you invited me in,[z] 36I needed clothes and you clothed me,[a] I was sick and you looked after me,[b] I was in prison and you came to visit me.'[c]

37"Then the righteous will answer him, 'Lord, when did we see you hungry and feed you, or thirsty and give you something to drink? 38When did we see you a stranger and invite you in, or needing clothes and clothe you? 39When did we see you sick or in prison and go to visit you?'

40"The King will reply, 'Truly I tell you, whatever you did for one of the least of

25:15 [n]Mt 18:24,25
25:19 [o]Mt 18:23
25:21 [p]ver 23; Mt 24:45,47; Lk 16:10
25:23 [q]ver 21
25:29 [r]Mt 13:12; Mk 4:25; Lk 8:18; 19:26
25:30 [s]S Mt 8:12
25:31 [t]S Lk 17:30 [u]Mt 19:28
25:32 [v]Mal 3:18 [w]Eze 34:17,20
25:34 [x]S Mt 3:2; 5:3, 10,19; 19:14; S Ac 20:32; 1Co 15:50; Gal 5:21; Jas 2:5 [y]Heb 4:3; 9:26; Rev 13:8; 17:8
25:35 [z]Job 31:32; Heb 13:2
25:36 [a]Isa 58:7; Eze 18:7; Jas 2:15,16 [b]Jas 1:27 [c]2Ti 1:16

---

for a unit of weight (about 75 pounds), then for a unit of coinage. The present-day use of "talent" to indicate an ability or gift is derived from this parable and often leads to a misunderstanding of the parable itself.
25:21 *faithful with a few … in charge of many.* Cf. 13:12; see notes on v. 29; Mk 4:25; Lk 19:26.
25:26 See note on Lk 19:22.
25:27 *bankers.* Sat at small tables and changed money (cf. 21:12).
25:29 The main point of the parable. Being ready for Christ's coming involves more than playing it safe and doing little or nothing. It demands the kind of service that produces results (see note on Lk 19:26).
25:30 *weeping and gnashing of teeth.* See note on 13:42.
25:31–46 The two most widely accepted interpretations of this judgment are: (1) It will occur at the beginning of an earthly millennial kingdom (vv. 31,34; see Rev 20:4 and note on 20:2). Its purpose will be to determine who will be allowed to enter the kingdom (v. 34). The basis for judgment will be the kind of treatment shown to the Jewish people ("these brothers and sisters of mine," v. 40) during the preceding great tribulation period (vv. 35–40,42–45). Ultimately, how one treats them will reveal whether or not one is saved (vv. 41,46). (2) The judgment referred to occurs at the great white throne at the end of the age (Rev 20:11–15). Its purpose will be to determine who will be allowed to enter the eternal kingdom of the saved and who will be consigned to eternal punishment in hell (vv. 34,46). The basis for judgment will be whether love is shown to God's people (see 1Jn 3:14–15). See note on v. 40.
25:31 *Son of Man.* See note on Mk 8:31. *in his glory.* See 16:27; 24:30. *angels.* See 13:41–42; 2Th 1:7; Rev 14:17–20. *sit on his glorious throne.* Not only as judge but also as king (vv. 34,40).
25:32 *All the nations.* Both Jews and Gentiles (see 28:19 and note). *separates the sheep from the goats.* Cf. 7:21–23; 13:40–43.
25:33 *on his right.* See Mk 10:37 and note.
25:34–40 Rewards in the kingdom of heaven are given to those who serve without thought of reward. There is no hint of merit here, for God gives out of grace, not debt.
25:34 *inheritance.* See Ac 20:32; Eph 1:14,18; 5:5; Col 1:12; 3:24; Heb 9:15; 1Pe 1:4. *kingdom.* See note on 3:2. *since the creation of the world.* Cf. Eph 1:4 and note.
25:40 *least of these brothers and sisters of mine.* To whom does

these brothers and sisters of mine, you did for me.'[d]

41 "Then he will say to those on his left, 'Depart from me,[e] you who are cursed, into the eternal fire[f] prepared for the devil and his angels.[g] 42 For I was hungry and you gave me nothing to eat, I was thirsty and you gave me nothing to drink, 43 I was a stranger and you did not invite me in, I needed clothes and you did not clothe me, I was sick and in prison and you did not look after me.'

44 "They also will answer, 'Lord, when did we see you hungry or thirsty or a stranger or needing clothes or sick or in prison, and did not help you?'

45 "He will reply, 'Truly I tell you, whatever you did not do for one of the least of these, you did not do for me.'[h]

46 "Then they will go away to eternal punishment, but the righteous to eternal life.[i]"[j]

The Plot Against Jesus

26:2-5pp — Mk 14:1,2; Lk 22:1,2

26 When Jesus had finished saying all these things,[k] he said to his disciples, 2 "As you know, the Passover[l] is two days away — and the Son of Man will be handed over to be crucified."

3 Then the chief priests and the elders of the people assembled[m] in the palace of the high priest, whose name was Caiaphas,[n] 4 and they schemed to arrest Jesus secretly and kill him.[o] 5 "But not during the festival," they said, "or there may be a riot[p] among the people."

Jesus Anointed at Bethany

26:6-13pp — Mk 14:3-9
26:6-13Ref — Lk 7:37,38; Jn 12:1-8

6 While Jesus was in Bethany[q] in the home of Simon the Leper, 7 a woman came to him with an alabaster jar of very expensive perfume, which she poured on his head as he was reclining at the table.

8 When the disciples saw this, they were indignant. "Why this waste?" they asked. 9 "This perfume could have been sold at a high price and the money given to the poor."

10 Aware of this, Jesus said to them, "Why are you bothering this woman? She has done a beautiful thing to me. 11 The poor you will always have with you,[a][r] but you will not always have me. 12 When she poured this perfume on my body, she did it to prepare me for burial.[s] 13 Truly I tell you, wherever this gospel is preached throughout the world, what she has done will also be told, in memory of her."

Judas Agrees to Betray Jesus

26:14-16pp — Mk 14:10,11; Lk 22:3-6

14 Then one of the Twelve — the one called Judas Iscariot[t] — went to the chief priests 15 and asked, "What are you willing to give me if I deliver him over to you?" So they counted out for him thirty pieces of silver.[u] 16 From then on Judas watched for an opportunity to hand him over.

The Last Supper

26:17-19pp — Mk 14:12-16; Lk 22:7-13
26:20-24pp — Mk 14:17-21
26:26-29pp — Mk 14:22-25; Lk 22:17-20; 1Co 11:23-25

17 On the first day of the Festival of Unleavened Bread,[v] the disciples came to Jesus and asked, "Where do you want us to make preparations for you to eat the Passover?"[w]

25:40 [d] S Mt 10:40,42; Heb 13:2
25:41 [e] S Mt 7:23 [f] Isa 66:24; Mt 3:12; S 5:22; Mk 9:43,48; Lk 3:17; Jude 7 [g] 2Pe 2:4
25:45 [h] Pr 14:31; 17:5
25:46 [i] Mt 19:29; Jn 3:15,16,36; 17:2,3; Ro 2:7; Gal 6:8; 1Jn 1:2; 5:11,13,20 [j] Da 12:2; Jn 5:29; Ac 24:15; Ro 2:7,8; Gal 6:8
26:1 [k] S Mt 7:28
26:2 [l] S Jn 11:55
26:3 [m] Ps 2:2 [n] ver 57; Lk 3:2; Jn 11:47-53; 18:13,14,24,28; Ac 4:6
26:4 [o] S Mt 12:14
26:5 [p] Mt 27:24
26:6 [q] S Mt 21:17
26:11 [r] Dt 15:11
26:12 [s] Jn 19:40
26:14 [t] ver 25,47; S Mt 10:4
26:15 [u] Ex 21:32; Zec 11:12
26:17 [v] Ex 12:18-20 [w] Dt 16:5-8

[a] *11* See Deut. 15:11.

Jesus refer? The principal views are: (1) all who are hungry, thirsty, poor, needy or otherwise distressed — but this seems too comprehensive; (2) apostles and other Christian missionaries — but this seems too restrictive; (3) the Jews mentioned in the first interpretation in the note on vv. 31 – 46; (4) Jesus' disciples (12:46 – 50; 28:8 – 10); (5) "God's people" mentioned in the second interpretation in the note on vv. 31 – 46.

25:41 *eternal fire prepared for the devil.* See Rev 20:10. *fire.* See Jude 7; Rev 19:20 and notes; 20:15.

25:46 *eternal punishment ... eternal life.* See Da 12:2; Jn 5:28 – 29; see also Jn 5:29; Ro 2:6 – 8; Gal 6:8 and notes. The parallelism between these two phrases prevents any weakening of the former.

26:2 *Passover.* See notes on Mk 14:1; Jn 2:13. *Son of Man.* See note on Mk 8:31.

26:3 *chief priests and the elders of the people.* The priestly and lay leadership of the Sanhedrin (see note on 2:4). *Caiaphas.* High priest AD 18 – 36 and the son-in-law of Annas (see Jn 18:13 and note), a former high priest, who served AD 6 – 15. In 1991 an ossuary (a limestone chest containing the bones of the dead) was found in Jerusalem inscribed with the name Caiaphas (see photo, p. 1643).

26:5 *there may be a riot.* Hundreds of thousands of Jewish pilgrims came to Jerusalem for Passover (see note on Mk 14:2), and riots were not unknown. The religious leaders (v. 3) knew that many people admired Jesus.

26:6 - 13 See note on Jn 12:1 – 11.

26:6 *Bethany.* See note on 21:17. *Simon the Leper.* Mentioned elsewhere only in Mk 14:3, though Simon was a common Jewish name in the first century. He was probably a well-known victim of leprosy who had been healed by Jesus.

26:7 *a woman.* Mary, sister of Martha and Lazarus (see Jn 12:3 and note). *alabaster jar.* Most alabaster of ancient times was actually marble (see note on Mk 14:3).

26:9 *given to the poor.* See note on Mk 14:5.

26:10 *beautiful.* The Greek word has an aesthetic as well as an ethical meaning.

26:11 *The poor you will always have with you.* See note on Mk 14:7.

26:12 *prepare me for burial.* See note on Mk 14:8.

26:14 *Iscariot.* See note on Mk 3:19. *chief priests.* See note on 2:4.

26:15 *thirty pieces of silver.* Equivalent to 120 denarii. Laborers customarily received one denarius for a day's work (20:1 – 16). See notes on 20:2; Zec 11:12.

26:17 *first day of the Festival of Unleavened Bread.* The 14th of

18 He replied, "Go into the city to a certain
man and tell him, 'The Teacher says: My
appointed time[x] is near. I am going to celebrate the Passover with my disciples at your
house.' " 19 So the disciples did as Jesus had
directed them and prepared the Passover.
20 When evening came, Jesus was reclining at the table with the Twelve. 21 And
while they were eating, he said, "Truly I
tell you, one of you will betray me."[y]
22 They were very sad and began to say
to him one after the other, "Surely you
don't mean me, Lord?"
23 Jesus replied, "The one who has
dipped his hand into the bowl with me
will betray me.[z] 24 The Son of Man will go
just as it is written about him.[a] But woe
to that man who betrays the Son of Man!
It would be better for him if he had not
been born."
25 Then Judas, the one who would betray him,[b] said, "Surely you don't mean
me, Rabbi?"[c]
Jesus answered, "You have said so."
26 While they were eating, Jesus took
bread, and when he had given thanks, he
broke it[d] and gave it to his disciples, saying, "Take and eat; this is my body."
27 Then he took a cup,[e] and when he had
given thanks, he gave it to them, saying,
"Drink from it, all of you. 28 This is my
blood of the[a] covenant,[f] which is poured
out for many for the forgiveness of sins.[g]
29 I tell you, I will not drink from this fruit
of the vine from now on until that day
when I drink it new with you[h] in my Father's kingdom."

30 When they had sung a hymn, they
went out to the Mount of Olives.[i]

Jesus Predicts Peter's Denial

26:31-35pp — Mk 14:27-31; Lk 22:31-34

31 Then Jesus told them, "This very
night you will all fall away on account of
me,[j] for it is written:

"'I will strike the shepherd,
and the sheep of the flock will be
scattered.'[b][k]

32 But after I have risen, I will go ahead of
you into Galilee."[l]
33 Peter replied, "Even if all fall away on
account of you, I never will."
34 "Truly I tell you," Jesus answered,
"this very night, before the rooster crows,
you will disown me three times."[m]
35 But Peter declared, "Even if I have to
die with you,[n] I will never disown you."
And all the other disciples said the same.

Gethsemane

26:36-46pp — Mk 14:32-42; Lk 22:40-46

36 Then Jesus went with his disciples to
a place called Gethsemane, and he said to
them, "Sit here while I go over there and
pray." 37 He took Peter and the two sons of
Zebedee[o] along with him, and he began to
be sorrowful and troubled. 38 Then he said
to them, "My soul is overwhelmed with
sorrow[p] to the point of death. Stay here
and keep watch with me."[q]

26:18 [x] Mk 14:35,41; Jn 7:6,8,30; 8:20; 12:23; 13:1; 17:1
26:21 [y] Lk 22:21-23; Jn 13:21
26:23 [z] Ps 41:9; Jn 13:18
26:24 [a] ver 31, 54,56; Isa 53; Da 9:26; Mk 9:12; Lk 24:25-27,46; Ac 17:2,3; 26:22,23; 1Pe 1:10,11
26:25 [b] S Mt 10:4 [c] S Mt 23:7
26:26 [d] S Mt 14:19
26:27 [e] 1Co 10:16
26:28 [f] Ex 24:6-8; Zec 9:11; Mal 2:5; Heb 9:20; 10:29; S 13:20 [g] S Mt 20:28; Mk 1:4
26:29 [h] Ac 10:41
26:30 [i] S Mt 21:1
26:31 [j] Mt 11:6; 13:21 [k] Zec 13:7; Jn 16:32
26:32 [l] Mt 28:7,10,16
26:34 [m] ver 75; Jn 13:38
26:35 [n] Jn 13:37
26:37 [o] S Mt 4:21
26:38 [p] S Jn 12:27 [q] ver 40,41

[a] 28 Some manuscripts *the new* [b] 31 Zech. 13:7

Nisan (March-April), it was also called the preparation of the Passover. The Passover meal was eaten the evening of the 14th after sunset — and therefore technically on the 15th, since the Jewish day ended at sunset. The Festival of Unleavened Bread lasted seven days, from the 15th to the 21st of Nisan (see Lev 23:5–6), but in the time of Christ the entire period, Nisan 14–21, was referred to under that name (see note on Mk 14:12).

26:18–30 These verses indicate that Jesus ate the Passover meal with his disciples the night before his crucifixion. For more information on the Lord's Supper, see notes on Mk 14:22,24.

26:18 *The Teacher says.* See note on Lk 22:11. *My appointed time.* Jesus' crucifixion.

26:19 *as Jesus had directed them.* See note on Lk 22:13. *prepared the Passover.* See note on Mk 14:15.

26:20 *When evening came.* See note on Mk 14:17. *reclining at the table.* See note on Mk 14:18.

26:21 *Truly I tell you.* See note on Mk 3:28.

26:23 *dipped his hand into the bowl with me.* It was the custom — still practiced by some in the Middle East — to take a piece of bread, or a piece of meat wrapped in bread, and dip it into a bowl of sauce (made of stewed fruit) on the table. *will betray me.* In that culture, as among Arabs today, to eat with a person was tantamount to saying, "I am your friend and will not hurt you." This fact made Judas's deed all the more despicable (cf. Ps 41:9 and note).

26:24 *as it is written about him.* See notes on Mk 14:21; Lk 24:44. *Son of Man.* See note on Mk 8:31.

26:26–28 See notes on Mk 14:22–24.

26:27 *took a cup.* See note on Lk 22:17.

26:28 *blood of the covenant . . . poured out for many.* See note on Mk 14:24.

26:29 *drink it new . . . in my Father's kingdom.* At the Messianic banquet (see Lk 22:16 and note).

26:30 *hymn.* The Passover fellowship was concluded with the second half of the Egyptian Hallel Psalms (Ps 115–118). Ps 113–114 were sung before the meal. *Mount of Olives.* See note on Mk 11:1.

26:31 *all fall away.* Not Peter only, but all the eleven (Judas had previously withdrawn, Jn 13:30). The meaning of the words "fall away" is seen in Peter's denial (vv. 69–75) and in the terrified flight of the other disciples (v. 56). *I will strike the shepherd.* See note on Zec 13:7.

26:32 *into Galilee.* Cf. 28:10,16–20; Mk 16:7; Jn 21:1–23.

26:34 *before the rooster crows.* The reference may be to the third of the Roman watches into which the night was divided (see note on 14:25; see also Mk 13:35 and note). Or it may simply refer to early morning when the rooster crows.

26:36 *Gethsemane.* The name means "oil press," a place for squeezing the oil from olives (see note on Mk 14:32).

26:37 *Peter and the two sons of Zebedee.* The latter were James and John. These three disciples seem to have been especially close to Jesus (see note on Mk 5:37).

39 Going a little farther, he fell with his
face to the ground and prayed, "My Father, if it is possible, may this cup[r] be tak-
en from me. Yet not as I will, but as you
will."[s]
40 Then he returned to his disciples and
found them sleeping. "Couldn't you men
keep watch with me[t] for one hour?" he
asked Peter. 41 "Watch and pray so that you
will not fall into temptation.[u] The spirit is
willing, but the flesh is weak."
42 He went away a second time and
prayed, "My Father, if it is not possible for
this cup to be taken away unless I drink it,
may your will be done."[v]
43 When he came back, he again found
them sleeping, because their eyes were
heavy. 44 So he left them and went away
once more and prayed the third time, saying the same thing.
45 Then he returned to the disciples and
said to them, "Are you still sleeping and
resting? Look, the hour[w] has come, and the
Son of Man is delivered into the hands of
sinners. 46 Rise! Let us go! Here comes my
betrayer!"

Jesus Arrested

26:47-56pp — Mk 14:43-50; Lk 22:47-53

47 While he was still speaking, Judas,[x]
one of the Twelve, arrived. With him was
a large crowd armed with swords and
clubs, sent from the chief priests and the
elders of the people. 48 Now the betrayer
had arranged a signal with them: "The
one I kiss is the man; arrest him." 49 Going
at once to Jesus, Judas said, "Greetings,
Rabbi!"[y] and kissed him.
50 Jesus replied, "Do what you came for,
friend."[a][z]
Then the men stepped forward, seized
Jesus and arrested him. 51 With that, one of
Jesus' companions reached for his sword,[a]
drew it out and struck the servant of the
high priest, cutting off his ear.[b]
52 "Put your sword back in its place,"
Jesus said to him, "for all who draw the
sword will die by the sword.[c] 53 Do you
think I cannot call on my Father, and he
will at once put at my disposal more than
twelve legions of angels?[d] 54 But how then
would the Scriptures be fulfilled[e] that say
it must happen in this way?"
55 In that hour Jesus said to the crowd,
"Am I leading a rebellion, that you have
come out with swords and clubs to capture
me? Every day I sat in the temple courts
teaching,[f] and you did not arrest me. 56 But
this has all taken place that the writings of
the prophets might be fulfilled."[g] Then all
the disciples deserted him and fled.

Jesus Before the Sanhedrin

26:57-68pp — Mk 14:53-65; Jn 18:12,13,19-24

57 Those who had arrested Jesus took
him to Caiaphas[h] the high priest, where
the teachers of the law and the elders had
assembled. 58 But Peter followed him at a
distance, right up to the courtyard of the
high priest.[i] He entered and sat down with
the guards[j] to see the outcome.
59 The chief priests and the whole Sanhedrin[k] were looking for false evidence
against Jesus so that they could put him to
death. 60 But they did not find any, though
many false witnesses[l] came forward.
Finally two[m] came forward 61 and declared, "This fellow said, 'I am able to destroy the temple of God and rebuild it in
three days.' "[n]
62 Then the high priest stood up and said
to Jesus, "Are you not going to answer?
What is this testimony that these men
are bringing against you?" 63 But Jesus remained silent.[o]

26:39 [r]S Mt 20:22 [s]ver 42; Ps 40:6-8; Isa 50:5; Mt 6:10; Jn 4:34; 5:30; 6:38 **26:40** [t]ver 38 **26:41** [u]Mt 6:13 **26:42** [v]S ver 39 **26:45** [w]S ver 18 **26:47** [x]S Mt 10:4 **26:49** [y]ver 25; S Mt 23:7 **26:50** [z]Mt 20:13; 22:12 **26:51** [a]Lk 22:36, 38

[b]Jn 18:10 **26:52** [c]Ge 9:6; Ex 21:12; Rev 13:10 **26:53** [d]2Ki 6:17; Da 7:10; Mt 4:11 **26:54** [e]S ver 24; S Mt 1:22 **26:55** [f]Mk 12:35; Lk 21:37; Jn 7:14, 28; 18:20 **26:56** [g]S ver 24; S Mt 1:22 **26:57** [h]S ver 3 **26:58** [i]ver 69; Mk 14:66; Lk 22:55; Jn 18:15 [j]Mk 15:16; Lk 11:21; Jn 7:32, 45, 46 **26:59** [k]S Mt 5:22 **26:60** [l]Ps 27:12; 35:11; Ac 6:13 [m]Dt 19:15 **26:61** [n]S Jn 2:19 **26:63** [o]S Mk 14:61

[a] 50 Or *"Why have you come, friend?"*

26:38–39 Jesus did not die serenely as many martyrs have. He was no mere martyr; he was the Lamb of God bearing the penalty of the sins of the entire human race. The wrath of God was turned loose on him. Only this can adequately explain what took place at Gethsemane.

26:38 *soul.* See 10:28 and note. *overwhelmed with sorrow.* See Isa 53:3 and note.

26:39 *cup.* A symbol of deep sorrow and suffering. Here it refers to his Father's face being turned away from him when he who had no sin was made sin (perhaps a sin offering) for us (see 27:46; 2Co 5:21 and note).

26:41 See note on Mk 14:38.

26:45 *the hour.* See note on Lk 22:53. *Son of Man.* See note on Mk 8:31.

26:47 *Judas.* See notes on Jn 6:70; 17:12. *large crowd armed with swords and clubs.* See note on Mk 14:43. *chief priests and the elders.* See notes on v. 3; 2:4.

26:48 *The one I kiss.* See note on Lk 22:47.

26:49 *Rabbi.* Hebrew word for "(my) teacher." *kissed him.* See notes on Mk 14:45; Lk 22:47.

26:50 *friend.* See note on 20:13.

26:51 *one of Jesus' companions.* Peter (see Jn 18:10 and note). *servant of the high priest.* Malchus (see Jn 18:10 and note). *cutting off his ear.* Perhaps Peter aimed at Malchus's head but missed and only succeeded in "cutting off his ear."

26:53 *legions.* A Roman legion had 6,000 soldiers.

26:54 *Scriptures be fulfilled.* In view of v. 56 probably a reference to Zec 13:7 (see notes on Mk 14:49; Lk 24:44).

26:55 Jesus protested the manner of his arrest. The crowd sent by the Sanhedrin (see note on Mk 14:55) had come after him as if he were a dangerous criminal or insurrectionist.

26:56 *disciples deserted him.* Contrast v. 35.

26:57—27:26 For a summary of the two stages (religious and civil) of the trial of Jesus see note on Mk 14:53—15:15.

26:57 *Caiaphas.* See v. 3; Jn 11:49 and notes. *teachers of the law.* See note on 2:4. *elders.* See notes on Ex 3:16; 2Sa 3:17.

26:59 *Sanhedrin.* See note on Mk 14:55.

26:61 *I am able to destroy the temple of God.* Possibly an intentional distortion of Jesus' words (see Mk 14:58; Jn 2:19 and notes).

The ossuary ("bone box") of Caiaphas was found in Jerusalem and dates to the first century. The inscription on the side of the box reads, "Joseph son of Caiaphas." Joseph Caiaphas, high priest from AD 18 to 36, is chiefly known for his involvement in the arrest of Jesus, trying Jesus for blasphemy and eventually handing him over to Pontius Pilate.

Z. Radovan/www.BibleLandPictures.com

The high priest said to him, "I charge
you under oath[p] by the living God:[q] Tell
us if you are the Messiah,[r] the Son of
God."[s]
64 "You have said so,"[t] Jesus replied.
"But I say to all of you: From now on you
will see the Son of Man sitting at the right
hand of the Mighty One[u] and coming on
the clouds of heaven."[a][v]
65 Then the high priest tore his clothes[w]
and said, "He has spoken blasphemy!
Why do we need any more witnesses?
Look, now you have heard the blasphemy. 66 What do you think?"
"He is worthy of death,"[x] they answered.
67 Then they spit in his face and struck
him with their fists.[y] Others slapped him
68 and said, "Prophesy to us, Messiah.
Who hit you?"[z]

26:63 [p] Lev 5:1 [q] S Mt 16:16 [r] Lk 22:67 [s] S Mt 4:3
26:64 [t] Mt 27:11; Lk 22:70 [u] S Mk 16:19 [v] S Rev 1:7
26:65 [w] S Mk 14:63
26:66 [x] Lev 24:16; Jn 19:7
26:67 [y] S Mt 16:21
26:68 [z] Lk 22:63-65

Peter Disowns Jesus

26:69-75pp — Mk 14:66-72; Lk 22:55-62; Jn 18:16-18,25-27

69 Now Peter was sitting out in the courtyard, and a servant girl came to him. "You
also were with Jesus of Galilee," she said.
70 But he denied it before them all. "I
don't know what you're talking about,"
he said.
71 Then he went out to the gateway,
where another servant girl saw him and
said to the people there, "This fellow was
with Jesus of Nazareth."
72 He denied it again, with an oath: "I
don't know the man!"
73 After a little while, those standing
there went up to Peter and said, "Surely
you are one of them; your accent gives
you away."
74 Then he began to call down curses, and
he swore to them, "I don't know the man!"
Immediately a rooster crowed. 75 Then
Peter remembered the word Jesus had
spoken: "Before the rooster crows, you
will disown me three times."[a] And he went
outside and wept bitterly.

Judas Hangs Himself

27 Early in the morning, all the chief
priests and the elders of the people made their plans how to have Jesus
executed.[b] 2 So they bound him, led him
away and handed him over[c] to Pilate the
governor.[d]
3 When Judas, who had betrayed him,[e]
saw that Jesus was condemned, he was
seized with remorse and returned the thirty pieces of silver[f] to the chief priests and
the elders. 4 "I have sinned," he said, "for I
have betrayed innocent blood."
"What is that to us?" they replied.
"That's your responsibility."[g]
5 So Judas threw the money into the
temple[h] and left. Then he went away and
hanged himself.[i]

26:75 [a] ver 34; Jn 13:38
27:1 [b] S Mt 12:14; Mk 15:1; Lk 22:66
27:2 [c] Mt 20:19 [d] Mk 15:1; Lk 13:1; Ac 3:13; 1Ti 6:13
27:3 [e] S Mt 10:4 [f] Mt 26:14,15
27:4 [g] ver 24
27:5 [h] Lk 1:9,21 [i] Ac 1:18

[a] 64 See Psalm 110:1; Daniel 7:13.

26:63 *I charge you under oath.* Jesus refused to answer the question of v. 62 (see v. 63a). But when the high priest used this form, Jesus was legally obliged to reply. *Messiah.* See note on 16:16.
26:64 This Son of Man saying brings together Ps 110:1 and Da 7:13. This combination indicates that Jesus will share God's rule in heaven and will judge all people. See Mt 17:5; 24:30 and notes.
26:65 *tore his clothes.* Ordinarily the high priest was forbidden by law to do this (Lev 10:6; 21:10), but this was considered a highly unusual circumstance. The high priest interpreted Jesus' answer in v. 64 as blasphemy (see note on Mk 14:64).
26:67 – 68 Mark (14:65) and Luke (22:64) report that they blindfolded Jesus, which explains the mocking command: "Prophesy ... Who hit you?"
26:73 *After a little while.* Lk 22:59 says "About an hour later." *your accent gives you away.* Peter had a Galilean accent that was conspicuous in Jerusalem.
27:1 *Early in the morning.* Continues the narrative from 26:68. The Sanhedrin could not have a legal session at night, so at daybreak they held a special meeting to make the death sentence (see 26:66) official. See notes on Mk 14:53 — 15:15; 15:1; Lk 22:66; Jn 18:28.
27:2 *handed him over to Pilate.* The Sanhedrin had been deprived by the Roman government of the right to carry out capital punishment, except in the case of a foreigner who entered the sacred precincts of the temple. So Jesus had to be handed over to Pilate for execution. For additional information about Pilate, see note on Lk 3:1.
27:3 – 10 See Ac 1:16 – 19.
27:3 *thirty pieces of silver.* See 26:15 and note.
27:5 *temple.* Probably the treasury room of the temple (see v. 6). *hanged himself.* See note on Ac 1:18.

6 The chief priests picked up the coins
and said, "It is against the law to put this
into the treasury, since it is blood money."
7 So they decided to use the money to buy
the potter's field as a burial place for foreigners. 8 That is why it has been called
the Field of Blood[j] to this day. 9 Then what
was spoken by Jeremiah the prophet was
fulfilled:[k] "They took the thirty pieces of
silver, the price set on him by the people
of Israel, 10 and they used them to buy the
potter's field, as the Lord commanded
me."[a][l]

Jesus Before Pilate

27:11-26pp — Mk 15:2-15; Lk 23:2,3,18-25; Jn 18:29-19:16

11 Meanwhile Jesus stood before the governor, and the governor asked him, "Are
you the king of the Jews?"[m]
"You have said so," Jesus replied.
12 When he was accused by the chief
priests and the elders, he gave no answer.[n] 13 Then Pilate asked him, "Don't
you hear the testimony they are bringing
against you?"[o] 14 But Jesus made no reply,[p]
not even to a single charge—to the great
amazement of the governor.
15 Now it was the governor's custom at
the festival to release a prisoner[q] chosen
by the crowd. 16 At that time they had a
well-known prisoner whose name was
Jesus[b] Barabbas. 17 So when the crowd had
gathered, Pilate asked them, "Which one
do you want me to release to you: Jesus
Barabbas, or Jesus who is called the Messiah?"[r] 18 For he knew it was out of self-
interest that they had handed Jesus over
to him.
19 While Pilate was sitting on the judge's
seat,[s] his wife sent him this message:
"Don't have anything to do with that innocent[t] man, for I have suffered a great
deal today in a dream[u] because of him."
20 But the chief priests and the elders
persuaded the crowd to ask for Barabbas
and to have Jesus executed.[v]
21 "Which of the two do you want me to
release to you?" asked the governor.
"Barabbas," they answered.
22 "What shall I do, then, with Jesus
who is called the Messiah?"[w] Pilate asked.
They all answered, "Crucify him!"
23 "Why? What crime has he committed?" asked Pilate.
But they shouted all the louder, "Crucify him!"
24 When Pilate saw that he was getting
nowhere, but that instead an uproar[x] was
starting, he took water and washed his
hands[y] in front of the crowd. "I am innocent of this man's blood,"[z] he said. "It is
your responsibility!"[a]
25 All the people answered, "His blood is
on us and on our children!"[b]
26 Then he released Barabbas to them.
But he had Jesus flogged,[c] and handed
him over to be crucified.

The Soldiers Mock Jesus

27:27-31pp — Mk 15:16-20

27 Then the governor's soldiers took
Jesus into the Praetorium[d] and gathered
the whole company of soldiers around
him. 28 They stripped him and put a scarlet
robe on him,[e] 29 and then twisted together
a crown of thorns and set it on his head.

27:8 [j] Ac 1:19 **27:9** [k] S Mt 1:22 **27:10** [l] Zec 11:12,13; Jer 32:6-9 **27:11** [m] S Mt 2:2 **27:12** [n] S Mk 14:61 **27:13** [o] Mt 26:62 **27:14** [p] S Mk 14:61 **27:15** [q] Jn 18:39 **27:17** [r] ver 22; Mt 1:16

27:19 [s] Jn 19:13 [t] ver 24 [u] Ge 20:6; Nu 12:6; 1Ki 3:5; Job 33:14-16; Mt 1:20; 2:12, 13,19,22 **27:20** [v] Ac 3:14 **27:22** [w] Mt 1:16 **27:24** [x] Mt 26:5 [y] Ps 26:6 [z] Dt 21:6-8 [a] ver 4 **27:25** [b] Jos 2:19; S Ac 5:28 **27:26** [c] Isa 53:5; Jn 19:1 **27:27** [d] Jn 18:28,33; 19:9 **27:28** [e] Jn 19:2

[a] *10* See Zech. 11:12,13; Jer. 19:1-13; 32:6-9.
[b] *16* Many manuscripts do not have *Jesus;* also in verse 17.

27:8 *Field of Blood.* Cf. "Valley of Slaughter" in Jer 19:6.
27:9 *Jeremiah.* The quotation that follows seems to combine Zec 11:12–13 and Jer 19:1–13 (or perhaps Jer 18:2–12 or 32:6–9). But Matthew attributes it to the better-known prophet Jeremiah, just as Mark (1:2–3) quotes Mal 3:1 and Isa 40:3 but attributes them both to the better-known prophet Isaiah (see note on Mk 1:2).
27:11 *governor.* Pontius Pilate (see note on v. 2). *king of the Jews.* See note on Jn 18:33.
27:14 *Jesus made no reply.* See 26:63; Mk 15:4; Isa 53:7 and notes. *amazement of the governor.* Probably because he had never seen such behavior before. He had no idea that Jesus was carrying out his Father's plan for the redemption of the world (see note on Mk 15:4).
27:15 *governor's custom.* Of which nothing is known outside the Gospels.
27:16 *well-known.* The Greek word here probably means "outstanding" or "notable" (cf. Ro 16:7). Barabbas had taken part in a rebellion (Lk 23:19; Jn 18:40), presumably against the Romans. So he would have been a folk hero among the Jews. See notes on Mk 15:7; Lk 23:18; Jn 18:40. Some manuscripts use Barabbas's full name, Jesus Barabbas, in vv. 16–17 (as in the NIV; see NIV text note on v. 16). If that is the correct reading, it sharpens the point of Pilate's question in v. 17.
27:19 Matthew is the only writer who records this incident. *dream.* Dreams play an important role in the life of Jesus in Matthew's Gospel (see 1:20; 2:12,13, 19,22).
27:24 *washed his hands.* See Dt 21:6; Ps 26:6 and notes; 73:13.
27:25 The people accept responsibility for their choice. Sadly, their words have often been inappropriately used to justify persecution of the Jewish people. If there was a fulfillment of their declaration, it was most likely in the destruction of Jerusalem in AD 70. All the following passages should be studied regarding responsibility for Christ's death on the cross: Isa 53:10; Ac 2:23; Jn 10:17–18; Heb 9:14; Mt 26:47,50,57,59,63–66; 27:1–2,20,22,26–27,31,41; Ro 5:8. Because of these and other similar Scriptures, a truly Biblical Christian should never be guilty of anti-Semitism.
27:26 *flogged.* Roman floggings were so brutal that sometimes the victim died before crucifixion (see note on Mk 15:15).
27:27 *Praetorium.* The governor's official residence in Jerusalem (see notes on Mk 15:16; Ac 23:25).
27:28 *scarlet robe.* The outer cloak of a Roman soldier. Mk 15:17,20; Jn 19:2,5 describe it as purple.
27:29 *crown of thorns.* See note on Mk 15:17. *staff.* A mock scepter. *Hail, king of the Jews!* See note on Mk 15:18.

They put a staff in his right hand. Then
they knelt in front of him and mocked
him. "Hail, king of the Jews!" they said.[f]
30 They spit on him, and took the staff and
struck him on the head again and again.[g]
31 After they had mocked him, they took
off the robe and put his own clothes on
him. Then they led him away to crucify
him.[h]

The Crucifixion of Jesus

27:33-44pp — Mk 15:22-32; Lk 23:33-43; Jn 19:17-24

32 As they were going out,[i] they met
a man from Cyrene,[j] named Simon,
and they forced him to carry the cross.[k]
33 They came to a place called Golgotha
(which means "the place of the skull").[l]
34 There they offered Jesus wine to drink,
mixed with gall;[m] but after tasting it, he
refused to drink it. 35 When they had crucified him, they divided up his clothes
by casting lots.[n] 36 And sitting down, they
kept watch[o] over him there. 37 Above
his head they placed the written charge
against him: THIS IS JESUS, THE KING OF THE
JEWS.

38 Two rebels were crucified with him,[p]
one on his right and one on his left.
39 Those who passed by hurled insults at
him, shaking their heads[q] 40 and saying,
"You who are going to destroy the temple
and build it in three days,[r] save yourself![s]
Come down from the cross, if you are the
Son of God!"[t] 41 In the same way the chief
priests, the teachers of the law and the
elders mocked him. 42 "He saved others,"
they said, "but he can't save himself! He's
the king of Israel![u] Let him come down
now from the cross, and we will believe[v]
in him. 43 He trusts in God. Let God rescue
him[w] now if he wants him, for he said, 'I
am the Son of God.'" 44 In the same way
the rebels who were crucified with him
also heaped insults on him.

27:29 [f] Isa 53:3; Jn 19:2,3 **27:30** [g] S Mt 16:21 **27:31** [h] Isa 53:7 **27:32** [i] Heb 13:12 [j] Ac 2:10; 6:9; 11:20; 13:1 [k] Mk 15:21; Lk 23:26 **27:33** [l] Jn 19:17 **27:34** [m] ver 48; Ps 69:21 **27:35** [n] Ps 22:18 **27:36** [o] ver 54 **27:38** [p] Isa 53:12 **27:39** [q] Ps 22:7; 109:25; La 2:15 **27:40** [r] S Jn 2:19 [s] ver 42 [t] Mt 4:3,6 **27:42** [u] Jn 1:49; 12:13 [v] S Jn 3:15 **27:43** [w] Ps 22:8

The Death of Jesus

27:45-56pp — Mk 15:33-41; Lk 23:44-49; Jn 19:29-30

45 From noon until three in the afternoon
darkness[x] came over all the land. 46 About
three in the afternoon Jesus cried out in a
loud voice, *"Eli, Eli,*[a] *lema sabachthani?"*
(which means "My God, my God, why
have you forsaken me?").[b][y]

47 When some of those standing there
heard this, they said, "He's calling Elijah."

48 Immediately one of them ran and got a
sponge. He filled it with wine vinegar,[z] put
it on a staff, and offered it to Jesus to drink.
49 The rest said, "Now leave him alone.
Let's see if Elijah comes to save him."

50 And when Jesus had cried out again
in a loud voice, he gave up his spirit.[a]

51 At that moment the curtain of the temple[b] was torn in two from top to bottom.
The earth shook, the rocks split[c] 52 and the
tombs broke open. The bodies of many
holy people who had died were raised to
life. 53 They came out of the tombs after
Jesus' resurrection and[c] went into the holy
city[d] and appeared to many people.

54 When the centurion and those with
him who were guarding[e] Jesus saw the
earthquake and all that had happened,
they were terrified, and exclaimed, "Surely
he was the Son of God!"[f]

55 Many women were there, watching from a distance. They had followed
Jesus from Galilee to care for his needs.[g]
56 Among them were Mary Magdalene,
Mary the mother of James and Joseph,[d]
and the mother of Zebedee's sons.[h]

The Burial of Jesus

27:57-61pp — Mk 15:42-47; Lk 23:50-56; Jn 19:38-42

57 As evening approached, there came
a rich man from Arimathea, named

27:45 [x] Am 8:9 **27:46** [y] Ps 22:1 **27:48** [z] ver 34; Ps 69:21 **27:50** [a] Jn 19:30 **27:51** [b] Ex 26:31-33; Heb 9:3,8; 10:19,20 [c] ver 54 **27:53** [d] S Mt 4:5 **27:54** [e] ver 36 [f] S Mt 4:3; 17:5 **27:55** [g] Lk 8:2,3 **27:56** [h] Mk 15:47; Lk 24:10; Jn 19:25

[a] 46 Some manuscripts *Eloi, Eloi* [b] 46 Psalm 22:1
[c] 53 Or *tombs, and after Jesus' resurrection they*
[d] 56 Greek *Joses,* a variant of *Joseph*

27:30–31 See Isa 50:6 and note.
27:30 *spit on him.* See note on Mk 15:19.
27:32 *they.* See v. 27. *Cyrene.* See note on Mk 15:21. *Simon … to carry the cross.* See note on Mk 15:21.
27:33 *Golgotha.* See note on Mk 15:22.
27:34 *mixed with gall.* Tradition says that the women of Jerusalem customarily furnished this pain-killing narcotic to prisoners who were crucified. Jesus refused to drink it because he wanted to be fully conscious until his death (v. 50).
27:35 *crucified.* See note on Mk 15:24. *casting lots.* Explained more precisely in Jn 19:23–24 (see notes there; see also NIV text note on Jn 19:24).
27:37 See notes on Mk 15:26; Lk 23:38; Jn 19:19.
27:38 *Two rebels.* See note on Mk 15:27.
27:39 *shaking their heads.* See Ps 22:7 and note.
27:41 *chief priests, the teachers of the law and the elders.* The Sanhedrin (see note on v. 1).
27:43 See Ps 22:8 and note.
27:46 *Eli, Eli, lema sabachthani?* Here Jesus spoke a dialect of Aramaic, which Matthew translates for his readers (see note on Mk 15:34).
27:47 *Elijah.* See note on Mk 15:35.
27:48 *sponge.* See note on Jn 19:29. *wine vinegar.* See notes on Mk 15:36; Lk 23:36; Jn 19:29.
27:49 See note on Mk 15:35.
27:50 *loud voice.* See note on Jn 19:30.
27:51 *curtain.* The curtain that separated the Holy Place from the Most Holy Place. The tearing of the curtain signified Christ's making it possible for believers to go directly into God's presence (see Mk 15:38; Lk 23:45; Heb 9:1–14; 10:14–22 and notes).
27:54 *centurion.* See note on 8:5. *Son of God.* See note on Lk 23:47.
27:55 *women … to care for his needs.* Women played a significant role in the ministry of Jesus (see Mk 15:41; Lk 23:49) and his disciples (see Lk 8:3 and note).
27:56 See notes on Mk 15:40; Lk 24:10.
27:57 *Arimathea.* A village in the hill country of Ephraim,

Joseph, who had himself become a disciple of Jesus. 58 Going to Pilate, he asked
for Jesus' body, and Pilate ordered that it
be given to him. 59 Joseph took the body,
wrapped it in a clean linen cloth, 60 and
placed it in his own new tomb[i] that he had
cut out of the rock. He rolled a big stone in
front of the entrance to the tomb and went
away. 61 Mary Magdalene and the other
Mary were sitting there opposite the tomb.

The Guard at the Tomb

62 The next day, the one after Preparation Day, the chief priests and the Pharisees went to Pilate. 63 "Sir," they said, "we
remember that while he was still alive that
deceiver said, 'After three days I will rise
again.'[j] 64 So give the order for the tomb to
be made secure until the third day. Otherwise, his disciples may come and steal the
body[k] and tell the people that he has been
raised from the dead. This last deception
will be worse than the first."
65 "Take a guard,"[l] Pilate answered. "Go,
make the tomb as secure as you know
how." 66 So they went and made the tomb
secure by putting a seal[m] on the stone[n] and
posting the guard.[o]

Jesus Has Risen

28:1-8pp — Mk 16:1-8; Lk 24:1-10; Jn 20:1-8

28 After the Sabbath, at dawn on the
first day of the week, Mary Magdalene[p] and the other Mary[q] went to look at
the tomb.
2 There was a violent earthquake,[r] for an
angel[s] of the Lord came down from heav-
en and, going to the tomb, rolled back the
stone[t] and sat on it. 3 His appearance was
like lightning, and his clothes were white
as snow.[u] 4 The guards were so afraid of him
that they shook and became like dead men.
5 The angel said to the women, "Do not
be afraid,[v] for I know that you are looking
for Jesus, who was crucified. 6 He is not
here; he has risen, just as he said.[w] Come
and see the place where he lay. 7 Then go
quickly and tell his disciples: 'He has risen
from the dead and is going ahead of you
into Galilee.[x] There you will see him.' Now
I have told you."
8 So the women hurried away from the
tomb, afraid yet filled with joy, and ran
to tell his disciples. 9 Suddenly Jesus met
them.[y] "Greetings," he said. They came to
him, clasped his feet and worshiped him.
10 Then Jesus said to them, "Do not be
afraid. Go and tell my brothers[z] to go to
Galilee; there they will see me."

The Guards' Report

11 While the women were on their way,
some of the guards[a] went into the city
and reported to the chief priests everything that had happened. 12 When the
chief priests had met with the elders and
devised a plan, they gave the soldiers a
large sum of money, 13 telling them, "You
are to say, 'His disciples came during the
night and stole him away[b] while we were
asleep.' 14 If this report gets to the governor,[c] we will satisfy him and keep you
out of trouble." 15 So the soldiers took the
money and did as they were instructed.
And this story has been widely circulated
among the Jews to this very day.

The Great Commission

16 Then the eleven disciples went to Galilee, to the mountain where Jesus had told

27:60 [i] Mt 27:66; 28:2; Mk 16:4; Ac 13:29
27:63 [j] S Mt 16:21
27:64 [k] Mt 28:13
27:65 [l] ver 66; Mt 28:11
27:66 [m] Da 6:17 [n] ver 60; Mt 28:2 [o] Mt 28:11
28:1 [p] Lk 8:2 [q] Mt 27:56
28:2 [r] Mt 27:51 [s] Jn 20:12; S Ac 5:19 [t] Mt 27:60
28:3 [u] Da 7:9; 10:6; Mk 9:3; S Jn 20:12
28:5 [v] ver 10; S Mt 14:27
28:6 [w] S Mt 16:21
28:7 [x] ver 10, 16; Mt 26:32
28:9 [y] Jn 20:14-18
28:10 [z] Mt 12:50; 25:40; Mk 3:34; Jn 20:17; Ro 8:29; Heb 2:11-13, 17
28:11 [a] Mt 27:65, 66
28:13 [b] Mt 27:64
28:14 [c] S Mt 27:2

---

about 20 miles northwest of Jerusalem; perhaps to be identified with Ramathaim, the birthplace of the prophet Samuel (see 1Sa 1:1 and note). *Joseph.* See notes on Lk 23:50; Jn 19:38.
27:58 *asked for Jesus' body.* See note on Lk 23:52.
27:60 *new tomb.* See note on Mk 15:46.
27:61 *the other Mary.* Presumably the mother of James and Joseph (v. 56).
27:62 *The next day, the one after Preparation Day.* Saturday, the Sabbath. Friday was the preparation day for the Sabbath (sunset Friday to sunset Saturday).
27:64 *This last deception will be worse than the first.* The first would be that Jesus was the Messiah, the second that he had risen as the Son of God.
27:65 *Take a guard.* Either of Roman soldiers or of their own temple police; 28:14 implies that they were answerable to Pilate ("the governor"), which may favor Roman soldiers. On the other hand, the fact that in 28:11 they "reported to the chief priests" (instead of to Pilate) may favor temple police, who would have been under the authority of the religious leaders. ("Take a guard" may also be rendered "You have a guard.")
28:1 *first day of the week.* See note on Lk 24:1. *the other Mary.* See note on 27:61. Mk 16:1 adds Salome, and Lk 24:10 adds Joanna.
28:2 *There was.* The sense is "Now there had been." The parallel accounts (Mk 16:2–6; Lk 24:1–7; Jn 20:1) make it clear that the events of vv. 2–4 occurred before the women actually arrived at the tomb. *violent earthquake.* Only Matthew mentions this earthquake and the one at Jesus' death (27:51,54).
28:6 *just as he said.* See 16:21 and note.
28:7 *going ahead of you into Galilee.* See 26:32 and note.
28:10 *my brothers.* His "disciples" (v. 16).
28:11–15 Only Matthew tells of the posting of the guard (27:62–66), and he follows up by telling about their report.
28:11 *reported to the chief priests.* See note on 27:65.
28:13 *His disciples … stole him away.* One of many human attempts to explain away Christ's resurrection. *while we were asleep.* It is more likely that Jewish temple police would be willing to admit to such dereliction of duty than Roman soldiers would.
28:14 See note on 27:65.
28:16–20 Christ's Great Commission for his church (cf. also Mk 16:15–18; Lk 24:46–48; Jn 17:18; 20:21; Ac 1:8 and relevant notes).
28:16 *eleven.* Judas had committed suicide (see 27:5 and note). *mountain.* Cf. note on 5:1. *had told them.* See v. 10.

The Garden Tomb, thought by many to fit the Bible's description of the tomb where Jesus' body was placed, is visited by hundreds of thousands of visitors each year. The Garden Tomb is typical of a first-century tomb with a groove for a stone that would be rolled in front of it to close it.

them to go.[d] 17 When they saw him, they
worshiped him; but some doubted. 18 Then
Jesus came to them and said, "All authority in heaven and on earth has been given
to me.[e] 19 Therefore go and make disciples
of all nations,[f] baptizing them in the name
of the Father and of the Son and of the
Holy Spirit,[g] 20 and teaching[h] them to obey
everything I have commanded you. And
surely I am with you[i] always, to the very
end of the age."[j]

28:16 [d] ver 7, 10; Mt 26:32 **28:18** [e] Da 7:13, 14; Lk 10:22; Jn 3:35; S 13:13; 17:2; 1Co 15:27; Eph 1:20-22; Php 2:9, 10 **28:19** [f] Isa 49:6; Mk 16:15, 16; Lk 24:47; Ac 1:8; 14:21 [g] Ac 1:8; 2:38; 8:16; Ro 6:3, 4; Gal 3:27; Col 2:12 **28:20** [h] Jn 14:26; Ac 2:42 [i] Dt 31:6; 1Ki 8:57; Hag 1:13; Mt 18:20; Ac 18:10 [j] Mt 13:39; 24:3

28:17 *some.* Probably of the 11 disciples, though it may include others as well. *doubted.* Belief in the resurrection was not instantaneous for them. After the traumatic experience of the crucifixion, it took time for the disciples to come to full faith (see Lk 24:10–11,25–26,36–47).

28:18 *authority.* See 10:1; see also 7:29; 16:28; Jn 17:2 and notes. *in heaven and on earth.* The scope of Christ's authority is the entire universe.

28:19–20 Christ's program of missions: "make disciples of all nations." It involves three steps: (1) "go," (2) "baptizing them" and (3) "teaching them to obey everything" Christ has commanded.

28:19 *disciples.* See 5:1 and note. *all nations.* Contrast 10:5–6 and note. *baptizing them.* As a sign of their union with and commitment to Christ (see notes on Ac 2:38; Ro 6:3–4). *Father … Son … Holy Spirit.* The doctrine of the Trinity means that there is one true God, existing eternally as three distinct persons: Father, Son and Holy Spirit (see 3:16–17 and note; 1Co 12:4–6; 2Co 13:14 and note; Eph 1:2–13; 4:4–6; 2Th 2:13 and note; Titus 3:4–6; 1Pe 1:2 and note; 1Jn 4:13–14; Rev 1:4–6 and NIV text note on 1:4).

28:20 *with you.* Matthew ends with the reassuring and empowering words of him who came to earth to be "God with us" (1:23). See note on 2Co 13:14.

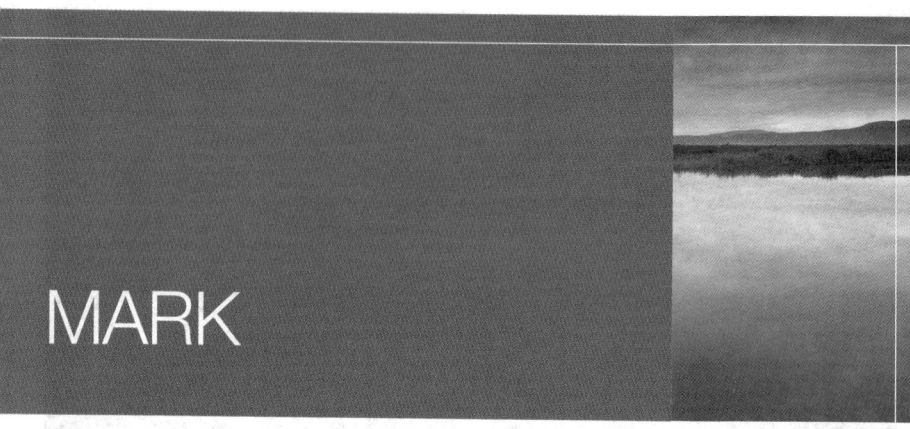

MARK

INTRODUCTION

Author

Although there is no direct internal evidence of authorship, it was the unanimous testimony of the early church that this Gospel was written by John Mark ("John, also called Mark," Ac 12:12,25; 15:37). The most important evidence comes from Papias (c. AD 140), who quotes an even earlier source as saying: (1) Mark was a close associate of Peter, from whom he received the tradition of the things said and done by the Lord (see 1Pe 5:13 and note); (2) this tradition did not come to Mark as a finished, sequential account of the life of our Lord, but as the preaching of Peter — preaching directed to the needs of the early Christian communities; (3) Mark accurately preserved this material. The conclusion drawn from this tradition is that the Gospel of Mark largely consists of the preaching of Peter arranged and shaped by Mark (see note on Ac 10:37).

John Mark in the NT

It is generally agreed that the Mark who is associated with Peter in the early non-Biblical tradition is also the John Mark of the NT. The first mention of him is in connection with his mother, Mary, who had a house in Jerusalem that served as a meeting place for believers (Ac 12:12). When Paul and Barnabas returned to Antioch from Jerusalem after the famine visit, Mark accompanied them (Ac 12:25). Mark next appears as a "helper" to Paul and Barnabas on their first missionary journey (Ac 13:5), but he deserted them at Perga in Pamphylia (see map, p. 1851) to return to Jerusalem (Ac 13:13). Paul must have been deeply disappointed with Mark's actions on this occasion, because when Barnabas proposed taking Mark on the second journey, Paul flatly refused, a refusal that broke up their working relationship (see Ac 15:36 – 39 and note on 15:39). Barnabas took Mark, who was his cousin (Col 4:10), and departed for Cyprus. No further mention is made of either of them in the book of Acts. Mark reappears in Paul's letter to the Colossians, written from Rome. Paul sends a greeting from

a **quick** look

Author:
John Mark

Audience:
Mostly Gentile Christians, probably in the church at Rome

Date:
Between the mid-50s and late 60s AD

Theme:
To encourage his readers to persevere through suffering and persecution, Mark presents Jesus as the Servant-Messiah and Son of God who died as a ransom for sinners.

Mark's Gospel emphasizes more what Jesus did than what he said. Mark moves quickly from one episode in Jesus' life and ministry to another.

Mark and adds: "You have received instructions about him; if he comes to you, welcome him" (Col 4:10; see Phm 24, written at about the same time). At this point Mark was apparently beginning to win his way back into Paul's confidence. By the end of Paul's life, Mark had fully regained Paul's favor (see 2Ti 4:11 and note).

Date of Composition

Some, who hold that Matthew and Luke used Mark as a major source, have suggested that Mark may have been composed in the 50s or early 60s. Others have felt that the content of the Gospel and statements made about Mark by the early church fathers indicate that the book was written shortly before the destruction of Jerusalem in AD 70. See essay and chart, pp. 1582 – 1583.

Place of Writing

According to early church tradition, Mark was written "in the regions of Italy" (Anti-Marcionite Prologue, a work possibly dating as early as the second century AD directed against the heretical views of Marcion) or, more specifically, in Rome (Irenaeus; Clement of Alexandria). These same authors closely associate Mark's writing of the Gospel with the apostle Peter. The above evidence is consistent with (1) the historical probability that Peter was in Rome during the last days of his life and was martyred there and (2) the Biblical evidence that Mark also was in Rome about the same time and was closely associated with Peter (see 2Ti 4:11; 1Pe 5:13, where the word "Babylon" may be a cryptogram for Rome; see also Introduction to 1 Peter: Place of Writing).

Recipients

The evidence points to the church at Rome, or at least to Gentile readers. Mark explains Jewish customs (7:2 – 4; 15:42), translates Aramaic words (3:17; 5:41; 7:11,34; 15:22,34) and seems to have a special interest in persecution and martyrdom (8:34 – 38; 13:9 – 13) — subjects of special concern to Roman believers (and to Peter as well; cf. 1 Peter). A Roman destination would explain the almost immediate acceptance of this Gospel and its rapid dissemination.

First-century fishing boat found in the shallows of the Sea of Galilee in 1986. Several of the apostles were fishermen before Jesus sent them out to "fish for people" (Mk 1:17).

Todd Bolen/www.BiblePlaces.com

Mosaic of Jesus healing a demon-possessed man (Mk 5:1 – 20)
Erich Lessing/Art Resource, NY

Occasion and Purpose

Since Mark's Gospel is traditionally associated with Rome, it may have been occasioned by the persecutions of the Roman church in the period c. AD 64 – 67. The famous fire of Rome in 64 — probably set by Nero himself but blamed on Christians — resulted in widespread persecution. Even martyrdom was not unknown among Roman believers. Mark may be writing to prepare his readers for such suffering by placing before them the life of our Lord. There are many references, both explicit and veiled, to suffering and discipleship throughout his Gospel (see 1:12 – 13; 3:22,30; 8:34 – 38; 10:30,33 – 34,45; 13:8 – 13).

Emphases

(1) *The cross.* Both the human cause (12:12; 14:1 – 2; 15:10) and the divine necessity (8:31; 9:31; 10:33 – 34) of the cross are emphasized by Mark.

(2) *Discipleship.* Special attention should be paid to the passages on discipleship that arise from Jesus' predictions of his passion (8:34 — 9:1; 9:35 — 10:31; 10:42 – 45).

(3) *The teachings of Jesus.* Although Mark records far fewer actual teachings of Jesus than the

other Gospel writers, there is a remarkable emphasis on Jesus as teacher. The words "teacher," "teach" or "teaching" and "Rabbi" are applied to Jesus in Mark 39 times.

(4) *The Messianic secret.* On several occasions Jesus warns his disciples or others to keep silent about who he is or what he has done (see 1:34,44 and notes; 3:12; 5:43; 7:36; 8:30; 9:9; see also note on Mt 8:4).

(5) *Son of God.* Although Mark emphasizes the humanity of Jesus (see 3:5; 6:6,31,34; 7:34; 8:12; 10:14; 11:12), he does not neglect his deity (see 1:1,11; 3:11; 5:7; 9:7; 12:1–11; 13:32; 15:39).

Special Characteristics

Mark's Gospel is a simple, succinct, unadorned, yet vivid account of Jesus' ministry, emphasizing more what Jesus did than what he said. Mark moves quickly from one episode in Jesus' life and ministry to another, often using the adverb "immediately" (see note on 1:12). The book as a whole is characterized as "the beginning of the good news" (1:1). The life, death and resurrection of Christ comprise the "beginning," of which the apostolic preaching in Acts is the continuation.

Outline

- I. The Beginnings of Jesus' Ministry (1:1–13)
  - A. His Forerunner (1:1–8)
  - B. His Baptism (1:9–11)
  - C. His Temptation (1:12–13)
- II. Jesus' Ministry in Galilee (1:14—6:29)
  - A. Early Galilean Ministry (1:14—3:12)
    1. Call of the first disciples (1:14–20)
    2. Miracles in Capernaum (1:21–34)
    3. Preaching and healing in Galilee (1:35–45)
    4. Ministry in Capernaum (2:1–22)
    5. Sabbath controversy (2:23—3:12)
  - B. Later Galilean Ministry (3:13—6:29)
    1. Choosing the 12 apostles (3:13–19)
    2. Teachings in Capernaum (3:20–35)
    3. Parables of the kingdom (4:1–34)
    4. Calming the Sea of Galilee (4:35–41)
    5. Healing a demon-possessed man (5:1–20)
    6. More Galilean miracles (5:21–43)
    7. Unbelief in Jesus' hometown (6:1–6)
    8. Six apostolic teams preach and heal in Galilee (6:7–13)
    9. King Herod's reaction to Jesus' ministry (6:14–29)
- III. Strategic Withdrawals from Galilee (6:30—9:29)
  - A. To the Eastern Shore of the Sea of Galilee (6:30–52)
  - B. To the Western Shore of the Sea (6:53—7:23)
  - C. To Syrian Phoenicia (7:24–30)
  - D. To the Region of the Decapolis (7:31—8:10)

   E. To the Vicinity of Caesarea Philippi (8:11 – 30)
   F. To the Mount of Transfiguration (8:31 — 9:29)
IV. Final Ministry in Galilee (9:30 – 50)
V. Jesus' Ministry in Judea and Perea (ch. 10)
   A. Teaching concerning Divorce (10:1 – 12)
   B. Teaching concerning Children (10:13 – 16)
   C. The Rich Young Man (10:17 – 31)
   D. A Request of Two Brothers (10:32 – 45)
   E. Restoration of Bartimaeus's Sight (10:46 – 52)
VI. The Passion of Jesus (chs. 11 – 15)
   A. The Entry of Jesus into Jerusalem as King (11:1 – 11)
   B. The Clearing of the Temple (11:12 – 19)
   C. Concluding Controversies with Jewish Leaders (11:20 — 12:44)
   D. The Olivet Discourse (ch. 13)
   E. The Anointing of Jesus (14:1 – 11)
   F. The Lord's Supper (14:12 – 26)
   G. The Arrest, Trial and Death of Jesus (14:27 — 15:47)
VII. The Resurrection of Jesus (ch. 16)

John the Baptist Prepares the Way

1:2-8pp — Mt 3:1-11; Lk 3:2-16

1 The beginning of the good news about
Jesus the Messiah,[a] the Son of God,[b][a]
2 as it is written in Isaiah the prophet:

"I will send my messenger ahead of you,
who will prepare your way"[c][b] —
3 "a voice of one calling in the
wilderness,
'Prepare the way for the Lord,
make straight paths for him.' "[d][c]

4 And so John the Baptist[d] appeared in the
wilderness, preaching a baptism of repentance[e] for the forgiveness of sins.[f] 5 The
whole Judean countryside and all the people of Jerusalem went out to him. Confessing their sins, they were baptized by him
in the Jordan River. 6 John wore clothing
made of camel's hair, with a leather belt
around his waist,[g] and he ate locusts[h] and
wild honey. 7 And this was his message:
"After me comes the one more powerful
than I, the straps of whose sandals I am
not worthy to stoop down and untie.[i] 8 I
baptize you with[e] water, but he will baptize you with[e] the Holy Spirit."[j]

1:1 [a]S Mt 4:3 **1:2** [b]Mal 3:1; Mt 11:10; Lk 7:27 **1:3** [c]Isa 40:3; Jn 1:23 **1:4** [d]S Mt 3:1 [e]ver 8; Jn 1:26, 33; Ac 1:5,22; 11:16; 13:24; 18:25; 19:3,4 [f]Lk 1:77 **1:6** [g]2Ki 1:8 [h]Lev 11:22 **1:7** [i]Ac 13:25 **1:8** [j]Isa 44:3; Joel 2:28; Jn 1:33; Ac 1:5; 2:4; 11:16; 19:4-6 **1:9** [k]S Mt 2:23 [l]S Mt 3:1 **1:10** [m]Jn 1:32 **1:11** [n]S Mt 3:17 [o]S Mt 3:17 **1:13** [p]Ex 24:18; 1Ki 19:8 [q]S Mt 4:10; Heb 4:15

The Baptism and Testing of Jesus

1:9-11pp — Mt 3:13-17; Lk 3:21,22
1:12,13pp — Mt 4:1-11; Lk 4:1-13

9 At that time Jesus came from Nazareth[k]
in Galilee and was baptized by John[l] in
the Jordan. 10 Just as Jesus was coming up
out of the water, he saw heaven being torn
open and the Spirit descending on him like
a dove.[m] 11 And a voice came from heaven:
"You are my Son,[n] whom I love; with you
I am well pleased."[o]
12 At once the Spirit sent him out into
the wilderness, 13 and he was in the wilderness forty days,[p] being tempted[f] by Satan.[q] He was with the wild animals, and
angels attended him.

[a] 1 Or *Jesus Christ. Messiah* (Hebrew) and *Christ* (Greek) both mean *Anointed One.* [b] 1 Some manuscripts do not have *the Son of God.* [c] 2 Mal. 3:1 [d] 3 Isaiah 40:3 [e] 8 Or *in* [f] 13 The Greek for *tempted* can also mean *tested.*

1:1 A summary of the main subject matter of Mark's Gospel (see Introduction: Special Characteristics). *The beginning.* Suggests the opening verse of Genesis (see Jn 1:1). *good news.* The meaning of "gospel," from the Old English *godspel,* "good story" or "good news," which accurately translates the Greek. The good news is that God has provided salvation through the life, death and resurrection of Jesus Christ. *Jesus.* See NIV text note on Mt 1:21. *Messiah.* See first NIV text note; see also 8:29 and note. *the Son of God.* See note on Jn 3:16.

1:2 *in Isaiah the prophet.* The quotation that immediately follows (see first two poetry lines) comes from Mal 3:1 (see note there) but is followed (v. 3) by one from Isa 40:3 (see note there). Isaiah here receives pride of place because he stands at the head of the prophetic canon, the division of the Hebrew Bible known as the Latter Prophets (see Introduction to Isaiah: Position in the Hebrew Bible; cf. Introduction to Joshua: Title and Theological Theme). See also note on Mt 27:9. Understanding the ministry of Jesus must begin with the OT. What Isaiah says about God applies to Jesus, his Son (v. 1). The passages cited speak of the messenger, the wilderness and the Lord, each of which is stressed in vv. 4–8.

1:4 *John ... appeared.* Mark, like John, has no nativity narrative, but begins with the ministry of John the Baptist. This is also where Peter begins in his proclamation of the gospel in Ac 10:37 (see note there; see also Introduction: Place of Writing). The name John means "The LORD is gracious." *wilderness.* The arid region west of the Dead Sea. *baptism.* John's practice of baptizing those who came to him in repentance was so characteristic of his ministry that he became known as "the Baptist" or "the Baptizer." He was preaching repentance-baptism, i.e., baptism that was preceded or accompanied by repentance. Baptism was not new to John's audience. They knew of baptism for Gentile converts but had not heard that the descendants of Abraham (Jews) needed to repent and be baptized. *repentance.* Involves deliberate turning from sin to righteousness, and John's emphasis on repentance recalls the preaching of the prophets (e.g., Hos 3:4–5). God always grants forgiveness when there is repentance.

1:5 *whole ... all.* Hyperbole, indicating the high interest created by John's preaching. For centuries Israel had had no prophet. *people of Jerusalem.* See note on Jn 7:25. *Jordan River.* The principal river in the Holy Land, beginning in the snows of Mount Hermon and ending in the Dead Sea. Its closest point to Jerusalem is about 20 miles.

1:6 *camel's hair ... leather belt.* Worn by Elijah and other prophets (see 2Ki 1:8 and note; cf. Zec 13:4). *locusts and wild honey.* See note on Mt 3:4.

1:7 *message.* Mark's account of John's message is brief (cf. Mt 3:7–12; Lk 3:7–17) and focuses on the coming of the powerful One. *sandals I am not worthy to ... untie.* See note on Jn 1:27.

1:8 *baptize you with the Holy Spirit.* See note on Mt 3:11.

1:9 *At that time.* Jesus began his public ministry c. AD 27 (see chart, p. 1636), when he was approximately 30 years old (Lk 3:23). As far as we know, he had spent most of his previous life in Nazareth. *Nazareth.* See notes on Mt 2:23; Lk 4:23. *baptized by John.* For the significance of Jesus' baptism, see Mt 3:15 and note.

1:10–11 All three persons of the Trinity are involved in Jesus' baptism: (1) the Father speaks, (2) the Son is baptized and (3) the Holy Spirit descends on the Son (see note on Mt 28:19).

1:10 *Spirit descending on him.* Jesus' anointing for ministry — an anointing he claimed in the synagogue at Nazareth (see Lk 4:18 and note). *like a dove.* Symbolizing the gentleness, purity and guilelessness of the Holy Spirit (see Mt 10:16; Lk 3:22 and note).

1:11 An allusion to Ps 2:7; Isa 42:1 and probably to Ge 22:2 (see note on Mt 3:17). *voice.* God sometimes spoke directly from heaven (see 9:7; Lk 3:22 and note; Jn 12:28–29; cf. Ex 19:3). *You are my Son.* In v. 1 Mark proclaims Jesus as the Son of God; here God the Father himself proclaims Jesus as his Son.

1:12 *At once.* A distinctive characteristic of Mark's style is his use (some 47 times) of a Greek word that has been variously translated "at once," "without delay," "immediately," "quickly," "just then" (see, e.g., vv. 18,20,23,28,42–43).

1:13 *forty.* See Mt 4:2 and note. *tempted.* See notes on Mt 4:1–11. *Satan.* See Ge 3:1; Job 1:6,9; Zec 3:1; Rev 2:9–10; 12:9–10 and notes. *wild animals.* In Jesus' day there were

Jesus Announces the Good News

1:16-20pp — Mt 4:18-22; Lk 5:2-11; Jn 1:35-42

14 After John[r] was put in prison, Jesus
went into Galilee,[s] proclaiming the good
news of God.[t] 15 "The time has come,"[u] he
said. "The kingdom of God has come near.
Repent and believe[v] the good news!"[w]

Jesus Calls His First Disciples

16 As Jesus walked beside the Sea of Galilee, he saw Simon and his brother Andrew casting a net into the lake, for they
were fishermen. 17 "Come, follow me,"
Jesus said, "and I will send you out to fish
for people." 18 At once they left their nets
and followed him.[x]
19 When he had gone a little farther, he
saw James son of Zebedee and his brother John in a boat, preparing their nets.
20 Without delay he called them, and they
left their father Zebedee in the boat with
the hired men and followed him.

Jesus Drives Out an Impure Spirit

1:21-28pp — Lk 4:31-37

21 They went to Capernaum, and when
the Sabbath came, Jesus went into the
synagogue and began to teach.[y] 22 The people were amazed at his teaching, because
he taught them as one who had authority, not as the teachers of the law.[z] 23 Just
then a man in their synagogue who was
possessed by an impure spirit cried out,
24 "What do you want with us,[a] Jesus of
Nazareth?[b] Have you come to destroy us?
I know who you are — the Holy One of
God!"[c]
25 "Be quiet!" said Jesus sternly. "Come
out of him!"[d] 26 The impure spirit shook
the man violently and came out of him
with a shriek.[e]
27 The people were all so amazed[f] that
they asked each other, "What is this? A
new teaching — and with authority! He
even gives orders to impure spirits and
they obey him." 28 News about him spread
quickly over the whole region[g] of Galilee.

Jesus Heals Many

1:29-31pp — Mt 8:14,15; Lk 4:38,39
1:32-34pp — Mt 8:16,17; Lk 4:40,41

29 As soon as they left the synagogue,[h]
they went with James and John to the
home of Simon and Andrew. 30 Simon's
mother-in-law was in bed with a fever,
and they immediately told Jesus about

1:14 [r] S Mt 3:1 [s] Mt 4:12 [t] Mt 4:23
1:15 [u] Ro 5:6; Gal 4:4; Eph 1:10 [v] S Jn 3:15 [w] Ac 20:21
1:18 [x] S Mt 4:19
1:21 [y] ver 39; S Mt 4:23; S Mk 10:1
1:22 [z] S Mt 7:28,29
1:24 [a] S Mt 8:29 [b] Mt 2:23; Lk 24:19; Jn 1:45,46; Ac 4:10; 24:5 [c] Ps 16:10; Isa 41:14,16, 20; Lk 1:35; Jn 6:69; Ac 3:14; 1Jn 2:20
1:25 [d] ver 34
1:26 [e] Mk 9:20
1:27 [f] Mk 10:24, 32
1:28 [g] S Mt 9:26
1:29 [h] ver 21,23

---

many more wild animals — including lions — in Israel than today. Only Mark reports their presence in this connection; he emphasizes that God kept Jesus safe in the wilderness. *angels attended him.* As they had attended Israel in the wilderness (see Ex 23:20,23; 32:34).

1:14 *After John was put in prison.* See Mt 4:12; 14:3; Lk 3:20 and notes. *good news of God.* The good news from, as well as about, God (see 1:1 and note).

1:15 *The time has come.* Not simply chronological time, but the decisive time for God's action. With the coming of the kingdom, God was doing something special. *kingdom of God.* See note on Mt 3:2. *has come near.* The coming of Christ (the King) brings the kingdom near to the people (see Lk 17:21 and note).

1:16 *Sea of Galilee.* A beautiful lake, almost 700 feet below sea level, 14 miles long and 6 miles wide, fed by the waters of the upper Jordan River. It was also called the Lake of Gennesaret (Lk 5:1) and the Sea of Tiberias (Jn 6:1; see NIV text note on Jn 21:1). In OT times it was known as the Sea of Kinnereth (see NIV text note on Nu 34:11) because it is shaped like a harp (see note on Dt 3:17). *Simon.* Probably a contraction of the OT name Simeon (see NIV text note on Ac 15:14). Jesus gave Simon the name Peter (see 3:16; see also Mt 16:18; Jn 1:42 and notes). *net.* See note on Mt 4:18.

1:17 *Come, follow me.* The call to discipleship is definite and demands a response of total commitment. This was not Jesus' first encounter with Simon and Andrew (see Jn 1:35 – 42). *send you out to fish for people.* As evangelists (see Lk 5:10).

1:21 *Capernaum.* See Mt 4:13; Lk 10:15 and notes. *Sabbath.* The seventh day of the week, the day of rest and worship (see 2:27; Ge 2:3; Ex 16:23; Isa 58:13 and notes). *synagogue.* A very important religious institution among the Jews of that day. Originating during the exile, it provided a place where Jews could study the Scriptures and worship God. A synagogue could be established in any town where there were at least ten married Jewish men. See note on Ac 13:14; see also essay, p. 1576, and model, p. 1710. *began to teach.* Jesus, like Paul (see Ac 13:14 – 15 and notes; 14:1; 17:2; 18:4), took advantage of the custom that allowed visiting teachers to participate in the worship service by invitation of the synagogue leaders (see Lk 4:16 – 17 and notes).

1:22 *amazed.* Mark frequently reported the amazement that Jesus' teaching and actions produced (see 2:12; 5:20,42; 6:2,51; 7:37; 10:26,32; 11:18; 12:17; 15:5). In these instances it was Christ's inherent authority that amazed. He did not quote human authorities, as did the teachers of the law, because his authority was directly from God (cf. Lk 2:46 – 48). *teachers of the law.* See note on Mt 2:4.

1:23 *man in their synagogue . . . cried out.* It was actually the demon who cried out (see 5:7 and note). *possessed by an impure spirit.* Demonic possession intended to torment and destroy those who are created in God's image, but the demon recognized that Jesus was a powerful adversary, capable of destroying the forces of Satan.

1:24 *us.* Although the man has only one demon, it speaks for the whole demonic realm, which quakes in fear at Jesus' presence. *Holy One of God.* A Messianic title affirming that Jesus is set apart for God's service and perhaps alluding to his divine origin (see Lk 1:35; 4:34; Jn 6:69). The title was perhaps used by the demons in accordance with the occult belief that the precise use of a person's name gave certain control over him (see 5:7).

1:25 *Be quiet!* Lit. "Be muzzled!" Jesus' superior power silences the shrieks of the demon-possessed man.

1:27 *with authority.* Jesus' authority in how he taught (v. 22) and in what he did (here) impressed the people.

1:29 *home of Simon and Andrew.* Jesus and the disciples probably went there for a meal, since the main Sabbath meal was served immediately following the synagogue service (see model, p. 1710).

1:30 *Simon's mother-in-law.* 1Co 9:5 speaks of Peter's being married.

her. 31 So he went to her, took her hand and helped her up.[i] The fever left her and she began to wait on them.

32 That evening after sunset the people brought to Jesus all the sick and demon-possessed.[j] 33 The whole town gathered at the door, 34 and Jesus healed many who had various diseases.[k] He also drove out many demons, but he would not let the demons speak because they knew who he was.[l]

Jesus Prays in a Solitary Place

1:35-38pp — Lk 4:42,43

35 Very early in the morning, while it was still dark, Jesus got up, left the house and went off to a solitary place, where he prayed.[m] 36 Simon and his companions went to look for him, 37 and when they found him, they exclaimed: "Everyone is looking for you!"

38 Jesus replied, "Let us go somewhere else — to the nearby villages — so I can preach there also. That is why I have come."[n] 39 So he traveled throughout Galilee, preaching in their synagogues[o] and driving out demons.[p]

Jesus Heals a Man With Leprosy

1:40-44pp — Mt 8:2-4; Lk 5:12-14

40 A man with leprosy[a] came to him and begged him on his knees,[q] "If you are willing, you can make me clean."

41 Jesus was indignant.[b] He reached out his hand and touched the man. "I am willing," he said. "Be clean!" 42 Immediately the leprosy left him and he was cleansed.

1:31 [i] S Lk 7:14
1:32 [j] S Mt 4:24
1:34 [k] S Mt 4:23 [l] Mk 3:12; Ac 16:17,18
1:35 [m] S Lk 3:21
1:38 [n] Isa 61:1
1:39 [o] S Mt 4:23 [p] S Mt 4:24
1:40 [q] Mk 10:17

1:44 [r] S Mt 8:4 [s] Lev 13:49 [t] Lev 14:1-32
1:45 [u] Lk 5:15,16 [v] Mk 2:13; Lk 5:17; Jn 6:2
2:2 [w] ver 13; Mk 1:45
2:3 [x] S Mt 4:24
2:5 [y] Lk 7:48
2:7 [z] Isa 43:25

43 Jesus sent him away at once with a strong warning: 44 "See that you don't tell this to anyone.[r] But go, show yourself to the priest[s] and offer the sacrifices that Moses commanded for your cleansing,[t] as a testimony to them." 45 Instead he went out and began to talk freely, spreading the news. As a result, Jesus could no longer enter a town openly but stayed outside in lonely places.[u] Yet the people still came to him from everywhere.[v]

Jesus Forgives and Heals a Paralyzed Man

2:3-12pp — Mt 9:2-8; Lk 5:18-26

2 A few days later, when Jesus again entered Capernaum, the people heard that he had come home. 2 They gathered in such large numbers[w] that there was no room left, not even outside the door, and he preached the word to them. 3 Some men came, bringing to him a paralyzed man,[x] carried by four of them. 4 Since they could not get him to Jesus because of the crowd, they made an opening in the roof above Jesus by digging through it and then lowered the mat the man was lying on. 5 When Jesus saw their faith, he said to the paralyzed man, "Son, your sins are forgiven."[y]

6 Now some teachers of the law were sitting there, thinking to themselves, 7 "Why does this fellow talk like that? He's blaspheming! Who can forgive sins but God alone?"[z]

[a] 40 The Greek word traditionally translated *leprosy* was used for various diseases affecting the skin.
[b] 41 Many manuscripts *Jesus was filled with compassion*

1:32 *evening.* See Lk 4:40 and note. *people brought.* They waited until the Sabbath was over ("after sunset") before carrying anything (see Jer 17:21–22).
1:34 *not let the demons speak.* See Introduction: Emphases. *because they knew who he was.* Luke says, "because they knew he was the Messiah" (Lk 4:41). Jesus probably wanted first to show by word and deed the kind of Messiah he was (in contrast to popular notions) before he clearly declared himself, and he would not let the demons frustrate this intent.
1:36 *companions.* Andrew, James and John (vv. 16,19,29), and perhaps also Philip and Nathanael (cf. Jn 1:43–45).
1:39 *throughout Galilee.* The first of what seem to be three preaching and healing tours of Galilee (second tour, Lk 8:1; third tour, Mk 6:6 and Mt 11:1).
1:40 *leprosy.* See NIV text note and Lev 13–14; see also note on Lev 13:2. *make me clean.* See notes on Lev 4:12; Mt 8:2.
1:41 *indignant.* Not at the man, but at the ravaging effect of the disease and the social isolation that resulted. *touched the man.* An act that brought defilement (Lev 5:2; 13:45–46). Jesus' compassion (see NIV text note) superseded ceremonial considerations.
1:44 *don't tell this to anyone.* See Introduction: Emphases; see also notes on Mt 8:4; 16:20; Lk 9:21. *go, show yourself to the priest.* Who would then pronounce him ceremonially clean (see, e.g., Lev 13:6,13,17,23; see also note on Lk 5:14). *testimony to them.* The sacrifices were to be evidence to the priests and the people that the cure was real and that Jesus respected the law. The healing was also a testimony to Jesus' divine power, since Jews believed that only God could cure leprosy (see 2Ki 5:1–14 and notes).
1:45 *no longer enter a town openly.* Jesus' growing popularity with the people (see v. 28; 3:7–8; Lk 7:17) and the increasing opposition from Jewish leaders (see 2:6–7,16,24; 3:2,6,22) sometimes made it necessary for him to withdraw from Galilee into surrounding territories.
2:1 *home.* When in Capernaum Jesus probably made his home at Peter's house (see 1:21,29).
2:2 *gathered in ... large numbers.* The same enthusiasm that greeted Jesus earlier (1:32–33,37) was evident at his return.
2:3 *paralyzed man.* Nothing definite can be said about the nature of the man's affliction beyond the fact that he could not walk. The determination of the four men to reach Jesus suggests that his condition was desperate.
2:4 *made an opening in the roof.* A typical house in the Middle East had a flat roof accessible by means of an outside staircase. The roof was often made of a thick layer of clay (packed with a stone roller), supported by mats of branches across wood beams.
2:5 *Jesus saw their faith.* Jesus recognized that the bold action of the paralyzed man and his friends gave evidence of faith. *Son, your sins are forgiven.* Jesus first met the man's deepest need: forgiveness.
2:7 *He's blaspheming! Who can forgive sins but God alone?* Jesus' claim to be able to forgive sins was a

8 Immediately Jesus knew in his spirit that this was what they were thinking in their hearts, and he said to them, "Why are you thinking these things? 9 Which is easier: to say to this paralyzed man, 'Your sins are forgiven,' or to say, 'Get up, take your mat and walk'? 10 But I want you to know that the Son of Man[a] has authority on earth to forgive sins." So he said to the man, 11 "I tell you, get up, take your mat and go home." 12 He got up, took his mat and walked out in full view of them all. This amazed everyone and they praised God,[b] saying, "We have never seen anything like this!"[c]

Jesus Calls Levi and Eats With Sinners

2:14-17pp — Mt 9:9-13; Lk 5:27-32

13 Once again Jesus went out beside the lake. A large crowd came to him,[d] and he began to teach them. 14 As he walked along, he saw Levi son of Alphaeus sitting at the tax collector's booth. "Follow me,"[e] Jesus told him, and Levi got up and followed him.

15 While Jesus was having dinner at Levi's house, many tax collectors and sinners were eating with him and his disciples, for there were many who followed him. 16 When the teachers of the law who were Pharisees[f] saw him eating with the sinners and tax collectors, they asked his disciples: "Why does he eat with tax collectors and sinners?"[g]

17 On hearing this, Jesus said to them, "It is not the healthy who need a doctor, but the sick. I have not come to call the righteous, but sinners."[h]

Jesus Questioned About Fasting

2:18-22pp — Mt 9:14-17; Lk 5:33-38

18 Now John's disciples and the Pharisees were fasting.[i] Some people came and asked Jesus, "How is it that John's disciples and the disciples of the Pharisees are fasting, but yours are not?"

19 Jesus answered, "How can the guests of the bridegroom fast while he is with them? They cannot, so long as they have him with them. 20 But the time will come when the bridegroom will be taken from them,[j] and on that day they will fast.

21 "No one sews a patch of unshrunk cloth on an old garment. Otherwise, the new piece will pull away from the old, making the tear worse. 22 And no one pours new wine into old wineskins. Other-

2:10 [a] S Mt 8:20 **2:12** [b] S Mt 9:8 [c] Mt 9:33 **2:13** [d] Mk 1:45; Lk 5:15; Jn 6:2 **2:14** [e] S Mt 4:19

2:16 [f] Ac 23:9 [g] S Mt 9:11 **2:17** [h] Lk 19:10; 1Ti 1:15 **2:18** [i] S Mt 6:16-18; Ac 13:2 **2:20** [j] Lk 17:22

claim to deity — which they considered to be blasphemous (see note on 14:64).

2:9 *Which is easier . . . ?* Jesus' point probably was that neither forgiving sins nor healing was easier. Both are equally impossible for people and equally easy for God.

2:10 *But I want you to know.* See note on Lk 5:24; spoken to the teachers of the law. The words "So he said to the man" explain a change in the persons addressed. It is clear that one purpose of miracles was to give evidence of Jesus' deity. For the use of miraculous signs in John's Gospel, see Jn 2:11; 20:30 – 31 and notes. *Son of Man.* See note on 8:31.

2:12 *This amazed everyone.* See note on 1:22.

2:14 *Levi son of Alphaeus.* Matthew (see Mt 9:9; 10:3). His given name was probably Levi (for the possible meaning of the name Levi, see NIV text note on Ge 29:34), and Matthew ("gift of the LORD") his apostolic name. *tax collector's booth.* Levi was a tax collector (see note on Lk 3:12) under Herod Antipas, tetrarch of Galilee. The tax collector's booth where Jesus found Levi was probably a toll booth on the major international road that went west from Damascus through Capernaum to the Mediterranean coast and then south to Egypt (see Isa 9:1 and note). *Levi got up and followed.* See note on Lk 5:28.

2:15 *tax collectors.* Jewish tax collectors were hated by most Jews and were regarded as outcasts. They could not serve as witnesses or as judges and were expelled from the synagogue. In the eyes of the Jewish community their disgrace extended to their families. See note on Mt 5:46. *sinners.* Notoriously evil people, as well as those who refused to follow the Mosaic law as interpreted by the teachers of the law. The term was commonly used of tax collectors, adulterers, robbers and the like. *were eating.* To eat with a person was a sign of friendship.

2:16 *teachers of the law who were Pharisees.* Not all teachers of the law were Pharisees — successors of the Hasidim, pious Jews who joined forces with the Maccabees during the struggle for freedom from Syrian oppression (166 – 142 BC). They were first called Pharisees during the reign of John Hyrcanus (135 – 105). Although some, no doubt, were godly, most of those who came into conflict with Jesus were hypocritical, envious, rigid and formalistic. According to Pharisaism, God's grace extended only to those who kept his law. See notes on Mt 2:4; 3:7.

2:17 *I have not come to call the righteous, but sinners.* Those who are self-righteous do not realize their need for salvation, but admitted sinners do.

2:18 *John's disciples.* John the Baptist's disciples may have been fasting because he was in prison (see 1:14), or this may have been a practice among them as an expression of repentance, intended to hasten the coming of redemption announced by John. *disciples of the Pharisees.* Pharisees as such were not teachers, but some were also "scribes" (teachers of the law), who often had disciples. Or perhaps the phrase is used in a nontechnical way to refer to people influenced by the Pharisees. *fasting.* In the Mosaic law only the fast of the Day of Atonement was required (see Lev 16:29,31 and note; 23:27 – 32; Nu 29:7). After the Babylonian exile four other yearly fasts were observed by the Jews (see Zec 7:5; 8:19 and notes). In Jesus' time the Pharisees fasted twice a week (see Lk 18:12 and note).

2:19 *How can the guests of the bridegroom fast while he is with them?* Jesus compared his disciples with the guests of a bridegroom. A Jewish wedding was a particularly joyous occasion, and the celebration associated with it often lasted a week. It was unthinkable to fast during such festivities, because fasting was associated with sorrow.

2:20 *bridegroom will be taken from them.* Jesus is the bridegroom who would be taken from them by death, and then fasting would be in order.

2:22 *new wineskins.* See note on Mt 9:17.

wise, the wine will burst the skins, and
both the wine and the wineskins will be
ruined. No, they pour new wine into new
wineskins."

Jesus Is Lord of the Sabbath

2:23-28pp — Mt 12:1-8; Lk 6:1-5
3:1-6pp — Mt 12:9-14; Lk 6:6-11

23 One Sabbath Jesus was going through
the grainfields, and as his disciples walked
along, they began to pick some heads of
grain.[k] 24 The Pharisees said to him, "Look,
why are they doing what is unlawful on
the Sabbath?"[l]

25 He answered, "Have you never read
what David did when he and his companions were hungry and in need? 26 In the
days of Abiathar the high priest,[m] he entered the house of God and ate the consecrated bread, which is lawful only for
priests to eat.[n] And he also gave some to
his companions."[o]

27 Then he said to them, "The Sabbath
was made for man,[p] not man for the Sabbath.[q] 28 So the Son of Man[r] is Lord even of
the Sabbath."

Jesus Heals on the Sabbath

3 Another time Jesus went into the synagogue,[s] and a man with a shriveled
hand was there. 2 Some of them were looking for a reason to accuse Jesus, so they
watched him closely[t] to see if he would
heal him on the Sabbath.[u] 3 Jesus said to
the man with the shriveled hand, "Stand
up in front of everyone."

4 Then Jesus asked them, "Which is lawful on the Sabbath: to do good or to do
evil, to save life or to kill?" But they remained silent.

5 He looked around at them in anger
and, deeply distressed at their stubborn
hearts, said to the man, "Stretch out your
hand." He stretched it out, and his hand
was completely restored. 6 Then the Pharisees went out and began to plot with the
Herodians[v] how they might kill Jesus.[w]

Crowds Follow Jesus

3:7-12pp — Mt 12:15,16; Lk 6:17-19

7 Jesus withdrew with his disciples to
the lake, and a large crowd from Galilee
followed.[x] 8 When they heard about all he
was doing, many people came to him from
Judea, Jerusalem, Idumea, and the regions
across the Jordan and around Tyre and Sidon.[y] 9 Because of the crowd he told his
disciples to have a small boat ready for
him, to keep the people from crowding
him. 10 For he had healed many,[z] so that

2:23 [k] Dt 23:25
2:24 [l] S Mt 12:2
2:26 [m] 1Ch 24:6; 2Sa 8:17 [n] Lev 24:5-9 [o] 1Sa 21:1-6
2:27 [p] Ex 23:12; Dt 5:14 [q] Col 2:16
2:28 [r] S Mt 8:20
3:1 [s] S Mt 4:23; Mk 1:21
3:2 [t] S Mt 12:10 [u] Lk 14:1
3:6 [v] Mt 22:16; Mk 12:13 [w] S Mt 12:14
3:7 [x] Mt 4:25
3:8 [y] S Mt 11:21
3:10 [z] S Mt 4:23

2:23 *pick some heads of grain.* There was nothing inherently wrong in the action itself, which comes under the provision of Dt 23:25.

2:24 *what is unlawful on the Sabbath.* According to Jewish tradition (in the Mishnah), harvesting (which is what Jesus' disciples technically were doing) was forbidden on the Sabbath. See Ex 34:21.

2:25 *what David did.* See 1Sa 21:1 – 6. The relationship between the OT incident and the apparent infringement of the Sabbath by the disciples lies in the fact that on both occasions godly men did something forbidden. Since, however, it is always "lawful to do good" (Mt 12:12) and to "save life" (Lk 6:9) — even on the Sabbath (3:4; see note there) — both David and the disciples were within the spirit of the law (see 1Sa 21:4 and note; Isa 58:6 – 7; Lk 13:10 – 17; 14:1 – 6).

2:26 *In the days of Abiathar the high priest.* According to 1Sa 21:1, Ahimelek, Abiathar's father (1Sa 22:20), was then high priest (see note on 2Sa 8:17). *house of God.* The tabernacle (see 1Sa 1:9 and note; 21:1). *consecrated bread.* See note on Mt 12:4.

2:27 *The Sabbath was made for man, not man for the Sabbath.* Jewish tradition had so multiplied the requirements and restrictions for keeping the Sabbath that the burden had become intolerable. Jesus cut across these traditions and emphasized the God-given purpose of the Sabbath — a day intended for the benefit of people (for spiritual, mental and physical restoration; see Ex 20:8 – 11).

2:28 See note on Lk 6:5.

3:1 – 6 A demonstration that Jesus is Lord of the Sabbath (see 2:28).

3:2 *Some of them.* The Pharisees (v. 6; cf. Lk 6:7). *to accuse Jesus.* Jesus' presence demanded a decision about his preaching, his acts and his person. The hostility, first seen in 2:6 – 7, continues to spread. See note on v. 6. *to see if he would heal him on the Sabbath.* An indication that the Pharisees believed in Jesus' power to perform miracles. The question was not "Could he?" but "Would he?" Jewish tradition prescribed that aid could be given the sick on the Sabbath only when the person's life was threatened, which obviously was not the case here. See notes on 2:25; Lk 13:14.

3:4 *to do good or to do evil, to save life or to kill?* Jesus asks: Which is better, to preserve life by healing or to destroy life by refusing to heal? The question is ironic since, whereas Jesus was ready to heal, the Pharisees were plotting to put him to death. It is obvious who was guilty of breaking the Sabbath. *they remained silent.* See 12:34.

3:5 *He looked around at them.* See note on Lk 6:10.

3:6 *the Pharisees … began to plot.* The decision to seek Jesus' death was not the result of this incident alone but was the response to a series of incidents (see 2:6 – 7,16 – 17,24). The plotting of the Pharisees and the Herodians is seen again on Tuesday of Passion Week (see 12:13 and note). *Herodians.* Evidently influential Jews who favored the Herodian dynasty, meaning they were supporters of Rome, from which the Herods received their authority. They joined the Pharisees in opposing Jesus because they feared he might have an unsettling political influence on the people. See Mt 22:15 – 17 and note.

3:8 Impressive evidence of Jesus' rapidly growing popularity among the people. This geographic list indicates that the crowds came not only from the areas in the vicinity of Capernaum but also from considerable distances. Mark tells of Jesus' work in all these regions except Idumea (see 1:14, Galilee; 5:1 and 10:1, the region across the Jordan; 7:24,31, Tyre and Sidon; 10:1, Judea; 11:11, Jerusalem). *Idumea.* The Greek form of Hebrew Edom, but here referring to an area south of Judea, not to earlier Edomite territory. See map, p. 1707.

those with diseases were pushing forward to touch him.[a] 11 Whenever the impure spirits saw him, they fell down before him and cried out, "You are the Son of God."[b] 12 But he gave them strict orders not to tell others about him.[c]

Jesus Appoints the Twelve

3:16-19pp — Mt 10:2-4; Lk 6:14-16; Ac 1:13

13 Jesus went up on a mountainside and called to him those he wanted, and they came to him.[d] 14 He appointed twelve[a][e] that they might be with him and that he might send them out to preach 15 and to have authority to drive out demons.[f] 16 These are the twelve he appointed: Simon (to whom he gave the name Peter),[g] 17 James son of Zebedee and his brother John (to them he gave the name Boanerges, which means "sons of thunder"), 18 Andrew, Philip, Bartholomew, Matthew, Thomas, James son of Alphaeus, Thaddaeus, Simon the Zealot 19 and Judas Iscariot, who betrayed him.

Jesus Accused by His Family and by Teachers of the Law

3:23-27pp — Mt 12:25-29; Lk 11:17-22
3:31-35pp — Mt 12:46-50; Lk 8:19-21

20 Then Jesus entered a house, and again a crowd gathered,[h] so that he and his disciples were not even able to eat.[i] 21 When his family[b] heard about this, they went to take charge of him, for they said, "He is out of his mind."[j]

22 And the teachers of the law who came down from Jerusalem[k] said, "He is possessed by Beelzebul![l] By the prince of demons he is driving out demons."[m]

3:10 [a] S Mt 9:20
3:11 [b] S Mt 4:3; Mk 1:23,24
3:12 [c] S Mt 8:4; Mk 1:24,25,34; Ac 16:17,18
3:13 [d] Mt 5:1
3:14 [e] S Mk 6:30
3:15 [f] S Mt 10:1
3:16 [g] Jn 1:42
3:20 [h] ver 7 [i] Mk 6:31
3:21 [j] Jn 10:20; Ac 26:24
3:22 [k] Mt 15:1 [l] Mt 10:25; 11:18; 12:24; Jn 7:20; 8:48, 52; 10:20 [m] Mt 9:34

23 So Jesus called them over to him and began to speak to them in parables:[n] "How can Satan[o] drive out Satan? 24 If a kingdom is divided against itself, that kingdom cannot stand. 25 If a house is divided against itself, that house cannot stand. 26 And if Satan opposes himself and is divided, he cannot stand; his end has come. 27 In fact, no one can enter a strong man's house without first tying him up. Then he can plunder the strong man's house.[p] 28 Truly I tell you, people can be forgiven all their sins and every slander they utter, 29 but whoever blasphemes against the Holy Spirit will never be forgiven; they are guilty of an eternal sin."[q]

30 He said this because they were saying, "He has an impure spirit."

31 Then Jesus' mother and brothers arrived.[r] Standing outside, they sent someone in to call him. 32 A crowd was sitting around him, and they told him, "Your mother and brothers are outside looking for you."

33 "Who are my mother and my brothers?" he asked.

34 Then he looked at those seated in a circle around him and said, "Here are my mother and my brothers! 35 Whoever does God's will is my brother and sister and mother."

The Parable of the Sower

4:1-12pp — Mt 13:1-15; Lk 8:4-10
4:13-20pp — Mt 13:18-23; Lk 8:11-15

4 Again Jesus began to teach by the lake.[s] The crowd that gathered around

3:23 [n] Mk 4:2 [o] S Mt 4:10
3:27 [p] Isa 49:24, 25
3:29 [q] Mt 12:31, 32; Lk 12:10
3:31 [r] ver 21
4:1 [s] Mk 2:13; 3:7

[a] 14 Some manuscripts *twelve — designating them apostles —* [b] 21 Or *his associates*

3:11 *impure spirits.* See note on 1:23. *You are the Son of God.* The impure spirits recognized who Jesus was, but they did not believe in him (see 1:24 and note).
3:12 *not to tell others about him.* See Introduction: Emphases. The time for revealing Jesus' identity had not yet come (see 1:34 and note; see also notes on Mt 8:4; 16:20), and demons were hardly the proper channel for such disclosure.
3:13 *mountainside.* Probably the hill country of Galilee around the lake. Lk 6:12 adds that he prayed.
3:14 *that they might be with him.* The training of the Twelve included not only instruction and practice in various forms of ministry but also — first and foremost — continuous association and intimate fellowship with Jesus himself.
3:16 – 19 See notes on Lk 6:14 – 16.
3:16 *Simon (to whom he gave the name Peter).* See note on 1:16.
3:17 *Boanerges.* One of many Aramaic words translated by Mark (see Introduction: Recipients). *sons of thunder.* Probably descriptive of their dispositions (see notes on 10:37; Lk 9:54).
3:18 *Thaddaeus.* Apparently the same as "Judas son of James" (Lk 6:16; Ac 1:13). *the Zealot.* See note on Mt 10:4.
3:19 *Iscariot.* Probably means "the man from Kerioth," perhaps the town of Kerioth Hezron (Jos 15:25), 12 miles south of Hebron. For Judas's betrayal of Jesus, see 14:10 – 11, 43 – 46.
3:20 *house.* Perhaps the home of Peter and Andrew (see 1:29; 2:1 and notes; see also model, p. 1710).
3:21 *his family ... went to take charge of him.* They may have come to Capernaum from Nazareth, about 30 miles away (see v. 31).
3:22 *who came down from Jerusalem.* See 7:1 and note. *Beelzebul.* See note on Mt 10:25.
3:23 *parables.* In this context the word is used in the general sense of comparisons (see note on 4:2).
3:24 *kingdom is divided against itself.* See note on Lk 11:17.
3:27 *enter a strong man's house ... plunder.* Jesus was doing this very thing when he freed people from Satan's control.
3:28 *Truly I tell you.* A solemn affirmation used by Jesus to strengthen his assertions (see 8:12; 9:1,41; 10:15,29; 11:23; 12:43; 13:30; 14:9,18,25,30; see also note on Jn 1:51).
3:29 *whoever blasphemes against the Holy Spirit will never be forgiven.* This sin is identified in v. 30 (cf. v. 22) — the teachers of the law attributed Jesus' healing to Satan's power rather than to the Holy Spirit (see note on Mt 12:31).
3:31 *Jesus' mother and brothers.* See note on Lk 8:19.
3:35 *Whoever does God's will.* Membership in God's spiritual family, evidenced by obedience to him, is more important than membership in our human families (see 10:30 and note).

him was so large that he got into a boat
and sat in it out on the lake, while all the
people were along the shore at the water's
edge. 2 He taught them many things by parables,[t] and in his teaching said: 3 "Listen!
A farmer went out to sow his seed.[u] 4 As
he was scattering the seed, some fell along
the path, and the birds came and ate it up.
5 Some fell on rocky places, where it did
not have much soil. It sprang up quickly, because the soil was shallow. 6 But
when the sun came up, the plants were
scorched, and they withered because they
had no root. 7 Other seed fell among thorns,
which grew up and choked the plants, so
that they did not bear grain. 8 Still other
seed fell on good soil. It came up, grew
and produced a crop, some multiplying
thirty, some sixty, some a hundred times."[v]

9 Then Jesus said, "Whoever has ears to
hear, let them hear."[w]

10 When he was alone, the Twelve and
the others around him asked him about
the parables. 11 He told them, "The secret
of the kingdom of God[x] has been given to
you. But to those on the outside[y] everything is said in parables 12 so that,

"'they may be ever seeing but never
perceiving,
and ever hearing but never
understanding;
otherwise they might turn and be
forgiven!'[a]"[z]

13 Then Jesus said to them, "Don't you
understand this parable? How then will
you understand any parable? 14 The farmer sows the word.[a] 15 Some people are
like seed along the path, where the word
is sown. As soon as they hear it, Satan[b]
comes and takes away the word that was
sown in them. 16 Others, like seed sown on
rocky places, hear the word and at once
receive it with joy. 17 But since they have
no root, they last only a short time. When
trouble or persecution comes because of
the word, they quickly fall away. 18 Still
others, like seed sown among thorns, hear
the word; 19 but the worries of this life, the
deceitfulness of wealth[c] and the desires
for other things come in and choke the
word, making it unfruitful. 20 Others, like
seed sown on good soil, hear the word,
accept it, and produce a crop—some thirty, some sixty, some a hundred times what
was sown."

A Lamp on a Stand

21 He said to them, "Do you bring in a
lamp to put it under a bowl or a bed? Instead, don't you put it on its stand?[d] 22 For
whatever is hidden is meant to be disclosed, and whatever is concealed is meant
to be brought out into the open.[e] 23 If anyone has ears to hear, let them hear."[f]

24 "Consider carefully what you hear,"
he continued. "With the measure you use,
it will be measured to you—and even
more.[g] 25 Whoever has will be given more;
whoever does not have, even what they
have will be taken from them."[h]

4:2 [t] ver 11; Mk 3:23 **4:3** [u] ver 26 **4:8** [v] Jn 15:5; Col 1:6 **4:9** [w] ver 23; S Mt 11:15 **4:11** [x] S Mt 3:2 [y] 1Co 5:12, 13; Col 4:5; 1Th 4:12; 1Ti 3:7 **4:12** [z] Isa 6:9, 10; S Mt 13:13-15 **4:14** [a] Mk 16:20; Lk 1:2; Ac 4:31; 8:4; 16:6; 17:11; Php 1:14 **4:15** [b] S Mt 4:10 **4:19** [c] Mt 19:23; 1Ti 6:9, 10, 17; 1Jn 2:15-17 **4:21** [d] S Mt 5:15 **4:22** [e] Jer 16:17; Mt 10:26; Lk 8:17; 12:2 **4:23** [f] ver 9; S Mt 11:15 **4:24** [g] S Mt 7:2 **4:25** [h] S Mt 25:29

[a] *12* Isaiah 6:9,10

4:1 *sat in it.* Sitting was the usual position for Jewish teachers (see 9:35; see also Mt 5:1; Lk 4:20 and notes).

4:2 *parables.* Usually stories out of ordinary life used to illustrate spiritual or moral truth, sometimes in the form of brief similes, comparisons (see note on 3:23), analogies or proverbial sayings. They tended to have a single main point, and not every detail was meant to have significance. See notes on Mt 13:3; Lk 8:4.

4:3–8 In that day seed was sown by hand—which, by its nature, scattered some seed on unproductive ground (see note on Lk 8:5).

4:3 *Listen!* This parable begins and ends (v. 9) with a call for careful attention, which suggests that its meaning is not self-evident. *sow his seed.* See note on Lk 8:5.

4:8 *multiplying ... a hundred times.* A hundredfold yield was an unusually productive harvest (see Ge 26:12–13). Harvest was a common figure for the consummation of God's kingdom (see Joel 3:13; Rev 14:15 and notes).

4:9 See note on Lk 8:8.

4:11 *secret of the kingdom of God.* In the NT "secret" refers to something God has revealed to his people. The secret (that which was previously unknown) is proclaimed to all, but only those who have faith understand. In this context the secret seems to be that the kingdom of God had drawn near (see v. 26; see also notes on 1:15; Mt 3:2) in the coming of Jesus Christ, the King.

4:12 *so that.* Jesus compares his preaching in parables to the ministry of Isaiah. Ironically, Isaiah's message was intended in part to further harden the Israelites' stubborn hearts and so fulfill God's promised judgment. In the same way, Jesus' parables blind the eyes of the religious leaders who have already rejected his kingdom message. In that very blindness, they will accomplish God's purpose of salvation through the death of the Messiah. See Isa 6:8–10 and notes on 6:8–10 and 6:9–10.

4:14 *the word.* The interpretation calls attention to the response to the word of God that Jesus has been preaching. In spite of many obstacles, God's word will accomplish his purpose (cf. Isa 55:11 and note).

4:17 *trouble or persecution.* See Introduction: Occasion and Purpose; see also 8:34–38; 10:30 and notes; 13:9–13.

4:19 *deceitfulness of wealth.* Prosperity tends to give a false sense of self-sufficiency, security and well-being (see 10:17–25 and notes; Dt 8:17–18; 32:15; Ecc 2:4–11; see also Lk 12:12–20; Jas 5:1–6 and notes).

4:20 *hundred times.* See v. 8 and note.

4:21 *Do you bring in a lamp ...?* As a lamp is placed to give, not hide, light, so Jesus, the light of the world (see Jn 8:12 and note), is destined to be revealed. *lamp.* See Mt 5:15 and note.

4:22 See note on Lk 8:17.

4:23 See note on Lk 8:8.

4:24 See note on Lk 8:18.

4:25 Those who have begun to understand and appropriate the truth of what Jesus was teaching will be granted fuller understanding in the future, but those

JERUSALEM DURING THE MINISTRY OF JESUS

Herod the Great (reigned 37–4 BC) rebuilt the temple and its surrounding walls and also built a palace, a fortress, a theater and a hippodrome (stadium) for horse and chariot races. He brought the city to the zenith of its architectural beauty and Roman cultural expression. This became Jerusalem in the time of Jesus.

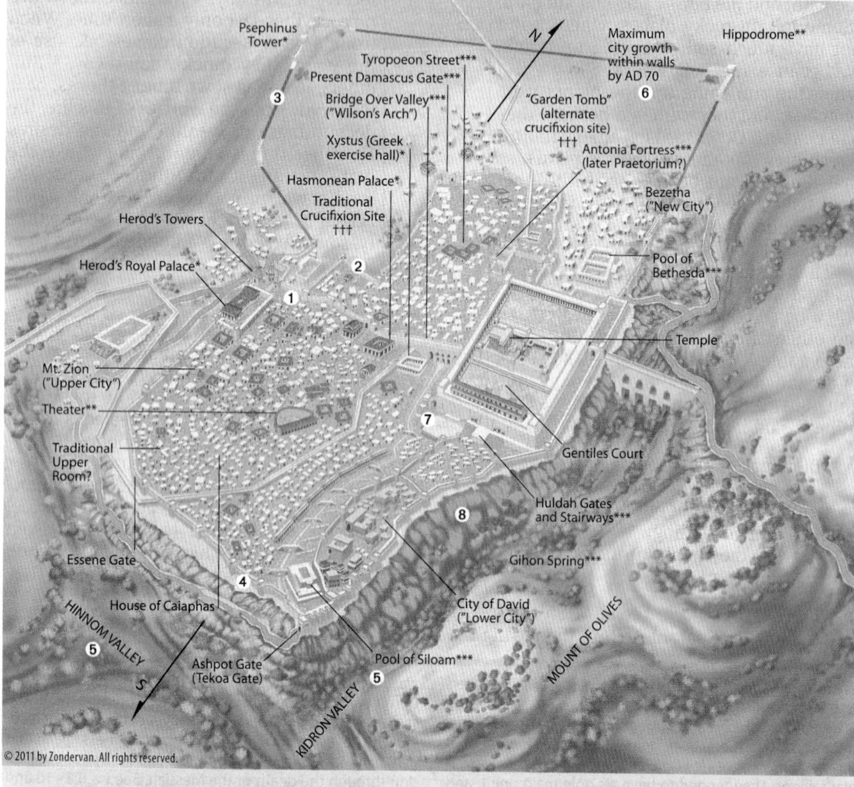

1 The **"FIRST WALL,"** so named by Josephus, encircled the city during the Hasmonean period, which began in 167 BC. After the revolt led by Judas Maccabeus in 167, Jerusalem expanded steadily in a period of independence under its own Jewish kings.

2 The **"SECOND WALL"** was built by Herod the Great or by earlier Hasmonean kings. Precise location is difficult to determine. This wall was put up around a market area in a valley, protecting it from raiding and looting, but was of questionable military value. At its eastern end, however, Herod built a military barracks (Antonia Fortress).

3 The **"THIRD WALL"** (shown with red line) was begun by Herod Agrippa I between AD 41 and 44 to enclose the growing northern suburbs, but the work was apparently stopped. Its construction was resumed, in haste, only after the First Jewish Revolt broke out in AD 66.

4 House of Caiaphas the high priest,* identified here with today's Church of St. Peter in Gallicantu.

5 Deep valleys on the east, south and west permitted urban expansion only to the north.

6 Maximum city growth within walls by AD 70.

7 Archaeological excavations have revealed a monumental stairway and the continuation of Tyropoeon Street,*** which lies along the valley called "Valley of the Cheesemongers" by Josephus.

8 The Siloam aqueduct-tunnel, 1,749′ long, was cut through solid bedrock, was 5′11″ high (average) and followed an "S" shaped course made necessary by engineering difficulties. It was dug by King Hezekiah and provided water during King Sennacherib's threat to lay siege to the city in 701 BC (2Ch 32:30). Water flows through it to this very day.

* Location generally known, but style of architecture is unknown; artist's concept only, and Roman architecture is assumed.
** Location and architecture unknown, but referred to in written history; shown here for illustrative purposes.
*** Ancient feature has remained, or appearance has been determined from evidence.

The Parable of the Growing Seed

26 He also said, "This is what the kingdom of God is like.[i] A man scatters seed
on the ground. 27 Night and day, whether he sleeps or gets up, the seed sprouts
and grows, though he does not know how.
28 All by itself the soil produces grain—
first the stalk, then the head, then the full
kernel in the head. 29 As soon as the grain
is ripe, he puts the sickle to it, because the
harvest has come."[j]

The Parable of the Mustard Seed

4:30-32pp — Mt 13:31,32; Lk 13:18,19

30 Again he said, "What shall we say the
kingdom of God is like,[k] or what parable
shall we use to describe it? 31 It is like a
mustard seed, which is the smallest of
all seeds on earth. 32 Yet when planted, it
grows and becomes the largest of all garden plants, with such big branches that
the birds can perch in its shade."

33 With many similar parables Jesus
spoke the word to them, as much as they
could understand.[l] 34 He did not say anything to them without using a parable.[m]
But when he was alone with his own disciples, he explained everything.

Jesus Calms the Storm

4:35-41pp — Mt 8:18,23-27; Lk 8:22-25

35 That day when evening came, he said
to his disciples, "Let us go over to the
other side." 36 Leaving the crowd behind,
they took him along, just as he was, in the
boat.[n] There were also other boats with
him. 37 A furious squall came up, and the
waves broke over the boat, so that it was
nearly swamped. 38 Jesus was in the stern,
sleeping on a cushion. The disciples woke
him and said to him, "Teacher, don't you
care if we drown?"

39 He got up, rebuked the wind and said
to the waves, "Quiet! Be still!" Then the
wind died down and it was completely
calm.

40 He said to his disciples, "Why are you
so afraid? Do you still have no faith?"[o]

41 They were terrified and asked each
other, "Who is this? Even the wind and the
waves obey him!"

Jesus Restores a Demon-Possessed Man

5:1-17pp — Mt 8:28-34; Lk 8:26-37
5:18-20pp — Lk 8:38,39

5 They went across the lake to the region of the Gerasenes.[a] 2 When Jesus
got out of the boat,[p] a man with an impure
spirit[q] came from the tombs to meet him.
3 This man lived in the tombs, and no one
could bind him anymore, not even with
a chain. 4 For he had often been chained
hand and foot, but he tore the chains apart

4:26 [i] S Mt 13:24
4:29 [j] Rev 14:15
4:30 [k] S Mt 13:24
4:33 [l] Jn 16:12
4:34 [m] S Jn 16:25
4:36 [n] ver 1; Mk 3:9; 5:2,21; 6:32,45
4:40 [o] Mt 14:31; Mk 16:14
5:2 [p] Mk 4:1 [q] Mk 1:23

[a] *1* Some manuscripts *Gadarenes;* other manuscripts *Gergesenes*

---

who have failed to appropriate it will experience no benefit from it.

4:26–29 Only Mark records this parable. Whereas the parable of the sower stresses the importance of proper soil for the growth of seed and the success of the harvest, here the mysterious power of the seed itself is emphasized. The gospel message contains its own power (cf. Ro 1:16).

4:26 *kingdom of God.* See note on v. 11.

4:29 *he puts the sickle to it, because the harvest has come.* A possible allusion to Joel 3:13 (see note there), where harvest is a figure for the consummation of God's kingdom.

4:30–34 The main point of this parable is that the kingdom of God seemingly had insignificant beginnings. It was introduced by the despised and rejected Jesus and his 12 unimpressive disciples. But a day will come when its true greatness and power will be seen by the whole world.

4:31 See notes on Mt 13:31–32.

4:34 *He did not say anything to them without using a parable.* Jesus used parables to illustrate truths, stimulate thinking and awaken spiritual perception. The people in general were not ready for the full truth of the gospel. When alone with his disciples Jesus taught more specifically, but even they usually needed to have things explained.

4:35–41 Although miracles are hard for people to accept today, the NT makes it clear that Jesus is Lord not only over his church but also over all creation.

4:35 *other side.* Jesus left the territory of Galilee to go to the "region of the Gerasenes" (5:1).

4:37 *furious squall came up.* Situated in a basin surrounded by mountains, the Sea of Galilee is particularly susceptible to sudden, violent storms. Cool air from the Mediterranean is drawn down through the narrow mountain passes and clashes with the hot, humid air lying over the lake.

4:38 *sleeping on a cushion.* The picture of Jesus, exhausted and asleep, is characteristic of Mark's human touch.

4:41 *Who is this?* In view of what Jesus had just done, the only answer to this rhetorical question was: He is the very Son of God! God's presence, as well as his power, was demonstrated (see Ps 65:6–7; 107:25–30 and notes; Pr 30:4). Mark indicates his answer to this question in the opening line of his Gospel (1:1). By such miracles Jesus sought to establish and increase the disciples' faith in his deity.

5:1–43 The stories of the healing of the demon-possessed man, Jairus's daughter and the woman with the hemorrhage all have to do with ceremonial uncleanness.

5:1 *across the lake.* The east side of the lake, a territory largely inhabited by Gentiles, as indicated by the presence of the large herd of pigs—animals Jews considered ceremonially unclean and therefore unfit to eat (see Isa 65:4 and note). *region of the Gerasenes.* Gerasa, located about 35 miles southeast of the Sea of Galilee (see map, p. 1663), may have had holdings on the eastern shore of the Sea, giving its name to a small village there now known as Khersa. About one mile south is a fairly steep slope within 40 yards of the shore, and about two miles from there are cavern tombs that appear to have been used as dwellings. See note on Lk 8:26.

5:2 *a man.* Mt 8:28 says there were two demon-possessed men (see note on Lk 8:27).

5:3 *lived in the tombs.* It was not unusual for the same cave to provide burial for the dead and shelter for the living. Very poor people often lived in such caves.

5:4 *often been chained.* Though the villagers no doubt

and broke the irons on his feet. No one was strong enough to subdue him. 5 Night and day among the tombs and in the hills he would cry out and cut himself with stones.

6 When he saw Jesus from a distance, he ran and fell on his knees in front of him. 7 He shouted at the top of his voice, "What do you want with me,[r] Jesus, Son of the Most High God?[s] In God's name don't torture me!" 8 For Jesus had said to him, "Come out of this man, you impure spirit!"

9 Then Jesus asked him, "What is your name?"

"My name is Legion,"[t] he replied, "for we are many." 10 And he begged Jesus again and again not to send them out of the area.

11 A large herd of pigs was feeding on the nearby hillside. 12 The demons begged Jesus, "Send us among the pigs; allow us to go into them." 13 He gave them permission, and the impure spirits came out and went into the pigs. The herd, about two thousand in number, rushed down the steep bank into the lake and were drowned.

14 Those tending the pigs ran off and reported this in the town and countryside, and the people went out to see what had happened. 15 When they came to Jesus, they saw the man who had been possessed by the legion[u] of demons,[v] sitting there, dressed and in his right mind; and they were afraid. 16 Those who had seen it told the people what had happened to the demon-possessed man—and told about the pigs as well. 17 Then the people began to plead with Jesus to leave their region.

18 As Jesus was getting into the boat, the man who had been demon-possessed begged to go with him. 19 Jesus did not let him, but said, "Go home to your own people and tell them[w] how much the Lord has done for you, and how he has had mercy on you." 20 So the man went away and began to tell in the Decapolis[a][x] how much Jesus had done for him. And all the people were amazed.

Jesus Raises a Dead Girl and Heals a Sick Woman

5:22-43pp — Mt 9:18-26; Lk 8:41-56

21 When Jesus had again crossed over by boat to the other side of the lake,[y] a large crowd gathered around him while he was by the lake.[z] 22 Then one of the synagogue leaders,[a] named Jairus, came, and when he saw Jesus, he fell at his feet. 23 He pleaded earnestly with him, "My little daughter is dying. Please come and put your hands on[b] her so that she will be healed and live." 24 So Jesus went with him.

A large crowd followed and pressed around him. 25 And a woman was there who had been subject to bleeding[c] for

5:7 [r] S Mt 8:29 [s] S Mt 4:3; Lk 1:32; 6:35; Ac 16:17; Heb 7:1 **5:9** [t] ver 15 **5:15** [u] ver 9 [v] ver 16, 18; S Mt 4:24 **5:19** [w] S Mt 8:4 **5:20** [x] Mt 4:25; Mk 7:31 **5:21** [y] Mt 9:1 [z] Mk 4:1 **5:22** [a] ver 35, 36, 38; Lk 13:14; Ac 13:15; 18:8, 17 **5:23** [b] Mt 19:13; Mk 6:5; 7:32; 8:23; 16:18; Lk 4:40; 13:13; S Ac 6:6 **5:25** [c] Lev 15:25-30

[a] *20* That is, the Ten Cities

chained him partly for their own protection, this harsh treatment added to his humiliation.

5:5 *cry out and cut himself with stones.* Every word in the story emphasizes the man's pathetic condition, as well as the purpose of demonic possession—to torment and destroy the divine likeness in which human beings are created (see Ge 1:26 and note).

5:6 *fell on his knees.* An act of homage rather than worship. The demon showed respect because he recognized that he was confronted by one greatly superior to him.

5:7 *What do you want with me . . . ?* Lit. "What to me and to you?" Similar expressions are found in the OT (e.g., 2Sa 16:10; 19:22), where they mean, "Mind your own business!" The demon was speaking, using the voice of the possessed man (see 1:23 and note). *Son of the Most High God.* See note on 1:24. *In God's name don't torture me!* The demon sensed that he was to be punished and used the strongest basis for an oath that he knew, though his appeal to God was strangely ironic.

5:9 *My name is Legion . . . for we are many.* A Roman legion was made up of 6,000 men. Here the term suggests that the man was possessed by numerous demons and perhaps also represents the many powers opposed to Jesus, who embodies the power of God (see 1:23–24 and notes).

5:10 *not to send them out of the area.* The demons were fearful of being sent into eternal punishment, i.e., "into the Abyss" (Lk 8:31; see note there).

5:11 *pigs.* See note on Lk 8:32.

5:13 *gave them permission.* See note on Mt 8:32.

5:16 *told about the pigs as well.* In addition to the remarkable change in the demon-possessed man, the drowning of the pigs seemed to be a major concern, no doubt because it was so dramatic and brought considerable financial loss to the owners.

5:17 *plead with Jesus to leave their region.* Fear of further loss may have motivated this response, but also the fact that a powerful force was at work in their midst, one that they could not comprehend.

5:19 *tell them how much the Lord has done for you.* This is in marked contrast to Jesus' exhortation to silence in the case of the man cleansed of leprosy (1:44; see 1:34; 3:12; Mt 8:4 and notes), perhaps because the healing of the demon-possessed man was in Gentile territory, where there was little danger that Messianic ideas about Jesus might be circulated (see Introduction: Emphases).

5:20 *Decapolis.* See note on Mt 4:25; see also map, p. 1663. *amazed.* See 1:22 and note.

5:21 *other side of the lake.* Jesus returned to the west side of the lake, perhaps to Capernaum.

5:22 *synagogue leaders.* A leader of the synagogue was a layman whose responsibilities were administrative and included such things as looking after the building and supervising the worship. Though there were exceptions (see Ac 13:14–15), most synagogues had only one ruler. Sometimes the title was honorary, with no administrative responsibilities assigned.

5:23 *is dying.* See note on Mt 9:18. *put your hands on her.* See note on Ac 6:6.

5:25 *bleeding for twelve years.* Probably a menstrual disorder. Her existence was wretched because she was shunned by

THE DECAPOLIS AND THE LANDS BEYOND THE JORDAN

- ✧ Cities of the Decapolis (Pliny)
- Territory under Antipas
- Territory under Philip
- Territory under governor of Judea
- Territory under proconsul of Syria

1 Place east of the Jordan River where John the Baptist was baptizing (Jn 1:28). Here at Bethany on the other side of the Jordan John saw Jesus and called him the "Lamb of God" (Jn 1:29,35).

2 Philip, Andrew and Peter were from Bethsaida (see Jn 1:44; 12:21 and note on 1:40). Jesus healed a blind man here (Mk 8:22). Feeding of the 5,000 took place near here (Lk 9:10).

3 Jesus and his disciples withdrew to Caesarea Philippi (Mt 16:13; Mk 8:27), and here Peter confessed that Jesus was the Messiah (Mt 16:15–16).

4 Paul was converted near Damascus and was brought blinded into the city (Ac 9:3,8; 22:6,11).

twelve years. 26 She had suffered a great
deal under the care of many doctors and
had spent all she had, yet instead of getting
better she grew worse. 27 When she heard
about Jesus, she came up behind him in
the crowd and touched his cloak, 28 because
she thought, "If I just touch his clothes,[d] I
will be healed." 29 Immediately her bleeding stopped and she felt in her body that
she was freed from her suffering.[e]
30 At once Jesus realized that power[f] had
gone out from him. He turned around in
the crowd and asked, "Who touched my
clothes?"
31 "You see the people crowding against
you," his disciples answered, "and yet you
can ask, 'Who touched me?' "
32 But Jesus kept looking around to see
who had done it. 33 Then the woman,
knowing what had happened to her, came
and fell at his feet and, trembling with
fear, told him the whole truth. 34 He said
to her, "Daughter, your faith has healed
you.[g] Go in peace[h] and be freed from your
suffering."
35 While Jesus was still speaking, some
people came from the house of Jairus,
the synagogue leader.[i] "Your daughter is
dead," they said. "Why bother the teacher
anymore?"
36 Overhearing[a] what they said, Jesus
told him, "Don't be afraid; just believe."
37 He did not let anyone follow him except Peter, James and John the brother of
James.[j] 38 When they came to the home of
the synagogue leader,[k] Jesus saw a commotion, with people crying and wailing
loudly. 39 He went in and said to them,
"Why all this commotion and wailing?
The child is not dead but asleep."[l] 40 But
they laughed at him.
After he put them all out, he took the
child's father and mother and the disciples
who were with him, and went in where
the child was. 41 He took her by the hand[m]
and said to her, *"Talitha koum!"* (which
means "Little girl, I say to you, get up!").[n]
42 Immediately the girl stood up and began to walk around (she was twelve years
old). At this they were completely astonished. 43 He gave strict orders not to let
anyone know about this,[o] and told them
to give her something to eat.

A Prophet Without Honor

6:1-6pp — Mt 13:54-58

6 Jesus left there and went to his hometown,[p] accompanied by his disciples.
2 When the Sabbath came,[q] he began to
teach in the synagogue,[r] and many who
heard him were amazed.[s]
"Where did this man get these things?"
they asked. "What's this wisdom that has
been given him? What are these remarkable miracles he is performing? 3 Isn't this
the carpenter? Isn't this Mary's son and
the brother of James, Joseph,[b] Judas and
Simon?[t] Aren't his sisters here with us?"
And they took offense at him.[u]
4 Jesus said to them, "A prophet is not
without honor except in his own town,
among his relatives and in his own
home."[v] 5 He could not do any miracles

5:28 [d] S Mt 9:20 **5:29** [e] ver 34 **5:30** [f] Lk 5:17; 6:19 **5:34** [g] S Mt 9:22 [h] S Ac 15:33 **5:35** [i] S ver 22 **5:37** [j] S Mt 4:21 **5:38** [k] S ver 22

5:39 [l] S Mt 9:24 **5:41** [m] Mk 1:31 [n] S Lk 7:14 **5:43** [o] S Mt 8:4 **6:1** [p] S Mt 2:23 **6:2** [q] Mk 1:21 [r] S Mt 4:23 [s] S Mt 7:28 **6:3** [t] S Mt 12:46 [u] Mt 11:6; Jn 6:61 **6:4** [v] Lk 4:24; Jn 4:44

[a] 36 Or *Ignoring* [b] 3 Greek *Joses*, a variant of *Joseph*

people generally, since anyone having contact with her was made ceremonially unclean (Lev 15:25–33).

5:26 *suffered a great deal under the care of many doctors.* The Jewish Talmud preserves a record of medicines and treatments prescribed for illnesses of this sort.

5:28 *If I just touch his clothes.* Although it needed to be bolstered by physical contact, her faith was rewarded (v. 34; cf. Ac 19:12). Instead of the unclean (the woman; see note on v. 25) making another (Jesus) impure through physical contact, with Jesus it was the reverse: The clean (Jesus) made the unclean (the woman) pure.

5:30 *power had gone out from him.* The woman was healed because God graciously determined to heal her through the power then active in Jesus.

5:32 *kept looking around to see who had done it.* Jesus would not allow the woman to recede into the crowd without publicly commending her faith and assuring her that she was permanently healed.

5:34 *healed.* The Greek for "healed" can also mean "saved." Here both physical healing ("be freed from your suffering") and spiritual salvation ("go in peace") are meant. The two also appear together in 2:1–12 (see note on 2:9); 3:1–6.

5:37 *Peter, James and John.* These three disciples had an especially close relationship to Jesus (see note on Ac 3:1).

5:38 *people crying and wailing loudly.* It was customary for professional mourners to be brought in at the time of death. In this case, however, it is not certain that enough time had elapsed for mourners to have been secured.

5:39 *not dead but asleep.* See note on Lk 8:52.

5:41 *Talitha koum!* Mark is the only Gospel writer who here preserves the original Aramaic—one of the languages of the Holy Land in the first century AD and probably the language Jesus and his disciples ordinarily spoke (they may also have spoken Hebrew and Greek).

5:42 *astonished.* See 1:22 and note.

5:43 *not to let anyone know.* In the vicinity of Galilee Jesus often cautioned people whom he healed not to spread the story of the miracle. His great popularity with the people, coupled with the growing opposition from the religious leaders, could have precipitated a crisis before Jesus' ministry was completed (see v. 19 and note; 7:36; 8:26).

6:1 *his hometown.* Nazareth (see notes on Mt 2:23; Lk 4:23).

6:2 *teach in the synagogue.* See 1:21 and note. *amazed.* See 1:22 and note.

6:3 *carpenter.* Matthew reports that Jesus was called "the carpenter's son" (Mt 13:55); only in Mark is Jesus himself referred to as a carpenter. The Greek word can also apply to a mason, smith or builder in general. The question is derogatory, meaning, "Isn't he a common worker with his hands like the rest of us?" *brother of James, Joseph, Judas and Simon.* See note on Lk 8:19. *they took offense at him.* They saw no reason to believe that he was different from them, much less that he was specially anointed by God.

there, except lay his hands on[w] a few sick
people and heal them. 6 He was amazed at
their lack of faith.

Jesus Sends Out the Twelve

6:7-11pp — Mt 10:1,9-14; Lk 9:1,3-5

Then Jesus went around teaching from
village to village.[x] 7 Calling the Twelve to
him,[y] he began to send them out two by
two[z] and gave them authority over impure
spirits.[a]

8 These were his instructions: "Take
nothing for the journey except a staff —
no bread, no bag, no money in your belts.
9 Wear sandals but not an extra shirt.
10 Whenever you enter a house, stay there
until you leave that town. 11 And if any
place will not welcome you or listen to
you, leave that place and shake the dust
off your feet[b] as a testimony against them."

12 They went out and preached that people should repent.[c] 13 They drove out many
demons and anointed many sick people
with oil[d] and healed them.

John the Baptist Beheaded

6:14-29pp — Mt 14:1-12
6:14-16pp — Lk 9:7-9

14 King Herod heard about this, for
Jesus' name had become well known.
Some were saying,[a] "John the Baptist[e] has
been raised from the dead, and that is why
miraculous powers are at work in him."

15 Others said, "He is Elijah."[f]

And still others claimed, "He is a prophet,[g] like one of the prophets of long ago."[h]

16 But when Herod heard this, he said,
"John, whom I beheaded, has been raised
from the dead!"

6:5 [w]S Mk 5:23
6:6 [x]Mt 9:35; Mk 1:39; Lk 13:22
6:7 [y]Mk 3:13 [z]Dt 17:6; Lk 10:1 [a]S Mt 10:1
6:11 [b]S Mt 10:14
6:12 [c]Lk 9:6
6:13 [d]S Jas 5:14
6:14 [e]S Mt 3:1
6:15 [f]Mal 4:5 [g]S Mt 21:11 [h]Mt 16:14; Mk 8:28
6:17 [i]Mt 4:12; 11:2; Lk 3:19,20
6:18 [j]Lev 18:16; 20:21
6:20 [k]S Mt 11:9
6:21 [l]Est 1:3; 2:18 [m]Lk 3:1
6:23 [n]Est 5:3,6; 7:2

17 For Herod himself had given orders to
have John arrested, and he had him bound
and put in prison.[i] He did this because of
Herodias, his brother Philip's wife, whom
he had married. 18 For John had been saying to Herod, "It is not lawful for you to
have your brother's wife."[j] 19 So Herodias
nursed a grudge against John and wanted to kill him. But she was not able to,
20 because Herod feared John and protected him, knowing him to be a righteous
and holy man.[k] When Herod heard John,
he was greatly puzzled[b]; yet he liked to
listen to him.

21 Finally the opportune time came. On
his birthday Herod gave a banquet[l] for his
high officials and military commanders
and the leading men of Galilee.[m] 22 When
the daughter of[c] Herodias came in and
danced, she pleased Herod and his dinner guests.

The king said to the girl, "Ask me for
anything you want, and I'll give it to you."
23 And he promised her with an oath,
"Whatever you ask I will give you, up to
half my kingdom."[n]

24 She went out and said to her mother,
"What shall I ask for?"

"The head of John the Baptist," she answered.

25 At once the girl hurried in to the king
with the request: "I want you to give me
right now the head of John the Baptist on
a platter."

26 The king was greatly distressed, but
because of his oaths and his dinner guests,

[a] 14 Some early manuscripts *He was saying*
[b] 20 Some early manuscripts *he did many things*
[c] 22 Some early manuscripts *When his daughter*

6:5 *He could not do any miracles there.* It was not that Jesus did not have power to perform miracles at Nazareth but that he chose not to in such a climate of unbelief (v. 6).
6:6 *He was amazed.* See note on Lk 7:9.
6:7 – 13 See note on Lk 9:1 – 6.
6:7 *the Twelve.* See notes on Ac 1:11; 1Co 15:5. *two by two.* The purpose of going in pairs may have been to bolster credibility by having the testimony of more than one witness (cf. Dt 17:6), as well as to provide mutual support during their training period.
6:8 *no bread, no bag, no money in your belts.* They were to depend entirely on the hospitality of those to whom they testified (see vv. 10 – 11; see also notes on Lk 9:3; 10:4).
6:9 *not an extra shirt.* At night an extra shirt was helpful as a covering to protect from the cold night air, and the implication here is that the disciples were to trust in God to provide lodging each night.
6:10 *stay there.* See note on Lk 9:4.
6:11 *shake the dust off your feet.* See notes on Mt 10:14; Lk 9:5.
6:12 – 13 *preached ... drove out many demons.* This mission marks the beginning of the disciples' own ministry in Jesus' name (see 3:14 – 15), and their message was precisely the same as his (1:15).
6:12 *repent.* See 1:4 and note.
6:13 *anointed many sick people with oil.* In the ancient world olive oil was widely used as a medicine (see Jas 5:14 and note).
6:14 *King Herod.* See note on Mt 14:1. Mark may here have used the title "king" sarcastically (since this Herod was actually a tetrarch; see chart, p. 1592), or perhaps he simply used Herod's popular title.
6:15 *He is Elijah.* See Mal 4:5 and note.
6:16 *John ... has been raised from the dead!* Herod, disturbed by an uneasy conscience and disposed to superstition, feared that John had come back to haunt him.
6:17 *John arrested ... and put in prison.* See 1:14 and note. Josephus says that John was imprisoned at Machaerus, a fortress in Perea on the eastern side of the Dead Sea (see map, p. 1707). *Herodias.* See note on Mt 14:3. *Philip's.* See note on Mt 14:3.
6:22 *daughter of Herodias.* See note on Mt 14:6.
6:23 *up to half my kingdom.* A proverbial reference to generosity, not to be taken literally (see Est 5:3,6). Generosity suited the occasion and would win the approval of the guests.
6:25 *platter.* See note on Mt 14:8.
6:26 *greatly distressed.* The Greek for this phrase is also used to describe Jesus' agony in Gethsemane (14:34, "overwhelmed with sorrow").

he did not want to refuse her. 27 So he immediately sent an executioner with orders to bring John's head. The man went, beheaded John in the prison, 28 and brought back his head on a platter. He presented it to the girl, and she gave it to her mother. 29 On hearing of this, John's disciples came and took his body and laid it in a tomb.

Jesus Feeds the Five Thousand

6:32-44pp — Mt 14:13-21; Lk 9:10-17; Jn 6:5-13
6:32-44Ref — Mk 8:2-9

30 The apostles[o] gathered around Jesus and reported to him all they had done and taught.[p] 31 Then, because so many people were coming and going that they did not even have a chance to eat,[q] he said to them, "Come with me by yourselves to a quiet place and get some rest."

32 So they went away by themselves in a boat[r] to a solitary place. 33 But many who saw them leaving recognized them and ran on foot from all the towns and got there ahead of them. 34 When Jesus landed and saw a large crowd, he had compassion on them, because they were like sheep without a shepherd.[s] So he began teaching them many things.

35 By this time it was late in the day, so his disciples came to him. "This is a remote place," they said, "and it's already very late. 36 Send the people away so that they can go to the surrounding countryside and villages and buy themselves something to eat."

37 But he answered, "You give them something to eat."[t]

They said to him, "That would take more than half a year's wages[a]! Are we to go and spend that much on bread and give it to them to eat?"

38 "How many loaves do you have?" he asked. "Go and see."

When they found out, they said, "Five—and two fish."[u]

39 Then Jesus directed them to have all the people sit down in groups on the green grass. 40 So they sat down in groups of hundreds and fifties. 41 Taking the five loaves and the two fish and looking up to heaven, he gave thanks and broke the loaves.[v] Then he gave them to his disciples to distribute to the people. He also divided the two fish among them all. 42 They all ate and were satisfied, 43 and the disciples picked up twelve basketfuls of broken pieces of bread and fish. 44 The number of the men who had eaten was five thousand.

Jesus Walks on the Water

6:45-51pp — Mt 14:22-32; Jn 6:15-21
6:53-56pp — Mt 14:34-36

45 Immediately Jesus made his disciples get into the boat[w] and go on ahead of

6:30 [o] Mt 10:2; Lk 9:10; 17:5; 22:14; 24:10; Ac 1:2,26 [p] Lk 9:10
6:31 [q] Mk 3:20
6:32 [r] ver 45; S Mk 4:36
6:34 [s] S Mt 9:36
6:37 [t] 2Ki 4:42-44
6:38 [u] Mt 15:34; Mk 8:5
6:41 [v] S Mt 14:19
6:45 [w] ver 32

[a] *37* Greek *take two hundred denarii*

6:30–44 The feeding of the 5,000 in Mark's Gospel begins with an elaborate introduction (vv. 30–38), is looked back to on two different occasions (v. 52; 8:17–19) and has a sequel in the feeding of the 4,000 (8:1–10).

6:30 *apostles.* In Mark's Gospel the word occurs only here and in 3:14 in some manuscripts (see NIV text note there). The apostles were Jesus' authorized agents or representatives (see Heb 3:1 and note). In the NT the word is sometimes used quite generally (see Jn 13:16, where the Greek *apostolos* is translated "messenger"). In the technical sense it is used (1) of the Twelve (Lk 6:13)—in which sense it is also applied to Paul (Ro 1:1)—and (2) of a larger group, including Barnabas (Ac 14:14), James the Lord's brother (Gal 1:19) and possibly Andronicus and Junia (Ro 16:7). *reported to him all they had done and taught.* Because he had commissioned them as his representatives. They were returning from what may have been a third preaching tour in Galilee (see vv. 12–13; 1:39 and notes).

6:32 *went away by themselves in a boat.* John reports that they went to the other side of the Sea of Galilee (Jn 6:1). Luke, more specifically, says they went to Bethsaida (Lk 9:10), which locates the feeding of the 5,000 on the northeast shore (see note on 7:24).

6:33 *ran on foot ... and got there ahead of them.* Perhaps a strong headwind slowed the boat down so that the people had time to go on foot around the lake and arrive before the boat.

6:37 *more than half a year's wages.* See NIV text note. The usual pay for a day's work was one denarius (see Mt 20:2 and note).

6:38 *loaves.* Barley loaves. Unlike our modern loaves, these were small and flat. One could easily eat several at a single meal (see note on Jn 6:9).

6:39 *green grass.* Grass is green around the Sea of Galilee after the late winter or early spring rains.

6:40 *groups of hundreds and fifties.* Recalls the order of the Mosaic camp in the wilderness (e.g., Ex 18:21).

6:42 *all ate and were satisfied.* Attempts to explain away this miracle (e.g., by suggesting that Jesus and his disciples shared their lunch and the crowd followed their good example) are inadequate. If Jesus was, as he claimed to be, the Son of God, the miracle presents no difficulties. God had promised that when the true Shepherd came, the wilderness would become rich pasture where the sheep would be gathered and fed (Eze 34:23–31). Jesus is the Shepherd who provides for all our needs, so that we lack nothing (cf. Ps 23:1).

6:43 *twelve basketfuls of broken pieces of bread and fish.* Bread was regarded by Jews as a gift of God, and it was required that scraps that fell on the ground during a meal be picked up. The fragments were collected in small wicker baskets that were carried as a part of daily attire. Each of the disciples returned with his basket full (see note on Mt 15:37).

6:44 *men.* Matthew adds "besides women and children" (Mt 14:21; see note there). *five thousand.* A number that could easily be calculated because of the division of the crowd into "groups of hundreds and fifties" (v. 40). The size of the crowd is amazing in light of the fact that the neighboring towns of Capernaum and Bethsaida probably had a population of only 2,000 to 3,000 each.

6:45 *go on ahead of him.* John indicates that the people were ready to take Jesus by force and make him king (see Jn 6:14–15 and note on 6:15), and Jesus therefore sent his disciples across the lake while he slipped away into the hills to pray (v. 46).

him to Bethsaida,[x] while he dismissed the
crowd. 46 After leaving them, he went up
on a mountainside to pray.[y]
47 Later that night, the boat was in the
middle of the lake, and he was alone on
land. 48 He saw the disciples straining at
the oars, because the wind was against
them. Shortly before dawn he went out to
them, walking on the lake. He was about
to pass by them, 49 but when they saw him
walking on the lake, they thought he was
a ghost.[z] They cried out, 50 because they all
saw him and were terrified.
Immediately he spoke to them and said,
"Take courage! It is I. Don't be afraid."[a]
51 Then he climbed into the boat[b] with
them, and the wind died down.[c] They
were completely amazed, 52 for they had
not understood about the loaves; their
hearts were hardened.[d]
53 When they had crossed over, they
landed at Gennesaret and anchored there.[e]
54 As soon as they got out of the boat, people recognized Jesus. 55 They ran throughout that whole region and carried the sick
on mats to wherever they heard he was.
56 And wherever he went — into villages,
towns or countryside — they placed the
sick in the marketplaces. They begged
him to let them touch even the edge of
his cloak,[f] and all who touched it were
healed.

That Which Defiles

7:1-23pp — Mt 15:1-20

7 The Pharisees and some of the teachers of the law who had come from
Jerusalem gathered around Jesus 2 and
saw some of his disciples eating food
with hands that were defiled,[g] that is, unwashed. 3 (The Pharisees and all the Jews
do not eat unless they give their hands a
ceremonial washing, holding to the tradition of the elders.[h] 4 When they come from
the marketplace they do not eat unless
they wash. And they observe many other
traditions, such as the washing of cups,
pitchers and kettles.[a])[i]
5 So the Pharisees and teachers of the
law asked Jesus, "Why don't your disciples live according to the tradition of the
elders[j] instead of eating their food with defiled hands?"
6 He replied, "Isaiah was right when he
prophesied about you hypocrites; as it is
written:

> " 'These people honor me with their lips,
> but their hearts are far from me.
> 7 They worship me in vain;
> their teachings are merely human rules.'[b][k]

8 You have let go of the commands of God
and are holding on to human traditions."[l]
9 And he continued, "You have a fine
way of setting aside the commands of God
in order to observe[c] your own traditions![m]
10 For Moses said, 'Honor your father and
mother,'[d][n] and, 'Anyone who curses their
father or mother is to be put to death.'[e][o]
11 But you say[p] that if anyone declares
that what might have been used to help
their father or mother is Corban (that is,

[a] 4 Some early manuscripts *pitchers, kettles and dining couches* [b] 6,7 Isaiah 29:13 [c] 9 Some manuscripts *set up* [d] 10 Exodus 20:12; Deut. 5:16 [e] 10 Exodus 21:17; Lev. 20:9

6:45 [x] S Mt 11:21 **6:46** [y] S Lk 3:21 **6:49** [z] Lk 24:37 **6:50** [a] S Mt 14:27 **6:51** [b] ver 32 [c] Mk 4:39 **6:52** [d] Mk 8:17-21 **6:53** [e] Jn 6:24, 25 **6:56** [f] S Mt 9:20 **7:2** [g] Ac 10:14, 28; 11:8; Ro 14:14 **7:3** [h] ver 5,8,9, 13; Lk 11:38 **7:4** [i] Mt 23:25; Lk 11:39 **7:5** [j] S ver 3; Gal 1:14; Col 2:8 **7:7** [k] Isa 29:13 **7:8** [l] S ver 3 **7:9** [m] S ver 3 **7:10** [n] Ex 20:12; Dt 5:16 [o] Ex 21:17; Lev 20:9 **7:11** [p] Mt 23:16, 18

6:46 *pray.* Mark's mention of Jesus' praying is further evidence of a crisis situation. On only three occasions in this Gospel (here; 1:35; 14:32 – 36) does Jesus withdraw to pray; each time a crisis is involved.

6:48 *Shortly before dawn.* Lit. "About the fourth watch of the night," 3:00 – 6:00 a.m. (see 13:35; Mt 14:25 and notes). *walking on the lake.* A special display of the majestic presence and power of the transcendent Lord, who rules over the sea (see Ps 89:9; Isa 51:10,15; Jer 31:35).

6:49 *a ghost.* Popular Jewish superstition held that the appearance of spirits during the night brought disaster. The disciples' terror was prompted by what they may have thought was a water spirit.

6:51 *amazed.* See 1:22 and note.

6:52 *they had not understood about the loaves.* If they had understood the feeding of the 5,000, they would not have been amazed at Jesus' walking on the water or his calming the waves. *hearts were hardened.* They were showing themselves to be similar to Jesus' opponents, who also exhibited hardness of heart (see 3:5; 8:17 – 21 and note on 8:16; Ex 4:21 and note).

6:53 *Gennesaret.* See note on Mt 14:34.

6:55 *carried the sick on mats.* See 2:3 – 4.

6:56 *touch even the edge of his cloak.* See note on 5:28.

7:1 *Pharisees … had come from Jerusalem.* Another delegation of fact-finding religious leaders from Jerusalem (see 3:22) sent to investigate the Galilean activities of Jesus (see 2:16; Mt 2:4 and notes).

7:3 *ceremonial washing.* See note on Jn 2:6. *tradition of the elders.* Considered to be binding (see v. 5 and note on Mt 15:2).

7:4 *marketplace.* Where Jews would come into contact with Gentiles, or with Jews who did not observe the ceremonial law, and thus become ceremonially unclean.

7:6 *Isaiah … prophesied.* Isaiah roundly denounced the religious leaders of his day (Isa 29:13), and Jesus quotes him to describe the tradition of the elders as "merely human rules" (v. 7). *hypocrites.* See Mt 6:2 and note.

7:8 *commands of God … human traditions.* Jesus clearly contrasts the two. God's commands are found in Scripture and are binding; the "tradition of the elders" (v. 3) is not Biblical and therefore not authoritative or binding.

7:10 The fifth commandment is cited in both its positive and negative forms.

7:11 *Corban.* A Hebrew/Aramaic word meaning "offering" (see note on Lev 1:2). By using this word in a religious vow an irresponsible Jewish son could formally dedicate to God (i.e., to the temple) his earnings that otherwise would have gone for the support of his parents. The money, however, did not necessarily have to go for religious purposes. The Corban formula was simply a means of circumventing the clear

devoted to God)— 12then you no longer let them do anything for their father or mother. 13Thus you nullify the word of God[q] by your tradition[r] that you have handed down. And you do many things like that."

14Again Jesus called the crowd to him and said, "Listen to me, everyone, and understand this. 15Nothing outside a person can defile them by going into them. Rather, it is what comes out of a person that defiles them." [16][a]

17After he had left the crowd and entered the house, his disciples asked him[s] about this parable. 18"Are you so dull?" he asked. "Don't you see that nothing that enters a person from the outside can defile them? 19For it doesn't go into their heart but into their stomach, and then out of the body." (In saying this, Jesus declared all foods[t] clean.)[u]

20He went on: "What comes out of a person is what defiles them. 21For it is from within, out of a person's heart, that evil thoughts come—sexual immorality, theft, murder, 22adultery, greed,[v] malice, deceit, lewdness, envy, slander, arrogance and folly. 23All these evils come from inside and defile a person."

Jesus Honors a Syrophoenician Woman's Faith

7:24-30pp — Mt 15:21-28

24Jesus left that place and went to the vicinity of Tyre.[b][w] He entered a house and did not want anyone to know it; yet he could not keep his presence secret. 25In fact, as soon as she heard about him, a woman whose little daughter was possessed by an impure spirit[x] came and fell at his feet. 26The woman was a Greek, born in Syrian Phoenicia. She begged Jesus to drive the demon out of her daughter.

27"First let the children eat all they want," he told her, "for it is not right to take the children's bread and toss it to the dogs."

28"Lord," she replied, "even the dogs under the table eat the children's crumbs."

29Then he told her, "For such a reply, you may go; the demon has left your daughter."

30She went home and found her child lying on the bed, and the demon gone.

Jesus Heals a Deaf and Mute Man

7:31-37pp — Mt 15:29-31

31Then Jesus left the vicinity of Tyre[y] and went through Sidon, down to the Sea of Galilee[z] and into the region of the Decapolis.[c][a] 32There some people brought to him a man who was deaf and could hardly talk,[b] and they begged Jesus to place his hand on[c] him.

33After he took him aside, away from the crowd, Jesus put his fingers into the man's ears. Then he spit[d] and touched the man's tongue. 34He looked up to heaven[e] and with a deep sigh[f] said to him, *"Eph-*

7:13 [q]S Heb 4:12 [r]S ver 3
7:17 [s]Mk 9:28
7:19 [t]Ro 14:1-12; Col 2:16; 1Ti 4:3-5 [u]S Ac 10:15
7:22 [v]Mt 20:15
7:24 [w]S Mt 11:21
7:25 [x]S Mt 4:24
7:31 [y]ver 24; S Mt 11:21 [z]S Mt 4:18 [a]Mt 4:25; Mk 5:20
7:32 [b]Mt 9:32; Lk 11:14 [c]S Mk 5:23
7:33 [d]Mk 8:23
7:34 [e]Mk 6:41; Jn 11:41 [f]Mk 8:12

[a] *16* Some manuscripts include here the words of 4:23.
[b] *24* Many early manuscripts *Tyre and Sidon*
[c] *31* That is, the Ten Cities

responsibility of children toward their parents as prescribed in the law. The teachers of the law held that the Corban oath was binding, even when uttered rashly. The practice was one of many traditions that adhered to the letter of the law while ignoring its spirit. *(that is, devoted to God).* By explaining this word, Mark reveals that he is addressing Gentile readers, probably Romans primarily (see Introduction: Recipients).

7:13 *you nullify the word of God by your tradition.* The teachers of the law appealed to Nu 30:1–2 in support of the Corban vow, but Jesus categorically rejects the practice of using one Biblical teaching to nullify another. The scribal interpretation of Nu 30:1–2 satisfied the letter of the passage but missed the meaning of the law as a whole. *nullify.* Cf. 2Co 4:2 and note.

7:19 *(In saying this, Jesus declared all foods clean.)* Mark adds this parenthetical comment to help his readers see the significance of Jesus' pronouncement for them (see Ac 10:9–16 and note on 10:14).

7:20 Jesus replaced the normal Jewish understandings of defilement with the truth that defilement comes from an impure heart, not the violation of external rules. Fellowship with God is not interrupted by unclean hands or food but by sin (see vv. 21–23 and note on Pr 4:23).

7:24 *Tyre.* A Gentile city located in Phoenicia (modern Lebanon), which bordered Galilee to the northwest (see map, p. 1670). A journey of about 30 miles from Capernaum would have brought Jesus "to the vicinity of Tyre." *did not want anyone to know.* Ever since the feeding of the 5,000 (6:30–44) Jesus and his disciples had been, for the most part, skirting the region of Galilee. His purpose was to avoid the opposition in Galilee and to secure opportunity to teach his disciples privately (9:30–31). The regions to which he withdrew were: (1) the northeast shore of the Sea of Galilee (6:30–53), (2) Phoenicia (7:24–30), (3) the Decapolis (7:31—8:10) and (4) Caesarea Philippi (8:27—9:32).

7:26 *Greek.* Here probably equivalent to "Gentile." *Syrian Phoenicia.* At that time Phoenicia belonged administratively to Syria. Mark possibly used the term to distinguish this woman from the Libyan Phoenicians of North Africa.

7:27 *take the children's bread and toss it to the dogs.* See note on Mt 15:26.

7:28 *Lord.* The only time in Mark's Gospel that Jesus is addressed as "Lord"—and this by a Syrian Phoenician woman.

7:31 *left the vicinity of Tyre and went through Sidon, down to the Sea of Galilee.* Apparently Jesus went north from Tyre to Sidon (about 25 miles) and then southeast through the territory of Herod Philip to the east side of the Sea of Galilee (see map, p. 1670). The route was circuitous—possibly to avoid entering Galilee, where Herod Antipas was in power (see 6:14–29) and where many people wanted to take Jesus by force and make him king (see Jn 6:14–15 and note on 6:15). Herod had intimated a hostile interest in Jesus (6:14–16). *Decapolis.* See notes on v. 24; Mt 4:25; see also map, p. 1663.

7:32 *place his hand on him.* In order to heal him (see 1:41; 5:23; Ac 6:6 and note).

7:33 *spit.* See 8:23; Jn 9:6 and note.

phatha!" (which means "Be opened!").
35 At this, the man's ears were opened,
his tongue was loosened and he began to
speak plainly.[g]
36 Jesus commanded them not to tell
anyone.[h] But the more he did so, the more
they kept talking about it. 37 People were
overwhelmed with amazement. "He has
done everything well," they said. "He even
makes the deaf hear and the mute speak."

Jesus Feeds the Four Thousand

8:1-9pp — Mt 15:32-39
8:1-9Ref — Mk 6:32-44
8:11-21pp — Mt 16:1-12

8 During those days another large crowd
gathered. Since they had nothing to
eat, Jesus called his disciples to him and
said, 2 "I have compassion for these people;[i] they have already been with me three
days and have nothing to eat. 3 If I send
them home hungry, they will collapse on
the way, because some of them have come
a long distance."
4 His disciples answered, "But where in
this remote place can anyone get enough
bread to feed them?"
5 "How many loaves do you have?"
Jesus asked.
"Seven," they replied.
6 He told the crowd to sit down on the
ground. When he had taken the seven
loaves and given thanks, he broke them
and gave them to his disciples to distribute
to the people, and they did so. 7 They had
a few small fish as well; he gave thanks
for them also and told the disciples to distribute them.[j] 8 The people ate and were
satisfied. Afterward the disciples picked
up seven basketfuls of broken pieces that
were left over.[k] 9 About four thousand were
present. After he had sent them away, 10 he
got into the boat with his disciples and
went to the region of Dalmanutha.
11 The Pharisees came and began to
question Jesus. To test him, they asked
him for a sign from heaven.[l] 12 He sighed
deeply[m] and said, "Why does this generation ask for a sign? Truly I tell you, no sign
will be given to it." 13 Then he left them,
got back into the boat and crossed to the
other side.

The Yeast of the Pharisees and Herod

14 The disciples had forgotten to bring
bread, except for one loaf they had with
them in the boat. 15 "Be careful," Jesus
warned them. "Watch out for the yeast[n] of
the Pharisees[o] and that of Herod."[p]
16 They discussed this with one another and said, "It is because we have no
bread."
17 Aware of their discussion, Jesus asked
them: "Why are you talking about having
no bread? Do you still not see or understand? Are your hearts hardened?[q] 18 Do
you have eyes but fail to see, and ears but
fail to hear? And don't you remember?

7:35 [g] Isa 35:5,6
7:36 [h] S Mt 8:4
8:2 [i] S Mt 9:36
8:7 [j] Mt 14:19
8:8 [k] ver 20
8:11 [l] S Mt 12:38
8:12 [m] Mk 7:34
8:15 [n] 1Co 5:6-8 [o] Lk 12:1 [p] S Mt 14:1; Mk 12:13
8:17 [q] Isa 6:9, 10; Mk 6:52

7:34 *Ephphatha!* An Aramaic word that Mark translates for his Gentile readers (see Introduction: Recipients).
7:35 *man's ears were opened … he began to speak plainly.* Jesus was doing what God had promised to do when he came to redeem his people (see Isa 35:5 – 6 and notes).
7:36 *not to tell anyone.* See 5:19,43; Mt 8:4; 16:20 and notes.
7:37 *overwhelmed with amazement.* See 1:22 and note.
8:1 – 10 Although there are striking similarities between this account and 6:34 – 44, they are two distinct incidents, as indicated by the fact that Jesus himself refers to two feedings (see vv. 18 – 20).
8:1 *another large crowd gathered.* Since this incident took place in the region of the Decapolis (see 7:31), the crowd may have been made up of both Jews and Gentiles.
8:2 *compassion for these people.* As Jesus had compassion because the people were "like sheep without a shepherd" (6:34), he now has compassion because they have been so long without food.
8:4 *where … can anyone get enough bread to feed them?* The disciples' question reflects their inadequacy and acknowledges that Jesus alone could feed the people. They had not forgotten his feeding of the 5,000 (6:34 – 44) and were probably simply giving back to him the task of procuring bread. Alternatively, their question may reveal their spiritual dullness — they were slow learners (see note on v. 16).
8:8 *seven basketfuls.* See note on Mt 15:37.
8:9 *four thousand.* See note on 6:44.
8:10 *Dalmanutha.* South of the Plain of Gennesaret (see note on Mt 14:34) a cave has been found bearing the name "Talmanutha," perhaps the spot where Jesus landed. Matthew says Jesus "went to the vicinity of Magadan" (Mt 15:39; see note there; see also map, p. 1776). Dalmanutha and Magadan (or Magdala), located on the western shore of the Sea of Galilee, may be names for the same place or for two places located close to each other.
8:11 *Pharisees.* See note on Mt 3:7. *sign from heaven.* The Pharisees wanted more compelling proof of Jesus' divine authority than his miracles, but he refused to perform such a sign because the request came from unbelief.
8:12 *Truly I tell you.* See note on 3:28.
8:13 *other side.* The eastern shore of the Sea of Galilee.
8:15 *yeast.* Here, as generally in the NT (Mt 16:6,11; Lk 12:1; see 1Co 5:6 – 8; Gal 5:9 and notes, but Mt 13:33 seems to be an exception — see note there), yeast is a symbol of evil or corruption. The metaphor includes the idea of a tiny amount of yeast being able to ferment a large amount of dough. In this context it refers to the evil disposition of both the Pharisees and Herod Antipas (see Lk 23:8 and note). The Pharisees asked Jesus to produce a sign, i.e., a proof of his divine authority (see note on v. 11).
8:16 Another possible reading of the Greek text could be translated: "They discussed with one another why they had no bread." According to this rendering the disciples were so concerned to find out who was to blame for not bringing more bread that they completely ignored Jesus' warning about the yeast of the Pharisees and of Herod. Such an understanding heightens Mark's depiction of the disciples as slow learners (see 4:13; 5:51 – 52; 7:18; 8:4,17 – 21 and note on 8:4; 9:32; 10:13 – 14,35 – 40).
8:17 *hearts hardened.* See v. 4; 6:52 and notes.
8:18 – 20 These verses indicate two feeding narratives (see note on vv. 1 – 10).

THE TERRITORIES OF TYRE AND SIDON

In a unique excursion into pagan and semipagan areas, Jesus visited the districts of Tyre and Sidon and the confederation of free cities called the Decapolis. He was called to minister to "the lost sheep of Israel" (Mt 15:24), but the phenomenal public attention in Galilee was intense. Even here his fame had spread, and he could not keep his presence secret. The commercially magnificent cities of Tyre and Sidon had been a source of cultural seductiveness and religious heterodoxy since the time of Jezebel. The cities had been heavily influenced by Hellenism; the sophistication of Greek culture was apparent in their coinage and architecture. Each was also a proud, historic center of Canaanite paganism, with tombs of ancient kings and temples to Melqart/Heracles, Astarte and various other deities.

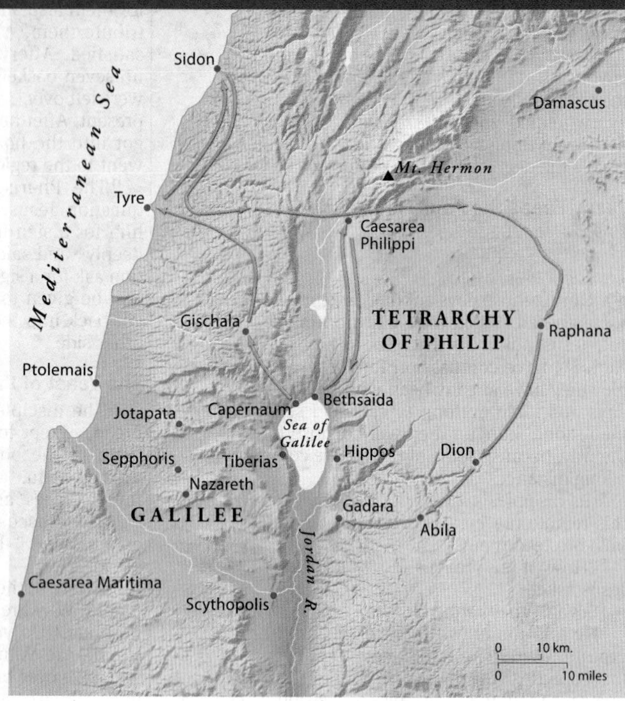

19When I broke the five loaves for the five
thousand, how many basketfuls of pieces
did you pick up?"
"Twelve,"[r] they replied.
20"And when I broke the seven loaves
for the four thousand, how many basketfuls of pieces did you pick up?"
They answered, "Seven."[s]
21He said to them, "Do you still not understand?"[t]

Jesus Heals a Blind Man at Bethsaida

22They came to Bethsaida,[u] and some
people brought a blind man[v] and begged
Jesus to touch him. 23He took the blind
man by the hand and led him outside the
village. When he had spit[w] on the man's
eyes and put his hands on[x] him, Jesus
asked, "Do you see anything?"
24He looked up and said, "I see people;
they look like trees walking around."
25Once more Jesus put his hands on the
man's eyes. Then his eyes were opened,
his sight was restored, and he saw everything clearly. 26Jesus sent him home, saying, "Don't even go into[a] the village."

Peter Declares That Jesus Is the Messiah

8:27-29pp — Mt 16:13-16; Lk 9:18-20

27Jesus and his disciples went on to the
villages around Caesarea Philippi. On the
way he asked them, "Who do people say
I am?"
28They replied, "Some say John the
Baptist;[y] others say Elijah;[z] and still others,
one of the prophets."

8:19 [r]Mt 14:20; Mk 6:41-44; Lk 9:17; Jn 6:13 **8:20** [s]ver 6-9; Mt 15:37 **8:21** [t]Mk 6:52 **8:22** [u]S Mt 11:21 [v]Mk 10:46; Jn 9:1 **8:23** [w]Mk 7:33 [x]S Mk 5:23 **8:28** [y]S Mt 3:1 [z]Mal 4:5

[a] 26 Some manuscripts *go and tell anyone in*

8:22 *Bethsaida.* See note on Mt 11:21.
8:23 *spit.* See 7:33 and note. *put his hands on him.* See 1:41; Ac 6:6 and note.
8:24 *like trees walking around.* The man had no doubt bumped into trees in his blindness; now he dimly sees something like tree trunks moving about.
8:25 *Once more Jesus put his hands on the man's eyes.* This second laying on of hands is unique in Jesus' healing ministry. It may symbolize that the disciples' spiritual sight is gradually increasing. *saw everything clearly.* Giving sight to the blind was another indication that Jesus was doing what God had promised to do when he came to bring salvation (see 7:35 and note).
8:26 *Don't even go into the village.* So as not to broadcast what Jesus had done for him and precipitate a crisis before Jesus had completed his ministry (see 5:19,43; Mt 8:4; 16:20 and notes).
8:27 *Caesarea Philippi.* See notes on 7:24; Mt 16:13.

29 "But what about you?" he asked.
"Who do you say I am?"
Peter answered, "You are the Messiah."[a]
30 Jesus warned them not to tell anyone
about him.[b]

Jesus Predicts His Death

8:31 — 9:1pp — Mt 16:21-28; Lk 9:22-27

31 He then began to teach them that the
Son of Man[c] must suffer many things[d] and
be rejected by the elders, the chief priests
and the teachers of the law,[e] and that he
must be killed[f] and after three days[g] rise
again.[h] 32 He spoke plainly[i] about this, and
Peter took him aside and began to rebuke
him.
33 But when Jesus turned and looked at
his disciples, he rebuked Peter. "Get behind
me, Satan!"[j] he said. "You do not
have in mind the concerns of God, but
merely human concerns."

The Way of the Cross

34 Then he called the crowd to him along
with his disciples and said: "Whoever
wants to be my disciple must deny themselves
and take up their cross and follow
me.[k] 35 For whoever wants to save their
life[a] will lose it, but whoever loses their
life for me and for the gospel will save it.[l]
36 What good is it for someone to gain the
whole world, yet forfeit their soul? 37 Or
what can anyone give in exchange for
their soul? 38 If anyone is ashamed of me
and my words in this adulterous and sinful
generation, the Son of Man[m] will be
ashamed of them[n] when he comes[o] in his
Father's glory with the holy angels."
9 And he said to them, "Truly I tell you,
some who are standing here will not
taste death before they see that the kingdom
of God has come[p] with power."[q]

The Transfiguration

9:2-8pp — Lk 9:28-36
9:2-13pp — Mt 17:1-13

2 After six days Jesus took Peter, James
and John[r] with him and led them up a
high mountain, where they were all alone.
There he was transfigured before them.
3 His clothes became dazzling white,[s] whiter
than anyone in the world could bleach
them. 4 And there appeared before them
Elijah and Moses, who were talking with
Jesus.
5 Peter said to Jesus, "Rabbi,[t] it is good
for us to be here. Let us put up three shelters
— one for you, one for Moses and one

8:29 [a] Jn 6:69; 11:27
8:30 [b] S Mt 8:4; 16:20; 17:9; Mk 9:9; Lk 9:21
8:31 [c] S Mt 8:20 [d] S Mt 16:21 [e] Mt 27:1,2 [f] Ac 2:23; 3:13 [g] S Mt 16:21 [h] S Mt 16:21
8:32 [i] Jn 18:20
8:33 [j] S Mt 4:10
8:34 [k] Mt 10:38; Lk 14:27
8:35 [l] S Jn 12:25
8:38 [m] S Mt 8:20 [n] Mt 10:33; Lk 12:9 [o] S 1Th 2:19
9:1 [p] Mk 13:30; Lk 22:18 [q] Mt 24:30; 25:31
9:2 [r] S Mt 4:21
9:3 [s] S Mt 28:3
9:5 [t] S Mt 23:7

[a] 35 The Greek word means either *life* or *soul;* also in verses 36 and 37.

8:29 *Messiah.* See note on Mt 16:16; a critical climax in Mark's Gospel as Peter, representing the apostles, recognizes Jesus as the promised Messiah. Yet his conception of the Messiah is about to be radically challenged (see notes on 8:31 — 10:52; 8:31; 8:32).

8:30 *not to tell anyone about him.* See v. 26 and note.

8:31 — 10:52 A new section begins in 8:31 and centers on three predictions of Jesus' death (8:31; 9:31; 10:33 – 34). It indicates a geographic shift from Galilee, where most of Jesus' public ministry reported by Mark took place, to Jerusalem and the closing days of Jesus' life on earth. In this section Jesus defines the true meaning of "Messiah" as the title applies to him (see note on v. 29).

8:31 *Son of Man.* Jesus' most common title for himself, used 81 times in the Gospels and never used by anyone but Jesus there. Elsewhere it is used by Stephen (Ac 7:56; see note there) and in John's vision (Rev 1:13). In Da 7:13 – 14 the Son of Man is pictured as a heavenly figure who in the end times is entrusted by God with authority, glory and sovereign power (see note on Da 7:13). That Jesus considered "Son of Man" to be a Messianic title is evident by his use of it here in juxtaposition to Peter's use of "Messiah" (v. 29; see note there). *must suffer.* As predicted, e.g., in Isa 52:13 — 53:12 (see note there and note on Lk 24:44; see also Mk 9:9,12,31; 10:33 – 34; 14:21,41 and relevant notes). *elders.* The lay members of the Sanhedrin, the high court of the Jews. *chief priests.* See note on Mt 2:4. These included the ruling high priest, Caiaphas; the former high priest, Annas; and the high priestly families. *teachers of the law.* See note on Mt 2:4. Representatives of the three groups mentioned here constituted the Sanhedrin.

8:32 *Peter ... began to rebuke him.* Suffering and rejection had no place in Peter's conception of the Messiah, and he rebuked Jesus for teaching what to him seemed not only inconceivable but also terribly wrong.

8:33 *Satan.* Peter's attempt to dissuade Jesus from going to the cross contained the same temptation Satan gave at the outset of Jesus' ministry (see Mt 4:8 – 10), so Jesus severely rebuked him.

8:34 *deny themselves.* Cease to make self the object of one's life and actions. *take up their cross.* The picture is of someone, already condemned, required to carry the beam of their own cross to the place of execution (see Jn 19:17 and note). Cross-bearing includes a willingness to suffer and die for the Lord's sake. *follow me.* Implying that his own death would be by crucifixion.

8:35 *save their life.* Physical life may be saved by denying Jesus, but eternal life will be lost. *loses their life.* Conversely, discipleship may result in the loss of physical life, but that loss is insignificant when compared with gaining eternal life (see note on Lk 9:24).

8:36 *whole world.* All the things that could possibly be achieved or acquired in this life. *their soul.* Eternal life (also in v. 37).

8:38 *ashamed of me and my words.* Contrast Ro 1:16. Those who are more concerned about fitting into and pleasing their own "adulterous and sinful generation" than about following and pleasing Christ will have no part in God's kingdom. *Son of Man.* See note on v. 31. *when he comes in his Father's glory.* The situation in which Jesus is rejected, humiliated and put to death will be reversed when he returns in glory as the Judge of all people (see 1Th 2:12 and note).

9:1 *Truly I tell you.* See note on 3:28. *not taste death before they see that the kingdom of God has come with power.* See note on Mt 16:28. *kingdom of God.* See note on Mt 3:2.

9:2 *After six days.* See note on Mt 17:1. *Peter, James and John.* See note on 5:37. *high mountain.* See note on Lk 9:28. *transfigured.* See note on Mt 17:2.

9:4 *Elijah and Moses.* See notes on Mt 17:3; Lk 9:30.

9:5 *Rabbi.* Hebrew for "(my) teacher." *three shelters.* Peter may

for Elijah." 6(He did not know what to say, they were so frightened.)

7Then a cloud appeared and covered them, and a voice came from the cloud:[u] "This is my Son, whom I love. Listen to him!"[v]

8Suddenly, when they looked around, they no longer saw anyone with them except Jesus.

9As they were coming down the mountain, Jesus gave them orders not to tell anyone[w] what they had seen until the Son of Man[x] had risen from the dead. 10They kept the matter to themselves, discussing what "rising from the dead" meant.

11And they asked him, "Why do the teachers of the law say that Elijah must come first?"

12Jesus replied, "To be sure, Elijah does come first, and restores all things. Why then is it written that the Son of Man[y] must suffer much[z] and be rejected?[a] 13But I tell you, Elijah has come,[b] and they have done to him everything they wished, just as it is written about him."

Jesus Heals a Boy Possessed by an Impure Spirit

9:14-28; 30-32pp — Mt 17:14-19; 22,23; Lk 9:37-45

14When they came to the other disciples, they saw a large crowd around them and the teachers of the law arguing with them. 15As soon as all the people saw Jesus, they were overwhelmed with wonder and ran to greet him.

16"What are you arguing with them about?" he asked.

17A man in the crowd answered, "Teacher, I brought you my son, who is possessed by a spirit that has robbed him of speech. 18Whenever it seizes him, it throws him to the ground. He foams at the mouth, gnashes his teeth and becomes rigid. I asked your disciples to drive out the spirit, but they could not."

19"You unbelieving generation," Jesus replied, "how long shall I stay with you? How long shall I put up with you? Bring the boy to me."

20So they brought him. When the spirit saw Jesus, it immediately threw the boy into a convulsion. He fell to the ground and rolled around, foaming at the mouth.[c]

21Jesus asked the boy's father, "How long has he been like this?"

"From childhood," he answered. 22"It has often thrown him into fire or water to kill him. But if you can do anything, take pity on us and help us."

23"'If you can'?" said Jesus. "Everything is possible for one who believes."[d]

24Immediately the boy's father exclaimed, "I do believe; help me overcome my unbelief!"

9:7 [u]Ex 24:16 [v]S Mt 3:17
9:9 [w]S Mk 8:30 [x]S Mt 8:20
9:12 [y]S Mt 8:20 [z]S Mt 16:21 [a]Lk 23:11
9:13 [b]S Mt 11:14
9:20 [c]Mk 1:26
9:23 [d]S Mt 21:21; Mk 11:23; Jn 11:40

have desired to erect new tents of meeting where God could again communicate with his people (see Ex 29:42). Or he may have been thinking of the booths used at the Festival of Tabernacles (see Lev 23:42 and note). In any case, he seemed eager to find fulfillment of the promised glory at that moment, prior to the sufferings that Jesus had announced as necessary.

9:7 *voice came from the cloud.* A cloud is frequently a symbol of God's presence to protect and guide (see note on Mt 17:5). *This is my Son, whom I love.* An allusion to Ps 2:7; Isa 42:1. *Listen to him!* The full sense includes obeying him. When God is involved, the only true hearing is obedient hearing (see Jas 1:22–25 and note on 1:25).

9:9 *not to tell anyone ... until.* See 5:19,43; Mt 8:4; 16:20 and notes. After Jesus' resurrection the disciples were to tell everyone what they had experienced, for Jesus' finished work would have demonstrated his true and full character as the Messiah. *Son of Man.* See note on 8:31.

9:10 *what "rising from the dead" meant.* As Jews they were familiar with the doctrine of the resurrection; it was the resurrection of the Son of Man that baffled them, because their theology had no place for a suffering and dying Messiah.

9:11 *Elijah must come first.* See note on Mt 17:10.

9:12 *Elijah does come first, and restores all things.* A reference to the coming of Elijah, or one like him, in preparation for the coming of the Messiah (see note on Mt 17:10). *Son of Man.* See note on 8:31. *must suffer much and be rejected.* Just as "Elijah" (John the Baptist; see note on v. 13) has been rejected (see note on Mt 17:12).

9:13 *Elijah has come.* A reference to John the Baptist (see Lk 1:17 and note). *they.* Herod and Herodias (see 6:17–29; Mt 14:3 and note). As Elijah was opposed by Ahab and Jezebel, so also John was opposed by a weak ruler and his wicked consort. *as it is written about him.* What Scripture says about Elijah in his relationship to Ahab and Jezebel (see 1Ki 19:1–10 and note on 19:3). There is no prediction of suffering associated with Elijah's ministry in the end times. However, what happened to Elijah under the threats of Jezebel foreshadowed what would happen to John the Baptist. The order of events suggested in vv. 11–13 is as follows: (1) Elijah ministered and suffered in the days of wicked Jezebel; (2) Elijah was a type of John the Baptist, who in turn suffered at the hands of Herodias; (3) the Son of Man suffered and was rejected a short time after John was beheaded.

9:14 *other disciples.* The nine besides Peter, James and John (see v. 2). *teachers of the law.* See note on Mt 2:4. If the transfiguration took place on Mount Hermon (see v. 2 and note), the presence of the teachers of the law so far north in the Holy Land would indicate their concern in monitoring the activities of Jesus.

9:17–18 See Mt 17:15,18 and notes.

9:18 Demonic possession was responsible for the boy's condition (see vv. 20,25–26).

9:19 *unbelieving generation.* Probably the referent should be restricted to the disciples. This cry of Jesus reveals his great disappointment with them (see note on 8:16).

9:22 *to kill him.* See note on 5:5.

9:23 *'If you can'?... Everything is possible for one who believes.* The question was not whether Jesus had the power to heal the boy but whether the father had faith to believe it. A person who truly believes will set no limits on what God can do.

9:24 *I do believe; help me overcome my unbelief!* Since human faith is never perfect, belief and unbelief are often mixed.

25When Jesus saw that a crowd was
running to the scene,[e] he rebuked the impure spirit. "You deaf and mute spirit," he
said, "I command you, come out of him
and never enter him again."
26The spirit shrieked, convulsed him violently and came out. The boy looked so
much like a corpse that many said, "He's
dead." 27But Jesus took him by the hand
and lifted him to his feet, and he stood up.
28After Jesus had gone indoors, his disciples asked him privately,[f] "Why couldn't
we drive it out?"
29He replied, "This kind can come out
only by prayer.[a]"

Jesus Predicts His Death a Second Time

9:33-37pp — Mt 18:1-5; Lk 9:46-48

30They left that place and passed
through Galilee. Jesus did not want anyone to know where they were, 31because
he was teaching his disciples. He said to
them, "The Son of Man[g] is going to be delivered into the hands of men. They will
kill him,[h] and after three days[i] he will
rise."[j] 32But they did not understand what
he meant[k] and were afraid to ask him
about it.
33They came to Capernaum.[l] When he
was in the house,[m] he asked them, "What
were you arguing about on the road?"
34But they kept quiet because on the way
they had argued about who was the greatest.[n]
35Sitting down, Jesus called the Twelve
and said, "Anyone who wants to be first
must be the very last, and the servant of
all."[o]
36He took a little child whom he placed
among them. Taking the child in his
arms,[p] he said to them, 37"Whoever welcomes one of these little children in my
name welcomes me; and whoever welcomes me does not welcome me but the
one who sent me."[q]

Whoever Is Not Against Us Is for Us

9:38-40pp — Lk 9:49,50

38"Teacher," said John, "we saw someone driving out demons in your name and
we told him to stop, because he was not
one of us."[r]
39"Do not stop him," Jesus said. "For no
one who does a miracle in my name can in
the next moment say anything bad about
me, 40for whoever is not against us is for
us.[s] 41Truly I tell you, anyone who gives
you a cup of water in my name because
you belong to the Messiah will certainly
not lose their reward.[t]

Causing to Stumble

42"If anyone causes one of these little ones — those who believe in me — to
stumble,[u] it would be better for them if
a large millstone were hung around their
neck and they were thrown into the sea.[v]
43If your hand causes you to stumble,[w]
cut it off. It is better for you to enter life
maimed than with two hands to go into
hell,[x] where the fire never goes out.[y] [44][b]

9:25 [e] ver 15 **9:28** [f] Mk 7:17 **9:31** [g] S Mt 8:20 [h] ver 12; Ac 2:23; 3:13 [i] S Mt 16:21 [j] S Mt 16:21 **9:32** [k] Lk 2:50; 9:45; 18:34; Jn 12:16 **9:33** [l] S Mt 4:13 [m] Mk 1:29 **9:34** [n] Lk 22:24 **9:35** [o] Mt 18:4; Mk 10:43; Lk 22:26 **9:36** [p] Mk 10:16 **9:37** [q] S Mt 10:40 **9:38** [r] Nu 11:27-29 **9:40** [s] Mt 12:30; Lk 11:23 **9:41** [t] S Mt 10:42 **9:42** [u] S Mt 5:29 [v] Mt 18:6; Lk 17:2 **9:43** [w] S Mt 5:29 [x] Mt 5:30; 18:8 [y] S Mt 25:41

[a] 29 Some manuscripts *prayer and fasting* [b] 44 Some manuscripts include here the words of verse 48.

9:25 *When Jesus saw that a crowd was running to the scene, he rebuked the impure spirit.* As much as possible, Jesus wanted to avoid further publicity.

9:29 *This kind.* Seems to suggest that there are different kinds of demons. *only by prayer.* The disciples apparently had taken for granted the power given to them or had come to believe that it was inherent in them. Lack of prayer indicated they had forgotten that their power over the demonic spirits came from trusting in Jesus and his power (see 3:15; 6:7,13; see also note on 6:12–13).

9:30 *passed through Galilee.* Jesus' public ministry in and around Galilee was now completed (see note on 7:24), and he was on his way to Jerusalem to suffer and die (see 10:32–34). As he had been doing for several months, Jesus continued to focus his teaching ministry on the Twelve (v. 31).

9:31 The second prediction of Jesus' death (see note on 8:31 — 10:52). *Son of Man.* See note on 8:31.

9:32 *they did not understand.* See v. 10; 8:32–33; Lk 24:44 and notes.

9:33–37 Parallel to 10:35–45 (see note there).

9:33 *Capernaum.* See Mt 4:13; Lk 10:15 and notes. *house.* Probably the one belonging to Peter and Andrew (see 1:29).

9:34 *they kept quiet.* No doubt due to embarrassment. *who was the greatest.* Questions of rank and status are normal and played an important role in the life of Jewish groups at this time, but they had no place in Jesus' value system (see v. 35; 10:42–44 and note on 10:43).

9:35 See note on Lk 9:48. *Sitting down.* See 4:1 and note.

9:38 *not one of us.* The man apparently was a believer, but he was not a member of the exclusive company of the Twelve. Nevertheless he acted in Jesus' name and had done what the disciples, on at least one occasion, had not been able to do (see vv. 14,28).

9:39 *Do not stop him.* Jesus' view of discipleship was far more inclusive than the narrow view held by the Twelve.

9:40 At first glance, this saying appears to contradict the one in Mt 12:30. There, however, reference is to those who vehemently opposed Jesus, whereas here it is to one who was in sympathy with Jesus and his ministry.

9:41 *Truly I tell you.* See note on 3:28. *gives you a cup of water.* God remembers even small acts of kindness extended to believers because they are believers (see note on Lk 9:50). *Messiah.* See 8:29 and note. *not lose their reward.* Have God's approval.

9:42 *little ones.* See Mt 18:6,10,14 and note; Lk 17:2. To cause believers to sin will bring serious judgment. *millstone.* A heavy stone slab used in grinding grain.

9:43 *cut it off.* Hyperbole, a figure of speech that exaggerates to make its point, is used here to emphasize the need for drastic action. Often sin can be conquered only by radical "spiritual surgery." *life.* Eternal life in the presence of God. *hell.* See Mt 5:22 and note.

45And if your foot causes you to stumble,[z] cut it off. It is better for you to enter
life crippled than to have two feet and be
thrown into hell.[a] [46][a] 47And if your eye
causes you to stumble,[b] pluck it out. It is
better for you to enter the kingdom of God
with one eye than to have two eyes and be
thrown into hell,[c] 48where

"'the worms that eat them do not
die,
and the fire is not quenched.'[b][d]

49Everyone will be salted[e] with fire.
50"Salt is good, but if it loses its saltiness, how can you make it salty again?[f]
Have salt among yourselves,[g] and be at
peace with each other."[h]

Divorce

10:1-12pp — Mt 19:1-9

10 Jesus then left that place and went
into the region of Judea and across
the Jordan.[i] Again crowds of people came
to him, and as was his custom, he taught
them.[j]
2Some Pharisees[k] came and tested him
by asking, "Is it lawful for a man to divorce his wife?"
3"What did Moses command you?" he
replied.
4They said, "Moses permitted a man to
write a certificate of divorce and send her
away."[l]
5"It was because your hearts were hard[m]
that Moses wrote you this law," Jesus replied. 6"But at the beginning of creation
God 'made them male and female.'[c][n] 7'For
this reason a man will leave his father and
mother and be united to his wife,[d] 8and
the two will become one flesh.'[e][o] So they
are no longer two, but one flesh. 9There-
fore what God has joined together, let no
one separate."
10When they were in the house again,
the disciples asked Jesus about this. 11He
answered, "Anyone who divorces his wife
and marries another woman commits
adultery against her.[p] 12And if she divorces her husband and marries another man,
she commits adultery."[q]

The Little Children and Jesus

10:13-16pp — Mt 19:13-15; Lk 18:15-17

13People were bringing little children to
Jesus for him to place his hands on them,
but the disciples rebuked them. 14When

9:45 [z] S Mt 5:29 [a] Mt 18:8 **9:47** [b] S Mt 5:29 [c] Mt 5:29; 18:9 **9:48** [d] Isa 66:24; S Mt 25:41 **9:49** [e] Lev 2:13 **9:50** [f] Mt 5:13; Lk 14:34, 35 [g] Col 4:6 [h] Ro 12:18; 2Co 13:11; 1Th 5:13 **10:1** [i] Mk 1:5; Jn 10:40; 11:7 [j] S Mt 4:23; Mk 2:13; 4:2; 6:6,34 **10:2** [k] Mk 2:16 **10:4** [l] Dt 24:1-4; Mt 5:31 **10:5** [m] Ps 95:8; Heb 3:15 **10:6** [n] Ge 1:27; 5:2 **10:8** [o] Ge 2:24; 1Co 6:16 **10:11** [p] S Lk 16:18 **10:12** [q] Ro 7:3; 1Co 7:10,11

[a] *46* Some manuscripts include here the words of verse 48. [b] *48* Isaiah 66:24 [c] *6* Gen. 1:27 [d] *7* Some early manuscripts do not have *and be united to his wife.* [e] *8* Gen. 2:24

9:47 *kingdom of God.* See note on Mt 3:2.

9:48 Isa 66:24 (see note there) speaks of the punishment for rebellion against God. As the final word of Isaiah's message, the passage became familiar as a picture of endless destruction. *worms that eat them do not die.* Worms were always present in the rubbish dump (see Mt 5:22 and note).

9:49 The saying may mean that everyone who enters hell will suffer its fire, or (if only loosely connected with the preceding) it may mean that every Christian in this life can expect to undergo the fire of suffering and purification.

9:50 *Salt is good.* The distinctive mark of discipleship typified by salt is allegiance to Jesus and the gospel (see 8:35,38; Mt 5:13 and notes). *be at peace with each other.* Strife is resolved and peace restored when we recognize in one another a common commitment to Jesus and the gospel.

10:1 *region of Judea.* The Greek and Roman equivalent to the OT land of Judah, essentially the southern part of the Holy Land (now exclusive of Idumea), which formerly had been the southern kingdom. For Jesus' ministry in Judea, see note on Lk 9:51. *Jordan.* See note on 1:5. Jesus' journey took him south from Capernaum, over the mountains of Samaria into Judea and then east across the Jordan into Perea, where Herod Antipas ruled (see note on Mt 14:1). For Jesus' ministry in Perea, see note on Lk 13:22.

10:2 *Pharisees.* See note on 2:16. *came and tested him.* The question of the Pharisees was hostile. It was for unlawful divorce and remarriage that John the Baptist denounced Herod Antipas and Herodias (see 6:17–18), and this rebuke cost him imprisonment and then his life. Jesus was now within Herod's jurisdiction, and the Pharisees may have hoped that Jesus' reply would cause the tetrarch to seize him as he had John. *Is it lawful … to divorce his wife?* Jews of that day generally agreed that divorce was lawful, the only debated issue being the proper grounds for it (see note on Mt 19:3).

10:5 *because your hearts were hard.* See 6:52 and note. Divorce was an accommodation to human weakness and was used to bring order in a society that had disregarded God's will, but it was not the standard God had originally intended, as vv. 6–9 clearly indicate. The purpose of Dt 24:1–4 (see note there) was not to make divorce acceptable but to reduce the hardship of its consequences.

10:6 *at the beginning of creation.* Jesus goes back to the time before human sin to show God's original intention. God instituted marriage as a great unifying blessing, bonding the male and female in his creation.

10:8 *no longer two, but one flesh.* The deduction drawn by Jesus affirms the ideal of the permanence of marriage.

10:9 *Therefore what God has joined together.* Jesus grounds the sanctity of marriage in the authority of God himself, and his "No" to divorce safeguards against human selfishness, which always threatens to destroy marriage.

10:11 *Anyone who divorces his wife.* In Jewish practice divorce was effected by the husband himself, not by a judicial authority or court. *commits adultery against her.* A simple declaration of divorce on the part of a husband could not release him from the divine law of marriage and its moral obligations. This enduring force of the marriage bond was unrecognized in rabbinic courts, where a certificate of divorce explicitly stated the right to remarry. Cf. Mt 19:3 and note; cf. also Mt 19:9, where an exception is mentioned. 1Co 7:15 may contain another exception (see notes on 1Co 7:12,15).

10:12 *she commits adultery.* In this historical and geographic context, Jesus' pronouncements confirm the bold denunciation by John the Baptist and equally condemn Herod Antipas and Herodias.

Jesus saw this, he was indignant. He said
to them, "Let the little children come to
me, and do not hinder them, for the kingdom of God belongs to such as these.[r]
15 Truly I tell you, anyone who will not receive the kingdom of God like a little child
will never enter it."[s] 16 And he took the
children in his arms,[t] placed his hands on
them and blessed them.

10:14 [r] S Mt 25:34 **10:15** [s] Mt 18:3 **10:16** [t] Mk 9:36 **10:17** [u] Mk 1:40 [v] Lk 10:25; S Ac 20:32

The Rich and the Kingdom of God

10:17-31pp — Mt 19:16-30; Lk 18:18-30

17 As Jesus started on his way, a man
ran up to him and fell on his knees[u] before him. "Good teacher," he asked, "what
must I do to inherit eternal life?"[v]
18 "Why do you call me good?" Jesus
answered. "No one is good — except God
alone. 19 You know the commandments:

10:14 *kingdom of God.* See note on Mt 3:2. *belongs to such as these.* The kingdom of God belongs to those who, like children, are prepared to receive the kingdom as a gift of God (see note on v. 15).

10:15 *Truly I tell you.* See note on 3:28. *like a little child.* The point of the comparison is the usual openness and receptivity of children. The kingdom of God must be received as a gift; it cannot be achieved by human effort. It can be entered only by those who know they are helpless, without claim or merit (see Mt 18:3; Lk 18:17 and notes).

10:16 *placed his hands on them and blessed them.* See note on Ac 6:6. Jesus visually demonstrated that the blessings of the kingdom are freely given.

10:17 *man.* Lk 18:18 calls him a "ruler," meaning he was probably a member of an official council or court, and Mt 19:20 says he was "young." *what must I do . . . ?* Cf. Ac 16:30 – 31 and notes. The rich man was thinking in terms of earning righteousness to merit eternal life, but Jesus taught that it was a gift to be received (see v. 15 and note). *eternal life.* See note on Mt 19:16.

10:18 *Why do you call me good?* Jesus was not denying his own goodness but was forcing the man to recognize that his only hope was in total reliance on God, who alone can give eternal life. He may also have been encouraging the young man to consider the full identity and nature of the One he was addressing.

DISCIPLESHIP AND SERVANT LEADERSHIP
THREE CYCLES OF EVENTS IN MARK

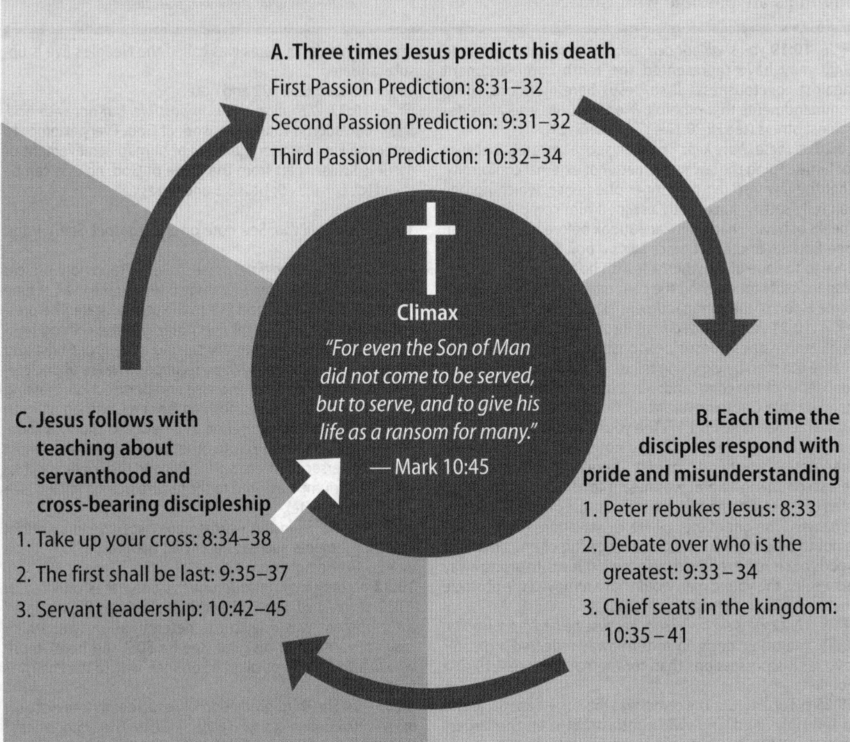

A. Three times Jesus predicts his death
First Passion Prediction: 8:31–32
Second Passion Prediction: 9:31–32
Third Passion Prediction: 10:32–34
Climax
"For even the Son of Man did not come to be served, but to serve, and to give his life as a ransom for many."
— Mark 10:45
B. Each time the disciples respond with pride and misunderstanding
1. Peter rebukes Jesus: 8:33
2. Debate over who is the greatest: 9:33 – 34
3. Chief seats in the kingdom: 10:35 – 41
C. Jesus follows with teaching about servanthood and cross-bearing discipleship
1. Take up your cross: 8:34–38
2. The first shall be last: 9:35–37
3. Servant leadership: 10:42–45

'You shall not murder, you shall not commit adultery, you shall not steal, you shall
not give false testimony, you shall not defraud, honor your father and mother.'[a]"[w]
20 "Teacher," he declared, "all these I
have kept since I was a boy."
21 Jesus looked at him and loved him.
"One thing you lack," he said. "Go, sell
everything you have and give to the poor,[x]
and you will have treasure in heaven.[y]
Then come, follow me."[z]
22 At this the man's face fell. He went
away sad, because he had great wealth.
23 Jesus looked around and said to his
disciples, "How hard it is for the rich[a] to
enter the kingdom of God!"
24 The disciples were amazed at his
words. But Jesus said again, "Children,
how hard it is[b] to enter the kingdom of
God![b] 25 It is easier for a camel to go through
the eye of a needle than for someone who
is rich to enter the kingdom of God."[c]
26 The disciples were even more amazed,
and said to each other, "Who then can be
saved?"
27 Jesus looked at them and said, "With
man this is impossible, but not with God;
all things are possible with God."[d]

10:19 [w] Ex 20:12-16; Dt 5:16-20 **10:21** [x] S Ac 2:45 [y] Mt 6:20; Lk 12:33 [z] S Mt 4:19 **10:23** [a] Ps 52:7; 62:10; Mk 4:19; 1Ti 6:9, 10, 17 **10:24** [b] Mt 7:13, 14; Jn 3:5 **10:25** [c] Lk 12:16-20; 16:19-31 **10:27** [d] S Mt 19:26 **10:28** [e] S Mt 4:19 **10:30** [f] Mt 6:33 [g] S Mt 12:32 [h] S Mt 25:46 **10:31** [i] S Mt 19:30 **10:32** [j] Mk 3:16-19 **10:33** [k] S Lk 9:51 [l] S Mt 8:20 [m] Mt 27:1, 2

28 Then Peter spoke up, "We have left
everything to follow you!"[e]
29 "Truly I tell you," Jesus replied, "no
one who has left home or brothers or sisters or mother or father or children or
fields for me and the gospel 30 will fail
to receive a hundred times as much[f] in
this present age: homes, brothers, sisters,
mothers, children and fields—along with
persecutions—and in the age to come[g]
eternal life.[h] 31 But many who are first will
be last, and the last first."[i]

Jesus Predicts His Death a Third Time

10:32-34pp — Mt 20:17-19; Lk 18:31-33

32 They were on their way up to Jerusalem, with Jesus leading the way, and
the disciples were astonished, while those
who followed were afraid. Again he took
the Twelve[j] aside and told them what was
going to happen to him. 33 "We are going
up to Jerusalem,"[k] he said, "and the Son
of Man[l] will be delivered over to the chief
priests and the teachers of the law.[m] They
will condemn him to death and will hand
him over to the Gentiles, 34 who will mock

[a] *19* Exodus 20:12-16; Deut. 5:16-20 [b] *24* Some manuscripts *is for those who trust in riches*

10:19 *you shall not defraud.* The prohibition of fraud may have represented the tenth commandment (against covetousness). If so, Jesus here mentions all six commandments that prohibit wrong actions and attitudes against others (see Ex 20:12–17; Dt 5:16–21).

10:20 *all these I have kept.* The man spoke sincerely, because for him keeping the law was a matter of external conformity. That the law also required inner obedience, which no one can fully satisfy, apparently escaped him completely. Paul speaks of having had a similar outlook before his conversion (see Php 3:6 and note). *since I was a boy.* Probably a reference to the age of 13, when a Jewish boy assumed personal responsibility for obeying the commandments and thus became a "son of the commandment(s)" (Aramaic *bar mitzvah*).

10:21 *Jesus ... loved him.* Jesus recognized the man's earnestness. Jesus' response was not intended to shame the man by exposing failure to understand the spiritual depth of the commandments but was an expression of genuine love. *One thing you lack ... Go, sell everything ... come, follow me.* See note on 1:17. The young man's primary problem was his wealth (see v. 22 and note), and therefore Jesus' prescription was to rid him of it. There is no indication that Jesus' command to him was meant for all Christians. It applies to those who have the same spiritual problem. *treasure in heaven.* The gift of eternal life, or salvation. This treasure is not to be earned by self-denial or giving of one's material goods but is to be received by following Jesus. In giving away his wealth, the young man would have removed the obstacle that kept him from trusting in Jesus.

10:22 *He went away sad, because he had great wealth.* The tragic decision to turn away reflected a greater love for his possessions than for eternal life (see 4:19 and note).

10:25 *eye of a needle.* The camel was the largest animal found in the Holy Land. The vivid contrast between the largest animal and the smallest opening represents what, humanly speaking, is impossible. The oft-repeated suggestion that one of Jerusalem's gates was called the Needle's Eye is unsubstantiated.

10:26 *amazed.* See 1:22 and note.

10:27 *With man this is impossible, but not with God.* Salvation is totally the work of God. Every attempt to enter the kingdom on the basis of human achievement or merit is futile. Apart from the grace of God, no one can be saved (cf. Eph 2:8–9; Titus 3:5 and notes).

10:28 See 1:18.

10:29 *Truly I tell you.* See note on 3:28. *gospel.* See 1:1 and note.

10:30 *hundred times as much.* See 4:8 and note. *present age ... age to come.* These two terms take in all of time from the fall of Adam and Eve to the eternal state. The present age is evil (see Gal 1:4 and note), but the coming righteous age will begin with the second advent of Christ and continue forever. *along with persecutions.* The life of discipleship is a combination of promise and persecution, blessing and suffering. God takes nothing from a Christian without making multiplied restoration in a new and glorious form. Paradoxically, fellowship with other believers develops most deeply in persecution. *eternal life.* Beyond the conflicts of history is the triumph assured to those who belong to God (see Mt 19:16 and note).

10:31 *first will be last.* A warning against pride in sacrificial accomplishments such as Peter had manifested (v. 28; see vv. 42–44 and note on v. 43).

10:32 *on their way up to Jerusalem.* See notes on Lk 9:51; 13:22. *astonished.* See 1:22 and note. Perhaps the disciples' astonishment was due to the determination with which Jesus proceeded to his goal (see Isa 50:7 and note). *those who followed.* Perhaps pilgrims on their way to the Passover in Jerusalem.

10:33–34 The third prediction of Jesus' death (see note on 8:31—10:52). *Gentiles, who will ... kill him.* The word "crucify" does not occur in any of the passion predictions in Mark's Gospel, but the statement that Jesus would be handed over

him and spit on him, flog him[n] and kill
him.[o] Three days later[p] he will rise."[q]

The Request of James and John

10:35-45pp — Mt 20:20-28

35 Then James and John, the sons of
Zebedee, came to him. "Teacher," they
said, "we want you to do for us whatever
we ask."
36 "What do you want me to do for
you?" he asked.
37 They replied, "Let one of us sit at your
right and the other at your left in your glory."[r]
38 "You don't know what you are asking,"[s] Jesus said. "Can you drink the cup[t]
I drink or be baptized with the baptism I
am baptized with?"[u]
39 "We can," they answered.
Jesus said to them, "You will drink the
cup I drink and be baptized with the baptism I am baptized with,[v] 40 but to sit at my
right or left is not for me to grant. These
places belong to those for whom they have
been prepared."
41 When the ten heard about this, they
became indignant with James and John.
42 Jesus called them together and said,
"You know that those who are regarded
as rulers of the Gentiles lord it over them,
and their high officials exercise authority over them. 43 Not so with you. Instead,
whoever wants to become great among
you must be your servant,[w] 44 and whoever wants to be first must be slave of all.
45 For even the Son of Man did not come
to be served, but to serve,[x] and to give his
life as a ransom for many."[y]

Blind Bartimaeus Receives His Sight

10:46-52pp — Mt 20:29-34; Lk 18:35-43

46 Then they came to Jericho. As Jesus
and his disciples, together with a large
crowd, were leaving the city, a blind man,
Bartimaeus (which means "son of Timae-
us"), was sitting by the roadside begging.
47 When he heard that it was Jesus of Nazareth,[z] he began to shout, "Jesus, Son of
David,[a] have mercy on me!"
48 Many rebuked him and told him to be
quiet, but he shouted all the more, "Son of
David, have mercy on me!"
49 Jesus stopped and said, "Call him."
So they called to the blind man, "Cheer
up! On your feet! He's calling you."
50 Throwing his cloak aside, he jumped to
his feet and came to Jesus.
51 "What do you want me to do for you?"
Jesus asked him.
The blind man said, "Rabbi,[b] I want to
see."
52 "Go," said Jesus, "your faith has
healed you."[c] Immediately he received his
sight and followed[d] Jesus along the road.

10:34 [n]S Mt 16:21 [o]Ac 2:23; 3:13 [p]S Mt 16:21 [q]S Mt 16:21 **10:37** [r]Mt 19:28 **10:38** [s]Job 38:2 [t]S Mt 20:22 [u]Lk 12:50 **10:39** [v]Ac 12:2; Rev 1:9 **10:43** [w]S Mk 9:35 **10:45** [x]S Mt 20:28 [y]S Mt 20:28 **10:47** [z]S Mk 1:24 [a]S Mt 9:27 **10:51** [b]S Mt 23:7 **10:52** [c]S Mt 9:22 [d]S Mt 4:19

to Gentiles to be killed by them suggests crucifixion, since this was the usual means of Roman execution of non-Romans. See note on Lk 24:44.

10:33 *Son of Man … chief priests … teachers of the law.* See notes on 8:31; Mt 2:4.

10:35–45 Parallel to 9:33–37. Both passages deal with true greatness, and both follow a prediction of Jesus' suffering and death. Both also show how spiritually undiscerning the disciples were (see note on 8:16).

10:35–36 *want … want.* James's and John's desire for position and power would be realized only if they willingly submitted to servanthood (see "wants … wants" in vv. 43–44).

10:35 *James and John, the sons of Zebedee.* See 1:19; 3:17.

10:37 *at your right and … at your left.* Positions of prestige and power.

10:38 *drink the cup I drink.* A Jewish expression that meant to share someone's fate. In the OT the cup of wine was a common metaphor for God's wrath against human sin and rebellion (see Jer 25:15–16 and notes; 49:12). Accordingly, the cup Jesus had to drink refers to divine punishment for sin that he bore for the redemption of the human race (see v. 45; 14:36 and notes). *be baptized with the baptism I am baptized with.* The image of baptism is parallel to that of the cup, referring to his suffering and death as a baptism (see Lk 12:50 and note; cf. Ro 6:3–4 for the figure).

10:40 *is not for me to grant.* Jesus would not usurp his Father's authority.

10:41 *the ten.* The other disciples. *indignant.* Possibly because they desired the positions of prestige and power for themselves.

10:43 *Not so with you.* Jesus overturns the value structure of the world. The life of discipleship is to be characterized by humble and loving service.

10:45 A key verse in Mark's Gospel. Jesus came to this world as a servant — indeed, *the* Servant — who would suffer and die for our redemption, as Isaiah clearly predicted (Isa 52:13 — 53:12). *Son of Man.* See note on 8:31. *did not come to be served, but to serve, and to give his life.* See note on Jn 13:5. *ransom.* Means "the price paid for release (from bondage)." Jesus gave his life to release us from bondage to sin and death. *for.* That is, "in place of," pointing to Christ's substitutionary death. *many.* In contrast to the one life given for our ransom. See note on Mt 20:28.

10:46 *Jericho.* A very ancient city located five miles west of the Jordan and about 15 miles northeast of Jerusalem. In Jesus' time OT Jericho was largely abandoned, but a new city, south of the old one, had been built by Herod the Great. *leaving the city.* Luke says Jesus "approached Jericho" (Lk 18:35). He may have been referring to the new Jericho, while Matthew (20:29) and Mark may have meant the old city. *blind man.* See Lk 18:35 and note. *begging.* The presence of a blind beggar just outside the city gates, on a road pilgrims followed on the way to Jerusalem, was a common sight in that day.

10:47 *Nazareth.* See note on Mt 2:23. *Son of David.* A Messianic title (see Isa 11:1–2; Jer 23:5–6; Eze 34:23–24; Mt 1:1; 9:27 and notes). Verses 47–48 are the only places in Mark where it is used to address Jesus. Its only other occurrence in Mark is in 12:35.

10:51 *What do you want …?* Jesus asks the blind man the same question he had asked James and John in v. 36, but he rightly gives the blind man what he requests; not so with the disciples, whose request is selfish. *Rabbi.* See notes on 11:21; Jn 20:16.

10:52 *your faith has healed you.* See 5:28 and note.

Jesus Comes to Jerusalem as King

11:1-10pp — Mt 21:1-9; Lk 19:29-38
11:7-10pp — Jn 12:12-15

11 As they approached Jerusalem and
came to Bethphage and Bethany[e]
at the Mount of Olives,[f] Jesus sent two of
his disciples, 2saying to them, "Go to the
village ahead of you, and just as you enter
it, you will find a colt tied there, which no
one has ever ridden.[g] Untie it and bring it
here. 3If anyone asks you, 'Why are you
doing this?' say, 'The Lord needs it and
will send it back here shortly.' "
4They went and found a colt outside in
the street, tied at a doorway.[h] As they untied it, 5some people standing there asked,
"What are you doing, untying that colt?"
6They answered as Jesus had told them to,
and the people let them go. 7When they
brought the colt to Jesus and threw their
cloaks over it, he sat on it. 8Many people
spread their cloaks on the road, while others spread branches they had cut in the
fields. 9Those who went ahead and those
who followed shouted,

"Hosanna![a]"

"Blessed is he who comes in the name
of the Lord!"[b][i]

10"Blessed is the coming kingdom of our
father David!"

"Hosanna in the highest heaven!"[j]

11Jesus entered Jerusalem and went into
the temple courts. He looked around at everything, but since it was already late, he
went out to Bethany with the Twelve.[k]

Jesus Curses a Fig Tree and Clears the Temple Courts

11:12-14pp — Mt 21:18-22
11:15-18pp — Mt 21:12-16; Lk 19:45-47; Jn 2:13-16
11:20-24pp — Mt 21:19-22

12The next day as they were leaving
Bethany, Jesus was hungry. 13Seeing in the
distance a fig tree in leaf, he went to find
out if it had any fruit. When he reached
it, he found nothing but leaves, because
it was not the season for figs.[l] 14Then he
said to the tree, "May no one ever eat fruit
from you again." And his disciples heard
him say it.
15On reaching Jerusalem, Jesus entered
the temple courts and began driving out
those who were buying and selling there.

11:1 [e]S Mt 21:17 [f]S Mt 21:1 **11:2** [g]Nu 19:2; Dt 21:3; 1Sa 6:7 **11:4** [h]Mk 14:16 **11:9** [i]Ps 118:25, 26; Mt 23:39 **11:10** [j]Lk 2:14 **11:11** [k]Mt 21:12, 17 **11:13** [l]Lk 13:6-9

[a] 9 A Hebrew expression meaning "Save!" which became an exclamation of praise; also in verse 10
[b] 9 Psalm 118:25,26

11:1 – 11 At this point a new section in the Gospel of Mark begins. Jesus arrives in Jerusalem, and the rest of his ministry takes place within the confines of the Holy City. Jesus' entry into Jerusalem as King, which inaugurates Passion Week, is a deliberate Messianic action, and the clue to its understanding is found in Zec 9:9 (quoted in Mt 21:5; Jn 12:15). Jesus purposefully offers himself as the Messiah, knowing that this will provoke Jewish leaders to take action against him.
11:1 *Bethphage.* See note on Mt 21:1 and map, p. 1687. *Bethany.* See note on Mt 21:17. *Mount of Olives.* Directly east of Jerusalem, it rises to a height of about 2,700 feet, some 200 feet higher than Mount Zion. Its summit commands a magnificent view of the city, and especially of the temple (now the site of the Dome of the Rock).
11:2 *the village ahead.* Probably Bethphage. *colt.* The Greek word can mean the young of any animal, but here it means the colt of a donkey (see Mt 21:2 and note; Jn 12:15). *which no one has ever ridden.* Unused animals were regarded as especially suitable for religious purposes (see Nu 19:2; Dt 21:3; 1Sa 6:7).
11:3 *If anyone asks you.* The message concerning the colt is not directed specifically to the owner but to anyone who might question the disciples' action. *Lord.* See note on Lk 19:31.
11:8 *branches.* The word means "leaves" or "leafy branches," which were readily available in nearby fields. Only John mentions palm branches (see Jn 12:13 and note), which may have come from Jericho, since they are not native to Jerusalem.
11:9 *Hosanna.* See NIV text note; see also note on Mt 21:9. *Blessed is he who comes.* A quotation of Ps 118:26 (see note there), one of the Hallel ("Praise") Psalms sung at Passover and especially fitting for this occasion.
11:10 *the coming kingdom of our father David.* The Messianic kingdom promised to David's son (see 2Sa 7:11 – 16 and notes).
11:11 *temple courts.* See note on Mt 4:5. *went out to Bethany.* Apparently Jesus spent each night through Thursday of Passion Week in Bethany (see note on Mt 21:17) at the home of his friends Mary, Martha and Lazarus (see v. 19; Jn 12:1 – 3).
11:12 *next day.* Monday of Passion Week.
11:13 *not the season for figs.* Fig trees around Jerusalem normally begin to get leaves in March or April but do not produce figs until their leaves are all out in June. This tree was an exception in that it was already, at Passover time, full of leaves.
11:14 *May no one ever eat fruit from you again.* Perhaps the incident was a parable of judgment, with the fig tree representing Israel (see Jer 24:1; Hos 9:10 and notes; Na 3:12). A tree full of leaves normally should have fruit, but this one was cursed because it had none. The fact that the clearing of the temple (vv. 15 – 19) is sandwiched between the two parts of the account of the fig tree (vv. 12 – 14,20 – 25) may underscore the theme of judgment (see v. 21 and note). The only application Jesus explicitly makes, however, is as an illustration of believing prayer (vv. 21 – 25).
11:15 – 19 All three Synoptic writers mention a clearing of the temple at the end of Jesus' ministry. Only John has one at the beginning. See notes on Mt 21:12 – 17; Jn 2:14 – 17.
11:15 *temple courts.* The court of the Gentiles, the only part of the temple in which Gentiles could worship God and gather for prayer (see v. 17 and note). *buying and selling.* Pilgrims coming to the Passover Festival needed animals that met the ritual requirements for sacrifice, and the vendors set up their animal pens and money tables in the court of the Gentiles. *tables of the money changers.* Pilgrims needed their money changed into the local currency because the annual temple tax had to be paid in that currency. Also, the Mishnah (see note on Mt 15:2) required currency from Tyre for some offerings. *those selling doves.* Doves were required for the purification of women (Lev 12:6; Lk 2:22 – 24), the cleansing of those with certain skin diseases (Lev 14:22 – 23), and other

He overturned the tables of the money
changers and the benches of those selling doves, 16 and would not allow anyone
to carry merchandise through the temple
courts. 17 And as he taught them, he said,
"Is it not written: 'My house will be called
a house of prayer for all nations'[a]?[m] But
you have made it 'a den of robbers.'[b]"[n]
18 The chief priests and the teachers of the
law heard this and began looking for a way
to kill him, for they feared him,[o] because the
whole crowd was amazed at his teaching.[p]
19 When evening came, Jesus and his
disciples[c] went out of the city.[q]
20 In the morning, as they went along,
they saw the fig tree withered from the
roots. 21 Peter remembered and said to
Jesus, "Rabbi,[r] look! The fig tree you
cursed has withered!"
22 "Have faith in God," Jesus answered.
23 "Truly[d] I tell you, if anyone says to this
mountain, 'Go, throw yourself into the
sea,' and does not doubt in their heart but
believes that what they say will happen,
it will be done for them.[s] 24 Therefore I tell
you, whatever you ask for in prayer, believe that you have received it, and it will
be yours.[t] 25 And when you stand praying,
if you hold anything against anyone, forgive them, so that your Father in heaven
may forgive you your sins."[u] [26][e]

The Authority of Jesus Questioned

11:27-33pp — Mt 21:23-27; Lk 20:1-8

27 They arrived again in Jerusalem, and
while Jesus was walking in the temple courts, the chief priests, the teachers
of the law and the elders came to him.
28 "By what authority are you doing these
things?" they asked. "And who gave you
authority to do this?"
29 Jesus replied, "I will ask you one
question. Answer me, and I will tell you
by what authority I am doing these things.
30 John's baptism — was it from heaven, or
of human origin? Tell me!"
31 They discussed it among themselves
and said, "If we say, 'From heaven,' he will
ask, 'Then why didn't you believe him?'
32 But if we say, 'Of human origin' . . ."
(They feared the people, for everyone held
that John really was a prophet.)[v]
33 So they answered Jesus, "We don't
know."
Jesus said, "Neither will I tell you by
what authority I am doing these things."

The Parable of the Tenants

12:1-12pp — Mt 21:33-46; Lk 20:9-19

12 Jesus then began to speak to them
in parables: "A man planted a vineyard.[w] He put a wall around it, dug a pit
for the winepress and built a watchtower. Then he rented the vineyard to some
farmers and moved to another place.
2 At harvest time he sent a servant to the

11:17 [m] Isa 56:7 [n] Jer 7:11 **11:18** [o] Mt 21:46; Mk 12:12; Lk 20:19 [p] S Mt 7:28 **11:19** [q] Lk 21:37 **11:21** [r] S Mt 23:7 **11:23** [s] S Mt 21:21 **11:24** [t] S Mt 7:7 **11:25** [u] S Mt 6:14 **11:32** [v] S Mt 11:9 **12:1** [w] Isa 5:1-7

[a] *17* Isaiah 56:7 [b] *17* Jer. 7:11 [c] *19* Some early manuscripts *came, Jesus* [d] *22,23* Some early manuscripts *"If you have faith in God," Jesus answered, 23"truly* [e] *26* Some manuscripts include here words similar to Matt. 6:15.

purposes (Lev 15:13 – 14,28 – 29). They were also the usual offering of the poor (Lev 5:7).

11:16 *to carry merchandise through the temple courts.* A detail found only in Mark. Apparently the temple area was being used as a shortcut between the city and the Mount of Olives. See note on v. 27.

11:17 *house of prayer for all nations.* Isa 56:7 assured godly Gentiles that they would be allowed to worship God in the temple. By allowing the court of the Gentiles to become a noisy, smelly marketplace, the Jewish religious leaders were interfering with God's provision. *den of robbers.* Not only because they took financial advantage of the people but also because they robbed the temple of its sanctity.

11:18 *chief priests ... teachers of the law.* See note on Mt 2:4. *began looking for a way to kill him.* See note on 3:6. They regarded Jesus as a dangerous threat to their whole way of life. *amazed.* See 1:22 and note.

11:19 *went out of the city.* To Bethany (see note on v. 11).

11:20 *In the morning.* Tuesday morning of Passion Week. *withered from the roots.* This detail indicates that the destruction was total (cf. Job 18:16) and that no one in the future would eat fruit from the tree. It served as a vivid warning of the judgment to come in AD 70 (see 13:2; Mt 24:2 and note).

11:21 *Rabbi.* Hebrew for "(my) teacher." *fig tree you cursed.* See note on v. 14. *has withered.* Perhaps prophetic of the fate of the Jewish authorities who were now about to reject their Messiah.

11:23 *Truly I tell you.* See note on 3:28. *this mountain ... into the sea.* The Mount of Olives, from which the Dead Sea is visible, or possibly Mount Zion, containing the temple (hinting at its destruction [13:2]). Cf. Mt 17:20 and note.

11:25 See Mt 6:14 – 15; 18:35 and note; cf. Eph 4:32 and note.

11:27 *temple courts.* Several courts surrounded the main temple buildings, including the court of the women, the court of the men (Israelite) and the court of the Gentiles (see vv. 16 – 17 and notes). *chief priests ... teachers of the law ... elders.* See notes on 8:31; Mt 2:4.

11:28 *authority.* The Sanhedrin was asking why Jesus performed what appeared to be an official act if he possessed no official status (see note on Lk 20:2).

11:30 *from heaven, or of human origin?* "Heaven" was a common Jewish substitute for the divine name to avoid a possible misuse of God's name (see Ex 20:7 and note; see also Introduction to Matthew: Recipients). Jesus' question implied that his authority, like that of John's baptism, came from God.

12:1 – 12 Many of Jesus' parables make one main point. This parable is rather complex, and the details fit the social situation in Jewish Galilee in the first century. Large estates, owned by absentee landlords, were put in the hands of local peasants who cultivated the land as tenant farmers. Jesus expands on the song of the vineyard in Isa 5:1 – 7 to portray Israel's religious leaders as wicked tenant farmers who abuse the owner's messengers (God's prophets) and ultimately kill the owner's son (Jesus). The parable exposed the planned attempt on Jesus' life, as well as God's judgment on the planners. See notes on Mt 21:35 – 37,41.

12:1 *them.* The representatives of the Sanhedrin mentioned

tenants to collect from them some of the fruit of the vineyard. 3 But they seized him, beat him and sent him away empty-handed. 4 Then he sent another servant to them; they struck this man on the head and treated him shamefully. 5 He sent still another, and that one they killed. He sent many others; some of them they beat, others they killed.

6 "He had one left to send, a son, whom he loved. He sent him last of all,[x] saying, 'They will respect my son.'

7 "But the tenants said to one another, 'This is the heir. Come, let's kill him, and the inheritance will be ours.' 8 So they took him and killed him, and threw him out of the vineyard.

9 "What then will the owner of the vineyard do? He will come and kill those tenants and give the vineyard to others. 10 Haven't you read this passage of Scripture:

" 'The stone the builders rejected
has become the cornerstone;[y]
11 the Lord has done this,
and it is marvelous in our eyes'[a]?"[z]

12 Then the chief priests, the teachers of the law and the elders looked for a way to arrest him because they knew he had spoken the parable against them. But they were afraid of the crowd;[a] so they left him and went away.[b]

Paying the Imperial Tax to Caesar

12:13-17pp — Mt 22:15-22; Lk 20:20-26

13 Later they sent some of the Pharisees and Herodians[c] to Jesus to catch him[d] in his words. 14 They came to him and said, "Teacher, we know that you are a man of integrity. You aren't swayed by others, because you pay no attention to who they are; but you teach the way of God in accordance with the truth. Is it right to pay the imperial tax[b] to Caesar or not? 15 Should we pay or shouldn't we?"

But Jesus knew their hypocrisy. "Why are you trying to trap me?" he asked. "Bring me a denarius and let me look at it." 16 They brought the coin, and he asked them, "Whose image is this? And whose inscription?"

"Caesar's," they replied.

17 Then Jesus said to them, "Give back to Caesar what is Caesar's and to God what is God's."[e]

And they were amazed at him.

Marriage at the Resurrection

12:18-27pp — Mt 22:23-33; Lk 20:27-38

18 Then the Sadducees,[f] who say there is no resurrection,[g] came to him with a question. 19 "Teacher," they said, "Moses wrote for us that if a man's brother dies and leaves a wife but no children, the man must marry the widow and raise up offspring for his brother.[h] 20 Now there were seven brothers. The first one married and died without leaving any children. 21 The second one married the widow, but he also died, leaving no child. It was the same with the third. 22 In fact, none of the seven left any children. Last of all, the woman died too. 23 At the resurrection[c] whose wife will she be, since the seven were married to her?"

24 Jesus replied, "Are you not in error because you do not know the Scriptures[i] or the power of God? 25 When the dead rise,

12:6 [x] Heb 1:1-3
12:10 [y] S Ac 4:11
12:11 [z] Ps 118:22,23
12:12 [a] S Mk 11:18 [b] Mt 22:22
12:13 [c] Mt 22:16; Mk 3:6 [d] S Mt 12:10
12:17 [e] Ro 13:7
12:18 [f] S Ac 4:1 [g] Ac 23:8; 1Co 15:12
12:19 [h] Dt 25:5
12:24 [i] 2Ti 3:15-17

[a] *11* Psalm 118:22,23 [b] *14* A special tax levied on subject peoples, not on Roman citizens [c] *23* Some manuscripts *resurrection, when people rise from the dead,*

in 11:27 (see note there). *parables.* See note on 4:2. *A man planted a vineyard.* The description reflects the language of Isa 5:1 – 2, where the vineyard clearly symbolizes Israel (see Isa 5:7). *watchtower.* See notes on Mt 21:33; Isa 5:2.
12:2 See note on Lk 20:10.
12:6 *son, whom he loved.* See 9:7 and note.
12:7 *inheritance will be ours.* Jewish law provided that a piece of property unclaimed by an heir would be declared ownerless and could then be claimed by others. The tenants assumed that the son came as heir to claim his property and that if he were slain they could claim the land.
12:10 *cornerstone.* See note on Ps 118:22.
12:13 – 17 This incident probably took place on Tuesday of Passion Week in one of the temple courts (see map, p. 1686).
12:13 *they.* See note on v. 1. *Pharisees.* See note on Mt 3:7. *Herodians.* See notes on 3:6; Mt 22:15 – 17. The plan to destroy Jesus, which had originated early in his Galilean ministry, had now matured and was gaining momentum in Jerusalem.
12:14 *pay the imperial tax to Caesar.* Subject peoples were required to pay a poll tax to the Roman emperor (see NIV text note). The tax was highly unpopular, and some Jews flatly refused to pay it, believing that payment was an admission of Roman right to rule. See note on Mt 22:15 – 17.
12:15 *hypocrisy.* See 7:6; Mt 5:18 – 20 and note; 6:2 and note; 23:13 – 36. *denarius.* See notes on 6:37; Mt 22:19.
12:17 *Give back to Caesar what is Caesar's.* See Mt 22:21 and note. There are obligations to the state that do not conflict with our obligations to God (see Ro 13:1 – 7; 1Ti 2:1 – 3; Titus 3:1 – 2; 1Pe 2:13 – 17 and notes). That a "denarius" (v. 15) belonged to Caesar was plainly marked in that on one side it bore a portrait of the emperor and on the other side an inscription that identified him. *to God what is God's.* Humans, who bear the image of God, owe to him their whole lives. *amazed.* See 1:22 and note.
12:18 *Sadducees.* A Jewish party that represented mainly the wealthy. Its members resided largely in Jerusalem and made the temple and its administration their primary interest. Though they were small in number, in Jesus' time they exerted powerful political and religious influence. *say there is no resurrection.* Their beliefs set them against the Pharisees and common Jewish piety (see notes on Mt 3:7; Lk 20:27; Ac 4:1; see also chart, p. 1631).
12:19 See note on Mt 22:24.
12:24 *you do not know the Scriptures.* Cf. v. 10; 2:25.
12:25 See note on Lk 20:36. In the resurrection there will be a new order of existence brought about by "the power of God"

they will neither marry nor be given in
marriage; they will be like the angels in
heaven.[j] 26 Now about the dead rising —
have you not read in the Book of Moses, in
the account of the burning bush, how God
said to him, 'I am the God of Abraham,
the God of Isaac, and the God of Jacob'[a]?[k]
27 He is not the God of the dead, but of the
living. You are badly mistaken!"

The Greatest Commandment

12:28-34pp — Mt 22:34-40

28 One of the teachers of the law[l] came
and heard them debating. Noticing that
Jesus had given them a good answer, he
asked him, "Of all the commandments,
which is the most important?"
29 "The most important one," answered
Jesus, "is this: 'Hear, O Israel: The Lord
our God, the Lord is one.[b] 30 Love the Lord
your God with all your heart and with all
your soul and with all your mind and
with all your strength.'[c][m] 31 The second is
this: 'Love your neighbor as yourself.'[d][n]
There is no commandment greater than
these."
32 "Well said, teacher," the man replied.
"You are right in saying that God is one
and there is no other but him.[o] 33 To love
him with all your heart, with all your understanding and with all your strength,
and to love your neighbor as yourself is
more important than all burnt offerings
and sacrifices."[p]
34 When Jesus saw that he had answered
wisely, he said to him, "You are not far

12:25 [j] 1Co 15:42, 49, 52
12:26 [k] Ex 3:6
12:28 [l] Lk 10:25-28; 20:39
12:30 [m] Dt 6:4, 5
12:31 [n] Lev 19:18; S Mt 5:43
12:32 [o] Dt 4:35, 39; Isa 45:6, 14; 46:9
12:33 [p] 1Sa 15:22; Hos 6:6; Mic 6:6-8; Heb 10:8
12:34 [q] S Mt 3:2 [r] Mt 22:46; Lk 20:40
12:35 [s] S Mt 26:55 [t] S Mt 9:27
12:36 [u] 2Sa 23:2 [v] Ps 110:1; S Mt 22:44
12:37 [w] Jn 12:9
12:39 [x] Lk 11:43

from the kingdom of God."[q] And from then
on no one dared ask him any more questions.[r]

Whose Son Is the Messiah?

12:35-37pp — Mt 22:41-46; Lk 20:41-44
12:38-40pp — Mt 23:1-7; Lk 20:45-47

35 While Jesus was teaching in the temple courts,[s] he asked, "Why do the teachers of the law say that the Messiah is the
son of David?[t] 36 David himself, speaking
by the Holy Spirit,[u] declared:

" 'The Lord said to my Lord:
"Sit at my right hand
until I put your enemies
under your feet." '[e][v]

37 David himself calls him 'Lord.' How then
can he be his son?"
The large crowd[w] listened to him with
delight.

Warning Against the Teachers of the Law

38 As he taught, Jesus said, "Watch out
for the teachers of the law. They like to
walk around in flowing robes and be greeted with respect in the marketplaces, 39 and
have the most important seats in the synagogues and the places of honor at banquets.[x] 40 They devour widows' houses and
for a show make lengthy prayers. These
men will be punished most severely."

[a] *26* Exodus 3:6 [b] *29* Or *The Lord our God is one Lord* [c] *30* Deut. 6:4,5 [d] *31* Lev. 19:18 [e] *36* Psalm 110:1

(v. 24; see 1Co 15:42 – 44 and note). *like the angels.* The basic characteristics of resurrection life will be fellowship with and service for God (see note on Heb 1:14).

12:26 – 27 Since God remains the God of the patriarchs, they must still be alive in their relationship to him.

12:26 *Book of Moses.* The Pentateuch, the first five books of the OT. *account of the burning bush.* A common way of referring to Ex 3:1 – 6 (cf. Ro 11:2, where "the passage about Elijah" refers to 1Ki 19:1 – 18).

12:28 *which is the most important?* Jewish rabbis counted 613 individual statutes in the law and attempted to differentiate between "heavy" (or "great") and "light" (or "little") commands.

12:29 – 31 Rabbi Hillel, a contemporary of Jesus, also stated that all the commandments are summarized in the call to love.

12:29 The OT citation came to be known as the *Shema*, named after the first word of Dt 6:4 (Hebrew for "Hear"). The *Shema* became the Jewish confession of faith, which was recited by pious Jews every morning and evening. To this day its recitation begins every synagogue service.

12:30 See notes on Dt 6:5; Mt 22:37; Lk 10:27.

12:31 According to Jesus, the second most important commandment (Lev 19:18) states that love for neighbor is an essential component of love for God (see Jn 13:34; 1Jn 4:19 – 21 and notes). *neighbor.* See Lk 10:25 – 37.

12:32 *Well said, teacher.* Cf. Lk 20:39 and note.

12:33 *more important than.* The comparison may have been suggested by the fact that the discussion took place in the temple courtyard (see 11:27 and note). *all burnt offerings and sacrifices.* See 1Sa 15:22; Isa 1:11 – 15; Hos 6:6; Mic 6:8 and notes.

12:34 *kingdom of God.* See note on Mt 3:2.

12:35 *Messiah.* See 8:29 and note. *son of David.* See note on 10:47. Most of the people knew that the Messiah was to be from the family of David.

12:36 *The Lord said to my Lord.* God said to David's Lord, i.e., David's superior — ultimately the Messiah (see note on Ps 110:1). The purpose of the quotation was to show that the Messiah was more than a descendant of David — he was David's Lord (see note on Lk 20:44).

12:37 See note on Lk 20:44.

12:38 *flowing robes.* The teachers of the law wore long robes that were fringed and almost reached to the ground.

12:39 *most important seats in the synagogues.* A reference to the bench that was in front of the "ark" containing the sacred scrolls. Those who sat there could be seen by all the worshipers in the synagogue.

12:40 *devour widows' houses.* Since the teachers of the law were not paid a regular wage, they were dependent on the generosity of patrons for their livelihood. Such a system was open to abuses, and widows were especially vulnerable to exploitation. *for a show make lengthy prayers.* See Mt 6:5 – 7. *punished most severely.* See note on Lk 20:47.

The Widow's Offering

12:41-44pp — Lk 21:1-4

41 Jesus sat down opposite the place
where the offerings were put[y] and watched
the crowd putting their money into the
temple treasury. Many rich people threw
in large amounts. 42 But a poor widow
came and put in two very small copper
coins, worth only a few cents.
43 Calling his disciples to him, Jesus
said, "Truly I tell you, this poor widow
has put more into the treasury than all the
others. 44 They all gave out of their wealth;
but she, out of her poverty, put in everything — all she had to live on."[z]

The Destruction of the Temple and Signs of the End Times

13:1-37pp — Mt 24:1-51; Lk 21:5-36

13 As Jesus was leaving the temple,
one of his disciples said to him,
"Look, Teacher! What massive stones!
What magnificent buildings!"
2 "Do you see all these great buildings?"
replied Jesus. "Not one stone here will be
left on another; every one will be thrown
down."[a]
3 As Jesus was sitting on the Mount of
Olives[b] opposite the temple, Peter, James,
John[c] and Andrew asked him privately,
4 "Tell us, when will these things happen?
And what will be the sign that they are all
about to be fulfilled?"
5 Jesus said to them: "Watch out that no
one deceives you.[d] 6 Many will come in my
name, claiming, 'I am he,' and will deceive
many. 7 When you hear of wars and rumors
of wars, do not be alarmed. Such things
must happen, but the end is still to come.
8 Nation will rise against nation, and kingdom against kingdom. There will be earthquakes in various places, and famines.
These are the beginning of birth pains.
9 "You must be on your guard. You will
be handed over to the local councils and
flogged in the synagogues.[e] On account of
me you will stand before governors and
kings as witnesses to them. 10 And the gospel must first be preached to all nations.
11 Whenever you are arrested and brought
to trial, do not worry beforehand about
what to say. Just say whatever is given
you at the time, for it is not you speaking,
but the Holy Spirit.[f]
12 "Brother will betray brother to death,
and a father his child. Children will rebel
against their parents and have them put to
death.[g] 13 Everyone will hate you because
of me,[h] but the one who stands firm to the
end will be saved.[i]
14 "When you see 'the abomination that
causes desolation'[a][j] standing where it[b]
does not belong — let the reader understand — then let those who are in Judea
flee to the mountains. 15 Let no one on the
housetop go down or enter the house to
take anything out. 16 Let no one in the field
go back to get their cloak. 17 How dreadful
it will be in those days for pregnant wom-

12:41 [y] 2Ki 12:9; Jn 8:20
12:44 [z] 2Co 8:12
13:2 [a] Lk 19:44
13:3 [b] S Mt 21:1 [c] S Mt 4:21
13:5 [d] ver 22; Jer 29:8; Eph 5:6; 2Th 2:3,10-12; 1Ti 4:1; 2Ti 3:13; 1Jn 4:6
13:9 [e] S Mt 10:17
13:11 [f] Mt 10:19,20; Lk 12:11,12
13:12 [g] Mic 7:6; Mt 10:21; Lk 12:51-53
13:13 [h] S Jn 15:21 [i] S Mt 10:22
13:14 [j] Da 9:27; 11:31; 12:11

[a] *14* Daniel 9:27; 11:31; 12:11 [b] *14* Or *he*

12:41 *temple treasury.* Located in the court of the women. Both men and women were allowed in this court, but women could go no farther into the temple buildings. It contained 13 trumpet-shaped receptacles for contributions brought by worshipers (see note on Lk 21:1).

12:42 *very small copper coins.* The smallest coins then in circulation in the Holy Land. Though her offering was meager, the widow brought "all she had" (v. 44; see 2Co 8:12 and note).

12:43 *Truly I tell you.* See note on 3:28.

13:1 - 37 Mark's version of the Olivet discourse (see note on Mt 24:1 — 25:46). It is the longest connected discourse in Mark's Gospel. The chapter falls into five sections: (1) Jesus' prophecy of the destruction of the temple, which gives rise to the disciples' questions (vv. 1 - 4); (2) warnings against deceivers, as well as false signs of the end (vv. 5 - 23); (3) the coming of the Son of Man (vv. 24 - 27); (4) the lesson of the fig tree (vv. 28 - 31); and (5) exhortation to watchfulness (vv. 32 - 37).

13:1 *massive stones.* According to Josephus (*Antiquities,* 15.11.3), they were white, and some of them were 37 feet long, 12 feet high and 18 feet wide. *magnificent buildings.* See note on Lk 21:5.

13:2 See note on Mt 24:2.

13:3 *Mount of Olives.* See note on 11:1; see also map, p. 1687. *Peter, James, John and Andrew.* See 1:16 - 20; 5:37 and note.

13:4 The disciples thought that the destruction of the temple would be one of the events that ushered in the end times (see Mt 24:3 and note). *sign.* The way by which the disciples might know that the destruction of the temple was about to take place and that the end of the age was approaching.

13:5 - 13 See Lk 21:8 - 19 and note on 21:9.

13:5 *Watch out.* It is clear from such commands as "Watch out" (see also vv. 35,37) and "You must be on your guard" (v. 9; see also vv. 23,33) that one of the main purposes of the Olivet discourse was to alert the disciples to the danger of deception.

13:6 *he.* That is, the Messiah.

13:7 *the end.* Not the destruction of Jerusalem but the end of the age (see Mt 24:3; Lk 21:9 and notes).

13:8 *birth pains.* See note on Mt 24:8.

13:9 *local councils.* See Mt 10:17 and note. *flogged.* Infraction of Jewish regulations was punishable by flogging, the maximum penalty being 39 strokes with a whip (see Dt 25:1 - 3 and note on 25:3; 2Co 11:23 - 24). *synagogues.* See note on 1:21.

13:10 *gospel.* See 1:1 and note. *first.* Before the end of the age (see Mt 24:14).

13:13 *stands firm to the end.* Such perseverance is a sure indication of salvation (cf. Heb 3:6,14 and notes; 6:11 - 12; 10:36).

13:14 *abomination that causes desolation.* See note on Mt 24:15. *standing where it does not belong.* Cf. 2Th 2:4 and note. *let the reader understand.* This may be Mark's own narrative comment alerting the reader to the imminent fulfillment of this prophecy in the destruction of Jerusalem (but see note on Mt 24:15). *flee to the mountains.* See note on Mt 24:16.

13:15 *housetop.* See notes on 2:4; Lk 17:31.

13:16 *cloak.* See note on Mt 5:40.

en and nursing mothers![k] 18 Pray that this
will not take place in winter, 19 because
those will be days of distress unequaled
from the beginning, when God created
the world,[l] until now—and never to be
equaled again.[m]
20 "If the Lord had not cut short those
days, no one would survive. But for the
sake of the elect, whom he has chosen,
he has shortened them. 21 At that time if
anyone says to you, 'Look, here is the
Messiah!' or, 'Look, there he is!' do not
believe it.[n] 22 For false messiahs and false
prophets[o] will appear and perform signs
and wonders[p] to deceive, if possible, even
the elect. 23 So be on your guard;[q] I have
told you everything ahead of time.
24 "But in those days, following that distress,

"'the sun will be darkened,
and the moon will not give its light;
25 the stars will fall from the sky,
and the heavenly bodies will be
shaken.'[a][r]

26 "At that time people will see the Son
of Man coming in clouds[s] with great power and glory. 27 And he will send his angels
and gather his elect from the four winds,
from the ends of the earth to the ends of
the heavens.[t]
28 "Now learn this lesson from the fig
tree: As soon as its twigs get tender and its
leaves come out, you know that summer is
near. 29 Even so, when you see these things
happening, you know that it[b] is near, right
at the door. 30 Truly I tell you, this generation[u] will certainly not pass away until
all these things have happened.[v] 31 Heaven
and earth will pass away, but my words
will never pass away.[w]

The Day and Hour Unknown

32 "But about that day or hour no one
knows, not even the angels in heaven,
nor the Son, but only the Father.[x] 33 Be on
guard! Be alert[c]![y] You do not know when
that time will come. 34 It's like a man going away: He leaves his house and puts
his servants[z] in charge, each with their assigned task, and tells the one at the door
to keep watch.
35 "Therefore keep watch because you
do not know when the owner of the house
will come back—whether in the evening,
or at midnight, or when the rooster crows,
or at dawn. 36 If he comes suddenly, do not
let him find you sleeping. 37 What I say to
you, I say to everyone: 'Watch!'"[a]

Jesus Anointed at Bethany

14:1-11pp—Mt 26:2-16
14:1,2,10,11pp—Lk 22:1-6
14:3-8Ref—Jn 12:1-8

14 Now the Passover[b] and the Festival of Unleavened Bread were only
two days away, and the chief priests and
the teachers of the law were scheming to

13:17 [k] Lk 23:29 **13:19** [l] Mk 10:6 [m] Da 9:26; 12:1; Joel 2:2 **13:21** [n] Lk 17:23; 21:8 **13:22** [o] S Mt 7:15 [p] S Jn 4:48; 2Th 2:9,10 **13:23** [q] 2Pe 3:17 **13:25** [r] Isa 13:10; 34:4; S Mt 24:29 **13:26** [s] S Rev 1:7 **13:27** [t] Zec 2:6 **13:30** [u] Lk 17:25 [v] Mk 9:1 **13:31** [w] S Mt 5:18 **13:32** [x] Ac 1:7; 1Th 5:1,2 **13:33** [y] 1Th 5:6 **13:34** [z] Mt 25:14 **13:37** [a] Lk 12:35-40 **14:1** [b] S Jn 11:55

[a] 25 Isaiah 13:10; 34:4 [b] 29 Or *he* [c] 33 Some manuscripts *alert and pray*

13:17 *pregnant women and nursing mothers.* Representative of anyone forced to flee under especially difficult circumstances.
13:18 *winter.* The time when heavy rains caused streams to become swollen and impossible to cross, preventing many from reaching a place of refuge.
13:19 *days of distress unequaled.* See note on Mt 24:21.
13:20 *cut short those days.* See note on Mt 24:22. *elect.* People of God.
13:21 *Messiah.* See 8:29 and note.
13:24–25 Imagery depicting the undoing of creation was commonly used by the OT prophets to describe God's awful judgment on a fallen world (see Isa 13:10; 24:21–23; 34:4; Eze 32:7; Joel 2:10,30–31; Am 8:9 and notes).
13:24 *in those days.* A common OT expression having to do with the Messianic age, the time of Israel's final redemption (see Jer 3:16,18; 31:29; 33:15–16; Joel 3:1; Zec 8:23; Heb 9:26 and note). *distress.* See v. 19 and note on Mt 24:21.
13:26 See Mt 24:30 and note. *Son of Man.* See note on 8:31. *coming in clouds with great power and glory.* A reference to Christ's second coming (see 8:38; Da 7:13; 2Th 1:6–10; Rev 19:11–16 and notes).
13:27 *angels.* Cf. Rev 14:14–16. *gather his elect.* In the OT, God is spoken of as gathering his scattered people (Dt 30:3–4; Isa 43:6; Jer 32:37; Eze 34:13; 36:24).
13:28 *fig tree.* See notes on 11:13; Lk 21:29.
13:29 *these things.* The signs listed in vv. 5–23 precede the destruction of Jerusalem and/or the end of the age. *it.* Probably a reference to the kingdom of God (see Lk 21:31) coming in the person of King Jesus (see NIV text note).
13:30 *Truly I tell you.* See note on 3:28. *generation.* See note on Lk 21:32.
13:32 *that day.* An OT expression (see Isa 2:11,17,20; Joel 1:15; Am 5:18; Mic 4:6; 1Th 5:2 and notes). *no one knows.* A specific outline of the future would be a hindrance, not a help, to faith. Certain signs have been given, but not for the purpose of making detailed, sequential predictions (see Ac 1:7; 1Th 5:1 and notes). *nor the Son.* While on earth, even Jesus lived by faith and in full dependence on the Spirit—as his servants must—and obedience was the hallmark of his ministry (see Heb 10:5–7 and note on 10:5).
13:35 *in the evening, or at midnight, or when the rooster crows, or at dawn.* The four watches of the night used by the Romans (see note on Mt 14:25).
13:37 *Watch!* See note on v. 5.
14:1–9 See note on Jn 12:1–11.
14:1 *Passover.* The festival commemorating the time when the angel of the Lord passed over the homes of the Hebrews rather than killing their firstborn sons as he did in the Egyptian homes (see Ex 12:11 and note). The lambs or kids used in the festival were killed on the 14th of Nisan (March-April), and the meal was eaten the same evening between sundown and midnight. Since the Jewish day began at sundown, the Passover Festival took place on the 15th of Nisan (see note on Jn 2:13). *Festival of Unleavened Bread.* This festival followed Passover and lasted seven days (see Ex 12:17; 23:15 and notes). *chief priests.* See note on 8:31. *teachers of the law.* See note on Mt 2:4.

Centuries-old olive trees in Gethsemane

arrest Jesus secretly and kill him.[c] 2 "But
not during the festival," they said, "or the
people may riot."
3 While he was in Bethany,[d] reclining at
the table in the home of Simon the Leper, a woman came with an alabaster jar
of very expensive perfume, made of pure
nard. She broke the jar and poured the
perfume on his head.[e]
4 Some of those present were saying indignantly to one another, "Why this waste
of perfume? 5 It could have been sold for
more than a year's wages[a] and the money
given to the poor." And they rebuked her
harshly.

6 "Leave her alone," said Jesus. "Why
are you bothering her? She has done a
beautiful thing to me. 7 The poor you will
always have with you,[b] and you can help
them any time you want.[f] But you will not
always have me. 8 She did what she could.
She poured perfume on my body beforehand to prepare for my burial.[g] 9 Truly I
tell you, wherever the gospel is preached
throughout the world,[h] what she has done
will also be told, in memory of her."
10 Then Judas Iscariot, one of the
Twelve,[i] went to the chief priests to betray

14:1 [c] S Mt 12:14
14:3 [d] S Mt 21:17
[e] Lk 7:37-39
14:7 [f] Dt 15:11
14:8 [g] Jn 19:40
14:9 [h] S Mt 24:14; Mk 16:15
14:10 [i] Mk 3:16-19

[a] 5 Greek *than three hundred denarii* [b] 7 See Deut. 15:11.

14:2 *not during the festival.* During Passover and the week-long Festival of Unleavened Bread, the population of Jerusalem increased from about 50,000 to a few hundred thousand. It would have been too risky to apprehend Jesus with so large and excitable a crowd present.

14:3–9 In John's Gospel this incident is placed before the beginning of Passion Week (see Jn 12:1–11 and note). Matthew and Mark may have placed it here to contrast the hatred of the religious leaders and the betrayal by Judas with the love and devotion of the woman who anointed Jesus.

14:3 *Bethany.* See note on Mt 21:17. *reclining at the table.* The usual posture for eating at a banquet. *Simon the Leper.* See note on Mt 26:6. *woman.* We know from Jn 12:3 that she was Mary, the sister of Martha and Lazarus. *alabaster jar.* A sealed flask with a long neck that was broken off when the contents were used and that contained enough ointment for one application. *nard.* See notes on SS 1:12; Jn 12:3. *poured the perfume on his head.* Anointing was a common custom at feasts (see Ps 23:5 and note). The woman's action expressed her deep devotion to Jesus.

14:4 *Some of those present.* Mt 26:8 identifies them as the disciples, while Jn 12:4–5 singles out Judas Iscariot.

14:5 *given to the poor.* It was a Jewish custom to give gifts to the poor on the evening of Passover (see Jn 13:29).

14:7 *The poor you will always have with you.* See Dt 15:11 and note. Jesus' statement did not express lack of concern for the poor, for their needs lay close to his heart (see Mt 6:2–4; Lk 4:18; 6:20; 14:13,21; 18:22; Jn 13:29). He was simply stating the truth.

14:8 *prepare for my burial.* It was a normal Jewish custom to anoint a dead body with aromatic oils in preparing it for burial (see 16:1 and note). Jesus seems to anticipate suffering a criminal's death, for only in that circumstance was there no anointing of the body.

14:9 *Truly I tell you.* See note on 3:28. *gospel.* See note on 1:1.

14:10 *Judas Iscariot.* See note on 3:19. *chief priests.* See note

Jesus to them.[j] 11 They were delighted to
hear this and promised to give him money.
So he watched for an opportunity to hand
him over.

The Last Supper

14:12-26pp — Mt 26:17-30; Lk 22:7-23
14:22-25pp — 1Co 11:23-25

12 On the first day of the Festival of Unleavened Bread, when it was customary
to sacrifice the Passover lamb,[k] Jesus' disciples asked him, "Where do you want us
to go and make preparations for you to eat
the Passover?"
13 So he sent two of his disciples, telling
them, "Go into the city, and a man carrying a jar of water will meet you. Follow
him. 14 Say to the owner of the house he
enters, 'The Teacher asks: Where is my
guest room, where I may eat the Passover
with my disciples?' 15 He will show you a
large room upstairs,[l] furnished and ready.
Make preparations for us there."
16 The disciples left, went into the city
and found things just as Jesus had told
them. So they prepared the Passover.
17 When evening came, Jesus arrived
with the Twelve. 18 While they were reclining at the table eating, he said, "Truly I tell
you, one of you will betray me — one who
is eating with me."
19 They were saddened, and one by one
they said to him, "Surely you don't mean
me?"
20 "It is one of the Twelve," he replied,
"one who dips bread into the bowl with
me.[m] 21 The Son of Man[n] will go just as it
is written about him. But woe to that man
who betrays the Son of Man! It would be
better for him if he had not been born."
22 While they were eating, Jesus took
bread, and when he had given thanks, he
broke it[o] and gave it to his disciples, saying, "Take it; this is my body."
23 Then he took a cup, and when he had
given thanks, he gave it to them, and they
all drank from it.[p]
24 "This is my blood of the[a] covenant,[q]
which is poured out for many," he said to
them. 25 "Truly I tell you, I will not drink
again from the fruit of the vine until that
day when I drink it new in the kingdom
of God."[r]
26 When they had sung a hymn, they
went out to the Mount of Olives.[s]

Jesus Predicts Peter's Denial

14:27-31pp — Mt 26:31-35

27 "You will all fall away," Jesus told
them, "for it is written:

> " 'I will strike the shepherd,
> and the sheep will be scattered.'[b][t]

28 But after I have risen, I will go ahead of
you into Galilee."[u]
29 Peter declared, "Even if all fall away,
I will not."
30 "Truly I tell you," Jesus answered,
"today — yes, tonight — before the rooster

14:10 [j] S Mt 10:4
14:12 [k] Ex 12:1-11; Dt 16:1-4; 1Co 5:7
14:15 [l] Ac 1:13
14:20 [m] Jn 13:18-27
14:21 [n] S Mt 8:20
14:22 [o] S Mt 14:19
14:23 [p] 1Co 10:16
14:24 [q] S Mt 26:28
14:25 [r] S Mt 3:2
14:26 [s] S Mt 21:1
14:27 [t] Zec 13:7
14:28 [u] Mk 16:7

[a] 24 Some manuscripts *the new* [b] 27 Zech. 13:7

on 8:31. This was an unexpected opportunity that they seized, even though they had intended not to apprehend Jesus during the festival (see v. 2 and note).
14:11 *money.* Thirty silver coins (see Mt 26:15 and note).
14:12 *first day of the Festival of Unleavened Bread.* Here the 14th of Nisan is meant because Passover lambs were killed on that day (Ex 12:6). The entire eight-day celebration was sometimes referred to as the Festival of Unleavened Bread. *make preparations.* These preparations would have included obtaining food for the meal, such as unleavened bread, wine, bitter herbs and a lamb.
14:13 *two of his disciples.* Peter and John (Lk 22:8). *man carrying a jar.* See note on Lk 22:10.
14:14 *The Teacher asks.* See note on Lk 22:11. *Where is my guest room . . . ?* It was a Jewish custom that anyone in Jerusalem who had a room available would give it upon request to a pilgrim to celebrate the Passover. Apparently Jesus had made previous arrangements with the owner of the house (cf. note on Ac 12:12).
14:16 *as Jesus had told them.* See note on Lk 22:13.
14:17 *evening.* Thursday of Passion Week.
14:18 *reclining at the table eating.* Originally the Passover meal was eaten standing (see Ex 12:11), but in Jesus' time it was customary to eat it while reclining (cf. v. 3 and note). *Truly I tell you.* See note on 3:28.
14:20 *dips bread into the bowl with me.* See note on Mt 26:23.
14:21 *Son of Man.* See note on 8:31. *as it is written about him.* Jesus may have had the "suffering servant" passage of Isa 52:13 — 53:12 in mind. See vv. 27,49 and note on Lk 24:44.
14:22 The NT gives four accounts of the Lord's Supper (here; Mt 26:26 – 28; Lk 22:19 – 20; 1Co 11:23 – 25). Matthew's account is very much like Mark's, and Luke's and Paul's have similarities. All the accounts include the taking of the bread; the thanksgiving or blessing; the breaking of the bread; the saying, "This is my body"; the taking of the cup; and the explanation of the relation of blood to the covenant. Only Paul and Luke record Jesus' command to continue to celebrate the Supper. *this is my body.* The bread represented his body, given for them (see 1Co 11:24 and note).
14:23 *had given thanks.* The word "Eucharist," often used to refer to the Lord's Supper, is derived from the Greek term used here.
14:24 *my blood of the covenant.* The cup represents the blood of Jesus, which, in turn, represents his poured-out life (i.e., his death). God's commitments to his people in the new covenant are possible only through Christ's atoning death (see Ex 24:6,8; Jer 31:31 – 34; Lk 22:20; Heb 8:8 – 12 and notes). *for many.* See Ro 5:15 and note.
14:25 *Truly I tell you.* See note on 3:28. *kingdom of God.* See note on Mt 3:2.
14:26 *hymn.* See note on Mt 26:30. *Mount of Olives.* See note on 11:1.
14:27 *You will all fall away.* Not that the disciples will lose their faith in Jesus but that their courage will fail and they will forsake him (see note on Mt 26:31).
14:28 *I will go ahead of you into Galilee.* See 16:7.
14:30 *Truly I tell you.* See note on 3:28. *crows twice.* See NIV text note here and on v. 72.

PASSION WEEK Bethany, the Mount of Olives and Jerusalem

The Roman road climbed steeply to the crest of the Mount of Olives, affording spectacular views of the Desert of Judea to the east and of Jerusalem across the Kidron Valley to the west.

1 **Arrival in Bethany**

FRIDAY (Jn 12:1)

Jesus arrived in Bethany six days before the Passover to spend some time with his friends, Mary, Martha and Lazarus. On the following Tuesday evening, while Jesus was still in Bethany, Mary anointed his feet with costly perfume as an act of humility. This tender expression indicated Mary's devotion to Jesus and her willingness to serve him.

2 **Sabbath—day of rest**

SATURDAY

Not mentioned in the Gospels.

The Lord spent the Sabbath day in traditional fashion with his friends.

3 **The "Triumphal" Entry**

SUNDAY (Mt 21:1–11; Mk 11:1–11; Lk 19:28–44; Jn 12:12–19)

On the first day of the week Jesus rode into Jerusalem on a donkey, fulfilling an ancient prophecy (Zec 9:9). The crowd welcomed him with the words of Ps 118:25–26, thus ascribing to him a Messianic title as the agent of the Lord, the coming King of Israel.

4 **Clearing of the temple**

MONDAY (Mt 21:12–17; Mk 11:15–18; Lk 19:45–48)

Jesus returned to the temple and found the court of the Gentiles full of traders and money changers making a large profit. Jesus drove them out and overturned their benches and tables.

5 **Day of controversy and parables**

TUESDAY (Mt 21:23—24:51; Mk 11:27—13:37; Lk 20:1—21:36)

IN JERUSALEM

Jesus evaded the traps set by the priests.

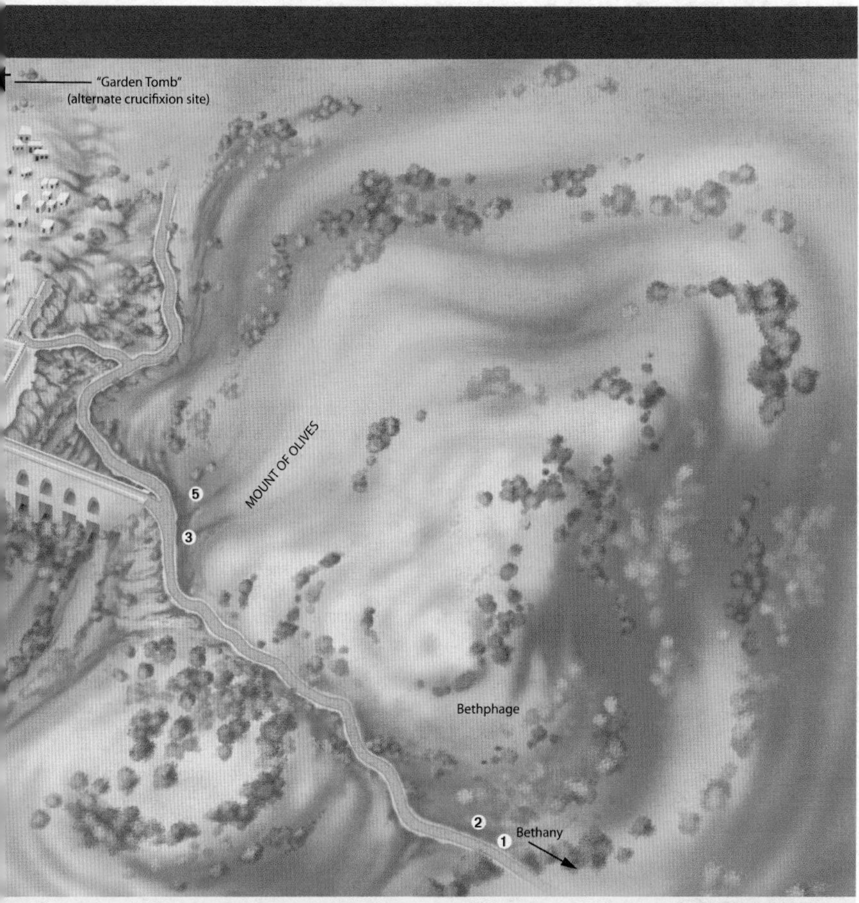

ON THE MOUNT OF OLIVES OVERLOOKING JERUSALEM

(Tuesday afternoon, exact location unknown)

Jesus taught in parables and warned the people against the Pharisees. He predicted the destruction of Herod's great temple and told his disciples about future events, including his own return.

Day of rest

WEDNESDAY

Although the Gospels do not mention this day, the counting of the days (Mk 14:1; Jn 12:1) seems to indicate that there was another day about which the Gospels record nothing.

6 **Passover, Last Supper**

THURSDAY (Mt 26:17–30; Mk 14:12–26; Lk 22:7–23)

In an upper room Jesus prepared both himself and his disciples for his death. He gave the Passover meal a new meaning. The loaf of bread and cup of wine represented his body soon to be sacrificed and his blood soon to be shed. And so he instituted the "Lord's Supper." After singing a hymn they went to Gethsemane, where Jesus prayed in agony, knowing what lay ahead for him.

7 **Crucifixion**

FRIDAY (Mt 27; Mk 15; Lk 22:66—23:56; Jn 18:28—19:37)

Following betrayal, arrest, desertion, false trials, denial, condemnation, beatings and mockery, Jesus was required to carry his cross to "the place of the skull" (Mt 27:33), where he was crucified with two other prisoners.

8 **In the tomb**

Jesus' body was placed in the tomb before 6:00 p.m. Friday evening, when the Sabbath began and all work stopped, and it lay in the tomb throughout the Sabbath.

9 **Resurrection**

SUNDAY (Mt 28:1–10; Mk 16:1–8; Lk 24:1–49; Jn 20)

Early in the morning, women went to the tomb and found that the stone closing the tomb's entrance had been rolled back. An angel told them Jesus was alive and gave them a message. Jesus appeared to Mary Magdalene in the garden, to Peter, to two disciples on the road to Emmaus and later that day to all the disciples but Thomas.

A HARMONISTIC OVERVIEW OF **JESUS' TRIALS**

PHASE	AUTHORITY/TIME/PLACE	EVENTS/JUDGMENT
The Jewish Trial		
1. First Jewish Phase (Jn 18:13–24)	Annas Thursday evening Annas's courtyard	Only John tells us that Jesus was originally sent to Annas, the former high priest and father-in-law of Caiaphas, for his initial questioning.
2. Second Jewish Phase (Mk 14:53–65; Mt 26:57–68; Lk 22:54)	Caiaphas and part of the Sanhedrin Thursday night Caiaphas's courtyard (Peter's denial begins here)	False witnesses are brought against Jesus. When asked if he is the Christ, the Son of God, he responds positively but defines his role as that of the Son of Man. He is accused of blasphemy, mocked and beaten.
3. Third Jewish Phase (Mk 15:1a; Mt 27:1; Lk 22:66–71)	The full Sanhedrin Friday, early morning	While all three Synoptics mention this phase of the trial, Luke alone describes Jesus' confession in terms similar to those recorded by Mark and Matthew the evening before.
The Roman Trial		
1. First Roman Phase (Mk 15:1b–5; Mt 27:2, 11–14; Lk 23:1–5; Jn 18:28–38)	Pilate Friday, early morning at the Praetorium	The Sanhedrin leads Jesus away to the governor Pilate, who asks him if he is the king of the Jews. Jesus responds positively. In John's account, Jesus explains that his kingdom is not of this world.
2. Second Roman Phase (Lk 23:6–12)	Herod Antipas Friday morning at Herod's palace	Luke alone records that when Pilate learned Jesus was from Galilee, he sent him to Herod, who was visiting Jerusalem. Herod questions Jesus without success, abuses him and returns him to Pilate.
3. Third Roman Phase (Mk 15:6–15; Mt 27:15–26; Lk 23:13–25)	Pilate Friday morning at the Praetorium	Holding to his custom to release a prisoner at Passover, Pilate attempts to free Jesus. Prompted by the chief priests, the crowds call for Barabbas's release and Jesus' crucifixion. Pilate scourges Jesus and turns him over for crucifixion.

crows twice[a] you yourself will disown me
three times."[v]
31 But Peter insisted emphatically, "Even
if I have to die with you,[w] I will never
disown you." And all the others said the
same.

Gethsemane

14:32-42pp — Mt 26:36-46; Lk 22:40-46

32 They went to a place called Gethsemane, and Jesus said to his disciples, "Sit
here while I pray." 33 He took Peter, James
and John[x] along with him, and he began to be deeply distressed and troubled.
34 "My soul is overwhelmed with sorrow to
the point of death,"[y] he said to them. "Stay
here and keep watch."
35 Going a little farther, he fell to the
ground and prayed that if possible the
hour[z] might pass from him. 36 "*Abba*,[b] Father,"[a] he said, "everything is possible for
you. Take this cup[b] from me. Yet not what
I will, but what you will."[c]
37 Then he returned to his disciples and

14:30 [v] ver 66-72; Lk 22:34; Jn 13:38
14:31 [w] Lk 22:33; Jn 13:37
14:33 [x] S Mt 4:21
14:34 [y] Jn 12:27
14:35 [z] ver 41; S Mt 26:18
14:36 [a] Ro 8:15; Gal 4:6 [b] S Mt 20:22 [c] S Mt 26:39

[a] 30 Some early manuscripts do not have *twice.*
[b] 36 Aramaic for *father*

14:32 *Gethsemane.* A "garden" (Jn 18:1) on the lower slopes of the Mount of Olives, one of Jesus' favorite places (see Lk 22:39 and note; Jn 18:2). The name is Hebrew and means "oil press," i.e., a place for squeezing the oil from olives. See photo, p. 1684.
14:33 *Peter, James and John.* See note on 5:37.
14:36 *Abba, Father.* Expressive of an especially close relationship to God (see also NIV text note). *this cup.* The chalice of death and of God's wrath that Jesus took from the Father's hand in fulfillment of his mission. What Jesus dreaded was not death as such but the manner of his death as the one who was taking "the sin of the world" (Jn 1:29) upon himself. See 10:38; Mt 26:39 and notes.

found them sleeping. "Simon," he said
to Peter, "are you asleep? Couldn't you
keep watch for one hour? 38 Watch and
pray so that you will not fall into temptation.[d] The spirit is willing, but the flesh is
weak."[e]
39 Once more he went away and prayed
the same thing. 40 When he came back, he
again found them sleeping, because their
eyes were heavy. They did not know what
to say to him.
41 Returning the third time, he said to
them, "Are you still sleeping and resting?
Enough! The hour[f] has come. Look, the
Son of Man is delivered into the hands of
sinners. 42 Rise! Let us go! Here comes my
betrayer!"

Jesus Arrested

14:43-50pp — Mt 26:47-56; Lk 22:47-50; Jn 18:3-11

43 Just as he was speaking, Judas,[g] one
of the Twelve, appeared. With him was a
crowd armed with swords and clubs, sent
from the chief priests, the teachers of the
law, and the elders.
44 Now the betrayer had arranged a
signal with them: "The one I kiss is the
man; arrest him and lead him away under guard." 45 Going at once to Jesus, Judas
said, "Rabbi!"[h] and kissed him. 46 The men
seized Jesus and arrested him. 47 Then one
of those standing near drew his sword and
struck the servant of the high priest, cutting off his ear.
48 "Am I leading a rebellion," said Jesus,
"that you have come out with swords and
clubs to capture me? 49 Every day I was
with you, teaching in the temple courts,[i]
and you did not arrest me. But the Scriptures must be fulfilled."[j] 50 Then everyone
deserted him and fled.[k]
51 A young man, wearing nothing but a
linen garment, was following Jesus. When
they seized him, 52 he fled naked, leaving
his garment behind.

Jesus Before the Sanhedrin

14:53-65pp — Mt 26:57-68; Jn 18:12,13,19-24
14:61-63pp — Lk 22:67-71

53 They took Jesus to the high priest,
and all the chief priests, the elders and the
teachers of the law came together. 54 Peter followed him at a distance, right into
the courtyard of the high priest.[l] There he
sat with the guards and warmed himself
at the fire.[m]
55 The chief priests and the whole Sanhedrin[n] were looking for evidence against
Jesus so that they could put him to death,
but they did not find any. 56 Many testified

14:38 [d] Mt 6:13 [e] Ro 7:22,23
14:41 [f] ver 35; S Mt 26:18
14:43 [g] S Mt 10:4
14:45 [h] S Mt 23:7
14:49 [i] S Mt 26:55 [j] Isa 53:7-12; S Mt 1:22
14:50 [k] ver 27
14:54 [l] S Mt 26:3 [m] Jn 18:18
14:55 [n] S Mt 5:22

14:37 *Simon.* See note on 1:16. Perhaps he is singled out because of his bold assertion that he would not fail Jesus (see vv. 29–31).

14:38 *fall into temptation.* Be attacked by temptation. Here the temptation is to be unfaithful in face of the threatening circumstances confronting them. *The spirit is willing.* The expression is taken from Ps 51:12 (see note on 51:10–12). When one's spirit is under God's control, it strives against human weakness.

14:41 *Son of Man.* See note on 8:31.

14:43 *Judas.* See note on 3:19. *crowd armed with swords and clubs.* Auxiliary police or servants of the court assigned to the task of maintaining public order beyond the precincts of the temple. Jn 18:3 indicates that at least some of the Roman cohort of soldiers were in the arresting group, along with officers of the temple guard. The fact that some carried clubs suggests that they were conscripted at the last moment. *chief priests … teachers of the law … elders.* See notes on 8:31; Mt 2:4. The warrant for Jesus' arrest had been issued by the Sanhedrin.

14:45 *Rabbi.* Hebrew for "(my) teacher." *kissed him.* A token of respect with which disciples customarily greeted their rabbi. See note on Lk 22:47.

14:47 *one of those standing near.* Peter (Jn 18:10). *servant of the high priest.* Malchus (Jn 18:10).

14:48 See note on Mt 26:55.

14:49 *temple courts.* See note on 11:27. *Scriptures must be fulfilled.* Perhaps a reference to Isa 53, or more particularly to Zec 13:7 (see note there), quoted by Jesus in v. 27 and fulfilled (at least in part) at this time (v. 50). See v. 21 and note.

14:50 *deserted him.* In fulfillment of vv. 27–31.

14:51 *young man.* Referred to only in Mark's Gospel. He is not specifically identified, but his anonymity may suggest that he was John Mark, writer of this Gospel (see Introduction: Author; John Mark in the NT). *linen garment.* Ordinarily the outer garment was made of wool. The fine linen garment left behind in the hand of a guard indicates that the youth was from a wealthy family.

14:52 *fled naked.* The absence of an undergarment suggests that he had dressed hastily to follow Jesus.

14:53 — 15:15 Jesus' trial took place in two stages: a Jewish trial and a Roman trial. By harmonizing the four Gospels, it becomes clear that each trial had three episodes. For the Jewish trial these were: (1) the preliminary hearing before Annas, the former high priest (reported only in Jn 18:12–14,19–23); (2) the trial before Caiaphas, the ruling high priest, and the Sanhedrin (14:53–65; see Mt 26:57–68; Lk 22:54–65; Jn 18:24); and (3) the final action of the council, which terminated its all-night session (15:1; see Mt 27:1; Lk 22:66–71). The three episodes of the Roman trial were: (1) the trial before Pilate (15:2–5; see Mt 27:11–26; Lk 23:1–5; Jn 18:28 — 19:16); (2) the trial before Herod Antipas (only in Lk 23:6–12); and (3) the trial before Pilate continued and concluded (15:6–15). Since Matthew, Mark and John give no account of Jesus before Herod Antipas, the trial before Pilate forms a continuous and uninterrupted narrative in these Gospels.

14:53 *high priest.* Caiaphas, son-in-law of Annas, the former high priest (see note on Jn 18:12). *all the chief priests, the elders and the teachers of the law.* The entire Sanhedrin (see note on v. 43; see also chart, p. 1688).

14:54 *courtyard of the high priest.* The Sanhedrin may have met at Caiaphas's house to ensure secrecy. *warmed himself at the fire.* See note on Jn 18:18.

14:55 *Sanhedrin.* The high court of the Jews. In NT times it was made up of three kinds of members: chief priests, elders and teachers of the law. Its total membership numbered 71, including the high priest, who was presiding officer (see note on Ac 5:21). Under Roman jurisdiction the Sanhedrin was given a great deal of authority, but it could not impose capital punishment (see Mt 27:2; Jn 18:31 and notes).

14:56 *Many testified falsely against him.* In Jewish judicial

falsely against him, but their statements
did not agree.
[57]Then some stood up and gave this
false testimony against him: [58]"We heard
him say, 'I will destroy this temple made
with human hands and in three days will
build another,[o] not made with hands.' "
[59]Yet even then their testimony did not
agree.
[60]Then the high priest stood up before
them and asked Jesus, "Are you not going to answer? What is this testimony
that these men are bringing against you?"
[61]But Jesus remained silent and gave no
answer.[p]
Again the high priest asked him, "Are
you the Messiah, the Son of the Blessed
One?"[q]
[62]"I am," said Jesus. "And you will see
the Son of Man sitting at the right hand of
the Mighty One and coming on the clouds
of heaven."[r]
[63]The high priest tore his clothes.[s] "Why
do we need any more witnesses?" he
asked. [64]"You have heard the blasphemy.
What do you think?"
They all condemned him as worthy of
death.[t] [65]Then some began to spit at him;
they blindfolded him, struck him with
their fists, and said, "Prophesy!" And the
guards took him and beat him.[u]

Peter Disowns Jesus

14:66-72pp — Mt 26:69-75; Lk 22:56-62; Jn 18:16-18,25-27

[66]While Peter was below in the courtyard,[v] one of the servant girls of the high
priest came by. [67]When she saw Peter
warming himself,[w] she looked closely at
him.
"You also were with that Nazarene,
Jesus,"[x] she said.
[68]But he denied it. "I don't know or understand what you're talking about,"[y] he
said, and went out into the entryway.[a]
[69]When the servant girl saw him there,
she said again to those standing around,
"This fellow is one of them." [70]Again he
denied it.[z]
After a little while, those standing near
said to Peter, "Surely you are one of them,
for you are a Galilean."[a]
[71]He began to call down curses, and he
swore to them, "I don't know this man
you're talking about."[b]
[72]Immediately the rooster crowed the
second time.[b] Then Peter remembered the
word Jesus had spoken to him: "Before
the rooster crows twice[c] you will disown
me three times."[c] And he broke down and
wept.

Jesus Before Pilate

15:2-15pp — Mt 27:11-26; Lk 23:2,3,18-25; Jn 18:29-19:16

15 Very early in the morning, the chief
priests, with the elders, the teachers of the law[d] and the whole Sanhedrin,[e]
made their plans. So they bound Jesus, led
him away and handed him over to Pilate.[f]

14:58 [o]S Jn 2:19 **14:61** [p]Isa 53:7; Mt 27:12, 14; Mk 15:5; Lk 23:9; Jn 19:9 [q]Mt 16:16; Jn 4:25,26 **14:62** [r]S Rev 1:7 **14:63** [s]Lev 10:6; 21:10; Nu 14:6; Ac 14:14 **14:64** [t]Lev 24:16 **14:65** [u]S Mt 16:21 **14:66** [v]ver 54 **14:67** [w]ver 54 [x]S Mk 1:24 **14:68** [y]ver 30, 72 **14:70** [z]ver 30, 68,72 [a]Ac 2:7 **14:71** [b]ver 30, 72 **14:72** [c]ver 30, 68 **15:1** [d]Mt 27:1; Lk 22:66 [e]S Mt 5:22 [f]S Mt 27:2

[a] 68 Some early manuscripts *entryway and the rooster crowed* [b] 72 Some early manuscripts do not have *the second time.* [c] 72 Some early manuscripts do not have *twice.*

procedure, witnesses functioned as the prosecution. *did not agree.* According to Dt 17:6 (see note there) a person could not be put to death except on the testimony of two or more witnesses.

14:58 This statement of Jesus is probably an allusion to what is reported in Jn 2:19 (see note there).

14:61 *remained silent.* See Isa 53:7 and note. *Messiah.* See first NIV text note on 1:1. *Son of the Blessed One.* "The Blessed One" was a way of referring to God without pronouncing his name (cf. note on 11:30). The title was therefore equivalent to "Son of God" (1:1; 15:39), though in this context it would seem not to refer to deity but to royal Messiahship, since in popular Jewish belief the Messiah was to be a man, not God.

14:62 See Mt 26:64 and note. *I am.* See Ex 3:14 and note; Jn 8:58–59 and note on 8:58. *Son of Man.* See note on 8:31. This Son of Man saying brings together Da 7:13 (see note there) and Ps 110:1 (see note there).

14:63 *tore his clothes.* A sign of great grief or shock (see Ge 37:29; 2Ki 18:37 and note; 19:1). In the case of the high priest it was a form of judicial act expressing the fact that he regarded Jesus' answer as blasphemous (see note on Mt 26:65).

14:64 *blasphemy.* Not only involved reviling the name of God (see Lev 24:10–16) but also included any affront to his majesty or authority (see Mk 2:7 and note; 3:28–29; Jn 5:18 and note; 10:33). Jesus' claim to be the Messiah and, in fact, to have majesty and authority belonging only to God was therefore regarded by Caiaphas as blasphemy, for which the Mosaic law prescribed death by stoning (Lev 24:16).

14:65 *began to spit at him ... struck him with their fists.* Conventional gestures of rejection and condemnation (see Nu 12:14; Dt 25:9; Job 30:10; Isa 50:6 and note). *blindfolded him.* A rabbinic interpretation of Isa 11:2–4 held that the Messiah could judge by smell without the aid of sight. *Prophesy!* Say who it was who struck you!

14:66 *below.* While Jesus was being beaten in an upstairs room of Caiaphas's house, Peter was below in the courtyard. *one of the servant girls.* The doorkeeper (see Jn 18:16; cf. Ac 12:3).

14:67 *Nazarene.* See note on Mt 2:23.

14:68 *I don't know or understand what you're talking about.* An expression used in Jewish law courts for a formal, legal denial.

14:70 *Galilean.* Peter's Galilean dialect showed him to be from Galilee, and his presence among the Judeans in the courtyard suggested he was a follower of Jesus.

14:72 *Before ... times.* See v. 30.

15:1 *Very early in the morning.* The working day of a Roman official began at daylight. *morning.* Friday of Passion Week. *Sanhedrin.* See note on 14:55. *made their plans.* Apparently to accuse Jesus before the civil authority for treason rather than blasphemy (see Lk 23:1–14 and note on 23:2). *Pilate.* See note on Lk 3:1.

2“Are you the king of the Jews?”[g] asked
Pilate.
“You have said so,” Jesus replied.
3The chief priests accused him of many
things. 4So again Pilate asked him, “Aren’t
you going to answer? See how many
things they are accusing you of.”
5But Jesus still made no reply,[h] and Pilate was amazed.
6Now it was the custom at the festival
to release a prisoner whom the people requested. 7A man called Barabbas was in
prison with the insurrectionists who had
committed murder in the uprising. 8The
crowd came up and asked Pilate to do for
them what he usually did.
9“Do you want me to release to you the
king of the Jews?”[i] asked Pilate, 10know-
ing it was out of self-interest that the chief
priests had handed Jesus over to him.
11But the chief priests stirred up the crowd
to have Pilate release Barabbas[j] instead.
12“What shall I do, then, with the one
you call the king of the Jews?” Pilate asked
them.
13“Crucify him!” they shouted.
14“Why? What crime has he committed?” asked Pilate.
But they shouted all the louder, “Crucify him!”
15Wanting to satisfy the crowd, Pilate
released Barabbas to them. He had Jesus
flogged,[k] and handed him over to be crucified.

15:2 [g]ver 9,12, 18,26; S Mt 2:2 **15:5** [h]S Mk 14:61 **15:9** [i]S ver 2 **15:11** [j]Ac 3:14

The Soldiers Mock Jesus

15:16-20pp — Mt 27:27-31

16The soldiers led Jesus away into
the palace[l] (that is, the Praetorium) and
called together the whole company of soldiers. 17They put a purple robe on him,
then twisted together a crown of thorns
and set it on him. 18And they began to
call out to him, “Hail, king of the Jews!”[m]
19Again and again they struck him on the
head with a staff and spit on him. Falling
on their knees, they paid homage to him.
20And when they had mocked him, they
took off the purple robe and put his own
clothes on him. Then they led him out[n] to
crucify him.

The Crucifixion of Jesus

15:22-32pp — Mt 27:33-44; Lk 23:33-43; Jn 19:17-24

21A certain man from Cyrene,[o] Simon,
the father of Alexander and Rufus,[p] was
passing by on his way in from the country,
and they forced him to carry the cross.[q]
22They brought Jesus to the place called
Golgotha (which means “the place of the
skull”). 23Then they offered him wine
mixed with myrrh,[r] but he did not take it.
24And they crucified him. Dividing up his

15:15 [k]Isa 53:6 **15:16** [l]Jn 18:28,33; 19:9 **15:18** [m]S ver 2 **15:20** [n]Heb 13:12 **15:21** [o]S Mt 27:32 [p]Ro 16:13 [q]Mt 27:32; Lk 23:26 **15:23** [r]ver 36; Ps 69:21; Pr 31:6

15:2 *king of the Jews.* See Jn 18:33–37 and notes on 18:33,36. *asked Pilate.* Judgment in a Roman court was the sole responsibility of the imperial magistrate.
15:3 *many things.* See Lk 23:2 and note. Multiple charges were common in criminal cases.
15:4 *Aren’t you going to answer?* If Jesus made no defense, according to Roman law Pilate would have to pronounce against him.
15:5 *made no reply.* See 14:61; Isa 53:7 and note.
15:6 *custom.* See note on Jn 18:39. *festival.* Passover (see 14:1–2 and notes).
15:7 *Barabbas.* See Mt 27:16–17 and note on 27:16; probably a member of the Zealots, a Jewish revolutionary group (see Mt 10:4; Jn 18:40; Ac 5:37 and note; see also chart, p. 1631). *uprising.* Under the Roman governors such revolts were common (see Lk 13:1).
15:13–14 *Crucify.* See note on v. 24.
15:15 *flogged.* The Romans used a whip made of several strips of leather, into which were embedded (near the ends) pieces of bone and lead. The Jews limited the number of stripes to a maximum of 40 (in practice to 39 in case of a miscount; see Dt 25:3 and note), but no such limitation was recognized by the Romans, and victims of Roman floggings often did not survive (cf. Ac 22:24 and note). *crucified.* The Roman historian Tacitus (*Annals*, 15.44) indicates that “Christus ... suffered the extreme penalty ... at the hands of ... Pontius Pilate.” See note on v. 24.
15:16 *Praetorium.* The word was used originally of a general’s tent or of the headquarters in a military camp (see note on v. 1). *whole company.* The soldiers quartered in the Praetorium were recruited from non-Jewish inhabitants of the Holy Land and assigned to the military governor.
15:17 *purple robe.* Probably an old military cloak, whose color suggested royalty (see Ex 25:4; Mt 27:28; Ac 16:14 and notes). *crown of thorns.* Made from the branches of a thorny tree, of which there were many in the Holy Land. Both robe and crown were parts of the mock royal attire placed on Jesus.
15:18 *Hail, king of the Jews!* A mocking salutation that corresponded to “Hail, Caesar!”
15:19 *spit on him.* Probably a parody on the kiss of homage that was customary when greeting royalty (see note on 14:65).
15:20 *mocked him.* Cf. Ps 22:6–7; Isa 50:6 and note.
15:21 *Cyrene.* See Ac 6:9 and note. *Simon, the father of Alexander.* A first-century AD ossuary (“bone box”; see note on Mt 26:3) bearing the inscription “Alexander (son) of Simon” was found recently in Jerusalem. *Simon.* Probably a Jew who was in Jerusalem to celebrate the Passover. *Alexander and Rufus.* Mentioned only by Mark, but referred to in such a way as to suggest that they were known by those to whom he wrote (cf. Ro 16:13). *carry the cross.* Men condemned to death were usually forced to carry a beam of the cross, often weighing 30 or 40 pounds, to the place of crucifixion. Jesus started out by carrying his (see Jn 19:17 and note), but he had been so weakened by flogging that Simon was pressed into service.
15:22 *the place of the skull.* It may have been a small hill that looked like a skull, or it may have been so named because of the many executions that took place there.
15:23 *wine mixed with myrrh.* The Talmud gives evidence that incense was mixed with wine to deaden pain (cf. Pr 31:6). Myrrh is a spice derived from plants native to the Arabian deserts and parts of Africa (see note on Ge 37:25).
15:24 *crucified.* A Roman means of execution in which the prisoner was nailed or tied to a stake or cross (see note on Jn 19:17). In the case of Jesus, heavy wrought-iron nails were driven through the wrists and the heel bones (see

clothes, they cast lots[s] to see what each
would get.
[25]It was nine in the morning when they
crucified him. [26]The written notice of the
charge against him read: THE KING OF THE
JEWS.[t]
[27]They crucified two rebels with him,
one on his right and one on his left. [28][a]
[29]Those who passed by hurled insults at
him, shaking their heads[u] and saying, "So!
You who are going to destroy the temple
and build it in three days,[v] [30]come down
from the cross and save yourself!" [31]In the
same way the chief priests and the teachers of the law mocked him[w] among themselves. "He saved others," they said, "but
he can't save himself! [32]Let this Messiah,[x]
this king of Israel,[y] come down now from
the cross, that we may see and believe."
Those crucified with him also heaped insults on him.

15:24 [s]Ps 22:18 **15:26** [t]S ver 2 **15:29** [u]Ps 22:7; 109:25 [v]S Jn 2:19 **15:31** [w]Ps 22:7 **15:32** [x]S Mk 14:61 [y]S ver 2 **15:33** [z]Am 8:9 **15:34** [a]Ps 22:1

The Death of Jesus

15:33-41pp — Mt 27:45-56; Lk 23:44-49; Jn 19:29-30

[33]At noon, darkness came over the
whole land until three in the afternoon.[z]
[34]And at three in the afternoon Jesus cried
out in a loud voice, *"Eloi, Eloi, lema sabachthani?"* (which means "My God, my
God, why have you forsaken me?").[b][a]
[35]When some of those standing near

[a] *28* Some manuscripts include here words similar to Luke 22:37. [b] *34* Psalm 22:1

Jn 20:25). If the victims lingered too long, death was hastened by breaking their legs (see Jn 19:31 and note). Archaeologists have discovered the bones of a crucified man, near Jerusalem, dating between AD 7 and 66, which shed light on the position of a person when nailed to a cross. Only slaves, the basest of criminals and offenders who were not Roman citizens were executed in this manner. First-century authors vividly describe the agony and disgrace of being crucified (see Php 2:8 and note). *Dividing up his clothes.* It was the accepted right of the executioner's squad to claim the minor possessions of the victim. Jesus' clothing probably consisted of an under and an outer garment, a belt, sandals and possibly a head covering (see note on Jn 19:18). *cast lots.* See Ps 22:18 and introduction to that psalm; see also Jn 19:23–24 and notes.
15:25 *nine in the morning.* See Lk 23:44; Jn 19:14 and notes.
15:26 *charge against him.* It was customary to write the charge on a wooden board that was carried before the victim as he walked to the place of execution, and then the board was affixed to the cross above his head. *THE KING OF THE JEWS.* The wording of the charge differs slightly in the Gospels, but all agree that Jesus was crucified for claiming to be the king of the Jews. One possible reconstruction of the original is THIS IS JESUS OF NAZARETH, THE KING OF THE JEWS (cf. Mt 27:37; Lk 23:38; Jn 19:19).
15:27 *two rebels.* Traditionally rendered "thieves," the Greek term signifies those guilty of insurrection.
15:29 See 14:58 and note.
15:32 *Messiah.* See first NIV text note on 1:1. *Those crucified with him.* One of the criminals later repented and asked to be included in Jesus' kingdom (Lk 23:39–43).
15:34 The words were spoken in a dialect of Aramaic, one of the languages commonly spoken in the Holy Land in Jesus'

A rolling-stone tomb in Israel, similar to the one in which Jesus was laid
www.HolyLandPhotos.org

heard this, they said, "Listen, he's calling
Elijah."
36Someone ran, filled a sponge with
wine vinegar,[b] put it on a staff, and offered it to Jesus to drink. "Now leave him
alone. Let's see if Elijah comes to take him
down," he said.
37With a loud cry, Jesus breathed his
last.[c]
38The curtain of the temple was torn
in two from top to bottom.[d] 39And when
the centurion,[e] who stood there in front of
Jesus, saw how he died,[a] he said, "Surely
this man was the Son of God!"[f]
40Some women were watching from a
distance.[g] Among them were Mary Magdalene, Mary the mother of James the younger and of Joseph,[b] and Salome.[h] 41In Galilee these women had followed him and
cared for his needs. Many other women
who had come up with him to Jerusalem
were also there.[i]

The Burial of Jesus

15:42-47pp — Mt 27:57-61; Lk 23:50-56; Jn 19:38-42

42It was Preparation Day (that is, the
day before the Sabbath).[j] So as evening
approached, 43Joseph of Arimathea, a
prominent member of the Council,[k] who
was himself waiting for the kingdom of
God,[l] went boldly to Pilate and asked for
Jesus' body. 44Pilate was surprised to hear
that he was already dead. Summoning the
centurion, he asked him if Jesus had already died. 45When he learned from the
centurion[m] that it was so, he gave the body
to Joseph. 46So Joseph bought some lin-
en cloth, took down the body, wrapped it
in the linen, and placed it in a tomb cut
out of rock. Then he rolled a stone against
the entrance of the tomb.[n] 47Mary Magdalene and Mary the mother of Joseph[o] saw
where he was laid.

Jesus Has Risen

16:1-8pp — Mt 28:1-8; Lk 24:1-10

16 When the Sabbath was over, Mary
Magdalene, Mary the mother of
James, and Salome bought spices[p] so that
they might go to anoint Jesus' body. 2Very
early on the first day of the week, just after sunrise, they were on their way to the
tomb 3and they asked each other, "Who
will roll the stone away from the entrance
of the tomb?"[q]
4But when they looked up, they saw
that the stone, which was very large, had
been rolled away. 5As they entered the
tomb, they saw a young man dressed in

15:36 [b] ver 23; Ps 69:21 **15:37** [c] Jn 19:30 **15:38** [d] Heb 10:19,20 **15:39** [e] ver 45 [f] Mk 1:1,11; 9:7; S Mt 4:3 **15:40** [g] Ps 38:11 [h] Mk 16:1; Lk 24:10; Jn 19:25 **15:41** [i] Mt 27:55,56; Lk 8:2,3 **15:42** [j] Mt 27:62; Jn 19:31 **15:43** [k] S Mt 5:22 [l] S Mt 3:2; Lk 2:25,38 **15:45** [m] ver 39 **15:46** [n] Mk 16:3 **15:47** [o] ver 40 **16:1** [p] Lk 23:56; Jn 19:39,40 **16:3** [q] Mk 15:46

[a] 39 Some manuscripts *saw that he died with such a cry*
[b] 40 Greek *Joses,* a variant of *Joseph;* also in verse 47

day. They reveal how deeply Jesus felt his abandonment by God as he bore "the sin of the world" (Jn 1:29; but see introduction to Ps 22 and note on Ps 22:1).

15:35 *Elijah.* The bystanders mistook the first words of Jesus' cry (*"Eloi, Eloi"*) to be a cry for Elijah. It was commonly believed that Elijah would come in times of critical need to protect the innocent and rescue the righteous (v. 36).

15:36 *wine vinegar.* A sour wine, the drink of laborers and common soldiers (see note on Lk 23:36).

15:37 *With a loud cry.* See note on Jn 19:30. The strength of the cry indicates that Jesus did not die the ordinary death of those crucified, who normally suffered long periods of complete agony, exhaustion and then unconsciousness before dying (see note on v. 24).

15:38 *curtain of the temple.* The curtain that separated the Holy Place from the Most Holy Place (see Ex 26:31–35; 26:31 and notes). The tearing of the curtain indicated that Christ had entered heaven itself for us so that we too may now enter God's presence (see Heb 9:8–10,12; 10:19–20 and notes). *torn.* At the beginning of Mark's Gospel, heaven was "torn" open (1:10), and the Father declared that Jesus was his Son (1:11). Now at the end, the temple curtain is "torn," and the centurion declares that Jesus is the Son of God (v. 39).

15:39 *centurion.* A commander of 100 men in the Roman army (see note on Ac 10:1). *saw how he died.* See note on v. 37. *Son of God.* See note on Mt 27:54.

15:40 *Mary Magdalene.* From 16:9; Lk 8:2 we learn that Jesus had driven seven demons out of her. *Mary the mother of James the younger and of Joseph.* See v. 47; 16:1. *Salome.* Probably the wife of Zebedee and the mother of James and John (see Mt 27:56).

15:41 *women had … cared for his needs.* See notes on Mt 27:55; Lk 8:3.

15:42 *Preparation Day.* Friday. Since it was now late in the afternoon, there was an urgency to get Jesus' body down from the cross before sundown, when the Sabbath began.

15:43 *Joseph.* See note on Lk 23:50. *Arimathea.* See note on Mt 27:57. *Council.* The Sanhedrin (see note on 14:55). *kingdom of God.* See note on Mt 3:2. *Pilate.* See note on v. 1. *asked for Jesus' body.* See note on Lk 23:52.

15:44 *surprised.* Crucified men often lived two or three days before dying, and the early death of Jesus was therefore extraordinary.

15:45 *gave the body to Joseph.* The release of the body of one condemned for high treason, and especially to someone who was not an immediate relative, was quite unusual.

15:46 *tomb cut out of rock.* Mt 27:60 states that the tomb belonged to Joseph and that it was new, i.e., it had not been used before. Its location was in a garden very near the site of the crucifixion (see Jn 19:41). There is archaeological evidence that the traditional site of the burial of Jesus (the Church of the Holy Sepulchre in Jerusalem) was a cemetery during the first century AD. *stone.* A "very large" (16:4) disc-shaped stone that rolled in a sloped channel.

16:1 *Sabbath was over.* About 6:00 p.m. Saturday evening. No purchases were possible on the Sabbath. *Mary Magdalene, Mary the mother of James, and Salome.* See note on 15:40. *spices.* Embalming was not practiced by the Jews. These spices were brought as an act of devotion and love (see note on Lk 23:56). *anoint Jesus' body.* The women had no expectation of Jesus' resurrection.

16:3 *Who will roll the stone away …?* Setting the large stone in place was a relatively easy task, but once it had slipped into the groove cut in bedrock in front of the entrance it was very difficult to remove. See photo, p. 1692.

16:5 *As they entered the tomb.* Inside the large opening of the facade of the tomb was a forechamber, at the back of which

a white robe[r] sitting on the right side, and they were alarmed.

6 "Don't be alarmed," he said. "You are looking for Jesus the Nazarene,[s] who was crucified. He has risen! He is not here. See the place where they laid him. 7 But go, tell his disciples and Peter, 'He is going ahead of you into Galilee. There you will see him,[t] just as he told you.' "[u]

8 Trembling and bewildered, the women went out and fled from the tomb. They said nothing to anyone, because they were afraid.[a]

[The earliest manuscripts and some other ancient witnesses do not have verses 9–20.]

9 When Jesus rose early on the first day of the week, he appeared first to Mary Magdalene,[v] out of whom he had driven seven demons. 10 She went and told those who had been with him and who were mourning and weeping. 11 When they heard that Jesus was alive and that she had seen him, they did not believe it.[w]

12 Afterward Jesus appeared in a different form to two of them while they were walking in the country.[x] 13 These returned and reported it to the rest; but they did not believe them either.

14 Later Jesus appeared to the Eleven as they were eating; he rebuked them for their lack of faith and their stubborn refusal to believe those who had seen him after he had risen.[y]

15 He said to them, "Go into all the world and preach the gospel to all creation.[z] 16 Whoever believes and is baptized will be saved, but whoever does not believe will be condemned.[a] 17 And these signs[b] will accompany those who believe: In my name they will drive out demons;[c] they will speak in new tongues;[d] 18 they will pick up snakes[e] with their hands; and when they drink deadly poison, it will not hurt them at all; they will place their hands on[f] sick people, and they will get well."

19 After the Lord Jesus had spoken to them, he was taken up into heaven[g] and he sat at the right hand of God.[h] 20 Then the disciples went out and preached everywhere, and the Lord worked with them and confirmed his word by the signs[i] that accompanied it.

16:5 [r] S Jn 20:12
16:6 [s] S Mk 1:24
16:7 [t] Jn 21:1-23 [u] Mk 14:28
16:9 [v] Mk 15:47; Jn 20:11-18
16:11 [w] ver 13, 14; Lk 24:11
16:12 [x] Lk 24:13-32
16:14 [y] Lk 24:36-43
16:15 [z] Mt 28:18-20; Lk 24:47,48; Ac 1:8
16:16 [a] Jn 3:16, 18,36; Ac 16:31
16:17 [b] S Jn 4:48 [c] Mk 9:38; Lk 10:17; Ac 5:16; 8:7; 16:18; 19:13-16 [d] Ac 2:4; 10:46; 19:6; 1Co 12:10, 28,30; 13:1; 14:2-39
16:18 [e] Lk 10:19; Ac 28:3-5 [f] S Ac 6:6
16:19 [g] Lk 24:50,51; Jn 6:62; Ac 1:9-11; 1Ti 3:16 [h] Ps 110:1; Mt 26:64; Ac 2:33; 5:31; Ro 8:34; Col 3:1; Heb 1:3; 12:2
16:20 [i] S Jn 4:48

[a] 8 Some manuscripts have the following ending between verses 8 and 9, and one manuscript has it after verse 8 (omitting verses 9-20): *Then they quickly reported all these instructions to those around Peter. After this, Jesus himself also sent out through them from east to west the sacred and imperishable proclamation of eternal salvation. Amen.*

---

a low, rectangular opening led to the burial chamber. *young man dressed in a white robe.* Mt 28:2 identifies him as an angel. See Lk 24:4 and note.

16:6 *the Nazarene.* Probably means "of Nazareth" (see note on Mt 2:23). *crucified.* See note on 15:24. *He has risen!* The climax of Mark's Gospel is the resurrection, without which Jesus' death, though noble, would be indescribably tragic (see 1Co 15:12–20 and notes). But in the resurrection he "was appointed the Son of God in power by his resurrection from the dead" (Ro 1:4; see NIV text note there).

16:7 *and Peter.* Jesus showed special concern for Peter, in view of his confident boasting and subsequent denials (14:29–31,66–72). *just as he told you.* See 14:28.

16:9–20 Serious doubt exists as to whether these verses belong to the Gospel of Mark. They are absent from important early manuscripts and display certain peculiarities of vocabulary, style and theological content that are unlike the rest of Mark. His Gospel probably ended at 16:8, or its original ending has been lost.

16:9 *Mary Magdalene.* See note on 15:40.

16:11,13 *did not believe.* See vv. 14,16; cf. Jn 20:24–29 and notes on 20:25,29.

16:12–13 A shortened account of the two men going to Emmaus (see Lk 24:13–35).

16:14 *the Eleven.* Judas Iscariot had committed suicide (see Mt 27:5 and note).

16:15–16 See the Great Commission in Mt 28:18–20 (see also note on Mt 28:19–20; cf. Lk 24:46–49; Jn 20:21–23; Ac 1:8).

16:16 *believes and is baptized.* See notes on 1:4; Ac 2:38; Ro 6:3–4.

16:18 *pick up snakes.* Cf. Paul in Ac 28:1–6. *drink deadly poison.* No occurrence of drinking deadly poison without harm is found in the NT.

16:19 *taken up into heaven.* The ascension was witnessed by the apostles (see Lk 24:51; Ac 1:9; cf. 1Ti 3:16 and note). *right hand of God.* See 14:62; Ps 110:1 and note.

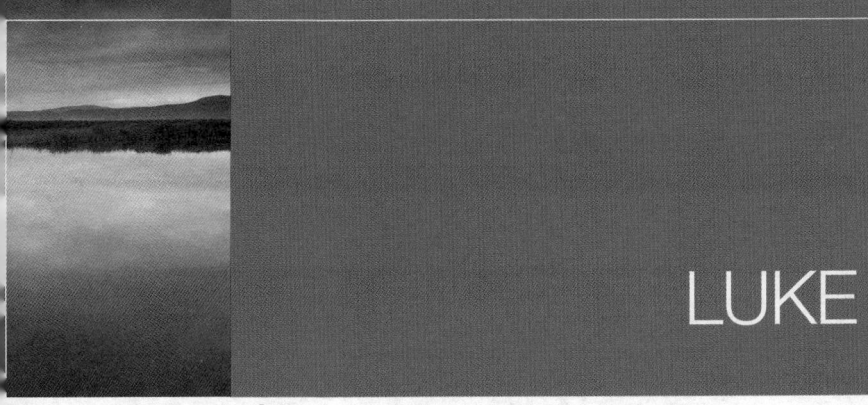

LUKE

INTRODUCTION

Author

The author's name does not appear in the book, but much internal and external evidence points to Luke. This Gospel is a companion volume to the book of Acts, and the language and structure of these two books indicate that both were written by the same person. They are addressed to the same individual, Theophilus, and the second volume refers to the first (Ac 1:1). Certain sections in Acts use the pronoun "we" (Ac 16:10 – 17; 20:5 – 15; 21:1 – 18; 27:1 — 28:16), indicating that the author was with Paul when the events described in these passages took place. By process of elimination, Paul's "dear friend Luke, the doctor" (Col 4:14) and "fellow worker" (Phm 24) becomes the most likely candidate. His authorship is supported by the uniform testimony of early Christian writings (e.g., the Muratorian Canon, AD 170, and the works of Irenaeus, c. 180).

Luke was probably a Gentile by birth, well educated in Greek culture, a physician by profession, a companion of Paul at various times from his second missionary journey to his final imprisonment in Rome and a loyal friend who remained with the apostle after others had deserted him (2Ti 4:11).

Antioch (of Syria) and Philippi are among the places suggested as his hometown.

Recipient and Purpose

The Gospel is specifically directed to Theophilus (1:3), whose name means "one who loves God" and almost certainly refers to a particular person rather than to lovers of God in general. The use of "most excellent" with the name further indicates an individual and supports the idea that he was a Roman official or at least of high position and wealth. He was possibly Luke's patron, responsible for seeing that the writings were copied and distributed. Such a dedication to the patron was common at that time.

Theophilus, however, was more than a patron. The message of this Gospel was intended for his own instruction (1:4), as well as for the instruction of those among whom the book would be

a **quick** look

Author:
Luke, a Gentile physician and missionary companion of Paul

Audience:
Addressed to Theophilus, but intended for all believers

Date:
Between the 60s and the 80s AD

Theme:
Luke presents Jesus as the Messiah and Lord whose life, death and resurrection make salvation available to all people everywhere.

Luke's writing is characterized by literary excellence, historical detail and warm, sensitive understanding of Jesus and those around him.

circulated. The fact that the Gospel was initially directed to Theophilus does not narrow or limit its purpose. It was written to strengthen the faith of all believers and to answer the attacks of unbelievers (see 1:1–4 and note). Luke wanted to show that the place of the Gentile Christian in God's kingdom is based on the teaching of Jesus. He wanted to commend the preaching of the gospel to the whole world.

Date and Place of Writing

The two most commonly suggested periods for dating the Gospel of Luke are: (1) AD 59–63, and (2) the 70s or the 80s (see essay and chart, pp. 1582–1583).

The place of writing is unknown, but Rome, Achaia, Ephesus and Caesarea have all been suggested. The place to which it was sent would, of course, depend on the residence of Theophilus. By its detailed designations of places in the Holy Land, the Gospel seems to be intended for readers who were unfamiliar with that land. Antioch, Achaia and Ephesus are possible destinations.

Style

Luke had outstanding command of the Greek language. His vocabulary is extensive and rich, and his style at times approaches that of classical Greek (as in the preface, 1:1–4), while at other times it is quite Semitic (1:5—2:52)—often like the Septuagint (the pre-Christian Greek translation of the OT).

Characteristics

The third Gospel presents the works and teachings of Jesus that are especially important for understanding the way of salvation. Its scope is complete from the birth of Christ to his ascension, its arrangement is orderly and it appeals to both Jews and Gentiles. The writing is characterized by literary excellence, historical detail and warm, sensitive understanding of Jesus and those around him.

Since the Synoptic Gospels (Matthew, Mark and Luke) report many of the same episodes in Jesus' life, one would expect much similarity in their accounts. The dissimilarities reveal the distinctive emphases of the separate writers. Luke's characteristic themes include: (1) universality, recognition of Gentiles as well as Jews in God's plan (see, e.g., 2:30–32 and notes on 2:31; 3:6); (2) emphasis on prayer, especially Jesus' praying before important occasions (see note on 3:21); (3) joy at the announcement of the gospel or "good news" (see note on 1:14); (4) special concern for the role of women (see, e.g., 8:1–3 and notes); (5) special interest in the poor and in issues of social justice (see note on 12:33); (6) concern for sinners (Jesus was viewed as a friend of sinners and tax collectors); (7) stress on the family circle (Jesus' activity included men, women and children, with the setting frequently in the home); (8) emphasis on the Holy Spirit (see note on 4:1); (9) inclusion of more parables than any other Gospel (see chart, p. 1736); and (10) emphasis on praising God (see 1:64; 24:53 and notes).

Sources

Although Luke acknowledges that many others had written about Jesus' life (1:1), he does not indicate that he relied solely on these reports for his own writing. He used personal investigation and arrangement, based on testimony from "eyewitnesses and servants of the word" (1:2)—including the preaching and oral accounts of the apostles. His language differences from the other Synop-

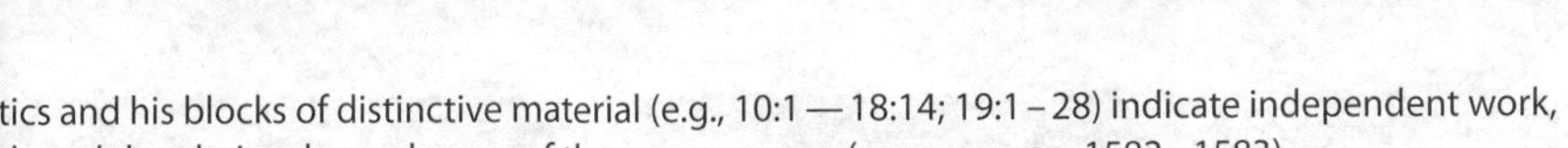

tics and his blocks of distinctive material (e.g., 10:1—18:14; 19:1-28) indicate independent work, though he obviously used some of the same sources (see essay, pp. 1582-1583).

Plan

Luke's account of Jesus' ministry can be divided into three major parts: (1) the events that occurred in and around Galilee (4:14—9:50), (2) those that took place in Judea and Perea (9:51—19:27) and (3) those of the final week in Jerusalem (19:28—24:53). Luke's uniqueness is especially seen in the amount of material devoted to Jesus' closing ministry in Judea and Perea, a section often called Jesus' "Journey to Jerusalem" or "The Travel Narrative." This material is predominantly made up of accounts of Jesus' discourses. Of the 28 parables that occur in Luke, 21 are found in 10:30—19:27. Of the 20 miracles recorded in Luke, only 5 appear in 9:51—19:27. The main theme of the teaching, parables and stories in this section is God's love for the lost: sinners, outcasts, Samaritans and people of low social status. Already in ch. 9 (see note on 9:51) Jesus is seen anticipating his final appearance in Jerusalem and his crucifixion (see note on 13:22).

The main theme of the Gospel is the nature of Jesus' Messiahship and mission, and a key verse is 19:10.

View overlooking the Sea of Galilee from the Mount of Beatitudes, where it is thought the Sermon on the Mount (Mt 5-7; cf. Luke's version of the sermon in Lk 6:20-49) was preached.

Jesus raised the widow's son at Nain (Lk 7:11).
www.HolyLandPhotos.org

Outline

I. The Preface (1:1 – 4)
II. The Births of John the Baptist and Jesus (1:5 — 2:52)
  A. The Annunciations (1:5 – 56)
  B. The Birth of John the Baptist (1:57 – 80)
  C. The Birth and Childhood of Jesus (ch. 2)
III. The Preparation of Jesus for His Public Ministry (3:1 — 4:13)
  A. His Forerunner (3:1 – 20)
  B. His Baptism (3:21 – 22)
  C. His Genealogy (3:23 – 38)
  D. His Temptation (4:1 – 13)
IV. His Ministry in Galilee (4:14 — 9:9)
  A. The Beginning of the Ministry in Galilee (4:14 – 41)
  B. The First Tour of Galilee (4:42 — 5:39)
  C. A Sabbath Controversy (6:1 – 11)
  D. The Choice of the 12 Apostles (6:12 – 16)
  E. The Sermon on the Plateau (6:17 – 49)
  F. Miracles in Capernaum and Nain (7:1 – 18)
  G. The Inquiry of John the Baptist (7:19 – 29)
  H. Jesus and the Pharisees (7:30 – 50)
  I. The Second Tour of Galilee (8:1 – 3)
  J. The Parables of the Kingdom (8:4 – 21)
  K. The Trip across the Sea of Galilee (8:22 – 39)
  L. The Third Tour of Galilee (8:40 — 9:9)

- V. His Withdrawal to Regions around Galilee (9:10 – 50)
  - A. To the Eastern Shore of the Sea of Galilee (9:10 – 17)
  - B. To Caesarea Philippi (9:18 – 50)
- VI. His Ministry in Judea (9:51 — 13:21)
  - A. Journey through Samaria to Judea (9:51 – 62)
  - B. The Mission of the 72 (10:1 – 24)
  - C. The Lawyer and the Parable of the Good Samaritan (10:25 – 37)
  - D. Jesus at Bethany with Mary and Martha (10:38 – 42)
  - E. Teachings in Judea (11:1 — 13:21)
- VII. His Ministry in and around Perea (13:22 — 19:27)
  - A. The Narrow Door (13:22 – 30)
  - B. Warning concerning Herod (13:31 – 35)
  - C. At a Pharisee's House (14:1 – 23)
  - D. The Cost of Discipleship (14:24 – 35)
  - E. The Parables of the Lost Sheep, the Lost Coin and the Lost Son (ch. 15)
  - F. The Parable of the Shrewd Manager (16:1 – 18)
  - G. The Rich Man and Lazarus (16:19 – 31)
  - H. Miscellaneous Teachings (17:1 – 10)
  - I. Ten Healed of Leprosy (17:11 – 19)
  - J. The Coming of the Kingdom (17:20 – 37)
  - K. The Persistent Widow (18:1 – 8)
  - L. The Pharisee and the Tax Collector (18:9 – 14)
  - M. Jesus and the Children (18:15 – 17)
  - N. The Rich Young Ruler (18:18 – 30)
  - O. Christ Foretells His Death (18:31 – 34)
  - P. A Blind Beggar Given His Sight (18:35 – 43)
  - Q. Jesus and Zacchaeus (19:1 – 10)
  - R. The Parable of the Ten Minas (19:11 – 27)
- VIII. His Last Days: Sacrifice and Triumph (19:28 — 24:53)
  - A. The Entry of Jesus into Jerusalem as King (19:28 – 44)
  - B. The Clearing of the Temple (19:45 – 48)
  - C. The Last Controversies with the Jewish Leaders (ch. 20)
  - D. The Olivet Discourse (ch. 21)
  - E. The Last Supper (22:1 – 38)
  - F. Jesus Praying in Gethsemane (22:39 – 46)
  - G. Jesus' Arrest (22:47 – 65)
  - H. Jesus on Trial (22:66 — 23:25)
  - I. The Crucifixion (23:26 – 56)
  - J. The Resurrection (24:1 – 12)
  - K. The Postresurrection Ministry (24:13 – 49)
  - L. The Ascension (24:50 – 53)

Introduction

1:1-4Ref — Ac 1:1

1 Many have undertaken to draw up an account of the things that have been fulfilled[a] among us, 2 just as they were handed down to us by those who from the first[a] were eyewitnesses[b] and servants of the word.[c] 3 With this in mind, since I myself have carefully investigated everything from the beginning, I too decided to write an orderly account[d] for you, most excellent[e] Theophilus,[f] 4 so that you may know the certainty of the things you have been taught.[g]

The Birth of John the Baptist Foretold

5 In the time of Herod king of Judea[h] there was a priest named Zechariah, who belonged to the priestly division of Abijah;[i] his wife Elizabeth was also a descendant of Aaron. 6 Both of them were righteous in the sight of God, observing all the Lord's commands and decrees blamelessly.[j] 7 But they were childless because Elizabeth was not able to conceive, and they were both very old.

8 Once when Zechariah's division was on duty and he was serving as priest before God,[k] 9 he was chosen by lot,[l] according to the custom of the priesthood, to go into the temple of the Lord and burn incense.[m] 10 And when the time for the burning of incense came, all the assembled worshipers were praying outside.[n]

11 Then an angel[o] of the Lord appeared to him, standing at the right side of the altar of incense.[p] 12 When Zechariah saw him, he was startled and was gripped with fear.[q] 13 But the angel said to him: "Do not be afraid,[r] Zechariah; your prayer has been heard. Your wife Elizabeth will bear you a son, and you are to call him John.[s] 14 He will be a joy and delight to you, and many will rejoice because of his birth,[t] 15 for he will be great in the sight of the Lord. He is never to take wine or other fermented drink,[u] and he will be filled with the Holy Spirit[v] even before he is born.[w] 16 He will bring back many of the people of Israel to the Lord their God. 17 And he will go on before the Lord,[x] in the spirit and power of Elijah,[y] to turn the hearts of the parents to their children[z] and the disobedient to the

[a] 1 Or *been surely believed*

1:2 [a] Mk 1:1; Jn 15:27; Ac 1:21,22 [b] Heb 2:3; 1Pe 5:1; 2Pe 1:16; 1Jn 1:1 [c] S Mk 4:14 **1:3** [d] Ac 11:4 [e] Ac 24:3; 26:25 [f] Ac 1:1 **1:4** [g] Jn 20:31; Ac 2:42 **1:5** [h] Mt 2:1 [i] 1Ch 24:10 **1:6** [j] Ge 6:9; Dt 5:33; 1Ki 9:4; Lk 2:25 **1:8** [k] 1Ch 24:19; 2Ch 8:14 **1:9** [l] Ac 1:26 [m] Ex 30:7,8; 1Ch 23:13; 2Ch 29:11; Ps 141:2 **1:10** [n] Lev 16:17 **1:11** [o] S Ac 5:19 [p] Ex 30:1-10 **1:12** [q] Jdg 6:22, 23; 13:22 **1:13** [r] ver 30; S Mt 14:27 [s] ver 60,63; S Mt 3:1 **1:14** [t] ver 58 **1:15** [u] Nu 6:3; Lev 10:9; Jdg 13:4; Lk 7:33 [v] ver 41, 67; Ac 2:4; 4:8, 31; 6:3,5; 9:17; 11:24; Eph 5:18; S Ac 10:44 [w] Jer 1:5; Gal 1:15 **1:17** [x] ver 76 [y] S Mt 11:14 [z] Mal 4:5,6

1:1 – 4 Using language similar to classical Greek, Luke begins with a formal preface, common to historical works of that time, in which he states his purpose for writing and identifies the recipient. He acknowledges other reports on the subject, shows the need for this new work and states his method of approach and sources of information.

1:1 *things ... fulfilled among us.* Things prophesied in the OT and now fully accomplished.

1:2 *handed down.* A technical term for passing on information as authoritative tradition (see 1Co 15:3 and note). *eyewitnesses and servants of the word.* Luke, though not an eyewitness himself, received testimony from those who were eyewitnesses and were dedicated to spreading the gospel. Apostolic preaching and interviews with other individuals associated with Jesus' ministry were available to him.

1:3 *carefully investigated.* Luke's account is characterized by a strong interest in historical accuracy. The account is complete, extending back to the very beginning of Jesus' earthly life. It has an orderly, meaningful arrangement. *most excellent.* Paul used this respectful term for governors Felix (Ac 24:3) and Festus (Ac 26:25). *Theophilus.* See Introduction: Recipient and Purpose.

1:4 *so that you may know.* Cf. John's purpose for writing (Jn 20:31; see note there).

1:5 *Herod king of Judea.* Herod the Great reigned 37 – 4 BC, and his kingdom also included Samaria, Galilee, Perea and Traconitis (see chart, p. 1592; see also note on Mt 2:1). The time referred to here is probably c. 7 – 6 BC. *Zechariah ... Elizabeth.* Both were of priestly descent from the line of Aaron. *priestly division of Abijah.* From the time of David the priests were organized into 24 divisions, and Abijah was one of the "heads of the priestly families" (Ne 12:12,17; see 1Ch 24:4,10 and notes).

1:6 *righteous ... blamelessly.* They were not sinless but were faithful and sincere in keeping God's commandments. Simeon (2:25) and Joseph (Mt 1:19) are given similar praise.

1:7 *childless.* See note on v. 25.

1:9 It was one of the priest's duties to keep the incense burning on the altar in front of the Most Holy Place. He supplied it with fresh incense before the morning sacrifice and again after the evening sacrifice (Ex 30:6 – 8). Ordinarily a priest would have this privilege very infrequently, and sometimes never, since duty assignments were determined by lot. *chosen by lot.* See notes on Ne 11:1; Pr 16:33; Jnh 1:7; Ac 1:26.

1:11 *angel of the Lord.* See v. 19; see also Ge 16:7 and note.

1:12 *fear.* A common reaction, as with Gideon (Jdg 6:22 – 23) and Manoah (Jdg 13:22).

1:13 *Do not be afraid.* This word of reassurance is given many times in both OT and NT (see, e.g., v. 30; 2:10 and note; 5:10; 8:50; 12:7,32; Ge 15:1; 21:17; 26:24; Dt 1:21 and note; Jos 1:9; 8:1 and note). *John.* The name (derived from Hebrew) means "The LORD is gracious" or "The LORD shows grace."

1:14 *joy.* A keynote of these opening chapters (vv. 44,47, 58; 2:10); this Gospel also closes with an expression of "great joy" (24:52).

1:15 *wine or other fermented drink.* It appears likely that John was to be subject to the Nazirite vow of abstinence from alcoholic drinks (see Nu 6:2 – 12 and notes). If so, he was a lifelong Nazirite, as were Samson (Jdg 13:4 – 7) and Samuel (1Sa 1:11). *filled with the Holy Spirit.* Consistent with his emphasis in his Gospel and in Acts (see note on 4:1), Luke's birth narratives stress the activity of the Holy Spirit (see vv. 35,41,67; 2:25 – 27). *even before he is born.* In the OT the Holy Spirit came upon individuals temporarily for some special task (see, e.g., Jdg 3:10 and note), but John was to be filled with the Spirit his entire life.

1:17 *Elijah.* John was not Elijah returning in the flesh (see Jn 1:21 and note), but he functioned like that OT preacher of repentance and was therefore a fulfillment of Mal 4:5 – 6 (see notes on Mal 4:5; Mt 11:14; 17:10). *to turn the hearts of the parents to their children.* See Mal 4:6 and note. True repentance results in reconciliation with others (see

wisdom of the righteous—to make ready a people prepared for the Lord."[a]

18 Zechariah asked the angel, "How can I be sure of this?[b] I am an old man and my wife is well along in years."[c]

19 The angel said to him, "I am Gabriel.[d] I stand in the presence of God, and I have been sent to speak to you and to tell you this good news. 20 And now you will be silent and not able to speak[e] until the day this happens, because you did not believe my words, which will come true at their appointed time."

21 Meanwhile, the people were waiting for Zechariah and wondering why he stayed so long in the temple. 22 When he came out, he could not speak to them. They realized he had seen a vision in the temple, for he kept making signs[f] to them but remained unable to speak.

23 When his time of service was completed, he returned home. 24 After this his wife Elizabeth became pregnant and for five months remained in seclusion. 25 "The Lord has done this for me," she said. "In these days he has shown his favor and taken away my disgrace[g] among the people."

The Birth of Jesus Foretold

26 In the sixth month of Elizabeth's pregnancy, God sent the angel Gabriel[h] to Nazareth,[i] a town in Galilee, 27 to a virgin pledged to be married to a man named Joseph,[j] a descendant of David. The virgin's name was Mary. 28 The angel went to her and said, "Greetings, you who are highly favored! The Lord is with you."

29 Mary was greatly troubled at his words and wondered what kind of greeting this might be. 30 But the angel said to her, "Do not be afraid,[k] Mary; you have found favor with God.[l] 31 You will conceive and give birth to a son, and you are to call him Jesus.[m] 32 He will be great and will be called the Son of the Most High.[n] The Lord God will give him the throne of his father David,[o] 33 and he will reign over Jacob's descendants forever; his kingdom[p] will never end."[q]

34 "How will this be," Mary asked the angel, "since I am a virgin?"

35 The angel answered, "The Holy Spirit will come on you,[r] and the power of the Most High[s] will overshadow you. So the holy one[t] to be born will be called[a] the Son of God.[u] 36 Even Elizabeth your relative is going to have a child[v] in her old age, and she who was said to be unable to conceive is in her sixth month. 37 For no word from God will ever fail."[w]

38 "I am the Lord's servant," Mary answered. "May your word to me be fulfilled." Then the angel left her.

Mary Visits Elizabeth

39 At that time Mary got ready and hurried to a town in the hill country of Judea,[x] 40 where she entered Zechariah's home

[a] 35 Or *So the child to be born will be called holy,*

1:17 [a] S Mt 3:3 **1:18** [b] Ge 15:8 [c] ver 34; Ge 17:17 **1:19** [d] ver 26; Da 8:16; 9:21 **1:20** [e] Ex 4:11; Eze 3:26 **1:22** [f] ver 62 **1:25** [g] Ge 30:23; Isa 4:1 **1:26** [h] S ver 19 [i] S Mt 2:23 **1:27** [j] Mt 1:16, 18,20; Lk 2:4 **1:30** [k] ver 13; S Mt 14:27 [l] Ge 6:8 **1:31** [m] Isa 7:14; Mt 1:21,25; Lk 2:21 **1:32** [n] ver 35, 76; S Mk 5:7 [o] S Mt 1:1 **1:33** [p] Mt 28:18 [q] 2Sa 7:16; Ps 89:3, 4; Isa 9:7; Jer 33:17; Da 2:44; 7:14, 27; Mic 4:7; Heb 1:8 **1:35** [r] Mt 1:18 [s] ver 32,76; S Mk 5:7 [t] S Mk 1:24 [u] S Mt 4:3 **1:36** [v] ver 24 **1:37** [w] S Mt 19:26 **1:39** [x] ver 65

3:8–9 and note on 3:9). *people prepared for the Lord.* John helped fulfill Isaiah's prophecy (see Isa 40:3–5 and notes), as Luke shows in 3:4–6.

1:18 *How can I be sure ...?* Like Abraham (see Ge 15:8 and note), Gideon (see Jdg 6:17 and note) and Hezekiah (2Ki 20:8), Zechariah asked for a sign (cf. 1Co 1:22).

1:19 *Gabriel.* The name can mean "God is my hero" or "Mighty man of God." Only two angels are identified by name in Scripture: Gabriel (Da 8:16; 9:21) and Michael (see Da 10:13,21 and note on 10:13; Jude 9; Rev 12:7 and note).

1:21 *the people were waiting for Zechariah.* They were waiting for him to come out of the Holy Place and pronounce the Aaronic blessing (see Nu 6:24–26 and notes).

1:23 *his time of service.* Each priest was responsible for a week's service at the temple once every six months. *home.* See v. 39.

1:24 *remained in seclusion.* Perhaps in devotion and gratitude that the Lord had taken away her childlessness.

1:25 *The Lord ... has shown his favor and taken away my disgrace.* Not only did lack of children deprive the parents of personal happiness, but it was generally considered to indicate divine disfavor and often brought social reproach (see Ge 16:2, Sarai; 25:21, Rebekah; 30:23, Rachel; 1Sa 1:1–18, Hannah; see also Lev 20:20–21; Ps 128:3; Jer 22:30).

1:26–35 This section speaks clearly of the virginal conception of Jesus (vv. 27,34–35; see Mt 1:18–25 and notes). The conception was the work of the Holy Spirit; the eternal second person of the Trinity, while remaining God, also "became flesh" (Jn 1:14; see note there). From conception he was fully God and fully man.

1:26 *Nazareth.* See note on Mt 2:23.

1:27 *pledged to be married.* See note on Mt 1:18.

1:28 *Greetings.* Ave in the Latin Vulgate (from which comes "Ave Maria").

1:31 *Jesus.* See Mt 1:21 and NIV text note for the meaning of this name.

1:32 *the Son of the Most High.* This title has two senses: (1) the divine Son of God and (2) the Messiah born in time. His Messiahship is clearly referred to in the following context (vv. 32b–33). *Most High.* A title frequently used of God in both the OT and NT (see vv. 35,76; 6:35; 8:28; Ge 14:19 and note; 2Sa 22:14; Ps 7:10,17). *throne.* Promised in the OT to the Messiah descended from David (see 2Sa 7:13,16; Ps 2:6–7; 89:25–27; Isa 9:6–7 and notes). *his father David.* Mary was a descendant of David, as was Joseph (see Mt 1:16 and note); so Jesus could rightly be called a "son" of David.

1:33 *forever.* See 2Sa 7:16; Ps 45:6 and notes; Rev 11:15. *his kingdom will never end.* Although Christ's role as mediator will one day be finished (see 1Co 15:24–28 and notes), the kingdom of the Father and Son, as one, will never end.

1:34 *How will this be ...?* Mary did not ask in disbelief, as Zechariah did (v. 20). See v. 45.

1:35 *holy one.* Jesus never sinned (see 2Co 5:21; Heb 4:15; 7:26 and notes; see also 1Pe 2:22; 1Jn 3:5).

1:36 *Elizabeth your relative.* It is not known whether she was a cousin, aunt or other relation.

and greeted Elizabeth. 41 When Elizabeth
heard Mary's greeting, the baby leaped in
her womb, and Elizabeth was filled with
the Holy Spirit.[y] 42 In a loud voice she exclaimed: "Blessed are you among wom-
en,[z] and blessed is the child you will bear!
43 But why am I so favored, that the mother
of my Lord[a] should come to me? 44 As soon
as the sound of your greeting reached my
ears, the baby in my womb leaped for joy.
45 Blessed is she who has believed that the
Lord would fulfill his promises to her!"

Mary's Song

1:46-53pp — 1Sa 2:1-10

46 And Mary said:

"My soul glorifies the Lord[b]
47 and my spirit rejoices in God my Savior,[c]
48 for he has been mindful
of the humble state of his servant.[d]
From now on all generations will call me blessed,[e]
49 for the Mighty One has done great things[f] for me—
holy is his name.[g]
50 His mercy extends to those who fear him,
from generation to generation.[h]
51 He has performed mighty deeds with his arm;[i]
he has scattered those who are proud in their inmost thoughts.[j]
52 He has brought down rulers from their thrones
but has lifted up the humble.[k]
53 He has filled the hungry with good things[l]
but has sent the rich away empty.
54 He has helped his servant Israel,
remembering to be merciful[m]

1:41 [y] S ver 15
1:42 [z] Jdg 5:24
1:43 [a] S Jn 13:13
1:46 [b] Ps 34:2,3
1:47 [c] Ps 18:46; Isa 17:10; 61:10; Hab 3:18; 1Ti 1:1; 2:3; 4:10
1:48 [d] ver 38; Ps 138:6 [e] Lk 11:27
1:49 [f] Ps 71:19 [g] Ps 111:9
1:50 [h] Ex 20:6; Ps 103:17
1:51 [i] Ps 98:1; Isa 40:10 [j] Ge 11:8; Ex 18:11; 2Sa 22:28; Jer 13:9; 49:16
1:52 [k] S Mt 23:12
1:53 [l] Ps 107:9
1:54 [m] Ps 98:3

55 to Abraham and his descendants[n] forever,
just as he promised our ancestors."

56 Mary stayed with Elizabeth for about
three months and then returned home.

The Birth of John the Baptist

57 When it was time for Elizabeth to
have her baby, she gave birth to a son.
58 Her neighbors and relatives heard that
the Lord had shown her great mercy, and
they shared her joy.
59 On the eighth day they came to circumcise[o] the child, and they were going to
name him after his father Zechariah, 60 but
his mother spoke up and said, "No! He is
to be called John."[p]
61 They said to her, "There is no one
among your relatives who has that name."
62 Then they made signs[q] to his father,
to find out what he would like to name
the child. 63 He asked for a writing tablet, and to everyone's astonishment he
wrote, "His name is John."[r] 64 Immediately his mouth was opened and his tongue
set free, and he began to speak,[s] praising
God. 65 All the neighbors were filled with
awe, and throughout the hill country of
Judea[t] people were talking about all these
things. 66 Everyone who heard this wondered about it, asking, "What then is this
child going to be?" For the Lord's hand
was with him.[u]

Zechariah's Song

67 His father Zechariah was filled with
the Holy Spirit[v] and prophesied:[w]

68 "Praise be to the Lord, the God of Israel,[x]
because he has come to his people
and redeemed them.[y]

1:55 [n] S Gal 3:16
1:59 [o] Ge 17:12; Lev 12:3; Lk 2:21; Php 3:5
1:60 [p] ver 13, 63; S Mt 3:1
1:62 [q] ver 22
1:63 [r] ver 13, 60; S Mt 3:1
1:64 [s] ver 20; Eze 24:27
1:65 [t] ver 39
1:66 [u] Ge 39:2; Ac 11:21
1:67 [v] S ver 15 [w] Joel 2:28
1:68 [x] Ge 24:27; 1Ki 8:15; Ps 72:18 [y] Ps 111:9; Lk 7:16

1:44 *for joy.* In some mysterious way the Holy Spirit produced this remarkable response in the unborn baby.

1:46–55 One of four hymns preserved in Lk 1–2 (see vv. 68–79; 2:14; 2:29–32 and notes). This hymn of praise is known as the Magnificat because in the Latin Vulgate translation the opening word is *Magnificat,* which means "glorifies." This song is like a psalm and should also be compared with the song of Hannah (1Sa 2:1–10; see note on 1Sa 2:1).

1:50 *those who fear him.* Those who revere God and live in harmony with his will (see notes on Ge 20:11; Pr 1:7).

1:51 *his arm.* A figurative description of God's powerful acts. God does not have a body; he is spirit (see Jn 4:24 and note).

1:53 *hungry.* Both physically and spiritually (Mt 5:6; Jn 6:35). The coming of God's kingdom will bring changes affecting every area of life.

1:54 *remembering to be merciful.* The song ends with an assurance that God will be true to his promises to his people (see Ge 22:16–18 and notes).

1:56 *three months.* Mary evidently remained with Elizabeth until John's birth and then returned to her home in Nazareth (see v. 36).

1:57–66 The birth of John the Baptist marks the fulfillment of the prophecy in vv. 5–25.

1:59 *name him after his father.* An accepted practice in that day, as seen in Josephus (*Life,* 1).

1:62 *they made signs to his father.* Apparently assuming that since he was mute he was also deaf.

1:63 *a writing tablet.* Probably a small wooden board covered with wax.

1:64 *praising God.* A common theme in Luke (2:13,20,28; 5:25–26; 7:16; 13:13; 17:15,18; 18:43; 19:37; 23:47; 24:53).

1:67 *filled with the Holy Spirit … prophesied.* Prophecy not only predicts but also proclaims God's word. Both Zechariah and Elizabeth (vv. 41–45) were enabled by the Holy Spirit to express what otherwise they could not have formulated.

1:68–79 This hymn is called the Benedictus ("Praise be") because the opening word in the Latin Vulgate translation is *Benedictus.* Whereas the Magnificat (see note on 1:46–55) is similar to a psalm, the Benedictus is more like a prophecy.

1:68 *redeemed them.* Not limited to national security (v. 71) but including moral and spiritual salvation (vv. 75,77).

69 He has raised up a horn[a][z] of salvation
for us
in the house of his servant David[a]
70 (as he said through his holy prophets
of long ago),[b]
71 salvation from our enemies
and from the hand of all who hate
us—
72 to show mercy to our ancestors[c]
and to remember his holy covenant,[d]
73 the oath he swore to our father
Abraham:[e]
74 to rescue us from the hand of our
enemies,
and to enable us to serve him[f]
without fear[g]
75 in holiness and righteousness[h] before
him all our days.

76 And you, my child, will be called a
prophet[i] of the Most High;[j]
for you will go on before the Lord to
prepare the way for him,[k]
77 to give his people the knowledge of
salvation
through the forgiveness of their
sins,[l]
78 because of the tender mercy of our
God,
by which the rising sun[m] will come
to us from heaven
79 to shine on those living in darkness
and in the shadow of death,[n]
to guide our feet into the path of
peace."[o]

80 And the child grew and became strong
in spirit[b];[p] and he lived in the wilderness
until he appeared publicly to Israel.

The Birth of Jesus

2 In those days Caesar Augustus[q] issued
a decree that a census should be taken
of the entire Roman world.[r] 2 (This was the
first census that took place while[c] Quirinius was governor of Syria.)[s] 3 And everyone
went to their own town to register.
4 So Joseph also went up from the town
of Nazareth in Galilee to Judea, to Bethlehem[t] the town of David, because he belonged to the house and line of David. 5 He
went there to register with Mary, who was
pledged to be married to him[u] and was expecting a child. 6 While they were there,
the time came for the baby to be born,
7 and she gave birth to her firstborn, a son.
She wrapped him in cloths and placed him
in a manger, because there was no guest
room available for them.
8 And there were shepherds living out in

[a] 69 *Horn* here symbolizes a strong king. [b] 80 Or *in the Spirit* [c] 2 Or *This census took place before*

1:69 [z] 1Sa 2:1, 10; 2Sa 22:3; Ps 18:2; 89:17; 132:17; Eze 29:21 [a] S Mt 1:1 **1:70** [b] Jer 23:5; Ac 3:21; Ro 1:2 **1:72** [c] Mic 7:20 [d] Ps 105:8, 9; 106:45; Eze 16:60 **1:73** [e] Ge 22:16-18 **1:74** [f] Heb 9:14 [g] 1Jn 4:18 **1:75** [h] Eph 4:24 **1:76** [i] S Mt 11:9 [j] ver 32, 35; S Mk 5:7 [k] ver 17; S Mt 3:3 **1:77** [l] Jer 31:34; Mt 1:21; Mk 1:4 **1:78** [m] Mal 4:2 **1:79** [n] Ps 107:14; Isa 9:2; 59:9; Mt 4:16; S Ac 26:18 [o] S Lk 2:14 **1:80** [p] Lk 2:40, 52 **2:1** [q] Mt 22:17; Lk 3:1 [r] S Mt 24:14 **2:2** [s] Mt 4:24; Ac 15:23,41; 21:3; Gal 1:21 **2:4** [t] S Jn 7:42 **2:5** [u] Lk 1:27

1:69 *horn.* Indicates strength (see NIV text note), as in the horn of an animal (Dt 33:17; Ps 22:21; Mic 4:13). Jesus, the Messiah from the house of David, has the power to save.

1:74 *to rescue us.* No doubt including liberation from all kinds of oppression and bondage as well as deliverance from sin.

1:76 *called a prophet of the Most High.* But Jesus will be called "the Son of the Most High" (see v. 32 and note). *prepare the way.* See notes on 3:4; Mal 3:1.

1:78 *the rising sun.* A reference to the coming of the Messiah (see also similar figures in Nu 24:17; Isa 9:2; 60:1; Mal 4:2–5 and notes). Zechariah not only praised his own son, the "prophet of the Most High" (vv. 76–77) but also gave honor to the coming Messiah (vv. 78–79). *will come to us.* God's coming (or visitation) occurs at the beginning (v. 68) and end of this hymn and is an important theme in Luke's Gospel (see 7:16; 19:44).

1:79 *those living in darkness.* The lost, separated from God (see Isa 9:1–2; Mt 4:15–16 and notes). *peace.* See note on 2:14.

1:80 *lived in the wilderness.* John's parents, old at his birth, probably died while he was young, and he apparently grew up in the Desert of Judea, which lies between Jerusalem and the Dead Sea. *until he appeared publicly.* John's preaching and announcing the coming of the Messiah marked his public appearance. He was about 30 years old when he began his ministry (see note on 3:23).

2:1–7 Jesus' birth marks the fulfillment of the prophecy in 1:26–38.

2:1 Luke takes special interest in relating his narrative to events of world history. *Caesar Augustus.* The first and (according to many) greatest Roman emperor (31 BC–AD 14). Having replaced the republic with an imperial form of government, he expanded the empire to include the entire Mediterranean world, established the famed *Pax Romana* ("Roman Peace") and ushered in the golden age of Roman literature and architecture. Augustus (which means "exalted") was a title conferred on him by the Roman senate in 27 BC. *census.* Used for military service and taxation. Jews, however, were exempt from Roman military service. God used the decree of a pagan emperor to fulfill the prophecy of Mic 5:2 (see note there; see also Mt 2:3–6). *Roman world.* See map, p. 2530, at the end of this study Bible.

2:2 *Quirinius.* This official appears to have been in office for two terms, first 6–4 BC and then AD 6–9. A census is associated with each term. This is the first; Ac 5:37 refers to the second. But see NIV text note.

2:3 *own town.* Probably the town of their ancestral origin.

2:4 *Nazareth ... Bethlehem.* Bethlehem, the town where David was born (1Sa 17:12; 20:6), was at least a three-day trip from Nazareth. *Judea.* The Roman designation for the southern part of the Holy Land, earlier included in the kingdom of Judah.

2:5 *with Mary.* Mary may also have been of the house of David and therefore required to enroll. In Syria, the Roman province in which the Holy Land was located, women 12 years of age and older were required to pay a poll tax and therefore to register. *pledged to be married.* See Mt 1:18 and note.

2:7 *cloths.* Strips of cloth were regularly used to wrap a newborn infant. *manger.* The feeding trough of the animals. This is the only indication that Christ was born in a stable. Very early tradition suggests that it was a cave, perhaps used as a stable.

2:8 *living out in the fields.* Does not necessarily mean it was summer, the dry season. The flocks reserved for temple sacrifice were kept in the fields near Bethlehem throughout the year. *keeping watch.* Against thieves and predatory animals.

the fields nearby, keeping watch over their
flocks at night. 9 An angel[v] of the Lord appeared to them, and the glory of the Lord
shone around them, and they were terrified. 10 But the angel said to them, "Do not
be afraid.[w] I bring you good news that will
cause great joy for all the people. 11 Today
in the town of David a Savior[x] has been
born to you; he is the Messiah,[y] the Lord.[z]
12 This will be a sign[a] to you: You will find
a baby wrapped in cloths and lying in a
manger."
13 Suddenly a great company of the
heavenly host appeared with the angel,
praising God and saying,

14 "Glory to God in the highest heaven,
and on earth peace[b] to those on
whom his favor rests."

15 When the angels had left them and
gone into heaven, the shepherds said to
one another, "Let's go to Bethlehem and
see this thing that has happened, which
the Lord has told us about."
16 So they hurried off and found Mary
and Joseph, and the baby, who was lying
in the manger.[c] 17 When they had seen him,
they spread the word concerning what had
been told them about this child, 18 and all

2:9 [v] S Ac 5:19 **2:10** [w] S Mt 14:27 **2:11** [x] S Mt 1:21; S Jn 3:17; 4:42; Ac 5:31; 13:23; S Ro 11:14; 1Ti 4:10; 1Jn 4:14 [y] Mt 1:16; 16:16, 20; Jn 11:27; Ac 2:36; 3:20; S 9:22 [z] S Jn 13:13 **2:12** [a] 1Sa 2:34; 10:7; 2Ki 19:29; Ps 86:17; Isa 7:14 **2:14** [b] Isa 9:6; 52:7; 53:5; Mic 5:5; Lk 1:79; S Jn 14:27; Ro 5:1; Eph 2:14,17 **2:16** [c] ver 7

2:9 *An angel of the Lord.* A designation used throughout the birth narratives (see 1:11 and note; Mt 1:20,24; 2:13,19). The angel in 1:11 is identified as Gabriel (1:19; see 1:26). Cf. Ge 16:7 and note.

2:10 *Do not be afraid.* Fear was the common reaction to angelic appearances (see note on 1:13), and encouragement was needed. *great joy.* See note on 1:14.

2:11 *town of David.* Bethlehem (v. 4). *Savior.* Many Jews were looking for a political leader to deliver them from Roman rule, while others were hoping for a savior to deliver them from sickness and physical hardship. But this announcement concerns the Savior who would deliver from sin and death (see Mt 1:21; Jn 4:42 and note). *the Messiah.* See second NIV text note on Mt 1:1. *the Lord.* A designation used of God and his "Anointed" (the Messiah) (see Ac 2:36; Php 2:11 and note on 2:9; 1Th 1:1 and note).

2:13,20 *praising God.* See 1:64 and note.

2:14 See note on 1:46–55. This brief hymn is called the Gloria in Excelsis Deo, from the first words of the Latin Vulgate translation (meaning "Glory to God in the Highest"). The angels recognized the glory and majesty of God by giving praise to him. *in the highest heaven.* Where God dwells (cf. Mt 6:9). *peace to those on whom his favor rests.* Peace is not assured to all, but only to those pleasing to God—the objects of his good pleasure (see Luke's use of the word "pleased" elsewhere: 3:22; 10:21; 12:32). The Roman world was experiencing the *Pax Romana* ("Roman Peace"), marked by external tranquillity. But the angels proclaimed a deeper, more lasting peace than that—a peace of mind and soul made possible by the Savior (v. 11). Peace with God is received by faith in Christ (see Ro 5:1 and note), and it is on believers that "his favor rests." The Davidic Messiah was called "Prince of Peace" (Isa 9:6; see note there), and Christ promised peace to his disciples (see Jn 14:27; Php 4:7 and notes). But Christ also brought conflict (the "sword"; see Mt 10:34 and note; cf. Lk 12:49), for peace with God involves opposition to Satan and his work (see Jas 4:7 and note).

MAIN ROMAN EMPERORS OF THE NEW TESTAMENT PERIOD

NAME	DATE	EVENTS UNDER THEIR REIGN
Caesar Augustus or Octavian	30 BC–AD 14	The emperor associated with the census at Jesus' birth (Lk 2:1). Demonstrating extraordinary skills as leader and administrator, Augustus inaugurated the *Pax Romana* ("Roman Peace"), an unprecedented period of peace and stability throughout the Mediterranean region. The freedom and relative safety of travel afforded by this peace would prove to be major factors for the rapid expansion of Christianity.
Tiberius	AD 14–37	Emperor during Jesus' public ministry (Lk 3:1). It was to him Jesus referred when he said, "Give back to Caesar what is Caesar's and to God what is God's" (see Mk 12:17 and note).
Caligula	AD 37–41	Provoked a crisis among the Jews by demanding that his image be set up in the Jerusalem temple. Agrippa I eventually convinced Caligula to cancel the order, and the emperor was assassinated before it was carried out. Paul may be alluding to this event as a type of the antichrist when he speaks of the "man of lawlessness" who "sets himself up in God's temple, proclaiming himself to be God" (2Th 2:3–4).
Claudius	AD 41–54	Expelled the Jews from Rome in AD 49, probably because of conflicts with Jewish Christians (Suetonius, *Life of Claudius* 25.4). Priscilla and Aquila came from Rome to Corinth at this time (Ac 18:2; cf. 11:28).
Nero	AD 54–68	The caesar to whom Paul appealed during his trial (Ac 25:10; 28:19). Later, in AD 64, Nero began the first major persecution against Christians, blaming them for a fire he was rumored to have set in Rome (Tacitus, *Annals* 15.44). Both Paul and Peter were probably martyred under Nero.
Vespasian	AD 69–79	Declared emperor while in Israel putting down the Jewish Revolt of AD 66–73. He returned to Rome, leaving his son Titus to complete the destruction of Jerusalem and the temple.
Domitian	AD 81–96	The second emperor (after Nero) to persecute the church. This persecution is likely the background to the book of Revelation.

THE HYMNS OF LUKE'S BIRTH NARRATIVE

SONG*	VERSES	SINGER	THEME
The *Magnificat*	1:46–55	Mary	God's exaltation of the lowly and humiliation of the mighty
The *Benedictus*	1:68–79	Zechariah	God's salvation through the Davidic Messiah, prepared for by John the Baptist
Gloria in Excelsis Deo	2:14	Angelic chorus	Glory to God; peace to the recipients of his grace
The *Nunc Dimittis*	2:29–32	Simeon	God's salvation as the glory of Israel and a light to the Gentiles

*Named for the first word(s) in the Latin translation.

who heard it were amazed at what the
shepherds said to them. 19 But Mary treasured up all these things and pondered
them in her heart.[d] 20 The shepherds returned, glorifying and praising God[e] for all
the things they had heard and seen, which
were just as they had been told.
21 On the eighth day, when it was time to
circumcise the child,[f] he was named Jesus,
the name the angel had given him before
he was conceived.[g]

Jesus Presented in the Temple

22 When the time came for the purification rites required by the Law of Moses,[h]
Joseph and Mary took him to Jerusalem to
present him to the Lord 23 (as it is written
in the Law of the Lord, "Every firstborn
male is to be consecrated to the Lord"[a]),[i]
24 and to offer a sacrifice in keeping with
what is said in the Law of the Lord: "a pair
of doves or two young pigeons."[b][j]
25 Now there was a man in Jerusalem
called Simeon, who was righteous and
devout.[k] He was waiting for the consolation of Israel,[l] and the Holy Spirit was on
him. 26 It had been revealed to him by the
Holy Spirit that he would not die before he
had seen the Lord's Messiah. 27 Moved by
the Spirit, he went into the temple courts.
When the parents brought in the child
Jesus to do for him what the custom of
the Law required,[m] 28 Simeon took him in
his arms and praised God, saying:

29 "Sovereign Lord, as you have promised,[n]
you may now dismiss[c] your servant
in peace.[o]
30 For my eyes have seen your salvation,[p]
31 which you have prepared in the
sight of all nations:
32 a light for revelation to the Gentiles,
and the glory of your people Israel."[q]

33 The child's father and mother marveled at what was said about him. 34 Then
Simeon blessed them and said to Mary, his
mother:[r] "This child is destined to cause
the falling[s] and rising of many in Israel, and to be a sign that will be spoken
against, 35 so that the thoughts of many
hearts will be revealed. And a sword will
pierce your own soul too."

2:19 [d] ver 51 **2:20** [e] S Mt 9:8 **2:21** [f] S Lk 1:59 [g] S Lk 1:31 **2:22** [h] Lev 12:2-8 **2:23** [i] Ex 13:2, 12, 15; Nu 3:13 **2:24** [j] Lev 12:8 **2:25** [k] Lk 1:6 [l] ver 38; Isa 52:9; Lk 23:51 **2:27** [m] ver 22 **2:29** [n] ver 26 [o] Ac 2:24 **2:30** [p] Isa 40:5; 52:10; Lk 3:6 **2:32** [q] Isa 42:6; 49:6; Ac 13:47; 26:23 **2:34** [r] S Mt 12:46 [s] Isa 8:14; Mt 21:44; 1Co 1:23; 2Co 2:16; Gal 5:11; 1Pe 2:7,8

[a] 23 Exodus 13:2,12 [b] 24 Lev. 12:8
[c] 29 Or *promised, / now dismiss*

2:19 *treasured up all these things ... in her heart.* Cf. v. 51.
2:21 *circumcise.* See Ge 17:10; Jn 7:22 and notes.
2:22 *purification.* Following the birth of a son, the mother had to wait 40 days before going to the temple to offer a sacrifice for her purification. If she could not afford a lamb and a pigeon (or dove), then two pigeons (or doves) would be acceptable (see Lev 12:2–8 and notes; cf. Lev 5:11). *to Jerusalem.* The distance from Bethlehem to Jerusalem was only about five miles. *present him to the Lord.* The firstborn of both people and animals were to be dedicated to the Lord (see v. 23; Ex 13:2–13 and notes). The animals were sacrificed, but the human beings were to serve God throughout their lives. The Levites actually served in the place of all the firstborn males in Israel (see Nu 3:11–13; 8:17–18).
2:25 *the consolation of Israel.* The comfort the Messiah would bring to his people at his coming (see vv. 26,38; 23:51; 24:21; Isa 40:1–2 and notes; Mt 5:4). *the Holy Spirit was on him.* Not in the way common to all believers after Pentecost. Simeon was given a special insight by the Spirit so that he would recognize the "Messiah" (v. 26; cf. 1:15 and note).
2:28 *praised God.* See 1:64 and note.
2:29–32 See note on 1:46–55. This hymn of Simeon has been called the *Nunc Dimittis*, from the first words of the Latin Vulgate translation, meaning "you may now dismiss."
2:31 *all nations.* As a Gentile himself, Luke was careful to emphasize the truth that salvation was offered to Gentiles (v. 32) as well as to Jews.
2:33 *child's father.* Luke, aware of the virgin birth of Jesus (1:26–35), is referring to Joseph as Jesus' legal father (see v. 41; Jn 1:45 and note).
2:34 *falling and rising of many in Israel.* Christ raises up those who believe in him but is a stumbling block for those who disbelieve (see 20:17–18 and note on 20:18; 1Co 1:23; 1Pe 2:6–8 and notes). *sign ... spoken against.* This somewhat enigmatic statement may mean that Jesus, a sign from God (v. 12; 11:30), would precipitate division, opposition and rejection.
2:35 *sword will pierce your own soul too.* The word "too" indicates that Mary, as well as Jesus, would suffer deep anguish — the first reference in this Gospel to Christ's suffering and death.

36 There was also a prophet,[t] Anna, the
daughter of Penuel, of the tribe of Asher.
She was very old; she had lived with her
husband seven years after her marriage,
37 and then was a widow until she was
eighty-four.[a u] She never left the temple but
worshiped night and day, fasting and praying.[v] 38 Coming up to them at that very moment, she gave thanks to God and spoke
about the child to all who were looking
forward to the redemption of Jerusalem.[w]
39 When Joseph and Mary had done everything required by the Law of the Lord,
they returned to Galilee to their own town
of Nazareth.[x] 40 And the child grew and became strong; he was filled with wisdom,
and the grace of God was on him.[y]

The Boy Jesus at the Temple

41 Every year Jesus' parents went to Jerusalem for the Festival of the Passover.[z]
42 When he was twelve years old, they
went up to the festival, according to the
custom. 43 After the festival was over,
while his parents were returning home,
the boy Jesus stayed behind in Jerusalem,
but they were unaware of it. 44 Thinking
he was in their company, they traveled on
for a day. Then they began looking for him
among their relatives and friends. 45 When
they did not find him, they went back to
Jerusalem to look for him. 46 After three
days they found him in the temple courts,
sitting among the teachers, listening to
them and asking them questions. 47 Everyone who heard him was amazed[a] at his
understanding and his answers. 48 When
his parents saw him, they were astonished. His mother[b] said to him, "Son, why
have you treated us like this? Your father[c]
and I have been anxiously searching for
you."
49 "Why were you searching for me?" he
asked. "Didn't you know I had to be in
my Father's house?"[b d] 50 But they did not
understand what he was saying to them.[e]
51 Then he went down to Nazareth with
them[f] and was obedient to them. But his
mother treasured all these things in her
heart.[g] 52 And Jesus grew in wisdom and
stature, and in favor with God and man.[h]

John the Baptist Prepares the Way

3:2-10pp — Mt 3:1-10; Mk 1:3-5
3:16,17pp — Mt 3:11,12; Mk 1:7,8

3 In the fifteenth year of the reign of Tiberius Caesar — when Pontius Pilate[i]
was governor of Judea, Herod[j] tetrarch of
Galilee, his brother Philip tetrarch of Iturea and Traconitis, and Lysanias tetrarch
of Abilene — 2 during the high-priesthood

2:36 [t] S Ac 21:9 **2:37** [u] 1Ti 5:9 [v] Ac 13:3; 14:23; 1Ti 5:5 **2:38** [w] ver 25; Isa 40:2; 52:9; Lk 1:68; 24:21 **2:39** [x] ver 51; S Mt 2:23 **2:40** [y] ver 52; Lk 1:80 **2:41** [z] Ex 23:15; Dt 16:1-8; Lk 22:8

2:47 [a] S Mt 7:28 **2:48** [b] S Mt 12:46 [c] Lk 3:23; 4:22 **2:49** [d] Jn 2:16 **2:50** [e] S Mk 9:32 **2:51** [f] ver 39; S Mt 2:23 [g] ver 19 **2:52** [h] ver 40; 1Sa 2:26; Pr 3:4; Lk 1:80 **3:1** [i] S Mt 27:2 [j] S Mt 14:1

[a] 37 Or *then had been a widow for eighty-four years.*
[b] 49 Or *be about my Father's business*

2:36 *prophet.* Other female prophets were Miriam (Ex 15:20), Deborah (Jdg 4:4), Huldah (2Ki 22:14) and the daughters of Philip (Ac 21:9). *Anna.* Greek *Hanna*; same name as OT Hannah (1Sa 1:2), which means "gracious." Hanna praised God for the child Jesus, as Hannah had praised God for the child Samuel (1Sa 2:1 – 10).
2:37 *never left the temple.* Herod's temple was quite large and included rooms for various uses, and Hanna may have been allowed to live in one of them. This statement, however, probably means that she spent her waking hours attending and worshiping in the temple.
2:38 *Jerusalem.* The holy city of God's chosen people; here it stands for Israel as a whole. See Introduction to Psalms: Theology: Major Themes, 7.
2:39 *they returned to Galilee.* Luke does not mention the coming of the Magi, the danger from Herod or the flight to and return from Egypt (cf. Mt 2:1 – 23).
2:41 *Festival of the Passover.* Annual attendance at three festivals by all adult males (normally accompanied by their families) was commanded in the law: Passover, Pentecost and Tabernacles (see notes on Ex 23:14 – 17; Dt 16:16). Distance prevented many from attending all three, but most Jews tried to be at Passover.
2:42 *twelve years old.* At age 12 boys began preparing to take their places in the religious community the following year.
2:46 *the teachers.* The rabbis, experts in Judaism.
2:49 *in my Father's house.* See NIV text note. Jesus pointed to his personal duty to his Father in heaven. He contrasted his "my Father" with Mary's "your father" (v. 48). At 12 years of age he was aware of his unique relationship to God, but he was also obedient to his earthly parents (v. 51).
2:52 Luke says of Jesus what is said of Samuel in 1Sa 2:26 (see note there). *Jesus grew.* Although Jesus was God, there is no indication that he had all knowledge and wisdom from birth. He seems to have matured like any other boy.
3:1 – 2 Ancient historians frequently dated an event by citing the year in the reign of the ruler at the time the event happened.
3:1 *fifteenth year.* Several possible dates could be indicated by this description, but the date AD 25 – 26 (Tiberius had authority in the provinces beginning in AD 11) best fits the chronology of the life of Christ. The other rulers named do not help pinpoint the beginning of John's ministry but only serve to indicate the general historical period. *Pontius Pilate.* The Roman governor of Judea from AD 26 to 36, whose official residence was in Caesarea on the Mediterranean coast. (In 1961 archaeologists unearthed a stone step in the Roman amphitheater in Caesarea contemporary with Pilate and bearing a Latin inscription that included these words: "Pontius Pilate, Prefect [Governor] of Judea"; see chart, p. 1810.) When he came to Jerusalem, he stayed in the magnificent palace built by Herod the Great, located southwest of the temple area. Mark calls this palace "the Praetorium" (Mk 15:16; see note there), and it was here that the Roman trial of Jesus took place (see note on Mk 14:53 — 15:15). *Herod tetrarch of Galilee.* At the death of Herod the Great (4 BC), his sons — Archelaus, Herod Antipas and Herod Philip — were given jurisdiction over his divided kingdom. Herod Antipas became the tetrarch of Galilee and Perea (see note on Mt 14:1). *Lysanias tetrarch of Abilene.* Nothing is known of this Lysanias beyond the fact that his name has been found in certain inscriptions (for Abilene, see map, p. 2524, at the end of this study Bible).
3:2 *the high-priesthood of Annas and Caiaphas.* Annas was high priest from AD 6 until he was deposed by the Roman official Gratus in 15. He was followed by his son Eleazar, his son-in-law Caiaphas and then four more sons.

THE HOLY LAND UNDER HEROD THE GREAT (37–4 BC)

Mediterranean Sea
Sidon
Tyre
Ptolemais
PHOENICIA
ULATHA
Abana R.
Damascus
Pharpar R.
Mt. Hermon
SYRIA
Caesarea Philippi (Paneas)
Meroth
ITUREANS
GAULANITIS
BATANEA
TRACONITIS
GALILEE
Sea of Galilee
Tiberias
Hippos
Dion
AURANITIS
Gaba
Sepphoris
Mt. Carmel
Jezreel Valley
Gadara
Caesarea Maritima (Strato's Tower)
Scythopolis
Pella
DECAPOLIS
SAMARIA
Sebaste (Samaria)
Gerasa
Jordan R.
Ammathus
Mt. Gerizim
Alexandrium
Joppa
Antipatris
PEREA
Phasaelis
Philadelphia
JUDEA
Jamnia
Jericho
Emmaus
Esbus
Jerusalem
Cypros
Azotus
Qumran
Bethlehem
Hyrcania
Ascalon
Herodium
Callirrhoe
Machaerus
Hebron
Gaza
Dead Sea
IDUMEA
Masada
Beersheba
NABATEANS

Qumran—site of Dead Sea Scrolls discovery and presumed home of Essene sect

Military colony founded by Herod
Herodian fortress
Herod's kingdom at the start of his reign
Additions to Herod's kingdom

0 10 km.
0 10 miles

of Annas and Caiaphas,[k] the word of God
came to John[l] son of Zechariah[m] in the
wilderness. 3 He went into all the country
around the Jordan, preaching a baptism
of repentance for the forgiveness of sins.[n]
4 As it is written in the book of the words
of Isaiah the prophet:

“A voice of one calling in the
wilderness,
‘Prepare the way for the Lord,
make straight paths for him.
5 Every valley shall be filled in,
every mountain and hill made low.
The crooked roads shall become
straight,
the rough ways smooth.
6 And all people will see God’s
salvation.’ ”[a][o]

7 John said to the crowds coming out to
be baptized by him, “You brood of vipers![p]
Who warned you to flee from the coming wrath?[q] 8 Produce fruit in keeping with
repentance. And do not begin to say to
yourselves, ‘We have Abraham as our father.’[r] For I tell you that out of these stones
God can raise up children for Abraham.
9 The ax is already at the root of the trees,
and every tree that does not produce good
fruit will be cut down and thrown into the
fire.”[s]
10 “What should we do then?”[t] the crowd
asked.
11 John answered, “Anyone who has two
shirts should share with the one who has
none, and anyone who has food should
do the same.”[u]
12 Even tax collectors came to be baptized.[v] “Teacher,” they asked, “what
should we do?”
13 “Don’t collect any more than you are
required to,”[w] he told them.
14 Then some soldiers asked him, “And
what should we do?”
He replied, “Don’t extort money and
don’t accuse people falsely[x]—be content
with your pay.”
15 The people were waiting expectantly and were all wondering in their hearts
if John[y] might possibly be the Messiah.[z]
16 John answered them all, “I baptize you
with[b] water.[a] But one who is more powerful than I will come, the straps of whose
sandals I am not worthy to untie. He will
baptize you with[b] the Holy Spirit and fire.[b]
17 His winnowing fork[c] is in his hand to
clear his threshing floor and to gather the
wheat into his barn, but he will burn up
the chaff with unquenchable fire.”[d] 18 And
with many other words John exhorted the
people and proclaimed the good news to
them.
19 But when John rebuked Herod[e] the tetrarch because of his marriage to Herodias, his brother’s wife, and all the other evil
things he had done, 20 Herod added this
to them all: He locked John up in prison.[f]

3:2 [k] S Mt 26:3 [l] S Mt 3:1 [m] Lk 1:13
3:3 [n] ver 16; S Mk 1:4
3:6 [o] Ps 98:2; Isa 40:3-5; 42:16; 52:10; Lk 2:30
3:7 [p] Mt 12:34; 23:33 [q] S Ro 1:18
3:8 [r] Isa 51:2; Lk 19:9; Jn 8:33, 39; Ac 13:26; Ro 4:1, 11, 12, 16, 17; 9:7, 8; Gal 3:7
3:9 [s] S Mt 3:10
3:10 [t] ver 12, 14; Ac 2:37; 16:30
3:11 [u] Isa 58:7; Eze 18:7
3:12 [v] Lk 7:29
3:13 [w] Lk 19:8
3:14 [x] Ex 23:1; Lev 19:11
3:15 [y] S Mt 3:1 [z] Jn 1:19, 20; Ac 13:25
3:16 [a] ver 3; S Mk 1:4 [b] Jn 1:26, 33; Ac 1:5; 2:3; 11:16; 19:4
3:17 [c] Isa 30:24 [d] Mt 13:30; S 25:41
3:19 [e] ver 1; S Mt 14:1
3:20 [f] S Mt 14:3, 4

[a] *6* Isaiah 40:3-5 [b] *16* Or *in*

Even though Rome had replaced Annas, the Jews continued to recognize his authority (see Jn 18:13; Ac 4:6 and notes), so Luke included his name as well as that of the Roman appointee, Caiaphas. *word of God.* The source of John’s preaching and authority for his baptizing. God’s message came to John as it came to the OT prophets (see Jer 1:2; Hos 1:1; Joel 1:1 and notes; see also Eze 1:3). *wilderness.* Refers to a desolate, uninhabited area, not necessarily a sandy, waterless place.

3:3 *baptism of repentance.* See note on Mt 3:11. John’s baptism represented a change of heart, which includes sorrow for sin and a determination to lead a holy life. *forgiveness of sins.* Christ would deliver the repentant person from sin’s penalty by dying on the cross.

3:4 *Prepare the way.* Before a king made a journey to a distant country, the roads he would travel were improved (see Isa 40:3 and note). Similarly, preparation for the Messiah was made in a moral and spiritual way by the ministry of John, which focused on repentance and forgiveness of sin and the need for a Savior.

3:6 *all people.* God’s salvation was to be made known to both Jews and Gentiles—a major theme of Luke’s Gospel (see note on 2:31).

3:7 *the coming wrath.* A reference to both the destruction of Jerusalem (21:20–23), which occurred in AD 70, and the final judgment (Jn 3:36). But see notes on 1Th 1:10; 5:9.

3:9 *ax ... at the root.* A symbolic way of saying that judgment is near for those who give no evidence of repentance. *fire.* A symbol of divine judgment (see Mt 7:19; 13:42 and note; see also La 1:13 and note).

3:11 *two shirts.* A “shirt” was something like a long undershirt. Since two such garments were not needed, the second should be given to a person in need of one (see 9:3 and note on Mk 6:9).

3:12 *tax collectors.* Taxes were collected for the Roman government by Jewish agents, who were especially detested for helping the pagan conqueror and for frequently defrauding their own people (see notes on 19:2,8; Mt 5:46; Mk 2:16).

3:14 *soldiers.* Limited military forces were allowed for certain Jewish leaders and institutions (such as those of Herod Antipas, the police guard of the temple and escorts for tax collectors). The professions of tax collector and soldier as such were not condemned, but the common unethical practices associated with them were.

3:16 *baptize you with the Holy Spirit.* Fulfilled at Pentecost (see Ac 1:5; 2:4,38 and notes). *and fire.* Here fire is associated with judgment (v. 17; see La 1:13 and note). See also the fire of Pentecost (see Ac 2:3 and note) and the fire of testing (see 1Co 3:13 and note).

3:17 *His winnowing fork.* See note on Ru 1:22. The chaff represents the unrepentant and the wheat the righteous. Many Jews thought that only pagans would be judged and punished when the Messiah came, but John declared that judgment would come to all who did not repent—including Jews.

3:19 *rebuked Herod ... because of his marriage to Herodias.* Herod Antipas had married the daughter of Aretas IV of Arabia but divorced her to marry his own niece, Herodias, who was already his brother’s (Herod Philip’s) wife (see Mt 14:3 and note; Mk 6:17).

3:20 *locked John up in prison.* According to Josephus, John was imprisoned in Machaerus, east of the Dead Sea (*Antiqui-*

The Baptism and Genealogy of Jesus

3:21,22pp — Mt 3:13-17; Mk 1:9-11
3:23-38pp — Mt 1:1-17

21 When all the people were being baptized, Jesus was baptized too. And as he
was praying,[g] heaven was opened 22 and
the Holy Spirit descended on him[h] in bodily form like a dove. And a voice came from
heaven: "You are my Son,[i] whom I love;
with you I am well pleased."[j]
23 Now Jesus himself was about thirty
years old when he began his ministry.[k] He
was the son, so it was thought, of Joseph,[l]

the son of Heli, 24 the son of Matthat,
the son of Levi, the son of Melki,
the son of Jannai, the son of Joseph,
25 the son of Mattathias, the son of Amos,
the son of Nahum, the son of Esli,
the son of Naggai, 26 the son of Maath,
the son of Mattathias, the son of Semein,
the son of Josek, the son of Joda,
27 the son of Joanan, the son of Rhesa,
the son of Zerubbabel,[m] the son of Shealtiel,
the son of Neri, 28 the son of Melki,
the son of Addi, the son of Cosam,
the son of Elmadam, the son of Er,
29 the son of Joshua, the son of Eliezer,
the son of Jorim, the son of Matthat,
the son of Levi, 30 the son of Simeon,
the son of Judah, the son of Joseph,
the son of Jonam, the son of Eliakim,
31 the son of Melea, the son of Menna,

3:21 [g] Mt 14:23; Mk 1:35; 6:46; Lk 5:16; 6:12; 9:18,28; 11:1 **3:22** [h] Isa 42:1; Jn 1:32,33; Ac 10:38 [i] S Mt 3:17 [j] S Mt 3:17 **3:23** [k] Mt 4:17; Ac 1:1 [l] Lk 1:27 **3:27** [m] Mt 1:12

3:31 [n] 2Sa 5:14; 1Ch 3:5 **3:33** [o] Ru 4:18-22; 1Ch 2:10-12 **3:34** [p] Ge 11:24, 26 **3:36** [q] Ge 11:12 [r] Ge 5:28-32 **3:37** [s] Ge 5:12-25 **3:38** [t] Ge 5:1, 2,6-9 **4:1** [u] ver 14, 18; S Lk 1:15, 35; 3:16,22; 10:21 [v] Lk 3:3, 21 [w] Eze 37:1; Lk 2:27 **4:2** [x] Ex 34:28; 1Ki 19:8 [y] Heb 4:15

the son of Mattatha, the son of Nathan,[n]
the son of David, 32 the son of Jesse,
the son of Obed, the son of Boaz,
the son of Salmon,[a] the son of Nahshon,
33 the son of Amminadab, the son of Ram,[b]
the son of Hezron, the son of Perez,[o]
the son of Judah, 34 the son of Jacob,
the son of Isaac, the son of Abraham,
the son of Terah, the son of Nahor,[p]
35 the son of Serug, the son of Reu,
the son of Peleg, the son of Eber,
the son of Shelah, 36 the son of Cainan,
the son of Arphaxad,[q] the son of Shem,
the son of Noah, the son of Lamech,[r]
37 the son of Methuselah, the son of Enoch,
the son of Jared, the son of Mahalalel,
the son of Kenan,[s] 38 the son of Enosh,
the son of Seth, the son of Adam,
the son of God.[t]

Jesus Is Tested in the Wilderness

4:1-13pp — Mt 4:1-11; Mk 1:12,13

4 Jesus, full of the Holy Spirit,[u] left the
Jordan[v] and was led by the Spirit[w] into
the wilderness, 2 where for forty days[x] he
was tempted[c] by the devil.[y] He ate nothing

[a] 32 Some early manuscripts *Sala* [b] 33 Some manuscripts *Amminadab, the son of Admin, the son of Arni*; other manuscripts vary widely. [c] 2 The Greek for *tempted* can also mean *tested.*

---

ties, 18.5.2; see map, p. 1707). This did not occur until sometime after the beginning of Jesus' ministry (see Jn 3:22–24), but Luke mentions it here in order to conclude this section on John's ministry before commencing his account of the beginning of Jesus' ministry (see also Mt 4:12; Mk 1:14). He later briefly alludes to John's death (9:7–9).

3:21 *baptized.* See note on Mt 3:15. *as he was praying.* Only Luke notes Jesus' praying at the time of his baptism. Jesus in prayer is one of the special themes of Luke (see 5:16; 6:12; 9:18,28–29; 11:1; 22:32,41; 23:34,46).

3:22 *Holy Spirit descended.* Luke specifies "in bodily form." To John it was a sign (see Jn 1:32–34; see also note on Mk 1:10). *my Son, whom I love.* See Ps 2:7 and note on 2:7–9; Isa 42:1; Heb 1:5 and note. Two other times the Gospel writers record the declarations of a voice from heaven referring to Jesus: (1) on the Mount of Transfiguration (9:35) and (2) in the temple courts during Jesus' final week (Jn 12:28).

3:23–38 There are several differences between Luke's genealogy and Matthew's (1:2–16). Matthew begins with Abraham (the father of the Jewish people), while Luke traces the line in the reverse order and goes back to Adam, showing Jesus' relationship to the whole human race (see note on 2:31). From Abraham to David, the genealogies of Matthew and Luke are almost the same, but from David on they are different. Many interpreters suggest that this is because Matthew traces the legal descent of the house of David, using only heirs to the throne, while Luke traces the direct bloodline of Joseph to David (see Introduction to 1 Chronicles: Genealogies) — perhaps the preferred view. Another common explanation is that Matthew follows the line of Joseph (Jesus' legal father through Solomon; see Mt 1:6–7, 16), while Luke emphasizes that of Mary (Jesus' blood relative through Nathan, v. 31). Although tracing a genealogy through the mother's side was unusual, so was the virgin birth. Luke's explanation here that Jesus was the son of Joseph, "so it was thought" (v. 23), brings to mind his explicit virgin birth statement (1:34–35) and suggests the importance of the role of Mary in Jesus' genealogy. However, this view is less likely since Luke here so explicitly names Joseph (v. 23), without any reference at all to Mary.

3:23 *about thirty years old.* Luke, a historian, relates the beginning of Jesus' public ministry both to world history (see vv. 1–2) and to the rest of Jesus' life. Thirty was the age when a Levite undertook his service (Nu 4:47) and when a man was considered mature. *so it was thought.* Luke had already affirmed the virgin birth (1:34–35) and here makes clear again that Joseph was not Jesus' physical father.

4:1 *full of the Holy Spirit.* Luke emphasizes the Holy Spirit not only in his Gospel (1:35,41,67; 2:25–27; 3:16,22; 4:14,18; 10:21; 11:13; 12:10,12) but also in Acts, where the Spirit is mentioned 57 times. *into the wilderness.* The Desert of Judea (see notes on 1:80; Mt 3:1).

4:2 *he was tempted.* See notes on Mt 4:1–11; 4:1; Heb 2:18; 4:15. Luke states that Jesus was tempted for the 40 days he was fasting, and the three specific temptations recounted in Matthew and Luke seem to have occurred at the close of this period — when Jesus' hunger was greatest and his resistance lowest. The sequence of the second and third temptations

during those days, and at the end of them
he was hungry.
3 The devil said to him, "If you are the
Son of God,[z] tell this stone to become
bread."
4 Jesus answered, "It is written: 'Man
shall not live on bread alone.'[a]"[a]
5 The devil led him up to a high place
and showed him in an instant all the kingdoms of the world.[b] 6 And he said to him,
"I will give you all their authority and
splendor; it has been given to me,[c] and I
can give it to anyone I want to. 7 If you
worship me, it will all be yours."
8 Jesus answered, "It is written: 'Worship the Lord your God and serve him
only.'[b]"[d]

4:3 [z] S Mt 4:3
4:4 [a] Dt 8:3
4:5 [b] S Mt 24:14
4:6 [c] Jn 12:31; 14:30; 1Jn 5:19
4:8 [d] Dt 6:13

[a] *4* Deut. 8:3 [b] *8* Deut. 6:13

---

differs in Matthew and Luke. Matthew probably followed the chronological order, since at the end of the mountain temptation (Matthew's third) Jesus told Satan to leave (Mt 4:10). To emphasize a certain point the Gospel writers often bring various events together, not intending to imply chronological sequence. Perhaps Luke's focus here is geographic, as he concludes with Jesus in Jerusalem.

4:3 *If you are.* See note on Mt 4:3. *tell this stone to become bread.* The devil always makes his temptations seem attractive.

4:6 *their authority . . . has been given to me.* Satan is elsewhere called "the prince of this world" (Jn 12:31), "the god of this age" (2Co 4:4) and "the ruler of the kingdom of

CAPERNAUM SYNAGOGUE

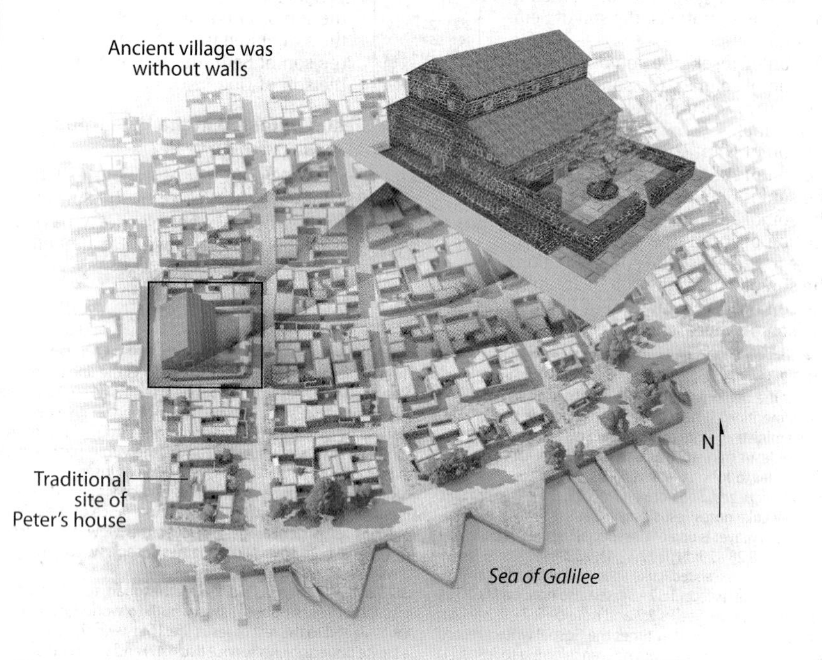

Ancient village was without walls
Traditional site of Peter's house
N
Sea of Galilee

Capernaum was more than a seaside fishing village in the days of Jesus. It was the place that Jesus chose to be the center of his ministry to the entire region of Galilee, and it possessed ideal characteristics as a point of dissemination for the gospel.

There were good reasons for this. The town itself was named Kephar Nahum, "village of [perhaps the prophet] Nahum," and was the centerpiece of a densely populated region having a bicultural flavor. On the one hand, there were numerous synagogues in Galilee (in addition to the one in Capernaum), where the ferment of Jewish religious life was profound. On the other hand, there was Hellenism, a pervasive culture already centuries old and potent in its paganism—a lifestyle that influenced manners, dress, architecture and political institutions as well.

Archaeological work at Capernaum has revealed a section of the pavement of a first-century synagogue below the still-existing ruins of the fourth-century one on the site. A private house later made into a church and a place of pilgrimage has yielded some evidence that may link it to the site of Simon Peter's house (Lk 4:38).

9The devil led him to Jerusalem and
had him stand on the highest point of the
temple. "If you are the Son of God," he
said, "throw yourself down from here.
10For it is written:

" 'He will command his angels
concerning you
to guard you carefully;
11 they will lift you up in their hands,
so that you will not strike your foot
against a stone.'[a]"[e]

12Jesus answered, "It is said: 'Do not
put the Lord your God to the test.'[b]"[f]
13When the devil had finished all this
tempting,[g] he left him[h] until an opportune
time.

Jesus Rejected at Nazareth

14Jesus returned to Galilee[i] in the power
of the Spirit, and news about him spread
through the whole countryside.[j] 15He was
teaching in their synagogues,[k] and everyone praised him.
16He went to Nazareth,[l] where he had
been brought up, and on the Sabbath day
he went into the synagogue,[m] as was his
custom. He stood up to read,[n] 17and the
scroll of the prophet Isaiah was handed
to him. Unrolling it, he found the place
where it is written:

18 "The Spirit of the Lord is on me,[o]
because he has anointed me
to proclaim good news[p] to the poor.
He has sent me to proclaim freedom
for the prisoners
and recovery of sight for the blind,
to set the oppressed free,
19 to proclaim the year of the Lord's
favor."[c][q]

20Then he rolled up the scroll, gave it
back to the attendant and sat down.[r] The
eyes of everyone in the synagogue were
fastened on him. 21He began by saying to
them, "Today this scripture is fulfilled[s] in
your hearing."
22All spoke well of him and were
amazed at the gracious words that came
from his lips. "Isn't this Joseph's son?"
they asked.[t]
23Jesus said to them, "Surely you will
quote this proverb to me: 'Physician, heal
yourself!' And you will tell me, 'Do here in
your hometown[u] what we have heard that
you did in Capernaum.' "[v]
24"Truly I tell you," he continued, "no
prophet is accepted in his hometown.[w]
25I assure you that there were many widows in Israel in Elijah's time, when the
sky was shut for three and a half years
and there was a severe famine throughout the land.[x] 26Yet Elijah was not sent
to any of them, but to a widow in Zarephath in the region of Sidon.[y] 27And there

[a] *11* Psalm 91:11,12 [b] *12* Deut. 6:16
[c] *19* Isaiah 61:1,2 (see Septuagint); Isaiah 58:6

4:11 [e]Ps 91:11, 12
4:12 [f]Dt 6:16
4:13 [g]Heb 4:15 [h]Jn 14:30
4:14 [i]Mt 4:12 [j]S Mt 9:26
4:15 [k]S Mt 4:23
4:16 [l]S Mt 2:23 [m]Mt 13:54 [n]S 1Ti 4:13
4:18 [o]S Jn 3:34 [p]Mk 16:15
4:19 [q]Lev 25:10; Isa 61:1,2; Ps 102:20; 103:6; Isa 42:7; 49:8,9; 58:6
4:20 [r]ver 17; S Mt 26:55
4:21 [s]S Mt 1:22
4:22 [t]Mt 13:54, 55; Jn 6:42; 7:15
4:23 [u]ver 16; S Mt 2:23 [v]Mk 1:21-28; 2:1-12
4:24 [w]Mt 13:57; Jn 4:44
4:25 [x]1Ki 17:1; 18:1; Jas 5:17, 18; Rev 11:6
4:26 [y]1Ki 17:8-16; S Mt 11:21

---

the air" (Eph 2:2) — but remains under God's sovereign power and control (cf. notes on 2Sa 24:1; Job 1:12; 2Co 4:4).

4:7 *worship me.* The devil was tempting Jesus to avoid the sufferings of the cross, which he came specifically to endure (see Mk 10:45 and note). The temptation offered an easy shortcut to world dominion.

4:9 *the highest point of the temple.* Either the southeast corner of the temple colonnade, from which there was a drop of some 100 feet to the Kidron Valley below, or the pinnacle of the temple proper. *temple.* See note on Mt 4:5. *If you are.* See note on Mt 4:3. *throw yourself down.* Satan was tempting Jesus to test God's faithfulness and to attract public attention dramatically.

4:10 *For it is written.* This time Satan also quoted Scripture, though he misused Ps 91:11–12.

4:12 Jesus answered with Scripture, as he had on each of the other two occasions, quoting from Deuteronomy (see NIV text notes here and on vv. 4,8).

4:13 *he left him until an opportune time.* Satan continued his testing throughout Jesus' ministry (see Mk 8:33 and note), culminating in the supreme test at Gethsemane.

4:14 *in the power of the Spirit.* See note on v. 1.

4:15 *was teaching in their synagogues.* See note on Mk 1:21.

4:16–30 Luke apparently moved the Nazareth sermon forward from a later point in Jesus' life (see Mk 6:1–6) to serve as an introduction and overview of Jesus' ministry. Notice that Jesus refers to his ministry in Capernaum (v. 23) even though he has not yet gone there according to Luke's Gospel (v. 31).

4:16 *as was his custom.* Jesus' custom of regular worship sets an example for all his followers. *to read.* Jesus probably read from Isaiah in Hebrew, and then he or someone else paraphrased it in Aramaic, one of the other common languages of the day.

4:17 *the scroll of the prophet Isaiah.* See essay, pp. 1574–1576. The books of the OT were written on scrolls, kept in a special place in the synagogue and handed to the reader by a special attendant. The passage Jesus read about the Messiah (Isa 61:1–2; see notes there) may have been one he chose to read, or it may have been the assigned passage for the day.

4:18 This verse tells of the Messiah's ministry of preaching and healing — to meet every human need. *he has anointed me.* Not with literal oil (see Ex 30:22–31), but with the Holy Spirit.

4:19 *the year of the Lord's favor.* Not a calendar year, but the period when salvation would be proclaimed — the Messianic age. This quotation from Isa 61:1–2 alludes to the Year of Jubilee (Lev 25:8–55), when once every 50 years slaves were freed, debts were canceled and ancestral property was returned to the original family. Isaiah predicted primarily the liberation of Israel from the future Babylonian exile, but Jesus proclaimed liberation from sin and all its consequences.

4:20 *sat down.* It was customary to stand while reading Scripture (v. 16; see Ne 8:3,5 and notes) but to sit while teaching (see 5:3; Mt 5:1 and note; 26:55; Mk 4:1; 9:35; Jn 8:2; Ac 16:13).

4:23 *hometown.* Nazareth (see v. 16). Although Jesus was born in Bethlehem, he was brought up in Nazareth, in Galilee (see 1:26; 2:39,51; Mt 2:23 and note). *Capernaum.* See note on Mt 4:13.

4:26–27 Mention of Jesus' reference to God's helping two non-Israelites (see 1Ki 17:7–24; 2Ki 5:1–19a and notes) reflects Luke's special concern for the Gentiles. Jesus'

were many in Israel with leprosy[a] in the time of Elisha the prophet, yet not one of them was cleansed — only Naaman the Syrian."[z]

28 All the people in the synagogue were furious when they heard this. 29 They got up, drove him out of the town,[a] and took him to the brow of the hill on which the town was built, in order to throw him off the cliff. 30 But he walked right through the crowd and went on his way.[b]

Jesus Drives Out an Impure Spirit

4:31-37pp — Mk 1:21-28

31 Then he went down to Capernaum,[c] a town in Galilee, and on the Sabbath he taught the people. 32 They were amazed at his teaching,[d] because his words had authority.[e]

33 In the synagogue there was a man possessed by a demon, an impure spirit. He cried out at the top of his voice, 34 "Go away! What do you want with us,[f] Jesus of Nazareth?[g] Have you come to destroy us? I know who you are[h] — the Holy One of God!"[i]

35 "Be quiet!" Jesus said sternly.[j] "Come out of him!" Then the demon threw the man down before them all and came out without injuring him.

36 All the people were amazed[k] and said to each other, "What words these are! With authority[l] and power he gives orders to impure spirits and they come out!" 37 And the news about him spread throughout the surrounding area.[m]

4:27 [z] 2Ki 5:1-14
4:29 [a] Nu 15:35; Ac 7:58; Heb 13:12
4:30 [b] Jn 8:59; 10:39
4:31 [c] ver 23; S Mt 4:13
4:32 [d] S Mt 7:28 [e] ver 36; Mt 7:29
4:34 [f] S Mt 8:29 [g] S Mk 1:24 [h] Jas 2:19 [i] ver 41; S Mk 1:24
4:35 [j] ver 39, 41; Mt 8:26; Lk 8:24
4:36 [k] S Mt 7:28 [l] ver 32; Mt 7:29; S Mt 10:1
4:37 [m] ver 14; S Mt 9:26
4:39 [n] ver 35,41
4:40 [o] S Mk 5:23 [p] S Mt 4:23
4:41 [q] S Mt 4:3 [r] S ver 35 [s] S Mt 8:4
4:43 [t] S Mt 3:2
4:44 [u] S Mt 4:23

Jesus Heals Many

4:38-41pp — Mt 8:14-17
4:38-43pp — Mk 1:29-38

38 Jesus left the synagogue and went to the home of Simon. Now Simon's mother-in-law was suffering from a high fever, and they asked Jesus to help her. 39 So he bent over her and rebuked[n] the fever, and it left her. She got up at once and began to wait on them.

40 At sunset, the people brought to Jesus all who had various kinds of sickness, and laying his hands on each one,[o] he healed them.[p] 41 Moreover, demons came out of many people, shouting, "You are the Son of God!"[q] But he rebuked[r] them and would not allow them to speak,[s] because they knew he was the Messiah.

42 At daybreak, Jesus went out to a solitary place. The people were looking for him and when they came to where he was, they tried to keep him from leaving them. 43 But he said, "I must proclaim the good news of the kingdom of God[t] to the other towns also, because that is why I was sent." 44 And he kept on preaching in the synagogues of Judea.[u]

Jesus Calls His First Disciples

5:1-11pp — Mt 4:18-22; Mk 1:16-20; Jn 1:40-42

5 One day as Jesus was standing by the Lake of Gennesaret,[b] the people were crowding around him and listening to the

[a] 27 The Greek word traditionally translated *leprosy* was used for various diseases affecting the skin. [b] 1 That is, the Sea of Galilee

point was that when Israel was in rebellion and rejected God's messengers of redemption (Elijah and Elisha), God caused non-Israelites to receive the covenant blessings that were properly Israel's. This is what aroused the anger of the crowd.

4:26 *Sidon.* One of the oldest Phoenician cities, 20 miles north of Tyre (see map, p. 1670). Jesus later healed a Gentile woman's daughter in this region (Mt 15:21 – 28).

4:28 *furious.* Because of Jesus' inclusion of Gentiles as recipients of God's blessings.

4:30 *walked right through the crowd.* Luke does not explain whether the escape was miraculous or simply the result of Jesus' commanding presence. In any case, his time (to die) had not yet come (see Jn 7:30 and note).

4:32 See note on Mk 1:22.

4:33 *possessed by a demon.* To pagans, "demon" meant a supernatural being, whether good or bad, but Luke makes it clear that this was an evil spirit. Such a demon could cause mental disorder (Jn 10:20), violent action (Lk 8:26 – 29), bodily disease (13:11,16) and rebellion against God (Rev 16:14).

4:34 *Holy One of God.* See note on Mk 1:24.

4:36 *amazed.* See v. 32 and note on Mk 1:22.

4:38 *synagogue.* See notes on Mt 4:13; Mk 1:21. *home of Simon.* See model, p. 1710. *Simon's mother-in-law.* Peter was married (see 1Co 9:5 and note). *high fever.* All three Synoptics tell of this miracle (Mt 8:14 – 15; Mk 1:29 – 31), but only Luke, the doctor, uses the more specific phrase "high fever."

4:40 *At sunset.* The Sabbath (v. 31) was over at sundown (about 6:00 p.m.). According to the tradition of the elders, Jews could not carry a burden or travel more than about two-thirds of a mile on the Sabbath. Only after sundown could they carry the sick to Jesus, and their eagerness is seen in the fact that they set out while the sun was still setting.

4:41 *because they knew he was the Messiah.* See note on Mk 1:34.

4:42 *solitary place.* Mark includes the words "where he prayed" (Mk 1:35).

4:43 *kingdom of God.* Luke's first use of this phrase; it occurs over 30 times in his Gospel. Some of its different meanings in the Bible are: the eternal kingship of God; the presence of the kingdom in the person of Jesus, the King; the approaching spiritual form of the kingdom; the future kingdom. See note on Mt 3:2.

4:44 This summary statement includes not only what has just been described (from v. 14 on) but also what lay ahead in Jesus' ministry. No express mention is made in the Synoptics of the early Judean ministry recorded in John (2:13 — 4:3), though it may be reflected in 13:34 (see note there) and Mt 23:37. *Judea.* Some manuscripts, as well as the parallel accounts (Mt 4:23; Mk 1:39), mention Galilee instead of Judea. In writing to a Gentile (see Introduction: Recipient and Purpose), Luke possibly used "Judea" to refer to the whole land of the Jews (see 23:5 and note; Ac 10:37; 11:1,29; 26:20).

5:1 *Lake of Gennesaret.* Luke is the only one who calls it this. The other Gospel writers call it the Sea of Galilee (see Mk 1:16

word of God.[v] 2He saw at the water's edge
two boats, left there by the fishermen,
who were washing their nets. 3He got
into one of the boats, the one belonging
to Simon, and asked him to put out a little
from shore. Then he sat down and taught
the people from the boat.[w]
4When he had finished speaking, he
said to Simon, "Put out into deep water,
and let down the nets for a catch."[x]
5Simon answered, "Master,[y] we've
worked hard all night and haven't caught
anything.[z] But because you say so, I will
let down the nets."
6When they had done so, they caught
such a large number of fish that their nets
began to break.[a] 7So they signaled their
partners in the other boat to come and
help them, and they came and filled both
boats so full that they began to sink.
8When Simon Peter saw this, he fell at
Jesus' knees and said, "Go away from me,
Lord; I am a sinful man!"[b] 9For he and
all his companions were astonished at the
catch of fish they had taken, 10and so were
James and John, the sons of Zebedee, Simon's partners.

Then Jesus said to Simon, "Don't be afraid;[c] from now on you will fish for people."
11So they pulled their boats up on
shore, left everything and followed him.[d]

5:1 [v]S Mk 4:14; S Heb 4:12 5:3 [w]Mt 13:2 5:4 [x]Jn 21:6 5:5 [y]Lk 8:24,45; 9:33,49; 17:13 [z]Jn 21:3 5:6 [a]Jn 21:11 5:8 [b]Ge 18:27; Job 42:6; Isa 6:5 5:10 [c]S Mt 14:27 5:11 [d]ver 28; S Mt 4:19 5:12 [e]S Mt 8:2

Jesus Heals a Man With Leprosy

5:12-14pp — Mt 8:2-4; Mk 1:40-44

12While Jesus was in one of the towns, a
man came along who was covered with leprosy.[ae] When he saw Jesus, he fell with his
face to the ground and begged him, "Lord,
if you are willing, you can make me clean."
13Jesus reached out his hand and
touched the man. "I am willing," he said.
"Be clean!" And immediately the leprosy
left him.
14Then Jesus ordered him, "Don't tell
anyone,[f] but go, show yourself to the
priest and offer the sacrifices that Moses
commanded[g] for your cleansing, as a testimony to them."
15Yet the news about him spread all the
more,[h] so that crowds of people came to
hear him and to be healed of their sicknesses. 16But Jesus often withdrew to
lonely places and prayed.[i]

5:14 [f]S Mt 8:4 [g]Lev 14:2-32 5:15 [h]S Mt 9:26 5:16 [i]S Lk 3:21 5:17 [j]Mt 15:1; Lk 2:46 [k]Mk 5:30; Lk 6:19 5:20 [l]Lk 7:48, 49

Jesus Forgives and Heals a Paralyzed Man

5:18-26pp — Mt 9:2-8; Mk 2:3-12

17One day Jesus was teaching, and
Pharisees and teachers of the law[j] were
sitting there. They had come from every
village of Galilee and from Judea and Jerusalem. And the power of the Lord was
with Jesus to heal the sick.[k] 18Some men
came carrying a paralyzed man on a mat
and tried to take him into the house to
lay him before Jesus. 19When they could
not find a way to do this because of the
crowd, they went up on the roof and lowered him on his mat through the tiles into
the middle of the crowd, right in front of
Jesus.
20When Jesus saw their faith, he said,
"Friend, your sins are forgiven."[l]
21The Pharisees and the teachers of the
law began thinking to themselves, "Who

[a] 12 The Greek word traditionally translated *leprosy* was used for various diseases affecting the skin.

and note), and John twice calls it the Sea of Tiberias (see Jn 6:1 and note; see also NIV text note on 21:1).

5:2 *washing their nets.* After each period of fishing the nets were washed, stretched and prepared for reuse.

5:3 *sat down.* The usual position for teaching (see note on 4:20). The boat provided an ideal arrangement, removed from the press of the crowd but near enough for Jesus to be seen and heard.

5:7 *their partners.* See v. 10.

5:8 *Go away from me, Lord.* The nearer people come to God, the more they feel their own sinfulness and unworthiness—as did Abraham (see Ge 18:27 and note), Job (see 42:6 and note) and Isaiah (6:5).

5:11 *left everything and followed him.* This was not the first time these men had been with Jesus (see Mk 1:17 and note; Jn 1:40–42; 2:1–2). Their periodic and loose association now became a closely knit fellowship as they followed the Master. The scene is the same as Mt 4:18–22 and Mk 1:16–20, but the accounts relate events from different hours of the morning.

5:12–16 The healing of the man with leprosy is described in all three of the Synoptic Gospels, but the setting is different in each.

5:12 *covered with leprosy.* See NIV text note; see also note on Lev 13:2. Luke alone notes the extent of his disease.

5:14 *Don't tell anyone.* See notes on Mt 8:4; 16:20. *but go, show yourself to the priest.* By this command Jesus urged the man to keep the law, to provide further proof for the actual healing, to testify to the authorities concerning his ministry and to supply ritual certification of cleansing so the man could be reinstated into society. *a testimony to them.* See note on Mk 1:44.

5:17 *Pharisees and teachers of the law.* See notes on Mt 2:4; 3:7; Mk 2:16. Opposition was rising in Galilee from these religious leaders. *Pharisees.* Mentioned here for the first time in Luke (see essay, p. 1576, and chart, p. 1631). Their name means "separated ones"; they numbered about 6,000 and were spread over the whole of the Holy Land. They were teachers in the synagogues, religious examples in the eyes of the people and self-appointed guardians of the law and its proper observance. They considered the interpretations and regulations handed down by tradition to be as authoritative as Scripture (Mk 7:8–13). Already Jesus had run counter to the Jewish leaders in Jerusalem (Jn 5:16–18). Now they came to a home in Capernaum (Mk 2:1–6) to hear and watch him. *teachers of the law.* "Scribes," who studied, interpreted and taught the law (both written and oral); see note on Ezr 7:6. The majority of these teachers belonged to the party of the Pharisees.

5:19 *roof.* See note on Mk 2:4. *tiles.* Probably ceiling tiles.

is this fellow who speaks blasphemy?
Who can forgive sins but God alone?"[m]
22 Jesus knew what they were thinking
and asked, "Why are you thinking these
things in your hearts? 23 Which is easier: to
say, 'Your sins are forgiven,' or to say, 'Get
up and walk'? 24 But I want you to know
that the Son of Man[n] has authority on earth
to forgive sins." So he said to the paralyzed
man, "I tell you, get up, take your mat and
go home." 25 Immediately he stood up in
front of them, took what he had been lying
on and went home praising God. 26 Everyone was amazed and gave praise to God.[o]
They were filled with awe and said, "We
have seen remarkable things today."

Jesus Calls Levi and Eats With Sinners

5:27-32pp — Mt 9:9-13; Mk 2:14-17

27 After this, Jesus went out and saw a
tax collector by the name of Levi sitting at
his tax booth. "Follow me,"[p] Jesus said to
him, 28 and Levi got up, left everything and
followed him.[q]
29 Then Levi held a great banquet for
Jesus at his house, and a large crowd of
tax collectors[r] and others were eating with
them. 30 But the Pharisees and the teachers
of the law who belonged to their sect[s] complained to his disciples, "Why do you eat
and drink with tax collectors and sinners?"[t]
31 Jesus answered them, "It is not the
healthy who need a doctor, but the sick.
32 I have not come to call the righteous, but
sinners to repentance."[u]

Jesus Questioned About Fasting

5:33-39pp — Mt 9:14-17; Mk 2:18-22

33 They said to him, "John's disciples[v]
often fast and pray, and so do the disciples
of the Pharisees, but yours go on eating
and drinking."
34 Jesus answered, "Can you make the
friends of the bridegroom[w] fast while he is
with them? 35 But the time will come when
the bridegroom will be taken from them;[x]
in those days they will fast."
36 He told them this parable: "No one
tears a piece out of a new garment to patch
an old one. Otherwise, they will have torn
the new garment, and the patch from the
new will not match the old. 37 And no one
pours new wine into old wineskins. Otherwise, the new wine will burst the skins;
the wine will run out and the wineskins
will be ruined. 38 No, new wine must be
poured into new wineskins. 39 And no one
after drinking old wine wants the new, for
they say, 'The old is better.' "

Jesus Is Lord of the Sabbath

6:1-11pp — Mt 12:1-14; Mk 2:23-3:6

6 One Sabbath Jesus was going through
the grainfields, and his disciples began
to pick some heads of grain, rub them in
their hands and eat the kernels.[y] 2 Some of
the Pharisees asked, "Why are you doing
what is unlawful on the Sabbath?"[z]
3 Jesus answered them, "Have you never read what David did when he and his
companions were hungry?[a] 4 He entered
the house of God, and taking the consecrated bread, he ate what is lawful only
for priests to eat.[b] And he also gave some
to his companions." 5 Then Jesus said to
them, "The Son of Man[c] is Lord of the Sabbath."
6 On another Sabbath[d] he went into the
synagogue and was teaching, and a man
was there whose right hand was shriveled.
7 The Pharisees and the teachers of the law

5:21 [m] Isa 43:25
5:24 [n] S Mt 8:20
5:26 [o] S Mt 9:8
5:27 [p] S Mt 4:19
5:28 [q] ver 11; S Mt 4:19
5:29 [r] Lk 15:1
5:30 [s] Ac 23:9 [t] S Mt 9:11
5:32 [u] S Jn 3:17
5:33 [v] Lk 7:18; Jn 1:35; 3:25,26
5:34 [w] Jn 3:29
5:35 [x] Lk 9:22; 17:22; Jn 16:5-7
6:1 [y] Dt 23:25
6:2 [z] S Mt 12:2
6:3 [a] 1Sa 21:6
6:4 [b] Lev 24:5,9
6:5 [c] S Mt 8:20
6:6 [d] ver 1

5:21 *this fellow ... speaks blasphemy.* See note on Mk 2:7. The Pharisees considered blasphemy to be the most serious sin anyone could commit (see note on Mk 14:64).
5:23 *Which is easier: to say ... ?* See notes on Mk 2:9–10.
5:24 *I want you to know.* Jesus' power to heal was a visible affirmation of his power to forgive sins. *Son of Man.* See note on Mk 8:31.
5:25 *praising God.* See v. 26; see also 1:64 and note.
5:27 *tax collector.* See note on 3:12. *Levi.* Another name for Matthew (6:15). *tax booth.* The place where customs were collected (see note on Mk 2:14).
5:28 *left everything and followed him.* Since Jesus had been ministering in Capernaum for some time, Levi probably had known him previously (see note on v. 11).
5:29 *great banquet.* When Levi began to follow Jesus, he did not do it secretly (cf. Jn 19:38 and note).
5:30 *Pharisees ... complained.* They probably stood outside and registered their complaints from a distance. *eat ... with tax collectors and sinners.* See note on Mk 2:15.
5:31 *not the healthy who need a doctor, but the sick.* Not to imply that the Pharisees were "the healthy" but that people must recognize themselves as sinners before they can be spiritually healed (see note on Mk 2:17).
5:33 *John's disciples ... fast and pray.* John the Baptist had grown up in the wilderness and learned to subsist on an austere diet of locusts and wild honey. His ministry was characterized by a sober message and a strenuous schedule. For a contrast between Jesus' ministry and John the Baptist's, see 7:24–28; Mt 11:1–19. The Pharisees also had rigorous lifestyles (see note on 18:12). But Jesus went to banquets, and his disciples enjoyed a freedom not known by the Pharisees. *fast.* See notes on 18:12; Mk 2:18. While Jesus rejected fasting legalistically for display (cf. Isa 58:3–11), he himself fasted privately and permitted voluntary use of fasting for spiritual benefit (Mt 4:2; 6:16–18).
5:35 See notes on Mk 2:19–20.
5:36 *parable.* See notes on Mt 13:3; Mk 4:2.
5:38 *new wineskins.* See note on Mt 9:17.
5:39 *The old is better.* Jesus was indicating the reluctance of some people to change from their traditional religious ways and try the gospel.
6:1 *going through the grainfields.* See note on Mk 2:23.
6:3 *what David did.* See note on Mk 2:25.
6:4 *consecrated bread.* See note on Mt 12:4.
6:5 *Son of Man.* See note on Mk 8:31. *Lord of the Sabbath.* Jesus has the authority to overrule human regulations con-

were looking for a reason to accuse Jesus,
so they watched him closely[e] to see if he
would heal on the Sabbath.[f] 8But Jesus
knew what they were thinking[g] and said
to the man with the shriveled hand, "Get
up and stand in front of everyone." So he
got up and stood there.
9Then Jesus said to them, "I ask you,
which is lawful on the Sabbath: to do good
or to do evil, to save life or to destroy it?"
10He looked around at them all, and
then said to the man, "Stretch out your
hand." He did so, and his hand was completely restored. 11But the Pharisees and
the teachers of the law were furious[h] and
began to discuss with one another what
they might do to Jesus.

The Twelve Apostles

6:13-16pp — Mt 10:2-4; Mk 3:16-19; Ac 1:13

12One of those days Jesus went out to a
mountainside to pray, and spent the night
praying to God.[i] 13When morning came,
he called his disciples to him and chose
twelve of them, whom he also designated apostles:[j] 14Simon (whom he named
Peter), his brother Andrew, James, John,
Philip, Bartholomew, 15Matthew,[k] Thomas,
James son of Alphaeus, Simon who was
called the Zealot, 16Judas son of James,
and Judas Iscariot, who became a traitor.

Blessings and Woes

6:20-23pp — Mt 5:3-12

17He went down with them and stood
on a level place. A large crowd of his disciples was there and a great number of people from all over Judea, from Jerusalem,
and from the coastal region around Tyre
and Sidon,[l] 18who had come to hear him
and to be healed of their diseases. Those
troubled by impure spirits were cured,
19and the people all tried to touch him,[m]
because power was coming from him and
healing them all.[n]
20Looking at his disciples, he said:

"Blessed are you who are poor,
for yours is the kingdom of God.[o]
21Blessed are you who hunger now,
for you will be satisfied.[p]
Blessed are you who weep now,
for you will laugh.[q]
22Blessed are you when people hate you,
when they exclude you[r] and insult you[s]
and reject your name as evil,
because of the Son of Man.[t]

23"Rejoice in that day and leap for joy,[u]
because great is your reward in heaven.
For that is how their ancestors treated the
prophets.[v]

24"But woe to you who are rich,[w]
for you have already received your
comfort.[x]
25Woe to you who are well fed now,
for you will go hungry.[y]
Woe to you who laugh now,
for you will mourn and weep.[z]
26Woe to you when everyone speaks well
of you,

6:7 [e]S Mt 12:10 [f]S Mt 12:2 **6:8** [g]S Mt 9:4 **6:11** [h]Jn 5:18 **6:12** [i]S Lk 3:21 **6:13** [j]S Mk 6:30 **6:15** [k]Mt 9:9 **6:17** [l]Mt 4:25; S Mt 11:21; Mk 3:7,8 **6:19** [m]S Mt 9:20 [n]Mk 5:30; Lk 5:17 **6:20** [o]S Mt 25:34 **6:21** [p]Isa 55:1, 2; Mt 5:6 [q]Isa 61:2,3; Mt 5:4; Rev 7:17 **6:22** [r]Jn 9:22; 16:2 [s]Isa 51:7 [t]S Jn 15:21 **6:23** [u]S Mt 5:12 [v]S Mt 5:12 **6:24** [w]Jas 5:1 [x]Lk 16:25 **6:25** [y]Isa 65:13 [z]Pr 14:13

---

cerning the Sabbath, such as those reflecting the interpretations of the Pharisees (see Mt 12:8; Mk 2:27 and note).

6:7 *to see if he would heal on the Sabbath.* See note on Mk 3:2.

6:8 *stand in front of everyone.* So there would be no question about the healing.

6:9 *which is lawful on the Sabbath ... ?* Jesus had been enduring questions and attacks from the Pharisees and now took the initiative by putting the questions to everyone in the synagogue (see note on Mk 3:4).

6:10 *He looked around at them.* Jesus wanted to see whether anyone objected to his question or the implied answer, but no one was bold enough to do so.

6:11 *were furious.* Because they could not withstand Jesus' reasoning. Already they were plotting to take his life (see Jn 5:18). See note on Mk 3:6.

6:12 Characteristically, Jesus spent the night in prayer before the important work of selecting his 12 apostles.

6:13 *he called his disciples.* Among those who came to hear Jesus was a group who regularly followed him and were committed to his teachings. At least 72 men were included, since this many disciples were sent out on an evangelistic campaign (10:1,17). Later, 120 believers waited and worshiped in Jerusalem following the ascension (Ac 1:15). From such disciples Jesus at this time chose 12 to be his apostles, a title meaning "ones sent with a special commission" (see notes on Mk 6:30; 1Co 1:1; Heb 3:1).

6:14 – 16 Lists of the apostles appear also in Mt 10:2 – 4; Mk 3:16 – 19; Ac 1:13. Although the order of the names varies, Peter is always first and Judas Iscariot last.

6:14 *Bartholomew.* Seems to be (in the Synoptics) the same as Nathanael (in John). Nathanael is associated with Philip in Jn 1:45.

6:15 *Matthew.* Another name for Levi (5:27). *James son of Alphaeus.* Probably the same as James the younger (Mk 15:40). *the Zealot.* See note on Mt 10:4.

6:16 *Judas son of James.* Another name for Thaddaeus (see Mt 10:3; Mk 3:18 and note). *Judas Iscariot.* Probably the only one from Judea, the rest coming from Galilee (see note on Mk 3:19).

6:17 *stood on a level place.* Perhaps a plateau, which would satisfy both this context and that in Mt 5:1 (see note on Mt 5:1 — 7:29). *Tyre and Sidon.* In Phoenicia (modern Lebanon); see notes on 4:26; 10:14; Mk 7:24,31; see also map, p. 1670.

6:20 – 49 Luke's Sermon on the Plateau, apparently parallel to Matthew's Sermon on the Mount (Mt 5 – 7). Although this sermon is much shorter than the one in Matthew, they both begin with the Beatitudes and end with the lesson of the builders. Some of Matthew's sermon is found in other portions of Luke (e.g., 11:2 – 4; 12:22 – 31,33 – 34), suggesting that the material may have been given on various occasions in Jesus' preaching.

6:20 – 23 See Mt 5:3 – 12 and notes. In Matthew's account Jesus speaks of poverty "in spirit" (Mt 5:3) and hunger "for righteousness" (Mt 5:6). Luke places a greater emphasis on material poverty as well. Those who are poor tend to look more strongly to God to meet all their needs.

6:24 – 26 This section is a point-by-point negative counterpart of vv. 20 – 22.

for that is how their ancestors
treated the false prophets.[a]

Love for Enemies

6:29,30pp — Mt 5:39-42

27 "But to you who are listening I say:
Love your enemies, do good to those who
hate you,[b] 28 bless those who curse you,
pray for those who mistreat you.[c] 29 If
someone slaps you on one cheek, turn
to them the other also. If someone takes
your coat, do not withhold your shirt from
them. 30 Give to everyone who asks you,
and if anyone takes what belongs to you,
do not demand it back.[d] 31 Do to others as
you would have them do to you.[e]
32 "If you love those who love you, what
credit is that to you?[f] Even sinners love
those who love them. 33 And if you do good
to those who are good to you, what credit
is that to you? Even sinners do that. 34 And
if you lend to those from whom you expect
repayment, what credit is that to you?[g]
Even sinners lend to sinners, expecting to
be repaid in full. 35 But love your enemies,
do good to them,[h] and lend to them without expecting to get anything back. Then
your reward will be great, and you will be
children[i] of the Most High,[j] because he is
kind to the ungrateful and wicked. 36 Be
merciful,[k] just as your Father[l] is merciful.

Judging Others

6:37-42pp — Mt 7:1-5

37 "Do not judge, and you will not be
judged.[m] Do not condemn, and you will
not be condemned. Forgive, and you will
be forgiven.[n] 38 Give, and it will be given
to you. A good measure, pressed down,
shaken together and running over, will be
poured into your lap.[o] For with the measure you use, it will be measured to you."[p]
39 He also told them this parable: "Can
the blind lead the blind? Will they not
both fall into a pit?[q] 40 The student is not
above the teacher, but everyone who is
fully trained will be like their teacher.[r]

6:26 [a] S Mt 7:15 **6:27** [b] ver 35; Mt 5:44; Ro 12:20 **6:28** [c] S Mt 5:44 **6:30** [d] Dt 15:7, 8, 10; Pr 21:26 **6:31** [e] Mt 7:12 **6:32** [f] Mt 5:46 **6:34** [g] Mt 5:42 **6:35** [h] ver 27 [i] S Ro 8:14 [j] S Mk 5:7 **6:36** [k] Jas 2:13 [l] Mt 5:48; 6:1; Lk 11:2; 12:32; Ro 8:15; Eph 4:6; 1Pe 1:17; 1Jn 1:3; 3:1 **6:37** [m] S Mt 7:1 [n] Mt 6:14 **6:38** [o] Ps 79:12; Isa 65:6,7 [p] S Mt 7:2 **6:39** [q] Mt 15:14 **6:40** [r] S Jn 13:16

41 "Why do you look at the speck of
sawdust in your brother's eye and pay no
attention to the plank in your own eye?
42 How can you say to your brother, 'Brother, let me take the speck out of your eye,'
when you yourself fail to see the plank in
your own eye? You hypocrite, first take the
plank out of your eye, and then you will
see clearly to remove the speck from your
brother's eye.

A Tree and Its Fruit

6:43,44pp — Mt 7:16,18,20

43 "No good tree bears bad fruit, nor does
a bad tree bear good fruit. 44 Each tree is
recognized by its own fruit.[s] People do not
pick figs from thornbushes, or grapes from
briers. 45 A good man brings good things
out of the good stored up in his heart, and
an evil man brings evil things out of the
evil stored up in his heart. For the mouth
speaks what the heart is full of.[t]

The Wise and Foolish Builders

6:47-49pp — Mt 7:24-27

46 "Why do you call me, 'Lord, Lord,'[u]
and do not do what I say?[v] 47 As for everyone who comes to me and hears my words
and puts them into practice,[w] I will show
you what they are like. 48 They are like a
man building a house, who dug down deep
and laid the foundation on rock. When a
flood came, the torrent struck that house
but could not shake it, because it was well
built. 49 But the one who hears my words
and does not put them into practice is like
a man who built a house on the ground
without a foundation. The moment the
torrent struck that house, it collapsed and
its destruction was complete."

The Faith of the Centurion

7:1-10pp — Mt 8:5-13

7 When Jesus had finished saying all
this[x] to the people who were listening,
he entered Capernaum. 2 There a centu-

6:44 [s] Mt 12:33 **6:45** [t] Pr 4:23; Mt 12:34,35; Mk 7:20 **6:46** [u] S Jn 13:13 [v] Mal 1:6; Mt 7:21 **6:47** [w] Lk 8:21; 11:28; Jas 1:22-25 **7:1** [x] Mt 7:28

6:27 *Love your enemies, do good.* The heart of Jesus' teaching is love. While the Golden Rule (v. 31) is sometimes expressed in negative form outside the Bible (see note on Mt 7:12), Jesus not only forbids treating others spitefully but also commands that we love everyone — even our enemies (see Mt 5:44 and note).

6:29 *turn to them the other also.* We are not to have a retaliatory attitude.

6:35 *Most High.* God (see Dt 32:8 and note).

6:36 *just as your Father is merciful.* God's perfection should be our example and goal (see Mt 5:48 and note).

6:37 *Do not judge.* Jesus did not relieve his followers of the need for discerning right and wrong (cf. vv. 43 – 45), but he condemned unjust and hypocritical judging of others (see note on Mt 7:1). *Forgive, and you will be forgiven.* See 11:4 and note.

6:38 See 2Co 8:1 – 5. *poured into your lap.* Probably refers to the way the outer garment was worn, leaving a fold over the belt that could be used as a large pocket to hold a measure of wheat.

6:41 *speck ... plank.* Jesus used hyperbole (a figure of speech that overstates for emphasis) to sharpen the contrast and to emphasize how foolish and hypocritical it is for us to criticize someone for a fault while remaining blind to our own considerable faults (see Mt 7:3 – 4 and note on 7:3).

6:42 *hypocrite.* See notes on 13:15; Mt 23:23; Ac 5:9.

6:43 – 45 Cf. Jas 3:11 – 12 and note.

6:46 – 49 See Mt 7:24 – 27 and notes.

6:47,49 *hears my words and puts them into practice ... does not put them into practice.* See Jas 1:22 – 25 and note on 1:25.

7:1 *Capernaum.* See note on Mt 4:13.

rion's servant, whom his master valued
highly, was sick and about to die. 3The
centurion heard of Jesus and sent some
elders of the Jews to him, asking him to
come and heal his servant. 4When they
came to Jesus, they pleaded earnestly with
him, "This man deserves to have you do
this, 5because he loves our nation and has
built our synagogue." 6So Jesus went with
them.

He was not far from the house when
the centurion sent friends to say to him:
"Lord, don't trouble yourself, for I do not
deserve to have you come under my roof.
7That is why I did not even consider myself worthy to come to you. But say the
word, and my servant will be healed.[y] 8For
I myself am a man under authority, with
soldiers under me. I tell this one, 'Go,'
and he goes; and that one, 'Come,' and he
comes. I say to my servant, 'Do this,' and
he does it."

9When Jesus heard this, he was amazed
at him, and turning to the crowd following
him, he said, "I tell you, I have not found
such great faith even in Israel." 10Then the
men who had been sent returned to the
house and found the servant well.

Jesus Raises a Widow's Son

7:11-16Ref — 1Ki 17:17-24; 2Ki 4:32-37; Mk 5:21-24,35-43; Jn 11:1-44

11Soon afterward, Jesus went to a town
called Nain, and his disciples and a large
crowd went along with him. 12As he approached the town gate, a dead person
was being carried out — the only son of
his mother, and she was a widow. And a
large crowd from the town was with her.
13When the Lord[z] saw her, his heart went
out to her and he said, "Don't cry."

14Then he went up and touched the
bier they were carrying him on, and the
bearers stood still. He said, "Young man,
I say to you, get up!"[a] 15The dead man sat
up and began to talk, and Jesus gave him
back to his mother.

16They were all filled with awe[b] and
praised God.[c] "A great prophet[d] has appeared among us," they said. "God has
come to help his people."[e] 17This news
about Jesus spread throughout Judea and
the surrounding country.[f]

Jesus and John the Baptist

7:18-35pp — Mt 11:2-19

18John's[g] disciples[h] told him about all
these things. Calling two of them, 19he
sent them to the Lord to ask, "Are you the
one who is to come, or should we expect
someone else?"

20When the men came to Jesus, they
said, "John the Baptist sent us to you to
ask, 'Are you the one who is to come, or
should we expect someone else?' "

21At that very time Jesus cured many
who had diseases, sicknesses[i] and evil
spirits, and gave sight to many who were
blind. 22So he replied to the messengers,
"Go back and report to John what you have
seen and heard: The blind receive sight,
the lame walk, those who have leprosy[a]

7:7 [y]Ps 107:20
7:13 [z]ver 19; Lk 10:1; 13:15; 17:5; 22:61; 24:34; Jn 11:2
7:14 [a]Mt 9:25; Mk 1:31; Lk 8:54; Jn 11:43; Ac 9:40
7:16 [b]Lk 1:65 [c]S Mt 9:8 [d]ver 39; S Mt 21:11 [e]Lk 1:68
7:17 [f]S Mt 9:26
7:18 [g]S Mt 3:1 [h]S Lk 5:33
7:21 [i]S Mt 4:23

[a] 22 The Greek word traditionally translated *leprosy* was used for various diseases affecting the skin.

7:2 *centurion's servant.* The centurion was probably a member of Herod Antipas's forces, which were organized in Roman fashion, ordinarily in companies of 100 men (see note on Mt 8:5). Roman centurions referred to in the NT showed characteristics to be admired (see, e.g., Ac 10:2 and note; 23:17–18; 27:43). This centurion showed genuine concern for his slave, and he was admired by the Jews, who spoke favorably of him even though he was a Gentile (see vv. 5,9).
7:3 *elders of the Jews.* Highly respected Jews of the community, though not necessarily rulers of the synagogue. They were willing to come and plead for the centurion. In Matthew's account (Mt 8:5–13) the centurion speaks with Jesus himself, while in Luke's account he speaks with Jesus through his friends (see note on Mt 8:5). Matthew often abbreviates in this way.
7:6 *I do not deserve to have you come under my roof.* See note on Mt 8:8.
7:9 Cf. note on Mt 8:11. *he was amazed.* The amazement of Jesus is only mentioned twice, here because of belief and at Nazareth because of unbelief (Mk 6:6; see note on Mk 6:5).
7:11 *Nain.* Mentioned only here. A small village located a few miles south of Nazareth still bears this name. It is generally accepted as the site where this incident took place. See photo, p. 1698.
7:14 *touched the bier.* By so doing Jesus risked ritual uncleanness (cf. Nu 19:16). *bier.* The man was probably carried on a bier in an open coffin, suggested by Jewish custom and the fact that he sat up in response to Jesus' command. This is the first of three instances of Jesus' raising someone from the dead, the others being Jairus's daughter (8:40–56) and Lazarus (Jn 11:38–44).
7:15 *gave him back to his mother.* Cf. 1Ki 17:23; 2Ki 4:36–37.
7:16 *praised God.* See 1:64 and note.
7:18 *John's disciples.* See note on 5:33; see also Mk 2:18. Despite John the Baptist's imprisonment, his disciples kept in contact with him and continued his ministry.
7:19 *should we expect someone else?* John had announced the coming of the Messiah, but now he himself had been languishing in prison for months, and the work of Jesus had not brought the results John apparently expected. His disappointment was natural. He wanted reassurance — and perhaps also wanted to urge Jesus to further action.
7:22 *report to John what you have seen and heard.* In answer, Jesus pointed to his healing and life-restoring miracles. He did not give promises but clearly observable evidence — evidence that reflected the predicted ministry of the Messiah. *the good news is proclaimed to the poor.* In Jesus' review of his works he used an ascending scale of impressive deeds, ending with the dead raised and the good news preached to the poor. In this way Jesus reminded John that these were the things predicted of the Messiah in the Scriptures (see Isa 29:18–21; 35:5–6 and notes; 61:1; Lk 4:18 and note).

are cleansed, the deaf hear, the dead are raised, and the good news is proclaimed to the poor.[j] 23 Blessed is anyone who does not stumble on account of me."

24 After John's messengers left, Jesus began to speak to the crowd about John: "What did you go out into the wilderness to see? A reed swayed by the wind? 25 If not, what did you go out to see? A man dressed in fine clothes? No, those who wear expensive clothes and indulge in luxury are in palaces. 26 But what did you go out to see? A prophet?[k] Yes, I tell you, and more than a prophet. 27 This is the one about whom it is written:

" 'I will send my messenger ahead of
you,
who will prepare your way before
you.'[a][l]

28 I tell you, among those born of women there is no one greater than John; yet the one who is least in the kingdom of God[m] is greater than he."

29 (All the people, even the tax collectors, when they heard Jesus' words, acknowledged that God's way was right, because they had been baptized by John.[n] 30 But the Pharisees and the experts in the law[o] rejected God's purpose for themselves, because they had not been baptized by John.)

31 Jesus went on to say, "To what, then, can I compare the people of this generation? What are they like? 32 They are like children sitting in the marketplace and calling out to each other:

" 'We played the pipe for you,
and you did not dance;
we sang a dirge,
and you did not cry.'

33 For John the Baptist came neither eating bread nor drinking wine,[p] and you say, 'He has a demon.' 34 The Son of Man came eating and drinking, and you say, 'Here is a glutton and a drunkard, a friend of tax collectors and sinners.'[q] 35 But wisdom is proved right by all her children."

Jesus Anointed by a Sinful Woman

7:37-39Ref — Mt 26:6-13; Mk 14:3-9; Jn 12:1-8
7:41,42Ref — Mt 18:23-34

36 When one of the Pharisees invited Jesus to have dinner with him, he went to the Pharisee's house and reclined at the table. 37 A woman in that town who lived a sinful life learned that Jesus was eating at the Pharisee's house, so she came there with an alabaster jar of perfume. 38 As she stood behind him at his feet weeping, she began to wet his feet with her tears. Then she wiped them with her hair, kissed them and poured perfume on them.

39 When the Pharisee who had invited him saw this, he said to himself, "If this man were a prophet,[r] he would know who is touching him and what kind of woman she is — that she is a sinner."

40 Jesus answered him, "Simon, I have something to tell you."

"Tell me, teacher," he said.

41 "Two people owed money to a certain moneylender. One owed him five hundred denarii,[b] and the other fifty. 42 Neither of them had the money to pay him back, so

7:22 [j] Isa 29:18, 19; 35:5,6; 61:1, 2; Lk 4:18 **7:26** [k] S Mt 11:9 **7:27** [l] Mal 3:1; Mt 11:10; Mk 1:2 **7:28** [m] S Mt 3:2 **7:29** [n] Mt 21:32; Mk 1:5; Lk 3:12 **7:30** [o] S Mt 22:35 **7:33** [p] Lk 1:15 **7:34** [q] Lk 5:29, 30; 15:1,2 **7:39** [r] ver 16; S Mt 21:11

[a] *27* Mal. 3:1 [b] *41* A denarius was the usual daily wage of a day laborer (see Matt. 20:2).

7:23 *anyone who does not stumble.* Jesus did not want discouragement and doubt to ensnare John.
7:24,26 *What did you go ... to see?* John was not a weak messenger, swayed by the pressures of human opinion. On the contrary, he was a true prophet.
7:26 *more than a prophet.* John was the unique prophet sent to prepare the way for the Messiah (v. 27).
7:28 *one who is least in the kingdom of God.* See note on Mt 11:11.
7:29 *tax collectors.* See note on Mt 5:46.
7:30 *experts in the law.* A designation used by Luke (see 10:25, 37; 11:45 – 46,52; 14:3; see also Mt 22:35) for the "scribes" (the teachers of the law), most of whom were Pharisees (see note on 5:17). *rejected God's purpose.* Tax collectors had shown their willingness to repent by accepting John's baptism, whereas the Pharisees showed their rejection of God's message by refusing to be baptized.
7:32 *like children sitting in the marketplace.* People had rejected both John and Jesus, but for different reasons — like children who refuse to play either a joyful game or a mournful one. They would not associate with John when he followed the strictest of rules or with Jesus when he freely associated with all kinds of people. *We played the pipe.* See note on Mt 11:17.
7:34 *Son of Man.* See note on Mk 8:31. *friend of tax collectors and sinners.* Jesus ate and talked with people who were religious and social outcasts. He even called a tax collector to be an apostle (5:27 – 32).
7:35 *wisdom is proved right by all her children.* In contrast to the rejection by foolish critics, spiritually wise persons could see that the ministries of both John and Jesus were godly, despite their differences. See note on Mt 11:19.
7:36 – 50 See note on Jn 12:1 – 11.
7:36 *one of the Pharisees.* See note on 5:17. His motive may have been to entrap Jesus rather than to learn from him.
7:37 *A woman ... who lived a sinful life.* She must have heard Jesus preach, and in repentance she determined to lead a new life. She came out of love and gratitude, in the understanding that she could be forgiven. *alabaster jar.* A long-necked, globular bottle. *perfume.* A perfumed ointment.
7:38 *stood behind him at his feet.* Jesus reclined on a couch with his feet extended away from the table, which made it possible for the woman to wipe his feet with her hair and still not disturb him. *poured perfume on them.* The anointing, perhaps originally intended for Jesus' head, was instead applied to his feet. A similar act was performed by Mary of Bethany just over a week before the crucifixion (see Jn 12:3 and note).
7:41 *five hundred denarii.* See NIV text note.

he forgave the debts of both. Now which
of them will love him more?"
43 Simon replied, "I suppose the one
who had the bigger debt forgiven."
"You have judged correctly," Jesus said.
44 Then he turned toward the woman and said to Simon, "Do you see this
woman? I came into your house. You did
not give me any water for my feet,[s] but
she wet my feet with her tears and wiped
them with her hair. 45 You did not give me
a kiss,[t] but this woman, from the time I
entered, has not stopped kissing my feet.
46 You did not put oil on my head,[u] but she
has poured perfume on my feet. 47 Therefore, I tell you, her many sins have been
forgiven — as her great love has shown.
But whoever has been forgiven little loves
little."
48 Then Jesus said to her, "Your sins are
forgiven."[v]
49 The other guests began to say among
themselves, "Who is this who even forgives sins?"
50 Jesus said to the woman, "Your faith
has saved you;[w] go in peace."[x]

The Parable of the Sower

8:4-15pp — Mt 13:2-23; Mk 4:1-20

8 After this, Jesus traveled about from
one town and village to another, proclaiming the good news of the kingdom
of God.[y] The Twelve were with him, 2 and
also some women who had been cured
of evil spirits and diseases: Mary (called
Magdalene)[z] from whom seven demons
had come out; 3 Joanna the wife of Chu-
za, the manager of Herod's[a] household;
Susanna; and many others. These women
were helping to support them out of their
own means.
4 While a large crowd was gathering and
people were coming to Jesus from town
after town, he told this parable: 5 "A farmer
went out to sow his seed. As he was scattering the seed, some fell along the path;
it was trampled on, and the birds ate it up.
6 Some fell on rocky ground, and when it
came up, the plants withered because they
had no moisture. 7 Other seed fell among
thorns, which grew up with it and choked
the plants. 8 Still other seed fell on good
soil. It came up and yielded a crop, a hundred times more than was sown."
When he said this, he called out, "Whoever has ears to hear, let them hear."[b]
9 His disciples asked him what this parable meant. 10 He said, "The knowledge
of the secrets of the kingdom of God has
been given to you,[c] but to others I speak
in parables, so that,

"'though seeing, they may not see;
though hearing, they may not
understand.'[a][d]

11 "This is the meaning of the parable:
The seed is the word of God.[e] 12 Those

7:44 [s] Ge 18:4; 19:2; 43:24; Jdg 19:21; Jn 13:4-14; 1Ti 5:10 **7:45** [t] Lk 22:47, 48; S Ro 16:16 **7:46** [u] Ps 23:5; Ecc 9:8 **7:48** [v] Mt 9:2 **7:50** [w] S Mt 9:22 [x] S Ac 15:33 **8:1** [y] S Mt 4:23

8:2 [z] Mt 27:55, 56 **8:3** [a] S Mt 14:1 **8:8** [b] S Mt 11:15 **8:10** [c] S Mt 13:11 [d] Isa 6:9; S Mt 13:13, 14 **8:11** [e] S Heb 4:12

[a] *10* Isaiah 6:9

7:44 *water for my feet.* The minimal gesture of hospitality.

7:47 *as her great love has shown.* Her love was evidence of her forgiveness, but not the basis for it. Verse 50 clearly states that she was saved by faith. See Eph 2:8 and note.

7:50 *Your faith has saved you.* Her sins were forgiven and she could experience God's peace (see 1:79 and note on 2:14).

8:1 *Jesus traveled about.* Jesus' ministry had been centered in Capernaum, and much of his preaching was in synagogues, but now he traveled again from town to town on a second tour of the Galilean countryside. For the first tour, see 4:43 – 44; Mt 4:23 – 25; Mk 1:38 – 39. For the third tour, see note on 9:1 – 6. *kingdom of God.* See note on 4:43.

8:2 *Mary (called Magdalene).* Her hometown was Magdala. She is not to be confused with the sinful woman of ch. 7 or Mary of Bethany (Jn 11:1).

8:3 *Susanna.* Nothing more is known of her. *helping to support them.* Jesus and his disciples did not provide for themselves by miracles but were supported by the service and means of such grateful people as these women.

8:4 *parable.* From this point on in Luke's Gospel Jesus used parables (see notes on Mt 13:3; Mk 4:2; see also Introduction: Characteristics) more extensively as a means of teaching. They were particularly effective and easy to remember because he used familiar scenes. Although parables clarified Jesus' teaching, they also included hidden meanings needing further explanation. These hidden meanings challenged the sincerely interested to further inquiry and taught truths that Jesus wanted to conceal from unbelievers (see v. 10 and note). From parables Jesus' enemies could find no direct statements to use against him. The parable of the sower is one of three parables recorded in each of the Synoptic Gospels (Mt 13:1 – 23; Mk 4:1 – 20). The others are those of the mustard seed (13:19; Mt 13:31 – 32; Mk 4:30 – 32) and of the vineyard (20:9 – 19; Mt 21:33 – 46; Mk 12:1 – 12).

8:5 *sow his seed.* In Eastern practice the seed was sometimes sown first and the field plowed afterward. Roads and pathways went directly through many fields, and the traffic made much of the surface too hard for seed to take root.

8:6 *on rocky ground.* On a thin layer of soil that covered solid rock. Any moisture that fell there soon evaporated, and the germinating seed withered and died (see Mt 13:5 – 6).

8:8 *a hundred times more.* Luke's version is more abbreviated than Matthew's (13:8) and Mark's (4:8), but the point is the same: The quantity of increase depends on the quality of soil. *let them hear.* A challenge for listeners to understand the message and appropriate it for themselves.

8:9 *His disciples.* They included "the Twelve and the others" (Mk 4:10).

8:10 *secrets of the kingdom of God.* Truths that can be known only by revelation from God (cf. Eph 3:3 and note; 1Pe 1:10 – 12). See note on Mk 4:11. *though seeing, they may not see.* This quotation from Isaiah (6:9) does not express a desire that some would not understand but simply states the sad truth that those who are not willing to receive Jesus' message will find the truth hidden from them. Their ultimate fate is implied in the fuller quotation in Mt 13:14 – 15 (see note on Mk 4:12).

8:11 *the word of God.* The message that comes from God.

along the path are the ones who hear, and
then the devil comes and takes away the
word from their hearts, so that they may
not believe and be saved. [13]Those on the
rocky ground are the ones who receive the
word with joy when they hear it, but they
have no root. They believe for a while,
but in the time of testing they fall away.[f]
[14]The seed that fell among thorns stands
for those who hear, but as they go on their
way they are choked by life's worries,
riches[g] and pleasures, and they do not mature. [15]But the seed on good soil stands for
those with a noble and good heart, who
hear the word, retain it, and by persevering produce a crop.

A Lamp on a Stand

[16]"No one lights a lamp and hides it
in a clay jar or puts it under a bed. Instead, they put it on a stand, so that those
who come in can see the light.[h] [17]For
there is nothing hidden that will not be
disclosed, and nothing concealed that
will not be known or brought out into
the open.[i] [18]Therefore consider carefully
how you listen. Whoever has will be giv-
en more; whoever does not have, even
what they think they have will be taken
from them."[j]

Jesus' Mother and Brothers

8:19-21pp — Mt 12:46-50; Mk 3:31-35

[19]Now Jesus' mother and brothers came
to see him, but they were not able to get
near him because of the crowd. [20]Some-
one told him, "Your mother and brothers[k]
are standing outside, wanting to see you."

8:13 [f]Mt 11:6 **8:14** [g]Mt 19:23; 1Ti 6:9,10,17 **8:16** [h]S Mt 5:15 **8:17** [i]Mt 10:26; Mk 4:22; Lk 12:2 **8:18** [j]S Mt 25:29 **8:20** [k]Jn 7:5

8:21 [l]Lk 6:47; 11:28; Jn 14:21 **8:24** [m]S Lk 5:5 [n]Lk 4:35,39, 41 [o]Ps 107:29; Jnh 1:15

[21]He replied, "My mother and brothers
are those who hear God's word and put it
into practice."[l]

Jesus Calms the Storm

8:22-25pp — Mt 8:23-27; Mk 4:36-41
8:22-25Ref — Mk 6:47-52; Jn 6:16-21

[22]One day Jesus said to his disciples,
"Let us go over to the other side of the
lake." So they got into a boat and set out.
[23]As they sailed, he fell asleep. A squall
came down on the lake, so that the boat
was being swamped, and they were in
great danger.
[24]The disciples went and woke him,
saying, "Master, Master,[m] we're going to
drown!"

He got up and rebuked[n] the wind and
the raging waters; the storm subsided, and
all was calm.[o] [25]"Where is your faith?" he
asked his disciples.

In fear and amazement they asked one
another, "Who is this? He commands even
the winds and the water, and they obey
him."

Jesus Restores a Demon-Possessed Man

8:26-37pp — Mt 8:28-34
8:26-39pp — Mk 5:1-20

[26]They sailed to the region of the Gerasenes,[a] which is across the lake from Galilee. [27]When Jesus stepped ashore, he was
met by a demon-possessed man from the
town. For a long time this man had not
worn clothes or lived in a house, but had

[a] 26 Some manuscripts *Gadarenes;* other manuscripts *Gergesenes;* also in verse 37

8:12 *may not believe.* The devil's purpose is that people will not hear with understanding and therefore will not appropriate the message and be saved.

8:13 *They believe for a while.* This kind of belief is superficial and does not save. It is similar to what James calls "dead" (Jas 2:17,26) or "useless" faith (Jas 2:20; see notes on Jas 2:14–26).

8:16 *lights a lamp.* Although Jesus couched much of his message in parables, he intended that the disciples make the truths known as widely as possible (see note on 11:33). *put it on a stand.* See note on Mt 5:15.

8:17 This verse explains v. 16. It is the destiny of the truth to be made known (cf. 12:2 and note). The disciples were to begin a proclamation that would become universal.

8:18 *consider carefully how you listen.* The disciples heard not only for themselves but also for those to whom they would minister (see Mk 4:24; cf. Jas 1:19–22). Truth that is not understood and appropriated will be lost (see 19:26; Php 3:16 and notes), but truth that is used will be multiplied.

8:19 *Jesus' mother and brothers came.* See note on Mk 3:21. More is known about their motive from Mk 3:21,31–32. The family, thinking he was "out of his mind" (Mk 3:21), probably wanted to get him away from his heavy schedule. *brothers.* Did not believe in Jesus at this time (Jn 7:5; see note on Jn 7:4). Various interpretations concerning their relationship to Jesus arose in the early church: They were sons of Joseph by a previous marriage (according to Epiphanius) or were cousins (said Jerome). The most natural conclusion (suggested by Helvidius) is that they were the sons of Joseph and Mary, younger half brothers of Jesus. Four of these brothers are named in Mk 6:3, where sisters are also mentioned. Since Joseph is not mentioned here, it is likely that he had died.

8:21 See Jas 1:22. Jesus' reply was not meant to reject his natural family but to emphasize the higher priority of his spiritual relationship to those who believed in him (see 11:28 and note).

8:22 *lake.* See 5:1 and note.

8:23 *squall.* See note on Mk 4:37.

8:26 *region of the Gerasenes.* The Gospels describe the location of this event in two ways: (1) the region of the Gerasenes (see note on Mk 5:1); (2) the region of the Gadarenes (see note on Mt 8:28). Some manuscripts of Matthew, Mark and Luke read "Gergesenes" (see NIV text note here), but this spelling may have been introduced in an attempt to resolve the differences.

8:27 *demon-possessed man.* See note on 4:33. Matthew (8:28) refers to two demon-possessed men, but Mark (5:2) and Luke probably mention only the one who was prominent and did the talking. *tombs.* An isolated burial ground avoided by most people (but see note on Mk 5:3).

lived in the tombs. 28 When he saw Jesus,
he cried out and fell at his feet, shouting
at the top of his voice, "What do you want
with me,[p] Jesus, Son of the Most High
God?[q] I beg you, don't torture me!" 29 For
Jesus had commanded the impure spirit to
come out of the man. Many times it had
seized him, and though he was chained
hand and foot and kept under guard, he
had broken his chains and had been driv-
en by the demon into solitary places.
30 Jesus asked him, "What is your
name?"
"Legion," he replied, because many
demons had gone into him. 31 And they
begged Jesus repeatedly not to order them
to go into the Abyss.[r]
32 A large herd of pigs was feeding there
on the hillside. The demons begged Jesus
to let them go into the pigs, and he gave
them permission. 33 When the demons
came out of the man, they went into the
pigs, and the herd rushed down the steep
bank into the lake[s] and was drowned.
34 When those tending the pigs saw
what had happened, they ran off and reported this in the town and countryside,
35 and the people went out to see what
had happened. When they came to Jesus,
they found the man from whom the demons had gone out, sitting at Jesus' feet,[t]
dressed and in his right mind; and they
were afraid. 36 Those who had seen it told
the people how the demon-possessed[u]
man had been cured. 37 Then all the people of the region of the Gerasenes asked
Jesus to leave them,[v] because they were
overcome with fear. So he got into the
boat and left.
38 The man from whom the demons
had gone out begged to go with him, but
Jesus sent him away, saying, 39 "Return
home and tell how much God has done
for you." So the man went away and told
all over town how much Jesus had done
for him.

8:28 [p] S Mt 8:29 [q] S Mk 5:7
8:31 [r] Rev 9:1, 2, 11; 11:7; 17:8; 20:1, 3
8:33 [s] ver 22, 23
8:35 [t] Lk 10:39
8:36 [u] S Mt 4:24
8:37 [v] Ac 16:39

Jesus Raises a Dead Girl and Heals a Sick Woman

8:40-56pp — Mt 9:18-26; Mk 5:22-43

40 Now when Jesus returned, a crowd
welcomed him, for they were all expecting him. 41 Then a man named Jairus, a
synagogue leader,[w] came and fell at Jesus'
feet, pleading with him to come to his
house 42 because his only daughter, a girl
of about twelve, was dying.
As Jesus was on his way, the crowds
almost crushed him. 43 And a woman was
there who had been subject to bleeding[x] for twelve years,[a] but no one could
heal her. 44 She came up behind him and
touched the edge of his cloak,[y] and immediately her bleeding stopped.
45 "Who touched me?" Jesus asked.
When they all denied it, Peter said,
"Master,[z] the people are crowding and
pressing against you."
46 But Jesus said, "Someone touched
me;[a] I know that power has gone out
from me."[b]
47 Then the woman, seeing that she
could not go unnoticed, came trembling
and fell at his feet. In the presence of all
the people, she told why she had touched
him and how she had been instantly
healed. 48 Then he said to her, "Daughter,
your faith has healed you.[c] Go in peace."[d]
49 While Jesus was still speaking, someone came from the house of Jairus, the
synagogue leader.[e] "Your daughter is
dead," he said. "Don't bother the teacher
anymore."
50 Hearing this, Jesus said to Jairus,
"Don't be afraid; just believe, and she will
be healed."
51 When he arrived at the house of Jairus, he did not let anyone go in with him
except Peter, John and James,[f] and the
child's father and mother. 52 Meanwhile,
all the people were wailing and mourning[g]

8:41 [w] ver 49; S Mk 5:22
8:43 [x] Lev 15:25-30
8:44 [y] S Mt 9:20
8:45 [z] S Lk 5:5
8:46 [a] Mt 14:36; Mk 3:10 [b] Lk 5:17; 6:19
8:48 [c] S Mt 9:22 [d] S Ac 15:33
8:49 [e] ver 41
8:51 [f] S Mt 4:21
8:52 [g] Lk 23:27

[a] 43 Many manuscripts *years, and she had spent all she had on doctors*

8:28 *Son of the Most High God.* Cf. 1:32 and note; 4:34. The title "Most High God" was commonly used by Gentiles (see Ge 14:19 and note; Ac 16:17); its use here perhaps indicates that this man was not a Jew (but see note on Mk 1:24). *don't torture me!* See Mk 1:24 and note.
8:30 *What is your name?* Jesus asked the man his name, but it was the demons who replied, thus showing they were in control. *Legion.* See note on Mk 5:9.
8:31 *Abyss.* A place of confinement for evil spirits and for Satan (see note on Rev 9:1).
8:32 *pigs.* Pigs were unclean to Jews, and eating them was forbidden (Lev 11:7–8), but this was the Decapolis, a predominantly Gentile territory. *he gave them permission.* See note on Mt 8:32.
8:39 *Return home and tell how much God has done for you.* Although the man wanted to follow Jesus, he was directed to make the miracle known in his own native territory. There was no danger here of interference with Jesus' ministry (see note on Mk 5:19).
8:41 *synagogue leader.* The leader was responsible for conducting services, selecting participants and maintaining order (see note on Mk 5:22).
8:43 *bleeding.* Probably a menstrual disorder that had made her ceremonially unclean (see Lev 15:19–30 and note on 15:25).
8:45 *Who touched me?* For the woman's good and for a testimony to the crowd, Jesus insisted that the miracle be made known.
8:46 *power has gone out.* See note on Mk 5:30.
8:48 *Daughter.* In the Gospel accounts this woman is the only individual Jesus addressed with this tender term (cf. 23:28). *Go in peace.* Cf. 7:50 and note.
8:50 *will be healed.* See note on Mk 5:34.
8:52 *wailing and mourning.* See note on Mk 5:38. *not dead but*

for her. "Stop wailing," Jesus said. "She is not dead but asleep."[h]

53 They laughed at him, knowing that she was dead. 54 But he took her by the hand and said, "My child, get up!"[i] 55 Her spirit returned, and at once she stood up. Then Jesus told them to give her something to eat. 56 Her parents were astonished, but he ordered them not to tell anyone what had happened.[j]

Jesus Sends Out the Twelve

9:3-5pp — Mt 10:9-15; Mk 6:8-11
9:7-9pp — Mt 14:1,2; Mk 6:14-16

9 When Jesus had called the Twelve together, he gave them power and authority to drive out all demons[k] and to cure diseases,[l] 2 and he sent them out to proclaim the kingdom of God[m] and to heal the sick. 3 He told them: "Take nothing for the journey — no staff, no bag, no bread, no money, no extra shirt.[n] 4 Whatever house you enter, stay there until you leave that town. 5 If people do not welcome you, leave their town and shake the dust off your feet as a testimony against them."[o] 6 So they set out and went from village to village, proclaiming the good news and healing people everywhere.

7 Now Herod[p] the tetrarch heard about all that was going on. And he was perplexed because some were saying that John[q] had been raised from the dead,[r] 8 others that Elijah had appeared,[s] and still others that one of the prophets of long ago had come back to life.[t] 9 But Herod said, "I beheaded John. Who, then, is this I hear such things about?" And he tried to see him.[u]

8:52 [h] S Mt 9:24
8:54 [i] S Lk 7:14
8:56 [j] S Mt 8:4
9:1 [k] S Mt 10:1 [l] S Mt 4:23; Lk 5:17
9:2 [m] S Mt 3:2
9:3 [n] Lk 10:4; 22:35
9:5 [o] S Mt 10:14
9:7 [p] S Mt 14:1 [q] S Mt 3:1 [r] ver 19
9:8 [s] S Mt 11:14 [t] ver 19; Jn 1:21
9:9 [u] Lk 23:8

Jesus Feeds the Five Thousand

9:10-17pp — Mt 14:13-21; Mk 6:32-44; Jn 6:5-13
9:13-17Ref — 2Ki 4:42-44

10 When the apostles[v] returned, they reported to Jesus what they had done. Then he took them with him and they withdrew by themselves to a town called Bethsaida,[w] 11 but the crowds learned about it and followed him. He welcomed them and spoke to them about the kingdom of God,[x] and healed those who needed healing.

12 Late in the afternoon the Twelve came to him and said, "Send the crowd away so they can go to the surrounding villages and countryside and find food and lodging, because we are in a remote place here."

13 He replied, "You give them something to eat."

They answered, "We have only five loaves of bread and two fish — unless we go and buy food for all this crowd." 14 (About five thousand men were there.)

But he said to his disciples, "Have them sit down in groups of about fifty each." 15 The disciples did so, and everyone sat down. 16 Taking the five loaves and the two fish and looking up to heaven, he gave thanks and broke them.[y] Then he gave them to the disciples to distribute to the people. 17 They all ate and were satisfied, and the disciples picked up twelve basketfuls of broken pieces that were left over.

Peter Declares That Jesus Is the Messiah

9:18-20pp — Mt 16:13-16; Mk 8:27-29
9:22-27pp — Mt 16:21-28; Mk 8:31 – 9:1

18 Once when Jesus was praying[z] in pri-

9:10 [v] S Mk 6:30 [w] S Mt 11:21
9:11 [x] ver 2; S Mt 3:2
9:16 [y] S Mt 14:19
9:18 [z] S Lk 3:21

---

asleep. Jesus meant that she was not permanently dead (see Jn 11:11 – 14 for a similar statement about Lazarus).
8:56 *ordered them not to tell.* See notes on Mt 8:4; Mk 5:43. Further publicity at this time concerning a raising from the dead would have been counterproductive to Jesus' ministry.
9:1 – 6 A new phase of Jesus' ministry began when he sent out the apostles to do the type of preaching, teaching and healing they had observed him doing (Mt 9:35). This was the third tour of Galilee by Jesus and his disciples (see note on 8:1). On the first tour Jesus traveled with the four fishermen; on the second all 12 were with him; on the third Jesus traveled alone after sending out the Twelve two by two.
9:1 *the Twelve.* The apostles (see 6:13 and note on Mk 6:30). *power and authority.* Special power to heal (see 5:17; 8:46; Mk 5:30 and note), authority in teaching and control over evil spirits. *demons.* Evil spirits (see note on 4:33).
9:3 *Take nothing.* No excess baggage that would encumber travel, not even the usual provisions. They were to be entirely dependent on the people with whom they were staying (see note on Mk 6:8).
9:4 *stay there.* They were not to move from house to house, seeking better lodging, but use only one home as headquarters while preaching in a community.
9:5 *shake the dust off your feet.* A sign of repudiation for their rejection of God's message and a gesture showing separation from everything associated with the place (see 10:11; see also notes on Mt 10:14; Ac 13:51).
9:7 *Herod the tetrarch.* See note on Mt 14:1. *John had been raised from the dead.* See note on Mk 6:16. Luke does not give details about John's death (see Mt 14:1 – 12; Mk 6:17 – 29), which occurred about this time, but simply notes that it had taken place (v. 9).
9:8 *Elijah had appeared.* See notes on 1:17; Mk 9:12.
9:9 *he tried to see him.* Herod's desire to see Jesus was not fulfilled until Jesus' trial (23:8 – 12).
9:10 – 17 The feeding of the 5,000 is the only miracle besides Jesus' resurrection that is reported in all four Gospels (see notes on Mk 6:30 – 44; Jn 6:1 – 14).
9:10 *Bethsaida.* See note on Mt 11:21. Jesus must have retired to a remote area near the town (v. 12).
9:12 *Late in the afternoon.* After the preaching and healing, the question was raised about food and lodging because they were in an isolated place. Jesus may have introduced the question (see Jn 6:5), but the Synoptics indicate that the disciples were also concerned.
9:14 *sit down in groups of about fifty.* See note on Mk 6:40.
9:17 *picked up twelve basketfuls of broken pieces.* This act served as an example of avoiding wastefulness and as a demonstration that everyone had been adequately fed (see note on Mk 6:43).

vate and his disciples were with him, he
asked them, "Who do the crowds say
I am?"
19 They replied, "Some say John the
Baptist;[a] others say Elijah; and still others,
that one of the prophets of long ago has
come back to life."[b]
20 "But what about you?" he asked.
"Who do you say I am?"
Peter answered, "God's Messiah."[c]

Jesus Predicts His Death

21 Jesus strictly warned them not to tell
this to anyone.[d] 22 And he said, "The Son
of Man[e] must suffer many things[f] and be
rejected by the elders, the chief priests and
the teachers of the law,[g] and he must be
killed[h] and on the third day[i] be raised to
life."[j]
23 Then he said to them all: "Whoever
wants to be my disciple must deny themselves and take up their cross daily and
follow me.[k] 24 For whoever wants to save
their life will lose it, but whoever loses their life for me will save it.[l] 25 What
good is it for someone to gain the whole
world, and yet lose or forfeit their very
self? 26 Whoever is ashamed of me and my
words, the Son of Man will be ashamed
of them[m] when he comes in his glory and
in the glory of the Father and of the holy
angels.[n]
27 "Truly I tell you, some who are standing here will not taste death before they
see the kingdom of God."

The Transfiguration

9:28-36pp — Mt 17:1-8; Mk 9:2-8

28 About eight days after Jesus said this,
he took Peter, John and James[o] with him
and went up onto a mountain to pray.[p]
29 As he was praying, the appearance of his
face changed, and his clothes became as
bright as a flash of lightning. 30 Two men,
Moses and Elijah, appeared in glorious
splendor, talking with Jesus. 31 They spoke
about his departure,[a][q] which he was about
to bring to fulfillment at Jerusalem. 32 Peter
and his companions were very sleepy,[r] but
when they became fully awake, they saw
his glory and the two men standing with
him. 33 As the men were leaving Jesus, Peter said to him, "Master,[s] it is good for us
to be here. Let us put up three shelters —
one for you, one for Moses and one for
Elijah." (He did not know what he was
saying.)
34 While he was speaking, a cloud appeared and covered them, and they were
afraid as they entered the cloud. 35 A voice
came from the cloud, saying, "This is my
Son, whom I have chosen;[t] listen to him."[u]

9:19 [a] S Mt 3:1 [b] ver 7,8 **9:20** [c] Jn 1:49; 6:66-69; 11:27 **9:21** [d] S Mk 8:30 **9:22** [e] S Mt 8:20 [f] S Mt 16:21 [g] Mt 27:1,2 [h] Ac 2:23; 3:13 [i] S Mt 16:21 [j] S Mt 16:21 **9:23** [k] Mt 10:38; Lk 14:27 **9:24** [l] S Jn 12:25 **9:26** [m] Mt 10:33; Lk 12:9; 2Ti 2:12 [n] S Mt 16:27 **9:28** [o] S Mt 4:21 [p] S Lk 3:21 **9:31** [q] 2Pe 1:15 **9:32** [r] Mt 26:43 **9:33** [s] S Lk 5:5 **9:35** [t] Isa 42:1 [u] S Mt 3:17

[a] 31 Greek *exodos*

9:18 *Who do the crowds say I am?* The report brought by the disciples was the same as the one that reached Herod (see vv. 7–8). This event occurred to the north, outside Herod's territory, in the vicinity of Caesarea Philippi (see Mt 16:13 and note; see also note on Mk 7:24).

9:20 *Peter answered.* He was the spokesman for the disciples. *God's Messiah.* See second NIV text note on Mt 1:1. This predicted Deliverer (the Messiah) had been desired for centuries (see notes on Mt 16:18; Mk 8:29; Jn 4:5).

9:21 *warned them not to tell.* The people had false notions about the Messiah and needed to be taught further before Jesus identified himself explicitly to the public. He had a crucial schedule to keep and could not be interrupted by premature reactions (see notes on Mt 8:4; 16:20; Mk 1:34).

9:22 *Son of Man.* See note on Mk 8:31. *must suffer.* Jesus' first explicit prediction of his death (for later references, see v. 44; 12:50; 17:25; 18:31–33; cf. 24:7,25–27,44–46 and note on 24:44).

9:23 *take up their cross daily.* To follow Jesus requires self-denial, complete dedication and willing obedience. Luke emphasizes continued action; "daily" is not mentioned explicitly in the parallel accounts (Mt 16:24–26; Mk 8:34). Disciples from Galilee knew what the cross meant, for hundreds of men had been executed by this means in their region.

9:24 *whoever loses their life for me.* A saying of Jesus found in all four Gospels and in two Gospels more than once (14:26–27; 17:33; Mt 10:38–39; 16:24–25; Mk 8:34–35; Jn 12:25 [see note there]). No other saying of Jesus is given such emphasis.

9:26 *Whoever is ashamed.* See 12:9; see also note on Mk 8:38.

9:27 See note on Mt 16:28. *kingdom of God.* See note on Mt 3:2.

9:28 *About eight days.* Frequently used to indicate a week (e.g., Jn 20:26 in the Greek; see note on Mt 17:1). *Peter, John and James.* These three were also with Jesus at the healing of Jairus's daughter (8:51) and in his last visit to Gethsemane (Mk 14:33). *onto a mountain.* Although Mount Tabor is the traditional site of the Mount of Transfiguration, its distance from Caesarea Philippi (the vicinity of the last scene), its height (about 1,800 feet) and its occupation by a fortress make it unlikely. Mount Hermon fits the context much better by being both closer and higher (over 9,000 feet; see Mk 9:2). *pray.* Again Luke points out the place of prayer in an important event.

9:30 *Moses and Elijah.* Moses, the great OT deliverer and lawgiver, and Elijah, the representative of the prophets. Moses' work had been finished by Joshua, Elijah's by Elisha (another form of the name Joshua). They now spoke with Jesus (whose Hebrew name was Joshua) concerning the "exodus" he was about to accomplish, by which he would deliver his people from the bondage of sin and bring to fulfillment the work of both Moses and Elijah (see notes on 1Ki 19:16; Mt 17:3).

9:31 *departure.* Greek *exodos,* a euphemism for Jesus' approaching death. It may also link Jesus' saving death and resurrection with God's saving of his people out of Egypt.

9:32 *sleepy.* Perhaps the event was at night. *saw his glory.* See note on Ex 33:18.

9:33 *three shelters.* Temporary structures to prolong the visit of the three important persons: lawgiver, prophet and Messiah. The idea was not appropriate, however, because Jesus had a work to finish in his few remaining days on earth (see note on Mk 9:5).

9:34–35 *cloud.* See Mt 17:5 and note.

9:35 *whom I have chosen.* Or "the Chosen One," related to a Jewish title found in Dead Sea Scrolls literature

36 When the voice had spoken, they found that Jesus was alone. The disciples kept this to themselves and did not tell anyone at that time what they had seen.[v]

Jesus Heals a Demon-Possessed Boy

9:37-42,43-45pp — Mt 17:14-18,22,23; Mk 9:14-27,30-32

37 The next day, when they came down from the mountain, a large crowd met him. 38 A man in the crowd called out, "Teacher, I beg you to look at my son, for he is my only child. 39 A spirit seizes him and he suddenly screams; it throws him into convulsions so that he foams at the mouth. It scarcely ever leaves him and is destroying him. 40 I begged your disciples to drive it out, but they could not."

41 "You unbelieving and perverse generation,"[w] Jesus replied, "how long shall I stay with you and put up with you? Bring your son here."

42 Even while the boy was coming, the demon threw him to the ground in a convulsion. But Jesus rebuked the impure spirit, healed the boy and gave him back to his father. 43 And they were all amazed at the greatness of God.

Jesus Predicts His Death a Second Time

While everyone was marveling at all that Jesus did, he said to his disciples, 44 "Listen carefully to what I am about to tell you: The Son of Man is going to be delivered into the hands of men."[x] 45 But they did not understand what this meant. It was hidden from them, so that they did not grasp it,[y] and they were afraid to ask him about it.

46 An argument started among the disciples as to which of them would be the greatest.[z] 47 Jesus, knowing their thoughts,[a] took a little child and had him stand beside him. 48 Then he said to them, "Whoever welcomes this little child in my name welcomes me; and whoever welcomes me welcomes the one who sent me.[b] For it is the one who is least among you all who is the greatest."[c]

49 "Master,"[d] said John, "we saw someone driving out demons in your name and we tried to stop him, because he is not one of us."

50 "Do not stop him," Jesus said, "for whoever is not against you is for you."[e]

Samaritan Opposition

51 As the time approached for him to be taken up to heaven,[f] Jesus resolutely set out for Jerusalem.[g] 52 And he sent messengers on ahead, who went into a Samaritan[h] village to get things ready for him; 53 but the people there did not welcome him, because he was heading for Jerusalem. 54 When the disciples James and John[i] saw this, they asked, "Lord, do you want us to call fire down from heaven to destroy them[a]?"[j] 55 But Jesus turned and rebuked them. 56 Then he and his disciples went to another village.

The Cost of Following Jesus

9:57-60pp — Mt 8:19-22

57 As they were walking along the road,[k] a man said to him, "I will follow you wherever you go."

58 Jesus replied, "Foxes have dens and birds have nests, but the Son of Man[l] has no place to lay his head."

59 He said to another man, "Follow me."[m]

9:36 [v] Mt 17:9 **9:41** [w] Dt 32:5 **9:44** [x] S ver 22 **9:45** [y] S Mk 9:32 **9:46** [z] Lk 22:24 **9:47** [a] S Mt 9:4 **9:48** [b] S Mt 10:40 [c] S Mk 9:35 **9:49** [d] S Lk 5:5 **9:50** [e] Mt 12:30; Lk 11:23 **9:51** [f] S Mk 16:19 [g] Lk 13:22; 17:11; 18:31; 19:28 **9:52** [h] S Mt 10:5 **9:54** [i] S Mt 4:21 [j] 2Ki 1:10,12 **9:57** [k] ver 51 **9:58** [l] S Mt 8:20 **9:59** [m] S Mt 4:19

[a] 54 Some manuscripts *them, just as Elijah did*

---

and possibly echoing Isa 42:1. See also 23:35. *have chosen.* Parallel to "love" (Mt 17:5; see Mt 3:17 and note; 2Pe 1:17).

9:39 *A spirit seizes him.* This evil spirit was causing seizures (Mt 17:15; see note on Mt 4:24) and a speechless condition (Mk 9:17). Evil spirits were responsible for many kinds of affliction (see note on 4:33).

9:44 Another prediction of Jesus' coming death (see note on v. 22), an indication of how it will be brought about (see 22:21).

9:46 *which ... would be the greatest.* A subject that arose on a number of occasions (see 22:24; see also Mk 10:35–45 and note on Mk 9:34).

9:48 *one who is least ... is the greatest.* People become great in God's sight as they sincerely and unpretentiously look away from self to revere him (see Mk 10:43 and note).

9:49 *not one of us.* Jesus shifts the pronoun to "you" in v. 50, which may mean that the man had a relationship to Jesus of which the disciples were unaware (see note on Mk 9:38).

9:50 *whoever is not against you is for you.* Spoken in the context of opposition to the disciples' work (cf. 11:23, set in a different context; see note there).

9:51 *taken up to heaven.* See 24:51; Ac 1:9. *set out for Jerusalem.* Lit. "set his face to go to Jerusalem" (cf. Isa 50:7). Luke emphasizes Jesus' determination to complete his mission (see note on 13:22). This is not a straight-line journey to Jerusalem but a new emphasis in Jesus' ministry to reach his Jerusalem goal (see Introduction: Plan).

9:52 *a Samaritan village.* Samaritans were particularly hostile to Jews who were on their way to observe religious festivals in Jerusalem. It was at least a three-day journey from Galilee to Jerusalem through Samaria, and Samaritans refused overnight shelter for the pilgrims. Because of this antipathy, Jews traveling between Galilee and Jerusalem frequently went on the east side of the Jordan River.

9:54 *call fire down.* As Elijah had (2Ki 1:9–16). James and John were known as "sons of thunder" (Mk 3:17; see note there).

9:55 *rebuked them.* See note on 2Ki 1:10.

9:57–62 The cost of being a true follower of Jesus. Neither hardships (vv. 57–58) nor bereavement (vv. 59–60) nor family ties (v. 61) should keep anyone from following him (v. 62).

9:57 *As they were walking.* Continuing their journey through Samaria to Jerusalem.

But he replied, "Lord, first let me go and
bury my father."
60 Jesus said to him, "Let the dead bury
their own dead, but you go and proclaim
the kingdom of God."[n]
61 Still another said, "I will follow you,
Lord; but first let me go back and say
goodbye to my family."[o]
62 Jesus replied, "No one who puts a
hand to the plow and looks back is fit for
service in the kingdom of God."

Jesus Sends Out the Seventy-Two

10:4-12pp — Lk 9:3-5
10:13-15,21,22pp — Mt 11:21-23,25-27
10:23,24pp — Mt 13:16,17

10 After this the Lord[p] appointed seventy-two[a] others[q] and sent them
two by two[r] ahead of him to every town
and place where he was about to go.[s] 2 He
told them, "The harvest is plentiful, but
the workers are few. Ask the Lord of the
harvest, therefore, to send out workers
into his harvest field.[t] 3 Go! I am sending
you out like lambs among wolves.[u] 4 Do
not take a purse or bag or sandals; and do
not greet anyone on the road.
5 "When you enter a house, first say,
'Peace to this house.' 6 If someone who
promotes peace is there, your peace will
rest on them; if not, it will return to you.
7 Stay there, eating and drinking whatever
they give you, for the worker deserves his
wages.[v] Do not move around from house
to house.
8 "When you enter a town and are welcomed, eat what is offered to you.[w] 9 Heal
the sick who are there and tell them, 'The
kingdom of God[x] has come near to you.'
10 But when you enter a town and are not
welcomed, go into its streets and say,
11 'Even the dust of your town we wipe
from our feet as a warning to you.[y] Yet be
sure of this: The kingdom of God has come
near.'[z] 12 I tell you, it will be more bearable
on that day for Sodom[a] than for that town.[b]
13 "Woe to you,[c] Chorazin! Woe to you,
Bethsaida! For if the miracles that were
performed in you had been performed in
Tyre and Sidon, they would have repented
long ago, sitting in sackcloth[d] and ashes.
14 But it will be more bearable for Tyre and
Sidon at the judgment than for you. 15 And
you, Capernaum,[e] will you be lifted to the
heavens? No, you will go down to Hades.[b]
16 "Whoever listens to you listens to me;
whoever rejects you rejects me; but whoever rejects me rejects him who sent me."[f]
17 The seventy-two[g] returned with joy
and said, "Lord, even the demons submit
to us in your name."[h]
18 He replied, "I saw Satan[i] fall like lightning from heaven.[j] 19 I have given you authority to trample on snakes[k] and scorpions and to overcome all the power of the
enemy; nothing will harm you. 20 However,
do not rejoice that the spirits submit to

9:60 [n] S Mt 3:2 **9:61** [o] 1Ki 19:20 **10:1** [p] S Lk 7:13 [q] Lk 9:1,2,51,52 [r] Mk 6:7 [s] Mt 10:1 **10:2** [t] Mt 9:37,38; Jn 4:35 **10:3** [u] Mt 10:16 **10:7** [v] S 1Ti 5:18 **10:8** [w] 1Co 10:27 **10:9** [x] S Mt 3:2 **10:11** [y] S Mt 10:14 [z] ver 9 **10:12** [a] S Mt 10:15 [b] Mt 11:24 **10:13** [c] Lk 6:24-26 [d] S Rev 11:3 **10:15** [e] S Mt 4:13 **10:16** [f] S Mt 10:40 **10:17** [g] ver 1 [h] S Mk 16:17 **10:18** [i] S Mt 4:10 [j] Isa 14:12; Rev 9:1; 12:8,9 **10:19** [k] Mk 16:18; Ac 28:3-5

[a] *1* Some manuscripts *seventy*; also in verse 17
[b] *15* That is, the realm of the dead

9:59 *bury my father.* If his father had already died, the man would have been occupied with the burial. But evidently he wanted to wait until after his father's death, which might have been years away. Jesus told him that the spiritually dead could bury the physically dead and that the spiritually alive should be busy proclaiming the kingdom of God (see Mt 8:21 – 22 and note on 8:22).

9:62 *looks back.* Cf. Jn 6:66; Php 3:13 and notes.

10:1 *appointed seventy-two.* Recorded only in Luke, though similar instructions were given to the Twelve (Mt 9:37 – 38; 10:7 – 16; Mk 6:7 – 11; cf. Lk 9:3 – 5). Certain differences in early manuscripts make it unclear as to whether the number was 72 or 70 (see NIV text note). Jesus covered Judea with his message (see note on 9:51) as thoroughly as he had Galilee. The number 72 (or 70) may be meant to signify the Gentile nations, since the table of nations in Ge 10 had 72 names (in the Greek OT; 70 in the Hebrew). Just as the first missionary journey of the Twelve signified the mission to Israel, so this mission signifies the mission to the Gentiles. *two by two.* During his ministry in Galilee, Jesus had also sent out the Twelve two by two (see 9:1 – 6; Mk 6:7 and notes), a practice continued in the early church (Ac 13:2; 15:27,39 – 40; 17:14; 19:22).

10:3 *lambs among wolves.* Cf. Mt 7:15; 10:16; Ac 20:29.

10:4 *Do not take a purse or bag or sandals.* They were to travel light, without moneybag, luggage or extra sandals (see note on 9:3). *do not greet anyone.* They were not to stop along the way to visit and exchange customary lengthy greetings. The mission was urgent.

10:7 *worker deserves … wages.* Cf. 1Co 9:3 – 12; 1Ti 5:18 and note. *Do not move around.* See note on 9:4.

10:9 *The kingdom of God has come near.* The heart of Jesus' message (see notes on 4:43; Mt 3:2).

10:11 *dust … we wipe from.* See note on 9:5.

10:12 *more bearable … for Sodom.* Although Sodom was so sinful that God destroyed it (see Ge 18:20 and note; 19:24 – 28; Jude 7 and note), the people who heard the message of Jesus and his disciples were even more accountable, because they had the gospel of the kingdom preached to them. *that day.* Judgment day.

10:13 *Chorazin … Bethsaida.* See note on Mt 11:21. *sackcloth and ashes.* See Mt 11:21; Rev 11:3 and notes.

10:14 *Tyre and Sidon.* Gentile cities in Phoenicia (see note on 6:17), north of Galilee, which had not had opportunity to witness Jesus' miracles and hear his preaching as had the people in most of Galilee (see note on v. 12).

10:15 *Capernaum.* Jesus' headquarters on the north shore of Galilee (see Mt 4:13 and note), whose inhabitants had many opportunities to see and hear him. Therefore the condemnation for their rejection was the greater.

10:18 *Satan fall.* Even the demons were driven out by the disciples (v. 17), which meant that Satan was suffering defeat (may echo the language of Isa 14:12; see note on Isa 14:12 – 15). *Satan.* See notes on Mk 1:13; 1Th 3:5.

10:19 *snakes and scorpions … power of the enemy.* The snakes and scorpions may represent evil spirits; the enemy is Satan himself.

10:20 One's salvation is more important than power to overcome the evil one or escape his harm. *your names are written.* Salvation is recorded in heaven (see Ps 69:28 and note; Da 12:1).

you, but rejoice that your names are written in heaven."[l]

21 At that time Jesus, full of joy through the Holy Spirit, said, "I praise you, Father, Lord of heaven and earth, because you have hidden these things from the wise and learned, and revealed them to little children.[m] Yes, Father, for this is what you were pleased to do.

22 "All things have been committed to me by my Father.[n] No one knows who the Son is except the Father, and no one knows who the Father is except the Son and those to whom the Son chooses to reveal him."[o]

23 Then he turned to his disciples and said privately, "Blessed are the eyes that see what you see. 24 For I tell you that many prophets and kings wanted to see what you see but did not see it, and to hear what you hear but did not hear it."[p]

The Parable of the Good Samaritan

10:25-28pp — Mt 22:34-40; Mk 12:28-31

25 On one occasion an expert in the law stood up to test Jesus. "Teacher," he asked, "what must I do to inherit eternal life?"[q]

26 "What is written in the Law?" he replied. "How do you read it?"

27 He answered, " 'Love the Lord your God with all your heart and with all your soul and with all your strength and with all your mind'[a];[r] and, 'Love your neighbor as yourself.'[b]"[s]

28 "You have answered correctly," Jesus replied. "Do this and you will live."[t]

29 But he wanted to justify himself,[u] so he asked Jesus, "And who is my neighbor?"

30 In reply Jesus said: "A man was going down from Jerusalem to Jericho, when he was attacked by robbers. They stripped him of his clothes, beat him and went away, leaving him half dead. 31 A priest happened to be going down the same road, and when he saw the man, he passed by on the other side.[v] 32 So too, a Levite, when he came to the place and saw him, passed by on the other side. 33 But a Samaritan,[w] as he traveled, came where the man was; and when he saw him, he took pity on him. 34 He went to him and bandaged his wounds, pouring on oil and wine. Then he put the man on his own donkey, brought him to an inn and took care of him. 35 The next day he took out two denarii[c] and gave them to the innkeeper. 'Look after him,' he said, 'and when I return, I will reimburse you for any extra expense you may have.'

36 "Which of these three do you think was a neighbor to the man who fell into the hands of robbers?"

37 The expert in the law replied, "The one who had mercy on him."

Jesus told him, "Go and do likewise."

At the Home of Martha and Mary

38 As Jesus and his disciples were on their way, he came to a village where a woman named Martha[x] opened her home to him. 39 She had a sister called Mary,[y] who sat at the Lord's feet[z] listening to what he said. 40 But Martha was distracted by all the preparations that had to be made. She came to him and asked, "Lord, don't you care[a] that my sister has left me to do the work by myself? Tell her to help me!"

41 "Martha, Martha," the Lord answered,

10:20 [l] S Rev 20:12 **10:21** [m] 1Co 1:26-29 **10:22** [n] S Mt 28:18 [o] Jn 1:18 **10:24** [p] 1Pe 1:10-12 **10:25** [q] Mt 19:16; Lk 18:18 **10:27** [r] Dt 6:5 [s] Lev 19:18; S Mt 5:43 **10:28** [t] S Ro 7:10 **10:29** [u] Lk 16:15

10:31 [v] Lev 21:1-3 **10:33** [w] S Mt 10:5 **10:38** [x] Jn 11:1; 12:2 **10:39** [y] Jn 11:1; 12:3 [z] Lk 8:35 **10:40** [a] Mk 4:38

[a] *27* Deut. 6:5 [b] *27* Lev. 19:18 [c] *35* A denarius was the usual daily wage of a day laborer (see Matt. 20:2).

10:21–22 See Mt 11:25–27 and notes.
10:23 *see what you see.* The Messiah and his saving work, for which they longed so much.
10:25 *expert in the law.* A scholar well versed in Scripture asked a common question (18:18; cf. Mt 22:35), either to take issue with Jesus or simply to see what kind of teacher he was. See note on 7:30.
10:27 *Love ... God ... Love your neighbor.* Elsewhere Jesus uses these words in reply to another question (see Mt 22:35–40; Mk 12:28–31 and notes), putting the same two Scriptures together (Dt 6:5; Lev 19:18). Whether a fourfold love (heart, soul, strength and mind, as here and in Mk 12:30) or threefold (Dt 6:5; Mt 22:37; Mk 12:33), the significance is that total devotion is demanded. *Love your neighbor.* James calls such neighborly love the "royal law" (Jas 2:8; see note there).
10:28 *will live.* Will have eternal life (v. 25).
10:29 *to justify himself.* The answer to his first question was obviously one he knew, so to gain credibility he asked for an interpretation. In effect he said, "But the real question is: Who is my neighbor?"
10:30 *Jerusalem to Jericho.* A distance of 17 miles and a descent from about 2,500 feet above sea level to about 800 feet below sea level. The road ran through rocky, desert country, which provided places for robbers to waylay defenseless travelers.
10:31–33 *priest... Levite... Samaritan.* It is significant that the person Jesus commended was neither the religious leader nor the lay associate but a hated foreigner. Jews viewed Samaritans as half-breeds, both physically (see note on Mt 10:5) and spiritually (see notes on Jn 4:20,22). Samaritans and Jews practiced open hostility (see note on 9:52), but Jesus asserted that love knows no national boundaries.
10:34 A demonstration of "Love your neighbor" (v. 27). *oil and wine.* For their healing effects (cf. Isa 1:6 and note; Mk 6:13; Jas 5:14 and note).
10:35 *two denarii.* Two days' wages, which would keep the man for up to two months in an inn.
10:36 *Which ... was a neighbor to the man ...?* The question now became: Which one proves he is the good neighbor by his actions?
10:38 *village.* Bethany, about two miles from Jerusalem, was the home of Mary and Martha (Jn 12:1–3; see note on Mt 21:17).

"you are worried[b] and upset about many things, 42 but few things are needed—or indeed only one.[a][c] Mary has chosen what is better, and it will not be taken away from her."

Jesus' Teaching on Prayer

11:2-4pp — Mt 6:9-13
11:9-13pp — Mt 7:7-11

11 One day Jesus was praying[d] in a certain place. When he finished, one of his disciples said to him, "Lord,[e] teach us to pray, just as John taught his disciples."

2 He said to them, "When you pray, say:

" 'Father,[b]
hallowed be your name,
your kingdom[f] come.[c]
3 Give us each day our daily bread.
4 Forgive us our sins,
for we also forgive everyone who
sins against us.[d][g]
And lead us not into temptation.[e]' "[h]

5 Then Jesus said to them, "Suppose you have a friend, and you go to him at midnight and say, 'Friend, lend me three loaves of bread; 6 a friend of mine on a journey has come to me, and I have no food to offer him.' 7 And suppose the one inside answers, 'Don't bother me. The door is already locked, and my children and I are in bed. I can't get up and give you anything.' 8 I tell you, even though he will not get up and give you the bread because of friendship, yet because of your shameless audacity[f] he will surely get up and give you as much as you need.[i]

9 "So I say to you: Ask and it will be given to you;[j] seek and you will find; knock and the door will be opened to you. 10 For everyone who asks receives; the one who seeks finds; and to the one who knocks, the door will be opened.

11 "Which of you fathers, if your son asks for[g] a fish, will give him a snake instead? 12 Or if he asks for an egg, will give him a scorpion? 13 If you then, though you are evil, know how to give good gifts to your children, how much more will your Father in heaven give the Holy Spirit to those who ask him!"

Jesus and Beelzebul

11:14,15,17-22,24-26pp — Mt 12:22,24-29,43-45
11:17-22pp — Mk 3:23-27

14 Jesus was driving out a demon that was mute. When the demon left, the man who had been mute spoke, and the crowd was amazed.[k] 15 But some of them said, "By Beelzebul,[l] the prince of demons, he is driving out demons."[m] 16 Others tested him by asking for a sign from heaven.[n]

17 Jesus knew their thoughts[o] and said to them: "Any kingdom divided against itself will be ruined, and a house divided against itself will fall. 18 If Satan[p] is divided against himself, how can his kingdom stand? I say this because you claim that I drive out demons by Beelzebul. 19 Now if I drive out demons by Beelzebul, by whom do your followers drive them out? So then, they will be your judges. 20 But if I drive out demons by the finger of God,[q] then the kingdom of God[r] has come upon you.

21 "When a strong man, fully armed, guards his own house, his possessions are

10:41 [b] Mt 6:25-34; Lk 12:11,22
10:42 [c] Ps 27:4
11:1 [d] S Lk 3:21 [e] S Jn 13:13
11:2 [f] S Mt 3:2
11:4 [g] Mt 18:35; Mk 11:25 [h] Mt 26:41; Jas 1:13
11:8 [i] Lk 18:1-6
11:9 [j] S Mt 7:7
11:14 [k] Mt 9:32, 33
11:15 [l] S Mk 3:22 [m] Mt 9:34
11:16 [n] S Mt 12:38
11:17 [o] S Mt 9:4
11:18 [p] S Mt 4:10
11:20 [q] Ex 8:19 [r] S Mt 3:2

[a] 42 Some manuscripts *but only one thing is needed*
[b] 2 Some manuscripts *Our Father in heaven*
[c] 2 Some manuscripts *come. May your will be done on earth as it is in heaven.*
[d] 4 Greek *everyone who is indebted to us*
[e] 4 Some manuscripts *temptation, but deliver us from the evil one*
[f] 8 Or *yet to preserve his good name*
[g] 11 Some manuscripts *for bread, will give him a stone? Or if he asks for*

11:1 *Jesus was praying.* Not only on special occasions (e.g., baptism, 3:21 [see note there]; choosing the Twelve, 6:12; Gethsemane, 22:41) but also as a regular practice (5:16; Mt 14:23; Mk 1:35; see Introduction: Characteristics). *teach us to pray.* The Lord's model prayer, given here in answer to a request, is similar to Mt 6:9-13, where it is part of the Sermon on the Mount. Six petitions are included in the prayer as given in the Sermon on the Mount by Matthew, whereas five appear in the prayer in Luke.

11:4 *Forgive us our sins.* Mt 6:12 has "debts," but the meaning is the same as "sins." Jesus taught this truth on other occasions as well (see Mt 18:35 and note; Mk 11:25; cf. Eph 4:32 and note).

11:5-13 Jesus now urged boldness in prayer (vv. 5-8) and gave assurance that God answers prayer (vv. 9-13). The argument is from the lesser to the greater (see v. 13).

11:13 *give the Holy Spirit.* Mt 7:11 has "give good gifts," meaning spiritual gifts. Luke emphasizes the work of the Spirit, who is one of the greatest of God's gifts.

11:14 *demon that was mute.* See note on 4:33. This evil spirit caused muteness. The probable parallel passage in Matthew (12:22-30; see also Mk 3:20-27) indicates that the man was also blind.

11:15 *Beelzebul, the prince of demons.* Satan (v. 18). See note on Mt 10:25.

11:16 *sign from heaven.* Jesus had just healed a mute. Here was their sign, and they would not recognize it (see Mk 8:11 and note).

11:17 *kingdom divided against itself.* If Satan gave power to Jesus, who opposed him in every way, he would be supporting an attack upon himself.

11:19 *by whom do your followers ...?* Jesus did not say whether the followers of the Pharisees (see Mt 12:24) actually drove out demons (see note on v. 24); but they claimed to drive them out by the power of God, and Jesus claimed the same. So to accuse Jesus of using Satanic power was implicitly to condemn their own followers as well. *your judges.* They will condemn you for your accusation against them.

11:20 *finger of God.* See Ex 8:19 and note. *the kingdom of God has come.* In the sense that the promised kingdom comes with Jesus (see notes on 4:43; 17:21); the powers of evil were being overthrown.

safe. 22But when someone stronger attacks
and overpowers him, he takes away the
armor in which the man trusted and divides up his plunder.
23"Whoever is not with me is against
me, and whoever does not gather with me
scatters.[s]
24"When an impure spirit comes out of
a person, it goes through arid places seeking rest and does not find it. Then it says,
'I will return to the house I left.' 25When
it arrives, it finds the house swept clean
and put in order. 26Then it goes and takes
seven other spirits more wicked than itself, and they go in and live there. And
the final condition of that person is worse
than the first."[t]
27As Jesus was saying these things, a
woman in the crowd called out, "Blessed
is the mother who gave you birth and
nursed you."[u]
28He replied, "Blessed rather are those
who hear the word of God[v] and obey it."[w]

The Sign of Jonah

11:29-32pp — Mt 12:39-42

29As the crowds increased, Jesus said,
"This is a wicked generation. It asks for a
sign,[x] but none will be given it except the
sign of Jonah.[y] 30For as Jonah was a sign
to the Ninevites, so also will the Son of
Man be to this generation. 31The Queen of
the South will rise at the judgment with
the people of this generation and condemn
them, for she came from the ends of the
earth to listen to Solomon's wisdom;[z] and
now something greater than Solomon is
here. 32The men of Nineveh will stand
up at the judgment with this generation
and condemn it, for they repented at the
preaching of Jonah;[a] and now something
greater than Jonah is here.

The Lamp of the Body

11:34,35pp — Mt 6:22,23

33"No one lights a lamp and puts it in
a place where it will be hidden, or under
a bowl. Instead they put it on its stand,
so that those who come in may see the
light.[b] 34Your eye is the lamp of your body.
When your eyes are healthy,[a] your whole
body also is full of light. But when they
are unhealthy,[b] your body also is full of
darkness. 35See to it, then, that the light
within you is not darkness. 36Therefore,
if your whole body is full of light, and no
part of it dark, it will be just as full of light
as when a lamp shines its light on you."

Woes on the Pharisees and the Experts in the Law

37When Jesus had finished speaking, a
Pharisee invited him to eat with him; so
he went in and reclined at the table.[c] 38But
the Pharisee was surprised when he noticed that Jesus did not first wash before
the meal.[d]
39Then the Lord[e] said to him, "Now
then, you Pharisees clean the outside of
the cup and dish, but inside you are full

11:23 [s] Mt 12:30; Mk 9:40; Lk 9:50 **11:26** [t] 2Pe 2:20 **11:27** [u] Lk 23:29 **11:28** [v] S Heb 4:12 [w] Pr 8:32; Lk 6:47; 8:21; Jn 14:21 **11:29** [x] ver 16; S Mt 12:38 [y] Jnh 1:17; Mt 16:4 **11:31** [z] 1Ki 10:1; 2Ch 9:1 **11:32** [a] Jnh 3:5 **11:33** [b] S Mt 5:15 **11:37** [c] Lk 7:36; 14:1 **11:38** [d] Mk 7:3,4 **11:39** [e] S Lk 7:13

[a] 34 The Greek for *healthy* here implies *generous*.
[b] 34 The Greek for *unhealthy* here implies *stingy*.

11:22 *someone stronger attacks.* Jesus was stronger than Beelzebul, and by his exorcism of demons he demonstrated that he had overpowered Satan and disarmed him. It was therefore foolish to suggest that Jesus had cast out demons by Satan's power.

11:23 The one who does not support Jesus opposes him, making neutrality impossible (see note on Mt 12:30). Even the worker in 9:50, whom the disciples described as "not one of us" (9:49), was apparently a believer, acting in Jesus' name (see note on Mk 9:38), and Jesus did not condemn him.

11:24 *impure spirit comes out.* Jesus is perhaps referring to the work of Jewish exorcists, who claimed to cast out demons (cf. v. 19 and note) but who rejected the kingdom of God and whose exorcisms were therefore ineffective. See Mt 12:43–45, where Jesus makes a similar comment about the Jewish nation of that day.

11:25 *finds the house swept clean.* The place had been cleaned up but left unoccupied. A life reformed but lacking God's presence and power is open to reoccupancy by evil.

11:28 *Blessed rather.* Jesus is not denying the blessedness of Mary. He is stressing that it is even more blessed to be his obedient follower.

11:29 *asks for a sign.* On several occasions Jews asked for miraculous signs (see v. 16; Mt 12:38; Mk 8:11 and notes), but Jesus rejected their requests because they had wrong motives.

11:30 *as Jonah was a sign.* Just as Jonah's preaching was a sign to the Ninevites, so Jesus' message of the kingdom was a sign to his generation. For a different application of Jonah as a sign, see Mt 12:40 and note.

11:31–32 *something greater than Solomon ... something greater than Jonah.* Jesus argued from the lesser to the greater. If the queen of Sheba responded positively to the wisdom of Solomon, and the people of Nineveh to the preaching of Jonah, how much more should the people of Jesus' day have responded to the ministry of Jesus, who is infinitely greater than Solomon or Jonah!

11:31 *The Queen of the South.* The queen of Sheba (see 1Ki 10:1–10 and notes).

11:33 *a bowl.* A container holding about one peck. *may see the light.* A lamp is meant to give light to those who are near it (see v. 36). Jesus had publicly exhibited the light of the gospel for all to see, but "a wicked generation" (v. 29) requested more spectacular signs. The problem was not with any failure on Jesus' part in giving light; it was with the faulty vision of his audience.

11:34 *lamp of your body.* See note on Mt 6:22. *your eyes are healthy.* Those asking for a sign do not need more light; they need good eyes to allow the light to enter. Cf. Mt 6:22–23 and notes.

11:38 *did not first wash.* Especially for ceremonial cleansing, not commanded in the law but added in the tradition of the Pharisees (cf. Mt 15:9 and note on Jn 2:6).

11:39 *clean the outside.* Engage in ceremonial washings of

of greed and wickedness.[f] 40 You foolish
people![g] Did not the one who made the
outside make the inside also? 41 But now
as for what is inside you—be generous
to the poor,[h] and everything will be clean
for you.[i]
42 "Woe to you Pharisees, because you
give God a tenth[j] of your mint, rue and
all other kinds of garden herbs, but you
neglect justice and the love of God.[k] You
should have practiced the latter without
leaving the former undone.[l]
43 "Woe to you Pharisees, because you
love the most important seats in the synagogues and respectful greetings in the
marketplaces.[m]
44 "Woe to you, because you are like unmarked graves,[n] which people walk over
without knowing it."
45 One of the experts in the law[o] answered him, "Teacher, when you say these
things, you insult us also."
46 Jesus replied, "And you experts in the
law, woe to you, because you load people
down with burdens they can hardly carry,
and you yourselves will not lift one finger
to help them.[p]
47 "Woe to you, because you build tombs
for the prophets, and it was your ancestors who killed them. 48 So you testify that
you approve of what your ancestors did;
they killed the prophets, and you build
their tombs.[q] 49 Because of this, God in his
wisdom[r] said, 'I will send them prophets
and apostles, some of whom they will kill
and others they will persecute.'[s] 50 Therefore this generation will be held responsible for the blood of all the prophets that
has been shed since the beginning of the
world, 51 from the blood of Abel[t] to the
blood of Zechariah,[u] who was killed between the altar and the sanctuary. Yes, I
tell you, this generation will be held responsible for it all.[v]
52 "Woe to you experts in the law, because you have taken away the key to
knowledge. You yourselves have not entered, and you have hindered those who
were entering."[w]
53 When Jesus went outside, the Pharisees and the teachers of the law began
to oppose him fiercely and to besiege him
with questions, 54 waiting to catch him in
something he might say.[x]

Warnings and Encouragements

12:2-9pp — Mt 10:26-33

12 Meanwhile, when a crowd of
many thousands had gathered, so
that they were trampling on one another,
Jesus began to speak first to his disciples,
saying: "Be[a] on your guard against the
yeast of the Pharisees, which is hypocrisy.[y] 2 There is nothing concealed that will
not be disclosed, or hidden that will not
be made known.[z] 3 What you have said in
the dark will be heard in the daylight, and
what you have whispered in the ear in the
inner rooms will be proclaimed from the
roofs.

11:39 [f] Mt 23:25,26; Mk 7:20-23 **11:40** [g] Lk 12:20; 1Co 15:36 **11:41** [h] Lk 12:33 [i] S Ac 10:15 **11:42** [j] Lk 18:12 [k] Dt 6:5; Mic 6:8 [l] Mt 23:23 **11:43** [m] Mt 23:6,7; Lk 14:7; 20:46 **11:44** [n] Mt 23:27 **11:45** [o] S Mt 22:35 **11:46** [p] S Mt 23:4 **11:48** [q] Mt 23:29-32; Ac 7:51-53 **11:49** [r] 1Co 1:24, 30; Col 2:3 [s] Mt 23:34 **11:51** [t] Ge 4:8 [u] 2Ch 24:20,21 [v] Mt 23:35,36 **11:52** [w] Mt 23:13 **11:54** [x] S Mt 12:10 **12:1** [y] Mt 16:6, 11,12 **12:2** [z] S Mk 4:22

[a] 1 *Or speak to his disciples, saying: "First of all, be*

the body. *greed and wickedness.* These Pharisees were more concerned about keeping ceremonies than about being moral (cf. Mk 7:20 and note).

11:40 *make the inside also.* The inside of a person (the heart and inner righteousness) is more important than the outside (ceremonial cleansing).

11:41 *everything will be clean.* Giving from the heart makes everything else right. If one gives to the poor, one's heart is no longer in the grip of "greed and wickedness" (v. 39).

11:42–52 Six woes pronounced by Jesus on the religious leaders (see note on Mt 23:13–32).

11:42 *tenth.* A tithe of all agricultural produce was required by OT law (see Dt 14:22–29 and note). *rue.* Strongly scented herbs with bitter leaves.

11:43 *most important seats in the synagogues.* See Mk 12:39 and note.

11:44 *unmarked graves.* The Jews whitewashed their tombs so that no one would accidentally touch them and be defiled (cf. Nu 19:16; Mt 23:27 and note). Just as touching a grave resulted in ceremonial uncleanness, so also being influenced by these misguided religious leaders could lead to moral uncleanness.

11:45 *experts in the law.* See note on 7:30.

11:46 *load people down.* By adding rules and regulations to the authentic law of Moses (see note on Mt 15:2) and doing nothing to help others keep them (Mt 23:4), while inventing ways for themselves to circumvent them (cf. Mt 11:28 and note).

11:47 *tombs for the prophets.* Outwardly these "experts in the law" (v. 46) appeared to honor the prophets in building or rebuilding memorials, but inwardly they rejected the Messiah the prophets announced. They lived in opposition to the teachings of the prophets, just as their ancestors had done.

11:49 *God in his wisdom said.* Not a quotation from the OT or any other known book. It may refer to God speaking through Jesus, or it may be referring in quotation form to God's decision to send prophets and apostles even though he knew they would be rejected.

11:51 *blood of Abel . . . Zechariah.* See note on Mt 23:35.

11:52 *key to knowledge.* The very persons who should have opened the people's minds concerning the law obscured their understanding by faulty interpretation and an erroneous system of theology. They kept themselves and the people in ignorance of the way of salvation, or, as Matthew's account puts it, they "shut the door of the kingdom of heaven in people's faces" (Mt 23:13).

11:54 *waiting to catch him.* The determination of the religious leaders to trap Jesus is evident throughout Luke (see 6:11 and note; 19:47–48; 20:19–20; 22:2).

12:1 *yeast of the Pharisees.* See note on Mk 8:15.

12:2 *nothing concealed that will not be disclosed.* In this context the meaning is that nothing hidden through hypocrisy will fail to be made known (cf. note on 8:17).

12:3 *inner rooms.* Storerooms were surrounded by other rooms so that no one could dig in from outside.

4 "I tell you, my friends,[a] do not be afraid of those who kill the body and after that can do no more. 5 But I will show you whom you should fear: Fear him who, after your body has been killed, has authority to throw you into hell. Yes, I tell you, fear him.[b] 6 Are not five sparrows sold for two pennies? Yet not one of them is forgotten by God. 7 Indeed, the very hairs of your head are all numbered.[c] Don't be afraid; you are worth more than many sparrows.[d]

8 "I tell you, whoever publicly acknowledges me before others, the Son of Man will also acknowledge before the angels of God.[e] 9 But whoever disowns me before others will be disowned[f] before the angels of God. 10 And everyone who speaks a word against the Son of Man[g] will be forgiven, but anyone who blasphemes against the Holy Spirit will not be forgiven.[h]

11 "When you are brought before synagogues, rulers and authorities, do not worry about how you will defend yourselves or what you will say,[i] 12 for the Holy Spirit will teach you at that time what you should say."[j]

The Parable of the Rich Fool

13 Someone in the crowd said to him, "Teacher, tell my brother to divide the inheritance with me."

14 Jesus replied, "Man, who appointed me a judge or an arbiter between you?" 15 Then he said to them, "Watch out! Be on your guard against all kinds of greed; life does not consist in an abundance of possessions."[k]

16 And he told them this parable: "The ground of a certain rich man yielded an abundant harvest. 17 He thought to himself, 'What shall I do? I have no place to store my crops.'

18 "Then he said, 'This is what I'll do. I will tear down my barns and build bigger ones, and there I will store my surplus grain. 19 And I'll say to myself, "You have plenty of grain laid up for many years. Take life easy; eat, drink and be merry."'

20 "But God said to him, 'You fool![l] This very night your life will be demanded from you.[m] Then who will get what you have prepared for yourself?'[n]

21 "This is how it will be with whoever stores up things for themselves but is not rich toward God."[o]

Do Not Worry

12:22-31pp — Mt 6:25-33

22 Then Jesus said to his disciples: "Therefore I tell you, do not worry about your life, what you will eat; or about your body, what you will wear. 23 For life is more than food, and the body more than clothes. 24 Consider the ravens: They do not sow or reap, they have no storeroom or barn; yet God feeds them.[p] And how much more valuable you are than birds! 25 Who of you by worrying can add a single hour to your life[a]? 26 Since you cannot do this very little thing, why do you worry about the rest?

27 "Consider how the wild flowers grow. They do not labor or spin. Yet I tell you, not even Solomon in all his splendor[q] was dressed like one of these. 28 If that is how God clothes the grass of the field, which is here today, and tomorrow is thrown into the fire, how much more will he clothe you—you of little faith![r] 29 And do not set your heart on what you will eat or drink; do not worry about it. 30 For the pagan world runs after all such things, and your Father[s] knows that you need them.[t] 31 But seek his kingdom,[u] and these things will be given to you as well.[v]

32 "Do not be afraid,[w] little flock, for

12:4 [a] Jn 15:14, 15 **12:5** [b] Heb 10:31 **12:7** [c] S Mt 10:30 [d] Mt 12:12 **12:8** [e] Lk 15:10 **12:9** [f] Mk 8:38; 2Ti 2:12 **12:10** [g] S Mt 8:20 [h] Mt 12:31,32; S 1Jn 5:16 **12:11** [i] Mt 10:17,19; Lk 21:12,14 **12:12** [j] Ex 4:12; Mt 10:20; Mk 13:11; Lk 21:15 **12:15** [k] Job 20:20; 31:24; Ps 62:10

12:20 [l] Jer 17:11; Lk 11:40 [m] Job 27:8 [n] Ps 39:6; 49:10 **12:21** [o] ver 33 **12:24** [p] Job 38:41; Ps 147:9 **12:27** [q] 1Ki 10:4-7 **12:28** [r] S Mt 6:30 **12:30** [s] S Lk 6:36 [t] Mt 6:8 **12:31** [u] S Mt 3:2 [v] Mt 19:29 **12:32** [w] S Mt 14:27

[a] 25 Or *single cubit to your height*

12:4 *after that can do no more.* Encouragement in the face of persecution (see Mt 10:28 and note).

12:5 *authority to throw you into hell.* God alone has this authority. The Greek word for "hell" is *ge(h)enna* (see note on Mt 5:22), not to be confused with Hades, the general name for the place of the dead. *fear him.* Respect his authority, stand in awe of his majesty and trust in him. Verses 6–7 give the basis for trust.

12:6 *five sparrows sold for two pennies.* God even cares for little birds, sold cheaply for food.

12:8 *acknowledges me.* When a person acknowledges that Jesus is the Messiah, the Son of God (see Mt 16:16; 1Jn 2:22 and notes), Jesus acknowledges that the individual is his loyal follower (cf. Mt 7:21).

12:9 *will be disowned.* See Mk 8:38; 2Ti 2:12 and notes; cf. Mt 7:21; 25:41–46. The same Greek word is used in Peter's denial (22:34, "deny"; 22:61, "disown").

12:10 *blasphemes against the Holy Spirit.* See notes on Mt 12:31; Mk 3:29.

12:12 *Holy Spirit will teach you … what you should say.* See Mt 10:19 and note.

12:13 *divide the inheritance.* Dt 21:17 (see note there) gave the general rule that an elder son received double a younger one's portion. Disputes over such matters were normally settled by rabbis. This man's request of Jesus was selfish and materialistic. There is no indication that the man had been listening seriously to what Jesus had been saying (cf. vv. 1–11). Jesus replied with a parable about the consequences of greed.

12:16 *parable.* See note on 8:4.

12:19 *eat … be merry.* See Isa 22:13 and note.

12:21 *rich toward God.* Cf. "treasures in heaven" (Mt 6:20; see note there; cf. Lk 12:34).

12:22 *do not worry.* See v. 29; see also Php 4:6–7 and notes.

12:27 *wild flowers.* See note on Mt 6:28.

12:28 See Mt 6:30 and note.

12:31 *seek his kingdom.* Since v. 32 suggests that Jesus is speaking to believers, who already possess the king-

your Father has been pleased to give you
the kingdom.[x] 33 Sell your possessions and
give to the poor.[y] Provide purses for yourselves that will not wear out, a treasure in
heaven[z] that will never fail, where no thief
comes near and no moth destroys.[a] 34 For
where your treasure is, there your heart
will be also.[b]

Watchfulness

12:35,36pp — Mt 25:1-13; Mk 13:33-37
12:39,40; 42-46pp — Mt 24:43-51

35 "Be dressed ready for service and
keep your lamps burning, 36 like servants
waiting for their master to return from a
wedding banquet, so that when he comes
and knocks they can immediately open
the door for him. 37 It will be good for
those servants whose master finds them
watching when he comes.[c] Truly I tell you,
he will dress himself to serve, will have
them recline at the table and will come
and wait on them.[d] 38 It will be good for
those servants whose master finds them
ready, even if he comes in the middle of
the night or toward daybreak. 39 But understand this: If the owner of the house
had known at what hour the thief[e] was
coming, he would not have let his house
be broken into. 40 You also must be ready,[f]
because the Son of Man will come at an
hour when you do not expect him."

41 Peter asked, "Lord, are you telling this
parable to us, or to everyone?"

42 The Lord[g] answered, "Who then is the
faithful and wise manager, whom the master puts in charge of his servants to give
them their food allowance at the proper
time? 43 It will be good for that servant
whom the master finds doing so when he
returns. 44 Truly I tell you, he will put him
in charge of all his possessions. 45 But suppose the servant says to himself, 'My master is taking a long time in coming,' and
he then begins to beat the other servants,
both men and women, and to eat and
drink and get drunk. 46 The master of that
servant will come on a day when he does
not expect him and at an hour he is not
aware of.[h] He will cut him to pieces and
assign him a place with the unbelievers.

47 "The servant who knows the master's
will and does not get ready or does not
do what the master wants will be beaten
with many blows.[i] 48 But the one who does
not know and does things deserving punishment will be beaten with few blows.[j]
From everyone who has been given much,
much will be demanded; and from the one
who has been entrusted with much, much
more will be asked.

Not Peace but Division

12:51-53pp — Mt 10:34-36

49 "I have come to bring fire on the
earth, and how I wish it were already kindled! 50 But I have a baptism[k] to undergo,
and what constraint I am under until it
is completed![l] 51 Do you think I came to
bring peace on earth? No, I tell you, but
division. 52 From now on there will be five
in one family divided against each other,
three against two and two against three.
53 They will be divided, father against son
and son against father, mother against
daughter and daughter against mother,
mother-in-law against daughter-in-law
and daughter-in-law against mother-in-
law."[m]

Interpreting the Times

54 He said to the crowd: "When you see

12:32 [x] S Mt 25:34
12:33 [y] S Ac 2:45 [z] S Mt 6:20 [a] S Jas 5:2
12:34 [b] Mt 6:21
12:37 [c] Mt 24:42, 46; 25:13 [d] S Mt 20:28
12:39 [e] Mt 6:19; 1Th 5:2; 2Pe 3:10; Rev 3:3; 16:15
12:40 [f] Mk 13:33; Lk 21:36
12:42 [g] S Lk 7:13
12:46 [h] ver 40
12:47 [i] Dt 25:2
12:48 [j] Lev 5:17; Nu 15:27-30
12:50 [k] Mk 10:38 [l] S Jn 19:30
12:53 [m] Mic 7:6; Mt 10:21

dom, this command probably means that Christians should seek the spiritual benefits of the kingdom rather than the material goods of the world (see Mt 6:33, which says, "seek *first* his kingdom" [emphasis added]).

12:33 *Sell your possessions.* Jesus does not instruct his disciples to sell all their possessions (see note on Mk 10:21). What is emphasized throughout this Gospel is that wealth is to be generously shared with the poor (see vv. 21 – 26). *give to the poor.* The danger of riches and the need for giving are characteristic themes in Luke (see 3:11; 6:30; 11:41 and note; 14:13 – 14; 16:9 and note; 18:22; 19:8). *treasure in heaven.* See v. 21 and note.

12:37 *dress himself to serve.* The master reverses the normal roles and serves the servants (cf. 22:27 and note on 22:26; Mk 10:45; Jn 13:5 – 14 and notes).

12:38 *middle of the night or toward daybreak.* Lit. "second or third watch." The second watch was 10:00 p.m. – 2:00 a.m., and the third watch was 2:00 a.m. – sunrise. Night was divided into four watches by the Romans (Mk 13:35) and three by the Jews (see Jdg 7:19 and note); see note on Mt 14:25. These were probably the last two of the Jewish watches. The banquet would have begun in the first watch (sunset – 10:00 p.m.).

12:40 Christ's return is certain, but the time is not known (see Mt 24:36; Mk 13:32 and note).

12:41 Jesus taught the people in parables but used a more direct approach with the disciples. However, he did not intend these warnings of watchfulness just for the disciples (see Mk 13:37). In the following verses he emphasizes the duty to fulfill responsibilities.

12:42 *wise manager.* An outstanding slave (v. 43) was sometimes left in charge of an estate (see 16:1 and note).

12:46 – 48 *cut him to pieces … beaten with many blows … beaten with few blows.* Three grades of punishment that the judge will mete out in proportion to both the privileges each person has enjoyed and one's response to those privileges (see Ro 2:12 – 16 and notes).

12:49 *fire.* Applied figuratively in different ways in the NT (see note on 3:16). Here it is associated with judgment (v. 49) and division (v. 51). Judgment falls on the wicked, who are separated from the righteous.

12:50 *baptism.* The suffering that Jesus was to endure on the cross (see note on Mk 10:38). *until it is completed.* The words from the cross would pronounce the completion (see Jn 19:28,30 and note). Jesus wished that the hour of suffering were already past.

a cloud rising in the west, immediately you say, 'It's going to rain,' and it does.[n] 55 And when the south wind blows, you say, 'It's going to be hot,' and it is. 56 Hypocrites! You know how to interpret the appearance of the earth and the sky. How is it that you don't know how to interpret this present time?[o]

57 "Why don't you judge for yourselves what is right? 58 As you are going with your adversary to the magistrate, try hard to be reconciled on the way, or your adversary may drag you off to the judge, and the judge turn you over to the officer, and the officer throw you into prison.[p] 59 I tell you, you will not get out until you have paid the last penny."[q]

Repent or Perish

13 Now there were some present at that time who told Jesus about the Galileans whose blood Pilate[r] had mixed with their sacrifices. 2 Jesus answered, "Do you think that these Galileans were worse sinners than all the other Galileans because they suffered this way?[s] 3 I tell you, no! But unless you repent, you too will all perish. 4 Or those eighteen who died when the tower in Siloam[t] fell on them—do you think they were more guilty than all the others living in Jerusalem? 5 I tell you, no! But unless you repent,[u] you too will all perish."

6 Then he told this parable: "A man had a fig tree growing in his vineyard, and he went to look for fruit on it but did not find any.[v] 7 So he said to the man who took care of the vineyard, 'For three years now I've been coming to look for fruit on this fig tree and haven't found any. Cut it down![w] Why should it use up the soil?'

8 " 'Sir,' the man replied, 'leave it alone for one more year, and I'll dig around it and fertilize it. 9 If it bears fruit next year, fine! If not, then cut it down.' "

Jesus Heals a Crippled Woman on the Sabbath

10 On a Sabbath Jesus was teaching in one of the synagogues,[x] 11 and a woman was there who had been crippled by a spirit for eighteen years.[y] She was bent over and could not straighten up at all. 12 When Jesus saw her, he called her forward and said to her, "Woman, you are set free from your infirmity." 13 Then he put his hands on her,[z] and immediately she straightened up and praised God.

14 Indignant because Jesus had healed on the Sabbath,[a] the synagogue leader[b] said to the people, "There are six days for work.[c] So come and be healed on those days, not on the Sabbath."

15 The Lord answered him, "You hypocrites! Doesn't each of you on the Sabbath untie your ox or donkey from the stall and lead it out to give it water?[d] 16 Then should not this woman, a daughter of Abraham,[e] whom Satan[f] has kept bound for eighteen long years, be set free on the Sabbath day from what bound her?"

17 When he said this, all his opponents were humiliated,[g] but the people were delighted with all the wonderful things he was doing.

The Parables of the Mustard Seed and the Yeast

13:18,19pp — Mk 4:30-32
13:18-21pp — Mt 13:31-33

18 Then Jesus asked, "What is the king-

12:54 [n] Mt 16:2
12:56 [o] Mt 16:3
12:58 [p] Mt 5:25
12:59 [q] Mt 5:26; Mk 12:42
13:1 [r] S Mt 27:2
13:2 [s] Jn 9:2,3
13:4 [t] Jn 9:7,11
13:5 [u] Mt 3:2; Ac 2:38
13:6 [v] Isa 5:2; Jer 8:13; Mt 21:19
13:7 [w] S Mt 3:10
13:10 [x] S Mt 4:23
13:11 [y] ver 16
13:13 [z] S Mk 5:23
13:14 [a] S Mt 12:2 [b] S Mk 5:22 [c] Ex 20:9
13:15 [d] Lk 14:5
13:16 [e] S Lk 3:8 [f] S Mt 4:10
13:17 [g] Isa 66:5

12:54–56 Wind from the west was from the Mediterranean Sea; from the south it was from the desert. Although people could use such indicators to forecast the weather, they could not recognize the signs of spiritual crisis, the coming of the Messiah, the threat of his death, the coming confrontation with Rome and the eternal consequences these events would have for their own lives.

12:57 *judge for yourselves.* Despite the insistence of the Pharisees, despite the Roman system and even despite the pressure of family, a person must accept God on his terms. The signs of the times called for immediate decision—before judgment came on the Jewish nation.

12:58 *be reconciled ... or.* Settle accounts before it is too late.

13:1 *Galileans whose blood Pilate had mixed with their sacrifices.* Pilate had evidently slaughtered some Galileans, perhaps during an act of protest in the temple. Such an action would be in line with Pilate's reputation for cruelty.

13:2,4 *worse sinners ... more guilty.* In ancient times it was often assumed that a calamity would befall only those who were extremely sinful (see Jn 9:2 and note; see also Job 4:7; 22:5, where Eliphaz falsely accused Job; see note on Job 22:5–11). But Jesus pointed out that all are sinners who must repent or face a fearful end.

13:4 *tower in Siloam.* Built into the southeast section of Jerusalem's wall (cf. note on Jn 9:7).

13:6 *fig tree.* Probably refers to the Jewish nation (see note on Mk 11:14), but it may also apply to an individual.

13:7 *For three years.* A period of ample opportunity.

13:11 *crippled by a spirit.* Various disorders were caused by evil spirits (see note on 4:33). The description of this woman's infirmity suggests that the bones of her spine were rigidly fused together.

13:12 *Woman.* See NIV text note on Jn 2:4. *set free.* The spirit had been cast out, and the woman was freed from her physical handicap.

13:13 *praised God.* See 1:64 and note.

13:14 *healed on the Sabbath.* A focal point of attack against Jesus was his conduct on the Sabbath (see 6:5; 14:5 and notes; Mt 12:1–8,11–12; Jn 5:10 and note; see also Ex 20:9–10). *synagogue leader.* See note on 8:41.

13:15 *hypocrites.* See note on Mt 6:2. *untie your ox.* They had more regard for the needs of an animal than for the far greater need of a human being. Jesus called his critics "hypocrites" because they pretended zeal for the law, but their motive was to attack him and his healing.

dom of God[h] like?[i] What shall I compare
it to? 19 It is like a mustard seed, which
a man took and planted in his garden. It
grew and became a tree,[j] and the birds
perched in its branches."[k]
20 Again he asked, "What shall I compare the kingdom of God to? 21 It is like
yeast that a woman took and mixed
into about sixty pounds[a] of flour until it
worked all through the dough."[l]

The Narrow Door

22 Then Jesus went through the towns
and villages, teaching as he made his way
to Jerusalem.[m] 23 Someone asked him,
"Lord, are only a few people going to be
saved?"
He said to them, 24 "Make every effort to
enter through the narrow door,[n] because
many, I tell you, will try to enter and will
not be able to. 25 Once the owner of the
house gets up and closes the door, you
will stand outside knocking and pleading,
'Sir, open the door for us.'
"But he will answer, 'I don't know you
or where you come from.'[o]
26 "Then you will say, 'We ate and drank
with you, and you taught in our streets.'
27 "But he will reply, 'I don't know you
or where you come from. Away from me,
all you evildoers!'[p]
28 "There will be weeping there, and
gnashing of teeth,[q] when you see Abraham, Isaac and Jacob and all the prophets
in the kingdom of God, but you yourselves
thrown out. 29 People will come from east
and west[r] and north and south, and will
take their places at the feast in the kingdom of God. 30 Indeed there are those who
are last who will be first, and first who
will be last."[s]

Jesus' Sorrow for Jerusalem

13:34,35pp — Mt 23:37-39
13:34,35Ref — Lk 19:41

31 At that time some Pharisees came to
Jesus and said to him, "Leave this place
and go somewhere else. Herod[t] wants to
kill you."
32 He replied, "Go tell that fox, 'I will
keep on driving out demons and healing
people today and tomorrow, and on the
third day I will reach my goal.'[u] 33 In any
case, I must press on today and tomorrow
and the next day—for surely no prophet[v]
can die outside Jerusalem!
34 "Jerusalem, Jerusalem, you who kill
the prophets and stone those sent to you,
how often I have longed to gather your
children together, as a hen gathers her
chicks under her wings,[w] and you were
not willing. 35 Look, your house is left to
you desolate.[x] I tell you, you will not see
me again until you say, 'Blessed is he who
comes in the name of the Lord.'[b]"[y]

Jesus at a Pharisee's House

14:8-10Ref — Pr 25:6,7

14 One Sabbath, when Jesus went to
eat in the house of a prominent
Pharisee,[z] he was being carefully watched.[a]
2 There in front of him was a man suffering from abnormal swelling of his body.
3 Jesus asked the Pharisees and experts in

13:18 [h] S Mt 3:2 [i] S Mt 13:24 **13:19** [j] Lk 17:6 [k] S Mt 13:32 **13:21** [l] 1Co 5:6 **13:22** [m] S Lk 9:51 **13:24** [n] Mt 7:13 **13:25** [o] Mt 7:23; 25:10-12 **13:27** [p] S Mt 7:23 **13:28** [q] S Mt 8:12 **13:29** [r] S Mt 8:11 **13:30** [s] S Mt 19:30 **13:31** [t] S Mt 14:1 **13:32** [u] S Heb 2:10 **13:33** [v] S Mt 21:11 **13:34** [w] S Mt 23:37 **13:35** [x] Jer 12:17; 22:5 [y] Ps 118:26; Lk 19:38 **14:1** [z] Lk 7:36; 11:37 [a] S Mt 12:10

[a] 21 Or about 27 kilograms [b] 35 Psalm 118:26

13:19 *mustard seed.* See notes on Mt 13:31–32; Mk 4:31. Elsewhere in Scripture, trees are sometimes used to symbolize great political powers (see Eze 17:23; 31:6; Da 4:11 and note).
13:21 *yeast.* See note on Mt 13:33. Its permeating quality is emphasized here as it works from the inside to affect all the dough. This parable speaks of the powerful influence of God's kingdom.
13:22 *Jerusalem.* Where he would die. Although Jesus was ministering throughout Perea, his eyes were constantly set on the Holy City and his ultimate destiny.
13:23 *only a few … saved?* Perhaps the questioner had observed that in spite of the very large crowds that came to hear Jesus' preaching and be healed, there were only a few followers who were loyal. Jesus did not answer directly but warned that many would try to enter after it was too late.
13:27 *I don't know you.* See Mt 7:23; 25:12.
13:29 *People … from east and west and north and south.* From the four corners of the world (Ps 107:3) and from among all people, including Gentiles. *feast in the kingdom of God.* See 14:15; Mt 8:11 and notes.
13:30 See Mt 19:30 and note.
13:31 *Herod wants to kill you.* See note on Mt 14:1. Jesus was probably in Perea, which was under Herod's jurisdiction (see note on 3:1). The Pharisees wanted to frighten Jesus into leaving this area and going to Judea.
13:32 *fox.* Perhaps indicating craftiness, but more likely referring to a worthless or pesky animal. *today and tomorrow.* In Semitic usage this phrase could refer to an indefinite but limited period of time. *reach my goal.* Jesus' life had a predetermined plan that would be carried out, and no harm could come to him until his purpose was accomplished (cf. 4:43; 9:22).
13:33 *outside Jerusalem.* Jesus' hour had not yet come (see 2:38; Jn 2:4 and note; cf. Jn 8:59; 10:39; 11:54). He would die in Jerusalem as had numerous prophets before him.
13:34 *how often I have longed to gather.* This lament over Jerusalem may suggest that Jesus was in Jerusalem more often than the Synoptic Gospels indicate (cf. Jn 2:13; 4:45; 5:1; 7:10; 10:22). However, the statement in vv. 34–35 may have been uttered some distance from Jerusalem, i.e., in Perea. According to Mt 23:37–38, the same utterance was spoken on Tuesday of Passion Week. Jesus repeated many of his teachings and sayings.
13:35 *house is left … desolate.* God will abandon his temple and his city (see 21:20,24; Jer 12:7; 22:5 and notes). *not see me again until.* See Zec 12:10 and note; Rev 1:7; cf. Isa 45:23; Ro 14:11; Php 2:10–11.
14:1 Of seven recorded miracles on the Sabbath, Luke includes five (4:31,38; 6:6; 13:14; here); the other two are Jn 5:10 (see note there); 9:14. Concerning the vigil of the Pharisees, see note on 13:14. Sabbath meals were prepared the day before.
14:2 *abnormal swelling of his body.* Perhaps edema, an

the law,[b] "Is it lawful to heal on the Sabbath or not?"[c] 4 But they remained silent. So taking hold of the man, he healed him and sent him on his way.

5 Then he asked them, "If one of you has a child[a] or an ox that falls into a well on the Sabbath day, will you not immediately pull it out?"[d] 6 And they had nothing to say.

7 When he noticed how the guests picked the places of honor at the table,[e] he told them this parable: 8 "When someone invites you to a wedding feast, do not take the place of honor, for a person more distinguished than you may have been invited. 9 If so, the host who invited both of you will come and say to you, 'Give this person your seat.' Then, humiliated, you will have to take the least important place. 10 But when you are invited, take the lowest place, so that when your host comes, he will say to you, 'Friend, move up to a better place.' Then you will be honored in the presence of all the other guests. 11 For all those who exalt themselves will be humbled, and those who humble themselves will be exalted."[f]

12 Then Jesus said to his host, "When you give a luncheon or dinner, do not invite your friends, your brothers or sisters, your relatives, or your rich neighbors; if you do, they may invite you back and so you will be repaid. 13 But when you give a banquet, invite the poor, the crippled, the lame, the blind,[g] 14 and you will be blessed. Although they cannot repay you, you will be repaid at the resurrection of the righteous."[h]

The Parable of the Great Banquet

14:16-24Ref — Mt 22:2-14

15 When one of those at the table with him heard this, he said to Jesus, "Blessed is the one who will eat at the feast[i] in the kingdom of God."[j]

16 Jesus replied: "A certain man was preparing a great banquet and invited many guests. 17 At the time of the banquet he sent his servant to tell those who had been invited, 'Come, for everything is now ready.'

18 "But they all alike began to make excuses. The first said, 'I have just bought a field, and I must go and see it. Please excuse me.'

19 "Another said, 'I have just bought five yoke of oxen, and I'm on my way to try them out. Please excuse me.'

20 "Still another said, 'I just got married, so I can't come.'

21 "The servant came back and reported this to his master. Then the owner of the house became angry and ordered his servant, 'Go out quickly into the streets and alleys of the town and bring in the poor, the crippled, the blind and the lame.'[k]

22 " 'Sir,' the servant said, 'what you ordered has been done, but there is still room.'

23 "Then the master told his servant, 'Go out to the roads and country lanes and compel them to come in, so that my house will be full. 24 I tell you, not one of those who were invited will get a taste of my banquet.' "[l]

The Cost of Being a Disciple

25 Large crowds were traveling with Jesus, and turning to them he said: 26 "If anyone comes to me and does not hate father and mother, wife and children, brothers and sisters — yes, even their

14:3 [b] S Mt 22:35 [c] S Mt 12:2
14:5 [d] Lk 13:15
14:7 [e] S Lk 11:43
14:11 [f] S Mt 23:12
14:13 [g] ver 21
14:14 [h] Ac 24:15
14:15 [i] Isa 25:6; Mt 26:29; Lk 13:29; Rev 19:9 [j] S Mt 3:2
14:21 [k] ver 13
14:24 [l] Mt 21:43; Ac 13:46

[a] 5 Some manuscripts *donkey*

excessive accumulation of fluid in the tissues and cavities of the body that indicates illness. The Greek for this word is a medical term found only here in the NT (see Introduction: Author).

14:3 *experts in the law.* See notes on 5:17; 7:30. By questioning them before the miracle, Jesus made it difficult for them to protest afterward.

14:5 *child.* See NIV text note. The reading "donkey" matches well with the "ox that falls into a well." But in Dt 5:14 the law is specified for both humans and animals; one category opens with "son" and another with "ox." Jesus' action was "unlawful" only according to rabbinic interpretations, not according to the Mosaic law itself (cf. note on Mk 2:25).

14:7 *places of honor.* Maneuvering for better seats may also have caused trouble at the Last Supper (22:24; see also 20:46; Mk 12:39 and note).

14:11 *humble themselves will be exalted.* A basic principle repeated often in the Bible (see 11:43; 18:14; 20:46; 2Ch 7:14 – 15; Pr 3:34; 25:6 – 7; Mt 18:4; 23:12; Jas 4:10; 1Pe 5:6).

14:14 *resurrection of the righteous.* All will be resurrected (see Da 12:2; Jn 5:28 – 29 and notes; Ac 24:15). Some hold that the resurrection of the righteous (1Co 15:23; 1Th 4:16; Rev 20:4 – 6) is distinct from the "general" resurrection (1Co 15:12,21; Heb 6:2; Rev 20:11 – 15). *the righteous.* Those who have been pronounced so by God on the basis of Christ's atonement (see Ro 1:17 and note) and who have evidenced their faith by their actions (cf. Mt 25:34 – 40).

14:15 *feast in the kingdom.* The great Messianic banquet to come. Association of the future kingdom with a feast was common (see 13:29; Isa 25:6 and note; Mt 8:11 and note; 25:1 – 10; 26:29 and note; Rev 19:9).

14:16 *Jesus replied.* Jesus used the man's remark as the occasion for a parable warning that not everyone would enter the kingdom. *great banquet.* See chart, p. 1736.

14:18 *bought a field.* The initial invitation must have been accepted, but when the final invitation came (by Jewish custom the announcement that came when the feast was ready), other interests took priority.

14:24 *those who were invited.* Without explicitly mentioning them, Jesus warned the Jewish religious leaders that those who refused the invitation to his Messianic banquet would not get one taste of it, but others would (see 20:9 – 19; see also note on Mt 21:41).

own life—such a person cannot be my
disciple.[m] 27 And whoever does not carry
their cross and follow me cannot be my
disciple.[n]
28 "Suppose one of you wants to build
a tower. Won't you first sit down and estimate the cost to see if you have enough
money to complete it? 29 For if you lay the
foundation and are not able to finish it,
everyone who sees it will ridicule you,
30 saying, 'This person began to build and
wasn't able to finish.'
31 "Or suppose a king is about to go to
war against another king. Won't he first
sit down and consider whether he is able
with ten thousand men to oppose the one
coming against him with twenty thousand? 32 If he is not able, he will send a
delegation while the other is still a long
way off and will ask for terms of peace.
33 In the same way, those of you who do
not give up everything you have cannot be
my disciples.[o]
34 "Salt is good, but if it loses its saltiness, how can it be made salty again?[p] 35 It
is fit neither for the soil nor for the manure
pile; it is thrown out.[q]
"Whoever has ears to hear, let them
hear."[r]

The Parable of the Lost Sheep

15:4-7pp — Mt 18:12-14

15 Now the tax collectors[s] and sinners
were all gathering around to hear
Jesus. 2 But the Pharisees and the teachers
of the law muttered, "This man welcomes
sinners and eats with them."[t]
3 Then Jesus told them this parable:[u]
4 "Suppose one of you has a hundred
sheep and loses one of them. Doesn't he
leave the ninety-nine in the open country
and go after the lost sheep until he finds
it?[v] 5 And when he finds it, he joyfully puts
it on his shoulders 6 and goes home. Then
he calls his friends and neighbors together
and says, 'Rejoice with me; I have found
my lost sheep.'[w] 7 I tell you that in the same
way there will be more rejoicing in heav-
en over one sinner who repents than over
ninety-nine righteous persons who do not
need to repent.[x]

The Parable of the Lost Coin

8 "Or suppose a woman has ten silver
coins[a] and loses one. Doesn't she light a
lamp, sweep the house and search carefully until she finds it? 9 And when she finds
it, she calls her friends and neighbors together and says, 'Rejoice with me; I have
found my lost coin.'[y] 10 In the same way, I
tell you, there is rejoicing in the presence
of the angels of God over one sinner who
repents."[z]

The Parable of the Lost Son

11 Jesus continued: "There was a man
who had two sons.[a] 12 The younger one
said to his father, 'Father, give me my
share of the estate.'[b] So he divided his
property[c] between them.
13 "Not long after that, the younger son
got together all he had, set off for a distant country and there squandered his
wealth[d] in wild living. 14 After he had spent
everything, there was a severe famine in
that whole country, and he began to be
in need. 15 So he went and hired himself
out to a citizen of that country, who sent

14:26 [m] Mt 10:37; S Jn 12:25 **14:27** [n] Mt 10:38; Lk 9:23 **14:33** [o] Php 3:7,8 **14:34** [p] Mk 9:50 **14:35** [q] Mt 5:13 [r] S Mt 11:15 **15:1** [s] Lk 5:29 **15:2** [t] S Mt 9:11 **15:3** [u] Mt 13:3 **15:4** [v] Ps 23; 119:176; Jer 31:10; Eze 34:11-16; Lk 5:32; 19:10 **15:6** [w] ver 9 **15:7** [x] ver 10 **15:9** [y] ver 6 **15:10** [z] ver 7 **15:11** [a] Mt 21:28 **15:12** [b] Dt 21:17 [c] ver 30 **15:13** [d] ver 30; Lk 16:1

[a] 8 Greek *ten drachmas,* each worth about a day's wages

14:26 *hate father and mother.* A vivid hyperbole, meaning that one must love Jesus even more than one's immediate family (see Mal 1:2–3 for another use of the figure). See Mt 10:37 and note on Mal 1:3.
14:27 *carry their cross.* See 9:23; Mt 10:38 and notes.
14:28 *estimate the cost.* Jesus did not want a blind, naive commitment that expected only blessings. As a builder estimates costs or a king evaluates military strength (v. 31), so people must consider what Jesus expects of his followers before they commit their lives to him.
14:33 *give up everything you have.* The cost, Jesus warned, is complete surrender to him (see Php 3:7–11).
14:34 *Salt is good.* See note on Mk 9:50.
15:1 *tax collectors and sinners.* See notes on 3:12; Mk 2:15.
15:2 *muttered.* Complained among themselves, but not openly. *eats with them.* More than simple association, eating with a person indicated acceptance and recognition (cf. Ps 41:9; Jn 13:18 and notes; Ac 11:3; 1Co 5:11 and note; Gal 2:12).
15:3 *this parable.* Jesus responded with a story that contrasted the love of God with the exclusiveness of the Pharisees (see chart, p. 1736).
15:4 *lost sheep.* The shepherd theme was familiar (see Ps 23; Isa 40:11; Eze 34:11–16 and notes).
15:6 *found my lost sheep.* See 19:10 and note.
15:7 *rejoicing in heaven.* God's joy over the sinner's repentance is set in stark contrast to the attitude of the Pharisees and the teachers of the law (v. 2). *righteous … do not need to repent.* Probably irony: those who think they are righteous (such as the Pharisees and the teachers of the law) and feel no need to repent.
15:8 *ten silver coins.* See NIV text note. A drachma was a Greek coin approximately equivalent to the Roman denarius, worth about an average day's wages (Mt 20:2). *search carefully.* Near Eastern houses frequently had no windows and only dirt floors, making the search for a single coin difficult.
15:12 *share of the estate.* The father might divide the inheritance (double to the older son; see 12:13; Dt 21:17 and notes) but retain the income from it until his death. But to give a younger son his portion of the inheritance upon request was highly unusual. Cf. Pr 20:21 and note.
15:13 *got together all he had.* The son's motive becomes apparent when he departs, taking with him all his possessions and leaving nothing behind to come back to. He wants to be free of parental restraint and to spend his share of the family wealth as he pleases. *wild living.* More specific in v. 30, though the older brother may have exaggerated because of his bitter attitude.

PARABLES OF JESUS

PARABLE	MATTHEW	MARK	LUKE	PARABLE	MATTHEW	MARK	LUKE
Lamp under a bowl	5:14–15	4:21–22	8:16; 11:33	Ten virgins	25:1–13		
Wise and foolish builders	7:24–27		6:47–49	Bags of gold (minas)	25:14–30		19:12–27
New cloth on an old coat	9:16	2:21	5:36	Sheep and goats	25:31–46		
New wine in old wineskins	9:17	2:22	5:37–38	Growing seed		4:26–29	
Sower and the soils	13:3–8,18–23	4:3–8,14–20	8:5–8,11–15	Watchful servants		13:35–37	12:35–40
Weeds	13:24–30,36–43			Moneylender			7:41–43
Mustard seed	13:31–32	4:30–32	13:18–19	Good Samaritan			10:30–37
Yeast	13:33		13:20–21	Friend in need			11:5–8
Hidden treasure	13:44			Rich fool			12:16–21
Valuable pearl	13:45–46			Unfruitful fig tree			13:6–9
Net	13:47–50			Lowest seat at the feast			14:7–14
Owner of a house	13:52			Great banquet			14:16–24
Lost sheep	18:12–14		15:4–7	Cost of discipleship			14:28–33
Unmerciful servant	18:23–34			Lost coin			15:8–10
Workers in the vineyard	20:1–16			Lost (prodigal) son			15:11–32
Two sons	21:28–32			Shrewd manager			16:1–8
Tenants	21:33–44	12:1–11	20:9–18	Rich man and Lazarus			16:19–31
Wedding banquet	22:2–14			Master and his servant			17:7–10
Fig tree	24:32–35	13:28–29	21:29–31	Persistent widow			18:2–8
Faithful and wise servant	24:45–51		12:42–48	Pharisee and tax collector			18:10–14

him to his fields to feed pigs.[e] 16He longed
to fill his stomach with the pods that the
pigs were eating, but no one gave him
anything.
17"When he came to his senses, he said,
'How many of my father's hired servants
have food to spare, and here I am starving
to death! 18I will set out and go back to
my father and say to him: Father, I have
sinned[f] against heaven and against you.
19I am no longer worthy to be called your
son; make me like one of your hired servants.' 20So he got up and went to his father.
"But while he was still a long way off,
his father saw him and was filled with compassion for him; he ran to his son, threw
his arms around him and kissed him.[g]
21"The son said to him, 'Father, I have
sinned against heaven and against you.[h]
I am no longer worthy to be called your
son.'
22"But the father said to his servants,
'Quick! Bring the best robe[i] and put it on
him. Put a ring on his finger[j] and sandals
on his feet. 23Bring the fattened calf and
kill it. Let's have a feast and celebrate.
24For this son of mine was dead and is
alive again;[k] he was lost and is found.' So
they began to celebrate.[l]
25"Meanwhile, the older son was in the
field. When he came near the house, he
heard music and dancing. 26So he called
one of the servants and asked him what
was going on. 27'Your brother has come,'
he replied, 'and your father has killed the
fattened calf because he has him back safe
and sound.'
28"The older brother became angry[m]
and refused to go in. So his father went

15:15 [e] Lev 11:7 **15:18** [f] Lev 26:40; Mt 3:2 **15:20** [g] Ge 45:14, 15; 46:29; Ac 20:37 **15:21** [h] Ps 51:4 **15:22** [i] Zec 3:4; Rev 6:11 [j] Ge 41:42 **15:24** [k] Eph 2:1, 5; 5:14; 1Ti 5:6 [l] ver 32 **15:28** [m] Jnh 4:1

15:15 *feed pigs.* The ultimate indignity for Jews; the work was abhorrent to them because pigs were ceremonially unclean animals (Lev 11:7).
15:16 *pods.* Probably seeds of the carob tree.
15:22–23 *best robe ... ring ... sandals ... feast.* Each was a sign of position and acceptance (cf. Ge 41:42 and note; Zec 3:4): a long robe of distinction, a signet ring of authority, sandals like a son (slaves went barefoot) and the fattened calf for a special occasion.
15:24 *lost.* See 19:10 and note.
15:28 *older brother.* The forgiving love of the father symbolizes the divine mercy of God, and the older brother's resentment is like the attitude of the Pharisees and teachers of the law who opposed Jesus (v. 2).

out and pleaded with him. 29 But he answered his father, 'Look! All these years
I've been slaving for you and never disobeyed your orders. Yet you never gave
me even a young goat so I could celebrate
with my friends. 30 But when this son of
yours who has squandered your property[n]
with prostitutes[o] comes home, you kill the
fattened calf for him!'
31 " 'My son,' the father said, 'you are always with me, and everything I have is
yours. 32 But we had to celebrate and be
glad, because this brother of yours was
dead and is alive again; he was lost and
is found.' "[p]

The Parable of the Shrewd Manager

16 Jesus told his disciples: "There was
a rich man whose manager was
accused of wasting his possessions.[q] 2 So
he called him in and asked him, 'What is
this I hear about you? Give an account of
your management, because you cannot be
manager any longer.'
3 "The manager said to himself, 'What
shall I do now? My master is taking away
my job. I'm not strong enough to dig, and
I'm ashamed to beg— 4 I know what I'll
do so that, when I lose my job here, people will welcome me into their houses.'
5 "So he called in each one of his master's debtors. He asked the first, 'How
much do you owe my master?'
6 " 'Nine hundred gallons[a] of olive oil,'
he replied.
"The manager told him, 'Take your bill,
sit down quickly, and make it four hundred and fifty.'
7 "Then he asked the second, 'And how
much do you owe?'
" 'A thousand bushels[b] of wheat,' he replied.
"He told him, 'Take your bill and make
it eight hundred.'
8 "The master commended the dishonest manager because he had acted shrewdly. For the people of this world[r] are more
shrewd[s] in dealing with their own kind
than are the people of the light.[t] 9 I tell
you, use worldly wealth[u] to gain friends
for yourselves, so that when it is gone, you
will be welcomed into eternal dwellings.[v]
10 "Whoever can be trusted with very little can also be trusted with much,[w] and
whoever is dishonest with very little will
also be dishonest with much. 11 So if you
have not been trustworthy in handling
worldly wealth,[x] who will trust you with
true riches? 12 And if you have not been
trustworthy with someone else's property,
who will give you property of your own?
13 "No one can serve two masters. Either
you will hate the one and love the other,
or you will be devoted to the one and despise the other. You cannot serve both God
and money."[y]
14 The Pharisees, who loved money,[z]
heard all this and were sneering at Jesus.[a]
15 He said to them, "You are the ones who
justify yourselves[b] in the eyes of others,
but God knows your hearts.[c] What people
value highly is detestable in God's sight.

Additional Teachings

16 "The Law and the Prophets were pro-

15:30 [n] ver 12, 13 [o] Pr 29:3 **15:32** [p] ver 24; Mal 3:17 **16:1** [q] Lk 15:13, 30
16:8 [r] Ps 17:14 [s] Ps 18:26 [t] Jn 12:36; Eph 5:8; 1Th 5:5 **16:9** [u] ver 11, 13 [v] Mt 19:21; Lk 12:33 **16:10** [w] Mt 25:21,23; Lk 19:17 **16:11** [x] ver 9,13 **16:13** [y] ver 9, 11; Mt 6:24 **16:14** [z] S 1Ti 3:3 [a] Lk 23:35 **16:15** [b] Lk 10:29 [c] S Rev 2:23

[a] 6 Or about 3,000 liters [b] 7 Or about 30 tons

15:29 *young goat.* Cheaper food than a fattened calf.

15:30 *this son of yours.* The older brother would not even recognize him as his brother, so bitter was his hatred.

15:31 *everything I have is yours.* The father loved both brothers. The parable shows a contrast between the self-centered exclusiveness of the Pharisees, who failed to understand God's love, and his joy over the repentance of sinners.

15:32 *dead and is alive.* A beautiful picture of the return of the younger son, which also pictures Christian conversion (see Ro 6:12–13 and note; Eph 2:1,5). The phrase "lost and is found" is often used to mean "perished and is saved" (see 19:10 and note; Mt 10:6; 18:12–14 and note).

16:1 *disciples.* Perhaps more than just the Twelve (see 6:13 and note; 10:1). *manager.* A steward who handled all the business affairs of the owner (cf. 1Co 4:1–2 and note on 4:1). *wasting.* He had squandered his master's possessions, just as the prodigal (wasteful) son had done (15:13).

16:3 *What shall I do now?* The dishonest manager (v. 8) had no scruples against using his position for his own benefit, even if it meant cheating his master. Knowing he would lose his job, the manager planned for his future by discounting the debts owed to his master in order to obligate the debtors to himself. Interpreters disagree as to whether his procedure of discounting was in itself dishonest. Was he giving away what really belonged to his master, or was he forgoing interest payments his master did not have a right to charge? Originally the manager may have overcharged the debtors, a common way of circumventing the Mosaic law that prohibited taking interest from fellow Jews (see Ex 22:25–27; Lev 25:36 and notes; Dt 23:19–20). So, to reduce the debts, he may have returned the figures to their initial amounts, which would both satisfy his master and gain the good favor of the debtors. In any event, the point remains the same: He was shrewd enough to use the means at his disposal to plan for his future well-being.

16:8 *people of the light.* God's people (see Jn 12:35–36; Eph 5:8; 1Th 5:5 and notes).

16:9 *use worldly wealth.* God's people should be alert to make use of what God has given them. *to gain friends.* By helping those in need, who in the future will show their gratitude when they welcome their benefactors into heaven ("eternal dwellings"). In this way worldly wealth may be wisely used to gain eternal benefit.

16:10 *trusted with much.* Cf. 19:17; Mt 25:21. Faithfulness is not determined by the amount entrusted but by the character of the person who uses it.

16:11 *true riches.* The things that belong to God's kingdom, in contrast to "worldly wealth."

16:13 *two masters.* See Mt 6:24; cf. Jas 4:4 and note.

claimed until John.[d] Since that time, the good news of the kingdom of God is being preached,[e] and everyone is forcing their way into it. 17 It is easier for heaven and earth to disappear than for the least stroke of a pen to drop out of the Law.[f]

18 "Anyone who divorces his wife and marries another woman commits adultery, and the man who marries a divorced woman commits adultery.[g]

The Rich Man and Lazarus

19 "There was a rich man who was dressed in purple and fine linen and lived in luxury every day.[h] 20 At his gate was laid a beggar[i] named Lazarus, covered with sores 21 and longing to eat what fell from the rich man's table.[j] Even the dogs came and licked his sores.

22 "The time came when the beggar died and the angels carried him to Abraham's side. The rich man also died and was buried. 23 In Hades, where he was in torment, he looked up and saw Abraham far away, with Lazarus by his side. 24 So he called to him, 'Father Abraham,[k] have pity on me and send Lazarus to dip the tip of his finger in water and cool my tongue, because I am in agony in this fire.'[l]

25 "But Abraham replied, 'Son, remember that in your lifetime you received your good things, while Lazarus received bad things,[m] but now he is comforted here and you are in agony.[n] 26 And besides all this, between us and you a great chasm has been set in place, so that those who want to go from here to you cannot, nor can anyone cross over from there to us.'

27 "He answered, 'Then I beg you, father, send Lazarus to my family, 28 for I have five brothers. Let him warn them,[o] so that they will not also come to this place of torment.'

29 "Abraham replied, 'They have Moses[p] and the Prophets;[q] let them listen to them.'

30 " 'No, father Abraham,'[r] he said, 'but if someone from the dead goes to them, they will repent.'

31 "He said to him, 'If they do not listen to Moses and the Prophets, they will not be convinced even if someone rises from the dead.' "

Sin, Faith, Duty

17 Jesus said to his disciples: "Things that cause people to stumble[s] are bound to come, but woe to anyone through whom they come.[t] 2 It would be better for them to be thrown into the sea with a millstone tied around their neck than to cause one of these little ones[u] to stumble.[v] 3 So watch yourselves.

"If your brother or sister[a] sins against you, rebuke them;[w] and if they repent, forgive them.[x] 4 Even if they sin against you seven times in a day and seven times come back to you saying 'I repent,' you must forgive them."[y]

5 The apostles[z] said to the Lord,[a] "Increase our faith!"

16:16 [d] Mt 5:17; 11:12,13 [e] S Mt 4:23 **16:17** [f] S Mt 5:18 **16:18** [g] Mt 5:31, 32; 19:9; Mk 10:11; Ro 7:2,3; 1Co 7:10,11 **16:19** [h] Eze 16:49 **16:20** [i] Ac 3:2 **16:21** [j] Mt 15:27; Lk 15:16 **16:24** [k] ver 30; S Lk 3:8 [l] S Mt 5:22 **16:25** [m] Ps 17:14 [n] Lk 6:21,24,25 **16:28** [o] Ac 2:40; 20:23; 1Th 4:6 **16:29** [p] S Lk 24:27,44; Jn 1:45; 5:45-47; Ac 15:21 [q] Lk 4:17; 24:27,44; Jn 1:45 **16:30** [r] ver 24; S Lk 3:8 **17:1** [s] S Mt 5:29 [t] Mt 18:7 **17:2** [u] Mk 10:24; Lk 10:21 [v] S Mt 5:29 **17:3** [w] S Mt 18:15 [x] Eph 4:32; Col 3:13 **17:4** [y] Mt 18:21,22 **17:5** [z] S Mk 6:30 [a] S Lk 7:13

[a] 3 The Greek word for *brother or sister* (*adelphos*) refers here to a fellow disciple, whether man or woman.

16:16 *until John.* The ministry of John the Baptist, which prepared the way for Jesus the Messiah, was the dividing line between the OT (the "Law and the Prophets") and the NT (see notes on Jer 31:31 – 34; Heb 8:6 – 12). *forcing their way.* The meaning is disputed, but it probably speaks of the fierce earnestness with which people were responding to the gospel of the kingdom. Multitudes were coming to hear Jesus and to receive his message.

16:17 The ministry of Jesus (introducing the new covenant era) was a fulfillment of the law (defining the old covenant era) in the most minute detail (cf. 21:33). *heaven and earth to disappear.* See Mk 13:24 – 25; 2Pe 3:7 and notes. *least stroke of a pen.* See Mt 5:17 – 18 and notes.

16:18 *divorces his wife.* See Mt 5:32; 19:3; Mk 10:11 – 12; 1Co 7:10 – 11 and notes. Jesus affirms the continuing authority of the law: For example, adultery was still adultery, still unlawful and still sinful. Matthew's treatment is fuller in that (1) it shows that this law was given because of hardened hearts in regard to divorce, and (2) it includes one exception as permissible grounds for divorce — sexual immorality (Mt 19:9).

16:19 *rich man.* Sometimes given the name Dives (from the Latin for "rich man"). *purple and fine linen.* Characteristic of costly garments.

16:20 *Lazarus.* Not the Lazarus Jesus raised from the dead (Jn 11:43 – 44). *covered with sores.* The Greek for this phrase is a common medical term found only here in the NT (see Introduction: Author).

16:22 The Talmud mentions both paradise (see 23:43 and note) and Abraham's side as the final home of the righteous. "Abraham's side" refers to the place of blessedness to which the righteous dead go. Its bliss is the quality of blessedness reserved for people like Abraham.

16:23 *Hades.* Here depicted as the place to which the wicked dead go and suffer torment.

16:28 *I have five brothers.* For the first time the rich man showed concern for others.

16:29 *Moses and the Prophets.* A way of designating the whole OT. The rich man had failed to pay attention to Scripture and its teaching (especially about helping the needy; see vv. 20 – 21) and feared his brothers would do the same. *listen to.* Hear and obey.

16:30 *someone from the dead.* The story may suggest that Lazarus was intended, but Luke's account seems to imply that Jesus was speaking also of his own resurrection (cf. v. 31; 9:22). If people's minds are closed and Scripture is rejected, no evidence — not even a resurrection — will change them.

17:2 *millstone.* A heavy stone for grinding grain. *little ones.* See Mt 18:6,10,14; Mk 9:42 and notes.

17:3 *brother or sister.* See Mt 18:15,17; Mk 3:35 and notes.

17:4 *seven times.* That is, forgiveness is to be unlimited (see notes on Ps 119:164; Mt 18:22; cf. Eph 4:32 and note).

17:5 *Increase our faith!* They felt incapable of measuring up to the standards set forth in vv. 1 – 4. They wanted greater faith to lay hold of the power to live up to Jesus' standards.

6 He replied, "If you have faith as small
as a mustard seed,[b] you can say to this
mulberry tree, 'Be uprooted and planted
in the sea,' and it will obey you.[c]
7 "Suppose one of you has a servant
plowing or looking after the sheep. Will he
say to the servant when he comes in from
the field, 'Come along now and sit down
to eat'? 8 Won't he rather say, 'Prepare my
supper, get yourself ready and wait on me[d]
while I eat and drink; after that you may
eat and drink'? 9 Will he thank the servant
because he did what he was told to do?
10 So you also, when you have done everything you were told to do, should say, 'We
are unworthy servants; we have only done
our duty.' "[e]

Jesus Heals Ten Men With Leprosy

11 Now on his way to Jerusalem,[f] Jesus
traveled along the border between Samaria and Galilee.[g] 12 As he was going into a
village, ten men who had leprosy[a][h] met
him. They stood at a distance[i] 13 and called
out in a loud voice, "Jesus, Master,[j] have
pity on us!"
14 When he saw them, he said, "Go,
show yourselves to the priests."[k] And as
they went, they were cleansed.
15 One of them, when he saw he was
healed, came back, praising God[l] in a
loud voice. 16 He threw himself at Jesus'
feet and thanked him—and he was a Samaritan.[m]
17 Jesus asked, "Were not all ten
cleansed? Where are the other nine? 18 Has
no one returned to give praise to God except this foreigner?" 19 Then he said to
him, "Rise and go; your faith has made
you well."[n]

17:6 [b] Mt 13:31; 17:20; Lk 13:19 [c] S Mt 21:21; Mk 9:23
17:8 [d] Lk 12:37
17:10 [e] 1Co 9:16
17:11 [f] S Lk 9:51 [g] Lk 9:51,52; Jn 4:3,4
17:12 [h] S Mt 8:2 [i] Lev 13:45,46
17:13 [j] S Lk 5:5
17:14 [k] Lev 14:2; Mt 8:4
17:15 [l] S Mt 9:8
17:16 [m] S Mt 10:5
17:19 [n] S Mt 9:22

The Coming of the Kingdom of God

17:26,27pp — Mt 24:37-39

20 Once, on being asked by the Pharisees
when the kingdom of God would come,[o]
Jesus replied, "The coming of the kingdom of God is not something that can be
observed, 21 nor will people say, 'Here it
is,' or 'There it is,'[p] because the kingdom
of God is in your midst."[b]
22 Then he said to his disciples, "The
time is coming when you will long to see
one of the days of the Son of Man,[q] but
you will not see it.[r] 23 People will tell you,
'There he is!' or 'Here he is!' Do not go
running off after them.[s] 24 For the Son of
Man in his day[c] will be like the lightning,[t]
which flashes and lights up the sky from
one end to the other. 25 But first he must
suffer many things[u] and be rejected[v] by
this generation.[w]
26 "Just as it was in the days of Noah,[x]
so also will it be in the days of the Son of
Man. 27 People were eating, drinking, marrying and being given in marriage up to
the day Noah entered the ark. Then the
flood came and destroyed them all.
28 "It was the same in the days of Lot.[y]
People were eating and drinking, buying
and selling, planting and building. 29 But
the day Lot left Sodom, fire and sulfur
rained down from heaven and destroyed
them all.
30 "It will be just like this on the day the
Son of Man is revealed.[z] 31 On that day no
one who is on the housetop, with possessions inside, should go down to get

17:20 [o] S Mt 3:2
17:21 [p] ver 23
17:22 [q] S Mt 8:20 [r] S Lk 5:35
17:23 [s] Mt 24:23; Lk 21:8
17:24 [t] Mt 24:27
17:25 [u] S Mt 16:21 [v] Lk 9:22; 18:32 [w] Mk 13:30; Lk 21:32
17:26 [x] Ge 6:5-8; 7:6-24
17:28 [y] Ge 19:1-28
17:30 [z] Mt 10:23; S 16:27; 24:3,27,37, 39; 25:31; S 1Co 1:7; S 1Th 2:19; 2Th 1:7; 2:8; 2Pe 3:4; S Rev 1:7

a 12 The Greek word traditionally translated *leprosy* was used for various diseases affecting the skin. *b* 21 Or *is within you* *c* 24 Some manuscripts do not have *in his day.*

17:6 See Mt 17:20 and note; Mk 11:23; see also notes on Mt 13:31–32; Mk 4:31.
17:7 *a servant.* A slave, used to illustrate performance of duty (cf. 12:37 and note).
17:11 *border between Samaria and Galilee.* From this point Jesus seems to have journeyed to Perea, where he ministered on his way south to Jerusalem (see notes on 9:51; 13:22).
17:14 *show yourselves to the priests.* Normal procedure after a cure (see Lev 13:2–3; 14:2–32).
17:15 *praising God.* See v. 18; see also 1:64 and note.
17:16 *Samaritan.* See note on 10:31–33. Normally Jews did not associate with Samaritans (see Jn 4:9 and note), but leprosy broke down some social barriers while erecting others (see notes on Lev 13:2,4, 45–46).
17:19 *your faith has made you well.* See Mt 9:22. The phrase may also be rendered "your faith has saved you" (7:50; see note on Mk 5:34). The fact that the Samaritan returned to thank Jesus may indicate that he had received salvation in addition to the physical healing all ten had received (cf. 7:50; 8:48,50 and notes).
17:20 *Pharisees.* See note on 5:17.
17:21 *the kingdom of God is in your midst.* The kingdom is present in the person of King Jesus (see note on 4:43).
17:22 *long to see.* In time of trouble, believers will desire to experience the day when Jesus returns in his glory and delivers his people from their distress.
17:23 *Do not go running off after them.* Do not leave your work in order to pursue predictions of Christ's second advent (see note on 1Th 4:11).
17:24 *like the lightning.* His coming will be sudden, unexpected and public (cf. 12:40 and note).
17:25 *he must suffer.* Jesus repeatedly foretold his coming death (see 5:35; 9:22,43–45 and note on 9:22; 12:50; 13:32–33; 18:32; 24:7; Mt 16:21; Mk 2:20 and note), which had to occur before his glorious return (see 1Pe 1:11 and note).
17:28 *in the days of Lot.* See Ge 18:16—19:28.
17:30 *Son of Man is revealed.* At Jesus' second coming he will be plainly visible to all (see 1Co 1:7; 2Th 1:7 and note; 1Pe 1:7,13; 4:13; Rev 1:7).
17:31 *on the housetop.* It was customary to relax on the flat rooftop. When the final hour comes, however, the individual there should not be thinking of going into the house to retrieve some material objects. Matthew and Mark refer similarly to flight at the fall of Jerusalem, and indirectly to the end time (Mt 24:17–18; Mk 13:15), but here the reference is explicitly to Jesus' return (see v. 30; cf. 21:21).

them. Likewise, no one in the field should go back for anything.[a] 32 Remember Lot's wife![b] 33 Whoever tries to keep their life will lose it, and whoever loses their life will preserve it.[c] 34 I tell you, on that night two people will be in one bed; one will be taken and the other left. 35 Two women will be grinding grain together; one will be taken and the other left."[d] [36][a]

37 "Where, Lord?" they asked.

He replied, "Where there is a dead body, there the vultures will gather."[e]

The Parable of the Persistent Widow

18 Then Jesus told his disciples a parable to show them that they should always pray and not give up.[f] 2 He said: "In a certain town there was a judge who neither feared God nor cared what people thought. 3 And there was a widow in that town who kept coming to him with the plea, 'Grant me justice[g] against my adversary.'

4 "For some time he refused. But finally he said to himself, 'Even though I don't fear God or care what people think, 5 yet because this widow keeps bothering me, I will see that she gets justice, so that she won't eventually come and attack me!' "[h]

6 And the Lord[i] said, "Listen to what the unjust judge says. 7 And will not God bring about justice for his chosen ones, who cry out[j] to him day and night? Will he keep putting them off? 8 I tell you, he will see that they get justice, and quickly. However, when the Son of Man[k] comes,[l] will he find faith on the earth?"

17:31 [a] Mt 24:17,18 **17:32** [b] Ge 19:26 **17:33** [c] S Jn 12:25 **17:35** [d] Mt 24:41 **17:37** [e] Mt 24:28 **18:1** [f] Isa 40:31; Lk 11:5-8; S Ac 1:14; S Ro 1:10; 12:12; Eph 6:18; Col 4:2; 1Th 5:17 **18:3** [g] Isa 1:17 **18:5** [h] Lk 11:8 **18:6** [i] S Lk 7:13 **18:7** [j] Ex 22:23; Ps 88:1; Rev 6:10 **18:8** [k] S Mt 8:20 [l] S Mt 16:27

18:9 [m] Lk 16:15 [n] Isa 65:5 **18:10** [o] Ac 3:1 **18:11** [p] Mt 6:5; Mk 11:25 **18:12** [q] Isa 58:3; Mt 9:14 [r] Mal 3:8; Lk 11:42 **18:13** [s] Isa 66:2; Jer 31:19; Lk 23:48 [t] Lk 5:32; 1Ti 1:15 **18:14** [u] S Mt 23:12 **18:17** [v] Mt 11:25; 18:3

The Parable of the Pharisee and the Tax Collector

9 To some who were confident of their own righteousness[m] and looked down on everyone else,[n] Jesus told this parable: 10 "Two men went up to the temple to pray,[o] one a Pharisee and the other a tax collector. 11 The Pharisee stood by himself[p] and prayed: 'God, I thank you that I am not like other people—robbers, evildoers, adulterers—or even like this tax collector. 12 I fast[q] twice a week and give a tenth[r] of all I get.'

13 "But the tax collector stood at a distance. He would not even look up to heaven, but beat his breast[s] and said, 'God, have mercy on me, a sinner.'[t]

14 "I tell you that this man, rather than the other, went home justified before God. For all those who exalt themselves will be humbled, and those who humble themselves will be exalted."[u]

The Little Children and Jesus

18:15-17pp — Mt 19:13-15; Mk 10:13-16

15 People were also bringing babies to Jesus for him to place his hands on them. When the disciples saw this, they rebuked them. 16 But Jesus called the children to him and said, "Let the little children come to me, and do not hinder them, for the kingdom of God belongs to such as these. 17 Truly I tell you, anyone who will not receive the kingdom of God like a little child[v] will never enter it."

[a] *36* Some manuscripts include here words similar to Matt. 24:40.

17:33 *whoever loses their life will preserve it.* See note on 9:24 (cf. Mt 10:39).

17:35 *taken.* Could refer to being "taken to/from destruction" or "taken into the kingdom." What is clear is that no matter how close two people may be in life, they have no guarantee of the same eternal destiny. One may go to judgment and condemnation, the other to salvation, reward and blessing.

17:37 *Where ... there the vultures will gather.* A proverb. See note on Mt 24:28. In response to the disciples' question, Jesus explains that these things will take place wherever there are people to whom the event pertains.

18:2 *nor cared what people thought.* The judge was unconcerned about the needs of others or about their opinion of him.

18:3 *widow.* Particularly helpless and vulnerable because she had no family to uphold her cause. Only justice and her own persistence were in her favor (cf. 1Ti 5:3 and note).

18:7 *will not God bring about justice ... ?* If an unworthy judge who feels no constraint of right or wrong is compelled by persistence to deal justly with a helpless individual, how much more will God answer prayer! *keep putting them off.* God will not delay his support of the chosen ones when they are right. He is not like the unjust judge, who had to be badgered until he wearied and gave in.

18:8 *will he find faith ... ?* Particularly faith that perseveres in prayer and loyalty (see Mt 24:12-13). Christ makes a second application that looks forward to the time of his second coming. A period of spiritual decline and persecution is assumed—a time that will require perseverance such as the widow demonstrated.

18:10 *to pray.* Periods for prayer were scheduled daily in connection with the morning and evening sacrifices. People could also go to the temple at any time for private prayer. *tax collector.* See note on Mt 5:46.

18:12 *fast twice a week.* Fasting was not commanded in the Mosaic law except for the fast on the annual Day of Atonement (see Mk 2:18 and note). However, the Pharisees also fasted on Mondays and Thursdays (see 5:33 and note; Mt 6:16; 9:14; Ac 27:9 and note). *a tenth of all I get.* As a typical first-century Pharisee, he tithed all that he acquired, not merely what he earned.

18:13 *beat his breast.* Cf. 23:48 and note. *have mercy on me.* The verb used here means "to be appeased/reconciled" (see note on 1Jn 2:2). The tax collector does not plead his good works but the mercy of God in forgiving his sin.

18:14 *justified before God.* God reckoned him to be righteous, i.e., his sins were forgiven and he was credited with righteousness—not his own (v. 9) but that which comes from God (see Ro 1:17 and note). *exalt ... humbled ... humble ... exalted.* See 14:11; Pr 3:34; 1Pe 5:5-6 and notes; see also Da 4:37; Jas 4:6.

18:17 *like a little child.* With humility, total dependence, full trust, frank openness and complete sincerity (see Mt 18:3; 19:14; Mk 10:14-15 and notes; cf. 1Pe 2:2).

The Rich and the Kingdom of God

18:18-30pp — Mt 19:16-29; Mk 10:17-30

18 A certain ruler asked him, "Good
teacher, what must I do to inherit eternal
life?"[w]
19 "Why do you call me good?" Jesus
answered. "No one is good—except God
alone. 20 You know the commandments:
'You shall not commit adultery, you shall
not murder, you shall not steal, you shall
not give false testimony, honor your father
and mother.'[a]"[x]
21 "All these I have kept since I was a
boy," he said.
22 When Jesus heard this, he said to
him, "You still lack one thing. Sell everything you have and give to the poor,[y] and
you will have treasure in heaven.[z] Then
come, follow me."
23 When he heard this, he became very
sad, because he was very wealthy. 24 Jesus
looked at him and said, "How hard it is
for the rich to enter the kingdom of God![a]
25 Indeed, it is easier for a camel to go
through the eye of a needle than for someone who is rich to enter the kingdom of
God."
26 Those who heard this asked, "Who
then can be saved?"
27 Jesus replied, "What is impossible
with man is possible with God."[b]
28 Peter said to him, "We have left all we
had to follow you!"[c]
29 "Truly I tell you," Jesus said to them,
"no one who has left home or wife or
brothers or sisters or parents or children
for the sake of the kingdom of God 30 will
fail to receive many times as much in this
age, and in the age to come[d] eternal life."[e]

Jesus Predicts His Death a Third Time

18:31-33pp — Mt 20:17-19; Mk 10:32-34

31 Jesus took the Twelve aside and told
them, "We are going up to Jerusalem,[f] and
everything that is written by the prophets[g] about the Son of Man[h] will be fulfilled.
32 He will be delivered over to the Gentiles.[i]
They will mock him, insult him and spit
on him; 33 they will flog him[j] and kill him.[k]
On the third day[l] he will rise again."[m]
34 The disciples did not understand
any of this. Its meaning was hidden from
them, and they did not know what he was
talking about.[n]

A Blind Beggar Receives His Sight

18:35-43pp — Mt 20:29-34; Mk 10:46-52

35 As Jesus approached Jericho,[o] a blind
man was sitting by the roadside begging.
36 When he heard the crowd going by, he
asked what was happening. 37 They told
him, "Jesus of Nazareth is passing by."[p]
38 He called out, "Jesus, Son of David,[q]
have mercy[r] on me!"
39 Those who led the way rebuked him
and told him to be quiet, but he shouted
all the more, "Son of David, have mercy
on me!"[s]
40 Jesus stopped and ordered the man to
be brought to him. When he came near,
Jesus asked him, 41 "What do you want me
to do for you?"
"Lord, I want to see," he replied.
42 Jesus said to him, "Receive your sight;
your faith has healed you."[t] 43 Immediately
he received his sight and followed Jesus,
praising God. When all the people saw it,
they also praised God.[u]

Zacchaeus the Tax Collector

19 Jesus entered Jericho[v] and was
passing through. 2 A man was there
by the name of Zacchaeus; he was a chief
tax collector and was wealthy. 3 He wanted
to see who Jesus was, but because he was
short he could not see over the crowd. 4 So
he ran ahead and climbed a sycamore-fig[w]
tree to see him, since Jesus was coming
that way.[x]

18:18 [w] Lk 10:25
18:20 [x] Ex 20:12-16; Dt 5:16-20; Ro 13:9
18:22 [y] S Ac 2:45 [z] S Mt 6:20
18:24 [a] Pr 11:28
18:27 [b] S Mt 19:26
18:28 [c] S Mt 4:19
18:30 [d] S Mt 12:32 [e] S Mt 25:46
18:31 [f] S Lk 9:51 [g] Ps 22; Isa 53 [h] S Mt 8:20
18:32 [i] Lk 23:1
18:33 [j] S Mt 16:21 [k] S Ac 2:23 [l] S Mt 16:21 [m] S Mt 16:21
18:34 [n] S Mk 9:32
18:35 [o] Lk 19:1
18:37 [p] Lk 19:4
18:38 [q] ver 39; S Mt 9:27 [r] Mt 17:15; Lk 18:13
18:39 [s] ver 38
18:42 [t] S Mt 9:22
18:43 [u] S Mt 9:8; Lk 13:17
19:1 [v] Lk 18:35
19:4 [w] 1Ki 10:27; 1Ch 27:28; Isa 9:10 [x] Lk 18:37

[a] 20 Exodus 20:12-16; Deut. 5:16-20

18:18-27 For this event, see notes on Mk 10:17-27.
18:18 *eternal life.* See note on Mt 19:16.
18:20 *You know the commandments.* See Ex 20:1-17; 20:2 and notes.
18:24 *kingdom of God.* See note on Mt 3:2.
18:30 *this age ... the age to come.* The present age of sin and misery and the future age to be inaugurated by the return of the Messiah (see Mk 10:30 and note).
18:31 *everything that is written by the prophets.* Sometimes referred to as the third prediction of Jesus' death, though the total number is more than three (see note on 17:25). The first distinct prediction is in 9:22 (see note there) and the second in 9:44 (see note there). The Messiah's death had been predicted and/or prefigured centuries before (see, e.g., 24:25-27; introduction to Ps 22; see also note on Isa 52:13—53:12; Zec 13:7 and note; Mt 26:24,31,54 and note on Lk 24:44). *Son of Man.* See note on Mk 8:31.
18:35 *approached Jericho.* See note on Mk 10:46. *blind man.* His name was Bartimaeus (Mk 10:46). Matthew reports that two blind men were healed (see note on Mt 20:30). Mark and Luke did not record the presence of the other.
18:38-39 *Son of David.* A Messianic title (see Mt 1:1 and note; 22:41-45; Mk 10:47 and note; 12:35; Jn 7:42; see also 2Sa 7:12-13; Ps 89:3-4; Am 9:11; Mt 12:23 and notes).
18:42 *your faith.* See note on 17:19.
18:43 *praising God ... praised God.* See 1:64 and note.
19:1 *entered Jericho.* See note on Mk 10:46. *passing through.* On his way to Jerusalem (see vv. 11,28).
19:2 *chief tax collector.* A position referred to only here in the Bible, probably designating one in charge of a district, with other tax collectors under him. The region was prosperous at this time, so it is no wonder that Zacchaeus had grown rich. See notes on 3:12; Mt 5:46; Mk 2:14-16.
19:4 *sycamore-fig tree.* A sturdy tree from 30 to 40 feet high,

5 When Jesus reached the spot, he looked up and said to him, "Zacchaeus, come down immediately. I must stay at your house today." 6 So he came down at once and welcomed him gladly.

7 All the people saw this and began to mutter, "He has gone to be the guest of a sinner."[y]

8 But Zacchaeus stood up and said to the Lord,[z] "Look, Lord! Here and now I give half of my possessions to the poor, and if I have cheated anybody out of anything,[a] I will pay back four times the amount."[b]

9 Jesus said to him, "Today salvation has come to this house, because this man, too, is a son of Abraham.[c] 10 For the Son of Man came to seek and to save the lost."[d]

The Parable of the Ten Minas

19:12-27Ref — Mt 25:14-30

11 While they were listening to this, he went on to tell them a parable, because he was near Jerusalem and the people thought that the kingdom of God[e] was going to appear at once.[f] 12 He said: "A man of noble birth went to a distant country to have himself appointed king and then to return. 13 So he called ten of his servants[g] and gave them ten minas.[a] 'Put this money to work,' he said, 'until I come back.'

14 "But his subjects hated him and sent a delegation after him to say, 'We don't want this man to be our king.'

15 "He was made king, however, and returned home. Then he sent for the servants to whom he had given the money, in order to find out what they had gained with it.

16 "The first one came and said, 'Sir, your mina has earned ten more.'

17 " 'Well done, my good servant!'[h] his master replied. 'Because you have been trustworthy in a very small matter, take charge of ten cities.'[i]

18 "The second came and said, 'Sir, your mina has earned five more.'

19 "His master answered, 'You take charge of five cities.'

20 "Then another servant came and said, 'Sir, here is your mina; I have kept it laid away in a piece of cloth. 21 I was afraid of you, because you are a hard man. You take out what you did not put in and reap what you did not sow.'[j]

22 "His master replied, 'I will judge you by your own words,[k] you wicked servant! You knew, did you, that I am a hard man, taking out what I did not put in, and reaping what I did not sow?[l] 23 Why then didn't you put my money on deposit, so that when I came back, I could have collected it with interest?'

24 "Then he said to those standing by, 'Take his mina away from him and give it to the one who has ten minas.'

25 " 'Sir,' they said, 'he already has ten!'

26 "He replied, 'I tell you that to everyone who has, more will be given, but as for the one who has nothing, even what they have will be taken away.[m] 27 But those enemies of mine who did not want me to be king over them — bring them here and kill them in front of me.' "

Jesus Comes to Jerusalem as King

19:29-38pp — Mt 21:1-9; Mk 11:1-10
19:35-38pp — Jn 12:12-15

28 After Jesus had said this, he went on ahead, going up to Jerusalem.[n] 29 As he ap-

19:7 [y] S Mt 9:11
19:8 [z] S Lk 7:13 [a] Lk 3:12, 13 [b] Ex 22:1; Lev 6:4, 5; Nu 5:7; 2Sa 12:6; Eze 33:14, 15
19:9 [c] S Lk 3:8
19:10 [d] Eze 34:12, 16; S Jn 3:17
19:11 [e] S Mt 3:2 [f] Lk 17:20; Ac 1:6
19:13 [g] Mk 13:34
19:17 [h] Pr 27:18 [i] Lk 16:10
19:21 [j] Mt 25:24
19:22 [k] 2Sa 1:16; Job 15:6 [l] Mt 25:26
19:26 [m] S Mt 25:29
19:28 [n] Mk 10:32; S Lk 9:51

[a] *13* A mina was about three months' wages.

with a short trunk and spreading branches, capable of holding a grown man. See note on Am 7:14.

19:5 *I must stay at your house.* Implies a divine necessity.

19:8 *four times.* The full repayment required under the law in case of theft (see Ex 22:1; 2Sa 12:6 and note).

19:9 *son of Abraham.* A true Jew — not only of the lineage of Abraham but one who also walks "in the footsteps" of Abraham's faith (Ro 4:12). Jesus recognized the tax collector as such, though Jewish society excluded him.

19:10 A key verse in Luke's Gospel. *Son of Man.* A Messianic title (see Introduction: Plan; see also note on Mk 8:31). *to seek and to save.* An important summary of Jesus' purpose — to bring salvation, meaning eternal life (18:18), and the kingdom of God (18:25). See note on 15:32.

19:11 *kingdom ... was going to appear.* They expected the Messiah to appear in power and glory and to set up his earthly kingdom, defeating all their political and military enemies.

19:12 *have himself appointed king.* A rather unusual procedure, but the Herods (see chart, pp. 1592 – 1593) did just that when they went to Rome to be appointed rulers over the Jews. Similarly, Jesus was soon to depart and in the future is to return as King. During his absence his servants are entrusted with their master's affairs (for a similar parable, see Mt 25:14 – 30).

19:13 *ten minas.* See NIV text note.

19:14 *sent a delegation.* Such an incident had occurred over 30 years earlier in the case of Archelaus (Josephus, *Wars,* 2.6.1; *Antiquities,* 17.9.3), as well as in a number of other instances. This aspect of the story may have been included to warn the Jews against rejecting Jesus as King.

19:22 *You knew ... that I am a hard man ...?* The master did not admit to the statement of the servant but repeated it in a question. If this was the opinion of the servant, he should have acted accordingly.

19:26 *more will be given ... what they have will be taken away.* See 8:18; 17:33 and notes; Mt 13:12. Those who seek spiritual gain in the gospel, for themselves and others, will become richer, and those who neglect or squander what is given them will become impoverished, losing even what they have.

19:27 *those enemies of mine ... kill them.* Perhaps a reference to Jerusalem's destruction in AD 70. The punishment of those who rebelled and actively opposed the king (see v. 14 and note) was much more severe than that of the negligent servant.

19:28 – 44 Jesus' entry into Jerusalem as King occurred on Sunday of Passion Week (see chart, p. 1638, and map, pp. 1686 – 1687; see also notes on Mt 21:1 – 9; Mk 11:1 – 10; Jn 12:12 – 15).

proached Bethphage and Bethany[o] at the
hill called the Mount of Olives,[p] he sent
two of his disciples, saying to them, 30 "Go
to the village ahead of you, and as you enter it, you will find a colt tied there, which
no one has ever ridden. Untie it and bring
it here. 31 If anyone asks you, 'Why are you
untying it?' say, 'The Lord needs it.' "
32 Those who were sent ahead went and
found it just as he had told them.[q] 33 As they
were untying the colt, its owners asked
them, "Why are you untying the colt?"
34 They replied, "The Lord needs it."
35 They brought it to Jesus, threw their
cloaks on the colt and put Jesus on it. 36 As
he went along, people spread their cloaks[r]
on the road.
37 When he came near the place where
the road goes down the Mount of Olives,[s]
the whole crowd of disciples began joyfully to praise God in loud voices for all the
miracles they had seen:

38 "Blessed is the king who comes in the
name of the Lord!"[a][t]

"Peace in heaven and glory in the
highest!"[u]

39 Some of the Pharisees in the crowd
said to Jesus, "Teacher, rebuke your disciples!"[v]
40 "I tell you," he replied, "if they keep
quiet, the stones will cry out."[w]
41 As he approached Jerusalem and saw
the city, he wept over it[x] 42 and said, "If
you, even you, had only known on this
day what would bring you peace—but
now it is hidden from your eyes. 43 The
days will come upon you when your enemies will build an embankment against
you and encircle you and hem you in on
every side.[y] 44 They will dash you to the
ground, you and the children within your
walls.[z] They will not leave one stone on
another,[a] because you did not recognize
the time of God's coming[b] to you."

19:29 [o] S Mt 21:17 [p] S Mt 21:1 **19:32** [q] Lk 22:13 **19:36** [r] 2Ki 9:13 **19:37** [s] S Mt 21:1 **19:38** [t] Ps 118:26; Lk 13:35 [u] S Lk 2:14 **19:39** [v] Mt 21:15,16 **19:40** [w] Hab 2:11 **19:41** [x] Isa 22:4; Lk 13:34,35 **19:43** [y] Isa 29:3; Jer 6:6; Eze 4:2; 26:8; Lk 21:20 **19:44** [z] Ps 137:9 [a] Lk 21:6 [b] 1Pe 2:12 **19:46** [c] Isa 56:7 [d] Jer 7:11 **19:47** [e] S Mt 26:55 [f] S Mt 12:14; Mk 11:18 **20:1** [g] S Mt 26:55 [h] Lk 8:1

Jesus at the Temple

19:45,46pp — Mt 21:12-16; Mk 11:15-18; Jn 2:13-16

45 When Jesus entered the temple courts,
he began to drive out those who were
selling. 46 "It is written," he said to them,
" 'My house will be a house of prayer'[b];[c]
but you have made it 'a den of robbers.'[c]"[d]
47 Every day he was teaching at the temple.[e] But the chief priests, the teachers of
the law and the leaders among the people
were trying to kill him.[f] 48 Yet they could
not find any way to do it, because all the
people hung on his words.

The Authority of Jesus Questioned

20:1-8pp — Mt 21:23-27; Mk 11:27-33

20 One day as Jesus was teaching the
people in the temple courts[g] and proclaiming the good news,[h] the chief priests

[a] 38 Psalm 118:26 [b] 46 Isaiah 56:7 [c] 46 Jer. 7:11

19:29 *Bethphage.* A village near the road going from Jericho to Jerusalem. *Bethany.* Another village about two miles southeast of Jerusalem (Jn 11:18) and the home of Mary, Martha and Lazarus. *Mount of Olives.* A ridge a little more than a mile long (see note on Mk 11:1). For the Mount of Olives, Bethany and Bethphage in relationship to Jerusalem, see map, pp. 1686–1687. *two of his disciples.* Not named here or in the parallel passages (Mt 21:1; Mk 11:1; cf. Jn 12:14).

19:30 *village.* Probably Bethphage. *colt.* In other accounts a donkey colt (Jn 12:15) is specified and the mother of the colt (Mt 21:7; see note there) with him. Luke uses a Greek word that the Septuagint (the pre-Christian Greek translation of the OT) frequently employed to translate the Hebrew for "donkey." Jesus chooses to enter Jerusalem this time mounted on a donkey to claim publicly that he was the chosen Son of David to sit on David's throne (see note on 1Ki 1:33), the one about whom the prophets had spoken (Zec 9:9; see note there). *which no one has ever ridden.* And thus available for sacred use (see note on Mk 11:2).

19:31 *The Lord.* Either God or, more likely, Jesus himself, here claiming his own unique status as Israel's Lord.

19:37 *praise God.* See 1:64 and note. *all the miracles.* The raising of Lazarus and the healing of blind Bartimaeus were recent examples, but included also would be the works recorded in John on various occasions in Jerusalem, as well as the whole of his ministry in Galilee (cf. Mt 21:14; Jn 12:17).

19:40 Perhaps an echo of Hab 2:11.

19:41 *he wept.* One of only two occasions when Jesus is said to have wept (see also Jn 11:35).

19:42 *peace.* That the Messiah would bring. *hidden.* Cf. 18:34.

19:43 *your enemies will build an embankment.* See 21:20 and note; fulfilled when the Romans took Jerusalem in AD 70, using an embankment to besiege the city. The description is reminiscent of OT predictions of an earlier destruction of Jerusalem (Isa 29:3; 37:33; Eze 4:1–3).

19:44 *the time of God's coming to you.* God came to the Jews in the person of Jesus the Messiah, but they failed to recognize him and rejected him (see Jn 1:10–11; cf. Lk 20:13–16).

19:45 Mark (11:11–17) makes clear that this clearing of the temple occurred the day after Jesus' entry into Jerusalem as King, i.e., on Monday of Passion Week. *temple courts.* The outer court (of the Gentiles), where animals for sacrifice were sold at unfair prices (see note on Mk 11:15). John records a clearing of the temple at the beginning of Jesus' ministry (Jn 2:13–25), but the Synoptics (see Mt 21:12–13; Mk 11:15–17) speak only of a clearing at the close of Jesus' ministry (see notes on Mt 21:12–17; Jn 2:14–17).

19:47 *chief priests.* See 3:2; 22:52; 23:4; 24:20; see also note on Mt 2:4. They were part of the Sanhedrin, the ruling Jewish council (see note on Mk 14:55). *were trying to kill him.* See 20:19–20 (cf. Jn 7:1; 11:53–57).

20:1 The events of 20:1—21:36 all occurred on Tuesday of Passion Week—a long day of controversy. *One day.* Not specified, but Mark's parallel accounts (Mk 11:19–20,27–33) indicate that this day (Tuesday) followed the clearing of the temple (Monday), which followed the "Triumphal" Entry (Sunday). See map, pp. 1686–1687. *chief priests.* See 19:47 and note. *teachers of the law.* See 5:30 and note on 5:17. *elders.* See note on Mt 15:2. Each of these groups was represented in the Jewish council, the Sanhedrin (see 22:66).

and the teachers of the law, together with
the elders, came up to him. 2 "Tell us by
what authority you are doing these things,"
they said. "Who gave you this authority?"[i]
3 He replied, "I will also ask you a question. Tell me: 4 John's baptism[j] — was it
from heaven, or of human origin?"
5 They discussed it among themselves
and said, "If we say, 'From heaven,' he
will ask, 'Why didn't you believe him?'
6 But if we say, 'Of human origin,' all the
people[k] will stone us, because they are
persuaded that John was a prophet."[l]
7 So they answered, "We don't know
where it was from."
8 Jesus said, "Neither will I tell you by
what authority I am doing these things."

The Parable of the Tenants

20:9-19pp — Mt 21:33-46; Mk 12:1-12

9 He went on to tell the people this parable: "A man planted a vineyard,[m] rented
it to some farmers and went away for a
long time.[n] 10 At harvest time he sent a servant to the tenants so they would give him
some of the fruit of the vineyard. But the
tenants beat him and sent him away empty-handed. 11 He sent another servant, but
that one also they beat and treated shamefully and sent away empty-handed. 12 He
sent still a third, and they wounded him
and threw him out.
13 "Then the owner of the vineyard said,
'What shall I do? I will send my son, whom
I love;[o] perhaps they will respect him.'
14 "But when the tenants saw him, they
talked the matter over. 'This is the heir,'
they said. 'Let's kill him, and the inheritance will be ours.' 15 So they threw him
out of the vineyard and killed him.
"What then will the owner of the vineyard do to them? 16 He will come and kill
those tenants[p] and give the vineyard to
others."
When the people heard this, they said,
"God forbid!"
17 Jesus looked directly at them and
asked, "Then what is the meaning of that
which is written:

> " 'The stone the builders rejected
> has become the cornerstone'[a]?[q]

18 Everyone who falls on that stone will be
broken to pieces; anyone on whom it falls
will be crushed."[r]
19 The teachers of the law and the chief
priests looked for a way to arrest him[s] immediately, because they knew he had spoken this parable against them. But they
were afraid of the people.[t]

Paying Taxes to Caesar

20:20-26pp — Mt 22:15-22; Mk 12:13-17

20 Keeping a close watch on him, they
sent spies, who pretended to be sincere.
They hoped to catch Jesus in something he
said,[u] so that they might hand him over to
the power and authority of the governor.[v]
21 So the spies questioned him: "Teacher,
we know that you speak and teach what is
right, and that you do not show partiality
but teach the way of God in accordance
with the truth.[w] 22 Is it right for us to pay
taxes to Caesar or not?"
23 He saw through their duplicity and
said to them, 24 "Show me a denarius.
Whose image and inscription are on it?"
"Caesar's," they replied.

20:2 [i] Jn 2:18; Ac 4:7; 7:27 **20:4** [j] S Mk 1:4 **20:6** [k] Lk 7:29 [l] S Mt 11:9 **20:9** [m] Isa 5:1-7 [n] Mt 25:14 **20:13** [o] S Mt 3:17 **20:16** [p] Lk 19:27 **20:17** [q] Ps 118:22; S Ac 4:11 **20:18** [r] Isa 8:14, 15 **20:19** [s] Lk 19:47 [t] S Mk 11:18 **20:20** [u] S Mt 12:10 [v] Mt 27:2 **20:21** [w] Jn 3:2

[a] *17* Psalm 118:22

20:2 *Who gave you this authority?* They had asked this of John the Baptist (Jn 1:19 – 25) and of Jesus early in his ministry (Jn 2:18 – 22). Here the reference is to the clearing of the temple, which not only defied the authority of the Jewish leaders but also hurt their monetary profits. The leaders may also have been looking for a way to discredit Jesus in the eyes of the people or raise suspicion of him as a threat to the authority of Rome.
20:4 *John's baptism ... from heaven, or of human origin?* By replying with a question, Jesus put the burden on his opponents — indicating only two alternatives: The work of John was either divinely inspired or humanly devised. By refusing to answer, they placed themselves in an awkward position. *from heaven.* See note on Mk 11:30.
20:10 *he sent a servant.* This parable (v. 9) is reminiscent of Isa 5:1 – 7 (see note on Isa 5:1). The servants who were sent to the tenants represent the prophets God sent in former times who were rejected (see Ne 9:26; Jer 7:25 and note; 25:4 – 7; Mt 23:34; Ac 7:52; Heb 11:36 – 38). *give him some of the fruit.* In accordance with a kind of sharecropping agreement, a fixed amount was due the landowner. At the proper time he would expect to receive his share.
20:13 *my son, whom I love.* The specific reference to the beloved son makes clearer the intended application of the son in the parable to the Son, Jesus Christ (see 3:22; Mt 17:5 and notes).
20:14 *Let's kill him.* Cf. 19:14. *inheritance will be ours.* See note on Mk 12:7.
20:16 *give the vineyard to others.* See note on Mt 21:41.
20:17 *cornerstone.* See Ac 4:11; Ro 9:33; 1Pe 2:7; see also note on Ps 118:22.
20:18 *will be broken to pieces.* As a pot dashed against a stone is broken, and as one lying beneath a falling stone is crushed, so those who reject Jesus the Messiah will be doomed (see Isa 8:14 and note; cf. Da 2:34 – 35,44; Lk 2:34).
20:19 *teachers of the law.* See note on Mt 2:4. For their opposition to Jesus, see 5:17,30 and note on 5:17; 9:22; 19:47; 22:2; 23:10.
20:20 *authority of the governor.* Fearing to take action themselves, the Jewish religious leaders hoped to draw from Jesus some statement that would bring action from the Roman officials and remove him from his contact with the people.
20:22 *pay taxes to Caesar.* See note on Mk 12:14. To agree to the taxes demanded by Caesar would disappoint the people, but to advise no payment would disturb the Roman officials. The questioners hoped to trap Jesus with this dilemma (see note on Mt 22:15 – 17).

25 He said to them, "Then give back to
Caesar what is Caesar's,[x] and to God what
is God's."
26 They were unable to trap him in what
he had said there in public. And astonished by his answer, they became silent.

The Resurrection and Marriage

20:27-40pp — Mt 22:23-33; Mk 12:18-27

27 Some of the Sadducees,[y] who say
there is no resurrection,[z] came to Jesus
with a question. 28 "Teacher," they said,
"Moses wrote for us that if a man's brother dies and leaves a wife but no children,
the man must marry the widow and raise
up offspring for his brother.[a] 29 Now there
were seven brothers. The first one married
a woman and died childless. 30 The second
31 and then the third married her, and in
the same way the seven died, leaving no
children. 32 Finally, the woman died too.
33 Now then, at the resurrection whose
wife will she be, since the seven were married to her?"
34 Jesus replied, "The people of this age
marry and are given in marriage. 35 But
those who are considered worthy of taking part in the age to come[b] and in the resurrection from the dead will neither marry
nor be given in marriage, 36 and they can
no longer die; for they are like the angels.
They are God's children,[c] since they are
children of the resurrection. 37 But in the
account of the burning bush, even Moses
showed that the dead rise, for he calls the
Lord 'the God of Abraham, and the God of
Isaac, and the God of Jacob.'[ad] 38 He is not
the God of the dead, but of the living, for
to him all are alive."

20:25 [x] Lk 23:2; Ro 13:7 **20:27** [y] S Ac 4:1 [z] Ac 23:8; 1Co 15:12 **20:28** [a] Dt 25:5 **20:35** [b] S Mt 12:32 **20:36** [c] S Jn 1:12 **20:37** [d] Ex 3:6

20:40 [e] Mt 22:46; Mk 12:34 **20:41** [f] S Mt 1:1 **20:43** [g] Ps 110:1; S Mt 22:44 **20:46** [h] S Lk 11:43 **21:1** [i] Mt 27:6; Jn 8:20

39 Some of the teachers of the law responded, "Well said, teacher!" 40 And no
one dared to ask him any more questions.[e]

Whose Son Is the Messiah?

20:41-47pp — Mt 22:41-23:7; Mk 12:35-40

41 Then Jesus said to them, "Why is it
said that the Messiah is the son of David?[f]
42 David himself declares in the Book of
Psalms:

"'The Lord said to my Lord:
"Sit at my right hand
43 until I make your enemies
a footstool for your feet."'[bg]

44 David calls him 'Lord.' How then can he
be his son?"

Warning Against the Teachers of the Law

45 While all the people were listening,
Jesus said to his disciples, 46 "Beware of
the teachers of the law. They like to walk
around in flowing robes and love to be
greeted with respect in the marketplaces and have the most important seats in
the synagogues and the places of hon-
or at banquets.[h] 47 They devour widows'
houses and for a show make lengthy
prayers. These men will be punished most
severely."

The Widow's Offering

21:1-4pp — Mk 12:41-44

21 As Jesus looked up, he saw the rich
putting their gifts into the temple
treasury.[i] 2 He also saw a poor widow put

[a] *37* Exodus 3:6 [b] *43* Psalm 110:1

20:24 *denarius.* A Roman coin worth about a day's wages (see note on Mt 22:19).
20:25 *to God what is God's.* See notes on Mt 22:21; Mk 12:17.
20:27 *Sadducees.* An aristocratic, politically minded group. They controlled the high priesthood at this time and held the majority of the seats in the Sanhedrin. They did not believe in the resurrection or an afterlife, and they rejected the oral tradition taught by the Pharisees (Josephus, *Antiquities,* 13.10.6). See notes on Ezr 7:2; Mt 2:4; 3:7; 22:23; Mk 12:18; Ac 4:1; see also essay, p. 1576, and chart, p. 1631.
20:28 *the man must marry the widow.* The levirate law (see note on Mt 22:24; cf. Ge 38:8 and note).
20:34–35 *this age ... the age to come.* See note on 18:30.
20:36 *like the angels.* The resurrection order cannot be assumed to follow present earthly lines. In the new age there will be no marriage, no procreation and no death (see note on Mk 12:25). *children of the resurrection.* Those who are to take part in the resurrection of the righteous (cf. Mk 12:18; Ac 4:1; 23:6 and notes).
20:37 *account of the burning bush.* Since Scripture chapters and verses were not used at the time of Christ, the passage was identified in this way, referring to Moses' experience with the burning bush (see Ex 3:2–6 and notes).
20:39 *Well said, teacher!* Even though there was great animosity against Jesus, the teachers of the law (who were Pharisees) sided with Jesus against the Sadducees on the matter of resurrection.
20:44 *David calls him 'Lord.'* Jesus' argument with the Jewish religious leaders is that since the Messiah is a descendant of David, how can this honored king refer to his offspring as Lord? Unless Jesus' opponents were ready to admit that the Messiah was also the divine Son of God, they could not answer his question. See notes on Ps 110:1; Mt 22:44; Mk 12:36.
20:46 *flowing robes ... important seats.* See notes on Mk 12:38–39.
20:47 *devour widows' houses.* They take advantage of this defenseless group by fraud and schemes for selfish gain. *punished most severely.* Cf. 12:46–48 and note. The higher the esteem received from others, the more severe the demands of true justice, and the more hypocrisy (Mt 23:1–36), the greater the condemnation.
21:1 *temple treasury.* In the court of women, east of Herod's temple, there were 13 boxes shaped like trumpets and positioned to receive the donations of the worshipers (see note on Mk 12:41).
21:2 *poor widow.* See 20:47 and note. *very small copper coins.* See note on Mk 12:42.

in two very small copper coins. 3 "Truly I tell you," he said, "this poor widow has put in more than all the others. 4 All these people gave their gifts out of their wealth; but she out of her poverty put in all she had to live on."[j]

The Destruction of the Temple and Signs of the End Times

21:5-36pp — Mt 24; Mk 13
21:12-17pp — Mt 10:17-22

5 Some of his disciples were remarking about how the temple was adorned with beautiful stones and with gifts dedicated to God. But Jesus said, 6 "As for what you see here, the time will come when not one stone will be left on another;[k] every one of them will be thrown down."

7 "Teacher," they asked, "when will these things happen? And what will be the sign that they are about to take place?"

8 He replied: "Watch out that you are not deceived. For many will come in my name, claiming, 'I am he,' and, 'The time is near.' Do not follow them.[l] 9 When you hear of wars and uprisings, do not be frightened. These things must happen first, but the end will not come right away."

10 Then he said to them: "Nation will rise against nation, and kingdom against kingdom.[m] 11 There will be great earthquakes, famines and pestilences in various places, and fearful events and great signs from heaven.[n]

12 "But before all this, they will seize you and persecute you. They will hand you over to synagogues and put you in prison, and you will be brought before kings and governors, and all on account of my name. 13 And so you will bear testimony to me.[o] 14 But make up your mind not to worry beforehand how you will defend yourselves.[p] 15 For I will give you[q] words and wisdom that none of your adversaries will be able to resist or contradict. 16 You will be betrayed even by parents, brothers and sisters, relatives and friends,[r] and they will put some of you to death. 17 Everyone will hate you because of me.[s] 18 But not a hair of your head will perish.[t] 19 Stand firm, and you will win life.[u]

20 "When you see Jerusalem being surrounded by armies,[v] you will know that its desolation is near. 21 Then let those who are in Judea flee to the mountains, let those in the city get out, and let those in the country not enter the city.[w] 22 For this is the time of punishment[x] in fulfillment[y] of all that has been written. 23 How dreadful it will be in those days for pregnant women and nursing mothers! There will be great distress in the land and wrath against this people. 24 They will fall by the sword and will be taken as prisoners to all the nations. Jerusalem will be trampled[z] on by the Gentiles until the times of the Gentiles are fulfilled.

25 "There will be signs in the sun, moon and stars. On the earth, nations will be in anguish and perplexity at the roaring and tossing of the sea.[a] 26 People will faint from terror, apprehensive of what is coming on

21:4 [j] 2Co 8:12
21:6 [k] Lk 19:44
21:8 [l] Lk 17:23
21:10 [m] 2Ch 15:6; Isa 19:2
21:11 [n] Isa 29:6; Joel 2:30
21:13 [o] Php 1:12
21:14 [p] Lk 12:11
21:15 [q] S Lk 12:12
21:16 [r] Lk 12:52,53
21:17 [s] S Jn 15:21
21:18 [t] S Mt 10:30
21:19 [u] S Mt 10:22
21:20 [v] S Lk 19:43
21:21 [w] Lk 17:31
21:22 [x] Isa 63:4; Da 9:24-27; Hos 9:7 [y] S Mt 1:22
21:24 [z] Isa 5:5; 63:18; Da 8:13; Rev 11:2
21:25 [a] 2Pe 3:10,12

21:3-4 See note on 2Co 8:12.
21:3 *Truly I tell you.* See note on Mk 3:28.
21:4 See Mk 12:44 and note on 12:42.
21:5-36 See note on Mk 13:1-37.
21:5 *how the temple was adorned.* "Whatever was not overlaid with gold was purest white" (Josephus, *Wars,* 5.5.6). Herod gave a golden vine for one of its decorations. Its grape clusters were as tall as a man.
21:6 *not one stone ... left.* Fulfilled in AD 70 when the Romans took Jerusalem and burned the temple (Mt 24:2; see note there).
21:7 *when ... ?* Mark reports that this question was asked by four disciples: Peter, James, John and Andrew (Mk 13:3). Matthew gives the question in a fuller form, including an inquiry for the sign of Jesus' coming and the end of the age (Mt 24:3; see note there). *what will be the sign ... ?* What would be the indication that these things are about to happen?
21:8 *I am he.* I am Jesus, the Messiah (having come a second time). *The time.* The end time.
21:9 *the end will not come right away.* Refers to the end of the age (see Mt 24:3,6). All the events listed in vv. 8-18 are characteristic of the entire present age, not just signs of the end of the age.
21:11 *signs from heaven.* See v. 25. For prophetic descriptions of celestial signs accompanying the day of the Lord, see note on Mk 13:24-25.
21:12 *hand you over to synagogues.* Synagogues were used not only for worship and school but also for community administration and for confinement of accused persons while awaiting trial (see note on Mk 13:9; cf. Mt 23:34).
21:15 *none ... will be able to resist.* See Ac 6:9-10.
21:18 Although persecution and death may come, God is in control, and the ultimate outcome will be eternal victory. *not a hair of your head will perish.* In view of v. 16, this cannot refer to physical safety. The figure indicates that there will be no real — i.e., spiritual and eternal — loss.
21:19 See note on Mk 13:13.
21:20 *surrounded by armies.* See 19:43 and note. The sign that the end was near (cf. v. 7 and note) would be the surrounding of Jerusalem with armies. Associated with this event would be the "abomination that causes desolation" (Mt 24:15; see note there).
21:21 *flee to the mountains.* When an army surrounds a city, it is natural to seek protection inside the walls, but Jesus directs his followers to seek the safety of the mountains because the city was doomed to destruction (see note on Mt 24:16).
21:22 *time of punishment.* God's retributive justice as the consequence of faithlessness (cf. Isa 63:4; Jer 5:29; Hos 9:7).
21:24 *times of the Gentiles.* The Gentiles would have both spiritual opportunities (see Mt 24:14 and note; Mk 13:10; cf. Lk 20:16; Ro 11:25 and note) and domination of Jerusalem, but these times will end when God's purpose for the Gentiles has been fulfilled.
21:27 See Mt 24:30 and note.

the world, for the heavenly bodies will be
shaken.[b] 27At that time they will see the
Son of Man[c] coming in a cloud[d] with power and great glory. 28When these things
begin to take place, stand up and lift up
your heads, because your redemption is
drawing near."[e]
29He told them this parable: "Look at
the fig tree and all the trees. 30When they
sprout leaves, you can see for yourselves
and know that summer is near. 31Even
so, when you see these things happening, you know that the kingdom of God[f]
is near.
32"Truly I tell you, this generation[g] will
certainly not pass away until all these
things have happened. 33Heaven and earth
will pass away, but my words will never
pass away.[h]
34"Be careful, or your hearts will be
weighed down with carousing, drunkenness and the anxieties of life,[i] and that
day will close on you suddenly[j] like a trap.
35For it will come on all those who live on
the face of the whole earth. 36Be always
on the watch, and pray[k] that you may be
able to escape all that is about to happen,
and that you may be able to stand before
the Son of Man."
37Each day Jesus was teaching at the
temple,[l] and each evening he went out[m]
to spend the night on the hill called the
Mount of Olives,[n] 38and all the people
came early in the morning to hear him at
the temple.[o]

21:26 [b]S Mt 24:29 **21:27** [c]S Mt 8:20 [d]S Rev 1:7 **21:28** [e]Lk 18:7 **21:31** [f]S Mt 3:2 **21:32** [g]Lk 11:50; 17:25 **21:33** [h]S Mt 5:18 **21:34** [i]Mk 4:19 [j]Lk 12:40,46; 1Th 5:2-7 **21:36** [k]Mt 26:41 **21:37** [l]S Mt 26:55 [m]Mk 11:19 [n]S Mt 21:1 **21:38** [o]Jn 8:2

22:1 [p]S Jn 11:55 **22:2** [q]S Mt 12:14 **22:3** [r]S Mt 4:10 [s]S Mt 10:4 **22:4** [t]ver 52; Ac 4:1; 5:24 **22:5** [u]Zec 11:12 **22:7** [v]Ex 12:18-20; Dt 16:5-8; S Mk 14:12 **22:8** [w]Ac 3:1, 11; 4:13, 19; 8:14

Judas Agrees to Betray Jesus

22:1,2pp — Mt 26:2-5; Mk 14:1,2,10,11

22 Now the Festival of Unleavened
Bread, called the Passover, was approaching,[p] 2and the chief priests and the
teachers of the law were looking for some
way to get rid of Jesus,[q] for they were
afraid of the people. 3Then Satan[r] entered
Judas, called Iscariot,[s] one of the Twelve.
4And Judas went to the chief priests and
the officers of the temple guard[t] and discussed with them how he might betray
Jesus. 5They were delighted and agreed
to give him money.[u] 6He consented, and
watched for an opportunity to hand Jesus
over to them when no crowd was present.

The Last Supper

22:7-13pp — Mt 26:17-19; Mk 14:12-16
22:17-20pp — Mt 26:26-29; Mk 14:22-25; 1Co 11:23-25
22:21-23pp — Mt 26:21-24; Mk 14:18-21; Jn 13:21-30
22:25-27pp — Mt 20:25-28; Mk 10:42-45
22:33,34pp — Mt 26:33-35; Mk 14:29-31; Jn 13:37,38

7Then came the day of Unleavened
Bread on which the Passover lamb had to
be sacrificed.[v] 8Jesus sent Peter and John,[w]
saying, "Go and make preparations for us
to eat the Passover."
9"Where do you want us to prepare for
it?" they asked.
10He replied, "As you enter the city, a
man carrying a jar of water will meet you.
Follow him to the house that he enters,
11and say to the owner of the house, 'The

21:28 *lift up your heads.* Do not be downcast at the appearance of these signs, but look up in joy, hope and trust (cf. Ps 24:7). *redemption.* Final, completed redemption (see Ro 8:23; Heb 9:28 and notes).

21:29 *Look at the fig tree.* The coming of spring is announced by the greening of the trees (cf. Mt 24:32–35; Mk 11:13 and note; 13:28–31). In a similar way, one can anticipate the coming of the kingdom when its signs are seen. But "kingdom" is used in different ways (see note on 4:43). The reference in v. 31 is to the future kingdom.

21:32 *this generation.* If reference here is to the destruction of Jerusalem that occurred about 40 years after Jesus spoke these words, "generation" is used in its ordinary sense of a normal life span. "All these things" would then have been fulfilled in the AD 70 destruction of Jerusalem. On the other hand, if reference here is to the second coming of Christ, "generation" might refer to a future generation alive at the beginning of "these things." It does not mean that Jesus had a mistaken notion that he was going to return immediately.

21:34 *that day.* When Christ returns and the future aspect of God's kingdom is inaugurated (cf. v. 31). *close on you suddenly.* Does not mean that Christ's second coming will be completely unannounced, since there will be introductory signs (vv. 28,31; cf. 1Th 5:1–3).

21:35 *whole earth.* The second coming of Christ will involve the whole of humankind, whereas the fall of Jerusalem did not.

21:36 *that you may be able to stand before the Son of Man.* Cf. 1Jn 2:28.

21:37 *Each day.* Each day during the final week of his life, from his "Triumphal" Entry to the time of the Passover (Sunday-Thursday). *Mount of Olives.* At Bethany (see notes on 19:29; Mt 21:17).

22:1 *Festival of Unleavened Bread ... Passover.* "Passover" was used in two different ways: (1) a specific meal begun at twilight on the 14th of Nisan (Lev 23:4–5) and (2) the week following the Passover meal (Eze 45:21), otherwise known as the Festival of Unleavened Bread, a week in which no leaven was allowed (see Ex 12:15 and note; 13:3–7; see also notes on Mk 14:1; Jn 2:13). By NT times the two names for the week-long festival were virtually interchangeable.

22:2 *the chief priests and the teachers of the law.* See 20:1 and note.

22:3 *Satan entered Judas.* In the Gospels this expression is used on two separate occasions: (1) before Judas went to the chief priests and offered to betray Jesus (here) and (2) during the Last Supper (Jn 13:27; see note there). Thus the Gospel writers depict Satan's control over Judas, who had never displayed strong commitment to Jesus (see Jn 13:2; see also notes on Jn 17:12; 1Co 15:2). *called Iscariot.* See Jn 6:71 and note.

22:4 *officers of the temple guard.* Jews, selected mostly from the Levites.

22:7 *Passover lamb had to be sacrificed.* On the 14th of Nisan between 2:30 and 5:30 p.m. in the court of the priests—Thursday of Passion Week.

22:10 *man carrying a jar.* It would have been unusual to see a man carrying a jar of water, since this was normally women's work.

Teacher asks: Where is the guest room, where I may eat the Passover with my disciples?' 12 He will show you a large room upstairs, all furnished. Make preparations there."

13 They left and found things just as Jesus had told them.[x] So they prepared the Passover.

14 When the hour came, Jesus and his apostles[y] reclined at the table.[z] 15 And he said to them, "I have eagerly desired to eat this Passover with you before I suffer.[a] 16 For I tell you, I will not eat it again until it finds fulfillment in the kingdom of God."[b]

17 After taking the cup, he gave thanks and said, "Take this and divide it among you. 18 For I tell you I will not drink again from the fruit of the vine until the kingdom of God comes."

19 And he took bread, gave thanks and broke it,[c] and gave it to them, saying, "This is my body given for you; do this in remembrance of me."

20 In the same way, after the supper he took the cup, saying, "This cup is the new covenant[d] in my blood, which is poured out for you.[a] 21 But the hand of him who is going to betray me is with mine on the table.[e] 22 The Son of Man[f] will go as it has been decreed.[g] But woe to that man who betrays him!" 23 They began to question among themselves which of them it might be who would do this.

24 A dispute also arose among them as to which of them was considered to be greatest.[h] 25 Jesus said to them, "The kings of the Gentiles lord it over them; and those who exercise authority over them call themselves Benefactors. 26 But you are not to be like that. Instead, the greatest among you should be like the youngest,[i] and the one who rules like the one who serves.[j] 27 For who is greater, the one who is at the table or the one who serves? Is it not the one who is at the table? But I am among you as one who serves.[k] 28 You are those who have stood by me in my trials. 29 And I confer on you a kingdom,[l] just as my Father conferred one on me, 30 so that you may eat and drink at my table in my kingdom[m] and sit on thrones, judging the twelve tribes of Israel.[n]

31 "Simon, Simon, Satan has asked[o] to sift all of you as wheat.[p] 32 But I have prayed for you,[q] Simon, that your faith may not fail. And when you have turned back, strengthen your brothers."[r]

22:13 [x] Lk 19:32
22:14 [y] S Mk 6:30 [z] Mt 26:20; Mk 14:17,18
22:15 [a] S Mt 16:21
22:16 [b] S Lk 14:15
22:19 [c] S Mt 14:19
22:20 [d] Ex 24:8; Isa 42:6; Jer 31:31-34; Zec 9:11; 2Co 3:6; Heb 8:6; 9:15
22:21 [e] Ps 41:9
22:22 [f] S Mt 8:20 [g] Ac 2:23; 4:28
22:24 [h] Mk 9:34; Lk 9:46
22:26 [i] 1Pe 5:5 [j] S Mk 9:35
22:27 [k] S Mt 20:28
22:29 [l] S Mt 25:34; 2Ti 2:12
22:30 [m] S Lk 14:15 [n] S Mt 19:28
22:31 [o] Job 1:6-12 [p] Am 9:9
22:32 [q] Jn 17:9, 15; S Ro 8:34 [r] Jn 21:15-17

[a] 19,20 Some manuscripts do not have *given for you . . . poured out for you.*

22:11 *The Teacher asks.* This form of address may have been chosen because the owner was a follower already known to Jesus.

22:13 *as Jesus had told them.* It may be that Jesus had made previous arrangements with the man in order to make sure that the Passover meal would not be interrupted. Since Jesus did not identify ahead of time just where he would observe Passover, Judas was unable to inform the enemy, who might have interrupted this important occasion.

22:14–30 It appears that Luke does not attempt to be strictly chronological in his account of the Last Supper. He records the most important part of the occasion first—the sharing of the bread and the cup. Then he tells of Jesus' comments about his betrayer and about the argument over who would be greatest, though both of these subjects seem to have been introduced earlier. John's Gospel (13:26–30), e.g., indicates that Judas had already left the room before the bread and cup of the Lord's Supper were shared, but Luke does not tell when he left.

22:14 *reclined at the table.* See note on Mk 14:18.

22:16 *until it finds fulfillment.* Jesus yearned to keep this Passover with his disciples because it was the last occasion before he himself was to be slain as the perfect "Passover lamb" (1Co 5:7; see note there) and thus fulfill this sacrifice for all time. Jesus would eat no more Passover meals until the coming of the future kingdom. After this he will renew fellowship with those who through the ages have commemorated the Lord's Supper. Finally, the fellowship will be consummated in the great Messianic "wedding supper" to come (Rev 19:9).

22:17 *After taking the cup.* Either the first of the four cups shared during regular observance of the Passover meal or the third cup.

22:18 *until the kingdom of God comes.* See notes on v. 16; 4:43.

22:19 *is.* Represents or signifies. *given for you.* Anticipating his substitutionary sacrifice on the cross. *in remembrance of me.* Just as the Passover was a constant reminder and proclamation of God's redemption of Israel from bondage in Egypt, so the keeping of Christ's command would be a remembering and proclaiming of the deliverance of believers from the bondage of sin through Christ's atoning work on the cross.

22:20 *after the supper.* Mentioned only here and in 1Co 11:25; see note on 1Co 11:23–26. *took the cup.* See note on Mk 14:24. *new covenant.* Promised through the prophet Jeremiah (see 31:31–34 and notes)—the fuller administration of God's saving grace, founded on and sealed by the death of Jesus ("in my blood"). See note on 1Co 11:25.

22:22 *as it has been decreed.* See Mt 26:24; Mk 14:21 and notes.

22:25 *Benefactors.* A title assumed by or conferred on rulers in Egypt, Syria and Rome as a display of honor, but frequently not representing actual service rendered.

22:26 *like the one who serves.* Jesus urges and exemplifies servant leadership—a trait that was as uncommon then as it is now (see Mk 10:45; Php 2:5,7 and notes).

22:27 *I am among you as one who serves.* See Jn 13:5 and note.

22:28 *in my trials.* Including temptations (cf. 4:13), hardships (9:58) and rejection (Jn 1:11).

22:29 *confer on you a kingdom.* The following context (v. 30) indicates that this kingdom is the future form of the kingdom (see notes on 4:43; Mt 3:2).

22:30 *sit on thrones.* As they shared in Jesus' trials, so they will share in his rule (see 2Ti 2:12 and note). *judging.* Leading or ruling (see NIV text note on Jdg 2:16). *twelve tribes of Israel.* See Mt 19:28.

22:31 *sift all of you.* Satan wanted to test the disciples, hoping to bring them to spiritual ruin.

33 But he replied, "Lord, I am ready to go
with you to prison and to death."[s]
34 Jesus answered, "I tell you, Peter, before the rooster crows today, you will deny
three times that you know me."
35 Then Jesus asked them, "When I sent
you without purse, bag or sandals,[t] did
you lack anything?"
"Nothing," they answered.
36 He said to them, "But now if you have
a purse, take it, and also a bag; and if you
don't have a sword, sell your cloak and
buy one. 37 It is written: 'And he was numbered with the transgressors'[a];[u] and I tell
you that this must be fulfilled in me. Yes,
what is written about me is reaching its
fulfillment."
38 The disciples said, "See, Lord, here
are two swords."
"That's enough!" he replied.

Jesus Prays on the Mount of Olives

22:40-46pp — Mt 26:36-46; Mk 14:32-42

39 Jesus went out as usual[v] to the Mount
of Olives,[w] and his disciples followed him.
40 On reaching the place, he said to them,
"Pray that you will not fall into temptation."[x] 41 He withdrew about a stone's
throw beyond them, knelt down[y] and
prayed, 42 "Father, if you are willing, take
this cup[z] from me; yet not my will, but
yours be done."[a] 43 An angel from heaven
appeared to him and strengthened him.[b]
44 And being in anguish, he prayed more
earnestly, and his sweat was like drops of
blood falling to the ground.[b]
45 When he rose from prayer and went
back to the disciples, he found them
asleep, exhausted from sorrow. 46 "Why
are you sleeping?" he asked them. "Get
up and pray so that you will not fall into
temptation."[c]

Jesus Arrested

22:47-53pp — Mt 26:47-56; Mk 14:43-50; Jn 18:3-11

47 While he was still speaking a crowd
came up, and the man who was called Judas, one of the Twelve, was leading them.
He approached Jesus to kiss him, 48 but
Jesus asked him, "Judas, are you betraying the Son of Man with a kiss?"
49 When Jesus' followers saw what was
going to happen, they said, "Lord, should
we strike with our swords?"[d] 50 And one of
them struck the servant of the high priest,
cutting off his right ear.
51 But Jesus answered, "No more of
this!" And he touched the man's ear and
healed him.
52 Then Jesus said to the chief priests,
the officers of the temple guard,[e] and the
elders, who had come for him, "Am I leading a rebellion, that you have come with
swords and clubs? 53 Every day I was with
you in the temple courts,[f] and you did not
lay a hand on me. But this is your hour[g] —
when darkness reigns."[h]

Peter Disowns Jesus

22:55-62pp — Mt 26:69-75; Mk 14:66-72; Jn 18:16-18,25-27

54 Then seizing him, they led him away
and took him into the house of the high
priest.[i] Peter followed at a distance.[j] 55 And

22:33 [s] Jn 11:16 **22:35** [t] Mt 10:9, 10; Lk 9:3; 10:4 **22:37** [u] Isa 53:12 **22:39** [v] Lk 21:37 [w] S Mt 21:1 **22:40** [x] Mt 6:13 **22:41** [y] Lk 18:11 **22:42** [z] S Mt 20:22 [a] S Mt 26:39 **22:43** [b] Mt 4:11; Mk 1:13

22:46 [c] ver 40 **22:49** [d] ver 38 **22:52** [e] ver 4 **22:53** [f] S Mt 26:55 [g] Jn 12:27 [h] Mt 8:12; Jn 1:5; 3:20 **22:54** [i] Mt 26:57; Mk 14:53 [j] Mt 26:58; Mk 14:54; Jn 18:15

a 37 Isaiah 53:12 *b 43,44* Many early manuscripts do not have verses 43 and 44.

22:34 See Mt 26:34; Jn 13:38 and notes.
22:36 *a purse ... a bag.* Cf. previous instructions (9:3; 10:4). Until now they had been dependent on generous hospitality, but future opposition would require them to be prepared to pay their own way. *buy one.* An extreme figure of speech (hyperbole) used to warn them of the perilous times about to come. They would need defense and protection, as Paul did when he appealed to Caesar (Ac 25:11; see note there) as the one who "bears the sword" (Ro 13:4).
22:37 *numbered with the transgressors.* Jesus was soon to be arrested as a criminal, in fulfillment of prophetic Scripture (see NIV text note; see also 24:44 and note), and his disciples would also be in danger for being his followers.
22:38 *"... two swords." "That's enough!"* Sensing that the disciples had taken him too literally, Jesus ironically closes the discussion with a curt "That's enough!" Not long after this, Peter was rebuked for using a sword (v. 50).
22:39 *Mount of Olives.* See 19:29 and note. Matthew specifies Gethsemane (Mt 26:36; see note there) and John, a garden (Jn 18:1). The place apparently was located on the lower slopes of the Mount of Olives.
22:40 *temptation.* Here refers to severe trial of the kind referred to in vv. 28 – 38, which might lead to a faltering of their faith.
22:42 *this cup.* The cup of suffering (see Mt 20:22; Mk 14:36 and notes; cf. Isa 51:17; Eze 23:31 and notes).
22:43 *angel.* Matthew and Mark tell of angels ministering to Jesus at the close of his fasting and temptations (Mt 4:11; Mk 1:13).
22:44 *drops of blood.* Probably perspiration in large drops like blood, or possibly the actual mingling of blood and sweat as in cases of extreme anguish, strain or sensitivity. Only Luke, the doctor, records this.
22:47 *crowd came up.* They were sent by the chief priests, elders (Mt 26:47) and teachers of the law (Mk 14:43; see note there), and they carried swords and clubs. Included was a detachment of soldiers with officials of the Jews (v. 52; Jn 18:3). *to kiss him.* This signal had been prearranged to identify Jesus to the authorities (Mt 26:48). It was unnecessary because Jesus identified himself (Jn 18:5), but Judas acted out his plan anyway.
22:50 *servant of the high priest.* Malchus by name; Simon Peter struck the blow (see Jn 18:10 and note).
22:51 *healed him.* Found only in Luke. Jesus rectified the wrong done by his follower. No faith on the part of Malchus was involved, but to allow such action would have been contrary to Jesus' own teaching.
22:52 See note on Mt 26:55.
22:53 *your hour.* The time appointed for Jesus' enemies to apprehend him, the time when the forces of darkness (the powers of evil) would do their worst to defeat God's plan.
22:54 *house of the high priest.* See notes on 3:2; Mk 14:53.

when some there had kindled a fire in the
middle of the courtyard and had sat down
together, Peter sat down with them. 56 A
servant girl saw him seated there in the
firelight. She looked closely at him and
said, "This man was with him."
57 But he denied it. "Woman, I don't
know him," he said.
58 A little later someone else saw him
and said, "You also are one of them."
"Man, I am not!" Peter replied.
59 About an hour later another asserted,
"Certainly this fellow was with him, for he
is a Galilean."[k]
60 Peter replied, "Man, I don't know
what you're talking about!" Just as he was
speaking, the rooster crowed. 61 The Lord[l]
turned and looked straight at Peter. Then
Peter remembered the word the Lord had
spoken to him: "Before the rooster crows
today, you will disown me three times."[m]
62 And he went outside and wept bitterly.

The Guards Mock Jesus

22:63-65pp — Mt 26:67,68; Mk 14:65; Jn 18:22,23

63 The men who were guarding Jesus
began mocking and beating him. 64 They
blindfolded him and demanded, "Prophesy! Who hit you?" 65 And they said many
other insulting things to him.[n]

Jesus Before Pilate and Herod

22:67-71pp — Mt 26:63-66; Mk 14:61-63; Jn 18:19-21
23:2,3pp — Mt 27:11-14; Mk 15:2-5; Jn 18:29-37
23:18-25pp — Mt 27:15-26; Mk 15:6-15; Jn 18:39 – 19:16

66 At daybreak the council[o] of the elders
of the people, both the chief priests and
the teachers of the law, met together,[p] and
Jesus was led before them. 67 "If you are
the Messiah," they said, "tell us."
Jesus answered, "If I tell you, you will
not believe me, 68 and if I asked you, you
would not answer.[q] 69 But from now on,
the Son of Man will be seated at the right
hand of the mighty God."[r]
70 They all asked, "Are you then the Son
of God?"[s]
He replied, "You say that I am."[t]
71 Then they said, "Why do we need any
more testimony? We have heard it from his
own lips."

23 Then the whole assembly rose and
led him off to Pilate.[u] 2 And they
began to accuse him, saying, "We have
found this man subverting our nation.[v] He
opposes payment of taxes to Caesar[w] and
claims to be Messiah, a king."[x]
3 So Pilate asked Jesus, "Are you the
king of the Jews?"
"You have said so," Jesus replied.
4 Then Pilate announced to the chief
priests and the crowd, "I find no basis for
a charge against this man."[y]
5 But they insisted, "He stirs up the
people all over Judea by his teaching. He
started in Galilee[z] and has come all the
way here."
6 On hearing this, Pilate asked if the man
was a Galilean.[a] 7 When he learned that
Jesus was under Herod's jurisdiction, he
sent him to Herod,[b] who was also in Jerusalem at that time.
8 When Herod saw Jesus, he was greatly
pleased, because for a long time he had
been wanting to see him.[c] From what he had

22:59 [k] Lk 23:6 **22:61** [l] S Lk 7:13 [m] ver 34 **22:65** [n] S Mt 16:21 **22:66** [o] S Mt 5:22 [p] Mt 27:1; Mk 15:1 **22:68** [q] Lk 20:3-8 **22:69** [r] S Mk 16:19 **22:70** [s] S Mt 4:3 [t] Mt 27:11; Lk 23:3 **23:1** [u] S Mt 27:2 **23:2** [v] ver 14 [w] Lk 20:22 [x] Jn 19:12 **23:4** [y] ver 14, 22,41; Mt 27:23; Jn 18:38; 1Ti 6:13; S 2Co 5:21 **23:5** [z] Mk 1:14 **23:6** [a] Lk 22:59 **23:7** [b] S Mt 14:1 **23:8** [c] Lk 9:9

22:57 *Woman.* See NIV text note on Jn 2:4.
22:59 *he is a Galilean.* Recognized by his accent (see Mt 26:73 and note) and identified by a relative of Malchus, the high priest's slave (see Jn 18:26 and note).
22:61 *The Lord ... looked straight at Peter.* Peter was outside in the enclosed courtyard, and perhaps Jesus was being taken from the trial by Caiaphas to the Sanhedrin when Jesus caught Peter's eye. *the word the Lord had spoken to him.* See v. 34.
22:64 *blindfolded him.* See note on Mk 14:65.
22:66 *At daybreak.* Only after daylight could a legal trial take place for the whole council (Sanhedrin) to pass the death sentence (see note on Mk 14:53 — 15:15).
22:67 *If you are the Messiah.* This demand is related to a question asked later: "Are you then the Son of God?" (v. 70).
22:69 *Son of Man.* See note on Mk 8:31. *seated at the right hand of ... God.* Jesus anticipates his ascension and glorification (see 24:50 – 53 and note on 24:51).
22:71 *We have heard it.* The reaction to Jesus' reply makes clear that his answer was a strong affirmative. Mark has simply, "I am" (Mk 14:62). Jesus' claim to have a position of authority at the right hand of God (v. 69) is taken as blasphemy by the council (v. 66).
23:1 *whole assembly.* The body of the Sanhedrin (see Mt 26:59; 27:1 and note; Mk 14:55 and note), which had met at the earliest hint of dawn (see 22:66 and note). *led him off to Pilate.* See note on Lk 3:1. *Pilate.* See note on Mk 15:1. The Roman governor had his main headquarters in Caesarea, but he was in Jerusalem during Passover to prevent trouble from the large number of Jews assembled for the occasion.
23:2 *subverting our nation.* Large crowds followed Jesus, but he was not misleading them or turning them against Rome. *opposes payment of taxes.* Another untrue charge (see 20:25 and note on Mt 22:21). *claims to be Messiah, a king.* Jesus claimed to be the Messiah, but not a political or military king, the kind Rome would be anxious to eliminate.
23:3 *You have said so.* Jesus somewhat indirectly affirms that he is a king, but then explains that his kingdom is not the kind that characterizes this world (see Jn 18:33 – 38 and notes).
23:5 *Judea.* May here refer to the whole of the land of the Jews (including Galilee) or to the southern section only, where the region of Judea proper was governed by Pilate (see note on 4:44).
23:7 *Herod's jurisdiction.* This Herod is Antipas, who ruled Galilee and Perea (see chart, p. 1592; see also note on 3:1). Although Pilate and Herod were rivals, Pilate did not want to handle this case; so he sent Jesus to Herod (cf. v. 12). *in Jerusalem.* Herod's main headquarters was in Tiberias on the Sea of Galilee; but, like Pilate, he had come to Jerusalem because of the crowds at Passover.
23:8 *wanting to see him.* Herod was worried about Jesus'

heard about him, he hoped to see him perform a sign of some sort. 9He plied him
with many questions, but Jesus gave him
no answer.[d] 10The chief priests and the
teachers of the law were standing there,
vehemently accusing him. 11Then Herod
and his soldiers ridiculed and mocked
him. Dressing him in an elegant robe,[e]
they sent him back to Pilate. 12That day
Herod and Pilate became friends[f]—before
this they had been enemies.
13Pilate called together the chief priests,
the rulers and the people, 14and said to
them, "You brought me this man as one
who was inciting the people to rebellion.
I have examined him in your presence
and have found no basis for your charges against him.[g] 15Neither has Herod, for
he sent him back to us; as you can see,
he has done nothing to deserve death.
16Therefore, I will punish him[h] and then
release him." [17][a]
18But the whole crowd shouted, "Away
with this man! Release Barabbas to us!"[i]
19(Barabbas had been thrown into prison for an insurrection in the city, and for
murder.)
20Wanting to release Jesus, Pilate appealed to them again. 21But they kept
shouting, "Crucify him! Crucify him!"
22For the third time he spoke to them:
"Why? What crime has this man committed? I have found in him no grounds for
the death penalty. Therefore I will have
him punished and then release him."[j]
23But with loud shouts they insistently
demanded that he be crucified, and their
shouts prevailed. 24So Pilate decided to
grant their demand. 25He released the man
who had been thrown into prison for insurrection and murder, the one they asked
for, and surrendered Jesus to their will.

The Crucifixion of Jesus

23:33-43pp — Mt 27:33-44; Mk 15:22-32; Jn 19:17-24

26As the soldiers led him away, they
seized Simon from Cyrene,[k] who was
on his way in from the country, and put
the cross on him and made him carry it
behind Jesus.[l] 27A large number of people followed him, including women who
mourned and wailed[m] for him. 28Jesus
turned and said to them, "Daughters of
Jerusalem, do not weep for me; weep for
yourselves and for your children.[n] 29For
the time will come when you will say,
'Blessed are the childless women, the
wombs that never bore and the breasts
that never nursed!'[o] 30Then

"'they will say to the mountains, "Fall
on us!"
and to the hills, "Cover us!"'[b][p]

31For if people do these things when the
tree is green, what will happen when it
is dry?"[q]
32Two other men, both criminals, were
also led out with him to be executed.[r]
33When they came to the place called the
Skull, they crucified him there, along with
the criminals—one on his right, the other
on his left. 34Jesus said, "Father,[s] forgive

23:9 [d]S Mk 14:61 **23:11** [e]Mk 15:17-19; Jn 19:2,3 **23:12** [f]Ac 4:27 **23:14** [g]S ver 4 **23:16** [h]ver 22; Mt 27:26; Jn 19:1; Ac 16:37; 2Co 11:23,24 **23:18** [i]Ac 3:13, 14 **23:22** [j]ver 16 **23:26** [k]S Mt 27:32 [l]Mk 15:21; Jn 19:17 **23:27** [m]Lk 8:52 **23:28** [n]Lk 19:41-44; 21:23,24 **23:29** [o]Mt 24:19 **23:30** [p]Isa 2:19; Hos 10:8; Rev 6:16 **23:31** [q]Eze 20:47 **23:32** [r]Isa 53:12; Mt 27:38; Mk 15:27; Jn 19:18 **23:34** [s]S Mt 11:25

[a] *17* Some manuscripts include here words similar to Matt. 27:15 and Mark 15:6. [b] *30* Hosea 10:8

---

popularity (see 9:9 and note) and had desired to kill him (see 13:31 and note), though the two had never met. There is no record that Jesus ever preached in Tiberias, where Herod's residence was located.
23:11 *elegant robe.* See note on Mk 15:17.
23:16 *I will punish him.* Although Pilate found Jesus "not guilty" as charged, he was willing to have him illegally beaten in order to satisfy the chief priests and the people and to warn against any possible trouble in the future. Scourging, though not intended to kill, was sometimes fatal (see note on Mk 15:15).
23:18 *Barabbas.* Means "son of Abba" (see Mt 27:16; Jn 18:40 and notes). Pilate offered a choice between Jesus and an obviously evil, dangerous criminal.
23:19 *insurrection ... murder.* This particular uprising is otherwise unknown, but, coupled with murder, it shows the gravity of his deeds (see Jn 18:40 and note).
23:22 *third time.* See vv. 4,14.
23:25 *surrendered Jesus.* Pilate had already handed Jesus over to the soldiers for scourging before he was convicted (Jn 19:1–5). He now handed him over for crucifixion.
23:26 *Simon.* His sons, Rufus and Alexander (see Mk 15:21 and note), must have been known in Christian circles at a later time, and perhaps were associated with the church at Rome (Ro 16:13). *Cyrene.* A leading city of Libya, west of Egypt (see note on Ac 6:9). *put the cross on him.* See note on Mk 15:21.
23:27–28 Found only in this Gospel. Luke emphasizes the role of women in the gospel story (see Introduction: Characteristics).
23:28 *weep for yourselves and for your children.* Because of the terrible suffering to befall Jerusalem about 40 years later, when the Romans would besiege the city and utterly destroy the temple.
23:29 *Blessed are the childless women.* It would be better not to have children than to have them experience such suffering. Cf. Jer 16:1–4; 1Co 7:25–35.
23:30 *Fall on us!* People would seek escape through destruction in death rather than endure continuing suffering and judgment (cf. Hos 10:8; Rev 6:16 and notes).
23:31 *tree is green ... dry.* If they treat the Messiah this way when the "tree" is well-watered and green, what will their plight be when he is withdrawn from them and they suffer for their rejection in the dry period?
23:33 *the Skull.* Latin *Calvaria,* hence the name "Calvary" (see note on Mk 15:22). *crucified.* See note on Mk 15:24.
23:34 *forgive them.* Cf. Ac 7:60 (Stephen). *they do not know what they are doing.* Cf. Ac 3:17 and note. *divided up his clothes.* Any possessions an executed person had with him were taken by the executioners. Unwittingly the soldiers (cf. Jn 19:23–24) were fulfilling the words of Ps 22:18 (but see introduction to Ps 22 and notes on Ps 22:17,20–21).

them, for they do not know what they are doing."[a][t] And they divided up his clothes by casting lots.[u]

35 The people stood watching, and the rulers even sneered at him.[v] They said, "He saved others; let him save himself if he is God's Messiah, the Chosen One."[w]

36 The soldiers also came up and mocked him.[x] They offered him wine vinegar[y] 37 and said, "If you are the king of the Jews,[z] save yourself."

38 There was a written notice above him, which read: THIS IS THE KING OF THE JEWS.[a]

39 One of the criminals who hung there hurled insults at him: "Aren't you the Messiah? Save yourself and us!"[b]

40 But the other criminal rebuked him. "Don't you fear God," he said, "since you are under the same sentence? 41 We are punished justly, for we are getting what our deeds deserve. But this man has done nothing wrong."[c]

42 Then he said, "Jesus, remember me when you come into your kingdom.[b]"[d]

43 Jesus answered him, "Truly I tell you, today you will be with me in paradise."[e]

The Death of Jesus

23:44-49pp — Mt 27:45-56; Mk 15:33-41; Jn 19:29-30

44 It was now about noon, and darkness came over the whole land until three in the afternoon,[f] 45 for the sun stopped shining. And the curtain of the temple[g] was torn in two.[h] 46 Jesus called out with a loud voice,[i] "Father, into your hands I commit my spirit."[c][j] When he had said this, he breathed his last.[k]

47 The centurion, seeing what had happened, praised God[l] and said, "Surely this was a righteous man." 48 When all the people who had gathered to witness this sight saw what took place, they beat their breasts[m] and went away. 49 But all those who knew him, including the women who had followed him from Galilee,[n] stood at a distance,[o] watching these things.

The Burial of Jesus

23:50-56pp — Mt 27:57-61; Mk 15:42-47; Jn 19:38-42

50 Now there was a man named Joseph, a member of the Council, a good and upright man, 51 who had not consented to their decision and action. He came from the Judean town of Arimathea, and he himself was waiting for the kingdom of God.[p] 52 Going to Pilate, he asked for Jesus' body. 53 Then he took it down, wrapped it in linen cloth and placed it in a tomb cut in the rock, one in which no one had yet been laid. 54 It was Preparation Day,[q] and the Sabbath was about to begin.

23:34 [t] S Mt 5:44 [u] Ps 22:18
23:35 [v] Ps 22:17 [w] Isa 42:1
23:36 [x] Ps 22:7 [y] Ps 69:21; Mt 27:48
23:37 [z] Lk 4:3,9
23:38 [a] S Mt 2:2
23:39 [b] ver 35, 37
23:41 [c] S ver 4
23:42 [d] S Mt 16:27
23:43 [e] 2Co 12:3,4; Rev 2:7
23:44 [f] Am 8:9
23:45 [g] Ex 26:31-33; Heb 9:3,8 [h] Heb 10:19,20
23:46 [i] Mt 27:50 [j] Ps 31:5; 1Pe 2:23 [k] Jn 19:30
23:47 [l] S Mt 9:8
23:48 [m] Lk 18:13
23:49 [n] Lk 8:2 [o] Ps 38:11
23:51 [p] Lk 2:25, 38
23:54 [q] Mt 27:62

[a] *34* Some early manuscripts do not have this sentence.
[b] *42* Some manuscripts *come with your kingly power*
[c] *46* Psalm 31:5

23:35 *the Chosen One.* See note on 9:35.
23:36 *wine vinegar.* A sour wine, the drink of laborers and common soldiers. Jesus refused a sedative drink (see Mt 27:34; Mk 15:23 and notes) but later was given the vinegar drink when he cried out in thirst (see Jn 19:28–30 and notes). Luke shows that it was offered in mockery.
23:38 *written notice.* Indicated the crime for which a person was dying. This was Pilate's way of mocking the Jewish leaders, as well as announcing what Jesus had been accused of. *KING OF THE JEWS.* See note on Mk 15:26.
23:39 *One of the criminals.* See note on Mk 15:32.
23:43 *paradise.* In the Septuagint (the pre-Christian Greek translation of the OT) the word designated a garden (Ge 2:8–10; cf. note on 2:8) or forest (see Ne 2:8 and note), but in the NT (used only here and in 2Co 12:4; Rev 2:7 [see note there]) it refers to the place of bliss and rest between death and resurrection (cf. Lk 16:22; 2Co 12:2).
23:44 *about noon ... three in the afternoon.* Lit. "about the sixth hour ... the ninth hour." Jesus had been put on the cross at 9:00 a.m. (see Mk 15:25). Cf. Jn 19:14 and note there.
23:45 *curtain of the temple.* The curtain between the Holy Place and the Most Holy Place. *was torn.* Its tearing symbolized Christ's opening the way directly to God (see Heb 9:3,8; 10:19–22 and notes on 10:19–20).
23:47 *praised God.* See 1:64 and note; either for having seen God publicly vindicate Jesus by mighty signs from heaven, or out of fear (see Mt 27:54) to appease the heavenly Judge and thus ward off a divine penalty for having carried out an unjust judgment. *this was a righteous man.* Or "this man was the Righteous One." Matthew and Mark report the centurion's words as "this man was the Son (or son) of God." "The Righteous One" and "the Son of God" would have been essentially equivalent terms. Similarly, "the son of God" and "a righteous man" would have been virtual equivalents. Which one the centurion intended is difficult to determine (see note on Mt 27:54). It seems clear, however, that the Gospel writers saw in his declaration a vindication of Jesus, and since the centurion was the Roman official in charge of the crucifixion his testimony was viewed as significant (see also the declarations of Pilate: vv. 4,14–15,22; Mt 27:23–24).
23:48 *beat their breasts.* A sign of anguish, grief or contrition (cf. 18:13).
23:49 *women ... from Galilee.* See Mk 15:40; Jn 19:25 and notes; cf. Lk 24:10 and note.
23:50 *Joseph, a member of the Council.* Either Joseph was not present at the meeting of the Sanhedrin (22:66), or he did not support the vote to have Jesus killed (see v. 51). Mk 14:64 suggests that he was not present, for the decision was supported by "all."
23:51 *Arimathea.* See note on Mt 27:57. *waiting for the kingdom of God.* See 2:25 and note.
23:52 The remains of an executed criminal often were left unburied or at best put in a dishonored place in a pauper's field. A near relative, such as a mother, might ask for the body, but it was a courageous gesture for Joseph, a member of the Sanhedrin, to ask for Jesus' body.
23:53 *in which no one had yet been laid.* Rock-hewn tombs were usually made to accommodate several bodies. This one, though finished, had not yet been used. See notes on 19:30; Mk 15:46.
23:54 *Preparation Day.* Friday, the day before the Sabbath, when preparation was made for keeping the Sabbath. It could be used for Passover preparation, but since in this instance it is followed by the Sabbath, it indicates Friday (see note on Mt 27:62).

55 The women who had come with Jesus from Galilee[r] followed Joseph and saw the tomb and how his body was laid in it. 56 Then they went home and prepared spices and perfumes.[s] But they rested on the Sabbath in obedience to the commandment.[t]

Jesus Has Risen

24:1-10pp — Mt 28:1-8; Mk 16:1-8; Jn 20:1-8

24 On the first day of the week, very early in the morning, the women took the spices they had prepared[u] and went to the tomb. 2 They found the stone rolled away from the tomb, 3 but when they entered, they did not find the body of the Lord Jesus.[v] 4 While they were wondering about this, suddenly two men in clothes that gleamed like lightning[w] stood beside them. 5 In their fright the women bowed down with their faces to the ground, but the men said to them, "Why do you look for the living among the dead? 6 He is not here; he has risen! Remember how he told you, while he was still with you in Galilee:[x] 7 'The Son of Man[y] must be delivered over to the hands of sinners, be crucified and on the third day be raised again.' "[z] 8 Then they remembered his words.[a]

9 When they came back from the tomb, they told all these things to the Eleven and to all the others. 10 It was Mary Magdalene, Joanna, Mary the mother of James, and the others with them[b] who told this to the apostles.[c] 11 But they did not believe[d] the women, because their words seemed to them like nonsense. 12 Peter, however, got up and ran to the tomb. Bending over, he saw the strips of linen lying by themselves,[e] and he went away,[f] wondering to himself what had happened.

On the Road to Emmaus

13 Now that same day two of them were going to a village called Emmaus, about seven miles[a] from Jerusalem.[g] 14 They were talking with each other about everything that had happened. 15 As they talked and discussed these things with each other, Jesus himself came up and walked along with them;[h] 16 but they were kept from recognizing him.[i]

17 He asked them, "What are you discussing together as you walk along?"

They stood still, their faces downcast. 18 One of them, named Cleopas,[j] asked him, "Are you the only one visiting Jerusalem who does not know the things that have happened there in these days?"

19 "What things?" he asked.

"About Jesus of Nazareth,"[k] they replied. "He was a prophet,[l] powerful in word and deed before God and all the people. 20 The

23:55 [r] ver 49 **23:56** [s] Mk 16:1; Lk 24:1 [t] Ex 12:16; 20:10 **24:1** [u] Lk 23:56 **24:3** [v] ver 23,24 **24:4** [w] S Jn 20:12 **24:6** [x] Mt 17:22, 23; Lk 9:22; 24:44 **24:7** [y] S Mt 8:20 [z] S Mt 16:21 **24:8** [a] Jn 2:22 **24:10** [b] Lk 8:1-3 [c] S Mk 6:30 **24:11** [d] Mk 16:11 **24:12** [e] Jn 20:3-7 [f] Jn 20:10 **24:13** [g] Mk 16:12 **24:15** [h] ver 36 **24:16** [i] Jn 20:14; 21:4 **24:18** [j] Jn 19:25 **24:19** [k] S Mk 1:24 [l] S Mt 21:11

a 13 Or about 11 kilometers

23:55 *women.* See v. 49 and note; cf. 8:2–3 and notes. They saw where Jesus was buried and would not mistake the location when they returned.
23:56 *spices and perfumes.* Yards of cloth and large quantities of spices were used in preparing a body for burial. Seventy-five pounds of myrrh and aloes were already used on that first evening (see Jn 19:39 and note). More was purchased for the return of the women after the Sabbath (see note on Mk 16:1).
24:1 *first day of the week.* By Jewish time, Sunday began at sundown on Saturday. The women bought spices after sunset on Saturday (see Mk 16:1 and note) and were ready to set out early the next day. When they started out, it was dark (see Jn 20:1 and note), and by the time they arrived at the tomb it was still early dawn (see Mt 28:1; Mk 16:2).
24:2 *the stone rolled away.* A tomb's entrance was ordinarily closed to keep vandals and animals from disturbing the bodies. This stone, however, had been sealed by Roman authority for a different reason (see Mt 27:62–66). See photo, p. 1692.
24:4 *two men.* They looked like men, but their clothes were remarkable (see 9:29; Ac 1:10 and note; 10:30 and note). Other reports referring to them call them angels (v. 23; see also Jn 20:12 and note). Although Matthew speaks of one angel, not two (Mt 28:2), and Mark of a young man in white (see Mk 16:5 and note), this is not strange because frequently only the spokesman is noted and an accompanying figure is not mentioned. Words and posture (seated, Jn 20:12; standing, Lk 24:4) often change in the course of events, so these variations are not necessarily contradictory. They are merely evidence of independent accounts.
24:6 *while ... in Galilee.* Jesus had predicted his death and resurrection on a number of occasions (see 9:22 and note), but the disciples failed to comprehend or accept what he was saying.
24:7 See vv. 25–27,44–46 and note on v. 44; 9:22; 17:25 and notes.
24:9 *to the Eleven and to all the others.* "Eleven" is sometimes used to refer to the group of apostles (Ac 1:26; 2:14) after the betrayal by Judas. Judas was dead at the time the apostles first met the risen Christ, but the group was still called the Twelve (Jn 20:24). The "others" included disciples who, for the most part, came from Galilee.
24:10 *Mary Magdalene.* See note on 8:2. She is named first in most of the lists of women (see Mt 27:56; Mk 15:40 and note; but cf. Jn 19:25) and was the first to see the risen Christ (Jn 20:13–18; see chart, p. 1754). *Joanna.* See 8:3. She is named only by Luke at this point (Mark is the only one who adds Salome at this time, Mk 16:1; see note on Mk 15:40). *Mary the mother of James.* See Mk 16:1. She is the "other Mary" of Mt 28:1 (see note there). The absence of the mother of Jesus is significant. She was probably with John (cf. Jn 19:27 and note).
24:12 *Peter ... ran.* John's Gospel (20:3–9) includes another disciple, John himself.
24:13 *two of them.* One was named Cleopas (v. 18). *Emmaus.* See map, p. 1770.
24:15 *Jesus ... came up and walked ... with them.* See chart, p. 1754.
24:16 *kept from recognizing him.* By special, divine intervention.
24:19 *prophet.* They had respect for Jesus as a man of God, but after his death they apparently were reluctant to call him the Messiah.

RESURRECTION APPEARANCES

APPEARANCE	PLACE	TIME	MATTHEW	MARK	LUKE	JOHN	ACTS	1 CO
The empty tomb	Jerusalem	Resurrection Sunday	28:1–10	16:1–8	24:1–12	20:1–9		
To Mary Magdalene in the garden	Jerusalem	Resurrection Sunday		16:9–11		20:11–18		
To other women	Jerusalem	Resurrection Sunday	28:9–10					
To two people going to Emmaus	Road to Emmaus	Resurrection Sunday		16:12–13	24:13–32			
To Peter	Jerusalem	Resurrection Sunday			24:34			15:5
To the ten disciples in the upper room	Jerusalem	Resurrection Sunday			24:36–43	20:19–25		
To the 11 disciples in the upper room	Jerusalem	Following Sunday		16:14		20:26–31		15:5
To seven disciples fishing	Sea of Galilee	Some time later				21:1–23		
To the 11 disciples on a mountain	Galilee	Some time later	28:16–20	16:15–18				
To more than 500	Unknown	Some time later						15:6
To James	Unknown	Some time later						15:7
To his disciples at his ascension	Mount of Olives	40 days after Jesus' resurrection			24:44–49		1:3–8	
To Paul	Damascus	Several years later					9:1–19 22:3–16 26:9–18	9:1

chief priests and our rulers[m] handed him
over to be sentenced to death, and they
crucified him; 21 but we had hoped that he
was the one who was going to redeem Israel.[n] And what is more, it is the third day[o]
since all this took place. 22 In addition,
some of our women amazed us.[p] They
went to the tomb early this morning 23 but
didn't find his body. They came and told
us that they had seen a vision of angels,
who said he was alive. 24 Then some of our
companions went to the tomb and found it
just as the women had said, but they did
not see Jesus."[q]
25 He said to them, "How foolish you
are, and how slow to believe all that the
prophets have spoken! 26 Did not the Messiah have to suffer these things and then
enter his glory?"[r] 27 And beginning with
Moses[s] and all the Prophets,[t] he explained
to them what was said in all the Scriptures
concerning himself.[u]
28 As they approached the village to
which they were going, Jesus continued
on as if he were going farther. 29 But they
urged him strongly, "Stay with us, for it is
nearly evening; the day is almost over." So
he went in to stay with them.
30 When he was at the table with them,
he took bread, gave thanks, broke it[v] and
began to give it to them. 31 Then their eyes
were opened and they recognized him,[w]

24:20 [m] Lk 23:13
24:21 [n] Lk 1:68; 2:38; 21:28 [o] S Mt 16:21
24:22 [p] ver 1-10
24:24 [q] ver 12
24:26 [r] Heb 2:10; 1Pe 1:11
24:27 [s] Ge 3:15; Nu 21:9; Dt 18:15 [t] Isa 7:14; 9:6; 40:10,11; 53; Eze 34:23; Da 9:24; Mic 7:20; Mal 3:1 [u] Jn 1:45
24:30 [v] S Mt 14:19
24:31 [w] ver 16

24:21 *to redeem Israel.* What they probably meant by this was "to set the Jewish nation free from bondage to Rome and so usher in the kingdom of God" (see 1:68; 2:38; 21:28,31 and note on 21:28; cf. Titus 2:14; 1Pe 1:18 and notes). *the third day.* A reference either to the Jewish belief that after the third day the soul left the body or to Jesus' remark that he would be resurrected on the third day (9:22).
24:23 *vision of angels.* See note on v. 4.
24:24 *some of our companions.* See v. 12 and note.
24:26 *suffer ... enter his glory.* See 1Pe 1:11 and note.
24:27 *Moses and all the Prophets.* A way of designating the whole of the OT Scriptures (see v. 44 and note; 16:16,29).
24:28 *as if he were going farther.* If they had not invited him in, he apparently would have continued on by himself.
24:31 *their eyes were opened.* Cf. v. 16; more than a matter of simple recognition.

and he disappeared from their sight.
32 They asked each other, "Were not our
hearts burning within us[x] while he talked
with us on the road and opened the Scriptures[y] to us?"
33 They got up and returned at once to
Jerusalem. There they found the Eleven
and those with them, assembled together 34 and saying, "It is true! The Lord[z] has
risen and has appeared to Simon."[a] 35 Then
the two told what had happened on the
way, and how Jesus was recognized by
them when he broke the bread.[b]

Jesus Appears to the Disciples

36 While they were still talking about
this, Jesus himself stood among them and
said to them, "Peace be with you."[c]
37 They were startled and frightened,
thinking they saw a ghost.[d] 38 He said to
them, "Why are you troubled, and why do
doubts rise in your minds? 39 Look at my
hands and my feet. It is I myself! Touch
me and see;[e] a ghost does not have flesh
and bones, as you see I have."
40 When he had said this, he showed
them his hands and feet. 41 And while they
still did not believe it because of joy and
amazement, he asked them, "Do you have
anything here to eat?" 42 They gave him a
piece of broiled fish, 43 and he took it and
ate it in their presence.[f]
44 He said to them, "This is what I told
you while I was still with you:[g] Everything
must be fulfilled[h] that is written about me
in the Law of Moses,[i] the Prophets[j] and
the Psalms."[k]
45 Then he opened their minds so they
could understand the Scriptures. 46 He told
them, "This is what is written: The Messiah
will suffer[l] and rise from the dead on the
third day,[m] 47 and repentance for the forgiveness of sins will be preached in his name[n] to
all nations,[o] beginning at Jerusalem.[p] 48 You
are witnesses[q] of these things. 49 I am going
to send you what my Father has promised;[r]
but stay in the city until you have been
clothed with power from on high."

The Ascension of Jesus

50 When he had led them out to the vicinity of Bethany,[s] he lifted up his hands
and blessed them. 51 While he was blessing them, he left them and was taken up
into heaven.[t] 52 Then they worshiped him
and returned to Jerusalem with great joy.
53 And they stayed continually at the temple,[u] praising God.

24:32 [x] Ps 39:3 [y] ver 27,45 **24:34** [z] S Lk 7:13 [a] 1Co 15:5 **24:35** [b] ver 30, 31 **24:36** [c] Jn 20:19,21, 26; S 14:27 **24:37** [d] Mk 6:49 **24:39** [e] Jn 20:27; 1Jn 1:1 **24:43** [f] Ac 10:41 **24:44** [g] Lk 9:45; 18:34 [h] S Mt 1:22; 16:21; Lk 9:22, 44; 18:31-33; 22:37 [i] S ver 27 [j] S ver 27 [k] Ps 2; 16; 22; 69; 72; 110; 118 **24:46** [l] S Mt 16:21 [m] S Mt 16:21 **24:47** [n] Ac 5:31; 10:43; 13:38 [o] Mt 28:19; Mk 13:10 [p] Isa 2:3 **24:48** [q] S Jn 15:27; Ac 1:8; 2:32; 4:20; 5:32; 13:31; 1Pe 5:1 **24:49** [r] S Jn 14:16; Ac 1:4 **24:50** [s] S Mt 21:17 **24:51** [t] 2Ki 2:11 **24:53** [u] S Ac 2:46

24:33 *the Eleven and those with them.* See note on v. 9.
24:34 *appeared to Simon.* See chart, p. 1754; see also 1Co 15:5 and note.
24:36 *Jesus himself stood among them.* Behind locked doors (Jn 20:19; see chart, p. 1754), indicating that his body was of a different order. It was his glorified resurrection body. *Peace be with you.* The traditional greeting, now given new significance by the resurrection.
24:39 *my hands and my feet.* Indicating that Jesus' heels as well as his wrists were nailed to the cross (see note on Mk 15:24; cf. Jn 20:20,27 and note on 20:20).
24:42 *a piece of broiled fish.* Demonstrating that he had a physical body that could consume food.
24:44 *Law of Moses, the Prophets and the Psalms.* The three parts of the Hebrew OT (Psalms was the most prominent book of the third section, called the Writings), indicating that the suffering, death (by execution) and resurrection of the Messiah were foreseen and foreshadowed in the OT Scriptures. Such a global claim sprang from the understanding that God, through the Messiah, came to bring about the full and final redemption of his people (e.g., 1:68) and the full and final restoration of all things (e.g., Ac 3:21). See notes on v. 46; Mt 16:21; Ac 2:23; 1Pe 1:11.
24:45 *opened their minds.* By explaining the OT Scriptures (cf. v. 27).
24:46 *suffer ... rise from the dead ... third day.* See 1Co 15:3–4. The OT depicts the Messiah as one who would suffer (see introduction to Ps 22; see also Isa 52:13—53:12) and rise from the dead on the third day (compare Ps 16:8–11 with Ac 2:23–33 and notes; see Isa 53:10–11 and notes; compare Jnh 1:17 with Mt 12:40 and note).
24:47 *repentance for the forgiveness of sins.* See Ac 5:31; 10:43; 13:38; 26:18. The prediction of Christ's death and resurrection (v. 46) is joined with the necessary human response (repentance) and the resulting benefit (forgiveness; cf. Isa 49:6; Ac 13:47; 26:22–23). *to all nations.* Prophesied also in Mk 13:10; cf. Mt 28:19–20 and note; Ac 10:34–35; 15:16–17; Ro 1:13–14; 4:16–17; 15:7–12. *beginning at Jerusalem.* See Ac 1:8 and note.
24:49 *what my Father has promised.* See Joel 2:28–32 and notes. The reference is to the coming power of the Spirit, fulfilled in Ac 2:4 (see also Ac 2:17–22 and notes).
24:50 *Bethany.* A village on the Mount of Olives (see notes on 19:29; Mt 21:17; see also map, p. 1687).
24:51 *taken up into heaven.* Different from his previous disappearances (4:30; 24:3; Jn 8:59). They saw him ascend into a cloud (see Ac 1:9; see also Ac 1:11–12 and notes).
24:53 *at the temple.* During the period of time immediately following Christ's ascension, the believers met continually at the temple (Ac 2:46; 3:1; 5:21,42), where many rooms were available for meetings (see note on 2:37). *praising God.* The Gospel of Luke begins (1:64; see note there) and ends (here) with praise to God in his temple. This Gospel also begins with the aged Zechariah's doubt (1:18) and unbelief (1:20) and ends with the disciples' worship of the risen and ascended Lord "with great joy" (v. 52; see 1:14 and note). Luke has fittingly prepared the way for what follows in his second volume (see Ac 1:1 and note).

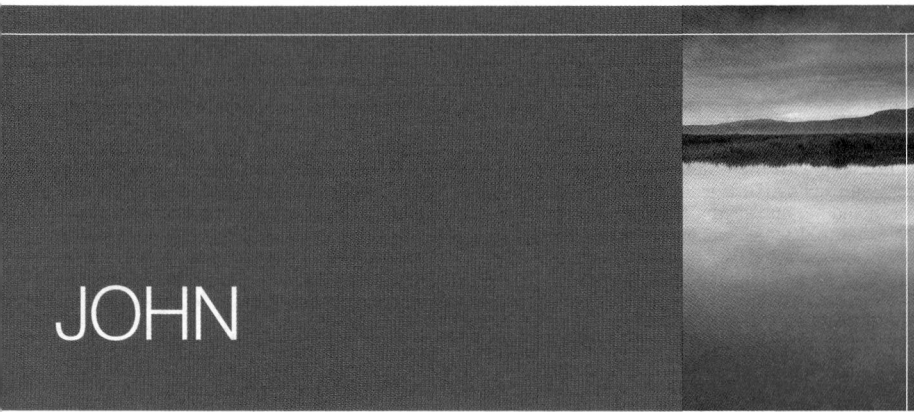

JOHN

INTRODUCTION

Author

The author is the apostle John, "the disciple whom Jesus loved" (13:23 [see note there]; 19:26; 20:2; 21:7,20,24). He was prominent in the early church but is not mentioned by name in this Gospel — which would be natural if he wrote it, but hard to explain otherwise. The author knew Jewish life well, as seen from references to popular Messianic speculations (see, e.g., 1:21 and note; 7:40 – 42); to the hostility between Jews and Samaritans (see 4:9 and note); and to Jewish customs, such as the duty of circumcision on the eighth day taking precedence over the prohibition of working on the Sabbath (see note on 7:22). He knew the geography of the Holy Land, locating Bethany about two miles from Jerusalem (11:18) and mentioning Cana, a village not referred to in any earlier writing known to us (2:1 [see note there]; 21:2). The Gospel of John has many touches that appear to reflect the recollections of an eyewitness — such as the house at Bethany being filled with the fragrance of the broken perfume jar (see 12:3 and note). Early writers such as Irenaeus and Tertullian say that John wrote this Gospel, and other evidence agrees (see Introduction to 1 John: Author).

a quick look

Author:
The apostle John

Audience:
Primarily Gentile believers and seeking unbelievers

Date:
Between AD 50 and 85

Theme:
John presents Jesus as the Word, the Messiah and the incarnate Son of God, who has come to reveal the Father and bring eternal life to all who believe in him.

Date

In general, two views of the dating of this Gospel have been advocated:

(1) The traditional view places it toward the end of the first century, c. AD 85 or later (see Introduction to 1 John: Date).

(2) More recently, some interpreters have suggested an earlier date, perhaps as early as the 50s and no later than 70.

The first view may be supported by reference to the statement of Clement of Alexandria (died between 211 and 216) that John wrote to supplement the accounts found in the other Gospels (Eusebius, *Ecclesiastical History*, 6.14.7), and thus his Gospel is later than the first three. It has also been argued that the seemingly more developed theology of the fourth Gospel indicates that it originated later.

> The literary style of this witness of Jesus is unique among the Gospels; here focus is on the "signs" of Jesus' identity and mission and on lengthy, theologically rich discourses.

The second view has found favor because it has been felt more recently that John wrote independently of the other Gospels (see essay and chart, pp. 1582 – 1583). This does not contradict the statement of Clement, referred to above. Also, those who hold this view point out that developed theology does not necessarily argue for a late origin. The theology of Romans (written c. 57) is every bit as developed as that in John. Further, the statement in 5:2 that there "is" (rather than "was") a pool "near the Sheep Gate" may suggest a time before 70, when Jerusalem was destroyed. Others, however, observe that John elsewhere sometimes used the present tense when speaking of the past.

Purpose and Emphases

John's Gospel is rather different from the other three. Whether or not he knew them (or any one of them) continues to be debated. In any event, his witness to Jesus goes its own way, highlighting matters that in the other Gospels remain implicit and underdeveloped. The literary style of this witness of Jesus is also unique among the Gospels; here focus is on the "signs" of Jesus' identity and mission (see note on 2:11) and on lengthy, theologically rich discourses. Some call chs. 1 – 11 the "Book of Signs" and chs. 12 – 21 the "Book of Glory."

View of the interior of a typical sheep pen. Jesus said, "I am the gate; whoever enters through me will be saved" (Jn 10:9).

www.HolyLandPhotos.org

Chapels located at "Bethany on the other side of the Jordan" (Jn 1:28), one of the possible sites of Jesus' baptism

John begins with the profound announcement that Jesus is the divine "Word" of self-revelation—who existed with God from the beginning and through whom God created all things. Jesus the "Word" became embodied (incarnated) as a human being to be the light of life for the world. After this comes the proclamation that this Jesus is the Son of God sent from the Father to finish the Father's work in the world (see 4:34 and note). God's own glory is made visible in him ("Anyone who has seen me has seen the Father," 14:9), and what he does glorifies the Father. In him the full grace and truth of God have shown themselves (cf. 1:17–18). Strikingly, a series of "I am" claims on Jesus' lips echo God's naming of himself in Ex 3:14, further strengthening the link between the Father and the Son (see 6:35 [see also note there]; 8:12; 8:58 [see also note there]; 9:5; 10:7,9,14; 11:25; 14:6; 15:1,5).

The words of 3:16 (see note there) nicely summarize this Gospel's central theme: "For God so loved the world that he gave his one and only Son, that whoever believes in him shall not perish but have eternal life." Although a variety of motivations for the composition of John's Gospel have been posited by interpreters (such as to supplement the other Gospels, to combat some form of heresy, or to oppose the continuing followers of John the Baptist), the author himself states his main purpose clearly in 20:31: "that you may believe that Jesus is the Messiah, the Son of God, and that by believing you may have life in his name."

For the main emphases of the book, see notes on 1:4,7,9,14,19,49; 2:4,11; 3:27; 4:34; 6:35; 13:1—17:26; 13:31; 17:1–2,5; 20:31.

Outline

- I. Prologue: The Word Became Flesh (1:1–18)
- II. The Beginning of Jesus' Ministry (1:19–51)
  - A. John the Baptist's Testimony about Jesus (1:19–34)
  - B. John's Disciples Follow Jesus (1:35–42)
  - C. Jesus Calls Philip and Nathanael (1:43–51)
- III. Jesus' Public Ministry: Signs and Discourses (chs. 2–11)
  - A. Changing Water into Wine (2:1–11)
  - B. Clearing the Temple (2:12–25)
  - C. Jesus Teaches Nicodemus (3:1–21)
  - D. John the Baptist's Final Testimony about Jesus (3:22–36)
  - E. Jesus and the Samaritans (4:1–42)
  - F. Healing of the Official's Son (4:43–54)
  - G. Jesus' Visit to Jerusalem at an Annual Festival (ch. 5)
  - H. Feeding the 5,000 and Jesus' Claim to Be the Bread of Life (ch. 6)
  - I. Jesus at the Festival of Tabernacles and Disputes over Who He Is (chs. 7–8)
  - J. Healing of the Man Born Blind (ch. 9)
  - K. Jesus Is the Good Shepherd (10:1–21)
  - L. Conflict at the Festival of Dedication over Jesus' Identity (10:22–42)
  - M. The Raising of Lazarus (ch. 11)
- IV. The Passion Week (chs. 12–19)
  - A. The Anointing of Jesus' Feet (12:1–11)
  - B. Jesus' Entry into Jerusalem as King (12:12–19)
  - C. Jesus Predicts His Death (12:20–36)
  - D. Belief and Unbelief among the Jews (12:37–50)
  - E. Jesus' Farewell Discourses and Prayer (chs. 13–17)
    - 1. At the Last Supper (chs. 13–14)
      - a. Jesus washes the disciples' feet (13:1–17)
      - b. Jesus predicts his betrayal (13:18–30)
      - c. Jesus predicts Peter's denial (13:31–38)
      - d. Jesus comforts his disciples (14:1–4)
      - e. Jesus is the way to the Father (14:5–14)
      - f. Jesus promises the Holy Spirit (14:15–30)
    - 2. On the way to Gethsemane (chs. 15–16)
      - a. The vine and the branches (15:1–17)
      - b. The world hates the disciples (15:18–25)
      - c. The work of the Holy Spirit (15:26—16:15)
      - d. The disciples' grief will turn to joy (16:16–33)

3. Jesus' prayer (ch. 17)
    a. For himself—that he be glorified (17:1–5)
    b. For his disciples (17:6–19)
    c. For all believers (17:20–26)

F. Jesus' Betrayal and Arrest (18:1–11)
G. Jesus' Trials before Jewish and Roman Officials (18:12–40)
H. Jesus' Crucifixion (19:1–27)
I. Jesus' Death and Burial (19:28–42)

V. Jesus' Resurrection (20:1–29)
VI. Statement of the Gospel's Purpose (20:30–31)
VII. Epilogue: Jesus' Recommissioning of the Disciples (ch. 21)

The Word Became Flesh

1 In the beginning was the Word,[a] and
the Word was with God,[b] and the
Word was God.[c] 2 He was with God in the
beginning.[d] 3 Through him all things were
made; without him nothing was made
that has been made.[e] 4 In him was life,[f]
and that life was the light[g] of all mankind.
5 The light shines in the darkness,[h] and the
darkness has not overcome[a] it.[i]
6 There was a man sent from God whose
name was John.[j] 7 He came as a witness
to testify[k] concerning that light, so that
through him all might believe.[l] 8 He himself was not the light; he came only as a
witness to the light.
9 The true light[m] that gives light to everyone[n] was coming into the world. 10 He was
in the world, and though the world was
made through him,[o] the world did not recognize him. 11 He came to that which was
his own, but his own did not receive him.[p]
12 Yet to all who did receive him, to those
who believed[q] in his name,[r] he gave the
right to become children of God[s] — 13 children born not of natural descent, nor of
human decision or a husband's will, but
born of God.[t]
14 The Word became flesh[u] and made
his dwelling among us. We have seen his
glory,[v] the glory of the one and only Son,
who came from the Father, full of grace[w]
and truth.[x]

[a] 5 Or *understood*

1:1 [a] Isa 55:11; Rev 19:13 [b] Jn 17:5; 1Jn 1:2 [c] Php 2:6 **1:2** [d] Ge 1:1; Jn 8:58; 17:5, 24; 1Jn 1:1; Rev 1:8 **1:3** [e] ver 10; 1Co 8:6; Col 1:16; Heb 1:2 **1:4** [f] S Jn 5:26; 6:57; 11:25; 14:6; Ac 3:15; Heb 7:16; 1Jn 1:1, 2; 5:20; Rev 1:18 [g] Ps 36:9; Jn 3:19; 8:12; 9:5; 12:46 **1:5** [h] Ps 18:28 [i] Jn 3:19 **1:6** [j] S Mt 3:1 **1:7** [k] ver 15, 19, 32; Jn 3:26; 5:33 [l] ver 12; S Jn 3:15 **1:9** [m] 1Jn 2:8 [n] Isa 49:6 **1:10** [o] S ver 3 **1:11** [p] Isa 53:3 **1:12** [q] ver 7; S Jn 3:15 [r] S 1Jn 3:23 [s] Dt 14:1; S Ro 8:14; 8:16, 21; Eph 5:1; 1Jn 3:1, 2 **1:13** [t] Jn 3:6; Titus 3:5; Jas 1:18; 1Pe 1:23; 1Jn 3:9; 4:7; 5:1, 4 **1:14** [u] Gal 4:4; Php 2:7, 8; 1Ti 3:16; Heb 2:14; 1Jn 1:1, 2; 4:2 [v] Ex 33:18; 40:34 [w] S Ro 3:24 [x] Jn 14:6

1:1 *In the beginning.* A deliberate echo of Ge 1:1 (see note there) to link God's action in behalf of the world through Jesus Christ (cf. 3:16) with his first work, the creation of the world. *Word.* Greek *logos,* a term Greeks used not only of the spoken word but also of the unspoken word, the word still in the mind — the reason. When they applied it to the universe, they meant the rational principle that governs all things. The Jews, however, used it to refer to the "word" of God by which he created the world and governs it (see the Septuagint [the pre-Christian Greek translation of the OT] rendering of Ps 33:6; 119:89; 147:15,18) and to refer to the law of God that he gave the Israelites to be their life (see Dt 32:47 and note on 30:20). Of the law the rabbis said that it was "created before the world," that it "lay on God's bosom while God sat on the throne of glory," that it was divine, that it was God's "firstborn" through whom he "created the heaven and the earth," that it is "light" and "life" for the world and that it "is truth." This Jewish use of *logos* as that which comes from God to fulfill his purpose in and for the world appears to lie behind the heavily freighted affirmation with which John begins his Gospel. *with God.* The Word was distinct from the Father. *was God.* Jesus was God in the fullest sense (see note on Ro 9:5). The prologue (vv. 1 – 18) begins and ends with a ringing affirmation of his deity (see note on v. 18).

1:4 *life.* One of the great concepts of this Gospel. The Greek word for "life" is found 36 times in John, while no other NT book uses it more than 17 times. Life is Christ's gift (10:28), and he, in fact, is "the life" (14:6). *light of all mankind.* This Gospel also links light with Christ, from whom comes all spiritual illumination. He is the "light of the world," who holds out wonderful hope for humanity (cf. 8:12 and note) and for the creation (see 3:16 and note). For an OT link between life and light, see Ps 27:1; 36:9 and notes.

1:5 *darkness.* The stark contrast between light and darkness is a striking theme in this Gospel (see, e.g., 12:35 – 36).

1:6 *John.* In this Gospel the name John always refers to John the Baptist.

1:7 *as a witness to testify.* John the Baptist's singular ministry was to testify about Jesus (10:41). "Witness" is another important concept in this Gospel. The Greek noun for "witness" or "testimony" is used 14 times (in Matthew not at all, in Mark three times, in Luke once) and the verb ("testify") 33 times (found once each in Matthew and Luke and not at all in Mark) — in both cases more often than anywhere else in the NT. John (the author) thereby emphasizes that the facts about Jesus are amply attested. *that through him all might believe.* People were not to believe "in" John the Baptist but "through" him. Similarly, the writer's purpose was to draw them to belief in Christ (20:31 [see note there]); he uses the Greek verb for "believe" about 100 times.

1:8 *He himself was not the light.* The greatness of John the Baptist caused some of his followers to have exaggerated ideas about him (see v. 21), but while Jesus affirms John's greatness (see Mt 11:11 and note), he also makes clear his limitations: John is "a lamp" (5:35) but not "the light."

1:9 John is referring to the incarnation of Christ. *world.* Another common word in John's writings, the Greek noun for "world" is found 78 times in this Gospel and 24 times in his letters (only 47 times in all of Paul's writings). It can mean the universe, the earth, the people on earth, most people, people opposed to God or the human system opposed to God's purposes. John emphasizes the word by repetition and moves without explanation from one meaning to another (see, e.g., 17:5,14 – 15 and notes).

1:12 *believed.* See v. 7; 20:31 and notes. *he gave the right.* Membership in God's family is by grace alone — the gift of God (see Eph 2:8 – 9 and notes). It is never a human achievement, as v. 13 emphasizes; yet the imparting of the gift is dependent on human reception of it, as the words "did receive" and "believed" make clear.

1:13 *born of God.* The "children of God" (v. 12) have been given a new openness to and relationship with God that was not theirs as a result of their natural birth (see 3:3,5; 2Co 5:17; Gal 6:15; Titus 3:5 and notes).

1:14 *flesh.* A strong, almost crude, word that stresses the reality of Christ's humanity. *made his dwelling among us. We have seen his glory.* Cf. 2Pe 1:16 – 18 and note on 1:16. The Greek verb translated "made his dwelling" is connected with the Greek noun meaning "tent/tabernacle" which, in turn, is associated with the Hebrew word for "tent/tabernacle." The verse would have reminded John's Jewish readers of the tent of meeting, which was filled with the glory of God (Ex 40:34 – 35). Christ revealed his glory to his disciples by the miracles he performed (see 2:11 and note) and by his death and resurrection. *grace and truth.* The corresponding Hebrew terms are often translated "(unfailing) love and faithfulness" (see notes on Ps 26:3; Pr 16:6). *grace.* A significant Christian concept (see notes on Jnh 4:2; Ro 1:7; Gal 1:3; Eph 1:2), though John never uses the word after the prologue (vv. 1 – 18). *truth.* John uses the Greek word for "truth" 25 times and links it closely with Jesus, who is the truth (see 14:6 and note).

15 (John testified[y] concerning him. He
cried out, saying, "This is the one I spoke
about when I said, 'He who comes after
me has surpassed me because he was before me.' ")[z] 16 Out of his fullness[a] we have
all received grace[b] in place of grace already
given. 17 For the law was given through
Moses;[c] grace and truth came through
Jesus Christ.[d] 18 No one has ever seen
God,[e] but the one and only Son, who is
himself God and[a][f] is in closest relationship
with the Father, has made him known.

John the Baptist Denies Being the Messiah

19 Now this was John's[g] testimony when
the Jewish leaders[b][h] in Jerusalem sent
priests and Levites to ask him who he
was. 20 He did not fail to confess, but confessed freely, "I am not the Messiah."[i]
21 They asked him, "Then who are you?
Are you Elijah?"[j]
He said, "I am not."
"Are you the Prophet?"[k]
He answered, "No."
22 Finally they said, "Who are you? Give
us an answer to take back to those who
sent us. What do you say about yourself?"
23 John replied in the words of Isaiah the
prophet, "I am the voice of one calling in
the wilderness,[l] 'Make straight the way for
the Lord.' "[c][m]
24 Now the Pharisees who had been sent
25 questioned him, "Why then do you baptize if you are not the Messiah, nor Elijah,
nor the Prophet?"
26 "I baptize with[d] water,"[n] John replied,
"but among you stands one you do not
know. 27 He is the one who comes after
me,[o] the straps of whose sandals I am not
worthy to untie."[p]
28 This all happened at Bethany on the
other side of the Jordan,[q] where John was
baptizing.

1:15 [y] ver 7 [z] ver 30; Mt 3:11 **1:16** [a] Eph 1:23; Col 1:19; 2:9 [b] S Ro 3:24 **1:17** [c] Dt 32:46; Jn 7:19 [d] ver 14 **1:18** [e] Ex 33:20; Jn 6:46; Col 1:15; 1Ti 6:16; 1Jn 4:12 [f] Jn 3:16, 18; 1Jn 4:9 **1:19** [g] S Mt 3:1 [h] Jn 2:18; 5:10, 16; 6:41, 52; 7:1; 10:24 **1:20** [i] Jn 3:28; Lk 3:15, 16 **1:21** [j] S Mt 11:14 [k] Dt 18:15
1:23 [l] Mt 3:1 [m] Isa 40:3 **1:26** [n] S Mk 1:4 **1:27** [o] ver 15, 30 [p] Mk 1:7 **1:28** [q] Jn 3:26; 10:40

[a] *18* Some manuscripts *but the only Son, who*
[b] *19* The Greek term traditionally translated *the Jews* (*hoi Ioudaioi*) refers here and elsewhere in John's Gospel to those Jewish leaders who opposed Jesus; also in 5:10, 15, 16; 7:1, 11, 13; 9:22; 18:14, 28, 36; 19:7, 12, 31, 38; 20:19.
[c] *23* Isaiah 40:3
[d] *26* Or *in*; also in verses 31 and 33 (twice)

1:15 *he was before me.* In ancient times the older person was given respect and regarded as greater than the younger. People would normally have ranked Jesus lower in respect than John, who was older. John the Baptist explains that this is only apparent, since Jesus, as the divine Word, existed before he was born on earth.

1:16 *grace in place of grace already given.* To the blessing that came through Moses has been added the greater blessing that has come through Jesus (see v. 17; see also Heb 1:1–4 and notes). Another possible interpretation of the Greek phrase is "grace on top of grace," meaning an abundance of grace.

1:18 *the one and only Son, who is himself God.* An explicit declaration of Christ's deity (see vv. 1,14 and notes; 3:16; see also note on Ro 9:5). *has made him known.* Sometimes in the OT people are said to have seen God (see, e.g., Ex 24:10 and note). But we are also told that no one can see God and live (Ex 33:20). Therefore, since no human being can see God as he really is, those who saw God saw him in a form he took upon himself temporarily for the occasion. Now, however, Christ "has made him known" (see 2Co 4:4; Col 1:15,19; 2:9 and notes).

1:19 *Jewish leaders.* See NIV text note. The Greek word for "Jews" occurs about 70 times in this Gospel. It is used in a favorable sense (e.g., 4:22) and in a neutral sense (e.g., 2:6). But generally John used it of the Jewish leaders who were hostile to Jesus (e.g., here; 5:10,16; 7:1, etc.). Here it refers to the delegation sent by the Sanhedrin to look into the activities of an unauthorized teacher. *Levites.* Descendants of the tribe of Levi, who were assigned to specific duties in connection with the tabernacle (Nu 3:17–37) and temple. They also had teaching responsibilities (2Ch 35:3; Ne 8:7–9), and it was probably in this role that they were sent with the priests to John the Baptist.

1:20 *I.* Emphatic, contrasting John the Baptist with someone else. Throughout the following verses this emphatic "I" occurs frequently, and almost invariably there is an implied contrast with Jesus, who is always given the higher place.

1:21 *Are you Elijah?... I am not.* The Jews remembered that Elijah had not died (2Ki 2:11) and believed that he would come back to earth to announce the end time. In this sense, John properly denied that he was Elijah. When Jesus later said the Baptist was Elijah (see Mt 11:14; 17:10 and notes), he meant it in the sense that John was a fulfillment of the prophecy of Mal 4:5 (see note there). *the Prophet.* The prophet of Dt 18:15 (see note there). The Jewish people expected a variety of persons to be associated with the coming of the Messiah. John the Baptist emphatically denies being "the Prophet." He had come to testify about Jesus, yet the people kept asking him about himself. His answers became progressively more terse.

1:23 The Baptist applied the prophecy of Isa 40:3 (see note there) to his own ministry of calling people to repent in preparation for the coming of the Messiah. The men of Qumran (the community that produced the Dead Sea Scrolls; see essay, pp. 1574–1576) applied the same words to themselves, but they prepared for the Lord's coming by isolating themselves from the world to secure their own salvation. John concentrated on helping people come to the Messiah (the Christ).

1:24 *Pharisees.* Members of the conservative religious party, who probed deeper than the rest of the delegation (v. 19). See notes on Mt 3:7; Mk 2:16; Lk 5:17; see also essay, p. 1576, and chart, p. 1631.

1:25 *the Messiah.* Means "the Anointed One." In OT times anointing signified being set apart for service, particularly as king (cf. 1Sa 16:1,13) or priest (Ex 28:41; 29:7; 30:30; 40:13,15). But people were looking for not just *an* anointed one but *the* Anointed One, the Messiah (cf. Mt 16:16 and note).

1:27 *whose sandals I am not worthy to untie.* A menial task, fit for a slave. Disciples would perform all sorts of service for their rabbis (teachers), but untying sandal straps was expressly excluded.

1:28 *Bethany.* The Bethany mentioned elsewhere in the Gospels was only about two miles from Jerusalem (see note on Mt 21:17). The precise site of this other Bethany is not known, except that it was located on the east side of the Jordan (see maps, pp. 1597, 1663; see also photo, p. 1758).

John Testifies About Jesus

29 The next day John saw Jesus coming
toward him and said, "Look, the Lamb
of God,[r] who takes away the sin of the
world![s] 30 This is the one I meant when I
said, 'A man who comes after me has surpassed me because he was before me.'[t] 31 I
myself did not know him, but the reason
I came baptizing with water was that he
might be revealed to Israel."
32 Then John gave this testimony: "I saw
the Spirit come down from heaven as a
dove and remain on him.[u] 33 And I myself
did not know him, but the one who sent
me to baptize with water[v] told me, 'The
man on whom you see the Spirit come
down and remain is the one who will baptize with the Holy Spirit.'[w] 34 I have seen and
I testify that this is God's Chosen One."[a][x]

John's Disciples Follow Jesus

1:40-42pp — Mt 4:18-22; Mk 1:16-20; Lk 5:2-11

35 The next day John[y] was there again
with two of his disciples. 36 When he saw
Jesus passing by, he said, "Look, the
Lamb of God!"[z]
37 When the two disciples heard him
say this, they followed Jesus. 38 Turning
around, Jesus saw them following and
asked, "What do you want?"
They said, "Rabbi"[a] (which means
"Teacher"), "where are you staying?"
39 "Come," he replied, "and you will
see."
So they went and saw where he was
staying, and they spent that day with him.
It was about four in the afternoon.

1:29 [r] ver 36; Ge 22:8; Isa 53:7; 1Pe 1:19; Rev 5:6; 13:8 [s] S Jn 3:17
1:30 [t] ver 15,27
1:32 [u] Mt 3:16
1:33 [v] S Mk 1:4 [w] S Mk 1:8
1:34 [x] ver 49; S Mt 4:3
1:35 [y] S Mt 3:1
1:36 [z] S ver 29
1:38 [a] ver 49; S Mt 23:7
1:41 [b] Jn 4:25
1:42 [c] Ge 17:5, 15; 32:28; 35:10 [d] Mt 16:18
1:43 [e] Mt 10:3; Jn 6:5-7; 12:21, 22; 14:8,9 [f] S Mt 4:19
1:44 [g] S Mt 11:21
1:45 [h] Jn 21:2 [i] S Lk 24:27 [j] S Lk 24:27 [k] S Mk 1:24 [l] Lk 3:23
1:46 [m] Jn 7:41, 42,52
1:47 [n] Ro 9:4,6 [o] Ps 32:2
1:49 [p] ver 38; S Mt 23:7

40 Andrew, Simon Peter's brother, was
one of the two who heard what John had
said and who had followed Jesus. 41 The
first thing Andrew did was to find his
brother Simon and tell him, "We have
found the Messiah" (that is, the Christ).[b]
42 And he brought him to Jesus.
Jesus looked at him and said, "You are
Simon son of John. You will be called[c] Cephas" (which, when translated, is Peter[b]).[d]

Jesus Calls Philip and Nathanael

43 The next day Jesus decided to leave
for Galilee. Finding Philip,[e] he said to him,
"Follow me."[f]
44 Philip, like Andrew and Peter, was
from the town of Bethsaida.[g] 45 Philip
found Nathanael[h] and told him, "We have
found the one Moses wrote about in the
Law,[i] and about whom the prophets also
wrote[j] — Jesus of Nazareth,[k] the son of Joseph."[l]
46 "Nazareth! Can anything good come
from there?"[m] Nathanael asked.
"Come and see," said Philip.
47 When Jesus saw Nathanael approaching, he said of him, "Here truly is an Israelite[n] in whom there is no deceit."[o]
48 "How do you know me?" Nathanael
asked.
Jesus answered, "I saw you while you
were still under the fig tree before Philip
called you."
49 Then Nathanael declared, "Rabbi,[p]

[a] *34* See Isaiah 42:1; many manuscripts *is the Son of God.* [b] *42* *Cephas* (Aramaic) and *Peter* (Greek) both mean *rock.*

1:29 *Lamb of God.* An expression found in the Bible only here and in v. 36. Many suggestions have been made as to which "lamb" John had in mind (e.g., the lamb offered at Passover or the lamb of Isa 53:7, of Jer 11:19, of Ge 22:8 or of Rev 5:6 [see note there]). It may be that John chose this unique way of referring to Jesus' mission to point both to the sacrificial offering that Jesus would become and to his subsequent conquest of all evil powers — the two ways by which he "takes away the sin of the world" (see 1Jn 2:2 and note).

1:31 *I ... did not know him.* Although John the Baptist was related to Jesus (Lk 1:36), he "lived in the wilderness until he appeared publicly to Israel" (Lk 1:80) and may not have known Jesus personally. But the words probably mean only that he did not know that Jesus was the Messiah until he saw the sign mentioned in vv. 32 – 33.

1:32 See note on Mt 3:15 for Jesus' baptism.

1:33 *baptize with the Holy Spirit.* John baptized with water, but Jesus would baptize with the Spirit — by which he would cause those who believe in him to participate in the powers and graces of the new life he came to give (see 20:22; Ac 1:5; 2:4; 11:15 – 16; 19:4 – 6; 1Co 12 – 14; Gal 3:5,14; 4:6; 5:16 – 25; Eph 1:13; 3:16; 5:18; Php 3:3; 1Th 4:8). *Holy Spirit.* His normal title in the NT, though it appears only here and in 14:26; 20:22 in this Gospel — emphasizing his holiness rather than his power or greatness.

1:34 *God's Chosen One.* See NIV text note.

1:35 *two.* One was Andrew (v. 40). The other is not named, but from early times it has been thought that he was the author of this Gospel. *his disciples.* In the sense that they had been baptized by John and looked to him as their religious teacher.

1:36 *Lamb of God.* See note on v. 29.

1:40 *Andrew.* One of the 12 apostles (Mt 10:2). He was from Bethsaida (v. 44) but later lived with Peter at Capernaum (Mk 1:29), where they fished for a living (Mt 4:18).

1:41 *the Messiah.* See note on v. 25.

1:42 *Simon son of John.* See note on Mt 16:17. *Cephas ... Peter.* See NIV text note. In the Gospels, Peter was anything but a rock; he was impulsive and unstable. In Acts, however, he was a pillar of the early church. Jesus named him not for what he was but for what, by God's grace, he would become (see Mt 16:18 and note).

1:44 *Bethsaida.* See note on Mt 11:21.

1:45 *the Law ... the prophets.* See note on Lk 24:44. *son of Joseph.* Not a denial of the virgin birth of Christ (see Mt 1:18,20,23,25 and note; Lk 1:26 – 35 and note). Joseph was Jesus' legal, though not his natural, father.

1:46 *Nazareth.* See 7:52; see also note on Mt 2:23.

1:47 *Here truly is an Israelite.* See 2:24 – 25.

1:48 *fig tree.* Its shade was a favorite place for study and prayer in hot weather.

1:49 *Rabbi.* Hebrew word for "(my) teacher." *the Son of God.* See vv. 14,18,34; 3:16 and note; 20:31. At the beginning of

THE SEVEN SIGNS OF JOHN'S GOSPEL

SIGN	VERSES
(1) Changing water into wine	2:1–11
(2) Healing an official's son	4:43–54
(3) Healing a disabled man at the Bethesda pool	5:1–15
(4) Feeding the 5,000	6:1–14
(5) Walking on water	6:16–21
(6) Healing the man born blind	9:1–12
(7) Raising Lazarus from the dead	11:1–44
Epilogue sign: the miraculous catch of fish	21:1–14

you are the Son of God;[q] you are the king
of Israel."[r]
50 Jesus said, "You believe[a] because I
told you I saw you under the fig tree. You
will see greater things than that." 51 He
then added, "Very truly I tell you,[b] you[b]
will see 'heaven open,[s] and the angels of
God ascending and descending[t] on'[c] the
Son of Man."[u]

Jesus Changes Water Into Wine

2 On the third day a wedding took
place at Cana in Galilee.[v] Jesus' mother[w] was there, 2 and Jesus and his disciples had also been invited to the wedding. 3 When the wine was gone, Jesus'
mother said to him, "They have no more
wine."
4 "Woman,[dx] why do you involve me?"[y]
Jesus replied. "My hour[z] has not yet
come."
5 His mother said to the servants, "Do
whatever he tells you."[a]
6 Nearby stood six stone water jars,
the kind used by the Jews for ceremonial washing,[b] each holding from twenty to
thirty gallons.[e]
7 Jesus said to the servants, "Fill the jars
with water"; so they filled them to the
brim.
8 Then he told them, "Now draw some
out and take it to the master of the banquet."
They did so, 9 and the master of the banquet tasted the water that had been turned
into wine.[c] He did not realize where it had
come from, though the servants who had
drawn the water knew. Then he called the
bridegroom aside 10 and said, "Everyone
brings out the choice wine first and then
the cheaper wine after the guests have had
too much to drink; but you have saved the
best till now."
11 What Jesus did here in Cana of Galilee
was the first of the signs[d] through which
he revealed his glory;[e] and his disciples
believed in him.[f]

[a] 50 Or *Do you believe . . . ?* [b] 51 The Greek is plural. [c] 51 Gen. 28:12 [d] 4 The Greek for *Woman* does not denote any disrespect. [e] 6 Or from about 75 to about 115 liters

1:49 [q] ver 34; S Mt 4:3 [r] S Mt 2:2; 27:42; Jn 12:13 **1:51** [s] S Mt 3:16 [t] Ge 28:12 [u] S Mt 8:20 **2:1** [v] Jn 4:46; 21:2 [w] S Mt 12:46 **2:4** [x] Jn 19:26 [y] S Mt 8:29 [z] S Mt 26:18 **2:5** [a] Ge 41:55 **2:6** [b] Mk 7:3,4; Jn 3:25 **2:9** [c] Jn 4:46 **2:11** [d] ver 23; Mt 12:38; Jn 3:2; S 4:48; 6:2,14,26,30; 12:37; 20:30 [e] Jn 1:14 [f] Ex 14:31

Jesus' ministry Nathanael acknowledged him with this meaningful title; later it was used in mockery (Mt 27:40; cf. Jn 19:7). Andrew's "the Messiah" (v. 41) and Nathanael's "the Son of God" together match Peter's "You are the Messiah, the Son of the living God" (Mt 16:16). *king of Israel.* See 12:13 and note. In Mk 15:32 "Messiah" and "king of Israel" are equated.

1:51 *Very truly I tell you.* See note on Mk 3:28; "truly I tell you" occurs more in this Gospel than in any other Gospel — and nowhere else in the NT. And John alone prefaces the phrase with "very" a total of 25 times. *heaven open.* In Jesus' ministry the disciples will see heaven's (God's) testimony about Jesus as plainly as if they heard an announcement from heaven concerning him. *the angels of God ascending and descending.* As in Jacob's dream (see Ge 28:12 and note), thus marking Jesus as God's stairway between heaven and earth, "the way and the truth and the life" (14:6). He is God's elect one through whom redemption comes to the world — perhaps identifying Jesus as "truly" *the* "Israelite" (v. 47). *Son of Man.* Jesus' favorite self-designation (see note on Mk 8:31).

2:1 *third day.* Cf. Ge 22:4 and note. *wedding.* Little is known of how a wedding was performed in the Holy Land in the first century, but clearly the feast was very important and might go on for a week. To fail in proper hospitality was a serious offense. *Cana.* Mentioned only in John's Gospel (v. 11; 4:46; 21:2). It was west of the Sea of Galilee, but the exact location is uncertain (see map, p. 1776).

2:3 *When the wine was gone.* More than a minor social embarrassment, since the family had an obligation to provide a feast of the socially required standard. There was no great variety in beverages, and people normally drank water or wine.

2:4 *Woman.* See NIV text note. *My hour has not yet come.* Several similar expressions scattered through this Gospel (see 7:6,8,30; 8:20 and notes) picture Jesus moving inevitably toward the destiny for which he had come: the time of his sacrificial death on the cross. At the crucifixion and resurrection Jesus' "hour" had truly come (see 12:23,27 and notes; 13:1; 16:32; 17:1).

2:6 *ceremonial washing.* Jews became ceremonially defiled during the normal circumstances of daily life and were cleansed by pouring water over their hands. For a lengthy feast with many guests a large amount of water was required for this purpose. *holding.* Refers to capacity, not to actual content.

2:8–9 *master of the banquet.* A function mentioned only here in the NT. Apparently he was one of the guests, charged with serving as master of ceremonies.

2:10 *too much to drink . . . you have saved the best.* Ordinarily, after the guests' taste buds were dulled, the "cheaper wine" was served.

2:11 *signs.* John always refers to Jesus' miracles as "signs," a word emphasizing the significance of the action rather than the marvel (see, e.g., 4:54; 6:14; 9:16; 11:47 and notes). There are seven (the number of completeness and perfection) such "signs" in the main body of this Gospel (see chart above; see also chart, p. 1765); the large catch of fish in 21:1–11 is in the epilogue (see Introduction: Outline;

MIRACLES OF JESUS

HEALING MIRACLES	MATTHEW	MARK	LUKE	JOHN
Man with leprosy	8:2–4	1:40–42	5:12–13	
Roman centurion's servant	8:5–13		7:1–10	
Peter's mother-in-law	8:14–15	1:30–31	4:38–39	
Two men from Gadara	8:28–34	5:1–15	8:27–35	
Paralyzed man	9:2–7	2:3–12	5:18–25	
Woman with bleeding	9:20–22	5:25–29	8:43–48	
Two blind men	9:27–31			
Mute, demon-possessed man	9:32–33			
Man with a shriveled hand	12:10–13	3:1–5	6:6–10	
Blind, mute, demon-possessed man	12:22		11:14	
Canaanite woman's daughter	15:21–28	7:24–30		
Demon-possessed boy	17:14–18	9:17–29	9:38–43	
Two blind men (including Bartimaeus)	20:29–34	10:46–52	18:35–43	
Deaf mute		7:31–37		
Demon-possessed man in synagogue		1:23–26	4:33–35	
Blind man at Bethsaida		8:22–26		
Crippled woman			13:11–13	
Man with abnormal swelling			14:1–4	
Ten men with leprosy			17:11–19	
The high priest's servant			22:50–51	
Official's son at Capernaum				4:46–54
Sick man at pool of Bethesda				5:1–9
Man born blind				9:1–7
MIRACLES SHOWING POWER OVER NATURE				
Calming the storm	8:23–27	4:37–41	8:22–25	
Walking on water	14:25	6:48–51		6:19–21
Feeding the 5,000	14:15–21	6:35–44	9:12–17	6:6–13
Feeding the 4,000	15:32–38	8:1–9		
Coin in fish's mouth	17:24–27			
Fig tree withered	21:18–22	11:12–14,20–25		
Large catch of fish			5:4–11	
Water turned into wine				2:1–11
Another large catch of fish				21:1–11
MIRACLES OF RAISING THE DEAD				
Jairus's daughter	9:18–19,23–25	5:22–24,38–42	8:41–42,49–56	
Widow's son at Nain			7:11–15	
Lazarus				11:1–44

12 After this he went down to Capernaum[g] with his mother[h] and brothers[i] and his disciples. There they stayed for a few days.

Jesus Clears the Temple Courts

2:14-16pp — Mt 21:12,13; Mk 11:15-17; Lk 19:45,46

13 When it was almost time for the Jewish Passover,[j] Jesus went up to Jerusalem.[k]
14 In the temple courts he found people selling cattle, sheep and doves,[l] and others sitting at tables exchanging money.[m] 15 So he made a whip out of cords, and drove all from the temple courts, both sheep and cattle; he scattered the coins of the money changers and overturned their tables.
16 To those who sold doves he said, "Get these out of here! Stop turning my Father's house[n] into a market!" 17 His disciples remembered that it is written: "Zeal for your house will consume me."[a][o]

2:12 [g] S Mt 4:13 [h] S Mt 12:46 [i] S Mt 12:46 **2:13** [j] S Jn 11:55 [k] Dt 16:1-6; Lk 2:41 **2:14** [l] Lev 1:14; Dt 14:26 [m] Dt 14:25 **2:16** [n] Lk 2:49 **2:17** [o] Ps 69:9

[a] *17* Psalm 69:9

cf. note on 6:35). They revealed Jesus' glory (see 1:14 and note) and likely also pointed to the fullness of the salvation he came to effect. In his account of Jesus' first display of "his glory" by providing an abundance of wine at a wedding feast, John probably was testifying that Christ's saving mission would culminate in the redemption of the creation from all its distresses, so that the wine of joy would flow fully, as the prophets had announced (see Isa 35:1–2; Joel 3:18; Am 9:13 and notes; cf. Ge 49:11 and note). *his disciples believed in him.* See 1:7; 20:31 and notes.

2:12 *went down.* Situated on the shore of the lake, Capernaum was at a lower level than Cana. *Capernaum.* See notes on Mt 4:13; Lk 10:15; see also model, p. 1710. *brothers.* See note on Lk 8:19.

2:13 *Passover.* See Ex 12 and notes on Ex 12:11–23; see also notes on Mt 26:17,18–30; Mk 14:1,12; Lk 22:1 and chart, pp. 188–189. Passover was one of the annual festivals that all Jewish men were required to celebrate in Jerusalem. See notes on 5:1; Dt 16:16.

2:14–17 Matthew, Mark and Luke record a clearing of the temple toward the end of Jesus' ministry (see note on Mt 21:12–17).

2:14 *cattle, sheep and doves.* Required for sacrifices. Jews who came great distances had to be able to buy sacrificial animals near the temple. The merchants, however, were selling them in the outer court of the temple itself, the one place where Gentiles could come to pray. *exchanging money.* Many coins had to be changed into currency acceptable to the temple authorities, which made money changers necessary (see note on Mk 11:15). They should not, however, have been working in the temple itself. See model below.

2:17 *His disciples remembered.* Probably after Jesus' crucifixion (see v. 22) — when Ps 69 struck them as a prophecy of his suffering at the hands of those his "zeal" for the true worship of God had deeply antagonized (see introduction to Ps 69).

A model of Herod's temple. The outer courts on either side are likely where Jesus found people selling cattle, sheep and doves, and others sitting at tables exchanging money (Jn 2:14).

Todd Bolen/www.BiblePlaces.com

18 The Jews[p] then responded to him,
"What sign[q] can you show us to prove
your authority to do all this?"[r]
19 Jesus answered them, "Destroy this
temple, and I will raise it again in three
days."[s]
20 They replied, "It has taken forty-six
years to build this temple, and you are
going to raise it in three days?" 21 But the
temple he had spoken of was his body.[t]
22 After he was raised from the dead, his
disciples recalled what he had said.[u] Then
they believed the scripture[v] and the words
that Jesus had spoken.
23 Now while he was in Jerusalem at the
Passover Festival,[w] many people saw the
signs[x] he was performing and believed[y] in
his name.[a] 24 But Jesus would not entrust
himself to them, for he knew all people. 25 He
did not need any testimony about mankind,[z]
for he knew what was in each person.[a]

Jesus Teaches Nicodemus

3 Now there was a Pharisee, a man
named Nicodemus[b] who was a member of the Jewish ruling council.[c] 2 He
came to Jesus at night and said, "Rabbi,[d]
we know[e] that you are a teacher who has
come from God. For no one could perform
the signs[f] you are doing if God were not
with him."[g]
3 Jesus replied, "Very truly I tell you, no
one can see the kingdom of God unless
they are born again.[b]"[h]
4 "How can someone be born when
they are old?" Nicodemus asked. "Surely
they cannot enter a second time into their
mother's womb to be born!"
5 Jesus answered, "Very truly I tell you,
no one can enter the kingdom of God unless they are born of water and the Spirit.[i]
6 Flesh gives birth to flesh, but the Spirit[c] gives birth to spirit.[j] 7 You should not
be surprised at my saying, 'You[d] must be
born again.' 8 The wind blows wherever it
pleases. You hear its sound, but you cannot tell where it comes from or where it is
going. So it is with everyone born of the
Spirit."[e][k]
9 "How can this be?"[l] Nicodemus asked.
10 "You are Israel's teacher,"[m] said Jesus,
"and do you not understand these things?
11 Very truly I tell you, we speak of what
we know,[n] and we testify to what we have
seen, but still you people do not accept
our testimony.[o] 12 I have spoken to you of
earthly things and you do not believe; how
then will you believe if I speak of heavenly
things? 13 No one has ever gone into heav-
en[p] except the one who came from heav-
en[q]—the Son of Man.[f][r] 14 Just as Moses
lifted up the snake in the wilderness,[s] so
the Son of Man must be lifted up,[g][t] 15 that
everyone who believes[u] may have eternal
life in him."[h][v]
16 For God so loved[w] the world that he
gave[x] his one and only Son,[y] that whoever

2:18 [p] S Jn 1:19 [q] S ver 11 [r] S Mt 12:38 **2:19** [s] S Mt 16:21; 26:61; 27:40; Mk 14:58; 15:29; Ac 6:14 **2:21** [t] 1Co 6:19 **2:22** [u] Lk 24:5-8; Jn 12:16; 14:26 [v] Ps 16:10; S Lk 24:27 **2:23** [w] ver 13 [x] S ver 11 [y] S Jn 3:15 **2:25** [z] Isa 11:3 [a] Dt 31:21; 1Ki 8:39; S Mt 9:4; Jn 6:61,64; 13:11 **3:1** [b] Jn 7:50; 19:39 [c] Lk 23:13 **3:2** [d] S Mt 23:7 [e] ver 11 [f] S Jn 2:11 [g] Jn 10:38; 14:10,11; Ac 2:22; 10:38 **3:3** [h] S Mt 3:2; S Jn 1:13 **3:5** [i] S Ac 22:16; Titus 3:5 **3:6** [j] S Jn 1:13; 1Co 15:50 **3:8** [k] 1Co 2:14-16 **3:9** [l] Jn 6:52,60 **3:10** [m] Lk 2:46 **3:11** [n] Jn 1:18; 7:16,17 [o] ver 32 **3:13** [p] Pr 30:4; Ac 2:34; Eph 4:8-10 [q] ver 31; Jn 6:38, 42; Heb 4:14; 9:24 [r] S Mt 8:20 **3:14** [s] Nu 21:8,9 [t] S Jn 12:32 **3:15** [u] ver 16,36; Ge 15:6; Nu 14:11; Mt 27:42; Mk 1:15; Jn 1:7, 12; 2:23; 5:24; 7:38; 20:29; Ac 13:39; 16:31; Ro 3:22; 10:9,10; 1Jn 5:1,5,10 [v] ver 16,36; S Mt 25:46; Jn 20:31 **3:16** [w] Ro 5:8; Eph 2:4; 1Jn 4:9,10 [x] Isa 9:6; Ro 8:32 [y] Ge 22:12; Jn 1:18

[a] *23* Or *in him* [b] *3* The Greek for *again* also means *from above*; also in verse 7. [c] *6* Or *but spirit* [d] *7* The Greek is plural. [e] *8* The Greek for *Spirit* is the same as that for *wind*. [f] *13* Some manuscripts *Man, who is in heaven* [g] *14* The Greek for *lifted up* also means *exalted*. [h] *15* Some interpreters end the quotation with verse 21.

2:19 *temple.* The Jews thought Jesus was referring to the literal temple, but John tells us that he was not (v. 21). Just a few years later Jesus was accused of saying that he would destroy the temple and raise it again (see Mt 26:61; Mk 14:58 and notes), and mockers repeated the charge as he hung on the cross (Mt 27:40; Mk 15:29). The same misunderstanding may have been behind the charge against Stephen (see Ac 6:13 and note).

2:20 *forty-six years.* The temple was not finally completed until AD 64. The meaning is that work had been going on for 46 years. Since it had begun c. 19 or 20 BC, the year of the event recorded here is c. AD 27 (see chart, p. 1636).

2:22 *recalled what he had said.* See 12:16; see also 14:26 and note. *Then they believed the scripture.* See 20:9 and note. It is not clear whether reference here is to a particular word from the OT (see, e.g., Ps 16:10; 17:15 and notes) or to the OT in general (cf. 1Co 15:4).

2:23 *Passover Festival.* See note on v. 13. *name.* See notes on Ps 5:11; Eze 20:9.

3:1 *Pharisee.* See notes on Mt 3:7; Mk 2:16; Lk 5:17.

3:2 *at night.* Perhaps Nicodemus was afraid to come by day. Or he may have wanted a long talk, which would have been difficult in the daytime with the crowds around Jesus.

3:3,7 *born again.* The Greek may also mean "born from above" (see NIV text note on v. 3). Both meanings are consistent with Jesus' redeeming work (see 1:13 and note).

3:5 *kingdom of God.* See note on Mt 3:2. *born of water and the Spirit.* A phrase understood in various ways: (1) It means much the same as "born of the Spirit" (v. 8; cf. 7:38–39; Titus 3:5 and notes). (2) Water here refers to purification. (3) Water refers to baptism—that of John (1:31) or that of Jesus and his disciples (see v. 22; 4:2 and notes). (4) Water refers to physical birth, specifically to the water of the amniotic sac (cf. vv. 4,6).

3:7 *You.* See NIV text note. This assertion applies to everyone, not just to Nicodemus. *must.* There are no exceptions. *born again.* See note on v. 3.

3:8 The Holy Spirit is sovereign. He works as he pleases in his renewal of human hearts.

3:11 *testimony.* See note on 1:7.

3:13 *Son of Man.* Jesus' favorite self-designation (see notes on Mk 8:31; Lk 19:10).

3:14 *Moses lifted up the snake.* See notes on Nu 21:8–9; 2Ki 18:4. *the Son of Man must be lifted up.* See 8:28; 12:32 and note; see also NIV text note.

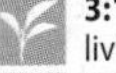

3:15–16 *believes.* See note on 1:7. *eternal life.* Life in living fellowship with God—both now and forever.

3:16 *God so loved the world.* The great truth that motivated God's plan of salvation (cf. 1Jn 4:9–10). "So" here means "in this way" rather than "so much." *world.* All people on earth—or perhaps all creation (see notes on 1:4,9). *gave his one and only Son.* Cf. Isa 9:6 ("a son is given," referring to the Messianic Son of David—who is also God's Son [see 2Sa

PERSONAL INTERVIEWS—PARALLELS IN JOHN 3 AND 4

NICODEMUS JOHN 3	THE SAMARITAN WOMAN JOHN 4
1. Jesus sparks interest with a spiritual metaphor: new birth (3:3).	**1.** Jesus sparks interest with a spiritual metaphor: living water (4:10).
2. Nicodemus is confused (3:4).	**2.** The woman is confused (4:11–12).
3. Jesus clarifies the spiritual significance (3:5).	**3.** Jesus clarifies the spiritual significance (4:13, 21–24).
4. More confusion by Nicodemus (3:9)	**4.** More confusion by the woman (4:15)
5. More clarification and a mild rebuke from Jesus (3:10–12)	**5.** More clarification and a mild rebuke from Jesus (4:21–24)
6. Jesus identifies himself as the Son of Man, the Son of God and the light (3:13–21).	**6.** Jesus identifies himself as the Messiah (4:26).

believes[z] in him shall not perish but have eternal life.[a] 17 For God did not send his Son into the world[b] to condemn the world, but to save the world through him.[c] 18 Whoever believes in him is not condemned,[d] but whoever does not believe stands condemned already because they have not believed in the name of God's one and only Son.[e] 19 This is the verdict: Light[f] has come into the world, but people loved darkness instead of light because their deeds were evil.[g] 20 Everyone who does evil hates the light, and will not come into the light for fear that their deeds will be exposed.[h] 21 But whoever lives by the truth comes into the light, so that it may be seen plainly that what they have done has been done in the sight of God.

John Testifies Again About Jesus

22 After this, Jesus and his disciples went out into the Judean countryside, where he spent some time with them, and baptized.[i] 23 Now John[j] also was baptizing at Aenon near Salim, because there was plenty of water, and people were coming and being baptized. 24 (This was before John was put in prison.)[k] 25 An argument developed between some of John's disciples and a certain Jew over the matter of ceremonial washing.[l] 26 They came to John and said to him, "Rabbi,[m] that man who was with you on the other side of the Jordan—the one you testified[n] about—look, he is baptizing, and everyone is going to him."

27 To this John replied, "A person can receive only what is given them from heaven. 28 You yourselves can testify that I said, 'I am not the Messiah but am sent ahead of him.'[o] 29 The bride belongs to the bridegroom.[p] The friend who attends the bridegroom waits and listens for him, and is full of joy when he hears the bridegroom's voice. That joy is mine, and it is now complete.[q] 30 He must become greater; I must become less."[a]

31 The one who comes from above[r] is above all; the one who is from the earth belongs to the earth, and speaks as one from the earth.[s] The one who comes from heaven is above all. 32 He testifies to

3:16 [z]S ver 15 [a]ver 36; Jn 6:29, 40; 11:25, 26 **3:17** [b]Jn 6:29, 57; 10:36; 11:42; 17:8, 21; 20:21 [c]Isa 53:11; S Mt 1:21; S Lk 2:11; 19:10; Jn 1:29; 12:47; S Ro 11:14; 1Ti 1:15; 2:5, 6; 1Jn 2:2; 3:5 **3:18** [d]Jn 5:24 [e]Jn 1:18; 1Jn 4:9 **3:19** [f]S Jn 1:4 [g]Ps 52:3; Jn 7:7 **3:20** [h]Eph 5:11, 13 **3:22** [i]Jn 4:2 **3:23** [j]S Mt 3:1 **3:24** [k]Mt 4:12; 14:3 **3:25** [l]Jn 2:6 **3:26** [m]S Mt 23:7 [n]Jn 1:7 **3:28** [o]Jn 1:20, 23 **3:29** [p]Mt 9:15 [q]Jn 16:24; 17:13; Php 2:2; 1Jn 1:4; 2Jn 12 **3:31** [r]ver 13 [s]Jn 8:23; 1Jn 4:5

[a] *30* Some interpreters end the quotation with verse 36.

7:14 and note]). See also 1:14,18 and notes; cf. Ge 22:2,16; Ro 8:32 and notes. Although believers are also called "sons" of God (2Co 6:18; Gal 4:4–6), Jesus is God's Son in a unique sense (see 20:31 and note).

3:18 *believes ... does not believe.* John is not speaking of momentary beliefs and doubts but of continuing, settled convictions. *name.* See 2:23 and note.

3:22 *baptized.* According to 4:2 only the disciples actually baptized.

3:23 *Aenon.* Possibly about eight miles south of Scythopolis (Beth Shan), west of the Jordan (see map, p. 1770).

3:24 See note on Lk 3:20.

3:25 *argument ... over ... ceremonial washing.* See 2:6 and note. The Dead Sea (Qumran) Scrolls (see essay, pp. 1574–1576) show that some Jews were deeply interested in the right way to achieve ceremonial purification.

3:26 *testified.* See note on 1:7. John's disciples knew that he had testified about Jesus, but they loved their master and were apparently envious of Jesus' success.

3:27 The words are true of both Jesus and John (and of everyone). Both had what God had given them, so there was no place for envy. *given.* The Greek verb is used 76 times in this Gospel, especially of the things the Father gives the Son.

3:29 *bridegroom.* The most important man at a wedding, referring here to Jesus. "The friend who attends the bridegroom" is there only to help him, which describes the role of John the Baptist. *full of joy.* Not because he was on center stage but because the bridegroom was there. John's joy was to hear of Jesus' success.

3:30 John the Baptist's pointed way of reaffirming his subordinate position.

3:31 *The one who comes from above.* Jesus, whose heavenly origin (see v. 13; 1Co 15:47) meant much to John. *the one*

what he has seen and heard,[t] but no one
accepts his testimony.[u] 33 Whoever has accepted it has certified that God is truthful.
34 For the one whom God has sent[v] speaks
the words of God, for God[a] gives the Spirit[w] without limit. 35 The Father loves the
Son and has placed everything in his
hands.[x] 36 Whoever believes in the Son has
eternal life,[y] but whoever rejects the Son
will not see life, for God's wrath remains
on them.

Jesus Talks With a Samaritan Woman

4 Now Jesus learned that the Pharisees
had heard that he was gaining and
baptizing more disciples than John[z]— 2 although in fact it was not Jesus who baptized, but his disciples. 3 So he left Judea[a]
and went back once more to Galilee.
4 Now he had to go through Samaria.[b]
5 So he came to a town in Samaria called
Sychar, near the plot of ground Jacob had
given to his son Joseph.[c] 6 Jacob's well
was there, and Jesus, tired as he was from
the journey, sat down by the well. It was
about noon.
7 When a Samaritan woman came to
draw water, Jesus said to her, "Will you
give me a drink?"[d] 8 (His disciples had
gone into the town[e] to buy food.)
9 The Samaritan woman said to him,
"You are a Jew and I am a Samaritan[f]
woman. How can you ask me for a drink?"
(For Jews do not associate with Samaritans.[b])
10 Jesus answered her, "If you knew the
gift of God and who it is that asks you for
a drink, you would have asked him and he
would have given you living water."[g]
11 "Sir," the woman said, "you have
nothing to draw with and the well is deep.
Where can you get this living water?
12 Are you greater than our father Jacob,
who gave us the well[h] and drank from it
himself, as did also his sons and his livestock?"
13 Jesus answered, "Everyone who
drinks this water will be thirsty again,
14 but whoever drinks the water I give
them will never thirst.[i] Indeed, the water I
give them will become in them a spring of
water[j] welling up to eternal life."[k]
15 The woman said to him, "Sir, give me
this water so that I won't get thirsty[l] and
have to keep coming here to draw water."
16 He told her, "Go, call your husband
and come back."
17 "I have no husband," she replied.
Jesus said to her, "You are right when
you say you have no husband. 18 The fact

3:32 [t] Jn 8:26; 15:15 [u] ver 11 **3:34** [v] S ver 17 [w] Isa 42:1; Mt 12:18; Lk 4:18; Ac 10:38 **3:35** [x] S Mt 28:18 **3:36** [y] S ver 15; Jn 5:24; 6:47 **4:1** [z] Jn 3:22, 26 **4:3** [a] Jn 3:22 **4:4** [b] S Mt 10:5 **4:5** [c] Ge 33:19; Jos 24:32 **4:7** [d] Ge 24:17; 1Ki 17:10 **4:8** [e] ver 5, 39 **4:9** [f] S Mt 10:5 **4:10** [g] Isa 44:3; 55:1; Jer 2:13; 17:13; Zec 14:8; Jn 7:37, 38; Rev 7:17; 21:6; 22:1, 17 **4:12** [h] ver 6 **4:14** [i] Jn 6:35 [j] Isa 12:3; 58:11; Jn 7:38 [k] S Mt 25:46 **4:15** [l] Jn 6:34

[a] 34 Greek *he* [b] 9 Or *do not use dishes Samaritans have used*

---

who is from the earth. A general expression that could apply to anyone, but here it particularly refers to John the Baptist.
3:32 *what he has seen and heard.* Jesus taught from divine experience. *no one.* Does not mean that no person accepted what he said (see v. 33) but that people in general refused his teaching.
3:33 *certified.* When people accept Christ's testimony, they accept the truth that Jesus came from heaven and that God was acting in him for the world's salvation. They thereby testify that God is truthful.
3:34 *the one whom God has sent.* Jesus as the sent one is a key theme in John's Gospel (e.g., 4:34; 17:3). *without limit.* Some hold that it is only to Jesus that the Spirit is given without limit. Others take the "he" (see NIV text note) as a reference to Christ's giving the Spirit without limit to believers.
3:36 *has.* Eternal life is a present possession, not something the believer will only obtain later (see note on v. 15). *God's wrath.* A strong expression, meaning that God is actively opposed to everything evil. The word "wrath" occurs only here in John's Gospel (see note on Ro 1:18). *remains.* No one who persists in rejecting the Son of God as Savior and Lord can expect God's wrath eventually to fade away. God's opposition to evil is both total and permanent.
4:1 *Pharisees.* These religious leaders took a close interest in John the Baptist (see 1:24 and note) and then also in Jesus.
4:2 The disciples did not baptize without Jesus' approval (see 3:2 and note).
4:3 *left Judea.* Success (which aroused opposition; see note on 7:1 — 8:59), not failure, led Jesus to leave Judea.
4:4 *had to go.* Perhaps the necessity lay in Jesus' mission rather than in geography. *Samaria.* Here the whole region, not simply the city. Jews often avoided Samaria by crossing the Jordan and traveling on the east side (see notes on Mt 10:5; Lk 9:52).
4:5 *Sychar.* A small village near Shechem. Jacob bought some land in the vicinity of Shechem (Ge 33:18 – 19), and it was apparently this land that he gave to Joseph (Ge 48:21 – 22). See map, p. 1770.
4:6 *Jacob's well.* Mentioned nowhere else in Scripture (see v. 11 and note).
4:7 *to draw water.* People normally drew water at the end of the day rather than in the heat of midday (see v. 6; Ge 24:11 and note). But the practice is attested by Josephus, who says that the young ladies whom Moses helped (Ex 2:15 – 17) came to draw water at noon.
4:9 *do not associate with.* The point of the NIV text note (and probably of the text) is that Jews would become ceremonially unclean if they used a drinking vessel handled by a Samaritan, since they held that all Samaritans were "unclean."
4:10 *gift.* The Greek for this word is used only here in this Gospel and emphasizes God's grace through Christ. Jesus gave life and gave it freely. *living water.* Not stagnant cistern water but fresh, flowing water, as of a spring or mountain stream, that revives and refreshes life. In 7:38 – 39 the term is explained as referring to the Holy Spirit, but here it refers to that which produces eternal life (see v. 14).
4:11 *deep.* Christian pilgrim sources as early as the fourth century mention a well in this area that was about 100 feet deep. When the present well was cleaned out in 1935, it was found to be 138 feet deep.
4:12 *our father Jacob.* Deep regard for the past prevented her from seeing the great opportunity of the present.
4:14 *welling up.* The expression is a vigorous one, with a meaning like "leaping up." Jesus was speaking of vigorous, abundant life (cf. 10:10).
4:15 Cf. the misunderstanding of Nicodemus (3:4). In both cases the way was opened for further instruction.

JESUS IN **JUDEA AND SAMARIA**

1 The most important port in the Holy Land in NT times

2 The birthplace of Jesus (Mt 2:1; Lk 2:4)

3 John the Baptist baptized here (Jn 3:23). Aenon was also the probable location of John's ministry.

4 Here Jesus talked with a Samaritan woman at Jacob's well (Jn 4:5).

5 The mountain referred to by the Samaritan woman at the well as the worship center for the Samaritans (Jn 4:20–23)

6 Jesus raised Lazarus from the dead (Jn 11:43–44). Here at Bethany Jesus was anointed in the house of Simon the Leper (Mt 26:6). It was also the scene of the ascension (Lk 24:50–51).

7 Jesus healed a blind man here at Jericho (Mt 20:29) and called Zacchaeus down from a tree (Lk 19:1). The Good Samaritan helped a traveler en route here (Lk 10:30).

8 Most important Biblical city. Jesus was crucified at Jerusalem as predicted (Mt 16:21; Mk 10:33; Lk 18:31).

9 The resurrected Jesus appeared to two people walking to Emmaus, and he ate with them there (Lk 24:13).

is, you have had five husbands, and the man you now have is not your husband. What you have just said is quite true."

19 "Sir," the woman said, "I can see that you are a prophet.[m] 20 Our ancestors worshiped on this mountain,[n] but you Jews claim that the place where we must worship is in Jerusalem."[o]

21 "Woman," Jesus replied, "believe me, a time is coming[p] when you will worship the Father neither on this mountain nor in Jerusalem.[q] 22 You Samaritans worship what you do not know;[r] we worship what we do know, for salvation is from the Jews.[s] 23 Yet a time is coming and has now come[t] when the true worshipers will worship the Father in the Spirit[u] and in truth, for they are the kind of worshipers the Father seeks. 24 God is spirit,[v] and his worshipers must worship in the Spirit and in truth."

25 The woman said, "I know that Messiah" (called Christ)[w] "is coming. When he comes, he will explain everything to us."

26 Then Jesus declared, "I, the one speaking to you—I am he."[x]

The Disciples Rejoin Jesus

27 Just then his disciples returned[y] and were surprised to find him talking with a woman. But no one asked, "What do you want?" or "Why are you talking with her?"

28 Then, leaving her water jar, the woman went back to the town and said to the people, 29 "Come, see a man who told me everything I ever did.[z] Could this be the Messiah?"[a] 30 They came out of the town and made their way toward him.

31 Meanwhile his disciples urged him, "Rabbi,[b] eat something."

32 But he said to them, "I have food to eat[c] that you know nothing about."

33 Then his disciples said to each other, "Could someone have brought him food?"

34 "My food," said Jesus, "is to do the will[d] of him who sent me and to finish his work.[e] 35 Don't you have a saying, 'It's still four months until harvest'? I tell you, open your eyes and look at the fields! They are ripe for harvest.[f] 36 Even now the one who reaps draws a wage and harvests[g] a crop for eternal life,[h] so that the sower and the reaper may be glad together. 37 Thus the saying 'One sows and another reaps'[i] is true. 38 I sent you to reap what you have not worked for. Others have done the hard

4:19 [m]S Mt 21:11 **4:20** [n]Dt 11:29; Jos 8:33 [o]Lk 9:53 **4:21** [p]Jn 5:28; 16:2 [q]Mal 1:11; 1Ti 2:8 **4:22** [r]2Ki 17:28-41 [s]Isa 2:3; Ro 3:1, 2; 9:4,5; 15:8,9 **4:23** [t]Jn 5:25; 16:32 [u]Php 3:3 **4:24** [v]Php 3:3 **4:25** [w]Mt 1:16; Jn 1:41 **4:26** [x]Jn 8:24; 9:35-37 **4:27** [y]ver 8 **4:29** [z]ver 17, 18 [a]Mt 12:23; Jn 7:26,31 **4:31** [b]S Mt 23:7 **4:32** [c]Job 23:12; Mt 4:4; Jn 6:27 **4:34** [d]S Mt 26:39 [e]S Jn 19:30 **4:35** [f]Mt 9:37; Lk 10:2 **4:36** [g]Ro 1:13 [h]S Mt 25:46 **4:37** [i]Job 31:8; Mic 6:15

4:18 *five husbands.* The Jews held that a woman might be divorced twice or at the most three times. If the Samaritans had the same standard, the woman's life had been exceedingly immoral. She probably had not married her present partner.

4:19 *you are a prophet.* Because of his special insight.

4:20 *this mountain.* Perhaps the woman did not like the way the conversation was going and so began to argue. The proper place of worship had long been a source of debate between Jews and Samaritans. Samaritans held that "this mountain" (Mount Gerizim) was especially sacred. Abraham and Jacob had built altars in the general vicinity (Ge 12:6–7; 33:18–20), and the people had been blessed from this mountain (Dt 11:29; 27:12). In the Samaritan Scriptures, Mount Gerizim (rather than Mount Ebal) was the mountain on which Moses had commanded an altar to be built (Dt 27:4–6). The Samaritans had built a temple on Mount Gerizim c. 400 BC, which the Jews destroyed c. 128. Both actions, of course, increased hostility between the two groups. See map, p. 1770.

4:22 *worship what you do not know.* The Samaritan Bible contained only the Pentateuch. Samaritans worshiped the true God, but their failure to accept much of his revelation meant that they knew little about him. *salvation is from the Jews.* The Messiah would come from God's historic people (see notes on Ro 1:16; 11:18).

4:24 *God is spirit … worship in the Spirit and in truth.* The place of worship is irrelevant, because true worship must be in keeping with God's nature, which is spirit. "True worshipers" (v. 23) must worship God in the power (enablement) of his Spirit and in accordance with truth. In John's Gospel truth is associated with Christ (see notes on 1:14; 14:6), a fact that has great importance for the proper understanding of Christian worship.

4:25 *Messiah … will explain everything.* The woman's last attempt to evade the issue. The matter was too important, she reasoned, for people like Jesus and herself to work out. Understanding would have to await the coming of the Messiah (see note on 1:25). The Samaritans expected a Messiah, but their rejection of all the inspired writings after the Pentateuch meant that they knew little about him. They thought of him mainly as a teacher.

4:26 *I am he.* The only occasion before his trial on which Jesus specifically said that he was the Messiah (but see Mk 9:41, "Messiah"). The term did not have the political overtones in Samaria that it had in Judea, which may be part of the reason Jesus used the designation here.

4:27 *were surprised.* Jewish religious teachers rarely spoke with women in public.

4:29 *everything I ever did.* An exaggeration, but it shows the impression Jesus made on her. *Could this be the Messiah?* Her question seems full of longing, as though she did not expect them to say "Yes," but she could not say "No."

4:32 Cf. Mt 4:4 and note.

4:33 A misunderstanding similar to that of the woman (see v. 15 and note).

4:34 *My food … is to do the will of him who sent me.* John often mentions that Jesus depended on the Father and did the work the Father sent him to do (see, e.g., 3:34; 5:30 and notes; 6:38; 8:26; 9:4; 10:37–38; 12:50 and note; 14:31 and note; 15:10; 17:4).

4:35 *four months until harvest.* Apparently a proverb that meant something like "Harvest cannot be rushed." But, while the crops must take their time ripening, in the fields that Jesus referred to the harvest is already ripe (cf. Mt 9:36–38).

4:36 *draws a wage.* The work, or at least part of it, had been done, and others were working hard. The disciples were not to think that the harvest was far off. Jesus was not speaking of grain but of the "crop for eternal life." There was urgency, for the crop would not wait. *glad together.* There is no competition among Christ's faithful servants, and sower and reaper share in the joy of the crop.

4:37 See 1Co 3:6–9.

4:38 *Others.* May refer to John the Baptist and his supporters, on whose work the apostles would build. Or perhaps Jesus was looking further back, to the prophets and other godly

work, and you have reaped the benefits of their labor."

Many Samaritans Believe

39 Many of the Samaritans from that town[j] believed in him because of the woman's testimony, "He told me everything I ever did."[k] 40 So when the Samaritans came to him, they urged him to stay with them, and he stayed two days. 41 And because of his words many more became believers.

42 They said to the woman, "We no longer believe just because of what you said; now we have heard for ourselves, and we know that this man really is the Savior of the world."[l]

Jesus Heals an Official's Son

43 After the two days[m] he left for Galilee. 44 (Now Jesus himself had pointed out that a prophet has no honor in his own country.)[n] 45 When he arrived in Galilee, the Galileans welcomed him. They had seen all that he had done in Jerusalem at the Passover Festival,[o] for they also had been there.

46 Once more he visited Cana in Galilee, where he had turned the water into wine.[p] And there was a certain royal official whose son lay sick at Capernaum. 47 When this man heard that Jesus had arrived in Galilee from Judea,[q] he went to him and begged him to come and heal his son, who was close to death.

48 "Unless you people see signs and wonders,"[r] Jesus told him, "you will never believe."

49 The royal official said, "Sir, come down before my child dies."

50 "Go," Jesus replied, "your son will live."

The man took Jesus at his word and departed. 51 While he was still on the way, his servants met him with the news that his boy was living. 52 When he inquired as to the time when his son got better, they said to him, "Yesterday, at one in the afternoon, the fever left him."

53 Then the father realized that this was the exact time at which Jesus had said to him, "Your son will live." So he and his whole household[s] believed.

54 This was the second sign[t] Jesus performed after coming from Judea to Galilee.

The Healing at the Pool

5 Some time later, Jesus went up to Jerusalem for one of the Jewish festivals. 2 Now there is in Jerusalem near the Sheep Gate[u] a pool, which in Aramaic[v] is called Bethesda[a] and which is surrounded by five covered colonnades. 3 Here a great number of disabled people used to lie—the blind, the lame, the paralyzed. [4][b] 5 One who was there had been an invalid for thirty-eight years. 6 When Jesus saw him lying there and learned that he had been in this condition for a long time, he asked him, "Do you want to get well?"

7 "Sir," the invalid replied, "I have no one to help me into the pool when the

4:39 [j] ver 5 [k] ver 29 **4:42** [l] S Lk 2:11 **4:43** [m] ver 40 **4:44** [n] Mt 13:57; Lk 4:24 **4:45** [o] Jn 2:23 **4:46** [p] Jn 2:1-11 **4:47** [q] ver 3, 54 **4:48** [r] Da 4:2, 3; S Jn 2:11; Ac 2:43; 14:3; Ro 15:19; 2Co 12:12; Heb 2:4

4:53 [s] S Ac 11:14 **4:54** [t] S ver 48; S Jn 2:11 **5:2** [u] Ne 3:1; 12:39 [v] Jn 19:13, 17, 20; 20:16; Ac 21:40; 22:2; 26:14

[a] 2 Some manuscripts *Bethzatha;* other manuscripts *Bethsaida* [b] 3,4 Some manuscripts include here, wholly or in part, *paralyzed—and they waited for the moving of the waters. [4]From time to time an angel of the Lord would come down and stir up the waters. The first one into the pool after each such disturbance would be cured of whatever disease they had.*

---

people of old. Either way, he expected the apostles to be reapers as well as sowers.

4:39 *that town.* Sychar (v. 5).

4:42 *the Savior of the world.* In the NT the expression occurs only here and in 1Jn 4:14. It points to the facts (1) that Jesus not only teaches but also saves and (2) that his salvation extends to the world (see note on 3:16).

4:44 *a prophet has no honor in his own country.* Nonetheless, Jesus went to Galilee, because he came to die for our salvation (cf. 1:29 and note; cf. also Lk 4:24).

4:45 *welcomed him.* The welcome of the Galileans actually was a kind of rejection, for they were interested only in Jesus' miracles. They were not welcoming the Messiah who could bring forgiveness of sins, but only a miracle worker who could meet all their physical needs and expectations. *all that he had done.* See 20:30 and note. *Passover Festival.* The one narrated in 2:13–25.

4:46 *royal official.* Evidently an officer in Herod's service.

4:48 *Unless you … see signs and wonders … you will never believe.* The general attitude of Galileans, not that of the official.

4:50 *your son will live.* Not simply a prophecy, but words of power. Jesus was healing, not forecasting a happy ending (see vv. 51,53).

4:53 *believed.* Cf. the aim of this Gospel (see 20:31 and note; see also Introduction: Purpose and Emphases).

4:54 *second sign.* This was the second time Jesus performed a sign after coming from Judea to Galilee (see 2:11 and note; see also chart, p. 1764).

5:1 *one of the Jewish festivals.* Probably Passover, Pentecost or Tabernacles. The identity of this festival is significant for the attempt to ascertain the number of Passovers included in Jesus' ministry, and thus the number of years his ministry lasted. John explicitly mentions at least three different Passovers: the first in 2:13,23 (see note on 2:13), the second in 6:4 and the third several times (e.g., in 11:55; 12:1), suggesting a public ministry lasting between two and three years. However, if the festival of 5:1 was a fourth Passover or assumes that a fourth Passover had come and gone, Jesus' ministry would have lasted between three and four years.

5:2 *there is.* Use of the present tense may mean that the pool was still in existence and that John wrote his Gospel before the destruction of Jerusalem. However, see Introduction: Date. *Bethesda.* The manuscripts have a variety of names (see NIV text note), but one of the Dead Sea Scrolls seems to show that Bethesda is the right name. The site is generally identified with the twin pools near the present-day Saint Anne's Church. There would have been a colonnade on each of the four sides and another between the two pools.

5:6 *Do you want to get well?* The man had not asked Jesus for help.

5:7 *when the water is stirred.* The man did not see Jesus as a

water is stirred. While I am trying to get
in, someone else goes down ahead of me."
8Then Jesus said to him, "Get up! Pick up
your mat and walk."[w] 9At once the man was
cured; he picked up his mat and walked.
The day on which this took place was
a Sabbath,[x] 10and so the Jewish leaders[y]
said to the man who had been healed, "It
is the Sabbath; the law forbids you to carry your mat."[z]
11But he replied, "The man who made
me well said to me, 'Pick up your mat and
walk.'"
12So they asked him, "Who is this fellow who told you to pick it up and walk?"
13The man who was healed had no idea
who it was, for Jesus had slipped away
into the crowd that was there.
14Later Jesus found him at the temple
and said to him, "See, you are well again.
Stop sinning[a] or something worse may
happen to you." 15The man went away
and told the Jewish leaders[b] that it was
Jesus who had made him well.

The Authority of the Son

16So, because Jesus was doing these
things on the Sabbath, the Jewish leaders
began to persecute him. 17In his defense
Jesus said to them, "My Father[c] is always
at his work[d] to this very day, and I too
am working." 18For this reason they tried
all the more to kill him;[e] not only was he
breaking the Sabbath, but he was even
calling God his own Father, making himself equal with God.[f]
19Jesus gave them this answer: "Very
truly I tell you, the Son can do nothing

5:8 [w] Mt 9:5,6 **5:9** [x] Mt 12:1-14; Jn 9:14 **5:10** [y] ver 16 [z] Ne 13:15-22; Jer 17:21; S Mt 12:2
5:14 [a] Mk 2:5; Jn 8:11 **5:15** [b] S Jn 1:19 **5:17** [c] Lk 2:49 [d] Jn 9:4; 14:10 **5:18** [e] S Mt 12:14 [f] Jn 10:30,33; 19:7

potential healer, and his mind was set on the supposed curative powers of the water.

5:9 *the man was cured.* Ordinarily, faith in Jesus was essential to the cure (e.g., Mk 5:34), but here the man did not even know who Jesus was (v. 13). So while Jesus usually healed in response to faith, he was not limited by a person's lack of it.

5:10 *the law forbids you to carry your mat.* It was not the law of Moses itself but their traditional interpretation of it that prohibited carrying loads of any kind on the Sabbath. The Jews had very strict regulations on keeping the Sabbath but also had many curious loopholes that their lawyers made full use of (cf. Mt 23:4). It is always lawful to do good and to save life—including on the Sabbath (see v. 17; 7:23; Lk 6:9; 13:15; 14:5 and notes).

5:12 *this fellow.* The Jews were contrasting the authority of the law of God, which in their view prohibited the action, and that of a mere man (as they considered Jesus to be) who permitted it.

5:14 *Stop sinning.* Implies that the man's sins had caused his disability. In 9:1 Jesus repudiates the idea that disabilities (such as blindness there) are always caused by sin, but he does not say they are never caused by sin. *something worse.* The eternal consequences of sin are more serious than any physical ailment.

5:16 *was doing.* The continuous action points to more than one incident, and the Jews (see note on 1:19) apparently discerned a pattern. *began to persecute him.* John does not tell us what form the persecution took.

5:17 *My Father is always at his work.* Jesus' justification for his action was his close relation to his Father. God does not stop his deeds of compassion on the Sabbath day, and neither did Jesus (see Mk 2:25 and note).

5:18 *his own Father.* Referring to a special relationship. The Jews did not object to the idea that God is the Father of all, but they strongly objected to Jesus' claim that he stood in a special relationship to the Father—a relationship so close as to make himself equal with God.

5:19 *can do nothing by himself.* Because of who and what he was, it was not possible for Jesus to act except in dependence on the Father (see 4:34 and note).

POSSIBLE CHRONOLOGY OF **JESUS' MINISTRY**

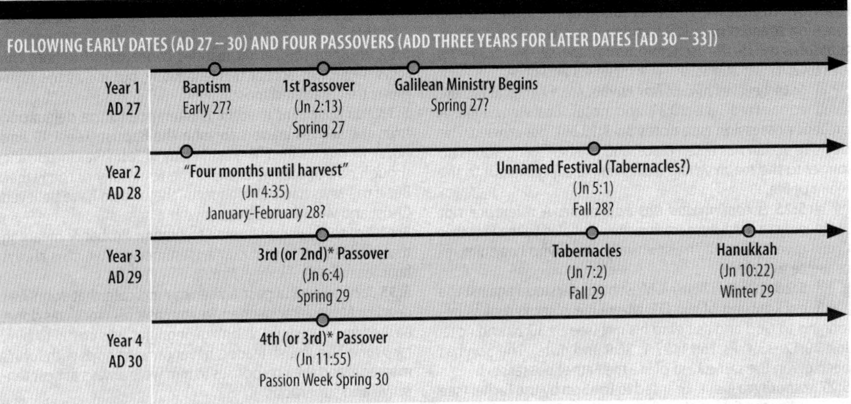

*Jesus' ministry would be reduced by one year (from AD 28 – 30) if the reference in John 4:35 is merely proverbial and if the unnamed festival of John 5:1 occurred in the fall or winter of the first year rather than the second.

by himself;[g] he can do only what he sees
his Father doing, because whatever the
Father does the Son also does. 20 For the
Father loves the Son[h] and shows him all
he does. Yes, and he will show him even
greater works than these,[i] so that you will
be amazed. 21 For just as the Father raises
the dead and gives them life,[j] even so the
Son gives life[k] to whom he is pleased to
give it. 22 Moreover, the Father judges no
one, but has entrusted all judgment to the
Son,[l] 23 that all may honor the Son just as
they honor the Father. Whoever does not
honor the Son does not honor the Father,
who sent him.[m]
24 "Very truly I tell you, whoever hears
my word and believes him who sent me[n]
has eternal life[o] and will not be judged[p]
but has crossed over from death to life.[q]
25 Very truly I tell you, a time is coming
and has now come[r] when the dead will
hear[s] the voice of the Son of God and
those who hear will live. 26 For as the Father
has life in himself, so he has granted
the Son also to have life[t] in himself. 27 And
he has given him authority to judge[u] because
he is the Son of Man.
28 "Do not be amazed at this, for a time
is coming[v] when all who are in their graves
will hear his voice 29 and come out—those
who have done what is good will rise to
live, and those who have done what is evil
will rise to be condemned.[w] 30 By myself
I can do nothing;[x] I judge only as I hear,
and my judgment is just,[y] for I seek not to
please myself but him who sent me.[z]

Testimonies About Jesus

31 "If I testify about myself, my testimony
is not true.[a] 32 There is another who
testifies in my favor,[b] and I know that his
testimony about me is true.
33 "You have sent to John and he has testified[c]
to the truth. 34 Not that I accept human
testimony;[d] but I mention it that you
may be saved.[e] 35 John was a lamp that
burned and gave light,[f] and you chose for
a time to enjoy his light.
36 "I have testimony weightier than that
of John.[g] For the works that the Father has
given me to finish—the very works that
I am doing[h]—testify that the Father has
sent me.[i] 37 And the Father who sent me

5:19 [g] ver 30; S Jn 14:24 **5:20** [h] Jn 3:35 [i] Jn 14:12 **5:21** [j] Ro 4:17; 8:11; 2Co 1:9; Heb 11:19 [k] Jn 11:25 **5:22** [l] ver 27; Ge 18:25; Jdg 11:27; Jn 9:39; S Ac 10:42 **5:23** [m] Lk 10:16; S 1Jn 2:23 **5:24** [n] S Mt 10:40; S Jn 3:15; S 3:17 [o] S Mt 25:46 [p] Jn 3:18 [q] 1Jn 3:14 **5:25** [r] Jn 4:23; 16:32 [s] Jn 8:43, 47 **5:26** [t] Dt 30:20; Job 10:12; 33:4; Ps 36:9; S Jn 1:4 **5:27** [u] S ver 22 **5:28** [v] Jn 4:21; 16:2 **5:29** [w] S Mt 25:46 **5:30** [x] ver 19 [y] Isa 28:6; Jn 8:16 [z] S Mt 26:39 **5:31** [a] Jn 8:14 **5:32** [b] ver 37; Jn 8:18

5:33 [c] S Jn 1:7 **5:34** [d] 1Jn 5:9 [e] Ac 16:30,31; Eph 2:8; Titus 3:5 **5:35** [f] Da 12:3; 2Pe 1:19 **5:36** [g] 1Jn 5:9 [h] Jn 14:11; 15:24 [i] S Jn 3:17

5:20 *the Father loves the Son.* Therefore the Father revealed to the Son his plans and purposes, and the Son obediently carried them out (see 17:4). *greater works.* The Son's activities in raising the dead and judging (see following verses).

5:21 *the Father raises the dead.* A firm belief among the Jews (except the Sadducees; see chart, p. 1631), who also held that the Father did not give this privilege to anyone else. Jesus claimed a prerogative that, according to his opponents, belonged only to God. *the Son gives life.* Probably refers to Christ's gift of abundant life here and now (10:10), though possibly also to the future resurrection (see 11:25 and note).

5:22 *entrusted all judgment to the Son.* The Jews believed that the Father is Judge of the world, so this teaching seemed heretical to them. For other NT assertions that Jesus will be the eschatological Judge, see Mt 25:31–33; Ac 10:42; 17:31; 2Co 5:10; 2Ti 4:1; 1Pe 4:5 and note.

5:24 *believes him … has eternal life.* Faith and life are connected (see 20:31 and note). *has eternal life.* A present possession (see notes on 3:15,36). *has crossed.* The decisive action has taken place, and the believer belongs no longer to the realm where death reigns supreme but to the realm of life.

5:25 *is coming and has now come.* A reference not only to the future resurrection but also to the fact that Christ gives life now. The spiritually dead who hear him receive life from him.

5:26 *has life in himself.* Must be understood against the background of the OT, where life is spoken of as belonging to God and as being his gift (see Dt 30:20 and note; Job 10:12; 33:4; Ps 16:11; 27:1; 36:9 and note). The Son has been given the same kind of life the Father possesses.

5:27 *authority to judge.* Granted to the Son by the Father (see v. 22 and note). *Son of Man.* See note on 1:51.

5:28–29 See Da 12:2 and note.

5:29 *done what is good … live … done what is evil … condemned.* As always in Scripture, judgment is based on what people have done in their lives (see Ro 2:6–8; Rev 20:12 and notes). Salvation, of course, is a gift from God in response to faith (see v. 24 and note), but true faith in Christ results in changed lives, lived in obedience to Christ as Lord (see Ro 10:9–10; Jas 2:14–26 and notes).

5:30 *By myself I can do nothing.* Jesus stresses his dependence on the Father (see note on v. 19). He judges only as he hears from the Father, which makes his judgment fair.

5:31–47 This section stresses the testimonies (see note on 1:7) of John the Baptist (v. 33), of the works of Jesus (v. 36), of God the Father (v. 37), of the Scriptures (v. 39) and of Moses (v. 46).

5:31 Jesus' testimony about himself required the support of all God's revelation. Otherwise, it would have been unacceptable.

5:32 *another.* The Father testifies concerning the Son. The Jews might not accept this testimony, but it was the testimony that mattered most.

5:33 *You have sent to John.* A reference to the delegation from the Jewish leaders to John the Baptist (see 1:19 and note). *he has testified.* The testimony of John was important, though not, of course, equal to the testimony of the Father. But if the Jews had believed John, they would have believed Christ and would have been saved.

5:34 *Not that I accept human testimony.* Probably meaning that he does not rely on human testimony—which is always fallible and often fickle (1Jn 5:9).

5:35 *John was.* The past tense may indicate that John was dead or at least imprisoned. In any case, his work was done. *burned and gave light.* John's giving light was costly to him. *for a time.* The Jewish leaders never came to grips with John's message, and their responses to him were always at best tentative and superficial.

5:36 *works.* The miracles of Jesus, which testified to what he is and to his divine mission (see 10:25 and note).

5:37 *the Father … has himself testified … his voice.* Probably a reference to God's voice in the Scriptures (see vv. 38–39).

has himself testified concerning me.[j] You
have never heard his voice nor seen his
form,[k] 38 nor does his word dwell in you,[l]
for you do not believe[m] the one he sent.[n]
39 You study[a] the Scriptures[o] diligently because you think that in them you have
eternal life.[p] These are the very Scriptures
that testify about me,[q] 40 yet you refuse to
come to me[r] to have life.
41 "I do not accept glory from human beings,[s] 42 but I know you. I know that you
do not have the love of God in your hearts.
43 I have come in my Father's name, and
you do not accept me; but if someone else
comes in his own name, you will accept
him. 44 How can you believe since you accept glory from one another but do not
seek the glory that comes from the only
God[b]?[t]
45 "But do not think I will accuse you
before the Father. Your accuser is Moses,[u]
on whom your hopes are set.[v] 46 If you believed Moses, you would believe me, for
he wrote about me.[w] 47 But since you do
not believe what he wrote, how are you
going to believe what I say?"[x]

Jesus Feeds the Five Thousand

6:1-13pp — Mt 14:13-21; Mk 6:32-44; Lk 9:10-17

6 Some time after this, Jesus crossed to
the far shore of the Sea of Galilee (that
is, the Sea of Tiberias), 2 and a great crowd
of people followed him because they saw
the signs[y] he had performed by healing the
sick. 3 Then Jesus went up on a mountainside[z] and sat down with his disciples. 4 The
Jewish Passover Festival[a] was near.
5 When Jesus looked up and saw a great
crowd coming toward him, he said to Philip,[b] "Where shall we buy bread for these
people to eat?" 6 He asked this only to test
him, for he already had in mind what he
was going to do.
7 Philip answered him, "It would take
more than half a year's wages[c] to buy
enough bread for each one to have a bite!"
8 Another of his disciples, Andrew, Simon Peter's brother,[c] spoke up, 9 "Here is
a boy with five small barley loaves and
two small fish, but how far will they go
among so many?"[d]
10 Jesus said, "Have the people sit
down." There was plenty of grass in that
place, and they sat down (about five thousand men were there). 11 Jesus then took
the loaves, gave thanks,[e] and distributed
to those who were seated as much as they
wanted. He did the same with the fish.
12 When they had all had enough to eat,
he said to his disciples, "Gather the pieces
that are left over. Let nothing be wasted."
13 So they gathered them and filled twelve
baskets with the pieces of the five barley
loaves left over by those who had eaten.
14 After the people saw the sign[f] Jesus
performed, they began to say, "Surely

5:37 [j] Jn 8:18 [k] Dt 4:12; 1Ti 1:17; S Jn 1:18 **5:38** [l] 1Jn 1:10; 2:14 [m] Isa 26:10 [n] S Jn 3:17 **5:39** [o] Ro 2:17, 18 [p] S Mt 25:46 [q] S Lk 24:27,44; Ac 13:27 **5:40** [r] Jn 6:44 **5:41** [s] ver 44 **5:44** [t] S Ro 2:29 **5:45** [u] Jn 9:28 [v] Ro 2:17 **5:46** [w] Ge 3:15; S Lk 24:27,44; Ac 26:22 **5:47** [x] Lk 16:29, 31 **6:2** [y] S Jn 2:11 **6:3** [z] ver 15 **6:4** [a] S Jn 11:55 **6:5** [b] S Jn 1:43 **6:8** [c] Jn 1:40 **6:9** [d] 2Ki 4:43 **6:11** [e] ver 23; S Mt 14:19 **6:14** [f] S Jn 2:11

[a] 39 Or *39 Study* [b] 44 Some early manuscripts *the Only One* [c] 7 Greek *take two hundred denarii*

God had also given his voice of approval at Jesus' baptism (see Mt 3:17 and note). *nor seen his form.* Probably refers to their lack of spiritual perception of who Jesus really is.

5:38 *you do not believe.* The Jews did not recognize what God was saying, as their failure to believe Jesus shows.

5:39 *You study the Scriptures diligently.* The Jewish leaders studied Scripture in minute detail. Despite their reverence for the very letter of Scripture (see notes on Mt 5:18–21), they did not recognize the one to whom Scripture bears supreme testimony (see Lk 24:44 and note).

5:41 Jesus did not accept the kind of human praise that his opponents prized (v. 44).

5:42 *love of God.* May mean God's love for them or theirs for God. Probably it is the latter.

5:43–44 The Jews whom Jesus was addressing had their attention firmly fixed on people. Their emphasis on self-seeking and on human praise showed that they did not accept the one who came from God, and therefore they missed the praise that comes from God.

5:43 *if someone else ... you will accept him.* See note on Zec 11:17.

5:45–47 The revelation God gave Moses is inseparable from the revelation God was giving through Jesus (see Lk 16:31; Ro 10:4 and note). Those who refused to believe the witness about Jesus in the earlier revelation would also reject the later revelation coming through him. To their surprise, he declared that his listeners had refused to believe both and should therefore be accused before God by Moses.

5:46 *he wrote about me.* The authors of the NT books sometimes expressly stressed and everywhere assumed that the OT, rightly read, pervasively points to Christ (see Lk 24:25–27,44–46 and note on 24:44). Here Jesus applies this truth specifically to the writings traditionally ascribed to Moses. He may have had Dt 18:15,18 especially in mind but probably was thinking more broadly of the whole scope of what the Pentateuch disclosed concerning God's saving program in history, which Jesus the Messiah came to complete.

6:1–15 The feeding of the 5,000 is the one miracle, apart from the resurrection, found in all four Gospels. It shows Jesus as the supplier of human need and also sets the stage for his testimony that he is the bread of life (v. 35).

6:1 *far shore.* The northeast shore, probably near Bethsaida (see Lk 9:10 and map, p. 1776). *Sea of Tiberias.* Probably the official Roman name of the Sea of Galilee (see note on Mk 1:16). The name came from the town of Tiberias (named after the emperor Tiberius), founded c. AD 20.

6:2 *signs.* See note on 2:11.

6:4 *Passover.* See notes on 2:13; 5:1.

6:5 *Philip.* Since he came from nearby Bethsaida (see 1:44 and note), it was appropriate to ask him.

6:9 *barley loaves.* Cheap bread, the food of the poor.

6:10 *about five thousand men.* Women and children were not included in this number (see Mt 14:21 and note).

6:12 *Gather the pieces.* See note on Mk 6:43.

6:13 *twelve baskets ... left over.* There was abundant supply (see note on Mk 6:43).

6:14 *sign ... Prophet.* It pointed people to the Son of Man and the food for eternal life that he gives (see v. 27 and note), but they thought only of the Prophet,

JESUS IN GALILEE

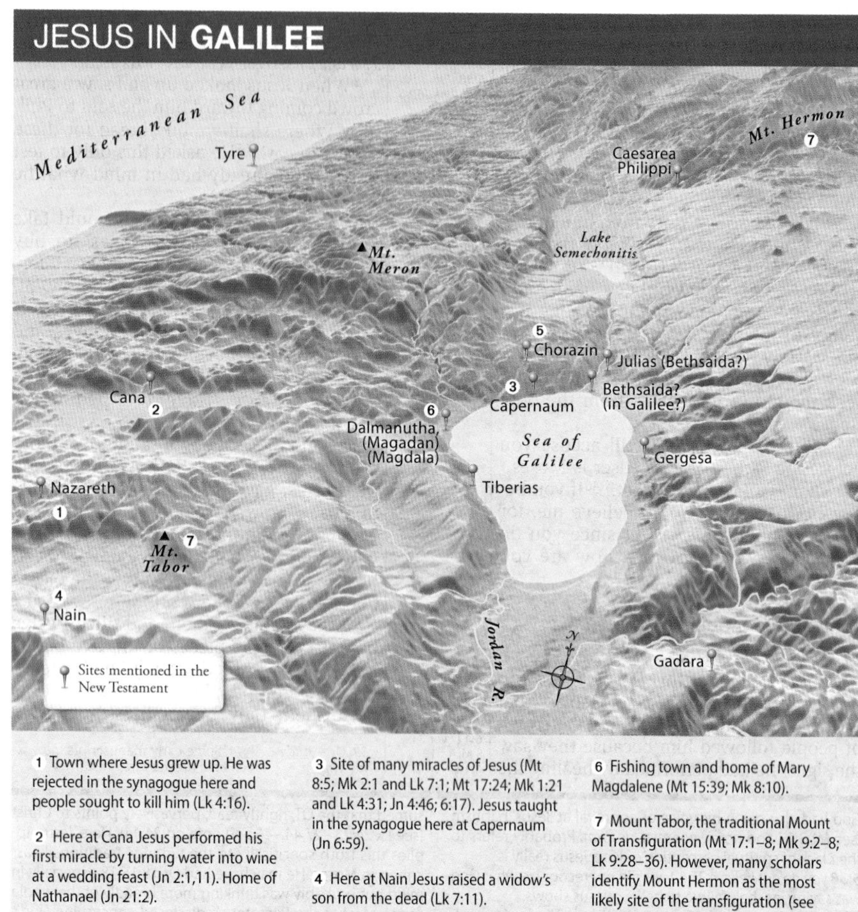

1 Town where Jesus grew up. He was rejected in the synagogue here and people sought to kill him (Lk 4:16).

2 Here at Cana Jesus performed his first miracle by turning water into wine at a wedding feast (Jn 2:1,11). Home of Nathanael (Jn 21:2).

3 Site of many miracles of Jesus (Mt 8:5; Mk 2:1 and Lk 7:1; Mt 17:24; Mk 1:21 and Lk 4:31; Jn 4:46; 6:17). Jesus taught in the synagogue here at Capernaum (Jn 6:59).

4 Here at Nain Jesus raised a widow's son from the dead (Lk 7:11).

5 One of the cities against which Jesus pronounced a woe (Mt 11:21; Lk 10:13).

6 Fishing town and home of Mary Magdalene (Mt 15:39; Mk 8:10).

7 Mount Tabor, the traditional Mount of Transfiguration (Mt 17:1–8; Mk 9:2–8; Lk 9:28–36). However, many scholars identify Mount Hermon as the most likely site of the transfiguration (see note on Lk 9:28).

this is the Prophet who is to come into
the world."[g] 15 Jesus, knowing that they
intended to come and make him king[h] by
force, withdrew again to a mountain by
himself.[i]

Jesus Walks on the Water

6:16-21pp — Mt 14:22-33; Mk 6:47-51

16 When evening came, his disciples
went down to the lake, 17 where they got
into a boat and set off across the lake
for Capernaum. By now it was dark,
and Jesus had not yet joined them. 18 A
strong wind was blowing and the waters grew rough. 19 When they had rowed
about three or four miles,[a] they saw
Jesus approaching the boat, walking on
the water;[j] and they were frightened.
20 But he said to them, "It is I; don't be
afraid."[k] 21 Then they were willing to take
him into the boat, and immediately the

6:14 [g] Dt 18:15, 18; Mt 11:3; S 21:11
6:15 [h] Jn 18:36 [i] Mt 14:23; Mk 6:46
6:19 [j] Job 9:8
6:20 [k] S Mt 14:27

[a] *19* Or about 5 or 6 kilometers

i.e., the prophet of Dt 18:15,18 who would be like Moses (see 1:21 and note). Through Moses, God had provided food and water for the people in the wilderness, and they expected the Prophet to do more than this.
6:15 *make him king by force.* Jesus rejected the widely held Jewish view of the Messiah's kingship (cf. notes on 18:36; Lk 24:21).
6:19 *three or four miles.* Mark says they were "in the middle of the lake" (Mk 6:47). *frightened.* They thought they were seeing a ghost (Mt 14:26).

boat reached the shore where they were heading.

22 The next day the crowd that had stayed on the opposite shore of the lake[l] realized that only one boat had been there, and that Jesus had not entered it with his disciples, but that they had gone away alone.[m] 23 Then some boats from Tiberias[n] landed near the place where the people had eaten the bread after the Lord had given thanks.[o] 24 Once the crowd realized that neither Jesus nor his disciples were there, they got into the boats and went to Capernaum in search of Jesus.

Jesus the Bread of Life

25 When they found him on the other side of the lake, they asked him, "Rabbi,[p] when did you get here?"

26 Jesus answered, "Very truly I tell you, you are looking for me,[q] not because you saw the signs[r] I performed but because you ate the loaves and had your fill. 27 Do not work for food that spoils, but for food that endures[s] to eternal life,[t] which the Son of Man[u] will give you. For on him God the Father has placed his seal[v] of approval."

28 Then they asked him, "What must we do to do the works God requires?"

29 Jesus answered, "The work of God is this: to believe[w] in the one he has sent."[x]

30 So they asked him, "What sign[y] then will you give that we may see it and believe you?[z] What will you do? 31 Our ancestors ate the manna[a] in the wilderness; as it is written: 'He gave them bread from heaven to eat.'[a]"[b]

32 Jesus said to them, "Very truly I tell you, it is not Moses who has given you the bread from heaven, but it is my Father who gives you the true bread from heaven. 33 For the bread of God is the bread that comes down from heaven[c] and gives life to the world."

34 "Sir," they said, "always give us this bread."[d]

35 Then Jesus declared, "I am[e] the bread of life.[f] Whoever comes to me will never go hungry, and whoever believes[g] in me will never be thirsty.[h] 36 But as I told you, you have seen me and still you do not believe. 37 All those the Father gives me[i] will come to me, and whoever comes to me I will never drive away. 38 For I have come down from heaven[j] not to do my will but to do the will[k] of him who sent me.[l] 39 And this is the will of him who sent me, that I shall lose none of all those he has given me,[m] but raise them up at the last day.[n] 40 For my Father's will is that everyone who looks to the Son[o] and believes in him shall have eternal life,[p] and I will raise them up at the last day."

[a] *31* Exodus 16:4; Neh. 9:15; Psalm 78:24,25

6:22 [l] ver 2 [m] ver 15-21 **6:23** [n] ver 1 [o] ver 11 **6:25** [p] S Mt 23:7 **6:26** [q] ver 24 [r] ver 30; S Jn 2:11 **6:27** [s] Isa 55:2 [t] ver 54; S Mt 25:46 [u] S Mt 8:20 [v] Ro 4:11; 1Co 9:2; 2Co 1:22; Eph 1:13; 4:30; 2Ti 2:19; Rev 7:3 **6:29** [w] 1Jn 3:23 [x] S Jn 3:17 **6:30** [y] S Jn 2:11 [z] S Mt 12:38 **6:31** [a] Nu 11:7-9 [b] Ex 16:4, 15; Ne 9:15; Ps 78:24; 105:40 **6:33** [c] ver 50; Jn 3:13,31 **6:34** [d] Jn 4:15 **6:35** [e] Ex 3:14; Jn 8:12; 10:7, 11; 11:25; 14:6; 15:1 [f] ver 48, 51 [g] S Jn 3:15 [h] Jn 4:14 **6:37** [i] ver 39; Jn 17:2,6,9,24 **6:38** [j] Jn 3:13, 31 [k] S Mt 26:39 [l] S Jn 3:17 **6:39** [m] Isa 27:3; Jer 23:4; Jn 10:28; 17:12; 18:9 [n] ver 40, 44,54 **6:40** [o] Jn 12:45 [p] S Mt 25:46

6:21 *immediately the boat reached the shore.* Some think that this was another miracle. In any event, the boat's safe arrival is implicitly credited to Jesus.

6:22–24 The crowd could not figure out what had happened to Jesus. But they wanted to see him again, so they looked for him in the most likely place, Capernaum (see note on 2:12).

6:27 *eternal life.* Not something to be achieved but to be received by faith in Christ (see vv. 28–29; 3:15 and notes). *Son of Man.* See note on Mk 8:31. Submission of the Son to the Father is one of John's major themes (see note on 4:34).

6:28 *What must we do . . . ?* They missed the point that eternal life is Christ's gift and were thinking in terms of achieving it by pious works (see Eph 2:8–9; Titus 3:5 and notes).

6:29 *work of God.* Believing in Jesus Christ is the indispensable "work" God calls for—the one that leads to eternal life (see 9:4 and note).

6:30 *What will you do?* They seek from Jesus a sign greater than the gift of manna that had accompanied Moses' ministry.

6:31 *manna.* A popular Jewish expectation was that when the Messiah came he would renew the sending of manna. The crowd probably reasoned that Jesus had done little compared to Moses. He had fed 5,000; Moses had fed a nation. He did it once; Moses did it for 40 years. He gave ordinary bread (see note on vv. 1–15; see also note on v. 14); Moses gave "bread from heaven" (see notes on Ex 16:4; Nu 11:7).

6:32 Jesus corrected them, pointing out that the manna in the wilderness did not come from Moses but from God and that the Father still "gives" (the present tense is important) the true bread from heaven (life through the Son).

6:33 *bread of God.* Jesus moved the discussion to something (and Someone) much more important than manna. *bread that comes down from heaven.* This affirmation is repeated six times in this context (here and in vv. 38,41,50–51,58), emphasizing Jesus' divine origin.

6:34 *this bread.* Probably another misunderstanding, like that by the woman at the well (see 4:15 and note; cf. also Nicodemus, 3:4). Their minds ran along materialistic lines.

6:35 *I am.* The first of seven (the number of completeness and perfection) self-descriptions of Jesus introduced by "I am" (see 8:12; [9:5;] 10:7,9; 10:11,14; 11:25; 14:6; 15:1,5; see also chart, p. 1786). In the Greek the words are solemnly emphatic and echo Ex 3:14 (see notes on Ex 3:12–15) and the seven "I am he" statements in Isaiah (41:4; 43:10,13,25; 46:4; 48:12; 51:12). Cf. note on 2:11. *the bread of life.* May mean "the bread that is living" and/or "the bread that gives life." What is implied in v. 33 is now made explicit, and it is repeated with minor variations in vv. 41,48,51.

6:36 Contrast 20:29.

6:37 God's action (see v. 44; 10:29; 17:6; 18:9 and notes), not ours (see v. 28 and note), is primary in salvation, and Christ's mercy is unfailing (see vv. 31–40; 10:28; 17:9,12,15,19 and notes on 17:12 and 17:19; 18:9).

6:38 *to do the will of him who sent me.* See note on 4:34.

6:39 *I shall lose none.* True believers will persevere because of Christ's firm hold on them (see 10:28–29; Php 1:6 and notes; cf. Heb 3:6,14 and notes; cf. also Introduction to Hebrews: Theme). *the last day.* An expression found only in John in the NT (see vv. 40,44,54). Jesus probably refers to the day of resurrection (v. 40) followed by judgment (cf. 5:25–30; 11:24; 12:48).

6:40 *eternal life.* See note on 3:15. *raise them up at the last day.* Death cannot destroy the life that Christ gives (see 11:25–26 and note on 11:25).

41 At this the Jews there began to grumble about him because he said, "I am
the bread that came down from heav-
en." 42 They said, "Is this not Jesus, the
son of Joseph,[q] whose father and mother
we know?[r] How can he now say, 'I came
down from heaven'?"[s]
43 "Stop grumbling among yourselves,"
Jesus answered. 44 "No one can come to
me unless the Father who sent me draws
them,[t] and I will raise them up at the last
day. 45 It is written in the Prophets: 'They
will all be taught by God.'[a][u] Everyone who
has heard the Father and learned from him
comes to me. 46 No one has seen the Father
except the one who is from God;[v] only he
has seen the Father. 47 Very truly I tell you,
the one who believes has eternal life.[w]
48 I am the bread of life.[x] 49 Your ancestors
ate the manna in the wilderness, yet they
died.[y] 50 But here is the bread that comes
down from heaven,[z] which anyone may
eat and not die. 51 I am the living bread[a]
that came down from heaven.[b] Whoever
eats this bread will live forever. This bread
is my flesh, which I will give for the life
of the world."[c]
52 Then the Jews[d] began to argue sharply
among themselves,[e] "How can this man
give us his flesh to eat?"
53 Jesus said to them, "Very truly I tell
you, unless you eat the flesh[f] of the Son
of Man[g] and drink his blood,[h] you have
no life in you. 54 Whoever eats my flesh
and drinks my blood has eternal life, and
I will raise them up at the last day.[i] 55 For
my flesh is real food and my blood is
real drink. 56 Whoever eats my flesh and
drinks my blood remains in me, and I in
them.[j] 57 Just as the living Father sent me[k]
and I live because of the Father, so the
one who feeds on me will live because of
me. 58 This is the bread that came down
from heaven. Your ancestors ate manna and died, but whoever feeds on this
bread will live forever."[l] 59 He said this
while teaching in the synagogue in Capernaum.

Many Disciples Desert Jesus

60 On hearing it, many of his disciples[m]
said, "This is a hard teaching. Who can
accept it?"[n]
61 Aware that his disciples were grumbling about this, Jesus said to them, "Does
this offend you?[o] 62 Then what if you see
the Son of Man[p] ascend to where he was
before![q] 63 The Spirit gives life;[r] the flesh
counts for nothing. The words I have spoken to you—they are full of the Spirit[b]
and life. 64 Yet there are some of you who
do not believe." For Jesus had known[s]
from the beginning which of them did not
believe and who would betray him.[t] 65 He
went on to say, "This is why I told you
that no one can come to me unless the
Father has enabled them."[u]
66 From this time many of his disciples[v]
turned back and no longer followed him.
67 "You do not want to leave too, do
you?" Jesus asked the Twelve.[w]
68 Simon Peter answered him,[x] "Lord, to
whom shall we go? You have the words
of eternal life.[y] 69 We have come to believe
and to know that you are the Holy One
of God."[z]
70 Then Jesus replied, "Have I not chosen you,[a] the Twelve? Yet one of you is

[a] 45 Isaiah 54:13 [b] 63 Or *are Spirit*; or *are spirit*

6:42 [q] Lk 4:22 [r] Jn 7:27,28 [s] ver 38,62 **6:44** [t] ver 65; Jer 31:3; Jn 12:32 **6:45** [u] Isa 54:13; Jer 31:33, 34; 1Co 2:13; 1Th 4:9; Heb 8:10,11; 10:16; 1Jn 2:27 **6:46** [v] S Jn 1:18; 5:37; 7:29 **6:47** [w] S Mt 25:46 **6:48** [x] ver 35,51 **6:49** [y] ver 31,58 **6:50** [z] ver 33 **6:51** [a] ver 35, 48 [b] ver 41,58 [c] Heb 10:10 **6:52** [d] S Jn 1:19 [e] Jn 7:43; 9:16; 10:19 **6:53** [f] Mt 26:26 [g] S Mt 8:20 [h] Mt 26:28 **6:54** [i] ver 39 **6:56** [j] Jn 15:4-7; 1Jn 2:24; 3:24; 4:15 **6:57** [k] S Jn 3:17 **6:58** [l] ver 49-51; Jn 3:36; 5:24 **6:60** [m] ver 66 [n] ver 52 **6:61** [o] Mt 13:57 **6:62** [p] S Mt 8:20 [q] S Mk 16:19; S Jn 3:13; 17:5 **6:63** [r] 2Co 3:6 **6:64** [s] S Jn 2:25 [t] S Mt 10:4 **6:65** [u] ver 37, 44; S Mt 13:11 **6:66** [v] ver 60 **6:67** [w] Mt 10:2 **6:68** [x] Mt 16:16 [y] ver 63; S Mt 25:46 **6:69** [z] S Mk 1:24; 8:29; Lk 9:20 **6:70** [a] Jn 15:16, 19

6:41 *the Jews there.* See note on 1:19.

6:44 *draws.* People do not come to Christ strictly on their own initiative; the Father draws them.

6:45 *the Prophets.* The section of the OT from which the quotation is taken (see note on Mt 5:17).

6:49 *they died.* Jesus' opponents had set their hearts (cf. v. 31 and note) on that which could neither give nor sustain spiritual life.

6:50 *eat and not die.* Jesus' gift is in contrast; the life he gives is eternal (see 11:26 and note).

6:51 *eats this bread.* By faith appropriates Jesus as the sustenance of one's life. *my flesh, which I will give.* Looking forward to Calvary. Providing eternal life would be costly to the Giver. *world.* See notes on 1:9; 4:42.

6:53–58 "Flesh" and "blood" here point to Christ as the crucified one and the source of life. Jesus speaks of faith's appropriation of himself as God's appointed sacrifice, not—at least not directly—of any ritual requirement.

6:54 *the last day.* See note on v. 39.

6:58 *bread that came down from heaven.* As in v. 49, the value of the manna is limited and is contrasted with the heavenly food Christ gives.

6:60 *hard.* Hard to accept, not hard to understand. The thought of eating the flesh of the Son of Man and drinking his blood was doubtless shocking to most of Jesus' Jewish hearers (see note on vv. 53–58).

6:62 *Son of Man.* See notes on Mk 8:31; Lk 6:5; 19:10. *ascend.* Probably refers to the series of events that began with the cross, where Jesus was glorified (see note on 7:39). *where he was before.* Referring to Jesus' heavenly preexistence (see 8:58; 17:5 and note).

6:63 Cf. 3:5–6,8. *are full of the Spirit and life.* Are the Spirit at work producing life.

6:65 Coming to Christ for salvation is never a merely human achievement (see vv. 37,39,44–45 and notes).

6:66 *From this time.* May also mean "For this reason." *many … turned back.* Jesus had already made clear what discipleship meant, and many were not ready to receive life in the way he taught.

6:68 As in the other Gospels, Peter acts as spokesman. *words of eternal life.* The expression is general. Peter was not speaking of a formula but of the thrust of Jesus' teaching. He perceived the truth of v. 63 (see note there).

6:69 *We have come to believe and to know.* Since the Greek verbs are in the perfect tense, they mean, "We have entered a state of belief and knowledge that has continued until the present time." *Holy One of God.* Applied to Jesus in Mk 1:24 (see note there); Lk 4:34 (cf. Ac 2:27).

a devil!"[b] 71 (He meant Judas, the son of
Simon Iscariot,[c] who, though one of the
Twelve, was later to betray him.)[d]

Jesus Goes to the Festival of Tabernacles

7 After this, Jesus went around in Galilee. He did not want[a] to go about in
Judea because the Jewish leaders[e] there
were looking for a way to kill him.[f] 2 But
when the Jewish Festival of Tabernacles[g]
was near, 3 Jesus' brothers[h] said to him,
"Leave Galilee and go to Judea, so that
your disciples there may see the works
you do. 4 No one who wants to become a
public figure acts in secret. Since you are
doing these things, show yourself to the
world." 5 For even his own brothers did not
believe in him.[i]

6 Therefore Jesus told them, "My time[j]
is not yet here; for you any time will do.
7 The world cannot hate you, but it hates
me[k] because I testify that its works are
evil.[l] 8 You go to the festival. I am not[b] going up to this festival, because my time[m]
has not yet fully come." 9 After he had said
this, he stayed in Galilee.

10 However, after his brothers had left for
the festival, he went also, not publicly, but
in secret. 11 Now at the festival the Jewish
leaders were watching for Jesus[n] and asking, "Where is he?"

12 Among the crowds there was widespread whispering about him. Some said,
"He is a good man."

Others replied, "No, he deceives the
people."[o] 13 But no one would say anything
publicly about him for fear of the leaders.[p]

Jesus Teaches at the Festival

14 Not until halfway through the festival
did Jesus go up to the temple courts and begin to teach.[q] 15 The Jews[r] there were amazed
and asked, "How did this man get such
learning[s] without having been taught?"[t]

16 Jesus answered, "My teaching is not
my own. It comes from the one who sent
me.[u] 17 Anyone who chooses to do the will
of God will find out[v] whether my teaching
comes from God or whether I speak on my
own. 18 Whoever speaks on their own does
so to gain personal glory,[w] but he who
seeks the glory of the one who sent him is
a man of truth; there is nothing false about
him. 19 Has not Moses given you the law?[x]
Yet not one of you keeps the law. Why are
you trying to kill me?"[y]

20 "You are demon-possessed,"[z] the

[a] *1* Some manuscripts *not have authority* [b] *8* Some manuscripts *not yet*

6:70 [b] Jn 13:27; 17:12 **6:71** [c] S Mt 26:14 [d] S Mt 10:4 **7:1** [e] S Jn 1:19 [f] ver 19,25; S Mt 12:14 **7:2** [g] Lev 23:34; Dt 16:16 **7:3** [h] S Mt 12:46 **7:5** [i] Ps 69:8; Mk 3:21 **7:6** [j] S Mt 26:18 **7:7** [k] Jn 15:18, 19 [l] Jn 3:19,20 **7:8** [m] ver 6; S Mt 26:18 **7:11** [n] Jn 11:56 **7:12** [o] ver 40,43 **7:13** [p] Jn 9:22; 12:42; 19:38; 20:19 **7:14** [q] ver 28; S Mt 26:55 **7:15** [r] S Jn 1:19 [s] Ac 26:24 [t] Mt 13:54 **7:16** [u] S Jn 14:24 **7:17** [v] Ps 25:14 **7:18** [w] Jn 5:41; 8:50,54 **7:19** [x] Dt 32:46; Jn 1:17 [y] ver 1; S Mt 12:14 **7:20** [z] S Mk 3:22

6:70 *a devil.* Judas (v. 71) would oppose Christ in the spirit of Satan.

6:71 *Iscariot.* Means "man from Kerioth" (in Judea; see Jos 15:25) and would apply equally to the father and the son (cf. 12:4). Judas seems to have been the only non-Galilean among the Twelve. *one of the Twelve.* Therefore one of the last persons likely to betray Jesus.

7:1—8:59 In chs. 7–8 John records strong opposition to Jesus, including repeated references to threats on his life (7:1,13,19,25,30,32,44; 8:37,40,59). The apostle seems to have gathered the major arguments against the Messiahship of Jesus and here answers them.

7:1 *After this.* Since 6:4 refers to the Passover Festival and 7:2 to the Festival of Tabernacles, the interval was about six months.

7:2 *Festival of Tabernacles.* The great festival in the Jewish year, celebrating the completion of harvest and commemorating God's goodness to the people during the wilderness wanderings (see Lev 23:33–43; Dt 16:13–15; Zec 14:16 and note). The name came from the leafy shelters in which people lived throughout the seven days of the festival.

7:3 *brothers.* See note on Lk 8:19.

7:4 It is not clear whether the brothers claimed some knowledge of Jesus' miracles that other people did not have or were suggesting that any claim to Messiahship must be decided in Jerusalem. Their advice was not given sincerely, for they did not yet believe in Jesus (v. 5).

7:6 *My time is not yet here.* Jesus moved in accordance with the will of God (see notes on 2:4; Ro 5:6).

7:7 *The world.* Either (1) people opposed to God or (2) the human system opposed to God's purposes (see note on 1Jn 2:15). The brothers belonged to the world and therefore could not be the objects of its hatred. Jesus, however, rebuked the world and was hated accordingly.

7:8 *not.* See NIV text note. Jesus was not refusing to go to the festival but refusing to go in the way his brothers suggested—as a pilgrim. When he went, it would be to deliver a prophetic message from God, for which he awaited the right time (see note on v. 6).

7:10 *not publicly.* Rejecting the brothers' suggestion to show himself (v. 4).

7:12 *whispering.* Because it was not safe to speak openly (cf. v. 13).

7:14 *halfway through the festival.* When the crowds would be at their maximum. Teaching in the temple courts at such a time would reach many.

7:15 *The Jews.* Distinct from "the crowds" (v. 12), who were also Jews (see note on 1:19). *without having been taught.* By a rabbi. Jesus had never been the disciple of a recognized Jewish teacher (see Ac 4:13 and note).

7:16 *not my own.* The Father, from whom he came, had been his "rabbi" (see note on 4:34).

7:17 *chooses to do the will of God.* Reflecting a whole attitude of life. A person sincerely set on doing God's will welcomes Jesus' teaching and believes in him (see 6:29 and note). *will find out.* Augustine commented, "Understanding is the reward of faith … What is 'If any man be willing to do his will'? It is the same thing as to believe."

7:18 *is a man of truth.* Or "is true." They should have recognized that Jesus was not self-seeking. In this Gospel, no one is spoken of as being "true" except God the Father (see 3:33 and note; 8:26) and Jesus (here). Once more John ranks Jesus with God.

7:19 *the law.* The Jews congratulated themselves on being the chosen recipients of the law, but Jesus told them that they all broke the law of which they were so proud (cf. Ro 2:17–29).

7:20 *You are demon-possessed.* The accusation of demonic possession is made elsewhere in John (e.g., 8:48–52; 10:20–21; cf. Mt 12:24–32; Mk 3:22–30). *crowd.* Probably the pilgrims who

crowd answered. "Who is trying to kill
you?"
21 Jesus said to them, "I did one miracle,[a] and you are all amazed. 22 Yet, because Moses gave you circumcision[b]
(though actually it did not come from
Moses, but from the patriarchs),[c] you circumcise a boy on the Sabbath. 23 Now if a
boy can be circumcised on the Sabbath so
that the law of Moses may not be broken,
why are you angry with me for healing a
man's whole body on the Sabbath? 24 Stop
judging by mere appearances, but instead
judge correctly."[d]

Division Over Who Jesus Is

25 At that point some of the people of
Jerusalem began to ask, "Isn't this the
man they are trying to kill?[e] 26 Here he is,
speaking publicly, and they are not saying
a word to him. Have the authorities[f] really
concluded that he is the Messiah?[g] 27 But
we know where this man is from;[h] when
the Messiah comes, no one will know
where he is from."
28 Then Jesus, still teaching in the temple courts,[i] cried out, "Yes, you know me,
and you know where I am from.[j] I am not
here on my own authority, but he who
sent me is true.[k] You do not know him,
29 but I know him[l] because I am from him
and he sent me."[m]
30 At this they tried to seize him, but no
one laid a hand on him,[n] because his hour
had not yet come.[o] 31 Still, many in the
crowd believed in him.[p] They said, "When
the Messiah comes, will he perform more
signs[q] than this man?"
32 The Pharisees heard the crowd whispering such things about him. Then the
chief priests and the Pharisees sent temple
guards to arrest him.
33 Jesus said, "I am with you for only a
short time,[r] and then I am going to the one
who sent me.[s] 34 You will look for me, but
you will not find me; and where I am, you
cannot come."[t]
35 The Jews said to one another, "Where
does this man intend to go that we cannot
find him? Will he go where our people live
scattered[u] among the Greeks,[v] and teach
the Greeks? 36 What did he mean when he
said, 'You will look for me, but you will
not find me,' and 'Where I am, you cannot
come'?"[w]
37 On the last and greatest day of the
festival,[x] Jesus stood and said in a loud
voice, "Let anyone who is thirsty come
to me and drink.[y] 38 Whoever believes[z] in
me, as Scripture has said,[a] rivers of living
water[b] will flow from within them."[a][c] 39 By
this he meant the Spirit,[d] whom those who
believed in him were later to receive.[e] Up
to that time the Spirit had not been given,
since Jesus had not yet been glorified.[f]

7:21 [a] ver 23; Jn 5:2-9 **7:22** [b] Lev 12:3 [c] Ge 17:10-14 **7:24** [d] 1Sa 16:7; Isa 11:3,4; Jn 8:15; 2Co 10:7 **7:25** [e] ver 1; S Mt 12:14 **7:26** [f] ver 48 [g] Jn 4:29 **7:27** [h] Mt 13:55; Lk 4:22; Jn 6:42 **7:28** [i] ver 14 [j] Jn 8:14 [k] Jn 8:26,42 **7:29** [l] S Mt 11:27 [m] S Jn 3:17 **7:30** [n] ver 32, 44; Jn 10:39 [o] S Mt 26:18 **7:31** [p] Jn 8:30; 10:42; 11:45; 12:11,42 [q] S Jn 2:11 **7:33** [r] Jn 12:35; 13:33; 16:16 [s] Jn 16:5,10, 17,28 **7:34** [t] ver 36; Jn 8:21; 13:33 **7:35** [u] S Jas 1:1 [v] Jn 12:20; Ac 17:4; 18:4 **7:36** [w] ver 34 **7:37** [x] Lev 23:36 [y] Isa 55:1; Rev 22:17 **7:38** [z] S Jn 3:15 [a] Isa 58:11 [b] S Jn 4:10 [c] S Jn 4:14 **7:39** [d] Joel 2:28; Jn 1:33; Ac 2:17,33 [e] S Jn 20:22 [f] Jn 12:23; 13:31,32

[a] *37,38* Or *me. And let anyone drink* [38]*who believes in me." As Scripture has said, "Out of him* (or *them*) *will flow rivers of living water."*

---

had come up to Jerusalem for the festival — different from "the Jewish leaders" who were trying to kill Jesus (v. 1) and the Jerusalem mob that knew of the plot (see v. 25 and note).

7:21 *one miracle.* Evidently that of healing the lame man (5:1–9), as the discussion about the Sabbath shows.

7:22 *circumcision.* The requirement of circumcision was included in the law Moses gave (see Ex 12:44,48 and note; Lev 12:3), yet it did not originate with Moses but went back to Abraham (see Ge 17:10–12 and notes). The Jews took such regulations as that in Lev 12:3 to mean that circumcision must be performed on the eighth day even if it was the Sabbath. This exception is of critical importance in understanding the controversy (v. 23). Jesus was not saying that the Sabbath should not be observed or that the Jewish regulations were too harsh. He was saying that his opponents did not understand what the Sabbath meant. The command to circumcise showed not only that work *might* sometimes be done on the Sabbath but that it *must* be done then. Deeds of mercy are in this category (see notes on 5:10; Mk 3:2).

7:25 *people of Jerusalem.* An expression found only here and in Mk 1:5 in the NT, probably referring to the Jerusalem mob (see note on v. 20). They did not originate the plot against Jesus, but they knew about it.

7:26 *Have the authorities really concluded . . . ?* In Greek, the question is in a form that expects a negative answer. *the Messiah.* See note on 1:25.

7:27 *no one will know where he is from.* Some Jews held that the OT gave the origin of the Messiah (cf. v. 42; Mt 2:4–6), but others believed that it did not.

7:28 *you know me.* Irony, because in a sense they knew Jesus and that he came from Nazareth, but in a deeper sense they did not know Jesus or the Father (see 8:19 and note). Jesus mentioned again his dependence on the Father (see 4:34 and note) and went on to declare that he had real knowledge of God and that they did not. Both his origin and mission were from God.

7:30 *they tried to seize him.* Jesus' enemies were powerless against him until his time came (see note on 2:4).

7:31 *crowd.* Of pilgrims (see note on v. 20). Many of them believed on the basis of the miraculous signs (cf. 6:26).

7:32 *Pharisees.* See note on Mt 3:7; see also essay, p. 1576, and chart, p. 1631. *chief priests.* See notes on Mt 2:4; Mk 8:31. There was only one ruling chief priest, but the Romans had deposed a number of chief priests, and these retained the title by courtesy.

7:33 *then I am going.* Jesus changed the topic from his miracles to his death, to which he referred enigmatically (v. 34).

7:35 *scattered among the Greeks.* From the time of the exile, many Jews lived outside the Holy Land and could be found in most cities throughout the Roman Empire.

7:37 *last . . . day of the festival.* Either the seventh or the eighth day: The Festival of Tabernacles lasted seven days (Lev 23:34; Dt 16:13,15) but had a "closing special assembly" on the eighth day (Lev 23:36). See note on Mk 14:12. *stood and said in a loud voice.* Teachers usually sat, so Jesus drew special attention to his message.

7:38 See NIV text note. *living water.* See note on 4:10.

7:39 *the Spirit.* Explaining the "living water" (v. 38). *had not been given.* In the manner in which he would be given at Pentecost (see Ac 2:1–2,4 and notes). *glorified.* Here probably refers to Jesus' crucifixion, resurrection and exaltation

40 On hearing his words, some of the
people said, "Surely this man is the Prophet."[g]
41 Others said, "He is the Messiah."
Still others asked, "How can the Messiah come from Galilee?[h] 42 Does not
Scripture say that the Messiah will come
from David's descendants[i] and from Bethlehem,[j] the town where David lived?"
43 Thus the people were divided[k] because
of Jesus. 44 Some wanted to seize him, but
no one laid a hand on him.[l]

Unbelief of the Jewish Leaders

45 Finally the temple guards went back
to the chief priests and the Pharisees,
who asked them, "Why didn't you bring
him in?"
46 "No one ever spoke the way this man
does,"[m] the guards replied.
47 "You mean he has deceived you
also?"[n] the Pharisees retorted. 48 "Have any
of the rulers or of the Pharisees believed in
him?[o] 49 No! But this mob that knows nothing of the law—there is a curse on them."
50 Nicodemus,[p] who had gone to Jesus
earlier and who was one of their own
number, asked, 51 "Does our law condemn
a man without first hearing him to find
out what he has been doing?"
52 They replied, "Are you from Galilee,
too? Look into it, and you will find that
a prophet does not come out of Galilee."[q]

[The earliest manuscripts and many other ancient witnesses do not have John 7:53—8:11. A few manuscripts include these verses, wholly or in part, after John 7:36, John 21:25, Luke 21:38 or Luke 24:53.]

8 *53 Then they all went home, 1 but Jesus went*
to the Mount of Olives.[r]
2 At dawn he appeared again in the temple
courts, where all the people gathered around
him, and he sat down to teach them.[s] *3 The*
teachers of the law and the Pharisees brought
in a woman caught in adultery. They made
her stand before the group 4 and said to Jesus,
"Teacher, this woman was caught in the act of
adultery. 5 In the Law Moses commanded us to
stone such women.[t] *Now what do you say?"*
6 They were using this question as a trap,[u] *in*
order to have a basis for accusing him.[v]
But Jesus bent down and started to write on
the ground with his finger. 7 When they kept on
questioning him, he straightened up and said

7:40 [g] S Mt 21:11 **7:41** [h] ver 52; Jn 1:46 **7:42** [i] S Mt 1:1 [j] Mic 5:2; Mt 2:5, 6; Lk 2:4 **7:43** [k] Jn 6:52; 9:16; 10:19 **7:44** [l] ver 30 **7:46** [m] S Mt 7:28 **7:47** [n] ver 12 **7:48** [o] Jn 12:42 **7:50** [p] Jn 3:1; 19:39
7:52 [q] ver 41 **8:1** [r] S Mt 21:1 **8:2** [s] ver 20; S Mt 26:55 **8:5** [t] Lev 20:10; Dt 22:22; Job 31:11 **8:6** [u] Mt 22:15, 18 [v] S Mt 12:10

(see note on 13:31). The fullness of the Spirit's work depends on Jesus' prior work of salvation.

7:40 *people.* The "crowd" of v. 20 (see note there). *the Prophet.* See 1:21 and note.

7:41 *from Galilee.* Typical irony by John. The crowd doubts that Jesus is the Messiah because he comes from Galilee instead of Bethlehem. Apparently they are not aware of his Bethlehem birth (see Mic 5:2; Mt 2:1; Lk 2:4 and notes).

7:42 *the Messiah will come from David's descendants and from Bethlehem.* See 1Sa 20:6; 2Sa 7:12–16 and notes; Ps 89:3–4; Mic 5:2. *from Bethlehem.* There were different ideas about the Messiah's place of origin (see v. 27 and note).

7:46 *guards.* They knew they would be in trouble for failing to make the arrest but did not mention the hostility of part of the crowd, which would have given them something of an excuse before the Pharisees. They were favorably impressed by the teaching of Jesus and were not inclined to cause him trouble.

7:47 *Pharisees retorted.* They must have been greatly irritated. Ordinarily the chief priests would have rebuked the temple guards.

7:49 *this mob.* The pilgrim crowd again (see note on v. 20). *knows nothing.* The Pharisees exaggerated the people's ignorance of Scripture (cf. v. 42). But the average Jew paid little attention to the minutiae that mattered so much to the Pharisees. The "tradition of the elders" (Mk 7:3) was too great a burden for people who earned their living by hard physical work, and consequently these regulations were widely disregarded.

7:50–51 There is irony here. The Pharisees implied that no leader believed in Jesus, yet Nicodemus, "a member of the Jewish ruling council" (3:1), spoke up. They called for people to observe the law, but Nicodemus pointed to their own disregard for the law in this instance.

7:52 *a prophet does not come out of Galilee.* See 1:46; see also note on Mt 2:23. They were angry—and wrong. Jonah came from Galilee, and perhaps other prophets had as well. Moreover, the Pharisees overlooked the right of God to raise up prophets from wherever he chooses.

7:53—8:11 This story probably did not belong originally to the Gospel of John. It is absent from almost all the early manuscripts, and those that include it sometimes place it elsewhere (e.g., after Lk 21:38). But the story may well be an authentic tradition about Jesus.

7:53 This verse (along with 8:1) shows that the story was originally attached to another narrative, since Jesus was not present at the meeting of the Sanhedrin described in vv. 45–52.

8:1 *Mount of Olives.* See notes on Zec 14:4; Mk 11:1; Lk 19:29; Ac 1:12.

8:3 *teachers of the law.* See notes on Mt 2:4; Mk 2:16; Lk 5:17. *a woman caught in adultery.* This sin cannot be committed alone, so the question arises as to why only one offender was brought. The incident may have been staged to trap Jesus (see v. 6 and note) and provision perhaps made for the man to escape. The woman's accusers must have been especially eager to humiliate her, since they could have kept her in private custody while they spoke to Jesus.

8:4 *caught in the act.* Mere compromising circumstances were not sufficient evidence; Jewish law required witnesses who had seen the act.

8:5 *to stone such women.* They altered the law a little. The manner of execution was not prescribed unless the woman was a betrothed virgin (Dt 22:23–24). And the law required the execution of both parties (Lev 20:10; Dt 22:22), not just the woman.

8:6 *using this question as a trap.* The Romans did not allow the Jews to carry out death sentences (see 18:31 and note), so if Jesus had said to stone her he could have been in conflict with the Romans. If he had said not to stone her he could have been accused of being unsupportive of the law. *write on the ground with his finger.* Some suggest that Jesus was writing an accusation against his accusers. A few later manuscripts add that he wrote "the sins of each of them" on the ground.

to them, "Let any one of you who is without sin be the first to throw a stone[w] at her."[x] 8Again he stooped down and wrote on the ground.

9At this, those who heard began to go away one at a time, the older ones first, until only Jesus was left, with the woman still standing there. 10Jesus straightened up and asked her, "Woman, where are they? Has no one condemned you?"

11"No one, sir," she said.

"Then neither do I condemn you,"[y] Jesus declared. "Go now and leave your life of sin."[z]

Dispute Over Jesus' Testimony

12When Jesus spoke again to the people, he said, "I am[a] the light of the world.[b] Whoever follows me will never walk in darkness, but will have the light of life."[c]

13The Pharisees challenged him, "Here you are, appearing as your own witness; your testimony is not valid."[d]

14Jesus answered, "Even if I testify on my own behalf, my testimony is valid, for I know where I came from and where I am going.[e] But you have no idea where I come from[f] or where I am going. 15You judge by human standards;[g] I pass judgment on no one.[h] 16But if I do judge, my decisions are true, because I am not alone. I stand with the Father, who sent me.[i] 17In your own Law it is written that the testimony of two witnesses is true.[j] 18I am one who testifies for myself; my other witness is the Father, who sent me."[k]

19Then they asked him, "Where is your father?"

"You do not know me or my Father,"[l] Jesus replied. "If you knew me, you would know my Father also."[m] 20He spoke these words while teaching[n] in the temple courts near the place where the offerings were put.[o] Yet no one seized him, because his hour had not yet come.[p]

Dispute Over Who Jesus Is

21Once more Jesus said to them, "I am going away, and you will look for me, and you will die[q] in your sin. Where I go, you cannot come."[r]

22This made the Jews ask, "Will he kill himself? Is that why he says, 'Where I go, you cannot come'?"

23But he continued, "You are from below; I am from above. You are of this world; I am not of this world.[s] 24I told you that you would die in your sins; if you do not believe that I am he,[t] you will indeed die in your sins."

25"Who are you?" they asked.

"Just what I have been telling you from the beginning," Jesus replied. 26"I have much to say in judgment of you. But he who sent me is trustworthy,[u] and what I have heard from him I tell the world."[v]

27They did not understand that he was telling them about his Father. 28So Jesus said, "When you have lifted up[a] the Son of Man,[w] then you will know that I am he and that I do nothing on my own but speak just what the Father has taught me.[x] 29The one who sent me is with me; he has not left me alone,[y] for I always do what

8:7 [w] Dt 17:7; Eze 16:40 [x] Ro 2:1,22 **8:11** [y] Jn 3:17 [z] Jn 5:14 **8:12** [a] S Jn 6:35 [b] S Jn 1:4 [c] Pr 4:18; Mt 5:14 **8:13** [d] Jn 5:31 **8:14** [e] Jn 13:3; 16:28 [f] Jn 7:28; 9:29 **8:15** [g] S Jn 7:24 [h] Jn 3:17 **8:16** [i] Jn 5:30 **8:17** [j] S Mt 18:16 **8:18** [k] Jn 5:37 **8:19** [l] Jn 16:3 [m] S 1Jn 2:23 **8:20** [n] S Mt 26:55 [o] Mk 12:41 [p] S Mt 26:18 **8:21** [q] Eze 3:18 [r] Jn 7:34; 13:33 **8:23** [s] Jn 3:31; 17:14 **8:24** [t] Jn 4:26; 13:19 **8:26** [u] Jn 7:28 [v] Jn 3:32; 15:15 **8:28** [w] S Jn 12:32 [x] S Jn 14:24 **8:29** [y] ver 16; Jn 16:32

[a] 28 The Greek for *lifted up* also means *exalted.*

8:7 *without sin.* The phrase is quite general and means "without any sin," not "without this sin." *be the first.* Jesus' answer disarmed them. Since he spoke of throwing a stone, he could not be accused of failure to uphold the law. But the qualification for throwing it prevented anyone from acting.
8:9 *began to go away.* Because they were not "without sin" (v. 7). *older ones.* They were the first to realize what was involved. But all the men were either conscience-stricken or afraid, and in the end only Jesus and the woman remained.
8:10 *Woman.* See NIV text note on 2:4.
8:11 *Go now and leave your life of sin.* Jesus did not condone what the woman had done.
8:12 *I am.* See note on 6:35. *the light.* See 1:4 and note; 9:5; 12:46. It is also true that "God is light" (1Jn 1:5). And as Jesus' followers reflect the light that comes from him, they too are "the light of the world" (Mt 5:14; cf. Php 2:15). *darkness.* Both the darkness of this world and that of Satan (cf. 3:19–21). *light of life.* "God is light" (1Jn 1:5), but Jesus is also the light from God that lights the way for life—as the pillar of fire lit the way for the Israelites (see Ex 13:21 and note; Ne 9:12). Cf. Ro 13:11–14; Eph 5:8–14; 1Th 5:4–8; 1Jn 1:5–7; 2:9–11.
8:13 *Pharisees.* See note on 7:32.
8:14 Jesus made two points: First, he was qualified to bear testimony, whereas the Pharisees were not; and he knew both his origin and his destination, whereas they knew neither. (See note on vv. 16–18 for the second point.)
8:15 The judgment of the Pharisees was limited and worldly. In the sense they meant, Jesus made it clear that he did not judge at all. In the proper sense, of course, he did judge (v. 26).
8:16–18 Jesus' second point was that his testimony was not unsupported: The Father was with him, so he and the Father were the two witnesses required by the law (see Dt 17:6 and note; 19:15).
8:16 *the Father, who sent me.* Jesus was always aware of his mission (see note on 4:34).
8:19 *If you knew me.* John makes it clear that the Word (Jesus) was with God and was God (see 1:1 and note) and revealed God (see 1:18 and note). Jesus here stresses that the Father is known through the Son and that to know the one is to know the other (see 14:7,10–11 and notes).
8:20 *his hour.* See note on 2:4.
8:23 Things other than death divide people (cf., e.g., v. 47; 3:31; 15:19 and note; 1Jn 3:10). *of.* Here denotes origin. Jesus was certainly *in* the world, but he was not *of* the world. They belonged to "this world"—Satan's domain (1Jn 5:19; cf. Jn 12:31; 14:30; 16:11).
8:24 *believe.* See note on 1:7. *I am.* Jesus echoes God's great affirmation about himself (see v. 58; 6:35; Ex 3:14 and notes).
8:28 *lifted up.* Normally used in the NT in the sense of "exalt" (see NIV text note), but John uses it of the crucifixion (see 3:14; 12:32 and notes). *Son of Man.* See note on Mk 8:31. *I am.* See notes on vv. 24,58.

pleases him."[z] 30 Even as he spoke, many
believed in him.[a]

Dispute Over Whose Children Jesus' Opponents Are

31 To the Jews who had believed him,
Jesus said, "If you hold to my teaching,[b]
you are really my disciples. 32 Then you
will know the truth, and the truth will set
you free."[c]
33 They answered him, "We are Abraham's descendants[d] and have never been
slaves of anyone. How can you say that we
shall be set free?"
34 Jesus replied, "Very truly I tell you, everyone who sins is a slave to sin.[e] 35 Now a
slave has no permanent place in the family, but a son belongs to it forever.[f] 36 So
if the Son sets you free,[g] you will be free
indeed. 37 I know that you are Abraham's
descendants. Yet you are looking for a way
to kill me,[h] because you have no room for
my word. 38 I am telling you what I have
seen in the Father's presence,[i] and you are
doing what you have heard from your father.[a]"[j]
39 "Abraham is our father," they answered.
"If you were Abraham's children,"[k] said
Jesus, "then you would[b] do what Abraham did. 40 As it is, you are looking for a
way to kill me,[l] a man who has told you
the truth that I heard from God.[m] Abraham
did not do such things. 41 You are doing the
works of your own father."[n]
"We are not illegitimate children," they
protested. "The only Father we have is
God himself."[o]

8:29 [z] Isa 50:5; Jn 4:34; 5:30; 6:38
8:30 [a] S Jn 7:31
8:31 [b] Jn 15:7; 2Jn 9
8:32 [c] ver 36; Ro 8:2; 2Co 3:17; Gal 5:1,13
8:33 [d] ver 37, 39; S Lk 3:8
8:34 [e] S Ro 6:16
8:35 [f] Gal 4:30
8:36 [g] ver 32
8:37 [h] ver 39,40
8:38 [i] Jn 5:19, 30; 14:10,24 [j] ver 41,44
8:39 [k] ver 37; S Lk 3:8
8:40 [l] S Mt 12:14 [m] ver 26
8:41 [n] ver 38, 44 [o] Isa 63:16; 64:8
8:42 [p] 1Jn 5:1 [q] S Jn 13:3 [r] Jn 7:28 [s] S Jn 3:17
8:44 [t] 1Jn 3:8 [u] ver 38,41 [v] Ge 3:4; 4:9; 2Ch 18:21; Ps 5:6; 12:2
8:45 [w] Jn 18:37
8:47 [x] Jn 18:37; 1Jn 4:6
8:48 [y] S Mt 10:5 [z] ver 52; S Mk 3:22
8:50 [a] ver 54; Jn 5:41
8:51 [b] Jn 11:26
8:52 [c] ver 48; S Mk 3:22

42 Jesus said to them, "If God were your
Father, you would love me,[p] for I have
come here from God.[q] I have not come on
my own;[r] God sent me.[s] 43 Why is my language not clear to you? Because you are
unable to hear what I say. 44 You belong
to your father, the devil,[t] and you want to
carry out your father's desires.[u] He was a
murderer from the beginning, not holding
to the truth, for there is no truth in him.
When he lies, he speaks his native language, for he is a liar and the father of
lies.[v] 45 Yet because I tell the truth,[w] you do
not believe me! 46 Can any of you prove me
guilty of sin? If I am telling the truth, why
don't you believe me? 47 Whoever belongs
to God hears what God says.[x] The reason
you do not hear is that you do not belong
to God."

Jesus' Claims About Himself

48 The Jews answered him, "Aren't we
right in saying that you are a Samaritan[y]
and demon-possessed?"[z]
49 "I am not possessed by a demon,"
said Jesus, "but I honor my Father and
you dishonor me. 50 I am not seeking glory for myself;[a] but there is one who seeks
it, and he is the judge. 51 Very truly I tell
you, whoever obeys my word will never
see death."[b]
52 At this they exclaimed, "Now we know
that you are demon-possessed![c] Abraham
died and so did the prophets, yet you say
that whoever obeys your word will never

[a] 38 Or *presence. Therefore do what you have heard from the Father.* [b] 39 Some early manuscripts *"If you are Abraham's children," said Jesus, "then*

8:30 *believed.* See 1:7; 20:31 and notes.

8:31 *believed.* Here seems to mean "made a formal profession of faith." Their words show that they were not true believers (see vv. 33,37).

8:32 *truth.* Closely connected with Jesus (see v. 36; 14:6 and note), it is not philosophical truth but the truth that leads to salvation. *free.* Freedom from sin, not from ignorance (see v. 36).

8:33 *have never been slaves.* Appears to be an amazing disregard of their Roman overlords — and their Egyptian, Assyrian, Babylonian, Persian and Syrian overlords as well. Perhaps they meant that they have always viewed themselves as the descendants of Abraham and heirs of the promises God made to him and so have never accepted servitude to others as their proper status.

8:34 *slave to sin.* Because sinners cannot break free by their own strength (see Ro 6:18 and note).

8:37 *you are looking for a way to kill me.* See note on 7:1 — 8:59.

8:38 Note the contrasts: "I ... you"; "seen ... heard"; "the Father ... your father." Not until later (see v. 44 and note) did Jesus say who their father was, but it is clear even at this point that it was neither God nor Abraham, as they claimed.

8:39 – 41 Their deeds revealed their parentage.

8:41 *illegitimate.* May have been a slander aimed at Jesus.

8:43 *my language.* The form of expression — the actual words. *what I say.* The content. These descendants of Abraham (v. 33) were so convinced of their own preconceptions that they did not really hear and understand what Jesus was saying (cf. v. 47).

8:44 *You belong to your father, the devil.* Jesus warned his Jewish opponents of the reality of Satan's murderous and deceitful influence. Since "salvation is from the Jews" (4:22; see note there), Jesus' words do not apply to the Jewish people as a whole. His warning should caution both Gentiles and Jews to follow Abraham's example (vv. 39 – 40; cf. Ro 4:16). *you want.* Points to determination of will. Their problem was basically spiritual, not intellectual. Being oriented toward Satan, they were bent on murder (v. 37) and eventually would succeed (v. 28). *truth.* Foreign to Satan and those who are his (see 14:6 and note).

8:46 *Can ... you prove me guilty of sin?* The asking of the question was more significant than the opponents' failure to answer, in that it showed that Jesus had a perfectly clear conscience.

8:47 *hears what God says.* See 10:3 – 4 and notes; 1Jn 4:6.

8:48 *Samaritan.* Possibly to suggest that he was lax in Jewish observances — "no better than a Samaritan" — or that he was a Samaritan by birth. *demon-possessed.* See 10:20 and note on 7:20.

8:51 *my word.* The whole of Jesus' message which, when accepted, brings deliverance from death.

taste death. 53 Are you greater than our father Abraham?[d] He died, and so did the
prophets. Who do you think you are?"
54 Jesus replied, "If I glorify myself,[e] my
glory means nothing. My Father, whom
you claim as your God, is the one who
glorifies me.[f] 55 Though you do not know
him,[g] I know him.[h] If I said I did not, I
would be a liar like you, but I do know
him and obey his word.[i] 56 Your father
Abraham[j] rejoiced at the thought of seeing
my day; he saw it[k] and was glad."
57 "You are not yet fifty years old," they
said to him, "and you have seen Abraham!"
58 "Very truly I tell you," Jesus answered,
"before Abraham was born,[l] I am!"[m] 59 At
this, they picked up stones to stone him,[n]
but Jesus hid himself,[o] slipping away from
the temple grounds.

Jesus Heals a Man Born Blind

9 As he went along, he saw a man blind
from birth. 2 His disciples asked him,
"Rabbi,[p] who sinned,[q] this man[r] or his parents,[s] that he was born blind?"
3 "Neither this man nor his parents
sinned," said Jesus, "but this happened so
that the works of God might be displayed in
him.[t] 4 As long as it is day,[u] we must do the
works of him who sent me. Night is coming, when no one can work. 5 While I am
in the world, I am the light of the world."[v]
6 After saying this, he spit[w] on the
ground, made some mud with the saliva,
and put it on the man's eyes. 7 "Go," he
told him, "wash in the Pool of Siloam"[x]
(this word means "Sent"). So the man
went and washed, and came home seeing.[y]
8 His neighbors and those who had formerly seen him begging asked, "Isn't this
the same man who used to sit and beg?"[z]
9 Some claimed that he was.
Others said, "No, he only looks like
him."
But he himself insisted, "I am the man."
10 "How then were your eyes opened?"
they asked.
11 He replied, "The man they call Jesus
made some mud and put it on my eyes.
He told me to go to Siloam and wash. So I
went and washed, and then I could see."[a]
12 "Where is this man?" they asked him.
"I don't know," he said.

The Pharisees Investigate the Healing

13 They brought to the Pharisees the
man who had been blind. 14 Now the day
on which Jesus had made the mud and
opened the man's eyes was a Sabbath.[b]
15 Therefore the Pharisees also asked him
how he had received his sight.[c] "He put
mud on my eyes," the man replied, "and I
washed, and now I see."
16 Some of the Pharisees said, "This man

8:53 [d] ver 39; Jn 4:12
8:54 [e] ver 50 [f] Jn 16:14; 17:1,5
8:55 [g] ver 19 [h] Jn 7:28,29 [i] Jn 15:10
8:56 [j] ver 37, 39; Ge 18:18 [k] S Mt 13:17
8:58 [l] S Jn 1:2 [m] Ex 3:14; 6:3
8:59 [n] Ex 17:4; Lev 24:16; 1Sa 30:6; Jn 10:31; 11:8 [o] Jn 12:36
9:2 [p] S Mt 23:7 [q] ver 34; Lk 13:2; Ac 28:4 [r] Eze 18:20 [s] Ex 20:5; Job 21:19
9:3 [t] Jn 11:4
9:4 [u] Jn 11:9; 12:35
9:5 [v] S Jn 1:4
9:6 [w] Mk 7:33; 8:23
9:7 [x] ver 11; 2Ki 5:10; Lk 13:4 [y] Isa 35:5; Jn 11:37
9:8 [z] Ac 3:2,10
9:11 [a] ver 7
9:14 [b] Mt 12:1-14; Jn 5:9
9:15 [c] ver 10

8:53 *Are you greater . . . ?* The question was framed to expect the answer "No." This is ironic, since Jesus was indeed far greater than Abraham, even as he was greater than Moses (see 6:30–35 and notes).

8:56 *my day.* All that was involved in the incarnation. Jesus probably was not referring to any one occasion but to Abraham's general joy in the fulfilling of the purposes of God in the Messiah, by which all nations on earth would receive blessing (see note on Ge 12:2–3). *he saw it.* In faith, from afar.

8:57 *not yet fifty years old.* A generous allowance for Jesus' maximum possible age. Jesus was "about" 30 when he began his ministry (see Lk 3:23 and note).

8:58 *Very truly I tell you.* See note on Mk 3:28. *I am!* A solemnly emphatic declaration echoing God's great affirmations in Ex 3:14 (see vv. 24,28; see also note on 6:35). Jesus did not say "I was" but "I am," expressing the eternity of his being and his oneness with the Father (see 1:1). With this climactic statement Jesus concludes his speech that began with the related claim, "I am the light of the world" (v. 12; see note there).

8:59 *to stone him.* Those who heard Jesus could not interpret his claim as other than blasphemy, for which stoning was the proper penalty (Lev 24:16). When Jesus declares "I am," there are only two possible responses: to reach for a rock or to fall at his feet. Unfortunately his enemies chose the former.

9:1–12 Jesus performed more miracles of this kind than of any other. Giving sight to the blind was predicted as a Messianic activity (see Isa 29:18; 35:5 and notes; 42:7). Thus these miracles were additional evidence that Jesus was the Messiah (see 20:31 and note).

9:2 *who sinned . . . ?* The rabbis had developed the principle that "there is no death without sin, and there is no suffering without iniquity" (cf. Introduction to Job: Theological Theme and Message). They were even capable of thinking that a child could sin in the womb or that its soul might have sinned in a preexistent state. They also held that terrible punishments came on certain people because of the sin of their parents. As the next verse shows, Jesus plainly contradicted these beliefs.

9:3 *works of God might be displayed.* Cf. 11:4,40 and note on 11:4.

9:4 *we.* Not Jesus only; his disciples share with him the responsibility of doing what God wants done. *Night is coming.* When Jesus, "the light of the world" (v. 5), will be taken away in death.

9:5 *the light of the world.* See note on 8:12.

9:6 Jesus used variety in his cures. He could turn even the dirt of the earth into a medium of restoration (cf. Mk 8:22–25).

9:7 *Pool of Siloam.* Until recent years the general site of the pool on the southern end of the main ridge on which Jerusalem was built was marked by a structure from the Byzantine period. In 2004, however, archaeologists identified nearby remains that proved to be the original Pool of Siloam of Jesus' day. The aqueduct leading into the pool served as part of the major water system developed by King Hezekiah (see notes on 2Ki 20:20; Ne 2:14; Job 28:10; Isa 8:6). *Sent.* Or "one who has been sent."

9:8 *begging.* About the only way blind people of that day could support themselves.

9:13 *Pharisees.* See note on 7:32.

9:14 *Sabbath.* Cf. 5:16 and the discussion that follows (see note on 5:10).

is not from God, for he does not keep the Sabbath."[d]

But others asked, "How can a sinner perform such signs?"[e] So they were divided.[f]

17 Then they turned again to the blind man, "What have you to say about him? It was your eyes he opened."

The man replied, "He is a prophet."[g]

18 They[h] still did not believe that he had been blind and had received his sight until they sent for the man's parents. 19 "Is this your son?" they asked. "Is this the one you say was born blind? How is it that now he can see?"

20 "We know he is our son," the parents answered, "and we know he was born blind. 21 But how he can see now, or who opened his eyes, we don't know. Ask him. He is of age; he will speak for himself." 22 His parents said this because they were afraid of the Jewish leaders,[i] who already had decided that anyone who acknowledged that Jesus was the Messiah would be put out[j] of the synagogue.[k] 23 That was why his parents said, "He is of age; ask him."[l]

24 A second time they summoned the man who had been blind. "Give glory to God by telling the truth,"[m] they said. "We know this man is a sinner."[n]

25 He replied, "Whether he is a sinner or not, I don't know. One thing I do know. I was blind but now I see!"

26 Then they asked him, "What did he do to you? How did he open your eyes?"

27 He answered, "I have told you already[o] and you did not listen. Why do you want to hear it again? Do you want to become his disciples too?"

28 Then they hurled insults at him and said, "You are this fellow's disciple! We are disciples of Moses![p] 29 We know that God spoke to Moses, but as for this fellow, we don't even know where he comes from."[q]

30 The man answered, "Now that is remarkable! You don't know where he comes from, yet he opened my eyes. 31 We know that God does not listen to sinners. He listens to the godly person who does his will.[r] 32 Nobody has ever heard of opening the eyes of a man born blind. 33 If this man were not from God,[s] he could do nothing."

34 To this they replied, "You were steeped in sin at birth;[t] how dare you lecture us!" And they threw him out.[u]

Spiritual Blindness

35 Jesus heard that they had thrown him out, and when he found him, he said, "Do you believe[v] in the Son of Man?"[w]

36 "Who is he, sir?" the man asked. "Tell me so that I may believe in him."[x]

37 Jesus said, "You have now seen him; in fact, he is the one speaking with you."[y]

38 Then the man said, "Lord, I believe," and he worshiped him.[z]

39 Jesus said,[a] "For judgment[a] I have come into this world,[b] so that the blind will see[c] and those who see will become blind."[d]

40 Some Pharisees who were with him heard him say this and asked, "What? Are we blind too?"[e]

41 Jesus said, "If you were blind, you

[a] *38,39* Some early manuscripts do not have *Then the man said . . . 39Jesus said.*

9:16 [d] S Mt 12:2 [e] S Jn 2:11 [f] S Jn 6:52 **9:17** [g] S Mt 21:11 **9:18** [h] S Jn 1:19 **9:22** [i] S Jn 7:13 [j] ver 34; Lk 6:22 [k] Jn 12:42; 16:2 **9:23** [l] ver 21 **9:24** [m] Jos 7:19 [n] ver 16 **9:27** [o] ver 15 **9:28** [p] Jn 5:45 **9:29** [q] Jn 8:14 **9:31** [r] Ge 18:23-32; Ps 34:15,16; 66:18; 145:19,20; Pr 15:29; Isa 1:15; 59:1,2; Jn 15:7; Jas 5:16-18; 1Jn 5:14,15 **9:33** [s] ver 16; Jn 3:2 **9:34** [t] ver 2 [u] ver 22,35; Isa 66:5 **9:35** [v] S Jn 3:15 [w] S Mt 8:20 **9:36** [x] Ro 10:14 **9:37** [y] Jn 4:26 **9:38** [z] Mt 28:9 **9:39** [a] S Jn 5:22 [b] Jn 3:19; 12:47 [c] Lk 4:18 [d] Mt 13:13 **9:40** [e] Ro 2:19

9:16 *Some ... others.* The first group started from their entrenched position and ruled out the possibility of Jesus being from God. The second started from the fact of the "signs" and ruled out the possibility of his being a sinner (cf. vv. 30–33 and notes).

9:17 *What have you to say about him?* It is curious that they put such a question to such a person; their doing so reflected their perplexity. *prophet.* Probably the highest designation the man could think of. He progressed in his thinking about Jesus: from a man (v. 11) to a prophet (v. 17), who might be followed by disciples (v. 27), to one "from God" (v. 33) to one who was properly to be worshiped (v. 38).

9:18 *They.* The Pharisees (see vv. 13,15–16; see also note on 1:19). In their prejudice they did not learn from the sign but tried to discredit the miracle.

9:21 *He is of age.* There was much to which the parents could not testify, but their emphasis on the son's responsibility showed their fear of getting involved.

9:22 *put out of the synagogue.* Excommunication is reported as early as the time of Ezra (10:8), but there is practically no information about the way it was practiced in NT times. The synagogue was the center of Jewish community life (see note on 6:59), so excommunication cut a person off from many social relationships (though, in some of its forms, at least in later times, not from worship).

9:24 *We.* Emphatic in the Greek.

9:27 *his disciples too.* The man already counted himself a disciple.

9:30–33 Good reasoning from an unschooled man.

9:31 *God does not listen to sinners.* Cf. the remark of some of the Pharisees in v. 16.

9:34 *threw him out.* May mean "expelled him from their assembly" or, more probably, "excommunicated him" (see note on v. 22; cf. note on 1Co 5:5).

9:35 *when he found him.* Jesus obviously had been looking for the man. *Son of Man.* See note on Mk 8:31.

9:36 The man was ready to follow any suggestion from his benefactor.

9:38 *I believe.* See notes on 1:7; 20:31. *he worshiped him.* The man was giving Jesus the reverence due to God.

9:39 It is unlikely that the conversation of vv. 35–38 took place in the presence of the Pharisees. The incident of vv. 39–41, therefore, probably occurred a little later. *For judgment.* In a sense Jesus did not come for judgment (see 3:17; 12:47 and note), but his coming divides people, and this always brings a type of judgment. Those who reject his gift end up "blind."

9:40 *Pharisees.* They found it incredible that anyone would consider them spiritually blind. See note on v. 13.

would not be guilty of sin; but now that
you claim you can see, your guilt remains.[f]

The Good Shepherd and His Sheep

10 "Very truly I tell you Pharisees,
anyone who does not enter the
sheep pen by the gate, but climbs in by
some other way, is a thief and a robber.[g]
2 The one who enters by the gate is the
shepherd of the sheep.[h] 3 The gatekeeper
opens the gate for him, and the sheep listen to his voice.[i] He calls his own sheep by
name and leads them out.[j] 4 When he has
brought out all his own, he goes on ahead
of them, and his sheep follow him because
they know his voice.[k] 5 But they will never follow a stranger; in fact, they will run
away from him because they do not recognize a stranger's voice." 6 Jesus used this
figure of speech,[l] but the Pharisees did not
understand what he was telling them.[m]
7 Therefore Jesus said again, "Very truly
I tell you, I am[n] the gate[o] for the sheep.
8 All who have come before me[p] are thieves
and robbers,[q] but the sheep have not listened to them. 9 I am the gate; whoever
enters through me will be saved.[a] They
will come in and go out, and find pasture.
10 The thief comes only to steal and kill
and destroy; I have come that they may
have life,[r] and have it to the full.[s]
11 "I am[t] the good shepherd.[u] The good
shepherd lays down his life for the sheep.[v]
12 The hired hand is not the shepherd and
does not own the sheep. So when he sees
the wolf coming, he abandons the sheep
and runs away.[w] Then the wolf attacks the
flock and scatters it. 13 The man runs away
because he is a hired hand and cares nothing for the sheep.
14 "I am the good shepherd;[x] I know my
sheep[y] and my sheep know me— 15 just
as the Father knows me and I know the
Father[z]—and I lay down my life for the
sheep.[a] 16 I have other sheep[b] that are not
of this sheep pen. I must bring them also.
They too will listen to my voice, and there
shall be one flock[c] and one shepherd.[d]
17 The reason my Father loves me is that

9:41 [f] Jn 15:22, 24
10:1 [g] ver 8, 10
10:2 [h] ver 11, 14; Mk 6:34
10:3 [i] ver 4, 5, 14, 16, 27 [j] ver 4, 5, 14, 16, 27
10:4 [k] S ver 3
10:6 [l] S Jn 16:25 [m] S Mk 9:32
10:7 [n] S Jn 6:35 [o] ver 9
10:8 [p] Jer 23:1, 2; Eze 34:2 [q] ver 1
10:10 [r] S Jn 1:4; 3:15, 16; 5:40; 20:31 [s] Ps 65:11; Ro 5:17
10:11 [t] S Jn 6:35 [u] ver 14; Ps 23:1; Isa 40:11; Eze 34:11-16, 23; Mt 2:6; Lk 12:32; Heb 13:20; 1Pe 2:25; 5:4; Rev 7:17 [v] ver 15, 17, 18; Jn 15:13; 1Jn 3:16
10:12 [w] Zec 11:16, 17
10:14 [x] S ver 11 [y] ver 27; Ex 33:12
10:15 [z] Mt 11:27 [a] ver 11, 17, 18
10:16 [b] Isa 56:8; Ac 10:34, 35 [c] Jn 11:52; 17:20, 21; Eph 2:11-19 [d] Eze 34:23; 37:24

SEVEN "I AM" STATEMENTS OF JOHN'S GOSPEL

1. The Bread of Life (6:35)
2. The Light of the World (8:12; 9:5)
3. The Gate (10:7)
4. The Good Shepherd (10:11,14)
5. The Resurrection and the Life (11:25)
6. The Way and the Truth and the Life (14:6)
7. The True Vine (15:1)

[a] 9 Or *kept safe*

9:41 The Pharisees' claim to sight showed their complete unawareness of their spiritual blindness and need. And, though they claimed to have sight, their actions were evidence of their blindness.

10:1–30 Should be understood in light of the OT (and ancient Near Eastern) concept of "shepherd," symbolizing a royal caretaker of God's people. God himself was called the "Shepherd of Israel" (Ps 80:1; see Ps 23:1 and note; Isa 40:10–11; Eze 34:11–16 and note on 34:2; Zec 10:2 and note), and he had given great responsibility to the leaders ("shepherds") of Israel, which they failed to respect. God denounced these false shepherds (see Isa 56:9–12; Eze 34) and promised to provide the true Shepherd, the Messiah, to care for the sheep (Eze 34:23).

10:1 *Very truly I tell you.* See note on Mk 3:28. *sheep pen.* An enclosure with only one entrance. Its walls kept the sheep from wandering away. See photo, p. 1757.

10:3 *gatekeeper.* Apparently in charge of a large sheep pen, where several flocks were kept. *his voice.* The sheep responded only to the voice of their own shepherd. *his own sheep.* Shepherds did not call sheep randomly, but only those that belonged to them.

10:4 *he goes on ahead.* Palestinian shepherds led their sheep (they did not drive them), and the sheep followed because they knew their own shepherd's voice.

10:6 *did not understand.* See 8:27; 12:16; Mk 8:16 and note; Lk 2:50; 9:45; 18:34.

10:7 *I am.* See note on 6:35.

10:8 *All … before me.* "False shepherds" like the Pharisees and the chief priests, not the true OT prophets (see note on vv. 1–30; cf. Zec 11:5,8 and notes).

10:9 *the gate.* The one way into salvation. Inside there is safety, and one is able to go out and find pasture, i.e., the supply of all needs.

10:10 *thief.* His interest is in himself. Christ's interest is in his sheep, whom he enables to have life to the full (see note on 1:4).

10:11 *I am.* See note on 6:35. *lays down his life.* Shepherds might risk danger for their sheep (see Ge 31:39; 1Sa 17:34–37), but they expected to come through alive. Jesus said that the good shepherd is willing to die for his sheep (cf. 15:13 and note; Isa 53:6–7).

10:12 *hired hand.* Interested in wages, not in the sheep (v. 13).

10:14 *I know … my sheep know.* A deep mutual knowledge, like that of the Father and the Son.

10:15 *I lay down my life.* See v. 11 and note; the fact of central importance.

10:16 *other sheep.* These already belonged to Christ, though they had not yet been brought to him. *not of this sheep pen.* Those outside Judaism. Here is a glimpse of the future worldwide scope of the church. *one flock.* All God's people have the same Shepherd (see 17:20–23).

10:17–18 That Christ would die for his people runs through this section of John's Gospel. Both the love and the plan of the Father are involved, as well as the au-

I lay down my life[e] — only to take it up
again. 18 No one takes it from me, but I lay
it down of my own accord.[f] I have authority to lay it down and authority to take it
up again. This command I received from
my Father."[g]
19 The Jews who heard these words were
again divided.[h] 20 Many of them said, "He
is demon-possessed[i] and raving mad.[j]
Why listen to him?"
21 But others said, "These are not the
sayings of a man possessed by a demon.[k]
Can a demon open the eyes of the blind?"[l]

Further Conflict Over Jesus' Claims

22 Then came the Festival of Dedication[a]
at Jerusalem. It was winter, 23 and Jesus
was in the temple courts walking in Solomon's Colonnade.[m] 24 The Jews[n] who were
there gathered around him, saying, "How
long will you keep us in suspense? If you
are the Messiah, tell us plainly."[o]
25 Jesus answered, "I did tell you,[p] but
you do not believe. The works I do in my
Father's name testify about me,[q] 26 but you
do not believe because you are not my
sheep.[r] 27 My sheep listen to my voice; I
know them,[s] and they follow me.[t] 28 I give
them eternal life,[u] and they shall never
perish;[v] no one will snatch them out of my
hand.[w] 29 My Father, who has given them
to me,[x] is greater than all[b];[y] no one can
snatch them out of my Father's hand. 30 I
and the Father are one."[z]
31 Again his Jewish opponents picked
up stones to stone him,[a] 32 but Jesus said
to them, "I have shown you many good
works from the Father. For which of these
do you stone me?"
33 "We are not stoning you for any good
work," they replied, "but for blasphemy, because you, a mere man, claim to be God."[b]
34 Jesus answered them, "Is it not written in your Law,[c] 'I have said you are
"gods"'[c]?[d] 35 If he called them 'gods,' to
whom the word of God[e] came — and Scripture cannot be set aside[f] — 36 what about
the one whom the Father set apart[g] as his
very own[h] and sent into the world?[i] Why
then do you accuse me of blasphemy because I said, 'I am God's Son'?[j] 37 Do not
believe me unless I do the works of my

10:17 [e] ver 11, 15,18 **10:18** [f] Mt 26:53 [g] Jn 15:10; Php 2:8; Heb 5:8 **10:19** [h] S Jn 6:52 **10:20** [i] S Mk 3:22 [j] 2Ki 9:11; Jer 29:26; Mk 3:21 **10:21** [k] S Mt 4:24 [l] Ex 4:11; Jn 9:32,33 **10:23** [m] Ac 3:11; 5:12 **10:24** [n] S Jn 1:19 [o] Lk 22:67; Jn 16:25,29 **10:25** [p] Jn 4:26; 8:58 [q] Jn 5:36; 14:11 **10:26** [r] Jn 8:47 **10:27** [s] ver 14 [t] ver 4 **10:28** [u] S Mt 25:46 [v] Isa 66:22 [w] S Jn 6:39 **10:29** [x] Jn 17:2, 6,24 [y] Jn 14:28 **10:30** [z] Dt 6:4; Jn 17:21-23 **10:31** [a] S Jn 8:59 **10:33** [b] Lev 24:16; Mt 26:63-66; Jn 5:18 **10:34** [c] Jn 8:17; 12:34; 15:25; Ro 3:19; 1Co 14:21 [d] Ps 82:6 **10:35** [e] S Heb 4:12 [f] S Mt 5:18 **10:36** [g] Jer 1:5 [h] Jn 6:69 [i] S Jn 3:17 [j] Jn 5:17,18

[a] *22* That is, Hanukkah [b] *29* Many early manuscripts *What my Father has given me is greater than all* [c] *34* Psalm 82:6

thority he gave to the Son. Christ obediently and voluntarily chose to die; otherwise, no one would have had the power to kill him (cf. Lk 23:46).

10:19 *divided.* See 7:43; 9:16.

10:20 *demon-possessed.* See note on 7:20.

10:21 See 9:16.

10:22 *Festival of Dedication.* The commemoration of the dedication (see NIV text note) of the temple by Judas Maccabeus in December, 165 BC, after it had been profaned by Antiochus IV Epiphanes (see essay, pp. 1571–1574). This was the last great deliverance the Jews had experienced. *It was winter.* A reference for those unfamiliar with the Jewish calendar (see bottom of chart, p. 188).

10:23 *Solomon's Colonnade.* See Ac 3:11 and note; 5:12. It was a roofed structure — somewhat similar to a Greek stoa — commonly but erroneously thought to date back to Solomon's time.

10:24 *If you are the Messiah.* Because of the different ideas about Messiahship then in vogue, it was not easy for Jews to resolve this critical issue. See notes on 1:25; 20:31.

10:25 *I did tell you.* Jesus had not specifically affirmed his Messiahship except to the Samaritan woman (see 4:26 and note). He may have meant here that the general thrust of his teaching made his claim clear or that such statements as that in 8:58 (see note there) were sufficient. Or he may have been referring to the evidence of his whole manner of life (including the miracles) — all he had done in the Father's name (for the name, see note on 2:23).

10:26 *not my sheep.* Their failure to believe arose from what they were.

10:27 *voice.* See v. 3 and note. *I know them.* See v. 14 and note. *they follow.* See v. 4 and note.

10:28 *eternal life.* Christ's gift (see note on 3:15). *never perish.* The Greek construction here is a strong denial that the sheep will ever perish. The sheep's security is in the power of the shepherd, who will let no one take them from him (see 3:16).

10:29 *My Father.* See note on 5:17. *no one can snatch them.* The Father's power ("hand") is greater than that of any enemy, making the sheep completely secure (cf. 17:11–12 and notes).

10:30 *one.* The Greek is neuter — "one thing," not "one person." The two are one in essence or nature, will and purpose, but they are not identical persons. This great truth is what warrants Jesus' "I am" declarations (see 6:35; 8:24,58; 17:21–22 and notes).

10:31 *his Jewish opponents.* See note on 1:19. *to stone him.* They took Jesus' words as blasphemy and therefore prepared to carry out the law (Lev 24:16), though without due process.

10:32 *good works.* See Mt 5:16; 1Ti 5:10,25; 6:18. Although the reference here includes Jesus' miracles, the underlying Greek words refer to works in general that are first of all fine and noble in character (see note on v. 38).

10:33 *blasphemy.* The Jewish leaders correctly understood the thrust of Jesus' words, but their preconceptions and unbelief prevented them from accepting his claim as true.

10:34 *your Law.* In its strictest sense the term meant the Pentateuch, but it was often used, as here, of the whole OT. *you are "gods."* The words Jesus quotes from Ps 82:6 (see note on 82:1) refer to the judges (or other leaders or rulers), whose tasks were divinely appointed (see Ex 22:28 and NIV text note; Dt 1:17; 16:18; 2Ch 19:6).

10:35 *Scripture cannot be set aside.* Jesus testified to the complete authority and reliability of the OT.

10:36 Jesus is making an argument from the lesser to the greater: If there is any sense in which humans can be spoken of as "gods" (as Ps 82:6 speaks of human rulers or judges), how much more may the term be used of him whom the Father set apart and sent!

10:37 *the works of my Father.* The kind of works of compassion that the Father himself does.

Father.[k] 38 But if I do them, even though
you do not believe me, believe the works,
that you may know and understand that
the Father is in me, and I in the Father."[l]
39 Again they tried to seize him,[m] but he
escaped their grasp.[n]
40 Then Jesus went back across the Jordan[o] to the place where John had been
baptizing in the early days. There he
stayed, 41 and many people came to him.
They said, "Though John never performed
a sign,[p] all that John said about this man
was true."[q] 42 And in that place many believed in Jesus.[r]

The Death of Lazarus

11 Now a man named Lazarus was
sick. He was from Bethany,[s] the
village of Mary and her sister Martha.[t]
2 (This Mary, whose brother Lazarus now
lay sick, was the same one who poured
perfume on the Lord and wiped his feet
with her hair.)[u] 3 So the sisters sent word
to Jesus, "Lord, the one you love[v] is sick."
4 When he heard this, Jesus said, "This
sickness will not end in death. No, it is for
God's glory[w] so that God's Son may be glorified through it." 5 Now Jesus loved Martha
and her sister and Lazarus. 6 So when he
heard that Lazarus was sick, he stayed where
he was two more days, 7 and then he said to
his disciples, "Let us go back to Judea."[x]
8 "But Rabbi,"[y] they said, "a short while
ago the Jews there tried to stone you,[z] and
yet you are going back?"
9 Jesus answered, "Are there not twelve
hours of daylight? Anyone who walks in
the daytime will not stumble, for they see
by this world's light.[a] 10 It is when a person
walks at night that they stumble, for they
have no light."
11 After he had said this, he went on to
tell them, "Our friend[b] Lazarus has fall-
en asleep;[c] but I am going there to wake
him up."
12 His disciples replied, "Lord, if he
sleeps, he will get better." 13 Jesus had
been speaking of his death, but his disciples thought he meant natural sleep.[d]
14 So then he told them plainly, "Lazarus is dead, 15 and for your sake I am glad
I was not there, so that you may believe.
But let us go to him."
16 Then Thomas[e] (also known as Didymus[a]) said to the rest of the disciples, "Let
us also go, that we may die with him."

Jesus Comforts the Sisters of Lazarus

17 On his arrival, Jesus found that Lazarus had already been in the tomb for four
days.[f] 18 Now Bethany[g] was less than two
miles[b] from Jerusalem, 19 and many Jews
had come to Martha and Mary to comfort
them in the loss of their brother.[h] 20 When
Martha heard that Jesus was coming, she
went out to meet him, but Mary stayed
at home.[i]

[a] *16 Thomas* (Aramaic) and *Didymus* (Greek) both mean *twin*. [b] *18* Or about 3 kilometers

10:37 [k] ver 25
10:38 [l] Jn 14:10,11,20; 17:21
10:39 [m] Jn 7:30 [n] Lk 4:30; Jn 8:59
10:40 [o] Jn 1:28
10:41 [p] S Jn 2:11 [q] Jn 1:26,27,30,34
10:42 [r] S Jn 7:31
11:1 [s] S Mt 21:17 [t] Lk 10:38
11:2 [u] Mk 14:3; Lk 7:38; Jn 12:3
11:3 [v] ver 5,36
11:4 [w] ver 40
11:7 [x] Jn 10:40
11:8 [y] S Mt 23:7 [z] Jn 8:59; 10:31
11:9 [a] Jn 9:4; 12:35
11:11 [b] ver 3 [c] S Mt 9:24
11:13 [d] Mt 9:24
11:16 [e] Mt 10:3; Jn 14:5; 20:24-28; 21:2; Ac 1:13
11:17 [f] ver 6,39
11:18 [g] ver 1; S Mt 21:17
11:19 [h] ver 31; Job 2:11
11:20 [i] Lk 10:38-42

10:38 *works.* Miracles were only a part of Jesus' works. It was Jesus' quality of life, not people's inability to explain his marvels, that he primarily spoke of here (see note on v. 32).
10:39 *they tried to seize him.* It is not clear whether this was to arrest him for trial or to take him out for stoning. *he escaped.* John does not say why they failed, but he often makes it clear that Jesus could not be killed before the appointed time (see note on 2:4; see also Lk 4:30 and note).
10:40 *where John had been baptizing.* See 1:28 and note.
10:41 *all that John said.* For John the Baptist as a witness, see 1:7 and note.
11:1 *Lazarus.* Mentioned only in chs. 11–12 of John's Gospel (the name is found also in the parable of Lk 16:19–31). The sisters are mentioned in Lk 10:38–42. *Bethany.* See map, p. 1770.
11:2 *poured perfume.* See 12:3 and note.
11:3 *the one you love.* The relationship must have been exceptionally close (see v. 36).
11:4 Cf. 9:3 and note on 9:2. *This sickness will not end in death.* Thus predicting the raising of Lazarus (v. 44), since Jesus already knew of his death (v. 14). In fact, Lazarus must have died shortly after the messengers left Bethany, accounting for the "four days" of vv. 17,39: one day for the journey of the messengers, the two days when Jesus remained where he was (see v. 6 and note) and a day for Jesus' journey to Bethany. But see note on v. 17. *glory.* See notes on 7:39; 12:41; 13:31. Here God's Son would be glorified through what happened to Lazarus, partly because the miracle displays the glory of God (who alone can raise the dead; see 5:21 and note) in Jesus (v. 40) and partly because it would help initiate events leading to the cross (vv. 46–53).
11:6 *he stayed.* Jesus moved as the Father directed, not as people (here Mary and Martha) wished (cf. 2:4 and note). *where he was.* In Perea, east of the Jordan River (10:40).
11:8 *the Jews there.* See note on 1:19. *tried to stone you.* See note on 10:31. There was clear danger in going into Judea.
11:9 *twelve hours.* Enough time for what must be done, but no time for waste.
11:11 *fallen asleep.* A euphemism for death, used by the unbelieving world as well as by Christians.
11:15 *believe.* See 1:7; 20:31 and notes.
11:16 *Thomas … Didymus.* The Aramaic word from which we get "Thomas" and the Greek word *Didymus* both mean "twin." Usually remembered for his doubting (see 20:24–25), he was also capable of devotion and courage, as here.
11:17 *four days.* See note on v. 4. Many Jews believed that the soul remained near the body for three days after death in the hope of returning to it. If this idea was in the minds of these people, they obviously thought all hope was gone—Lazarus was irrevocably dead.
11:18 *Bethany.* See note on Mt 21:17.
11:19 *to comfort them.* Jewish custom provided for three days of very heavy mourning, then four of heavy mourning, followed by lighter mourning for the remainder of 30 days. It was usual for friends to visit the family to comfort them.
11:20 *she went out to meet him.* Perhaps because as the older sister Martha was the hostess.

Roman catacomb fresco depicting the raising of Lazarus (Jn 11)

Z. Radovan/www.BibleLandPictures.com

21 "Lord," Martha said to Jesus,
"if you had been here, my brother
would not have died.[j] 22 But I know
that even now God will give you
whatever you ask."[k]
23 Jesus said to her, "Your brother
will rise again."
24 Martha answered, "I know he
will rise again in the resurrection[l]
at the last day."[m]
25 Jesus said to her, "I am[n] the
resurrection and the life.[o] The one
who believes[p] in me will live, even
though they die; 26 and whoever
lives by believing[q] in me will never
die.[r] Do you believe this?"
27 "Yes, Lord," she replied, "I believe that you are the Messiah,[s] the
Son of God,[t] who is to come into
the world."[u]
28 After she had said this, she went back
and called her sister Mary aside. "The
Teacher[v] is here," she said, "and is asking for you." 29 When Mary heard this, she
got up quickly and went to him. 30 Now
Jesus had not yet entered the village, but
was still at the place where Martha had
met him.[w] 31 When the Jews who had been
with Mary in the house, comforting her,[x]
noticed how quickly she got up and went
out, they followed her, supposing she was
going to the tomb to mourn there.
32 When Mary reached the place where
Jesus was and saw him, she fell at his feet
and said, "Lord, if you had been here, my
brother would not have died."[y]
33 When Jesus saw her weeping, and the
Jews who had come along with her also
weeping, he was deeply moved[z] in spirit and troubled.[a] 34 "Where have you laid
him?" he asked.

"Come and see, Lord," they replied.
35 Jesus wept.[b]
36 Then the Jews said, "See how he
loved him!"[c]
37 But some of them said, "Could not he
who opened the eyes of the blind man[d]
have kept this man from dying?"[e]

Jesus Raises Lazarus From the Dead

38 Jesus, once more deeply moved,[f]
came to the tomb. It was a cave with a
stone laid across the entrance.[g] 39 "Take
away the stone," he said.
"But, Lord," said Martha, the sister of
the dead man, "by this time there is a bad
odor, for he has been there four days."[h]
40 Then Jesus said, "Did I not tell you
that if you believe,[i] you will see the glory
of God?"[j]

11:21 [j] ver 32, 37
11:22 [k] ver 41,42
11:24 [l] Da 12:2; Jn 5:28,29; Ac 24:15 [m] Jn 6:39,40
11:25 [n] S Jn 6:35 [o] S Jn 1:4 [p] S Jn 3:15
11:26 [q] S Jn 3:15 [r] S Mt 25:46
11:27 [s] S Lk 2:11 [t] S Mt 4:3 [u] Jn 6:14
11:28 [v] Mt 26:18; Jn 13:13
11:30 [w] ver 20
11:31 [x] ver 19
11:32 [y] ver 21
11:33 [z] ver 38 [a] S Jn 12:27
11:35 [b] Lk 19:41
11:36 [c] ver 3
11:37 [d] Jn 9:6,7 [e] ver 21,32 **11:38** [f] ver 33 [g] Mt 27:60; Lk 24:2; Jn 20:1 **11:39** [h] ver 17 **11:40** [i] ver 23-25 [j] ver 4

11:21 Repeated by Mary in v. 32. Perhaps the sisters had said this to one another often as they awaited Jesus' arrival.

11:22 *whatever you ask.* This comment seems to mean that Martha hoped for an immediate resurrection, in spite of the fact that Lazarus's body had already begun to decay. Nothing is too difficult for God to do (see Ge 18:14; Jer 32:17,27 and notes).

11:25 *I am.* See note on 6:35. *life.* See note on 1:4. Jesus was saying more than that he gives resurrection and life. In some way these are identified with him, and his nature is such that final death is impossible for him. He is life (see 14:6 and note; Ac 3:15; Heb 7:16 and note). *The one who believes in me will live.* See note on 1:7. Jesus not only is life, but he also conveys life to believers so that death will never triumph over them (cf. 1Co 15:57 and note).

11:26 *never die.* Believers may die physically but, as those who have eternal life, their physical death is not their ultimate end (v. 25). Death cannot destroy the life Christ gives.

11:27 *I believe.* Martha is often remembered for her shortcoming recorded in Lk 10:40–41. But she was a woman of faith, as this magnificent declaration shows.

11:28 *The Teacher.* A significant description to be given by a woman. The rabbis would not teach women (see 4:27 and note), but Jesus taught them frequently (see, e.g., Lk 10:38–42).

11:31 *to mourn there.* Wailing at a tomb was common, and the Jews immediately thought this was in Mary's mind. Because they followed her, Jesus got maximum publicity.

11:32 Cf. v. 21.

11:33 *weeping.* Both times the word denotes a loud expression of grief, i.e., "wailing." *troubled.* See notes on 12:27; 13:21.

11:35 *wept.* The Greek for this word is not the one for loud grief, as in v. 33, but one that denotes quiet weeping, i.e., "shed tears."

11:36 Cf. v. 5.

11:37 Their position was like that of Martha (v. 21) and Mary (v. 32), but they based it on Jesus' ability to give sight to the blind (cf. ch. 9).

11:38 *once more deeply moved.* See v. 33. *cave with a stone laid across the entrance.* This type of burial place was not uncommon in the Holy Land at this time, especially for the wealthy (cf. 20:1 and notes on Mk 15:46; Lk 24:2).

11:39 *four days.* See notes on vv. 4,17.

11:40 *glory.* See note on v. 4; see also photo above.

41So they took away the stone. Then
Jesus looked up[k] and said, "Father,[l] I thank
you that you have heard me. 42I knew that
you always hear me, but I said this for the
benefit of the people standing here,[m] that
they may believe that you sent me."[n]
43When he had said this, Jesus called in
a loud voice, "Lazarus, come out!"[o] 44The
dead man came out, his hands and feet
wrapped with strips of linen,[p] and a cloth
around his face.[q]

Jesus said to them, "Take off the grave clothes and let him go."

The Plot to Kill Jesus

45Therefore many of the Jews who had
come to visit Mary,[r] and had seen what
Jesus did,[s] believed in him.[t] 46But some of
them went to the Pharisees and told them
what Jesus had done. 47Then the chief
priests and the Pharisees[u] called a meeting[v] of the Sanhedrin.[w]

"What are we accomplishing?" they
asked. "Here is this man performing many
signs.[x] 48If we let him go on like this, everyone will believe in him, and then the
Romans will come and take away both our
temple and our nation."
49Then one of them, named Caiaphas,[y]
who was high priest that year,[z] spoke up,
"You know nothing at all! 50You do not
realize that it is better for you that one
man die for the people than that the whole
nation perish."[a]
51He did not say this on his own, but as
high priest that year he prophesied that
Jesus would die for the Jewish nation,
52and not only for that nation but also
for the scattered children of God, to bring
them together and make them one.[b] 53So
from that day on they plotted to take his
life.[c]
54Therefore Jesus no longer moved
about publicly among the people of Judea.[d] Instead he withdrew to a region near
the wilderness, to a village called Ephraim, where he stayed with his disciples.
55When it was almost time for the Jewish Passover,[e] many went up from the
country to Jerusalem for their ceremonial
cleansing[f] before the Passover. 56They kept
looking for Jesus,[g] and as they stood in
the temple courts they asked one another,
"What do you think? Isn't he coming to
the festival at all?" 57But the chief priests
and the Pharisees had given orders that
anyone who found out where Jesus was
should report it so that they might arrest
him.

Jesus Anointed at Bethany

12:1-8Ref — Mt 26:6-13; Mk 14:3-9; Lk 7:37-39

12 Six days before the Passover,[h] Jesus
came to Bethany,[i] where Lazarus
lived, whom Jesus had raised from the
dead. 2Here a dinner was given in Jesus'
honor. Martha served,[j] while Lazarus was
among those reclining at the table with
him. 3Then Mary took about a pint[a] of
pure nard, an expensive perfume;[k] she

11:41 [k] Jn 17:1 [l] S Mt 11:25 **11:42** [m] Jn 12:30 [n] S Jn 3:17 **11:43** [o] S Lk 7:14 **11:44** [p] Jn 19:40 [q] Jn 20:7 **11:45** [r] ver 19 [s] Jn 2:23 [t] Ex 14:31; S Jn 7:31 **11:47** [u] ver 57 [v] Mt 26:3 [w] S Mt 5:22 [x] S Jn 2:11 **11:49** [y] S Mt 26:3 [z] ver 51; Jn 18:13,14 **11:50** [a] Jn 18:14 **11:52** [b] Isa 49:6; Jn 10:16 **11:53** [c] S Mt 12:14 **11:54** [d] Jn 7:1 **11:55** [e] Ex 12:13,23, 27; Mt 26:1,2; Mk 14:1; Jn 13:1 [f] 2Ch 30:17,18 **11:56** [g] Jn 7:11 **12:1** [h] S Jn 11:55 [i] S Mt 21:17 **12:2** [j] Lk 10:38-42 **12:3** [k] Mk 14:3

[a] 3 Or about 0.5 liter

11:44 *strips of linen.* Narrow strips, like bandages. Sometimes a shroud was used (see note on 19:40). *a cloth.* A separate item.
11:45 *many of the Jews ... believed in him.* Perhaps some who had been opposed to Jesus now became believers (see notes on 1:7,19; 20:31).
11:46 *Pharisees.* See note on 7:32.
11:47 *the chief priests and the Pharisees.* In all four Gospels the Pharisees appear as Jesus' principal opponents throughout his public ministry. But they lacked political power, and it is the chief priests (see note on Mt 2:4) who were prominent in the events that led to Jesus' crucifixion. Here both groups are associated in a meeting of the Sanhedrin (see note on Mk 14:55). They did not deny the reality of the miraculous signs (see note on 2:11), but they did not understand their meaning, for they failed to believe.
11:49 *Caiaphas.* High priest c. AD 18–36. He was the son-in-law of Annas (see 18:13; Mt 26:3; Lk 3:2 and notes), who had been deposed from the high priesthood by the Romans in AD 15. *high priest that year.* Probably means simply that he was high priest at that time. *You know nothing at all!* A remark typical of Sadducean rudeness (Caiaphas, as high priest, was a Sadducee). Josephus says that Sadducees "in their dealings with their peers are as rude as to foreigners." For Sadducees, see note on Mt 3:7.
11:50 *better.* Caiaphas was concerned with political expediency, not with guilt and innocence. He believed that one man, no matter how innocent, should perish rather than that the nation be put in jeopardy. Ironically in AD 70 the nation still perished.
11:51 *as high priest.* Caiaphas was not a private citizen but God's high priest, and God overruled in what he said. *that year.* See note on v. 49. *prophesied.* His words were true in a way he could not imagine. Prophecy in Scripture is the impartation of divinely revealed truth. In reality Caiaphas's words meant that Jesus' death would be for the nation, not by way of removing political trouble but by taking away the sins of those who believed in him.
11:52 *for the scattered children of God.* Jesus' death would have effects far beyond the nation (cf. 1:29; 3:16; 4:42; 10:16 and notes).
11:54 *he withdrew.* Jesus was not to die before his "hour" (see note on 2:4), but he would not act imprudently. Knowing the attitude of his opponents, he withdrew. He would die for others, but in his own time, not that of his enemies.
11:55 *Passover.* See notes on 2:13; 5:1. *ceremonial cleansing.* Especially important at a time like Passover, because without it, it would not be possible to keep the festival (see 2:6; 18:28; 1Co 11:28 and notes).
11:56 *Isn't he coming ... ?* The question expected the answer "No."
12:1–11 All four Gospels have an account of a woman anointing Jesus. John's account seems to tell of the same incident recorded in Mt 26:6–13 and Mk 14:3–9, while that in Lk 7:36–50 is probably a different event (see notes on all these passages).
12:1 *Bethany.* See note on Mt 21:17.
12:3 *nard.* The name of both a plant and the fragrant oil it yielded. Since it was very expensive, Mary's act of devotion

poured it on Jesus' feet and wiped his feet
with her hair.[l] And the house was filled
with the fragrance of the perfume.
4 But one of his disciples, Judas Iscariot,
who was later to betray him,[m] objected,
5 "Why wasn't this perfume sold and the
money given to the poor? It was worth a
year's wages.[a]" 6 He did not say this because he cared about the poor but because
he was a thief; as keeper of the money
bag,[n] he used to help himself to what was
put into it.
7 "Leave her alone," Jesus replied. "It
was intended that she should save this
perfume for the day of my burial.[o] 8 You
will always have the poor among you,[b p]
but you will not always have me."
9 Meanwhile a large crowd of Jews
found out that Jesus was there and came,
not only because of him but also to see
Lazarus, whom he had raised from the
dead.[q] 10 So the chief priests made plans
to kill Lazarus as well, 11 for on account of
him[r] many of the Jews were going over to
Jesus and believing in him.[s]

Jesus Comes to Jerusalem as King

12:12-15pp — Mt 21:4-9; Mk 11:7-10; Lk 19:35-38

12 The next day the great crowd that
had come for the festival heard that Jesus
was on his way to Jerusalem. 13 They took
palm branches[t] and went out to meet him,
shouting,

"Hosanna![c]"

"Blessed is he who comes in the name
of the Lord!"[d u]

"Blessed is the king of Israel!"[v]

14 Jesus found a young donkey and sat on
it, as it is written:

15 "Do not be afraid, Daughter Zion;
see, your king is coming,
seated on a donkey's colt."[e w]

16 At first his disciples did not understand all this.[x] Only after Jesus was glorified[y] did they realize that these things had
been written about him and that these
things had been done to him.
17 Now the crowd that was with him[z]
when he called Lazarus from the tomb
and raised him from the dead continued to
spread the word. 18 Many people, because
they had heard that he had performed
this sign,[a] went out to meet him. 19 So the
Pharisees said to one another, "See, this is
getting us nowhere. Look how the whole
world has gone after him!"[b]

Jesus Predicts His Death

20 Now there were some Greeks[c] among
those who went up to worship at the festival. 21 They came to Philip, who was from
Bethsaida[d] in Galilee, with a request. "Sir,"
they said, "we would like to see Jesus."

12:3 [l] Jn 11:2 **12:4** [m] S Mt 10:4 **12:6** [n] Jn 13:29 **12:7** [o] Jn 19:40 **12:8** [p] Dt 15:11 **12:9** [q] Jn 11:43, 44 **12:11** [r] ver 17, 18; Jn 11:45 [s] S Jn 7:31 **12:13** [t] Lev 23:40 [u] Ps 118:25,26 [v] S Jn 1:49 **12:15** [w] Zec 9:9 **12:16** [x] S Mk 9:32 [y] ver 23; Jn 2:22; 7:39 **12:17** [z] Jn 11:42 **12:18** [a] ver 11; Lk 19:37 **12:19** [b] Jn 11:47,48 **12:20** [c] Jn 7:35; Ac 11:20 **12:21** [d] S Mt 11:21

[a] 5 Greek *three hundred denarii* [b] 8 See Deut. 15:11. [c] 13 A Hebrew expression meaning "Save!" which became an exclamation of praise [d] 13 Psalm 118:25,26 [e] 15 Zech. 9:9

---

was costly. It was also an unusual act, both because she poured the oil on Jesus' feet (normally it was poured on the head) and because she used her hair to wipe them (a respectable woman did not ordinarily unbind her hair in public). Further, it showed her humility, for it was a servant's work to attend to the feet (see notes on 1:27; 13:5).
12:4 *Judas Iscariot.* See notes on 6:71; 17:12.
12:5 *money given to the poor.* See note on Mk 14:5.
12:6 *thief.* The one passage from which we learn that Judas was dishonest. Yet he must have been thought to be a man of some reliability, for he was keeper of the money bag.
12:7 *save.* Probably the meaning is "save for this purpose." Perfume was normally associated with festivity, but it was also used in burials (see 19:39–40), and Jesus links it with his burial, which Mary's act unwittingly anticipates.
12:8 *You will always have the poor among you.* See note on Mk 14:7.
12:9 *Jews.* See note on 1:19.
12:10 The Jewish leaders previously had spoken of the death of one man (see 11:50 and note), but now they wanted another death. Sin grows (cf. Jas 1:15).
12:12 *great crowd.* Pilgrims who had gathered for the Passover Festival. Many of the pilgrims had doubtless seen and heard Jesus in Galilee, and they welcomed the opportunity to proclaim him as the Messiah.
12:13 *palm branches.* See note on Mk 11:8. They were used in celebration of victory and were symbols of Jewish nationalism. John saw a multitude with palm branches in heaven (Rev 7:9). *Hosanna!* See NIV text note; see also note on Mt 21:9. *name.* See note on 2:23. *Blessed is the king of Israel!* The people's addition to the words of the psalm, which John alone records. It reflects his special interest in Jesus' royalty, which he brings out throughout the passion narrative.
12:14 *donkey.* See notes on Zec 9:9; Mt 21:2,7; Mk 11:2; Lk 19:30.
12:15 *Daughter Zion.* A personification of Jerusalem (see note on 2Ki 19:21).
12:16 An example of the meaning of 16:13. *glorified.* See notes on v. 41; 11:4; 13:31. Only after the crucifixion and the coming of the Holy Spirit did the disciples appreciate the meaning of the prophecy and its fulfillment.
12:19 *Pharisees.* See note on 7:32. *whole world has gone after him!* A good example of hyperbole in the Bible.
12:20 *Greeks.* Probably "God-fearers," people attracted to Judaism by its monotheism and morality, but repelled by its nationalism and requirements such as circumcision. They worshiped in the synagogues but did not become converts to Judaism (cf. note on Ac 16:14).
12:21 *Philip.* A Greek name, which may be why they came to this disciple (though he was not the only one of the Twelve to have a Greek name). *Bethsaida.* See note on Mt 11:21. *to see.* Means "to have an interview with." After v. 22 John records no more about these Greeks (yet see note on v. 32). He regarded their coming, but not their conversation with Jesus, as important. Jesus came to die for the world, and the coming of these Gentiles indicates the scope of the effectiveness of his approaching crucifixion.

22 Philip went to tell Andrew; Andrew and
Philip in turn told Jesus.
23 Jesus replied, "The hour[e] has come for
the Son of Man to be glorified.[f] 24 Very truly I tell you, unless a kernel of wheat falls
to the ground and dies,[g] it remains only a
single seed. But if it dies, it produces many
seeds. 25 Anyone who loves their life will
lose it, while anyone who hates their life
in this world will keep it[h] for eternal life.[i]
26 Whoever serves me must follow me; and
where I am, my servant also will be.[j] My
Father will honor the one who serves me.
27 "Now my soul is troubled,[k] and what
shall I say? 'Father,[l] save me from this
hour'?[m] No, it was for this very reason I
came to this hour. 28 Father, glorify your
name!"

Then a voice came from heaven,[n] "I
have glorified it, and will glorify it again."
29 The crowd that was there and heard it
said it had thundered; others said an angel
had spoken to him.
30 Jesus said, "This voice was for your
benefit,[o] not mine. 31 Now is the time for
judgment on this world;[p] now the prince
of this world[q] will be driven out. 32 And I,
when I am lifted up[a] from the earth,[r] will
draw all people to myself."[s] 33 He said this
to show the kind of death he was going
to die.[t]
34 The crowd spoke up, "We have heard
from the Law[u] that the Messiah will remain forever,[v] so how can you say, 'The
Son of Man[w] must be lifted up'?[x] Who is
this 'Son of Man'?"
35 Then Jesus told them, "You are going
to have the light[y] just a little while longer. Walk while you have the light,[z] before
darkness overtakes you.[a] Whoever walks
in the dark does not know where they
are going. 36 Believe in the light while you
have the light, so that you may become
children of light."[b] When he had finished
speaking, Jesus left and hid himself from
them.[c]

Belief and Unbelief Among the Jews

37 Even after Jesus had performed so
many signs[d] in their presence, they still
would not believe in him. 38 This was to
fulfill the word of Isaiah the prophet:

> "Lord, who has believed our message
> and to whom has the arm of the
> Lord been revealed?"[b][e]

39 For this reason they could not believe,
because, as Isaiah says elsewhere:

> 40 "He has blinded their eyes
> and hardened their hearts,

12:23 [e] S Mt 26:18 [f] Jn 13:32; 17:1 **12:24** [g] 1Co 15:36 **12:25** [h] Mt 10:39; Mk 8:35; Lk 14:26; 17:33 [i] S Mt 25:46 **12:26** [j] Jn 14:3; 17:24; 2Co 5:8; Php 1:23; 1Th 4:17 **12:27** [k] Mt 26:38, 39; Jn 11:33, 38; 13:21 [l] S Mt 11:25 [m] ver 23 **12:28** [n] S Mt 3:17 **12:30** [o] Ex 19:9; Jn 11:42 **12:31** [p] Jn 16:11 [q] Jn 14:30; 16:11; 2Co 4:4; Eph 2:2; 1Jn 4:4; 5:19 **12:32** [r] ver 34; Isa 11:10; Jn 3:14; 8:28 [s] Jn 6:44 **12:33** [t] Jn 18:32; 21:19 **12:34** [u] S Jn 10:34 [v] Ps 110:4; Isa 9:7; Eze 37:25; Da 7:14 [w] S Mt 8:20 [x] Jn 3:14 **12:35** [y] ver 46 [z] Eph 5:8 [a] 1Jn 1:6; 2:11 **12:36** [b] ver 46; S Lk 16:8 [c] Jn 8:59 **12:37** [d] S Jn 2:11 **12:38** [e] Isa 53:1; Ro 10:16

[a] 32 The Greek for *lifted up* also means *exalted.*
[b] 38 Isaiah 53:1

12:22 *Andrew.* See note on 1:40.
12:23 *The hour has come.* The hour to which everything else led (see note on 2:4). *glorified.* Jesus was speaking about his death on the cross and his subsequent resurrection and exaltation (see notes on v. 41; 11:4; 13:31).
12:24 *if it dies, it produces.* The principle of life through death is seen in the plant world. The kernel must perish as a kernel if there is to be a plant.
12:25 *anyone who hates their life … will keep it.* To love one's life here and now — to concentrate on one's own success — is to lose what truly matters (cf. Mk 8:34 – 35; Lk 9:23 – 24 and notes). Supremely, of course, the principle is seen in the cross of Jesus. *hates.* Love for God must be such that all other loves are, by comparison, hatred (see notes on Mal 1:3; Lk 14:26). *eternal life.* See note on 3:15.
12:27 *troubled.* John's equivalent to the agony in Gethsemane described in the other Gospels (see Mt 26:38 – 39 and notes; Mk 14:34 – 36; Lk 22:42 and note). *this hour.* Jesus faced the prospect of becoming sin (or a sin offering) for sinful people (see 2Co 5:21 and note). He considered praying for God to save him from this death but refused to do so, because the very reason he had come was to die for sinners.
12:28 *Father, glorify your name!* His prayer was not for deliverance but for the Father to be glorified (cf. Mt 6:9 and note). The voice from heaven gave the answer. *name.* See note on 2:23.
12:31 *judgment on this world.* The cross was God's judgment on the world. *prince of this world.* Satan (see 16:11). The cross would seem to be his triumph; in fact, it was his defeat. Out of it would flow the greatest good ever to come to the world.
12:32 *lifted up.* See NIV text note. Jesus refers here first of all to his crucifixion (see v. 33), but he most likely refers also to his resurrection and ascension into heaven to reign at God's right hand (see v. 41; 3:14 and notes; see also 8:28; cf. Ac 2:33; 5:31, where "exalted" renders the same Greek word). *all people.* Christ will draw people to himself, without regard for nationality, ethnic affiliation or status. It is significant that Greek Gentiles were present on this occasion (see v. 20 and note).
12:34 *the Law.* Here seems to mean OT Scripture in general (see note on 10:34), the reference being to passages such as Ps 89:30 – 37; 110:4; Isa 9:7 (see notes there; see also note on Lk 24:44). *the Messiah.* See note on 1:25. *Son of Man.* The only place in the Gospels where anyone other than Jesus used the expression, and even here Jesus is being quoted (see note on Mk 8:31).
12:35 – 36 *light.* Closely identified with Jesus, as seen from the call to believe in the light (see notes on 1:4; 8:12).
12:37 *they still would not believe.* God's ancient people should have responded when God sent his Messiah. They should have seen the significance of the signs he did.
12:39 *could not believe.* Does not mean that the people in question had no choice. They purposely rejected God and chose evil, and v. 40 explains that God in turn brought on them a judicial blinding of eyes and hardening of hearts. Yet many Jewish leaders did believe in Jesus as the Messiah (see v. 42 and note).
12:40 These words from Isa 6:10 (see note there) are quoted by Jesus (see Mt 13:13 – 14; Mk 4:12; Lk 8:10) and by Paul (Ac 28:26 – 27). See notes on Mk 4:12; Lk 8:11.

so they can neither see with their eyes,
nor understand with their hearts,
nor turn — and I would heal them."[a][f]
41 Isaiah said this because he saw Jesus'
glory[g] and spoke about him.[h]
42 Yet at the same time many even
among the leaders believed in him.[i] But
because of the Pharisees[j] they would not
openly acknowledge their faith for fear
they would be put out of the synagogue;[k]
43 for they loved human praise[l] more than
praise from God.[m]
44 Then Jesus cried out, "Whoever believes in me does not believe in me only,
but in the one who sent me.[n] 45 The one
who looks at me is seeing the one who
sent me.[o] 46 I have come into the world as
a light,[p] so that no one who believes in me
should stay in darkness.
47 "If anyone hears my words but does
not keep them, I do not judge that person. For I did not come to judge the world,
but to save the world.[q] 48 There is a judge
for the one who rejects me and does not
accept my words; the very words I have
spoken will condemn them[r] at the last day.
49 For I did not speak on my own, but the
Father who sent me commanded me[s] to
say all that I have spoken. 50 I know that
his command leads to eternal life.[t] So
whatever I say is just what the Father has
told me to say."[u]

Jesus Washes His Disciples' Feet

13 It was just before the Passover Festival.[v] Jesus knew that the hour
had come[w] for him to leave this world and
go to the Father.[x] Having loved his own
who were in the world, he loved them to
the end.
2 The evening meal was in progress, and
the devil had already prompted Judas, the
son of Simon Iscariot, to betray Jesus.[y]
3 Jesus knew that the Father had put all
things under his power,[z] and that he had
come from God[a] and was returning to
God; 4 so he got up from the meal, took off
his outer clothing, and wrapped a towel
around his waist.[b] 5 After that, he poured
water into a basin and began to wash his
disciples' feet,[c] drying them with the towel
that was wrapped around him.
6 He came to Simon Peter, who said to

12:40 [f] Isa 6:10; S Mt 13:13,15 **12:41** [g] Isa 6:1-4 [h] Lk 24:27 **12:42** [i] ver 11; Jn 7:48 [j] S Jn 7:13 [k] Jn 9:22 **12:43** [l] 1Sa 15:30 [m] S Ro 2:29 **12:44** [n] S Mt 10:40; Jn 5:24 **12:45** [o] S Jn 14:9 **12:46** [p] S Jn 1:4 **12:47** [q] S Jn 3:17 **12:48** [r] Jn 5:45 **12:49** [s] Jn 14:31 **12:50** [t] S Mt 25:46 [u] S Jn 14:24 **13:1** [v] S Jn 11:55 [w] S Mt 26:18 [x] Jn 16:28 **13:2** [y] S Mt 10:4 **13:3** [z] S Mt 28:18 [a] Jn 8:42; 16:27, 28,30; 17:8 **13:4** [b] S Mt 20:28 **13:5** [c] S Lk 7:44

[a] 40 Isaiah 6:10

12:41 *saw Jesus' glory.* Isaiah spoke primarily of the glory of God (Isa 6:3; see notes on Eze 1:28; 43:2). John spoke of the glory of Jesus and made no basic distinction between the two, attesting Jesus' oneness with God (cf. Heb 1:6,10 and notes). The thought of glory here is complex. There is the idea of majesty, and there is also the idea (which meant so much to John) that Jesus' death on the cross and his subsequent resurrection and exaltation show his real glory. Isaiah foresaw the rejection of Christ, as the passages quoted (Isa 53:1; 6:10) show. He spoke of the Messiah both in the words about blind eyes and hard hearts, on the one hand, and about healing, on the other. This is the cross and this is glory, for the cross, resurrection and exaltation portray both suffering and healing, rejection and triumph, humiliation and glory.

12:42 *many ... leaders believed.* John does not give a picture of unrelieved gloom. Many Jewish leaders believed (see note on 1:7), though they remained secret believers for fear of excommunication (see note on 9:22). Two such cases in this Gospel are Nicodemus and Joseph of Arimathea (see 3:1–2; 19:38–39 and notes).

12:44 *cried out.* The words are given special emphasis by being spoken in a loud voice. *believes in me.* John ends his story of the public ministry of Jesus with an appeal for belief (see notes on 1:7; 20:31; see also Introduction: Purpose and Emphases). He does not say when Jesus spoke these words (they may have been uttered earlier), but they are a fitting close to this part of his account. *the one who sent me.* Jesus' mission, as well as the inseparability of the Father and the Son, are stressed throughout this Gospel (see note on 4:34).

12:46 *I have come into the world.* Points to both Jesus' preexistence and his mission. *light.* See vv. 35–36 and note.

12:47 *to judge.* Not the purpose of Jesus' coming (3:17–18), but judgment is the other side of salvation. It is not the purpose of the sun's shining to cast shadows, but when the sun shines, shadows are inevitable.

12:49 *the Father ... commanded me to say all that I have spoken.* Jesus' hearers have a great responsibility. His "words" (v. 48) are what the Father commanded him to say. To reject them, therefore, is to reject God.

12:50 *eternal life.* See note on 3:15. *So.* Jesus said what he did in order to fulfill the will of the Father — a wonderful note on which to end the account of Jesus' public ministry (see v. 44 and note).

13:1 — 17:26 John has by far the longest account of the upper room, though curiously he says nothing about the institution of the Lord's Supper. Still we owe to him most of our information about what our Lord said to his disciples on that fateful night. One feature of the farewell discourses is Jesus' emphasis on love. The Greek noun *agape* ("love") and the verb *agapao* ("love") occur only 8 times in chs. 1–12 but 31 times in chs. 13–17. Chs. 13–14 take place at the Last Supper, while the discourses in chs. 15–16 are probably uttered on the way to Gethsemane (note "let us leave" in 14:31 [see note there]).

13:1 *Passover Festival.* See notes on 2:13; 5:1; see also notes on Ex 12:11–26. *the hour.* See note on 2:4. *he loved them to the end.* See 10:11,15,17; 15:13 and note.

13:2 *evening meal.* Some believe that this feast was a fellowship meal eaten sometime before the Passover Festival. This would mean that the Last Supper could not have been the Passover meal, as the Synoptic Gospels clearly indicate. However, this meal may have been the Passover Festival itself, in which case the accounts of the Synoptics and John would agree. *the devil.* See v. 27. *Judas ... Iscariot.* See note on 6:71.

13:3 *the Father had put all things under his power.* John again emphasizes the fulfillment of God's plan and Jesus' control of the situation. *was returning to God.* See 20:17 and note.

13:5 *began to wash his disciples' feet.* A menial task (see note on 1:27), normally performed by a servant. On this occasion there was no servant, and no one else volunteered. Jesus' action was during the meal, not upon arrival, and was done deliberately to emphasize a point. It was a lesson in humility, but it also set forth the principle of selfless service that was so soon to be exemplified in the cross. John alone tells of this incident, but Luke says that in rebuking

him, "Lord, are you going to wash my
feet?"
7 Jesus replied, "You do not realize now
what I am doing, but later you will understand."[d]
8 "No," said Peter, "you shall never wash
my feet."
Jesus answered, "Unless I wash you,
you have no part with me."
9 "Then, Lord," Simon Peter replied,
"not just my feet but my hands and my
head as well!"
10 Jesus answered, "Those who have had
a bath need only to wash their feet; their
whole body is clean. And you are clean,[e]
though not every one of you."[f] 11 For he
knew who was going to betray him,[g] and
that was why he said not every one was
clean.
12 When he had finished washing their
feet, he put on his clothes and returned to
his place. "Do you understand what I have
done for you?" he asked them. 13 "You
call me 'Teacher'[h] and 'Lord,'[i] and rightly so, for that is what I am. 14 Now that
I, your Lord and Teacher, have washed
your feet, you also should wash one another's feet.[j] 15 I have set you an example
that you should do as I have done for you.[k]
16 Very truly I tell you, no servant is greater than his master,[l] nor is a messenger
greater than the one who sent him. 17 Now
that you know these things, you will be
blessed if you do them.[m]

Jesus Predicts His Betrayal

18 "I am not referring to all of you;[n] I
know those I have chosen.[o] But this is to
fulfill this passage of Scripture:[p] 'He who
shared my bread[q] has turned[a][r] against
me.'[b][s]
19 "I am telling you now before it happens, so that when it does happen you
will believe[t] that I am who I am.[u] 20 Very
truly I tell you, whoever accepts anyone I
send accepts me; and whoever accepts me
accepts the one who sent me."[v]
21 After he had said this, Jesus was troubled in spirit[w] and testified, "Very truly I
tell you, one of you is going to betray me."[x]
22 His disciples stared at one another, at
a loss to know which of them he meant.
23 One of them, the disciple whom Jesus
loved,[y] was reclining next to him. 24 Simon
Peter motioned to this disciple and said,
"Ask him which one he means."
25 Leaning back against Jesus, he asked
him, "Lord, who is it?"[z]
26 Jesus answered, "It is the one to
whom I will give this piece of bread when
I have dipped it in the dish." Then, dip-

[a] 18 Greek *has lifted up his heel*   [b] 18 Psalm 41:9

13:7 [d] ver 12
13:10 [e] Jn 15:3 [f] ver 18
13:11 [g] S Mt 10:4
13:13 [h] Mt 26:18; Jn 11:28 [i] S Mt 28:18; Lk 1:43; 2:11; 6:46; 11:1; Ac 10:36; Ro 10:9,12; 14:9; 1Co 12:3; Php 2:11; Col 2:6
13:14 [j] 1Pe 5:5
13:15 [k] S Mt 11:29; S 1Ti 4:12
13:16 [l] Mt 10:24; Lk 6:40; Jn 15:20
13:17 [m] Mt 7:24, 25; Lk 11:28; Jas 1:25
13:18 [n] ver 10 [o] Jn 15:16,19 [p] S Mt 1:22 [q] Mt 26:23 [r] Jn 6:70 [s] Ps 41:9
13:19 [t] Jn 14:29; 16:4 [u] Jn 4:26; 8:24
13:20 [v] S Mt 10:40
13:21 [w] S Jn 12:27 [x] Mt 26:21
13:23 [y] Jn 19:26; 20:2; 21:7,20
13:25 [z] Mt 26:22; Jn 21:20

the disciples over a quarrel concerning who would be the greatest, Jesus said, "I am among you as one who serves" (Lk 22:27). Jesus' life of service would culminate on the cross (see Php 2:5–8 and notes).

13:8 *No.* Characteristically, Peter objected, though apparently no one else did. His actions reflect a mixture of humility (he did not want Jesus to perform this lowly service for him) and pride (he tried to dictate to Jesus; see also Mt 16:21–23). *Unless I wash you.* Jesus' reply looks beyond the incident to what it symbolizes: Peter needed a spiritual cleansing. The external washing was a picture of cleansing from sin.

13:9 *my hands and my head.* Peter's response was wholehearted, but he was still dictating to Jesus.

13:10 *only to wash their feet.* A man would bathe himself before going to a feast. When he arrived, he only needed to wash his feet to be entirely clean again.

13:11 *he knew.* Again John emphasizes Jesus' command of the situation.

13:13 *Teacher ... Lord.* An instructor would normally be called "Teacher," but "Lord" referred to one occupying the supreme place. Jesus accepted both titles.

13:14–15 Some Christians believe that Christ intended to institute a foot-washing ordinance to be practiced regularly. Most Christians, however, interpret Christ's action here as providing an example of humble service. Cf. 1Ti 5:10 and note.

13:14 *wash one another's feet.* Christians should be willing to perform the most menial services for one another. Cf. Gal 5:13 and note.

13:16 With minor variations this saying, which Jesus used often, is found in 15:20; Mt 10:24; Lk 6:40 (cf. Mk 10:43–45; Lk 22:27).

13:17 *blessed if you do them.* Cf. Eze 33:32 and note; Jas 1:22–25; 4:17.

13:18 *not referring to all of you.* Jesus was leading up to his prediction of the betrayal (see v. 21 and note). *shared my bread.* To eat bread together was a mark of close fellowship (see note on Ps 41:9). *turned against.* Lit. "lifted up his heel against." The idiom may be derived from a horse's preparing to kick, or perhaps something like shaking off the dust from one's feet (see Lk 9:5 and note).

13:19 *so that ... you will believe.* See note on 12:44. Jesus' concern was for the disciples, not himself. *I am who I am.* An emphatic form of speech, such as that in 8:58 (see note there). Cf. Ex 3:14–15 and notes.

13:20 *anyone I send ... the one who sent me.* Jesus' mission is a common theme in this Gospel (see notes on 4:34; 12:44; 17:3–4,18), and now the mission of his followers is linked with it (cf. 20:21).

13:21 *troubled.* See 11:33 and note. Though he knew of it long before it happened, Jesus was grieved by the betrayal of a friend.

13:22 *at a loss.* The disciples' astonishment shows that Judas had concealed his contacts with the high priests. No one suspected him (see v. 28), but all seem to have thought that the betrayal would be involuntary (see Mk 14:19).

13:23 *the disciple whom Jesus loved.* Usually thought to be John, the author of this Gospel (see Introduction: Author). The expression does not, of course, mean that Jesus did not love the others but that he had a special bond with this man. *reclining.* At a dinner, guests reclined on couches, leaning on the left elbow with the head toward the table (cf. note on Mk 14:18).

13:26 *the one to whom I ... give ... bread ... dipped ... in the dish.* Evidently Judas was near Jesus, possibly in the seat of

ping the piece of bread, he gave it to Judas,[a] the son of Simon Iscariot. 27 As soon
as Judas took the bread, Satan entered
into him.[b]
So Jesus told him, "What you are about
to do, do quickly." 28 But no one at the
meal understood why Jesus said this to
him. 29 Since Judas had charge of the money,[c] some thought Jesus was telling him to
buy what was needed for the festival,[d] or
to give something to the poor.[e] 30 As soon
as Judas had taken the bread, he went out.
And it was night.[f]

Jesus Predicts Peter's Denial

13:37,38pp — Mt 26:33-35; Mk 14:29-31; Lk 22:33,34

31 When he was gone, Jesus said, "Now
the Son of Man[g] is glorified[h] and God is
glorified in him.[i] 32 If God is glorified in
him,[a] God will glorify the Son in himself,[j]
and will glorify him at once.
33 "My children, I will be with you only
a little longer. You will look for me, and
just as I told the Jews, so I tell you now:
Where I am going, you cannot come.[k]
34 "A new command[l] I give you: Love
one another.[m] As I have loved you, so you
must love one another.[n] 35 By this everyone
will know that you are my disciples, if you
love one another."[o]
36 Simon Peter asked him, "Lord, where
are you going?"[p]
Jesus replied, "Where I am going, you
cannot follow now,[q] but you will follow
later."[r]
37 Peter asked, "Lord, why can't I follow
you now? I will lay down my life for you."
38 Then Jesus answered, "Will you really lay down your life for me? Very truly I
tell you, before the rooster crows, you will
disown me three times![s]

Jesus Comforts His Disciples

14 "Do not let your hearts be troubled.[t] You believe[u] in God[b];[v] believe
also in me. 2 My Father's house has many
rooms; if that were not so, would I have
told you that I am going there[w] to prepare
a place for you? 3 And if I go and prepare a
place for you, I will come back[x] and take
you to be with me that you also may be
where I am.[y] 4 You know the way to the
place where I am going."

Jesus the Way to the Father

5 Thomas[z] said to him, "Lord, we don't
know where you are going, so how can we
know the way?"
6 Jesus answered, "I am[a] the way[b] and
the truth[c] and the life.[d] No one comes to
the Father except through me.[e] 7 If you
really know me, you will know[c] my Father

13:26 [a] S Mt 10:4 **13:27** [b] Lk 22:3 **13:29** [c] Jn 12:6 [d] ver 1 [e] Jn 12:5 **13:30** [f] Lk 22:53 **13:31** [g] S Mt 8:20 [h] Jn 7:39; 12:23 [i] Jn 14:13; 17:4; 1Pe 4:11 **13:32** [j] Jn 17:1 **13:33** [k] S Jn 7:33, 34 **13:34** [l] Jn 15:12; 1Jn 2:7-11; 3:11 [m] Lev 19:18; 1Th 4:9; 1Pe 1:22 [n] Jn 15:12; Eph 5:2; 1Jn 4:10, 11 **13:35** [o] 1Jn 3:14; 4:20 **13:36** [p] Jn 16:5 [q] ver 33; Jn 14:2 [r] Jn 21:18, 19; 2Pe 1:14 **13:38** [s] Jn 18:27 **14:1** [t] ver 27 [u] S Jn 3:15 [v] Ps 4:5 **14:2** [w] Jn 13:33, 36; 16:5 **14:3** [x] ver 18, 28; S Mt 16:27 [y] S Jn 12:26 **14:5** [z] S Jn 11:16 **14:6** [a] S Jn 6:35 [b] Jn 10:9; Eph 2:18; Heb 10:20 [c] Jn 1:14 [d] S Jn 1:4 [e] Ac 4:12

[a] 32 Many early manuscripts do not have *If God is glorified in him.* [b] 1 Or *Believe in God* [c] 7 Some manuscripts *If you really knew me, you would know*

---

honor. John used Judas's full name (see note on 6:71) in recording this solemn moment.

13:27 *As soon as Judas took the bread.* Evidently the critical moment. If the giving of the bread to Judas was a mark of honor, it also seems to have been a final appeal — which Judas did not accept. *Satan.* The name is used only here in John (cf. v. 2; see notes on Job 1:6; Zec 3:1; Rev 12:9 – 10). *do quickly.* Jesus' words once more indicate his control. He would die as he directed, not as his opponents determined.

13:29 *the festival.* See v. 1 and note on v. 2. *the poor.* See 12:5 and note on Mk 14:5.

13:30 *night.* In light of John's emphasis on the conflict between light and darkness, this may have been more than a time note — picturing also the darkness of Judas's soul (cf. notes on 1:4; 8:12; Isa 60:2).

13:31 *Son of Man.* See note on Mk 8:31. *glorified.* See v. 32 and note on 7:39. Here the idea of glory includes a reference to Jesus' sacrificial death on the cross and the glorious salvation that would result. *God is glorified in him.* The glory of the Father is closely bound to that of the Son.

13:34 *A new command.* In a sense it was an old one (see Lev 19:18 and note), but for Christ's disciples it was new, because it was the mark of their special bond, created by Christ's great love for them (cf. Mt 22:37,39; Mk 12:31; Lk 10:27 and notes). *As I have loved you.* Our standard is Christ's love for us.

13:35 *love.* The distinguishing mark of Christ's followers (cf. 1Jn 3:23; 4:7 – 8,11 – 12,19 – 21).

13:36 *where are you going?* Peter seems to have ignored Jesus' words about love and to have been more concerned about his Master's departure. In Jesus' reply "you" is singular and thus personal to Peter, whereas in v. 33 the word is plural.

13:37 *I will lay down my life.* Words similar to those of the good shepherd in 10:11. Peter was characteristically sure of himself, when in fact he would not at this time lay down his life for Jesus (though later he would; see 21:18 – 19 and notes). Exactly the opposite would be true.

13:38 *you will disown me three times.* Peter's denial is prophesied in all four Gospels (Mt 26:33 – 35; Mk 14:29 – 31; Lk 22:31 – 34).

14:1 *Do not ... be troubled.* The apostles had just received disturbing news (13:33,36). *You believe in God; believe also in me.* Jesus' antidote for a troubled heart (cf. Ps 56:3 – 4; Isa 26:3 – 4).

14:2 *My Father's house.* Heaven. *many rooms.* Lit. "many dwelling places," implying permanence and plenty of room.

14:3 *I will come back.* Jesus comes in several ways, but the primary reference here is to his second advent (cf. Rev 22:7,12,20).

14:4 *way.* See v. 6 and note.

14:5 *Thomas.* He was honest and plainly told the Lord he did not understand (see note on 11:16).

14:6 *I am.* See note on 6:35. *the way.* To God. Jesus is not one way among many but the only way (see Ac 4:12; Heb 10:19 – 20 and notes). In the early church, Christianity was sometimes called "the Way" (see, e.g., Ac 9:2 and note). *the truth.* A key emphasis in this Gospel (see note on 1:14). *the life.* See note on 1:4. Very likely the statement means "I am the way (to the Father) in that I am the truth and the life" (cf. 17:3).

14:7 *me ... my Father.* Once more Jesus stresses the intimate connection between the Father and himself. Jesus brought a full revelation of the Father (see 1:18 and note), so the apostles had real knowledge of him (see note on 8:19).

as well.[f] From now on, you do know him
and have seen him."
8 Philip[g] said, "Lord, show us the Father
and that will be enough for us."
9 Jesus answered: "Don't you know me,
Philip, even after I have been among you
such a long time? Anyone who has seen
me has seen the Father.[h] How can you say,
'Show us the Father'? 10 Don't you believe
that I am in the Father, and that the Father
is in me?[i] The words I say to you I do not
speak on my own authority.[j] Rather, it is
the Father, living in me, who is doing his
work. 11 Believe me when I say that I am
in the Father and the Father is in me; or at
least believe on the evidence of the works
themselves.[k] 12 Very truly I tell you, whoever believes[l] in me will do the works I
have been doing,[m] and they will do even
greater things than these, because I am going to the Father. 13 And I will do whatever
you ask[n] in my name, so that the Father
may be glorified in the Son. 14 You may ask
me for anything in my name, and I will
do it.

Jesus Promises the Holy Spirit

15 "If you love me, keep my commands.[o]
16 And I will ask the Father, and he will
give you another advocate[p] to help you
and be with you forever— 17 the Spirit of
truth.[q] The world cannot accept him,[r] because it neither sees him nor knows him.
But you know him, for he lives with you
and will be[a] in you. 18 I will not leave you
as orphans;[s] I will come to you.[t] 19 Before
long, the world will not see me anymore,
but you will see me.[u] Because I live, you
also will live.[v] 20 On that day[w] you will realize that I am in my Father,[x] and you are
in me, and I am in you.[y] 21 Whoever has
my commands and keeps them is the one
who loves me.[z] The one who loves me will
be loved by my Father,[a] and I too will love
them and show myself to them."
22 Then Judas[b] (not Judas Iscariot) said,
"But, Lord, why do you intend to show
yourself to us and not to the world?"[c]
23 Jesus replied, "Anyone who loves me
will obey my teaching.[d] My Father will
love them, and we will come to them and
make our home with them.[e] 24 Anyone
who does not love me will not obey my
teaching. These words you hear are not
my own; they belong to the Father who
sent me.[f]
25 "All this I have spoken while still
with you. 26 But the Advocate,[g] the Holy
Spirit, whom the Father will send in my

[a] 17 Some early manuscripts *and is*

14:7 [f] Jn 1:18; S 1Jn 2:23 **14:8** [g] S Jn 1:43 **14:9** [h] Isa 9:6; Jn 1:14; 12:45; 2Co 4:4; Php 2:6; Col 1:15; Heb 1:3 **14:10** [i] ver 11, 20; Jn 10:38; 17:21 [j] S ver 24 **14:11** [k] Jn 5:36; 10:38 **14:12** [l] Mt 21:21 [m] Lk 10:17 **14:13** [n] S Mt 7:7 **14:15** [o] ver 21, 23; Ps 103:18; Jn 15:10; 1Jn 2:3-5; 3:22, 24; 5:3; 2Jn 6; Rev 12:17; 14:12 **14:16** [p] ver 26; Jn 15:26; 16:7 **14:17** [q] Jn 15:26; 16:13; 1Jn 4:6; 5:6 [r] 1Co 2:14 **14:18** [s] 1Ki 6:13 [t] ver 3, 28; S Mt 16:27 **14:19** [u] Jn 7:33, 34; 16:16 [v] Jn 6:57 **14:20** [w] Jn 16:23, 26 [x] ver 10, 11; Jn 10:38; 17:21 [y] S Ro 8:10 **14:21** [z] S ver 15 [a] Dt 7:13; Jn 16:27; 1Jn 2:5 **14:22** [b] Lk 6:16; Ac 1:13 [c] Ac 10:41 **14:23** [d] S ver 15 [e] S Ro 8:10 **14:24** [f] ver 10; Dt 18:18; Jn 5:19; 7:16; 8:28; 12:49, 50 **14:26** [g] ver 16; Jn 15:26; 16:7

14:9 *Anyone who has seen me has seen the Father.* See 1:18 and note.

14:10 *I do not speak on my own authority.* Jesus' teaching was not of human origin, and there was an inseparable connection between his words and his work.

14:11 *Believe ... that I am in the Father and the Father is in me.* Saving faith is trust in a person, but it must also have factual content. Faith includes believing that Jesus is one with the Father (see 17:21–22 and notes).

14:12 *Very truly I tell you.* See note on Mk 3:28. *greater things.* These depended on Jesus' going to the Father, because they are works done in the strength of the Holy Spirit, whom Jesus would send from the Father (see vv. 16–17; 15:26 and notes). Cf. Col 1:6 and note.

14:13 *in my name.* Not simply prayer that mentions Jesus' name but prayer in accordance with all that the person who bears the name is (see note on 2:23). It is prayer aimed at carrying forward the work Jesus did—prayer that he himself will answer (see also v. 14).

14:15 *love ... keep.* Love, like faith (see Jas 2:14–26 and notes), cannot be separated from obedience (see vv. 21,23–24).

14:16 *the Father ... will give you.* The first of a series of important passages about the Holy Spirit (see v. 26; 15:26; 16:7–15 and notes), the gift of the Father. *another.* Besides Jesus. *advocate.* A legal term, but with a broader meaning than "counsel for the defense" (see 1Jn 2:1 and note). It referred to any person who helped someone in trouble with the law. The Spirit will always stand by Christ's people.

14:17 *Spirit of truth.* In essence and in action the Spirit is characterized by truth. He brings people to the truth of God. All three persons of the Trinity are linked with truth. See also the Father (see 4:24 and note; cf. Ps 31:5; Isa 65:16 and note) and the Son (see v. 6 and note). *The world.* Which takes no notice of the Spirit of God (see notes on 1:9; 1Co 2:14). But the Spirit was "with" Jesus' disciples and would be "in" them. Many believe the latter relationship (indwelling) specifically anticipates the coming of the Holy Spirit on the day of Pentecost (see Ac 1:2; 2:4,17,38 and notes; cf. Ro 8:9 and note).

14:18 *I will come to you.* The words relate to the coming of the Spirit, but Jesus also speaks of his own appearances after the resurrection and at his second coming (see vv. 3,19,28 and note on v. 3; 16:22 and note).

14:19 *world ... but you.* The cross separated the world (those who would not see Jesus thereafter) from the disciples (who would). *Because I live, you also will live.* The life of the Christian always depends on the life of Christ (see 1:4; 3:15; 10:10; Php 1:21 and notes).

14:20 *On that day you will realize.* The resurrection would radically change their thinking.

14:21 *keeps ... loves.* Love for Christ and keeping his commands cannot be separated (see note on v. 15). *loved by my Father ... I too will love them.* The love of the Father cannot be separated from that of the Son.

14:22 *Judas (not Judas Iscariot).* See Lk 6:16 and note. *why ...?* Judas (and, for that matter, the other apostles) probably looked for Jesus to fulfill popular Messianic expectations. It was not easy, therefore, to understand how that would mean showing himself to the disciples but not to the world.

14:23 *loves ... obey ... love.* Again love and obedience are linked (see vv. 15,21; 15:10 and notes).

14:24 Once more the close relationship between Jesus' words and the Father's is stressed (see v. 10; 7:16).

14:26 *Advocate.* See note on v. 16. *Holy Spirit.* See 1:33 and note. *whom the Father will send.* Both the Father

name,[h] will teach you all things[i] and will
remind you of everything I have said to
you.[j] 27 Peace I leave with you; my peace I
give you.[k] I do not give to you as the world
gives. Do not let your hearts be troubled[l]
and do not be afraid.
28 "You heard me say, 'I am going away
and I am coming back to you.'[m] If you
loved me, you would be glad that I am
going to the Father,[n] for the Father is greater than I.[o] 29 I have told you now before
it happens, so that when it does happen
you will believe.[p] 30 I will not say much
more to you, for the prince of this world[q]
is coming. He has no hold over me, 31 but
he comes so that the world may learn that
I love the Father and do exactly what my
Father has commanded me.[r]
"Come now; let us leave.

The Vine and the Branches

15 "I am[s] the true vine,[t] and my Father is the gardener. 2 He cuts off
every branch in me that bears no fruit,[u]
while every branch that does bear fruit[v]
he prunes[a] so that it will be even more
fruitful. 3 You are already clean because of
the word I have spoken to you.[w] 4 Remain
in me, as I also remain in you.[x] No branch
can bear fruit by itself; it must remain in
the vine. Neither can you bear fruit unless
you remain in me.
5 "I am the vine; you are the branches.
If you remain in me and I in you, you will
bear much fruit;[y] apart from me you can
do nothing. 6 If you do not remain in me,
you are like a branch that is thrown away
and withers; such branches are picked up,
thrown into the fire and burned.[z] 7 If you
remain in me[a] and my words remain in
you, ask whatever you wish, and it will
be done for you.[b] 8 This is to my Father's
glory,[c] that you bear much fruit, showing
yourselves to be my disciples.[d]
9 "As the Father has loved me,[e] so have
I loved you. Now remain in my love. 10 If
you keep my commands,[f] you will remain in my love, just as I have kept my
Father's commands and remain in his
love. 11 I have told you this so that my joy
may be in you and that your joy may be
complete.[g] 12 My command is this: Love

14:26 [h] Ac 2:33 [i] Jn 16:13; 1Jn 2:20,27 [j] Jn 2:22 **14:27** [k] Nu 6:26; Ps 85:8; Mal 2:6; S Lk 2:14; 24:36; Jn 16:33; Php 4:7; Col 3:15 [l] ver 1 **14:28** [m] ver 2-4, 18; S Mt 16:27 [n] Jn 5:18 [o] Jn 10:29 **14:29** [p] Jn 13:19; 16:4 **14:30** [q] S Jn 12:31 **14:31** [r] Jn 10:18; 12:49 **15:1** [s] S Jn 6:35 [t] Ps 80:8-11; Isa 5:1-7 **15:2** [u] ver 6; S Mt 3:10 [v] Ps 92:14; Mt 3:8; 7:20; Gal 5:22; Eph 5:9; Php 1:11 **15:3** [w] Jn 13:10; 17:17; Eph 5:26 **15:4** [x] S Jn 6:56 **15:5** [y] ver 16 **15:6** [z] ver 2; Eze 15:4; S Mt 3:10 **15:7** [a] ver 4; S Jn 6:56 [b] S Mt 7:7 **15:8** [c] S Mt 9:8 [d] Jn 8:31 **15:9** [e] Jn 17:23,24,26 **15:10** [f] S Jn 14:15 **15:11** [g] S Jn 3:29

[a] 2 The Greek for *he prunes* also means *he cleans.*

---

and the Son are involved in the sending (see 15:26 and note). *name.* See notes on v. 13; 2:23. *remind you of everything I have said to you.* Crucial for the life of the church—and for the writing of the NT.

14:27 *Peace ... my peace.* A common Hebrew greeting (see 20:19,21,26 and note on 20:19), which Jesus uses here in an unusual way. The term speaks, in effect, of the salvation that Christ's redemptive work will achieve for his disciples—total well-being and inner rest of spirit, in fellowship with God. All true peace is his gift, which the repetition emphasizes. *I do not give ... as the world gives.* In its greetings of peace the world can only express a longing or wish. But Jesus' peace is real and present (see 16:33 and note). *troubled.* See note on v. 1.

14:28 *heard me say.* Cf. v. 3. *the Father is greater than I.* Revealing the subordinate role Jesus accepted as a necessary part of the incarnation. The statement must be understood in the light of the unity between the Father and the Son (see 10:30 and note).

14:30 *prince of this world.* See note on 12:31. *has no hold over me.* Satan has a hold over people because of their fallen state. Since Christ was sinless, Satan could have no hold over him.

14:31 *I ... do exactly what my Father has commanded me.* Jesus had stressed the importance of his followers being obedient (see vv. 15,21,23 and notes), and he set the example. With these words he goes to fulfill his mission (chs. 18–19). Cf. 4:34; 17:4 and notes. *let us leave.* Probably means "let us leave the upper room (see note on 13:1—17:26) and proceed to Gethsemane" (see 18:1).

15:1 *I am.* See note on 6:35. *the true vine.* The vine is frequently used in the OT as a symbol of Israel (see, e.g., Ps 80:8–16; Isa 5:1–7; Jer 2:21 and notes). When this imagery is used, Israel is often shown as lacking in some way. Jesus, however, is "the true vine."

15:2 *cuts off.* A reference to judgment (see note on v. 6). *prunes.* Pruning produces fruitfulness. In the NT the figure of good fruit represents the product of a godly life (see Mt 3:8; 7:16–20) or virtues of character (see Gal 5:22–23; Eph 5:9; Php 1:11 and notes).

15:3 *clean.* See NIV text note on v. 2. *the word.* Sums up the message of Jesus.

15:4 *Remain in me.* The believer has no fruitfulness apart from union and fellowship with Christ. A branch out of contact with the vine is lifeless.

15:5 *I am the vine.* See note on v. 1. The repetition gives emphasis. *remain in me and I in you.* A living union with Christ is absolutely necessary; without it there is nothing. *apart from me you can do nothing.* Cf. Php 4:13 (see note there).

15:6 *thrown into the fire and burned.* Judged (see note on v. 2). In light of such passages as 6:39; 10:27–29 (see notes there), these branches probably do not represent true believers. Genuine salvation is evidenced by a life of fruitfulness (see notes on vv. 2,4,10; see also Heb 6:9, "things that have to do with salvation," and note there; cf. Mt 7:19–23).

15:7 *my words remain in you.* It is impossible to pray correctly apart from knowing and believing the teachings of Christ. *ask whatever you wish.* See 14:13; 1Jn 5:14 and notes.

15:8 *to my Father's glory.* The Father is glorified in the work of the Son (see 13:31 and note), and he is also glorified in the fruit-bearing of disciples (see Mt 7:20; Lk 6:43–45).

15:10 *keep ... as I have kept.* Again the importance of obedience (cf. 14:15,21,23), and again the example of Christ (see 14:31 and note). *my love ... his love.* See vv. 12,14. Obedience and love go together (see 14:15,21,23; 1Jn 2:5 and notes; 5:2–3).

15:11 *joy.* Mentioned previously in this Gospel only in 3:29, but one of the characteristic notes of the upper room discourse (see 16:22,24 and note on 16:22; 17:13). The Christian way is never dreary, for Jesus desires his disciples' joy to be complete (see also Introduction to Philippians: Characteristics, 4; see also Php 4:4; 1Th 5:16; 1Jn 1:4 and notes).

each other as I have loved you.[h] 13 Greater love has no one than this: to lay down one's life for one's friends.[i] 14 You are my friends[j] if you do what I command.[k] 15 I no longer call you servants, because a servant does not know his master's business. Instead, I have called you friends, for everything that I learned from my Father I have made known to you.[l] 16 You did not choose me, but I chose you and appointed you[m] so that you might go and bear fruit[n]—fruit that will last—and so that whatever you ask in my name the Father will give you.[o] 17 This is my command: Love each other.[p]

The World Hates the Disciples

18 "If the world hates you,[q] keep in mind that it hated me first. 19 If you belonged to the world, it would love you as its own. As it is, you do not belong to the world, but I have chosen you[r] out of the world. That is why the world hates you.[s] 20 Remember what I told you: 'A servant is not greater than his master.'[a][t] If they persecuted me, they will persecute you also.[u] If they obeyed my teaching, they will obey yours also. 21 They will treat you this way because of my name,[v] for they do not know the one who sent me.[w] 22 If I had not come and spoken to them,[x] they would not be guilty of sin; but now they have no excuse for their sin.[y] 23 Whoever hates me hates my Father as well. 24 If I had not done among them the works no one else did,[z] they would not be guilty of sin.[a] As it is, they have seen, and yet they have hated both me and my Father. 25 But this is to fulfill what is written in their Law:[b] 'They hated me without reason.'[b][c]

The Work of the Holy Spirit

26 "When the Advocate[d] comes, whom I will send to you from the Father[e]—the Spirit of truth[f] who goes out from the Father—he will testify about me.[g] 27 And you also must testify,[h] for you have been with me from the beginning.[i]

16 "All this[j] I have told you so that you will not fall away.[k] 2 They will put you out of the synagogue;[l] in fact, the time is coming when anyone who kills you will think they are offering a service to God.[m] 3 They will do such things because they have not known the Father or me.[n] 4 I have told you this, so that when their time comes you will remember[o] that I warned you about them. I did not tell you this from the beginning because I was with you,[p] 5 but now I am going to him who sent me.[q] None of you asks me, 'Where are you going?'[r] 6 Rather, you

[a] *20* John 13:16 [b] *25* Psalms 35:19; 69:4

15:12 [h] ver 17; S Jn 13:34 **15:13** [i] Ge 44:33; Jn 10:11; Ro 5:7,8 **15:14** [j] Job 16:20; Pr 18:24; Lk 12:4 [k] Mt 12:50 **15:15** [l] Jn 8:26 **15:16** [m] ver 19; Jn 13:18 [n] ver 5 [o] S Mt 7:7 **15:17** [p] ver 12 **15:18** [q] Isa 66:5; Jn 7:7; 1Jn 3:13 **15:19** [r] ver 16 [s] Jn 17:14 **15:20** [t] S Jn 13:16 [u] 2Ti 3:12 **15:21** [v] Isa 66:5; Mt 5:10,11; 10:22; Lk 6:22; Ac 5:41; 1Pe 4:14; Rev 2:3 [w] Jn 16:3 **15:22** [x] Eze 2:5; 3:7 [y] Jn 9:41; Ro 1:20; 2:1 **15:24** [z] Jn 5:36 [a] Jn 9:41 **15:25** [b] S Jn 10:34 [c] Ps 35:19; 69:4; 109:3 **15:26** [d] Jn 14:16 [e] Jn 14:26; 16:7 [f] S Jn 14:17 [g] 1Jn 5:7 **15:27** [h] S Lk 24:48; Jn 21:24; 1Jn 1:2; 4:14 [i] S Lk 1:2

16:1 [j] Jn 15:18-27 [k] Mt 11:6 **16:2** [l] Jn 9:22; 12:42 [m] Isa 66:5; Ac 26:9,10; Rev 6:9 **16:3** [n] Jn 15:21; 17:25; 1Jn 3:1 **16:4** [o] Jn 13:19; 14:29 [p] Jn 15:27 **16:5** [q] ver 10,17,28; Jn 7:33 [r] Jn 13:36; 14:5

15:13 Christ's love was demonstrated not only in his words but also in his sacrificial death (see Eph 5:25 and note).

15:15 *servants ... friends.* A servant is simply an agent, doing what his master commands and often not understanding his master's purpose. But Jesus takes his friends into his confidence. *everything ... I have made known to you.* From 16:12 we learn that though Jesus had let his disciples know as much as they were able to absorb of the Father's plan, the revelation was not yet complete. The Spirit would make other things known in due course (see 16:12–13 and notes).

15:16 *I chose you ... bear fruit ... ask.* Disciples normally chose the particular rabbi to whom they wanted to be attached, but it was not so with Jesus' disciples. He chose them, and for a purpose—the bearing of fruit (see v. 2 and note). We usually desire a strong prayer life in order that we may be fruitful, but here it is the other way around. Jesus enables us to bear fruit, and then the Father will hear our prayers. *in my name.* See notes on 2:23; 14:13.

15:18–19 *world.* Here refers to the human system that opposes God's purpose (see note on 1:9).

15:21 *They will treat you this way.* Because Christians do not belong to the world, persecution from the world is inevitable. The basic reason is the world's ignorance and rejection of the Father (cf. 16:3). *name.* See note on 2:23.

15:22 *no excuse.* Privilege and responsibility go together. The Jews had had the great privilege of having the Son of God among them—in addition to having received God's special revelation in the OT. Those who rejected him were totally guilty and without excuse. If he had not come to them, they would still have been sinners, but they would not have been guilty of rejecting him directly (see v. 24).

15:23 Contrast 13:20.

15:25 *to fulfill what is written.* See note on Ps 35:19. In the end God's purpose is always accomplished, despite the belief of those who reject Jesus that they have successfully opposed it. *Law.* See notes on 10:34; 12:34.

15:26 *Advocate.* See note on 14:16. *I will send.* See notes on 14:16,26. *Spirit of truth.* See note on 14:17. *goes out from the Father.* Probably refers to the Spirit's being sent to do the Father's work on earth rather than to his eternal relationship with the Father. *testify.* See note on 1:7.

15:27 *you also.* Emphatic. Believers bear their testimony to Christ in the power of the Spirit (see Ac 1:8 and note). But it is *their* testimony, and *they* are responsible for bearing it. *from the beginning.* The apostles bore the definitive testimony, for they were uniquely chosen and taught by Christ and were eyewitnesses of his glory (see Lk 24:48; Ac 10:39,41).

16:2 *put you out of the synagogue.* See note on 9:22. *a service to God.* Religious people have often persecuted others in the strong conviction that they were doing God's will (see Ac 26:9–11; Gal 1:13–14).

16:3 *the Father.* See note on 5:17. *or me.* Again the Father and the Son are linked. Not to know Christ is to be ignorant of the Father (see 14:7,10–11; 17:6–7,22–23,26 and notes).

16:5 *None of you asks me, 'Where are you going?'* Peter had asked such a question (13:36) but quickly turned his attention to another subject. His concern had been with what would happen to himself and the others and not with where Jesus was going.

are filled with grief[s] because I have said
these things. 7 But very truly I tell you, it
is for your good that I am going away.
Unless I go away, the Advocate[t] will not
come to you; but if I go, I will send him
to you.[u] 8 When he comes, he will prove
the world to be in the wrong about sin
and righteousness and judgment: 9 about
sin,[v] because people do not believe in me;
10 about righteousness,[w] because I am going to the Father,[x] where you can see me
no longer; 11 and about judgment, because
the prince of this world[y] now stands condemned.

12 "I have much more to say to you,
more than you can now bear.[z] 13 But when
he, the Spirit of truth,[a] comes, he will
guide you into all the truth.[b] He will not
speak on his own; he will speak only what
he hears, and he will tell you what is yet
to come. 14 He will glorify me because it is
from me that he will receive what he will
make known to you. 15 All that belongs to
the Father is mine.[c] That is why I said the
Spirit will receive from me what he will
make known to you."

The Disciples' Grief Will Turn to Joy

16 Jesus went on to say, "In a little while[d]
you will see me no more, and then after a
little while you will see me."[e]

17 At this, some of his disciples said
to one another, "What does he mean
by saying, 'In a little while you will see
me no more, and then after a little while
you will see me,'[f] and 'Because I am
going to the Father'?"[g] 18 They kept asking, "What does he mean by 'a little
while'? We don't understand what he is
saying."

19 Jesus saw that they wanted to ask him
about this, so he said to them, "Are you
asking one another what I meant when
I said, 'In a little while you will see me
no more, and then after a little while you
will see me'? 20 Very truly I tell you, you
will weep and mourn[h] while the world rejoices. You will grieve, but your grief will
turn to joy.[i] 21 A woman giving birth to a
child has pain[j] because her time has come;
but when her baby is born she forgets the
anguish because of her joy that a child is
born into the world. 22 So with you: Now is
your time of grief,[k] but I will see you again[l]
and you will rejoice, and no one will take
away your joy.[m] 23 In that day[n] you will no
longer ask me anything. Very truly I tell
you, my Father will give you whatever you
ask in my name.[o] 24 Until now you have
not asked for anything in my name. Ask
and you will receive,[p] and your joy will be
complete.[q]

16:6 [s] ver 22 **16:7** [t] Jn 14:16, 26; 15:26 [u] Jn 7:39; 14:26 **16:9** [v] Jn 15:22 **16:10** [w] Ac 3:14; 7:52; Ro 1:17; 3:21, 22; 1Pe 3:18 [x] S ver 5 **16:11** [y] S Jn 12:31 **16:12** [z] Mk 4:33; 1Co 3:2 **16:13** [a] S Jn 14:17 [b] Ps 25:5; Jn 14:26 **16:15** [c] Jn 17:10 **16:16** [d] S Jn 7:33 [e] ver 22; Jn 14:18-24 **16:17** [f] ver 16 [g] ver 5 **16:20** [h] Mk 16:10; Lk 23:27 [i] Jn 20:20 **16:21** [j] Isa 13:8; 21:3; 26:17; Mic 4:9; 1Th 5:3 **16:22** [k] ver 6 [l] ver 16 [m] ver 20; Jer 31:12 **16:23** [n] ver 26; Jn 14:20 [o] S Mt 7:7 **16:24** [p] S Mt 7:7 [q] S Jn 3:29

16:6 *you are filled with grief.* Because of his announced departure.

16:7 *Unless I go away.* Jesus did not say why the Spirit would not come until he went away but clearly taught that his saving work on the cross was necessary before the sending of the Spirit. *Advocate.* See note on 14:16. *I will send him.* See note on 14:26.

16:8 *he will prove the world to be in the wrong.* The work the Spirit does in the world; the NT normally speaks of his work in believers.

16:9 *about sin.* Apart from the Spirit's convicting work, people can never see themselves as sinners. *because people do not believe.* May mean that their sin is their failure to believe or that their unbelief is a classic example of sin. John may have had both of these in mind.

16:10 *about righteousness.* The righteousness brought about by Christ's sacrificial death (see Ro 1:17; 3:21–24 and notes). *because I am going to the Father.* The ascension, which as part of Christ's exaltation placed God's seal of approval on Christ's redemptive act.

16:11 *about judgment.* Jesus was speaking of the defeat of Satan, which was a form of judgment, not simply a victory. More than power is in question. God acts with justice. *because the prince of this world now stands condemned.* See note on 12:31.

16:12 *more than you can now bear.* This may mean "more than you can understand now," or "more than you can perform without the Spirit's help" (to live out Christ's teaching requires the enabling presence of the Spirit).

16:13 *Spirit of truth.* See note on 14:17. *only what he hears.* We are not told whether he hears from the Father or the Son, but it obviously does not matter, for the verse stresses the close relationship among the three. *what is yet to come.* Probably means the whole Christian way or revelation (presented and preserved in the apostolic writings), still future at the time Jesus spoke.

16:14 *glorify me.* See note on 1:14. The Spirit draws no attention to himself but promotes the glory of Christ.

16:15 *All that belongs to the Father is mine.* Cf. 17:10. The three persons of the Trinity are closely related.

16:16 *a little while ... a little while.* Few doubt that the first phrase refers to the interval before the crucifixion. But interpretations differ as to whether the second refers to the interval preceding the resurrection, the coming of the Spirit or the second coming of Christ. It seems that the language here best fits the resurrection (see v. 22 and note).

16:17 *going to the Father.* See v. 10 and note. Jesus had not linked this with "a little while," but the apostles saw them as connected.

16:20 *weep.* The same verb for loud wailing as in 11:33 (see note there), which carries the idea of deep sorrow and its outward expression.

16:21 *A woman giving birth.* Giving birth usually causes both pain and joy (cf. Isa 26:17–19; 66:7–14; Hos 13:13–14).

16:22 *I will see you again.* As in v. 16, probably a reference to Jesus' appearances after his resurrection. *no one will take away your joy.* The resurrection would change things permanently, bringing a joy that cannot be removed by the world's assaults (see note on 15:11).

16:23 *you will no longer ask me anything.* Seems to mean asking for information (rather than asking in prayer), which would not be necessary after the resurrection. Jesus then moved on to the subject of prayer. However, Jesus may have been saying that though his disciples previously had been praying to him, after his death and resurrection they were to go directly to the Father and pray in his (Christ's) name (see vv. 24,26–27 and notes). *name.* See notes on 2:23; 14:13.

16:24 *Until now.* Previously they had asked the Father or

25 “Though I have been speaking figuratively,[r] a time is coming[s] when I will no longer use this kind of language but will tell you plainly about my Father. 26 In that day you will ask in my name.[t] I am not saying that I will ask the Father on your behalf. 27 No, the Father himself loves you because you have loved me[u] and have believed that I came from God.[v] 28 I came from the Father and entered the world; now I am leaving the world and going back to the Father.”[w]

29 Then Jesus’ disciples said, “Now you are speaking clearly and without figures of speech.[x] 30 Now we can see that you know all things and that you do not even need to have anyone ask you questions. This makes us believe[y] that you came from God.”[z]

31 “Do you now believe?” Jesus replied. 32 “A time is coming[a] and in fact has come when you will be scattered,[b] each to your own home. You will leave me all alone.[c] Yet I am not alone, for my Father is with me.[d]

33 “I have told you these things, so that in me you may have peace.[e] In this world you will have trouble.[f] But take heart! I have overcome[g] the world.”

Jesus Prays to Be Glorified

17 After Jesus said this, he looked toward heaven[h] and prayed:

“Father, the hour has come.[i] Glorify your Son, that your Son may glorify you.[j] 2 For you granted him authority over all people[k] that he might give eternal life[l] to all those you have given him.[m] 3 Now this is eternal life: that they know you,[n] the only true God, and Jesus Christ, whom you have sent.[o] 4 I have brought you glory[p] on earth by finishing the work you gave me to do.[q] 5 And now, Father, glorify me[r] in your presence with the glory I had with you[s] before the world began.[t]

Jesus Prays for His Disciples

6 “I have revealed you[a][u] to those whom you gave me[v] out of the world. They were yours; you gave them to me and they have obeyed your word. 7 Now they know that everything you have given me comes from you. 8 For I gave them the words you gave me[w] and they accepted them. They knew with certainty that I came from you,[x] and they believed that you sent me.[y]

16:25 [r] ver 29; Ps 78:2; Eze 20:49; Mt 13:34; Mk 4:33,34; Jn 10:6 [s] ver 2 **16:26** [t] ver 23, 24 **16:27** [u] Jn 14:21, 23 [v] ver 30; S Jn 13:3 **16:28** [w] ver 5, 10,17; Jn 13:3 **16:29** [x] S ver 25 **16:30** [y] 1Ki 17:24 [z] ver 27; S Jn 13:3 **16:32** [a] ver 2, 25 [b] Mt 26:31 [c] Mt 26:56 [d] Jn 8:16,29 **16:33** [e] S Jn 14:27 [f] Jn 15:18-21 [g] Ro 8:37; 1Jn 4:4; 5:4; Rev 2:7,11,17, 26; 3:5,12,21; 21:7 **17:1** [h] Jn 11:41 [i] S Mt 26:18 [j] Jn 12:23; 13:31,32 **17:2** [k] S Mt 28:18 [l] S Mt 25:46 [m] ver 6,9, 24; Da 7:14; Jn 6:37,39 **17:3** [n] S Php 3:8 [o] ver 8,18,21, 23,25; S Jn 3:17 **17:4** [p] Jn 13:31 [q] S Jn 19:30 **17:5** [r] ver 1 [s] Php 2:6 [t] S Jn 1:2 **17:6** [u] ver 26; Jn 1:18 [v] S ver 2 **17:8** [w] ver 14,26; S Jn 14:24 [x] S Jn 13:3 [y] ver 3,18,21,23, 25; S Jn 3:17

[a] 6 Greek *your name*

Christ, but they had not asked the Father in Christ’s name. *your joy.* See note on 15:11.

16:25 *I have been speaking figuratively.* Throughout the discourse, not just in the immediately preceding words. *a time is coming.* After the resurrection.

16:26 *in my name.* See notes on 2:23; 14:13. *I am not saying that I will ask.* Not a contradiction of Ro 8:34; Heb 7:25; 1Jn 2:1 (see notes there). Those passages mean that Christ’s presence in heaven as the crucified and risen Lord is itself an intercession. Here the teaching is that there will be no need for him to make petitions in our behalf.

16:27 *the Father himself loves you.* Christ is explaining why the disciples can come directly to the Father in prayer: They have loved and trusted in Jesus, and in love God will hear their requests in Jesus’ name.

16:29 *without figures of speech.* See v. 25 and note.

16:30 *believe that you came from God.* Two recurring themes of this Gospel: believing (see note on 1:7) and Jesus’ coming from God (see notes on 4:34; 17:3,8).

16:32 *you will be scattered.* The disciples had faith, but not enough to stand firm in the face of disaster. Jesus knew they would fail (see Mt 26:31 and note; cf. Zec 13:7 and note); however, his church is not built on people’s strength but on God’s ability to use people even after they have failed.

16:33 Notice the contrasts: between “in me” and “in this world” (see note on 1:9) and between “peace” and “trouble.” *I have overcome.* Just before his death Jesus affirms his final victory.

17:1–26 Jesus’ longest recorded prayer—sometimes called his “High Priestly Prayer.”

17:1 *he looked toward heaven.* The customary attitude in prayer (11:41; Ps 123:1; Mk 7:34), though sometimes Jesus prostrated himself (see Mt 26:39; see also note on 1Ch 17:16). *Father.* Used of God in John’s Gospel about 120 times. *the hour.* See note on 2:4. *Glorify … glorify.* See notes on 1:14; 7:39; 13:31. The glory of the Father and that of the Son are closely connected, and the death by which Jesus would glorify God would lead to eternal life for believers (v. 2).

17:2 *granted.* The act of giving is stressed in this chapter (vv. 4,6–9,11–12,14,22,24); see note on 3:27. *eternal life.* See note on 3:15. *those you have given him.* Again God’s initiative in salvation is stressed (see vv. 6,12; 6:37,39,44 and notes).

17:3 *eternal life … know you.* Eternal life is not just a future inheritance but also a present possession—available because of our relationship with the Father through the Son. John’s Gospel stresses this latter sense. *sent.* Again the mission of Jesus is mentioned (see 3:34; 4:34; 13:20 and notes).

17:4 *I have brought you glory.* Christ’s mission was not self-centered. *the work you gave me.* Jesus emphasized the supreme place of the Father (see note on 4:34).

17:5 *glorify me … with the glory I had with you.* Jesus asks the Father to return him to his previous position of glory, to exchange humiliation for glorification. This occurred at Christ’s resurrection and exaltation to God’s right hand. *world.* The universe (see notes on v. 14; 1:9). The Greek word for “world” occurs 18 times in this prayer.

17:6 *I have revealed you.* See NIV text note and notes on 2:23; 14:13; cf. 1:18. *those whom you gave me.* Again the divine initiative (see note on v. 2).

17:7 *everything … comes from you.* Only as people see the Father at work in Jesus do they have a proper concept of God. The disciples had at last reached this understanding. Cf. Jas 1:17.

17:8 Three things about the disciples are mentioned: (1) They accepted the teaching (unlike the Pharisees and others who heard it but did not receive it). (2) They knew with certainty Jesus’ divine origin. Acceptance of that revela-

9 I pray for them.[z] I am not praying for
the world, but for those you have given
me,[a] for they are yours. 10 All I have is
yours, and all you have is mine.[b] And
glory has come to me through them.
11 I will remain in the world no longer,
but they are still in the world,[c] and I
am coming to you.[d] Holy Father, protect them by the power of[a] your name,
the name you gave me, so that they
may be one[e] as we are one.[f] 12 While
I was with them, I protected them
and kept them safe by[b] that name you
gave me. None has been lost[g] except
the one doomed to destruction[h] so that
Scripture would be fulfilled.[i]
13 "I am coming to you now,[j] but
I say these things while I am still in
the world, so that they may have the
full measure of my joy[k] within them.
14 I have given them your word and
the world has hated them,[l] for they
are not of the world any more than
I am of the world.[m] 15 My prayer is
not that you take them out of the
world but that you protect them from
the evil one.[n] 16 They are not of the
world, even as I am not of it.[o] 17 Sanctify them by[c] the truth; your word
is truth.[p] 18 As you sent me into the
world,[q] I have sent them into the
world.[r] 19 For them I sanctify myself,
that they too may be truly sanctified.[s]

Jesus Prays for All Believers

20 "My prayer is not for them alone.
I pray also for those who will believe
in me through their message, 21 that
all of them may be one,[t] Father, just
as you are in me and I am in you.[u]
May they also be in us so that the
world may believe that you have sent
me.[v] 22 I have given them the glory that you gave me,[w] that they may
be one as we are one[x]— 23 I in them
and you in me—so that they may be
brought to complete unity. Then the
world will know that you sent me[y]
and have loved them[z] even as you
have loved me.

[a] 11 Or Father, keep them faithful to *[b] 12 Or kept them faithful to* *[c] 17 Or them to live in accordance with*

17:9 [z] Lk 22:32 [a] S ver 2 **17:10** [b] Jn 16:15 **17:11** [c] Jn 13:1 [d] ver 13; Jn 7:33 [e] ver 21-23; Ps 133:1 [f] Jn 10:30 **17:12** [g] S Jn 6:39 [h] Jn 6:70 [i] S Mt 1:22 **17:13** [j] ver 11 [k] S Jn 3:29 **17:14** [l] Jn 15:19 [m] ver 16; Jn 8:23 **17:15** [n] S Mt 5:37 **17:16** [o] ver 14 **17:17** [p] S Jn 15:3; 2Sa 7:28; 1Ki 17:24 **17:18** [q] ver 3, 8, 21, 23, 25; S Jn 3:17 [r] Jn 20:21 **17:19** [s] ver 17 **17:21** [t] Jer 32:39 [u] ver 11; Jn 10:38 [v] ver 3, 8, 18, 23, 25; S Jn 3:17 **17:22** [w] Jn 1:14 [x] S Jn 14:20 **17:23** [y] ver 3, 8, 18, 21, 25; S Jn 3:17 [z] Jn 16:27

tion led them further into truth. (3) They believed (see notes on 1:7,12; 20:31).

17:9 *not ... for the world.* The only prayer Jesus could pray for the world was that it cease to be worldly (i.e., opposed to God), and this he did pray (vv. 21,23).

17:11 *Holy Father.* A form of address found only here in the NT (but cf. 1Pe 1:16; Rev 4:8 and notes). The name suggests both remoteness and nearness; God is both awe-inspiring (see Lev 11:44 and note) and loving. *protect them by the power of your name.* Cf. 1Sa 17:45; Ps 5:11; 20:7–8; Pr 18:10; Eze 20:9 and notes. *that they may be one.* The latter part of the prayer strongly emphasizes unity. Here the unity is already given, not something to be achieved. The meaning is "that they continually be one" rather than "that they become one." The unity is to be like that between the Father and the Son. It is much more than unity of organization, but the church's present divisions are the result of the failures of Christians.

17:12 *I protected them.* Christ's power is adequate for every need (cf. 1Pe 1:5 and note). *the one doomed to destruction.* Lit. "the son of destruction" (see 2Th 2:3 and note), i.e., one belonging to the sphere of damnation and destined for destruction (but predestination is not in view here). Reference is to Judas Iscariot (see 13:18 and note).

17:13 *my joy.* See note on 15:11.

17:14 *the world.* The world that is hostile to God and God's people (see notes on v. 5; 1:9). *not of the world.* They do not have the mindset of the world, i.e., hostility to God, for they have been "born of the Spirit" (3:8) and are "children of God" (1:12).

17:15 *not that you take them out of the world.* The world is where Jesus' disciples are to do their work; Jesus does not wish them to be taken from it until that work is done (see v. 18). *the evil one.* Satan, who is especially active in the world (Mt 6:13; 1Jn 5:19), making God's protection indispensable.

17:17 *Sanctify.* See v. 19; 1Co 1:2 and notes. *the truth; your word.* Sanctification and revelation (as recorded in the word of God) go together (cf. 1Pe 2:2 and note). For the relationship between Christ's teaching and truth, see 8:31–32 and note on 8:32.

17:18 *As you sent me ... I have sent them.* Jesus' mission is one of the dominant themes of this Gospel and is given as the pattern for his followers (see v. 3 and note). *into the world.* We may long for heaven, but it is on earth that our work is done (cf. 20:21).

17:19 *I sanctify myself.* This statement appears to be unparalleled. In the Septuagint (the pre-Christian Greek translation of the OT) the verb is used of consecrating priests (Ex 28:41) and sacrifices (Ex 28:38; Nu 18:9). Jesus solemnly "sanctifies" (i.e., "sets apart") himself to do God's will, which at this point meant his death. *that they too may be ... sanctified.* Jesus died on the cross not only to save us but also to consecrate us to God's service (see note on 1Co 1:2).

17:20 *those who will believe in me.* Jesus had just spoken of the mission and the sanctification of his followers (vv. 18–19). He was confident that they would spread the gospel, and he prayed for those who would believe as a result. All future believers are included in this prayer.

17:21 *that all of them may be one.* See note on v. 11. *Father.* See note on v. 1. *that the world may believe.* The unity of believers should have an effect on outsiders, to convince them of the mission of Christ. Jesus' prayer is a rebuke of the groundless and often bitter divisions among believers.

17:22 *glory.* See note on v. 1. Believers are to be characterized by humility and service, just as Christ was, and it is on them that God's glory rests. *that they may be one as we are one.* Again the Lord emphasized the importance of unity among his followers, and again the standard is the unity of the Father and the Son.

17:23 *I in them and you in me.* There are two indwellings here: that of the Son in believers and that of the Father in the Son. It is because the latter is a reality that the former can take place. *complete unity.* Again the emphasis on unity has an evangelistic aim. This time it is connected not only with the mission of Jesus but also with God's love for people and for Christ.

24 "Father, I want those you have
given me[a] to be with me where I am,[b]
and to see my glory,[c] the glory you
have given me because you loved me
before the creation of the world.[d]
25 "Righteous Father, though the
world does not know you,[e] I know
you, and they know that you have
sent me.[f] 26 I have made you[a] known
to them,[g] and will continue to make
you known in order that the love you
have for me may be in them[h] and that
I myself may be in them."

Jesus Arrested

18:3-11pp — Mt 26:47-56; Mk 14:43-50; Lk 22:47-53

18 When he had finished praying,
Jesus left with his disciples and
crossed the Kidron Valley.[i] On the other
side there was a garden,[j] and he and his
disciples went into it.[k]
2 Now Judas, who betrayed him, knew
the place, because Jesus had often met
there with his disciples.[l] 3 So Judas came
to the garden, guiding[m] a detachment of
soldiers and some officials from the chief
priests and the Pharisees.[n] They were carrying torches, lanterns and weapons.
4 Jesus, knowing all that was going to
happen to him,[o] went out and asked them,
"Who is it you want?"[p]
5 "Jesus of Nazareth,"[q] they replied.
"I am he," Jesus said. (And Judas the
traitor was standing there with them.)
6 When Jesus said, "I am he," they drew
back and fell to the ground.
7 Again he asked them, "Who is it you
want?"[r]
"Jesus of Nazareth," they said.
8 Jesus answered, "I told you that I am
he. If you are looking for me, then let
these men go." 9 This happened so that
the words he had spoken would be fulfilled: "I have not lost one of those you
gave me."[b s]
10 Then Simon Peter, who had a sword,
drew it and struck the high priest's servant, cutting off his right ear. (The servant's name was Malchus.)
11 Jesus commanded Peter, "Put your
sword away! Shall I not drink the cup[t] the
Father has given me?"
12 Then the detachment of soldiers with
its commander and the Jewish officials[u]
arrested Jesus. They bound him 13 and
brought him first to Annas, who was the
father-in-law of Caiaphas,[v] the high priest
that year. 14 Caiaphas was the one who had
advised the Jewish leaders that it would
be good if one man died for the people.[w]

17:24 [a] S ver 2 [b] S Jn 12:26 [c] Jn 1:14 [d] ver 5; S Mt 25:34; S Jn 1:2 **17:25** [e] Jn 15:21; 16:3 [f] ver 3,8,18,21,23; S Jn 3:17; 16:27 **17:26** [g] ver 6 [h] Jn 15:9 **18:1** [i] 2Sa 15:23 [j] ver 26; S Mt 21:1 [k] Mt 26:36 **18:2** [l] Lk 21:37; 22:39 **18:3** [m] Ac 1:16 [n] ver 12 **18:4** [o] Jn 6:64; 13:1,11 [p] ver 7 **18:5** [q] S Mk 1:24 **18:7** [r] ver 4 **18:9** [s] S Jn 6:39 **18:11** [t] S Mt 20:22 **18:12** [u] ver 3 **18:13** [v] ver 24; S Mt 26:3 **18:14** [w] Jn 11:49-51

[a] 26 Greek *your name* [b] 9 John 6:39

17:24 *Father.* See note on v. 1. *I want.* Means "I will that." Jesus said, "I will"—his last will and testament for his followers. Where he himself was concerned, he prayed, "not what I will, but what you will" (Mk 14:36). *to be with me.* The Christian's greatest blessing (see 14:3; 1Th 4:17 and note). *my glory.* Perhaps used here to refer to Jesus' eternal splendor (see 1Jn 3:2). Or Jesus' prayer may have been that in the life to come they might fully appreciate the glory of his lowly service (cf. Eph 2:7).
17:25 *Righteous Father.* A form of address found only here in the NT (cf. note on "Holy Father" in v. 11). *they know.* They did not know God directly and personally, but they knew that God had sent Christ. To recognize God in Christ's mission is a great advance over anything the world can know.
17:26 *made you known to them.* See 16:3 and note.
18:1 *crossed the Kidron Valley.* East of Jerusalem (see map, pp. 1686–1687).
18:3 *Judas.* See note on 6:71. *officials from the chief priests and the Pharisees.* Equivalent to the temple guard sent by the Sanhedrin (see notes on Mt 2:4; 3:7; Mk 14:55). *torches.* Resinous pieces of wood fastened together. *lanterns.* Terra-cotta holders into which household lamps could be inserted.
18:4 *knowing all that was going to happen to him.* Jesus was not taken by surprise.
18:5 *I am.* See 6:35; 8:58 and notes. *with them.* John does not let us forget where Judas belonged.
18:6 *fell to the ground.* They came to arrest a meek peasant and instead were met in the dim light by a majestic and powerful person.
18:8 *I am.* The threefold repetition (vv. 5,6,8) emphasizes the solemn words. *let these men go.* Jesus cared for the disciples even as he was going to his death. Twice he had made the arresting party say plainly that he was the one they wanted (vv. 4–5,7).
18:9 *would be fulfilled.* Words normally used in quoting Scripture, and Jesus' words are on the same level (see 6:39; 17:12 and notes).
18:10 *Simon Peter.* It is to John that we owe the information that the man with the sword (the Greek for this word refers to a short sword) was Peter and that the man he wounded was named Malchus.
18:11 *the cup.* Often points to suffering (see Ps 75:8; Eze 23:31 and note) and the wrath of God (see notes on Ps 16:5; Isa 51:17; Jer 25:15; Ro 1:18; Rev 14:10). *the Father has given me.* The Synoptic Gospels also speak of the cup at the time of Jesus' prayer at Gethsemane (see Mt 26:39; Mk 14:36; Lk 22:42 and notes), and John says it came from the Father. God was in control.
18:12 *bound him.* The reason for the bonds is not clear. Perhaps their use was standard procedure, much like the modern use of handcuffs.
18:13 *Annas.* Had been deposed from the high priesthood by the Romans in AD 15 but was probably still regarded by many as the true high priest (see note on Lk 3:2). In Jewish law no one could be sentenced on the day their trial was held. The two examinations—this one (mentioned only by John; see note on Mk 14:53—15:15) and the one before Caiaphas—may have been conducted to give some form of legitimacy to what was done. *high priest that year.* See note on 11:49.
18:14 *Caiaphas ... had advised the Jewish leaders.* A reference to 11:49–50 (see notes there). For John it was this unconscious prophecy that mattered most about Caiaphas. John may also have been hinting that a fair trial could not be expected from a man who had already said that putting Jesus to death was expedient.

Peter's First Denial

18:16-18pp — Mt 26:69,70; Mk 14:66-68; Lk 22:55-57

15 Simon Peter and another disciple were
following Jesus. Because this disciple was
known to the high priest,[x] he went with
Jesus into the high priest's courtyard,[y]
16 but Peter had to wait outside at the door.
The other disciple, who was known to the
high priest, came back, spoke to the servant girl on duty there and brought Peter in.
17 "You aren't one of this man's disciples
too, are you?" she asked Peter.
He replied, "I am not."[z]
18 It was cold, and the servants and officials stood around a fire[a] they had made to
keep warm. Peter also was standing with
them, warming himself.[b]

The High Priest Questions Jesus

18:19-24pp — Mt 26:59-68; Mk 14:55-65; Lk 22:63-71

19 Meanwhile, the high priest questioned
Jesus about his disciples and his teaching.
20 "I have spoken openly to the world,"
Jesus replied. "I always taught in synagogues[c] or at the temple,[d] where all the
Jews come together. I said nothing in secret.[e] 21 Why question me? Ask those who
heard me. Surely they know what I said."
22 When Jesus said this, one of the officials[f] nearby slapped him in the face.[g] "Is
this the way you answer the high priest?"
he demanded.

18:15 [x]S Mt 26:3 [y]Mt 26:58; Mk 14:54; Lk 22:54 **18:17** [z]ver 25 **18:18** [a]Jn 21:9 [b]Mk 14:54,67 **18:20** [c]S Mt 4:23 [d]Mt 26:55 [e]Jn 7:26 **18:22** [f]ver 3 [g]Mt 16:21; Jn 19:3

18:23 [h]Mt 5:39; Ac 23:2-5 **18:24** [i]ver 13; S Mt 26:3 **18:25** [j]ver 18 [k]ver 17 **18:26** [l]ver 10 [m]ver 1 **18:27** [n]Jn 13:38 **18:28** [o]S Mt 27:2 [p]ver 33; Jn 19:9 [q]Jn 11:55

23 "If I said something wrong," Jesus replied, "testify as to what is wrong. But if I
spoke the truth, why did you strike me?"[h]
24 Then Annas sent him bound to Caiaphas[i] the high priest.

Peter's Second and Third Denials

18:25-27pp — Mt 26:71-75; Mk 14:69-72; Lk 22:58-62

25 Meanwhile, Simon Peter was still
standing there warming himself.[j] So they
asked him, "You aren't one of his disciples
too, are you?"
He denied it, saying, "I am not."[k]
26 One of the high priest's servants, a
relative of the man whose ear Peter had
cut off,[l] challenged him, "Didn't I see you
with him in the garden?"[m] 27 Again Peter
denied it, and at that moment a rooster
began to crow.[n]

Jesus Before Pilate

18:29-40pp — Mt 27:11-18,20-23; Mk 15:2-15; Lk 23:2,3,18-25

28 Then the Jewish leaders took Jesus
from Caiaphas to the palace of the Roman
governor.[o] By now it was early morning,
and to avoid ceremonial uncleanness they
did not enter the palace,[p] because they
wanted to be able to eat the Passover.[q]
29 So Pilate came out to them and asked,
"What charges are you bringing against
this man?"
30 "If he were not a criminal," they replied,

18:15 *another disciple.* Perhaps John himself. *known to the high priest.* Refers to more than casual acquaintance; he had entrée into the high priest's house and could bring Peter in.
18:16 *servant girl.* All four Gospels tell us that Peter's first challenge (v. 17) came from a slave girl, the most unimportant person imaginable.
18:17 The form of the girl's question implied a negative answer, and Peter capitalized on that by saying, "I am not." The other Gospels seem to indicate that the other denials followed immediately, but it is likely that there were intervals during which other things happened (see Lk 22:58–59).
18:18 *Peter also was standing with them.* On a cold night he would have been conspicuous if he had stayed away from the fire.
18:19 *questioned.* Not legal, since witnesses were supposed to be brought in first to establish guilt. The accused were not required to prove their innocence. Perhaps Annas regarded this as a preliminary inquiry, not a trial.
18:20 *I have spoken openly.* It should not have been difficult to find witnesses (v. 21). *nothing in secret.* Not a denial that he taught the disciples privately, but a denial that he had secretly taught them subversive teaching different from his public message.
18:22 *slapped.* Another illegality. The Greek word apparently means a blow with the open hand—a slap.
18:23 *testify.* A legal term, indicating an invitation to act in proper legal form. John stresses the importance of testimony throughout his Gospel (see note on 1:7).
18:25 *they asked him.* Some find a difficulty in that Mt 26:71 says another girl asked this question, whereas Mk 14:69 says it was the same girl and Lk 22:58 that it was a man. But with a group of servants talking around a fire, several would doubtless take up and repeat such a question, which could be the meaning of John's "they." As on the first occasion (v. 17) the question anticipated the answer "No." The servants probably did not really expect to find a follower of Jesus in the high priest's courtyard, but the question seemed worth asking.
18:26 *a relative.* Another piece of information we owe to John. A relative would have a deeper interest in the swordsman than other people had. But the light in the garden would have been dim, as in the courtyard (a charcoal fire glows, but does not have flames). *Didn't I see you . . . ?* Expecting the answer "Yes."
18:27 *a rooster began to crow.* The fulfillment of the prophecy in 13:38 (see note there).
18:28 *Roman governor.* John says little about the Jewish phase of Jesus' trial but much about the Roman trial (see note on Mk 14:53—15:15). It is possible that John was in the Praetorium, the governor's official residence, for this trial. *early morning.* The chief priests evidently held a second session of the Sanhedrin after daybreak to give some appearance of legality to what they did (Mk 15:1). This occasion would have been immediately after that, perhaps between 6:00 a.m. and 7:00 a.m. *ceremonial uncleanness.* A result of entering a Gentile residence. *to eat the Passover.* This appears to contradict the Synoptic Gospels, which have Jesus eating the Passover meal the night before. Here are two possible solutions: (1) Some say different Jewish groups ate the Passover meal at different times. (2) The term "Passover" may be used here to refer to the whole festival of Passover and Unleavened Bread, which lasted seven days and included a number of meals.
18:29 *Pilate.* The Roman governor (see note on Mk 15:1). He

"we would not have handed him over to
you."
31 Pilate said, "Take him yourselves and
judge him by your own law."
"But we have no right to execute anyone," they objected. 32 This took place to
fulfill what Jesus had said about the kind
of death he was going to die.[r]
33 Pilate then went back inside the palace,[s] summoned Jesus and asked him,
"Are you the king of the Jews?"[t]
34 "Is that your own idea," Jesus asked,
"or did others talk to you about me?"
35 "Am I a Jew?" Pilate replied. "Your
own people and chief priests handed you
over to me. What is it you have done?"
36 Jesus said, "My kingdom[u] is not of
this world. If it were, my servants would
fight to prevent my arrest by the Jewish
leaders.[v] But now my kingdom is from another place."[w]
37 "You are a king, then!" said Pilate.
Jesus answered, "You say that I am a
king. In fact, the reason I was born and
came into the world is to testify to the
truth.[x] Everyone on the side of truth listens to me."[y]
38 "What is truth?" retorted Pilate. With
this he went out again to the Jews gathered there and said, "I find no basis for a
charge against him.[z] 39 But it is your custom for me to release to you one prisoner
at the time of the Passover. Do you want
me to release 'the king of the Jews'?"
40 They shouted back, "No, not him!
Give us Barabbas!" Now Barabbas had
taken part in an uprising.[a]

Jesus Sentenced to Be Crucified

19:1-16pp — Mt 27:27-31; Mk 15:16-20

19 Then Pilate took Jesus and had
him flogged.[b] 2 The soldiers twisted together a crown of thorns and put it
on his head. They clothed him in a purple
robe 3 and went up to him again and again,
saying, "Hail, king of the Jews!"[c] And they
slapped him in the face.[d]
4 Once more Pilate came out and said
to the Jews gathered there, "Look, I am
bringing him out[e] to you to let you know
that I find no basis for a charge against
him."[f] 5 When Jesus came out wearing the
crown of thorns and the purple robe,[g] Pilate said to them, "Here is the man!"
6 As soon as the chief priests and their
officials saw him, they shouted, "Crucify!
Crucify!"
But Pilate answered, "You take him and
crucify him.[h] As for me, I find no basis for
a charge against him."[i]
7 The Jewish leaders insisted, "We have
a law, and according to that law he must
die,[j] because he claimed to be the Son of
God."[k]
8 When Pilate heard this, he was even
more afraid, 9 and he went back inside the
palace.[l] "Where do you come from?" he
asked Jesus, but Jesus gave him no answer.[m] 10 "Do you refuse to speak to me?"

18:32 [r] Mt 20:19; 26:2; Jn 3:14; 8:28; 12:32,33
18:33 [s] ver 28, 29; Jn 19:9 [t] Lk 23:3; S Mt 2:2
18:36 [u] S Mt 3:2 [v] Mt 26:53 [w] Lk 17:21; Jn 6:15
18:37 [x] Jn 3:32 [y] Jn 8:47; 1Jn 4:6
18:38 [z] S Lk 23:4
18:40 [a] Ac 3:14
19:1 [b] Dt 25:3; Isa 50:6; 53:5; Mt 27:26
19:3 [c] Mt 27:29 [d] Jn 18:22
19:4 [e] Jn 18:38 [f] ver 6; S Lk 23:4
19:5 [g] ver 2
19:6 [h] Ac 3:13 [i] ver 4; S Lk 23:4
19:7 [j] Lev 24:16 [k] Mt 26:63-66; Jn 5:18; 10:33
19:9 [l] Jn 18:33 [m] S Mk 14:61

showed himself tolerant of Jewish ways. *What charges . . . ?* A normal question at the beginning of a trial, but it was difficult to answer, because the Jews had no charge that would stand up in a Roman court of law.

18:31 *Take him yourselves.* In other words, no Roman charge, no Roman trial. *no right to execute anyone.* They were looking for an execution, not a fair trial. The restriction was important, for otherwise Rome's supporters could be quietly removed by local legal executions. Sometimes the Romans seem to have tolerated local executions (e.g., of Stephen, Ac 7), but normally they retained the right to inflict the death penalty.

18:32 *the kind of death he was going to die.* Cf. 12:32–33 and "must" in 12:34. Jewish execution was by stoning, but Jesus' death was to be by crucifixion, whereby he would bear the curse (see Dt 21:22–23 and notes). The Romans, not the Jews, had to put Jesus to death. God was overruling in the whole process.

18:33 *Are you the king of the Jews?* Pilate's first words to Jesus, identical in all four Gospels.

18:34 *Is that your own idea . . . ?* If so, Pilate's question (v. 33) had meant, "Are you a rebel?" If the question had originated with the Jews, it meant, "Are you the Messianic King?"

18:36 *My kingdom.* Jesus agrees that he has a kingdom but asserts that it is not the kind of kingdom that has soldiers to fight for it. It was not built, nor is it maintained, by military might.

18:37 *to testify to the truth.* Two of this Gospel's important ideas (see 1:7; 1:14; 14:6 and notes).

18:38 *What is truth?* Pilate may have been jesting and meant "What does truth matter?" Or he may have been serious and meant "It is not easy to find truth. What is it?" Either way, it was clear to him that Jesus was no rebel. *I find no basis for a charge against him.* Repeated in 19:4,6 (see note on 19:6). Teaching the truth was not a criminal offense.

18:39 *your custom.* Prisoners are known to have been released on special occasions in other places. *king of the Jews.* John keeps his emphasis on the note of royalty. Pilate may have hoped that the use of the title would influence the people toward the way he wanted them to decide.

18:40 *Barabbas.* A rebel and a murderer (see Lk 23:19 and note on 23:18). The name is Aramaic and means "son of Abba," i.e., "son of the father"; in place of this man, the "Son of the Father" died (see note on Mt 27:16).

19:1 Pilate hoped a flogging would satisfy the Jews and enable him to release Jesus (see note on Mk 15:15).

19:2 *thorns.* A general term relating to any thorny plant (see note on Mk 15:17). *purple.* A color used by royalty.

19:6 *You . . . crucify him.* The petulant utterance of an exasperated man, for the Jews could not carry out this form of execution. *I find no basis for a charge against him.* For the third time Pilate proclaimed Jesus' innocence (see 18:38 and note; 19:4). Luke also records this threefold proclamation (Lk 23:4,14,22).

19:7 *he must die.* Apparently referring to the penalty for blasphemy (Lev 24:16).

19:8 *even more afraid.* Pilate was evidently superstitious, and this charge frightened him.

19:9 *Jesus gave him no answer.* The reason is not clear since Jesus had answered other questions readily. Perhaps Pilate would not have understood the answer or would not have believed it.

Pilate said. "Don't you realize I have power either to free you or to crucify you?"

11 Jesus answered, "You would have no power over me if it were not given to you from above.[n] Therefore the one who handed me over to you[o] is guilty of a greater sin."

12 From then on, Pilate tried to set Jesus free, but the Jewish leaders kept shouting, "If you let this man go, you are no friend of Caesar. Anyone who claims to be a king[p] opposes Caesar."

13 When Pilate heard this, he brought Jesus out and sat down on the judge's seat[q] at a place known as the Stone Pavement (which in Aramaic[r] is Gabbatha). 14 It was the day of Preparation[s] of the Passover; it was about noon.[t]

"Here is your king,"[u] Pilate said to the Jews.

15 But they shouted, "Take him away! Take him away! Crucify him!"

"Shall I crucify your king?" Pilate asked.

"We have no king but Caesar," the chief priests answered.

16 Finally Pilate handed him over to them to be crucified.[v]

The Crucifixion of Jesus

19:17-24pp — Mt 27:33-44; Mk 15:22-32; Lk 23:33-43

So the soldiers took charge of Jesus. 17 Carrying his own cross,[w] he went out to the place of the Skull[x] (which in Aramaic[y] is called Golgotha). 18 There they crucified him, and with him two others[z] — one on each side and Jesus in the middle.

19 Pilate had a notice prepared and fastened to the cross. It read: JESUS OF NAZARETH,[a] THE KING OF THE JEWS.[b] 20 Many of the Jews read this sign, for the place where Jesus was crucified was near the city,[c] and the sign was written in Aramaic, Latin and Greek. 21 The chief priests of the Jews protested to Pilate, "Do not write 'The King of the Jews,' but that this man claimed to be king of the Jews."[d]

22 Pilate answered, "What I have written, I have written."

23 When the soldiers crucified Jesus, they took his clothes, dividing them into four shares, one for each of them, with the undergarment remaining. This garment was seamless, woven in one piece from top to bottom.

24 "Let's not tear it," they said to one another. "Let's decide by lot who will get it."

This happened that the scripture might be fulfilled[e] that said,

> "They divided my clothes among them
> and cast lots for my garment."[a][f]

So this is what the soldiers did.

19:11 [n] S Ro 13:1 [o] Jn 18:28-30; Ac 3:13 **19:12** [p] Lk 23:2 **19:13** [q] Mt 27:19 [r] S Jn 5:2 **19:14** [s] Mt 27:62 [t] Mk 15:25 [u] ver 19, 21 **19:16** [v] Mt 27:26; Mk 15:15; Lk 23:25 **19:17** [w] Ge 22:6; Lk 14:27; 23:26

[x] Lk 23:33 [y] S Jn 5:2 **19:18** [z] Lk 23:32 **19:19** [a] S Mk 1:24 [b] ver 14, 21 **19:20** [c] Heb 13:12 **19:21** [d] ver 14 **19:24** [e] ver 28, 36, 37; S Mt 1:22 [f] Ps 22:18

[a] *24* Psalm 22:18

19:10 *I have power.* Pilate was incredulous and very conscious of his authority. His second question indicates his personal responsibility for crucifying Jesus.
19:11 Jesus' last words to Pilate. *from above.* All earthly authority comes ultimately from God (cf. Ro 13:14 and note). *greater sin.* That of Caiaphas (not Judas, who was only a means). But "greater" implies that there was a lesser sin, so Pilate's sin was also real.
19:12 *no friend of Caesar.* Some people had official status as "Friends of Caesar," but the term seems to be used here in the general sense. There was an implied threat that if he released Jesus, Pilate would be accused before Caesar. His record was such that he could not face such a prospect without concern.
19:13 *the Stone Pavement.* Not a translation of *Gabbatha,* which seems to mean "the hill of the house," but a different name for the same place.
19:14 *day of Preparation.* Probably does not mean preparation for the Passover celebration, which has already taken place (see note on 18:28), but rather preparation for the Sabbath of Passover week. Normally Friday was the day people prepared for the Sabbath. *about noon.* Lit. "about the sixth hour." Mk 15:25 says that Jesus was crucified at "nine in the morning" (lit. "the third hour"). It is possible that Mark's Gospel contains a copyist's error, for the Greek numerals for three and six could be confused. Or it may be that John was using Roman time, in which case the appearance before Pilate would have been at 6:00 a.m. and the crucifixion at 9:00 a.m. (the third hour according to Jewish reckoning; see Mk 15:33). For other time references, see Mt 27:45–46; Mk 15:33–34; Lk 23:44 and note. *Here is your king.* John does not let us forget the sovereignty of Jesus. Pilate did not mean the expression seriously, but the author of this Gospel did. *the Jews.* See note on 1:19.
19:15 *We have no king but Caesar.* More irony. They rejected any suggestion that they were rebels against Rome but expressed the truth of their spiritual condition.
19:17 *Carrying his own cross.* A cross might be shaped like a *T,* an *X,* a *Y* or an *I,* as well as in the traditional form. A condemned man would normally carry a beam of it to the place of execution. Somewhere along the way Simon of Cyrene took Jesus' cross (see Mk 15:21 and note), probably because Jesus was weakened by the flogging. *Golgotha.* "Calvary" comes from a Latin word that has the same meaning (see Mk 15:22 and note).
19:18 *they crucified him.* See note on Mk 15:24. As with the scourging, John describes this horror with one Greek word. None of the Gospel writers dwells on the physical sufferings of Jesus. *one on each side.* Perhaps meant as a final insult, but it brings out the important truth that in his death Jesus was identified with sinners (see note on Mk 15:27).
19:19 *a notice.* A placard stating the crime for which someone was executed was often fastened to his cross. *THE KING OF THE JEWS.* Again the royalty theme.
19:20 *Aramaic.* One of the languages of the Jewish people at that time (along with Hebrew). *Latin.* The official language of Rome. *Greek.* The common language of communication throughout the empire. The threefold inscription may account for the slight differences in wording in the four Gospels.
19:22 Pilate had to have a sufficient reason for the execution, and he was not above mocking the Jews, but for John his insistence may also have served to underscore that Jesus' kingship is final and unalterable.
19:23 *undergarment.* A type of shirt, reaching from the neck to the knees or ankles. *seamless.* Therefore too valuable to be cut up.
19:24 See introduction to Ps 22 and notes on Ps 22:17,20–21.

25 Near the cross[g] of Jesus stood his
mother,[h] his mother's sister, Mary the wife
of Clopas, and Mary Magdalene.[i] 26 When
Jesus saw his mother[j] there, and the disciple whom he loved[k] standing nearby, he
said to her, "Woman,[a] here is your son,"
27 and to the disciple, "Here is your mother." From that time on, this disciple took
her into his home.

The Death of Jesus

19:29,30pp — Mt 27:48,50; Mk 15:36,37; Lk 23:36

28 Later, knowing that everything had
now been finished,[l] and so that Scripture would be fulfilled,[m] Jesus said, "I
am thirsty." 29 A jar of wine vinegar[n] was
there, so they soaked a sponge in it, put
the sponge on a stalk of the hyssop plant,
and lifted it to Jesus' lips. 30 When he had
received the drink, Jesus said, "It is finished."[o] With that, he bowed his head and
gave up his spirit.
31 Now it was the day of Preparation,[p]
and the next day was to be a special Sabbath. Because the Jewish leaders did not
want the bodies left on the crosses[q] during
the Sabbath, they asked Pilate to have the
legs broken and the bodies taken down.
32 The soldiers therefore came and broke
the legs of the first man who had been
crucified with Jesus, and then those of the
other.[r] 33 But when they came to Jesus and
found that he was already dead, they did
not break his legs. 34 Instead, one of the
soldiers pierced[s] Jesus' side with a spear,
bringing a sudden flow of blood and water.[t] 35 The man who saw it[u] has given
testimony, and his testimony is true.[v] He
knows that he tells the truth, and he testifies so that you also may believe. 36 These
things happened so that the scripture
would be fulfilled:[w] "Not one of his bones
will be broken,"[b][x] 37 and, as another scripture says, "They will look on the one they
have pierced."[c][y]

The Burial of Jesus

19:38-42pp — Mt 27:57-61; Mk 15:42-47; Lk 23:50-56

38 Later, Joseph of Arimathea asked Pilate for the body of Jesus. Now Joseph
was a disciple of Jesus, but secretly because he feared the Jewish leaders.[z] With
Pilate's permission, he came and took the
body away. 39 He was accompanied by Nicodemus,[a] the man who earlier had visited
Jesus at night. Nicodemus brought a mixture of myrrh and aloes, about seventy-
five pounds.[d] 40 Taking Jesus' body, the
two of them wrapped it, with the spices,
in strips of linen.[b] This was in accordance
with Jewish burial customs.[c] 41 At the place
where Jesus was crucified, there was a
garden, and in the garden a new tomb, in
which no one had ever been laid. 42 Because it was the Jewish day of Preparation[d] and since the tomb was nearby,[e] they
laid Jesus there.

[a] *26* The Greek for *Woman* does not denote any disrespect. [b] *36* Exodus 12:46; Num. 9:12; Psalm 34:20 [c] *37* Zech. 12:10 [d] *39* Or about 34 kilograms

19:25 [g] Mt 27:55,56 [h] S Mt 12:46 [i] Lk 24:18 **19:26** [j] S Mt 12:46 [k] S Jn 13:23 **19:28** [l] S ver 30; Jn 13:1 [m] ver 24,36,37; S Mt 1:22 **19:29** [n] Ps 69:21 **19:30** [o] Lk 12:50; Jn 4:34; 17:4 **19:31** [p] ver 14, 42 [q] Dt 21:23; Jos 8:29; 10:26, 27 **19:32** [r] ver 18 **19:34** [s] Zec 12:10; Rev 1:7 [t] 1Jn 5:6,8 **19:35** [u] S Lk 24:48 [v] Jn 15:27; 21:24 **19:36** [w] ver 24,28, 37; S Mt 1:22 [x] Ex 12:46; Nu 9:12; Ps 34:20 **19:37** [y] Zec 12:10; Rev 1:7 **19:38** [z] S Jn 7:13 **19:39** [a] Jn 3:1; 7:50 **19:40** [b] Lk 24:12; Jn 11:44; 20:5,7 [c] Mt 26:12 **19:42** [d] ver 14, 31 [e] ver 20,41

19:25 *Clopas.* Mentioned only here in the NT. *Mary Magdalene.* Appears in the crucifixion and resurrection story in all four Gospels, but apart from that we read of her only in Lk 8:2–3 (see note on 8:2).
19:26 *disciple whom he loved.* John (see note on 13:23). *Woman.* See NIV text note.
19:27 *took her into his home.* And so took responsibility for her. It may be that Jesus' brothers still did not believe in him (see 7:5).
19:28 *I am thirsty.* May refer to Ps 69:21 (see note there; cf. Ps 22:15).
19:29 *wine vinegar.* Equivalent to cheap wine, the drink of ordinary people (see notes on Mk 15:36; Lk 23:36). *hyssop.* The name given to a number of plants (see note on Ex 12:22).
19:30 *It is finished.* Apparently the loud cry of Mt 27:50; Mk 15:37. Jesus died as a victor and had "finished" (v. 28) what he came to do (cf. 17:4). *gave up his spirit.* An unusual way of describing death, perhaps suggesting an act of will (cf. 10:17–18 and note).
19:31 *Preparation.* See note on v. 14. *a special Sabbath.* The Sabbath that fell at Passover time. The Passover meal had been eaten on Thursday evening, the day of Preparation was Friday and the Sabbath came on Saturday. *the Jewish leaders.* See note on 1:19. *to have the legs broken.* To hasten death, because the victim then could not put any weight on his legs, and breathing would be difficult.
19:34 *pierced Jesus' side.* Probably to make doubly sure that Jesus was dead, but perhaps simply an act of brutality (see v. 37; Isa 53:5; Zec 12:10; cf. Ps 22:16). *blood and water.* The result of the spear piercing the pericardium (the sac that surrounds the heart) and the heart itself.
19:35 *The man who saw it.* Either John himself or someone he regarded as reliable. Obviously he considered the incident important and comments that it was well attested. *testifies ... believe.* See note on 1:7.
19:36–37 *scripture.* Again John observes God's overruling in the fulfillment of Scripture. It was extraordinary that Jesus was the only one of the three whose legs were not broken and that he suffered an unusual spear thrust that did not break a bone.
19:38 See note on Lk 23:52. *Joseph.* A rich disciple (Mt 27:57), and a member of the Sanhedrin who had not agreed to Jesus' condemnation (Lk 23:51; see note on 23:50). *Arimathea.* See note on Mt 27:57. *secretly.* It would have been hard for a member of the Sanhedrin to support Jesus' cause openly. Jesus' closest followers all ran away (see Mk 14:50 and note), and it was left to Joseph and Nicodemus to provide for his burial. *With Pilate's permission.* Otherwise people could take away their crucified friends before they died and revive them.
19:39 *Nicodemus.* John alone tells us that he joined Joseph in the burial. *seventy-five pounds.* A very large amount, such as was used in royal burials (cf. 2Ch 16:14).
19:40 *strips of linen.* Thin strips like bandages. There was also a shroud, a large sheet (Mt 27:59; Mk 15:46; Lk 23:53).
19:41 *new tomb.* Joseph's own tomb (Mt 27:60).
19:42 *Preparation.* See note on v. 14. *nearby.* Haste was necessary, since it was near sunset, when the Sabbath would start and no work could be done.

The Empty Tomb

20:1-8pp — Mt 28:1-8; Mk 16:1-8; Lk 24:1-10

20 Early on the first day of the week, while it was still dark, Mary Magdalene[f] went to the tomb and saw that the stone had been removed from the entrance.[g] 2 So she came running to Simon Peter and the other disciple, the one Jesus loved,[h] and said, "They have taken the Lord out of the tomb, and we don't know where they have put him!"[i]

3 So Peter and the other disciple started for the tomb.[j] 4 Both were running, but the other disciple outran Peter and reached the tomb first. 5 He bent over and looked in[k] at the strips of linen[l] lying there but did not go in. 6 Then Simon Peter came along behind him and went straight into the tomb. He saw the strips of linen lying there, 7 as well as the cloth that had been wrapped around Jesus' head.[m] The cloth was still lying in its place, separate from the linen. 8 Finally the other disciple, who had reached the tomb first,[n] also went inside. He saw and believed. 9 (They still did not understand from Scripture[o] that Jesus had to rise from the dead.)[p] 10 Then the disciples went back to where they were staying.

Jesus Appears to Mary Magdalene

11 Now Mary stood outside the tomb crying. As she wept, she bent over to look into the tomb[q] 12 and saw two angels in white,[r] seated where Jesus' body had been, one at the head and the other at the foot.

13 They asked her, "Woman, why are you crying?"[s]

"They have taken my Lord away," she said, "and I don't know where they have put him."[t] 14 At this, she turned around and saw Jesus standing there,[u] but she did not realize that it was Jesus.[v]

15 He asked her, "Woman, why are you crying?[w] Who is it you are looking for?"

Thinking he was the gardener, she said, "Sir, if you have carried him away, tell me where you have put him, and I will get him."

16 Jesus said to her, "Mary."

She turned toward him and cried out in Aramaic,[x] "Rabboni!"[y] (which means "Teacher").

17 Jesus said, "Do not hold on to me, for I have not yet ascended to the Father. Go instead to my brothers[z] and tell them, 'I am ascending to my Father[a] and your Father, to my God and your God.' "

18 Mary Magdalene[b] went to the disciples[c] with the news: "I have seen the Lord!" And she told them that he had said these things to her.

Jesus Appears to His Disciples

19 On the evening of that first day of the week, when the disciples were together, with the doors locked for fear of the Jewish leaders,[d] Jesus came and stood among

20:1 [f] ver 18; Lk 8:2; Jn 19:25 [g] Mt 27:60,66
20:2 [h] S Jn 13:23 [i] ver 13
20:3 [j] Lk 24:12
20:5 [k] ver 11 [l] S Jn 19:40
20:7 [m] Jn 11:44
20:8 [n] ver 4
20:9 [o] Mt 22:29; Jn 2:22 [p] Lk 24:26,46; Ac 2:24
20:11 [q] ver 5
20:12 [r] Mt 28:2, 3; Mk 16:5; Lk 24:4; Ac 1:10; S 5:19; 10:30
20:13 [s] ver 15 [t] ver 2
20:14 [u] Mk 16:9 [v] Lk 24:16; Jn 21:4
20:15 [w] ver 13
20:16 [x] S Jn 5:2 [y] S Mt 23:7
20:17 [z] S Mt 28:10 [a] Jn 7:33
20:18 [b] S ver 1 [c] Lk 24:10,22,23
20:19 [d] S Jn 7:13

20:1 *while it was still dark.* Mark says it was "just after sunrise" (Mk 16:2). Perhaps the women came in groups, with Mary Magdalene coming very early. Or John may refer to the time of leaving home, Mark to that of arrival at the tomb. *Mary Magdalene.* See note on 19:25; cf. Mk 16:9.
20:2 *Simon Peter.* Despite his denials, he was still the leading figure among the disciples. *the one Jesus loved.* John (see note on 13:23). *we.* Indicates that there were others with Mary (see Mt 28:1; Mk 16:1; Lk 24:10), though John does not identify them. *have put him.* Mary had no thought of resurrection.
20:7 *still lying in its place.* An orderly arrangement, not in disarray, as would have resulted from a grave robbery.
20:8 *He saw and believed.* Cf. v. 29. John did not say what he believed, but it must have been that Jesus was resurrected.
20:9 *Scripture.* First they came to know of the resurrection through what they saw in the tomb; only later did they see it in Scripture. It is obvious they did not make up a story of resurrection to fit a preconceived understanding of Scriptural prophecy. *had to rise.* It was in Scripture and thus the will of God.
20:11 *Mary.* Perhaps Jesus appeared first to Mary because she needed him most at that time. *crying.* As in 11:33 (see note there), it means "wailing," a loud expression of grief.
20:12 *two angels.* Matthew has one angel (Mt 28:2), Mark a young man (Mk 16:5) and Luke two men who were angels (Lk 24:4,23). See note on Lk 24:4.
20:13 *Woman.* See NIV text note on 2:4.
20:14 *did not realize that it was Jesus.* A number of times the risen Jesus was not recognized (21:4; Mt 28:17; Lk 24:16,37). He may have looked different, or he may intentionally have prevented recognition (see note on Lk 24:16).
20:16 *Mary.* Cf. 10:3–4. *Rabboni.* A strengthened form of *Rabbi,* and in the NT found elsewhere only in Mk 10:51 (in the Greek). Although the word means "(my) teacher," there are few if any examples of its use in ancient Judaism as a form of address other than in calling on God in prayer. However, John's explanation casts doubt on any thought that Mary intended to address Jesus as God here.
20:17 *I have not yet ascended.* See 13:3. The meaning appears to be that the ascension was still some time off. Mary would have opportunity to see Jesus again, so she need not cling to him. Alternatively, Jesus may be reminding Mary that after his crucifixion she cannot have him with her except through the Holy Spirit (see 16:5–16). *my brothers.* Probably the disciples (see v. 18; Mk 3:35 and note). The members of his family did not believe in him (see 7:5 and note on 7:4), though they became disciples not long after this (see Ac 1:14 and note). *my Father and your Father.* God is Father both of Christ and of believers, but in different senses (see 1:12,14,18,34; 3:16 and note).
20:18 *have seen the Lord.* Although Mary was the first to see the risen Lord, others would soon follow (see vv. 20,25,29; see also chart, p. 1754).
20:19 See Lk 24:36 and note. *disciples.* Probably includes others besides the apostles, "the Twelve" (v. 24). *the Jewish leaders.* See note on 1:19. *Peace be with you!* The normal Hebrew greeting (cf. Da 10:19). Because of their behavior the previous Friday, they may have expected rebuke and censure; but Jesus calmed their fears (see note on 14:27).

them and said, "Peace[e] be with you!"[f]
20 After he said this, he showed them his
hands and side.[g] The disciples were overjoyed[h] when they saw the Lord.
21 Again Jesus said, "Peace be with you![i]
As the Father has sent me,[j] I am sending
you."[k] 22 And with that he breathed on
them and said, "Receive the Holy Spirit.[l]
23 If you forgive anyone's sins, their sins
are forgiven; if you do not forgive them,
they are not forgiven."[m]

Jesus Appears to Thomas

24 Now Thomas[n] (also known as Didymus[a]), one of the Twelve, was not with
the disciples when Jesus came. 25 So the
other disciples told him, "We have seen
the Lord!"

But he said to them, "Unless I see the
nail marks in his hands and put my finger
where the nails were, and put my hand
into his side,[o] I will not believe."[p]

26 A week later his disciples were in the
house again, and Thomas was with them.
Though the doors were locked, Jesus came
and stood among them and said, "Peace[q]
be with you!"[r] 27 Then he said to Thomas, "Put your finger here; see my hands.
Reach out your hand and put it into my
side. Stop doubting and believe."[s]
28 Thomas said to him, "My Lord and
my God!"
29 Then Jesus told him, "Because you
have seen me, you have believed;[t] blessed
are those who have not seen and yet have
believed."[u]

20:19 [e] S Jn 14:27 [f] ver 21,26; Lk 24:36-39 **20:20** [g] Lk 24:39,40; Jn 19:34 [h] Jn 16:20,22 **20:21** [i] ver 19 [j] S Jn 3:17 [k] Mt 28:19; Jn 17:18 **20:22** [l] Jn 7:39; Ac 2:38; 8:15-17; 19:2; Gal 3:2 **20:23** [m] Mt 16:19; 18:18 **20:24** [n] S Jn 11:16 **20:25** [o] ver 20 [p] Mk 16:11 **20:26** [q] S Jn 14:27 [r] ver 21 **20:27** [s] ver 25; Lk 24:40 **20:29** [t] S Jn 3:15 [u] 1Pe 1:8

20:30 [v] S Jn 2:11 [w] Jn 21:25 **20:31** [x] S Jn 3:15; 19:35 [y] S Mt 4:3 [z] S Mt 25:46 **21:1** [a] ver 14; Jn 20:19,26 [b] Jn 6:1 **21:2** [c] S Jn 11:16 [d] Jn 1:45 [e] Jn 2:1 [f] S Mt 4:21 **21:3** [g] Lk 5:5 **21:4** [h] Lk 24:16; Jn 20:14 **21:6** [i] Lk 5:4-7 **21:7** [j] S Jn 13:23

The Purpose of John's Gospel

30 Jesus performed many other signs[v] in
the presence of his disciples, which are
not recorded in this book.[w] 31 But these are
written that you may believe[b][x] that Jesus is
the Messiah, the Son of God,[y] and that by
believing you may have life in his name.[z]

Jesus and the Miraculous Catch of Fish

21 Afterward Jesus appeared again to
his disciples,[a] by the Sea of Galilee.[c][b] It happened this way: 2 Simon Peter,
Thomas[c] (also known as Didymus[a]), Nathanael[d] from Cana in Galilee,[e] the sons of
Zebedee,[f] and two other disciples were together. 3 "I'm going out to fish," Simon Peter told them, and they said, "We'll go with
you." So they went out and got into the
boat, but that night they caught nothing.[g]
4 Early in the morning, Jesus stood on
the shore, but the disciples did not realize
that it was Jesus.[h]
5 He called out to them, "Friends,
haven't you any fish?"

"No," they answered.
6 He said, "Throw your net on the right
side of the boat and you will find some."
When they did, they were unable to haul the
net in because of the large number of fish.[i]
7 Then the disciple whom Jesus loved[j]
said to Peter, "It is the Lord!" As soon as
Simon Peter heard him say, "It is the Lord,"
he wrapped his outer garment around him

[a] 24 *Thomas* (Aramaic) and *Didymus* (Greek) both mean *twin*. [b] 31 Or *may continue to believe* [c] 1 Greek *Tiberias*

20:20 *his hands and side.* Where the wounds were (John does not refer to the wounds in the feet). According to Lk 24:37 they thought they were seeing a ghost. Jesus was clearly identifying himself.
20:21 *Peace be with you!* See note on v. 19. *I am sending you.* See note on 17:18.
20:22 *Receive the Holy Spirit.* Thus anticipating what happened 50 days later on the day of Pentecost (see Ac 2:2,4,14,17,33,38 and notes). The disciples needed God's help to carry out the commission they had just been given.
20:23 Lit. "If you forgive anyone their sins, they have (already) been forgiven; if you do not forgive, they have not been forgiven." The intent of this word of Jesus has been much debated, but it seems right to say that God does not forgive people's sins because the apostles (or we) do so, nor does he withhold forgiveness because the apostles (or we) do. However, through the Holy Spirit (v. 22) the apostles and all believers do participate in Christ's saving mission, which has as one of its crucial effects God's forgiveness of the sins of all who repent and believe in Jesus as God's Son and the Savior of the world (cf. Mt 16:19 and note; 18:18 and NIV text note).
20:24 *Thomas.* See note on 11:16.
20:25 *Unless I see … and put … I will not believe.* Hard-headed skepticism can scarcely go further than this.
20:26 *Peace.* See vv. 19,21 and note on 14:27.
20:28 *My Lord and my God!* To acknowledge Jesus as Lord and God is the high point of faith (see note on 1:1).
20:29 *those who have not seen and yet have believed.* Would have been very few at this time (see v. 8 and note). All whom John mentions had seen in some sense. The words, of course, apply to future believers as well.
20:30 *signs.* See note on 2:11. John had selected from among many. *in the presence of his disciples.* Those who could testify to what he had done. John again stresses testimony (see note on 1:7).
20:31 *that you may believe.* Expresses John's evangelistic purpose. *believe.* See note on 1:7. *Jesus is the Messiah, the Son of God.* Faith has content. *the Messiah.* See note on 1:25. This whole Gospel is written to show the truth of Jesus' Messiahship and to present him as the Son of God, so that the readers may believe in him. *Son of God.* See 3:16 and note. *that by believing you may have life.* Another expression of purpose—to bring about faith that leads to life (see notes on 1:4; 3:15–16). *name.* Represents all that he is and stands for (see note on 2:23).
21:1 *Galilee.* Lit. "Tiberias" (see NIV text note; see also note on 6:1).
21:2 *Simon Peter.* See note on Mk 1:16. *Thomas.* See note on 11:16. *sons of Zebedee.* James and John, not named in this Gospel (see Mt 4:21).
21:3 *that night.* Nighttime was favored by fishermen in ancient times (as Aristotle, e.g., informs us).
21:4 *did not realize that it was Jesus.* Cf. Mary Magdalene (see note on 20:14).
21:7 *disciple whom Jesus loved.* See note on 13:23. *his outer garment.* It is curious that he put on this garment (the word appears only here in the NT) preparatory to jumping into the

(for he had taken it off) and jumped into
the water. 8 The other disciples followed in
the boat, towing the net full of fish, for
they were not far from shore, about a hundred yards.[a] 9 When they landed, they saw
a fire[k] of burning coals there with fish on
it,[l] and some bread.

10 Jesus said to them, "Bring some of
the fish you have just caught." 11 So Simon Peter climbed back into the boat and
dragged the net ashore. It was full of large
fish, 153, but even with so many the net
was not torn. 12 Jesus said to them, "Come
and have breakfast." None of the disciples dared ask him, "Who are you?" They
knew it was the Lord. 13 Jesus came, took
the bread and gave it to them, and did the
same with the fish.[m] 14 This was now the
third time Jesus appeared to his disciples[n]
after he was raised from the dead.

Jesus Reinstates Peter

15 When they had finished eating, Jesus
said to Simon Peter, "Simon son of John,
do you love me more than these?"

"Yes, Lord," he said, "you know that I
love you."[o]

Jesus said, "Feed my lambs."[p]

16 Again Jesus said, "Simon son of John,
do you love me?"

He answered, "Yes, Lord, you know that
I love you."

Jesus said, "Take care of my sheep."[q]

17 The third time he said to him, "Simon
son of John, do you love me?"

Peter was hurt because Jesus asked him
the third time, "Do you love me?"[r] He said,
"Lord, you know all things;[s] you know
that I love you."

Jesus said, "Feed my sheep.[t] 18 Very truly I tell you, when you were younger you
dressed yourself and went where you wanted; but when you are old you will stretch
out your hands, and someone else will
dress you and lead you where you do not
want to go." 19 Jesus said this to indicate the
kind of death[u] by which Peter would glorify
God.[v] Then he said to him, "Follow me!"[w]

20 Peter turned and saw that the disciple
whom Jesus loved[x] was following them.
(This was the one who had leaned back
against Jesus at the supper and had said,
"Lord, who is going to betray you?")[y]
21 When Peter saw him, he asked, "Lord,
what about him?"

22 Jesus answered, "If I want him to remain alive until I return,[z] what is that to
you? You must follow me."[a] 23 Because of
this, the rumor spread among the believers[b] that this disciple would not die. But
Jesus did not say that he would not die; he
only said, "If I want him to remain alive
until I return, what is that to you?"

24 This is the disciple who testifies to
these things[c] and who wrote them down.
We know that his testimony is true.[d]

25 Jesus did many other things as well.[e]
If every one of them were written down, I
suppose that even the whole world would
not have room for the books that would
be written.

21:9 [k] Jn 18:18 [l] ver 10,13 **21:13** [m] ver 9 **21:14** [n] Jn 20:19,26 **21:15** [o] Mt 26:33,35; Jn 13:37 [p] Lk 12:32 **21:16** [q] 2Sa 5:2; Eze 34:2; Mt 2:6; S Jn 10:11; Ac 20:28; 1Pe 5:2,3 **21:17** [r] Jn 13:38 [s] Jn 16:30 [t] S ver 16 **21:19** [u] Jn 12:33; 18:32 [v] Jn 13:36; 2Pe 1:14 [w] S Mt 4:19 **21:20** [x] ver 7; S Jn 13:23 [y] Jn 13:25 **21:22** [z] S Mt 16:27 [a] ver 19; S Mt 4:19 **21:23** [b] S Ac 1:16 **21:24** [c] S Jn 15:27 [d] Jn 19:35 **21:25** [e] Jn 20:30

[a] *8* Or about 90 meters

water. But Jews regarded a greeting as a religious act that could be done only when one was clothed. Peter may have been preparing himself to greet the Lord.

21:9 *burning coals.* Lit. "charcoal," as in 18:18 ("fire"; see note on 18:26). Thus the charcoal "fire" is present at both Peter's denials and his restoration.

21:11 *Peter … dragged the net ashore.* Appears to mean that Peter headed up the effort, for the whole group had not been able previously to haul the net into the boat (v. 6). *the net was not torn.* In contrast to the nets mentioned in Lk 5:6.

21:14 *third time.* The third appearance to a group of disciples (20:19–23,24–29), though there had been other appearances to individuals.

21:15–17 *love.* The Greek word for "love" in Jesus' first two questions is different from that in his third question and in all Peter's answers. It is uncertain whether a distinction in meaning is intended since John often used synonyms for stylistic reasons (e.g., "Feed my lambs" [v. 15], "Take care of my sheep" [v. 16] and "Feed my sheep" [v. 17]). Also, no distinction is made between these two words elsewhere in this Gospel. The more important point is that Peter's threefold denial of Jesus (18:16–18,25–27) is now reversed with Peter's threefold affirmation of his love for Jesus.

21:15 *more than these.* May mean "more than you love these men" or "more than these men love me" or "more than you love these things" (i.e., the fishing gear). Perhaps the second is best, for Peter had claimed a devotion above that of the others (Mt 26:33; Mk 14:29; cf. Jn 13:37). Peter did not take up the comparison, and Jesus did not explain it. *Feed my lambs.* Cf. "Take care of my sheep" (v. 16) and "Feed my sheep" (v. 17); cf. 1Pe 5:1–4 and notes.

21:17 *you know all things.* Peter's replies stress Christ's knowledge, not his own grasp of the situation.

21:18 *Very truly I tell you.* See note on Mk 3:28. *stretch out your hands.* The early church understood this as a prophecy of crucifixion.

21:19 *the kind of death.* Peter would be a martyr. Tradition indicates that he was crucified upside down.

21:20 *disciple whom Jesus loved.* See note on 13:23. *was following.* He was doing what Peter was twice told to do (vv. 19,22). *at the supper.* See 13:23–25.

21:22 *until I return.* A clear declaration of the second coming (see 14:3 and note).

21:24 *disciple who testifies.* Testimony is important throughout this Gospel (see note on 1:7). We now learn that it was the beloved disciple who was the witness behind the account. *these things.* Must refer to the whole book. *who wrote them down.* The beloved disciple was not only the witness but also the actual author. *We know.* Evidently written by contemporaries in a position to know the truth.

21:25 *many other things.* As in 20:30 (see note there) we are assured that the author has been selective. *even the whole world would not have room.* Hyperbole (for another example of this figure of speech, see Lk 14:26 and note). Our historical knowledge of Jesus is at best partial, but we have been given all we need to know.

MAJOR ARCHAEOLOGICAL FINDS RELATING TO THE NEW TESTAMENT

SITE OR ARTIFACT	LOCATION — ISRAEL	RELATING SCRIPTURE
Caiaphas ossuary	Jerusalem	Mt 26:3
Herod's temple	Jerusalem	Lk 1:9
Herod's winter palace	Jericho	Mt 2:4
The Herodium (site of Herod's tomb)	Near Bethlehem	Mt 2:19
Masada	Near western shore of Dead Sea	Cf. Lk 21:20
Early synagogue	Capernaum	Mt 4:13; Mk 1:21
Pool of Siloam	Jerusalem	Jn 9:7
Pool of Bethesda	Jerusalem	Jn 5:2
Pilate inscription	Caesarea	Lk 3:1
Inscription: Gentile entrance to temple sanctuary	Jerusalem	Ac 21:27–29
Skeletal remains of crucified man	Jerusalem	Mk 15:24
Peter's house	Capernaum	Mt 4:13; Lk 4:38
Jacob's well	Nablus	Jn 4:5–6

Heel bone of crucified man from the first century, found in an ossuary in Jerusalem in 1968

Z. Radovan/www.BibleLandPictures.com

Masada, located near the western shore of the Dead Sea. Herod the Great fortified Masada c. 37–31 BC as a refuge in the event of a revolt. The fortress became the last holdout of the Jewish zealots in the war against the Romans (AD 66–73).

© Michael Melford/National Geographic Stock

MAJOR ARCHAEOLOGICAL FINDS (CONT.)

SITE OR ARTIFACT	LOCATION — ASIA MINOR	RELATING SCRIPTURE
Derbe inscription	Kerti Hüyük	Ac 14:20
Sergius Paulus inscription	Kythraia, Cyprus	Ac 13:6–7
Zeus altar (Satan's throne?)	Pergamum	Rev 2:13
Fourth-century BC walls	Assos	Ac 20:13–14
Artemis temple and altar	Ephesus	Ac 19:27–28
Ephesian theater	Ephesus	Ac 19:29
Silversmith shops	Ephesus	Ac 19:24
Artemis statues	Ephesus	Ac 19:35

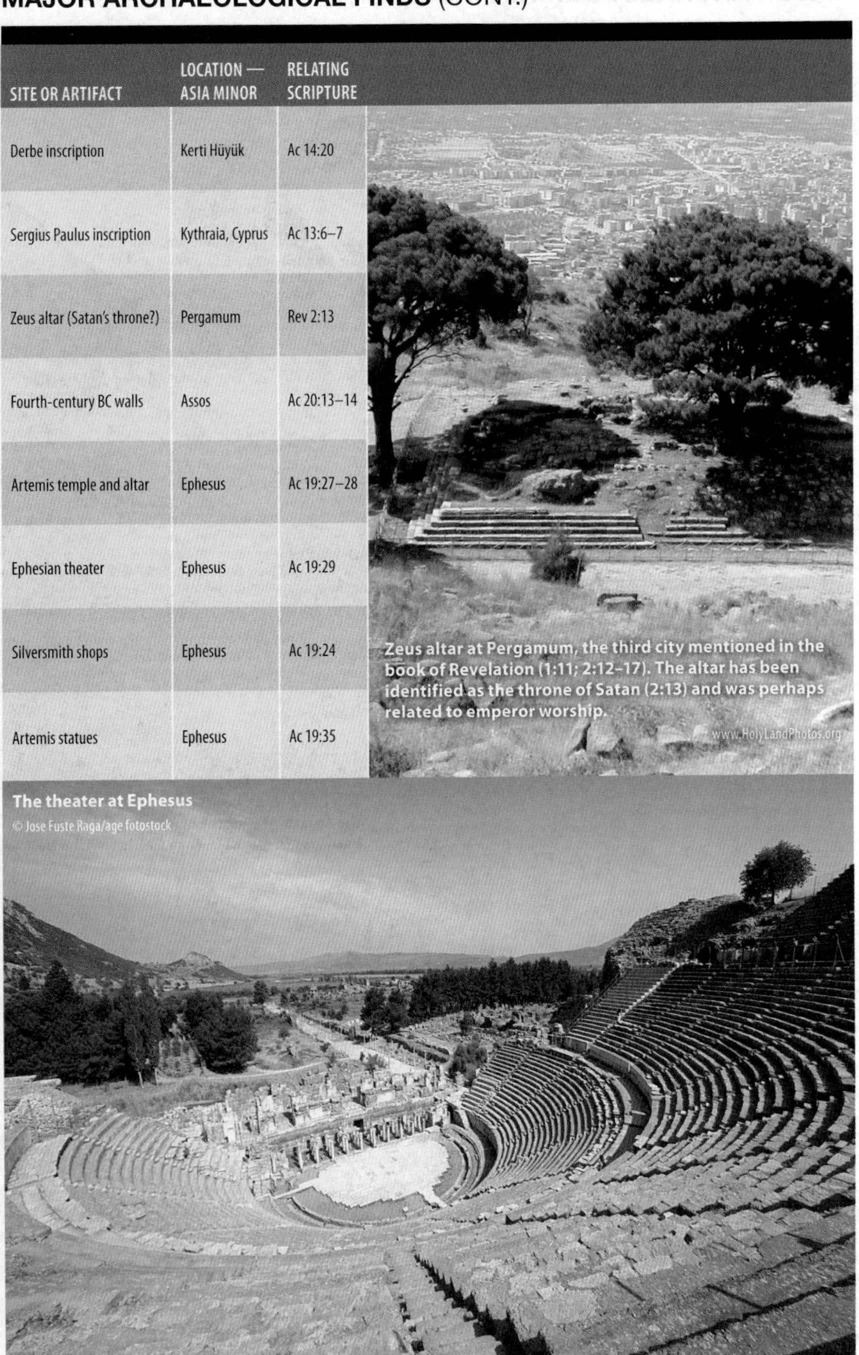

Zeus altar at Pergamum, the third city mentioned in the book of Revelation (1:11; 2:12–17). The altar has been identified as the throne of Satan (2:13) and was perhaps related to emperor worship.

www.HolyLandPhotos.org

The theater at Ephesus

© Jose Fuste Raga/age fotostock

MAJOR ARCHAEOLOGICAL FINDS (CONT.)

SITE OR ARTIFACT	LOCATION — GREECE	RELATING SCRIPTURE
Erastus inscription	Corinth	Ro 16:23
Synagogue inscription	Corinth	Ac 18:4
Meat market inscription	Corinth	1Co 10:25
Cult dining rooms (in Asclepius and Demeter temples)	Corinth	1Co 8:10; 10:14
Court (bema)	Corinth	Ac 18:12
Marketplace (bema)	Philippi	Ac 16:19
Starting gate for races	Isthmia	1Co 9:24,26
Gallio inscription	Delphi	Ac 18:12
Egnatian Way	Neapolis (Kavalla), Philippi, Amphipolis, Apollonia, Thessalonica	Cf. Ac 16:11–12; 17:1
Politarch inscription	Thessalonica	Ac 17:6

The Gallio inscription found at Delphi mentions Lucius Junius Gallio and indicates that he was the proconsul of Achaia. He is also listed as a "friend of Caesar," which dates his governorship to AD 51/52. He is the same Gallio mentioned in Acts 18:12: "While Gallio was proconsul of Achaia, the Jews of Corinth made a united attack on Paul and brought him to the place of judgment."

Todd Bolen/www.BiblePlaces.com

The Corinthian court (bema) may have been the "place of judgment" (Ac 18:12) where Paul was brought before Gallio in AD 51/52.

© 1995 Phoenix Data Systems

MAJOR ARCHAEOLOGICAL FINDS (CONT.)

SITE OR ARTIFACT	LOCATION — ITALY	RELATING SCRIPTURE
Tomb of Augustus	Rome	Lk 2:1
Mamertine Prison	Rome	2Ti 1:16–17; 2:9; 4:6–8
Appian Way	Puteoli to Rome	Ac 28:13–16
Golden House of Nero	Rome	Cf. Ac 25:10; 1Pe 2:13
Arch of Titus	Rome	Cf. Lk 19:43–44; 21:6,20

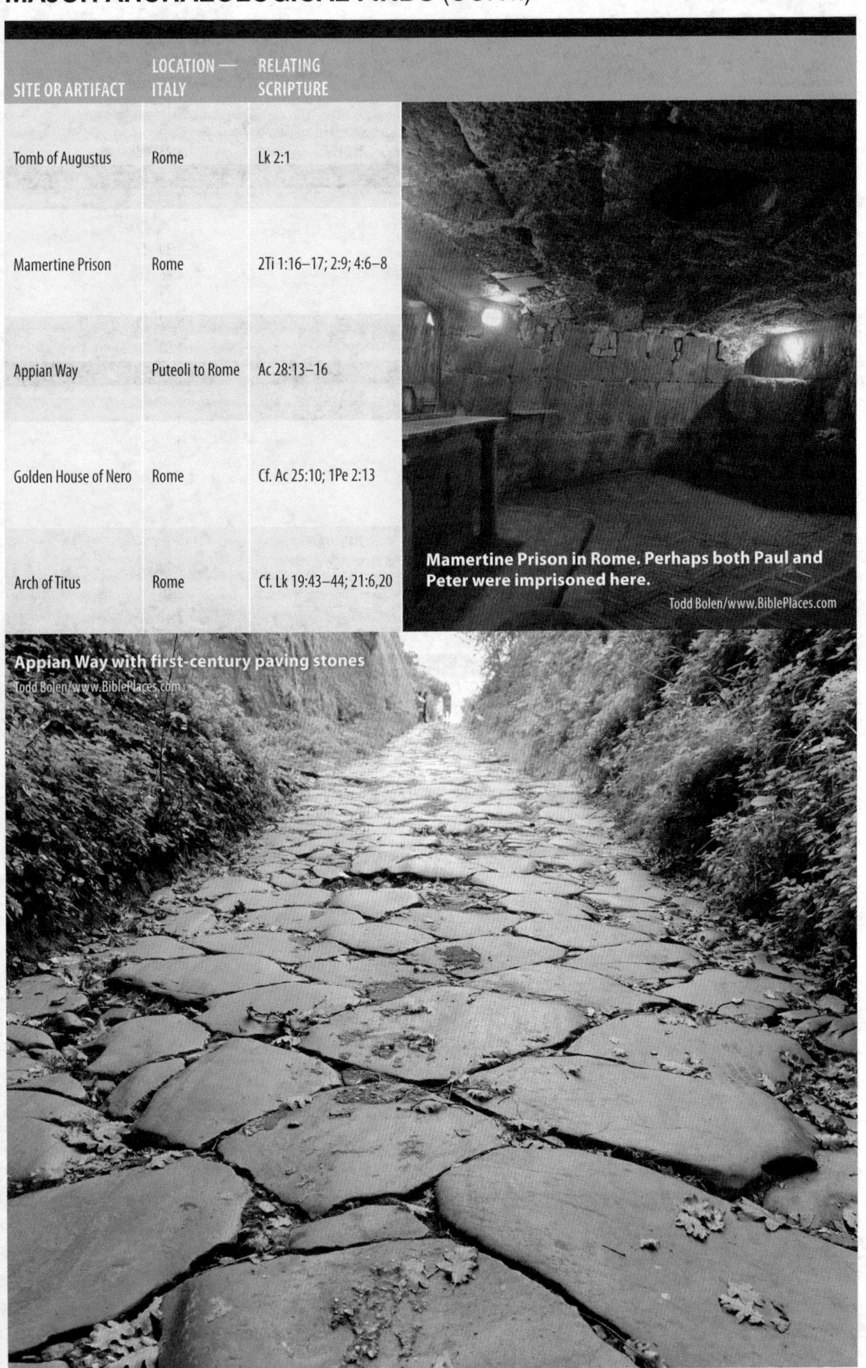

Mamertine Prison in Rome. Perhaps both Paul and Peter were imprisoned here.
Todd Bolen/www.BiblePlaces.com

Appian Way with first-century paving stones
Todd Bolen/www.BiblePlaces.com

A HARMONY OF THE GOSPELS

	MATTHEW	MARK	LUKE	JOHN
A Preview of Who Jesus Is				
Luke's purpose in writing a Gospel			1:1–4	
John's prologue: Jesus Christ, the preexistent Word incarnate				1:1–18
Genealogies of Jesus	1:1–17		3:23b–38	
The Early Years of John the Baptist				
John's birth foretold to Zechariah			1:5–25	
Jesus' birth foretold to Mary			1:26–38	
Mary's visit to Elizabeth, and Elizabeth's song			1:39–45	
Mary's song of joy			1:46–56	
John's birth			1:57–66	
Zechariah's prophetic song			1:67–79	
John's growth and early life			1:80	
The Early Years of Jesus Christ				
Circumstances of Jesus' birth explained to Joseph	1:18–25			
Birth of Jesus			2:1–7	
Praise of the angels, and witness of the shepherds			2:8–20	
Circumcision of Jesus			2:21	
Jesus presented in the temple with the homage of Simeon and Anna			2:22–38	
Visit of the Magi	2:1–12			
Escape into Egypt, and murder of boys in Bethlehem	2:13–18			
Return to Nazareth	2:19–23		2:39	
Growth and early life of Jesus			2:40	
Jesus' first Passover in Jerusalem			2:41–50	
Jesus' growth to adulthood			2:51–52	
The Public Ministry of John the Baptist				
His ministry launched		1:1	3:1–2	
His person, proclamation and baptism	3:1–6	1:2–6	3:3–6	
His messages to the Pharisees, Sadducees, crowds, tax collectors and soldiers	3:7–10		3:7–14	
His description of Christ	3:11–12	1:7–8	3:15–18	
The End of John's Ministry and the Beginning of Christ's Public Ministry				
Jesus' baptism by John	3:13–17	1:9–11	3:21–23a	
Jesus' temptation in the wilderness	4:1–11	1:12–13	4:1–13	
John's testimony about himself to the priests and Levites				1:19–28
John's testimony to Jesus as the Son of God				1:29–34
Jesus' first followers				1:35–51
Jesus' first miracle: water becomes wine				2:1–11
Jesus' first stay in Capernaum with his relatives and early disciples				2:12
First clearing of the temple at the Passover				2:13–22
Early response to Jesus' miracles				2:23–25
Nicodemus's interview with Jesus				3:1–21
John superseded by Jesus				3:22–36
Jesus' departure from Judea	4:12	1:14a	3:19–20; 4:14a	4:1–4
Discussion with a Samaritan woman				4:5–26
Challenge of a spiritual harvest				4:27–38
Evangelization of Sychar				4:39–42
Arrival in Galilee				4:43–45
The Ministry of Christ in Galilee				
Opposition at Home and a New Headquarters				
Nature of the Galilean ministry	4:17	1:14b–15	4:14b–15	
Child at Capernaum healed by Jesus while at Cana				4:46–54
Ministry and rejection at Nazareth			4:16–31a	
Move to Capernaum	4:13–16			

[This is a tentative harmony only, since some sequences are debatable.]

A HARMONY OF THE GOSPELS (CONT.)

	MATTHEW	MARK	LUKE	JOHN
Disciples Called and Ministry Throughout Galilee				
Call of the four	4:18–22	1:16–20	5:1–11	
Teaching in the synagogue of Capernaum authenticated by healing a demon-possessed man		1:21–28	4:31b–37	
Peter's mother-in-law and others healed	8:14–17	1:29–34	4:38–41	
Tour of Galilee with Simon and others	4:23–25	1:35–39	4:42–44	
Healing of a man with leprosy, followed by much publicity	8:2–4	1:40–45	5:12–16	
Forgiving and healing of a paralyzed man	9:1–8	2:1–12	5:17–26	
Call of Matthew	9:9	2:13–14	5:27–28	
Banquet at Matthew's house	9:10–13	2:15–17	5:29–32	
With three parables Jesus defends his disciples for feasting instead of fasting	9:14–17	2:18–22	5:33–39	
Sabbath Controversies and Withdrawals				
Jesus heals an invalid on the Sabbath			5:1–9	
Effort to kill Jesus for breaking the Sabbath and saying he was equal with God				5:10–18
Discourse demonstrating the Son's equality with the Father				5:19–47
Controversy over disciples' picking grain on the Sabbath	12:1–8	2:23–28	6:1–5	
Healing of a man's shriveled hand on the Sabbath	12:9–14	3:1–6	6:6–11	
Withdrawal to the Sea of Galilee with large crowds from many places	12:15–21	3:7–12		
Appointment of the Twelve and Sermon on the Mount				
Twelve apostles chosen		3:13–19	6:12–16	
Setting of the Sermon	5:1–2		6:17–19	
Blessings of those who inherit the kingdom and woes to those who do not	5:3–12		6:20–26	
Responsibility while awaiting the kingdom	5:13–16			
Law, righteousness and the kingdom	5:17–20			
Six contrasts in interpreting the law	5:21–48		6:27–30,32–36	
Three hypocritical "acts of righteousness" to be avoided	6:1–18			
Three prohibitions against avarice, harsh judgment and unwise exposure of sacred things	6:19—7:6		6:37–42	
Application and conclusion	7:7–27		6:31,43–49	
Reaction of the crowds	7:28—8:1			
Growing Fame and Emphasis on Repentance				
A centurion's faith and the healing of his servant	8:5–13		7:1–10	
A widow's son raised at Nain			7:11–17	
John the Baptist's relationship to the kingdom	11:2–19		7:18–35	
Woes to Chorazin and Bethsaida for failure to repent	11:20–30			
Jesus' feet anointed by a sinful but contrite woman			7:36–50	
First Public Rejection by Jewish Leaders				
A tour with the Twelve and other followers			8:1–3	
Blasphemous accusation by the teachers of the law and Pharisees	12:22–37	3:20–30		
Request for a sign refused	12:38–45			
Announcement of new spiritual kinship	12:46–50	3:31–35	8:19–21	
Secrets About the Kingdom Given in Parables				
TO THE CROWDS BY THE SEA				
The setting of the parables	13:1–3a	4:1–2	8:4	
The parable of the sower	13:3b–23	4:3–25	8:5–18	
The parable of the growing seed		4:26–29		
The parable of the weeds	13:24–30			
The parable of the mustard seed	13:31–32	4:30–32		
The parable of the yeast	13:33–35	4:33–34		
TO THE DISCIPLES IN THE HOUSE				
The parable of the weeds explained	13:36–43			
The parable of the hidden treasure	13:44			
The parable of the valuable pearl	13:45–46			
The parable of the net	13:47–50			
The parable of the house owner	13:51–53			

A HARMONY OF THE GOSPELS (CONT.)

	MATTHEW	MARK	LUKE	JOHN
Continuing Opposition				
Crossing the lake and calming the storm	8:18,23–27	4:35–41	8:22–25	
Healing the Gerasene demon-possessed men and resultant opposition	8:28–34	5:1–20	8:26–39	
Return to Galilee, healing of a woman who touched Jesus' garment and raising of Jairus's daughter	9:18–26	5:21–43	8:40–56	
Three miracles of healing, and another blasphemous accusation	9:27–34			
Final visit to unbelieving Nazareth	13:54–58	6:1–6a		
Final Galilean Campaign				
Shortage of workers	9:35–38	6:6b		
Commissioning of the Twelve	10:1–42	6:7–11	9:1–5	
Workers sent out	11:1	6:12–13	9:6	
Herod Antipas's mistaken identification of Jesus	14:1–2	6:14–16	9:7–9	
Earlier imprisonment and beheading of John the Baptist	14:3–12	6:17–29		
THE MINISTRY OF CHRIST AROUND GALILEE				
Lesson on the Bread of Life				
Return of the workers		6:30	9:10a	
Withdrawal from Galilee	14:13–14	6:31–34	9:10b–11	6:1–3
Feeding the 5,000	14:15–21	6:35–44	9:12–17	6:4–13
A premature attempt to make Jesus king blocked	14:22–23	6:45–46		6:14–15
Walking on the water during a storm on the lake	14:24–33	6:47–52		6:16–21
Healings at Gennesaret	14:34–36	6:53–56		
Discourse on the true bread of life				6:22–59
Defection among the disciples				6:60–71
Lesson on the Yeast of the Pharisees, Sadducees and Herodians				
Conflict over the tradition of ceremonial uncleanness	15:1–3a,7–9b, 3b–6,10-20	7:1–23		7:1
Ministry to a believing Greek woman in Tyre and Sidon	15:21–28	7:24–30		
Healings in the Decapolis	15:29–31	7:31–37		
Feeding the 4,000 in the Decapolis	15:32–38	8:1–9a		
Return to Galilee, and encounter with the Pharisees and Sadducees	15:39—16:4	8:9b–12		
Warning about the error of the Pharisees, Sadducees and Herodians	16:5–12	8:13–21		
Healing a blind man at Bethsaida		8:22–26		
Lesson of Messiahship Learned and Confirmed				
Peter's identification of Jesus as the Christ, and first prophecy of the church	16:13–20	8:27–30	9:18–21	
First direct prediction of the rejection, crucifixion and resurrection	16:21–26	8:31–37	9:22–25	
Coming of the Son of Man and judgment	16:27–28	8:38—9:1	9:26–27	
Transfiguration of Jesus	17:1–8	9:2–8	9:28–36a	
Discussion of resurrection, Elijah and John the Baptist	17:9–13	9:9–13	9:36b	
Lessons on Responsibility to Others				
Healing of a demon-possessed boy, and unbelief rebuked	17:14–20	9:14–29	9:37–43a	
Second prediction of Jesus' death and resurrection	17:22–23	9:30–32	9:43b–45	
Payment of temple tax	17:24–27			
Rivalry over greatness in the kingdom	18:1–5	9:33–37	9:46–48	
Warning against causing believers to sin	18:6–14	9:38–50	9:49–50	
Treatment and forgiveness of a sinning brother or sister	18:15–35			
Journey to Jerusalem for the Feast of Tabernacles				
Complete commitment required of followers	8:19–22		9:57–62	
Ridicule by Jesus' half brothers				7:2–9
Journey through Samaria			9:51–56	7:10
THE LATER JUDEAN MINISTRY OF CHRIST				
Ministry Beginning at the Feast of Tabernacles				
Mixed reaction to Jesus' teaching and miracles				7:11–31
Frustrated attempt to arrest Jesus				7:32–52

A HARMONY OF THE GOSPELS (CONT.)

	MATTHEW	MARK	LUKE	JOHN
Jesus' forgiveness of a woman caught in adultery				[7:53—8:11]
Conflict over Jesus' claim to be the light of the world				8:12–20
Jesus' relationship to God the Father				8:21–30
Jesus' relationship to Abraham, and attempted stoning				8:31–59
Healing of a man born blind				9:1–7
Response of the blind man's neighbors				9:8–12
Examination and excommunication of the blind man by the Pharisees				9:13–34
Jesus' identification of himself to the blind man				9:35–38
Spiritual blindness of the Pharisees				9:39–41
Allegory of the good shepherd and the thief				10:1–18
Further division among the Jews				10:19–21
Private Lessons on Loving Service and Prayer				
Commissioning of the 72			10:1–16	
Return of the 72			10:17–24	
Parable of the Good Samaritan			10:25–37	
Jesus' visit with Mary and Martha			10:38–42	
Lesson on how to pray, and the parable of the bold friend			11:1–13	
Second Debate with the Teachers of the Law and the Pharisees				
A third blasphemous accusation, and a second debate			11:14–36	
Woes to the Pharisees and the teachers of the law while eating with a Pharisee			11:37–54	
Warning the disciples about hypocrisy			12:1–12	
Warning about greed and trust in wealth			12:13–34	
Warning against being unprepared for the Son of Man's coming			12:35–48	
Warning about the coming division			12:49–53	
Warning against failing to discern the present time			12:54–59	
Two alternatives: repent or perish			13:1–9	
Opposition from a synagogue ruler for healing a woman on the Sabbath			13:10–21	
Another attempt to stone or arrest Jesus for blasphemy at the Festival of Dedication				10:22–39
THE MINISTRY OF CHRIST IN AND AROUND PEREA				
Principles of Discipleship				
From Jerusalem to Perea				10:40–42
Question about salvation and entering the kingdom			13:22–30	
Anticipation of Jesus' coming death, and his sorrow over Jerusalem			13:31–35	
Healing of a man with abnormal swelling while eating with a prominent Pharisee on the Sabbath, and three parables suggested by the occasion			14:1–24	
Cost of discipleship			14:25–35	
Parables in defense of association with sinners			15:1–32	
Parable to teach the proper use of money			16:1–13	
Parable to teach the danger of wealth			16:14–31	
Four lessons on discipleship			17:1–10	
Sickness and death of Lazarus				11:1–16
Lazarus raised from the dead				11:17–44
Decision of the Sanhedrin to put Jesus to death				11:45–54
Teaching While on Final Journey to Jerusalem				
Healing of ten lepers while passing through Samaria and Galilee			17:11–21	
Instructions regarding the Son of Man's coming			17:22–37	
Two parables on prayer: the persistent widow, and the Pharisee and the tax collector			18:1–14	
Conflict with Pharisees' teaching on divorce	19:1–12	10:1–12		
Example of little children in relation to the kingdom	19:13–15	10:13–16	18:15–17	
Riches and the kingdom	19:16–30	10:17–31	18:18–30	
Parable of the landowner's sovereignty	20:1–16			
Third prediction of Jesus' death and resurrection	20:17–19	10:32–34	18:31–34	
Warning against ambitious pride	20:20–28	10:35–45		
Healing of blind Bartimaeus and his companion	20:29–34	10:46–52	18:35–43	

A HARMONY OF THE GOSPELS (CONT.)

	MATTHEW	MARK	LUKE	JOHN
Salvation of Zacchaeus			19:1–10	
Parable to teach responsibility while the kingdom is delayed			19:11–28	
THE FORMAL PRESENTATION OF CHRIST TO ISRAEL AND THE RESULTING CONFLICT				
"Triumphal" Entry and the Fig Tree				
Arrival at Bethany				11:55—12:1, 9–11
"Triumphal" Entry into Jerusalem	21:1–3, 6–7, 4–5, 8–11, 14–17	11:1–11	19:29–44	12:12–19
Cursing of the fig tree for having leaves but no figs	21:18–19a	11:12–14		
Second clearing of the temple	21:12–13	11:15–18	19:45–48	
Request of some Greeks to see Jesus, and necessity of the Son of Man's being lifted up				12:20–36a
Different responses to Jesus, and Jesus' response to the crowds				12:36b–50
Withered fig tree and the lesson on faith	21:19b–22	11:19–25	21:37–38	
Official Challenge to Christ's Authority				
Questioning of Jesus' authority by the chief priests, teachers of the law and elders	21:23–27	11:27–33	20:1–8	
Jesus' response with his own question and three parables	21:28—22:14	12:1–12	20:9–19	
Attempts by Pharisees and Herodians to trap Jesus with a question about paying taxes to Caesar	22:15–22	12:13–17	20:20–26	
Sadducees' puzzling question about the resurrection	22:23–33	12:18–27	20:27–40	
A Pharisee's legal question	22:34–40	12:28–34		
Christ's Response to His Enemies' Challenges				
Christ's relationship to David as son and Lord	22:41–46	12:35–37	20:41–44	
Seven woes against the teachers of the law and Pharisees	23:1–36	12:38–40	20:45–47	
Jesus' sorrow over Jerusalem	23:37–39			
A poor widow's gift of all she had		12:41–44	21:1–4	
PROPHECIES IN PREPARATION FOR THE DEATH OF CHRIST				
The Olivet Discourse: Jesus Speaks Prophetically about the Temple and His Own Second Coming				
Setting of the discourse	24:1–3	13:1–4	21:5–7	
Beginning of birth pains	24:4–14	13:5–13	21:8–19	
Abomination that causes desolation, and subsequent distress	24:15–28	13:14–23	21:20–24	
Coming of the Son of Man	24:29–31	13:24–27	21:25–27	
Signs of nearness but unknown time	24:32–41	13:28–32	21:28–33	
Five parables to teach watchfulness and faithfulness	24:42—25:30	13:33–37	21:34–36	
Judgment at the Son of Man's coming	25:31–46			
Arrangements for Betrayal				
Plot by the Sanhedrin to arrest and kill Jesus	26:1–5	14:1–2	22:1–2	
Mary's anointing of Jesus for burial	26:6–13	14:3–9		12:2–8
Judas's agreement to betray Jesus	26:14–16	14:10–11	22:3–6	
The Last Supper				
Preparation for the Passover meal	26:17–19	14:12–16	22:7–13	
Beginning of the Passover meal, and dissension among the disciples over greatness	26:20	14:17	22:14–16, 24–30	
Washing the disciples' feet				13:1–20
Identification of the betrayer	26:21–25	14:18–21	22:21–23	13:21–30
Prediction of Peter's denial	26:31–35	14:27–31	22:31–38	13:31–38
Conclusion of the meal, and the Lord's Supper instituted (1Co 11:23–26)	26:26–29	14:22–25	22:17–20	
Discourse and Prayers from the Upper Room to Gethsemane				
Questions about his destination, the Father and the Holy Spirit answered				14:1–31

A HARMONY OF THE GOSPELS (CONT.)

	MATTHEW	MARK	LUKE	JOHN
The vine and the branches				15:1–17
Opposition from the world				15:18—16:4
Coming and ministry of the Spirit				16:5–15
Prediction of joy over Jesus' resurrection				16:16–22
Promise of answered prayer and peace				16:23–33
Jesus' prayer for himself, his disciples and all who believe				17:1–26
Jesus' three agonizing prayers in Gethsemane	26:30,36–46	14:26,32–42	22:39–46	18:1
THE DEATH OF CHRIST				
Betrayal and Arrest				
Jesus betrayed, arrested and forsaken	26:47–56	14:43–52	22:47–53	18:2–12
Trial				
First Jewish phase, before Annas				18:13–14, 19–23
Second Jewish phase, before Caiaphas and the Sanhedrin	26:57,59–68	14:53,55–65	22:54a,63–65	18:24
Peter's denials	26:58,69–75	14:54,66–72	22:54b–62	18:15–18, 25–27
Third Jewish phase, before the Sanhedrin	27:1	15:1a	22:66–71	
Remorse and suicide of Judas Iscariot (Ac 1:18–19)	27:3–10			
First Roman phase, before Pilate	27:2,11–14	15:1b–5	23:1–5	18:28–38
Second Roman phase, before Herod Antipas			23:6–12	
Third Roman phase, before Pilate	27:15–26	15:6–15	23:13–25	18:39—19:16a
Crucifixion				
Mockery by the Roman soldiers	27:27–30	15:16–19		
Journey to Golgotha	27:31–34	15:20–23	23:26–33a	19:16b–17
First three hours of crucifixion	27:35–44	15:24–32	23:33b–43	19:18,23–24, 19–22,25–27
Last three hours of crucifixion	27:45–50	15:33–37	23:44–45a,46	19:28–30
Witness of Jesus' death	27:51–56	15:38–41	23:45b,47–49	
Burial				
Certification of Jesus' death, and procurement of his body	27:57–58	15:42–45	23:50–52	19:31–38
Jesus' body placed in a tomb	27:59–60	15:46	23:53–54	19:39–42
The tomb watched by the women and guarded by the soldiers	27:61–66	15:47	23:55–56	
THE RESURRECTION AND ASCENSION OF CHRIST				
The Empty Tomb				
The tomb visited by the women	28:1	16:1		
The stone rolled away	28:2–4			
The tomb found to be empty by the women	28:5–8	16:2–8	24:1–8	20:1
The tomb found to be empty by Peter and John			24:9–12	20:2–10
The Resurrection Appearances				
Appearance to Mary Magdalene		[16:9–11]		20:11–18
Appearance to the other women	28:9–10			
Report of the soldiers to the Jewish authorities	28:11–15			
Appearance to the two disciples traveling to Emmaus		[16:12–13]	24:13–32	
Report of the two disciples to the rest (1Co 15:5a)			24:33–35	
Appearance to the ten assembled disciples		[16:14]	24:36–43	20:19–25
Appearance to the eleven assembled disciples (1Co 15:5b)				20:26–31
Appearance to the seven disciples while they were fishing				21:1–25
Appearance to the Eleven in Galilee (1Co 15:6)	28:16–20	[16:15–18]		
Appearance to James, Jesus' brother (1Co 15:7)				
Appearance to the disciples in Jerusalem (Ac 1:3–8)			24:44–49	
The Ascension				
Christ's parting blessing and departure (Ac 1:9–12)		[16:19–20]	24:50–53	

ACTS

INTRODUCTION

Author

Although the author does not name himself, both external and internal evidence leads to the conclusion that the author was Luke.

The earliest of the external testimonies appears in the Muratorian Canon (c. AD 170), where the explicit statement is made that Luke was the author of both the third Gospel and the "Acts of All the Apostles." Eusebius (c. 325) lists information from numerous sources to identify the author of these books as Luke (*Ecclesiastical History*, 3.4).

Within the writing itself are some clues as to who the author was:

(1) *A companion of Paul.* In the description of the happenings in Acts, certain passages make use of the pronoun "we." At these points the author includes himself as a companion of Paul in his travels (16:10 – 17; 20:5 — 21:18; 27:1 — 28:16; see notes on 16:10,17; 27:1). A historian as careful with details as this author proves to be would have good reason for choosing to use "we" in some places and "they" elsewhere. The author was therefore probably present with Paul at the particular events described in the "we" sections.

These "we" passages include the period of Paul's two-year imprisonment at Rome (ch. 28). During this time Paul wrote, among other letters, Philemon and Colossians. In them he sends greetings from his companions, and Luke is included among them (see Col 4:9 – 17 and notes; Phm 23 – 24). In fact, after eliminating those who, for one reason or another, would not fit the requirements for the author of Acts, Luke is left as the most likely candidate.

(2) *A physician.* Paul describes Luke as a "doctor" in Col 4:14 (see note there). Although it cannot be proved that the author of Acts was a physician simply from his vocabulary, the words he uses and the traits and education reflected in his writings fit well his role as a physician (see, e.g., note on 28:6). It is true that the doctor of the first century did not have as specialized a vocabulary as that of doctors today, but there are some usages in Luke and Acts that seem to suggest that a medical man could have been the author of these books.

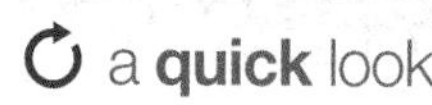

Author:
Luke, a Gentile physician and missionary companion of Paul

Audience:
Addressed to Theophilus, but intended for all believers

Date:
About AD 63 or later

Theme:
Luke shows how the gospel spread rapidly from Jerusalem to the whole Roman Empire, and from its Jewish roots to the Gentile world.

Date

Two main dates have been suggested for the writing of this book: (1) c. AD 63, soon after the last event recorded in the book, and (2) c. 70 or even later.

The earlier date is supported by:

(1) *Silence about later events.* While arguments from silence are not conclusive, it is perhaps significant that the book contains no allusion to events that happened after the close of Paul's two-year imprisonment in Rome: e.g., the burning of Rome and the persecution of the Christians there (AD 64), the martyrdom of Peter and Paul (possibly 67) and the destruction of Jerusalem (70).

(2) *No outcome of Paul's trial.* If Luke knew the outcome of the trial Paul was waiting for (see 28:30 and note), why did he not record it at the close of Acts? Perhaps it was because he had brought the history up to date.

Those who prefer the later date hold that 1:8 (see note there) reveals one of the purposes Luke had in writing his history and shows that this purpose influenced the way the book ended. Luke wanted to show how the church penetrated the world of his day in ever-widening circles (Jerusalem, Judea, Samaria, the ends of the earth) until it reached Rome, the world's political and cultural center. On this understanding, mention of the martyrdom of Paul (c. AD 67) and of the destruction of Jerusalem (70) was not pertinent. This would allow for the writing of Acts c. 70 or even later.

Recipient

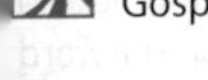

The recipient of the book, Theophilus, is the same person addressed in the first volume, the Gospel of Luke (see Introduction to Luke: Recipient and Purpose).

Importance

The book of Acts provides a bridge for the writings of the NT. As a second volume to Luke's Gospel, it joins what Jesus "began to do and to teach" (1:1; see note there) as told in the Gospels with what he continued to do and teach through the apostles' preaching and the establishment of the church. Besides linking the Gospel narratives on the one hand and the apostolic letters on the other, it supplies an account of the life of Paul, from which we can learn the setting for his letters. Geographically, its story spans the lands between Jerusalem, where the church began, and Rome, the political center of the empire. Historically, it provides a selective account of the first 30 years of the church. It is also a bridge that ties the church in its beginning with each succeeding age. The book reveals the potential of the church when it is guided and empowered by the Holy Spirit.

Theme and Purpose

The theme of the work is best summarized in 1:8 (see note there). It was ordinary procedure for a historian at this time to begin a second volume by summarizing the first volume and indicating the contents anticipated in his second volume. Luke summarized his first volume in 1:1 – 3; the theme of his second volume is presented in the words of Jesus: "You will be my witnesses in Jerusalem, and in all Judea and Samaria, and to the ends of the earth" (1:8). This is, in effect, an outline of the book of Acts (see Plan and Outline).

Harbor of Attalia near Perga (Ac 13:13; 14:25), where Paul stopped on his first missionary journey
www.HolyLandPhotos.org

The main purposes of the book appear to be:

(1) *To demonstrate the unstoppable progress of the gospel.* This progress is both geographic and ethnic. Luke seeks to show how the gospel moved from its Jewish roots in Jerusalem outward into the Gentile world. His overriding purpose is to demonstrate that the advance of the church is the work of God and the fulfillment of his plan to bring salvation to the ends of the earth. The church, made up of Jews and Gentiles and empowered and guided by the Holy Spirit, represents the people of God in the present age.

(2) *To present a history.* The significance of Acts as a historical account of Christian origins should not be underestimated. It tells of the founding of the church, the spread of the gospel, the beginnings of congregations, and evangelistic efforts in the apostolic pattern. One of the unique aspects of Christianity is its firm historical foundation. The life and teachings of Jesus Christ are established in the four Gospel narratives, and the book of Acts provides a coordinated account of the beginning and spread of the church as the result of the work of the risen Lord and the Holy Spirit through the apostles.

(3) *To give a defense.* One finds embedded in Acts a record of Christian defenses made to both Jews (e.g., 4:8 – 12) and Gentiles (e.g., 25:8 – 11), with the underlying purposes of confirmation for believers and conversion of unbelievers. It shows how the early church coped with pagan and Jewish thought, the Roman government and Hellenistic society.

Characteristics

 (1) *Accurate historical detail.* The account covers a period of about 30 years and reaches across the lands from Jerusalem to Rome. Luke's description of these times and places is filled with

As a second volume to Luke's Gospel, the book of Acts joins what Jesus "began to do and to teach" as told in the Gospels with what he continued to do and teach through the apostles' preaching and the establishment of the church.

all kinds of people and cultures, a variety of governmental administrations, court scenes in Caesarea, and dramatic events involving such centers as Antioch, Ephesus, Athens, Corinth and Rome. Barbarian country districts and Jewish centers are included as well. Yet in each instance archaeological findings reveal that Luke uses the proper terms for the time and place being described. Hostile criticism has not succeeded in disproving the accuracy of Luke's political and geographic designations (see chart, pp. 1810–1813, and maps and archaeological notes scattered throughout the book).

(2) *Literary excellence.* Not only does Luke have a large vocabulary compared with other NT writers, but he also uses these words in literary styles that fit the cultural settings of the events he is recording. At times he employs fine literary Greek; at other times the Palestinian Aramaic of the first century shows through his expressions. This is an indication of Luke's careful practice of using language appropriate to the time and place being described. Aramaisms are used when Luke is describing happenings that took place in the Holy Land (chs. 1–12). When, however, Paul departs for Hellenistic lands beyond the territories where Aramaic-speaking people live, Aramaisms cease.

(3) *Dramatic description.* Luke's skillful use of speeches contributes to the drama of his narrative. Not only are they carefully spaced and well balanced between Peter and Paul, but the speeches of a number of other individuals add variety and vividness to the account (see 5 below). Luke's use of details brings the action to life. Nowhere in ancient literature is there an account of a shipwreck superior to Luke's with its nautical details (ch. 27). The book is vivid and fast-moving throughout.

(4) *Realistic portrayal of the church.* Luke demonstrates the veracity of his account by recording the failures as well as the successes, the bad as well as the good, in the early church. Not only is the discontent between the Hellenistic Jews and the Hebraic Jews recorded (see 6:1 and note) but also the discord between Paul and Barnabas (see 15:39 and note). Divisions and differences are recognized (15:2; 21:20–21).

(5) *Effective use of speeches.* One of the distinguishing features of the book of Acts is its speeches. They may be classified as follows: (1) evangelistic—two types: to Jews and God-fearers (2:14–40; 3:12–26; 4:8–12; 5:29–32; 10:34–43; 13:16–41), to pagans (17:22–31); (2) deliberative (1:16–17,20–22; 15:7–11,13–21); (3) apologetic (7:2–52; 22:1–21; 23:1–6; 24:10–21; 25:8,10; 26:2–23; 28:17–20,21–22,25–28); (4) hortatory (20:18–35).

The speeches are obviously not verbatim reports; any of them can be read in a few minutes. We know, e.g., that Paul sometimes preached for several hours (see 20:7,9; 28:23). However, studies of these speeches (speakers, audiences, circumstances, language and style of writing) give us reason to believe that they are accurate summaries of what was actually said.

Plan and Outline

Luke weaves together different interests and emphases as he relates the beginnings and expansion of the church. The design of his book revolves around (1) key persons: Peter and Paul; (2) important topics and events: the role of the Holy Spirit, pioneer missionary outreach to new fields, conversions, the growth of the church and life in the Christian community; (3) significant problems: conflict between Jews and Gentiles, persecution of the church by some Jewish elements, trials before Jews and Romans, confrontations with Gentiles and other hardships in the ministry; (4) geographic advances: five significant stages (see the quotations in the outline; see also map, p. 1849; cf. note on 1:8).

- I. Peter and the Beginnings of the Church in the Holy Land (chs. 1–12)
  - A. "Throughout Judea, Galilee and Samaria" (1:1—9:31; see 9:31 and note)
    1. Introduction (1:1–2)
    2. Christ's resurrection ministry (1:3–11)
    3. The period of waiting for the Holy Spirit (1:12–26)
    4. The filling with the Spirit (ch. 2)
    5. The healing of the lame man and the resultant arrest of Peter and John (3:1—4:31)
    6. The community of goods (4:32—5:11)
    7. The arrest of the 12 apostles (5:12–42)
    8. The choice of the Seven (6:1–7)
    9. Stephen's arrest and martyrdom (6:8—7:60)
    10. The scattering of the Jerusalem believers (8:1–4)
    11. Philip's ministry (8:5–40)
        - a. In Samaria (8:5–25)
        - b. To the Ethiopian eunuch (8:26–40)
    12. Saul's conversion (9:1–31)
  - B. "As far as Phoenicia, Cyprus and Antioch" (9:32—12:25; see 11:19 and note)
    1. Peter's ministry on the Mediterranean coast (9:32—11:18)
        - a. To Aeneas and Dorcas (9:32–43)
        - b. To Cornelius (10:1—11:18)
    2. The new Gentile church in Antioch (11:19–30)
    3. Herod's persecution of the church and his subsequent death (ch. 12)
- II. Paul and the Expansion of the Church from Antioch to Rome (chs. 13–28)
  - A. "Throughout the region of Phrygia and Galatia" (13:1—15:35; see 16:6 and note)
    1. Paul's first missionary journey (chs. 13–14)
    2. The Jerusalem conference (15:1–35)
  - B. "Over to Macedonia" (15:36—21:16; see 16:9 and note)
    1. Paul's second missionary journey (15:36—18:22)
    2. Paul's third missionary journey (18:23—21:16)
  - C. "To Rome" (21:17—28:31; see 28:14 and note)
    1. Paul's imprisonment in Jerusalem (21:17—23:35)
        - a. Arrest (21:17—22:29)
        - b. Trial before the Sanhedrin (22:30—23:11)
        - c. Transfer to Caesarea (23:12–35)
    2. Paul's imprisonment in Caesarea (chs. 24–26)
        - a. Trial before Felix (ch. 24)
        - b. Trial before Festus (25:1–12)
        - c. Hearing before Festus and Agrippa (25:13—26:32)
    3. Voyage to Rome (27:1—28:15)
    4. Two years under house arrest in Rome (28:16–31)

Jesus Taken Up Into Heaven

1 In my former book,[a] Theophilus, I
wrote about all that Jesus began to do
and to teach[b] 2until the day he was tak-
en up to heaven,[c] after giving instructions[d]
through the Holy Spirit to the apostles[e] he
had chosen.[f] 3After his suffering, he presented himself to them and gave many
convincing proofs that he was alive. He appeared to them[g] over a period of forty days
and spoke about the kingdom of God.[h]
4On one occasion, while he was eating
with them, he gave them this command:
"Do not leave Jerusalem, but wait[i] for the
gift my Father promised, which you have
heard me speak about.[j] 5For John baptized
with[a] water,[k] but in a few days you will be
baptized with[a] the Holy Spirit."[l]

6Then they gathered around him and
asked him, "Lord, are you at this time going to restore[m] the kingdom to Israel?"

7He said to them: "It is not for you to
know the times or dates the Father has set
by his own authority.[n] 8But you will receive power when the Holy Spirit comes
on you;[o] and you will be my witnesses[p] in
Jerusalem, and in all Judea and Samaria,[q]
and to the ends of the earth."[r]

9After he said this, he was taken up[s] before their very eyes, and a cloud hid him
from their sight.

10They were looking intently up into the
sky as he was going, when suddenly two
men dressed in white[t] stood beside them.
11"Men of Galilee,"[u] they said, "why do
you stand here looking into the sky? This
same Jesus, who has been taken from you
into heaven, will come back[v] in the same
way you have seen him go into heaven."

Matthias Chosen to Replace Judas

12Then the apostles returned to Jerusalem[w] from the hill called the Mount of Olives,[x] a Sabbath day's walk[b] from the city.
13When they arrived, they went upstairs to
the room[y] where they were staying. Those
present were Peter, John, James and Andrew; Philip and Thomas, Bartholomew
and Matthew; James son of Alphaeus
and Simon the Zealot, and Judas son of
James.[z] 14They all joined together constantly in prayer,[a] along with the women[b]

[a] *5* Or *in* [b] *12* That is, about 5/8 mile or about 1 kilometer

1:1 [a]Lk 1:1-4 [b]Lk 3:23 **1:2** [c]ver 9,11; S Mk 16:19 [d]Mt 28:19,20 [e]S Mk 6:30 [f]Jn 13:18; 15:16,19 **1:3** [g]Mt 28:17; Lk 24:34, 36; Jn 20:19, 26; 21:1,14; 1Co 15:5-7 [h]S Mt 3:2 **1:4** [i]Ps 27:14 [j]Lk 24:49; Jn 14:16; Ac 2:33 **1:5** [k]S Mk 1:4 [l]S Mk 1:8 **1:6** [m]Mt 17:11; Ac 3:21 **1:7** [n]Dt 29:29; Ps 102:13; Mt 24:36 **1:8** [o]Ac 2:1-4 [p]S Lk 24:48 [q]Ac 8:1-25 [r]S Mt 28:19 **1:9** [s]ver 2; S Mk 16:19 **1:10** [t]S Jn 20:12 **1:11** [u]Ac 2:7 [v]S Mt 16:27 **1:12** [w]Lk 24:52 [x]S Mt 21:1 **1:13** [y]Ac 9:37; 20:8 [z]Mt 10:2-4; Mk 3:16-19; Lk 6:14-16 **1:14** [a]Ac 2:42; 4:24; 6:4; S Lk 18:1; S Ro 1:10 [b]Lk 23:49,55

1:1 *my former book.* The Gospel of Luke. Acts was addressed to the same patron, Theophilus (see Introduction to Luke: Recipient and Purpose). *began to do and to teach.* An apt summation of Luke's Gospel, implying that Jesus' work continues in Acts through his own personal interventions and the ministry of the Holy Spirit (see note on Lk 24:53).

1:2 *taken up to heaven.* Jesus' ascent to heaven was the last scene of Luke's Gospel (24:50–52) and is the opening scene of this second volume (vv. 6–11). The ascension occurred 40 days after the resurrection (v. 3). *through the Holy Spirit.* Jesus' postresurrection instruction of his apostles was carried on through the Holy Spirit, and succeeding statements make it clear that what the apostles were to accomplish was likewise to be done through the Spirit (vv. 4–5,8; see Lk 24:49 and note; Jn 20:22; see also Introduction to Judges: Themes and Theology). Luke characteristically stresses the Holy Spirit's work and enabling power (e.g., v. 8; 2:4,17; 4:8,31; 5:3; 6:3,5; 7:55; 8:16; 9:17,31; 10:44; 13:2,4; 15:28; 16:6; 19:2,6; see note on Lk 4:1).

1:3 *many convincing proofs.* See the resurrection appearances (Mt 28:1–20; Lk 24:1–53; Jn 20:1–29; 1Co 15:3–8). *kingdom of God.* The heart of Jesus' preaching (see notes on Mt 3:2; Lk 4:43).

1:4 *the gift my Father promised.* Luke views the coming of the Holy Spirit on the day of Pentecost as the birth of the church and the dawn of the new era of salvation through Jesus the Messiah (see Lk 3:16; 24:49 and notes; Jn 14:26; 15:26–27; 16:12–13).

1:5 *John baptized with water.* See Lk 3:16 and note. *in a few days.* The day of Pentecost came ten days later, when the baptism with the Holy Spirit occurred (2:1–4).

1:6 *restore the kingdom to Israel?* Like their fellow countrymen, they were looking for the deliverance of the people of Israel from foreign domination and for the establishment of an earthly kingdom. The reference to the coming of the Spirit had caused them to wonder if the new age was about to dawn.

1:7 *the times or dates.* The elapsing time or the character of coming events (see Mk 13:32; 1Th 5:1 and notes).

1:8 A virtual outline of Acts: The apostles were to be witnesses in Jerusalem (chs. 1–7), Judea and Samaria (chs. 8–9) and the ends of the earth—including Caesarea, Antioch, Asia Minor, Greece and Rome (chs. 10–28). However, they were not to begin this staggering task until they had been equipped with the power of the Spirit (vv. 4–5). *my witnesses.* An important theme throughout Acts (2:32; 3:15; 5:32; 10:39; 13:31; 22:15). *Judea.* The region in which Jerusalem was located. *Samaria.* The adjoining region to the north.

1:9 *taken up.* See v. 2; Ge 5:24 and notes. *a cloud hid him.* See Mt 17:5 and note.

1:10 *two men dressed in white.* Cf. Jn 20:12.

1:11 *Men of Galilee.* All of the Twelve were from Galilee except Judas, and he was no longer present. *in the same way.* In the same resurrection body and in clouds and with "great glory" (Mt 24:30; see note there).

1:12 *Mount of Olives.* The ascension occurred on the eastern slope of the mount between Jerusalem and Bethany (Lk 19:28–29,37; see notes on Zec 14:4; Mk 11:1; Lk 19:29; 24:50). *Sabbath day's walk.* See NIV text note. This distance was drawn from rabbinical reasoning based on several OT passages (Ex 16:29; Nu 35:5; Jos 3:4). A faithful Jew was to travel no farther on the Sabbath.

1:13 *room.* Probably an upper room of a large house, such as the one where the Last Supper was held (Mk 14:15) or that of Mary, the mother of Mark (see note on 12:12). *Bartholomew.* Apparently John calls him Nathanael (see Jn 1:45–49; 21:2). *James son of Alphaeus.* The same as James the younger (Mk 15:40). *Zealot.* See note on Mt 10:4. *Judas son of James.* Not Judas Iscariot, but the same person as Thaddaeus (see note on Mt 10:3).

1:14 *with the women.* Possibly wives of the apostles (cf. 1Co 9:5 and note) and those listed as ministering to Jesus (Mt 27:55; Lk 8:2–3; 24:22). *Mary the mother of Jesus.* Last mentioned here in Scripture. *brothers.* See note on Lk

COUNTRIES OF PEOPLE MENTIONED AT PENTECOST

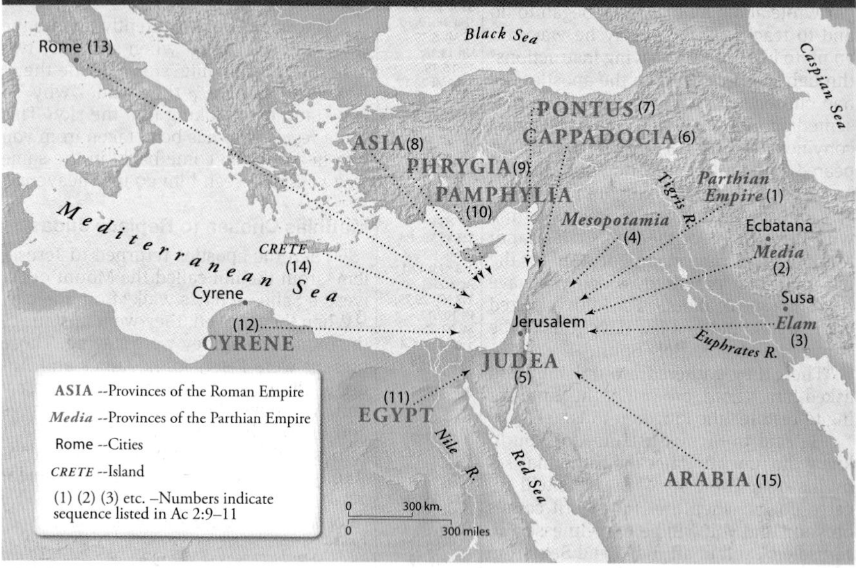

ASIA --Provinces of the Roman Empire
Media --Provinces of the Parthian Empire
Rome --Cities
CRETE --Island
(1) (2) (3) etc. –Numbers indicate sequence listed in Ac 2:9–11

and Mary the mother of Jesus, and with
his brothers.[c]
[15]In those days Peter stood up among
the believers (a group numbering about a
hundred and twenty) [16]and said, "Brothers and sisters,[a][d] the Scripture had to be
fulfilled[e] in which the Holy Spirit spoke
long ago through David concerning Judas,[f]
who served as guide for those who arrested Jesus. [17]He was one of our number[g]
and shared in our ministry."[h]
[18](With the payment[i] he received for his
wickedness, Judas bought a field;[j] there he
fell headlong, his body burst open and all
his intestines spilled out. [19]Everyone in Jerusalem heard about this, so they called
that field in their language[k] Akeldama,
that is, Field of Blood.)
[20]"For," said Peter, "it is written in the
Book of Psalms:

"'May his place be deserted;
let there be no one to dwell in it,'[b][l]

and,

"'May another take his place of
leadership.'[c][m]

[21]Therefore it is necessary to choose one of
the men who have been with us the whole
time the Lord Jesus was living among us,
[22]beginning from John's baptism[n] to the
time when Jesus was taken up from us.
For one of these must become a witness[o]
with us of his resurrection."
[23]So they nominated two men: Joseph
called Barsabbas (also known as Justus)

1:14 [c]S Mt 12:46
1:16 [d]Ac 6:3; 11:1,12,29; 14:2; 18:18, 27; 21:7; S 22:5; S Ro 7:1 [e]ver 20; S Mt 1:22 [f]S Mt 10:4
1:17 [g]Jn 6:70, 71 [h]ver 25
1:18 [i]Mt 26:14, 15 [j]Mt 27:3-10
1:19 [k]S Jn 5:2
1:20 [l]Ps 69:25 [m]Ps 109:8
1:22 [n]S Mk 1:4 [o]ver 8; S Lk 24:48

[a] *16* The Greek word for *brothers and sisters* (*adelphoi*) refers here to believers, both men and women, as part of God's family; also in 6:3; 11:29; 12:17; 16:40; 18:18, 27; 21:7, 17; 28:14, 15. [b] *20* Psalm 69:25 [c] *20* Psalm 109:8

8:19. These brothers would include James, who later became a leader in the Jerusalem church (12:17; 15:13; 21:18; Gal 1:19; 2:9; see Introduction to James: Author).

1:16 *the Scripture had to be fulfilled.* For the Scripture referred to, see NIV text notes on v. 20. Both before and after Christ came, numerous psalms were viewed as Messianic. What happened in the psalmist's experience was typical of the experiences of the Messiah. No doubt Jesus' instruction in Lk 24:27,45–47 included these Scriptures.

1:18 *Judas bought a field.* Judas bought the field indirectly: The money he returned to the priests (Mt 27:3) was used to purchase the potter's field (Mt 27:7). *fell headlong.* Mt 27:5 reports that Judas hanged himself. It appears that when the body finally fell, either because of decay or because someone cut it down, it was in a decomposed condition and so broke open in the middle.

1:20 *it is written.* Two passages of Scripture (see NIV text notes) were put together to suggest that Judas had left a vacancy that had to be filled (see notes on Ps 69:25; 109:8).

1:21 *was living among us.* Ministered publicly (cf. 9:28).

1:22 *a witness with us of his resurrection.* Apparently several met this requirement. On this occasion, however, the believers were selecting someone to become an official witness to the resurrection, i.e., someone to help proclaim and oversee the apostles' teaching about Jesus for the church—thus, a 12th apostle (v. 25).

1:23 *Barsabbas.* Means "son of (the) Sabbath." This patronymic was used for two early Jewish Christians, possibly brothers.

and Matthias. 24Then they prayed,[p] "Lord,
you know everyone's heart.[q] Show us[r]
which of these two you have chosen 25to
take over this apostolic ministry, which
Judas left to go where he belongs." 26Then
they cast lots, and the lot fell to Matthias;
so he was added to the eleven apostles.[s]

The Holy Spirit Comes at Pentecost

2 When the day of Pentecost[t] came, they
were all together[u] in one place. 2Sud-
denly a sound like the blowing of a violent wind came from heaven and filled
the whole house where they were sitting.[v]
3They saw what seemed to be tongues of
fire that separated and came to rest on
each of them. 4All of them were filled with
the Holy Spirit[w] and began to speak in other tongues[ax] as the Spirit enabled them.
5Now there were staying in Jerusalem
God-fearing[y] Jews from every nation under
heaven. 6When they heard this sound, a
crowd came together in bewilderment, because each one heard their own language
being spoken. 7Utterly amazed,[z] they
asked: "Aren't all these who are speaking Galileans?[a] 8Then how is it that each
of us hears them in our native language?
9Parthians, Medes and Elamites; residents
of Mesopotamia, Judea and Cappado-
cia,[b] Pontus[c] and Asia,[bd] 10Phrygia[e] and
Pamphylia,[f] Egypt and the parts of Libya
near Cyrene;[g] visitors from Rome 11(both
Jews and converts to Judaism); Cretans
and Arabs — we hear them declaring the
wonders of God in our own tongues!"
12Amazed and perplexed, they asked one
another, "What does this mean?"
13Some, however, made fun of them and
said, "They have had too much wine."[h]

Peter Addresses the Crowd

14Then Peter stood up with the Eleven,
raised his voice and addressed the crowd:

1:24 [p] Ac 6:6; 13:3; 14:23 **1:24** [q] Ac 15:8; S Rev 2:23 [r] 1Sa 14:41 **1:26** [s] Ac 2:14 **2:1** [t] Lev 23:15, 16; Ac 20:16; 1Co 16:8 [u] Ac 1:14 **2:2** [v] Ac 4:31 **2:4** [w] S Lk 1:15 [x] S Mk 16:17 **2:5** [y] Lk 2:25; Ac 8:2 **2:7** [z] ver 12 [a] Ac 1:11 **2:9** [b] 1Pe 1:1 [c] Ac 18:2; 1Pe 1:1 [d] Ac 16:6; 19:10; Ro 16:5; 1Co 16:19; 2Co 1:8; Rev 1:4 **2:10** [e] Ac 16:6; 18:23 [f] Ac 13:13; 14:24; 15:38 [g] S Mt 27:32 **2:13** [h] 1Co 14:23; Eph 5:18

[a] 4 Or *languages*; also in verse 11 [b] 9 That is, the Roman province by that name

One was Joseph (here); the other was Judas, a prophet in Jerusalem who was sent to Antioch with Silas (15:22,32). *Justus.* Joseph's Hellenistic name. Nothing more is known of him.
1:26 *cast lots.* See Pr 16:33 and note. By casting lots they submitted the decision to the ascended Lord. The use of rocks or sticks to designate the choice was common (see 1Ch 26:13 – 16; see also notes on Ne 11:1; Jnh 1:7). This is the Bible's last mention of casting lots.
2:1 *day of Pentecost.* The 50th day after the Sabbath of Passover week (Lev 23:15 – 16), thus the first day of the week. Pentecost is also called the Festival of Weeks (Dt 16:10), the Festival of Harvest (Ex 23:16) and the day of firstfruits (Nu 28:26). See chart, pp. 188 – 189. In Judaism, Pentecost was traditionally seen as the day Moses received the law. Now it will be seen as the day the Spirit came to fulfill God's promise as given in the Law and the Prophets. *they were all together.* The nearest antecedent of "they" is the 11 apostles (plus Matthias), but the reference is probably to all those mentioned in 1:13 – 15. *in one place.* Evidently not the upstairs room where they were staying (1:13) but perhaps some place in the temple precincts, for the apostles were "continually at the temple" when it was open (Lk 24:53; see note there).
2:2 *violent wind.* Breath or wind is a symbol of the Spirit of God (see Eze 37:9,14; Jn 3:8). The coming of the Spirit is marked by audible (wind) and visible (fire) signs. *whole house.* May refer to the temple (cf. 7:47).
2:3 *tongues.* A descriptive metaphor appropriate to the context, in which several languages are about to be spoken. *fire.* A symbol of the divine presence (see Ex 3:2 and note), it was also associated with judgment (see Mt 3:12 and note).
2:4 *All of them.* Could refer either to the apostles or to the 120. Those holding that the 120 are meant point to the fulfillment of Joel's prophecy (vv. 17 – 18) as involving more than the 12 apostles. The nearest reference, however, is to the apostles (see note on v. 1), and the narrative continues with Peter and the 11 standing to address the crowd (v. 14). *filled with the Holy Spirit.* A fulfillment of 1:4 – 5,8; see also Jesus' promise in Lk 24:49 and note there (cf. Jn 14:16 – 18; 20:22 and note). Their spirits were completely under the control of the Holy Spirit; their words were his words. *in other tongues.* The Spirit enabled them to speak in languages they had not previously learned (see NIV text note). Two other examples of speaking in tongues are found in Acts (see 10:46; 19:6 and note). One extended NT passage deals with this spiritual gift (1Co 12 – 14). Not all agree, however, that these other passages refer to speaking in known languages. The gift had particular relevance here, where people of different nationalities and languages were gathered.
2:5 *God-fearing Jews.* Devout Jews from different parts of the world but assembled now in Jerusalem either as pilgrims attending the Festival of Pentecost or as current residents (cf. Lk 2:25).
2:6 *heard their own language.* These Jews heard the apostles speak in languages native to the different places from which they had come (see map, p. 1826).
2:9 *Parthians.* Inhabitants of the territory from the Tigris River to India. *Medes.* Media lay east of Mesopotamia, northwest of Persia and south-southwest of the Caspian Sea. *Elamites.* Elam was north of the Persian Gulf, bounded on the west by the Tigris. *Mesopotamia.* Between the Euphrates and Tigris Rivers. *Judea.* The homeland of the Jews, perhaps used here in the OT sense "from the Wadi of Egypt to … the Euphrates" (Ge 15:18), including Galilee. *Cappadocia, Pontus and Asia.* Districts in Asia Minor. *Asia.* See note on 2Co 1:8.
2:10 *Phrygia and Pamphylia.* Districts in Asia Minor. *Egypt.* Jews had lived in Egypt since the sixth century BC. Two out of the five districts of Alexandria were Jewish. *Libya.* A region west of Egypt. *Cyrene.* The capital of a district of Libya called Cyrenaica. *Rome.* Thousands of Jews lived in Rome.
2:11 *converts to Judaism.* Gentiles who undertook the full observance of the Mosaic law were received into full fellowship with the Jews. *Cretans.* Represented an island lying south-southeast of Greece. *Arabs.* From a region to the east. The kingdom of the Nabatean Arabs lay between the "Red Sea" and the Euphrates, with Petra as its capital. *we hear them declaring.* Not a miracle of hearing but of speaking. The believers were declaring God's wonders in the native languages of the various visiting Jews (see map, p. 1826).
2:14 – 40 The pattern and themes of the message that follows became common in the early church: (1) an explanation of events (vv. 14 – 21); (2) the gospel of Jesus Christ — his death, resurrection and exaltation (vv. 22 – 36); (3) an exhortation to repentance and baptism (vv. 37 – 40). The outline of this sermon is similar to those in chs. 3; 10; 13.
2:14 *with the Eleven.* The apostles had been baptized with the Holy Spirit and had spoken in other languages to various

"Fellow Jews and all of you who live in Jerusalem, let me explain this to you; listen carefully to what I say. 15 These people are not drunk, as you suppose. It's only nine in the morning![i] 16 No, this is what was spoken by the prophet Joel:

17 " 'In the last days, God says,
I will pour out my Spirit on all people.[j]
Your sons and daughters will prophesy,[k]
your young men will see visions,
your old men will dream dreams.
18 Even on my servants, both men and women,
I will pour out my Spirit in those days,
and they will prophesy.[l]
19 I will show wonders in the heavens above
and signs on the earth below,[m]
blood and fire and billows of smoke.
20 The sun will be turned to darkness
and the moon to blood[n]
before the coming of the great and glorious day of the Lord.
21 And everyone who calls
on the name of the Lord[o] will be saved.'[a][p]

22 "Fellow Israelites, listen to this: Jesus of Nazareth[q] was a man accredited by God to you by miracles, wonders and signs,[r] which God did among you through him,[s] as you yourselves know. 23 This man was handed over to you by God's deliberate plan and foreknowledge;[t] and you, with the help of wicked men,[b] put him to death by nailing him to the cross.[u] 24 But God raised him from the dead,[v] freeing him from the agony of death, because it was impossible for death to keep its hold on him.[w] 25 David said about him:

" 'I saw the Lord always before me.
Because he is at my right hand,
I will not be shaken.
26 Therefore my heart is glad and my tongue rejoices;
my body also will rest in hope,
27 because you will not abandon me to the realm of the dead,
you will not let your holy one see decay.[x]
28 You have made known to me the paths of life;
you will fill me with joy in your presence.'[c][y]

2:15 [i] 1Th 5:7 **2:17** [j] Nu 11:25; Isa 44:3; Eze 39:29; Jn 7:37-39; Ac 10:45 [k] S Ac 21:9 **2:18** [l] Ac 21:9-12 **2:19** [m] Lk 21:11 **2:20** [n] S Mt 24:29 **2:21** [o] Ge 4:26; 26:25; Ps 105:1; Ac 9:14; 1Co 1:2; 2Ti 2:22 [p] Joel 2:28-32; Ro 10:13 **2:22** [q] S Mk 1:24 [r] S Jn 4:48 [s] S Jn 3:2 **2:23** [t] Isa 53:10; Ac 3:18; 4:28 [u] Mt 16:21; Lk 24:20; Ac 3:13 **2:24** [v] ver 32; Ac 13:30,33,34,37; 17:31; Ro 6:4; 8:11; 10:9; 1Co 6:14; 15:15; Eph 1:20; Col 2:12; Heb 13:20; 1Pe 1:21 [w] Jn 20:9 **2:27** [x] ver 31; Ac 13:35 **2:28** [y] Ps 16:8-11

[a] *21* Joel 2:28-32 [b] *23* Or *of those not having the law* (that is, Gentiles) [c] *28* Psalm 16:8-11 (see Septuagint)

groups. Now they stood with Peter, who served as their spokesman.

2:15 *only nine in the morning!* On a festival day such as Pentecost, Jews would not break their fast until at least 10:00 a.m. So it was extremely unlikely that a group of men would be drunk at such an early hour.

2:17–18 *all people ... sons ... daughters ... young men ... old men ... men ... women.* The Spirit is bestowed on all, irrespective of gender, age and rank.

2:17 *last days.* See Isa 2:2 and note; Hos 3:5; Mic 4:1; see also notes on 1Ti 4:1; 2Ti 3:1; Heb 1:2; 1Pe 1:20; 1Jn 2:18. In the passage quoted from Joel, the Hebrew has "afterward" and the Septuagint (the pre-Christian Greek translation of the OT) "after these things." Peter interprets Joel 2:28–32 as referring specifically to the latter days of the new covenant (see Jer 31:33–34; Eze 36:26–27; 39:29), in contrast to the former days of the old covenant. The age of Messianic fulfillment has arrived. *my Spirit.* See note on 1:2.

2:18 *they will prophesy.* See 1Co 12:10 and note.

2:19–20 See notes on Joel 2:30–31; Mk 13:24–25.

2:21 *everyone who calls.* Cf. v. 39; includes faith and response rather than merely using words (Mt 7:21).

2:22 *accredited ... by miracles, wonders and signs.* The mighty works done by Jesus were signs that the Messiah had come.

2:23 *God's deliberate plan and foreknowledge.* God's purpose revealed through the prophets was that the Messiah must suffer and die (see 17:2–3; 26:22–23; Lk 24:25–26,45–46; cf. 1Pe 1:11 and note). *wicked men.* See NIV text note; here, however, the Gentiles were acting in an evil way.

2:24 *it was impossible for death to keep its hold on him.* See v. 36; Ro 1:4 and note; 1Co 15:12–20.

2:27 *not abandon me to the realm of the dead.* David referred ultimately to the Messiah (v. 31). God would not allow his physical body to decompose. See note on Ps 16:9–11.

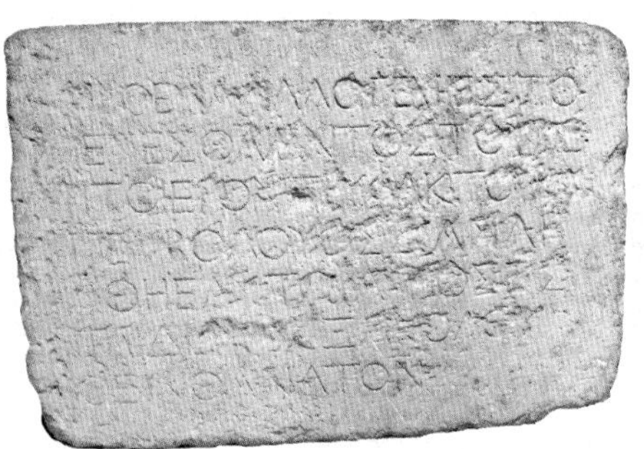

This Greek inscription, dated to the first century AD, was originally mounted on the balustrade (fence) around the Jerusalem temple. The inscription reads, "Foreigners must not enter inside the balustrade or into the forecourt around the sanctuary. Whoever is caught will have himself to blame for his ensuing death." The good news of Jesus Christ challenged this exclusionary message. In Acts the gospel is proclaimed to the whole world.

Todd Bolen/www.BiblePlaces.com

29 "Fellow Israelites,[z] I can tell you confidently that the patriarch[a] David died and was buried,[b] and his tomb is here[c] to this day. 30 But he was a prophet and knew that God had promised him on oath that he would place one of his descendants on his throne.[d] 31 Seeing what was to come, he spoke of the resurrection of the Messiah, that he was not abandoned to the realm of the dead, nor did his body see decay.[e] 32 God has raised this Jesus to life,[f] and we are all witnesses[g] of it. 33 Exalted[h] to the right hand of God,[i] he has received from the Father[j] the promised Holy Spirit[k] and has poured out[l] what you now see and hear. 34 For David did not ascend to heaven, and yet he said,

"'The Lord said to my Lord:
"Sit at my right hand
35 until I make your enemies
a footstool for your feet."'[a][m]

36 "Therefore let all Israel be assured of this: God has made this Jesus, whom you crucified, both Lord[n] and Messiah."[o]

37 When the people heard this, they were cut to the heart and said to Peter and the other apostles, "Brothers, what shall we do?"[p]

38 Peter replied, "Repent and be baptized,[q] every one of you, in the name of Jesus Christ for the forgiveness of your sins.[r] And you will receive the gift of the Holy Spirit.[s] 39 The promise is for you and your children[t] and for all who are far off[u]—for all whom the Lord our God will call."

40 With many other words he warned them; and he pleaded with them, "Save yourselves from this corrupt generation."[v] 41 Those who accepted his message were baptized, and about three thousand were added to their number[w] that day.

The Fellowship of the Believers

42 They devoted themselves to the apostles' teaching[x] and to fellowship, to the breaking of bread[y] and to prayer.[z] 43 Everyone was filled with awe at the many wonders and signs performed by the apostles.[a] 44 All the believers were together and had everything in common.[b] 45 They sold property and possessions to give to anyone who had need.[c] 46 Every day they continued to meet together in the temple courts.[d] They broke bread[e] in their homes and ate together with glad and sincere hearts, 47 praising God and enjoying the

[a] *35* Psalm 110:1

2:29 [z] S Ac 22:5 [a] Ac 7:8,9 [b] 1Ki 2:10; Ac 13:36 [c] Ne 3:16 **2:30** [d] S Mt 1:1 **2:31** [e] Ps 16:10 **2:32** [f] S ver 24 [g] S Lk 24:48 **2:33** [h] S Php 2:9 [i] S Mk 16:19 [j] Ac 1:4 [k] Jn 7:39; 14:26; 15:26 [l] Ac 10:45 **2:35** [m] Ps 110:1; S Mt 22:44 **2:36** [n] S Mt 28:18 [o] S Lk 2:11 **2:37** [p] Lk 3:10, 12,14; Ac 16:30 **2:38** [q] ver 41; Ac 8:12,16,36, 38; 9:18; 10:48; 16:15,33; 19:5; 22:16; Col 2:12 [r] Jer 36:3; Mk 1:4; S Lk 24:47; Ac 3:19 [s] S Jn 20:22 **2:39** [t] Isa 44:3; 65:23 [u] Isa 57:19; Ac 10:45; Eph 2:13 **2:40** [v] Dt 32:5; Php 2:15 **2:41** [w] ver 47; Ac 4:4; 5:14; 6:1,7; 9:31,35, 42; 11:21,24; 14:1,21; 16:5; 17:12 **2:42** [x] Mt 28:20 [y] S Mt 14:19 [z] S Ac 1:14 **2:43** [a] Ac 5:12 **2:44** [b] Ac 4:32 **2:45** [c] Mt 19:21; Lk 12:33; 18:22; Ac 4:34,35; 6:1 **2:46** [d] Lk 24:53; Ac 3:1; 5:21,42 [e] ver 42; S Mt 14:19

2:29 *his tomb is here.* The tomb of David could be seen in Jerusalem. It still contained the remains of David's body. The words of Ps 16:8–11 did not fully apply to him.

2:30 *one of his descendants on his throne.* An allusion to Ps 132:11.

2:33 *Exalted to the right hand of God.* See notes on Lk 22:69; Heb 1:2–3. *promised Holy Spirit.* See note on 1:4. *has poured out.* See v. 17; Joel 2:28.

2:34 *The Lord said to my Lord.* The Lord (God) said to my Lord (the Son of David, the Messiah). According to Peter, David referred to his descendant with uncommon respect because he, through the inspiration of the Spirit, recognized how great and divine he would be (Mt 22:41–45). Not only was he to be resurrected (vv. 31–32) but he was also to be exalted to God's right hand (vv. 33–35). And his presence there was now being demonstrated by the sending of the Holy Spirit (v. 33; Jn 16:7). See Lk 20:42 and note on Ps 110:1; see also introduction to that psalm.

2:37 *cut to the heart.* Because they now realized the enormity of their guilt.

2:38 *Repent and be baptized.* Repentance was important in the message of the forerunner, John the Baptist (Mk 1:4; Lk 3:3), in the preaching of Jesus (Mk 1:15; Lk 13:3) and in the directions Jesus left just before his ascension (Lk 24:47). So also baptism was important to John the Baptist (Mk 1:4), in the instructions of Jesus (Mt 28:18–19) and in the preaching recorded in Acts—where it was associated with belief (8:12; 18:8), acceptance of the word (v. 41) and repentance (here). *in the name of Jesus Christ.* Not a contradiction to the fuller formula given in Mt 28:19. In Acts the abbreviated form emphasizes the distinctive quality of this baptism, for Jesus is now included in a way that he was not in John's baptism (19:4–5). *for the forgiveness of your sins.* Not that baptism effects forgiveness. Rather, forgiveness comes through that which is symbolized by baptism (see Ro 6:3–4; 1Pe 3:21 and notes). *Holy Spirit.* Two gifts are now given: the forgiveness of sins (see also 22:16) and the Holy Spirit. The promise of the indwelling gift of the Holy Spirit is given to all Christians (cf. Ro 8:9–11 and note on 8:9; 1Co 12:13 and note).

2:41 *their number.* The number of believers.

2:42 *apostles' teaching.* Included all that Jesus himself taught (Mt 28:20), especially the gospel, which was centered in his death, burial and resurrection (see vv. 23–24; 3:15; 4:10; 1Co 15:1–4). It was a unique teaching in that it came from God and was clothed with the authority conferred on the apostles (2Co 13:10; 1Th 4:2). Today it is available in the books of the NT. *fellowship.* The corporate fellowship of believers in worship. *breaking of bread.* Although this phrase is used of an ordinary meal in v. 46 (see Lk 24:30,35), the Lord's Supper seems to be indicated here (see note on 20:7; cf. 1Co 10:16; 11:20). *prayer.* Acts emphasizes the importance of prayer in the Christian life—private as well as public (1:14; 3:1; 6:4; 10:4,31; 12:5; 16:13,16).

2:44 *believers were together.* The unity of the early church (see 4:32; Jn 17:11,21–23; Ro 15:5; Eph 4:1–16; Php 2:1–4 and notes). *everything in common.* See 4:34–35. This was a voluntary sharing to provide for those who did not have enough for the essentials of living (see good and bad examples of sharing, 4:36—5:9).

2:46 *temple courts.* Probably Solomon's Colonnade (see 3:11 and note; 5:12). *broke bread in their homes.* Here the daily life of Christians is described, distinguishing their activity in the temple from that in their homes, where they ate their meals—not the Lord's Supper (see note on v. 42)—with gladness and generosity. *glad and sincere hearts.* The fellowship, oneness and sharing enjoyed in the early church are fruits of the Spirit. Joy is to be the mood of the believer (see note on 16:34).

2:47 *praising God.* See 3:8–9; 4:21; 10:46; 11:18; 21:20; emphasized also in Luke's Gospel (see notes on Lk 1:64; 24:53).

favor of all the people.[f] And the Lord added to their number[g] daily those who were being saved.

Peter Heals a Lame Beggar

3 One day Peter and John[h] were going up to the temple[i] at the time of prayer — at three in the afternoon.[j] 2 Now a man who was lame from birth[k] was being carried to the temple gate[l] called Beautiful, where he was put every day to beg[m] from those going into the temple courts. 3 When he saw Peter and John about to enter, he asked them for money. 4 Peter looked straight at him, as did John. Then Peter said, "Look at us!" 5 So the man gave them his attention, expecting to get something from them.

6 Then Peter said, "Silver or gold I do not have, but what I do have I give you. In the name of Jesus Christ of Nazareth,[n] walk." 7 Taking him by the right hand, he helped him up, and instantly the man's feet and ankles became strong. 8 He jumped to his feet and began to walk. Then he went with them into the temple courts, walking and jumping,[o] and praising God. 9 When all the people[p] saw him walking and praising God, 10 they recognized him as the same man who used to sit begging at the temple gate called Beautiful,[q] and they were filled with wonder and amazement at what had happened to him.

Peter Speaks to the Onlookers

11 While the man held on to Peter and John,[r] all the people were astonished and came running to them in the place called Solomon's Colonnade.[s] 12 When Peter saw this, he said to them: "Fellow Israelites, why does this surprise you? Why do you stare at us as if by our own power or godliness we had made this man walk? 13 The God of Abraham, Isaac and Jacob,[t] the God of our fathers,[u] has glorified his servant Jesus. You handed him over[v] to be killed, and you disowned him before Pilate,[w] though he had decided to let him go.[x] 14 You disowned the Holy[y] and Righteous One[z] and asked that a murderer be released to you.[a] 15 You killed the author of life, but God raised him from the dead.[b] We are witnesses[c] of this. 16 By faith in the name of Jesus,[d] this man whom you see and know was made strong. It is Jesus' name and the faith that comes through him that has completely healed him, as you can all see.

17 "Now, fellow Israelites,[e] I know that you acted in ignorance,[f] as did your leaders.[g] 18 But this is how God fulfilled[h] what he had foretold[i] through all the prophets,[j] saying that his Messiah would suffer.[k] 19 Repent, then, and turn to God, so that your sins may be wiped out,[l] that times of refreshing may come from the Lord, 20 and that he may send the Messiah,[m] who has been appointed for you — even Jesus. 21 Heaven must receive him[n] until the time comes for God to restore everything,[o] as he promised long ago through his holy prophets.[p] 22 For Moses said, 'The Lord your God

2:47 [f] S Ro 14:18 [g] S ver 41 **3:1** [h] S Lk 22:8 [i] Ac 2:46 [j] Ps 55:17; Ac 10:30 **3:2** [k] Ac 14:8 [l] Lk 16:20 [m] Jn 9:8 **3:6** [n] ver 16; S Mk 1:24 **3:8** [o] Isa 35:6; Ac 14:10 **3:9** [p] Ac 4:16,21 **3:10** [q] ver 2 **3:11** [r] S Lk 22:8 [s] Jn 10:23; Ac 5:12 **3:13** [t] Ex 3:6 [u] Ac 5:30; 7:32; 22:14 [v] Ac 2:23 [w] S Mt 27:2 [x] S Lk 23:4 **3:14** [y] S Mk 1:24; Ac 4:27 [z] Ac 7:52 [a] Mk 15:11; Lk 23:18-25 **3:15** [b] S Ac 2:24 [c] S Lk 24:48 **3:16** [d] ver 6 **3:17** [e] S Ac 22:5 [f] Lk 23:34 [g] Ac 13:27 **3:18** [h] S Mt 1:22 [i] Ac 2:23 [j] S Lk 24:27 [k] Ac 17:2,3; 26:22,23 **3:19** [l] Ps 51:1; Isa 43:25; 44:22; S Ac 2:38 **3:20** [m] S Lk 2:11 **3:21** [n] Ac 1:11 [o] Mt 17:11; Ac 1:6 [p] Lk 1:70

3:1 *Peter and John.* Among the foremost apostles (Gal 2:9). Along with John's brother, James, they had been especially close to Jesus (Mk 9:2; 13:3; 14:33; Lk 22:8). Arrested together (4:3), they were also together in Samaria (8:14). *time of prayer.* The three stated times of prayer for later Judaism were mid-morning (the third hour, 9:00 a.m.), the time of the evening sacrifice (the ninth hour, 3:00 p.m.) and sunset.
3:2 *gate called Beautiful.* The favorite entrance to the temple court, it was probably the bronze-sheathed gate that is elsewhere called the Nicanor Gate. Apparently it led from the court of the Gentiles to the court of women, east of the temple.
3:6 *In the name of Jesus Christ.* Not by power of their own, but by the authority of the Messiah.
3:7 *he helped him up.* But he had faith to be healed (v. 16).
3:8 *into the temple courts.* From the outer court (for Gentiles also) into the court of women, containing the treasury (Mk 12:41 – 44), and then into the court of Israel (see map, p. 2525, at the end of this study Bible). From the outer court, nine gates led into the inner courts.
3:11 *Solomon's Colonnade.* A porch along the inner side of the wall enclosing the outer court, with rows of 27-foot-high stone columns and a roof of cedar (see note on Jn 10:23).
3:12 – 26 See note on 2:14 – 40.
3:13 *his servant Jesus.* A reminder of the suffering servant prophesied in Isa 52:13 — 53:12 (see Mt 12:18; Ac 4:27,30). *disowned him.* Voted against Jesus, spurned him, denied him and refused to acknowledge him as the true Messiah. *Pilate . . . had decided to let him go.* See Jn 19:12.
3:14 *Holy . . . One.* Cf. note on Lev 11:44. *Righteous One.* For this description of the Messiah elsewhere, see 7:52; 22:14; cf. 1Jn 2:1. *murderer.* Barabbas (see Lk 23:18 and note).
3:15 *You killed . . . God raised . . . We are witnesses.* A recurring theme in the speeches of Acts (see 2:23 – 24; 4:10; 5:30 – 32; 10:39 – 41; 13:28 – 29; cf. 1Co 15:1 – 4).
3:17 *you acted in ignorance.* They did not know that Jesus was the true Messiah (see Lk 23:34). Nevertheless, God will be generous in his mercy if they only repent and turn to him (see v. 19 and note).
3:18 *foretold through all the prophets.* Echoes what Jesus had said (Lk 24:26 – 27). The suffering was prophesied (compare Isa 53:7 – 8 with Ac 8:32 – 33; Ps 2:1 – 2 with Ac 4:25 – 26; Ps 22:1 with Mt 27:46; see also Lk 24:44; 1Pe 1:11 and notes).
3:19 *Repent.* Repentance is a change of mind and will arising from sorrow for sin and leading to transformation of life (see notes on 2:38; Lk 3:3). *turn to God.* Subsequent to repentance and not completely identical with it. See 11:21 ("believed and turned") and 26:20 ("repent and turn"; see also 9:35; 14:15; 15:19; 26:18; 28:27). In the strictest sense, repentance is turning from sin, and faith is turning to God. However, the word "turn" is not always used with such precision. *your sins . . . wiped out.* Your sins will be forgiven as a result of repentance.

will raise up for you a prophet like me
from among your own people; you must
listen to everything he tells you.[q] 23 Anyone
who does not listen to him will be completely cut off from their people.'[a][r]
24 "Indeed, beginning with Samuel,
all the prophets[s] who have spoken have
foretold these days. 25 And you are heirs[t]
of the prophets and of the covenant[u] God
made with your fathers. He said to Abraham, 'Through your offspring all peoples
on earth will be blessed.'[b][v] 26 When God
raised up[w] his servant, he sent him first[x]
to you to bless you by turning each of you
from your wicked ways."

Peter and John Before the Sanhedrin

4 The priests and the captain of the temple guard[y] and the Sadducees[z] came
up to Peter and John while they were
speaking to the people. 2 They were greatly disturbed because the apostles were
teaching the people, proclaiming in Jesus
the resurrection of the dead.[a] 3 They seized
Peter and John and, because it was evening, they put them in jail[b] until the next
day. 4 But many who heard the message
believed; so the number of men who believed grew[c] to about five thousand.
5 The next day the rulers,[d] the elders and
the teachers of the law met in Jerusalem.
6 Annas the high priest was there, and so
were Caiaphas,[e] John, Alexander and others of the high priest's family. 7 They had
Peter and John brought before them and
began to question them: "By what power
or what name did you do this?"
8 Then Peter, filled with the Holy Spirit,[f] said to them: "Rulers and elders of the
people![g] 9 If we are being called to account
today for an act of kindness shown to a
man who was lame[h] and are being asked
how he was healed, 10 then know this, you
and all the people of Israel: It is by the
name of Jesus Christ of Nazareth,[i] whom
you crucified but whom God raised from
the dead,[j] that this man stands before you
healed. 11 Jesus is

> " 'the stone you builders rejected,
> which has become the cornerstone.'[c][k]

12 Salvation is found in no one else, for
there is no other name under heaven given
to mankind by which we must be saved."[l]
13 When they saw the courage of Peter
and John[m] and realized that they were unschooled, ordinary men,[n] they were astonished and they took note that these men
had been with Jesus.[o] 14 But since they
could see the man who had been healed
standing there with them, there was nothing they could say. 15 So they ordered them
to withdraw from the Sanhedrin[p] and then
conferred together. 16 "What are we going to do with these men?"[q] they asked.

3:22 [q] Dt 18:15, 18; Ac 7:37 **3:23** [r] Dt 18:19 **3:24** [s] S Lk 24:27 **3:25** [t] Ac 2:39 [u] Ro 9:4,5 [v] Ge 12:3; 22:18; 26:4; 28:14 **3:26** [w] ver 22; S Ac 2:24 [x] Ac 13:46; Ro 1:16 **4:1** [y] Lk 22:4 [z] Mt 3:7; 16:1, 6; 22:23,34; Ac 5:17; 23:6-8 **4:2** [a] Ac 17:18 **4:3** [b] Ac 5:18 **4:4** [c] S Ac 2:41 **4:5** [d] Lk 23:13 **4:6** [e] S Mt 26:3 **4:8** [f] S Lk 1:15 [g] ver 5; Lk 23:13 **4:9** [h] Ac 3:6 **4:10** [i] S Mk 1:24 [j] S Ac 2:24 **4:11** [k] Ps 118:22; Isa 28:16; Zec 10:4; Mt 21:42; Eph 2:20; 1Pe 2:7 **4:12** [l] S Mt 1:21; Jn 14:6; Ac 10:43; S Ro 11:14; 1Ti 2:5 **4:13** [m] S Lk 22:8 [n] Mt 11:25 [o] Mk 3:14 **4:15** [p] S Mt 5:22 **4:16** [q] Jn 11:47

[a] *23* Deut. 18:15,18,19 [b] *25* Gen. 22:18; 26:4 [c] *11* Psalm 118:22

3:22,26 *raise up ... raised up.* Christ is the fulfillment of prophecies made relative to Moses, David and Abraham. He was to be a prophet like Moses (vv. 22–23), he was foretold in Samuel's declarations concerning David (v. 24; see note there) and he was to bring blessing to all people as promised to Abraham (vv. 25–26).

3:24 *beginning with Samuel, all the prophets ... foretold.* Samuel anointed David to be king and spoke of the establishment of his kingdom (1Sa 16:13; cf. 13:14; 15:28; 28:17). Nathan's prophecy (2Sa 7:12–16) was ultimately Messianic (see Ac 13:22–23,34; Heb 1:5).

3:25 *offspring.* The word is singular, ultimately signifying Christ (see Gal 3:16).

4:1 *priests.* Those who were serving that week in the temple precincts (see note on Lk 1:23). *captain of the temple guard.* A member of one of the leading priestly families; next in rank to the high priest (see 5:24,26; Lk 22:4,52). *Sadducees.* A Jewish sect whose members came from the priestly line and controlled the temple. They did not believe in the resurrection or a personal Messiah but held that the Messianic age—an ideal time—was then present and must be preserved. The high priest, one of their number, presided over the Sanhedrin (see 5:17; 23:6–8; Mt 22:23–33). See notes on Ezr 7:2; Mt 3:7; Mk 12:18; Lk 20:27; see also essay, p. 1576, and chart, p. 1631.

4:2 *in Jesus.* On the basis of Jesus' resurrection.

4:3 *evening.* The evening sacrifices ended about 4:00 p.m., and the temple gates would be closed at that time. Any judgments involving life and death must be begun and concluded in daylight hours.

4:4 *men.* Lit. "males." *five thousand.* A growth from the 3,000 at Pentecost (2:41); see later growth (5:14; 6:7).

4:5 *rulers, the elders and the teachers of the law.* The three groups making up the Sanhedrin, Israel's supreme court (see Lk 22:66; see also notes on Mt 2:4; 15:2; Mk 2:16; 14:55; Lk 5:17).

4:6 *Annas.* High priest AD 6–15, but deposed by the Romans and succeeded by his son, Eleazar, then by his son-in-law, Caiaphas (18–36), who was also called Joseph. However, Annas was still recognized by the Jews as high priest (Lk 3:2; cf. Jn 18:13, 24). *John.* May be Jonathan, son of Annas, who was appointed high priest in AD 36. Others suggest that it was Johanan ben Zakkai, who became the president of the Great Synagogue after the fall of Jerusalem. *Alexander.* Not further identified.

4:8 *filled with the Holy Spirit.* See note on 2:4.

4:10 *Jesus Christ of Nazareth.* See Mt 2:23 and note.

4:11 *the stone ... rejected.* Fulfillment of prophecy was an important element in early Christian sermons and defenses. Jesus had also used Ps 118:22 (Mt 21:42; see 1Pe 2:7 and cf. Ro 9:33; Isa 28:16). *cornerstone.* See note on Ps 118:22.

4:12 *no other name.* See 10:43; Jn 14:6; 1Ti 2:5; see also NIV text note on Mt 1:21.

4:13 *courage.* A certain boldness characterized by the assurance, authority and forthrightness of the apostles (2:29; 4:29; 28:31), and shared by the believers (4:31). *unschooled, ordinary men.* Peter and John had not been trained in the rabbinic schools, nor did they hold official positions in recognized religious circles. *took note that these men had been with Jesus.* Probably because they were displaying some of his power and authority (cf. Mk 1:22 and note; 3:14).

4:15 *Sanhedrin.* See notes on v. 5; 5:21; Mk 14:55.

"Everyone living in Jerusalem knows they
have performed a notable sign,[r] and we
cannot deny it. 17But to stop this thing
from spreading any further among the
people, we must warn them to speak no
longer to anyone in this name."

18Then they called them in again and
commanded them not to speak or teach
at all in the name of Jesus.[s] 19But Peter
and John replied, "Which is right in God's
eyes: to listen to you, or to him?[t] You be the
judges! 20As for us, we cannot help speaking[u] about what we have seen and heard."[v]

21After further threats they let them
go. They could not decide how to punish
them, because all the people[w] were praising God[x] for what had happened. 22For the
man who was miraculously healed was
over forty years old.

The Believers Pray

23On their release, Peter and John went
back to their own people and reported all
that the chief priests and the elders had
said to them. 24When they heard this,
they raised their voices together in prayer
to God.[y] "Sovereign Lord," they said, "you
made the heavens and the earth and the
sea, and everything in them.[z] 25You spoke
by the Holy Spirit through the mouth of
your servant, our father David:[a]

"'Why do the nations rage
and the peoples plot in vain?
26The kings of the earth rise up
and the rulers band together
against the Lord
and against his anointed one.[a][b][b]

27Indeed Herod[c] and Pontius Pilate[d] met
together with the Gentiles and the people of Israel in this city to conspire against
your holy servant Jesus,[e] whom you
anointed. 28They did what your power and
will had decided beforehand should happen.[f] 29Now, Lord, consider their threats
and enable your servants to speak your
word with great boldness.[g] 30Stretch out
your hand to heal and perform signs and
wonders[h] through the name of your holy
servant Jesus."[i]

31After they prayed, the place where
they were meeting was shaken.[j] And they
were all filled with the Holy Spirit[k] and
spoke the word of God[l] boldly.[m]

The Believers Share Their Possessions

32All the believers were one in heart
and mind. No one claimed that any of
their possessions was their own, but they
shared everything they had.[n] 33With great
power the apostles continued to testify[o] to
the resurrection[p] of the Lord Jesus. And
God's grace[q] was so powerfully at work in
them all 34that there were no needy persons among them. For from time to time
those who owned land or houses sold
them,[r] brought the money from the sales
35and put it at the apostles' feet,[s] and it
was distributed to anyone who had need.[t]

36Joseph, a Levite from Cyprus, whom
the apostles called Barnabas[u] (which
means "son of encouragement"), 37sold
a field he owned and brought the money
and put it at the apostles' feet.[v]

Ananias and Sapphira

5 Now a man named Ananias, together with his wife Sapphira, also sold

4:16 [r] Ac 3:6-10 **4:18** [s] Am 7:13; Ac 5:40 **4:19** [t] Ac 5:29 **4:20** [u] Job 32:18; Jer 20:9; Am 3:8 [v] S Lk 24:48 **4:21** [w] Ac 5:26 [x] S Mt 9:8 **4:24** [y] S Ac 1:14 [z] Ne 9:6; Job 41:11; Isa 37:16 **4:25** [a] Ac 1:16 **4:26** [b] Ps 2:1,2; Da 9:25; Lk 4:18; Ac 10:38; Heb 1:9 **4:27** [c] S Mt 14:1 [d] S Mt 27:2; Lk 23:12 [e] ver 30; Ac 3:13,14 **4:28** [f] Ac 2:23 **4:29** [g] ver 13, 31; Ps 138:3; Ac 9:27; 13:46; 14:3; 28:31; Eph 6:19; Php 1:14 **4:30** [h] S Jn 4:48 [i] ver 27 **4:31** [j] Ac 2:2 [k] S Lk 1:15 [l] S Heb 4:12 [m] S ver 29 **4:32** [n] Ac 2:44 **4:33** [o] S Lk 24:48 [p] Ac 1:22 [q] S Ro 3:24 **4:34** [r] Mt 19:21; Ac 2:45 **4:35** [s] ver 37; Ac 5:2 [t] Ac 2:45; 6:1 **4:36** [u] Ac 9:27; 11:22,30; 13:2; 1Co 9:6; Gal 2:1,9,13 **4:37** [v] ver 35; Ac 5:2

[a] *26* That is, Messiah or Christ [b] *26* Psalm 2:1,2

4:19 See note on Ro 13:3.
4:20 *cannot help speaking.* See 5:29; cf. Jer 20:9 and note.
4:22 *forty years old.* Normally healing at such an advanced age (for that time) did not take place.
4:23 *went back.* Probably to the same upper room where the apostles had met before (1:13) and where the congregation may have continued to meet (12:12).
4:24 *Sovereign Lord.* See Lk 2:29.
4:27 *Herod.* Herod Antipas, tetrarch of Galilee and Perea (Lk 23:7–15; see chart, p. 1592). *Pontius Pilate.* Roman governor of Judea (see Lk 3:1 and note).
4:28 *decided beforehand.* Not that God had compelled them to act as they did, but he willed to use them and their freely chosen acts to accomplish his saving purpose (see 2:23).
4:30 *holy servant.* See note on 3:13.
4:31 *was shaken.* An immediate sign that the prayers had been heard (see 16:26). *filled with the Holy Spirit.* See note on 2:4. *spoke the word of God.* They continued preaching the gospel despite the warnings of the council (see note on v. 13).
4:32 *one in heart and mind.* In complete accord, extending to their attitude toward personal possessions (see 2:44 and note).
4:33 *testify to the resurrection.* As significant as the death of Christ was, the most compelling event was the resurrection—an event about which the disciples could not keep silent.
4:34 *those who owned land or houses sold them.* See note on 2:44.
4:36 *Levite.* Although Levites owned no inherited land in the Holy Land, these regulations may not have applied to the Levites in other countries, such as Cyprus. So perhaps Barnabas sold land he owned in Cyprus and brought the proceeds to the apostles (v. 37). Or he may have been married, and the land sold may have been from his wife's property. It is also possible that the prohibition against Levite ownership of land in the Holy Land was no longer observed. *Cyprus.* An island in the eastern part of the Mediterranean Sea. Jews had settled there from Maccabean times. *Barnabas.* Used here as a good example of giving. In this way Luke introduces the one who will become an important companion of Paul (see 13:1–4). For other significant contributions of this greathearted leader to the life and ministry of the early church, see 9:27; 11:22,25; 15:37–39.
5:1 *Ananias ... Sapphira.* Given as bad examples of sharing (Barnabas was the good example; see note on 4:36). Love of praise for (pretended) generosity and love for money led to the first recorded sin in the life of the church. It is a warning to the readers that "God cannot be mocked" (Gal

a piece of property. 2 With his wife's full
knowledge he kept back part of the money
for himself,[w] but brought the rest and put
it at the apostles' feet.[x]
3 Then Peter said, "Ananias, how is it
that Satan[y] has so filled your heart[z] that
you have lied to the Holy Spirit[a] and have
kept for yourself some of the money you
received for the land?[b] 4 Didn't it belong to
you before it was sold? And after it was
sold, wasn't the money at your disposal?[c] What made you think of doing such
a thing? You have not lied just to human
beings but to God."[d]
5 When Ananias heard this, he fell down
and died.[e] And great fear[f] seized all who
heard what had happened. 6 Then some
young men came forward, wrapped up
his body,[g] and carried him out and buried him.
7 About three hours later his wife came
in, not knowing what had happened. 8 Peter asked her, "Tell me, is this the price
you and Ananias got for the land?"
"Yes," she said, "that is the price."[h]
9 Peter said to her, "How could you conspire to test the Spirit of the Lord?[i] Listen!
The feet of the men who buried your husband are at the door, and they will carry
you out also."
10 At that moment she fell down at his
feet and died.[j] Then the young men came
in and, finding her dead, carried her out
and buried her beside her husband.[k]
11 Great fear[l] seized the whole church and
all who heard about these events.

The Apostles Heal Many

12 The apostles performed many signs
and wonders[m] among the people. And all
the believers used to meet together[n] in Solomon's Colonnade.[o] 13 No one else dared
join them, even though they were highly
regarded by the people.[p] 14 Nevertheless,
more and more men and women believed
in the Lord and were added to their number.[q] 15 As a result, people brought the sick
into the streets and laid them on beds and
mats so that at least Peter's shadow might
fall on some of them as he passed by.[r]
16 Crowds gathered also from the towns
around Jerusalem, bringing their sick and
those tormented by impure spirits, and all
of them were healed.[s]

The Apostles Persecuted

17 Then the high priest and all his associates, who were members of the party[t] of
the Sadducees,[u] were filled with jealousy.
18 They arrested the apostles and put them
in the public jail.[v] 19 But during the night
an angel[w] of the Lord opened the doors
of the jail[x] and brought them out.[y] 20 "Go,
stand in the temple courts," he said, "and
tell the people all about this new life."[z]
21 At daybreak they entered the temple
courts, as they had been told, and began
to teach the people.
When the high priest and his associates[a]
arrived, they called together the Sanhedrin[b] — the full assembly of the elders of Israel — and sent to the jail for the apostles.

5:2 [w] Jos 7:11 [x] Ac 4:35,37 **5:3** [y] S Mt 4:10 [z] Jn 13:2, 27 [a] ver 9 [b] Dt 23:21 **5:4** [c] Dt 23:22 [d] Lev 6:2 **5:5** [e] ver 10; Ps 5:6 [f] ver 11 **5:6** [g] Jn 19:40 **5:8** [h] ver 2 **5:9** [i] ver 3 **5:10** [j] ver 5 [k] ver 6 **5:11** [l] ver 5; Ac 19:17

5:12 [m] S Jn 4:48; Ac 2:43 [n] Ac 4:32 [o] Jn 10:23; Ac 3:11 **5:13** [p] Ac 2:47; 4:21 **5:14** [q] S Ac 2:41 **5:15** [r] Ac 19:12 **5:16** [s] Mt 8:16; S Mk 16:17 **5:17** [t] Ac 15:5 [u] S Ac 4:1 **5:18** [v] Ac 4:3 **5:19** [w] Ge 16:7; Ex 3:2; Mt 1:20; 2:13,19; 28:2; Lk 1:11; 2:9; S Jn 20:12; Ac 8:26; 10:3; 12:7,23; 27:23 [x] Ac 16:26 [y] Ps 34:7 **5:20** [z] Jn 6:63, 68 **5:21** [a] Ac 4:5,6 [b] ver 27,34,41; S Mt 5:22

6:7). Compare this divine judgment at the beginning of the church era with God's judgments on Nadab and Abihu (Lev 10:2), on Achan (Jos 7:25) and on Uzzah (2Sa 6:7).

5:2 *kept back part.* They had a right to keep back whatever they chose, but to make it appear that they had given all when they had not was sinful.

5:3 *Satan has so filled your heart.* The continuing activity of Satan is noted (see Lk 22:3; Jn 13:2,27; 1Pe 5:8). *lied to the Holy Spirit.* A comparison with v. 4 shows that the Holy Spirit is regarded as God himself present with his people.

5:9 *test the Spirit of the Lord.* If no dire consequences had followed this act of sin, the results among the believers would have been serious when the deceit became known. Not only would dishonesty appear profitable, but the conclusion that the Spirit could be deceived would follow. It was important to set the course properly at the outset in order to leave no doubt that God will not tolerate such hypocrisy and deceit (see vv. 2,8).

5:11 See v. 5. *church.* The first use of the term in Acts. It can denote either the local congregation (8:1; 11:22; 13:1) or the universal church (see 20:28). The Greek word for "church" (*ekklesia*) was already being used for political and other assemblies (see 19:32,41) and, in the Septuagint (the pre-Christian Greek translation of the OT), for Israel when gathered in religious assembly.

5:12 *Solomon's Colonnade.* See note on 3:11.

5:13 *No one else dared join them.* Because of the fate of Ananias and his wife, no pretenders or halfhearted followers risked identification with the believers. Luke cannot mean that no one joined the Christian community, since v. 14 indicates that many were coming to Christ.

5:14 *more men and women believed.* See 4:4. This is the first specific mention of women believing (cf. 8:3,12; 9:2; 13:50; 16:1,13–14; 17:4,12,34; 18:2; 21:5; but cf. also 1:14).

5:15 *Peter's shadow.* Parallels such items as Paul's handkerchiefs (19:12) and the edge of Jesus' cloak (Mt 9:20) — not that any of these material objects had magical qualities, but the least article or shadow represented a direct means of contact with Jesus or his apostles.

5:17 *high priest.* The official high priest recognized by Rome was Caiaphas, but the Jews considered Annas, Caiaphas's father-in-law, to be the actual high priest since the high priesthood was to be held for life (see note on 4:6). *his associates.* His family members. *party of the Sadducees.* See note on 4:1.

5:18 *in the public jail.* To await trial the next day.

5:19 *angel of the Lord.* This phrase is used four other times in Acts: (1) Stephen speaks of him (7:30–38); (2) he guides Philip (8:26); (3) he liberates Peter (12:7–10); and (4) he strikes down Herod (12:23). See also Mt 1:20–24; 2:13,19; 28:2; Lk 1:11–38; 2:9 and notes on Ge 16:7; 2Ki 1:3; Ps 34:7; Zec 1:8.

5:20 *all about this new life.* The good news of eternal life in all its fullness (see Jn 6:68; Ro 6:4; 2Co 5:17; Php 1:21 and notes).

5:21 *Sanhedrin.* The supreme Jewish court, consisting of 70 to 100 men (71 being the proper number). They sat in a semicircle, backed by three rows of disciples of the learned men

22 But on arriving at the jail, the officers did not find them there.[c] So they went back and reported, 23 "We found the jail securely locked, with the guards standing at the doors; but when we opened them, we found no one inside." 24 On hearing this report, the captain of the temple guard and the chief priests[d] were at a loss, wondering what this might lead to.

25 Then someone came and said, "Look! The men you put in jail are standing in the temple courts teaching the people." 26 At that, the captain went with his officers and brought the apostles. They did not use force, because they feared that the people[e] would stone them.

27 The apostles were brought in and made to appear before the Sanhedrin[f] to be questioned by the high priest. 28 "We gave you strict orders not to teach in this name,"[g] he said. "Yet you have filled Jerusalem with your teaching and are determined to make us guilty of this man's blood."[h]

29 Peter and the other apostles replied: "We must obey God rather than human beings![i] 30 The God of our ancestors[j] raised Jesus from the dead[k]—whom you killed by hanging him on a cross.[l] 31 God exalted him to his own right hand[m] as Prince and Savior[n] that he might bring Israel to repentance and forgive their sins.[o] 32 We are witnesses of these things,[p] and so is the Holy Spirit,[q] whom God has given to those who obey him."

33 When they heard this, they were furious[r] and wanted to put them to death. 34 But a Pharisee named Gamaliel,[s] a teacher of the law,[t] who was honored by all the people, stood up in the Sanhedrin and ordered that the men be put outside for a little while. 35 Then he addressed the Sanhedrin: "Men of Israel, consider carefully what you intend to do to these men. 36 Some time ago Theudas appeared, claiming to be somebody, and about four hundred men rallied to him. He was killed, all his followers were dispersed, and it all came to nothing. 37 After him, Judas the Galilean appeared in the days of the census[u] and led a band of people in revolt. He too was killed, and all his followers were scattered. 38 Therefore, in the present case I advise you: Leave these men alone! Let them go! For if their purpose or activity is of human origin, it will fail.[v] 39 But if it is from God, you will not be able to stop these men; you will only find yourselves fighting against God."[w]

40 His speech persuaded them. They called the apostles in and had them flogged.[x] Then they ordered them not to speak in the name of Jesus, and let them go.

41 The apostles left the Sanhedrin, rejoicing[y] because they had been counted worthy of suffering disgrace for the Name.[z] 42 Day after day, in the temple courts[a] and from house to house, they never stopped teaching and proclaiming the good news[b] that Jesus is the Messiah.[c]

The Choosing of the Seven

6 In those days when the number of disciples was increasing,[d] the Hellenistic Jews[a][e] among them complained against the Hebraic Jews because their widows[f]

5:22 [c] Ac 12:18, 19
5:24 [d] Ac 4:1
5:26 [e] Ac 4:21
5:27 [f] S Mt 5:22
5:28 [g] Ac 4:18 [h] Mt 23:35; 27:25; Ac 2:23, 36; 3:14, 15; 7:52
5:29 [i] Ex 1:17; Ac 4:19
5:30 [j] S Ac 3:13 [k] S Ac 2:24 [l] Ac 10:39; 13:29; Gal 3:13
5:31 [m] S Mk 16:19 [n] S Lk 2:11 [o] S Mt 1:21; Mk 1:4; Lk 24:47; Ac 2:38; 3:19; 10:43
5:32 [p] S Lk 24:48 [q] Jn 15:26
5:33 [r] Ac 2:37; 7:54
5:34 [s] Ac 22:3 [t] Lk 2:46; 5:17
5:37 [u] Lk 2:1, 2
5:38 [v] Mt 15:13
5:39 [w] 2Ch 13:12; Pr 21:30; Isa 46:10; Ac 7:51; 11:17
5:40 [x] S Mt 10:17
5:41 [y] S Mt 5:12 [z] S Jn 15:21
5:42 [a] S Ac 2:46 [b] S Ac 13:32 [c] S Ac 9:22
6:1 [d] S Ac 2:41 [e] Ac 9:29 [f] Ac 9:39, 41; 1Ti 5:3

[a] *1* That is, Jews who had adopted the Greek language and culture

(cf. 4:13 and note), with the clerks of the court standing in front. See note on Mk 14:55.

5:24 *captain of the temple guard.* See note on 4:1.

5:28 *make us guilty of this man's blood.* Probably a reference to the apostles' repeated declaration that some of the Jews and some of their leaders had killed Jesus (2:23; 3:13–15; 4:10–11; cf. Mt 27:25).

5:29 See 4:19 and note.

5:30 *cross.* See Jn 19:17; 1Pe 2:24 and notes; see also Dt 21:22–23. Like its Hebrew counterpart, the Greek for this word could refer to a tree, a pole, a wooden beam (or "cross") or some similar object.

5:32 *so is the Holy Spirit . . . given to those who obey him.* See Jn 15:26–27. The disciples' testimony was directed and confirmed by the Holy Spirit, who convicts the world through the word (Jn 16:8–11) and is given to those who respond to God with faith and obedience (Ro 1:5; see note on Ac 6:7).

5:34 *a Pharisee named Gamaliel.* The most famous Jewish teacher of his time and traditionally listed among the "heads of the schools." Possibly he was the grandson of Hillel. Like Hillel (see note on Mt 19:3), he was moderate in his views, a characteristic that is apparent in his cautious recommendation on this occasion. Saul (Paul) was one of his students (22:3).

5:36 *Theudas.* Unknown, though Josephus mentions another man by this name who appeared about ten years later.

5:37 *Judas the Galilean.* The Jewish historian Josephus refers to him as a man from Gamala in Gaulanitis who refused to give tribute to Caesar. His revolt was crushed, but a movement, started in his time, may have lived on in the party of the Zealots (see 1:13 and note on Mt 10:4). *days of the census.* Not the first census of Quirinius, noted by Luke in his Gospel (see Lk 2:2 and note), but the one in AD 6.

5:39 *not . . . stop these men.* Gamaliel's words proved prophetic and serve as thematic for Acts. Since nothing can stop the church throughout Acts, it is proven to be the work of God.

5:40 *flogged.* Beaten with the Jewish penalty of "forty lashes minus one" (2Co 11:24).

6:1 *the number of disciples was increasing.* A considerable length of time may have transpired since the end of ch. 5. The church continued to grow (see 5:14), but this gave rise to inevitable problems, both from within (6:1–7) and from without (6:8—7:60). At this stage of its development, the church was entirely Jewish in its composition. However, there were two groups of Jews within the fellowship: (1) *Hellenistic Jews.* Those born in lands other than the Holy Land who spoke the Greek language and were more Grecian than Hebraic in their attitudes and outlook (see NIV text note). (2) *Hebraic Jews.* Those who spoke Palestinian Ara-

were being overlooked in the daily distribution of food.[g] 2So the Twelve gathered all the disciples[h] together and said,
"It would not be right for us to neglect
the ministry of the word of God[i] in order
to wait on tables. 3Brothers and sisters,[j]
choose seven men from among you who
are known to be full of the Spirit[k] and wisdom. We will turn this responsibility over
to them[l] 4and will give our attention to
prayer[m] and the ministry of the word."
5This proposal pleased the whole group.
They chose Stephen,[n] a man full of faith
and of the Holy Spirit;[o] also Philip,[p] Proc-
orus, Nicanor, Timon, Parmenas, and Nicolas from Antioch, a convert to Judaism.
6They presented these men to the apostles, who prayed[q] and laid their hands on
them.[r]
7So the word of God spread.[s] The number of disciples in Jerusalem increased
rapidly,[t] and a large number of priests became obedient to the faith.

6:1 [g] Ac 4:35
6:2 [h] S Ac 11:26 [i] S Heb 4:12
6:3 [j] S Ac 1:16 [k] S Lk 1:15 [l] Ex 18:21; Ne 13:13
6:4 [m] S Ac 1:14
6:5 [n] ver 8; Ac 7:55-60; 11:19; 22:20 [o] S Lk 1:15 [p] Ac 8:5-40; 21:8
6:6 [q] S Ac 1:24 [r] Nu 8:10; 27:18; Ac 9:17; 19:6; 28:8; 1Ti 4:14; S Mk 5:23
6:7 [s] Ac 12:24; 19:20 [t] S Ac 2:41
6:8 [u] S Jn 4:48
6:9 [v] S Mt 27:32 [w] Ac 15:23,41; 22:3; 23:34 [x] S Ac 2:9
6:10 [y] Lk 21:15
6:11 [z] 1Ki 21:10 [a] Mt 26:59-61
6:12 [b] S Mt 5:22
6:13 [c] Ex 23:1; Ps 27:12 [d] Mt 24:15; Ac 7:48; 21:28

Stephen Seized

8Now Stephen, a man full of God's
grace and power, performed great wonders and signs[u] among the people. 9Op-
position arose, however, from members of
the Synagogue of the Freedmen (as it was
called)—Jews of Cyrene[v] and Alexandria
as well as the provinces of Cilicia[w] and
Asia[x]—who began to argue with Stephen.
10But they could not stand up against the
wisdom the Spirit gave him as he spoke.[y]
11Then they secretly[z] persuaded some
men to say, "We have heard Stephen
speak blasphemous words against Moses
and against God."[a]
12So they stirred up the people and the
elders and the teachers of the law. They
seized Stephen and brought him before
the Sanhedrin.[b] 13They produced false witnesses,[c] who testified, "This fellow never
stops speaking against this holy place[d] and

---

maic and/or Hebrew and preserved Jewish culture and customs. *daily distribution of food.* Help was needed by widows who had no one to care for them and so became the church's responsibility (cf. 4:35; 11:28–29; see also 1Ti 5:3–16).

6:2 *the Twelve.* At this early stage, the apostles were responsible for church life in general, including the ministry of the word of God and the care of the needy. *to wait on tables.* To preside over the distribution of charitable gifts. The early church was concerned not only about a spiritual ministry ("ministry of the word" and "prayer"; see v. 4) but also about a material ministry.

6:3 *choose seven men.* The church elected them (v. 5), and the apostles ordained them ("laid their hands on them," v. 6). In this way they were appointed to their work. *full of the Spirit.* See note on 2:4.

6:5 *They chose Stephen … Nicolas.* It is significant that all seven of the men chosen had Greek names. The murmuring had come from the Greek-speaking segment of the church; those elected to care for the work came from their number so as to represent their interests fairly. Only Stephen and Philip of the Seven receive further notice (Stephen, 6:8—7:60; Philip, 8:5–40; 21:8–9). *from Antioch, a convert to Judaism.* It is significant that a convert to Judaism was included in the number and that Luke points out his place of origin as Antioch, the city to which the gospel was soon to be taken and which was to become the headquarters for the forthcoming Gentile missionary effort.

6:6 *prayed and laid their hands on them.* Laying on of hands was used in the OT period to confer blessing (Ge 48:13–20), to transfer guilt from sinner to sacrifice (Lev 1:4) and to commission a person for a new responsibility (Nu 27:23). In the NT period, laying on of hands was observed in healing (28:8; Mk 1:41), blessing (Mk 10:16), ordaining or commissioning (Ac 6:6; 13:3; 1Ti 5:22) and imparting of spiritual gifts (Ac 8:17; 19:6; 1Ti 4:14; 2Ti 1:6). These seven men were appointed to responsibilities turned over to them by the Twelve. The Greek word used to describe their responsibility ("wait on") is the verb from which the noun "deacon" comes. Later one reads of deacons in Php 1:1; 1Ti 3:8–13. The Greek noun for "deacon" can also be translated "minister" or "servant." The men appointed on this occasion were simply called the Seven (21:8), just as the apostles were called the Twelve. It is disputed whether the Seven were the first deacons or whether the office of deacon arose later (see note on 1Ti 3:8).

6:7 One of a series of progress reports given periodically throughout the book of Acts (1:15; 2:41; 4:4; 5:14; 6:7; 9:31; 12:24; 16:5; 19:20; 28:31). *a large number of priests.* Though involved by lineage and life service in the priestly observances of the old covenant, they accepted the preaching of the apostles, which proclaimed a sacrifice that made the old sacrifices unnecessary (see Heb 8:13 and note; 10:1–4, 11–14). *became obedient to the faith.* Responded to the commands of the gospel. To believe is to obey God. Faith itself is obedience, but faith also produces obedience (Ro 1:5; Eph 2:8–10; Jas 2:14–26).

6:8 *great wonders and signs.* Until now, Acts told of only the apostles working miracles (2:43; 3:4–8; 5:12). But now, after the laying on of the apostles' hands, Stephen too is reported as working miraculous signs. Philip also will soon do the same (8:6).

6:9 *Freedmen.* Persons who had been freed from slavery. They came from different Hellenistic areas. *Cyrene.* The chief city in Libya and north Africa (see notes on 2:10; Mk 15:21), halfway between Alexandria and Carthage. One of its population groups was Jewish (see 11:19–21). *Alexandria.* Capital of Egypt and second only to Rome in the empire. Two out of five districts in Alexandria were Jewish. *Cilicia.* A Roman province in the southeast corner of Asia Minor, adjoining Syria. Tarsus, the birthplace of Saul, was one of its principal towns. *Asia.* A Roman province in the western part of Asia Minor. Ephesus, where Saul (Paul) later ministered for a few years, was its capital. *began to argue.* Since Saul was from Tarsus, this may have been the synagogue he attended, and he may have been among those who argued with Stephen. He was present when Stephen was stoned (7:58).

6:11 *blasphemous words against Moses and against God.* Since Stephen declared that the worship of God was no longer to be restricted to the temple (7:48–49), his opponents twisted these words to trump up an accusation that Stephen was attacking the temple, the law, Moses and, ultimately, God.

6:12 *the elders and the teachers of the law.* See notes on Mt 2:4; 15:2; Mk 2:16; Lk 5:17. *Sanhedrin.* See note on Mk 14:55.

6:13 *speaking against this holy place and against the law.* Similar to the charges brought against Christ (see Mt 26:61).

against the law. 14 For we have heard him
say that this Jesus of Nazareth will destroy
this place[e] and change the customs Moses
handed down to us."[f]
15 All who were sitting in the Sanhedrin[g]
looked intently at Stephen, and they saw
that his face was like the face of an angel.

Stephen's Speech to the Sanhedrin

7 Then the high priest asked Stephen,
"Are these charges true?"
2 To this he replied: "Brothers and fathers,[h] listen to me! The God of glory[i] appeared to our father Abraham while he
was still in Mesopotamia, before he lived
in Harran.[j] 3 'Leave your country and your
people,' God said, 'and go to the land I will
show you.'[a][k]
4 "So he left the land of the Chaldeans
and settled in Harran. After the death of
his father, God sent him to this land where
you are now living.[l] 5 He gave him no inheritance here,[m] not even enough ground to
set his foot on. But God promised him that
he and his descendants after him would
possess the land,[n] even though at that time
Abraham had no child. 6 God spoke to him
in this way: 'For four hundred years your
descendants will be strangers in a country
not their own, and they will be enslaved
and mistreated.[o] 7 But I will punish the nation they serve as slaves,' God said, 'and
afterward they will come out of that country and worship me in this place.'[b][p] 8 Then
he gave Abraham the covenant of circumcision.[q] And Abraham became the father
of Isaac and circumcised him eight days
after his birth.[r] Later Isaac became the father of Jacob,[s] and Jacob became the father of the twelve patriarchs.[t]
9 "Because the patriarchs were jealous
of Joseph,[u] they sold him as a slave into
Egypt.[v] But God was with him[w] 10 and rescued him from all his troubles. He gave
Joseph wisdom and enabled him to gain
the goodwill of Pharaoh king of Egypt. So
Pharaoh made him ruler over Egypt and
all his palace.[x]
11 "Then a famine struck all Egypt and
Canaan, bringing great suffering, and our
ancestors could not find food.[y] 12 When Jacob heard that there was grain in Egypt,
he sent our forefathers on their first visit.[z] 13 On their second visit, Joseph told
his brothers who he was,[a] and Pharaoh
learned about Joseph's family.[b] 14 After
this, Joseph sent for his father Jacob and
his whole family,[c] seventy-five in all.[d]
15 Then Jacob went down to Egypt, where
he and our ancestors died.[e] 16 Their bodies
were brought back to Shechem and placed
in the tomb that Abraham had bought
from the sons of Hamor at Shechem for a
certain sum of money.[f]

6:14 [e] S Jn 2:19 [f] Ac 15:1; 21:21; 26:3; 28:17 **6:15** [g] S Mt 5:22 **7:2** [h] Ac 22:1 [i] Ps 29:3 [j] Ge 11:31; 15:7 **7:3** [k] Ge 12:1 **7:4** [l] Ge 12:5 **7:5** [m] Heb 11:13 [n] Ge 12:7; 17:8; 26:3 **7:6** [o] Ex 1:8-11; 12:40 **7:7** [p] Ge 15:13, 14; Ex 3:12 **7:8** [q] Ge 17:9-14 [r] Ge 21:2-4 [s] Ge 25:26 [t] Ge 29:31-35; 30:5-13,17-24; 35:16-18,22-26 **7:9** [u] Ge 37:4, 11 [v] Ge 37:28; Ps 105:17 [w] Ge 39:2,21, 23; Hag 2:4 **7:10** [x] Ge 41:37-43; Ps 105:20-22 **7:11** [y] Ge 41:54 **7:12** [z] Ge 42:1,2 **7:13** [a] Ge 45:1-4 [b] Ge 45:16 **7:14** [c] Ge 45:9, 10 [d] Ge 46:26, 27; Ex 1:5; Dt 10:22 **7:15** [e] Ge 46:5-7; 49:33; Ex 1:6 **7:16** [f] Ge 23:16-20; 33:18, 19; 50:13; Jos 24:32

[a] *3* Gen. 12:1 [b] *7* Gen. 15:13,14

Stephen may have referred to Jesus' words as recorded in Jn 2:19 (see note there), and the words may have been misunderstood or purposely misinterpreted (v. 14), as at the trial of Jesus. *holy place.* The temple in Jerusalem.

7:1 *high priest.* Probably Caiaphas (see Mt 26:57–66), but see note on 4:6; cf. Jn 18:19, 24. *Are these charges true?* See notes on 6:11,13.

7:2–53 See Introduction: Characteristics, 5 (*Effective use of speeches*). Since the author of Acts gives more space to Stephen's speech than to any other, it is safe to assume that he considered it particularly important. Broadly speaking, it is not meant to be a personal defense with the hope of conciliating Stephen's accusers (see vv. 51–52) but a history of Israel's failures. It deals with the three great pillars of Jewish piety: (1) the land (vv. 2–36), (2) the law (vv. 37–43) and (3) the temple (vv. 44–50), and ends with a resounding denunciation of Stephen's accusers (vv. 51–52). Stephen indicts Israel's leaders for rejecting God's messengers in the past and now rejecting Jesus, "the Righteous One" (v. 52).

7:2 *Abraham ... in Mesopotamia, before he lived in Harran.* Abraham's call came in Ur, not Harran (cf. Ge 12:1 and note; 15:7; Ne 9:7). Or perhaps he was called first in Ur and then later his call was renewed in Harran (see note on Jer 15:19–21).

7:4 *land of the Chaldeans.* A district in southern Babylonia, the name was later applied to a region that included all of Babylonia (see map, p. 2515, at the end of this study Bible). *After the death of his father.* Ge 11:26 does not mean that all three sons—Abraham, Nahor and Haran—were born to Terah in the same year when he was 70 years old. See Ge 11:26—12:1. It may be that Haran was Terah's firstborn and that Abraham was born 60 years later. Thus the death of Terah at 205 years of age could have occurred just before Abraham, at 75, left Harran.

7:6 *four hundred years.* A round number for the length of Israel's stay in Egypt (Ex 12:40–41 has 430 years). That four generations would represent considerably less than 400 years is not a necessary conclusion (see note on Ge 15:16). Ex 6:16–20 makes Moses the great-grandson of Levi, son of Jacob and brother of Joseph. This would make four generations from Levi to Moses. But in 1Ch 7:22–27 a list of ten names represents the generations between Ephraim, the son of Joseph, and Joshua. The ten generations at 40 years each would equal 400 years, the same period of time noted as four generations. But one list is abbreviated and the other gives a fuller genealogy.

7:8 *covenant of circumcision.* See notes on Ge 17:10–11. The essential conditions for the religion of the Israelites were already fulfilled long before the temple was built and their present religious customs began. *twelve patriarchs.* See Ge 35:23–26.

7:9 *they sold him.* Israel consistently rejected God's favored individuals. Stephen builds his case about Jesus' rejection by noting Joseph's rejection by his brothers (Ge 37:12–36).

7:13 *second visit.* See Ge 43.

7:14 *Jacob and his whole family, seventy-five in all.* Although the Hebrew Bible uses the number 70 (see Ge 46:26–27 and note on 46:27; Ex 1:5; Dt 10:22), the pre-Christian Greek translation of the OT (the Septuagint) adds at Ge 46:20 the names of one son of Manasseh, two of Ephraim, and one grandson of each. This makes the number 75 and is the number that Stephen uses.

7:16 Stephen brings together OT accounts of two land purchases (by Abraham and Jacob) and two burial places

17 “As the time drew near for God to fulfill his promise to Abraham, the number of
our people in Egypt had greatly increased.[g]
18 Then ‘a new king, to whom Joseph
meant nothing, came to power in Egypt.’[ah]
19 He dealt treacherously with our people
and oppressed our ancestors by forcing
them to throw out their newborn babies
so that they would die.[i]
20 “At that time Moses was born, and he
was no ordinary child.[b] For three months
he was cared for by his family.[j] 21 When
he was placed outside, Pharaoh’s daughter
took him and brought him up as her own
son.[k] 22 Moses was educated in all the wisdom of the Egyptians[l] and was powerful in
speech and action.
23 “When Moses was forty years old, he
decided to visit his own people, the Israelites. 24 He saw one of them being mistreated by an Egyptian, so he went to his
defense and avenged him by killing the
Egyptian. 25 Moses thought that his own
people would realize that God was using him to rescue them, but they did not.
26 The next day Moses came upon two Israelites who were fighting. He tried to reconcile them by saying, ‘Men, you are brothers; why do you want to hurt each other?’
27 “But the man who was mistreating the
other pushed Moses aside and said, ‘Who
made you ruler and judge over us?[m] 28 Are
you thinking of killing me as you killed
the Egyptian yesterday?’[c] 29 When Moses
heard this, he fled to Midian, where he
settled as a foreigner and had two sons.[n]
30 “After forty years had passed, an angel
appeared to Moses in the flames of a burning bush in the desert near Mount Sinai.
31 When he saw this, he was amazed at the
sight. As he went over to get a closer look,
he heard the Lord say:[o] 32 ‘I am the God of
your fathers,[p] the God of Abraham, Isaac
and Jacob.’[d] Moses trembled with fear and
did not dare to look.[q]
33 “Then the Lord said to him, ‘Take off
your sandals, for the place where you are
standing is holy ground.[r] 34 I have indeed
seen the oppression of my people in Egypt.
I have heard their groaning and have come
down to set them free. Now come, I will
send you back to Egypt.’[es]
35 “This is the same Moses they had
rejected with the words, ‘Who made
you ruler and judge?’[t] He was sent to be
their ruler and deliverer by God himself,
through the angel who appeared to him in
the bush. 36 He led them out of Egypt[u] and
performed wonders and signs[v] in Egypt,
at the Red Sea[w] and for forty years in the
wilderness.[x]
37 “This is the Moses who told the Israelites, ‘God will raise up for you a prophet
like me from your own people.’[fy] 38 He was
in the assembly in the wilderness, with
the angel[z] who spoke to him on Mount
Sinai, and with our ancestors;[a] and he received living words[b] to pass on to us.[c]
39 “But our ancestors refused to obey
him. Instead, they rejected him and in
their hearts turned back to Egypt.[d] 40 They
told Aaron, ‘Make us gods who will go
before us. As for this fellow Moses who
led us out of Egypt — we don’t know what
has happened to him!’[ge] 41 That was the
time they made an idol in the form of a

7:17 [g] Ex 1:7; Ps 105:24 **7:18** [h] Ex 1:8 **7:19** [i] Ex 1:10-22 **7:20** [j] Ex 2:2; Heb 11:23 **7:21** [k] Ex 2:3-10 **7:22** [l] 1Ki 4:30; Isa 19:11 **7:27** [m] Ge 19:9; Nu 16:13 **7:29** [n] Ex 2:11-15 **7:31** [o] Ex 3:1-4 **7:32** [p] S Ac 3:13 [q] Ex 3:6 **7:33** [r] Ex 3:5; Jos 5:15 **7:34** [s] Ex 3:7-10 **7:35** [t] ver 27 **7:36** [u] Ex 12:41; 33:1 [v] Ex 11:10; S Jn 4:48 [w] Ex 14:21 [x] Ex 15:25; 17:5,6 **7:37** [y] Dt 18:15, 18; Ac 3:22 **7:38** [z] ver 53 [a] Ex 19:17; Lev 27:34 [b] Dt 32:45-47; Heb 4:12 [c] Ro 3:2 **7:39** [d] Nu 14:3,4 **7:40** [e] Ex 32:1,23

[a] 18 Exodus 1:8 [b] 20 Or *was fair in the sight of God* [c] 28 Exodus 2:14 [d] 32 Exodus 3:6 [e] 34 Exodus 3:5,7,8,10 [f] 37 Deut. 18:15 [g] 40 Exodus 32:1

(at Hebron and Shechem). According to the OT, Abraham purchased land at Hebron (Ge 23:17 – 18), where he (Ge 25:9 – 11), Isaac (Ge 35:29) and Jacob (Ge 50:13) were buried. Jacob bought land at Shechem (Ge 33:19), where Joseph was later buried (Jos 24:32). Josephus preserves a tradition that Joseph's brothers were buried at Hebron. Stephen's rhetorical device (by which he recalls that Jacob and the 12 patriarchs were not buried in Egypt but in Canaan) is strange to modern ears but would have been well understood by his hearers.

7:18 *a new king, to whom Joseph meant nothing.* See note on Ex 1:8.

7:22 *Moses was educated in all the wisdom of the Egyptians.* Not explicitly stated in the OT but to be expected if he grew up in the household of the pharaoh's daughter. Both Philo and Josephus speak of Moses' great learning. *was powerful in speech.* See Ex 4:10 and note.

7:23 *Moses was forty.* Moses was 80 years old when sent to speak before the pharaoh (Ex 7:7) and 120 years old when he died (Dt 34:7). Stephen's words agree with a tradition that at Moses' first departure from Egypt he was 40 years of age.

7:29 *fled to Midian.* Rejected by his own people, Moses feared that they would inform the Egyptians, and this led to his flight to Midian, the land flanking the Gulf of Aqaba on both sides (see Ex 2:15 and note). *had two sons.* Gershom and Eliezer (Ex 2:22; 18:3 – 4; 1Ch 23:15).

7:30 *After forty years.* Plus the 40 years of v. 23, making the 80 years of Ex 7:7. *Mount Sinai.* Called Horeb in Ex 3:1 (see note there).

7:35 *the same Moses … sent to be their ruler and deliverer.* The Israelites rejected Moses, their deliverer, just as the Jews of Stephen's day were rejecting Jesus, their deliverer. Yet both were sent by God. *angel who appeared to him in the bush.* See Ex 3:2.

7:37 *prophet like me.* See 3:22 – 23; see also notes on Dt 18:15; 34:10,12.

7:38 *assembly.* The assembled Israelites. *angel who spoke to him.* According to Jewish interpretation at that time, the law was given to Moses by angel mediation — after the manner of the original call of Moses (see Ex 3:2; see also v. 53; Gal 3:19; Heb 2:2). *he received living words to pass on to us.* Moses was the mediator between God and Israel on Mount Sinai.

7:39 *refused to obey him.* Another rejection of God's representative and his commands.

7:40 *Make us gods.* While Moses was on Sinai receiving the law, the people made the golden calf, rejecting God and his representative (Ex 32:1). The people had not traveled far from the idolatry of Egypt.

calf. They brought sacrifices to it and reveled in what their own hands had made.[f]
42 But God turned away from them[g] and
gave them over to the worship of the sun,
moon and stars.[h] This agrees with what is
written in the book of the prophets:

"'Did you bring me sacrifices and
offerings
forty years in the wilderness, people
of Israel?
43 You have taken up the tabernacle of
Molek
and the star of your god Rephan,
the idols you made to worship.
Therefore I will send you into exile'[a][i]
beyond Babylon.

44 "Our ancestors had the tabernacle of
the covenant law[j] with them in the wilderness. It had been made as God directed Moses, according to the pattern he had
seen.[k] 45 After receiving the tabernacle,
our ancestors under Joshua brought it
with them when they took the land from
the nations God drove out before them.[l]
It remained in the land until the time of
David,[m] 46 who enjoyed God's favor and
asked that he might provide a dwelling
place for the God of Jacob.[b][n] 47 But it was
Solomon who built a house for him.[o]
48 "However, the Most High[p] does not
live in houses made by human hands.[q] As
the prophet says:

49 "'Heaven is my throne,
and the earth is my footstool.[r]
What kind of house will you build for me?
says the Lord.
Or where will my resting place be?
50 Has not my hand made all these
things?'[c][s]

51 "You stiff-necked people![t] Your hearts[u]
and ears are still uncircumcised. You are
just like your ancestors: You always resist the Holy Spirit! 52 Was there ever a
prophet your ancestors did not persecute?[v]
They even killed those who predicted the
coming of the Righteous One. And now
you have betrayed and murdered him[w]—
53 you who have received the law that
was given through angels[x] but have not
obeyed it."

The Stoning of Stephen

54 When the members of the Sanhedrin
heard this, they were furious[y] and gnashed
their teeth at him. 55 But Stephen, full of
the Holy Spirit,[z] looked up to heaven and
saw the glory of God, and Jesus standing
at the right hand of God.[a] 56 "Look," he
said, "I see heaven open[b] and the Son of
Man[c] standing at the right hand of God."
57 At this they covered their ears and,
yelling at the top of their voices, they all
rushed at him, 58 dragged him out of the
city[d] and began to stone him.[e] Meanwhile,
the witnesses[f] laid their coats[g] at the feet
of a young man named Saul.[h]
59 While they were stoning him, Stephen
prayed, "Lord Jesus, receive my spirit."[i]
60 Then he fell on his knees[j] and cried out,
"Lord, do not hold this sin against them."[k]
When he had said this, he fell asleep.[l]
8 And Saul[m] approved of their killing
him.

The Church Persecuted and Scattered

On that day a great persecution broke
out against the church in Jerusalem,

7:41 [f] Ex 32:4-6; Ps 106:19,20; Rev 9:20
7:42 [g] Jos 24:20; Isa 63:10 [h] Jer 19:13
7:43 [i] Am 5:25-27
7:44 [j] Ex 38:21; Nu 1:50; 17:7 [k] Ex 25:8,9,40
7:45 [l] Jos 3:14-17; 18:1; 23:9; 24:18; Ps 44:2 [m] 2Sa 7:2,6
7:46 [n] 2Sa 7:8-16; 1Ki 8:17; Ps 132:1-5
7:47 [o] 1Ki 6:1-38
7:48 [p] S Mk 5:7 [q] 1Ki 8:27; 2Ch 2:6
7:49 [r] Mt 5:34,35
7:50 [s] Isa 66:1,2
7:51 [t] Ex 32:9; 33:3,5 [u] Lev 26:41; Dt 10:16; Jer 4:4; 9:26
7:52 [v] S Mt 5:12 [w] Ac 3:14; 1Th 2:15
7:53 [x] ver 38; Gal 3:19; Heb 2:2
7:54 [y] Ac 5:33
7:55 [z] S Lk 1:15 [a] S Mk 16:19
7:56 [b] S Mt 3:16 [c] S Mt 8:20
7:58 [d] Lk 4:29 [e] Lev 24:14,16 [f] Dt 17:7 [g] Ac 22:20 [h] Ac 8:1
7:59 [i] Ps 31:5; Lk 23:46
7:60 [j] Lk 22:41; Ac 9:40 [k] S Mt 5:44 [l] S Mt 9:24
8:1 [m] Ac 7:58

[a] 43 Amos 5:25-27 (see Septuagint) [b] 46 Some early manuscripts *the house of Jacob* [c] 50 Isaiah 66:1,2

7:42 *God … gave them over.* See note on Ro 1:24. *sun, moon and stars.* See note on Jer 19:13.
7:43 Stephen quotes Am 5:25–27 as translated in the Septuagint, except that he replaces Damascus with Babylon in view of the fact that the final exile of Israel from the promised land was carried out by the Babylonians (Amos was speaking first of the Assyrian exile of the northern kingdom). *Molek … Rephan.* See note on Am 5:26. *Molek.* See note on Lev 18:21.
7:44–50 Because he had been accused of "speaking against this holy place" (6:13), Stephen concludes his recital with a word about the sanctuary. Presumably, he had been preaching that the risen Christ had now replaced the temple as the mediation of God's saving presence among his people and as the one (the "place") through whom they (and "all nations," Mk 11:17) could come to God in prayer (see note on 6:13).
7:44 *tabernacle of the covenant law.* So called by Stephen because the primary contents of the wilderness tabernacle were the ark of the covenant and the two covenant tablets it contained, which were called "the covenant law" (see Ex 25:16,21 and notes).
7:49 Isa 66:1–2 reminded Israel that all creation is the temple that God himself had made. Stephen recalls that word to remind his hearers that ultimately God builds his own temple.
7:51 *hearts and ears … uncircumcised.* Although the men were physically circumcised, they were acting like the uncircumcised pagans of the nations around them. They were not truly consecrated to the Lord.
7:52 *Righteous One.* See 3:14 and note.
7:53 *law that was given through angels.* See note on v. 38.
7:55 *full of the Holy Spirit.* See note on 2:4; see also 6:5. *glory of God.* See note on Lk 2:9.
7:56 *Son of Man.* See note on Mk 8:31. *standing at the right hand of God.* Cf. Ps 110:1 and note; Mk 14:62; Lk 22:69; Heb 1:2–3 and note. The significance of Jesus' "standing" is debated, though it may picture Stephen's acceptance by the heavenly Judge and underscore the truth of his message.
7:58 *laid their coats at the feet of … Saul.* Some have thought that this marked Saul as being in charge of the execution. In any case, it is Luke's way of introducing the main character of the second section of the book (chs. 13–28).
7:60 *do not hold this sin against them.* Cf. Jesus' words in Lk 23:34. *fell asleep.* See note on Jn 11:11.
8:1 *approved.* See 22:20 and note. *all except the apostles.* For the apostles to stay in Jerusalem would be an encouragement to those in prison and a center of appeal to those scat-

and all except the apostles
were scattered[n] throughout
Judea and Samaria.[o] 2God-
ly men buried Stephen and
mourned deeply for him.
3But Saul[p] began to destroy
the church.[q] Going from
house to house, he dragged
off both men and women
and put them in prison.

Philip in Samaria

4Those who had been scat-
tered[r] preached the word
wherever they went.[s] 5Phil-
ip[t] went down to a city in
Samaria and proclaimed the
Messiah there. 6When the
crowds heard Philip and
saw the signs he performed,
they all paid close attention
to what he said. 7For with
shrieks, impure spirits came
out of many,[u] and many who
were paralyzed or lame were
healed.[v] 8So there was great
joy in that city.

Simon the Sorcerer

9Now for some time a
man named Simon had prac-
ticed sorcery[w] in the city and
amazed all the people of Samaria. He boasted that he
was someone great,[x] 10and
all the people, both high
and low, gave him their attention and exclaimed, "This man is rightly called the
Great Power of God."[y] 11They followed
him because he had amazed them for a
long time with his sorcery. 12But when
they believed Philip as he proclaimed the
good news of the kingdom of God[z] and
the name of Jesus Christ, they were baptized,[a] both men and women. 13Simon
himself believed and was baptized. And
he followed Philip everywhere, astonished
by the great signs and miracles[b] he saw.
14When the apostles in Jerusalem heard
that Samaria[c] had accepted the word of
God,[d] they sent Peter and John[e] to Samaria. 15When they arrived, they prayed for
the new believers there that they might

PHILIP'S AND PETER'S MISSIONARY JOURNEYS

8:1 [n]ver 4; Ac 11:19 [o]Ac 9:31 **8:3** [p]Ac 7:58 [q]Ac 9:1, 13, 21; 22:4, 19; 26:10, 11; 1Co 15:9; Gal 1:13, 23; Php 3:6; 1Ti 1:13 **8:4** [r]ver 1 [s]Ac 15:35 **8:5** [t]Ac 6:5; 21:8

8:7 [u]S Mk 16:17 [v]S Mt 4:24 **8:9** [w]Ac 13:6 [x]Ac 5:36 **8:10** [y]Ac 14:11; 28:6 **8:12** [z]S Mt 3:2 [a]S Ac 2:38 **8:13** [b]ver 6; Ac 19:11 **8:14** [c]ver 1 [d]S Heb 4:12 [e]S Lk 22:8

tered. The church now went underground. *scattered throughout Judea and Samaria.* The beginning of the fulfillment of the commission in 1:8—not by the church's plan, but by events beyond the believers' control. See map, p. 1849.
8:3 *began to destroy.* See 22:4. The Greek underlying this phrase sometimes describes the ravages of wild animals.
8:4 *preached the word.* Many witnesses to the gospel went everywhere proclaiming the good news. The number of witnesses multiplied, and the territory covered was expanded greatly (cf. 11:19–20).
8:5 *Philip.* One of the Seven in the Jerusalem church (6:3,5; see note on 6:6), who now becomes an evangelist, proclaiming the Christ (Messiah); see also 21:8. Philip is an example of one of those who were scattered. *a city in Samaria.* Some manuscripts have "the city of Samaria," a reference to the old capital Samaria, renamed Sebaste or Neapolis (modern Nablus).
8:9 *Simon.* In early Christian literature the "sorcerer" (Simon Magus) is described as the arch-heretic of the church and the "father" of Gnostic teaching. *sorcery.* See note on 2Ki 17:17.
8:10 *the Great Power of God.* Simon claimed to be either God himself or, more likely, his chief representative.
8:13 *Simon himself believed and was baptized.* It is difficult to know whether Simon's faith was genuine. Even though Luke says Simon believed, Peter's statement that Simon had no part in the apostles' ministry because his heart was not "right before God" (v. 21) casts doubt on the authenticity of his faith.
8:14 *Samaria.* That is, some of its citizens. Cf. 1:8. *had accepted the word of God.* Were obedient to the gospel proclaimed by Philip. *sent Peter and John.* The Jerusalem church assumed the responsibility of inspecting new evangelistic efforts and the communities of believers they produced (see 11:22).

receive the Holy Spirit,[f] 16 because the
Holy Spirit had not yet come on any of
them;[g] they had simply been baptized in
the name of the Lord Jesus.[h] 17 Then Peter
and John placed their hands on them,[i] and
they received the Holy Spirit.[j]
18 When Simon saw that the Spirit was
given at the laying on of the apostles'
hands, he offered them money 19 and said,
"Give me also this ability so that everyone
on whom I lay my hands may receive the
Holy Spirit."
20 Peter answered: "May your money
perish with you, because you thought you
could buy the gift of God with money![k]
21 You have no part or share[l] in this ministry, because your heart is not right[m] before God. 22 Repent[n] of this wickedness and
pray to the Lord in the hope that he may
forgive you for having such a thought in
your heart. 23 For I see that you are full of
bitterness and captive to sin."
24 Then Simon answered, "Pray to the
Lord for me[o] so that nothing you have said
may happen to me."
25 After they had further proclaimed
the word of the Lord[p] and testified about
Jesus, Peter and John returned to Jerusalem, preaching the gospel in many Samaritan villages.[q]

Philip and the Ethiopian

26 Now an angel[r] of the Lord said to
Philip,[s] "Go south to the road — the desert
road — that goes down from Jerusalem to
Gaza." 27 So he started out, and on his way
he met an Ethiopian[a][t] eunuch,[u] an important official in charge of all the treasury
of the Kandake (which means "queen of
the Ethiopians"). This man had gone to
Jerusalem to worship,[v] 28 and on his way
home was sitting in his chariot reading the
Book of Isaiah the prophet. 29 The Spirit
told[w] Philip, "Go to that chariot and stay
near it."
30 Then Philip ran up to the chariot and
heard the man reading Isaiah the prophet.
"Do you understand what you are reading?" Philip asked.
31 "How can I," he said, "unless someone explains it to me?" So he invited Philip to come up and sit with him.
32 This is the passage of Scripture the eunuch was reading:

"He was led like a sheep to the
slaughter,
and as a lamb before its shearer is
silent,
so he did not open his mouth.
33 In his humiliation he was deprived of
justice.
Who can speak of his
descendants?
For his life was taken from the
earth."[b][x]

34 The eunuch asked Philip, "Tell me,
please, who is the prophet talking about,
himself or someone else?" 35 Then Philip
began[y] with that very passage of Scripture[z]
and told him the good news[a] about Jesus.
36 As they traveled along the road, they
came to some water and the eunuch said,
"Look, here is water. What can stand
in the way of my being baptized?"[b] [37][c]
38 And he gave orders to stop the chariot.
Then both Philip and the eunuch went
down into the water and Philip baptized
him. 39 When they came up out of the water, the Spirit of the Lord suddenly took
Philip away,[c] and the eunuch did not see
him again, but went on his way rejoicing.

8:15 [f] S Jn 20:22 **8:16** [g] S Ac 10:44; 19:2 [h] Mt 28:19; S Ac 2:38 **8:17** [i] S Ac 6:6 [j] S Jn 20:22 **8:20** [k] 2Ki 5:16; Da 5:17; Mt 10:8; Ac 2:38 **8:21** [l] Ne 2:20 [m] Ps 78:37 **8:22** [n] Ac 2:38 **8:24** [o] Ex 8:8; Nu 21:7; 1Ki 13:6; Jer 42:2 **8:25** [p] S Ac 13:48 [q] ver 40 **8:26** [r] S Ac 5:19 [s] Ac 6:5 **8:27** [t] Ps 68:31; 87:4; Zep 3:10 [u] Isa 56:3-5 [v] 1Ki 8:41-43; Jn 12:20
8:29 [w] Ac 10:19; 11:12; 13:2; 20:23; 21:11 **8:33** [x] Isa 53:7,8 **8:35** [y] Mt 5:2 [z] Lk 24:27; Ac 17:2; 18:28; 28:23 [a] S Ac 13:32 **8:36** [b] S Ac 2:38; 10:47 **8:39** [c] 1Ki 18:12; 2Ki 2:16; Eze 3:12,14; 8:3; 11:1,24; 43:5; 2Co 12:2; 1Th 4:17; Rev 12:5

[a] *27* That is, from the southern Nile region
[b] *33* Isaiah 53:7,8 (see Septuagint)
[c] *37* Some manuscripts include here *Philip said, "If you believe with all your heart, you may." The eunuch answered, "I believe that Jesus Christ is the Son of God."*

8:16 *not yet come on any of them.* Since the day of Pentecost, those who "belong to Christ" (Ro 8:9) also have the Holy Spirit. But the Spirit had not yet been made manifest to the Christians in Samaria by the usual signs. This deficiency was now graciously supplied (v. 17).
8:17 *placed their hands on them.* See v. 18; 19:1 – 7; cf. 2Ti 1:6; see also note on 6:6.
8:18 *he offered them money.* Simon had boasted before of having great powers (see v. 10 and note), and now he tried to buy the magical power he believed the apostles possessed.
8:23 *full of bitterness.* See Dt 29:18. *captive to sin.* See Ro 6:20.
8:26 *an angel of the Lord.* Cf. v. 29; see note on 5:19. *from Jerusalem to Gaza.* A distance of about 50 miles (see map, p. 1839).
8:27 *an Ethiopian.* Ethiopia corresponded in this period to Nubia (Meroe), from the upper Nile region at the first cataract (Aswan) to Khartoum. *Kandake.* The traditional title of the queen mother, responsible for performing the secular duties of the reigning king — who was thought to be too sacred for such activities. *gone to Jerusalem to worship.* If not a full-fledged convert to Judaism (Dt 23:1), the Ethiopian was a Gentile God-fearer (see note on 10:2).
8:30 *heard the man reading.* It was customary practice to read aloud.
8:34 *who is the prophet talking about . . . ?* Beginning with Isa 53 (see v. 35), Philip may have identified the suffering servant with the Davidic Messiah of Isa 11 or with the Son of Man (Da 7:13).
8:35 *good news.* The way of salvation through Jesus Christ (see note on Mk 1:1).
8:36 *they came to some water.* There were several possibilities: a brook in the Valley of Elah (which David crossed to meet Goliath, 1Sa 17:40); the Wadi el-Hasi just north of Gaza; water from a spring or one of the many pools in the area.
8:39 *rejoicing.* Joy is associated with salvation in Acts (see note on 16:34).
8:40 *Azotus.* OT Ashdod (see 1Sa 5:1), one of the five Philistine cities (see map, p. 359). It was about 19 miles from Gaza and 60 miles from Caesarea (see map, p. 1839). *Caesarea.* Rebuilt by Herod and with an excellent harbor, it served as the headquarters of the Roman governors. The account leaves Philip in Caesarea at this time; his next appearance is 20 years later, and he is still located in the same place (21:8).

40 Philip, however, appeared at Azotus and traveled about, preaching the gospel in all the towns[d] until he reached Caesarea.[e]

Saul's Conversion

9:1-19pp — Ac 22:3-16; 26:9-18

9 Meanwhile, Saul was still breathing out murderous threats against the Lord's disciples.[f] He went to the high priest 2 and asked him for letters to the synagogues in Damascus,[g] so that if he found any there who belonged to the Way,[h] whether men or women, he might take them as prisoners to Jerusalem. 3 As he neared Damascus on his journey, suddenly a light from heaven flashed around him.[i] 4 He fell to the ground and heard a voice[j] say to him, "Saul, Saul, why do you persecute me?"

5 "Who are you, Lord?" Saul asked.

"I am Jesus, whom you are persecuting," he replied. 6 "Now get up and go into the city, and you will be told what you must do."[k]

7 The men traveling with Saul stood there speechless; they heard the sound[l] but did not see anyone.[m] 8 Saul got up from the ground, but when he opened his eyes he could see nothing.[n] So they led him by the hand into Damascus. 9 For three days he was blind, and did not eat or drink anything.

10 In Damascus there was a disciple named Ananias. The Lord called to him in a vision,[o] "Ananias!"

"Yes, Lord," he answered.

11 The Lord told him, "Go to the house of Judas on Straight Street and ask for a man from Tarsus[p] named Saul, for he is praying. 12 In a vision he has seen a man named Ananias come and place his hands on[q] him to restore his sight."

13 "Lord," Ananias answered, "I have heard many reports about this man and all the harm he has done to your holy people[r] in Jerusalem.[s] 14 And he has come here with authority from the chief priests[t] to arrest all who call on your name."[u]

15 But the Lord said to Ananias, "Go! This man is my chosen instrument[v] to proclaim my name to the Gentiles[w] and their kings[x] and to the people of Israel. 16 I will show him how much he must suffer for my name."[y]

17 Then Ananias went to the house and entered it. Placing his hands on[z] Saul, he said, "Brother Saul, the Lord — Jesus, who appeared to you on the road as you were coming here — has sent me so that you may see again and be filled with the Holy Spirit."[a] 18 Immediately, something like scales fell from Saul's eyes, and he could see again. He got up and was baptized,[b] 19 and after taking some food, he regained his strength.

Saul in Damascus and Jerusalem

Saul spent several days with the disciples[c] in Damascus.[d] 20 At once he began to preach in the synagogues[e] that Jesus is the Son of God.[f] 21 All those who heard

8:40 [d] ver 25 [e] Ac 10:1,24; 12:19; 21:8,16; 23:23,33; 25:1,4,6,13 **9:1** [f] S Ac 8:3 **9:2** [g] Isa 17:1; Jer 49:23 [h] Ac 19:9,23; 22:4; 24:14,22 **9:3** [i] 1Co 15:8 **9:4** [j] Isa 6:8 **9:6** [k] ver 16; Eze 3:22 **9:7** [l] Jn 12:29 [m] Da 10:7 **9:8** [n] ver 18 **9:10** [o] Ac 10:3,17,19; 12:9; 16:9,10; 18:9 **9:11** [p] ver 30; Ac 11:25; 21:39; 22:3 **9:12** [q] S Mk 5:23 **9:13** [r] ver 32; Ac 26:10; Ro 1:7; 15:25,26,31; 16:2,15; Eph 1:1; Php 1:1 [s] S Ac 8:3 **9:14** [t] ver 2,21 [u] S Ac 2:21 **9:15** [v] Ac 13:2; Ro 1:1; Gal 1:15; 1Ti 1:12 [w] Ro 11:13; 15:15,16; Gal 1:16; 2:7,8 [x] Ac 25:22,23; 26:1 **9:16** [y] Ac 20:23; 21:11; 2Co 6:4-10; 11:23-27; 2Ti 1:8; 2:3,9 **9:17** [z] S Ac 6:6 [a] S Lk 1:15 **9:18** [b] S Ac 2:38 **9:19** [c] S Ac 11:26 [d] Ac 26:20 **9:20** [e] Ac 13:5,14; 14:1; 17:2,10,17; 18:4,19; 19:8 [f] S Mt 4:3

9:1 *Saul.* Introduced at the stoning of Stephen (7:58), he was born in Tarsus and trained under Gamaliel (22:3). See notes on Ro 1:1; Php 3:4 – 14. *murderous threats.* We do not know that Saul was directly involved in the death of anyone other than Stephen (8:1), but there appear to have been similar cases (22:4; 26:10). *high priest.* Probably Caiaphas (see note on 4:6) and the members of the Sanhedrin, who had authority over Jews both in Judea and elsewhere.

9:2 *Damascus.* See map, p. 1842. Located in the Roman province of Syria, it was the nearest important city outside the Holy Land. It also had a large Jewish population. The distance from Jerusalem to Damascus was about 150 miles, four to six days' travel. *the Way.* A name for Christianity occurring a number of times in Acts (16:17; 18:25 – 26; 19:9,23; 22:4; 24:14,22; see 2Pe 2:2). Jesus called himself "the way" (Jn 14:6). *prisoners to Jerusalem.* Where the full authority of the Sanhedrin could be exercised in trial for either acquittal or death.

9:3 *a light from heaven.* "About noon" (26:13).

9:4 *why do you persecute me?* To persecute the church is to persecute Christ, for the church is his body (see 1Co 12:27; Eph 1:22 – 23).

9:5 *Who are you, Lord?* In rabbinic tradition such a voice from heaven would have been understood as the voice of God himself. The solemn repetition of Saul's name (v. 4) and the bright light (v. 3) suggested to him that he was in the presence of deity.

9:7 *heard the sound.* Those with Saul "heard the sound" but "did not understand" what the voice was saying (22:9; cf. Da 10:7).

9:10 *Ananias.* This Ananias is mentioned elsewhere only in 22:12. His was a common name (5:1; 23:2). The Greek form is derived from the Hebrew name Hananiah, meaning "The LORD is gracious/shows grace" (see Da 1:6 and note).

9:11 *Straight Street.* Probably followed the same route of the long, straight street that today runs through the city from east to west. It is a decided contrast to the numerous crooked streets of the city (see map, p. 1842). *Tarsus.* See note on 22:3. *praying.* Prayer is often associated with visions in Luke and Acts (see 10:9 – 11; Lk 1:10; 3:21; 9:28).

9:13 *your holy people.* See v. 32 and notes on Ro 1:7; Php 1:1.

9:15 *to the Gentiles.* See Ro 1:13 – 14. *their kings.* Agrippa (26:1) and Caesar at Rome (25:11 – 12; 28:19).

9:16 *how much he must suffer.* See 2Co 11:23 – 28 and notes.

9:17 *Jesus, who appeared to you.* The Damascus road experience was not merely a vision. The resurrected Christ actually appeared to Saul, and on this fact Saul based his qualification to be an apostle (see 1Co 9:1 and note; 15:8).

9:20 *At once.* Following his baptism (v. 18). *synagogues.* It became Saul's regular practice to preach at every opportunity in the synagogues (13:5; 14:1; 17:1 – 2,10; 18:4,19; 19:8). *Jesus is the Son of God.* Saul's message was a declaration of what he himself had become convinced of on the Damascus road: Christ's deity and Messiahship.

him were astonished and asked, "Isn't
he the man who raised havoc in Jerusalem among those who call on this name?[g]
And hasn't he come here to take them as
prisoners to the chief priests?"[h] 22 Yet Saul
grew more and more powerful and baffled
the Jews living in Damascus by proving
that Jesus is the Messiah.[i]
23 After many days had gone by, there
was a conspiracy among the Jews to kill
him,[j] 24 but Saul learned of their plan.[k]
Day and night they kept close watch on
the city gates in order to kill him. 25 But
his followers took him by night and lowered him in a basket through an opening
in the wall.[l]
26 When he came to Jerusalem,[m] he
tried to join the disciples, but they were
all afraid of him, not believing that he
really was a disciple. 27 But Barnabas[n] took
him and brought him to the apostles. He
told them how Saul on his journey had
seen the Lord and that the Lord had spoken to him,[o] and how in Damascus he had
preached fearlessly in the name of Jesus.[p]
28 So Saul stayed with them and moved
about freely in Jerusalem, speaking boldly
in the name of the Lord. 29 He talked and

9:21 [g] S Ac 8:3 [h] ver 14
9:22 [i] S Lk 2:11; Ac 5:42; 17:3; 18:5,28
9:23 [j] S Ac 20:3
9:24 [k] Ac 20:3, 19; 23:16,30
9:25 [l] 1Sa 19:12; 2Co 11:32,33
9:26 [m] Ac 22:17; 26:20; Gal 1:17, 18
9:27 [n] S Ac 4:36 [o] ver 3-6 [p] ver 20,22

9:22 *Messiah.* See second NIV text note on Mt 1:1.
9:23 *After many days.* Three years (Gal 1:17–18). It is probable that the major part of this period was spent in Arabia, away from Damascus, though the borders of Arabia extended to the environs of Damascus. *conspiracy among the Jews to kill him.* Upon Saul's return to Damascus, the governor under Aretas gave orders for his arrest (2Co 11:32; see note there). The absence of Roman coins minted in Damascus between AD 34 and 62 may indicate that Aretas was in control during that period.
9:25 *lowered him in a basket.* See 2Co 11:33 (cf. Jos 2:15; 1Sa 19:12).
9:26 *he came to Jerusalem.* From Gal 1:19 we learn that the only apostles Paul met were Peter and James, the Lord's brother. James was not one of the Twelve, but he held a position in Jerusalem comparable to that of an apostle (see Gal 2:9).
9:27 *Barnabas.* See note on 4:36.
9:29 *He talked and debated.* Formerly Saul was arguing against Christ; now he is forcefully presenting Jesus as the Messiah.

ROMAN DAMASCUS

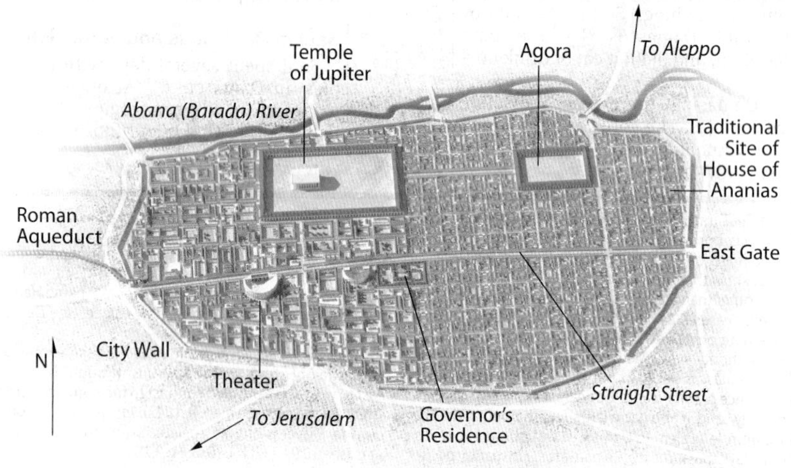

Damascus represented much more to Saul, the strict Pharisee, than any other stop on his campaign of repression. It was the hub of a vast commercial network with far-flung lines of caravan trade reaching into north Syria, Mesopotamia, Anatolia, Persia and Arabia. If the new "Way" of Christianity flourished in Damascus, it would quickly reach all these places. From the viewpoint of the Sanhedrin and of Saul, the archpersecutor, it had to be stopped in Damascus.

The dominant political figure at the time of Paul's escape from Damascus (2Co 11:32-33) was Aretas IV, king of the Nabateans (9 BC–AD 40), though normally the Decapolis cities were attached to the province of Syria and were thus under the influence of Rome.

The city itself was a veritable oasis, situated in a plain watered by the Biblical rivers Abana and Pharpar (see note on 2Ki 5:12; see also map, p. 1707). Roman architecture overlaid the Hellenistic town plan with a great temple to Jupiter and a mile-long colonnaded street, the "Straight Street" of Ac 9:11. The city gates and a section of the town wall may still be seen today, as well as the lengthy bazaar that runs along the line of the ancient street.

debated with the Hellenistic Jews,[a][q] but
they tried to kill him.[r] 30 When the believers[s] learned of this, they took him down
to Caesarea[t] and sent him off to Tarsus.[u]
31 Then the church throughout Judea,
Galilee and Samaria[v] enjoyed a time of
peace and was strengthened. Living in the
fear of the Lord and encouraged by the
Holy Spirit, it increased in numbers.[w]

Aeneas and Dorcas

32 As Peter traveled about the country,
he went to visit the Lord's people[x] who
lived in Lydda. 33 There he found a man
named Aeneas, who was paralyzed and
had been bedridden for eight years. 34 "Aeneas," Peter said to him, "Jesus Christ
heals you.[y] Get up and roll up your mat."
Immediately Aeneas got up. 35 All those
who lived in Lydda and Sharon[z] saw him
and turned to the Lord.[a]
36 In Joppa[b] there was a disciple named
Tabitha (in Greek her name is Dorcas); she
was always doing good[c] and helping the
poor. 37 About that time she became sick
and died, and her body was washed and
placed in an upstairs room.[d] 38 Lydda was
near Joppa; so when the disciples[e] heard
that Peter was in Lydda, they sent two
men to him and urged him, "Please come
at once!"
39 Peter went with them, and when he
arrived he was taken upstairs to the room.
All the widows[f] stood around him, crying and showing him the robes and other
clothing that Dorcas had made while she
was still with them.
40 Peter sent them all out of the room;[g]
then he got down on his knees[h] and
prayed. Turning toward the dead woman,
he said, "Tabitha, get up."[i] She opened
her eyes, and seeing Peter she sat up. 41 He
took her by the hand and helped her to
her feet. Then he called for the believers,
especially the widows, and presented her
to them alive. 42 This became known all
over Joppa, and many people believed in
the Lord.[j] 43 Peter stayed in Joppa for some
time with a tanner named Simon.[k]

Cornelius Calls for Peter

10 At Caesarea[l] there was a man named
Cornelius, a centurion in what was
known as the Italian Regiment. 2 He and all
his family were devout and God-fearing;[m]
he gave generously to those in need and

9:29 [q] Ac 6:1 [r] 2Co 11:26 **9:30** [s] S Ac 1:16 [t] S Ac 8:40 [u] S ver 11 **9:31** [v] Ac 8:1 [w] S Ac 2:41 **9:32** [x] S ver 13 **9:34** [y] Ac 3:6, 16; 4:10 **9:35** [z] 1Ch 5:16; 27:29; SS 2:1; Isa 33:9; 35:2; 65:10 [a] S Ac 2:41 **9:36** [b] Jos 19:46; 2Ch 2:16; Ezr 3:7; Jnh 1:3; Ac 10:5 [c] 1Ti 2:10; Titus 3:8 **9:37** [d] Ac 1:13; 20:8 **9:38** [e] S Ac 11:26 **9:39** [f] Ac 6:1; 1Ti 5:3 **9:40** [g] Mt 9:25 [h] Lk 22:41; Ac 7:60 [i] S Lk 7:14 **9:42** [j] S Ac 2:41 **9:43** [k] Ac 10:6 **10:1** [l] S Ac 8:40 **10:2** [m] ver 22, 35; Ac 13:16, 26

[a] *29* That is, Jews who had adopted the Greek language and culture

---

9:30 *Caesarea.* See note on 8:40. *Tarsus.* Saul's birthplace (see note on 22:3).

9:31 *church.* The whole Christian body, including Christians in the districts of Judea, Galilee and Samaria. The singular thus does not here refer to the various congregations but to the church as a whole (see note on 5:11). *encouraged by the Holy Spirit.* The work of the Spirit is particularly noted throughout the book of Acts (see 13:2 and note on 1:2). This is why the book is sometimes called the Acts of the Holy Spirit.

9:32 *Lydda.* A town two or three miles north of the road connecting Joppa and Jerusalem. Lydda is about 12 miles from Joppa.

9:33 *Aeneas.* Since Peter was there to visit the believers, Aeneas was probably one of the Christians.

9:35 *Sharon.* The fertile plain of Sharon runs about 50 miles along the Mediterranean coast, roughly from Joppa to Caesarea. The reference here, however, may be to a village in the neighborhood of Lydda instead of to a district (an Egyptian papyrus refers to a town by that name in the Holy Land).

9:36 *Joppa.* About 38 miles from Jerusalem, the main seaport of Judea. Today it is known as Jaffa and is a suburb of Tel Aviv.

9:37 *body was washed.* In preparation for burial, a custom common to both Jews (Purification of the Dead; Mishnah, *Shabbat* 23.5) and Greeks. *upstairs room.* If burial was delayed, it was customary to lay the body in an upper room. In Jerusalem the body had to be buried the day the person died, but outside Jerusalem up to three days might be allowed for burial.

9:38 *near Joppa.* See note on v. 32. *come at once!* Whether for consolation or for a miracle, Peter was urged to hurry in order to arrive before the burial.

9:40 *sent them all out.* Cf. 1Ki 17:23; 2Ki 4:33. Peter had been present on all three occasions recorded in Scripture when Jesus raised individuals from the dead (Mt 9:25; Lk 7:11–17; Jn 11:1–44). As when Jesus raised Jairus's daughter, the crowd in the room was told to leave. Unlike Jesus, however, Peter knelt and prayed.

9:42 *many people believed.* Cf. Jn 12:11.

9:43 *a tanner.* Occupations were frequently used with personal names to further identify individuals (see 16:14; 18:3; 19:24; 2Ti 4:14), but in this case it is especially significant. A tanner was involved in treating the skins of dead animals, thus contacting the unclean according to Jewish law, so Simon was despised by many. Peter's decision to stay with him shows already a willingness to reject Jewish prejudice and helps to prepare the way for his coming vision and the mission to the Gentiles.

10:1 *Caesarea.* Located 30 miles north of Joppa and named in honor of Augustus Caesar, it was the headquarters for the Roman forces of occupation (see also note on 8:40). *Cornelius.* A Latin name made popular when Cornelius Sulla liberated some 10,000 slaves over 100 years earlier. These had all taken his family name, Cornelius. *centurion.* Commanded a military unit that normally numbered at least 100 men (see note on Mt 8:5). The Roman legion (about 6,000 men) was divided into ten regiments, each of which had a designation. This was the "Italian" (another was the "Imperial," or "Augustan," 27:1). A centurion commanded about a sixth of a regiment. Centurions were carefully selected; all of them mentioned in the NT appear to have had noble qualities (e.g., Lk 7:5). The Roman centurions provided necessary stability to the entire Roman system.

10:2 *devout.* In spite of all his good deeds, Cornelius needed to hear the way of salvation from a human messenger. The role of the angel (v. 3) was to bring Cornelius and Peter together (cf. 8:26; 9:10). *God-fearing.* The term used of one who was not a full-fledged convert to Judaism but who believed in one God and respected the moral and ethical teachings of the Jews.

TIMELINE OF **PAUL'S LIFE**

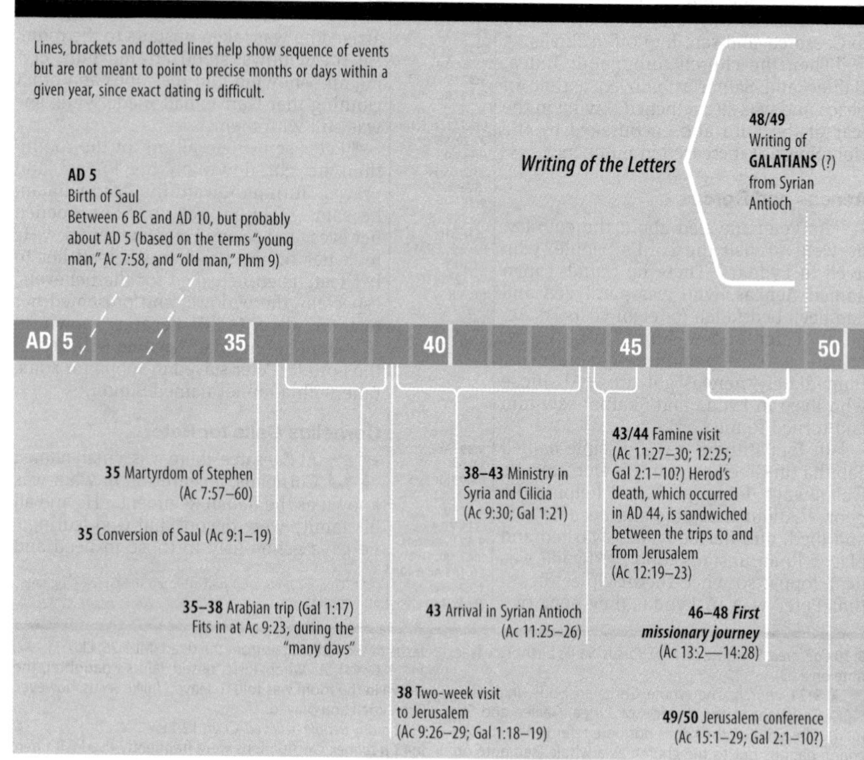

prayed to God regularly. [3]One day at about
three in the afternoon[n] he had a vision.[o] He
distinctly saw an angel[p] of God, who came
to him and said, "Cornelius!"
[4]Cornelius stared at him in fear. "What
is it, Lord?" he asked.
The angel answered, "Your prayers and
gifts to the poor have come up as a memorial
offering[q] before God.[r] [5]Now send
men to Joppa[s] to bring back a man named
Simon who is called Peter. [6]He is staying
with Simon the tanner,[t] whose house is
by the sea."
[7]When the angel who spoke to him had
gone, Cornelius called two of his servants
and a devout soldier who was one of his
attendants. [8]He told them everything that
had happened and sent them to Joppa.[u]

Peter's Vision

10:9-32Ref — Ac 11:5-14

[9]About noon the following day as they
were on their journey and approaching the
city, Peter went up on the roof[v] to pray.
[10]He became hungry and wanted something
to eat, and while the meal was being
prepared, he fell into a trance.[w] [11]He
saw heaven opened[x] and something like
a large sheet being let down to earth by
its four corners. [12]It contained all kinds

10:3 [n]Ps 55:17; Ac 3:1 [o]S Ac 9:10 [p]S Ac 5:19 **10:4** [q]Ps 20:3; S Mt 10:42; 26:13 [r]Rev 8:4 **10:5** [s]S Ac 9:36 **10:6** [t]Ac 9:43 **10:8** [u]S Ac 9:36 **10:9** [v]S Mt 24:17 **10:10** [w]Ac 22:17 **10:11** [x]S Mt 3:16

10:3 *about three in the afternoon.* Another indication that Cornelius followed Jewish religious practices. Three in the afternoon was a Jewish hour of prayer (see 3:1)—the hour of the evening incense. *a vision.* Not a dream or trance but a revelation through an angel to Cornelius while he was at prayer (see v. 30; see also note on 9:11).
10:4 *have come up.* Like the smoke of a sacrifice (see Ps 141:2; Php 4:18 and note; Heb 13:15–16). *memorial offering.* A portion of the grain offering burned on the altar was called a "memorial" (Lev 2:2).
10:5–6 *Joppa ... Simon the tanner.* See notes on 9:36,43.
10:9 *roof to pray.* It was customary for eastern houses to have flat roofs with outside stairways. The roof was used as a convenient place for relaxation and privacy (see Mk 2:4 and note).
10:10 *fell into a trance.* A state of mind God produced and used to communicate with Peter. It was not merely imagination or a dream. Peter's consciousness was heightened to receive the vision from God.

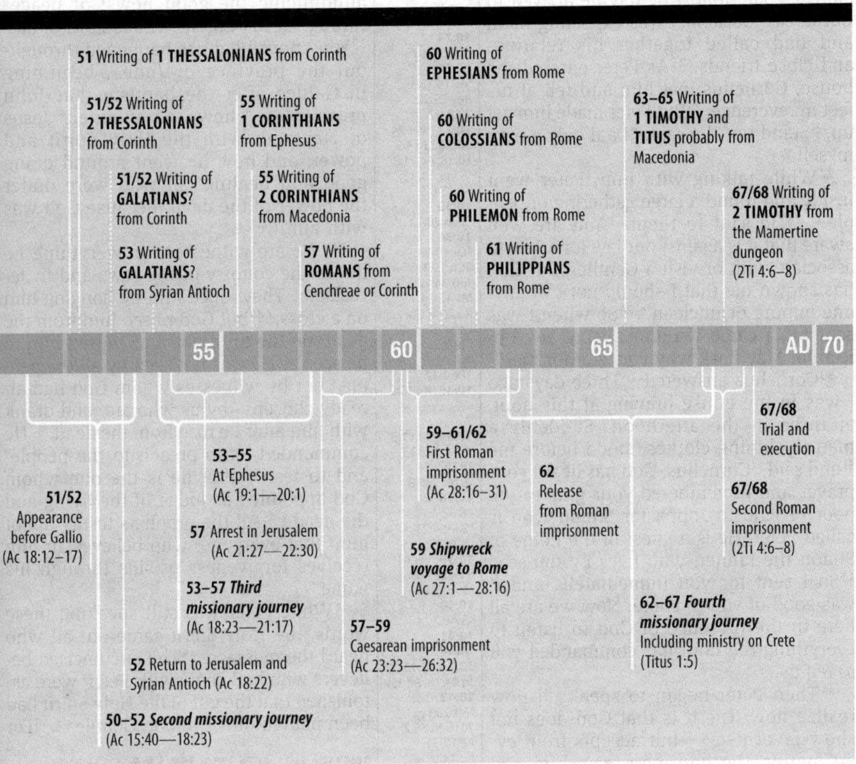

of four-footed animals, as well as reptiles
and birds. 13 Then a voice told him, "Get
up, Peter. Kill and eat."
14 "Surely not, Lord!"[y] Peter replied. "I
have never eaten anything impure or unclean."[z]
15 The voice spoke to him a second time,
"Do not call anything impure that God has
made clean."[a]
16 This happened three times, and immediately the sheet was taken back to heaven.
17 While Peter was wondering about the
meaning of the vision,[b] the men sent by
Cornelius[c] found out where Simon's house
was and stopped at the gate. 18 They called
out, asking if Simon who was known as
Peter was staying there.
19 While Peter was still thinking about
the vision,[d] the Spirit said[e] to him, "Simon, three[a] men are looking for you. 20 So
get up and go downstairs. Do not hesitate
to go with them, for I have sent them."[f]
21 Peter went down and said to the men,
"I'm the one you're looking for. Why have
you come?"
22 The men replied, "We have come from
Cornelius the centurion. He is a righteous
and God-fearing man,[g] who is respected
by all the Jewish people. A holy angel
told him to ask you to come to his house
so that he could hear what you have to
say."[h] 23 Then Peter invited the men into
the house to be his guests.

Peter at Cornelius's House

The next day Peter started out with them,

[a] *19* One early manuscript *two;* other manuscripts do not have the number.

10:14 [y] Ac 9:5 [z] Lev 11:4-8, 13-20; 20:25; Dt 14:3-20; Eze 4:14
10:15 [a] ver 28; Ge 9:3; Mt 15:11; Lk 11:41; Ac 11:9; Ro 14:14,17, 20; 1Co 10:25; 1Ti 4:3,4; Titus 1:15
10:17 [b] S Ac 9:10 [c] ver 7,8
10:19 [d] S Ac 9:10 [e] S Ac 8:29
10:20 [f] Ac 15:7-9
10:22 [g] ver 2 [h] Ac 11:14

10:12 *all kinds of four-footed animals.* Including animals both clean and unclean, according to Lev 11.
10:14 *Surely not, Lord!* So deeply ingrained was the observance of the laws of clean and unclean that Peter refused to obey immediately. *impure or unclean.* Anything common (impure) was forbidden by the law to be eaten (cf. Ezr 4:14).
10:15 *God has made clean.* Jesus had already laid the groundwork for setting aside the laws of clean and unclean food (Mt 15:11; see also 1Ti 4:3–5).
10:16 *three times.* To make a strong impression on Peter.
10:23 *invited the men into the house.* By providing lodging for them, Peter was already taking the first step toward

and some of the believers[i] from Joppa went
along.[j] 24 The following day he arrived in
Caesarea.[k] Cornelius was expecting them
and had called together his relatives
and close friends. 25 As Peter entered the
house, Cornelius met him and fell at his
feet in reverence. 26 But Peter made him get
up. "Stand up," he said, "I am only a man
myself."[l]
27 While talking with him, Peter went
inside and found a large gathering of people.[m] 28 He said to them: "You are well
aware that it is against our law for a Jew to
associate with or visit a Gentile.[n] But God
has shown me that I should not call anyone impure or unclean.[o] 29 So when I was
sent for, I came without raising any objection. May I ask why you sent for me?"
30 Cornelius answered: "Three days ago
I was in my house praying at this hour,
at three in the afternoon. Suddenly a
man in shining clothes[p] stood before me
31 and said, 'Cornelius, God has heard your
prayer and remembered your gifts to the
poor. 32 Send to Joppa for Simon who is
called Peter. He is a guest in the home of
Simon the tanner, who lives by the sea.'
33 So I sent for you immediately, and it
was good of you to come. Now we are all
here in the presence of God to listen to
everything the Lord has commanded you
to tell us."
34 Then Peter began to speak: "I now
realize how true it is that God does not
show favoritism[q] 35 but accepts from every nation the one who fears him and
does what is right.[r] 36 You know the message[s] God sent to the people of Israel,
announcing the good news[t] of peace[u]
through Jesus Christ, who is Lord of all.[v]
37 You know what has happened throughout the province of Judea, beginning
in Galilee after the baptism that John
preached— 38 how God anointed[w] Jesus
of Nazareth with the Holy Spirit and
power, and how he went around doing
good and healing[x] all who were under
the power of the devil, because God was
with him.[y]
39 "We are witnesses[z] of everything he
did in the country of the Jews and in Jerusalem. They killed him by hanging him
on a cross,[a] 40 but God raised him from the
dead[b] on the third day and caused him to
be seen. 41 He was not seen by all the people,[c] but by witnesses whom God had already chosen—by us who ate[d] and drank
with him after he rose from the dead. 42 He
commanded us to preach to the people[e]
and to testify that he is the one whom
God appointed as judge of the living and
the dead.[f] 43 All the prophets testify about
him[g] that everyone[h] who believes[i] in him
receives forgiveness of sins through his
name."[j]
44 While Peter was still speaking these
words, the Holy Spirit came on[k] all who
heard the message. 45 The circumcised believers who had come with Peter[l] were astonished that the gift of the Holy Spirit had
been poured out[m] even on Gentiles.[n] 46 For

10:23 [i] S Ac 1:16 [j] ver 45; Ac 11:12 **10:24** [k] S Ac 8:40 **10:26** [l] Ac 14:15; Rev 19:10; 22:8,9 **10:27** [m] ver 24 **10:28** [n] Jn 4:9; 18:28; Ac 11:3 [o] S ver 14,15; Ac 15:8,9 **10:30** [p] S Jn 20:12 **10:34** [q] Dt 10:17; 2Ch 19:7; Job 34:19; Mk 12:14; Ro 2:11; Gal 2:6; Eph 6:9; Col 3:25; Jas 2:1; 1Pe 1:17 **10:35** [r] Ac 15:9 **10:36** [s] 1Jn 1:5 [t] S Ac 13:32 [u] S Lk 2:14 [v] S Mt 28:18 **10:38** [w] S Ac 4:26 [x] S Mt 4:23 [y] S Jn 3:2 **10:39** [z] ver 41; S Lk 24:48 [a] S Ac 5:30 **10:40** [b] S Ac 2:24 **10:41** [c] Jn 14:17, 22 [d] Lk 24:43; Jn 21:13; Ac 1:4 **10:42** [e] Mt 28:19, 20 [f] S Jn 5:22; Ac 17:31; Ro 14:9; 2Co 5:10; 2Ti 4:1; 1Pe 4:5 **10:43** [g] Isa 53:11; Ac 26:22 [h] Ac 15:9 [i] S Jn 3:15 [j] S Lk 24:27 **10:44** [k] Ac 8:15,16; 11:15; 15:8; 19:6; S Lk 1:15 **10:45** [l] ver 23 [m] Ac 2:33,38 [n] Ac 11:18; 15:8

accepting Gentiles. Such intimate relationship with Gentiles was contrary to prescribed Jewish practice. *The next day.* It was too late in the day to start out on the long journey to Caesarea (see note on v. 1). *some of the believers.* Six in number (11:12), they were "circumcised believers" (10:45; see also note on 11:1).

10:26 *I am only a man.* Possibly Cornelius was only intending to honor Peter as one having a rank superior to his own, since he was God's messenger. But Peter allowed no chance for misunderstanding—he was not to be worshiped as more than a created being (cf. 14:11–15).

10:28 *God has shown me.* Peter recognized that his vision had deeper significance than declaring invalid the distinction between clean and unclean meat; he saw that the barrier between Jew and Gentile had been removed (see Eph 2:11–22).

10:30 *a man in shining clothes.* Common language to describe an angel when appearing in the form of a man (see 1:10 and note; Mt 28:3; Mk 16:5; Jn 20:12).

10:34 *God does not show favoritism.* God does not favor individuals because of their station in life, their nationality or their material possessions (see Ro 2:11; Jas 2:1 and notes; see also Dt 10:17–19; Job 34:19; 2Co 19:17; Eph 6:9; Col 3:25; 1Pe 1:17). He does, however, respect their character and judge their work. This is evident because God "accepts from every nation the one who fears him and does what is right" (v. 35). Cornelius already worshiped the true God, but this was not enough: He lacked faith in Christ (v. 36).

10:36 *people of Israel.* The first recipients of the "message," but it was not restricted to them, as the phrase "Lord of all" indicates (see Jn 3:16; Ro 1:16). *peace.* Between God and humans (see Ro 5:1 and note). *Lord of all.* Lord of both Jew and Gentile (see vv. 34–35), so the gospel is for all people.

10:37 *after the baptism that John preached.* Similar to the outline of Mark's Gospel, Peter's sermon begins with John's baptism and continues to the resurrection of Jesus. This is significant since the early church fathers viewed Mark as the interpreter of Peter (see Introduction to Mark: Author). See previous summaries of Peter's preaching (2:14–41; 3:12–26; 4:8–12; 5:29–32); see also note on 2:14–40.

10:38 *how God anointed Jesus.* See Isa 61:1–3; Lk 4:18–21.

10:39 *hanging him on a cross.* See note on 5:30.

10:41 *who ate and drank.* Those who ate with Jesus after he rose from the dead received unmistakable evidence of his bodily resurrection (see Lk 24:42–43; Jn 21:12–15).

10:43 *All the prophets testify about him.* See Lk 24:44 and note.

10:44 *the Holy Spirit came on.* See 8:16 and note.

10:45 *astonished … even on Gentiles.* Apparently the early Jewish Christians failed to understand that the gospel was for Gentiles as well as for Jews, and that they would share alike in the benefits of redemption. Gentile converts to Judaism, however, were accepted (see 6:5).

they heard them speaking in tongues[a][o]
and praising God.
Then Peter said, 47 "Surely no one can
stand in the way of their being baptized
with water.[p] They have received the Holy
Spirit just as we have."[q] 48 So he ordered
that they be baptized in the name of Jesus
Christ.[r] Then they asked Peter to stay with
them for a few days.

Peter Explains His Actions

11 The apostles and the believers[s]
throughout Judea heard that the
Gentiles also had received the word of
God.[t] 2 So when Peter went up to Jerusalem, the circumcised believers[u] criticized
him 3 and said, "You went into the house of
uncircumcised men and ate with them."[v]
4 Starting from the beginning, Peter told
them the whole story: 5 "I was in the city
of Joppa praying, and in a trance I saw
a vision.[w] I saw something like a large
sheet being let down from heaven by its
four corners, and it came down to where I
was. 6 I looked into it and saw four-footed
animals of the earth, wild beasts, reptiles
and birds. 7 Then I heard a voice telling
me, 'Get up, Peter. Kill and eat.'
8 "I replied, 'Surely not, Lord! Nothing
impure or unclean has ever entered my
mouth.'
9 "The voice spoke from heaven a second time, 'Do not call anything impure
that God has made clean.'[x] 10 This happened three times, and then it was all
pulled up to heaven again.
11 "Right then three men who had been
sent to me from Caesarea[y] stopped at the
house where I was staying. 12 The Spirit
told[z] me to have no hesitation about going
with them.[a] These six brothers[b] also went
with me, and we entered the man's house.
13 He told us how he had seen an angel[c]
appear in his house and say, 'Send to Joppa for Simon who is called Peter. 14 He will
bring you a message[d] through which you
and all your household[e] will be saved.'
15 "As I began to speak, the Holy Spirit came on[f] them as he had come on us
at the beginning.[g] 16 Then I remembered
what the Lord had said: 'John baptized
with[b] water,[h] but you will be baptized
with[b] the Holy Spirit.'[i] 17 So if God gave
them the same gift[j] he gave us[k] who believed in the Lord Jesus Christ, who was I
to think that I could stand in God's way?"
18 When they heard this, they had no
further objections and praised God, saying, "So then, even to Gentiles God has
granted repentance that leads to life."[l]

The Church in Antioch

19 Now those who had been scattered by
the persecution that broke out when Stephen was killed[m] traveled as far as Phoenicia, Cyprus and Antioch,[n] spreading the
word only among Jews. 20 Some of them,
however, men from Cyprus[o] and Cyrene,[p]
went to Antioch[q] and began to speak to
Greeks also, telling them the good news[r]
about the Lord Jesus. 21 The Lord's hand
was with them,[s] and a great number of
people believed and turned to the Lord.[t]

10:46 [o] S Mk 16:17 **10:47** [p] Ac 8:36 [q] S Jn 20:22; Ac 11:17 **10:48** [r] S Ac 2:38 **11:1** [s] S Ac 1:16 [t] S Heb 4:12 **11:2** [u] Ac 10:45 **11:3** [v] Ac 10:25, 28; Gal 2:12 **11:5** [w] S Ac 9:10; 10:9-32 **11:9** [x] S Ac 10:15 **11:11** [y] S Ac 8:40 **11:12** [z] S Ac 8:29 [a] Ac 15:9; Ro 3:22 [b] ver 1, 29; S Ac 1:16 **11:13** [c] S Ac 5:19 **11:14** [d] Ac 10:36 [e] Jn 4:53; Ac 16:15, 31-34; 18:8; 1Co 1:11, 16 **11:15** [f] S Ac 10:44 [g] Ac 2:4 **11:16** [h] S Mk 1:4 [i] S Mk 1:8 **11:17** [j] Ac 2:38 [k] Ac 10:45, 47 **11:18** [l] Ro 10:12, 13; 2Co 7:10 **11:19** [m] Ac 8:1, 4 [n] ver 26, 27; Ac 13:1; 14:26; 18:22; Gal 2:11 **11:20** [o] Ac 4:36 [p] S Mt 27:32 [q] S ver 19 [r] S Ac 13:32 **11:21** [s] Lk 1:66 [t] S Ac 2:41

[a] *46 Or other languages* [b] *16 Or in*

10:46 *speaking in tongues.* The same experience the disciples had at Pentecost (2:4,11), as well as "some disciples" at Ephesus (19:1,6).
10:47 *no one can stand in the way of their being baptized with water.* The Gentiles had received the same gift (11:17) as the Jewish believers; they spoke in tongues as did the Jewish Christians on the day of Pentecost. This was unavoidable evidence that the invitation to the kingdom was open to Gentiles as well as to Jews.
11:1 *believers.* Lit. "brothers." At times "brothers" is used to refer to those of common Jewish lineage (2:29; 7:2), but in Christian contexts it denotes those united in Christ (6:3; 10:23; see note on Ro 1:13). In matters of deep concern, the "apostles" did not act alone. The divine will gave guidance, and the apostles interpreted and exhorted, but the consent of the whole church was sought ("the whole group," 6:5; "apostles and the believers," here; "the church," 11:22; "the church and the apostles and elders," 15:4; cf. 15:22).
11:2 *circumcised believers.* Jewish Christians.
11:3 *uncircumcised men.* The Gentiles who would not observe the laws of clean and unclean food and would violate Jewish regulations concerning food preparation. *ate with them.* See Lk 15:2 and note.
11:4–17 See notes on 10:1–23,28–33.
11:14 *you and all your household.* Not only the family but also slaves and employed individuals under Cornelius's authority (see note on Ge 6:18).
11:17 *stand in God's way.* Peter could not deny the Gentiles the invitation to be baptized (10:47) and to enjoy full fellowship in Christ with all believers. The Jewish believers were compelled to recognize that God was going to save Gentiles on equal terms with Jews. By divine action rather than by human choice, the door was being opened to Gentiles.
11:18 *repentance that leads to life.* A change of one's attitude toward sin, which leads to a turning from sin to God and results in eternal life (see note on 2:38).
11:19 *persecution that broke out when Stephen was killed.* See 8:1–4 and notes. *Phoenicia.* A country about 15 miles wide and 120 miles long, stretching along the northeastern Mediterranean coast (modern Lebanon). Its important cities were Tyre and Sidon. *Cyprus.* An island in the northeastern Mediterranean; the home of Barnabas (4:36). *Antioch.* The third city of the Roman Empire (after Rome and Alexandria). It was 15 miles inland from the northeast corner of the Mediterranean. The first largely Gentile local church was located here, and it was from this church that Paul's three missionary journeys were launched (13:1–4; 15:40; 18:23).
11:20 *Cyrene.* See note on 2:10. *Greeks.* Not Greek-speaking Jews, but Gentiles.
11:21 *Lord's hand.* Indicates the presence of the Lord's power to assist and bless (see 4:30; Lk 1:16; but see also Ac 13:11), sometimes evidenced by signs and wonders (cf. Ex 8:19).

22 News of this reached the church in Jerusalem, and they sent Barnabas[u] to Antioch. 23 When he arrived and saw what
the grace of God had done,[v] he was glad
and encouraged them all to remain true to
the Lord with all their hearts.[w] 24 He was
a good man, full of the Holy Spirit[x] and
faith, and a great number of people were
brought to the Lord.[y]
25 Then Barnabas went to Tarsus[z] to look
for Saul, 26 and when he found him, he
brought him to Antioch. So for a whole year
Barnabas and Saul met with the church and
taught great numbers of people. The disciples[a] were called Christians first[b] at Antioch.
27 During this time some prophets[c] came
down from Jerusalem to Antioch. 28 One
of them, named Agabus,[d] stood up and
through the Spirit predicted that a severe
famine would spread over the entire Roman world.[e] (This happened during the
reign of Claudius.)[f] 29 The disciples,[g] as
each one was able, decided to provide
help[h] for the brothers and sisters[i] living in
Judea. 30 This they did, sending their gift to
the elders[j] by Barnabas[k] and Saul.[l]

Peter's Miraculous Escape From Prison

12 It was about this time that King
Herod[m] arrested some who belonged
to the church, intending to persecute them.
2 He had James, the brother of John,[n] put
to death with the sword.[o] 3 When he saw
that this met with approval among the
Jews,[p] he proceeded to seize Peter also.
This happened during the Festival of Unleavened Bread.[q] 4 After arresting him, he
put him in prison, handing him over to
be guarded by four squads of four soldiers
each. Herod intended to bring him out for
public trial after the Passover.[r]
5 So Peter was kept in prison, but the
church was earnestly praying to God for
him.[s]
6 The night before Herod was to bring
him to trial, Peter was sleeping between
two soldiers, bound with two chains,[t] and
sentries stood guard at the entrance. 7 Suddenly an angel[u] of the Lord appeared and
a light shone in the cell. He struck Peter
on the side and woke him up. "Quick, get
up!" he said, and the chains fell off Peter's
wrists.[v]
8 Then the angel said to him, "Put on
your clothes and sandals." And Peter did
so. "Wrap your cloak around you and follow me," the angel told him. 9 Peter followed him out of the prison, but he had

11:22 [u] S Ac 4:36 **11:23** [v] Ac 13:43; 14:26; 15:40; 20:24 [w] Ac 14:22 **11:24** [x] S Lk 1:15 [y] S Ac 2:41 **11:25** [z] S Ac 9:11 **11:26** [a] ver 29; Ac 6:1,2; 9:19, 26,38; 13:52 [b] Ac 26:28; 1Pe 4:16 **11:27** [c] Ac 13:1; 15:32; 1Co 11:4; 12:28,29; 14:29,32,37; S Eph 4:11 **11:28** [d] Ac 21:10 [e] S Mt 24:14 [f] Ac 18:2 **11:29** [g] S ver 26 [h] Ro 15:26; 2Co 8:1-4; 9:2 [i] ver 1,12; S Ac 1:16 **11:30** [j] Ac 14:23; 15:2,22; 20:17; 1Ti 5:17; Titus 1:5; Jas 5:14; 1Pe 5:1; 2Jn 1 [k] S Ac 4:36 [l] Ac 12:25 **12:1** [m] S Mt 14:1 **12:2** [n] S Mt 4:21 [o] Mk 10:39 **12:3** [p] Ac 24:27; 25:9 [q] Ex 12:15; 23:15; Ac 20:6 **12:4** [r] S Jn 11:55 **12:5** [s] S Ac 1:14; Ro 15:30,31; Eph 6:18 **12:6** [t] Ac 21:33 **12:7** [u] S Ac 5:19 [v] Ps 107:14; Ac 16:26

11:22 *Barnabas.* See notes on 4:36; 9:27. *Antioch.* See note on v. 19. The sending of Barnabas was apparently in keeping with the Jerusalem church's policy of sending leaders to check on new ministries that came to their attention (see 8:14).

11:23 *he ... encouraged them.* His name means "son of encouragement" (4:36; see note there).

11:24 *full of the Holy Spirit and faith.* See the description of Stephen (6:5).

11:25 *Tarsus.* See 9:11,30 and note on 22:3.

11:26 *whole year.* Luke notes definite periods of time (18:11; 19:8,10; 24:27; 28:30). *Christians.* Whether adopted by believers or invented by enemies as a term of reproach, it is an apt title for those "belonging to Christ" (the meaning of the term). It occurs elsewhere in Scripture only in 26:28; 1Pe 4:16.

11:27 *prophets.* The first mention of the gift of prophecy in Acts. Prophets preach, exhort, explain or, as in this case, foretell (see 13:1; 15:32; 19:6; 21:9–10; Ro 12:6; 1Co 12:10; 13:2,8; 14:3,6,29–37; see also notes on Jnh 3:2; Zec 1:1; Eph 4:11).

11:28 *Agabus.* Later foretells Paul's imprisonment (21:10). In Acts, prophets are engaged in foretelling (v. 27; 21:9–10) at least as often as in forthtelling (15:32). *Claudius.* Emperor of Rome (AD 41–54).

11:29 *as each one was able.* Cf. 2Co 8:3.

11:30 *elders.* First reference to them in Acts (see notes on 1Ti 3:1; 5:17). Since the apostles are not mentioned, they may have been absent from Jerusalem at this time.

12:1 *about this time.* Some hold that the events recorded in ch. 12 group together matters concerning Herod Agrippa I (see below; see also chart, p. 1593) and may not be in strict chronological order. For example, the arrival of Barnabas and Saul in Jerusalem (11:30) may have followed Herod's persecution and Peter's release from prison. Since the date of Herod's death was AD 44, these events would probably have occurred in 43. According to this view, the famine of 11:28 occurred c. 46, following Herod's death (v. 23). Others hold that such juggling of events is unnecessary. Thus the relief gift of 11:30 came before Herod's death in 44, and the return of Barnabas and Saul (v. 25) followed Herod's death. According to the former view, the Jerusalem visit of Gal 2:1–10 was the famine visit of v. 25; 11:30. According to the latter view, the Gal 2:1 visit was the Jerusalem council visit of 15:1–29 (see chart, pp. 1844–1845). *King Herod.* Agrippa I, grandson of Herod the Great (see notes on Mt 2:1; 14:1) and son of Aristobulus. He was a nephew of Herod Antipas, who had beheaded John the Baptist (Mt 14:3–12) and had tried Jesus (Lk 23:8–12). When Antipas was exiled, Agrippa received his tetrarchy, as well as those of Philip and Lysanias (see Lk 3:1 and note). In AD 41 Judea and Samaria were added to his realm.

12:2 *James.* Brother of John the apostle and son of Zebedee (Mt 4:21). This event took place about ten years after Jesus' death and resurrection. Jesus had warned of their coming suffering (Mt 20:20–23). *death with the sword.* Beheaded, like John the Baptist.

12:3 *Festival of Unleavened Bread.* See notes on Mk 14:1; Lk 22:1.

12:4 *four squads.* One company of four soldiers for each of the four watches of the night (see note on Mt 14:25). *Passover.* Another way of referring to the whole week of the festival (see note on Lk 22:1).

12:7 *angel of the Lord.* See note on 5:19. *a light shone.* Reflecting the glory of the Lord (see 7:55 and note).

12:9 *prison.* Probably the Antonia Fortress, located at the northwest corner of the temple—the "barracks" where Paul was later held (see 21:34). See model, p. 1850.

THE SPREAD OF THE GOSPEL

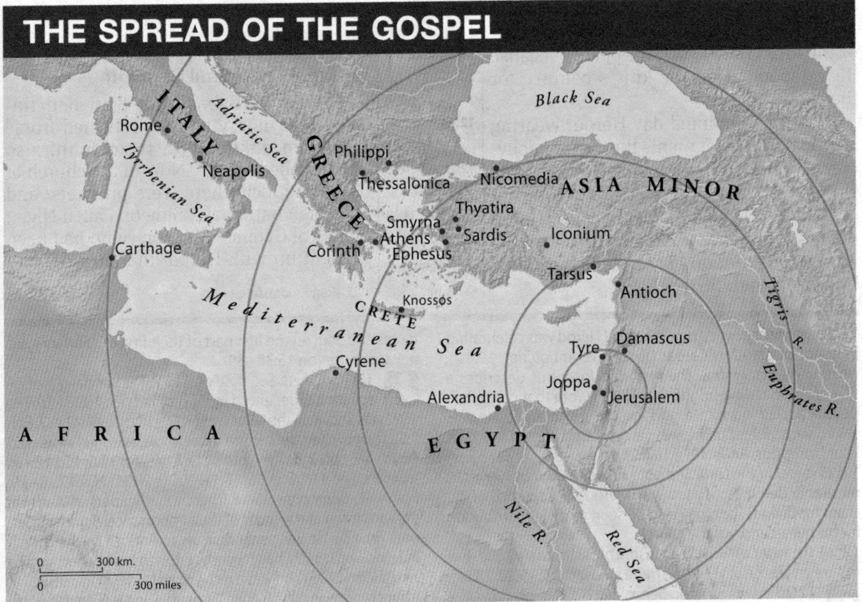

no idea that what the angel was doing was
really happening; he thought he was seeing a vision.[w] 10They passed the first and
second guards and came to the iron gate
leading to the city. It opened for them by
itself,[x] and they went through it. When
they had walked the length of one street,
suddenly the angel left him.
11Then Peter came to himself[y] and
said, "Now I know without a doubt that
the Lord has sent his angel and rescued
me[z] from Herod's clutches and from everything the Jewish people were hoping
would happen."
12When this had dawned on him, he went
to the house of Mary the mother of John,
also called Mark,[a] where many people had
gathered and were praying.[b] 13Peter knocked
at the outer entrance, and a servant named
Rhoda came to answer the door.[c] 14When
she recognized Peter's voice, she was so
overjoyed[d] she ran back without opening it
and exclaimed, "Peter is at the door!"
15"You're out of your mind," they told
her. When she kept insisting that it was
so, they said, "It must be his angel."[e]
16But Peter kept on knocking, and when
they opened the door and saw him, they
were astonished. 17Peter motioned with
his hand[f] for them to be quiet and described how the Lord had brought him
out of prison. "Tell James[g] and the other
brothers and sisters[h] about this," he said,
and then he left for another place.
18In the morning, there was no small
commotion among the soldiers as to what
had become of Peter. 19After Herod had a
thorough search made for him and did not
find him, he cross-examined the guards
and ordered that they be executed.[i]

Herod's Death

Then Herod went from Judea to Caesarea[j] and stayed there. 20He had been quarreling with the people of Tyre and Sidon;[k]
they now joined together and sought an

12:9 [w]S Ac 9:10 **12:10** [x]Ac 5:19; 16:26 **12:11** [y]Lk 15:17 [z]Ps 34:7; Da 3:28; 6:22; 2Co 1:10; 2Pe 2:9 **12:12** [a]ver 25; Ac 13:5,13; 15:37,39; Col 4:10; 2Ti 4:11; Phm 24; 1Pe 5:13 [b]ver 5 **12:13** [c]Jn 18:16,17 **12:14** [d]Lk 24:41 **12:15** [e]S Mt 18:10 **12:17** [f]Ac 13:16; 19:33; 21:40 [g]S Ac 15:13 [h]S Ac 1:16 **12:19** [i]Ac 16:27 [j]S Ac 8:40 **12:20** [k]S Mt 11:21

12:12 *Mary.* The aunt of Barnabas (see Col 4:10). Apparently her home was a gathering place for Christians. It may have been the location of the upper room where the Last Supper was held (see Mk 14:13–15; see also Ac 1:13 and note) and the place of prayer in 4:31. *John ... Mark.* See note on v. 25.
12:13 *Rhoda.* A hired servant, but in sympathy with the family and the church.
12:15 *his angel.* Reflects the belief that everyone has a personal angel who ministers to them (cf. Mt 18:10 and note; Heb 1:14).
12:16 *they were astonished.* Though they had been "earnestly praying to God for him" (v. 5).
12:17 *James.* The Lord's brother, a leader in the Jerusalem church (see Gal 1:19 and note). James, the brother of John, had been killed (see v. 2).
12:19 *Caesarea.* Not only a headquarters for Roman governors, but Agrippa used it as his capital when no governors were assigned to Judea (see notes on 8:40; 10:1).
12:20 *Tyre and Sidon.* The leading cities of Phoenicia (Lebanon today). They were dependent on the grainfields of Galilee for their food. *Blastus.* The treasurer; not otherwise known.

audience with him. After securing the support of Blastus, a trusted personal servant of the king, they asked for peace, because they depended on the king's country for their food supply.[l]

21 On the appointed day Herod, wearing his royal robes, sat on his throne and delivered a public address to the people. 22 They shouted, "This is the voice of a god, not of a man." 23 Immediately, because Herod did not give praise to God, an angel[m] of the Lord struck him down,[n] and he was eaten by worms and died.

12:20 [l] 1Ki 5:9, 11; Eze 27:17
12:23 [m] S Ac 5:19 [n] 1Sa 25:38; 2Sa 24:16, 17; 2Ki 19:35
12:24 [o] S Heb 4:12 [p] Ac 6:7; 19:20
12:25 [q] S Ac 4:36 [r] Ac 11:30 [s] S ver 12
13:1 [t] S Ac 11:19 [u] S Ac 11:27 [v] S Eph 4:11 [w] S Ac 4:36 [x] S Mt 27:32 [y] S Mt 14:1

24 But the word of God[o] continued to spread and flourish.[p]

Barnabas and Saul Sent Off

25 When Barnabas[q] and Saul had finished their mission,[r] they returned from[a] Jerusalem, taking with them John, also
13 called Mark.[s] 1 Now in the church at
Antioch[t] there were prophets[u] and teachers:[v] Barnabas,[w] Simeon called Niger, Lucius of Cyrene,[x] Manaen (who had been brought up with Herod[y] the tetrarch) and

[a] 25 Some manuscripts *to*

12:21 *On the appointed day.* A festival Herod was celebrating in honor of Claudius Caesar (Josephus, *Antiquities,* 19.8.2). *wearing his royal robes.* The historian Josephus describes a silver robe, dazzling bright, that Herod wore that day. When people acclaimed him a god, he did not deny it. He was seized with violent pains, was carried out and died five days later (Josephus, *Antiquities,* 19.8.2).
12:23 *angel of the Lord.* See note on v. 7. *eaten by worms.* A miserable death associated with Herod's acceptance of acclaim for divinity, but may also be seen as divine retribution for his persecution of the church.
12:24 *the word of God ... flourish.* Third summary report of progress (see 6:7; 9:31). Three more follow (16:5; 19:20; 28:31).
12:25 *John ... Mark.* See v. 12. He was perhaps the young man who fled on the night of Jesus' arrest (Mk 14:51–52). He wrote the second Gospel (see Introduction to Mark: Author; John Mark in the NT) and accompanied Barnabas and Saul on the first part of their first missionary journey (see notes on 15:38–39).
13:1 *prophets.* See note on 11:27. The special gift of inspiration experienced by OT prophets (Dt 18:18–20; 2Pe 1:21) was known in the NT as well (2:17–18; 1Co 14:29–32; Eph 3:5). The prophets are second to the apostles in Paul's lists (1Co 12:28–29; Eph 2:20; 4:11; but cf. Lk 11:49; Ro 12:6; 1Co 12:10). *teachers.* See 11:26; 15:35; 18:11; 20:20; 28:31; 1Co 12:28–29; Eph 4:11. *Barnabas ... Saul.* The church leaders at Antioch, perhaps listed in the order of their importance. *Barnabas.* See note on 4:36. He was sent originally to Antioch by the church in Jerusalem (11:22), had recently returned from taking alms to Jerusalem (12:25) and was a recognized leader in the church at Antioch. *Simeon called Niger.* "Simeon" suggests Jewish background; in that case, "Niger" (Latin for "black") may indicate his dark complexion. *Lucius of Cyrene.* Lucius is a Latin name. In the second group of preachers coming to Antioch, some were from

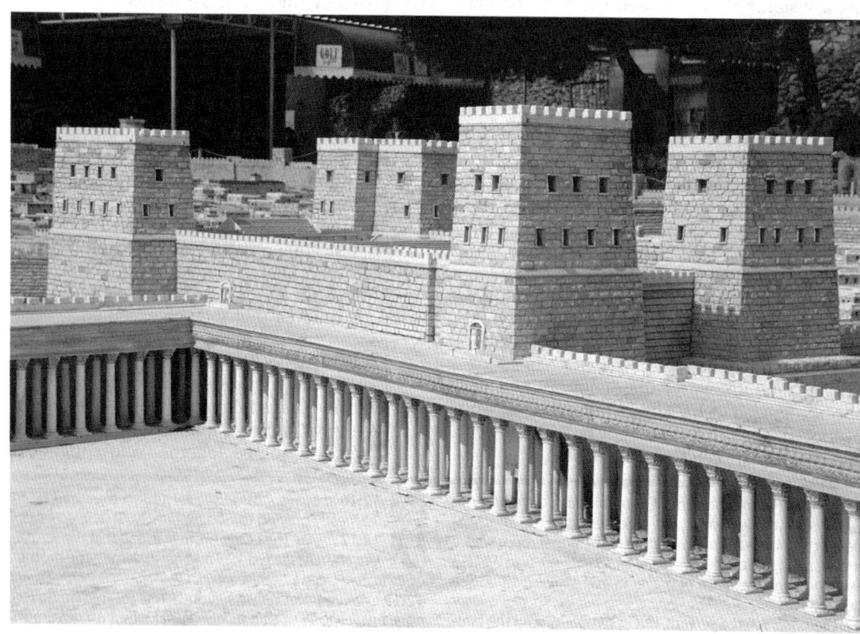

Built by Herod the Great (37–4 BC), the Antonia Fortress overlooked the northwest corner of the temple mount (cf. note on Ac 12:9).

Saul. [2]While they were worshiping the Lord and fasting, the Holy Spirit said,[z] "Set apart for me Barnabas and Saul for the work[a] to which I have called them."[b] [3]So after they had fasted and prayed, they placed their hands on them[c] and sent them off.[d]

On Cyprus

[4]The two of them, sent on their way by the Holy Spirit,[e] went down to Seleucia and sailed from there to Cyprus.[f] [5]When they arrived at Salamis, they proclaimed the word of God[g] in the Jewish synagogues.[h] John[i] was with them as their helper.

[6]They traveled through the whole island until they came to Paphos. There they met a Jewish sorcerer[j] and false prophet[k] named Bar-Jesus, [7]who was an attendant of the proconsul,[l] Sergius Paulus. The proconsul, an intelligent man, sent for Barnabas and Saul because he wanted to hear the word of God. [8]But Elymas the sorcerer[m] (for that is what his name means) opposed them and tried to turn the proconsul[n] from the faith.[o] [9]Then Saul, who was also called Paul, filled with the Holy Spirit,[p] looked straight at Elymas and said, [10]"You are a child of the devil[q] and an enemy of everything that is right! You are full of all kinds of deceit and trickery. Will you never stop perverting the right ways of the Lord?[r] [11]Now the hand of the Lord is against you.[s] You are going to be blind for a time, not even able to see the light of the sun."[t]

Immediately mist and darkness came over him, and he groped about, seeking

PAUL'S FIRST MISSIONARY JOURNEY c. AD 46–48 (Ac 13:4–14:28)

13:2 [z]S Ac 8:29 [a]Ac 14:26 [b]Ac 9:15; 22:21 **13:3** [c]S Ac 6:6 [d]Ac 14:26 **13:4** [e]ver 2,3 [f]Ac 4:36 **13:5** [g]S Heb 4:12 [h]S Ac 9:20 [i]S Ac 12:12 **13:6** [j]Ac 8:9 [k]S Mt 7:15 **13:7** [l]ver 8, 12; Ac 18:12; 19:38 **13:8** [m]Ac 8:9 [n]S ver 7 [o]Isa 30:11; Ac 6:7 **13:9** [p]S Lk 1:15 **13:10** [q]Mt 13:38; Jn 8:44 [r]Hos 14:9 **13:11** [s]Ex 9:3; 1Sa 5:6, 7; Ps 32:4 [t]Ge 19:10, 11; 2Ki 6:18

Cyrene (11:20), capital of Libya (see 6:9 and note). *Manaen.* In Hebrew, Menahem. He was the foster brother or intimate friend of Herod Antipas.

13:2 *worshiping the Lord and fasting.* Paul's first missionary journey did not result from a planning session but from the Spirit's initiative as the leaders worshiped (see v. 4). The communication from the Holy Spirit may have come through the prophets.

13:3 *placed their hands on them.* For the purpose of separating the two for the designated work (see 14:26 for the completion of the mission). Fasting and prayer accompany this appointment (see 14:23; cf. Lk 2:37).

13:4—14:28 Paul's first missionary journey (see map above).

13:4 See map, pp. 2528–2529, at the end of this study Bible. *Seleucia.* The seaport of Antioch (16 miles to the west, and 5 miles upstream from the mouth of the Orontes River). *Cyprus.* Many Jews lived there, and the gospel had already been preached there (11:19–20; see note on 11:19).

13:5 *Salamis.* A town on the east coast of the central plain of Cyprus, near modern Famagusta. *John.* John Mark, a cousin of Barnabas (see 12:25; Col 4:10 and note). *helper.* In what way we are not told. Some hold that he served as a catechist for new converts, but Luke seems to use the term in a broader sense (see 26:16; Lk 1:2 ["servants"]).

13:6 *Paphos.* At the western end of Cyprus, nearly 100 miles from Salamis. It was the headquarters for Roman rule. *Bar-Jesus.* "Bar" is Aramaic for "son of"; "Jesus" is derived from the Greek for "Joshua" (see NIV text note on Mt 1:21).

13:7 *proconsul.* Since Cyprus was a Roman senatorial province, a proconsul was assigned to it. *Sergius Paulus.* See chart, p. 1811.

13:8 *Elymas.* A Semitic name meaning "sorcerer" or "magician" or "wise man" (probably a self-assumed designation).

13:9 *Saul … called Paul.* The names mean "asked [of God]" and "little" respectively. It was customary to have a given name, in this case Saul (Hebrew, Jewish background), and a later name, in this case Paul (Roman, Hellenistic background). From now on Saul is called Paul in Acts. This may be due to Saul's success in preaching to Paulus or to the fact that he is now entering the Gentile phase of his ministry. The order in which they are mentioned now changes from "Barnabas and Saul" to "Paul and Barnabas." Upon their return to the Jerusalem church, however, the order reverts to "Barnabas and Paul" (15:12).

13:11 *hand of the Lord.* See note on 11:21. *You are going to be blind.* Cf. Paul's experience in 9:8–18.

someone to lead him by the hand. 12 When the proconsul[u] saw what had happened, he believed, for he was amazed at the teaching about the Lord.

In Pisidian Antioch

13 From Paphos,[v] Paul and his companions sailed to Perga in Pamphylia,[w] where John[x] left them to return to Jerusalem. 14 From Perga they went on to Pisidian Antioch.[y] On the Sabbath[z] they entered the synagogue[a] and sat down. 15 After the reading from the Law[b] and the Prophets, the leaders of the synagogue sent word to them, saying, "Brothers, if you have a word of exhortation for the people, please speak."

16 Standing up, Paul motioned with his hand[c] and said: "Fellow Israelites and you Gentiles who worship God, listen to me! 17 The God of the people of Israel chose our ancestors; he made the people prosper during their stay in Egypt; with mighty power he led them out of that country;[d] 18 for about forty years he endured their conduct[a][e] in the wilderness;[f] 19 and he overthrew seven nations in Canaan,[g] giving their land to his people[h] as their inheritance.[i] 20 All this took about 450 years.

"After this, God gave them judges[j] until the time of Samuel the prophet.[k] 21 Then the people asked for a king,[l] and he gave them Saul[m] son of Kish, of the tribe of Benjamin,[n] who ruled forty years. 22 After removing Saul,[o] he made David their king.[p] God testified concerning him: 'I have found David son of Jesse, a man after my own heart;[q] he will do everything I want him to do.'[r]

23 "From this man's descendants[s] God has brought to Israel the Savior[t] Jesus,[u] as he promised.[v] 24 Before the coming of Jesus, John preached repentance and baptism to all the people of Israel.[w] 25 As John was completing his work,[x] he said: 'Who do you suppose I am? I am not the one you are looking for.[y] But there is one coming after me whose sandals I am not worthy to untie.'[z]

26 "Fellow children of Abraham[a] and you God-fearing Gentiles, it is to us that this message of salvation[b] has been sent. 27 The people of Jerusalem and their rulers did not recognize Jesus,[c] yet in condemning him they fulfilled the words of the prophets[d] that are read every Sabbath. 28 Though they found no proper ground for a death sentence, they asked Pilate to have him executed.[e] 29 When they had carried out all that was written about him,[f] they took him down from the cross[g] and laid him in a tomb.[h] 30 But God raised him from the dead,[i] 31 and for many days he was seen by those who had traveled with him from Galilee to Jerusalem.[j] They are now his witnesses[k] to our people.

32 "We tell you the good news:[l] What

[a] *18* Some manuscripts *he cared for them*

13:12 [u] S ver 7 **13:13** [v] ver 6 [w] S Ac 2:10 [x] S Ac 12:12 **13:14** [y] Ac 14:19,21 [z] ver 27,42,44; Ac 16:13; 18:4 [a] S Ac 9:20 **13:15** [b] Ac 15:21 **13:16** [c] S Ac 12:17 **13:17** [d] Ex 6:6,7; Dt 7:6-8 **13:18** [e] Dt 1:31 [f] Nu 14:33; Ps 95:10; Ac 7:36 **13:19** [g] Dt 7:1 [h] Jos 19:51; Ac 7:45 [i] Ps 78:55 **13:20** [j] Jdg 2:16 [k] 1Sa 3:19,20; Ac 3:24 **13:21** [l] 1Sa 8:5,19 [m] 1Sa 10:1 [n] 1Sa 9:1,2 **13:22** [o] 1Sa 15:23,26 [p] 1Sa 16:13; Ps 89:20 [q] 1Sa 13:14; Jer 3:15 [r] Isa 44:28 **13:23** [s] S Mt 1:1 [t] S Lk 2:11 [u] Mt 1:21 [v] ver 32; 2Sa 7:11; 22:51; Jer 30:9 **13:24** [w] S Mk 1:4 **13:25** [x] Ac 20:24 [y] Jn 1:20 [z] Mt 3:11; Jn 1:27 **13:26** [a] S Lk 3:8; S Ac 22:5 [b] Ac 4:12; 28:28 **13:27** [c] Ac 3:17 [d] S Lk 24:27; S Mt 1:22 **13:28** [e] Mt 27:20-25; Ac 3:14 **13:29** [f] S Mt 1:22; Lk 18:31 [g] S Ac 5:30 [h] Lk 23:53 **13:30** [i] S Mt 16:21; 28:6; S Ac 2:24 **13:31** [j] Mt 28:16 [k] S Lk 24:48 **13:32** [l] Isa 40:9; 52:7; Ac 5:42; 8:35; 10:36; 14:7,15,21; 17:18

13:12 *he believed.* He was convinced by the miracle and the message.

13:13 *Perga in Pamphylia.* Perga was the capital of Pamphylia, a coastal province of Asia Minor between the provinces of Lycia and Cilicia, and was 5 miles inland and 12 miles east of the important seaport Attalia (see map, p. 1851). *John left them.* See 12:25 and note. Homesickness to get back to Jerusalem, an illness of Paul necessitating a change in plans and a trip to Galatia, and a change in leadership from Barnabas to Paul have all been suggested as reasons for John Mark's return. Paul's dissatisfaction with his departure is noted later (15:37–39).

13:14–41 Paul and Barnabas in the synagogue of Pisidian Antioch. Paul's first recorded synagogue sermon in Acts sets the pattern for the rest of his ministry. When most of the Jews reject the gospel, he turns to the Gentiles (see vv. 45–48; Ro 1:16). The sermon moves carefully through Israel's history until David and then jumps one thousand years forward to the fulfillment in David's greater Son, Jesus the Messiah. For another account of a synagogue service, see Lk 4:16–21.

13:14 *Pisidian.* See note on 14:24. *Antioch.* Named after Antiochus, king of Syria after the death of Alexander the Great. It was 110 miles from Perga, 3,600 feet above sea level and at the hub of good roads and trade. The city had a large Jewish population. It was a Roman colony, which meant that a contingent of retired military men was settled there. They were given free land and were made citizens of the city of Rome, with all the accompanying privileges. *synagogue.* Paul's regular practice was to begin his preaching in the synagogue, as long as the Jews would allow it (see v. 5; 14:1; 17:1,10,17; 18:4,19; 19:8). His reason for doing so was grounded in his understanding of God's redemptive plan (see v. 46; Ro 1:16 and note; 2:9–10 and note on 2:9; see also Ro 9–11). He was not neglecting his Gentile mission, for the God-fearers ("Gentiles who worship God," v. 16; see note on 10:2) were part of the audience. Moreover, the synagogue provided a ready-made preaching situation with a building, regularly scheduled meetings and a people who knew the OT Scriptures. It was customary to invite visitors, and especially visiting rabbis (such as Paul), to address the gathering.

13:15 *the Law and the Prophets.* Sections from the OT were read, followed by exposition and exhortation. *leaders of the synagogue.* See note on Mk 5:22. *word of exhortation.* See Introduction to Hebrews: Literary Form.

13:20 *about 450 years.* The 400 years of the "stay in Egypt" (v. 17; see note on 7:6) plus the 40 years in the wilderness and the time between the crossing of the Jordan and the distribution of the land (see Jos 14–19).

13:23 *as he promised.* See, e.g., Isa 11:1–16.

13:25 *John ... said.* See Mt 3:11; Mk 1:7; Lk 3:16; Jn 1:20,27.

13:26 *God-fearing Gentiles.* See note on v. 14.

13:27 *fulfilled the words of the prophets.* See Lk 24:44 and note.

13:28 *no proper ground for a death sentence.* Cf. Jn 19:4 and note.

13:29–31 *cross ... tomb ... God raised ... witnesses.* See note on 3:15.

13:31 *many days.* Forty days (see 1:3).

God promised our ancestors[m] 33 he has
fulfilled for us, their children, by raising
up Jesus.[n] As it is written in the second
Psalm:

> "'You are my son;
> today I have become your father.'[a][o]

34 God raised him from the dead so that
he will never be subject to decay. As God
has said,

> "'I will give you the holy and sure
> blessings promised to David.'[b][p]

35 So it is also stated elsewhere:

> "'You will not let your holy one see
> decay.'[c][q]

36 "Now when David had served God's
purpose in his own generation, he fell
asleep;[r] he was buried with his ancestors[s] and his body decayed. 37 But the one
whom God raised from the dead[t] did not
see decay.
38 "Therefore, my friends, I want you to
know that through Jesus the forgiveness of
sins is proclaimed to you.[u] 39 Through him
everyone who believes[v] is set free from every sin, a justification you were not able
to obtain under the law of Moses.[w] 40 Take
care that what the prophets have said does
not happen to you:

> 41 "'Look, you scoffers,
> wonder and perish,
> for I am going to do something in your
> days
> that you would never believe,
> even if someone told you.'[d]"[x]

42 As Paul and Barnabas were leaving
the synagogue,[y] the people invited them
to speak further about these things on
the next Sabbath. 43 When the congregation was dismissed, many of the Jews and
devout converts to Judaism followed Paul
and Barnabas, who talked with them and
urged them to continue in the grace of
God.[z]
44 On the next Sabbath almost the whole
city gathered to hear the word of the Lord.
45 When the Jews saw the crowds, they
were filled with jealousy. They began
to contradict what Paul was saying[a] and
heaped abuse[b] on him.
46 Then Paul and Barnabas answered
them boldly: "We had to speak the word
of God to you first.[c] Since you reject it and
do not consider yourselves worthy of eternal life, we now turn to the Gentiles.[d] 47 For
this is what the Lord has commanded us:

> "'I have made you[e] a light for the
> Gentiles,[e]
> that you[e] may bring salvation to the
> ends of the earth.'[f]"[f]

48 When the Gentiles heard this, they
were glad and honored the word of the
Lord;[g] and all who were appointed for
eternal life believed.
49 The word of the Lord[h] spread through
the whole region. 50 But the Jewish leaders incited the God-fearing women of high
standing and the leading men of the city.
They stirred up persecution against Paul
and Barnabas, and expelled them from
their region.[i] 51 So they shook the dust off
their feet[j] as a warning to them and went
to Iconium.[k] 52 And the disciples[l] were
filled with joy and with the Holy Spirit.[m]

In Iconium

14 At Iconium[n] Paul and Barnabas
went as usual into the Jewish synagogue.[o] There they spoke so effectively
that a great number[p] of Jews and Greeks
believed. 2 But the Jews who refused to believe stirred up the other Gentiles and poisoned their minds against the brothers.[q]

13:32 [m] Ac 26:6; Ro 1:2; 4:13; 9:4 **13:33** [n] S Ac 2:24 [o] Ps 2:7; S Mt 3:17 **13:34** [p] Isa 55:3 **13:35** [q] Ps 16:10; Ac 2:27 **13:36** [r] S Mt 9:24 [s] 2Sa 7:12; 1Ki 2:10; 2Ch 29:28; Ac 2:29 **13:37** [t] S Ac 2:24 **13:38** [u] S Lk 24:47; Ac 2:38 **13:39** [v] S Jn 3:15 [w] S Ro 3:28 **13:41** [x] Hab 1:5 **13:42** [y] ver 14 **13:43** [z] S Ac 11:23; 14:22; S Ro 3:24 **13:45** [a] S 1Th 2:16 [b] Ac 18:6; 1Pe 4:4; Jude 10 **13:46** [c] ver 26; Ac 3:26 [d] Mt 21:41; Ac 18:6; 22:21; 26:20; 28:28; Ro 11:11 **13:47** [e] S Lk 2:32 [f] Isa 49:6 **13:48** [g] ver 49; Ac 8:25; 15:35, 36; 19:10, 20 **13:49** [h] S ver 48 **13:50** [i] S 1Th 2:16 **13:51** [j] S Mt 10:14 [k] Ac 14:1, 19, 21; 16:2; 2Ti 3:11 **13:52** [l] S Ac 11:26 [m] S Lk 1:15 **14:1** [n] S Ac 13:51 [o] S Ac 9:20 [p] S Ac 2:41 **14:2** [q] S Ac 1:16

[a] 33 Psalm 2:7 [b] 34 Isaiah 55:3 [c] 35 Psalm 16:10 (see Septuagint) [d] 41 Hab. 1:5 [e] 47 The Greek is singular. [f] 47 Isaiah 49:6

13:33 *today I have become your father.* Here refers to the resurrection of Jesus (see NIV text note here and note on Ps 2:7–9; cf. Ro 1:4).
13:35 *not let your holy one see decay.* Quoted also in Peter's sermon at Pentecost (see notes on 2:27; Ps 16:10).
13:39 *justification.* Combines two aspects: (1) the forgiveness of sins (here); (2) the gift of righteousness (see Ro 3:21–22 and note on 3:24).
13:43 *continue in the grace of God.* See Titus 2:11–12 and note on 2:12.
13:46 *had to speak ... to you first.* Because the gospel came from and was directed to the Jews first, and because Paul was himself a Jew with great compassion for his people (Ro 1:16; 9:1–5; 10:1–3). See note on v. 14.
13:47 *you.* See NIV text note; see also 9:15–16; 22:14–15,21; 26:15–18. Paul extends the prophetic word concerning the Messianic "servant" (Isa 49:6) to those who continue that servant's mission (cf. Isa 54:17 and note).
13:48 *all who were appointed for eternal life believed.* Possession of eternal life involves both human faith and divine appointment.
13:51 *shook the dust.* To show the severance of responsibility and the repudiation of those who had rejected their message and had brought suffering to the servants of the Lord (see note on Lk 9:5). *Iconium.* Modern Konya; it was an important crossroads and agricultural center in the central plain of the province of Galatia.
13:52 *filled ... with the Holy Spirit.* See notes on 2:4; Eph 5:18.
14:1 *went as usual into the ... synagogue.* See note on 13:14. *great number.* At first there was good success, then bitter opposition from the Jews (v. 2). But these evidently failed in their initial attempt, for Paul and Barnabas remained there a considerable time (v. 3). A second wave of persecution was planned, involving violence (v. 5).

3 So Paul and Barnabas spent considerable
time there, speaking boldly[r] for the Lord,
who confirmed the message of his grace by
enabling them to perform signs and wonders.[s] 4 The people of the city were divided;
some sided with the Jews, others with the
apostles.[t] 5 There was a plot afoot among
both Gentiles and Jews,[u] together with their
leaders, to mistreat them and stone them.[v]
6 But they found out about it and fled[w] to
the Lycaonian cities of Lystra and Derbe
and to the surrounding country, 7 where
they continued to preach[x] the gospel.[y]

In Lystra and Derbe

8 In Lystra there sat a man who was
lame. He had been that way from birth[z]
and had never walked. 9 He listened to
Paul as he was speaking. Paul looked directly at him, saw that he had faith to be
healed[a] 10 and called out, "Stand up on
your feet!"[b] At that, the man jumped up
and began to walk.[c]
11 When the crowd saw what Paul had
done, they shouted in the Lycaonian language, "The gods have come down to us
in human form!"[d] 12 Barnabas they called
Zeus, and Paul they called Hermes because he was the chief speaker.[e] 13 The
priest of Zeus, whose temple was just outside the city, brought bulls and wreaths to
the city gates because he and the crowd
wanted to offer sacrifices to them.
14 But when the apostles Barnabas and
Paul heard of this, they tore their clothes[f]
and rushed out into the crowd, shouting:
15 "Friends, why are you doing this? We too
are only human,[g] like you. We are bringing
you good news,[h] telling you to turn from
these worthless things[i] to the living God,[j]
who made the heavens and the earth[k] and
the sea and everything in them.[l] 16 In the
past, he let[m] all nations go their own way.[n]
17 Yet he has not left himself without testimony:[o] He has shown kindness by giving
you rain from heaven and crops in their
seasons;[p] he provides you with plenty
of food and fills your hearts with joy."[q]
18 Even with these words, they had difficulty keeping the crowd from sacrificing
to them.
19 Then some Jews[r] came from Antioch
and Iconium[s] and won the crowd over.
They stoned Paul[t] and dragged him outside the city, thinking he was dead. 20 But
after the disciples[u] had gathered around
him, he got up and went back into the
city. The next day he and Barnabas left
for Derbe.

The Return to Antioch in Syria

21 They preached the gospel[v] in that city
and won a large number[w] of disciples.
Then they returned to Lystra, Iconium[x]
and Antioch, 22 strengthening the disciples and encouraging them to remain true
to the faith.[y] "We must go through many
hardships[z] to enter the kingdom of God,"
they said. 23 Paul and Barnabas appointed elders[aa] for them in each church and,

[a] 23 Or *Barnabas ordained elders*; or *Barnabas had elders elected*

14:3 [r] S Ac 4:29 [s] S Jn 4:48 **14:4** [t] Ac 17:4,5; 28:24 **14:5** [u] S Ac 20:3 [v] ver 19 **14:6** [w] Mt 10:23 **14:7** [x] Ac 16:10 [y] ver 15,21; S Ac 13:32 **14:8** [z] Ac 3:2 **14:9** [a] Mt 9:28, 29; 13:58 **14:10** [b] Eze 2:1 [c] Ac 3:8 **14:11** [d] Ac 8:10; 28:6 **14:12** [e] Ex 7:1 **14:14** [f] S Mk 14:63 **14:15** [g] S Ac 10:26 [h] ver 7,21; S Ac 13:32 [i] 1Sa 12:21; 1Th 1:9 [j] S Mt 16:16 [k] Ge 1:1 [l] Ps 146:6; Rev 14:7 **14:16** [m] Ac 17:30 [n] Ps 81:12; Mic 4:5 **14:17** [o] Ro 1:20 [p] Dt 11:14; Job 5:10; Ps 65:10 [q] Ps 4:7 **14:19** [r] Ac 13:45 [s] S Ac 13:51 [t] 2Co 11:25; 2Ti 3:11 **14:20** [u] ver 22, 28; S Ac 11:26 **14:21** [v] S Ac 13:32 [w] S Ac 2:41 [x] S Ac 13:51 **14:22** [y] Ac 11:23; 13:43 [z] Jn 16:33; 1Th 3:3; 2Ti 3:12 **14:23** [aa] S Ac 11:30

14:3 *confirmed ... by ... signs and wonders.* A major purpose of miracles was to confirm the truth of the words and the approval of God (cf. 2:22 and note).

14:4 *apostles.* Both Paul and Barnabas are called apostles (see v. 14; see also note on Mk 6:30). The term is used here not of the Twelve but in the broader sense to refer to persons sent on a mission, i.e., missionaries (see 13:2–3).

14:5 *stone them.* A Jewish mode of execution for blasphemy (see note on Jn 10:31). Probably mob action was planned here.

14:6 *Lycaonian cities.* Lycaonia was a district east of Pisidia, north of the Taurus Mountains. It was part of the Roman province of Galatia. *Lystra.* A Roman colony (see note on 13:14) and probable home of Timothy (see 16:1 and note—though he was known in Iconium as well [see 16:2]), it was about 20 miles from Iconium and 130 miles from Antioch. *Derbe.* About 60 miles from Lystra; home of Gaius (see 20:4 and note on 14:20).

14:12 *Zeus ... Hermes.* Zeus was the patron god of Lystra, and his temple was there. People who had come to bring sacrifices to Zeus apparently decided to make an offering to Paul and Barnabas instead. The identification of Zeus with Barnabas may indicate that his appearance was more imposing, and Paul was identified as the god Hermes (the Roman Mercury) because he was the spokesman (see 28:6). This incident may have been occasioned by an ancient legend that told of a supposed visit to the same general area by Zeus and Hermes. The two were, however, not recognized by anyone except an old couple. So the people of Lystra were determined not to allow such an oversight to happen again.

14:13 *city gates.* The Greek for this expression can refer to the temple gates, the city gates or house gates.

14:14 *tore their clothes.* A Jewish way of expressing great anguish (see Ge 37:29,34 and note on 37:34).

14:15 *worthless things.* Used in the OT to denote false gods (see 1Sa 12:21).

14:16 See 17:30 and note.

14:19 *They stoned Paul.* Inside the city rather than at the usual place of execution outside the walls (7:58; see Gal 6:17 and note).

14:20 *disciples had gathered around him.* Young Timothy may have been present (see 2Ti 3:10–11 and note on 3:11). *got up ... next day ... left.* Luke's description of Paul's quick recovery from stoning suggests a miracle (cf. 28:5–6). *Derbe.* A border town in the southeastern part of the Lycaonian region of Galatia (see note on v. 6). An inscription naming the city has been discovered about 30 miles east of what was previously thought to be the city site.

14:21 *they returned.* Not by the shorter route through the Taurus Mountains but to the cities where they had established churches (see v. 22).

14:22 *many hardships.* See Php 1:29 and note.

14:23 *appointed.* The Greek for this word (used also in 2Co 8:19) can mean (1) to stretch out the hand, (2) to appoint by

with prayer and fasting,[b] committed them to the Lord,[c] in whom they had put their trust. 24 After going through Pisidia, they came into Pamphylia,[d] 25 and when they had preached the word in Perga, they went down to Attalia.

26 From Attalia they sailed back to Antioch,[e] where they had been committed to the grace of God[f] for the work they had now completed.[g] 27 On arriving there, they gathered the church together and reported all that God had done through them[h] and how he had opened a door[i] of faith to the Gentiles. 28 And they stayed there a long time with the disciples.[j]

The Council at Jerusalem

15 Certain people[k] came down from Judea to Antioch and were teaching the believers:[l] "Unless you are circumcised,[m] according to the custom taught by Moses,[n] you cannot be saved." 2 This brought Paul and Barnabas into sharp dispute and debate with them. So Paul and Barnabas were appointed, along with some other believers, to go up to Jerusalem[o] to see the apostles and elders[p] about this question. 3 The church sent them on their way, and as they traveled through Phoenicia[q] and Samaria, they told how the Gentiles had been converted.[r] This news made all the believers very glad. 4 When they came to Jerusalem, they were welcomed by the church and the apostles and elders, to whom they reported everything God had done through them.[s]

5 Then some of the believers who belonged to the party[t] of the Pharisees[u] stood up and said, "The Gentiles must be circumcised and required to keep the law of Moses."[v]

6 The apostles and elders met to consider this question. 7 After much discussion, Peter got up and addressed them: "Brothers, you know that some time ago God made a choice among you that the Gentiles might hear from my lips the message of the gospel and believe.[w] 8 God, who knows the heart,[x] showed that he accepted them by giving the Holy Spirit to them,[y] just as he did to us. 9 He did not discriminate between us and them,[z] for he purified their hearts by faith.[a] 10 Now then, why do you try to test God[b] by putting on the necks of Gentiles a yoke[c] that neither we nor our ancestors have been able to bear? 11 No! We believe it is through the grace[d] of our Lord Jesus that we are saved, just as they are."

12 The whole assembly became silent as they listened to Barnabas and Paul telling about the signs and wonders[e] God had

14:23 [b] Ac 13:3 [c] Ac 20:32
14:24 [d] S Ac 2:10
14:26 [e] S Ac 11:19 [f] S Ac 11:23 [g] Ac 13:1,3
14:27 [h] Ac 15:4, 12; 21:19 [i] 1Co 16:9; 2Co 2:12; Col 4:3; Rev 3:8
14:28 [j] S Ac 11:26
15:1 [k] ver 24; Gal 2:12 [l] S Ac 1:16 [m] ver 5; Gal 5:2,3 [n] S Ac 6:14
15:2 [o] Gal 2:2 [p] S Ac 11:30
15:3 [q] Ac 11:19 [r] Ac 14:27
15:4 [s] ver 12; Ac 14:27; 21:19
15:5 [t] Ac 5:17 [u] Mt 3:7 [v] ver 1
15:7 [w] Ac 10:1-48
15:8 [x] S Rev 2:23 [y] S Ac 10:44,47
15:9 [z] Ac 10:28, 34; 11:12 [a] Ac 10:43
15:10 [b] Ac 5:9 [c] S Mt 23:4; Gal 5:1
15:11 [d] S Ro 3:24; Gal 2:16; Eph 2:5-8
15:12 [e] S Jn 4:48

---

show of hands or (3) to appoint or elect without regard to the method. In 6:6 the appointment of the Seven included selection by the church and presentation to the apostles, who prayed and laid their hands on them. Because these were new churches, at least partly pagan in background, Paul and Barnabas may have both selected and appointed the elders. See NIV text note.

14:24 *Pisidia.* A district about 120 miles long and 50 miles wide, north of Pamphylia (13:13–14). Bandits frequented the region (see perhaps 2Co 11:26). *Pamphylia.* A district 80 miles long and 20 miles at the widest part, on the southern coast of Asia Minor. After AD 74 Pisidia was included in the Roman province of Pamphylia (see 13:13).

14:25 *Perga.* See note on 13:13. *Attalia.* The best harbor on the coast of Pamphylia (see 13:13). See photo, p. 1822.

14:26 *Antioch.* See 11:20; see also note on 11:19.

14:27 *opened a door of faith.* God had brought Gentiles to faith—had, as it were, opened the door for them to believe (cf. 11:18).

14:28 *long time.* Probably more than a year.

15:1 *Certain people.* Probably from "the party of the Pharisees" (v. 5). These were believers who insisted that before anyone could become a true Christian they must keep the law of Moses, and the test of such compliance was circumcision. *from Judea.* Meant that these Judaizers (or legalists) were given a hearing, not that they correctly represented the apostles and elders of Jerusalem (cf. v. 24).

15:2 *go up to Jerusalem.* See notes on 12:1; Gal 2:1. Those who hold that Gal 2:1–10 refers to the famine visit of 11:27–30 and 12:25 argue that since Gal 2:2 says that the visit mentioned there was occasioned by a revelation, it must refer to Agabus's prediction of the coming famine (11:27–28). Those who believe that Gal 2:1–10 refers to the Jerusalem council visit of 15:1–22 assert that the famine visit occurred at the time of Herod Agrippa's death in AD 44 (11:27–30; 12:25). Thus Saul's conversion, which was 14 years earlier (Gal 2:1), would have occurred in 30, the probable year of Christ's crucifixion—which obviously seems too early.

15:4–22 The sequence of meetings described in vv. 4–22 is: (1) a general meeting of welcome and report (vv. 4–5); (2) a meeting of the leaders (perhaps to one side) while the church was still assembled (vv. 6–11); (3) a meeting of the apostles, the elders and the whole assembly (vv. 12–22).

15:4 The first meeting was a report, cordially received, about the work done among the Gentiles.

15:5 *believers who belonged to the party of the Pharisees.* Some Pharisees became Christians and brought their Judaic beliefs with them. They believed that Gentiles must first become converts to Judaism and be circumcised (see v. 1), and then they would be eligible to be saved by faith. Perhaps some of them had gone to Antioch and now returned to present their case.

15:7 *Peter got up.* After a period of considerable discussion by the apostles and elders, Peter addressed them. *Gentiles might hear.* Peter's argument was his own experience: God had sent him to preach to the Gentiles (see 10:28–29 and note on 10:28).

15:8 *giving the Holy Spirit to them.* The irrefutable proof of God's acceptance (see 8:15–17; 10:44,47 and notes; 11:17–18).

15:9 *purified their hearts by faith.* Peter's way of saying what Paul affirmed (Ro 5:1; cf. Gal 2:15–16).

15:10 *yoke.* The law (see Gal 5:1 and note; cf. Mt 11:28–29 and notes).

15:11 *through the grace of our Lord.* No circumcision was required. *we are saved, just as they are.* See Ro 3:9.

15:12 *assembly became silent.* See note on vv. 4–22. Apparently the people had remained in place while the apostles

done among the Gentiles through them.[f]
13 When they finished, James[g] spoke up.
"Brothers," he said, "listen to me. 14 Simon[a] has described to us how God first
intervened to choose a people for his
name from the Gentiles.[h] 15 The words of
the prophets are in agreement with this,
as it is written:

16 " 'After this I will return
and rebuild David's fallen tent.
Its ruins I will rebuild,
and I will restore it,
17 that the rest of mankind may seek the
Lord,
even all the Gentiles who bear my
name,
says the Lord, who does these things'[b][i]—
18 things known from long ago.[c][j]

19 "It is my judgment, therefore, that we
should not make it difficult for the Gentiles who are turning to God. 20 Instead
we should write to them, telling them to
abstain from food polluted by idols,[k] from
sexual immorality,[l] from the meat of strangled animals and from blood.[m] 21 For the
law of Moses has been preached in every
city from the earliest times and is read in
the synagogues on every Sabbath."[n]

The Council's Letter to Gentile Believers

22 Then the apostles and elders,[o] with
the whole church, decided to choose some
of their own men and send them to Antioch[p] with Paul and Barnabas. They chose
Judas (called Barsabbas) and Silas,[q] men
who were leaders among the believers.
23 With them they sent the following letter:

The apostles and elders, your brothers,

To the Gentile believers in Antioch,[r] Syria[s] and Cilicia:[t]

Greetings.[u]

24 We have heard that some went
out from us without our authorization
and disturbed you, troubling your
minds by what they said.[v] 25 So we all
agreed to choose some men and send
them to you with our dear friends
Barnabas and Paul— 26 men who
have risked their lives[w] for the name
of our Lord Jesus Christ. 27 Therefore
we are sending Judas and Silas[x] to
confirm by word of mouth what we
are writing. 28 It seemed good to the
Holy Spirit[y] and to us not to burden
you with anything beyond the following requirements: 29 You are to abstain
from food sacrificed to idols, from
blood, from the meat of strangled animals and from sexual immorality.[z]
You will do well to avoid these things.

Farewell.

15:12 [f] ver 4; Ac 14:27; 21:19 **15:13** [g] Ac 12:17; 21:18; 1Co 15:7; Gal 1:19; 2:9,12 **15:14** [h] 2Pe 1:1 **15:17** [i] Am 9:11,12 **15:18** [j] Isa 45:21 **15:20** [k] 1Co 8:7-13; 10:14-28; Rev 2:14,20 [l] 1Co 10:7,8; Rev 2:14,20 [m] ver 29; Ge 9:4; Lev 3:17; 7:26; 17:10-13; 19:26; Dt 12:16,23 **15:21** [n] Ac 13:15; 2Co 3:14,15 **15:22** [o] S Ac 11:30 [p] S Ac 11:19 [q] ver 27,32,40; Ac 16:19,25,29; 2Co 1:19; 1Th 1:1; 2Th 1:1; 1Pe 5:12 **15:23** [r] ver 1; S Ac 11:19 [s] S Lk 2:2 [t] ver 41; S Ac 6:9 [u] Ac 23:25,26; Jas 1:1 **15:24** [v] ver 1; Gal 1:7; 5:10 **15:26** [w] Ac 9:23-25; 14:19; 1Co 15:30 **15:27** [x] S ver 22 **15:28** [y] Ac 5:32 **15:29** [z] ver 20; Ac 21:25

[a] *14* Greek *Simeon,* a variant of *Simon;* that is, Peter
[b] *17* Amos 9:11,12 (see Septuagint)
[c] *17,18* Some manuscripts *things'— / 18the Lord's work is known to him from long ago*

---

and elders met. The assembly had not remained quiet during that time, but now it became silent to listen to the leaders. *Barnabas and Paul.* The order here (see also 13:7; 14:12,14) puts Barnabas first (perhaps reflecting his importance in Jerusalem), whereas in the account of the missionary journey the order was usually "Paul and Barnabas" after the events on the island of Cyprus (13:42–43,46,50; 14:1,3,20,23). *signs and wonders.* See 8:19–20; 14:3.

15:13 *James.* The Lord's brother (see note on 12:17; see also Introduction to James: Author). His argument added proof from Scripture.

15:14 *Simon.* Peter (see v. 7). James uses Peter's Hebrew name in its Hebrew form (Simeon; see NIV text note). *a people for his name.* A new community largely made up of Gentiles but including Jews as well (see Jn 10:16 and note; cf. 1Pe 2:9–10).

15:15 *prophets.* Specifically Am 9:11–12 (see NIV text note on Am 9:12).

15:16 *After this I will return.* Some have taken this quotation from Amos as setting forth a sequence of the end times, including (1) the church age (taking out "a people for his name," v. 14), (2) the restoration of Israel as a nation (v. 16) and (3) the final salvation of the Gentiles (vv. 17–18). Others declare that the quotation merely confirms God's intent to save Gentiles.

15:18 *from long ago.* Since OT times (see Ro 15:9 and note).

15:19 *not make it difficult.* Circumcision was not required, but four stipulations were laid down (see note on v. 20). These were in areas where the Gentiles had particular weaknesses and where the Jews were particularly repulsed by Gentile violations. It would help both the individual and the relationship between Gentile and Jew if these requirements were observed. They involved divine directives that the Jews believed were given before the Mosaic laws.

15:20 *food polluted by idols.* See v. 29; 1Co 8:7–13; Rev 2:14, 20. *sexual immorality.* A sin taken too lightly by the Greeks and also associated with certain pagan religious festivals. *meat of strangled animals.* Thus retaining the blood that was forbidden to be eaten (see Ge 9:4). *blood.* Expressly forbidden in Jewish law (see Lev 17:10–12). Reference here may be to consuming blood apart from meat.

15:22 *apostles and elders, with the whole church.* Apparently there was unanimous agreement with the choice of messengers and with the contents of the letter (vv. 23–29). *Judas (called Barsabbas).* The same surname as that of Joseph Barsabbas (see 1:23 and note). The two may have been brothers. *Silas.* A leader in the Jerusalem church, a prophet (v. 32), a Roman citizen (16:37–38) and Paul's companion on his second missionary journey (15:40).

15:23 *in Antioch, Syria and Cilicia.* Antioch was the leading city of the combined provinces of Syria and Cilicia.

15:26 *risked their lives.* See 13:15; 14:2,5,19.

15:28 *seemed good to the Holy Spirit and to us.* Prior authority is given to the Spirit (whose working in the assembly is thus claimed), but there was also agreement among the apostles, elders and brothers (vv. 22–23).

15:29 *abstain from food … sexual immorality.* See note on v. 20.

30 So the men were sent off and went
down to Antioch, where they gathered
the church together and delivered the letter. 31 The people read it and were glad for
its encouraging message. 32 Judas and Silas,[a] who themselves were prophets,[b] said
much to encourage and strengthen the believers. 33 After spending some time there,
they were sent off by the believers with
the blessing of peace[c] to return to those
who had sent them. [34][a] 35 But Paul and
Barnabas remained in Antioch, where they
and many others taught and preached[d] the
word of the Lord.[e]

Disagreement Between Paul and Barnabas

36 Some time later Paul said to Barnabas, "Let us go back and visit the believers
in all the towns[f] where we preached the
word of the Lord[g] and see how they are
doing." 37 Barnabas wanted to take John,
also called Mark,[h] with them, 38 but Paul
did not think it wise to take him, because
he had deserted them[i] in Pamphylia and
had not continued with them in the work.
39 They had such a sharp disagreement
that they parted company. Barnabas took
Mark and sailed for Cyprus, 40 but Paul
chose Silas[j] and left, commended by the
believers to the grace of the Lord.[k] 41 He
went through Syria[l] and Cilicia,[m] strengthening the churches.[n]

15:32 [a]S ver 22 [b]S Ac 11:27 **15:33** [c]1Sa 1:17; Mk 5:34; Lk 7:50; Ac 16:36; 1Co 16:11 **15:35** [d]Ac 8:4 [e]S Ac 13:48 **15:36** [f]Ac 13:4, 13,14,51; 14:1,6,24,25 [g]S Ac 13:48 **15:37** [h]S Ac 12:12 **15:38** [i]Ac 13:13 **15:40** [j]S ver 22 [k]S Ac 11:23 **15:41** [l]ver 23; S Lk 2:2 [m]S Ac 6:9 [n]Ac 16:5

16:1 [o]Ac 14:6 [p]Ac 17:14; 18:5; 19:22; 20:4; Ro 16:21; 1Co 4:17; 16:10; 2Co 1:1, 19; Php 1:1; 2:19; Col 1:1; 1Th 1:1; 3:2,6; 2Th 1:1; 1Ti 1:2, 18; 2Ti 1:2,5,6; Phm 1 [q]2Ti 1:5 **16:2** [r]ver 40; S Ac 1:16 [s]S Ac 13:51 **16:3** [t]Gal 2:3 **16:4** [u]S Ac 11:30 [v]Ac 15:2

Timothy Joins Paul and Silas

16 Paul came to Derbe and then to
Lystra,[o] where a disciple named
Timothy[p] lived, whose mother was Jewish and a believer[q] but whose father was
a Greek. 2 The believers[r] at Lystra and Iconium[s] spoke well of him. 3 Paul wanted to
take him along on the journey, so he circumcised him because of the Jews who
lived in that area, for they all knew that
his father was a Greek.[t] 4 As they traveled
from town to town, they delivered the decisions reached by the apostles and elders[u]
in Jerusalem[v] for the people to obey.[w] 5 So
the churches were strengthened[x] in the
faith and grew daily in numbers.[y]

Paul's Vision of the Man of Macedonia

6 Paul and his companions traveled
throughout the region of Phrygia[z] and Galatia,[a] having been kept by the Holy Spirit
from preaching the word in the province
of Asia.[b] 7 When they came to the border
of Mysia, they tried to enter Bithynia,
but the Spirit of Jesus[c] would not allow
them to. 8 So they passed by Mysia and

[a] 34 Some manuscripts include here *But Silas decided to remain there.*

[w]Ac 15:28,29 **16:5** [x]Ac 9:31; 15:41 [y]S Ac 2:41 **16:6** [z]Ac 2:10; 18:23 [a]Ac 18:23; Gal 1:2; 3:1 [b]S Ac 2:9 **16:7** [c]Ro 8:9; Gal 4:6; Php 1:19; 1Pe 1:11

15:32 *prophets.* One of the primary functions of prophets in the early church was, as here indicated, to encourage and strengthen believers (see notes on 11:27; 1Co 14:3).

15:33 *those who had sent them.* The Jerusalem church (see v. 22).

15:36 *towns where we preached the word.* Towns of the first missionary journey (see 13:4—14:26).

15:38 *he had deserted them.* Mark had turned back at Perga and did not go to Antioch, Iconium, Lystra and Derbe (see note on 13:13).

15:39—18:22 Paul's second missionary journey (see map, pp. 2528–2529, at the end of this study Bible; see also map, p. 1858).

15:39–40 *Barnabas took Mark … Paul chose Silas.* Thus the end result of the disagreement between Paul and Barnabas was four missionaries instead of two (cf. Ge 50:20 and note; Ro 8:28).

15:39 *they parted company.* Barnabas and Mark do not appear again in Acts. However, in 1Co 9:6 Paul names Barnabas as setting a noble example in working to support himself. Also in Gal 2:11–13 another scene is described in Antioch that includes Barnabas. Mark evidently returned from his work with Barnabas and became associated with Peter (see 1Pe 5:13 and note). During Paul's first imprisonment, Mark was included in Paul's group (see Col 4:10; Phm 24). By the end of Paul's life he came to admire Mark so much that he requested him to come to be with him during his final days (see 2Ti 4:11 and note; see also Introduction to Mark: John Mark in the NT). *Cyprus.* The island of Barnabas's birthplace (4:36).

15:40 *Silas.* Had returned to Jerusalem with Judas after delivering the Jerusalem letter (vv. 32–33). His presence in Antioch now indicates that, after reporting to those who had sent him, he came back to Antioch to participate in the church's work there.

16:1 *Derbe.* See notes on 14:6,20. Paul had approached Derbe on the first trip from the opposite direction, so the order of towns is reversed here. *Lystra.* See note on 14:6. *Timothy.* See Introduction to 1 Timothy: Recipient. Since Paul addressed him as a young man some 15 years later (see 1Ti 4:12), he must have been in his teens at this time. *father was a Greek.* Statements concerning his mother's faith (here and in 2Ti 1:5) and silence concerning any faith on his father's part suggest that the father was neither a convert to Judaism nor a believer in Christ.

16:3 *he circumcised him.* As a matter of expediency so that his work among the Jews might be more effective. This was different from Titus's case (see Gal 2:3), where circumcision was refused because some were demanding it as necessary for salvation.

16:6 *his companions.* Silas and Timothy. *Phrygia.* The district was formerly the Hellenistic territory of Phrygia, but it had more recently been divided between the Roman provinces of Asia and Galatia. Iconium and Antioch were in Galatian Phrygia. *Galatia.* The name had been used to denote the Hellenistic kingdom, but in 25 BC it had been expanded considerably to become the Roman province of that name. *Asia.* This, too, had been a smaller area formerly but now was a Roman province including the Hellenistic districts of Mysia, Lydia, Caria and parts of Phrygia.

16:7 *Mysia.* In the northwest part of the province of Asia. Luke uses these old Hellenistic names, but Paul preferred the provincial (Roman) names. *Bithynia.* A senatorial province formed after 74 BC, it was east of Mysia. *Spirit of Jesus.* The

PAUL'S SECOND MISSIONARY JOURNEY

c. AD 49–52 (Ac 15:39–18:22)

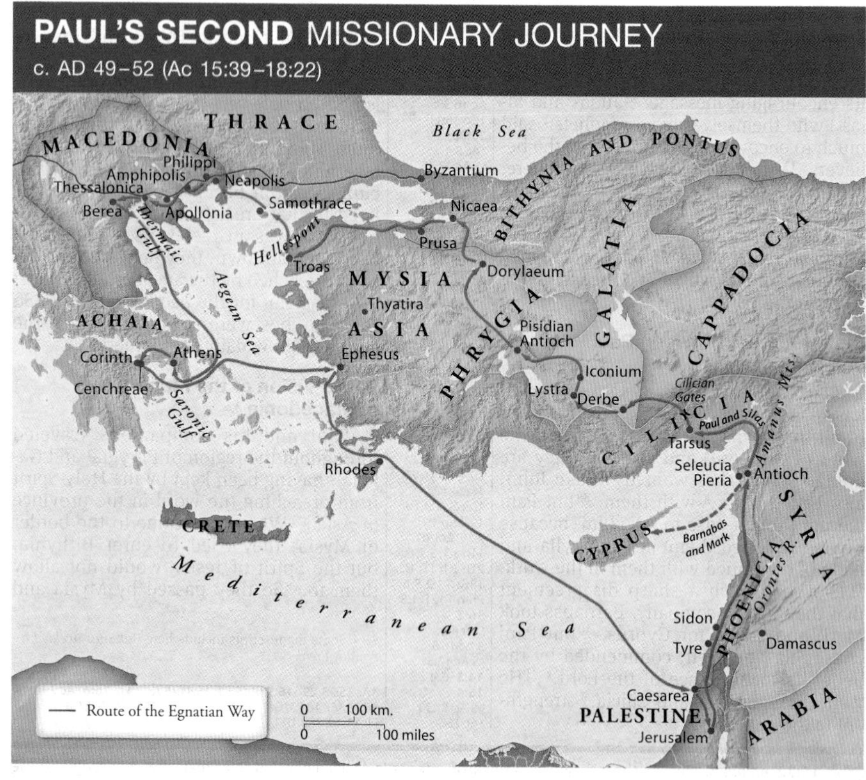

went down to Troas.[d] 9During the night
Paul had a vision[e] of a man of Macedonia[f]
standing and begging him, "Come over
to Macedonia and help us." 10After Paul
had seen the vision, we[g] got ready at once
to leave for Macedonia, concluding that
God had called us to preach the gospel[h]
to them.

16:8 [d] ver 11; Ac 20:5; 2Co 2:12; 2Ti 4:13 **16:9** [e] S Ac 9:10 [f] Ac 19:21, 29; 20:1, 3; Ro 15:26; 1Co 16:5; 1Th 1:7, 8 **16:10** [g] ver 10-17; Ac 20:5-15; 21:1-18; 27:1-28:16 [h] Ac 14:7 **16:11** [i] S ver 8 **16:12** [j] Ac 20:6; Php 1:1; 1Th 2:2

Lydia's Conversion in Philippi

11From Troas[i] we put out to sea and
sailed straight for Samothrace, and the next
day we went on to Neapolis. 12From there
we traveled to Philippi,[j] a Roman colony

identification of the "Spirit of Jesus" with the "Spirit of God" ("Holy Spirit," v. 6) is a clear indication that Jesus is truly God. Cf. Ro 8:9. *not allow.* The Spirit may have led in any of a number of ways: vision, circumstances, good sense or use of the prophetic gift.

16:8 *Troas.* Located ten miles from ancient Troy. Alexandria Troas (its full name) was a Roman colony and an important seaport for connections between Macedonia and Greece on the one hand and Asia Minor on the other. Paul returned to Troas following his work in Ephesus on his third journey (see 2Co 2:12). At some time—on Paul's second journey or on his third—a church was started there, for Paul ministered to believers in Troas when he returned from his third journey on his way to Jerusalem (20:5–12).

16:9 *vision.* One of the ways God gave direction (cf. 10:3). *man of Macedonia.* Macedonia had become a Roman province in 148 BC. There is no indication that the man of the vision is Luke, as some have suggested, but he does join the group at this point.

16:10 *we got ready.* This is where the "we" passages of Acts begin (see Introduction: Author). The conclusion is that Luke is informing the reader that he had joined the party at Troas.

16:11 *Samothrace.* An island in the northeastern Aegean Sea. It was a convenient place for boats to anchor rather than risk sailing at night. *Neapolis.* The seaport for Philippi, ten miles away; modern Kavalla.

16:12 *Philippi.* A city in eastern Macedonia named after Philip II, father of Alexander the Great (see map above). Since it was a Roman colony, it was independent of provincial administration and had a governmental organization modeled after that of Rome (see note on 13:14). Many retired legionnaires from the Roman army settled there, but few Jews. See Introduction to Philippians: Recipients. *leading city.* Thessalonica was the capital of Macedonia. But Macedonia had four districts, and Philippi was in the first of these. Amphipolis, however, was the first city of that district. Luke may have intended to say that Philippi was "a" leading city (there is no article in the Greek), or that it was the first city reached from the border, or that its fame and significance made it truly the leading city of the area.

and the leading city of that district[a] of Macedonia.[k] And we stayed there several days.
13 On the Sabbath[l] we went outside the
city gate to the river, where we expected
to find a place of prayer. We sat down and
began to speak to the women who had
gathered there. 14 One of those listening
was a woman from the city of Thyatira[m]
named Lydia, a dealer in purple cloth. She
was a worshiper of God. The Lord opened
her heart[n] to respond to Paul's message.
15 When she and the members of her
household[o] were baptized,[p] she invited us
to her home. "If you consider me a believer in the Lord," she said, "come and stay
at my house." And she persuaded us.

Paul and Silas in Prison

16 Once when we were going to the place
of prayer,[q] we were met by a female slave
who had a spirit[r] by which she predicted
the future. She earned a great deal of money for her owners by fortune-telling. 17 She
followed Paul and the rest of us, shouting,
"These men are servants of the Most High
God,[s] who are telling you the way to be
saved." 18 She kept this up for many days.
Finally Paul became so annoyed that he
turned around and said to the spirit, "In
the name of Jesus Christ I command you
to come out of her!" At that moment the
spirit left her.[t]
19 When her owners realized that their
hope of making money[u] was gone, they
seized Paul and Silas[v] and dragged[w] them
into the marketplace to face the authorities. 20 They brought them before the magistrates and said, "These men are Jews,
and are throwing our city into an uproar[x]
21 by advocating customs unlawful for us
Romans[y] to accept or practice."[z]
22 The crowd joined in the attack against
Paul and Silas, and the magistrates ordered them to be stripped and beaten
with rods.[a] 23 After they had been severely flogged, they were thrown into prison,
and the jailer[b] was commanded to guard
them carefully. 24 When he received these
orders, he put them in the inner cell and
fastened their feet in the stocks.[c]
25 About midnight[d] Paul and Silas[e] were
praying and singing hymns[f] to God, and
the other prisoners were listening to them.
26 Suddenly there was such a violent earthquake that the foundations of the prison
were shaken.[g] At once all the prison doors
flew open,[h] and everyone's chains came
loose.[i] 27 The jailer woke up, and when
he saw the prison doors open, he drew
his sword and was about to kill himself
because he thought the prisoners had escaped.[j] 28 But Paul shouted, "Don't harm
yourself! We are all here!"
29 The jailer called for lights, rushed in
and fell trembling before Paul and Silas.[k]
30 He then brought them out and asked,
"Sirs, what must I do to be saved?"[l]
31 They replied, "Believe[m] in the Lord
Jesus, and you will be saved[n]—you and
your household."[o] 32 Then they spoke the
word of the Lord to him and to all the
others in his house. 33 At that hour of the

16:12 [k] S ver 9 **16:13** [l] S Ac 13:14 **16:14** [m] Rev 1:11; 2:18, 24 [n] Lk 24:45 **16:15** [o] S Ac 11:14 [p] S Ac 2:38 **16:16** [q] ver 13 [r] Dt 18:11; 1Sa 28:3,7 **16:17** [s] S Mk 5:7 **16:18** [t] S Mk 16:17 **16:19** [u] ver 16; Ac 19:25,26 [v] S Ac 15:22 [w] Ac 8:3; 17:6; 21:30; Jas 2:6 **16:20** [x] Ac 17:6 **16:21** [y] ver 12 [z] Est 3:8 **16:22** [a] 2Co 11:25; 1Th 2:2 **16:23** [b] ver 27, 36 **16:24** [c] Job 13:27; 33:11; Jer 20:2, 3; 29:26 **16:25** [d] Ps 119:55,62 [e] S Ac 15:22 [f] S Eph 5:19 **16:26** [g] Ac 4:31 [h] Ac 5:19; 12:10 [i] Ac 12:7 **16:27** [j] Ac 12:19 **16:29** [k] S Ac 15:22 **16:30** [l] Ac 2:37 **16:31** [m] S Jn 3:15 [n] S Ro 11:14 [o] S Ac 11:14

[a] 12 The text and meaning of the Greek for *the leading city of that district* are uncertain.

16:13 *place of prayer.* There were so few Jews in Philippi that there was no synagogue (ten married men were required), so the Jews who were there met for prayer along the banks of the Gangites River (see map, p. 1998). It was customary for such places of prayer to be located outdoors near running water.

16:14 *Thyatira.* In the Roman province of Asia, 20 miles southeast of Pergamum (in the Hellenistic kingdom of Lydia; see map, p. 1858; see also map, pp. 2528–2529, at the end of this study Bible). It was famous for its dyeing works, and especially for its royal purple (crimson). See Rev 1:11 and note on Rev 2:18. *Lydia.* A businesswoman. Her name may be associated with her place of origin, the Hellenistic district of Lydia. *worshiper of God.* Lydia was a Gentile who, like Cornelius (see 10:2), believed in the true God and followed the moral teachings of Scripture. She had not, however, become a full convert to Judaism. *opened her heart.* After the resurrection the minds of the disciples were opened to understand the Scriptures (Lk 24:45); similarly, Lydia's heart was opened to respond to the gospel message of Paul.

16:15 *come and stay at my house.* Cf. Lk 19:5.

16:16 *spirit by which she predicted the future.* A demonic "python" spirit. The python was a mythical snake worshiped at Delphi and associated with the Delphic oracle. The term "python" came to be used of the persons through whom the python spirit supposedly spoke. Since such persons spoke involuntarily, the term "ventriloquist" was used to describe them. To what extent she actually predicted the future is not known.

16:17 *rest of us.* The "we" section (see note on v. 10) ends here and begins again in 20:5. *Most High God.* A title used by the man possessed by an impure spirit (Mk 5:7). It was a common title among both Jews (see Nu 24:16; Isa 14:14; Da 3:26) and Greeks (found in inscriptions). But the title is not used of God in the NT by Christians or Jews (though cf. Ac 7:48).

16:20 *magistrates.* The Greek term *strategos* (Latin *praetor*), not the usual word but a term of courtesy used in some Roman colonies, such as Philippi.

16:23 *flogged.* See note on Mk 15:15.

16:24 *inner cell … stocks.* Used not only for extra security but also for torture.

16:27 *about to kill himself.* If a prisoner escaped, the life of the guard was demanded in his place (see 12:19). To take his own life would shorten the shame and distress.

16:30 *what must I do to be saved?* The jailer had heard that these were preachers of a way of salvation (v. 17). Now with the earthquake and his own impending death, he wanted to know about the way.

16:31 *Believe in the Lord Jesus.* A concise statement of the way of salvation (see 10:43).

16:32 *word of the Lord.* See 10:36. Paul and Silas explained the gospel more thoroughly to the jailer and to all the other members of his household, and they all believed in Christ and were saved (v. 34).

night[p] the jailer took them and washed
their wounds; then immediately he and all
his household were baptized.[q] 34 The jailer brought them into his house and set a
meal before them; he[r] was filled with joy
because he had come to believe in God—
he and his whole household.
35 When it was daylight, the magistrates
sent their officers to the jailer with the order: "Release those men." 36 The jailer[s] told
Paul, "The magistrates have ordered that
you and Silas be released. Now you can
leave. Go in peace."[t]
37 But Paul said to the officers: "They
beat us publicly without a trial, even
though we are Roman citizens,[u] and threw
us into prison. And now do they want to
get rid of us quietly? No! Let them come
themselves and escort us out."
38 The officers reported this to the magistrates, and when they heard that Paul
and Silas were Roman citizens, they were
alarmed.[v] 39 They came to appease them
and escorted them from the prison, requesting them to leave the city.[w] 40 After
Paul and Silas came out of the prison, they
went to Lydia's house,[x] where they met
with the brothers and sisters[y] and encouraged them. Then they left.

In Thessalonica

17 When Paul and his companions
had passed through Amphipolis
and Apollonia, they came to Thessalonica,[z] where there was a Jewish synagogue.
2 As was his custom, Paul went into the
synagogue,[a] and on three Sabbath[b] days
he reasoned with them from the Scriptures,[c] 3 explaining and proving that the
Messiah had to suffer[d] and rise from the
dead.[e] "This Jesus I am proclaiming to
you is the Messiah,"[f] he said. 4 Some of
the Jews were persuaded and joined Paul
and Silas,[g] as did a large number of God-
fearing Greeks and quite a few prominent
women.
5 But other Jews were jealous; so they
rounded up some bad characters from
the marketplace, formed a mob and started a riot in the city.[h] They rushed to Jason's[i] house in search of Paul and Silas
in order to bring them out to the crowd.[a]
6 But when they did not find them, they
dragged[j] Jason and some other believers[k]
before the city officials, shouting: "These
men who have caused trouble all over the
world[l] have now come here,[m] 7 and Jason has welcomed them into his house.
They are all defying Caesar's decrees, saying that there is another king, one called
Jesus."[n] 8 When they heard this, the crowd
and the city officials were thrown into turmoil. 9 Then they made Jason[o] and the others post bond and let them go.

In Berea

10 As soon as it was night, the believers

16:33 [p] ver 25 [q] S Ac 2:38 **16:34** [r] S Ac 11:14 **16:36** [s] ver 23, 27 [t] S Ac 15:33 **16:37** [u] Ac 22:25-29 **16:38** [v] Ac 22:29 **16:39** [w] Mt 8:34; Lk 8:37 **16:40** [x] ver 14 [y] ver 2; S Ac 1:16 **17:1** [z] ver 11, 13; Php 4:16; 1Th 1:1; 2Th 1:1; 2Ti 4:10 **17:2** [a] S Ac 9:20 [b] S Ac 13:14 [c] Ac 8:35; 18:28 **17:3** [d] Lk 24:26; Ac 3:18 [e] Lk 24:46; S Ac 2:24 [f] S Ac 9:22 **17:4** [g] S Ac 15:22 **17:5** [h] ver 13; S 1Th 2:16 [i] Ro 16:21 **17:6** [j] S Ac 16:19 [k] S Ac 1:16 [l] S Mt 24:14 [m] Ac 16:20 **17:7** [n] Lk 23:2; Jn 19:12 **17:9** [o] ver 5

[a] 5 Or *the assembly of the people*

16:33 *that hour of the night.* "About midnight" (v. 25).

16:34 *brought them into his house.* Cf. v. 15. *filled with joy.* The consistent consequence of conversion, regardless of circumstances (see note on 8:39).

16:35 *magistrates.* See note on v. 20.

16:37 *without a trial.* Public beating for a Roman citizen (see v. 38) would have been illegal, let alone beating without a trial (see 22:25 and note). *Let them come themselves.* Paul and Silas were not asking for an escort to salve their injured pride as much as they were establishing their innocence for the sake of the church in Philippi and its future.

17:1 *Amphipolis ... Thessalonica.* The Egnatian Way crossed the whole of present-day northern Greece east-west and included Philippi, Amphipolis, Apollonia and Thessalonica on its route. At several locations, such as Neapolis (modern Kavalla), Philippi and Apollonia, the road is still visible today. If a person traveled about 30 miles a day, each city could be reached after one day's journey. *Thessalonica.* About 100 miles from Philippi. It was the capital of the province of Macedonia and had a population of more than 200,000, including a colony of Jews (and a synagogue). All these contributed to Paul's decision to preach there. See Introduction to 1 Thessalonians: Thessalonica: The City and the Church.

17:2 *synagogue.* See note on 13:14. *three Sabbath days.* These two weeks represent the time spent in the synagogue reasoning with the Jews, not Paul's total time in Thessalonica. An analysis of the Thessalonian letters reveals that Paul had taught them much more doctrine than would have been possible in two or three weeks.

17:3 *explaining.* Lk 24:45 uses the same Greek verb (there translated "opened") in describing Jesus' making clear to two of his disciples the teaching of Scripture concerning his death and resurrection (see Lk 24:27,44 and note on 24:44).

17:4 *God-fearing Greeks.* See notes on 10:2; 16:14. *prominent women.* Perhaps the wives of the leading men of the city, but women who deserve notice and position in their own right (see also v. 12).

17:5 *were jealous.* Because of the large number of people (including some Jews, many God-fearing Gentiles and many prominent women) who responded to Paul's ministry (cf. 13:45). *Jason's house.* Paul had probably been staying there.

17:6 *city officials.* The Greek term *politarch* (lit. "city ruler"), used here and in v. 8, is found nowhere else in Greek literature, but it was discovered in 1835 in a Greek inscription on an arch that had spanned the Egnatian Way on the west side of Thessalonica. (The arch was destroyed in 1867, but the block with the inscription was rescued and is now in the British Museum in London.) The term has since been found in many other inscriptions in surrounding towns of Macedonia, as well as elsewhere.

17:7 *defying Caesar's decrees.* Blasphemy was the gravest accusation for a Jew, but treason—to support a rival king above Caesar—was the worst accusation for a Roman. Cf. the charge against Jesus that he claimed to be king (see Jn 18:12).

17:9 *post bond.* Jason was forced to guarantee a peaceful, quiet community, or he would face the confiscation of his properties and perhaps even death.

sent Paul and Silas[p] away to Berea.[q] On
arriving there, they went to the Jewish
synagogue.[r] 11 Now the Berean Jews were
of more noble character than those in
Thessalonica,[s] for they received the message with great eagerness and examined
the Scriptures[t] every day to see if what
Paul said was true.[u] 12 As a result, many
of them believed, as did also a number of
prominent Greek women and many Greek
men.[v]
13 But when the Jews in Thessalonica
learned that Paul was preaching the word
of God at Berea,[w] some of them went there
too, agitating the crowds and stirring them
up. 14 The believers[x] immediately sent
Paul to the coast, but Silas[y] and Timothy[z]
stayed at Berea. 15 Those who escorted
Paul brought him to Athens[a] and then left
with instructions for Silas and Timothy to
join him as soon as possible.[b]

In Athens

16 While Paul was waiting for them in
Athens, he was greatly distressed to see
that the city was full of idols. 17 So he
reasoned in the synagogue[c] with both
Jews and God-fearing Greeks, as well
as in the marketplace day by day with
those who happened to be there. 18 A
group of Epicurean and Stoic philosophers began to debate with him. Some
of them asked, "What is this babbler
trying to say?" Others remarked, "He
seems to be advocating foreign gods."
They said this because Paul was preaching the good news[d] about Jesus and the
resurrection.[e] 19 Then they took him and
brought him to a meeting of the Areopagus,[f] where they said to him, "May we
know what this new teaching[g] is that you
are presenting? 20 You are bringing some
strange ideas to our ears, and we would
like to know what they mean." 21 (All the
Athenians[h] and the foreigners who lived
there spent their time doing nothing but
talking about and listening to the latest
ideas.)
22 Paul then stood up in the meeting of
the Areopagus[i] and said: "People of Athens! I see that in every way you are very
religious.[j] 23 For as I walked around and
looked carefully at your objects of worship, I even found an altar with this inscription: TO AN UNKNOWN GOD. So you are
ignorant of the very thing you worship[k]—
and this is what I am going to proclaim
to you.
24 "The God who made the world and
everything in it[l] is the Lord of heaven
and earth[m] and does not live in temples
built by human hands.[n] 25 And he is not
served by human hands, as if he needed
anything. Rather, he himself gives everyone life and breath and everything else.[o]
26 From one man he made all the nations,

17:10 [p]S Ac 15:22 [q]ver 13; Ac 20:4 [r]S Ac 9:20
17:11 [s]S ver 1 [t]Lk 16:29; Jn 5:39 [u]Dt 29:29
17:12 [v]S Ac 2:41
17:13 [w]S Heb 4:12
17:14 [x]S Ac 9:30 [y]S Ac 15:22 [z]S Ac 16:1
17:15 [a]ver 16, 21,22; Ac 18:1; 1Th 3:1 [b]Ac 18:5
17:17 [c]S Ac 9:20
17:18 [d]S Ac 13:32 [e]ver 31,32; Ac 4:2
17:19 [f]ver 22 [g]Mk 1:27
17:21 [h]S ver 15
17:22 [i]ver 19 [j]ver 16
17:23 [k]Jn 4:22
17:24 [l]Isa 42:5; Ac 14:15 [m]Dt 10:14; Isa 66:1,2; Mt 11:25 [n]1Ki 8:27; Ac 7:48
17:25 [o]Ps 50:10-12; Isa 42:5

17:10 *Paul and Silas.* Timothy was probably left at Philippi, later rejoining Paul and Silas at Berea (compare v. 10 with v. 14). *Berea.* Modern Verria, located 50 miles from Thessalonica in another district of Macedonia. *synagogue.* See note on 13:14.

17:11 *Berean Jews.* Luke includes a Berean, Sopater, son of Pyrrhus, in the list of delegates who accompanied Paul to Jerusalem to deliver the contributions for the poor (see 20:4 and note).

17:14 *coast.* One might conclude that Paul went by boat to Athens. But the road to Athens is also a coastal road, and Paul may have walked the distance after having been escorted to the coast (some 20 miles). In any event, Christian companions stayed with him until reaching Athens.

17:15 *Athens.* Five centuries before Paul, Athens had been at the height of its glory in art, philosophy and literature. She had retained her reputation in philosophy through the years and still maintained a leading university in Paul's day. See map, p. 1858.

17:17 *synagogue.* See note on 13:14. *God-fearing Greeks.* See note on 10:2.

17:18 *Epicurean ... philosophers.* Originally they taught that the supreme good is happiness—but not mere momentary pleasure or temporary gratification. By Paul's time, however, this philosophy had degenerated into a more sensual system of thought. *Stoic philosophers.* They taught that people should live in accord with nature, recognize their own self-sufficiency and independence and suppress their desires. At its best, Stoicism had some admirable qualities, but, like Epicureanism, by Paul's time it had degenerated into a system of pride. *babbler.* The Greek word meant "seed picker," a bird picking up seeds here and there. Then it came to refer to the loafer in the marketplace who picked up whatever scraps of learning he could find and paraded them without digesting them himself.

17:19 *Areopagus.* Means "hill of Ares." Ares was the Greek god of thunder and war (the Roman equivalent was Mars). The Areopagus was located just west of the acropolis and south of the Agora and had once been the site of the meeting of the Court or Council of the Areopagus. Earlier the Council governed a Greek city-state, but by NT times the Areopagus retained authority only in the areas of religion and morals and met in the Royal Portico at the northwest corner of the Agora. The Council members considered themselves the custodians of teachings that introduced new religions and foreign gods.

17:22 *religious.* Or "superstitious." The Greek for this word could be used either to congratulate people or to criticize them, depending on whether those using it included themselves in the circle of individuals they were describing. The Athenians would not know which meaning to take until Paul continued. In this context it is clear that Paul wanted to be complimentary in order to gain a hearing.

17:23 *TO AN UNKNOWN GOD.* The Greeks were fearful of offending any god by failing to give him or her attention; so they felt they could cover any omissions by the label "unknown god." Other Greek writers confirm that such altars could be seen in Athens—a striking point of contact for Paul.

17:24 *The God who made the world.* Thus a personal Creator, in contrast with the views of pantheistic Stoicism. *does not live in temples built by human hands.* Cf. Stephen's similar declaration in his famous speech (7:28); cf. also 1Ki 8:27.

17:26 *From one man he made all the nations.* All people are of

that they should inhabit the whole earth;
and he marked out their appointed times
in history and the boundaries of their
lands.[p] 27 God did this so that they would
seek him and perhaps reach out for him
and find him, though he is not far from
any one of us.[q] 28 'For in him we live and
move and have our being.'[a][r] As some of
your own poets have said, 'We are his offspring.'[b]
29 "Therefore since we are God's offspring, we should not think that the divine
being is like gold or silver or stone—an
image made by human design and skill.[s]
30 In the past God overlooked[t] such ignorance,[u] but now he commands all people
everywhere to repent.[v] 31 For he has set a
day when he will judge[w] the world with
justice[x] by the man he has appointed.[y] He
has given proof of this to everyone by raising him from the dead."[z]
32 When they heard about the resurrection of the dead,[a] some of them sneered,
but others said, "We want to hear you
again on this subject." 33 At that, Paul left
the Council. 34 Some of the people became
followers of Paul and believed. Among
them was Dionysius, a member of the Areopagus,[b] also a woman named Damaris,
and a number of others.

17:26 [p] Dt 32:8; Job 12:23 **17:27** [q] Dt 4:7; Isa 55:6; Jer 23:23, 24 **17:28** [r] Dt 30:20; Job 12:10; Da 5:23 **17:29** [s] Isa 40:18-20; Ro 1:23 **17:30** [t] Ac 14:16; Ro 3:25 [u] ver 23; 1Pe 1:14 [v] Lk 24:47; Titus 2:11, 12 **17:31** [w] S Mt 10:15 [x] Ps 9:8; 96:13; 98:9 [y] S Ac 10:42 [z] S Ac 2:24 **17:32** [a] ver 18, 31 **17:34** [b] ver 19, 22

18:1 [c] S Ac 17:15 [d] Ac 19:1; 1Co 1:2; 2Co 1:1, 23; 2Ti 4:20 **18:2** [e] ver 19, 26; Ro 16:3; 1Co 16:19; 2Ti 4:19 [f] Ac 11:28 **18:3** [g] Ac 20:34; 1Co 4:12; 1Th 2:9; 2Th 3:8

In Corinth

18 After this, Paul left Athens[c] and
went to Corinth.[d] 2 There he met
a Jew named Aquila, a native of Pontus,
who had recently come from Italy with his
wife Priscilla,[e] because Claudius[f] had ordered all Jews to leave Rome. Paul went
to see them, 3 and because he was a tentmaker as they were, he stayed and worked
with them.[g] 4 Every Sabbath[h] he reasoned
in the synagogue,[i] trying to persuade Jews
and Greeks.
5 When Silas[j] and Timothy[k] came from
Macedonia,[l] Paul devoted himself exclusively to preaching, testifying to the Jews
that Jesus was the Messiah.[m] 6 But when
they opposed Paul and became abusive,[n]
he shook out his clothes in protest[o] and
said to them, "Your blood be on your own
heads![p] I am innocent of it.[q] From now on
I will go to the Gentiles."[r]
7 Then Paul left the synagogue and went
next door to the house of Titius Justus, a
worshiper of God.[s] 8 Crispus,[t] the synagogue

[a] *28* From the Cretan philosopher Epimenides
[b] *28* From the Cilician Stoic philosopher Aratus

18:4 [h] S Ac 13:14 [i] S Ac 9:20 **18:5** [j] S Ac 15:22 [k] S Ac 16:1 [l] S Ac 16:9; 17:14, 15 [m] S Ac 9:22 **18:6** [n] S Ac 13:45 [o] S Mt 10:14 [p] 2Sa 1:16; Eze 33:4 [q] Eze 3:17-19; Ac 20:26 [r] S Ac 13:46 **18:7** [s] Ac 16:14 **18:8** [t] 1Co 1:14

---

one family (whether Athenians or Romans, Greeks or barbarians, Jews or Gentiles). *marked out their appointed times.* He planned the exact times when nations should emerge and decline. *boundaries of their lands.* He also planned the specific area to be occupied by each nation. He is God, the Designer (things were not left to Chance, as the Epicureans [see note on v. 18] thought).

17:28 *some of your own poets.* There are two quotations here: (1) "In him we live and move and have our being," from the Cretan poet Epimenides (c. 600 BC) in his *Cretica,* and (2) "We are his offspring," from the Cilician Stoic (see note on v. 18) poet Aratus (c. 315–240) in his *Phaenomena,* as well as from Cleanthes (331–233) in his *Hymn to Zeus.* Paul quotes Greek poets elsewhere as well (see 1Co 15:33; Titus 1:12 and notes).

17:30 *overlooked such ignorance.* God had not judged them for worshiping false gods in their ignorance, but now the situation has changed (see v. 31).

17:31 *the man he has appointed.* Jesus, the Son of Man (see Da 7:13; cf. Mt 25:31–46; Jn 5:22–23; Ac 10:42).

17:32–34 Three responses to Paul's sermon: (1) Some rejected ("sneered"), (2) some procrastinated ("We want to hear you again"), (3) some accepted ("became followers of Paul and believed").

17:32 *resurrection of the dead.* Immortality of the soul was accepted by the Greeks, but not resurrection of a dead body.

17:33 *the Council.* The meeting of the Areopagites.

17:34 *Dionysius.* Later tradition states, though it cannot be proved, that he became bishop of Athens. *Damaris.* Some have suggested that she must have been a foreign, educated woman to have been present at a public meeting such as the Areopagus. It is also possible that she was a God-fearing Gentile who had heard Paul at the synagogue (v. 17).

18:1 *went to Corinth.* Either by land along the isthmus (a distance of about 50 miles) or by sea from Piraeus, the port of Athens, to Cenchreae, on the eastern shore of the isthmus of Corinth. See Introduction to 1 Corinthians: The City of Corinth; see also map, p. 1920.

18:2 *Aquila ... Priscilla.* Since no mention is made of a conversion and since a partnership is established in work (see v. 3), it is likely that they were already Christians. They may have been converted in Rome by those returning from Pentecost or by others at a later time (see vv. 18–19; 1Co 16:9; Ro 16:3–4). *Pontus.* In the northeastern region of Asia Minor, a province lying along the Black Sea between Bithynia and Armenia (see 2:9). *Claudius.* Emperor of Rome (AD 41–54). *ordered all Jews to leave Rome.* Recorded in Suetonius (*Claudius,* 25). The expulsion order was given, Suetonius writes, because of "their [the Jews'] continual tumults instigated by Chrestus" (a common misspelling of "Christ"). If "Chrestus" refers to Christ, the riots obviously were "about" him rather than led "by" him.

18:3 *tentmaker.* Paul would have been taught this trade as a youth. It was the Jewish custom to provide manual training for sons, whether rich or poor.

18:4 *synagogue.* See note on 13:14.

18:5 *Silas and Timothy came from Macedonia.* Paul instructed these two to come to him at Athens (17:15). Evidently they did (see 1Th 3:1–2), but they may have been sent back to Macedonia almost immediately to check on the churches—perhaps Silas to Philippi and Timothy to Thessalonica.

18:7 *Titius Justus.* Titius was a common Roman name. Justus is used to distinguish him from the Titus of 2Co 2:13; 7:13–14; 8:16,23. *worshiper of God.* Like Titus (see Gal 2:3), an uncircumcised Gentile, but attending the synagogue.

18:8 *Crispus.* Paul baptized him (1Co 1:14). *synagogue leader.* See note on 13:15.

leader,[u] and his entire household[v] believed
in the Lord; and many of the Corinthians
who heard Paul believed and were baptized.
9 One night the Lord spoke to Paul in a
vision:[w] "Do not be afraid;[x] keep on speaking, do not be silent. 10 For I am with you,[y]
and no one is going to attack and harm
you, because I have many people in this
city." 11 So Paul stayed in Corinth for a
year and a half, teaching them the word
of God.[z]
12 While Gallio was proconsul[a] of Achaia,[b] the Jews of Corinth made a united attack on Paul and brought him to the place
of judgment. 13 "This man," they charged,
"is persuading the people to worship God
in ways contrary to the law."
14 Just as Paul was about to speak, Gallio said to them, "If you Jews were making a complaint about some misdemeanor
or serious crime, it would be reasonable
for me to listen to you. 15 But since it involves questions about words and names
and your own law[c]—settle the matter
yourselves. I will not be a judge of such
things." 16 So he drove them off. 17 Then
the crowd there turned on Sosthenes[d] the
synagogue leader[e] and beat him in front
of the proconsul; and Gallio showed no
concern whatever.

Priscilla, Aquila and Apollos

18 Paul stayed on in Corinth for some
time. Then he left the brothers and sisters[f] and sailed for Syria,[g] accompanied by
Priscilla and Aquila.[h] Before he sailed, he
had his hair cut off at Cenchreae[i] because
of a vow he had taken.[j] 19 They arrived at
Ephesus,[k] where Paul left Priscilla and Aquila. He himself went into the synagogue
and reasoned with the Jews. 20 When they
asked him to spend more time with them,
he declined. 21 But as he left, he promised,
"I will come back if it is God's will."[l] Then
he set sail from Ephesus. 22 When he landed at Caesarea,[m] he went up to Jerusalem
and greeted the church and then went
down to Antioch.[n]
23 After spending some time in Antioch,
Paul set out from there and traveled from
place to place throughout the region of Galatia[o] and Phrygia,[p] strengthening all the
disciples.[q]
24 Meanwhile a Jew named Apollos,[r] a
native of Alexandria, came to Ephesus.[s]
He was a learned man, with a thorough
knowledge of the Scriptures. 25 He had
been instructed in the way of the Lord, and
he spoke with great fervor[a][t] and taught
about Jesus accurately, though he knew
only the baptism of John.[u] 26 He began to
speak boldly in the synagogue. When Priscilla and Aquila[v] heard him, they invited

[a] 25 Or *with fervor in the Spirit*

18:8 [u] S Mk 5:22 [v] S Ac 11:14 **18:9** [w] S Ac 9:10 [x] S Mt 14:27 **18:10** [y] S Mt 28:20 **18:11** [z] S Heb 4:12 **18:12** [a] Ac 13:7, 8,12; 19:38 [b] ver 27; Ro 15:26; 1Co 16:15; 2Co 9:2; 1Th 1:7,8 **18:15** [c] Ac 23:29; 25:11,19 **18:17** [d] 1Co 1:1 [e] ver 8 **18:18** [f] ver 27; S Ac 1:16 [g] S Lk 2:2 [h] S ver 2 [i] Ro 16:1 [j] Nu 6:2,5,18; Ac 21:24 **18:19** [k] ver 21, 24; Ac 19:1,17, 26; 1Co 15:32; 16:8; Eph 1:1; 1Ti 1:3; Rev 1:11; 2:1 **18:21** [l] Ro 1:10; 15:32; 1Co 4:19; Jas 4:15 **18:22** [m] S Ac 8:40 [n] S Ac 11:19 **18:23** [o] S Ac 16:6 [p] Ac 2:10; 16:6 [q] Ac 14:22; 15:32,41 **18:24** [r] Ac 19:1; 1Co 1:12; 3:5,6, 22; 4:6; 16:12; Titus 3:13 [s] S ver 19 **18:25** [t] Ro 12:11 [u] S Mk 1:4 **18:26** [v] S ver 2

18:9 *in a vision.* Paul had seen the Lord in a resurrection body at his conversion (9:4–6; 1Co 15:8) and in the temple at Jerusalem in a trance (22:17–18). Now he sees him in a vision (see 23:11).

18:10 *I have many people.* Corinth was a large, strategic, political, commercial and religious center. It was important that a strong church be established there (see note on v. 1).

18:11 *a year and a half.* During this time he may also have taken the gospel to the neighboring districts of Achaia (see 2Co 1:1 and note).

18:12 *Gallio.* The brother of Seneca, the philosopher, who was the tutor of Nero. Gallio was admired as a man of exceptional fairness and calmness. From an inscription found at Delphi (see map, pp. 2528–2529, at the end of this study Bible), it is known that Gallio was proconsul of Achaia in AD 51–52. This information enables us to date Paul's visit to Corinth on his second journey as well as his writing of the Thessalonian letters (see Introduction to 1 Thessalonians: Author, Date and Place of Writing; see also chart, p. 1812).

18:13 *contrary to the law.* The Jews were claiming that Paul was advocating a religion not recognized by Roman law as Judaism was. If he had been given the opportunity to speak, he could have argued that the gospel he was preaching was the faith of his fathers (see 24:14–15; 26:6–7) and thus authorized by Roman law.

18:17 *the crowd there turned on Sosthenes.* It is not clear whether the Greeks beat Sosthenes, seeing the occasion as an opportunity to vent their feelings against the Jews, or the Jews beat their own synagogue ruler because he was unsuccessful in presenting their case—probably the former. A Sosthenes is included with Paul in the writing of 1 Corinthians (1:1). Perhaps he was the second ruler of the synagogue at Corinth to become a Christian in response to Paul's preaching (see v. 8).

18:18 *Priscilla and Aquila.* The order of the names used here (but cf. v. 2) may indicate the prominent role of Priscilla or her higher social position (see Ro 16:3; 2Ti 4:19). *vow he had taken.* Grammatically this could refer to Aquila, but the emphasis on Paul and his activity makes Paul more probable. It was probably a temporary Nazirite vow (see Nu 6:1–21). Different vows were frequently taken to express thanks for deliverance from grave dangers. Shaving the head marked the end of a vow.

18:19 *Ephesus.* Leading commercial city of Asia Minor, the capital of provincial Asia and the warden of the temple of Artemis (Diana). See Introduction to Ephesians: The City of Ephesus; see also map, p. 1982. *synagogue.* See note on 13:14.

18:23—21:17 Paul's third missionary journey (see map, pp. 2528–2529, at the end of this study Bible; see also map, p. 1864; cf. maps, pp. 1851, 1858).

18:23 *region of Galatia and Phrygia.* The use of the phrase may indicate the southern part of Galatia in the Phrygian area (see note on 16:6).

18:24 *Alexandria.* In Egypt—where the OT had been translated into Greek (the Septuagint; see essay, p. 1574). The second most important city in the Roman Empire, it had a large Jewish population. *the Scriptures.* The pre-Christian Greek translation of the OT.

18:25 *baptism of John.* It was not in the name of Jesus (see also 19:2–4). Apollos had an incomplete knowledge of Jesus. Perhaps he knew that Jesus was the Messiah, but not about Christian baptism and the coming of the Spirit at Pentecost.

him to their home and explained to him
the way of God more adequately.
27 When Apollos wanted to go to Achaia,[w] the brothers and sisters[x] encouraged
him and wrote to the disciples there to
welcome him. When he arrived, he was
a great help to those who by grace had
believed. 28 For he vigorously refuted his
Jewish opponents in public debate, proving from the Scriptures[y] that Jesus was the
Messiah.[z]

18:27 [w]S ver 12 [x]ver 18; S Ac 1:16 **18:28** [y]Ac 8:35; 17:2 [z]ver 5; S Ac 9:22

19:1 [a]S Ac 18:24 [b]S Ac 18:1 [c]S Ac 18:19 **19:2** [d]S Jn 20:22

Paul in Ephesus

19 While Apollos[a] was at Corinth,[b]
Paul took the road through the interior and arrived at Ephesus.[c] There he
found some disciples 2 and asked them,
"Did you receive the Holy Spirit[d] when[a]
you believed?"
They answered, "No, we have not even
heard that there is a Holy Spirit."

[a] 2 Or *after*

18:27 *Achaia.* The Roman province with Corinth as its capital. **18:28** *the Scriptures.* See Lk 24:44 and note. The Greek OT was read and known in Corinth (see note on v. 24). Apollos's Christian exposition of the Greek Scriptures put him above both Paul and Peter in the eyes of some in the Corinthian church (see 1Co 1:12 and note).

19:1 *Apollos was at Corinth.* Apollos was introduced at Ephesus (18:24) in the absence of Paul; he moved to Corinth before Paul returned to Ephesus. But later Apollos came back to Ephesus during Paul's ministry there (see 1Co 16:12). *through the interior.* Not the lower direct route down the Lycus and Meander Valleys but the upper Phrygian route, approaching Ephesus from a more northerly direction. If Paul got to northern Galatia, which is unlikely, it must have been on one of these trips through the interior (see 16:6; 18:23 and notes). *Ephesus.* See note on 18:19. *some disciples.* These 12 (v. 7) seem to have been followers of Jesus, but indirectly through John the Baptist or some of his followers. Or perhaps they had received their teaching from Apollos himself in his earlier state of partial understanding (see 18:26 and note on 18:25). Like Apollos, they had a limited understanding of the gospel.

19:2 *receive the Holy Spirit.* Paul finds that they were not informed about the Holy Spirit at all (vv. 3–6).

PAUL'S THIRD MISSIONARY JOURNEY
c. AD 53–57 (Ac 18:23–21:17)

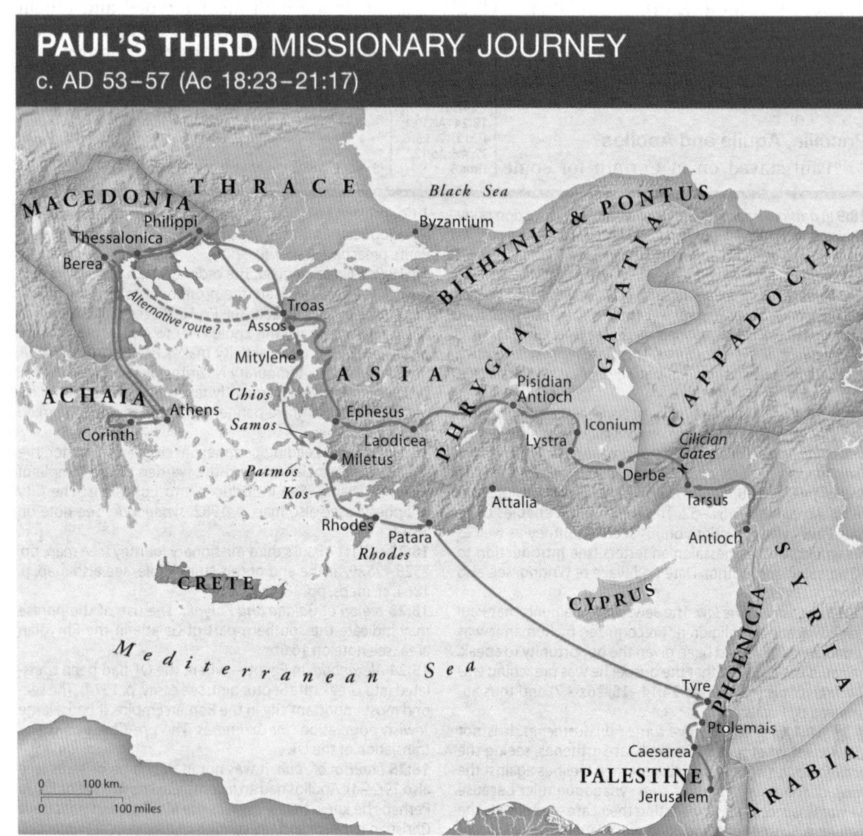

3 So Paul asked, "Then what baptism did
you receive?"
"John's baptism," they replied.
4 Paul said, "John's baptism[e] was a baptism of repentance. He told the people to
believe in the one coming after him, that
is, in Jesus."[f] 5 On hearing this, they were
baptized in the name of the Lord Jesus.[g]
6 When Paul placed his hands on them,[h]
the Holy Spirit came on them,[i] and they
spoke in tongues[a][j] and prophesied. 7 There
were about twelve men in all.
8 Paul entered the synagogue[k] and spoke
boldly there for three months, arguing persuasively about the kingdom of God.[l] 9 But
some of them[m] became obstinate; they refused to believe and publicly maligned the
Way.[n] So Paul left them. He took the disciples[o] with him and had discussions daily
in the lecture hall of Tyrannus. 10 This went
on for two years,[p] so that all the Jews and
Greeks who lived in the province of Asia[q]
heard the word of the Lord.[r]
11 God did extraordinary miracles[s]
through Paul, 12 so that even handkerchiefs and aprons that had touched him
were taken to the sick, and their illnesses
were cured[t] and the evil spirits left them.
13 Some Jews who went around driving
out evil spirits[u] tried to invoke the name
of the Lord Jesus over those who were demon-possessed. They would say, "In the
name of the Jesus[v] whom Paul preaches, I
command you to come out." 14 Seven sons
of Sceva, a Jewish chief priest, were doing this. 15 One day the evil spirit answered
them, "Jesus I know, and Paul I know
about, but who are you?" 16 Then the man
who had the evil spirit jumped on them
and overpowered them all. He gave them
such a beating that they ran out of the
house naked and bleeding.
17 When this became known to the
Jews and Greeks living in Ephesus,[w] they
were all seized with fear,[x] and the name
of the Lord Jesus was held in high honor.
18 Many of those who believed now came
and openly confessed what they had done.
19 A number who had practiced sorcery
brought their scrolls together and burned
them publicly. When they calculated the
value of the scrolls, the total came to fifty thousand drachmas.[b] 20 In this way the
word of the Lord[y] spread widely and grew
in power.[z]
21 After all this had happened, Paul
decided[c] to go to Jerusalem,[a] passing
through Macedonia[b] and Achaia.[c] "After
I have been there," he said, "I must visit
Rome also."[d] 22 He sent two of his helpers,[e] Timothy[f] and Erastus,[g] to Macedonia,
while he stayed in the province of Asia[h] a
little longer.

The Riot in Ephesus

23 About that time there arose a great
disturbance about the Way.[i] 24 A silversmith named Demetrius, who made silver shrines of Artemis, brought in a lot

[a] 6 Or *other languages* [b] 19 A drachma was a silver coin worth about a day's wages. [c] 21 Or *decided in the Spirit*

19:4 [e] S Mk 1:4 [f] Jn 1:7 **19:5** [g] S Ac 2:38 **19:6** [h] S Ac 6:6 [i] S Ac 10:44 [j] S Mk 16:17 **19:8** [k] S Ac 9:20 [l] S Mt 3:2; Ac 28:23 **19:9** [m] Ac 14:4 [n] ver 23; S Ac 9:2 [o] ver 30; S Ac 11:26 **19:10** [p] Ac 20:31 [q] ver 22, 26, 27; S Ac 2:9 [r] S Ac 13:48 **19:11** [s] Ac 8:13 **19:12** [t] Ac 5:15 **19:13** [u] Mt 12:27 [v] Mk 9:38 **19:17** [w] S Ac 18:19 [x] Ac 5:5, 11 **19:20** [y] S Ac 13:48 [z] Ac 6:7; 12:24 **19:21** [a] Ac 20:16, 22; 21:4, 12, 15; Ro 15:25 [b] S Ac 16:9 [c] S Ac 18:12 [d] Ro 15:24, 28 **19:22** [e] Ac 13:5 [f] S Ac 16:1 [g] Ro 16:23; 2Ti 4:20 [h] ver 10, 26, 27; S Ac 2:9 **19:23** [i] S Ac 9:2

19:4 *John's baptism.* See notes on Mt 3:11,15. *baptism of repentance.* A summation of John's teaching. It was preparatory and provisional, stressing human sinfulness and thus creating a sense of need for the gospel. John's baptism looked forward to Jesus, who by his death would make possible the forgiveness of sins (see note on Mk 1:4).
19:6 *placed his hands on them.* See note on 6:6. *Holy Spirit came on them … spoke in tongues and prophesied.* The same experience the disciples had at Pentecost (2:4,11) and the Gentiles had in Caesarea (10:46).
19:8 *three months.* Much longer than the three Sabbaths in Thessalonica (17:2), but the same approach: Jews first, then Greeks (see note on 13:14). *kingdom of God.* See notes on Mt 3:2; Lk 4:43.
19:9 *the Way.* See note on 9:2. *lecture hall of Tyrannus.* Probably a school used regularly by Tyrannus, a philosopher or rhetorician. Instruction was probably given in the cooler, morning hours. One Greek manuscript of this verse adds that Paul did his instructing from 11:00 a.m. to 4:00 p.m. This would have been the hot time of the day, but the hall was available and the people were not at their regular work.
19:10 *two years.* Two years and three months (see v. 8) was the longest stay in one missionary location that Luke records. By Jewish reckoning, any part of a year is considered a year; so this period can be spoken of as three years (20:31). *all … in the province of Asia heard.* One of the elements of Paul's missionary strategy is seen here. Many of the cities where Paul planted churches were strategic centers that, when evangelized, served as focal points from which the gospel radiated out to the surrounding areas (see note on Col 4:13). Other examples are Antioch in Pisidia (see 13:14 and note), Thessalonica (see 17:1 and note), Athens (see 17:15 and note) and Corinth (see 18:1).
19:12 *handkerchiefs.* Probably used by Paul in his trade of leatherworking: one for tying around his head, the other around his waist. Cf. 5:15 and note.
19:14 *Sceva, a Jewish chief priest.* May have been related to the high priestly family of Jerusalem. But more likely he took this title himself to make further impression with his magical wiles. Drawn by Paul's ability to drive out evil spirits, Jewish exorcists wanted to copy his work (cf. 8:9–24; 13:6).
19:19 *scrolls.* Such documents, bearing alleged magical formulas and secret information, have been unearthed. Ephesus was a center for magical incantations. *fifty thousand drachmas.* The high price (see NIV text note) was not due to the quality of the books but to the supposed power gained by their secret rigmarole of words and names.
19:21 *Macedonia and Achaia.* See notes on 1Th 1:7–8; see also map, p. 1864.
19:22 *Erastus.* An important Corinthian figure, at one time "the city's director of public works" (see note on Ro 16:23). At this point he returns to Corinth by way of Macedonia with Timothy.
19:23 *the Way.* See 9:2 and note.
19:24 *silversmith named Demetrius.* Each trade had its guild, and Demetrius was probably a responsible leader of the guild for the manufacture of silver shrines and images.

of business for the craftsmen there. 25He
called them together, along with the workers in related trades, and said: "You know,
my friends, that we receive a good income
from this business.[j] 26And you see and
hear how this fellow Paul has convinced
and led astray large numbers of people
here in Ephesus[k] and in practically the
whole province of Asia.[l] He says that gods
made by human hands are no gods at all.[m]
27There is danger not only that our trade
will lose its good name, but also that the
temple of the great goddess Artemis will
be discredited; and the goddess herself,
who is worshiped throughout the province
of Asia and the world, will be robbed of
her divine majesty."
28When they heard this, they were furious and began shouting: "Great is Artemis of the Ephesians!"[n] 29Soon the whole
city was in an uproar. The people seized
Gaius[o] and Aristarchus,[p] Paul's traveling
companions from Macedonia,[q] and all
of them rushed into the theater together. 30Paul wanted to appear before the
crowd, but the disciples[r] would not let
him. 31Even some of the officials of the
province, friends of Paul, sent him a message begging him not to venture into the
theater.
32The assembly was in confusion: Some
were shouting one thing, some another.[s]
Most of the people did not even know why
they were there. 33The Jews in the crowd
pushed Alexander to the front, and they
shouted instructions to him. He motioned[t]
for silence in order to make a defense before the people. 34But when they realized
he was a Jew, they all shouted in unison
for about two hours: "Great is Artemis of
the Ephesians!"[u]
35The city clerk quieted the crowd and
said: "Fellow Ephesians,[v] doesn't all the
world know that the city of Ephesus is
the guardian of the temple of the great Artemis and of her image, which fell from
heaven? 36Therefore, since these facts are
undeniable, you ought to calm down and
not do anything rash. 37You have brought
these men here, though they have neither
robbed temples[w] nor blasphemed our goddess. 38If, then, Demetrius and his fellow
craftsmen[x] have a grievance against anybody, the courts are open and there are
proconsuls.[y] They can press charges. 39If
there is anything further you want to bring
up, it must be settled in a legal assembly. 40As it is, we are in danger of being
charged with rioting because of what happened today. In that case we would not be
able to account for this commotion, since
there is no reason for it." 41After he had
said this, he dismissed the assembly.

Through Macedonia and Greece

20 When the uproar had ended, Paul
sent for the disciples[z] and, after
encouraging them, said goodbye and set
out for Macedonia.[a] 2He traveled through
that area, speaking many words of encouragement to the people, and finally arrived
in Greece, 3where he stayed three months.
Because some Jews had plotted against
him[b] just as he was about to sail for

19:25 [j] Ac 16:16, 19,20
19:26 [k] S Ac 18:19 [l] S Ac 2:9 [m] Dt 4:28; Ps 115:4; Isa 44:10-20; Jer 10:3-5; Ac 17:29; 1Co 8:4; Rev 9:20
19:28 [n] S Ac 18:19
19:29 [o] Ac 20:4; Ro 16:23; 1Co 1:14 [p] Ac 20:4; 27:2; Col 4:10; Phm 24 [q] S Ac 16:9
19:30 [r] S Ac 11:26
19:32 [s] Ac 21:34
19:33 [t] S Ac 12:17
19:34 [u] ver 28
19:35 [v] S Ac 18:19
19:37 [w] Ro 2:22
19:38 [x] ver 24 [y] Ac 13:7,8,12; 18:12
20:1 [z] S Ac 11:26 [a] S Ac 16:9
20:3 [b] ver 19; Ac 9:23,24; 14:5; 23:12, 15,30; 25:3; 2Co 11:26; S 1Th 2:16

Artemis. The Greek name for the Roman goddess Diana. The Ephesian Artemis, however, was very different from the Greco-Roman goddess. She had taken on the characteristics of Cybele, the mother goddess of fertility worshiped in Asia Minor. A meteorite may be the basis of the many-breasted image of heavenly workmanship claimed for Artemis (v. 35). Reproductions of the original image from the time of the emperor Domitian (AD 81 – 96) have been found in Ephesus.
19:25 *good income.* Since the temple of Artemis was one of the seven wonders of the ancient world, people came from far and wide to view it. Their purchase of silver shrines and images produced a lucrative business for the craftsmen.
19:27 *temple of the great goddess.* See map, p. 1982. The temple was the glory of Ephesus: 425 feet long and 220 feet wide, having 127 white marble columns 62 feet high and less than 4 feet apart. In the inner sanctuary was the many-breasted image supposedly dropped from heaven.
19:29 *Gaius.* See note on 20:4. *Aristarchus.* Traveled later with Paul from Corinth to Jerusalem (20:3 – 4) and also accompanied Paul on the voyage from Jerusalem to Rome (27:1 – 2; see Col 4:10 and note).
19:31 *officials of the province.* Greek *Asiarchon,* members of a council of men of wealth and influence elected to promote the worship of the emperor. Paul had friends in this highest circle.
19:33 *Alexander.* Pushed forward by the Jews either to make clear the disassociation of the Jews from the Christians and/or to accuse the Christians further of an offense against the Greeks. The crowd recognized that the Jews were not worshipers of Artemis any more than the Christians were.
19:35 *city clerk.* The secretary of the city who published the decisions of the civic assembly. He was the most important local official and the chief executive officer of the assembly, acting as go-between for Ephesus and the Roman authorities. *fell from heaven.* See note on v. 24.
19:38 *courts ... proconsuls.* Probably general terms, not intended to refer to more than one court or one proconsul. As capital city of the province of Asia, Ephesus was the headquarters for the proconsul.
19:39 *legal assembly.* The regular civil meeting, ordinarily held three times a month.
20:1 *said goodbye and set out.* Paul wanted to: (1) leave Ephesus, (2) preach in Troas on his way to Macedonia, (3) meet Titus at Troas with a report from Corinth (see 2Co 2:12 – 13 and note on 2:12) and (4) continue collecting the offering for Judea (see 1Co 16:1 – 4; 2Co 8:1 — 9:15; Ro 15:25 – 28). *Macedonia.* Where Paul probably wrote 2 Corinthians (see 2Co 7:5; 8:1; 9:4; see also chart, p. 1845).
20:2 *He traveled through that area.* May cover a considerable period. He may have gone to Illyricum (see Ro 15:19 and note) at this time.
20:3 *three months.* Probably a reference to the stay in Corinth, the capital of Achaia. These would be the winter months when ships did not sail regularly. Paul probably wrote Romans at this time (see Introduction to Romans: Occasion). *plotted against him.* The Jews were determined to take Paul's

Syria,[c] he decided to go back through Macedonia.[d] 4 He was accompanied by Sopater
son of Pyrrhus from Berea, Aristarchus[e]
and Secundus from Thessalonica,[f] Gaius[g]
from Derbe, Timothy[h] also, and Tychicus[i]
and Trophimus[j] from the province of Asia.[k]
5 These men went on ahead and waited for
us[l] at Troas.[m] 6 But we sailed from Philippi[n] after the Festival of Unleavened Bread,
and five days later joined the others at Troas,[o] where we stayed seven days.

Eutychus Raised From the Dead at Troas

7 On the first day of the week[p] we came
together to break bread.[q] Paul spoke to
the people and, because he intended to
leave the next day, kept on talking until
midnight. 8 There were many lamps in the
upstairs room[r] where we were meeting.
9 Seated in a window was a young man
named Eutychus, who was sinking into a
deep sleep as Paul talked on and on. When
he was sound asleep, he fell to the ground
from the third story and was picked up
dead. 10 Paul went down, threw himself on
the young man[s] and put his arms around
him. "Don't be alarmed," he said. "He's
alive!"[t] 11 Then he went upstairs again and
broke bread[u] and ate. After talking until
daylight, he left. 12 The people took the
young man home alive and were greatly
comforted.

Paul's Farewell to the Ephesian Elders

13 We went on ahead to the ship and
sailed for Assos, where we were going to
take Paul aboard. He had made this arrangement because he was going there
on foot. 14 When he met us at Assos, we
took him aboard and went on to Mitylene. 15 The next day we set sail from there
and arrived off Chios. The day after that
we crossed over to Samos, and on the
following day arrived at Miletus.[v] 16 Paul
had decided to sail past Ephesus[w] to avoid
spending time in the province of Asia,[x] for
he was in a hurry to reach Jerusalem,[y] if
possible, by the day of Pentecost.[z]

20:3 [c] S Lk 2:2 [d] S Ac 16:9
20:4 [e] S Ac 19:29 [f] S Ac 17:1 [g] S Ac 19:29 [h] S Ac 16:1 [i] Eph 6:21; Col 4:7; Titus 3:12 [j] Ac 21:29; 2Ti 4:20 [k] S Ac 2:9
20:5 [l] S Ac 16:10 [m] S Ac 16:8
20:6 [n] S Ac 16:12 [o] S Ac 16:8
20:7 [p] 1Co 16:2; Rev 1:10 [q] S Mt 14:19
20:8 [r] Ac 1:13; 9:37
20:10 [s] 1Ki 17:21; 2Ki 4:34 [t] Mt 9:23,24
20:11 [u] ver 7; S Mt 14:19
20:15 [v] ver 17; 2Ti 4:20
20:16 [w] S Ac 18:19 [x] S Ac 2:9 [y] S Ac 19:21 [z] S Ac 2:1

---

life; also, at this time he was carrying the offering for the Christians in Judea, so there would have been a temptation for theft as well. The port at Cenchreae would have provided a convenient place for Paul's enemies to detect him as he entered a ship to embark for Syria.

20:4 These men seem to be the delegates appointed to accompany Paul and the money given for the needy in Judea (see note on 2Co 8:23). Three were from Macedonia, two from Galatia and two from Asia. Luke may have joined them at Philippi ("we sailed," v. 6; see note on 16:10). *Sopater.* May be the same as Sosipater (Ro 16:21). *Aristarchus.* See note on 19:29. *Secundus.* Not mentioned elsewhere. His name means "second," as Tertius (see Ro 16:22) means "third" and Quartus (see Ro 16:23) means "fourth." *Gaius from Derbe.* A Gaius from Macedonia was associated with Aristarchus (see 19:29), but the grouping of the names in pairs (after the reference to Sopater) indicates that this Gaius was associated with Roman Galatia and is different from the Macedonian Gaius. *Timothy.* May have represented more than one particular church. He was from Lystra but had been responsible for working in other churches (1Co 16:10–11; Php 2:19–23). He had been sent to Macedonia before Paul left Ephesus (19:22). *Tychicus.* A constant help to Paul, especially in association with the churches of Asia (Eph 6:21–22; Col 4:7–9; 2Ti 4:12; Titus 3:12). *Trophimus.* Appears again in 21:29 (see 2Ti 4:20). He was an Ephesian, and it is implied that he was a Gentile.

20:5 *Troas.* Was to be the rendezvous for Paul and those who went on ahead by sea from Neapolis, the seaport of Philippi (16:11). Paul and his immediate companions stayed in Philippi before sailing a week later.

20:6 *from Philippi.* From the seaport, Neapolis, about ten miles away. *Festival of Unleavened Bread.* Began with Passover and lasted a week. Paul spent the period in Philippi. Formerly he had hoped to reach Jerusalem sooner (see 19:21), but now he hoped to arrive there for Pentecost (see 20:16). *five days later.* The voyage from Neapolis to Troas took five days. It had taken about two days the other direction (16:11). *seven days.* Although Paul was in a hurry to arrive at Jerusalem by Pentecost, he remained for seven days at Troas. This might have been because of a ship schedule, but more likely the delay was in order to meet with the believers on the first day of the week to break bread.

20:7 *first day of the week.* Sunday. Although some maintain that they met on Saturday evening, since the Jewish day began at six o'clock the previous evening, there is no indication that Luke is using the Jewish method of reporting time to tell of happenings in this Hellenistic city. *break bread.* Here indicates the Lord's Supper, since breaking bread was the express purpose for this formal gathering. The Lord's Supper had been commanded (Lk 22:19) and was observed regularly (see 2:42 and note). *kept on talking until midnight.* All the speeches of Paul as recorded in Acts are short, indicating that they are summaries (see Introduction: Characteristics).

20:9 *Eutychus.* A name common among the Freedmen class (see note on 6:9).

20:10 *He's alive!* As Peter had raised Tabitha (9:40), so Paul raised Eutychus.

20:13 *Assos.* On the opposite side of the peninsula from Troas—about 20 miles away by land. The coastline, however, was about 40 miles. Thus Paul was not far behind the ship that sailed around the peninsula.

20:14 *Mitylene.* After the first day of sailing, they put into this harbor on the southeast shore of the island of Lesbos.

20:15 *Chios.* The second night they spent off the shore of this larger island, which lay along the west coast of Asia Minor (see map, p. 1864). *Samos.* Crossing the mouth of the bay that leads to Ephesus, they came on the third day to Samos, one of the most important islands in the Aegean. *Miletus.* About 35 miles south of Ephesus, the destination of the ship Paul was on. He would have had to change ships to put into Ephesus, which would have lost time (see v. 16). If he had come to Ephesus, he would have had to visit a number of families, which would have taken more time. If trouble should arise, such as the riot of a year ago (19:23–41), even more time would be lost. This could not be risked.

20:16 *by the day of Pentecost.* Fifty days from Passover. Five days plus seven days (v. 6) plus four days (vv. 13–15) had already gone by, leaving only about two-thirds of the time for the remainder of the trip. *Pentecost.* See note on 2:1.

17From Miletus,[a] Paul sent to Ephesus
for the elders[b] of the church. 18When they
arrived, he said to them: "You know how
I lived the whole time I was with you,[c]
from the first day I came into the province
of Asia.[d] 19I served the Lord with great humility and with tears[e] and in the midst of
severe testing by the plots of my Jewish
opponents.[f] 20You know that I have not
hesitated to preach anything[g] that would
be helpful to you but have taught you publicly and from house to house. 21I have declared to both Jews[h] and Greeks that they
must turn to God in repentance[i] and have
faith in our Lord Jesus.[j]
22"And now, compelled by the Spirit, I
am going to Jerusalem,[k] not knowing what
will happen to me there. 23I only know
that in every city the Holy Spirit warns
me[l] that prison and hardships are facing
me.[m] 24However, I consider my life worth
nothing to me;[n] my only aim is to finish
the race[o] and complete the task[p] the Lord
Jesus has given me[q]—the task of testifying to the good news of God's grace.[r]
25"Now I know that none of you among
whom I have gone about preaching the
kingdom[s] will ever see me again.[t] 26There-
fore, I declare to you today that I am innocent of the blood of any of you.[u] 27For
I have not hesitated to proclaim to you
the whole will of God.[v] 28Keep watch over
yourselves and all the flock[w] of which the
Holy Spirit has made you overseers.[x] Be
shepherds of the church of God,[a][y] which
he bought[z] with his own blood.[b][a] 29I know
that after I leave, savage wolves[b] will come
in among you and will not spare the flock.[c]
30Even from your own number men will
arise and distort the truth in order to draw
away disciples[d] after them. 31So be on your
guard! Remember that for three years[e] I
never stopped warning each of you night
and day with tears.[f]
32"Now I commit you to God[g] and to the
word of his grace, which can build you
up and give you an inheritance[h] among all
those who are sanctified.[i] 33I have not coveted anyone's silver or gold or clothing.[j]
34You yourselves know that these hands
of mine have supplied my own needs and
the needs of my companions.[k] 35In everything I did, I showed you that by this kind
of hard work we must help the weak, remembering the words the Lord Jesus himself said: 'It is more blessed to give than
to receive.'"
36When Paul had finished speaking, he
knelt down with all of them and prayed.[l]
37They all wept as they embraced him and
kissed him.[m] 38What grieved them most
was his statement that they would never
see his face again.[n] Then they accompanied him to the ship.[o]

On to Jerusalem

21 After we[p] had torn ourselves away
from them, we put out to sea and
sailed straight to Kos. The next day we
went to Rhodes and from there to Patara.
2We found a ship crossing over to Phoenicia,[q] went on board and set sail. 3After

20:17 [a] ver 15 [b] S Ac 11:30 **20:18** [c] Ac 18:19-21; 19:1-41 [d] S Ac 2:9 **20:19** [e] Ps 6:6 [f] S ver 3 **20:20** [g] ver 27; Ps 40:10; Jer 26:2; 42:4 **20:21** [h] Ac 18:5 [i] S Ac 2:38 [j] Ac 24:24; 26:18; Eph 1:15; Col 2:5; Phm 5 **20:22** [k] ver 16 **20:23** [l] S Ac 8:29; 21:4 [m] S Ac 9:16 **20:24** [n] Ac 21:13 [o] 2Ti 4:7 [p] 2Co 4:1 [q] Gal 1:1; Titus 1:3 [r] S Ac 11:23 **20:25** [s] S Mt 4:23 [t] ver 38 **20:26** [u] Eze 3:17-19; Ac 18:6 **20:27** [v] S ver 20 **20:28** [w] ver 29; S Jn 21:16 [x] S 1Ti 3:1 [y] S 1Co 10:32 [z] S 1Co 6:20 [a] S Ro 3:25 **20:29** [b] Eze 34:5; Mt 7:15 [c] ver 28 **20:30** [d] S Ac 11:26 **20:31** [e] Ac 19:10 [f] ver 19 **20:32** [g] Ac 14:23 [h] S Eph 1:14; S Mt 25:34; Col 1:12; 3:24; Heb 9:15; 1Pe 1:4 [i] Ac 26:18

[a] 28 Many manuscripts *of the Lord* [b] 28 Or *with the blood of his own Son.*

20:33 [j] 1Sa 12:3; 1Co 9:12; 2Co 2:17; 7:2; 11:9; 12:14-17; 1Th 2:5 **20:34** [k] S Ac 18:3 **20:36** [l] Lk 22:41; Ac 9:40; 21:5 **20:37** [m] S Lk 15:20 **20:38** [n] ver 25 [o] Ac 21:5 **21:1** [p] S Ac 16:10 **21:2** [q] Ac 11:19

20:17 *elders of the church.* The importance of the leadership of elders has been evident throughout Paul's ministry. He had delivered the famine gift from the church at Antioch to the elders of the Jerusalem church (11:30). He had appointed elders on his first missionary journey (see 14:23) and had addressed the holders of this office later in Philippi (Php 1:1, "overseers"). He requested the Ephesian elders to meet with him on this solemn occasion (see v. 28). Some years later he wrote down instructions about the elders' qualifications (1Ti 3; Titus 1; see chart, p. 2041).
20:19 *with tears.* See v. 31. Paul's ministry at Ephesus was conducted with emotional fervency and a sense of urgency.
20:22 *compelled by the Spirit.* Paul did not go to Jerusalem against the direction of the Spirit, as some have suggested, but because of the guidance of the Spirit. People pleaded with him not to go (21:4,12), not because the Spirit prohibited his going but because the Spirit revealed the capture that awaited him there (21:11–12).
20:24 *finish the race.* See 2Ti 4:7 and note.
20:25 *none of you … will ever see me again.* Not a message from God but what Paul anticipated. He had been mistaken before in his plans: He had intended to stay in Ephesus until Pentecost but had to leave earlier (see v. 1; 1Co 16:8–9). His prophetic power was not used to foresee his own future, just as his healing power was not used to heal his own disease (see 2Co 12:7–9). As it turned out, Paul evidently did revisit Ephesus (see 1Ti 1:3). *kingdom.* See notes on Mt 3:2; Lk 4:43.
20:28 *overseers. Be shepherds.* The "elders" (v. 17) were called "overseers" and told to pastor ("shepherd") the flock—demonstrating that the same men could be called "elders," "overseers" or "pastors." *his own blood.* See NIV text note; the reading there refers to the sacrificial death of God's own Son.
20:29 *wolves.* See Lk 10:3 and note.
20:31 *three years.* See note on 19:10.
20:32 *inheritance.* See 1Pe 1:4 and note. *sanctified.* See note on 1Co 1:2.
20:34 *supplied my own needs.* Paul had worked in Thessalonica (1Th 2:9) and Corinth (Ac 18:3).
20:35 *remembering the words the Lord Jesus himself said.* A formula regularly used in the early church to introduce a quotation from Jesus (1 Clement 46:7). This is a rare instance of a saying of Jesus not found in the canonical Gospels.
20:38 *never see his face again.* See v. 25 and note.
21:1 *sailed straight to Kos.* Favorable winds took them to a stopping place for the night at this island. *Rhodes.* The leading city on the island of Rhodes, once noted for its harbor colossus, one of the seven wonders of the ancient world (but demolished over two centuries before Paul arrived there). It took them a day to get to Rhodes. *Patara.* On the southern coast of Lycia. Paul changed ships from a vessel that hugged

sighting Cyprus and passing to the south
of it, we sailed on to Syria.[r] We landed at
Tyre, where our ship was to unload its cargo. 4 We sought out the disciples[s] there and
stayed with them seven days. Through the
Spirit[t] they urged Paul not to go on to Jerusalem. 5 When it was time to leave, we left
and continued on our way. All of them, including wives and children, accompanied
us out of the city, and there on the beach
we knelt to pray.[u] 6 After saying goodbye to
each other, we went aboard the ship, and
they returned home.

7 We continued our voyage from Tyre[v]
and landed at Ptolemais, where we greeted the brothers and sisters[w] and stayed
with them for a day. 8 Leaving the next
day, we reached Caesarea[x] and stayed at
the house of Philip[y] the evangelist,[z] one of
the Seven. 9 He had four unmarried daughters who prophesied.[a]

10 After we had been there a number
of days, a prophet named Agabus[b] came
down from Judea. 11 Coming over to us,
he took Paul's belt, tied his own hands
and feet with it and said, "The Holy Spirit
says,[c] 'In this way the Jewish leaders in
Jerusalem will bind[d] the owner of this belt
and will hand him over to the Gentiles.' "[e]

12 When we heard this, we and the people there pleaded with Paul not to go up to
Jerusalem. 13 Then Paul answered, "Why
are you weeping and breaking my heart? I
am ready not only to be bound, but also to
die[f] in Jerusalem for the name of the Lord
Jesus."[g] 14 When he would not be dissuad-

21:3 [r] S Lk 2:2 **21:4** [s] S Ac 11:26 [t] ver 11; Ac 20:23 **21:5** [u] Lk 22:41; Ac 9:40; 20:36 **21:7** [v] Ac 12:20 [w] S Ac 1:16 **21:8** [x] S Ac 8:40 [y] Ac 6:5; 8:5-40 [z] Eph 4:11; 2Ti 4:5 **21:9** [a] Ex 15:20; Jdg 4:4; Ne 6:14; Lk 2:36; Ac 2:17; 1Co 11:5 **21:10** [b] Ac 11:28 **21:11** [c] S Ac 8:29 [d] ver 33 [e] 1Ki 22:11; Isa 20:2-4; Jer 13:1-11; Mt 20:19 **21:13** [f] Ac 20:24 [g] S Jn 15:21; S Ac 9:16 **21:14** [h] Ru 1:18 [i] S Mt 26:39 **21:15** [j] S Ac 19:21 **21:16** [k] S Ac 8:40 [l] ver 3,4 **21:17** [m] S Ac 9:30 [n] Ac 15:4 **21:18** [o] S Ac 15:13 [p] S Ac 11:30 **21:19** [q] Ac 14:27; 15:4, 12 [r] Ac 1:17 **21:20** [s] Ac 22:3; Ro 10:2; Gal 1:14;

ed, we gave up[h] and said, "The Lord's will
be done."[i]

15 After this, we started on our way up
to Jerusalem.[j] 16 Some of the disciples from
Caesarea[k] accompanied us and brought us
to the home of Mnason, where we were to
stay. He was a man from Cyprus[l] and one
of the early disciples.

Paul's Arrival at Jerusalem

17 When we arrived at Jerusalem, the
brothers and sisters[m] received us warmly.[n] 18 The next day Paul and the rest of
us went to see James,[o] and all the elders[p]
were present. 19 Paul greeted them and
reported in detail what God had done
among the Gentiles[q] through his ministry.[r]

20 When they heard this, they praised
God. Then they said to Paul: "You see,
brother, how many thousands of Jews
have believed, and all of them are zealous[s] for the law.[t] 21 They have been informed that you teach all the Jews who
live among the Gentiles to turn away from
Moses,[u] telling them not to circumcise
their children[v] or live according to our
customs.[w] 22 What shall we do? They will
certainly hear that you have come, 23 so do
what we tell you. There are four men with
us who have made a vow.[x] 24 Take these
men, join in their purification rites[y] and
pay their expenses, so that they can have
their heads shaved.[z] Then everyone will

Php 3:6 [t] Ac 15:1,5 **21:21** [u] ver 28 [v] Ac 15:19-21; 1Co 7:18, 19 [w] S Ac 6:14 **21:23** [x] Nu 6:2,5,18; Ac 18:18 **21:24** [y] ver 26; Ac 24:18 [z] Ac 18:18

the shore of Asia Minor to one going directly to Tyre and Phoenicia.

21:3 *Cyprus.* See 13:4 and note. *Tyre.* Paul had passed through this Phoenician area at least once before (15:3; cf. Mk 7:24).

21:4 *seven days.* These, added to the 29 days since the Passover in Philippi, would leave only two weeks until Pentecost. *urged Paul not to go.* The Spirit warned of the coming trials in store for Paul at Jerusalem (20:23). Because of these warnings, Paul's Christian friends urged him not to go on, knowing that trials lay ahead. But Paul felt "compelled by the Spirit" to go (20:22; see note there).

21:7 *Ptolemais.* The modern city of Akko, north of and across the bay from Mount Carmel. It was one day's journey from Tyre on the north and 35 miles to Caesarea on the south.

21:8 *Caesarea.* A Gentile city, the capital of Roman Judea (see note on 10:1). *Philip the evangelist.* Philip's evangelistic work may have focused on Caesarea for almost 25 years (see note on 8:40). "Evangelist" is a title used only here and in Eph 4:11; 2Ti 4:5.

21:9 *unmarried daughters.* They may have been dedicated in a special way to serving the Lord (cf. 1Co 7:34). *prophesied.* See 1Co 11:5; 12:8–10; cf. Lk 2:36. For OT prophetesses, see Ex 15:20; Jdg 4:4; 2Ki 22:14; Ne 6:14; Isa 8:3 and note.

21:10 *prophet named Agabus.* Evidently he held the office of prophet, as Philip held the office of evangelist (v. 8). This is the same prophet who had been in Antioch prophesying the coming famine in Jerusalem some 15 years earlier (11:27–29).

21:12 *we and the people there.* Now Luke, in the company of travelers with Paul, joins in urging Paul not to go to Jerusalem.

21:13 *to die.* Cf. Php 1:21 and note.

21:14 *Lord's will be done.* May mean that they finally recognized that it was the Lord's will for Paul to go to Jerusalem.

21:16 *Mnason.* Must have been a disciple of some means to be able to accommodate Paul and a group of about nine men traveling with him.

21:17 *arrived at Jerusalem.* No more than a day or two before Pentecost. *the brothers and sisters received us warmly.* May indicate the grateful reception of the offering as well.

21:18 *James.* The brother of the Lord, author of the letter of James and leader of the church in Jerusalem (see Gal 1:19 and note; 2:9).

21:23 *made a vow.* They were evidently under the temporary Nazirite vow and became unclean before the completion time of the vow (perhaps from contact with a dead body); cf. Nu 6:2–12.

21:24 *purification rites.* In some instances the rites included the offering of sacrifices. Such rites were observed by choice by some Jewish Christians but were not required of Christians, whether Jew or Gentile. *pay their expenses.* Paul's part in sponsoring these men would include (1) paying part or all of the expenses of the sacrificial victims (in this case eight pigeons and four lambs, Nu 6:9–12) and (2) going to the temple to notify the priest when their days of purification would be fulfilled so the priests would be prepared to sacrifice their offerings (v. 26). *living in obedience to the law.* Paul had earlier taken a vow himself (see 18:18 and note), he had been a Jew

know there is no truth in these reports
about you, but that you yourself are living in obedience to the law. 25 As for the
Gentile believers, we have written to them
our decision that they should abstain from
food sacrificed to idols, from blood, from
the meat of strangled animals and from
sexual immorality."[a]
26 The next day Paul took the men and
purified himself along with them. Then he
went to the temple to give notice of the
date when the days of purification would
end and the offering would be made for
each of them.[b]

Paul Arrested

27 When the seven days were nearly
over, some Jews from the province of Asia
saw Paul at the temple. They stirred up the
whole crowd and seized him,[c] 28 shouting,
"Fellow Israelites, help us! This is the man
who teaches everyone everywhere against
our people and our law and this place.
And besides, he has brought Greeks into
the temple and defiled this holy place."[d]
29 (They had previously seen Trophimus[e]
the Ephesian[f] in the city with Paul and assumed that Paul had brought him into the
temple.)
30 The whole city was aroused, and the
people came running from all directions.
Seizing Paul,[g] they dragged him[h] from the
temple, and immediately the gates were
shut. 31 While they were trying to kill him,
news reached the commander of the Roman troops that the whole city of Jerusalem was in an uproar. 32 He at once took
some officers and soldiers and ran down
to the crowd. When the rioters saw the
commander and his soldiers, they stopped
beating Paul.[i]
33 The commander came up and arrested him and ordered him to be bound[j]
with two[k] chains.[l] Then he asked who he
was and what he had done. 34 Some in the
crowd shouted one thing and some another,[m] and since the commander could not
get at the truth because of the uproar, he
ordered that Paul be taken into the barracks.[n] 35 When Paul reached the steps,[o]
the violence of the mob was so great he
had to be carried by the soldiers. 36 The
crowd that followed kept shouting, "Get
rid of him!"[p]

Paul Speaks to the Crowd

22:3-16pp — Ac 9:1-22; 26:9-18

37 As the soldiers were about to take
Paul into the barracks,[q] he asked the commander, "May I say something to you?"
"Do you speak Greek?" he replied.
38 "Aren't you the Egyptian who started a
revolt and led four thousand terrorists out
into the wilderness[r] some time ago?"[s]
39 Paul answered, "I am a Jew, from Tarsus[t] in Cilicia,[u] a citizen of no ordinary
city. Please let me speak to the people."
40 After receiving the commander's permission, Paul stood on the steps and motioned[v] to the crowd. When they were all
22 silent, he said to them in Aramaic[a]:[w] 1 "Brothers and fathers,[x] listen
now to my defense."
2 When they heard him speak to them in
Aramaic,[y] they became very quiet.
Then Paul said: 3 "I am a Jew,[z] born in

21:25 [a] Ac 15:20,29
21:26 [b] Nu 6:13-20; Ac 24:18
21:27 [c] Jer 26:8; Ac 24:18; 26:21; S 1Th 2:16
21:28 [d] Mt 24:15; Ac 6:13; 24:5,6
21:29 [e] Ac 20:4; 2Ti 4:20 [f] S Ac 18:19
21:30 [g] Ac 26:21 [h] S Ac 16:19
21:32 [i] Ac 23:27
21:33 [j] ver 11 [k] Ac 12:6 [l] Ac 20:23; 22:29; Eph 6:20; 2Ti 2:9
21:34 [m] Ac 19:32 [n] ver 37; Ac 22:24; 23:10, 16,32
21:35 [o] ver 40
21:36 [p] Lk 23:18; Jn 19:15; Ac 22:22
21:37 [q] S ver 34
21:38 [r] Mt 24:26 [s] Ac 5:36
21:39 [t] S Ac 9:11 [u] S Ac 6:9
21:40 [v] S Ac 12:17 [w] S Jn 5:2
22:1 [x] Ac 7:2
22:2 [y] Ac 21:40; S Jn 5:2
22:3 [z] Ac 21:39

[a] 40 Or possibly *Hebrew*; also in 22:2

to the Jews (see 1Co 9:20–21), and Timothy had been circumcised (see 16:3 and note). However, Paul was very careful not to sacrifice Christian principle in any act of obedience to the law (e.g., he would not have Titus circumcised, Gal 2:3).
21:25 See 15:23–29 and notes.
21:27 *seven days.* Cf. Nu 6:9. These were the days required for purification, shaving their heads at the altar, the sacrifice of a sin offering and burnt offering for each and announcing the completion to the priests. *Jews from the province of Asia.* Paul had suffered already from the hands of Asian Jews (20:19).
21:28 *teaches ... against our people and our law and this place.* Cf. the accusations brought against Stephen in 6:13. *brought Greeks into the temple.* Explicitly forbidden according to inscribed stone markers (still in existence; see chart, p. 1810). Any Gentiles found within the bounds of the court of Israel would be killed. But there is no evidence that Paul had brought anyone other than Jews into the area.
21:29 *Trophimus.* See 20:4 and note. Paul probably did not take him into the forbidden area. If he had, they should have attacked Trophimus rather than Paul.
21:30 *gates were shut.* By order of the temple officer to prevent further trouble inside the sacred precincts.
21:31 *commander.* Greek *chiliarch* (a commander of 1,000 [a regiment]), Claudius Lysias by name (23:26), who was stationed at the Fortress of Antonia (see note on v. 37).
21:32 *some officers.* Centurions. Since the plural is used, it is likely that at least two centurions and 200 soldiers were involved.
21:33 *two chains.* Probably his hands were chained to a soldier on either side.
21:34 *barracks.* See note on 12:9.
21:37 *barracks.* The Fortress of Antonia was connected to the northern end of the temple area by two flights of steps. The tower overlooked the temple area.
21:38 *the Egyptian who started a revolt.* Josephus tells of an Egyptian false prophet who some years earlier had led 4,000 (Josephus, through a misreading of a Greek capital letter, says 30,000) out to the Mount of Olives. Roman soldiers killed hundreds, but the leader escaped. *terrorists.* The Greek here is a loanword from Latin *sicarii,* meaning "dagger-men," who were violent assassins.
21:39 *Tarsus.* See note on 22:3.
21:40 *Aramaic.* More likely Aramaic than Hebrew (see NIV text note), since Aramaic was the most commonly used language among Palestinian Jews.
22:1 *Brothers.* See note on 11:1.
22:2 *Aramaic.* See note on 21:40. Actually, if he had spoken in Hebrew, they would have become even quieter in order not to miss a single word, because it would have been more difficult for them to understand.

Tarsus[a] of Cilicia,[b] but brought up in this
city. I studied under[c] Gamaliel[d] and was
thoroughly trained in the law of our ancestors.[e] I was just as zealous[f] for God as
any of you are today. 4 I persecuted[g] the
followers of this Way[h] to their death, arresting both men and women and throwing them into prison,[i] 5 as the high priest
and all the Council[j] can themselves testify.
I even obtained letters from them to their
associates[k] in Damascus,[l] and went there
to bring these people as prisoners to Jerusalem to be punished.

6 "About noon as I came near Damascus, suddenly a bright light from heaven
flashed around me.[m] 7 I fell to the ground
and heard a voice say to me, 'Saul! Saul!
Why do you persecute me?'

8 " 'Who are you, Lord?' I asked.

" 'I am Jesus of Nazareth,[n] whom you are
persecuting,' he replied. 9 My companions
saw the light,[o] but they did not understand
the voice[p] of him who was speaking to me.

10 " 'What shall I do, Lord?' I asked.

" 'Get up,' the Lord said, 'and go into
Damascus. There you will be told all that
you have been assigned to do.'[q] 11 My companions led me by the hand into Damascus, because the brilliance of the light had
blinded me.[r]

12 "A man named Ananias came to see
me.[s] He was a devout observer of the law
and highly respected by all the Jews living there.[t] 13 He stood beside me and said,
'Brother Saul, receive your sight!' And at
that very moment I was able to see him.

14 "Then he said: 'The God of our ancestors[u] has chosen you to know his will
and to see[v] the Righteous One[w] and to hear
words from his mouth. 15 You will be his
witness[x] to all people of what you have
seen[y] and heard. 16 And now what are you
waiting for? Get up, be baptized[z] and wash
your sins away,[a] calling on his name.'[b]

17 "When I returned to Jerusalem[c] and
was praying at the temple, I fell into a
trance[d] 18 and saw the Lord speaking to
me. 'Quick!' he said. 'Leave Jerusalem
immediately, because the people here will
not accept your testimony about me.'

19 " 'Lord,' I replied, 'these people know
that I went from one synagogue to another
to imprison[e] and beat[f] those who believe
in you. 20 And when the blood of your martyr[a] Stephen was shed, I stood there giving
my approval and guarding the clothes of
those who were killing him.'[g]

21 "Then the Lord said to me, 'Go; I will
send you far away to the Gentiles.' "[h]

Paul the Roman Citizen

22 The crowd listened to Paul until he
said this. Then they raised their voices and
shouted, "Rid the earth of him![i] He's not
fit to live!"[j]

23 As they were shouting and throwing
off their cloaks[k] and flinging dust into the
air,[l] 24 the commander ordered that Paul be
taken into the barracks.[m] He directed[n] that
he be flogged and interrogated in order
to find out why the people were shouting

[a] 20 Or *witness*

22:3 [a] S Ac 9:11 [b] S Ac 6:9 [c] Lk 10:39 [d] Ac 5:34 [e] Ac 26:5 [f] 1Ki 19:10; S Ac 21:20 **22:4** [g] S Ac 8:3 [h] S Ac 9:2 [i] ver 19,20 **22:5** [j] Lk 22:66 [k] S Ac 1:16; 2:29; 13:26; 23:1; 28:17,21; S Ro 7:1; 9:3 [l] Ac 9:2 **22:6** [m] Ac 9:3 **22:8** [n] S Mk 1:24 **22:9** [o] Ac 26:13 [p] Ac 9:7 **22:10** [q] Ac 16:30 **22:11** [r] Ac 9:8 **22:12** [s] Ac 9:17 [t] Ac 10:22 **22:14** [u] S Ac 3:13 [v] S 1Co 15:8 [w] Ac 7:52 **22:15** [x] Ac 23:11; 26:16 [y] ver 14 **22:16** [z] S Ac 2:38 [a] Lev 8:6; Ps 51:2; Eze 36:25; Jn 3:5; 1Co 6:11; Eph 5:26; Titus 3:5; Heb 10:22; 1Pe 3:21 [b] Ro 10:13 **22:17** [c] Ac 9:26 [d] Ac 10:10 **22:19** [e] ver 4; S Ac 8:3 [f] S Mt 10:17 **22:20** [g] Ac 7:57-60; 8:1 **22:21** [h] S Ac 9:15; S 13:46 **22:22** [i] Ac 21:36 [j] Ac 25:24 **22:23** [k] Ac 7:58 [l] 2Sa 16:13 **22:24** [m] S Ac 21:34 [n] ver 29

22:3 *born in Tarsus.* Paul had citizenship in Tarsus (21:39) as well as being a Roman citizen. "No ordinary city" (21:39) was used by Euripides to describe Athens. Tarsus was 10 miles inland on the Cydnus River and 30 miles from the mountains, which were cut by a deep, narrow gorge called the Cilician Gates. It was an important commercial center, university city and crossroads of travel. *brought up in this city.* Paul must have come to Jerusalem at an early age. Another translation ("brought up in this city at the feet of Gamaliel, being thoroughly trained according to the law of our fathers") would suggest that Paul came to Jerusalem when he was old enough to begin training under Gamaliel. *Gamaliel.* The most honored rabbi of the first century. Possibly he was the grandson of Hillel (see also 5:34–40).

22:4 *I persecuted the followers.* See 9:1–4. *this Way.* See 9:2 and note.

22:5 *high priest.* Caiaphas, the high priest over 20 years earlier, was now dead, and Ananias was high priest (see 23:2 and note); but the records of the high priest would show Paul's testimony to be true. *Council.* The Sanhedrin (see Mk 14:55 and note).

22:6–21 The fact that the account of Paul's conversion occurs three times in Acts (9:1–22; here; 26:9–18) confirms its importance for Luke. See note on Ge 24:34–49 for this common feature of ancient storytelling.

22:6 *About noon.* A detail not included in the earlier account (9:1–22).

22:8 *Who are you, Lord?* See note on 9:5. *persecuting.* See note on 9:4.

22:9 *did not understand the voice.* They heard the sound (9:7) but did not understand what was said.

22:12 *Ananias ... devout observer of the law.* Important to this audience (see note on Lk 1:6).

22:14 *to see the Righteous One.* Cf. 3:14; Lk 23:47 and notes. To see the resurrected Jesus was all-important to Paul (see 26:16; 1Co 9:1; 15:8). It was that experience that had convinced him of the truth of the gospel and that became the foundation of his theology.

22:16 *wash your sins away.* Baptism is the outward sign of an inward work of grace. The reality and the symbol are closely associated in the NT (see 2:38; Titus 3:5; 1Pe 3:21 and notes). The outward rite, however, does not produce the inward grace (cf. Ro 2:28–29; Eph 2:8–9; Php 3:4–9). See note on Ro 6:3–4.

22:17 *When I returned to Jerusalem.* Refers to the visit described in 9:26; Gal 1:17–18. *at the temple, I fell into a trance.* See Peter's trance (10:10; 11:5; cf. 2Co 12:3). Paul was not a blasphemer of the temple but continued to hold it in high honor.

22:20 *giving my approval.* Does not necessarily mean that Paul had to be a member of the Sanhedrin, though some have thought so (see note on 26:10). He could show his approval by allowing them to put their cloaks at his feet.

22:24 *commander.* See note on 21:31. *barracks.* See note on 21:37. *that he be flogged.* Not with the rod, as at Philippi

at him like this. 25 As they stretched him
out to flog him, Paul said to the centurion
standing there, "Is it legal for you to flog
a Roman citizen who hasn't even been
found guilty?"[o]
26 When the centurion heard this, he
went to the commander and reported it.
"What are you going to do?" he asked.
"This man is a Roman citizen."
27 The commander went to Paul and
asked, "Tell me, are you a Roman citizen?"
"Yes, I am," he answered.
28 Then the commander said, "I had to
pay a lot of money for my citizenship."
"But I was born a citizen," Paul replied.
29 Those who were about to interrogate
him[p] withdrew immediately. The commander himself was alarmed when he
realized that he had put Paul, a Roman
citizen,[q] in chains.[r]

Paul Before the Sanhedrin

30 The commander wanted to find out
exactly why Paul was being accused by
the Jews.[s] So the next day he released him[t]
and ordered the chief priests and all the
members of the Sanhedrin[u] to assemble.
Then he brought Paul and had him stand
before them.
23 Paul looked straight at the Sanhedrin[v] and said, "My brothers,[w] I
have fulfilled my duty to God in all good
conscience[x] to this day." 2 At this the high
priest Ananias[y] ordered those standing
near Paul to strike him on the mouth.[z]
3 Then Paul said to him, "God will strike
you, you whitewashed wall![a] You sit there
to judge me according to the law, yet you
yourself violate the law by commanding
that I be struck!"[b]
4 Those who were standing near Paul
said, "How dare you insult God's high
priest!"
5 Paul replied, "Brothers, I did not realize that he was the high priest; for it is
written: 'Do not speak evil about the ruler
of your people.'[a]"[c]
6 Then Paul, knowing that some of them
were Sadducees[d] and the others Pharisees,
called out in the Sanhedrin, "My brothers,[e]
I am a Pharisee,[f] descended from Pharisees. I stand on trial because of the hope
of the resurrection of the dead."[g] 7 When
he said this, a dispute broke out between
the Pharisees and the Sadducees, and the
assembly was divided. 8 (The Sadducees
say that there is no resurrection,[h] and that
there are neither angels nor spirits, but the
Pharisees believe all these things.)
9 There was a great uproar, and some of
the teachers of the law who were Pharisees[i] stood up and argued vigorously. "We
find nothing wrong with this man,"[j] they
said. "What if a spirit or an angel has spoken to him?"[k] 10 The dispute became so violent that the commander was afraid Paul
would be torn to pieces by them. He ordered the troops to go down and take him
away from them by force and bring him
into the barracks.[l]

22:25 [o] Ac 16:37 **22:29** [p] ver 24 [q] ver 24,25; Ac 16:38 [r] S Ac 21:33 **22:30** [s] Ac 23:28 [t] Ac 21:33 [u] S Mt 5:22 **23:1** [v] Ac 22:30 [w] S Ac 22:5 [x] Ac 24:16; 1Co 4:4; 2Co 1:12; 1Ti 1:5,19; 3:9; 2Ti 1:3; Heb 9:14; 10:22; 13:18; 1Pe 3:16,21 **23:2** [y] Ac 24:1 [z] Jn 18:22 **23:3** [a] Mt 23:27 [b] Lev 19:15; Dt 25:1,2; Jn 7:51 **23:5** [c] Ex 22:28 **23:6** [d] ver 7, 8; S Ac 4:1 [e] S Ac 22:5 [f] Ac 26:5; Php 3:5 [g] Ac 24:15,21; 26:8 **23:8** [h] Mt 22:23; 1Co 15:12 **23:9** [i] Mk 2:16 [j] ver 29; Jer 26:16; S Lk 23:4; Ac 25:25; 26:31; 28:18 [k] Ac 22:7, 17,18 **23:10** [l] S Ac 21:34

[a] 5 Exodus 22:28

(16:22–24), but with the scourge, a merciless instrument of torture. It was legal to use it to force a confession from a slave or foreigner but never from a Roman citizen. The scourge consisted of a whip of leather thongs with pieces of bone or metal attached to the ends (cf. Mk 15:15 and note).

22:25 *they stretched him out.* The Greek word used for tying a person to a post for whipping. *centurion.* See note on 10:1. *Roman citizen.* According to Roman law, all Roman citizens were assured exclusion from all degrading forms of punishment: beating with rods, scourging, crucifixion.

22:28 *pay a lot of money.* There were three ways to obtain Roman citizenship: (1) receive it as a reward for some outstanding service to Rome; (2) buy it at a considerable price; (3) be born into a family of Roman citizens. How Paul's father or an earlier ancestor had gained citizenship, no one knows. By 171 BC a large number of Jews were citizens of Tarsus, and in the time of Pompey (106–48) some of these could have received Roman citizenship as well.

22:29 *alarmed.* Cf. the same reaction of the magistrates in Philippi (16:38).

22:30 *he released him.* Paul was no longer bound, and presumably he would have been free completely if the Sanhedrin had not wished to detain him. *chief priests.* Those of the high priestly line of descent (mainly Sadducees; see note on Mt 2:4), but the Sanhedrin now included a considerable number of Pharisees. These men constituted the ruling body of the Jews. The Jewish court was respected by the Roman governor, whose approval had to be obtained before sentencing to capital punishment.

23:1 *Sanhedrin.* See notes on 5:21; 22:30. *brothers.* Fellow Jews (see note on 11:1). *good conscience.* A consistent claim of Paul (see 24:16; Ro 9:1; 1Co 4:4; 2Co 1:12; 2Ti 1:3).

23:2 *Ananias.* High priest AD 47–59, son of Nebedaeus. He is not to be confused with the high priest Annas (AD 6–15; see note on Lk 3:2). Ananias was noted for cruelty and violence. When the revolt against Rome broke out, he was assassinated by his own people.

23:3 *whitewashed wall!* Having an attractive exterior but filled with unclean contents, such as tombs holding dead bodies (see Mt 23:27); or walls that look substantial but fall before the winds (see Eze 13:10–12). It is a metaphor for a hypocrite.

23:5 *I did not realize that he was the high priest.* Explained in different ways: (1) Paul had poor eyesight (suggested by such passages as Gal 4:15; 6:11 [see note there]) and failed to see that the one who presided was the high priest. (2) He failed to discern that the one who presided was the high priest because on some occasions others had sat in his place. (3) He was using pure irony: A true high priest would not give such an order. (4) He refused to acknowledge that Ananias was the high priest under these circumstances.

23:6 *Sadducees.* See note on 4:1. They denied the resurrection, as well as the existence of angels and spirits (v. 8). *Pharisees.* See notes on Mt 3:7; Mk 2:16; Lk 5:17.

23:10 *commander.* See note on 21:31. *barracks.* See note on 21:37.

11 The following night the Lord stood
near Paul and said, "Take courage![m] As
you have testified about me in Jerusalem,
so you must also testify in Rome."[n]

The Plot to Kill Paul

12 The next morning some Jews formed
a conspiracy[o] and bound themselves with
an oath not to eat or drink until they had
killed Paul.[p] 13 More than forty men were
involved in this plot. 14 They went to the
chief priests and the elders and said, "We
have taken a solemn oath not to eat anything until we have killed Paul.[q] 15 Now
then, you and the Sanhedrin[r] petition the
commander to bring him before you on
the pretext of wanting more accurate information about his case. We are ready to
kill him before he gets here."
16 But when the son of Paul's sister
heard of this plot, he went into the barracks[s] and told Paul.
17 Then Paul called one of the centurions and said, "Take this young man
to the commander; he has something to
tell him." 18 So he took him to the commander.
The centurion said, "Paul, the prisoner,[t]
sent for me and asked me to bring this
young man to you because he has something to tell you."
19 The commander took the young man
by the hand, drew him aside and asked,
"What is it you want to tell me?"
20 He said: "Some Jews have agreed to
ask you to bring Paul before the Sanhedrin[u] tomorrow on the pretext of wanting
more accurate information about him.[v]
21 Don't give in to them, because more
than forty[w] of them are waiting in ambush
for him. They have taken an oath not to
eat or drink until they have killed him.[x]
They are ready now, waiting for your consent to their request."
22 The commander dismissed the young
man with this warning: "Don't tell anyone
that you have reported this to me."

Paul Transferred to Caesarea

23 Then he called two of his centurions
and ordered them, "Get ready a detachment of two hundred soldiers, seventy
horsemen and two hundred spearmen[a] to
go to Caesarea[y] at nine tonight.[z] 24 Provide
horses for Paul so that he may be taken
safely to Governor Felix."[a]
25 He wrote a letter as follows:

26 Claudius Lysias,

To His Excellency,[b] Governor Felix:

Greetings.[c]

27 This man was seized by the Jews
and they were about to kill him,[d] but
I came with my troops and rescued
him,[e] for I had learned that he is a Roman citizen.[f] 28 I wanted to know why
they were accusing him, so I brought
him to their Sanhedrin.[g] 29 I found that
the accusation had to do with questions about their law,[h] but there was
no charge against him[i] that deserved
death or imprisonment. 30 When I was
informed[j] of a plot[k] to be carried out
against the man, I sent him to you at
once. I also ordered his accusers[l] to
present to you their case against him.

31 So the soldiers, carrying out their
orders, took Paul with them during the
night and brought him as far as Antipatris. 32 The next day they let the cavalry[m]
go on with him, while they returned to the
barracks.[n] 33 When the cavalry[o] arrived in
Caesarea,[p] they delivered the letter to the
governor[q] and handed Paul over to him.
34 The governor read the letter and asked

23:11 [m] S Mt 14:27 [n] Ac 19:21; 28:23
23:12 [o] S Ac 20:3 [p] ver 14,21,30; Ac 25:3
23:14 [q] ver 12
23:15 [r] ver 1; Ac 22:30
23:16 [s] ver 10; S Ac 21:34
23:18 [t] S Eph 3:1
23:20 [u] ver 1 [v] ver 14,15
23:21 [w] ver 13 [x] ver 12,14
23:23 [y] S Ac 8:40 [z] ver 33
23:24 [a] ver 26, 33; Ac 24:1-3, 10; 25:14
23:26 [b] Lk 1:3; Ac 24:3; 26:25 [c] Ac 15:23
23:27 [d] Ac 21:32 [e] Ac 21:33 [f] Ac 22:25-29
23:28 [g] Ac 22:30
23:29 [h] Ac 18:15; 25:19 [i] S ver 9
23:30 [j] ver 20, 21 [k] S Ac 20:3 [l] ver 35; Ac 24:19; 25:16
23:32 [m] ver 23 [n] S Ac 21:34
23:33 [o] ver 23, 24 [p] S Ac 8:40 [q] ver 26

[a] *23* The meaning of the Greek for this word is uncertain.

23:11 *the Lord stood near.* In times of crisis and need for strength, Paul was given help (see 18:9; 22:18; 27:23; cf. 2Co 12:7–10 and notes).
23:12 *bound themselves with an oath.* These men were probably from the Zealots or the "terrorists" (see 21:38 and note) later responsible for revolt against Rome.
23:17 *centurions.* See note on 10:1.
23:22 *Don't tell anyone.* For the young man's own safety and because of the commander's plans to transfer Paul under cover of night (see v. 23).
23:23 *soldiers … horsemen … spearmen.* Heavily armed infantry, cavalry and lightly armed soldiers. The commander assigned 470 men to protect Paul, the Roman citizen (cf. 22:25–29)—but the Greek for "spearmen" is an obscure word that could perhaps be translated "additional mounts and pack animals" (see NIV text note).
23:24 *Governor Felix.* See note on v. 34.
23:27 *for I had learned that he is a Roman citizen.* Inserted to gain the commander's favor with Rome, but not a true statement, because the commander did not learn of Paul's citizenship until he was about to scourge him to gain information.
23:29 Cf. the false charge made against Paul before Gallio in Corinth (18:13–16).
23:30 *ordered his accusers to present to you their case.* He anticipated that the order would be given by the time the letter was delivered.
23:31 *Antipatris.* Rebuilt by Herod the Great and named for his father (Antipater). It was a military post between Samaria and Judea—30 miles from Jerusalem.
23:33 *Caesarea.* The headquarters of Roman rule for Samaria and Judea—28 miles from Antipatris (see note on 8:40).
23:34 *The governor.* Antonius Felix. The emperor Claudius had appointed him governor of Judea c. AD 52, a time when Felix's brother was the emperor's favorite minister. The brothers had formerly been slaves, then Freedmen, then high officials in government. The historian Tacitus

what province he was from. Learning that
he was from Cilicia,[r] 35he said, "I will hear
your case when your accusers[s] get here."
Then he ordered that Paul be kept under
guard[t] in Herod's palace.

Paul's Trial Before Felix

24 Five days later the high priest Ananias[u] went down to Caesarea with
some of the elders and a lawyer named
Tertullus, and they brought their charges[v]
against Paul before the governor.[w] 2When
Paul was called in, Tertullus presented
his case before Felix: "We have enjoyed
a long period of peace under you, and
your foresight has brought about reforms
in this nation. 3Everywhere and in every
way, most excellent[x] Felix, we acknowledge this with profound gratitude. 4But in
order not to weary you further, I would
request that you be kind enough to hear
us briefly.

5"We have found this man to be a troublemaker, stirring up riots[y] among the
Jews[z] all over the world. He is a ringleader
of the Nazarene[a] sect[b] 6and even tried to
desecrate the temple;[c] so we seized him.
[7][a] 8By examining him yourself you will
be able to learn the truth about all these
charges we are bringing against him."

9The other Jews joined in the accusation,[d] asserting that these things were true.

10When the governor[e] motioned for him
to speak, Paul replied: "I know that for a
number of years you have been a judge
over this nation; so I gladly make my defense. 11You can easily verify that no more
than twelve days[f] ago I went up to Jerusalem to worship. 12My accusers did not find
me arguing with anyone at the temple,[g] or
stirring up a crowd[h] in the synagogues or
anywhere else in the city. 13And they cannot prove to you the charges they are now
making against me.[i] 14However, I admit
that I worship the God of our ancestors[j] as
a follower of the Way,[k] which they call a
sect.[l] I believe everything that is in accordance with the Law and that is written in
the Prophets,[m] 15and I have the same hope
in God as these men themselves have, that
there will be a resurrection[n] of both the
righteous and the wicked.[o] 16So I strive always to keep my conscience clear[p] before
God and man.

17"After an absence of several years, I
came to Jerusalem to bring my people gifts
for the poor[q] and to present offerings. 18I
was ceremonially clean[r] when they found
me in the temple courts doing this. There
was no crowd with me, nor was I involved
in any disturbance.[s] 19But there are some
Jews from the province of Asia,[t] who ought
to be here before you and bring charges if
they have anything against me.[u] 20Or these
who are here should state what crime they
found in me when I stood before the Sanhedrin— 21unless it was this one thing I

23:34 [r]S Ac 6:9; 21:39 **23:35** [s]ver 30; Ac 24:19; 25:16 [t]Ac 24:27 **24:1** [u]Ac 23:2 [v]Ac 23:30,35 [w]S Ac 23:24 **24:3** [x]Lk 1:3; Ac 23:26; 26:25 **24:5** [y]Ac 16:20; 17:6 [z]Ac 21:28 [a]S Mk 1:24 [b]ver 14; Ac 26:5; 28:22 **24:6** [c]Ac 21:28 **24:9** [d]S 1Th 2:16 **24:10** [e]S Ac 23:24 **24:11** [f]Ac 21:27; ver 1 **24:12** [g]Ac 25:8; 28:17 [h]ver 18 **24:13** [i]Ac 25:7 **24:14** [j]S Ac 3:13 [k]S Ac 9:2 [l]S ver 5 [m]Ac 26:6,22; 28:23 **24:15** [n]Ac 23:6; 28:20 [o]S Mt 25:46 **24:16** [p]S Ac 23:1 **24:17** [q]Ac 11:29,30; Ro 15:25-28, 31; 1Co 16:1-4, 15; 2Co 8:1-4; Gal 2:10 **24:18** [r]Ac 21:26 [s]ver 12 **24:19** [t]S Ac 2:9 [u]Ac 23:30

[a] *6-8* Some manuscripts include here *him, and we would have judged him in accordance with our law. 7But the commander Lysias came and took him from us with much violence, 8ordering his accusers to come before you.*

said of Felix, "He held the power of a tyrant with the disposition of a slave." He married three queens in succession, one of whom was Drusilla (see note on 24:24). *from Cilicia.* If Paul had come from a province nearby, Felix might have turned him over for trial under another's jurisdiction.

23:35 *Herod's palace.* Erected as a royal residence by Herod the Great but now used as a Roman praetorium—the headquarters of the local Roman governor. Praetoria were located in Rome (Php 1:13), Ephesus, Jerusalem (Jn 18:28; see note there), Caesarea and other parts of the empire.

24:1 *Five days later.* After the departure from Jerusalem. This would allow just enough time for a messenger to go from Caesarea to Jerusalem, the Sanhedrin to appoint their representatives, and the appointees to make the return journey to Caesarea. *Ananias.* See note on 23:2. The high priest himself made the 60-mile journey to supervise the case personally. *elders.* The Sanhedrin was made up of 71 elders. The designation was used of both the religious and the political councils. See notes on Ex 3:16; 2Sa 3:17; Joel 1:2; Mt 15:2. *lawyer.* Lit. "orator." In a court trial one trained in forensic rhetoric would serve as an attorney at law. *Tertullus.* A common variant of the name Tertius. Possibly he was a Roman but more likely a Hellenistic Jew familiar with the procedures of the Roman court.

24:2–3 *long period of peace … with profound gratitude.* The expected eulogy with which to introduce a speech before a judge. In his six years in office Felix had eliminated bands of robbers, thwarted organized assassins and crushed a movement led by an Egyptian (see note on 21:38). But in general his record was not good. He was recalled by Rome two years later because of misrule. His reforms and improvements are hard to identify historically.

24:5 *troublemaker … ringleader of the Nazarene sect.* To excite dissension in the empire was treason against Caesar. To be a leader of a religious sect without Roman approval was contrary to law. *Nazarene sect.* Christianity.

24:6 *tried to desecrate the temple.* The charge is now qualified as merely an attempt (see 21:28 and note).

24:10 Paul's reserved introduction lacks the flattery employed by Tertullus (vv. 2–4).

24:11 *twelve days ago.* Paul answers each accusation. He was not a troublemaker, and he had not been involved in disturbances. He had but recently arrived in Jerusalem. He had spent five days in Caesarea and nearly seven in Jerusalem.

24:14 *worship … God … as a follower of the Way.* Paul admits to his part in the Way, but he still believes the Law and the Prophets. He shares the same hope as the Jews—resurrection and judgment (v. 15).

24:16 *conscience clear.* See note on 23:1.

24:17 *to bring my people gifts for the poor.* The only explicit reference in Acts to the collection that was so important to Paul (see note on 20:4). *to present offerings.* May refer to Paul's help in sponsoring those who were fulfilling their vows (see 21:24 and note). He also may have intended to present offerings for himself.

24:19 *Jews from the province of Asia.* See 21:27–29. The absence of these Asian Jews would seem to suggest that they could not substantiate their accusations.

shouted as I stood in their presence: 'It is concerning the resurrection of the dead that I am on trial before you today.' "[v]

22 Then Felix, who was well acquainted with the Way,[w] adjourned the proceedings. "When Lysias the commander comes," he said, "I will decide your case." 23 He ordered the centurion to keep Paul under guard[x] but to give him some freedom[y] and permit his friends to take care of his needs.[z]

24 Several days later Felix came with his wife Drusilla, who was Jewish. He sent for Paul and listened to him as he spoke about faith in Christ Jesus.[a] 25 As Paul talked about righteousness, self-control[b] and the judgment[c] to come, Felix was afraid[d] and said, "That's enough for now! You may leave. When I find it convenient, I will send for you." 26 At the same time he was hoping that Paul would offer him a bribe, so he sent for him frequently and talked with him.

27 When two years had passed, Felix was succeeded by Porcius Festus,[e] but because Felix wanted to grant a favor to the Jews,[f] he left Paul in prison.[g]

Paul's Trial Before Festus

25 Three days after arriving in the province, Festus[h] went up from Caesarea[i] to Jerusalem, 2 where the chief priests and the Jewish leaders appeared before him and presented the charges against Paul.[j] 3 They requested Festus, as a favor to them, to have Paul transferred to Jerusalem, for they were preparing an ambush to kill him along the way.[k] 4 Festus answered, "Paul is being held[l] at Caesarea,[m] and I myself am going there soon. 5 Let some of your leaders come with me, and if the man has done anything wrong, they can press charges against him there."

6 After spending eight or ten days with them, Festus went down to Caesarea. The next day he convened the court[n] and ordered that Paul be brought before him.[o] 7 When Paul came in, the Jews who had come down from Jerusalem stood around him. They brought many serious charges against him,[p] but they could not prove them.[q]

8 Then Paul made his defense: "I have done nothing wrong against the Jewish law or against the temple[r] or against Caesar."

9 Festus, wishing to do the Jews a favor,[s] said to Paul, "Are you willing to go up to Jerusalem and stand trial before me there on these charges?"[t]

Roman coin with the portrait of Emperor Nero (AD 54–68), who was known for torturing and executing Christians of the early church.
Z. Radovan/www.BibleLandPictures.com

24:21 [v] Ac 23:6 **24:22** [w] S Ac 9:2 **24:23** [x] Ac 23:35 [y] Ac 28:16 [z] Ac 23:16; 27:3 **24:24** [a] S Ac 20:21 **24:25** [b] Gal 5:23; 1Th 5:6; 1Pe 4:7; 5:8; 2Pe 1:6 [c] Ac 10:42 [d] Jer 36:16 **24:27** [e] Ac 25:1, 4,9,14 [f] Ac 12:3; 25:9 [g] Ac 23:35; 25:14 **25:1** [h] S Ac 24:27 [i] S Ac 8:40 **25:2** [j] ver 15; Ac 24:1 **25:3** [k] S Ac 20:3 **25:4** [l] Ac 24:23 [m] S Ac 8:40 **25:6** [n] ver 17 [o] ver 10 **25:7** [p] Mk 15:3; Lk 23:2,10; Ac 24:5,6 [q] Ac 24:13 **25:8** [r] Ac 6:13; 24:12; 28:17 **25:9** [s] Ac 24:27; 12:3 [t] ver 20

24:21 *concerning the resurrection.* Paul again introduces the point of contention between the Pharisees and Sadducees (see 23:6–8; see also chart, p. 1631).
24:22 *well acquainted with the Way.* Felix could not have governed Judea and Samaria for six years without becoming familiar with the place and activities of the Christians.
24:23 *to give him some freedom.* Perhaps Paul was under house arrest similar to what he would experience while awaiting trial in Rome (28:30–31)—in recognition of the fact that he was a Roman citizen who had not been found guilty of any crime.
24:24 *Drusilla.* Felix's third wife, daughter of Herod Agrippa I. At age 15 she married Azizus, king of Emesa, but deserted him for Felix a year later. Her son, also named Agrippa, died in the eruption of Vesuvius (AD 79).
24:25 *Felix was afraid.* Hearing of "righteousness, self-control and the judgment," Felix looked at his past life and was filled with fear. He had a spark of sincerity and concern. *When I find it convenient.* Lust, pride, greed and selfish ambition made it continually inconvenient to change.
24:26 *offer him a bribe.* Felix supposed that Paul had access to considerable funds. He had heard of his bringing an offering to the Jewish Christians in Jerusalem (see v. 17 and note). So he wanted Paul to give him money in order to secure his release. Paul no longer had the money, nor would he offer a bribe if he had it.
24:27 *Felix was succeeded by … Festus.* Felix was recalled to Rome in AD 59/60 to answer for disturbances and irregularities in his rule, such as his handling of riots between Jewish and Syrian inhabitants. Festus is not mentioned in existing historical records before his arrival in Judea. He died in office after two years, but his record for that time shows wisdom and honesty superior to both his predecessor, Felix, and his successor, Albinus. *to grant a favor to the Jews.* Felix did not want to incite more anger among the Jews, whom he would be facing in Roman court shortly. To release Paul from prison would do just that.
25:1 *from Caesarea to Jerusalem.* Sixty miles, a two-day trip. Festus was anxious to go immediately to the center of Jewish rule and worship.
25:2 *chief priests and the Jewish leaders.* The Sanhedrin (see note on Mk 14:55).
25:3 *ambush.* Probably the same group that had earlier made a vow to take Paul's life (see 23:12 and note).
25:6 *convened the court.* To make his decision binding as a formal ruling.
25:7 *charges … they could not prove.* Again, as in the first hearing, Paul's adversaries produced no witnesses or evidence of any kind (see 24:2–9).
25:8 *nothing … against the Jewish law.* Paul had respect for the law (see Ro 7:12; 8:3–4; 1Co 9:20 and note). *against the temple.* See notes on 21:28–29. Paul had not defied its customs by taking Trophimus into forbidden areas (21:29). Jesus had prophesied its destruction, but he was not responsible for its plight (Lk 21:5–6). *against Caesar.* Paul proclaimed the kingdom of God, but not as a political rival of Rome (cf. 17:6–7). He advocated respect for law and order (see Ro 13:1–7) and prayer for civil rulers (see 1Ti 2:1–2).
25:9 *Are you willing to go up to Jerusalem …?* Obviously not. Festus had said that the trial would be before him; so Paul

10 Paul answered: "I am now standing
before Caesar's court, where I ought to be
tried. I have not done any wrong to the
Jews,[u] as you yourself know very well. 11 If,
however, I am guilty of doing anything deserving death, I do not refuse to die. But
if the charges brought against me by these
Jews are not true, no one has the right to
hand me over to them. I appeal to Caesar!"[v]
12 After Festus had conferred with his
council, he declared: "You have appealed
to Caesar. To Caesar you will go!"

Festus Consults King Agrippa

13 A few days later King Agrippa and
Bernice arrived at Caesarea[w] to pay their
respects to Festus. 14 Since they were
spending many days there, Festus discussed Paul's case with the king. He said:
"There is a man here whom Felix left as
a prisoner.[x] 15 When I went to Jerusalem,
the chief priests and the elders of the Jews
brought charges against him[y] and asked
that he be condemned.
16 "I told them that it is not the Roman
custom to hand over anyone before they
have faced their accusers and have had an
opportunity to defend themselves against
the charges.[z] 17 When they came here with
me, I did not delay the case, but convened
the court the next day and ordered the
man to be brought in.[a] 18 When his accusers got up to speak, they did not charge
him with any of the crimes I had expected.
19 Instead, they had some points of dispute[b]
with him about their own religion[c] and
about a dead man named Jesus who Paul
claimed was alive. 20 I was at a loss how to
investigate such matters; so I asked if he
would be willing to go to Jerusalem and
stand trial there on these charges.[d] 21 But
when Paul made his appeal to be held over
for the Emperor's decision, I ordered him
held until I could send him to Caesar."[e]
22 Then Agrippa said to Festus, "I would
like to hear this man myself."
He replied, "Tomorrow you will hear
him."[f]

Paul Before Agrippa

26:12-18pp — Ac 9:3-8; 22:6-11

23 The next day Agrippa and Bernice[g]
came with great pomp and entered the
audience room with the high-ranking
military officers and the prominent men of
the city. At the command of Festus, Paul
was brought in. 24 Festus said: "King Agrippa, and all who are present with us, you
see this man! The whole Jewish community[h] has petitioned me about him in Jerusalem and here in Caesarea, shouting that he
ought not to live any longer.[i] 25 I found he
had done nothing deserving of death,[j] but
because he made his appeal to the Emper-
or[k] I decided to send him to Rome. 26 But I
have nothing definite to write to His Majesty about him. Therefore I have brought
him before all of you, and especially before you, King Agrippa, so that as a result
of this investigation I may have something
to write. 27 For I think it is unreasonable to
send a prisoner on to Rome without spec-
ifying the charges against him."

25:10 [u] ver 8 **25:11** [v] ver 21, 25; Ac 26:32; 28:19 **25:13** [w] S Ac 8:40 **25:14** [x] Ac 24:27 **25:15** [y] ver 2; Ac 24:1 **25:16** [z] ver 4, 5; Ac 23:30 **25:17** [a] ver 6, 10 **25:19** [b] Ac 18:15; 23:29 [c] Ac 17:22 **25:20** [d] ver 9 **25:21** [e] ver 11, 12 **25:22** [f] Ac 9:15 **25:23** [g] ver 13; Ac 26:30 **25:24** [h] ver 2, 3, 7 [i] Ac 22:22 **25:25** [j] S Ac 23:9 [k] S ver 11

insisted that he was then standing in the Roman civil court (v. 10). He wanted to keep his trial there rather than suffer at the hands of a Jewish religious court. As a Roman citizen, he could refuse to go to a local provincial court; instead, he looked to a higher Roman court.

25:11 *I appeal to Caesar!* Nero had become the emperor by this time. It was the right of every Roman citizen to have his case heard before Caesar himself (or his representative) in Rome. This was the highest court of appeal, and winning such a case could have led to more than just Paul's acquittal. It could have resulted in official recognition of Christianity as distinct from Judaism.

25:12 *his council.* The officials and legal experts who made up the advisory council for the Roman governor.

25:13 *King Agrippa.* Herod Agrippa II. He was 17 years old at the death of his father in AD 44 (12:23). Being too young to succeed his father, he was replaced by Roman governors. Eight years later, however, a gradual extension of territorial authority began. Ultimately he ruled over territory north and northeast of the Sea of Galilee, over several Galilean cities and over some cities in Perea. At the Jewish revolt, when Jerusalem fell, he was on the side of the Romans. He died c. AD 100 — the last of the Herods. *Bernice.* The oldest daughter of Agrippa I, she was 16 years old at his death. When only 13, she married her uncle, Herod of Chalcis, and had two sons. When Herod died, she lived with her brother, Agrippa II. To silence rumors that she was living in incest with her brother, she married Polemon, king of Cilicia, but left him soon afterward to return to Agrippa. She became the mistress of the emperor Vespasian's son Titus but was later ignored by him. *to pay their respects.* It was customary for rulers to pay a complimentary visit to a new ruler at the time of his assignment. It was advantageous to each that they get along (cf. Herod Antipas and Pilate, Lk 23:6 – 12).

25:19 *religion.* Or "superstition," the same word used by Paul in 17:22 (see note there).

25:22 *I would like to hear.* Agrippa had been wishing to hear Paul (cf. Antipas wanting to see Jesus, Lk 9:9; 23:8).

25:23 *audience room.* Not the judgment hall, for this was not a court trial. It was in an auditorium appropriate for the pomp of the occasion, with a king, his sister, the Roman governor and the outstanding leaders of both the Jews and the Roman government present. *high-ranking military officers.* Five regiments were stationed at Caesarea, so their five commanders would have been in attendance (see note on 21:31).

25:26 *I have nothing definite.* Festus was required to send Caesar an explicit report on the case when an appeal was made. He hoped for some help from Agrippa in this matter. This was not an official trial but a special hearing to satisfy the curiosity of Agrippa and provide an assessment for Festus. *especially before you, King Agrippa.* He would be sensitive to differences between Pharisees and Sadducees, expectations of the Messiah, differences between Jews and Christians, and Jewish customs pertinent to these problems (see 26:2 – 3 and note on 26:3).

26 Then Agrippa said to Paul, “You
have permission to speak for yourself.”[l]
So Paul motioned with his hand[m] and began his defense: 2 “King Agrippa, I consider
myself fortunate to stand before you[n] today
as I make my defense against all the accusations of the Jews,[o] 3 and especially so because you are well acquainted with all the
Jewish customs[p] and controversies.[q] Therefore, I beg you to listen to me patiently.
4 “The Jewish people all know the way
I have lived ever since I was a child,[r] from
the beginning of my life in my own country, and also in Jerusalem. 5 They have
known me for a long time[s] and can testify,
if they are willing, that I conformed to the
strictest sect[t] of our religion, living as a
Pharisee.[u] 6 And now it is because of my
hope[v] in what God has promised our ancestors[w] that I am on trial today. 7 This is
the promise our twelve tribes[x] are hoping
to see fulfilled as they earnestly serve God
day and night.[y] King Agrippa, it is because
of this hope that these Jews are accusing
me.[z] 8 Why should any of you consider it
incredible that God raises the dead?[a]
9 “I too was convinced[b] that I ought to do
all that was possible to oppose[c] the name
of Jesus of Nazareth.[d] 10 And that is just
what I did in Jerusalem. On the authority
of the chief priests I put many of the Lord’s
people[e] in prison,[f] and when they were
put to death, I cast my vote against them.[g]
11 Many a time I went from one synagogue
to another to have them punished,[h] and I
tried to force them to blaspheme. I was so
obsessed with persecuting them that I even
hunted them down in foreign cities.
12 “On one of these journeys I was going
to Damascus with the authority and commission of the chief priests. 13 About noon,
King Agrippa, as I was on the road, I saw
a light from heaven, brighter than the sun,
blazing around me and my companions.
14 We all fell to the ground, and I heard
a voice[i] saying to me in Aramaic,[a][j] ‘Saul,
Saul, why do you persecute me? It is hard
for you to kick against the goads.’
15 “Then I asked, ‘Who are you, Lord?’
“ ‘I am Jesus, whom you are persecuting,’
the Lord replied. 16 ‘Now get up and stand
on your feet.[k] I have appeared to you to
appoint you as a servant and as a witness
of what you have seen and will see of me.[l]
17 I will rescue you[m] from your own people
and from the Gentiles.[n] I am sending you to
them 18 to open their eyes[o] and turn them
from darkness to light,[p] and from the power
of Satan to God, so that they may receive
forgiveness of sins[q] and a place among
those who are sanctified by faith in me.’[r]
19 “So then, King Agrippa, I was not disobedient[s] to the vision from heaven. 20 First
to those in Damascus,[t] then to those in
Jerusalem[u] and in all Judea, and then to
the Gentiles,[v] I preached that they should
repent[w] and turn to God and demonstrate
their repentance by their deeds.[x] 21 That is
why some Jews seized me[y] in the temple
courts and tried to kill me.[z] 22 But God has
helped me to this very day; so I stand here
and testify to small and great alike. I am
saying nothing beyond what the prophets
and Moses said would happen[a]— 23 that
the Messiah would suffer[b] and, as the first
to rise from the dead,[c] would bring the
message of light to his own people and to
the Gentiles.”[d]

26:1 [l] Ac 9:15; 25:22 [m] S Ac 12:17 **26:2** [n] Ps 119:46 [o] Ac 24:1,5; 25:2,7,11 **26:3** [p] ver 7; S Ac 6:14 [q] Ac 25:19 **26:4** [r] Gal 1:13, 14; Php 3:5 **26:5** [s] Ac 22:3 [t] S Ac 24:5 [u] Ac 23:6; Php 3:5 **26:6** [v] Ac 23:6; 24:15; 28:20 [w] S Ac 13:32; Ro 15:8 **26:7** [x] Jas 1:1 [y] 1Th 3:10; 1Ti 5:5 [z] ver 2 **26:8** [a] Ac 23:6 **26:9** [b] 1Ti 1:13 [c] Jn 16:2 [d] S Jn 15:21 **26:10** [e] S Ac 9:13 [f] S Ac 8:3; 9:2,14,21 [g] Ac 22:20 **26:11** [h] S Mt 10:17 **26:14** [i] Ac 9:7 [j] S Jn 5:2 **26:16** [k] Eze 2:1; Da 10:11 [l] Ac 22:14,15 **26:17** [m] Jer 1:8, 19 [n] S Ac 9:15; S 13:46 **26:18** [o] Isa 35:5 [p] Ps 18:28; Isa 42:7, 16; Eph 5:8; Col 1:13; 1Pe 2:9 [q] Lk 24:47; Ac 2:38 [r] S Ac 20:21,32 **26:19** [s] Isa 50:5 **26:20** [t] Ac 9:19-25 [u] Ac 9:26-29; 22:17-20 [v] S Ac 9:15; S 13:46 [w] Ac 3:19 [x] Jer 18:11; 35:15; Mt 3:8; Lk 3:8

[a] 14 Or *Hebrew*

26:21 [y] Ac 21:27,30 [z] Ac 21:31 **26:22** [a] S Lk 24:27,44; Ac 10:43; 24:14 **26:23** [b] S Mt 16:21 [c] 1Co 15:20,23; Col 1:18; Rev 1:5 [d] S Lk 2:32

26:1 *permission to speak.* Agrippa gave the permission because Festus allowed him to have charge of the hearing.
26:3 *well acquainted with all the Jewish customs.* Agrippa as king controlled the temple treasury and the investments of the high priest and could appoint the high priest. He was consulted by the Romans on religious matters. This is one of the reasons Festus wanted him to assess Paul (see note on 25:26).
26:5 *living as a Pharisee.* Cf. Gal 1:14; Php 3:4–6.
26:6 *my hope in what God has promised.* Including God’s kingdom, the Messiah and the resurrection (see v. 8).
26:8 Paul had been speaking to Agrippa but at this point must have addressed others as well, such as Festus and the commanders (see note on 21:31), who did not believe in the resurrection. Agrippa was also allied with the Sadducees, whom he appointed high priests, and probably rejected both the resurrection of Christ and resurrection in general.
26:10 *I cast my vote against them.* Does not necessarily mean that Paul was a member of the Sanhedrin (see note on 22:20). He may have been appointed to a commission to carry out the prosecution (see v. 12).
26:11 *force them to blaspheme.* He tried to force them either to curse Jesus or to confess publicly that Jesus is the Son of God, in which case they could be condemned for blasphemy, a sufficient cause for death (see Mt 26:63–66).
26:12 *I was going to Damascus.* Again Paul gives an account of his conversion (see 9:1–19; 22:4–21 and notes).
26:14 *I heard a voice.* See notes on 9:7; 22:9. *to kick against the goads.* A Greek proverb for useless resistance—the ox succeeds only in hurting itself.
26:17 *to them.* Not only to the Jews but also to the Gentiles (see 22:21; Gal 1:15–16). His mission was from God (Gal 1:1).
26:18 *from darkness to light.* A figure especially characteristic of Paul (see Ro 13:12; 2Co 4:6; Eph 5:8–14; Col 1:13; 1Th 5:5). *Satan.* See Mt 16:23; 1Jn 3:8 and notes. *sanctified.* See note on 1Co 1:2.
26:20 *demonstrate … repentance by … deeds.* Works do not secure salvation either before or after conversion, but they are a sign of the reality of repentance (cf. 3:19 and note).
26:22 *the prophets and Moses.* The OT Scriptures (see Lk 24:27,44 and note on 24:44).
26:23 *the first to rise from the dead.* The firstfruits of the dead—to die no more (see 1Co 15:20; Col 1:18 and notes). *to the Gentiles.* Cf. Isa 49:6.

24 At this point Festus interrupted Paul's
defense. "You are out of your mind,[e]
Paul!" he shouted. "Your great learning[f] is
driving you insane."
25 "I am not insane, most excellent[g] Festus," Paul replied. "What I am saying is
true and reasonable. 26 The king is familiar
with these things,[h] and I can speak freely
to him. I am convinced that none of this
has escaped his notice, because it was not
done in a corner. 27 King Agrippa, do you
believe the prophets? I know you do."
28 Then Agrippa said to Paul, "Do you
think that in such a short time you can
persuade me to be a Christian?"[i]
29 Paul replied, "Short time or long—I
pray to God that not only you but all who
are listening to me today may become
what I am, except for these chains."[j]
30 The king rose, and with him the governor and Bernice[k] and those sitting with
them. 31 After they left the room, they began saying to one another, "This man is
not doing anything that deserves death or
imprisonment."[l]
32 Agrippa said to Festus, "This man
could have been set free[m] if he had not appealed to Caesar."[n]

26:24 [e] S Jn 10:20; S 1Co 4:10 [f] Jn 7:15
26:25 [g] S Ac 23:26
26:26 [h] ver 3
26:28 [i] Ac 11:26
26:29 [j] S Ac 21:33
26:30 [k] Ac 25:23
26:31 [l] S Ac 23:9
26:32 [m] Ac 28:18 [n] S Ac 25:11

27:1 [o] S Ac 16:10 [p] Ac 18:2; 25:12, 25 [q] Ac 10:1
27:2 [r] S Ac 2:9 [s] S Ac 19:29 [t] S Ac 16:9 [u] S Ac 17:1
27:3 [v] Mt 11:21 [w] ver 43 [x] Ac 24:23; 28:16
27:4 [y] ver 7
27:5 [z] S Ac 6:9 [a] S Ac 2:10
27:6 [b] Ac 28:11 [c] ver 1; Ac 18:2; 25:12, 25
27:7 [d] ver 4 [e] ver 12, 13, 21; Titus 1:5

Paul Sails for Rome

27 When it was decided that we[o]
would sail for Italy,[p] Paul and some
other prisoners were handed over to a centurion named Julius, who belonged to the
Imperial Regiment.[q] 2 We boarded a ship
from Adramyttium about to sail for ports
along the coast of the province of Asia,[r]
and we put out to sea. Aristarchus,[s] a Macedonian[t] from Thessalonica,[u] was with us.
3 The next day we landed at Sidon;[v] and
Julius, in kindness to Paul,[w] allowed him to
go to his friends so they might provide for
his needs.[x] 4 From there we put out to sea
again and passed to the lee of Cyprus because the winds were against us.[y] 5 When
we had sailed across the open sea off the
coast of Cilicia[z] and Pamphylia,[a] we landed at Myra in Lycia. 6 There the centurion
found an Alexandrian ship[b] sailing for Italy[c] and put us on board. 7 We made slow
headway for many days and had difficulty
arriving off Cnidus. When the wind did
not allow us to hold our course,[d] we sailed
to the lee of Crete,[e] opposite Salmone. 8 We
moved along the coast with difficulty and
came to a place called Fair Havens, near
the town of Lasea.

26:24 *You are out of your mind.* See Jn 10:20; cf. 1Co 14:23. The governor felt that Paul's education and reading of the sacred Scriptures had led him to a mania about prophecy and resurrection.
26:26 *not done in a corner.* This gospel is based on actual events, lived out in historical times and places. The king must himself attest to the truth of what Paul has affirmed.
26:27 *do you believe the prophets?* King Agrippa was faced with a dilemma. If he said "Yes," Paul would press him to recognize their fulfillment in Jesus; if he said "No," he would be in trouble with the devout Jews, who accepted the message of the prophets as the very word of God.
26:28 *in such a short time you can persuade me to be a Christian?* His question is an evasion of Paul's question and an answer to what he anticipates Paul's next question will be. His point is that he will not be persuaded by such a brief statement. *Christian.* See note on 11:26.
26:29 *these chains.* Paul was still bound as a prisoner.
26:31 *not doing anything that deserves death or imprisonment.* Luke calls attention to the officials' agreement on Paul's innocence (cf. Herod's and Pilate's agreement on Jesus' innocence in Lk 23:13–15).
27:1 See map, pp. 2528–2529, at the end of this study Bible; see also map, p. 1879. *we would sail.* The "we" narrative (see note on 16:10) begins again (the last such reference appeared in 21:18). Probably Luke had spent the two years of Paul's Caesarean imprisonment nearby, and now he joins those ready to sail. *centurion named Julius.* Otherwise unknown. Perhaps he was given the specific duties of an imperial courier, which included delivering prisoners for trial. *Imperial Regiment.* The Roman legions were designated by number, and each of the regiments also had designations. The identification "Augustan," or "Imperial" (belonging to the empire), was common (see note on 10:1).
27:2 *Adramyttium.* A harbor on the west coast of the province of Asia, southeast of Troas, east of Assos. *ports along the coast.* At one of these stops Julius would plan to transfer to a ship going to Rome. *Aristarchus.* See 19:29 and note; see also Phm 24, which indicates that he was in Rome with Paul later.
27:3 *Sidon.* About 70 miles north of Caesarea.
27:4 *the lee of Cyprus.* They sought the protecting shelter of the island by sailing north on the eastern side of the island, then west along the northern side. *winds were against us.* Prevailing winds in summer were westerly.
27:5 *Cilicia and Pamphylia.* Adjoining provinces on the southern shore of Asia Minor. From Sidon to Myra along this coast would normally be a voyage of 10 to 15 days. *Myra in Lycia.* The growing importance of the city of Myra was associated with the development of navigation. Instead of hugging the coast from point to point, more ships were daring to run directly from Alexandria in Egypt to harbors like Myra on the southern coast of Asia Minor. It was considerably out of the way on the trip to Rome from Egypt, but the prevailing westerly wind would not allow a direct voyage toward the west. Myra became an important grain-storage city as well.
27:6 *Alexandrian ship.* A ship from Egypt (with grain cargo, v. 38) bound for Rome. Paul and the others could have remained on the first ship and continued up the coast to Macedonia, then taken the land route over the Egnatian Way across Greece and on to Rome, entering Italy at the port of Brundisium. But Julius chose to change ships here, accepting the opportunity of a direct voyage to Rome. Some suggest that Aristarchus from Macedonia stayed with the first ship and went to his home area to tell of Paul's coming imprisonment in Rome. If so, he later joined Paul in Rome (see note on v. 2).
27:7 *Cnidus.* From Myra to Cnidus at the southwest point of Asia Minor was about 170 miles. The trip probably took another 10 to 15 days. *Crete.* An island 160 miles long. Rather than cross the open sea to Greece, the ship was forced to bear south, seeking to sail west with the protection of the island of Crete on the north ("to the lee of Crete"). *Salmone.* A promontory on the northeast point of Crete.
27:8 *Fair Havens ... Lasea.* The former was a port about midway on the southern coast of Crete, and the latter was a city about five miles away (see inset map, p. 1879).

9 Much time had been lost, and sailing
had already become dangerous because by
now it was after the Day of Atonement.[a][f] So
Paul warned them, 10 "Men, I can see that
our voyage is going to be disastrous and
bring great loss to ship and cargo, and to
our own lives also."[g] 11 But the centurion, instead of listening to what Paul said, followed
the advice of the pilot and of the owner of
the ship. 12 Since the harbor was unsuitable
to winter in, the majority decided that we
should sail on, hoping to reach Phoenix and
winter there. This was a harbor in Crete,[h]
facing both southwest and northwest.

27:9 [f] Lev 16:29-31; 23:27-29; Nu 29:7
27:10 [g] ver 21
27:12 [h] S ver 7
27:14 [i] Mk 4:37
27:16 [j] ver 30

The Storm

13 When a gentle south wind began to
blow, they saw their opportunity; so they
weighed anchor and sailed along the shore
of Crete. 14 Before very long, a wind of
hurricane force,[i] called the Northeaster,
swept down from the island. 15 The ship
was caught by the storm and could not
head into the wind; so we gave way to
it and were driven along. 16 As we passed
to the lee of a small island called Cauda,
we were hardly able to make the lifeboat[j]

[a] 9 That is, Yom Kippur

27:9 *Atonement.* The Jewish Day of Atonement fell in the latter part of September or in October. The usual sailing season by Jewish calculation lasted from Pentecost (May-June) to Tabernacles, which was five days after Atonement. The Romans considered sailing after Sept. 15 doubtful and after Nov. 11 suicidal.
27:12 *Phoenix.* A major city that served as a wintering place, having a harbor with protection against the storms.
27:13–44 Luke's magnificent account of the storm at sea is possibly intended to be more than just an interesting story well told. Here at the climax of his account of the spread of the gospel from Jerusalem to Rome, especially through the labors of the apostle Paul, he provides in cameo an exquisite depiction of the state of the world seen from the perspective of Paul's gospel: The peoples of the world (represented by the ship's passengers) stand under the threat of God's judgment (represented by the terrible storm), with Paul and what he represents being their only hope. On board are representatives of the world's economic, military and political powers and those skilled in navigating the sea, but none of these can master the raging storm to save themselves or their possessions. They escape only as they follow Paul's instructions. Cf. note on Jnh 1:4–16.
27:14 *Northeaster.* A typhoon-like, east-northeast wind (the Euroquilo), which drove the ship away from its destination (see inset map below).
27:16 *Cauda.* About 23 miles from Crete. This provided enough shelter to make preparation against the storm. *to*

PAUL'S JOURNEY TO **ROME** c. AD 59–60 (Ac 27:1–28:16)

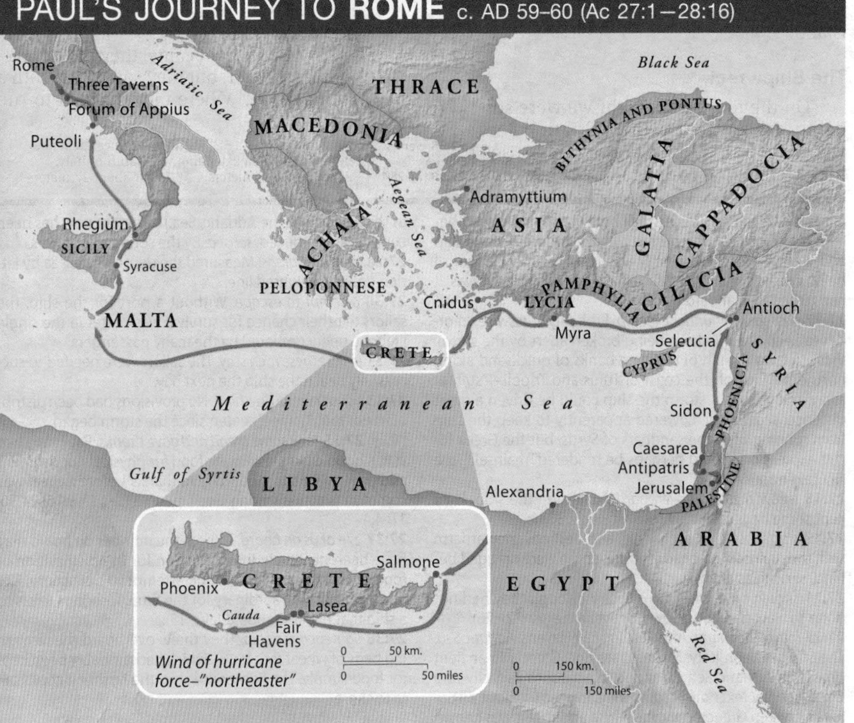

secure, 17so the men hoisted it aboard.
Then they passed ropes under the ship itself to hold it together. Because they were
afraid they would run aground[k] on the
sandbars of Syrtis, they lowered the sea
anchor[a] and let the ship be driven along.
18We took such a violent battering from
the storm that the next day they began to
throw the cargo overboard.[l] 19On the third
day, they threw the ship's tackle overboard with their own hands. 20When neither sun nor stars appeared for many days
and the storm continued raging, we finally
gave up all hope of being saved.
21After they had gone a long time without food, Paul stood up before them and
said: "Men, you should have taken my
advice[m] not to sail from Crete;[n] then you
would have spared yourselves this damage
and loss. 22But now I urge you to keep up
your courage,[o] because not one of you will
be lost; only the ship will be destroyed.
23Last night an angel[p] of the God to whom
I belong and whom I serve[q] stood beside
me[r] 24and said, 'Do not be afraid, Paul.
You must stand trial before Caesar;[s] and
God has graciously given you the lives of
all who sail with you.'[t] 25So keep up your
courage,[u] men, for I have faith in God that
it will happen just as he told me.[v] 26Nev-
ertheless, we must run aground[w] on some
island."[x]

The Shipwreck

27On the fourteenth night we were still
being driven across the Adriatic[b] Sea,
when about midnight the sailors sensed
they were approaching land. 28They took
soundings and found that the water was
a hundred and twenty feet[c] deep. A short
time later they took soundings again and
found it was ninety feet[d] deep. 29Fear-
ing that we would be dashed against
the rocks, they dropped four anchors
from the stern and prayed for daylight.
30In an attempt to escape from the ship,
the sailors let the lifeboat[y] down into the
sea, pretending they were going to lower
some anchors from the bow. 31Then Paul
said to the centurion and the soldiers,
"Unless these men stay with the ship,
you cannot be saved."[z] 32So the soldiers
cut the ropes that held the lifeboat and
let it drift away.
33Just before dawn Paul urged them
all to eat. "For the last fourteen days," he
said, "you have been in constant suspense
and have gone without food—you haven't
eaten anything. 34Now I urge you to take
some food. You need it to survive. Not
one of you will lose a single hair from his
head."[a] 35After he said this, he took some
bread and gave thanks to God in front of
them all. Then he broke it[b] and began to
eat. 36They were all encouraged[c] and ate
some food themselves. 37Altogether there
were 276 of us on board. 38When they had
eaten as much as they wanted, they lightened the ship by throwing the grain into
the sea.[d]
39When daylight came, they did not recognize the land, but they saw a bay with a
sandy beach,[e] where they decided to run

27:17 [k] ver 26, 39
27:18 [l] ver 19, 38; Jnh 1:5
27:21 [m] ver 10 [n] S ver 7
27:22 [o] ver 25, 36
27:23 [p] S Ac 5:19 [q] Ro 1:9 [r] Ac 18:9; 23:11; 2Ti 4:17
27:24 [s] Ac 23:11 [t] ver 44
27:25 [u] ver 22, 36 [v] Ro 4:20,21
27:26 [w] ver 17, 39 [x] Ac 28:1
27:30 [y] ver 16
27:31 [z] ver 24
27:34 [a] S Mt 10:30
27:35 [b] S Mt 14:19
27:36 [c] ver 22, 25
27:38 [d] ver 18; Jnh 1:5
27:39 [e] Ac 28:1

[a] *17* Or *the sails* [b] *27* In ancient times the name referred to an area extending well south of Italy. [c] *28* Or about 37 meters [d] *28* Or about 27 meters

make the lifeboat secure. A small boat was being towed behind the ship. It was interfering with the progress of the ship and with the steering. It may also have been in danger of being crushed against the ship in the wind and the waves. It had to be taken aboard (v. 17).
27:17 *passed ropes under the ship.* Probably crosswise, in order to keep the ship from being broken apart by the storm. *Syrtis.* A long stretch of desolate banks of quicksand along northern Africa off the coast of Tunis and Tripoli—still far away, but in such a storm the ship could be driven a great distance. *sea anchor.* Lowered apparently to keep the ship from running onto the sandbars of Syrtis, but the Greek for this expression should perhaps be rendered "mainsail" (see NIV text note).
27:18 *throw the cargo overboard.* To lighten the ship. They kept some bags of grain, however (see v. 38).
27:19 *ship's tackle.* Spars, planks and perhaps the yardarm with the mainsail attached. At times these were dragged behind, serving as a brake.
27:21 *should have taken my advice.* Although they had not done so, Paul had good news for everyone (vv. 22–26).
27:27 *fourteenth night.* After leaving Fair Havens. *Adriatic Sea.* The sea between Italy, Malta, Crete and Greece. In ancient times the Adriatic Sea extended as far south as Sicily and Crete (see NIV text note). (Some think this sea included all the area between Greece, Italy and Africa and that it was known as the Adrian, not the Adriatic, Sea.) Its extent now has been considerably reduced. *sensed.* By the sound of breakers.
27:28 *took soundings.* Measured the depth of the sea by letting down a weighted line.
27:30 *attempt to escape.* Without a port for the ship, the sailors felt their chance for survival was better in the single lifeboat, unencumbered by the many passengers.
27:31 *Unless these men stay.* The sailors were needed to successfully beach the ship the next day.
27:33 *haven't eaten anything.* No provisions had been distributed nor regular meals eaten since the storm began.
27:35 *took some bread and gave thanks.* Paul gave two good examples: He ate food for physical nourishment and gave thanks to God. To give thanks before a meal was common practice among God's people (see Lk 9:16; 24:30; 1Ti 4:4–5).
27:37 *276 of us on board.* To note the number on board may have been necessary in preparation for the distribution of food or perhaps for the coming attempt to get ashore. The number is not extraordinary for the time. Josephus refers to a ship that had 600 aboard (*Life,* 15).
27:38 *lightened the ship.* They threw overboard the remaining bags of wheat (see v. 18), which had probably been kept for food supply. The lighter the ship, the farther it could sail in to shore.

the ship aground if they could. 40 Cutting
loose the anchors,[f] they left them in the
sea and at the same time untied the ropes
that held the rudders. Then they hoisted
the foresail to the wind and made for the
beach. 41 But the ship struck a sandbar
and ran aground. The bow stuck fast and
would not move, and the stern was broken
to pieces by the pounding of the surf.[g]
42 The soldiers planned to kill the prisoners to prevent any of them from swimming
away and escaping. 43 But the centurion
wanted to spare Paul's life[h] and kept them
from carrying out their plan. He ordered
those who could swim to jump overboard
first and get to land. 44 The rest were to get
there on planks or on other pieces of the
ship. In this way everyone reached land
safely.[i]

Paul Ashore on Malta

28 Once safely on shore, we[j] found out
that the island[k] was called Malta.
2 The islanders showed us unusual kindness. They built a fire and welcomed us
all because it was raining and cold. 3 Paul
gathered a pile of brushwood and, as he
put it on the fire, a viper, driven out by the
heat, fastened itself on his hand. 4 When
the islanders saw the snake hanging from
his hand,[l] they said to each other, "This
man must be a murderer; for though he
escaped from the sea, the goddess Justice
has not allowed him to live."[m] 5 But Paul
shook the snake off into the fire and suffered no ill effects.[n] 6 The people expected
him to swell up or suddenly fall dead; but
after waiting a long time and seeing nothing unusual happen to him, they changed
their minds and said he was a god.[o]
7 There was an estate nearby that belonged to Publius, the chief official of the
island. He welcomed us to his home and
showed us generous hospitality for three
days. 8 His father was sick in bed, suffering from fever and dysentery. Paul went
in to see him and, after prayer,[p] placed his
hands on him[q] and healed him.[r] 9 When
this had happened, the rest of the sick on
the island came and were cured. 10 They
honored us[s] in many ways; and when we
were ready to sail, they furnished us with
the supplies we needed.

Paul's Arrival at Rome

11 After three months we put out to sea
in a ship that had wintered in the island—
it was an Alexandrian ship[t] with the figurehead of the twin gods Castor and Pollux. 12 We put in at Syracuse and stayed
there three days. 13 From there we set sail
and arrived at Rhegium. The next day the
south wind came up, and on the following
day we reached Puteoli. 14 There we found
some brothers and sisters[u] who invited us
to spend a week with them. And so we
came to Rome. 15 The brothers and sisters[v]
there had heard that we were coming, and
they traveled as far as the Forum of Appius and the Three Taverns to meet us. At

27:40 [f] ver 29 **27:41** [g] 2Co 11:25 **27:43** [h] ver 3 **27:44** [i] ver 22, 31 **28:1** [j] S Ac 16:10 [k] Ac 27:26,39 **28:4** [l] Mk 16:18 [m] Lk 13:2,4

28:5 [n] Lk 10:19 **28:6** [o] Ac 14:11 **28:8** [p] Jas 5:14, 15 [q] S Ac 6:6 [r] Ac 9:40 **28:10** [s] Ps 15:4 **28:11** [t] Ac 27:6 **28:14** [u] S Ac 1:16 **28:15** [v] S Ac 1:16

27:40 *untied the ropes that held the rudders.* In order to lower the stern rudders into place so the ship could be steered toward the sandy shore. Ancient ships had a steering oar on either side of the stern.

27:42 *soldiers planned to kill the prisoners.* If a prisoner escaped, the life of his guard was taken in his place. The soldiers did not want to risk having a prisoner escape (see 16:27 and note).

27:43 Once more the centurion (Julius, v. 3; see also note on v. 1) is to be admired for stopping this plan and trusting the prisoners.

28:1 *Malta.* Known as Melita by the Greeks and Romans. It was included in the province of Sicily and is located 58 miles south of that large island.

28:2 *islanders.* Lit. "barbarians"; all non-Greek-speaking people were called this by Greeks. Far from being uncivilized tribesmen, they were Phoenician in ancestry and used a Phoenician dialect but were thoroughly Romanized. *raining and cold.* It was the end of October or the beginning of November.

28:3 *a viper.* Must have been known to the islanders to be poisonous.

28:6 *to swell up.* The usual medical term for inflammation; it is used only by Luke in the NT (see Introduction to Luke: Author). *said he was a god.* Parallel to the Lystrans' attempt to worship Paul and Barnabas (14:11–18).

28:7 *Publius.* A Roman name, but the first name and not the family name. It must have been what the islanders called him. *chief official.* The "first man" of Malta, a technical term for the top authority. Luke's designation is accurate here, as elsewhere, even though the Greek term used is not a common one. Cf. also "proconsul" (Greek *anthypatos,* 13:7), "magistrates" (Greek *strategoi,* 16:20), "city officials" (Greek *politarchas,* 17:6), "officials of the province" (Greek *Asiarchon,* 19:31). *for three days.* Probably until they could find more permanent housing for the winter (see v. 11).

28:11 *After three months.* They had to remain here until the sailing season opened in late February or early March. *figurehead.* A carving mounted at the prow of the ship. *Castor and Pollux.* The two "sons of Zeus" (Greek *Dioscuroi*), the guardian deities of sailors.

28:12 *Syracuse.* The leading city on the island of Sicily, situated on the east coast.

28:13 *Rhegium.* A town on the coast of Italy, near the southwestern tip and close to the narrowest point of the strait separating that country from Sicily, opposite Messina. Around the promontory north of the town was the whirlpool of Charybdis and the rock of Scylla. Coming from his triumph in Judea, the general Titus landed here on his way to Rome. *Puteoli.* Modern Pozzuoli, almost 200 miles from Rhegium. It was situated in the northern part of the Bay of Naples and was the chief port of Rome, though 75 miles away. The population included Jews as well as Christians.

28:14 *spend a week.* Either the centurion had business to care for or he was free to delay the journey at Paul's request (see 27:42–43; see also 27:3). *Rome.* See map, p. 1883.

28:15 *Forum of Appius.* A small town 43 miles from Rome, noted for its wickedness. Some Roman Christians came this

the sight of these people Paul thanked God
and was encouraged. 16 When we got to
Rome, Paul was allowed to live by himself,
with a soldier to guard him.[w]

Paul Preaches at Rome Under Guard

17 Three days later he called together the
local Jewish leaders.[x] When they had assembled, Paul said to them: "My brothers,[y] although I have done nothing against
our people[z] or against the customs of our
ancestors,[a] I was arrested in Jerusalem
and handed over to the Romans. 18 They
examined me[b] and wanted to release me,[c]
because I was not guilty of any crime deserving death.[d] 19 The Jews objected, so I
was compelled to make an appeal to Caesar.[e] I certainly did not intend to bring any
charge against my own people. 20 For this
reason I have asked to see you and talk
with you. It is because of the hope of Israel[f] that I am bound with this chain."[g]

21 They replied, "We have not received
any letters from Judea concerning you,
and none of our people[h] who have come
from there has reported or said anything
bad about you. 22 But we want to hear what
your views are, for we know that people
everywhere are talking against this sect."[i]

23 They arranged to meet Paul on a certain day, and came in even larger numbers
to the place where he was staying. He witnessed to them from morning till evening,
explaining about the kingdom of God,[j]
and from the Law of Moses and from the

28:16 [w] Ac 24:23; 27:3 **28:17** [x] Ac 25:2 [y] S Ac 22:5 [z] S Ac 25:8 [a] S Ac 6:14 **28:18** [b] Ac 22:24 [c] Ac 26:31, 32 [d] S Ac 23:9 **28:19** [e] S Ac 25:11 **28:20** [f] Ac 26:6, 7 [g] S Ac 21:33 **28:21** [h] S Ac 22:5 **28:22** [i] S Ac 24:5, 14 **28:23** [j] S Mt 3:2; Ac 19:8 [k] S Ac 8:35 [l] Ac 17:3 **28:24** [m] Ac 14:4; 17:4, 5 **28:25** [n] S Heb 3:7 **28:27** [o] Ps 119:70 [p] Isa 6:9, 10; S Mt 13:15 **28:28** [q] Lk 2:30 [r] S Ac 13:46 **28:31** [s] ver 23; S Mt 4:23 [t] S Ac 4:29

Prophets[k] he tried to persuade them about
Jesus.[l] 24 Some were convinced by what
he said, but others would not believe.[m]
25 They disagreed among themselves and
began to leave after Paul had made this
final statement: "The Holy Spirit spoke
the truth to your ancestors when he said[n]
through Isaiah the prophet:

26 " 'Go to this people and say,
"You will be ever hearing but never
understanding;
you will be ever seeing but never
perceiving."
27 For this people's heart has become
calloused;[o]
they hardly hear with their ears,
and they have closed their eyes.
Otherwise they might see with their
eyes,
hear with their ears,
understand with their hearts
and turn, and I would heal them.'[a][p]

28 "Therefore I want you to know that
God's salvation[q] has been sent to the Gentiles,[r] and they will listen!" [29][b]
30 For two whole years Paul stayed there
in his own rented house and welcomed
all who came to see him. 31 He proclaimed
the kingdom of God[s] and taught about the
Lord Jesus Christ—with all boldness[t] and
without hindrance!

[a] 27 Isaiah 6:9,10 (see Septuagint) [b] 29 Some manuscripts include here *After he said this, the Jews left, arguing vigorously among themselves.*

far to meet Paul. Beyond this they would not be certain of the way he would come. *Three Taverns.* A town 33 miles from Rome. Other Roman believers met Paul here. The term "tavern" was used to designate any kind of shop.

28:16 *live by himself.* "In his own rented house" (v. 30). He had committed no flagrant crime and was not politically dangerous. So he was allowed to have his own living quarters, but a guard was with him at all times, perhaps chained to him (Eph 6:20; Php 1:13–14,17; Col 4:3,18; Phm 10,13).

28:17 *Jewish leaders.* The decree of the emperor Claudius (see 18:2 and note) had been allowed to lapse, and Jews had returned to Rome with their leaders. *My brothers.* An epithet that recognized the common Jewish blood he shared with them. Cf. the usage in v. 15, referring to brothers ("believers") in Christ (see note on 11:1).

28:20 *hope of Israel.* See note on 26:6.

28:22 *we want to hear … your views.* The Jews in Rome were well aware of the dispute over whether Jesus was the Messiah. They wanted to hear Paul's presentation, and he was eager to present it before the arrival of adverse opinions from the Jewish leaders of Jerusalem.

28:23 *Law of Moses … Prophets.* The OT Scriptures (see Lk 24:27,44 and note on 24:44).

28:26–27 This OT passage (Isa 6:9–10; see notes there) was quoted by Jesus (see Mt 13:14–15; Mk 4:12; Lk 8:10; Jn 12:39–40 and notes) to make a similar point. Paul, too, had alluded to it in his letter to the Romans (Ro 11:8). The theme of the rejection of the gospel by many in Israel has been an important one throughout Acts (see note on 13:14–31).

28:28 *God's salvation has been sent to the Gentiles.* The main theme of the book of Acts. The gospel is meant for all. And Paul was a chosen vessel to carry the message to Gentiles as well as to Jews (see 9:15 and note; Ro 1:13; 11:13 and note).

28:30 *two whole years.* Paul served the Lord (v. 31) during the full period of waiting for his accusers to press the trial in Rome. There are a number of indications that he was released from this imprisonment: (1) Acts stops abruptly at this time. (2) Paul wrote to churches expecting to visit them soon, so he must have anticipated a release (see Php 2:24; Phm 22). (3) A number of the details in the Pastoral Letters do not fit into the historical setting given in the book of Acts. These details indicate a return to Asia Minor, Crete and Greece after the events at the close of Acts. (4) Tradition indicates that Paul went to Spain. Even if he did not go, the very fact that a tradition arose suggests a time when he could have taken that journey. See map and accompanying text, pp. 2038–2039.

28:31 Acts ends on a triumphant note (just as Luke's Gospel does; see Lk 24:50–53). Despite being under house arrest Paul is preaching and teaching in Rome, the capital city of the Roman Empire—"with all boldness and without hindrance" (see 1:8 and note).

ROME IN THE TIME OF PAUL

In terms of political importance, geographic position and sheer magnificence, the superlative city of the empire was Rome, the capital.

Located on a series of jutting foothills and low-lying eminences (the "seven hills"; see note on Rev 17:9) east of a bend in the Tiber River some 18 miles from the Mediterranean, Rome was celebrated for its impressive public buildings, aqueducts, baths, theaters and thoroughfares, many of which led from distant provinces. The city of the first Christian century had spread far beyond its fourth-century BC Servian walls and lay unwalled, secure in its greatness.

The most prominent features were the Capitoline hill, with temples to Jupiter and Juno, and the nearby Palatine, adorned with imperial palaces, including Nero's Golden House. Both hills overlooked the Roman Forum, the hub of the entire empire (see map below).

Alternatively described as the glorious crowning achievement of humankind and as the sewer of the universe to which all the scum from every corner of the empire flowed, Rome had reasons for both civic pride in its architecture and shame for staggering urban social problems not unlike those of cities today.

The apostle Paul entered the city from the south on the Appian Way. He first lived under house arrest and then, after a period of freedom, as a condemned prisoner (perhaps in the Mamertine dungeon near the Forum). Remarkably, Paul was able to proclaim the gospel among all classes of people, from the palace to the prison. According to tradition, he was executed at a spot on the Ostian Way outside Rome in AD 68.

The Neronian persecution in AD 64 was a transparent attempt by the emperor to throw the blame on Christians for the great fire that destroyed large parts of the city. The populace, however, blamed Nero and felt sorry for those unjustly tortured in the arena (cf. Tacitus, *Annals*, 15.44).

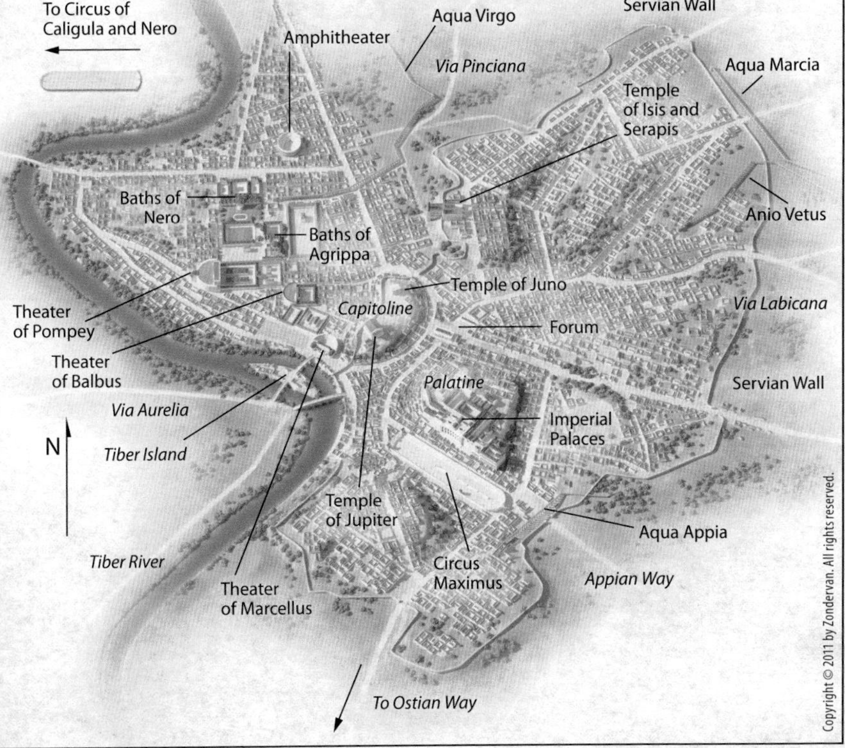

THE LETTERS AND REVELATION

The rest of the NT is primarily made up of letters, or epistles, written by Paul, James, Peter, John and Jude (the authorship of Hebrews is uncertain). The books of Romans through Thessalonians are letters from the apostle Paul to particular churches and situations in the latter half of the first century AD. These situations range from eating food sacrificed to idols and dealing with sexual immorality to specific doctrines and teachings relevant to what the churches were facing.

The Pastoral Letters are Paul's special instructions to Timothy and Titus as church leaders (see essay, p. 2033). Along with Philemon, these letters are addressed to individuals rather than churches (though they have wider intended audiences). It is in these books that we see Paul at his most personal and vulnerable.

The General Letters are the books of James through Jude (see essay, p. 2087). These letters were written by various authors, generally follow a typical epistolary form (like other letters) and were addressed to specific situations. The book of Revelation may also be viewed as a kind of letter, as it begins with letters to seven churches in western Asia Minor (modern-day Turkey). However, it is also classified as apocalyptic literature (see Introduction to Revelation: Literary Form), in which symbolism and vivid language are used to describe the cosmic conflict between good and evil, as well as the ultimate triumph of the Lamb (Rev 17:14).

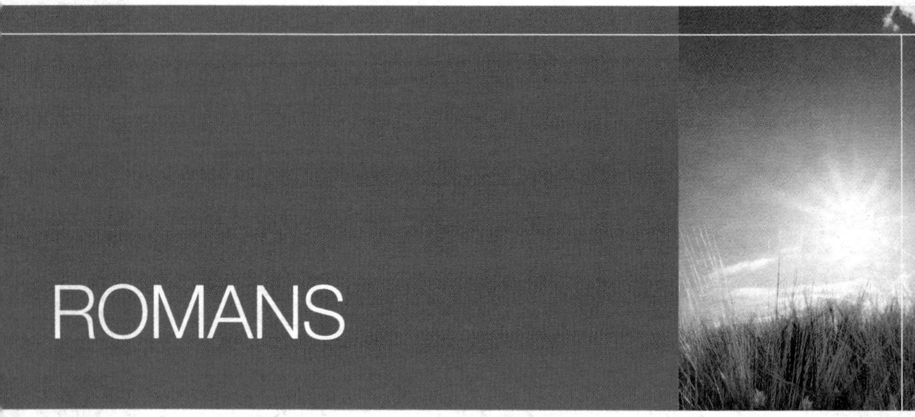

ROMANS

INTRODUCTION

Author

The writer of this letter was the apostle Paul (see 1:1 and note). No voice from the early church was ever raised against his authorship. The letter contains a number of historical references that agree with known facts of Paul's life. The doctrinal content of the book is typical of Paul, which is evident from a comparison with other letters he wrote.

Date and Place of Writing

The book was probably written in the early spring of AD 57 (see chart, p. 1845). Very likely Paul was on his third missionary journey, ready to return to Jerusalem with an offering from the mission churches for poverty-stricken believers in Jerusalem (see 15:25–27 and notes). In 15:26 it is suggested that Paul had already received contributions from the churches of Macedonia and Achaia, so he either was at Corinth or had already been there. Since he had not yet been at Corinth (on his third missionary journey) when he wrote 1 Corinthians (cf. 1Co 16:1–4) and the collection issue had still not been resolved when he wrote 2 Corinthians (2Co 8–9), the writing of Romans must follow that of 1,2 Corinthians (dated c. 55).

The most likely place of writing is either Corinth or Cenchreae (about six miles away) because of references to Phoebe of Cenchreae (see 16:1 and note) and to Gaius, Paul's host (see 16:23 and note), who was probably a Corinthian (see 1Co 1:14). Erastus (see 16:23 and note) may also have been a Corinthian (see 2Ti 4:20).

a quick look

Author:
The apostle Paul

Audience:
The church in Rome, predominantly Gentile but including a minority of Jews

Date:
About AD 57

Theme:
Paul writes to the church in Rome to present his basic statement of the gospel: God's plan of salvation for all peoples, Jew and Gentile alike.

Recipients

The original recipients of the letter were Christians living in Rome (1:7). Ch. 16 suggests that there were at least five house churches (16:5,10,11,14,15) in the city. The believers in Rome were predominantly Gentile (see 1:5–6,14–16). Jews, however, must have constituted a substantial minority of the congregation (see 4:1; chs. 9 – 11; see also notes on 1:13; 14:1). Perhaps Paul originally sent the entire letter to the Roman church, after which he or someone else used a shorter form (chs. 1 – 14 or 1 – 15) for more general distribution. See note on 2Pe 3:15; see also map, p. 1883.

Major Theme

Paul's primary theme in Romans is the basic gospel, God's plan of salvation and righteousness for all humankind, Jew and Gentile alike (see 1:16 – 17 and notes). Although justification by faith has been suggested by some as the theme, it would seem that a broader theme states the message of the book more adequately. "The righteousness of God" (1:17) includes justification by faith, but it also embraces such related ideas as guilt, sanctification and security.

Purposes

Paul's purposes for writing this letter were varied:

(1) He wrote to prepare the way for his coming visit to Rome and his proposed mission to Spain (1:10 – 15; 15:22 – 29).

(2) He wrote to present the basic system of salvation to a church that had not received the teaching of an apostle before.

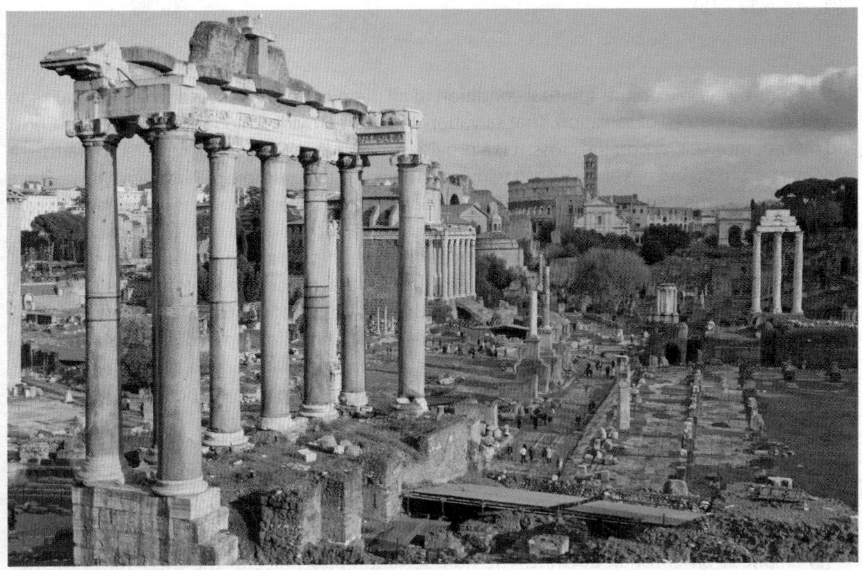

The Forum: the economic, social, religious and cultural center of ancient Rome

Paul shows that Israel has a place in God's sovereign redemptive plan. Now she consists of only a remnant, allowing for the conversion of the Gentiles, but the time will come when "all Israel will be saved."

(3) He sought to explain the relationship between Jew and Gentile in God's overall plan of redemption. There was evidently tension in the church between the Jewish and Gentile Christians, in part over the question of whether to keep dietary laws and sacred days (see 14:1 – 6 and note on 14:1). The Jewish Christians were being rejected by the larger Gentile group in the church (see 14:1 and note) because the Jewish believers still felt constrained to observe dietary laws and sacred days (14:2 – 6).

Occasion

When Paul wrote this letter, he was probably at Corinth (see Ac 20:2 – 3 and notes) on his third missionary journey. His work in the eastern Mediterranean was almost finished (see 15:18 – 23), and he greatly desired to visit the Roman church (see 1:11 – 12; 15:23 – 24). At this time, however, he could not go to Rome because he felt he must personally deliver the collection taken among the Gentile churches for the poverty-stricken Christians of Jerusalem (see 15:25 – 28 and notes). So instead of going to Rome, he sent a letter to prepare the Christians there for his intended visit in connection with a mission to Spain (see 15:23 – 24 and note on 15:24). For many years Paul had wanted to visit Rome to minister there (see 1:13 – 15), and this letter served as a careful and systematic theological introduction to that hoped-for personal ministry. Since he was not acquainted directly with the Roman church, he says little about its problems (but see 14:1 — 15:13; cf. also 13:1 – 7; 16:17 – 18).

Contents

Paul begins by surveying the spiritual condition of all people. He finds Jews and Gentiles alike to be sinners and in need of salvation. That salvation has been provided by God through Jesus Christ and his redemptive work on the cross. It is a provision, however, that must be received by faith — a principle by which God has always dealt with humankind, as the example of Abraham shows. Since salvation is only the beginning of Christian experience, Paul moves on to show how believers are freed from sin, law and death — a provision made possible by their union with Christ in both death and resurrection and by the indwelling presence and power of the Holy Spirit. Paul then shows that Israel too, though presently in a state of unbelief, has a place in God's sovereign redemptive plan. Now she consists of only a remnant, allowing for the conversion of the Gentiles, but the time will come when "all Israel will be saved" (11:26; see note there). The letter concludes with an appeal to the readers to work out their Christian faith in practical ways, both in the church and in the world. None of Paul's other letters states so profoundly the content of the gospel and its implications for both the present and the future.

Special Characteristics

(1) *The most systematic of Paul's letters.* It reads more like an elaborate theological essay than a letter.

(2) *Emphasis on Christian doctrine.* The number and importance of the theological themes touched upon are impressive: sin and death, salvation, grace, faith, righteousness, justification, sanctification, redemption, resurrection and glorification.

(3) *Widespread use of OT quotations.* Although Paul regularly quotes from the OT in his letters, in Romans the argument is sometimes carried along by such quotations (see especially chs. 9 – 11).

(4) *Deep concern for Israel.* Paul writes about Israel's present status, their relationship to the Gentiles and their final salvation (chs. 9 – 11).

Outline

- I. Introduction (1:1 – 15)
- II. Theme: The Righteousness of God (1:16 – 17)
- III. The Unrighteousness of All People (1:18 — 3:20)
  - A. Gentiles (1:18 – 32)
  - B. Jews (2:1 — 3:8)
  - C. Summary: All People (3:9 – 20)
- IV. God's Righteousness Imputed: Justification (3:21 — 5:21)
  - A. Through Christ (3:21 – 26)
  - B. Received by Faith (3:27 — 4:25)
    1. The principle established (3:27 – 31)
    2. The principle illustrated (ch. 4)
  - C. The Fruits of Righteousness (5:1 – 11)
  - D. Summary: Humanity's Unrighteousness Contrasted with God's Gift of Righteousness (5:12 – 21)
- V. God's Righteousness Imparted: Sanctification (chs. 6 – 8)
  - A. Freedom from Sin's Tyranny (ch. 6)
  - B. Freedom from the Law's Condemnation (ch. 7)
  - C. Life in the Power of the Holy Spirit (ch. 8)
- VI. God's Righteousness Vindicated: The Justice of His Way with Israel (chs. 9 – 11)
  - A. The Justice of God's Rejection of Israel (9:1 – 29)
  - B. The Cause of That Rejection (9:30 — 10:21)
  - C. The Rejection Is Neither Complete Nor Final (ch. 11)
    1. Even now there is a remnant (11:1 – 10)
    2. The rejection is only temporary (11:11 – 24)
    3. God's ultimate purpose is mercy (11:25 – 36)
- VII. Righteousness Practiced (12:1 — 15:13)
  - A. In the Body — the Church (ch. 12)
  - B. In the World (ch. 13)
  - C. Among Weak and Strong Christians (14:1 — 15:13)
- VIII. Conclusion (15:14 – 33)
- IX. Commendation, Greetings and Doxology (ch. 16)

1 Paul, a servant of Christ Jesus, called
to be an apostle[a] and set apart[b] for the
gospel of God[c]— 2 the gospel he promised
beforehand[d] through his prophets[e] in the
Holy Scriptures[f] 3 regarding his Son, who
as to his earthly life[a][g] was a descendant
of David,[h] 4 and who through the Spirit of
holiness was appointed the Son of God in
power[b][i] by his resurrection from the dead:[j]
Jesus Christ our Lord.[k] 5 Through him we
received grace[l] and apostleship to call all
the Gentiles[m] to the obedience that comes
from[c] faith[n] for his name's sake. 6 And you
also are among those Gentiles who are
called to belong to Jesus Christ.[o]

7 To all in Rome who are loved by God[p]
and called to be his holy people:[q]

Grace and peace to you from God our
Father and from the Lord Jesus Christ.[r]

Paul's Longing to Visit Rome

8 First, I thank my God through Jesus
Christ for all of you,[s] because your faith is
being reported all over the world.[t] 9 God,
whom I serve[u] in my spirit in preaching
the gospel of his Son, is my witness[v] how
constantly I remember you 10 in my prayers
at all times;[w] and I pray that now at last by
God's will[x] the way may be opened for me
to come to you.[y]

11 I long to see you[z] so that I may impart
to you some spiritual gift[a] to make you
strong— 12 that is, that you and I may be
mutually encouraged by each other's faith.
13 I do not want you to be unaware,[b] brothers and sisters,[d][c] that I planned many times
to come to you (but have been prevented
from doing so until now)[d] in order that I
might have a harvest among you, just as I
have had among the other Gentiles.

14 I am obligated[e] both to Greeks and
non-Greeks, both to the wise and the foolish. 15 That is why I am so eager to preach
the gospel also to you who are in Rome.[f]

16 For I am not ashamed of the gospel,[g]
because it is the power of God[h] that brings

1:1 [a] S 1Co 1:1 [b] S Ac 9:15 [c] Ro 15:16; S 2Co 2:12; 11:7; 1Th 2:8, 9; 1Pe 4:17 **1:2** [d] S Ac 13:32; Titus 1:2 [e] Lk 1:70; Ro 3:21 [f] Gal 3:8 **1:3** [g] S Jn 1:14; Ro 9:5 [h] S Mt 1:1 **1:4** [i] S Mt 4:3 [j] S Ac 2:24 [k] 1Co 1:2 **1:5** [l] 1Ti 1:14 [m] S Ac 9:15 [n] Ac 6:7; Ro 16:26 **1:6** [o] Jude 1; Rev 17:14 **1:7** [p] Ro 8:39; 1Th 1:4 [q] S Ac 9:13 [r] 1Co 1:3; Eph 1:2; 1Ti 1:2; Titus 1:4; 1Pe 1:2 **1:8** [s] 1Co 1:4; Eph 1:16; 1Th 2:13; 2Th 1:3; 2Ti 1:3 [t] S Ro 10:18; 16:19 **1:9** [u] 2Ti 1:3 [v] Job 16:19; Jer 42:5; 2Co 1:23; Gal 1:20; Php 1:8; 1Th 2:5, 10

[a] 3 Or *who according to the flesh* [b] 4 Or *was declared with power to be the Son of God* [c] 5 Or *that is*
[d] 13 The Greek word for *brothers and sisters* (*adelphoi*) refers here to believers, both men and women, as part of God's family; also in 7:1, 4; 8:12, 29; 10:1; 11:25; 12:1; 15:14, 30; 16:14, 17.

1:10 [w] 1Sa 12:23; S Lk 18:1; S Ac 1:14; Eph 1:16; Php 1:4; Col 1:9; 2Th 1:11; 2Ti 1:3; Phm 4 [x] S Ac 18:21 [y] ver 13; Ro 15:32 **1:11** [z] Ro 15:23 [a] 1Co 1:7; 12:1-31 **1:13** [b] S Ro 11:25 [c] S Ro 7:1 [d] Ro 15:22, 23 **1:14** [e] 1Co 9:16 **1:15** [f] Ro 15:20 **1:16** [g] 2Ti 1:8 [h] 1Co 1:18

1:1 *Paul.* See note on Ac 13:9. In ancient times writers put their names at the beginning of letters. For the story of Paul's ministry, see Ac 9:1 – 30 and note on 9:1; 13:1 — 28:31; for his autobiographical accounts see 2Co 6:3 – 10; 11:21 — 12:10; Gal 1:13 – 24; Php 3:4 – 14; 1Ti 1:12 – 16. *servant.* The Greek for this word means (1) a "slave," who completely belongs to his owner and has no freedom to leave, or (2) a "servant," who willingly chooses to serve his master. See notes on Ex 14:31; Ps 18 title; Isa 41:8 – 9; 42:1. *apostle.* One specially commissioned by Christ (see notes on Mk 6:30; 1Co 1:1; Heb 3:1). *set apart.* See Gal 1:15 and note. *gospel.* See note on Mk 1:1.

1:2 *prophets.* Not just the writers of the prophetic books, for the whole OT prophesied about Jesus (see Lk 24:27,44 – 47 and notes). *Holy Scriptures.* The OT.

1:3 – 4 These verses are often considered to be an early Christian creedal hymn, which Paul cites to show that he and the Roman believers share a common faith.

1:3 *regarding his Son.* The central figure of the gospel is Jesus, in and through whom all the promises of the OT are fulfilled (see Lk 24:27,44 – 47 and notes; cf. 2Co 1:20 and note). *descendant of David.* See Mt 1:1,16; 9:27; Mk 10:47; Jn 7:42 and notes.

1:4 *Son of God.* See Jn 3:16 and note. *his resurrection.* The authentication of Jesus' divine nature and the focal point of the apostolic proclamation (see Ac 2:14 – 40; 4:33 and notes).

1:7 *his holy people.* All Christians are "holy" in that they are positionally "set apart" to God and are experientially being made increasingly "holy" by the Holy Spirit (see note on 1Co 1:2). *Grace and peace.* The initial greeting used by both Paul and Peter in all their letters. It combines the traditional Greek ("greetings"; related to the Greek word for "grace") and Hebrew ("peace") greetings but links them expressly with the only true source of "grace" (in the sense of God's unmerited favor, especially that which comes to sinful humanity through the saving work of Christ) and "peace" (the total well-being and security that only God can provide and that he does provide fully only to those who are at peace with him; see 5:1; Php 4:7 and notes; Gal 1:3; Eph 1:2; see also Jn 14:27; 20:19 and notes). This greeting is echoed in the conclusions of Paul's and Peter's letters, so that these letters stand framed in what amounts to an apostolic benediction on those who are addressed. Cf. Ex 34:6 – 7 and note. *Lord Jesus Christ.* See note on 1Th 1:1.

1:8 *thank.* Paul often began his letters with thanks (see 1Co 1:4; Eph 1:16; Php 1:3 – 4 and note; Col 1:3 and note; 1Th 1:2; 2Th 1:3; 2Ti 1:3; Phm 4). *through Jesus Christ.* The Christian must go through Christ not only for requests to God (see Jn 15:16) but also to give thanks. *all over the world.* Every place where the gospel has been preached.

1:9 *gospel of his Son.* The same as the "gospel of God" (v. 1).

1:10 *way may be opened.* See 15:23 – 29.

1:12 *mutually.* Paul's genuine humility is seen in his desire to be ministered to by the believers at Rome, as well as to minister to them.

1:13 *brothers and sisters.* See NIV text note; see also note on Ac 11:1. *harvest.* New converts, as well as spiritual growth by those already converted. *among you . . . among the other Gentiles.* Suggests that the church at Rome was predominantly Gentile.

1:14 *Greeks.* Those Gentiles who spoke Greek or followed the Greek way of life, even though they may have been Latin-speaking citizens of the Roman Empire. *non-Greeks.* Lit. "barbarians," a word that probably imitated the unintelligible sound of their languages to Greek ears. They were the "other Gentiles" (v. 13) to whom Paul ministered.

1:16 – 17 The theme of the entire book.

1:16 *not ashamed.* Not even in the capital city of the Roman Empire (see v. 15). *gospel.* See note on Mk 1:1. *power.* The message of the gospel has divine "power" to save "everyone who believes" (see 1Co 1:18,24; cf. 1Pe 1:23 and note). *first.* Not only in time but also in privilege. "Salvation is from the Jews" (Jn 4:22), and the Messiah was a Jew. The "very words of God" (3:2), the covenants, law, temple worship, revelation of the divine glory and Messianic prophecies came to them

salvation to everyone who believes:[i] first
to the Jew,[j] then to the Gentile.[k] 17 For in
the gospel the righteousness of God is revealed[l]—a righteousness that is by faith[m]
from first to last,[a] just as it is written: "The
righteous will live by faith."[b n]

God's Wrath Against Sinful Humanity

18 The wrath of God[o] is being revealed
from heaven against all the godlessness
and wickedness of people, who suppress
the truth by their wickedness, 19 since what
may be known about God is plain to them,
because God has made it plain to them.[p]
20 For since the creation of the world God's
invisible qualities—his eternal power and
divine nature—have been clearly seen, being understood from what has been made,[q]
so that people are without excuse.[r]

21 For although they knew God, they neither glorified him as God nor gave thanks
to him, but their thinking became futile
and their foolish hearts were darkened.[s]
22 Although they claimed to be wise, they
became fools[t] 23 and exchanged the glory
of the immortal God for images[u] made to
look like a mortal human being and birds
and animals and reptiles.

24 Therefore God gave them over[v] in the
sinful desires of their hearts to sexual impurity for the degrading of their bodies
with one another.[w] 25 They exchanged the
truth about God for a lie,[x] and worshiped
and served created things[y] rather than the
Creator—who is forever praised.[z] Amen.[a]

26 Because of this, God gave them over[b]
to shameful lusts.[c] Even their women exchanged natural sexual relations for unnatural ones.[d] 27 In the same way the men also
abandoned natural relations with women
and were inflamed with lust for one another. Men committed shameful acts with
other men, and received in themselves the
due penalty for their error.[e]

28 Furthermore, just as they did not think
it worthwhile to retain the knowledge of
God, so God gave them over[f] to a depraved
mind, so that they do what ought not to
be done. 29 They have become filled with
every kind of wickedness, evil, greed and
depravity. They are full of envy, murder,
strife, deceit and malice. They are gossips,[g] 30 slanderers, God-haters, insolent,
arrogant and boastful; they invent ways
of doing evil; they disobey their parents;[h]
31 they have no understanding, no fidelity,
no love,[i] no mercy. 32 Although they know
God's righteous decree that those who do
such things deserve death,[j] they not only
continue to do these very things but also
approve[k] of those who practice them.

God's Righteous Judgment

2 You, therefore, have no excuse,[l] you
who pass judgment on someone else,
for at whatever point you judge another,

[a] *17* Or *is from faith to faith* [b] *17* Hab. 2:4

1:16 [i] S Jn 3:15 [j] Ac 3:26; 13:46 [k] S Ac 13:46; Ro 2:9,10 **1:17** [l] Ro 3:21; Php 3:9 [m] S Ro 9:30 [n] Hab 2:4; Gal 3:11; Heb 10:38 **1:18** [o] Jn 3:36; Ro 5:9; Eph 5:6; Col 3:6; 1Th 1:10; Rev 19:15 **1:19** [p] Ac 14:17 **1:20** [q] Ps 19:1-6 [r] Ro 2:1 **1:21** [s] Ge 8:21; Jer 2:5; 17:9; Eph 4:17,18 **1:22** [t] 1Co 1:20, 27; 3:18,19 **1:23** [u] Dt 4:16, 17; Ps 106:20; Jer 2:11; Ac 17:29 **1:24** [v] ver 26, 28; Ps 81:12; Eph 4:19 [w] 1Pe 4:3 **1:25** [x] Isa 44:20 [y] Jer 10:14; 13:25; 16:19, 20 [z] Ro 9:5; 2Co 11:31 [a] S Ro 11:36

1:26 [b] ver 24, 28 [c] Eph 4:19; 1Th 4:5 [d] Lev 18:22,23 **1:27** [e] Lev 18:22; 20:13; 1Co 6:18 **1:28** [f] ver 24,26 **1:29** [g] 2Co 12:20; 1Ti 5:13; Jas 3:2; 3Jn 10 **1:30** [h] 2Ti 3:2 **1:31** [i] 2Ti 3:3 **1:32** [j] S Ro 6:23 [k] Ps 50:18; Lk 11:48; Ac 8:1; 22:20 **2:1** [l] Ro 1:20

(9:3–5; see notes there). These privileges, however, were not extended to the Jews because of their superior merit or because of God's partiality toward them (cf. Dt 7:7–11 and note on Dt 4:37). It was necessary that the invasion of this world by the gospel begin at a particular point with a particular people, who in turn were responsible to carry that gospel to the other nations (see 2:9 and note).

1:17 *righteousness.* The state of being in a right relationship with God (see notes on 2:13; 3:21,24).

1:18—3:20 In developing the theme of the righteousness of God (1:17; 3:21—5:21), Paul sets the stage by showing that all have sinned and therefore need the righteousness that only God can provide. He shows the sin of the Gentiles (1:18–32) and the sin of the Jews (2:1—3:8) and then summarizes the sin of all—Gentile and Jew alike (3:9–20).

1:18–20 No one—not even one who has not heard of the Bible or of Christ—has an excuse for not honoring God, because the whole created world reveals him.

1:18 *wrath of God.* Not a petulant, irrational burst of anger, such as humans often exhibit, but a holy, just revulsion against what is contrary to and opposes his holy nature and will. *is being revealed.* God's wrath is not limited to the end-time judgment of the wicked (1Th 1:10; Rev 19:15; 20:11–15). Here the wrath of God is his abandonment of the wicked to their sins (vv. 24–32). *the truth.* The truth about God revealed in the creation order.

1:21 *knew God.* From seeing his revelation in creation (vv. 19–20). The fact that these people were idolaters (v. 23) and knew God only through the creation order indicates that they were Gentiles. *gave thanks.* For earthly blessings, such as sun, rain and crops (see Mt 5:45 and note; Ac 14:17).

1:23 *glory.* God's unique majesty (see Isa 40:5 and note; 48:11; see also Eze 1:28; 43:2 and notes), of which fallen humankind has lost sight and for which people have substituted deities of their own devising, patterned after various creatures (see Ps 106:20 and note).

1:24,26,28 *God gave them over.* God allowed sin to run its course as an act of judgment.

1:25 *Amen.* Can mean either "Yes indeed, it is so" or "So be it" (see 9:5; 11:36; 15:33; 16:27; see also note on Dt 27:15; cf. 1Ki 1:36).

1:26 *their women.* Not necessarily their wives.

1:27 Homosexual practice is sinful in God's eyes. The OT also condemns the practice (see Lev 18:22; 20:13).

1:28 *knowledge of God.* See vv. 19,21. *depraved mind.* The intent precedes the act (see v. 21; Mk 7:20–23).

1:29–31 A list of vices similar to those found in 13:13; Mk 7:21–22; 1Co 5:10–11; 6:9–10; 2Co 12:20–21; Gal 5:19–21; Eph 4:31; 5:3–5; Col 3:5,8; 1Ti 1:9–10; 2Ti 3:2–5; Rev 21:8; 22:15.

1:32 *they know.* Their outrageous conduct was not due to total ignorance of what God required but to self-will and rebellion. *approve.* The extreme of sin is applauding, rather than regretting, the sins of others (see Ps 1:1; 1Co 15:33 and notes).

2:1–16 In this section Paul sets forth principles that govern God's judgment. God judges (1) according to truth (v. 2), (2) according to deeds (vv. 6–11) and (3) according to the light a person has (vv. 12–15). These principles lay the groundwork for Paul's discussion of the guilt of the Jews (vv. 17–29).

2:1 *no excuse.* Cf. 1:20. Paul's teaching about judging agrees

The Colosseum in Rome, one of the most impressive reminders of the might of the Roman Empire

you are condemning yourself, because you
who pass judgment do the same things.[m]
2 Now we know that God's judgment
against those who do such things is based
on truth. 3 So when you, a mere human
being, pass judgment on them and yet do
the same things, do you think you will escape God's judgment? 4 Or do you show
contempt for the riches[n] of his kindness,[o]
forbearance[p] and patience,[q] not realizing
that God's kindness is intended to lead
you to repentance?[r]
5 But because of your stubbornness and
your unrepentant heart, you are storing
up wrath against yourself for the day of
God's wrath[s], when his righteous judgment[t] will be revealed. 6 God "will repay
each person according to what they have
done."[a][u] 7 To those who by persistence in
doing good seek glory, honor[v] and immortality,[w] he will give eternal life.[x] 8 But for
those who are self-seeking and who reject
the truth and follow evil,[y] there will be
wrath and anger.[z] 9 There will be trouble
and distress for every human being who
does evil:[a] first for the Jew, then for the
Gentile;[b] 10 but glory, honor and peace for
everyone who does good: first for the Jew,
then for the Gentile.[c] 11 For God does not
show favoritism.[d]
12 All who sin apart from the law will
also perish apart from the law, and all who
sin under the law[e] will be judged by the
law. 13 For it is not those who hear the law
who are righteous in God's sight, but it
is those who obey[f] the law who will be
declared righteous. 14 (Indeed, when Gentiles, who do not have the law, do by nature things required by the law,[g] they are
a law for themselves, even though they do
not have the law. 15 They show that the requirements of the law are written on their
hearts, their consciences also bearing witness, and their thoughts sometimes accusing them and at other times even defending them.) 16 This will take place on the day
when God judges people's secrets[h] through
Jesus Christ,[i] as my gospel[j] declares.

2:1 [m] 2Sa 12:5-7; S Mt 7:1,2
2:4 [n] Ro 9:23; 11:33; Eph 1:7, 18; 2:7; 3:8, 16; Col 2:2
[o] Ro 11:22
[p] Ro 3:25
[q] Ex 34:6; Ro 9:22; 1Ti 1:16; 1Pe 3:20; 2Pe 3:15
[r] 2Pe 3:9
2:5 [s] Ps 110:5; Rev 6:17
[t] Jude 6
2:6 [u] Ps 62:12; S Mt 16:27
2:7 [v] ver 10
[w] 1Co 15:53, 54; 2Ti 1:10
[x] S Mt 25:46
2:8 [y] 2Th 2:12
[z] Eze 22:31
2:9 [a] Ps 32:10
[b] ver 10; Ro 1:16
2:10 [c] ver 9; Ro 1:16
2:11
[d] S Ac 10:34
2:12 [e] Ro 3:19; 6:14; 1Co 9:20, 21; Gal 4:21; 5:18; S Ro 7:4
2:13 [f] Jas 1:22, 23,25
2:14 [g] Ac 10:35
2:16
[h] Ecc 12:14; 1Co 4:5
[i] Ac 10:42
[j] Ro 16:25; 2Ti 2:8

[a] 6 Psalm 62:12; Prov. 24:12

with that of Jesus (see note on Mt 7:1), who did not condemn judging as such, but hypocritical judging. *you who pass judgment.* A warning that had special relevance for Jews, who were inclined to look down on Gentiles because of their ignorance of God's revelation in the OT and because of their immoral lives.

2:2 *we know.* An expression Paul frequently used, assuming that the persons addressed agreed with the statement that followed (see 3:19; 6:6,9; 7:14; 8:22,28; 1Co 8:1,4; 2Co 5:1; 1Ti 1:8).

2:3 Jesus also condemned such judgmental acts (see Mt 7:3 and note; cf. Lk 18:9).

2:4 The purpose of God's kindness is to give opportunity for repentance (see 2Pe 3:9 and note). The Jews had misconstrued his patience to be a lack of intent to judge.

2:5 *day of God's wrath.* See v. 8; judgment in the end times, in contrast to the judgment discussed in 1:18–32.

2:6–7 Paul is not contradicting his continual emphasis in all his writings, including Romans, that people are saved not by what they do but by faith in what Christ has done for them. Paul is referring to "persistence in doing good" as the proof of genuine faith (see Gal 5:6; Jas 2:14–26 and notes).

2:8 *wrath and anger.* On the day of final judgment.

2:9 *first for the Jew.* With spiritual privilege comes spiritual responsibility (see Am 3:2 and note; Lk 12:48; cf. Ro 1:16 and note).

2:11 A basic teaching of both the OT and the NT.

2:12 *law.* The Mosaic law. "All who sin apart from the law" refers to Gentiles. God judges according to the light available to people. Gentiles will not be condemned for not obeying a law they did not possess. Their judgment will be on other grounds (see v. 15; 1:18–20 and note; cf. Am 1:3—2:3).

2:13 *will be declared righteous.* At God's pronouncement of acquittal on judgment day (see note on 3:24).

2:14 *by nature.* By natural impulse, without the external constraint of the Mosaic law. *things required by the law.* Does not mean that pagans fulfilled the requirements of the Mosaic law but refers to practices in pagan society that agreed with the law, such as caring for the sick and elderly, honoring parents and condemning adultery. *law for themselves.* The moral nature of pagans, enlightened by conscience (v. 15), functioned for them as the Mosaic law did for the Jews.

2:16 See Ecc 12:14 and note. This verse should be read with v. 13, as the parentheses around vv. 14–15 indicate. *my gospel.* See 16:25 and note.

The Jews and the Law

17 Now you, if you call yourself a Jew; if you rely on the law and boast in God;[k] 18 if you know his will and approve of what is superior because you are instructed by the law; 19 if you are convinced that you are a guide for the blind, a light for those who are in the dark, 20 an instructor of the foolish, a teacher of little children, because you have in the law the embodiment of knowledge and truth— 21 you, then, who teach others, do you not teach yourself? You who preach against stealing, do you steal?[l] 22 You who say that people should not commit adultery, do you commit adultery? You who abhor idols, do you rob temples?[m] 23 You who boast in the law,[n] do you dishonor God by breaking the law? 24 As it is written: "God's name is blasphemed among the Gentiles because of you."[a][o]

25 Circumcision has value if you observe the law,[p] but if you break the law, you have become as though you had not been circumcised.[q] 26 So then, if those who are not circumcised keep the law's requirements,[r] will they not be regarded as though they were circumcised?[s] 27 The one who is not circumcised physically and yet obeys the law will condemn you[t] who, even though you have the[b] written code and circumcision, are a lawbreaker.

28 A person is not a Jew who is one only outwardly,[u] nor is circumcision merely outward and physical.[v] 29 No, a person is a Jew who is one inwardly; and circumcision is circumcision of the heart,[w] by the Spirit,[x] not by the written code.[y] Such a person's praise is not from other people, but from God.[z]

God's Faithfulness

3 What advantage, then, is there in being a Jew, or what value is there in circumcision? 2 Much in every way![a] First of all, the Jews have been entrusted with the very words of God.[b]

3 What if some were unfaithful?[c] Will their unfaithfulness nullify God's faithfulness?[d] 4 Not at all! Let God be true,[e] and every human being a liar.[f] As it is written:

> "So that you may be proved right when
> you speak
> and prevail when you judge."[c][g]

5 But if our unrighteousness brings out God's righteousness more clearly,[h] what shall we say? That God is unjust in bringing his wrath on us? (I am using a human argument.)[i] 6 Certainly not! If that were so, how could God judge the world?[j] 7 Someone might argue, "If my falsehood enhances God's truthfulness and so increases his glory,[k] why am I still condemned as a sinner?"[l] 8 Why not say—as some slanderously claim that we say—"Let us do evil that good may result"?[m] Their condemnation is just!

No One Is Righteous

9 What shall we conclude then? Do we have any advantage?[n] Not at all! For we have already made the charge that Jews and Gentiles alike are all under the power of sin.[o] 10 As it is written:

a 24 Isaiah 52:5 (see Septuagint); Ezek. 36:20,22
b 27 Or *who, by means of a*
c 4 Psalm 51:4

2:17 [k] ver 23; Jer 8:8; Mic 3:11; Jn 5:45; Ro 9:4 **2:21** [l] Mt 23:3,4 **2:22** [m] Ac 19:37 **2:23** [n] S ver 17 **2:24** [o] Isa 52:5; Eze 36:22; 2Pe 2:2 **2:25** [p] ver 13, 27; Gal 5:3 [q] Jer 4:4; 9:25,26 **2:26** [r] Ro 8:4 [s] S 1Co 7:19 **2:27** [t] Mt 12:41, 42 **2:28** [u] Mt 3:9; Jn 8:39; Ro 9:6, 7 [v] Gal 6:15 **2:29** [w] Dt 30:6 [x] Php 3:3; Col 2:11 [y] Ro 7:6; 2Co 3:6 [z] Jn 5:44; 12:43; 1Co 4:5; 2Co 10:18; Gal 1:10; 1Th 2:4; 1Pe 3:4 **3:2** [a] Ro 9:4, 5 [b] Dt 4:8; Ps 147:19; Ac 7:38 **3:3** [c] Ro 10:16; Heb 4:2 [d] 2Ti 2:13 **3:4** [e] Jn 3:33 [f] Ps 116:11 [g] Ps 51:4 **3:5** [h] Ro 5:8 [i] Ro 6:19; Gal 3:15 **3:6** [j] Ge 18:25; Ro 2:16 **3:7** [k] ver 4 [l] Ro 9:19 **3:8** [m] Ro 6:1 **3:9** [n] ver 1 [o] ver 19,23; 1Ki 8:46; 2Ch 6:36; Ps 106:6; Ro 5:12; 11:32; Gal 3:22

2:17–24 The presentation takes the form of a dialogue. Paul knew how a self-righteous Jew thought, for he had been one himself. He cites one advantage after another that Jews regarded as unqualified assets. But those assets became liabilities when there was no correspondence between profession and practice. Paul applied to the Jew the principles of judgment set forth in vv. 1–16 (see note on those verses).

2:19–20 *the blind ... little children.* Gentiles, to whom Jews regarded themselves as vastly superior because they (the Jews) possessed the Mosaic law.

2:22 *do you rob temples?* See Ac 19:37. This could refer literally to robbing temples (large amounts of wealth were often stored in pagan temples). Or it could refer to sacrilege in general.

2:25 *Circumcision.* The sign of the covenant that God made with Israel (see Ge 17:11 and note; Lev 12:3) and a pledge of the covenant blessing (see 4:11 and note). The Jews had come to regard circumcision as a guarantee of God's favor.

2:27 If a Gentile's deeds excelled those of a Jew in righteousness, that very fact condemned the Jew, who had an immeasurably better set of standards in the law of Moses.

2:29 *by the Spirit.* The true sign of belonging to God is not an outward mark on the physical body but the regenerating power of the Holy Spirit within (see Titus 3:5 and note)—what Paul meant by "circumcision of the heart" (see 4:9–12; Dt 30:6 and notes on Ge 17:10; Jer 4:4). *praise is not from other people, but from God.* Cf. Jn 5:41,44; 12:43; 1Co 4:3–5 and notes on 4:3,5.

3:2 *First of all.* Paul does not discuss the other advantages of being a Jew until 9:4–5 (see notes there). *entrusted.* The advantage of having the very words of God involves a duty. *very words of God.* The OT.

3:3 *God's faithfulness.* God is faithful to his promises and would punish Israel for their unbelief (v. 5; see 2Ti 2:13 and note).

3:4 God's punishment of sin exhibits his faithfulness to his righteous character.

3:5 *brings out God's righteousness.* By contrast, in showing it up against the dark background of human sin. *human argument.* "Human" in the sense of its weakness and absurdity.

3:6 *judge.* On judgment day. *world.* All moral creatures (also in v. 19)—a more limited reference than in 1:20.

3:8 *Let us do evil that good may result.* Paul deals with this issue more fully in ch. 6.

3:9 *Do we have any advantage?* Are Jews better than Gentiles in the sight of God? *all under the power of sin.* Nine times in four verses (vv. 9–12) Paul mentions the universality of sin ("all," two times; "no one," four times; "not even one," two times; "together," once). *under the power of sin.* And its condemnation.

3:10–18 An impressive series of OT citations that underscores Paul's claim that both Jews and Gentiles are totally under the

"There is no one righteous, not even
one;
11 there is no one who understands;
there is no one who seeks God.
12 All have turned away,
they have together become
worthless;
there is no one who does good,
not even one."[ap]
13 "Their throats are open graves;
their tongues practice deceit."[bq]
"The poison of vipers is on their
lips."[cr]
14 "Their mouths are full of cursing
and bitterness."[ds]
15 "Their feet are swift to shed blood;
16 ruin and misery mark their ways,
17 and the way of peace they do not
know."[et]
18 "There is no fear of God before their
eyes."[fu]

19 Now we know that whatever the law
says,[v] it says to those who are under the
law,[w] so that every mouth may be silenced[x]
and the whole world held accountable to
God.[y] 20 Therefore no one will be declared
righteous in God's sight by the works of
the law;[z] rather, through the law we become conscious of our sin.[a]

Righteousness Through Faith

21 But now apart from the law the righteousness of God[b] has been made known,
to which the Law and the Prophets testify.[c] 22 This righteousness[d] is given through
faith[e] in[g] Jesus Christ[f] to all who believe.[g]
There is no difference between Jew and
Gentile,[h] 23 for all have sinned[i] and fall
short of the glory of God, 24 and all are
justified[j] freely by his grace[k] through the
redemption[l] that came by Christ Jesus.
25 God presented Christ as a sacrifice of
atonement,[hm] through the shedding of his
blood[n]—to be received by faith. He did

3:12 [p] Ps 14:1-3; 53:1-3; Ecc 7:20 **3:13** [q] Ps 5:9 [r] Ps 140:3 **3:14** [s] Ps 10:7 **3:17** [t] Isa 59:7,8 **3:18** [u] Ps 36:1 **3:19** [v] S Jn 10:34 [w] S Ro 2:12 [x] Ps 63:11; 107:42; Eze 16:63 [y] ver 9 **3:20** [z] Ac 13:39; Gal 2:16 [a] S Ro 4:15 **3:21** [b] Isa 46:13; Jer 23:6; Ro 1:17; 9:30 [c] Ac 10:43; Ro 1:2 **3:22** [d] Ro 1:17 [e] S Ro 9:30 [f] Gal 2:16; 3:22 [g] S Jn 3:15; Ro 4:11; 10:4 [h] Ro 10:12; Gal 3:28; Col 3:11 **3:23** [i] S ver 9 **3:24** [j] S Ro 4:25 [k] Jn 1:14,16, 17; Ro 4:16; 5:21; 6:14; 11:5; 2Co 12:9; Eph 2:8; 4:7; Titus 2:11; Heb 4:16 [l] Ps 130:7; 1Co 1:30; Gal 4:5; Eph 1:7,14; Col 1:14; Heb 9:12 **3:25** [m] Ex 25:17; Lev 16:10; Ps 65:3; Heb 2:17; 9:28; 1Jn 4:10 [n] Ac 20:28; Ro 5:9; Eph 1:7; Heb 9:12,14; 13:12; 1Pe 1:19; Rev 1:5

[a] *12* Psalms 14:1-3; 53:1-3; Eccles. 7:20
[b] *13* Psalm 5:9 [c] *13* Psalm 140:3 [d] *14* Psalm 10:7 (see Septuagint) [e] *17* Isaiah 59:7,8
[f] *18* Psalm 36:1 [g] *22* Or *through the faithfulness of*
[h] *25* The Greek for *sacrifice of atonement* refers to the atonement cover on the ark of the covenant (see Lev. 16:15,16).

power of sin. Several factors explain why the citations are not always verbatim: (1) NT citations sometimes gave the general sense and were not meant to be word-for-word. (2) Quotation marks were not used in Greek. (3) The citations were often taken from the pre-Christian Greek translation (the Septuagint) of the Hebrew OT, because Greek readers were not familiar with the Hebrew Bible. (4) Sometimes the NT writer, in order to drive home his point, would purposely (under the inspiration of the Holy Spirit) enlarge, abbreviate or adapt an OT passage or combine two or more passages.

3:11 *understands.* About God and what is right.

3:12 *All have turned away.* See Isa 53:6 and note.

3:13 *open graves.* Expressing the corruption of the heart.

3:15 See Pr 1:16; 4:27; 6:18.

3:18 *fear of God.* Awesome reverence for God; the source of all godliness (see notes on Ge 20:11; Pr 1:7).

3:19 *we know.* See note on 2:2. *law.* The OT (as in Jn 10:34; 15:25; 1Co 14:21). *those who are under the law.* Jews. *every mouth ... whole world.* Jews as well as Gentiles are guilty.

3:20 *declared righteous.* See notes on v. 24; 2:13. *we become conscious of our sin.* According to Paul, this is one of the primary purposes of the law (see 7:7 and note).

3:21—5:21 Having shown that all (both Gentiles and Jews) are unrighteous (1:18—3:20), Paul now shows that God has provided a righteousness for humankind.

3:21 *But now.* There are two possible meanings: (1) temporal—all of time is divided into two periods, and in the "now" period the righteousness of God has been made known; (2) logical—the contrast is between the righteousness gained by observing the law (which is impossible, v. 20) and the righteousness provided by God. *apart from the law.* Apart from keeping the law. *the Law and the Prophets testify.* See Ge 15:6; Ps 32:1–2; Hab 2:4; Mt 5:17 and notes.

3:22 *no difference between Jew and Gentile.* See 10:12 and note.

3:23 *the glory of God.* What God intended humans to be. The glory mankind had before the fall (see Ge 1:26–28; Ps 8:4–8 and notes; cf. Eph 4:24; Col 3:10) believers will again have through Christ (see Heb 2:5–9 and notes).

3:24 *justified.* Paul uses the Greek verb for "justified" 27 times, mostly in Romans and Galatians. It is translated "justify" in all cases except two (2:13; 3:20, where it is translated "declared righteous"). The term describes what happens when people believe in Christ as their Savior: From the negative viewpoint, God declares them to be not guilty; from the positive viewpoint, he declares them to be righteous. He cancels the guilt of their sin and credits righteousness to them. Paul emphasizes two points in this regard: (1) No one lives a perfectly good, holy, righteous life. On the contrary, "there is no one righteous" (v. 10), and "all have sinned and fall short of the glory of God" (v. 23). "Therefore no one will be declared righteous in God's sight by the works of the law" (v. 20). (2) But even though all are sinners, God will declare those who put their trust in Jesus not guilty but righteous. This legal declaration is valid because Christ died to pay the penalty for our sin and lived a life of perfect righteousness that can in turn be imputed to us. This is the central theme of Romans and is stated in the theme verse, 1:17 ("the righteousness of God ... by faith"). Christ's righteousness (his obedience to God's law and his sacrificial death) will be credited to believers as their own. Paul uses the Greek for "credited" ten times in ch. 4 alone. *freely by his grace.* The central thought in justification is that, although people clearly and totally deserve to be declared guilty (vv. 9–19), God declares them righteous because of their trust in Christ. This is stated in several ways here: (1) "freely" (as a gift, for nothing), (2) "by his grace," (3) "through the redemption that came by Christ Jesus" and (4) "by faith" (v. 25). *redemption.* A word taken from the slave market—the basic idea is that of obtaining release by payment of a ransom. Paul uses this word to refer to release from guilt, with its liability for judgment, and to deliverance from slavery to sin, because Christ in his death paid the ransom to set us free.

3:25 *sacrifice of atonement.* The Greek for this phrase speaks of a sacrifice that satisfies the righteous wrath of God. Without this appeasement all people are justly destined for eternal punishment. See note on 1Jn 2:2. *through ... his blood ... received by faith.* Saving faith looks to Jesus Christ and his sacrificial death for us.

this to demonstrate his righteousness,
because in his forbearance he had left
the sins committed beforehand unpunished[o]— 26 he did it to demonstrate his
righteousness at the present time, so as
to be just and the one who justifies those
who have faith in Jesus.
27 Where, then, is boasting?[p] It is excluded. Because of what law? The law that requires works? No, because of the law that
requires faith. 28 For we maintain that a
person is justified by faith apart from the
works of the law.[q] 29 Or is God the God of
Jews only? Is he not the God of Gentiles
too? Yes, of Gentiles too,[r] 30 since there
is only one God, who will justify the circumcised by faith and the uncircumcised
through that same faith.[s] 31 Do we, then,
nullify the law by this faith? Not at all!
Rather, we uphold the law.

Abraham Justified by Faith

4 What then shall we say[t] that Abraham, our forefather according to the
flesh,[u] discovered in this matter? 2 If, in
fact, Abraham was justified by works, he
had something to boast about—but not
before God.[v] 3 What does Scripture say?
"Abraham believed God, and it was credited to him as righteousness."[a][w]
4 Now to the one who works, wages are
not credited as a gift[x] but as an obligation. 5 However, to the one who does not
work but trusts God who justifies the ungodly, their faith is credited as righteousness.[y] 6 David says the same thing when
he speaks of the blessedness of the one
to whom God credits righteousness apart
from works:

7 "Blessed are those
whose transgressions are forgiven,
whose sins are covered.
8 Blessed is the one
whose sin the Lord will never count
against them."[b][z]

9 Is this blessedness only for the circumcised, or also for the uncircumcised?[a] We
have been saying that Abraham's faith
was credited to him as righteousness.[b]
10 Under what circumstances was it credited? Was it after he was circumcised, or
before? It was not after, but before! 11 And
he received circumcision as a sign, a seal
of the righteousness that he had by faith
while he was still uncircumcised.[c] So then,
he is the father[d] of all who believe[e] but
have not been circumcised, in order that
righteousness might be credited to them.
12 And he is then also the father of the circumcised who not only are circumcised
but who also follow in the footsteps of the
faith that our father Abraham had before
he was circumcised.
13 It was not through the law that Abraham and his offspring received the promise[f] that he would be heir of the world,[g]
but through the righteousness that comes

3:25 [o] Ac 14:16; 17:30 **3:27** [p] Ro 2:17, 23; 4:2; 1Co 1:29-31; Eph 2:9 **3:28** [q] ver 20, 21; Ac 13:39; Gal 2:16; 3:11; Eph 2:9; Jas 2:20,24,26 **3:29** [r] Ac 10:34, 35; Ro 9:24; 10:12; 15:9; Gal 3:28 **3:30** [s] Ro 4:11, 12; Gal 3:8 **4:1** [t] S Ro 8:31 [u] S Lk 3:8 **4:2** [v] 1Co 1:31 **4:3** [w] ver 5,9, 22; Ge 15:6; Gal 3:6; Jas 2:23 **4:4** [x] Ro 11:6 **4:5** [y] ver 3,9,22; S Ro 9:30 **4:8** [z] Ps 32:1, 2; 103:12; 2Co 5:19 **4:9** [a] Ro 3:30 [b] S ver 3 **4:11** [c] Ge 17:10, 11 [d] ver 16, 17; S Lk 3:8 [e] S Ro 3:22 **4:13** [f] S Ac 13:32; Gal 3:16,29 [g] Ge 17:4-6

[a] 3 Gen. 15:6; also in verse 22 [b] 8 Psalm 32:1,2

3:25b–26 The sins of God's people, punished symbolically in the animal sacrifices of the OT period, were totally punished in the once-for-all sacrifice of Christ on the cross.

3:28 *by faith.* When Luther translated this passage, he added the word "alone," which, though not in the Greek, accurately reflects the meaning (see note on Jas 2:14–26).

3:30 *only one God.* By appealing to the first article of Jewish faith ("the LORD is one," Dt 6:4; see note there), Paul argues that there is only one way of salvation for both Jew ("circumcised") and Gentile ("uncircumcised"), namely, faith in Christ.

3:31 Paul anticipated being charged with antinomianism (against law): If justification comes by faith alone, then is not the law rejected? He gives a more complete answer in chs. 6–7 and reasserts the validity of the law in 13:8–10.

4:1 *Abraham, our forefather.* The great patriarch of the Jewish nation, the true example of a justified person (see Jas 2:21–23 and notes). The Jews of Jesus' time used Abraham as an example of justification by works, but Paul holds him up as a shining example of righteousness by faith (see vv. 9,22 and note on v. 22; cf. Gal 3:7–9 and notes).

4:2 *If ... Abraham was justified by works.* Many of Paul's Jewish contemporaries held that Abraham was justified by works (in the Apocrypha, see Ecclesiasticus 44:21), but the fact is that he was not (see v. 3), and therefore all boasting on his part is excluded.

4:3 The reference is to Ge 15:6 (see note there), where nothing is mentioned about works (see note on 3:21). *credited.* Abraham had kept no law, rendered no service and performed no ritual that earned credit to his account before God. His belief in God, who had made promises to him, was credited to him as righteousness.

4:6–8 God does not continue to credit unrighteousness to sinners who repent, but forgives them when they confess (see Ps 32:3–5 and notes; Eze 18:23,27–28,32 and notes on 18:23 and 18:32; 33:14–16).

4:9 See 3:30 and note.

4:10 *not after, but before!* Abraham was declared righteous (Ge 15:6) some 14 years before he was circumcised (Ge 17:24,26). See Gal 3:17 for a similar statement.

4:11 *sign.* Circumcision was, among other things, the outward sign of the righteousness that God had credited to Abraham for his faith (see Ge 17:11 and note). *So then.* Abraham is the "father" of believing Gentiles (the uncircumcised), because he believed and was justified before the rite of circumcision (the mark of Jews) was instituted.

4:12 *father of the circumcised.* Abraham is also the father of believing Jews. Thus his story shows that for Jew and Gentile alike there is only one way of justification—the way of faith.

4:13 *not through the law.* Not on the condition that the promise be merited by works of the law. *his offspring.* All those of whom Abraham is said to be father (vv. 11–12). *heir of the world.* "World" here refers to the creation, as in 1:20. No express mention of this heirship is made in the Genesis account of Abraham. He is promised "offspring like the dust of the earth" (Ge 13:16), possession of the land of Canaan (Ge 12:7; 13:14–15; 15:7,18–21; 17:8) and blessing through him (see Ge 12:2–3 and note; 18:18) or his offspring (Ge 22:18)

by faith.[h] 14 For if those who depend on the
law are heirs, faith means nothing and the
promise is worthless,[i] 15 because the law
brings wrath.[j] And where there is no law
there is no transgression.[k]
16 Therefore, the promise comes by faith,
so that it may be by grace[l] and may be
guaranteed[m] to all Abraham's offspring—
not only to those who are of the law but
also to those who have the faith of Abraham. He is the father of us all.[n] 17 As it
is written: "I have made you a father of
many nations."[a][o] He is our father in the
sight of God, in whom he believed—the
God who gives life[p] to the dead and calls[q]
into being things that were not.[r]
18 Against all hope, Abraham in hope believed and so became the father of many
nations,[s] just as it had been said to him,
"So shall your offspring be."[b][t] 19 Without
weakening in his faith, he faced the fact
that his body was as good as dead[u]—since
he was about a hundred years old[v]—and
that Sarah's womb was also dead.[w] 20 Yet he
did not waver through unbelief regarding
the promise of God, but was strengthened[x]
in his faith and gave glory to God,[y] 21 being fully persuaded that God had power to
do what he had promised.[z] 22 This is why
"it was credited to him as righteousness."[a]
23 The words "it was credited to him" were
written not for him alone, 24 but also for
us,[b] to whom God will credit righteousness—for us who believe in him[c] who
raised Jesus our Lord from the dead.[d] 25 He
was delivered over to death for our sins[e]
and was raised to life for our justification.[f]

Peace and Hope

5 Therefore, since we have been justified[g] through faith,[h] we[c] have peace[i]
with God through our Lord Jesus Christ,[j]
2 through whom we have gained access[k]
by faith into this grace in which we now
stand.[l] And we[d] boast in the hope[m] of
the glory of God. 3 Not only so, but we[d]
also glory in our sufferings,[n] because we
know that suffering produces perseverance;[o] 4 perseverance, character; and character, hope. 5 And hope[p] does not put us

[a] *17* Gen. 17:5 [b] *18* Gen. 15:5 [c] *1* Many manuscripts *let us* [d] *2,3* Or *let us*

4:13 [h] S Ro 9:30 **4:14** [i] Gal 3:18 **4:15** [j] Ro 7:7-25; 1Co 15:56; 2Co 3:7; Gal 3:10; S Ro 7:12 [k] Ro 3:20; 5:13; 7:7 **4:16** [l] S Ro 3:24 [m] Ro 15:8 [n] ver 11; S Lk 3:8; S Gal 3:16 **4:17** [o] Ge 17:5 [p] S Jn 5:21 [q] Isa 48:13 [r] 1Co 1:28 **4:18** [s] ver 17 [t] Ge 15:5 **4:19** [u] Heb 11:11, 12 [v] Ge 17:17 [w] Ge 18:11 **4:20** [x] 1Sa 30:6 [y] S Mt 9:8 **4:21** [z] Ge 18:14; S Mt 19:26 **4:22** [a] S ver 3 **4:24** [b] Ps 102:18; Hab 2:2; Ro 15:4; 1Co 9:10; 10:11; 2Ti 3:16, 17 [c] Ro 10:9; 1Pe 1:21 [d] S Ac 2:24 **4:25** [e] Isa 53:5,6; Ro 5:6,8; 8:32; 2Co 5:21 [f] Isa 53:11; Ro 3:24; 5:1,9,16,18; 8:30; 1Co 6:11; 2Co 5:15 **5:1** [g] S Ro 4:25 [h] S Ro 3:28 [i] S Lk 2:14 [j] ver 10 **5:2** [k] Eph 2:18; 3:12 [l] 1Co 15:1 [m] S Heb 3:6 **5:3** [n] S Mt 5:12 [o] S Heb 10:36 **5:5** [p] Php 1:20; S Heb 3:6; 1Jn 3:2,3

---

for all peoples on earth. But since, as Genesis already makes clear, God purposed through Abraham and his offspring to work out the destiny of the whole world, it was implicit in the promises to Abraham that he and his offspring would "inherit the land" (see Ps 37:9,11,22,29,34 and note on 37:9; Mt 5:5). The full realization of this awaits the consummation of the Messianic kingdom at Christ's return.

4:14 *those who depend on the law.* Those whose claim to the inheritance is based on obedience to the law. *promise.* See note on v. 13.

4:15 *the law brings wrath.* The law, because it reveals and even stimulates sin (see 7:7–11), produces wrath, not promise. *transgression.* Overstepping a clearly defined line. Where there is no law there is still sin, but it does not have the character of transgression.

4:16 A summary of the thought of vv. 11–12. For the close correlation between faith and grace, see 3:24–25; Eph 2:8–9 and notes. *those who are of the law.* Jewish Christians. *those who have the faith of Abraham.* Gentile Christians who share Abraham's faith but who, like Abraham, do not possess the law.

4:17 *in the sight of God.* God considers Abraham the father of Jews and believing Gentiles alike, no matter how others (especially the Jews) may see him. *the God who gives life to the dead.* The main reference is to the birth of Isaac through Abraham and Sarah, both of whom were far past the age of childbearing (see Ge 18:11). Secondarily Paul alludes also to the resurrection of Christ (see vv. 24–25 and notes). *calls into being things that were not.* God has the ability to create out of nothing, as he demonstrated in the birth of Isaac.

4:18 *Against all hope ... in hope believed.* When all hope, as a human possibility, failed, Abraham placed his hope in God.

4:19 *Without weakening in his faith.* Abraham had some anxious moments (see Ge 17:17–18), but God did not count these against him. *faced the fact.* Faith does not refuse to face reality but looks beyond all difficulties to God and his promises. *Sarah's womb was also dead.* Sarah was ten years younger than Abraham (see Ge 17:17) but well past the age of bearing children.

4:20 *gave glory to God.* Because Abraham had faith to believe that God would do what he promised. Whereas works are human attempts to establish a claim on God, faith brings glory to him.

4:22 *This is why.* Abraham's faith was "credited to him as righteousness" because it was true faith, i.e., complete confidence in God's promise.

4:23 *not for him alone.* Abraham's experience was not private or individual but had broad implications. If justification by faith was true for him, it is universally true.

4:24 *but also for us.* As Abraham was justified because he believed in a God who brought life from the dead, so we will be justified by believing "in him who raised Jesus our Lord from the dead" (see 10:9 and note).

4:25 These words, which reflect the Septuagint (Greek) translation of Isa 53:12, are probably quoted from a Christian confessional formula. *justification.* See 3:24 and note.

5:1 *peace with God.* Not merely a subjective feeling (peace of mind) but primarily an objective status, a new relationship with God: Once we were his enemies, but now we are his friends (see v. 10 and note; Eph 2:16; Col 1:21–22).

5:2 *access.* Jesus ushers us into the presence of God. The heavy curtain (of the temple) that separated us from God and God from us has been removed (see notes on Mt 27:51; Heb 10:19–22). *hope of the glory of God.* Our confidence that the purpose for which God created us will be ultimately realized (see note on 3:23).

5:3 *glory in our sufferings.* Not "because of" but "in." Paul does not advocate a morbid view of life but a joyous and triumphant one (see Jas 1:2 and note).

5:4 Christians can rejoice in suffering because they know that it is not meaningless. Part of God's purpose is to produce character in his children (see Jas 1:3).

5:5 *hope.* The believer's hope is not to be equated with unfounded optimism. On the contrary, it is the confi-

to shame, because God's love[q] has been poured out into our hearts through the Holy Spirit,[r] who has been given to us.
6 You see, at just the right time,[s] when we were still powerless,[t] Christ died for the ungodly.[u] 7 Very rarely will anyone die for a righteous person, though for a good person someone might possibly dare to die. 8 But God demonstrates his own love for us in this: While we were still sinners, Christ died for us.[v]
9 Since we have now been justified[w] by his blood,[x] how much more shall we be saved from God's wrath[y] through him! 10 For if, while we were God's enemies,[z] we were reconciled[a] to him through the death of his Son, how much more, having been reconciled, shall we be saved through his life![b] 11 Not only is this so, but we also boast in God through our Lord Jesus Christ, through whom we have now received reconciliation.[c]

Death Through Adam, Life Through Christ

12 Therefore, just as sin entered the world through one man,[d] and death through sin,[e] and in this way death came to all people, because all sinned[f]—
13 To be sure, sin was in the world before the law was given, but sin is not charged against anyone's account where there is no law.[g] 14 Nevertheless, death reigned from the time of Adam to the time of Moses, even over those who did not sin by breaking a command, as did Adam,[h] who is a pattern of the one to come.[i]
15 But the gift is not like the trespass. For if the many died by the trespass of the one man,[j] how much more did God's grace and the gift that came by the grace of the one man, Jesus Christ,[k] overflow to the many! 16 Nor can the gift of God be compared with the result of one man's sin: The judgment followed one sin and brought condemnation, but the gift followed many trespasses and brought justification. 17 For if, by the trespass of the one man, death[l] reigned through that one man, how much more will those who receive God's abundant provision of grace and of the gift of righteousness reign in life[m] through the one man, Jesus Christ!

5:5 [q] ver 8; Jn 3:16; Ro 8:39 [r] Ac 2:33; 10:45; Titus 3:5,6
5:6 [s] Mk 1:15; Gal 4:4; Eph 1:10 [t] ver 8, 10 [u] Ro 4:25
5:8 [v] Jn 3:16; 15:13; 1Pe 3:18; 1Jn 3:16; 4:10
5:9 [w] S Ro 4:25 [x] S Ro 3:25 [y] S Ro 1:18
5:10 [z] Ro 11:28; Col 1:21 [a] ver 11; Ro 11:15; 2Co 5:18, 19; Col 1:20, 22 [b] Ro 8:34; Heb 7:25
5:11 [c] S ver 10
5:12 [d] ver 15, 16,17; Ge 3:1-7; 1Co 15:21, 22 [e] ver 14,18; Ge 2:17; 3:19; S Ro 6:23 [f] S Ro 3:9
5:13 [g] S Ro 4:15
5:14 [h] Ge 3:11, 12 [i] 1Co 15:22, 45
5:15 [j] ver 12, 18,19 [k] Ac 15:11
5:17 [l] S ver 12 [m] Jn 10:10

---

dent expectation and blessed assurance of our future destiny and is based on God's love, which is revealed to us by the Holy Spirit and objectively demonstrated to us in the death of Christ. Paul has moved from faith (v. 1) to hope (vv. 2,4–5) to love (here; see 1Co 13:13; 1Th 1:3 and notes). *has been poured out.* The verb indicates a present status resulting from a past action. When we first believed in Christ, the Holy Spirit poured out his love in our hearts, and his love for us continues to dwell in us. *who has been given to us.* All true believers have the gift of the Spirit (see 8:9 and note).

5:6 *the right time.* The appointed moment in God's redemptive plan (see Mk 1:15 and note). *Christ died for the ungodly.* Christ's love is grounded in God's free grace and is not the result of any inherent worthiness found in its objects (humankind). In fact, it is lavished on us in spite of our undesirable character.

5:7 *righteous person ... good person.* "Righteous" and "good" may be synonymous terms, or "righteous" may refer to moral uprightness while "good" goes beyond this to genuine concern for others. Of course, we were neither righteous nor good, but sinners, when Christ died for us (see v. 8; 3:10–12).

5:9 *by his blood.* By laying down his life as a sacrifice—a reference to Christ's death for our sins (see 3:25 and note). *God's wrath.* The final judgment, as the verb "shall be saved" makes clear (see note on 1:18; cf. 1Th 1:9–10 and notes).

5:10 *God's enemies.* Humans are enemies of God, not the reverse. Thus the hostility must be removed from humans if reconciliation is to be accomplished. God took the initiative in bringing this about through the death of his Son (see v. 11; Col 1:21–22 and note on 1:20). *reconciled.* To reconcile is "to put an end to hostility," and is closely related to the term "justify," as the parallelism in vv. 9–10 indicates:

v. 9	v. 10
justified	reconciled
by his blood	through the death of his Son
shall we be saved	shall we be saved

saved through his life. A reference to the unending life and ministry of the resurrected Christ for his people (see Heb 7:25 and note). Since we were reconciled when we were God's enemies, we will be saved because Christ lives to keep us. See notes on 2Co 5:18,21.

5:11 *we have now received reconciliation.* Reconciliation, like justification (v. 1), is a present reality for Christians and is something to rejoice about (see Col 1:20 and note).

5:12–21 A contrast between Adam and Christ. Adam introduced sin and death into the world; Christ brought righteousness and life. The comparison begun in v. 12 is completed in v. 18; these two verses summarize the whole passage. These two men also sum up the message of the book up to this point. Adam stands for humanity's condemnation (1:18—3:20); Christ stands for the believer's justification (3:21—5:11).

5:12 *death.* Physical death is the penalty for sin. It is also the symbol of spiritual death—ultimate separation from God (Rev 20:15; 21:8). *because all sinned.* Not a repetition of 3:23. The context shows that Adam's sin involved the rest of humankind in condemnation (vv. 18–19) and death (v. 15). We do not start life with even the possibility of living it sinlessly; we begin it as sinners by nature (see Ge 8:21; Ps 51:5; 58:3 and notes; Eph 2:3).

5:13 *sin is not charged against anyone's account.* In the period when there was no (Mosaic) law, people were not charged with sin in the sense of "breaking a command" (v. 14).

5:14 *pattern.* Adam by his sin brought universal ruin on the human race. In this act he is the prototype of Christ, who through one righteous act (v. 18) brought universal blessing. The analogy is one of contrast.

5:15 *the many.* The same as "all people" in v. 12 (see Isa 53:11; Mk 10:45). *how much more.* A theme that runs through this section. God's grace is infinitely greater for good than is Adam's sin for evil.

5:16 *gift of God.* Salvation and "righteousness" (v. 17). *many trespasses.* The sins of the succeeding generations.

5:17 *will ... reign in life.* The future reign of believers with Jesus Christ (see 2Ti 2:12 and note; Rev 20:4,6; 22:5).

18Consequently, just as one trespass resulted in condemnation for all people,[n] so
also one righteous act resulted in justification[o] and life[p] for all people. 19For just as
through the disobedience of the one man[q]
the many were made sinners,[r] so also
through the obedience[s] of the one man the
many will be made righteous.
20The law was brought in so that the
trespass might increase.[t] But where sin increased, grace increased all the more,[u] 21so
that, just as sin reigned in death,[v] so also
grace[w] might reign through righteousness
to bring eternal life[x] through Jesus Christ
our Lord.

Dead to Sin, Alive in Christ

6 What shall we say, then?[y] Shall we
go on sinning so that grace may increase?[z] 2By no means! We are those
who have died to sin;[a] how can we live
in it any longer? 3Or don't you know that
all of us who were baptized[b] into Christ
Jesus were baptized into his death? 4We
were therefore buried with him through
baptism into death[c] in order that, just as
Christ was raised from the dead[d] through
the glory of the Father, we too may live a
new life.[e]
5For if we have been united with him
in a death like his, we will certainly also
be united with him in a resurrection like
his.[f] 6For we know that our old self[g] was
crucified with him[h] so that the body ruled
by sin[i] might be done away with,[a] that we
should no longer be slaves to sin[j]— 7be-
cause anyone who has died has been set
free from sin.[k]
8Now if we died with Christ, we believe
that we will also live with him.[l] 9For we
know that since Christ was raised from the
dead,[m] he cannot die again; death no longer has mastery over him.[n] 10The death he
died, he died to sin[o] once for all;[p] but the
life he lives, he lives to God.
11In the same way, count yourselves
dead to sin[q] but alive to God in Christ

[a] 6 Or *be rendered powerless*

5:18 [n]S ver 12 [o]S Ro 4:25 [p]Isa 53:11 **5:19** [q]ver 12 [r]S Ro 3:9 [s]S Php 2:8 **5:20** [t]Ro 3:20; 7:7,8; Gal 3:19 [u]Ro 6:1; 1Ti 1:13,14 **5:21** [v]ver 12, 14; S Ro 6:16 [w]S Ro 3:24 [x]S Mt 25:46 **6:1** [y]S Ro 8:31 [z]ver 15; Ro 3:5,8 **6:2** [a]S ver 6; ver 10,11; S ver 18; Ro 8:13; Col 3:3, 5; 1Pe 2:24 **6:3** [b]S Mt 28:19 **6:4** [c]S ver 6 [d]S Ac 2:24 [e]Ro 7:6; S 2Co 5:17; Eph 4:22-24; Col 3:10 **6:5** [f]ver 4, 8; Ro 8:11; 2Co 4:10; Eph 2:6; Php 3:10,11; Col 2:12; 3:1; 2Ti 2:11 **6:6** [g]S Gal 5:24; Eph 4:22; Col 3:9 [h]S ver 2; ver 3-8; 2Co 4:10; Gal 2:20; 5:24; 6:14; Php 3:10; Col 2:12,20; 3:3 [i]Ro 7:24 [j]S ver 16 **6:7** [k]S ver 18 **6:8** [l]S ver 5 **6:9** [m]ver 4; S Ac 2:24 [n]Rev 1:18 **6:10** [o]S ver 2 [p]S Heb 7:27 **6:11** [q]S ver 2

5:18 *life for all.* Contrast v. 12; does not mean that everyone eventually will be saved, but that salvation is available to all (see 1Jn 2:2 and note). To be effective, God's gracious gift must be received (see v. 17).

5:19 *made righteous.* A reference to a person's status before God (see v. 17; 2Co 5:21 and note), not to a change in character. The latter (the doctrine of sanctification) is developed in chs. 6–8.

5:20 *law was brought in.* Not to bring about redemption but to point out the need for it. The law made sin even more sinful by revealing what sin is in stark contrast to God's holiness.

6:1—8:39 In 3:21—5:21 Paul explains how God has provided for our redemption and justification. He next explains the doctrine of sanctification—the process by which believers grow to maturity in Christ. He treats this subject in three parts: (1) freedom from sin's tyranny (ch. 6), (2) freedom from the law's condemnation (ch. 7) and (3) life in the power of the Holy Spirit (ch. 8).

6:1 *Shall we go on sinning so that grace may increase?* This question arose out of what Paul had just said in 5:20: "Where sin increased, grace increased all the more." His answer is "By no means!" (v. 2). Then he explains his answer.

6:2 *died to sin.* The reference is to an event in the past and is explained in v. 3.

6:3-4 The when and how of the Christian's death to sin. In NT times baptism so closely followed conversion that the two were considered part of one event (see Ac 2:38 and note). So although baptism is not a means by which we enter into a vital faith relationship with Jesus Christ, it is closely associated with faith (see 1Pe 3:21 and note). Baptism depicts graphically what happens as a result of the Christian's union with Christ, which comes with faith—through faith we are united with Christ, just as through our natural birth we are united with Adam. As we fell into sin and became subject to death in father Adam, so we now have died and been raised again with Christ—which baptism symbolizes.

6:3 *know.* Three key words in this chapter are "know" (here and in vv. 6,9), "offer" (vv. 13,16,19) and "obey" (vv. 12, 16–17).

6:4 *buried with him through baptism into death.* Amplified in vv. 5–7. *through the glory of the Father.* By the power of God. God's glory is his divine excellence, his perfection. Any one of his attributes is a manifestation of his excellence. Thus his power is a manifestation of his glory, as is his righteousness (see 3:23 and note). Glory and power are often closely related in the Bible (see Ps 145:11; Col 1:11; 1Pe 4:11; Rev 1:6; 4:11; 5:12–13; 7:12; 19:1). *live a new life.* Amplified in vv. 8–10.

6:6 *our old self.* Our unregenerate self; what we once were in Adam (1Co 15:22; see note there; see also Ro 5:12–21 and note). *crucified with him.* See vv. 7,8,11,12–13; Gal 2:20 and notes. *body ruled by sin.* The self in its pre-Christian state, dominated by sin. This is a figurative expression in which the old self is personified. It is a "body" that can be put to death. For the believer, this old self has been "rendered powerless" (see NIV text note) so that it can no longer enslave us to sin—whatever lingering vitality it may yet exert in its death throes.

6:7 *has died.* The believer's death with Christ to sin's ruling power (see v. 3). *set free from sin.* Not sinless, but free from sin's shackles and power.

6:8 As resurrection followed death in the experience of Christ, so the believer who dies with Christ is raised to a new quality of life here and now. Resurrection in the sense of a new birth is already a fact, and it increasingly exerts itself in the believer's life.

6:10 *he died to sin once for all.* See Heb 9:12 and note. In his death Christ (for the sake of sinners) submitted to the "reign" of sin (5:21); but his death broke the judicial link between sin and death, and he passed forever from the sphere of sin's "reign." Having been raised from the dead, he now lives forever to glorify God. *to God.* For the glory of God.

6:11 *count yourselves.* The first step toward victory over sin in the life of believers (for the succeeding steps, see note on vv. 12–13). They are dead to sin and alive to God, and by faith they are to live in the light of this truth.

Jesus. 12 Therefore do not let sin
reign[r] in your mortal body so that
you obey its evil desires. 13 Do not
offer any part of yourself to sin as
an instrument of wickedness,[s] but
rather offer yourselves to God as
those who have been brought from
death to life; and offer every part
of yourself to him as an instrument
of righteousness.[t] 14 For sin shall
no longer be your master,[u] because
you are not under the law,[v] but under grace.[w]

Slaves to Righteousness

15 What then? Shall we sin because we are not under the law
but under grace?[x] By no means!
16 Don't you know that when you
offer yourselves to someone as
obedient slaves, you are slaves of
the one you obey[y]—whether you
are slaves to sin,[z] which leads to
death,[a] or to obedience, which
leads to righteousness? 17 But
thanks be to God[b] that, though you
used to be slaves to sin,[c] you have
come to obey from your heart the
pattern of teaching[d] that has now
claimed your allegiance. 18 You
have been set free from sin[e] and have become slaves to righteousness.[f]
19 I am using an example from everyday
life[g] because of your human limitations.
Just as you used to offer yourselves as
slaves to impurity and to ever-increasing
wickedness, so now offer yourselves as
slaves to righteousness[h] leading to holiness. 20 When you were slaves to sin,[i] you
were free from the control of righteousness.[j] 21 What benefit did you reap at that
time from the things you are now ashamed
of? Those things result in death![k] 22 But
now that you have been set free from
sin[l] and have become slaves of God,[m] the

A Jewish *mikveh*, or ritual bath, south of the temple mount. These baths were used by worshipers to cleanse themselves ceremonially before entering the temple. "Don't you know that all of us who were baptized into Christ Jesus were baptized into his death? We were therefore buried with him through baptism into death in order that, just as Christ was raised from the dead through the glory of the Father, we too may live a new life" (Ro 6:3–4). Just as ancient worshipers entered a *mikveh* unclean and came out clean, so those who are baptized in Christ have a new life.

www.HolyLandPhotos.org

6:12 [r]ver 16 **6:13** [s]ver 16, 19; Ro 7:5 [t]Ro 12:1; 2Co 5:14, 15; 1Pe 2:24 **6:14** [u]S ver 16 [v]S Ro 2:12 [w]S Ro 3:24 **6:15** [x]ver 1, 14 **6:16** [y]2Pe 2:19 [z]ver 6, 12, 14, 17, 20; Ge 4:7; Ps 51:5; 119:133; Jn 8:34; Ro 5:21; 7:14, 23, 25; 8:2; 2Pe 2:19 [a]S ver 23 **6:17** [b]Ro 1:8; S 2Co 2:14 [c]S ver 16 [d]2Ti 1:13 **6:18** [e]S ver 2; ver 7, 22; Ro 8:2; 1Pe 4:1; S ver 16 [f]S ver 22 **6:19** [g]Ro 3:5; Gal 3:15 [h]S ver 13; S ver 22 **6:20** [i]S ver 16 [j]ver 16 **6:21** [k]S ver 23 **6:22** [l]S ver 18 [m]ver 18, 19; Ro 7:25; 1Co 7:22; Eph 6:6; 1Pe 2:16

---

in Christ. The first occurrence in Romans of this phrase, which is found often in Paul's writings. True believers are "in Christ" because they have died with Christ and have been raised to new life with him. See note on Eph 1:1.

6:12–13 A call for Christians to become in practice what they already are in their status before God—dead to sin (see vv. 5–7) and alive to God (see vv. 8–10). The second step toward victory over sin is refusal to let sin reign in one's life (v. 12). The third step is to offer oneself to God (v. 13).

6:13 *offer.* Put yourselves in the service of, perhaps also echoing the language of sacrifice. *every part of yourself.* All the separate capacities of your being (also in v. 19).

6:14 *sin shall no longer be your master.* Paul conceived of sin as a power that enslaves, and so personified it (see Ps 19:13). *not under the law.* The meaning is not that Christians have been freed from all moral authority. They have, however, been freed from the law in the manner in which God's people were under law in the OT era. Law provides no enablement to resist the power of sin; it only condemns the sinner. But grace enables. *under grace.* For the disciplinary aspect of grace, see Titus 2:11–12 and notes.

6:15–23 The question raised here seems to come from those who are afraid that the doctrine of justification by faith alone will remove all moral restraint. Paul rejects such a suggestion and shows that Christians do not throw morality to the winds. To the contrary, they exchange sin for righteousness as their master.

6:16 The contrast between sin and obedience suggests that sin is by nature disobedience to God.

6:17 *have come to obey from your heart.* Christian obedience is not forced or legalistic, but willing. *pattern of teaching.* May refer to a summary of the moral and ethical teachings of Christ that was given to new converts in the early church.

6:18 *slaves to righteousness.* Christians have changed masters. Whereas they were formerly slaves to sin (vv. 16–17), now they become slaves (willing servants) to righteousness.

6:19 *I am using an example from everyday life.* Paul apologizes for using an imperfect analogy. The word "slave" when applied to Christians, who are free in Christ, naturally presents problems.

6:22 *set free from sin.* See note on v. 6. *holiness.* Slavery to God produces holiness, and the end of the process is eternal life (viewed not in its present sense but in its final, future sense). There is no eternal life without holiness (see Heb 12:14). Those who have been justified will surely give

benefit you reap leads to holiness, and the result is eternal life.[n] 23 For the wages of sin is death,[o] but the gift of God is eternal life[p] in[a] Christ Jesus our Lord.

Released From the Law, Bound to Christ

7 Do you not know, brothers and sisters[q]—for I am speaking to those who know the law—that the law has authority over someone only as long as that person lives? 2 For example, by law a married woman is bound to her husband as long as he is alive, but if her husband dies, she is released from the law that binds her to him.[r] 3 So then, if she has sexual relations with another man while her husband is still alive, she is called an adulteress.[s] But if her husband dies, she is released from that law and is not an adulteress if she marries another man.

4 So, my brothers and sisters, you also died to the law[t] through the body of Christ,[u] that you might belong to another,[v] to him who was raised from the dead, in order that we might bear fruit for God. 5 For when we were in the realm of the flesh,[b][w] the sinful passions aroused by the law[x] were at work in us,[y] so that we bore fruit for death.[z] 6 But now, by dying to what once bound us, we have been released from the law[a] so that we serve in the new way of the Spirit, and not in the old way of the written code.[b]

The Law and Sin

7 What shall we say, then?[c] Is the law sinful? Certainly not![d] Nevertheless, I would not have known what sin was had it not been for the law.[e] For I would not have known what coveting really was if the law had not said, "You shall not covet."[c][f] 8 But sin, seizing the opportunity afforded by the commandment,[g] produced in me every kind of coveting. For apart from the law, sin was dead.[h] 9 Once I was alive apart from the law; but when the commandment came, sin sprang to life and I died. 10 I found that the very commandment that was intended to bring life[i] actually brought death. 11 For sin, seizing the opportunity afforded by the commandment,[j] deceived me,[k] and through the commandment put me to death. 12 So then, the law is holy, and the commandment is holy, righteous and good.[l]

a 23 Or *through* *b* 5 In contexts like this, the Greek word for *flesh* (*sarx*) refers to the sinful state of human beings, often presented as a power in opposition to the Spirit. *c* 7 Exodus 20:17; Deut. 5:21

6:22 [n] S Mt 25:46 **6:23** [o] ver 16, 21; Ge 2:17; Pr 10:16; Eze 18:4; Ro 1:32; S 5:12; 7:5, 13; 8:6, 13; Gal 6:7, 8; Jas 1:15 [p] S Mt 25:46 **7:1** [q] S Ac 1:16; S 22:5; Ro 1:13; 1Co 1:10; 5:11; 6:6; 14:20, 26; Gal 3:15; 6:18 **7:2** [r] 1Co 7:39 **7:3** [s] S Lk 16:18 **7:4** [t] ver 6; S Ro 6:6; 8:2; Gal 2:19; 3:23-25; 4:31; 5:1 [u] Col 1:22 [v] Gal 2:19, 20 **7:5** [w] S Gal 5:24 [x] Ro 7:7-11 [y] Ro 6:13 [z] S Ro 6:23 **7:6** [a] S ver 4 [b] Ro 2:29; 2Co 3:6 **7:7** [c] S Ro 8:31 [d] S ver 12 [e] S Ro 4:15 [f] Ex 20:17; Dt 5:21 **7:8** [g] ver 11 [h] S Ro 4:15 **7:10** [i] Lev 18:5; Lk 10:26-28; S Ro 10:5; Gal 3:12 **7:11** [j] ver 8 [k] Ge 3:13 **7:12** [l] ver 7, 13, 14, 16; Ro 8:4; Gal 3:21; 1Ti 1:8; S Ro 4:15

---

evidence of that fact by the presence of holiness in their lives. For other occurrences of the word "holiness," see v. 19; 1Co 1:30 and note on 1:2; 1Ti 2:15; Heb 12:14. For "holy," see Lev 11:44 and note; 1Th 4:4,7. For "sanctified," see 1Th 4:3. For "sanctifying work," see 2Th 2:13; 1Pe 1:2 and note.

6:23 Two kinds of servitude are contrasted here. One brings death as its wages; the other results in eternal life, not as wages earned or merited but as a gift of God (cf. Eph 2:8–9 and notes). For the contrast between wages and gift, see 4:4. *eternal life.* See Jn 17:3.

7:1 *the law.* Perhaps Paul has in mind the Mosaic law, but his concern here is with the fundamental character of law as such.

7:2–3 These verses illustrate the principle set down in v. 1. Death decisively changes a person's relationship to the law.

7:4 *So.* Paul now draws the conclusion from the principle stated in v. 1 and illustrated in vv. 2–3. *died to the law.* The law's power to condemn no longer threatens believers, whose death here is to be understood in terms of 6:2–7. There, however, they die to sin; here they die to the law. The result is that the law has no more hold on them. *through the body of Christ.* His physical body (self) crucified. *belong to another.* The resurrected Christ (see 6:5; cf. Titus 2:14; 1Pe 2:9 and note). The purpose of this union is to produce the fruit of holiness.

7:5 *in the realm of the flesh.* A condition, so far as Christians are concerned, that belongs to the past—the unregenerate state (cf. 1Co 6:11; Gal 5:19–23 and notes). *aroused by the law.* The law not only reveals sin; it also stimulates it. The natural human tendency is to desire the forbidden thing. *death.* Physical death and, beyond that, spiritual death—final separation from God (see note on 5:12)—were the fruit of our union with the law (cf. note on v. 4).

7:6 *what once bound us.* The law (see later in this verse, as well as v. 4). *released from the law.* In the sense of its condemnation (see note on v. 4). *new way of the Spirit.* See note on 8:4. *old way of the written code.* Life under the OT law.

7:7 *Is the law sinful?* This question was occasioned by the remarks about the law in vv. 4–6. *I.* Paul seems to be using the first person pronoun of himself, but also as representative of people in general (vv. 7–12) and of Christians in particular (vv. 13–25). *I would not have known what sin was.* The law fulfilled the important function of revealing the presence and fact of sin.

7:8 *opportunity afforded by the commandment.* See note on v. 5. *sin was dead.* Not nonexistent but not fully perceived (see 5:13 and note).

7:9 *Once I was alive.* Paul reviews his own experience from the vantage point of his present understanding. Before he realized that the law condemned him to death, he was alive. Reference is to the time either before his *bar mitzvah* (see below) or before his conversion, when the true rigor of the law became clear to him (cf. Lk 18:20–21; see Php 3:6 and note). *when the commandment came.* When Paul came to the realization that he stood guilty before the law—a reference either to his *bar mitzvah,* when he, at age 13, assumed full responsibility for the law, or to the time when he became aware of the full force of the law (at his conversion). *I died.* Paul came to realize he was condemned to death, because law reveals sin, and sin's wages is death (see 6:23 and note).

7:10 *was intended to bring life.* See Lev 18:5 and note. As it worked out in Paul's experience, the law became the avenue through which sin entered generally. Instead of giving life, the law brought condemnation; instead of producing holiness, it stimulated sin.

7:12 *the law is holy.* Despite the despicable use that sin made of the law, the law was not to blame. The law is God's and as such is "holy, righteous and good."

13 Did that which is good, then, become
death to me? By no means! Nevertheless,
in order that sin might be recognized as
sin, it used what is good[m] to bring about
my death,[n] so that through the commandment sin might become utterly sinful.
14 We know that the law is spiritual; but
I am unspiritual,[o] sold[p] as a slave to sin.[q]
15 I do not understand what I do. For what
I want to do I do not do, but what I hate I
do.[r] 16 And if I do what I do not want to do,
I agree that the law is good.[s] 17 As it is, it is
no longer I myself who do it, but it is sin
living in me.[t] 18 For I know that good itself
does not dwell in me, that is, in my sinful
nature.[a][u] For I have the desire to do what
is good, but I cannot carry it out. 19 For I do
not do the good I want to do, but the evil I
do not want to do—this I keep on doing.[v]
20 Now if I do what I do not want to do, it
is no longer I who do it, but it is sin living
in me that does it.[w]
21 So I find this law at work:[x] Although
I want to do good, evil is right there with
me. 22 For in my inner being[y] I delight in
God's law;[z] 23 but I see another law at work
in me, waging war[a] against the law of my
mind and making me a prisoner of the
law of sin[b] at work within me. 24 What a
wretched man I am! Who will rescue me
from this body that is subject to death?[c]
25 Thanks be to God, who delivers me
through Jesus Christ our Lord![d]
So then, I myself in my mind am a slave
to God's law,[e] but in my sinful nature[b] a
slave to the law of sin.[f]

Life Through the Spirit

8 Therefore, there is now no condemnation[g] for those who are in Christ
Jesus,[h] 2 because through Christ Jesus[i] the
law of the Spirit who gives life[j] has set
you[c] free[k] from the law of sin[l] and death.
3 For what the law was powerless[m] to do
because it was weakened by the flesh,[d][n]
God did by sending his own Son in the

a 18 Or *my flesh* *b* 25 Or *in the flesh* *c* 2 The Greek is singular; some manuscripts *me* *d* 3 In contexts like this, the Greek word for *flesh* (*sarx*) refers to the sinful state of human beings, often presented as a power in opposition to the Spirit; also in verses 4-13.

7:13 [m] S ver 12 [n] S Ro 6:23 **7:14** [o] 1Co 3:1 [p] 1Ki 21:20, 25; 2Ki 17:17 [q] S Ro 6:16 **7:15** [r] ver 19; Gal 5:17 **7:16** [s] S ver 12 **7:17** [t] ver 20 **7:18** [u] ver 25; S Gal 5:24 **7:19** [v] ver 15 **7:20** [w] ver 17 **7:21** [x] ver 23,25 **7:22** [y] Eph 3:16 [z] Ps 1:2; 40:8 **7:23** [a] Gal 5:17; Jas 4:1; 1Pe 2:11 [b] S Ro 6:16 **7:24** [c] Ro 6:6; 8:2 **7:25** [d] S 2Co 2:14 [e] S Ro 6:22 [f] S Ro 6:16 **8:1** [g] ver 34 [h] ver 39; S Ro 16:3 **8:2** [i] Ro 7:25 [j] 1Co 15:45 [k] Jn 8:32,36; S Ro 6:18 [l] S Ro 6:16; S 7:4

8:3 [m] Heb 7:18; 10:1-4 [n] Ro 7:18,19; S Gal 5:24

7:13–25 Whether Paul is describing a Christian or non-Christian experience has been hotly debated through the centuries. That he is speaking of the non-Christian life is suggested by: (1) the use of phrases such as "sold as a slave to sin" (v. 14), "I know that good itself does not dwell in me" (v. 18) and "What a wretched man I am!" (v. 24)—which do not seem to describe Christian experience; (2) the contrast between ch. 7 and ch. 8, making it difficult for the other view to be credible; (3) the problem of the value of conversion if one ends up in spiritual misery. In favor of the view that Paul is describing Christian experience are: (1) the use of the present tense throughout the passage; (2) Paul's humble opinion of himself (v. 18); (3) his high regard for God's law (vv. 14,16); (4) the location of this passage in the section of Romans where Paul is dealing with sanctification—the growth of the Christian in holiness.

7:13 Sin used a holy thing (law) for an unholy end (death). By this fact the contemptible nature of sin is revealed.

7:14 *spiritual.* The law had its origin in God. *I am.* The personal pronoun and the verb, taken together, suggest that Paul is describing his present (Christian) experience. *unspiritual.* Even believers have the seeds of rebellion in their hearts. *sold as a slave to sin.* A phrase so strong that many refuse to accept it as descriptive of a Christian. However, it may graphically point out the failure even of Christians to meet the radical ethical and moral demands of the gospel. It also points up the persistent nature of sin. Cf. Paul's statement in 1Ti 1:15: "sinners—of whom I am the worst" (see note there).

7:15 *I do not understand.* The struggle within creates tension, ambivalence and confusion (cf. Gal 5:16–17 and notes).

7:16 *I agree that the law is good.* Even when Paul is rebellious and disobedient, the Holy Spirit reveals to him the essential goodness of the law.

7:17 *no longer I myself who do it.* Not an attempt to escape moral responsibility but a statement of the great control sin can have over a Christian's life.

7:18 *good itself does not dwell in me.* A reference to Paul's fallen nature, as the last phrase of the sentence indicates.

7:20 *sin ... does it.* See note on v. 17.

7:21 *law.* Here means "principle."

7:22 *I delight in God's law.* The Mosaic law or God's law generally. It is difficult to see how a non-Christian could say this.

7:23 *another law.* A principle or force at work in Paul, preventing him from giving obedience to God's law. *law of my mind.* His desire to obey God's law. *law of sin.* Essentially the same as "another law," mentioned above.

7:24 *body that is subject to death.* Figurative for the body of sin (see 6:6; 8:10 and notes) that hung on him like a corpse and from which he could not gain freedom.

7:25 The first half of this verse is the answer to the question raised in v. 24—deliverance comes, not through legalistic effort, but through Christ (see 8:2 and note). The last half is a summary of vv. 13–24. *I myself.* The real self—the inner being that delights in God's law (see v. 22 and note). *slave to the law of sin.* Christians must reckon with the enslaving power of their sinfulness (see note on v. 23) as long as they live—until "the redemption of our bodies" (8:23).

8:1 *condemnation.* The law brings condemnation and death because it points out, stimulates and condemns sin. But the Christian is no longer "under the law" (6:14; see note there). *in Christ Jesus.* United with him, as explained in 6:1–10 (see note on 6:11; see also Eph 1:1; Php 2:1 and notes).

8:2 *law of the Spirit who gives life.* The controlling power of the Holy Spirit, who is life-giving (see 1:16 and note). Paul uses the word "law" in several different ways in Romans—to mean, e.g., a controlling power (here); God's law (2:17–20; 9:31; 10:3–5); the Pentateuch (3:21b); the OT as a whole (see 3:19 and note); and a principle (3:27). *law of sin and death.* The controlling power of sin, which ultimately produces death (see 7:24 and note).

8:3 *powerless to do.* The law was not able to overcome sin (cf. Heb 7:18 and note). It could point out, condemn and even stimulate sin, but it could not remove it, and it could not enable believers to obey that law perfectly (see note on v. 4, "according to the Spirit," which presents the Holy Spirit as our great enabler). *in the likeness of sinful flesh.* Christ in his incarnation became truly human, but, unlike all other humans, was sinless (see note on Mt 4:1–11). *in the flesh.* Probably referring to Christ's human body (on the cross).

likeness of sinful flesh[o] to be a sin offering.[a][p] And so he condemned sin in the
flesh, 4 in order that the righteous requirement[q] of the law might be fully met in us,
who do not live according to the flesh but
according to the Spirit.[r]
5 Those who live according to the flesh
have their minds set on what the flesh desires;[s] but those who live in accordance
with the Spirit have their minds set on
what the Spirit desires.[t] 6 The mind governed by the flesh is death,[u] but the mind
governed by the Spirit is life[v] and peace.
7 The mind governed by the flesh is hostile
to God;[w] it does not submit to God's law,
nor can it do so. 8 Those who are in the
realm of the flesh[x] cannot please God.
9 You, however, are not in the realm of
the flesh[y] but are in the realm of the Spirit, if indeed the Spirit of God lives in you.[z]
And if anyone does not have the Spirit of
Christ,[a] they do not belong to Christ. 10 But
if Christ is in you,[b] then even though your
body is subject to death because of sin,
the Spirit gives life[b] because of righteousness. 11 And if the Spirit of him who raised
Jesus from the dead[c] is living in you, he
who raised Christ from the dead will also
give life to your mortal bodies[d] because of[c]
his Spirit who lives in you.
12 Therefore, brothers and sisters, we
have an obligation — but it is not to the
flesh, to live according to it.[e] 13 For if you
live according to the flesh, you will die;[f]
but if by the Spirit you put to death the
misdeeds of the body,[g] you will live.[h]
14 For those who are led by the Spirit of
God[i] are the children of God.[j] 15 The Spirit[k]
you received does not make you slaves,
so that you live in fear again;[l] rather, the
Spirit you received brought about your
adoption to sonship.[d] And by him we cry,
"Abba,[e] Father."[m] 16 The Spirit himself testifies with our spirit[n] that we are God's
children.[o] 17 Now if we are children, then
we are heirs[p] — heirs of God and co-heirs
with Christ, if indeed we share in his sufferings[q] in order that we may also share
in his glory.[r]

8:3 [o]S Php 2:7 [p]Heb 2:14,17 **8:4** [q]Ro 2:26 [r]S Gal 5:16 **8:5** [s]Gal 5:19-21 [t]Gal 5:22-25 **8:6** [u]S Ro 6:23 [v]ver 13; Gal 6:8 **8:7** [w]Jas 4:4 **8:8** [x]S Gal 5:24 **8:9** [y]S Gal 5:24 [z]ver 11; 1Co 6:19; 2Ti 1:14 [a]Jn 14:17; S Ac 16:7; 1Jn 4:13 **8:10** [b]ver 9; Ex 29:45; Jn 14:20,23; 2Co 13:5; Gal 2:20; Eph 3:17; Col 1:27; Rev 3:20 **8:11** [c]S Ac 2:24 [d]Jn 5:21; S Ro 6:5 **8:12** [e]ver 4; S Gal 5:24 **8:13** [f]S Ro 6:23 [g]S Ro 6:2 [h]ver 6; Gal 6:8 **8:14** [i]S Gal 5:18 [j]ver 19; Hos 1:10; Mal 3:17; Mt 5:9; S Jn 1:12; Gal 3:26; 4:5; Eph 1:5; Rev 21:7 **8:15** [k]S Jn 20:22 [l]S 2Ti 1:7 [m]Mk 14:36; Gal 4:5,6

Present Suffering and Future Glory

18 I consider that our present sufferings
are not worth comparing with the glory
that will be revealed in us.[s] 19 For the creation waits in eager expectation for the
children of God[t] to be revealed. 20 For the
creation was subjected to frustration, not
by its own choice, but by the will of the

[a] 3 Or *flesh, for sin* [b] 10 Or *you, your body is dead because of sin, yet your spirit is alive* [c] 11 Some manuscripts *bodies through* [d] 15 The Greek word for *adoption to sonship* is a term referring to the full legal standing of an adopted male heir in Roman culture; also in verse 23. [e] 15 Aramaic for *father*

8:16 [n]2Co 1:22; Eph 1:13 [o]S ver 14; S Jn 1:12 **8:17** [p]S Ac 20:32; Gal 3:29; 4:7; Eph 3:6; Titus 3:7 [q]S 2Co 1:5 [r]2Ti 2:12; 1Pe 4:13 **8:18** [s]2Co 4:17; 1Pe 4:13; 5:1 **8:19** [t]S ver 14

8:4 *righteous requirement of the law.* The law still plays a role in the life of a believer — not, however, as a means of salvation but as a moral and ethical guide, obeyed out of love for God and by the power that the Spirit provides. This is the fulfillment of Jer 31:31 – 34 (a prophecy of the new covenant; see notes there). *fully met.* Lit. "fulfilled." God's aim in sending his Son was that believers might be enabled to embody the true and full intentions of the law. *according to the Spirit.* How the law's "righteous requirement" can be fully met — by no longer letting the flesh hold sway but by yielding to the directing and empowering ministry of the Holy Spirit.

8:5 – 8 Two mindsets are described here: that of the flesh and that of the Spirit. The former leads to death, the latter to life and peace. The flesh is bound up with death (v. 6), hostility to God (v. 7), insubordination (v. 7) and unacceptability to God (v. 8).

8:9 Paul makes it unmistakably clear that "the Spirit of God lives in" every believer.

8:10 *your body is subject to death because of sin.* Even a Christian's body is subject to physical death, the consequence of sin. *the Spirit gives life.* See v. 2 and note. On this reading, "body" is understood as in 7:24. For another reading, see NIV text note. *because of righteousness.* Christians are indwelt by the life-giving Spirit as a result of their justification.

8:11 For the close connection between the resurrection of Christ and that of believers, see 1Co 6:14; 15:20,23; 2Co 4:14; Php 3:21; 1Th 4:14 and notes. *give life to your mortal bodies.* The resurrection of our bodies is guaranteed to believers by the indwelling presence of the Holy Spirit — whose presence is evidenced by a Spirit-controlled life (vv. 4 – 9), which in turn provides assurance that our resurrection is certain even now.

8:14 *children of God.* God is the Father of all in the sense that he created all and his love and providential care are extended to all (see Mt 5:45 and note). But not all are his children. Jesus said to the unbelieving Jews of his day, "You belong to your father, the devil" (Jn 8:44; see note there). People become children of God through faith in God's unique Son (see Jn 1:12 and note), and being led by God's Spirit is the hallmark of this relationship.

8:15 *adoption to sonship.* See NIV text note. The Greek word for this phrase occurs four other times in the NT (v. 23; 9:4; Gal 4:5 [see note there]; Eph 1:5). Adoption was common among the Greeks and Romans, who granted the adopted son all the privileges of a natural son, including inheritance rights. Christians are adopted sons by grace; Christ, however, is God's Son by nature. *Abba, Father.* Expressive of an especially close relationship to God (see also NIV text note).

8:16 *testifies with our spirit.* The inner testimony of the Holy Spirit to our relationship to Christ.

8:17 *heirs.* Those who have already entered, at least partially, into the possession of their inheritance. *co-heirs with Christ.* Everything really belongs to Christ, but by grace we share in what is his. *if indeed we share in his sufferings.* The meaning is not that there is some doubt about sharing Christ's glory. Rather, despite the fact that Christians presently suffer, they are assured a future entrance into their inheritance.

8:19 *creation.* Both animate and inanimate, but exclusive of human beings (see vv. 22 – 23, where "whole creation" and "we ourselves" are contrasted). *children of God to be revealed.* Christians are already children of God, but the full manifestation of all that this means will not come until the end (see 1Jn 3:1 – 2).

8:20 *was subjected to frustration.* A reference to Ge 3:17 – 19.

one who subjected it,[u] in hope [21]that[a] the
creation itself will be liberated from its
bondage to decay[v] and brought into the
freedom and glory of the children of God.[w]
[22]We know that the whole creation has
been groaning[x] as in the pains of childbirth right up to the present time. [23]Not
only so, but we ourselves, who have the
firstfruits of the Spirit,[y] groan[z] inwardly as
we wait eagerly[a] for our adoption to sonship, the redemption of our bodies.[b] [24]For
in this hope we were saved.[c] But hope that
is seen is no hope at all.[d] Who hopes for
what they already have? [25]But if we hope
for what we do not yet have, we wait for
it patiently.[e]
[26]In the same way, the Spirit helps us in
our weakness. We do not know what we
ought to pray for, but the Spirit[f] himself intercedes for us[g] through wordless groans.
[27]And he who searches our hearts[h] knows
the mind of the Spirit, because the Spirit
intercedes[i] for God's people in accordance
with the will of God.
[28]And we know that in all things God
works for the good[j] of those who love him,
who[b] have been called[k] according to his
purpose.[l] [29]For those God foreknew[m] he
also predestined[n] to be conformed to the
image of his Son,[o] that he might be the
firstborn[p] among many brothers and sisters. [30]And those he predestined,[q] he also
called;[r] those he called, he also justified;[s]
those he justified, he also glorified.[t]

More Than Conquerors

[31]What, then, shall we say in response
to these things?[u] If God is for us,[v] who can
be against us?[w] [32]He who did not spare his
own Son,[x] but gave him up for us all—
how will he not also, along with him,
graciously give us all things? [33]Who will
bring any charge[y] against those whom God
has chosen? It is God who justifies. [34]Who
then is the one who condemns?[z] No one.
Christ Jesus who died[a]—more than that,
who was raised to life[b]—is at the right
hand of God[c] and is also interceding for
us.[d] [35]Who shall separate us from the
love of Christ?[e] Shall trouble or hardship

8:20 [u]Ge 3:17-19; 5:29 **8:21** [v]Ac 3:21; 2Pe 3:13; Rev 21:1 [w]S Jn 1:12 **8:22** [x]Jer 12:4 **8:23** [y]S 2Co 5:5 [z]2Co 5:2, 4 [a]ver 19; Gal 5:5 [b]ver 11; Php 3:21 **8:24** [c]1Th 5:8; Titus 3:7 [d]S 2Co 4:18 **8:25** [e]Ps 37:7 **8:26** [f]ver 15,16 [g]Eph 6:18 **8:27** [h]S Rev 2:23 [i]S ver 34 **8:28** [j]Ge 50:20; Isa 38:17; Jer 29:11 [k]ver 30; Ro 11:29; 1Co 1:9; Gal 1:6, 15; Eph 4:1, 4; 1Th 2:12; 2Ti 1:9; Heb 9:15; 1Pe 2:9; 2Pe 1:10 [l]Eph 1:11; 3:11; Heb 6:17 **8:29** [m]Ro 11:2; 1Pe 1:2 [n]Eph 1:5, 11 [o]1Co 15:49; 2Co 3:18; Php 3:21; 1Jn 3:2 [p]S Col 1:18 **8:30** [q]Eph 1:5, 11 [r]S ver 28 [s]S Ro 4:25 [t]Ro 9:23 **8:31** [u]Ro 4:1; 6:1; 7:7; 9:14, 30 [v]Ex 3:12; Isa 41:10; Hag 1:13 [w]Ps 56:9; 118:6; Isa 8:10; Jer 20:11; Heb 13:6 **8:32** [x]Ge 22:13; Mal 3:17; Jn 3:16; Ro 5:8 **8:33** [y]Isa 50:8, 9 **8:34** [z]ver 1 [a]Ro 5:6-8 [b]S Ac 2:24 [c]S Mk 16:19 [d]ver 27; Job 16:20; Isa 53:12; Heb 7:25; 9:24; 1Jn 2:1 **8:35** [e]ver 37-39

[a] *20,21* Or *subjected it in hope.* [21]*For* [b] *28* Or *that all things work together for good to those who love God, who;* or *that in all things God works together with those who love him to bring about what is good—with those who*

in hope. A possible allusion to the promise of Ge 3:15 (see note there).
8:21 *will be liberated from its bondage to decay.* The physical universe is not destined for destruction (annihilation) but for renewal (see 2Pe 3:13 and note; Rev 21:1). And living things will no longer be subject to death and decay, as they are today.
8:22 *has been groaning.* Creation is personified as a woman in labor waiting for the birth of her child.
8:23 *firstfruits of the Spirit.* Believers' possession of the Holy Spirit is not only evidence of their present salvation (vv. 14,16) but also a pledge of their future inheritance—and not only a pledge but also the down payment on that inheritance (see 2Co 1:22; 5:5 and notes; Eph 1:14). *firstfruits.* See Ex 23:19 and note; cf. 1Co 15:20 and note. *our adoption to sonship.* See note on v. 15. Christians are already God's children, but this is a reference to the full realization of our inheritance in Christ. *redemption of our bodies.* The resurrection, as the final stage of our adoption. The first stage was God's predestination of our adoption (see Eph 1:5); the second is our present inclusion as children of God (see v. 14; Gal 3:25–26 and notes).
8:24 *in this hope.* We are saved by faith (see Eph 2:8 and note), not hope; but hope accompanies salvation.
8:26 *In the same way.* As hope sustains believers when they suffer, so the Holy Spirit helps them when they pray. *through wordless groans.* In v. 23 it is the believer who groans; here it is the Holy Spirit. Whether Paul means words that are unspoken or words that cannot be expressed in human language is not clear—probably the former, though v. 27 seems to suggest the latter.
8:27 The relationship between the Holy Spirit and God the Father is so close that the Holy Spirit's prayers need not be audible. God knows his every thought.
8:28 *the good.* That which conforms us "to the image of his Son" (v. 29). *called.* Effectual calling: the call of God to which there is invariably a positive response.
8:29 *foreknew.* Some insist that the knowledge here is not abstract but is couched in love and mixed with purpose. They hold that God not only knew us before we had any knowledge of him but that he also knew us, in the sense of choosing us by his grace, before the foundation of the world (see Eph 1:4; 2Ti 1:9 and notes). Others believe that Paul here refers to the fact that in eternity past God knew those who by faith would become his people. *predestined.* Predestination here is to moral conformity to the likeness of his Son. *that he might be the firstborn among many brothers and sisters.* The reason God foreknew, predestined and conformed believers to Christ's likeness is that the Son might hold the position of highest honor in the great family of God.
8:30 *predestined ... glorified.* The sequence by which God carries out his predestination. *glorified.* Since this final stage is firmly grounded in God's set purpose, it is as certain as if it had already happened.
8:31 *If.* That is, "Since."
8:32 The argument (from the greater to the lesser) here is similar to that in 5:9–10. If God gave the supreme gift of his Son to save us, he will certainly also give whatever is necessary to bring to fulfillment the work begun at the cross. See note on Ge 22:16.
8:33–34 A court of law is in mind. No charge can be brought against the Christian because God has already pronounced a verdict of not guilty.
8:34 *Who then is the one who condemns?* Echoes the language of Isa 50:9. Paul gives three reasons why no one can condemn God's elect: (1) Christ died for us; (2) Christ is alive and seated at the right hand of God, the position of power; (3) Christ is interceding for us (see Heb 7:25; 1Jn 2:1 and notes).
8:35–39 Paul shows his readers that suffering does not separate believers from Christ but actually carries them along toward their ultimate goal.

or persecution or famine or nakedness or
danger or sword?[f] 36 As it is written:

"For your sake we face death all day long;
we are considered as sheep to be slaughtered."[a][g]

37 No, in all these things we are more than
conquerors[h] through him who loved us.[i]
38 For I am convinced that neither death
nor life, neither angels nor demons,[b] neither the present nor the future,[j] nor any
powers,[k] 39 neither height nor depth, nor
anything else in all creation, will be able
to separate us from the love of God[l] that is
in Christ Jesus our Lord.[m]

Paul's Anguish Over Israel

9 I speak the truth in Christ—I am not
lying,[n] my conscience confirms[o] it
through the Holy Spirit— 2 I have great
sorrow and unceasing anguish in my
heart. 3 For I could wish that I myself[p] were
cursed[q] and cut off from Christ for the sake
of my people,[r] those of my own race,[s] 4 the
people of Israel.[t] Theirs is the adoption to
sonship;[u] theirs the divine glory,[v] the covenants,[w] the receiving of the law,[x] the temple worship[y] and the promises.[z] 5 Theirs are
the patriarchs,[a] and from them is traced
the human ancestry of the Messiah,[b] who
is God over all,[c] forever praised![c][d] Amen.

God's Sovereign Choice

6 It is not as though God's word[e] had
failed. For not all who are descended from
Israel are Israel.[f] 7 Nor because they are his
descendants are they all Abraham's children. On the contrary, "It is through Isaac
that your offspring will be reckoned."[d][g]
8 In other words, it is not the children by
physical descent who are God's children,[h]
but it is the children of the promise who
are regarded as Abraham's offspring.[i] 9 For
this was how the promise was stated: "At
the appointed time I will return, and Sarah
will have a son."[e][j]

10 Not only that, but Rebekah's children
were conceived at the same time by our
father Isaac.[k] 11 Yet, before the twins were
born or had done anything good or bad[l]—

8:35 [f] 1Co 4:11; 2Co 11:26,27 8:36 [g] Ps 44:22; 1Co 4:9; 15:30,31; 2Co 4:11; 6:9; 11:23 8:37 [h] 1Co 15:57 [i] Ro 5:8; Gal 2:20; Eph 5:2; Rev 1:5; 3:9 8:38 [j] 1Co 3:22 [k] Eph 1:21; Col 1:16; 1Pe 3:22 8:39 [l] S Ro 5:8 [m] ver 1; S Ro 16:3 9:1 [n] Ps 15:2; 2Co 11:10; Gal 1:20; 1Ti 2:7 [o] S Ro 1:9 9:3 [p] Ex 32:32 [q] 1Co 12:3; 16:22 [r] S Ac 22:5 [s] Ro 11:14 9:4 [t] ver 6 [u] Ex 4:22; 6:7; Dt 7:6 [v] Heb 9:5 [w] Ge 17:2; Dt 4:13; Ac 3:25; Eph 2:12 [x] Ps 147:19 [y] Heb 9:1 [z] S Ac 13:32; S Gal 3:16 9:5 [a] Ro 11:28 [b] Mt 1:1-16; Ro 1:3 [c] Jn 1:1; Col 2:9 [d] Ro 1:25; 2Co 11:31 9:6 [e] S Heb 4:12 [f] Ro 2:28,29; Gal 6:16 9:7 [g] Ge 21:12; Heb 11:18 9:8 [h] S Ro 8:14 [i] S Gal 3:16 9:9 [j] Ge 18:10,14 9:10 [k] Ge 25:21 9:11 [l] ver 16

[a] 36 Psalm 44:22 [b] 38 Or *nor heavenly rulers*
[c] 5 Or *Messiah, who is over all. God be forever praised!* Or *Messiah. God who is over all be forever praised!*
[d] 7 Gen. 21:12 [e] 9 Gen. 18:10,14

8:36 Ps 44:22 (see note there) is quoted to show that suffering has always been part of the experience of God's people (see Php 1:29 and note).
8:37 *who loved us.* Referring especially to Christ's death on the cross (see note on Ge 22:16; see also Gal 2:20; Eph 5:25 and notes).
8:39 *neither height nor depth.* It is impossible to get beyond God's loving reach (see Eph 3:17–19). *nor anything else in all creation.* Includes all created things. Only God is not included, and he is the one who has justified us (see note on vv. 33–34).
9:1—11:36 God's way with Israel. Among other matters, Paul addresses three urgent questions occasioned by the rejection of the gospel by many (most?) Jews in Paul's day: (1) Has the word of God to Israel concerning her salvation come to nothing? (2) Has God completely and finally rejected his people Israel? (3) Is the gospel incapable of saving the Jews? His answer to all three is an emphatic "No!" See Introduction: Contents; Outline.
9:1 *through the Holy Spirit.* Conscience is a reliable guide only when enlightened by the Holy Spirit.
9:3 *cursed.* The Greek for this word is *anathema,* and it means delivered over to the wrath of God for eternal destruction (see 1Co 12:3; 16:22; Gal 1:8 and notes). Such was Paul's great love for his fellow Jews. For a similar expression of love, see Ex 32:32.
9:4 *people of Israel.* The descendants of Jacob (who was renamed Israel by God; see Ge 32:28 and note). The name was used of the entire nation (see Jdg 5:7), then of the northern kingdom after the nation was divided (see 1Ki 12), the southern kingdom being called Judah. During the intertestamental period and later in NT times, Jews in the Holy Land used the title to indicate that they were the chosen people of God. Its use here is especially relevant because Paul is about to show that, despite Israel's unbelief and disobedience, God's promises to her are still valid. *adoption to sonship.* Israel had been accepted as God's son (see Ex 4:22; Jer 31:9; Hos 11:1 and notes). *glory.* The evidence of the presence of God among his people (see Ex 16:7,10; Lev 9:6,23; Nu 16:19). *covenants.* For example, the Abrahamic (Ge 15:17–21; 17:1–8); the Mosaic (Ex 19:5; 24:1–4), renewed on the plains of Moab (Dt 29:1–15), at Mounts Ebal and Gerizim (Jos 8:30–35) and at Shechem (Jos 24); the Phinehas or Levitical (Nu 25:12–13; Jer 33:21; Mal 2:4–5); the Davidic (2Sa 7; 23:5; Ps 89:3–4,28–29; 132:11–12); and the new (prophesied in Jer 31:31–34). See chart, p. 23. *promises.* Especially those made to Abraham (see Ge 12:7; 13:14–17; see also 17:5–8; 22:16–18 and notes) but also including the many OT Messianic promises (see, e.g., 2Sa 7:12,16; Ps 110; Isa 9:6–7; Jer 23:5; 31:31–34; Eze 34:23–24; 37:24; Da 9:25–27; Mic 5:1–4; Zec 9:9–10 and notes).
9:5 *patriarchs.* Abraham, Isaac, Jacob and his sons. *the Messiah, who is God.* A statement affirming the deity of Jesus the Messiah (but see NIV text note for other possibilities). For other passages explicitly or implicitly affirming the deity of Christ, see 1:4; 10:9; Mt 1:23; 28:19; Lk 1:35; 5:20–21; Jn 1:1,3,10,14,18; 5:18; 8:58; 20:28; 2Co 13:14; Php 2:6; Col 1:15–20; 2:9; Titus 2:13; Heb 1:2–3,6,8; 2Pe 1:1; Rev 1:13–18; 22:13 and relevant notes.
9:6 *God's word.* His clearly stated purpose, which has not failed, because "not all who are descended from Israel are Israel." Paul is not denying the election of all Israel (as a nation) but stating that within Israel there is a separation, that of unbelieving Israel and believing Israel. Physical descent is no guarantee of a place in God's spiritual family.
9:7 *descendants.* Physical descendants (e.g., Ishmael and his offspring).
9:8 *children by physical descent.* Those merely biologically descended from Abraham. *God's children.* See v. 4. Not all Israelites were God's children (see Jn 8:44 and note). The reference is to the Israel of faith.
9:11 *done anything good or bad.* God's choice of Jacob was based on sovereign freedom, not on the fulfillment of any

in order that God's purpose[m] in election
might stand: 12 not by works but by him
who calls—she was told, "The older will
serve the younger."[an] 13 Just as it is written:
"Jacob I loved, but Esau I hated."[bo]
14 What then shall we say?[p] Is God unjust? Not at all![q] 15 For he says to Moses,

"I will have mercy on whom I have
mercy,
and I will have compassion on
whom I have compassion."[cr]

16 It does not, therefore, depend on human
desire or effort, but on God's mercy.[s] 17 For
Scripture says to Pharaoh: "I raised you up
for this very purpose, that I might display
my power in you and that my name might
be proclaimed in all the earth."[dt] 18 Therefore God has mercy on whom he wants
to have mercy, and he hardens whom he
wants to harden.[u]
19 One of you will say to me:[v] "Then why
does God still blame us?[w] For who is able
to resist his will?"[x] 20 But who are you, a
human being, to talk back to God?[y] "Shall
what is formed say to the one who formed
it,[z] 'Why did you make me like this?' "[ea]
21 Does not the potter have the right to
make out of the same lump of clay some
pottery for special purposes and some for
common use?[b]

22 What if God, although choosing to
show his wrath and make his power
known, bore with great patience[c] the objects of his wrath—prepared for destruction?[d] 23 What if he did this to make the
riches of his glory[e] known to the objects of
his mercy, whom he prepared in advance
for glory[f]— 24 even us, whom he also
called,[g] not only from the Jews but also
from the Gentiles?[h] 25 As he says in Hosea:

"I will call them 'my people' who are
not my people;
and I will call her 'my loved one'
who is not my loved one,"[fi]

26 and,

"In the very place where it was said to
them,
'You are not my people,'
there they will be called 'children of
the living God.' "[gj]

27 Isaiah cries out concerning Israel:

"Though the number of the Israelites
be like the sand by the sea,[k]
only the remnant will be saved.[l]

9:11 [m] Ro 8:28
9:12 [n] Ge 25:23
9:13 [o] Mal 1:2,3
9:14 [p] S Ro 8:31 [q] 2Ch 19:7
9:15 [r] Ex 33:19
9:16 [s] Eph 2:8; Titus 3:5
9:17 [t] Ex 9:16; 14:4; Ps 76:10
9:18 [u] Ex 4:21; 7:3; 14:4, 17; Dt 2:30; Jos 11:20; Ro 11:25
9:19 [v] Ro 11:19; 1Co 15:35; Jas 2:18 [w] Ro 3:7 [x] 2Sa 16:10; 2Ch 20:6; Da 4:35
9:20 [y] Job 1:22; 9:12; 40:2 [z] Isa 64:8; Jer 18:6 [a] Isa 29:16; 45:9; 10:15
9:21 [b] 2Ti 2:20
9:22 [c] S Ro 2:4 [d] Pr 16:4
9:23 [e] S Ro 2:4 [f] Ro 8:30
9:24 [g] S Ro 8:28 [h] S Ro 3:29
9:25 [i] Hos 2:23; 1Pe 2:10
9:26 [j] Hos 1:10; S Mt 16:16; S Ro 8:14
9:27 [k] Ge 22:17; Hos 1:10 [l] 2Ki 19:4; Jer 44:14; 50:20; Joel 2:32; Ro 11:5

[a] *12* Gen. 25:23 [b] *13* Mal. 1:2,3 [c] *15* Exodus 33:19
[d] *17* Exodus 9:16 [e] *20* Isaiah 29:16; 45:9
[f] *25* Hosea 2:23 [g] *26* Hosea 1:10

prior conditions. *God's purpose in election.* God's purpose embodied in his election (see note on Eph 1:4).

9:12 *not by works but by him who calls.* Before Rebekah's children were even born, God made a choice—a choice obviously not based on works. *calls.* See 8:28 and note.

9:13 *Jacob I loved, but Esau I hated.* Equivalent to "Jacob I chose, but Esau I rejected" (cf. Lk 14:26 and note). In vv. 6–13 Paul is clearly dealing with personal and not national election—he is not portraying the nation Israel (Jacob) over the nation Edom (Esau)—though Mal 1:2–3 (see NIV text note here) does speak of the nations. Paul's intention is evident in light of the problem he is addressing: How can God's promise stand when so many who comprise Israel (in the OT collective sense) are unbelieving and therefore cut off? See ch. 11 and notes.

9:14 *Is God unjust?* Unjust to elect on the basis of his sovereign freedom, as with Jacob and Esau.

9:15 Paul denies injustice in God's dealing with Isaac and Ishmael, and Jacob and Esau, by appealing to God's sovereign right to dispense mercy as he chooses.

9:16 *It.* God's choice, which is not controlled in any way by human beings. However, Paul makes it clear that the basis for Israel's rejection was her unbelief (see vv. 30–32 and notes).

9:17 *Pharaoh.* The pharaoh of the exodus. *raised you up.* Made you ruler of Egypt. *my name.* The character of God, particularly as revealed in the exodus (see Ex 15:13–18; Jos 2:10–11; 9:9; 1Sa 4:8).

9:18 The first part of this verse again echoes Ex 33:19 (see v. 15) and the last part such texts as Ex 7:3; 9:12; 14:4,17, in which God is said to harden the hearts of the pharaoh and the Egyptians (see Ex 4:21 and note). *on whom he wants to have mercy.* Cannot mean that God is arbitrary in his mercy, because Paul ultimately bases God's rejection of Israel on her unbelief (see vv. 30–32).

9:19 Someone may object: "If God determines whose heart is hardened and whose is not, how can he blame anyone for hardening their heart?"

9:20 *who are you, a human being, to talk back to God?* Cf. Ecc 8:4. Paul is not silencing all human questioning of God, but he is speaking to those with an impenitent, God-defying attitude who want to make God answerable to them for what he does and who, by their questions, defame the character of God.

9:21 The analogy between God and the potter and between a human being and a pot should not be pressed to the extreme. The main point is the sovereign freedom of God in dealing with people (cf. Jer 18:1–10 and notes).

9:22–23 An illustration of the principle stated in v. 21. The emphasis is on God's mercy, not his wrath.

9:22 No one can call God to account for what he does. But he does not exercise his freedom of choice arbitrarily, and he shows great patience even toward the objects of his wrath. In light of 2:4 (see note there), the purpose of such patience is to bring about repentance.

9:23 *glory.* See note on 3:23.

9:25–26 In the original context these passages from Hosea refer to the spiritual restoration of Israel. But Paul finds in them the principle that God is a saving, forgiving, restoring God, who delights to take those who are "not my people" and make them "my people." Paul then applies this principle to Gentiles, whom God makes his people by sovereignly grafting them into covenant relationship (see ch. 11).

9:27–29 Isa 10:22–23 and 1:9 (see NIV text notes here) indicate that only a small remnant will survive from the great multitude of Israelites. God's calling includes both Jews and Gentiles (see v. 24), but the vast majority are Gentiles, as v. 30 suggests.

28 For the Lord will carry out
his sentence on earth with speed
and finality."[a][m]

29 It is just as Isaiah said previously:

"Unless the Lord Almighty[n]
had left us descendants,
we would have become like Sodom,
we would have been like
Gomorrah."[b][o]

Israel's Unbelief

30 What then shall we say?[p] That the
Gentiles, who did not pursue righteousness, have obtained it, a righteousness
that is by faith;[q] 31 but the people of Israel,
who pursued the law as the way of righteousness,[r] have not attained their goal.[s]
32 Why not? Because they pursued it not
by faith but as if it were by works. They
stumbled over the stumbling stone.[t] 33 As
it is written:

"See, I lay in Zion a stone that causes
people to stumble
and a rock that makes them fall,
and the one who believes in him will
never be put to shame."[c][u]

10 Brothers and sisters, my heart's
desire[v] and prayer to God for the
Israelites is that they may be saved. 2 For
I can testify about them that they are zealous[w] for God, but their zeal is not based

9:28 [m] Isa 10:22,23 **9:29** [n] Jas 5:4 [o] Isa 1:9; Ge 19:24-29; Dt 29:23; Isa 13:19; Jer 50:40 **9:30** [p] S Ro 8:31 [q] Ro 1:17; 3:22; 4:5,13; 10:6; Gal 2:16; Php 3:9; Heb 11:7 **9:31** [r] Dt 6:25; Isa 51:1; Ro 10:2,3; 11:7 [s] Gal 5:4 **9:32** [t] 1Pe 2:8 **9:33** [u] Isa 8:14; 28:16; Ro 10:11; 1Pe 2:6,8 **10:1** [v] Ps 20:4 **10:2** [w] S Ac 21:20

[a] 28 Isaiah 10:22,23 (see Septuagint) [b] 29 Isaiah 1:9 [c] 33 Isaiah 8:14; 28:16

9:30—10:21 The cause of the rejection of Israel.

9:30-32 A new step in Paul's argument: The reason for Israel's rejection lay in the nature of her disobedience—she failed to obey her own God-given law, which in reality was pointing to Christ. She pursued the law—yet not by faith but by works. Thus the real cause of Israel's rejection was that she failed to believe.

9:31 *the law as the way of righteousness.* Paul does not reject obedience to the law but righteousness by works, the attempt to use the law to put God in one's debt.

9:32 *not by faith.* The failure of Israel was not that she pursued the wrong thing (i.e., righteous standing before God), but that she pursued it by works in a futile effort to merit God's favor rather than pursuing it by faith. *stumbling stone.* Jesus the Messiah. God's rejection of Israel was not arbitrary but was based on Israel's rejection of God's way of gaining righteousness (faith).

9:33 Isa 8:14 and 28:16 (see NIV text note here), which are here combined, apparently were commonly used by early Christians in defense of Jesus' Messiahship (see 1Pe 2:4,6-8; see also Ps 118:22 and note; Lk 20:17-18).

10:1 *prayer to God for the Israelites.* Paul often prayed for the churches (see Eph 1:15-23; 3:14-21; Php 1:9-11; Col 1:3-14; 1Th 1:2-3; 2Th 1:3,11-12). Here he prays for the salvation of his fellow "Israelites."

10:2 *zealous for God.* The Jews' zeal for God (see Ac 21:20; 22:3; Gal 1:14) was commendable in that God was its object, but it was flawed because it was not based on right knowledge about God's way of salvation. Paul, before his conversion, was an example of such zeal (see Gal 1:14 and note).

The Circus Maximus in Rome. Little remains of what was once a huge chariot racing stadium during Paul's time.

on knowledge. 3 Since they did not know
the righteousness of God and sought to
establish their own, they did not submit
to God's righteousness.[x] 4 Christ is the culmination of the law[y] so that there may be
righteousness for everyone who believes.[z]
5 Moses writes this about the righteousness that is by the law: "The person who
does these things will live by them."[a][a]
6 But the righteousness that is by faith[b]
says: "Do not say in your heart, 'Who will
ascend into heaven?' "[b][c] (that is, to bring
Christ down) 7 "or 'Who will descend into
the deep?' "[c][d] (that is, to bring Christ up
from the dead).[e] 8 But what does it say?
"The word is near you; it is in your mouth
and in your heart,"[d][f] that is, the message concerning faith that we proclaim:
9 If you declare[g] with your mouth, "Jesus
is Lord,"[h] and believe[i] in your heart that
God raised him from the dead,[j] you will
be saved.[k] 10 For it is with your heart that
you believe and are justified, and it is with
your mouth that you profess your faith
and are saved. 11 As Scripture says, "Anyone who believes in him will never be put
to shame."[e][l] 12 For there is no difference between Jew and Gentile[m]—the same Lord
is Lord of all[n] and richly blesses all who
call on him, 13 for, "Everyone who calls on
the name of the Lord[o] will be saved."[f][p]

Bronze statue of a Roman chariot pulled by two galloping horses (first century BC), similar to what would have been used in the Circus Maximus

Roman chariot pulled by two galloping horses, Gallo-Roman (first century BC)/ Musee Municipal, Laon, France/Giraudon/The Bridgeman Art Library

14 How, then, can they call on the one
they have not believed in? And how can
they believe in the one of whom they have
not heard? And how can they hear with-

[a] *5* Lev. 18:5 [b] *6* Deut. 30:12 [c] *7* Deut. 30:13 [d] *8* Deut. 30:14 [e] *11* Isaiah 28:16 (see Septuagint) [f] *13* Joel 2:32

10:3 [x] Ro 1:17; S 9:31 **10:4** [y] Gal 3:24; Ro 7:1-4 [z] S Ro 3:22 **10:5** [a] Lev 18:5; Dt 4:1; 6:24; Ne 9:29; Pr 19:16; Isa 55:3; Eze 20:11, 13, 21; S Ro 7:10 **10:6** [b] S Ro 9:30 [c] Dt 30:12 **10:7** [d] Dt 30:13 [e] S Ac 2:24 **10:8** [f] Dt 30:14 **10:9** [g] Mt 10:32 [h] S Jn 13:13 [i] S Jn 3:15 [j] S Ac 2:24 [k] S Ro 11:14 **10:11** [l] Isa 28:16; Ro 9:33 **10:12** [m] S Ro 3:22, 29 [n] S Mt 28:18 **10:13** [o] S Ac 2:21 [p] Joel 2:32

10:3 *the righteousness of God.* Righteous standing based on faith (see 1:17 and note), which comes from God as a gift and cannot be earned by human works. *their own.* Righteous standing based on their own efforts.

10:4 *Christ is the culmination of the law.* Although the Greek for "culmination" (*telos*) can mean either (1) "termination," "cessation," or (2) "goal," "culmination," "fulfillment," it seems best here to understand it in the latter sense. Christ is the fulfillment of the law (see Mt 5:17 and note) in the sense that he brought it to completion by obeying perfectly its demands and by fulfilling its types and prophecies. Christians are no longer "under the law" (6:14; see note there), since Christ has freed them from its condemnation, but the law still plays a role in their lives. They are liberated by the Holy Spirit to fulfill its moral demands (see 8:4 and note). *righteousness.* The righteous standing before God that Christ makes available to everyone who believes (see notes on 1:17; 3:24).

10:5 *The person who does these things will live by them.* Paul quotes Lev 18:5 (see note there; see also Dt 6:25 and note), which speaks of the righteousness to which Israel was called under the Sinaitic covenant.

10:6–7 The Scripture here quoted by Paul (Dt 30:12–14) was frequently quoted (sometimes rather loosely) in Jewish circles for various purposes. Paul uses it to sharpen the contrast between "the righteousness that is by the law" (v. 5) and "the righteousness that is by faith." He takes a word that originally referred to the Mosaic law that was given as the way to life and applies it to the gospel of Christ as the way to life. In the case of Christ, just as in the case of the law, the way to life is accessible without any superhuman effort on the part of people. They do not have to bring the transcended Christ down from heaven, and they do not have to raise a dead Christ from the dead; he is accessible through the gospel proclaimed by the apostle.

10:8 *The word is near you.* In the OT passage (Dt 30:14; see note on 30:12,14) the "word" is God's word as found in the law. Paul takes the passage and applies it to the gospel, "the message concerning faith"—the main point being the accessibility of the gospel. Righteousness is gained by faith, not by deeds, and is readily available to anyone who will receive it freely from God through Christ.

10:9 *Jesus is Lord.* This affirmation, the earliest Christian confession of faith (see also 1Co 12:3 and note), served as the Christian equivalent of the Jewish *Shema* (see Dt 6:4–9; Mk 12:29; Jas 2:19 and notes). It was probably used at baptisms. In view of the fact that "Lord" is used over 6,000 times in the Septuagint (the pre-Christian Greek translation of the OT) to translate the name of Israel's God (Yahweh), it is clear that Paul, when using this title for Jesus, is affirming that, in Jesus, the God of Israel was himself present among his people. *in your heart.* In Biblical terms the heart is not merely the seat of the emotions and affections but also of the intellect and will (see Ps 4:7 and note). *God raised him from the dead.* A bedrock truth of Christian doctrine (see 1Co 15:4,14,17) and the central thrust of apostolic preaching (see, e.g., note on Ac 2:14–40; see also Ac 3:15 and note; 4:10; 10:40). Christians believe not only that Jesus lived but also that he still lives. *will be saved.* This may include final salvation—salvation at the last day (see Heb 9:28 and note).

10:10 Salvation involves inward belief ("with your heart") as well as outward confession ("with your mouth").

10:12 *no difference between Jew and Gentile.* In the sense that both are on the same footing as far as salvation is concerned (see v. 13; 3:22).

10:13 Peter cited this same passage (Joel 2:32) on the day of Pentecost (see Ac 2:21 and note).

10:14–15 Since it might be argued that Jews had never had a fair opportunity to hear and respond to the gospel, Paul, by

out someone preaching to them? 15 And
how can anyone preach unless they are
sent? As it is written: “How beautiful are
the feet of those who bring good news!”[aq]
16 But not all the Israelites accepted the
good news.[r] For Isaiah says, “Lord, who
has believed our message?”[bs] 17 Consequently, faith comes from hearing the message,[t] and the message is heard through
the word about Christ.[u] 18 But I ask: Did
they not hear? Of course they did:

“Their voice has gone out into all the
earth,
their words to the ends of the world.”[cv]

19 Again I ask: Did Israel not understand?
First, Moses says,

“I will make you envious[w] by those
who are not a nation;
I will make you angry by a nation
that has no understanding.”[dx]

20 And Isaiah boldly says,

“I was found by those who did not
seek me;
I revealed myself to those who did
not ask for me.”[ey]

21 But concerning Israel he says,

“All day long I have held out my hands
to a disobedient and obstinate people.”[fz]

The Remnant of Israel

11 I ask then: Did God reject his people? By no means![a] I am an Israelite myself, a descendant of Abraham,[b]
from the tribe of Benjamin.[c] 2 God did not
reject his people,[d] whom he foreknew.[e]
Don’t you know what Scripture says in the
passage about Elijah—how he appealed to
God against Israel: 3 “Lord, they have killed
your prophets and torn down your altars;
I am the only one left, and they are trying
to kill me”[g]?[f] 4 And what was God’s answer
to him? “I have reserved for myself seven
thousand who have not bowed the knee to
Baal.”[hg] 5 So too, at the present time there
is a remnant[h] chosen by grace.[i] 6 And if by
grace, then it cannot be based on works;[j]
if it were, grace would no longer be grace.
7 What then? What the people of Israel
sought so earnestly they did not obtain.[k]
The elect among them did, but the others
were hardened,[l] 8 as it is written:

“God gave them a spirit of stupor,
eyes that could not see
and ears that could not hear,[m]
to this very day.”[in]

9 And David says:

“May their table become a snare and a
trap,
a stumbling block and a retribution
for them.
10 May their eyes be darkened so they
cannot see,[o]
and their backs be bent forever.”[jp]

Ingrafted Branches

11 Again I ask: Did they stumble so as
to fall beyond recovery? Not at all![q] Rather, because of their transgression, salva-

10:15 [q] Isa 52:7; Na 1:15
10:16 [r] Heb 4:2 [s] Isa 53:1; Jn 12:38
10:17 [t] Gal 3:2, 5 [u] Col 3:16
10:18 [v] Ps 19:4; S Mt 24:14; Ro 1:8; Col 1:6, 23; 1Th 1:8
10:19 [w] Ro 11:11, 14 [x] Dt 32:21
10:20 [y] Isa 65:1; Ro 9:30
10:21 [z] Isa 65:2; Jer 35:17
11:1 [a] Lev 26:44; 1Sa 12:22; Ps 94:14; Jer 31:37; 33:24-26 [b] 2Co 11:22 [c] Php 3:5
11:2 [d] S ver 1 [e] S Ro 8:29
11:3 [f] 1Ki 19:10, 14
11:4 [g] 1Ki 19:18
11:5 [h] S Ro 9:27 [i] S Ro 3:24
11:6 [j] Ro 4:4
11:7 [k] Ro 9:31 [l] ver 25; S Ro 9:18
11:8 [m] S Mt 13:13-15 [n] Dt 29:4; Isa 29:10
11:10 [o] ver 8 [p] Ps 69:22, 23
11:11 [q] ver 1

a 15 Isaiah 52:7 *b* 16 Isaiah 53:1 *c* 18 Psalm 19:4 *d* 19 Deut. 32:21 *e* 20 Isaiah 65:1 *f* 21 Isaiah 65:2 *g* 3 1 Kings 19:10,14 *h* 4 1 Kings 19:18 *i* 8 Deut. 29:4; Isaiah 29:10 *j* 10 Psalm 69:22,23

means of a series of rhetorical questions, states (in reverse order) the conditions necessary to call on Christ and be saved: (1) a preacher sent from God, (2) proclamation of the message, (3) hearing the message, (4) believing the message.

10:15 *How beautiful are the feet of those who bring good news!* The quotation is from Isa 52:7 (see note there), which refers to those who bring the exiles the good news of their imminent release from captivity in Babylonia. Here it is applied to gospel preachers, who bring the good news of release from captivity to sin.

10:18 *Their voice … world.* The quotation is from Ps 19:4 (see note there), which refers to the testimony of the heavens to the glory of God. Here “their voice” is applied to gospel preachers and is used to show that Israel cannot offer the excuse that she did not have opportunity to hear, since preachers went everywhere. These words (originally used to describe God’s revelation in nature) aptly describe the widespread preaching of the gospel.

10:19 *Did Israel not understand?* The quotation that follows (from Dt 32:21; see note there) answers this question by suggesting that the Gentiles, whom the Jews considered to be spiritually unenlightened, understood. Surely if Gentiles understood the message, Jews could have. *those who are not a nation.* The Gentiles, those who are not a nation of God’s forming in the sense that Israel was.

10:21 The responsibility for Israel’s rejection as a nation rested with Israel herself. She had failed to meet God’s requirement, namely, faith. Yet, as Isa 65:2 stated, God continued to reach out in love to the people of Israel in spite of their disobedience.

11:1 *reject.* Totally reject. There has always been a faithful remnant among the Jewish people (see note on 9:1—11:36).

11:2 *whom he foreknew.* See note on 8:29.

11:5 *remnant.* As it was in Elijah’s day, so it was in Paul’s day. Despite widespread apostasy, a faithful remnant of Jews remained. *chosen by grace.* The grounds for the existence of the remnant was not their good works but God’s grace.

11:7 *What the people of Israel sought so earnestly.* A righteous standing before God, which eluded the greater part of Israel. *The elect.* The faithful remnant among the Jews. *others were hardened.* Because they refused the way of faith (see 9:30–32 and notes), God made them impervious to spiritual truth (see notes on v. 25; Isa 6:8–10; Mk 4:12; Lk 8:10)—a judicial hardening of Israel.

11:8 *to this very day.* The spiritual dullness of the Jews had continued from Isaiah’s day to Paul’s day.

11:9–10 The passage from Ps 69:22–23 (see notes there) was probably originally spoken by David concerning his enemies; Paul uses it to describe the results of God’s hardening.

11:11 *their transgression.* The Jews’ rejection of the gospel. *make Israel envious.* See v. 14; 10:19 and note; see also notes on 1Ki 17:16; 2Ki 5:14; Lk 4:26–27.

tion has come to the Gentiles[r] to make
Israel envious.[s] 12 But if their transgression means riches for the world, and their
loss means riches for the Gentiles,[t] how
much greater riches will their full inclusion bring!
13 I am talking to you Gentiles. Inasmuch as I am the apostle to the Gentiles,[u]
I take pride in my ministry 14 in the hope
that I may somehow arouse my own people to envy[v] and save[w] some of them. 15 For
if their rejection brought reconciliation[x] to
the world, what will their acceptance be
but life from the dead?[y] 16 If the part of the
dough offered as firstfruits[z] is holy, then
the whole batch is holy; if the root is holy,
so are the branches.
17 If some of the branches have been
broken off,[a] and you, though a wild olive shoot, have been grafted in among the
others[b] and now share in the nourishing
sap from the olive root, 18 do not consider yourself to be superior to those other
branches. If you do, consider this: You do
not support the root, but the root supports
you.[c] 19 You will say then, "Branches were
broken off so that I could be grafted in."
20 Granted. But they were broken off because of unbelief, and you stand by faith.[d]
Do not be arrogant,[e] but tremble.[f] 21 For if
God did not spare the natural branches, he
will not spare you either.
22 Consider therefore the kindness[g] and
sternness of God: sternness to those who
fell, but kindness to you, provided that
you continue[h] in his kindness. Otherwise,
you also will be cut off.[i] 23 And if they do
not persist in unbelief, they will be grafted
in, for God is able to graft them in again.[j]
24 After all, if you were cut out of an olive
tree that is wild by nature, and contrary to
nature were grafted into a cultivated olive
tree,[k] how much more readily will these,
the natural branches, be grafted into their
own olive tree!

All Israel Will Be Saved

25 I do not want you to be ignorant[l] of
this mystery,[m] brothers and sisters, so that

11:11 [r] S Ac 13:46 [s] ver 14; Ro 10:19 **11:12** [t] ver 25 **11:13** [u] S Ac 9:15 **11:14** [v] ver 11; Ro 10:19; 1Co 10:33; 1Th 2:16 [w] S Mt 1:21; S Lk 2:11; S Jn 3:17; Ac 4:12; 16:31; 1Co 1:21; 1Ti 2:4; Titus 3:5 **11:15** [x] S Ro 5:10 [y] Lk 15:24,32 **11:16** [z] Lev 23:10,17; Nu 15:18-21 **11:17** [a] Jer 11:16; Jn 15:2 [b] Ac 2:39; Eph 2:11-13 **11:18** [c] Jn 4:22 **11:20** [d] 1Co 10:12; 2Co 1:24 [e] 1Ti 6:17 [f] 1Pe 1:17 **11:22** [g] Ro 2:4 [h] 1Co 15:2; Col 1:23; Heb 3:6 [i] Jn 15:2 **11:23** [j] 2Co 3:16 **11:24** [k] Jer 11:16 **11:25** [l] Ro 1:13; 1Co 10:1; 12:1; 2Co 1:8; 1Th 4:13 [m] S Ro 16:25

11:12 *riches for the world.* Equivalent to "riches for the Gentiles," a reference to the abundant benefits of salvation already enjoyed by believing Gentiles, which had come about because of the rejection of the gospel by the Jews. That rejection caused the apostles to turn to the Gentiles (see Ac 13:46–48; 18:6). *their loss.* Equivalent to "their transgression" (see note on v. 11), but focusing on the loss that this transgression entailed. *greater riches.* See note on v. 15. *their full inclusion.* The salvation of Israel (see vv. 26–27 and notes; see also the "full number of the Gentiles," v. 25).

11:13 *apostle to the Gentiles.* See 1:5; 15:9,12,16 and notes; Ac 9:15; Gal 1:16; 2:7,9 and note on 2:7; see also Eph 2:11–22; 3:3,6,10 and notes.

11:15 *their rejection.* God's temporary and partial exclusion of the Jews (see v. 25 and note). *reconciliation to the world.* Somewhat equivalent to "riches for the world" (see note on v. 12). *life from the dead.* Equivalent to "greater riches" in v. 12. The sequence of redemptive events is: The "transgression" and "loss" (v. 12) of Israel leads to the salvation of the Gentiles, which leads to the jealousy or envy of Israel, which leads to the "full inclusion" (v. 12) of Israel when the hardening is removed, which leads to even more riches for the Gentiles. But what are the "greater riches" (v. 12) for the Gentiles, which Paul describes here as "life from the dead"? Three views may be suggested: (1) an unprecedented spiritual awakening in the world; (2) the consummation of redemption at the resurrection of the dead; (3) a figurative expression describing the conversion of the Jews as a joyful and glorious event (like resurrection)—which will result in even greater blessing for the world. Of these three views the first seems least likely, since, before Israel's spiritual rebirth, the fullness of the Gentiles will already have come in (see v. 25). Since the Gentile mission will then be complete, there seems to be no place for a period of unprecedented spiritual awakening. The second view also seems unlikely, since the context suggests nothing about bodily resurrection.

11:16 The first half of this verse is a reference to Nu 15:17–21. Part of the dough made from the first of the harvested grain (firstfruits) was offered to the Lord. This consecrated the whole batch. *firstfruits.* The patriarchs (cf. Ex 23:19 and note). *whole batch.* The Jewish people. *holy.* Not that all Jews are righteous (i.e., saved) but that God will be true to his promises concerning them (see 3:3–4 and notes). Paul foresaw a future for Israel, even though she was for a time set aside. *root.* The patriarchs. *branches.* The Jewish people.

11:17 *branches.* Individual Jews. *wild olive shoot.* Gentile Christians. *grafted in.* The usual procedure was to insert a shoot or slip of a cultivated tree into a common or wild one. In vv. 17–24, however, the metaphor is used, "contrary to nature" (v. 24), of grafting a wild olive branch (the Gentiles) into the cultivated olive tree. Such a procedure is unnatural, which is precisely the point. Normally, such a graft would be unfruitful. *olive root.* The patriarchs. The whole olive tree (v. 24) represents the people of God (cf. Jer 11:16).

11:18 *the root supports you.* The salvation of Gentile Christians is dependent on the Jews, especially the patriarchs (e.g., the Abrahamic covenant). See Jn 4:22 and note.

11:19 *Branches.* Unbelieving Jews.

11:20 *tremble.* On the fear of God, see note on Ge 20:11; see also Pr 1:7 and note; 3:7; Php 2:12–13; Heb 4:1, "be careful"; 1Pe 1:17.

11:22 *kindness and sternness of God.* Any adequate doctrine of God must include these two elements. When we ignore his kindness, God seems a ruthless tyrant; when we ignore his sternness, he seems a doting Father.

11:23 *God is able to graft them in again.* Paul holds out hope for the Jews—God is able (see Mk 10:27 and note).

11:24 *contrary to nature.* Paul recognized that such grafting was not commonly practiced (see note on v. 17). The inclusion of Gentiles in the family of God is "contrary to nature" (see Eph 2:12 and note). Obviously, the reasoning in this verse is more theological than horticultural. It would be difficult horticulturally to graft broken branches back into the parent tree, but the Jews really "belong" (historically and theologically) to the parent tree. Thus they will "much more readily ... be grafted into their own olive tree" (see note on v. 17).

11:25 *mystery.* The so-called mystery religions of Paul's day used the Greek word (*mysterion*) in the sense of something that was to be revealed only to the initiated. Paul himself, however, used it to refer to something formerly hidden or obscure but now revealed by God for all to know

you may not be conceited:[n] Israel has experienced a hardening[o] in part until the
full number of the Gentiles has come in,[p]
26 and in this way[a] all Israel will be saved.[q]
As it is written:

"The deliverer will come from
Zion;
he will turn godlessness away from
Jacob.
27 And this is[b] my covenant with
them
when I take away their sins."[c][r]

28 As far as the gospel is concerned, they
are enemies[s] for your sake; but as far as
election is concerned, they are loved on
account of the patriarchs,[t] 29 for God's gifts
and his call[u] are irrevocable.[v] 30 Just as you
who were at one time disobedient[w] to God
have now received mercy as a result of
their disobedience, 31 so they too have now
become disobedient in order that they too
may now[d] receive mercy as a result of
God's mercy to you. 32 For God has bound
everyone over to disobedience[x] so that he
may have mercy on them all.

11:25 [n]Ro 12:16 [o]ver 7; S Ro 9:18 [p]Lk 21:24
11:26 [q]Isa 45:17; Jer 31:34
11:27 [r]Isa 59:20,21; 27:9; Heb 8:10,12
11:28 [s]Ro 5:10 [t]Dt 7:8; 10:15; Ro 9:5
11:29 [u]S Ro 8:28 [v]S Heb 7:21
11:30 [w]S Eph 2:2
11:32 [x]S Ro 3:9
11:33 [y]S Ro 2:4 [z]Ps 92:5; Eph 3:10; Col 2:3 [a]Job 5:9; 11:7; Ps 139:6; Ecc 8:17; Isa 40:28
11:34 [b]Isa 40:13,14; Job 15:8; 36:22; Jer 23:18; 1Co 2:16
11:35 [c]Job 41:11; 35:7
11:36 [d]1Co 8:6; 11:12; Col 1:16; Heb 2:10

Doxology

33 Oh, the depth of the riches[y] of the
wisdom and[e] knowledge of God![z]
How unsearchable his judgments,
and his paths beyond tracing out![a]
34 "Who has known the mind of the Lord?
Or who has been his counselor?"[f][b]
35 "Who has ever given to God,
that God should repay them?"[g][c]
36 For from him and through him and for
him are all things.[d]
To him be the glory forever! Amen.[e]

A Living Sacrifice

12 Therefore, I urge you,[f] brothers
and sisters, in view of God's mercy, to offer your bodies as a living sacrifice,[g] holy and pleasing to God—this is
your true and proper worship. 2 Do not
conform[h] to the pattern of this world,[i] but

[a] *26* Or *and so* [b] *27* Or *will be* [c] *27* Isaiah 59:20,21; 27:9 (see Septuagint); Jer. 31:33,34 [d] *31* Some manuscripts do not have *now.* [e] *33* Or *riches and the wisdom and the* [f] *34* Isaiah 40:13 [g] *35* Job 41:11

[e]Ro 16:27; Eph 3:21; 1Ti 1:17; 1Pe 5:11; Jude 25; Rev 5:13; 7:12 **12:1** [f]Eph 4:1; 1Pe 2:11 [g]Ro 6:13,16,19; 1Co 6:20; 1Pe 2:5 **12:2** [h]1Pe 1:14 [i]1Co 1:20; 2Co 10:2; 1Jn 2:15

---

and understand (see 16:25; 1Co 2:7 and note; 4:1; 13:2; 14:2; 15:51 and note; Eph 1:9; 3:3,9 and note on 3:3; 5:32 and note; 6:19; Col 1:26–27 and notes; 2:2; 4:3; 2Th 2:7 and note; 1Ti 3:9,16). The word is used of (1) the incarnation (1Ti 3:16; see note there); (2) the death of Christ (1Co 2:1, NIV text note; 2:7, "God's wisdom, a mystery"); (3) God's purpose to sum up all things in Christ (Eph 1:9–10), and especially to include both Jews and Gentiles in the NT church (Eph 3:3–6); (4) the change that will take place at the resurrection (1Co 15:51); and (5) the plan of God by which both Jew and Gentile, after a period of disobedience by both, will by his mercy be included in his kingdom (here). *so that you may not be conceited.* God's merciful plan to include the Gentiles in his great salvation plan should humble them, not fill them with arrogance. *in part.* Israel's hardening is partial, not total. *until.* Israel's hardening is temporary, not permanent. *full number of the Gentiles.* The total number of the elect Gentiles.

11:26 *and in this way.* An emphatic statement that this is the way all Israel will be saved. *all Israel.* Three main interpretations of this phrase are: (1) the total number of elect Jews of every generation (equivalent to the "full inclusion" of Israel [v. 12; see note there], which is analogous to the "full number of the Gentiles" [v. 25; see note there]); (2) the total number of the elect, both Jews and Gentiles, of every generation; (3) the great majority of Jews of the final generation. *will be saved.* The salvation of the Jews will, of course, be on the same basis as anyone's salvation: personal faith in Jesus Christ, crucified and risen from the dead. *The deliverer will come from Zion.* The quotation is from Isa 59:20, where the deliverer ("Redeemer") seems to refer to God. The Talmud (a Jewish collection of religious instruction) understood the text to be a reference to the Messiah, and Paul appears to use it in this way. *Zion.* See notes on Gal 4:26; Heb 12:22.

11:27 *covenant.* The new covenant of Jer 31:31–34 (see notes there). *when I take away their sins.* See Jer 31:34; Zec 13:1 and note. Just as salvation for Gentiles involves forgiveness of sins, so the Jews, when they are saved, are forgiven by the mercy of God—his forgiveness based only on their repentance and faith (see v. 23; Zec 12:10—13:1 and notes).

11:28 *they are enemies.* Only temporarily. *for your sake.* Explained in v. 11. *loved on account of the patriarchs.* Not because any merit was passed on from the patriarchs to the Jewish people as a whole, but because God in love chose Israel, and that choice was "irrevocable" (v. 29).

11:29 *God's gifts and his call are irrevocable.* God does not change his mind with reference to his call. Even though Israel is presently in a state of unbelief, God's purpose will be fulfilled in her.

11:32 *everyone.* Both groups under discussion (Jews and Gentiles). There has been a period of disobedience for each in order that God may have mercy on them all. Paul is in no way teaching universal salvation.

11:33–36 The doxology that ends this section of Romans is the natural outpouring of Paul's praise to God, whose wisdom and knowledge brought about his great plan for the salvation of both Jews and Gentiles.

12:1—15:33 Paul now turns to the practical application of all he has said previously in the letter. This does not mean that he has not said anything about Christian living up to this point. Chs. 6–8 have touched on this already, but now Paul goes into detail to show that Jesus Christ is to be Lord of every area of life. These chapters are not a postscript to the great theological discussions in chs. 1–11. In a real sense the entire letter has been directed toward the goal of showing that God demands our action as well as our believing and thinking. Faith expresses itself in obedience (see notes on Jas 2:14–26).

12:1 *Therefore, I urge you.* Paul draws an important inference from the truth set forth in chs. 1–11. *God's mercy.* Much of the letter has been concerned with demonstrating this. *your bodies.* See 6:13 and note. *living sacrifice.* In contrast to dead animal sacrifices, or perhaps "living" in the sense of having the new life of the Holy Spirit (see 6:4; 8:2 and note). *true and proper worship.* Not merely ritual activity but the involvement of heart, mind and will in worship and obedient service.

12:2 *this world.* With all its evil and corruption (see Gal 1:4; 1Jn 2:15 and notes). *be transformed.* Here a process, not a single event. The same Greek word is used in the

be transformed by the renewing of your
mind.[j] Then you will be able to test and
approve what God's will is[k]—his good,
pleasing[l] and perfect will.

Humble Service in the Body of Christ

3 For by the grace given me[m] I say to every one of you: Do not think of yourself
more highly than you ought, but rather
think of yourself with sober judgment, in
accordance with the faith God has distributed to each of you. 4 For just as each of
us has one body with many members, and
these members do not all have the same
function,[n] 5 so in Christ we, though many,
form one body,[o] and each member belongs
to all the others. 6 We have different gifts,[p]
according to the grace given to each of us.
If your gift is prophesying,[q] then prophesy in accordance with your[a] faith;[r] 7 if it is
serving, then serve; if it is teaching, then
teach;[s] 8 if it is to encourage, then give encouragement;[t] if it is giving, then give generously;[u] if it is to lead,[b] do it diligently; if
it is to show mercy, do it cheerfully.

Love in Action

9 Love must be sincere.[v] Hate what is
evil; cling to what is good.[w] 10 Be devoted
to one another in love.[x] Honor one another
above yourselves.[y] 11 Never be lacking in
zeal, but keep your spiritual fervor,[z] serving the Lord. 12 Be joyful in hope,[a] patient
in affliction,[b] faithful in prayer.[c] 13 Share
with the Lord's people who are in need.[d]
Practice hospitality.[e]
14 Bless those who persecute you;[f] bless
and do not curse. 15 Rejoice with those who
rejoice; mourn with those who mourn.[g]
16 Live in harmony with one another.[h] Do
not be proud, but be willing to associate
with people of low position.[c] Do not be
conceited.[i]
17 Do not repay anyone evil for evil.[j] Be

[a] *6* Or *the* [b] *8* Or *to provide for others*
[c] *16* Or *willing to do menial work*

12:2 [j] Eph 4:23 [k] S Eph 5:17 [l] S 1Ti 5:4 **12:3** [m] Ro 15:15; 1Co 15:10; Gal 2:9; Eph 3:7; 4:7; 1Pe 4:10,11 **12:4** [n] 1Co 12:12-14; Eph 4:16 **12:5** [o] 1Co 6:15; 10:17; 12:12, 20,27; Eph 2:16; 4:4,25; 5:30; Col 3:15 **12:6** [p] 1Co 7:7; 12:4,8-10 [q] S Eph 4:11 [r] 1Pe 4:10,11 **12:7** [s] S Eph 4:11 **12:8** [t] Ac 11:23; 13:15; 15:32 [u] 2Co 8:2; 9:5-13 **12:9** [v] 2Co 6:6; 1Ti 1:5 [w] Ps 97:10; Am 5:15; 1Th 5:21,22 **12:10** [x] Ps 133:1; 1Th 4:9; Heb 13:1; 1Pe 1:22 [y] Php 2:3 **12:11** [z] Ac 18:25 **12:12** [a] Ro 5:2 [b] Heb 10:32,36 [c] S Lk 18:1 **12:13** [d] S Ac 24:17 [e] 2Ki 4:10; Job 31:32; 1Ti 3:2; 5:10; Heb 13:2; 1Pe 4:9 **12:14** [f] S Mt 5:44 **12:15** [g] Job 30:25 **12:16** [h] S Ro 15:5 [i] ver 3; Ps 131:1; Isa 5:21; Jer 45:5; Ro 11:25 **12:17** [j] ver 19; Pr 20:22; 24:29

transfiguration narratives (Mt 17:2–8; Mk 9:2–8) and in 2Co 3:18 (see note there). *mind.* Thought and will as they relate to morality (see 1:28; Eph 4:23). *Then.* After the spiritual transformation just described has taken place. *God's will.* What God wants from the believer here and now. *good.* That which leads to the spiritual and moral growth of the Christian. *pleasing.* To God, not necessarily to us. *perfect.* No improvement can be made on the will of God.

12:3 *in accordance with the faith.* The power given by God to each believer to fulfill various ministries in the church (see vv. 4–8 and notes). *God has distributed.* Since the power comes from God, there can be no basis for a superior attitude or self-righteousness.

12:4–8 Paul likens Christians to members of a human body. There are many members and each has a different function, but all are needed for the health of the body. The emphasis is on unity within diversity (see 1Co 12:12–31 and notes).

12:5 *in Christ.* The key to Paul's concept of Christian unity. It is only in Jesus Christ that any unity in the church is possible. True unity is spiritually based. See note on 6:11.

12:6 *gifts.* Greek *charismata,* referring to special gifts of grace—freely given by God to his people to meet the needs of the body (see notes on 1Co 1:7; 12:4). *prophesying.* See notes on 1Co 12:10; 14:1–5. *then prophesy.* There is to be no false modesty that denies the existence of gifts or refuses to use them. *in accordance with your faith.* Probably means about the same thing as "in accordance with the faith" in v. 3 (see note there).

12:7 *serving.* Any kind of service needed by the body of Christ or by any of its members. *teaching.* See notes on 1Co 12:28; Eph 4:11.

12:8 *to encourage.* Exhorting others with an uplifting, cheerful call to worthwhile accomplishment. The teacher often carried out this function. In teaching, believers are shown what they must do; in encouraging, they are helped to do it. *giving.* Giving what is one's own, or possibly distributing what has been given by others. *lead ... diligently.* Possibly a reference to an elder. The Ephesian church had elders by about this time (see Ac 20:17; 1Ti 5:17 and notes). *show mercy.* Caring for the sick, the poor and the aged. *cheerfully.* Serving the needy should be a delight, not a chore (cf. 2Co 9:7).

12:9 *Love.* Believers' love for fellow Christians and perhaps also for other people. *sincere.* True love, not pretense. In view of the preceding paragraph, with its emphasis on social concern, the love Paul speaks of here is not mere emotion but love in action, as delineated in the rest of the chapter (cf. Jas 2:1–4,14–17; 1Jn 3:16–18; 4:19–21). *evil ... good.* See Am 5:15. "Evil" and "good" frame vv. 9–21.

12:10 *love.* Love within the family of God. *Honor one another above yourselves.* Only a mind renewed by the Holy Spirit (see v. 2) could possibly do this (see Php 2:3 and note).

12:11 *spiritual fervor.* Lit. "fervent in spirit." If "spirit" means "Holy Spirit" here, the reference would be to the fervor the Holy Spirit provides.

12:12 *Be joyful in hope.* The certainty of the Christian's hope is a cause for joy (see 5:5 and note; see also 8:16–25; 1Pe 1:3–9). *patient.* Enduring triumphantly—necessary for Christians, because affliction is their inevitable experience (see Jn 16:33; 2Ti 3:12 and notes). *faithful in prayer.* One must not only pray in hard times but also maintain communion with God through prayer at all times (see Lk 18:1; 1Th 5:17 and note).

12:13 *Share with the Lord's people.* The Christian has social responsibility to all people, but especially to other believers (see Gal 6:10; 1Ti 5:8).

12:14 *Bless those who persecute you.* Paul is echoing Jesus' teaching (see Mt 5:44 and note; Lk 6:28 and note on 6:27).

12:15 Identification with others in their joys and in their sorrows is a Christian's privilege and responsibility.

12:17 *Do not repay anyone evil for evil.* See Mt 5:39–42,44–45; 1Th 5:15; 1Pe 3:9 and notes. *Be careful to do what is right in the eyes of everyone.* A possible reflection of Pr 3:4 in the Septuagint (the pre-Christian Greek translation of the OT). Christian conduct should never betray the high moral standards of the gospel, or it will provoke the disdain of unbelievers and bring the gospel into disrepute (see 2Co 8:21 and note; 1Ti 3:7).

careful to do what is right in the eyes of
everyone.[k] 18If it is possible, as far as it
depends on you, live at peace with everyone.[l] 19Do not take revenge,[m] my dear
friends, but leave room for God's wrath,
for it is written: "It is mine to avenge; I
will repay,"[a][n] says the Lord. 20On the contrary:

"If your enemy is hungry, feed him;
if he is thirsty, give him something
to drink.
In doing this, you will heap burning
coals on his head."[b][o]

21Do not be overcome by evil, but overcome evil with good.

Submission to Governing Authorities

13 Let everyone be subject to the governing authorities,[p] for there is no
authority except that which God has established.[q] The authorities that exist have
been established by God. 2Consequently,
whoever rebels against the authority is rebelling against what God has instituted,[r]
and those who do so will bring judgment
on themselves. 3For rulers hold no terror
for those who do right, but for those who
do wrong. Do you want to be free from
fear of the one in authority? Then do what
is right and you will be commended.[s] 4For
the one in authority is God's servant for
your good. But if you do wrong, be afraid,
for rulers do not bear the sword for no
reason. They are God's servants, agents of
wrath to bring punishment on the wrongdoer.[t] 5Therefore, it is necessary to submit
to the authorities, not only because of possible punishment but also as a matter of
conscience.[u]

6This is also why you pay taxes,[v] for the
authorities are God's servants, who give
their full time to governing. 7Give to everyone what you owe them: If you owe
taxes, pay taxes;[w] if revenue, then revenue; if respect, then respect; if honor, then
honor.

Love Fulfills the Law

8Let no debt remain outstanding, except
the continuing debt to love one another,
for whoever loves others has fulfilled the
law.[x] 9The commandments, "You shall not
commit adultery," "You shall not murder,"
"You shall not steal," "You shall not covet,"[c][y] and whatever other command there
may be, are summed up[z] in this one command: "Love your neighbor as yourself."[d][a]
10Love does no harm to a neighbor. Therefore love is the fulfillment of the law.[b]

The Day Is Near

11And do this, understanding the present time: The hour has already come[c] for
you to wake up from your slumber,[d] because our salvation is nearer now than

12:17 [k]2Co 8:21 **12:18** [l]S Mk 9:50; S Ro 14:19 **12:19** [m]ver 17; Lev 19:18; Pr 20:22; 24:29 [n]Dt 32:35; Ge 50:19; 1Sa 26:10; Ps 94:1; Jer 51:36 **12:20** [o]Pr 25:21, 22; Ex 23:4; Mt 5:44; Lk 6:27 **13:1** [p]Titus 3:1; 1Pe 2:13,14 [q]Da 2:21; 4:17; Jn 19:11 **13:2** [r]Ex 16:8 **13:3** [s]1Pe 2:14 **13:4** [t]1Th 4:6 **13:5** [u]Pr 24:21, 22 **13:6** [v]Mt 22:17 **13:7** [w]Mt 17:25; 22:17,21; Lk 23:2 **13:8** [x]ver 10; S Mt 5:43; Jn 13:34; Col 3:14 **13:9** [y]Ex 20:13-15,17; Dt 5:17-19,21 [z]Mt 7:12 [a]Lev 19:18; S Mt 5:43 **13:10** [b]S ver 8; ver 9 **13:11** [c]1Co 7:29-31; 10:11; Jas 5:8; 1Pe 4:7; 1Jn 2:18; Rev 22:10 [d]Eph 5:14; 1Th 5:5,6

[a] *19* Deut. 32:35 [b] *20* Prov. 25:21,22
[c] *9* Exodus 20:13-15,17; Deut. 5:17-19,21
[d] *9* Lev. 19:18

12:18 *If it is possible . . . live at peace.* Jesus pronounced a blessing on peacemakers (see Mt 5:9 and note), and believers are to cultivate peace with everyone to the extent that such peace depends on them (see Jas 3:18 and note).
12:20 *heap burning coals on his head.* Doing good to one's enemy (v. 21), instead of trying to take revenge, may bring about their repentance (see note on Pr 25:22).
12:21 *evil . . . good.* See note on v. 9.
13:1 *be subject to.* A significant theme in vv. 1–7. *governing authorities.* The civil rulers, all of whom were probably pagans at the time Paul was writing. Christians may have been tempted not to submit to them and to claim allegiance only to Christ. *established by God.* Even the possibility of a persecuting state did not shake Paul's conviction that civil government is ordained by God (see 1Pe 2:13–17 and notes).
13:2 *judgment.* Either divine judgment or, more likely, punishment by the governing authorities, since v. 3 ("For") explains this verse; see also v. 4.
13:3 *do what is right and you will be commended.* Paul is not stating that this will always be true but is describing the proper, ideal function of rulers. When civil rulers overstep their proper function, the Christian is to obey God rather than human authorities (see Ac 4:19; 5:29).
13:4 *God's servant.* In the order of divine providence the ruler is God's servant (see Isa 45:1 and note). *good.* Rulers exist for the benefit of society—to protect the general public by maintaining good order. *sword.* The symbol of Roman authority on both the national and the international levels. Here we find the Biblical principle of using force for the maintenance of good order.
13:5 *as a matter of conscience.* Civil authorities are ordained by God, and in order to maintain a good conscience Christians must duly honor them.
13:6 *you pay taxes.* Because rulers are God's agents, who function for the benefit of society in general.
13:8 *continuing debt.* To love is the one debt that is never paid off. No matter how much people have loved, they are under obligation to keep on loving. *one another.* Includes not only fellow Christians but all people, as the second half of the verse makes clear ("loves others"). *the law.* The Mosaic law, which lays down both moral and social responsibilities.
13:9 Further explains the last statement of v. 8, namely, that love of neighbor encompasses all our social responsibilities. *your neighbor.* Jesus taught that our neighbor is anyone in need (see Lk 10:25–36 and notes), which is probably the idea Paul has in mind here. *as yourself.* Not a command to love ourselves but a recognition of the fact that we naturally do so (cf. Eph 5:33).
13:11–14 In this section, as in other NT passages, the certain coming of the end of the present age is used to provide motivation for godly living (see, e.g., Mt 25:31–46; Mk 13:33–37; Lk 21:36; Php 4:5; 1Th 5:6,8; Titus 2:11–14; Jas 5:7–11; 2Pe 3:11–14; 1Jn 2:28; 3:2–3).
13:11 *present time.* The time of salvation, the closing period of the present age, before the consummation of the kingdom. *The hour.* The time for action. *our salvation.* The full realization of salvation at the second coming of Jesus Christ (see 8:23; Heb 9:28; 1Pe 1:5 and notes). *is nearer now.* Every day brings us closer to the second advent of Christ.

when we first believed. 12 The night is nearly over; the day is almost here.[e] So let us put aside the deeds of darkness[f] and put on the armor[g] of light. 13 Let us behave decently, as in the daytime, not in carousing and drunkenness,[h] not in sexual immorality and debauchery, not in dissension and jealousy.[i] 14 Rather, clothe yourselves with the Lord Jesus Christ,[j] and do not think about how to gratify the desires of the flesh.[a][k]

The Weak and the Strong

14 Accept the one whose faith is weak,[l] without quarreling over disputable matters. 2 One person's faith allows them to eat anything, but another, whose faith is weak, eats only vegetables.[m] 3 The one who eats everything must not treat with contempt[n] the one who does not, and the one who does not eat everything must not judge[o] the one who does, for God has accepted them. 4 Who are you to judge someone else's servant?[p] To their own master, servants stand or fall. And they will stand, for the Lord is able to make them stand.

5 One person considers one day more sacred than another;[q] another considers every day alike. Each of them should be fully convinced in their own mind. 6 Whoever regards one day as special does so to the Lord. Whoever eats meat does so to the Lord, for they give thanks to God;[r] and whoever abstains does so to the Lord and gives thanks to God. 7 For none of us lives for ourselves alone,[s] and none of us dies for ourselves alone. 8 If we live, we live for the Lord; and if we die, we die for the Lord. So, whether we live or die, we belong to the Lord.[t] 9 For this very reason, Christ died and returned to life[u] so that he might be the Lord of both the dead and the living.[v]

10 You, then, why do you judge your brother or sister[b]? Or why do you treat them with contempt?[w] For we will all stand before God's judgment seat.[x] 11 It is written:

> "'As surely as I live,'[y] says the Lord,
> 'every knee will bow before me;
> every tongue will acknowledge
> God.'"[c][z]

12 So then, each of us will give an account of ourselves to God.[a]

13:12 [e] Heb 10:25; 1Jn 2:8 [f] Eph 5:11 [g] Eph 6:11, 13; 1Th 5:8 **13:13** [h] S Eph 5:18 [i] Lk 21:34; Gal 5:20, 21; Eph 5:18; 1Pe 4:3 **13:14** [j] Gal 3:27; Eph 4:24; Col 3:10, 12 [k] S Gal 5:24 **14:1** [l] Ro 15:1; 1Co 8:9-12; 9:22 **14:2** [m] ver 14 **14:3** [n] ver 10; Lk 18:9 [o] ver 10, 13; Col 2:16 **14:4** [p] S Mt 7:1 **14:5** [q] Gal 4:10; Col 2:16 **14:6** [r] S Mt 14:19; 1Co 10:30, 31; 1Ti 4:3, 4 **14:7** [s] 2Co 5:15; Gal 2:20 **14:8** [t] Php 1:20 **14:9** [u] Rev 1:18; 2:8 [v] S Ac 10:42; 2Co 5:15 **14:10** [w] ver 3; S Mt 7:1 [x] S 2Co 5:10 **14:11** [y] Isa 49:18 [z] Isa 45:23; Php 2:10, 11 **14:12** [a] Mt 12:36; 1Pe 4:5

[a] *14* In contexts like this, the Greek word for *flesh* (*sarx*) refers to the sinful state of human beings, often presented as a power in opposition to the Spirit.
[b] *10* The Greek word for *brother or sister* (*adelphos*) refers here to a believer, whether man or woman, as part of God's family; also in verses 13, 15 and 21.
[c] *11* Isaiah 45:23

13:12 *The night.* The present evil age. *is nearly over; the day is almost here.* A clear example of the NT teaching of the imminence of the end times (see 1Co 7:29; Php 4:5; Jas 5:9; 1Pe 4:7; 1Jn 2:18 and notes). These texts do not mean that the early Christians believed that Jesus would return within a few years (and thus were mistaken). Rather, they regarded the death and resurrection of Christ as the crucial events of history that began the last days (see Heb 1:1–2 and notes). Since the next great event in God's redemptive plan is the second coming of Jesus Christ, "the night," no matter how long it may chronologically last, is "nearly over." *the day.* The appearing of Jesus Christ, which ushers in the consummation of the kingdom.

13:13 See 1:29–31 and note.

13:14 *clothe yourselves with the Lord Jesus Christ.* See Gal 3:27. Paul exhorts believers to display outwardly what has already taken place inwardly (see Col 3:1–10 and notes)—including practicing all the virtues associated with Christ. *clothe ... with.* See note on Ps 109:29.

14:1—15:13 Cf. 1Co 8:1—11:1 and notes.

14:1 *whose faith is weak.* Probably Jewish Christians at Rome who were continuing to observe the hallmarks of Jewish identity, such as dietary restrictions and the keeping of the Sabbath and other special days. Their concern was not the same as that of the Judaizers of Galatia. The Judaizers thought they could put God in their debt by works of righteousness and were trying to force this heretical teaching on the Galatian churches, but the "weak" Roman Christians did neither. They were wrestling with the status of OT regulations under the new covenant inaugurated by the coming of Christ. *without quarreling over disputable matters.* Fellowship among Christians is not to be based on everyone's agreement on disputable questions. Christians do not agree on all matters pertaining to the Christian life, nor do they need to.

14:2 *One person's faith.* In contrast, Paul now describes the "strong" (15:1) Christian. Here faith is used in the sense of assurance or confidence. The strong Christian's understanding of the gospel allows them to recognize that one's dietary choices have no spiritual significance.

14:4 *someone else's.* God's. A Christian is not to reject a fellow Christian, who is also a servant of God. *To their own master, servants stand or fall.* The "weak" Christian is not the master of the "strong" Christian, nor is the "strong" the master of the "weak." God is Master, and to him alone all believers are responsible.

14:5 *one day more sacred than another.* Some feel that this refers primarily to the Sabbath, but it is probably a reference to all the special days of the OT ceremonial law. *considers every day alike.* All days are to be dedicated to God through holy living and godly service. *fully convinced in their own mind.* The importance of personal conviction in disputable matters of conduct runs through this passage (see vv. 14,16, 22–23).

14:6 The motivation behind the actions of both the strong and the weak is to be the same: Both should want to serve the Lord and give thanks for his provision.

14:7 *none of us lives for ourselves alone.* The reference is to Christians. We live not to please ourselves but to please the Lord. *none of us dies for ourselves alone.* Even in death the important thing is one's relationship to the Lord. Paul repeats the truths of this verse in v. 8.

14:9 *Lord.* See note on 10:9. Christ's Lordship over both the dead and the living arises out of his death and resurrection.

14:10 *why do you judge your brother or sister?* Addressed to weak Christians. *why do you treat them with contempt?* Addressed to strong Christians. *we will all.* Refers to every Christian. *God's judgment seat.* All Christians will be judged, and the judgment will be based on works (see 2Co 5:10 and note; cf. 1Co 3:10–15 and notes).

14:12 See Ecc 12:14 and note.

13 Therefore let us stop passing judgment[b] on one another. Instead, make up
your mind not to put any stumbling block
or obstacle in the way of a brother or sister.[c]
14 I am convinced, being fully persuaded in
the Lord Jesus, that nothing is unclean in
itself.[d] But if anyone regards something as
unclean, then for that person it is unclean.[e]
15 If your brother or sister is distressed because of what you eat, you are no longer
acting in love.[f] Do not by your eating destroy someone for whom Christ died.[g]
16 Therefore do not let what you know is
good be spoken of as evil.[h] 17 For the kingdom of God is not a matter of eating and
drinking,[i] but of righteousness, peace[j] and
joy in the Holy Spirit,[k] 18 because anyone
who serves Christ in this way is pleasing to
God and receives human approval.[l]
19 Let us therefore make every effort to
do what leads to peace[m] and to mutual edification.[n] 20 Do not destroy the work of God
for the sake of food.[o] All food is clean,[p] but
it is wrong for a person to eat anything
that causes someone else to stumble.[q] 21 It
is better not to eat meat or drink wine or
to do anything else that will cause your
brother or sister to fall.[r]

22 So whatever you believe about these
things keep between yourself and God.
Blessed is the one who does not condemn[s]
himself by what he approves. 23 But whoever has doubts[t] is condemned if they eat,
because their eating is not from faith; and
everything that does not come from faith
is sin.[a]

15 We who are strong ought to bear
with the failings of the weak[u] and
not to please ourselves. 2 Each of us should
please our neighbors for their good,[v] to
build them up.[w] 3 For even Christ did not
please himself[x] but, as it is written: "The
insults of those who insult you have fallen
on me."[b][y] 4 For everything that was written
in the past was written to teach us,[z] so
that through the endurance taught in the
Scriptures and the encouragement they
provide we might have hope.
5 May the God who gives endurance and
encouragement give you the same attitude
of mind[a] toward each other that Christ

[a] 23 Some manuscripts place 16:25-27 here; others after 15:33. [b] 3 Psalm 69:9

14:13 [b] ver 1; S Mt 7:1 [c] S 2Co 6:3 **14:14** [d] ver 20; S Ac 10:15 [e] 1Co 8:7 **14:15** [f] Eph 5:2 [g] ver 20; 1Co 8:11 **14:16** [h] 1Co 10:30 **14:17** [i] 1Co 8:8 [j] Isa 32:17 [k] Ro 15:13; Gal 5:22 **14:18** [l] Lk 2:52; Ac 24:16; 2Co 8:21 **14:19** [m] Ps 34:14; Ro 12:18; 1Co 7:15; 2Ti 2:22; Heb 12:14 [n] Ro 15:2; 1Co 14:3-5, 12, 17, 26; 2Co 12:19; Eph 4:12, 29 **14:20** [o] ver 15 [p] ver 14; S Ac 10:15 [q] ver 13; 1Co 8:9-12 **14:21** [r] S Mt 5:29 **14:22** [s] 1Jn 3:21 **14:23** [t] ver 5 **15:1** [u] Ro 14:1; 1Th 5:14

15:2 [v] S 1Co 10:24 [w] S Ro 14:19 **15:3** [x] 2Co 8:9 [y] Ps 69:9 **15:4** [z] S Ro 4:23, 24 **15:5** [a] Ro 12:16; 1Co 1:10; 2Co 13:11; Eph 4:3; Php 2:2; Col 3:14; 1Pe 3:8

14:13 *Instead.* The words that immediately follow are addressed to strong Christians. *obstacle.* Something that causes one to fall into sin.

14:14 *I am convinced, being fully persuaded in the Lord Jesus.* Now that Paul was a Christian, the old food taboos no longer applied (see Mk 7:19–20; Ac 10:15,28 and notes). *nothing is unclean in itself.* For Paul's teaching elsewhere on this subject, see 1Ti 4:4; Titus 1:15 and note. *if anyone regards something as unclean, then for that person it is unclean.* Not to be generalized to mean that sin is only a matter of subjective opinion or conscience. Paul is not discussing conduct that in the light of Scripture is clearly sinful but conduct concerning which Christians may legitimately differ (in this case, food regulations). With regard to such matters, decisions should be guided by conscience.

14:15 *love.* The key to proper settlement of disputes. *someone for whom Christ died.* Christ so valued weak Christians that he died for them. Surely strong Christians ought to be willing to make adjustments in their own behavior for the sake of such fellow believers (see 1Co 8:11–13; 10:23, 28–29,32–33 and notes).

14:16 *what you know is good.* From your own understanding of Christian liberty. *be spoken of as evil.* To exercise freedom without responsibility can lead to evil results.

14:17 *kingdom of God.* See notes on Mt 3:2; Lk 4:43. *is not a matter of eating and drinking.* To be concerned with such trivial matters is to miss completely the essence of Christian living. *righteousness.* Righteous living. Paul's concern for the moral and ethical dimension of the Christian life stands out in all his letters. *peace.* See 5:1 and note. *joy in the Holy Spirit.* Joy given by the Holy Spirit (see Gal 5:22–23).

14:19 *mutual edification.* The spiritual building up of individual Christians and of the church (see 1:11–12 and note on 1:12).

14:20 *work of God.* The weak Christian who as a redeemed person is God's work and one in whom God continues to work (cf. Eph 2:10). *causes someone else to stumble.* Paul recognizes a strong Christian's right to certain freedoms, but qualifies this with the principle of regard for a weak Christian's scruples.

14:22 *keep between yourself and God.* Strong Christians are not required to go against their convictions or change their standards. Yet they are not to flaunt their Christian freedom but to keep it a private matter. *what he approves.* Probably a reference to the eating of certain foods.

14:23 *everything.* The matters discussed above, namely, conduct about which there can be legitimate differences of opinion among Christians. *faith.* Here the conviction that one's action is in keeping with God's will.

15:1 *We who are strong.* Paul identifies himself with the strong Christians, those whose personal convictions allow them more freedom than the weak. *to bear.* Not merely to tolerate or put up with but to uphold lovingly. *failings.* Not sins, since in the matters under discussion there is no clear guidance in Scripture. *not to please ourselves.* Not that Christians should never please themselves, but that they should not insist on doing what they want without regard to the scruples of other Christians.

15:3 *Christ did not please himself.* He came to do the will of the Father, not his own will (see Jn 4:34 and note). This involved suffering and even death (see Mt 20:28; Mk 10:45; 2Co 8:9; Php 2:5–8 and notes). *The insults of those who insult you have fallen on me.* In the psalm quoted (69:9; see note there) "you" refers to God and "me" refers to the righteous sufferer, whom Paul identifies with Christ. The quotation serves to show how Christ did not please himself but voluntarily bore human hostility toward God.

15:4 Here Paul defends his application of Ps 69:9 to Christ. In so doing, he states a great truth concerning the purpose of Scripture: It was written for our instruction, so that as we patiently endure we might be encouraged to hold fast our hope in Christ (see 1Co 10:6,11).

15:5 *the same attitude of mind toward each other that Christ Jesus had.* Not that believers should all come to

Jesus had, 6 so that with one mind and one
voice you may glorify[b] the God and Father[c]
of our Lord Jesus Christ.
7 Accept one another,[d] then, just as
Christ accepted you, in order to bring
praise to God. 8 For I tell you that Christ
has become a servant of the Jews[ae] on behalf of God's truth, so that the promises[f]
made to the patriarchs might be confirmed
9 and, moreover, that the Gentiles[g] might
glorify God[h] for his mercy. As it is written:

> "Therefore I will praise you among the
> Gentiles;
> I will sing the praises of your name."[bi]

10 Again, it says,

> "Rejoice, you Gentiles, with his people."[cj]

11 And again,

> "Praise the Lord, all you Gentiles;
> let all the peoples extol him."[dk]

12 And again, Isaiah says,

> "The Root of Jesse[l] will spring up,
> one who will arise to rule over the
> nations;
> in him the Gentiles will hope."[em]

13 May the God of hope fill you with all
joy and peace[n] as you trust in him, so that
you may overflow with hope by the power
of the Holy Spirit.[o]

15:6 [b] Ps 34:3 [c] Rev 1:6 **15:7** [d] Ro 14:1 **15:8** [e] Mt 15:24; Ac 3:25,26 [f] 2Co 1:20 **15:9** [g] S Ro 3:29 [h] S Mt 9:8 [i] 2Sa 22:50; Ps 18:49 **15:10** [j] Dt 32:43; Isa 66:10 **15:11** [k] Ps 117:1 **15:12** [l] S Rev 5:5 [m] Isa 11:10; Mt 12:21 **15:13** [n] Ro 14:17 [o] ver 19; 1Co 2:4; 4:20; 1Th 1:5

15:14 [p] Eph 5:9 [q] S 2Co 8:7; 2Pe 1:12 **15:15** [r] S Ro 12:3 **15:16** [s] S Ac 9:15 [t] ver 19; S Ro 1:1 [u] Isa 66:20 **15:17** [v] Php 3:3 [w] Heb 2:17 **15:18** [x] Ac 15:12; 21:19; Ro 1:5 [y] Ro 16:26 **15:19** [z] S Jn 4:48; Ac 19:11 [a] S ver 13 [b] Ac 22:17-21 [c] S 2Co 2:12

Paul the Minister to the Gentiles

14 I myself am convinced, my brothers
and sisters, that you yourselves are full
of goodness,[p] filled with knowledge[q] and
competent to instruct one another. 15 Yet
I have written you quite boldly on some
points to remind you of them again, because of the grace God gave me[r] 16 to be
a minister of Christ Jesus to the Gentiles.[s]
He gave me the priestly duty of proclaiming the gospel of God,[t] so that the Gentiles
might become an offering[u] acceptable to
God, sanctified by the Holy Spirit.
17 Therefore I glory in Christ Jesus[v] in
my service to God.[w] 18 I will not venture
to speak of anything except what Christ
has accomplished through me in leading
the Gentiles[x] to obey God[y] by what I have
said and done— 19 by the power of signs
and wonders,[z] through the power of the
Spirit of God.[a] So from Jerusalem[b] all the
way around to Illyricum, I have fully proclaimed the gospel of Christ.[c] 20 It has always been my ambition to preach the gospel[d] where Christ was not known, so that
I would not be building on someone else's
foundation.[e] 21 Rather, as it is written:

[a] *8* Greek *circumcision* [b] *9* 2 Samuel 22:50; Psalm 18:49 [c] *10* Deut. 32:43 [d] *11* Psalm 117:1 [e] *12* Isaiah 11:10 (see Septuagint)

15:20 [d] Ro 1:15 [e] 2Co 10:15,16

---

the same conclusions on the matters of conscience discussed above, but that they might agree to disagree in love (cf. Eph 4:1–6; Php 2:1–5 and notes).

15:7 *just as Christ accepted you.* See 14:3; see also 14:4,15 and notes.

15:8 *Christ has become a servant of the Jews.* Clearly revealed in his earthly ministry. He was sent to the Jewish people and largely limited his ministry to them (see Mt 15:24). God gave a special priority, so far as the gospel is concerned, to the Jews (see 1:16 and note; 3:1–8; see also 9:4–5 and notes). *promises made to the patriarchs.* The covenant promises made to Abraham (Ge 12:1–3; 17:7; 18:19; 22:18), Isaac (Ge 26:3–4) and Jacob (Ge 28:13–15; 46:2–4; see chart, p. 23).

15:9 *that the Gentiles might glorify God.* From the beginning, God's redemptive work in and for Israel had in view the redemption of the Gentiles (see Ge 12:2–3 and note). They would both see God's mighty and gracious acts for his people and hear the praises of God's people as they celebrated what God had done for them (a common theme in the Psalms; see Paul's quotations in vv. 9b–12 and note on Ps 9:1). Thus they would come to know the true God and glorify him for his mercy (see notes on Ps 46:10; 47:9). God's greatest and climactic act for Israel's salvation was the sending of the Messiah to fulfill the promises made to the patriarchs and so to gather in the great harvest of the Gentiles.

15:10 See note on Dt 32:43.

15:12 *Root of Jesse.* Jesse was the father of David (see 1Sa 16:5–13; Mt 1:6), and the Messiah was the "Son of David" (see Mt 1:1 and note; 21:9; see also Isa 11:1; Rev 5:5 and notes). *in him the Gentiles will hope.* The Gentile mission of the early church was a fulfillment of this prophecy (Isa 11:10; see note there), as is the continuing evangelization of the nations (cf. Isa 42:4 and note).

15:13 *God of hope.* Any hope the Christian has comes from God (see note on 5:5). *by the power of the Holy Spirit.* Hope cannot be conjured up by human effort; it is God's gift by his Spirit (see 8:24–25).

15:15 *to remind you of them again.* Since Paul had never preached or taught in Rome, he may be referring to Christian doctrine generally known in the church.

15:16 *minister of Christ Jesus to the Gentiles.* See notes on 11:13; Gal 2:7. *priestly duty of proclaiming the gospel.* Paul's priestly function was different from that of the Levitical priests. They were involved with the rituals of the temple, whereas he preached the gospel. *an offering acceptable to God, sanctified by the Holy Spirit.* The offering Paul brought to God was the Gentile church. *sanctified.* See note on 1Co 1:2.

15:17 *I glory.* Paul was not boasting of his own achievements but of what Christ had accomplished through him (v. 18).

15:19 *signs and wonders.* See Ac 14:8–10; 16:16–18, 25–26; 20:9–12; 28:8–9; 2Co 12:12 and note; Heb 2:4 and note. *from Jerusalem.* The home of the mother church, where the gospel originated and its dissemination began (see Ac 1:8 and note; see also map, p. 1849, and Introduction to Acts: Plan and Outline). *Illyricum.* A Roman province north of Macedonia (present-day Albania, Serbia and Montenegro [the former Yugoslavia]). Acts mentions nothing of Paul's ministry there, and perhaps all he means is that he reached the border. *I have fully proclaimed the gospel.* Not everyone in the eastern Mediterranean had heard the gospel, but Paul believed that his work there had been completed and it was time to move on to other places.

15:20 *not be building on someone else's foundation.* Rather, Paul wanted to lay foundations on which others could build (see 1Co 3:6,10 and notes).

"Those who were not told about him
will see,
and those who have not heard will
understand."[a][f]

22 This is why I have often been hindered
from coming to you.[g]

Paul's Plan to Visit Rome

23 But now that there is no more place
for me to work in these regions, and since
I have been longing for many years to visit
you,[h] 24 I plan to do so when I go to Spain.[i]
I hope to see you while passing through
and to have you assist[j] me on my journey there, after I have enjoyed your company for a while. 25 Now, however, I am
on my way to Jerusalem[k] in the service[l]
of the Lord's people[m] there. 26 For Macedonia[n] and Achaia[o] were pleased to make
a contribution for the poor among the
Lord's people in Jerusalem.[p] 27 They were
pleased to do it, and indeed they owe it to
them. For if the Gentiles have shared in
the Jews' spiritual blessings, they owe it to
the Jews to share with them their material
blessings.[q] 28 So after I have completed this
task and have made sure that they have received this contribution, I will go to Spain[r]
and visit you on the way. 29 I know that
when I come to you,[s] I will come in the
full measure of the blessing of Christ.
30 I urge you, brothers and sisters, by
our Lord Jesus Christ and by the love of
the Spirit,[t] to join me in my struggle by
praying to God for me.[u] 31 Pray that I may
be kept safe[v] from the unbelievers in Judea and that the contribution[w] I take to
Jerusalem may be favorably received by
the Lord's people[x] there, 32 so that I may
come to you[y] with joy, by God's will,[z] and
in your company be refreshed.[a] 33 The God
of peace[b] be with you all. Amen.

Personal Greetings

16 I commend[c] to you our sister Phoebe, a deacon[b,c] of the church in
Cenchreae.[d] 2 I ask you to receive her in
the Lord[e] in a way worthy of his people[f]
and to give her any help she may need
from you, for she has been the benefactor
of many people, including me.

3 Greet Priscilla[d] and Aquila,[g] my co-
workers[h] in Christ Jesus.[i] 4 They
risked their lives for me. Not only I
but all the churches of the Gentiles
are grateful to them.
5 Greet also the church that meets at their
house.[j]
Greet my dear friend Epenetus, who
was the first convert[k] to Christ in the
province of Asia.[l]
6 Greet Mary, who worked very hard for
you.
7 Greet Andronicus and Junia, my fellow
Jews[m] who have been in prison with
me.[n] They are outstanding among[e]
the apostles, and they were in Christ[o]
before I was.

15:21 [f]Isa 52:15
15:22 [g]Ro 1:13
15:23 [h]Ac 19:21; Ro 1:10,11
15:24 [i]ver 28 [j]1Co 16:6; Titus 3:13
15:25 [k]S Ac 19:21 [l]S Ac 24:17 [m]S Ac 9:13
15:26 [n]S Ac 16:9 [o]S Ac 18:12 [p]S Ac 24:17
15:27 [q]1Co 9:11
15:28 [r]ver 24
15:29 [s]Ro 1:10, 11
15:30 [t]Gal 5:22; Col 1:8 [u]2Co 1:11; Col 4:12
15:31 [v]2Co 1:10; 2Th 3:2; 2Ti 3:11; 2Pe 2:9 [w]ver 25; S Ac 24:17 [x]S Ac 9:13
15:32 [y]Ro 1:10, 13 [z]S Ac 18:21 [a]1Co 16:18; Phm 7
15:33 [b]Ro 16:20; 2Co 13:11; Php 4:9; 1Th 5:23; 2Th 3:16; Heb 13:20
16:1 [c]S 2Co 3:1 [d]Ac 18:18
16:2 [e]Php 2:29 [f]S Ac 9:13
16:3 [g]S Ac 18:2 [h]S Php 2:25 [i]ver 7,9,10; Ro 8:1,39; 1Co 1:30; 2Co 5:17; Gal 1:22; 5:6; Eph 1:13
16:5 [j]1Co 16:19; Col 4:15; Phm 2 [k]1Co 16:15 [l]S Ac 2:9
16:7 [m]ver 11,21 [n]Col 4:10; Phm 23 [o]S ver 3

[a] 21 Isaiah 52:15 (see Septuagint) [b] 1 Or *servant* [c] 1 The word *deacon* refers here to a Christian designated to serve with the overseers/elders of the church in a variety of ways; similarly in Phil. 1:1 and 1 Tim. 3:8,12. [d] 3 Greek *Prisca,* a variant of *Priscilla* [e] 7 Or *are esteemed by*

15:22 *hindered from coming to you.* Paul's great desire to complete the missionary task in the eastern Mediterranean had prevented him from making a trip to Rome.
15:23 *no more place for me to work.* Because of the principle stated in v. 20. *longing for many years to visit you.* See 1:11–15.
15:24 *to have you assist me on my journey there.* Paul wanted to use the Roman church as a base of operations for a mission to Spain (see also v. 28). *enjoyed your company for a while.* More than a quick stop at Rome was contemplated (see 1:11–12).
15:25 *in the service of the Lord's people there.* Paul wanted to present the gift (see v. 26) personally to the Jerusalem church. The gift needed interpretation. It was not merely money; it represented the love and concern of the Gentile churches for their Jewish brothers and sisters in Christ. *the Lord's people.* See note on 1:7.
15:26 *Macedonia and Achaia.* See note on 1Th 1:7. *contribution.* See 1Co 16:1–4; 2Co 8:1—9:15 and notes.
15:27 *Jews' spiritual blessings.* Especially Christ and the gospel.
15:28 *this contribution.* The collection from the Gentile churches.
15:31 *Pray that I may be kept safe from the unbelievers in Judea.* Paul wanted to go to Jerusalem. The delivery of the collection was important to him, but he had received warnings about what might happen to him there (see Ac 20:22–23 and note on 20:22). *may be favorably received.* Perhaps a reference to the way in which the money was to be distributed—often a delicate and difficult task.
15:32 *in your company be refreshed.* See 1:11–12.
15:33 *God of peace.* See notes on 5:1; 1Th 5:23.
16:1 *our sister.* In the sense of being a fellow believer. *Phoebe.* Probably the carrier of the letter to Rome (cf. v. 2). *deacon.* See NIV text note; one who serves or ministers in any way. When church related, as it is here, it probably refers to a specific office—woman deacon or deaconess. *Cenchreae.* A port located about six miles east of Corinth on the Saronic Gulf.
16:3 *Priscilla and Aquila.* Close friends of Paul, who worked in the same trade of tentmaking (see Ac 18:2–3 and notes).
16:4 *risked their lives for me.* There is no other record of this in the NT or elsewhere, but it must have been widely known, as the last part of the verse indicates (cf. Php 2:25–30 and notes).
16:6 *Mary.* Six persons are known by this name in the NT. This one is unknown apart from this reference.
16:7 *Junia.* A feminine name. Andronicus and Junia may have been husband and wife (cf. Priscilla and Aquila [v. 3] and probably Philologus and Julia [v. 15]). *among the apostles.* Two possible interpretations are: (1) "Apostles" is used in a wider sense than the Twelve—to include preachers of the gospel recognized by the churches (see Ac 14:4,14 and note on 14:4; 1Th 2:6). (2) "Apostles" is here preceded by the

8 Greet Ampliatus, my dear friend
in the Lord.
9 Greet Urbanus, our co-worker
in Christ,[p] and my dear friend
Stachys.
10 Greet Apelles, whose fidelity to
Christ has stood the test.[q]
Greet those who belong to the
household[r] of Aristobulus.
11 Greet Herodion, my fellow Jew.[s]
Greet those in the household[t]
of Narcissus who are in the
Lord.
12 Greet Tryphena and Tryphosa,
those women who work hard
in the Lord.
Greet my dear friend Persis, another woman who has worked
very hard in the Lord.
13 Greet Rufus,[u] chosen[v] in the Lord, and
his mother, who has been a mother
to me, too.
14 Greet Asyncritus, Phlegon, Hermes, Patrobas, Hermas and the other brothers
and sisters with them.
15 Greet Philologus, Julia, Nereus and his
sister, and Olympas and all the Lord's
people[w] who are with them.[x]
16 Greet one another with a holy kiss.[y]
All the churches of Christ send greetings.

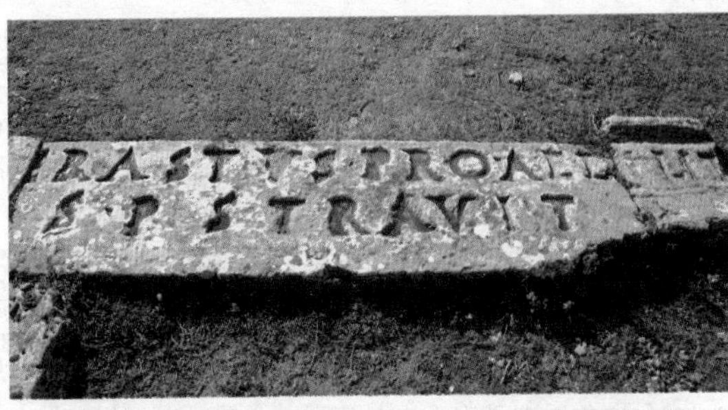

A Latin inscription in Corinth dating to the mid-first century AD mentions an "Erastus," probably the same Erastus mentioned by Paul (Ro 16:23). The inscription reads: "Erastus, in return for his aedileship, laid [this pavement] at his own expense."

www.HolyLandPhotos.org

17 I urge you, brothers and sisters,
to watch out for those who cause divisions and put obstacles in your way that
are contrary to the teaching you have
learned.[z] Keep away from them.[a]
18 For
such people are not serving our Lord
Christ,[b] but their own appetites.[c] By
smooth talk and flattery they deceive[d] the
minds of naive people.
19 Everyone has
heard[e] about your obedience, so I rejoice
because of you; but I want you to be wise
about what is good, and innocent about
what is evil.[f]
20 The God of peace[g] will soon crush[h] Satan[i] under your feet.
The grace of our Lord Jesus be with
you.[j]
21 Timothy,[k] my co-worker, sends his
greetings to you, as do Lucius,[l] Jason[m] and
Sosipater, my fellow Jews.[n]
22 I, Tertius, who wrote down this letter,
greet you in the Lord.
23 Gaius,[o] whose hospitality I and the
whole church here enjoy, sends you his
greetings.
Erastus,[p] who is the city's director of
public works, and our brother Quartus
send you their greetings. [24][a]

16:9 [p] S ver 3 **16:10** [q] S ver 3 [r] S Ac 11:14 **16:11** [s] ver 7,21 [t] S Ac 11:14 **16:13** [u] Mk 15:21 [v] S 2Jn 1 **16:15** [w] ver 2; S Ac 9:13 [x] ver 14 **16:16** [y] 1Co 16:20; 2Co 13:12; 1Th 5:26; 1Pe 5:14 **16:17** [z] Gal 1:8, 9; 1Ti 1:3; 6:3 [a] Mt 18:15-17; 1Co 5:11; 2Th 3:6, 14; 2Ti 3:5; Titus 3:10; 2Jn 10 **16:18** [b] Ro 14:18 [c] Php 3:19 [d] 2Sa 15:6; Ps 12:2; Isa 30:10; Col 2:4 **16:19** [e] Ro 1:8

[a] 24 Some manuscripts include here *May the grace of our Lord Jesus Christ be with all of you. Amen.*

[f] S 1Co 14:20 **16:20** [g] S Ro 15:33 [h] Ge 3:15 [i] S Mt 4:10 [j] 2Co 13:14; S Gal 6:18; 1Th 5:28; Rev 22:21 **16:21** [k] S Ac 16:1 [l] Ac 13:1 [m] Ac 17:5 [n] ver 7,11 **16:23** [o] S Ac 19:29 [p] Ac 19:22; 2Ti 4:20

definite article; this may indicate that the Twelve are in view. If that is the case, the meaning would be that these two persons were outstanding "in the opinion of" the apostles.
16:8 – 10 *Ampliatus ... Urbanus ... Stachys ... Apelles.* All common slave names found in the imperial household.
16:10 *Aristobulus.* Perhaps refers to the grandson of Herod the Great and brother of Herod Agrippa I.
16:11 *Narcissus.* Sometimes identified with Tiberius Claudius Narcissus, a wealthy freedman of the Roman emperor Tiberius.
16:12 *Tryphena and Tryphosa.* Perhaps sisters, even twins, because it was common for such persons to be given names from the same root. *Persis.* Means "Persian woman."
16:14 – 15 None of these persons can be further identified, except that they were slaves or freedmen in the Roman church.
16:16 *holy kiss.* See 1Co 16:20; 2Co 13:12; 1Th 5:26 and notes; 1Pe 5:14. Justin Martyr (AD 150) tells us that the holy kiss was a regular part of the worship service in his day. It is still a practice in some churches.
16:17 – 20 Throughout these verses there are echoes of the story of the fall in Ge 2 – 3.
16:17 *those who cause divisions and put obstacles in your way.* Who these people were we cannot tell, but some of their characteristics are mentioned in v. 18.
16:19 *wise about what is good.* Christians are to be experts in doing good.
16:20 *God of peace.* See 15:33 and note; cf. note on 1:7. *will soon crush Satan.* A reference to Satan's final doom (see Ge 3:15 and note). For "soon," see note on 13:12. *grace.* See note on 1:7. *with you.* See note on 2Co 13:14.
16:21 *Jason.* Possibly the Jason mentioned in Ac 17:5 – 9. *Sosipater.* Probably Sopater, son of Pyrrhus, from Berea (see Ac 20:4 and note).
16:22 *I, Tertius, who wrote down this letter.* He had functioned as Paul's secretary.
16:23 *Gaius.* Usually identified with Titius Justus, a God-fearer, in whose house Paul stayed while in Corinth (see Ac 18:7 and note; 1Co 1:14). His full name would be Gaius Titius Justus. *here.* In Corinth. *Erastus.* At Corinth archaeologists have discovered a reused block of stone in a paved square, with the Latin inscription: "Erastus, in return for his aedileship, laid [this pavement] at his own expense." This may refer to the Erastus mentioned here. If it does, it is the earliest reference to a Christian by name outside the NT. He may also be the same person referred to in Ac 19:22 and 2Ti 4:20 (see notes there), though it is difficult to be certain because the name was fairly common. *Quartus.* Means "fourth (son)."

25 Now to him who is able[q] to establish
you in accordance with my gospel,[r] the
message I proclaim about Jesus Christ, in
keeping with the revelation of the mystery[s]
hidden for long ages past, 26 but now revealed and made known through the prophetic writings[t] by the command of the
eternal God, so that all the Gentiles might
come to the obedience that comes from[a]
faith[u]— 27 to the only wise God be glory
forever through Jesus Christ! Amen.[v]

16:25 [q] 2Co 9:8; Eph 3:20; Jude 24 [r] Ro 2:16; 2Ti 2:8 [s] Isa 48:6; Eph 1:9; 3:3-6, 9; Col 1:26,27; 2:2; 1Ti 3:16 **16:26** [t] Ro 1:2 [u] Ro 1:5 **16:27** [v] S Ro 11:36

[a] *26* Or *that is*

16:25 *my gospel.* Not a gospel different from that preached by others, but a gospel Paul received by direct revelation (see Gal 1:12 and note on 1:11). *message I proclaim about Jesus Christ.* A description of the gospel; it is about Jesus Christ, who embodies its content (see 1:3; 1Co 15:3–4 and notes). *mystery.* See note on 11:25. *for long ages.* From eternity past (see 1Co 2:7 and note).

16:26 *revealed and made known through the prophetic writings.* See 1:2 and note. *all the Gentiles.* The universality of the gospel (see Mt 28:19 and note).

16:27 *to … God be glory.* The ultimate purpose of all things (see 11:36; Ps 29:1–2; 86:9,12; 96:7–8; 115:1; Lk 2:14 and note; 1Co 10:31 and note; Eph 1:12,14; Rev 5:13; 7:12; 15:4; 19:1,7).

1 CORINTHIANS

INTRODUCTION

Author and Date

Paul is acknowledged as the author both by the letter itself (1:1 – 2; 16:21) and by the early church fathers. His authorship was attested by Clement of Rome as early as AD 96, and today practically all NT interpreters concur. The letter was written c. 55 (see chart, p. 1845) toward the close of Paul's three-year residency in Ephesus (see 16:5 – 9; Ac 20:31). It is clear from his reference to staying at Ephesus until Pentecost (16:8) that he intended to remain there somewhat less than a year when he wrote 1 Corinthians.

The City of Corinth

Corinth was a thriving city; at that time it was the chief city of Greece both commercially and politically. See map and model, p. 1920.

(1) *Its commerce.* Located just off the Corinthian isthmus (see map, p. 1864), it was a crossroads for travelers and traders. It had two harbors: (a) Cenchreae, six miles to the east on the Saronic Gulf, and (b) Lechaion, a mile and a half to the north on the Corinthian Gulf. Goods were transported across the isthmus on the Diolkos, a stone road by which smaller ships could be hauled fully loaded across the isthmus, and by which cargoes of larger ships could be transported by wagons from one side to the other. Trade flowed through the city from Italy and Spain (to the west) and from Asia Minor, Phoenicia and Egypt (to the east).

(2) *Its culture.* Although Corinth was not a university town like Athens, it was nevertheless characterized by typical Greek culture. Its people were interested in Greek philosophy and placed a high premium on wisdom.

(3) *Its religion.* Corinth contained at least 12 temples. Whether they were all in use during Paul's time is not known for certain. About a fourth of a mile north of the theater stood the temple of Asclepius, the god of healing, and the sixth-

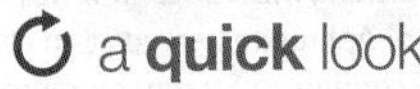

a **quick** look

Author:
The apostle Paul

Audience:
Believers at Corinth whose church was torn apart by factions and spiritual immaturity

Date:
AD 55

Theme:
Paul addresses problems in the church and answers questions from the church.

century BC temple of Apollo was located in the middle of the city. In addition, the Jews established a synagogue there, the inscribed lintel of which has been found and placed in the museum at old Corinth.

CORINTH IN THE TIME OF PAUL

The city of Corinth, perched astride the narrow isthmus connecting the Greek mainland with the Peloponnese, was one of the dominant commercial centers of the Mediterranean world as early as the eighth century BC.

No city in Greece was more favorably situated for land and sea trade. With a high, strong citadel at its back, it lay between the Saronic Gulf and the Ionian Sea, with ports at Lechaion and Cenchreae. A *diolkos*, or stone road for the overland transport of ships and/or offloaded cargo, linked the two seas. Crowning the Acrocorinth was the temple of Aphrodite, served at an earlier time, according to Strabo, by more than 1,000 pagan priestess-prostitutes.

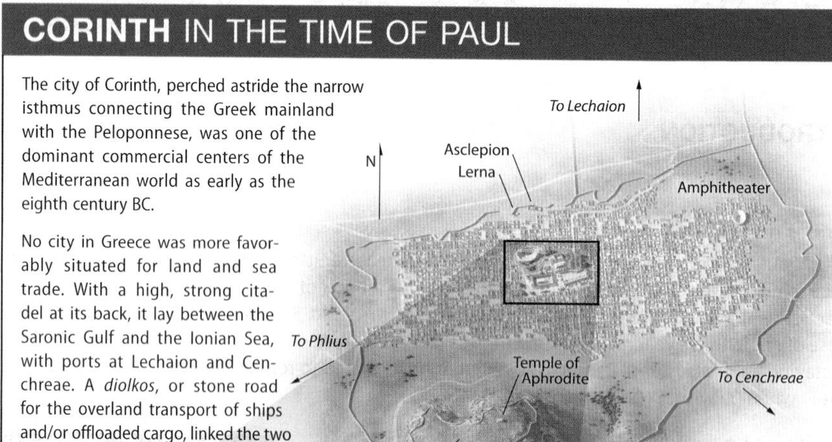

By the time the gospel reached Corinth in the spring of AD 52, the city had a proud history of leadership in the Achaian League, and a spirit of revived Hellenism under Roman domination after 44 BC, following the destruction of the city by Mummius in 146 BC.

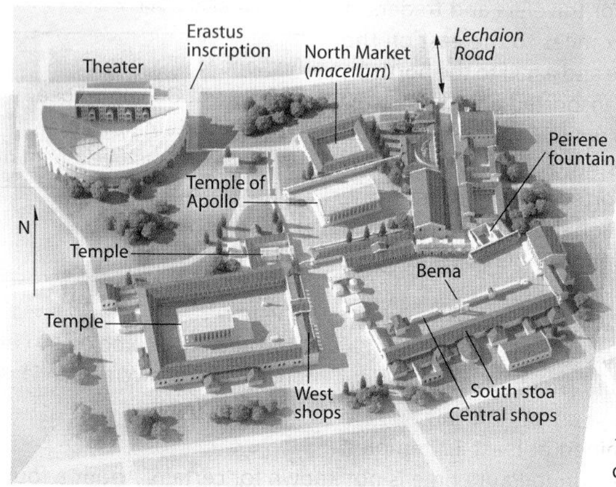

Paul's lengthy stay in Corinth brought him directly in contact with the major monuments of the *agora*, many of which still survive. The fountain-house of the spring *Peirene*, the temple of Apollo, the *macellum* (or meat market; 1Co 10:25), the theater and the bema (Ac 18:12) all played a part in the experience of the apostle. An inscription from the theater names the city official Erastus, probably the friend of Paul mentioned in Ro 16:23 (see note there).

Paul reveals a true pastor's heart as he deals with problems of Christian conduct in the church at Corinth.

(4) *Its immorality.* As a crossroads of commerce and trade, Corinth was plagued by immoral behavior. The worship of Aphrodite fostered prostitution in the name of religion. At one time 1,000 sacred prostitutes are said to have served her temple, though such claims are associated with old Corinth, destroyed two centuries before Paul. So widely known did the immorality of Corinth become that the Greek verb "to Corinthianize" came to mean "to practice sexual immorality." In a setting like this it is no wonder that the Corinthian church was plagued with numerous problems.

Occasion and Purposes

Paul had received information from several sources concerning the conditions existing in the church at Corinth. Some members of the household of Chloe had informed him of the factions that had developed in the church (1:11). There were three individuals — Stephanas, Fortunatus and Achaicus — who had come to Paul in Ephesus to make some contribution to his ministry (16:17), but whether these were the ones from Chloe's household we do not know.

Some of those who had come had brought disturbing information concerning moral irregularities in the church (chs. 5 – 6). Immorality had plagued the Corinthian assembly almost from the beginning. From 5:9 – 10 it is apparent that Paul had written previously concerning moral laxness. He had urged believers "not to associate with sexually immoral people" (5:9). Because of misunderstanding he now finds it necessary to clarify his instruction (5:10 – 11) and to urge immediate and drastic action (5:3 – 5,13).

Other Corinthian visitors had brought a letter from the church that requested counsel on several subjects (see 7:1 and note; cf. 8:1; 12:1; 16:1).

It is clear that although the church was gifted (see 1:4 – 7), it was immature and unspiritual (3:1 – 4). Paul's purposes for writing were: (1) to instruct and restore the church in its areas of weakness, correcting erroneous practices such as divisions (1:10 — 4:21), immorality (ch. 5; 6:12 – 20), litigation in pagan courts (6:1 – 8) and abuse of the Lord's Supper (11:17 – 34); (2) to correct false teaching concerning the resurrection (ch. 15); (3) to answer questions addressed to Paul in the letter that had been brought to him (see previous paragraph); and perhaps also (4) to call the church to obedience in the light of a growing challenge to Paul's authority — an issue that would provide the immediate context for 2 Corinthians.

Theme

The letter revolves around the theme of problems in the church with respect to Christian conduct. It thus has to do with progressive sanctification, the continuing development of one's holy character. Obviously Paul was personally concerned with the Corinthians' problems, revealing a true pastor's heart.

Relevance

This letter continues to be timely for the church today, both to instruct and to inspire. Christians are still powerfully influenced by their cultural environment, and most of the questions and problems that confronted the church at Corinth are still very much with us — problems like immaturity, instability, divisions, jealousy and envy, lawsuits, marital difficulties, sexual immorality and the misuse of spiritual gifts. Yet in spite of this concentration on problems, Paul's letter contains some of the most familiar and beloved chapters in the entire Bible — e.g., ch. 13 (on love) and ch. 15 (on resurrection).

Outline

- I. Introduction (1:1 – 9)
- II. Divisions in the Church (1:10 — 4:21)
  - A. The Fact of the Divisions (1:10 – 17)
  - B. The Causes of the Divisions (1:18 — 4:13)
    1. A wrong conception of the Christian message (1:18 — 3:4)
    2. A wrong conception of Christian ministry and ministers (3:5 — 4:5)
    3. A wrong conception of the Christian (4:6 – 13)
  - C. The Exhortation to End the Divisions (4:14 – 21)

View of Corinth. In the foreground is the north market, in the distance is the temple of Apollo, and on the horizon is the Acrocorinth.

III. Moral and Ethical Disorders in the Life of the Church (chs. 5 – 6)
   A. Laxity in Church Discipline (ch. 5)
   B. Lawsuits before Non-Christian Judges (6:1 – 11)
   C. Sexual Immorality (6:12 – 20)
IV. Instruction on Marriage (ch. 7)
   A. General Principles (7:1 – 7)
   B. The Problems of the Married (7:8 – 24)
   C. The Problems of the Unmarried (7:25 – 40)
V. Instruction on Questionable Practices (8:1 — 11:1)
   A. The Principles Involved (ch. 8)
   B. The Principles Illustrated (ch. 9)
   C. A Warning from the History of Israel (10:1 – 22)
   D. The Principles Applied (10:23 — 11:1)
VI. Instruction on Public Worship (11:2 — 14:40)
   A. Propriety in Worship (11:2 – 16)
   B. The Lord's Supper (11:17 – 34)
   C. Spiritual Gifts (chs. 12 – 14)
      1. The test of the gifts (12:1 – 3)
      2. The unity of the gifts (12:4 – 11)
      3. The diversity of the gifts (12:12 – 31a)
      4. The necessity of exercising the gifts in love (12:31b — 13:13)
      5. The superiority of prophecy over tongues (14:1 – 25)
      6. Rules governing public worship (14:26 – 40)
VII. Instruction on the Resurrection (ch. 15)
   A. The Certainty of the Resurrection (15:1 – 34)
   B. The Consideration of Certain Objections (15:35 – 57)
   C. The Concluding Appeal (15:58)
VIII. Conclusion: Practical and Personal Matters (ch. 16)

1 Paul, called to be an apostle[a] of Christ Jesus by the will of God,[b] and our brother Sosthenes,[c]

2 To the church of God[d] in Corinth,[e] to those sanctified in Christ Jesus and called[f] to be his holy people, together with all those everywhere who call on the name[g] of our Lord Jesus Christ—their Lord and ours:

3 Grace and peace to you from God our Father and the Lord Jesus Christ.[h]

Thanksgiving

4 I always thank my God for you[i] because of his grace given you in Christ Jesus. 5 For in him you have been enriched[j] in every way—with all kinds of speech and with all knowledge[k]— 6 God thus confirming our testimony[l] about Christ among you. 7 Therefore you do not lack any spiritual gift[m] as you eagerly wait for our Lord Jesus Christ to be revealed.[n] 8 He will also keep you firm to the end, so that you will be blameless[o] on the day of our Lord Jesus Christ.[p] 9 God is faithful,[q] who has called you[r] into fellowship with his Son, Jesus Christ our Lord.[s]

A Church Divided Over Leaders

10 I appeal to you, brothers and sisters,[a][t] in the name of our Lord Jesus Christ, that all of you agree with one another in what you say and that there be no divisions among you,[u] but that you be perfectly united[v] in mind and thought. 11 My brothers and sisters, some from Chloe's household[w] have informed me that there are quarrels among you. 12 What I mean is this: One of you says, "I follow Paul";[x] another, "I follow Apollos";[y] another, "I follow Cephas[b]";[z] still another, "I follow Christ."

13 Is Christ divided? Was Paul crucified for you? Were you baptized in the name of Paul?[a] 14 I thank God that I did not baptize any of you except Crispus[b] and Gaius,[c] 15 so no one can say that you were baptized in my name. 16 (Yes, I also baptized the household[d] of Stephanas;[e] beyond that, I don't remember if I baptized anyone else.) 17 For Christ did not send me to baptize,[f] but to preach the gospel—not with wisdom[g] and eloquence, lest the cross of Christ be emptied of its power.

[a] *10* The Greek word for *brothers and sisters* (*adelphoi*) refers here to believers, both men and women, as part of God's family; also in verses 11 and 26; and in 2:1; 3:1; 4:6; 6:8; 7:24, 29; 10:1; 11:33; 12:1; 14:6, 20, 26, 39; 15:1, 6, 50, 58; 16:15, 20. [b] *12* That is, Peter

1:1 [a] Ro 1:1; Eph 1:1; 2Ti 1:1 [b] S 2Co 1:1 [c] Ac 18:17 **1:2** [d] S 1Co 10:32 [e] S Ac 18:1 [f] Ro 1:7 [g] S Ac 2:21 **1:3** [h] S Ro 1:7 **1:4** [i] S Ro 1:8 **1:5** [j] 2Co 9:11 [k] S 2Co 8:7 **1:6** [l] 2Th 1:10; 1Ti 2:6; Rev 1:2 **1:7** [m] Ro 1:11; 1Co 12:1-31 [n] S Mt 16:27; S Lk 17:30; 1Th 1:10; S 2:19; Titus 2:13; Jas 5:7, 8; 1Pe 1:13; 2Pe 3:12; S Rev 1:7 **1:8** [o] S 1Th 3:13 [p] Am 5:18; 1Co 5:5; Php 1:6, 10; 2:16; 1Th 5:2 **1:9** [q] Dt 7:9; Isa 49:7; 1Co 10:13; 1Th 5:24; 2Th 3:3; 2Ti 2:13; Heb 10:23; 11:11 [r] S Ro 8:28 [s] 1Jn 1:3 **1:10** [t] S Ro 7:1 [u] 1Co 11:18 [v] S Ro 15:5

1:11 [w] S Ac 11:14 **1:12** [x] 1Co 3:4, 22 [y] S Ac 18:24 [z] Jn 1:42; 1Co 3:22; 9:5 **1:13** [a] S Mt 28:19 **1:14** [b] Ac 18:8 [c] S Ac 19:29 **1:16** [d] S Ac 11:14 [e] 1Co 16:15 **1:17** [f] Jn 4:2; S Ac 2:38 [g] 1Co 2:1, 4, 13

1:1 *Paul.* See note on Ro 1:1. *apostle of Christ Jesus.* See notes on Mk 6:30; Heb 3:1. Paul uses this title in all his letters (except Philippians, 1,2 Thessalonians and Philemon) to establish his authority as Christ's messenger—an authority that had been challenged (see ch. 9; 2Co 11). He reinforces his authority by adding "by the will of God" (see 15:9–11; Ac 9:1–16; 13:2; 18:9–10; 22:6–21; 26:12–18). *Sosthenes.* Perhaps the synagogue ruler at Corinth who was assaulted by the Greeks (Ac 18:17). If so, he obviously became a Christian—possibly while Paul was preaching at Corinth (Ac 18:18) or during Apollos's ministry there (Ac 19:1).

1:2 *church of God.* Used only by Paul and only in Ac 20:28, here and in 2Co 1:1. Its OT counterpart is the expression "assembly (or community) of the LORD" (Dt 23:1; see Nu 16:3; 20:4; 1Ch 28:8). *sanctified in Christ Jesus.* Consecrated to the service of God through Christ's saving action in their lives—as Jesus had "sanctified" himself (see Jn 17:19 and note; see also Jn 17:17 and NIV text note). Such consecration to God's service marks them as "holy" (set apart for God; see Ex 3:5; 19:6; Ro 6:22 and notes) and requires that they be morally "holy" (see Lev 11:44 and note). *everywhere.* See note on 1Th 1:8.

1:3 *Grace and peace.* See Ro 1:7 and note. *Lord Jesus Christ.* See note on 1Th 1:1.

1:4 *thank.* See Ro 1:8 and note.

1:5 *speech and … knowledge.* Gifts of the Spirit (see 12:8–10 and notes; see also 2Co 8:7).

1:6 *confirming.* Paul's preaching about Christ had been accepted by the Corinthians, and their changed lives had proved it to be true.

1:7 *any spiritual gift.* Probably refers to the spiritual gifts of chs. 12–14. According to those chapters, a "spiritual" gift is some capability given through the Holy Spirit that enables one to minister to the needs of Christ's body, the church (see 12:7–11; 14:3,12,17). The Greek word used here stresses that it is a gift of grace.

1:8 *He.* God the Father (see v. 9). *end.* Of the age, when Christ comes again. *on the day of our Lord Jesus Christ.* When he returns (v. 7; see Php 1:6 and note).

1:9 *God is faithful.* He may be trusted to do what he has promised (see 1Th 5:24 and note), namely, to keep believers "firm to the end" (v. 8; see note there).

1:10 *brothers and sisters.* See NIV text note. *perfectly united.* See 10:17 and note; Ro 15:5–6; Eph 4:3–6 and note on 4:3; Php 2:1–2 and notes. Jesus prayed for such unity (see Jn 17:11,21–23 and notes).

1:11 *quarrels.* See Gal 5:20; 2Ti 2:24; Jas 4:1–2.

1:12 *Apollos.* He had carried on a fruitful ministry in Corinth (see Ac 18:24—19:1 and notes). *Cephas.* See NIV text notes here and on Jn 1:42. Those who followed Cephas in Corinth were probably Jewish Christians.

1:13 *Is Christ divided?* See 12:12–13 and notes. *baptized.* Cf. Ro 6:3–4 and note.

1:14 *Crispus.* Probably the synagogue ruler mentioned in Ac 18:8. *Gaius.* Probably the Gaius referred to in Ro 16:23.

1:16 *household.* Other examples of households being baptized are those of Cornelius (Ac 10:24,48), Lydia (Ac 16:15) and the Philippian jailer (Ac 16:33–34). The term may include family members, servants or anyone else who lived in the house (cf. Ge 17:12–13,23). *household of Stephanas.* See 16:15 and note.

1:17 *not … to baptize.* Paul is not minimizing baptism; rather, he is asserting that his God-given task was primarily to preach. Jesus (Jn 4:2) and Peter (Ac 10:48) also had others baptize for them. *wisdom and eloquence.* Lit. "wisdom of speech." Paul's mission was not to couch the gospel in the language of a trained orator, one who applied the special rhetorical techniques of persuasion that had been developed

Christ Crucified Is God's Power and Wisdom

18 For the message of the cross is foolishness[h] to those who are perishing,[i] but to us who are being saved[j] it is the power of God.[k] 19 For it is written:

"I will destroy the wisdom of the wise;
the intelligence of the intelligent I will frustrate."[a][l]

20 Where is the wise person?[m] Where is the teacher of the law? Where is the philosopher of this age?[n] Has not God made foolish[o] the wisdom of the world? 21 For since in the wisdom of God the world[p] through its wisdom did not know him, God was pleased through the foolishness of what was preached to save[q] those who believe.[r] 22 Jews demand signs[s] and Greeks look for wisdom, 23 but we preach Christ crucified:[t] a stumbling block[u] to Jews and foolishness[v] to Gentiles, 24 but to those whom God has called,[w] both Jews and Greeks, Christ the power of God[x] and the wisdom of God.[y] 25 For the foolishness[z] of God is wiser than human wisdom, and the weakness[a] of God is stronger than human strength.

26 Brothers and sisters, think of what you were when you were called.[b] Not many of you were wise[c] by human standards; not many were influential; not many were of noble birth. 27 But God chose[d] the foolish[e] things of the world to shame the wise; God chose the weak things of the world to shame the strong. 28 God chose the lowly things of this world and the despised things—and the things that are not[f]—to nullify the things that are, 29 so that no one may boast before him.[g] 30 It is because of him that you are in Christ Jesus,[h] who has become for us wisdom from God—that is, our righteousness,[i] holiness[j] and redemption.[k] 31 Therefore, as it is written: "Let the one who boasts boast in the Lord."[b][l]

2 And so it was with me, brothers and sisters. When I came to you, I did not come with eloquence or human wisdom[m] as I proclaimed to you the testimony about God.[c] 2 For I resolved to know nothing while I was with you except Jesus Christ and him crucified.[n] 3 I came to you[o] in weakness[p] with great fear and trembling.[q] 4 My message and my preaching were not

1:18 [h] ver 21, 23,25; 1Co 2:14 [i] 2Co 2:15; 4:3; 2Th 2:10 [j] Ac 2:47 [k] ver 24; Ro 1:16 **1:19** [l] Isa 29:14 **1:20** [m] Isa 19:11,12 [n] 1Co 2:6,8; 3:18; 2Co 4:4; Gal 1:4 [o] ver 27; Job 12:17; Isa 44:25; Jer 8:9; Ro 1:22; 1Co 3:18,19 **1:21** [p] ver 27, 28; 1Co 6:2; 11:32 [q] S Ro 11:14 [r] S Ro 3:22 **1:22** [s] S Mt 12:38; S Jn 2:11; S 4:48 **1:23** [t] 1Co 2:2; Gal 3:1 [u] S Lk 2:34 [v] S ver 18 **1:24** [w] S Ro 8:28 [x] ver 18; Ro 1:16 [y] ver 30; S Col 2:3 **1:25** [z] S ver 18 [a] 2Co 13:4 **1:26** [b] S Ro 8:28 [c] ver 20 **1:27** [d] Jas 2:5 [e] ver 20; Ro 1:22; 1Co 3:18,19 **1:28** [f] Ro 4:17 **1:29** [g] Eph 2:9 **1:30** [h] S Ro 16:3 [i] Jer 23:5,6; 33:16; 2Co 5:21; Php 3:9 [j] 1Co 1:2 [k] S Ro 3:24 **1:31** [l] Jer 9:23,24; Ps 34:2; 44:8; 2Co 10:17 **2:1** [m] ver 4,13; 1Co 1:17 **2:2** [n] Gal 6:14; 1Co 1:23 **2:3** [o] Ac 18:1-18 [p] 1Co 4:10; 9:22; 2Co 11:29,30; 12:5,9,10; 13:9 [q] S 2Co 7:15

[a] *19* Isaiah 29:14 [b] *31* Jer. 9:24 [c] *1* Some manuscripts *proclaimed to you God's mystery*

---

by the rabbis among the Jews and by the philosophers among the Greeks. *emptied of its power.* On the hearers. The heart of the gospel message would not be affected by such preaching.

1:19 Paul loosely quotes the Septuagint (pre-Christian Greek) translation of God's word to Jerusalem in Isa 29:14 and has God speak these words again in a new context. *the wise.* Aristides said that on every street in Corinth one met a so-called wise man, who had his own solutions to humanity's problems.

1:20 *the wise person.* Probably a reference to Gentile philosophers in general. *teacher of the law.* See note on Mt 2:4. *philosopher of this age.* Probably refers to the Greek sophists, who engaged in long and subtle disputes. *God made foolish the wisdom of the world.* All humanly devised philosophical and ideological systems end in meaninglessness because they have a wrong concept of God and his revelation.

1:21 *wisdom ... foolishness.* Jesus expresses a similar thought in Lk 10:21. It is God's intention that worldly wisdom should not be the means of knowing him. *foolishness of what was preached.* Not that preaching is foolish, but that the message being preached (Christ crucified) is viewed by "the world" (both Jews and Greeks) as foolish.

1:22 *Jews demand signs.* They want to see a display of divine power effecting their deliverance (see Mt 12:38; 16:1,4; Mk 8:11–12; Jn 2:18; 6:30). *Greeks look for wisdom.* Specifically, they look for the kind of insight into the workings of the world that would relieve humanity of its woes.

1:23 *Christ crucified.* See 2:2. *stumbling block to Jews.* They expected a triumphant, political Messiah (see Ac 1:6 and note), not a crucified one. For use of the metaphor "stumbling block" in reference to the Jews, see Ro 11:9; cf. Ro 9:32–33; 1Pe 2:8. *foolishness to Gentiles.* Greeks and Romans were sure that no reputable person would be crucified, so it was unthinkable that one who was crucified as a criminal could be the world's Savior.

1:24 *power.* See Ro 1:4,16. *wisdom.* See v. 30. The crucified Christ is the power and the wisdom of God that saves.

1:26–31 The Corinthian Christians were living proof that salvation does not depend on anything in themselves, so that those who are saved can only "boast in the Lord" (v. 31). Their salvation did not spring from the cleverness of human intellect or the centers of human power but from the free grace of God. Compare Paul's elaboration of this theme with the song of Hannah (1Sa 2:1–10) and the song of Mary (Lk 1:46–55).

1:30 *because of him ... you are in Christ.* It is God who has called you to union and communion with Christ. *in Christ.* See note on Eph 1:1. *righteousness.* It is by faith in Christ that we are justified (declared righteous); see Ro 3:24 and note; 5:19. *holiness.* See note on v. 2. *redemption.* See note on Ro 3:24.

1:31 See Jer 9:24 and note.

2:1 *brothers and sisters.* See NIV text note on 1:10. *When I came to you.* On his initial trip to Corinth c. AD 51 (Ac 18). *not with eloquence or human wisdom.* See note on 1:17.

2:2 *know nothing ... except Jesus Christ.* Paul resolved to make Christ the sole subject of his teaching and preaching while he was with them. *Jesus Christ.* See 1:30. *him crucified.* See 1:17–18,23.

2:4 *not with wise and persuasive words.* This does not give preachers a license to neglect study and preparation. Paul's letters reveal a great deal of knowledge in many areas of learning, and his eloquence is apparent in his address before the Areopagus (see Ac 17:22–31 and notes). Paul's point is that unless the Holy Spirit works in a listener's heart, the wisdom and eloquence of a preacher are ineffective. Paul's confidence as a preacher did not rest on intellectual and oratorical ability, as did that of the Jewish rabbis

with wise and persuasive words,[r] but with
a demonstration of the Spirit's power,[s] 5so
that your faith might not rest on human
wisdom, but on God's power.[t]

God's Wisdom Revealed by the Spirit

6We do, however, speak a message of
wisdom among the mature,[u] but not the
wisdom of this age[v] or of the rulers of this
age, who are coming to nothing.[w] 7No, we
declare God's wisdom, a mystery[x] that has
been hidden[y] and that God destined for
our glory before time began. 8None of the
rulers of this age[z] understood it, for if they
had, they would not have crucified the
Lord of glory.[a] 9However, as it is written:

> "What no eye has seen,
> what no ear has heard,
> and what no human mind has
> conceived"[a] —
> the things God has prepared for
> those who love him —[b]

10these are the things God has revealed[c] to
us by his Spirit.[d]

The Spirit searches all things, even the
deep things of God. 11For who knows a
person's thoughts[e] except their own spirit[f] within them? In the same way no one
knows the thoughts of God except the
Spirit of God. 12What we have received is
not the spirit[g] of the world,[h] but the Spirit
who is from God, so that we may understand what God has freely given us. 13This
is what we speak, not in words taught us
by human wisdom[i] but in words taught
by the Spirit, explaining spiritual realities with Spirit-taught words.[b] 14The person without the Spirit does not accept the
things that come from the Spirit of God[j]
but considers them foolishness,[k] and cannot understand them because they are
discerned only through the Spirit. 15The
person with the Spirit[l] makes judgments
about all things, but such a person is not
subject to merely human judgments, 16for,

> "Who has known the mind of the Lord
> so as to instruct him?"[c][m]

But we have the mind of Christ.[n]

The Church and Its Leaders

3 Brothers and sisters, I could not address you as people who live by the
Spirit[o] but as people who are still worldly[p] — mere infants[q] in Christ. 2I gave you
milk, not solid food,[r] for you were not
yet ready for it.[s] Indeed, you are still not
ready. 3You are still worldly. For since
there is jealousy and quarreling[t] among
you, are you not worldly? Are you not
acting like mere humans? 4For when one
says, "I follow Paul," and another, "I follow Apollos,"[u] are you not mere human
beings?

5What, after all, is Apollos?[v] And what
is Paul? Only servants,[w] through whom
you came to believe — as the Lord has

[a] 9 Isaiah 64:4 [b] 13 Or *Spirit, interpreting spiritual truths to those who are spiritual* [c] 16 Isaiah 40:13

2:4 [r] ver 1 [s] S Ro 15:13 **2:5** [t] 2Co 4:7; 6:7 **2:6** [u] Eph 4:13; Php 3:15; Col 4:12; Heb 5:14; 6:1; Jas 1:4 [v] ver 8; S 1Co 1:20 [w] Ps 146:4 **2:7** [x] ver 1 [y] Ro 16:25 **2:8** [z] ver 6; S 1Co 1:20 [a] Ps 24:7; Ac 7:2; Jas 2:1 **2:9** [b] Isa 64:4; 65:17 **2:10** [c] S Mt 13:11; 2Co 12:1,7; Gal 1:12; 2:2; Eph 3:3,5 [d] Jn 14:26 **2:11** [e] Jer 17:9 [f] Pr 20:27 **2:12** [g] Ro 8:15 [h] 1Co 1:20,27; Jas 2:5 **2:13** [i] ver 1,4; 1Co 1:17 **2:14** [j] Jn 14:17 [k] S 1Co 1:18 **2:15** [l] 1Co 3:1; Gal 6:1 **2:16** [m] Isa 40:13; S Ro 11:34 [n] Jn 15:15 **3:1** [o] 1Co 2:15 [p] Ro 7:14; 1Co 2:14 [q] 1Co 14:20 **3:2** [r] Heb 5:12-14; 1Pe 2:2 [s] Jn 16:12 **3:3** [t] Ro 13:13; 1Co 1:11; Gal 5:20 **3:4** [u] 1Co 1:12

3:5 [v] S Ac 18:24 [w] 1Co 4:1; 2Co 6:4; Eph 3:7; Col 1:23,25

---

and the Greek orators (see note on 1:17). *demonstration.* The Greek word is used of producing proofs in an argument in court. Paul's preaching was marked by the convincing demonstration of the power of the Holy Spirit.

2:6 *mature.* Wise, developed Christians; contrast the "infants" mentioned in 3:1 (see Heb 5:11 — 6:3 and notes).

2:7 *mystery.* Cf. Ro 11:25; Eph 3:3; 1Ti 3:16 and notes. The secret, or "mystery," was once hidden but is now known because God has revealed it to his people (v. 10). To unbelievers it is still hidden. *for our glory.* God's wisdom will cause every believer to share eventually in Christ's glory (see Ro 8:17 and note). *before time began.* See Ro 8:29 – 30; Eph 1:4; 2Ti 1:9 and notes; see also Jn 17:24.

2:8 *rulers of this age.* Such as the chief priests (Lk 24:20), Pilate and Herod Antipas (cf. Ac 4:27). *crucified the Lord of glory.* The cross is here contrasted with the majesty of the victim.

2:9 *things God has prepared.* Probably not to be limited to either present or future blessing; both are involved (cf. vv. 7,12).

2:10 *Spirit searches all things.* Not in order to know them, for he knows all things. Instead, he comprehends the depth of God's nature and his plans of grace, so that he is fully competent to make the revelation claimed here. *deep things of God.* See Ro 11:33 – 36 and note; cf. Rev 2:24.

2:12 *spirit of the world.* Cf. v. 6 ("wisdom of this age"); the spirit of human wisdom as alienated from God — the attitude of the flesh (see Ro 8:5 – 8 and note).

2:13 *words taught by the Spirit.* The message Paul proclaimed was expressed in words given by the Holy Spirit. Thus spiritual truth was aptly combined with Spirit-taught words (but see NIV text note).

2:14 — 3:4 This passage explains why many fail to apprehend true wisdom (2:9). It is because such wisdom is perceived only by the Spirit-enlightened (mature) Christian (2:14 – 16; cf. v. 6). The Corinthians, however, were still worldly (infant) believers (3:1 – 4), and the proof of their immaturity was their division over human leaders (3:3 – 4).

2:14 *person without the Spirit.* Described in Jude 19 as one who follows "mere natural instincts" (cf. Ro 8:9). The non-Christian is governed in thought and life by an unrenewed, worldly heart. Such persons are yet untouched by the Holy Spirit and are not equipped to receive appreciatively truth that comes from the Spirit. They need the new birth (see Jn 3:8; Titus 3:5 and notes). *foolishness.* See 1:18.

2:15 *person with the Spirit.* Renewed by the Spirit (mature, v. 6). *not subject to merely human judgments.* One who does not have the Spirit is not qualified to judge anyone who has the Spirit. Thus believers are not rightfully subject to the opinions of unbelievers.

3:1 *Brothers and sisters.* See NIV text note on 1:10. *people who live by the Spirit.* See note on 2:15. *worldly.* See note on 2:14 — 3:4.

3:2 *milk, not solid food.* See Heb 5:12 – 14 and notes.

3:3 *like mere humans.* Like people of the world instead of people of God. They were following merely human standards.

3:4 *I follow Paul . . . Apollos.* See 1:12.

assigned to each his task. 6 I planted the
seed,[x] Apollos watered it, but God has
been making it grow. 7 So neither the one
who plants nor the one who waters is anything, but only God, who makes things
grow. 8 The one who plants and the one
who waters have one purpose, and they
will each be rewarded according to their
own labor.[y] 9 For we are co-workers in
God's service;[z] you are God's field,[a] God's
building.[b]
10 By the grace God has given me,[c] I laid
a foundation[d] as a wise builder, and someone else is building on it. But each one
should build with care. 11 For no one can
lay any foundation other than the one already laid, which is Jesus Christ.[e] 12 If anyone builds on this foundation using gold,
silver, costly stones, wood, hay or straw,
13 their work will be shown for what it is,[f]
because the Day[g] will bring it to light. It
will be revealed with fire, and the fire will
test the quality of each person's work.[h] 14 If
what has been built survives, the builder
will receive a reward.[i] 15 If it is burned up,
the builder will suffer loss but yet will be
saved—even though only as one escaping
through the flames.[j]
16 Don't you know that you yourselves
are God's temple[k] and that God's Spirit
dwells in your midst?[l] 17 If anyone destroys
God's temple, God will destroy that person; for God's temple is sacred, and you
together are that temple.

3:6 [x] Ac 18:4-11; 1Co 4:15; 9:1; 15:1 **3:8** [y] ver 14; Ps 18:20; 62:12; Mt 25:21; 1Co 9:17 **3:9** [z] Mk 16:20; 2Co 6:1; 1Th 3:2 [a] Isa 61:3 [b] Eph 2:20-22; 1Pe 2:5 **3:10** [c] S Ro 12:3 [d] Ro 15:20; S Eph 2:20 **3:11** [e] Isa 28:16; Eph 2:20 **3:13** [f] 1Co 4:5 [g] S 1Co 1:8; 2Th 1:7-10; 2Ti 1:12,18; 4:8 [h] Nu 31:22,23; Jer 23:28,29; Mal 3:3; S 2Th 1:7 **3:14** [i] S ver 8 **3:15** [j] Jude 23 **3:16** [k] 1Co 6:19; 2Co 6:16; Eph 2:21,22; Heb 3:6 [l] S Ro 8:9 **3:18** [m] Isa 5:21; 1Co 8:2; Gal 6:3 [n] S 1Co 1:20 **3:19** [o] ver 18; Ro 1:22; 1Co 1:20,27 [p] Job 5:13 **3:20** [q] Ps 94:11 **3:21** [r] 1Co 4:6 [s] Ro 8:32 **3:22** [t] ver 5,6 [u] S 1Co 1:12 [v] Ro 8:38 **3:23** [w] 1Co 15:23; 2Co 10:7;

18 Do not deceive yourselves. If any of
you think you are wise[m] by the standards
of this age,[n] you should become "fools"
so that you may become wise. 19 For the
wisdom of this world is foolishness[o] in
God's sight. As it is written: "He catches
the wise in their craftiness"[a];[p] 20 and again,
"The Lord knows that the thoughts of the
wise are futile."[b][q] 21 So then, no more boasting about human leaders![r] All things are
yours,[s] 22 whether Paul or Apollos[t] or Cephas[c][u] or the world or life or death or the
present or the future[v]—all are yours, 23 and
you are of Christ,[w] and Christ is of God.

The Nature of True Apostleship

4 This, then, is how you ought to regard
us: as servants[x] of Christ and as those
entrusted[y] with the mysteries[z] God has revealed. 2 Now it is required that those who
have been given a trust must prove faithful. 3 I care very little if I am judged by
you or by any human court; indeed, I do
not even judge myself. 4 My conscience[a] is
clear, but that does not make me innocent.[b]
It is the Lord who judges me.[c] 5 Therefore
judge nothing[d] before the appointed time;
wait until the Lord comes.[e] He will bring
to light[f] what is hidden in darkness and

[a] *19* Job 5:13 [b] *20* Psalm 94:11 [c] *22* That is, Peter

Gal 3:29 **4:1** [x] S 1Co 3:5 [y] 1Co 9:17; Titus 1:7 [z] S Ro 16:25 **4:4** [a] S Ac 23:1 [b] Ro 2:13 [c] 2Co 10:18 **4:5** [d] S Mt 7:1,2 [e] S 1Th 2:19 [f] Job 12:22; Ps 90:8; 1Co 3:13

3:6 *I planted.* See Ac 18:4–11. Paul's work was of a pioneer nature, preaching where no one had ever preached before (see 2Co 10:13–16; Ro 15:20–21). *Apollos watered.* See Ac 18:24–28. Apollos worked in the established church, teaching and encouraging the converts Paul had won.
3:9 *God's field.* The people are God's farmland. *God's building.* They are also depicted as God's temple (vv. 16–17). Paul's choice of metaphors accords with the fact that in the ancient world planting the land and building a house (or city or temple) were traditionally the two basic focal points of human industry.
3:10 *I laid a foundation.* By preaching Christ and him crucified (2:2). *someone else.* Apollos—and possibly others.
3:12 *If anyone builds.* Reference is to those whose position in the church is that of "builders." *gold, silver, costly stones.* Precious, durable work that stands the test of divine judgment; symbolic of pure Christian doctrine and living. *wood, hay or straw.* Worthless work that will not stand the test; symbolic of someone's teaching and life that merely confuses or actually misleads believers.
3:13 Cf. 4:5; 2Co 5:10 and note. *the Day.* See 1:8 and note. *fire.* God's judgment. The work of some believers will stand the test while that of others will disappear—emphasizing the importance of teaching the pure word of God.
3:15 *loss.* Of reward (v. 14). *as one escaping through the flames.* Perhaps a Greek proverbial phrase, meaning "by a narrow escape," with one's work burned up by the fire of God's holy justice and judgment (cf. Zec 3:2 and note).
3:16 *God's temple.* Here Paul speaks of the church as "God's temple" (see Eph 2:21–22 and notes). He says, "You yourselves (plural) are God's temple (singular)," and the "you" of v. 17 is also plural. In 6:19 he speaks of each Christian as a temple of the Holy Spirit.
3:17 *God will destroy that person.* Such a foolish laborer is not one of the Lord's true servants and suffers a worse end than the "builder" of v. 15. In the context of chs. 1–4 Paul here refers to people who tear the local church apart by factions and quarrels concerning their understanding of the gospel (1:11–12). *sacred.* Holy, set apart for God's use and glory (see note on 1:2); so do not desecrate the church by breaking it up into various factions.
3:18 *become "fools."* Turn away from human wisdom (from being "wise by the standards of this age"). Cf. 1:18. *become wise.* Cf. 1:21,24 and notes.
3:21 *about human leaders.* About being some particular "builder's" disciple (see 1:12 and note; 3:4; cf. 1:31; 4:6). *All things are yours.* Because of their relationship to God through Christ (v. 23), they are heirs of all things (see Ro 8:17 and note)—heirs of the ministries of all those who faithfully promote the gospel, and also of everything over which God and Christ hold sovereign rule, namely, all those things that the philosophers of this world claim to have mastered by their wisdom.
3:23 *you are of Christ.* You are united with and belong to Christ (see 1:30 and note). *Christ is of God.* Christ is in union with God the Father (see Jn 10:30 and note).
4:1 *those entrusted.* The Greek underlying this phrase means "house manager" or "steward." *mysteries.* Things that human wisdom could not discover but that are now revealed by God to his people (see 2:7 and note).
4:5 *appointed time.* When God will judge believers (see 3:13 and note). *expose the motives.* Cf. 1Sa 16:7; 1Ki 8:39; 1Ch 28:9; Ps 139:23–24; Pr 16:2; 21:2; Lk 16:15; Heb 4:12–13.

will expose the motives of the heart. At that time each will receive their praise from God.[g]

6 Now, brothers and sisters, I have applied these things to myself and Apollos for your benefit, so that you may learn from us the meaning of the saying, "Do not go beyond what is written."[h] Then you will not be puffed up in being a follower of one of us over against the other.[i] 7 For who makes you different from anyone else? What do you have that you did not receive?[j] And if you did receive it, why do you boast as though you did not?

8 Already you have all you want! Already you have become rich![k] You have begun to reign—and that without us! How I wish that you really had begun to reign so that we also might reign with you! 9 For it seems to me that God has put us apostles on display at the end of the procession, like those condemned to die[l] in the arena. We have been made a spectacle[m] to the whole universe, to angels as well as to human beings. 10 We are fools for Christ,[n] but you are so wise in Christ![o] We are weak, but you are strong![p] You are honored, we are dishonored! 11 To this very hour we go hungry and thirsty, we are in rags, we are brutally treated, we are homeless.[q] 12 We work hard with our own hands.[r] When we are cursed, we bless;[s] when we are persecuted,[t] we endure it; 13 when we are slandered, we answer kindly. We have become the scum of the earth, the garbage[u] of the world—right up to this moment.

4:5 [g]S Ro 2:29 **4:6** [h]1Co 1:19, 31; 3:19,20 [i]1Co 1:12; 3:4 **4:7** [j]Jn 3:27; Ro 12:3,6 **4:8** [k]Rev 3:17, 18 **4:9** [l]S Ro 8:36 [m]Ps 71:7; Heb 10:33 **4:10** [n]S 1Co 1:18; Ac 17:18; 26:24 [o]1Co 3:18; 2Co 11:19 [p]S 1Co 2:3 **4:11** [q]Ro 8:35; 2Co 11:23-27 **4:12** [r]S Ac 18:3 [s]Ro 12:14; 1Pe 3:9 [t]S Mt 5:44 **4:13** [u]Jer 20:18; La 3:45

4:14 [v]1Co 6:5; 15:34; 2Th 3:14 [w]S 1Th 2:11 **4:15** [x]S ver 14 [y]1Co 9:12,14, 18,23; 15:1 **4:16** [z]1Co 11:1; Php 3:17; 4:9; 1Th 1:6; 2Th 3:7,9 **4:17** [a]1Co 16:10 [b]S Ac 16:1 [c]S 1Ti 1:2 [d]S 1Co 7:17 **4:18** [e]Jer 43:2 [f]ver 21 **4:19** [g]1Co 16:5, 6; 2Co 1:15,16 [h]S Ac 18:21 **4:20** [i]Ro 14:17 [j]S Ro 15:13 **4:21** [k]2Co 1:23; 2:1; 13:2,10 **5:1** [l]Lev 18:8; Dt 22:30; 27:20 **5:2** [m]2Co 7:7-11 [n]ver 13 **5:3** [o]Col 2:5; 1Th 2:17

Paul's Appeal and Warning

14 I am writing this not to shame you[v] but to warn you as my dear children.[w] 15 Even if you had ten thousand guardians in Christ, you do not have many fathers, for in Christ Jesus I became your father[x] through the gospel.[y] 16 Therefore I urge you to imitate me.[z] 17 For this reason I have sent to you[a] Timothy,[b] my son[c] whom I love, who is faithful in the Lord. He will remind you of my way of life in Christ Jesus, which agrees with what I teach everywhere in every church.[d]

18 Some of you have become arrogant,[e] as if I were not coming to you.[f] 19 But I will come to you very soon,[g] if the Lord is willing,[h] and then I will find out not only how these arrogant people are talking, but what power they have. 20 For the kingdom of God is not a matter of[i] talk but of power.[j] 21 What do you prefer? Shall I come to you with a rod of discipline,[k] or shall I come in love and with a gentle spirit?

Dealing With a Case of Incest

5 It is actually reported that there is sexual immorality among you, and of a kind that even pagans do not tolerate: A man is sleeping with his father's wife.[l] 2 And you are proud! Shouldn't you rather have gone into mourning[m] and have put out of your fellowship[n] the man who has been doing this? 3 For my part, even though I am not physically present, I am with you in spirit.[o] As one who is pres-

4:6 *brothers and sisters.* See NIV text note on 1:10. *these things.* See 3:5—4:5. *what is written.* The Corinthian believers should view even Paul and Apollos in light of what the OT has to say about human weakness and limitations. *puffed up.* Pride is one of the root causes of divisions.
4:8 Paul uses irony and sarcasm here to get the Corinthians to see how poor they really are in comparison with apostles because of their haughtiness and spiritual immaturity. *have become rich.* Cf. 1:5; 2Co 9:11. *have begun to reign.* They think they already participate fully in Christ's reign (see Ro 5:17 and note; 2Ti 2:12) and have no need of an apostle's ministry.
4:9 *apostles.* See note on 1:1. *spectacle.* "Theater" is derived from the Greek word used here. Paul refers to the triumphal procession of a victorious Roman general with captives of war bringing up the rear—men condemned to die in the arena in mortal combat with gladiators or with ferocious beasts. He pictures all the world and even angels looking on while the apostles are brought in last to fight to the death.
4:10 More irony. *wise ... strong.* Paul uses different Greek words here from those in 1:24.
4:11–13 A graphic description of Paul's condition right up to the writing of this letter.
4:12 *We work hard with our own hands.* Paul was a tentmaker by trade (see Ac 18:3 and note; cf. 1Co 9:6,18; Ac 20:34–35). *we bless.* See Mt 5:44; Lk 6:28; Ro 12:14 and note. *endure it.* Instead of retaliating.
4:14 *my dear children.* See v. 15.
4:15 *guardians.* See Gal 3:24 and note. *your father.* Cf. 3:6,10.
4:16 *imitate me.* See 11:1 and note.
4:17 *I have sent to you Timothy.* Apparently Timothy had already begun his journey to Corinth by way of Macedonia (see 16:10 and note).
4:18 *Some of you.* Some of the Corinthians who were trying to undercut Paul's authority (see 9:1–3) were teaching that he was unstable (see 2Co 1:17 and note) and that his ministry was worthless (see 2Co 10:10 and note; cf. 12:11–12 and notes).
4:19 *arrogant.* See 5:2 and note.
4:20 *kingdom of God.* God's present reign in the lives of his people (cf. note on Mt 3:2)—that dynamic new life in Christ (see 2Co 5:17 and note), the power of the new birth (Jn 3:3–8), showing itself in a humble life, dedicated to Christ and his mission. *not ... of talk but of power.* Empty talk is contrasted with the genuine power of the Holy Spirit. *power.* Paul returns to the Greek word he used in 1:24.
4:21 *with a rod of discipline.* See 2Co 1:28; 2:1; 13:2,10 and notes.
5:1 *even pagans do not tolerate.* The Roman orator Cicero states that incest was practically unheard of in Roman society. *his father's wife.* That this expression was used rather than "his mother" suggests that the woman was his stepmother. The OT prohibited such sexual relations (see Lev 18:8; Dt 22:30 and notes).
5:2 *proud.* Evidently proud of their liberty—a distortion of grace (cf. Ro 6:1–2 and note on 6:1). *put out of your fellowship.* Excommunicated from the church (cf. Jn 9:22).
5:3 *in the name of our Lord Jesus.* By his authority.

ent with you in this way, I have already
passed judgment in the name of our Lord
Jesus[p] on the one who has been doing
this. 4 So when you are assembled and I
am with you in spirit, and the power of
our Lord Jesus is present, 5 hand this man
over[q] to Satan[r] for the destruction of the
flesh,[a,b] so that his spirit may be saved on
the day of the Lord.[s]
6 Your boasting is not good.[t] Don't
you know that a little yeast[u] leavens the
whole batch of dough?[v] 7 Get rid of the old
yeast, so that you may be a new unleavened batch—as you really are. For Christ,
our Passover lamb, has been sacrificed.[w]
8 Therefore let us keep the Festival, not
with the old bread leavened with malice
and wickedness, but with the unleavened
bread[x] of sincerity and truth.
9 I wrote to you in my letter not to associate[y] with sexually immoral people—
10 not at all meaning the people of this
world[z] who are immoral, or the greedy
and swindlers, or idolaters. In that case
you would have to leave this world. 11 But
now I am writing to you that you must
not associate with anyone who claims to
be a brother or sister[c][a] but is sexually immoral or greedy, an idolater[b] or slanderer,
a drunkard or swindler. Do not even eat
with such people.[c]
12 What business is it of mine to judge
those outside[d] the church? Are you not to
judge those inside?[e] 13 God will judge those
outside. "Expel the wicked person from
among you."[d][f]

Lawsuits Among Believers

6 If any of you has a dispute with another, do you dare to take it before the
ungodly for judgment instead of before the
Lord's people?[g] 2 Or do you not know that
the Lord's people will judge the world?[h]
And if you are to judge the world, are you
not competent to judge trivial cases? 3 Do
you not know that we will judge angels?

5:3 [p] 2Th 3:6
5:5 [q] 1Ti 1:20 [r] S Mt 4:10 [s] S 1Co 1:8
5:6 [t] Jas 4:16 [u] Mt 16:6,12 [v] Gal 5:9
5:7 [w] Ex 12:3-6, 21; Mk 14:12; 1Pe 1:19
5:8 [x] Ex 12:14, 15; Dt 16:3
5:9 [y] Eph 5:11; 2Th 3:6,14
5:10 [z] 1Co 10:27
5:11 [a] S Ro 7:1 [b] 1Co 10:7,14 [c] S Ro 16:17
5:12 [d] S Mk 4:11 [e] ver 3-5; 1Co 6:1-4
5:13 [f] Dt 13:5; 17:7; 19:19; 22:21,24; 24:7; Jdg 20:13
6:1 [g] Mt 18:17
6:2 [h] Mt 19:28; Lk 22:30; 1Co 5:12

[a] 5 In contexts like this, the Greek word for *flesh* (*sarx*) refers to the sinful state of human beings, often presented as a power in opposition to the Spirit. [b] 5 Or *of his body* [c] 11 The Greek word for *brother or sister* (*adelphos*) refers here to a believer, whether man or woman, as part of God's family; also in 8:11, 13. [d] 13 Deut. 13:5; 17:7; 19:19; 21:21; 22:21,24; 24:7

5:4 *the power of our Lord Jesus is present.* Jesus' power is present through his word and his Holy Spirit.

5:5 *hand this man over to Satan.* Abandon this sinful man to the devil, that he may afflict him as he pleases. This abandonment to Satan was to be accomplished not by some magical incantation but by expelling the man from the church (see v. 13; see also vv. 2,7,11). To expel him was to put him out in the devil's territory, severed from any connection with God's people (cf. note on 1Ti 1:20). *for the destruction of the flesh.* So that being officially ostracized from the church will cause the man such anguish that he will repent and forsake his wicked way. For an alternative interpretation, see second NIV text note. In the latter view, Satan is allowed to bring physical affliction on the man, which would bring him to repentance. *his spirit ... saved.* Cf. 3:15. *day of the Lord.* When Christ returns (see 1:7).

5:6 *a little yeast ... the whole batch of dough.* To illustrate Christian holiness and discipline, Paul alludes to the prohibition against the use of leaven (or yeast) in the bread eaten in the Passover Festival (see Ex 12:15 and note). Yeast in Scripture usually symbolizes evil or sin (see Mk 8:15 and note), and the church here is called on to get rid of the yeast of sin (v. 8) because its members are an unleavened batch of dough—new creations in Christ (see 2Co 5:17 and note).

5:7 *Get rid of the old yeast.* Perhaps refers to the Passover custom of sweeping all the (leavened) bread crumbs out of one's house before preparing the Passover meal. *a new unleavened batch—as you really are.* Already sanctified in God's sight (see 1:2 and note; 6:11), Paul calls on them to become holy in conduct. *Christ, our Passover lamb.* In his death on the cross, Christ fulfilled the true meaning of the Jewish sacrifice of the Passover lamb (cf. Jn 1:29 and note). Christ, the Lamb of God, was crucified on Passover day, a celebration that began the evening before when the Passover meal was eaten (cf. Ex 12:8).

5:8 *let us keep the Festival.* Keeping the Festival of Unleavened Bread (which followed Passover; see chart, pp. 188–189) symbolized living the Christian life in holy dedication to God and not getting involved in such sins as malice, wickedness and incestuous relations.

5:9 *I wrote to you in my letter.* Paul here clarifies a previous letter (one not preserved). Some in the Corinthian church mistook that letter to mean that on separating from sin, they should disassociate themselves from all immoral persons, including non-Christian people. Instead, Paul meant that they should separate from immoral persons who were affiliated with the church (vv. 10–11).

5:10–11 See note on Ro 1:29–31.

5:11 *Do not even eat with such people.* Calling oneself a Christian while continuing to live an immoral life is reprehensible and degrading and gives a false testimony to Christ. If the true Christian has intimate association with someone who does this, the non-Christian world may assume that the church approves such immoral, ungodly living, and thus the name of Christ would be dishonored. Questions could arise concerning the true character of the Christian's own testimony (cf. Ro 16:17–18; see also 2Th 3:6,14–15 and notes).

5:12 *judge those inside.* The church is to exercise spiritual discipline over the professing believers in the church (cf. Mt 18:15–18), but it is not to attempt to judge those outside its membership. There are governing authorities in place to judge them (see Ro 13:1–5 and notes), and their ultimate judge is God (v. 13; cf. Rev 20:11–15).

6:1 *a dispute with another.* Paul seems to be talking about various kinds of civil court cases here (cf. the phrase "rather be cheated," v. 7), not criminal cases that should be handled by the state (Ro 13:3–4). *before the Lord's people.* The Corinthians should take their civil cases before qualified Christians for settlement. In Paul's day the Romans allowed the Jews to apply their own law in such matters, and since the Romans did not yet consider Christians as a separate class from the Jews, Christians no doubt had the same rights.

6:2 *the Lord's people will judge the world.* As those who share in Christ's reign (cf. Mt 19:28; 2Ti 2:12; Rev 20:4). *competent to judge trivial cases.* Paul views believers as fully competent to judge cases where Christians have claims against each other, because they view matters from a godly vantage point. In comparison with their future role in the judgment of the world and of angels (v. 3), judgments concerning things of this life are insignificant.

6:3 *we will judge angels.* Cf. 2Pe 2:4,9; Jude 6.

How much more the things of this life!
4Therefore, if you have disputes about such
matters, do you ask for a ruling from those
whose way of life is scorned in the church?
5I say this to shame you.[i] Is it possible that
there is nobody among you wise enough
to judge a dispute between believers?[j]
6But instead, one brother[k] takes another to
court—and this in front of unbelievers![l]
7The very fact that you have lawsuits
among you means you have been completely defeated already. Why not rather
be wronged? Why not rather be cheated?[m] 8Instead, you yourselves cheat and
do wrong, and you do this to your brothers and sisters.[n] 9Or do you not know that
wrongdoers will not inherit the kingdom
of God?[o] Do not be deceived:[p] Neither the
sexually immoral nor idolaters nor adulterers[q] nor men who have sex with men[ar]
10nor thieves nor the greedy nor drunkards
nor slanderers nor swindlers[s] will inherit
the kingdom of God. 11And that is what
some of you were.[t] But you were washed,[u]
you were sanctified,[v] you were justified[w] in
the name of the Lord Jesus Christ and by
the Spirit of our God.

Sexual Immorality

12"I have the right to do anything," you
say—but not everything is beneficial.[x]
"I have the right to do anything"—but I
will not be mastered by anything. 13You
say, "Food for the stomach and the stomach for food, and God will destroy them
both."[y] The body, however, is not meant
for sexual immorality but for the Lord,[z]
and the Lord for the body. 14By his power
God raised the Lord from the dead,[a] and
he will raise us also.[b] 15Do you not know
that your bodies are members of Christ
himself?[c] Shall I then take the members
of Christ and unite them with a prostitute? Never! 16Do you not know that he
who unites himself with a prostitute is one
with her in body? For it is said, "The two
will become one flesh."[bd] 17But whoever
is united with the Lord is one with him
in spirit.[ce]
18Flee from sexual immorality.[f] All other sins a person commits are outside the
body, but whoever sins sexually, sins
against their own body.[g] 19Do you not
know that your bodies are temples[h] of the
Holy Spirit, who is in you, whom you have
received from God? You are not your own;[i]

[a] 9 The words *men who have sex with men* translate two Greek words that refer to the passive and active participants in homosexual acts. [b] *16* Gen. 2:24 [c] *17* Or *in the Spirit*

6:5 [i]S 1Co 4:14 [j]Ac 1:15 **6:6** [k]S Ro 7:1 [l]2Co 6:14,15; 1Ti 5:8 **6:7** [m]Mt 5:39, 40 **6:8** [n]1Th 4:6 **6:9** [o]S Mt 25:34 [p]Job 13:9; 1Co 15:33; Gal 6:7; Jas 1:16 [q]Lev 18:20; Dt 22:22 [r]Lev 18:22 **6:10** [s]1Ti 1:10; Rev 21:8; 22:15 **6:11** [t]S Eph 2:2 [u]S Ac 22:16 [v]1Co 1:2 [w]S Ro 4:25 **6:12** [x]1Co 10:23 **6:13** [y]Col 2:22 [z]ver 15,19; Ro 12:1 **6:14** [a]S Ac 2:24 [b]S Ro 6:5; Eph 1:19,20; 1Th 4:16 **6:15** [c]S Ro 12:5 **6:16** [d]Ge 2:24; Mt 19:5; Eph 5:31 **6:17** [e]Jn 17:21-23; Ro 8:9-11; Gal 2:20 **6:18** [f]ver 9; 1Co 5:1; 2Co 12:21; Gal 5:19; Eph 5:3; 1Th 4:3,4; Heb 13:4 [g]Ro 6:12 **6:19** [h]Jn 2:21 [i]Ro 14:7,8

6:4 *those whose way of life is scorned in the church.* The verse asks ironically whether believers should submit their cases to pagan judges, who really are not qualified to decide on cases between Christians.

6:7 *completely defeated already.* Most likely by greed, retaliation and hatred, instead of practicing unselfishness, forgiveness and love—even willingness to suffer loss.

6:9–10 See Ro 1:29–31 and note.

6:9 *not inherit the kingdom of God.* See Eph 5:5. *sexually immoral.* Paul here identifies two kinds of sexually immoral persons: "adulterers" and "men who have sex with men." In Ro 1:26 he adds the category of women who practice homosexuality. People who engage in such practices, as well as the other offenders listed in vv. 9–10, are explicitly excluded from God's kingdom (but see next note).

6:11 *some of you were. But.* God, however, does save and sanctify people like those described in vv. 9–10. *sanctified.* See 1:2 and note. *justified.* See Ro 3:24 and note.

6:12 *"I have the right to do anything."* Paul is quoting some in the Corinthian congregation who boasted that they had a right to do anything they pleased (see v. 13; 7:1; 10:23 and notes). The apostle counters by observing that such "freedom" of action may not benefit the Christian. *not be mastered by anything.* One may become enslaved by those actions in which one "freely" chooses to indulge.

6:13 *"Food for the stomach and the stomach for food, and God will destroy them both."* Paul quotes some Corinthians again who were claiming that as the physical acts of eating and digesting food have no bearing on one's inner spiritual life, so the physical act of promiscuous sexual activity does not affect one's spiritual life. *The body … is not meant for sexual immorality but for the Lord.* Some Corinthians claimed that there was no resurrection of the body (15:12), so it did not matter what one did with it. Paul here declares the dignity of the human body: It is intended for the Lord and will be raised. Although granting that food and the stomach are transitory, Paul denies that what one does with one's body is unimportant. This is particularly true of the use of sex, which the Lord has appointed for use in the man-woman relationship in marriage (see 7:2–5; cf. Heb 13:4).

6:14 *God raised the Lord … us also.* As an illustration of God's high regard for the body, Paul cites the resurrection of Christ's body and, eventually, of the believer's body (see 15:51–53; 1Th 4:16–17). A body destined for resurrection should not be used for immorality.

6:15 *members of Christ.* See 12:27. It is not merely the spirit that is a member of Christ's body; it is the whole person, consisting of spirit and body. This fact gives dignity to the human body.

6:16 *one with her in body.* In a sexual relationship the two bodies become one (cf. Ge 2:24; Mt 19:4–5), and a new human being may emerge from the sexual union. Sexual relations outside the marriage bond are a gross perversion of the divinely established marriage union.

6:17 *one with him in spirit.* There is a higher union than the marriage bond: the believer's spiritual union with Christ, which is the perfect model for the kind of unity that should mark the marriage relationship (cf. Eph 5:21–33 and notes on 5:23,32).

6:18 *Flee.* The Greek for this imperative may suggest that one must continually run away from sexual sinning (advice particularly needed in Corinth). Cf. Ge 39:12; 2Ti 2:22. *whoever sins sexually, sins against their own body.* The body is a temple of the Holy Spirit (v. 19); thus to use it in prostitution (see notes on Ge 20:9; Ex 34:15) disgraces God's temple.

6:19 *your bodies are temples of the Holy Spirit.* Cf. note on 3:16. Their bodies are therefore sacred and are to be

20 you were bought at a price.[j] Therefore honor God with your bodies.[k]

Concerning Married Life

7 Now for the matters you wrote about: "It is good for a man not to have sexual relations with a woman."[l] 2 But since sexual immorality is occurring, each man should have sexual relations with his own wife, and each woman with her own husband. 3 The husband should fulfill his marital duty to his wife,[m] and likewise the wife to her husband. 4 The wife does not have authority over her own body but yields it to her husband. In the same way, the husband does not have authority over his own body but yields it to his wife. 5 Do not deprive each other except perhaps by mutual consent and for a time,[n] so that you may devote yourselves to prayer. Then come together again so that Satan[o] will not tempt you[p] because of your lack of self-control. 6 I say this as a concession, not as a command.[q] 7 I wish that all of you were as I am.[r] But each of you has your own gift from God; one has this gift, another has that.[s]

8 Now to the unmarried[a] and the widows I say: It is good for them to stay unmarried, as I do.[t] 9 But if they cannot control themselves, they should marry,[u] for it is better to marry than to burn with passion.

10 To the married I give this command (not I, but the Lord): A wife must not separate from her husband.[v] 11 But if she does, she must remain unmarried or else be reconciled to her husband.[w] And a husband must not divorce his wife.

12 To the rest I say this (I, not the Lord):[x] If any brother has a wife who is not a believer and she is willing to live with him, he must not divorce her. 13 And if a woman has a husband who is not a believer and he is willing to live with her, she must not divorce him. 14 For the unbelieving husband has been sanctified through his wife, and the unbelieving wife has been sanctified through her believing husband. Otherwise your children would be unclean, but as it is, they are holy.[y]

15 But if the unbeliever leaves, let it be so. The brother or the sister is not bound in such circumstances; God has called us to live in peace.[z] 16 How do you know, wife, whether you will save[a] your husband?[b] Or, how do you know, husband, whether you will save your wife?

Concerning Change of Status

17 Nevertheless, each person should live as a believer in whatever situation the

6:20 [j] Ps 74:2; S Mt 20:28; Ac 20:28; 1Co 7:23; Rev 5:9; 14:4 [k] Php 1:20
7:1 [l] ver 8, 26
7:3 [m] Ex 21:10; 1Pe 3:7
7:5 [n] Ex 19:15; 1Sa 21:4, 5 [o] S Mt 4:10 [p] 1Th 3:5
7:6 [q] 2Co 8:8
7:7 [r] ver 8; 1Co 9:5 [s] Mt 19:11, 12; Ro 12:6; 1Co 12:4, 11
7:8 [t] ver 1, 26
7:9 [u] 1Ti 5:14
7:10 [v] Mal 2:14-16; S Lk 16:18
7:11 [w] ver 39; Ro 7:2, 3
7:12 [x] ver 6, 10; 2Co 11:17
7:14 [y] Mal 2:15
7:15 [z] S Ro 14:19; 1Co 14:33
7:16 [a] S Ro 11:14 [b] 1Pe 3:1

[a] 8 Or *widowers*

treated as sacred (holy). Christians should also realize that by the Spirit's presence and power they can be helped against such sins as sexual immorality (Ro 8:9). *not your own.* Cf. 1Pe 2:9 and note.

6:20 *bought at a price.* See 7:23 and note. *honor God with your bodies.* Cf. 10:31; Ro 6:12–13 and notes.

7:1 *matters you wrote about.* The Corinthians had written Paul, asking him a number of vexing questions (see 8:1; 12:1; 16:1). *"It is good for a man not to have sexual relations with a woman."* The best understanding of this statement is that Paul is again (see notes on 6:12–13,18) quoting a slogan of the Corinthians. He refutes this idea in v. 2 by stating that sexual relations have their proper expression in marriage.

7:3 *fulfill . . . marital duty.* Married couples should have regular sexual relations. Permanent abstention deprives the other partner of his or her natural right.

7:4 *In the same way.* Both husband and wife have conjugal rights and exclusive possession of the other in this area.

7:5 *Do not deprive each other.* Of sexual fulfillment. *Satan . . . not tempt you because of your lack of self-control.* The Christian deprived of regular sexual activity with his or her marriage partner may be tempted by Satan to sexual immorality. The normal God-given sexual drive in the human being is strong.

7:6 *I say this.* See v. 2. *concession, not as a command.* Although marriage is desirable and according to God's plan, it is not mandatory under all circumstances (see vv. 25–38).

7:7 *as I am.* Unmarried. Paul views his celibate lifestyle as a "gift from God" that made it possible for him to accept his unmarried state and use it in the service of his Lord.

7:10 *I give this command (not I, but the Lord).* Paul is citing a command from the Lord Jesus during his earthly ministry that married couples must stay together (Mt 5:32; 19:3–9; Mk 10:2–12; Lk 16:18). Paul probably heard about such commands from other disciples (cf. Gal 1:18–19).

7:11 *But if she does, she must remain unmarried or else be reconciled.* Paul argues that in the light of Christ's command she (or he) is not to marry again. Rather, the separated or divorced couple is to be reconciled. Clearly the ideal is that marriage should not be permanently disrupted.

7:12 *I say this (I, not the Lord).* Paul is not saying that his words do not carry divine authority (he is writing inspired Scripture), but only that Jesus did not directly address this issue (see v. 40 and note). *any brother has a wife . . . not a believer.* The apostle is talking here (and in v. 13) about couples already married, when one of them becomes a Christian. If at all possible, they should remain together, unless the unbeliever, whether man or woman, refuses to remain (v. 15).

7:14 *sanctified through his wife . . . sanctified through her believing husband.* These words of Paul are among those that are "hard to understand" (2Pe 3:16). Paul here affirms that, within the marriage relationship, unbelieving marriage partners in some sense participate with their believing spouse in the quality of being consecrated to God's service ("sanctified"; see 1:2 and note)—at least to the effect that the children born of their union are "holy" (consecrated to God's service). Some believe that such children are called holy because they are included with their parents in the new covenant in Christ, just as the children of Abraham were included in the covenant with their father (and so were circumcised).

7:15 *The brother or the sister is not bound in such circumstances.* The believer is not under obligation to try to continue living with the unbeliever. *live in peace.* If the unbeliever were forced to live with the believer, there would be no peace in the home.

7:17 *live . . . in whatever situation the Lord has assigned to them.* Christians are to live confidently for the Lord

Lord has assigned to them, just as God
has called them.[c] This is the rule I lay
down in all the churches.[d] 18 Was a man
already circumcised when he was called?
He should not become uncircumcised.
Was a man uncircumcised when he was
called? He should not be circumcised.[e]
19 Circumcision is nothing and uncircumcision is nothing.[f] Keeping God's commands
is what counts. 20 Each person should remain in the situation they were in when
God called them.[g]

21 Were you a slave when you were
called? Don't let it trouble you—although
if you can gain your freedom, do so. 22 For
the one who was a slave when called to
faith in the Lord is the Lord's freed person;[h] similarly, the one who was free
when called is Christ's slave.[i] 23 You were
bought at a price;[j] do not become slaves of
human beings. 24 Brothers and sisters, each
person, as responsible to God, should remain in the situation they were in when
God called them.[k]

Concerning the Unmarried

25 Now about virgins: I have no command from the Lord,[l] but I give a judgment as one who by the Lord's mercy[m] is
trustworthy. 26 Because of the present crisis, I think that it is good for a man to
remain as he is.[n] 27 Are you pledged to a
woman? Do not seek to be released. Are
you free from such a commitment? Do not
look for a wife.[o] 28 But if you do marry, you
have not sinned;[p] and if a virgin marries,
she has not sinned. But those who marry
will face many troubles in this life, and I
want to spare you this.

29 What I mean, brothers and sisters, is
that the time is short.[q] From now on those
who have wives should live as if they do
not; 30 those who mourn, as if they did not;
those who are happy, as if they were not;
those who buy something, as if it were not
theirs to keep; 31 those who use the things
of the world, as if not engrossed in them.
For this world in its present form is passing away.[r]

32 I would like you to be free from concern. An unmarried man is concerned
about the Lord's affairs[s]—how he can
please the Lord. 33 But a married man
is concerned about the affairs of this
world—how he can please his wife—
34 and his interests are divided. An unmarried woman or virgin is concerned about
the Lord's affairs: Her aim is to be devoted
to the Lord in both body and spirit.[t] But
a married woman is concerned about the
affairs of this world—how she can please
her husband. 35 I am saying this for your
own good, not to restrict you, but that you
may live in a right way in undivided[u] devotion to the Lord.

36 If anyone is worried that he might not
be acting honorably toward the virgin he
is engaged to, and if his passions are too
strong[a] and he feels he ought to marry,
he should do as he wants. He is not sin-

7:17 [c] Ro 12:3 [d] 1Co 4:17; 14:33; 2Co 8:18; 11:28 **7:18** [e] Ac 15:1,2 **7:19** [f] Ro 2:25-27; Gal 5:6; 6:15; Col 3:11 **7:20** [g] ver 24 **7:22** [h] Jn 8:32, 36 [i] S Ro 6:22 **7:23** [j] S 1Co 6:20 **7:24** [k] ver 20 **7:25** [l] ver 6; 2Co 8:8 [m] 2Co 4:1; 1Ti 1:13,16 **7:26** [n] ver 1,8 **7:27** [o] ver 20,21 **7:28** [p] ver 36 **7:29** [q] ver 31; S Ro 13:11,12 **7:31** [r] ver 29; S Heb 12:27 **7:32** [s] 1Ti 5:5 **7:34** [t] Lk 2:37 **7:35** [u] Ps 86:11

[a] 36 Or *if she is getting beyond the usual age for marriage*

---

in whatever station in life God has placed them. See v. 18 for an example. No change of status that anyone brings about by their own action can advance their salvation.

7:18 *circumcised ... uncircumcised.* Jew ... Gentile. In the religious sphere, Christian Jews should not undo their circumcision, and Christian Gentiles should not yield to Jewish pressure for circumcision (cf. Ac 15:1–5; Gal 5:1–3).

7:19 See Gal 5:6 and note.

7:21 *Were you a slave ...?* In the social and economic sphere, Christian slaves should live contentedly in their situation, realizing that they have become free in Christ (v. 22; Jn 8:32,36). *if you can gain your freedom, do so.* If Christian slaves have an opportunity to get their freedom, they should take advantage of it. In the Roman Empire slaves were sometimes freed by Roman patricians. There is nothing wrong with seeking to improve one's social condition, but this will have no bearing on one's standing with God.

7:22 *is the Lord's freed person.* Has been set free from bondage to sin (see Ro 6:18,22; Heb 9:15 and notes; cf. Jn 8:34,36; 1Pe 2:16) and is therefore free to serve Christ as his "slave"—just as the Israelites were set free from Egyptian bondage so that in freedom they could become the servant people of God (see Ex 6:6–7; 19:4–6).

7:23 *bought at a price ... not ... slaves of human beings.* Christians in all stations of life should realize that their ultimate allegiance is to Christ, who bought them with his blood (see 6:20; 1Pe 1:18–19 and note on 1:18).

7:25 *Now about virgins.* Paul answers another major question the Corinthians had asked (v. 1). *I give a judgment as one who ... is trustworthy.* Paul is not giving a direct command from Jesus here (as in v. 10; cf. Ac 20:35 and note). In this matter, which is not a question of right and wrong, Paul expresses his own judgment. Even though he puts it this way, he is certainly not denying that he wrote under the influence of divine inspiration (see v. 40 and note). And since he writes under inspiration, what he recommends is clearly the better course of action.

7:26 *present crisis.* Probably a reference to the pressures in the Christian life in an immoral and particularly hostile environment (cf. vv. 2,28; 5:1; 2Ti 3:12). Paul's recommendation here (see also v. 27) does not apply to all times and all situations.

7:28 *many troubles.* Times of suffering and persecution for Christ, when being married would mean even greater hardship in taking care of one's family.

7:29–31 Christians already live under the foreshadowings of Christ's return, when the world in its present form will pass away. For this reason, believers should not treat present realities as having ultimate significance.

7:29 *brothers and sisters.* See note on Ro 1:13.

7:31 *this world ... is passing away.* Cf. 1Jn 2:17.

7:34 *his interests are divided.* He cannot give undistracted service to Christ (v. 35). This is particularly true in times of persecution.

7:36 *not ... acting honorably toward the virgin he is engaged to ... passions are too strong ... They should get married.* In

ning.[v] They should get married. 37 But the man who has settled the matter in his own mind, who is under no compulsion but has control over his own will, and who has made up his mind not to marry the virgin—this man also does the right thing. 38 So then, he who marries the virgin does right,[w] but he who does not marry her does better.[a]

39 A woman is bound to her husband as long as he lives.[x] But if her husband dies, she is free to marry anyone she wishes, but he must belong to the Lord.[y] 40 In my judgment,[z] she is happier if she stays as she is—and I think that I too have the Spirit of God.

Concerning Food Sacrificed to Idols

8 Now about food sacrificed to idols:[a] We know that "We all possess knowledge."[b] But knowledge puffs up while love builds up. 2 Those who think they know something[c] do not yet know as they ought to know.[d] 3 But whoever loves God is known by God.[b][e]

4 So then, about eating food sacrificed to idols:[f] We know that "An idol is nothing at all in the world"[g] and that "There is no God but one."[h] 5 For even if there are so-called gods,[i] whether in heaven or on earth (as indeed there are many "gods" and many "lords"), 6 yet for us there is but one God,[j] the Father,[k] from whom all things came[l] and for whom we live; and there is but one Lord,[m] Jesus Christ, through whom all things came[n] and through whom we live.

7 But not everyone possesses this knowledge.[o] Some people are still so accustomed to idols that when they eat sacrificial food they think of it as having been sacrificed to a god, and since their conscience is weak,[p] it is defiled. 8 But food does not bring us near to God;[q] we are no worse if we do not eat, and no better if we do.

9 Be careful, however, that the exercise of your rights does not become a stumbling block[r] to the weak.[s] 10 For if someone with a weak conscience sees you, with all your knowledge, eating in an idol's temple, won't that person be emboldened to eat what is sacrificed to idols?[t] 11 So this weak brother or sister, for whom Christ died, is destroyed[u] by your knowledge.

7:36 [v] ver 28 **7:38** [w] Heb 13:4 **7:39** [x] Ro 7:2,3 [y] 2Co 6:14 **7:40** [z] ver 25 **8:1** [a] ver 4,7, 10; Ac 15:20 [b] Ro 15:14 **8:2** [c] 1Co 3:18 [d] 1Co 13:8,9,12; 1Ti 6:4 **8:3** [e] Jer 1:5; Ro 8:29; Gal 4:9 **8:4** [f] ver 1,7, 10; Ex 34:15 [g] Ac 14:15; 1Co 10:19; Gal 4:8 [h] ver 6; Dt 6:4; Ps 86:10; Eph 4:6; 1Ti 2:5 **8:5** [i] 2Th 2:4 **8:6** [j] S ver 4 [k] Mal 2:10 [l] S Ro 11:36 [m] Eph 4:5 [n] S Jn 1:3 **8:7** [o] ver 1 [p] Ro 14:14; 1Co 10:28 **8:8** [q] Ro 14:17 **8:9** [r] S 2Co 6:3; Gal 5:13 [s] Ro 14:1 **8:10** [t] ver 1,4,7 **8:11** [u] Ro 14:15, 20

[a] 36-38 Or *36If anyone thinks he is not treating his daughter properly, and if she is getting along in years* (or *if her passions are too strong*), *and he feels she ought to marry, he should do as he wants. He is not sinning. He should let her get married. 37But the man who has settled the matter in his own mind, who is under no compulsion but has control over his own will, and who has made up his mind to keep the virgin unmarried—this man also does the right thing. 38So then, he who gives his virgin in marriage does right, but he who does not give her in marriage does better.* [b] 2,3 An early manuscript and another ancient witness *think they have knowledge do not yet know as they ought to know. 3But whoever loves truly knows.*

---

the light of hostility toward believers in Corinth, a man might refrain from marrying his fiancée. But if he then realizes that his (or her) "passions are too strong" and the situation thus seems unfair, it is perfectly proper for them to get married.

7:37 *has control over his own will … does the right thing.* The man who determines that there is no need for him to marry his fiancée under the circumstances has made a good decision too (v. 38). Paul may be referring to a man who has control of his passions, as in v. 7 (cf. v. 9).

7:39 *bound to her husband as long as he lives.* Marriage is a lifelong union (yet see the exception clause in Mt 19:9 and note on 19:3). *if her husband dies.* Death breaks the marriage bond, and a Christian is then free to marry another Christian ("but he must belong to the Lord").

7:40 *as she is.* A widow. *I think that I too have the Spirit of God.* Paul writes as one convinced that he is guided by the Holy Spirit.

8:1—11:1 Cf. Ro 14:1—15:13 and notes.

8:1 *Now about food.* Another matter the Corinthians had written about (see 7:1 and note). *sacrificed to idols.* Offered on pagan altars. Meat left over from a sacrifice might be eaten by the priests, eaten by the offerer and his friends at a feast in the temple (see note on v. 10) or sold in the public meat market. Some Christians felt that if they ate such meat they participated in pagan worship and thus compromised their testimony for Christ. Other Christians did not feel this way. *knowledge.* Explained in vv. 2–6. *knowledge puffs up.* It fills one with false pride. *love builds up.* Explained in vv. 7–13.

8:2 *do not yet know.* Even the wisest and most knowledgeable among Christians have only limited knowledge. God is the only one who knows all (cf. Ro 11:33–36).

8:3 *whoever loves God is known by God.* Not their knowledge as such but their love for God is what counts; their love is a manifestation that God has accepted them and has dealt with them as among his own (see Gal 4:9). The background of Paul's assertion is very likely the OT use of Hebrew *yada'* ("to know") in such passages as Ge 18:19 ("have chosen"); 2Sa 7:20; Ps 1:6 ("watches over"); Am 3:2 ("have I chosen"); Na 1:7 ("cares for").

8:4 *An idol is nothing.* It represents no real god and possesses no power (see Ps 115:4–7; 135:15–17; Isa 44:12–20). But there are demons behind them (10:20).

8:5 *so-called gods.* The gods of Greek and Roman mythology.

8:6 *one God.* See Dt 6:4 and note. *from whom all things came … through whom all things came.* See Heb 2:10. God the Father is the ultimate source of all creation (Ac 4:24; Ro 11:36). God the Son is the dynamic one through whom, with the Father, all things came into existence (see Jn 1:3; Col 1:16 and note; Heb 1:2).

8:7 *possesses this knowledge.* Knows that an idol is an empty symbol, representing no real divine being. *sacrificed to a god.* Sacrificed to the god the idol represents. *since their conscience is weak, it is defiled.* They think that in eating meat sacrificed on pagan altars they have involved themselves in pagan worship and thus have sinned against Christ.

8:9 *your rights.* To eat meat sacrificed to idols because you know that an idol is nothing (v. 4). *the weak.* Those Christians whose consciences are weak, who think it is wrong to eat meat sacrificed to idols.

8:10 *your knowledge.* See vv. 1,4,8. *eating in an idol's temple.* At the site of ancient Corinth, archaeologists have discovered two temples containing rooms apparently used for pagan feasts where meat offered to idols was eaten. To such feasts Christians may have been invited by pagan friends.

12 When you sin against them[v] in this way
and wound their weak conscience, you sin
against Christ.[w] 13 Therefore, if what I eat
causes my brother or sister to fall into sin,
I will never eat meat again, so that I will
not cause them to fall.[x]

Paul's Rights as an Apostle

9 Am I not free?[y] Am I not an apostle?[z]
Have I not seen Jesus our Lord?[a] Are
you not the result of my work in the Lord?[b]
2 Even though I may not be an apostle to
others, surely I am to you! For you are the
seal[c] of my apostleship in the Lord.
3 This is my defense to those who sit in
judgment on me. 4 Don't we have the right
to food and drink?[d] 5 Don't we have the
right to take a believing wife[e] along with
us, as do the other apostles and the Lord's
brothers[f] and Cephas[a]?[g] 6 Or is it only I and
Barnabas[h] who lack the right to not work
for a living?
7 Who serves as a soldier[i] at his own expense? Who plants a vineyard[j] and does
not eat its grapes? Who tends a flock and
does not drink the milk? 8 Do I say this
merely on human authority? Doesn't the
Law say the same thing? 9 For it is written
in the Law of Moses: "Do not muzzle an
ox while it is treading out the grain."[b][k] Is it
about oxen that God is concerned?[l] 10 Surely he says this for us, doesn't he? Yes, this
was written for us,[m] because whoever
plows and threshes should be able to do
so in the hope of sharing in the harvest.[n]

8:12 [v] Mt 18:6 [w] Mt 25:40,45 **8:13** [x] S Mt 5:29 **9:1** [y] ver 19 [z] S 1Co 1:1; 2Co 12:12 [a] S 1Co 15:8 [b] 1Co 3:6; 4:15 **9:2** [c] 2Co 3:2,3 **9:4** [d] ver 14; S Ac 18:3 **9:5** [e] 1Co 7:7, 8 [f] S Mt 12:46 [g] S 1Co 1:12 **9:6** [h] S Ac 4:36 **9:7** [i] 2Ti 2:3, 4 [j] Dt 20:6; Pr 27:18; 1Co 3:6,8 **9:9** [k] Dt 25:4; 1Ti 5:18 [l] Dt 22:1-4; Pr 12:10 **9:10** [m] S Ro 4:23, 24 [n] Pr 11:25; 2Ti 2:6 **9:11** [o] ver 14; Ro 15:27; Gal 6:6 **9:12** [p] ver 15, 18; S Ac 18:3 [q] 2Co 6:3; 11:7-12 **9:13** [r] Lev 6:16, 26; Dt 18:1 **9:14** [s] S 1Ti 5:18 **9:15** [t] ver 12, 18; S Ac 18:3 [u] 2Co 11:9,10 **9:16** [v] Ro 1:14; Ac 9:15; 26:16-18 **9:17** [w] 1Co 3:8, 14 [x] 1Co 4:1; Gal 2:7; Col 1:25 **9:18** [y] 2Co 11:7; 12:13 [z] ver 12, 15 **9:19** [a] ver 1

11 If we have sown spiritual seed among
you, is it too much if we reap a material harvest from you?[o] 12 If others have this
right of support from you, shouldn't we
have it all the more?
But we did not use this right.[p] On the
contrary, we put up with anything rather
than hinder[q] the gospel of Christ.
13 Don't you know that those who serve
in the temple get their food from the temple, and that those who serve at the altar
share in what is offered on the altar?[r] 14 In
the same way, the Lord has commanded
that those who preach the gospel should
receive their living from the gospel.[s]
15 But I have not used any of these
rights.[t] And I am not writing this in the
hope that you will do such things for me,
for I would rather die than allow anyone
to deprive me of this boast.[u] 16 For when I
preach the gospel, I cannot boast, since
I am compelled to preach.[v] Woe to me if
I do not preach the gospel! 17 If I preach
voluntarily, I have a reward;[w] if not voluntarily, I am simply discharging the trust
committed to me.[x] 18 What then is my
reward? Just this: that in preaching the
gospel I may offer it free of charge,[y] and
so not make full use of my rights[z] as a
preacher of the gospel.

Paul's Use of His Freedom

19 Though I am free[a] and belong to no
one, I have made myself a slave to every-

[a] 5 That is, Peter [b] 9 Deut. 25:4

8:12 *wound their weak conscience.* Eating meat offered to idols when they feel it is wrong tends to blunt their consciences, so that doing what is wrong becomes much easier. The result may be moral tragedy. *you sin against Christ.* Cf. Mt 10:40; 18:5; Mk 9:37; Lk 9:48; Ro 14:15 and note; 14:19–20.

8:13 *I will never eat meat again.* Paul presents himself as an example for the church (cf. Ro 14:21).

9:1 *Am I not free?* Do I not have the rights that any Christian has? *Am I not an apostle?* Some at Corinth (2Co 12:11–12) questioned Paul's genuine apostleship. To certify his apostleship Paul gives this proof: that he has seen the Lord Jesus (Ac 9:1–9; 22:6–16; 26:12–18), as was true of the other apostles (Ac 1:21–22). Furthermore, he adds that his ministry has produced true spiritual fruit (the Corinthians) for the Lord, which should confirm to them that he is indeed an apostle.

9:4 *right to food and drink.* Paul and Barnabas, as God's workers, have a right to have their food and other physical needs supplied at the church's expense (cf. vv. 6,13–14).

9:5 *take a believing wife along with us.* Paul asserts his right to be married, if he wishes. This does not mean that he was married, as some have imagined (see 7:7 and note). Other apostles, including Peter (see Mk 1:30), had wives.

9:9 *Is it about oxen ...?* See 1Ti 5:18. In the Mosaic law that Paul quotes (Dt 25:4), God was indeed concerned about oxen that labored for their owners (cf. Jnh 4:11 and note). But this law was also illustrative of a basic principle of justice that God was teaching Israel and "us" (v. 10), a principle with greater moral weight when persons are involved than when farm animals are involved.

9:11 *material harvest.* Food, lodging and pay supplied by the Corinthians (cf. Gal 6:6). Paul here sets forth the principle that those who serve the church should be supported by the church (cf. Php 4:14–19).

9:12 *did not use this right.* The point of Paul's discussion in ch. 9. He had numerous rights that he did not claim because of his love for the Corinthians. Thus ch. 9 is an extended personal illustration of the practice advocated in ch. 8. Because of love for others, believers should be ready to surrender their rights (see Ro 14:15 and note).

9:13 *those who serve in the temple.* The Corinthian believers would understand this illustration not only from their knowledge of the OT (cf. Lev 7:28–36; Nu 18:8–20) but also from the practice in pagan temples in Greece and Rome.

9:15 *this boast.* That he had preached the gospel without charge, so that they could not say that they had paid him for it.

9:16 *I am compelled to preach.* The Lord had laid on Paul the necessity of preaching the gospel (Ac 9:1–16; 26:16–18; see also Jer 20:9 and note). *Woe to me.* Cf. v. 27 and note.

9:18 *my reward ... in preaching the gospel.* Paul's reward in preaching is not material things but the boasting that he has preached to the Corinthians without charge and has not taken advantage of the rights he deserves: food and drink, shelter and pay (vv. 3–12).

9:19 *I have made myself a slave to everyone.* Not only did Paul not use his right to material support in preaching the gospel but he also deprived himself—curtailed his personal privileges and social and religious rights—in dealing with different kinds of people. *to win.* To bring to Christ.

one,[b] to win as many as possible.[c] 20 To the Jews I became like a Jew, to win the Jews.[d] To those under the law I became like one under the law (though I myself am not under the law),[e] so as to win those under the law. 21 To those not having the law I became like one not having the law[f] (though I am not free from God's law but am under Christ's law),[g] so as to win those not having the law. 22 To the weak I became weak, to win the weak.[h] I have become all things to all people[i] so that by all possible means I might save some.[j] 23 I do all this for the sake of the gospel, that I may share in its blessings.

9:19 [b] 2Co 4:5; Gal 5:13 [c] Mt 18:15; 1Pe 3:1 **9:20** [d] Ac 16:3; 21:20-26; Ro 11:14 [e] S Ro 2:12 **9:21** [f] Ro 2:12, 14 [g] Gal 6:2 **9:22** [h] S Ro 14:1; S 1Co 2:3 [i] 1Co 10:33 [j] S Ro 11:14

Late Hellenistic period statue of running athlete. A victor's crown can be seen on his head. Athletics were very popular during Paul's lifetime and made for an appropriate metaphor to the Christian life. "Do you not know that in a race all the runners run, but only one gets the prize? Run in such a way as to get the prize. Everyone who competes in the games goes into strict training. They do it to get a crown that will not last, but we do it to get a crown that will last forever" (1Co 9:24–25).

Todd Bolen/www.BiblePlaces.com

The Need for Self-Discipline

24 Do you not know that in a race all the runners run, but only one gets the prize?[k] Run[l] in such a way as to get the prize. 25 Everyone who competes in the games goes into strict training. They do it to get a crown[m] that will not last, but we do it to get a crown that will last forever.[n] 26 Therefore I do not run like someone running aimlessly;[o] I do not fight like a boxer beating the air.[p] 27 No, I strike a blow to my body[q] and make it my slave so that after I have preached to others, I myself will not be disqualified for the prize.[r]

Warnings From Israel's History

10 For I do not want you to be ignorant[s] of the fact, brothers and sisters, that our ancestors were all under the cloud[t] and that they all passed through the sea.[u] 2 They were all baptized into[v] Moses in the cloud and in the sea. 3 They all ate the same spiritual food[w] 4 and drank the same spiritual drink; for they drank from the spiritual rock[x] that accompanied them, and that rock was Christ. 5 Nevertheless, God was

9:24 [k] Php 3:14; Col 2:18 [l] ver 25, 26; Gal 2:2; 5:7; Php 2:16; 2Ti 4:7; Heb 12:1 **9:25** [m] 2Ti 2:5 [n] 2Ti 4:8; Jas 1:12; 1Pe 5:4; Rev 2:10; 3:11 **9:26** [o] S ver 24 [p] 1Ti 6:12 **9:27** [q] Ro 8:13 [r] ver 24 **10:1** [s] S Ro 11:25 [t] Ex 13:21; Ps 105:39 [u] Ex 14:22, 29; Ps 66:6 **10:2** [v] Ro 6:3 **10:3** [w] S Jn 6:31 **10:4** [x] Ex 17:6; Nu 20:11; Ps 78:15; 105:41

9:20 *those under the law.* Those under the OT law and religious practices (the Jews). *I became like one under the law.* For the Jews' sake Paul conformed to the Jewish law (see Ac 16:3; 18:18 and notes; 21:20–26 and notes on 21:23–24).

9:21 *those not having the law.* Those who had not been raised under the OT law (the Gentiles). *I became like one not having the law.* Paul accommodated himself to Gentile culture when it did not violate his allegiance to Christ, though he still reckoned that he was under God's law and Christ's law. (By "Christ's law" Paul is probably referring to Christ's teachings, though the term is not necessarily restricted to them.)

9:22 *the weak.* Those whose consciences are weak (8:9–12). *I became weak.* Paul did not exercise his Christian freedom in such things as eating meat sacrificed to idols (8:9,13).

9:23 *share in its blessings.* Paul's hope concerning the manner of his own participation in the future glory of believers is linked with the faithfulness with which he carried out the apostolic mission Christ gave him (cf. v. 27 and note; see 2Co 3:1–3; 5:10; Php 2:16; 1Th 2:19–20 and notes).

9:24 *race ... runners.* The Corinthians were familiar with the foot races in their own Isthmian games, which occurred every other year and were second only to the Olympic games in importance. *prize.* In ancient times the prize was a perishable wreath (v. 25). See photo above.

9:25 *crown that will last forever.* See 1Pe 5:4 and note; cf. 1Th 2:19 and note. See also photo above.

9:26 *not ... running aimlessly.* See Php 3:14 and note.

9:27 *I strike a blow to my body and make it my slave.* Here Paul uses the figure of boxing to represent the Christian life. He does not aimlessly beat the air, but he severely disciplines his own body in serving Christ. *not be disqualified for the prize.* Paul realizes that he must with rigor serve the Lord and battle against sin. If he fails in this, he may be excluded from the reward (see 3:10–15).

10:1 *the cloud ... the sea.* These two watery entities had played a central role in God's deliverance of Israel out of Egypt through his servant Moses (the cloud signifying God's guidance [see Ex 13:21; 40:36–37; Nu 9:17,21; 10:11–12; 14:14; Ne 9:12,19; Ps 78:14] and the sea signifying God's climactic act of deliverance in which he brought his people safely through the sea but brought judgment on the Egyptians [see Ex 14:1 — 15:20; Dt 11:4; Jos 2:10; Ne 9:9,11; Ps 66:6; 77:16,19; 78:13,53; 106:9–11; 136:13–15; Isa 43:16–17; 51:10; 63:11–13]). The Israelites' journey, guided by the cloud, and their safe passage through the sea under the ministry of Moses united them with God's servant Moses in the working out of God's redemptive program (see v. 2 and note).

10:2 *baptized.* Figurative language Paul used to depict Israel's union with Moses in God's redemptive program is analogous in important ways to the Christian's union with Christ in his death and resurrection, as signified by Christian baptism (see Ro 6:3–4 and note).

10:3–4 *spiritual food ... spiritual drink.* The manna and the water from the rock (Ex 16:2–36; 17:1–7; Nu 20:2–11; 21:16) are used as figures representing the spiritual sustenance that God continually provides for his people — as signified in the Lord's Supper.

10:4 *that rock was Christ.* The rock, from which the water came, and the manna are here viewed by Paul as symbolic of the spiritual sustenance God's people experienced already in the wilderness through Christ, the bread of life and the water of life (see Jn 4:14; 6:30–35 and notes). For Christ's presence with God's people already in the wilderness, cf. 8:6 and note.

10:5 *God was not pleased with most of them.* In spite of the remarkable privileges given to the Israelites (vv. 1–4), they failed to obey God, thus incurring his

not pleased with most of them; their bodies were scattered in the wilderness.[y]
6 Now these things occurred as examples[z] to keep us from setting our hearts
on evil things as they did. 7 Do not be
idolaters,[a] as some of them were; as it is
written: "The people sat down to eat and
drink and got up to indulge in revelry."[ab]
8 We should not commit sexual immorality, as some of them did — and in one day
twenty-three thousand of them died.[c] 9 We
should not test Christ,[bd] as some of them
did — and were killed by snakes.[e] 10 And do
not grumble, as some of them did[f] — and
were killed[g] by the destroying angel.[h]
11 These things happened to them as examples[i] and were written down as warnings for us,[j] on whom the culmination
of the ages has come.[k] 12 So, if you think
you are standing firm,[l] be careful that you
don't fall! 13 No temptation[c] has overtaken
you except what is common to mankind.
And God is faithful;[m] he will not let you be
tempted[c] beyond what you can bear.[n] But
when you are tempted,[c] he will also provide a way out so that you can endure it.

Idol Feasts and the Lord's Supper

14 Therefore, my dear friends,[o] flee
from idolatry.[p] 15 I speak to sensible people; judge for yourselves what I say. 16 Is
not the cup of thanksgiving for which we
give thanks a participation in the blood of
Christ? And is not the bread that we break[q]
a participation in the body of Christ?[r] 17 Because there is one loaf, we, who are many,
are one body,[s] for we all share the one loaf.
18 Consider the people of Israel: Do not
those who eat the sacrifices[t] participate in
the altar? 19 Do I mean then that food sacrificed to an idol is anything, or that an idol
is anything?[u] 20 No, but the sacrifices of pagans are offered to demons,[v] not to God,
and I do not want you to be participants
with demons. 21 You cannot drink the cup
of the Lord and the cup of demons too;
you cannot have a part in both the Lord's
table and the table of demons.[w] 22 Are we
trying to arouse the Lord's jealousy?[x] Are
we stronger than he?[y]

The Believer's Freedom

23 "I have the right to do anything," you
say — but not everything is beneficial.[z]
"I have the right to do anything" — but

[a] 7 Exodus 32:6 [b] 9 Some manuscripts *test the Lord* [c] 13 The Greek for *temptation* and *tempted* can also mean *testing* and *tested.*

10:5 [y] Nu 14:29; Heb 3:17; Jude 5 **10:6** [z] ver 11 **10:7** [a] ver 14 [b] Ex 32:4,6,19 **10:8** [c] Nu 25:1-9 **10:9** [d] Ex 17:2; Ps 78:18; 95:9; 106:14 [e] Nu 21:5,6 **10:10** [f] Nu 16:41; 17:5,10 [g] Nu 16:49 [h] Ex 12:23; 1Ch 21:15; Heb 11:28 **10:11** [i] ver 6 [j] S Ro 4:24 [k] S Ro 13:11 **10:12** [l] Ro 11:20; 2Co 1:24 **10:13** [m] S 1Co 1:9 [n] 2Pe 2:9 **10:14** [o] Heb 6:9; 1Pe 2:11; 1Jn 2:7; Jude 3 [p] ver 7; 1Jn 5:21 **10:16** [q] S Mt 14:19 [r] Mt 26:26-28; 1Co 11:23-25 **10:17** [s] S Ro 12:5 **10:18** [t] Lev 7:6,14,15 **10:19** [u] S 1Co 8:4 **10:20** [v] Lev 17:7; Dt 32:17; Ps 106:37; Rev 9:20 **10:21** [w] 2Co 6:15,16 **10:22** [x] Dt 32:16,21; 1Ki 14:22; Ps 78:58; Jer 44:8 [y] Ecc 6:10; Isa 45:9 **10:23** [z] 1Co 6:12

displeasure. Of the adults who came out of Egypt, only Caleb and Joshua were allowed to enter Canaan (Nu 14:22–24,28–35; Dt 1:34–36; Jos 1:1–2; 14:6–14).

10:6 *as they did.* What Paul has in mind is described in vv. 7–10.

10:7 *idolaters.* Referring to the incident of the golden calf (Ex 32:1–6). The people ate a ritual meal sacrificed to an idol (cf. ch. 8).

10:8 Refers to Israel's participation in the worship of the Baal of Peor and the sexual practices associated with that worship (see Nu 25:1–9). *twenty-three thousand.* The Hebrew and Greek (Septuagint) texts of Nu 25:9 have 24,000. It is clear that Paul is not striving for exactness but is only speaking approximately. First-century writers were not as concerned about being precise as twenty-first-century authors often are.

10:10 *do not grumble.* As in Nu 16:41. *destroying angel.* Paul links the angel who brought the plague of Nu 16:46–50—because of the grumbling of the Israelites against Moses and Aaron (Nu 16:41)—with the destroying angel of Ex 12:23.

10:11 *written down as warnings.* See Ro 15:4 and note. *culmination of the ages.* The period of time inaugurated by Christ's death and resurrection and continuing into the future until Christ's second coming and beyond. It is the period of fulfillment when all that God has been doing for his people throughout all previous ages comes to its fruition in the Messiah.

10:13 *temptation.* Temptation in itself is not sin. Jesus was tempted (Mt 4:1–11). Yielding to temptation is sin. The Greek for "temptation" and "tempted" can also mean "testing" and "tested," so Paul may have been speaking of "testing" with its accompanying temptation (see Mt 6:13 and note). *endure it.* Through God's enablement to resist the temptation to sin or to endure the trial without falling.

10:14 *flee from idolatry.* Like that described in Ex 32:1–6. Corinthian Christians had come out of a background of paganism. Temples for the worship of Apollo, Asclepius, Demeter, Aphrodite and other pagan gods and goddesses were seen daily by the Corinthians as they engaged in the activities of everyday life. The worship of Aphrodite was a particularly strong temptation (see note on 6:18; cf. 1Jn 5:21 and note).

10:16 *cup of thanksgiving.* The cup of wine that Christians drink during the celebration of the Lord's Supper (see Mt 26:27–28; Mk 14:23–24 and note; Lk 22:20). Drinking the wine of the Lord's Supper as an act of faith is a claim of personal participation in the benefits of Christ's shed blood. *bread that we break.* The loaf of bread that is broken and eaten during the Lord's Supper (see Mt 26:26; Mk 14:22 and note; Lk 22:19 and note). *participation in the body of Christ.* The sense is similar to Paul's statement concerning "participation in the blood of Christ."

10:17 *one loaf.* The act of many believers partaking of one loaf of bread symbolizes the unity of the body of Christ, the church, which is nourished by the one bread of life (cf. Jn 6:33–58).

10:18 *those who eat the sacrifices participate in the altar.* When the people of Israel ate part of the sacrifice made at the altar (Lev 7:15; 8:31; Dt 12:17–18), they participated with the altar in consuming the sacrifices. What was consumed on the altar (with fire) was Yahweh's portion.

10:19 *Do I mean ... that an idol is anything?* See 8:4–6 and notes.

10:20 *offered to demons.* In reality, demons (not gods) were the objects of idol worship. God's people are warned that if they do eat meat sacrificed to idols, they should not eat it with pagans in their temple feasts, for to do so is to become "participants with demons."

10:22 *arouse the Lord's jealousy.* By sharing in pagan idolatry and worship (cf. Ex 20:5 and note).

10:23 *not everything is constructive.* See 6:12 and note. Personal freedom and desire for one's rights are not the only considerations. One must also consider "the good of others" (v. 24; cf. 8:1; Gal 6:2).

not everything is constructive. 24 No one
should seek their own good, but the good
of others.[a]
25 Eat anything sold in the meat market
without raising questions of conscience,[b]
26 for, "The earth is the Lord's, and everything in it."[ac]
27 If an unbeliever invites you to a meal
and you want to go, eat whatever is put
before you[d] without raising questions of
conscience. 28 But if someone says to you,
"This has been offered in sacrifice," then
do not eat it, both for the sake of the one
who told you and for the sake of conscience.[e] 29 I am referring to the other person's conscience, not yours. For why is my
freedom[f] being judged by another's conscience? 30 If I take part in the meal with
thankfulness, why am I denounced because of something I thank God for?[g]
31 So whether you eat or drink or whatever you do, do it all for the glory of God.[h]
32 Do not cause anyone to stumble,[i] whether Jews, Greeks or the church of God[j]—
33 even as I try to please everyone in every
way.[k] For I am not seeking my own good
but the good of many,[l] so that they may
be saved.[m] 1 Follow my example,[n] as
I follow the example of Christ.[o]

11

On Covering the Head in Worship

2 I praise you[p] for remembering me in
everything[q] and for holding to the traditions just as I passed them on to you.[r] 3 But
I want you to realize that the head of every
man is Christ,[s] and the head of the woman
is man,[bt] and the head of Christ is God.[u]
4 Every man who prays or prophesies[v] with
his head covered dishonors his head. 5 But
every woman who prays or prophesies[w]
with her head uncovered dishonors her
head—it is the same as having her head
shaved.[x] 6 For if a woman does not cover

[a] 26 Psalm 24:1   [b] 3 Or *of the wife is her husband*

10:24 [a] ver 33; S Ro 15:1, 2; 1Co 13:5; Php 2:4, 21 **10:25** [b] S Ac 10:15; 1Co 8:7 **10:26** [c] Ps 24:1; Ex 9:29; 19:5; Job 41:11; Ps 50:12; 1Ti 4:4 **10:27** [d] Lk 10:7 **10:28** [e] 1Co 8:7, 10-12 **10:29** [f] 1Co 9:1, 19 **10:30** [g] S Ro 14:6 **10:31** [h] Zec 14:21; Col 3:17; 1Pe 4:11 **10:32** [i] S Mt 5:29; Ac 24:16; S 2Co 6:3 [j] Ac 20:28; 1Co 1:2; 11:16, 22; 15:9; 1Ti 3:5, 15 **10:33** [k] Ro 15:2; 1Co 9:22 [l] S ver 24 [m] S Ro 11:14

11:1 [n] S 1Co 4:16 [o] Ro 15:3; 1Pe 2:21 **11:2** [p] ver 17, 22 [q] 1Co 4:17 [r] ver 23; 1Co 15:2, 3; 2Th 2:15; 3:6 **11:3** [s] S Eph 1:22 [t] Ge 3:16; Eph 5:23 [u] 1Co 3:23 **11:4** [v] S Ac 11:27 **11:5** [w] S Ac 21:9 [x] Dt 21:12

10:25 *Eat anything sold in the meat market.* Even if it has been sacrificed to an idol, because out in the public market it has lost its pagan religious significance.

10:26 A quotation from Ps 24:1 used at Jewish mealtimes as a blessing (cf. Ps 50:12; 89:11).

10:27 *eat whatever is put before you.* Whether or not it might be meat sacrificed to idols, ask no questions. As long as the subject has not been brought up, you are free to eat the meat.

10:28 *for the sake of the one who told you.* If the meat has been identified as meat sacrificed to idols and you eat it, the informant might think you condone or even are willing to participate in the worship of idols. *for the sake of conscience.* So as not to cause someone else (v. 29) to think it is all right to eat meat sacrificed to idols even though they have doubts about it.

10:29 *my freedom.* Cf. Ro 14:16 and note. The exercise of one's personal freedom is to be governed by whether the action will bring glory to God, whether it will build up the church of God and whether it will encourage the unsaved to receive Christ as Savior and Lord (vv. 31–33).

10:30 *something I thank God for.* Paul could thank God for meat sacrificed to idols, for the idol is nothing and the meat is a part of God's created world.

10:31 *all for the glory of God.* The all-inclusive principle that governs the discussion in chs. 8–10 is that God should be glorified in everything the Christian does (see note on Ro 16:27).

10:32 *Do not cause anyone to stumble.* Living to glorify God will result in doing what is beneficial for others, whether Christians ("the church of God") or non-Christians ("Jews, Greeks").

10:33 *please everyone in every way.* Paul will do nothing that might hinder someone else from receiving the salvation proclaimed in his gospel. *that they may be saved.* See 9:22.

11:1 Notice the order: (1) Christ is the supreme example (cf. 1Pe 2:21); (2) Christ's apostle follows his example ("as I follow"); (3) we are to follow the apostle's example.

11:3–16 The subject of this section is propriety in public worship. Clearly Paul is concerned that the proper relationship between husbands and wives be reflected in public worship; however, much remains uncertain. As in the previous section, he desires that all be done to the glory of God (10:31).

11:3 Some understand the term "head" to refer primarily to the concept of honor, in that one's physical head is the seat of one's honor (cf. vv. 4–5). Thus as Christ honored God, each man is to honor Christ, and each woman is to honor her husband. Others see in the word "head" the idea of authority (which would also include the concept of honor). They point out that Paul clearly uses the term in the sense of authority in Eph 1:21–22 ("under his feet"; "head over everything"), in Eph 5:22–23 (where headship is seen in a context of submission) and in Col 1:18; 2:10. Thus as Christ has authority over "every man" and is therefore to be honored by them, so the husband holds a position of authority and is therefore to be honored by his wife. See note on 15:28.

11:4–7 See NIV text note for another interpretation of this passage related to hair length rather than head covering.

11:4 The first use of "head" in this verse refers to a man's physical head; the second refers to his spiritual Head (Christ)—or perhaps is intended in a double sense. In the culture of Paul's day, men uncovered their heads in worship to signify their respect for and submission to deity. When a man prayed or prophesied with his head covered, he failed to show the proper attitude toward Christ. *prophesies.* See 12:10 and note.

11:5–6 Paul's message to women was: Show respect for and submission to your husband by covering your head during public worship. Some do not see in these verses a temporary cultural significance to the covering/uncovering of the head. They insist that since Paul referred to the order of creation (vv. 7–9), his directive is not to be restricted to his time. Thus women of all times should wear a head covering.

Others find a lasting principle in the passage requiring wives, in all ways, to show respect for husbands by submitting to their authority—not merely by a particular style of attire but by godly lives. Man, who was created first, is to have authority over his wife (see 1Ti 2:11–14), who was made out of his body (Ge 2:21–24) to be his helper and companion (Ge 2:20). She is to honor her husband by submitting to him as her head (see v. 3).

Still others see these verses not as a mandate for all marriages but as reflecting marriage relationships at that time

her head, she might as well have her hair cut off; but if it is a disgrace for a woman to have her hair cut off or her head shaved, then she should cover her head.

7 A man ought not to cover his head,[a] since he is the image[y] and glory of God; but woman is the glory of man. 8 For man did not come from woman, but woman from man;[z] 9 neither was man created for woman, but woman for man.[a] 10 It is for this reason that a woman ought to have authority over her own[b] head, because of the angels. 11 Nevertheless, in the Lord woman is not independent of man, nor is man independent of woman. 12 For as woman came from man, so also man is born of woman. But everything comes from God.[b]

13 Judge for yourselves: Is it proper for a woman to pray to God with her head uncovered? 14 Does not the very nature of things teach you that if a man has long hair, it is a disgrace to him, 15 but that if a woman has long hair, it is her glory? For long hair is given to her as a covering. 16 If anyone wants to be contentious about this, we have no other practice—nor do the churches of God.[c]

Correcting an Abuse of the Lord's Supper

11:23-25pp — Mt 26:26-28; Mk 14:22-24; Lk 22:17-20

17 In the following directives I have no praise for you,[d] for your meetings do more harm than good. 18 In the first place, I hear that when you come together as a church, there are divisions[e] among you, and to some extent I believe it. 19 No doubt there have to be differences among you to show which of you have God's approval.[f] 20 So then, when you come together, it is not the Lord's Supper you eat, 21 for when you are eating, some of you go ahead with your own private suppers.[g] As a result, one person remains hungry and another gets drunk. 22 Don't you have homes to eat and drink in? Or do you despise the church of God[h] by humiliating those who have nothing?[i] What shall I say to you? Shall I praise you?[j] Certainly not in this matter!

23 For I received from the Lord[k] what I also passed on to you:[l] The Lord Jesus, on the night he was betrayed, took bread, 24 and when he had given thanks, he broke it and said, "This is my body,[m] which is for you; do this in remembrance of me." 25 In the same way, after supper he took the cup, saying, "This cup is the new covenant[n] in my blood;[o] do this, whenever you drink it, in remembrance of me."

11:7 [y] Ge 1:26; 5:1; 9:6; Jas 3:9
11:8 [z] Ge 2:21-23; 1Ti 2:13
11:9 [a] Ge 2:18
11:12 [b] S Ro 11:36
11:16 [c] S 1Co 7:17; S 10:32
11:17 [d] ver 2, 22
11:18 [e] 1Co 1:10-12; 3:3
11:19 [f] 1Jn 2:19
11:21 [g] 2Pe 2:13; Jude 12
11:22 [h] S 1Co 10:32 [i] Jas 2:6 [j] ver 2, 17
11:23 [k] Gal 1:12 [l] S ver 2
11:24 [m] 1Co 10:16
11:25 [n] S Lk 22:20 [o] 1Co 10:16

[a] 4-7 Or *4 Every man who prays or prophesies with long hair dishonors his head. 5 But every woman who prays or prophesies with no covering of hair dishonors her head—she is just like one of the "shorn women." 6 If a woman has no covering, let her be for now with short hair; but since it is a disgrace for a woman to have her hair shorn or shaved, she should grow it again. 7 A man ought not to have long hair* [b] 10 Or *have a sign of authority on her*

in Corinth and therefore giving a reason why the women there should have covered their heads (v. 10). They point to vv. 11–12 as a contrast, emphasizing equality and mutual dependence between men and women who are "in the Lord" (v. 11; see Gal 3:28; 1Pe 3:7).

11:10 Paul's meaning here is obscure. *have authority over her own head.* See NIV text note, which is understood by some to refer to the woman's authority as co-ruler with man in the creation (Ge 1:26–27). Others take the phrase to refer to the man's authority as properly recognized by the woman in her head covering. Still others understand Paul as viewing the woman's head covering as a symbol of protection against the influence of fallen angels. *angels.* Perhaps mentioned here because they are interested in all aspects of the Christian's salvation and are sensitive to decorum in worship (cf. Eph 3:10 and note). But see previous entry.

11:13–14 *proper ... the very nature of things.* Believers must be conscious of how their actions appear in their culture, in light of what is considered to be honorable behavior.

11:16 In worship services, Paul and the churches in general followed the common custom of the men wearing short hair and the women long hair. Paul was basing his remarks, particularly in vv. 13–16, on common custom in the churches.

11:17 *no praise.* Contrast v. 2.

11:18 *divisions.* Paul had already dealt with one aspect of these divisions (1:10–17).

11:19 *God's approval.* As deplorable as factions may be, they serve one good purpose: They distinguish those who are faithful and true in God's sight.

11:20 *not the Lord's Supper you eat.* Their intention was to eat the Lord's Supper, but it was profaned by their gluttony and discrimination.

11:21 *remains hungry ... gets drunk.* The early church held the *agape* ("love") feast in connection with the Lord's Supper (cf. 2Pe 2:13 and note; Jude 12). Perhaps the meal was something like a present-day potluck dinner. In good Greek style they brought food for all to share, the rich bringing more and the poor less, but because of their cliques the rich ate much and the poor were left hungry.

11:22 *Shall I praise you?* See v. 17.

11:23–26 Observe the similarity of Paul's words here with Mt 26:26–29; Mk 14:22–25; and especially Lk 22:17–20.

11:23 *I received from the Lord.* Paul does not necessarily mean that he received the message about the Lord's Supper directly from Christ. The information probably was passed on to him by others who had heard it from Jesus (see 15:3 and note; cf. 7:10 and note).

11:24 *had given thanks.* The Jewish practice at meals. This makes it a true Eucharist ("thanksgiving"). *is.* See note on Lk 22:19. *my body.* The broken bread is a symbol of Christ's body "given" for sinners (Lk 22:19; see note there). *for you.* See note on Lk 22:19. *in remembrance of me.* As the Festival of Passover was a commemorative meal (see Ex 12:14), so also the Lord's Supper is a memorial supper, recalling and portraying Christ's death for sinners.

11:25 *after supper.* After the Passover supper. The Lord's Supper was first celebrated by Jesus in connection with the Passover meal (cf. Mt 26:18–30 and parallels in Mark and Luke). *cup.* A symbol of the new covenant in Jesus' blood (see Mk 14:24 and note; Lk 22:20; cf. Jer 31:31–34). (The old covenant was the Mosaic or Sinaitic covenant; see

26 For whenever you eat this bread and
drink this cup, you proclaim the Lord's
death until he comes.[p]
27 So then, whoever eats the bread or
drinks the cup of the Lord in an unworthy
manner will be guilty of sinning against
the body and blood of the Lord.[q] 28 Everyone ought to examine themselves[r] before
they eat of the bread and drink from the
cup. 29 For those who eat and drink without discerning the body of Christ eat and
drink judgment on themselves. 30 That is
why many among you are weak and sick,
and a number of you have fallen asleep.[s]
31 But if we were more discerning with regard to ourselves, we would not come under such judgment.[t] 32 Nevertheless, when
we are judged in this way by the Lord, we
are being disciplined[u] so that we will not
be finally condemned with the world.[v]
33 So then, my brothers and sisters, when
you gather to eat, you should all eat together. 34 Anyone who is hungry[w] should eat
something at home,[x] so that when you meet
together it may not result in judgment.
And when I come[y] I will give further directions.

11:26 [p]S 1Co 1:7 **11:27** [q]Heb 10:29 **11:28** [r]2Co 13:5 **11:30** [s]S Mt 9:24 **11:31** [t]Ps 32:5; 1Jn 1:9 **11:32** [u]Ps 94:12; 118:18; Pr 3:11, 12; Heb 12:7-10; Rev 3:19 [v]Jn 15:18,19 **11:34** [w]ver 21 [x]ver 22 [y]S 1Co 4:19

12:1 [z]Ro 1:11; 1Co 1:7; 14:1, 37 [a]S Ro 11:25 **12:2** [b]S Eph 2:2 [c]Ps 115:5; Jer 10:5; Hab 2:18,19 **12:3** [d]Ro 9:3; 1Co 16:22 [e]S Jn 13:13 [f]1Jn 4:2,3 **12:4** [g]ver 8-11; Ro 12:4-8; Eph 4:11; Heb 2:4 **12:6** [h]S Php 2:13 [i]Eph 4:6

Concerning Spiritual Gifts

12 Now about the gifts of the Spirit,[z] brothers and sisters, I do not
want you to be uninformed.[a] 2 You know
that when you were pagans,[b] somehow or
other you were influenced and led astray
to mute idols.[c] 3 Therefore I want you to
know that no one who is speaking by the
Spirit of God says, "Jesus be cursed,"[d] and
no one can say, "Jesus is Lord,"[e] except by
the Holy Spirit.[f]
4 There are different kinds of gifts, but
the same Spirit[g] distributes them. 5 There
are different kinds of service, but the same
Lord. 6 There are different kinds of working, but in all of them and in everyone[h] it
is the same God[i] at work.
7 Now to each one the manifestation of
the Spirit is given for the common good.[j]
8 To one there is given through the Spirit
a message of wisdom,[k] to another a message of knowledge[l] by means of the same
Spirit, 9 to another faith[m] by the same Spirit, to another gifts of healing[n] by that one

12:7 [j]1Co 14:12; Eph 4:12 **12:8** [k]1Co 2:6 [l]S 2Co 8:7 **12:9** [m]Mt 17:19,20; 1Co 13:2 [n]ver 28,30; Mt 10:1

Ex 24:3–8 and notes on 24:6,8.) By the use of this covenant sign God signifies his bestowal of salvation upon his people, sealed and paid for by the shedding of Jesus' blood.

11:26 *whenever you eat ... and drink.* The Lord's Supper should be held periodically, but there is no explicit instruction as to how often. *you proclaim the Lord's death.* The Lord's Supper is never celebrated apart from a proclamation of "Christ crucified" (1:23; cf. 2:2). *until he comes.* Cf. Mt 26:29 and note.

11:27 *in an unworthy manner.* In the unloving and self-centered manner that characterized some of the Corinthians at their unruly *agape* supper (vv. 20–22; see note on v. 21).

11:28 *examine themselves.* All participants should test the attitude of their own hearts and actions and their awareness of the significance of the Supper, thus making the Supper, under God, a spiritual means of grace.

11:29 *without discerning the body of Christ.* The word "body" may refer to either the Lord's physical body or the church as the body of Christ (see 12:13,27 and notes). The first view means that the person partakes of the Lord's Supper without recognizing that it symbolizes Christ's crucified body. But in that case, why is the blood not mentioned? The second view means that the participant is not aware of the nature of the church as the body of Christ, resulting in the self-centered actions of vv. 20–21. *judgment.* Not God's eternal judgment, which is to come on the unbeliever, but such disciplinary judgment as physical sickness and death (v. 30).

11:30 *have fallen asleep.* See Jn 11:11 and note.

11:32 *disciplined.* As God's redeemed children we are disciplined—just as parents discipline their children (see Heb 12:5–11 and notes).

11:33 *gather to eat.* Another reference to the *agape* fellowship meal (see note on v. 21). Each person was to exercise restraint and wait to eat with the others. Those who are too hungry should satisfy their hunger at home and not bring selfish and discriminatory practices into the church (v. 34).

12:1 *Now about.* Suggests Paul is answering another question raised by the Corinthians in their letter (cf. 7:1; 8:1; 16:1). *gifts of the Spirit.* See 1:7 and note.

12:2 *led astray to mute idols.* At one time the Corinthians had been led by various influences to worship mute idols (see 8:4–6 and notes), but now they are to be led by the Holy Spirit.

12:3 *"Jesus be cursed" ... "Jesus is Lord."* Those who are regenerated by the Holy Spirit cannot pronounce a curse on Jesus; rather, they are the only ones who can confess from the heart, "Jesus is Lord" (cf. Jn 20:28; 1Jn 4:2–3). The Greek word for "Lord" here is used in the pre-Christian Greek translation of the OT (the Septuagint) to translate the Hebrew name *Yahweh* ("the LORD"). See note on Ro 10:9.

12:4–6 *same Spirit ... same Lord ... same God.* These verses, reflecting the Trinity (see note on Mt 28:19), show the diversity and unity of spiritual gifts.

12:4 *gifts.* Gifts of grace produced by the indwelling Holy Spirit. See note on v. 1.

12:5 *service.* The Greek word in its various forms is used to indicate service to the Christian community, such as serving tables (Ac 6:2–3); it is also the word used in the early church for the office of deacon (Php 1:1).

12:6 *working.* The Greek word indicates power in operation that produces obvious results.

12:7 *to each one the manifestation ... given for the common good.* Every member of the body of Christ has been given some spiritual gift that is an evidence of the Spirit's working in their lives. All the gifts are intended to build up the members of the Christian community (see 1Pe 4:10–11). They are not to be used for selfish advantage, as some in the Corinthian community apparently were doing.

12:8 *To one ... to another.* Not everyone has the same gift or all the gifts. *message of wisdom ... knowledge.* Gifts that meet the need of the Christian community when knowledge or wisdom is required to make decisions or to choose proper courses of action.

12:9 *faith.* Not saving faith, which all Christians possess, but faith to meet a specific need within the body of Christ. *gifts of healing.* Lit. "gifts of healings." The double plural may suggest different kinds of illnesses and the various ways God heals them.

Spirit, 10 to another miraculous powers,[o] to
another prophecy,[p] to another distinguishing between spirits,[q] to another speaking
in different kinds of tongues,[a][r] and to still
another the interpretation of tongues.[a]
11 All these are the work of one and the
same Spirit,[s] and he distributes them to
each one, just as he determines.

Unity and Diversity in the Body

12 Just as a body, though one, has many
parts, but all its many parts form one
body,[t] so it is with Christ.[u] 13 For we were
all baptized[v] by[b] one Spirit[w] so as to form
one body—whether Jews or Gentiles,
slave or free[x]—and we were all given the
one Spirit to drink.[y] 14 Even so the body is
not made up of one part but of many.[z]
15 Now if the foot should say, "Because
I am not a hand, I do not belong to the
body," it would not for that reason stop
being part of the body. 16 And if the ear
should say, "Because I am not an eye, I do
not belong to the body," it would not for
that reason stop being part of the body.
17 If the whole body were an eye, where
would the sense of hearing be? If the
whole body were an ear, where would the
sense of smell be? 18 But in fact God has
placed[a] the parts in the body, every one of
them, just as he wanted them to be.[b] 19 If
they were all one part, where would the
body be? 20 As it is, there are many parts,
but one body.[c]
21 The eye cannot say to the hand, "I
don't need you!" And the head cannot say
to the feet, "I don't need you!" 22 On the
contrary, those parts of the body that seem
to be weaker are indispensable, 23 and the
parts that we think are less honorable we
treat with special honor. And the parts
that are unpresentable are treated with
special modesty, 24 while our presentable
parts need no special treatment. But God
has put the body together, giving greater
honor to the parts that lacked it, 25 so that
there should be no division in the body,
but that its parts should have equal concern for each other. 26 If one part suffers,
every part suffers with it; if one part is
honored, every part rejoices with it.
27 Now you are the body of Christ,[d] and

12:10 [o] ver 28-30; Gal 3:5 [p] S Eph 4:11 [q] 1Jn 4:1 [r] S Mk 16:17 **12:11** [s] S ver 4 **12:12** [t] S Ro 12:5 [u] ver 27 **12:13** [v] S Mk 1:8 [w] Eph 2:18 [x] Gal 3:28; Col 3:11 [y] Jn 7:37-39 **12:14** [z] ver 12, 20 **12:18** [a] ver 28 [b] ver 11 **12:20** [c] ver 12, 14; S Ro 12:5 **12:27** [d] Eph 1:23; 4:12; Col 1:18,24

[a] *10* Or *languages*; also in verse 28 [b] *13* Or *with*; or *in*

12:10 *miraculous powers.* Lit. "deeds of power." In Scripture, miracles are events that in the eyes of those who experienced and/or witnessed them clearly evidenced God's power purposefully at work in a way beyond the usual or the expected. *prophecy.* A message imparted to a believer by the Holy Spirit. It may be a prediction (cf. Agabus, Ac 11:28 [see note there]; 21:10–11) or an indication of the will of God in a given situation (cf. 14:1–5,29–30 and notes; Ac 13:1–2 and note on 13:1). *distinguishing between spirits.* Since there can also be false prophecies that come from evil spirits, this gift is necessary in order for the church to distinguish the true from the false (cf. 1Jn 4:1–6). *different kinds of tongues.* Since the Greek word for "tongues" is elsewhere used to refer to "languages" or "dialects," some understand it to refer here to the ability to speak in human languages not learned by other means, as the apostles did on the day of Pentecost (see Ac 2:4,6,11 and notes; cf. also 1Co 14:9–10). Others believe that in chs. 12–14 the term "tongues" refers to both earthly and heavenly languages, including ecstatic languages of praise and prayer (see 13:1; 14:2,10 and notes). *interpretation of tongues.* The ability to make intelligible the sense of what is spoken in a tongue so that hearers can understand and be edified (cf. 14:5,13,27–28).

12:11 *as he determines.* The Holy Spirit sovereignly determines which gift or gifts each believer should have.

12:12 *one … many parts.* This example illustrates the unity and diversity of the different spiritual gifts exercised by God's people, who are all members of the one body of Christ. *with Christ.* With Christ's body, the church, of which he is the head (Eph 1:22–23; cf. Ro 12:4–8 and notes).

12:13 Cf. Ro 6:3–4 and note. *all baptized by one Spirit so as to form one body.* Regenerated by the Holy Spirit (Jn 3:3,5) and united with Christ as part of his body. *Jews or Gentiles.* In Christ there is no ethnic or cultural distinction (see Gal 3:28 and note). *slave or free.* No social distinction. *all given the one Spirit to drink.* God has given all his people the Holy Spirit to indwell them (6:19) so that their lives may overflow with the fruit of the Spirit (Gal 5:22–23; cf. Jn 7:37–39).

12:14–20 Addressed mainly to those who feel that their gifts are inferior and unimportant. Apparently the more spectacular gifts (such as tongues) had been glorified in the Corinthian church, making those who did not have them feel inferior.

12:14 See Ro 12:4–8. As the human body must have diversity to work effectively as a whole, so the members of Christ's body have diverse gifts, the use of which can help bring about the accomplishment of Christ's united purpose.

12:18 Paul stresses the sovereign purpose of God in diversifying the parts of the body; by implication he is saying that God has arranged that different Christians in the body of Christ exercise different spiritual gifts, not the same gift. And this diversity is intended to accomplish God's unified purpose. God's method employs diversity to create unity.

12:21–26 Addressed mainly to those who feel that their gifts are superior and most important (see note on vv. 14–20). These verses provide another indication that some gifts, like tongues, had been magnified as being preeminent.

12:21 The principle here is the interdependence of the parts of the body in the one whole. Christians in the body of Christ are mutually dependent as they exercise their distinctive functions.

12:22 *weaker are indispensable.* Christians who seem to have less important functions in the body of Christ are actually indispensable.

12:23 Christians should give "special honor" and support to those in the church who have ordinary gifts.

12:24 Persons with more spectacular gifts do not need to be given special honor.

12:25 *no division.* See 1:10–12.

12:26 *every part suffers.* In the body of Christ if one Christian suffers, all the Christians are affected (cf. Ac 12:1–5—the martyrdom of James and the imprisonment of Peter).

12:27 *you are the body of Christ.* Addressed to the local church at Corinth. Each local church is the body of Christ, just as the universal church is Christ's body.

each one of you is a part of it.[e] 28 And
God has placed in the church[f] first of all
apostles,[g] second prophets,[h] third teachers, then miracles, then gifts of healing,[i]
of helping, of guidance,[j] and of different
kinds of tongues.[k] 29 Are all apostles? Are
all prophets? Are all teachers? Do all work
miracles? 30 Do all have gifts of healing?
Do all speak in tongues[a]?[l] Do all interpret?
31 Now eagerly desire[m] the greater gifts.

Love Is Indispensable

And yet I will show you the most excellent way.

13 If I speak in the tongues[b][n] of men
or of angels, but do not have love,
I am only a resounding gong or a clanging cymbal. 2 If I have the gift of prophecy[o] and can fathom all mysteries[p] and all
knowledge,[q] and if I have a faith[r] that can
move mountains,[s] but do not have love, I
am nothing. 3 If I give all I possess to the
poor[t] and give over my body to hardship
that I may boast,[c][u] but do not have love, I
gain nothing.

4 Love is patient,[v] love is kind. It does
not envy, it does not boast, it is not
proud.[w] 5 It does not dishonor others, it is
not self-seeking,[x] it is not easily angered,[y]
it keeps no record of wrongs.[z] 6 Love does
not delight in evil[a] but rejoices with the
truth.[b] 7 It always protects, always trusts,
always hopes, always perseveres.[c]
8 Love never fails. But where there are
prophecies,[d] they will cease; where there
are tongues,[e] they will be stilled; where
there is knowledge, it will pass away. 9 For
we know in part[f] and we prophesy in part,
10 but when completeness comes,[g] what is
in part disappears. 11 When I was a child,
I talked like a child, I thought like a child,
I reasoned like a child. When I became a
man, I put the ways of childhood[h] behind
me. 12 For now we see only a reflection as
in a mirror;[i] then we shall see face to face.[j]

[a] 30 Or *other languages* [b] 1 Or *languages*
[c] 3 Some manuscripts *body to the flames*

12:27 [e]S Ro 12:5 **12:28** [f]S 1Co 10:32 [g]S Eph 4:11 [h]S Eph 4:11 [i]ver 9 [j]Ro 12:6-8 [k]ver 10; S Mk 16:17 **12:30** [l]ver 10 **12:31** [m]1Co 14:1,39 **13:1** [n]ver 8; S Mk 16:17 **13:2** [o]ver 8; S Eph 4:11; S Ac 11:27 [p]1Co 14:2 [q]S 2Co 8:7 [r]1Co 12:9 [s]Mt 17:20; 21:21 **13:3** [t]Lk 19:8; S Ac 2:45 [u]Da 3:28 **13:4** [v]1Th 5:14 [w]1Co 5:2 **13:5** [x]S 1Co 10:24 [y]S Mt 5:22 [z]Job 14:16,17; Pr 10:12; 17:9; 1Pe 4:8 **13:6** [a]2Th 2:12 [b]2Jn 4; 3Jn 3,4 **13:7** [c]ver 8,13 **13:8** [d]ver 2 [e]ver 1 **13:9** [f]ver 12; S 1Co 8:2 **13:10** [g]Php 3:12 **13:11** [h]Ps 131:2 **13:12** [i]Job 26:14; 36:26 [j]Ge 32:30; Job 19:26; 1Jn 3:2

12:28 The list here differs somewhat from that in vv. 8 – 10 (see notes there). Paul notes three of the gifts of Eph 4:11 (see note there), then five of the spiritual gifts listed in vv. 8 – 10. The apostles and prophets were part of the foundation of the church (see Mt 16:18; Eph 2:20 and notes), and teaching was associated with the pastoral office (see Eph 4:11 and note; 1Ti 3:2). These three gifts are listed as "first," "second" and "third," indicating their importance in the church. The rest of the list is introduced with "then," indicating the variety that follows. Paul's lists of spiritual gifts seem to be largely random samples. Apart from v. 28a he does not rank them in importance since he has already insisted that all gifts are important (vv. 21 – 26). *apostles.* Those chosen by Christ during his earthly ministry to be with him and to go out and preach (Mk 3:14). They were also to be witnesses of the resurrection (Ac 1:21 – 22). The term was occasionally used in a broader sense (see Mk 6:30; Ac 14:4 and notes). *miracles … healing … tongues.* See notes on vv. 9 – 10. *helping.* Any act of helping others may be the product of a spiritual gift (see Ro 12:6 – 8 and notes), though the primary reference here is probably to a ministry to the poor, needy, sick and distressed (cf. Ac 6:1 – 6). *guidance.* Those with the gift of guidance (or administration) were enabled by the Holy Spirit to organize and project plans and spiritual programs in the church.

12:29 – 30 *Are all apostles …?* Expects a negative answer. Christians have different gifts, and no one gift should be expected by everyone, nor should one person be expected to have all the gifts.

12:31 *eagerly desire the greater gifts.* See 14:1 – 5 and notes. *the most excellent way.* Paul now shows the right way to exercise all spiritual gifts — the way of love. He does not identify love as a gift; rather, it is a fruit of the Spirit (Gal 5:22).

13:1 – 3 *tongues … prophecy … faith … give.* Paul selects four gifts as examples. He declares that even their most spectacular manifestations mean nothing unless motivated by love.

13:1 *tongues of men or of angels.* Paul uses hyperbole. Even if he could speak not only the various languages of human beings but even the languages used by angels — if he did not speak in love, it would be nothing but noise. *love.* The Greek for this word (*agape*) indicates a selfless concern for the welfare of others. It is like Christ's love manifested on the cross (cf. Jn 3:16; 13:34 – 35; Eph 5:25; 1Jn 3:16).

13:2 *all mysteries and all knowledge.* Again Paul uses hyperbole to express the amount of understanding possessed. Even if he is gifted with unlimited knowledge — if he does not possess and exercise that knowledge in love, he is nothing. *faith that can move mountains.* A special capacity to trust God to remove or overcome overwhelming threats or insurmountable obstacles (cf. Zec 4:7; Mt 17:20 and notes). Again Paul uses hyperbole.

13:3 *give over my body to hardship.* A reference to bodily sufferings (cf. 2Co 11:23 – 29; 12:10 and notes; cf. also NIV text note). Even such suffering, if not motivated by love, accomplishes nothing.

13:4 – 7 Love is now described both positively and negatively.

13:4 *not proud.* See 8:1 and note.

13:5 *It does not dishonor others.* Perhaps an indirect reference to their unruly and dishonorable conduct in worship (11:18 – 22).

13:6 *does not delight in evil.* As they were doing in ch. 5.

13:8 *never fails.* Never comes to an end, is never replaced by anything else (see v. 13 and note). *prophecies … will cease; … tongues … will be stilled; … knowledge … will pass away.* These three will cease because they are limited in nature (v. 9) and will be unnecessary when what is complete has come (v. 10).

13:10 *completeness.* The Greek for this word can mean "end," "fulfillment," "completeness" or "maturity." In this context the contrast is between the partial and the complete. Verse 12 seems to indicate that Paul is here speaking of either Christ's second coming or a believer's death, when they will see Christ "face to face" (v. 12).

13:12 *we see only a reflection as in a mirror.* The imagery is of a polished metal (probably bronze) mirror in which one could perceive only an imperfect reflection (cf. Jas 1:23) — in contrast to seeing the Lord directly and clearly in the new creation. *know fully … fully known.* The Christian will know the Lord to the fullest extent possible for a finite being, similar to the way the Lord knows the Christian — fully and

Now I know in part; then I shall know fully, even as I am fully known.[k]
13 And now these three remain: faith, hope and love.[l] But the greatest of these is love.[m]

Intelligibility in Worship

14 Follow the way of love[n] and eagerly desire[o] gifts of the Spirit,[p] especially prophecy.[q] 2 For anyone who speaks in a tongue[a][r] does not speak to people but to God. Indeed, no one understands them;[s] they utter mysteries[t] by the Spirit. 3 But the one who prophesies speaks to people for their strengthening,[u] encouraging[v] and comfort. 4 Anyone who speaks in a tongue[w] edifies[x] themselves, but the one who prophesies[y] edifies the church. 5 I would like every one of you to speak in tongues,[b] but I would rather have you prophesy.[z] The one who prophesies is greater than the one who speaks in tongues,[b] unless someone interprets, so that the church may be edified.[a]

6 Now, brothers and sisters, if I come to you and speak in tongues, what good will I be to you, unless I bring you some revelation[b] or knowledge[c] or prophecy or word of instruction?[d] 7 Even in the case of lifeless things that make sounds, such as the pipe or harp, how will anyone know what tune is being played unless there is a distinction in the notes? 8 Again, if the trumpet does not sound a clear call, who will get ready for battle?[e] 9 So it is with you. Unless you speak intelligible words with your tongue, how will anyone know what you are saying? You will just be speaking into the air. 10 Undoubtedly there are all sorts of languages in the world, yet none of them is without meaning. 11 If then I do not grasp the meaning of what someone is saying, I am a foreigner to the speaker, and the speaker is a foreigner to me.[f] 12 So it is with you. Since you are eager for gifts of the Spirit,[g] try to excel in those that build up[h] the church.

13 For this reason the one who speaks in a tongue should pray that they may interpret what they say.[i] 14 For if I pray in a tongue, my spirit prays,[j] but my mind is unfruitful. 15 So what shall I do? I will pray with my spirit,[k] but I will also pray

13:12 [k] 1Co 8:3; Gal 4:9 **13:13** [l] Ro 5:2-5; Gal 5:5,6; Eph 4:2-5; Col 1:4,5; 1Th 1:3; 5:8; Heb 6:10-12 [m] Mt 22:37-40; 1Co 16:14; Gal 5:6; 1Jn 4:7-12,16 **14:1** [n] 1Co 16:14 [o] ver 39; 1Co 12:31 [p] S 1Co 12:1 [q] ver 39; S Eph 4:11 **14:2** [r] S Mk 16:17 [s] ver 6-11,16 [t] 1Co 13:2 **14:3** [u] ver 4, 5,12,17,26; S Ro 14:19 [v] ver 31 **14:4** [w] S Mk 16:17 [x] S ver 3 [y] S 1Co 13:2 **14:5** [z] Nu 11:29 [a] S ver 3 **14:6** [b] ver 26; Eph 1:17 [c] S 2Co 8:7 [d] Ro 6:17 **14:8** [e] Nu 10:9; Jer 4:19 **14:11** [f] Ge 11:7

[a] 2 Or *in another language*; also in verses 4, 13, 14, 19, 26 and 27 [b] 5 Or *in other languages*; also in verses 6, 18, 22, 23 and 39

14:12 [g] S 1Co 12:1 [h] S ver 3 **14:13** [i] ver 5 **14:14** [j] ver 2 **14:15** [k] ver 2,14

---

infinitely. This will not be true until the Lord returns or the believer sees him "face to face" at death.

13:13 *remain.* Now and forever. *faith, hope and love.* See 1Th 1:3 and note. *the greatest of these is love.* True because God is love (1Jn 4:8) and has communicated his love to us (1Jn 4:10) and commands us to love one another (Jn 13:34–35; cf. Ro 13:10; 1Co 8:1; Gal 5:6; Eph 4:16; 5:20; Php 1:9; Col 3:14; 1Pe 4:8). Love supersedes the gifts because it outlasts them all. Long after these sought-after gifts are no longer necessary, love will still be the governing principle that controls all that God and his redeemed people are and do.

14:1–5 The basic principle Paul insists on is that whatever is done in the church must contribute to the edification (building up) of the body. This is in keeping with the declaration in 12:7 that gifts are "given for the common good." It also is in agreement with the principle of love (ch. 13). What is spoken in the church, then, must be intelligible—it must be spoken in the vernacular language or at least be interpreted in the vernacular. Prophecy is therefore more desirable than tongues (unless an interpreter is present) because prophecy is spoken in the native language of the listeners.

14:1 *way of love … gifts of the Spirit.* Love is the means by which such gifts are made effective. *prophecy.* See note on 12:10.

14:2 *tongue.* See NIV text note. The hearers cannot understand what those who speak in a tongue are saying. Therefore what they say is a mystery unless it is interpreted. Only God understands it.

14:3 In prophesying the speaker can strengthen, encourage and comfort others (see 12:7 and note).

14:4 *edifies themselves.* It is a personal edification in the area of the emotions, of deepening conviction, of fuller commitment and greater love.

14:5 *like … you to speak in tongues.* Paul was not opposed to tongues-speaking if it was practiced properly. *The one who prophesies is greater.* Because those who prophesy serve the common good more effectively since what they say can be understood and thus edifies the church. *unless someone interprets.* If speakers in tongues also have the gift of interpretation, their speaking is as beneficial as prophecy, for then it can be understood (see v. 13).

14:6 *what good will I be …?* It would be useless to speak in tongues unless, by interpretation, one brings the church something understandable and edifying.

14:7 *pipe or harp.* Instruments that were well known in Greece. *distinction in the notes.* For a person to recognize the tune and to understand and appreciate it, there must be a variety of notes so arranged as to create a meaningful tune. One note repeated monotonously cannot accomplish this.

14:8 *trumpet … ready for battle.* All Greeks would be acquainted with the use of the trumpet for battle signals (cf. Homer's *Iliad,* 18.219), and the Jews would be familiar with the use of the ram's horn (Nu 10:9; Jos 6:4,9). Again, the notes sounded must convey a message.

14:9 *speak intelligible words.* Speak in the vernacular language of the listeners rather than in a tongue (or else provide an interpretation).

14:10 *all sorts of languages.* Some see vv. 10–11 as an indication that the tongues of chs. 12–14 were languages otherwise unknown to the speakers.

14:12 *excel in those that build up the church.* The basic principle of ch. 14.

14:14 *mind is unfruitful.* When a person speaks in tongues or prays in tongues, the human mind does not produce the language.

14:15–17 *pray … sing … praising God … say "Amen" … thanksgiving.* Elements employed in OT (1Ch 16:36; Ne 5:13; 8:6; Ps 104:33; 136:1; 148:1) and NT (Ro 11:36; Eph 5:18–20) worship. "Amen," meaning "It is true" or "So be it," is the believer's confession of agreement with and commitment to the words spoken (see Ro 1:25 and note). Thus it is important that a message in tongues be interpreted.

14:15 *pray with my spirit … with my understanding … sing with my spirit … with my understanding.* May mean that Paul will

with my understanding; I will sing[l] with
my spirit, but I will also sing with my understanding. 16 Otherwise when you are
praising God in the Spirit, how can someone else, who is now put in the position of
an inquirer,[a] say "Amen"[m] to your thanksgiving,[n] since they do not know what you
are saying? 17 You are giving thanks well
enough, but no one else is edified.[o]
18 I thank God that I speak in tongues
more than all of you. 19 But in the church I
would rather speak five intelligible words
to instruct others than ten thousand words
in a tongue.[p]
20 Brothers and sisters, stop thinking like
children.[q] In regard to evil be infants,[r] but
in your thinking be adults. 21 In the Law[s]
it is written:

"With other tongues
and through the lips of foreigners
I will speak to this people,
but even then they will not listen
to me,[t]
says the Lord."[b]

22 Tongues, then, are a sign, not for believers but for unbelievers; prophecy,[u]
however, is not for unbelievers but for
believers. 23 So if the whole church comes
together and everyone speaks in tongues,
and inquirers or unbelievers come in,

14:15 [l] S Eph 5:19 **14:16** [m] Dt 27:15-26; 1Ch 16:36; Ne 8:6; Ps 106:48; Rev 5:14; 7:12 [n] S Mt 14:19; 1Co 11:24 **14:17** [o] S ver 3 **14:19** [p] ver 6 **14:20** [q] 1Co 3:11; Eph 4:14; Heb 5:12, 13; 1Pe 2:2 [r] Jer 4:22; Mt 10:16; Ro 16:19 **14:21** [s] ver 34; S Jn 10:34 [t] Dt 28:49; Isa 28:11,12 **14:22** [u] ver 1 **14:23** [v] Ac 2:13 **14:25** [w] Ro 2:16 [x] Isa 45:14; Zec 8:23 **14:26** [y] S Ro 7:1 [z] 1Co 12:7-10 [a] S Eph 5:19 [b] ver 6 [c] ver 2 [d] 1Co 12:10 [e] S Ro 14:19 **14:29** [f] ver 32, 37; S 1Co 13:2 [g] 1Co 12:10

will they not say that you are out of your
mind?[v] 24 But if an unbeliever or an inquirer comes in while everyone is prophesying, they are convicted of sin and are
brought under judgment by all, 25 as the
secrets[w] of their hearts are laid bare. So
they will fall down and worship God, exclaiming, "God is really among you!"[x]

Good Order in Worship

26 What then shall we say, brothers and
sisters?[y] When you come together, each of
you[z] has a hymn,[a] or a word of instruction,[b] a revelation, a tongue[c] or an interpretation.[d] Everything must be done so
that the church may be built up.[e] 27 If anyone speaks in a tongue, two—or at the
most three—should speak, one at a time,
and someone must interpret. 28 If there is
no interpreter, the speaker should keep
quiet in the church and speak to himself
and to God.
29 Two or three prophets[f] should speak,
and the others should weigh carefully
what is said.[g] 30 And if a revelation comes
to someone who is sitting down, the first
speaker should stop. 31 For you can all
prophesy in turn so that everyone may be

[a] *16* The Greek word for *inquirer* is a technical term for someone not fully initiated into a religion; also in verses 23 and 24. [b] *21* Isaiah 28:11,12

---

sometimes pray or sing with his spirit in a tongue; at other times he will pray or sing with his understanding in his own language. Others believe that Paul was declaring his intention to pray or sing with both understanding and spirit at the same time.

14:19 *But in the church.* Some believe that an interpretation is unnecessary when the gift of tongues is being used as a private prayer language. They base such a distinction on v. 18 (see v. 14) when compared with the phrase "in the church."

14:20 *In regard to evil be infants.* Just as in the case of infants, have no evil desires or wrong motives in wanting to excel in spiritual gifts (such as speaking in tongues) as an end in itself.

14:21–22 The passage from Isa 28 indicates that the foreign language of the Assyrians was a sign to unbelieving Israel that judgment was coming on them. Paul deduced from this fact that tongues were intended to be a sign of judgment for unbelievers (cf. v. 22 and note), as, e.g., in Ac 2:4–12. Similarly, prophecy was for the benefit of believers (v. 22) since it communicated revealed truth to those disposed to receive it (cf. Mt 13:11–16).

14:21 *the Law.* See Jn 10:34; 12:34 and note; 15:25; Ro 3:19 and note.

14:22 *Tongues ... a sign, not for believers.* Because they do not need a sign of God's judgment as unbelievers do.

14:23 *inquirers.* Perhaps those who had become "inquirers" concerning the gospel but as yet did not really understand (see v. 16 and NIV text note there). *unbelievers.* Those who have made no movement toward saving faith. The context is a meeting of the church in which everyone is speaking in tongues, with the result that general confusion reigns. *out of your mind.* The visitors will be repulsed by the confusion, and the phenomenon meant to be an impressive sign will have a negative effect on the unsaved.

14:24 *everyone is prophesying.* Prophecy, spoken in the vernacular language and intended for believers, turns out to have a positive effect on unbelievers because they hear and understand and are convicted of their sins. (Yet see restrictions on prophesying in vv. 29–32 and notes there.)

14:26–27 *each of you ... anyone ... someone.* The stress here is again on the diversity and yet complementary nature of spiritual gifts. It is also apparent that every member could participate in worship, not just certain leaders or officers.

14:26 *a hymn, or a word of instruction, a revelation, a tongue or an interpretation.* Elements that made up the worship service at Corinth (see note on vv. 15–17). Some of these elements (the hymn and the word of instruction) came from OT and synagogue worship (see Lk 4:16–22). All parts of Christian worship should be edifying to the church ("that the church may be built up").

14:27–28 Three restrictions are placed on speaking in a tongue "in the church" (v. 28): (1) Only two or three should do so in a meeting. (2) They should do so one at a time. (3) There must be interpretation.

14:28 *the speaker should keep quiet.* The implication seems to be that it was up to the one speaking in a tongue in the Corinthian church to make certain that there was in the audience someone to interpret his message.

14:29 *Two or three prophets should speak.* Apparently in turn (v. 31), as with those who speak in tongues (v. 27). *weigh carefully.* Judge. The prophets themselves were to decide whether the messages of their fellow prophets were valid (see note on v. 32).

14:30 *a revelation.* Prophecies referred to in chs. 12–14 could come through any member of the church (vv. 26,29–31) and were intended for particular persons in particular circumstances; the "revelation" they contained could be a prediction (Agabus, Ac 11:28; 21:10–11), a divine directive (Ac 13:1–2) or a message designed to strengthen, encourage or comfort (v. 3).

instructed and encouraged. 32 The spirits
of prophets are subject to the control of
prophets.[h] 33 For God is not a God of disorder[i] but of peace[j]—as in all the congregations[k] of the Lord's people.[l]
34 Women[a] should remain silent in the
churches. They are not allowed to speak,[m]
but must be in submission,[n] as the law[o]
says. 35 If they want to inquire about something, they should ask their own husbands
at home; for it is disgraceful for a woman
to speak in the church.[b]
36 Or did the word of God[p] originate
with you? Or are you the only people it
has reached? 37 If anyone thinks they are a
prophet[q] or otherwise gifted by the Spirit,[r]
let them acknowledge that what I am writing to you is the Lord's command.[s] 38 But if
anyone ignores this, they will themselves
be ignored.[c]
39 Therefore, my brothers and sisters,
be eager[t] to prophesy,[u] and do not forbid speaking in tongues. 40 But everything
should be done in a fitting and orderly[v]
way.

The Resurrection of Christ

15 Now, brothers and sisters, I want
to remind you of the gospel[w] I
preached to you,[x] which you received and
on which you have taken your stand. 2 By
this gospel you are saved,[y] if you hold
firmly[z] to the word I preached to you. Otherwise, you have believed in vain.
3 For what I received[a] I passed on to you[b]
as of first importance[d]: that Christ died
for our sins[c] according to the Scriptures,[d]
4 that he was buried,[e] that he was raised[f]

14:32 [h] 1Jn 4:1 **14:33** [i] ver 40 [j] S Ro 15:33 [k] S 1Co 7:17; S 10:32 [l] S Ac 9:13 **14:34** [m] 1Co 11:5,13 [n] S Eph 5:22; 1Ti 2:11,12 [o] ver 21; Ge 3:16 **14:36** [p] S Heb 4:12 **14:37** [q] S Ac 11:27; 1Co 13:2; 2Co 10:7 [r] 1Co 2:15; S 12:1 [s] 1Jn 4:6 **14:39** [t] ver 1; 1Co 12:31 [u] ver 1; S Eph 4:11 **14:40** [v] ver 33; Col 2:5 **15:1** [w] Isa 40:9; Ro 2:16 [x] S 1Co 3:6; S Gal 1:8 **15:2** [y] Ro 1:16 [z] S Ro 11:22 **15:3** [a] Gal 1:12 [b] S 1Co 11:2 [c] Isa 53:5; Jn 1:29; S Gal 1:4; 1Pe 2:24 [d] S Mt 26:24; S Lk 24:27; S 24:44; Ac 17:2; 26:22,23 **15:4** [e] Mt 27:59,60 [f] S Ac 2:24

[a] 33,34 Or *peace. As in all the congregations of the Lord's people, 34women* [b] 34,35 In a few manuscripts these verses come after verse 40. [c] 38 Some manuscripts *But anyone who is ignorant of this will be ignorant* [d] 3 Or *you at the first*

14:32 *control of prophets.* Prophecy (and tongues as well) was not an uncontrollable emotional ecstasy. Paul insists that these gifts should be controlled by the recipients themselves (vv. 15,26–32). See notes on vv. 27–29.
14:33 *God ... of peace.* See 1Th 5:23 and note. *disorder.* Paul was concerned that disorderly and unregulated worship at Corinth would bring discredit on the name of the God who had called them in Christ to peace and unity. *in all the congregations of the Lord's people.* A unique expression in the NT that stresses the universality and commonality of the whole visible church of God on earth. All congregations are to obey the directives that follow.
14:34–35 See note on 11:3–16. Some believe that in light of 11:3 there is a God-ordained order that is to be the basis for administration and authority. Women are to be in submission to their husbands, both at home (see Eph 5:22) and in the church (see v. 34; 1Ti 2:11–12), regardless of their particular culture. According to this view, a timeless order was established at creation (see note on 11:5–6).

Others maintain that Paul's concern here is that the church be strengthened (v. 26) by believers showing respect for others (see vv. 30–31) and for God (see v. 33) as they exercise their spiritual gifts. Such respect must necessarily take account of accepted social practices. If within a particular social order it is considered disgraceful for a woman to speak in church—and it was in this case (v. 35)—then she shows disrespect by doing so and should remain silent. There were occasions, though—even in their culture—for women to speak in church. For example, in 11:5 Paul assumes that women pray and prophesy in public worship. Thus his purpose, according to this view, was not to define the role of women but to establish a fitting (vv. 34–35) and orderly (vv. 27–31) way of worship (v. 40).

Still others say that in this context Paul is discussing primarily the disruption of worship by women who become involved in noisy discussions surrounding tongues-speaking and prophecy. Instead of publicly clamoring for explanations, the wives were to discuss matters with their husbands at home (cf. v. 35). Paul does not altogether forbid women to speak in church (see 11:5). What he is forbidding is the disorderly speaking indicated in these verses.
14:34 *as the law says.* Cf. Ge 3:16; 1Pe 3:6 and note.
14:36 Paul asks these rhetorical questions sarcastically, suggesting that the Corinthians were following their own practice in these matters rather than conforming to God's word.
14:37 *the Lord's command.* Paul's commands are the Lord's commands and are to be followed. In a situation where so much stress was being placed on gifts, Paul insists that any genuinely gifted person will recognize the apostle's God-given authority.
14:38 *will themselves be ignored.* By Paul and the churches, or by God.
14:39 *brothers and sisters.* See NIV text note on 1:10. *do not forbid speaking in tongues.* Paul's solution to the tongues problem in the Corinthian church was not to forbid tongues but to correct the improper use of the gift.
14:40 *a fitting and orderly way.* As spelled out in vv. 26–35.
15:1–58 When Paul began this letter to the Corinthians, he foregrounded the cross of Christ (1:17–18)—"we preach Christ crucified" (1:23); "I resolved to know nothing while I was with you except Jesus Christ and him crucified" (2:2; cf. 15:3–4). Now, as he nears the end of his letter, he develops at length the essential truth of Christ's resurrection, a reality assumed throughout the letter as a whole.
15:1,50 *brothers and sisters.* See NIV text note on 1:10.
15:1 *gospel.* See note on Mk 1:1.
15:2 *if you hold firmly.* See Heb 3:14 and note. *believed in vain.* The gospel Paul preached is the good news of victory over sin through the saving effects of Christ's death by crucifixion and of his triumph over death in his resurrection. "Christ crucified" (1:23) and "raised from the dead" (15:20) is the only hope for sinful mortals to "inherit the kingdom of God" (v. 50; see vv. 53–57).
15:3 *what I received I passed on to you as of first importance.* Here Paul links himself with early Christian tradition. He was not its originator, nor did he receive it directly from the Lord. His source was other Christians. The verbs he uses are technical terms for receiving and transmitting tradition (see note on 11:23). What follows is the heart of the gospel: that Christ died for our sins (not for his own sins; cf. Heb 7:27), that he was buried (confirmation that he had really died) and that he was raised from the dead. *according to the Scriptures.* Paul probably had in mind Isa 53:5–6,11–12, but he may also have been thinking of the Passover sacrifice and other sin offerings of the OT sacrificial system (see chart, p. 164).
15:4 *on the third day.* Cf. Mt 12:40. The Jews counted parts of

on the third day[g] according to the Scriptures,[h] 5 and that he appeared to Cephas,[a][i]
and then to the Twelve.[j] 6 After that, he appeared to more than five hundred of the
brothers and sisters at the same time, most
of whom are still living, though some
have fallen asleep.[k] 7 Then he appeared to
James,[l] then to all the apostles,[m] 8 and last
of all he appeared to me also,[n] as to one
abnormally born.

9 For I am the least of the apostles[o] and
do not even deserve to be called an apostle, because I persecuted[p] the church of
God.[q] 10 But by the grace[r] of God I am what
I am, and his grace to me[s] was not without effect. No, I worked harder than all
of them[t]—yet not I, but the grace of God
that was with me.[u] 11 Whether, then, it is I
or they,[v] this is what we preach, and this
is what you believed.

The Resurrection of the Dead

12 But if it is preached that Christ has
been raised from the dead,[w] how can
some of you say that there is no resurrection[x] of the dead?[y] 13 If there is no resurrection of the dead, then not even Christ has
been raised. 14 And if Christ has not been
raised,[z] our preaching is useless and so is
your faith. 15 More than that, we are then
found to be false witnesses about God, for
we have testified about God that he raised
Christ from the dead.[a] But he did not raise
him if in fact the dead are not raised. 16 For
if the dead are not raised, then Christ has
not been raised either. 17 And if Christ
has not been raised, your faith is futile;
you are still in your sins.[b] 18 Then those
also who have fallen asleep[c] in Christ are
lost. 19 If only for this life we have hope
in Christ, we are of all people most to be
pitied.[d]

20 But Christ has indeed been raised
from the dead,[e] the firstfruits[f] of those
who have fallen asleep.[g] 21 For since death
came through a man,[h] the resurrection of
the dead[i] comes also through a man. 22 For
as in Adam all die, so in Christ all will be
made alive.[j] 23 But each in turn: Christ, the
firstfruits;[k] then, when he comes,[l] those
who belong to him.[m] 24 Then the end will
come, when he hands over the kingdom[n]

[a] 5 That is, Peter

15:4 [g] S Mt 16:21 [h] Jn 2:21,22; Ac 2:25,30,31 **15:5** [i] Lk 24:34 [j] Mk 16:14; Lk 24:36-43 **15:6** [k] ver 18, 20; S Mt 9:24 **15:7** [l] S Ac 15:13 [m] Lk 24:33,36, 37; Ac 1:3,4 **15:8** [n] Ac 9:3-6, 17; 1Co 9:1; Gal 1:16 **15:9** [o] 2Co 12:11; Eph 3:8; 1Ti 1:15 [p] S Ac 8:3 [q] S 1Co 10:32 **15:10** [r] S Ro 3:24 [s] S Ro 12:3 [t] 2Co 11:23; Col 1:29 [u] S Php 2:13 **15:11** [v] Gal 2:6 **15:12** [w] ver 4 [x] S Jn 11:24 [y] Ac 17:32; 23:8; 2Ti 2:18 **15:14** [z] 1Th 4:14 **15:15** [a] S Ac 2:24 **15:17** [b] S Ro 4:25 **15:18** [c] ver 6, 20; S Mt 9:24 **15:19** [d] S 1Co 4:9 **15:20** [e] 1Pe 1:3 [f] ver 23; S Ac 26:23 [g] ver 6,18; S Mt 9:24 **15:21** [h] S Ro 5:12 [i] ver 12 **15:22** [j] Ro 5:14-18; S 1Co 6:14 **15:23** [k] ver 20 [l] ver 52; S 1Th 2:19 [m] S 1Co 3:23 **15:24** [n] Da 2:44; 7:14,27; 2Pe 1:11

---

days as whole days. Thus the three days would include part of Friday afternoon, all of Saturday, and Sunday morning. A similar way of reckoning time is seen in Jn 20:26 (lit. "after eight days," NIV "a week later"); two Sundays are implied, one at each end of the expression. *according to the Scriptures.* Here Paul may have had in mind Ps 16:8–11; Isa 53:10–12; cf. Jnh 1:17; Lk 24:44 and note.

15:5–8 Six resurrection appearances of Christ are listed here. The Gospels tell of others (see chart, p. 1754).

15:5 *Cephas … the Twelve.* See NIV text note. The appearance to Peter is the one mentioned in Lk 24:34, which occurred on Easter Sunday. The appearance to the Twelve seems to have taken place on Sunday evening (see Lk 24:36–43; Jn 20:19–23). "The Twelve" seems to be a conventional way of referring to the group of original apostles, even though Judas was no longer with them.

15:6 *more than five hundred … at the same time.* This appearance may be the one in Galilee recorded in Mt 28:10,16–20, where the Eleven and possibly more met the risen Lord. *some have fallen asleep.* See Jn 11:11; 1Th 4:13 and notes.

15:7 *James.* Since this James is listed in addition to the apostles, he is not James the son of Zebedee or James the son of Alphaeus (Mt 10:2–3). This is James, the half brother of Jesus (Mt 13:55), who did not believe in Christ before the resurrection (Jn 7:5) but afterward joined the apostolic band (Ac 1:14) and later became prominent in the Jerusalem church (Ac 15:13). It is not clear in Scripture when and where this appearance to James occurred. *to all the apostles.* Probably the same as "the Twelve" in v. 5 (but see also Ac 1:6–11).

15:8 *last of all.* See Ac 9:1–8. This appearance to Paul came several years after the resurrection (perhaps c. AD 33). *one abnormally born.* Paul was not part of the original group of apostles. He had not lived with Christ as the others had. His entry into the apostolic office was thus not "normal." Furthermore, at his conversion he was abruptly snatched from his former way of life (Ac 9:3–6).

15:9 *I persecuted.* See 1Ti 1:13 and note. *church of God.* In persecuting the church, he was actually persecuting Christ (see Ac 9:4 and note).

15:12–19 Some at Corinth were saying that there was no resurrection of the body, and Paul draws out the implications of this false contention.

15:12 *Christ has been raised.* Paul uses the same verb form (that expresses the certainty of Christ's bodily resurrection) a total of seven times in this passage (vv. 4,12,13,14,16,17,20).

15:19 If faith in Christ brings benefits only for the present life and not deliverance from the ultimate "wages of sin" (Ro 6:23), then believers are worse off (because they are deluded) than those who live "without hope and without God in the world" (Eph 2:12).

15:20 *But Christ has indeed been raised.* Paul's categorical conclusion based on his evidence set forth in vv. 3–8. *firstfruits.* The first sheaf of the harvest given to the Lord as a token that all the harvest belonged to him and would be dedicated to him through dedicated lives (see Ex 23:19; Lev 2:12 and notes). So Christ, who has been raised, is the guarantee of the resurrection of all of God's redeemed people (cf. 1Th 4:13–18 and notes).

15:21 *death came through a man.* Through Adam (see Ge 3:17–19; Ro 5:12 and note). *the resurrection of the dead comes also through a man.* Through Christ, the second Adam, "the last Adam" (v. 45; cf. Ro 5:12–21 and note).

15:22 *in Adam all die.* All who are "in Adam"—i.e., his descendants—suffer death. *in Christ all will be made alive.* All who are "in Christ"—i.e., who are related to him by faith—will be made alive at the resurrection (cf. Jn 5:25; Ro 5:17–18; 1Th 4:16–17 and note; Rev 20:6).

15:23 *each in turn.* Christ, the firstfruits, was raised in his own time in history (c. AD 30), and those who are identified with Christ by faith will be raised at his second coming. His resurrection is the pledge that ours will follow.

15:24 *the end.* The second coming of Christ and all the events accompanying it. This includes his handing

to God the Father after he has destroyed
all dominion, authority and power.[o] 25 For
he must reign[p] until he has put all his enemies under his feet.[q] 26 The last enemy to
be destroyed is death.[r] 27 For he "has put
everything under his feet."[a][s] Now when it
says that "everything" has been put under
him, it is clear that this does not include
God himself, who put everything under
Christ.[t] 28 When he has done this, then the
Son himself will be made subject to him
who put everything under him,[u] so that
God may be all in all.[v]

29 Now if there is no resurrection, what
will those do who are baptized for the dead?
If the dead are not raised at all, why are
people baptized for them? 30 And as for us,
why do we endanger ourselves every hour?[w]
31 I face death every day[x]—yes, just as surely as I boast about you in Christ Jesus our
Lord. 32 If I fought wild beasts[y] in Ephesus[z]
with no more than human hopes, what
have I gained? If the dead are not raised,

> "Let us eat and drink,
> for tomorrow we die."[b][a]

33 Do not be misled:[b] "Bad company corrupts good character."[c][c] 34 Come back to
your senses as you ought, and stop sinning; for there are some who are ignorant
of God[d]—I say this to your shame.[e]

The Resurrection Body

35 But someone will ask,[f] "How are the
dead raised? With what kind of body will
they come?"[g] 36 How foolish![h] What you
sow does not come to life unless it dies.[i]
37 When you sow, you do not plant the
body that will be, but just a seed, perhaps
of wheat or of something else. 38 But God
gives it a body as he has determined, and
to each kind of seed he gives its own body.[j]
39 Not all flesh is the same: People have
one kind of flesh, animals have another,

15:24 [o] Ro 8:38
15:25 [p] Isa 9:7; 52:7 [q] ver 27; S Mt 22:44
15:26 [r] 2Ti 1:10; Rev 20:14; 21:4
15:27 [s] ver 25; Ps 8:6; S Mt 22:44 [t] S Mt 28:18
15:28 [u] Php 3:21 [v] 1Co 3:23
15:30 [w] 2Co 11:26
15:31 [x] S Ro 8:36
15:32 [y] 2Co 1:8 [z] S Ac 18:19 [a] Isa 22:13; Lk 12:19
15:33 [b] S 1Co 6:9 [c] Pr 22:24,25
15:34 [d] S Gal 4:8 [e] S 1Co 4:14
15:35 [f] Ro 9:19 [g] Eze 37:3
15:36 [h] Lk 11:40; 12:20 [i] Jn 12:24
15:38 [j] Ge 1:11

[a] *27* Psalm 8:6 [b] *32* Isaiah 22:13 [c] *33* From the Greek poet Menander

---

over the kingdom to the Father, following his destroying all dominion, authority and power of the persons and forces opposing him.

15:25 *For he must reign.* During this process of Christ's destroying all dominion and handing over the kingdom to the Father, Christ must reign (Rev 20:1–6). Some take this to mean that Christ will literally reign with his people for 1,000 years on the earth (cf. Isa 2:2–4; Mic 4:1–5). Others believe that this refers to Christ's reign over the course of history and in the lives of his people, who are spiritually raised, or born again. This reign is viewed as continuing throughout the present age. *under his feet.* An OT figure for complete conquest. Verse 25 is an allusion to Ps 110:1 (cf. Mt 22:44; Ac 2:34; Heb 1:13 and notes).

15:26 *last enemy.* For death as enemy, see Ps 49:14; Jer 9:21 and notes. The final destruction of death (cf. 2Ti 1:10) will occur as the climax of events when Christ returns (see Rev 20:14; 21:4).

15:27 *everything under his feet.* An allusion to Ps 8:6. For another reading of Ps 8 as ultimately a word about Jesus Christ, see Heb 2:5–9 and notes.

15:28 *the Son himself will be made subject to him.* The Son will be made subject to the Father in the sense that, administratively, after he subjects all things to his power he will then turn it all over to God the Father, the administrative head. This is not to suggest that the Son is in any way inferior to the Father. All three persons of the Trinity are equal in deity and in dignity. The subordination referred to is one of function (see Jn 4:34; 5:19; 7:16 and notes). The Father is supreme in the Trinity; the Son carries out the Father's will; the Spirit is sent by the Father and the Son to vitalize life, communicate God's truth, apply his salvation to people and enable them to obey God's will. *so that God may be all in all.* The triune God will be shown to be supreme and sovereign in all things (cf. 3:21 and note).

15:29 *those ... who are baptized for the dead.* The present tense suggests that at Corinth people were currently being baptized for the dead. But because Paul does not give any more information about the practice, many attempts have been made to interpret the concept. Three of these are: (1) Living believers were being baptized for believers who died before they were baptized, so that they too, in this way, would not miss out on baptism. (2) Christians were being baptized in anticipation of the resurrection of the dead. (3) New converts were being baptized to fill the ranks of Christians who had died. At any rate, Paul mentions this custom almost in passing, using it in his arguments substantiating the resurrection of the dead but without necessarily approving the practice. The passage will likely remain obscure.

15:30 *why do we endanger ourselves every hour?* Cf. 2Co 11:23–29.

15:31 *I face death every day.* Paul faced the reality of death daily (cf. 2Co 4:8–12; 11:23–26), and he wanted the Corinthians to know it. *boast about you.* About their conversion and growth in grace—in spite of their failures (cf. 1Th 2:20).

15:32 *I fought wild beasts in Ephesus.* This statement can be taken literally or figuratively. But since Ac 19 makes no mention of Paul suffering imprisonment and having to face the lions in Ephesus, it is more likely that the expression means that the enemies in Ephesus were as ferocious as wild beasts. *"Let us eat and drink, for tomorrow we die."* See Isa 22:13; an alternative philosophy of life if there is no resurrection.

15:33 A quotation from the Greek comedy *Thais* written by the Greek poet Menander, whose writings the Corinthians would know (see NIV text note). The application of the quotation is that those who are teaching that there is no resurrection (v. 12) are the "bad company" and that they are corrupting the "good character" of those who hold to the correct doctrine. Cf. Ps 1:1; Pr 22:24–25 and notes.

15:34 *stop sinning.* The sin of denying that there is a resurrection and thus doubting even the resurrection of Christ, all of which had a negative effect on the lives they were living. *some who are ignorant of God.* Even in the Corinthian church. This, Paul says, is a shameful situation.

15:35–49 In discussing the nature of the resurrection body, Paul compares it to plant life (vv. 36–38), to fleshly beings (v. 39) and to celestial and earthly physical bodies (vv. 40–41).

15:36–38 Plant organisms, though organized similarly in their own order, are different; the seed sown is related to the new plant that sprouts, but the new sprout has a different and genuinely new body that God has given it.

15:39 *Not all flesh is the same.* Although there is much that is similar in the organizational character of fleshly beings, each species is different: humans, animals, birds, fish.

birds another and fish another. 40 There are
also heavenly bodies and there are earthly
bodies; but the splendor of the heavenly
bodies is one kind, and the splendor of the
earthly bodies is another. 41 The sun has
one kind of splendor,[k] the moon another and the stars another;[l] and star differs
from star in splendor.
42 So will it be[m] with the resurrection of
the dead.[n] The body that is sown is perishable, it is raised imperishable;[o] 43 it is
sown in dishonor, it is raised in glory;[p] it
is sown in weakness, it is raised in power;
44 it is sown a natural body, it is raised a
spiritual body.[q]
If there is a natural body, there is also a
spiritual body. 45 So it is written: "The first
man Adam became a living being"[a];[r] the
last Adam,[s] a life-giving spirit.[t] 46 The spiritual did not come first, but the natural, and
after that the spiritual.[u] 47 The first man was
of the dust of the earth;[v] the second man is
of heaven.[w] 48 As was the earthly man, so
are those who are of the earth; and as is
the heavenly man, so also are those who
are of heaven.[x] 49 And just as we have borne
the image of the earthly man,[y] so shall we[b]
bear the image of the heavenly man.[z]
50 I declare to you, brothers and sisters,
that flesh and blood[a] cannot inherit the
kingdom of God,[b] nor does the perishable
inherit the imperishable.[c] 51 Listen, I tell
you a mystery:[d] We will not all sleep,[e] but
we will all be changed[f]— 52 in a flash, in
the twinkling of an eye, at the last trumpet. For the trumpet will sound,[g] the dead[h]
will be raised imperishable, and we will be
changed. 53 For the perishable[i] must clothe
itself with the imperishable,[j] and the mortal with immortality. 54 When the perishable
has been clothed with the imperishable,
and the mortal with immortality, then the
saying that is written will come true: "Death
has been swallowed up in victory."[c][k]

55 "Where, O death, is your victory?
Where, O death, is your sting?"[d][l]

56 The sting of death is sin,[m] and the power
of sin is the law.[n] 57 But thanks be to God![o]
He gives us the victory through our Lord
Jesus Christ.[p]
58 Therefore, my dear brothers and sisters, stand firm. Let nothing move you.
Always give yourselves fully to the work
of the Lord,[q] because you know that your
labor in the Lord is not in vain.[r]

The Collection for the Lord's People

16 Now about the collection[s] for the
Lord's people:[t] Do what I told the
Galatian[u] churches to do. 2 On the first day

[a] *45* Gen. 2:7 [b] *49* Some early manuscripts *so let us* [c] *54* Isaiah 25:8 [d] *55* Hosea 13:14

15:41 [k] Ps 19:4-6 [l] Ps 8:1,3 **15:42** [m] Da 12:3; Mt 13:43 [n] ver 12 [o] ver 50, 53,54 **15:43** [p] Php 3:21; Col 3:4 **15:44** [q] ver 50 **15:45** [r] Ge 2:7 [s] Ro 5:14 [t] Jn 5:21; 6:57, 58; Ro 8:2 **15:46** [u] ver 44 **15:47** [v] Ge 2:7; 3:19; Ps 90:3 [w] Jn 3:13,31 **15:48** [x] Php 3:20,21 **15:49** [y] Ge 5:3 [z] S Ro 8:29 **15:50** [a] Eph 6:12; Heb 2:14 [b] S Mt 25:34 [c] ver 42,53,54 **15:51** [d] 1Co 13:2; 14:2 [e] S Mt 9:24 [f] 2Co 5:4; Php 3:21 **15:52** [g] S Mt 24:31 [h] Jn 5:25 **15:53** [i] ver 42, 50,54 [j] 2Co 5:2,4 **15:54** [k] Isa 25:8; Heb 2:14; Rev 20:14 **15:55** [l] Hos 13:14 **15:56** [m] S Ro 5:12 [n] S Ro 4:15 **15:57** [o] S 2Co 2:14 [p] Ro 8:37; Heb 2:14,15 **15:58** [q] 1Co 16:10 [r] Isa 65:23 **16:1** [s] S Ac 24:17 [t] S Ac 9:13 [u] S Ac 16:6

15:40–41 Here the analogy involves inanimate objects of creation: the sun, moon and stars with their differing splendor and the earthly bodies (possibly the great mountains, canyons and seas) with their splendor. In it all, God can take similar physical material and organize it differently to accomplish his purpose.

15:42–44 In applying these analogies, the apostle says that in the case of the resurrection of the dead God will take a perishable, dishonorable, weak (and sinful) body—"a natural body" characterized by sin—and in the resurrection make it an imperishable, glorious, powerful body, fit to live eternally with God. There is continuity, but there is also change.

15:44–49 The contrast here between the natural body and the spiritual body again follows from their two representatives (see notes on vv. 21–22). One is the first Adam, who had a natural body of the dust of the ground (Ge 2:7) and through whom a natural body is given to his descendants. The other is the last Adam, Christ, the life-giving spirit (cf. Jn 5:26) who through his death and resurrection will at the second coming give his redeemed people a spiritual body similar to his resurrected, glorified body (cf. Lk 24:36–43; Php 3:21 and notes; 1Jn 3:2).

15:50 Paul's final argument about the resurrection of the body: God's redeemed people must have newly organized, imperishable bodies to live with him. "Flesh and blood" stands for the perishable, corrupt, weak, sinful state of human beings (see note on Gal 1:16).

15:51 *mystery.* Things about the resurrection body that were not understood but are now revealed (see note on Ro 11:25). *We will not all sleep.* Some believers will not experience death and the grave (see 1Th 4:15 and note).

15:52 *in a flash.* The change to an imperishable body will occur instantly at the great trumpet call that announces the consummation of redemption (see Mt 24:31; 1Th 4:16–17).

15:53–54 *clothe itself with … clothed with.* See note on Ps 109:29.

15:56 *The sting of death is sin.* It was sin that brought humanity under death's power (see Ro 5:12–21 and notes). *the power of sin is the law.* The law of God gives sin its power, for it reveals our sin and condemns us because of our sin (cf. Ro 7:7–12 and notes).

15:57 *victory through our Lord Jesus Christ.* Victory over the condemnation for sin that the law brought (v. 56) and over death and the grave (vv. 54–55), through the death and resurrection of Christ (cf. Ro 4:25).

15:58 *Therefore.* Because of Christ's resurrection and ours, we know that serving him is not empty, useless activity. *your labor in the Lord is not in vain.* All our efforts in service to Christ are invested in his winning cause. He will also reward us at his second coming (Mt 25:21; Lk 19:17; cf. 1Co 2:7; 2Co 4:17 and notes).

16:1 *Now about.* Again an answer to one of the questions of the Corinthians (cf. 7:1; 8:1; 12:1). *collection.* Cf. 2Co 8–9; Ro 15:25–28. *the Lord's people.* His people at Jerusalem (cf. v. 3; Ro 15:26). *Galatian churches.* The fact that the Galatian and Macedonian churches (2Co 8:1; 9:1–4) are involved, along with the Corinthians, indicates that the collection of this offering was quite widespread. The Jerusalem believers may have become poverty-stricken because of the famine recorded in Ac 11:28 (c. AD 44 or 46) or because of the persecution of Jerusalem Christians (cf. Ac 8:1).

16:2 *On the first day of every week, each one of you should set aside.* Every Sunday believers were to bring

of every week,[v] each one of you should
set aside a sum of money in keeping with
your income, saving it up, so that when I
come no collections will have to be made.[w]
3 Then, when I arrive, I will give letters of
introduction to the men you approve[x] and
send them with your gift to Jerusalem. 4 If
it seems advisable for me to go also, they
will accompany me.

Personal Requests

5 After I go through Macedonia, I will
come to you[y]—for I will be going through
Macedonia.[z] 6 Perhaps I will stay with you
for a while, or even spend the winter, so
that you can help me on my journey,[a]
wherever I go. 7 For I do not want to see
you now and make only a passing visit;
I hope to spend some time with you, if
the Lord permits.[b] 8 But I will stay on at
Ephesus[c] until Pentecost,[d] 9 because a great
door for effective work has opened to me,[e]
and there are many who oppose me.
10 When Timothy[f] comes, see to it that
he has nothing to fear while he is with
you, for he is carrying on the work of the
Lord,[g] just as I am. 11 No one, then, should
treat him with contempt.[h] Send him on
his way[i] in peace[j] so that he may return
to me. I am expecting him along with the
brothers.
12 Now about our brother Apollos:[k] I
strongly urged him to go to you with the
brothers. He was quite unwilling to go now,
but he will go when he has the opportunity.
13 Be on your guard; stand firm[l] in the
faith; be courageous; be strong.[m] 14 Do everything in love.[n]
15 You know that the household of Stephanas[o] were the first converts[p] in Achaia,[q] and they have devoted themselves to
the service[r] of the Lord's people.[s] I urge
you, brothers and sisters, 16 to submit[t] to
such people and to everyone who joins
in the work and labors at it. 17 I was glad
when Stephanas, Fortunatus and Achaicus arrived, because they have supplied
what was lacking from you.[u] 18 For they
refreshed[v] my spirit and yours also. Such
men deserve recognition.[w]

Final Greetings

19 The churches in the province of Asia[x]
send you greetings. Aquila and Priscilla[a][y]
greet you warmly in the Lord, and so does

[a] 19 Greek *Prisca,* a variant of *Priscilla*

16:2 [v] Ac 20:7 [w] 2Co 9:4,5 **16:3** [x] 2Co 3:1; 8:18,19 **16:5** [y] S 1Co 4:19 [z] S Ac 16:9 **16:6** [a] Ro 15:24; Titus 3:13 **16:7** [b] S Ac 18:21 **16:8** [c] S Ac 18:19 [d] S Ac 2:1 **16:9** [e] S Ac 14:27 **16:10** [f] S Ac 16:1 [g] 1Co 15:58 **16:11** [h] 1Ti 4:12 [i] 2Co 1:16; 3Jn 6 [j] S Ac 15:33 **16:12** [k] S Ac 18:24 **16:13** [l] 1Co 1:8; 2Co 1:21; Gal 5:1; Php 1:27; 1Th 3:8; S Titus 1:9 [m] S Eph 6:10 **16:14** [n] 1Co 14:1 **16:15** [o] 1Co 1:16 [p] Ro 16:5 [q] S Ac 18:12 [r] S Ac 24:17 [s] S Ac 9:13 **16:16** [t] 1Th 5:12; Heb 13:17 **16:17** [u] 2Co 11:9; Php 2:30 **16:18** [v] Ro 15:32; Phm 7 [w] Php 2:29 **16:19** [x] S Ac 2:9 [y] S Ac 18:2

---

what they had set aside for the Lord's work—an amount proportionate to their income. Since it was to be brought on Sunday, the day when Christians gathered for worship (see Ac 20:7; Rev 1:10 and notes), it was probably collected at the worship service rather than at home. Justin Martyr indicates (in his *Apology,* 1.67–68) that in his time (c. AD 150) offerings were brought to the church on Sundays.

16:3 For proper financial accountability and responsibility these approved men would act as auditors and guardians of the funds the Corinthians gave (cf. 2Co 8:16–21 and notes).

16:4 *If it seems advisable for me to go also.* Possibly to take care of important missionary business or to be there to explain about the gift when it arrives.

16:5 *After I go through Macedonia.* After leaving Ephesus (v. 8), where he was when he wrote 1 Corinthians, Paul planned to go up to Macedonia, no doubt to visit the Philippians and others in northern Greece, and then to Corinth. He had originally planned to go to Corinth first and then to Macedonia but thought it best to change his plans (see 2Co 1:12—2:4).

16:6 *even spend the winter.* Probably the three-month stay in Greece mentioned in Ac 20:3 (see note there). *help me on my journey.* With supplies and equipment, and certainly with prayers and goodwill. However, Paul had indicated earlier in the letter (9:7–12) that he did not want to be a financial burden to them.

16:8 *until Pentecost.* The 50th day (Pentecost means "50") after Passover, when the Jews celebrated the Festival of Firstfruits (Lev 23:10–16)—late spring.

16:9 *many who oppose me.* Probably a reference to the pagan craftsmen who made the silver shrines of Artemis and to the general populace whom they had stirred up (Ac 19:23–34).

16:10 *When Timothy comes.* In Ac 19:22 Paul sends Timothy (and Erastus) into Macedonia, after which Timothy was to go on to Corinth (1Co 4:17). *see to it that he has nothing to fear.* Timothy seems to have been somewhat timid (see 1Ti 4:12; 2Ti 1:7 and notes), and Paul wants the Corinthians to treat him kindly.

16:11,23 *peace . . . grace.* See note on Ro 1:7.

16:11 *brothers.* Possibly including Erastus (cf. Ac 19:22), who was a believer from Corinth and "the city's director of public works" (Ro 16:23; see note there).

16:12 *Now about . . . Apollos.* The Corinthians had asked Paul about Apollos (cf. the similar words, "now about," in 7:1 ["now for the matters"]; 8:1; 12:1; 16:1) and his coming to see them. For other words about Apollos, see 1:12; 3:4–6,22; 4:6; cf. Ac 18:24,27; 19:1; Titus 3:13.

16:15 *household of Stephanas.* Some of the few people Paul baptized at Corinth (1:16). They were among the first converts in Achaia (Greece), along with the few individuals in Athens who had believed a short time earlier (Ac 17:34). *service.* The whole household of Stephanas was serving.

16:17 These were probably the ones who had brought to the apostle the letter from the Corinthians referred to in 7:1. Their coming "supplied what was lacking" from the Corinthians, i.e., the affection of these three brothers supplied the affection Paul desired from the whole Corinthian church.

16:18 *refreshed my spirit and yours.* Perhaps through their willingness to come to get Paul's advice and to bring it back to Corinth. At least a new relationship between Paul and the Corinthians was in the making.

16:19 *province of Asia.* The Roman province (in present-day western Turkey) in which Ephesus and the surrounding cities were located (see Ac 19:10 and note; see also map, p. 2153). During Paul's long ministry in Ephesus, all in the province of Asia heard the word. The churches of Colossae, Laodicea and Hierapolis (cf. Col 4:13–16; Rev 1:11), which were located on the border of the province of Asia, may be included in the greetings, along with the other churches of Rev 2–3 (see map, p. 2153). *Aquila and Priscilla.* They had helped Paul found the church at Corinth (Ac 18:1–4). *warmly in the Lord.* Enthusiastically, as fellow believers. *the church that meets at*

the church that meets at their house.[z] 20 All
the brothers and sisters here send you
greetings. Greet one another with a holy
kiss.[a]
21 I, Paul, write this greeting in my own
hand.[b]
22 If anyone does not love the Lord,[c] let
that person be cursed![d] Come, Lord[a]![e]
23 The grace of the Lord Jesus be with you.[f]
24 My love to all of you in Christ Jesus.
Amen.[b]

16:19 [z]S Ro 16:5 **16:20** [a]S Ro 16:16 **16:21** [b]Gal 6:11; Col 4:18; 2Th 3:17; Phm 19 **16:22** [c]Eph 6:24 [d]Ro 9:3 [e]Rev 22:20 **16:23** [f]S Ro 16:20

[a] *22* The Greek for *Come, Lord* reproduces an Aramaic expression (*Marana tha*) used by early Christians.
[b] *24* Some manuscripts do not have *Amen.*

---

their house. Aquila and Priscilla had left Corinth with Paul and had gone to Ephesus (Ac 18:18–19). Evidently they were still there, and a church was meeting at their house; it now sends greetings. House churches were common in this early period (cf. Ro 16:3–5; Phm 2).

16:20 *holy kiss.* See notes on 2Co 13:12; Ro 16:16. The kiss of mutual respect and love in the Lord was evidently the public practice of early Christians—from a practice that was customary in the ancient East. Such a practice may have been used in the first-century AD synagogue—men kissing men, and women kissing women—and it would have been natural for the practice to have been continued in the early Jewish-Gentile churches.

16:21 *greeting in my own hand.* Paul now signs this letter, as was his habit (see Gal 6:11; Col 4:18; Phm 19), a mark of the authenticity of the letter (2Th 3:17). Someone else had been penning the letter for him up to this point (cf. Ro 16:22).

16:22 *let that person be cursed!* May those who have not come to love the Lord Jesus Christ in response to the preaching of the gospel experience God's displeasure and wrath (see Jn 3:36 and note). Paul's curse is based on God as witness to the unbelievers' essential lack of love for the Lord Jesus and of obedience to God (cf. Gal 1:8–9; Ro 9:3 and note). *Come, Lord!* See NIV text note; an expression used by the early church as a cry that the second coming of Christ may soon take place (Rev 22:20).

16:23 The apostle's usual benediction (see Gal 6:18; Eph 6:24; Php 4:23); a longer Trinitarian benediction is found in 2Co 13:14 (see note there). *grace.* See note on vv. 11,23. *with you.* See note on 2Co 13:14.

16:24 Although he has been severe with the Corinthians, Paul wants them to know that he loves them as believers in Christ Jesus. *in Christ Jesus.* See note on Eph 1:1.

2 CORINTHIANS

INTRODUCTION

Author

Paul is the author of this letter (see 1:1; 10:1). It is stamped with his style and contains more autobiographical material than any of his other writings.

Date

The available evidence indicates that the year AD 55 is a reasonable estimate for the writing of this letter. From 1Co 16:5 – 8 it may be concluded that 1 Corinthians was written from Ephesus before Pentecost (in the late spring) and that 2 Corinthians may have been written later that same year before the onset of winter. 2Co 2:13; 7:5 indicate that it was probably written from Macedonia (see chart, p. 1845).

Recipients

The opening greeting of the letter states that it was addressed to the church in Corinth and to Christians throughout Achaia (the Roman province comprising all of Greece south of Macedonia; see map, p. 1864).

Occasion

It seems that Paul wrote at least four letters to the church at Corinth: (1) the letter referred to in 1Co 5:9 (see note there); (2) 1 Corinthians; (3) the severe letter (see 2Co 2:3 – 4; see also below); (4) 2 Corinthians. After writing 1 Corinthians Paul continued his ministry at Ephesus until he heard that his letter had not completely accomplished its purpose. A group of men had come to Corinth who presented themselves as apostles. They were false teachers who were challenging, among other things, Paul's personal integrity and his authority as an apostle (see 11:4; 12:11).

In the face of this serious situation, Paul decided to make a quick trip to Corinth (12:4; 13:1 – 2) to see whether he could remedy the situation. The visit turned out to be painful and did

a quick look

Author:
The apostle Paul

Audience:
The church in Corinth

Date:
AD 55

Theme:
Paul encourages the Corinthian believers to be reconciled with him and to reject false apostles who are challenging his authority and creating dissension in the church.

not accomplish its purpose. So when Paul returned to Ephesus, he wrote the Corinthians a severe letter "out of great distress and anguish of heart and with many tears" (2:4), probably sending it by Titus (12:18). This letter is now lost, though some identify it with 2Co 10 – 13.

After writing the severe letter, Paul had second thoughts. He was deeply concerned about how the Corinthians might react to it. So after the riot caused by Demetrius and his fellow silversmiths (see Ac 19:23 – 41), he left Ephesus and set out for Macedonia by way of Troas. He expected to meet Titus in Troas to get news of the effect of his severe letter on the Corinthian church, but Titus was not there (see 2Co 2:12 – 13). Still deeply concerned and despite the fact that the Lord had opened up an opportunity to preach the gospel at Troas, Paul said goodbye to the believers there and moved on to Macedonia, where he met Titus. To his relief, the news from the Corinthian church was basically good. The severe letter had brought its intended results (7:5 – 16). The encouraging report of Titus concerning the improved situation at Corinth was the immediate occasion of the writing of 2 Corinthians.

How, then, does one explain the harsh tone of chs. 10 – 13, which is so different from the rest of the letter? Some think that when Paul had just completed writing the first nine chapters, a report came to him that a strong and vocal minority was still causing trouble at Corinth. So before sending off the letter he added the last four chapters to address this troublemaking group. Others hold that chs. 10 – 13 were written some time after Paul had sent the first nine chapters and that they constitute a separate letter that was later attached to 2 Corinthians. There is, however, no manuscript evidence that warrants splitting 2 Corinthians into two parts.

Ancient lighthouse at Patara. Paul stopped at Patara (Ac 21:1) on his way back to Jerusalem after his third missionary journey.

www.HolyLandPhotos.org

Paul writes to explain to the Corinthian believers the true nature (its joys, sufferings and rewards) and high calling of Christian ministry.

Purposes

Because of the occasion that prompted this letter, Paul had a number of purposes in mind:

(1) To express the comfort and joy he felt because the Corinthians had responded favorably to his severe letter (1:3 – 4; 7:8 – 9,12 – 13).

(2) To let them know about the trouble he had gone through in the province of Asia (1:8 – 11).

(3) To explain why he had changed his travel plans (1:12—2:4).

(4) To ask them to forgive the offending party (2:5 – 11).

(5) To warn them not to be "yoked together with unbelievers" (6:14—7:1).

(6) To explain to them the true nature (its joys, sufferings and rewards) and high calling of Christian ministry. This is the so-called great digression, but it turns out to be in some ways the most important section of the letter (2:14—7:4; see notes on 2:14; 7:4 – 5).

(7) To teach the Corinthians about the grace of giving and to make sure that they complete the collection for the impoverished Christians at Jerusalem (chs. 8 – 9).

(8) To deal with the minority opposition in the church (chs. 10 – 13).

(9) To prepare the Corinthians for his upcoming visit (12:14; 13:1 – 3,10).

Structure

The structure of the letter relates primarily to Paul's impending third visit to Corinth. The letter falls naturally into three sections:

(1) Paul explains the reason for the changes in his itinerary (chs. 1 – 7).

(2) Paul encourages the Corinthians to complete their collection in preparation for his arrival (chs. 8 – 9).

(3) Paul stresses the certainty of his coming, his authenticity as an apostle and his readiness to exercise discipline if necessary (chs. 10 – 13).

Unity

Some have questioned the unity of this letter (see Occasion), but it forms a coherent whole, as the structure shows (see Structure; see also Outline). Tradition has been unanimous in affirming its unity (the early church fathers, e.g., knew the letter only in its present form). Furthermore, none of the early Greek manuscripts break up the book.

Outline

I. Apologetic: Paul's Explanation of His Conduct and Apostolic Ministry (chs. 1 – 7)
   A. Greetings (1:1 – 2)
   B. Thanksgiving for Divine Comfort in Affliction (1:3 – 11)
   C. The Integrity of Paul's Motives and Conduct (1:12—2:4)
   D. Forgiving the Offending Party at Corinth (2:5 – 11)
   E. God's Direction in Ministry (2:12 – 17)
   F. The Corinthian Believers—a Letter from Christ (3:1 – 11)
   G. Seeing the Glory of God with Unveiled Faces (3:12—4:6)
   H. Treasure in Clay Jars (4:7 – 16a)

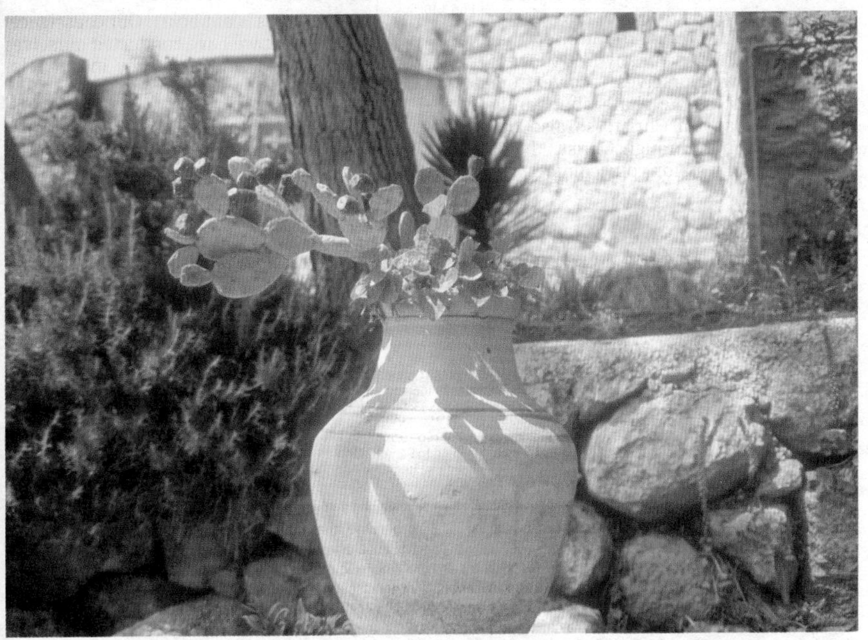

Clay jar containing a sabra cactus near Bethany. "We have this treasure in jars of clay" (2Co 4:7).

- I. The Prospect of Death and What It Means for the Christian (4:16b — 5:10)
- J. The Ministry of Reconciliation (5:11 — 6:10)
- K. A Spiritual Father's Appeal to His Children (6:11 — 7:4)
- L. The Meeting with Titus (7:5 – 16)

II. Hortatory: The Collection for the Christians at Jerusalem (chs. 8 – 9)
- A. Generosity Encouraged (8:1 – 15)
- B. Titus and His Companions Sent to Corinth (8:16 — 9:5)
- C. Results of Generous Giving (9:6 – 15)

III. Polemical: Paul's Vindication of His Apostolic Authority (chs. 10 – 13)
- A. Paul's Defense of His Apostolic Authority and the Area of His Mission (ch. 10)
- B. Paul Forced into Foolish Boasting (chs. 11 – 12)
- C. Final Warnings (13:1 – 10)
- D. Conclusion, Final Greetings and Benediction (13:11 – 14)

1 Paul, an apostle[a] of Christ Jesus by the
will of God,[b] and Timothy[c] our brother,

To the church of God[d] in Corinth,[e] together with all his holy people throughout
Achaia:[f]

2 Grace and peace to you from God our
Father and the Lord Jesus Christ.[g]

Praise to the God of All Comfort

3 Praise be to the God and Father of our
Lord Jesus Christ,[h] the Father of compassion and the God of all comfort, 4 who
comforts us[i] in all our troubles, so that
we can comfort those in any trouble with
the comfort we ourselves receive from
God. 5 For just as we share abundantly
in the sufferings of Christ,[j] so also our
comfort abounds through Christ. 6 If we
are distressed, it is for your comfort and
salvation;[k] if we are comforted, it is for
your comfort, which produces in you patient endurance of the same sufferings we
suffer. 7 And our hope for you is firm, because we know that just as you share in
our sufferings,[l] so also you share in our
comfort.

8 We do not want you to be uninformed,[m] brothers and sisters,[a] about the
troubles we experienced[n] in the province
of Asia.[o] We were under great pressure,
far beyond our ability to endure, so that
we despaired of life itself. 9 Indeed, we felt
we had received the sentence of death.
But this happened that we might not rely
on ourselves but on God,[p] who raises the
dead.[q] 10 He has delivered us from such a
deadly peril,[r] and he will deliver us again.
On him we have set our hope[s] that he will
continue to deliver us, 11 as you help us
by your prayers.[t] Then many will give
thanks[u] on our behalf for the gracious favor granted us in answer to the prayers
of many.

Paul's Change of Plans

12 Now this is our boast: Our conscience[v]
testifies that we have conducted ourselves
in the world, and especially in our relations with you, with integrity[b][w] and godly
sincerity.[x] We have done so, relying not on
worldly wisdom[y] but on God's grace. 13 For
we do not write you anything you cannot
read or understand. And I hope that, 14 as
you have understood us in part, you will
come to understand fully that you can
boast of us just as we will boast of you in
the day of the Lord Jesus.[z]

15 Because I was confident of this, I
wanted to visit you[a] first so that you might
benefit twice.[b] 16 I wanted to visit you
on my way[c] to Macedonia[d] and to come
back to you from Macedonia, and then to
have you send me on my way[e] to Judea.[f]

[a] 8 The Greek word for *brothers and sisters* (*adelphoi*) refers here to believers, both men and women, as part of God's family; also in 8:1; 13:11. [b] 12 Many manuscripts *holiness*

1:1 [a] S 1Co 1:1 [b] 1Co 1:1; Eph 1:1; Col 1:1; 2Ti 1:1 [c] S Ac 16:1 [d] S 1Co 10:32 [e] S Ac 18:1 [f] S Ac 18:12 **1:2** [g] S Ro 1:7 **1:3** [h] Eph 1:3; 1Pe 1:3 **1:4** [i] Isa 49:13; 51:12; 66:13; 2Co 7:6, 7, 13 **1:5** [j] Ro 8:17; 2Co 4:10; Gal 6:17; Php 3:10; Col 1:24; 1Pe 4:13 **1:6** [k] 2Co 4:15 **1:7** [l] S ver 5 **1:8** [m] S Ro 11:25 [n] 1Co 15:32 [o] S Ac 2:9 **1:9** [p] Jer 17:5, 7 [q] S Jn 5:21 **1:10** [r] S Ro 15:31 [s] 1Ti 4:10 **1:11** [t] Ro 15:30; Php 1:19 [u] 2Co 4:15; 9:11 **1:12** [v] S Ac 23:1 [w] 1Th 2:10 [x] 2Co 2:17 [y] 1Co 1:17; 2:1, 4, 13 **1:14** [z] S 1Co 1:8 **1:15** [a] S 1Co 4:19 [b] Ro 1:11, 13; 15:29 **1:16** [c] 1Co 16:5-7 [d] S Ac 16:9 [e] 1Co 16:11; 3Jn 6 [f] Ac 19:21

1:1 *Paul.* See note on Ro 1:1. *apostle ... by the will of God.* See 1Co 1:1 and note. *Timothy.* Evidently with Paul when this letter was written, but not necessarily a co-author. *our brother.* Our fellow believer, our brother in Christ (see Ac 9:17; Heb 2:11 and note). *church of God.* The community of believers, the local representatives of the universal church (see note on 1Co 1:2). *Corinth.* See Introduction to 1 Corinthians: The City of Corinth; see also map, p. 1920. *his holy people.* See note on Ro 1:7. *Achaia.* Greece, as distinct from Macedonia in the north (see map, p. 1864). Though the letter deals particularly with the situation in Corinth, it was also intended for Christians elsewhere in Greece. Presumably copies of the letter would be made in Corinth and circulated to them.

1:2 *Grace and peace.* See note on Ro 1:7. *Lord Jesus Christ.* Also occurs at the end of this letter (13:14); see note on 1Th 1:1.

1:3 *God and Father of our Lord Jesus Christ.* See note on Eph 1:3. *comfort.* Consolation and encouragement. This comfort flows to believers when they suffer for Jesus' sake, and it equips them to comfort others who are in trouble (vv. 4–7).

1:4 *all our troubles.* See, e.g., vv. 8–11 and note on v. 9; 4:8–12 and note on 4:10; 6:4–10; 11:23–28 and notes on 11:24–25; 11:25; Gal 6:17 and note.

1:5 *share ... in the sufferings of Christ.* See 4:10; Gal 6:17; Php 3:10 and notes.

1:6 *patient endurance.* See Ro 5:3–5; 2Pe 1:5–11 and notes.

1:7 *share in our sufferings, so also ... in our comfort.* See Ro 12:15; 1Co 12:26 and notes.

1:8 *We.* Throughout this letter Paul uses the editorial plural (we, us, our, ourselves). Except where the context indicates otherwise, these plurals should be understood as referring to Paul alone. *brothers and sisters.* See NIV text note. *province of Asia.* A Roman province in western Asia Minor, present-day Turkey (see map, p. 1851).

1:9 Paul's hardships were so life-threatening that he regarded his survival and recovery as tantamount to being raised from the dead. *rely ... on God.* A key principle of this letter. God's grace is all-sufficient; Christ strengthens us when we are weak (see 12:9–10; Php 4:13 and notes).

1:10 *hope.* See note on Eph 1:18.

1:11 *you help us by your prayers.* Cf. Ro 15:31; Eph 6:19–20.

1:12 In defending his trustworthiness against the slanders being spread about him, Paul appeals to the witness of his own conscience and to the Corinthians' firsthand knowledge of his character. He had spent 18 months with them when he first came to Corinth (Ac 18:11), so they could not plead ignorance of his integrity.

1:14 *day of the Lord Jesus.* Time of his return (cf. 1Th 2:19–20).

1:15 *you might benefit twice.* Here and in v. 16 Paul refers to his change of itinerary. Originally he had planned to cross over by sea from Ephesus to Corinth, visiting the Corinthians before traveling north to Macedonia, and then, returning from Macedonia, to visit them a second time, thus giving them the benefit of two short visits. This was when he was on good terms with them. What probably occurred was that he paid them a quick visit directly from Ephesus, a visit he had not contemplated and that proved to be "painful" (2:1; see note there). That visit then gave rise to his letter that caused them sorrow (see 7:8–9 and note).

1:16 *Macedonia.* See notes on v. 1; Php 4:15.

17 Was I fickle when I intended to do this?
Or do I make my plans in a worldly manner[g] so that in the same breath I say both
"Yes, yes" and "No, no"?
18 But as surely as God is faithful,[h] our
message to you is not "Yes" and "No."
19 For the Son of God,[i] Jesus Christ, who
was preached among you by us—by me
and Silas[a][j] and Timothy[k]—was not "Yes"
and "No," but in him it has always[l] been
"Yes." 20 For no matter how many promises[m] God has made, they are "Yes" in
Christ. And so through him the "Amen"[n] is
spoken by us to the glory of God.[o] 21 Now it
is God who makes both us and you stand
firm[p] in Christ. He anointed[q] us, 22 set his
seal[r] of ownership on us, and put his Spirit in our hearts as a deposit, guaranteeing
what is to come.[s]
23 I call God as my witness[t]—and I stake
my life on it—that it was in order to spare
you[u] that I did not return to Corinth. 24 Not
that we lord it over[v] your faith, but we
work with you for your joy, because it is
2 by faith you stand firm.[w] 1 So I made
up my mind that I would not make another painful visit to you.[x] 2 For if I grieve
you,[y] who is left to make me glad but you
whom I have grieved? 3 I wrote as I did,[z]
so that when I came I would not be distressed[a] by those who should have made
me rejoice. I had confidence[b] in all of you,
that you would all share my joy. 4 For I
wrote you[c] out of great distress and anguish of heart and with many tears, not to
grieve you but to let you know the depth
of my love for you.

Forgiveness for the Offender

5 If anyone has caused grief,[d] he has not
so much grieved me as he has grieved
all of you to some extent—not to put it
too severely. 6 The punishment[e] inflicted on him by the majority is sufficient.
7 Now instead, you ought to forgive and
comfort him,[f] so that he will not be overwhelmed by excessive sorrow. 8 I urge you,
therefore, to reaffirm your love for him.
9 Another reason I wrote you[g] was to see
if you would stand the test and be obedient in everything.[h] 10 Anyone you forgive, I
also forgive. And what I have forgiven—if
there was anything to forgive—I have forgiven in the sight of Christ for your sake,
11 in order that Satan[i] might not outwit us.
For we are not unaware of his schemes.[j]

Ministers of the New Covenant

12 Now when I went to Troas[k] to preach
the gospel of Christ[l] and found that the

[a] 19 Greek *Silvanus*, a variant of *Silas*

1:17 [g] 2Co 10:2, 3; 11:18 **1:18** [h] S 1Co 1:9 **1:19** [i] S Mt 4:3 [j] S Ac 15:22 [k] S Ac 16:1 [l] Heb 13:8 **1:20** [m] Ro 15:8 [n] S 1Co 14:16 [o] Ro 15:9 **1:21** [p] S 1Co 16:13 [q] 1Jn 2:20, 27 **1:22** [r] Ge 38:18; Eze 9:4; Hag 2:23 [s] S 2Co 5:5 **1:23** [t] S Ro 1:9 [u] 1Co 4:21; 2Co 2:1, 3; 13:2, 10 **1:24** [v] 1Pe 5:3 [w] Ro 11:20; 1Co 15:1 **2:1** [x] S 2Co 1:23 **2:2** [y] 2Co 7:8 **2:3** [z] ver 4, 9; 2Co 7:8, 12 [a] 2Co 12:21 [b] 2Co 7:16; 8:22; Gal 5:10; 2Th 3:4; Phm 21 **2:4** [c] ver 3, 9; 2Co 7:8, 12 **2:5** [d] 1Co 5:1, 2 **2:6** [e] 1Co 5:4, 5; 2Co 7:11 **2:7** [f] Gal 6:1; Eph 4:32; Col 3:13 **2:9** [g] ver 3, 4; 2Co 7:8, 12 [h] 2Co 7:15; 10:6 **2:11** [i] S Mt 4:10 [j] Lk 22:31; 2Co 4:4; 1Pe 5:8, 9 **2:12** [k] S Ac 16:8 [l] S Ro 1:1; 2Co 4:3, 4; 8:18; 9:13; 1Th 3:2

1:17 Paul's opponents in Corinth had been attempting to persuade the Christians there that this change of plan was evidence that his word was not to be trusted, that he was fickle and unreliable. The two rhetorical questions are in effect his denial that he acts lightly and that he says "Yes" and "No" at the same time, so that it is impossible to know what he means. In any case, his plan to visit the Corinthians had not been abandoned; it had simply been modified.

1:18 – 19 *not "Yes" and "No."* Paul now appeals to the gospel message he had preached to them. Believing it, they had found it to be true and free from ambiguity, and by their experience of its dynamic power they had proved it to be one great affirmative in Christ.

1:19 *who was preached among you.* During Paul's first visit to Corinth (see Ac 18:5). *Silas.* See Ac 15:22 and note.

1:20 *"Amen."* The "Amen" uttered by the congregation at the end of an offering of prayer or praise (cf. 1Co 14:16 and note on 14:15 – 17).

1:21 *anointed us.* See Ex 29:7 and note; 1Sa 16:13; Isa 61:1.

1:22 *seal.* See notes on Hag 2:23; Eph 1:13; cf. Eph 4:30. *deposit.* A part given as a guarantee that the whole will be forthcoming (see Ro 8:23 and note). The first installment of a sum of money that has been inherited, e.g., assures the recipient that the whole will be received.

1:23 *to spare you.* Paul's change of plans for visiting the Corinthian Christians had been motivated not by a fickle and insensitive attitude but by love and concern for them.

2:1 *another painful visit.* Paul had already made one painful visit to Corinth, and he wanted to avoid another such visit, though he was ready to assert his authority if it should prove necessary (cf. 13:2). This former visit could not have been the one he made to Corinth at the time when the church there was founded in response to the preaching of the gospel (cf. Ac 18). Therefore he must have paid a second visit, which is confirmed by 12:14 and 13:1, where he states that the visit he is now about to make will be his third. The second visit probably took place between the writing of 1 and 2 Corinthians, though some hold that it occurred before 1 Corinthians was written.

2:3 – 4 See Introduction: Occasion.

2:5 – 11 Speaks of a particular person who has been the cause of serious offense in Corinth and upon whom church discipline has been imposed. Paul admonishes the Corinthians that because the offender has shown genuine sorrow and repentance for his sin, the punishment should be discontinued and he should be lovingly restored to their fellowship. The offense in question probably took place during Paul's intermediate visit to Corinth (see note on v. 1) and may have been the occasion for his writing the severe letter demanding the punishment of the offender (see note on vv. 3 – 4). Another view is that Paul refers to the incident recorded in 1Co 5.

2:7 *comfort.* See 1:3 – 7 and note on 1:3.

2:11 *Satan.* See Mt 16:23; 1Jn 3:8 and notes. *his schemes.* See Ge 3:1; Lk 22:31; Jn 8:44 and notes; see also 1Pe 5:8.

2:12 *I went to Troas.* Paul had traveled up from Ephesus to Troas, a city on the Aegean coast (see Ac 16:8 and note; see also map, p. 1858), hoping to find Titus there and to receive news from him about the Corinthian church. But Titus, who Paul presumably knew would be following the same route in reverse, did not arrive in Troas; so Paul, anxious for news from Corinth, "went on to Macedonia" (v. 13), perhaps to the city of Philippi (see map, p. 1858). *opened a door.* See Ac 14:27; Rev 3:8 and notes; see also 1Co 16:9; Col 4:3.

Lord had opened a door[m] for me, 13 I still
had no peace of mind,[n] because I did not
find my brother Titus[o] there. So I said
goodbye to them and went on to Macedonia.[p]
14 But thanks be to God,[q] who always
leads us as captives in Christ's triumphal
procession and uses us to spread the aroma[r] of the knowledge[s] of him everywhere.
15 For we are to God the pleasing aroma[t] of
Christ among those who are being saved
and those who are perishing.[u] 16 To the
one we are an aroma that brings death;[v] to
the other, an aroma that brings life. And
who is equal to such a task?[w] 17 Unlike so
many, we do not peddle the word of God
for profit.[x] On the contrary, in Christ we
speak before God with sincerity,[y] as those
sent from God.[z]

3 Are we beginning to commend ourselves[a] again? Or do we need, like
some people, letters of recommendation[b]
to you or from you? 2 You yourselves are
our letter, written on our hearts, known
and read by everyone.[c] 3 You show that
you are a letter from Christ, the result
of our ministry, written not with ink but
with the Spirit of the living God,[d] not on
tablets of stone[e] but on tablets of human
hearts.[f]
4 Such confidence[g] we have through
Christ before God. 5 Not that we are competent in ourselves[h] to claim anything for
ourselves, but our competence comes
from God.[i] 6 He has made us competent as
ministers of a new covenant[j]—not of the
letter[k] but of the Spirit; for the letter kills,
but the Spirit gives life.[l]

2:12 [m] S Ac 14:27 **2:13** [n] 2Co 7:5 [o] 2Co 7:6, 13; 8:6, 16, 23; 12:18; Gal 2:1, 3; Titus 1:4 [p] S Ac 16:9 **2:14** [q] Ro 6:17; 7:25; 1Co 15:57; 2Co 9:15 [r] Eze 20:41; Eph 5:2; Php 4:18 [s] S 2Co 8:7 **2:15** [t] S ver 14; Ge 8:21; Ex 29:18; Nu 15:3 [u] S 1Co 1:18 **2:16** [v] S Lk 2:34; Jn 3:36 [w] 2Co 3:5, 6 **2:17** [x] S Ac 20:33; 2Co 4:2; 1Th 2:5 [y] 1Co 5:8 [z] 2Co 1:12; 12:19 **3:1** [a] Ro 16:1; 2Co 5:12; 10:12, 18; 12:11 [b] Ac 18:27; Ro 16:1; 1Co 16:3 **3:2** [c] 1Co 9:2 **3:3** [d] S Mt 16:16 [e] ver 7; Ex 24:12; 31:18; 32:15, 16 [f] Pr 3:3; 7:3; Jer 31:33; Eze 36:26 **3:4** [g] S Eph 3:12 **3:5** [h] 2Co 2:16 [i] 1Co 15:10 **3:6** [j] S Lk 22:20 [k] Ro 2:29; 7:6 [l] Jn 6:63

2:13 *my brother.* Cf. 8:23. *Titus.* See Introduction to Titus: Recipient. Paul held Titus in high esteem; he entrusted Titus with the organization of the collection of funds in Corinth for the relief of the poverty-stricken Christians of Jerusalem (see 8:6 and note), and he chose him to bear this letter to the Corinthian Christians (see 8:16–17 and note on 8:16).

2:14 At this point Paul breaks off the narrative of his itinerary and in a characteristic manner begins a lengthy digression (the narrative is not resumed until 7:5; see note there). The digression, however, is relevant to the main tenor of this letter, for it is an outpouring of triumphant faith in praise of the adequacy of God's grace for every situation. *leads us as captives in Christ's triumphal procession.* A victorious Roman general would lead his soldiers and their captives in festive procession, while the people watched and applauded and the air was filled with the sweet smell released by the burning of spices in the streets (cf. note on 1Co 4:9). *everywhere.* Cf. note on 1Th 1:8.

2:16 *aroma that brings death … aroma that brings life.* As the gospel aroma is released in the world through Christian testimony, it is always sweet-smelling, even though it may be differently received. Ultimately there are two kinds of people: "those who are being saved and those who are perishing" (v. 15). To the latter, testifying Christians are the smell of death, not because the gospel message has become evil-smelling or death-dealing but because in rejecting the life-giving grace of God unbelievers choose death for themselves. To those who welcome the gospel of God's grace, Christians with their testimony are the fragrance of life. *who is equal to such a task?* For the answer, see 3:4–5.

2:17 *peddle the word of God for profit.* Paul is referring to false teachers who had infiltrated the Corinthian church. Such persons—themselves insincere, self-sufficient and boastful—artfully presented themselves in a persuasive manner, and their chief interest was to take money from gullible church members (cf. Mic 3:5,11). Paul, by contrast, had preached the gospel sincerely and free of charge, taking care not to be a financial burden to the Corinthian believers (see 11:7–9; 1Co 9:11–15 and notes).

3:1 *Are we beginning to commend ourselves again?* Paul realizes that virtually everything he wrote or said was liable to be twisted by the false teachers in Corinth. *letters of recommendation.* The appearance of vagrant impostors led to the need for letters of recommendation. Paul needed no such confirmation, but others, including the Corinthian intruders, did need authentication and often resorted to unscrupulous methods for obtaining or forging such letters.

3:2 *known and read by everyone.* Because of the power of the gospel demonstrated by their transformed lives.

3:3 *letter from Christ.* Paul is no more than an instrument in the hands of the Master. *written not with ink.* As a parchment or papyrus document would be—but ink fades and may easily be deleted or blocked out. *with the Spirit of the living God.* The Spirit is himself life and therefore life-giving (v. 6), and the life he gives is eternal and without defect. *not on tablets of stone.* As at Sinai (see note on v. 6). *on tablets of human hearts.* See Jer 31:33; Eze 11:19; 36:26 and notes. Paul explains the significance of this contrast between the old and the new covenants in vv. 7–18.

3:4–5 Answers the question raised in 2:16.

3:6 *ministers of.* Those who serve the cause of (see Ro 15:16; Col 1:7; 4:7; 1Ti 4:6). Paul will return to the theme of "this ministry" in 4:1. *new covenant.* Here Paul takes up the theme suggested by the mention of "tablets of human hearts" (v. 3; see note there). See Heb 8–10. Paul's reference to "ministers of a new covenant," in contrast to the "ministry that brought death" (v. 7), may have been occasioned by his opponents in Corinth who were Judaizers, perhaps those who claimed to be associated with Peter (see 1Co 1:12 and note) and who are referred to as Hebrews in 11:22 (see note there). *the letter.* The Ten Commandments, originally written on the two tablets of stone (see Ex 24:12; 31:18 and note). *the Spirit.* The writing of the law "with the Spirit of the living God … on tablets of human hearts" (v. 3; see note there), which was the promise of the new covenant as foretold by the prophets (see Jer 31:31–34 and notes). *the letter kills, but the Spirit gives life.* Does not mean that the external, literal sense of Scripture is deadly or unprofitable while the inner, spiritual sense is vital. "The letter" is synonymous with the law as an external standard before which all people, because they are lawbreakers, stand guilty and condemned to death. Therefore it is described as the "ministry that brought death" (v. 7) and the "ministry that brought condemnation" (v. 9). On the other hand, the Spirit who "gives life" writes that same law inwardly "on tablets of human hearts" (v. 3; see note there). He thus provides believers with love for God's law, which previously they had hated, and with power to keep it, which previously they had not possessed.

The Greater Glory of the New Covenant

7 Now if the ministry that brought
death,[m] which was engraved in letters on
stone, came with glory, so that the Israelites could not look steadily at the face
of Moses because of its glory,[n] transitory
though it was, 8 will not the ministry of
the Spirit be even more glorious? 9 If the
ministry that brought condemnation[o] was
glorious, how much more glorious is the
ministry that brings righteousness![p] 10 For
what was glorious has no glory now in
comparison with the surpassing glory.
11 And if what was transitory came with
glory, how much greater is the glory of
that which lasts!

12 Therefore, since we have such a
hope,[q] we are very bold.[r] 13 We are not like
Moses, who would put a veil over his face[s]
to prevent the Israelites from seeing the
end of what was passing away. 14 But their
minds were made dull,[t] for to this day the
same veil remains when the old covenant[u]
is read.[v] It has not been removed, because
only in Christ is it taken away. 15 Even to
this day when Moses is read, a veil covers their hearts. 16 But whenever anyone
turns to the Lord,[w] the veil is taken away.[x]
17 Now the Lord is the Spirit,[y] and where
the Spirit of the Lord is, there is freedom.[z]
18 And we all, who with unveiled faces
contemplate[a][a] the Lord's glory,[b] are being
transformed into his image[c] with ever-
increasing glory, which comes from the
Lord, who is the Spirit.

Present Weakness and Resurrection Life

4 Therefore, since through God's mercy[d] we have this ministry, we do not
lose heart.[e] 2 Rather, we have renounced
secret and shameful ways;[f] we do not use
deception, nor do we distort the word of
God.[g] On the contrary, by setting forth
the truth plainly we commend ourselves
to everyone's conscience[h] in the sight of
God. 3 And even if our gospel[i] is veiled,[j] it
is veiled to those who are perishing.[k] 4 The
god[l] of this age[m] has blinded[n] the minds of

[a] 18 Or *reflect*

3:7 [m]ver 9; S Ro 4:15 [n]ver 13; Ex 34:29-35; Isa 42:21 **3:9** [o]ver 7; Dt 27:26 [p]Ro 1:17; 3:21,22 **3:12** [q]Ro 5:4, 5; 8:24,25 [r]S Ac 4:29 **3:13** [s]ver 7; Ex 34:33 **3:14** [t]Ro 11:7, 8; 2Co 4:4 [u]Ac 13:15; 15:21 [v]ver 6 **3:16** [w]Ro 11:23 [x]Ex 34:34; Isa 25:7 **3:17** [y]Isa 61:1, 2; Gal 4:6,7 [z]S Jn 8:32 **3:18** [a]1Co 13:12 [b]Jn 17:22, 24; 2Co 4:4,6 [c]S Ro 8:29 **4:1** [d]1Co 7:25; 1Ti 1:13, 16 [e]ver 16; Ps 18:45; Isa 40:31 **4:2** [f]Ro 6:21; S 1Co 4:5 [g]2Co 2:17; S Heb 4:12 [h]2Co 5:11 **4:3** [i]S 2Co 2:12 [j]2Co 3:14 [k]S 1Co 1:18 **4:4** [l]S Jn 12:31 [m]S 1Co 1:20 [n]2Co 3:14

3:7–18 Paul is defending his ministry of the new covenant in Christ (cf. v. 6 and note) and here compares the experiences of Moses, who mediated the old covenant of Sinai, and his own as a minister of the new covenant. But he now applies the word "ministry" (v. 7) to the law that was "engraved in letters on stone" (v. 7) and to the Spirit, who writes "on tablets of human hearts" (v. 3; see note there). The point of comparison is the fading glory that shone on Moses' face and the "ever-increasing glory" (v. 18; see note there) reflected in the faces of those who minister the new covenant.

3:7 *came with glory.* The law of the old covenant given at Sinai was in no way bad or evil; on the contrary, Paul describes it elsewhere as holy, righteous, good and spiritual (Ro 7:12,14). The evil is in the hearts and deeds of people who, as lawbreakers, bring upon themselves the condemnation of the law and the penalty of death—and the law engraved on stone could not purge away that evil. *its glory.* The glory of God surrounded the giving of the law and was reflected on the face of Moses when he descended from the mountain (see Ex 34:29–30).

3:8–9 *ministry of the Spirit ... brings righteousness.* Giving life instead of death (cf. Isa 46:13 and note).

3:11 *what was transitory.* The old covenant of Sinai, which was not to endure forever. In due course it was superseded by the unfading and much more glorious radiance belonging to the new covenant (see Heb 8 and notes on 8:7–13).

3:13 *Moses, who would put a veil over his face.* See Ex 34:33–35 and note on 34:33. The purpose of the veil was to prevent the Israelites from seeing the fading of the glory.

3:14 *to this day the same veil remains.* The veil that prevented the Israelites from seeing the fading of the glory on Moses' face kept them from recognizing the temporary and inadequate character of the "old covenant" (see chart, p. 23)—a "veil" that is removed only in Christ.

3:17 *the Lord is the Spirit.* This statement should be linked with what was said at the end of v. 6: "the Spirit gives life." Only by turning to the Lord Jesus Christ (v. 16) can the condemnation and the sentence of death pronounced by the law on the lawbreaker be annulled and replaced by the free, life-giving grace of the new covenant. *where the Spirit of the Lord is, there is freedom.* See Jn 8:33,36 and note on 8:32. The "new covenant" (v. 6) promised an inward transformation through the Holy Spirit (see Jer 31:31–34; Eze 36:27; Joel 2:2–29 and notes).

3:18 *with unveiled faces.* In contrast to Moses (v. 13). *transformed into his image with ever-increasing glory.* Christ himself is the glory of God in the fullness of its radiance (see Heb 1:2–3 and note); his is the eternal and unfading glory, which he had with the Father "before the world began" (Jn 17:5). Cf. Ro 8:29; 12:2 and notes.

4:1 *this ministry.* See 3:6 and note. *not lose heart.* When God through his mercy calls and commissions his servants, he also supplies the strength necessary for them to persevere in the face of hardship and persecution.

4:2 *renounced secret and shameful ways.* Paul is referring to the false teachers in Corinth. By contrast, he is able to appeal to the conscience of every one of them and also to his own integrity "in the sight of God," because his practice was always that of setting forth the truth plainly, i.e., without obscuring it or resorting to deception (cf. 1:12,18–24 and note on 1:12).

4:3 *gospel is veiled.* See 3:13–18 and notes.

4:4 *god of this age.* The devil, who is the archenemy of God and the unseen power behind all unbelief and ungodliness. Those who follow him have in effect made him their god. *this age.* Used in contrast to the future, eternal age when God's creation will be forever purged of all that now mars and defiles it. Paul calls it the "present evil age" in Gal 1:4 (see note there). *blinded the minds of unbelievers.* Paul continues to use the imagery of the veil that covers the divine glory so that those who reject the gospel fail to see that glory (3:13–18). *image of God.* Christ, the incarnate Son, authentically displays God to us (see Col 1:15 and note). He is the image of God in which humanity was originally created (see Ge 1:26 and note) and into which redeemed humanity is being gloriously transformed (3:18) until at last, when Christ comes again at the end of this age, we who believe will "be like him" (1Jn 3:2).

unbelievers, so that they cannot see the
light of the gospel that displays the glory
of Christ,[o] who is the image of God.[p] 5 For
what we preach is not ourselves,[q] but Jesus
Christ as Lord,[r] and ourselves as your servants[s] for Jesus' sake. 6 For God, who said,
"Let light shine out of darkness,"[a][t] made
his light shine in our hearts[u] to give us the
light of the knowledge of God's glory displayed in the face of Christ.[v]
7 But we have this treasure in jars of clay[w]
to show that this all-surpassing power is
from God[x] and not from us. 8 We are hard
pressed on every side,[y] but not crushed;
perplexed,[z] but not in despair; 9 persecuted,[a] but not abandoned;[b] struck down, but
not destroyed.[c] 10 We always carry around
in our body the death of Jesus,[d] so that the
life of Jesus may also be revealed in our
body.[e] 11 For we who are alive are always
being given over to death for Jesus' sake,[f]
so that his life may also be revealed in our
mortal body. 12 So then, death is at work in
us, but life is at work in you.[g]
13 It is written: "I believed; therefore I
have spoken."[b][h] Since we have that same
spirit of[c] faith,[i] we also believe and therefore speak, 14 because we know that the one
who raised the Lord Jesus from the dead[j]
will also raise us with Jesus[k] and present us
with you to himself.[l] 15 All this is for your
benefit, so that the grace that is reaching
more and more people may cause thanksgiving[m] to overflow to the glory of God.
16 Therefore we do not lose heart.[n]
Though outwardly we are wasting away,
yet inwardly[o] we are being renewed[p] day
by day. 17 For our light and momentary
troubles are achieving for us an eternal
glory that far outweighs them all.[q] 18 So
we fix our eyes not on what is seen, but
on what is unseen,[r] since what is seen is
temporary, but what is unseen is eternal.

Awaiting the New Body

5 For we know that if the earthly[s] tent[t]
we live in is destroyed, we have a
building from God, an eternal house
in heaven, not built by human hands.
2 Meanwhile we groan,[u] longing to be
clothed instead with our heavenly dwelling,[v] 3 because when we are clothed, we
will not be found naked. 4 For while we are

4:4 [o] ver 6 [p] S Jn 14:9 **4:5** [q] 1Co 1:13 [r] 1Co 1:23 [s] 1Co 9:19 **4:6** [t] Ge 1:3; Ps 18:28 [u] 2Pe 1:19 [v] ver 4 **4:7** [w] Job 4:19; Isa 64:8; 2Ti 2:20 [x] Jdg 7:2; 1Co 2:5; 2Co 6:7 **4:8** [y] 2Co 7:5 [z] Gal 4:20 **4:9** [a] Jn 15:20; Ro 8:35 [b] Heb 13:5 [c] Ps 37:24; Pr 24:16 **4:10** [d] S Ro 6:6; S 2Co 1:5 [e] S Ro 6:5 **4:11** [f] Ro 8:36 **4:12** [g] 2Co 13:9 **4:13** [h] Ps 116:10 [i] 1Co 12:9 **4:14** [j] S Ac 2:24 [k] 1Th 4:14 [l] Eph 5:27; Col 1:22; Jude 24 **4:15** [m] 2Co 1:11; 9:11 **4:16** [n] ver 1; Ps 18:45 [o] Ro 7:22 [p] Ps 103:5; Isa 40:31; Col 3:10 **4:17** [q] Ps 30:5; Ro 8:18; 1Pe 1:6,7 **4:18** [r] 2Co 5:7; Ro 8:24; Heb 11:1 **5:1** [s] 1Co 15:47 [t] Isa 38:12; 2Pe 1:13,14 **5:2** [u] ver 4; Ro 8:23 [v] ver 4; 1Co 15:53,54

[a] *6* Gen. 1:3 [b] *13* Psalm 116:10 (see Septuagint)
[c] *13* Or *Spirit-given*

4:5 *preach ... not ourselves.* As did the false teachers, puffed up with self-importance (cf. 1Co 2:2 and note).

4:6 *"Let light shine out of darkness."* God said this at the creation (see Ge 1:2–4 and notes) and says it again in the new creation or new birth (see 5:17; Jn 3:3 and notes; 1Pe 1:3), as the darkness of sin is dispelled by the light of the gospel. *the light of the knowledge of God's glory.* The light that now shines in Paul's heart (qualifying him to be a proclaimer of Christ) is the knowledge of God's glory as it was displayed in the face of Christ—who has come from the glorious presence of God in heaven (see Jn 1:14 and note).

4:7 *this treasure.* The gospel. *jars of clay.* Treasures were concealed in clay jars, which had little value or beauty and did not attract attention to themselves and their contents. Here they represent Paul's human frailty and unworthiness. *all-surpassing power is from God and not from us.* The idea that the absolute insufficiency of human beings reveals the total sufficiency of God pervades this letter.

4:8–12 See 11:23–26 and notes.

4:10 *We always carry around in our body the death of Jesus.* The frailty of the "clay jar" of Paul's humanity (v. 7) is plainly seen in the constant hardships and persecutions with which he is buffeted for the sake of the gospel and through which he shares in Christ's suffering (see 1:5; Ro 8:17; Php 3:10; Col 1:24 and notes). *that the life of Jesus may also be revealed in our body.* Refers to Christ's resurrection life and power (see Php 3:10 and note). Once again (see v. 7 and note), human weakness provides the occasion for the triumph of divine power.

4:12 *death.* See 1Co 15:31 and note. *life.* See v. 10 and note.

4:13 *"I believed; therefore I have spoken."* Faith leads to testimony. Paul therefore tirelessly labored and journeyed to bring the gospel message to others.

4:14 *one who raised the Lord Jesus.* God (Ac 2:24). *raise us with Jesus.* See Ro 8:11; 1Co 15:20 and notes.

4:16 *we do not lose heart.* Repeating the statement in v. 1. The intervening paragraphs explain why the apostle continues to have a cheerful heart, and the rest of the chapter summarizes the argument he has developed. *wasting away.* Because of the hardships to which he is subjected. *being renewed.* Because of the flame of resurrection life burning within.

4:17 *light and momentary troubles.* Seen from the perspective of eternity, the Christian's difficulties diminish in importance. *eternal glory that far outweighs them all.* By comparison, the eternal glory is far greater than all the suffering one may face in this life (see Ro 8:17–18 and note on 8:17).

4:18 *what is seen ... what is unseen.* The experiences and circumstances of this present life are visible to the Christian; but these are merely temporary and fleeting. To fix our eyes on them would cause us to "lose heart" (vv. 1,16). By contrast the unseen realities, which are no less real for being invisible (cf. Heb 11:1,7,26–27), are eternal and imperishable. Accordingly, we look up and away from the impermanent appearances of this present world scene (see Php 3:20; Heb 12:2 and notes).

5:1 *earthly tent we live in.* Our present body (see Jn 1:14 and note; 2Pe 1:13). As a tent is a temporary and flimsy abode, so our bodies are frail, vulnerable and wasting away (see 4:10–12,16 and notes). *a building from God, an eternal house in heaven.* A solid structure—permanent, not temporary. This is one of the eternal realities that are as yet "unseen" (4:18). *not built by human hands.* The work of God, and therefore perfect and permanent (see Heb 9:11 and note).

5:2 *Meanwhile.* As we await the Lord's return. *we groan.* Because we long for the perfection that will be ours when we put on the glorious spiritual body (cf. 1Co 15:42–49 and notes). *clothed instead with our heavenly dwelling.* The eternal dwelling provided by God is pictured as a garment (see v. 4).

5:3 *naked.* Without the clothing of a body, which is the state of those whose earthly dwelling has been dismantled by death (see v. 8 and note).

5:4 *what is mortal.* Our present mortal body. *swallowed up by*

in this tent, we groan[w] and are burdened,
because we do not wish to be unclothed
but to be clothed instead with our heavenly dwelling,[x] so that what is mortal may be
swallowed up by life. 5 Now the one who
has fashioned us for this very purpose is
God, who has given us the Spirit as a deposit, guaranteeing what is to come.[y]
6 Therefore we are always confident and
know that as long as we are at home in the
body we are away from the Lord. 7 For we
live by faith, not by sight.[z] 8 We are confident, I say, and would prefer to be away
from the body and at home with the Lord.[a]
9 So we make it our goal to please him,[b]
whether we are at home in the body or
away from it. 10 For we must all appear before the judgment seat of Christ, so that
each of us may receive what is due us[c] for
the things done while in the body, whether good or bad.

The Ministry of Reconciliation

11 Since, then, we know what it is to fear
the Lord,[d] we try to persuade others. What
we are is plain to God, and I hope it is
also plain to your conscience.[e] 12 We are
not trying to commend ourselves to you
again,[f] but are giving you an opportunity
to take pride in us,[g] so that you can answer those who take pride in what is seen
rather than in what is in the heart. 13 If we
are "out of our mind,"[h] as some say, it is
for God; if we are in our right mind, it is
for you. 14 For Christ's love compels us, because we are convinced that one died for
all, and therefore all died.[i] 15 And he died
for all, that those who live should no longer live for themselves[j] but for him who
died for them[k] and was raised again.
16 So from now on we regard no one
from a worldly[l] point of view. Though
we once regarded Christ in this way, we
do so no longer. 17 Therefore, if anyone is
in Christ,[m] the new creation[n] has come:[a]
The old has gone, the new is here![o] 18 All
this is from God,[p] who reconciled us to
himself through Christ[q] and gave us the
ministry of reconciliation: 19 that God
was reconciling the world to himself in
Christ, not counting people's sins against

[a] 17 Or *Christ, that person is a new creation.*

5:4 [w] ver 2; Ro 8:23 [x] ver 2; 1Co 15:53,54 **5:5** [y] Ro 8:23; 2Co 1:22; Eph 1:13,14 **5:7** [z] 1Co 13:12; S 2Co 4:18 **5:8** [a] S Jn 12:26 **5:9** [b] Ro 14:18; Eph 5:10; Col 1:10; 1Th 4:1 **5:10** [c] S Mt 16:27; Ac 10:42; Ro 2:16; 14:10; Eph 6:8 **5:11** [d] Job 23:15; Heb 10:31; 12:29; Jude 23 [e] 2Co 4:2 **5:12** [f] S 2Co 3:1 [g] 2Co 1:14 **5:13** [h] 2Co 11:1, 16,17; 12:11 **5:14** [i] Ro 6:6, 7; Gal 2:20; Col 3:3 **5:15** [j] Ro 14:7-9 [k] Ro 4:25 **5:16** [l] 2Co 10:4; 11:18 **5:17** [m] S Ro 16:3 [n] S Jn 1:13; S Ro 6:4; Gal 6:15 [o] Isa 65:17; Rev 21:4,5 **5:18** [p] S Ro 11:36 [q] S Ro 5:10

life. By our participation in the resurrection life of Jesus (see 4:10 and note) our mortal being is "swallowed up by life," not by death. Paul reverses the age-old imagery of death and the grave being the great swallower (see Ps 49:14 and note), as did Isaiah (see Isa 25:8; see also 1Co 15:54).

5:5 *God ... has given us the Spirit.* The Holy Spirit applies the benefits of Christ's redeeming work to the hearts of believers and makes his resurrection power a reality of their daily experience (cf. 4:10–16 and notes). This guarantees their eventual transformation into the likeness of Christ's glorified body (see Php 3:21 and note). *deposit.* See 1:22 and note.

5:6 *at home in the body ... away from the Lord.* Still living here in our earthly dwelling (see v. 1 and note); it does not mean that we are deprived of the Lord's spiritual presence with us in our daily lives.

5:7 *by faith, not by sight.* See 4:18 and note; cf. 1Co 13:12 and note.

5:8 *away from the body ... at home with the Lord.* The situation of believers after death, when they are no longer living in their mortal bodies (see Php 1:23 and note).

5:9 *whether we are at home in the body or away from it.* Whether we will still be alive or will already be with the Lord.

5:10 *appear before the judgment seat of Christ.* To give an accounting of what we have done with our lives as Christians (cf. 1Co 3:11–15 and note on 3:13). *things done while in the body.* Although the body is wasting away, we are responsible for our actions while in it.

5:11 *fear the Lord.* As the one to whom we are accountable (v. 10; see Ge 20:11; Pr 1:7 and notes). *we try to persuade others.* Paul needs to persuade some members of the Corinthian church that he, not any of the false teachers who have invaded their ranks, is their authentic apostle.

5:12 *take pride in what is seen.* The pretension of the false apostles is a superficial front; their concern is not with spirituality that is true and deep but with money (see 2:17 and note), popularity and self-importance.

5:13 *"out of our mind" ... in our right mind.* Perhaps Paul's enemies were asserting that he was suffering from religious mania—what they regarded as his insane way of life. If this is what it means to be out of his mind, Paul does not deny it, for this whole letter shows how willingly and joyfully he endured affliction for the gospel (see 12:10). On the other hand, there was nothing that could be called eccentric about his manner of presenting the gospel to the Corinthians, for he had been sensible and sober-minded, avoiding flowery rhetoric and all forms of sensationalism (see 1Co 2:1–5 and notes).

5:14 *Christ's love.* As shown in his death for us, though some hold that the meaning here is "our love for Christ." *one.* The incarnate Son. *therefore all died.* Because Christ died for all, he involved all in his death. For some his death would confirm their own death, but for others (those who by faith would become united with him) his death was their death to sin and self, so that they now live in and with the resurrected Christ (v. 15; see Ro 6:1–11). However, some hold that Paul is not speaking specifically here about the scope of Christ's atonement but about the effect of Christ's death on the Christian life. Thus "all" would refer not to every human being but only to believers.

5:16 *we once regarded Christ in this way.* Paul admits that before his conversion he held views of Christ that were "worldly"—based on purely human considerations.

5:17 *in Christ.* United with Christ through faith in him and commitment to him (see Ro 6:11; Eph 1:1; Php 2:1 and notes). *new creation.* Redemption is the restoration and fulfillment of God's purposes in creation (see 4:6 and note), and this takes place in Christ, through whom all things were made (see Col 1:16 and note; Heb 1:2) and in whom all things are restored or created anew (cf. Ro 8:19–23; Eph 2:10).

5:18 *All this is from God.* God takes the initiative in redemption (see Jn 3:16; Ro 5:8; Eph 2:8–10 and notes), and he sustains it and brings it to completion (see Php 1:6 and note). *ministry of reconciliation.* We who are the recipients of divine reconciliation have the privilege and obligation of now being "Christ's ambassadors" (v. 20), God's instruments to proclaim the "message of reconciliation" (v. 19) throughout the world. *reconciliation.* See Ro 5:10–11 and notes.

them.[r] And he has committed to us the
message of reconciliation. 20We are therefore Christ's ambassadors,[s] as though God
were making his appeal through us.[t] We
implore you on Christ's behalf: Be reconciled to God.[u] 21God made him who had
no sin[v] to be sin[a] for us, so that in him we
might become the righteousness of God.[w]

6 As God's co-workers[x] we urge you not
to receive God's grace in vain.[y] 2For
he says,

> "In the time of my favor I heard you,
> and in the day of salvation I helped
> you."[b][z]

I tell you, now is the time of God's favor,
now is the day of salvation.

Paul's Hardships

3We put no stumbling block in anyone's
path,[a] so that our ministry will not be discredited. 4Rather, as servants of God we
commend ourselves in every way: in great
endurance; in troubles, hardships and distresses; 5in beatings, imprisonments[b] and riots; in hard work, sleepless nights and hunger;[c] 6in purity, understanding, patience and
kindness; in the Holy Spirit[d] and in sincere
love;[e] 7in truthful speech[f] and in the power of God;[g] with weapons of righteousness[h]
in the right hand and in the left; 8through
glory and dishonor,[i] bad report[j] and good
report; genuine, yet regarded as impostors;[k]
9known, yet regarded as unknown; dying,[l]
and yet we live on;[m] beaten, and yet not
killed; 10sorrowful, yet always rejoicing;[n]
poor, yet making many rich;[o] having nothing,[p] and yet possessing everything.[q]

11We have spoken freely to you, Corinthians, and opened wide our hearts to you.[r]
12We are not withholding our affection from
you, but you are withholding yours from
us. 13As a fair exchange—I speak as to my
children[s]—open wide your hearts[t] also.

Warning Against Idolatry

14Do not be yoked together[u] with unbelievers.[v] For what do righteousness and
wickedness have in common? Or what
fellowship can light have with darkness?[w]
15What harmony is there between Christ
and Belial[c]?[x] Or what does a believer[y] have
in common with an unbeliever?[z] 16What
agreement is there between the temple of
God and idols?[a] For we are the temple[b] of
the living God.[c] As God has said:

> "I will live with them
> and walk among them,
> and I will be their God,
> and they will be my people."[d][d]

17Therefore,

> "Come out from them[e]
> and be separate,
> says the Lord.

[a] *21* Or *be a sin offering* [b] *2* Isaiah 49:8
[c] *15* Greek *Beliar*, a variant of *Belial* [d] *16* Lev. 26:12; Jer. 32:38; Ezek. 37:27

5:19 [r]S Ro 4:8 **5:20** [s]2Co 6:1; Eph 6:20 [t]ver 18 [u]Isa 27:5 **5:21** [v]Heb 4:15; 7:26; 1Pe 2:22, 24; 1Jn 3:5 [w]S Ro 1:17; S 1Co 1:30 **6:1** [x]S 1Co 3:9; 2Co 5:20 [y]1Co 15:2 **6:2** [z]Isa 49:8; Ps 69:13; Isa 55:6 **6:3** [a]S Mt 5:29; Ro 14:13, 20; 1Co 8:9, 13; 9:12; 10:32 **6:5** [b]Ac 16:23; 2Co 11:23-25 [c]1Co 4:11 **6:6** [d]1Co 2:4; 1Th 1:5 [e]Ro 12:9; 1Ti 1:5 **6:7** [f]2Co 4:2 [g]2Co 4:7 [h]Ro 13:12; 2Co 10:4; Eph 6:10-18 **6:8** [i]1Co 4:10 [j]1Co 4:13 [k]Mt 27:63 **6:9** [l]S Ro 8:36 [m]2Co 1:8-10; 4:10, 11 **6:10** [n]S Mt 5:12; 2Co 7:4; Php 2:17; 4:4; Col 1:24; 1Th 1:6 [o]2Co 8:9 [p]Ac 3:6 [q]Ro 8:32; 1Co 3:21 **6:11** [r]2Co 7:3 **6:13** [s]S 1Th 2:11 [t]2Co 7:2 **6:14** [u]Ge 24:3; Dt 22:10; 1Co 5:9, 10 [v]1Co 6:6 [w]Eph 5:7, 11; 1Jn 1:6 **6:15** [x]1Co 10:21 [y]Ac 5:14 [z]1Co 6:6 **6:16** [a]1Co 10:21 [b]S 1Co 3:16 [c]S Mt 16:16 [d]Lev 26:12; Jer 32:38; Eze 37:27; Rev 21:3 **6:17** [e]Rev 18:4

5:20 *Christ's ambassadors.* The honor of Christ and his church is in his ambassadors' hands. He expects them to represent him well. People will think more highly or less highly of Christ and his church based on the effectiveness of his ambassadors' service.

5:21 A summary of the gospel. Christ, the only entirely righteous one, took our sin upon himself at Calvary and endured the punishment we deserved (see NIV text note), namely, death and separation from God. Thus, by a marvelous exchange, he made it possible for us to receive his righteousness and thereby be reconciled to God (cf. 1Co 1:30 and note).

6:1 *to receive God's grace in vain.* To live for oneself (see 5:15) is one way to do this.

6:2 *time of my favor … day of salvation.* An affirmation that is true in a general sense of all God's saving acts in the history of his people, but that finds its particular fulfillment in this present age of grace between the two comings of Christ. *now.* Underscores the urgency of the divine invitation (see Ps 32:6 and note).

6:4–10 See note on 1:4.

6:4 *as servants of God we commend ourselves.* Paul commends himself again inasmuch as the gospel he preached in Corinth is at stake; but in contrast to the false apostles who were no better than self-servers, he does so as God's servant.

6:5 *imprisonments.* See, e.g., Ac 16:23; Eph 3:1; Php 1:13–14; Col 4:18; 2Ti 1:16; Phm 1.

6:7 *weapons of righteousness.* Cf. Eph 6:14–17 and notes.

6:10 *making many rich.* True wealth does not consist in worldly possessions but in being "rich toward God" (Lk 12:21). Believers, even if they have nothing of this world's goods, nevertheless have everything in him who is Lord of all (cf. 1Co 1:4–5; 3:21–23; Eph 2:7; 3:8; Php 4:19 and note; Col 2:3).

6:11–13 Paul has always been completely open and sincere in his relations with the Christians in Corinth (cf. 1:12–14; 4:2 and note), but the false apostles among them have been trying to persuade them that Paul does not really love them. Now the apostle tenderly appeals to these Corinthians, who are the beneficiaries of his love for them (cf. 11:11).

6:14 *Do not be yoked together with unbelievers.* Cf. Dt 22:10. For the Corinthian believers to cooperate with false teachers, who are in reality servants of Satan, notwithstanding their charming and persuasive ways (see 11:13–14 and notes), is to become unequally yoked, destroying the harmony and fellowship that unite true believers in Christ. *what fellowship can light have with darkness?* See 4:6 and note.

6:15 *Belial.* Satan (see Dt 13:13 and note).

6:16 *agreement … between the temple of God and idols.* There can be no reversion to or compromise with the idolatry they have forsaken for the gospel (cf. 1Th 1:9). *temple of the living God.* Built of "living stones," namely, Christian believers (1Pe 2:5; see note there); therefore it is all the more important that they form no defiling and unholy alliances (cf. 1Co 6:19–20). *their God … my people.* The supreme OT affirmation of covenant relationship between God and his people (see Jer 7:23; Hos 1:9; Zec 8:8 and notes).

6:17 *Come out from them.* See Rev 18:4 and note.

Touch no unclean thing,
and I will receive you."[a][f]

18 And,

"I will be a Father to you,
and you will be my sons and
daughters,[g]
says the Lord Almighty."[b][h]

7 Therefore, since we have these promises,[i] dear friends,[j] let us purify ourselves from everything that contaminates
body and spirit, perfecting holiness[k] out of
reverence for God.

Paul's Joy Over the Church's Repentance

2 Make room for us in your hearts.[l] We
have wronged no one, we have corrupted
no one, we have exploited no one. 3 I do
not say this to condemn you; I have said
before that you have such a place in our
hearts[m] that we would live or die with you.
4 I have spoken to you with great frankness; I take great pride in you.[n] I am greatly encouraged;[o] in all our troubles my joy
knows no bounds.[p]
5 For when we came into Macedonia,[q]
we had no rest, but we were harassed
at every turn[r]—conflicts on the outside,
fears within.[s] 6 But God, who comforts the
downcast,[t] comforted us by the coming of
Titus,[u] 7 and not only by his coming but
also by the comfort you had given him.
He told us about your longing for me, your
deep sorrow, your ardent concern for me,
so that my joy was greater than ever.
8 Even if I caused you sorrow by my letter,[v] I do not regret it. Though I did regret
it—I see that my letter hurt you, but only
for a little while— 9 yet now I am happy, not
because you were made sorry, but because
your sorrow led you to repentance. For you
became sorrowful as God intended and so
were not harmed in any way by us. 10 Godly sorrow brings repentance that leads to
salvation[w] and leaves no regret, but worldly sorrow brings death. 11 See what this
godly sorrow has produced in you: what
earnestness, what eagerness to clear yourselves, what indignation, what alarm, what
longing, what concern,[x] what readiness to
see justice done. At every point you have
proved yourselves to be innocent in this
matter. 12 So even though I wrote to you,[y] it
was neither on account of the one who did
the wrong[z] nor on account of the injured
party, but rather that before God you could
see for yourselves how devoted to us you
are. 13 By all this we are encouraged.
In addition to our own encouragement,
we were especially delighted to see how
happy Titus[a] was, because his spirit has
been refreshed by all of you. 14 I had boasted to him about you,[b] and you have not
embarrassed me. But just as everything
we said to you was true, so our boasting
about you to Titus[c] has proved to be true
as well. 15 And his affection for you is all
the greater when he remembers that you
were all obedient,[d] receiving him with
fear and trembling.[e] 16 I am glad I can have
complete confidence in you.[f]

The Collection for the Lord's People

8 And now, brothers and sisters, we
want you to know about the grace that
God has given the Macedonian[g] churches.

[a] *17* Isaiah 52:11; Ezek. 20:34,41 [b] *18* 2 Samuel 7:14; 7:8

6:17 [f] Isa 52:11; Eze 20:34,41 **6:18** [g] Ex 4:22; 2Sa 7:14; 1Ch 17:13; Isa 43:6; S Ro 8:14 [h] 2Sa 7:8 **7:1** [i] 2Co 6:17, 18 [j] S 1Co 10:14 [k] 1Th 4:7; 1Pe 1:15,16 **7:2** [l] 2Co 6:12, 13 **7:3** [m] 2Co 6:11, 12; Php 1:7 **7:4** [n] ver 14; 2Co 8:24 [o] ver 13 [p] S 2Co 6:10 **7:5** [q] 2Co 2:13; S Ac 16:9 [r] 2Co 4:8 [s] Dt 32:25 **7:6** [t] 2Co 1:3, 4 [u] ver 13; S 2Co 2:13 **7:8** [v] 2Co 2:2,4 **7:10** [w] Ac 11:18 **7:11** [x] ver 7 **7:12** [y] ver 8; 2Co 2:3,9 [z] 1Co 5:1,2 **7:13** [a] ver 6; S 2Co 2:13 **7:14** [b] ver 4 [c] ver 6 **7:15** [d] 2Co 2:9; 10:6 [e] Ps 55:5; 1Co 2:3; Php 2:12 **7:16** [f] S 2Co 2:3 **8:1** [g] S Ac 16:9

7:1 *holiness.* See 1Co 1:2; Ex 3:5; Lev 11:44; Ro 6:22; 1Th 4:7 and notes; Heb 12:14.
7:2 *Make room for us in your hearts.* Resumes the thought of 6:13 after a brief digression. *We have … exploited no one.* Implies that Paul had been accused by the false teachers of being unjust, destructive and fraudulent—the very things they themselves were guilty of. Cf. 1Sa 12:3 and note.
7:3 Again Paul declares the depth of his affection for the Corinthian believers and appeals to them to respond by displaying their love for him (cf. 6:11–13 and note).
7:4 *great frankness … my joy knows no bounds.* The long digression that started at 2:14 (see note there) concludes here on this note of exhilaration. The news he had been so anxiously awaiting from Corinth has turned out to be reassuring, and Paul is overjoyed to receive it.
7:5 *we.* Paul and Titus. Here Paul resumes the account he began in 2:12–13, where he described how his hopes of meeting Titus in Troas were disappointed and how, restless for news, he had decided to press on into Macedonia. He now explains that on reaching Macedonia, he was at last comforted by the arrival of Titus, who had been well received in Corinth and was able to assure Paul (see v. 7) of the "longing" and "ardent concern" of the Corinthian Christians for him and of the "deep sorrow" they had expressed because of the grief they had caused him. Consequently, his "joy was greater than ever" (v. 7). *Macedonia.* See notes on 1:1; Php 4:15.
7:6 *God … comforts the downcast.* See 1:3 and note; cf. Ps 42:5,11; 43:5. *Titus.* See Introduction to Titus: Recipient.
7:8 Paul regretted the necessity of writing a letter to the Corinthians that caused them sorrow. *my letter.* Some think Paul here refers either to 1 Corinthians or to 2Co 10–13 (see Introduction: Occasion), but more likely he refers to a letter now lost that he wrote shortly after his "painful visit" (2:1; see note there).
7:10 *Godly sorrow … worldly sorrow.* The former manifests itself by repentance and the experience of divine grace; the latter brings death because, instead of being God-centered sorrow over the wickedness of sin, it is self-centered sorrow over the painful consequences of sin.
7:15 *you were all obedient.* This seems to indicate that when Titus left Corinth to report to Paul, there was no strong opposition party (see note on 10:1).
8:1—9:15 Paul addresses the question of the collection of money for the distressed believers in Jerusalem, which the Corinthians had started but not completed.
8:1 *grace.* The "grace of giving" on the part of believers (v. 7) is more than matched by the self-giving "grace of our Lord Jesus Christ" (v. 9).

2 In the midst of a very severe trial, their overflowing joy and their extreme poverty welled up in rich generosity.[h] 3 For I testify that they gave as much as they were able,[i] and even beyond their ability. Entirely on their own, 4 they urgently pleaded with us for the privilege of sharing[j] in this service[k] to the Lord's people.[l] 5 And they exceeded our expectations: They gave themselves first of all to the Lord, and then by the will of God also to us. 6 So we urged[m] Titus,[n] just as he had earlier made a beginning, to bring also to completion[o] this act of grace on your part. 7 But since you excel in everything[p]—in faith, in speech, in knowledge,[q] in complete earnestness and in the love we have kindled in you[a]—see that you also excel in this grace of giving.

8 I am not commanding you,[r] but I want to test the sincerity of your love by comparing it with the earnestness of others. 9 For you know the grace[s] of our Lord Jesus Christ,[t] that though he was rich, yet for your sake he became poor,[u] so that you through his poverty might become rich.[v]

10 And here is my judgment[w] about what is best for you in this matter. Last year you were the first not only to give but also to have the desire to do so.[x] 11 Now finish the work, so that your eager willingness[y] to do it may be matched by your completion of it, according to your means. 12 For if the willingness is there, the gift is acceptable according to what one has,[z] not according to what one does not have.

13 Our desire is not that others might be relieved while you are hard pressed, but that there might be equality. 14 At the present time your plenty will supply what they need,[a] so that in turn their plenty will supply what you need. The goal is equality, 15 as it is written: "The one who gathered much did not have too much, and the one who gathered little did not have too little."[b][b]

Titus Sent to Receive the Collection

16 Thanks be to God,[c] who put into the heart[d] of Titus[e] the same concern I have for you. 17 For Titus not only welcomed our appeal, but he is coming to you with much enthusiasm and on his own initiative.[f] 18 And we are sending along with him the brother[g] who is praised by all the churches[h] for his service to the gospel.[i] 19 What is more, he was chosen by the churches to accompany us[j] as we carry the offering, which we administer in order to honor the Lord himself and to show our eagerness to help.[k] 20 We want to avoid any criticism of the way we administer this liberal gift. 21 For we are taking pains to do what is right, not only in the eyes of the Lord but also in the eyes of man.[l]

22 In addition, we are sending with them our brother who has often proved to us in many ways that he is zealous, and now even more so because of his great confidence in you. 23 As for Titus,[m] he is my partner[n] and co-worker[o] among you; as for our brothers,[p] they are representatives of the churches and an honor to Christ. 24 Therefore show these men the proof of

8:2 [h] Ex 36:5; 2Co 9:11
8:3 [i] 1Co 16:2
8:4 [j] ver 1 [k] S Ac 24:17 [l] S Ac 9:13
8:6 [m] ver 17; 2Co 12:18 [n] ver 16, 23; S 2Co 2:13 [o] ver 10, 11
8:7 [p] 2Co 9:8 [q] Ro 15:14; 1Co 1:5; 12:8; 13:1, 2; 14:6
8:8 [r] 1Co 7:6
8:9 [s] S Ro 3:24 [t] 2Co 13:14 [u] Mt 20:28; Php 2:6-8 [v] 2Co 6:10
8:10 [w] 1Co 7:25, 40 [x] 1Co 16:2, 3; 2Co 9:2
8:11 [y] ver 12, 19; Ex 25:2; 2Co 9:2
8:12 [z] Mk 12:43, 44; 2Co 9:7
8:14 [a] Ac 4:34; 2Co 9:12
8:15 [b] Ex 16:18
8:16 [c] S 2Co 2:14 [d] Rev 17:17 [e] S 2Co 2:13
8:17 [f] ver 6
8:18 [g] 2Co 12:18 [h] S 1Co 7:17 [i] S 2Co 2:12
8:19 [j] Ac 14:23; 1Co 16:3, 4 [k] ver 11, 12
8:21 [l] Ro 12:17; S 14:18; S Titus 2:14
8:23 [m] S 2Co 2:13 [n] Phm 17 [o] S Php 2:25 [p] ver 18, 22

[a] 7 Some manuscripts *and in your love for us*
[b] 15 Exodus 16:18

8:2 *overflowing joy.* In the blessings of the gospel.

8:5 *gave themselves first of all to the Lord.* The true basis of all Christian giving. God's grace makes a difference in the lives and attitudes of his people—a central theme of this letter (cf. 12:9–10).

8:6 *we urged Titus.* The collection had been started in Corinth under the direction of Titus during the previous year (see v. 10; 9:2) but had slowed down or come to a standstill. Paul is now sending Titus back to them, bearing this present letter, for the purpose of completing this "act of grace."

8:7 *you excel in everything.* Cf. 1Co 1:4–7.

8:8 *I am not commanding you.* True charity and generosity cannot be commanded. *sincerity of your love.* They can prove this by giving selflessly and spontaneously. *earnestness of others.* The remarkable example of the Macedonian churches (vv. 1–5).

8:9 *though he was rich … he became poor.* The eternal Son, in his incarnation and atoning death, emptied himself of his riches (see Php 2:7 and note). *through his poverty might become rich.* The supreme example and incentive for all genuine Christian generosity. *rich.* Cf. Pr 3:9–10 and note on 3:10; 10:22 and note; Eph 1:3; 1Pe 1:3–5.

8:11 The work they had started "last year" with "desire" (v. 10) needs to be completed (see note on v. 6).

8:12 *according to what one has.* See v. 11. What matters is the willingness, no matter how small the amount that can be afforded (see Mk 12:41–44 and note on 12:42). The mechanics of the collection being made in Corinth had been proposed by Paul in his earlier letter (see 1Co 16:1–2 and notes).

8:13–15 Paul's desire is that believers throughout the whole Christian community share what they have with believers who are in need so that a measure of equality is maintained within the church—so that, as with Israel in the wilderness (see Ex 16:18 and note), there would be no one who has "too much" and no one who has "too little" (v. 15).

8:16–17 Titus had established a relationship of trust and affection with the Corinthians (see 7:6–7,13–15). He had organized the collection when it was started the previous year (see note on v. 6).

8:18 *brother.* Perhaps Luke or Barnabas.

8:19 Paul provides a good example of the care that church leaders should take in handling money (see 1Co 16:3–4 and note on 16:3).

8:20 It is important not only that God sees but also that people see (cf. vv. 19,21) that one is carrying on the Lord's work in an ethical way.

8:21 *taking pains to do what is right.* Paul is the victim of disgraceful slander (implied by 12:17–18; see note on 12:16; see also Introduction: Purposes), but the integrity of his representatives (see v. 23 and note) reflects well on his own integrity.

8:22 *our brother.* This second brother is also anonymous (cf. v. 18 and note).

8:23 *partner and co-worker.* See 2:13 and note. *representatives of the churches.* Duly elected delegates of the churches at

your love and the reason for our pride in
you,[q] so that the churches can see it.
9 There is no need[r] for me to write to
you about this service[s] to the Lord's
people.[t] 2 For I know your eagerness to
help,[u] and I have been boasting[v] about it
to the Macedonians, telling them that since
last year[w] you in Achaia[x] were ready to
give; and your enthusiasm has stirred most
of them to action. 3 But I am sending the
brothers[y] in order that our boasting about
you in this matter should not prove hollow,
but that you may be ready, as I said you
would be.[z] 4 For if any Macedonians[a] come
with me and find you unprepared, we—
not to say anything about you—would be
ashamed of having been so confident. 5 So
I thought it necessary to urge the brothers[b]
to visit you in advance and finish the arrangements for the generous gift you had
promised. Then it will be ready as a generous gift,[c] not as one grudgingly given.[d]

Generosity Encouraged

6 Remember this: Whoever sows sparingly will also reap sparingly, and whoever sows generously will also reap generously.[e] 7 Each of you should give what
you have decided in your heart to give,[f]
not reluctantly or under compulsion,[g] for
God loves a cheerful giver.[h] 8 And God
is able[i] to bless you abundantly, so that
in all things at all times, having all that
you need,[j] you will abound in every good
work. 9 As it is written:

> "They have freely scattered their gifts[k]
> to the poor;
> their righteousness endures forever."[a][l]

8:24 q 2Co 7:4, 14; 9:2
9:1 r 1Th 4:9
s S Ac 24:17
t S Ac 9:13
9:2 u 2Co 8:11, 12,19 v 2Co 7:4, 14; 8:24
w 2Co 8:10
x S Ac 18:12
9:3 y 2Co 8:23
z 1Co 16:2
9:4 a Ro 15:26
9:5 b ver 3
c Php 4:17
d 2Co 12:17,18
9:6 e Pr 11:24, 25; 22:9; Gal 6:7,9
9:7 f Ex 25:2; 2Co 8:12
g Dt 15:10
h Ro 12:8
9:8 i Eph 3:20
j Php 4:19
9:9 k Mal 3:10
l Ps 112:9
9:10 m Isa 55:10
n Hos 10:12
9:11 o 1Co 1:5
p ver 5
q 2Co 1:11; 4:15
9:12 r 2Co 8:14
s S 2Co 1:11
9:13 t S 2Co 8:4
u S Mt 9:8
v S Heb 3:1
w S 2Co 2:12
x ver 5
9:15
y S 2Co 2:14
z Ro 5:15,16
10:1 a Mt 11:29
b Gal 5:2; Eph 3:1
10:2
c S 1Co 4:21
d Ro 12:2
10:3 e ver 2
10:4 f S 2Co 6:7
g 1Co 2:5 h ver 8; Jer 1:10; 23:29; 2Co 13:10

10 Now he who supplies seed to the sower
and bread for food[m] will also supply and
increase your store of seed and will enlarge the harvest of your righteousness.[n]
11 You will be enriched[o] in every way so
that you can be generous[p] on every occasion, and through us your generosity will
result in thanksgiving to God.[q]
12 This service that you perform is not
only supplying the needs[r] of the Lord's
people but is also overflowing in many
expressions of thanks to God.[s] 13 Because
of the service[t] by which you have proved
yourselves, others will praise God[u] for the
obedience that accompanies your confession[v] of the gospel of Christ,[w] and for your
generosity[x] in sharing with them and with
everyone else. 14 And in their prayers for
you their hearts will go out to you, because of the surpassing grace God has giv-
en you. 15 Thanks be to God[y] for his indescribable gift![z]

Paul's Defense of His Ministry

10 By the humility and gentleness[a] of
Christ, I appeal to you—I, Paul,[b]
who am "timid" when face to face with
you, but "bold" toward you when away!
2 I beg you that when I come I may not
have to be as bold[c] as I expect to be toward some people who think that we
live by the standards of this world.[d] 3 For
though we live in the world, we do not
wage war as the world does.[e] 4 The weapons we fight with[f] are not the weapons of
the world. On the contrary, they have divine power[g] to demolish strongholds.[h] 5 We

[a] 9 Psalm 112:9

large (so that they could not be dismissed as cronies chosen by Paul alone); see note on Ac 20:4. *an honor to Christ.* By their outstanding faithfulness.

9:2 *Macedonians … Achaia.* See 1:1 and note.

9:5 *generous gift, not … grudgingly given.* See vv. 6–7,11.

9:6 Probably a well-known proverb. For a similar principle, cf. Pr 11:24–25; 22:8–9; Lk 6:38; Gal 6:7.

9:8 *bless you abundantly … all things … all times … all that you need … abound in every good work.* Through his abounding grace (see v. 14 and note) God can enable each Christian to abound in generous deeds (see v. 11).

9:9–10 *righteousness.* See note on Ps 1:5.

9:10 The God who is the ultimate source of the physical food that sustains all human life is the same God who supplies the spiritual nourishment that enables believers to flourish and serve.

9:12 *not only supplying the needs of the Lord's people.* The effect of generous giving on the part of the Corinthians will extend beyond Jerusalem to the church as a whole, causing widespread prayer and praise to be offered (see vv. 11,13–14).

9:14 *the surpassing grace God has given you.* Displayed in this unselfish demonstration of their loving concern for fellow believers who are in desperate need.

9:15 *indescribable gift.* His own Son (see Jn 3:16 and note). God is the first giver; he selflessly gives himself to us in the person of his Son, and all true Christian giving is our grateful response (cf. 8:9 and note; 1Jn 4:9–11).

10:1—13:14 See Introduction: Occasion. From the mild tone of the first nine chapters of this letter, it appears that most of the Corinthian believers had been won over to Paul (cf. 7:6–16) after having been alienated by his opponents. In this final section, however, Paul deals firmly with the slanders that have been spread against him in Corinth by the remaining opposition. Those who wish to discredit him have been saying that he is bold at a distance, threatening in his letters to take severe disciplinary action (cf., e.g., his warning that, if necessary, he will come "with a rod of discipline" [1Co 4:21]). But they say that he will not dare to be anything but weak and indecisive if he is present with them in person—in short, that he does not have the apostolic authority he claims to have. Paul is ready to prove otherwise, should the occasion demand, when he comes to Corinth for the third time (see 10:6,10–11 and note on 10:10).

10:1 *humility and gentleness of Christ.* An indication of his own affectionate desire to show these same qualities when present with them.

10:4 *weapons we fight with.* Paul is prepared for warfare; his weapons, however, are not the weapons prized by this fallen world and fashioned by human pride (cf. 1:17; 4:2). *strongholds.* Of "arguments" and "every pretension" (v. 5) defiantly raised "against the knowledge of God" (cf. Ro 1:18–23),

demolish arguments and every pretension
that sets itself up against the knowledge of
God,[i] and we take captive every thought to
make it obedient[j] to Christ. 6 And we will
be ready to punish every act of disobedience, once your obedience is complete.[k]
7 You are judging by appearances.[a][l] If
anyone is confident that they belong to
Christ,[m] they should consider again that
we belong to Christ just as much as they
do.[n] 8 So even if I boast somewhat freely
about the authority the Lord gave us[o] for
building you up rather than tearing you
down,[p] I will not be ashamed of it. 9 I do
not want to seem to be trying to frighten
you with my letters. 10 For some say, "His
letters are weighty and forceful, but in
person he is unimpressive[q] and his speaking amounts to nothing."[r] 11 Such people
should realize that what we are in our letters when we are absent, we will be in our
actions when we are present.
12 We do not dare to classify or compare
ourselves with some who commend themselves.[s] When they measure themselves by
themselves and compare themselves with
themselves, they are not wise. 13 We, however, will not boast beyond proper limits,
but will confine our boasting to the sphere
of service God himself has assigned to us,[t]
a sphere that also includes you. 14 We are
not going too far in our boasting, as would
be the case if we had not come to you, for
we did get as far as you[u] with the gospel
of Christ.[v] 15 Neither do we go beyond our
limits[w] by boasting of work done by others.[x] Our hope is that, as your faith continues to grow,[y] our sphere of activity among
you will greatly expand, 16 so that we can
preach the gospel[z] in the regions beyond
you.[a] For we do not want to boast about
work already done in someone else's territory. 17 But, "Let the one who boasts boast
in the Lord."[b][b] 18 For it is not the one who
commends himself[c] who is approved, but
the one whom the Lord commends.[d]

Paul and the False Apostles

11 I hope you will put up with[e] me in a
little foolishness.[f] Yes, please put up
with me! 2 I am jealous for you with a godly
jealousy. I promised you to one husband,[g]
to Christ, so that I might present you[h] as
a pure virgin to him. 3 But I am afraid that
just as Eve was deceived by the serpent's
cunning,[i] your minds may somehow be led
astray from your sincere and pure devotion
to Christ. 4 For if someone comes to you
and preaches a Jesus other than the Jesus
we preached,[j] or if you receive a different
spirit[k] from the Spirit you received, or a dif-

[a] 7 Or *Look at the obvious facts* [b] 17 Jer. 9:24

10:5 [i] Isa 2:11, 12; 1Co 1:19 [j] 2Co 9:13 **10:6** [k] 2Co 2:9; 7:15 **10:7** [l] S Jn 7:24; 2Co 5:12 [m] 1Co 1:12; S 3:23; 14:37 [n] 2Co 11:23 **10:8** [o] ver 13, 15 [p] ver 4; Jer 1:10; 2Co 13:10 **10:10** [q] ver 1; 1Co 2:3; Gal 4:13, 14 [r] 1Co 1:17; 2Co 11:6 **10:12** [s] ver 18; S 2Co 3:1 **10:13** [t] ver 15, 16; S Ro 12:3 **10:14** [u] S 1Co 3:6 [v] S 2Co 2:12 **10:15** [w] ver 13 [x] Ro 15:20 [y] 2Th 1:3 **10:16** [z] S Ro 1:1; S 2Co 2:12 [a] S Ac 19:21 **10:17** [b] Jer 9:24; Ps 34:2; 44:8; 1Co 1:31 **10:18** [c] ver 12 [d] S Ro 2:29 **11:1** [e] ver 4, 19, 20; Mt 17:17 [f] ver 16, 17, 21; 2Co 5:13 **11:2** [g] Hos 2:19; Eph 5:26, 27 [h] S 2Co 4:14 **11:3** [i] Ge 3:1-6, 13; 1Ti 2:14; Rev 12:9 **11:4** [j] 1Co 3:11 [k] Ro 8:15

among which are the faulty reasonings by which the false apostles have been trying to shake the faith of the Christians in Corinth (see 1Co 2:13–14).

10:6 *every act of disobedience.* On the part of the interlopers and those who sided with them.

10:7 *belong to Christ.* Probably echoes the claim to superior spirituality by the Christ party (see 1Co 1:12) and the false teachers in Corinth. Paul, who had dramatically encountered and been commissioned by the risen Lord (see Ac 9:3–9; 22:6–11; 26:12–18) and who had received the gospel he preached "by revelation from Jesus Christ" (Gal 1:12; cf. 2Co 12:2–7), asserts that he belongs to Christ "just as much."

10:8 *authority ... for building you up.* The primary purpose of Paul's apostolic authority is constructive, not destructive (see 13:10).

10:9 *frighten you with my letters.* See 2:3–4 and note; 7:8–9; chs. 10–13; 1Co 4:14–21.

10:10 *His letters are weighty and forceful.* Paul had already written at least three letters to Corinth (see Introduction: Occasion). *his speaking amounts to nothing.* See note on 10:1—13:14. Paul's adversaries used a professional type of oratory designed to extract money from their gullible audiences. But Paul's manner of speaking was plain, straightforward and free from artificiality—and also "free of charge" (11:7; see note there), which meant that, if his slanderous opponents were to be believed, what he said was worthless. But Paul proclaimed the message of Christ crucified, and the transformed lives of the Corinthian believers testified to the divine power with which he spoke (cf. 1Co 2:1–5 and notes).

10:12 *they measure themselves by themselves.* The false teachers in Corinth behave as though there is no standard of comparison higher than themselves, but Paul boasts only "in the Lord" (v. 17; cf. 1Co 1:31 [see note there]).

10:13 *the sphere of service God himself has assigned to us.* The picture may be that of an athletic contest in which lanes are marked out for the different runners. In that case, "sphere of service" should be rendered "lane"—as should also "sphere of activity" (v. 15) and "territory" (v. 16). In intruding themselves into Corinth, the false apostles had crossed into Paul's "lane." Others understand the Greek word in question to refer to an assigned sphere of authority.

10:16 *regions beyond.* Perhaps Spain (see Ro 15:24,28).

10:17 See 1Co 1:31 and note. *boast in the Lord.* Boast in what Jesus Christ has done either for us (see Gal 6:14) or through us (see Ro 15:18; cf. Ac 14:27).

11:1 *foolishness.* In order to compare his own ministry with that of the false apostles, Paul has to speak about himself, which inevitably seems like foolish boasting.

11:2 *godly jealousy.* Paul cannot bear the thought that there might be any rival to Christ and his gospel. *I promised you to one husband.* As their spiritual father (cf. 6:13), Paul has promised the Corinthian believers to Christ, who is frequently depicted in the NT as the bridegroom, with the church portrayed as his bride (see Mt 9:15; Jn 3:29 and note; Eph 5:23–32 and notes; Rev 19:7–9; 21:2). *pure virgin.* Undefiled by the doctrines of false teachers (see vv. 3–4).

11:3 *deceived by the serpent's cunning.* See Ge 3:1–7 and note on 3:1.

11:4 *a Jesus other than the Jesus we preached.* A Jesus cast in the mold of Judaistic teachings (Paul's opponents were Jews; see v. 22). *different spirit.* A spirit of bondage, fear and worldliness (cf. Ro 8:15; 1Co 2:12 and note; Gal 2:4; Col 2:20–23 and note on 2:23) instead of a spirit of freedom, love, joy, peace and power (cf. 3:17; Ro 14:17 and notes; Gal 2:4; 5:1,22; Eph 3:20; Col 1:11; 2Ti 1:7). *different gospel.* Cf. Gal 1:6–9. *you put*

ferent gospel[l] from the one you accepted,
you put up with it[m] easily enough.
5I do not think I am in the least inferior
to those "super-apostles."[a][n] 6I may indeed
be untrained as a speaker,[o] but I do have
knowledge.[p] We have made this perfectly
clear to you in every way. 7Was it a sin[q]
for me to lower myself in order to elevate
you by preaching the gospel of God[r] to you
free of charge?[s] 8I robbed other churches
by receiving support from them[t] so as to
serve you. 9And when I was with you and
needed something, I was not a burden to
anyone, for the brothers who came from
Macedonia supplied what I needed.[u] I
have kept myself from being a burden to
you[v] in any way, and will continue to do
so. 10As surely as the truth of Christ is in
me,[w] nobody in the regions of Achaia[x] will
stop this boasting[y] of mine. 11Why? Because I do not love you? God knows[z] I do![a]
12And I will keep on doing what I am
doing in order to cut the ground from under those who want an opportunity to be
considered equal with us in the things
they boast about. 13For such people are
false apostles,[b] deceitful[c] workers, masquerading as apostles of Christ.[d] 14And no
wonder, for Satan[e] himself masquerades
as an angel of light. 15It is not surprising,
then, if his servants also masquerade as
servants of righteousness. Their end will
be what their actions deserve.[f]

Paul Boasts About His Sufferings

16I repeat: Let no one take me for a fool.[g]
But if you do, then tolerate me just as
you would a fool, so that I may do a little
boasting. 17In this self-confident boasting
I am not talking as the Lord would,[h] but
as a fool.[i] 18Since many are boasting in the
way the world does,[j] I too will boast.[k] 19You
gladly put up with[l] fools since you are so
wise![m] 20In fact, you even put up with[n] anyone who enslaves you[o] or exploits you or
takes advantage of you or puts on airs or
slaps you in the face. 21To my shame I admit that we were too weak[p] for that!
Whatever anyone else dares to boast
about—I am speaking as a fool—I also
dare to boast about.[q] 22Are they Hebrews?
So am I.[r] Are they Israelites? So am I.[s] Are
they Abraham's descendants? So am I.[t]
23Are they servants of Christ?[u] (I am out
of my mind to talk like this.) I am more. I
have worked much harder,[v] been in prison
more frequently,[w] been flogged more severely,[x] and been exposed to death again

[a] 5 Or *to the most eminent apostles*

11:4 [l] Gal 1:6-9 [m] S ver 1
11:5 [n] 2Co 12:11; Gal 2:6
11:6 [o] S 1Co 1:17 [p] S 2Co 8:7; Eph 3:4
11:7 [q] 2Co 12:13 [r] S Ro 1:1 [s] 1Co 9:18
11:8 [t] Php 4:15, 18
11:9 [u] Php 4:15, 18 [v] 2Co 12:13, 14,16
11:10 [w] S Ro 9:1 [x] S Ac 18:12 [y] 1Co 9:15
11:11 [z] ver 31; S Ro 1:9 [a] 2Co 12:15
11:13 [b] S Mt 7:15 [c] Titus 1:10 [d] Rev 2:2
11:14 [e] S Mt 4:10
11:15 [f] S Mt 16:27; Php 3:19
11:16 [g] ver 1
11:17 [h] 1Co 7:12,25 [i] ver 21
11:18 [j] 2Co 5:16; 10:4 [k] ver 21; Php 3:3,4
11:19 [l] S ver 1 [m] 1Co 4:10
11:20 [n] S ver 1 [o] Gal 2:4; 4:9; 5:1
11:21 [p] 2Co 10:1,10 [q] ver 17,18; Php 3:4
11:22 [r] Php 3:5 [s] Ro 9:4; 11:1 [t] S Lk 3:8; Ro 11:1 **11:23** [u] S 1Co 3:5 [v] S 1Co 15:10 [w] Ac 16:23; 2Co 6:4,5 [x] Ac 16:23; 2Co 6:4,5

up with it easily enough. They have been undiscerningly tolerant of these deceivers in their midst.

11:5 *"super-apostles."* Paul's sarcastic way of referring to the false apostles who had infiltrated the Corinthian church and were in reality not apostles at all, except in their own arrogantly inflated opinion of themselves (cf. 10:12 and note).

11:6 *I may ... be untrained as a speaker.* I do not use the skills, references and flourishes of professional rhetoric (see 10:10 and note). *I do have knowledge.* As the Corinthian believers well knew, Paul had knowledge of Christ that was true, powerful and God-given.

11:7 *free of charge.* Another slanderous criticism made by Paul's adversaries was that his refusal to accept payment for his instruction proved that it was worth nothing. This accusation at the same time helped to cloak their own grasping character, since their method of operation was to demand payment for their "professional" services. Paul, his enemies said, was lowering himself by breaking the rule that teachers should receive payment in proportion to the worth of their performance (cf. 1Co 9:3–14).

11:8 *robbed other churches.* Accepted freely given support from established congregations.

11:9 *burden.* A financial liability (see 2:17 and note). This reinforced his teaching that the gospel of Jesus Christ is a free gift (see Ro 6:23 and note). *brothers who came from Macedonia.* Silas and Timothy brought gifts from the churches there (Ac 18:5), particularly from the church at Philippi (Php 4:15).

11:10 *Achaia.* See note on 1:1.

11:12 *I will keep on.* Paul will not be deterred from presenting the gospel without charge. *equal.* In financial matters.

11:13 *masquerading as apostles of Christ.* Now Paul exposes these would-be "super-apostles" (v. 5; see note there) as "false apostles" and servants of Satan (v. 14) who are covering up their true identity.

11:14 *as an angel of light.* Though in reality he is the prince of darkness (cf. Col 1:12–13 and notes).

11:16 *Let no one take me for a fool.* See note on v. 1.

11:18 *boast.* By speaking of the nature of his apostolic ministry.

11:19 *You gladly put up with fools.* Resumes the implied rebuke of v. 4 and has the same ironic tone. There it was a matter of their readiness to tolerate false teaching; here it is a matter of their willingness to put up with disgraceful treatment by these false teachers.

11:20 *enslaves you.* By imposing human rules (cf. Gal 5:1 and note). *exploits you.* See Mk 12:40 and note. *takes advantage of you.* Thanks to the Corinthians' lack of discernment and their readiness to be impressed by outward show and clever talk. *puts on airs.* For the purpose of lording it over the members of the church (cf. 1:24). *slaps you in the face.* Using physical violence to cow them into submission.

11:21 *too weak for that.* Compared with the self-seeking crudeness of the impostors, Paul's conduct may well be considered weak—but he is probably speaking ironically here.

11:22 *Hebrews ... Israelites ... Abraham's descendants.* The claims implied here on the part of the false apostles indicate that they were Jews who felt superior to Gentile Christians. Thus it is probable that they were Judaizers, wishing to impose distinctive Jewish practices on Gentile converts. This, of course, was not Paul's position (see Ro 2:28–29; 1Co 12:13; Gal 3:28–29; Eph 2:11–18; Col 3:11 and note). For Paul's claim, see Ac 22:3–5; 26:4–5; Php 3:5–6.

11:23 *servants of Christ.* Paul is not granting their claim to be servants of Christ (cf. vv. 13–15). Indeed, the consideration of the nature of his ministry and its cost to him in suffering will show that he is more a servant of Christ than any or all of them. *exposed to death again and again.* Cf. 4:8–11.

and again.[y] 24 Five times I received from the
Jews the forty lashes[z] minus one. 25 Three
times I was beaten with rods,[a] once I was
pelted with stones,[b] three times I was shipwrecked,[c] I spent a night and a day in the
open sea, 26 I have been constantly on the
move. I have been in danger from rivers,
in danger from bandits, in danger from
my fellow Jews,[d] in danger from Gentiles;
in danger in the city,[e] in danger in the
country, in danger at sea; and in danger
from false believers.[f] 27 I have labored and
toiled[g] and have often gone without sleep;
I have known hunger and thirst and have
often gone without food;[h] I have been
cold and naked. 28 Besides everything else,
I face daily the pressure of my concern for
all the churches.[i] 29 Who is weak, and I do
not feel weak?[j] Who is led into sin,[k] and I
do not inwardly burn?

30 If I must boast, I will boast[l] of the
things that show my weakness.[m] 31 The
God and Father of the Lord Jesus, who is
to be praised forever,[n] knows[o] that I am not
lying. 32 In Damascus the governor under
King Aretas had the city of the Damascenes
guarded in order to arrest me.[p] 33 But I was
lowered in a basket from a window in the
wall and slipped through his hands.[q]

Paul's Vision and His Thorn

12 I must go on boasting.[r] Although
there is nothing to be gained, I will
go on to visions and revelations[s] from the
Lord. 2 I know a man in Christ[t] who fourteen years ago was caught up[u] to the third
heaven.[v] Whether it was in the body or out
of the body I do not know—God knows.[w]
3 And I know that this man—whether in
the body or apart from the body I do not
know, but God knows— 4 was caught up[x]
to paradise[y] and heard inexpressible things,
things that no one is permitted to tell. 5 I will
boast about a man like that, but I will not
boast about myself, except about my weaknesses.[z] 6 Even if I should choose to boast,[a]
I would not be a fool,[b] because I would be
speaking the truth. But I refrain, so no one
will think more of me than is warranted by
what I do or say, 7 or because of these surpassingly great revelations.[c] Therefore, in
order to keep me from becoming conceited,
I was given a thorn in my flesh,[d] a messenger of Satan,[e] to torment me. 8 Three times I
pleaded with the Lord to take it away from
me.[f] 9 But he said to me, "My grace[g] is sufficient for you, for my power[h] is made perfect
in weakness.[i]"[j] Therefore I will boast all the
more gladly about my weaknesses, so that
Christ's power may rest on me. 10 That is
why, for Christ's sake, I delight[k] in weaknesses, in insults, in hardships,[l] in persecutions,[m] in difficulties. For when I am weak,
then I am strong.[n]

Paul's Concern for the Corinthians

11 I have made a fool of myself,[o] but you
drove me to it. I ought to have been commended by you, for I am not in the least

11:23 [y]S Ro 8:36 **11:24** [z]Dt 25:3 **11:25** [a]Ac 16:22 [b]Ac 14:19 [c]Ac 27:1-44 **11:26** [d]S Ac 20:3 [e]Ac 21:31 [f]Gal 2:4 **11:27** [g]S Ac 18:3; Col 1:29 [h]1Co 4:11,12; 2Co 6:5 **11:28** [i]S 1Co 7:17 **11:29** [j]S Ro 14:1; S 1Co 2:3 [k]S Mt 5:29 **11:30** [l]ver 16; Gal 6:14; 2Co 12:5,9 [m]S 1Co 2:3 **11:31** [n]Ro 1:25; 9:5 [o]ver 11; S Ro 1:9 **11:32** [p]Ac 9:24 **11:33** [q]Ac 9:25 **12:1** [r]ver 5, 9; 2Co 11:16, 30 [s]ver 7; S 1Co 2:10 **12:2** [t]S Ro 16:3 [u]ver 4; S Ac 8:39 [v]Eph 4:10 [w]2Co 11:11 **12:4** [x]ver 2 [y]Lk 23:43; Rev 2:7 **12:5** [z]ver 9,10; S 1Co 2:3 **12:6** [a]2Co 10:8 [b]ver 11; 2Co 11:16 **12:7** [c]ver 1; S 1Co 2:10 [d]Nu 33:55 [e]S Mt 4:10 **12:8** [f]Mt 26:39, 44 **12:9** [g]S Ro 3:24 [h]S Php 4:13 [i]S 1Co 2:3 [j]1Ki 19:12 **12:10** [k]S Mt 5:12 [l]2Co 6:4 [m]2Th 1:4 [n]2Co 13:4 **12:11** [o]2Co 11:1

11:24–25 *lashes ... rods.* Eight floggings are mentioned here, five at the hands of Jewish authorities (cf. Dt 25:3; Mk 15:15 and notes) and three at the hands of Roman authorities. On these occasions the Romans used rods (see Ac 16:22). The three beatings with rods took place despite the fact that Paul, a Roman citizen, was legally protected from such punishment (cf. Ac 16:37; 22:25 and notes).

11:25 *pelted with stones.* A traditional manner of Jewish execution (cf. Jn 8:59; Ac 7:57–59; 14:19–20). *shipwrecked.* Only one shipwreck is recorded in Acts, but it took place after the writing of this letter (Ac 27:39–44). The three shipwrecks referred to here could have taken place during the voyages mentioned in Ac 9:30; 11:25–26; 13:4,13; 14:26; 16:11; 18:18–19,21–22.

11:26 *in danger from bandits.* See note on Ac 14:24.

11:28–29 Paul felt the weakness of any Corinthian believer who was weak. If any of them was led into sin, Paul burned with indignation against the person responsible but also experienced the shame of the offense and longed for the restoration of the one who had stumbled.

11:30 *I will boast of the things that show my weakness.* His weakness opens the way for him to boast about the strength of God's grace in his life (see 12:9–10 and notes).

11:32–33 Paul relates this incident here because it was another example of the humiliation ("weakness," v. 30) he suffered.

11:32 *Damascus.* See note on Ac 9:2; see also map, p. 1842. *King Aretas.* See note on Ac 9:23. Aretas IV, father-in-law of Herod Antipas, ruled over the Nabatean Arabs from c. 9 BC to AD 40. The Roman emperor Caligula may have given Damascus back to Aretas, since it was once part of his territory.

11:33 *from a window.* See Ac 9:25. For similar escapes, see Jos 2:15; 1Sa 19:12.

12:2,4 *caught up to the third heaven ... caught up to paradise.* Paul is unsure whether this remarkable experience included his body or took place in separation from it (cf. Eze 8:3 and note). The "third heaven" designates a place beyond the earth's atmosphere and beyond the planets and stars to the presence of God himself. Thus the risen and glorified Lord Jesus is said to have passed "through the heavens" (see Heb 4:14; see also note and NIV text note there), and now, having "ascended higher than all the heavens" (Eph 4:10), to be "exalted above the heavens" (Heb 7:26). The term "paradise" (see Ne 2:8; Lk 23:43; Rev 2:7 and notes) is synonymous with the third heaven, where believers who have died are "at home with the Lord" (5:8 [see note there]; cf. "with Christ," Php 1:23).

12:2 *a man in Christ.* Paul himself. *fourteen years ago.* Early in his ministry, before his first missionary journey (Ac 13:4—14:28).

12:7 *revelations.* See v. 1. *thorn in my flesh.* The nature of this affliction is unknown. *messenger of Satan.* A further description of Paul's thorn (cf. Job 2:7 and note).

12:9 *My grace is sufficient for you.* A better solution than to remove Paul's thorn. Human weakness provides the ideal opportunity for the display of divine power.

12:10 Cf. Php 4:13 and note. The classic example of power in weakness is the cross of Christ (cf. 13:4).

12:11 *made a fool of myself.* See note on 11:1. *you drove me to it.* The Corinthian Christians have put Paul under pressure to

inferior to the "super-apostles,"[a][p] even
though I am nothing.[q] 12 I persevered in
demonstrating among you the marks of a
true apostle, including signs, wonders and
miracles.[r] 13 How were you inferior to the
other churches, except that I was never a
burden to you?[s] Forgive me this wrong![t]
14 Now I am ready to visit you for the
third time,[u] and I will not be a burden to
you, because what I want is not your possessions but you. After all, children should
not have to save up for their parents,[v] but
parents for their children.[w] 15 So I will very
gladly spend for you everything I have and
expend myself as well.[x] If I love you more,[y]
will you love me less? 16 Be that as it may, I
have not been a burden to you.[z] Yet, crafty
fellow that I am, I caught you by trickery!
17 Did I exploit you through any of the men
I sent to you? 18 I urged[a] Titus[b] to go to you
and I sent our brother[c] with him. Titus did
not exploit you, did he? Did we not walk
in the same footsteps by the same Spirit?
19 Have you been thinking all along that
we have been defending ourselves to you?
We have been speaking in the sight of
God[d] as those in Christ; and everything
we do, dear friends,[e] is for your strengthening.[f] 20 For I am afraid that when I come[g]
I may not find you as I want you to be, and
you may not find me as you want me to
be.[h] I fear that there may be discord,[i] jealousy, fits of rage, selfish ambition,[j] slander,[k] gossip,[l] arrogance[m] and disorder.[n] 21 I
am afraid that when I come again my God
will humble me before you, and I will be
grieved[o] over many who have sinned earlier[p] and have not repented of the impurity,
sexual sin and debauchery[q] in which they
have indulged.

12:11 [p] 2Co 11:5 [q] 1Co 15:9,10
12:12 [r] S Jn 4:48
12:13 [s] ver 14; 1Co 9:12,18 [t] 2Co 11:7
12:14 [u] 2Co 13:1 [v] 1Co 4:14,15 [w] Pr 19:14
12:15 [x] Php 2:17; 1Th 2:8 [y] 2Co 11:11
12:16 [z] 2Co 11:9
12:18 [a] 2Co 8:6,16 [b] S 2Co 2:13 [c] 2Co 8:18
12:19 [d] Ro 9:1 [e] S 1Co 10:14 [f] S Ro 14:19; 2Co 10:8
12:20 [g] 2Co 2:1-4 [h] 1Co 4:21 [i] 1Co 1:11; 3:3 [j] Gal 5:20 [k] Ro 1:30 [l] S Ro 1:29 [m] 1Co 4:18 [n] 1Co 14:33
12:21 [o] 2Co 2:1,4 [p] 2Co 13:2 [q] S 1Co 6:18
13:1 [r] 2Co 12:14 [s] Dt 19:15; S Mt 18:16
13:2 [t] ver 10 [u] 2Co 1:23 [v] 2Co 12:21
13:3 [w] Mt 10:20; 1Co 5:4
13:4 [x] 1Co 1:25; Php 2:7,8; 1Pe 3:18 [y] Ro 1:4; 6:4; 1Co 6:14 [z] ver 9; S 1Co 2:3 [a] S Ro 6:5
13:5 [b] 1Co 11:28 [c] La 3:40; Jn 6:6 [d] S Ro 8:10
13:9 [e] S 1Co 2:3 [f] 2Co 4:12 [g] ver 11; Eph 4:13 **13:10** [h] S 2Co 1:23 [i] 2Co 10:8

Final Warnings

13 This will be my third visit to you.[r]
"Every matter must be established
by the testimony of two or three witnesses."[b][s] 2 I already gave you a warning when
I was with you the second time. I now repeat it while absent:[t] On my return I will
not spare[u] those who sinned earlier[v] or any
of the others, 3 since you are demanding
proof that Christ is speaking through me.[w]
He is not weak in dealing with you, but is
powerful among you. 4 For to be sure, he
was crucified in weakness,[x] yet he lives by
God's power.[y] Likewise, we are weak[z] in
him, yet by God's power we will live with
him[a] in our dealing with you.
5 Examine yourselves[b] to see whether you are in the faith; test yourselves.[c]
Do you not realize that Christ Jesus is
in you[d]—unless, of course, you fail the
test? 6 And I trust that you will discover
that we have not failed the test. 7 Now we
pray to God that you will not do anything
wrong—not so that people will see that
we have stood the test but so that you will
do what is right even though we may seem
to have failed. 8 For we cannot do anything
against the truth, but only for the truth.
9 We are glad whenever we are weak[e] but
you are strong;[f] and our prayer is that you
may be fully restored.[g] 10 This is why I
write these things when I am absent, that
when I come I may not have to be harsh[h]
in my use of authority—the authority the
Lord gave me for building you up, not for
tearing you down.[i]

[a] *11* *Or the most eminent apostles* [b] *1* Deut. 19:15

write about himself as he did because they had accepted the claims of the "super-apostles" (see 11:5 and note) who had invaded their ranks, challenging Paul's apostolic authority.
12:12 *signs, wonders and miracles.* See Heb 2:4 and note. By implication, false teachers had come to Corinth without these apostolic signs.
12:13 *never a burden to you.* See 11:9 and note; see also notes on 11:7,12. *Forgive me this wrong!* Irony—resuming the line of discussion in 11:7–12.
12:14 *third time.* See 2:1 and note; 13:1. *children.* Cf. 6:13. Paul is their spiritual father.
12:16 *I caught you by trickery!* Sarcastically echoes another of the slanders being made against Paul by the false apostles: that he was exploiting them by the trick of organizing a collection for the poverty-stricken Christians in Jerusalem—contributions that would never reach their intended destination because they went into Paul's own pocket (v. 17).
12:18 *Titus ... our brother.* See notes on 8:6,16–17,18,23.
12:19 *speaking in the sight of God as those in Christ.* See 1Co 4:3–4 and note on 4:3. *everything we do ... is for your strengthening.* See 10:8 and note.
12:20–21 See Ro 1:29–31 and note.
12:20 The church at Corinth was immature, unspiritual, disorganized and schismatic (see 1Co 3:1–4 and notes).
12:21 *sinned earlier ... sexual sin and debauchery.* See 1Co 5:1,11; 6:13,16,18–19 and notes.
13:1 *third visit.* See 2:1 and note; 12:14. *two or three witnesses.* Cf. Dt 17:6 and note.
13:2 *those who sinned earlier.* See 12:21 and note. *any of the others.* Probably the Corinthians who had sided with the false teachers.
13:3 *demanding proof that Christ is speaking through me.* See note on 10:10.
13:4 *crucified in weakness.* See 12:10 and note; cf. 8:9; Php 2:6–8.
13:5 *Examine yourselves ... test yourselves.* Cf. 2Pe 1:10–11 and notes.
13:7 *do what is right.* Then there will be no need for Paul to give evidence of his authority by taking disciplinary action when he comes to them.
13:8 *we cannot do anything against the truth.* Paul can exercise his apostolic authority only in a way that supports the truth.
13:9 *are weak.* Have no need to give proof of his apostolic strength (cf. 12:9–10 and notes). *strong.* In the truth. *fully restored.* See Gal 6:1 and note.
13:10 *building you up, not ... tearing you down.* See 10:8 and note.

Final Greetings

[11]Finally, brothers and sisters,[j] rejoice!
Strive for full restoration, encourage one
another, be of one mind, live in peace.[k] And
the God of love[l] and peace[m] will be with
you.
[12]Greet one another with a holy kiss.[n]
[13]All God's people here send their greetings.[o]
[14]May the grace of the Lord Jesus
Christ,[p] and the love of God,[q] and the fellowship of the Holy Spirit[r] be with you
all.

13:11 [j] 1Th 4:1; 2Th 3:1 [k] S Mk 9:50 [l] 1Jn 4:16 [m] S Ro 15:33; Eph 6:23 **13:12** [n] S Ro 16:16 **13:13** [o] Php 4:22 **13:14** [p] S Ro 16:20; 2Co 8:9 [q] Ro 5:5; Jude 21 [r] Php 2:1

13:11–13 These concluding exhortations and greetings exhibit a note of confidence.
13:11,14 *peace ... grace.* See note on Ro 1:7.
13:11 *brothers and sisters.* See note on Ro 1:13. *full restoration.* See v. 9 and note. *encourage one another.* See 1Co 14:3; Heb 10:22–25 and notes. *be of one mind.* See Php 2:2 and note. *live in peace.* See Mt 5:9; Ro 12:18; Jas 3:18 and notes. *God of love.* See 1Jn 4:8 and note. *God of ... peace.* See 1Th 5:23 and note; Heb 13:20.
13:12 *holy kiss.* See 1Co 16:20; Ro 16:16 and notes.
13:13 *God's people.* See note on Ro 1:7.

13:14 This benediction is Trinitarian in form and has ever since been a part of Christian worship tradition (see Mt 28:19 and note). *grace of ... Christ.* See 8:9 and note. *love of God.* See Jn 3:16; 1Jn 4:8–10 and notes; see also Ro 5:8. *fellowship of the Holy Spirit.* See note on Php 2:1. *with you.* This phrase or its equivalent ("with your spirit" [Php 4:23; see note there; see also Gal 6:18; 2Ti 4:22; Phm 25]) occurs near the end of all of Paul's letters except Ephesians. Its OT counterpart is the Immanuel theme—"God with us"—and its equivalents (see Ge 26:3; Isa 7:14; Rev 21:3 and notes).

GALATIANS

INTRODUCTION

Author

The opening verse identifies the author of Galatians as the apostle Paul (see note on Ro 1:1). Apart from a few nineteenth-century interpreters, no one has seriously questioned his authorship.

Date and Destination

The date of Galatians depends to a great extent on the destination of the letter. There are two main views:

(1) *The North Galatian theory.* This older view holds that the letter was addressed to churches located in north-central Asia Minor, where the Gauls had settled when they invaded the area in the third century BC. It is held that Paul visited this area on his second missionary journey, though Acts contains no reference to such a visit. Galatians, it is maintained, was written between AD 53 and 57 from Ephesus or Macedonia, sometime during or after Paul's second missionary journey.

(2) *The South Galatian theory.* According to this view, Galatians was written to churches in the southern area of the Roman province of Galatia (Antioch, Iconium, Lystra and Derbe) that Paul had founded on his first missionary journey. If this is the case, Galatians could be Paul's earliest letter. Some believe that Galatians was written from Syrian Antioch in 48–49 after Paul's first journey and before the Jerusalem council meeting (Ac 15). Others say that Galatians was written in Syrian Antioch or Corinth between 51 and 53 (see chart, pp. 1844–1845).

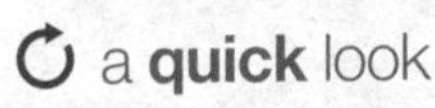

a quick look

Author:
The apostle Paul

Audience:
Churches in southern Galatia, and perhaps northern Galatia, founded by Paul during his missionary journey

Date:
AD 48, or in the 50s

Theme:
Paul writes to counter the claims of legalistic Judaizers who were telling the Galatian believers that they must be circumcised and keep the law of Moses in order to be saved.

Occasion and Purpose

Judaizers were Jewish Christians who believed, among other things, that a number of the ceremonial practices of the OT were still binding on the NT church. Following Paul's successful campaign in Galatia, they insisted that Gentile converts to

Christianity abide by certain OT rites, especially circumcision. They may have been motivated by a desire to avoid persecution from zealous Jews who objected to their fraternizing with Gentiles (see 6:12). The Judaizers argued that Paul was not an authentic apostle and that out of a desire to make the message more appealing to Gentiles he had removed from the gospel certain legal requirements.

Paul responded by clearly establishing his apostolic authority and thereby substantiating the gospel he preached. By introducing additional requirements for justification (e.g., works of the law), his adversaries had perverted the gospel of grace and, unless prevented, would bring Paul's converts into the bondage of legalism. It is by grace through faith alone that people are justified, and it is by faith alone that they are to live out their new life in the freedom of the Spirit.

Theological Teaching

Galatians stands as an eloquent and vigorous apologetic for the essential NT truth that people are justified by faith in Jesus Christ — by nothing less and nothing more — and that they are sanctified

Basilica of St. Paul in Pisidian Antioch, built in the fourth century AD. Paul preached one of his sermons in the synagogue at Antioch (Ac 13:13–43).

www.HolyLandPhotos.org

The Judaizers argued that Paul was not an authentic apostle and that out of a desire to make the message more appealing to Gentiles he had removed from the gospel certain legal requirements.

not by legalistic works but by the obedience that comes from faith in God's work for them, in them and through them by the grace and power of Christ and the Holy Spirit. It was the rediscovery of the basic message of Galatians (and Romans) that brought about the Protestant Reformation. Galatians is often referred to as "Luther's book," because Martin Luther relied so strongly on this letter in all his preaching, teaching and writing against the prevailing theology of his day. It is also referred to as the "Magna Carta of Christian Liberty." A key verse is 2:16 (see note there).

Outline

- I. Introduction (1:1 – 10)
  - A. Greetings (1:1 – 5)
  - B. Denunciation (1:6 – 10)
- II. Personal: Authentication of the Apostle of Liberty and Faith (1:11 — 2:21)
  - A. Paul's Gospel Was Received by Special Revelation (1:11 – 12)
  - B. Paul's Gospel Was Independent of the Jerusalem Apostles and the Judean Churches (1:13 — 2:21)
    1. Evidenced by his early activities as a Christian (1:13 – 17)
    2. Evidenced by his first visit to Jerusalem after becoming a Christian (1:18 – 24)
    3. Evidenced by his second visit to Jerusalem (2:1 – 10)
    4. Evidenced by his rebuke of Peter at Antioch (2:11 – 21)
- III. Doctrinal: Justification of the Doctrine of Liberty and Faith (chs. 3 – 4)
  - A. The Galatians' Experience of the Gospel (3:1 – 5)
  - B. The Experience of Abraham (3:6 – 9)
  - C. The Curse of the Law (3:10 – 14)
  - D. The Priority of the Promise (3:15 – 18)
  - E. The Purpose of the Law (3:19 – 25)
  - F. Children, Not Slaves (3:26 — 4:7)
  - G. The Danger of Turning Back (4:8 – 11)
  - H. Appeal to Embrace the Freedom of God's Children (4:12 – 20)
  - I. God's Children Are Children of the Free Woman (4:21 – 31)
- IV. Practical: Practice of the Life of Liberty and Faith (5:1 — 6:10)
  - A. Exhortation to Freedom (5:1 – 12)
  - B. Life by the Spirit, Not by the Flesh (5:13 – 26)
  - C. Call for Mutual Help (6:1 – 10)
- V. Conclusion and Benediction (6:11 – 18)

1 Paul, an apostle[a]—sent not from men
nor by a man,[b] but by Jesus Christ[c]
and God the Father,[d] who raised him from
the dead[e]— 2 and all the brothers and sisters[a] with me,[f]

To the churches in Galatia:[g]

3 Grace and peace to you from God our
Father and the Lord Jesus Christ,[h] 4 who
gave himself for our sins[i] to rescue us from
the present evil age,[j] according to the will
of our God and Father,[k] 5 to whom be glory
for ever and ever. Amen.[l]

No Other Gospel

6 I am astonished that you are so quickly
deserting the one who called[m] you to live
in the grace of Christ and are turning to
a different gospel[n]— 7 which is really no
gospel at all. Evidently some people are
throwing you into confusion[o] and are trying to pervert[p] the gospel of Christ. 8 But
even if we or an angel from heaven should
preach a gospel other than the one we
preached to you,[q] let them be under God's
curse![r] 9 As we have already said, so now I
say again: If anybody is preaching to you a
gospel other than what you accepted,[s] let
them be under God's curse!
10 Am I now trying to win the approval
of human beings, or of God? Or am I trying to please people?[t] If I were still trying
to please people, I would not be a servant
of Christ.

Paul Called by God

11 I want you to know, brothers and sisters,[u] that the gospel I preached[v] is not of
human origin. 12 I did not receive it from
any man,[w] nor was I taught it; rather, I received it by revelation[x] from Jesus Christ.[y]
13 For you have heard of my previous
way of life in Judaism,[z] how intensely I
persecuted the church of God[a] and tried
to destroy it.[b] 14 I was advancing in Judaism beyond many of my own age among
my people and was extremely zealous[c] for
the traditions of my fathers.[d] 15 But when
God, who set me apart from my mother's
womb[e] and called me[f] by his grace, was
pleased 16 to reveal his Son in me so that
I might preach him among the Gentiles,[g]
my immediate response was not to consult
any human being.[h] 17 I did not go up to
Jerusalem to see those who were apostles
before I was, but I went into Arabia. Later
I returned to Damascus.[i]

[a] 2 The Greek word for *brothers and sisters* (*adelphoi*) refers here to believers, both men and women, as part of God's family; also in verse 11; and in 3:15; 4:12, 28, 31; 5:11, 13; 6:1, 18.

1:1 [a]S 1Co 1:1 [b]ver 11,12 [c]ver 15,16; S Ac 9:15; 20:24 [d]ver 15,16; S Ac 9:15; 20:24 [e]S Ac 2:24
1:2 [f]Php 4:21 [g]S Ac 16:6
1:3 [h]S Ro 1:7
1:4 [i]S Mt 20:28; S Ro 4:25; S 1Co 15:3; Gal 2:20 [j]S 1Co 1:20 [k]S Php 4:20
1:5 [l]S Ro 11:36
1:6 [m]ver 15; S Ro 8:28 [n]2Co 11:4
1:7 [o]Ac 15:24; Gal 5:10 [p]Jer 23:16,36
1:8 [q]ver 11, 16; 1Co 15:1; 2Co 11:4; Gal 2:2 [r]Ro 9:3
1:9 [s]Ro 16:17
1:10 [t]S Ro 2:29
1:11 [u]1Co 15:1 [v]S ver 8
1:12 [w]ver 1 [x]ver 16; S 1Co 2:10 [y]1Co 11:23; 15:3
1:13 [z]Ac 26:4, 5 [a]S 1Co 10:32 [b]S Ac 8:3
1:14 [c]S Ac 21:20 [d]Mt 15:2
1:15 [e]Isa 49:1, 5; Jer 1:5 [f]S Ac 9:15; S Ro 8:28
1:16 [g]S Ac 9:15; Gal 2:9 [h]Mt 16:17
1:17 [i]Ac 9:2,19-22

1:1 *Paul.* See note on Ro 1:1. *apostle.* One sent on a mission with full authority of representation; an ambassador (see note on 1Co 1:1). *raised him from the dead.* The resurrection is the central affirmation of the Christian faith (see Ac 17:18; Ro 1:4; 1Co 15:20; 1Pe 1:3), and because Paul had seen the risen Christ he was qualified to be an apostle (see Ac 1:22 and note; 2:32; 1Co 15:8).

1:2 *brothers and sisters.* See NIV text note. *churches.* This was a circular letter to several congregations. *Galatia.* The term occurs three times in the NT (and "Galatian" once [1Co 16:1]). In 2Ti 4:10 the reference is uncertain. In 1Pe 1:1 it refers to the northern area of Asia Minor occupied by the Gauls. Here (and in 1Co 16:1) Paul probably uses the term to refer to the Roman province of Galatia and an additional area to the south, through which he traveled on his first missionary journey (Ac 13:14—14:23). See Introduction: Date and Destination.

1:3 *Grace and peace.* See note on Ro 1:7. *Lord Jesus Christ.* Also occurs at the end of this letter (6:18); see note on 1Th 1:1.

1:4 *for our sins.* See Mt 1:21; Jn 1:29; 1Co 15:3; 1Pe 2:24 and note. *present evil age.* The present period of the world's history (see note on 2Co 4:4). In contrast to the age to come (the climax of the Messianic age), this present age is characterized by wickedness (Eph 2:1–2; 6:12).

1:5 For other doxologies, see, e.g., Ro 9:5; 11:36; 16:27; Eph 3:21; 1Ti 1:17.

1:6 *so quickly.* So soon after your conversion. *one who called you.* God. *grace of Christ.* The test of a pure, unadulterated gospel.

1:7 *no gospel at all.* Because it lacks the heart of the gospel—the good news of God's marvelous grace in Christ (see notes on Mk 1:1; 1Co 15:3). *some people.* The Judaizers (see Introduction: Occasion and Purpose).

1:8 *under God's curse.* The Greek word (*anathema*) originally referred to a pagan temple offering in payment for a vow. Later it came to represent a curse (see v. 9; Ro 9:3 and note; 1Co 12:3; 16:22).

1:10 *servant of Christ.* Paul once wore the "yoke of slavery" (5:1) but having been set free from sin by the redemption that is in Christ, he became a slave of righteousness, a slave of God (see Ro 6:18,22 and note on 6:18).

1:11 *I want you to know, brothers and sisters.* A similar phrase is found in 1Co 15:1, where Paul sets forth the gospel he received. *the gospel I preached.* Called "my gospel" in Ro 2:16; 16:25 (see note there).

1:12 *received it by revelation.* See Eph 3:2–6.

1:13 *Judaism.* The Jewish faith and way of life that developed during the period between the OT and the NT. The term is derived from Judah, the southern kingdom that came to an end in the sixth century BC with the exile into Babylonia (see essay, p. 1576). *church of God.* The NT counterpart of the OT assembly (see Nu 16:21) or community of the Lord (Nu 20:4).

1:14 *zealous.* See Php 3:6. *traditions of my fathers.* Traditions orally transmitted from previous generations and contrasted with the written law of Moses. Cf. the "tradition of the elders" (see note on Mt 15:2).

1:15 *set me apart from my mother's womb.* See Isa 49:1; Jer 1:5; Ro 1:1.

1:16 *Gentiles.* Lit. "nations" or "peoples." The term commonly designated foreigners—hence pagans, or the non-Jewish world. *any human being.* Lit. "flesh and blood"—in the NT usually with the implication of human weakness or ignorance (see Mt 16:17; 1Co 15:50 and note). Paul received his message from God (vv. 11–12).

1:17 *Jerusalem.* The religious center of Judaism and the birthplace of Christianity. *Arabia.* The Nabatean kingdom in Transjordan, stretching southward from Damascus toward the Arabian peninsula. *Damascus.* The capital of ancient Syria (Aram in the OT). Paul had been converted en route from

18 Then after three years,[j] I went up to
Jerusalem[k] to get acquainted with Cephas[a]
and stayed with him fifteen days. 19 I saw
none of the other apostles—only James,[l]
the Lord's brother. 20 I assure you before
God[m] that what I am writing you is no lie.[n]
21 Then I went to Syria[o] and Cilicia.[p] 22 I
was personally unknown to the churches
of Judea[q] that are in Christ.[r] 23 They only
heard the report: "The man who formerly
persecuted us is now preaching the faith[s]
he once tried to destroy."[t] 24 And they
praised God[u] because of me.

Paul Accepted by the Apostles

2 Then after fourteen years, I went up
again to Jerusalem,[v] this time with
Barnabas.[w] I took Titus[x] along also. 2 I went
in response to a revelation[y] and, meeting
privately with those esteemed as leaders, I
presented to them the gospel that I preach
among the Gentiles.[z] I wanted to be sure
I was not running and had not been running my race[a] in vain. 3 Yet not even Titus,[b]
who was with me, was compelled to be
circumcised, even though he was a Greek.[c]
4 This matter arose because some false believers[d] had infiltrated our ranks to spy on[e]
the freedom[f] we have in Christ Jesus and
to make us slaves. 5 We did not give in to
them for a moment, so that the truth of
the gospel[g] might be preserved for you.

6 As for those who were held in high
esteem[h]—whatever they were makes no
difference to me; God does not show favoritism[i]—they added nothing to my
message.[j] 7 On the contrary, they recognized that I had been entrusted with the
task[k] of preaching the gospel to the uncircumcised,[b][l] just as Peter[m] had been to
the circumcised.[c] 8 For God, who was at
work in Peter as an apostle[n] to the circumcised, was also at work in me as an
apostle[o] to the Gentiles. 9 James,[p] Cephas[d][q]
and John, those esteemed as pillars,[r] gave
me and Barnabas[s] the right hand of fellowship when they recognized the grace
given to me.[t] They agreed that we should
go to the Gentiles,[u] and they to the circumcised. 10 All they asked was that we should
continue to remember the poor,[v] the very
thing I had been eager to do all along.

Paul Opposes Cephas

11 When Cephas[w] came to Antioch,[x] I opposed him to his face, because he stood
condemned. 12 For before certain men
came from James,[y] he used to eat with
the Gentiles.[z] But when they arrived, he

[a] 18 That is, Peter [b] 7 That is, Gentiles [c] 7 That is, Jews; also in verses 8 and 9 [d] 9 That is, Peter; also in verses 11 and 14

1:18 [j] Ac 9:22, 23 [k] Ac 9:26,27 **1:19** [l] Mt 13:55; S Ac 15:13 **1:20** [m] S Ro 1:9 [n] S Ro 9:1 **1:21** [o] S Lk 2:2 [p] S Ac 6:9 **1:22** [q] 1Th 2:14 [r] S Ro 16:3 **1:23** [s] Ac 6:7 [t] S Ac 8:3 **1:24** [u] S Mt 9:8 **2:1** [v] Ac 15:2 [w] S Ac 4:36 [x] S 2Co 2:13 **2:2** [y] S 1Co 2:10 [z] Ac 15:4,12 [a] S 1Co 9:24 **2:3** [b] ver 1; S 2Co 2:13 [c] Ac 16:3; 1Co 9:21 **2:4** [d] S Ac 1:16; 2Co 11:26 [e] Jude 4 [f] Gal 5:1,13 **2:5** [g] ver 14 **2:6** [h] ver 2 [i] S Ac 10:34; S Rev 2:23 [j] 1Co 15:11 **2:7** [k] 1Th 2:4; 1Ti 1:11 [l] S Ac 9:15 [m] ver 9,11,14 **2:8** [n] Ac 1:25 [o] S 1Co 1:1 **2:9** [p] S Ac 15:13 [q] ver 7,11, 14 [r] 1Ti 3:15; Rev 3:12 [s] ver 1; S Ac 4:36 [t] S Ro 12:3 [u] S Ac 9:15 **2:10** [v] S Ac 24:17 **2:11** [w] ver 7,9,14 [x] S Ac 11:19 **2:12** [y] S Ac 15:13 [z] Ac 11:3

Jerusalem to Damascus (see Ac 9:1–9 and note on 9:2; see also map, p. 1842).

1:18 *after three years.* From the time of his departure into Arabia. The text does not say he spent the three years in Arabia. *I went up to Jerusalem.* Probably the visit referred to in Ac 9:26–30, though some equate it with the one in Ac 11:30. *Cephas.* See NIV text note; from the Aramaic word for "stone" (see Mt 16:18 and note). The name highlights a like quality in the bearer (see note on Jn 1:42).

1:19 *James.* See Introduction to James: Author. In Ac 21:18 this James appears to be the leader of the elders in the Jerusalem church. *the Lord's brother.* See note on Lk 8:19.

1:21 *Syria and Cilicia.* Provinces in Asia Minor (see map, p. 1851). Specifically, Paul went to Tarsus (see Ac 9:30 and note), his hometown in Cilicia.

2:1 *after fourteen years.* Probably from the date of Paul's conversion. *I went up again to Jerusalem.* According to some, the visit mentioned in Ac 11:30; according to others, the one in Ac 15:1–4 (see notes on Ac 12:1; 15:2). *Barnabas.* Means "one who encourages." His given name was Joseph, and he was a Levite from the island of Cyprus (see Ac 4:36 and note) and Paul's companion on the first missionary journey (Ac 13:1—14:28). *Titus.* A Gentile Christian who served as Paul's delegate to Corinth (see 2Co 2:13; 7:6–7; 8:6,16; 12:18) and later was left in Crete to oversee the church there (see Titus 1:5; see also Introduction to Titus: Recipient).

2:2 *those esteemed as leaders.* Paul recognized their authority and is probably referring to James, Peter and John (v. 9; cf. v. 6). *had not been running my race in vain.* Cf. 1Co 15:58; Php 2:16.

2:4 *false believers.* Judaizers who held that Gentile converts should be circumcised and obey the law of Moses (cf. Ac 15:5; 2Co 11:26). *spy on.* Used in the Septuagint (the pre-Christian Greek translation of the OT) in 2Sa 10:3 and 1Ch 19:3 of spying out a territory. *freedom.* See 5:1,13; Ro 6:18,20,22; 8:2. "Free" and "freedom" are key words in Galatians, occurring 11 times (here; 3:28; 4:22,23,26,30,31; 5:1 [twice],13 [twice]).

2:6 *those who were held in high esteem.* See note on v. 2. *not show favoritism.* Cf. Dt 10:17; 1Sa 16:7; Lk 20:21; Jas 2:1.

2:7 *to the uncircumcised.* That is, Gentiles. Paul's ministry was not exclusively to them. In fact, he regularly went first to the synagogue when arriving in a new location (see note on Ac 13:14). He did, however, consider himself to be foremost an apostle to the Gentiles (see Ro 11:13 and note).

2:9 *James.* See note on 1:19. His name may have been mentioned first because he played a dominant role in the Jerusalem council (Ac 15:12–21). *pillars.* A common metaphor for those who represent and strongly support an institution. *right hand of fellowship.* A common practice among both Jews and Greeks, indicating a pledge of friendship. *grace.* The entrusting to Paul of the gospel to the Gentiles (see v. 7).

2:10 Paul already had been involved in a trip to Jerusalem to help the impoverished Christians there (see Ac 11:29–30). He would make another visit for the same purpose at the end of his third missionary journey (see Ac 24:17 and note; Ro 15:25–27; 1Co 16:3–4; 2Co 9).

2:11 *Antioch.* The leading city of Roman Syria and third leading city of the empire (after Rome and Alexandria; see map, p. 1879). From it Paul had been sent out on his missionary journeys (see Ac 13:1–3; 14:26). *stood condemned.* For yielding to the pressure of the circumcision party (the Judaizers), thus going against what he knew to be right.

2:12 *circumcision group.* Judaizers, who believed that circumcision was necessary for salvation (cf. Ac 10:45; 11:2; Ro 4:12).

began to draw back and separate himself from the Gentiles because he was afraid of those who belonged to the circumcision group.[a] 13 The other Jews joined him in his hypocrisy, so that by their hypocrisy even Barnabas[b] was led astray.

14 When I saw that they were not acting in line with the truth of the gospel,[c] I said to Cephas[d] in front of them all, "You are a Jew, yet you live like a Gentile and not like a Jew.[e] How is it, then, that you force Gentiles to follow Jewish customs?[f]

15 "We who are Jews by birth[g] and not sinful Gentiles[h] 16 know that a person is not justified by the works of the law,[i] but by faith in Jesus Christ.[j] So we, too, have put our faith in Christ Jesus that we may be justified by faith in[a] Christ and not by the works of the law, because by the works of the law no one will be justified.[k]

17 "But if, in seeking to be justified in Christ, we Jews find ourselves also among the sinners,[l] doesn't that mean that Christ promotes sin? Absolutely not![m] 18 If I rebuild what I destroyed, then I really would be a lawbreaker.

19 "For through the law I died to the law[n] so that I might live for God.[o] 20 I have been crucified with Christ[p] and I no longer live, but Christ lives in me.[q] The life I now live in the body, I live by faith in the Son of God,[r] who loved me[s] and gave himself for me.[t] 21 I do not set aside the grace of God, for if righteousness could be gained through the law,[u] Christ died for nothing!"[b]

2:12 [a] Ac 10:45; 11:2
2:13 [b] ver 1; S Ac 4:36
2:14 [c] ver 5 [d] ver 7, 9, 11 [e] Ac 10:28 [f] ver 12
2:15 [g] Php 3:4, 5 [h] 1Sa 15:18; Lk 24:7
2:16 [i] S Ro 3:28 [j] S Ro 9:30 [k] S Ro 3:28; S 4:25
2:17 [l] ver 15 [m] Gal 3:21
2:19 [n] S Ro 7:4 [o] Ro 6:10, 11, 14; 2Co 5:15
2:20 [p] S Ro 6:6 [q] S Ro 8:10; 1Pe 4:2 [r] S Mt 4:3 [s] S Ro 8:37 [t] S Gal 1:4
2:21 [u] Gal 3:21

3:1 [v] Lk 24:25 [w] S Ac 16:6 [x] Gal 5:7 [y] 1Co 1:23
3:2 [z] S Jn 20:22 [a] ver 5, 10; Gal 2:16 [b] Ro 10:17; Heb 4:2
3:5 [c] 1Co 12:10 [d] ver 2, 10; Gal 2:16
3:6 [e] Ge 15:6; S Ro 4:3
3:7 [f] ver 9 [g] S Lk 3:8
3:8 [h] Ge 12:3; 18:18; 22:18; 26:4; Ac 3:25
3:9 [i] ver 7; Ro 4:16 [j] Ro 4:18-22
3:10 [k] ver 2, 5; Gal 2:16 [l] ver 13; S Ro 4:15

Faith or Works of the Law

3 You foolish[v] Galatians![w] Who has bewitched you?[x] Before your very eyes Jesus Christ was clearly portrayed as crucified.[y] 2 I would like to learn just one thing from you: Did you receive the Spirit[z] by the works of the law,[a] or by believing what you heard?[b] 3 Are you so foolish? After beginning by means of the Spirit, are you now trying to finish by means of the flesh?[c] 4 Have you experienced[d] so much in vain—if it really was in vain? 5 So again I ask, does God give you his Spirit and work miracles[c] among you by the works of the law, or by your believing what you heard?[d] 6 So also Abraham "believed God, and it was credited to him as righteousness."[e][e]

7 Understand, then, that those who have faith[f] are children of Abraham.[g] 8 Scripture foresaw that God would justify the Gentiles by faith, and announced the gospel in advance to Abraham: "All nations will be blessed through you."[f][h] 9 So those who rely on faith[i] are blessed along with Abraham, the man of faith.[j]

10 For all who rely on the works of the law[k] are under a curse,[l] as it is written: "Cursed is everyone who does not contin-

[a] 16 Or *but through the faithfulness of . . . justified on the basis of the faithfulness of* [b] 21 Some interpreters end the quotation after verse 14. [c] 3 In contexts like this, the Greek word for *flesh* (*sarx*) refers to the sinful state of human beings, often presented as a power in opposition to the Spirit. [d] 4 Or *suffered* [e] 6 Gen. 15:6 [f] 8 Gen. 12:3; 18:18; 22:18

2:13 *other Jews.* Jewish Christians not associated with the circumcision party but whom Peter's behavior had led astray. *hypocrisy.* See note on Mt 6:2.
2:14 *you live like a Gentile.* You do not observe Jewish customs, especially dietary restrictions (see v. 12). Peter evidently responded well to Paul's rebuke, since there is no historical evidence of continuing rivalry between the two (see 2Pe 3:15).
2:16 A key verse in Galatians (see Introduction: Theological Teaching). Three times it tells us that no one is justified by observing the law, and three times it underscores the indispensable requirement of placing one's faith in Christ. *not justified by the works of the law.* Paul is not depreciating the law itself, for he clearly maintained that God's law is "holy, righteous and good" (Ro 7:12; see note there). He is arguing against an illegitimate use of the OT law that made the observance of that law the grounds of acceptance with God. *but by faith in Jesus.* The essence of the gospel message (see Ro 3:20,28; Php 3:9; see also notes on Ro 3:24,28). Faith is the means by which justification is received, not its basis (cf. notes on Eph 2:8–9; Jas 2:14–26).
2:17 See Ro 6:1 and note.
2:19 *I died to the law.* See v. 20; see also note on Ro 7:4.
2:20 *crucified with Christ.* The believer identifies with Christ in Christ's death and resurrection, leaving their old life behind and sharing in Christ's resurrection life (see 5:24; Ro 6:7–8 and notes). *gave himself for me.* See 1:4; 1Ti 2:6; Titus 2:14.
2:21 *Christ died for nothing.* To mingle legalism (or works) with grace distorts grace and makes a mockery of the cross.
3:1 *foolish.* They were not mentally deficient but simply failed to use their powers of perception (see Lk 24:25; Ro 1:14; 1Ti 6:9; Titus 3:3). *Who . . . ?* Obviously legalistic Judaizers. *portrayed as crucified.* See 1Co 1:23; 2:2. The verb means "to publicly portray or placard." Cf. the bronze snake that Moses displayed on a pole (Nu 21:9).
3:2 *the Spirit.* A major theme in Galatians from this point on (Paul refers to the Holy Spirit 16 times).
3:3 *beginning by means of the Spirit . . . finish by means of the flesh?* Both salvation and sanctification are the work of the Holy Spirit. *the flesh.* A reference to human nature in its unregenerate weakness (see NIV text note). Trying to achieve righteousness by works, including circumcision, was a part of life in the "flesh."
3:4 *if it really was in vain.* Paul hopes that those who have been misled will return to the true gospel.
3:7 *children of Abraham.* Abraham was the physical and spiritual father of the Jewish race (see Jn 8:33,39,53; Ac 7:2; Ro 4:12). Here all believers (Jews and Gentiles) are called his spiritual children (see notes on Ro 4:11–12). They are also referred to as the "seed" (v. 29) or "descendants" (Heb 2:16) of Abraham.
3:8 *Scripture foresaw.* A personification of Scripture that calls attention to its divine origin (see 1Ti 5:18).
3:9 *Abraham, the man of faith.* Paul develops this theme at length in Ro 4; see also Heb 11:8–19.
3:10 *rely on the works of the law.* The reference is to legalists—those who refuse God's offer of grace and insist on pursuing righteousness through works. *under a curse.* Because no one under the law ever perfectly kept the law.

ue to do everything written in the Book of
the Law."[am] 11 Clearly no one who relies on
the law is justified before God,[n] because
"the righteous will live by faith."[bo] 12 The
law is not based on faith; on the contrary,
it says, "The person who does these things
will live by them."[cp] 13 Christ redeemed us
from the curse of the law[q] by becoming a
curse for us, for it is written: "Cursed is
everyone who is hung on a pole."[dr] 14 He
redeemed us in order that the blessing giv-
en to Abraham might come to the Gentiles
through Christ Jesus,[s] so that by faith we
might receive the promise of the Spirit.[t]

The Law and the Promise

15 Brothers and sisters,[u] let me take an
example from everyday life. Just as no one
can set aside or add to a human covenant
that has been duly established, so it is in
this case. 16 The promises were spoken to
Abraham and to his seed.[v] Scripture does
not say "and to seeds," meaning many
people, but "and to your seed,"[ew] meaning one person, who is Christ. 17 What
I mean is this: The law, introduced 430
years[x] later, does not set aside the covenant previously established by God and
thus do away with the promise. 18 For if the
inheritance depends on the law, then it no
longer depends on the promise;[y] but God
in his grace gave it to Abraham through a
promise.
19 Why, then, was the law given at all? It
was added because of transgressions[z] until the Seed[a] to whom the promise referred
had come. The law was given through angels[b] and entrusted to a mediator.[c] 20 A mediator,[d] however, implies more than one
party; but God is one.
21 Is the law, therefore, opposed to the
promises of God? Absolutely not![e] For if
a law had been given that could impart
life, then righteousness would certainly
have come by the law.[f] 22 But Scripture has
locked up everything under the control of
sin,[g] so that what was promised, being
given through faith in Jesus Christ, might
be given to those who believe.

Children of God

23 Before the coming of this faith,[f] we
were held in custody[h] under the law,
locked up until the faith that was to come
would be revealed.[i] 24 So the law was our
guardian until Christ came[j] that we might
be justified by faith.[k] 25 Now that this faith
has come, we are no longer under a guardian.[l]
26 So in Christ Jesus you are all children
of God[m] through faith, 27 for all of you who
were baptized into Christ[n] have clothed

[a] *10* Deut. 27:26 [b] *11* Hab. 2:4 [c] *12* Lev. 18:5
[d] *13* Deut. 21:23 [e] *16* Gen. 12:7; 13:15; 24:7
[f] *22,23* Or *through the faithfulness of Jesus . . . 23Before faith came*

3:10 [m] Dt 27:26; Jer 11:3 **3:11** [n] S Ro 3:28 [o] Hab 2:4; S Ro 9:30; Heb 10:38 **3:12** [p] Lev 18:5; S Ro 10:5 **3:13** [q] Gal 4:5 [r] Dt 21:23; S Ac 5:30 **3:14** [s] Ro 4:9, 16 [t] ver 2; Joel 2:28; S Jn 20:22; S Ac 2:33 **3:15** [u] S Ro 7:1 **3:16** [v] Ge 17:19; Ps 132:11; Mic 7:20; Lk 1:55; Ro 4:13, 16; 9:4, 8; Gal 3:29; 4:28 [w] Ge 12:7; 13:15; 17:7, 8, 10; 24:7 **3:17** [x] Ge 15:13, 14; Ex 12:40; Ac 7:6 **3:18** [y] Ro 4:14 **3:19** [z] Ro 5:20 [a] ver 16 [b] Dt 33:2; Ac 7:53 [c] Ex 20:19; Dt 5:5 **3:20** [d] 1Ti 2:5; Heb 8:6; 9:15; 12:24 **3:21** [e] Gal 2:17; S Ro 7:12 [f] Gal 2:21 **3:22** [g] Ro 3:9-19; 11:32 **3:23** [h] Ro 11:32 [i] ver 25 **3:24** [j] ver 19; Ro 10:4; S 4:15 [k] Gal 2:16 **3:25** [l] S Ro 7:4 **3:26** [m] S Ro 8:14 **3:27** [n] S Mt 28:19

God's blessing has never been earned but has always been freely given. *everything.* See Jas 2:10 and note.
3:11 *will live.* Means here (and in v. 12) almost the same thing as "will be justified."
3:12 See note on Lev 18:5.
3:13 *Christ redeemed us.* See 4:5; Eph 1:7 and note. *pole.* Used in classical Greek of poles on which bodies were impaled (cf. Est 2:23 and note); here of the cross (see Ac 5:30 and note; 1Pe 2:24).
3:14 *blessing given to Abraham.* See v. 8; Ro 4:1–5. *promise of the Spirit.* See Eze 36:26; 37:14; 39:29; Jn 14:16–17; cf. Eph 1:13.
3:15 *Brothers and sisters.* See NIV text note on 1:2. *human covenant.* The Greek word normally indicates a last will or testament, which is probably the legal instrument Paul is referring to here. But in the Septuagint (the pre-Christian Greek translation of the OT) it had been widely used of God's covenant with his people (see also Mt 26:28; Lk 1:72; Ac 3:25; 7:8; 2Co 3:14; Heb 8:9), so Paul's choice of analogy was apt for his purpose.
3:16 *promises.* See notes on Ro 4:13; 9:4.
3:17 *430 years.* See Ex 12:40–41. The period in Egypt is designated in round numbers as "four hundred years" in Ge 15:13; Ac 7:6 (see note there).
3:19 *was added.* From the time of Abraham, the promise covenanted to him (Ge 12:2–3,7; 15:18–20; 17:4–8) had stood at the center of God's relationship with his people. After the exodus the law contained in the Sinaitic covenant (Ex 19–24) became an additional element in that relationship—what Jeremiah by implication called the "old covenant" when he brought God's promise of a "new covenant" (Jer 31:31–34). *because of transgressions.* To make them known, even to increase them (see Ro 4:15; 7:7–11 and notes). *the Seed.* Christ (v. 16). *through angels.* See Ac 7:38,53 and note on 7:38. *mediator.* Moses (see note on v. 20).
3:20 The Sinaitic covenant was a formal arrangement of mutual commitments between God and Israel, with Moses as the mediator. But since the promise God covenanted with Abraham involved commitment only from God's side (and God is one; see note on Dt 6:4), no mediator was involved.
3:21 The reason the law is not opposed to the promise is that, although in itself it cannot save, it serves to reveal sin, which alienates God from humans, and to show the need for the salvation that the promise offers.
3:23 *this faith.* In Christ (v. 22). *held in custody under the law.* To be a prisoner of sin (v. 22) and a prisoner of law amounts to much the same, because law reveals and stimulates sin (see v. 19 and note; cf. Col 2:20).
3:24 *was our guardian.* The expression translates the Greek *paidagogos* (from which "pedagogue" is derived). It refers to the personal slave-attendant who accompanied a freeborn boy wherever he went and exercised a certain amount of discipline over him. His function was more like that of a babysitter than a teacher (see 1Co 4:15, "guardians").
3:25–26 By adoption, the justified believer is a full adult heir in God's family, with all the attendant rights and privileges (4:1–7; Ro 8:14–17).
3:27 *baptized into Christ.* See Ro 6:3–11; 1Co 12:13 and note. *clothed . . . with.* See note on Ps 109:29.

yourselves with Christ.[o] 28 There is neither Jew nor Gentile, neither slave nor free,[p] nor is there male and female,[q] for you are all one in Christ Jesus.[r] 29 If you belong to Christ,[s] then you are Abraham's seed,[t] and heirs[u] according to the promise.[v]

4 What I am saying is that as long as an heir is underage, he is no different from a slave, although he owns the whole estate. 2 The heir is subject to guardians and trustees until the time set by his father. 3 So also, when we were underage, we were in slavery[w] under the elemental spiritual forces[a] of the world.[x] 4 But when the set time had fully come,[y] God sent his Son,[z] born of a woman,[a] born under the law,[b] 5 to redeem[c] those under the law, that we might receive adoption[d] to sonship.[b][e] 6 Because you are his sons, God sent the Spirit of his Son[f] into our hearts,[g] the Spirit who calls out, *"Abba,*[c] Father."[h] 7 So you are no longer a slave, but God's child; and since you are his child, God has made you also an heir.[i]

Paul's Concern for the Galatians

8 Formerly, when you did not know God,[j] you were slaves[k] to those who by nature are not gods.[l] 9 But now that you know God—or rather are known by God[m]—how is it that you are turning back to those weak and miserable forces[d]? Do you wish to be enslaved[n] by them all over again?[o] 10 You are observing special days and months and seasons and years![p] 11 I fear for you, that somehow I have wasted my efforts on you.[q]

12 I plead with you, brothers and sisters,[r] become like me, for I became like you. You did me no wrong. 13 As you know, it was because of an illness[s] that I first preached the gospel to you, 14 and even though my illness was a trial to you, you did not treat me with contempt or scorn. Instead, you welcomed me as if I were an angel of God, as if I were Christ Jesus himself.[t] 15 Where, then, is your blessing of me now? I can testify that, if you could have done so, you would have torn out your eyes and given them to me. 16 Have I now become your enemy by telling you the truth?[u]

17 Those people are zealous to win you over, but for no good. What they want is to alienate you from us, so that you may have zeal for them.[v] 18 It is fine to be zealous, provided the purpose is good, and to be so always, not just when I am with you.[w] 19 My dear children,[x] for whom I am again in the pains of childbirth until Christ

3:27 [o] S Ro 13:14 **3:28** [p] 1Co 12:13; Col 3:11 [q] Ge 1:27; 5:2; Joel 2:29 [r] Jn 10:16; 17:11; Eph 2:14,15 **3:29** [s] S 1Co 3:23 [t] ver 16; S Lk 3:8 [u] S Ro 8:17 [v] ver 16 **4:3** [w] ver 8,9, 24,25; Gal 2:4 [x] Col 2:8,20 **4:4** [y] Mk 1:15; Ro 5:6; Eph 1:10 [z] S Jn 3:17 [a] S Jn 1:14 [b] Lk 2:27 **4:5** [c] S Ro 3:24 [d] Jn 1:12 [e] S Ro 8:14 **4:6** [f] S Ac 16:7 [g] Ro 5:5 [h] Ro 8:15,16 **4:7** [i] S Ro 8:17 **4:8** [j] Ro 1:28; 1Co 1:21; 15:34; 1Th 4:5; 2Th 1:8 [k] S ver 3 [l] 2Ch 13:9; Isa 37:19; Jer 2:11; 5:7; 16:20; 1Co 8:4,5 **4:9** [m] 1Co 8:3 [n] S ver 3 [o] Col 2:20 **4:10** [p] Ro 14:5; Col 2:16 **4:11** [q] 1Th 3:5 **4:12** [r] S Ro 7:1; Gal 6:18 **4:13** [s] 1Co 2:3 **4:14** [t] Mt 10:40 **4:16** [u] Am 5:10 **4:17** [v] Gal 2:4,12 **4:18** [w] ver 13,14 **4:19** [x] S 1Th 2:11

[a] 3 Or *under the basic principles* [b] 5 The Greek word for *adoption to sonship* is a legal term referring to the full legal standing of an adopted male heir in Roman culture. [c] 6 Aramaic for *Father* [d] 9 Or *principles*

3:28 Unity in Christ transcends ethnic, social and gender distinctions (see Ro 10:12; 1Co 12:13; Eph 2:15–16).

3:29 Christians are Abraham's true, spiritual descendants.

4:1 *underage.* Minors. Contrast with "adults" in 1Co 14:20 ("mature" in Php 3:15).

4:2 *guardians.* A broader term than the one used in 3:24. See Mt 20:8 ("foreman"); Lk 8:3 ("manager").

4:3 *in slavery.* See note on 3:23. *elemental spiritual forces.* See Col 2:8 and note.

4:4 *time had fully come.* The time "set" (v. 2) by God for his children to become adult sons and heirs. *God sent his Son.* See Jn 1:14; 3:16; Ro 1:1–6; 1Jn 4:14. *born of a woman.* Showing that Christ was truly human. *born under the law.* Subject to the Jewish law.

4:5 *those under the law.* Those under the authority of the law of Moses (cf. notes on 5:18; Ro 6:14; 1Co 9:20). *adoption to sonship.* See NIV text note; see also Ro 8:15, where "sonship" is contrasted with "slaves" (cf. Eph 1:5 and note). God takes into his family as fully recognized sons and heirs both Jews (those who had been under the law) and Gentiles who believe in Christ.

4:6 *Spirit of his Son.* A new "guardian" (v. 2), identified as the "Spirit of God" and "Spirit of Christ" in Ro 8:9 (see Ro 8:2; Eph 1:13–14). *calls out.* The Greek for this phrase is a vivid verb expressing deep emotion, often used of an inarticulate cry. In Mt 27:50 it is used of Jesus' final cry on the cross. *Abba, Father.* Expressive of an especially close relationship to God (see also NIV text note).

4:8 *when you did not know God.* See 1Co 12:2; 1Th 4:5. *are not gods.* When the Galatians were pagans, they thought that the beings they worshiped were gods; but when they became Christians they learned better (see 1Co 8:5 and note).

4:9 *turning back.* See 3:1–3. *weak and miserable forces.* See note on v. 3. *enslaved ... again.* Legalistic trust in rituals, in moral achievement, in the law, in good works or even in cold, dead orthodoxy may indicate a relapse into second childhood on the part of those who should be knowing and enjoying the freedom of full-grown sons and heirs.

4:10 *special days.* Such as the Sabbath and the Day of Atonement (tenth day of Tishri; see Lev 16:29–34), which had never been, and can never be, in themselves means of salvation or sanctification. *months and seasons.* Such as New Moons (see Nu 28:11–15; Isa 1:13–14), Passover (Ex 12:18) and Firstfruits (Lev 23:10). *years.* Such as the sabbath year (see Lev 25:4). The Pharisees meticulously observed all these in an attempt to gain merit before God.

4:11 *wasted my efforts.* Due to their return to Pharisaic legalism.

4:12 *brothers and sisters.* See NIV text note on 1:2.

4:13 *illness.* On the basis of v. 15; 6:11 (see note there), some suggest it was eye trouble. Others have suggested malaria or epilepsy. *first preached.* When Paul visited Galatia on his first missionary journey (Ac 13:14—14:23; see map, p. 1851).

4:14 *you welcomed me.* He implies that under the influence of Judaizers they have changed their attitude toward him.

4:15 *torn out your eyes.* A hyperbole indicating their willingness, for his benefit, to part with that which was most precious to them.

4:16 *your enemy.* Telling the truth sometimes results in loss of friends. *the truth.* The good news about God's grace in Christ.

4:17 *Those people.* Judaizers (see 2:4,12).

4:19 *My dear children.* For Paul's affectionate relationship to his converts, see Ac 20:37–38; Php 4:1; 1Th 2:7–8. The expression occurs only here in Paul's writings but is common in

is formed in you,[y] 20how I wish I could be
with you now and change my tone, because I am perplexed about you!

Hagar and Sarah

21Tell me, you who want to be under
the law,[z] are you not aware of what the
law says? 22For it is written that Abraham
had two sons, one by the slave woman[a]
and the other by the free woman.[b] 23His
son by the slave woman was born according to the flesh,[c] but his son by the free
woman was born as the result of a divine
promise.[d]

24These things are being taken figuratively: The women represent two covenants. One covenant is from Mount Sinai
and bears children who are to be slaves:
This is Hagar. 25Now Hagar stands for
Mount Sinai in Arabia and corresponds to the present city of Jerusalem, because she is in slavery
with her children. 26But the Jerusalem that is above[e] is free, and she
is our mother. 27For it is written:

"Be glad, barren woman,
you who never bore a child;
shout for joy and cry aloud,
you who were never in labor;
because more are the children
of the desolate woman
than of her who has a
husband."[a][f]

28Now you, brothers and sisters,
like Isaac, are children of promise.[g]
29At that time the son born according to the flesh[h] persecuted the son
born by the power of the Spirit.[i] It
is the same now. 30But what does Scripture say? "Get rid of the slave woman and
her son, for the slave woman's son will
never share in the inheritance with the
free woman's son."[b][j] 31Therefore, brothers and sisters, we are not children of the
slave woman,[k] but of the free woman.[l]

Freedom in Christ

5 It is for freedom that Christ has set us
free.[m] Stand firm,[n] then, and do not let
yourselves be burdened again by a yoke
of slavery.[o]

2Mark my words! I, Paul, tell you that if
you let yourselves be circumcised,[p] Christ
will be of no value to you at all. 3Again I

4:19 [y] Ro 8:29; Eph 4:13 **4:21** [z] S Ro 2:12 **4:22** [a] Ge 16:15 [b] Ge 21:2 **4:23** [c] ver 28, 29; Ro 9:7,8 [d] Ge 17:16-21; 18:10-14; 21:1; Heb 11:11 **4:26** [e] Heb 12:22; Rev 3:12; 21:2,10 **4:27** [f] Isa 54:1 **4:28** [g] ver 23; S Gal 3:16 **4:29** [h] ver 23 [i] Ge 21:9 **4:30** [j] Ge 21:10 **4:31** [k] S Ro 7:4 [l] ver 22 **5:1** [m] ver 13; Jn 8:32; Gal 2:4; S Ro 7:4 [n] S 1Co 16:13 [o] S Mt 23:4; Gal 2:4 **5:2** [p] ver 3,6,11,12; Ac 15:1

[a] *27* Isaiah 54:1 [b] *30* Gen. 21:10

SLAVERY AND **FREEDOM**

SLAVERY	FREEDOM
Hagar was a slave woman.	Sarah was a "free" wife.
Ishmael was born of the flesh, a trademark of the Judaizers (6:13–14).	Isaac was born through promise (4:23) and the Spirit (4:29).
Mount Sinai, Jerusalem of the Judaizers (4:25), is a symbol of slavery.	Mount Zion (4:26; Heb 12:22) stands for joyous freedom (based on Isa 54:1).
"Ishmael" is in slavery and opposes his brother.	"Isaac" (Paul and his converts) suffers persecution (6:12–13).
The Judaizers are to be refused since Ishmael did not gain an inheritance (4:30).	Paul's gospel connects believers with the "free woman" and the promise of liberty (4:31).

John's (e.g., Jn 13:33; 1Jn 2:1; 3:7). *until Christ is formed in you.* The goal of Paul's ministry (see Ro 8:29; Eph 4:13,15; Col 1:27).
4:21 *under the law.* See note on v. 5.
4:22 *two sons.* Ishmael was born to the slave woman, Hagar (Ge 16:1 - 16), and Isaac to the free woman, Sarah (Ge 21:2 - 5).
4:23 *promise.* See Ge 17:19; 18:10 - 15 and note on 18:10; cf. Ro 9:6 - 9.
4:24 *These things are being taken figuratively.* The Sarah-Hagar account is an allegory not in the sense that it was nonhistorical but in the sense that Paul uses the events to illustrate a theological truth. *covenant.* See note on 3:15. *Mount Sinai.* Where the old covenant was established, with its law governing Israel's life (see Ex 19:2; 20:1 - 17).
4:25 *corresponds to the present city of Jerusalem.* Jerusalem can be equated with Mount Sinai because it represents the center of Judaism.
4:26 *the Jerusalem that is above.* Rabbinical teaching held that the Jerusalem above was the heavenly archetype that in the Messianic period would be let down to earth (cf. Rev 21:2). Here it refers to the heavenly city of God, in which Christ reigns and of which Christians are citizens, in contrast to the "present city of Jerusalem" (v. 25). *our mother.* See note on 2Sa 20:19. As citizens of the heavenly Jerusalem, Christians are her children.
4:27 Paul applies Isaiah's joyful promise (see Isa 54:1 and note) to exiled Jerusalem (in her exile "barren" of children) to the ingathering of believers through the gospel, by which "Jerusalem's" children have become many.
4:28 *children of promise.* Children by virtue of God's promise (see 3:29; Ro 9:8).
4:29 *persecuted the son born by the power of the Spirit.* Suggested by Ge 21:9 (see note there); cf. Ps 83:5 - 6. *the same now.* See Ac 13:50; 14:2 - 5,19; 1Th 2:14 - 16.
4:30 *Get rid of the slave woman.* Sarah's words in Ge 21:10 were used by Paul as the Scriptural basis for teaching the Galatians to put the Judaizers out of the church.
4:31 *we are not children of the slave woman.* The believer is not enslaved to the law but is a child of promise and lives by faith (cf. 3:7,29).
5:1 *freedom.* Emphasized by its position in the Greek sentence. The freedom spoken of here is freedom from the yoke of the law. *burdened.* Cf. Mt 11:28 - 30 and notes on 11:29 - 30. *yoke of slavery.* The burden of the rigorous demands of the law as the means for gaining God's favor — an intolerable burden for sinful humanity (see Ac 15:10 - 11).
5:2 As a condition for God's acceptance, circumcision impeded the development of the Christian life through trusting in Christ.
5:3 *obligated to obey the whole law.* The OT law is a unit; submission to it cannot be selective (see Jas 2:10 and note).

ACTS OF THE FLESH
AND HARVEST OF THE SPIRIT

ACTS OF THE FLESH	HARVEST OF THE SPIRIT
Sexual immorality, impurity and debauchery	Love, joy, peace
Idolatry and witchcraft	Forbearance, kindness, goodness
Hatred, discord, jealousy, fits of rage	Faithfulness, gentleness, self-control
Selfish ambition, dissensions, factions	
Envy, drunkenness, orgies, and the like	

Adapted from *Zondervan Illustrated Bible Backgrounds Commentary: NT*: Vol. 3 by CLINTON E. ARNOLD.

declare to every man who lets himself be
circumcised that he is obligated to obey
the whole law.[q] 4You who are trying to be
justified by the law[r] have been alienated
from Christ; you have fallen away from
grace.[s] 5For through the Spirit we eagerly
await by faith the righteousness for which
we hope.[t] 6For in Christ Jesus[u] neither circumcision nor uncircumcision has any
value.[v] The only thing that counts is faith
expressing itself through love.[w]
7You were running a good race.[x] Who
cut in on you[y] to keep you from obeying
the truth? 8That kind of persuasion does
not come from the one who calls you.[z] 9"A
little yeast works through the whole batch
of dough."[a] 10I am confident[b] in the Lord
that you will take no other view.[c] The one
who is throwing you into confusion,[d] whoever that may be, will have to pay
the penalty. 11Brothers and sisters,
if I am still preaching circumcision,
why am I still being persecuted?[e]
In that case the offense[f] of the
cross has been abolished. 12As for
those agitators,[g] I wish they would
go the whole way and emasculate
themselves!

Life by the Spirit

13You, my brothers and sisters,
were called to be free.[h] But do not
use your freedom to indulge the
flesh[a];[i] rather, serve one another[j]
humbly in love. 14For the entire
law is fulfilled in keeping this one
command: "Love your neighbor as
yourself."[bk] 15If you bite and devour each
other, watch out or you will be destroyed
by each other.
16So I say, walk by the Spirit,[l] and you
will not gratify the desires of the flesh.[m]
17For the flesh desires what is contrary to
the Spirit, and the Spirit what is contrary
to the flesh.[n] They are in conflict with each
other, so that you are not to do whatever[c]
you want.[o] 18But if you are led by the Spirit,[p] you are not under the law.[q]
19The acts of the flesh are obvious: sex-

5:3 [q]Ro 2:25; Gal 3:10; Jas 2:10 **5:4** [r]S Ro 3:28 [s]Heb 12:15; 2Pe 3:17 **5:5** [t]Ro 8:23, 24 **5:6** [u]S Ro 16:3 [v]S 1Co 7:19 [w]1Th 1:3; Jas 2:22 **5:7** [x]S 1Co 9:24 [y]Gal 3:1 **5:8** [z]S Ro 8:28 **5:9** [a]1Co 5:6 **5:10** [b]S 2Co 2:3 [c]Php 3:15 [d]ver 12; Gal 1:7 **5:11** [e]Gal 4:29; 6:12 [f]S Lk 2:34 **5:12** [g]ver 10 **5:13** [h]S ver 1 [i]S ver 24; 1Co 8:9; 1Pe 2:16 [j]1Co 9:19; 2Co 4:5; Eph 5:21 **5:14** [k]Lev 19:18; S Mt 5:43; Gal 6:2 **5:16** [l]ver 18, 25; Ro 8:2, 4-6, 9, 14; S 2Co 5:17 [m]S ver 24 **5:17** [n]Ro 8:5-8 [o]Ro 7:15-23 **5:18** [p]S ver 16 [q]S Ro 2:12; 1Ti 1:9

[a] 13 In contexts like this, the Greek word for *flesh* (*sarx*) refers to the sinful state of human beings, often presented as a power in opposition to the Spirit; also in verses 16, 17, 19 and 24; and in 6:8. [b] 14 Lev. 19:18 [c] 17 Or *you do not do what*

5:4 *fallen away from grace.* Placed yourself outside the scope of divine favor, because gaining God's favor by observing the law and receiving it by grace are mutually exclusive (see 2:2 and note; cf. 3:3 and note).
5:5 *righteousness for which we hope.* A reference to God's final verdict of "not guilty," assured presently to the believer by faith and by the sanctifying work of the Holy Spirit. This is one of the few eschatological statements in Galatians.
5:6 *neither circumcision nor uncircumcision has any value.* See v. 2; 2:21; 6:15; 1Co 7:19. *faith expressing itself through love.* Faith is not mere intellectual assent (see Jas 2:18–19) but a living trust in God's grace that expresses itself in acts of love (see 1Th 1:3).
5:7 *were running a good race.* Before the Judaizers hindered them. Paul was fond of depicting the Christian life as a race (see, e.g., 2:2; 1Co 9:24–27 and note on 9:27; Php 2:16; 2Ti 4:7).
5:8 *persuasion.* By the Judaizers.
5:9 A proverb used here to stress the pervasive effect of Judaism. When the word "yeast" in the Bible is used as a symbol, it indicates evil or the corrupting influence of false teaching (see note on Mk 8:15), except in Mt 13:33 (see note there).
5:11 *Brothers and sisters.* See NIV text note on 1:2. *why am I still being persecuted?* Because human pride refuses to acknowledge that it is incapable of doing anything to merit salvation. Paul's preaching excluded circumcision and obedience to the law as a means of justification and focused instead on Christ's finished work on the cross. This was an offense to the Judaizers and continues to be so to many people in our own day (see Ro 9:32–33 and note on 9:32; 1Co 1:23 and note).
5:12 *emasculate themselves.* Paul's sarcasm is evident (cf. Php 3:2).
5:13 *do not use your freedom to indulge the flesh.* See Ro 6:1 and note. True Christian liberty is not license to sin but freedom to serve God and one another in love (see 1Pe 2:16 and note).
5:14 *entire law is fulfilled.* Doing to others what you would have them do to you expresses the spirit and intention of "the Law and the Prophets" (Mt 7:12; cf. Mk 12:31; cf. also Ro 13:8–10 and notes on 13:8–9).
5:15 *bite and devour each other.* The opposite of vv. 13–14. Seeking to attain status with God and human beings by mere observance of the law breeds a self-righteous, critical spirit.
5:16 *walk.* Present tense—"go on walking" (used of habitual conduct). Living by the promptings and power of the Spirit is the key to conquering sinful desires (see v. 25 and note; Ro 8:2–4).
5:17 *in conflict with each other.* Cf. Ro 7:13–25; 1Pe 2:11 and notes.
5:18 *led by the Spirit.* See Ro 8:14. *not under the law.* Not under the bondage of trying to please God by minute observance of the law for salvation or sanctification (see Ro 6:14 and note).
5:19–21 See Ro 1:29–31 and note.

ual immorality,[r] impurity and debauchery; 20 idolatry and witchcraft; hatred,
discord, jealousy, fits of rage, selfish ambition, dissensions, factions 21 and envy;
drunkenness, orgies, and the like.[s] I warn
you, as I did before, that those who live
like this will not inherit the kingdom of
God.[t]
22 But the fruit[u] of the Spirit is love,[v] joy,
peace,[w] forbearance, kindness, goodness,
faithfulness, 23 gentleness and self-control.[x] Against such things there is no law.[y]
24 Those who belong to Christ Jesus have
crucified the flesh[z] with its passions and
desires.[a] 25 Since we live by the Spirit,[b] let
us keep in step with the Spirit. 26 Let us not
become conceited,[c] provoking and envying each other.

5:19 [r] S 1Co 6:18 **5:21** [s] Mt 15:19; Ro 13:13 [t] S Mt 25:34 **5:22** [u] Mt 7:16-20; Eph 5:9 [v] Col 3:12-15 [w] Mal 2:6 **5:23** [x] S Ac 24:25 [y] ver 18 **5:24** [z] ver 13, 16-21; S Ro 6:6; 7:5, 18; 8:3-5, 8, 9, 12, 13; 13:14; Gal 6:8; Col 2:11 [a] ver 16, 17 **5:25** [b] S ver 16 **5:26** [c] Php 2:3

Doing Good to All

6 Brothers and sisters, if someone is
caught in a sin, you who live by the
Spirit[d] should restore[e] that person gently.
But watch yourselves, or you also may
be tempted. 2 Carry each other's burdens,
and in this way you will fulfill the law of
Christ.[f] 3 If anyone thinks they are something[g] when they are not, they deceive

6:1 [d] 1Co 2:15; 3:1 [e] S Mt 18:15; S 2Co 2:7 **6:2** [f] 1Co 9:21; Jas 2:8 **6:3** [g] Ro 12:3; 1Co 8:2

5:22–23 For other lists of virtues, see 2Co 6:6–10; Eph 4:2; 5:9; Php 4:8–9; Col 3:12–15. Christian character is produced by the Holy Spirit, not by the mere moral discipline of trying to live by the law. Paul makes it clear that justification by faith does not result in libertinism. The indwelling Holy Spirit produces Christian virtues in the believer's life (see chart below).
5:22 *fruit of the Spirit.* Compare the singular "fruit" with the plural "acts" (v. 19).
5:23 *no law.* See 1Ti 1:9.
5:24 *crucified the flesh.* See 2:20; 6:14 and notes.
5:25 *keep in step with.* Or "walk in line with," a different Greek verb from "walk by" in v. 16.
6:1 *Brothers and sisters.* See NIV text note on 1:2. *you who live by the Spirit.* Contrast with 1Co 3:1–3. *restore.* See note on 2Co 13:9. The Greek for this verb is used elsewhere in the NT for mending nets (Mk 1:19) and bringing factions together (1Co 1:10).
6:2 *Carry each other's burdens.* The emphasis is on moral burdens or weaknesses (see v. 1; Ro 15:1–3). *law of Christ.* See 1Co 9:21 and note.

THE FRUIT OF THE **SPIRIT**

The aspects of the fruit of the Spirit advocated by Paul in Galatians 5:22–23 occur not only here but also elsewhere in the Scriptures. Most of the attributes are those by which God himself lives.

ASPECT	GK NUMBER*	DEFINITION	ATTRIBUTE OF GOD	ATTRIBUTE FOR CHRISTIANS
love	26	sacrificial, unmerited deeds to help a needy person	Ex 34:6; Jn 3:16; Ro 5:8; 1Jn 4:8,16	Jn 13:34–35; Ro 12:9,10; 1Pe 1:22; 1Jn 4:7,11–12,21
joy	5915	an inner happiness not dependent on outward circumstances	Ps 104:31; Isa 62:5; Lk 15:7,10	Dt 12:7,12,18; Ps 64:10; Isa 25:9; Php 4:4; 1Pe 1:8
peace	1645	harmony in all relationships	Isa 9:6–7; Eze 34:25; Jn 14:27; Heb 13:20	Isa 26:3; Ro 5:1; 12:18; 14:17; Eph 2:14–17
forbearance	3429	putting up with others, even when one is severely tried	Ro 9:22; 1Ti 1:16; 1Pe 3:20; 2Pe 3:9,15	Eph 4:2; Col 1:11; Heb 6:12; Jas 5:7–8,10
kindness	5983	doing thoughtful deeds for others	Ro 2:4; 11:22; Eph 2:7; Titus 3:4	1Co 13:4; Eph 4:32; Col 3:12
goodness	20	showing generosity to others	Ne 9:25,35; Ps 31:19; Mk 10:18	Ro 15:14; Eph 5:9; 2Th 1:11
faithfulness	4411	trustworthiness and reliability	Ps 33:4; 1Co 1:9; 10:13; Heb 10:23; 1Jn 1:9	Lk 16:10–12; 2Th 1:4; 2Ti 4:7; Titus 2:10
gentleness	4559	meekness and humility	Zec 9:9; Mt 11:29	Isa 66:2; Mt 5:5; Eph 4:2; Col 3:12
self-control	1602	victory over sinful desires		Pr 16:32; Titus 1:8; 2:12; 1Pe 5:8–9; 2Pe 1:6

*The numbers refer to the Greek dictionary entry numbers in Goodrick & Kohlenberger, *The NIV Exhaustive Concordance*.

themselves.[h] 4Each one should test their
own actions. Then they can take pride
in themselves alone,[i] without comparing
themselves to someone else,[j] 5for each one
should carry their own load.[k] 6Neverthe-
less, the one who receives instruction in
the word should share all good things with
their instructor.[l]

7Do not be deceived:[m] God cannot be
mocked. A man reaps what he sows.[n]
8Whoever sows to please their flesh,[o] from
the flesh will reap destruction;[p] whoever
sows to please the Spirit, from the Spirit
will reap eternal life.[q] 9Let us not become
weary in doing good,[r] for at the proper time
we will reap a harvest if we do not give up.[s]
10Therefore, as we have opportunity, let us
do good[t] to all people, especially to those
who belong to the family[u] of believers.

Not Circumcision but the New Creation

11See what large letters I use as I write
to you with my own hand![v]

12Those who want to impress people by
means of the flesh[w] are trying to compel
you to be circumcised.[x] The only reason
they do this is to avoid being persecuted[y]
for the cross of Christ. 13Not even those
who are circumcised keep the law,[z] yet
they want you to be circumcised that they
may boast about your circumcision in the
flesh.[a] 14May I never boast except in the
cross of our Lord Jesus Christ,[b] through
which[a] the world has been crucified to
me, and I to the world.[c] 15Neither circumcision nor uncircumcision means anything;[d] what counts is the new creation.[e]
16Peace and mercy to all who follow this
rule—to[b] the Israel of God.

17From now on, let no one cause me
trouble, for I bear on my body the marks[f]
of Jesus.

18The grace of our Lord Jesus Christ[g]
be with your spirit,[h] brothers and sisters.
Amen.

[a] 14 Or *whom* [b] 16 Or *rule and to*

6:3 [h] 1Co 3:18 **6:4** [i] 2Co 13:5 [j] 2Co 10:12 **6:5** [k] ver 2; Jer 31:30 **6:6** [l] 1Co 9:11, 14; 1Ti 5:17,18 **6:7** [m] S 1Co 6:9 [n] Pr 22:8; Jer 34:17; Hos 10:12,13; 2Co 9:6 **6:8** [o] S Gal 5:24 [p] Job 4:8; Hos 8:7; S Ro 6:23 [q] Jas 3:18 **6:9** [r] 1Co 15:58; 2Co 4:1 [s] Job 42:12; Ps 126:5; Heb 12:3; Rev 2:10 **6:10** [t] Pr 3:27; S Titus 2:14 [u] Eph 2:19; 1Pe 4:17 **6:11** [v] S 1Co 16:21 **6:12** [w] Mt 23:25, 26 [x] Ac 15:1 [y] Gal 5:11 **6:13** [z] Ro 2:25 [a] Php 3:3 **6:14** [b] 1Co 2:2 [c] S Ro 6:2,6 **6:15** [d] S 1Co 7:19 [e] S 2Co 5:17 **6:17** [f] Isa 44:5; S 2Co 1:5; 11:23 **6:18** [g] S Ro 16:20 [h] Php 4:23; 2Ti 4:22; Phm 25

6:4 *Each one should test their own actions.* The emphasis here is on personal responsibility (see 1Co 11:28; 2Co 13:5).
6:5 *carry their own load.* The "for" at the beginning of the verse connects it with v. 4. Each of us is responsible before God. The reference may be to the future judgment (the Greek verb is in the future tense), when every Christian will give an account to God (see Ro 14:10,12 and note on 14:10; 2Co 5:10 and note).
6:6 *share all good things.* See Php 4:14–19; 1Ti 5:17 and note.
6:7 *reaps what he sows.* See 2Co 9:6. As vv. 8–9 show, the principle applies not only negatively but also positively.
6:8 See Ro 8:13. *destruction.* See 5:19–21. *eternal life.* In 5:21 Paul speaks of inheriting "the kingdom of God" and here of reaping "eternal life." The first focuses on the realm (sphere, context) that will be inherited (as Israel inherited the promised land); the second focuses on the blessed life that will be enjoyed in that realm (see Jn 3:15–16 and note).
6:10 *especially to those who belong to the family of believers.* See 1Ti 5:8.
6:11 *large letters.* May have been for emphasis or, as some have suggested, because Paul had poor eyesight (see note on 4:13). *with my own hand.* The letter up to this point had probably been dictated to a scribe, after which Paul took the pen in his own hand and finished the letter (cf. Ro 16:22; 2Th 3:17 and notes).
6:12 *compel you to be circumcised.* Cf. 2:3. *to avoid being persecuted.* By advocating circumcision (see 5:11) the Judaizers were less apt to experience opposition from the Jewish opponents of Christianity. They were thinking only of themselves. See Introduction: Occasion and Purpose.
6:14 *never boast except in the cross.* See 1Co 1:31; 2:2. *world.* All that is against God (see notes on Jn 1:9; 1Jn 2:15). *crucified to me, and I to the world.* See 2:19–20; 5:24.
6:15 *new creation.* In Christ the redeemed undergo a transformation that results in an entirely new being. Creation again takes place (see 2Co 5:17 and note).
6:16,18 *Peace ... grace.* See note on Ro 1:7.
6:16 *Peace and mercy.* Cf. Ps 125:5; 128:6. *this rule.* See vv. 14–15. *Israel of God.* In contrast to "Israel according to flesh" (a literal rendering of the Greek for "people of Israel" in 1Co 10:18), the NT church, made up of believing Jews and Gentiles, is the new seed of Abraham and the heir according to the promise (3:29; cf. Ro 9:6; Php 3:3)—though some limit the phrase here to Christian Jews (see NIV text note).
6:17 *marks of Jesus.* In ancient times the Greek word for "marks" was used for the brand that identified slaves or animals. Paul's suffering (stoning, Ac 14:19; beatings, Ac 16:22; 2Co 11:25; illness, 2Co 12:7; Gal 4:13–14) marked him as a "servant of Christ" (1:10; cf. 2Co 4:10).
6:18 *be with your spirit.* Be with you (see 2Co 13:14 and note). *brothers and sisters.* See NIV text note on 1:2. *Amen.* A word of confirmation often used at the close of a doxology or benediction.

EPHESIANS

INTRODUCTION

Author, Date and Place of Writing

The author identifies himself as Paul (1:1; 3:1; cf. 3:7,13; 4:1; 6:19 – 20). Some have taken the absence of the usual personal greetings and the verbal similarity of many parts to Colossians, among other reasons, as grounds for doubting authorship by the apostle Paul. However, this was probably a circular letter, intended for other churches in addition to the one in Ephesus (see notes on 1:1,15; 6:21 – 23). Paul may have written it about the same time as Colossians, c. AD 60, while he was in prison at Rome (see 3:1; 4:1; 6:20; see also chart, p. 1845).

The City of Ephesus

Ephesus was the most important city in western Asia Minor (now Turkey). It had a harbor that at that time opened into the Cayster River (see map, p. 1982), which in turn emptied into the Aegean Sea (see map, p. 2153). Because it was also at an intersection of major trade routes, Ephesus became a commercial center. It boasted a pagan temple dedicated to the Roman goddess Diana (Greek *Artemis*); cf. Ac 19:23 – 31. Paul made Ephesus his base of operations for over two years, during which he and his associates evangelized western Asia Minor (Ac 19:10), and the church there apparently flourished for some time, but later needed the warning of Rev 2:1 – 7. All seven churches of Revelation may have been founded by Paul and his associates during the two years and three months Paul spent in Ephesus (see note on Ac 19:10; see also Introduction to Colossians: Colossae: The Town and the Church).

Theological Message

Unlike several of the other letters Paul wrote, Ephesians does not address any particular error or heresy. Paul wrote to expand the horizons of his readers, so that they might understand better the dimensions of God's eternal purpose and grace and come to appreciate the high goals God has for the church.

Author:
The apostle Paul

Audience:
Believers in the church at Ephesus and probably other Christians in western Asia Minor

Date:
About AD 60

Theme:
Paul summarizes his gospel of salvation by grace through faith alone and describes the nature and role of the church in God's eternal plan.

Paul writes to expand the horizons of his readers, so that they might understand better the dimensions of God's eternal purpose and grace and come to appreciate the high goals God has for the church.

The letter opens with a sequence of statements about God's blessings, which are interspersed with a remarkable variety of expressions drawing attention to God's wisdom, forethought and purpose. Paul emphasizes that we have been saved, not only for our personal benefit, but also to bring praise and glory to God. The climax of God's purpose, "when the times reach their fulfillment," is to bring all things in the universe together under Christ (1:10). It is crucially important that Christians realize this, so in 1:15 – 23 Paul prays for their understanding (a second prayer occurs in 3:14 – 21).

EPHESUS IN THE TIME OF PAUL

The Roman province of Asia with its many splendid cities was one of the jewels on a belt of Roman lands encircling the Mediterranean.

Located on the most direct sea and land route to the eastern provinces of the empire, Ephesus was an emporium that had few equals anywhere in the world. Certainly no city in Asia was more famous or more populous. It ranked with Rome, Corinth, Antioch and Alexandria among the foremost urban centers of the empire.

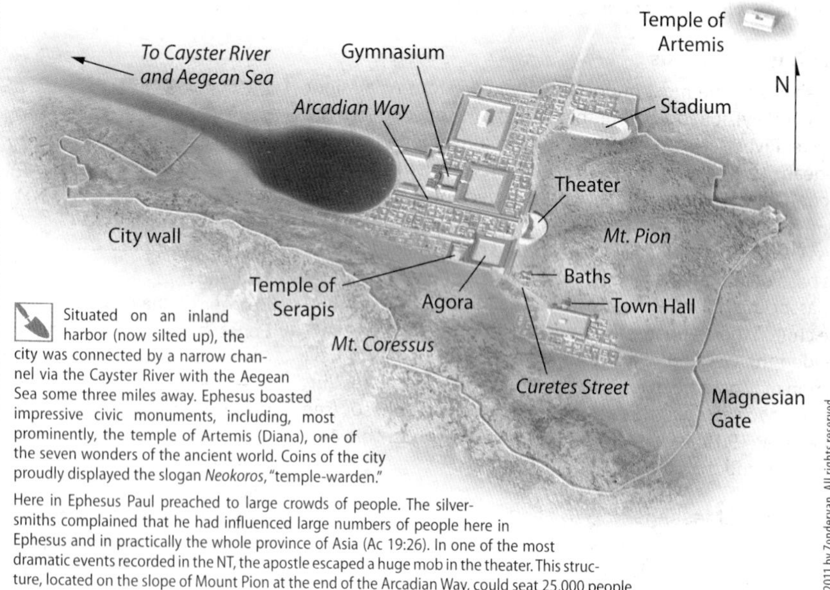

Situated on an inland harbor (now silted up), the city was connected by a narrow channel via the Cayster River with the Aegean Sea some three miles away. Ephesus boasted impressive civic monuments, including, most prominently, the temple of Artemis (Diana), one of the seven wonders of the ancient world. Coins of the city proudly displayed the slogan *Neokoros*, "temple-warden."

Here in Ephesus Paul preached to large crowds of people. The silversmiths complained that he had influenced large numbers of people here in Ephesus and in practically the whole province of Asia (Ac 19:26). In one of the most dramatic events recorded in the NT, the apostle escaped a huge mob in the theater. This structure, located on the slope of Mount Pion at the end of the Arcadian Way, could seat 25,000 people.

Other places doubtless familiar to the apostle were the Commercial Agora, the Magnesian Gate, the Town Hall and Curetes Street.

Library of Celsus at Ephesus, built during the period AD 110 – 135

© Cornel Achirei/www.BigStockPhoto.com

Having explained God's great goals for the church, Paul proceeds to show the steps toward their fulfillment. First, God has reconciled individuals to himself as an act of grace (2:1 – 10). Second, God has reconciled these saved individuals to each other, Christ having broken down the barriers through his own death (2:11 – 22). But God has done something even beyond this: He has united these reconciled individuals in one body, the church. This is a "mystery" not fully known until it was revealed to Paul (3:1 – 6). Now Paul is able to state even more clearly what God has intended for the church, namely, that it be the means by which he displays his "manifold wisdom" to the "rulers and authorities in the heavenly realms" (3:7 – 13). It is clear through the repetition of "heavenly realms" (1:3,20; 2:6; 3:10; 6:12) that Christian existence is not merely on an earthly plane. It receives its meaning and significance from heaven, where Christ is exalted at the right hand of God (1:20).

Nevertheless, that life is lived out on earth, where the practical daily life of the believer continues to work out the purposes of God. The ascended Lord gave "gifts" to the members of his church to enable them to minister to one another and so promote unity and maturity (4:1 – 16). The unity of the church under the headship of Christ foreshadows the uniting of "all things in heaven and on earth under Christ" (1:10). The new life of purity and mutual deference stands in contrast to the old way of life without Christ (4:17 — 6:9). Those who are "strong in the Lord" have victory over the evil one in the great spiritual conflict, especially through the power of prayer (6:10 – 20; see note on 1:3).

Outline

I. Greetings (1:1 – 2)
II. The Divine Purpose: The Glory and Headship of Christ (1:3 – 14)
III. Prayer That Christians May Realize God's Purpose and Power (1:15 – 23)
IV. Steps Toward the Fulfillment of God's Purpose (chs. 2 – 3)
   A. Salvation of Individuals by Grace through Faith (2:1 – 10)
   B. Reconciliation of Jew and Gentile through the Cross (2:11 – 18)
   C. Uniting of Jew and Gentile in One Household (2:19 – 22)
   D. Revelation of God's Wisdom through the Church (3:1 – 13)
   E. Prayer for Deeper Experience of God's Fullness (3:14 – 21)
V. Practical Ways to Fulfill God's Purpose in the Church (4:1 — 6:20)
   A. Unity (4:1 – 6)
   B. Maturity (4:7 – 16)
   C. Renewal of Personal Life (4:17 — 5:20)
   D. Deference in Personal Relationships (5:21 — 6:9)
      1. Principle (5:21)
      2. Husbands and wives (5:22 – 33)
      3. Children and parents (6:1 – 4)
      4. Slaves and masters (6:5 – 9)
   E. Strength for Spiritual Conflict (6:10 – 20)
VI. Conclusion, Final Greetings and Benediction (6:21 – 24)

View toward the now-silted harbor from the theater at Ephesus
www.HolyLandPhotos.org

1

Paul, an apostle[a] of Christ Jesus by the
will of God,[b]

To God's holy people[c] in Ephesus,[a][d] the
faithful[e] in Christ Jesus:

2 Grace and peace to you from God our
Father and the Lord Jesus Christ.[f]

Praise for Spiritual Blessings in Christ

3 Praise be to the God and Father of our
Lord Jesus Christ,[g] who has blessed us
in the heavenly realms[h] with every spiritual blessing in Christ. 4 For he chose us[i]
in him before the creation of the world[j]
to be holy and blameless[k] in his sight. In
love[l] 5 he[b] predestined[m] us for adoption to
sonship[c][n] through Jesus Christ, in accordance with his pleasure[o] and will— 6 to
the praise of his glorious grace,[p] which he
has freely given us in the One he loves.[q]
7 In him we have redemption[r] through
his blood,[s] the forgiveness of sins, in accordance with the riches[t] of God's grace
8 that he lavished on us. With all wisdom
and understanding, 9 he[d] made known to
us the mystery[u] of his will according to
his good pleasure, which he purposed[v] in
Christ, 10 to be put into effect when the
times reach their fulfillment[w]—to bring
unity to all things in heaven and on earth
under Christ.[x]
11 In him we were also chosen,[e] having

1:1 [a]S 1Co 1:1 [b]S 2Co 1:1 [c]S Ac 9:13 [d]S Ac 18:19 [e]Col 1:2
1:2 [f]S Ro 1:7
1:3 [g]2Co 1:3; 1Pe 1:3 [h]ver 20; Eph 2:6; 3:10; 6:12
1:4 [i]2Th 2:13 [j]S Mt 25:34 [k]Lev 11:44; 20:7; 2Sa 22:24; Ps 15:2; Eph 5:27; Col 1:22 [l]Eph 4:2,15,16
1:5 [m]ver 11; Ro 8:29,30 [n]S Ro 8:14,15 [o]Lk 12:32; 1Co 1:21; Col 1:19
1:6 [p]ver 12,14 [q]Mt 3:17
1:7 [r]ver 14; S Ro 3:24 [s]S Ro 3:25 [t]S Ro 2:4
1:9 [u]S Ro 16:25 [v]S ver 11
1:10 [w]Mk 1:15; Ro 5:6; Gal 4:4 [x]Col 1:20

[a] *1* Some early manuscripts do not have *in Ephesus.*
[b] *4,5* Or *sight in love.* [5]*He*
[c] *5* The Greek word for *adoption to sonship* is a legal term referring to the full legal standing of an adopted male heir in Roman culture.
[d] *8,9* Or *us with all wisdom and understanding.* [9]*And he*
[e] *11* Or *were made heirs*

1:1 *Paul.* See note on Ro 1:1. *apostle ... by the will of God.* See 1Co 1:1 and note. Paul not only stresses his authority under God but also anticipates the strong emphasis he will make later in this chapter and book on God's sovereign plan and purpose. *God's holy people.* Those God has called to be his own people, i.e., all Christians (see vv. 15,18). The Greek word for this phrase carried the idea of dedication to a deity (see note on Ro 1:7). *in Ephesus.* See NIV text note. The book may have been intended as a circular letter to several churches, including the one at Ephesus (see notes on v. 15; 6:21–23; Ac 19:10). *in Christ Jesus.* This phrase (or a similar one) occurs ten times in vv. 1–13. It refers to the spiritual union of Christ with believers, which Paul often symbolizes by the metaphor "body of Christ" (see, e.g., v. 23; 2:16; 4:4,12,16; 5:23,30).

1:2 *Grace and peace.* See note on Ro 1:7. Paul uses the word "grace" 12 times and "peace" 8 times in Ephesians. *Lord Jesus Christ.* Also occurs at the end of this letter (6:23–24); see note on 1Th 1:1.

1:3–14 All one sentence in Greek, this section is often called a "doxology" because it recites what God has done and is an expression of worship to honor him. Paul speaks first of the blessings we have through the Father (vv. 3–6), then of those that come through the Son (vv. 7–12) and finally of those through the Holy Spirit (vv. 13–14).

1:3 *Father of our Lord Jesus Christ.* Jesus' relation to God the Father is unique (see Jn 20:17 and note). *blessed ... blessing.* Jewish people used the word "bless" to express both God's kindness to us and our thanks or praise to him. *heavenly realms.* Occurs five times in Ephesians, emphasizing Paul's perception that in the exaltation of Christ (his resurrection and enthronement at God's right hand) and in the Christian's union with the exalted Christ ultimate issues are involved—issues that pertain to the divine realm and that in the final analysis are worked out in and from that realm. At stake are God's eternal eschatological purpose (3:11) and the titanic conflict between God and the powerful spiritual forces arrayed against him—a purpose and a conflict that come to focus in the history of redemption. Here (v. 3) Paul asserts that through their union with the exalted Christ, Christians have already been made beneficiaries of every spiritual blessing that belongs to and comes from the heavenly realm. In vv. 20–22 he proclaims Christ's exaltation to that realm and his elevation over all other powers and titles, so that he rules over all for the sake of his church. According to 2:6, those who have been made alive with Christ (2:5) share in Christ's exaltation and enthronement in heaven. Thus (3:10) by the gathering of Gentiles and Jews into one body of Christ (the church), God triumphantly displays his "manifold wisdom" to the "rulers and authorities" in the heavenly realms. As a result, the spiritual struggle of believers here and now is not so much against "flesh and blood" as against the great spiritual forces that wage war against God in heaven (see 6:12 and note).

1:4 *chose.* Divine election is a frequent theme in Paul's letters (Ro 8:29–33; 9:6–26; 11:5,7,28; 16:13; Col 3:12; 1Th 1:4; 2Th 2:13; Titus 1:1). In this chapter it is emphasized in the following ways: (1) "he chose us" (here); (2) "he predestined us" (v. 5); (3) "we were also chosen" (v. 11); (4) "having been predestined" (v. 11). *before the creation of the world.* Cf. Jn 17:24. *holy and blameless.* See 5:27 for the same pair of words. Holiness is the result—not the basis—of God's choosing. It refers both to the holiness imparted to the believer because of Christ and to the believer's personal sanctification (see notes on Ex 3:5; Lev 11:44; 1Co 1:2). *In love.* See NIV text note on vv. 4–5; cf. 3:17; 4:2,15–16; 5:2.

1:5 *adoption to sonship.* See Ro 8:15 and note.

1:6 *to the praise of his glorious grace.* See vv. 12,14. Election by grace is for God's glory.

1:7–8 *the riches of God's grace that he lavished on us.* Cf. "what great love the Father has lavished on us" (1Jn 3:1).

1:7 *redemption.* See v. 14; 4:30; see also Ro 3:24; Titus 2:14 and notes. The Ephesians were familiar with the Greco-Roman practice of redemption: Slaves were freed by the payment of a ransom. Similarly, the ransom necessary to free sinners from the bondage of sin and the resulting curse imposed by the law (see Gal 3:13) was the death of Christ (called here "his blood"). *through his blood.* Cf. 2:13; 1Pe 1:18–19.

1:9 *mystery.* See notes on Ro 11:25; Col 1:26.

1:10 *to bring ... under Christ.* Paul uses a significant term here that not only has the idea of leadership but also was often used of adding up a column of figures. A contemporary way of putting it might be to say that in a world of confusion, where things do not "add up" or make sense, we look forward to the time when everything will be brought into meaningful relationship under the headship of Christ.

1:11 *In him.* Christ is the center of God's plan. Whether the universe or the individual Christian is in view, only

been predestined[y] according to the plan
of him who works out everything in
conformity with the purpose[z] of his will,
12 in order that we, who were the first to
put our hope in Christ, might be for the
praise of his glory.[a] 13 And you also were
included in Christ[b] when you heard the
message of truth,[c] the gospel of your salvation. When you believed, you were
marked in him with a seal,[d] the promised
Holy Spirit,[e] 14 who is a deposit guaranteeing our inheritance[f] until the redemption[g]
of those who are God's possession—to
the praise of his glory.[h]

Thanksgiving and Prayer

15 For this reason, ever since I heard about
your faith in the Lord Jesus[i] and your love
for all God's people,[j] 16 I have not stopped
giving thanks for you,[k] remembering you
in my prayers.[l] 17 I keep asking that the God
of our Lord Jesus Christ, the glorious Father,[m] may give you the Spirit[a] of wisdom[n]
and revelation, so that you may know him
better. 18 I pray that the eyes of your heart
may be enlightened[o] in order that you may
know the hope to which he has called[p] you,
the riches[q] of his glorious inheritance[r] in his
holy people,[s] 19 and his incomparably great
power for us who believe. That power[t] is
the same as the mighty strength[u] 20 he exerted when he raised Christ from the dead[v]
and seated him at his right hand[w] in the
heavenly realms,[x] 21 far above all rule and
authority, power and dominion,[y] and every
name[z] that is invoked, not only in the present age but also in the one to come.[a] 22 And
God placed all things under his feet[b] and
appointed him to be head[c] over everything
for the church, 23 which is his body,[d] the
fullness of him[e] who fills everything in every way.[f]

Made Alive in Christ

2 As for you, you were dead in your
transgressions and sins,[g] 2 in which
you used to live[h] when you followed the
ways of this world[i] and of the ruler of the
kingdom of the air,[j] the spirit who is now
at work in those who are disobedient.[k] 3 All
of us also lived among them at one time,[l]
gratifying the cravings of our flesh[b][m] and

[a] *17* Or *a spirit* [b] *3* In contexts like this, the Greek word for *flesh* (*sarx*) refers to the sinful state of human beings, often presented as a power in opposition to the Spirit.

1:11 [y] ver 5; Ro 8:29,30 [z] ver 9; Ro 8:28; Eph 3:11; Heb 6:17 **1:12** [a] ver 6,14 **1:13** [b] S Ro 16:3 [c] Eph 4:21; Col 1:5 [d] Eph 4:30 [e] Jn 14:16,17 **1:14** [f] S Ac 20:32; S 2Co 5:5 [g] ver 7; S Ro 3:24 [h] ver 6,12 **1:15** [i] S Ac 20:21 [j] S Col 1:4 **1:16** [k] S Ro 1:8 [l] S Ro 1:10 **1:17** [m] Jn 20:17; Ro 15:6; Rev 1:6 [n] Ex 28:3; Isa 11:2; Php 1:9; Col 1:9 **1:18** [o] Job 42:5; 2Co 4:6; Heb 6:4 [p] S Ro 8:28 [q] ver 7; S Ro 2:4 [r] ver 11 [s] Col 1:12 **1:19** [t] Eph 3:7; Col 1:29 [u] Isa 40:26; Eph 6:10 **1:20** [v] S Ac 2:24 [w] S Mk 16:19 [x] S ver 3 **1:21** [y] Eph 3:10; Col 1:16 [z] Php 2:9,10 [a] S Mt 12:32 **1:22** [b] S Mt 22:44; S 28:18 [c] 1Co 11:3; Eph 4:15; 5:23; Col 1:18; 2:19 **1:23** [d] S 1Co 12:27 [e] S Jn 1:16; Eph 3:19 [f] Eph 4:10 **2:1** [g] ver 5; Col 2:13 **2:2** [h] ver 3, 11-13; Ro 11:30; 1Co 6:11; 5:8; Col 3:7; Titus 3:3; 1Pe 4:3 [i] Ro 12:2 [j] S Jn 12:31 [k] Eph 5:6 **2:3** [l] S ver 2 [m] S Gal 5:24

---

in relationship to Christ is there a meaningful future. Paul goes on to speak, not of the world as a whole, but of those who respond to God's call. *predestined.* See vv. 4–5; see also Ro 8:29–30 and notes.

1:12 *we, who were the first to put our hope in Christ.* Probably a reference to those Jews who, like Paul, had become believers before many Gentiles had.

1:13 *And you also.* Probably refers to the majority of the Ephesians, who were Gentiles. *message of truth.* See 2Ti 2:15 and note. *marked … with a seal.* In those days a seal denoted ownership and security.

1:14 *deposit.* See note on Ro 8:23. *inheritance.* See Col 1:12; see also Heb 9:15; 1Pe 1:4 and notes.

1:15 *ever since I heard.* This sounds strange from one who had spent a few years in Ephesus. He may be referring to a greatly enlarged church there, many members of which Paul did not know, or, if Ephesians was intended as a circular letter (see note on v. 1), he may be referring to news from the whole area, only a part of which he had visited.

1:17 *God of our Lord Jesus Christ.* See note on v. 3. *Spirit of wisdom and revelation.* The focus of the prayer. *him.* God the Father.

1:18 *eyes of your heart.* Your mind or understanding or inner awareness. *hope.* Has an objective quality of certainty (see Ro 5:5 and note). It is the assurance of eternal life guaranteed by the present possession of the Holy Spirit (see v. 14). *called.* See Ro 8:28 and note; Php 3:14; 2Ti 1:9; Heb 3:1. *his glorious inheritance in his holy people.* Either the inheritance we have from God (see v. 14; Col 1:12) or the inheritance God receives, i.e., the believers themselves (cf. Ps 2:8; Isa 53:10). *his holy people.* See note on v. 1.

1:19 In this verse Paul piles term upon term to emphasize that the extraordinary, divine power by which Jesus Christ was raised (v. 20) is the same power at work in and through believers (see Php 3:10 and note; cf. also Ps 77:16–19 and note).

1:20 *right hand.* The symbolic place of highest honor and authority.

1:21 *all rule … every name that is invoked.* Including whatever supernatural beings his contemporaries might conceive of, for in his day many people believed not only in the existence of angels and demons but also in that of other beings. Christ is above them all. *the present age … the one to come.* See Mt 12:32. Like the rabbinic teachers of his day, Paul distinguishes between the present age, which is evil, and the future age when the Messiah will consummate his kingdom and there will be a completely righteous society on earth.

1:22 *under his feet.* Ps 8:5–6 emphasizes the destiny of human beings, and Heb 2:6–9 shows that ultimately it is the Son of Man who rules over everything (cf. Heb 10:13). *head.* Christ is not only head of the church but also head over everything (see note on v. 10).

1:23 *his body.* See 2:16; 4:4,12,16; 5:23,30. *fullness … fills.* The church is the fullness of Christ probably in the sense that it is filled by him who fills all things.

2:1–10 In ch. 1 Paul wrote of the great purposes and plan of God, culminating in the universal headship of Christ (1:10,22), all of which is to be for "the praise of his glory" (1:14). He now proceeds to explain the steps by which God will accomplish his purposes, beginning with the salvation of individuals.

2:1 A description of their past moral and spiritual condition, separated from the life of God (cf. Col 1:21).

2:2 *ruler.* Satan (cf. Jn 14:30, "prince"). *air.* Satan is no mere earthbound enemy (cf. 6:12). *spirit.* Satan is a created, but not a human, being (cf. Job 1:6; Eze 28:15; see note on Isa 14:12–15).

2:3 *All of us.* Jews and Gentiles. *deserving of wrath.* See Jn 3:36 and note; Ro 1:18–20; 2:5; 9:22.

following its desires and thoughts. Like
the rest, we were by nature deserving of
wrath. 4 But because of his great love for
us,[n] God, who is rich in mercy, 5 made us
alive with Christ even when we were dead
in transgressions[o]—it is by grace you
have been saved.[p] 6 And God raised us up
with Christ[q] and seated us with him[r] in
the heavenly realms[s] in Christ Jesus, 7 in
order that in the coming ages he might
show the incomparable riches of his
grace,[t] expressed in his kindness[u] to us in
Christ Jesus. 8 For it is by grace[v] you have
been saved,[w] through faith[x]—and this is
not from yourselves, it is the gift of God—
9 not by works,[y] so that no one can boast.[z]
10 For we are God's handiwork,[a] created[b]
in Christ Jesus to do good works,[c] which
God prepared in advance for us to do.

Jew and Gentile Reconciled Through Christ

11 Therefore, remember that formerly[d] you who are Gentiles by birth and
called "uncircumcised" by those who call
themselves "the circumcision" (which is
done in the body by human hands)[e]—
12 remember that at that time you were
separate from Christ, excluded from citizenship in Israel and foreigners[f] to the
covenants of the promise,[g] without hope[h]
and without God in the world. 13 But now
in Christ Jesus you who once[i] were far
away have been brought near[j] by the
blood of Christ.[k]

14 For he himself is our peace,[l] who has
made the two groups one[m] and has destroyed the barrier, the dividing wall of
hostility, 15 by setting aside in his flesh[n]
the law with its commands and regulations.[o] His purpose was to create in himself one[p] new humanity out of the two,
thus making peace, 16 and in one body to
reconcile both of them to God through
the cross,[q] by which he put to death their
hostility. 17 He came and preached peace[r]
to you who were far away and peace to
those who were near.[s] 18 For through him
we both have access[t] to the Father[u] by one
Spirit.[v]

2:4 [n]S Jn 3:16 **2:5** [o]ver 1; Ps 103:12 [p]ver 8; Jn 5:24; S Ac 15:11 **2:6** [q]S Ro 6:5 [r]Eph 1:20 [s]S Eph 1:3 **2:7** [t]S Ro 2:4 [u]Titus 3:4 **2:8** [v]S Ro 3:24 [w]ver 5 [x]S Ro 9:30 **2:9** [y]Dt 9:5; Ro 4:2; 2Ti 1:9; Titus 3:5 [z]1Co 1:29 **2:10** [a]Isa 29:23; 43:7; 60:21 [b]Eph 4:24 [c]S Titus 2:14 **2:11** [d]S ver 2 [e]Col 2:11 **2:12** [f]Isa 14:1; 65:1 [g]Gal 3:17 [h]1Th 4:13 **2:13** [i]S ver 2 [j]ver 17 [k]Col 1:20 **2:14** [l]ver 15; S Jn 14:27 [m]1Co 12:13; Eph 3:6 **2:15** [n]Col 1:21, 22 [o]Col 2:14 [p]Gal 3:28 **2:16** [q]2Co 5:18; Col 1:20,22 **2:17** [r]S Lk 2:14 [s]ver 13; Ps 148:14; Isa 57:19 **2:18** [t]Eph 3:12 [u]Col 1:12 [v]1Co 12:13; Eph 4:4

2:5 *made us alive with Christ.* This truth is expanded in Ro 6:1–10 (see notes there).

2:6 *heavenly realms.* See note on 1:3. *in Christ Jesus.* Through our union with Christ (see note on 1:1).

2:7 *coming ages.* Cf. 1:21; refers to the future of eternal blessing with Christ. *show.* Or "exhibit" or "prove."

2:8 A major passage for understanding God's grace, i.e., his kindness, unmerited favor and forgiving love. *you have been saved.* "Saved" has a wide range of meanings. It includes salvation from God's wrath, which we all had incurred by our sinfulness. The tense of the verb (also in v. 5) suggests a completed action with emphasis on its present effect. *through faith.* See Ro 3:21–31 (and notes on that passage), which establishes the necessity of faith in Christ as the only means of being made right with God. *not from yourselves.* No human effort can contribute to our salvation; it is the gracious gift of God (see Titus 3:5 and note).

2:9 *not by works.* One cannot earn salvation by "the works of the law" (Ro 3:20,28; cf. Jas 2:14–26 and notes). Such a legalistic approach to salvation (or sanctification) is consistently condemned in Scripture (see Gal 2:16 and note). *no one can boast.* No one can take credit for his or her salvation. Cf. 1Co 1:26–31; 2Co 5:17 and notes.

2:10 *handiwork.* The Greek for this word sometimes has the connotation of a "work of art." *good works.* The outworking of grace (see Titus 3:8; see also Introduction to Titus: Distinctive Characteristics). *prepared in advance.* Carries forward the theme of God's sovereign purpose and planning, seen in ch. 1 (see, e.g., 1:4 and note).

2:11–22 From the salvation of individuals, Paul moves to another aspect of salvation in which God reconciles Jews and Gentiles, previously hostile peoples, not only to himself but also to each other through Christ (vv. 11–16). Even more than that, God unites these now reconciled people in one body, a truth introduced in vv. 19–22 and explained in ch. 3.

2:11–12 Refers to the state of those without Christ, described in vv. 1–10.

2:11 *you who are Gentiles.* Most of the Ephesians (cf. 1:13, "And you also"). *"uncircumcised"… "the circumcision."* The rite of circumcision was applied to every Jewish male who was eight days old (see Ge 17:12 and note); so this physical act ("done in the body by human hands") was a clear mark of distinction between Jew and Gentile, in which Jewish people naturally took pride.

2:12 *at that time.* Before salvation, in contrast to "But now" (v. 13). *separate from Christ… without God.* All these expressions emphasize the distance of unbelieving Gentiles from Israel, as well as from Christ. *covenants.* God had promised blessings to and through the Jewish people (see note on Ro 9:4).

2:13 *But now.* Not only contrasts with "at that time" (v. 12) but also introduces the contrast between "from Christ" (v. 12) and "in Christ" (here). *blood of Christ.* Expresses the violent death of Christ as he poured out his lifeblood as a sacrifice for us (see 1:7; Heb 9:11–13 and notes).

2:14 *two groups.* Believing Jews and believing Gentiles. *barrier… dividing wall.* Possibly an allusion to the barricade in the Jerusalem temple area that marked the limit to which a Gentile might go (see note on Ac 21:28). It is used here to describe the total religious isolation Jews and Gentiles experienced from each other. *hostility.* Between Jews and Gentiles.

2:15 *setting aside… the law.* Since Mt 5:17 and Ro 3:31 teach that God's moral standard expressed in the OT law is not changed by the coming of Christ, what is abolished here is probably the effect of the specific "commands and regulations" in separating Jews from Gentiles, whose nonobservance of the Jewish law renders them ritually unclean (cf. Col 2:13–14). *in his flesh.* Probably refers to the death of Christ (cf. note on Ro 8:3). *one new humanity.* The united body of believers, the church.

2:16 *one body.* While this could possibly mean the body of Christ offered on the cross (cf. "in his flesh," v. 15), it probably refers to the "one new humanity" just mentioned, the body of believers.

2:17 *far away… near.* Gentiles and Jews, respectively.

19 Consequently, you are no longer foreigners and strangers,[w] but fellow citizens[x]
with God's people and also members of
his household,[y] 20 built[z] on the foundation[a]
of the apostles and prophets,[b] with Christ
Jesus himself[c] as the chief cornerstone.[d]
21 In him the whole building is joined together and rises to become a holy temple[e]
in the Lord. 22 And in him you too are being built together to become a dwelling in
which God lives by his Spirit.[f]

God's Marvelous Plan for the Gentiles

3 For this reason I, Paul, the prisoner[g] of
Christ Jesus for the sake of you Gentiles—
2 Surely you have heard about the administration of God's grace that was given
to me[h] for you, 3 that is, the mystery[i] made
known to me by revelation,[j] as I have already written briefly. 4 In reading this,
then, you will be able to understand my
insight[k] into the mystery of Christ, 5 which
was not made known to people in other
generations as it has now been revealed
by the Spirit to God's holy apostles and
prophets.[l] 6 This mystery is that through
the gospel the Gentiles are heirs[m] together with Israel, members together of one
body,[n] and sharers together in the promise
in Christ Jesus.[o]
7 I became a servant of this gospel[p] by
the gift of God's grace given me[q] through
the working of his power.[r] 8 Although I am
less than the least of all the Lord's people,[s]
this grace was given me: to preach to the
Gentiles[t] the boundless riches of Christ,[u]
9 and to make plain to everyone the administration of this mystery,[v] which for
ages past was kept hidden in God, who
created all things. 10 His intent was that

2:19 [w] ver 12 [x] Php 3:20 [y] Gal 6:10 **2:20** [z] 1Co 3:9 [a] Mt 16:18; 1Co 3:10; Rev 21:14 [b] S Eph 4:11 [c] 1Co 3:11 [d] S Ac 4:11; 1Pe 2:4-8 **2:21** [e] 1Co 3:16, 17 **2:22** [f] 1Co 3:16 **3:1** [g] Ac 23:18; Eph 4:1; 2Ti 1:8; Phm 1,9 **3:2** [h] Col 1:25 **3:3** [i] S Ro 16:25 [j] S 1Co 2:10 **3:4** [k] 2Co 11:6 **3:5** [l] Ro 16:26; S Eph 4:11 **3:6** [m] S Ro 8:17 [n] Eph 2:15,16 [o] Eze 47:22 **3:7** [p] S 1Co 3:5 [q] S Ro 12:3 [r] Eph 1:19; Col 1:29 **3:8** [s] S 1Co 15:9 [t] S Ac 9:15 [u] S Ro 2:4 **3:9** [v] S Ro 16:25

2:19 *Consequently.* Paul indicates that the unity described in vv. 19–22 is based on what Christ did through his death, described in vv. 14–18. *you.* The Gentiles at Ephesus are particularly in view here. *citizens … household.* Familiar imagery. The household in ancient times was what we today might call an "extended family."

2:20 *foundation.* Further metaphorical language to convey the idea of a solid, integrated structure. *apostles and prophets.* Probably refers to the founding work of the early Christian apostles and prophets as they preached and taught God's word (cf. Mt 16:18 and note; 1Co 3:10–11). *cornerstone.* Isa 28:16, which uses the same term in its pre-Christian Greek translation (the Septuagint), refers to a foundation with a "tested" stone at the corner.

2:21 *joined together.* Cf. 4:16 for the same word. Both passages speak of the close relationship between believers. *rises.* The description of a building under construction conveys the sense of the dynamic growth of the church. *holy temple.* Paul now uses the metaphor of a temple, thereby indicating the purpose ("to become") for which God has established his church (see 1Co 3:16 and note).

2:22 *dwelling.* The church is to be a people or community in whom the Holy Spirit dwells (cf. 2Co 6:16 and note).

3:1–13 Having saved people individually by his grace (2:1–10), and having reconciled them to each other, as well as to himself, through the sacrificial death of Christ (2:11–22), God also now unites them on an equal basis in one body, the church. This step in God's eternal plan was not fully revealed in previous times. Paul calls it a "mystery" (v. 3; see note there).

3:1 *For this reason.* Because of all that God has done, explained in the preceding several verses. *prisoner.* Apparently Paul was under house arrest at this time (see Ac 28:16,30 and note on 28:16). *of Christ.* Paul's physical imprisonment was because he obeyed Christ in spite of opposition. After this verse Paul breaks his train of thought to explain the "mystery" (v. 4). He resumes his initial thought in v. 14.

3:2 *Surely you have heard.* Most of the Ephesians would have heard of Paul's ministry because of his long stay there earlier. However, if this was a circular letter (see note on 1:1), the other churches may not have known much about it. *administration.* Paul unfolds God's administrative plan for the church and for the universe in this letter (see especially 1:3–12). He has been given a significant responsibility in the execution of this plan.

3:3 *mystery.* A truth known only by divine revelation (v. 5; see Ro 16:25; see also notes on Ro 11:25; Col 1:26). Here the word "mystery" has the special meaning of the private, wise plan of God, which in Ephesians relates primarily to the unification of believing Jews and Gentiles in the new body, the church (see v. 6). It may be thought of as a secret that is temporarily hidden, but more than that, it is a plan God is actively working out and revealing stage by stage (cf. 1:9–10; Rev 10:7). *by revelation.* See Gal 1:12. *as I have already written briefly.* May refer to 1:9–10.

3:5 *not made known to people in other generations.* See note on v. 6. *holy.* Set apart for God's service. *apostles and prophets.* See note on 2:20. Although Paul was the chief recipient, others received this revelation also.

3:6 *heirs.* See note on 1:18; cf. Gal 3:26–29 and notes. *together … together … together.* The repetition of this word indicates the unique aspect of the mystery that was not previously known: the equality and mutuality that Gentiles had with Jews in the church, the one body. That Gentiles would turn to the God of Israel and be saved was prophesied in the OT (see Ro 15:9–12); that they would come into an organic unity with believing Jews on an equal footing was unexpected.

3:7 *God's grace given me.* See v. 2 and note.

3:8 *less than the least.* Cf. 1Ti 1:15 and note. Paul never ceased to be amazed that one so unworthy as he should have been chosen for so high a task. His modesty was genuine, even though we may disagree with his self-evaluation. *grace.* In this case, a special endowment that brings responsibility for service. *to preach.* Parallels "to make plain" (v. 9). *boundless.* Far beyond what we can know, but not beyond our appreciation—at least in part (cf. Ro 11:33).

3:9 *administration of this mystery.* See v. 2 and note; cf. v. 3 and note.

3:10 *now.* In contrast to the "ages past" (v. 9). *through the church.* The fact that God had done the seemingly impossible—reconciling and organically uniting Jews and Gentiles in the church—makes the church the perfect means of displaying God's wisdom. *manifold.* Multifaceted (in the way that many facets of a diamond reflect and enhance its beauty). *rulers and authorities.* Christ had ascended over all these (1:20–21; cf. 1Pe 3:19–20a and note). It is a staggering thought that the church on earth is observed, so to speak, by these spiritual powers and that to the degree the church is

now, through the church, the manifold
wisdom of God[w] should be made known[x]
to the rulers and authorities[y] in the heavenly realms,[z] 11 according to his eternal
purpose[a] that he accomplished in Christ
Jesus our Lord. 12 In him and through faith
in him we may approach God[b] with freedom and confidence.[c] 13 I ask you, therefore, not to be discouraged because of my
sufferings for you, which are your glory.

A Prayer for the Ephesians

14 For this reason I kneel[d] before the Father, 15 from whom every family[a] in heav-
en and on earth derives its name. 16 I pray
that out of his glorious riches[e] he may
strengthen you with power[f] through his
Spirit in your inner being,[g] 17 so that Christ
may dwell in your hearts[h] through faith.
And I pray that you, being rooted[i] and established in love, 18 may have power, together with all the Lord's holy people,[j] to
grasp how wide and long and high and
deep[k] is the love of Christ, 19 and to know
this love that surpasses knowledge[l] — that
you may be filled[m] to the measure of all
the fullness of God.[n]
20 Now to him who is able[o] to do immeasurably more than all we ask[p] or imagine,
according to his power[q] that is at work
within us, 21 to him be glory in the church
and in Christ Jesus throughout all generations, for ever and ever! Amen.[r]

Unity and Maturity in the Body of Christ

4 As a prisoner[s] for the Lord, then, I urge
you to live a life worthy[t] of the calling[u]
you have received. 2 Be completely humble and gentle; be patient, bearing with
one another[v] in love.[w] 3 Make every effort
to keep the unity[x] of the Spirit through the
bond of peace.[y] 4 There is one body[z] and
one Spirit,[a] just as you were called to one
hope when you were called[b]; 5 one Lord,[c]
one faith, one baptism; 6 one God and Father of all,[d] who is over all and through all
and in all.[e]
7 But to each one of us[f] grace[g] has been
given[h] as Christ apportioned it. 8 This is
why it[b] says:

"When he ascended on high,
he took many captives[i]
and gave gifts to his people."[c][j]

3:10 [w] S Ro 11:33; 1Co 2:7 [x] 1Pe 1:12 [y] Eph 1:21; 6:12; Col 2:10, 15 [z] S Eph 1:3 **3:11** [a] S Eph 1:11 **3:12** [b] Eph 2:18 [c] 2Co 3:4; Heb 3:14; 4:16; 10:19, 35; 1Jn 2:28; 3:21; 4:17 **3:14** [d] Php 2:10 **3:16** [e] ver 8; S Ro 2:4 [f] S Php 4:13 [g] Ro 7:22 **3:17** [h] S Ro 8:10 [i] Col 2:7 **3:18** [j] Eph 1:15 [k] Job 11:8, 9; Ps 103:11 **3:19** [l] Php 4:7 [m] Col 2:10 [n] Eph 1:23 **3:20** [o] Ro 16:25; 2Co 9:8 [p] 1Ki 3:13 [q] ver 7 **3:21** [r] S Ro 11:36 **4:1** [s] S Eph 3:1 [t] Php 1:27; Col 1:10; 1Th 2:12 [u] S Ro 8:28 **4:2** [v] Col 3:12, 13 [w] ver 15, 16; Eph 1:4 **4:3** [x] S Ro 15:5 [y] Col 3:15

[a] *15* The Greek for *family* (*patria*) is derived from the Greek for *father* (*pater*). [b] *8* Or *God* [c] *8* Psalm 68:18

4:4 [z] S Ro 12:5 [a] 1Co 12:13; Eph 2:18 [b] S Ro 8:28 **4:5** [c] 1Co 8:6 **4:6** [d] Dt 6:4; Zec 14:9 [e] S Ro 11:36 **4:7** [f] 1Co 12:7, 11 [g] S Ro 3:24 [h] S Ro 12:3 **4:8** [i] Col 2:15 [j] Ps 68:18

spiritually united it portrays to them the wisdom of God. This thought may be essential in understanding the meaning of "calling" in 4:1. *heavenly realms.* See note on 1:3.

3:11 *eternal purpose.* The effective headship of Christ over a united church is in preparation for his ultimate assumption of headship over the universe (1:10).

3:12 See Heb 4:16; 10:19–22 and notes.

3:14–21 Paul now expresses a prayer that grows out of his awareness of all that God is doing in believers. God's key gifts are "power" (vv. 16,18,20) and "love" (vv. 17–19).

3:14 *For this reason.* Resumes the thought of v. 1. *I kneel.* Expresses deep emotion and reverence, as people in Paul's day usually stood to pray (see note on 1Ch 17:16).

3:15 *family.* The word in Greek is similar to the word for "father" (see NIV text note), so it can be said that the "family" derives its name (and being) from the "father." God is our Father, and we can commit our prayers to him in confidence.

3:16 *inner being.* See v. 17; 2Co 4:16 and notes.

3:17 *dwell.* Be completely at home. Christ was already present in the Ephesian believers' lives (cf. Ro 8:9). *hearts.* The whole inner being.

3:18 Cf. Ro 8:35–39.

3:19 *surpasses knowledge.* Not unknowable, but so great that it cannot be completely known. *fullness.* God, who is infinite in all his attributes, allows us to draw on his resources — in this case, his love.

3:20 *immeasurably more.* Has specific reference to the matters presented in this section of Ephesians but is not limited to these. *his power.* See 1:19–21.

3:21 *to him be glory.* The ultimate goal of our existence (see 1:6 and note). *in the church and in Christ Jesus.* A remarkable parallel. God has called the church to an extraordinary position and vocation (cf. v. 10; 4:1).

4:1–32 The chapter begins (v. 2) and ends (v. 32) with exhortations to love and forgive one another.

4:1–16 So far Paul has taught that God brought Jew and Gentile into a new relationship to each other in the church and that he called the church to display his wisdom. Paul now shows how God made provision for those in the church to live and work together in unity and to grow together into maturity.

4:1 *prisoner.* See note on 3:1. *calling.* See 3:10,21 and notes.

4:3 *keep the unity.* Which God produced through the reconciling death of Christ (see 2:14–22). It is the heavy responsibility of Christians to keep that unity from being disturbed.

4:4 *one hope.* Has different aspects (e.g., 1:5,10; 2:7), but it is still one hope, tied to the glorious future of Christ, in which all believers share (cf. Ro 5:2–5; Col 1:27 and notes).

4:5 *one baptism.* Probably not the baptism of the Spirit (see 1Co 12:13), which was inward and therefore invisible, but water baptism (see note on Ro 6:3–4). Since Paul apparently has in mind that which identifies all believers as belonging together, he would naturally refer to that church ordinance in which every new convert participated publicly. At that time it was a more obvious common mark of identification of Christians than it is now, when it is celebrated in different ways and often only seen by those in the church.

4:7 *grace.* See 3:7–8.

4:8 Ps 68:18 (see note there) speaks of God's triumphant ascension to his throne in the temple at Jerusalem (symbolic of his heavenly throne). Paul applies this to Christ's triumphal ascension into heaven. Where the psalm states further that God "received gifts from people," Paul apparently takes his cue from certain rabbinic interpretations current in his day that read the Hebrew preposition for "from" in the sense of "to" (a meaning it often has) and the verb for "received" in the sense of "take and give" (a meaning it sometimes has — but with a different preposition; see Ge 15:9; 18:5; 27:13; Ex 25:2; 1Ki 17:10–11). *captives.*

9 (What does "he ascended" mean except that he also descended to the lower,
earthly regions[a]? 10 He who descended is
the very one who ascended[k] higher than
all the heavens, in order to fill the whole
universe.)[l] 11 So Christ himself gave[m] the
apostles,[n] the prophets,[o] the evangelists,[p]
the pastors and teachers,[q] 12 to equip his
people for works of service, so that the
body of Christ[r] may be built up[s] 13 until
we all reach unity[t] in the faith and in the
knowledge of the Son of God[u] and become
mature,[v] attaining to the whole measure of
the fullness of Christ.[w]
14 Then we will no longer be infants,[x]
tossed back and forth by the waves,[y] and
blown here and there by every wind of
teaching and by the cunning and craftiness of people in their deceitful scheming.[z]
15 Instead, speaking the truth in love,[a] we
will grow to become in every respect the
mature body of him who is the head,[b] that
is, Christ. 16 From him the whole body,
joined and held together by every supporting ligament, grows[c] and builds itself up[d]
in love,[e] as each part does its work.

Instructions for Christian Living

17 So I tell you this, and insist on it in the
Lord, that you must no longer[f] live as the
Gentiles do, in the futility of their thinking.[g] 18 They are darkened in their understanding[h] and separated from the life of
God[i] because of the ignorance that is in
them due to the hardening of their hearts.[j]
19 Having lost all sensitivity,[k] they have giv-
en themselves over[l] to sensuality[m] so as to
indulge in every kind of impurity, and they
are full of greed.

4:10 [k] Pr 30:1-4 [l] Eph 1:23 **4:11** [m] ver 8 [n] 1Co 12:28; Eph 2:20; 3:5; 2Pe 3:2; Jude 17 [o] S Ac 11:27; Ro 12:6; 1Co 12:10,28; 13:2,8; 14:1, 39; Eph 2:20; 3:5; 2Pe 3:2 [p] Ac 21:8; 2Ti 4:5 [q] Ac 13:1; Ro 2:21; 12:7; 1Co 12:28; 14:26; 1Ti 1:7; Jas 3:1 **4:12** [r] S 1Co 12:27 [s] S Ro 14:19 **4:13** [t] ver 3, 5 [u] S Php 3:8 [v] S 1Co 2:6; Col 1:28 [w] Jn 1:16; Eph 1:23; 3:19 **4:14** [x] S 1Co 14:20 [y] Isa 57:20; Jas 1:6 [z] Eph 6:11

[a] 9 Or *the depths of the earth*

4:15 [a] ver 2, 16; Eph 1:4 [b] S Eph 1:22 **4:16** [c] Col 2:19 [d] 1Co 12:7 [e] ver 2, 15; Eph 1:4 **4:17** [f] Eph 2:2 [g] Ro 1:21 **4:18** [h] Dt 29:4; Ro 1:21 [i] Eph 2:12 [j] 2Co 3:14 **4:19** [k] 1Ti 4:2 [l] Ro 1:24 [m] Col 3:5; 1Pe 4:3

Paul probably applies this to the spiritual enemies Christ defeated at the cross.

4:9 *ascended ... descended.* Although Paul quoted from the psalm to introduce the idea of the "gifts to his people," he takes the opportunity to remind his readers of Christ's coming to earth (his incarnation) and his subsequent resurrection and ascension. This passage probably does not teach, as some think and as some translations suggest, that Christ descended into hell.

4:11 *Christ himself gave.* The quotation from Ps 68 has its ultimate meaning when applied to Christ as the ascended Lord, who himself has given gifts. *apostles.* Mentioned here because of their role in establishing the church (see 2:20). For qualifications of the initial group of apostles, see Ac 1:21 – 22; see also notes on Mk 6:30; Ro 1:1; 1Co 1:1; Heb 3:1. In a broader sense, Paul was also an apostle (see 1:1). *prophets.* People to whom God made known a message for his people that was appropriate to their particular need or situation (see Ac 11:27; 1Co 12:10 and notes). *evangelists.* See Ac 21:8; 1Co 1:17. While the other gifted people helped it grow through edification, the evangelists helped the church grow by augmentation. Since the objective mentioned in v. 12 is "to equip his people for works of service," we may assume that evangelists, among their various ministries, helped other Christians in their testimony. *pastors and teachers.* Because of the Greek grammatical construction, it is clear that these groups of gifted people are closely related. Those who have pastoral care for God's people (the image is that of shepherding) will naturally provide "food" from the Scriptures (teaching). They will be especially gifted as teachers (cf. 1Ti 3:2).

4:12 *to equip his people for works of service.* Those mentioned in v. 11 were not to do all the work for the people but were to train the people to do the work themselves. *so that the body of Christ may be built up.* See v. 16. Spiritual gifts are for the body, the church, and are not to be exercised individualistically. "Built up" reflects the imagery of 2:19 – 22. Both concepts — body and building — occurring together emphasize the key idea of growth.

4:13 *until.* Expresses not merely duration but also purpose. *unity.* Carries forward the ideal of vv. 1 – 6. *in the faith.* Here "faith" refers to the Christians' common conviction about Christ and the doctrines concerning him, as the following words make clear (cf. also "the apostles' teaching" in Ac 2:42). *knowledge of the Son of God.* Unity is not just a matter of a loving attitude or religious feeling; it is also a matter of truth and a common understanding about God's Son. *mature ... fullness of Christ.* Not the maturity of doctrinal conviction just mentioned, nor a personal maturity that includes the ability to relate well to other people (cf. vv. 2 – 3), but the maturity of the perfectly balanced character of Christ.

4:14 *infants.* Contrast the maturity of v. 13 (cf. 1Co 3:1). *tossed.* The nautical imagery pictures the instability of those who are not strong Christians (cf. Jas 1:6). *teaching.* Then, as now, there were many distorted teachings and heresies that would easily throw the immature off course. *cunning ... craftiness ... deceitful scheming.* Sometimes those who try to draw people away from the Christian faith are not innocently misguided but deliberately deceitful and evil (cf. 1Ti 4:1 – 2).

4:15 *speaking the truth in love.* A truthful and loving manner of life is implied. *grow ... head.* A slightly different restatement of v. 13, based now on the imagery of Christ as the head of the body, which is the church. Paul thus speaks primarily of corporate maturity. It is the "body of Christ" that is to be "built up" (v. 12). In v. 13 "we all" are to become "mature."

4:16 Further details of the imagery of the body growing under the direction of the head. The parts of the body help each other in the growing process, picturing the mutual ministries of God's people spoken of in vv. 11 – 13 (cf. Ro 12:3 – 8). *love.* Maturity and unity are impossible without it (cf. vv. 2,15).

4:17 — 5:20 Paul has just discussed unity and maturity as twin goals for the church, which God has brought into existence through the death of Christ. He now goes on to show that purity is also essential among those who belong to him.

4:17 *futility of their thinking.* Life without God is intellectually frustrating, useless and meaningless (see, e.g., Ecc 1:2 and note; Ro 1:21).

4:18 *darkened in their understanding.* Continues the idea of a futile thought life. *hardening of their hearts.* Moral unresponsiveness (see note on v. 19).

4:19 *have given themselves over.* Just as the pharaoh's heart was hardened reciprocally by himself and by God (see Ex 7 – 11; see also note on Ex 4:21), so here the Gentiles have given themselves over to a sinful kind of life, while Ro 1:24,26,28 says that God gave them over to that life.

20 That, however, is not the way of life
you learned 21 when you heard about
Christ and were taught in him in accordance with the truth that is in Jesus. 22 You
were taught, with regard to your former
way of life, to put off[n] your old self,[o] which
is being corrupted by its deceitful desires;[p]
23 to be made new in the attitude of your
minds;[q] 24 and to put on[r] the new self,[s] created to be like God in true righteousness
and holiness.[t]
25 Therefore each of you must put off
falsehood and speak truthfully[u] to your
neighbor, for we are all members of one
body.[v] 26 "In your anger do not sin"[a];[w] Do
not let the sun go down while you are
still angry, 27 and do not give the devil a
foothold.[x] 28 Anyone who has been stealing must steal no longer, but must work,[y]
doing something useful with their own
hands,[z] that they may have something to
share with those in need.[a]
29 Do not let any unwholesome talk
come out of your mouths,[b] but only what
is helpful for building others up[c] according to their needs, that it may benefit
those who listen. 30 And do not grieve the
Holy Spirit of God,[d] with whom you were
sealed[e] for the day of redemption.[f] 31 Get
rid of[g] all bitterness, rage and anger, brawling and slander, along with every form of
malice.[h] 32 Be kind and compassionate to
one another,[i] forgiving each other, just as
in Christ God forgave you.[j]
5 1 Follow
God's example,[k] therefore, as dearly loved children[l] 2 and walk in the way
of love, just as Christ loved us[m] and gave
himself up for us[n] as a fragrant offering
and sacrifice to God.[o]
3 But among you there must not be even
a hint of sexual immorality,[p] or of any kind
of impurity, or of greed,[q] because these
are improper for God's holy people. 4 Nor
should there be obscenity, foolish talk[r] or
coarse joking, which are out of place, but
rather thanksgiving.[s] 5 For of this you can
be sure: No immoral, impure or greedy
person—such a person is an idolater[t]—
has any inheritance[u] in the kingdom of

4:22 [n] ver 25, 31; Col 3:5, 8,9; Jas 1:21; 1Pe 2:1 [o] S Ro 6:6 [p] Jer 17:9; Heb 3:13 **4:23** [q] Ro 12:2; Col 3:10 **4:24** [r] S Ro 13:14 [s] S Ro 6:4 [t] Eph 2:10 **4:25** [u] Ps 15:2; Lev 19:11; Zec 8:16; Col 3:9 [v] S Ro 12:5 **4:26** [w] Ps 4:4; S Mt 5:22 **4:27** [x] 2Co 2:10, 11 **4:28** [y] Ac 20:35 [z] 1Th 4:11 [a] Gal 6:10 **4:29** [b] Mt 12:36; Eph 5:4; Col 3:8 [c] S Ro 14:19 **4:30** [d] Isa 63:10; 1Th 5:19 [e] 2Co 1:22; 5:5; Eph 1:13 [f] Ro 8:23 **4:31** [g] S ver 22 [h] Col 3:8; 1Pe 2:1 **4:32** [i] 1Pe 3:8 [j] Mt 6:14, 15; Col 3:12, 13 **5:1** [k] Mt 5:48; Lk 6:36 [l] S Jn 1:12 **5:2** [m] S Jn 13:34 [n] ver 25; S Gal 1:4; 2:20 [o] Heb 7:27 **5:3** [p] S 1Co 6:18 [q] Col 3:5 **5:4** [r] Eph 4:29 [s] S ver 20 **5:5** [t] Col 3:5 [u] S Ac 20:32

[a] *26* Psalm 4:4 (see Septuagint)

4:20 *you.* Emphatic in the Greek text.
4:21 *truth that is in Jesus.* The wording and the use of the name Jesus (rather than Christ) suggest that Paul is referring to the embodiment of truth in Jesus' earthly life.
4:22 *former way of life.* Described in 2:1–3. *old self.* Probably means the kind of person the Christian used to be (cf. 1Co 6:11 and note). The old lifestyle resulted from deceitful desires.
4:23 *minds.* Cf. the evil thoughts of unbelievers (vv. 17–18).
4:24 *new self, created to be like God.* Since the new self is created, it cannot refer to the indwelling Christ, but refers to the kind of person he produces in the new believer. Nor is it some kind of new essential nature of the believer, because that would have been brought into existence at his new birth. In contrast, this is a new way of life that one not only "puts on" positionally at conversion (note the past tense in the parallel in Col 3:9–10) but is also urged to "put on" experientially as a Christian (see note on Ro 6:12–13).
4:25 *truthfully.* Cf. vv. 15,21. "Speak truthfully to your neighbor" echoes Zec 8:16. *neighbor.* Probably means fellow Christians in this context.
4:26 *In your anger.* Christians do not lose their emotions at conversion, but their emotions should be purified. Some anger is sinful, some is not (see Ps 4:4 and note). *Do not let the sun go down.* No anger is to outlast the day.
4:27 *devil.* Personal sin is usually due to our evil desires (see Jas 1:14) rather than to direct tempting by the devil. However, Satan can use our sins—especially those, like anger, that are against others—to bring about greater evil, such as divisions among Christians.
4:28 *steal no longer ... work ... have something to share.* It is not enough to cease from sin; one must do good. The former thief must now help those in need (cf. 1Th 4:11–12; 2Th 3:6–13).
4:29 *only what is helpful.* An exhortation parallel to the previous one. Christians not only stop saying unwholesome things; they also begin to say things that will help build others up (cf. 1Co 14:3).
4:30 *grieve.* By sin, such as "unwholesome talk" (v. 29) and the sins mentioned in v. 31. The verb also demonstrates that the Holy Spirit is a person, not just an influence, for only a person can be grieved. *sealed.* See note on 1:13. *day of redemption.* See 1:14; 1Pe 1:5 and notes.
4:31 *bitterness ... malice.* Such things grieve the Holy Spirit. This continues the instruction concerning one's speech (v. 29). See note on Ro 1:29–31.
4:32 *kind and compassionate.* The opposite of the negative qualities of v. 31. *forgiving.* This basic Christian attitude, which is a result of being forgiven in Christ, along with being kind and compassionate, brings to others what we have received from God (see Col 3:13; cf. Hos 1–3 and note on 3:1).
5:1 *Follow God's example.* One way of imitating God is to have a forgiving spirit (4:32). The way we imitate our Lord is to act "just as" (v. 2; 4:32) he did. The sacrificial way Jesus expressed his love for us is not only the means of salvation (as seen in ch. 2) but also an example of the way we are to live for the sake of others.
5:2 *Christ loved us and gave himself up for us.* See v. 25 and note. *fragrant offering.* In the OT the offering of a sacrifice pleased the Lord so much that it was described as a "pleasing aroma" (Ge 8:21 [see note there]; Ex 29:18,25,41; Lev 1:9,13,17).
5:3–5 See note on Ro 1:29–31.
5:3 *not ... even a hint.* See v. 12. *any kind of impurity, or of greed.* Paul moves from specifically sexual sins to more general sins, such as greed. These include sexual lust but refer to other kinds of excessive desire as well. *God's holy people.* See 2:21; 1Co 1:2 and note.
5:4 *foolish talk or coarse joking.* The context and the word "obscenity" indicate that it is not humor as such but off-color jokes and the like that are out of place. *thanksgiving.* See v. 20; 1Th 5:18. By being grateful for all that God has given us, we can displace evil thoughts and words.
5:5 *immoral, impure or greedy.* See v. 3. *idolater.* Cf. Col 3:5. The greedy want things more than they want God and put things in place of God, thereby committing idolatry. *inheritance.* Those who persist in sexual and other kinds of greed have excluded God, who therefore excludes them from the kingdom (but see notes on 1Co 6:9,11).

Christ and of God.[a][v] 6 Let no one deceive
you[w] with empty words, for because of
such things God's wrath[x] comes on those
who are disobedient.[y] 7 Therefore do not
be partners with them.
8 For you were once[z] darkness, but now
you are light in the Lord. Live as children
of light[a] 9 (for the fruit[b] of the light consists in all goodness,[c] righteousness and
truth) 10 and find out what pleases the
Lord.[d] 11 Have nothing to do with the fruitless deeds of darkness,[e] but rather expose
them. 12 It is shameful even to mention
what the disobedient do in secret. 13 But
everything exposed by the light[f] becomes
visible—and everything that is illuminated becomes a light. 14 This is why it is said:

"Wake up, sleeper,[g]
rise from the dead,[h]
and Christ will shine on you."[i]

15 Be very careful, then, how you live[j]—
not as unwise but as wise, 16 making the
most of every opportunity,[k] because the
days are evil.[l] 17 Therefore do not be foolish, but understand what the Lord's will
is.[m] 18 Do not get drunk on wine,[n] which
leads to debauchery. Instead, be filled
with the Spirit,[o] 19 speaking to one another
with psalms, hymns, and songs from the
Spirit.[p] Sing and make music from your
heart to the Lord, 20 always giving thanks[q]
to God the Father for everything, in the
name of our Lord Jesus Christ.

Instructions for Christian Households

5:22-6:9pp — Col 3:18-4:1

21 Submit to one another[r] out of reverence for Christ.
22 Wives, submit yourselves to your own

[a] 5 Or *kingdom of the Messiah and God*

5:5 [v] S Mt 25:34 **5:6** [w] S Mk 13:5 [x] S Ro 1:18 [y] Eph 2:2 **5:8** [z] S Eph 2:2 [a] Jn 8:12; S Lk 16:8; S Ac 26:18 **5:9** [b] Mt 7:16-20; Gal 5:22 [c] Ro 15:14 **5:10** [d] S 1Ti 5:4 **5:11** [e] Ro 13:12; 2Co 6:14 **5:13** [f] Jn 3:20, 21 **5:14** [g] Ro 13:11 [h] Isa 26:19; Jn 5:25 [i] Isa 60:1; Mal 4:2 **5:15** [j] ver 2 **5:16** [k] Col 4:5 [l] Eph 6:13 **5:17** [m] Ro 12:2; Col 1:9; 1Th 4:3 **5:18** [n] Lev 10:9; Pr 20:1; Isa 28:7; Ro 13:13 [o] S Lk 1:15 **5:19** [p] Ps 27:6; 95:2; Ac 16:25; 1Co 14:15, 26; Col 3:16 **5:20** [q] ver 4; Job 1:21; Ps 34:1; Col 3:17; Heb 13:15 **5:21** [r] Gal 5:13; 1Pe 5:5

5:6 *God's wrath.* See Zec 1:2; Ro 1:18 and notes.

5:7 *partners.* Although Christians live in normal social relationships with others, as did the Lord Jesus (Lk 5:30–32; 15:1–2), they are not to participate in the sinful lifestyle of unbelievers (cf. 2Co 6:14 and note).

5:8 *darkness ... light.* This section emphasizes the contrast between light and darkness, showing that those who belong to him who is "light" (1Jn 1:5), i.e., pure and true, not only have their lives illumined by him but also are the means of introducing that light into the dark areas of human conduct (cf. Mt 5:14).

5:9 *fruit of the light.* A mixed metaphor, but the meaning is clear. Light is productive (consider the effect of light on plant growth), and those who live in God's light produce the fruit of moral and ethical character (cf. Gal 5:22–23), while those who live in darkness do not (see v. 11).

5:11 *Have nothing to do with.* See v. 7. *expose.* Light, by nature, exposes what is in darkness, and the contrast shows sin for what it really is.

5:12 *shameful ... to mention.* Christians should not dwell on the evils that their lives are exposing in others.

5:13 *everything exposed ... everything ... illuminated.* Paul seems to be stressing the all-pervasive nature of the light of God and its inevitable effect.

5:14 *it is said.* What follows may well be a hymn used by early Christians (see note on Col 3:16). *sleeper ... dead.* Two images that describe a sinner (cf. 2:1 and note). *Christ will shine on you.* With his life-giving light (cf. 2Co 4:4–6 and notes).

5:15 *unwise ... wise.* Cf. Jas 3:13–17. Having emphasized the contrast between light and darkness, Paul now turns to the contrast between wisdom and foolishness.

5:16 *opportunity.* The foolish person has no strategy for life and misses opportunities to live for God in an evil environment (see Col 4:5).

5:17 *foolish ... understand.* The contrast continues. The foolish not only miss opportunities to make wise use of time; they have a more fundamental problem: They do not understand what God's purposes are for humankind and for Christians. God's purposes are a basic theme in Ephesians (see ch. 1).

5:18 *be filled.* The Greek present tense is used here to indicate that the filling of the Spirit is not a once-for-all experience. Repeatedly, as the occasion requires, the Spirit empowers for worship, service and testimony. The contrast between being filled with wine and filled with the Spirit is obvious. But there is something in common that enables Paul to make the contrast, namely, that people can be under an influence that affects them, whether of wine or of the Spirit. Since Col 3:15—4:1 is very similar to Eph 5:18—6:9, we may assume that Paul intends to convey a basically similar thought in the introductory sentences to each passage. When he speaks here of being filled with the Spirit and when he speaks in Colossians of being under the rule of the peace of Christ and indwelt by the "message" of Christ, he means being under God's control. The effect of this control is essentially the same in both passages: a happy, mutual encouragement to praise God and a healthy, mutual relationship with people. See note on v. 21.

5:19 *psalms ... songs.* Every kind of appropriate song—whether psalms like those of the OT or hymns directed to God or to others that Christians were accustomed to singing—could provide a means for praising and thanking God (v. 20). Actually, however, all three terms may refer to different types of psalms (see note on Col 3:16). *songs from the Spirit.* Songs prompted by the Spirit.

5:20 *always giving thanks.* See Col 2:7; 3:15; 4:2; 1Th 5:18.

5:21—6:9 In chs. 2–4 Paul showed the way God brought believing Jews and Gentiles together into a new relationship in Christ. In 4:1–6 he stressed the importance of unity. Now he shows how believers, filled with the Spirit, can live together in a practical way in various human relationships. This list of mutual responsibilities is similar to the pattern found in Col 3:18—4:1; 1Pe 2:13—3:12; cf. Ro 13:1–10.

5:21 *Submit to one another.* Goes equally well with both the preceding and the following sections, but it is especially basic to the following paragraphs. Paul will show how, in each relationship, each partner can have a conciliatory attitude that will help that relationship. The Greek grammar indicates that this mutual submission is associated with the filling of the Spirit in v. 18. The command "be filled" (v. 18) is followed by a series of participles in the Greek: speaking (v. 19), singing (v. 19), making music (v. 19), giving thanks (v. 20) and submitting (v. 21).

5:22 *Wives, submit.* An aspect of the mutual submission

husbands[s] as you do to the Lord.[t] 23 For
the husband is the head of the wife as
Christ is the head of the church,[u] his body,
of which he is the Savior. 24 Now as the
church submits to Christ, so also wives
should submit to their husbands[v] in everything.
25 Husbands, love your wives,[w] just as
Christ loved the church and gave himself
up for her[x] 26 to make her holy,[y] cleansing[a]
her by the washing[z] with water through
the word, 27 and to present her to himself[a]
as a radiant church, without stain or wrinkle or any other blemish, but holy and
blameless.[b] 28 In this same way, husbands
ought to love their wives[c] as their own
bodies. He who loves his wife loves himself. 29 After all, no one ever hated their
own body, but they feed and care for their
body, just as Christ does the church—
30 for we are members of his body.[d] 31 "For
this reason a man will leave his father
and mother and be united to his wife, and
the two will become one flesh."[b][e] 32 This
is a profound mystery—but I am talking
about Christ and the church. 33 However,
each one of you also must love his wife[f]
as he loves himself, and the wife must respect her husband.

6 Children, obey your parents in the
Lord, for this is right.[g] 2 "Honor your
father and mother"—which is the first
commandment with a promise— 3 "so
that it may go well with you and that you
may enjoy long life on the earth."[c][h]
4 Fathers,[d] do not exasperate your children;[i] instead, bring them up in the training and instruction of the Lord.[j]
5 Slaves, obey your earthly masters with
respect[k] and fear, and with sincerity of
heart,[l] just as you would obey Christ.[m]
6 Obey them not only to win their favor
when their eye is on you, but as slaves of
Christ,[n] doing the will of God from your

5:22 [s]Ge 3:16; 1Co 14:34; Col 3:18; 1Ti 2:12; Titus 2:5; 1Pe 3:1,5,6 [t]Eph 6:5
5:23 [u]S Eph 1:22
5:24 [v]S ver 22
5:25 [w]ver 28, 33; Col 3:19 [x]S ver 2
5:26 [y]Jn 17:19; Heb 2:11; 10:10,14; 13:12 [z]S Ac 22:16
5:27 [a]S 2Co 4:14 [b]Eph 1:4
5:28 [c]ver 25
5:30 [d]S Ro 12:5; S 1Co 12:27
5:31 [e]Ge 2:24; Mt 19:5; 1Co 6:16
5:33 [f]ver 25
6:1 [g]Pr 6:20; Col 3:20
6:3 [h]Ex 20:12; Dt 5:16
6:4 [i]Col 3:21 [j]Ge 18:19; Dt 6:7; Pr 13:24; 22:6
6:5 [k]1Ti 6:1; Titus 2:9; 1Pe 2:18 [l]Col 3:22 [m]Eph 5:22
6:6 [n]S Ro 6:22

WHY THERE WASN'T A **MASSIVE SLAVE REVOLT** IN THE FIRST CENTURY

There is no evidence in ancient literature of a slave rebellion with the abolition of slavery as its goal. Why? Not only was Roman-era slavery a nonracial institution (there were slaves of all races), but most slaves could reasonably expect emancipation by the time they reached 30 years of age. Nor was the work of a slave limited to hard labor; slaves worked in a variety of different occupations—including household management, teaching, business and industry—and many even owned property. Because of the poverty of many free laborers, the economic and living conditions of slaves were often far better. This led many free laborers to sell themselves into slavery as a means of economic advancement.This is not to deny that slavery was essentially an ungodly structure that deprived a person of freedom and dignity. It is simply to affirm that Roman-era slavery did not share all of the same features of New World slavery that would ignite a rebellion.

[a] 26 Or *having cleansed* [b] 31 Gen. 2:24
[c] 3 Deut. 5:16 [d] 4 Or *Parents*

taught in v. 21. *as you do to the Lord.* Does not put a woman's husband in the place of the Lord but shows rather that a woman ought to submit to her husband as an act of service to the Lord.

5:23 *head of the wife.* See 1Co 11:3 and note. *as Christ.* The analogy between the relationship of Christ to the church and that of the husband to the wife is basic to the entire passage. *his body.* See 2:16; 4:4,12,16.

5:25 *Husbands.* Paul now shows that this is not a one-sided submission but a reciprocal relationship. *love.* Explained by what follows. *Christ loved the church and gave himself up for her.* Not only the expression of our Lord's love but also an example of how the husband ought to devote himself to his wife's good. To give oneself up to death for the beloved is a more extreme expression of devotion than the wife is called upon to make (cf. Jn 15:13 and note).

5:26 *washing with water through the word.* Many attempts have been made to see marriage customs or liturgical symbolism in these words. One thing is clear: Jesus died not only to bring forgiveness but also to effect a new life of holiness in the church, which is his "bride." A study of the concepts of washing, of water and of the word should include reference to Jn 3:5 (see note there); 15:3; see also Titus 3:5; Heb 10:22; Jas 1:18; 1Pe 1:23; 3:21 and notes.

5:27 *holy and blameless.* See 1:4 and note.

5:28–29 *as their own bodies ... loves himself ... their own body.* The basis for such expressions and for the teaching of these verses is the quotation from Ge 2:24 in v. 31. If the husband and wife become "one flesh," then for the man to love his wife is to love one who has become part of himself.

5:32 *mystery.* See note on Ro 11:25. The profound truth of the union of Christ and his "bride," the church, is beyond unaided human understanding. It is not that the relationship of husband and wife provides an illustration of the union of Christ and the church but that the basic reality is the latter, with marriage a human echo of that relationship.

5:33 *love ... respect.* A rephrasing and summary of the whole passage.

6:1 *obey your parents.* Cf. Pr 30:17; Col 3:20 and note; 2Ti 3:2. *in the Lord.* In fellowship with the Lord and in obedience to him.

6:2–3 *Honor your father ... on the earth.* In Dt 5:16 (see Ex 20:12), where this commandment occurs, the "promise" was expressed in terms of the anticipated occupation of the "land," i.e., Canaan. That specific application was, of course, not appropriate to the Ephesians, so the more general application is made here.

6:4 *do not exasperate.* Fathers must surrender any right they may feel they have to act unreasonably toward their children.

6:5 *Slaves.* Both the OT and the NT included regulations for societal situations such as slavery and divorce (see Dt 24:1–4), which were the results of the hardness of hearts (Mt 19:8). Such regulations did not encourage or condone such situations but were divinely given, practical ways of dealing with the realities of the day. Cf. 1Co 7:21 and note; Phm 16.

heart. 7Serve wholeheartedly, as if you were serving the Lord, not people,[o] 8because you know that the Lord will reward each one for whatever good they do,[p] whether they are slave or free.

9And masters, treat your slaves in the same way. Do not threaten them, since you know that he who is both their Master and yours[q] is in heaven, and there is no favoritism[r] with him.

The Armor of God

10Finally, be strong in the Lord[s] and in his mighty power.[t] 11Put on the full armor of God,[u] so that you can take your stand against the devil's schemes. 12For our struggle is not against flesh and blood,[v] but against the rulers, against the authorities,[w] against the powers[x] of this dark world and against the spiritual forces of evil in the heavenly realms.[y] 13Therefore put on the full armor of God,[z] so that when the day of evil comes, you may be able to stand your ground, and after you have done everything, to stand. 14Stand firm then, with the belt of truth buckled around your waist,[a] with the breastplate of righteousness in place,[b] 15and with your feet fitted with the readiness that comes from the gospel of peace.[c] 16In addition to all this, take up the shield of faith,[d] with which you can extinguish all the flaming arrows of the evil one.[e] 17Take the helmet of salvation[f] and the sword of the Spirit,[g] which is the word of God.[h]

18And pray in the Spirit[i] on all occasions[j] with all kinds of prayers and requests.[k] With this in mind, be alert and always keep on praying[l] for all the Lord's people. 19Pray also for me,[m] that whenever I speak, words may be given me so that I will fearlessly[n] make known the mystery[o] of the gospel, 20for which I am an ambassador[p] in chains.[q] Pray that I may declare it fearlessly, as I should.

SPIRITUAL WARFARE IMAGERY

IMAGE	BACKGROUND	SPIRITUAL WEAPON
1. Belt . . . buckled around your waist	Isa 11:5	Truth
2. Breastplate	Isa 59:17	Righteousness
3. Feet fitted	Isa 52:7	Gospel of peace
4. Shield	Ps 35:2; Isa 21:5 — 23 times in the OT	Faith
5. Helmet	Isa 59:17	Salvation
6. Sword	Isa 49:2 — 178 times in the OT	Spirit/Word of God/Prayer

Adapted from *Zondervan Illustrated Bible Backgrounds Commentary: NT*: Vol. 3 by CLINTON E. ARNOLD. Ephesians—Copyright © 2002 by Clinton E. Arnold, p. 335. Used by permission of Zondervan.

6:7 [o]Col 3:23 **6:8** [p]S Mt 16:27; Col 3:24 **6:9** [q]Job 31:13, 14 [r]S Ac 10:34 **6:10** [s]2Sa 10:12; Ps 27:14; Hag 2:4; 1Co 16:13; 2Ti 2:1 [t]Eph 1:19 **6:11** [u]ver 13; Ro 13:12; 1Th 5:8 **6:12** [v]1Co 15:50; Heb 2:14 [w]Eph 1:21; 3:10 [x]Ro 8:38 [y]S Eph 1:3 **6:13** [z]ver 11; S 2Co 6:7 **6:14** [a]Isa 11:5 [b]Ps 132:9; Isa 59:17; 1Th 5:8 **6:15** [c]Isa 52:7; Ro 10:15 **6:16** [d]1Jn 5:4 [e]S Mt 5:37 **6:17** [f]Isa 59:17 [g]Isa 49:2 [h]S Heb 4:12 **6:18** [i]Ro 8:26, 27 [j]S Lk 18:1 [k]Mt 26:41; Php 1:4; 4:6 [l]S Ac 1:14; Col 1:3 **6:19** [m]S 1Th 5:25 [n]S Ac 4:29 [o]S Ro 16:25 **6:20** [p]2Co 5:20 [q]S Ac 21:33

6:8 *the Lord will reward.* Probably a reference to the believer's final reward (see 1Co 3:10–15; 2Co 5:10 and notes).

6:9 *masters.* Once again Paul stresses reciprocal attitudes (cf. 5:21—6:4). See Titus 2:9 and note. *their Master and yours.* Cf. Ro 14:4 and note. *no favoritism with him.* See Ac 10:34 and note.

6:10–20 Paul's scope in Ephesians has been cosmic. From the very beginning he has drawn attention to the unseen world (see note on 1:3; see also 1:10,20–23; 2:6; 6:10), and now he describes the spiritual battle that takes place against evil "in the heavenly realms" (v. 12).

6:10 *strong . . . power.* Implies that human effort is inadequate but that God's power is invincible.

6:12 *not against flesh and blood.* A caution against lashing out against human opponents as though they were the real enemy and also against assuming that the battle can be fought using merely human resources. *rulers . . . forces.* Cf. Paul's earlier allusions to powerful beings in the unseen world (see notes on 1:21; 3:10). *heavenly realms.* See note on 1:3.

6:13–14 *stand your ground . . . Stand firm.* In this context the imagery is not that of a massive invasion of the domain of evil but of individual soldiers withstanding assault.

6:14 *belt of truth.* Cf. the symbolic clothing of the Messiah in Isa 11:5. Character, not brute force, wins the battle, just as in the case of the Messiah. *breastplate of righteousness.* Here again, the warriors' character is their defense. God himself is symbolically described as putting on a breastplate of righteousness when he goes forth to bring about justice (see Isa 59:17 and note).

6:15 *feet fitted with the readiness.* Whereas the description of the messenger's feet in Isa 52:7 reflects the custom of running barefooted, here the message of the gospel is picturesquely connected with the protective and supportive footgear of the Roman soldier. *gospel of peace.* An expression found only here in the Bible (cf. 2:14–16; Ro 5:1 and note).

6:16 *shield of faith . . . extinguish . . . flaming arrows.* Describes the large Roman shield covered with leather, which could be soaked in water and used to put out flame-tipped arrows.

6:17–18 *sword of the Spirit . . . pray in the Spirit.* Reminders that the battle is spiritual and must be fought in God's strength, depending on the word and on God through prayer.

6:17 *helmet of salvation.* Isa 59:17 has similar language, along with the breastplate imagery (see note on v. 14). The helmet protected the soldier and, under certain circumstances, helmets provided a striking symbol of military victory.

6:18 *pray in the Spirit.* Pray with the help of the Spirit (cf. Ro 8:26 and note). *the Lord's people.* See note on 1:1.

6:19 *mystery.* See 3:3,9 and note on 3:3.

6:20 *in chains.* See Php 1:7,13 and note; Col 4:3; Phm 10,13.

Final Greetings

[21]Tychicus,[r] the dear brother and faithful servant in the Lord, will tell you everything, so that you also may know how I
am and what I am doing. [22]I am sending
him to you for this very purpose, that you
may know how we are,[s] and that he may
encourage you.[t]

[23]Peace[u] to the brothers and sisters,[a]
and love with faith from God the Father
and the Lord Jesus Christ. [24]Grace to all
who love our Lord Jesus Christ with an
undying love.[b]

6:21 [r] S Ac 20:4
6:22 [s] Col 4:7-9 [t] Col 2:2; 4:8
6:23 [u] Gal 6:16; 2Th 3:16; 1Pe 5:14

[a] *23* The Greek word for *brothers and sisters* (*adelphoi*) refers here to believers, both men and women, as part of God's family. [b] *24* Or *Grace and immortality to all who love our Lord Jesus Christ.*

6:21–23 Paul concludes with greetings that lack personal references such as are usually found in his letters. This is understandable if Ephesians is a circular letter (see note on 1:1).
6:21 *Tychicus.* An associate of Paul who traveled as his representative (cf. Col 4:7; 2Ti 4:12; Titus 3:12).
6:23–24 *Peace ... Grace.* See note on Ro 1:7.
6:23 *brothers and sisters.* See NIV text note.
6:24 *love our Lord Jesus.* Cf. Jn 14:15,21,23; 21:15–17 and notes.

PHILIPPIANS

INTRODUCTION

Author, Date and Place of Writing

The early church was unanimous in its testimony that Philippians was written by the apostle Paul (see 1:1). Internally, the letter reveals the stamp of genuineness. The many personal references of the author fit what we know of Paul from other NT books.

It is evident that Paul wrote the letter from prison (see 1:13 – 14). Some have argued that this imprisonment took place in Ephesus, perhaps c. AD 53 – 55; others put it in Caesarea c. 57 – 59. Best evidence, however, favors Rome as the place of origin and the date as c. 61 (see chart, p. 1845). This fits well with the account of Paul's house arrest in Ac 28:14 – 31. When he wrote Philippians, he was not in the Mamertine dungeon as he may have been when he wrote 2 Timothy. He was in his own rented house, where for two years he was free to impart the gospel to all who came to him.

Purpose

Paul's primary purpose in writing this letter was to thank the Philippians for the gift they had sent him upon learning of his detention at Rome (1:5; 4:10 – 19). However, he makes use of this occasion to fulfill several other desires: (1) to report on his own circumstances (1:12 – 26; 4:10 – 19); (2) to encourage the Philippians to stand firm in the face of persecution and to rejoice — regardless of circumstances (1:27 – 30; 4:4); (3) to exhort them to humility and unity (2:1 – 11; 4:2 – 5); (4) to commend Timothy and Epaphroditus to the Philippian church (2:19 – 30); and (5) to warn the Philippians against the Judaizers (legalists) and antinomians (libertines) among them (ch. 3).

Recipients

The city of Philippi (see map, p. 1998) was named after King Philip II of Macedon, father of Alexander the Great. It was a prosperous Roman colony, which meant that the citizens of Philippi were also citizens of the city of Rome itself. They prided themselves on being Romans (see Ac 16:21), dressed like Romans and often spoke Latin. No doubt this was the background

Author:
The apostle Paul

Audience:
The believers at Philippi, a prosperous Roman colony

Date:
About AD 61

Theme:
Paul writes to encourage the Christians at Philippi to live joyfully in every circumstance.

Paul wrote to thank the Philippians for the gift they had sent him and to encourage them to stand firm in the face of persecution and to rejoice — regardless of circumstances.

for Paul's reference to the believer's heavenly citizenship (3:20 – 21). Many of the Philippians were retired military men who had been given land in the vicinity and who in turn served as a military presence in this frontier city. That Philippi was a Roman colony may explain why there were not enough Jews there to permit the establishment of a synagogue and why Paul does not quote the OT in the Philippian letter (but see 1:19; Job 13:16 and notes).

Characteristics

(1) Philippians contains no OT quotations (but see note on Job 13:16).

(2) It is a missionary thank-you letter in which the missionary reports on the progress of his work.

(3) It manifests a particularly vigorous type of Christian living: (1) self-humbling (2:1 – 4); (2) pressing toward the goal (3:13 – 14); (3) lack of anxiety (4:6); and (4) ability to do all things (4:13; but see note there).

(4) It is outstanding as the NT letter of joy; the word "joy" in its various forms occurs some 16 times.

(5) It contains one of the most profound Christological passages in the NT (2:5 – 11). Yet even here Paul's purpose is not to teach theology alone, but to call the church to unity on the basis of the humility and servanthood of Jesus Christ.

Byzantine and Roman remains at Philippi. Paul visited the city on his second and third missionary journeys. He was imprisoned here with Silas during the second journey (Ac 16:16 – 40).

PHILIPPI IN THE TIME OF PAUL

The Roman colony of Philippi (*Colonia Augusta Julia Philippensis*) was an important city in Macedonia, located on the main highway leading from the eastern provinces to Rome. This road, the Egnatian Way, ran along the north side of the city's forum and was the chief cause of its prosperity and political importance. Ten miles east on the coast was Neapolis, the place where Paul landed after sailing from Troas in response to the Macedonian vision.

As a prominent city of the gold-producing region of Macedonia, Philippi had a proud history. Named originally after Philip II, the father of Alexander the Great, the city was later honored with the names of Julius Caesar and Augustus. Many Italian settlers from the legions swelled the ranks of citizens and made Philippi vigorous and polyglot. It grew from a small settlement to a city of dignity and privilege. Among its highest honors was the *ius Italicum*, by which it enjoyed rights legally equivalent to those of Italian cities.

Ruins of the theater, the acropolis, the forum, the baths and the commemorative arch (about a mile west of the city) have been found. A little farther beyond the arch at the Gangites River is the place where Paul addressed some God-fearing women and where Lydia was converted (Ac 16:13-15).

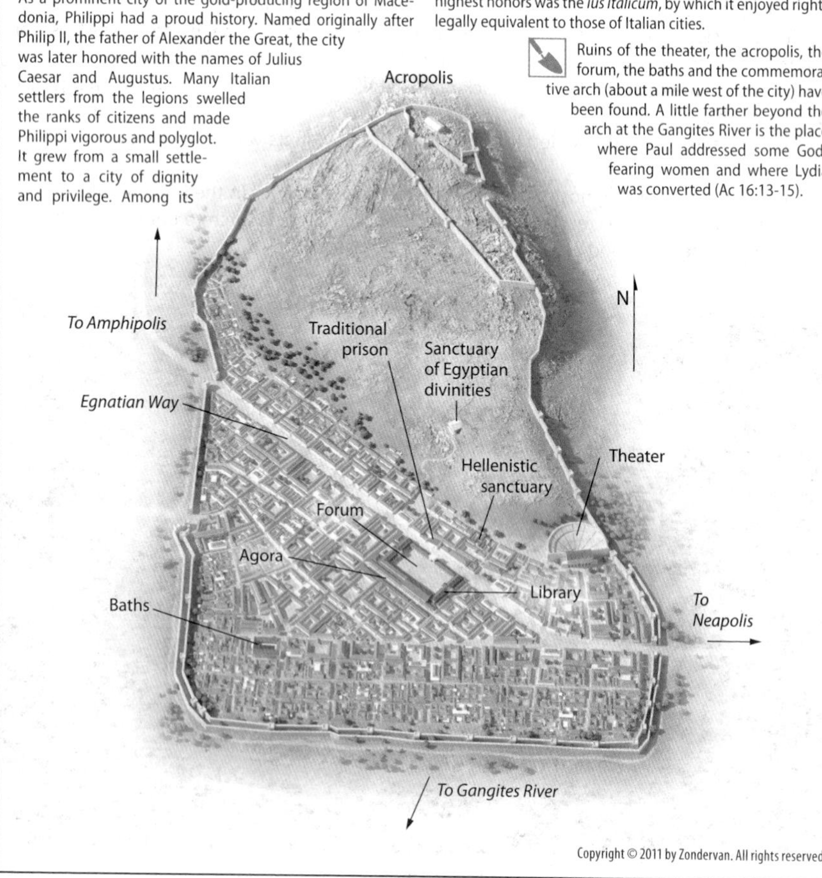

Outline

I. Greetings (1:1 – 2)
II. Thanksgiving and Prayer for the Philippians (1:3 – 11)
III. Paul's Personal Circumstances (1:12 – 26)
IV. Exhortations (1:27 — 2:18)
  A. Living a Life Worthy of the Gospel (1:27 – 30)
  B. Following the Servant Attitude of Christ (2:1 – 18)
V. Paul's Associates in the Gospel (2:19 – 30)
  A. Timothy (2:19 – 24)
  B. Epaphroditus (2:25 – 30)
VI. Warnings against Judaizers and Antinomians (ch. 3)
  A. Against Judaizers or Legalists (3:1 – 16)
  B. Against Antinomians or Libertines (3:17 – 21)
VII. Final Exhortations, Thanks and Conclusion (ch. 4)
  A. Exhortations concerning Various Aspects of the Christian Life (4:1 – 9)
  B. Concluding Testimony and Repeated Thanks (4:10 – 20)
  C. Final Greetings and Benediction (4:21 – 23)

1 Paul and Timothy,[a] servants of Christ
Jesus,

To all God's holy people[b] in Christ Jesus
at Philippi,[c] together with the overseers[d]
and deacons[a]:[e]

2Grace and peace to you from God our
Father and the Lord Jesus Christ.[f]

Thanksgiving and Prayer

3I thank my God every time I remember
you.[g] 4In all my prayers for all of you, I always pray[h] with joy 5because of your partnership[i] in the gospel from the first day[j]
until now, 6being confident of this, that
he who began a good work in you will
carry it on to completion[k] until the day of
Christ Jesus.[l]

7It is right[m] for me to feel this way about
all of you, since I have you in my heart[n]
and, whether I am in chains[o] or defending[p]
and confirming the gospel, all of you share
in God's grace with me. 8God can testify[q]
how I long for all of you with the affection
of Christ Jesus.

9And this is my prayer: that your love[r]
may abound more and more in knowledge
and depth of insight,[s] 10so that you may be
able to discern what is best and may be
pure and blameless for the day of Christ,[t]
11filled with the fruit of righteousness[u] that
comes through Jesus Christ—to the glory
and praise of God.

Paul's Chains Advance the Gospel

12Now I want you to know, brothers
and sisters,[b] that what has happened to
me has actually served to advance the
gospel. 13As a result, it has become clear
throughout the whole palace guard[c] and
to everyone else that I am in chains[v] for
Christ. 14And because of my chains,[w] most
of the brothers and sisters have become

1:1 [a]S Ac 16:1; 2Co 1:1 [b]S Ac 9:13 [c]S Ac 16:12 [d]S 1Ti 3:1 [e]1Ti 3:8 **1:2** [f]S Ro 1:7 **1:3** [g]S Ro 1:8 **1:4** [h]S Ro 1:10 **1:5** [i]Ac 2:42; Php 4:15 [j]Ac 16:12-40 **1:6** [k]Ps 138:8 [l]ver 10; S 1Co 1:8 **1:7** [m]2Pe 1:13 [n]2Co 7:3 [o]ver 13,14, 17; S Ac 21:33 [p]ver 16 **1:8** [q]S Ro 1:9 **1:9** [r]1Th 3:12 [s]S Eph 1:17 **1:10** [t]ver 6; S 1Co 1:8 **1:11** [u]S Jas 3:18 **1:13** [v]ver 7,14, 17; S Ac 21:33 **1:14** [w]ver 7,13, 17; S Ac 21:33

[a] *1* The word *deacons* refers here to Christians designated to serve with the overseers/elders of the church in a variety of ways; similarly in Romans 16:1 and 1 Tim. 3:8,12. [b] *12* The Greek word for *brothers and sisters* (*adelphoi*) refers here to believers, both men and women, as part of God's family; also in verse 14; and in 3:1, 13, 17; 4:1, 8, 21. [c] *13* Or *whole palace*

1:1–2 As in all his letters, Paul follows the conventional letter format of his day, with its three elements: (1) identification of the sender, (2) identification of the recipients and (3) greeting.

1:1 *Paul.* See note on Ro 1:1. *Timothy.* See Introduction to 1 Timothy: Recipient. Timothy is identified with the contents of the letter as Paul's associate, but not as coauthor. *servants.* See Ro 1:1 and note; Titus 1:1; Jas 1:1; 2Pe 1:1; Jude 1; Rev 1:1. In Paul's case, this designation brings out an essential aspect of the more usual identification of himself as "apostle." *God's holy people.* See Ro 1:7 and note. *in Christ.* See note on Eph 1:1. *Philippi.* See Introduction: Recipients. *overseers and deacons.* The only place in Paul's writings where church officers as a group are singled out as recipients of a letter. *overseers.* See note on 1Ti 3:1. *deacons.* See note on 1Ti 3:8.

1:2 *Grace and peace.* See note on Ro 1:7. *Lord Jesus Christ.* Also occurs at the end of this letter (4:23); see note on 1Th 1:1.

1:3–4 *I thank my God … prayers for … you … with joy.* Prayers of joyful thanksgiving for his readers' response to the gospel are a hallmark of the opening sentences of Paul's letters (see Ro 1:8; 1Co 1:4; Col 1:3; 1Th 1:2; 2Th 1:3; 2Ti 1:3; Phm 4).

1:5 *your partnership in the gospel.* The basis of Paul's prayerful thanksgiving is not only their reception of the gospel but also their active support of his ministry (see 4:15 and note). *from the first day.* When Paul first came to Philippi (Ac 16:12). *now.* Toward the close (see 2:24 and note) of Paul's first Roman imprisonment (see Ac 28:16–31).

1:6 *work in you.* Paul is confident not only of what God has done "for" the readers in forgiving their sins but also of what he has done "in" them (see v. 11). "Work" refers to God's activity in saving them. *day of Christ Jesus.* His return, when their salvation will be brought to completion (see 1:10; 2:16; 1Co 1:8; 5:5; 2Co 1:14). It is God who initiates salvation, who continues it and who will one day bring it to its consummation.

1:7 *in chains.* See note on Eph 6:20. *share in God's grace.* Not even imprisonment and persecution can change such sharing. Even in Paul's imprisonment the Philippian Christians willingly identified themselves with Paul by sending Epaphroditus and their financial gifts (2:25–30; 4:18). They had become one with Paul in his apostolic commission to preach the gospel (see v. 5).

1:8 *affection of Christ Jesus.* The deep yearning and intense, compassionate love exhibited by Jesus himself and now fostered in Paul by his union with Christ. This affection reaches out to all, impartially and without exception.

1:9 *abound more and more.* Real love requires growth and maturation (see 1Th 3:12; 4:10; 2Th 1:3). *in knowledge.* The way love grows (cf. Col 1:9). *depth of insight.* Practical discernment and sensitivity. Christian love is not mere sentiment; it is rooted in knowledge and understanding.

1:10 *discern what is best.* Christians are to approve (and practice) what is morally and ethically superior. *pure and blameless.* The goal of Christians in this life is to be without any mixture of evil and not open to censure because of moral or spiritual failure. *for the day of Christ.* Then the goal will be perfectly realized (see note on v. 6), and then Christians must give an account (see 2Co 5:10 and note; Ro 14:10,12 and note on 14:10).

1:11 *filled with the fruit of righteousness.* What is expected of all Christians (cf. Mt 5:20–48; Heb 12:11; Jas 3:18; see also Am 6:12; Gal 5:22–23). *through Jesus Christ.* Produced by Christ (in union with him) through the work of the Holy Spirit (cf. Jn 15:5; Eph 2:10). *to the glory and praise of God.* The ultimate goal of all that God does in believers (see Eph 1:6,12,14).

1:12 *brothers and sisters.* See NIV text note. *what has happened to me.* Paul's detainment in a Roman prison. *advance the gospel.* Instead of hindering the gospel, Paul's imprisonment had served to make it known.

1:13 *clear … chains for Christ.* It has become apparent to all who know of Paul's situation that he is imprisoned not because he is guilty of a crime but on account of his stand for the gospel. *whole palace guard.* A contingent of soldiers, numbering several thousand, many of whom would have had personal contact with Paul or would have been assigned individually to guard him during the course of his imprisonment (see Ac 28:16,30). *chains.* Either actual chains or a broader reference to his sufferings and imprisonment (see v. 14).

1:14 *brothers and sisters … proclaim the gospel without fear.* The unexpected result of Paul's imprisonment.

confident in the Lord and dare all the more
to proclaim the gospel without fear.[x]
15 It is true that some preach Christ
out of envy and rivalry, but others out of
goodwill. 16 The latter do so out of love,
knowing that I am put here for the defense
of the gospel.[y] 17 The former preach Christ
out of selfish ambition,[z] not sincerely, supposing that they can stir up trouble for me
while I am in chains.[a] 18 But what does it
matter? The important thing is that in every way, whether from false motives or
true, Christ is preached. And because of
this I rejoice.
Yes, and I will continue to rejoice, 19 for I
know that through your prayers[b] and God's
provision of the Spirit of Jesus Christ[c] what
has happened to me will turn out for my
deliverance.[a][d] 20 I eagerly expect[e] and hope
that I will in no way be ashamed, but will
have sufficient courage[f] so that now as always Christ will be exalted in my body,[g]
whether by life or by death.[h] 21 For to me,
to live is Christ[i] and to die is gain. 22 If I
am to go on living in the body, this will
mean fruitful labor for me. Yet what shall
I choose? I do not know! 23 I am torn between the two: I desire to depart[j] and be
with Christ,[k] which is better by far; 24 but
it is more necessary for you that I remain
in the body. 25 Convinced of this, I know
that I will remain, and I will continue with
all of you for your progress and joy in the
faith, 26 so that through my being with you
again your boasting in Christ Jesus will
abound on account of me.

Life Worthy of the Gospel

27 Whatever happens, conduct yourselves in a manner worthy[l] of the gospel
of Christ. Then, whether I come and see
you or only hear about you in my absence,
I will know that you stand firm[m] in the one
Spirit,[b] striving together[n] as one for the
faith of the gospel 28 without being frightened in any way by those who oppose
you. This is a sign to them that they will
be destroyed, but that you will be saved—
and that by God. 29 For it has been granted to you[o] on behalf of Christ not only to
believe in him, but also to suffer[p] for him,
30 since you are going through the same

1:14 [x] S Ac 4:29 **1:16** [y] ver 7,12 **1:17** [z] Php 2:3 [a] ver 7,13,14; S Ac 21:33 **1:19** [b] 2Co 1:11 [c] S Ac 16:7 [d] Phm 22 **1:20** [e] Ro 8:19 [f] ver 14 [g] 1Co 6:20 [h] Ro 14:8 **1:21** [i] Gal 2:20 **1:23** [j] 2Ti 4:6 [k] S Jn 12:26 **1:27** [l] S Eph 4:1 [m] S 1Co 16:13 [n] Jude 3 **1:29** [o] Mt 5:11,12; Ac 5:41 [p] S Ac 14:22

[a] 19 Or *vindication*; or *salvation* [b] 27 Or *in one spirit*

1:16 *The latter do so out of love.* Those who preach with a right motive recognize the true reason for Paul's imprisonment, already expressed earlier in v. 13, and are encouraged to take the same bold stand that he has taken.

1:17 *The former preach Christ out of selfish ambition.* Those who preach with wrong, insincere motives do so out of a sense of competition with Paul and so think they are making his imprisonment more difficult to bear. *not sincerely.* Not from pure motives.

1:18 *whether from false motives or true, Christ is preached.* These preachers are not to be viewed as being heretical. Their message is true, even though their motives are not pure. The gospel has its objectivity and validity apart from those who proclaim it; the message is more than the medium. *I rejoice ... will continue to rejoice.* An example of the kind of vigorous Christian experience Paul expressed. He was under arrest, and fellow Christians sought, by their preaching, to add to his difficulties; yet he kept on rejoicing.

1:19 *Spirit of Jesus Christ.* The Holy Spirit is not only the Spirit of God the Father (Ro 8:9,14; 1Co 2:10–11,14) but also the Spirit of Christ, the second person of the Trinity (Ac 16:7; Ro 8:9; Gal 4:6). He is sent by the Father (Jn 14:16–17,26; Gal 4:6) and by the Son (Jn 15:26; 16:7). *turn out for my deliverance.* Either Paul's release from prison (see v. 25; 2:24) or, in view of the immediately following verses, the deliverance brought to the believer by death (cf. Ro 8:38–39). Verse 25, however, seems to point to the former interpretation (see note there). See Job 13:16 and note.

1:20 *ashamed ... sufficient courage.* The circumstances of imprisonment, with all its attendant suffering and oppression, constitute a real temptation for Paul to abandon the gospel and his resolute service for Christ. *my body.* Where the exalted Christ dwells by his Spirit and is at work (cf. Ro 8:9–10), and so is exalted by what Paul does. *whether by life or by death.* Whether his service for Christ continues or ends in death.

1:21 *to live is Christ.* Christ was the source and secret of Paul's continual joy (even in prison), for Paul's life found all its meaning in Christ (see 3:7–11). *gain.* Verse 23 specifies that the gain brought by death is being "with Christ," so that here Paul is saying that his ultimate concern and most precious possession, both now and forever, is Christ and his relationship to him.

1:22 *fruitful labor.* The spread of the gospel and the upbuilding of the church.

1:23–24 *depart and be with Christ ... remain in the body.* Either alternative was a good one. While mysteries remain, this passage clearly teaches that when believers die they are with Christ, apart from the body (see 2Co 5:6,8–9).

1:23 *better by far.* Being with Christ after death must involve some kind of conscious presence and fellowship (cf. 2Co 5:6,8 and note on 5:8).

1:24 *necessary for you.* Paul puts the needs of those he ministers to ahead of his personal preference.

1:25 *I will remain.* It is possible that Paul was later released from prison (see map and accompanying text, p. 2038). *progress ... in the faith.* The Christian life is to be one of joyful growth and advance (see note on v. 9).

1:26 *your boasting in Christ Jesus ... on account of me.* Paul's conduct of his ministry among the Philippians will be a reason for their rejoicing in what Christ is doing among them.

1:27 *worthy of the gospel.* Appropriate to the standards and goals given with the gospel. *in the one Spirit.* In the Spirit's enablement (but see NIV text note). *striving together as one.* Particularly where the gospel is under attack, Christians need each other and must stand together.

1:28 *sign.* Persistent opposition to the church and the gospel is a sure sign of eventual destruction, since it involves rejection of the only way of salvation. By the same token, when Christians are persecuted for their faith, this is a sign of the genuineness of their salvation (see 2Th 1:5 and note).

1:29 *granted ... to suffer.* Given as a gift or privilege. Christian suffering, as well as faith, is a blessing (cf. Mt 5:11–12; Ac 5:41; Jas 1:2; 1Pe 4:14). The Christian life is to be a "not only ... but also" proposition: not only believing but also suffering.

1:30 *same struggle.* Their common involvement with Paul, in

struggle[q] you saw[r] I had, and now hear[s]
that I still have.

Imitating Christ's Humility

2 Therefore if you have any encouragement from being united with Christ, if
any comfort from his love, if any common
sharing in the Spirit,[t] if any tenderness
and compassion,[u] 2 then make my joy complete[v] by being like-minded,[w] having the
same love, being one[x] in spirit and of one
mind. 3 Do nothing out of selfish ambition
or vain conceit.[y] Rather, in humility value
others above yourselves,[z] 4 not looking to
your own interests but each of you to the
interests of the others.[a]
5 In your relationships with one another,
have the same mindset as Christ Jesus:[b]

6 Who, being in very nature[a] God,[c]
did not consider equality with God[d]
something to be used to his
own advantage;
7 rather, he made himself nothing[e]
by taking the very nature[b] of a
servant,[f]
being made in human likeness.[g]
8 And being found in appearance as a man,
he humbled himself
by becoming obedient to death[h] —
even death on a cross![i]

9 Therefore God exalted him[j] to the
highest place
and gave him the name that is above
every name,[k]
10 that at the name of Jesus every knee
should bow,[l]
in heaven and on earth and under
the earth,[m]
11 and every tongue acknowledge that
Jesus Christ is Lord,[n]
to the glory of God the Father.

1:30 [q] 1Th 2:2; Heb 10:32 [r] Ac 16:19-40 [s] ver 13 **2:1** [t] 2Co 13:14 [u] Col 3:12 **2:2** [v] S Jn 3:29 [w] Php 4:2 [x] S Ro 15:5 **2:3** [y] Gal 5:26 [z] Ro 12:10; 1Pe 5:5 **2:4** [a] S 1Co 10:24 **2:5** [b] S Mt 11:29 **2:6** [c] Jn 1:1; S 14:9 [d] Jn 5:18 **2:7** [e] 2Co 8:9 [f] S Mt 20:28 [g] S Jn 1:14; Ro 8:3; Heb 2:17 **2:8** [h] S Mt 26:39; Jn 10:18; Ro 5:19; Heb 5:8 [i] S 1Co 1:23 **2:9** [j] Isa 52:13; 53:12; Da 7:14; Ac 2:33; Heb 2:9 [k] Eph 1:20,21 **2:10** [l] Ps 95:6; Isa 45:23; Ro 14:11 [m] Mt 28:18; Eph 1:10; Col 1:20 **2:11** [n] S Jn 13:13

[a] 6 Or *in the form of* [b] 7 Or *the form*

conflict with those who oppose the gospel. *you saw.* When Paul and Silas first visited Philippi and were imprisoned (see Ac 16:19–40).

2:1 *united with Christ.* Or "united in Christ." In Paul's teaching, this personal union is the basic reality of salvation. To be in Christ is to be saved. It is to be in intimate personal relationship with Christ the Savior. From this relationship flow all the particular benefits and fruits of salvation, such as encouragement (see, e.g., 3:8–10; Ro 8:1; 2Co 5:17; Gal 2:20). *comfort from his love.* The comforting knowledge and assurance that come from God's love in Christ, demonstrated especially in Christ's death for the forgiveness of sins and eternal life (see Jn 3:16; Ro 5:8; 8:38–39; 1Jn 3:16; 4:9–10,16). *common sharing in the Spirit.* The fellowship among believers produced by the Spirit, who indwells each of them (see 2Co 13:14). *tenderness and compassion.* Christians are to have intense care and deep sympathy for each other (see 1:8 and note; Col 3:12). All these benefits—encouragement, comfort, fellowship, tenderness and compassion—are viewed by Paul as present realities for the Philippians.

2:2 *like-minded ... same love ... one in spirit and of one mind.* Emphasizes the unity that should exist among Christians. *like-minded.* Not uniformity in thought but the common disposition to work together and serve one another—the "mindset" of Christ (v. 5; see 4:2; Ro 12:16; 15:5 and note; 2Co 13:11).

2:3 *selfish ambition or vain conceit.* The mortal enemies of unity and harmony in the church (cf. 1:17; see Gal 5:20, where "selfish ambition" is listed among the "acts of the flesh"). *humility.* Required for Christian unity. This is the mindset of those who are not conceited but who have a right attitude toward themselves and others. *value others above yourselves.* Not that everyone else is superior or more talented, but that Christian love sees others as worthy of preferential treatment (see Ro 12:10 and note; Gal 5:13; Eph 5:21; 1Pe 5:5 and note).

2:4 *your own interests.* These are proper, but only if there is equal concern for the interests of others (cf. Ro 15:1 and note).

2:5 *have the same mindset as Christ Jesus.* In spite of all that is unique and radically different about the person and work of Christ (see vv. 6–11), Christians are to have his attitude of self-sacrificing humility and love for others (see vv. 2–4; Mt 11:29; Jn 13:12–17).

2:6–11 The poetic character of these verses is apparent. Many view them as an early Christian hymn (see note on Col 3:16), taken over and perhaps modified by Paul. If so, they nonetheless express his convictions. The subjects of this passage are Christ's humiliation (vv. 6–8) and exaltation (vv. 9–11).

2:6 *in very nature God.* Affirming that Jesus is fully God (see Ro 9:5 and note). *nature.* Essential form (see NIV text note), the sum of those qualities that make God specifically God. *equality with God.* The status and privileges that inevitably follow from being in very nature God. *something to be used to his own advantage.* Perhaps something to be forcibly retained—the glory Christ had with the Father before his incarnation. But he did not consider that high position to be something he could not give up. On the other hand, it may be something still to be attained, like a prize, as if he did not yet possess it.

2:7 *made himself nothing.* Or "emptied himself." He did this, not by giving up deity, but by laying aside his glory (see Jn 17:5) and submitting to the humiliation of becoming a man (see 2Co 8:9 and note). Jesus is truly God and truly man. Another view is that he emptied himself, not of deity itself, but of its prerogatives—the high position and glory of deity. *nature of a servant.* Emphasizes the full reality of his servant identity (see Mk 10:45 and note). As a servant, he was always submissive to the will of the Father (see Lk 22:42; Jn 4:34 and note).

2:8 *appearance as a man.* Not only was Jesus "like" a human being (v. 7), but he also took on the actual outward characteristics of a man (see Jn 1:14; Ro 8:3; Heb 2:17 and notes). *humbled himself.* See v. 7; 2Co 8:9. *obedient.* How Jesus humbled himself (cf. Heb 5:7–8). A "servant" (v. 7) obeys. *to death.* Stresses both the totality and the climax of Jesus' obedience. *on a cross.* Heightens Jesus' humiliation; he died as someone cursed (see Gal 3:13; Heb 12:2). Crucifixion was the most degrading form of execution that could be inflicted on a person.

2:9 *exalted.* See Mt 28:18; Ac 2:33; cf. Isa 52:13. *the name ... above every name.* Reference is doubtless to the office or rank conferred on Jesus—his glorious position ("Lord," v. 11), not his proper name (cf. Eph 1:21; Heb 1:4–5 and notes).

2:10–11 *bow ... acknowledge.* See Isa 45:23 and note. God's design is that all people everywhere should worship and serve Jesus as Lord. Ultimately all will acknowledge him as Lord (see Ro 14:9), whether willingly or not.

2:10 *at the name of Jesus.* In honor of his exalted position as "Lord" (v. 11; see v. 9 and note).

Do Everything Without Grumbling

12 Therefore, my dear friends, as you
have always obeyed—not only in my
presence, but now much more in my absence—continue to work out your salvation with fear and trembling,[o] 13 for it is
God who works in you[p] to will and to act
in order to fulfill his good purpose.[q]
14 Do everything without grumbling[r] or
arguing, 15 so that you may become blameless[s] and pure, "children of God[t] without
fault in a warped and crooked generation."[a][u] Then you will shine among them
like stars in the sky 16 as you hold firmly
to the word of life. And then I will be able
to boast on the day of Christ[v] that I did
not run[w] or labor in vain.[x] 17 But even if I
am being poured out like a drink offering[y]
on the sacrifice[z] and service coming from
your faith, I am glad and rejoice with all
of you.[a] 18 So you too should be glad and
rejoice with me.

Timothy and Epaphroditus

19 I hope in the Lord Jesus to send Timothy[b] to you soon,[c] that I also may be
cheered when I receive news about you.
20 I have no one else like him,[d] who will
show genuine concern for your welfare.
21 For everyone looks out for their own interests,[e] not those of Jesus Christ. 22 But
you know that Timothy has proved himself, because as a son with his father[f] he
has served with me in the work of the
gospel. 23 I hope, therefore, to send him
as soon as I see how things go with me.[g]
24 And I am confident[h] in the Lord that I
myself will come soon.
25 But I think it is necessary to send
back to you Epaphroditus, my brother,
co-worker[i] and fellow soldier,[j] who is also
your messenger, whom you sent to take
care of my needs.[k] 26 For he longs for all of
you[l] and is distressed because you heard
he was ill. 27 Indeed he was ill, and almost
died. But God had mercy on him, and not
on him only but also on me, to spare me
sorrow upon sorrow. 28 Therefore I am all
the more eager to send him,[m] so that when
you see him again you may be glad and I
may have less anxiety. 29 So then, welcome
him in the Lord with great joy, and honor
people like him,[n] 30 because he almost died
for the work of Christ. He risked his life to
make up for the help you yourselves could
not give me.[o]

[a] *15* Deut. 32:5

2:12 [o] S 2Co 7:15 **2:13** [p] Ezr 1:5; 1Co 12:6; 15:10; Gal 2:8; Heb 13:21 [q] Eph 1:5 **2:14** [r] 1Co 10:10; 1Pe 4:9 **2:15** [s] S 1Th 3:13 [t] Mt 5:45, 48; Eph 5:1 [u] Ac 2:40 **2:16** [v] S 1Co 1:8 [w] S 1Co 9:24 [x] 1Th 2:19 **2:17** [y] 2Co 12:15; 2Ti 4:6 [z] Ro 15:16 [a] S 2Co 6:10 **2:19** [b] S Ac 16:1 [c] ver 23 **2:20** [d] 1Co 16:10 **2:21** [e] S 1Co 10:24 **2:22** [f] 1Co 4:17; 1Ti 1:2 **2:23** [g] ver 19 **2:24** [h] Php 1:25 **2:25** [i] Ro 16:3, 9,21; 2Co 8:23; Php 4:3; Col 4:11; Phm 1 [j] Phm 2 [k] Php 4:18 **2:26** [l] Php 1:8 **2:28** [m] ver 25 **2:29** [n] 1Co 16:18; 1Ti 5:17 **2:30** [o] 1Co 16:17

2:12 *Therefore.* Because of Christ's incomparable example (vv. 5–11). *obeyed.* The commands of God as passed on to the Philippians by Paul (see Ro 1:5; 15:18; 2Co 10:5–6). *my presence.* During the course of Paul's second (see Ac 16:12–40) and third (see Ac 20:1–3,6) missionary journeys. *work out your salvation.* Work it out to the finish; not a reference to the attempt to earn one's salvation by works, but a reference to the expression of one's salvation in spiritual growth and development. Salvation is not merely a gift received once for all; it expresses itself in an ongoing process in which the believer is strenuously involved (cf. Mt 24:13; 1Co 9:24–27; Heb 3:14; 6:9–11; 2Pe 1:5–8)—the process of perseverance, humble service, spiritual growth and maturation. *fear and trembling.* Not because of doubt or anxiety; rather, the reference is to an active reverence and a singleness of purpose in response to God's grace.

2:13 *God … works in you.* See Col 1:29 and note. *to will and to act.* Intention, or faith, and our obedience cannot be separated (cf. Gal 5:6 and note; Jas 2:18,20,22).

2:14–17 Some things involved in working out our salvation.

2:14 *grumbling.* Being discontented with God's will is an expression of unbelief that prevents one from doing what pleases God (v. 13; cf. 1Co 10:10 and note). *arguing.* Over debatable points that do not need to be settled for the good of the church (see 2Ti 2:23; Titus 3:9).

2:15 *blameless and pure … without fault.* Not absolute, sinless perfection, but wholehearted, unmixed devotion to doing God's will (see 1:10 and note). *warped and crooked generation.* A description of the unbelieving world (see Ac 2:40; Eph 2:1–3; cf. Mt 17:17). *shine among them like stars.* The contrast, like light in darkness, that Christians are to be to the world around them (cf. Mt 5:15–16).

2:16 *boast.* Not out of pride or a sense of self-accomplishment, but because of what God has done through Paul (see 1Th 2:19). *day of Christ.* See note on 1:6. *in vain.* Cf. 1Co 9:24–27 and notes.

2:17–18 *I … rejoice … you too should … rejoice.* Christian joy ought always to be mutual.

2:17 *I am being poured out.* The reference may be to his entire ministry as one large thanksgiving sacrifice. However, it is more probable that Paul refers to his present imprisonment, which may end in a martyr's death. His life would then be poured out as a drink offering accompanying the sacrificial service of the Philippians. *like a drink offering.* The OT background is the daily sacrifices in Ex 29:38–41. *coming from your faith.* Genuine faith is active and working (see note on v. 13).

2:19–23 Paul plans to send Timothy, who is with him in Rome (see 1:1 and note), to discover and report on conditions in the Philippian church.

2:20 *I have no one else like him.* Timothy was a good example of the kind of person envisioned in the exhortation of v. 4.

2:21 A sharp contrast between Timothy and Paul's other associates—an outstanding commendation for one so young (see 1Ti 4:12 and note).

2:22 *as a son with his father.* This relationship between Timothy and Paul is developed at length in 1,2 Timothy. *served.* Like Jesus and Paul, Timothy had a servant attitude.

2:24 Paul anticipates his release in the near future (see 1:25).

2:25–30 Epaphroditus, after a close brush with death (vv. 27,30), is being sent home to Philippi.

2:25 *messenger.* A broader use of the Greek word often translated "apostle," applied here to Epaphroditus as a representative of the Philippian church (cf. 2Co 8:23).

2:27 Cf. 1:21–26.

2:28 *anxiety.* The legitimate cares and concerns that come with the Christian life and the gospel ministry (see note on 4:6; cf. 2Co 4:8; 11:28).

2:29 *in the Lord.* As a fellow believer (see Ro 16:2).

No Confidence in the Flesh

3 Further, my brothers and sisters, rejoice in the Lord! It is no trouble for
me to write the same things to you again,[p]
and it is a safeguard for you. 2 Watch out
for those dogs,[q] those evildoers, those
mutilators of the flesh. 3 For it is we who
are the circumcision,[r] we who serve God
by his Spirit, who boast in Christ Jesus,[s]
and who put no confidence in the flesh—
4 though I myself have reasons for such
confidence.[t]
If someone else thinks they have reasons to put confidence in the flesh, I have
more: 5 circumcised[u] on the eighth day, of
the people of Israel,[v] of the tribe of Benjamin,[w] a Hebrew of Hebrews; in regard
to the law, a Pharisee;[x] 6 as for zeal,[y] persecuting the church;[z] as for righteousness
based on the law,[a] faultless.
7 But whatever were gains to me I now
consider loss[b] for the sake of Christ. 8 What
is more, I consider everything a loss because of the surpassing worth of knowing[c] Christ Jesus my Lord, for whose sake
I have lost all things. I consider them
garbage, that I may gain Christ[d] 9 and be
found in him, not having a righteousness
of my own that comes from the law,[e] but
that which is through faith in[a] Christ—the
righteousness[f] that comes from God on the
basis of faith.[g] 10 I want to know[h] Christ—
yes, to know the power of his resurrection
and participation in his sufferings,[i] becoming like him in his death,[j] 11 and so, somehow, attaining to the resurrection[k] from
the dead.
12 Not that I have already obtained all
this, or have already arrived at my goal,[l]
but I press on to take hold[m] of that for
which Christ Jesus took hold of me.[n]
13 Brothers and sisters, I do not consider
myself yet to have taken hold of it. But one
thing I do: Forgetting what is behind[o] and

[a] 9 Or *through the faithfulness of*

3:1 [p] Php 2:18
3:2 [q] Ps 22:16, 20; Rev 22:15
3:3 [r] Ro 2:28, 29; Gal 6:15; Col 2:11 [s] Ro 15:17; Gal 6:14
3:4 [t] 2Co 11:21
3:5 [u] S Lk 1:59 [v] 2Co 11:22 [w] Ro 11:1 [x] Ac 23:6
3:6 [y] S Ac 21:20 [z] S Ac 8:3 [a] ver 9; Ro 10:5
3:7 [b] Mt 13:44; Lk 14:33
3:8 [c] ver 10; Jer 9:23, 24; Jn 17:3; Eph 4:13; S 2Pe 1:2 [d] Ps 73:25
3:9 [e] ver 6; Ro 10:5 [f] Jer 33:16 [g] S Ro 9:30
3:10 [h] S ver 8 [i] S 2Co 1:5 [j] S Ro 6:3-5
3:11 [k] S Jn 11:24; S Ro 6:5; Rev 20:5,6
3:12 [l] 1Co 13:10 [m] 1Ti 6:12 [n] Ac 9:5,6
3:13 [o] Lk 9:62

3:1 *rejoice in the Lord!* See 4:4 and note. *same things ... again.* Matters taken up in the verses that follow, which Paul had previously dealt with either orally when he was in Philippi or perhaps in an earlier letter. *safeguard.* Where serious error is present, there is safety in repetition.

3:2 *dogs.* A harsh word for Paul's opponents, showing their aggressive opposition to the gospel, the seriousness of their error and its destructive, "devouring" results (cf. Gal 5:15). Their teaching was probably similar to what Paul had to oppose in the Galatian churches (see Introduction to Galatians: Occasion and Purpose). *mutilators.* Again a strong, painfully vivid term; the false teachers have so distorted the meaning of circumcision (cf. v. 3) that it has become nothing more than a useless cutting of the body.

3:3 *circumcision.* Its true, inner meaning is realized only in believers, who worship God with genuine spiritual worship and who glory in Christ as their Savior rather than trusting in their own human effort (cf. Ro 2:28–29 and note on 2:29; Col 2:11–13; see also Dt 30:6; Eze 36:26). *boast ... no confidence.* Everyone is a "boaster," either in Christ or in themselves. *flesh.* Weak human nature (see Gal 3:3 and note).

3:4–14 Paul's personal testimony, a model for every believer; one of the most significant autobiographical sections in his letters (see note on Ro 1:1; cf. Ac 22:1–21; 26:1–23).

3:4–6 Paul's pre-Christian confidence, rooted in his Jewish heritage, privileges and attainments.

3:5 *eighth day.* See Ge 17:12 and note. *of the people of Israel.* Paul was born a Jew and was not a convert to Judaism. *tribe of Benjamin.* Paul's Jewish roots were deep and indisputable. Jerusalem, the Holy City, lay on the border of the tribal territory of Benjamin. *Hebrew of Hebrews.* In language, attitudes and lifestyle (see Ac 22:2–3; Gal 1:14). *Pharisee.* See note on Mt 3:7.

3:6 *righteousness based on the law.* Righteousness produced by using the law as an attempt to merit God's approval and blessing (cf. v. 9)—a use of the law strongly opposed by Paul as contrary to the gospel itself (see Ro 3:27–28; 4:1–5; Gal 2:16 and note; 3:10–12 and note on 3:10). *faultless.* In terms of legalistic standards of scrupulous external conformity to the letter of the law.

3:7–14 Paul's confidence in Christ.

3:7 *whatever.* The things mentioned in vv. 5–6. *gains ... loss.* The great reversal in Paul—begun on the road to Damascus (see Ac 9:3–16)—from being self-centered to being centered in Christ.

3:8 *knowing Christ Jesus.* Not only a knowledge of facts but a knowledge gained through experience that, in its surpassing greatness, transforms the entire person (see 2Co 5:17 and note). The following verses spell this out. *garbage.* What Paul now has as a Christian is not merely preferable or a better alternative; in contrast, his former way of life was worthless and despicable (cf. Eph 2:3–7).

3:9 *be found in him.* Union with Christ (see note on 2:1; cf. 1Co 1:30)—not simply an experience in the past but a present, continuing relationship. *righteousness ... from the law.* See note on v. 6. *righteousness ... through faith.* A principal benefit of union with Christ (see Ro 3:21–22; 1Co 1:30; Gal 2:16 and note).

3:10 *know Christ.* See 1:20–21 and notes. As in v. 8, this knowledge is not merely factual; it includes the experience of "the power of his resurrection" (see Eph 1:17–20), of "participation in his sufferings" (cf. Ac 9:16) and of being "like him in his death" (see 2Co 4:7–12; 12:9–10). Believers already share positionally in Christ's death and resurrection (cf. Ro 6:2–13; Gal 2:20; 5:24; 6:14; Eph 2:6; Col 2:12–13; 3:1). In v. 10, however, Paul speaks of the actual experience of Christ's resurrection power and of suffering with and for him, even to the point of death.

3:11 *somehow.* Not an indication of doubt or uncertainty, but an indication of humility because Paul does not want to be guilty of presumption. *resurrection.* The great personal anticipation of every believer (see Da 12:2; Jn 5:29; Ac 24:15; 1Co 15:23; 1Th 4:16).

3:12–14 The Christian life is like a race; elsewhere Paul uses athletic imagery in a similar way (1Co 9:24–27; 1Ti 6:12; 2Ti 4:7–8; cf. Mt 24:13; Heb 12:1).

3:12 *take hold ... took hold of me.* Paul's goal is Christ's goal for him, and Christ supplies the resources for him to "press on toward the goal" (v. 14; cf. 2:12–13).

3:13 *Forgetting.* Not losing all memory of his sinful past (see vv. 4–6) but leaving it behind him as done with and settled.

straining toward what is ahead, 14 I press
on[p] toward the goal to win the prize[q] for
which God has called[r] me heavenward in
Christ Jesus.

Following Paul's Example

15 All of us, then, who are mature[s] should
take such a view of things.[t] And if on some
point you think differently, that too God
will make clear to you.[u] 16 Only let us live
up to what we have already attained.

17 Join together in following my example,[v] brothers and sisters, and just as you
have us as a model, keep your eyes on
those who live as we do.[w] 18 For, as I have
often told you before and now tell you
again even with tears,[x] many live as enemies of the cross of Christ.[y] 19 Their destiny[z] is destruction, their god is their stomach,[a] and their glory is in their shame.[b]
Their mind is set on earthly things.[c] 20 But
our citizenship[d] is in heaven.[e] And we eagerly await a Savior from there, the Lord
Jesus Christ,[f] 21 who, by the power[g] that
enables him to bring everything under his
control, will transform our lowly bodies[h]
so that they will be like his glorious body.[i]

Closing Appeal for Steadfastness and Unity

4 Therefore, my brothers and sisters,
you whom I love and long for,[j] my joy
and crown, stand firm[k] in the Lord in this
way, dear friends!

2 I plead with Euodia and I plead with
Syntyche to be of the same mind[l] in the
Lord. 3 Yes, and I ask you, my true companion, help these women since they have
contended at my side in the cause of the
gospel, along with Clement and the rest of
my co-workers,[m] whose names are in the
book of life.[n]

Final Exhortations

4 Rejoice in the Lord always. I will say
it again: Rejoice![o] 5 Let your gentleness be

3:14 [p] Heb 6:1 [q] 1Co 9:24 [r] S Ro 8:28 **3:15** [s] S 1Co 2:6 [t] Gal 5:10 [u] Eph 1:17; 1Th 4:9 **3:17** [v] S 1Co 4:16 [w] S 1Ti 4:12 **3:18** [x] Ac 20:31 [y] Gal 6:12 **3:19** [z] Ps 73:17 [a] Ro 16:18 [b] Ro 6:21; Jude 13 [c] Ro 8:5,6; Col 3:2 **3:20** [d] Eph 2:19 [e] Col 3:1; Heb 12:22 [f] S 1Co 1:7 **3:21** [g] Eph 1:19 [h] 1Co 15:43-53 [i] Ro 8:29; Col 3:4 **4:1** [j] Php 1:8 [k] S 1Co 16:13 **4:2** [l] Php 2:2 **4:3** [m] S Php 2:25 [n] S Rev 20:12 **4:4** [o] Ps 85:6; 97:12; Hab 3:18; S Mt 5:12; Ro 12:12; Php 3:1

3:14 *prize.* The winner of the Greek races received a wreath of leaves and sometimes a cash award (see 1Co 9:24 and note); the Christian receives an award of everlasting glory. *heavenward.* Paul's ultimate aspirations are found not in this life but in heaven, because Christ is there (see Col 3:1–2).

3:15 *mature.* Those who have made reasonable progress in spiritual growth and stability (see 1Co 2:6 and note; 3:1–3; Heb 5:14 and note). *such a view.* That expressed in vv. 12–14: There are heights yet to be scaled; do not become complacent. *think differently.* If the readers accept the view set forth in vv. 12–14 and yet fail to agree in some lesser point, God will clarify the matter for them.

3:16 *live up to what … already attained.* Put into practice the truth they have already comprehended. We are responsible for the truth we currently possess.

3:17 *following my example.* As Paul follows the example of Christ (see 1Co 11:1 and note). *keep your eyes on those who live.* The lifestyles Christians lead ought to be models worth following.

3:18 *told you before.* See v. 1. *with tears.* Cf. Ac 20:19,31. *live as enemies of the cross.* In glaring contrast to Paul's conduct (v. 10) and to the truth of the gospel.

3:19 *destruction.* The opposite of salvation. *god … stomach.* A deep self-centeredness; their appetites and desires come first (see Ro 16:18). *earthly things.* They have set their minds on the things of this life (see Col 3:1–2 and note on 3:1); they are antinomians (libertines), the opposite of the legalists of v. 2.

3:20 *citizenship.* Philippi was a Roman colony (see Introduction: Recipients), and its people were proud of their Roman citizenship. But Paul points to a higher citizenship. In this world Christians are strangers and foreigners, fully involved in it but not of it (cf. Jn 17:14–15 and notes; 1Co 7:29–31 and note on 7:29; 1Pe 2:11 and note). *in heaven.* Where Christ is (see Gal 4:26 and note); contrast the "earthly things" of v. 19 (cf. Eph 2:6; Col 3:1–4). *eagerly await … from there.* See Ro 8:19; 1Co 1:7; 1Th 1:9–10; 2Ti 4:8.

3:21 *power … under his control.* Christ's present power, earned by his obedience to death (see 2:8) and received in his resurrection and ascension, is universal and absolute (see Mt 28:18; 1Co 15:27; Eph 1:20–22). *will transform.* By the Holy Spirit at the resurrection (see Ro 8:11 and note). *our lowly bodies.* Subject to weakness, decay and death, due to sin (see Ro 8:10,20–23; 1Co 15:42–44 and note). *like his glorious body.* See Ro 8:29; 1Jn 3:2. The resurrection body, received already by Christ, who is the "firstfruits," will be received by believers in the future resurrection "harvest" (see 1Co 15:20,49). It is "spiritual," i.e., transformed by the power of the Holy Spirit (see 1Co 15:44,46).

4:1 *love and long for.* See notes on 1:8; 2:1. *my joy and crown.* True not only now, but especially when Christ returns (see 1Th 2:19 and note). *stand firm.* In the midst of present struggles for the sake of the gospel (cf. 1:27–30; 1Co 15:58). *in this way.* Refers to the closing statements of ch. 3. In the face of libertine practices (3:18–19), the Philippians should follow Paul's example (3:17), having their minds set on heavenly things (3:20–21).

4:2–3 The disagreement between Euodia and Syntyche is serious enough to be mentioned in a letter to be read publicly, but Paul seems confident that "these women" (v. 3) will be reconciled. His handling of the situation is a model of tact—he does not take sides but encourages others closer to the situation to promote reconciliation (see 2:2 and note).

4:3 *at my side … my co-workers.* Those associated with the apostle in the cause of the gospel (women as well as men) are his equals, not subordinates (cf. 2:25; Ro 16:3,9,21; Phm 24). *Clement.* Not mentioned elsewhere in the NT. *the rest of my co-workers.* Not mentioned individually because they are known to God and their names are entered in the book of life, the heavenly register of the elect (see note on Rev 3:5).

4:4 *Rejoice in the Lord.* See 3:1. *always.* Under all kinds of circumstances, including suffering (see Hab 3:17–18 and note; Jas 1:2; 1Pe 4:13).

4:5 *gentleness.* Christlike consideration for others (cf. 2Co 10:1). This quality is especially essential in church leaders (see 1Ti 3:3; Titus 3:2, "considerate"). *near.* See Ro 13:11 and note; cf. Jas 5:8–9 and note on 5:9; Rev 22:7,12,20. The next great event in God's prophetic schedule is Christ's return. The whole period from Christ's first coming to the consummation of the kingdom is viewed in the NT as the last time (see 1Jn 2:18 and note). From God's vantage point, a thousand years are as a day (see 2Pe 3:8 and note). Thus there is a sense in which, for every generation, the Lord's coming is near.

evident to all. The Lord is near.[p] 6 Do not be anxious about anything,[q] but in every situation, by prayer and petition, with thanksgiving, present your requests to God.[r] 7 And the peace of God,[s] which transcends all understanding,[t] will guard your hearts and your minds in Christ Jesus.

8 Finally, brothers and sisters, whatever is true, whatever is noble, whatever is right, whatever is pure, whatever is lovely, whatever is admirable—if anything is excellent or praiseworthy—think about such things. 9 Whatever you have learned or received or heard from me, or seen in me—put it into practice.[u] And the God of peace[v] will be with you.

Thanks for Their Gifts

10 I rejoiced greatly in the Lord that at last you renewed your concern for me.[w] Indeed, you were concerned, but you had no opportunity to show it. 11 I am not saying this because I am in need, for I have learned to be content[x] whatever the circumstances. 12 I know what it is to be in need, and I know what it is to have plenty. I have learned the secret of being content in any and every situation, whether well fed or hungry,[y] whether living in plenty or in want.[z] 13 I can do all this through him who gives me strength.[a]

14 Yet it was good of you to share[b] in my troubles. 15 Moreover, as you Philippians know, in the early days[c] of your acquaintance with the gospel, when I set out from Macedonia,[d] not one church shared with me in the matter of giving and receiving, except you only;[e] 16 for even when I was in Thessalonica,[f] you sent me aid more than once when I was in need.[g] 17 Not that I desire your gifts; what I desire is that more be credited to your account.[h] 18 I have received full payment and have more than enough. I am amply supplied, now that I have received from Epaphroditus[i] the gifts you sent. They are a fragrant[j] offering, an acceptable sacrifice, pleasing to God. 19 And my God will meet all your needs[k] according to the riches of his glory[l] in Christ Jesus.

4:5 [p] Ps 119:151; 145:18; Heb 10:37; Jas 5:8,9 **4:6** [q] Mt 6:25-34 [r] Eph 6:18; 1Ti 2:1 **4:7** [s] Isa 26:3; S Jn 14:27 [t] Eph 3:19 **4:9** [u] S 1Co 4:16 [v] S Ro 15:33 **4:10** [w] 2Co 11:9 **4:11** [x] 1Ti 6:6,8; Heb 13:5 **4:12** [y] S 1Co 4:11 [z] 2Co 11:9 **4:13** [a] 2Co 12:9; Eph 3:16; Col 1:11; 1Ti 1:12; 2Ti 4:17 **4:14** [b] Php 1:7 **4:15** [c] Php 1:5 [d] S Ac 16:9 [e] 2Co 11:8,9 **4:16** [f] S Ac 17:1 [g] 1Th 2:9 **4:17** [h] 1Co 9:11,12 **4:18** [i] Php 2:25 [j] S 2Co 2:14 **4:19** [k] Ps 23:1; 2Co 9:8 [l] S Ro 2:4

4:6 *anxious.* Self-centered, counterproductive worry, not legitimate cares and concerns for the spread of the gospel (see 2:28 and note; 2Co 11:28; see also Mt 6:25–31; 1Pe 5:7). *in every situation, by prayer.* Anxiety and prayer are two great opposing forces in Christian experience. *thanksgiving.* The antidote to worry (along with prayer and petition).

4:7 *peace of God.* Not merely a psychological state of mind, but an inner tranquillity based on peace with God—the peaceful state of those whose sins are forgiven (cf. Jn 14:27; Ro 5:1 and note). The opposite of anxiety, it is the tranquillity that comes when believers commit all their cares to God in prayer and worry about them no more. *transcends all understanding.* The full dimensions of God's love and care are beyond human comprehension (see Eph 3:18–20). *guard ... hearts ... minds.* A military concept depicting a sentry standing guard. God's "protective custody" of those who are in Christ Jesus extends to the core of their beings and to their deepest intentions (cf. 1Pe 1:5 and note).

4:8 *true ... praiseworthy.* Paul understood the influence of one's thoughts on one's life. What people allow to occupy their minds will sooner or later determine their speech and action. Paul's exhortation to "think about such things" is followed by a second exhortation, "put it into practice" (v. 9). The combination of virtues listed in vv. 8–9 is sure to produce a wholesome thought pattern, which in turn will result in a life of moral and spiritual excellence (see note on Gal 5:22–23).

4:9 *seen in me.* See note on 3:17. *God of peace.* See note on 1Th 5:23; cf. the "peace of God" (v. 7).

4:10 *at last ... no opportunity.* The delay in sending gifts to Paul was not the fault of the Philippians, nor was it because they were lacking in concern for him (cf. 2Co 11:9). Perhaps Paul's uncertain itinerary prior to his arrival at Rome or the lack of an available messenger had prevented the Philippians from showing their concern.

4:11 *content whatever the circumstances.* Paul genuinely appreciates the gifts from Philippi (see vv. 14,18), but he is not ultimately dependent on them (cf. 1Ti 6:6–8).

4:12 *content ... whether well fed ... whether living in plenty.* Prosperity, too, can be a source of discontent.

4:13 *all this.* All those circumstances that Paul has just spoken of in vv. 11–12. *him who gives me strength.* Christ. Union with the living, exalted Christ is the secret of being content (v. 12) and the source of Paul's abiding strength (see especially 2Co 12:9–10; see also Jn 15:5; Eph 3:16–17; Col 1:11).

4:14 *share.* The Philippians' gifts are a means of involving them in Paul's troubles (cf. Heb 10:33).

4:15 *early days.* During Paul's second missionary journey, when he first preached in Philippi (see Ac 16:12–40). *set out.* For the south (Achaia), where Athens and Corinth were located (see Ac 17:14–16; 18:1–4). *Macedonia.* The northern part of modern-day Greece, where Berea and Thessalonica, as well as Philippi, were located (see map, p. 1858). *shared with me in the matter of.* Or "participated with me in an account of." Paul uses commercial language to describe "giving and receiving" (credit and debit) between the Philippians and himself (see "credited to your account," v. 17). Yet this commercial imagery is plainly transcended by the mutual concern and self-sacrifice of their relationship. *except you only.* The generosity of the Philippian church is unique and unmatched (cf. 2Co 8:1–5).

4:16 *when I was in Thessalonica.* While he was still in Macedonia (see Ac 17:1–9). *aid more than once.* The gifts sent to Rome through Epaphroditus are the latest in a long and consistent pattern of generosity (cf. 2Co 8:1–5).

4:17 *credited to your account.* See note on v. 15. The "investment value" of the Philippians' gift is not primarily what Paul received but the "spiritual dividends" they received.

4:18 *a fragrant offering, an acceptable sacrifice.* The OT background is the sacrifice, not of atonement for sin, but of thanksgiving and praise (cf. Lev 7:12–15; Ro 12:1; Eph 5:2 and note; Heb 13:15–16 and note on 13:15). *acceptable ... pleasing to God.* Because of Christ's work for us (see 1Pe 2:5) and God's work in us (see Php 2:13).

4:19 *my.* A personal touch (cf. "my God" in 1:3). *will meet.* A promise given to a church that had sacrificially given to meet Paul's need. *your needs.* Paul is concerned not only about his own situation but also about that of the Philippians. *the riches of his glory in Christ Jesus.* The

20 To our God and Father[m] be glory for
ever and ever. Amen.[n]

Final Greetings

21 Greet all God's people in Christ Jesus.
The brothers and sisters who are with me[o]
send greetings. 22 All God's people[p] here
send you greetings, especially those who
belong to Caesar's household.
23 The grace of the Lord Jesus Christ[q] be
with your spirit.[r] Amen.[a]

4:20 [m]Gal 1:4; 1Th 1:3; 3:11, 13 [n]S Ro 11:36
4:21 [o]Gal 1:2
4:22 [p]S Ac 9:13
4:23 [q]S Ro 16:20 [r]S Gal 6:18

[a] *23* Some manuscripts do not have *Amen.*

true measure of God's blessings to the church (cf. Eph 1:18; 3:16–20).
4:20 Paul cannot hold back a doxology, especially as he considers the truth of v. 19.
4:21–22 Final greetings are a typical feature of Paul's letters (see, e.g., Ro 16:3–16,21–23; 1Co 16:19–20; 2Co 13:12–13; Col 4:10–12,14–15,18).
4:21 *God's people.* See note on Ro 1:7. *brothers and sisters who are with me.* Paul's fellow workers at Rome, especially Timothy (see 1:1,14,16).
4:22 *Caesar's household.* Not blood relatives of the emperor but those employed (slaves or freedmen) in or around the palace area (cf. "palace guard," 1:13).
4:23 A typical closing benediction of Paul. *grace.* See note on Ro 1:7. *be with your spirit.* See note on Gal 6:18.

COLOSSIANS

INTRODUCTION

Author, Date and Place of Writing

That Colossians is a genuine letter of Paul (1:1) is usually not disputed. In the early church, all who speak on the subject of authorship ascribe it to Paul. In the nineteenth century, however, some thought that the heresy refuted in ch. 2 was second-century Gnosticism. But a careful analysis of ch. 2 shows that the heresy referred to there is noticeably less developed than the Gnosticism of leading Gnostic teachers of the second and third centuries. Also, the seeds of what later became the full-blown Gnosticism of the second century were present in the first century and already making inroads into the churches. Consequently, it is not necessary to date Colossians in the second century at a time too late for Paul to have written the letter.

Instead, it is to be dated during Paul's first imprisonment in Rome, where he spent at least two years under house arrest (see Ac 28:16 – 31). Some have argued that Paul wrote Colossians from Ephesus or Caesarea, but most of the evidence favors Rome as the place where he penned all the Prison Letters (Ephesians, Colossians, Philippians and Philemon). Colossians should be dated c. AD 60, in the same year as Ephesians and Philemon (see chart, p. 1845).

Colossae: The Town and the Church

Several hundred years before Paul's day, Colossae had been a leading city in Asia Minor (present-day Turkey). It was located on the Lycus River and on the great east-west trade route leading from Ephesus on the Aegean Sea to the Euphrates River (see map, p. 1864). By the first century AD Colossae was diminished to a second-rate market town, which had been surpassed long before in power and importance by the neighboring towns of Laodicea and Hierapolis (see 4:13).

What gave Colossae NT importance, however, was the fact that during Paul's three-year ministry in Ephesus, Epaphras had been converted and had carried the gospel to Colossae (cf. 1:7 – 8; Ac 19:10). The young church that resulted then became the target

Author:
The apostle Paul

Audience:
The believers at Colossae, a church perhaps planted by Paul's coworker, Epaphras

Date:
About AD 60

Theme:
Paul writes to demonstrate that Christ is supreme over every human philosophy and accomplishment.

of heretical attack, which led to Epaphras's visit to Paul in Rome and ultimately to the penning of the Colossian letter.

Perhaps as a result of the efforts of Epaphras or other converts of Paul, Christian churches had also been established in Laodicea and Hierapolis. Some of them were house churches (see 4:15; Phm 2). Most likely all of them were primarily Gentile.

The Colossian Heresy

In his Colossian letter, Paul never explicitly describes the false teaching he opposes. The nature of the heresy (or heresies) must be inferred from statements he made in opposition to the false teachers. An analysis of his refutation suggests that their teachings were diverse in nature. Some of the elements were:

(1) *Ceremonialism.* It held to strict rules about the kinds of food and drink that were permissible, about religious festivals (2:16 – 17) and about circumcision (2:11; 3:11).

(2) *Asceticism.* "Do not handle! Do not taste! Do not touch!" (2:21; cf. 2:23).

(3) *Worship of (or with) angels.* See 2:18 and note.

Unexcavated tell at Colossae. A tell is a mound of ancient ruins including several layers built over each other through time.

To refute the Colossian heresy, Paul exalts Christ as the very image of God, the Creator, the head of the church, the first to be resurrected, the fullness of deity in bodily form, and the one who reconciles all things to God.

(4) *Devaluing the person and work of Christ.* This is implied in Paul's emphasis on the supremacy of Christ (1:15 – 20; 2:2 – 3,9).

(5) *Secret knowledge.* The later Gnostics boasted of this (see 2:18 and Paul's emphasis in 2:2 – 3 on Christ, "in whom are hidden all the treasures of wisdom").

(6) *Reliance on human wisdom and tradition.* See 2:4,8.

These elements seem to fall into two categories, Jewish and proto-Gnostic. It is likely, therefore, that the false teaching at Colossae was a mixture of an extreme form of Judaism and an early stage of Gnosticism (see Introduction to 1 John: Gnosticism; see also note on 2:23).

Purpose and Theme

Paul's purpose is to refute the Colossian heresy. To accomplish this goal, he exalts Christ as the very image of God (1:15), the Creator (1:16), the preexistent sustainer of all things (1:17), the head of the church (1:18), the first to be resurrected (1:18), the fullness of deity in bodily form (1:19; 2:9) and the one who reconciles all things to God (1:20 – 22). Thus Christ is completely adequate: "In Christ you have been brought to fullness" (2:10). At the same time, Paul exposes the false teachers' view of Christ as altogether deficient. It was a hollow and deceptive philosophy (2:8), lacking any ability to restrain the flesh (2:23).

The theme of Colossians is the complete adequacy of Christ, as contrasted with the emptiness of mere human philosophy.

Outline

- I. Introduction (1:1 – 14)
  - A. Greetings (1:1 – 2)
  - B. Thanksgiving (1:3 – 8)
  - C. Prayer (1:9 – 14)
- II. The Supremacy of Christ (1:15 – 23)
- III. Paul's Labor for the Church (1:24 — 2:7)
  - A. His Ministry for the Sake of the Church (1:24 – 29)
  - B. His Concern for the Spiritual Welfare of His Readers (2:1 – 7)
- IV. Freedom from Human Regulations through Life with Christ (2:8 – 23)
  - A. Warning to Guard against the False Teachers (2:8 – 15)
  - B. Pleas to Reject the False Teachers (2:16 – 19)
  - C. An Analysis of the Heresy (2:20 – 23)
- V. Rules for Holy Living (3:1 — 4:6)
  - A. The Old Self and the New Self (3:1 – 17)
  - B. Rules for Christian Households (3:18 — 4:1)
  - C. Further Instructions (4:2 – 6)
- VI. Final Greetings and Benediction (4:7 – 18)

1 Paul, an apostle[a] of Christ Jesus by the
will of God,[b] and Timothy[c] our brother,

2 To God's holy people in Colossae, the
faithful brothers and sisters[a] in Christ:

Grace[d] and peace to you from God our
Father.[b e]

Thanksgiving and Prayer

3 We always thank God,[f] the Father of
our Lord Jesus Christ, when we pray for
you, 4 because we have heard of your faith
in Christ Jesus and of the love[g] you have
for all God's people[h]— 5 the faith and love
that spring from the hope[i] stored up for
you in heaven[j] and about which you have
already heard in the true message[k] of the
gospel 6 that has come to you. In the same
way, the gospel is bearing fruit[l] and growing throughout the whole world[m]—just as
it has been doing among you since the
day you heard it and truly understood
God's grace. 7 You learned it from Epaphras,[n] our dear fellow servant,[c] who is a
faithful minister[o] of Christ on our[d] behalf,
8 and who also told us of your love in the
Spirit.[p]

9 For this reason, since the day we heard
about you,[q] we have not stopped praying for you.[r] We continually ask God to
fill you with the knowledge of his will[s]
through all the wisdom and understanding that the Spirit gives,[e t] 10 so that you
may live a life worthy[u] of the Lord and
please him[v] in every way: bearing fruit in
every good work, growing in the knowledge of God,[w] 11 being strengthened with
all power[x] according to his glorious might
so that you may have great endurance
and patience,[y] 12 and giving joyful thanks
to the Father,[z] who has qualified you[f] to
share in the inheritance[a] of his holy people in the kingdom of light.[b] 13 For he has
rescued us from the dominion of darkness[c] and brought us into the kingdom[d]
of the Son he loves,[e] 14 in whom we have
redemption,[f] the forgiveness of sins.[g]

1:1 [a] S 1Co 1:1 [b] S 2Co 1:1 [c] S Ac 16:1 **1:2** [d] Col 4:18 [e] S Ro 1:7 **1:3** [f] S Ro 1:8 **1:4** [g] Gal 5:6 [h] S Ac 9:13; Eph 1:15; Phm 5 **1:5** [i] ver 23; 1Th 5:8; Titus 1:2 [j] 1Pe 1:4 [k] S 2Ti 2:15 **1:6** [l] Jn 15:16 [m] ver 23; S Ro 10:18 **1:7** [n] Col 4:12; Phm 23 [o] Col 4:7 **1:8** [p] Ro 15:30 **1:9** [q] ver 4; Eph 1:15 [r] S Ro 1:10 [s] S Eph 5:17 [t] S Eph 1:17 **1:10** [u] S Eph 4:1 [v] S 2Co 5:9 [w] ver 6 **1:11** [x] S Php 4:13 [y] Eph 4:2 **1:12** [z] Eph 5:20 [a] S Ac 20:32 [b] S Ac 26:18 **1:13** [c] S Ac 26:18 [d] 2Pe 1:11 [e] Mt 3:17 **1:14** [f] S Ro 3:24 [g] Eph 1:7

[a] 2 The Greek word for *brothers and sisters* (*adelphoi*) refers here to believers, both men and women, as part of God's family; also in 4:15.
[b] 2 Some manuscripts *Father and the Lord Jesus Christ*
[c] 7 Or *slave* [d] 7 Some manuscripts *your* [e] 9 Or *all spiritual wisdom and understanding* [f] 12 Some manuscripts *us*

1:1 *Paul.* It was customary to put the writer's name at the beginning of a letter. For more information on Paul, see notes on Ac 13:9; Ro 1:1. *apostle ... by the will of God.* See 1Co 1:1 and note. *Christ.* Paul is very Christ-centered, as seen by this short letter, in which he uses the title "Christ" 29 times and the title "Lord" (alone) 9 times. *Timothy.* Paul also mentions Timothy in 2 Corinthians, Philippians, 1,2 Thessalonians and Philemon, but Paul is really the sole author, as seen by the constant use of the pronoun "I" (see especially 4:18).

1:2 *holy people.* Because of Christ's substitutionary death for the Colossian believers, they are declared holy in the sight of God, and because of the Holy Spirit's work they are continuing to be made holy in their lives (see notes on Ro 1:7; 6:22; 1Co 1:2). *faithful.* See 1:7; 4:7,9. *brothers and sisters.* See NIV text note. *in Christ.* Paul mentions the spiritual union with Christ 12 times in Colossians (see note on Eph 1:1). *Grace and peace.* See note on Ro 1:7.

1:3 *We.* Paul and Timothy (v. 1). *thank God.* Every one of Paul's letters, except Galatians, begins with thanks or praise (see note on Php 1:3–4). In Colossians thanks is an important theme (see v. 12; 2:7; 3:15–17; 4:2). In the Bible humans are never thanked for their faith and love, but rather for God, who is the source of these virtues. *Lord Jesus Christ.* See note on 1Th 1:1.

1:4 *God's people.* The Greek word for this phrase is sometimes rendered "saints," meaning "holy people" (v. 2) or "people set apart to God" (see note on Ro 1:7; see also Preface at the front of this study Bible).

1:5 The three great Christian virtues of faith, love and hope appear also in Ro 5:2–5; 1Co 13:13; Gal 5:5–6; 1Th 1:3; 5:8; Heb 10:22–24. *hope.* Not wishful thinking but a confident expectation (see Ro 5:5 and note). For this unusual thought of faith and love coming from hope, see Titus 1:2. *true message.* The "gospel" (see Eph 1:13; 2Ti 2:15).

1:6 *throughout the whole world.* Hyperbole, to dramatize the rapid spread of the gospel into every quarter of the Roman Empire within three decades of Pentecost (see v. 23; Ro 1:8 and note; 10:18; 16:19). In refutation of the charge of the false teachers, Paul insists that the Christian faith is not merely local or regional but worldwide.

1:7 *Epaphras.* A native (4:12) and probably founder of the Colossian church, and an evangelist in nearby Laodicea and Hierapolis (4:13). Paul loved and admired him, calling him a "fellow prisoner" (Phm 23), his "dear fellow servant" and "a faithful minister of Christ." Epaphras was the one who told Paul at Rome about the Colossian church problem and thereby stimulated him to write this letter (vv. 4,8). His name, a shortened form of Epaphroditus (from "Aphrodite," the Greek goddess of love), suggests that he was a convert from paganism. He is not the Epaphroditus of Php 2:25; 4:18.

1:8 *your love in the Spirit.* The Holy Spirit is the source of all Christian love (see Ro 5:5; Gal 5:22–23 and notes).

1:9 *knowledge of his will.* Biblical knowledge is not merely the possession of facts. Rather, knowledge and wisdom in the Bible are practical, having to do with godly living. This is borne out by vv. 10–12, where knowledge, wisdom and understanding result in a life worthy of the Lord.

1:10 *live a life.* This phrase (lit. "walk") is linked to 2:6; 3:7; 4:5 ("act") by the same Greek verb. *bearing fruit ... growing.* Cf. v. 6.

1:12 *inheritance.* See 1Pe 1:4 and note. *light.* Often symbolizes holiness (see 1Jn 1:5 and note), truth (Ps 119:105,130; 2Co 4:6), glory (Isa 60:1–3; 1Ti 6:16) and life (Jn 1:4). Accordingly, God (1Jn 1:5), Christ (Jn 8:12) and the Christian (Eph 5:8) are characterized by light. The "kingdom of light" is the opposite of the "dominion of darkness" (v. 13). See also note on Ps 27:1.

1:13 *kingdom.* Does not here refer to a territory but to the authority, rule or sovereign power of a king. Here it means that the Christian is no longer under the dominion of evil (darkness) but under the benevolent rule of God's Son.

1:14 *redemption.* Deliverance and freedom from the penalty of sin by the payment of a ransom—the substitutionary death of Christ (see Ro 3:24; Eph 1:7 and notes).

The Supremacy of the Son of God

[15]The Son is the image[h] of the invisible
God,[i] the firstborn[j] over all creation. [16]For
in him all things were created:[k] things in
heaven and on earth, visible and invisible,
whether thrones or powers or rulers or
authorities;[l] all things have been created
through him and for him.[m] [17]He is before
all things,[n] and in him all things hold together. [18]And he is the head[o] of the body,
the church;[p] he is the beginning and the
firstborn[q] from among the dead,[r] so that
in everything he might have the supremacy. [19]For God was pleased[s] to have all his
fullness[t] dwell in him, [20]and through him
to reconcile[u] to himself all things, whether
things on earth or things in heaven,[v] by
making peace[w] through his blood,[x] shed
on the cross.
[21]Once you were alienated from God
and were enemies[y] in your minds[z] because
of[a] your evil behavior. [22]But now he has
reconciled[a] you by Christ's physical body[b]
through death to present you[c] holy in his
sight, without blemish and free from accusation[d]— [23]if you continue[e] in your faith,
established[f] and firm, and do not move
from the hope[g] held out in the gospel. This

1:15 [h]S Jn 14:9 [i]S Jn 1:18; 1Ti 1:17; Heb 11:27 [j]S ver 18 **1:16** [k]S Jn 1:3 [l]Eph 1:20,21 [m]S Ro 11:36 **1:17** [n]S Jn 1:2 **1:18** [o]S Eph 1:22 [p]ver 24; S 1Co 12:27 [q]ver 15; Ps 89:27; Ro 8:29; Heb 1:6 [r]Ac 26:23; Rev 1:5 **1:19** [s]S Eph 1:5 [t]S Jn 1:16 **1:20** [u]S Ro 5:10 [v]Eph 1:10 [w]S Lk 2:14 [x]Eph 2:13 **1:21** [y]Ro 5:10 [z]Eph 2:3 **1:22** [a]ver 20; S Ro 5:10 [b]Ro 7:4 [c]S 2Co 4:14 [d]Eph 1:4; 5:27 **1:23** [e]S Ro 11:22 [f]Eph 3:17 [g]ver 5

[a] 21 Or *minds, as shown by*

1:15–20 Perhaps an early Christian hymn (see note on 3:16) on the supremacy of Christ—used here by Paul to counteract the false teaching at Colossae. It is divided into two parts: (1) Christ's supremacy in creation (vv. 15–17); (2) Christ's supremacy in redemption (vv. 18–20).

1:15 *image.* Christ is called the "image of God" here and in 2Co 4:4 (see note there). In Heb 1:3 he is described as the "radiance of God's glory and the exact representation of his being." This figure of the image suggests two truths: (1) God is invisible ("No one has ever seen God," Jn 1:18); and (2) Christ, who is the eternal Son of God and who became the God-man, reflects and reveals him (see also Jn 1:18; 14:9). *firstborn over all creation.* Just as the firstborn son had certain privileges and rights in the Biblical world, so also Christ has certain rights in relation to all creation—priority, preeminence and sovereignty (vv. 16–18).

1:16 *thrones or powers or rulers or authorities.* Angels (see Eph 6:12 and note). An angelic hierarchy figured prominently in the Colossian heresy (see Introduction: The Colossian Heresy). *all things have been created through him.* See Jn 1:3. Seven times in vv. 15–20 Paul mentions "all creation," "all things" and "everything," thus stressing that Christ is supreme over all.

1:17 *He is before all things.* Referring to time, as in Jn 1:1–2; 8:58. *in him all things hold together.* See Heb 1:3 and note (item 5).

1:18 *head.* Christ is supreme in the church as the one on whom it is dependent (see notes on 1Co 11:3; Eph 1:22). *beginning.* Of the new creation. *firstborn.* Christ was the first to rise from the dead with a resurrection body. Elsewhere Paul calls him the "firstfruits of those who have fallen asleep" (1Co 15:20). Others who were raised from the dead (2Ki 4:35; Lk 7:15; Jn 11:44; Ac 9:36–41; 20:7–12) were raised only to die again.

1:19 *fullness.* Part of the technical vocabulary of some Gnostic philosophies. In these systems it meant the sum of the supernatural forces controlling the fate of people. For Paul "fullness" meant the totality of God with all his powers and attributes (see 2:9 and note).

1:20 *reconcile to himself all things.* Does not mean that Christ by his death has saved all people. Scripture speaks of an eternal hell and makes clear that only believers are saved. When Adam and Eve sinned, not only was the harmony between God and human beings destroyed, but also disorder came into creation (Ro 8:19–22). So when Christ died on the cross, he made peace possible between God and humans, and he restored in principle the harmony in the physical world, though the full realization of the latter will come only when Christ returns (see Ro 8:21 and note).

1:22 *death.* Christ's death.

1:23 *every creature.* See note on v. 6.

LETTER TO COLOSSAE

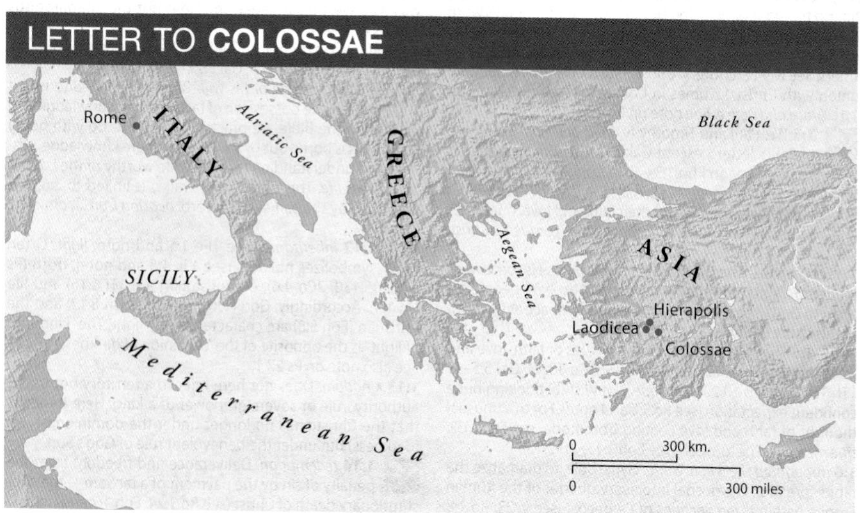

is the gospel that you heard and that has
been proclaimed to every creature under
heaven,[h] and of which I, Paul, have become a servant.[i]

Paul's Labor for the Church

[24]Now I rejoice[j] in what I am suffering
for you, and I fill up in my flesh what is
still lacking in regard to Christ's afflictions,[k] for the sake of his body, which is
the church.[l] [25]I have become its servant[m]
by the commission God gave me[n] to present to you the word of God[o] in its fullness— [26]the mystery[p] that has been kept
hidden for ages and generations, but is
now disclosed to the Lord's people. [27]To
them God has chosen to make known[q]
among the Gentiles the glorious riches[r] of
this mystery, which is Christ in you,[s] the
hope of glory.
[28]He is the one we proclaim, admonishing[t] and teaching everyone with all
wisdom,[u] so that we may present everyone fully mature[v] in Christ. [29]To this end
I strenuously[w] contend[x] with all the energy
Christ so powerfully works in me.[y]

2 I want you to know how hard I am
contending[z] for you and for those at
Laodicea,[a] and for all who have not met
me personally. [2]My goal is that they may
be encouraged in heart[b] and united in
love, so that they may have the full riches of complete understanding, in order
that they may know the mystery[c] of God,
namely, Christ, [3]in whom are hidden all
the treasures of wisdom and knowledge.[d]
[4]I tell you this so that no one may deceive
you by fine-sounding arguments.[e] [5]For
though I am absent from you in body, I
am present with you in spirit[f] and delight
to see how disciplined[g] you are and how
firm[h] your faith in Christ[i] is.

Spiritual Fullness in Christ

[6]So then, just as you received Christ
Jesus as Lord,[j] continue to live your lives in
him, [7]rooted[k] and built up in him, strengthened in the faith as you were taught,[l] and
overflowing with thankfulness.
[8]See to it that no one takes you captive
through hollow and deceptive philosophy,[m] which depends on human tradition
and the elemental spiritual forces[a] of this
world[n] rather than on Christ.

1:23 [h]ver 6; S Ro 10:18 [i]ver 25; S 1Co 3:5 **1:24** [j]S 2Co 6:10 [k]S 2Co 1:5 [l]S 1Co 12:27 **1:25** [m]ver 23; S 1Co 3:5 [n]Eph 3:2 [o]S Heb 4:12 **1:26** [p]S Ro 16:25 **1:27** [q]S Mt 13:11 [r]S Ro 2:4 [s]S Ro 8:10 **1:28** [t]Col 3:16 [u]1Co 2:6, 7 [v]Mt 5:48; Eph 5:27 **1:29** [w]1Co 15:10; 2Co 11:23 [x]Col 2:1 [y]Eph 1:19; 3:7 **2:1** [z]Col 1:29; 4:12 [a]Col 4:13, 15, 16; Rev 1:11; 3:14 **2:2** [b]Eph 6:22; Col 4:8 [c]S Ro 16:25 **2:3** [d]Isa 11:2; Jer 23:5; Ro 11:33; 1Co 1:24, 30 **2:4** [e]S Ro 16:18 **2:5** [f]1Co 5:4; 1Th 2:17

[a] 8 Or *the basic principles*; also in verse 20

[g]1Co 14:40 [h]1Pe 5:9 [i]S Ac 20:21 **2:6** [j]S Jn 13:13; Col 1:10 **2:7** [k]Eph 3:17 [l]Eph 4:21 **2:8** [m]1Ti 6:20 [n]ver 20; Gal 4:3

1:24 *what I am suffering.* During his mission to the Gentiles Paul experienced all kinds of affliction (see 2Co 11:23–27), but here he was probably referring especially to his imprisonment. *fill up … what is still lacking.* Does not mean that there was a deficiency in the atoning sacrifice of Christ. Rather, it means that Paul suffered afflictions because he was preaching the good news of Christ's atonement. Christ suffered on the cross to atone for sin, and Paul filled up Christ's afflictions by experiencing the added sufferings necessary to carry this good news to a lost world (cf. Mt 5:11–12; Ac 5:41).

1:25 *commission.* The task with which he was entrusted (see 1Co 9:17). *to present … the word of God in its fullness.* The meaning seems to be that the word of God is brought to completion, i.e., to its intended purpose, only when it is proclaimed (cf. Isa 55:11). Paul's commission to bring the word to completion, therefore, required him to make the word of God heard in Colossae, as well as elsewhere. See Ro 15:19 for a similar statement.

1:26 *mystery.* The purpose of God, unknown to humans except by revelation. This word was a popular, pagan religious term used in the mystery religions to refer to secret information available only to an exclusive group of people. Paul changes that meaning radically by always combining it with words such as "disclosed" (here), "made known" (Eph 1:9), "make plain" (Eph 3:9) and "revelation" (Ro 16:25; see note there). The Christian mystery is not secret knowledge for a few. It is a revelation of divine truths—once hidden but now openly proclaimed.

1:27 *Gentiles … Christ in you.* The mystery is the fact that Christ indwells Gentiles, for it had not been previously revealed that the Gentiles would be admitted to the church on equal terms with Israel (see note on Eph 3:6). *glory.* The glorious future prepared by God for his people (see 3:4; Ro 5:2 and note; 8:17–18; 1Co 2:7 and note; 15:42–44 and note; 2Co 4:17 and note; 1Th 2:12; 2Th 2:14; 2Ti 2:10; Heb 2:10; 1Pe 5:1,4 and note on 5:1).

1:28 *fully mature.* Employed by the mystery religions and the Gnostics to describe those who had become possessors of the secrets or knowledge boasted of by the particular religion (see Introduction to 1 John: Gnosticism). But in Christ every believer is one of the "mature."

1:29 An example of the combination of human effort and divine help (see Php 2:12–13 and notes).

2:1 *I am contending.* Probably a reference to Paul's prayers and inner conflicts and concerns for the Colossians. *Laodicea.* This letter was to be read to the church there too (4:16). Laodicea (near modern Denizli) was only about 11 miles northwest of Colossae (see map, p. 2012).

2:2 *mystery.* See notes on 1:26; Ro 11:25.

2:3 *knowledge.* Paul stressed knowledge in this letter (v. 2; 1:9–10) because he was refuting a heresy that emphasized knowledge as the means of salvation (see Introduction to 1 John: Gnosticism). Paul insisted that the Christian, not the Gnostic, possessed genuine knowledge.

2:5 *absent … in body, … present … in spirit.* Cf. 1Co 5:3.

2:6–7 Cf. Eph 3:16–19.

2:6 *live … in him.* The believer's intimate, spiritual, living union with Christ is mentioned repeatedly in this letter (see, e.g., vv. 7,10–13,20; 1:2,27–28; 3:1,3).

2:7 *overflowing with thankfulness.* See Eph 5:20 and note.

2:8 *elemental spiritual forces of this world.* If the NIV text note rendering is correct, this phrase (which occurs also in v. 20; Gal 4:3,9) refers to false, worldly, elementary religious teachings. Paul was counteracting the Colossian heresy, which, in part, taught that for salvation one needed to combine faith in Christ with secret knowledge and with human regulations concerning such physical and external practices as circumcision, eating and drinking and observance of religious festivals. On the other hand, if the translation in the main NIV text is correct, it refers to evil spiritual powers (cf. Ro 8:38–39; 1Co 15:24; cf. also Eph 6:10–18; Col 2:15; 1Pe 3:19–20a and notes).

9 For in Christ all the fullness[o] of the Deity lives in bodily form, 10 and in Christ you have been brought to fullness. He is the head[p] over every power and authority.[q] 11 In him you were also circumcised[r] with a circumcision not performed by human hands. Your whole self ruled by the flesh[a][s] was put off when you were circumcised by[b] Christ, 12 having been buried with him in baptism,[t] in which you were also raised with him[u] through your faith in the working of God, who raised him from the dead.[v]

13 When you were dead in your sins[w] and in the uncircumcision of your flesh, God made you[c] alive[x] with Christ. He forgave us all our sins,[y] 14 having canceled the charge of our legal indebtedness,[z] which stood against us and condemned us; he has taken it away, nailing it to the cross.[a] 15 And having disarmed the powers and authorities,[b] he made a public spectacle of them, triumphing over them[c] by the cross.[d]

Freedom From Human Rules

16 Therefore do not let anyone judge you[d] by what you eat or drink,[e] or with regard to a religious festival,[f] a New Moon celebration[g] or a Sabbath day.[h] 17 These are a shadow of the things that were to come;[i] the reality, however, is found in Christ. 18 Do not let anyone who delights in false humility[j] and the worship of angels disqualify you.[k] Such a person also goes into great detail about what they have seen; they are puffed up with idle notions by their unspiritual mind. 19 They have lost connection with the head,[l] from whom the whole body,[m] supported and held together by its ligaments and sinews, grows as God causes it to grow.[n]

20 Since you died with Christ[o] to the elemental spiritual forces of this world,[p] why, as though you still belonged to the world, do you submit to its rules:[q] 21 "Do not handle! Do not taste! Do not touch!"? 22 These rules, which have to do with things that are all destined to perish[r] with use, are based on merely human commands and teachings.[s] 23 Such regulations indeed have an appearance of wisdom, with their self-

2:9 [o] S Jn 1:16 **2:10** [p] S Eph 1:22 [q] S Mt 28:18 **2:11** [r] Ro 2:29; Php 3:3 [s] S Gal 5:24 **2:12** [t] S Mt 28:19 [u] S Ro 6:5 [v] S Ac 2:24 **2:13** [w] Eph 2:1, 5 [x] Eph 2:5 [y] Eph 4:32 **2:14** [z] Eph 2:15 [a] 1Pe 2:24 **2:15** [b] ver 10; Eph 6:12 [c] Mt 12:29; Lk 10:18; Jn 12:31 **2:16** [d] Ro 14:3, 4 [e] Mk 7:19; Ro 14:17 [f] Lev 23:2; Ro 14:5 [g] 1Ch 23:31 [h] Mk 2:27, 28; Gal 4:10 **2:17** [i] Heb 8:5; 10:1 **2:18** [j] ver 23 [k] 1Co 9:24; Php 3:14 **2:19** [l] S Eph 1:22 [m] S 1Co 12:27 [n] Eph 4:16 **2:20** [o] S Ro 6:6 [p] ver 8; Gal 4:3, 9 [q] ver 14, 16 **2:22** [r] 1Co 6:13 [s] Isa 29:13; Mt 15:9; Titus 1:14

[a] *11* In contexts like this, the Greek word for *flesh* (*sarx*) refers to the sinful state of human beings, often presented as a power in opposition to the Spirit; also in verse 13. [b] *11* Or *put off in the circumcision of* [c] *13* Some manuscripts *us* [d] *15* Or *them in him*

2:9 *fullness of the Deity.* See note on 1:19. The declaration that the very essence of deity was present in totality in Jesus' human body was a direct refutation of Gnostic teaching.

2:10–15 Here Paul declares that the Christian is complete in Christ, rather than being deficient as the Gnostics claimed. This completeness includes the putting off of the flesh (v. 11), resurrection from spiritual death (vv. 12–13), forgiveness (v. 13) and deliverance from legalistic requirements (v. 14) and from evil spirit beings (v. 15).

2:10 *head.* Cf. 1:18 and note; see Eph 1:19–22 and notes.

2:11–12 *circumcision ... baptism.* In the Israelite faith, circumcision was a sign that the individual stood in covenant relation with God. While this is the only reference where circumcision is associated with baptism, some see the passage as implying that, for the Christian, water baptism is the parallel sign of the covenant relationship.

2:12 See Ro 6:3–4 and notes.

2:13 Cf. Eph 2:1–9 and notes.

2:14 *the charge of our legal indebtedness.* A business term, meaning a certificate of indebtedness in the debtor's handwriting. Paul uses it as a designation for the Mosaic law, with all its regulations, under which everyone is a debtor to God.

2:15 *having disarmed.* Not only did God cancel out the accusations of the law against the Christian, but he also conquered and disarmed the evil angels (powers and authorities, 1:16; Eph 6:12), who entice people to follow asceticism and false teachings about Christ. The picture is of conquered soldiers stripped of their clothes, as well as their weapons, to symbolize their total defeat. *triumphing over them.* Lit. "leading them in a triumphal procession." The metaphor recalls a Roman general leading his captives through the streets of his city for all the citizens to see as evidence of his complete victory (see 2Co 2:14 and note). That Christ triumphed over the devil and his cohorts is seen from Mt 12:29; Lk 10:18; Ro 16:20.

2:16 Cf. Paul's exhortations to the Roman church (Ro 14:1—15:13); cf. also 1Co 8–10.

2:17 *shadow ... reality.* The ceremonial laws of the OT are here referred to as shadows (cf. Heb 8:5; 10:1) because they symbolically depicted the coming of Christ; so any insistence on the observance of such ceremonies is a failure to recognize that their fulfillment has already taken place. This element of the Colossian heresy was combined with a rigid asceticism, as vv. 20–21 reveal.

2:18 *false humility.* Humility in which one delights is of necessity mock humility. *worship of angels.* Second-century Gnosticism conceived of a list of spirit beings who had emanated from God and through whom God may be approached. Or the phrase may mean "participating in worship together with angels" (see Introduction: The Colossian Heresy). *disqualify.* This term pictures an umpire or referee who excludes from competition any athlete who fails to follow the rules. The Colossians were not to permit any false teacher to deny the reality of their salvation because they were not delighting in mock humility and in the worship of angelic beings. *what they have seen.* Probably refers to professed visions by the false teachers.

2:19 *lost connection with the head.* The central error of the Colossian heresy is a defective view of Christ, in which he is believed to be less than deity (see v. 9; 1:19).

2:20 *elemental spiritual forces.* See note on v. 8.

2:21 *Do not handle ... taste ... touch!* The strict ascetic nature of the heresy is seen here. These prohibitions seem to carry OT ceremonial laws to the extreme.

2:23 A rather detailed analysis of the Colossian heresy: (1) It appeared to set forth an impressive system of religious philosophy. (2) It was, however, a system created by the false teachers themselves ("self-imposed"), rather than being of divine origin. (3) The false teachers attempted to parade their humility. (4) This may have been done by a harsh asceticism that brutally misused the body. Paul's analysis is that such

imposed worship, their false humility[t] and
their harsh treatment of the body, but they
lack any value in restraining sensual indulgence.

Living as Those Made Alive in Christ

3 Since, then, you have been raised
with Christ,[u] set your hearts on things
above, where Christ is, seated at the right
hand of God.[v] 2Set your minds on things
above, not on earthly things.[w] 3For you
died,[x] and your life is now hidden with
Christ in God. 4When Christ, who is your[a]
life,[y] appears,[z] then you also will appear
with him in glory.[a]
5Put to death,[b] therefore, whatever belongs to your earthly nature:[c] sexual immorality,[d] impurity, lust, evil desires and
greed,[e] which is idolatry.[f] 6Because of
these, the wrath of God[g] is coming.[b] 7You
used to walk in these ways, in the life you
once lived.[h] 8But now you must also rid
yourselves[i] of all such things as these: anger, rage, malice, slander,[j] and filthy language from your lips.[k] 9Do not lie to each
other,[l] since you have taken off your old
self[m] with its practices 10and have put on
the new self,[n] which is being renewed[o] in

2:23 [t]ver 18
3:1 [u]S Ro 6:5 [v]S Mk 16:19
3:2 [w]Php 3:19, 20
3:3 [x]S Ro 6:2; 2Co 5:14
3:4 [y]Gal 2:20 [z]1Co 1:7 [a]1Pe 1:13; 1Jn 3:2
3:5 [b]S Ro 6:2; S Eph 4:22 [c]S Gal 5:24 [d]S 1Co 6:18 [e]Eph 5:3 [f]Gal 5:19-21; Eph 5:5
3:6 [g]S Ro 1:18
3:7 [h]S Eph 2:2
3:8 [i]S Eph 4:22 [j]Eph 4:31 [k]Eph 4:29
3:9 [l]S Eph 4:22, 25 [m]S Ro 6:6
3:10 [n]S Ro 6:4; S 13:14 [o]Ro 12:2; S 2Co 4:16; Eph 4:23 [p]Eph 2:10
3:11 [q]Ro 10:12; 1Co 12:13 [r]S 1Co 7:19 [s]Gal 3:28 [t]Eph 1:23
3:12 [u]ver 10 [v]Php 2:3 [w]2Co 6:6; Gal 5:22,23;

knowledge in the image of its Creator.[p]
11Here there is no Gentile or Jew,[q] circumcised or uncircumcised,[r] barbarian, Scythian, slave or free,[s] but Christ is all,[t] and
is in all.
12Therefore, as God's chosen people,
holy and dearly loved, clothe yourselves[u]
with compassion, kindness, humility,[v]
gentleness and patience.[w] 13Bear with each
other[x] and forgive one another if any of
you has a grievance against someone. Forgive as the Lord forgave you.[y] 14And over
all these virtues put on love,[z] which binds
them all together in perfect unity.[a]
15Let the peace of Christ[b] rule in your
hearts, since as members of one body[c] you
were called to peace.[d] And be thankful.
16Let the message of Christ[e] dwell among
you richly as you teach and admonish one
another with all wisdom[f] through psalms,[g]
hymns, and songs from the Spirit, singing to God with gratitude in your hearts.[h]
17And whatever you do,[i] whether in word

[a] 4 Some manuscripts *our* [b] 6 Some early manuscripts *coming on those who are disobedient*

Eph 4:2 **3:13** [x]Eph 4:2 [y]Eph 4:32 **3:14** [z]1Co 13:1-13 [a]S Ro 15:5 **3:15** [b]S Jn 14:27 [c]S Ro 12:5 [d]S Ro 14:19 **3:16** [e]Ro 10:17 [f]Col 1:28 [g]Ps 47:7 [h]S Eph 5:19 **3:17** [i]1Co 10:31

practices are worthless because they totally fail to control sinful desires. *self-imposed worship.* The false teachers themselves had created the regulations of their heretical system. They were not from God.

3:1 *then.* "Then" (or "therefore") links the doctrinal section of the letter with the practical section, just as it does in Ro 12:1; Eph 4:1; Php 4:1. *you have been raised.* Verses 1–10 set forth what has been described as the indicative and the imperative (standing and state) of the Christian. The indicative statements describe believers in Christ: They are dead (v. 3); they have been raised with Christ (v. 1); they are with Christ in heaven ("hidden with Christ," v. 3); they have "taken off [the] old self" (v. 9); and they have "put on the new self" (v. 10). The imperative statements indicate what believers are to do as a result: set their hearts (or minds) on things above (vv. 1–2); put to death practices that belong to their earthly nature (v. 5); and rid themselves of practices that characterized the unregenerate self (v. 8). In summary, they are called upon to become in daily experience what they are in Christ (cf. Ro 6:1–13).

3:4 *appears.* Refers to Christ's second coming (see 1Jn 3:2).

3:5,8 See note on Ro 1:29–31.

3:6 *wrath of God.* See notes on Zec 1:2; Ro 1:18. God is unalterably opposed to sin and will invariably make sure that it is justly punished.

3:9–10 *taken off ... put on.* As one takes off dirty clothes and puts on clean ones, so Christians, individually and collectively, are called upon to renounce their evil ways and live in accordance with the rules of Christ's kingdom (see vv. 12–14; cf. Ro 13:12; Gal 3:27; cf. also Eph 4:22–24 and notes).

3:10 *renewed.* See 2 Co 5:17. *knowledge.* See 1:10; 2:2–3 and note on 2:3. *image of its Creator.* See note on Ge 1:26.

3:11 *barbarian.* Someone who did not speak Greek and was thought to be uncivilized. *Scythian.* Scythians were known especially for their brutality and were considered by others as little better than wild beasts. They came originally from what is today south Russia. *Christ is all, and is in all.* Christ transcends all barriers and unifies people from all cultures, races and nations. Such distinctions are no longer significant. Christ alone matters (see Gal 3:28 and note).

3:12 *God's chosen people.* Israel was called this (Dt 4:37), and so is the Christian community (1Pe 2:9; see note there). Divine election is a frequent theme in Paul's letters (see note on Eph 1:4), but the Bible never teaches that it dulls human responsibility. On the contrary, as this verse shows, it is precisely because Christians have been "chosen" for eternal salvation that they must put forth every effort to live the godly life. For Paul, divine sovereignty and human responsibility go hand in hand. *clothe ... with.* See note on Ps 109:29.

3:14 See 1Co 13:13 and note.

3:15 *peace of Christ.* The attitude of peace that Christ alone gives—in place of the attitude of bitterness and quarrelsomeness. This attitude is to "rule" (lit. "function like an umpire") in all human relationships (cf. Mt 10:34 and note). *be thankful.* See Eph 5:20 and note.

3:16 *message of Christ.* Refers especially to Christ's teaching, which in the time of the Colossians was transmitted orally. But by implication it includes the OT as well as the NT. *psalms, hymns, and songs from the Spirit.* Some of the most important doctrines were expressed in Christian hymns preserved for us now only in Paul's letters (1:15–20; Eph 5:14; Php 2:6–11; 1Ti 3:16). "Psalms" refers to the OT psalms (see Lk 20:42; 24:44; Ac 1:20; 13:33), some of which may have been set to music by the church. "Psalm" could also describe a song newly composed for Christian worship (cf. 1Co 14:26, where "hymn" is lit. "psalm" in the Greek text). A "hymn" was a song of praise, especially used in a celebration (see Mt 26:30 and note; Heb 2:12), much like the OT psalms that praised God for all that he is. A "song" recounted the acts of God and praised him for them (see Rev 5:9 and note; 15:3), much like the OT psalms that thanked God for all that he had done. See Eph 5:19 and note.

or deed, do it all in the name of the Lord Jesus, giving thanks[j] to God the Father through him.

Instructions for Christian Households

3:18-4:1pp — Eph 5:22-6:9

18 Wives, submit yourselves to your husbands,[k] as is fitting in the Lord.
19 Husbands, love your wives and do not be harsh with them.
20 Children, obey your parents in everything, for this pleases the Lord.
21 Fathers,[a] do not embitter your children, or they will become discouraged.
22 Slaves, obey your earthly masters in everything; and do it, not only when their eye is on you and to curry their favor, but with sincerity of heart and reverence for the Lord. 23 Whatever you do, work at it with all your heart, as working for the Lord, not for human masters, 24 since you know that you will receive an inheritance[l] from the Lord as a reward.[m] It is the Lord Christ you are serving. 25 Anyone who does wrong will be repaid for their wrongs, and there is no favoritism.[n]

4 Masters, provide your slaves with what is right and fair,[o] because you know that you also have a Master in heaven.

Further Instructions

2 Devote yourselves to prayer,[p] being watchful and thankful. 3 And pray for us, too, that God may open a door[q] for our message, so that we may proclaim the mystery[r] of Christ, for which I am in chains.[s] 4 Pray that I may proclaim it clearly, as I should. 5 Be wise[t] in the way you act toward outsiders;[u] make the most of every opportunity.[v] 6 Let your conversation be always full of grace,[w] seasoned with salt,[x] so that you may know how to answer everyone.[y]

Final Greetings

7 Tychicus[z] will tell you all the news about me. He is a dear brother, a faithful minister and fellow servant[b][a] in the Lord. 8 I am sending him to you for the express purpose that you may know about our[c] circumstances and that he may encourage your hearts.[b] 9 He is coming with Onesimus,[c] our faithful and dear brother, who is one of you.[d] They will tell you everything that is happening here.

10 My fellow prisoner Aristarchus[e] sends you his greetings, as does Mark,[f] the cousin of Barnabas.[g] (You have received instructions about him; if he comes to you, welcome him.) 11 Jesus, who is called Justus, also sends greetings. These are the only Jews[d] among my co-workers[h] for the kingdom of God, and they have proved a comfort to me. 12 Epaphras,[i] who is one of you[j] and a servant of Christ Jesus, sends greetings. He is always wrestling in prayer for you,[k] that you may stand firm in all the will of God, mature[l] and fully assured. 13 I vouch for him that he is working hard for you and for those at Laodicea[m] and Hierapolis. 14 Our dear friend Luke,[n] the

3:17 [j] S Eph 5:20 **3:18** [k] S Eph 5:22 **3:24** [l] S Ac 20:32 [m] S Mt 16:27 **3:25** [n] S Ac 10:34 **4:1** [o] Lev 25:43, 53 **4:2** [p] S Lk 18:1 **4:3** [q] S Ac 14:27 [r] S Ro 16:25 [s] S Ac 21:33 **4:5** [t] Eph 5:15 [u] S Mk 4:11 [v] Eph 5:16 **4:6** [w] Eph 4:29 [x] Mk 9:50 [y] 1Pe 3:15 **4:7** [z] S Ac 20:4 [a] Eph 6:21, 22; Col 1:7 **4:8** [b] Eph 6:21, 22; Col 2:2 **4:9** [c] Phm 10 [d] ver 12 **4:10** [e] S Ac 19:29 [f] S Ac 12:12 [g] S Ac 4:36 **4:11** [h] S Php 2:25 **4:12** [i] Col 1:7; Phm 23 [j] ver 9 [k] S Ro 15:30 [l] S 1Co 2:6 **4:13** [m] S Col 2:1 **4:14** [n] 2Ti 4:11; Phm 24

[a] 21 Or *Parents* [b] 7 Or *slave*; also in verse 12
[c] 8 Some manuscripts *that he may know about your*
[d] 11 Greek *only ones of the circumcision group*

3:18—4:1 See Eph 5:22—6:9 and notes.
3:20 *in everything.* In everything not sinful (see Ac 5:29).
3:22—4:1 Paul neither condones slavery nor sanctions revolt against masters. Rather, he calls on both slaves and masters to show Christian principles in their relationship and thus to attempt to change the institution from within (see note on 1Co 7:21). The reason Paul writes more about slaves and masters than about wives, husbands, children and fathers may be that the slave Onesimus (4:9) is going along with Tychicus to deliver this Colossian letter and the letter to Philemon, Onesimus's master, who also lives in Colossae.
3:24 *inheritance.* See 1Pe 1:4; Heb 9:15 and notes.
3:25 *no favoritism.* See Ac 10:34 and note.
4:2 *Devote yourselves to prayer.* See notes on Lk 11:1; Ac 2:42; Ro 12:12; 1Th 5:17. *being watchful.* Being spiritually alert. *being … thankful.* See Eph 5:20 and note.
4:3 *mystery.* See notes on 1:26–27; Ro 11:25.
4:5 *outsiders.* Non-Christians (see 1Co 5:12–13; 1Th 4:12; 1Ti 3:7). *make the most of every opportunity.* See Eph 5:16 and note.
4:6 *seasoned with salt.* Salt is a preservative and is tasty. Similarly, the Christian's conversation is to be wholesome and helpful (see 3:8; Eph 4:29).
4:7 *Tychicus.* See note on Eph 6:21.
4:9–17 Onesimus (v. 9), Aristarchus (v. 10), Mark (v. 10), Epaphras (v. 12), Luke (v. 14), Demas (v. 14) and Archippus (v. 17) are mentioned in Philemon. This suggests that the letters to Colossae and Philemon were written at the same time and place.
4:9 *Onesimus.* See Introduction to Philemon: Recipient, Background and Purpose.
4:10 *Aristarchus.* A Macedonian who is mentioned three times in Acts: (1) He was with Paul during the Ephesian riot (Ac 19:29) and therefore was known in Colossae. (2) Both he and Tychicus (Ac 20:4) were with Paul in Greece. (3) He accompanied Paul on his trip to Rome (Ac 27:2). *Mark.* The author of the second Gospel. Against Barnabas's advice, Paul refused to take Mark on the second missionary journey because Mark had "deserted" him at Pamphylia (see Ac 15:38 and note). But now — about 12 years later — the difficulties seem to have been ironed out, because Paul, both here and in Phm 24 (sent at the same time to Philemon, who was in Colossae), sends Mark's greetings. About five years later, Paul even writes that Mark "is helpful to me in my ministry" (2Ti 4:11). See note on Ac 15:39.
4:13 *Hierapolis.* A town in Asia Minor (present-day Turkey), about 6 miles from Laodicea (see map, p. 2012) and 14 miles from Colossae. Its church may have been founded during Paul's three-year stay in Ephesus (Ac 19; see note on Ac 19:10), but probably not by Paul himself (cf. 2:1).
4:14 *Luke.* Wrote about Paul in the book of Acts, having often accompanied him on his travels (see note on Ac 16:10). He was with Paul in Rome during his imprisonment (Ac 28), where this letter was written. *Demas.* A Christian worker who would later desert Paul (2Ti 4:10).

doctor, and Demas[o] send greetings. 15 Give
my greetings to the brothers and sisters at
Laodicea,[p] and to Nympha and the church
in her house.[q]
16 After this letter has been read to you,
see that it is also read[r] in the church of the
Laodiceans and that you in turn read the
letter from Laodicea.
17 Tell Archippus:[s] "See to it that you
complete the ministry you have received
in the Lord."[t]
18 I, Paul, write this greeting in my own
hand.[u] Remember[v] my chains.[w] Grace be
with you.[x]

4:14 [o] 2Ti 4:10; Phm 24 **4:15** [p] S Col 2:1 [q] S Ro 16:5 **4:16** [r] 2Th 3:14; S 1Ti 4:13 **4:17** [s] Phm 2 [t] 2Ti 4:5 **4:18** [u] S 1Co 16:21 [v] Heb 13:3 [w] S Ac 21:33 [x] 1Ti 6:21; 2Ti 4:22; Titus 3:15; Heb 13:25

4:15 *church in her house.* For the most part the early church had no buildings, so it usually met for worship and instruction in homes. It often centered around one family, as, e.g., Priscilla and Aquila (Ro 16:5; 1Co 16:19), Philemon (Phm 2) and Mary, the mother of John Mark (Ac 12:12).
4:16 *After this letter has been read to you.* The practice of the early church was to read Paul's letters aloud to the assembled congregation. *letter from Laodicea.* Probably not a letter by the Laodiceans. Rather, it was likely one that the Laodiceans were to lend to the Colossians—a letter that Paul had originally written to the Laodiceans. This may have been a fourth letter (in addition to Ephesians, Colossians and Philemon) that Tychicus carried to this area in what is present-day Turkey. Or it could have been Paul's letter to the Ephesians—a circular letter making the rounds from Ephesus to Laodicea to Colossae (see Introduction to Ephesians: Author, Date and Place of Writing).
4:17 *Archippus.* Phm 2 calls him Paul's "fellow soldier."
4:18 Paul's custom was to dictate his letters (see Ro 16:22) and pen a few greetings himself (1Co 16:21; Gal 6:11; 2Th 3:17; Phm 19). His personal signature was the guarantee of the genuineness of the letter. *Grace.* See note on Ro 1:7. *with you.* See note on 2Co 13:14.

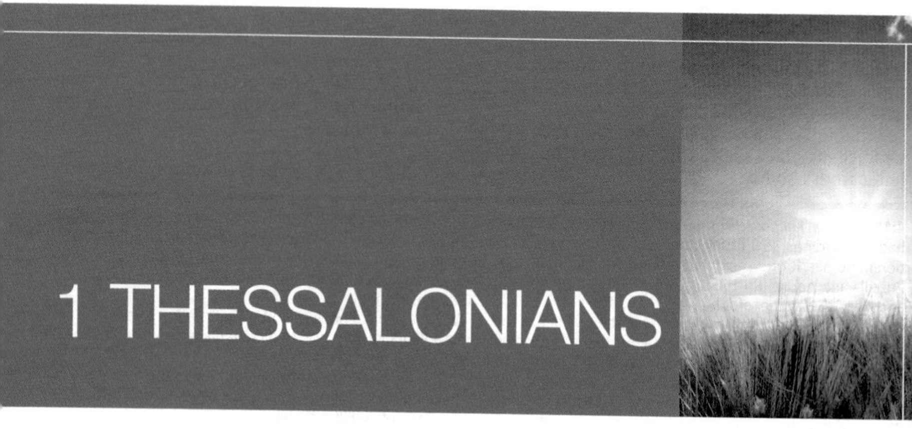

1 THESSALONIANS

INTRODUCTION

Background of the Thessalonian Letters

It is helpful to trace the locations of Paul and his companions that relate to the Thessalonian correspondence. The travels were as follows:

(1) Paul, Silas and Timothy established the church in Thessalonica on Paul's second missionary journey (Ac 17:1 – 9).

(2) Because of persecution, Paul and Silas fled from Thessalonica to Berea. Since Timothy is not mentioned (see Ac 17:10 and note), it is possible that he stayed in Thessalonica or went back to Philippi and then rejoined Paul and Silas in Berea (Ac 17:14).

(3) Paul fled to Athens from Berean persecution, leaving Silas and Timothy in Berea (see Ac 17:14).

(4) Paul sent word back, instructing Silas and Timothy to come to him in Athens (see Ac 17:15; see also note on 1Th 3:1 – 2).

(5) Timothy rejoined Paul at Athens and was sent back to Thessalonica (see 3:1 – 5). Since Silas is not mentioned, it has been conjectured that he went back to Philippi when Timothy went to Thessalonica (see note on 3:1 – 2).

(6) Paul moved on to Corinth (see Ac 18:1).

(7) Silas and Timothy came to Paul in Corinth (see 3:6; Ac 18:5).

(8) Paul wrote 1 Thessalonians and sent it to the church.

(9) Sometime later (perhaps AD 51/52) he sent 2 Thessalonians in response to further information about the church there.

Author, Date and Place of Writing

Both external and internal evidence (see 1:1; 2:18) support the view that Paul wrote 1 Thessalonians (from Corinth; see note on 3:1 – 2). Early church writers are agreed on the matter, with testimonies beginning as early as AD 140 (Marcion). Paul's known characteristics are apparent in the letter (3:1 – 2,8 – 11 compared with Ac 15:36; 2Co 11:28). Historical allusions in the book fit Paul's life as recounted in Acts (2:14 – 16

a quick look

Author:
The apostle Paul

Audience:
The largely Gentile church in Thessalonica, founded by Paul

Date:
About AD 51

Theme:
Paul praises the Thessalonian believers for their spiritual maturity and perseverance, and he encourages them to further growth in view of Christ's imminent return.

compared with Ac 17:5 – 10; 3:6 compared with Ac 17:15 – 16). In the face of such evidence, few have ever rejected authorship by Paul.

This epistle is generally dated c. AD 51 (see chart, p. 1845). Weighty support for this date was found in an inscription discovered at Delphi, Greece (see map, pp. 2528 – 2529, at the end of this study Bible), that dates Gallio's proconsulship to c. 51 – 52 and thus places Paul at Corinth at the same time (see Ac 18:12 – 17 and note on 18:12; see also chart, p. 1812). Except for the possibility of an early date for Galatians (48 – 49?), 1 Thessalonians is Paul's earliest canonical letter.

Thessalonica: The City and the Church

Thessalonica was a bustling seaport city at the head of the Thermaic Gulf (see photo below). It was an important communication and trade center, located at the junction of the great Egnatian Way and the road leading north to the Danube. It was the largest city in Macedonia and was also the capital of its province.

The background of the Thessalonian church is found in Ac 17:1 – 9. Since Paul began his ministry there in the Jewish synagogue, it is reasonable to assume that the new church included some Jews. However, 1:9 – 10 and Ac 17:4 seem to indicate that the church was largely Gentile in membership.

Looking south at the eastern edge of the Thessaloniki Bay. During the days of Paul, Thessalonica was the capital city of Macedonia. He visited there on his second and third missionary journeys.

www.HolyLandPhotos.org

Paul writes to encourage the new converts in their trials and to give assurance concerning the future of believers who die before Christ returns.

View of the Taurus mountains through the Cilician Gates. Paul passed through here on his second and third missionary journeys. The church at Thessalonica was founded during Paul's second journey.

Purpose

Paul had left Thessalonica abruptly (see Ac 17:5 – 10) after a rather brief stay. Recent converts from paganism (1:9) were thus left with little external support in the midst of persecution. Paul's purpose in writing this letter was to praise the new converts for their perseverance and to encourage them in their trials (3:3 – 5), to give instruction concerning godly living (4:1 – 12) and to give assurance concerning the future of believers who die before Christ returns (4:13 – 18; see Themes; see also notes on 4:13,15).

Themes

The central theme of the letter is Paul's encouragement for the church at Thessalonica, which is thriving in spite of persecution. A strong secondary theme in both Thessalonian letters, however, is eschatology (doctrine of last things). Every chapter of 1 Thessalonians ends with a reference to the second coming of Christ, with ch. 4 giving it major consideration (1:9 – 10; 2:19 – 20; 3:13; 4:13 – 18; 5:23 – 24). Thus, the second coming permeates 1 Thessalonians, and the two letters are often designated as the eschatological letters of Paul.

Outline

I. Thanksgiving for the Thessalonians (ch. 1)
  A. The Grounds for Thanksgiving (1:1 – 4)
  B. The Genuineness of the Grounds (1:5 – 10)
II. Defense of the Apostolic Actions and Absence (chs. 2 – 3)
  A. Defense of the Apostolic Actions (2:1 – 16)
  B. Defense of the Apostolic Absence (2:17 — 3:10)
  C. The Prayer (3:11 – 13)
III. Exhortations to the Thessalonians (4:1 — 5:22)
  A. Primarily concerning Personal Life (4:1 – 12)
  B. Concerning the Coming of Christ (4:13 — 5:11)
  C. Primarily concerning Church Life (5:12 – 22)
IV. Concluding Prayer, Greetings and Benediction (5:23 – 28)

1 Paul, Silas[a][a] and Timothy,[b]

To the church of the Thessalonians[c] in
God the Father and the Lord Jesus Christ:

Grace and peace to you.[d]

Thanksgiving for the Thessalonians' Faith

2 We always thank God for all of you[e] and
continually mention you in our prayers.[f]
3 We remember before our God and Father[g]
your work produced by faith,[h] your labor
prompted by love,[i] and your endurance inspired by hope[j] in our Lord Jesus Christ.
4 For we know, brothers and sisters[b]
loved by God,[k] that he has chosen you,
5 because our gospel[l] came to you not simply with words but also with power,[m] with
the Holy Spirit and deep conviction. You
know[n] how we lived among you for your
sake. 6 You became imitators of us[o] and
of the Lord, for you welcomed the message in the midst of severe suffering[p] with
the joy[q] given by the Holy Spirit.[r] 7 And so
you became a model[s] to all the believers
in Macedonia[t] and Achaia.[u] 8 The Lord's
message[v] rang out from you not only in
Macedonia and Achaia—your faith in God
has become known everywhere.[w] Therefore we do not need to say anything about
it, 9 for they themselves report what kind
of reception you gave us. They tell how
you turned[x] to God from idols[y] to serve the
living and true God,[z] 10 and to wait for his
Son from heaven,[a] whom he raised from
the dead[b]—Jesus, who rescues us from
the coming wrath.[c]

Paul's Ministry in Thessalonica

2 You know, brothers and sisters, that
our visit to you[d] was not without results.[e] 2 We had previously suffered[f] and
been treated outrageously in Philippi,[g] as
you know, but with the help of our God
we dared to tell you his gospel in the face
of strong opposition.[h] 3 For the appeal we

1:1 [a] S Ac 15:22 [b] S Ac 16:1; 2Th 1:1 [c] S Ac 17:1 [d] S Ro 1:7 **1:2** [e] S Ro 1:8; Eph 5:20 [f] S Ro 1:10 **1:3** [g] S Php 4:20 [h] Gal 5:6; 2Th 1:11; Jas 2:14-26 [i] 1Th 3:6; 2Th 1:3; S 1Co 13:13 [j] Ro 8:25 **1:4** [k] Col 3:12; 2Th 2:13 **1:5** [l] S 2Co 2:12; 2Th 2:14 [m] Ro 1:16; S Ro 15:13 [n] 1Th 2:10 **1:6** [o] S 1Co 4:16 [p] Ac 17:5-10 [q] S 2Co 6:10 [r] Ac 13:52 **1:7** [s] S 1Ti 4:12 [t] S Ac 16:9 [u] S Ac 18:12 **1:8** [v] 2Th 3:1 [w] Ro 1:8 **1:9** [x] Ac 14:15 [y] 1Co 12:2; Gal 4:8 [z] S Mt 16:16 **1:10** [a] S 1Co 1:7

[a] *1* Greek *Silvanus*, a variant of *Silas* [b] *4* The Greek word for *brothers and sisters* (*adelphoi*) refers here to believers, both men and women, as part of God's family; also in 2:1, 9, 14, 17; 3:7; 4:1, 10, 13; 5:1, 4, 12, 14, 25, 27.

[b] S Ac 2:24 [c] S Ro 1:18 **2:1** [d] 1Th 1:5,9 [e] 2Th 1:10 **2:2** [f] Ac 14:19; 16:22; Php 1:30 [g] S Ac 16:12 [h] Ac 17:1-9

1:1 *Paul.* See note on Ro 1:1. *Silas.* See note on Ac 15:22. He accompanied Paul on most of his second missionary journey (Ac 15:39—18:22). *Timothy.* See Introduction to 1 Timothy: Recipient. Both he and Silas helped Paul found the Thessalonian church (see Ac 17:1–14). *in.* Indicates the vital union and living relationship that Christians have with the Father and the Son (see Jn 14:23; 17:21). The close connection between the Father and the Son points to the Trinitarian relationship (see 3:11; 2Th 1:2,8,12; 2:16; 3:5). *Lord Jesus Christ.* Occurs also at the end of this letter (5:28). For the meanings of "Lord," "Jesus" and "Christ," see NIV text notes on Mt 1:1,21; see also notes on Lk 2:11; Ro 10:9; 1Co 12:3; Php 2:9–11. *Grace and peace.* See note on Ro 1:7.

1:2 *thank.* See note on Php 1:3–4.

1:3 The triad of faith, hope and love is found often in the NT (5:8; Ro 5:2–5; 1Co 13:13; Gal 5:5–6; Col 1:4–5; Heb 6:10–12; 10:22–24; 1Pe 1:3–8,21–22). *work produced by faith.* Faith produces action (see Ro 1:5; 16:26; Gal 5:6 and note; 2Th 1:11; Jas 2:14–26 and note). *labor prompted by love.* See Heb 6:10. *hope.* Not unfounded wishful thinking but firm confidence in our Lord Jesus Christ and his return (v. 10). See Heb 6:18–20 and notes on Ro 5:5; Col 1:5.

1:4 *know.* The reasons for Paul's conviction regarding their election are stated in vv. 5–10. *brothers and sisters.* United to each other through union with Christ (see NIV text note). This phrase (including its singular form) is used 28 times in the two letters to the Thessalonians. *loved ... chosen.* Both words speak of God's electing love (see Col 3:12 and note; 2Th 2:13; see also note on Eph 1:4).

1:5 *our gospel.* The gospel preached by Paul, Silas and Timothy (see Ro 16:25 and note). It is first of all God the Father's (2:8), because he originated it, and Christ's (3:2), because it springs from his atoning death. *power.* The power that delivered them from spiritual bondage. That power is from the Holy Spirit (see Ro 15:13,18–19; 1Co 2:4–5), but it also resides in the gospel itself (see Ro 1:16). *deep conviction.* Such conviction, on the part of both the preachers and the Thessalonians, was also from the Holy Spirit.

1:6 *imitators.* The order in Christian imitation: (1) Believers in Macedonia and Achaia imitated the Thessalonians (v. 7), just as the Thessalonians imitated the churches in Judea (2:14); (2) the Thessalonians imitated Paul, just as the Corinthians did (1Co 4:6; 11:1) and just as all believers were to imitate their leaders (2Th 3:7,9; 1Ti 4:12; Titus 2:7; 1Pe 5:3); (3) Paul imitated Christ (1Co 11:1), as did the Thessalonians (here); (4) all were to imitate God (Eph 5:1). *severe suffering.* Such as recorded in Ac 17:5–14 (see also 1Th 2:14).

1:7 *Macedonia and Achaia.* The two Roman provinces into which Greece was then divided (see Ac 19:21; Ro 15:26; see also map, p. 2039). *Macedonia.* See note on Php 4:15.

1:8 *everywhere.* In every place they visited or knew about (see Ro 1:8 and note; 1Co 1:2; 2Co 2:14; 1Ti 2:8). The news spread because of Thessalonica's strategic location (see Introduction: Thessalonica: The City and the Church).

1:9–10 Three marks of true conversion: (1) turning from idols, (2) serving God and (3) waiting for Christ to return. In his two short letters to the Thessalonians, Paul speaks much about the second coming of Christ (v. 10; 2:19; 3:13; 4:13—5:4; 2Th 1:7–10; 2:1–12).

1:10 *wrath.* See note on Ro 1:18. Some see a reference here to the final judgment (see 2:16; Ro 2:5 and notes), while others think it refers to a future period of tribulation (described in Rev 6–18; see 1Th 5:9; Rev 6:16).

2:1–12 A manual for a minister: (1) His *message* is God's good news ("gospel," v. 2). (2) His *motive* is not impurity (v. 3), pleasing people (v. 4), greed (v. 5) or seeking praise from people (v. 6), but pleasing God (v. 4). (3) His *manner* is not one of trickery (v. 3), flattery (v. 5) or a cover-up (v. 5), but of courage (v. 2), gentleness (v. 7), love (vv. 8,11), toil (v. 9) and holiness (v. 10).

2:1 *You know.* The local church could refute the accusation of insincerity that evidently had been leveled against Paul (v. 3).

2:2 *treated outrageously.* Paul was deeply hurt by the way he had been treated in the city of Philippi (see Ac 16:19–40).

2:3 *impure motives.* See Php 1:15–18 and notes on 1:17–18. *trick.* The Greek for this word was originally used of a lure for

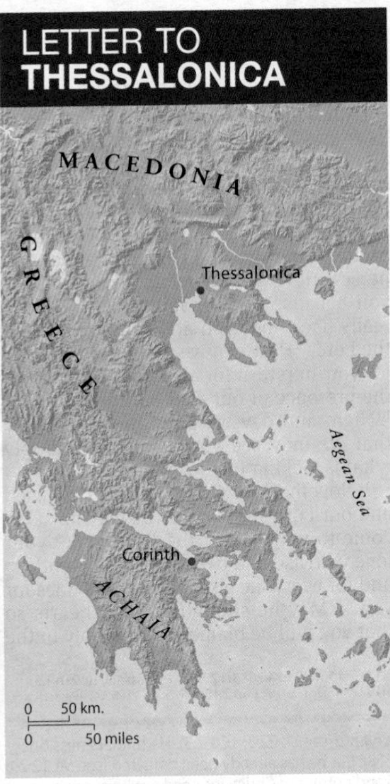

make does not spring from error or impure
motives,[i] nor are we trying to trick you.[j]
4On the contrary, we speak as those approved by God to be entrusted with the
gospel.[k] We are not trying to please people[l] but God, who tests our hearts.[m] 5You
know we never used flattery, nor did we
put on a mask to cover up greed[n]—God
is our witness.[o] 6We were not looking
for praise from people,[p] not from you or
anyone else, even though as apostles[q] of
Christ we could have asserted our authority.[r] 7Instead, we were like young children[a] among you.

Just as a nursing mother cares for her
children,[s] 8so we cared for you. Because
we loved you so much, we were delighted
to share with you not only the gospel of
God[t] but our lives as well.[u] 9Surely you
remember, brothers and sisters, our toil
and hardship; we worked[v] night and day
in order not to be a burden to anyone[w]
while we preached the gospel of God to
you. 10You are witnesses,[x] and so is God,[y]
of how holy,[z] righteous and blameless we
were among you who believed. 11For you
know that we dealt with each of you as a
father deals with his own children,[a] 12en-
couraging, comforting and urging you to
live lives worthy[b] of God, who calls[c] you
into his kingdom and glory.

13And we also thank God continually[d]
because, when you received the word of
God,[e] which you heard from us, you accepted it not as a human word, but as it
actually is, the word of God, which is indeed at work in you who believe. 14For
you, brothers and sisters, became imitators[f] of God's churches in Judea,[g] which
are in Christ Jesus: You suffered from
your own people[h] the same things those
churches suffered from the Jews 15who
killed the Lord Jesus[i] and the prophets[j]
and also drove us out. They displease God
and are hostile to everyone 16in their effort to keep us from speaking to the Gentiles[k] so that they may be saved. In this
way they always heap up their sins to the
limit.[l] The wrath of God has come upon
them at last.[b]

2:3 [i] 2Co 2:17 [j] 2Co 4:2 **2:4** [k] Gal 2:7; 1Ti 1:11 [l] S Ro 2:29 [m] S Rev 2:23 **2:5** [n] S Ac 20:33 [o] ver 10; S Ro 1:9 **2:6** [p] Jn 5:41, 44 [q] 1Co 9:1,2 [r] 2Co 11:7-11 **2:7** [s] S ver 11 **2:8** [t] S Ro 1:1 [u] 2Co 12:15; 1Jn 3:16 **2:9** [v] S Ac 18:3 [w] S 2Co 11:9; 2Th 3:8 **2:10** [x] 1Th 1:5 [y] ver 5; S Ro 1:9 [z] 2Co 1:12 **2:11** [a] ver 7; 1Co 4:14; Gal 4:19; S 1Ti 1:2; Phm 10; S 1Jn 2:1 **2:12** [b] S Eph 4:1 [c] S Ro 8:28 **2:13** [d] 1Th 1:2; S Ro 1:8 [e] S Heb 4:12 **2:14** [f] 1Th 1:6 [g] Gal 1:22 [h] Ac 17:5; 2Th 1:4 **2:15** [i] Lk 24:20; Ac 2:23 [j] S Mt 5:12 **2:16** [k] Ac 13:45, 50; 17:5; S 20:3; 21:27; 24:9 [l] Mt 23:32

[a] 7 Some manuscripts *were gentle* [b] 16 Or *them fully*

---

catching fish; it came to refer to any sort of cunning used for profit.

2:4 *our hearts.* Not simply our emotions, but also our intellects and wills (see note on Ps 4:7).

2:5 *mask to cover up greed.* Personal profit was never Paul's aim (see Ac 20:33; 2Co 2:17 and note).

2:6 *apostles.* See note on Mk 6:30. *our authority.* Apostles were entitled to be supported by the church (see 1Co 9:3–14; 2Co 11:7–11). Paul did not always take advantage of the right but insisted that he had it.

2:7 *as a nursing mother.* See v. 11, where Paul also applies the metaphor of a father to himself.

2:9 *toil and hardship.* Greeks despised manual labor and viewed it as fit only for slaves, but Paul was not ashamed of doing any sort of work that would help further the gospel. He did not want to be unduly dependent on others (see 2Th 3:8).

2:11 *as a father.* See note on v. 7.

2:12 *live lives worthy of God.* See Eph 4:1. *calls.* See notes on 1:4; Ro 8:28. *kingdom.* The chief subject of Jesus' teaching (see notes on Mt 3:2; Lk 4:43). Paul did not use this term often but used it once to sum up the message of his preaching (Ac 20:25; cf. Ac 28:31). *glory.* God's splendor and majesty revealed to us at the consummation of his kingdom (see Mk 8:38; Ro 5:2; 8:18; cf. Eze 43:2 and note; 1Jn 3:2).

2:13 *not as a human word.* Not tailored to fit the popular knowledge of the day.

2:14 *imitators.* See note on 1:6. *You suffered from your own people.* At the time of Paul's initial visit to Thessalonica, persecution instigated by the Jews apparently was carried out by Gentiles (see Ac 17:5–9). *Jews.* Although Paul had great love and deep concern for the salvation of those of his own race (see Ro 9:1–3; 10:1), he did not fail to rebuke harshly Jews who persecuted the church.

2:15 *prophets.* Throughout OT history, Israelites had persecuted their prophets (cf. Ac 7:52). *drove us out.* See Ac 9:23–25,29–30; 13:50–51; 14:5–6,19; 17:10,13–14.

2:16 *wrath of God has come.* The eschatological wrath, the final outpouring of God's anger upon sinful humanity (see 1:10 and note). It is spoken of as already present, either because it had been partially experienced by the Jews or because of its absolute certainty.

Paul's Longing to See the Thessalonians

17 But, brothers and sisters, when we
were orphaned by being separated from
you for a short time (in person, not in
thought),[m] out of our intense longing we
made every effort to see you.[n] 18 For we
wanted to come to you—certainly I, Paul,
did, again and again—but Satan[o] blocked
our way.[p] 19 For what is our hope, our joy,
or the crown[q] in which we will glory[r] in
the presence of our Lord Jesus when he
comes?[s] Is it not you? 20 Indeed, you are
our glory[t] and joy.

3 So when we could stand it no longer,[u]
we thought it best to be left by ourselves in Athens.[v] 2 We sent Timothy,[w] who
is our brother and co-worker[x] in God's
service in spreading the gospel of Christ,[y]
to strengthen and encourage you in your
faith, 3 so that no one would be unsettled
by these trials.[z] For you know quite well
that we are destined for them.[a] 4 In fact,
when we were with you, we kept telling
you that we would be persecuted. And it
turned out that way, as you well know.[b]
5 For this reason, when I could stand it
no longer,[c] I sent to find out about your
faith.[d] I was afraid that in some way the
tempter[e] had tempted you and that our labors might have been in vain.[f]

Timothy's Encouraging Report

6 But Timothy[g] has just now come to
us from you[h] and has brought good news
about your faith and love.[i] He has told us
that you always have pleasant memories
of us and that you long to see us, just
as we also long to see you.[j] 7 Therefore,
brothers and sisters, in all our distress and
persecution we were encouraged about
you because of your faith. 8 For now we
really live, since you are standing firm[k] in
the Lord. 9 How can we thank God enough
for you[l] in return for all the joy we have in
the presence of our God because of you?[m]
10 Night and day we pray[n] most earnestly
that we may see you again[o] and supply
what is lacking in your faith.

11 Now may our God and Father[p] himself
and our Lord Jesus clear the way for us to
come to you. 12 May the Lord make your
love increase and overflow for each other[q]
and for everyone else, just as ours does for
you. 13 May he strengthen your hearts so
that you will be blameless[r] and holy in the

2:17 [m] 1Co 5:3; Col 2:5 [n] 1Th 3:10 **2:18** [o] S Mt 4:10 [p] Ro 1:13; 15:22 **2:19** [q] Isa 62:3; Php 4:1 [r] 2Co 1:14 [s] S Mt 16:27; S Lk 17:30; S 1Co 1:7; 4:5; 1Th 3:13; 2Th 1:8-10; 1Pe 1:7; 1Jn 2:28; S Rev 1:7 **2:20** [t] 2Co 1:14 **3:1** [u] ver 5 [v] S Ac 17:15 **3:2** [w] S Ac 16:1 [x] S 1Co 3:9 [y] S 2Co 2:12 **3:3** [z] Mk 4:17; Jn 16:33; Ro 5:3; 2Co 1:4; 4:17; 2Ti 3:12 [a] S Ac 9:16; 14:22 **3:4** [b] 1Th 2:14 **3:5** [c] ver 1 [d] ver 2 [e] Mt 4:3 [f] Gal 2:2; Php 2:16 **3:6** [g] S Ac 16:1 [h] Ac 18:5 [i] 1Th 1:3 [j] 1Th 2:17,18 **3:8** [k] S 1Co 16:13 **3:9** [l] 1Th 1:2 [m] 1Th 2:19,20 **3:10** [n] 2Ti 1:3 [o] 1Th 2:17

3:11 [p] ver 13; S Php 4:20 **3:12** [q] Php 1:9; 1Th 4:9,10; 2Th 1:3 **3:13** [r] Ps 15:2; 1Co 1:8; Php 2:15; 1Th 5:23; 1Ti 6:14; 2Pe 3:14

2:17 *orphaned.* Paul is like a mother (v. 7), a father (v. 11) and now an orphan.
2:18 *Satan blocked our way.* Cf. Introduction to Job: Theme and Message; cf. also note on Eph 1:3.
2:19 *crown.* Not a royal crown, but a wreath used on festive occasions or as the prize in the Greek games (see 2Ti 4:8 and note; Jas 1:12; 1Pe 5:4; Rev 2:10 and note). *when he comes.* See 3:13; 4:15; 5:23; 2Th 2:1,8. The expression was used regarding the arrival of a great person, as on a royal visit.
2:20 *you are our glory and joy.* True both now (cf. Php 4:1) and when Christ returns.
3:1–2 Paul first went to Athens alone, then sent to Berea for Silas and Timothy (Ac 17:14–15). It is not clear whether Silas, as instructed (Ac 17:15), came to Athens with Timothy. However, when Timothy later returned from Thessalonica to Paul, who was now at Corinth, Silas came with him (Ac 18:5). See Introduction: Background of the Thessalonian Letters.
3:1 *we.* An editorial "we," referring to Paul alone.
3:2 *co-worker in God's service.* A striking way of viewing Christian service, found also in 1Co 3:9. *gospel of Christ.* See notes on 1:5; Mk 1:1. *strengthen.* In Greek classical literature the word was generally used in the literal sense of putting a buttress on a building. In the NT it is mainly used figuratively, as here.
3:3 *trials.* The opposition and persecution suffered by the Thessalonian converts. *we are destined for them.* Christians must expect troubles (see Mk 4:17; Jn 16:33; Ac 14:22; Php 1:29; 2Ti 3:12; cf. 1Pe 2:21 and note), but these are not disasters, for they advance God's purposes (see Ac 11:19; Ro 5:3; 2Co 1:4; 4:17 and note).
3:5 *I.* Paul uses the Greek emphatic pronoun (elsewhere used only in 2:18) to bring out his deep concern. *tempter.* Satan is spoken of in every major division of the NT. He is supreme among evil spirits (see Jn 12:31; 16:11; Eph 2:2). His activities can affect the physical (see 2Co 12:7) and the spiritual (see Mt 13:39; Mk 4:15; 2Co 4:4 and note). He tempted Jesus (Mt 4:1–11) and continues to tempt Jesus' servants (see Lk 22:3; 1Co 7:5). He hinders missionary work (2:18). But he has already been defeated (see Mt 12:29; Col 2:15 and note), and Christians need not be overwhelmed by him (see Eph 6:16). His final overthrow is certain (see Rev 20:10).
3:6 *brought good news.* The only place where the Greek for this phrase is used by Paul for anything other than the gospel. Three things caused him joy: (1) "your faith"—a right attitude toward God; (2) "your ... love"—a right attitude toward others; (3) "you long to see us"—a right attitude toward Paul.
3:9 *thank God.* The preceding shows that Paul's work of evangelism had been effective. He might have congratulated himself on work well done, but instead he thanked God for the joy he had from what God had done.
3:10 *Night and day.* Not prayer at two set times, but frequent prayer (see 1:2–3). *most earnestly.* Translates a strong and unusual Greek compound word (found elsewhere in the NT only in 5:13; Eph 3:20) that brings out Paul's passionate longing. *what is lacking.* Some of the things lacking were of a practical nature, such as moral (4:1–12) and disciplinary matters (5:12–24). Others were doctrinal, such as confusion over Christ's return (4:13—5:11). *your faith.* The fifth time in the chapter that Paul speaks of their faith (see vv. 2,5–7).
3:11 In the middle of a letter Paul frequently breaks into prayer (e.g., Eph 1:15–23; 3:14–21; Php 1:9–11; Col 1:9–12). For the link between Father and Son, see note on 1:1.
3:12 *Lord.* In Paul's writings this usually means Jesus rather than the Father.
3:13 *strengthen.* See note on v. 2. *holy.* The basic idea is "set apart [for God]" (see notes on Ex 3:5; Lev 11:44; Ro 6:22; Eph 1:1). Here it refers to the completed process of sanctification (see note on 1Co 1:2). *holy ones.* Used of the saints (Christians) in many NT passages (see note on Ro 1:7). Here it may mean the departed saints who will return with Jesus, the angels (see Mk 8:38) or, more probably, both.

presence of our God and Father[s] when our
Lord Jesus comes[t] with all his holy ones.[u]

Living to Please God

4 As for other matters, brothers and sisters,[v] we instructed you how to live[w]
in order to please God,[x] as in fact you are
living. Now we ask you and urge you in
the Lord Jesus to do this more and more.
2 For you know what instructions we gave
you by the authority of the Lord Jesus.
3 It is God's will[y] that you should be
sanctified: that you should avoid sexual immorality;[z] 4 that each of you should
learn to control your own body[aa] in a way
that is holy and honorable, 5 not in passionate lust[b] like the pagans,[c] who do not
know God;[d] 6 and that in this matter no
one should wrong or take advantage of a
brother or sister.[b][e] The Lord will punish[f]
all those who commit such sins,[g] as we
told you and warned you before. 7 For God
did not call us to be impure, but to live a
holy life.[h] 8 Therefore, anyone who rejects
this instruction does not reject a human
being but God, the very God who gives
you his Holy Spirit.[i]
9 Now about your love for one another[j]
we do not need to write to you,[k] for you
yourselves have been taught by God[l] to
love each other.[m] 10 And in fact, you do love
all of God's family throughout Macedonia.[n]
Yet we urge you, brothers and sisters, to do
so more and more,[o] 11 and to make it your
ambition to lead a quiet life: You should
mind your own business and work with
your hands,[p] just as we told you, 12 so that
your daily life may win the respect of outsiders[q] and so that you will not be dependent on anybody.

Believers Who Have Died

13 Brothers and sisters, we do not want
you to be uninformed[r] about those who
sleep in death,[s] so that you do not grieve
like the rest of mankind, who have no
hope.[t] 14 For we believe that Jesus died
and rose again,[u] and so we believe that
God will bring with Jesus those who have
fallen asleep in him.[v] 15 According to the

3:13 [s] ver 11; S Php 4:20 [t] S 1Th 2:19 [u] Mt 25:31; 2Th 1:7
4:1 [v] 2Co 13:11; 2Th 3:1 [w] S Eph 4:1 [x] S 2Co 5:9
4:3 [y] S Eph 5:17 [z] S 1Co 6:18
4:4 [a] 1Co 7:2,9
4:5 [b] Ro 1:26 [c] Eph 4:17 [d] S Gal 4:8
4:6 [e] Lev 25:17; 1Co 6:8 [f] Dt 32:35; Ps 94:1; Ro 2:5-11; 12:19; Heb 10:30,31 [g] Heb 13:4
4:7 [h] Lev 11:44; 1Pe 1:15
4:8 [i] Eze 36:27; Ro 5:5; 2Co 1:22; Gal 4:6; 1Jn 3:24
4:9 [j] S Ro 12:10 [k] 1Th 5:1 [l] S Jn 6:45 [m] S Jn 13:34
4:10 [n] S Ac 16:9 [o] S 1Th 3:12
4:11 [p] Eph 4:28; 2Th 3:10-12
4:12 [q] S Mk 4:11
4:13 [r] S Ro 11:25 [s] S Mt 9:24 [t] Eph 2:12
4:14 [u] Ro 14:9; 1Co 15:3,4; 2Co 5:15 [v] 1Co 15:18

[a] 4 Or *learn to live with your own wife*; or *learn to acquire a wife*   [b] 6 The Greek word for *brother or sister* (*adelphos*) refers here to a believer, whether man or woman, as part of God's family.

4:1 *live.* Lit. "walk." Paul uses this metaphor often of the Christian way (see Ro 6:4; 2Co 5:7; Eph 4:1; 5:15; Col 1:10, "live a life"; 2:6; 4:5, "act"). It points to steady progress. *we ask you and urge you.* Paul is not arrogant, but he does speak with authority in the Lord Jesus. He has the "mind of Christ" (1Co 2:16).

4:2 *instructions.* Used of authoritative commands and has a military ring ("orders," Ac 5:28; 16:24).

4:3 *sanctified.* See note on 3:13. *sexual immorality.* In the first century moral standards were generally very low, and chastity was regarded as an unreasonable restriction. Paul, however, would not compromise God's clear and demanding standards. The warning was needed, for Christians were not immune to the temptation (see 1Co 5:1).

4:5 *like the pagans.* See Ro 1:24–27. The Christian is to be different. *who do not know God.* See 2Th 1:8 and note; Gal 4:8; cf. Ps 79:6–7 and note.

4:6 *wrong … sister.* Sexual sin harms others besides those who engage in it. In adultery, e.g., the spouse is always wronged. Premarital sex wrongs the future partner by robbing him or her of the virginity that ought to be brought to marriage. *The Lord will punish.* A motive for chastity.

4:7 Another reason for chastity is God's call to holiness (see Heb 12:14; 1Pe 1:6 and notes).

4:8 *God who gives you his Holy Spirit.* Still another reason for chastity is that sexual sin is against God (see Ge 39:9 and note), who gives the Holy Spirit to believers for their sanctification. To live in sexual immorality is to reject God, specifically in regard to the Holy Spirit (cf. 1Co 6:12–20 and notes).

4:9 *love for one another.* Translates *philadelphia,* a Greek word that outside the NT almost without exception denoted the mutual love of children of the same father. In the NT it always means love of fellow believers in Christ, all of whom have the same heavenly Father. *taught by God.* Cf. Isa 54:13; Jn 6:45; 1Co 2:13.

4:11 *mind your own business.* Some Thessalonians, probably because of idleness, were taking undue interest in other people's affairs (see 2Th 3:11 and note). *work with your hands.* The Greeks in general thought manual labor degrading and fit only for slaves. Christians took seriously the need for earning their own living, but some of the Thessalonians, perhaps as a result of their belief in the imminent return of Christ (see 2Th 3:11), were neglecting work and relying on others to support them.

4:12 *not be dependent on anybody.* Or "have need of nothing." Both meanings are true and significant. Christians in need because of their idleness are not obedient Christians (cf. Titus 3:14).

4:13 *those who sleep in death.* For the Christian, sleep is a particularly apt metaphor for death, since death's finality and horror are removed by the assurance of resurrection. Some of the Thessalonians seem to have misunderstood Paul and thought all believers would live until Christ returns. When some died, the question arose, "Will those who have died have part in that great day?" See note on v. 15. *who have no hope.* Inscriptions on tombs and references in literature show that first-century pagans viewed death with horror, as the end of everything. The Christian attitude was in strong contrast (see 1Co 15:55–57; Php 1:20–23).

4:14 *died.* Paul does not say that Christ "slept," perhaps to underscore the fact that he bore the full horror of death so that those who believe in him would not have to. *rose again.* For the importance of the resurrection, see 1Co 15, especially vv. 14,17–22. *those who have fallen asleep in him.* Believers who have died trusting in Jesus.

4:15 *According to the Lord's word.* The doctrine mentioned here is not recorded in the Gospels and was either a direct revelation to Paul or something Jesus said that Christians passed on orally. *we who are still alive.* Those believers who will be alive when Christ returns. "We" does not necessarily mean that Paul thought that he would be alive then. He often identified himself with those he wrote to or about. Elsewhere he says that God will raise "us" at that time (1Co 6:14; 2Co 4:14). *will certainly not precede.* The Thessalonians had evidently been concerned that those among them who

Lord's word, we tell you that we who are still alive, who are left until the coming of the Lord,[w] will certainly not precede those who have fallen asleep.[x] 16 For the Lord himself will come down from heaven,[y] with a loud command, with the voice of the archangel[z] and with the trumpet call of God,[a] and the dead in Christ will rise first.[b] 17 After that, we who are still alive and are left[c] will be caught up together with them in the clouds[d] to meet the Lord in the air. And so we will be with the Lord[e] forever. 18 Therefore encourage one another[f] with these words.

The Day of the Lord

5 Now, brothers and sisters, about times and dates[g] we do not need to write to you,[h] 2 for you know very well that the day of the Lord[i] will come like a thief in the night.[j] 3 While people are saying, "Peace and safety,"[k] destruction will come on them suddenly,[l] as labor pains on a pregnant woman, and they will not escape.[m]

4 But you, brothers and sisters, are not in darkness[n] so that this day should surprise you like a thief.[o] 5 You are all children of the light[p] and children of the day. We do not belong to the night or to the darkness. 6 So then, let us not be like others, who are asleep,[q] but let us be awake[r] and sober.[s] 7 For those who sleep, sleep at night, and those who get drunk, get drunk at night.[t] 8 But since we belong to the day,[u] let us be sober, putting on faith and love as a breastplate,[v] and the hope of salvation[w] as a helmet.[x] 9 For God did not appoint us to suffer wrath[y] but to receive salvation through our Lord Jesus Christ.[z] 10 He died for us so that, whether we are awake or asleep, we may live together with him.[a] 11 Therefore encourage one another[b] and build each other up,[c] just as in fact you are doing.

Final Instructions

12 Now we ask you, brothers and sisters, to acknowledge those who work hard[d] among you, who care for you in the Lord[e] and who admonish you. 13 Hold them in the highest regard in love be-

4:15 [w] S 1Co 1:7 [x] 1Co 15:52
4:16 [y] S Mt 16:27 [z] Jude 9 [a] S Mt 24:31 [b] 1Co 15:23; 2Th 2:1; Rev 14:13
4:17 [c] 1Co 15:52 [d] Ac 1:9; S Ac 8:39; S Rev 1:7; 11:12 [e] S Jn 12:26
4:18 [f] 1Th 5:11
5:1 [g] Ac 1:7 [h] 1Th 4:9
5:2 [i] S 1Co 1:8 [j] S Lk 12:39
5:3 [k] Jer 4:10; 6:14; Eze 13:10 [l] Job 15:21; Ps 35:8; 55:15; Isa 29:5; 47:9, 11 [m] 2Th 1:9
5:4 [n] S Ac 26:18; 1Jn 2:8 [o] ver 2
5:5 [p] S Lk 16:8
5:6 [q] Ro 13:11 [r] S Mt 25:13 [s] S Ac 24:25
5:7 [t] Ac 2:15; Ro 13:13; 2Pe 2:13
5:8 [u] ver 5 [v] S Eph 6:14 [w] Ro 8:24 [x] Isa 59:17; Eph 6:17
5:9 [y] 1Th 1:10 [z] 2Th 2:13, 14
5:10 [a] Ro 14:9; 2Co 5:15
5:11 [b] 1Th 4:18 [c] Eph 4:29
5:12 [d] Ro 16:6,12; 1Co 15:10 [e] 1Ti 5:17; Heb 13:17

had died would miss their place in the great events when the Lord comes, and Paul assures them this will not be the case.

4:16 *the Lord himself.* See Ac 1:11. *archangel.* The only named archangel in the Bible is Michael (Jude 9; see Da 10:13). In Scripture, Gabriel is simply called an angel (Lk 1:19,26). *will rise first.* Before the ascension of believers mentioned in the next verse.

4:17 *we who are still alive.* See note on v. 15. *caught up.* The only place in the NT where a "rapture" (from Latin *raptus*) is clearly referred to. Christians debate whether the rapture will take place before, after or in the middle of a future period of great tribulation. Whichever view is taken, the rapture will not be silent or secret, since it is accompanied by "a loud command ... the voice of the archangel and ... the trumpet call of God" (v. 16). *in the clouds.* Cf. Ac 1:9 and note. *with the Lord.* The chief hope of the believer (see 5:10; Jn 14:3; 2Co 5:8; Php 1:23; Col 3:4).

4:18 *encourage one another.* The primary purpose of vv. 13–18 is not to give a chronology of future events, though that is involved, but to urge mutual encouragement, as shown here and in v. 13.

5:1 *times and dates.* See Ac 1:6–7. There have always been some Christians who try to fix the date of our Lord's return, but apparently the Thessalonians were not among them.

5:2 *day of the Lord.* See 1Co 5:5. The expression goes back to Am 5:18 (see note there). In the OT it is a time when God will come and intervene with judgment and/or blessing (see note on Joel 1:15). In the NT the thought of judgment continues (see Ro 2:5; 2Pe 2:9), but it is also the "day of redemption" (Eph 4:30); the "day of God" (2Pe 3:12) or of Christ (1Co 1:8; Php 1:6); and the "last day" (Jn 6:39), the "great Day" (Jude 6) or simply "the day" (2Th 1:10). It is the consummation of all things. There will be some preliminary signs (e.g., 2Th 2:3), but for unbelievers the coming will be as unexpected as that of a thief in the night (cf. Mt 24:43–44; Lk 12:39–40; 2Pe 3:10; Rev 3:3; 16:15).

5:3 *destruction.* Not annihilation, but exclusion from the Lord's presence (see 2Th 1:9 and note); thus the ruin of life and all its proud accomplishments. *suddenly.* Paul stresses the surprise of unbelievers. He uses a word found elsewhere in the NT only in Lk 21:34. *labor pains.* Here the idea is not the pain of childbirth so much as the suddenness and inevitability of such pains. *not.* An emphatic double negative in the Greek, a construction Paul uses only four times in all his writings.

5:4 *darkness.* Believers no longer live in darkness, nor are they of the darkness (v. 5). See Ac 26:18; 2Co 6:14; see also 1Jn 1:5–7 and notes. *thief.* See note on v. 2.

5:5 *children of ... children of.* Echoes Hebrew idiom, in which to be the "children of" a quality meant to be characterized by that quality. Christians do not simply live in the light; they are characterized by light.

5:6 *asleep.* Unbelievers are spiritually insensitive, but this kind of sleep is not for "children of the light" (v. 5). *be awake.* Lit. "watch," which is in keeping with the emphasis Paul is placing on Christ's coming (cf. Mt 24:42–43; 25:13; Mk 13:34–37). *sober.* A contrast with the conduct mentioned in v. 7.

5:8 *the day.* A reference to the light that characterizes Christians; perhaps it refers also to the coming of Christ (see v. 2 and note). *breastplate ... helmet.* Paul also uses the metaphor of armor in Ro 13:12; 2Co 6:7; 10:4; Eph 6:13–17 (see notes on Eph 6:14,17). He does not consistently attach a particular virtue to each piece of armor; it is the general idea of equipment for battle that is pictured. For the triad of faith, hope and love, see 1:3 and note.

5:9 *appoint.* God's appointment, not human choice, is the significant thing. *wrath.* See note on 1:10. *salvation.* Our final, completed salvation.

5:10 *are awake or asleep.* That is, live or die; or, if the sense is moral, are alert or carnal (see v. 6). *with him.* To be Christ's is to have entered a relationship that nothing can destroy.

5:11 *build ... up.* The verb basically applies to building houses, but Paul frequently used it for Christians being edified.

5:12 *those who work hard among you.* Not much is known about the organization and leadership of the church at this period, but the reference is possibly to elders (cf. Heb 13:7,17 and notes).

5:13 *because of their work.* Not merely because of personal attachment or respect for their high position,

cause of their work. Live in peace with
each other.[f] 14 And we urge you, brothers
and sisters, warn those who are idle[g] and
disruptive, encourage the disheartened,
help the weak,[h] be patient with everyone. 15 Make sure that nobody pays back
wrong for wrong,[i] but always strive to do
what is good for each other[j] and for everyone else.
16 Rejoice always,[k] 17 pray continually,[l]
18 give thanks in all circumstances;[m] for
this is God's will for you in Christ Jesus.
19 Do not quench the Spirit.[n] 20 Do not
treat prophecies[o] with contempt 21 but test
them all;[p] hold on to what is good,[q] 22 reject every kind of evil.

5:13 [f]S Mk 9:50 **5:14** [g]2Th 3:6, 7,11 [h]Ro 14:1; 1Co 8:7-12 **5:15** [i]Ro 12:17; 1Pe 3:9 [j]Eph 4:32 **5:16** [k]Php 4:4 **5:17** [l]S Lk 18:1 **5:18** [m]S Eph 5:20 **5:19** [n]Eph 4:30 **5:20** [o]1Co 14:1-40 **5:21** [p]1Co 14:29; 1Jn 4:1 [q]Ro 12:9 **5:23** [r]S Ro 15:33 [s]Heb 4:12 [t]S 1Th 3:13 [u]S 1Th 2:19

23 May God himself, the God of peace,[r]
sanctify you through and through. May
your whole spirit, soul[s] and body be kept
blameless[t] at the coming of our Lord Jesus
Christ.[u] 24 The one who calls[v] you is faithful,[w] and he will do it.[x]

25 Brothers and sisters, pray for us.[y]
26 Greet all God's people with a holy kiss.[z]
27 I charge you before the Lord to have this
letter read to all the brothers and sisters.[a]
28 The grace of our Lord Jesus Christ be
with you.[b]

5:24 [v]S Ro 8:28 [w]S 1Co 1:9 [x]Nu 23:19; Php 1:6 **5:25** [y]Eph 6:19; Col 4:3; 2Th 3:1; Heb 13:18 **5:26** [z]S Ro 16:16 **5:27** [a]2Th 3:14; S 1Ti 4:13 **5:28** [b]S Ro 16:20

---

but in appreciation for their work. *Live in peace.* The words apply to Christian relationships in general, but here they probably refer especially to right relations between leaders and those under them (cf. Ro 14:17,19).

5:14 *those who are idle.* It seems that some Thessalonians were so sure the second coming was close that they had given up their jobs in order to prepare for it, but Paul says they should work (see 2Th 3:10–11 and notes). *the disheartened … the weak.* These are to be helped, not rejected, by the strong (cf. Ro 14:1–15; 1Co 8:13 and note).

5:15 *pays back.* Retaliation is never a Christian option (cf. Ro 12:17 and note). Christians are called to forgive (see Mt 5:38–42; 18:21–35; Eph 4:32 and note).

5:16 See Php 4:4 and note.

5:17 For the practice of continual (or regular) prayer, see 1:3; 2:13; Ro 1:9–10; Eph 6:18; Col 1:3; 2Ti 1:3.

5:18 *give thanks.* See Eph 5:20 and note.

5:19 *quench the Spirit.* Paul may be warning against a mechanical attitude toward worship that discourages the expression of the gifts of the Spirit in the local assembly (see v. 20).

5:20 *prophecies.* For the gift of prophecy, see Ro 12:6; 1Co 12:10,28 and note on 12:10; 13:2; 14; Eph 4:11. For the function of prophecies, see 1Co 14:3.

5:21 *test them all.* The approval of prophecy (v. 20) does not mean that anyone who claims to speak in the name of the Lord is to be accepted without question. Paul does not say what specific tests are to be applied, but he is clear that every teaching must be tested — surely his audience must be in agreement with his gospel (cf. 1Co 14:29–33 and notes).

5:23 A typical prayer. *God of peace.* A fitting reference to God in view of vv. 12–15. But Paul often refers to God in this way near the end of his letters (see Ro 1:7 and note; 15:33; 16:20; 1Co 14:33; 2Co 13:11; Php 4:9; cf. 2Th 3:16). See also Heb 13:20–21. *sanctify.* See 1Co 1:2 and note. *your whole spirit, soul and body.* Paul emphasizes the whole person without attempting to differentiate various parts (see Heb 4:12 and note).

5:24 Paul's confidence rests in the nature of God (cf. Ge 18:25 and note), who can be relied on to complete what he begins (see Nu 23:19; Php 1:6 and notes).

5:26 *all.* Paul sent a warm greeting to everyone, even those he had corrected. *holy kiss.* A kiss was a normal greeting of that day, similar to our modern handshake (see Ro 16:16; 1Co 16:20; 2Co 13:12 and notes; cf. "kiss of love," 1Pe 5:14).

5:27 *I charge you.* Surprisingly strong language, meaning "I put you on oath" — used only here in the NT. Paul clearly wanted every member of the church to read or hear his letter and to know of his concern and advice for them.

5:28 Paul always ended his letters with a benediction of grace for his readers, sometimes adding other blessings, as in 2Co 13:14. *grace.* See note on Ro 1:7. *Lord Jesus Christ.* See note on 1:1. *with you.* See note on 2Co 13:14.

2 THESSALONIANS

INTRODUCTION

Author, Date and Place of Writing

Paul's authorship of 2 Thessalonians has been questioned more often than that of 1 Thessalonians, in spite of the fact that it has more support from early Christian writers. Objections are based on internal factors rather than on the adequacy of the statements of the church fathers. It is thought that there are differences in the vocabulary (ten words not used elsewhere), in the style (it is said to be unexpectedly formal) and in the eschatology (the doctrine of the "man of lawlessness" is not taught elsewhere). These minor differences, however, are not sufficient to overturn the united testimony of the early church.

Because of its similarity to 1 Thessalonians, this epistle was probably written soon after the first letter. The situation in the church seems to have been much the same. Paul probably penned it (see 1:1; 3:17) c. AD 51 or 52 in Corinth, after Silas and Timothy had returned from delivering 1 Thessalonians (see chart, p. 1845; see also Introduction to 1 Thessalonians).

Purpose

Inasmuch as the situation in the Thessalonian church has not changed substantially, Paul's purpose in writing is very much the same as in his first letter to its members. He writes (1) to encourage persecuted believers (1:4 – 10), (2) to correct a misunderstanding concerning the Lord's return (2:1 – 12) and (3) to exhort the Thessalonians to be steadfast and to work for a living (2:13 — 3:15).

Theme

Like 1 Thessalonians, this letter deals extensively with eschatology (see Introduction to 1 Thessalonians: Themes). In fact, in 2 Thessalonians 18 out of 47 verses deal with this subject.

Author:
The apostle Paul

Audience:
The church at Thessalonica

Date:
About AD 51 or 52

Theme:
Paul writes to correct a misunderstanding concerning the Lord's return and to exhort the Thessalonian believers to be steadfast and to work for a living.

Like 1 Thessalonians, this letter deals extensively with eschatology.

Thessalonian odeum, a small theater where musicians and orators performed

Todd Bolen/www.BiblePlaces.com

Outline

I. Introduction (ch. 1)
   A. Greetings (1:1 – 2)
   B. Thanksgiving for the Thessalonians' Faith, Love and Perseverance (1:3 – 10)
   C. Intercession for Their Spiritual Progress (1:11 – 12)

II. Instruction (ch. 2)
   A. Prophecy regarding the Day of the Lord (2:1 – 12)
   B. Thanksgiving for Their Election and Calling (Their Position) (2:13 – 15)
   C. Prayer for Their Service and Testimony (Their Practice) (2:16 – 17)

III. Injunctions (ch. 3)
   A. Call to Prayer (3:1 – 5)
   B. Charge to Discipline the Disorderly and Lazy (3:6 – 15)
   C. Conclusion, Final Greetings and Benediction (3:16 – 18)

1 Paul, Silas[a][a] and Timothy,[b]

To the church of the Thessalonians[c] in
God our Father and the Lord Jesus Christ:

2 Grace and peace to you from God the
Father and the Lord Jesus Christ.[d]

Thanksgiving and Prayer

3 We ought always to thank God for
you,[e] brothers and sisters,[b] and rightly so,
because your faith is growing more and
more, and the love all of you have for one
another is increasing.[f] 4 Therefore, among
God's churches we boast[g] about your perseverance and faith[h] in all the persecutions
and trials you are enduring.[i]
5 All this is evidence[j] that God's judgment is right, and as a result you will be
counted worthy[k] of the kingdom of God, for
which you are suffering. 6 God is just:[l] He
will pay back trouble to those who trouble you[m] 7 and give relief to you who are
troubled, and to us as well. This will happen when the Lord Jesus is revealed from
heaven[n] in blazing fire[o] with his powerful
angels.[p] 8 He will punish[q] those who do not
know God[r] and do not obey the gospel of
our Lord Jesus.[s] 9 They will be punished
with everlasting destruction[t] and shut out
from the presence of the Lord[u] and from the
glory of his might[v] 10 on the day[w] he comes
to be glorified[x] in his holy people and to
be marveled at among all those who have
believed. This includes you, because you
believed our testimony to you.[y]
11 With this in mind, we constantly pray
for you,[z] that our God may make you worthy[a] of his calling,[b] and that by his power he
may bring to fruition your every desire for
goodness[c] and your every deed prompted
by faith.[d] 12 We pray this so that the name
of our Lord Jesus may be glorified in you,[e]
and you in him, according to the grace of
our God and the Lord Jesus Christ.[c]

The Man of Lawlessness

2 Concerning the coming of our Lord
Jesus Christ[f] and our being gathered
to him,[g] we ask you, brothers and sisters,
2 not to become easily unsettled or alarmed

1:1 [a]S Ac 15:22 [b]S Ac 16:1; 1Th 1:1 [c]S Ac 17:1 **1:2** [d]S Ro 1:7 **1:3** [e]S Ro 1:8; Eph 5:20 [f]S 1Th 3:12 **1:4** [g]2Co 7:14 [h]1Th 1:3 [i]1Th 1:6; 2:14; S 3:3 **1:5** [j]Php 1:28 [k]Lk 20:35 **1:6** [l]Lk 18:7, 8 [m]Ro 12:19; Col 3:25; S Rev 6:10 **1:7** [n]S Lk 17:30 [o]Heb 10:27; S 12:29; 2Pe 3:7; S Rev 1:14 [p]Jude 14 **1:8** [q]Ps 79:6; Isa 66:15; Jer 10:25 [r]S Gal 4:8 [s]Ro 2:8; S 2Co 2:12 **1:9** [t]Php 3:19; 1Th 5:3; 2Pe 3:7 [u]2Ki 17:18 [v]Isa 2:10, 19; 2Th 2:8 **1:10** [w]1Co 3:13 [x]Jn 17:10 [y]1Co 1:6 **1:11** [z]S Ro 1:10 [a]ver 5 [b]S Ro 8:28 [c]Ro 15:14 [d]1Th 1:3 **1:12** [e]Isa 24:15; Php 2:9-11 **2:1** [f]S 1Th 2:19 [g]Mk 13:27; 1Th 4:15-17

[a] *1* Greek *Silvanus,* a variant of *Silas* [b] *3* The Greek word for *brothers and sisters* (*adelphoi*) refers here to believers, both men and women, as part of God's family; also in 2:1, 13, 15; 3:1, 6, 13. [c] *12* Or *God and Lord, Jesus Christ*

1:1–2 See note on 1Th 1:1.
1:1 *Paul.* See note on Ro 1:1. *Lord Jesus Christ.* Occurs also at the end of this letter (3:18). See note on 1Th 1:1.
1:2 *Grace and peace.* See note on Ro 1:7.
1:3 *ought.* Paul is obliged to give thanks where it is due (cf. 1Th 1:7–8; see note on Php 1:3–4). *brothers and sisters.* See NIV text note. *faith … love.* Two virtues that Paul had been pleased to acknowledge in the Thessalonian church (see 1Th 3:6–7 and note on 3:6) but that were also somewhat lacking (see 1Th 3:10,12 and note on 3:10). *is increasing.* The same verb Paul had used in his prayer that its members' love might grow (1Th 3:12).
1:4 *we.* Emphatic, "we ourselves." Paul seems to imply that it was unusual for the founders of a church to boast about it, though others might do so (cf. 1Th 1:9). But the Thessalonians were so outstanding that Paul departed from normal practice. *persecutions and trials.* See 1Th 1:6; 2:14; 3:3.
1:5 *evidence that God's judgment is right.* The evidence was in the way the Thessalonians endured trials. The judgment on them was right because God did not leave them to their own resources. He provided strength to endure, and this in turn produced spiritual and moral character. It also proved that God was on their side and gave a warning to their persecutors (cf. Php 1:28 and note). *kingdom of God.* See notes on 1Th 2:12; Mt 3:2.
1:6 *God is just.* The justice of God brings punishment on unrepentant sinners (cf. Mk 9:47–48; Lk 13:3–5), and it may be in the here and now (see Ro 1:24,26,28 and note) as well as on judgment day.
1:7 *give relief.* Retribution involves not only punishment of the evil but also relief for the righteous. *us as well.* Paul was no academic theologian writing in comfort from a distance; rather, he was suffering just as they were. *revealed.* Christ is now hidden, and many people even deny his existence. But at his second coming he will be seen by everyone for who he is. *blazing fire.* He comes to punish wickedness (see Rev 19:12; cf. Isa 66:15; Rev 1:14). *his powerful angels.* Perhaps a class of angels (such a group is mentioned in apocalyptic writings) given special power to do God's will (cf. Rev 19:14 and note).
1:8 *do not know God.* Does not refer to those who have never heard of the true God but to those who refuse to recognize him (cf. 2:10,12 and note on 2:10; Ro 1:28). *do not obey.* The gospel invites acceptance, and rejection is disobedience to a royal invitation.
1:9 *destruction.* Since salvation implies resurrection of the body, annihilation cannot be in mind here (see 1Th 5:3 and note). The word means something like "complete ruin" (see Mt 7:13 and note). Here it means being shut out from Christ's presence. This eternal separation is the penalty of sin and the essence of hell (cf. Rev 20:14–15; 21:8,27).
1:10 *the day.* See note on 1Th 5:2. *glorified in his holy people.* Not simply "among" but "in" them. His glory is seen in what they are. *holy people.* See note on 1Th 3:13. *our testimony.* The preaching of the gospel is essentially bearing testimony to what God has done in Christ.
1:11 *constantly pray.* See notes on 1Th 5:17; Col 4:2. *desire for goodness … deed prompted by faith.* God initiates every such "desire" and every act "prompted by faith" (see 1Th 1:3 and note); Paul prays accordingly that he will bring them to fulfillment.
1:12 *name.* In ancient times one's name was often more than a personal label; it summed up what a person was. *Lord Jesus may be glorified in you.* Paul looks for glory to be ascribed to Christ because of all he will do in the lives of the Thessalonian Christians (see v. 10 and note). *and you in him.* Christians will share in Christ's glory by virtue of their union with him (cf. Jn 15:4 and note; 17:21).
2:1 *coming.* See 1Th 2:19 and note. The second coming of Christ is the principal topic of 2 Thessalonians. What Paul wrote was supplemental to his oral teaching and the instructions contained in his earlier letter. *gathered to him.* See 1Th 4:17 and note.
2:2 *unsettled.* The Greek for this verb was often used of a ship adrift from its mooring and suggests lack of stability.

by the teaching allegedly from us—whether by a prophecy or by word of mouth or
by letter[h]—asserting that the day of the
Lord[i] has already come.[j] 3 Don't let anyone
deceive you[k] in any way, for that day will
not come until the rebellion[l] occurs and
the man of lawlessness[a] is revealed,[m] the
man doomed to destruction. 4 He will oppose and will exalt himself over everything
that is called God[n] or is worshiped, so that
he sets himself up in God's temple, proclaiming himself to be God.[o]
5 Don't you remember that when I was
with you I used to tell you these things?[p]
6 And now you know what is holding him
back,[q] so that he may be revealed at the
proper time. 7 For the secret power of lawlessness is already at work; but the one
who now holds it back[r] will continue to
do so till he is taken out of the way. 8 And
then the lawless one will be revealed,[s]
whom the Lord Jesus will overthrow with
the breath of his mouth[t] and destroy by
the splendor of his coming.[u] 9 The coming
of the lawless one will be in accordance
with how Satan[v] works. He will use all
sorts of displays of power through signs
and wonders[w] that serve the lie, 10 and all
the ways that wickedness deceives those
who are perishing.[x] They perish because
they refused to love the truth and so be
saved.[y] 11 For this reason God sends them[z]
a powerful delusion[a] so that they will believe the lie[b] 12 and so that all will be condemned who have not believed the truth
but have delighted in wickedness.[c]

Stand Firm

13 But we ought always to thank God
for you,[d] brothers and sisters loved by
the Lord, because God chose you as firstfruits[b][e] to be saved[f] through the sanctifying work of the Spirit[g] and through belief in the truth. 14 He called you[h] to this
through our gospel,[i] that you might share
in the glory of our Lord Jesus Christ.
15 So then, brothers and sisters, stand
firm[j] and hold fast to the teachings[c] we

2:2 [h] ver 15; 2Th 3:17 [i] S 1Co 1:8 [j] 2Ti 2:18 **2:3** [k] S Mk 13:5 [l] Mt 24:10-12 [m] ver 8; Da 7:25; 8:25; 11:36; Rev 13:5,6 **2:4** [n] 1Co 8:5 [o] Isa 14:13,14; Eze 28:2 **2:5** [p] 1Th 3:4 **2:6** [q] ver 7 **2:7** [r] ver 6 **2:8** [s] S ver 3 [t] Isa 11:4; Rev 2:16; 19:15 [u] S Lk 17:30 **2:9** [v] S Mt 4:10 [w] Mt 24:24; Rev 13:13; S Jn 4:48 **2:10** [x] S 1Co 1:18 [y] Pr 4:6; Jn 3:17-19 **2:11** [z] Ro 1:28 [a] Mt 24:5; S Mk 13:5 [b] Ro 1:25 **2:12** [c] Ro 1:32; 2:8 **2:13** [d] S Ro 1:8 [e] Eph 1:4 [f] 1Th 5:9 [g] 1Pe 1:2 **2:14** [h] S Ro 8:28; S 11:29 [i] 1Th 1:5 **2:15** [j] S 1Co 16:13

[a] 3 Some manuscripts *sin* [b] 13 Some manuscripts *because from the beginning God chose you* [c] 15 Or *traditions*

alarmed. Jesus issued a similar instruction, using the same verb (Mk 13:7). *teaching allegedly from us.* Paul seems to be uncertain about what was disturbing them, so he uses a general expression. *prophecy.* Lit. "spirit," denoting a revelation inspired by either the Holy Spirit or some other spirit. *word of mouth.* Perhaps referring to a sermon or other oral communication. *letter.* A forgery. *day of the Lord.* See 1Th 5:2 and note. *has already come.* Obviously Christ's climactic return had not occurred, but Paul was combating the idea that the final days had begun and their completion would be imminent.
2:3 *the rebellion.* At the last time there will be a falling away from the faith (see Mt 24:10–12; 1Ti 4:1). But here Paul is speaking of a specific act of rebellion that embodies the supreme opposition of evil to the things of God. *the man of lawlessness.* The leader of the forces of evil at the last time. Only here is he called by this name. John tells us of many "antichrists" (1Jn 2:18), and this may be the worst of them—the antichrist of Rev 13—though Paul's description of the man of lawlessness has some distinctive features. He is not Satan, because he is clearly distinguished from him in v. 9. *revealed.* Since the Greek for this word is from the same root as that used of Jesus Christ in 1:7, it may indicate something supernatural. *doomed to destruction.* For all his proud claims, his final overthrow is certain. The same expression is used of Judas Iscariot (see Jn 17:12).
2:4 *everything that is called God or is worshiped.* He is not merely a political or military man but claims a place above every god and everything associated with worship. He even claims to be God (cf. Da 11:36–37 and note on 11:36; Rev 13:5–8). *God's temple.* Apparently refers to the temple in Jerusalem (cf. Mt 24:15 and note).
2:6 *what is holding him back.* The expression is neuter, but the masculine equivalent is in v. 7. There have been many suggestions as to the identity of this restrainer: (1) the Roman state with its emperor, (2) Paul's missionary work, (3) the Jewish nation, (4) the principle of law and government embodied in the state, (5) the Holy Spirit or (6) the restraining ministry of the Holy Spirit through the church, etc.
2:7 *secret power.* Or "mystery" (see note on Ro 11:25). The term is most often used in reference to the gospel or some aspect of it. The expression here, however, indicates that we know something about evil only as God reveals it. This evil is already at work and will continue until the restrainer is removed at the end time.
2:8 *the lawless one will be revealed.* Evidently refers to some supernatural aspects of his appearing (see v. 9). *overthrow with the breath of his mouth.* Despite his impressiveness (v. 4), the man of lawlessness will be easily destroyed by Christ (cf. Da 11:45; Rev 19:20). *splendor.* In 2Ti 1:10 ("appearing") the Greek for this word refers to Jesus' first coming, but everywhere else in the NT to his second coming.
2:9 *coming.* The same Greek word used of Christ's coming in v. 8. Satan empowers the lawless one with signs and wonders (cf. Mt 24:24). *the lie.* See v. 11 and note.
2:10 *deceives.* The aim of the miracles of v. 9. *refused.* Their unbelief was willful and intentional. *truth.* Often closely connected with Jesus (see Jn 14:6 and note; Eph 4:21) and with the gospel (see Gal 2:5; Eph 1:13).
2:11 *For this reason.* Because of their deliberate rejection of the truth (v. 10). *God sends them a powerful delusion.* God uses sin to punish the sinful (cf. Ro 1:24–28). *the lie.* Not just any lie, but the great lie that the man of lawlessness is God (v. 4).
2:13 *we ought always to thank God for you.* See 1:3 and note. *loved by the Lord … God chose.* For the connection between God's love and election, see Col 3:12; 1Th 1:4; see also note on Eph 1:4. *sanctifying work.* A necessary aspect of salvation, not something reserved for special Christians (see 1Th 3:13; 4:3; 1Co 1:2 and notes). *truth.* See note on v. 10. All three persons of the Trinity are mentioned in this verse (see note on 1Th 1:1).
2:14 *called … through our gospel.* The past tense refers to the time when the Thessalonians were converted, but the divine call is a present reality in 1Th 5:24. *our gospel.* See note on 1Th 1:5. *glory of our Lord Jesus Christ.* Cf. 1Th 2:12 and note. Ultimately there is no glory other than God's (cf. Heb 1:2–3 and note).
2:15 *teachings.* Lit. "traditions." Until the NT was written, essential Christian teaching was passed on in the "traditions," just as rabbinic law was (see Mt 15:2 and note); it could be either oral or written. In 1Co 15:3 (see note there) Paul uses the technical words for receiving and passing on traditions.

passed on to you,[k] whether by word of
mouth or by letter.
16 May our Lord Jesus Christ himself and
God our Father,[l] who loved us[m] and by his
grace gave us eternal encouragement and
good hope, 17 encourage[n] your hearts and
strengthen[o] you in every good deed and word.

Request for Prayer

3 As for other matters, brothers and sisters,[p] pray for us[q] that the message
of the Lord[r] may spread rapidly and be
honored, just as it was with you.[s] 2 And
pray that we may be delivered from wicked and evil people,[t] for not everyone has
faith. 3 But the Lord is faithful,[u] and he
will strengthen you and protect you from
the evil one.[v] 4 We have confidence[w] in the
Lord that you are doing and will continue
to do the things we command. 5 May the
Lord direct your hearts[x] into God's love
and Christ's perseverance.

Warning Against Idleness

6 In the name of the Lord Jesus Christ,[y]
we command you, brothers and sisters, to
keep away from[z] every believer who is idle
and disruptive[a] and does not live according
to the teaching[a] you received from us.[b] 7 For
you yourselves know how you ought to follow our example.[c] We were not idle when
we were with you, 8 nor did we eat anyone's
food without paying for it. On the contrary,
we worked[d] night and day, laboring and
toiling so that we would not be a burden
to any of you. 9 We did this, not because we
do not have the right to such help,[e] but in
order to offer ourselves as a model for you
to imitate.[f] 10 For even when we were with
you,[g] we gave you this rule: "The one who
is unwilling to work[h] shall not eat."
11 We hear that some among you are idle
and disruptive. They are not busy; they are
busybodies.[i] 12 Such people we command
and urge in the Lord Jesus Christ[j] to settle
down and earn the food they eat.[k] 13 And
as for you, brothers and sisters, never tire
of doing what is good.[l]
14 Take special note of anyone who does
not obey our instruction in this letter. Do
not associate with them,[m] in order that
they may feel ashamed.[n] 15 Yet do not regard them as an enemy, but warn them as
you would a fellow believer.[o]

Final Greetings

16 Now may the Lord of peace[p] himself
give you peace at all times and in every
way. The Lord be with all of you.[q]
17 I, Paul, write this greeting in my own
hand,[r] which is the distinguishing mark in
all my letters. This is how I write.
18 The grace of our Lord Jesus Christ be
with you all.[s]

2:15 [k] S 1Co 11:2 **2:16** [l] S Php 4:20 [m] S Jn 3:16 **2:17** [n] 1Th 3:2 [o] 2Th 3:3 **3:1** [p] 1Th 4:1 [q] S 1Th 5:25 [r] 1Th 1:8 [s] 1Th 2:13 **3:2** [t] S Ro 15:31 **3:3** [u] S 1Co 1:9 [v] S Mt 5:37 **3:4** [w] S 2Co 2:3 **3:5** [x] 1Ch 29:18 **3:6** [y] 1Co 5:4 [z] ver 14; S Ro 16:17 [a] ver 7,11 [b] S 1Co 11:2 **3:7** [c] ver 9; S 1Co 4:16 **3:8** [d] S Ac 18:3; Eph 4:28 **3:9** [e] 1Co 9:4-14 [f] ver 7; S 1Co 4:16 **3:10** [g] 1Th 3:4 [h] 1Th 4:11 **3:11** [i] ver 6,7; 1Ti 5:13 **3:12** [j] 1Th 4:1 [k] 1Th 4:11; Eph 4:28 **3:13** [l] Gal 6:9 **3:14** [m] ver 6; S Ro 16:17 [n] S 1Co 4:14 **3:15** [o] Gal 6:1; 1Th 5:14; Phm 16 **3:16** [p] S Ro 15:33 [q] Ru 2:4 **3:17** [r] S 1Co 16:21 **3:18** [s] S Ro 16:20

[a] 6 Or *tradition*

2:16–17 There is a similar prayer in the first letter (1Th 3:11–13).
2:17 *encourage ... strengthen.* Also used together in 1Th 3:2. The prayer is for inner strength that will produce results in both action and speech.
3:1 *As for other matters.* In 1Th 5:25 Paul asked simply for prayer; here he mentions specifics. *just as it was with you.* Lit. "just as also with you." The expression is general enough to cover the present as well as the past (cf. 1Th 2:13).
3:2 For Paul's difficulties at Corinth (where he wrote this letter), see Ac 18:12–13.
3:3 *faithful.* In the Greek text the word immediately follows "faith" (v. 2), putting the faithfulness of the Lord in sharp contrast with the lack of faith in people (cf. 1Co 1:9 and note; 10:13; 2Co 1:18). *the evil one.* Satan (see Mt 6:13 and note).
3:5 *hearts.* See note on 1Th 2:4. *God's love.* Paul is about to rebuke the idle and is here reminding them of God's love. There should be no hard feelings among those who owe everything to the love of God. *Christ's perseverance.* The endurance he so marvelously displayed in his incarnate life on earth (see Heb 12:1–3 and notes).
3:6 *the name.* See 1:12 and note. *command.* An authoritative word with a military ring. *keep away.* Not withdrawal of all contact but withholding of close fellowship. Idleness is sinful and disruptive, but those guilty of it are still brothers and sisters in Christ (v. 15). *idle.* The problem was mentioned in the first letter (4:11–12; 5:14; see notes there), and evidently had worsened. Paul takes it seriously and gives more attention to it in this letter than to anything else but the second coming. *teaching.* See 2:15 and note.
3:7 *follow our example.* See 1Th 1:6 and note.
3:8 *eat ... food.* A Hebraism for "make a living" (see, e.g., Ge 3:19; Am 7:12). Paul is not saying that he never accepted hospitality but that he had not depended on other people for his living (see 1Th 2:9 and note).
3:9 *the right.* See note on 1Th 2:6.
3:10 Pagan parallels are in the form of "Anyone who does not work does not eat." But Paul uses an imperative: lit. "let him (or them) not eat."
3:11 *busybodies.* Worse than being idle, they were interfering with other people's affairs, a problem to which idleness often leads.
3:12 *settle down.* Not going about as useless "busybodies" (v. 11).
3:14 Paul realizes that some may not heed his letter. *associate with.* The Greek for this phrase is an unusual double compound, meaning "mix up together with" (used elsewhere in the NT only in 1Co 5:9,11—of a similar withdrawal of close fellowship). It indicates a disassociation that will bring the person back to a right attitude. *feel ashamed.* And repent. The aim is not punishment but restoration to fellowship.
3:15 Discipline in the church should be carried out lovingly and gently (cf. Gal 6:1), never harshly. *warn.* See 1Th 5:12, where the Greek for this verb is translated "admonish." *fellow believer.* Lit. "brother." See note on Ro 1:13.
3:16,18 *peace ... grace.* See note on Ro 1:7.
3:16 *Lord of peace.* The more usual phrase is "God of peace" (see note on 1Th 5:23). *all of you.* Even the disorderly.
3:17 Paul normally dictated his letters (cf. Ro 16:22), but toward the end of some of them he added a brief word in his own handwriting (see 1Co 16:21 and note; Gal 6:11; Col 4:18). Here he tells us that this practice was his distinguishing mark.
3:18 See 1Th 5:28 and note. Paul has criticized his offenders, but his last prayer is for everyone. *Lord Jesus Christ.* See note on 1:1. *with you.* See note on 2Co 13:14.

THE PASTORAL LETTERS

"Pastoral" characterizes the contents of 1,2 Timothy and Titus. These letters provide instruction concerning the care of the churches.

Biblical interpreters have raised more doubts about the authenticity of the Pastoral Letters than about any of the other letters of Paul:

(1) The events mentioned in the Pastorals cannot be fitted into the account of Paul's life and ministry in Acts.
(2) The theology is different from that found in the other letters of Paul, and the church organization is more advanced.
(3) The vocabulary and style of writing are not characteristic of Paul.

Although these may appear to be formidable objections to authorship by Paul, there are satisfactory answers:

(1) Paul's death is not reported in Ac 28. In all probability he was released from prison and went on another mission (see map and accompanying text, pp. 2038 – 2039), during which there was adequate time for the historical events mentioned in the Pastoral Letters to take place.
(2) The theology is consistent with that found in other letters of Paul, and the church organization in the Pastorals is no more advanced than that found, e.g., in Philippians (see 1:1 and note).
(3) While the scope of these letters is too limited to draw any firm conclusions about authorship based on vocabulary and style, these features of the Pastorals can be satisfactorily accounted for by considering the different circumstances, addressees and subject matter Paul is dealing with.

Certain themes and phrases recur throughout the Pastoral Letters: (1) God the Savior (see note on Titus 1:3); (2) sound doctrine, faith and teaching (see note on Titus 1:9); (3) godliness (see note on 1Ti 2:2); (4) controversies (1Ti 1:4; 6:4; 2Ti 2:23; Titus 3:9); (5) trustworthy sayings (see note on 1Ti 1:15).

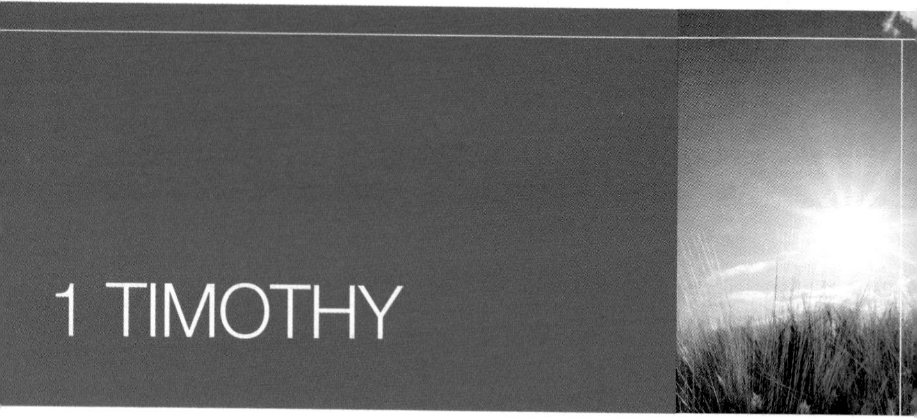

1 TIMOTHY

INTRODUCTION

Author

Both early tradition and the greetings of the Pastoral Letters (1,2 Timothy; Titus) themselves claim Paul as their author (1:1; 2Ti 1:1; Titus 1:1). Some objections have been raised in recent years on the basis of an alleged uncharacteristic vocabulary and style (see, e.g., notes on 1:15; 2:2), but other evidence still convincingly supports Paul's authorship. See essay, p. 2033.

Background and Purpose

During his fourth missionary journey (see map, pp. 2038–2039), Paul had instructed Timothy to care for the church at Ephesus (1:3) while he went on to Macedonia. When he realized that he might not return to Ephesus in the near future (3:14–15), he wrote this first letter to Timothy to develop the charge he had given his young assistant (1:3,18), to refute false teachings (1:3–7; 4:1–8; 6:3–5,20–21) and to supervise the affairs of the growing Ephesian church (church worship, ch. 2; the appointment of qualified church leaders, 3:1–13; 5:17–25).

A major problem in the Ephesian church was a heresy that combined Gnosticism (see Introduction to 1 John: Gnosticism), decadent Judaism (1:3–7) and false asceticism (4:1–5).

Date

1 Timothy was written sometime after the events of Ac 28 (c. AD 63–65; see chart, p. 1845), at least eight years after Paul's three-year stay in Ephesus (see Ac 19:10 and note).

Recipient

As the greeting indicates (1:2), Paul is writing to Timothy, a native of Lystra (in modern Turkey). Timothy's father was Greek, while his mother was a Jewish Christian (Ac 16:1). From childhood he had been taught the OT (2Ti 1:5; 3:15). Paul called him "my true son in the faith" (1:2; see note there), perhaps having led him to faith in Christ during his first visit

a quick look

Author:
The apostle Paul

Audience:
Timothy, one of Paul's closest associates, but no doubt intended also to be read to the whole church in Ephesus

Date:
About AD 64

Theme:
Paul writes to instruct Timothy concerning the care of the church at Ephesus.

Paul's admiration of Timothy is seen in the letter to the Philippians, where Paul speaks highly of his younger associates.

to Lystra (see photo below). At the time of his second visit Paul invited Timothy to join him on his missionary travels, circumcising him so that his Greek ancestry would not be a liability in working with the Jews (Ac 16:3). Timothy helped Paul evangelize Macedonia and Achaia (Ac 17:14 – 15; 18:5) and was with him during much of his long preaching ministry at Ephesus (Ac 19:22). He traveled with him from Ephesus to Macedonia to Corinth (see Ac 20:3 and note), back to Macedonia, and to Asia Minor (Ac 20:1 – 6). He may even have accompanied him all the way to Jerusalem. He was with Paul during the apostle's first Roman imprisonment (Php 1:1; Col 1:1; Phm 1).

Following Paul's release (after Ac 28) Timothy again traveled with him but eventually stayed at Ephesus to deal with the problems there, while Paul went on to Macedonia. Paul's closeness to and admiration of Timothy are seen in Paul's naming him as the co-sender of six of his letters (2 Corinthians, Philippians, Colossians, 1,2 Thessalonians and Philemon) and in his speaking highly of him to the Philippians (Php 2:19 – 22). At the end of Paul's life he requested Timothy to join him at Rome (2Ti 4:9,21). According to Heb 13:23, Timothy himself was imprisoned and subsequently released — whether at Rome or elsewhere, we do not know.

Timothy was not an apostle. It may be best to regard him as an apostolic representative, delegated to carry out special work (cf. Titus 1:5).

Unexcavated tell at Lystra, Timothy's hometown. Paul visited Lystra during his first missionary journey. Timothy joined his missionary team on the second journey (Ac 16:1 – 3).

Todd Bolen/www.BiblePlaces.com

Outline

I. Greetings (1:1 – 2)
II. Warning against False Teachers (1:3 – 11)
   A. The Nature of the Heresy (1:3 – 7)
   B. The Purpose of the Law (1:8 – 11)
III. The Lord's Grace to Paul (1:12 – 17)
IV. The Purpose of Paul's Instructions to Timothy (1:18 – 20)
V. Instructions concerning Church Administration (chs. 2 – 3)
   A. Public Worship (ch. 2)
      1. Prayer in public worship (2:1 – 8)
      2. Women in public worship (2:9 – 15)
   B. Qualifications for Church Officers (3:1 – 13)
      1. Overseers (3:1 – 7)
      2. Deacons (3:8 – 13)
   C. Purpose of These Instructions (3:14 – 16)
VI. Instructions concerning False Teaching (ch. 4)
   A. False Teaching Described (4:1 – 5)
   B. Methods of Dealing with It Explained (4:6 – 16)
VII. Instructions concerning Different Groups in the Church (5:1 — 6:2)
   A. The Older and the Younger (5:1 – 2)
   B. Widows (5:3 – 16)
   C. Elders (5:17 – 25)
   D. Slaves (6:1 – 2)
VIII. Miscellaneous Matters (6:3 – 19)
   A. False Teachers (6:3 – 5)
   B. Love of Money (6:6 – 10)
   C. Charge to Timothy (6:11 – 16)
   D. The Rich (6:17 – 19)
IX. Concluding Appeal and Benediction (6:20 – 21)

1 Paul, an apostle of Christ Jesus by the
command of God[a] our Savior[b] and of
Christ Jesus our hope,[c]
2 To Timothy[d] my true son[e] in the faith:
Grace, mercy and peace from God the
Father and Christ Jesus our Lord.[f]

Timothy Charged to Oppose False Teachers

3 As I urged you when I went into Macedonia,[g] stay there in Ephesus[h] so that you
may command certain people not to teach
false doctrines[i] any longer 4 or to devote
themselves to myths[j] and endless genealogies.[k] Such things promote controversial
speculations[l] rather than advancing God's
work—which is by faith. 5 The goal of
this command is love, which comes from
a pure heart[m] and a good conscience[n] and
a sincere faith.[o] 6 Some have departed from
these and have turned to meaningless talk.
7 They want to be teachers[p] of the law, but
they do not know what they are talking
about or what they so confidently affirm.[q]
8 We know that the law is good[r] if one
uses it properly. 9 We also know that the
law is made not for the righteous[s] but
for lawbreakers and rebels,[t] the ungodly
and sinful, the unholy and irreligious, for
those who kill their fathers or mothers,
for murderers, 10 for the sexually immoral, for those practicing homosexuality, for
slave traders and liars and perjurers—and
for whatever else is contrary to the sound
doctrine[u] 11 that conforms to the gospel
concerning the glory of the blessed God,
which he entrusted to me.[v]

The Lord's Grace to Paul

12 I thank Christ Jesus our Lord, who has
given me strength,[w] that he considered me
trustworthy, appointing me to his service.[x]
13 Even though I was once a blasphemer
and a persecutor[y] and a violent man, I
was shown mercy[z] because I acted in ignorance and unbelief.[a] 14 The grace of our
Lord was poured out on me abundantly,[b]
along with the faith and love that are in
Christ Jesus.[c]
15 Here is a trustworthy saying[d] that deserves full acceptance: Christ Jesus came
into the world to save sinners[e]—of whom
I am the worst. 16 But for that very reason I
was shown mercy[f] so that in me, the worst
of sinners, Christ Jesus might display his
immense patience[g] as an example for those
who would believe[h] in him and receive
eternal life.[i] 17 Now to the King[j] eternal, immortal,[k] invisible,[l] the only God,[m] be honor
and glory for ever and ever. Amen.[n]

The Charge to Timothy Renewed

18 Timothy, my son,[o] I am giving you
this command in keeping with the prophecies once made about you,[p] so that by
recalling them you may fight the battle
well,[q] 19 holding on to faith and a good

1:1 [a]S 2Co 1:1; Titus 1:3 [b]S Lk 1:47 [c]Col 1:27 **1:2** [d]S Ac 16:1 [e]ver 18; 1Co 4:17; S 1Th 2:11; 2Ti 1:2; Titus 1:4 [f]S Ro 1:7 **1:3** [g]S Ac 16:9 [h]S Ac 18:19 [i]Gal 1:6,7; 1Ti 6:3 **1:4** [j]1Ti 4:7; 2Ti 4:4; Titus 1:14 [k]Titus 3:9 [l]S 2Ti 2:14 **1:5** [m]2Ti 2:22 [n]S Ac 23:1; 1Ti 4:2 [o]Gal 5:6; 2Ti 1:5 **1:7** [p]S Eph 4:11 [q]Job 38:2 **1:8** [r]Ro 7:12 **1:9** [s]Gal 5:23 [t]Gal 3:19 **1:10** [u]1Ti 6:3; 2Ti 1:13; 4:3; Titus 1:9; 2:1 **1:11** [v]Gal 2:7; 1Th 2:4; Titus 1:3 **1:12** [w]S Php 4:13 [x]S Ac 9:15 **1:13** [y]S Ac 8:3 [z]ver 16 [a]Ac 26:9 **1:14** [b]2Co 4:15 [c]2Ti 1:13; S 1Th 1:3 **1:15** [d]1Ti 3:1; 4:9; 2Ti 2:11; Titus 3:8 [e]Mk 2:17; S Jn 3:17 **1:16** [f]ver 13 [g]S Ro 2:4 [h]S Jn 3:15 [i]S Mt 25:46 **1:17** [j]Rev 15:3 [k]1Ti 6:16 [l]S Col 1:15 [m]Jude 25 [n]S Ro 11:36 **1:18** [o]S ver 2 [p]1Ti 4:14 [q]1Ti 6:12; 2Ti 2:3; 4:7

1:1 *Paul.* See note on Ro 1:1. *apostle.* One specially commissioned by Christ (see 1Co 1:1 and note). *God our Savior.* See Titus 1:3 and note. *Christ Jesus our hope.* See Col 1:27; Titus 2:13; Heb 6:18–19; 1Jn 3:3 and notes. *hope.* Expresses absolute certainty, not a mere wish (see note on Eph 1:18).
1:2 *true son in the faith.* Spiritual son (see 1:18; 1Co 4:17; 2Ti 1:2; 2:1; Phm 10). *Grace … peace.* See note on Ro 1:7. *mercy.* See Ro 9:22–23 and note; included only here and in 2Ti 1:2 in the greetings of Paul's letters.
1:3–11 In this section, along with 4:1–8; 6:3–5,20–21, Paul warns against heretical teachers in the Ephesian church. They are characterized by (1) teaching "false doctrines" (v. 3; see 6:3); (2) building up endless, far-fetched, fictitious stories based on obscure genealogical points (v. 4; 4:7); (3) being argumentative (v. 4; 6:4); (4) using talk that was "meaningless" (v. 6); (5) wanting to be teachers of the OT law (v. 7); (6) being conceited (v. 7; 6:4); (7) not knowing what they were talking about (v. 7; 6:4); (8) teaching ascetic practices (4:3); and (9) using their positions of religious leadership for "financial gain" (6:5). These heretics probably were forerunners of the Gnostics (see 6:20 and note).
1:3 *I went into Macedonia.* Since this incident is not recorded in Acts, it probably occurred after Ac 28, between Paul's first and second Roman imprisonments (see Introduction: Recipient). *Macedonia.* See note on Php 4:15. *stay there in Ephesus.* And do the Lord's work in the Ephesian church—which was well established by this time. Paul had an extensive ministry there on his third missionary journey about eight years earlier (Ac 19:1—20:1). *Ephesus.* See Introduction to Ephesians: The City of Ephesus; see also map, p. 1982.
1:4 *myths.* Perhaps mythical stories built on OT history ("genealogies") that later developed into intricate Gnostic philosophical systems (see Introduction to 1 John: Gnosticism).
1:5 *pure heart.* See 2Ti 2:22; Ps 24:4 and note; 51:10; cf. Mt 5:8.
1:8 *the law is good.* See Ro 7:7–12 and note on 7:12.
1:9–10 See note on Ro 1:29–31.
1:10 *sound doctrine.* See Titus 1:9 and note.
1:11 *gospel.* See Mk 1:1 and note. *entrusted.* See 6:20; 1Co 9:17; Gal 2:7; 1Th 2:4; 2Ti 1:14.
1:12 *Christ … has given me strength.* See 2Co 12:9–10; Php 4:13 and notes. *appointing me to his service.* See v. 1 and note.
1:13 *a blasphemer and a persecutor and a violent man.* See Ac 9:1; 22:4–5,19; 26:10–11 and note on 26:11.
1:14 *faith and love … in Christ.* See 2Ti 1:13 and note.
1:15 *Here is a trustworthy saying.* A clause found nowhere else in the NT but used five times in the Pastorals (here; 3:1; 4:9; 2Ti 2:11; Titus 3:8) to identify a key teaching. *of whom I am the worst.* The closer one gets to a holy God, the more the magnitude of one's sin becomes evident (cf. Isa 6:5; see 1Co 15:9; Eph 3:8 and note).
1:16 *eternal life.* See Jn 3:15 and note.
1:17 *invisible.* See Col 1:15 and note.
1:18 *son.* See v. 2 and note. *prophecies once made about you.* In the early church God revealed his will in various matters through prophets (see Ac 13:1–3, where prophets had an active role in sending Paul and Barnabas on their mission to the Gentiles). In Timothy's case a prophecy may have occurred at the time of or before his ordination (4:14), perhaps about 12 years earlier on Paul's second missionary journey (see Ac 16:1–3). *fight the battle well.* See 6:12; 2Ti 2:3; 4:7 and note.

conscience,[r] which some have rejected and
so have suffered shipwreck with regard to
the faith.[s] 20 Among them are Hymenaeus[t]
and Alexander,[u] whom I have handed over
to Satan[v] to be taught not to blaspheme.

Instructions on Worship

2 I urge, then, first of all, that petitions,
prayers,[w] intercession and thanksgiving be made for all people— 2 for kings
and all those in authority,[x] that we may live
peaceful and quiet lives in all godliness[y]
and holiness. 3 This is good, and pleases[z]
God our Savior,[a] 4 who wants[b] all people[c] to
be saved[d] and to come to a knowledge of
the truth.[e] 5 For there is one God[f] and one

1:19 [r] ver 5; S Ac 23:1 [s] 1Ti 6:21; 2Ti 2:18
1:20 [t] 2Ti 2:17 [u] 2Ti 4:14 [v] 1Co 5:5
2:1 [w] Eph 6:18
2:2 [x] Ezr 6:10; Ro 13:1 [y] 1Ti 3:16; 4:7,8; 6:3,5,6,11; 2Ti 3:5; Titus 1:1
2:3 [z] S 1Ti 5:4 [a] S Lk 1:47
2:4 [b] Eze 18:23,32; 33:11 [c] 1Ti 4:10; Titus 2:11; 2Pe 3:9 [d] S Jn 3:17; S Ro 11:14 [e] 2Ti 2:25; Titus 1:1; Heb 10:26
2:5 [f] Dt 6:4; Ro 3:29,30; 10:12

1:20 *Hymenaeus.* See 2Ti 2:17–18. *Alexander.* Perhaps the Alexander of 2Ti 4:14. *handed over to Satan.* Such action would protect the church from false teaching and also discipline the offenders (see Mt 18:17 and note). Paul had excluded these two men from the church, which was considered a sanctuary from Satan's power. Out in the world, away from the fellowship and care of the church, they would be "taught" (the Greek word means basically "to discipline") "not to blaspheme." The purpose of such drastic action was more remedial than punitive. For a similar situation, see 1Co 5:5,13 and note on 5:5.

2:1–2 *prayers … for kings and all those in authority.* See Jer 29:7; 1Pe 2:13 and note. The notorious Roman emperor Nero (AD 54–68) was in power when Paul wrote these words.

2:2 *godliness.* A key word (along with "godly") in the Pastorals, occurring ten times (here; 3:16; 4:7–8; 6:3,5–6,11; 2Ti 3:5; Titus 1:1), but nowhere else in the writings of Paul. It implies a good and holy life, with special emphasis on its source, a deep reverence for God.

2:3 *God our Savior.* See Titus 1:3 and note.

2:4 *wants all people to be saved.* God desires the salvation of all people (cf. 2Pe 3:9 and note). On the other hand, the Bible indicates that God chooses some (not all) people to be saved (see 4:10; Ro 8:29 and notes).

2:5 *there is one God.* The basic belief of Judaism (see Dt 6:4

PAUL'S FOURTH MISSIONARY JOURNEY c. AD 62–68

It is clear from Ac 13:1—21:17 that Paul went on three missionary journeys. There is also reason to believe that he made a fourth journey after his release from the Roman imprisonment recorded in Ac 28. The conclusion that such a journey did indeed take place is based on: (1) Paul's declared intention to go to Spain (Ro 15:24,28), (2) Eusebius's implication that Paul was released following his first Roman imprisonment (*Ecclesiastical History*, 2.22.2–3) and (3) statements in early Christian literature that he took the gospel as far as Spain (Clement of Rome, *Epistle to the Corinthians*, ch. 5; *Actus Petri Vercellenses*, chs. 1–3; Muratorian Canon, lines 34–39).

The places Paul may have visited after his release from prison are indicated by statements of intention in his earlier writings and by subsequent mention in the Pastoral Letters. The order of his travel cannot be determined with certainty, but the itinerary below seems likely.

1. **ROME**—released from prison in AD 62
2. **SPAIN**—62–64 (Ro 15:24,28)
3. **CRETE**—64–65 (Titus 1:5)
4. **MILETUS**—65 (2Ti 4:20)
5. **COLOSSAE**—66 (Phm 22)
6. **EPHESUS**—66 (1Ti 1:3)
7. **PHILIPPI**—66 (Php 2:23–24; 1Ti 1:3)
8. **NICOPOLIS**—66–67 (Titus 3:12)
9. **ROME**—67 (2Ti 1:17)
10. Martyrdom—67/68 (2Ti 4:6)

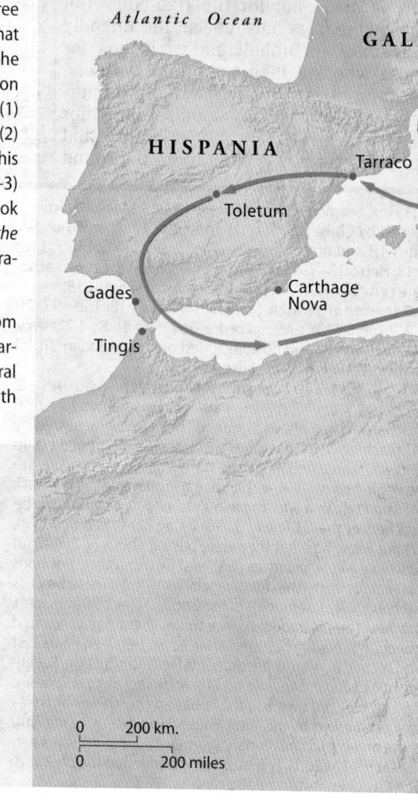

mediator[g] between God and mankind, the man Christ Jesus,[h] 6 who gave himself as a ransom[i] for all people. This has now been witnessed to[j] at the proper time.[k] 7 And for this purpose I was appointed a herald and an apostle—I am telling the truth, I am not lying[l]—and a true and faithful teacher[m] of the Gentiles.[n]
8 Therefore I want the men everywhere to pray, lifting up holy hands[o] without anger or disputing. 9 I also want the women to dress modestly, with decency and propriety, adorning themselves, not with elaborate hairstyles or gold or pearls or expensive clothes,[p] 10 but with good deeds,[q] appropriate for women who profess to worship God.
11 A woman[a] should learn in quietness

2:5 [g] S Gal 3:20 [h] Ro 1:3 2:6 [i] S Mt 20:28 [j] S 1Co 1:6 [k] 1Ti 6:15; Titus 1:3 2:7 [l] S Ro 9:1 [m] 2Ti 1:11 [n] S Ac 9:15 2:8 [o] Ps 24:4; 63:4; 134:2; 141:2; Lk 24:50 2:9 [p] 1Pe 3:3 2:10 [q] Pr 31:13

[a] *11* Or *wife*; also in verse 12

and note), which every Jew confessed daily in the *Shema* (see Mk 12:29 and note). *mediator.* One who represents God to humans and humans to God—and who removes all alienation between them by offering himself as "a ransom for all" (v. 6). Cf. Jn 14:6; Heb 8:6 and notes.
2:6 *ransom.* See Mt 20:28 and note. *witnessed.* Refers to the apostolic testimony that Christ gave himself as the ransom. *proper time.* See Gal 4:4 and note.
2:7 *for this purpose.* To testify that, through his death, Christ has bridged the gap between God and human beings and made salvation available to all. *herald.* See 2Ti 1:11; one who with authority makes a public proclamation. *apostle.* See 1Co 1:1 and note.
2:8 *men.* The Greek for this word does not refer to humankind (as in vv. 5–6) but to males as distinct from females. Women also prayed in public, however (see 1Co 11:5 and note).
2:9–14 Some maintain that Paul's teaching about women here is historically conditioned, not universal and timeless. Others view these verses as unaffected by the historical situation and therefore applicable to every age.
2:9 Not a total ban on the wearing of jewelry or braided hair. Rather, Paul was expressing caution in a society where such things were signs of extravagant luxury and proud personal display.
2:10 See 1Pe 3:3–5 and note on 3:3.

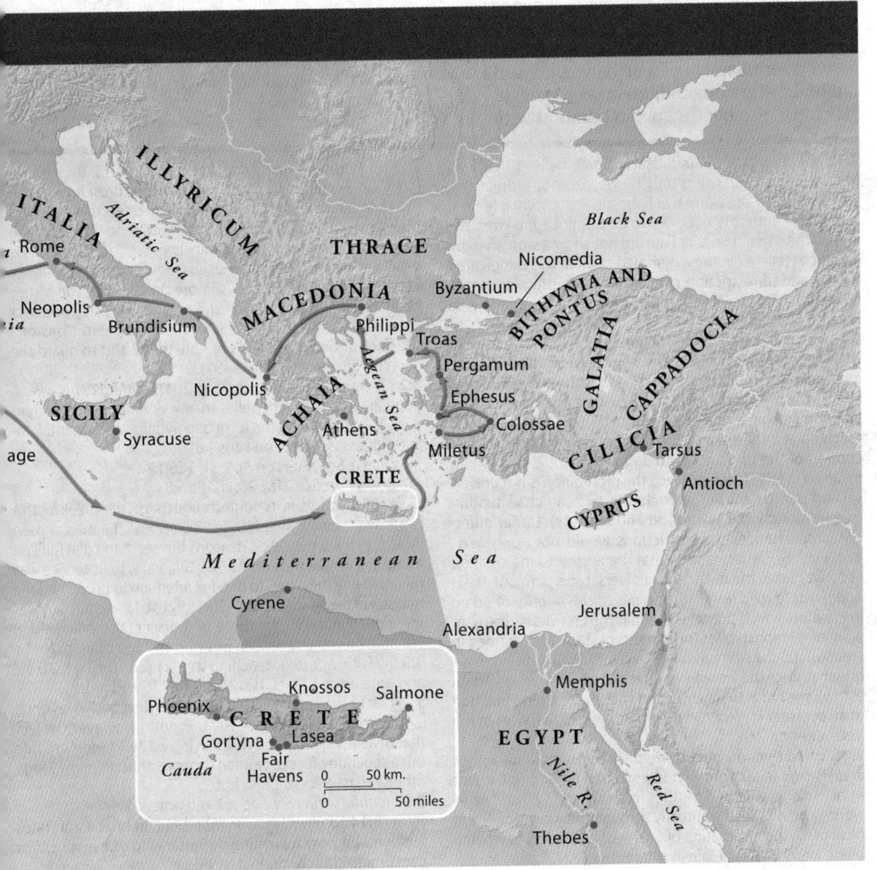

and full submission.[r] 12 I do not permit
a woman to teach or to assume authority over a man;[a] she must be quiet.[s] 13 For
Adam was formed first, then Eve.[t] 14 And
Adam was not the one deceived; it was the
woman who was deceived and became
a sinner.[u] 15 But women[b] will be saved
through childbearing—if they continue
in faith, love[v] and holiness with propriety.

Qualifications for Overseers and Deacons

3 Here is a trustworthy saying:[w] Whoever aspires to be an overseer[x] desires a noble task. 2 Now the overseer is to
be above reproach,[y] faithful to his wife,[z]
temperate,[a] self-controlled, respectable,
hospitable,[b] able to teach,[c] 3 not given to
drunkenness,[d] not violent but gentle, not
quarrelsome,[e] not a lover of money.[f] 4 He
must manage his own family well and see
that his children obey him, and he must
do so in a manner worthy of full[c] respect.[g]
5 (If anyone does not know how to manage
his own family, how can he take care of
God's church?)[h] 6 He must not be a recent
convert, or he may become conceited[i] and
fall under the same judgment[j] as the devil.
7 He must also have a good reputation with
outsiders,[k] so that he will not fall into disgrace and into the devil's trap.[l]
8 In the same way, deacons[d][m] are to be
worthy of respect, sincere, not indulging
in much wine,[n] and not pursuing dishonest gain. 9 They must keep hold of the deep
truths of the faith with a clear conscience.[o]
10 They must first be tested;[p] and then if
there is nothing against them, let them
serve as deacons.
11 In the same way, the women[e] are to be
worthy of respect, not malicious talkers[q] but
temperate[r] and trustworthy in everything.
12 A deacon must be faithful to his wife[s]
and must manage his children and his
household well.[t] 13 Those who have served
well gain an excellent standing and great
assurance in their faith in Christ Jesus.

Reasons for Paul's Instructions

14 Although I hope to come to you soon,
I am writing you these instructions so that,

2:11 [r] 1Pe 3:3,4 **2:12** [s] S Eph 5:22 **2:13** [t] Ge 2:7, 22; 1Co 11:8 **2:14** [u] Ge 3:1-6, 13; 2Co 11:3 **2:15** [v] 1Ti 1:14 **3:1** [w] S 1Ti 1:15 [x] Ac 20:28; Php 1:1; Titus 1:7 **3:2** [y] Titus 1:6-8 [z] ver 12 [a] ver 11; Titus 2:2 [b] S Ro 12:13 [c] 2Ti 2:24 **3:3** [d] Titus 1:7 [e] 2Ti 2:24 [f] Lk 16:14; 1Ti 6:10; 2Ti 3:2; Heb 13:5; 1Pe 5:2 **3:4** [g] ver 12; Titus 1:6 **3:5** [h] S 1Co 10:32 **3:6** [i] 1Ti 6:4; 2Ti 3:4 [j] S 2Pe 2:4 **3:7** [k] S Mk 4:11 [l] 2Ti 2:26 **3:8** [m] Php 1:1 [n] 1Ti 5:23; Titus 1:7; 2:3 **3:9** [o] S Ac 23:1 **3:10** [p] 1Ti 5:22 **3:11** [q] 2Ti 3:3; Titus 2:3 [r] ver 2 **3:12** [s] ver 2 [t] ver 4

[a] *12* Or *over her husband* [b] *15* Greek *she* [c] *4* Or *him with proper* [d] *8* The word *deacons* refers here to Christians designated to serve with the overseers/elders of the church in a variety of ways; similarly in verse 12; and in Romans 16:1 and Phil. 1:1. [e] *11* Possibly deacons' wives or women who are deacons

2:12 *not permit a woman to teach.* Some believe that Paul here prohibited teaching only by women not properly instructed, i.e., by the women at Ephesus. Such women tended to exercise authority over, i.e., to be domineering over, the men. Others maintain that Paul did not allow a woman to be an official teacher in the assembled church. This is indicated by the added restriction concerning exercising "authority over a man" (a male), i.e., functioning as an overseer (see note on 3:1).

2:13–14 Paul based the restrictions on Ge 2–3. Some argue that "for" does not express the reason for woman's silence and submission but is used only as a connective word, as in v. 5. The meaning, then, would be that Adam's priority in creation illustrates the present situation of male priority in teaching at Ephesus, and Eve's deception illustrates the deception of the untrained and aggressive Ephesian women involved in false teaching. Thus the prohibition is not universal and permanent but restricted to this church's situation (see Introduction: Background and Purpose). Under different circumstances the restrictions would not apply (e.g., 1Co 11:1–5). Others believe that the appeal to the creation account makes the restrictions universal and permanent: (1) *Adam was formed first.* Paul appeals to the priority of Adam in creation, which predates the fall. Thus he views the man-woman relationship set forth in this passage as grounded in creation. (2) *the woman ... was deceived.* Paul appears to argue that since the woman was deceived (and then led Adam astray), she is not to be entrusted with the teaching function of an overseer (or elder) in the public worship services of the assembled church.

2:15 *saved through childbearing.* Three possible meanings are: (1) This speaks of the godly woman finding fulfillment in her role as wife and mother in the home; (2) it refers to women being saved spiritually through the most significant birth of all, the incarnation of Christ; or (3) it refers to women being kept physically safe in childbirth.

3:1 *trustworthy saying.* See note on 1:15. *overseer.* In Greek culture the word was used of a presiding official in a civic or religious organization. Here it refers to a man who oversees a local congregation. The equivalent word from the Jewish background of Christianity is "elder." The terms "overseer" and "elder" are often used interchangeably (see Ac 20:17,28; Titus 1:5–7; see also note on 1Pe 5:2). The duties of an overseer were to teach and preach (3:2; 5:17), to direct the affairs of the church (3:5; 5:17), to shepherd ("pastor") the flock of God (Ac 20:28; see note there) and to guard the church from error (Ac 20:28–31).

3:2 *overseer is to be.* See chart, p. 2041. *faithful to his wife.* A general principle that applies to any violation of God's marriage law, whether in the form of polygamy or of marital unfaithfulness (see note on Titus 1:6).

3:5 *church.* See notes on Ac 9:31; 2Co 1:1.

3:7 *devil's trap.* See 2Ti 2:26; cf. 1Pe 5:8.

3:8 *deacons.* In its nontechnical usage, the Greek for this word means simply "one who serves." The men chosen in Ac 6:1–6 are not called deacons but seem to have fulfilled a similar role (see note on Ac 6:6). Generally, their service was meant to free the elders to give full attention to prayer and the ministry of the word (Ac 6:2,4). The only two local church offices mentioned in the NT are those of overseer (also called elder; see note on v. 1) and deacon (see Php 1:1). See chart, p. 2041.

3:9 *the faith.* Apostolic teaching (see 4:1,6; 6:10,12, 21; 2Ti 4:7 and note; Titus 1:13; cf. 1Co 15:3; 2Th 2:15 and notes).

3:11 *the women.* Could refer to (1) deacons' wives or (2) women deacons (see NIV text note). However, the fact that deacons are referred to again in vv. 12–13 seems to rule out a separate office of women deacons, though many judge otherwise (see Ro 16:1 and note).

3:12 *faithful to his wife.* See v. 2 and note.

3:14 *I am writing ... so that.* Here, in brief, Paul states his purpose for writing the letter—to give instructions concerning church conduct (v. 15).

15 if I am delayed, you will know how people ought to conduct themselves in God's
household, which is the church[u] of the living God,[v] the pillar and foundation of the
truth. 16 Beyond all question, the mystery[w]
from which true godliness[x] springs is great:

He appeared in the flesh,[y]
  was vindicated by the Spirit,[a]
was seen by angels,
  was preached among the nations,[z]
was believed on in the world,
  was taken up in glory.[a]

4 The Spirit[b] clearly says that in later
times[c] some will abandon the faith and
follow deceiving spirits[d] and things taught
by demons. 2 Such teachings come through
hypocritical liars, whose consciences have

3:15 [u] ver 5; S 1Co 10:32 [v] S Mt 16:16 **3:16** [w] S Ro 16:25 [x] S 1Ti 2:2 [y] S Jn 1:14 [z] Ps 9:11; Col 1:23 [a] S Mk 16:19 **4:1** [b] Jn 16:13; S Ac 8:29; 1Co 2:10 [c] 2Ti 3:1; 2Pe 3:3 [d] S Mk 13:5

[a] 16 Or *vindicated in spirit*

3:15 *God's household.* The family of God, made up of believers. *pillar and foundation of the truth.* See 2Ti 2:19 and note.
3:16 *mystery from which true godliness springs.* See Ro 11:25; Col 1:26 and notes. The phrase means the "revealed secret of true piety," i.e., the secret that produces piety in people. That secret, as the following words indicate, is none other than Jesus Christ. His incarnation, in all its aspects (particularly his saving work), is the source of genuine piety. The words are printed in poetic form and probably come from an early creedal hymn (see note on Col 3:16). *godliness.* See 2:2 and note. *vindicated by the Spirit.* The Holy Spirit enabled Jesus to drive out demons (see Mt 12:28) and perform miracles. Most important, the Spirit raised Jesus from the dead (see Ro 1:4; cf. 1Pe 3:18 and note) and thereby vindicated him, showing that he was indeed the Son of God. *seen by angels.* At his resurrection (Mt 28:2) and ascension (Ac 1:10; see note there). *taken up in glory.* See Lk 24:51; Ac 1:9–12 and notes.
4:1,6 *the faith.* See note on 3:9.
4:1 *The Spirit clearly says.* As, e.g., in Mk 13:22; Ac 20:29–30; 2Th 2:3. Paul, however, is perhaps speaking here of a specific revelation made to him by the Spirit. *later times.* The time beginning with the first coming of the Messiah (see Jas 5:3 and note). That Paul is not referring only to the time immediately prior to Christ's second coming is obvious from his assumption in v. 7 that the false teachings were already present at the time of his writing.

QUALIFICATIONS FOR **ELDERS/OVERSEERS AND DEACONS**

QUALIFICATION	TITLE	SCRIPTURE	QUALIFICATION	TITLE	SCRIPTURE
Self-controlled	ELDER	1Ti 3:2; Titus 1:8	Disciplined	ELDER	Titus 1:8
Hospitable	ELDER	1Ti 3:2; Titus 1:8	Above reproach (blameless)	ELDER DEACON	1Ti 3:2; Titus 1:6 1Ti 3:9
Able to teach	ELDER	1Ti 3:2; 5:17; Titus 1:9	Faithful to his wife	ELDER DEACON	1Ti 3:2; Titus 1:6 1Ti 3:12
Not violent but gentle	ELDER	1Ti 3:3; Titus 1:7	Temperate	ELDER DEACON	1Ti 3:2; Titus 1:7 1Ti 3:8
Not quarrelsome	ELDER	1Ti 3:3	Respectable	ELDER DEACON	1Ti 3:2 1Ti 3:8
Not a lover of money	ELDER	1Ti 3:3	Not given to drunkenness	ELDER DEACON	1Ti 3:3; Titus 1:7 1Ti 3:8
Not a recent convert	ELDER	1Ti 3:6	Manages his own family well	ELDER DEACON	1Ti 3:4 1Ti 3:12
Has a good reputation with outsiders	ELDER	1Ti 3:7	Sees that his children obey him	ELDER DEACON	1Ti 3:4–5; Titus 1:6 1Ti 3:12
Not overbearing	ELDER	Titus 1:7	Does not pursue dishonest gain	ELDER DEACON	Titus 1:7 1Ti 3:8
Not quick-tempered	ELDER	Titus 1:7	Holds to the truth	ELDER DEACON	Titus 1:9 1Ti 3:9
Loves what is good	ELDER	Titus 1:8	Sincere	DEACON	1Ti 3:8
Upright, holy	ELDER	Titus 1:8	Tested	DEACON	1Ti 3:10

been seared as with a hot iron.[e] 3They forbid people to marry[f] and order them to abstain from certain foods,[g] which God created[h] to be received with thanksgiving[i] by those who believe and who know the truth. 4For everything God created is good,[j] and nothing is to be rejected[k] if it is received with thanksgiving, 5because it is consecrated by the word of God[l] and prayer.

6If you point these things out to the brothers and sisters,[a] you will be a good minister of Christ Jesus, nourished on the truths of the faith[m] and of the good teaching that you have followed.[n] 7Have nothing to do with godless myths and old wives' tales;[o] rather, train yourself to be godly.[p] 8For physical training is of some value, but godliness has value for all things,[q] holding promise for both the present life[r] and the life to come.[s] 9This is a trustworthy saying[t] that deserves full acceptance. 10That is why we labor and strive, because we have put our hope in the living God,[u] who is the Savior of all people,[v] and especially of those who believe.

11Command and teach these things.[w] 12Don't let anyone look down on you[x] because you are young, but set an example[y] for the believers in speech, in conduct, in love, in faith[z] and in purity. 13Until I come,[a] devote yourself to the public reading of Scripture,[b] to preaching and to teaching. 14Do not neglect your gift, which was given you through prophecy[c] when the body of elders[d] laid their hands on you.[e]

15Be diligent in these matters; give yourself wholly to them, so that everyone may see your progress. 16Watch your life and doctrine closely. Persevere in them, because if you do, you will save[f] both yourself and your hearers.

Widows, Elders and Slaves

5 Do not rebuke an older man[g] harshly,[h] but exhort him as if he were your father. Treat younger men[i] as brothers, 2older women as mothers, and younger women as sisters, with absolute purity.

3Give proper recognition to those widows who are really in need.[j] 4But if a widow has children or grandchildren, these should learn first of all to put their religion into practice by caring for their own family and so repaying their parents and grandparents,[k] for this is pleasing to God.[l] 5The widow who is really in need[m] and left all alone puts her hope in God[n] and continues night and day to pray[o] and to ask God for help. 6But the widow who lives for pleasure is dead even while she lives.[p] 7Give the people these instructions,[q] so that no one may be open to blame. 8Anyone who does not provide for their relatives, and especially for their own household, has denied[r] the faith and is worse than an unbeliever.

9No widow may be put on the list of widows unless she is over sixty, has

4:2 [e] Eph 4:19 **4:3** [f] Heb 13:4 [g] Col 2:16 [h] Ge 1:29; 9:3 [i] ver 4; Ro 14:6; 1Co 10:30 **4:4** [j] Ge 1:10, 12, 18, 21, 25, 31; Mk 7:18, 19; Ro 14:14-18 [k] S Ac 10:15 **4:5** [l] S Heb 4:12 **4:6** [m] 1Ti 1:10 [n] 2Ti 3:15 **4:7** [o] 1Ti 1:4; 2Ti 2:16 [p] S 1Ti 2:2 **4:8** [q] 1Ti 6:6 [r] Ps 37:9, 11; Pr 22:4; Mt 6:33; Mk 10:29, 30 [s] Mk 10:29, 30 **4:9** [t] S 1Ti 1:15 **4:10** [u] S Mt 16:16 [v] S Lk 1:47; S 2:11 **4:11** [w] 1Ti 5:7; 6:2 **4:12** [x] S 2Ti 1:7; Titus 2:15 [y] Php 3:17; 1Th 1:7; 2Th 3:9; Titus 2:7; 1Pe 5:3 [z] 1Ti 1:14 **4:13** [a] 1Ti 3:14 [b] Lk 4:16; Ac 13:14-16; Col 4:16; 1Th 5:27 **4:14** [c] 1Ti 1:18 [d] S Ac 11:30 [e] S Ac 6:6; 2Ti 1:6 **4:16** [f] S Ro 11:14 **5:1** [g] Titus 2:2 [h] Lev 19:32 [i] Titus 2:6 **5:3** [j] ver 5, 16 **5:4** [k] ver 8; Eph 6:1, 2 [l] Ro 12:2; Eph 5:10; 1Ti 2:3 **5:5** [m] ver 3, 16 [n] 1Co 7:34; 1Pe 3:5 [o] Lk 2:37; S Ro 1:10 **5:6** [p] S Lk 15:24 **5:7** [q] 1Ti 4:11; 6:2 **5:8** [r] 2Pe 2:1; Jude 4

[a] 6 The Greek word for *brothers and sisters* (*adelphoi*) refers here to believers, both men and women, as part of God's family.

4:3 This unbiblical asceticism arose out of the mistaken belief that the material world was evil—a central belief of the Gnostic heresy (see Introduction to 1 John: Gnosticism).

4:4 *everything God created is good.* See Ge 1:4,10,12,18,21,25,31 and note on 1:4; see also Titus 1:15 and note.

4:6 *brothers and sisters.* See NIV text note. *good teaching that you have followed.* Even from early childhood (see 2Ti 3:15 and note).

4:7 *myths.* See 1:4 and note. *train yourself to be godly.* See 2:2 and note. Godliness requires self-discipline.

4:9 *trustworthy saying.* See note on 1:15. Here the expression probably refers back to the seemingly proverbial statement in v. 8. The words "labor and strive" in v. 10 may refer to the training mentioned in vv. 7b–8.

4:10 *hope.* See note on 1:1. *Savior of all.* Obviously this does not mean that God saves every person from eternal punishment, for such universalism would contradict the clear testimony of Scripture. God is, however, the Savior of all in that he offers salvation to all and saves all who come to him (all "who believe").

4:12 *because you are young.* Cf. Jer 1:7 and note. Timothy was probably in his mid-30s or younger, and in that day such an influential position was not usually held by a man so young. For this reason his leadership may have been called into question. *example.* See Titus 2:7–8 and note.

4:13 *Until I come.* Paul's journey had taken him from Ephesus to Macedonia (see map, p. 2039), but he hoped to rejoin Timothy soon at Ephesus (3:14).

4:14 *through prophecy.* See 1:18 and note. *laid their hands on you.* As an act of commissioning to service (see Ac 6:6; Heb 6:1–2 and notes).

4:16 *you will save . . . your hearers.* God alone saves, but Christians can be God's instruments to bring about the salvation of others.

5:3 *Give proper recognition to those widows.* Probably refers to taking care of them, including the giving of material support. Widows were particularly vulnerable in ancient societies because pensions, government assistance, life insurance and the like were not available to them.

5:4 *put their religion into practice.* See Jas 1:22–27; 2:14–26 and note.

5:5 For an example of such a widow, see Lk 2:36–38.

5:6 *dead even while she lives.* Dead spiritually, while living physically.

5:8 *the faith.* See note on 3:9. Apostolic teaching emphasized social responsibility. *worse than an unbeliever.* Even in the pagan world of that time, people generally took care of their family members.

5:9 The church in Ephesus seems to have maintained a "list of widows" supported by the church. While there is no evidence of an order of widows comparable to that of the overseers, it appears that those on the list were expected to devote themselves to prayer (v. 5) and good deeds (v. 10).

been faithful to her husband, 10 and is well known for her good deeds,[s] such as bringing up children, showing hospitality,[t] washing the feet[u] of the Lord's people, helping those in trouble[v] and devoting herself to all kinds of good deeds.

11 As for younger widows, do not put them on such a list. For when their sensual desires overcome their dedication to Christ, they want to marry. 12 Thus they bring judgment on themselves, because they have broken their first pledge. 13 Besides, they get into the habit of being idle and going about from house to house. And not only do they become idlers, but also busybodies[w] who talk nonsense,[x] saying things they ought not to. 14 So I counsel younger widows to marry,[y] to have children, to manage their homes and to give the enemy no opportunity for slander.[z] 15 Some have in fact already turned away to follow Satan.[a]

16 If any woman who is a believer has widows in her care, she should continue to help them and not let the church be burdened with them, so that the church can help those widows who are really in need.[b]

17 The elders[c] who direct the affairs of the church well are worthy of double honor,[d] especially those whose work is preaching and teaching. 18 For Scripture says, "Do not muzzle an ox while it is treading out the grain,"[ae] and "The worker deserves his wages."[bf] 19 Do not entertain an accusation against an elder[g] unless it is brought by two or three witnesses.[h] 20 But those elders who are sinning you are to reprove[i] before everyone, so that the others may take warning.[j] 21 I charge you, in the sight of God and Christ Jesus[k] and the elect angels, to keep these instructions without partiality, and to do nothing out of favoritism.

22 Do not be hasty in the laying on of hands,[l] and do not share in the sins of others.[m] Keep yourself pure.[n]

23 Stop drinking only water, and use a little wine[o] because of your stomach and your frequent illnesses.

24 The sins of some are obvious, reaching the place of judgment ahead of them; the sins of others trail behind them. 25 In the same way, good deeds are obvious, and even those that are not obvious cannot remain hidden forever.

6 All who are under the yoke of slavery should consider their masters worthy of full respect,[p] so that God's name and our teaching may not be slandered.[q] 2 Those who have believing masters should not show them disrespect just because they are fellow believers.[r] Instead, they should serve them even better because their masters are dear to them as fellow believers and are devoted to the welfare[c] of their slaves.

False Teachers and the Love of Money

These are the things you are to teach and insist on.[s] 3 If anyone teaches otherwise[t] and does not agree to the sound instruction[u] of our Lord Jesus Christ and to godly teaching, 4 they are conceited[v] and understand nothing. They have an unhealthy interest in controversies and quarrels about words[w] that result in

5:10 [s] Ac 9:36; 1Ti 6:18; 1Pe 2:12 [t] S Ro 12:13 [u] S Lk 7:44 [v] ver 16
5:13 [w] 2Th 3:11 [x] S Ro 1:29
5:14 [y] 1Co 7:9 [z] 1Ti 6:1
5:15 [a] S Mt 4:10
5:16 [b] ver 3-5
5:17 [c] S Ac 11:30 [d] Php 2:29; 1Th 5:12
5:18 [e] Dt 25:4; 1Co 9:7-9 [f] Lk 10:7; Lev 19:13; Dt 24:14, 15; Mt 10:10; 1Co 9:14
5:19 [g] S Ac 11:30 [h] S Mt 18:16
5:20 [i] 2Ti 4:2; Titus 1:13; 2:15 [j] Dt 13:11
5:21 [k] 1Ti 6:13; 2Ti 4:1
5:22 [l] S Ac 6:6 [m] Eph 5:11 [n] Ps 18:26
5:23 [o] 1Ti 3:8
6:1 [p] S Eph 6:5 [q] 1Ti 5:14; Titus 2:5,8
6:2 [r] Phm 16 [s] 1Ti 4:11
6:3 [t] 1Ti 1:3 [u] S 1Ti 1:10
6:4 [v] 1Ti 3:6; 2Ti 3:4 [w] S 2Ti 2:14

[a] *18* Deut. 25:4 [b] *18* Luke 10:7 [c] *2* Or *and benefit from the service*

5:10 *washing the feet of the Lord's people.* A menial task, but necessary in NT times because of dusty roads and the wearing of sandals (see Jn 13:14). *the Lord's people.* See note on Col 1:4.

5:12 *broken their first pledge.* Perhaps when a widow was added to the list she pledged special devotion to Christ, which would be diminished by remarriage. Or Paul may be referring to the believer's basic trust in Christ, which a widow would compromise by marrying outside the faith.

5:13 *busybodies.* See 2Th 3:11 and note.

5:15 *Satan.* See notes on Job 1:6; Mt 16:23; 1Th 3:5; 1Jn 3:8; Rev 12:9–10.

5:17 All elders were to exercise leadership (3:4–5) and to teach and preach (3:2), and all were to receive honor. But those who excelled in leadership were to be counted "worthy of double honor." This was especially true of those who labored at teaching and preaching. (The Greek word translated "work" refers to toil.) That such honor should include financial support is indicated by the two illustrations in v. 18.

5:18 *Scripture.* The use of this term for both an OT (Dt 25:4) and a NT (Lk 10:7) passage shows that by this time portions of the NT (or what ultimately became a part of the NT) were considered to be equal in authority to the OT Scriptures (see 2Pe 3:16 and note). *Do not muzzle ... grain.* See 1Co 9:9–11 and notes on 9:9,11.

5:19 *two or three witnesses.* Cf. Dt 17:6 and note.

5:20 *those elders who are sinning.* The context indicates that Paul is speaking of the discipline of elders.

5:21 *elect angels.* Chosen angels, in contrast to Satan and the other fallen angels. *do nothing out of favoritism.* See Ex 23:3; Lev 19:15; Dt 1:17; 16:19; Job 13:10; Pr 18:5; 24:23; 28:21; Mal 2:9; Jas 2:1,9; 3:7. Cf. note on Ac 10:34.

5:22 *Do not be hasty in the laying on of hands.* Paul is speaking about the ordination of elders (see 4:14 and note), which should not be done until candidates have had time to prove themselves. *do not share in the sins of others.* Do not ordain a person unworthy of the office of elder. *Keep yourself pure.* Probably refers here to refusal to become involved in the ordination of an unworthy man.

5:23 *Stop drinking only water.* A parenthetical comment in Paul's discussion of elders. In view of Timothy's physical ailments, and perhaps because safe drinking water was often difficult to find, Paul advised him to drink "a little wine."

5:24–25 *sins of some ... good deeds.* Paul advises being alert to hidden sins, as well as to good deeds, in the lives of candidates for ordination.

6:1 *slavery.* See notes on 1Co 7:21; Eph 6:5; Col 3:22—4:1; see also Phm 16.

6:2b *These ... things.* Paul's preceding instructions.

6:3–5 Paul returns to the subject of 1:3 (see note on 1:3–11).

6:3 *sound instruction ... godly.* See essay, p. 2033.

envy, strife, malicious talk, evil suspicions
5and constant friction between people of
corrupt mind, who have been robbed of
the truth[x] and who think that godliness is
a means to financial gain.
6But godliness with contentment[y] is
great gain.[z] 7For we brought nothing into
the world, and we can take nothing out
of it.[a] 8But if we have food and clothing,
we will be content with that.[b] 9Those who
want to get rich[c] fall into temptation and
a trap[d] and into many foolish and harmful
desires that plunge people into ruin and
destruction. 10For the love of money[e] is a
root of all kinds of evil. Some people, eager for money, have wandered from the
faith[f] and pierced themselves with many
griefs.[g]

Final Charge to Timothy

11But you, man of God,[h] flee from all
this, and pursue righteousness, godliness,[i]
faith, love,[j] endurance and gentleness.
12Fight the good fight[k] of the faith. Take
hold of[l] the eternal life[m] to which you were
called when you made your good confession[n] in the presence of many witnesses.
13In the sight of God, who gives life to everything, and of Christ Jesus, who while
testifying before Pontius Pilate[o] made the
good confession,[p] I charge you[q] 14to keep
this command without spot or blame[r] until the appearing of our Lord Jesus Christ,[s]
15which God will bring about in his own
time[t]—God, the blessed[u] and only Ruler,[v] the King of kings and Lord of lords,[w]
16who alone is immortal[x] and who lives
in unapproachable light,[y] whom no one
has seen or can see.[z] To him be honor and
might forever. Amen.[a]

17Command those who are rich[b] in this
present world not to be arrogant nor to put
their hope in wealth,[c] which is so uncertain, but to put their hope in God,[d] who
richly provides us with everything for our
enjoyment.[e] 18Command them to do good,
to be rich in good deeds,[f] and to be generous and willing to share.[g] 19In this way
they will lay up treasure for themselves[h]
as a firm foundation for the coming age,
so that they may take hold of[i] the life that
is truly life.
20Timothy, guard what has been entrusted[j] to your care. Turn away from godless chatter[k] and the opposing ideas of
what is falsely called knowledge, 21which
some have professed and in so doing have
departed from the faith.[l]
Grace be with you all.[m]

6:5 [x]2Ti 3:8; Titus 1:15 **6:6** [y]Php 4:11; Heb 13:5 [z]1Ti 4:8 **6:7** [a]Job 1:21; Ps 49:17; Ecc 5:15 **6:8** [b]Pr 30:8; Heb 13:5 **6:9** [c]Pr 15:27; 28:20 [d]1Ti 3:7 **6:10** [e]S 1Ti 3:3 [f]ver 21; Jas 5:19 [g]Jos 7:21 **6:11** [h]2Ti 3:17 [i]ver 3,5, 6; S 1Ti 2:2 [j]1Ti 1:14; 2Ti 2:22; 3:10 **6:12** [k]1Co 9:25, 26; S 1Ti 1:18 [l]ver 19; Php 3:12 [m]S Mt 25:46 [n]S Heb 3:1 **6:13** [o]Jn 18:33-37 [p]ver 12 [q]1Ti 5:21; 2Ti 4:1 **6:14** [r]S 1Th 3:13 [s]S 1Co 1:7; 2Ti 1:10; 4:1,8 **6:15** [t]1Ti 2:6; Titus 1:3 [u]1Ti 1:11 [v]1Ti 1:17 [w]Dt 10:17; Ps 136:3; Da 2:47; Rev 1:5; 17:14; 19:16 **6:16** [x]1Ti 1:17 [y]Ps 104:2; 1Jn 1:7 [z]S Jn 1:18 [a]S Ro 11:36 **6:17** [b]ver 9 [c]Ps 62:10; Jer 49:4; Lk 12:20,21 [d]1Ti 4:10 [e]Ac 14:17 **6:18** [f]S 1Ti 5:10 [g]Ro 12:8, 13; Eph 4:28 **6:19** [h]S Mt 6:20 [i]ver 12; Php 3:12 **6:20** [j]2Ti 1:12,14 [k]2Ti 2:16 **6:21** [l]ver 10; 2Ti 2:18 [m]S Col 4:18

6:5 *robbed of the truth.* They had once known the truth but had been led into error. *who think that godliness is a means to financial gain.* See notes on 2Co 2:17; 11:7.
6:7 *take nothing out of it.* See Ps 49:17.
6:8 See Php 4:11–12 and notes.
6:9 See Lk 12:13–21 and note on 12:13.
6:10,12,21 *the faith.* See note on 3:9.
6:12 *Fight the good fight.* See 1:18 and note. *Take hold of ... eternal life.* Timothy had possessed eternal life since he had first been saved, but Paul urges him to claim its benefits in greater fullness (see vv. 17–19 and note on 4:16). *when you made your good confession.* Perhaps a reference to Timothy's confession of faith at his baptism during Paul's first missionary journey.
6:13 *who while testifying before Pontius Pilate made the good confession.* Probably a reference to Jesus' statements recorded in Jn 18:34–37; 19:11.
6:14 *this command.* Perhaps the whole charge given to Timothy to preach the gospel and care for the church (see v. 20)—though the preceding context may indicate that Paul used the singular "command" to sum up the various commands listed in vv. 11–12.
6:15 *in his own time.* Just as Jesus' first coming occurred at the precise time God wanted (Gal 4:4), so also his second coming will be at God's appointed time. *King of kings and Lord of lords.* See Rev 17:14 and note; 19:16.
6:16 *whom no one has seen or can see.* See Jn 1:18 and note.
6:17–19 See note on v. 12.
6:19 *lay up treasure.* See Mt 6:19–21 and note; 19:21; Lk 12:33 and note.
6:20 *what has been entrusted to your care.* The gospel (see 2Ti 1:14). *what is falsely called knowledge.* Perhaps a reference to an early form of the heresy of Gnosticism, which taught that one may be saved by knowledge. (The term "Gnosticism" comes from the Greek word for knowledge; see Introduction to 1 John: Gnosticism.)
6:21 *Grace.* See note on Ro 1:7. *with you.* See note on 2Co 13:14. *you all.* The plural indicates that Paul expects his letter to Timothy to be read to the entire Ephesian congregation (see note on 2Ti 4:22).

2 TIMOTHY

INTRODUCTION

Author, Date and Setting

See essay, p. 2033. After Paul's release from prison in Rome in AD 62 (Ac 28) and after his fourth missionary journey (see map and accompanying text, pp. 2038 – 2039), during which he wrote 1 Timothy and Titus, Paul was again imprisoned under Emperor Nero c. 66 – 67. It was during this time that he wrote 2 Timothy (see chart, p. 1845). In contrast to his first imprisonment, when he lived in a "rented house" (Ac 28:30; see note there), he now languished in a cold dungeon (see 4:13 and note), chained like a common criminal (1:16; 2:9). His friends even had a hard time finding out where he was being kept (1:17). Paul knew that his work was done and that his life was nearly at an end (4:6 – 8).

Reasons for Writing

Paul had three reasons for writing to Timothy at this time:

(1) Paul was lonely. Phygelus and Hermogenes, "everyone in the province of Asia" (1:15), and Demas (4:10) had all deserted him. Crescens, Titus and Tychicus were away (4:10 – 12), and only Luke was with him (4:11). Paul wanted very much for Timothy to join him also. Timothy was his co-worker (Ro 16:21), who "as a son with his father" (Php 2:22 ; see note there) had served closely with Paul (see 1Co 4:17). Of him Paul could say, "I have no one else like him" (Php 2:20). Paul longed for Timothy (1:4) and twice asked him to come soon (4:9,21). For more information on Timothy, see Introduction to 1 Timothy: Recipient.

(2) Paul was concerned about the welfare of the churches during this time of persecution under Nero, and he admonished Timothy to guard the gospel (1:14), to persevere in it (3:14), to keep on preaching it (4:2) and, if necessary, to suffer for it (1:8; 2:3).

(3) Paul wanted to write to the Ephesian church through his letter to Timothy (see note on 4:22).

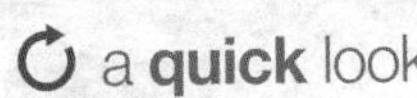

Author:
The apostle Paul

Audience:
Paul's disciple Timothy, who was ministering in Ephesus

Date:
About AD 66–67

Theme:
Facing imminent death, Paul encourages Timothy to carry on the ministry and faithfully guard the gospel.

Paul is concerned about the welfare of the churches during this time of persecution under Nero, and he admonishes Timothy to keep on preaching the gospel and, if necessary, to suffer for it.

Outline

- I. Introduction (1:1–4)
- II. Paul's Concern for Timothy (1:5–14)
- III. Paul's Situation (1:15–18)
- IV. Special Instructions to Timothy (ch. 2)
  - A. Call for Endurance (2:1–13)
  - B. Warning about Foolish Controversies (2:14–26)
- V. Warning about the Last Days (ch. 3)
  - A. Terrible Times (3:1–9)
  - B. Means of Combating Them (3:10–17)
- VI. Paul's Departing Remarks (4:1–8)
  - A. Charge to Preach the Word (4:1–5)
  - B. Paul's Victorious Prospect (4:6–8)
- VII. Final Requests, Greetings and Benediction (4:9–22)

Temple of Hadrian (second century AD) at Ephesus. Paul wrote this letter to Timothy, who was serving in Ephesus.

1 Paul, an apostle[a] of Christ Jesus by
the will of God,[b] in keeping with the
promise of life that is in Christ Jesus,[c]

2 To Timothy,[d] my dear son:[e]

Grace, mercy and peace from God the
Father and Christ Jesus our Lord.[f]

Thanksgiving

3 I thank God,[g] whom I serve, as my ancestors did, with a clear conscience,[h] as
night and day I constantly remember you
in my prayers.[i] 4 Recalling your tears,[j] I
long to see you,[k] so that I may be filled
with joy. 5 I am reminded of your sincere
faith,[l] which first lived in your grandmother Lois and in your mother Eunice[m] and, I
am persuaded, now lives in you also.

Appeal for Loyalty to Paul and the Gospel

6 For this reason I remind you to fan
into flame the gift of God, which is in you
through the laying on of my hands.[n] 7 For
the Spirit God gave us does not make us
timid,[o] but gives us power,[p] love and self-
discipline. 8 So do not be ashamed[q] of the
testimony about our Lord or of me his
prisoner.[r] Rather, join with me in suffering for the gospel,[s] by the power of God.
9 He has saved[t] us and called[u] us to a holy
life—not because of anything we have
done[v] but because of his own purpose and
grace. This grace was given us in Christ
Jesus before the beginning of time, 10 but
it has now been revealed[w] through the appearing of our Savior, Christ Jesus,[x] who
has destroyed death[y] and has brought life
and immortality to light through the gospel. 11 And of this gospel[z] I was appointed[a] a herald and an apostle and a teacher.[b] 12 That is why I am suffering as I am.
Yet this is no cause for shame,[c] because
I know whom I have believed, and am
convinced that he is able to guard[d] what I
have entrusted to him until that day.[e]
13 What you heard from me,[f] keep[g] as
the pattern[h] of sound teaching,[i] with faith
and love in Christ Jesus.[j] 14 Guard[k] the
good deposit that was entrusted to you—
guard it with the help of the Holy Spirit
who lives in us.[l]

Examples of Disloyalty and Loyalty

15 You know that everyone in the province of Asia[m] has deserted me,[n] including
Phygelus and Hermogenes.
16 May the Lord show mercy to the
household of Onesiphorus,[o] because he
often refreshed me and was not ashamed[p]
of my chains.[q] 17 On the contrary, when he
was in Rome, he searched hard for me until he found me. 18 May the Lord grant that
he will find mercy from the Lord on that
day![r] You know very well in how many
ways he helped me[s] in Ephesus.[t]

1:1 [a]S 1Co 1:1 [b]S 2Co 1:1 [c]Eph 3:6; Titus 1:2; 1Ti 6:19 **1:2** [d]S Ac 16:1 [e]S 1Ti 1:2 [f]S Ro 1:7 **1:3** [g]S Ro 1:8 [h]S Ac 23:1 [i]S Ro 1:10 **1:4** [j]Ac 20:37 [k]2Ti 4:9 **1:5** [l]1Ti 1:5 [m]Ac 16:1; 2Ti 3:15 **1:6** [n]S Ac 6:6; 1Ti 4:14 **1:7** [o]Jer 42:11; Ro 8:15; 1Co 16:10, 11; 1Ti 4:12; Heb 2:15 [p]Isa 11:2 **1:8** [q]ver 12, 16; Mk 8:38 [r]S Eph 3:1 [s]2Ti 2:3,9; 4:5 **1:9** [t]S Ro 11:14 [u]S Ro 8:28 [v]S Eph 2:9 **1:10** [w]Eph 1:9 [x]S 1Ti 6:14 [y]1Co 15:26,54 **1:11** [z]ver 8 [a]S Ac 9:15 [b]1Ti 2:7 **1:12** [c]ver 8, 16; Mk 8:38 [d]ver 14; 1Ti 6:20 [e]ver 18; S 1Co 1:8; 2Ti 4:8 **1:13** [f]2Ti 2:2 [g]S Titus 1:9 [h]Ro 6:17 [i]S 1Ti 1:10 [j]S 1Th 1:3; 1Ti 1:14

1:14 [k]ver 12 [l]S Ro 8:9 **1:15** [m]S Ac 2:9 [n]2Ti 4:10,11,16 **1:16** [o]2Ti 4:19 [p]ver 8, 12; Mk 8:38 [q]S Ac 21:33 **1:18** [r]S ver 12 [s]Heb 6:10 [t]S Ac 18:19

1:1 *Paul.* See note on Ro 1:1. *apostle.* See note on 1Co 1:1. *in keeping with the promise of life.* God's choice of Paul to be an apostle was in keeping with that promise, because apostles were appointed to preach and explain the good news that eternal life is available to all who will receive it through faith in Christ.
1:2 *Timothy, my dear son.* See note on 1Ti 1:2. *Grace ... peace.* See note on Ro 1:7. *mercy.* See 1Ti 1:2 and note.
1:3 *thank God ... in my prayers.* See note on Php 1:3–4.
1:4 *Recalling your tears.* Perhaps refers to Timothy's tears when Paul left for Macedonia (see 1Ti 1:3 and note). *long to see you.* See 4:9,21.
1:5 *your grandmother Lois ... your mother Eunice.* According to Ac 16:1, Timothy's mother was a Jewish Christian. Here we learn that his grandmother too was a Christian. Timothy's father, however, was a Greek and apparently an unbeliever (Ac 16:1).
1:6 *fan into flame the gift of God.* Gifts are not given in full bloom; they need to be developed through use. *through the laying on of my hands.* See 1Ti 4:14 and note. Paul was God's instrument through whom the gift came from the Holy Spirit to Timothy (see note on 1Ti 1:18).
1:7 *timid.* Apparently lack of confidence was a serious problem for Timothy (see 1Co 16:10–11 and note on 16:10; 1Ti 4:12).
1:8 *do not be ashamed.* Cf. v. 12; Ro 1:16 and note.
1:9 *called us to a holy life.* See Eph 1:4 and note; 1Th 4:7. *not because of anything we have done but because of his own purpose and grace.* Salvation is by grace alone and is based not on human effort but on God's saving plan and the gracious gift of his Son (see Ro 3:28; see also Eph 2:8–9; Titus 3:5 and notes). *before the beginning of time.* God's plan to save lost sinners was made in eternity past (see Eph 1:4; 1Pe 1:20 and notes; Rev 13:8).
1:10 *Christ ... has destroyed death.* See 1Co 15:26,54–57 and notes on 15:26,56,57. *has brought life and immortality to light.* Implying that before Jesus came, the certainty of life after death was somewhat shrouded in darkness (see Ps 11:7; Ecc 3:21; Isa 26:19; Da 12:2 and notes). *gospel.* See note on Mk 1:1.
1:11 *a herald and an apostle.* See 1Ti 2:7 and note.
1:12 *no cause for shame.* Cf. v. 8 and note. *what I have entrusted to him.* Probably Paul's commitment to Christ and his gospel (cf. v. 14; 1Ti 6:20 and notes). *that day.* The day of judgment.
1:13 *sound teaching.* See Titus 1:9 and note. *faith and love in Christ.* See 1Ti 1:14; faith and love through union with Christ—another way of saying "Christian faith and love."
1:14 *good deposit ... entrusted to you.* The gospel (see note on v. 12). Paul gives the same command in 1Ti 6:20. *Holy Spirit who lives in us.* See Ro 5:5; 1Co 6:19 and notes; see also Ro 8:9.
1:15 *everyone.* Probably a deliberate exaggeration to express widespread desertion. *province of Asia.* Timothy was in Ephesus, the capital of the Roman province of Asia (see Introduction to Ephesians: The City of Ephesus; see also map, p. 1982).
1:16 *Onesiphorus.* He and his family probably lived in Ephesus (v. 18; 4:19).
1:17 *Rome.* See Introduction: Author, Date and Setting; cf. v. 8; 2:9.
1:18 *that day.* The day of judgment (see v. 12). *he helped me in Ephesus.* Either on Paul's third missionary journey (see map, p. 1864) or on his fourth (see map, pp. 2038–2039).

The Appeal Renewed

2 You then, my son,[u] be strong[v] in the
grace that is in Christ Jesus. 2And
the things you have heard me say[w] in the
presence of many witnesses[x] entrust to reliable people who will also be qualified
to teach others. 3Join with me in suffering,[y] like a good soldier[z] of Christ Jesus.
4No one serving as a soldier gets entangled in civilian affairs, but rather tries to
please his commanding officer. 5Similarly,
anyone who competes as an athlete does
not receive the victor's crown[a] except by
competing according to the rules. 6The
hardworking farmer should be the first to
receive a share of the crops.[b] 7Reflect on
what I am saying, for the Lord will give
you insight into all this.
8Remember Jesus Christ, raised from
the dead,[c] descended from David.[d] This
is my gospel,[e] 9for which I am suffering[f]
even to the point of being chained[g] like a
criminal. But God's word[h] is not chained.
10Therefore I endure everything[i] for the
sake of the elect,[j] that they too may obtain
the salvation[k] that is in Christ Jesus, with
eternal glory.[l]
11Here is a trustworthy saying:[m]

If we died with him,
we will also live with him;[n]
12if we endure,
we will also reign with him.[o]
If we disown him,
he will also disown us;[p]
13if we are faithless,
he remains faithful,[q]
for he cannot disown himself.

Dealing With False Teachers

14Keep reminding God's people of these
things. Warn them before God against
quarreling about words;[r] it is of no value, and only ruins those who listen. 15Do
your best to present yourself to God as
one approved, a worker who does not
need to be ashamed and who correctly
handles the word of truth.[s] 16Avoid godless chatter,[t] because those who indulge
in it will become more and more ungodly. 17Their teaching will spread like gan-
grene. Among them are Hymenaeus[u] and
Philetus, 18who have departed from the
truth. They say that the resurrection has
already taken place,[v] and they destroy the
faith of some.[w] 19Nevertheless, God's solid
foundation stands firm,[x] sealed with this
inscription: "The Lord knows those who
are his,"[y] and, "Everyone who confesses
the name of the Lord[z] must turn away
from wickedness."
20In a large house there are articles not

2:1 [u] S 1Ti 1:2 [v] S Eph 6:10 **2:2** [w] 2Ti 1:13 [x] 1Ti 6:12 **2:3** [y] ver 9; 2Ti 1:8; 4:5 [z] S 1Ti 1:18 **2:5** [a] S 1Co 9:25 **2:6** [b] 1Co 9:10 **2:8** [c] S Ac 2:24 [d] S Mt 1:1 [e] Ro 2:16; 16:25 **2:9** [f] S Ac 9:16 [g] S Ac 21:33 [h] S Heb 4:12 **2:10** [i] Col 1:24 [j] Titus 1:1 [k] 2Co 1:6 [l] 2Co 4:17; 1Pe 5:10 **2:11** [m] S 1Ti 1:15 [n] Ro 6:2-11 **2:12** [o] Ro 8:17; 1Pe 4:13 [p] Mt 10:33 **2:13** [q] Ro 3:3; S 1Co 1:9 **2:14** [r] ver 23; 1Ti 1:4; 6:4; Titus 3:9 **2:15** [s] Eph 1:13; Col 1:5; Jas 1:18 **2:16** [t] Titus 3:9; 1Ti 6:20 **2:17** [u] 1Ti 1:20 **2:18** [v] 2Th 2:2 [w] 1Ti 1:19; 6:21 **2:19** [x] Isa 28:16 [y] Ex 33:12; Nu 16:5; Jn 10:14; 1Co 8:3; Gal 4:9 [z] 1Co 1:2

2:1 *my son.* See 1Ti 1:2 and note. *strong in the grace … in Christ.* Enabling power comes from a relationship to Christ (see 2Co 12:9–10; Eph 6:10 and notes).

2:2 *the things you have heard me say in the presence of many witnesses.* Refers to Paul's preaching and teaching, which Timothy had heard repeatedly on Paul's missionary journeys. *reliable people.* People characterized by trustworthiness, dependability and faithfulness (cf. Mt 25:21,23 and notes on 25:21; Lk 12:42; 1Co 4:2; Eph 6:21; Col 1:7; 4:7; 1Ti 1:12; 1Pe 4:10; 3Jn 3; Rev 2:10,13; 13:10; 14:12; 17:14; cf. also Ps 4:3 and note).

2:3–6 Paul gives three examples for Timothy to follow: (1) a soldier who wants to please his commander, (2) an athlete who follows the rules of the game and (3) a farmer who works hard.

2:5 *victor's crown.* Cf. 1Co 9:25 and note.

2:6 *receive a share of the crops.* In this illustration, as in the previous two (soldier, vv. 3–4; athlete, v. 5), the main lesson is that dedicated effort will be rewarded (see 1Ti 5:17 and note).

2:8 *raised from the dead, descended from David.* Christ's resurrection proclaims his deity, and his descent from David shows his humanity; both truths are basic to the gospel. Since Christ is God, his death has infinite value; since he is human, he could rightfully become our substitute.

2:9 *chained like a criminal.* Apparently Paul was awaiting execution (see 4:6 and note).

2:10 *I endure everything for the sake of the elect.* No suffering is too great if it brings about the salvation of God's chosen ones who will yet believe. *in Christ.* See notes on 1:13; Eph 1:1. *eternal glory.* The final state of salvation.

2:11–13 Probably an early Christian hymn. The point to which Paul appeals is that suffering for Christ will be followed by glory (see Ro 8:17–18).

2:11 *trustworthy saying.* See note on 1Ti 1:15. *If we died with him, we will also live with him.* The Greek grammatical construction here assumes that we "died with" Christ in the past, when he died for us on the cross. We are therefore assured that we will also live with him eternally (cf. Ro 6:2–11).

2:12 *if we endure, we will also reign.* Faithfully bearing up under suffering and trial will result in reward when Christ returns (see Ro 8:17 and note). *If we disown him.* See Mt 10:33.

2:13 *he remains faithful.* See La 3:22–23; Ro 3:3–4 and notes.

2:14–18 The wording of vv. 14–16 indicates that the heresy mentioned here is an early form of Gnosticism—the same as that dealt with in 1 Timothy and Titus (see note on 1Ti 1:3–11 and Introduction to 1 John: Gnosticism). Two leaders of this heresy, Hymenaeus (see 1Ti 1:20) and Philetus (v. 17), denied bodily resurrection (v. 18) and probably asserted that there is only spiritual resurrection (similar to the error mentioned in 1Co 15:12–19; see notes there). Gnosticism interpreted resurrection allegorically, not literally.

2:15 *ashamed.* See 1:8 and note. *word of truth.* The gospel (Eph 1:13; Col 1:5), whose truth Timothy was to believe and obey and whose contents he was therefore to preach (4:2).

2:16 *godless chatter.* See note on 1Ti 1:3–11.

2:19 *God's solid foundation.* The church, which upholds the truth (1Ti 3:15). In spite of the heresy of Hymenaeus and Philetus (v. 17), Timothy should be heartened to know that the church is God's solid foundation. There are two inscriptions on it: One stresses the security of the church ("The Lord knows those who are his"; here "know," as often in the Bible, means to be intimately acquainted with), while the other emphasizes human responsibility ("Everyone who confesses the name of the Lord must turn away from wickedness"). *sealed.* The church is owned and securely protected by God (see Eph 1:13 and note).

only of gold and silver, but also of wood
and clay; some are for special purposes
and some for common use.[a] 21 Those who
cleanse themselves from the latter will be
instruments for special purposes, made
holy, useful to the Master and prepared to
do any good work.[b]

22 Flee the evil desires of youth and pursue righteousness, faith, love[c] and peace,
along with those who call on the Lord[d]
out of a pure heart.[e] 23 Don't have anything to do with foolish and stupid arguments, because you know they produce
quarrels.[f] 24 And the Lord's servant must
not be quarrelsome but must be kind to
everyone, able to teach, not resentful.[g]
25 Opponents must be gently instructed,
in the hope that God will grant them repentance leading them to a knowledge of
the truth,[h] 26 and that they will come to
their senses and escape from the trap of
the devil,[i] who has taken them captive to
do his will.

3 But mark this: There will be terrible
times in the last days.[j] 2 People will
be lovers of themselves, lovers of money,[k]
boastful, proud,[l] abusive,[m] disobedient to
their parents,[n] ungrateful, unholy, 3 without love, unforgiving, slanderous, without
self-control, brutal, not lovers of the good,
4 treacherous,[o] rash, conceited,[p] lovers
of pleasure rather than lovers of God—
5 having a form of godliness[q] but denying
its power. Have nothing to do with such
people.[r]

6 They are the kind who worm their way[s]
into homes and gain control over gullible
women, who are loaded down with sins
and are swayed by all kinds of evil desires,
7 always learning but never able to come
to a knowledge of the truth.[t] 8 Just as Jannes and Jambres opposed Moses,[u] so also
these teachers oppose[v] the truth. They are
men of depraved minds,[w] who, as far as
the faith is concerned, are rejected. 9 But
they will not get very far because, as in
the case of those men,[x] their folly will be
clear to everyone.

A Final Charge to Timothy

10 You, however, know all about my
teaching,[y] my way of life, my purpose,
faith, patience, love, endurance, 11 persecutions, sufferings—what kinds of
things happened to me in Antioch,[z] Iconium[a] and Lystra,[b] the persecutions I endured.[c] Yet the Lord rescued[d] me from all
of them.[e] 12 In fact, everyone who wants
to live a godly life in Christ Jesus will be
persecuted,[f] 13 while evildoers and impostors will go from bad to worse,[g] deceiving and being deceived.[h] 14 But as for you,
continue in what you have learned and
have become convinced of, because you
know those from whom you learned it,[i]
15 and how from infancy[j] you have known
the Holy Scriptures,[k] which are able to
make you wise[l] for salvation through
faith in Christ Jesus. 16 All Scripture is
God-breathed[m] and is useful for teaching,[n] rebuking, correcting and training in
righteousness,[o] 17 so that the servant of

2:20 [a] Ro 9:21 **2:21** [b] 2Co 9:8; Eph 2:10; 2Ti 3:17 **2:22** [c] 1Ti 1:14; 6:11 [d] S Ac 2:21 [e] 1Ti 1:5 **2:23** [f] S ver 14 **2:24** [g] 1Ti 3:2,3 **2:25** [h] S 1Ti 2:4 **2:26** [i] 1Ti 3:7 **3:1** [j] 1Ti 4:1; 2Pe 3:3 **3:2** [k] S 1Ti 3:3 [l] Ro 1:30 [m] 2Pe 2:10-12 [n] Ro 1:30 **3:4** [o] Ps 25:3 [p] 1Ti 3:6; 6:4 **3:5** [q] S 1Ti 2:2 [r] S Ro 16:17 **3:6** [s] Jude 4

3:7 [t] S 1Ti 2:4 **3:8** [u] Ex 7:11 [v] Ac 13:8 [w] 1Ti 6:5 **3:9** [x] Ex 7:12; 8:18; 9:11 **3:10** [y] 1Ti 4:6 **3:11** [z] Ac 13:14, 50 [a] S Ac 13:51 [b] Ac 14:6 [c] 2Co 11:23-27 [d] S Ro 15:31 [e] Ps 34:19 **3:12** [f] Jn 15:20; S Ac 14:22 **3:13** [g] 2Ti 2:16 [h] S Mk 13:5 **3:14** [i] 2Ti 1:13 **3:15** [j] 2Ti 1:5 [k] Jn 5:39 [l] Dt 4:6; Ps 119:98,99 **3:16** [m] 2Pe 1:20, 21 [n] S Ro 4:23, 24 [o] Dt 29:29

2:21 *made holy.* Set apart to God for use in his service (see 1Co 1:2; 1Pe 1:16 and notes).
2:22 *youth.* See 1Ti 4:12 and note. *peace.* See Ro 12:16. *pure heart.* See 1Ti 1:5 and note.
2:23 The Gnostic heresy is in view again (see note on vv. 14–18).
2:24 *Lord's servant.* Seems to refer primarily to a person who, like Timothy, is set aside for special service. *able to teach.* Cf. note on 1Ti 3:1.
2:25 *repentance.* See Mt 4:17 and note. *knowledge of the truth.* See 1Ti 2:4.
2:26 *trap of the devil.* See 1Ti 3:7; cf. Eph 6:11; 1Pe 5:8.
3:1 *last days.* The Messianic era, the time beginning with Christ's first coming (see 1Ti 4:1; Heb 1:1–2 and notes; 1Pe 1:20). That "the last days" in this passage does not refer only to the time just prior to Christ's return is apparent from Paul's command to Timothy to "have nothing to do" (v. 5) with the unbelieving and unfaithful people who characterize this time.
3:2–5 For similar lists of vices, see note on Ro 1:29–31.
3:2 *lovers of money.* See 1Ti 6:9–10,17–18.
3:5 *godliness.* See 1Ti 2:2 and note.
3:6 *gullible women.* Unstable women who are guilt-ridden because of their sins, torn by lust and victims of various false teachers ("always learning," v. 7, but never coming to a saving knowledge of Christ).
3:8 *Jannes and Jambres.* According to Jewish tradition, they were the Egyptian court magicians who opposed Moses (see Ex 7:11 and note).
3:11 *Antioch, Iconium and Lystra.* Three cities in the Roman province of Galatia (see map, p. 1858) that Paul visited on his first and second missionary journeys (see Ac 13:14,51; 14:6 and notes). Since Timothy was from Lystra (Ac 16:1), he would have known firsthand of Paul's sufferings in that region. *the Lord rescued me from all of them.* Even from execution by stoning (see Ac 14:19–20 and notes).
3:12 See Mt 10:22; Ac 14:22; Php 1:29 and note; 1Pe 4:12. *in Christ.* See notes on 1:13; Eph 1:1.
3:14 *those from whom you learned it.* Perhaps a reference to Paul, as well as to Timothy's mother and grandmother (see 1:5 and note).
3:15 *from infancy you have known the Holy Scriptures.* A Jewish boy formally began to study the OT when he was five years old. Timothy was taught at home by his mother and grandmother even before he reached this age (see 1:5 and note).
3:16 *All Scripture.* The primary reference is to the OT, since some of the NT books had not even been written at this time. (See 1Ti 5:18 and note for indications that some NT books—or material ultimately included in the NT—were already considered equal in authority to the OT Scriptures.) *God-breathed.* Paul affirms God's active involvement in the writing of Scripture, an involvement so powerful and pervasive that what is written is the infallible and authoritative word of God (see 2Pe 1:20–21 and notes).
3:17 *servant of God.* Lit. "man of God" (see NIV text note). Paul calls Timothy a "man of God" in 1Ti 6:11.

God[a][p] may be thoroughly equipped for every good work.[q]

4 In the presence of God and of Christ Jesus, who will judge the living and the dead,[r] and in view of his appearing[s] and his kingdom, I give you this charge:[t] 2 Preach[u] the word;[v] be prepared in season and out of season; correct, rebuke[w] and encourage[x]—with great patience and careful instruction. 3 For the time will come when people will not put up with sound doctrine.[y] Instead, to suit their own desires, they will gather around them a great number of teachers to say what their itching ears want to hear.[z] 4 They will turn their ears away from the truth and turn aside to myths.[a] 5 But you, keep your head in all situations, endure hardship,[b] do the work of an evangelist,[c] discharge all the duties of your ministry.

6 For I am already being poured out like a drink offering,[d] and the time for my departure is near.[e] 7 I have fought the good fight,[f] I have finished the race,[g] I have kept the faith. 8 Now there is in store for me[h] the crown of righteousness,[i] which the Lord, the righteous Judge, will award to me on that day[j]—and not only to me, but also to all who have longed for his appearing.[k]

3:17 [p] 1Ti 6:11 [q] 2Ti 2:21
4:1 [r] S Ac 10:42 [s] ver 8; S 1Ti 6:14 [t] 1Ti 5:21; 6:13
4:2 [u] 1Ti 4:13 [v] Gal 6:6 [w] 1Ti 5:20; Titus 1:13; 2:15 [x] Titus 2:15
4:3 [y] S 1Ti 1:10 [z] Isa 30:10
4:4 [a] S 1Ti 1:4
4:5 [b] 2Ti 1:8; 2:3,9 [c] Ac 21:8; Eph 4:11
4:6 [d] Nu 15:1-12; 28:7,24; Php 2:17 [e] Php 1:23
4:7 [f] S 1Ti 1:18 [g] S 1Co 9:24; Ac 20:24
4:8 [h] Col 1:5; 1Pe 1:4 [i] S 1Co 9:25 [j] S 2Ti 1:12 [k] S 1Ti 6:14
4:9 [l] ver 21; Titus 3:12
4:10 [m] Col 4:14; Phm 24 [n] 1Jn 2:15 [o] S Ac 17:1 [p] S Ac 16:6 [q] S 2Co 2:13
4:11 [r] Col 4:14; Phm 24 [s] 2Ti 1:15 [t] S Ac 12:12
4:12 [u] S Ac 20:4

Personal Remarks

9 Do your best to come to me quickly,[l] 10 for Demas,[m] because he loved this world,[n] has deserted me and has gone to Thessalonica.[o] Crescens has gone to Galatia,[p] and Titus[q] to Dalmatia. 11 Only Luke[r] is with me.[s] Get Mark[t] and bring him with you, because he is helpful to me in my ministry. 12 I sent Tychicus[u] to Ephesus.[v] 13 When you come, bring the cloak that I left with Carpus at Troas,[w] and my scrolls, especially the parchments.

14 Alexander[x] the metalworker did me a great deal of harm. The Lord will repay him for what he has done.[y] 15 You too should be on your guard against him, because he strongly opposed our message.

16 At my first defense, no one came to my support, but everyone deserted me. May it not be held against them.[z] 17 But the Lord stood at my side[a] and gave me strength,[b] so that through me the message might be fully proclaimed and all the Gentiles might hear it.[c] And I was delivered

[a] 17 *Or that you, a man of God,*

[v] S Ac 18:19 **4:13** [w] S Ac 16:8 **4:14** [x] Ac 19:33; 1Ti 1:20 [y] Ps 28:4; 109:20; Ro 2:6; 12:19 **4:16** [z] Ac 7:60 **4:17** [a] Ac 23:11 [b] S Php 4:13 [c] S Ac 9:15

4:1 Paul states his charge to Timothy, aware that he does so in the presence of God the Father and of Christ, who will judge everyone. He is also keenly aware of the twin facts of Christ's return ("his appearing") and the coming establishment of God's kingdom in its fullest expression. Timothy was to view a charge so given as of utmost importance. *Jesus, who will judge.* See Mt 25:31–33; see also Jn 5:22; Jas 5:9; 1Pe 4:5 and notes.

4:2 *be prepared.* Be ready in any situation to speak the needed word, whether of correction, of rebuke or of encouragement.

4:3 *sound doctrine.* See Titus 1:9 and note. *itching ears.* Ears that want to be "scratched" by words in keeping with one's evil desires.

4:4 *myths.* See 1Ti 1:4 and note.

4:6 *drink offering.* The offering of wine poured out to the Lord (see Nu 15:1–12; 28:7). Paul views his approaching death as the pouring out of his life as an offering to Christ (see Php 2:17 and note). *my departure.* His impending death in AD 67/68 (see chart, p. 1845; cf. Php 1:23).

4:7 Paul looks back over 30 years of labor as an apostle (c. AD 36–67/68). Like an athlete who had engaged successfully in a contest ("fought the good fight"; see note on 1Ti 1:18), he had "finished the race" and "kept the faith," i.e., had carefully preserved the deposit of Christian truth. *the faith.* See note on 1Ti 3:9.

4:8 *crown of righteousness.* Continuing with the same figure of speech, Paul uses the metaphor of the wreath given to the winner of a race (see 1Co 9:25 and note). He could be referring to (1) a crown given as a reward for a righteous life, (2) a crown consisting of righteousness or (3) a crown given righteously (justly) by the righteous Judge. *that day.* The day of Christ's second coming ("appearing"; see v. 1).

4:10 *Demas.* See Col 4:14 and note; Phm 24. *Thessalonica.* See Introduction to 1 Thessalonians: Thessalonica: The City and the Church; see also photo, p. 2019. *Galatia.* Either the northern area of Asia Minor (Gaul) or a Roman province in what is now central Turkey (see note on Gal 1:2). *Titus.* See Introduction to Titus: Recipient. *Dalmatia.* Also known as Illyricum (Ro 15:19; see map, pp. 2528–2529, at the end of this study Bible).

4:11 *Mark.* See Introduction to Mark: Mark in the NT. John Mark had deserted Paul and Barnabas on their first missionary journey (Ac 13:13). After Paul refused to take Mark on the second journey, Barnabas separated from Paul, taking Mark with him on a mission to Cyprus (Ac 15:36–41). Ultimately Mark proved himself to Paul, indicated by his presence with Paul during Paul's first Roman imprisonment (Col 4:10; Phm 24) and by Paul's request here for Timothy to bring Mark with him to Rome.

4:12 *Tychicus.* See Ac 20:4; Eph 6:21 and notes.

4:13 *cloak.* For protection against the cold dampness (see Introduction: Author, Date and Setting). It was probably a heavy, sleeveless, outer garment, circular in shape with a hole in the middle for one's head. *Troas.* See Ac 16:8 and note; see also map, p. 2039. *scrolls, especially the parchments.* The scrolls (see note on Ex 17:14) were made of leather or papyrus, and the parchments were made of the skins of animals. The latter may have been copies of parts of the OT.

4:14 *Alexander the metalworker.* Perhaps the Alexander mentioned in 1Ti 1:20.

4:16 *my first defense.* The first court hearing of Paul's present case, not his defense on the occasion of his first imprisonment (Ac 28).

4:17 *through me the message might be fully proclaimed.* Even in these dire circumstances Paul used the occasion to testify about Jesus Christ in the imperial court (cf. Ac 16:25; cf. also Php 1:12–14 and notes). *delivered from the lion's mouth.* Since, as a Roman citizen, Paul could not be thrown to the lions in the amphitheater, this must be a figurative way of saying that his first hearing did not result in an immediate guilty verdict.

from the lion's mouth.[d] 18 The Lord will
rescue me from every evil attack[e] and will
bring me safely to his heavenly kingdom.[f]
To him be glory for ever and ever. Amen.[g]

Final Greetings

19 Greet Priscilla[a] and Aquila[h] and the
household of Onesiphorus.[i] 20 Erastus[j]
stayed in Corinth, and I left Trophimus[k]
sick in Miletus.[l] 21 Do your best to get here
before winter.[m] Eubulus greets you, and
so do Pudens, Linus, Claudia and all the
brothers and sisters.[b]
22 The Lord be with your spirit.[n] Grace
be with you all.[o]

4:17 [d] 1Sa 17:37; Ps 22:21; Da 6:22; 1Co 15:32 **4:18** [e] Ps 121:7; 2Pe 2:9 **4:18** [f] ver 1 [g] S Ro 11:36 **4:19** [h] S Ac 18:2 [i] 2Ti 1:16 **4:20** [j] Ac 19:22 [k] Ac 20:4; 21:29 [l] Ac 20:15, 17

[a] *19* Greek *Prisca,* a variant of *Priscilla* [b] *21* The Greek word for *brothers and sisters* (*adelphoi*) refers here to believers, both men and women, as part of God's family.

4:21 [m] ver 9; Titus 3:12 **4:22** [n] S Gal 6:18 [o] S Col 4:18

4:18 *will rescue me from every evil attack.* Since Paul fully expected to die soon (see v. 6 and note), the rescue he speaks of here is spiritual, not physical. *heavenly kingdom.* Heaven itself.

4:19 *Priscilla and Aquila.* See Ac 18:2,18; 1Co 16:19 and notes. *Onesiphorus.* See 1:16 and note.

4:20 *Erastus.* See Ro 16:23 and note. *Corinth.* See Introduction to 1 Corinthians: The City of Corinth; see also map, p. 1920. *Trophimus.* See note on Ac 20:4. *Miletus.* A seaport on the coast of Asia Minor about 35 miles south of Ephesus (see map, p. 2039). See Ac 20:15 and note.

4:21 *Linus.* Early tradition says he was bishop of Rome after the deaths of Peter and Paul. *brothers and sisters.* See NIV text note.

4:22 *be with your spirit.* See note on Gal 6:18. *Grace.* See note on Ro 1:7. *with you.* See note on 2Co 13:14. *you.* As at the end of 1 Timothy (see note on 1Ti 6:21), "you" here is plural (hence NIV "you all"), showing that the letter was intended for public use. The word "your" in the first part of the verse, however, is singular, indicating that it was addressed to Timothy alone.

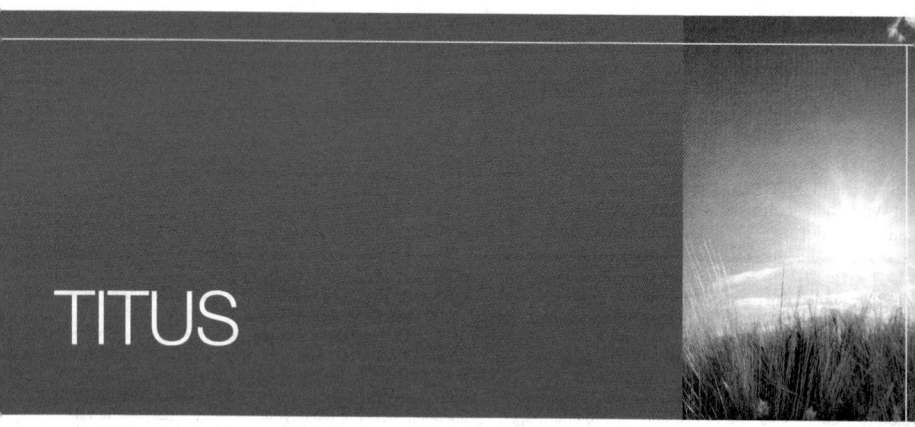

TITUS

INTRODUCTION

Author

See essay, p. 2033. The author is Paul (see 1:1 and note; see also Introduction to 1 Timothy: Author).

Recipient

The letter is addressed to Titus, one of Paul's converts (see 1:4 and note) and a considerable help to Paul in his ministry. When Paul left Antioch to discuss the gospel with the Jerusalem leaders, he took Titus with him (Gal 2:1 – 3); acceptance of Titus (a Gentile) as a Christian without circumcision vindicated Paul's stand there (Gal 2:3 – 5). Presumably Titus, who is not referred to in Acts (but is mentioned 13 times in the rest of the NT), worked with Paul at Ephesus during his third missionary journey (see map, p. 1864). It is likely that he was the bearer of Paul's severe letter to the Corinthian church (see Introduction to 2 Corinthians: Occasion). Paul was concerned about the possible negative reaction of the Corinthian church to his severe letter, so he arranged to meet Titus at Troas (2Co 2:12 – 13). When Titus did not appear, Paul traveled on to Macedonia. There he met Titus and with great relief heard the good news that the worst of the trouble was over at Corinth (2Co 7:6 – 7,13 – 14). Titus, accompanied by two Christian brothers, was the bearer of 2 Corinthians (2Co 8:23) and was given the responsibility for making final arrangements for the collection, begun a year earlier, in Corinth (see 2Co 8:6,16 – 17 and notes).

Following Paul's release from his first Roman imprisonment (Ac 28), he and Titus worked briefly in Crete (1:5), after which he commissioned Titus to remain there as his representative and complete some needed work (1:5; 2:15; 3:12 – 13). Paul asked Titus to meet him at Nicopolis (see map, p. 2039) when a replacement arrived (see 3:12 and note). Later, Titus went on a mission to Dalmatia (see 2Ti 4:10 and note), the last word we hear about him in the NT. Considering the assignments given him, he obviously was a capable and resourceful leader.

a **quick** look

Author:
The apostle Paul

Audience:
Titus, a trusted Gentile companion of Paul

Date:
About AD 63–65

Theme:
Paul writes to instruct Titus concerning the care of the church on the island of Crete.

The letter is addressed to Titus, one of Paul's converts and a considerable help to Paul in his ministry. When Paul left Antioch to discuss the gospel with the Jerusalem leaders, he took Titus with him.

Crete

The fourth largest island in the Mediterranean Sea, Crete lies directly south of the Aegean Sea (see map and inset, p. 2039; see also photo below; cf. note on 1Sa 30:14; cf. also Paul's experiences there in Ac 27:7–13). In NT times life in Crete had sunk to a deplorable moral level. The dishonesty, gluttony and laziness of its inhabitants were proverbial (1:12).

Occasion and Purpose

Apparently Paul introduced Christianity in Crete when he and Titus visited the island, after which he left Titus there to organize the converts. Paul evidently sent the letter with Zenas and Apollos, who were on a journey that took them through Crete (3:13), to give Titus personal authorization and guidance in meeting opposition (1:5; 2:1,7–8,15; 3:9), instructions about faith and conduct, and warnings about false teachers. Paul also informed Titus of his future plans for him (3:12).

Place and Date of Writing

Paul may have written from Macedonia, for he had not yet reached Nicopolis (see 3:12). The letter was written after he was released from his first Roman imprisonment (Ac 28), probably between AD 63 and 65 (see chart, p. 1845)—or possibly at a later date if he wrote after his planned trip to Spain (see Ro 15:24 and note; see also map and accompanying text, pp. 2038–2039).

Harbor on the island of Crete, where Paul had left Titus to oversee the church

Distinctive Characteristics

Especially significant, considering the nature of the Cretan heresy, are the repeated emphases on loving and doing and teaching "what is good" (1:8,16; 2:3,7,14; 3:1,8,14) and the classic summaries of Christian doctrine, stressing the grace of God (2:11 – 14; 3:4 – 7).

Outline

- I. Greetings (1:1 – 4)
- II. Concerning Elders (1:5 – 9)
  - A. Reasons for Leaving Titus in Crete (1:5)
  - B. Qualifications of Elders (1:6 – 9)
- III. Concerning False Teachers (1:10 – 16)
- IV. Concerning Various Groups in the Congregations (ch. 2)
  - A. The Instructions to Different Groups (2:1 – 10)
  - B. The Foundation for Christian Living (2:11 – 14)
  - C. The Duty of Titus (2:15)
- V. Concerning Believers in General (3:1 – 8)
  - A. Obligations as Citizens (3:1 – 2)
  - B. Motives for Godly Conduct (3:3 – 8)
- VI. Concerning Response to Spiritual Error (3:9 – 11)
- VII. Conclusion, Final Greetings and Benediction (3:12 – 15)

Basilica of Titus on Crete

www.HolyLandPhotos.org

1 Paul, a servant of God[a] and an apostle[b] of Jesus Christ to further the faith
of God's elect and their knowledge of the
truth[c] that leads to godliness[d]— 2 in the
hope of eternal life,[e] which God, who does
not lie,[f] promised before the beginning of
time,[g] 3 and which now at his appointed
season[h] he has brought to light[i] through
the preaching entrusted to me[j] by the command of God[k] our Savior,[l]

4 To Titus,[m] my true son[n] in our common
faith:

Grace and peace from God the Father
and Christ Jesus our Savior.[o]

Appointing Elders Who Love What Is Good

1:6-8Ref— 1Ti 3:2-4

5 The reason I left you in Crete[p] was
that you might put in order what was left
unfinished and appoint[a] elders[q] in every
town, as I directed you. 6 An elder must
be blameless,[r] faithful to his wife, a man
whose children believe[b] and are not open
to the charge of being wild and disobedient. 7 Since an overseer[s] manages God's
household,[t] he must be blameless—not
overbearing, not quick-tempered, not giv-
en to drunkenness, not violent, not pursuing dishonest gain.[u] 8 Rather, he must be
hospitable,[v] one who loves what is good,[w]
who is self-controlled,[x] upright, holy and
disciplined. 9 He must hold firmly[y] to the
trustworthy message as it has been taught,
so that he can encourage others by sound
doctrine[z] and refute those who oppose it.

Rebuking Those Who Fail to Do Good

10 For there are many rebellious people,
full of meaningless talk[a] and deception, especially those of the circumcision group.[b]
11 They must be silenced, because they are
disrupting whole households[c] by teaching
things they ought not to teach—and that
for the sake of dishonest gain. 12 One of
Crete's own prophets[d] has said it: "Cretans[e] are always liars, evil brutes, lazy

1:1 [a] Ro 1:1; Jas 1:1 [b] S 1Co 1:1 [c] S 1Ti 2:4 [d] S 1Ti 2:2 **1:2** [e] Titus 3:7; 2Ti 1:1 [f] Nu 23:19; Heb 6:18 [g] 2Ti 1:9 **1:3** [h] 1Ti 2:6; 6:15 [i] 2Ti 1:10 [j] S 1Ti 1:11 [k] S 2Co 1:1; 1Ti 1:1 [l] S Lk 1:47 **1:4** [m] S 2Co 2:13 [n] S 1Ti 1:2 [o] S Ro 1:7 **1:5** [p] Ac 27:7 [q] S Ac 11:30 **1:6** [r] S 1Th 3:13; 1Ti 3:2 **1:7** [s] S 1Ti 3:1 [t] 1Co 4:1 [u] S 1Ti 3:3,8 **1:8** [v] S Ro 12:13 [w] 2Ti 3:3 [x] Titus 2:2,5,6,12 **1:9** [y] S 1Co 16:13; 1Ti 1:19; 2Ti 1:13; 3:14 [z] S 1Ti 1:10 **1:10** [a] 1Ti 1:6 [b] Ac 10:45; 11:2 **1:11** [c] 1Ti 5:13 **1:12** [d] Ac 17:28 [e] Ac 2:11

[a] 5 Or *ordain* [b] 6 Or *children are trustworthy*

1:1 *Paul.* See note on Ro 1:1. *servant of God.* Only here does Paul call himself a servant of God; elsewhere he says "servant of Christ" (Ro 1:1; Gal 1:10; Php 1:1). James uses both terms of himself (Jas 1:1). *servant.* See note on Ro 1:1. *apostle.* See note on 1Co 1:1. *to further the faith ... and their knowledge.* Paul's appointed mission as God's servant and Christ's apostle—further explained in v. 2 (see Ac 9:15; 22:15; 26:16–18). *godliness.* See 1Ti 2:2 and note.

1:2 *hope.* See Col 1:5 and note. *eternal life.* See note on Jn 3:15. *does not lie.* In contrast to the Cretans (v. 12)—and the devil (Jn 8:44). *before the beginning of time.* See 2Ti 1:9 and note.

1:3 *appointed season.* Crucial events in God's program occur at his designated times in history (see 1Ti 2:6; 6:15 and notes). *the preaching.* The authoritative message that centers in Christ. *God our Savior.* Three times in the letter God the Father is called Savior (here; 2:10; 3:4; see also 1Ti 1:1; 2:3; 4:10), and three times Jesus is called Savior (v. 4; 2:13; 3:6; see also 2Ti 1:10).

1:4 *my true son.* Titus, like Timothy (1Ti 1:2), was a spiritual son, having been converted through Paul's ministry. Onesimus was also called a son by Paul (Phm 10). *true.* Genuine. *our common faith.* The faith shared by all true believers. *Grace and peace.* See note on Ro 1:7. *Savior.* In all of Paul's other greetings Jesus is called "Lord." Paul uses "Savior" 12 times in all his letters, half of the references being in Titus.

1:5 *left you in Crete.* Implies that Paul and Titus had been together in Crete, a ministry not mentioned in Acts. On his voyage to Rome, Paul visited Crete briefly as a prisoner (Ac 27:7–8), but now that he had been released from his first Roman imprisonment he was free to travel wherever he wished (see 3:12 and note). *appoint elders.* Though Paul and Titus may already have preached in Crete, they had not had time to organize churches. The appointing of elders is consistent with Paul's usual practice (see Ac 14:23 and note).

1:6–9 1Ti 3:1–7 gives a parallel list of qualifications for elders, but the two lists reflect the different situations in which Timothy and Titus ministered. See chart, p. 2041.

1:6 *faithful to his wife.* Since elders, by definition, were chosen from among the older men of the congregation, Paul assumed they already would be married and have children. A qualified unmarried man was not necessarily barred. It is also improbable that the standard forbids an elder to remarry if his wife dies (cf. Ro 7:2–3; 1Co 7:39). The most likely meaning is simply that a faithful, monogamous married life must be maintained. See note on 1Ti 3:2.

1:7 *overseer.* The use of "elder" in v. 5 and "overseer" (or "bishop") in v. 7 indicates that the terms were used interchangeably (cf. Ac 20:17,28; see note on 1Pe 5:2). "Elder" indicates qualification (maturity and experience), while "overseer" indicates responsibility (watching over God's flock).

1:8 *self-controlled.* A virtue much needed in Crete (see vv. 10–14); Paul refers to it five times in two chapters (here; 2:2,5,6,12). *disciplined.* Possessing the inner strength to control one's desires and actions.

1:9 *sound doctrine.* Correct teaching, in keeping with that of the apostles (see 1Ti 1:10; 6:3; 2Ti 1:13; 4:3). The teaching is called "sound" not only because it builds up in the faith but also because it protects against the corrupting influence of false teachers. Soundness of doctrine, faith and speech is a basic concern in all the Pastoral Letters (1,2 Timothy; Titus). In them, this use of "sound" occurs eight times (here; v. 13; 2:1,2; 1Ti 1:10; 6:3; 2Ti 1:13; 4:3), but it is found nowhere else in Paul's writings.

1:10 *rebellious.* Against the word of God and against Paul and Titus as the Lord's authoritative ministers. These troublemakers had three main characteristics: (1) They belonged to the "circumcision group," like the people of Gal 2:12, believing that, for salvation or sanctification or both, it was necessary to be circumcised and to keep the Jewish ceremonial law (see Introduction to Galatians: Occasion and Purpose). (2) They held to unscriptural "Jewish myths" (v. 14) and "genealogies" (3:9; see 1Ti 1:4 and note). (3) They were ascetics (vv. 14–15), having scruples against things that God declared to be good. These characteristics somewhat parallel the Colossian heresy (see Introduction to Colossians: The Colossian Heresy). *full of meaningless talk.* Paul used similar language in writing to Timothy about this kind of person (1Ti 1:6).

1:12 The quotation is from the poet Epimenides, a sixth-century BC native of Crete, who was held in high esteem by the Cretans. He was credited with several predictions that

gluttons."[a] 13This saying is true. Therefore
rebuke[f] them sharply, so that they will be
sound in the faith[g] 14and will pay no attention to Jewish myths[h] or to the merely
human commands[i] of those who reject the
truth.[j] 15To the pure, all things are pure,[k]
but to those who are corrupted and do
not believe, nothing is pure.[l] In fact, both
their minds and consciences are corrupted.[m] 16They claim to know God, but by
their actions they deny him.[n] They are detestable, disobedient and unfit for doing
anything good.[o]

1:13 [f]S 1Ti 5:20 [g]Titus 2:2 **1:14** [h]S 1Ti 1:4 [i]S Col 2:22 [j]2Ti 4:4 **1:15** [k]Ps 18:26; Mt 15:10,11; Mk 7:14-19; Ac 10:9-16,28; Col 2:20-22 [l]Ro 14:14,23 [m]1Ti 6:5 **1:16** [n]Jer 5:2; 12:2; 1Jn 2:4 [o]Hos 8:2,3

Doing Good for the Sake of the Gospel

2 You, however, must teach what is appropriate to sound doctrine.[p] 2Teach
the older men[q] to be temperate,[r] worthy

[a] 12 From the Cretan philosopher Epimenides

2:1 [p]S 1Ti 1:10 **2:2** [q]1Ti 5:1 [r]1Ti 3:2

were fulfilled. For other uses of pagan sayings by Paul, see Ac 17:28; 1Co 15:33 and notes. In Greek literature "to Cretanize" meant to lie.

1:13 *the faith.* See note on 1Ti 3:9.

1:14 *Jewish myths.* See note on v. 10.

1:15 *To the pure, all things are pure.* To Christians, who have been purified by the atoning death of Christ, "everything God created is good, and nothing is to be rejected if it is received with thanksgiving" (1Ti 4:4; see note there). *to those who are corrupted and do not believe, nothing is pure.* Unbelievers, especially ascetics with unbiblical scruples against certain foods, marriage and the like (cf. Col 2:21; 1Ti 4:3 and notes), do not enjoy the freedom of true Christians, who receive all God's creation with thanksgiving. Instead, they set up arbitrary, human prohibitions against what they consider to be impure (see Mt 15:10–11,16–20; Ac 10:9–16; Ro 14:20). The principle of this verse does not conflict with the many NT teachings against practices that are morally and spiritually wrong. *consciences.* See 1Ti 4:2–3.

1:16 *by their actions they deny him.* The false teachers stood condemned by the test of personal conduct. *good.* See Introduction: Distinctive Characteristics. Right knowledge is extremely important because it "leads to godliness" (v. 1). Paul maintained a balance between doctrine and practice.

2:1 *You.* Emphatic, contrasting the work of Titus with that of the false teachers just denounced (1:10–16). *sound doctrine.* See 1:9 and note.

2:2–10 Sound doctrine demands right conduct of all believers, regardless of age, gender or position.

2:2 Older men, as leaders, were to be moral and spiritual examples. *temperate.* Instead of being "lazy gluttons," as were Cretans in general (1:12), these older believers were to be responsible and sensible.

TITUS MINISTERED ON THE ISLAND OF CRETE

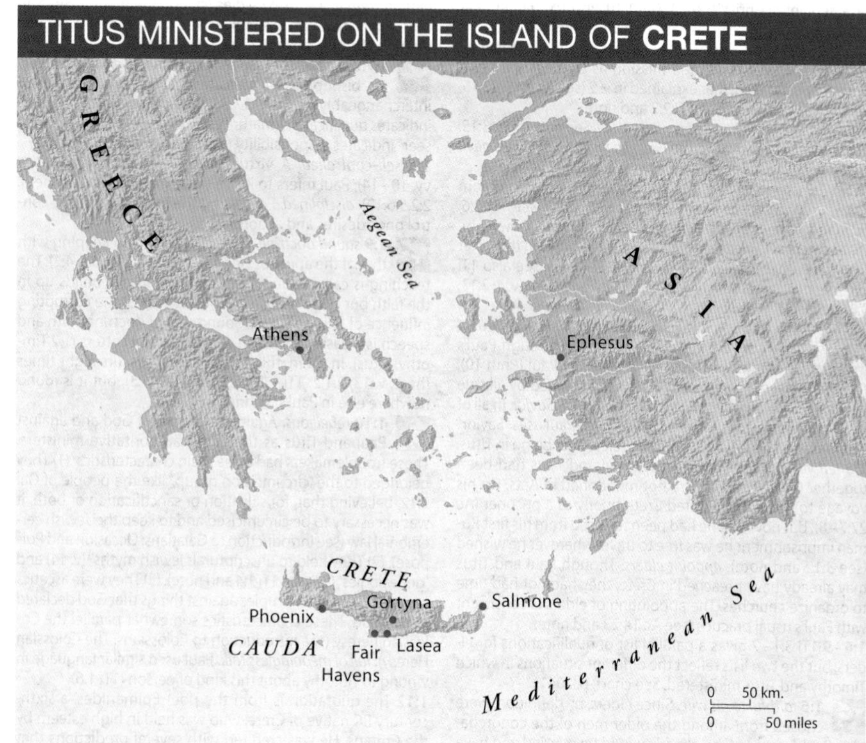

of respect, self-controlled,[s] and sound in
faith,[t] in love and in endurance.
3 Likewise, teach the older women to
be reverent in the way they live, not to be
slanderers[u] or addicted to much wine,[v] but
to teach what is good. 4 Then they can urge
the younger women[w] to love their husbands
and children, 5 to be self-controlled[x] and
pure, to be busy at home,[y] to be kind, and
to be subject to their husbands,[z] so that no
one will malign the word of God.[a]
6 Similarly, encourage the young men[b] to
be self-controlled.[c] 7 In everything set them
an example[d] by doing what is good.[e] In
your teaching show integrity, seriousness
8 and soundness of speech that cannot be
condemned, so that those who oppose
you may be ashamed because they have
nothing bad to say about us.[f]
9 Teach slaves to be subject to their masters in everything,[g] to try to please them,
not to talk back to them, 10 and not to steal
from them, but to show that they can be
fully trusted, so that in every way they will
make the teaching about God our Savior[h]
attractive.[i]
11 For the grace[j] of God has appeared[k]
that offers salvation to all people.[l] 12 It
teaches us to say "No" to ungodliness
and worldly passions,[m] and to live self-
controlled,[n] upright and godly lives[o] in
this present age, 13 while we wait for the
blessed hope—the appearing[p] of the glory
of our great God and Savior, Jesus Christ,[q]
14 who gave himself for us[r] to redeem us
from all wickedness[s] and to purify[t] for
himself a people that are his very own,[u]
eager to do what is good.[v]
15 These, then, are the things you should
teach. Encourage and rebuke with all authority. Do not let anyone despise you.

Saved in Order to Do Good

3 Remind the people to be subject to rulers and authorities,[w] to be obedient,
to be ready to do whatever is good,[x] 2 to
slander no one,[y] to be peaceable and considerate, and always to be gentle toward
everyone.
3 At one time[z] we too were foolish, disobedient, deceived and enslaved by all
kinds of passions and pleasures. We lived
in malice and envy, being hated and hating one another. 4 But when the kindness[a]
and love of God our Savior[b] appeared,[c]

2:2 [s]ver 5,6, 12; Titus 1:8 [t]Titus 1:13 **2:3** [u]1Ti 3:11 [v]1Ti 3:8 **2:4** [w]1Ti 5:2 **2:5** [x]ver 2,6, 12; Titus 1:8 [y]1Ti 5:14 [z]S Eph 5:22 [a]1Ti 6:1; S Heb 4:12 **2:6** [b]1Ti 5:1 [c]ver 2,5,12; Titus 1:8 **2:7** [d]S 1Ti 4:12 [e]S ver 14 **2:8** [f]S 1Pe 2:12 **2:9** [g]S Eph 6:5 **2:10** [h]S Lk 1:47 [i]Mt 5:16 **2:11** [j]S Ro 3:24 [k]2Ti 1:10 [l]S 1Ti 2:4 **2:12** [m]Titus 3:3 [n]ver 2,5, 6; Titus 1:8 [o]2Ti 3:12 **2:13** [p]S 1Co 1:7; S 1Ti 6:14 [q]2Pe 1:1 **2:14** [r]S Mt 20:28 [s]S Mt 1:21 [t]Heb 1:3; 1Jn 1:7 [u]Ex 19:5; Dt 4:20; 14:2; Ps 135:4; Mal 3:17; 1Pe 2:9 [v]ver 7; Pr 16:7; Mt 5:16; 2Co 8:21; Eph 2:10; Titus 3:1,8,14; 1Pe 2:12,15; 3:13
3:1 [w]Ro 13:1; 1Pe 2:13,14 [x]S 2Ti 2:21; S Titus 2:14 **3:2** [y]Eph 4:31
3:3 [z]S Eph 2:2 **3:4** [a]Eph 2:7 [b]S Lk 1:47 [c]Titus 2:11

2:3 *Likewise.* The same moral standards applied to women as to men. *not to be slanderers.* Slanderous talk apparently was a common vice among Cretan women. *addicted to much wine.* Cf. 1:7; 1Ti 3:3,8.

2:4 *love their husbands.* Just as husbands are exhorted (Eph 5:25) to love their wives.

2:5 *subject to their husbands.* See Eph 5:22 and note; Col 3:18; 1Pe 3:1 and note. *no one will malign the word of God.* Indicating Paul's deep spiritual concern behind these ethical instructions. See also vv. 8,10, dealing with his concern that Christian living should help rather than hinder the spread of the gospel.

2:7–8 Perhaps Titus was still a young man and was not yet well respected by the Cretan churches. The demands on a leader are all-inclusive, involving not only his word but also his lifestyle (see Jas 3:1 and note).

2:7 *good.* See Introduction: Distinctive Characteristics.

2:9–10 Instructions for a distinct group in the churches. Slavery was a basic element of Roman society, and the impact of Christianity upon slaves was a vital concern. Guidance for the conduct of Christian slaves was essential (see Eph 6:5 and note).

2:9 *masters.* The Greek for this word, from which our English term "despot" is derived, indicates the owner's absolute authority over his slave. Roman slaves had no legal rights, their fates being entirely in their masters' hands (see note on Col 3:22—4:1).

2:10 *make the teaching … attractive.* Christian slaves could give a unique and powerful testimony to the gospel by their willing faithfulness and obedience to their masters.

2:11–14 A powerful statement that concisely describes the effect grace should have on believers. It encourages rejection of ungodliness and leads to holier living—in keeping with Paul's repeated insistence that profession of Christ be accompanied by godly living (vv. 1–2,4–5,10; 3:8).

2:11 *For.* Introduces the doctrinal basis for the ethical demands just stressed. Right conduct must be founded on right doctrine. *grace of God.* The undeserved love God showed us in Christ while we were still sinners and his enemies (Ro 5:6–10) and by which we are saved, apart from any moral achievements or religious acts on our part (see 3:5; Eph 2:8–9 and notes). But this same grace instructs us that our salvation should produce good works (see v. 14 and note; Eph 2:10).

2:12 *teaches us.* The word translated "teaches" refers to more than instruction; it includes the whole process of training a child—instruction, encouragement, correction and discipline. *this present age.* See 2Co 4:4 and note.

2:13 *the blessed hope—the appearing of the glory.* The second coming (see 1Ti 6:14; 2Ti 4:1; see also note on 2Ti 4:8). *our great God and Savior, Jesus Christ.* It is possible to translate this phrase "the great God and our Saviour, Jesus Christ" (KJV), but the NIV rendering better represents the Greek construction and is an explicit testimony to the deity of Christ (see Ro 9:5 and note).

2:14 Salvation involves the double work of redeeming us from guilt and judgment (see Ro 3:24 and note) and of producing moral purity and helpful service to others (see Introduction: Distinctive Characteristics).

2:15 A summary of Titus's responsibility and authority. *things.* The content of the whole chapter.

3:1–2 NT teaching is not confined to the area of personal salvation but includes much instruction about practical living. Although believers are citizens of heaven (see Php 3:20 and note), they must also submit themselves to earthly government (see Ro 13:1–7; 1Pe 2:13–17 and notes) and help promote the well-being of the community.

3:1 *rulers and authorities.* The terms refer to all forms and levels of human government (cf. Eph 3:10; 6:12 for application to angels). *good.* See Introduction: Distinctive Characteristics.

3:3 Cf. Eph 2:1–3.

3:4 *kindness and love of God.* The reasons why God did not simply banish fallen human beings but acted to save them (cf. 2:11).

5 he saved us,[d] not because of righteous
things we had done,[e] but because of his
mercy.[f] He saved us through the washing[g] of rebirth and renewal[h] by the Holy
Spirit, 6 whom he poured out on us[i] generously through Jesus Christ our Savior, 7 so
that, having been justified by his grace,[j]
we might become heirs[k] having the hope[l]
of eternal life.[m] 8 This is a trustworthy saying.[n] And I want you to stress these things,
so that those who have trusted in God may
be careful to devote themselves to doing
what is good.[o] These things are excellent
and profitable for everyone.
9 But avoid[p] foolish controversies and
genealogies and arguments and quarrels[q]
about the law,[r] because these are unprofitable and useless.[s] 10 Warn a divisive person once, and then warn them a second
time. After that, have nothing to do with
them.[t] 11 You may be sure that such people
are warped and sinful; they are self-con-
demned.

Final Remarks

12 As soon as I send Artemas or Tychicus[u] to you, do your best to come to me at
Nicopolis, because I have decided to winter there.[v] 13 Do everything you can to help
Zenas the lawyer and Apollos[w] on their
way and see that they have everything
they need. 14 Our people must learn to devote themselves to doing what is good,[x] in
order to provide for urgent needs and not
live unproductive lives.
15 Everyone with me sends you greetings. Greet those who love us in the faith.[y]
Grace be with you all.[z]

3:5 [d] S Ro 11:14 [e] S Eph 2:9 [f] 1Pe 1:3 [g] S Ac 22:16 [h] Ro 12:2
3:6 [i] S Ro 5:5
3:7 [j] S Ro 3:24 [k] S Ro 8:17 [l] Ro 8:24 [m] S Mt 25:46; Titus 1:2
3:8 [n] S 1Ti 1:15 [o] S Titus 2:14
3:9 [p] 2Ti 2:16 [q] S 2Ti 2:14 [r] Titus 1:10-16 [s] 2Ti 2:14
3:10 [t] S Ro 16:17
3:12 [u] S Ac 20:4 [v] 2Ti 4:9,21
3:13 [w] S Ac 18:24
3:14 [x] S Titus 2:14
3:15 [y] 1Ti 1:2 [z] S Col 4:18

3:5 *saved us ... because of his mercy.* Salvation is not achieved by human effort or merit but comes through God's mercy alone (see Da 9:18; Eph 2:8–9 and notes). *washing of rebirth.* A reference to new birth, of which baptism (among other things) is a sign. It cannot mean that baptism is necessary for regeneration, since the NT plainly teaches that the new birth is an act of God's Spirit (see, e.g., Jn 3:5) and is not effected or achieved by ceremony. *renewal by the Holy Spirit.* The new birth and the indwelling of the Holy Spirit are central to the gospel message (see Lk 3:16; Ro 8:1–2 and note on 8:2).
3:6 *whom he poured out on us generously.* Cf. Ro 5:5.
3:7 *justified by his grace.* See Ro 3:24 and note. *heirs.* See Ro 8:17 and note. *hope.* See notes on Ro 5:5; Col 1:5.
3:8 *trustworthy saying.* See note on 1Ti 1:15. Here the phrase refers to the doctrinal summary in vv. 4–7. *good.* See Introduction: Distinctive Characteristics.
3:9 *genealogies.* See note on 1Ti 1:4. *about the law.* A reference to the situation described in 1:10–16. A similar problem existed in Ephesus (see 1Ti 1:3–7 and note on 1:3–11).
3:11 Stubborn refusal to listen to correction reveals inner perversion.
3:12 *Tychicus.* Paul's trusted co-worker, who on various occasions traveled with or for Paul (see Ac 20:4; Eph 6:21 and notes). *Nicopolis.* Means "city of victory." Several cities had this name, but the reference here is apparently to the city in Epirus on the western shore of Greece (see map, p. 2039). *decided to winter there.* Indicates that Paul had not arrived there when he wrote and that he was still free to travel at will, not yet having been imprisoned in Rome for the second time.
3:13 *Zenas the lawyer.* If he was a Jewish convert, "lawyer" means that he was an expert in the Mosaic law; if he was a Gentile convert, that he was a Roman jurist. *Apollos.* A native of Alexandria and one of Paul's well-known co-workers (Ac 18:24–28; 19:1; 1Co 1:12; 3:4–6,22; 16:12). The two travelers apparently brought the letter from Paul.
3:14 *good.* See Introduction: Distinctive Characteristics. *provide for urgent needs.* See 1Ti 5:8; cf. 2Th 3:10–12.
3:15 *Grace.* See note on Ro 1:7. *with you.* See note on 2Co 13:14.

PHILEMON

INTRODUCTION

Author, Date and Place of Writing

Paul wrote this short letter (see vv. 1,9,19) probably at the same time as Colossians (c. AD 60; see Introduction to Colossians: Author, Date and Place of Writing) and sent it to Colossae with the same travelers, Onesimus and Tychicus. He apparently wrote both letters from prison in Rome, though possibly from Ephesus (see Introduction to Philippians: Author, Date and Place of Writing; see also chart, p. 1845).

Recipient, Background and Purpose

Paul wrote this letter to Philemon, a believer in Colossae who, along with others, was a slave owner (cf. Col 4:1; for slavery in the NT, see note on Eph 6:5). One of his slaves, Onesimus, had apparently stolen from him (cf. v. 18) and then run away, which under Roman law was punishable by death. But Onesimus met Paul and through his ministry became a Christian (see v. 10). Now he was willing to return to his master, and Paul writes this personal appeal to ask that he be accepted as a Christian brother (see v. 16).

Approach and Structure

To win Philemon's willing acceptance of Onesimus, Paul writes in a very tactful and warmhearted manner. The appeal (vv. 4 – 21) is organized in a way prescribed by ancient Greek and Roman teachers: to build rapport (vv. 4 – 10), to persuade the mind (vv. 11 – 19) and to move the emotions (vv. 20 – 21). The name Onesimus is not mentioned until the rapport has been built (v. 10), and the appeal itself is stated only near the end of the section to persuade the mind (v. 17).

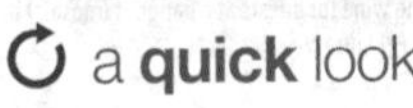

a **quick** look

Author:
The apostle Paul

Audience:
Philemon and the members of the church at Colossae

Date:
About AD 60

Theme:
Paul urges Philemon to show grace to Onesimus, his runaway slave.

Outline

I. Greetings (1 – 3)
II. Thanksgiving and Prayer (4 – 7)
III. Paul's Plea for Onesimus (8 – 21)
IV. Final Request, Greetings and Benediction (22 – 25)

Mosaic of slaves pouring wine for guests at a banquet (third century AD). In Philemon, Paul makes a plea on behalf of Onesimus, Philemon's slave.

Servants pouring wine for guests at a banquet (mosaic) by Roman (third century AD) Musee National du Bardo, Le Bardo, Tunisia/Ancient Art and Architecture Collection Ltd./ The Bridgeman Art Library

1 Paul, a prisoner[a] of Christ Jesus, and
Timothy[b] our brother,[c]

To Philemon our dear friend and fellow
worker[d]— 2 also to Apphia our sister and
Archippus[e] our fellow soldier[f]—and to the
church that meets in your home:[g]

3 Grace and peace to you[a] from God our
Father and the Lord Jesus Christ.[h]

Thanksgiving and Prayer

4 I always thank my God[i] as I remember
you in my prayers,[j] 5 because I hear about
your love for all his holy people[k] and your
faith in the Lord Jesus.[l] 6 I pray that your
partnership with us in the faith may be
effective in deepening your understanding
of every good thing we share for the sake
of Christ. 7 Your love has given me great
joy and encouragement,[m] because you,
brother, have refreshed[n] the hearts of the
Lord's people.

Paul's Plea for Onesimus

8 Therefore, although in Christ I could be
bold and order you to do what you ought
to do, 9 yet I prefer to appeal to you[o] on
the basis of love. It is as none other than
Paul—an old man and now also a prisoner[p] of Christ Jesus— 10 that I appeal to
you for my son[q] Onesimus,[b][r] who became
my son while I was in chains.[s] 11 Formerly
he was useless to you, but now he has become useful both to you and to me.

12 I am sending him—who is my very
heart—back to you. 13 I would have liked
to keep him with me so that he could take
your place in helping me while I am in
chains[t] for the gospel. 14 But I did not want
to do anything without your consent, so
that any favor you do would not seem
forced[u] but would be voluntary. 15 Perhaps
the reason he was separated from you for
a little while was that you might have him
back forever— 16 no longer as a slave,[v] but
better than a slave, as a dear brother.[w] He
is very dear to me but even dearer to you,
both as a fellow man and as a brother in
the Lord.

1 [a]ver 9,23; S Eph 3:1 [b]S Ac 16:1 [c]2Co 1:1 [d]S Php 2:25 **2** [e]Col 4:17 [f]Php 2:25 [g]S Ro 16:5 **3** [h]S Ro 1:7 **4** [i]S Ro 1:8 [j]S Ro 1:10 **5** [k]S Col 1:4; 1Th 3:6 [l]S Ac 20:21 **7** [m]2Co 7:4; 13 [n]ver 20; Ro 15:32; 1Co 16:18 **9** [o]1Co 1:10 [p]ver 1,23; S Eph 3:1 **10** [q]S 1Th 2:11 [r]Col 4:9 [s]S Ac 21:33 **13** [t]ver 10; S Ac 21:33 **14** [u]2Co 9:7; 1Pe 5:2 **16** [v]1Co 7:22 [w]Mt 23:8; S Ac 1:16; 1Ti 6:2

[a] *3* The Greek is plural; also in verses 22 and 25; elsewhere in this letter "you" is singular.
[b] *10 Onesimus* means *useful.*

1–2 Although Paul writes together with Timothy and although he addresses the entire church in Colossae, in this very personal letter to Philemon he uses "I," rather than "we," and "you" (singular, except in vv. 22,25).

1 *Paul.* See note on Ro 1:1. *prisoner.* See Eph 3:1; Php 1:13 and notes. *Timothy.* See note on Col 1:1; see also Introduction to 1 Timothy: Recipient. *Philemon.* A Christian living in Colossae or nearby and the owner of the slave Onesimus.

2 *Apphia.* Probably Philemon's wife. *Archippus.* See Col 4:17.

3 *Grace ... peace.* See note on Ro 1:7. *Lord Jesus Christ.* Occurs also at the end of this letter (v. 25). See note on 1Th 1:1.

4 *thank ... remember you in my prayers.* See Php 1:3–4 and note.

5 See Col 1:4. *his holy people.* See notes on Ro 1:7; Eph 1:1; Col 1:4.

7 *hearts.* Figurative for the emotions of pity and love (see vv. 12,20; cf. also Ps 4:7 and note).

10 *my son.* See note on 1Ti 1:2. *Onesimus.* See NIV text note; see also Introduction: Recipient, Background and Purpose.

11 *useless ... useful.* A wordplay on the meaning of Onesimus's name (see NIV text note on v. 10).

13 *in chains for the gospel.* See v. 1 and note.

16 *no longer as a slave.* Although not explicitly calling for

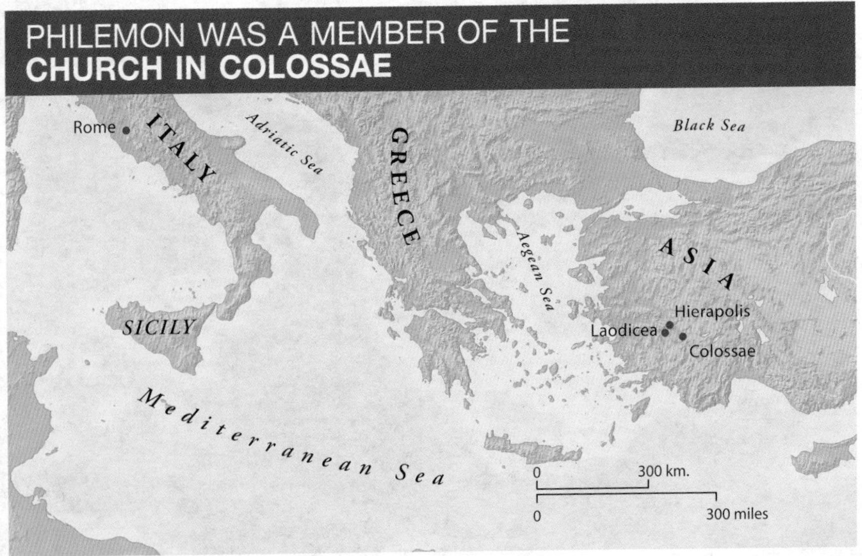

[17]So if you consider me a partner,[x] welcome him as you would welcome me. [18]If
he has done you any wrong or owes you
anything, charge it to me.[y] [19]I, Paul, am
writing this with my own hand.[z] I will pay
it back—not to mention that you owe me
your very self. [20]I do wish, brother, that
I may have some benefit from you in the
Lord; refresh[a] my heart in Christ. [21]Con-
fident[b] of your obedience, I write to you,
knowing that you will do even more than
I ask.

[22]And one thing more: Prepare a guest
room for me, because I hope to be[c] restored to you in answer to your prayers.[d]

[23]Epaphras,[e] my fellow prisoner[f] in
Christ Jesus, sends you greetings. [24]And
so do Mark,[g] Aristarchus,[h] Demas[i] and
Luke, my fellow workers.[j]
[25]The grace of the Lord Jesus Christ be
with your spirit.[k]

17 [x]2Co 8:23 **18** [y]Ge 43:9 **19** [z]S 1Co 16:21 **20** [a]ver 7; 1Co 16:18 **21** [b]S 2Co 2:3 **22** [c]Php 1:25; 2:24; Heb 13:19 [d]2Co 1:11; Php 1:19 **23** [e]Col 1:7 [f]ver 1; Ro 16:7; Col 4:10 **24** [g]S Ac 12:12 [h]S Ac 19:29 [i]Col 4:14; 2Ti 4:10 [j]ver 1 **25** [k]S Gal 6:18

Onesimus's release, Paul is implicitly undermining the institution of slavery. Cf. 1Ti 6:2.

17–19 Martin Luther said, "Even as Christ did for us with God the Father, thus Paul also does for Onesimus with Philemon."

19 *writing this with my own hand.* See 1Co 16:21 and note. *owe me your very self.* Paul had probably led Philemon to faith in Christ.

20 *I … my.* Both pronouns are emphatic, making an obvious allusion to v. 7. *benefit.* The Greek for this word is another play on the name Onesimus.

21 *even more than I ask.* Perhaps suggesting that Philemon set Onesimus free.

22 *one thing more.* It was not unusual for an ancient letter, though occasioned by one matter, to also include another matter. Often, as here, the second matter had to do with how and when the author planned to meet the recipient again.

23 *Epaphras.* See Col 1:7 and note; 4:12.

24 *Mark, Aristarchus.* See note on Col 4:10. *Demas and Luke.* See note on Col 4:14.

25 *grace.* See note on Ro 1:7. *be with your spirit.* See note on Gal 6:18.

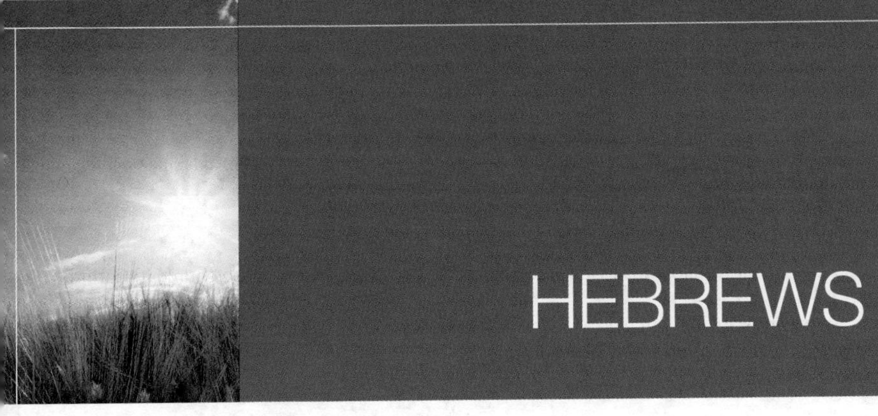

HEBREWS

INTRODUCTION

Author

The writer of this letter does not identify himself, but he was obviously well known to the original recipients. Though for some 1,200 years (from c. AD 400 to 1600) the book was commonly called "The Epistle of Paul to the Hebrews," there was no agreement in the earliest centuries regarding its authorship. Since the Reformation it has been widely recognized that Paul could not have been the writer. There is no disharmony between the teaching of Hebrews and that of Paul's letters, but the specific emphases and writing styles are markedly different. Contrary to Paul's usual practice, the author of Hebrews nowhere names himself in the letter. The readers, however, certainly knew who he was, as evidenced by his personal comments (13:18,22,24). We know that the author was a man from 11:32 (see note there). Moreover, the statement "This salvation, which was first announced by the Lord, was confirmed to us by those who heard him" (2:3), indicates that the author had neither been with Jesus during his earthly ministry nor received special revelation directly from the risen Lord, as Paul had (Gal 1:11–12).

The earliest suggestion of authorship is found in Tertullian's *De Pudicitia,* 20 (c. 200), in which he quotes from "an epistle to the Hebrews under the name of Barnabas." From the letter itself it is clear that the writer must have had authority in the apostolic church and was an intellectual Hebrew Christian, well versed in the OT. Barnabas meets these requirements. He was a Jew of the priestly tribe of Levi (Ac 4:36) who became a close friend of Paul after the latter's conversion. Under the guidance of the Holy Spirit, the church at Antioch commissioned Barnabas and Paul for the work of evangelism and sent them off on the first missionary journey (Ac 13:1–4).

The other leading candidate for authorship is Apollos, whose name was first suggested by Martin Luther and who is favored by many interpreters today. Apollos, an Alexandrian by birth, was also a Jewish Christian with notable intellectual and oratorical abilities. Luke tells us that "he was a learned man, with a thorough knowledge of the Scriptures" (Ac 18:24). We

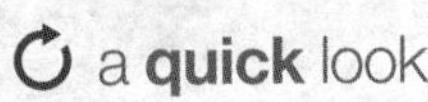

a **quick** look

Author:
Unknown; possibly Apollos or Barnabas

Audience:
Primarily Jewish Christians

Date:
About AD 67–70

Theme:
The author demonstrates the absolute supremacy and sufficiency of Jesus Christ as revealer and mediator of God's grace.

also know that Apollos was associated with Paul in the early years of the church in Corinth (1Co 1:12; 3:4–6,22).

Two things are evident: The author was a master of the Greek language of his day, and he was thoroughly acquainted with the pre-Christian Greek translation of the OT (the Septuagint), which he regularly quotes.

Date

Hebrews was probably written before the destruction of Jerusalem and the temple in AD 70 because: (1) If it had been written after this date, the author almost certainly would have mentioned the temple's destruction and the end of the Jewish sacrificial system; and (2) the author consistently uses the Greek present tense when speaking of the temple and the priestly activities connected with it (see 5:1–3; 7:23,27; 8:3–5; 9:6–9,13,25; 10:1,3–4,8,11; 13:10–11). However, he describes the wilderness tabernacle, not the Jerusalem temple.

Recipients

The letter was addressed primarily to Jewish converts who were familiar with the OT and who were being tempted to revert to Judaism or to Judaize the gospel (cf. Gal 2:14). The destination of the letter is probably either the Holy Land or Rome, the latter being the most likely. The letter is first attested by Clement of Rome (c. AD 96), and the statement "Those from Italy send you their greetings" (13:24) sounds like Romans living elsewhere sending their greetings home.

A collection of swords and daggers, most of which are double-edged. Hebrews 4:12 reminds us that the word of God is "sharper than any double-edged sword."

Réunion des Musées Nationaux/Art Resource, NY

Theme

The theme of Hebrews is the absolute supremacy and sufficiency of Jesus Christ as revealer and mediator of God's grace. The prologue (1:1–4) presents Christ as God's full and final revelation, far surpassing the revelation given in the OT. The prophecies and promises of the OT are fulfilled in the "new covenant" (or "new testament"), of which Christ is the mediator. From the OT itself, Christ is shown to be superior to the ancient prophets, to angels, to Moses (the mediator of the former covenant) and to Aaron and his priestly descendants. Hebrews could be called "the

From the Old Testament itself, Christ is shown to be superior to the ancient prophets, to angels, to Moses (the mediator of the former covenant) and to Aaron and his priestly descendants.

book of better things" since the two Greek words for "better" and "superior" occur 15 times in the letter (1:4 [twice]; 6:9; 7:19,22; 8:6 [3 times]; 9:23; 10:34; 11:4,16,35,40; 12:24; see chart, p. 2069). A striking feature of this presentation of the gospel is the unique manner in which the author employs expositions of eight specific passages of the OT Scriptures:

(1) 2:5 – 9: Exposition of Ps 8:4 – 6
(2) 3:7 — 4:13: Exposition of Ps 95:7 – 11
(3) 4:14 — 7:28: Exposition of Ps 110:4
(4) 8:1 — 10:18: Exposition of Jer 31:31 – 34
(5) 10:1 – 10: Exposition of Ps 40:6 – 8
(6) 10:32 — 12:3: Exposition of Hab 2:3 – 4
(7) 12:4 – 13: Exposition of Pr 3:11 – 12
(8) 12:18 – 24: Exposition of Ex 19:10 – 23

Practical applications of this theme are given throughout the book. The readers are told that there can be no turning back to or continuation of the old Jewish system, which has been superseded by the unique priesthood of Christ. God's people must now look only to him, whose atoning death, resurrection and ascension have opened the way into the true, heavenly sanctuary of God's presence. To "ignore so great a salvation" (2:3) or to give up the pursuit of holiness (12:10,14) is to face the anger of the "living God" (10:31). Five times the author weaves into his presentation of the gospel stern warnings (see note on 2:1 – 4) and reminds his readers of the divine judgment that came on the rebellious generation of Israelites in the wilderness (see 3:16 – 19 and note).

Stone anchor used by Greek and Roman ships. "We have this hope as an anchor for the soul, firm and secure" (Heb 6:19).
Todd Bolen/www.BiblePlaces.com

Literary Form

Hebrews is commonly referred to as a letter, though it does not have the typical form of a letter. It ends like a letter (13:22 – 25) but begins more like an essay or sermon (1:1 – 4). The author does not identify himself or those addressed, which letter writers normally did. And he offers no manner of greeting, such as is usually found at the beginning of ancient letters. Rather, he begins with a magnificent statement about Jesus Christ. He calls his work a "word of exhortation" (13:22), the conventional designation given to a sermon in a synagogue service (see Ac 13:15). Like a sermon, Hebrews is full of encouragement, exhortations and stern warnings. It is likely that the author used sermonic materials and sent them out in a modified letter form.

Outline

I. Prologue: The Superiority of God's New Revelation (1:1–4)

II. The Superiority of Christ to Leading Figures under the Old Covenant (1:5—7:28)
   - A. Christ Is Superior to the Angels (1:5—2:18)
     1. Scriptural proof of his superiority (1:5–14)
     2. Exhortation not to ignore the revelation of God in his Son (2:1–4)
     3. Jesus was made lower than the angels for a little while (2:5–9)
     4. Having been made like us, Jesus was enabled to save us (2:10–18)
   - B. Christ Is Superior to Moses (3:1—4:13)
     1. Demonstration of Christ's superiority (3:1–6)
     2. Exhortation to enter Sabbath-rest (3:7—4:13)
   - C. Christ Is Superior to the Aaronic Priests (4:14—7:28)
     1. Jesus is the great high priest (4:14–16)
     2. Qualifications of a priest (5:1–10)
     3. Exhortation to press on toward maturity (5:11—6:12)
     4. The certainty of God's promise (6:13–20)
     5. Christ's superior priestly order (ch. 7)

III. The Superior Sacrificial Work of Our High Priest (8:1—10:18)
   - A. A New Sanctuary and a New Covenant (ch. 8)
   - B. The Old Sanctuary (9:1–10)
   - C. The Better Sacrifice (9:11—10:18)

IV. A Call to Follow Jesus Faithfully and with Perseverance (10:19—12:29)
   - A. Having Confidence to Enter the Sanctuary (10:19–25)
   - B. A Warning against Persistence in Sin (10:26–31)
   - C. Persevering in Faith under Pressure (10:32—12:3)
     1. As in the past, so in the future (10:32–39)
     2. Faith and its many outstanding examples (ch. 11)
     3. Jesus, the supreme example (12:1–3)
   - D. Encouragement to Persevere in the Face of Hardship (12:4–13)
   - E. Exhortation to Holy Living (12:14–17)
   - F. Crowning Motivation and Warning (12:18–29)

V. Conclusion (ch. 13)
   - A. Rules for Christian Living (13:1–17)
   - B. Request for Prayer (13:18–19)
   - C. Benediction (13:20–21)
   - D. Personal Remarks (13:22–23)
   - E. Greetings and Final Benediction (13:24–25)

God's Final Word: His Son

1 In the past God spoke[a] to our ancestors through the prophets[b] at many
times and in various ways,[c] 2 but in these
last days[d] he has spoken to us by his Son,[e]
whom he appointed heir[f] of all things,
and through whom[g] also he made the universe.[h] 3 The Son is the radiance of God's
glory[i] and the exact representation of his
being,[j] sustaining all things[k] by his powerful word. After he had provided purification for sins,[l] he sat down at the right hand
of the Majesty in heaven.[m] 4 So he became
as much superior to the angels as the name
he has inherited is superior to theirs.[n]

The Son Superior to Angels

5 For to which of the angels did God ever
say,

"You are my Son;
today I have become your Father"[a]?[o]

Or again,

"I will be his Father,
and he will be my Son"[b]?[p]

6 And again, when God brings his firstborn[q] into the world,[r] he says,

"Let all God's angels worship
him."[c][s]

7 In speaking of the angels he says,

"He makes his angels spirits,
and his servants flames of fire."[d][t]

8 But about the Son he says,

"Your throne, O God, will last for
ever and ever;[u]
a scepter of justice will be the
scepter of your kingdom.
9 You have loved righteousness and
hated wickedness;
therefore God, your God, has set
you above your companions[v]
by anointing you with the oil[w] of
joy."[e][x]

1:1 [a] Jn 9:29; Heb 2:2,3; 4:8; 12:25 [b] Lk 1:70; Ac 2:30 [c] Nu 12:6,8 **1:2** [d] Dt 4:30; Heb 9:26; 1Pe 1:20 [e] ver 5; S Mt 3:17; Heb 3:6; 5:8; 7:28 [f] Ps 2:8; Mt 11:27; S 28:18 [g] S Jn 1:3 [h] Heb 11:3 **1:3** [i] Jn 1:14 [j] S Jn 14:9 [k] Col 1:17 [l] Titus 2:14; Heb 7:27; 9:11-14 [m] S Mk 16:19 **1:4** [n] Eph 1:21; Php 2:9,10; Heb 8:6 **1:5** [o] Ps 2:7; S Mt 3:17 [p] 2Sa 7:14 **1:6** [q] Jn 3:16; S Col 1:18 [r] Heb 10:5 [s] Dt 32:43 (LXX and DSS); Ps 97:7 **1:7** [t] Ps 104:4 **1:8** [u] S Lk 1:33 **1:9** [v] Php 2:9 [w] Isa 61:1,3 [x] Ps 45:6,7

[a] 5 Psalm 2:7 [b] 5 2 Samuel 7:14; 1 Chron. 17:13 [c] 6 Deut. 32:43 (see Dead Sea Scrolls and Septuagint) [d] 7 Psalm 104:4 [e] 9 Psalm 45:6,7

1:1 *In the past.* In contrast to "in these last days" (v. 2), the Messianic era inaugurated by the incarnation (see Ac 2:17; 1Ti 4:1; 1Jn 2:18 and notes). *God spoke.* Cf. "he has spoken" (v. 2). God is the ultimate author of both the OT and the NT. *to our ancestors.* In contrast to "to us" (v. 2). *through the prophets.* All OT writers are here viewed as prophets in that their testimony was preparation for the coming of Christ; cf. "by his Son" (v. 2), a new and unique category of revelation in contrast to that of the prophets. *at many times and in various ways.* The OT revelation was occasional and lacking in finality.

1:2–3 The superiority of God's revelation through his Son (see Introduction: Theme) is demonstrated by seven great descriptive statements about him: (1) *appointed heir of all things.* The incarnate Son, having performed the work of redemption, was gloriously exalted to the position of the firstborn heir of God, i.e., he received the inheritance of God's estate ("all things"). See Ro 8:17. (2) *through whom also he made the universe.* See Jn 1:3; 1Co 8:6; Col 1:16 and note. (3) *radiance of God's glory.* As the brilliance of the sun is inseparable from the sun itself, so the Son's radiance is inseparable from deity, for he himself is God, the second person of the Trinity (see Jn 1:14,18 and notes). (4) *exact representation of his being.* Jesus is not merely an image or reflection of God. Because the Son himself is God (see note on Ro 9:5), he is the absolutely authentic representation of God's being (see Jn 14:9; Col 1:15 and note). (5) *sustaining all things.* Christ is not like Atlas, the mythical Greek god who held the world on his shoulders. The Son dynamically holds together all that has been created through him (Col 1:17). (6) *provided purification for sins.* Through his redeeming death on the cross (see 7:27; 9:12; Titus 2:14 and notes). (7) *sat down at the right hand of the Majesty in heaven.* Being seated at God's right hand indicates that Christ is actively ruling with God as Lord over all (see v. 13; 8:1; 10:12; 12:2; Mt 26:64; Ac 2:23; 5:34; Ro 8:34; Eph 1:20; Col 3:1; 1Pe 3:22).

1:2 *these last days.* The time when all that was promised and worked toward in the OT was coming to fulfillment (see v. 1; Jas 5:3; 2Pe 3:3 and notes; see also 1Pe 1:20; Jude 18).

1:4 *superior to the angels.* See Introduction: Theme. To most Jews angels were exalted beings, especially revered because they were involved in giving the law at Sinai (see 2:2), and to the Jews the law was God's supreme revelation. The Dead Sea Scrolls reflect the expectation that the archangel Michael would be the supreme figure in the Messianic kingdom (cf. Rev 12:7 and note). *name.* Cf. Php 2:9 and note. What follows indicates that this name was "Son"—a name to which no angel could lay claim.

1:5–14 Christ's superiority to angels is documented by seven OT quotations (see NIV text notes), showing that he is God's Son, that he is worshiped by angels and that, though he is God, he is distinguished from the Father.

1:5 *You are my Son; today I have become your Father.* This passage (Ps 2:7) is quoted in Ac 13:33 as fulfilled in Christ's resurrection. Jesus did not become the Son of God at this time but was appointed Son of God "in power" at his resurrection (Ro 1:4). *I will be his Father, and he will be my Son.* Jews acknowledged 2Sa 7:14 (of which this passage is a quotation) and Ps 2 to be Messianic in their ultimate application (see Lk 1:32–33 and notes). This royal personage is neither an angel nor an archangel; he is God's Son.

1:6 *firstborn.* See Col 1:15 and note. *Let all God's angels worship him.* The author quotes a line that was in his Greek version of Deuteronomy (see NIV text note). This statement, which in the OT refers to the Lord God (Yahweh), is here applied to Christ, giving clear indication of his full deity. The very beings with whom Christ is being compared are commanded to proclaim his superiority by worshiping him.

1:7 *He makes his angels spirits, and his servants flames of fire.* Ps 104:4 speaks of the storm wind and the lightning as agents of God's purposes. The Septuagint (the pre-Christian Greek translation of the OT), which the author of Hebrews quotes as the version familiar to his readers, reflects the developing doctrine of angels during the period between the OT and the NT. *angels.* English "angel" comes from the Greek word *angelos,* which means "messenger" or "agent." The Hebrew word most often translated "angel" has essentially the same meaning.

1:8 *But about the Son he says, "Your throne, O God, will last for ever"* ... The author selects a passage that intimates the deity of the Messianic (and Davidic) King, further demonstrating the Son's superiority over angels (see Ps 45:6 and note).

10 He also says,

"In the beginning, Lord, you laid the
foundations of the earth,
and the heavens are the work of
your hands.[y]
11 They will perish, but you remain;
they will all wear out like a
garment.[z]
12 You will roll them up like a robe;
like a garment they will be changed.
But you remain the same,[a]
and your years will never end."[a][b]

13 To which of the angels did God ever say,

"Sit at my right hand[c]
until I make your enemies
a footstool[d] for your feet"[b]?[e]

14 Are not all angels ministering spirits[f]
sent to serve those who will inherit[g] salvation?[h]

Warning to Pay Attention

2 We must pay the most careful attention, therefore, to what we have heard,
so that we do not drift away.[i] 2 For since
the message spoken[j] through angels[k] was
binding, and every violation and disobedience received its just punishment,[l] 3 how
shall we escape if we ignore so great a salvation?[m] This salvation, which was first
announced by the Lord,[n] was confirmed
to us by those who heard him.[o] 4 God also
testified to it by signs, wonders and various miracles,[p] and by gifts of the Holy
Spirit[q] distributed according to his will.[r]

Jesus Made Fully Human

5 It is not to angels that he has subjected the world to come, about which we
are speaking. 6 But there is a place where
someone[s] has testified:

"What is mankind that you are mindful
of them,
a son of man that you care for him?[t]
7 You made them a little[c] lower than the
angels;
you crowned them with glory and
honor
8 and put everything under their
feet."[d,e][u]

In putting everything under them,[f] God
left nothing that is not subject to them.[f]
Yet at present we do not see everything
subject to them.[f] 9 But we do see Jesus,
who was made lower than the angels for a

1:10 [y] Ps 8:6; Zec 12:1 **1:11** [z] Isa 34:4; 51:6; S Heb 12:27 **1:12** [a] Heb 13:8 [b] Ps 102:25-27 **1:13** [c] ver 3; S Mk 16:19 [d] Jos 10:24; Heb 10:13 [e] Ps 110:1; S Mt 22:44 **1:14** [f] Ps 91:11; 103:20; Da 7:10 [g] Mt 25:34; Mk 10:17; S Ac 20:32 [h] S Ro 11:14; Heb 2:3; 5:9; 9:28 **2:1** [i] S Ro 11:22 **2:2** [j] S Heb 1:1 [k] Dt 33:2; Ac 7:53; Gal 3:19 [l] Heb 10:28 **2:3** [m] Heb 10:29; 12:25 [n] Heb 1:2 [o] S Lk 1:2 **2:4** [p] Mk 16:20; S Jn 4:48 [q] S 1Co 12:4 [r] S Eph 1:5 **2:6** [s] Heb 4:4 [t] Job 7:17; Ps 144:3 **2:8** [u] Ps 8:4-6; S Mt 22:44

[a] 12 Psalm 102:25-27 [b] 13 Psalm 110:1
[c] 7 Or *them for a little while* [d] 6-8 Psalm 8:4-6
[e] 7,8 Or *⁷You made him a little lower than the angels;/ you crowned him with glory and honor/ ⁸and put everything under his feet."* [f] 8 Or *him*

1:10 *In the beginning, Lord, you laid the foundations of the earth.* As in v. 6, a passage addressed to Yahweh ("Lord") is applied to the Son.

1:13 *Sit at my right hand.* See note on vv. 2–3. Ps 110 is applied repeatedly to Jesus in Hebrews (vv. 3,13; 5:6,10; 6:20; 7:3,11,17,21; 8:1; 10:12–13; 12:2).

1:14 *ministering spirits.* See v. 7. Christ reigns; angels minister as those sent to serve.

2:1–4 The first of five warnings strategically positioned throughout the letter (see 3:7—4:13; 6:4–8; 10:26–31; 12:25–29). The author sternly warns that a return to Jewish practices is a denial of Christ's atoning work on the cross and so would have dire consequences.

2:1 *what we have heard.* The message of the gospel, including that of Christ's person as the God-man and his redemptive work on the cross. *drift away.* From the greater revelation given through the Son.

2:2 *the message spoken through angels.* The law given through Moses at Sinai (see Ac 7:38 and note).

2:3 *how shall we escape ...?* See 12:25. *so great a salvation.* The argument here is from the lesser to the greater and assumes that the gospel is greater than the law. Thus, if disregard for the law brought certain punishment, disregard for the gospel will bring even greater punishment. *confirmed to us by those who heard him.* The eyewitnesses, chiefly the apostles (see Ac 1:21–22 and note on 1:22; 1Jn 1:1 and note; cf. 2Pe 1:16 and note), had vouched for the message first announced by Christ. The author himself apparently was neither an apostle nor an eyewitness (see Introduction: Author).

2:4 *signs, wonders and various miracles.* God added his confirmation to the gospel message through supernatural acts such as healing the sick (see Ac 3:7–9,11–12,16; 5:12–16; 9:32–41; 14:3,8–9; 19:11–12; 28:8–9). *gifts of the Holy Spirit.* Such as the gift of tongues (see Ac 2:4–12). *distributed according to his will.* See 1Co 12:4–11.

2:5–9 An exposition of Ps 8:4–6, which continues to show Christ's superiority over the angels—in him humanity's appointed role as ruler (under God) over God's other creatures (cf. Ge 1:26,28 and notes) comes to ultimate fulfillment (see notes on Ps 8:4–6; Eph 1:22).

2:5 *It is not to angels that he has subjected the world to come.* Christ, as bearer of the new revelation (see 1:2–3 and note), is superior to angels who had participated in bringing the revelation at Sinai (see 2:2 and note).

2:6–8 Awed by the marvelous order and immensity of God's handiwork in the celestial universe, the psalmist marveled at the high dignity God had bestowed on puny mortals by entrusting them with dominion over the other creatures (see Ge 1:26–28 and notes).

2:7 *angels.* The author here quotes his Greek version of the Psalter, which renders the common Hebrew word for "God" or "gods" in this way in Ps 8:5 (see NIV text note there), as it does the Hebrew for "sons of God" in Job 1:6; 2:1 (see NIV text notes there).

2:8 *everything.* God's purpose from the beginning was that humanity should be sovereign in the creaturely realm, subject only to God. Due to sin, that purpose of God has not yet been fully realized. Indeed, humans are themselves "in slavery" (v. 15).

2:9 *Jesus ... now crowned with glory and honor.* See 10:13 and note. Ps 8 is here applied to Jesus in particular. As forerunner of humanity's restored dominion over the earth, he was made lower than the angels for a while (see NIV text note on v. 7 and on vv. 6–8) but is now crowned with glory and honor at God's right hand. By his perfect life, his death on the cross and his exaltation, he has made possible for redeemed humanity the ultimate fulfillment of Ps 8 in the future kingdom.

THE **"GREATER THANS"** IN HEBREWS

One of the author's main points in Hebrews is that Jesus is greater than all those things associated with the Jewish religion and way of life. Sometimes he actually uses the words "greater than"; sometimes he does not. But in all cases the theme is clear.

THEME	PASSAGE IN HEBREWS
Jesus is greater than the prophets.	1:1–3
Jesus is greater than the angels.	1:4–14; 2:5
Jesus is greater than Moses.	3:1–6
Jesus is greater than Joshua.	4:6–11
Jesus is greater than the Aaronic high priests.	5:1–10; 7:26—8:2
Jesus is greater than the Levitical priests.	6:20—7:25
Jesus as the high priest in the order of Melchizedek is greater than Abraham.	7:1–10
Jesus' ministry is greater than the tabernacle ministry.	8:3–6; 9:1–28
Jesus' new covenant is greater than the old covenant.	8:7–13
Jesus' sacrifice is greater than the OT sacrifices.	10:1–14
Experiencing Jesus is greater than the experience on Mount Sinai.	12:18–24

little while, now crowned with glory and
honor[v] because he suffered death,[w] so that
by the grace of God he might taste death
for everyone.[x]
10 In bringing many sons and daughters
to glory, it was fitting that God, for whom
and through whom everything exists,[y]
should make the pioneer of their salvation
perfect through what he suffered.[z] 11 Both
the one who makes people holy[a] and those
who are made holy[b] are of the same family. So Jesus is not ashamed to call them
brothers and sisters.[ac] 12 He says,

> "I will declare your name to my
> brothers and sisters;
> in the assembly I will sing your
> praises."[bd]

13 And again,

> "I will put my trust in him."[ce]

And again he says,

> "Here am I, and the children God has
> given me."[df]

14 Since the children have flesh and
blood,[g] he too shared in their humanity[h] so
that by his death he might break the power[i] of him who holds the power of death—
that is, the devil[j]— 15 and free those who
all their lives were held in slavery by their

2:9 [v] ver 7; Ac 3:13; S Php 2:9 [w] Php 2:7-9 [x] 2Co 5:15 **2:10** [y] S Ro 11:36 [z] Lk 24:26; Heb 5:8, 9; 7:28 **2:11** [a] Heb 13:12 [b] S Eph 5:26 [c] S Mt 28:10 **2:12** [d] Ps 22:22; 68:26 **2:13** [e] Isa 8:17 [f] Isa 8:18; Jn 10:29 **2:14** [g] 1Co 15:50; Eph 6:12 [h] S Jn 1:14 [i] Ge 3:15; 1Co 15:54-57; 2Ti 1:10 [j] 1Jn 3:8

[a] *11* The Greek word for *brothers and sisters* (*adelphoi*) refers here to believers, both men and women, as part of God's family; also in verse 12; and in 3:1, 12; 10:19; 13:22. [b] *12* Psalm 22:22 [c] *13* Isaiah 8:17 [d] *13* Isaiah 8:18

2:10 *many sons and daughters to glory.* Those who believe in Christ are made God's children through his only Son (cf. Jn 1:12–13; Ro 8:14–23 and notes on 8:14–15,17,23; Gal 3:26; 4:5 and note; Eph 4:5; 5:1; 1Jn 3:1–2). *make ... perfect through what he suffered.* It was through Christ's suffering that God fully qualified him as the one sent to carry out his redemptive mission, specifically the priestly aspects of that mission (see v. 17 and note; see also 5:9; 7:28). *pioneer.* The Greek word often expresses the idea of "originator, founder." It was also applied to a leader, ruler or prince. In the present context, it perhaps has the sense of "champion"—the one who came to the aid of those enslaved to "him who holds the power of death" (v. 14; cf. v. 15; 12:2 and note; Ac 3:15; 5:31 ["Prince"]).

2:11 *who makes people holy ... who are made holy.* Christ became a human being to identify himself with humans and, by his substitutionary sacrifice on the cross, to restore their lost holiness. *holy.* See 1Co 1:2 and note.

2:12 *I will declare your name to my brothers and sisters.* A quotation from Ps 22:22, a psalm describing the sufferings of God's righteous servant (see introduction to Ps 22). The key phrase is "my brothers and sisters," seen here as coming from the lips of the triumphant Messiah. *brothers and sisters.* See NIV text note on v. 11.

2:13 *I will put my trust in him.* An expression of true dependence on God, perfectly exemplified in Christ. In him humanity is seen as it was intended to be. *Here am I, and the children God has given me.* Also seen ultimately as an utterance of the incarnate Son. The Father's children are given to the Son to be his brothers and sisters (see v. 11; cf. Mt 12:50).

2:14 *him who holds the power of death.* Satan wields the power of death only insofar as he induces people to sin and to come under sin's penalty, which is death (see Ro 5:12; 6:23 and notes).

2:15 *free.* See 1Co 15:54–57 and notes on 15:56–57; Rev 1:18.

fear[k] of death. 16For surely it is not angels
he helps, but Abraham's descendants.[l]
17For this reason he had to be made like
them,[a][m] fully human in every way, in order that he might become a merciful[n] and
faithful high priest[o] in service to God,[p] and
that he might make atonement for the sins
of the people.[q] 18Because he himself suffered when he was tempted, he is able to
help those who are being tempted.[r]

Jesus Greater Than Moses

3 Therefore, holy brothers and sisters,[s]
who share in the heavenly calling,[t]
fix your thoughts on Jesus, whom we
acknowledge[u] as our apostle and high
priest.[v] 2He was faithful to the one who
appointed him, just as Moses was faithful in all God's house.[w] 3Jesus has been
found worthy of greater honor than Moses,[x] just as the builder of a house has
greater honor than the house itself. 4For
every house is built by someone, but God
is the builder of everything.[y] 5"Moses was
faithful as a servant[z] in all God's house,"[b][a]
bearing witness to what would be spoken
by God in the future. 6But Christ is faithful as the Son[b] over God's house. And we
are his house,[c] if indeed we hold firmly[d]
to our confidence and the hope[e] in which
we glory.

2:15 [k]S 2Ti 1:7
2:16 [l]S Lk 3:8
2:17 [m]ver 14; S Php 2:7 [n]Heb 5:2 [o]Heb 3:1; 4:14, 15; 5:5, 10; 7:26, 28; 8:1, 3; 9:11 [p]Heb 5:1 [q]S Ro 3:25
2:18 [r]Heb 4:15
3:1 [s]Heb 2:11 [t]S Ro 8:28 [u]1Ti 6:12; Heb 4:14; 10:23; 2Co 9:13 [v]S Heb 2:17
3:2 [w]ver 5; Nu 12:7
3:3 [x]Dt 34:12
3:4 [y]Ge 1:1
3:5 [z]Ex 14:31 [a]ver 2; Nu 12:7
3:6 [b]S Heb 1:2 [c]S 1Co 3:16; 1Ti 3:15 [d]ver 14; S Ro 11:22; Heb 4:14 [e]Ro 5:2; Heb 6:11, 18, 19; 7:19; 11:1
3:7 [f]Ac 28:25; Heb 9:8; 10:15
3:8 [g]ver 15; Heb 4:7
3:9 [h]Nu 14:33; Dt 1:3; Ac 7:36
3:11 [i]Dt 1:34, 35 [j]Heb 4:3, 5 [k]Ps 95:7-11
3:12 [l]S Mt 16:16

Warning Against Unbelief

7So, as the Holy Spirit says:[f]

"Today, if you hear his voice,
8 do not harden your hearts[g]
as you did in the rebellion,
during the time of testing in the
wilderness,
9where your ancestors tested and
tried me,
though for forty years they saw
what I did.[h]
10That is why I was angry with that
generation;
I said, 'Their hearts are always
going astray,
and they have not known my
ways.'
11So I declared on oath in my anger,[i]
'They shall never enter my
rest.'[j]"[c][k]

12See to it, brothers and sisters, that
none of you has a sinful, unbelieving heart
that turns away from the living God.[l] 13But
encourage one another daily,[m] as long as
it is called "Today," so that none of you
may be hardened by sin's deceitfulness.[n]

[a] *17* Or *like his brothers* [b] *5* Num. 12:7
[c] *11* Psalm 95:7-11

3:13 [m]Heb 10:24, 25 [n]Jer 17:9; Eph 4:22

2:16 *Abraham's descendants.* Christ came to redeem Abraham's descendants—those who have Abraham's faith (see Ge 12:2–3; Ro 4:11,16; 9:8; Gal 3:29 and notes).
2:17 *merciful and faithful high priest.* See v. 18; 5:2. *high priest.* In Israel the high priest was the head of the priestly order and the only one who could enter into the very presence of God in the Most Holy Place in the temple—to "make atonement" for the people of God (see 9:7 and note; 13:11; Lev 16:1–34 and note). *make atonement.* In order for Christ to turn aside the wrath of God against guilty sinners, he had to become one with them and die as a substitute for them (see notes on Lev 16:20–22; 17:11; Mk 10:45; Ro 3:25; 1Jn 2:2).
2:18 *he was tempted.* See note on 4:15.
3:1–6 The faithful high priest who is worthy of our trust because he is greater than Moses.
3:1 *holy.* See note on 1Co 1:2. *brothers and sisters.* See NIV text note on 2:11. *share in the heavenly calling.* That is, participate (see note on v. 14) in the invitation to enter into and enjoy the presence of God (see 11:16; 12:22 and notes). *apostle.* Means "one who is sent" (see note on Mk 6:30). Jesus repeatedly spoke of himself as having been sent into the world by the Father (e.g., Mt 10:40; 15:24; Mk 9:37; Lk 9:48; Jn 4:34; 5:24,30,36–38; 6:38). He is the supreme apostle, the one from whom all other apostleship flows. *high priest.* See note on 2:17.
3:2 A comparison of Christ and Moses, both of whom were sent by the Father to lead his people—the one to lead them from bondage under the pharaoh to the promised land, the other to lead them from bondage under the devil (2:14–15) to the Sabbath-rest promised to those who believe (4:3,9). The analogy focuses on faithful stewardship.
3:3 *the builder … has greater honor than the house.* Jesus is the actual builder of the house (or household; see v. 6 and note), whereas Moses was simply a part of it.
3:4 *God is the builder of everything.* Jesus is here equated with God, making it beyond question that Christ is greater than Moses.
3:5–6 *a servant in all God's house … the Son over God's house.* The superiority of Christ over Moses (see Introduction: Theme) is shown in two comparisons: (1) Moses was a *servant*, whereas Christ is the *Son*, and (2) Moses was *in* God's house, i.e., a part of it, whereas Christ is *over* God's house. Both were faithful.
3:5 *faithful … in all God's house.* See Nu 12:7 and note.
3:6 *we are his house.* The house is made up of God's people, his household (see Eph 2:19; 1Pe 2:5 and notes). *if indeed we hold firmly to our confidence.* Failure to persevere reveals that a person is actually not a child of God, whereas perseverance is the hallmark of his children (cf. 10:35–36). *hope.* Assurance of free access to God (see v. 1; 6:18–19 and notes; 11:1; Ro 5:2 and note). *glory.* Rejoice (cf. Gal 6:14; cf. also 1Co 1:29,31; 2Co 10:17; Eph 2:9).
3:7—4:13 An exposition of Ps 95:7–11, stressing Christ's superiority over Moses, and a warning (the second; see note on 2:1–4) against disobedience and unbelief.
3:7–11 This quotation from Ps 95:7–11 summarizes the inglorious history of Israel under Moses' leadership in the wilderness. Three time periods are alluded to: that of the exodus, that of the psalmist and that of the writing of Hebrews. The example of Israel under Moses was used by the psalmist to warn the Israelites of his day against unbelief and disobedience. Similarly the author of Hebrews recalls the psalmist's words to warn the readers of this letter.
3:7 *Holy Spirit.* For the Holy Spirit as the speaker in (OT) Scripture, see 9:8; 10:15; Mk 12:36; Ac 1:16; 4:25; 21:11; 28:25; 1Pe 1:12; see also 2Pe 1:20–21 and notes; cf. 2Ti 3:16 and note.
3:13 *as long as it is called "Today."* See 4:7.

14 We have come to share in Christ, if indeed we hold[o] our original conviction firmly to the very end.[p] 15 As has just been said:

> "Today, if you hear his voice,
> do not harden your hearts
> as you did in the rebellion."[aq]

16 Who were they who heard and rebelled? Were they not all those Moses led out of Egypt?[r] 17 And with whom was he angry for forty years? Was it not with those who sinned, whose bodies perished in the wilderness?[s] 18 And to whom did God swear that they would never enter his rest[t] if not to those who disobeyed?[u] 19 So we see that they were not able to enter, because of their unbelief.[v]

A Sabbath-Rest for the People of God

4 Therefore, since the promise of entering his rest still stands, let us be careful that none of you be found to have fallen short of it.[w] 2 For we also have had the good news proclaimed to us, just as they did; but the message they heard was of no value to them, because they did not share the faith of those who obeyed.[bx] 3 Now we who have believed enter that rest, just as God has said,

> "So I declared on oath in my anger,
> 'They shall never enter my rest.' "[cy]

And yet his works have been finished since the creation of the world. 4 For somewhere he has spoken about the seventh day in these words: "On the seventh day God rested from all his works."[dz] 5 And again in the passage above he says, "They shall never enter my rest."[a]

6 Therefore since it still remains for some to enter that rest, and since those who formerly had the good news proclaimed to them did not go in because of their disobedience,[b] 7 God again set a certain day, calling it "Today." This he did when a long time later he spoke through David, as in the passage already quoted:

> "Today, if you hear his voice,
> do not harden your hearts."[ac]

8 For if Joshua had given them rest,[d] God would not have spoken[e] later about another day. 9 There remains, then, a Sabbath-rest for the people of God; 10 for anyone who enters God's rest also rests from their works,[ef] just as God did from his.[g] 11 Let us, therefore, make every effort to enter that rest, so that no one will perish by following their example of disobedience.[h]

12 For the word of God[i] is alive[j] and active.[k] Sharper than any double-edged sword,[l] it penetrates even to dividing soul

3:14 [o] ver 6 [p] S Eph 3:12 **3:15** [q] ver 7, 8; Ps 95:7,8; Heb 4:7 **3:16** [r] Nu 14:2 **3:17** [s] Nu 14:29; Ps 106:26; 1Co 10:5 **3:18** [t] Nu 14:20-23; Dt 1:34,35 [u] Heb 4:6 **3:19** [v] Ps 78:22; 106:24; Jn 3:36 **4:1** [w] Heb 12:15 **4:2** [x] 1Th 2:13 **4:3** [y] Ps 95:11; Dt 1:34,35; Heb 3:11 **4:4** [z] Ge 2:2,3; Ex 20:11 **4:5** [a] Ps 95:11; S ver 3 **4:6** [b] ver 11; Heb 3:18 **4:7** [c] Ps 95:7,8; Heb 3:7,8,15 **4:8** [d] Jos 22:4 [e] S Heb 1:1 **4:10** [f] Lev 23:3; Rev 14:13 [g] ver 4 **4:11** [h] ver 6; Heb 3:18 **4:12** [i] S Mk 4:14; Lk 5:1; 11:28; Jn 10:35; Ac 12:24; 1Th 2:13; 2Ti 2:9; 1Pe 1:23; 1Jn 2:14; Rev 1:2, 9 [j] Ac 7:38; 1Pe 1:23 [k] Isa 55:11; Jer 23:29; 1Th 2:13 [l] Eph 6:17; S Rev 1:16

a 15,7 Psalm 95:7,8 *b* 2 Some manuscripts *because those who heard did not combine it with faith*
c 3 Psalm 95:11; also in verse 5 *d* 4 Gen. 2:2
e 10 Or *labor*

3:14 *to share in Christ.* To belong to him and participate in the blessings he gives (cf. v. 1). *hold ... firmly to the very end.* Cf. v. 6; 6:11; Mt 10:22; 24:13; Mk 13:13; Ro 2:26; cf. also 1Co 1:8. *our original conviction.* And the faith commitment we made on the basis of that conviction.

3:16–19 The argument is pursued with a series of rhetorical questions. The important truths are that the people who failed to enter Canaan were the ones who had heard God's promise concerning the land and that they refused to believe and to act on what God had promised—an action described as rebellion (v. 16), sin (v. 17), disobedience (v. 18) and unbelief (v. 19). Consequently, God in his anger closed the doors of Canaan in the face of that whole generation of Israelites (Nu 14:21–35).

4:1 *promise of entering his rest.* See Ex 33:14; Dt 3:20 and note. *still stands.* God's promise to bring his people into circumstances of "rest" in his creation, while conditional, was open-ended. It was grounded in God's covenanted promises to Abraham (see Ge 15:12–21; 17:1–8; 22:15–18), was later reinforced by God's covenant with David (see 2Sa 7:5–16 and notes; cf. 1Ki 5:4 and note) and eventually came to be focused on the Messiah (see Isa 11:1–9 and notes). Through the Messiah's reign, God's promise of rest will ultimately be fulfilled in the new creation (see Isa 65:17; 66:22; Rev 21:4).

4:3 *we who have believed enter that rest.* Just as entering into rest in Canaan demanded faith in God's promise, so the ultimate "Sabbath-rest" (v. 9) is entered only by faith in the person and work of Jesus Christ. *his works have been finished since the creation of the world.* God rested from his work on the seventh day of creation (see v. 4; Ge 2:2), and thus his rest is already a reality. The rest God calls us to enter (vv. 10–11) is not our rest but his rest, which he invites us to share.

4:6–8 Israel's going into Canaan under Joshua was a partial and temporary entering of God's rest. That, however, was not the end of entering, as shown in the continuing invitation of Ps 95:7–8.

4:7 *calling it "Today."* See 3:13.

4:9 *There remains, then, a Sabbath-rest.* God's rest may still be entered by faith in his Son. Since the pre-Christian Greek translation of the OT (the Septuagint), which the author and his readers knew well, made no verbal distinction between the Sabbath "rest" (Hebrew *shabbat* [see, e.g., Ge 2:3 and note; Ex 20:11; 23:12]) and the rest that Israel, if faithful, was to experience every day in the promised land (Hebrew *nuaḥ/menuḥah* [see, e.g., Ex 31:14–15; Dt 3:20]), the writer associates these two in a way that suggests he saw in the weekly Sabbath-rest a sign and pledge of the promised life of rest. The fact that neither the Hebrew nor the Septuagint made any verbal distinction between God's "rest" in Ps 95:11 and his "resting place" in Ps 132:14; Isa 66:1 (see note on Ps 132:8) may have reinforced this striking conceptual association.

4:10 *rests from their works.* Believers cease their efforts to gain salvation by their own works and rest in the finished work of Christ on the cross. The believer's final rest may also be in view here (see Rev 14:13).

4:11 *make every effort.* Not a call to earn one's salvation by works but an exhortation to enter Sabbath-rest by faith and not follow Israel's sad example in the wilderness.

4:12–13 The reasons for giving serious attention to the exhortation of v. 11.

4:12 *word of God.* God's truth was revealed by Jesus (the

and spirit, joints and marrow; it judges
the thoughts and attitudes of the heart.[m]
13 Nothing in all creation is hidden from
God's sight.[n] Everything is uncovered and
laid bare before the eyes of him to whom
we must give account.

Jesus the Great High Priest

14 Therefore, since we have a great high
priest[o] who has ascended into heaven,[a][p]
Jesus the Son of God,[q] let us hold firmly
to the faith we profess.[r] 15 For we do not
have a high priest[s] who is unable to empathize with our weaknesses, but we have
one who has been tempted in every way,
just as we are[t]—yet he did not sin.[u] 16 Let
us then approach[v] God's throne of grace
with confidence,[w] so that we may receive
mercy and find grace to help us in our
time of need.

5 Every high priest is selected from
among the people and is appointed to
represent the people in matters related to
God,[x] to offer gifts and sacrifices[y] for sins.[z]
2 He is able to deal gently with those who
are ignorant and are going astray,[a] since he
himself is subject to weakness.[b] 3 This is
why he has to offer sacrifices for his own
sins, as well as for the sins of the people.[c]
4 And no one takes this honor on himself,
but he receives it when called by God, just
as Aaron was.[d]
5 In the same way, Christ did not take
on himself the glory[e] of becoming a high
priest.[f] But God said[g] to him,

"You are my Son;
today I have become your
Father."[b][h]

6 And he says in another place,

"You are a priest forever,
in the order of Melchizedek."[i][c][j]

7 During the days of Jesus' life on earth,
he offered up prayers and petitions[k] with
fervent cries and tears[l] to the one who
could save him from death, and he was
heard[m] because of his reverent submission.[n] 8 Son[o] though he was, he learned
obedience from what he suffered[p] 9 and,
once made perfect,[q] he became the source
of eternal salvation for all who obey him
10 and was designated by God to be high
priest[r] in the order of Melchizedek.[s]

[a] 14 Greek *has gone through the heavens*
[b] 5 Psalm 2:7 [c] 6 Psalm 110:4

4:12 [m] 1Co 14:24,25 **4:13** [n] Ps 33:13-15; Pr 5:21; Jer 16:17; 23:24; Da 2:22 **4:14** [o] S Heb 2:17 [p] Heb 6:20; 8:1; 9:24 [q] S Mt 4:3 [r] S Heb 3:1 **4:15** [s] S Heb 2:17 [t] Heb 2:18 [u] S 2Co 5:21 **4:16** [v] S Heb 7:19 [w] S Eph 3:12 **5:1** [x] Heb 2:17 [y] Heb 8:3; 9:9 [z] Heb 7:27 **5:2** [a] Isa 29:24; Heb 2:18; 4:15 [b] Heb 7:28 **5:3** [c] Lev 9:7; 16:6; Heb 7:27; 9:7 **5:4** [d] Ex 28:1; Nu 14:40; 18:7 **5:5** [e] Jn 8:54 [f] S Heb 2:17 [g] S Heb 1:1 [h] Ps 2:7; S Mt 3:17 **5:6** [i] ver 10; Ge 14:18; Heb 6:20; 7:1-22 [j] Ps 110:4; Heb 7:17,21 **5:7** [k] Lk 22:41-44 [l] Mt 27:46, 50; Lk 23:46 [m] Ps 22:24 [n] Mk 14:36 **5:8** [o] S Heb 1:2 [p] S Php 2:8 **5:9** [q] S Heb 2:10 **5:10** [r] ver 5; S Heb 2:17 [s] S ver 6

incarnate Word; see Jn 1:1,14), but it has also been given verbally, the word referred to here. This dynamic word of God is active in accomplishing God's purposes (see Ps 19:7–11; 107:20; 147:15,18; Isa 40:8; 55:11; Gal 3:8; Eph 5:26; Jas 1:18; 1Pe 1:23). The author of Hebrews describes it as a "living" power that judges as with an all-seeing eye, penetrating a person's innermost being. *soul and spirit, joints and marrow.* The totality and depth of one's being (see 1Th 5:23 and note).

4:13 *Nothing in all creation is hidden from God's sight.* The author associates the activity of the word with the activity of God, as though they are one and the same—which in a sense they are.

4:14—7:28 An exposition of Ps 110:4, stressing Christ's superiority over Aaron because his is a better priesthood (see Introduction: Theme; see also chart, p. 2069).

4:14 *great high priest.* See 2:17 and note; 3:1. *into heaven.* As the Aaronic high priest on the Day of Atonement passed from the sight of the people into the Most Holy Place (see Lev 16:15,17), so Jesus passed from the sight of his watching disciples, ascending "through the heavens" into the heavenly sanctuary (see NIV text note), his work of atonement accomplished (Ac 1:9–11). *hold firmly to the faith we profess.* Suggests that the readers were in danger of letting their faith slip (see similar admonitions in 2:1; 3:6,14).

4:15 *tempted in every way, just as we are.* See 2:18. The author stresses the parallel between Christ's temptations and ours. He did not have each temptation we have but experienced the whole range of our temptations. *yet he did not sin.* The way in which Christ's temptations were different from ours was in the results—his temptations never led to sin (see Mt 4:1–11 and notes).

4:16 *Let us then approach.* Because Christ, our high priest, has experienced human temptation, he stands ready to give immediate and sympathetic help when we are tempted (see 2:10 and note).

5:1–4 The high-priestly office had two specific qualifications: (1) The high priest had to be "selected from among the people" (v. 1) and thus be able to represent them before God, and (2) he had to "be called by God" (v. 4).

5:1 *high priest.* See note on 2:17. *gifts and sacrifices.* See 8:3; 9:9 and notes on Lev 1:2; 2:1; see also chart, p. 164.

5:2 *those who are ignorant and are going astray.* See Ps 119:176 and note. Contrast the unintentional sin (see Lev 4 and note on 4:2; Nu 15:22–29 and note on 15:22) with defiant rebellion against God (see Nu 15:30–31 and note on 15:30; cf. Heb 6:4–6; 10:26–31 and notes).

5:4 *no one takes this honor on himself.* In Christ's day the high-priestly office was in the hands of a family that had bought control of it.

5:5 *Christ did not take on himself the glory of becoming a high priest.* The Son was appointed by the Father, as the two passages cited here show (Ps 2:7; 110:4). *today I have become your Father.* See 1:5; Ps 2:7–9 and notes; cf. Ro 1:4.

5:6 *in the order of Melchizedek.* See notes on 7:3; Ge 14:20; Ps 110:4.

5:7 *prayers ... tears.* The principal reference here is to Christ's agony in Gethsemane and on Golgotha. *to the one who could save him from death.* To the Father. Jesus did not shrink from physical suffering and death but from the indescribable agony of taking humankind's sin on himself (cf. Mt 27:46). Although he asked that the cup of suffering might be taken from him, he did not waver in his determination to fulfill the Father's will (see Mt 26:36–46 and note on 26:38–39). *he was heard.* His prayer was granted by the Father, who saved him from death—through resurrection.

5:8 *Son though he was.* Though he was *God's* Son (see 1:2–3). *learned obedience.* Learned experientially what his full obedience to God's will for humankind entailed for him. *from what he suffered.* Especially in the ordeal of his atoning death, by which "he became the source of eternal salvation for all who obey him" (v. 9).

5:9 *made perfect.* See 2:10 and note.

Warning Against Falling Away

6:4-6Ref — Heb 10:26-31

11 We have much to say about this, but it is hard to make it clear to you because you no longer try to understand. 12 In fact, though by this time you ought to be teachers, you need someone to teach you the elementary truths[t] of God's word all over again. You need milk, not solid food![u] 13 Anyone who lives on milk, being still an infant,[v] is not acquainted with the teaching about righteousness. 14 But solid food is for the mature,[w] who by constant use have trained themselves to distinguish good from evil.[x]

6 Therefore let us move beyond[y] the elementary teachings[z] about Christ and be taken forward to maturity, not laying again the foundation of repentance from acts that lead to death,[a][a] and of faith in God, 2 instruction about cleansing rites,[b][b] the laying on of hands,[c] the resurrection of the dead,[d] and eternal judgment. 3 And God permitting,[e] we will do so.

4 It is impossible for those who have once been enlightened,[f] who have tasted the heavenly gift,[g] who have shared in the Holy Spirit,[h] 5 who have tasted the goodness[i] of the word of God[j] and the powers of the coming age 6 and who have fallen[c] away, to be brought back to repentance.[k] To their loss they are crucifying the Son of God[l] all over again and subjecting him to public disgrace. 7 Land that drinks in the rain often falling on it and that produces a crop useful to those for whom it is farmed receives the blessing of God. 8 But land that produces thorns and thistles is worthless and is in danger of being cursed.[m] In the end it will be burned.

9 Even though we speak like this, dear friends,[n] we are convinced of better things in your case — the things that have to do with salvation. 10 God is not unjust; he will not forget your work and the love you have shown him as you have helped his people and continue to help them.[o] 11 We want each of you to show this same diligence to the very end, so that what you hope[p] for may be fully realized. 12 We do not want you to become lazy, but to

5:12 [t] Heb 6:1 [u] 1Co 3:2; 1Pe 2:2 **5:13** [v] S 1Co 14:20 **5:14** [w] S 1Co 2:6 [x] Isa 7:15 **6:1** [y] Php 3:12-14 [z] Heb 5:12 [a] Heb 9:14 **6:2** [b] Jn 3:25 [c] S Ac 6:6 [d] S Ac 2:24; Ac 17:18,32 **6:3** [e] Ac 18:21 **6:4** [f] Heb 10:32 [g] Eph 2:8 [h] Gal 3:2 **6:5** [i] Ps 34:8 [j] S Heb 4:12 **6:6** [k] 2Pe 2:21; 1Jn 5:16 [l] S Mt 4:3 **6:8** [m] Ge 3:17, 18; Isa 5:6; 27:4 **6:9** [n] S 1Co 10:14 **6:10** [o] S Mt 10:40,42; 1Th 1:3 **6:11** [p] S Heb 3:6

[a] 1 Or *from useless rituals* [b] 2 Or *about baptisms* [c] 6 Or *age,* [6] *if they fall*

5:11 *much to say about this.* About Christ's eternal priesthood "in the order of Melchizedek" (v. 10; see ch. 7). *you no longer try to understand.* Instead of progressing in the Christian life, the readers had become spiritually sluggish and mentally lazy (6:12).

5:12 *by this time.* They were not recent converts. *elementary truths of God's word.* Such as those listed in 6:1 – 2 (see note there). Having taken the first steps toward becoming (mature) Christians, they had slipped back to where they started. *solid food.* Advanced teaching, such as that given in ch. 7.

5:14 *mature.* Those who had progressed in spiritual life and had become Christians of sound judgment and discernment. *distinguish good from evil.* Something neither physical nor spiritual infants can do.

6:1 – 2 *not laying again the foundation.* Six fundamental doctrines are mentioned: (1) *repentance.* The change of mind that causes one to turn away from sin (see note on Mt 4:17). (2) *faith in God.* The counterpart of repentance. As repentance is turning away from sin, faith is turning to God (cf. 1Th 1:9). (3) *instruction about cleansing rites.* If the NIV text note rendering is correct, reference is probably to different baptisms with which the readers were familiar, such as Jewish baptism of converts to Judaism, John the Baptist's baptism, and the baptism commanded by Jesus (see Mt 28:19 and note). If the NIV main text translation is correct ("cleansing rites"), reference is probably to the ceremonial or ritual washings as practiced in first-century Judaism (cf. 9:10; Mk 7:3 – 5; Jn 2:6 and note; Jas 4:8 and note). (4) *laying on of hands.* Sometimes followed baptism (Ac 8:17). Otherwise laying on of hands was practiced in connection with ordaining or commissioning (Ac 6:6; see note there), healing the sick (see Mk 6:5; Lk 4:40; Ac 28:8) and bestowal of blessing (see Mt 19:13 – 15). (5) *resurrection of the dead.* The resurrection of all people in the last days (see Jn 5:25 – 29; 11:25; 2Co 4:14). (6) *eternal judgment.* Either the fact of God's judgment or the verdict that determines the eternal condition of those judged.

6:1 *elementary teachings about Christ.* See note on 5:12. *acts that lead to death.* Lit. "dead works"; deeds or useless rituals that cannot impart life (see 9:14).

6:3 A common expression of dependence on the will of God (cf. 1Co 16:7; Jas 4:13 – 15). Only the Lord can open minds and hearts and bring spiritual maturity.

6:4 – 8 The third warning (see note on 2:1 – 4).

6:4 – 6 The most common interpretations of this difficult passage are: (1) It refers to Christians who actually lose their salvation. (2) It is a hypothetical argument to warn immature Hebrew Christians (5:11 – 14) that they must progress to maturity (see v. 1) or else experience divine discipline or judgment (see vv. 7 – 8). (3) It refers to professing Christians whose apostasy proves that their faith was not genuine (cf. 1Jn 2:19). This view sees chs. 3 – 4 as a warning based on the rebellion of the Israelites in the wilderness. As Israel could not enter the promised land after exploring the region and tasting its fruit, so the professing Hebrew Christians would not be able to repent if they adamantly turned against "the light" they had received. According to this interpretation, such expressions as "enlightened," "tasted the heavenly gift" and "shared in the Holy Spirit" indicate that such persons had come under the influence of God's covenant blessings and had professed to turn from darkness to light but were in danger of a public and final rejection of Christ, proving they had never been regenerated (see 10:26 – 31 and notes; cf. 2Pe 2:20 – 22 and notes).

6:5 *the coming age.* See Mk 10:30 and note; 1Ti 6:19.

6:7 – 8 A short parable graphically illustrating the warning just given (cf. Mt 13:3 – 23).

6:8 *be burned.* Cf. 10:27; Jn 15:6 and notes.

6:9 *convinced of better things … that have to do with salvation.* Although the author has suggested the possibility that some of his readers may still be unsaved, he is confident that God has been at work among them. Changed lives and works of love (v. 10) suggest that most of them were indeed regenerated.

6:11 *to the very end.* A call for perseverance in faith as an evidence of salvation. *that what you hope for may be fully realized.* See 3:6 and note; 11:1; 2Co 13:5; 2Pe 1:10 and note.

6:12 *lazy.* See 5:11 and note. *those who through faith and patience inherit what has been promised.* For examples, see ch. 11.

imitate[q] those who through faith and patience[r] inherit what has been promised.[s]

The Certainty of God's Promise

13 When God made his promise to Abraham, since there was no one greater for him to swear by, he swore by himself,[t] 14 saying, "I will surely bless you and give you many descendants."[a][u] 15 And so after waiting patiently, Abraham received what was promised.[v]

16 People swear by someone greater than themselves, and the oath confirms what is said and puts an end to all argument.[w] 17 Because God wanted to make the unchanging[x] nature of his purpose very clear to the heirs of what was promised,[y] he confirmed it with an oath. 18 God did this so that, by two unchangeable things in which it is impossible for God to lie,[z] we who have fled to take hold of the hope[a] set before us may be greatly encouraged. 19 We have this hope as an anchor for the soul, firm and secure. It enters the inner sanctuary behind the curtain,[b] 20 where our forerunner, Jesus, has entered on our behalf.[c] He has become a high priest[d] forever, in the order of Melchizedek.[e]

Melchizedek the Priest

7 This Melchizedek was king of Salem[f] and priest of God Most High.[g] He met Abraham returning from the defeat of the kings and blessed him,[h] 2 and Abraham gave him a tenth of everything. First, the name Melchizedek means "king of righteousness"; then also, "king of Salem" means "king of peace." 3 Without father or mother, without genealogy,[i] without beginning of days or end of life, resembling the Son of God,[j] he remains a priest forever.

4 Just think how great he was: Even the patriarch[k] Abraham gave him a tenth of the plunder![l] 5 Now the law requires the descendants of Levi who become priests to collect a tenth from the people[m] — that is, from their fellow Israelites — even though they also are descended from Abraham. 6 This man, however, did not trace his descent from Levi, yet he collected a tenth from Abraham and blessed[n] him who had the promises.[o] 7 And without doubt the lesser is blessed by the greater. 8 In the one case, the tenth is collected by people who die; but in the other case, by him who is declared to be living.[p] 9 One might even say that Levi, who collects the tenth, paid the tenth through Abraham, 10 because when Melchizedek met Abraham, Levi was still in the body of his ancestor.

Jesus Like Melchizedek

11 If perfection could have been attained through the Levitical priesthood — and indeed the law given to the people[q] estab-

6:12 [q] Heb 13:7 [r] 2Th 1:4; Jas 1:3; Rev 13:10; 14:12 [s] Heb 10:36 **6:13** [t] Ge 22:16; Lk 1:73 **6:14** [u] Ge 22:17 **6:15** [v] Ge 21:5 **6:16** [w] Ex 22:11 **6:17** [x] ver 18; Ps 110:4 [y] Ro 4:16; Heb 11:9 **6:18** [z] Nu 23:19; Titus 1:2 [a] S Heb 3:6 **6:19** [b] Lev 16:2; Heb 9:2, 3, 7 **6:20** [c] S Heb 4:14 [d] S Heb 2:17 [e] S Heb 5:6 **7:1** [f] Ps 76:2 [g] S Mk 5:7 [h] ver 6; Ge 14:18-20 **7:3** [i] ver 6 [j] S Mt 4:3 **7:4** [k] Ac 2:29 [l] Ge 14:20 **7:5** [m] Nu 18:21, 26 **7:6** [n] Ge 14:19, 20 [o] Ro 4:13 **7:8** [p] Heb 5:6; 6:20 **7:11** [q] ver 18, 19; Heb 8:7

[a] *14* Gen. 22:17

6:13 *God made his promise to Abraham.* The promise of many descendants was made with an oath to emphasize its unchanging character (see Ge 22:16 – 18). Ordinarily the swearing of an oath belongs to our fallen human situation, in which a person's word is not always trustworthy (cf. Mt 5:23 – 26 and note). God's swearing of an oath was a condescension to human frailty, thus making his word, which in itself is absolutely trustworthy, doubly dependable (see v. 18 and note).
6:15 *after waiting patiently.* For 25 years (see Ge 12:3 – 4; 21:5). *received what was promised.* The birth of his son Isaac (Ge 17:2; 18:10; 21:5).
6:18 *two unchangeable things.* God's promise, which in itself is absolutely trustworthy, and God's oath confirming that promise (see note on v. 13). *be greatly encouraged.* Since we look back on the fulfillment of the promise that Abraham saw only in anticipation (see 11:13; Jn 8:56 and notes).
6:19 *as an anchor for the soul, firm and secure.* Like an anchor holding a ship safely in position, our hope in Christ guarantees our safety. *inner sanctuary behind the curtain.* Whereas the ship's anchor goes down to the ocean bed, the Christian's anchor goes up into the true, heavenly sanctuary.
6:20 *a high priest forever, in the order of Melchizedek.* The grand theme that the author introduced briefly in 5:6 – 10 and now develops in ch. 7. *high priest.* See note on 2:17.
7:1 *Melchizedek.* See Ge 14:18 – 20 and notes; cf. Ps 110:4 and note. *king ... and priest.* Of particular significance is Melchizedek's holding both offices, one of the ways in which he is treated here as a prefiguration of Christ (see notes on Zec 4:14; 6:13). *Salem.* Jerusalem (see note on Ge 14:18).
7:2 *king of righteousness ... king of peace.* Messianic titles (see Isa 9:6 – 7; Jer 23:5 – 6 and notes).
7:3 *Without father ... or end of life.* Ge 14:18 – 20, contrary to the practice elsewhere in the early chapters of Genesis, does not mention Melchizedek's parentage and children, or his birth and death. That he was a real, historical figure is clear, but the author of Hebrews (in accordance with Jewish interpretation) uses the silence of Scripture about Melchizedek's genealogy to portray him as a prefiguration of Christ. Melchizedek's priesthood anticipates Christ's eternal existence and his unending priesthood. Some believe the appearance of Melchizedek to Abraham was a manifestation of Christ before his incarnation, but the comparison "resembling the Son of God" argues against such an interpretation.
7:4 *think how great he was.* The one who collects a tithe is greater than the one who pays it, and "the lesser is blessed by the greater" (v. 7). In both ways Melchizedek was greater than Abraham.
7:8 *In the one case.* In the case of the Aaronic priests. *in the other case.* In the case of Melchizedek.
7:11 *the law given.* The law of Moses and the priesthood went together. All the people without exception were sinners, subject to the law's condemnation, and thus were in need of a priestly system to mediate between them and God. *in the order of Melchizedek, not in the order of Aaron.* Implies that the Aaronic (or Levitical) priesthood was imperfect but that Melchizedek's was perfect. The announcement of a coming one who would be a priest forever (Ps 110:4) was written midway in the history of the Levitical priesthood — which could be understood as a hint that the existing system was to give way to something better.

lished that priesthood — why was there
still need for another priest to come,[r] one
in the order of Melchizedek,[s] not in the
order of Aaron? 12 For when the priesthood
is changed, the law must be changed also.
13 He of whom these things are said belonged to a different tribe,[t] and no one
from that tribe has ever served at the altar.[u] 14 For it is clear that our Lord descended from Judah,[v] and in regard to that tribe
Moses said nothing about priests. 15 And
what we have said is even more clear if
another priest like Melchizedek appears,
16 one who has become a priest not on the
basis of a regulation as to his ancestry but
on the basis of the power of an indestructible life. 17 For it is declared:

"You are a priest forever,
in the order of Melchizedek."[a][w]

18 The former regulation is set aside because it was weak and useless[x] 19 (for the
law made nothing perfect),[y] and a better
hope[z] is introduced, by which we draw
near to God.[a]
20 And it was not without an oath! Others became priests without any oath, 21 but
he became a priest with an oath when
God said to him:

"The Lord has sworn
and will not change his mind:[b]
'You are a priest forever.' "[a][c]

22 Because of this oath, Jesus has become
the guarantor of a better covenant.[d]
23 Now there have been many of those
priests, since death prevented them from
continuing in office; 24 but because Jesus
lives forever, he has a permanent priesthood.[e] 25 Therefore he is able to save[f] completely[b] those who come to God[g] through
him, because he always lives to intercede
for them.[h]
26 Such a high priest[i] truly meets our
need — one who is holy, blameless, pure,
set apart from sinners,[j] exalted above the
heavens.[k] 27 Unlike the other high priests,
he does not need to offer sacrifices[l] day
after day, first for his own sins,[m] and then
for the sins of the people. He sacrificed
for their sins once for all[n] when he offered
himself.[o] 28 For the law appoints as high
priests men in all their weakness;[p] but the
oath, which came after the law, appointed the Son,[q] who has been made perfect[r]
forever.

The High Priest of a New Covenant

8 Now the main point of what we are
saying is this: We do have such a high
priest,[s] who sat down at the right hand
of the throne of the Majesty in heaven,[t]
2 and who serves in the sanctuary, the true

a 17,21 Psalm 110:4 *b* 25 Or *forever*

7:11 [r] Heb 10:1 [s] ver 17; S Heb 5:6 **7:13** [t] ver 11 [u] ver 14 **7:14** [v] Isa 11:1; Mt 1:3; 2:6; Lk 3:33; Rev 5:5 **7:17** [w] Ps 110:4; ver 21; S Heb 5:6 **7:18** [x] Ro 8:3 **7:19** [y] ver 11; Ro 3:20; 7:7, 8; Gal 3:21; Heb 9:9; 10:1 [z] S Heb 3:6 [a] ver 25; Heb 4:16; 10:1, 22; Jas 4:8 **7:21** [b] Nu 23:19; 1Sa 15:29; Mal 3:6; Ro 11:29 [c] Ps 110:4; S Heb 5:6 **7:22** [d] S Lk 22:20 **7:24** [e] ver 28 **7:25** [f] S Ro 11:14 [g] S ver 19 [h] S Ro 8:34 **7:26** [i] S Heb 2:17 [j] S 2Co 5:21 [k] S Heb 4:14 **7:27** [l] Heb 5:1 [m] S Heb 5:3 [n] Ro 6:10; Heb 9:12, 26, 28; 10:10; 1Pe 3:18 [o] Eph 5:2; Heb 9:14, 28 **7:28** [p] Heb 5:2 [q] S Heb 1:2 [r] S Heb 2:10 **8:1** [s] S Heb 2:17 [t] S Mk 16:19; S Heb 4:14

7:16 *become a priest not on the basis of a regulation as to his ancestry.* In the law of Moses the priestly function was restricted to the family of Aaron from the tribe of Levi (see Ex 28:1–4; 40:12–15; Nu 3:10), but Jesus came from the nonpriestly tribe of Judah (vv. 14–15). *power of an indestructible life.* According to Ps 110:4 the priest in the order of Melchizedek is "a priest forever." This is what Jesus became as a result of the act of God's power that raised him from the dead as the eternal victor over death.
7:18 *The former regulation … was weak and useless.* The law is holy and good (Ro 7:12), but it could neither give the ability to fulfill its demands nor provide the atonement necessary for those who violated it (v. 19a).
7:19 The law was only preparatory (see Gal 3:23–24 and notes) and brought nothing to fulfillment (see Mt 5:17 and note). *better hope.* The new covenant is better because it assures us of complete redemption and brings us into the very presence of God. See 3:6 and note; see also Introduction: Theme; chart, p. 2069.
7:20 No divine oath was associated with the establishment of the Levitical priesthood.
7:21 *with an oath.* For the significance of the oath, see 6:17.
7:22 *better covenant.* See chs. 8–10; see also Introduction: Theme.
7:23 *death prevented them from continuing in office.* Impermanence was further evidence of the imperfection of the Levitical order.
7:25 *completely.* May include the ideas of completeness and permanence (see NIV text note). *always lives to intercede.* His people will never be without a priest to represent them in the very presence of God, interceding on their behalf (see 1Jn 2:1–2 and notes; cf. Jn 17:6–26).
7:26 *high priest.* See note on 2:17. *meets our need.* Of salvation from sin and its consequences.
7:27 *day after day.* A reference to the endless repetition of sacrifices throughout the year (see Ex 29:36–42), evidence that these sacrifices never effectively and finally atoned for sin. *first for his own sins.* Christ's priesthood is superior because he has no personal sins for which sacrifice had to be made (see Lev 9:8 and note). *once for all.* A key phrase in Hebrews (see 9:12,26 and note on 9:12; 10:2,10). *offered himself.* Levitical priests offered up only animals; our high priest offered himself, the perfect substitute for us.
7:28 *men in all their weakness.* Because (1) they are mortal and therefore impermanent, v. 23; (2) they are sinful, v. 27; and (3) they could only offer animals, which could never provide a genuine substitute for human beings made in the image of God (see Ge 1:26–28 and notes). *made perfect forever.* In regard to his appointed mission (see 2:10; 5:9 and notes).
8:1—10:18 The argument of this section grows out of an exposition of Jer 31:31–34 and demonstrates that Christ is the mediator of a "better covenant" (7:22).
8:1 See note on 1:2–3. *high priest.* See note on 2:17.
8:2 *true tabernacle.* In contrast to the tabernacle erected by Moses, which was an imperfect and impermanent copy of the heavenly one. *set up by the Lord, not by a mere human being.* The heavenly sanctuary built by God corresponds to the Most Holy Place, the innermost sanctuary in Moses' tabernacle, into which the high priest briefly entered with the blood of atonement once a year (see Lev 16:13–15,34). In the heavenly sanctuary, however, our great high priest dwells eternally as our intercessor (7:25).

tabernacle[u] set up by the Lord, not by a mere human being.

3 Every high priest[v] is appointed to offer both gifts and sacrifices,[w] and so it was necessary for this one also to have something to offer.[x] 4 If he were on earth, he would not be a priest, for there are already priests who offer the gifts prescribed by the law.[y] 5 They serve at a sanctuary that is a copy[z] and shadow[a] of what is in heaven. This is why Moses was warned[b] when he was about to build the tabernacle: "See to it that you make everything according to the pattern shown you on the mountain."[ac] 6 But in fact the ministry Jesus has received is as superior to theirs as the covenant[d] of which he is mediator[e] is superior to the old one, since the new covenant is established on better promises.

7 For if there had been nothing wrong with that first covenant, no place would have been sought for another.[f] 8 But God found fault with the people and said[b]:

"The days are coming, declares the Lord,
when I will make a new covenant[g]
with the people of Israel
and with the people of Judah.
9 It will not be like the covenant
I made with their ancestors[h]
when I took them by the hand
to lead them out of Egypt,
because they did not remain faithful to my covenant,
and I turned away from them,
declares the Lord.
10 This is the covenant[i] I will establish
with the people of Israel
after that time, declares the Lord.
I will put my laws in their minds
and write them on their hearts.[j]
I will be their God,
and they will be my people.[k]
11 No longer will they teach their neighbor,
or say to one another, 'Know the Lord,'
because they will all know me,[l]
from the least of them to the greatest.
12 For I will forgive their wickedness
and will remember their sins no more."[m][cn]

13 By calling this covenant "new,"[o] he has made the first one obsolete;[p] and what is obsolete and outdated will soon disappear.

Worship in the Earthly Tabernacle

9 Now the first covenant had regulations for worship and also an earthly sanctuary.[q] 2 A tabernacle[r] was set up. In its first room were the lampstand[s] and the table[t] with its consecrated bread;[u] this was called the Holy Place.[v] 3 Behind the second curtain was a room called the Most Holy Place,[w] 4 which had the golden altar of incense[x] and the gold-covered ark of the covenant.[y] This ark contained the gold jar of

8:2 [u] Heb 9:11, 24 **8:3** [v] S Heb 2:17 [w] Heb 5:1; 9:9 [x] Heb 9:14 **8:4** [y] Heb 5:1; 9:9 **8:5** [z] Heb 9:23 [a] Col 2:17; Heb 10:1 [b] Heb 11:7; 12:25 [c] Ex 25:40 **8:6** [d] ver 8, 13; S Lk 22:20 [e] S Gal 3:20 **8:7** [f] Heb 7:11, 18; 10:1 **8:8** [g] ver 6, 13; S Lk 22:20 **8:9** [h] Ex 19:5,6; 20:1-17 **8:10** [i] Ro 11:27 [j] 2Co 3:3; Heb 10:16 [k] Eze 11:20; Zec 8:8 **8:11** [l] Isa 54:13; S Jn 6:45 **8:12** [m] Heb 10:17 [n] Ro 11:27 **8:13** [o] ver 6, 8; S Lk 22:20 [p] 2Co 5:17 **9:1** [q] Ex 25:8 **9:2** [r] Ex 25:8, 9 [s] Ex 25:31-39 [t] Ex 25:23-29 [u] Ex 25:30; Lev 24:5-8 [v] Ex 26:33, 34 **9:3** [w] Ex 26:31-33 **9:4** [x] Ex 30:1-5 [y] Ex 25:10-22

[a] *5* Exodus 25:40 [b] *8* Some manuscripts may be translated *fault and said to the people.* [c] *12* Jer. 31:31-34

8:3 *gifts and sacrifices.* See 5:1 and note.
8:4 *priests who offer the gifts.* The present tense of the verb "offer," here and elsewhere in the letter, indicates that the temple in Jerusalem was still standing. This letter, therefore, must have been written prior to the temple's destruction in AD 70 (see Introduction: Date).
8:5 *copy and shadow of what is in heaven.* An implication the author draws from the words of Ex 25:40. *make everything according to the pattern.* Because both the tabernacle and its ministry were intended to symbolize the only way sinners may approach a holy God and find forgiveness.
8:6 *mediator.* Cf. 1Ti 2:5 and note. In Hebrews "mediator" is always "of a new [superior/better] covenant" (9:15; 12:24; see 7:22; 8:6). The role of "mediator" here appears to be not that of instituting the covenant but of guaranteeing that the covenant promises are fulfilled (cf. 7:22), that the promised deliverance is actually accomplished (cf. Moses' mediatorial acts in Ex 32:31–32; 33:12–23; 34:5–10; Nu 14:13–20).
8:7 *if there had been nothing wrong with that first covenant.* The line of argument here is similar to that in 7:11, where the Levitical priestly order is shown to be inferior because it was replaced by the order of Melchizedek. Similarly, if the Sinaitic covenant were without defect, there would have been no need to replace it with a new covenant.
8:8–12 A quotation from Jer 31:31–34 (see note there) containing a prophetic announcement and definition of the new covenant, which was to be different from the Sinaitic covenant (v. 9). Its superior benefits are: (1) God's laws will become inner principles (v. 10a) that enable his people to delight in doing his will (cf. Eze 36:26–27; Ro 8:2–4 and notes); (2) God and his people will have intimate fellowship (v. 10b); (3) sinful ignorance of God will be removed forever (v. 11); and (4) forgiveness of sins will be an everlasting reality (v. 12).
8:10 *their God . . . my people.* See note on Zec 8:8.
8:13 *obsolete and outdated.* The Sinaitic covenant—but not the Abrahamic covenant (cf. Ro 4:16–17; chs. 9–11; Gal 3:7–9,14,16–18; Eph 2:12).
9:1 *first covenant.* The covenant made at Sinai (see 8:13 and note).
9:2 *A tabernacle was set up.* The tabernacle built under Moses. *lampstand.* Made of hammered gold and placed at the south side of the Holy Place (Ex 40:24), it had seven lamps that were kept burning every night (Ex 25:31–40; 27:21). *the table with its consecrated bread.* Made of acacia wood overlaid with gold (Ex 25:23–30), it stood on the north side of the Holy Place (Ex 40:22). On it were twelve loaves, replaced every Sabbath and arranged in two stacks of six (Lev 24:5–8).
9:4 *which had the golden altar of incense.* Although the altar of incense stood in the Holy Place, the author describes it as belonging to the Most Holy Place. His purpose was to show its close relationship to the inner sanctuary and the ark of the covenant (see 1Ki 6:22 and note). On the Day of Atonement the high priest took incense from this altar, along with the blood of the sin offering, into the Most Holy Place (Lev

According to Hebrews 9:1–10, the tabernacle represented the "first covenant" mediated through Moses, but its external regulations applied only until the "new order" brought about by Jesus.

manna,[z] Aaron's staff that had budded,[a]
and the stone tablets of the covenant.[b]
5 Above the ark were the cherubim of the
Glory,[c] overshadowing the atonement cover.[d] But we cannot discuss these things in
detail now.
6 When everything had been arranged
like this, the priests entered regularly[e] into
the outer room to carry on their ministry.
7 But only the high priest entered[f] the inner room,[g] and that only once a year,[h] and
never without blood,[i] which he offered for
himself[j] and for the sins the people had
committed in ignorance.[k] 8 The Holy Spirit
was showing[l] by this that the way[m] into
the Most Holy Place had not yet been disclosed as long as the first tabernacle was
still functioning. 9 This is an illustration[n]
for the present time, indicating that the
gifts and sacrifices being offered[o] were not
able to clear the conscience[p] of the worshiper. 10 They are only a matter of food[q]
and drink[r] and various ceremonial washings[s]—external regulations[t] applying until
the time of the new order.

The Blood of Christ

11 But when Christ came as high priest[u]
of the good things that are now already
here,[a][v] he went through the greater and
more perfect tabernacle[w] that is not made
with human hands,[x] that is to say, is not a
part of this creation. 12 He did not enter by
means of the blood of goats and calves;[y]
but he entered the Most Holy Place[z] once
for all[a] by his own blood,[b] thus obtaining[b] eternal redemption. 13 The blood of
goats and bulls[c] and the ashes of a heifer[d]
sprinkled on those who are ceremonially

9:4 [z] Ex 16:32, 33 [a] Nu 17:10 [b] Ex 31:18; 32:15 **9:5** [c] Ex 25:17-19 [d] Ex 25:20-22; 26:34 **9:6** [e] Nu 28:3 **9:7** [f] Lev 16:11-19 [g] ver 2,3 [h] Lev 16:34 [i] Lev 16:11, 14 [j] Lev 16:11; Heb 5:2,3 [k] Heb 5:2,3 **9:8** [l] S Heb 3:7 [m] Jn 14:6; Heb 10:19,20 **9:9** [n] Heb 10:1 [o] Heb 5:1; 8:3 [p] S Heb 7:19 **9:10** [q] Lev 11:2-23 [r] Nu 6:3; Col 2:16 [s] Lev 11:25,28, 40 [t] Heb 7:16 **9:11** [u] S Heb 2:17 [v] Heb 10:1 [w] ver 24; Heb 8:2 [x] S Jn 2:19 **9:12** [y] ver 19; Lev 16:6, 15; Heb 10:4 [z] ver 24 [a] ver 26, 28; S Heb 7:27 [b] ver 14; S Ro 3:25 **9:13** [c] Heb 10:4 [d] Nu 19:9, 17, 18

[a] 11 Some early manuscripts *are to come*
[b] 12 Or *blood, having obtained*

16:12–14). *ark of the covenant.* A chest made of acacia wood, overlaid inside and out with gold (Ex 25:10–16). *manna ... staff ... tablets.* See notes on Ex 16:33–34; see also Nu 17:8–10.
9:5 *cherubim of the Glory.* Two winged figures made of pure gold, of one piece with the atonement cover, or mercy seat, and standing at either end of it. It was between them that the glory of God's presence appeared (Ex 25:17–22; Lev 16:2; Nu 7:89). *atonement cover.* Fitting exactly over the top of the ark of the covenant, it was a slab of pure gold on which the blood of the sin offering was sprinkled by the high priest on the Day of Atonement (Lev 16:14–15).
9:7 *only once a year.* On the Day of Atonement (*Yom Kippur*), the tenth day of the seventh month (Lev 16:29,34). For a description of its ritual, see Lev 16 and notes. *sins ... committed in ignorance.* See 5:2 and note.
9:8 *Holy Spirit.* See 3:7 and note. *as long as the first tabernacle was still functioning.* As long as the Mosaic system with its imperfect priesthood and sacrifice remained in effect (8:7–8,13).
9:9 *an illustration for the present time.* The Mosaic tabernacle and its temple replacement, though superseded, still provided instruction through their typical (symbolic) significance and were reminders that returning to the old order was useless, since it could not deal effectively with sin. *gifts and sacrifices.* See 5:1 and note. See model above.
9:10 *the new order.* The new covenant era, with its new priesthood, new sanctuary and new sacrifice, all introduced by Christ (see Introduction: Theme), is superior to the old covenant era.
9:11 *not a part of this creation.* It was not an earthly tabernacle but the heavenly sanctuary of God's presence (v. 24; 8:2).
9:12 *blood of goats and calves.* See note on Lev 17:11. *he entered ... once for all.* Not repeatedly, year after year, as did the Levitical high priests. Christ's sacrifice was perfect, because it was completely effective and did not need to be repeated. After he had obtained eternal redemption, Christ ascended into the true heavenly sanctuary.
9:13 *blood of goats and bulls.* As on the Day of Atonement. *ashes of a heifer.* As prescribed in Nu 19 for those who became ceremonially unclean as a result of contact with a corpse. *outwardly clean.* Such sprinkling, since it was only external, could not cleanse a person from sin.

unclean sanctify them so that they are
outwardly clean. 14How much more, then,
will the blood of Christ, who through the
eternal Spirit[e] offered himself[f] unblemished to God, cleanse our consciences[g]
from acts that lead to death,[a][h] so that we
may serve the living God![i]
15For this reason Christ is the mediator[j]
of a new covenant,[k] that those who are
called[l] may receive the promised[m] eternal
inheritance[n] — now that he has died as a
ransom to set them free from the sins committed under the first covenant.[o]
16In the case of a will,[b] it is necessary
to prove the death of the one who made
it, 17because a will is in force only when
somebody has died; it never takes effect
while the one who made it is living. 18This
is why even the first covenant was not put
into effect without blood.[p] 19When Moses
had proclaimed[q] every command of the
law to all the people, he took the blood of
calves,[r] together with water, scarlet wool
and branches of hyssop, and sprinkled the
scroll and all the people.[s] 20He said, "This
is the blood of the covenant, which God
has commanded you to keep."[c][t] 21In the
same way, he sprinkled with the blood
both the tabernacle and everything used in
its ceremonies. 22In fact, the law requires
that nearly everything be cleansed with
blood,[u] and without the shedding of blood
there is no forgiveness.[v]
23It was necessary, then, for the copies[w]
of the heavenly things to be purified with
these sacrifices, but the heavenly things
themselves with better sacrifices than
these. 24For Christ did not enter a sanctuary made with human hands that was only
a copy of the true one;[x] he entered heav-
en itself,[y] now to appear for us in God's
presence.[z] 25Nor did he enter heaven to
offer himself again and again, the way the
high priest enters the Most Holy Place[a] every year with blood that is not his own.[b]
26Otherwise Christ would have had to suffer many times since the creation of the
world.[c] But he has appeared[d] once for all[e]
at the culmination of the ages to do away
with sin by the sacrifice of himself.[f] 27Just
as people are destined to die once,[g] and after that to face judgment,[h] 28so Christ was
sacrificed once[i] to take away the sins of
many; and he will appear a second time,[j]
not to bear sin,[k] but to bring salvation[l] to
those who are waiting for him.[m]

Christ's Sacrifice Once for All

10 The law is only a shadow[n] of the
good things[o] that are coming — not
the realities themselves.[p] For this reason it
can never, by the same sacrifices repeated endlessly year after year, make perfect[q]
those who draw near to worship.[r] 2Other-
wise, would they not have stopped being
offered? For the worshipers would have
been cleansed once for all, and would no
longer have felt guilty for their sins.[s] 3But
those sacrifices are an annual reminder
of sins.[t] 4It is impossible for the blood of
bulls and goats[u] to take away sins.[v]

9:14 [e] 1Pe 3:18 [f] S Eph 5:2 [g] Ps 51:2; 65:3; Jer 33:8; Zec 13:1; S Titus 2:14; Heb 10:2, 22 [h] Heb 6:1 [i] S Mt 16:16 **9:15** [j] S Gal 3:20 [k] S Lk 22:20 [l] S Ro 8:28; S 11:29 [m] Heb 6:15; 10:36 [n] S Ac 20:32 [o] Heb 7:22 **9:18** [p] Ex 24:6-8 **9:19** [q] Heb 1:1 [r] ver 12 [s] Ex 24:6-8 **9:20** [t] Ex 24:8; S Mt 26:28 **9:22** [u] Ex 29:21; Lev 8:15 [v] Lev 17:11 **9:23** [w] Heb 8:5 **9:24** [x] Heb 8:2 [y] ver 12; S Heb 4:14 [z] S Ro 8:34 **9:25** [a] Heb 10:19 [b] ver 7,8 **9:26** [c] Heb 4:3 [d] 1Jn 3:5 [e] ver 12, 28; S Heb 7:27 [f] ver 12 **9:27** [g] Ge 3:19 [h] 2Co 5:10 **9:28** [i] ver 12, 26; S Heb 7:27 [j] S Mt 16:27 [k] 1Pe 2:24 [l] Heb 5:9 [m] S 1Co 1:7 **10:1** [n] Col 2:17; Heb 8:5 [o] Heb 9:11 [p] Heb 9:23 [q] ver 4, 11; S Heb 7:19 [r] S Heb 7:19 **10:2** [s] Heb 9:9 **10:3** [t] Lev 16:34; Heb 9:7 **10:4** [u] Heb 9:12, 13 [v] ver 1, 11

[a] 14 Or *from useless rituals* [b] 16 Same Greek word as *covenant*; also in verse 17 [c] 20 Exodus 24:8

9:14 *through the eternal Spirit.* An unusual expression that is much debated but probably refers to the Holy Spirit, who empowered Jesus to fulfill his mission (see Mt 3:16 and note). *offered himself.* He was the one who offered the sacrifice, and he was the sacrifice itself. *unblemished.* See Lev 22:19 – 21; 1Pe 1:18 – 19 and note on 1:19. *cleanse our consciences.* Remove sin's defilement from the very core of our beings. *acts that lead to death.* See 6:1 and note.

9:15 *mediator.* See 8:6 and note. *new covenant.* See 7:22; 8:6,13. *the promised eternal inheritance.* Specified in Jer 31:31 – 34 (see note on 8:8 – 12). On the basis of Christ's atoning death, this inheritance has become real for those who are called by God (cf. Ro 8:28). *as a ransom.* See Mk 10:45 and note.

9:16 *will.* Translates the same Greek word as that for "covenant" (v. 15), but here and in v. 17 used in the sense of a last will and testament. (Verse 18 returns to the concept of covenant.) Beneficiaries have no claim on the benefits assigned to them in a will until the testator dies (v. 17). Since Christ's death has been duly attested, "the promised eternal inheritance" (v. 15) is available to his beneficiaries.

9:18 – 20 For the ceremony referred to here, see Ex 24:4 – 8.

9:18 *without blood.* Without death — the death of the calves from which Moses took blood to seal the old covenant.

9:21 See, e.g., Lev 8:10,19,30.

9:22 See note on Lev 17:11.

9:23 *copies of the heavenly things.* See 8:5. Whereas it was necessary for the earthly sanctuary to be purified with animal sacrifices, it was necessary for the heavenly sanctuary to be purified with the better sacrifice of Christ himself.

9:24 *now to appear for us in God's presence.* See 7:25; 1Jn 2:1 and notes. Christ also "has appeared" (v. 26), and "he will appear" (v. 28).

9:26 *culmination of the ages.* His coming has ushered in the great Messianic era, toward which all history has moved (see notes on 1:1 – 2).

9:28 *appear a second time.* See, e.g., Mt 24:3 – 21; 25:31 – 46; Jn 14:3; 1Co 1:7; 15:23; 1Th 2:19; 4:13 – 18; 2Th 1:7; Titus 2:13; 2Pe 3:4; Rev 3:11; 19:11 – 16. *to bring salvation.* The consummation of the salvation purchased for us on the cross (see, e.g., Ro 8:29 – 30; Php 3:20 – 21; 1Jn 3:2). *waiting for him.* As the Israelites on the Day of Atonement waited for the high priest to reappear after ministering in the Most Holy Place, bringing assurance that their sins had been atoned for (cf. 2Ti 4:8; Titus 2:13).

10:1 – 10 An exposition of Ps 40:6 – 8 (see notes there).

10:1 *The law.* Together with the Levitical priesthood to which it was closely linked under the Mosaic system (see note on 7:11). *only a shadow.* The sacrifices prescribed by the law prefigured Christ's ultimate sacrifice. Thus they were repeated year after year, the very repetition bearing testimony that the perfect, sin-removing sacrifice had not yet been offered. *never . . . make perfect.* See v. 14 and note.

10:4 *impossible for the blood of bulls and goats to take away*

5 Therefore, when Christ came into the
world,[w] he said:

"Sacrifice and offering you did not
desire,
but a body you prepared for me;[x]
6 with burnt offerings and sin offerings
you were not pleased.
7 Then I said, 'Here I am—it is written
about me in the scroll[y]—
I have come to do your will, my
God.' "[az]

8 First he said, "Sacrifices and offerings,
burnt offerings and sin offerings you did
not desire, nor were you pleased with
them"[a]—though they were offered in
accordance with the law. 9 Then he said,
"Here I am, I have come to do your will."[b]
He sets aside the first to establish the second. 10 And by that will, we have been
made holy[c] through the sacrifice of the
body[d] of Jesus Christ once for all.[e]
11 Day after day every priest stands and
performs his religious duties; again and
again he offers the same sacrifices,[f] which
can never take away sins.[g] 12 But when this
priest had offered for all time one sacrifice
for sins,[h] he sat down at the right hand of
God,[i] 13 and since that time he waits for his
enemies to be made his footstool.[j] 14 For by
one sacrifice he has made perfect[k] forever
those who are being made holy.[l]

10:5 [w]Heb 1:6 [x]Heb 2:14; 1Pe 2:24
10:7 [y]Ezr 6:2; Jer 36:2 [z]Ps 40:6-8; S Mt 26:39
10:8 [a]ver 5,6; S Mk 12:33
10:9 [b]ver 7
10:10 [c]ver 14; S Eph 5:26 [d]Heb 2:14; 1Pe 2:24 [e]S Heb 7:27
10:11 [f]Heb 5:1 [g]ver 1,4
10:12 [h]Heb 5:1 [i]S Mk 16:19
10:13 [j]Jos 10:24; Heb 1:13
10:14 [k]ver 1 [l]ver 10; S Eph 5:26
10:15 [m]S Heb 3:7
10:16 [n]Jer 31:33; Heb 8:10
10:17 [o]Jer 31:34; Heb 8:12
10:19 [p]S Eph 3:12 [q]Lev 16:2; Eph 2:18; Heb 9:8,12,25
10:20 [r]Heb 9:8 [s]Heb 6:19; 9:3
10:21 [t]S Heb 2:17 [u]S Heb 3:6
10:22 [v]ver 1; S Heb 7:19 [w]Eph 3:12 [x]Eze 36:25; Heb 9:14; 12:24; 1Pe 1:2

15 The Holy Spirit also testifies[m] to us
about this. First he says:

16 "This is the covenant I will make with
them
after that time, says the Lord.
I will put my laws in their hearts,
and I will write them on their
minds."[bn]

17 Then he adds:

"Their sins and lawless acts
I will remember no more."[co]

18 And where these have been forgiven,
sacrifice for sin is no longer necessary.

A Call to Persevere in Faith

19 Therefore, brothers and sisters, since
we have confidence[p] to enter the Most
Holy Place[q] by the blood of Jesus, 20 by a
new and living way[r] opened for us through
the curtain,[s] that is, his body, 21 and since
we have a great priest[t] over the house of
God,[u] 22 let us draw near to God[v] with a sincere heart and with the full assurance that
faith brings,[w] having our hearts sprinkled
to cleanse us from a guilty conscience[x]
and having our bodies washed with pure

[a] *7* Psalm 40:6-8 (see Septuagint) [b] *16* Jer. 31:33 [c] *17* Jer. 31:34

sins. An animal cannot be an adequate substitute for a human being.

10:5–6 The different Greek terms used for Levitical sacrifices represent four of the five types of offerings prescribed by the Mosaic law (Lev 1–7), namely, fellowship, grain, burnt and sin (see chart, p. 164).

10:5 *when Christ came into the world, he said.* The words of this psalm of David (40:6–8) express Christ's obedient submission to the Father in coming to earth. The Mosaic sacrifices are replaced by submissive obedience to the will of God (v. 7).

10:6 *you were not pleased.* See 1Sa 15:22; Ps 40:6 and notes.

10:7 *to do your will.* The will of the Father was the Son's consuming concern (see Lk 22:42; Jn 4:34 and note).

10:9 *He sets aside the first to establish the second.* His perfect sacrifice, offered in complete submission to God's will, supersedes and therefore replaces all previous sacrifices as the means by which sinners are made holy.

10:10,14 *made holy.* Cleansed from all sin (forgiven and purified) and consecrated to God's service (see note on 1Co 1:2).

10:10 *once for all.* Contrast v. 1 (see note there; see also v. 12 and 7:27 and note).

10:11–12 A contrast between standing and sitting. The Levitical priest always stood, because his work was never finished (see 7:27 and note).

10:12 *for all time.* See 7:27 and note. *sat down at the right hand of God.* See note on vv. 11–12; see also 1:13 and note.

10:13 Having offered, as priest, the all-sufficient sacrifice, Jesus now sits enthroned as king, looking forward to the ultimate triumph over all that opposes his rule (see 1:3 and note; cf. Rev 5:6–14 and note on 5:6; cf. also Rev 7:10,17; 11:15; 19:11–21; 20:4).

10:14 *made perfect.* The one "made perfect" (5:9; see 7:28 and note; see also 2:10) has "made" sinners "perfect" in regard to God's will for their holiness.

10:15 *Holy Spirit.* See 3:7 and note.

10:16–18 The two quotations included here are from Jer 31:31–34 (already cited in 8:8–12). The new covenant guarantees that sins will be completely forgiven (v. 17), with the result that no additional sacrifice for sins is needed (v. 18).

10:19 *confidence to enter the Most Holy Place.* See vv. 13–14 and notes.

10:20 *the curtain, that is, his body.* Having sacrificed himself in his body on the cross, Jesus, our high priest, entered the Most Holy Place (see 6:19 and note; cf. 9:11 and note), and he made sinners "perfect" in holiness (see v. 14 and note) so that they too may enter through the curtain—his sacrificed and resurrected body being for us the "new and living way" (cf. Mt 27:51; Mk 15:38 and notes).

10:22–25 Five exhortations spring from Jesus' provision for our reconciliation to his Father: (1) "Let us draw near to God." (2) "Let us hold unswervingly to . . . hope." (3) "Let us consider how we may spur one another on." (4) "Not giving up meeting together." (5) "Encouraging one another." For the triad of faith, hope and love in vv. 22–24, see note on 1Th 1:3.

10:22 Four conditions are given for drawing "near to God": (1) *a sincere heart.* Undivided allegiance in the inner being. (2) *full assurance that faith brings.* Faith that knows no hesitation in trusting in and following Christ. (3) *hearts sprinkled . . . from a guilty conscience.* Total freedom from a sense of guilt, a freedom based on the once-for-all sacrifice of Christ. (4) *bodies washed with pure water.* Very likely both "hearts sprinkled" and "bodies washed" allude to Christian baptism (cf. Mt 28:19) and the cleansing from sin through the sacrificial death of Christ that it signifies (see Ro 6:3–11

water.[y] 23 Let us hold unswervingly to the
hope[z] we profess,[a] for he who promised
is faithful.[b] 24 And let us consider how we
may spur one another on toward love and
good deeds,[c] 25 not giving up meeting together,[d] as some are in the habit of doing,
but encouraging one another[e]—and all
the more as you see the Day approaching.[f]
26 If we deliberately keep on sinning[g] after we have received the knowledge of the
truth,[h] no sacrifice for sins is left, 27 but
only a fearful expectation of judgment
and of raging fire[i] that will consume the
enemies of God. 28 Anyone who rejected
the law of Moses died without mercy on
the testimony of two or three witnesses.[j]
29 How much more severely do you think
someone deserves to be punished who
has trampled the Son of God[k] underfoot,[l]
who has treated as an unholy thing the
blood of the covenant[m] that sanctified
them,[n] and who has insulted the Spirit[o] of
grace?[p] 30 For we know him who said, "It is
mine to avenge; I will repay,"[aq] and again,
"The Lord will judge his people."[br] 31 It is
a dreadful thing[s] to fall into the hands[t] of
the living God.[u]
32 Remember those earlier days after
you had received the light,[v] when you endured in a great conflict full of suffering.[w]
33 Sometimes you were publicly exposed to
insult and persecution;[x] at other times you
stood side by side with those who were so
treated.[y] 34 You suffered along with those
in prison[z] and joyfully accepted the confiscation of your property, because you knew
that you yourselves had better and lasting
possessions.[a] 35 So do not throw away your
confidence;[b] it will be richly rewarded.
36 You need to persevere[c] so that when
you have done the will of God, you will
receive what he has promised.[d] 37 For,

"In just a little while,
he who is coming[e] will come
and will not delay."[cf]

38 And,

"But my righteous[d] one will live by
faith.[g]
And I take no pleasure
in the one who shrinks back."[eh]

39 But we do not belong to those who
shrink back and are destroyed, but to
those who have faith and are saved.

Faith in Action

11 Now faith is confidence in what
we hope for[i] and assurance about
what we do not see.[j] 2 This is what the ancients were commended for.[k]
3 By faith we understand that the universe was formed at God's command,[l] so
that what is seen was not made out of
what was visible.
4 By faith Abel brought God a better offering than Cain did. By faith he was commended[m] as righteous, when God spoke
well of his offerings.[n] And by faith Abel
still speaks, even though he is dead.[o]
5 By faith Enoch was taken from this life,
so that he did not experience death: "He

[a] *30* Deut. 32:35 [b] *30* Deut. 32:36; Psalm 135:14 [c] *37* Isaiah 26:20; Hab. 2:3 [d] *38* Some early manuscripts *But the righteous* [e] *38* Hab. 2:4 (see Septuagint)

10:22 [y]S Ac 22:16 **10:23** [z]S Heb 3:6 [a]S Heb 3:1 [b]S 1Co 1:9 **10:24** [c]S Titus 2:14 **10:25** [d]Ac 2:42 [e]Heb 3:13 [f]S 1Co 3:13 **10:26** [g]Ex 21:14; Nu 15:30; Heb 5:2; 6:4-8; 2Pe 2:20 [h]S 1Ti 2:4 **10:27** [i]Isa 26:11; 2Th 1:7; Heb 9:27; 12:29 **10:28** [j]Dt 17:6, 7; S Mt 18:16; Heb 2:2 **10:29** [k]S Mt 4:3 [l]Heb 6:6 [m]S Mt 26:28 [n]1Co 6:11; Rev 1:5 [o]Eph 4:30; Heb 6:4 [p]Heb 2:3; 12:25 **10:30** [q]Dt 32:35; Ro 12:19 [r]Dt 32:36; Ps 135:14 **10:31** [s]S 2Co 5:11 [t]Isa 19:16 [u]S Mt 16:16 **10:32** [v]Heb 6:4 [w]Php 1:29, 30 **10:33** [x]1Co 4:9 [y]Php 4:14; 1Th 2:14 **10:34** [z]Heb 13:3 [a]Heb 11:16; 1Pe 1:4, 5 **10:35** [b]S Eph 3:12 **10:36** [c]Ro 5:3; Heb 12:1; Jas 1:3, 4, 12; 5:11; 2Pe 1:6

[d]Heb 6:15; 9:15 **10:37** [e]Mt 11:3 [f]Rev 22:20 **10:38** [g]Ro 1:17; Gal 3:11 [h]Hab 2:3, 4 **11:1** [i]S Heb 3:6 [j]S 2Co 4:18 **11:2** [k]ver 4, 39 **11:3** [l]Ge 1; Jn 1:3; Heb 1:2; 2Pe 3:5 **11:4** [m]ver 2, 39 [n]Ge 4:4; 1Jn 3:12 [o]Heb 12:24

---

and notes). For OT background, see Eze 36:25 and note; see also Lev 14:9; 15:13; 16:4,24,26; Nu 19:19; cf. Zec 13:1.
10:23 *hope we profess.* See 3:6; 6:18–19 and notes. *he who promised is faithful.* Cf. 2Ti 2:13.
10:25 *not giving up meeting together.* The Greek word translated "giving up" speaks of desertion and abandonment (see Mt 27:46; 2Co 4:9; 2Ti 4:10,16). *the Day.* Of the Lord's return (see 1Th 5:2,4; 2Th 1:10; 2:2; 2Pe 3:10).
10:26–31 The fourth warning (see note on 2:1–4). This warning is especially to persons ("some," v. 25) deserting the Christian assembly. See 6:4–8, where the same spiritual condition is discussed (see also notes there).
10:26 *deliberately keep on sinning.* Committing the sin of apostasy (see v. 29; see also note on 5:2). The OT background is Nu 15:27–31. *no sacrifice for sins is left.* To reject Christ's sacrifice for sins is to reject the only sacrifice; there is no other.
10:27 *judgment and ... raging fire.* See 12:29; 2Th 1:6–9 and notes. For fire as the instrument of divine judgment, see La 1:13 and note.
10:28 See Dt 17:6 and note.
10:29 *blood of the covenant.* See 9:20 and note on 9:18; 13:20; see also Mt 26:28; Mk 14:24 and note.
10:31 See 12:29.
10:32—12:3 An exposition of Hab 2:3–4.
10:32 *those earlier days.* Presumably following their first enthusiastic response to the gospel, when they had unflinchingly suffered loss and persecution and were deeply concerned for each other.
10:34 *better and lasting possessions.* Such as salvation in Christ and future reward (see 11:10,16,35; 13:14 and notes).
10:38 *my righteous one will live by faith.* See note on Hab 2:4.
10:39 *shrink back and are destroyed.* The opposite of "have faith and are saved." The author is confident that those to whom he is writing are, for the most part, among the saved (see 6:9 and note).
11:1—12:3 Encouragements to persevere in faith.
11:2 *the ancients.* Heroes of faith in the pre-Christian era, such as those listed in this chapter. *were commended for.* Repeated in v. 39, thus framing the chapter with a key thematic emphasis.
11:4 See Ge 4:2–5. *commended as righteous.* The chief reason for the acceptance of Abel's sacrifice was that he offered it "by faith." It is implied that Cain's sacrifice was rejected because he offered it without faith, as a mere formality (see note on Ge 4:3–4; see also 1Jn 3:12).
11:5 *Enoch.* See Ge 5:18–24. *taken him away.* To God's presence (see note on Ge 5:24; cf. Ps 49:15; 73:24).

could not be found, because God had taken him away."[a][p] For before he was taken, he was commended as one who pleased God. 6 And without faith it is impossible to please God, because anyone who comes to him[q] must believe that he exists and that he rewards those who earnestly seek him.

7 By faith Noah, when warned about things not yet seen,[r] in holy fear built an ark[s] to save his family.[t] By his faith he condemned the world and became heir of the righteousness that is in keeping with faith.[u]

8 By faith Abraham, when called to go to a place he would later receive as his inheritance,[v] obeyed and went,[w] even though he did not know where he was going. 9 By faith he made his home in the promised land[x] like a stranger in a foreign country; he lived in tents,[y] as did Isaac and Jacob, who were heirs with him of the same promise.[z] 10 For he was looking forward to the city[a] with foundations,[b] whose architect and builder is God.[c] 11 And by faith even Sarah, who was past childbearing age,[d] was enabled to bear children[e] because she[b] considered him faithful[f] who had made the promise. 12 And so from this one man, and he as good as dead,[g] came descendants as numerous as the stars in the sky and as countless as the sand on the seashore.[h]

13 All these people were still living by faith when they died. They did not receive the things promised;[i] they only saw them and welcomed them from a distance,[j] admitting that they were foreigners and strangers on earth.[k] 14 People who say such things show that they are looking for a country of their own. 15 If they had been thinking of the country they had left, they would have had opportunity to return.[l] 16 Instead, they were longing for a better country—a heavenly one.[m] Therefore God is not ashamed[n] to be called their God,[o] for he has prepared a city[p] for them.

17 By faith Abraham, when God tested him, offered Isaac as a sacrifice.[q] He who had embraced the promises was about to sacrifice his one and only son, 18 even though God had said to him, "It is through Isaac that your offspring will be reckoned."[c][r] 19 Abraham reasoned that God could even raise the dead,[s] and so in a manner of speaking he did receive Isaac back from death.

20 By faith Isaac blessed Jacob and Esau in regard to their future.[t]

21 By faith Jacob, when he was dying, blessed each of Joseph's sons,[u] and worshiped as he leaned on the top of his staff.

22 By faith Joseph, when his end was near, spoke about the exodus of the Israelites from Egypt and gave instructions concerning the burial of his bones.[v]

23 By faith Moses' parents hid him for three months after he was born,[w] because they saw he was no ordinary child, and they were not afraid of the king's edict.[x]

24 By faith Moses, when he had grown up, refused to be known as the son of

11:5 [p]Ge 5:21-24 **11:6** [q]Heb 7:19 **11:7** [r]S ver 1 [s]Ge 6:13-22 [t]1Pe 3:20 [u]Ge 6:9; Eze 14:14,20; S Ro 9:30 **11:8** [v]Ge 12:7 [w]Ge 12:1-4; Ac 7:2-4 **11:9** [x]Ac 7:5 [y]Ge 12:8; 18:1, 9 [z]Heb 6:17 **11:10** [a]Heb 12:22; 13:14 [b]Rev 21:2,14 [c]ver 16 **11:11** [d]Ge 17:17-19; 18:11-14 [e]Ge 21:2 [f]S 1Co 1:9 **11:12** [g]Ro 4:19 [h]Ge 22:17 **11:13** [i]ver 39 [j]S Mt 13:17 [k]Ge 23:4; Lev 25:23; Php 3:20; 1Pe 1:17; 2:11 **11:15** [l]Ge 24:6-8 **11:16** [m]2Ti 4:18 [n]Mk 8:38 [o]Ge 26:24; 28:13; Ex 3:6, 15 [p]ver 10; Heb 13:14 **11:17** [q]Ge 22:1-10; Jas 2:21 **11:18** [r]Ge 21:12; Ro 9:7 **11:19** [s]Ro 4:21; S Jn 5:21 **11:20** [t]Ge 27:27-29, 39,40

[a] 5 Gen. 5:24 [b] 11 Or *By faith Abraham, even though he was too old to have children—and Sarah herself was not able to conceive—was enabled to become a father because he* [c] 18 Gen. 21:12

11:21 [u]Ge 48:1,8-22 **11:22** [v]Ge 50:24,25; Ex 13:19; Jos 24:32 **11:23** [w]Ex 2:2 [x]Ex 1:16,22

11:6 *without faith it is impossible to please God.* That Enoch pleased God is proof of his faith. *believe that he exists.* Faith must have an object, and the proper object of genuine faith is God. *who earnestly seek him.* Cf. Jer 29:13.

11:7 *Noah.* See Ge 5:28—9:29. *By his faith he condemned.* When the flood came, God's word was proved to be true, Noah's faith was vindicated, and the world's unbelief was judged. *righteousness that is in keeping with faith.* Noah expressed complete trust in God and his word, even when it related to "things not yet seen" (see v. 1; cf. vv. 26–27; Jn 20:29 and note), namely, the coming flood. Thus Noah also fitted the description of God's righteous ones who live by faith (10:38).

11:8 *Abraham.* Presented in the NT as the outstanding example of those who live "by faith" and as the "father of all who believe" (Ro 4:11; see Ro 4:12,16; Gal 3:7,9,29). *called.* See Ge 12:1–3. His faith expressed itself in obedience (see note on Ge 12:4). *a place he would later receive.* Canaan.

11:10 *city with foundations.* Speaks of permanence, in contrast to the tents in which the patriarch lived (v. 9). This city is "the heavenly Jerusalem" (12:22), "the city that is to come" (13:14), "the new Jerusalem" (Rev 21:2; see 21:2–4,9–27). *builder.* See v. 16; cf. Eph 2:19–22; 1Pe 2:4–5 and notes; cf. also Ps 147:2 and note on Isa 62:5.

11:11 *Sarah ... was past childbearing age.* See Ge 11:30; 18:11–12 and notes.

11:12 *as good as dead.* Because he was 100 years old (see Ge 21:5; Ro 4:19). *stars in the sky ... sand on the seashore.* See Ge 13:16 and note; 15:5; 22:17; 26:4; 1Ki 4:20 and note.

11:13 *saw them and welcomed them from a distance.* By faith they saw—dimly—the realities to which the promises pointed and were sure that what they hoped for would ultimately be theirs (see v. 1). *foreigners and strangers on earth.* As were the patriarchs in Canaan (see Ge 17:8; 23:4; 28:4). Their true home was the future city of God (see vv. 10,16).

11:14 *country of their own.* A country in which they would no longer be "foreigners and strangers" (v. 13). "Country" and "city" (v. 16) were virtually interchangeable since a country was viewed as an extension of its royal city.

11:16 *prepared a city for them.* See v. 10 and note.

11:17 See Ge 22. *his one and only son.* See Ge 22:2,12,16 and notes.

11:19 Cf. Ge 22:13 and note.

11:20 See Ge 27:27–40.

11:21 See 48:9–20. *worshiped ... staff.* See Ge 47:31 and note.

11:22 See Ge 50:24–25. Jacob (v. 21) and Joseph are additional examples of those whose faith is no less strong at death than in life (v. 13).

11:23 See Ex 2:2–3; Ac 7:20–44. *Moses' parents.* See Ex 6:20; Nu 26:58–59. *no ordinary child.* See note on Ex 2:2. *were not afraid.* At least to the extent that they were ready to defy the king's edict. *king's edict.* To kill all Israelite males at birth (Ex 1:16,22).

11:24 *son of Pharaoh's daughter.* See Ex 2:5,10,15 and notes.

Pharaoh's daughter.[y] 25 He chose to be
mistreated[z] along with the people of God
rather than to enjoy the fleeting pleasures
of sin. 26 He regarded disgrace[a] for the
sake of Christ[b] as of greater value than the
treasures of Egypt, because he was looking ahead to his reward.[c] 27 By faith he
left Egypt,[d] not fearing the king's anger;
he persevered because he saw him who is
invisible. 28 By faith he kept the Passover
and the application of blood, so that the
destroyer[e] of the firstborn would not touch
the firstborn of Israel.[f]

29 By faith the people passed through
the Red Sea as on dry land; but when
the Egyptians tried to do so, they were
drowned.[g]

30 By faith the walls of Jericho fell, after
the army had marched around them for
seven days.[h]

31 By faith the prostitute Rahab, because
she welcomed the spies, was not killed
with those who were disobedient.[ai]

32 And what more shall I say? I do not
have time to tell about Gideon,[j] Barak,[k]
Samson[l] and Jephthah,[m] about David[n] and
Samuel[o] and the prophets, 33 who through
faith conquered kingdoms,[p] administered
justice, and gained what was promised;
who shut the mouths of lions,[q] 34 quenched
the fury of the flames,[r] and escaped the
edge of the sword;[s] whose weakness was
turned to strength;[t] and who became powerful in battle and routed foreign armies.[u]
35 Women received back their dead, raised
to life again.[v] There were others who were
tortured, refusing to be released so that
they might gain an even better resurrection.
36 Some faced jeers and flogging,[w] and even
chains and imprisonment.[x] 37 They were put
to death by stoning;[by] they were sawed in
two; they were killed by the sword.[z] They
went about in sheepskins and goatskins,[a]
destitute, persecuted and mistreated—
38 the world was not worthy of them. They
wandered in deserts and mountains, living
in caves[b] and in holes in the ground.

39 These were all commended[c] for their

11:24 [y] Ex 2:10, 11
11:25 [z] ver 37
11:26 [a] Heb 13:13 [b] Lk 14:33 [c] Heb 10:35
11:27 [d] Ex 12:50, 51
11:28 [e] 1Co 10:10 [f] Ex 12:21-23
11:29 [g] Ex 14:21-31
11:30 [h] Jos 6:12-20
11:31 [i] Jos 2:1, 9-14; 6:22-25; Jas 2:25
11:32 [j] Jdg 6-8 [k] Jdg 4-5 [l] Jdg 13-16 [m] Jdg 11-12 [n] 1Sa 16:1, 13 [o] 1Sa 1:20
11:33 [p] 2Sa 8:1-3 [q] Da 6:22
11:34 [r] Da 3:19-27 [s] Ex 18:4 [t] 2Ki 20:7 [u] Jdg 15:8
11:35 [v] 1Ki 17:22, 23; 2Ki 4:36, 37
11:36 [w] Jer 20:2; 37:15 [x] Ge 39:20

[a] 31 Or *unbelieving* [b] 37 Some early manuscripts *stoning; they were put to the test;*

11:37 [y] 2Ch 24:21 [z] 1Ki 19:10; Jer 26:23 [a] 2Ki 1:8 **11:38** [b] 1Ki 18:4; 19:9 **11:39** [c] ver 2, 4

11:25 *pleasures of sin.* The luxury and prestige of Egypt's royal palace.

11:26 *for the sake of Christ.* Although Moses' understanding of the details of Israel's promised future was extremely limited, he chose to be associated with the people through whom that future was to be realized. The author of Hebrews here concretizes that future in the person of the Messiah he is proclaiming as the one through whom God has guaranteed the promised future. *treasures of Egypt.* The priceless treasures of King Tutankhamun's tomb alone included several thousand pounds of pure gold.

11:27 *By faith he left Egypt.* Probably referring to his flight to Midian when he was 40 years old (see Ex 2:11–15 and note; Ac 7:23–29). *not fearing the king's anger.* Exodus indicates that Moses was afraid (Ex 2:14) but does not expressly say of whom (but see note on Ac 7:29). And it tells us that he fled from the pharaoh when the pharaoh tried to kill him (Ex 2:15) but does not expressly say that he fled out of fear. The author of Hebrews capitalizes on these features of the account to highlight the fact that, in his fleeing from the pharaoh, Moses was sustained by his trust in God that the liberation of Israel would come and that he would have some part in it. *he persevered.* For 40 years in Midian (Ac 7:30). *saw him who is invisible.* See vv. 1,6; see also Ro 1:20; Col 1:15 and note; 1Ti 1:17.

11:28 See Ex 12:1–30.

11:29 See Ex 14–15. The third and final 40-year period of Moses' life was spent leading the Israelites through the wilderness. At the age of 120 years he died in Moab (Dt 34:1–7).

11:30–31 See Jos 2; 6.

11:30 *Jericho.* The first obstacle to Israel's conquest of the promised land under Joshua's leadership was captured by faith without a battle.

11:31 *By faith.* See Jos 6:9–11. *prostitute.* A designation of this Canaanite's way of life within Canaanite society. *welcomed the spies.* See Jas 2:25.

11:32–38 There were many more heroes of faith before the coming of Christ, and much more could be written about them. Only a small sampling is given, representing all types of men and women of faith. The great quality they had in common was that of overcoming "through faith" (v. 33).

11:32 *to tell.* Translates the masculine form of a Greek verb, indicating that the author of Hebrews was a man (see Introduction: Author). *Gideon, Barak, Samson and Jephthah.* See Jdg 4–8; 11–16; 1Sa 12:11 and NIV text notes. *Samuel and the prophets.* For Samuel being counted as the first among the prophets, see Ac 3:24; 13:20; cf. Ps 99:6; Jer 15:1 and notes.

11:33 *conquered kingdoms.* See, e.g., David's conquests (2Sa 5:6–25; 8:1–14; 10:1–19; 12:26–31). *administered justice.* See, e.g., Samuel (1Sa 12:3–5); David (2Sa 8:15); Solomon (1Ki 3:9,12,16–28). *gained what was promised.* May refer to Israel's circumstances of rest in the promised land to which Solomon refers in 1Ki 5:4 (see note there); see also Jos 23:14; 24:8–13; 2Ch 20:30 (see note there). *shut the mouths of lions.* See, e.g., Daniel in the lions' den (Da 6).

11:34 *quenched the fury of the flames.* See, e.g., Daniel's friends, Shadrach, Meshach and Abednego, in the "blazing furnace" (Da 3:6,11,15,17,20–21,23,26; see note on 3:17). *escaped the ... sword.* See, e.g., David (1Sa 17:45–49); Elijah (2Ki 1); Elisha (2Ki 6:31); Jeremiah (Jer 26:7–24). *weakness was turned to strength.* See, e.g., Samson (Jdg 16:21–30); Hannah (1Sa 1); Jeremiah (Jer 1:6–10).

11:35 *Women received back their dead.* Cf. the widow of Zarephath (1Ki 17:17–24) and the Shunammite woman (2Ki 4:8–36). *were tortured, refusing to be released so that they might gain an even better resurrection.* Strongly reminiscent of the heroic Maccabean Jewish patriots of the second century BC (in the Apocrypha, see 2 Maccabees 7).

11:36 *jeers and flogging.* See, e.g., Jeremiah (Jer 20:2,7–8). *imprisonment.* See, e.g., Jeremiah (Jer 37:15–16).

11:37 *They were put to death by stoning.* See, e.g., Zechariah, the son of Jehoiada the priest, who was stoned to death for declaring the truth (2Ch 24:21). *sawed in two.* Perhaps refers to Isaiah, who, according to tradition, met this kind of death under wicked King Manasseh (see Introduction to Isaiah: Author).

11:39 *all commended for their faith.* See v. 2 and note. They

faith, yet none of them received what had
been promised,[d] [40]since God had planned
something better for us so that only together with us[e] would they be made perfect.[f]

12 Therefore, since we are surrounded
by such a great cloud of witness-
es, let us throw off everything that hinders
and the sin that so easily entangles. And
let us run[g] with perseverance[h] the race
marked out for us, [2]fixing our eyes on
Jesus,[i] the pioneer[j] and perfecter of faith.
For the joy set before him he endured the
cross,[k] scorning its shame,[l] and sat down
at the right hand of the throne of God.[m]
[3]Consider him who endured such opposition from sinners, so that you will not
grow weary[n] and lose heart.

God Disciplines His Children

[4]In your struggle against sin, you have
not yet resisted to the point of shedding
your blood.[o] [5]And have you completely
forgotten this word of encouragement that
addresses you as a father addresses his
son? It says,

"My son, do not make light of the
Lord's discipline,
and do not lose heart[p] when he
rebukes you,
[6]because the Lord disciplines the one he
loves,[q]
and he chastens everyone he accepts
as his son."[a][r]

11:39 [d]ver 13; Heb 10:36
11:40 [e]Rev 6:11 [f]S Heb 2:10
12:1 [g]S 1Co 9:24 [h]S Heb 10:36
12:2 [i]Ps 25:15 [j]Heb 2:10 [k]Php 2:8, 9; Heb 2:9 [l]Heb 13:13 [m]S Mk 16:19
12:3 [n]Gal 6:9; Rev 2:3
12:4 [o]Heb 10:32-34; 13:13
12:5 [p]ver 3
12:6 [q]Ps 94:12; 119:75; Rev 3:19 [r]Pr 3:11,12
12:7 [s]Dt 8:5; 2Sa 7:14; Pr 13:24
12:8 [t]1Pe 5:9
12:9 [u]Nu 16:22; 27:16; Rev 22:6 [v]Isa 38:16
12:10 [w]S 2Pe 1:4
12:11 [x]Isa 32:17; Jas 3:17,18
12:12 [y]Isa 35:3
12:13 [z]Pr 4:26 [a]Gal 6:1
12:14 [b]S Ro 14:19 [c]Ro 6:22 [d]S Mt 5:8
12:15 [e]Gal 5:4; Heb 3:12; 4:1 [f]Dt 29:18
12:16 [g]S 1Co 6:18

[7]Endure hardship as discipline; God is
treating you as his children.[s] For what children are not disciplined by their father?
[8]If you are not disciplined—and everyone
undergoes discipline[t]—then you are not
legitimate, not true sons and daughters at
all. [9]Moreover, we have all had human fathers who disciplined us and we respected
them for it. How much more should we
submit to the Father of spirits[u] and live![v]
[10]They disciplined us for a little while as
they thought best; but God disciplines us
for our good, in order that we may share
in his holiness.[w] [11]No discipline seems
pleasant at the time, but painful. Later
on, however, it produces a harvest of righteousness and peace[x] for those who have
been trained by it.
[12]Therefore, strengthen your feeble arms
and weak knees.[y] [13]"Make level paths for
your feet,"[b][z] so that the lame may not be
disabled, but rather healed.[a]

Warning and Encouragement

[14]Make every effort to live in peace with
everyone[b] and to be holy;[c] without holiness no one will see the Lord.[d] [15]See to
it that no one falls short of the grace of
God[e] and that no bitter root[f] grows up to
cause trouble and defile many. [16]See that
no one is sexually immoral,[g] or is godless
like Esau, who for a single meal sold his

[a] *5,6* Prov. 3:11,12 (see Septuagint) [b] *13* Prov. 4:26

---

were commended by the Holy Spirit in the Scriptural accounts (see 3:7 and note).

11:40 *God had planned something better.* The fulfillment for them, as for us, is in Christ, who is "the resurrection and the life" (Jn 11:25–26). *only together with us would they be made perfect.* All persons of faith who had gone before focused their faith on God and his promises. The fulfillment of God's promises to them has now come in Jesus Christ, and their redemption too is now complete in him.

12:1 *surrounded by such a great cloud of witnesses.* The imagery suggests an athletic contest in a great amphitheater. The witnesses are the heroes of the past who have just been mentioned (ch. 11). They are not spectators but inspiring examples. The Greek word translated "witnesses" is the origin of the English word "martyr" and means "testifiers, witnesses." They bear testimony to the power of faith and to God's faithfulness. *run with perseverance.* See Ac 20:24; 1Co 9:24–26; Gal 2:2; 5:7; Php 2:16; 2Ti 4:7. The Christian life is pictured as a long-distance race rather than a short sprint.

12:2 *pioneer and perfecter of faith.* That is, the beginner (cf. note on 2:10) and completer of faith—the One who went ahead of all believers in their faith and led on to its definitive goal, hence the perfect embodiment of faith and the supreme model for faith. *joy set before him.* His glorification at the Father's "right hand" (see note on 1:2–3, item 7; cf. Isa 53:10–12 and notes). *endured the cross.* See Php 2:8 and note. *scorning its shame.* As with Christ, the humiliation of our present suffering for the gospel's sake is far outweighed by the prospect of future glory (see Mt 5:10–12; Ro 8:18; 2Co 4:17; 1Pe 4:13; 5:1,10).

12:3 *Consider him.* He suffered infinitely more than any of his disciples is asked to suffer—a great encouragement for us when we are weary and tempted to become discouraged. *not grow weary.* See Gal 6:9; Rev 2:3; cf. Isa 40:28–31.

12:4–13 Encouragement to persevere in the face of hardship: an exposition of Pr 3:11–12.

12:5 *the Lord's discipline.* Suffering and persecution should be seen as corrective and instructive training for our spiritual development as God's children.

12:6 *chastens.* The Greek for this verb means "to whip." God chastens us in order to correct our faults.

12:7 *treating you as his children.* God's discipline is evidence that we are his children. Far from being a reason for despair, discipline is a basis for encouragement and perseverance (v. 10).

12:11 *produces a harvest of righteousness.* When received submissively (see v. 9), discipline is wholesome and beneficial.

12:12 See Isa 35:3.

12:13 *Make level paths.* A call for upright conduct that will help, rather than hinder, the spiritual and moral welfare of others, especially the "lame" who waver in the Christian faith.

12:14–17 Exhortation to holy living (see 4:1; 6:4–8; Gal 5:4 and note).

12:14 *without holiness no one will see the Lord.* Cf. 1Pe 1:15–16 and note on 1:16; see also 1Co 1:2 and note; cf. 1Jn 3:2–3.

12:15 *falls short of the grace of God.* Or "fails to lay hold of" God's grace (see 6:4–8 and notes). *bitter root.* Pride, animosity, rivalry or anything else harmful to others.

12:16 *godless like Esau.* See Ge 25:29–34. He had no appreciation for true values (cf. Php 3:19). He "despised his birthright" (Ge 25:34) by valuing food for his stomach more highly than his birthright.

inheritance rights as the oldest son.[h] 17Afterward, as you know, when he wanted to inherit this blessing, he was rejected. Even though he sought the blessing with tears,[i] he could not change what he had done.

The Mountain of Fear and the Mountain of Joy

18You have not come to a mountain that can be touched and that is burning with fire; to darkness, gloom and storm;[j] 19to a trumpet blast[k] or to such a voice speaking words[l] that those who heard it begged that no further word be spoken to them,[m] 20because they could not bear what was commanded: "If even an animal touches the mountain, it must be stoned to death."[an] 21The sight was so terrifying that Moses said, "I am trembling with fear."[bo]

22But you have come to Mount Zion,[p] to the city[q] of the living God,[r] the heavenly Jerusalem.[s] You have come to thousands upon thousands of angels in joyful assembly, 23to the church of the firstborn,[t] whose names are written in heaven.[u] You have come to God, the Judge of all,[v] to the spirits of the righteous made perfect,[w] 24to Jesus the mediator[x] of a new covenant, and to the sprinkled blood[y] that speaks a better word than the blood of Abel.[z]

25See to it that you do not refuse[a] him who speaks.[b] If they did not escape when they refused him who warned[c] them on earth, how much less will we, if we turn away from him who warns us from heaven?[d] 26At that time his voice shook the earth,[e] but now he has promised, "Once more I will shake not only the earth but also the heavens."[cf] 27The words "once more" indicate the removing of what can be shaken[g]—that is, created things—so that what cannot be shaken may remain.

28Therefore, since we are receiving a kingdom that cannot be shaken,[h] let us be thankful, and so worship God acceptably with reverence and awe,[i] 29for our "God is a consuming fire."[dj]

Concluding Exhortations

13 Keep on loving one another as brothers and sisters.[k] 2Do not forget to show hospitality to strangers,[l] for by so doing some people have shown hospitality to angels without knowing it.[m] 3Continue to remember those in prison[n] as if you were together with them in pris-

12:16 [h] Ge 25:29-34 **12:17** [i] Ge 27:30-40 **12:18** [j] Ex 19:12-22; 20:18; Dt 4:11 **12:19** [k] Ex 20:18 [l] Dt 4:12 [m] Ex 20:19; Dt 5:5,25; 18:16 **12:20** [n] Ex 19:12,13 **12:21** [o] Dt 9:19 **12:22** [p] Isa 24:23; 60:14; Rev 14:1 [q] Heb 11:10; 13:14 [r] S Mt 16:16 [s] S Gal 4:26 **12:23** [t] Ex 4:22 [u] S Rev 20:12 [v] Ge 18:25; Ps 94:2 [w] Php 3:12 **12:24** [x] S Gal 3:20 [y] Heb 9:19; 10:22; 1Pe 1:2 [z] Ge 4:10; Heb 11:4 **12:25** [a] Heb 3:12 [b] S Heb 1:1 [c] Heb 8:5; 11:7 [d] Dt 18:19; Heb 2:2,3; 10:29 **12:26** [e] Ex 19:18 [f] Hag 2:6 **12:27** [g] Isa 34:4; 54:10; 1Co 7:31; Heb 1:11, 12; 2Pe 3:10; 1Jn 2:17 **12:28** [h] Ps 15:5; Da 2:44 [i] Mal 2:5; 4:2; Heb 13:15 **12:29** [j] Ex 24:17; Dt 4:24; 9:3; Ps 97:3; Isa 33:14; S 2Th 1:7 **13:1** [k] S Ro 12:10 **13:2** [l] Job 31:32; Mt 25:35; S Ro 12:13 [m] Ge 18:1-33; 19:1-3 **13:3** [n] Mt 25:36; Col 4:18; Heb 10:34

[a] *20* Exodus 19:12,13 [b] *21* See Deut. 9:19. [c] *26* Haggai 2:6 [d] *29* Deut. 4:24

12:17 *blessing.* Of the firstborn. The readers may have contemplated compromising their faith in order to gain relief from persecution. But to trade their spiritual birthright for temporary ease in this world would deprive them of Christ's blessing. *he was rejected.* Because he only regretted his loss and did not repent of his sin (Ge 27). His sorrow was not "godly sorrow" that "brings repentance that leads to salvation," but "worldly sorrow" that "brings death" (2Co 7:10). *with tears.* Not tears of repentance. See Ge 27:34–38. *could not change what he had done.* Cf. 6:4–6 and note.

12:18–29 Crowning motivation and warning (the fifth; see note on 2:1–4—including an exposition of Ex 19:10–23 in vv. 18–24).

12:18–21 These verses recall the awesome occasion when the law was given at Mount Sinai (see Ex 19:10–25; Dt 4:11–12; 5:22–26).

12:22 *Mount Zion.* Not the literal Mount Zion (Jerusalem, or its southeast portion), but the heavenly city of God and those who dwell there with him (see 11:10,13–16; 13:14; Php 3:20). The circumstances under which the old covenant was given (vv. 18–21) and the features of the new covenant (vv. 22–24) point out the utter contrast between the two covenants and lay the foundation for one more warning and exhortation to those still thinking of returning to Judaism. *thousands upon thousands of angels.* See Rev 5:11–12.

12:23 *church of the firstborn.* Believers in general who make up the church: (1) Reference cannot be to the angels since these have just been mentioned (v. 22). (2) "Firstborn" cannot refer to Christ (though he is called firstborn, 1:6; Ro 8:29; Col 1:15–18; Rev 1:5), since here the Greek word is plural. (3) The fact that the names of these "firstborn" are recorded in heaven reminds us of the redeemed (see Rev 3:5; 13:8; 17:8; 20:12; 21:27). The designation of them as "firstborn" suggests their privileged position as heirs together with Christ, the supreme firstborn and "heir of all things" (Heb 1:2). *God, the Judge of all.* See 4:13; Ro 14:10–12; 1Co 3:10–15; 2Co 5:10; Rev 20:11–15. *spirits of the righteous made perfect.* For the most part, these were pre-Christian believers such as Abel (11:4) and Noah (11:7). They are referred to as "spirits" because they are waiting for the resurrection and as "righteous" because God credited their faith to them as righteousness, as he did to Abraham (see Ge 15:6; Ro 4:3 and notes). Actual justification was not accomplished, however, until Christ made it complete by his death on the cross (see 11:40; Ro 3:24–26 and note; 4:23–25).

12:24 *mediator of a new covenant.* See 8:6 and note. *better word than the blood of Abel.* Abel's blood cried out for justice and retribution (see Ge 4:10 and note), whereas the blood of Jesus shed on the cross speaks of forgiveness and reconciliation (see 9:12 and note; 10:19; Col 1:20; 1Jn 1:7).

12:25–29 The fifth warning (see note on 2:1–4).

12:25 *him who speaks.* God. *warned them on earth.* At Sinai. *him who warns us from heaven.* Christ, who is both from and in heaven (1:1–3; 4:14; 6:20; 7:26; 9:24). Since we have greater revelation, we have greater responsibility and therefore greater danger (see 2:2–3 and notes).

12:26 *shook the earth.* See Ex 19:18; cf. Jdg 5:4–5; Ps 68:7–8.

12:27 *once more.* During the great end-time upheavals associated with the second advent of Christ (see Mt 24:29; Mk 13:24–25 and note; Lk 21:11,25; Ac 2:20). *what cannot be shaken.* The "kingdom" (v. 28).

12:28 *worship God acceptably.* See Jn 4:19–24; Ro 12:1.

12:29 *"God is a consuming fire."* See NIV text note; cf. 10:27 and note; Ex 24:17; Dt 9:3; 1Co 3:10 and note.

13:2 *show hospitality to strangers.* See Mt 25:35. *strangers.* Members of the Christian community not personally known. *shown hospitality to angels without knowing it.* As did Abraham (Ge 18), Gideon (Jdg 6) and Manoah (Jdg 13).

13:3 *remember those in prison…and those who are mistreated.*

on, and those who are mistreated as if you
yourselves were suffering.
4 Marriage should be honored by all,[o]
and the marriage bed kept pure, for God
will judge the adulterer and all the sexually immoral.[p] 5 Keep your lives free from the
love of money[q] and be content with what
you have,[r] because God has said,

"Never will I leave you;
never will I forsake you."[a][s]

6 So we say with confidence,

"The Lord is my helper; I will not be
afraid.
What can mere mortals do to me?"[b][t]

7 Remember your leaders,[u] who spoke
the word of God[v] to you. Consider the outcome of their way of life and imitate[w] their
faith. 8 Jesus Christ is the same yesterday
and today and forever.[x]
9 Do not be carried away by all kinds of
strange teachings.[y] It is good for our hearts
to be strengthened[z] by grace, not by eating
ceremonial foods,[a] which is of no benefit
to those who do so.[b] 10 We have an altar
from which those who minister at the tabernacle[c] have no right to eat.[d]
11 The high priest carries the blood of animals into the Most Holy Place as a sin offering,[e] but the bodies are burned outside
the camp.[f] 12 And so Jesus also suffered
outside the city gate[g] to make the people
holy[h] through his own blood.[i] 13 Let us,
then, go to him[j] outside the camp, bearing
the disgrace he bore.[k] 14 For here we do not
have an enduring city,[l] but we are looking
for the city that is to come.[m]
15 Through Jesus, therefore, let us
continually offer to God a sacrifice[n] of
praise—the fruit of lips[o] that openly profess his name. 16 And do not forget to do
good and to share with others,[p] for with
such sacrifices[q] God is pleased.
17 Have confidence in your leaders[r] and
submit to their authority, because they
keep watch over you[s] as those who must
give an account. Do this so that their work
will be a joy, not a burden, for that would
be of no benefit to you.
18 Pray for us.[t] We are sure that we have
a clear conscience[u] and desire to live honorably in every way. 19 I particularly urge
you to pray so that I may be restored to
you soon.[v]

Benediction and Final Greetings

20 Now may the God of peace,[w] who
through the blood of the eternal covenant[x]

[a] 5 Deut. 31:6 [b] 6 Psalm 118:6,7

13:4 [o] Mal 2:15; 1Co 7:38; 1Ti 4:3 [p] Dt 22:22; 1Co 6:9; Rev 22:15 **13:5** [q] S 1Ti 3:3 [r] Php 4:11; 1Ti 6:6,8 [s] Dt 31:6,8; Jos 1:5 **13:6** [t] Ps 118:6,7 **13:7** [u] ver 17, 24; 1Co 16:16 [v] S Heb 4:12 [w] Heb 6:12 **13:8** [x] Ps 102:27; Heb 1:12 **13:9** [y] Eph 4:14 [z] Col 2:7 [a] Col 2:16 [b] Heb 9:10 **13:10** [c] Heb 8:5 [d] 1Co 9:13; 10:18 **13:11** [e] Lev 16:15 [f] Ex 29:14; Lev 4:12,21; 9:11; 16:27 **13:12** [g] Jn 19:17 [h] S Eph 5:26 [i] S Ro 3:25 **13:13** [j] Lk 9:23 [k] Heb 11:26 **13:14** [l] Heb 12:27 [m] Php 3:20; Heb 11:10, 27; 12:22 **13:15** [n] 1Pe 2:5 [o] Isa 57:19; Hos 14:2 **13:16** [p] Ro 12:13 [q] Php 4:18 **13:17** [r] ver 7, 24 [s] Isa 62:6; Ac 20:28 **13:18** [t] S 1Th 5:25 [u] S Ac 23:1 **13:19** [v] Phm 22 **3:20** [w] S Ro 15:33 [x] Ge 9:16; 17:7,13,19; Isa 55:3; 61:8; Eze 37:26; S Mt 26:28

Especially fellow believers (see 10:32–34; Mt 25:36; 1Co 12:26).

13:4 *Marriage should be honored.* See 1Co 6:13–18; 7:1–15; Eph 5:26–31; 1Ti 4:3. *marriage bed kept pure.* See Ex 20:14 and note. *adulterer and ... sexually immoral.* See 1Co 6:9.

13:5 *love of money.* See Lk 12:15,21; Php 4:10–13; 1Ti 6:6–10,17–19. *be content.* See Php 4:11–12; 1Ti 6:8.

13:7–17 A unit framed by the exhortation to "remember your [past] leaders ... and imitate their faith" and the exhortation to "have confidence in your [present] leaders and submit to their authority."

13:7 *leaders, who spoke the word of God.* See 2:3; 5:12. *Consider the outcome of their way of life.* Consider how they persevered in their faith and entered into the promised inheritance (see 6:12). *imitate their faith.* See 6:12; Eph 5:1; 1Th 1:6 and notes; cf. 1Co 4:16.

13:8 *Jesus Christ is the same.* A confession of the changelessness of Christ, no doubt related to the preceding verse. The substance of their former leaders' faith was the unchanging Christ. *yesterday.* Probably the days of Christ's life on earth, when the eyewitnesses observed him (2:3). *today.* The Christ whom the eyewitnesses saw was still the same, and what they had said about him was still true. *forever.* And it will always be true. To compromise his absolute supremacy by returning to the inferior Aaronic priesthood and sacrifices (see chs. 5–10) is to undermine the gospel.

13:9 *not by eating ceremonial foods.* As the legalistic Judaizers were teaching. The old Mosaic order was done away with at the cross and must not be revived.

13:10 *We have an altar.* Probably refers to the cross, which marked the end of the whole Aaronic priesthood and its replacement by the order of Melchizedek, of which Christ is the unique and only priest. *no right to eat.* The priests could not eat the sacrifice on the Day of Atonement, but we can partake of our sacrifice, so to speak—through spiritual reception of Christ by faith (see Jn 6:48–58). We have a higher privilege than the priests under the old covenant had.

13:11 *burned outside the camp.* See Lev 4:12 and note; 16:27.

13:12 *Jesus also suffered outside the city gate.* Christ's death outside Jerusalem represented the removal of sin, as had the removal of the bodies of sacrificial animals outside the camp of Israel.

13:13 *go to him outside the camp.* Calls for separation from Judaism to Christ. As he died in disgrace outside the city, so the readers should be willing to be disgraced by turning unequivocally from Judaism to Christ (cf. Ac 5:41).

13:14 *city that is to come.* See notes on 11:10,14,16.

13:15 *sacrifice of praise.* Cf. Ro 12:1. For the OT background, see notes on Lev 3:1; Ps 7:17; cf. Ps 51:17 and note.

13:16 *sacrifices.* See Php 4:18 and note.

13:17 *your leaders.* Their present leaders, as distinct from their first ones, now dead, mentioned in v. 7 (see note on vv. 7–17). *submit to their authority.* Dictatorial leadership is not condoned by this command (see 2Co 10:8 and note), but respect for authority, orderliness and discipline in the church are taught throughout the NT.

13:19 *restored to you soon.* The identity and whereabouts of the writer are not known to us, but "restored" suggests that somehow he had been delayed in visiting those to whom he was writing, perhaps by his current ministry. That he was not under arrest is clear from v. 23.

13:20,25 *peace ... Grace.* See note on Ro 1:7.

13:20–21 This benediction provides a fitting conclusion to the letter.

13:20 *God of peace.* A title for God used frequently in benedictions (see Ro 15:33; 16:20; Php 4:9; 1Th 5:23

brought back from the dead[y] our Lord
Jesus, that great Shepherd of the sheep,[z]
21 equip you with everything good for
doing his will,[a] and may he work in us[b]
what is pleasing to him,[c] through Jesus
Christ, to whom be glory for ever and ever.
Amen.[d]

22 Brothers and sisters, I urge you to bear
with my word of exhortation, for in fact I
have written to you quite briefly.[e]
23 I want you to know that our brother
Timothy[f] has been released. If he arrives
soon, I will come with him to see you.
24 Greet all your leaders[g] and all the
Lord's people. Those from Italy[h] send you
their greetings.
25 Grace be with you all.[i]

13:20 [y] S Ac 2:24 [z] S Jn 10:11
13:21 [a] 2Co 9:8 [b] S Php 2:13 [c] 1Jn 3:22 [d] S Ro 11:36
13:22 [e] 1Pe 5:12
13:23 [f] S Ac 16:1
13:24 [g] ver 7,17 [h] Ac 18:2
13:25 [i] S Col 4:18

---

and note). *blood of.* See 10:29 and note. *eternal covenant.* The new covenant (see note on 8:8–12). What Jeremiah designates as the new covenant in 31:31 he describes as everlasting in 32:40 (cf. Isa 55:3; 61:8 and notes). *great Shepherd.* See, e.g., Ps 23; Isa 40:11; Eze 34:11–16,23; 37:24; Jn 10:2–3,11,14,27; 1Pe 2:25; 5:4.

13:21 *everything good.* Such as faith, faithfulness, obedience and perseverance.

13:22–25 A postscript.

13:22 *Brothers and sisters.* See NIV text note on 2:11. *word of exhortation.* See Introduction: Literary Form. The main thrust of the letter is to go on in Christian maturity and not fall away from Christ. *quite briefly.* Compared to the lengthy treatise that would be necessary to explain adequately the superiority of Christ (see 11:32 and note on 11:32–38).

13:23 *Timothy.* See Introduction to 1 Timothy: Recipient.

13:24 *leaders.* Mentioned in v. 17. *Those from Italy.* From this brief greeting no firm conclusion can be drawn concerning the source or destination of this "letter." The writer may simply be passing on to his readers greetings from some Italian believers who are with him.

13:25 *with you.* Cf. note on 2Co 13:14.

THE GENERAL LETTERS

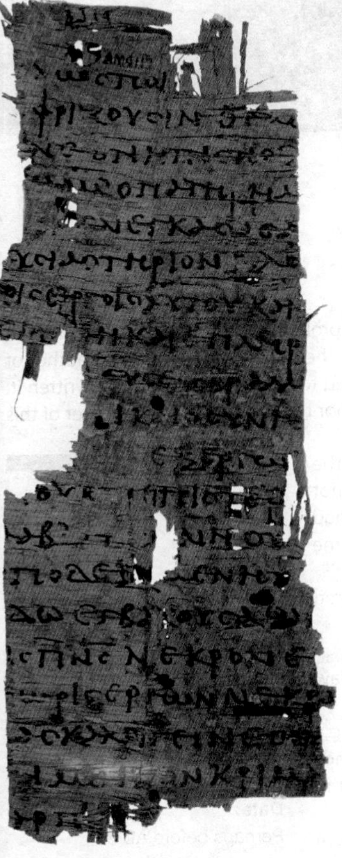

The seven letters following Hebrews — James; 1,2 Peter; 1,2,3 John; Jude — have often been designated as the General Letters. This term goes back to the early church historian Eusebius (c. AD 265 – 340), who in his *Ecclesiastical History* (2:23 – 25) first referred to these seven letters as the Catholic Letters, using the word "catholic" in the sense of "universal."

The letters so designated may be said to be, for the most part, addressed to general audiences rather than to specific persons or localized groups. The only exceptions are 2 and 3 John, which are written to individuals or a specific church. In contrast to these general letters, Paul addresses his letters to individual churches (such as Philippians), small groups of churches (such as Galatians) or individuals (such as Timothy or Titus).

As Eusebius noted long ago, one interesting fact connected with the General Letters is that most of them were at one time among the disputed books of the NT. James, 2 Peter, 2 John, 3 John and Jude were all questioned extensively before being admitted to the canon of Scripture.

Recto side of P.Oxy. IX 1171. This earliest manuscript containing the letter of James dates to the third century AD.

Princeton University Library

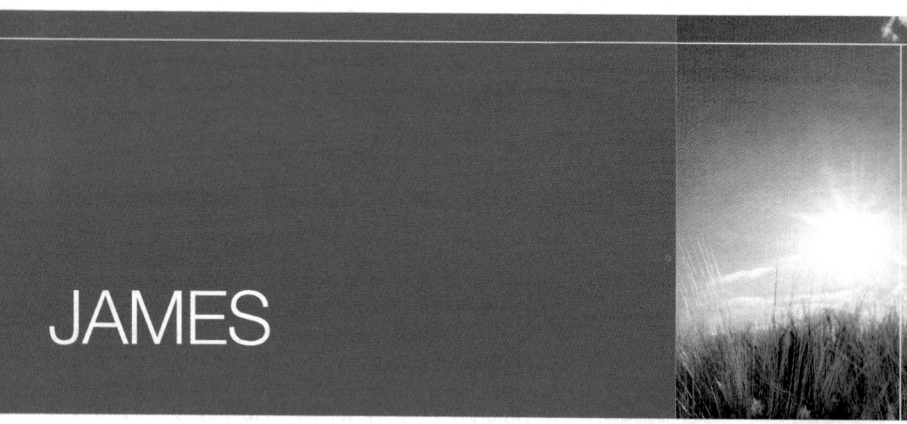

JAMES

INTRODUCTION

Author

The author identifies himself as James (1:1); he was probably the brother of Jesus and the leader of the Jerusalem council (Ac 15). Four men in the NT have this name. The author of this letter could not have been the apostle James, who died too early (AD 44) to have written it. The other two men named James had neither the stature nor the influence that the writer of this letter had.

James was one of several brothers of Jesus, probably the oldest since he heads the list in Mt 13:55. At first he did not believe in Jesus and even challenged him and misunderstood his mission (Jn 7:2–5). After Jesus' resurrection, James became very prominent in the Jerusalem church:

(1) James was one of the select individuals Christ appeared to after his resurrection (see 1Co 15:7 and note).

(2) Paul called him a "pillar" of the church (Gal 2:9).

(3) Paul, on his first postconversion visit to Jerusalem, saw James (Gal 1:19).

(4) Paul did the same on his last visit (Ac 21:18).

(5) When Peter was rescued from prison, he told his friends to tell James, presumably because James was a key leader in the church (Ac 12:17).

(6) James was a leader in the important council of Jerusalem (Ac 15:13).

(7) Jude could identify himself simply as "a brother of James" (Jude 1:1), so well known was James. James was martyred c. AD 62, an event recorded by the Jewish historian Josephus (*Antiquities*, 20.9.1).

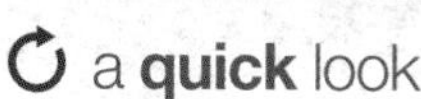

a quick look

Author:
James, a leader of the Jerusalem church

Audience:
Jewish Christians, perhaps Jerusalem believers scattered after Stephen's death

Date:
Perhaps before AD 50

Theme:
James emphasizes vital Christianity characterized by good deeds and faith that works.

Date

Some date the letter in the early 60s. There are indications, however, that it was written before AD 50:

(1) Its distinctively Jewish nature suggests that it was composed when the church was still predominantly Jewish.

Vineyard in Galilee. James uses common images such as grapevines to illustrate spiritual truths (3:12).

(2) It reflects a simple church order — officers of the church are called "elders" (5:14) and "teachers" (3:1).

(3) No reference is made to the controversy over Gentile circumcision.

(4) The Greek term *synagoge* ("synagogue" or "meeting") is used to designate the meeting or meeting place of the church (2:2).

If this early dating is correct, this letter is the earliest of all the NT writings — with the possible exception of Galatians (see Introduction to Galatians: Date and Destination).

Recipients

The recipients are identified explicitly only in 1:1: "the twelve tribes scattered among the nations." Some hold that this expression refers to Christians in general, but the term "twelve tribes" would more naturally apply to Jewish Christians. Furthermore, a Jewish audience would be more in keeping with the obviously Jewish nature of the letter (e.g., the use of the Hebrew title for God, *kyrios sabaoth*, "Lord Almighty," 5:4). That the recipients were Christians is clear from 2:1; 5:7 – 8. It has been plausibly suggested that these were believers from the early Jerusalem church who, after Stephen's death, were scattered as far as Phoenicia, Cyprus and Syrian Antioch (see Ac 8:1; 11:19

and notes). This would account for James's references to trials and oppression, his intimate knowledge of the readers and the authoritative nature of the letter. As leader of the Jerusalem church, James wrote as pastor to instruct and encourage his dispersed people in the face of their difficulties (see essay, p. 2087).

Theme

The central theme of James is "faith that works." The letter is concerned primarily with practical matters related to the Christian's walk (or lifestyle). How does faith work itself out in a Christian's life? "Faith without deeds is dead," James says (2:26). There is no such thing as true faith that does not express itself in a life of godliness. For the relationship between James and Paul on faith and works, see notes on 2:14–26 and 2:21.

Distinctive Characteristics

Characteristics that make the letter distinctive are: (1) its unmistakably Jewish nature; (2) its emphasis on vital Christianity, characterized by good deeds and a faith that works (genuine faith must and will be accompanied by a consistent lifestyle); (3) its simple organization; (4) its familiarity with

Rough waves on the Sea of Galilee. "The one who doubts is like a wave of the sea, blown and tossed by the wind" (Jas 1:6).

Todd Bolen/www.BiblePlaces.com

James writes as pastor to instruct and encourage his dispersed people in the face of their difficulties.

Jesus' teachings preserved in the Sermon on the Mount (compare 2:5 with Mt 5:3; 3:10 – 12 with Mt 7:15 – 20; 3:18 with Mt 5:9; 5:2 – 3 with Mt 6:19 – 20; 5:12 with Mt 5:33 – 37); (5) its similarity to OT wisdom writings such as Proverbs (see essay, p. 786); (6) its excellent Greek.

Outline

I. Greetings (1:1)
II. Trials and Temptations (1:2 – 18)
  A. The Testing of Faith (1:2 – 12)
  B. The Source of Temptation (1:13 – 18)
III. Listening and Doing (1:19 – 27)
IV. Favoritism Forbidden (2:1 – 13)
V. Faith and Deeds (2:14 – 26)
VI. Taming the Tongue (3:1 – 12)
VII. Two Kinds of Wisdom (3:13 – 18)
VIII. Warning against Worldliness (ch. 4)
  A. Quarrelsomeness (4:1 – 3)
  B. Spiritual Unfaithfulness (4:4)
  C. Pride (4:5 – 10)
  D. Slander (4:11 – 12)
  E. Boasting (4:13 – 17)
IX. Warning to Rich Oppressors (5:1 – 6)
X. Miscellaneous Exhortations (5:7 – 20)
  A. Concerning Patience in Suffering (5:7 – 11)
  B. Concerning Oaths (5:12)
  C. Concerning the Prayer of Faith (5:13 – 18)
  D. Concerning Those Who Wander from the Truth (5:19 – 20)

1 James,[a] a servant of God[b] and of the Lord Jesus Christ,

To the twelve tribes[c] scattered[d] among the nations:

Greetings.[e]

Trials and Temptations

2 Consider it pure joy, my brothers and sisters,[a] whenever you face trials of many kinds,[f] 3 because you know that the testing of your faith[g] produces perseverance.[h] 4 Let perseverance finish its work so that you may be mature[i] and complete, not lacking anything. 5 If any of you lacks wisdom, you should ask God,[j] who gives generously to all without finding fault, and it will be given to you.[k] 6 But when you ask, you must believe and not doubt,[l] because the one who doubts is like a wave of the sea, blown and tossed by the wind. 7 That person should not expect to receive anything from the Lord. 8 Such a person is double-minded[m] and unstable[n] in all they do.

9 Believers in humble circumstances ought to take pride in their high position.[o] 10 But the rich should take pride in their humiliation—since they will pass away like a wild flower.[p] 11 For the sun rises with scorching heat[q] and withers[r] the plant; its blossom falls and its beauty is destroyed.[s] In the same way, the rich will fade away even while they go about their business.

12 Blessed is the one who perseveres under trial[t] because, having stood the test, that person will receive the crown of life[u] that the Lord has promised to those who love him.[v]

13 When tempted, no one should say, "God is tempting me." For God cannot be tempted by evil, nor does he tempt anyone; 14 but each person is tempted when they are dragged away by their own[w] evil desire and enticed. 15 Then, after desire has conceived, it gives birth to sin;[x] and sin, when it is full-grown, gives birth to death.[y]

16 Don't be deceived,[z] my dear brothers and sisters.[a] 17 Every good and perfect gift is from above,[b] coming down from the Father of the heavenly lights,[c] who does not change[d] like shifting shadows. 18 He chose to give us birth[e] through the word of truth,[f] that we might be a kind of firstfruits[g] of all he created.

Listening and Doing

19 My dear brothers and sisters,[h] take note of this: Everyone should be quick to listen, slow to speak[i] and slow to become angry, 20 because human anger[j] does not

[a] *2* The Greek word for *brothers and sisters* (*adelphoi*) refers here to believers, both men and women, as part of God's family; also in verses 16 and 19; and in 2:1, 5, 14; 3:10, 12; 4:11; 5:7, 9, 10, 12, 19.

1:1 [a] S Ac 15:13 [b] Ro 1:1; Titus 1:1 [c] Ac 26:7 [d] Dt 32:26; Jn 7:35; 1Pe 1:1 [e] Ac 15:23 **1:2** [f] ver 12; S Mt 5:12; Heb 10:34; 12:11 **1:3** [g] 1Pe 1:7 [h] S Heb 10:36 **1:4** [i] S 1Co 2:6 **1:5** [j] 1Ki 3:9, 10; Pr 2:3-6 [k] Ps 51:6; Da 1:17; 2:21; S Mt 7:7 **1:6** [l] S Mt 21:21; Mk 11:24 **1:8** [m] Ps 119:113; Jas 4:8 [n] 2Pe 2:14; 3:16 **1:9** [o] S Mt 23:12 **1:10** [p] Job 14:2; Ps 103:15, 16; Isa 40:6, 7; 1Co 7:31; 1Pe 1:24 **1:11** [q] Mt 20:12 [r] Ps 102:4, 11 [s] Isa 40:6-8 **1:12** [t] ver 2; Ge 22:1; Jas 5:11; 1Pe 3:14 [u] S 1Co 9:25 [v] Ex 20:6; 1Co 2:9; 8:3; Jas 2:5 **1:14** [w] Pr 19:3 **1:15** [x] Ge 3:6; Job 15:35; Ps 7:14; Isa 59:4 [y] S Ro 6:23 **1:16** [z] S 1Co 6:9 [a] ver 19; Jas 2:5 **1:17** [b] Ps 85:12; Jn 3:27; Jas 3:15, 17 [c] Ge 1:16; Ps 136:7; Da 2:22; 1Jn 1:5 [d] Nu 23:19; Ps 102:27; Mal 3:6 **1:18** [e] S Jn 1:13 [f] S 2Ti 2:15 [g] Jer 2:3; Rev 14:4 **1:19** [h] ver 16; Jas 2:5 [i] Pr 10:19; Jas 3:3-12 **1:20** [j] S Mt 5:22

1:1 *James.* See Introduction: Author. *servant.* See note on Ro 1:1. *twelve tribes.* See Introduction: Recipients.

1:2–3 *trials ... testing ... produces perseverance.* This, together with similar language in v. 12, forms a frame around James's word about trials.

1:2 *joy.* See Mt 5:11–12; Ac 5:41; Ro 5:3 and note; Php 4:4 and note; 1Pe 1:6. *brothers and sisters.* See NIV text note. James addresses the readers as "brothers and sisters" 15 times in this short letter. He has many rebukes for them, but he chides them in brotherly love. *trials.* The same Greek root lies behind the word "trials" here and the word "tempted" in v. 13. In vv. 2–3 the emphasis is on difficulties that come from outside; in vv. 13–15 it is on inner moral trials, such as temptation to sin.

1:5 *wisdom.* Enables one to face trials with "pure joy" (v. 2). Wisdom is not just acquired information but practical insight with spiritual implications (see 3:13–18; Pr 1:2–4 and note on 1:2; 2:10–15; 4:5–9; 9:10–12).

1:6 *wave of the sea.* See Eph 4:14 and note; see also photo, p. 2090.

1:9–10 *Believers in humble circumstances ... the rich.* Christians who experience poverty are to take pride in their high position (v. 9) as believers (see 2:5). Wealthy believers, on the other hand, should take pride not in their possessions but in the fact that God has humbled them and given them a godly value system, so that they now realize how transitory life and wealth are (v. 10).

1:10 *pass away like a wild flower.* See Job 14:2; Ps 103:15; Isa 40:6–7; 1Pe 1:24; cf. Lk 12:15,20–21; 1Ti 6:8–10,17–19.

1:11 *will fade away.* Cf. 4:14 and note.

1:12 *Blessed.* See Jer 17:7–8; Mt 5:3–12; see also notes on Ps 1:1; Mt 5:3; Rev 1:3. *perseveres under trial.* See vv. 2–4 and note on vv. 2–3. *crown.* The Greek for this word was the usual term for the wreath placed on the head of a victorious athlete or military leader (see 1Co 9:25; 2Ti 4:8; 1Pe 5:4; Rev 2:10 and notes). *life.* Eternal life, as the future tense of the verb ("will receive") indicates.

1:13 *tempted.* In vv. 13–14 the verb refers to temptations that test one's moral strength to resist sin (see note on Mt 4:1). *God cannot be tempted.* Because God in his very nature is holy, there is nothing in him for sin to appeal to. *nor does he tempt anyone.* See note on Ge 22:1.

1:14 *dragged away ... and enticed.* Words commonly used to describe hunting methods, used here metaphorically of how evil desire operates (cf. 2Pe 2:14 and note). *evil desire.* A person's innate tendency to sin (cf. Jer 17:9).

1:15 The three stages—desire, sin, death—are seen in the temptations of Eve (Ge 3:6–22) and David (2Sa 11:2–17).

1:17 *Every good and perfect gift is from above.* See v. 5; 3:17. *Father of ... lights.* God is the Creator of the heavenly bodies, which give light to the earth, but, unlike them, he does not change.

1:18 *birth.* Not a reference to creation but to regeneration (see Jn 3:3,5,7 and notes). *word of truth.* The proclamation of the gospel (see 1Pe 1:23–25 and note on 1:23). *firstfruits.* See Lev 23:9–14 and chart, pp. 188–189. Just as the first sheaf of the harvest was an indication that the whole harvest would eventually follow, so the early Christians were an indication that a great number of people would eventually be born again (cf. 1Co 15:20 and note).

1:19 *Everyone should be ... slow to speak.* See v. 26.

produce the righteousness that God desires. 21 Therefore, get rid of[k] all moral filth and the evil that is so prevalent and humbly accept the word planted in you,[l] which can save you.

22 Do not merely listen to the word, and so deceive yourselves. Do what it says.[m] 23 Anyone who listens to the word but does not do what it says is like someone who looks at his face in a mirror 24 and, after looking at himself, goes away and immediately forgets what he looks like. 25 But whoever looks intently into the perfect law that gives freedom,[n] and continues in it—not forgetting what they have heard, but doing it—they will be blessed in what they do.[o]

26 Those who consider themselves religious and yet do not keep a tight rein on their tongues[p] deceive themselves, and their religion is worthless. 27 Religion that God our Father accepts as pure and faultless is this: to look after[q] orphans and widows[r] in their distress and to keep oneself from being polluted by the world.[s]

Favoritism Forbidden

2 My brothers and sisters, believers in our glorious[t] Lord Jesus Christ must not show favoritism.[u] 2 Suppose a man comes into your meeting wearing a gold ring and fine clothes, and a poor man in filthy old clothes also comes in. 3 If you show special attention to the man wearing fine clothes and say, "Here's a good seat for you," but say to the poor man, "You stand there" or "Sit on the floor by my feet," 4 have you not discriminated among yourselves and become judges[v] with evil thoughts?

5 Listen, my dear brothers and sisters:[w] Has not God chosen those who are poor in the eyes of the world[x] to be rich in faith[y] and to inherit the kingdom[z] he promised those who love him?[a] 6 But you have dishonored the poor.[b] Is it not the rich who are exploiting you? Are they not the ones who are dragging you into court?[c] 7 Are they not the ones who are blaspheming the noble name of him to whom you belong?

8 If you really keep the royal law found in Scripture, "Love your neighbor as yourself,"[a][d] you are doing right. 9 But if you show favoritism,[e] you sin and are convicted by the law as lawbreakers.[f] 10 For whoever keeps the whole law and yet stumbles[g] at just one point is guilty of breaking all of it.[h] 11 For he who said, "You shall not commit adultery,"[b][i] also said, "You shall not murder."[c][j] If you do not commit adultery but do commit murder, you have become a lawbreaker.

12 Speak and act as those who are going to be judged[k] by the law that gives freedom,[l] 13 because judgment without mercy will be shown to anyone who has not been merciful.[m] Mercy triumphs over judgment.

[a] *8* Lev. 19:18 [b] *11* Exodus 20:14; Deut. 5:18
[c] *11* Exodus 20:13; Deut. 5:17

1:21 [k] S Eph 4:22 [l] Eph 1:13 **1:22** [m] S Mt 7:21; Jas 2:14-20 **1:25** [n] Ps 19:7; Jn 8:32; Gal 2:4; Jas 2:12 [o] S Jn 13:17 **1:26** [p] Ps 34:13; 39:1; 141:3; Jas 3:2-12; 1Pe 3:10 **1:27** [q] Mt 25:36 [r] Dt 14:29; Job 31:16,17,21; Ps 146:9; Isa 1:17,23 [s] Ro 12:2; Jas 4:4; 2Pe 1:4; 2:20 **2:1** [t] Ac 7:2; 1Co 2:8 [u] ver 9; Dt 1:17; Lev 19:15; Pr 24:23; S Ac 10:34 **2:4** [v] S Jn 7:24 **2:5** [w] Jas 1:16,19 [x] Job 34:19; 1Co 1:26-28 [y] Lk 12:21; Rev 2:9 [z] S Mt 25:34 [a] S Jas 1:12 **2:6** [b] 1Co 11:22 [c] Ac 8:3; 16:19 **2:8** [d] Lev 19:18; S Mt 5:43 **2:9** [e] ver 1 [f] Dt 1:17 **2:10** [g] Jas 3:2 [h] Mt 5:19; Gal 3:10; 5:3 **2:11** [i] Ex 20:14; Dt 5:18 [j] Ex 20:13; Dt 5:17 **2:12** [k] S Mt 16:27 [l] S Jas 1:25 **2:13** [m] Mt 5:7; 9:13; 12:7; 18:32-35; Lk 6:37

1:21 *word.* Of God (cf. 1Pe 1:23). *save you.* Here eschatological (future) salvation is primarily in view (cf. Heb 1:14; 9:28 and note).

1:25 *perfect law.* The moral and ethical teaching of Christianity, which is based on the OT moral law, as embodied in the Ten Commandments (see Ps 19:7) but brought to completion (perfection) by Jesus Christ (see notes on Mt 5:17; Ro 10:4). *freedom.* In contrast to the sinner, who is a slave to sin (see Jn 8:34 and note), obeying the moral law gives Christians the joyous freedom to be what they were created for (see 2:12).

1:26–27 An example of a person not doing the word and of one doing it.

1:26 *religious.* Refers to the outward acts of religion: e.g., giving to the needy, fasting and public acts of praying and worshiping (see Mt 6:1–18 and note on 6:1). *keep a tight rein on their tongues.* See 3:1–12.

1:27 See Jer 22:16 and note. *orphans and widows.* See notes on Ex 22:21–27; Isa 1:17. *world.* Not the world of nature but the world of people in their rebellion against and alienation from God (see 1Jn 2:15 and note).

2:1 *believers … must not show favoritism.* God does not show favoritism (see note on Ac 10:34)—nor should believers (see vv. 5–13 and note; see also note on 1Ti 5:21). *glorious.* See Jn 1:14; Heb 1:3 and notes.

2:2 *meeting.* The Greek for this term is the origin of the English word "synagogue."

2:4 *judges with evil thoughts.* Cf. Lev 19:15.

2:5–13 James gives three arguments against showing favoritism to the rich: (1) The rich persecute the poor—the believers (vv. 5–7). (2) Favoritism violates the royal law of love and thus is sin (vv. 8–11). (3) Favoritism will be judged (vv. 12–13).

2:5 *Has not God chosen those who are poor … ?* Cf. Lk 6:20 and note on 6:20–23; 1Co 1:26–31. *kingdom.* The kingdom that is entered by the new birth (see note on 1:18) and that will be consummated in the future (Mt 25:34,46; see note on Mt 3:2).

2:8 *royal law.* The law of love (see Lev 19:18 and note) is called "royal" because it is the supreme law that is the source of all other laws governing human relationships. It is the summation of all such laws (see Mt 22:36–40; Ro 13:8–10 and notes on 13:8–9).

2:10 *guilty of breaking all.* The law is the expression of the character and will of God; therefore to violate one part of the law is to violate God's will and thus his whole law (cf. Mt 5:18–19; 23:23).

2:11 James may have chosen these two commandments because both violate the law of love to one's neighbor (v. 8).

2:12 *judged.* This judgment is not for determining eternal destiny, for James is speaking to believers (v. 1), whose destiny is already determined (see Jn 5:24 and note). Rather, it is for giving rewards to believers (see 1Co 3:12–15; 2Co 5:10; Rev 22:12 and notes). *law that gives freedom.* The royal law of love (v. 8).

2:13 *Mercy triumphs over judgment.* If people are merciful, God will be merciful on the day of judgment (see Pr 21:13; Mt 5:7; 6:14–15; 18:21–35).

Faith and Deeds

14 What good is it, my brothers and sisters, if someone claims to have faith but
has no deeds?[n] Can such faith save them?
15 Suppose a brother or a sister is without
clothes and daily food.[o] 16 If one of you
says to them, "Go in peace; keep warm
and well fed," but does nothing about
their physical needs, what good is it?[p] 17 In
the same way, faith by itself, if it is not accompanied by action, is dead.[q]
18 But someone will say, "You have faith;
I have deeds."
Show me your faith without deeds,[r] and
I will show you my faith[s] by my deeds.[t]
19 You believe that there is one God.[u] Good!
Even the demons believe that[v]—and
shudder.
20 You foolish person, do you want evidence that faith without deeds is useless[a]?[w] 21 Was not our father Abraham considered righteous for what he did when he
offered his son Isaac on the altar?[x] 22 You
see that his faith and his actions were
working together,[y] and his faith was made
complete by what he did.[z] 23 And the scripture was fulfilled that says, "Abraham believed God, and it was credited to him as
righteousness,"[b][a] and he was called God's
friend.[b] 24 You see that a person is considered righteous by what they do and not by
faith alone.
25 In the same way, was not even Rahab
the prostitute considered righteous for
what she did when she gave lodging to
the spies and sent them off in a different
direction?[c] 26 As the body without the spirit
is dead, so faith without deeds is dead.[d]

Taming the Tongue

3 Not many of you should become
teachers,[e] my fellow believers, because you know that we who teach will be
judged[f] more strictly.[g] 2 We all stumble[h] in
many ways. Anyone who is never at fault
in what they say[i] is perfect,[j] able to keep
their whole body in check.[k]
3 When we put bits into the mouths of
horses to make them obey us, we can turn
the whole animal.[l] 4 Or take ships as an example. Although they are so large and are
driven by strong winds, they are steered
by a very small rudder wherever the pilot wants to go. 5 Likewise, the tongue is a
small part of the body, but it makes great
boasts.[m] Consider what a great forest is set
on fire by a small spark. 6 The tongue also
is a fire,[n] a world of evil among the parts
of the body. It corrupts the whole body,[o]
sets the whole course of one's life on fire,
and is itself set on fire by hell.[p]
7 All kinds of animals, birds, reptiles and
sea creatures are being tamed and have
been tamed by mankind, 8 but no human
being can tame the tongue. It is a restless
evil, full of deadly poison.[q]
9 With the tongue we praise our Lord
and Father, and with it we curse human
beings, who have been made in God's

2:14 [n] Mt 7:26; Jas 1:22-25 **2:15** [o] Mt 25:35, 36 **2:16** [p] Lk 3:11; 1Jn 3:17, 18 **2:17** [q] ver 20, 26; Gal 5:6 **2:18** [r] Ro 3:28 [s] Heb 11 [t] Mt 7:16, 17; Jas 3:13 **2:19** [u] Dt 6:4; Mk 12:29; 1Co 8:4-6 [v] Mt 8:29; Lk 4:34 **2:20** [w] ver 17, 26 **2:21** [x] Ge 22:9, 12 **2:22** [y] Heb 11:17 [z] 1Th 1:3 **2:23** [a] Ge 15:6; S Ro 4:3 [b] 2Ch 20:7; Isa 41:8 **2:25** [c] S Heb 11:31 **2:26** [d] ver 17, 20 **3:1** [e] S Eph 4:11 [f] S Mt 7:1 [g] Ro 2:21 **3:2** [h] 1Ki 8:46; Ro 3:9-20; Jas 2:10; 1Jn 1:8 [i] Ps 39:1; Pr 10:19; 1Pe 3:10 [j] S Mt 12:37 [k] Jas 1:26 **3:3** [l] Ps 32:9 **3:5** [m] Ps 12:3, 4; 73:8, 9 **3:6** [n] Pr 16:27 [o] Mt 15:11, 18, 19 [p] S Mt 5:22 **3:8** [q] Ps 140:3; Ro 3:13

[a] *20* Some early manuscripts *dead* [b] *23* Gen. 15:6

2:14–26 In vv. 14–20,24,26 "faith" is not used in the sense of genuine, saving faith. Rather, it is demonic (v. 19), useless (v. 20) and dead (v. 26). It is a mere intellectual acceptance of certain truths without trust in Christ as Savior. James is also not saying that a person is saved by works and not by genuine faith. Rather, he is saying, to use Martin Luther's words, that people are justified (declared righteous before God) by faith alone, but not by a faith that is alone. Genuine faith will produce good deeds, but only faith in Christ saves (see note on v. 21). (For more information on justification, see note on Ro 3:24.)

2:15–16 This illustration of false faith is parallel to the illustration of false love found in 1Jn 3:17 (see note there). The latter passage calls for love in action; this one calls for faith in action. Cf. Pr 3:27–28.

2:18 *You have faith; I have deeds.* The false claim is that there are "faith" Christians and "deeds" Christians, i.e., that faith and deeds can exist independently of each other. *Show me your faith without deeds.* Irony; James denies the possibility of this.

2:19 *there is one God.* A declaration of monotheism that reflects the well-known Jewish creed called in Hebrew the *Shema*, "Hear" (Dt 6:4 [see notes on 6:4–9]; Mk 12:29 [see note there]).

2:21 Apart from its context, this verse might seem to contradict Paul's teaching that people are saved by faith and not by good deeds (see Ro 3:28 and note; Gal 2:15–16 and note on 2:16). But James means only that righteous action is evidence of genuine faith—not that it saves, for the verse (Ge 15:6; see note there) that he cites (v. 23) to substantiate his point says, "Abram believed the LORD, and he credited it [i.e., faith, not works] to him as righteousness." Furthermore, Abraham's act of faith recorded in Ge 15:6 occurred before he offered up Isaac, which was only a proof of the genuineness of his faith. As Paul wrote, "The only thing that counts is faith expressing itself through love" (Gal 5:6; see note there). Faith that saves produces good deeds (cf. Eph 2:10; Titus 3:8).

2:23 *God's friend.* This designation (see 2Ch 20:7 and note on Ge 18:17) further describes Abraham's relationship to God as one of complete acceptance (cf. Jn 15:13–15).

2:24 *not by faith alone.* Not by an intellectual assent to certain truths (see note on 2:14–26).

2:25 *Rahab the prostitute.* James does not approve Rahab's occupation. He merely commends her for her faith (see also Heb 11:31 and note), which she demonstrated by helping the spies (Jos 2).

3:1 *judged more strictly.* Because teachers have great influence, they will be held more accountable (cf. Mt 23:1–33; Lk 20:46–47; Heb 13:17).

3:2 *perfect.* Since the tongue is so difficult to control, those who control it perfectly gain control of themselves in all other areas of life as well.

3:6 *world of evil.* Like the world in its fallenness. *corrupts the whole body.* Because the tongue is the cause of so many sins (cf. Mk 7:20–23). *set on fire by hell.* A figurative and forceful way of saying that the source of the tongue's evil is the devil (see Jn 8:44 and note). *hell.* See notes on Mt 5:22; Lk 16:23.

3:9 *in God's likeness.* Since humans have been made "in God's

likeness.[r] 10 Out of the same mouth come
praise and cursing. My brothers and sisters, this should not be. 11 Can both fresh
water and salt water flow from the same
spring? 12 My brothers and sisters, can a
fig tree bear olives, or a grapevine bear
figs?[s] Neither can a salt spring produce
fresh water.

Two Kinds of Wisdom

13 Who is wise and understanding
among you? Let them show it[t] by their
good life, by deeds[u] done in the humility that comes from wisdom. 14 But if you
harbor bitter envy and selfish ambition[v]
in your hearts, do not boast about it or
deny the truth.[w] 15 Such "wisdom" does
not come down from heaven[x] but is earthly, unspiritual, demonic.[y] 16 For where you
have envy and selfish ambition,[z] there you
find disorder and every evil practice.
17 But the wisdom that comes from heav-
en[a] is first of all pure; then peace-loving,[b]
considerate, submissive, full of mercy[c] and
good fruit, impartial and sincere.[d] 18 Peacemakers[e] who sow in peace reap a harvest
of righteousness.[f]

Submit Yourselves to God

4 What causes fights and quarrels[g]
among you? Don't they come from
your desires that battle[h] within you? 2 You
desire but do not have, so you kill.[i] You
covet but you cannot get what you want,
so you quarrel and fight. You do not have
because you do not ask God. 3 When you
ask, you do not receive,[j] because you ask
with wrong motives,[k] that you may spend
what you get on your pleasures.

4 You adulterous[l] people,[a] don't you
know that friendship with the world[m]
means enmity against God?[n] Therefore,
anyone who chooses to be a friend of the
world becomes an enemy of God.[o] 5 Or
do you think Scripture says without reason that he jealously longs for the spirit
he has caused to dwell in us[b]?[p] 6 But he
gives us more grace. That is why Scripture says:

> "God opposes the proud
> but shows favor to the humble."[c][q]

7 Submit yourselves, then, to God. Resist the devil,[r] and he will flee from you.
8 Come near to God and he will come near
to you.[s] Wash your hands,[t] you sinners,
and purify your hearts,[u] you double-minded.[v] 9 Grieve, mourn and wail. Change
your laughter to mourning and your joy
to gloom.[w] 10 Humble yourselves before the
Lord, and he will lift you up.[x]
11 Brothers and sisters, do not slander
one another.[y] Anyone who speaks against
a brother or sister[d] or judges them[z] speaks
against the law[a] and judges it. When you
judge the law, you are not keeping it,[b] but
sitting in judgment on it. 12 There is only
one Lawgiver and Judge,[c] the one who is
able to save and destroy.[d] But you — who
are you to judge your neighbor?[e]

[a] 4 An allusion to covenant unfaithfulness; see Hosea 3:1. [b] 5 Or *that the spirit he caused to dwell in us envies intensely;* or *that the Spirit he caused to dwell in us longs jealously* [c] 6 Prov. 3:34 [d] 11 The Greek word for *brother or sister* (*adelphos*) refers here to a believer, whether man or woman, as part of God's family.

3:9 [r] Ge 1:26, 27; 1Co 11:7 **3:12** [s] Mt 7:16 **3:13** [t] Jas 2:18 [u] S 1Pe 2:12 **3:14** [v] ver 16; 2Co 12:20 [w] Jas 5:19 **3:15** [x] ver 17; Jas 1:17 [y] 1Ti 4:1 **3:16** [z] ver 14; Gal 5:20, 21 **3:17** [a] 1Co 2:6; Jas 1:17 [b] Heb 12:11 [c] Lk 6:36 [d] Ro 12:9 **3:18** [e] Mt 5:9; S Ro 14:19 [f] Pr 11:18; Isa 32:17; Hos 10:12; Php 1:11 **4:1** [g] Titus 3:9 [h] S Ro 7:23 **4:2** [i] Mt 5:21, 22; Jas 5:6; 1Jn 3:15 **4:3** [j] Ps 18:41; S Mt 7:7 [k] Ps 66:18; 1Jn 3:22; 5:14 **4:4** [l] Isa 54:5; Jer 3:20; Hos 2:2-5; 3:1; 9:1 [m] S Jas 1:27 [n] Ro 8:7; 1Jn 2:15 [o] Jn 15:19 **4:5** [p] 1Co 6:19 **4:6** [q] Pr 3:34; S Mt 23:12 **4:7** [r] Eph 4:27; 6:11; 1Pe 5:6-9 **4:8** [s] Ps 73:28; Zec 1:3; Mal 3:7; Heb 7:19 [t] Isa 1:16 [u] Ps 24:4; Jer 4:14 [v] Ps 119:113; Jas 1:8 **4:9** [w] Lk 6:25 **4:10** [x] ver 6; Job 5:11; 1Pe 5:6 **4:11** [y] Ro 1:30; 2Co 12:20; 1Pe 2:1 [z] S Mt 7:1 [a] Jas 2:8 [b] Jas 1:22 **4:12** [c] Isa 33:22; S Jas 5:9 [d] Mt 10:28 [e] S Mt 7:1

likeness" (see Ge 1:26–27 and notes), to curse a human being is to show contempt for God (see Ge 9:6 and note).

3:11–12 Only a renewed heart can produce pure speech.

3:13 *wisdom.* See note on 1:5.

3:15 *from heaven.* From God (see 1:5; 1Co 2:6–16; see also Da 4:26 and note).

3:16 *disorder.* Cf. "God is not a God of disorder but of peace" (1Co 14:33; see note there).

3:17 *impartial.* See 2:1–13; see also note on 1Ti 5:21.

3:18 *Peacemakers.* Contrast v. 16. Discord cannot produce conduct pleasing to God. Cf. Mt 5:9 and note.

4:2 *kill.* Some hold that this word is here used figuratively (cf. Mt 5:21–22) for "hate." Others hold that it should be understood straightforwardly to describe what can happen when covetous desire is sufficiently frustrated (see, e.g., Ahab's murder of Naboth, 1Ki 21:1–16; David's murder of Uriah, 2Sa 11).

4:4 *adulterous people.* Those who are spiritually unfaithful, who love the world rather than God. For spiritual adultery, see Ex 34:15 and note. *world.* See note on 1:27.

4:5 *Scripture.* The passage James had in mind is not known. *he jealously longs for the spirit he has caused to dwell in us.* God jealously longs for our faithfulness and love (see v. 4). In this case the Scripture referred to may be Ex 20:5 (see note there). Regarding the two alternative translations (see NIV text note), the opening words of the first ("the spirit he caused to dwell in us"), if correct, would allude to God's creation of Adam (see Ge 2:7 and note). Because of the fall (Ge 3), a person's spirit "envies intensely," but God's grace (v. 6) is able to overcome human envy. The second, if correct, refers to the Holy Spirit and makes him the subject. The Holy Spirit longs jealously for our full devotion.

4:6 See 1Pe 5:5, which also quotes Pr 3:34.

4:7–10 These verses contain ten commands, each of which is so stated in Greek that it calls for immediate action in rooting out the sinful attitude of pride.

4:7 *Resist the devil.* See Eph 6:10–20 and note; 1Pe 5:8–9.

4:8 *Wash your hands.* Before the OT priests ministered to God in the tabernacle, they had to wash their hands and feet at the bronze basin as a symbol of spiritual cleansing (Ex 30:17–21). For the imagery of "clean hands and a pure heart," see Ps 24:4 and note.

4:9 *Grieve, mourn and wail.* Repent.

4:10 See Mt 23:12; Lk 14:11 and note; 1Pe 5:6.

4:11 *speaks against a brother or sister … speaks against the law.* See note on 2:8; see also Ex 20:16 and note; Ps 15:3; 50:19–20; Pr 6:16,19 and note. To speak against a Christian brother or sister is to scorn the law of love.

Boasting About Tomorrow

13 Now listen,[f] you who say, "Today or tomorrow we will go to this or that city, spend a year there, carry on business and make money."[g] 14 Why, you do not even know what will happen tomorrow. What is your life? You are a mist that appears for a little while and then vanishes.[h] 15 Instead, you ought to say, "If it is the Lord's will,[i] we will live and do this or that." 16 As it is, you boast in your arrogant schemes. All such boasting is evil.[j] 17 If anyone, then, knows the good they ought to do and doesn't do it, it is sin for them.[k]

Warning to Rich Oppressors

5 Now listen,[l] you rich people,[m] weep and wail[n] because of the misery that is coming on you. 2 Your wealth has rotted, and moths have eaten your clothes.[o] 3 Your gold and silver are corroded. Their corrosion will testify against you and eat your flesh like fire. You have hoarded wealth in the last days.[p] 4 Look! The wages you failed to pay the workers[q] who mowed your fields are crying out against you. The cries[r] of the harvesters have reached the ears of the Lord Almighty.[s] 5 You have lived on earth in luxury and self-indulgence. You have fattened yourselves[t] in the day of slaughter.[a][u] 6 You have condemned and murdered[v] the innocent one,[w] who was not opposing you.

Patience in Suffering

7 Be patient, then, brothers and sisters, until the Lord's coming.[x] See how the farmer waits for the land to yield its valuable crop, patiently waiting[y] for the autumn and spring rains.[z] 8 You too, be patient and stand firm, because the Lord's coming[a] is near.[b] 9 Don't grumble against one another, brothers and sisters,[c] or you will be judged. The Judge[d] is standing at the door![e]

10 Brothers and sisters, as an example of patience in the face of suffering, take the prophets[f] who spoke in the name of the Lord. 11 As you know, we count as blessed[g] those who have persevered. You have heard of Job's perseverance[h] and have seen what the Lord finally brought about.[i] The Lord is full of compassion and mercy.[j]

12 Above all, my brothers and sisters, do not swear—not by heaven or by earth or by anything else. All you need to say is a simple "Yes" or "No." Otherwise you will be condemned.[k]

The Prayer of Faith

13 Is anyone among you in trouble? Let them pray.[l] Is anyone happy? Let them sing songs of praise.[m] 14 Is anyone among

[a] 5 Or *yourselves as in a day of feasting*

4:13 [f] Jas 5:1 [g] Pr 27:1; Lk 12:18-20 **4:14** [h] Job 7:7; Ps 39:5; 102:3; 144:4; Isa 2:22 **4:15** [i] S Ac 18:21 **4:16** [j] 1Co 5:6 **4:17** [k] Lk 12:47; Jn 9:41 **5:1** [l] Jas 4:13 [m] Lk 6:24; 1Ti 6:9; Jas 2:2-6 [n] Isa 13:6; Eze 30:2 **5:2** [o] Job 13:28; Ps 39:11; Isa 50:9; Mt 6:19,20 **5:3** [p] ver 7,8 **5:4** [q] Lev 19:13; Jer 22:13; Mal 3:5 [r] Dt 24:15 [s] Ro 9:29 **5:5** [t] Eze 16:49; Am 6:1; Lk 16:19 [u] Jer 12:3; 25:34 **5:6** [v] Jas 4:2 [w] Heb 10:38 **5:7** [x] S 1Co 1:7 [y] Gal 6:9 [z] Dt 11:14; Jer 5:24; Joel 2:23 **5:8** [a] S 1Co 1:7 [b] S Ro 13:11 **5:9** [c] Jas 4:11 [d] Ps 94:2; 1Co 4:5; Jas 4:12; 1Pe 4:5 [e] Mt 24:33 **5:10** [f] S Mt 5:12 **5:11** [g] Mt 5:10 [h] Job 1:21,22; 2:10; S Heb 10:36 [i] Job 42:10,12-17 [j] Ex 34:6; Nu 14:18; Ps 103:8 **5:12** [k] Mt 5:34-37 **5:13** [l] Ps 50:15 [m] Col 3:16

4:13—5:6 Jas 4:13–17 is addressed to traveling merchants and condemns arrogance; 5:1–6 is a warning to wealthy landowners about their improper use of wealth.
4:14 *mist.* Cf. "shadow" (1Ch 29:15), "breath" (Job 7:7), "cloud" (Job 7:9) and "evening shadow" (Ps 102:11).
5:1 *rich.* These (as also in 2:2,6) are not Christians, for James warns them to repent and weep because of the coming misery. Verses 1–6 are similar to OT declarations of judgment against pagan nations, interspersed in books otherwise addressed to God's people (Isa 13–23; Jer 46–51; Eze 25–32; Am 1:3—2:16; Zep 2:4–15).
5:2 *clothes.* One of the forms of wealth in the ancient world (see Jdg 14:12–13 and note on 14:12; Ac 20:33).
5:3 *corrosion.* The result of hoarding. It will both testify against and judge the selfish rich. *last days.* See notes on Ac 2:17; 1Ti 4:1; 2Ti 3:1; Heb 1:1–2; 1Jn 2:18.
5:4 *the Lord Almighty.* See notes on Ge 17:1; 1Sa 1:3.
5:5 *luxury and self-indulgence.* See Lk 16:19–31. *the day of slaughter.* The day of judgment. The wicked rich are like cattle that continue to fatten themselves on the very day they are to be slaughtered, totally unaware of their coming destruction.
5:6 *condemned.* Probably through control of the courts by the rich and powerful.
5:7–8 *Be patient.* Resist resentment and retaliation (see v. 9).
5:7 *then.* Refers back to vv. 1–6. Since the believers are suffering at the hands of the wicked rich, they are to look forward patiently to the Lord's return. *autumn and spring rains.* In Israel the autumn rains come in October and November, soon after the grain is sown, and the spring rains come in March and April, just prior to harvest (Dt 11:14; Jer 5:24; Hos 6:3; Joel 2:23).
5:9 *Don't grumble.* James calls for patience toward believers as well as unbelievers (vv. 7–8). *The Judge is standing at the door!* A reference to Christ's second coming (see vv. 7–8) and the judgment associated with it. The NT insistence on imminence (see Ro 13:12 and note; Heb 10:25; 1Pe 4:7; Rev 22:20) arises from the teaching that the "last days" began with the incarnation. We have been living in the "last days" (v. 3) ever since (see notes on Heb 1:1–2). The next great event in redemptive history is Christ's second coming. The NT does not say when it will take place, but its certainty is never questioned, and believers are consistently admonished to watch for it. It was in this light that James expected the imminent return of Christ.
5:10 *as an example of patience in . . . suffering, take the prophets.* Cf. Mt 5:12; 23:31; Ac 7:52.
5:11 *Job's perseverance.* Not "patience." Job was not patient (Job 3; 12:1–3; 16:1–3; 21:4), but he persevered (Job 1:20–22; 2:9–10; 13:15). This is the only place in the NT where Job is mentioned, though Job 5:13 is quoted in 1Co 3:19.
5:12 *do not swear.* James's words are very close to Christ's (Mt 5:33–37; see note there). James is not condemning the taking of solemn oaths, such as God's before Abraham (see Heb 6:13 and note) or Jesus' before Caiaphas (Mt 26:63–64) or Paul's (Ro 1:9; 9:1). Rather, he is condemning the flippant use of God's name or a sacred object to guarantee the truth of what is spoken.
5:14 *elders.* See notes on 1Ti 3:1; 5:17. *church.* See note on Mt 16:18. *oil.* One of the best-known ancient medicines (referred to by Philo, Pliny and the physician Galen; see also Isa 1:6 and note; Lk 10:34). Some believe that James may be using the term medicinally in this passage. Others, however, regard its

you sick? Let them call the elders[n] of the
church to pray over them and anoint them
with oil[o] in the name of the Lord. 15 And
the prayer offered in faith[p] will make the
sick person well; the Lord will raise them
up. If they have sinned, they will be forgiven. 16 Therefore confess your sins[q] to
each other and pray for each other so that
you may be healed.[r] The prayer of a righteous person is powerful and effective.[s]
17 Elijah was a human being, even as we
are.[t] He prayed earnestly that it would not
rain, and it did not rain on the land for
three and a half years.[u] 18 Again he prayed,
and the heavens gave rain, and the earth
produced its crops.[v]
19 My brothers and sisters, if one of
you should wander from the truth[w] and
someone should bring that person back,[x]
20 remember this: Whoever turns a sinner
from the error of their way will save[y] them
from death and cover over a multitude of
sins.[z]

5:14 [n]S Ac 11:30 [o]Ps 23:5; Isa 1:6; Mk 6:13; 16:18; Lk 10:34 **5:15** [p]Jas 1:6 **5:16** [q]Mt 3:6; Ac 19:18 [r]Heb 12:13; 1Pe 2:24 [s]S Mt 7:7; S Jn 9:31 **5:17** [t]Ac 14:15 [u]1Ki 17:1; Lk 4:25 **5:18** [v]1Ki 18:41-45 **5:19** [w]Jas 3:14 [x]S Mt 18:15 **5:20** [y]S Ro 11:14 [z]1Pe 4:8

use here as an aid to faith, an outward sign of the healing to be brought about by God in response to "prayer offered in faith" (v. 15; see Mk 6:13 and note).
5:17 *Elijah … prayed.* That Elijah prayed may be assumed from 1Ki 17:1; 18:41–46. The three and a half years (see also Lk 4:25) are probably a round number (half of seven), based on 1Ki 18:1 (see note there; cf. Rev 11:1–6 and notes).
5:19 *brothers and sisters.* See NIV text note on 1:2. *wander from the truth.* The wanderer is either a professing Christian whose faith is not genuine (cf. Heb 6:4–8 and note on 6:4–6; 2Pe 2:20–22 and notes) or a sinning Christian who needs to be restored. For the former, the death spoken of in v. 20 is the "second death" (Rev 21:8); for the latter, it is physical death (cf. 1Co 11:29–32 and notes). See note on 1Jn 5:16.
5:20 *cover over … sins.* The sins of the wanderer will be forgiven by God (see Pr 10:12 and note).

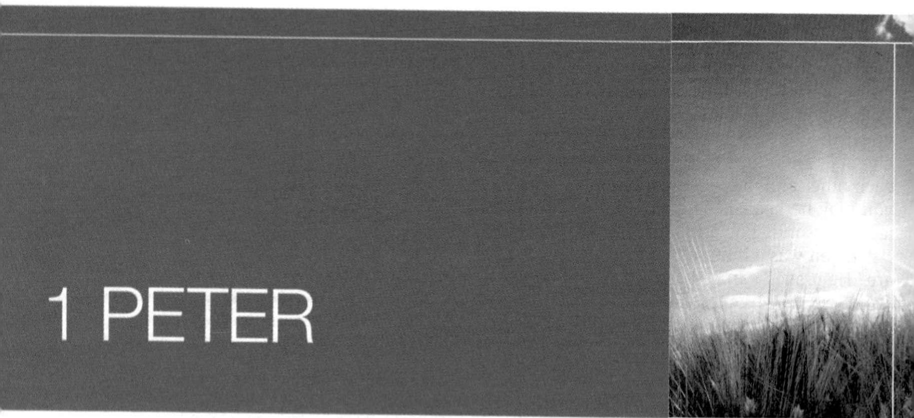

1 PETER

INTRODUCTION

Author and Date

The author identifies himself as the apostle Peter (1:1), and the contents and character of the letter support his authorship (see notes on 1:12; 4:13; 5:1 – 2,5,13). Moreover, the letter reflects the history and terminology of the Gospels and Acts (notably Peter's speeches). Its themes and concepts reflect Peter's experiences and his associations in the period of our Lord's earthly ministry and in the apostolic age. That he was acquainted, e.g., with Paul and his letters is made clear in 2Pe 3:15 – 16 (see notes there); Gal 1:18; 2:1 – 21 and elsewhere. Coincidences in thought and expression with Paul's writings are therefore not surprising.

From the beginning, 1 Peter was recognized as authoritative and as the work of the apostle Peter. The earliest reference to it may be 2Pe 3:1 (see note there), where Peter himself refers to a former letter he had written. 1 Clement (AD 95) seems to indicate acquaintance with 1 Peter. Polycarp, a disciple of the apostle John, makes use of 1 Peter in his letter to the Philippians. The author of the Gospel of Truth (140 – 150) was acquainted with 1 Peter. Eusebius (fourth century) indicated that its authorship by Peter was universally received.

The letter was explicitly ascribed to Peter by that group of church fathers whose testimonies appear in the attestation of so many of the genuine NT writings, namely, Irenaeus (AD 140 – 203), Tertullian (150 – 222), Clement of Alexandria (155 – 215) and Origen (185 – 253). It is thus clear that Peter's authorship of the book has early and strong support.

Nevertheless, some claim that the idiomatic Greek of this letter is beyond Peter's competence. But in his time Aramaic, Hebrew and Greek were used in the Holy Land, and he may well have been acquainted with more than one language. That he was not a professionally trained scribe (Ac 4:13) does not mean that he was unacquainted with Greek; in fact, as a Galilean fisherman he in all likelihood did use it. Even if he had not known

a quick look

Author:
The apostle Peter

Audience:
Gentile and Jewish believers in Pontus, Galatia, Cappadocia, western Asia Minor and Bithynia

Date:
About AD 60 to 64

Theme:
Peter gives instructions on holy living for those suffering persecution.

First Peter has been characterized as a letter of suffering and persecution, of suffering and glory, of hope, of pilgrimage, of courage, and as a letter dealing with the true grace of God.

it in the earliest days of the church, he may have acquired it as an important aid to his apostolic ministry in the decades that intervened between that time and the writing of 1 Peter.

It is true, however, that the Greek of 1 Peter is good, literary Greek, and even though Peter could no doubt speak Greek, as so many in the Mediterranean world could, it is unlikely that he would write such polished Greek. It is precisely at this point that Peter's remark in 5:12 (see note there) concerning Silas may be significant. Here the apostle claims that he wrote "with the help of" (more lit. "through" or "by means of") Silas. This phrase cannot refer merely to Silas as a letter carrier. Thus Silas was the intermediate agent in writing. Some have claimed that Silas's qualifications for recording Peter's letter in literary Greek are found in Ac 15:22 – 29. It is known that a secretary in those days often composed documents in good Greek for those who did not have the language facility to do so. Thus in 1 Peter it is possible that Silas's Greek may be seen, while in 2 Peter it may be Peter's rough Greek that appears.

Some also maintain that the book reflects a situation that did not exist until after Peter's death, suggesting that the persecution referred to in 4:14 – 16; 5:8 – 9 is descriptive of Domitian's reign (AD 81 – 96). However, the situation that was developing in Nero's time (54 – 68) is just as adequately described by those verses.

1 Peter was written to the churches in Asia Minor (see 1:1), including Cappadocia, seen here. Cappadocia is known for these strange rock formations, into which local peoples carved subterranean towns, seeking shelter from the conquerors.

A modern Syrian shepherd with his sheep. Jesus is referred to as the "Chief Shepherd" in 1 Peter 5:4 (see note there).

The book can be satisfactorily dated in the early 60s. It cannot be placed earlier than 60 since it shows familiarity with Paul's Prison Letters (e.g., Colossians and Ephesians, which are to be dated no earlier than 60): Compare 1:1 – 3 with Eph 1:1 – 3; 2:18 with Col 3:22; 3:1 – 6 with Eph 5:22 – 24. Furthermore, it cannot be dated later than 67/68, since Peter was martyred during Nero's reign.

Place of Writing

In 5:13 Peter indicates that he was "in Babylon" when he wrote 1 Peter. Although a number of other possibilities have been proposed (e.g., [1] an Egyptian "Babylon," which was then a Roman military post, [2] a Mesopotamian Babylon, still occupied, but not by many Jews, according to Josephus, and [3] Jerusalem, symbolically called "Babylon"), the long-held tradition that Peter was referring to Rome (cf. Rev 14:8; 17:9 – 10 and notes) is still the most likely, and most widely held, view today.

Recipients

See note on 1:1.

Themes

Although many theological themes are woven throughout the work, the central theme, and one that the author repeatedly returns to, is the exhortation to stand firm in the faith in the face of suffering and persecution. Every chapter refers to suffering: 1:6 – 9; 2:19 – 25; 3:8 – 22; 4:1 – 2,12 – 19; 5:1,10. The ultimate example of righteous suffering is Christ himself (2:21 – 25; 3:18; 4:1,13; 5:1).

Peter also says that he has written "encouraging you and testifying that this is the true grace of God" (5:12). The letter includes a series of exhortations (imperatives) that run from 1:13 to 5:11.

Outline

- I. Greetings (1:1 – 2)
- II. Praise to God for His Grace and Salvation (1:3 – 12)
- III. Exhortations to Holiness of Life (1:13 — 5:11)
  - A. The Requirement of Holiness (1:13 — 2:3)
  - B. The Position of Believers (2:4 – 12)
    - 1. A spiritual house (2:4 – 8)
    - 2. A chosen people (2:9 – 10)
    - 3. Foreigners and strangers (2:11 – 12)
  - C. Submission to Authority (2:13 — 3:7)
    - 1. Submission to rulers (2:13 – 17)
    - 2. Submission to masters (2:18 – 20)
    - 3. Christ's example of submission (2:21 – 25)
    - 4. Submission of wives to husbands (3:1 – 6)
    - 5. The corresponding duty of husbands (3:7)
  - D. Duties of All (3:8 – 17)
  - E. Christ's Example (3:18 — 4:6)
  - F. Conduct in View of the End of All Things (4:7 – 11)
  - G. Conduct of Those Who Suffer for Christ (4:12 – 19)
  - H. Conduct of Elders (5:1 – 4)
  - I. Conduct of the Young (5:5 – 11)
- IV. The Purpose of the Letter (5:12)
- V. Final Greetings and Benediction (5:13 – 14)

1 Peter, an apostle of Jesus Christ,[a]

To God's elect,[b] exiles[c] scattered[d]
throughout the provinces of Pontus,[e] Galatia,[f] Cappadocia, Asia and Bithynia,[g] 2who
have been chosen according to the foreknowledge[h] of God the Father, through the
sanctifying work of the Spirit,[i] to be obedient[j] to Jesus Christ and sprinkled with
his blood:[k]

Grace and peace be yours in abundance.[l]

Praise to God for a Living Hope

3Praise be to the God and Father of our
Lord Jesus Christ![m] In his great mercy[n] he
has given us new birth[o] into a living hope[p]
through the resurrection of Jesus Christ
from the dead,[q] 4and into an inheritance[r]
that can never perish, spoil or fade.[s] This
inheritance is kept in heaven for you,[t] 5who
through faith are shielded by God's power[u]
until the coming of the salvation[v] that is
ready to be revealed[w] in the last time. 6In
all this you greatly rejoice,[x] though now
for a little while[y] you may have had to suffer grief in all kinds of trials.[z] 7These have
come so that the proven genuineness[a] of
your faith—of greater worth than gold,
which perishes even though refined by
fire[b]—may result in praise, glory and hon-
or[c] when Jesus Christ is revealed.[d] 8Though
you have not seen him, you love him; and
even though you do not see him now, you
believe in him[e] and are filled with an inexpressible and glorious joy, 9for you are
receiving the end result of your faith, the
salvation of your souls.[f]

10Concerning this salvation, the prophets, who spoke[g] of the grace that was to
come to you,[h] searched intently and with
the greatest care,[i] 11trying to find out the
time and circumstances to which the Spirit of Christ[j] in them was pointing when
he predicted[k] the sufferings of the Messiah
and the glories that would follow. 12It was

1:1 [a] 2Pe 1:1 [b] Mt 24:22 [c] S Heb 11:13 [d] S Jas 1:1 [e] Ac 2:9; 18:2 [f] S Ac 16:6 [g] Ac 16:7 **1:2** [h] Ro 8:29 [i] 2Th 2:13 [j] ver 14,22 [k] Heb 10:22; 12:24 [l] S Ro 1:7 **1:3** [m] 2Co 1:3; Eph 1:3 [n] Titus 3:5 [o] ver 23; S Jn 1:13 [p] ver 13,21; S Heb 3:6 [q] 1Co 15:20; 1Pe 3:21 **1:4** [r] S Ac 20:32; S Ro 8:17 [s] 1Pe 5:4 [t] Col 1:5; 2Ti 4:8 **1:5** [u] 1Sa 2:9; Jn 10:28 [v] S Ro 11:14 [w] S Ro 8:18 **1:6** [x] Ro 5:2 [y] 1Pe 5:10 [z] Jas 1:2; 1Pe 4:12 **1:7** [a] Jas 1:3 [b] Job 23:10; Ps 66:10; Pr 17:3; Isa 48:10 [c] 2Co 4:17 [d] ver 13; S 1Th 2:19; 1Pe 4:13 **1:8** [e] Jn 20:29 **1:9** [f] Ro 6:22 **1:10** [g] S Mt 26:24 [h] ver 13 [i] S Mt 13:17 **1:11** [j] S Ac 16:7; 2Pe 1:21 [k] S Mt 26:24

1:1 *Peter.* See Introduction: Author and Date; see also notes on Mt 16:18; Jn 1:42. *apostle.* See notes on Mk 6:30; 1Co 1:1; Heb 3:1. *elect.* See note on Eph 1:4. *exiles.* People temporarily residing on earth but whose home is in heaven (cf. 1Ch 29:15; Ps 39:12 and note; Heb 13:14). *scattered throughout ... Pontus ... Bithynia.* Jewish and Gentile Christians scattered throughout much of western Asia Minor (see map, p. 1858). People from this area were in Jerusalem on the day of Pentecost (see Ac 2:9–11 and map, p. 1826). Paul preached and taught in some of these provinces (see, e.g., Ac 16:6; 18:23 and notes; 19:10,26).

1:2 *chosen.* See note on Eph 1:4. *foreknowledge.* See note on Ro 8:29. *Father ... Spirit ... Jesus Christ.* All three persons of the Trinity (see note on Mt 28:19) are involved in the redemption of the elect (see note on Eph 1:3–14). *sanctifying work.* See notes on 1Co 1:2; 2Th 2:13. The order of the terms employed suggests that the sanctifying work of the Spirit referred to here is the influence of the Spirit that draws one from sin toward holiness. Peter says the Spirit's sanctifying leads to obedient, saving faith and cleansing from sin (see note on 1Co 7:14). *obedient to Jesus Christ.* God's choice is designed to bring this about. *sprinkled with his blood.* The benefits of Christ's redemption are applied to his people (cf. Ex 24:4–8; Isa 52:15; Heb 9:11–14,18–28). *Grace and peace.* See note on Ro 1:7.

1:3 *Praise be to the God and Father of our Lord Jesus Christ!* See Eph 1:3 and note. *Lord Jesus Christ.* See note on 1Th 1:1. *mercy.* See Ro 9:22–23; Titus 3:5 and notes. *new birth.* See Jn 3:3–8 and note on 3:3. *living hope.* In spite of the frequent suffering and persecution mentioned in this letter (v. 6; 2:12,18–25; 3:13–18; 4:1,4,12–19; 5:1,7–10), hope is such a key thought in it (the word itself is used here and in vv. 13,21; 3:5,15) that it may be called a letter of hope in the midst of suffering (see Introduction: Themes). In the Bible, hope is not wishful thinking but a confident expectation, much like faith that is directed toward the future (see note on Eph 1:18). *resurrection of Jesus Christ.* Secures for his people their new birth and the hope that they will be resurrected just as he was (see 1Co 15:20–23 and notes on 15:20,23).

1:4 *into an inheritance.* Believers are born again not only to a hope but also to the inheritance that is the substance of that hope. The inheritance is eternal—in its essence (it is not subject to decay) and in its preservation (it is divinely kept for us). See Heb 9:15 and note.

1:5 *through faith ... by God's power.* There are two sides to the perseverance of Christians. They are shielded (1) by God's power and (2) by their own faith. Thus they are never kept contrary to their will nor apart from God's activity. *salvation.* See note on 2Ti 1:9. The Bible speaks of salvation as (1) past—when a person first believes (see, e.g., Titus 3:5), (2) present—the continuing process of salvation, or sanctification (see vv. 2,9 and note on v. 2; Lev 11:44 and note; 1Co 1:18) and (3) future—when Christ returns and salvation, or sanctification, is completed through glorification (here; see also Ro 8:23,30; 13:11; Heb 9:28; Jas 1:21 and notes).

1:7 *proven genuineness of your faith.* See Ro 5:3; Jas 1:2–4. Not only is the faith itself precious, but Peter's words indicate that the trial of faith is also valuable. Believers will share in the "praise, glory and honor" of God (see 5:4; 1Co 4:5).

1:8 *though you do not see him now, you believe.* Similar to Jesus' saying in Jn 20:29, on an occasion when Peter was present.

1:9 *souls.* Implies the whole person. Peter is not excluding the glorified body from heaven.

1:10 *prophets ... searched intently.* Inspiration (see 2Pe 1:21 and note) did not bestow omniscience. The prophets probably did not always understand the full significance of all the words they spoke (see v. 11). *grace that was to come to you.* The "salvation" they were already experiencing (see also v. 9). For the "grace" of ultimate redemption, see v. 13 and note.

1:11 *Spirit of Christ.* The Holy Spirit is called this because Christ sent him (see Jn 16:7) and ministered through him (see Lk 4:14,18). *the sufferings of the Messiah and the glories.* A theme running through the Bible (see, e.g., Ps 22; Isa 52:13—53:12; Zec 9:9–10; 13:7; Mt 16:21–27; 17:22–23; 20:18–19; Lk 24:26,46; Jn 2:19; Ac 3:17–21; Php 2:5–11; 1Ti 3:16; cf. Lk 9:26; 21:27) and a basic concept in this letter (vv. 18–21; 3:17–22; 4:12–16; 5:1,4,9–10). Those who are united to Christ will also, after suffering, enter into glory. And they will benefit in the midst of their present sufferings from his having already entered into glory (3:21–22).

1:12 *Holy Spirit sent from heaven.* By Christ, on the day of Pentecost (see Ac 2:33), at which Peter was present. God the Father also sent the Spirit (see Jn 14:16,26).

revealed to them that they were not serving themselves but you,[l] when they spoke
of the things that have now been told you
by those who have preached the gospel to
you[m] by the Holy Spirit sent from heaven.[n]
Even angels long to look into these things.

Be Holy

13 Therefore, with minds that are alert
and fully sober,[o] set your hope[p] on the
grace to be brought to you[q] when Jesus
Christ is revealed at his coming.[r] 14 As obedient[s] children, do not conform[t] to the evil
desires you had when you lived in ignorance.[u] 15 But just as he who called you is
holy, so be holy in all you do;[v] 16 for it is
written: "Be holy, because I am holy."[a][w]
17 Since you call on a Father[x] who judges
each person's work[y] impartially,[z] live out
your time as foreigners[a] here in reverent
fear.[b] 18 For you know that it was not with
perishable things such as silver or gold
that you were redeemed[c] from the empty way of life[d] handed down to you from
your ancestors, 19 but with the precious
blood[e] of Christ, a lamb[f] without blemish

[a] *16* Lev. 11:44,45; 19:2

1:12 [l]S Ro 4:24 [m]ver 25 [n]S Lk 24:49 **1:13** [o]S Ac 24:25 [p]ver 3,21; S Heb 3:6 [q]ver 10 [r]ver 7; S 1Co 1:7 **1:14** [s]ver 2, 22 [t]Ro 12:2 [u]Eph 4:18 **1:15** [v]Isa 35:8; 1Th 4:7; 1Jn 3:3 **1:16** [w]Lev 11:44,45; 19:2; 20:7 **1:17** [x]S Mt 6:9 [y]S Mt 16:27 [z]S Ac 10:34 [a]S Heb 11:13 [b]Heb 12:28 **1:18** [c]S Mt 20:28; S 1Co 6:20 [d]Gal 4:3 **1:19** [e]S Ro 3:25 [f]S Jn 1:29

1:13 *with minds that are alert.* A graphic call for mental action. In the language of the first century it meant that the readers should literally gather up their long, flowing garments and be ready for physical action (cf. Jer 1:17 and note). *set your hope on.* The first of a long series of exhortations (actually imperatives) that end at 5:11 (see Introduction: Themes). *grace to be brought to you.* The final state of complete blessedness and deliverance from sin. Peter later indicates that a major purpose of this letter is to encourage and testify regarding "the true grace of God" (5:12; cf. also 5:10).

1:14 *children.* Christians, born into the family of God (see v. 23), are children of their heavenly Father (v. 17) and can pray, "Our Father in heaven" (Mt 6:9). Believers are also described as being adopted into God's family (see Ro 8:15 and note).

1:16 *Be holy, because I am holy.* To be holy is to be set apart—separated from sin and impurity and set apart to God (see notes on Ex 3:5; Lev 11:44; Ro 6:22; 1Co 1:2). The complete moral perfection of God, whose eyes are too pure to look with favor on evil (Hab 1:13), should move his people to strive for moral purity. 1 Peter is a letter of practical earnestness, filled with exhortations and encouragements.

1:17 *impartially.* See Ac 10:34 and note. *foreigners.* See note on v. 1. *reverent fear.* Not terror, but wholesome reverence and respect for God, which is the basis for all godly living (cf. Pr 1:7 and note).

1:18 *redeemed.* In the Bible, to redeem someone usually means to rescue them from some bad situation (e.g., Israel from Egyptian bondage [Ex 6:6; 15:15], the psalmist from the threat of death [Ps 26:11] or from enemies [Ps 31:5]). Often this comes at a cost to the one who redeems. In the Greco-Roman world slaves could be redeemed by the payment of a price, either by someone else or by the slaves themselves. Jesus redeems believers (see Ro 3:24 and note; Titus 2:14) at the cost of his blood (see v. 19; Eph 1:7 and note; Rev 5:9), i.e., his death (see Mt 20:28; Heb 9:15 and notes; cf. Gal 3:13). The result is the "forgiveness of sins" (Col 1:14) and justification (see Ro 3:24 and note). *empty way of life ... from your ancestors.* Some maintain that the recipients must have been pagans because the NT stresses the emptiness of pagan life (see Ro 1:21; Eph 4:17 and note). Others think they were Jews since Jews were traditionalists who stressed the influence of the father as teacher in the home. In the light of the context of the whole letter, probably both Jews and Gentiles are addressed.

1:19 *lamb.* The OT sacrifices were types (foreshadowings) of Christ, depicting the ultimate and only effective sacrifice. Thus Christ is the Passover lamb (see 1Co 5:7 and note) who takes away the sin of the world (see Jn 1:29 and note). *without blemish or defect.* See Heb 9:14 and note; see also Introduction to Leviticus: Theological Themes.

PETER WROTE THIS LETTER TO PROVINCES IN ASIA MINOR

Adriatic Sea
Black Sea
Rome
ITALY
BITHYNIA
PONTUS
Troas
ASIA
Aegean Sea
GALATIA
CAPPADOCIA
Athens
Ephesus
SYRIA
0 300 km.
0 300 miles
Mediterranean Sea

or defect.[g] 20 He was chosen before the creation of the world,[h] but was revealed in
these last times[i] for your sake. 21 Through
him you believe in God,[j] who raised him
from the dead[k] and glorified him,[l] and so
your faith and hope[m] are in God.
22 Now that you have purified[n] yourselves by obeying[o] the truth so that you
have sincere love for each other, love one
another deeply,[p] from the heart.[a] 23 For you
have been born again,[q] not of perishable
seed, but of imperishable,[r] through the living and enduring word of God.[s] 24 For,

"All people are like grass,
and all their glory is like the flowers
of the field;
the grass withers and the flowers fall,
25 but the word of the Lord endures
forever."[b][t]

And this is the word that was preached
to you.

2 Therefore, rid yourselves[u] of all malice and all deceit, hypocrisy, envy,
and slander[v] of every kind. 2 Like newborn
babies, crave pure spiritual milk,[w] so that
by it you may grow up[x] in your salvation,
3 now that you have tasted that the Lord
is good.[y]

The Living Stone and a Chosen People

4 As you come to him, the living
Stone[z]—rejected by humans but chosen
by God[a] and precious to him— 5 you also,
like living stones, are being built[b] into a
spiritual house[c][c] to be a holy priesthood,[d]
offering spiritual sacrifices acceptable to
God through Jesus Christ.[e] 6 For in Scripture it says:

"See, I lay a stone in Zion,
a chosen and precious cornerstone,[f]
and the one who trusts in him
will never be put to shame."[d][g]

[a] 22 Some early manuscripts *from a pure heart* [b] 25 Isaiah 40:6-8 (see Septuagint) [c] 5 Or *into a temple of the Spirit* [d] 6 Isaiah 28:16

1:19 [g] Ex 12:5 **1:20** [h] Eph 1:4; S Mt 25:34 [i] Heb 9:26 **1:21** [j] Ro 4:24; 10:9 [k] S Ac 2:24 [l] Php 2:7-9; Heb 2:9 [m] ver 3, 13; S Heb 3:6 **1:22** [n] Jas 4:8 [o] ver 2, 14 [p] S Jn 13:34; S Ro 12:10 **1:23** [q] ver 3; S Jn 1:13 [r] Jn 1:13 [s] S Heb 4:12 **1:25** [t] Isa 40:6-8; S Jas 1:10, 11 **2:1** [u] S Eph 4:22 [v] S Jas 4:11 **2:2** [w] 1Co 3:2; Heb 5:12, 13 [x] Eph 4:15, 16 **2:3** [y] Ps 34:8; Heb 6:5 **2:4** [z] ver 7 [a] Isa 42:1 **2:5** [b] Pr 9:1; 1Co 3:9; Eph 2:20-22 [c] 1Ti 3:15 [d] ver 9; Ex 19:6; Isa 61:6; Rev 1:6; 5:10; 20:6 [e] Php 4:18; Heb 13:15 **2:6** [f] Eph 2:20 [g] Isa 28:16; Ro 9:32, 33; 10:11

1:20 *chosen.* Some think the Greek for this word means "foreknown," i.e., God knew before creation that it would be necessary for Christ to redeem human beings (cf. Rev 13:8), but he has revealed Christ in these last times. Others interpret the word as meaning that in eternity past God chose Christ as Redeemer. *these last times.* See note on Jas 5:3.

1:22 *sincere love.* See Ro 12:9 and note. *love one another.* A command no doubt based on Jn 13:34–35 (see notes there). See also 1Th 4:9–10 (and note on 4:9), where, like Peter, Paul commends his readers for their love of fellow believers and then urges them to love still more (see Mt 5:43–44; Jas 2:8 and notes). *deeply.* Fervently.

1:23 *born again … through the … word of God.* The new birth comes about through the direct action of the Holy Spirit (see Jn 3:5; Titus 3:5 and notes), but the word of God also plays an important role (see Jas 1:18), for it presents the gospel to sinners and calls on them to repent and believe in Christ (see v. 25). *perishable seed … imperishable.* In this context the seed is doubtless the word of God, which is imperishable, living and enduring.

1:25 *the word … endures forever.* The main point of the quotation here.

2:1 *Therefore.* Connects the exhortations that follow with 1:23–25; compare "born again" (1:23) with "newborn babies" (2:2).

2:2 *crave.* The unrestrained hunger of a healthy baby provides an example of the kind of eager desire for spiritual food that ought to mark the believer. *spiritual milk.* Probably referring to God's word (1:23,25). The author is speaking figuratively. Milk is not to be understood here as in 1Co 3:2; Heb 5:12–14—in unfavorable contrast to solid food—but as an appropriate nourishment for babies. *grow up.* The Greek for this phrase is the standard term for the desirable growth of children (cf. 2Pe 3:18).

2:3 *have tasted.* The tense of the Greek verb used here suggests that an initial act of tasting is referred to. Since this taste has proved satisfactory, the believers are urged to long for additional spiritual food.

2:4 *living Stone.* Christ (see vv. 6–8 and NIV text notes; cf. Mt 21:42; Mk 12:10–11; Lk 20:17; Ac 4:11; Ro 9:33). The Stone is living in that it is personal. Furthermore, he is a life-giving Stone. Christ as the Son of God has life in himself (see Jn 1:4; 5:26 and notes). See also "living water" (Jn 4:10–14 [see note on 4:10]; 7:38), "living bread" (Jn 6:51 [see note on 6:35]) and "living way" (Heb 10:20). *rejected by humans but chosen by God.* Peter repeatedly makes a contrast in Acts between the hostility of unbelievers toward Jesus and God's exaltation of him (Ac 2:22–36; 3:13–15; 4:10–11; 10:39–42).

2:5 *living stones.* Believers derive their life from Christ, who is the original living Stone, the "life-giving spirit" (1Co 15:45) to whom they have come (v. 4). These references to stones may reflect Jesus' words to Peter in Mt 16:18 (see note there). *spiritual house.* The house is spiritual in a metaphorical sense, but also in that it is formed and indwelt by the Spirit of God. Every stone in the house has been made alive by the Holy Spirit, sent by the exalted living Stone, Jesus Christ (cf. Ac 2:33). The OT temple provides the background of this passage (cf. Jn 2:19; 1Co 3:16; Eph 2:19–22 and notes). *holy priesthood.* The whole body of believers. As priests, believers are to (1) reflect the holiness of God and that of their high priest (see 1:15; Heb 7:26; 10:10 and note; and note on 10:10,14), (2) offer spiritual sacrifices (here), (3) intercede for others before God and (4) represent God before them. *spiritual sacrifices.* The NT refers to a variety of offerings: bodies offered to God (Ro 12:1), offerings of money or material goods (Php 4:18; Heb 13:16), sacrifices of praise to God (Heb 13:15) and sacrifices of doing good (Heb 13:16). *acceptable to God.* Through the work of our Mediator, Jesus Christ (cf. Jn 14:6). Believers are living stones that make up a spiritual temple in which, as a holy priesthood, they offer up spiritual sacrifices.

2:6 *precious cornerstone.* See Ps 118:22 and note; Mt 21:42; Mk 12:10; Lk 20:17; Ac 4:11 and note. This is an obvious reference to Christ, as vv. 6b–8 make clear. The cornerstone, which determined the design and orientation of the building, was the most significant stone in the structure. The picture that Peter creates is of a structure made up of believers ("living stones," v. 5), the design and orientation of which are all in keeping with Christ, the cornerstone. *the one who trusts in him.* Two attitudes toward the cornerstone are evident: (1) Some trust in him; (2) others reject him (v. 7) and, as a result, stumble and fall (v. 8).

7 Now to you who believe, this stone is
precious. But to those who do not believe,[h]

"The stone the builders rejected[i]
has become the cornerstone,"[a][j]

8 and,

"A stone that causes people to stumble
and a rock that makes them fall."[b][k]

They stumble because they disobey the
message—which is also what they were
destined for.[l]

9 But you are a chosen people,[m] a royal priesthood,[n] a holy nation,[o] God's special possession,[p] that you may declare the
praises of him who called you out of darkness into his wonderful light.[q] 10 Once you
were not a people, but now you are the
people of God;[r] once you had not received
mercy, but now you have received mercy.

Living Godly Lives in a Pagan Society

11 Dear friends,[s] I urge you, as foreigners
and exiles,[t] to abstain from sinful desires,[u]
which wage war against your soul.[v] 12 Live
such good lives among the pagans that,
though they accuse you of doing wrong,
they may see your good deeds[w] and glorify
God[x] on the day he visits us.
13 Submit yourselves for the Lord's sake
to every human authority:[y] whether to the
emperor, as the supreme authority, 14 or to
governors, who are sent by him to punish those who do wrong[z] and to commend
those who do right.[a] 15 For it is God's will[b]
that by doing good you should silence
the ignorant talk of foolish people.[c] 16 Live
as free people,[d] but do not use your freedom as a cover-up for evil;[e] live as God's
slaves.[f] 17 Show proper respect to everyone, love the family of believers,[g] fear
God, honor the emperor.[h]
18 Slaves, in reverent fear of God submit yourselves to your masters,[i] not only
to those who are good and considerate,[j]
but also to those who are harsh. 19 For it is
commendable if someone bears up under
the pain of unjust suffering because they
are conscious of God.[k] 20 But how is it to
your credit if you receive a beating for doing wrong and endure it? But if you suffer
for doing good and you endure it, this is
commendable before God.[l] 21 To this[m] you
were called,[n] because Christ suffered for
you,[o] leaving you an example,[p] that you
should follow in his steps.

a 7 Psalm 118:22 *b* 8 Isaiah 8:14

2:7 [h] 2Co 2:16 [i] ver 4 [j] Ps 118:22; S Ac 4:11 **2:8** [k] Isa 8:14; S Lk 2:34 [l] Ro 9:22 **2:9** [m] Dt 10:15; 1Sa 12:22 [n] ver 5 [o] Ex 19:6; Dt 7:6; Isa 62:12 [p] S Titus 2:14 [q] S Ac 26:18 **2:10** [r] Hos 1:9, 10; 2:23; Ro 9:25, 26 **2:11** [s] S 1Co 10:14 [t] S Heb 11:13 [u] Ro 13:14; Gal 5:16 [v] Jas 4:1 **2:12** [w] Php 2:15; Titus 2:8; S Titus 2:14; 1Pe 3:16 [x] S Mt 9:8 **2:13** [y] Ro 13:1; Titus 3:1 **2:14** [z] Ro 13:4 [a] Ro 13:3 **2:15** [b] 1Pe 3:17; 4:19 [c] S ver 12 **2:16** [d] S Jn 8:32 [e] Gal 5:13 [f] S Ro 6:22 **2:17** [g] S Ro 12:10 [h] Pr 24:21; Ro 13:7 **2:18** [i] S Eph 6:5 [j] Jas 3:17 **2:19** [k] 1Pe 3:14, 17 **2:20** [l] 1Pe 3:17 **2:21** [m] S Ac 14:22; Php 1:29; 1Pe 3:9 [n] S Ro 8:28 [o] 1Pe 3:18; 4:1, 13 [p] S Mt 11:29; 16:24

2:8 *what they were destined for.* Some see here an indication that some people are destined to fall and be lost. Others say that unbelievers are destined to be lost because God in his foreknowledge (cf. 1:2 and note) saw them as unbelievers. Still others hold that Peter means that unbelief is destined to result in eternal destruction.

2:9 *chosen people.* See Eph 1:4 and note; Isa 43:10,20; 44:1–2. As Israel was called God's chosen people in the OT, so in the NT believers are designated as chosen, or elect. *royal priesthood.* See notes on v. 5; Ex 19:6; cf. Isa 61:6. *holy nation.* Cf. Dt 28:9. *God's special possession.* See Ex 19:5 and note. Though once not the people of God, they are now the recipients of God's mercy (cf. Hos 1:6–10 and note on 1:10; Ro 9:25–26 and note; 10:19). *declare the praises of him.* See Isa 43:21; Ac 2:11.

2:10 See notes on Hos 1:6,9; 2:1,22; Ro 9:25–26. In Hosea it is Israel who is not God's people; in Romans it is the Gentiles to whom Paul applies Hosea's words; in 1 Peter the words are applied to both.

2:11 *foreigners and exiles.* See note on 1:1. As foreigners and exiles on earth, whose citizenship is in heaven, they are to be separated from the corruption of the world, not yielding to its destructive sinful desires.

2:12 *see your good deeds.* Deeds that can be seen to be good (cf. Mt 5:16). The Greek word translated "see" refers to a careful watching, over a period of time. The pagans' evaluation is not a snap judgment. *the day he visits us.* Perhaps the day of judgment and ensuing punishment, or possibly the day when God visits a person with salvation. The believer's good life may then influence the unbeliever to repent and believe.

2:13—3:6 Peter urges that Christians submit to all legitimate authorities, whether or not the persons exercising authority are believers. The recognition of properly constituted authority is necessary for the greatest good of the largest number of people, and it is necessary to best fulfill the will of God in the world.

2:13 *every human authority.* Such authority depends on God for its existence (see Ro 13:1–2 and note on 13:1). Indirectly, when people disobey a human ruler they disobey God, who ordained the system of human government (cf. Ro 13:2). *emperor.* When Peter wrote, the emperor was the godless, brutal Nero, who ruled from AD 54 to 68 (see Introduction: Author and Date). Of course, obedience to the emperor must never be in violation of the law of God (to see this basic principle in action, cf. Ac 4:19; 5:29).

2:15 *silence the ignorant talk.* Good citizenship counters false charges made against Christians and thus commends the gospel to unbelievers (cf. Titus 2:7–8).

2:16 *Live as free people.* Does not authorize rebellion against constituted authority but urges believers freely to submit to God and to earthly authorities (as long as such submission does not conflict with the law of God). *as a cover-up for evil.* Genuine freedom is the freedom to serve God, a freedom exercised under law. Liberty is not license to do as we please.

2:17 *proper respect to everyone.* Because every human being bears the image of God. *fear God.* See note on 1:17.

2:18 *Slaves.* Household servants, whatever their particular training and functions. The context indicates that Peter is addressing Christian slaves. NT writers do not attack slavery as an institution (see note on Eph 6:5), but the NT contains the principles that ultimately uprooted slavery (see Phm 16). Peter's basic teachings on the subject may apply to employer-employee relations today (see Eph 6:5–8; Col 3:22–25; 1Ti 6:1–2; Titus 2:9–10).

2:19 *conscious of God.* As submission to duly constituted authority is "for the Lord's sake" (v. 13; cf. Eph 6:7–8), so one will submit to the point of suffering unjustly if it is God's will.

2:21 *To this you were called.* The patient endurance of injustice is part of God's plan for the Christian. It was an important feature of the true grace of God experienced

22 "He committed no sin,[q]
and no deceit was found in his
mouth."[a][r]

23 When they hurled their insults at him,[s]
he did not retaliate; when he suffered, he
made no threats.[t] Instead, he entrusted
himself[u] to him who judges justly.[v] 24 "He
himself bore our sins"[w] in his body on the
cross,[x] so that we might die to sins[y] and
live for righteousness; "by his wounds you
have been healed."[z] 25 For "you were like
sheep going astray,"[b][a] but now you have
returned to the Shepherd[b] and Overseer of
your souls.[c]

3 Wives, in the same way submit yourselves[d] to your own husbands[e] so that,
if any of them do not believe the word,
they may be won over[f] without words by
the behavior of their wives, 2 when they
see the purity and reverence of your lives.
3 Your beauty should not come from outward adornment, such as elaborate hairstyles and the wearing of gold jewelry or
fine clothes.[g] 4 Rather, it should be that of
your inner self,[h] the unfading beauty of a
gentle and quiet spirit, which is of great
worth in God's sight.[i] 5 For this is the way
the holy women of the past who put their
hope in God[j] used to adorn themselves.[k]
They submitted themselves to their own
husbands, 6 like Sarah, who obeyed Abraham and called him her lord.[l] You are her
daughters if you do what is right and do
not give way to fear.

7 Husbands,[m] in the same way be considerate as you live with your wives, and
treat them with respect as the weaker partner and as heirs with you of the gracious
gift of life, so that nothing will hinder your
prayers.

Suffering for Doing Good

8 Finally, all of you, be like-minded,[n] be
sympathetic, love one another,[o] be com-

2:22 [q] S 2Co 5:21 [r] Isa 53:9 **2:23** [s] Heb 12:3; 1Pe 3:9 [t] Isa 53:7 [u] Lk 23:46 [v] Ps 9:4 **2:24** [w] Isa 53:4, 11; Heb 9:28 [x] S Ac 5:30 [y] S Ro 6:2 [z] Dt 32:39; Ps 103:3; Isa 53:5; Heb 12:13; Jas 5:16 **2:25** [a] Isa 53:6 [b] S Jn 10:11 [c] Job 10:12 **3:1** [d] 1Pe 2:18 [e] S Eph 5:22 [f] 1Co 7:16; 9:19 **3:3** [g] Isa 3:18-23; 1Ti 2:9 **3:4** [h] Ro 7:22; Eph 3:16 [i] S Ro 2:29 **3:5** [j] 1Ti 5:5 [k] Est 2:15 **3:6** [l] Ge 18:12 **3:7** [m] Eph 5:25-33; Col 3:19

[a] *22* Isaiah 53:9 [b] *24,25* Isaiah 53:4,5,6 (see Septuagint)

3:8 [n] S Ro 15:5 [o] S Ro 12:10

---

by the readers (5:12). *Christ suffered for you.* Cf. Isa 52:13—53:12. Christ is the supreme example of suffering evil for doing good. His experience as the suffering Servant-Savior transforms the sufferings of his followers from misery into privilege (cf. Ac 5:41).

2:22 Scripture declares the sinlessness of Christ in the clearest of terms, allowing for no exception (see 1:19; Ac 3:14 and note; 2Co 5:21; Heb 4:15; 7:26; 1Jn 3:5). *no deceit.* Cf. v. 1; 3:10.

2:23 Prominent examples of our Lord's silent submission are found in Mt 27:12–14,34–44 (see also parallels in the other Gospels). *entrusted himself.* Cf. 4:19.

2:24 *bore our sins.* See Isa 53:12. Although dealing with the example set by Christ, Peter touches also on the redemptive work of Christ, which has significance far beyond that of setting an example. Peter here points to the substitutionary character of the atonement. Christ, like the sacrificial lamb of the OT, died for our sins, the innocent for the guilty (see Ro 5:6; 1Jn 2:2 and notes). *cross.* See note on Ac 5:30; see also Ac 10:39; 13:29; Gal 3:13 and note. *that we might die to sins and live for righteousness.* Cf. Ro 6:3–14. Peter stresses the bearing of the cross on our sanctification. As a result of Christ's death on the cross, believers are positionally dead to sin so that they may live new lives and present themselves to God as instruments of righteousness (see note on Ro 6:11–13). *you have been healed.* See Isa 53:5 and note; not generally viewed as a reference to physical healing, though some believe that such healing was included in the atonement (cf. Isa 53:4 and note; Mt 8:16–17). Others see spiritual healing in this passage. It is another way of asserting that Christ's death brings salvation to those who trust in him.

2:25 *Shepherd.* A concept raised here in connection with the allusion to the wandering sheep of Isa 53. The sheep had wandered from their shepherd, and to their Shepherd (Christ) they have now returned. See note on Ps 23:1; see also Eze 34:23–24 and notes; Jn 10:11,14 and note on Heb 13:20. *Overseer.* Christ (cf. 5:2,4 and note on 5:2; Ac 20:28). Elders are to be both shepherds and overseers, i.e., they are to look out for the welfare of the flock. These are not two separate offices or functions; the second term is a further explanation of the first.

3:1–6 Instructions to wives (cf. Ge 3:16; 1Co 11:3 and notes; Eph 5:22–24 and note on 5:22; Col 3:18; 1Ti 2:9–10; Titus 2:5).

3:1 *in the same way.* As believers are to submit to government authorities (2:13–17) and as slaves are to submit to masters (2:18–25). *submit yourselves.* The same Greek verb as is used in 2:13,18, a term that calls for submission to a recognized authority. Inferiority is not implied by this passage. The submission is one of role or function necessary for the orderly operation of the home. *the word.* The gospel message. *without words.* Believing wives are not to rely on argumentation to win their unbelieving husbands, but on the quality of their lives. "Actions speak louder than words."

3:2 *purity and reverence.* Their lives are to be marked by a moral purity that springs from reverence toward God.

3:3 *elaborate hairstyles ... jewelry.* See 1Ti 2:9 and note; extreme coiffures and gaudy exhibits of jewelry. Christian women should not rely on such extremes of adornment for beauty. *clothes.* The Greek for this word simply means "garment," but in this context expensive garments are meant (hence "fine clothes").

3:5 *holy women of the past.* The standards stated by Peter are not limited to any particular time or culture.

3:6 *called him her lord.* An expression of the submission called for in v. 1 (see Ge 18:12). *her daughters ... fear.* Christian women become daughters of Sarah as they become like her in doing good and in not fearing any potential disaster but trusting in God (cf. Pr 3:25–27).

3:7 *weaker partner.* Not a reference to moral stamina, strength of character or mental capacity, but most likely to sheer physical strength. *heirs with you of the gracious gift of life.* Women experience the saving grace of God on equal terms with men (see Gal 3:28 and note). *hinder your prayers.* Spiritual fellowship, with God and with one another, may be hindered by disregarding God's instruction concerning husband-wife relationships.

3:8–12 In 2:11–17 Peter addressed all his readers, and in 2:18–25 he spoke directly to slaves; in 3:1–6 he addressed wives and in 3:7 husbands. Now he encourages all his readers to develop virtues appropriate in their relations with others (see "all of you," v. 8).

3:8 *be like-minded.* See Ro 12:16; Php 2:2 and note. *be sym-*

passionate and humble.[p] 9Do not repay
evil with evil[q] or insult with insult.[r] On
the contrary, repay evil with blessing,[s] because to this[t] you were called[u] so that you
may inherit a blessing.[v] 10For,

"Whoever would love life
and see good days
must keep their tongue from evil
and their lips from deceitful speech.
11They must turn from evil and do good;
they must seek peace and pursue it.
12For the eyes of the Lord are on the
righteous
and his ears are attentive to their
prayer,
but the face of the Lord is against
those who do evil."[a][w]

13Who is going to harm you if you
are eager to do good?[x] 14But even if you
should suffer for what is right, you are
blessed.[y] "Do not fear their threats[b]; do
not be frightened."[c][z] 15But in your hearts
revere Christ as Lord. Always be prepared
to give an answer[a] to everyone who asks
you to give the reason for the hope[b] that
you have. But do this with gentleness and
respect, 16keeping a clear conscience,[c] so
that those who speak maliciously against
your good behavior in Christ may be
ashamed of their slander.[d] 17For it is better,
if it is God's will,[e] to suffer for doing good[f]
than for doing evil. 18For Christ also suffered once[g] for sins,[h] the righteous for the
unrighteous, to bring you to God.[i] He was
put to death in the body[j] but made alive
in the Spirit.[k] 19After being made alive,[d]
he went and made proclamation to the
imprisoned spirits[l]— 20to those who were
disobedient long ago when God waited patiently[m] in the days of Noah while the ark
was being built.[n] In it only a few people,
eight in all,[o] were saved[p] through water,

3:8 [p] Eph 4:2; 1Pe 5:5 **3:9** [q] Ro 12:17; 1Th 5:15 [r] 1Pe 2:23 [s] S Mt 5:44 [t] S 1Pe 2:21 [u] S Ro 8:28 [v] Heb 6:14 **3:12** [w] Ps 34:12-16 **3:13** [x] S Titus 2:14 **3:14** [y] ver 17; 1Pe 2:19, 20; 4:15,16 [z] Isa 8:12,13 **3:15** [a] Col 4:6 [b] S Heb 3:6 **3:16** [c] ver 21; S Ac 23:1 [d] 1Pe 2:12,15 **3:17** [e] 1Pe 2:15; 4:19 [f] 1Pe 2:20; 4:15,16 **3:18** [g] S Heb 7:27 [h] 1Pe 2:21; 4:1, 13 [i] S Ro 5:2 [j] Col 1:22; 1Pe 4:1 [k] 1Pe 4:6 **3:19** [l] 1Pe 4:6 **3:20** [m] S Ro 2:4 [n] Ge 6:3,5,13,14 [o] Ge 8:18 [p] Heb 11:7

[a] 12 Psalm 34:12-16 [b] 14 Or *fear what they fear* [c] 14 Isaiah 8:12 [d] 18,19 Or *but made alive in the spirit, 19in which also*

pathetic. See Ro 12:15; 1Co 12:26 and notes. *love one another.* See 1Th 4:9 and note; Heb 13:1. *be compassionate.* See Col 3:12. *humble.* See Php 2:6–8 and notes.

3:9 See 2:23; Ro 12:17–21 and notes.

3:10–12 Peter introduces this quotation from Ps 34 with the explanatory conjunction "for," showing that he views the quotation as giving reasons for obeying the exhortation of v. 9. According to the psalmist, (1) those who do such things will find life to be most gratifying (v. 10), (2) their days will be good (v. 10), (3) God's eyes will ever be on them to bless them (v. 12) and (4) God's ears will be ready to hear their prayer (v. 12).

3:12 *face of the Lord.* See Ps 13:1 and note.

3:13 *Who … harm you …?* As a general rule, people are not harmed for acts of kindness. This is especially true if one is an enthusiast ("eager") for doing good.

3:14 *even if you should suffer.* In the Greek, this conditional clause is the furthest removed from stating a reality. Suffering for righteousness is a remote possibility, but even if it does occur, it brings special blessing to the sufferer (see Mt 5:10–12). *Do not fear their threats.* In Isaiah's context (see NIV text note) God's people are not to view things as unbelievers do. They are not to make worldly judgments or be afraid of the enemies of God. Instead, they are to fear God (see Isa 8:13).

3:15 *revere Christ as Lord.* An exhortation to the readers to make an inner commitment to Christ. Then they need not be speechless when called on to defend their faith. Instead, there will be a readiness to answer. *Always be prepared to give an answer.* Among other things, this requires a knowledge of God's word. *hope.* See Ro 5:5 and note. *with gentleness and respect.* The Christian is always to be a gentleman or gentle woman, even when opposed by unbelievers. Our apologetic ("answer") is always to be given with love, never in degrading terms.

3:16 *ashamed of their slander.* Because it is shown to be obviously untrue and because the believer's loving attitude puts the opponent's bitterness in a bad light.

3:18 *once.* See Heb 9:28. *the righteous for the unrighteous.* Peter, like Paul in Php 2:5–11, refers to Jesus as an example of the type of conduct that should characterize the Christian. We are to be ready to suffer for doing good (vv. 13–14,17). The thought of Christ's suffering and death, however, leads Peter to comment on what occurred after Christ's death—which leads to tangential remarks about preaching to the spirits in prison and about baptism (see vv. 19–21). *made alive in the Spirit.* Referring to the resurrection. Elsewhere the resurrection is attributed to the Father (Ac 2:32; Gal 1:1; Eph 1:20) and to the Son (Jn 10:17–18). If the NIV text note is correct, the reference would be to Christ's own spirit, through which also he "made proclamation to the imprisoned spirits" (v. 19).

3:19–20a Three main interpretations of this passage have been suggested: (1) Some hold that in his preincarnate state Christ went and preached through Noah to the wicked generation of that time. (2) Others argue that between his death and resurrection Christ went to the prison where fallen angels are incarcerated and there preached to the angels who are said to have left their proper state and married human women during Noah's time (cf. Ge 6:1–4; 2Pe 2:4; Jude 6). The "sons of God" in Ge 6:2,4 are said to have been angels, as they are in Job 1:6; 2:1 (see NIV text notes there). The message he preached to these evil angels was probably a declaration of victory. (3) Still others say that between death and resurrection Christ went to the place of the dead and preached to the spirits of Noah's wicked contemporaries. What he proclaimed may have been the gospel, or it may have been a declaration of victory for Christ and doom for his hearers.

The weakness of the first view is that it does not relate the event to Christ's death and resurrection, as the context seems to do. The main problem with the second view is that it assumes sexual relations between angels and women, and such physical relations may not be possible for angels since they are spirits (see note on Ge 6:2). A major difficulty with the third view is that the term "spirits" is only used of human beings when qualifying terms are added. Otherwise the term seems restricted to supernatural beings.

Perhaps a more satisfactory view would be to translate v. 19: "And in that [resurrection] state, by means of (his) ascension [see v. 22, where the same Greek verb form is used of Christ's ascension] he made proclamation to the imprisoned spirits." The latter phrase most likely refers to the disobedient spirits ("angels, authorities and powers," v. 22). Thus Christ's ascension "into heaven" (v. 22) was itself a victory proclamation to them (cf. Eph 3:10 and note).

21 and this water symbolizes baptism that now saves you[q] also — not the removal of dirt from the body but the pledge of a clear conscience[r] toward God.[a] It saves you by the resurrection of Jesus Christ,[s] 22 who has gone into heaven[t] and is at God's right hand[u] — with angels, authorities and powers in submission to him.[v]

Living for God

4 Therefore, since Christ suffered in his body,[w] arm yourselves also with the same attitude, because whoever suffers in the body is done with sin.[x] 2 As a result, they do not live the rest of their earthly lives for evil human desires,[y] but rather for the will of God. 3 For you have spent enough time in the past[z] doing what pagans choose to do — living in debauchery, lust, drunkenness, orgies, carousing and detestable idolatry.[a] 4 They are surprised that you do not join them in their reckless, wild living, and they heap abuse on you.[b] 5 But they will have to give account to him who is ready to judge the living and the dead.[c] 6 For this is the reason the gospel was preached even to those who are now dead,[d] so that they might be judged according to human standards in regard to the body, but live according to God in regard to the spirit.

7 The end of all things is near.[e] Therefore be alert and of sober mind[f] so that you may pray. 8 Above all, love each other deeply,[g] because love covers over a multitude of sins.[h] 9 Offer hospitality[i] to one another without grumbling.[j] 10 Each of you

3:21 [q] S Ac 22:16 [r] ver 16; S Ac 23:1 [s] 1Pe 1:3
3:22 [t] S Heb 4:14 [u] S Mk 16:19 [v] S Mt 28:18; S Ro 8:38
4:1 [w] S 1Pe 2:21 [x] S Ro 6:18
4:2 [y] Ro 6:2; 1Pe 1:14
4:3 [z] S Eph 2:2 [a] S Ro 13:13
4:4 [b] 1Pe 3:16
4:5 [c] S Ac 10:42
4:6 [d] 1Pe 3:19
4:7 [e] S Ro 13:11 [f] S Ac 24:25
4:8 [g] S 1Pe 1:22 [h] Pr 10:12; Jas 5:20
4:9 [i] S Ro 12:13 [j] Php 2:14

[a] *21* Or *but an appeal to God for a clear conscience*

3:21 *water symbolizes baptism.* There is a double figure here. The flood symbolizes baptism, and baptism symbolizes salvation achieved through "the washing of rebirth" (Titus 3:5; see note there). The flood was a figure of baptism in that in both instances the water that spoke of judgment (in the flood the death of the wicked, in baptism the death of Christ and the believer) is the water that saves. Baptism is a symbol of salvation in that it depicts Christ's death, burial and resurrection and our identification with him in these experiences (see Ro 6:4). *now saves you also.* In reality, believers are saved by what baptism symbolizes — Christ's death and resurrection. The symbol and the reality are so closely related that the symbol is sometimes used to refer to the reality (see note on Ro 6:3 – 4). *pledge of a clear conscience toward God.* The act of baptism is a commitment on the part of believers in all good conscience to make sure that what baptism symbolizes will become a reality in their lives. *saves you by the resurrection of Jesus Christ.* In the final analysis people are saved not by any ritual but by the supernatural power of the resurrection.
3:22 *gone into heaven.* See Ac 1:9 – 11. *at God's right hand.* See Heb 1:3 and note; 12:2. *angels, authorities and powers.* See vv. 19 – 20a; Eph 1:21; 6:12 and notes.
4:1 *Therefore.* Since 3:19 – 22 is parenthetical, 4:1 ties directly back to 3:18. The aspect of Christ's suffering that these passages stress is suffering unjustly because one has done good. Furthermore, it is physical suffering — "in his body." *arm yourselves also with the same attitude.* Believers are to be prepared also to suffer unjustly and to face such abuse with Christ's attitude — with his willingness to suffer for doing good. (For a similar principle in Paul's writings, see Php 2:5 – 11.) *because . . . is done with sin.* Such suffering enables believers to straighten out their priorities. Sinful desires and practices that once seemed important seem insignificant when one's life is in jeopardy. Serious suffering for Christ advances the progress of sanctification.
4:2 *for evil human desires . . . for the will of God.* Now that Christ's attitude prevails, God's will is the determining factor in life.
4:3 *time in the past.* The time before conversion (see Eph 2:1 – 3 and note on 2:1). *pagans.* Lit. "the Gentiles." Along with the term "idolatry," this suggests that at least some of the readers were Gentiles (see note on 1:1) who had been converted from a pagan lifestyle.
4:4 *They are surprised . . . and they heap abuse on you.* Godly living can bring persecution (see 2Ti 3:12 and note).
4:5 *have to give account.* See Mt 12:36; Ac 17:31; Ro 2:5,16 and note on 2:5. *him who is ready to judge.* In the NT both the Father and the Son are said to be judge on the great, final judgment day. The Father is the ultimate source of judgment, but he will delegate judgment to the Son (cf. Jn 5:27; Ac 17:31 and notes). *the living and the dead.* Those alive and those dead when the final judgment day dawns.
4:6 *For this is the reason.* The reason referred to is expressed in the latter part of the verse (in the "so that" clause), not in the preceding verse. *was preached even to those who are now dead.* This preaching was a past event. The word "now" does not occur in the Greek, but it is necessary to make it clear that the preaching was done not after these people had died but while they were still alive. (There will be no opportunity for people to be saved after death; see Heb 9:27.) *that they might be judged according to human standards in regard to the body.* The first reason that the gospel was preached to those now dead. Some say that this judgment is that to which all people must submit, either in this life (see Jn 5:24) or in the life to come (see v. 5). The gospel is preached to people in this life so that in Christ's death they may receive judgment now and avoid judgment to come. Others hold that these people are judged according to human standards by the pagan world, which does not understand why God's people no longer follow its sinful way of life (see vv. 2 – 4). So also the world misunderstood Christ (see Ac 2:22 – 24,36; 3:13 – 15; 5:30 – 32; 7:51 – 53). *but live according to God in regard to the spirit.* The second reason that the gospel was preached to those now dead. Some believe this means that all gospel preaching has as its goal that the hearers may live as God lives — eternally — and that this life is given by the Holy Spirit. Others maintain that it means that the ultimate reason for the preaching of the gospel is that God's people, even though the wicked world may abuse them and put them to death, will have eternal life, which the Holy Spirit imparts.
4:7 *The end . . . is near.* See note on Jas 5:9. *Therefore.* Anticipating the end times, particularly Christ's return, should influence believers' attitudes, actions and relationships (see 2Pe 3:11 – 14 and notes). *be alert and of sober mind.* Cf. 1:13; 5:8; 1Th 5:6. *so that you may pray.* Cf. 3:7 and note; 1Co 7:5.
4:8 *love each other deeply.* See 1Th 4:9; 2Pe 1:7 and notes; 1Jn 4:7 – 11. *love covers over . . . sins.* See Jas 5:20 and note. Love forgives again and again (see Mt 18:21 – 22 and note on 18:22; 1Co 13:5; Eph 4:32 and note).
4:9 *Offer hospitality.* See Ro 12:13 and note; 1Ti 3:2; 5:10; Titus 1:8; Heb 13:2 and note; 3Jn 5 – 8.
4:10 *use whatever gift you have received.* See Ro 12:4 – 8; 1Co 12:7 – 11 and notes.

Bust of Nero as a young man. Nero was the Roman emperor from AD 54 to 68 and was known for his persecution of Christians.

should use whatever gift you have received
to serve others,[k] as faithful[l] stewards of
God's grace in its various forms. 11 If anyone speaks, they should do so as one who
speaks the very words of God.[m] If anyone
serves, they should do so with the strength
God provides,[n] so that in all things God
may be praised[o] through Jesus Christ. To
him be the glory and the power for ever
and ever. Amen.[p]

4:10 [k]Ro 12:6,7 [l]1Co 4:2
4:11 [m]1Th 2:4 [n]Eph 6:10 [o]1Co 10:31 [p]S Ro 11:36
4:12 [q]1Pe 1:6,7
4:13 [r]S Mt 5:12 [s]S 2Co 1:5 [t]Ro 8:17; 1Pe 1:7; 5:1
4:14 [u]S Jn 15:21 [v]Mt 5:11
4:16 [w]Ac 5:41
4:17 [x]Jer 25:29; Eze 9:6; Am 3:2; 1Ti 3:15 [y]2Th 1:8
4:18 [z]Pr 11:31; Lk 23:31
4:19 [a]1Pe 2:15; 3:17
5:1 [b]S Ac 11:30 [c]S Lk 24:48 [d]1Pe 1:5,7; 4:13; Rev 1:9
5:2 [e]S Jn 21:16

Suffering for Being a Christian

12 Dear friends, do not be surprised at
the fiery ordeal that has come on you[q]
to test you, as though something strange
were happening to you. 13 But rejoice[r] inasmuch as you participate in the sufferings of
Christ,[s] so that you may be overjoyed when
his glory is revealed.[t] 14 If you are insulted because of the name of Christ,[u] you are
blessed,[v] for the Spirit of glory and of God
rests on you. 15 If you suffer, it should not
be as a murderer or thief or any other kind
of criminal, or even as a meddler. 16 However, if you suffer as a Christian, do not be
ashamed, but praise God that you bear that
name.[w] 17 For it is time for judgment to begin with God's household;[x] and if it begins
with us, what will the outcome be for those
who do not obey the gospel of God?[y] 18 And,

"If it is hard for the righteous to be
saved,
what will become of the ungodly
and the sinner?"[a][z]

19 So then, those who suffer according
to God's will[a] should commit themselves
to their faithful Creator and continue to
do good.

To the Elders and the Flock

5 To the elders among you, I appeal as a
fellow elder[b] and a witness[c] of Christ's
sufferings who also will share in the glory to be revealed:[d] 2 Be shepherds of God's
flock[e] that is under your care, watching

[a] *18* Prov. 11:31 (see Septuagint)

4:11 *very words.* The Greek for this phrase is used to refer to the Scriptures or to words God has spoken (see Ac 7:38; Ro 3:2 and note). *To him be the glory.* See 1Co 1:26–31 and note; Jude 24–25.
4:12 *do not be surprised at the fiery ordeal.* See 1:6–7 and note on 1:7; 2:20–21 and note on 2:21.
4:13 *rejoice inasmuch as you participate in the sufferings of Christ.* See Col 1:24 and note. Peter once rebelled against the idea that Christ would suffer (see Mt 16:21–23).
4:14 *insulted because of the name of Christ.* See Mt 5:11–12; Jn 15:18–20; Ac 5:41; 14:22; Ro 8:17 and note; 2Co 1:5; Php 3:10 and note; 2Ti 3:12 and note.
4:16 *Christian.* See note on Ac 11:26.
4:17 *judgment to begin with God's household.* The persecutions that believers were undergoing were divinely sent judgment intended to purify God's people. *the outcome . . . for those who do not obey the gospel.* If God brings judgment on his own people, how much more serious will the judgment be that he will bring on unbelievers!
5:1 *fellow elder.* See notes on Ex 3:16; 2Sa 3:17; Ac 20:17; 1Ti 3:1; 5:17. Peter, who identified himself as an apostle at the beginning of his letter (1:1), chooses now to identify himself with the elders of the churches (cf. 2Jn 1; 3Jn 1). This would be heartening to them in light of their great responsibilities and the difficult situation faced by the churches. The churches for which these elders were responsible were scattered across much of Asia Minor (see 1:1 and note), so if Peter was a local church officer he must have been officially related to one of them. *witness of Christ's sufferings.* Peter had been with Jesus from the early days of his ministry and was a witness of all its phases and aspects, including the climactic events of his suffering (cf. Mt 26:58; Mk 14:54; Lk 22:60–62; Jn 18:10–11,15–16). In this letter he bears notable witness to Christ's sufferings (see 2:21–24) and obeys his command in Ac 1:8. *share in the glory to be revealed.* See Ro 8:18. Peter witnessed Christ's glory in his ministry in general (see Jn 1:14; 2:11), and, as one present at the transfiguration (see 2Pe 1:16 and note; Mt 16:27; 17:8), he had already seen the glory of Christ's coming kingdom. In God's appointed time, just as Christ suffered and entered into glory, so all his people, after their sufferings, will participate in his future glory (see vv. 4,10).
5:2 *Be shepherds of God's flock.* A metaphor that our Lord himself had employed (Lk 15:3–7; Jn 10:1–18) and that must have been etched on Peter's mind (see Jn 21:15–17; cf. 1Pe 2:25). Peter is fulfilling Christ's command to feed his sheep as he writes this letter. What he writes to the elders is reminiscent of Paul's farewell address to the Ephesian elders (especially Ac 20:28; see note there). The term "shepherd" is an OT metaphor as well (see Eze 34:1–10, where the Lord holds the leaders of Israel responsible for failing to care for the flock). *watching over.* Or "overseeing." The same term is used in Ac 20:28; Php 1:1; 1Ti 3:2; Titus 1:7. See note on 1Ti 3:1. It is clear from this passage, as well as from

over them — not because you must, but
because you are willing, as God wants you
to be;[f] not pursuing dishonest gain,[g] but
eager to serve; 3 not lording it over[h] those
entrusted to you, but being examples[i] to
the flock. 4 And when the Chief Shepherd[j]
appears, you will receive the crown of glory[k] that will never fade away.[l]
5 In the same way, you who are younger,
submit yourselves[m] to your elders. All of
you, clothe yourselves with humility[n] toward one another, because,

> "God opposes the proud
> but shows favor to the humble."[a][o]

6 Humble yourselves, therefore, under
God's mighty hand, that he may lift you
up in due time.[p] 7 Cast all your anxiety on
him[q] because he cares for you.[r]
8 Be alert and of sober mind.[s] Your enemy the devil prowls around[t] like a roaring lion[u] looking for someone to devour.
9 Resist him,[v] standing firm in the faith,[w]
because you know that the family of believers throughout the world is undergoing
the same kind of sufferings.[x]
10 And the God of all grace, who called
you[y] to his eternal glory[z] in Christ, after
you have suffered a little while,[a] will himself restore you and make you strong,[b]
firm and steadfast. 11 To him be the power
for ever and ever. Amen.[c]

Final Greetings

12 With the help of Silas,[b][d] whom I regard as a faithful brother, I have written
to you briefly,[e] encouraging you and testifying that this is the true grace of God.
Stand fast in it.[f]
13 She who is in Babylon, chosen together with you, sends you her greetings, and
so does my son Mark.[g] 14 Greet one another with a kiss of love.[h]
Peace[i] to all of you who are in Christ.

[a] 5 Prov. 3:34 [b] 12 Greek *Silvanus*, a variant of *Silas*

5:2 [f] 2Co 9:7; Phm 14 [g] S 1Ti 3:3 **5:3** [h] Eze 34:4; Mt 20:25-28 [i] S 1Ti 4:12 **5:4** [j] S Jn 10:11 [k] S 1Co 9:25 [l] 1Pe 1:4 **5:5** [m] Eph 5:21 [n] 1Pe 3:8 [o] Pr 3:34; S Mt 23:12 **5:6** [p] Job 5:11; Jas 4:10 **5:7** [q] Ps 37:5; Mt 6:25 [r] Ps 55:22; Heb 13:5 **5:8** [s] S Ac 24:25 [t] Job 1:7 [u] 2Ti 4:17 **5:9** [v] S Jas 4:7 [w] Col 2:5 [x] S Ac 14:22 **5:10** [y] S Ro 8:28 [z] 2Co 4:17; 2Ti 2:10 [a] 1Pe 1:6 [b] Ps 18:32; 2Th 2:17 **5:11** [c] S Ro 11:36 **5:12** [d] S Ac 15:22 [e] Heb 13:22 [f] S 1Co 16:13 **5:13** [g] S Ac 12:12 **5:14** [h] S Ro 16:16 [i] S Eph 6:23

Ac 20:17,28, that the terms "elder," "overseer" and "shepherd" (pastor) all apply to one office (see note on Titus 1:7).
5:3 *not lording it over those entrusted to you.* Cf. Mt 16:24–27; Mk 10:42–45; Php 2:6–11; 2Th 3:9. Although Peter has full apostolic authority (see v. 1), he does not lord it over his readers in this letter but exemplifies the virtues he recommends.
5:4 *Chief Shepherd.* Christ. When he returns, he will reward those who have served as shepherds under him. See photo, p. 2100. *never fade away.* See 1:4 and note.
5:5 *submit yourselves.* The theme that runs throughout 2:13—3:6. *your elders.* See v. 1 and note; or "those who are older." *clothe yourselves with humility toward one another.* Peter may have had in mind the footwashing scene of Jn 13, in which he figured prominently. Although he was at first rebellious, he writes now with understanding (see Jn 13:7). *clothe ... with.* See note on Ps 109:29.
5:6 See Lk 14:11 and note. *lift you up in due time.* His help will come at just the right time (cf. Heb 4:16 and note).
5:7 See Php 4:6–7 and notes; cf. Ps 55:22.
5:8 *Be alert and of sober mind.* Cf. 1:13; 4:7; 1Th 5:6. *devil.* See 2Co 4:4; 1Jn 3:8 and notes.
5:9 *Resist him.* See Jas 4:7 and note. *family of believers.* See note on Ac 11:1. They are not isolated; they belong to a fellowship of suffering.
5:10,12,14 *grace ... grace ... Peace.* See note on Ro 1:7.
5:10 *God of all grace.* Cf. 1:10,13 and notes.
5:12 *With the help of Silas.* Silas may have been the bearer of the letter to its destination. He may also have been a scribe who recorded what Peter dictated or who aided, as an informed and intelligent secretary, in the phrasing of Peter's thoughts (see Introduction: Author and Date). *encouraging ... grace of God.* See Introduction: Themes.
5:13 *She.* Perhaps a Christian congregation (see 2Jn 1 and note). *Babylon.* See Introduction: Place of Writing. *chosen.* See note on Eph 1:4. *my son Mark.* Peter regards Mark with such warmth and affection that he calls him his son. It is possible that Peter had led Mark to faith in Christ (cf. 1Ti 1:2 and note). Early Christian tradition closely associates Mark and Peter (see Introduction to Mark: Author).
5:14 *kiss.* See note on 1Co 16:20. *Peace to all ... in Christ.* Spiritual well-being and blessedness to all who are united to Christ. Peter thus ends with a reference to the union of believers with Christ (see note on Eph 1:1), a concept fundamental to the understanding of the whole letter.

2 PETER

INTRODUCTION

Author

The author identifies himself as Simon Peter (1:1). He uses the first person singular pronoun in a highly personal passage (1:12 – 15) and claims to be an eyewitness of the transfiguration (1:16 – 18 [see note on 1:16]; cf. Mt 17:1 – 5). He asserts that this is his second letter to the readers (3:1) and refers to Paul as "our dear brother" (3:15; see note there). In short, the letter claims to be Peter's, and its character is compatible with that claim.

Although 2 Peter was not as widely known and recognized in the early church as 1 Peter, some may have used and accepted it as authoritative as early as the second century and perhaps even in the latter part of the first century (1 Clement [AD 95] may allude to it). It was not ascribed to Peter until Origen's time (185 – 253), and he seems to reflect some doubt concerning it. Eusebius (265 – 340) placed it among the questioned books, though he admits that most accept it as from Peter. After Eusebius's time, it seems to have been quite generally accepted as canonical.

In recent centuries, however, its genuineness has been challenged by a considerable number of interpreters. One of the objections that has been raised is the difference in style from that of 1 Peter. But the difference is not absolute; there are noteworthy similarities in vocabulary and in other matters. In fact, no other known writing is as much like 1 Peter as 2 Peter. The differences that do exist may be accounted for by variations in subject matter, in the form and purpose of the letters, in the time and circumstances of writing, in sources used or models followed and in scribes who may have been employed. Perhaps most significant is the statement in 1Pe 5:12 that Silas assisted in the writing of 1 Peter. No such statement is made concerning 2 Peter, which may explain its noticeable difference in style (see Introduction to 1 Peter: Author and Date).

Other objections arise from a secular reconstruction of early Christian history or misunderstandings or misconstructions of the available data. For example, some argue that the reference to Paul's letters in 3:15 – 16 indicates an advanced date for this book — beyond Peter's lifetime. But it is quite possible that

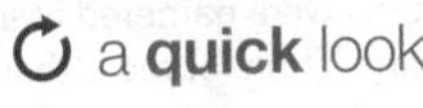

Author:
The apostle Peter

Audience:
Christians in western Asia Minor

Date:
Between AD 65 and 68

Theme:
Peter teaches how to deal with false teachers and evildoers who have come into the church.

Aerial view of Mount Tabor, a possible site for Jesus' transfiguration. Peter refers to this event in 2 Peter 1:17 – 18.

Paul's letters were gathered at an early date, since some of them had been in existence and perhaps in circulation for more than ten years (Thessalonians by as much as 15 years) prior to Peter's death. Besides, what Peter says may only indicate that he was acquainted with some of Paul's letters (communication in the Roman world and in the early church was good), not that there was a formal, ecclesiastical collection of them.

Date

2 Peter was written toward the end of Peter's life (cf. 1:12 – 15), after he had written a prior letter (3:1) to the same readers (probably 1 Peter). Since Peter was martyred during the reign of Nero, his death must have occurred prior to AD 68, so it is very likely that he wrote 2 Peter between 65 and 68.

Some have argued that this date is too early for the writing of 2 Peter, but nothing in the book requires a later date. The error combated is comparable to the kind of heresy present in the first century. To insist that the second chapter was directed against second-century Gnosticism is to assume more than the contents of the chapter warrant. While the heretics referred to in 2 Peter may well have been among the forerunners of second-century Gnostics, nothing is said of them that would not fit into the later years of Peter's life.

Some have suggested a later date because they interpret the reference to the "ancestors" in 3:4 to mean an earlier Christian generation. However, the word is most naturally interpreted as the OT patriarchs (cf. Jn 6:31; Ac 3:13; Heb 1:1). Similarly, reference to Paul and his letters (3:15 – 16; see Author) does not require a date beyond Peter's lifetime.

2 Peter and Jude

There are conspicuous similarities between 2 Peter and Jude (compare 2Pe 2 with Jude 4 – 18), but there are also significant differences. It has been suggested that one borrowed from the other or that they both drew on a common source. If there is borrowing, it is not a slavish borrowing but one that adapts to suit the writer's purpose. While many have insisted that Jude used Peter, it is more reasonable to assume that the longer letter (Peter) incorporated much of the shorter (Jude). Such borrowing is fairly common in ancient writings. For example, many believe that Paul used parts of early hymns in Php 2:6 – 11 and 1Ti 3:16.

Purpose

In his first letter Peter feeds Christ's sheep by instructing them how to deal with persecution from outside the church (see 1Pe 4:12); in this second letter he teaches them how to deal with false teachers and evildoers who have come into the church (see 2:1; 3:3 – 4 and notes). While the

Remains of the fifth-century church built over a house believed to have been Peter's at Capernaum

www.HolyLandPhotos.org

Peter's purpose is to stimulate Christian growth, to combat false teaching and to encourage watchfulness for the Lord's certain return.

particular situations naturally call for variations in content and emphasis, in both letters Peter as a pastor ("shepherd") of Christ's sheep (see Jn 21:15 – 17) seeks to commend to his readers a wholesome combination of Christian faith and practice. More specifically, his purpose is threefold: (1) to stimulate Christian growth (ch. 1), (2) to combat false teaching (ch. 2) and (3) to encourage watchfulness in view of the Lord's certain return (ch. 3).

Outline

- I. Greetings (1:1 – 2)
- II. Exhortation to Growth in Christian Virtues (1:3 – 11)
  - A. The Divine Enablement (1:3 – 4)
  - B. The Call for Growth (1:5 – 7)
  - C. The Value of Such Growth (1:8 – 11)
- III. The Purpose and Authentication of Peter's Message (1:12 – 21)
  - A. His Aim in Writing (1:12 – 15)
  - B. The Basis of His Authority (1:16 – 21)
- IV. Warning against False Teachers (ch. 2)
  - A. Their Coming Predicted (2:1 – 3a)
  - B. Their Judgment Assured (2:3b – 9)
  - C. Their Characteristics Set Forth (2:10 – 22)
- V. The Fact of Christ's Return (3:1 – 16)
  - A. Peter's Purpose in Writing Restated (3:1 – 2)
  - B. The Coming of Scoffers (3:3 – 7)
  - C. The Certainty of Christ's Return (3:8 – 10)
  - D. Exhortations Based on the Fact of Christ's Return (3:11 – 16)
- VI. Conclusion and Doxology (3:17 – 18)

1 Simon Peter, a servant[a] and apostle of
Jesus Christ,[b]

To those who through the righteousness[c] of our God and Savior Jesus Christ[d]
have received a faith as precious as ours:

2 Grace and peace be yours in abundance[e] through the knowledge of God and
of Jesus our Lord.[f]

Confirming One's Calling and Election

3 His divine power[g] has given us everything we need for a godly life through our
knowledge of him[h] who called us[i] by his
own glory and goodness. 4 Through these
he has given us his very great and precious promises,[j] so that through them you
may participate in the divine nature,[k] having escaped the corruption in the world
caused by evil desires.[l]
5 For this very reason, make every effort
to add to your faith goodness; and to goodness, knowledge;[m] 6 and to knowledge,
self-control;[n] and to self-control, perseverance;[o] and to perseverance, godliness;[p]
7 and to godliness, mutual affection; and to
mutual affection, love.[q] 8 For if you possess
these qualities in increasing measure, they
will keep you from being ineffective and
unproductive[r] in your knowledge of our
Lord Jesus Christ.[s] 9 But whoever does not
have them is nearsighted and blind,[t] forgetting that they have been cleansed from
their past sins.[u]
10 Therefore, my brothers and sisters,[a]
make every effort to confirm your calling[v]
and election. For if you do these things,
you will never stumble,[w] 11 and you will receive a rich welcome into the eternal kingdom[x] of our Lord and Savior Jesus Christ.[y]

Prophecy of Scripture

12 So I will always remind you of these
things,[z] even though you know them and
are firmly established in the truth[a] you
now have. 13 I think it is right to refresh
your memory[b] as long as I live in the tent

[a] 10 The Greek word for *brothers and sisters* (*adelphoi*) refers here to believers, both men and women, as part of God's family.

1:1 [a] Ro 1:1 [b] 1Pe 1:1 [c] Ro 3:21-26 [d] Titus 2:13 **1:2** [e] S Ro 1:7 [f] ver 3,8; 2Pe 2:20; 3:18; S Php 3:8 **1:3** [g] 1Pe 1:5 [h] S ver 2 [i] S Ro 8:28 **1:4** [j] 2Co 7:1 [k] Eph 4:24; Heb 12:10; 1Jn 3:2 [l] Jas 1:27; 2Pe 2:18-20 **1:5** [m] S ver 2; Col 2:3 **1:6** [n] S Ac 24:25 [o] S Heb 10:36 [p] ver 3 **1:7** [q] S Ro 12:10; 1Th 3:12 **1:8** [r] Jn 15:2; Col 1:10; Titus 3:14 [s] S ver 2 **1:9** [t] 1Jn 2:11 [u] Eph 5:26; S Mt 1:21 **1:10** [v] S Ro 8:28 [w] Ps 15:5; 2Pe 3:17; Jude 24

1:11 [x] Ps 145:13; 2Ti 4:18 [y] 2Pe 2:20; 3:18 **1:12** [z] Php 3:1; 1Jn 2:21; Jude 5 [a] 2Jn 2 **1:13** [b] 2Pe 3:1

1:1 *Simon Peter.* See Introduction to 1 Peter: Author; Date; see also notes on Mt 16:18; Jn 1:42. *servant.* See note on Ro 1:1. *apostle.* See notes on Mk 6:30; 1Co 1:1; Heb 3:1. *To those.* Probably the same people as those in 1Pe 1:1. *God and Savior Jesus Christ.* Assumes that Jesus is both God and Savior. For other passages that ascribe deity to Christ, see note on Ro 9:5. *have received.* God in his justice ("righteousness") imparts to people the ability to believe. *a faith.* Not here a body of truth to be believed—the faith—but the act of believing, or the God-given capacity to trust in Christ for salvation.
1:2 *Grace and peace.* See note on Ro 1:7. *knowledge of God and of Jesus.* The concept of Christian knowledge is prominent in 2 Peter (see vv. 3,5,8 and note on v. 3; 3:18 and note). Peter was combating heretical teaching, and one of the best antidotes for heresy is true knowledge.
1:3 *everything we need for a godly life.* God has made available all that we need spiritually through our knowledge of him. If 2 Peter was written to combat an incipient Gnosticism, the apostle may be insisting that the knowledge possessed by those in apostolic circles was entirely adequate to meet their spiritual needs. No secret, esoteric knowledge is necessary for salvation (see Introduction to 1 John: Gnosticism). *godly.* True godliness is a genuine reverence toward God that governs one's attitude toward every aspect of life (see 1Ti 2:2 and note). *glory and goodness.* The excellence of God: "Glory" expresses the excellence of his being—his attributes and essence; "goodness" depicts excellence expressed in deeds—virtue in action. God uses both to bring about our salvation.
1:4 *Through these.* Through God's excellence—internal and external—he has given us great promises. Their nature is suggested in the words that follow: participation in the divine nature and escape from worldly corruption. *participate in the divine nature.* Does not indicate that Christians become divine in any sense, but only that we are indwelt by God through his Holy Spirit (see Jn 14:16–17 and notes). Our humanity and his deity, as well as the human personality and the divine, remain distinct and separate. *world.* See note on Jn 1:9. *evil desires.* See 2:10 and note.

1:5–9 The virtues that will produce a well-rounded, fruitful Christian life (see Gal 5:22–23 and note).
1:5 *faith.* The root of the Christian life (see v. 1 and note). *goodness.* Cf. v. 3 and note. *knowledge.* See notes on vv. 2–3.
1:6 *self-control.* According to many of the false teachers, knowledge made self-control unnecessary; according to Peter, Christian knowledge leads to self-control (cf. Pr 25:28; Gal 5:23).
1:7 *mutual affection.* Warmhearted affection toward all in the family of faith. *love.* The kind of outgoing, selfless attitude that leads one to sacrifice for the good of others (see note on 1Pe 4:8).
1:8 *if you possess these qualities.* Peter does not mean to imply that the believer is to cultivate each listed quality in turn, one after the other, until all have been perfected. Instead, they are all to be cultivated simultaneously. *increasing measure.* Peter has continuing spiritual growth in mind (cf. 3:18; 1Pe 2:2; Php 3:10; 1Th 3:12). *keep you from being … unproductive in your knowledge.* Christians' knowledge should affect the way they live. It does not set them free from moral restraints, as the heretics taught (see Introduction to 1 John: Gnosticism). Rather, it produces holiness and all such virtues (cf. Col 1:9–12).
1:9 *nearsighted and blind.* Since one cannot be both at the same time, Peter may have in mind a possible alternative meaning for "nearsighted," namely, "to shut the eyes." Such people are blind because they have closed their eyes to the truth (see 1Jn 2:11).
1:10 *brothers and sisters.* See NIV text note. *confirm your calling and election.* By cultivating the qualities listed in vv. 5–7, they and others can be assured that God has chosen them and called them (cf. Mt 7:20; Gal 5:6; Jas 2:18 and notes). When God elects and calls, it is to obedience and holiness (see 1Pe 1:2; Eph 1:3–6 and notes), and these fruits confirm their divine source. *never stumble.* Those who in this way give evidence of their faith will never cease to persevere.
1:11 *receive a rich welcome.* By producing the fruits Peter is commending to them (see vv. 5–10). *eternal kingdom.* Eternal life (cf. Mt 25:46).
1:12 See Ro 15:15; Php 3:1; 1Jn 2:21.
1:13 *tent of this body.* See Jn 1:14; 2Co 5:1 and notes.

of this body,[c] 14 because I know that I will
soon put it aside,[d] as our Lord Jesus Christ
has made clear to me.[e] 15 And I will make
every effort to see that after my departure[f]
you will always be able to remember these
things.
16 For we did not follow cleverly devised
stories when we told you about the coming of our Lord Jesus Christ in power,[g]
but we were eyewitnesses of his majesty.[h]
17 He received honor and glory from God
the Father when the voice came to him
from the Majestic Glory, saying, "This is
my Son, whom I love; with him I am well
pleased."[a][i] 18 We ourselves heard this voice
that came from heaven when we were
with him on the sacred mountain.[j]
19 We also have the prophetic message
as something completely reliable,[k] and you
will do well to pay attention to it, as to a
light[l] shining in a dark place, until the day
dawns[m] and the morning star[n] rises in your
hearts.[o] 20 Above all, you must understand[p]
that no prophecy of Scripture came about
by the prophet's own interpretation of
things. 21 For prophecy never had its origin
in the human will, but prophets, though
human, spoke from God[q] as they were carried along by the Holy Spirit.[r]

False Teachers and Their Destruction

2 But there were also false prophets[s]
among the people, just as there will
be false teachers among you.[t] They will
secretly introduce destructive heresies,
even denying the sovereign Lord[u] who
bought them[v]—bringing swift destruction
on themselves. 2 Many will follow their depraved conduct[w] and will bring the way of
truth into disrepute. 3 In their greed[x] these
teachers will exploit you[y] with fabricated
stories. Their condemnation has long been
hanging over them, and their destruction
has not been sleeping.
4 For if God did not spare angels when
they sinned,[z] but sent them to hell,[b] putting them in chains of darkness[c] to be held

1:13 [c] Isa 38:12; 2Co 5:1,4 **1:14** [d] 2Ti 4:6 [e] Jn 13:36; 21:18,19 **1:15** [f] Lk 9:31 **1:16** [g] Mk 13:26; 14:62 [h] Mt 17:1-8 **1:17** [i] S Mt 3:17 **1:18** [j] Mt 17:6 **1:19** [k] 1Pe 1:10, 11 [l] Ps 119:105 [m] Lk 1:78 [n] Rev 22:16 [o] 2Co 4:6 **1:20** [p] 2Pe 3:3 **1:21** [q] 2Ti 3:16 [r] 2Sa 23:2; Ac 1:16; 3:18; 1Pe 1:11 **2:1** [s] Dt 13:1-3; Jer 6:13; S Mt 7:15 [t] 1Ti 4:1 [u] Jude 4 [v] S 1Co 6:20 **2:2** [w] Jude 4 **2:3** [x] ver 14 [y] 2Co 2:17; 1Th 2:5 **2:4** [z] Ge 6:1-4

[a] 17 Matt. 17:5; Mark 9:7; Luke 9:35 [b] 4 Greek *Tartarus* [c] 4 Some manuscripts *in gloomy dungeons*

1:14 *Christ has made clear to me.* Either the revelation recorded in Jn 21:18–19 (see notes there) or a subsequent one.
1:15 *departure.* Greek *exodos* ("exodus"), a euphemism for death also in Lk 9:31 (see note there). *always be able to remember these things.* An aim that was realized, whether intentionally or unintentionally, through the Gospel of Mark, which early tradition connected with Peter.
1:16 *cleverly devised stories.* Peter's message was based on his eyewitness account of the supernatural events that marked the life of Jesus. It was not made up of myths and imaginative stories, as was the message of the heretics of 2:3 (see note there). *coming of our Lord Jesus Christ.* In Christ's transfiguration the disciples received a foretaste of what his coming will be like when he returns to establish his eternal kingdom (see Mt 16:28 and note). *eyewitnesses of his majesty.* A reference to Christ's transfiguration (see vv. 17–18; Mt 16:28—17:8).
1:18 *sacred mountain.* See note on Lk 9:28.
1:19–21 Peter's message rests on two solid foundations: (1) the voice from God at the transfiguration (vv. 16–18) and (2) the still more significant testimony of Scripture (vv. 19–21). An alternative, but less probable, view is that the apostles' testimony to the transfiguration fulfills and thus confirms the Scriptures that predicted such things.
1:19 *morning star.* See Rev 22:16; cf. Nu 24:17 and note.
1:20 Two major views of this verse are: (1) No prophecy is to be privately or independently interpreted (cf. the false teachers in 3:16). The Holy Spirit, Scripture itself and the church should be included in the interpretative process. (2) No prophecy originated through the prophet's own interpretation (the sense of the NIV). The preceding and following contexts indicate that this view is probably to be preferred. In vv. 16–18 the subject discussed is the origin of the apostolic message. Did it come from human imaginings, or was it from God? In v. 21 again the subject is origin. No prophecy of Scripture arose from a merely human interpretation of things. This understanding of v. 20 is further supported by the explanatory "For" with which v. 21 begins. Verse 21 explains v. 20 by restating its content and then affirming God as the origin of prophecy.
1:21 *carried along by the Holy Spirit.* See 2Ti 3:16 and note. In the production of Scripture both God and humans were active participants. God was the source of the content of Scripture, so that what it says is what God has said. But the human authors also spoke actively; they were more than recorders, yet what they said came from God. Although actively speaking, "they were carried along by the Holy Spirit."
2:1 *false prophets.* See 1Ki 18:19; Isa 9:13–17; Jer 5:31; 14:14; 23:30–32 and note on 23:31; Mic 3:5,7 and notes. *there will be false teachers among you.* Numerous NT passages warn of false teachers who are already present or yet to come (see Mt 24:4–5,11; Ac 20:29–30; Gal 1:6–9; Php 3:2; Col 2:4,8,18,20–23; 2Th 2:1–3; 1Ti 1:3–7; 4:1–3; 2Ti 3:1–8; 1Jn 2:18–19,22–23; 2Jn 7–11; Jude 3–4). *destructive heresies.* Divisive opinions or teachings that result in the moral and spiritual destruction of those who accept them. *sovereign Lord who bought them.* See Jude 4 and note; does not necessarily mean that the false teachers were believers. Christ's death paid the penalty for their sin, but it would not become effective for their salvation unless they trusted in Christ as Savior. (However, see vv. 20–22, where it is obvious that the heretics had at least professed knowing the Lord.) *swift destruction.* Not immediate physical calamity but sudden doom, whether at death or at the Lord's second coming (cf. Mt 24:50–51; 2Th 1:9 and note).
2:2 *depraved conduct.* Open, extreme immorality not held in check by any sense of shame. *way of truth.* See Ps 119:30. The Christian faith is not only correct doctrine but also correct living.
2:3 *In their greed.* They will be motivated by a desire for money (see 2Co 2:17 and note) and will commercialize the Christian faith to their own selfish advantage. *fabricated stories.* See note on 1:16. *condemnation has long been hanging over them.* Long ago, in OT times, their condemnation was declared (see vv. 4–9 for OT examples of the fact that judgment is coming on the wicked). *destruction has not been sleeping.* Although delay makes it seem that they have escaped God's judgment, destruction is a reality that is sure to come upon them.
2:4–8 Three examples showing that God will rescue the godly and destroy the wicked.
2:4 *angels when they sinned.* Some believe this sin was the one referred to in Ge 6:2, where the sons of God are said to

for judgment;[a] 5 if he did not spare the ancient world[b] when he brought the flood on
its ungodly people,[c] but protected Noah, a
preacher of righteousness, and seven others;[d] 6 if he condemned the cities of Sodom
and Gomorrah by burning them to ashes,[e]
and made them an example[f] of what is going to happen to the ungodly;[g] 7 and if he
rescued Lot,[h] a righteous man, who was
distressed by the depraved conduct of the
lawless[i] 8 (for that righteous man,[j] living
among them day after day, was tormented
in his righteous soul by the lawless deeds
he saw and heard)— 9 if this is so, then
the Lord knows how to rescue the godly
from trials[k] and to hold the unrighteous
for punishment on the day of judgment.[l]
10 This is especially true of those who follow the corrupt desire[m] of the flesh[a] and
despise authority.

Bold and arrogant, they are not afraid to
heap abuse on celestial beings;[n] 11 yet even
angels, although they are stronger and
more powerful, do not heap abuse on such
beings when bringing judgment on them
from[b] the Lord.[o] 12 But these people blaspheme in matters they do not understand.
They are like unreasoning animals, creatures of instinct, born only to be caught
and destroyed, and like animals they too
will perish.[p]

13 They will be paid back with harm for
the harm they have done. Their idea of
pleasure is to carouse in broad daylight.[q]
They are blots and blemishes, reveling in
their pleasures while they feast with you.[c r]
14 With eyes full of adultery, they never
stop sinning; they seduce[s] the unstable;[t]
they are experts in greed[u]—an accursed
brood![v] 15 They have left the straight way
and wandered off to follow the way of Balaam[w] son of Bezer,[d] who loved the wages
of wickedness. 16 But he was rebuked for

2:4 [a] 1Ti 3:6; Jude 6; Rev 20:1,2 **2:5** [b] 2Pe 3:6 [c] Ge 6:5-8:19 [d] Heb 11:7; 1Pe 3:20 **2:6** [e] Ge 19:24,25 [f] Nu 26:10; Jude 7 [g] Mt 10:15; 11:23,24; Ro 9:29 **2:7** [h] Ge 19:16 [i] 2Pe 3:17 **2:8** [j] Heb 11:4 **2:9** [k] Ps 37:33; S Ro 15:31; Rev 3:10 [l] S Mt 10:15 **2:10** [m] 2Pe 3:3; Jude 16,18 [n] Jude 8 **2:11** [o] Jude 9 **2:12** [p] Ps 49:12; Jude 10 **2:13** [q] S Ro 13:13; 1Th 5:7 [r] 1Co 11:20,21; Jude 12 **2:14** [s] ver 18 [t] Jas 1:8; 2Pe 3:16 [u] ver 3 [v] Eph 2:3 **2:15** [w] Nu 22:4-20; 31:16; Dt 23:4; Jude 11; Rev 2:14

[a] *10* In contexts like this, the Greek word for *flesh* (*sarx*) refers to the sinful state of human beings, often presented as a power in opposition to the Spirit; also in verse 18. [b] *11* Many manuscripts *beings in the presence of* [c] *13* Some manuscripts *in their love feasts* [d] *15* Greek *Bosor*

have intermarried with human daughters, meaning (according to this view) that angels married human women. The offspring of those marriages are said to have been the Nephilim (Ge 6:4; see notes on Ge 6:2,4). But since it appears impossible for angels, who are spirits, to have sexual relations with women, the sin referred to in this verse probably occurred before the fall of Adam and Eve. The angels who fell became the devil and the evil angels (probably the demons and evil spirits referred to in the NT). *sent them to hell.* See NIV text note. *Tartarus* was the term used by the Greeks to designate the place where the most wicked spirits were sent to be punished. Why some evil angels are imprisoned and others are free to serve Satan as demons is not explained in Scripture. *judgment.* The final judgment, probably associated with the "great white throne" judgment of Rev 20:11–15.

2:5 *ungodly people.* See Ge 6:5,11–12. *preacher of righteousness.* A description of Noah found nowhere else in Scripture. However, similar descriptions are used of him in Josephus (*Antiquities*, 1.3.1), *1 Clement* (7.6; 9.4) and the *Sibylline Oracles* (1.128–29). *seven others.* Noah's wife, three sons and three daughters-in-law (Noah was the eighth; see 1Pe 3:20).

2:6 *condemned the cities of Sodom and Gomorrah.* See Ge 19.

2:7 *distressed by the depraved conduct.* See Ge 19:4–9. How Lot could be so distressed, how he could be called a "righteous man" and yet offer to turn over his two daughters to the wicked townsmen to be sexually abused is difficult to understand apart from a knowledge of the code of honor characteristic of that day (see note on Ge 19:8).

2:9 States the point made in vv. 4–8—the wicked whose coming Peter predicts will surely be punished.

2:10 *This is especially true.* The heretics of Peter's day are certain to come under judgment for two main reasons: (1) They "follow the corrupt desire of the flesh," referring to inordinate sexual indulgence (see v. 18; 1:4; 3:3). (2) They "despise authority." *heap abuse on celestial beings.* A specific example of despising authority. This could refer to the slander of earthly dignitaries such as church leaders, which might well be expected from such shameless peddlers of error. On the other hand, it could refer to the blaspheming of angels, as the NIV text suggests. This view seems more likely since the parallel passage in Jude 8–10 is speaking of angels.

2:11 *angels . . . do not heap abuse on.* Even good angels, who might have more right to do so because of their greater power, do not bring such accusations against inferior, evil angels.

2:12 *matters they do not understand.* The heresy to which Peter refers may have been an early form of second-century Gnosticism (see Introduction to 1 John: Gnosticism) that claimed to possess special, esoteric knowledge. If so, it is ironic that those who professed special knowledge acted out of abysmal ignorance, and the result was arrogant blasphemy. *like unreasoning animals.* A scathing denunciation. They are like irrational animals, whose lives are guided by mere instinct and who are born merely to be slaughtered. Destruction is their final lot.

2:13 *carouse in broad daylight.* See 1Th 5:7. Even the pagan world carried on its corrupt practices under cover of darkness, but these heretics were utterly shameless. *in their pleasures while they feast with you.* See NIV text note. Jude 12 without doubt reads "love feasts," which may well have been the intended reading here. These false teachers seem to have been involved in the sacred feasts of brotherly love that, in the early church, accompanied the Lord's Supper. In fact, it appears that they injected their carousing into these holy observances and delighted in their shameless acts (cf. 1Co 11:17–22,27–34 and notes on 11:20–22).

2:14 *eyes full of adultery.* Lit. "eyes full of an adulterous woman," which means that they desired every woman they saw, viewing her as a potential sexual partner (see Job 31:1; Mt 5:28 and notes). *never stop sinning.* Their eyes serve as constant instruments of lust. *seduce the unstable.* For a parallel use of the Greek for "seduce," see Jas 1:14 and note. It depicts the fisherman who attempts to lure and catch fish with bait. *experts in greed.* The Greek text implies that they had exercised themselves like an athlete, not in physical activity but in greed.

2:15 *way of Balaam son of Bezer.* See Nu 22–24. Balaam was bent on cursing Israel, though God had forbidden it. He wanted the money Balak offered him. Similarly, these false teachers apparently were guilty of attempting to extract money from naive listeners. For a donkey to rebuke the prophet's madness (v. 16) reflects not only on the foolishness of Balaam but also on that of the false teachers of Peter's day.

his wrongdoing by a donkey—an animal
without speech—who spoke with a human voice and restrained the prophet's
madness.[x]
17 These people are springs without water[y] and mists driven by a storm. Blackest
darkness is reserved for them.[z] 18 For they
mouth empty, boastful words[a] and, by appealing to the lustful desires of the flesh,
they entice people who are just escaping[b]
from those who live in error. 19 They promise them freedom, while they themselves
are slaves of depravity—for "people are
slaves to whatever has mastered them."[c]
20 If they have escaped the corruption of
the world by knowing[d] our Lord and Savior Jesus Christ[e] and are again entangled
in it and are overcome, they are worse off
at the end than they were at the beginning.[f] 21 It would have been better for them
not to have known the way of righteousness, than to have known it and then to
turn their backs on the sacred command
that was passed on to them.[g] 22 Of them
the proverbs are true: "A dog returns to its
vomit,"[a][h] and, "A sow that is washed returns to her wallowing in the mud."

The Day of the Lord

3 Dear friends,[i] this is now my second
letter to you. I have written both of
them as reminders[j] to stimulate you to
wholesome thinking. 2 I want you to recall
the words spoken in the past by the holy
prophets[k] and the command given by our
Lord and Savior through your apostles.[l]
3 Above all, you must understand that
in the last days[m] scoffers will come, scoff-
ing and following their own evil desires.[n]
4 They will say, "Where is this 'coming' he
promised?[o] Ever since our ancestors died,
everything goes on as it has since the beginning of creation."[p] 5 But they deliberately forget that long ago by God's word[q]

2:16 [x] Nu 22:21-30 **2:17** [y] Jude 12 [z] Jude 13 **2:18** [a] Jude 16 [b] ver 20; 2Pe 1:4 **2:19** [c] S Ro 6:16 **2:20** [d] S 2Pe 1:2 [e] 2Pe 1:11; 3:18 [f] Mt 12:45 **2:21** [g] Eze 18:24; Heb 6:4-6; 10:26,27 **2:22** [h] Pr 26:11 **3:1** [i] S 1Co 10:14 [j] 2Pe 1:13 **3:2** [k] Lk 1:70; Ac 3:21 [l] S Eph 4:11 **3:3** [m] 1Ti 4:1; 2Ti 3:1 [n] 2Pe 2:10; Jude 18 **3:4** [o] Isa 5:19; Eze 12:22; Mt 24:48; S Lk 17:30 [p] Mk 10:6 **3:5** [q] Ge 1:6,9; Heb 11:3

[a] *22* Prov. 26:11

2:17 *springs without water.* A picture of cruel deception. The thirsty traveler comes to the spring expecting cool, refreshing water but finds it dry (see Jer 15:18 and note). So the false teachers promise satisfying truth but in reality have nothing to offer. *mists driven by a storm.* Gone before a drop of moisture falls. *Blackest darkness.* Their destiny is hell.

2:18 *mouth empty, boastful words.* Words that sound impressive to the new convert but in reality have nothing to offer. *lustful desires.* See v. 10 and note. *entice.* See note on v. 14 ("seduce"). *people who are just escaping.* New converts who have just broken away from pagan friends. Thus the depraved false teachers prey on new converts, who have not yet had a chance to develop spiritual resistance.

2:19 *They promise them freedom.* Probably freedom from moral restraint (cf. 1Co 6:12–13; Gal 5:13 and notes). The very ones who promise freedom from bondage to rules and regulations are themselves slaves of depravity. Freedom from law resulted in bondage to sin, and liberty was turned into license.

2:20–22 Some point to this passage as clear proof that genuinely saved persons may lose their salvation. They know the Lord; they escape the world's corruption; they know the way of righteousness. Then they turn away from the message and go back to their old way of life. Their knowledge is said to have been genuine; their change of life was real; and their return to their old way of life was not superficial. Others insist that their knowledge of the Lord and of the way of righteousness could not have been genuine. If such people had been truly regenerated, they would have persevered in their faith. It is argued that the teaching of Jn 10:27–30 (especially v. 28) and Ro 8:28–39 makes it clear that no genuinely saved person can be lost. Thus, according to this view, the persons described here could not have been genuinely saved. See v. 22 and note; 1Jn 2:19.

2:20 *If they have escaped the corruption of the world.* A reference to false teachers who had once apparently been believers in Christ. Their professed knowledge of Christ had at least produced a change in lifestyle. *again entangled in it and are overcome.* A complete return to the old, sinful pattern of life.

2:21 *better … not to have known the way of righteousness.* Knowledge of the way increases people's responsibility and their hardness of heart if they then reject it. In its early days, Christianity was known as "the Way" (Ac 9:2 [see note there]; 19:9,23; 22:4; 24:14,22). *sacred command.* The whole Christian message that people are commanded to receive (cf. note on Jude 3).

2:22 *A dog returns … A sow … returns.* In both cases the nature of the animal is not changed. The sow returns to the mud because by nature it is still a sow. The change was merely cosmetic.

3:1 *second letter.* The first letter may have been 1 Peter, though there is some reason to doubt this identification. For example, 1 Peter cannot be very accurately described as a reminder. *reminders.* See 1:12–13,15.

3:2 *holy prophets.* OT personages. *command.* See note on 2:21. *your apostles.* Peter places the OT prophets and the NT apostles on an equal plane. Both are vehicles of God's sacred truth. Peter, being one of the apostles, can speak with knowledge and authority as a representative of the apostolic group.

3:3 *last days.* An expression that refers to the whole period introduced by Christ's first coming. These days are last in comparison to OT days, which were preliminary and preparatory (see notes on Heb 1:1–2). Also, the Christian era is the time of the beginnings of prophetic fulfillment. *scoffers will come.* Perhaps the same false teachers described in ch. 2 (e.g., they follow their own evil desires; cf. 2:10,18–19). In ch. 3, however, the emphasis is on Christ's return. These people may have been early Gnostics who resisted the idea of a time of judgment and moral accountability. *evil desires.* See 2:10 and note.

3:4 *he.* Christ. *Ever since our ancestors died.* Either the first Christians to die after Christ's death and resurrection (e.g., Stephen, James the brother of John and other early Christian leaders who had died; cf. Heb 13:7 and note) or the OT patriarchs (see Introduction: Date). *everything goes on as it has.* Their argument against Christ's return was: Since it has not occurred up to this time, it will never occur. That nature is not subject to divine intervention, they say, has been proved by observation (1) of the period since the ancestors died—perhaps 30 years—and (2) of the period since creation.

3:5 *they deliberately forget.* Ignoring the flood as a divine intervention was not an oversight; it was deliberate. They did not want to face up to the fallacy in their argument. *God's word.* Of command, such as "Let there be light" (Ge 1:3). *earth was formed out of water and by water.* See Ge 1:6–10 (see also

the heavens came into being and the earth
was formed out of water and by water.[r]
6By these waters also the world of that
time[s] was deluged and destroyed.[t] 7By the
same word the present heavens and earth
are reserved for fire,[u] being kept for the
day of judgment[v] and destruction of the
ungodly.

8But do not forget this one thing, dear
friends: With the Lord a day is like a thousand years, and a thousand years are like
a day.[w] 9The Lord is not slow in keeping
his promise,[x] as some understand slow-
ness. Instead he is patient[y] with you, not
wanting anyone to perish, but everyone to
come to repentance.[z]

10But the day of the Lord will come like
a thief.[a] The heavens will disappear with
a roar;[b] the elements will be destroyed by
fire,[c] and the earth and everything done in
it will be laid bare.[a][d]

11Since everything will be destroyed in
this way, what kind of people ought you
to be? You ought to live holy and godly
lives 12as you look forward[e] to the day of
God and speed its coming.[b][f] That day will
bring about the destruction of the heavens
by fire, and the elements will melt in the
heat.[g] 13But in keeping with his promise we
are looking forward to a new heaven and
a new earth,[h] where righteousness dwells.

14So then, dear friends, since you are
looking forward to this, make every effort to be found spotless, blameless[i] and
at peace with him. 15Bear in mind that
our Lord's patience[j] means salvation,[k]
just as our dear brother Paul also wrote
you with the wisdom that God gave him.[l]
16He writes the same way in all his letters,
speaking in them of these matters. His

3:5 [r]Ps 24:2
3:6 [s]2Pe 2:5 [t]Ge 7:21,22
3:7 [u]ver 10, 12; S 2Th 1:7 [v]S Mt 10:15
3:8 [w]Ps 90:4
3:9 [x]Hab 2:3; Heb 10:37 [y]S Ro 2:4 [z]S 1Ti 2:4; Rev 2:21
3:10 [a]S Lk 12:39 [b]Isa 34:4 [c]ver 7, 12; S 2Th 1:7 [d]Mt 24:35; S Heb 12:27; Rev 21:1
3:12 [e]S 1Co 1:7 [f]Ps 50:3 [g]ver 10
3:13 [h]Isa 65:17; 66:22; Rev 21:1
3:14 [i]S 1Th 3:13
3:15 [j]S Ro 2:4 [k]ver 9 [l]Eph 3:3

[a] 10 Some manuscripts *be burned up* [b] 12 Or *as you wait eagerly for the day of God to come*

notes there), where the waters on earth were separated from the atmospheric waters of the heavens, and the mountains then appeared, causing the earthly waters to be gathered into oceans.

3:6 *By these waters also the world ... was deluged and destroyed.* Peter points out the fallacy of the scoffers' argument. There has been a divine intervention since the time of creation, namely, the flood (see note on Ge 6:17).

3:7 *By the same word.* The word of God that brought the world into existence (v. 5) and that brought watery destruction on the wicked of Noah's day will bring fiery destruction on the world that exists today and on its wicked people.

3:8 *a thousand years are like a day.* Cf. Ps 90:4–5 and note. God does not view time as humans do. He stands above time, with the result that when time is seen in the light of eternity, an age appears no longer than one short day and a day seems no shorter than a long age. Since time is purely relative with God, he waits patiently while human beings stew with impatience.

3:9 God's seeming delay in bringing about the consummation of all things is a result not of indifference but of patience in waiting for all who will come to repentance. Thus the scoffers are wrong on two points: (1) They fail to recognize that all things have not continued without divine intervention since creation (the flood was an intervention, vv. 4–6). (2) They misunderstand the reason for apparent divine delay (God is a long-suffering God). *repentance.* See Mt 4:17; Mk 1:4 and note.

3:10 *day of the Lord.* See notes on Isa 2:11,17,20; Joel 1:15; Am 5:18; 1Th 5:2. *like a thief.* Suddenly and unexpectedly. *The heavens will disappear with a roar.* Apocalyptic language, common to books like Daniel and Revelation. Due to the figurative nature of such writings, we must not expect complete literalism but recognize it as an attempt to describe the indescribable, a task as impossible as it would have been for a first-century writer to describe the phenomena of our atomic age. What may be referred to is the destruction of the atmospheric heavens with a great rushing sound (see v. 12). *elements.* Refers either to the heavenly bodies or to the physical elements—in the first century, such things as earth, air, fire and water. *fire.* See vv. 7,12. *earth ... laid bare.* See NIV text note. Either the earth and its contents will disappear and not be seen anymore, or the earth and all human works will appear before God's judgment seat (cf. 1Co 3:13,15 and notes).

3:11 *Since everything will be destroyed.* The transitory nature of the present form of the material universe ought to make a difference in one's system of values and one's priorities. The result should be lives of holiness (separated from sin and to God) and godliness (devoted to the worship and service of God). Cf. 1:13–16; Mt 25:13; 1Th 5:6,8,11.

3:12 *the day of God.* Apparently synonymous with "the day of the Lord" (see v. 10 and note) since it is characterized by the same kind of events. Cf. Rev 16:14. *speed its coming.* That day may be hastened by God's people as they speed up the accomplishment of his purposes. Since he is waiting for all who will come to repentance (v. 9), the sooner believers bring others to the Savior the sooner that day will dawn (cf. Ac 3:19–20). Prayer also serves to hasten the day (Mt 6:10), as does holy living (v. 11). *destruction of the heavens.* See v. 10. *elements will melt in the heat.* See v. 10; Isa 34:4 and notes.

3:13 *his promise.* New heavens and a new earth are promised by Isaiah (65:17; 66:22). This promise is confirmed by Rev 21:1. *where righteousness dwells.* Righteousness will dwell there as a permanent resident. Cf. Isa 11:4–5; 45:8; Da 9:24 and notes.

3:14,18 *peace ... grace.* See note on Ro 1:7.

3:14 *spotless, blameless.* Cf. 1Pe 1:19, where the same two Greek words are applied to Christ. *at peace with him.* Believers have peace with God as a result of being justified by faith (see Ro 5:1 and note), but they may displease him by failing to live as he desires and thus not receive his commendation and his reward when he returns (cf. 1Co 3:10–15; 2Co 5:10 and notes).

3:15 *our Lord's patience means salvation.* See v. 9 and note. *our dear brother Paul.* Peter expresses warmth in his reference to Paul. The unity of teaching and purpose that governed their relationship, abundantly attested in Paul's letters and the book of Acts, is confirmed here by Peter. It has been suggested that what Paul wrote to the recipients of 2 Peter may have been a copy of Romans, which was sent to the churches as a circular letter (see Introduction to Romans: Recipients; see also note on 1Pe 1:1).

3:16 *writes the same way in all his letters.* Peter may be referring in general to the exhortations to holy living in vv. 11–14, which parallel many passages in Paul's writings. *ignorant and unstable people.* The ignorant are simply the unlearned who have not been taught basic apostolic teaching and thus may be easily led astray (cf. 2:14 and note). *other Scriptures.* Peter

letters contain some things that are hard
to understand, which ignorant and unstable[m] people distort,[n] as they do the other
Scriptures,[o] to their own destruction.
17 Therefore, dear friends, since you
have been forewarned, be on your guard[p]
so that you may not be carried away by
the error[q] of the lawless[r] and fall from your
secure position.[s] 18 But grow in the grace[t]
and knowledge[u] of our Lord and Savior
Jesus Christ.[v] To him be glory both now
and forever! Amen.[w]

3:16 [m] Jas 1:8; 2Pe 2:14 [n] Ps 56:5; Jer 23:36 [o] ver 2 **3:17** [p] 1Co 10:12 [q] 2Pe 2:18 [r] 2Pe 2:7 [s] Rev 2:5

3:18 [t] S Ro 3:24 [u] S 2Pe 1:2 [v] 2Pe 1:11; 2:20 [w] S Ro 11:36

placed Paul's writings on the same level of authority as the God-breathed writings of the OT (see 1:21; 2Ti 3:16 and notes).
3:17 *you have been forewarned.* That false teachers are coming (cf. ch. 2).

3:18 *grow in ... knowledge.* Peter concludes by again stressing knowledge (see 1:2–3 and notes; see also 1:5), probably as an antidote to the false teachers who boasted in their esoteric knowledge.

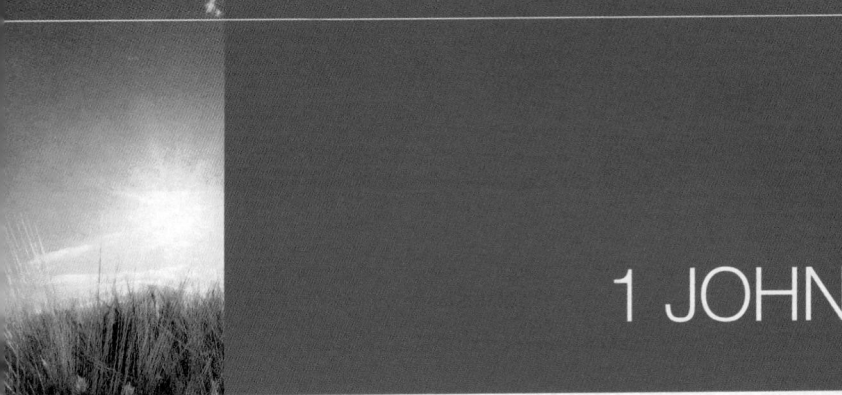

INTRODUCTION

Author

The author is John, son of Zebedee (see Mk 1:19 – 20) — the apostle and the author of the Gospel of John and Revelation (see Introductions to both books: Author). He was a fisherman, one of Jesus' inner circle (together with James and Peter), and "the disciple whom Jesus loved" (Jn 13:23; see note there). He may have been a first cousin of Jesus. (John's mother may have been Salome, possibly a sister of Mary; cf. Mt 27:56; Mk 15:40 and note; 16:1; Jn 19:25. This view assumes that "his mother's sister" in Jn 19:25 refers to Salome; some further assume that "Mary the wife of Clopas" there stands in apposition to "his mother's sister," which would mean that this Mary and Salome were one and the same person.)

Unlike most NT letters, 1 John does not tell us who its author is. The earliest identification of him comes from the church fathers: Irenaeus (c. AD 140 – 203), Clement of Alexandria (c. 150 – 215), Tertullian (c. 155 – 222) and Origen (c. 185 – 253) all designated the writer as the apostle John. As far as we know, no one else was suggested by the early church.

This traditional identification is confirmed by evidence in the letter itself:

(1) The style of the Gospel of John is markedly similar to that of this letter. Both are written in simple Greek and use contrasting figures, such as light and darkness, life and death, truth and lies, love and hate.

(2) Similar phrases and expressions, such as those found in the following passages, are striking:

1 John	*Gospel of John*
1:1	1:1,14
1:4	16:24
1:6 – 7	3:19 – 21
2:7	13:34 – 35
3:8	8:44

a **quick** look

Author:
The apostle John

Audience:
Believers in western Asia Minor

Date:
Between AD 85 and 95

Theme:
John writes to assure believers of the certainty of their faith and to refute heretical doctrines teaching that Jesus was not fully human and fully divine.

1 John	*Gospel of John*
3:14	5:24
4:6	8:47
4:9	1:14,18; 3:16
5:9	5:32,37
5:12	3:36

(3) The mention of eyewitness testimony (1:1 – 4) harmonizes with the fact that John was a follower of Christ from the earliest days of his ministry.

(4) The authoritative manner that pervades the letter — seen in its commands (2:15,24,28; 4:1; 5:21), its firm assertions (2:6; 3:14; 4:12) and its pointed identification of error (1:6,8; 2:4,22) — is what would be expected from an apostle.

(5) The suggestions of advanced age (addressing his readers as "children," 2:1,28; 3:7) agree with early church tradition concerning John's age when he wrote the books known to be his.

(6) The harsh description of the heretics as antichrists (2:18), liars (2:22) and children of the devil (3:10) is consistent with Jesus' characterization of John as a son of thunder (see Mk 3:17 and note).

(7) The indications of a close relationship with the Lord (1:1; 2:5 – 6,24,27 – 28) fit the descriptions of "the disciple whom Jesus loved" and the one who reclined "next to him" (Jn 13:23).

Date

The letter is difficult to date with precision, but factors such as (1) evidence from early Christian writers (Irenaeus and Clement of Alexandria), (2) the early form of Gnosticism reflected in the letter's denunciations and (3) indications of the advanced age of John suggest a date late in the first century. Since the author of 1 John seems to build on concepts and themes found in the fourth Gospel (see 1Jn 2:7 – 11), it is reasonable to date the letter somewhere between AD 85 and 95, after the writing of the Gospel, which may have been written c. 85 (see Introduction to John: Date), and before the writing of Revelation, which may have been written c. 95 (see Introduction to Revelation: Date).

Recipients

1Jn 2:12 – 14,19; 3:1; 5:13 make it clear that this letter was addressed to believers. But the letter itself does not indicate who they were or where they lived. The fact that it mentions no one by name suggests that it was a circular letter sent to Christians in a number of places. Evidence from early Christian writers places the apostle John in Ephesus during most of his later years (c. AD 70 – 100). The earliest confirmed use of 1 John was in the Roman province of Asia (in modern Turkey), where Ephesus was located. Clement of Alexandria indicates that John ministered in the various churches scattered throughout that province. It may be assumed, therefore, that 1 John was sent to the churches of the Roman province of Asia (see map, pp. 2528 – 2529, at the end of this study Bible).

Gnosticism

One of the most dangerous heresies of the first two centuries of the church was Gnosticism. Its central teaching was that spirit is good and matter is evil. From this unbiblical dualism flowed five important errors:

Ruins of the Basilica of St. John near Ephesus. The traditional grave of John is under the square platform at bottom right.

(1) The human body, which is matter, is therefore evil. It is to be contrasted with God, who is wholly spirit and therefore good.

(2) Salvation is the escape from the body, achieved not by faith in Christ but by special knowledge (the Greek word for "knowledge" is *gnosis,* hence Gnosticism).

(3) Christ's true humanity was denied in two ways: (a) Some said that Christ only "seemed" to have a body, a view called Docetism, from the Greek *dokeo* ("to seem"), and (b) others said that the divine Christ joined the man Jesus at baptism and left him before he died, a view called Cerinthianism, after its most prominent spokesman, Cerinthus. This view may be the background of much of 1 John (see 1:1; 2:22; 4:2 – 3 and notes).

(4) Some said that since the body was considered evil, it was to be treated harshly. This ascetic form of Gnosticism may be the background of part of the letter to the Colossians (see Col 2:21,23 and notes).

(5) Paradoxically, this dualism sometimes also led to licentiousness. The reasoning was that since matter — and not the breaking of God's law (1Jn 3:4) — was considered evil, breaking God's law was of no moral consequence.

The Gnosticism addressed in the NT was an early form of the heresy, not the intricately developed system of the second and third centuries. In addition to that seen in Colossians and in John's letters, acquaintance with early Gnosticism may be reflected in 1,2 Timothy, Titus and 2 Peter and perhaps 1 Corinthians.

Occasion and Purpose

Former members of John's churches had abandoned the true faith (2:18 – 19), causing doubt in the churches and fear of further desertions. These false teachers were apparently following an early form of Gnostic teaching of the Cerinthian variety (see Gnosticism). This heresy was also libertine, throwing off moral restraints.

Consequently, John wrote this letter with two basic purposes in mind: (1) to expose these false teachers (see 2:26 and note) and (2) to give believers assurance of salvation (see 5:13 and note). In keeping with his intention to combat Gnostic teachers, John specifically struck at their total lack of morality (3:8 – 10), and by giving eyewitness testimony to the incarnation he sought to confirm his readers' belief in the incarnate Christ (1:3). John set forth several key tests of authentic Christian faith: (1) belief that Jesus is the Messiah, the Son of God (2:18 – 28; 3:23 — 4:6; 4:14 – 15; 5:1,5);

A view of the road from the Ephesus theater toward the now-silted harbor. John spent most of his later years in Ephesus and wrote his letters from there.

Z. Radovan/www.BibleLandPictures.com

By giving eyewitness testimony to the incarnation, John seeks to confirm his readers' belief in the incarnate Christ.

(2) obedience to Christ's commands (1:5—2:6; 2:29—3:10; 3:22–24; 5:4–21); and (3) love for brothers and sisters in Christ (2:7–17; 3:10–24; 4:7—5:3). These are the indispensable hallmarks of true believers. Success in this would give the writer joy (1:4).

Outline*

I. Introduction: The Reality of the Incarnation (1:1–4)
II. The Christian Life as Fellowship with the Father and the Son (1:5—2:28)
   A. Ethical Tests of Fellowship (1:5—2:11)
      1. Moral likeness (1:5–7)
      2. Confession of sin (1:8—2:2)
      3. Obedience (2:3–6)
      4. Love for fellow believers (2:7–11)
   B. Two Digressions (2:12–17)
   C. Christological Test of Fellowship (2:18–28)
      1. Contrast: apostates versus believers (2:18–21)
      2. Person of Christ: the crux of the test (2:22–23)
      3. Persistent belief: key to continuing fellowship (2:24–28)
III. The Christian Life as Divine Sonship (2:29—4:6)
   A. Ethical Tests of Sonship (2:29—3:24)
      1. Righteousness (2:29—3:10a)
      2. Love (3:10b–24)
   B. Christological Tests of Sonship (4:1–6)
IV. The Christian Life as an Integration of the Ethical and the Christological (4:7—5:12)
   A. The Ethical Test: Love (4:7—5:5)
      1. The source of love (4:7–16)
      2. The fruit of love (4:17–19)
      3. The relationship of love for God and love for one's fellow Christians (4:20—5:1)
      4. Obedience: the evidence of love for God's children (5:2–5)
   B. The Christological Test (5:6–12)
V. Conclusion: Great Christian Certainties (5:13–21)

The Incarnation of the Word of Life

1 That which was from the beginning,[a]
which we have heard, which we have
seen with our eyes,[b] which we have looked
at and our hands have touched[c]—this we
proclaim concerning the Word of life. [2]The
life appeared;[d] we have seen it and testify
to it,[e] and we proclaim to you the eternal
life,[f] which was with the Father and has
appeared to us. [3]We proclaim to you what
we have seen and heard,[g] so that you also
may have fellowship with us. And our fellowship is with the Father and with his
Son, Jesus Christ.[h] [4]We write this[i] to make
our[a] joy complete.[j]

Light and Darkness, Sin and Forgiveness

[5]This is the message we have heard[k]
from him and declare to you: God is light;[l]
in him there is no darkness at all. [6]If we
claim to have fellowship with him and yet
walk in the darkness,[m] we lie and do not
live out the truth.[n] [7]But if we walk in the
light,[o] as he is in the light, we have fellowship with one another, and the blood of
Jesus, his Son, purifies us from all[b] sin.[p]
[8]If we claim to be without sin,[q] we deceive ourselves and the truth is not in us.[r]
[9]If we confess our sins, he is faithful and
just and will forgive us our sins[s] and purify us from all unrighteousness.[t] [10]If we
claim we have not sinned,[u] we make him
out to be a liar[v] and his word is not in us.[w]

2 My dear children,[x] I write this to you
so that you will not sin. But if anybody does sin, we have an advocate[y] with
the Father—Jesus Christ, the Righteous
One. [2]He is the atoning sacrifice for our
sins,[z] and not only for ours but also for the
sins of the whole world.[a]

Love and Hatred for Fellow Believers

[3]We know[b] that we have come to know
him[c] if we keep his commands.[d] [4]Whoever
says, "I know him,"[e] but does not do what
he commands is a liar, and the truth is not
in that person.[f] [5]But if anyone obeys his

[a] 4 Some manuscripts *your* [b] 7 Or *every*

1:1 [a]S Jn 1:2 [b]S Lk 24:48; Jn 1:14; 19:35; Ac 4:20; 2Pe 1:16; 1Jn 4:14 [c]Jn 20:27 **1:2** [d]Jn 1:1-4; 11:25; 14:6; 1Ti 3:16; 1Pe 1:20; 1Jn 3:5,8 [e]S Jn 15:27 [f]S Mt 25:46 **1:3** [g]S ver 1 [h]1Co 1:9 **1:4** [i]1Jn 2:1 [j]S Jn 3:29 **1:5** [k]1Jn 3:11 [l]1Ti 6:16 **1:6** [m]Jn 3:19-21; 8:12; 2Co 6:14; Eph 5:8; 1Jn 2:11 [n]Jn 3:19-21; 1Jn 2:4; 4:20 **1:7** [o]Isa 2:5 [p]Heb 9:14; Rev 1:5; 7:14 **1:8** [q]Pr 20:9; Jer 2:35; Ro 3:9-19; Jas 3:2 [r]Jn 8:44; 1Jn 2:4 **1:9** [s]Ps 32:5; 51:2; Pr 28:13 [t]ver 7; Mic 7:18-20; Heb 10:22 **1:10** [u]ver 8 [v]1Jn 5:10 [w]Jn 5:38; 1Jn 2:14 **2:1** [x]ver 12,13,28; 1Jn 3:7,18; 4:4; 5:21; S 1Th 2:11 [y]S Ro 8:34; 1Ti 2:5 **2:2** [z]Ro 3:25; 1Jn 4:10 [a]S Mt 1:21; S Jn 3:17 **2:3** [b]ver 5; 1Jn 3:24; 4:13; 5:2 [c]S ver 4 [d]S Jn 14:15 **2:4** [e]ver 3; Titus 1:16; 1Jn 3:6; 4:7,8 [f]1Jn 1:6,8

1:1–4 The introduction to this letter deals with the same subject and uses several of the same words as the introduction to John's Gospel (1:1–4)—"beginning," "Word," "life," "with."

1:1 *was from the beginning.* Has always existed. *we.* John and the other apostles. *heard … seen … looked at … touched.* The apostle had made a careful examination of "the Word of life." He testifies that the one who has existed from eternity "became flesh" (Jn 1:14; see note there)—i.e., a flesh-and-blood man. He was truly divine and truly human. At the outset, John contradicts the heresy of the Gnostics (see Introduction: Gnosticism). *Word of life.* The one who is life and reveals life (see v. 2 and note). "Word" here speaks of revelation (see note on Jn 1:1).

1:2 *The life … the eternal life.* Christ. He is called "the life" because he is the living one who has life in himself (see Jn 1:4; 11:25; 14:6 and notes). He is also the source of life and sovereign over life (5:11). The letter begins and ends (5:20) with the theme of eternal life (see Jn 17:3 and note).

1:3 *fellowship with us.* Participation with us (vicariously) in our experience of hearing, seeing and touching the incarnate Christ (v. 1). Fellowship (Greek *koinonia*) is the spiritual union of the believer with Christ—as described in the figures of the vine and branches (Jn 15:1–5) and the body and the head (1Co 12:12; Col 1:18)—as well as communion with the Father and with fellow believers (see vv. 6–7).

1:4 *our joy complete.* John's joy in the Lord could not be complete unless his readers shared the true knowledge of the Christ (see 2Jn 12; cf. Php 2:2).

1:5 *from him.* From Christ. *light … darkness.* Light represents what is good, true and holy, while darkness represents what is evil and false (see Jn 3:19–21).

1:6–7 *walk in the darkness … in the light.* Two lifestyles—one characterized by wickedness and error, the other by holiness and truth.

1:6 *we.* John and his readers. *to have fellowship with him.* To be in living, spiritual union with God. *walk.* A metaphor for living. *truth.* See note on Jn 1:14.

1:7 *sin.* A key word in 1 John, occurring 27 times in the Greek.

1:9 *faithful and just.* Here the phrase is virtually a single concept (faithful-and-just). It indicates that God's response toward those who confess their sins will be in accordance with his nature and his gracious commitment to his people (see Ps 143:1; Zec 8:8 and note; cf. Pr 28:13 and note). *faithful.* To his promise to forgive (see Jer 31:34; Mic 7:18–20; Heb 10:22–23 and notes). *will forgive us.* Will provide the forgiveness that restores the communion with God that had been interrupted by sin (as requested in the Lord's Prayer, Mt 6:12).

1:10 *we have not sinned.* Gnostics denied that their immoral actions were sinful.

2:1 *dear children.* John, the aged apostle, often used this expression of endearment (vv. 12,28; 3:7,18; 4:4; 5:21; the term in 2:18 translates a different Greek word). *advocate.* Refers to someone who speaks in court in behalf of a defendant (see note on Jn 14:16). *Righteous One.* In God's court the defender must be, and is, sinless (cf. Ac 3:14 and note).

2:2 *atoning sacrifice for our sins.* God's holiness demands punishment for human sin. God, therefore, out of love (4:10; Jn 3:16), sent his Son to make substitutionary atonement for the believer's sin. In this way the Father's wrath is satisfied; his wrath against the Christian's sin has been turned away and directed toward Christ. See note on Ro 3:25. *for the sins of the whole world.* Forgiveness through Christ's atoning sacrifice is not limited to one particular group only; it has worldwide application (see Jn 1:29). It must, however, be received by faith (see Jn 3:16). Thus this verse does not teach universalism (that all people ultimately will be saved), but that God is an impartial God.

2:3 *know.* Forty-two times 1 John uses two Greek verbs normally translated "know." One of these verbs is related to the name of the Gnostics, the heretical sect that claimed to have a special knowledge (Greek *gnosis*) of God (see Introduction: Gnosticism). *keep his commands.* Does not mean that only those who never disobey (1:8–9) know God, but simply refers to those whose lives are characterized by obedience.

2:5 *love for God is truly made complete in them.* The NIV main text translation ("love for God") means that our

word,[g] love for God[a] is truly made complete in them.[h] This is how we know[i] we
are in him: 6 Whoever claims to live in him
must live as Jesus did.[j]
7 Dear friends,[k] I am not writing you a
new command but an old one, which you
have had since the beginning.[l] This old
command is the message you have heard.
8 Yet I am writing you a new command;[m]
its truth is seen in him and in you, because the darkness is passing[n] and the true
light[o] is already shining.[p]
9 Anyone who claims to be in the light
but hates a brother or sister[b][q] is still in the
darkness.[r] 10 Anyone who loves their brother and sister[c] lives in the light,[s] and there
is nothing in them to make them stumble.[t]
11 But anyone who hates a brother or sister[u] is in the darkness and walks around
in the darkness.[v] They do not know where
they are going, because the darkness has
blinded them.[w]

Reasons for Writing

12 I am writing to you, dear children,[x]
because your sins have been forgiven
on account of his name.[y]
13 I am writing to you, fathers,
because you know him who is from
the beginning.[z]
I am writing to you, young men,
because you have overcome[a] the evil
one.[b]

2:5 [g]S Jn 14:15 [h]1Jn 4:12 [i]S ver 3 **2:6** [j]S Mt 11:29 **2:7** [k]S 1Co 10:14 [l]ver 24; 1Jn 3:11,23; 4:21; 2Jn 5,6 **2:8** [m]S Jn 13:34 [n]Ro 13:12; Heb 10:25 [o]Jn 1:9 [p]Eph 5:8; 1Th 5:5 **2:9** [q]ver 11; Lev 19:17; 1Jn 3:10,15, 16; 4:20,21 [r]1Jn 1:5 **2:10** [s]1Jn 3:14 [t]ver 11; Ps 119:165 **2:11** [u]S ver 9 [v]S 1Jn 1:6 [w]Jn 11:9; 12:35 **2:12** [x]S ver 1 [y]S 1Jn 3:23 **2:13** [z]S Jn 1:1 [a]S Jn 16:33 [b]ver 14; S Mt 5:37 **2:14** [c]S ver 1 [d]S Jn 1:1 [e]Eph 6:10 [f]S Heb 4:12 [g]S Jn 5:38; 1Jn 1:10 [h]S ver 13 **2:15** [i]Ro 12:2 [j]Jas 4:4 **2:16** [k]Ge 3:6; Ro 13:14; Eph 2:3 [l]Pr 27:20 **2:17** [m]S Heb 12:27 [n]Mt 12:50 **2:18** [o]S Ro 13:11

14 I write to you, dear children,[c]
because you know the Father.
I write to you, fathers,
because you know him who is from
the beginning.[d]
I write to you, young men,
because you are strong,[e]
and the word of God[f] lives in you,[g]
and you have overcome the evil
one.[h]

On Not Loving the World

15 Do not love the world or anything in
the world.[i] If anyone loves the world, love
for the Father[d] is not in them.[j] 16 For everything in the world—the lust of the flesh,[k]
the lust of the eyes,[l] and the pride of life—
comes not from the Father but from the
world. 17 The world and its desires pass
away,[m] but whoever does the will of God[n]
lives forever.

Warnings Against Denying the Son

18 Dear children, this is the last hour;[o]
and as you have heard that the antichrist

[a] 5 Or *word, God's love* [b] 9 The Greek word for *brother or sister* (*adelphos*) refers here to a believer, whether man or woman, as part of God's family; also in verse 11; and in 3:15, 17; 4:20; 5:16. [c] 10 The Greek word for *brother and sister* (*adelphos*) refers here to a believer, whether man or woman, as part of God's family; also in 3:10; 4:20, 21. [d] 15 Or *world, the Father's love*

---

love for God becomes complete when it expresses itself in acts of obedience (see 3:16–18). The NIV text note rendering means that God's love for the believer is made complete when it moves the believer to acts of obedience (see 4:12). *in him.* Spiritual union with God (see Jn 17:21; Eph 1:1 and note).

2:7–8 *new command.* See Jn 13:34–35 and notes. The Biblical command to love was old (see Lev 19:18; see also Mt 22:39–40). But its newness is seen in: (1) the new and dramatic illustration of divine love on the cross; (2) Christ's exposition of the OT law (see Mt 5), which seemed new to Christ's hearers; and (3) the daily experience of believers as they grow in love for each other.

2:7 *Dear friends.* Like "dear children" (see note on v. 1), a favorite term of John (used ten times in two letters: here; 3:2,21; 4:1,7,11; 3Jn 1,2,5,11). *since the beginning.* The beginning of their Christian experience, when they first heard the gospel.

2:8 *true light.* Used in the NT only here and in Jn 1:9 (see note on Jn 1:4), this phrase refers to the gospel of Jesus Christ, who is the light of the world (see Jn 8:12 and note; cf. 2Co 4:6 and note).

2:9–10 *hates … loves.* In the Bible hatred and love as moral qualities are not primarily emotions but attitudes expressed in actions (see 3:15–16).

2:9 *light … darkness.* See note on 1:5. *brother or sister.* See note on Ro 1:13.

2:10 *stumble.* Into sin.

2:12–14 *I am writing to you … because.* By extended repetition in these verses, John assures his readers that, in spite of the rigorous tests contained in the letter, he is confident of their salvation. *dear children … fathers … young men.* As elsewhere in this letter, "dear children" probably refers to all John's readers (see note on v. 1), including fathers and young people. The terms "fathers" and "young men" may, however, describe two different levels of spiritual maturity. Some hold that all three terms refer to levels of spiritual maturity.

2:12 *his name.* Jesus (see 3:23; 5:13; see also note on Ac 4:12).

2:13–14 *him who is from the beginning.* Christ (see note on 1:1).

2:15 *world.* Not the world of people (Jn 3:16) or the created world (Jn 17:24), but here the world, or realm, of sin (v. 16; see Jas 4:4 and note), which is controlled by Satan and organized against God and righteousness (see note on Jn 1:9). *love for the Father.* Cf. 2:5 and note.

2:18 *last hour.* With other NT writers, John viewed the whole period beginning with Christ's first coming as the last days (see Ac 2:17; 2Ti 3:1 and note). They understood this to be the "last" of the days because neither former prophecy nor new revelation concerning the history of salvation indicated the coming of another era before the return of Christ. The word "last" in "last days," "last times" and "last hour" also expresses a sense of urgency and imminence (see Heb 1:2 and note). The Christian is to be alert, waiting for the return of Christ (Mt 25:1–13). *the antichrist … many antichrists.* John assumed his readers knew that a great enemy of God and his people would arise before Christ's return. That person is called "antichrist" (here), "the man of lawlessness" (2Th 2:3; but see note there) and "the beast" (Rev 13:1–10). But prior to him there will be many antichrists. These are characterized by the following: (1) They deny the incarnation (see 4:2 and note; 2Jn 7) and that Jesus is the divine Christ (v. 22); (2) they deny the Father (v. 22); (3) they do not have the Father (v. 23); (4) they are liars (v. 22) and deceivers (2Jn 7); (5) they

is coming,[p] even now many antichrists
have come.[q] This is how we know it is the
last hour. 19They went out from us,[r] but
they did not really belong to us. For if they
had belonged to us, they would have remained with us; but their going showed
that none of them belonged to us.[s]
20But you have an anointing[t] from the
Holy One,[u] and all of you know the truth.[a][v]
21I do not write to you because you do not
know the truth, but because you do know
it[w] and because no lie comes from the
truth. 22Who is the liar? It is whoever denies that Jesus is the Christ. Such a person
is the antichrist—denying the Father and
the Son.[x] 23No one who denies the Son has
the Father; whoever acknowledges the Son
has the Father also.[y]
24As for you, see that what you have
heard from the beginning[z] remains in you.
If it does, you also will remain in the Son
and in the Father.[a] 25And this is what he
promised us—eternal life.[b]
26I am writing these things to you about
those who are trying to lead you astray.[c]
27As for you, the anointing[d] you received
from him remains in you, and you do
not need anyone to teach you. But as his
anointing teaches you about all things[e] and
as that anointing is real, not counterfeit—
just as it has taught you, remain in him.[f]

God's Children and Sin

28And now, dear children,[g] continue in
him, so that when he appears[h] we may be
confident[i] and unashamed before him at
his coming.[j]
29If you know that he is righteous,[k] you
know that everyone who does what is
right has been born of him.[l]
3 See what great love[m] the Father has lavished on us, that we should be called
children of God![n] And that is what we are!
The reason the world does not know us is
that it did not know him.[o] 2Dear friends,[p]
now we are children of God,[q] and what we
will be has not yet been made known. But
we know that when Christ appears,[b][r] we
shall be like him,[s] for we shall see him as
he is.[t] 3All who have this hope in him purify themselves,[u] just as he is pure.[v]
4Everyone who sins breaks the law; in
fact, sin is lawlessness.[w] 5But you know
that he appeared so that he might take
away our sins.[x] And in him is no sin.[y] 6No
one who lives in him keeps on sinning.[z]
No one who continues to sin has either
seen him[a] or known him.[b]
7Dear children,[c] do not let anyone lead
you astray.[d] The one who does what is
right is righteous, just as he is righteous.[e]
8The one who does what is sinful is of the
devil,[f] because the devil has been sinning
from the beginning. The reason the Son

[a] 20 Some manuscripts *and you know all things*
[b] 2 Or *when it is made known*

2:18 [p]ver 22; 1Jn 4:3; 2Jn 7 [q]1Jn 4:1 **2:19** [r]Ac 20:30 [s]1Co 11:19 **2:20** [t]ver 27; 2Co 1:21 [u]S Mk 1:24 [v]Jer 31:34; Mt 13:11; Jn 14:26 **2:21** [w]2Pe 1:12; Jude 5 **2:22** [x]1Jn 4:3; 2Jn 7 **2:23** [y]Jn 8:19; 14:7; 1Jn 4:15; 5:1; 2Jn 9 **2:24** [z]S ver 7 [a]Jn 14:23; 15:4; 1Jn 1:3; 2Jn 9 **2:25** [b]S Mt 25:46 **2:26** [c]1Jn 3:7 **2:27** [d]ver 20 [e]1Co 2:12 [f]Jn 15:4 **2:28** [g]S ver 1 [h]Col 3:4; 1Jn 3:2 [i]S Eph 3:12 [j]S 1Th 2:19 **2:29** [k]1Jn 3:7 [l]S Jn 1:13 **3:1** [m]S Jn 3:16 [n]ver 2,10; S Jn 1:12 [o]Jn 15:21; 16:3 **3:2** [p]S 1Co 10:14 [q]ver 1,10; S Jn 1:12 [r]Col 3:4; 1Jn 2:28 [s]Ro 8:29; 2Pe 1:4 [t]Ps 17:15; Jn 17:24; 2Co 3:18

3:3 [u]2Co 7:1; 2Pe 3:13,14 [v]Ps 18:26 **3:4** [w]1Jn 5:17 **3:5** [x]ver 8; S Jn 3:17 [y]S 2Co 5:21 **3:6** [z]ver 9; 1Jn 5:18 [a]3Jn 11 [b]S 1Jn 2:4 **3:7** [c]S 1Jn 2:1 [d]1Jn 2:26 [e]1Jn 2:29 **3:8** [f]ver 10; Jn 8:44

---

are many (v. 18); (6) in John's day they left the church because they had nothing in common with believers (v. 19). The antichrists referred to in John's letter were the early Gnostics. The "anti" in "antichrist" means "against" (cf. 2Th 2:4 and note; Rev 13:6–7; cf. also Mt 24:4–5,10–11,15,23–24).

2:19 The occasion of the letter (see Introduction: Occasion and Purpose).

2:20 *anointing.* The Holy Spirit (see v. 27; Jn 14:16–17; 15:26; 16:13; Ac 10:38). *Holy One.* Either Jesus Christ (Mk 1:24; Jn 6:69; Ac 2:27; 3:14; 22:14) or the Father (2Ki 19:22; Job 6:10).

2:22 *Jesus is the Christ.* See note on Mt 16:16. The man Jesus is the divine Messiah (see the parallel confession in 5:5; see also Introduction: Gnosticism and note on 5:6).

2:23 See 2Jn 9 for the same thought.

2:25 *eternal life.* See Jn 3:15 and note; cf. Mt 19:16 and note.

2:26 One of the statements of purpose for the letter (see Introduction: Occasion and Purpose).

2:27 *anointing.* See note on v. 20. *do not need anyone to teach you.* Since the Bible constantly advocates teaching (Mt 28:20; 1Co 12:28; Eph 4:11; Col 3:16; 1Ti 4:11; 2Ti 2:2,24), John is not ruling out human teachers. At the time when he wrote, however, Gnostic teachers were insisting that the teaching of the apostles was to be supplemented with the "higher knowledge" that they (the Gnostics) claimed to possess. John's response was that what the readers were taught under the Spirit's ministry through the apostles was not only adequate but the only reliable truth. See the promise of the new covenant in Jer 31:34 (see also note there). *teaches you.* The teaching ministry of the Holy Spirit (what is commonly called illumination) does not involve revelation of new truth or the explanation of all difficult passages of Scripture to our satisfaction. Rather, it is the development of the capacity to appreciate and appropriate God's truth already revealed—making the Bible meaningful in thought and daily living. *all things.* All things necessary to know for salvation and Christian living.

2:28 *continue in him.* See "remains in" (vv. 24,27). *confident.* See 3:21; 4:17; 5:14.

2:29 *he … him.* God the Father. *does what is right.* Those who are born again are marked by righteous conduct.

3:1 *children of God.* See note on Jn 1:12.

3:2 *we shall be like him.* Cf. Ro 8:29; 1Co 15:49; Php 3:21.

3:3 *hope.* Not a mere wish, but unshakable confidence concerning the future (see Ro 5:5 and note). *purify themselves.* By turning from sin.

3:5 *take away our sins.* See Jn 1:29 and note. *in him is no sin.* Amply confirmed elsewhere in the NT (see 2Co 5:21; Heb 4:15 and notes; 1Pe 3:18).

3:6 *No one … keeps on sinning.* John is not asserting sinless perfection (see 1:8–10; 2:1) but explaining that the believer's life is characterized not by sin but by doing what is right.

3:8 *devil.* In this short letter John says much about the devil: (1) He is called "the devil" (here) and "the evil one" (v. 12; 2:13–14; 5:18–19). (2) He "has been sinning from the beginning" (here), i.e., from the time he first rebelled against God, before the fall of Adam and Eve (see Jn 8:44 and note). (3) He is the instigator of human sin, and those who continue to sin belong to him (vv. 8,12) and are his children (v. 10). (4) He is in the world (4:3) and has "the whole world"

of God[g] appeared was to destroy the devil's work.[h] 9 No one who is born of God[i]
will continue to sin,[j] because God's seed[k]
remains in them; they cannot go on sinning, because they have been born of God.
10 This is how we know who the children
of God[l] are and who the children of the
devil[m] are: Anyone who does not do what
is right is not God's child, nor is anyone
who does not love[n] their brother and sister.[o]

More on Love and Hatred

11 For this is the message you heard[p]
from the beginning:[q] We should love one
another.[r] 12 Do not be like Cain, who belonged to the evil one[s] and murdered his
brother.[t] And why did he murder him?
Because his own actions were evil and
his brother's were righteous.[u] 13 Do not
be surprised, my brothers and sisters,[a] if
the world hates you.[v] 14 We know that we
have passed from death to life,[w] because
we love each other. Anyone who does not
love remains in death.[x] 15 Anyone who
hates a brother or sister[y] is a murderer,[z]
and you know that no murderer has eternal life residing in him.[a]
16 This is how we know what love is:
Jesus Christ laid down his life for us.[b]
And we ought to lay down our lives for
our brothers and sisters.[c] 17 If anyone has
material possessions and sees a brother or
sister in need but has no pity on them,[d]
how can the love of God be in that person?[e]
18 Dear children,[f] let us not love with words
or speech but with actions and in truth.[g]
19 This is how we know that we belong
to the truth and how we set our hearts at
rest in his presence: 20 If our hearts condemn us, we know that God is greater
than our hearts, and he knows everything.
21 Dear friends,[h] if our hearts do not condemn us, we have confidence before God[i]
22 and receive from him anything we ask,[j]
because we keep his commands[k] and do
what pleases him.[l] 23 And this is his command: to believe[m] in the name of his Son,
Jesus Christ,[n] and to love one another as
he commanded us.[o] 24 The one who keeps
God's commands[p] lives in him,[q] and he in
them. And this is how we know that he
lives in us: We know it by the Spirit he
gave us.[r]

On Denying the Incarnation

4 Dear friends,[s] do not believe every
spirit,[t] but test the spirits to see whether they are from God, because many false
prophets have gone out into the world.[u]
2 This is how you can recognize the Spirit of God: Every spirit that acknowledges
that Jesus Christ has come in the flesh[v] is
from God,[w] 3 but every spirit that does not
acknowledge Jesus is not from God. This
is the spirit of the antichrist,[x] which you
have heard is coming and even now is already in the world.[y]
4 You, dear children,[z] are from God and
have overcome them,[a] because the one

3:8 [g] S Mt 4:3 [h] Heb 2:14 **3:9** [i] S Jn 1:13 [j] ver 6; Ps 119:3; 1Jn 5:18 [k] 1Pe 1:23 **3:10** [l] ver 1, 2; S Jn 1:12 [m] ver 8 [n] 1Jn 4:8 [o] S 1Jn 2:9 **3:11** [p] 1Jn 1:5 [q] S 1Jn 2:7 [r] Jn 13:34,35; 15:12; 1Jn 4:7, 11,21; 2Jn 5 **3:12** [s] S Mt 5:37 [t] Ge 4:8 [u] Ps 38:20; Pr 29:10 **3:13** [v] Jn 15:18, 19; 17:14 **3:14** [w] Jn 5:24 [x] S 1Jn 2:9 **3:15** [y] S 1Jn 2:9 [z] Mt 5:21, 22; Jn 8:44 [a] Gal 5:20,21; Rev 21:8 **3:16** [b] Jn 10:11 [c] Jn 15:13; Php 2:17; 1Th 2:8 **3:17** [d] Dt 15:7, 8; Jas 2:15,16 [e] 1Jn 4:20 **3:18** [f] S 1Jn 2:1 [g] Eze 33:31; Ro 12:9 **3:21** [h] S 1Co 10:14 [i] S Eph 3:12; 1Jn 5:14 **3:22** [j] S Mt 7:7 [k] S Jn 14:15 [l] Jn 8:29; Heb 13:21 **3:23** [m] Jn 6:29 [n] S Lk 24:47; Jn 1:12; 3:18; 20:31; 1Co 6:11; 1Jn 5:13 [o] S Jn 13:34 **3:24** [p] 1Jn 2:3 [q] 1Jn 2:6;

[a] *13* The Greek word for *brothers and sisters* (*adelphoi*) refers here to believers, both men and women, as part of God's family; also in verse 16.

4:15 [r] 1Th 4:8; 1Jn 4:13 **4:1** [s] S 1Co 10:14 [t] Jer 29:8; 1Co 12:10; 2Th 2:2 [u] S Mt 7:15; 1Jn 2:18 **4:2** [v] S Jn 1:14; 1Jn 2:23 [w] 1Co 12:3 **4:3** [x] 1Jn 2:22; 2Jn 7 [y] 1Jn 2:18 **4:4** [z] S 1Jn 2:1 [a] S Jn 16:33

of unbelievers under his control (5:19). (5) But he cannot lay hold of believers to harm them (5:18). (6) On the contrary, Christians will overcome him (2:13–14; 4:4), and Christ will destroy his work (cf. Ro 16:20 and note; Heb 2:14).

3:9 *God's seed.* The picture is of human reproduction, in which the sperm (the Greek for "seed" is *sperma*) bears the life principle and transfers the paternal characteristics. *cannot go on sinning.* Not a complete cessation of sin, but a life that is not characterized by sin.

3:11 *from the beginning.* See note on 2:7. *love one another.* See note on 4:7—5:3.

3:12 *Cain.* See Heb 11:4 and note.

3:13 *brothers and sisters.* See NIV text note.

3:15 *hates.* See note on 2:9–10. *murderer.* See Jas 4:2 and note.

3:17–18 See Jas 2:14–17 and note on 2:15–16.

3:17 *love of God.* God's kind of love, which he pours out in the believer's heart (see Ro 5:5 and note) and which in turn enables the Christian to love fellow believers. Or it may speak of the believer's love for God.

3:20 *God is greater than our hearts.* An oversensitive conscience can be quieted by the knowledge that God himself has declared active love to be an evidence of salvation. He knows the hearts of all—whether, in spite of shortcomings, they have been born of him.

3:23 This command has two parts: (1) Believe in Christ (see Jn 6:29 and note), and (2) love each other (see Jn 13:34–35 and notes). The first part is developed in 4:1–6 and the second part in 4:7–12.

3:24 *We know it by the Spirit.* See Ro 8:16 and note.

4:1 *spirit.* A person moved by a spirit, whether by the Holy Spirit or an evil one. *test the spirits.* Cf. 1Th 5:21 and note. (Mt 7:1 does not refer to such testing or judgment; it speaks of self-righteous moral judgment of others.) *false prophets.* A true prophet speaks from God, being "carried along by the Holy Spirit" (2Pe 1:21; see note there). False prophets, such as the Gnostics of John's day, speak under the influence of spirits alienated from God. Christ warned against false prophets (see Mt 7:15 and note; Mk 13:22), as did Paul (see 1Ti 4:1 and note) and Peter (see 2Pe 2:1 and note).

4:2 *acknowledges.* Not only knows intellectually—for demons know, and shudder (Jas 2:19; cf. Mk 1:24)—but also confesses publicly (cf. Ro 10:9–10 and notes). *Jesus Christ has come in the flesh.* See note on 1:1. Thus John excludes the Gnostics, especially the Cerinthians, who taught that the divine Christ came upon the human Jesus at his baptism and then left him at the cross, so that it was only the man Jesus who died (see Introduction: Gnosticism).

4:3 *does not acknowledge Jesus.* The incarnate Jesus Christ of 1:2 (see note on 2:18).

4:4 *from God.* An abbreviated form of the expression "born of God" (2:29; 3:9–10). *them.* The false prophets (v. 1), who were inspired by the spirit of the antichrist (v. 3). *the one*

who is in you[b] is greater than the one who
is in the world.[c] 5 They are from the world[d]
and therefore speak from the viewpoint of
the world, and the world listens to them.
6 We are from God, and whoever knows
God listens to us; but whoever is not from
God does not listen to us.[e] This is how we
recognize the Spirit[a] of truth[f] and the spirit
of falsehood.[g]

God's Love and Ours

7 Dear friends, let us love one another,[h]
for love comes from God. Everyone who
loves has been born of God[i] and knows
God.[j] 8 Whoever does not love does not
know God, because God is love.[k] 9 This is
how God showed his love among us: He
sent his one and only Son[l] into the world
that we might live through him.[m] 10 This
is love: not that we loved God, but that
he loved us[n] and sent his Son as an atoning sacrifice for our sins.[o] 11 Dear friends,[p]
since God so loved us,[q] we also ought to
love one another.[r] 12 No one has ever seen
God;[s] but if we love one another, God lives
in us and his love is made complete in us.[t]
13 This is how we know[u] that we live in
him and he in us: He has given us of his
Spirit.[v] 14 And we have seen and testify[w]
that the Father has sent his Son to be the
Savior of the world.[x] 15 If anyone acknowledges that Jesus is the Son of God,[y] God
lives in them and they in God.[z] 16 And so
we know and rely on the love God has
for us.
God is love.[a] Whoever lives in love lives
in God, and God in them.[b] 17 This is how
love is made complete[c] among us so that
we will have confidence[d] on the day of
judgment:[e] In this world we are like Jesus.
18 There is no fear in love. But perfect love
drives out fear,[f] because fear has to do
with punishment. The one who fears is
not made perfect in love.
19 We love because he first loved us.[g]
20 Whoever claims to love God yet hates
a brother or sister[h] is a liar.[i] For whoever
does not love their brother and sister,
whom they have seen,[j] cannot love God,
whom they have not seen.[k] 21 And he has
given us this command:[l] Anyone who
loves God must also love their brother
and sister.[m]

Faith in the Incarnate Son of God

5 Everyone who believes[n] that Jesus is
the Christ[o] is born of God,[p] and everyone who loves the father loves his child as
well.[q] 2 This is how we know[r] that we love
the children of God:[s] by loving God and
carrying out his commands. 3 In fact, this
is love for God: to keep his commands.[t]
And his commands are not burdensome,[u]
4 for everyone born of God[v] overcomes[w]
the world. This is the victory that has
overcome the world, even our faith. 5 Who

[a] 6 Or *spirit*

4:4 [b] Ro 8:31 [c] 2Ki 6:16; S Jn 12:31 **4:5** [d] Jn 15:19; 17:14,16 **4:6** [e] Jn 8:47 [f] S Jn 14:17 [g] S Mk 13:5 **4:7** [h] S 1Jn 3:11 [i] S Jn 1:13 [j] S 1Jn 2:4 **4:8** [k] ver 7,16 **4:9** [l] Jn 1:18 [m] Jn 3:16,17; 1Jn 5:11 **4:10** [n] Ro 5:8,10 [o] S Ro 3:25 **4:11** [p] S 1Co 10:14 [q] S Jn 3:16 [r] Jn 15:12; S 1Jn 3:11 **4:12** [s] S Jn 1:18 [t] ver 17; 1Jn 2:5 **4:13** [u] S 1Jn 2:3 [v] 1Jn 3:24 **4:14** [w] S Jn 15:27 [x] S Lk 2:11; S Jn 3:17 **4:15** [y] S 1Jn 2:23; 5:5 [z] 1Jn 3:24 **4:16** [a] ver 8 [b] ver 12,13; 1Jn 3:24 **4:17** [c] ver 12; 1Jn 2:5 [d] S Eph 3:12 [e] S Mt 10:15 **4:18** [f] Ro 8:15 **4:19** [g] ver 10 **4:20** [h] S 1Jn 2:9 [i] S 1Jn 1:6; 2:4 [j] 1Jn 3:17 [k] ver 12; S Jn 1:18 **4:21** [l] 1Jn 2:7 [m] S Mt 5:43; S 1Jn 2:9 **5:1** [n] S Jn 3:15 [o] 1Jn 2:22; 4:2,15 [p] S Jn 1:13; S 1Jn 2:23 [q] Jn 8:42 **5:2** [r] S 1Jn 2:3 [s] 1Jn 3:14 **5:3** [t] S Jn 14:15 [u] Mt 11:30; 23:4 **5:4** [v] S Jn 1:13 [w] S Jn 16:33

who is in the world. The devil (see Jn 12:31 and note). In v. 3 "world" means the inhabited earth; in vv. 4–5 it means the community, or system, of those not born of God—including the antichrists (see note on Jn 1:9).

4:6 *Spirit of truth.* Cf. 5:6 and note; see note on Jn 14:17.

4:7—5:3 The word "love" in its various forms is used 43 times in the letter, 32 times in this short section.

4:8 *does not know God.* Only those who are to some degree like him truly know him. *God is love.* In his essential nature and in all his actions, God is loving (see also v. 16). John similarly affirms that God is spirit (see Jn 4:24 and note) and light (see 1:5 and note), as well as righteous (2:29; 3:7), holy (2:20), powerful or great (4:4), faithful (see 1:9 and note), true (5:20) and just (1:9).

4:9 *one and only Son.* See Jn 1:18; 3:16 and notes.

4:10 *atoning sacrifice for our sins.* See note on 2:2.

4:12 *No one has ever seen God.* See note on Jn 1:18. Since our love has its source in God's love, his love reaches full expression (is made complete) when we love fellow Christians. Thus the God whom "no one has ever seen" is seen in those who love, because God lives in them.

4:13–14 *Spirit ... Father ... Son.* See note on Mt 28:19.

4:13 *has given us of his Spirit.* See 3:24 and note.

4:16 *God is love.* See note on v. 8.

4:17 *like Jesus.* The fact that we are like Christ in love is a sign that God, who is love, lives in us; therefore we may have confidence on the day of judgment that we are saved.

4:18 *no fear in love.* There is no fear of God's judgment because genuine love confirms salvation.

4:19 All love comes ultimately from God; genuine love is never self-generated by his creatures.

4:21 *this command.* See Jn 13:34 and note. *Anyone who loves God must also love their brother and sister.* See 3:16–18; Jas 2:14–17.

5:1 *Everyone who believes that Jesus is the Christ is born of God.* Faith in Jesus as the Messiah is a sign of being born again, just as love is (4:7). *the Christ.* See note on 2:22. *everyone who loves the father loves his child as well.* John wrote at a time when members of a family were closely associated as a unit under the headship of the father. He could therefore use the family as an illustration to show that anyone who loves God the Father will naturally love God's children.

5:3 *this is love for God: to keep his commands.* Cf. Jn 14:15,21 and notes. *his commands are not burdensome.* Not because the commands themselves are light or easy to obey but, as John explains in v. 4, because of the new birth. The one born of God by faith is enabled by the Holy Spirit to obey.

5:4 *overcomes ... has overcome.* To overcome the world is to gain victory over its sinful pattern of life, which is another way of describing obedience to God (v. 3). Such obedience is not impossible for believers because they have been born again and the Holy Spirit dwells within them and gives them strength. John speaks of two aspects of victory: (1) the initial victory of turning in faith from the world to God ("has overcome"); (2) the continuing, day-by-day victory of Christian living ("overcomes"). *world.* See note on 2:15.

5:5 *Son of God.* For parallel confessions, see 2:22; 4:2; 5:1 and notes.

is it that overcomes the world? Only the
one who believes that Jesus is the Son of
God.[x]
6This is the one who came by water and
blood[y]—Jesus Christ. He did not come by
water only, but by water and blood. And
it is the Spirit who testifies, because the
Spirit is the truth.[z] 7For there are three[a]
that testify: 8the[a] Spirit, the water and
the blood; and the three are in agreement.
9We accept human testimony,[b] but God's
testimony is greater because it is the testimony of God,[c] which he has given about
his Son. 10Whoever believes in the Son
of God accepts this testimony.[d] Whoever
does not believe God has made him out
to be a liar,[e] because they have not believed the testimony God has given about
his Son. 11And this is the testimony: God
has given us eternal life,[f] and this life is in
his Son.[g] 12Whoever has the Son has life;
whoever does not have the Son of God
does not have life.[h]

Concluding Affirmations

13I write these things to you who believe in the name of the Son of God[i] so
that you may know that you have eternal
life.[j] 14This is the confidence[k] we have in
approaching God: that if we ask anything
according to his will, he hears us.[l] 15And
if we know that he hears us—whatever
we ask—we know[m] that we have what we
asked of him.[n]
16If you see any brother or sister commit a sin that does not lead to death, you
should pray and God will give them life.[o]
I refer to those whose sin does not lead to
death. There is a sin that leads to death.[p] I
am not saying that you should pray about
that.[q] 17All wrongdoing is sin,[r] and there is
sin that does not lead to death.[s]
18We know that anyone born of God[t]
does not continue to sin; the One who
was born of God keeps them safe, and the
evil one[u] cannot harm them.[v] 19We know
that we are children of God,[w] and that the
whole world is under the control of the
evil one.[x] 20We know also that the Son of
God has come[y] and has given us understanding,[z] so that we may know him who
is true.[a] And we are in him who is true by
being in his Son Jesus Christ. He is the
true God and eternal life.[b]
21Dear children,[c] keep yourselves from
idols.[d]

[a] 7,8 Late manuscripts of the Vulgate *testify in heaven: the Father, the Word and the Holy Spirit, and these three are one. 8And there are three that testify on earth: the* (not found in any Greek manuscript before the fourteenth century)

5:5 [x]ver 1; S 1Jn 2:23 **5:6** [y]Jn 19:34 [z]S Jn 14:17 **5:7** [a]S Mt 18:16 **5:9** [b]Jn 5:34 [c]Mt 3:16,17; Jn 5:32,37; 8:17,18 **5:10** [d]Ro 8:16; Gal 4:6 [e]Jn 3:33; 1Jn 1:10 **5:11** [f]S Mt 25:46 [g]S Jn 1:4 **5:12** [h]Jn 3:15, 16,36 **5:13** [i]S 1Jn 3:23 [j]ver 11; S Mt 25:46 **5:14** [k]S Eph 3:12; 1Jn 3:21 [l]S Mt 7:7 **5:15** [m]ver 18, 19,20 [n]1Ki 3:12 **5:16** [o]Jas 5:15 [p]Ex 23:21; Heb 6:4-6; 10:26 [q]Jer 7:16; 14:11 **5:17** [r]1Jn 3:4 [s]ver 16; 1Jn 2:1 **5:18** [t]S Jn 1:13 [u]S Mt 5:37 [v]Jn 14:30 **5:19** [w]1Jn 4:6 [x]Jn 12:31; 14:30; 17:15 **5:20** [y]ver 5 [z]Lk 24:45 [a]Jn 17:3 [b]ver 11; S Mt 25:46 **5:21** [c]S 1Jn 2:1 [d]1Co 10:14; 1Th 1:9

5:6 *water and blood.* Water symbolizes Jesus' baptism, and blood symbolizes his death. These are mentioned because Jesus' ministry began at his baptism and ended at his death. John may be reacting to the Gnostic heretics of his day (see Introduction: Gnosticism) who said that Jesus was born only a man and remained so until his baptism. At that time, they maintained, the Messiah (the Son of God) descended on the human Jesus but left him before his suffering on the cross—so that it was only the man Jesus who died. Throughout this letter John has been insisting that Jesus Christ is God as well as man (1:1–4; 4:2; 5:5). He now asserts that it was this God-man Jesus Christ who came into our world, was baptized and died. Jesus was the Son of God not only at his baptism but also at his death (v. 6b). This truth is extremely important, because, if Jesus died only as a man, his sacrificial atonement (2:2; 4:10) would not have been sufficient to take away the guilt of human sin. *the Spirit who testifies.* The Holy Spirit testifies that Jesus is the Son of God in two ways: (1) The Spirit descended on Jesus at his baptism (Jn 1:32–34), and (2) he continues to confirm in the hearts of believers the apostolic testimony that Jesus' baptism and death verify that he is the Messiah, the Son of God (see 2:27; 1Co 12:3 and notes; cf. Ro 8:16 and note).
5:7 *three.* The OT law required "two or three witnesses" (Dt 17:6; see note there). At the end of this verse, some older English versions add the words found in the NIV text note. But the addition is not found in any Greek manuscript or NT translation prior to the fourteenth century.
5:9 *God's testimony.* The Holy Spirit's testimony, mentioned in vv. 6–8.
5:11 *has given us eternal life.* As a present possession (see notes on Jn 3:15,36).
5:13 Another statement of the letter's purpose (see 2:26 and note). See Introduction: Occasion and Purpose.
5:14 *if we ask anything according to his will.* Cf. Lk 22:42. For another condition for prayer, see 3:21–22.
5:16 Verses 16–17 illustrate the kind of petition we can be sure God will answer (see vv. 14–15). *sin that leads to death.* In the context of this letter directed against Gnostic teaching, which denied the incarnation and threw off all moral restraints, it is probable that the "sin that leads to death" refers to the Gnostics' adamant and persistent denial of the truth and to their shameless immorality. This kind of unrepentant sin leads to spiritual death. Another view is that this is sin that results in physical death. It is held that because a believer continues to sin, God in judgment takes his or her life (cf. 1Co 11:30). In either case, "sin that does not lead to death" is of a less serious nature.
5:18–20 *We know.* The letter ends with three striking statements affirming the truths that "we know" and summarizing some of the letter's major themes.
5:18 *the One who was born of God.* Jesus, the Son of God.
5:20 *him who is true.* God the Father. *He is the true God.* Could refer to either God the Father or God the Son. *eternal life.* The letter began with this theme (1:1–2) and now ends with it.
5:21 *idols.* False gods, as opposed to the one true God (v. 20).

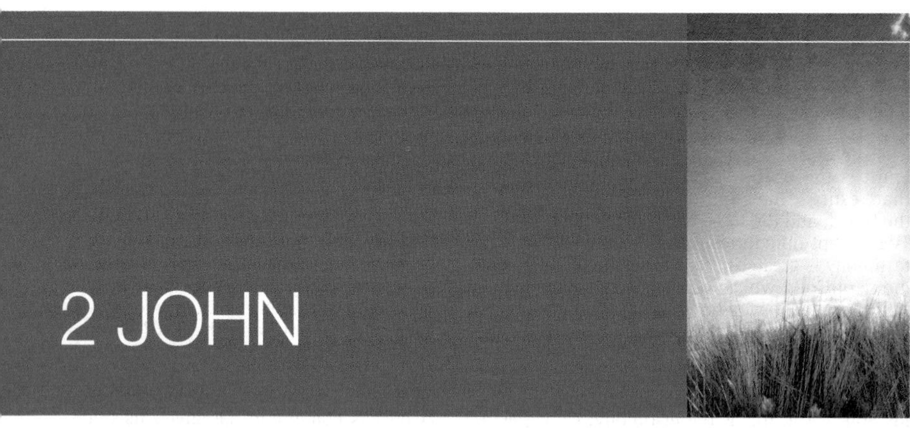

INTRODUCTION

Author

The author is John the apostle. Obvious similarities to 1 John and the Gospel of John suggest that the same person wrote all three books. Compare the following:

2Jn 5	1Jn 2:7	Jn 13:34 – 35
2Jn 6	1Jn 5:3	Jn 14:23
2Jn 7	1Jn 4:2 – 3	
2Jn 12	1Jn 1:4	Jn 15:11; 16:24

See Introductions to 1 John and the Gospel of John: Author.

Date

The letter was probably written about the same time as 1 John (AD 85 – 95), as the above comparisons suggest (see Introduction to 1 John: Date).

Occasion and Purpose

During the first two centuries the gospel was taken from place to place by traveling evangelists and teachers. Believers customarily took these missionaries into their homes and gave them provisions for their journey when they left. Since Gnostic teachers also relied on this practice (see note on 3Jn 5), 2 John was written to urge discernment in supporting traveling teachers; otherwise, someone might unintentionally contribute to the propagation of heresy rather than truth.

a **quick** look

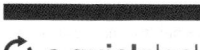

Author:
The apostle John

Audience:
The "lady chosen by God," probably a local church in western Asia Minor

Date:
Between AD 85 and 95

Theme:
John writes to urge discernment in supporting traveling teachers, since false teachers were also traveling and teaching heresy.

Outline

I. Greetings (1 – 3)
II. Commendation (4)
III. Exhortation and Warning (5 – 11)
IV. Conclusion and Final Greetings (12 – 13)

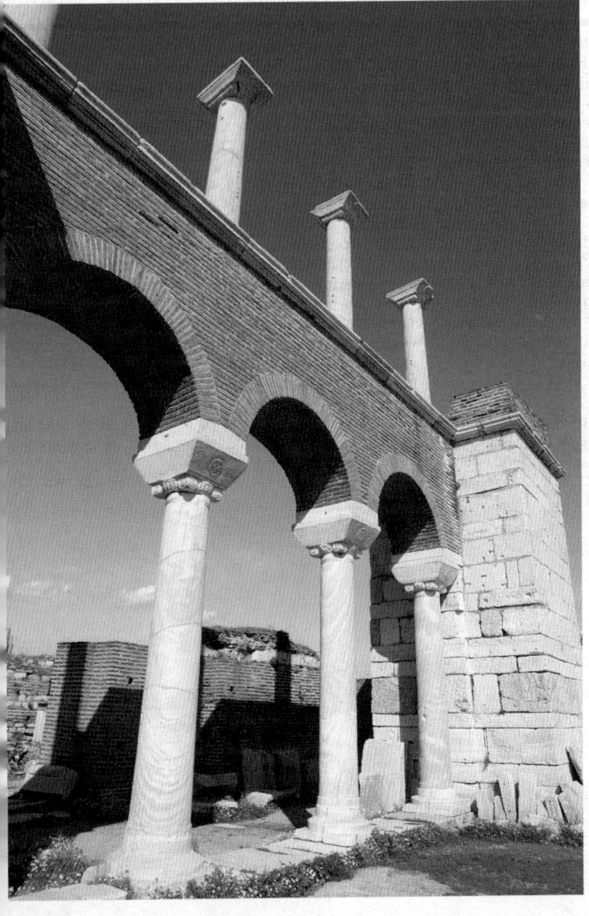

The ruins of St. John's Basilica, located near Ephesus, constructed in the fifth century AD by Emperor Justinian. It stands on what is believed to be the burial site of John the apostle.

1 The elder,[a]

To the lady chosen by God[b] and to her
children, whom I love in the truth[c]—and
not I only, but also all who know the
truth[d]— 2 because of the truth,[e] which
lives in us[f] and will be with us forever:

3 Grace, mercy and peace from God the
Father and from Jesus Christ,[g] the Father's
Son, will be with us in truth and love.

4 It has given me great joy to find some
of your children walking in the truth,[h] just
as the Father commanded us. 5 And now,
dear lady, I am not writing you a new
command but one we have had from the
beginning.[i] I ask that we love one another.
6 And this is love:[j] that we walk in obedience to his commands.[k] As you have heard
from the beginning,[l] his command is that
you walk in love.
7 I say this because many deceivers, who
do not acknowledge Jesus Christ[m] as coming in the flesh,[n] have gone out into the
world.[o] Any such person is the deceiver
and the antichrist.[p] 8 Watch out that you do
not lose what we[a] have worked for, but
that you may be rewarded fully.[q] 9 Anyone
who runs ahead and does not continue
in the teaching of Christ[r] does not have
God; whoever continues in the teaching
has both the Father and the Son.[s] 10 If anyone comes to you and does not bring this
teaching, do not take them into your house
or welcome them.[t] 11 Anyone who welcomes them shares[u] in their wicked work.
12 I have much to write to you, but I do
not want to use paper and ink. Instead, I
hope to visit you and talk with you face to
face,[v] so that our joy may be complete.[w]

13 The children of your sister, who is
chosen by God,[x] send their greetings.

[a] 8 Some manuscripts *you*

1 [a] S Ac 11:30; 3Jn 1 [b] ver 13; Ro 16:13; 1Pe 5:13 [c] ver 3 [d] Jn 8:32; 1Ti 2:4
2 [e] 2Pe 1:12 [f] Jn 14:17; 1Jn 1:8
3 [g] S Ro 1:7
4 [h] 3Jn 3,4
5 [i] S 1Jn 2:7
6 [j] 1Jn 2:5 [k] S Jn 14:15 [l] S 1Jn 2:7
7 [m] 1Jn 2:22; 4:2,3 [n] S Jn 1:14 [o] 1Jn 4:1 [p] S 1Jn 2:18
8 [q] S Mt 10:42; Mk 10:29, 30; 1Co 3:8; Heb 10:35,36; 11:26
9 [r] Jn 8:31 [s] S 1Jn 2:23
10 [t] S Ro 16:17
11 [u] 1Ti 5:22
12 [v] 3Jn 13,14 [w] S Jn 3:29
13 [x] ver 1

1 *elder.* See note on 1Ti 3:1. In his later years John functioned as an elder, perhaps of the Ephesian church. The apostle Peter held a similar position (see 1Pe 5:1 and note). *lady chosen.* Either an unknown Christian woman in the province of Asia or a figurative designation of a local church there (see v. 13). *her children.* Children of that Christian lady or members of that local church. *truth.* See note on Jn 1:14.
3 *Grace ... peace.* See note on Ro 1:7. *mercy.* See Ro 9:22–23 and note.
5 *new command.* See note on 1Jn 2:7–8.
6 *from the beginning.* See note on 1Jn 2:7.
7–11 This section deals with the basic Gnostic heresy attacked in 1 John, namely, that the Son of God did not become flesh (see Jn 1:14 and note) but that he temporarily came upon the man Jesus between his baptism and crucifixion (see Introduction to 1 John: Gnosticism).
7 *Jesus Christ as coming in the flesh.* See 1Jn 4:2–3 and note. *antichrist.* See note on 1Jn 2:18.
8 *worked for ... rewarded.* Work faithfully accomplished on earth brings future reward (see Mk 9:41; 10:29–30; Lk 19:16–19; Heb 11:26; cf. 1Co 3:10–15; 2Co 5:10 and notes).
9 *runs ahead.* A reference to the Gnostics, who believed that they had advanced beyond the teaching of the apostles. *teaching of Christ.* The similarity of this letter to 1 John, the nature of the heresy combated and the immediate context suggest that John is not referring to teaching given by Christ but to true teaching about Christ as the incarnate God-man (see 1Jn 2:23). *whoever continues in the teaching has ... the Son.* See 1Jn 5:12.
10 *take them into your house.* A reference to the housing and feeding of traveling teachers (see Introduction: Occasion and Purpose). The instruction does not prohibit greeting or even inviting a person into one's home for conversation. John was warning against providing food and shelter, since this would be an investment in the "wicked work" of false teachers and would give public approval (see v. 11).
12 *paper and ink.* Paper was made from papyrus reeds, which were readily available and cheap. The ink (the Greek for this word comes from a word that means "black") was made by mixing carbon, water and gum or oil. *that our joy may be complete.* See 1Jn 1:4 and note.
13 *sister, who is chosen.* May be taken literally to designate another Christian woman or figuratively to refer to another local church (see note on v. 1).

3 JOHN

INTRODUCTION

Author

The author is John the apostle. In the first verses of both 2 John and 3 John the author identifies himself as "the elder." Note other similarities: "love in the truth" (v. 1 of both letters), "walking in the truth" (v. 4 of both letters) and the similar conclusions. See Introductions to 1 John and the Gospel of John: Author.

Date

The letter was probably written about the same time as 1 and 2 John (AD 85 – 95). See Introduction to 1 John: Date.

Occasion and Purpose

See Introduction to 2 John: Occasion and Purpose. Itinerant teachers sent out by John were rejected in one of the churches in the province of Asia by a dictatorial leader, Diotrephes, who even excommunicated members who showed hospitality to John's messengers. John wrote this letter to commend Gaius for supporting the teachers and, indirectly, to warn Diotrephes.

Outline

I. Greetings (1 – 2)
II. Commendation of Gaius (3 – 8)
III. Condemnation of Diotrephes (9 – 10)
IV. Exhortation to Gaius (11)
V. Example of Demetrius (12)
VI. Conclusion, Benediction and Final Greetings (13 – 14)

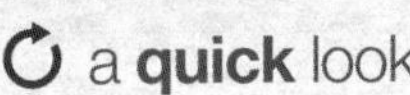

Author:
The apostle John

Audience:
Gaius, perhaps a leader of one of the churches in western Asia Minor

Date:
Between AD 85 and 95

Theme:
John writes this letter to commend Gaius for supporting traveling teachers and to rebuke Diotrephes for refusing to welcome them.

Aerial view of Ephesus. John lived here after the destruction of Jerusalem in AD 70. Church tradition indicates that he also died here c. AD 100.

1 The elder,[a]

To my dear friend Gaius, whom I love
in the truth.

2 Dear friend, I pray that you may enjoy
good health and that all may go well with
you, even as your soul is getting along
well. 3 It gave me great joy when some
believers[b] came and testified about your
faithfulness to the truth, telling how you
continue to walk in it.[c] 4 I have no greater joy than to hear that my children[d] are
walking in the truth.[e]
5 Dear friend, you are faithful in what
you are doing for the brothers and sisters,[a][f] even though they are strangers to
you.[g] 6 They have told the church about
your love. Please send them on their way[h]
in a manner that honors[i] God. 7 It was for
the sake of the Name[j] that they went out,
receiving no help from the pagans.[k] 8 We
ought therefore to show hospitality to
such people so that we may work together
for the truth.
9 I wrote to the church, but Diotrephes,
who loves to be first, will not welcome
us. 10 So when I come,[l] I will call attention
to what he is doing, spreading malicious
nonsense about us. Not satisfied with that,
he even refuses to welcome other believers.[m] He also stops those who want to do
so and puts them out of the church.[n]
11 Dear friend, do not imitate what is evil
but what is good.[o] Anyone who does what
is good is from God.[p] Anyone who does
what is evil has not seen God.[q] 12 Demetrius is well spoken of by everyone[r] — and
even by the truth itself. We also speak well
of him, and you know that our testimony
is true.[s]
13 I have much to write you, but I do not
want to do so with pen and ink. 14 I hope
to see you soon, and we will talk face to
face.[t]

Peace to you.[u] The friends here send
their greetings. Greet the friends there by
name.[v]

1 [a] S Ac 11:30; 2Jn 1
3 [b] ver 5, 10; S Ac 1:16 [c] 2Jn 4
4 [d] S 1Jn 2:1 [e] ver 3
5 [f] S ver 3 [g] Ro 12:13; Heb 13:2
6 [h] 1Co 16:11; 2Co 1:16 [i] S Eph 4:1
7 [j] S Jn 15:21 [k] Ac 20:33, 35
10 [l] ver 14; 2Jn 12 [m] ver 5 [n] Jn 9:22, 34
11 [o] Ps 34:14; 37:27 [p] 1Jn 2:29 [q] 1Jn 3:6, 9, 10
12 [r] 1Ti 3:7 [s] Jn 19:35; 21:24
14 [t] 2Jn 12 [u] S Ro 1:7; S Eph 6:23 [v] Jn 10:3

[a] 5 The Greek word for *brothers and sisters* (*adelphoi*) refers here to believers, both men and women, as part of God's family.

1 *The elder.* See note on 2Jn 1. *dear friend.* A favorite term of John (see note on 1Jn 2:7). *Gaius.* A Christian in one of the churches of the province of Asia. Gaius was a common Roman name. This letter presents two good examples (Gaius [vv. 3–8] and Demetrius [v. 12]) and one bad example (Diotrephes [see vv. 9–10 and notes]). *truth.* See note on Jn 1:14.
3–4 *your faithfulness to the truth … you continue to walk in it … walking in the truth.* See 2Jn 4.
4 *my children.* Perhaps John's converts, or believers currently under his spiritual guidance (see 1Jn 2:1 and note).
5 *doing for the brothers and sisters.* The early church provided hospitality and support for missionaries. See Introduction to 2 John: Occasion and Purpose; see also note on 2Jn 10. *brothers and sisters.* See NIV text note.
7 *Name.* See note on Ac 4:12. Today Orthodox Jews often address God by the title *Ha-Shem* ("The Name").
8 *show hospitality.* See v. 5; 1Pe 4:9 and notes.
9 *I wrote.* A previous letter of the apostle that is now lost. *church.* Some identify this church with the chosen lady of 2Jn 1. *Diotrephes.* A church leader who was exercising dictatorial power in the church. He must have had considerable influence since he was able to exclude people from the church fellowship (v. 10). See Introduction: Occasion and Purpose.
10 *spreading malicious nonsense.* See Pr 18:8; 2Th 3:11 and notes; 1Ti 5:13.
11 *does what is good.* The continual practice of good, not merely doing occasional good deeds (cf. Ro 12:21). *has not seen God.* See 1Jn 3:6.
12 *Demetrius is well spoken of.* In contrast to Diotrephes (see vv. 9–10 and notes; see also note on v. 1). Demetrius may have been the bearer of this letter. *even by the truth itself.* Possibly in some sense the gospel personified.
13–14 See 2Jn 12–13 for a similar conclusion (see also notes there).
14 *Peace to you.* Not a prayer or wish but a benedictory pronouncement (see note on Ro 1:7).

JUDE

INTRODUCTION

Author

The author identifies himself as Jude (v. 1), which is another form of the Hebrew name Judah (Greek "Judas"), a common name among the Jews. Of those so named in the NT, the ones most likely to be author of this letter are: (1) Judas the apostle (see Lk 6:16; Ac 1:13 and note) — not Judas Iscariot — and (2) Judas the brother of the Lord (Mt 13:55; Mk 6:3). The latter is more likely. For example, the author does not claim to be an apostle and even seems to separate himself from the apostles (v. 17). Furthermore, he describes himself as a "brother of James" (v. 1). Ordinarily a person in Jude's day would describe himself as someone's son rather than as someone's brother. The reason for the exception here may have been James's prominence in the church at Jerusalem (see Introduction to James: Author).

Although neither Jude nor James describes himself as a brother of the Lord, others did not hesitate to speak of them in this way (see Mt 13:55; Jn 7:3 – 10; Ac 1:14; 1Co 9:5; Gal 1:19). Apparently they themselves did not ask to be heard because of the special privilege they had as members of the household of Joseph and Mary.

Possible references to the letter of Jude or quotations from it are found at a very early date: e.g., in Clement of Rome (c. AD 96). Clement of Alexandria (155 – 215), Tertullian (150 – 222) and Origen (185 – 253) accepted it; it was included in the Muratorian Canon (c. 170) and was accepted by Athanasius (298 – 373) and by the Council of Carthage (397). Eusebius (265 – 340) listed the letter among the questioned books, though he recognized that many considered it as coming from Jude.

According to Jerome and Didymus, some did not accept the letter as canonical because of the manner in which it uses noncanonical literature (see notes on vv. 9,14). But an inspired author may legitimately make use of such literature — whether for illustrative purposes or for appropriation of historically reliable or otherwise acceptable material — and such use does not necessarily endorse that literature as inspired. Under the

a **quick** look

Author:
Most likely Jude, the brother of Jesus

Audience:
Christians who are being threatened by false teachers

Date:
Between AD 65 and 80

Theme:
Jude writes to warn Christians about false teachers who are trying to convince them that being saved by grace gives them license to sin.

influence of the Spirit the church came to the conviction that the authority of God stands behind the letter of Jude. The fact that the letter was questioned and tested but nonetheless was finally accepted by the churches indicates the strength of its claims to authenticity.

Date

There is nothing in the letter that requires a date beyond the lifetime of Jude, the brother of the Lord. The error the author is combating, like that in 2 Peter, is not the heretical teaching of the second century but that which could and did develop at an early date (cf. Ac 20:29 – 30; Ro 6:1; 1Co 5:1 – 11; 2Co 12:21; Gal 5:13; Eph 5:3 – 17; 1Th 4:6). (See also Introduction to 2 Peter: Date.) There is, moreover, nothing in the letter that requires a date after the time of the apostles, as some have argued. It may even be that Jude's readers had heard some of the apostles speak (see vv. 17 – 18). Likewise, the use of the word "faith" in the objective sense of the body of truth believed (v. 3) does not require a late dating of the letter. It was used in such a sense as early as Gal 1:23.

Sunset over the Sea of Galilee. Jude 13 compares false teachers to "wild waves of the sea."

The question of the relationship between Jude and 2 Peter has a bearing on the date of Jude. If 2Pe 2 makes use of Jude — a commonly accepted view (see Introduction to 2 Peter: 2 Peter and Jude) — then Jude is to be dated prior to 2 Peter, probably c. AD 65. Otherwise, a date as late as c. 80 would be possible.

PARALLELS BETWEEN JUDE AND 2 PETER

JUDE		2 PETER
4	The false teachers' "condemnation" from the past	2:3
4	The false teachers "deny" our "Sovereign [and] Lord"	2:1
6	Angels confined for judgment	2:4
7	Sodom and Gomorrah as examples of judgment on gross evil	2:6
8	The false teachers "reject [Jude] / despise [2Pe] authority"; they "heap abuse on celestial beings"	2:10
9	Angels do not "condemn . . . for slander [Jude] / heap abuse . . . when bringing judgment [2Pe]"	2:11
12	The false teachers are "blemishes"	2:13
12	Jude: "clouds without rain, blown along by the wind"; 2Pe: "springs without water and mists driven by a storm"	2:17
18	"Scoffers" following "their own evil [2Pe] / ungodly [Jude] desires"	3:3

Recipients

The description of those to whom Jude addressed his letter is very general (see v. 1). It could apply to Jewish Christians, Gentile Christians or both. Their location is not indicated. It should not be assumed that, since 2Pe 2 and Jude 4–18 appear to describe similar situations, they were both written to the same people. The kind of heresy depicted in these two passages was widespread (see Date).

Occasion and Purpose

Although Jude was very eager to write to his readers about salvation, he felt that he must instead warn them about certain immoral men circulating among them who were perverting the grace of God (see v. 4 and note). Apparently these false teachers were trying to convince believers that being saved by grace gave them license to sin since their sins would no longer be held against them. Jude thought it imperative that his readers be on guard against such men and be prepared to oppose their perverted teaching with the truth about God's saving grace.

It has generally been assumed that these false teachers were Gnostics. Although this identification is no doubt correct, they must have been forerunners of fully developed, second-century Gnosticism (see Introduction to 2 Peter: Date).

Jude thinks it imperative that his readers be on guard and be prepared to oppose false teaching with the truth about God's grace.

Outline

I. Greetings (1 – 2)
II. Occasion for the Letter (3 – 4)
    A. The Change of Subject (3)
    B. The Reason for the Change: The Presence of Godless Apostates (4)
III. Warning against False Teachers (5 – 16)
    A. Historical Examples of the Judgment of Apostates (5 – 7)
        1. Unbelieving Israel (5)
        2. Angels who fell (6)
        3. Sodom and Gomorrah (7)
    B. Description of the Apostates of Jude's Day (8 – 16)
        1. Their slanderous speech deplored (8 – 10)
        2. Their character graphically portrayed (11 – 13)
        3. Their destruction prophesied (14 – 16)
IV. Exhortation to Believers (17 – 23)
V. Concluding Doxology (24 – 25)

1 Jude,[a] a servant of Jesus Christ[b] and a
brother of James,

To those who have been called,[c] who
are loved in God the Father and kept for[a]
Jesus Christ:[d]

2 Mercy, peace[e] and love be yours in
abundance.[f]

The Sin and Doom of Ungodly People

3 Dear friends,[g] although I was very eager to write to you about the salvation we
share,[h] I felt compelled to write and urge
you to contend[i] for the faith[j] that was once
for all entrusted to God's holy people.[k]
4 For certain individuals whose condemnation was written about[b] long ago have
secretly slipped in among you.[l] They are
ungodly people, who pervert the grace of
our God into a license for immorality and
deny Jesus Christ our only Sovereign and
Lord.[m]
5 Though you already know all this,[n] I
want to remind you[o] that the Lord[c] at one
time delivered his people out of Egypt, but
later destroyed those who did not believe.[p]
6 And the angels who did not keep their
positions of authority but abandoned their
proper dwelling—these he has kept in
darkness, bound with everlasting chains
for judgment on the great Day.[q] 7 In a similar way, Sodom and Gomorrah[r] and the
surrounding towns[s] gave themselves up to
sexual immorality and perversion. They
serve as an example of those who suffer
the punishment of eternal fire.[t]
8 In the very same way, on the strength
of their dreams these ungodly people pollute their own bodies, reject authority and
heap abuse on celestial beings.[u] 9 But even
the archangel[v] Michael,[w] when he was disputing with the devil about the body of
Moses,[x] did not himself dare to condemn
him for slander but said, "The Lord rebuke

[a] *1* Or *by*; or *in* [b] *4* Or *individuals who were marked out for condemnation* [c] *5* Some early manuscripts *Jesus*

1 [a]Mt 13:55; Jn 14:22; Ac 1:13 [b]Ro 1:1 [c]Ro 1:6,7 [d]Jn 17:12
2 [e]Gal 6:16; 1Ti 1:2 [f]S Ro 1:7
3 [g]S 1Co 10:14 [h]Titus 1:4 [i]1Ti 6:12 [j]ver 20; Ac 6:7 [k]S Ac 9:13
4 [l]Gal 2:4 [m]Titus 1:16; 2Pe 2:1; 1Jn 2:22
5 [n]S 1Jn 2:20 [o]2Pe 1:12,13; 3:1,2 [p]Nu 14:29; Dt 1:32; 2:15; Ps 106:26; 1Co 10:1-5; Heb 3:16,17
6 [q]S 2Pe 2:4,9
7 [r]S Mt 10:15 [s]Dt 29:23 [t]S Mt 25:41; 2Pe 3:7
8 [u]2Pe 2:10
9 [v]1Th 4:16 [w]Da 10:13,21; 12:1; Rev 12:7 [x]Dt 34:6

1 *servant.* See note on Ro 1:1. *brother of James.* See Introduction: Author. *called.* See note on Ro 8:28. *loved in God.* See Jn 3:16; Ro 8:28–39. *kept for Jesus Christ.* He who holds the whole universe together (see Col 1:17; Heb 1:3) will see that God's children are kept in the faith and that they reach their eternal inheritance (see Jn 6:37–40; 17:11–12; 1Pe 1:3–5).

2 *Mercy.* See Ge 19:16; Ro 9:22–23; Titus 3:5 and notes. *peace.* See note on Ro 1:7.

3 *Dear friends.* See vv. 17,20; see also note on 2Pe 3:1. *the salvation we share.* Jude's original intention was to write a general treatment of the doctrine of salvation, probably dealing with such subjects as human sin and guilt, God's love and grace, the forgiveness of sins and the changed lifestyle that follows new birth. *the faith.* Here used of the body of truth held by believers everywhere—the gospel and all its implications (see Introduction: Date; see also 1Ti 4:6). This truth was under attack and had to be defended. *once for all entrusted.* The truth has finality and is not subject to change. *God's holy people.* See notes on Ro 1:7; Eph 1:1; Col 1:4.

4 *For.* Introduces the reason Jude felt impelled to change the subject of his letter (see Introduction: Occasion and Purpose). *whose condemnation was written about.* The reference may be to OT denunciations of ungodly people or to Enoch's prophecy (vv. 14–15). Or Jude may mean that judgment has long been about to fall on them because of their sin (see 2Pe 2:3 and note—which may be a clarification of this clause). *ungodly people.* See vv. 15,18. *pervert the grace of our God into a license for immorality.* They assume that salvation by grace gives them the right to sin without restraint, either because God in his grace will freely forgive all their sins or because sin, by contrast, magnifies the grace of God (cf. Ro 5:20; 6:1 and note). *deny … our only Sovereign and Lord.* The Greek term translated "Sovereign" describes power without limit, or absolute domination. The Greek construction indicates that both "Sovereign" and "Lord" refer to the same person, and this verse, as well as the parallel passage (2Pe 2:1), clearly states that that person is Christ.

5–7 Three examples of divine judgment (see Introduction: Outline).

5 *destroyed those who did not believe.* They did not believe that God would give them the land of Canaan; consequently all unbelieving adults died in the wilderness without entering the promised land (see Nu 14:29–30; Dt 1:32–36; 2:15; 1Co 10:1–5 and note on 10:5; Heb 3:16–19 and note).

6 *angels.* See note on 2Pe 2:4. *positions of authority.* See note on 2Pe 2:4. God had assigned differing areas of responsibility and authority to each of the angels (see Da 10:20–21, where the various princes may be angels assigned to various nations). Some of these angels refused to maintain their assignments and thus became the devil and his angels (cf. Mt 25:41). *their proper dwelling.* Angels apparently were assigned specific locations, as well as responsibilities. Some assume that they left the heavenly realm and came to earth (see note on 2Pe 2:4). *kept … bound … for judgment.* See note on 2Pe 2:4. *the great Day.* The final judgment.

7 *In a similar way.* Does not mean that the sin of Sodom and Gomorrah was the same as that of the angels or vice versa. This phrase is used to introduce the third illustration of the fact that God will see to it that the unrighteous will be consigned to eternal punishment on judgment day. *perversion.* Lit. "went after other flesh"; more specifically, homosexual practices (see Ge 19:5 and note). *serve as an example of … punishment of eternal fire.* God destroyed Sodom and Gomorrah by pouring out "burning sulfur" (Ge 19:24)—a foretaste of the eternal fire that is to come.

8 *their dreams.* The godless people were referred to as having "dreams" either (1) because they claimed to receive revelations or, more likely, (2) because in their passion they were out of touch with truth and reality (they were "dreamers"). *pollute their own bodies.* Probably a reference to the homosexual practices in Sodom and Gomorrah (see vv. 4,7; 1Co 6:9,18 and note on 6:9). *reject authority.* See note on 2Pe 2:10. *heap abuse on celestial beings.* See note on 2Pe 2:10.

9 According to several church fathers, this verse is based on a noncanonical work called The Testament of Moses (approximately the first century AD). Other NT quotations from, or allusions to, non-Biblical works include Paul's quotations of Aratus (see Ac 17:28 and note), Menander (see 1Co 15:33 and note) and Epimenides (see Titus 1:12 and note). Such usage in no way suggests that the quotations, or the books from which they were taken, are divinely inspired. It only means that the Biblical author found the quotations to be a helpful confirmation, clarification or illustration.

you!"[a][y] 10 Yet these people slander whatever they do not understand, and the very
things they do understand by instinct—as
irrational animals do—will destroy them.[z]
11 Woe to them! They have taken the
way of Cain;[a] they have rushed for profit
into Balaam's error;[b] they have been destroyed in Korah's rebellion.[c]
12 These people are blemishes at your love
feasts,[d] eating with you without the slightest qualm—shepherds who feed only themselves.[e] They are clouds without rain,[f] blown
along by the wind;[g] autumn trees, without
fruit and uprooted[h]—twice dead. 13 They
are wild waves of the sea,[i] foaming up their
shame;[j] wandering stars, for whom blackest
darkness has been reserved forever.[k]
14 Enoch,[l] the seventh from Adam,
prophesied about them: "See, the Lord is
coming[m] with thousands upon thousands
of his holy ones[n] 15 to judge[o] everyone, and
to convict all of them of all the ungodly
acts they have committed in their ungodliness, and of all the defiant words ungodly sinners have spoken against him."[b][p]
16 These people are grumblers[q] and faultfinders; they follow their own evil desires;[r]
they boast[s] about themselves and flatter
others for their own advantage.

9 [y] Zec 3:2
10 [z] 2Pe 2:12
11 [a] Ge 4:3-8; Heb 11:4; 1Jn 3:12 [b] S 2Pe 2:15 [c] Nu 16:1-3, 31-35
12 [d] 2Pe 2:13; 1Co 11:20-22 [e] Eze 34:2,8, 10 [f] Pr 25:14; 2Pe 2:17 [g] Eph 4:14 [h] Mt 15:13
13 [i] Isa 57:20 [j] Php 3:19 [k] 2Pe 2:17
14 [l] Ge 5:18,21-24 [m] S Mt 16:27 [n] Dt 33:2; Da 7:10; Zec 14:5; Heb 12:22
15 [o] 2Pe 2:6-9 [p] 1Ti 1:9
16 [q] 1Co 10:10 [r] ver 18; 2Pe 2:10 [s] 2Pe 2:18
17 [t] S Eph 4:11 [u] Heb 2:3; 2Pe 3:2
18 [v] 1Ti 4:1; 2Ti 3:1; 2Pe 3:3 [w] ver 16; 2Pe 2:1; 3:3

A Call to Persevere

17 But, dear friends, remember what the
apostles[t] of our Lord Jesus Christ foretold.[u]
18 They said to you, "In the last times[v] there
will be scoffers who will follow their own
ungodly desires."[w] 19 These are the people
who divide you, who follow mere natural
instincts and do not have the Spirit.[x]
20 But you, dear friends, by building
yourselves up[y] in your most holy faith[z] and
praying in the Holy Spirit,[a] 21 keep yourselves in God's love as you wait[b] for the
mercy of our Lord Jesus Christ to bring
you to eternal life.[c]
22 Be merciful to those who doubt;

[a] 9 Jude is alluding to the Jewish *Testament of Moses* (approximately the first century A.D.). [b] 14,15 From the Jewish *First Book of Enoch* (approximately the first century B.C.)

19 [x] 1Co 2:14,15 20 [y] Col 2:7; 1Th 5:11 [z] ver 3 [a] Eph 6:18
21 [b] Titus 2:13; Heb 9:28; 2Pe 3:12 [c] S Mt 25:46

---

10 *whatever they do not understand.* See note on 2Pe 2:12; cf. 1Co 2:14. *irrational animals.* See note on 2Pe 2:12.

11 Three OT examples of the kind of persons Jude warns his readers about. *Woe to them!* A warning that judgment is coming (see Mt 23:13, 15–16,23,25,27,29). *way of Cain.* The way of selfishness and greed (see note on Ge 4:3–4) and the way of hatred and murder (see 1Jn 3:12). *Balaam's error.* The error of consuming greed (see note on 2Pe 2:15). *Korah's rebellion.* Korah rose up against God's appointed leadership (see Nu 16). Jude may be suggesting that the false teachers of his day were rebelling against church leadership (cf. 3Jn 9–10).

12–13 These verses contain six graphic metaphors: (1) *blemishes at your love feasts.* See note on 2Pe 2:13. (2) *shepherds who feed only themselves.* Instead of feeding the sheep for whom they are responsible (see Eze 34:8–10). (3) *clouds without rain.* Like clouds promising moisture for the parched land, the false teachers promise soul-satisfying truth, but in reality they have nothing to offer. (4) *autumn trees, without fruit and uprooted—twice dead.* Though the trees ought to be heavy with fruit. (5) *wild waves of the sea.* As wind-tossed waves constantly churn up rubbish, so these apostates continually stir up moral filth (see Isa 57:20). (6) *wandering stars.* As shooting stars appear in the sky only to fly off into eternal oblivion, so these false teachers are destined for the darkness of eternal hell.

14 *Enoch, the seventh from Adam.* Not the Enoch in the line of Cain (Ge 4:17) but the one in the line of Seth (Ge 5:18–24; 1Ch 1:1–3). He was seventh if Adam is counted as the first. The quotation is from the book of Enoch, which purports to have been written by the Enoch of Ge 5 but actually did not appear until the first century BC. The book of Enoch was a well-respected writing in NT times. That it was not canonical does not mean that it contained no truth; nor does Jude's quotation of the book mean that he considered it inspired (see Introduction: Author; see also note on v. 9). *the Lord is coming.* Jude uses the quotation to refer to Christ's second coming and to his judgment of the wicked (see 2Th 1:6–10). *holy ones.* Probably angels (see Da 4:13–17; 2Th 1:7). However, some think they are raptured believers who are returning with the Lord (see 1Th 3:13 and note).

15 *ungodly … ungodliness … ungodly.* The repetition and the awesome judgment scene that is depicted emphasize the condemnation of the false teachers in v. 4 (see note there).

16 *These people.* The ungodly people first mentioned in v. 4 and subsequently referred to repeatedly as "these people" (vv. 10,12,19; cf. v. 8). They are the libertine false teachers who pervert the grace of God.

17 *remember what the apostles … foretold.* The coming of these godless people should not take believers by surprise, for it had been predicted by the apostles (Ac 20:29; 1Ti 4:1; 2Ti 3:1–5; 2Pe 2:1–3; 3:2–3).

18 *They said.* The Greek for this phrase indicates that the apostles repeatedly warned that such godless apostates would come. *last times.* See note on Jas 5:3. *scoffers.* In both 2Pe 3:3 and Jude the scoffers are said to be characterized by selfish lusts ("desires").

19 *people who divide you.* At the very least this phrase means that they were divisive, creating factions in the church—the usual practice of heretics. Or Jude may be referring to the later Gnostics' division of people into the spiritual (the Gnostics) and the sensual (those for whom there is no hope). *follow mere natural instincts.* An ironic description of the false teachers, who labeled others as sensual (see 1Co 2:14 and note). *do not have the Spirit.* Rather than being the spiritual ones—the privileged elite class the Gnostics claimed to be—Jude denies that they even possess the Spirit. A person who does not have the Spirit is clearly not saved (see Ro 8:9).

20 *But you, dear friends.* In contrast to the ungodly false teachers, about whom this letter speaks at length. *most holy faith.* See note on v. 3. *in the Holy Spirit.* According to the Spirit's promptings and with the power of the Spirit (see Ro 8:26–27; Gal 4:6; Eph 6:17–18 and notes).

21 *keep yourselves in God's love.* God both keeps believers in his love (see Ro 8:35–39 and notes) and enables them to keep themselves in his love. *eternal life.* See Jn 3:15 and note.

22–23 *those who doubt … others.* Perhaps those who have come under the influence of the apostates.

23 save others by snatching them from the
fire;[d] to others show mercy, mixed with
fear—hating even the clothing stained by
corrupted flesh.[a][e]

Doxology

24 To him who is able[f] to keep you from
stumbling and to present you before his
glorious presence[g] without fault[h] and
with great joy— 25 to the only God[i] our
Savior be glory, majesty, power and authority, through Jesus Christ our Lord,
before all ages, now and forevermore![j]
Amen.[k]

23 [d] Am 4:11; Zec 3:2-5; 1Co 3:15 [e] Rev 3:4 **24** [f] S Ro 16:25 [g] S 2Co 4:14 [h] Col 1:22 **25** [i] Jn 5:44; 1Ti 1:17 [j] Heb 13:8 [k] S Ro 11:36

[a] *22,23* The Greek manuscripts of these verses vary at several points.

23 *save others by snatching them from the fire.* Rescuing them from the verge of destruction (see Am 4:11; Zec 3:2; 1Co 3:15 and notes). *mercy, mixed with fear.* Even in showing mercy one may be trapped by the allurement of sin. *clothing stained by corrupted flesh.* The wicked are pictured as being so corrupt that even their garments are polluted by their sinful flesh.

24–25 After all the attention necessarily given in this letter to the ungodly and their works of darkness, Jude concludes by focusing attention on God, who is fully able to keep those who put their trust in him.

REVELATION

INTRODUCTION

Author

Four times the author identifies himself as John (1:1,4,9; 22:8). From as early as Justin Martyr in the second century AD it has been held that this John was the apostle, the son of Zebedee (see Mt 10:2). The book itself reveals that the author was a Jew, well versed in Scripture, a church leader who was well known to the seven churches of Asia Minor, and a deeply religious person fully convinced that the Christian faith would soon triumph over the demonic forces at work in the world.

In the third century, however, an African bishop named Dionysius compared the language, style and thought of the Apocalypse (Revelation) with that of the other writings of John and decided that the book could not have been written by the apostle John. He suggested that the author was a certain John the Presbyter (or Elder), whose name appears elsewhere in ancient writings. Although many today follow Dionysius in his view of authorship, the external evidence seems to support the traditional view.

Date

Revelation was written when Christians were entering a time of persecution. The two periods most often mentioned are the latter part of Nero's reign (AD 54–68; see 13:18 and note) and the latter part of Domitian's reign (81–96). Most interpreters date the book c. 95.

Occasion

Since Roman authorities at this time were beginning to enforce emperor worship, Christians — who held that Christ, not Caesar, was Lord — were facing increasing hostility. The believers at Smyrna are warned against coming opposition (2:10), and the church at Philadelphia is told of an hour of trial coming on the world (3:10). Antipas has already given his life (2:13), along with others (6:9). John has been exiled to the island of Patmos

a **quick** look

Author:
The apostle John

Audience:
Seven churches in western Asia Minor

Date:
About AD 95

Theme:
John writes to encourage the faithful to stand firm against persecution and compromise in the light of the imminent return of Christ to deliver the righteous and judge the wicked.

Monastery of St. John on the island of Patmos

(probably the site of a Roman penal colony) for his activities as a Christian missionary (1:9). Some within the church are advocating a policy of compromise (2:14–15,20), which has to be corrected before its subtle influence can undermine the determination of believers to stand fast in the perilous days that lie ahead.

Purpose

John writes to encourage the faithful to resist staunchly the demands of emperor worship. He informs his readers that the final showdown between God and Satan is imminent. Satan will increase his persecution of believers, but they must stand fast, even to death. They are sealed against any spiritual harm and will soon be vindicated when Christ returns, when the wicked are forever destroyed, and when God's people enter an eternity of glory and blessedness.

Literary Form

For an adequate understanding of Revelation, the reader must recognize that it is a distinct kind of literature. Revelation is apocalyptic, a kind of writing that is highly symbolic. Although its visions often seem bizarre to the Western reader, the book fortunately provides a number of clues for its

Revelation is apocalyptic,
a kind of writing that is highly symbolic.

own interpretation (e.g., stars are angels, lampstands are churches, 1:20; "the great prostitute," 17:1, is "Babylon" [Rome?], 17:5,18; and the heavenly Jerusalem is the wife of the Lamb, 21:9 – 10).

Distinctive Feature

A distinctive feature is the frequent use of the number seven (52 times). There are seven beatitudes (see note on 1:3), seven churches (1:4,11), seven spirits (1:4), seven golden lampstands (1:12), seven stars (1:16), seven seals (5:1), seven horns and seven eyes (5:6), seven trumpets (8:2), seven thunders (10:3), seven signs (12:1,3; 13:13 – 14; 15:1; 16:14; 19:20), seven crowns (12:3), seven plagues (15:6), seven golden bowls (15:7), seven hills (17:9) and seven kings (17:10), as well as other sevens. Symbolically, the number seven stands for completeness.

Interpretation

Interpreters of Revelation normally fall into four groups:

(1) *Preterists* understand the book primarily in terms of its first-century setting, claiming that most of its events have already taken place.

(2) *Historicists* take it as describing the long chain of events from Patmos to the end of history.

(3) *Futurists* place the book primarily in the end times.

(4) *Idealists* view it as symbolic pictures of such timeless truths as the victory of good over evil.

Island of Patmos, where John was exiled and received his revelation

Fortunately, the fundamental truths of Revelation do not depend on adopting a particular point of view. They are available to anyone who will read the book for its overall message and resist the temptation to become overly enamored with the details.

Outline

I. Introduction (1:1 – 8)
  A. Prologue (1:1 – 3)
  B. Greetings and Doxology (1:4 – 8)
II. Jesus among the Seven Churches (1:9 – 20)
III. The Letters to the Seven Churches (chs. 2 – 3)
  A. Ephesus (2:1 – 7)
  B. Smyrna (2:8 – 11)
  C. Pergamum (2:12 – 17)
  D. Thyatira (2:18 – 29)
  E. Sardis (3:1 – 6)
  F. Philadelphia (3:7 – 13)
  G. Laodicea (3:14 – 22)
IV. The Throne, the Scroll and the Lamb (chs. 4 – 5)
  A. The Throne in Heaven (ch. 4)
  B. The Seven-Sealed Scroll (5:1 – 5)
  C. The Lamb Slain (5:6 – 14)
V. The Seven Seals (6:1 — 8:1)
  A. First Seal: The White Horse (6:1 – 2)
  B. Second Seal: The Red Horse (6:3 – 4)
  C. Third Seal: The Black Horse (6:5 – 6)
  D. Fourth Seal: The Pale Horse (6:7 – 8)
  E. Fifth Seal: The Souls under the Altar (6:9 – 11)
  F. Sixth Seal: The Great Earthquake (6:12 – 17)
  G. The Sealing of the 144,000 (7:1 – 8)
  H. The Great Multitude (7:9 – 17)
  I. Seventh Seal: Silence in Heaven (8:1)
VI. The Seven Trumpets (8:2 — 11:19)
  A. Introduction (8:2 – 5)
  B. First Trumpet: Hail and Fire Mixed with Blood (8:6 – 7)
  C. Second Trumpet: A Mountain Thrown into the Sea (8:8 – 9)
  D. Third Trumpet: The Star Wormwood (8:10 – 11)
  E. Fourth Trumpet: A Third of the Sun, Moon and Stars Struck (8:12 – 13)
  F. Fifth Trumpet: The Plague of Locusts (9:1 – 12)
  G. Sixth Trumpet: Release of the Four Angels (9:13 – 21)
  H. The Angel and the Little Scroll (ch. 10)
  I. The Two Witnesses (11:1 – 14)
  J. Seventh Trumpet: Judgments and Rewards (11:15 – 19)

- VII. Interlude: Persecution, Deliverance and Judgment (chs. 12 – 14)
  - A. The Woman and the Dragon (ch. 12)
  - B. The Two Beasts (ch. 13)
  - C. The Lamb and the 144,000 (14:1 – 5)
  - D. The Harvest of the Earth (14:6 – 20)
- VIII. The Seven Bowls (chs. 15 – 16)
  - A. Introduction: The Song of Moses and the Seven Angels with the Seven Plagues (ch. 15)
  - B. First Bowl: Ugly and Painful Sores (16:1 – 2)
  - C. Second Bowl: Sea Turns to Blood (16:3)
  - D. Third Bowl: Rivers and Springs of Water Become Blood (16:4 – 7)
  - E. Fourth Bowl: Sun Scorches People with Fire (16:8 – 9)
  - F. Fifth Bowl: Darkness (16:10 – 11)
  - G. Sixth Bowl: Euphrates River Dries Up (16:12 – 16)
  - H. Seventh Bowl: Tremendous Earthquake (16:17 – 21)
- IX. The Destruction of Babylon and the Coming of the New Jerusalem (17:1 — 22:5)
  - A. The Destruction of Babylon (17:1 — 19:5)
    1. The great prostitute described (ch. 17)
    2. The fall of Babylon (ch. 18)
    3. Praise for Babylon's fall (19:1 – 5)
  - B. Praise for the Wedding of the Lamb (19:6 – 10)
  - C. The Return of Christ (19:11 – 21)
  - D. The Thousand Years (20:1 – 6)
  - E. Satan's Doom (20:7 – 10)
  - F. Great White Throne Judgment (20:11 – 15)
  - G. The Coming of the New Jerusalem (22:1 — 22:5)
    1. The new heaven and new earth (21:1 – 8)
    2. The new Jerusalem (21:9 – 27)
    3. Eden restored (22:1 – 5)
- X. Conclusion and Benediction (22:6 – 21)

Prologue

1 The revelation from Jesus Christ,
which God gave[a] him to show his
servants what must soon take place.[b] He
made it known by sending his angel[c] to his
servant John,[d] 2 who testifies to everything
he saw—that is, the word of God[e] and
the testimony of Jesus Christ.[f] 3 Blessed is
the one who reads aloud the words of this
prophecy, and blessed are those who hear
it and take to heart what is written in it,[g]
because the time is near.[h]

Greetings and Doxology

4 John,

To the seven churches[i] in the province
of Asia:

Grace and peace to you[j] from him who
is, and who was, and who is to come,[k] and
from the seven spirits[a][l] before his throne,
5 and from Jesus Christ, who is the faithful
witness,[m] the firstborn from the dead,[n] and
the ruler of the kings of the earth.[o]

To him who loves us[p] and has freed
us from our sins by his blood,[q] 6 and has
made us to be a kingdom and priests[r] to
serve his God and Father[s]—to him be glory and power for ever and ever! Amen.[t]

7 "Look, he is coming with the clouds,"[b][u]
and "every eye will see him,
even those who pierced him";[v]
and all peoples on earth "will
mourn[w] because of him."[c]
So shall it be! Amen.

8 "I am the Alpha and the Omega,"[x] says
the Lord God, "who is, and who was, and
who is to come,[y] the Almighty."[z]

John's Vision of Christ

9 I, John,[a] your brother and companion
in the suffering[b] and kingdom[c] and patient
endurance[d] that are ours in Jesus, was on
the island of Patmos because of the word
of God[e] and the testimony of Jesus.[f] 10 On
the Lord's Day[g] I was in the Spirit,[h] and I
heard behind me a loud voice like a trumpet,[i] 11 which said: "Write on a scroll what
you see[j] and send it to the seven churches:[k]
to Ephesus,[l] Smyrna,[m] Pergamum,[n] Thyatira,[o] Sardis,[p] Philadelphia[q] and Laodicea."[r]
12 I turned around to see the voice that
was speaking to me. And when I turned
I saw seven golden lampstands,[s] 13 and
among the lampstands[t] was someone like
a son of man,[d][u] dressed in a robe reaching

[a] 4 That is, the sevenfold Spirit [b] 7 Daniel 7:13
[c] 7 Zech. 12:10 [d] 13 See Daniel 7:13.

1:1 [a]Jn 12:49; 17:8 [b]ver 19; Da 2:28,29; Rev 22:6 [c]Rev 22:16 [d]ver 4,9; Rev 22:8 **1:2** [e]ver 9; S Heb 4:12 [f]ver 9; 1Co 1:6; Rev 6:9; 12:17; 19:10 **1:3** [g]Lk 11:28; Rev 22:7 [h]S Ro 13:11 **1:4** [i]ver 11,20 [j]S Ro 1:7 [k]ver 8; Rev 4:8; 11:17; 16:5 [l]Isa 11:2; Rev 3:1; 4:5; 5:6 **1:5** [m]Isa 55:4; Jn 18:37; Rev 3:14 [n]Ps 89:27; Col 1:18 [o]S 1Ti 6:15 [p]S Ro 8:37 [q]S Ro 3:25 **1:6** [r]S 1Pe 2:5; Rev 5:10; 20:6 [s]Ro 15:6 [t]S Ro 11:36 **1:7** [u]Da 7:13; S Mt 16:27; 24:30; 26:64; S Lk 17:30; S 1Co 1:7; S 1Th 2:19; 4:16,17 [v]Jn 19:34,37 [w]Zec 12:10; Mt 24:30 **1:8** [x]S ver 17; Rev 21:6; 22:13 [y]S ver 4 [z]Rev 4:8; 15:3; 19:6

1:9 [a]ver 1 [b]S Ac 14:22; 2Co 1:7; Php 4:14 [c]ver 6 [d]2Ti 2:12 [e]ver 2; S Heb 4:12 [f]S ver 2 **1:10** [g]Ac 20:7 [h]Rev 4:2; 17:3; 21:10 [i]Ex 20:18; Rev 4:1 **1:11** [j]ver 19 [k]ver 4,20 [l]S Ac 18:19 [m]Rev 2:8 [n]Rev 2:12 [o]Ac 16:14; Rev 2:18,24 [p]Rev 3:1 [q]Rev 3:7 [r]S Col 2:1; Rev 3:14 **1:12** [s]ver 20; Ex 25:31-40; Zec 4:2; Rev 2:1 **1:13** [t]Rev 2:1 [u]Eze 1:26; Da 7:13; 10:16; Rev 14:14

1:1 *revelation.* Apocalypse ("unveiling" or "disclosure"). *servants.* All believers. *soon take place.* See v. 3; 22:6–7,10,20. *his angel.* A mediating angel. "Angel(s)" occurs over 80 times in Revelation. *John.* See Introduction: Author.

1:3 *Blessed.* The first of seven beatitudes in the book (see 14:13; 16:15; 19:9; 20:6; 22:7,14). "Blessed" means much more than "happy." It describes the favorable circumstance granted by God to a person (see notes on Ps 1:1; Mt 5:3). *prophecy.* Includes not only foretelling the future but also proclaiming any word from God—whether command, instruction, history or prediction (see 1Co 14:3 and note). *time is near.* See note on Jas 5:9.

1:4 *seven churches.* Located about 50 miles apart, forming a circle in Asia moving clockwise north from Ephesus and coming around full circle from Laodicea (east of Ephesus; see map, p. 2153). They were perhaps postal centers serving seven geographic regions. Apparently the entire book of Revelation (including the seven letters) was sent to each church (see v. 11). See note on 2:1—3:22. *Asia.* A Roman province lying in modern western Turkey. *Grace and peace.* See note on Ro 1:7. *who is ... was ... is to come.* A paraphrase of the divine name from Ex 3:14–15. Cf. Heb 13:8. *seven spirits.* See NIV text note; see also Zec 4:2 and note and cf. 4:10.

1:5–6 *has freed us ... has made us.* Emphasizes these blessings as present possessions already enjoyed by the believer (see also 5:9–10).

1:6 *a kingdom and priests.* This OT designation of Israel (see notes on Ex 19:6; Zec 3) is applied in the NT to the church (1Pe 2:5,9).

1:7 *coming with the clouds.* See Mt 24:30 and note. *pierced.* See Ps 22:16; Isa 53:5; Zec 12:10; Jn 19:34,37. *So shall it be! Amen.* A double affirmation.

1:8 *the Alpha and the Omega.* The first and last letters of the Greek alphabet. God is the beginning and the end (see 21:6). He sovereignly rules over all human history. In 22:13 Jesus applies the same title to himself; see also "the First and the Last" (v. 17; 2:8; 22:13). *Almighty.* Nine of the 12 occurrences of this term in the NT are in Revelation (here; 4:8; 11:17; 15:3; 16:7,14; 19:6,15; 21:22). The other three are in Ro 9:29; 2Co 6:18; Jas 5:4.

1:9 *suffering ... kingdom ... patient endurance.* Three pivotal themes in Revelation: (1) suffering (2:9–10,22; 7:14), (2) kingdom (11:15; 12:10; 16:10; 17:12,17–18), (3) patient endurance (2:2–3,19; 3:10; 13:10; 14:12). *Patmos.* A small (four by eight miles), rocky island in the Aegean Sea some 50 miles southwest of Ephesus, off the coast of modern Turkey (see map, p. 2153; see also photo, p. 2147). It probably served as a Roman penal settlement. Eusebius, the "father of church history" (AD 265–340), reports that John was released from Patmos under the emperor Nerva (96–98).

1:10 *the Lord's Day.* A technical term for the first day of the week—so named because Jesus rose from the dead on that day. It was also the day on which the Christians met (see Ac 20:7) and took up collections (see 1Co 16:2). *in the Spirit.* In a state of spiritual exaltation by the power of the Spirit—not a dream, but a vision like Peter's in Ac 10:10.

1:11 *scroll.* Pieces of papyrus or parchment sewn together and rolled on a spindle (see note on Ex 17:14). The book form was not invented until about the second century AD. *seven churches.* See note on v. 4.

1:12 *seven.* See Introduction: Distinctive Feature. *golden lampstands.* The seven churches (see v. 20).

1:13 *son of man.* See notes on Da 7:13; Mk 8:31. *robe ... to his feet.* The high priest wore a full-length robe (Ex 28:4; 29:5).

down to his feet[v] and with a golden sash around his chest.[w] 14 The hair on his head was white like wool, as white as snow, and his eyes were like blazing fire.[x] 15 His feet were like bronze glowing in a furnace,[y] and his voice was like the sound of rushing waters.[z] 16 In his right hand he held seven stars,[a] and coming out of his mouth was a sharp, double-edged sword.[b] His face was like the sun[c] shining in all its brilliance.

17 When I saw him, I fell at his feet[d] as though dead. Then he placed his right hand on me[e] and said: "Do not be afraid.[f] I am the First and the Last.[g] 18 I am the Living One; I was dead,[h] and now look, I am alive for ever and ever![i] And I hold the keys of death and Hades.[j]

19 "Write, therefore, what you have seen,[k] what is now and what will take place later. 20 The mystery of the seven stars that you saw in my right hand[l] and of the seven golden lampstands[m] is this: The seven stars are the angels[a] of the seven churches,[n] and the seven lampstands are the seven churches.[o]

To the Church in Ephesus

2 "To the angel[b] of the church in Ephesus[p] write:

These are the words of him who holds the seven stars in his right hand[q] and walks among the seven golden lampstands.[r] 2 I know your deeds,[s] your hard work and your perseverance. I know that you cannot tolerate wicked people, that you have tested[t] those who claim to be apostles but are not, and have found them false.[u] 3 You have persevered and have endured hardships for my name,[v] and have not grown weary.

4 Yet I hold this against you: You have forsaken the love you had at first.[w] 5 Consider how far you have fallen! Repent[x] and do the things you did at first. If you do not repent, I will come to you and remove your lampstand[y] from its place. 6 But you have this in your favor: You hate the practices of the Nicolaitans,[z] which I also hate.

7 Whoever has ears, let them hear[a] what the Spirit says to the churches. To the one who is victorious,[b] I will give the right to eat from the tree of life,[c] which is in the paradise[d] of God.

1:13 [v] Isa 6:1 [w] Da 10:5; Rev 15:6 **1:14** [x] Da 7:9; 10:6; Rev 2:18; 19:12 **1:15** [y] Eze 1:7; Da 10:6; Rev 2:18 [z] Eze 43:2; Rev 14:2; 19:6 **1:16** [a] ver 20; Rev 2:1; 3:1 [b] Isa 1:20; 49:2; Heb 4:12; Rev 2:12, 16; 19:15,21 [c] Jdg 5:31; Mt 17:2 **1:17** [d] Eze 1:28; Da 8:17,18 [e] Da 8:18 [f] S Mt 14:27 [g] Isa 41:4; 44:6; 48:12; Rev 2:8; 22:13 **1:18** [h] Ro 6:9; Rev 2:8 [i] Dt 32:40; Da 4:34; 12:7; Rev 4:9,10; 10:6; 15:7 [j] Rev 9:1; 20:1 **1:19** [k] ver 11; Hab 2:2 **1:20** [l] S ver 16 [m] S ver 12 [n] ver 4,11 [o] Mt 5:14,15 **2:1** [p] S Ac 18:19 [q] Rev 1:16 [r] Rev 1:12,13 **2:2** [s] ver 19; Rev 3:1,8,15 [t] 1Jn 4:1 [u] 2Co 11:13 **2:3** [v] S Jn 15:21 **2:4** [w] Jer 2:2; Mt 24:12 **2:5** [x] ver 16,22; Rev 3:3,19 [y] Rev 1:20 **2:6** [z] ver 15 **2:7** [a] S Mt 11:15; ver 11,17,29; Rev 3:6,13,22; 13:9 [b] S Jn 16:33 [c] Ge 2:9; 3:22-24; Rev 22:2,14,19 [d] Lk 23:43

[a] 20 Or *messengers* [b] 1 Or *messenger*; also in verses 8, 12 and 18

Reference to Christ as high priest is supported by the reference to the golden sash around his chest.

1:14 *white like wool.* Cf. Da 7:9; Isa 1:18. The hoary head suggests wisdom and dignity (Lev 19:32; Pr 16:31). *eyes ... like blazing fire.* Penetrating insight (see 4:6).

1:16 *sharp, double-edged sword.* Like a long Thracian sword (also in 2:12,16; 6:8; 19:15,21). The sword in 6:4; 13:10,14 was a small sword or dagger. The sword symbolizes Christ's word of divine judgment (see Isa 49:2; Heb 4:12).

1:17 *fell at his feet.* A sign of great respect and awe (4:10; 5:8; 7:11; 19:10; 22:8). *I am.* See note on Jn 6:35. *the First and the Last.* Essentially the same as "the Alpha and the Omega" (v. 8; cf. Isa 44:6; 48:12).

1:18 *Living One.* Based on OT references to the "living God" (e.g., Jos 3:10; Ps 42:2; 84:2). In contrast to the dead gods of paganism, Christ possesses life in his essential nature (cf. Jn 1:4 and note). *keys of death and Hades.* Absolute control over their domain (see Mt 16:18 and note).

1:19 Many see a threefold division in this verse and take it as a clue to the entire structure of the book. "What you have seen" would be the inaugural vision of ch. 1; "what is now" would be the letters to the seven churches (chs. 2–3); "what will take place later" would be everything from ch. 4 on. An alternative interpretation sees the initial clause as the essential unit (it parallels v. 11), followed by two explanatory clauses. The sense would be: "Write, therefore, what you are about to see, i.e., both what is now and what will take place later." Some who hold the latter view make no attempt to outline the book on this basis, maintaining that there is a mixture of "now" and "later" throughout.

1:20 The first of several places where the symbols are interpreted (see also 17:15,18). *angels.* Either (1) heavenly messengers or (2) earthly messengers/ministers (see NIV text note).

2:1—3:22 Some take the seven letters as a preview of church history in its downward course toward Laodicean lukewarmness. Others interpret them as characteristic of various kinds of Christian congregations that have existed from John's day until the present time. In either case, they were historical churches in Asia Minor (see map, p. 2153; see also map, pp. 2528–2529, at the end of this study Bible). A general pattern in the letters is character of Christ, commendation, complaint, correction and conclusion.

2:1 *angel.* See note on 1:20. *Ephesus.* See Introduction to Ephesians: The City of Ephesus. *holds the seven stars.* See 1:16,20. *seven golden lampstands.* See 1:12,20.

2:2 *tested.* The necessity of testing for correct doctrine and dependable advice was widely recognized in the early church (see 1Co 14:29; 1Th 5:21; 1Jn 4:1).

2:4 *the love you had at first.* For Christ and/or for one another.

2:5 *remove your lampstand.* Immediate judgment.

2:6 *Nicolaitans.* A heretical sect within the church that had worked out a compromise with the pagan society. Its adherents apparently taught that spiritual liberty gave them sufficient leeway to practice idolatry and immorality. Tradition identifies them with "Nicolas from Antioch, a convert to Judaism" (Ac 6:5), who was one of the first seven deacons in the Jerusalem church—though the evidence is merely circumstantial. A similar group at Pergamum held the teaching of Balaam (vv. 14–15), and some at Thyatira were followers of the woman Jezebel (v. 20). From their heretical tendencies it would appear that all three groups were Nicolaitans or at least part of the same sect.

2:7 *To the one who is victorious.* The challenge to be victorious in the battle against evil (see 12:11) occurs in each letter (here; vv. 11,17,26; 3:5,12,21). *paradise.* Originally a Persian word for a pleasure garden (see note on Lk 23:43). In Revelation it symbolizes the eschatological state in which

To the Church in Smyrna

8 “To the angel of the church in Smyrna[e]
write:

These are the words of him who is
the First and the Last,[f] who died and
came to life again.[g] 9 I know your afflictions and your poverty—yet you
are rich![h] I know about the slander
of those who say they are Jews and
are not,[i] but are a synagogue of Satan.[j] 10 Do not be afraid of what you
are about to suffer. I tell you, the devil
will put some of you in prison to test
you,[k] and you will suffer persecution
for ten days.[l] Be faithful,[m] even to the
point of death, and I will give you life
as your victor’s crown.[n]

11 Whoever has ears, let them hear[o]
what the Spirit says to the churches.
The one who is victorious will not be
hurt at all by the second death.[p]

To the Church in Pergamum

12 “To the angel of the church in Pergamum[q] write:

These are the words of him who
has the sharp, double-edged sword.[r]
13 I know where you live—where Satan has his throne. Yet you remain
true to my name. You did not renounce your faith in me,[s] not even in
the days of Antipas, my faithful witness,[t] who was put to death in your
city—where Satan lives.[u]

2:8 [e] Rev 1:11 [f] S Rev 1:17 [g] Rev 1:18 **2:9** [h] 2Co 6:10; Jas 2:5 [i] Rev 3:9 [j] ver 13,24; S Mt 4:10 **2:10** [k] Rev 3:10 [l] Da 1:12, 14 [m] ver 13; Rev 17:14 [n] S Mt 10:22; S 1Co 9:25 **2:11** [o] S ver 7 [p] Rev 20:6,14; 21:8 **2:12** [q] Rev 1:11 [r] ver 16; S Rev 1:16 **2:13** [s] Rev 14:12 [t] Rev 1:5; 11:3 [u] ver 9,24; S Mt 4:10

God and believers are restored to the perfect fellowship that existed before sin entered the world.

2:8 *Smyrna.* A proud and beautiful Asian city (modern Izmir) closely aligned with Rome and eager to meet its demands for emperor worship. This plus a large and actively hostile Jewish population made it extremely difficult to live there as a Christian. Polycarp, the most famous of the early martyrs, was bishop of Smyrna. *the First and the Last.* See note on 1:17. *died ... came to life.* See 1:18 and note.

2:9 *who say they are Jews.* See Ro 2:28–29. *Satan.* See notes on Mt 16:23; 1Jn 3:8.

2:10 *devil.* Greek *diabolos,* meaning “accuser” or “adversary.” *persecution.* See the warnings by Jesus (Jn 15:20) and Paul (2Ti 3:12). *ten days.* Probably indicates a limited period of suffering. *life as your victor’s crown.* The crown that is eternal life. “Crown” does not refer to a royal crown (12:3; 13:1; 19:12) but to the garland or wreath awarded to the winner in athletic contests (3:11; 4:4,10; 6:2; 9:7; 12:1; 14:14).

2:11 *The one who is victorious.* See note on v. 7. *second death.* The lake of fire (20:14; see 20:6; 21:8).

2:12 *Pergamum.* Modern Bergama; the ancient capital of Asia, built on a cone-shaped hill rising 1,000 feet above the surrounding valley. Its name in Greek means “citadel.” See map, p. 2153. *double-edged sword.* See note on 1:16.

2:13 *where Satan has his throne.* Satan “ruled” from Pergamum in that it was the official center of emperor

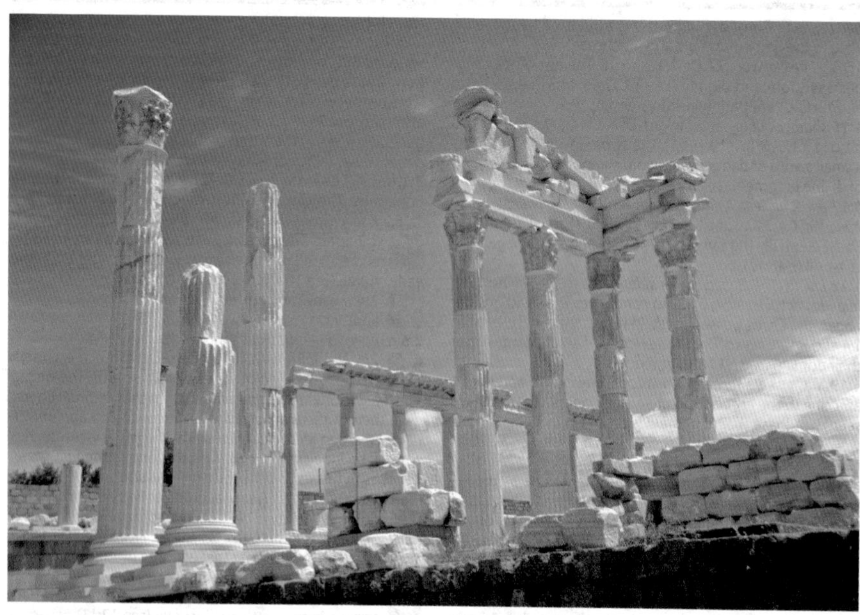

The impressive temple of Trajan, built on the Acropolis at Pergamum, for the worship of the Roman emperor Trajan

[14]Nevertheless, I have a few
things against you:[v] There are
some among you who hold to
the teaching of Balaam,[w] who
taught Balak to entice the Israelites to sin so that they ate
food sacrificed to idols[x] and
committed sexual immorali-
ty.[y] [15]Likewise, you also have
those who hold to the teaching
of the Nicolaitans.[z] [16]Repent[a]
therefore! Otherwise, I will
soon come to you and will fight
against them with the sword of
my mouth.[b]
[17]Whoever has ears, let them
hear[c] what the Spirit says to the
churches. To the one who is
victorious,[d] I will give some of
the hidden manna.[e] I will also
give that person a white stone
with a new name[f] written on it,
known only to the one who receives it.[g]

To the Church in Thyatira

[18]"To the angel of the church in
Thyatira[h] write:

These are the words of the
Son of God,[i] whose eyes are
like blazing fire and whose feet
are like burnished bronze.[j] [19]I
know your deeds,[k] your love
and faith, your service and
perseverance, and that you are
now doing more than you did
at first.
[20]Nevertheless, I have this against
you: You tolerate that woman Jezebel,[l] who calls herself a prophet. By
her teaching she misleads my servants into sexual immorality and the
eating of food sacrificed to idols.[m] [21]I
have given her time[n] to repent of her
immorality, but she is unwilling.[o] [22]So
I will cast her on a bed of suffering,
and I will make those who commit
adultery[p] with her suffer intensely,
unless they repent of her ways. [23]I
will strike her children dead. Then all
the churches will know that I am he

THE SEVEN CHURCHES OF REVELATION

ASIA
Aegean Sea
Pergamum
Thyatira
Sardis
Smyrna
Philadelphia
CHIOS
Ephesus
SAMOS
Laodicea
Miletus
PATMOS
LYCIA
KOS
Cnidus
Patara
Rhodes
RHODES
Mediterranean Sea
CRETE
0 50 km.
0 50 miles
• Seven churches of Revelation 1–3

2:14 [v]ver 20 [w]S 2Pe 2:15 [x]S Ac 15:20 [y]1Co 6:13 **2:15** [z]ver 6 **2:16** [a]S ver 5 [b]2Th 2:8; S Rev 1:16 **2:17** [c]S ver 7 [d]S Jn 16:33 [e]Jn 6:49, 50 [f]Isa 56:5; 62:2; 65:15 [g]Rev 19:12 **2:18** [h]ver 24; Ac 16:14; Rev 1:11 [i]S Mt 4:3 [j]S Rev 1:14, 15 **2:19** [k]S ver 2 **2:20** [l]1Ki 16:31; 21:25; 2Ki 9:7 [m]ver 14; S Ac 15:20 **2:21** [n]Ro 2:4; 2Pe 3:9 [o]Ro 2:5; Rev 9:20; 16:9, 11 **2:22** [p]Rev 17:2; 18:9

worship in Asia. *Antipas.* First martyr of Asia. According to tradition he was slowly roasted to death in a bronze kettle during the reign of Domitian (81–96). *faithful witness.* The Lord's title in 1:5.

2:14 *teaching of Balaam.* Balaam advised the Midianite women how to lead the Israelites astray (Nu 25:1–2; 31:16; cf. Jude 11 and notes on Nu 22:5,8). He is a fitting prototype of corrupt teachers who deceive believers into compromise with worldliness. *food sacrificed to idols ... immorality.* See Ac 15:20,29.

2:15 *Nicolaitans.* See note on v. 6.

2:16 *sword of my mouth.* The long sword (see note on 1:16).

2:17 *victorious.* See note on v. 7. *hidden manna.* The heavenly food available to the believer who overcomes (cf. Ps 78:24), in contrast to the unclean food of the Balaamites. *white stone.* Certain kinds of stones were used as tokens for various purposes. In the context of a Messianic banquet the white stone was probably for the purpose of admission. *new name.* The name of the victor (see Isa 62:2; 65:15).

2:18 *Thyatira.* Modern Akhisar. Founded by Seleucus I (311–280 BC) as a military outpost, it was noted for its many trade guilds. Lydia, "a dealer in purple cloth," was from Thyatira (see note on Ac 16:14). *eyes ... like blazing fire.* See note on 1:14; cf. Da 10:6. *burnished bronze.* A refined alloy of copper or bronze with metallic zinc (see 1:15).

2:20 *Jezebel.* See 1Ki 16:31; 2Ki 9:22,30–37. The name is used here as an epithet for a prominent woman in the congregation who undermined loyalty to God by promoting tolerance toward pagan practices. *sexual immorality ... food sacrificed to idols.* See v. 14.

2:22 *bed of suffering.* Disease was often considered as appropriate punishment for sins (cf. 1Co 11:29–30).

2:23 *her children.* Jezebel is the spiritual mother of all who pursue antinomian (libertine) doctrines. *he who*

who searches hearts and minds,[q] and
I will repay each of you according to
your deeds.[r]
24 Now I say to the rest of you in
Thyatira, to you who do not hold to
her teaching and have not learned
Satan's so-called deep secrets, 'I will
not impose any other burden on you,[s]
25 except to hold on to what you have[t]
until I come.'[u]
26 To the one who is victorious[v] and
does my will to the end,[w] I will give
authority over the nations[x]— 27 that
one 'will rule them with an iron scepter[y] and will dash them to pieces like
pottery'[a][z]—just as I have received
authority from my Father. 28 I will
also give that one the morning star.[a]
29 Whoever has ears, let them hear[b]
what the Spirit says to the churches.

To the Church in Sardis

3 "To the angel[b] of the church in Sardis[c]
write:

These are the words of him who
holds the seven spirits[c][d] of God and
the seven stars.[e] I know your deeds;[f]
you have a reputation of being
alive, but you are dead.[g] 2 Wake up!
Strengthen what remains and is about
to die, for I have found your deeds
unfinished in the sight of my God.
3 Remember, therefore, what you have
received and heard; hold it fast, and
repent.[h] But if you do not wake up, I
will come like a thief,[i] and you will
not know at what time[j] I will come
to you.

4 Yet you have a few people in Sardis who have not soiled their clothes.[k]
They will walk with me, dressed in
white,[l] for they are worthy. 5 The one
who is victorious[m] will, like them, be
dressed in white.[n] I will never blot
out the name of that person from the
book of life,[o] but will acknowledge
that name before my Father[p] and his
angels. 6 Whoever has ears, let them
hear[q] what the Spirit says to the
churches.

To the Church in Philadelphia

7 "To the angel of the church in Philadelphia[r] write:

These are the words of him who is
holy[s] and true,[t] who holds the key of
David.[u] What he opens no one can
shut, and what he shuts no one can
open. 8 I know your deeds.[v] See, I
have placed before you an open door[w]
that no one can shut. I know that you
have little strength, yet you have kept
my word and have not denied my
name.[x] 9 I will make those who are of
the synagogue of Satan,[y] who claim
to be Jews though they are not,[z] but
are liars—I will make them come and
fall down at your feet[a] and acknowledge that I have loved you.[b] 10 Since
you have kept my command to endure patiently, I will also keep you[c]
from the hour of trial that is going to

a 27 Psalm 2:9 *b* 1 Or *messenger;* also in verses 7 and 14 *c* 1 That is, the sevenfold Spirit

2:23 [q] 1Sa 16:7; 1Ki 8:39; Ps 139:1, 2, 23; Pr 21:2; Jer 17:10; Lk 16:15; Ro 8:27; 1Th 2:4 [r] S Mt 16:27
2:24 [s] Ac 15:28
2:25 [t] Rev 3:11 [u] S Mt 16:27
2:26 [v] S Jn 16:33 [w] Mt 10:22 [x] Ps 2:8; Rev 3:21
2:27 [y] Rev 12:5; 19:15 [z] Ps 2:9; Isa 30:14; Jer 19:11
2:28 [a] Rev 22:16
2:29 [b] S ver 7
3:1 [c] Rev 1:11 [d] S Rev 1:4 [e] S Rev 1:16 [f] S Rev 2:2 [g] 1Ti 5:6
3:3 [h] S Rev 2:5 [i] S Lk 12:39 [j] Lk 12:39
3:4 [k] Jude 23 [l] ver 5, 18; Rev 4:4; 6:11; 7:9, 13, 14; 19:14
3:5 [m] S Jn 16:33 [n] S ver 4 [o] S Rev 20:12 [p] Mt 10:32
3:6 [q] S Rev 2:7
3:7 [r] Rev 1:11 [s] S Mk 1:24 [t] 1Jn 5:20; Rev 6:10; 19:11 [u] Isa 22:22; Mt 16:19
3:8 [v] S Rev 2:2 [w] S Ac 14:27 [x] Rev 2:13
3:9 [y] Rev 2:9 [z] Rev 2:9 [a] Isa 49:23 [b] Isa 43:4; S Ro 8:37
3:10 [c] 2Pe 2:9

---

searches hearts and minds. Cf. Ps 7:9; Pr 24:12; Jer 11:20; 17:10. "Minds" (lit. "kidneys") probably refers here to the will and the affections; "hearts" may designate the center of rational life. *according to your deeds.* Judgment based on works is taught by Jesus (Mt 16:27) and Paul (Ro 2:6), as well as John (Rev 18:6; 20:12–13; 22:12).
2:24 *Satan's so-called deep secrets.* Later Gnosticism (see Introduction to 1 John: Gnosticism) taught that in order to defeat Satan one had to enter his stronghold, i.e., experience evil deeply.
2:26 *victorious.* See note on v. 7.
2:27 *rule.* Lit. "shepherd" (a common metaphor for "rule"). *iron scepter.* Symbolic of the strength of his rule (see 12:5; 19:15).
2:28 *morning star.* Cf. 22:16 and note; Da 12:3.
3:1 *Sardis.* Modern Sart. Capital of the ancient kingdom of Lydia, it was a city of great wealth and fame. The acropolis was a natural citadel on the northern spur of Mount Tmolus. It rose 1,500 feet above the lower valley. *seven spirits of God.* See 1:4 and note. *seven stars.* See 1:20 and note.
3:3 *come like a thief.* Not a reference to the second coming of Christ, because here his coming depends on the church's refusal to repent. Elsewhere in the NT the clause refers to the second advent (16:15; Mt 24:42–44; 1Th 5:2; 2Pe 3:10).
3:4 *dressed in white.* Description of the redeemed (3:18; 6:11; 7:9,13–14; cf. 4:4; 19:14).
3:5 *victorious.* See note on 2:7. *book of life.* A divine ledger is first mentioned in Ex 32:32–33 (see note on Ps 69:28; cf. Da 12:1). It was a register of all citizens in the kingdom community. To have one's name erased from this book would indicate loss of citizenship (see 13:8; 17:8; 20:12,15; 21:27; Php 4:3).
3:7 *Philadelphia.* Modern Alashehir; a city of commercial importance conveniently located as the gateway to the high central plateau of the Roman province of Asia. The name means "brotherly love" and commemorates the loyalty and devotion of Attalus II (220–130 BC), the city's cofounder, to his brother Eumenes II. *holy and true.* See 6:10. For God as the Holy One, see Isa 40:25; Hab 3:2–3; Mk 1:24; see also notes on Ex 3:5; Lev 11:44. *key of David.* Christ is the Davidic Messiah with authority to control entrance to the kingdom (see Isa 22:22; Mt 16:19).
3:8 *open door.* Either the door of opportunity or the door to the kingdom. The context favors the latter.
3:9 *synagogue of Satan.* A bold metaphor directed against unbelieving and hostile Jews. Cf. Jesus' scathing rebuke in Jn 8:44; see also 2Co 11:14–15. The Jewish synagogue was a gathering place for worship, study and communal activities. *claim to be Jews.* See Ro 2:28–29. *fall down at your feet.* An appropriate act of worship in the Near East (see Isa 45:14; 60:14; cf. Ac 10:25; Php 2:10; see also note on Rev 1:17).
3:10 *keep you from.* The Greek for this phrase can mean either "keep you from undergoing" or "keep you through." *hour of trial.* The period of testing that precedes the consummation of

Remains of the temple of Artemis at Sardis

come on the whole world[d] to test[e] the
inhabitants of the earth.[f]
11 I am coming soon.[g] Hold on to
what you have,[h] so that no one will
take your crown.[i] 12 The one who is
victorious[j] I will make a pillar[k] in the
temple of my God. Never again will
they leave it. I will write on them the
name of my God[l] and the name of the
city of my God,[m] the new Jerusalem,[n]
which is coming down out of heaven
from my God; and I will also write on
them my new name. 13 Whoever has
ears, let them hear[o] what the Spirit
says to the churches.

To the Church in Laodicea

14 "To the angel of the church in Laodicea[p]
write:

These are the words of the Amen,
the faithful and true witness,[q] the ruler of God's creation.[r] 15 I know your
deeds,[s] that you are neither cold nor
hot.[t] I wish you were either one or
the other! 16 So, because you are lukewarm — neither hot nor cold — I am
about to spit you out of my mouth.
17 You say, 'I am rich; I have acquired
wealth and do not need a thing.'[u]
But you do not realize that you are
wretched, pitiful, poor, blind and naked.[v] 18 I counsel you to buy from me
gold refined in the fire,[w] so you can
become rich; and white clothes[x] to
wear, so you can cover your shameful
nakedness;[y] and salve to put on your
eyes, so you can see.
19 Those whom I love I rebuke and
discipline.[z] So be earnest and repent.[a]
20 Here I am! I stand at the door[b] and

3:10 [d] S Mt 24:14 [e] Rev 2:10 [f] Rev 6:10; 8:13; 11:10; 13:8, 14; 17:8 **3:11** [g] S Mt 16:27 [h] Rev 2:25 [i] S 1Co 9:25 **3:12** [j] S Jn 16:33 [k] Gal 2:9 [l] Rev 14:1; 22:4 [m] Eze 48:35 [n] Gal 4:26; Rev 21:2, 10 **3:13** [o] S Rev 2:7 **3:14** [p] S Col 2:1; Rev 1:11 [q] Jn 18:37; Rev 1:5 [r] Pr 8:22; Jn 1:3; Col 1:16, 18 **3:15** [s] S Rev 2:2 [t] Ro 12:11 **3:17** [u] Hos 12:8; 1Co 4:8 [v] Pr 13:7 **3:18** [w] S 1Pe 1:7 [x] S ver 4 [y] Rev 16:15 **3:19** [z] Dt 8:5; Pr 3:12; 1Co 11:32; Heb 12:5, 6 [a] S Rev 2:5 **3:20** [b] Mt 24:33; Jas 5:9

the kingdom (see 13:5 – 10; Mt 24:4 – 28; cf. Da 12:1; Mk 13:19; 2Th 2:1 – 12). *inhabitants of the earth.* See 6:10 and note.
3:11 *I am coming soon.* Cf. 1:1; 22:7,12,20 (see note on Jas 5:9). *crown.* See 2:10 and note.
3:12 *victorious.* See note on 2:7. *temple.* See note on 7:15. *name of my God.* See 14:1; 22:4. *new Jerusalem.* See 21:2,10. *write on them my new name.* Names revealed character. Christ's new name symbolizes all that he is by virtue of his redemptive work for humankind. This awaits the second advent.
3:14 *Laodicea.* Near modern Denizli. The wealthiest city in Phrygia during Roman times, it was widely known for its banking establishments, medical school and textile industry. Its major weakness was lack of an adequate water supply. Each of these characteristics is reflected in the letter. *the Amen.* Isa 65:16 speaks of "the God of the Amen," i.e., "the one true God." As a personal designation it describes one who is totally trustworthy and faithful. *faithful and true witness.* See 1:5; 19:11. *ruler.* The Greek word can mean first in point of time ("beginning") or first in rank ("ruler").
3:16 *lukewarm — neither hot nor cold.* "Hot" may refer to the hot, medicinal waters of nearby Hierapolis. The church in Laodicea supplied neither healing for the spiritually sick nor refreshment for the spiritually weary. *spit.* Lit. "vomit."
3:18 Refers to three items in which Laodicea took great pride: financial wealth, an extensive textile industry and a famous eye salve.
3:19 *whom I love I … discipline.* See Job 5:17; Ps 94:12; Pr 3:11 – 12; 1Co 11:32; Heb 12:5 – 11 and relevant notes.
3:20 *I stand at the door and knock.* Usually taken as a picture of Christ knocking on the door of the individual unbeliever's

knock. If anyone hears my voice and
opens the door,[c] I will come in[d] and eat
with that person, and they with me.
21 To the one who is victorious,[e] I
will give the right to sit with me on
my throne,[f] just as I was victorious[g]
and sat down with my Father on
his throne. 22 Whoever has ears, let
them hear[h] what the Spirit says to the
churches."

The Throne in Heaven

4 After this I looked, and there before
me was a door standing open[i] in heav-
en. And the voice I had first heard speaking to me like a trumpet[j] said, "Come up
here,[k] and I will show you what must
take place after this."[l] 2 At once I was in
the Spirit,[m] and there before me was a
throne in heaven[n] with someone sitting
on it. 3 And the one who sat there had the
appearance of jasper[o] and ruby.[p] A rainbow[q] that shone like an emerald[r] encircled
the throne. 4 Surrounding the throne were
twenty-four other thrones, and seated on
them were twenty-four elders.[s] They were
dressed in white[t] and had crowns of gold
on their heads. 5 From the throne came
flashes of lightning, rumblings and peals
of thunder.[u] In front of the throne, seven
lamps[v] were blazing. These are the sev-
en spirits[a][w] of God. 6 Also in front of the
throne there was what looked like a sea of
glass,[x] clear as crystal.
In the center, around the throne, were
four living creatures,[y] and they were covered with eyes, in front and in back.[z] 7 The
first living creature was like a lion, the second was like an ox, the third had a face
like a man, the fourth was like a flying
eagle.[a] 8 Each of the four living creatures[b]
had six wings[c] and was covered with eyes
all around,[d] even under its wings. Day and
night[e] they never stop saying:

"'Holy, holy, holy
is the Lord God Almighty,'[b][f]
who was, and is, and is to come."[g]

9 Whenever the living creatures give glory,
honor and thanks to him who sits on the
throne[h] and who lives for ever and ever,[i]
10 the twenty-four elders[j] fall down before
him[k] who sits on the throne[l] and worship
him who lives for ever and ever. They lay
their crowns before the throne and say:

11 "You are worthy, our Lord and God,
to receive glory and honor and power,[m]

[a] 5 That is, the sevenfold Spirit [b] 8 Isaiah 6:3

3:20 [c] Lk 12:36 [d] S Ro 8:10 **3:21** [e] S Jn 16:33 [f] S Mt 19:28 [g] Rev 5:5 **3:22** [h] S Rev 2:7 **4:1** [i] S Mt 3:16 [j] Rev 1:10 [k] Rev 11:12 [l] Rev 1:19; 22:6 **4:2** [m] S Rev 1:10 [n] ver 9, 10; 1Ki 22:19; Isa 6:1; Eze 1:26-28; Da 7:9; Rev 20:11 **4:3** [o] Rev 21:11 [p] Rev 21:20 [q] Eze 1:28; Rev 10:1 [r] Rev 21:19 **4:4** [s] ver 10; Rev 5:6, 8, 14; 11:16; 19:4 [t] S Rev 3:4, 5 **4:5** [u] Ex 19:16; Rev 8:5; 11:19; 16:18 [v] Zec 4:2 [w] S Rev 1:4 **4:6** [x] Rev 15:2 [y] ver 8, 9; Eze 1:5; Rev 5:6; 6:1; 7:11; 14:3; 15:7; 19:4 [z] Eze 1:18; 10:12 **4:7** [a] Eze 1:10; 10:14 **4:8** [b] S ver 6 [c] Isa 6:2 [d] Eze 1:18 [e] Rev 14:11 [f] Isa 6:3; S Rev 1:8 [g] S Rev 1:4 **4:9** [h] ver 2; Ps 47:8; S Rev 5:1 [i] S Rev 1:18 **4:10** [j] S ver 4 [k] Dt 33:3; Rev 5:8, 14; 7:11; 11:16 [l] S ver 2 **4:11** [m] Rev 1:6; 5:12

heart. In context, however, the self-deluded members of the congregation are being addressed.

3:21 *victorious.* See note on 2:7. *sit with me on my throne.* See 20:4,6; Mt 19:28; 2Ti 2:12.

4:1—5:14 These two chapters constitute an introduction to chs. 6–20. In the throne room of heaven, the Lamb assumes the responsibility of initiating the great final conflict with the forces of evil, the end of which will see the Lamb triumphant and the devil consigned to the lake of fire.

4:1 *Come up here.* Similarly, Moses was called up on Mount Sinai to receive divine direction (Ex 19:20,24). Cf. also the heavenly ascent of the two witnesses (11:12). Some interpreters find the rapture of the church in this verse. *what must take place after this.* See 1:1,19; Da 2:28–29,45.

4:2 *in the Spirit.* In a state of heightened spiritual awareness by the power of the Spirit (see note on 1:10; see also 17:3; 21:10). *throne in heaven.* The depiction of God ruling from his throne in heaven is a regular feature of the OT (e.g., Ps 47:8; Isa 6:1).

4:3 *jasper ... ruby ... emerald.* Since God dwells in "unapproachable light" and is one "whom no one has seen or can see" (1Ti 6:16), he is described in terms of the reflected brilliance of precious stones—an emerald rainbow around the throne (cf. Eze 1:26–28).

4:4 *twenty-four elders.* Representative of either the whole company of believers in heaven or an exalted angelic order worshiping and serving God there (see vv. 9–11; 5:5–14; 7:11–17; 11:16–18; 14:3; 19:4). The number 24 is often understood to reflect the 12 Israelite tribes of the OT and the 12 apostles of the NT.

4:5 *flashes of lightning ... thunder ... blazing.* Symbolic of the awesome majesty and power of God (cf. the manifestation of God at Sinai, Ex 19:16–19; cf. also the conventional OT depiction of God's coming in mighty power to deliver his people, Ps 18:12–15; 77:18). In Revelation, thunder and lightning always mark an important event connected with the heavenly temple (8:5; 11:19; 16:18). *seven spirits.* See note on 1:4; "seven" symbolizes fullness, completeness or perfection.

4:6 *sea of glass.* See 15:2. The source of the imagery may be Eze 1:22 (cf. Ex 24:10), but it is also possible that it is the basin in the heavenly temple (cf. 11:19; 14:15,17; 15:5–6,8; 16:1,17), whose counterpart in the earthly temple was referred to as the Sea (1Ki 7:23–25; 2Ki 16:17; 2Ch 4:2,4,10,15; Jer 27:19). Other features of the temple in heaven are: the lamps (v. 5), the altar (6:9), the altar of incense (8:3) and the ark of the covenant (11:19). *four living creatures.* An exalted order of angelic beings whose task is to guard the heavenly throne and lead in worship and adoration of God. *covered with eyes.* Nothing escapes their attention.

4:7 Ezekiel in a vision also saw four living creatures, each of which had four faces—human in front, lion on the right, ox on the left and eagle behind (Eze 1:6,10). In John's vision the creatures were in the form of a lion, an ox and a flying eagle, and one had a face like that of a man.

4:8 *six wings.* This feature of the living creatures and the praise they speak seem to be modeled after the seraphim of Isa 6:2–3; thus the living creatures combine features of the cherubim of Eze 1 and 10 (see note on v. 7) and the seraphim of Isa 6. *Holy, holy, holy.* See note on Isa 6:3. Rev 4:8 is the first of five praise hymns in chs. 4–5: 4:8; 4:11; 5:9–10; 5:12; 5:13. The first two are directed to God the Father, the next two to God the Son, and the final one to both. *was ... is ... is to come.* An expansion of the divine name in Ex 3:14–15 (see note on Rev 1:4). God's power and holiness extend from eternity past to eternity yet to come (cf. Isa 41:4).

4:10 *lay their crowns.* Acknowledgment that God alone is worthy of ultimate praise and worship.

4:11 *you created all things.* See Ge 1.

for you created all things,
and by your will they were
created
and have their being."[n]

The Scroll and the Lamb

5 Then I saw in the right hand of him
who sat on the throne[o] a scroll with
writing on both sides[p] and sealed[q] with
seven seals. 2 And I saw a mighty angel[r] proclaiming in a loud voice, "Who
is worthy to break the seals and open
the scroll?" 3 But no one in heaven or on
earth or under the earth could open the
scroll or even look inside it. 4 I wept and
wept because no one was found who was
worthy to open the scroll or look inside.
5 Then one of the elders said to me, "Do
not weep! See, the Lion[s] of the tribe of Judah,[t] the Root of David,[u] has triumphed.
He is able to open the scroll and its seven
seals."
6 Then I saw a Lamb,[v] looking as if it
had been slain, standing at the center of
the throne, encircled by the four living
creatures[w] and the elders.[x] The Lamb had
seven horns and seven eyes,[y] which are
the seven spirits[a][z] of God sent out into all
the earth. 7 He went and took the scroll
from the right hand of him who sat on the
throne.[a] 8 And when he had taken it, the
four living creatures[b] and the twenty-four
elders[c] fell down before the Lamb. Each
one had a harp[d] and they were holding
golden bowls full of incense, which are the
prayers[e] of God's people. 9 And they sang a
new song, saying:[f]

"You are worthy[g] to take the scroll
and to open its seals,
because you were slain,
and with your blood[h] you purchased[i]
for God
persons from every tribe and
language and people and
nation.[j]
10 You have made them to be a kingdom
and priests[k] to serve our God,
and they will reign[b] on the earth."[l]

11 Then I looked and heard the voice of
many angels, numbering thousands upon
thousands, and ten thousand times ten
thousand.[m] They encircled the throne and
the living creatures[n] and the elders.[o] 12 In a
loud voice they were saying:

"Worthy is the Lamb,[p] who was
slain,[q]
to receive power and wealth and
wisdom and strength
and honor and glory and praise!"[r]

13 Then I heard every creature in heaven
and on earth and under the earth[s] and on
the sea, and all that is in them, saying:

"To him who sits on the throne[t] and to
the Lamb[u]
be praise and honor and glory and
power,
for ever and ever!"[v]

14 The four living creatures[w] said, "Amen,"[x]
and the elders[y] fell down and worshiped.[z]

4:11 [n]Ac 14:15; Rev 10:6
5:1 [o]ver 7, 13; Rev 4:2,9; 6:16 [p]Eze 2:9, 10 [q]Isa 29:11; Da 12:4
5:2 [r]Rev 10:1
5:5 [s]Ge 49:9 [t]S Heb 7:14 [u]Isa 11:1, 10; Ro 15:12; Rev 22:16
5:6 [v]ver 8,9, 12,13; S Jn 1:29 [w]S Rev 4:6 [x]S Rev 4:4 [y]Zec 4:10 [z]S Rev 1:4
5:7 [a]S ver 1
5:8 [b]S Rev 4:6 [c]S Rev 4:4 [d]Rev 14:2; 15:2 [e]Ps 141:2; Rev 8:3,4
5:9 [f]Ps 40:3; 98:1; 149:1; Isa 42:10; Rev 14:3,4 [g]Rev 4:11 [h]Heb 9:12 [i]S 1Co 6:20 [j]S Rev 13:7
5:10 [k]S 1Pe 2:5 [l]Rev 3:21; 20:4
5:11 [m]Da 7:10; Heb 12:22; Jude 14 [n]S Rev 4:6 [o]S Rev 4:4
5:12 [p]ver 13 [q]ver 9 [r]Rev 1:6; 4:11
5:13 [s]ver 3; Php 2:10 [t]S ver 1,7 [u]ver 6; Rev 6:16; 7:10 [v]1Ch 29:11; Mal 1:6; 2:2; S Ro 11:36
5:14 [w]S Rev 4:6 [x]Rev 4:9 [y]S Rev 4:4 [z]Rev 4:10

[a] *6* That is, the sevenfold Spirit [b] *10* Some manuscripts *they reign*

5:1 *scroll.* See note on 1:11; cf. the little scroll of 10:2,8–10. *writing on both sides.* Like the stone tablets of the OT covenant law (see Ex 32:15 and note; Eze 2:9–10). The fibers of a papyrus scroll run horizontally on the inside, which makes writing easier than on the reverse side (where the fibers are vertical). *sealed with seven seals.* Indicating absolute inviolability (cf. Isa 29:11; Da 12:4).
5:2 *mighty angel.* Powerful enough to address his challenge to the whole creation (cf. 10:1; 18:21 and the angel with great authority and splendor in 18:2).
5:3 *heaven … earth … under the earth.* A conventional phrase used to express the universality of the proclamation—no creature was worthy. It is not intended to teach a threefold division of the universe (cf. Ex 20:4; Php 2:10).
5:5 *Lion of the tribe of Judah.* A Messianic title taken from Ge 49:8–10, where Judah is named a "lion's cub" and promised the right to rule "until he to whom it belongs shall come" (see also Eze 21:27). *Root of David.* See Isa 11:1,10, which looks forward to the ideal king in the line of David. The title is interpreted Messianically in Ro 15:12.
5:6 *Lamb.* Pictured as the sacrifice for sin ("slain"; cf. Isa 53:7; Jn 1:29) and as the mighty conqueror (17:14). Revelation uses a special word for "lamb" (29 times in Revelation and only once elsewhere in the NT—Jn 21:15). The idea of the lamb as a victorious military leader seems to come from the apocalyptic tradition (1 Enoch 90:9; Testament of Joseph 19:8). *as if it had been slain.* Bearing the marks of its slaughter—he has come to power through his death. *seven horns.* The horn is an ancient Jewish symbol for power or strength (cf. Dt 33:17). The fourth beast of Da 7:7,20 had ten horns (cf. Da 8:3,5). Seven horns would symbolize full strength. *seven spirits.* See note on 4:5.
5:8 *harp.* An ancient stringed instrument (not the large modern harp) used especially to accompany songs (Ps 33:2). *bowls full of incense.* The bowl was a flat, shallow cup. Incense was a normal feature of Hebrew ritual (see Dt 33:10; cf. Ps 141:2; Rev 8:3–4). *prayers of God's people.* In later Jewish thought angels often present to God the prayers of God's people (Tobit 12:15; 3 Baruch 11). *God's people.* See notes on Ro 1:7; Eph 1:1; Col 1:4.
5:9 *new song.* Cf. 14:3; Ps 96:1; 144:9; Isa 42:10. In the OT a new song celebrated a new act of divine deliverance or blessing (see Ps 33:3 and note). That is also its sense here; notice the theme of the song. *with your blood you purchased … persons.* The sacrificial death of Christ is central to NT teaching (see Mk 10:45; 1Co 6:20).
5:10 *have made them.* See note on 1:6. *kingdom and priests.* See note on 1:6. *reign on the earth.* See 2:26–27; 20:4,6; 22:5.
5:11 *thousands upon thousands.* A rhetorical phrase for an indefinitely large number (see Da 7:10; cf. Heb 12:22).
5:12 *power … praise!* See David's farewell prayer in 1Ch 29:10–19. The attributes increase from three in 4:11 to four in 5:13 to seven in 5:12; 7:12.
5:13 *heaven … earth … under the earth.* See note on v. 3.

The Seals

6 I watched as the Lamb[a] opened the
first of the seven seals.[b] Then I heard
one of the four living creatures[c] say in a
voice like thunder,[d] "Come!" 2 I looked,
and there before me was a white horse![e]
Its rider held a bow, and he was given a
crown,[f] and he rode out as a conqueror
bent on conquest.[g]
3 When the Lamb opened the second
seal, I heard the second living creature[h]
say, "Come!" 4 Then another horse came
out, a fiery red one.[i] Its rider was given
power to take peace from the earth[j] and to
make people kill each other. To him was
given a large sword.
5 When the Lamb opened the third
seal, I heard the third living creature[k] say,
"Come!" I looked, and there before me
was a black horse![l] Its rider was holding
a pair of scales in his hand. 6 Then I heard
what sounded like a voice among the four
living creatures,[m] saying, "Two pounds[a] of
wheat for a day's wages,[b] and six pounds[c]
of barley for a day's wages,[b][n] and do not
damage[o] the oil and the wine!"
7 When the Lamb opened the fourth
seal, I heard the voice of the fourth living creature[p] say, "Come!" 8 I looked, and
there before me was a pale horse![q] Its rider was named Death, and Hades[r] was following close behind him. They were given
power over a fourth of the earth to kill by
sword, famine and plague, and by the wild
beasts of the earth.[s]

9 When he opened the fifth seal, I saw
under[t] the altar[u] the souls of those who
had been slain[v] because of the word of
God[w] and the testimony they had maintained. 10 They called out in a loud voice,
"How long,[x] Sovereign Lord,[y] holy and
true,[z] until you judge the inhabitants of
the earth[a] and avenge our blood?"[b] 11 Then
each of them was given a white robe,[c] and
they were told to wait a little longer, until
the full number of their fellow servants,
their brothers and sisters,[d] were killed just
as they had been.[d]
12 I watched as he opened the sixth seal.
There was a great earthquake.[e] The sun
turned black[f] like sackcloth[g] made of goat
hair, the whole moon turned blood red,
13 and the stars in the sky fell to earth,[h] as
figs drop from a fig tree[i] when shaken by a
strong wind. 14 The heavens receded like a
scroll being rolled up,[j] and every mountain
and island was removed from its place.[k]
15 Then the kings of the earth, the princes, the generals, the rich, the mighty, and
everyone else, both slave and free,[l] hid in
caves and among the rocks of the mountains.[m] 16 They called to the mountains and
the rocks, "Fall on us[n] and hide us[e] from

[a] 6 Or about 1 kilogram [b] 6 Greek *a denarius* [c] 6 Or about 3 kilograms [d] 11 The Greek word for *brothers and sisters* (*adelphoi*) refers here to believers, both men and women, as part of God's family; also in 12:10; 19:10. [e] 16 See Hosea 10:8.

6:1 [a] S Rev 5:6 [b] Rev 5:1 [c] S Rev 4:6,7 [d] Rev 14:2; 19:6 **6:2** [e] Zec 1:8; 6:3; Rev 19:11 [f] Zec 6:11; Rev 14:14; 19:12 [g] Ps 45:4 **6:3** [h] Rev 4:7 **6:4** [i] Zec 1:8; 6:2 [j] Mt 10:34 **6:5** [k] Rev 4:7 [l] Zec 6:2 **6:6** [m] S Rev 4:6, 7 [n] Eze 4:16 [o] Rev 7:1,3; 9:4 **6:7** [p] Rev 4:7 **6:8** [q] Zec 6:3 [r] Hos 13:14; Rev 1:18; 20:13, 14 [s] Jer 15:2,3; 24:10; Eze 5:12, 17 **6:9** [t] Ex 29:12; Lev 4:7 [u] Rev 14:18; 16:7 [v] Rev 20:4 [w] Ro 1:2; S Heb 4:12 **6:10** [x] Ps 119:84; Zec 1:12 [y] Lk 2:29; 2Pe 2:1 [z] S Rev 3:7 [a] S Rev 3:10 [b] Dt 32:43; 2Ki 9:7; Ps 79:10; Rev 16:6; 18:20; 19:2 **6:11** [c] S Rev 3:4 [d] Heb 11:40 **6:12** [e] Ps 97:4; Isa 29:6; Eze 38:19; Rev 8:5; 11:13; 16:18 [f] S Mt 24:29 [g] Isa 50:3 **6:13** [h] S Mt 24:29; Rev 8:10; 9:1 [i] Isa 34:4 **6:14** [j] S 2Pe 3:10; Rev 20:11; 21:1 [k] Ps 46:2; Isa 54:10; Jer 4:24; Eze 38:20; Na 1:5; Rev 16:20; 21:1 **6:15** [l] Rev 19:18 [m] Isa 2:10,19,21 **6:16** [n] Hos 10:8; Lk 23:30

6:1 *Lamb.* See v. 16; see also 5:6 and note. *seven seals.* The first of three sevenfold numbered series of judgments (cf. the seven trumpets in chs. 8–9 and the seven bowls in ch. 16). *four living creatures.* See 4:6–7 and notes.
6:2 *white horse.* The imagery of the "four horsemen of the Apocalypse" comes from Zec 1:8–17; 6:1–8 (see note on Zec 6:2–3). The colors in Revelation correspond to the character of the rider: White symbolizes conquest. Major interpretations of the rider on the white horse are: (1) Christ (cf. 19:11), (2) the antichrist and (3) the spirit of conquest. The latter establishes a more natural sequence with the other three riders (which symbolize bloodshed, famine and death). *bow.* A battle weapon.
6:4 *another horse … a fiery red one.* Symbolizing bloodshed and war (cf. Zec 1:8; 6:2). *people kill each other.* If the white horse is conquest from without, the red horse may be internal revolution. *sword.* See note on 1:16.
6:5 *black horse.* Symbolizing famine (cf. Zec 6:2,6). The sequence is thus conquest, bloodshed, famine. *pair of scales.* A balance beam with scales hung from either end. Weights were originally stones.
6:6 *wheat … barley.* One quart of wheat would be enough for only one person. Three quarts of the less nutritious barley would be barely enough for a small family. Famine had inflated prices to at least ten times their normal level. *oil and the wine.* Sets limits on the destruction by the rider of the black horse. The roots of the olive and vine go deeper and would not be immediately affected by a limited drought.
6:8 *pale horse.* Describes the ashen appearance of the dead; it symbolizes death. *Hades.* Generally equivalent to Hebrew *Sheol* (see 1:18; 20:13–14; see also note on Mt 16:18). *sword … wild beasts.* See Eze 5:16–17 and note.
6:9 *under the altar.* In OT ritual the blood of the slaughtered animal was poured out at the base of the altar (Ex 29:12; Lev 4:7).
6:10 *inhabitants of the earth.* A regular designation in Revelation for humankind in its hostility to God (see 3:10; 8:13; 11:10; 13:8,12; 17:2,8). *avenge our blood.* See Dt 32:35 and note.
6:11 *white robe.* Symbol of blessedness and purity (see 3:5,18; 4:4; 7:9,13; 19:14). *until the full number … were killed.* Jewish thought held that God rules the world according to a predetermined time schedule (see 2 Esdras 4:35–37) and that the end awaits the death of a certain number of the righteous (1 Enoch 47:4). *brothers and sisters.* See note on Ro 1:13.
6:12 *earthquake.* A regular feature of divine visitation (see Ex 19:18; Isa 2:19; Hag 2:6). *sackcloth.* See note on 11:3. *moon turned blood red.* See Joel 2:31, quoted by Peter in his Pentecost sermon (Ac 2:20).
6:13 *stars … fell.* One of the signs immediately preceding the coming of the Son of Man (Mk 13:25–26). *figs.* Green figs appearing in the winter and easily blown from the tree, which at that season has no leaves.
6:14 *heavens receded like a scroll.* See Isa 34:4 and note. *every mountain and island was removed.* Perhaps suggested by Jer 4:24 or Na 1:5; see 16:20; 20:11.
6:15 *generals.* A general was a Roman officer who commanded a cohort, i.e., about 1,000 men. *hid in caves.* See Jer 4:29.
6:16 *wrath of the Lamb.* Only here is wrath attributed to the Lamb, but it is related to God's wrath (see "their wrath" in

the face of him who sits on the throne[o]
and from the wrath of the Lamb! 17 For the
great day[p] of their[a] wrath has come, and
who can withstand it?"[q]

144,000 Sealed

7 After this I saw four angels standing
at the four corners[r] of the earth, holding back the four winds[s] of the earth to
prevent[t] any wind from blowing on the
land or on the sea or on any tree. 2 Then
I saw another angel coming up from the
east, having the seal[u] of the living God.[v]
He called out in a loud voice to the four
angels who had been given power to harm
the land and the sea:[w] 3 "Do not harm[x] the
land or the sea or the trees until we put a
seal on the foreheads[y] of the servants of
our God." 4 Then I heard the number[z] of
those who were sealed: 144,000[a] from all
the tribes of Israel.

5 From the tribe of Judah 12,000 were
sealed,
from the tribe of Reuben 12,000,
from the tribe of Gad 12,000,
6 from the tribe of Asher 12,000,
from the tribe of Naphtali 12,000,
from the tribe of Manasseh 12,000,
7 from the tribe of Simeon 12,000,
from the tribe of Levi 12,000,
from the tribe of Issachar 12,000,
8 from the tribe of Zebulun 12,000,
from the tribe of Joseph 12,000,
from the tribe of Benjamin 12,000.

The Great Multitude in White Robes

9 After this I looked, and there before me
was a great multitude that no one could
count, from every nation, tribe, people
and language,[b] standing before the throne[c]
and before the Lamb. They were wearing white robes[d] and were holding palm
branches in their hands. 10 And they cried
out in a loud voice:

"Salvation belongs to our God,[e]
who sits on the throne,[f]
and to the Lamb."

11 All the angels were standing around the
throne and around the elders[g] and the four
living creatures.[h] They fell down on their
faces[i] before the throne and worshiped
God, 12 saying:

"Amen!
Praise and glory
and wisdom and thanks and honor
and power and strength
be to our God for ever and ever.
Amen!"[j]

13 Then one of the elders asked me,
"These in white robes[k]—who are they,
and where did they come from?"
14 I answered, "Sir, you know."
And he said, "These are they who have
come out of the great tribulation; they
have washed their robes[l] and made them
white in the blood of the Lamb.[m] 15 Therefore,

"they are before the throne of God[n]
and serve him[o] day and night in his
temple;[p]
and he who sits on the throne[q]
will shelter them with his presence.[r]

6:16 [o] S Rev 5:1 **6:17** [p] Joel 1:15; 2:1,2,11,31; Zep 1:14,15; Rev 16:14 [q] Ps 76:7; Na 1:6; Mal 3:2 **7:1** [r] Isa 11:12 [s] Jer 49:36; Eze 37:9; Da 7:2; Zec 6:5; Mt 24:31 [t] S Rev 6:6 **7:2** [u] Rev 9:4 [v] S Mt 16:16 [w] ver 1 **7:3** [x] S Rev 6:6 [y] Eze 9:4; Rev 9:4; 14:1; 22:4 **7:4** [z] Rev 9:16 [a] Rev 14:1,3 **7:9** [b] S Rev 13:7 [c] ver 15 [d] S Rev 3:4 **7:10** [e] Ps 3:8; Rev 12:10; 19:1 [f] S Rev 5:1 **7:11** [g] S Rev 4:4 [h] S Rev 4:6 [i] S Rev 4:10 **7:12** [j] S Ro 11:36; Rev 5:12-14 **7:13** [k] S Rev 3:4 **7:14** [l] Rev 22:14 [m] Heb 9:14; 1Jn 1:7; Rev 12:11 **7:15** [n] ver 9 [o] Rev 22:3 [p] Rev 11:19 [q] S Rev 5:1 [r] Isa 4:5,6; Rev 21:3

[a] 17 Some manuscripts *his*

---

v. 17). God's wrath is a subject that permeates NT teaching and is both present (see Ro 1:18 and note) and future (see 19:15). It is prophesied in the OT (Zep 1:14–18; Na 1:6; Mal 3:2).

7:1–17 Ch. 7 separates the final seal (8:1) from the preceding six (the same feature is found in the trumpet sequence; see 10:1—11:13). Ch. 7 contains two visions: (1) the sealing of the 144,000 (vv. 1–8) and (2) the innumerable multitude (vv. 9–17).

7:1 *four winds.* Destructive agents of God (see Jer 49:36).

7:2 *seal of the living God.* Ancient documents were folded and tied, and a lump of clay was pressed over the knot. The sender would then stamp the hardening clay with his signet ring or roll it with a cylinder seal, which authenticated and protected the contents. The sealing in ch. 7 results in the name of the Lord being stamped on the forehead of his followers (see 9:4; 14:1; cf. 22:4). Its primary purpose is to protect the people of God in the coming judgments. For the background see Eze 9:4, where the mark was the Hebrew letter *Taw,* made like an *X* or + (see also note on Eze 9:4).

7:4 *144,000.* Some find here a reference to members of actual Jewish tribes, the faithful Jewish remnant of the "great tribulation" (v. 14). Others take the passage as symbolic of all the faithful believers who live during the period of tribulation.

7:5 *Judah.* Perhaps listed before Reuben, his older brother, because the Messiah belonged to the tribe of Judah (but see note on Ge 37:21).

7:6 *Manasseh.* One of the two Joseph tribes (Ephraim and Manasseh), yet mentioned separately, probably to make up 12 tribes since Dan is omitted. This omission is due perhaps to Dan's early connection with idolatry (Jdg 18:30), or to a tradition that the antichrist was to come from that tribe.

7:9 *great multitude.* Identified in v. 14 as those who have come out of the "great tribulation." *every nation, tribe, people and language.* All four are mentioned together also in 5:9; 11:9; 13:7; 14:6. Cf. 10:11; 17:15, in which one of the four is changed. *palm branches.* Used for festive occasions (see Lev 23:40; Jn 12:13).

7:10 *Salvation belongs to our God.* See Ge 49:18 ("deliverance"); Jnh 2:9.

7:11 *elders.* See note on 4:4. *four living creatures.* See note on 4:6.

7:12 *Praise … strength.* The sevenfold list of attributes expresses complete or perfect praise (see note on 5:12).

7:13 *white robes.* See note on 6:11.

7:14 *the great tribulation.* The period of final hostility prior to Christ's return (cf. Mt 24:21 and note). Some hold that the beginning of this hostility was already being experienced by the church of John's day (cf. 1Jn 2:18 and note).

7:15 *temple.* All 16 references to the temple in Revelation use the word that designates the temple proper rather than the

THE CHURCH AND THE TRIBULATION

Revelation provides a mixed portrait regarding the subject of Christians and tribulation. John himself was suffering on Patmos, while Antipas had already been martyred in Pergamum. The believers in Smyrna and Philadelphia had been persecuted, and those in Smyrna were about to endure even more trials. The picture here in Revelation 7 shows many whose blood had been shed for their faith. However, the four other churches in Asia had yet to experience significant tribulation.

In the modern church three main views of the tribulation are currently taught. Pretribulationists believe that the rapture of the church will occur before the great tribulation. The invitation to John to "come up" to heaven in Revelation 4:1 is seen as a type of the rapture. Because the church is not mentioned in chapters 4–18, it must therefore be absent when the seal, trumpet and bowl judgments fall upon the earth.

Midtribulationalists hold that the church will be on earth during the first half of the great tribulation, but at its midpoint (after three and a half years) the church will be raptured. Thus, the church is spared the more severe judgments of divine wrath that will come upon the earth.

Posttribulationists believe that the rapture will not occur until the great tribulation is over. Christians will be on earth during the judgments described in Revelation but will be protected, even as Israel was during the plagues that came upon Egypt. Regardless of one's perspective, we must all heed the warning with which Jesus prepared his church: "In the world you have tribulation, but take courage; I have overcome the world" (Jn 16:33 NASB).

16 'Never again will they hunger;
never again will they thirst.[s]
The sun will not beat down on
them,'[a]
nor any scorching heat.[t]
17 For the Lamb at the center of the
throne
will be their shepherd;[u]
'he will lead them to springs of living
water.'[a][v]
'And God will wipe away every tear
from their eyes.'[b]"[w]

The Seventh Seal and the Golden Censer

8 When he opened the seventh seal,[x]
there was silence in heaven for about
half an hour.
2 And I saw the seven angels[y] who stand
before God, and seven trumpets were giv-
en to them.[z]
3 Another angel,[a] who had a golden censer, came and stood at the altar. He was
given much incense to offer, with the
prayers of all God's people,[b] on the golden
altar[c] in front of the throne. 4 The smoke of
the incense, together with the prayers of
God's people, went up before God[d] from
the angel's hand. 5 Then the angel took
the censer, filled it with fire from the altar,[e] and hurled it on the earth; and there
came peals of thunder,[f] rumblings, flashes
of lightning and an earthquake.[g]

The Trumpets

6 Then the seven angels who had the
seven trumpets[h] prepared to sound them.
7 The first angel[i] sounded his trumpet,
and there came hail and fire[j] mixed with
blood, and it was hurled down on the
earth. A third[k] of the earth was burned up,

7:16 [s] Jn 6:35 [t] Isa 49:10 **7:17** [u] S Jn 10:11 [v] S Jn 4:10 [w] Isa 25:8; 35:10; 51:11; 65:19; Rev 21:4 **8:1** [x] Rev 6:1 **8:2** [y] ver 6-13; Rev 9:1, 13; 11:15 [z] S Mt 24:31 **8:3** [a] Rev 7:2 [b] Rev 5:8 [c] ver 5; Ex 30:1-6; Heb 9:4; Rev 9:13 **8:4** [d] Ps 141:2 **8:5** [e] Lev 16:12, 13 [f] S Rev 4:5 [g] S Rev 6:12 **8:6** [h] S ver 2 **8:7** [i] S ver 2 [j] Eze 38:22 [k] ver 7-12; Rev 9:15, 18; 12:4

[a] *16,17* Isaiah 49:10 [b] *17* Isaiah 25:8

larger precincts. It is the place where God's presence dwells. Thus no longer may only one tribe (Levites) go into God's presence, but all believers serve God there, for they have been made priests in God's service (see 1:6; 5:10; 20:6). *shelter them with his presence.* The imagery would evoke memories of the tabernacle in the wilderness (Lev 26:11–13).
7:17 *shepherd.* Ancient kings often referred to themselves as the shepherds of their people (see Ps 23:1 and note).
8:1 *silence in heaven.* A dramatic pause before the next series of plagues—the final act of the drama is left undisclosed here, reserved to be presented later.
8:2 *seven trumpets.* In OT times the trumpet served to announce important events and give signals in time of war. The seven trumpets of Rev 8–9; 11:15–19 announce a series of plagues more severe than the seals but not as completely devastating as the bowls (ch. 16).
8:3 *censer.* A firepan used to hold live charcoal for the burning of incense (cf. Ex 27:3; 1Ki 7:50). *with the prayers.* Most translations consider the incense to be mingled "with" prayers. The Greek for this phrase also allows a translation that takes the incense "to be" the prayers ("incense . . . consisting of the prayers").
8:4 Although the angel is involved in presenting to God the prayers of God's people, he does not make them acceptable. The Jewish apocalyptic concept of angels as mediators finds no place in the NT. Angels did function as mediators in the old covenant era (see Ac 7:38 and note), but there is no record of such a mediatorial function on the part of angels in the new covenant era.
8:5 *thunder . . . earthquake.* See note on 4:5.
8:7 *hail and fire mixed with blood.* Cf. the imagery of the seventh plague on Egypt (Ex 9:13–25; cf. Eze 38:22). *A third of the earth was burned up.* This fraction indicates that the punishment announced by the trumpets is not yet complete and

a third of the trees were burned up, and all
the green grass was burned up.[l]
8 The second angel sounded his trumpet,
and something like a huge mountain,[m] all
ablaze, was thrown into the sea. A third[n]
of the sea turned into blood,[o] 9 a third[p] of
the living creatures in the sea died, and a
third of the ships were destroyed.
10 The third angel sounded his trumpet,
and a great star, blazing like a torch, fell
from the sky[q] on a third of the rivers and
on the springs of water[r]— 11 the name of
the star is Wormwood.[a] A third[s] of the waters turned bitter, and many people died
from the waters that had become bitter.[t]
12 The fourth angel sounded his trumpet, and a third of the sun was struck, a
third of the moon, and a third of the stars,
so that a third[u] of them turned dark.[v] A
third of the day was without light, and
also a third of the night.[w]
13 As I watched, I heard an eagle that
was flying in midair[x] call out in a loud
voice: "Woe! Woe! Woe[y] to the inhabitants of the earth,[z] because of the trumpet
blasts about to be sounded by the other
three angels!"
9 The fifth angel sounded his trumpet,
and I saw a star that had fallen from
the sky to the earth.[a] The star was given
the key[b] to the shaft of the Abyss.[c] 2 When
he opened the Abyss, smoke rose from it
like the smoke from a gigantic furnace.[d]
The sun and sky were darkened[e] by the
smoke from the Abyss.[f] 3 And out of the
smoke locusts[g] came down on the earth
and were given power like that of scorpions[h] of the earth. 4 They were told not to
harm[i] the grass of the earth or any plant
or tree,[j] but only those people who did not
have the seal of God on their foreheads.[k]
5 They were not allowed to kill them but
only to torture them for five months.[l] And
the agony they suffered was like that of
the sting of a scorpion[m] when it strikes.
6 During those days people will seek death
but will not find it; they will long to die,
but death will elude them.[n]
7 The locusts looked like horses prepared for battle.[o] On their heads they wore
something like crowns of gold, and their
faces resembled human faces.[p] 8 Their hair
was like women's hair, and their teeth
were like lions' teeth.[q] 9 They had breastplates like breastplates of iron, and the
sound of their wings was like the thundering of many horses and chariots rushing
into battle.[r] 10 They had tails with stingers,
like scorpions, and in their tails they had
power to torment people for five months.[s]
11 They had as king over them the angel
of the Abyss,[t] whose name in Hebrew[u] is

8:7 [l] Rev 9:4
8:8 [m] Jer 51:25
[n] S ver 7
[o] Rev 16:3
8:9 [p] S ver 7
8:10 [q] Isa 14:12; Rev 6:13; 9:1
[r] Rev 14:7; 16:4
8:11 [s] S ver 7
[t] Jer 9:15; 23:15
8:12 [u] S ver 7
[v] Ex 10:21-23; Rev 6:12,13
[w] Eze 32:7
8:13 [x] Rev 14:6; 19:17
[y] Rev 9:12; 11:14; 12:12
[z] S Rev 3:10
9:1 [a] Rev 8:10
[b] Rev 1:18
[c] ver 2,11; S Lk 8:31
9:2 [d] Ge 19:28; Ex 19:18
[e] Joel 2:2,10
[f] ver 1,11; S Lk 8:31
9:3 [g] Ex 10:12-15 [h] ver 5,10
9:4 [i] S Rev 6:6
[j] Rev 8:7
[k] S Rev 7:2,3
9:5 [l] ver 10 [m] ver 3
9:6 [n] Job 3:21; 7:15; Jer 8:3; Rev 6:16
9:7 [o] Joel 2:4
[p] Da 7:8
9:8 [q] Joel 1:6
9:9 [r] Joel 2:5
9:10 [s] ver 3,5,19
9:11 [t] ver 1, 2; S Lk 8:31
[u] Rev 16:16

[a] *11* Wormwood is a bitter substance.

final (the same fraction appears in each of the next three plagues: vv. 8–9,10–11,12). A smaller fraction (a fourth) of devastation accompanied the opening of the fourth seal (6:8).
8:8 *sea turned into blood.* Reminiscent of the first plague on Egypt (Ex 7:20–21). This is an eschatological judgment rather than natural pollution resulting from widespread volcanic upheavals.
8:10 *great star ... fell.* See notes on 6:13; 9:1.
8:11 *Wormwood.* A plant with a strong, bitter taste (see NIV text note). It is used here as a metaphor for calamity and sorrow (see Pr 5:3–4; Jer 9:15; La 3:19). It is not poisonous, but its bitterness suggests death. *waters turned bitter.* The reverse of the miracle at Marah, where bitter waters were made sweet (Ex 15:25).
8:12 *a third of the sun was struck.* In the ninth plague on Egypt, thick darkness covered the land for three days (Ex 10:21–23). References to the Egyptian plagues suggest that in Revelation we have the final exodus of God's people from the bondage of a world controlled by hostile powers.
8:13 *Woe! Woe! Woe ...!* These three woes correspond to the three final trumpet plagues (see 9:12; 11:14 [10:1—11:13 is an interlude]; the seven bowl judgments of chs. 15–16 apparently constitute the third woe). The woes fall on the unbelieving world (the phrase "the inhabitants of the earth" refers to the wicked; see note on 6:10), not on the righteous (9:4; but see note there).
9:1 *star that had fallen.* The star in 8:10 was part of a cosmic disturbance; here the star is a divine agent, probably an angel (cf. 20:1). *Abyss.* Conceived of as the subterranean abode of demonic hordes and Satan (see 20:1–3; Lk 8:31). This Greek word means "very deep" or "bottomless" and is used in the Septuagint (the pre-Christian Greek translation of the OT) to translate the Hebrew word for the primeval deep (see Ge 1:2; 7:11; Pr 8:28). Eight of the nine NT occurrences of the Greek word *Abyss* are in Revelation.
9:3 *locusts.* For background, see the plague of locusts in Ex 10:1–20. Joel 1:2—2:11 interprets the locust plague as a foreshadowing of the devastations that accompany the day of the Lord. Locusts traveled in enormous swarms and could strip a land of all vegetation. In 1866, 200,000 people died in a famine in Algiers following a locust plague. *scorpions.* Large, spiderlike organisms that injure or kill by means of a poisonous barb in the tail.
9:4 *people who did not have the seal of God.* Apparently it is only the first woe that does not affect the "servants of ... God" (7:3; see 7:14; 12:17 and note; 13:7). Cf. the Israelites, who were protected from the Egyptian plagues (Ex 8:22; 9:4,26; 10:23; 11:7).
9:5 *five months.* A limited period of time suggested by the life cycle of the locust or the dry season (spring through late summer, about five months), in which the danger of a locust invasion is always present.
9:6 *seek death but will not find it.* Cf. Hos 10:8 (quoted in Lk 23:30). Cornelius Gallus, a Roman poet living in the first century BC, wrote: "Worse than any wound is the wish to die and yet not be able to do so." Cf. Paul's attitude toward death in Php 1:20–24 (see notes there).
9:7 *human faces.* The locusts appear to have the cunning of intelligent beings. They do not simply use brute force.
9:8 *women's hair.* Perhaps a reference to long antennae. *lions' teeth.* Cruel, inhumane.
9:9 *breastplates.* The breastplate was a coat of mail that protected the front. *like breastplates of iron.* Probably thin iron pieces riveted to a leather base.
9:10 *five months.* See note on v. 5.
9:11 *Abaddon.* A personification of destruction (cf. Pr 15:11).

Abaddon[v] and in Greek is Apollyon (that
is, Destroyer).
12 The first woe is past; two other woes
are yet to come.[w]
13 The sixth angel sounded his trumpet,
and I heard a voice coming from the four
horns[x] of the golden altar that is before
God.[y] 14 It said to the sixth angel who had
the trumpet, "Release the four angels[z]
who are bound at the great river Euphrates."[a] 15 And the four angels who had been
kept ready for this very hour and day and
month and year were released[b] to kill a
third[c] of mankind.[d] 16 The number of the
mounted troops was twice ten thousand
times ten thousand. I heard their number.[e]
17 The horses and riders I saw in my vision looked like this: Their breastplates
were fiery red, dark blue, and yellow as
sulfur. The heads of the horses resembled
the heads of lions, and out of their mouths[f]
came fire, smoke and sulfur.[g] 18 A third[h] of
mankind was killed[i] by the three plagues
of fire, smoke and sulfur[j] that came out of
their mouths. 19 The power of the horses
was in their mouths and in their tails; for
their tails were like snakes, having heads
with which they inflict injury.
20 The rest of mankind who were not
killed by these plagues still did not repent[k] of the work of their hands;[l] they did
not stop worshiping demons,[m] and idols
of gold, silver, bronze, stone and wood—
idols that cannot see or hear or walk.[n]
21 Nor did they repent[o] of their murders,
their magic arts,[p] their sexual immorality[q]
or their thefts.

The Angel and the Little Scroll

10 Then I saw another mighty angel[r] coming down from heaven.[s]
He was robed in a cloud, with a rainbow[t]
above his head; his face was like the sun,[u]
and his legs were like fiery pillars.[v] 2 He
was holding a little scroll,[w] which lay open
in his hand. He planted his right foot on
the sea and his left foot on the land,[x]
3 and he gave a loud shout like the roar
of a lion.[y] When he shouted, the voices
of the seven thunders[z] spoke. 4 And when
the seven thunders spoke, I was about to
write;[a] but I heard a voice from heaven[b]
say, "Seal up what the seven thunders
have said and do not write it down."[c]
5 Then the angel I had seen standing on
the sea and on the land[d] raised his right
hand to heaven.[e] 6 And he swore[f] by him
who lives for ever and ever,[g] who created
the heavens and all that is in them, the
earth and all that is in it, and the sea and
all that is in it,[h] and said, "There will be
no more delay![i] 7 But in the days when
the seventh angel is about to sound his
trumpet,[j] the mystery[k] of God will be ac-

9:11 [v]Job 26:6; 28:22; 31:12; Ps 88:11 **9:12** [w]S Rev 8:13 **9:13** [x]Ex 30:1-3 [y]Rev 8:3 **9:14** [z]Rev 7:1 [a]Ge 15:18; Dt 1:7; Jos 1:4; Isa 11:15; Rev 16:12 **9:15** [b]Rev 20:7 [c]S Rev 8:7 [d]ver 18 **9:16** [e]Rev 5:11; 7:4 **9:17** [f]Rev 11:5 [g]ver 18; Ps 11:6; Isa 30:33; Eze 38:22; Rev 14:10; 19:20; 20:10; 21:8 **9:18** [h]S Rev 8:7 [i]ver 15 [j]S ver 17 **9:20** [k]S Rev 2:21 [l]Dt 4:28; 31:29; Jer 1:16; Mic 5:13; Ac 7:41 [m]S 1Co 10:20 [n]Ps 115:4-7; 135:15-17; Da 5:23 **9:21** [o]S Rev 2:21 [p]Isa 47:9, 12; Rev 18:23 [q]Rev 17:2, 5 **10:1** [r]Rev 5:2 [s]Rev 18:1; 20:1 [t]Eze 1:28; Rev 4:3 [u]Mt 17:2; Rev 1:16 [v]Rev 1:15 **10:2** [w]ver 8-10; Rev 5:1 [x]ver 5, 8 **10:3** [y]Hos 11:10 [z]Rev 4:5 **10:4** [a]Rev 1:11, 19 [b]ver 8 [c]Da 8:26; 12:4, 9; Rev 22:10 **10:5** [d]ver 1, 2 [e]Dt 32:40; Da 12:7 **10:6** [f]Ge 14:22; Ex 6:8; Nu 14:30 [g]S Rev 1:18 [h]Ps 115:15; 146:6; Rev 4:11; 14:7 [i]Rev 16:17 **10:7** [j]S Mt 24:31 [k]S Ro 16:25

9:12 *first woe.* See note on 8:13.

9:13 *horns of the golden altar.* See 8:3–5. The horns were projections at the four corners of the altar (Ex 27:2). Those fleeing judgment could seek mercy by taking hold of the horns (1Ki 1:50–51; 2:28; see note on Am 3:14).

9:14 *four angels.* Apparently in charge of the demonic horsemen (vv. 15–19). *Euphrates.* See note on Ge 15:18.

9:15 *hour . . . day . . . month . . . year.* Apocalyptic thought views God as acting according to an exact timetable.

9:16 *twice ten thousand times ten thousand.* The reference is most likely general, intending an incalculable host rather than a specific number (cf. Ps 68:17; Da 7:10; Rev 5:11 and note).

9:17 *breastplates.* See note on v. 9. *out of their mouths came fire.* Cf. the two witnesses in 11:5.

9:19 *tails were like snakes, having heads.* Emphasizes the demonic origin of the horses (cf. 12:9).

9:20 *still did not repent.* Suggests that the purpose of the extreme suffering of some was to call the others to repentance (cf. v. 21; 2:21; 16:9,11; cf. also Am 4:6–11 and note). *demons.* Spiritual beings in league with Satan and exerting an evil influence on human affairs (cf. 12:7–9; Dt 4:28; Ps 115:5–7; Lk 4:33 and note; 1Co 10:20; Eph 6:10–18).

9:21 *Nor did they repent.* See 16:9,11. Even physical pain will not change the rebellious heart. *magic arts.* Involved the mixing of various ingredients (the Greek for this phrase is *pharmakon,* from which comes the English "pharmacy") for magical purposes. Believers at Ephesus publicly burned their books of magic, valued at 50,000 drachmas (Ac 19:19). (A drachma was a silver coin worth about a day's wages.)

10:1—11:13 The second interlude (see note on 7:1–17).

10:1 *mighty angel.* Perhaps the angel of 5:2. *robed in a cloud.* See Mt 17:5; 24:30 and notes. *rainbow.* Cf. Eze 1:26–28. The rainbow became a sign of God's pledge never to destroy the earth again by a flood (see Ge 9:8–17 and note on 9:13). *legs were like fiery pillars.* Since the exodus supplies background for this central part of Revelation (see note on 8:12), this feature may recall the pillars of fire and cloud that guided (Ex 13:21–22) and protected (Ex 14:19,24) the Israelites during their wilderness journey.

10:2 *little scroll.* Not the same as the scroll of destiny in ch. 5, since that scroll was intended to reveal its contents and this scroll was to be eaten. Furthermore, the term "little scroll" sets off this particular scroll from all others. *right foot on the sea . . . left foot on the land.* Indicates his tremendous size and symbolizes that his coming has to do with the destiny of all creation (cf. v. 6).

10:3 *seven thunders.* In 8:5; 11:19; 16:18 thunder is connected with divine punishment. Here, too, it anticipates the judgment to fall on those who refuse God's love and grace.

10:4 *Seal up.* In Da 8:26; 12:4,9 the prophecies are sealed until the last times, when they will be opened. What the seven thunders said will not be revealed until their proper time. Cf. the angel's instructions in 22:10 not to seal the prophecies of Revelation.

10:5 *raised his right hand.* A part of oath taking (see Ge 14:22–23; Dt 32:40).

10:6 *him who lives for ever and ever.* Of special encouragement in a context of impending martyrdom (cf. 1:18; 4:9–10; 15:7). *no more delay.* The martyrs in 6:9–11 were told to rest for a while, but now the end has come (cf. Da 12:1; Mk 13:19).

10:7 *mystery of God.* In apocalyptic thought mysteries were secrets preserved in heaven and revealed to the apocalyptist.

complished, just as he announced to his
servants the prophets."[l]
8 Then the voice that I had heard from
heaven[m] spoke to me once more: "Go, take
the scroll[n] that lies open in the hand of the
angel who is standing on the sea and on
the land."
9 So I went to the angel and asked him
to give me the little scroll. He said to me,
"Take it and eat it. It will turn your stomach sour, but 'in your mouth it will be as
sweet as honey.'[a]"[o] 10 I took the little scroll
from the angel's hand and ate it. It tasted as sweet as honey in my mouth,[p] but
when I had eaten it, my stomach turned
sour. 11 Then I was told, "You must prophesy[q] again about many peoples, nations,
languages and kings."[r]

The Two Witnesses

11 I was given a reed like a measuring rod[s] and was told, "Go and
measure the temple of God and the altar,
with its worshipers. 2 But exclude the outer court;[t] do not measure it, because it
has been given to the Gentiles.[u] They will
trample on the holy city[v] for 42 months.[w]
3 And I will appoint my two witnesses,[x]
and they will prophesy for 1,260 days,[y]
clothed in sackcloth."[z] 4 They are "the two
olive trees"[a] and the two lampstands, and
"they stand before the Lord of the earth."[b][b]
5 If anyone tries to harm them, fire comes
from their mouths and devours their enemies.[c] This is how anyone who wants to
harm them must die.[d] 6 They have power
to shut up the heavens[e] so that it will not
rain during the time they are prophesying;[f]
and they have power to turn the waters
into blood[g] and to strike the earth with every kind of plague as often as they want.
7 Now when they have finished their testimony, the beast[h] that comes up from the
Abyss[i] will attack them,[j] and overpower

[a] 9 Ezek. 3:3 [b] 4 See Zech. 4:3,11,14.

10:7 [l] Am 3:7
10:8 [m] ver 4
[n] ver 2
10:9 [o] Jer 15:16; Eze 2:8-3:3
10:10 [p] S ver 9
10:11 [q] Eze 37:4, 9 [r] Da 3:4; S Rev 13:7
11:1 [s] Eze 40:3; Rev 21:15
11:2 [t] Eze 40:17, 20 [u] Lk 21:24 [v] S Rev 21:2 [w] ver 3; Da 7:25; 12:7; Rev 12:6, 14; 13:5
11:3 [x] Rev 1:5; 2:13 [y] S ver 2 [z] Ge 37:34; 2Sa 3:31; Ne 9:1; Jnh 3:5
11:4 [a] Ps 52:8; Jer 11:16; Zec 4:3,11 [b] Zec 4:14
11:5 [c] 2Sa 22:9; 2Ki 1:10; Jer 5:14; Rev 9:17,18 [d] Nu 16:29,35
11:6 [e] S Lk 4:25 [f] ver 3 [g] Ex 7:17, 19; Rev 8:8
11:7 [h] Rev 13:1-4 [i] S Lk 8:31 [j] Da 7:21; Rev 13:7

THE TRUMPET AND BOWL JUDGMENTS AND THE EGYPTIAN PLAGUES

The Exodus tradition is an important background for Revelation. The Passover typology was initially introduced in 5:6 when John sees a slain Lamb. The two witnesses, like Moses, were empowered to turn the waters into blood and to strike the earth with plagues (11:6). The song of Moses also became the song of the Lamb (15:3). The plagues against Egypt provide a prophetic background for the serial judgments of the seven trumpets and the seven bowls, with six of the ten being replicated in Revelation. Like Exodus, Revelation's judgments are arranged in increasing degrees of intensity. Like the pharaoh whose heart became hardened (Ex 7–14), the inhabitants of the earth refuse to repent (Rev 9:20–21; 16:9,11).

Here the mystery is that God has won the victory over the forces of evil and will reign for ever and ever (cf. 11:15).
10:9 *Take it and eat it.* Grasp and digest fully the contents of the scroll (cf. Ps 119:103). *turn your stomach sour.* The message of the little scroll (11:1–13) will involve suffering—the bad news. *in your mouth ... sweet as honey.* God's eternal purposes will experience no further delay—the good news.
10:11 *prophesy again.* The prophecies following the sounding of the seventh trumpet in 11:15. *peoples ... kings.* See note on 7:9.
11:1 *reed.* A bamboo-like cane that often reached a height of 20 feet and grew in abundance in the waters along the banks of the Jordan. Straight and light, the reed was a convenient measuring rod (see Eze 40:3; Zec 2:1–2). *temple.* See note on 7:15, though here the sanctuary on earth is what is measured. Some hold that the symbolic reference is to the believing church, others that it refers to believing Israel. Some representatives of the latter view believe that "temple" should be understood more literally as a future rebuilt temple. *altar.* The context of worship suggests that this is the altar of burnt offering, where sacrifices were offered.
11:2 *outer court.* The court of the Gentiles, approximately 26 acres. *trample on the holy city.* Cf. Ps 79:1; Isa 63:18; Lk 21:24. *42 months.* Three and a half years. Some find the background for this period in the time of Jewish suffering under the Syrian tyrant, Antiochus Epiphanes (168–165 BC). Others point out that, whereas the temple was desolated for three years under Antiochus, the figure used in Revelation is three and a half years, which no doubt looks back to the dividing of the 70th "seven" (Da 9:27) into two equal parts. The same time period is also designated as 1,260 days (v. 3; 12:6) and as "a time, times and half a time" (12:14; cf. Da 7:25; 12:7). This period of time evidently became a conventional symbol for a limited period of unrestrained wickedness.
11:3 *two witnesses.* Modeled after Moses and Elijah (see notes on vv. 5–6). They may symbolize testifying believers in the final period before Christ returns, or they may be two actual individuals who will be martyred for the proclamation of the truth. *1,260 days.* See note on v. 2. These are months of 30 days each (42 months x 30 days = 1,260 days). *sackcloth.* See 6:12; a coarse, dark cloth woven from the hair of goats or camels. It was worn as a sign of mourning and penitence (Joel 1:13; Jnh 3:5–6; Mt 11:21; see note on Ge 37:34).
11:4 The imagery emphasizes that the power for effective testimony is supplied by the Spirit of God (see notes on Zec 4).
11:5 *fire comes ... and devours.* Cf. Elijah's encounters with the messengers of Ahaziah (2Ki 1:10,12).
11:6 *power to shut up the heavens.* Cf. the drought in the days of Elijah (1Ki 17:1; see also Lk 4:25; Jas 5:17). *waters into blood.* God used Moses to bring the same plague on the Egyptians (Ex 7:17–21).
11:7 *the beast.* First mention of the major opponent of God's people in the final days (see chs. 13; 17). That he comes up from the Abyss (see note on 9:1) indicates his demonic

and kill them. 8Their bodies will lie in the
public square of the great city[k] — which
is figuratively called Sodom[l] and Egypt —
where also their Lord was crucified.[m] 9For
three and a half days some from every
people, tribe, language and nation[n] will
gaze on their bodies and refuse them
burial.[o] 10The inhabitants of the earth[p]
will gloat over them and will celebrate by
sending each other gifts,[q] because these
two prophets had tormented those who
live on the earth.

11But after the three and a half days[r] the
breath[a] of life from God entered them,[s]
and they stood on their feet, and terror
struck those who saw them. 12Then they
heard a loud voice from heaven saying to
them, "Come up here."[t] And they went up
to heaven in a cloud,[u] while their enemies
looked on.

13At that very hour there was a severe
earthquake[v] and a tenth of the city collapsed. Seven thousand people were killed
in the earthquake, and the survivors were
terrified and gave glory[w] to the God of
heaven.[x]

14The second woe has passed; the third
woe is coming soon.[y]

The Seventh Trumpet

15The seventh angel sounded his trumpet,[z] and there were loud voices[a] in heav-
en, which said:

"The kingdom of the world has become
the kingdom of our Lord and of his
Messiah,[b]
and he will reign for ever and ever."[c]

16And the twenty-four elders,[d] who were
seated on their thrones before God, fell on
their faces[e] and worshiped God, 17saying:

"We give thanks[f] to you, Lord God
Almighty,[g]
the One who is and who was,[h]
because you have taken your great
power
and have begun to reign.[i]
18The nations were angry,[j]
and your wrath has come.
The time has come for judging the
dead,[k]
and for rewarding your servants the
prophets[l]
and your people who revere your name,
both great and small[m] —
and for destroying those who destroy
the earth."

19Then God's temple[n] in heaven was
opened, and within his temple was seen
the ark of his covenant.[o] And there came
flashes of lightning, rumblings, peals of
thunder,[p] an earthquake and a severe hailstorm.[q]

The Woman and the Dragon

12 A great sign[r] appeared in heaven:[s] a
woman clothed with the sun, with
the moon under her feet and a crown of
twelve stars[t] on her head. 2She was pregnant and cried out in pain[u] as she was
about to give birth. 3Then another sign

[a] *11* Or *Spirit* (see Ezek. 37:5,14)

11:8 [k]Rev 16:19 [l]Isa 1:9; Jer 23:14; Eze 16:46 [m]Heb 13:12 **11:9** [n]S Rev 13:7 [o]Ps 79:2,3 **11:10** [p]S Rev 3:10 [q]Ne 8:10,12; Est 9:19,22 **11:11** [r]ver 9 [s]Eze 37:5,9,10,14 **11:12** [t]Rev 4:1 [u]2Ki 2:11; Ac 1:9 **11:13** [v]S Rev 6:12 [w]Rev 14:7; 16:9; 19:7 [x]Rev 16:11 **11:14** [y]S Rev 8:13 **11:15** [z]S Mt 24:31 [a]Rev 16:17; 19:1 [b]Rev 12:10 [c]Ps 145:13; Da 2:44; 7:14,27; Mic 4:7; Zec 14:9; Lk 1:33 **11:16** [d]S Rev 4:4 [e]S Rev 4:10 **11:17** [f]Ps 30:12 [g]S Rev 1:8 [h]S Rev 1:4 [i]Rev 19:6 **11:18** [j]Ps 2:1 [k]Rev 20:12 [l]Rev 10:7 [m]S Rev 19:5 **11:19** [n]Rev 15:5,8 [o]Ex 25:10-22; 2Ch 5:7; Heb 9:4 [p]S Rev 4:5 [q]Rev 16:21 **12:1** [r]ver 3 [s]Rev 11:19 [t]Ge 37:9 **12:2** [u]Isa 26:17; Gal 4:19

---

character. *kill them.* They will suffer the same fate as their Lord (see v. 8).

11:8 *Their bodies will lie in the public square.* In the Near East the denial of burial was a flagrant violation of decency. *great city.* Probably Jerusalem, though some say Rome, Babylon or some other city. It may be symbolic of the world opposed to God (see 16:19; 17:18; 18:10,16,18–19,21). Sodom (see similarly Isa 1:10) refers to its low level of morality (cf. Ge 19:4–11), and Egypt emphasizes oppression and slavery. Some say that Jesus could have been crucified in Rome in the sense that her power extended throughout the known world and was immediately responsible for Christ's execution.

11:9 *three and a half days.* A short time when compared with the three and a half years of their ministry. *refuse them burial.* See note on v. 8.

11:11 *breath of life from God entered them.* A dramatic validation of the true faith (cf. Eze 37:5,10).

11:12 *went up to heaven in a cloud.* Cf. 1Th 4:17. *enemies looked on.* Cf. 1:7.

11:13 *earthquake.* See notes on 6:12; Eze 38:19. *gave glory to the God of heaven.* Not an act of repentance but the terrified realization that Christ, not the antichrist, is the true Lord of all.

11:14 *second woe.* Cf. 9:12.

11:15 *seventh angel sounded.* The series of trumpet blasts is now continued (see 9:13) and completed. *kingdom of our Lord.* Cf. Ex 15:18; Ps 10:16; Zec 14:9. *of our Lord and of his Messiah.* Cf. Ps 2:2 and note.

11:16 *twenty-four elders.* See note on 4:4.

11:17 *One who is and who was.* In 1:4,8; 4:8 he is also the one "who is to come." This is now omitted because his reign is here pictured as having begun.

11:18 *nations were angry.* See Ps 48:4. *your wrath.* See note on 6:16. God's wrath triumphs in 14:10–11; 16:15–21; 20:8–9. *judging the dead.* Anticipated in 6:10, carried out in 20:11–15. *your servants the prophets.* See Da 9:6,10; Am 3:7; Zec 1:6.

11:19 *God's temple in heaven.* The sanctuary in heaven (3:12; 7:15; 15:5–8) as distinguished from the sanctuary on earth (11:1). *ark of his covenant.* The OT ark, a chest of acacia wood (Dt 10:1–2), symbolized the throne or presence of God among his people. It was probably destroyed when Nebuzaradan destroyed the temple in Jerusalem (2Ki 25:8–10). In the NT it symbolizes God's faithfulness in keeping covenant with his people. *lightning ... hailstorm.* See note on 4:5.

12:1 *sign.* An extraordinary spectacle or event that points beyond itself (cf. Lk 21:11,25; Ac 2:19). *a woman clothed with the sun.* Perhaps a symbolic reference to the believing Messianic community (see v. 5), though some believe "woman" refers specifically to Israel (see note on v. 7; for the imagery, cf. Ge 37:9–10). *twelve stars.* Cf. the 12 tribes of Israel.

12:2 *cried out in pain.* Cf. the similar language describing the rebirth of Jerusalem in Isa 66:7 (see Mic 4:10).

12:3 *red dragon.* Identified in v. 9 (cf. 20:2). Dragons abound

appeared in heaven:[v] an enormous red
dragon[w] with seven heads[x] and ten horns[y]
and seven crowns[z] on its heads. 4 Its tail
swept a third[a] of the stars out of the sky
and flung them to the earth.[b] The dragon stood in front of the woman who was
about to give birth, so that it might devour her child[c] the moment he was born.
5 She gave birth to a son, a male child, who
"will rule all the nations with an iron scepter."[a][d] And her child was snatched up[e] to
God and to his throne. 6 The woman fled
into the wilderness to a place prepared for
her by God, where she might be taken care
of for 1,260 days.[f]

7 Then war broke out in heaven. Michael[g] and his angels fought against the dragon,[h] and the dragon and his angels[i] fought
back. 8 But he was not strong enough, and
they lost their place in heaven. 9 The great
dragon was hurled down—that ancient
serpent[j] called the devil,[k] or Satan,[l] who
leads the whole world astray.[m] He was
hurled to the earth,[n] and his angels with
him.

10 Then I heard a loud voice in heaven[o]
say:

"Now have come the salvation[p] and
the power
and the kingdom of our God,
and the authority of his Messiah.
For the accuser of our brothers and
sisters,[q]
who accuses them before our God
day and night,
has been hurled down.
11 They triumphed over[r] him
by the blood of the Lamb[s]
and by the word of their testimony;[t]
they did not love their lives so much
as to shrink from death.[u]
12 Therefore rejoice, you heavens[v]
and you who dwell in them!
But woe[w] to the earth and the sea,[x]
because the devil has gone down to
you!
He is filled with fury,
because he knows that his time is
short."

13 When the dragon[y] saw that he had
been hurled to the earth, he pursued the
woman who had given birth to the male
child.[z] 14 The woman was given the two
wings of a great eagle,[a] so that she might
fly to the place prepared for her in the wilderness, where she would be taken care
of for a time, times and half a time,[b] out
of the serpent's reach. 15 Then from his
mouth the serpent[c] spewed water like a
river, to overtake the woman and sweep
her away with the torrent. 16 But the earth
helped the woman by opening its mouth
and swallowing the river that the dragon
had spewed out of his mouth. 17 Then the
dragon was enraged at the woman and
went off to wage war[d] against the rest of
her offspring[e]—those who keep God's
commands[f] and hold fast their testimony
about Jesus.[g]

The Beast out of the Sea

13 The dragon[b] stood on the shore of
the sea. And I saw a beast coming
out of the sea.[h] It had ten horns and sev-
en heads,[i] with ten crowns on its horns,

[a] 5 Psalm 2:9 [b] 1 Some manuscripts *And I*

12:3 [v] ver 1; Rev 15:1 [w] ver 9,13,16,17; Rev 13:1 [x] Rev 13:1; 17:3,7,9 [y] Da 7:7,20; Rev 13:1; 17:3,7,12,16 [z] Rev 19:12 **12:4** [a] S Rev 8:7 [b] Da 8:10 [c] Mt 2:16 **12:5** [d] Ps 2:9; Rev 2:27; 19:15 [e] S Ac 8:39 **12:6** [f] S Rev 11:2 **12:7** [g] S Jude 9 [h] ver 3 [i] Mt 25:41 **12:9** [j] ver 15; Ge 3:1-7 [k] Mt 25:41; Rev 20:2 [l] S Mt 4:10 [m] Rev 20:3,8,10 [n] Lk 10:18; Jn 12:31 **12:10** [o] Rev 11:15 [p] Rev 7:10 [q] Job 1:9-11; Zec 3:1; 1Pe 5:8 **12:11** [r] S Jn 16:33; Rev 15:2 [s] S Rev 7:14 [t] Rev 6:9 [u] Lk 14:26; Rev 2:10 **12:12** [v] Ps 96:11; Isa 44:23; 49:13; Rev 18:20 [w] S Rev 8:13 [x] Rev 10:6 **12:13** [y] ver 3 [z] ver 5 **12:14** [a] Ex 19:4 [b] S Rev 11:2 **12:15** [c] ver 9 **12:17** [d] Rev 11:7; 13:7 [e] Ge 3:15 [f] S Jn 14:15 [g] S Rev 1:2

13:1 [h] Da 7:1-6; Rev 15:2; 16:13 [i] S Rev 12:3

in the mythology of ancient peoples (Leviathan in Canaanite lore and Set-Typhon, the red crocodile, in Egypt). In the OT they are normally used metaphorically to depict the enemies of God and of Israel (see Ps 74:14; Isa 27:1; Eze 29:3). *seven heads.* See 13:1; 17:9–11 and notes. *ten horns.* Symbolizing great power (see 13:1; 17:12 and note).

12:5 *a son, a male child.* The Messiah. *iron scepter.* See note on 2:27. *snatched up to God.* The ascension of Christ.

12:6 *wilderness.* Not a wasteland but a place of spiritual refuge (cf. Hos 2:14). *1,260 days.* The time of spiritual protection corresponds to the time of persecution (see note on 11:2; cf. 13:5).

12:7 *Michael.* An archangel who defeats Satan in heavenly warfare. In Da 12:1 he is the protector of Israel who will deliver her from tribulation in the last days (cf. vv. 13–17).

12:9 *dragon was hurled … to the earth.* Not the original casting of Satan out of heaven, but his final exclusion—an explanation of his intense hostility against God's people in the last days (vv. 12–17). *devil, or Satan.* See notes on 2:9–10. *leads … astray.* Cf. 2Co 11:3; see also Lk 22:31; Jn 13:2.

12:10 *accuser.* See Job 1:9–11 and notes on 1:6; Mt 16:23; 1Jn 3:8; see also Zec 3:1. Satan (v. 9) in Hebrew means "accuser" or "adversary."

12:11 *blood of the Lamb.* See note on 5:9; see also 1:5; 7:14.

12:12 *his time is short.* The period of final, intense hostility of Satan toward the people of God.

12:13–16 Cf. the similarity to the exodus.

12:14 *wilderness.* See note on v. 6. *a time, times and half a time.* One year plus two years plus half a year (see note on 11:2).

12:16 *earth helped … by opening its mouth.* Cf. Nu 16:30–33, where the earth opened and swallowed Korah's men.

12:17 *rest of her offspring.* Believers in general, as contrasted with Christ, the male child of vv. 5,13.

13:1 *beast coming out of the sea.* First mentioned in 11:7. According to some, the beast symbolizes the Roman Empire, the deification of secular authority. According to others, he is the final, personal antichrist. According to still others, the beast symbolizes anti-Christian political power that came to expression in the Roman Empire of John's day, that continues in various ways down through the present era and that will become manifest in the political power of the final antichrist (see note on 14:8). The background seems to be Daniel's vision of the four great beasts (Da 7:2–7). For the interpreting angel's explanation of the beast, see 17:8–12 and notes on 17:9,10,12. *sea.* See 17:15. *ten horns.* See 17:12 and note. *blasphemous name.* Roman emperors tended to assume titles of deity. Domitian, e.g., was addressed as *Dominus et Deus noster* ("Our Lord and God").

and on each head a blasphemous name.[j]
2 The beast I saw resembled a leopard,[k] but
had feet like those of a bear[l] and a mouth
like that of a lion.[m] The dragon gave the
beast his power and his throne and great
authority.[n] 3 One of the heads of the beast
seemed to have had a fatal wound, but
the fatal wound had been healed.[o] The
whole world was filled with wonder[p] and
followed the beast. 4 People worshiped the
dragon because he had given authority
to the beast, and they also worshiped the
beast and asked, "Who is like[q] the beast?
Who can wage war against it?"
5 The beast was given a mouth to utter
proud words and blasphemies[r] and to exercise its authority for forty-two months.[s]
6 It opened its mouth to blaspheme God,
and to slander his name and his dwelling place and those who live in heaven.[t]
7 It was given power to wage war[u] against
God's holy people and to conquer them.
And it was given authority over every
tribe, people, language and nation.[v] 8 All
inhabitants of the earth[w] will worship the
beast — all whose names have not been
written in the Lamb's book of life,[x] the
Lamb[y] who was slain from the creation of
the world.[a][z]
9 Whoever has ears, let them hear.[a]

10 "If anyone is to go into captivity,
into captivity they will go.
If anyone is to be killed[b] with the
sword,
with the sword they will be killed."[c][b]

This calls for patient endurance and faithfulness[c] on the part of God's people.[d]

13:1 [j] Da 11:36; Rev 17:3 **13:2** [k] Da 7:6 [l] Da 7:5 [m] Da 7:4 [n] Rev 2:13; 16:10 **13:3** [o] ver 12,14 [p] Rev 17:8 **13:4** [q] Ex 15:11 **13:5** [r] Da 7:8, 11,20,25; 11:36; 2Th 2:4 [s] S Rev 11:2 **13:6** [t] Rev 12:12 **13:7** [u] Da 7:21; Rev 11:7 [v] Rev 5:9; 7:9; 10:11; 17:15 **13:8** [w] ver 12, 14; S Rev 3:10 [x] S Rev 20:12 [y] S Jn 1:29 [z] S Mt 25:34 **13:9** [a] S Rev 2:7 **13:10** [b] Jer 15:2; 43:11 [c] S Heb 6:12 [d] Rev 14:12 **13:11** [e] ver 1,2 [f] Rev 16:13 **13:12** [g] ver 4 [h] ver 14; Rev 19:20 [i] ver 15; Rev 14:9,11; 16:2; 19:20; 20:4 [j] ver 3 **13:13** [k] S Mt 24:24 [l] 1Ki 18:38; 2Ki 1:10; Lk 9:54; Rev 20:9 **13:14** [m] 2Th 2:9, 10 [n] Rev 12:9 [o] S Rev 3:10 [p] ver 3,12 **13:15** [q] S ver 12 [r] Da 3:3-6 **13:16** [s] S Rev 19:5 [t] Rev 7:3; 14:9; 20:4

The Beast out of the Earth

11 Then I saw a second beast, coming
out of the earth.[e] It had two horns like a
lamb, but it spoke like a dragon.[f] 12 It exercised all the authority[g] of the first beast
on its behalf,[h] and made the earth and
its inhabitants worship the first beast,[i]
whose fatal wound had been healed.[j]
13 And it performed great signs,[k] even
causing fire to come down from heaven[l]
to the earth in full view of the people.
14 Because of the signs[m] it was given power to perform on behalf of the first beast,
it deceived[n] the inhabitants of the earth.[o]
It ordered them to set up an image in hon-
or of the beast who was wounded by the
sword and yet lived.[p] 15 The second beast
was given power to give breath to the image of the first beast, so that the image
could speak and cause all who refused
to worship[q] the image to be killed.[r] 16 It
also forced all people, great and small,[s]
rich and poor, free and slave, to receive
a mark on their right hands or on their
foreheads,[t] 17 so that they could not buy
or sell unless they had the mark,[u] which
is the name of the beast or the number of
its name.[v]
18 This calls for wisdom.[w] Let the person
who has insight calculate the number of
the beast, for it is the number of a man.[d][x]
That number is 666.

[a] 8 Or *written from the creation of the world in the book of life belonging to the Lamb who was slain*
[b] 10 Some manuscripts *anyone kills*
[c] 10 Jer. 15:2
[d] 18 Or *is humanity's number*

13:17 [u] Rev 14:9 [v] ver 18; Rev 14:11; 15:2 **13:18** [w] Rev 17:9 [x] Rev 15:2; 21:17

13:2 *leopard ... bear ... lion.* John's beast combined characteristics of Daniel's four beasts (Da 7:4–6). *dragon.* See note on 12:3.
13:3 *fatal wound ... healed.* Emphasizes the tremendous recuperative power of the beast. *whole world was filled with wonder.* See 17:8 for a similar reaction.
13:5–6 Cf. Da 11:36–39 and note on 11:36.
13:5 *was given.* Four times in the Greek text of vv. 5–7 the passive "was given" occurs, either emphasizing the subordinate role of the beast (see vv. 2,4) or indicating that even the beast operates under the authority granted to it by God (the verbs in vv. 2,4 are active, while the verbs here are passive). *forty-two months.* See note on 11:2.
13:7 *wage war.* See 12:17; see also Da 7:7.
13:8 *book of life.* See note on 3:5; cf. 20:12,15. *Lamb who was slain.* See note on 5:6; cf. Isa 53:7; Jn 1:29,36. *slain from the creation of the world.* The death of Christ was a redemptive event decreed from eternity. See, however, NIV text note, which affirms that believers' names were written in the book of life from eternity (cf. 17:8).
13:11 *a second beast, coming out of the earth.* According to some he symbolizes religious power in the service of secular authorities. According to others he is the personal false prophet (see 16:13; 19:20; 20:10). *two horns like a lamb.* He attempts to appear gentle and harmless. *spoke like a dragon.* See Jesus' warning in Mt 7:15 about ravenous wolves that come in sheep's clothing.
13:12 *exercised all the authority of the first beast.* The trinity of evil is now complete. The beast from the earth is under the authority of the beast from the sea. The latter is subject to the dragon. Satan, secular power and religious compromise (or Satan, the antichrist and the false prophet) join against the cause of God: Father, Son and Holy Spirit.
13:13 *great signs.* See the warning in Dt 13:1–3; see also Mt 24:24; 2Th 2:9; cf. Rev 19:20. *fire ... from heaven.* See 1Ki 18:24–39.
13:14 *set up an image.* Cf. Da 3:1–11; 2Th 2:4.
13:15 *the image could speak.* Belief in statues that could speak is widely attested in ancient literature. Ventriloquism and other forms of deception were common.
13:16 *mark.* Whatever its origin — possibly the branding of slaves or enemy soldiers, the sealing and stamping of official documents or the sign of the cross on the forehead of a new Christian — the mark of the beast apparently symbolized allegiance to the demands of emperor worship. In the final days of the antichrist it will be the ultimate test of loyalty (cf. v. 17; 14:9,11; 15:2; 16:2; 19:20; 20:4). It imitates the sealing of the servants of God in ch. 7.
13:17 *buy or sell.* Economic boycott against all faithful believers. *number of its name.* In ancient times the letters of the alphabet served for numbers. Riddles using numerical equivalents for names were popular.
13:18 *666.* Various schemes for decoding these numbers result in such names as Euanthas, Lateinos and Nero Caesar.

The Lamb and the 144,000

14 Then I looked, and there before me
was the Lamb,[y] standing on Mount
Zion,[z] and with him 144,000[a] who had
his name and his Father's name[b] written
on their foreheads.[c] 2 And I heard a sound
from heaven like the roar of rushing waters[d] and like a loud peal of thunder.[e] The
sound I heard was like that of harpists
playing their harps.[f] 3 And they sang a new
song[g] before the throne and before the four
living creatures[h] and the elders.[i] No one
could learn the song except the 144,000[j]
who had been redeemed from the earth.
4 These are those who did not defile themselves with women, for they remained virgins.[k] They follow the Lamb wherever he
goes.[l] They were purchased from among
mankind[m] and offered as firstfruits[n] to God
and the Lamb. 5 No lie was found in their
mouths;[o] they are blameless.[p]

The Three Angels

6 Then I saw another angel flying in mid-
air,[q] and he had the eternal gospel to proclaim to those who live on the earth[r]—to
every nation, tribe, language and people.[s]
7 He said in a loud voice, "Fear God[t] and
give him glory,[u] because the hour of his
judgment has come. Worship him who
made[v] the heavens, the earth, the sea and
the springs of water."[w]
8 A second angel followed and said,
" 'Fallen! Fallen is Babylon the Great,'[a][x]
which made all the nations drink the maddening wine of her adulteries."[y]
9 A third angel followed them and said
in a loud voice: "If anyone worships the
beast[z] and its image[a] and receives its mark
on their forehead[b] or on their hand, 10 they,
too, will drink the wine of God's fury,[c]
which has been poured full strength into
the cup of his wrath.[d] They will be tormented with burning sulfur[e] in the presence of the holy angels and of the Lamb.
11 And the smoke of their torment will rise
for ever and ever.[f] There will be no rest
day or night[g] for those who worship the
beast and its image,[h] or for anyone who receives the mark of its name."[i] 12 This calls
for patient endurance[j] on the part of the
people of God[k] who keep his commands[l]
and remain faithful to Jesus.
13 Then I heard a voice from heaven say,
"Write this: Blessed are the dead who die
in the Lord[m] from now on."
"Yes," says the Spirit,[n] "they will rest
from their labor, for their deeds will follow them."

Harvesting the Earth and Trampling the Winepress

14 I looked, and there before me was a
white cloud,[o] and seated on the cloud was

a 8 Isaiah 21:9

14:1 y S Rev 5:6 z Ps 2:6; Heb 12:22 a ver 3; Rev 7:4 b Rev 3:12; 22:4 c S Rev 7:3 **14:2** d S Rev 1:15 e Rev 6:1 f Rev 5:8; 15:2 **14:3** g S Rev 5:9 h S Rev 4:6 i S Rev 4:4 j ver 1 **14:4** k 2Co 11:2; Rev 3:4 l Rev 7:17 m Rev 5:9 n Jer 2:3; Jas 1:18 **14:5** o Ps 32:2; Zep 3:13; Jn 1:47; 1Pe 2:22 p Eph 5:27 **14:6** q Rev 8:13; 19:17 r S Rev 3:10 s S Rev 13:7 **14:7** t Ps 34:9; Rev 15:4 u S Rev 11:13 v S Rev 10:6 w Rev 8:10; 16:4 **14:8** x Isa 21:9; Jer 51:8; Rev 16:19; 17:5; 18:2,10 y Rev 17:2,4; 18:3,9 **14:9** z S Rev 13:12 a Rev 13:14 b S Rev 13:16 **14:10** c Isa 51:17; Jer 25:15 d Jer 51:7; Rev 18:6 e S Rev 9:17 **14:11** f Isa 34:10; Rev 19:3 g Rev 4:8 h ver 9; S Rev 13:12 i Rev 13:17 **14:12** j S Heb 6:12 k Rev 13:10 l S Jn 14:15 **14:13** m 1Co 15:18; 1Th 4:16 n Rev 2:7; 22:17 **14:14** o Mt 17:5

Others take 666 as a symbol for a trinity of evil and imperfection—each digit falls short of the perfect number 7.

14:1 *Lamb.* See note on 5:6. *Mount Zion.* In the OT it was first the fortress of the pre-Israelite city of Jerusalem (2Sa 5:7), captured by David and established as his capital. Later it became a virtual synonym for Jerusalem. In Revelation, as in Heb 12:22–24, it is the heavenly Jerusalem, the eternal dwelling place of God and his people (cf. Gal 4:26). It comes down to the new earth in 21:2–3. *144,000.* See note on 7:4. *name.* Contrast 13:16–18.

14:2 *harps.* See note on 5:8.

14:3 *new song.* See note on 5:9. The theme is deliverance.

14:4 *not defile themselves with women.* Probably a symbolic description of believers who kept themselves from defiling relationships with the pagan world system (cf. note on Ex 34:15). *follow the Lamb.* As his disciples (see Mt 19:21; Mk 8:34). *firstfruits.* See Lev 23:9–14. The word is used figuratively in the NT for the first converts in an area (Ro 16:5) and the first to rise from the dead (1Co 15:20). In Revelation believers are considered as a choice offering to God and the Lamb.

14:5 *No lie.* Contrast Ro 1:25; 2Th 2:9–12 and note on 2:11; cf. Isa 53:9.

14:6 *eternal gospel.* The content of this "good news" is perhaps found in v. 7.

14:7 *him who made the heavens.* See Ex 20:11; Ps 146:6.

14:8 *Babylon the Great.* Ancient Babylon in Mesopotamia was the political, commercial and religious center of a world empire. It was noted for its luxury and moral decadence. The title "Babylon the Great" is taken from Da 4:30. According to some it is used in Revelation (e.g., here and in 16:19; 17:5; 18:2,10,21) for Rome as the center of opposition to God and his people. According to others it represents the whole political, economic and religious system of the world in general under the rule of the antichrist (see note on 13:1). According to still others it is to be understood as literal Babylon—rebuilt and restored. Babylon's fall is proclaimed in Isa 13:17,19–20; 21:9; Jer 50:39; 51:8. *maddening wine of her adulteries.* Here Babylon (Rome?) is pictured as a prostitute whose illicit relations are achieved by intoxication (see note on Ex 34:15).

14:10 *cup of his wrath.* In the OT God's wrath is commonly pictured as a cup of wine to be drunk (Ps 75:8; Isa 51:17; Jer 25:15). It is not the outworking of impersonal laws of retribution but the response of a righteous God to those who refuse his love and grace. *burning sulfur.* Sodom and Gomorrah were destroyed by a rain of burning sulfur (Ge 19:24). Ps 11:6 speaks of a similar fate for the wicked. The figure occurs elsewhere in the OT and the Apocrypha. It is used several times in the final chapters of Revelation (19:20; 20:10; 21:8).

14:11 *torment ... for ever and ever.* Revelation offers no support for the doctrine of the annihilation of the wicked (also compare 19:20 with 20:10).

14:13 *Blessed.* The second beatitude (see note on 1:3).

14:14 *seated on the cloud.* Cf. Mt 17:5; 24:30 and notes. *son of man.* See 1:13 and notes on Da 7:13; Mk 8:31. *crown of gold.* A victory wreath of gold. See note on 2:10 for the comparison between the victory crown and the royal crown. *sickle.* The Israelite sickle used for cutting grain was normally a flint or iron blade attached to a curved shaft of wood or bone.

one like a son of man[a][p] with a
crown[q] of gold on his head and a
sharp sickle in his hand. 15 Then
another angel came out of the
temple[r] and called in a loud
voice to him who was sitting on
the cloud, "Take your sickle[s] and
reap, because the time to reap
has come, for the harvest[t] of the
earth is ripe." 16 So he who was
seated on the cloud swung his
sickle over the earth, and the
earth was harvested.
17 Another angel came out of
the temple in heaven, and he
too had a sharp sickle.[u] 18 Still
another angel, who had charge
of the fire, came from the altar[v]
and called in a loud voice to
him who had the sharp sickle,
"Take your sharp sickle[w] and
gather the clusters of grapes
from the earth's vine, because
its grapes are ripe." 19 The angel
swung his sickle on the earth, gathered
its grapes and threw them into the great
winepress of God's wrath.[x] 20 They were
trampled in the winepress[y] outside the
city,[z] and blood[a] flowed out of the press,
rising as high as the horses' bridles for a
distance of 1,600 stadia.[b]

Seven Angels With Seven Plagues

15 I saw in heaven another great and
marvelous sign:[b] seven angels[c] with
the seven last plagues[d]—last, because with
them God's wrath is completed. 2 And I
saw what looked like a sea of glass[e] glowing with fire and, standing beside the sea,
those who had been victorious[f] over the
beast[g] and its image[h] and over the number
of its name.[i] They held harps[j] given them
by God 3 and sang the song of God's servant[k] Moses[l] and of the Lamb:[m]

"Great and marvelous are your
deeds,[n]
Lord God Almighty.[o]
Just and true are your ways,[p]
King of the nations.[c]
4 Who will not fear you, Lord,[q]
and bring glory to your name?[r]
For you alone are holy.
All nations will come
and worship before you,[s]
for your righteous acts[t] have been
revealed."[d]

A winepress at Neot Kedumim shows the flat surface where grapes would be trampled, and the storage units in the foreground into which the juice would flow. The winepress is used as a metaphor for the harvest of the earth in the end times (Rev 14:20).

Todd Bolen/www.BiblePlaces.com

14:14 [p]Da 7:13; S Rev 1:13 [q]S Rev 6:2 **14:15** [r]ver 17; Rev 11:19 [s]ver 18; Joel 3:13; Mk 4:29 [t]Jer 51:33 **14:17** [u]S ver 15 **14:18** [v]Rev 6:9; 8:5; 16:7 [w]S ver 15 **14:19** [x]Rev 19:15 **14:20** [y]ver 19; Isa 63:3; Joel 3:13; Rev 19:15 [z]Heb 13:12; Rev 11:8 [a]Ge 49:11; Dt 32:14 **15:1** [b]Rev 12:1, 3 [c]ver 6-8; Rev 16:1; 17:1; 21:9 [d]Lev 26:21; Rev 9:20 **15:2** [e]Rev 4:6 [f]Rev 12:11 [g]Rev 13:1 [h]Rev 13:14 [i]Rev 13:17 [j]Rev 5:8; 14:2 **15:3** [k]Jos 1:1 [l]Ex 15:1 [m]S Rev 5:9 [n]Ps 111:2 [o]S Rev 1:8 [p]Ps 145:17 **15:4** [q]Jer 10:7 [r]Ps 86:9 [s]Isa 66:23 [t]Rev 19:8

[a] *14* See Daniel 7:13. [b] *20* That is, about 180 miles or about 300 kilometers [c] *3* Some manuscripts *ages* [d] *3,4* Phrases in this song are drawn from Psalm 111:2,3; Deut. 32:4; Jer. 10:7; Psalms 86:9; 98:2.

14:15 *harvest of the earth.* Symbolizes in a general way the coming judgment (see v. 19; Mt 13:30,40–42). Some interpreters think it refers to the ingathering of the righteous at the return of Christ (but note the following verses).
14:18 *another angel, who had charge of the fire.* The angel of 8:3–5. Fire is commonly associated with judgment (see La 1:13 and note; Mt 18:8; Lk 9:54; 2Th 1:7). *sharp sickle.* The context suggests (in contrast to the sickle of v. 14) the smaller grape-knife with which the farmer cut the clusters of grapes from the vine.
14:19 *winepress.* A rock-hewn trough about eight feet square with a channel leading to a lower and smaller trough. Grapes were thrown into the upper vat and tramped with bare feet. The juice was collected in the lower vat (see note on Hag 2:16). At times mechanical pressure was added. The treading of grapes was a common OT figure for the execution of divine wrath (see Isa 63:3; La 1:15; Joel 3:13 and note). See photo above; see also photos, p. 820.
14:20 *outside the city.* Bloodshed would defile the city (see Joel 3:12–14; Zec 14:1–4; cf. Heb 13:12). *1,600 stadia.* See NIV text note; the approximate length of the Holy Land from north to south.
15:1–8 Introduces the last of the three sevenfold series of judgments—the bowls of wrath (see note on 8:2).
15:1 *God's wrath.* See note on 6:16.
15:2 *sea of glass.* See note on 4:6. *victorious over the beast.* Cf. the victory of God's people over the devil in 12:11. *number of its name.* See notes on 13:16–18. *harps.* See note on 5:8.
15:3–4 See Jer 10:7 and note.
15:3 *song of … Moses.* See Ex 15; Dt 32. Ex 15:1–18 was sung on Sabbath evenings in the synagogue to celebrate Israel's great deliverance from Egypt. *and of the Lamb.* The risen Lord triumphed over his enemies (including death and Hades, 1:18) in securing spiritual deliverance for his followers (cf. Ps 22). *Great and marvelous are your deeds.* See Ex 15:11; Ps 92:5; 111:2. *Almighty.* See note on 1:8. *King of the nations.* See Jer 10:10; cf. 1Ti 1:17.
15:4 Universal recognition of God is taught in both the OT (Ps 86:9; Isa 45:22–23; Mal 1:11) and the NT (Php 2:9–11).

5 After this I looked, and I saw in heaven
the temple[u]—that is, the tabernacle of the
covenant law[v]—and it was opened.[w] 6 Out
of the temple[x] came the seven angels with
the seven plagues.[y] They were dressed
in clean, shining linen[z] and wore golden
sashes around their chests.[a] 7 Then one of
the four living creatures[b] gave to the seven
angels[c] seven golden bowls filled with the
wrath of God, who lives for ever and ever.[d]
8 And the temple was filled with smoke[e]
from the glory of God and from his power,
and no one could enter the temple[f] until
the seven plagues of the seven angels were
completed.

The Seven Bowls of God's Wrath

16 Then I heard a loud voice from the
temple[g] saying to the seven angels,[h] "Go, pour out the seven bowls of
God's wrath on the earth."[i]
2 The first angel went and poured out his
bowl on the land,[j] and ugly, festering sores[k]
broke out on the people who had the mark
of the beast and worshiped its image.[l]
3 The second angel poured out his bowl
on the sea, and it turned into blood like
that of a dead person, and every living
thing in the sea died.[m]
4 The third angel poured out his bowl on
the rivers and springs of water,[n] and they
became blood.[o] 5 Then I heard the angel in
charge of the waters say:

"You are just in these judgments,[p]
O Holy One,[q]
you who are and who were;[r]
6 for they have shed the blood of your
holy people and your prophets,[s]
and you have given them blood to
drink[t] as they deserve."

7 And I heard the altar[u] respond:

"Yes, Lord God Almighty,[v]
true and just are your judgments."[w]

8 The fourth angel[x] poured out his bowl on
the sun,[y] and the sun was allowed to scorch
people with fire.[z] 9 They were seared by the
intense heat and they cursed the name of
God,[a] who had control over these plagues,
but they refused to repent[b] and glorify him.[c]
10 The fifth angel poured out his bowl
on the throne of the beast,[d] and its kingdom was plunged into darkness.[e] People gnawed their tongues in agony 11 and
cursed[f] the God of heaven[g] because of
their pains and their sores,[h] but they refused to repent of what they had done.[i]
12 The sixth angel poured out his bowl
on the great river Euphrates,[j] and its water
was dried up to prepare the way[k] for the
kings from the East.[l] 13 Then I saw three
impure spirits[m] that looked like frogs;[n]
they came out of the mouth of the dragon,[o] out of the mouth of the beast[p] and out
of the mouth of the false prophet.[q] 14 They
are demonic spirits[r] that perform signs,[s]
and they go out to the kings of the whole
world,[t] to gather them for the battle[u] on
the great day[v] of God Almighty.

15 "Look, I come like a thief![w] Blessed
is the one who stays awake[x] and remains clothed, so as not to go naked
and be shamefully exposed."[y]

16 Then they gathered the kings together[z]
to the place that in Hebrew[a] is called Armageddon.[b]

15:5 [u] Rev 11:19 [v] Ex 38:21; Nu 1:50 [w] S Mt 3:16 **15:6** [x] Rev 14:15 [y] S ver 1 [z] Eze 9:2; Da 10:5 [a] Rev 1:13 **15:7** [b] S Rev 4:6 [c] S ver 1 [d] S Rev 1:18 **15:8** [e] Isa 6:4 [f] Ex 40:34, 35; 1Ki 8:10, 11; 2Ch 5:13, 14 **16:1** [g] Rev 11:19 [h] S Rev 15:1 [i] ver 2-21; Ps 79:6; Zep 3:8 **16:2** [j] Rev 8:7 [k] ver 11; Ex 9:9-11; Dt 28:35 [l] Rev 13:15-17; 14:9 **16:3** [m] Ex 7:17-21; Rev 8:8, 9; Rev 11:6 **16:4** [n] Rev 8:10 [o] Ex 7:17-21 **16:5** [p] Rev 15:3 [q] Rev 15:4 [r] S Rev 1:4; Rev 6:10 **16:6** [s] Lk 11:49-51 [t] Isa 49:26; Rev 17:6; 18:24 **16:7** [u] Rev 6:9; 14:18 [v] S Rev 1:8 [w] Rev 15:3; 19:2 **16:8** [x] Rev 8:12 [y] Rev 6:12 [z] Rev 14:18 **16:9** [a] ver 11, 21 [b] S Rev 2:21 [c] S Rev 11:13 **16:10** [d] Rev 13:2 [e] Ex 10:21-23; Isa 8:22; Rev 8:12; 9:2 **16:11** [f] ver 9, 21 [g] Rev 11:13 [h] ver 2 [i] S Rev 2:21 **16:12** [j] S Rev 9:14 [k] Isa 11:15, 16 [l] Isa 41:2; 46:11 **16:13** [m] Rev 18:2 [n] Ex 8:6 [o] S Rev 12:3 [p] S Rev 13:1 [q] Rev 19:20; 20:10 **16:14** [r] 1Ti 4:1 [s] S Mt 24:24 [t] S Mt 24:14 [u] Rev 17:14; 19:19; 20:8 [v] S Rev 6:17 **16:15** [w] S Lk 12:39 [x] Lk 12:37 [y] Rev 3:18 **16:16** [z] ver 14 [a] Rev 9:11 [b] Jdg 5:19; 2Ki 23:29, 30; Zec 12:11

15:5 *tabernacle of the covenant law.* The dwelling place of God during the wilderness wandering of the Israelites (see Ex 40:34–35). It was so named because the ancient tent contained the two tablets of the covenant law brought down from Mount Sinai (Ex 32:15; 38:21; Dt 10:5).
15:6 *seven plagues.* The last series of plagues (see v. 1). *golden sashes.* Symbolic of royal and priestly functions.
15:7 *wrath of God.* Cf. 2Th 1:7–9.
15:8 *filled with smoke.* Cf. Ex 40:34; 1Ki 8:10–11; Eze 44:4. Smoke symbolizes the power and glory of God. *no one could enter the temple.* Both tabernacle and temple provide illustrations: with reference to Moses, Ex 40:35; with reference to the priests, 2Ch 5:14.
16:2 *land.* Compare the first four bowls (vv. 2–9) with the first four trumpets (8:7–12). *ugly, festering sores.* Cf. the boils and abscesses of the sixth Egyptian plague (Ex 9:9–11; see also Job 2:7–8,13). *mark of the beast.* See 13:16 and note.
16:4 *rivers and springs of water.* Cf. 8:10–11; see also Ps 78:44.
16:5 *you who are and who were.* See note on 11:17; cf. Ex 3:14.
16:6 *given them blood to drink.* Punishment is tailored to fit the crime (see Isa 49:26; cf. Pr 26:27; Ob 15; Gal 6:7 and notes).
16:7 *altar.* Personified.
16:8 *fire.* Often connected with judgment in Scripture (see note on 14:18; see also Dt 28:22; 1Co 3:13; 2Pe 3:7).
16:9 *refused to repent.* In 11:13 the nations were dazzled into homage by the great earthquake. Here they mock and blaspheme God's name (see 13:6).
16:10 *throne of the beast.* Cf. Satan's throne in 2:13. "Throne" occurs 42 times in Revelation. The other 40 references are to the throne of God. *darkness.* Cf. Ex 10:21–23. *gnawed their tongues.* Cf. the scene in 6:15–17.
16:11 *God of heaven.* Used in Da 2:44 of the sovereign God, who destroys the kingdoms of the world and establishes his own universal and eternal reign.
16:12 *Euphrates.* See note on Ge 15:18. *kings from the East.* Evidently Parthian rulers (17:15—18:24), to be distinguished from the "kings of the whole world" (v. 14) who wage the final war against Christ and the armies of heaven (19:11–21).
16:13 *frogs.* Cf. Ex 8:2,6. Lev 11:10 classifies the frog as an unclean animal. The imagery suggests the deceptive propaganda that will, in the last days, lead people to accept and support the cause of evil. *dragon … beast … false prophet.* The evil trinity.
16:14 *signs.* Cf. 13:13. *kings of the whole world.* See 6:15. *great day of God.* See 19:11–21 for this battle.
16:15 *Blessed.* The third beatitude (see note on 1:3).
16:16 *Armageddon.* Probably stands for Har Mageddon, "the

Aerial view of Megiddo. According to Revelation 16:16 the final battle between Christ and the antichrist will occur in "the place that in Hebrew is called Armageddon," which many believe to be Megiddo.

17 The seventh angel poured out his bowl
into the air,[c] and out of the temple[d] came a
loud voice[e] from the throne, saying, "It is
done!"[f] 18 Then there came flashes of lightning, rumblings, peals of thunder[g] and a
severe earthquake.[h] No earthquake like it
has ever occurred since mankind has been
on earth,[i] so tremendous was the quake.
19 The great city[j] split into three parts, and
the cities of the nations collapsed. God remembered[k] Babylon the Great[l] and gave
her the cup filled with the wine of the fury
of his wrath.[m] 20 Every island fled away
and the mountains could not be found.[n]
21 From the sky huge hailstones,[o] each
weighing about a hundred pounds,[a] fell
on people. And they cursed God[p] on account of the plague of hail,[q] because the
plague was so terrible.

Babylon, the Prostitute on the Beast

17 One of the seven angels[r] who had
the seven bowls[s] came and said to
me, "Come, I will show you the punishment[t] of the great prostitute,[u] who sits by
many waters.[v] 2 With her the kings of the
earth committed adultery, and the inhabitants of the earth were intoxicated with
the wine of her adulteries."[w]
3 Then the angel carried me away in
the Spirit[x] into a wilderness.[y] There I saw
a woman sitting on a scarlet[z] beast that
was covered with blasphemous names[a]
and had seven heads and ten horns.[b] 4 The
woman was dressed in purple and scarlet, and was glittering with gold, precious
stones and pearls.[c] She held a golden cup[d]
in her hand, filled with abominable things
and the filth of her adulteries.[e] 5 The name
written on her forehead was a mystery:[f]

BABYLON THE GREAT[g]
THE MOTHER OF PROSTITUTES[h]
AND OF THE ABOMINATIONS OF THE EARTH.

[a] *21* Or about 45 kilograms

16:17 [c] Eph 2:2 [d] Rev 14:15 [e] Rev 11:15 [f] Rev 21:6 **16:18** [g] S Rev 4:5 [h] S Rev 6:12 [i] Da 12:1; Mt 24:21 **16:19** [j] S Rev 17:18 [k] Rev 18:5 [l] S Rev 14:8 [m] Rev 14:10 **16:20** [n] S Rev 6:14 **16:21** [o] Eze 13:13; 38:22; Rev 8:7; 11:19 [p] ver 9, 11 [q] Ex 9:23-25 **17:1** [r] S Rev 15:1 [s] Rev 15:7 [t] Rev 16:19 [u] ver 5, 15, 16; Isa 23:17; Rev 19:2 [v] Jer 51:13 **17:2** [w] S Rev 14:8 **17:3** [x] S Rev 1:10 [y] Rev 12:6, 14 [z] Rev 18:12, 16 [a] Rev 13:1 [b] S Rev 12:3 **17:4** [c] Eze 28:13; Rev 18:16 [d] Jer 51:7; Rev 18:6 [e] ver 2; S Rev 14:8 **17:5** [f] ver 7 [g] S Rev 14:8 [h] ver 1, 2

mountain of Megiddo" (see note on Jdg 5:19). Many see no specific geographic reference in the designation and take it to be a symbol of the final overthrow of evil by God. Others understand it more literally. See photo above.
16:17 *temple.* See 15:5 – 6. *It is done!* The last of the seven bowls of divine wrath has now been poured out.
16:19 *great city.* See 11:8; 17:18 and notes.
16:21 *plague of hail.* Cf. Ex 9:18 – 26.
17:1 — 22:5 The destruction of Babylon (17:1 — 19:5) and the coming of the new creation and the new Jerusalem in which Eden is restored (21:1 — 22:5) — together with visionary depictions of decisive redemptive events that culminate in the latter state (19:6 — 20:15).
17:1 — 18:24 See note on 14:8.
17:1 *seven angels.* Cf. 15:1; 16. *great prostitute.* See v. 18 for the angel's own identification of this symbol. In v. 5 the prostitute is named "Babylon the Great." *sits by many waters.* See v. 15; Ps 137:1; Jer 51:13.
17:2 *wine of her adulteries.* See note on 14:8; cf. 18:3; Isa 23:17; Jer 51:7.
17:3 *in the Spirit.* In a state of spiritual ecstasy by the power of the Spirit (see notes on 1:10; 4:2; see also 21:10). *scarlet beast.* The beast that rose out of the sea in ch. 13. The color scarlet is similar to that of the red dragon in 12:3 (cf. v. 4). *blasphemous names.* See note on 13:1.
17:5 *BABYLON THE GREAT.* See note on 14:8.

[6]I saw that the woman was drunk with the blood of God's holy people,[i] the blood of those who bore testimony to Jesus.

When I saw her, I was greatly astonished. [7]Then the angel said to me: "Why are you astonished? I will explain to you the mystery[j] of the woman and of the beast she rides, which has the seven heads and ten horns.[k] [8]The beast, which you saw, once was, now is not, and yet will come up out of the Abyss[l] and go to its destruction.[m] The inhabitants of the earth[n] whose names have not been written in the book of life[o] from the creation of the world will be astonished[p] when they see the beast, because it once was, now is not, and yet will come.

[9]"This calls for a mind with wisdom.[q] The seven heads[r] are seven hills on which the woman sits. [10]They are also seven kings. Five have fallen, one is, the other has not yet come; but when he does come, he must remain for only a little while. [11]The beast who once was, and now is not,[s] is an eighth king. He belongs to the seven and is going to his destruction.

[12]"The ten horns[t] you saw are ten kings who have not yet received a kingdom, but who for one hour[u] will receive authority as kings along with the beast. [13]They have one purpose and will give their power and authority to the beast.[v] [14]They will wage war[w] against the Lamb, but the Lamb will triumph over[x] them because he is Lord of lords and King of kings[y]—and with him will be his called, chosen[z] and faithful followers."

[15]Then the angel said to me, "The waters[a] you saw, where the prostitute sits, are peoples, multitudes, nations and languages.[b] [16]The beast and the ten horns[c] you saw will hate the prostitute.[d] They will bring her to ruin[e] and leave her naked;[f] they will eat her flesh[g] and burn her with fire.[h] [17]For God has put it into their hearts[i] to accomplish his purpose by agreeing to hand over to the beast their royal authority,[j] until God's words are fulfilled.[k] [18]The woman you saw is the great city[l] that rules over the kings of the earth."

Lament Over Fallen Babylon

18 After this I saw another angel[m] coming down from heaven.[n] He had great authority, and the earth was illuminated by his splendor.[o] [2]With a mighty voice he shouted:

"'Fallen! Fallen is Babylon the Great!'[a][p]
She has become a dwelling for
demons
and a haunt for every impure spirit,[q]
a haunt for every unclean bird,
a haunt for every unclean and
detestable animal.[r]
[3]For all the nations have drunk
the maddening wine of her adulteries.[s]
The kings of the earth committed
adultery with her,[t]
and the merchants of the earth
grew rich[u] from her excessive
luxuries."[v]

Warning to Escape Babylon's Judgment

[4]Then I heard another voice from heaven say:

"'Come out of her, my people,'[b][w]
so that you will not share in her sins,
so that you will not receive any of
her plagues;[x]
[5]for her sins are piled up to heaven,[y]
and God has remembered[z] her crimes.

[a] *2* Isaiah 21:9 [b] *4* Jer. 51:45

17:6 [i]Rev 16:6; 18:24 **17:7** [j]ver 5 [k]ver 3; S Rev 12:3 **17:8** [l]S Lk 8:31 [m]Rev 13:10 [n]S Rev 3:10 [o]S Rev 20:12 [p]Rev 13:3 **17:9** [q]Rev 13:18 [r]ver 3 **17:11** [s]ver 8 **17:12** [t]S Rev 12:3 [u]Rev 18:10, 17,19 **17:13** [v]ver 17 **17:14** [w]S Rev 16:14 [x]S Jn 16:33 [y]S 1Ti 6:15 [z]Mt 22:14 **17:15** [a]ver 1; Isa 8:7; Jer 47:2 [b]S Rev 13:7 **17:16** [c]S Rev 12:3 [d]ver 1 [e]Rev 18:17,19 [f]Eze 16:37,39 [g]Rev 19:18 [h]Rev 18:8 **17:17** [i]2Co 8:16 [j]ver 13 [k]Jer 39:16; Rev 10:7 **17:18** [l]Rev 16:19; 18:10,18,19,21 **18:1** [m]Rev 17:1 [n]Rev 10:1; 20:1 [o]Eze 43:2 **18:2** [p]S Rev 14:8 [q]Rev 16:13 [r]Isa 13:21,22; 34:11,13-15; Jer 50:39; 51:37; Zep 2:14, 15 **18:3** [s]S Rev 14:8 [t]Rev 17:2 [u]ver 11,15,23; Eze 27:9-25 [v]ver 7,9 **18:4** [w]Isa 48:20; Jer 50:8; 51:6, 9,45; 2Co 6:17 [x]Ge 19:15 **18:5** [y]2Ch 28:9; Ezr 9:6; Jer 51:9 [z]Rev 16:19

17:6 *God's holy people ... those who bore testimony.* See 6:9. *God's holy people.* See note on 5:8.
17:7 *mystery.* See note on 10:7.
17:8 *once was, now is not, and yet will come.* An obvious imitation of the description of the Lamb (1:18; 2:8). Cf. the description of God in 1:4,8; 4:8. Here the phrase seems to mean that the beast appeared once, is not presently evident, but will in the future again make his presence known. Evil is persistent. *Abyss.* See note on 9:1. *go to its destruction.* Although evil is real and persistent, there is no uncertainty about its ultimate fate. *book of life.* See note on 3:5.
17:9 *seven hills.* It is perhaps significant that Rome began as a network of seven hill settlements on the east bank of the Tiber River (see map, p. 1883). Her designation as the city on seven hills is commonplace among Roman writers (e.g., Virgil, Martial, Cicero).
17:10 *seven kings.* That seven heads symbolize both seven hills and seven kings illustrates the fluidity of apocalyptic symbolism—unless the hills are figurative for royal (or political) power. *Five ... one ... the other.* Taken (1) as seven actual Roman emperors, (2) as seven secular empires or (3) symbolically as the power of the Roman Empire as a whole.
17:11 *now is not.* Cf. 13:3. *eighth king.* The antichrist, who plays the role of a king ("belongs to the seven") but is in reality part of the cosmic struggle between God and Satan.
17:12 *ten kings.* Since they are said to have not yet received royal power, they seem to belong to the future. They are likely symbolic and represent the totality of political powers that will align themselves with the beast. *one hour.* A short time.
17:14 *Lamb will triumph.* See 5:6 and note. *Lord of lords and King of kings.* Emphasizes the supreme sovereignty of the Lamb (cf. 5:6 and note;19:16; Dt 10:17; Ps 136:2–3; Da 2:47; 1Ti 6:15).
17:18 *great city.* Cf. 16:19; 17:1; see notes on 11:8; 14:8.
18:1 *great authority.* See note on 5:2. *earth was illuminated by his splendor.* Cf. Ex 34:29–35; Ps 104:2; Eze 43:1–5; 1Ti 6:16.
18:2 *Fallen is Babylon.* Cf. Isa 21:9; Jer 51:8; see notes on 11:8; 14:8.
18:3 *wine of her adulteries.* See note on 14:8.
18:4 *Come out of her.* A common prophetic warning (cf. Isa 52:11; Jer 51:45; 2Co 6:14—7:1).

6 Give back to her as she has given;
pay her back[a] double[b] for what she has done.
Pour her a double portion from her own cup.[c]
7 Give her as much torment and grief
as the glory and luxury she gave herself.[d]
In her heart she boasts,
'I sit enthroned as queen.
I am not a widow;[a]
I will never mourn.'[e]
8 Therefore in one day[f] her plagues will overtake her:
death, mourning and famine.
She will be consumed by fire,[g]
for mighty is the Lord God who judges her.

Threefold Woe Over Babylon's Fall

9 "When the kings of the earth who
committed adultery with her[h] and shared
her luxury[i] see the smoke of her burning,[j]
they will weep and mourn over her.[k] 10 Terrified at her torment, they will stand far
off[l] and cry:

" 'Woe! Woe to you, great city,[m]
you mighty city of Babylon!
In one hour[n] your doom has come!'

11 "The merchants[o] of the earth will weep
and mourn[p] over her because no one buys
their cargoes anymore[q]— 12 cargoes of gold,
silver, precious stones and pearls; fine lin-
en, purple, silk and scarlet cloth; every sort
of citron wood, and articles of every kind
made of ivory, costly wood, bronze, iron
and marble;[r] 13 cargoes of cinnamon and
spice, of incense, myrrh and frankincense,
of wine and olive oil, of fine flour and
wheat; cattle and sheep; horses and carriages; and human beings sold as slaves.[s]
14 "They will say, 'The fruit you longed
for is gone from you. All your luxury and
splendor have vanished, never to be recovered.' 15 The merchants who sold these
things and gained their wealth from her[t]
will stand far off,[u] terrified at her torment.
They will weep and mourn[v] 16 and cry out:

" 'Woe! Woe to you, great city,[w]
dressed in fine linen, purple and scarlet,
and glittering with gold, precious stones and pearls![x]
17 In one hour[y] such great wealth has been brought to ruin!'[z]

"Every sea captain, and all who travel by ship, the sailors, and all who earn
their living from the sea,[a] will stand far
off.[b] 18 When they see the smoke of her
burning,[c] they will exclaim, 'Was there
ever a city like this great city[d]?'[e] 19 They
will throw dust on their heads,[f] and with
weeping and mourning[g] cry out:

" 'Woe! Woe to you, great city,[h]
where all who had ships on the sea
became rich through her wealth!
In one hour she has been brought to ruin!'[i]

20 "Rejoice over her, you heavens![j]
Rejoice, you people of God!
Rejoice, apostles and prophets!
For God has judged her
with the judgment she imposed on you."[k]

The Finality of Babylon's Doom

21 Then a mighty angel[l] picked up a
boulder the size of a large millstone and
threw it into the sea,[m] and said:

"With such violence
the great city[n] of Babylon will be thrown down,
never to be found again.
22 The music of harpists and musicians,
pipers and trumpeters,
will never be heard in you again.[o]
No worker of any trade
will ever be found in you again.
The sound of a millstone
will never be heard in you again.[p]
23 The light of a lamp
will never shine in you again.
The voice of bridegroom and bride
will never be heard in you again.[q]

[a] 7 See Isaiah 47:7,8.

18:6 [a] Ps 137:8; Jer 50:15, 29 [b] Isa 40:2 [c] Rev 14:10; 16:19; 17:4 **18:7** [d] Eze 28:2-8 [e] Ps 10:6; Isa 47:7,8; Zep 2:15 **18:8** [f] ver 10; Isa 9:14; 47:9; Jer 50:31,32 [g] Rev 17:16 **18:9** [h] ver 3; Rev 14:8; 17:2,4 [i] ver 3,7 [j] ver 18; Rev 14:11; 19:3 [k] Jer 51:8; Eze 26:17,18 **18:10** [l] ver 15, 17 [m] ver 16, 19 [n] ver 17; Rev 17:12 **18:11** [o] Eze 27:27 [p] ver 15,19; Eze 27:31 [q] S ver 3 **18:12** [r] Eze 27:12-22; Rev 17:4 **18:13** [s] Eze 27:13; 1Ti 1:10 **18:15** [t] S ver 3 [u] ver 10,17 [v] ver 11,19; Eze 27:31 **18:16** [w] ver 10, 19 [x] Rev 17:4 **18:17** [y] ver 10; Rev 17:12 [z] Rev 17:16 [a] Eze 27:28-30 [b] ver 10,15 **18:18** [c] ver 9; Rev 19:3 [d] S Rev 17:18 [e] Eze 27:32; Rev 13:4 **18:19** [f] Jos 7:6; La 2:10; Eze 27:30 [g] ver 11,15; Eze 27:31 [h] ver 10,16; Rev 17:18 [i] Rev 17:16 **18:20** [j] Jer 51:48; S Rev 12:12 [k] Rev 19:2 **18:21** [l] Rev 5:2; 10:1 [m] Jer 51:63 [n] S Rev 17:18 **18:22** [o] Isa 24:8; Eze 26:13 [p] Jer 25:10 **18:23** [q] Jer 7:34; 16:9; 25:10

18:6 *double.* In full, sufficiently (see note on Isa 40:2). *her own cup.* See 17:4.
18:7 *I am not a widow.* A claim that the men of Babylon have not died on battlefields.
18:9–20 Three groups lament: (1) kings (v. 9), (2) merchants (v. 11) and (3) seamen (v. 17). The passage is modeled after Ezekiel's lament over Tyre (Eze 27). Of the 29 commodities in vv. 12–13 there are 15 also listed in Eze 27:12–22.
18:9 *kings … weep and mourn over her.* Probably because of their own great financial loss (see v. 11).
18:10 *one hour.* Repeated in vv. 17,19; cf. note on 17:12.
18:12 *purple.* An expensive dye since it must be extracted a drop at a time from the murex shellfish. *citron wood.* An expensive dark wood from north Africa—used for inlay work in costly furniture. *marble.* Used to decorate public buildings and the homes of the very rich.
18:13 *myrrh and frankincense.* Brought by the Magi as gifts for the infant Jesus (Mt 2:11).
18:17 *sea captain.* The pilot of the ship rather than the owner. Both are mentioned in Ac 27:11.
18:19 *throw dust on their heads.* An act of sorrow and dismay (see Eze 27:30). *In one hour.* See vv. 10,17.
18:20 *God has judged her with the judgment she imposed on you.* The scales of justice will be balanced (see note on Ob 15).
18:21 *large millstone.* Similar to the large millstone of Mk 9:42, which was actually a "donkey millstone" (one large enough to require a donkey to turn it).

Your merchants were the world's
important people.[r]
By your magic spell[s] all the nations
were led astray.
24 In her was found the blood of prophets
and of God's holy people,[t]
of all who have been slaughtered on
the earth."[u]

Threefold Hallelujah Over Babylon's Fall

19 After this I heard what sounded like the roar of a great multitude[v] in heaven shouting:

"Hallelujah![w]
Salvation[x] and glory and power[y] belong
to our God,
2 for true and just are his judgments.[z]
He has condemned the great
prostitute[a]
who corrupted the earth by her
adulteries.
He has avenged on her the blood of his
servants."[b]

3 And again they shouted:

"Hallelujah![c]
The smoke from her goes up for ever
and ever."[d]

4 The twenty-four elders[e] and the four living creatures[f] fell down[g] and worshiped God, who was seated on the throne. And they cried:

"Amen, Hallelujah!"[h]

5 Then a voice came from the throne, saying:

"Praise our God,
all you his servants,[i]
you who fear him,
both great and small!"[j]

18:23 [r]ver 3; Isa 23:8 [s]Na 3:4 **18:24** [t]Rev 16:6; 17:6 [u]Jer 51:49; Mt 23:35 **19:1** [v]ver 6; Rev 11:15 [w]ver 3,4,6 [x]Rev 7:10; 12:10 [y]Rev 4:11; 7:12 **19:2** [z]Rev 16:7 [a]S Rev 17:1 [b]S Rev 6:10 **19:3** [c]ver 1,4,6 [d]Isa 34:10; Rev 14:11 **19:4** [e]S Rev 4:4 [f]S Rev 4:6 [g]S Rev 4:10 [h]ver 1,3,6 **19:5** [i]Ps 134:1 [j]ver 18; Ps 115:13; Rev 11:18; 13:16; 20:12 **19:6** [k]ver 1; Rev 11:15 [l]S Rev 1:15 [m]ver 1,3,4 [n]S Rev 1:8 [o]Rev 11:15 **19:7** [p]S Rev 11:13 [q]ver 9; Mt 22:2; 25:10; Eph 5:32 [r]Rev 21:2,9; 22:17 **19:8** [s]ver 14; Rev 15:6 [t]Isa 61:10; Eze 44:17; Zec 3:4; Rev 15:4 **19:9** [u]ver 10 [v]Rev 1:19 [w]Lk 14:15 [x]Rev 21:5; 22:6 **19:10** [y]Rev 22:8 [z]Ac 10:25, 26; Rev 22:9 [a]S Rev 1:2 **19:11** [b]S Mt 3:16 [c]ver 19, 21; Rev 6:2 [d]Rev 3:14 [e]Ex 15:3; Ps 96:13;

6 Then I heard what sounded like a great multitude,[k] like the roar of rushing waters[l] and like loud peals of thunder, shouting:

"Hallelujah![m]
For our Lord God Almighty[n] reigns.[o]
7 Let us rejoice and be glad
and give him glory![p]
For the wedding of the Lamb[q] has come,
and his bride[r] has made herself
ready.
8 Fine linen,[s] bright and clean,
was given her to wear."

(Fine linen stands for the righteous acts[t] of God's holy people.)

9 Then the angel said to me,[u] "Write this:[v] Blessed are those who are invited to the wedding supper of the Lamb!"[w] And he added, "These are the true words of God."[x]
10 At this I fell at his feet to worship
him.[y] But he said to me, "Don't do that!
I am a fellow servant with you and with
your brothers and sisters who hold to the
testimony of Jesus. Worship God![z] For it is
the Spirit of prophecy who bears testimony to Jesus."[a]

The Heavenly Warrior Defeats the Beast

11 I saw heaven standing open[b] and there
before me was a white horse, whose rider[c] is called Faithful and True.[d] With justice he judges and wages war.[e]
12 His eyes
are like blazing fire,[f] and on his head are
many crowns.[g] He has a name written on
him[h] that no one knows but he himself.[i]
13 He is dressed in a robe dipped in blood,[j]
and his name is the Word of God.[k]
14 The
armies of heaven were following him,
riding on white horses and dressed in fine

Isa 11:4 **19:12** [f]S Rev 1:14 [g]Rev 6:2; 12:3 [h]ver 16 [i]S Rev 2:17 **19:13** [j]Isa 63:2,3 [k]Jn 1:1

18:24 *blood of prophets.* See 6:10; 17:6; 19:2; cf. Eze 24:7. *prophets ... God's holy people.* Probably not two distinct groups: The first may be a special class within the second (cf. the order in 16:6). *God's holy people.* See note on Col 1:4.

19:1 *great multitude.* See note on 7:9. *Hallelujah!* Occurs four times in vv. 1–6 but nowhere else in the NT. It is derived from two Hebrew words meaning "Praise the LORD" (see NIV text note on Ps 135:1).

19:2 *great prostitute.* See 17:1,5,18; see also 14:8 and note. *avenged on her the blood of his servants.* See the prayer in 6:10; cf. 16:6; 18:20.

19:3 *Hallelujah!* Although this word of praise to the Lord occurs four times (vv. 1,3,4,6; see note on v. 1), the NIV sectional heading above ch. 19 ("Threefold Hallelujah") is still correct because this one in v. 3 actually goes with the one in v. 1 (note "again" here) and is uttered by the same group (identified and introduced as a "great multitude"). The other two instances are introduced in vv. 4,6. Cf. the "Threefold Woe" in 18:10,16,19.

19:4 *twenty-four elders and the four living creatures.* See notes on 4:4,6.

19:7 *wedding of the Lamb.* The imagery of a wedding to express the intimate relationship between God and his people ("his bride") has its roots in the prophetic literature of the OT (e.g., Isa 54:5–7; Hos 2:19). Cf. the NT usage (Mt 22:2–14; see 2Co 11:2 and note; Eph 5:25–27,32).

19:9 *Blessed.* The fourth beatitude (see note on 1:3). *wedding supper.* See Mt 8:11; Lk 14:15; 22:16 and notes.

19:10 *fell at his feet.* See note on 1:17; cf. Ac 10:25. *Spirit of prophecy.* Probably means that the message attested by Jesus is that which the Spirit takes and puts in the mouth of Christian prophets.

19:11 *white horse.* Probably not the white horse of 6:2 (see note there). The context here indicates that the rider is Christ returning as Warrior-Messiah-King.

19:12 *name written.* A secret name whose meaning is veiled from all created beings.

19:13 *robe dipped in blood.* Either the blood of the enemy shed in conflict (cf. 14:14–20; Isa 63:1–3) or the blood of Christ shed to atone for sin.

19:14 *armies of heaven.* Angelic beings (cf. Dt 33:2; Ps 68:17); probably also believers (cf. 17:14).

linen,[l] white[m] and clean. 15 Coming out of his mouth is a sharp sword[n] with which to strike down[o] the nations. "He will rule them with an iron scepter."[a][p] He treads the winepress[q] of the fury of the wrath of God Almighty. 16 On his robe and on his thigh he has this name written:[r]

KING OF KINGS AND LORD OF LORDS.[s]

17 And I saw an angel standing in the sun, who cried in a loud voice to all the birds[t] flying in midair,[u] "Come,[v] gather together for the great supper of God,[w] 18 so that you may eat the flesh of kings, generals, and the mighty, of horses and their riders, and the flesh of all people,[x] free and slave,[y] great and small."[z]

19 Then I saw the beast[a] and the kings of the earth[b] and their armies gathered together to wage war against the rider on the horse[c] and his army. 20 But the beast was captured, and with it the false prophet[d] who had performed the signs[e] on its behalf.[f] With these signs he had deluded[g] those who had received the mark of the beast[h] and worshiped its image.[i] The two of them were thrown alive into the fiery lake[j] of burning sulfur.[k] 21 The rest were killed with the sword[l] coming out of the mouth of the rider on the horse,[m] and all the birds[n] gorged themselves on their flesh.

The Thousand Years

20 And I saw an angel coming down out of heaven,[o] having the key[p] to the Abyss[q] and holding in his hand a great chain. 2 He seized the dragon, that ancient serpent, who is the devil, or Satan,[r] and bound him for a thousand years.[s] 3 He threw him into the Abyss,[t] and locked and sealed[u] it over him, to keep him from deceiving the nations[v] anymore until the thousand years were ended. After that, he must be set free for a short time.

4 I saw thrones[w] on which were seated those who had been given authority to judge.[x] And I saw the souls of those who had been beheaded[y] because of their testimony about Jesus[z] and because of the word of God.[a] They[b] had not worshiped the beast[b] or its image and had not received its mark on their foreheads or their hands.[c] They came to life and reigned[d] with Christ a thousand years. 5 (The rest of the dead did not come to life until the thousand years were ended.) This is the first resurrection.[e] 6 Blessed[f] and holy are those who share in the first resurrection. The second death[g] has no power over them, but they will be priests[h] of God and of Christ and will reign with him[i] for a thousand years.

The Judgment of Satan

7 When the thousand years are over,[j] Satan will be released from his prison 8 and will go out to deceive the nations[k] in the

[a] 15 Psalm 2:9 [b] 4 Or *God; I also saw those who*

19:14 [l] ver 8 [m] S Rev 3:4 **19:15** [n] ver 21; S Rev 1:16 [o] Isa 11:4; 2Th 2:8 [p] Ps 2:9; Rev 2:27; 12:5 [q] S Rev 14:20 **19:16** [r] ver 12 [s] S 1Ti 6:15 **19:17** [t] ver 21 [u] Rev 8:13; 14:6 [v] Jer 12:9; Eze 39:17 [w] Isa 34:6; Jer 46:10 **19:18** [x] Eze 39:18-20 [y] Rev 6:15 [z] S ver 5 **19:19** [a] S Rev 13:1 [b] Rev 16:14,16 [c] ver 11,21 **19:20** [d] Rev 16:13 [e] S Mt 24:24 [f] Rev 13:12 [g] Rev 13:14 [h] Rev 13:16 [i] Rev 13:15 [j] Da 7:11; Rev 20:10, 14,15; 21:8 [k] S Rev 9:17 **19:21** [l] ver 15; S Rev 1:16 [m] ver 11,19 [n] ver 17 **20:1** [o] Rev 10:1; 18:1 [p] Rev 1:18 [q] S Lk 8:31 **20:2** [r] S Mt 4:10 [s] Isa 24:22; S 2Pe 2:4 **20:3** [t] ver 1 [u] Da 6:17; Mt 27:66 [v] ver 8, 10; Rev 12:9 **20:4** [w] Da 7:9 [x] Mt 19:28; Rev 3:21 [y] Rev 6:9 [z] S Rev 1:2 [a] S Heb 4:12 [b] S Rev 13:12 [c] S Rev 13:16 [d] ver 6; Rev 22:5 **20:5** [e] ver 6; Lk 14:14; Php 3:11; 1Th 4:16 **20:6** [f] Rev 14:13 [g] S Rev 2:11 [h] S 1Pe 2:5 [i] ver 4; Rev 22:5 **20:7** [j] ver 2 **20:8** [k] ver 3,10; Rev 12:9

19:15 *sharp sword.* See note on 1:16. *iron scepter.* See note on 2:27. *treads the winepress of the ... wrath of God.* Cf. Isa 63:3 and note. *winepress.* See note on 14:19.
19:16 *KING OF KINGS.* See note on 17:14.
19:17 *great supper of God.* A grim contrast to the "wedding supper of the Lamb" (v. 9; cf. Eze 39:17–20).
19:19 See 16:16 and note.
19:20 *beast ... false prophet.* See notes on 13:1,11. *fiery lake of burning sulfur.* See 20:10,14–15; 21:8. Punishment by fire is prominent in both Biblical (see, e.g., note on La 1:13) and non-Biblical (Jewish) writings (e.g., 1 Enoch 54:1). Although the designation *gehenna* is not used here, this is what John refers to (see note on Mt 5:22). Originally the site of a shrine where human sacrifices were offered (2Ki 16:3; 23:10; Jer 7:31), it came to be equated with the "hell" of final judgment in apocalyptic literature.
19:21 *birds gorged themselves.* The "great supper of God" of vv. 17–18.
20:1—22:21 These last three chapters reflect many of the subjects and themes of the first three chapters of Genesis (see Introduction to Genesis: Literary Features).
20:1 *Abyss.* See note on 9:1.
20:2 *dragon.* See note on 12:3. *ancient serpent.* See 12:15; Ge 3:1–5. *thousand years.* The millennium (from the Latin *mille,* "thousand," and *annus,* "year"). It is taken literally by some as 1,000 actual years, while others interpret it metaphorically as a long but undetermined period of time. There are three basic approaches to the subject of the millennium: (1) Amillennialism: The millennium describes the present reign of Christ in heaven over his realm (Mt 28:18–20), along with the souls of deceased believers, and in the hearts and lives of living believers on earth (see also note on 1Co 15:25). The present form of God's kingdom will be followed by Christ's return, the general resurrection, the final judgment and Christ's continuing reign over the perfect kingdom on the new earth in the eternal state. (2) Premillennialism: The present form of God's kingdom is moving toward a grand climax when Christ will return, the first resurrection will occur and his kingdom will find expression in a literal, visible reign of peace and righteousness on the earth in space-time history. After the final resurrection, the last judgment and the renewal of the heavens and the earth, this future, temporal kingdom will merge into the eternal kingdom, and the Lord will reign forever on the new earth. (3) Postmillennialism: The world will eventually be Christianized through the preaching of the gospel, resulting in a long period of peace and prosperity called the millennium. This future period will close with Christ's second coming, the resurrection of the dead, the final judgment and the eternal state.
20:3 *free for a short time.* See vv. 7–10.
20:4 *souls of those who had been beheaded.* See 6:9–11. *its mark.* See note on 13:16. *came to life.* The "first resurrection" (v. 5).
20:5 *rest of the dead.* Either the wicked or everyone except the martyrs (see v. 4).
20:6 *Blessed.* The fifth beatitude (see note on 1:3). *second death.* Defined in v. 14 as the "lake of fire" (cf. 21:8).
20:7 *thousand years.* See note on v. 2.
20:8 *Gog and Magog.* Symbolize the nations of the world as

four corners of the earth[l]—Gog and Magog[m]—and to gather them for battle.[n] In number they are like the sand on the seashore.[o] 9 They marched across the breadth of the earth and surrounded[p] the camp of God's people, the city he loves.[q] But fire came down from heaven[r] and devoured them. 10 And the devil, who deceived them,[s] was thrown into the lake of burning sulfur,[t] where the beast[u] and the false prophet[v] had been thrown. They will be tormented day and night for ever and ever.[w]

The Judgment of the Dead

11 Then I saw a great white throne[x] and him who was seated on it. The earth and the heavens fled from his presence,[y] and there was no place for them. 12 And I saw the dead, great and small,[z] standing before the throne, and books were opened.[a] Another book was opened, which is the book of life.[b] The dead were judged[c] according to what they had done[d] as recorded in the books. 13 The sea gave up the dead that were in it, and death and Hades[e] gave up the dead[f] that were in them, and each person was judged according to what they had done.[g] 14 Then death[h] and Hades[i] were thrown into the lake of fire.[j] The lake of fire is the second death.[k] 15 Anyone whose name was not found written in the book of life[l] was thrown into the lake of fire.

A New Heaven and a New Earth

21 Then I saw "a new heaven and a new earth,"[a][m] for the first heaven and the first earth had passed away,[n] and there was no longer any sea. 2 I saw the Holy City,[o] the new Jerusalem, coming down out of heaven from God,[p] prepared as a bride[q] beautifully dressed for her husband. 3 And I heard a loud voice from the throne saying, "Look! God's dwelling place is now among the people, and he will dwell with them.[r] They will be his people, and God himself will be with them and be their God.[s] 4 'He will wipe every tear from their eyes.[t] There will be no more death'[b][u] or mourning or crying or pain,[v] for the old order of things has passed away."[w]

5 He who was seated on the throne[x] said, "I am making everything new!"[y] Then he said, "Write this down, for these words are trustworthy and true."[z]

6 He said to me: "It is done.[a] I am the Alpha and the Omega,[b] the Beginning and the End. To the thirsty I will give water without cost[c] from the spring of the water of life.[d] 7 Those who are victorious[e] will inherit all this, and I will be their God and they will be my children.[f] 8 But the cowardly, the unbelieving, the vile, the murderers, the sexually immoral, those who practice magic arts, the idolaters and all liars[g]—they will be consigned to the fiery lake of burning sulfur.[h] This is the second death."[i]

The New Jerusalem, the Bride of the Lamb

9 One of the seven angels who had the seven bowls full of the seven last plagues[j] came and said to me, "Come, I will show you the bride,[k] the wife of the Lamb." 10 And he carried me away[l] in the Spirit[m] to a mountain great and high, and showed me the Holy City, Jerusalem, coming down out of heaven from God.[n] 11 It shone with the glory of God,[o] and its brilliance was like that of a very precious jewel, like a jasper,[p] clear as crystal.[q] 12 It had a great,

[a] 1 Isaiah 65:17 [b] 4 Isaiah 25:8

20:8 [l] Isa 11:12; Eze 7:2; Rev 7:1 [m] Eze 38:2; 39:1 [n] S Rev 16:14 [o] Eze 38:9, 15; Heb 11:12 **20:9** [p] Eze 38:9, 16 [q] Ps 87:2 [r] Eze 38:22; 39:6; S Rev 13:13 **20:10** [s] ver 3, 8; Rev 12:9; 19:20 [t] S Rev 9:17 [u] Rev 16:13 [v] Rev 16:13 [w] Rev 14:10, 11 **20:11** [x] S Rev 4:2 [y] S Rev 6:14 **20:12** [z] S Rev 19:5 [a] Da 7:10 [b] ver 15; Ex 32:32; Dt 29:20; Da 12:1; Mal 3:16; Lk 10:20; Rev 3:5; 21:27 [c] Rev 11:18 [d] Jer 17:10; S Mt 16:27 **20:13** [e] Rev 1:18; 6:8 [f] Isa 26:19 [g] S Mt 16:27 **20:14** [h] 1Co 15:26 [i] ver 13 [j] S Rev 19:20 [k] S Rev 2:11 **20:15** [l] S ver 12 **21:1** [m] S 2Pe 3:13 [n] S Rev 6:14 **21:2** [o] ver 10; Ne 11:18; Isa 52:1; Rev 11:2; 22:19 [p] ver 10; Heb 11:10; 12:22; Rev 3:12 [q] S Rev 19:7 **21:3** [r] Ex 25:8; 2Ch 6:18; Eze 48:35; Zec 2:10 [s] S 2Co 6:16 **21:4** [t] S Rev 7:17 [u] Isa 25:8; 1Co 15:26; Rev 20:14 [v] Isa 35:10; 65:19 [w] S 2Co 5:17

21:5 [x] Rev 4:9; 20:11 [y] ver 4 [z] Rev 19:9; 22:6 **21:6** [a] Rev 16:17 [b] Rev 1:8; 22:13 [c] Isa 55:1 [d] S Jn 4:10 **21:7** [e] S Jn 16:33 [f] ver 3; 2Sa 7:14; 2Co 6:16; S Ro 8:14 **21:8** [g] ver 27; Ps 5:6; 1Co 6:9; Heb 12:14; Rev 22:15 [h] S Rev 9:17 [i] S Rev 2:11 **21:9** [j] S Rev 15:1, 6, 7 [k] S Rev 19:7 **21:10** [l] Eze 40:2; Rev 17:3 [m] S Rev 1:10 [n] S ver 2 **21:11** [o] ver 23; Isa 60:1, 2; Eze 43:2; Rev 15:8; 22:5 [p] ver 18, 19; Rev 4:3 [q] Rev 4:6

---

they band together for a final assault on God. The OT background is Eze 38–39.

20:10 *tormented day and night.* See note on 14:11; cf. 14:10.

20:12 *book of life.* See note on 3:5. *judged according to what they had done.* The principle of judgment on the basis of works is taught in Ps 62:12; Jer 17:10; Ro 2:6; 1Pe 1:17 and elsewhere.

20:13 *death and Hades.* See 6:8 and note.

20:14–15 *lake of fire.* See note on 19:20.

21:2—22:5 The "Holy City" combines elements of Jerusalem, the temple and the Garden of Eden (see Introduction to Genesis: Literary Features).

21:2 *new Jerusalem.* See "the Jerusalem that is above" (Gal 4:26; see also note there). *bride.* See note on 19:7.

21:3 *God's dwelling place.* See Lev 26:11–12; Eze 37:27; 2Co 6:16; Eph 2:21–22. *among ... with ... with.* The most eloquent culmination of the Immanuel theme (see 2Co 13:14 and note). *his people ... their God.* The deepest expression of the intimate fellowship that God had promised to those in covenant relationship with him (see Zec 8:8 and note).

21:4 *wipe every tear.* See 7:17; Isa 25:8.

21:6 *the Alpha and the Omega.* See note on 1:8. *water of life.* Cf. Ps 36:9; Jn 4:10,14 and notes.

21:7 *victorious.* Cf. the emphasis on victory in the seven letters (2:7,11,17,26; 3:5,12,21).

21:8 *cowardly ... liars.* See note on Ro 1:29–31. "Cowardly" heads the list because it stands opposed to the faithfulness of those "who are victorious" (v. 7). *magic arts.* Cf. Ac 19:19. The magical tradition in ancient times called for the mixing of various herbs to ward off evil. *fiery lake of burning sulfur.* See note on 19:20.

21:9 *seven last plagues.* See 15:1.

21:10 *in the Spirit.* See notes on 1:10; 4:2; 17:3.

21:12 *twelve gates.* See Eze 48:30–35. The number 12 probably emphasizes the continuity of the NT church and the OT people of God. See v. 14, where the 12 foundations bear the names of the 12 apostles; see also 4:4 and note.

high wall with twelve gates,[r] and with
twelve angels at the gates. On the gates
were written the names of the twelve tribes
of Israel.[s] 13There were three gates on the
east, three on the north, three on the south
and three on the west. 14The wall of the
city had twelve foundations,[t] and on them
were the names of the twelve apostles[u] of
the Lamb.
15The angel who talked with me had a
measuring rod[v] of gold to measure the city,
its gates[w] and its walls. 16The city was laid
out like a square, as long as it was wide.
He measured the city with the rod and
found it to be 12,000 stadia[a] in length, and
as wide and high as it is long. 17The angel
measured the wall using human[x] measurement, and it was 144 cubits[b] thick.[c] 18The
wall was made of jasper,[y] and the city of
pure gold, as pure as glass.[z] 19The foundations of the city walls were decorated
with every kind of precious stone.[a] The
first foundation was jasper,[b] the second
sapphire, the third agate, the fourth emerald, 20the fifth onyx, the sixth ruby,[c] the
seventh chrysolite, the eighth beryl, the
ninth topaz, the tenth turquoise, the eleventh jacinth, and the twelfth amethyst.[d]
21The twelve gates[d] were twelve pearls,[e]
each gate made of a single pearl. The great
street of the city was of gold, as pure as
transparent glass.[f]
22I did not see a temple[g] in the city, because the Lord God Almighty[h] and the
Lamb[i] are its temple. 23The city does not
need the sun or the moon to shine on it,
for the glory of God[j] gives it light,[k] and the
Lamb[l] is its lamp. 24The nations will walk
by its light, and the kings of the earth will
bring their splendor into it.[m] 25On no day
will its gates[n] ever be shut,[o] for there will
be no night there.[p] 26The glory and hon-
or of the nations will be brought into it.[q]
27Nothing impure will ever enter it, nor
will anyone who does what is shameful or
deceitful,[r] but only those whose names are
written in the Lamb's book of life.[s]

21:12 [r]ver 15,21, 25; Rev 22:14 [s]Eze 48:30-34 **21:14** [t]S Eph 2:20; Heb 11:10 [u]Ac 1:26; Eph 2:20 **21:15** [v]Eze 40:3; Rev 11:1 [w]S ver 12 **21:17** [x]Rev 13:18 **21:18** [y]S ver 11 [z]ver 21 **21:19** [a]Ex 28:17-20; Isa 54:11,12; Eze 28:13 [b]S ver 11 **21:20** [c]Rev 4:3 **21:21** [d]S ver 12 [e]Isa 54:12 [f]ver 18 **21:22** [g]Jn 4:21, 23 [h]S Rev 1:8 [i]S Rev 5:6 **21:23** [j]S ver 11 [k]Isa 24:23; 60:19,20; Rev 22:5 [l]S Rev 5:6 **21:24** [m]ver 26; Isa 60:3,5 **21:25** [n]S ver 12 [o]Isa 60:11 [p]Zec 14:7; Rev 22:5 **21:26** [q]ver 24 **21:27** [r]Isa 52:1; Joel 3:17; Rev 22:14,15 [s]S Rev 20:12

22:1 [t]Ps 36:8; 46:4 [u]ver 17; S Jn 4:10 [v]Rev 4:6 [w]Eze 47:1; Zec 14:8 **22:2** [x]S Rev 2:7 [y]Eze 47:12 **22:3** [z]Zec 14:11 [a]Rev 7:15 **22:4** [b]S Mt 5:8 [c]S Rev 7:3 **22:5** [d]Rev 21:25; Zec 14:7 [e]Isa 60:19, 20; Rev 21:23 [f]Da 7:27; Rev 20:4 **22:6** [g]Rev 1:1 [h]Rev 21:5 [i]1Co 14:32;

Eden Restored

22 Then the angel showed me the river[t] of the water of life,[u] as clear as
crystal,[v] flowing[w] from the throne of God
and of the Lamb 2down the middle of
the great street of the city. On each side
of the river stood the tree of life,[x] bearing
twelve crops of fruit, yielding its fruit every month. And the leaves of the tree are
for the healing of the nations.[y] 3No longer
will there be any curse.[z] The throne of God
and of the Lamb will be in the city, and
his servants will serve him.[a] 4They will see
his face,[b] and his name will be on their
foreheads.[c] 5There will be no more night.[d]
They will not need the light of a lamp or
the light of the sun, for the Lord God will
give them light.[e] And they will reign for
ever and ever.[f]

John and the Angel

6The angel said to me,[g] "These words
are trustworthy and true.[h] The Lord, the
God who inspires the prophets,[i] sent his
angel[j] to show his servants the things that
must soon take place."

7"Look, I am coming soon![k] Blessed[l] is
the one who keeps the words of the prophecy written in this scroll."[m]

8I, John, am the one who heard and saw
these things.[n] And when I had heard and
seen them, I fell down to worship at the
feet[o] of the angel who had been showing
them to me. 9But he said to me, "Don't
do that! I am a fellow servant with you
and with your fellow prophets and with all
who keep the words of this scroll.[p] Worship God!"[q]
10Then he told me, "Do not seal up[r] the

[a] *16* That is, about 1,400 miles or about 2,200 kilometers
[b] *17* That is, about 200 feet or about 65 meters
[c] *17* Or *high* [d] *20* The precise identification of some of these precious stones is uncertain.

Heb 12:9 [j]ver 16; Rev 1:1 **22:7** [k]ver 12,20; S Mt 16:27 [l]Rev 1:3; 16:15 [m]ver 10,18,19 **22:8** [n]S Rev 1:1 [o]Rev 19:10 **22:9** [p]ver 10, 18,19 [q]Rev 19:10 **22:10** [r]Da 8:26; Rev 10:4

21:15 *measure the city.* Cf. Eze 40–41. In Rev 11 the measuring was to ensure protection; here it serves to show the size and symmetry of the eternal dwelling place of the faithful.
21:16 *length . . . wide . . . high.* Thus a perfect cube, as was the Most Holy Place of the tabernacle and the temple.
21:17 *144 cubits.* See NIV text note.
21:20 See NIV text note.
21:27 *Lamb's book of life.* See note on 3:5.
22:1 *river of the water of life.* The description of the river here seems to combine elements taken from the description of Eden (Ge 2:8–14) and the river flowing from the new temple seen by Ezekiel (Eze 47:1–12), as well as certain new elements.
22:2 *tree of life.* See v. 14; Ge 2:9; 3:22; Eze 47:12.
22:4 *They will see his face.* In ancient times criminals were banished from the presence of the king (Est 7:8; cf. 2Sa 14:24). One blessing of eternity will be to see the Lord face to face (cf. 1Co 13:12; 1Jn 3:2). *his name.* See note on 3:12.
22:5 *they will reign.* See 5:10; 20:6; Da 7:18,27.
22:6 *his servants.* See v. 3. *things that must soon take place.* See 1:1,19.
22:7 *I am coming soon!* See vv. 12,20; 2:16; 3:11. *Blessed.* The sixth beatitude (see note on 1:3).
22:8 *fell down to worship.* See note on 1:17.
22:9 *Don't do that!* The episode (here and in 19:10) is no doubt included to remind the reader/listener that the worship of any created being — no matter how noble — is a form of idolatry, a vice sternly warned against (v. 15; 21:8; see notes on Ge 20:9; Ex 34:15).
22:10 *Do not seal up the words.* Contrast Da 12:4.

words of the prophecy of this scroll,[s] because the time is near.[t] 11 Let the one who
does wrong continue to do wrong; let the
vile person continue to be vile; let the one
who does right continue to do right; and
let the holy person continue to be holy."[u]

Epilogue: Invitation and Warning

12 "Look, I am coming soon![v] My reward
is with me,[w] and I will give to each person
according to what they have done.[x] 13 I am
the Alpha and the Omega,[y] the First and
the Last,[z] the Beginning and the End.[a]
14 "Blessed are those who wash their
robes,[b] that they may have the right to the
tree of life[c] and may go through the gates[d]
into the city.[e] 15 Outside[f] are the dogs,[g]
those who practice magic arts, the sexually immoral, the murderers, the idolaters
and everyone who loves and practices
falsehood.
16 "I, Jesus,[h] have sent my angel[i] to give
you[a] this testimony for the churches.[j] I am
the Root[k] and the Offspring of David,[l] and
the bright Morning Star."[m]

22:10 [s] ver 7,18,19 [t] S Ro 13:11 **22:11** [u] Eze 3:27; Da 12:10 **22:12** [v] ver 7, 20; S Mt 16:27 [w] Isa 40:10; 62:11 [x] S Mt 16:27 **22:13** [y] Rev 1:8 [z] S Rev 1:17 [a] Rev 21:6 **22:14** [b] Rev 7:14 [c] S Rev 2:7 [d] S Rev 21:12 [e] S Rev 21:27 **22:15** [f] Dt 23:18; 1Co 6:9,10; Gal 5:19-21; Col 3:5,6; Rev 21:8 [g] Php 3:2 **22:16** [h] Rev 1:1 [i] ver 6 [j] Rev 1:4 [k] S Rev 5:5 [l] S Mt 1:1 [m] 2Pe 1:19; Rev 2:28 **22:17** [n] Rev 2:7; 14:13 [o] S Rev 19:7 [p] S Jn 4:10 **22:18** [q] ver 7, 10, 19 [r] Dt 4:2; 12:32; Pr 30:6 [s] Rev 15:6-16:21 **22:19** [t] Dt 4:2; 12:32; Pr 30:6 [u] ver 7,10,18 [v] S Rev 2:7 **22:20** [w] Rev 1:2 [x] ver 7,12; S Mt 16:27 [y] 1Co 16:22 **22:21** [z] S Ro 16:20

17 The Spirit[n] and the bride[o] say, "Come!"
And let the one who hears say, "Come!"
Let the one who is thirsty come; and let
the one who wishes take the free gift of
the water of life.[p]

18 I warn everyone who hears the words
of the prophecy of this scroll:[q] If anyone
adds anything to them,[r] God will add to
that person the plagues described in this
scroll.[s] 19 And if anyone takes words away[t]
from this scroll of prophecy,[u] God will take
away from that person any share in the
tree of life[v] and in the Holy City, which are
described in this scroll.
20 He who testifies to these things[w] says,
"Yes, I am coming soon."[x]
Amen. Come, Lord Jesus.[y]
21 The grace of the Lord Jesus be with
God's people.[z] Amen.

[a] *16* The Greek is plural.

22:11 "The time is near" (v. 10), so it is too late to change. The unrepentant must now face the consequences of their actions (see v. 12).
22:12 *I am coming soon!* See vv. 7,20; 2:16; 3:11. *according to what they have done.* See notes on 2:23; 20:12.
22:13 *the Alpha and the Omega.* See note on 1:8.
22:14 *Blessed.* The last of the seven beatitudes (see note on 1:3). *wash their robes.* "In the blood of the Lamb" (7:14).
22:15 *dogs … falsehood.* See note on Ro 1:29–31. *dogs.* A term applied to all types of ceremonially impure persons. In Dt 23:18 it designates a male prostitute.
22:16 *my angel.* Cf. 1:1. *the Root and the Offspring of David.* See note on 5:5; cf. Isa 11:1,10; Ro 1:3. *bright Morning Star.* See Nu 24:17 and note.
22:18–19 Cf. the commands in Dt 4:2; 12:32. The warning here relates specifically to the book of Revelation.
22:20 *I am coming soon.* See vv. 7,12; 2:16; 3:11. *Come, Lord Jesus.* See note on 1Co 16:22.
22:21 *grace.* See note on Ro 1:7. *with.* See note on 2Co 13:14. *Amen.* See notes on Dt 27:15; Ro 1:25.

STUDY HELPS

TABLE OF WEIGHTS AND MEASURES

	Biblical Unit	Approximate American Equivalent	Approximate Metric Equivalent
Weights	talent (60 minas)	75 pounds	34 kilograms
	mina (50 shekels)	1 1/4 pounds	560 grams
	shekel (2 bekas)	2/5 ounce	11.5 grams
	pim (2/3 shekel)	1/4 ounce	7.8 grams
	beka (10 gerahs)	1/5 ounce	5.7 grams
	gerah	1/50 ounce	0.6 gram
	daric	1/3 ounce	8.4 grams
Length	cubit	18 inches	45 centimeters
	span	9 inches	23 centimeters
	handbreadth	3 inches	7.5 centimeters
	stadion (pl. stadia)	600 feet	183 meters
Capacity			
Dry Measure	cor [homer] (10 ephahs)	6 bushels	220 liters
	lethek (5 ephahs)	3 bushels	110 liters
	ephah (10 omers)	3/5 bushel	22 liters
	seah (1/3 ephah)	7 quarts	7.5 liters
	omer (1/10 ephah)	2 quarts	2 liters
	cab (1/18 ephah)	1 quart	1 liter
Liquid Measure	bath (1 ephah)	6 gallons	22 liters
	hin (1/6 bath)	1 gallon	3.8 liters
	log (1/72 bath)	1/3 quart	0.3 liter

The figures of the table are calculated on the basis of a shekel equaling 11.5 grams, a cubit equaling 18 inches and an ephah equaling 22 liters. The quart referred to is either a dry quart (slightly larger than a liter) or a liquid quart (slightly smaller than a liter), whichever is applicable. The ton referred to in the footnotes is the American ton of 2,000 pounds. These weights are calculated relative to the particular commodity involved. Accordingly, the same measure of capacity in the text may be converted into different weights in the footnotes.

This table is based upon the best available information, but it is not intended to be mathematically precise; like the measurement equivalents in the footnotes, it merely gives approximate amounts and distances. Weights and measures differed somewhat at various times and places in the ancient world. There is uncertainty particularly about the ephah and the bath; further discoveries may shed more light on these units of capacity.

REVISED SPELLING OF PROPER NAMES

1984 NIV	2011 NIV
Abib	Aviv
Abimelech	Abimelek
Acbor	Akbor
Acco	Akko
Acsah	Aksah
Acshaph	Akshaph
Aczib	Akzib
Adrammelech	Adrammelek
Ahimelech	Ahimelek
Ahisamach	Ahisamak
Allammelech	Allammelek
Anammelech	Anammelek
Asshur	Ashur
Asshurites	Ashurites
Athach	Athak
Baca	Baka
Bacuth	Bakuth
Becorath	Bekorath
Beracah	Berakah
Beth Car	Beth Kar
Bicri	Bikri
Cabbon	Kabbon
Cabul	Kabul
Calcol	Kalkol
Calno	Kalno
Calneh	Kalneh
Candace	Kandake
Canneh	Kanneh
Carshena	Karshena
Carcas	Karkas
Carmi	Karmi
Casiphia	Kasiphia
Casluhites	Kasluhites
Cenchrea	Cenchreae
Col-Hozeh	Kol-Hozeh
Colosse	Colossae
Conaniah	Konaniah
Cos	Kos
Cozbi	Kozbi
Cozeba	Kozeba
Cun	Kun

1984 NIV	2011 NIV
Cuthah	Kuthah
Ebed-Melech	Ebed-Melek
Elimelech	Elimelek
Erech	Uruk
Eshcol	Eshkol
Eshtarah	Eshterah
Evil-Merodach	Awel-Marduk
Goiim	Goyim
Hacaliah	Hakaliah
Hacmoni	Hakmoni
Hadrach	Hadrak
Hanoch	Hanok
Hathach	Hathak
Haran	Harran
Hatticon	Hattikon
Hazazon Tamar	Hazezon Tamar
Helech	Helek
Iim	Iyim
Iscah	Iskah
Isshiah	Ishiah
Jaakanites	Bene Jaakan
Jacan	Jakan
Jecoliah	Jekoliah
Jehucal	Jehukal
Josech	Josek
Kios	Chios
Kittim	Kittites
Korazin	Chorazin
Lecah	Lekah
Maacah	Maakah
Macbannai	Makbannai
Macbenah	Makbenah
Macnadebai	Maknadebai
Malcam	Malkam
Malluch	Malluk
Maoch	Maok
Marcaboth	Markaboth
Meconah	Mekonah
Melech	Melek
Memucan	Memukan
Merodach-Baladan	Marduk-Baladan

1984 NIV	2011 NIV
Meshech	Meshek
Mica	Mika
Micmash	Mikmash
Micmethah	Mikmethah
Micri	Mikri
Milcah	Milkah
Milcom	Milkom
Mithcah	Mithkah
Mizraim	Egypt
Molech	Molek
Nacon	Nakon
Nathan-Melech	Nathan-Melek
Neco	Necho
Nisroch	Nisrok
Ocran	Okran
Parnach	Parnak
Pasach	Pasak
Racal	Rakal
Recab	Rekab
Recabites	Rekabites
Recah	Rekah

1984 NIV	2011 NIV
Regem-Melech	Regem-Melek
Rodanim	Rodanites
Sabteca	Sabteka
Sacar	Sakar
Salecah	Salekah
Secacah	Sekakah
Secu	Seku
Shecaniah	Shekaniah
Sheshach	Sheshak
Shobach	Shobak
Shophach	Shophak
Sibbecai	Sibbekai
Soco	Soko
Socoh	Sokoh
Succoth	Sukkoth
Ucal	Ukal
Zaccai	Zakkai
Zaccur	Zakkur
Zeboiim	Zeboyim
Zicri	Zikri

INDEX TO TOPICS

—Wanted to kill Shimei . . . 2Sa 16:5–12
—Fought against Absalom . . . 2Sa 18:2,5,12
—Fought against Sheba . . . 2Sa 20:1–6,10
—Fought against Philistines . . . 2Sa 21:15–17

ABNER

—Cousin of Saul . . . 1Sa 14:50
—Commander of Saul's army . . . 1Sa 17:55–57
—Chided by David for carelessness . . . 1Sa 26:5–16
—Made Ish-Bosheth king after Saul . . . 2Sa 2:8–10
—Defeated by David's men . . . 2Sa 2:12–17
—Defected to David . . . 2Sa 3:8–21
—Killed by Joab and Abishai . . . 2Sa 3:22–39

ABORTION

A. Law regarding accidental loss of a child . . . Ex 21:22
B. What is said about a fetus
—It is called a child . . . Mt 1:20
—It has conscious awareness . . . Lk 1:36,41,44
—Sinful nature is present at conception . . . Ps 51:5
C. How God relates to a fetus
—God cares for a conceived child . . . Isa 46:3
—God forms a child . . . Ps 139:13–15; Isa 44:2,24
—God plans a child's life . . . Ps 139:16; Isa 49:1; Jer 1:5; Gal 1:15

ABRAHAM

A. Family data
—Line of Shem . . . 1Ch 1:24–27
—Son of Terah . . . Ge 11:26–27
—Original name: Abram . . . Ge 11:27
—Husband of Sarai . . . Ge 11:29
—Father of Ishmael with Hagar . . . Ge 16:1–4,15–16
—Father of Isaac with Sarah . . . Ge 21:1–3
—Father of many children with Keturah . . . Ge 25:1–4
—Died at 175 years old . . . Ge 25:7–8
B. Covenant with the Lord
1. Called while in Ur . . . Ge 12:1–3; Ac 7:2–4
2. Received promises
—Land and descendants . . . Ge 13:14–17; Ge 15:18–21; Ge 22:15–18
—A son by Sarah . . . Ge 17:16; Ge 18:9–15
3. Given circumcision as a sign . . . Ge 17:1–14,23–27; Ro 4:9–12
4. Declared righteous through faith . . . Ge 15:6; Ro 4:3,20–24; Gal 3:6–9
5. Covenant sealed by sacrifice . . . Ge 15:8–21
6. Name changed to Abraham . . . Ge 17:5; Ne 9:7
7. Covenant remembered . . . Lk 1:68–75; Heb 6:13–15
C. Travels and significant events
—Left Ur . . . Ge 11:31
—Went to Canaan . . . Ge 12:1–6; Ac 7:2–4
—Deceived Pharaoh about Sarai . . . Ge 12:10–20
—Divided land with Lot, settled in Hebron . . . Ge 13:1–18
—Rescued Lot from four kings . . . Ge 14:1–16
—Blessed by Melchizedek . . . Ge 14:17–20; Heb 7:1–7
—Declared righteous through faith . . . Ge 15:6
—Fathered Ishmael with Hagar . . . Ge 16:1–16
—Entertained three visitors . . . Ge 18:1–15
—Interceded for the city of Sodom . . . Ge 18:16–33
—Deceived Abimelek about Sarah . . . Ge 20:1–10
—Fathered Isaac with Sarah . . . Ge 21:1–3
—Sent Hagar and Ishmael away . . . Ge 21:8–21; Gal 4:22–30
—Made a covenant with Abimelek . . . Ge 21:22–32
—Tested by command to sacrifice Isaac . . . Ge 22:1–18; Heb 11:17–19
—Bought field for Sarah's burial . . . Ge 23:1–20
—Secured wife for Isaac . . . Ge 24:1–67
—Fathered children with Keturah . . . Ge 25:1–6
—Died . . . Ge 25:7–11
D. Titles ascribed to him
—Mighty prince . . . Ge 23:5–6
—Servant of God . . . Ge 26:24
—Friend of God . . . Isa 41:8; Jas 2:23
—Prophet . . . Ge 20:7
—Father of Israel . . . Ex 3:15; Mt 3:9
—Father of all believers . . . Ro 4:11–12,16; Gal 3:7
E. Significance in New Testament
—Jesus is a son of Abraham . . . Mt 1:1
—His true seed is Christ . . . Gal 3:15–16,29
—Jesus preceded him . . . Jn 8:57–58
—Rejoiced to see Jesus' day . . . Jn 8:56
—Showed greatness of Christ by giving a tithe to Melchizedek . . . Heb 7:4–10
—Lived by faith . . . Heb 11:8–12, 17–19
—Believed in the power of the resurrection . . . Ro 4:17–21
—Became the father of believers . . . Ro 4:11–12; Gal 3:7
—His faith preceded the law . . . Ro 4:9–11,13–16; Gal 3:17–19
—Got rid of the children of the slave woman . . . Gal 4:21–31
—Demonstrated faith by works . . . Jas 2:20–24

ABSALOM

—Son of David by Maakah . . . 2Sa 3:3; 1Ch 3:2
—Killed Amnon for rape of Tamar . . . 2Sa 13:23–33
—Fled to Geshur . . . 2Sa 13:36–38
—Allowed by David to return . . . 2Sa 14:1–24
—Reconciled with David . . . 2Sa 14:28–33
—Rebelled against David . . . 2Sa 15:1–12
—David fled from him . . . 2Sa 15:13–37
—Accepted the advice of Hushai . . . 2Sa 16:15–17:23
—Fought against David's men . . . 2Sa 18:1–8
—Killed by Joab . . . 2Sa 18:9–18
—Mourned by David . . . 2Sa 18:19–19:8

ACCESS TO GOD

A. The command to approach God
—In the Old Testament . . . Isa 55:6; Am 5:4,6
—In the New Testament . . . Mt 7:7; Lk 11:9; Jas 4:8
B. How can we approach God?
1. From God's standpoint
—The Father draws us to himself . . . Jn 6:44
—Jesus is the way to the Father . . . Jn 14:6; Ro 5:2; Eph 3:12; 1Pe 3:18
—The Spirit enables us to come near . . . Eph 2:18
2. From our standpoint
—We must believe . . . Ro 5:2; Heb 11:6
—We must live clean, obedient lives . . . Ps 24:3–5; Mt 5:8
—We must pray to the Father . . . Mt 6:6
—We must call upon God's name . . . Ps 145:18
C. Promises to those who approach God
—We will find God . . . Dt 4:29; 2Ch 15:2
—God will listen to us . . . 2Ki 13:4
—God will forgive us . . . 2Ch 7:14
—God will make a covenant with us . . . Isa 55:3

—God will bless us . . . Ps 65:4
—We can have confidence before God . . . Eph 3:12; Heb 4:16; 1Jn 5:14

See also PRAYER

ACHAN

—Son of Karmi, of tribe of Judah . . . Jos 7:1
—Stole things from Jericho . . . Jos 7:1
—His sin caused defeat at Ai . . . Jos 7:3–12
—His sin revealed . . . Jos 7:13–23
—Stoned to death . . . Jos 7:24–26
—A lesson for Israel . . . Jos 22:18–20

ACHISH

—King of Gath before whom David feigned insanity . . . 1Sa 21:10–15
—Gave David town of Ziklag . . . 1Sa 27:1–7
—Trusted David . . . 1Sa 27:10–12
—Philistines asked him to expel David . . . 1Sa 29:1–11
—Still king in time of Solomon . . . 1Ki 2:39–40

ADAM

A. The first Adam
1. The creation of Adam
—Made in God's image . . . Ge 1:26–27
—Made from dust of the earth . . . Ge 2:7
—Became a living being . . . Ge 2:7; 1Co 15:45
—Woman was created from him . . . Ge 2:21–23
2. The work of Adam
—Was placed in Eden . . . Ge 2:8
—Took care of Eden . . . Ge 2:15
—Named the animals . . . Ge 2:19–20
—Work cursed after the fall . . . Ge 3:17–19
—Was banished from Eden . . . Ge 3:23–24
3. Marriage of Adam and Eve
—Was established by God . . . Ge 2:23–24
—Eve tempted her husband . . . Ge 3:6; 1Ti 2:14
—Adam blamed Eve . . . Ge 3:12
—Adam and Eve had children . . . Ge 4:1–2; Ge 4:25–5:4
4. Temptation and fall of Adam
—God warned Adam not to sin . . . Ge 2:16–17
—Adam disobeyed God . . . Ge 3:1–6
—God pronounced punishment . . . Ge 3:16–19
—Adam died . . . Ge 5:5
—Sin and death passed on to all humans . . . Ro 5:12,15–17,19
—God condemns us for Adam's sin . . . Ro 5:16,18
B. The second Adam (Christ) . . . 1Co 15:45
1. Prophecy concerning him in Eden . . . Ge 3:15
2. Christ as the second Adam
—Descended from the first Adam . . . Lk 3:23–38
—Obedient to God's will . . . Ro 5:19
—Victorious over the devil . . . Mt 4:1–11; 1Jn 3:8
3. Results for believers
—They receive righteousness and life . . . Ro 5:15–18; 1Co 15:22
—They will receive new bodies like his . . . 1Co 15:46–49; Php 3:20–21

ADONIJAH

—Son of David by Haggith . . . 2Sa 3:4; 1Ch 3:2
—Attempted to be king after David . . . 1Ki 1:5–27
—David made Solomon king instead . . . 1Ki 1:28–53
—Wanted Abishag as wife . . . 1Ki 2:13–22
—Killed at Solomon's command . . . 1Ki 2:23–25

ADOPTION

—Becoming someone's child by a legal act
A. In human relationships
—Abram wants to adopt . . . Ge 15:2–4
—Pharaoh's daughter adopts Moses . . . Ex 2:10
—Mordecai adopts Esther . . . Est 2:7
—A wife adopts a maid's son . . . Ge 16:1–3; Ge 30:1–5; Ge 30:9–12
B. In the God-man relationship
1. It is rooted in God's eternal love . . . Eph 1:4–5; Ro 8:29; 1Jn 3:1
2. Israel is God's adopted son . . . Ex 4:22–23; Dt 14:2; Jer 31:9; Hos 11:1; Ro 9:4
3. Christians are God's adopted children
—We become children by God's grace . . . Eph 1:5–6
—We become children through faith in Christ . . . Jn 1:12–13; Gal 3:26
—We can call God Father . . . Mt 6:9; Ro 8:15; Gal 4:6–7
—We become siblings of Christ . . . Mk 3:34–35; Heb 2:11–12
—We are united as one body in Christ . . . Eph 2:11–13,19; Eph 3:6
—Our adoption is completed only at the resurrection . . . Ro 8:19,23; 1Jn 3:2
4. Results of being God's children
—We receive the rights of inheritance . . . Ro 8:17; Gal 4:7
—We must walk in light . . . Jn 12:35–36; Eph 5:8–10; 1Th 5:4–5
—We must live as obedient children . . . 1Pe 1:14–16
—We must live in peace . . . Mt 5:9; Eph 2:17–19
—We must live in love . . . Mt 5:44–45; Lk 6:35
—We must separate ourselves from evil . . . 2Co 6:17–18; Php 2:15
—We are subject to God's discipline . . . Heb 12:5–11
—We can expect suffering . . . Ro 8:18,22

ADULLAM

—A city in southwest Judah . . . Jos 15:21,33,35
—Judah married a woman from there . . . Ge 38:1–2
—David hid his followers in a cave near it . . . 1Sa 22:1–2
—David's men risked getting water from Bethlehem . . . 2Sa 23:13–17; 1Ch 11:15–19
—Fortified by Rehoboam . . . 2Ch 11:5–10
—Judgment prophesied against it . . . Mic 1:15
—Established again after the exile . . . Ne 11:30

ADULTERY

—Sexual unfaithfulness to one's spouse
A. Related theme
ADULTERY is a theme of Hosea . . . Hos 4:13
B. Old Testament perspective
1. Laws against adultery
—In the Ten Commandments . . . Ex 20:14; Dt 5:18
—Various laws on adultery . . . Lev 20:10; Nu 5:12–31; Dt 22:22–24
2. Examples of adultery
—Judah and Tamar . . . Ge 38:15–18
—David and Bathsheba . . . 2Sa 11:2–5
—Others in Judah . . . Jer 5:7–9; Jer 29:23
3. Characteristics of adultery
—Is a sin against one's spouse and God . . . Ge 39:7–9; 2Sa 12:13; Ps 51:4
—Is personally dangerous . . . Pr 2:16–19; Pr 6:25–29,32
—Defiles a whole nation . . . Jer 3:1; Jer 23:10–15; Eze 33:26

C. New Testament perspective
1. The sin of adultery
—Starts in a sinful heart ... Mt 15:19
—Considered a sinful action ... Ro 7:2–3
Jas 2:11
2Pe 2:14
—Sinful even in thought ... Mt 5:27–28
—Remarriage as adultery ... Mt 5:31–32
Mt 19:8–9
2. Results of adultery
—Leads to God's judgment ... Heb 13:4
—Leads to exclusion from the kingdom ... Gal 5:19–21
1Co 6:9
Rev 22:15
3. Pardon promised for adulterers ... Jn 8:3–11
1Co 6:11
D. Spiritual adultery
—References in the Old Testament ... Jer 3:6–10,20
Eze 16:32–35
Hos 1:2
—References in the New Testament ... Mt 12:39
Jas 4:4
—God judges spiritual adultery ... Jer 5:11–17
Eze 16:37–42
Mk 8:38
—God desires faithfulness to Christ ... 2Co 11:2
See also MARRIAGE

AFFLICTION
See PAIN

AGABUS
—A prophet in the early church ... Ac 11:27–28
—Predicted a severe famine for the world ... Ac 11:28
—Predicted Paul's arrest in Jerusalem ... Ac 21:10–11

AGAG
—King of Amalekites; spared by Saul ... 1Sa 15:7–9,20
—Killed by Samuel ... 1Sa 15:32–33

AGRIPPA
—King who visited Festus ... Ac 25:13–22
—Paul spoke before him ... Ac 25:23–26:23
—Paul invited him to believe ... Ac 26:25–27
—Rejected the gospel ... Ac 26:28
—Declared Paul innocent ... Ac 26:31–32

AHAB
A. Personal data
—Son of Omri; king of Israel ... 1Ki 16:28–29
—Husband of Jezebel ... 1Ki 16:31
B. Significant events
—Promoted Baal worship ... 1Ki 16:31–33
—Opposed by Elijah ... 1Ki 17:1
—Contest on Mount Carmel ... 1Ki 18:16–39
—Defeated Ben-Hadad ... 1Ki 20:1–34
—Coveted Naboth's vineyard ... 1Ki 21:1–16
—Fought against king of Aram ... 1Ki 22:29–30
—Accidentally killed in battle ... 1Ki 22:34–38
C. Prophesied against
—By an unnamed prophet ... 1Ki 20:35–43
—By Elijah ... 1Ki 21:17–29
—By Micaiah ... 1Ki 22:9–28
D. Subsequent history
—Elisha told Jehu to destroy Ahab's family ... 2Ki 9:6–10
—House of Ahab destroyed ... 2Ki 10:1–17
—Name became a symbol of wickedness ... 2Ch 21:6,13
2Ch 22:3–4
Mic 6:16

AHAZ
—Son of Jotham; king of Judah ... 2Ki 16:1
2Ch 28:1
—Worshiped idols ... 2Ki 16:1–4,10–18
2Ch 28:1–4,22–25
—Fought against Aram and Israel ... 2Ki 16:5–6
Isa 7:1
—Defeated by Aram and Israel ... 2Ch 28:5–15
—Fought against Edom and Philistia ... 2Ch 28:16–19
—Sought help from Assyria ... 2Ki 16:7–9
—Refused a sign from the Lord ... Isa 7:2–17
—His death ... 2Ki 16:19–20

AHAZIAH
A. Son of Ahab; king of Israel ... 1Ki 22:51
—Worshiped idols ... 1Ki 22:52–53
—Made an alliance with Jehoshaphat ... 2Ch 20:36–37
—Died while seeking advice from Baal ... 2Ki 1:1–17
B. Son of Jehoram; king of Judah ... 2Ki 8:25–26
2Ch 22:1–2
—Worshiped idols ... 2Ki 8:27
2Ch 22:3–4
—Allied with Joram, king of Israel ... 2Ki 8:28–29
—Killed by Jehu while visiting Joram ... 2Ki 9:14–29
2Ch 22:1–9
—Only surviving son was Joash ... 2Ki 11:1–3

AHIMELEK
A. Priest at Nob during Saul's time ... 1Sa 21:1
—Gave David consecrated bread ... 1Sa 21:2–6
—Gave David Goliath's sword ... 1Sa 21:8–9
—Betrayed to Saul by Doeg ... 1Sa 22:9–16
—Killed by Doeg with other priests ... 1Sa 22:17–19
—Son Abiathar escaped to join David ... 1Sa 22:20–23
B. Grandson of Ahimelek ... 2Sa 8:17
—Co-priest with Zadok during David's reign ... 1Ch 18:16
1Ch 24:6,31
C. One of David's warriors ... 1Sa 26:6

AHITHOPHEL
—A counselor of David ... 2Sa 15:12
—Joined Absalom against David ... 2Sa 15:31–37
—Advised Absalom ... 2Sa 16:15–23
—Absalom rejected his counsel ... 2Sa 17:1–14
—Committed suicide ... 2Sa 17:23

AI
—A city in Palestine, east of Bethel ... Jos 7:2
—Abram built an altar near there ... Ge 12:8
—Joshua's troops were initially defeated there ... Jos 7:3–5
—After Achan's death, Ai was destroyed ... Jos 8:1–29
—Later rebuilt, with Israelites settling there ... Ezr 2:2,28

ALCOHOL
A. Terms used in the Bible
—Beer and wine ... 1Sa 1:15
Pr 31:4,6
—Fermented drink ... Nu 6:3
Jdg 13:4,7
—Mixed wine ... Pr 9:2
Pr 23:30
—Old wine and new wine ... Am 9:13
Lk 5:37–39
B. Various uses for alcohol
—In family meals ... Ge 27:25
—In public feasting ... Est 1:7–8,10
Da 5:1–4
—At weddings ... Jn 2:3
—As an offering to God ... Ex 29:38,40
Lev 23:12–13
—As a tithe ... Dt 12:17
Ne 13:5
—In barter exchange ... 2Ch 2:10
—As a commodity for commerce ... Eze 27:18
—As medicine ... Lk 10:34
1Ti 5:23
—As a drug for pain ... Pr 31:6
Mk 15:23
—As a means to become drunk ... Ge 9:20–21
C. Positive aspects of alcohol
—A blessing from God ... Joel 2:19
—Can help one celebrate ... Jn 2:1–11
—Can give enjoyment ... Ps 104:15
Zec 9:17
—Can aid in happiness ... Ecc 10:19

—Can help to refresh someone 2Sa 16:2
—Can help one's health 1Ti 5:23
D. Dangers of using alcohol
—Loosens morals Ge 9:21–22
—Inflames an individual Isa 5:11–12
—Destroys health 1Sa 25:36–37
—Impairs judgment Pr 31:4–5
Isa 28:7
—Raises tempers Pr 20:1
—Leads to poverty Pr 23:21
—Leads to sorrow Pr 23:29–30
—Creates disunity in the church 1Co 11:18–21
E. Drunkenness forbidden Isa 5:11–12,22
Ro 13:13
1Co 5:11
1Co 6:9–10
Eph 5:18
F. Symbolic uses of alcohol
—Symbolizes the blood of Christ Mt 26:27–29
—Symbolizes the gospel of salvation Isa 55:1
—Symbolizes the judgment of God Ps 75:8
Jer 25:15–16
Rev 14:10
—Symbolizes the sins of the antichrist Rev 17:2
Rev 18:3

ALIEN

—A citizen of one country residing in another
A. Aliens within the nation of Israel
1. Who were they?
—Those leaving Egypt with Israelites Ex 12:38
—Unconquered nations in Canaan Jos 9:26–27
1Ki 9:20–21
—Captives taken in war Dt 21:10–11
—Slaves purchased Lev 25:44–46
—Foreigners hired in Israel 1Ki 9:27
—Foreigners attracted to Israel 2Ch 6:32–33
2. How were they to be treated?
—God had a special love for them Dt 10:18
Ps 146:9
—They were not to be oppressed Ex 22:21
Ex 23:9
Lev 19:33–34
—They enjoyed equal protection Lev 24:22
Lev 25:35
Dt 1:16–17
Dt 24:17–21
—They shared equal responsibility Ex 20:8–10
Nu 15:14–16
—Israel condemned for oppressing them Ps 94:6
Eze 22:7,29
B. God's people as aliens
1. In the Old Testament
—Abraham in Canaan Ge 17:8
Ge 23:4
—Jacob in Canaan Ge 28:4
—Moses in Midian Ex 18:3
—Israelites in Egypt Ge 15:13
Ex 23:9
—Israelites in Canaan Lev 25:23
1Ch 29:15
Ps 39:12
Ps 119:19
—Israelites in Babylon La 5:2
—Their true homeland was elsewhere Heb 11:13–15
2. In the New Testament
—We are called foreigners 1Pe 1:17
1Pe 2:11
—We are not part of this world Jn 17:14,16
—Our true home is heaven Php 3:20–21
Col 3:1,3
Heb 11:16
—We must not love the world Ro 12:2
1Jn 2:15–17
—We may not alienate people in the church Eph 2:19–22
Heb 13:1–2

ALTAR

A. Altars used in pagan religions
1. Such altars built Ex 32:5
1Ki 16:32–33
1Ki 18:26
Ac 17:23
2. Such altars destroyed
—At God's command Ex 34:13
Dt 7:5
—By Moses Ex 32:20
—By Gideon Jdg 6:25–28
—By all the Israelites 2Ki 11:18
2Ch 31:1
—By various kings 2Ki 18:4
2Ki 23:12
2Ch 14:3,5
—By the Lord himself Hos 10:2
B. Altars used in the worship of the Lord
1. Such altars built or rebuilt by:
—Noah Ge 8:20
—Abram Ge 12:7–8
Ge 13:18
—Isaac Ge 26:25
—Jacob Ge 35:6–7
—Moses Ex 17:15
—Joshua Jos 8:30
—Gideon Jdg 6:24
—Samuel 1Sa 7:17
—Saul 1Sa 14:35
—David 2Sa 24:25
—Solomon 2Ch 8:12
—Asa 2Ch 15:8
—Elijah 1Ki 18:30–32
—Hezekiah's men 2Ch 29:18
—Manasseh 2Ch 33:16
—Jeshua and Zerubbabel Ezr 3:2–3
2. Altars located in
—The tabernacle Ex 37:25–38:7
—Solomon's temple 2Ch 4:1,19
—The second temple Ezr 7:17
—Ezekiel's temple Eze 43:13–27
—Herod's temple Lk 1:11
3. Purpose of altars to the Lord
—To sacrifice to the Lord Ge 8:20
Ge 12:7–8
—To make atonement for God's people Lev 16:18–20
—To burn incense to the Lord Ex 30:1–10
—To function as memorials Ex 17:15
Jos 22:26–27
4. Altars in the Christian religion
—Christ's cross is our altar Heb 13:10–12
—No need for sacrifice after Christ came Heb 9:6–15,23–28
Heb 10:1–18
—The heavenly altar of incense Rev 6:9
Rev 8:3–5

AMALEKITES

A. Their identity
—The descendants of Amalek, grandson of Esau Ge 36:15–16
—Lived in the Negev (south Canaan) Nu 13:29
B. Their wars
—Defeated by Kedorlaomer and his allies Ge 14:5–7
—Defeated by Israelites in the desert Ex 17:8–13
—Defeated the disobedient Israelites Nu 14:41–45
—Allied with Eglon against Israelites Jdg 3:12–13
—Allied with Midianites against Israelites Jdg 6:3,33
—Defeated by Gideon Jdg 7:12,22–24
—Defeated by King Saul 1Sa 14:47–48
1Sa 15:1–9
—King Agag killed by Samuel 1Sa 15:32–33
—Defeated by David 1Sa 27:8–9
1Sa 30:1–19
—An Amalekite soldier killed King Saul 2Sa 1:4–15
C. Important data concerning them
—They had no fear of God Dt 25:17–18

—Moses prophesied their complete destruction ...... Ex 17:14
Dt 25:17–19
—Balaam predicted their destruction .... Nu 24:20
—Destruction completed by the Simeonites.......... 1Ch 4:42–43

AMASA
—Nephew of David.................................. 1Ch 2:17
—Commander of Absalom's forces.................... 2Sa 17:25
—Came back to David............................... 2Sa 19:13
—Killed by Joab................................... 2Sa 20:4–13

AMAZIAH
A. Son of Joash; king of Judah..................... 2Ki 14:1–2
—Killed his father's assassins.................... 2Ki 14:5–6
—Raised a large army.............................. 2Ch 25:5–6
—Defeated Edom 2Ki 14:7
2Ch 25:7–13
—Worshiped Edom's gods 2Ch 25:14
—Rebuked by a prophet............................. 2Ch 25:15–16
—Defeated by Israel 2Ki 14:8–14
2Ch 25:17–24
—Killed by conspirators 2Ch 25:27
B. Idolatrous priest who opposed Amos.............. Am 7:10–17

AMBITION
—A goal one sets in life
A. Related theme
PRIORITIES is a theme of Haggai.................... Hag 1:4
B. Examples of proper ambitions
—Witnessing to unbelievers .... Ro 15:20
—Being fully devoted to the Lord.................. 1Co 7:32,34
—Desiring the greater gifts, especially love 1Co 12:31–13:7
—Pleasing God in everything 2Co 5:9
—Striving for perfection, unity and peace......... 2Co 13:11
—Forging ahead in service to Christ............... Php 3:12–14
—Leading a quiet, diligent life 1Th 4:11
—Pursuing righteousness and godliness............. 1Ti 6:11
2Ti 2:22
C. Examples of improper ambitions
—Competing with others in the kingdom............. Mk 10:35–45
Php 1:15,17
—Serving one's own selfish wants .... Php 2:3
Jas 2:14–16
—Seeking riches 1Ki 3:7–12
Lk 12:13–21
1Ti 6:9–10
—Attempting to glorify oneself .... Ge 11:3–4
Da 4:28–30
—Attempting to displace God....................... Eze 28:2
2Th 2:3–4

See also PRIDE

AMMONITES
A. Their identity
—Descendants of Ben-Ammi, son of Lot.............. Ge 19:38
—Related to the Moabites.......................... Ge 19:36–38
—Given land east of the Jordan .... Dt 2:19
Dt 3:16
—Served the god Molek............................. 1Ki 11:7,33
B. Significant Ammonites
—Nahash: besieged Jabesh.......................... 1Sa 11:1–2
—Hanun: opposed David 2Sa 10:1–4
—Zelek: one of David's mighty men 1Ch 11:39
—Naamah: the mother of Rehoboam 1Ki 14:21,31
—Zabad: conspired against Joash................... 2Ch 24:26
—Tobiah: opposed Nehemiah .... Ne 2:10,19
Ne 4:3,7–8
C. Their wars
—Allied with Eglon against Israelites............. Jdg 3:12–13
—Allied with Philistines against Israelites....... Jdg 10:7–9,17–18
—Defeated by Jephthah............................. Jdg 11:4–33
—Defeated by Saul 1Sa 11:1–11
1Sa 14:47
—Defeated by David's army......................... 2Sa 10:1–14
2Sa 12:26–31
1Ch 19:1–15
1Ch 20:1
—Allied with Moabites against Jehoshaphat 2Ch 20:1
—They and Moabites destroyed each other........... 2Ch 20:22–24
—Defeated by Uzziah............................... 2Ch 26:8
—Defeated by Jotham 2Ch 27:5
—Allied against Jehoiakim 2Ki 24:1–2
—Plotted against rebuilding of Jerusalem .... Ne 2:19
Ne 4:1–3,7–8
D. Important data concerning them
1. During the time of Moses and Joshua
—Not attacked by the Israelites .... Dt 2:19,37
—Refused to give food to Israelites .... Dt 23:4
—Not allowed to join the Israelites............... Dt 23:4
Ne 13:1–8
—Half of their land given to Gad.................. Jos 13:25
2. During the time of the kings
—Israelites worshiped their gods.................. Jdg 10:6
1Ki 11:5,7
—David used them to kill Uriah.................... 2Sa 12:9
—Solomon intermarried with them................... 1Ki 11:1
1Ki 14:21
3. Numerous Jews intermarried with them............ Ezr 9:1
Ne 13:23–27
4. Prophecies concerning their destruction......... Isa 11:12–14
Jer 49:1–5
Eze 21:28–32
Eze 25:1–7
Am 1:13–15
Zep 2:8–11

AMNON
—Firstborn of David 2Sa 3:2
—Raped Tamar 2Sa 13:1–19
—Killed by Absalom 2Sa 13:20–29
—David mourned for him............................ 2Sa 13:37

AMON
A. Son of Manasseh; king of Judah 2Ki 21:18–19
—Promoted idolatry................................ 2Ki 21:20–22
—Assassinated..................................... 2Ki 21:23–24
B. Ruler of city of Samaria under Ahab............. 1Ki 22:26
2Ch 18:25

AMORITES
A. Their identity
—Descendants of Canaan, grandson of Noah .... Ge 10:6,15–16
—One of the Canaanite nations..................... Ex 33:2
—Lived in hill country, east of the Jordan .... Nu 13:29
Jos 2:10
—Boundaries given................................. Jos 12:2–5
B. Significant Amorites
—Mamre, Eshkol, Aner: friends of Abram .... Ge 14:13
—Sihon and Og: fought against Israelites.......... Nu 21:21,33
Dt 4:46–47
C. Their wars
—Defeated by Kedorlaomer and his allies........... Ge 14:5–7
—Sihon and Og defeated by the Israelites.......... Nu 21:21–31
—They defeated disobedient Israelites .... Dt 1:42–45
—Five Amorite kings defeated by Joshua .... Jos 10:5–26
D. Important data concerning them
1. Exceptionally sinful............................ Ge 15:16
2Ki 21:11
2. God promised their land to the Israelites....... Ex 3:8,17
Ex 34:11
3. Political relationship with Israelites
—Land given to tribe of Reuben.................... Jos 13:15,21
—Israelites told to destroy them.................. Dt 7:1–6
Dt 20:16–18
—Israelites did not destroy them .... Jos 13:2,4
Jdg 1:34–36
—Amorites and Israelites at peace 1Sa 7:14
—Became slaves of Israelites...................... 1Ki 9:20–21
2Ch 8:7–8
4. Religious relationship with Israelites
—Israelites must not worship their gods........... Jos 24:14–15
—Israelites worshiped their gods.................. Jdg 6:10
5. Intermarried with the Israelites .... Jdg 3:5–6
Ezr 9:1–2

AMOS

A. Prophet from Tekoa ... Am 1:1
—Originally a farmer and shepherd ... Am 7:14
—Confronted the prophet Amaziah ... Am 7:10–17
B. Ancestor of Jesus ... Lk 3:25

ANANIAS

A. Husband of Sapphira ... Ac 5:1
—Kept back part of their money ... Ac 5:2
—Died for lying to God ... Ac 5:3–10
B. Disciple in Damascus who baptized Saul/Paul ... Ac 9:10–17
—Commissioned Paul ... Ac 22:12–16
C. High priest at Paul's arrest ... Ac 23:2; Ac 24:1

ANCESTRY

—Those from whom one has descended
A. Related theme
GENEALOGY is a theme of 1 Chronicles ... 1Ch 9:1
B. Physical ancestry of the Israelites
—Genealogies were important ... Ge 5:1–32; Ge 46:8–26; 1Ch 1:1–9:44; Ezr 2:3–61; Mt 1:1–17; Lk 3:23–38
—Priests had to prove ancestry ... Ezr 2:62; Ne 7:64
—Israelites proud of Abraham as father ... Isa 41:8; Isa 51:2; Lk 3:8; Jn 8:31–33
C. Ancestry of Jesus
—A descendant of Adam ... Lk 3:38
—A descendant of Abraham ... Mt 1:1; Ro 9:5
—A descendant of David ... Mt 1:1; Ro 1:3
D. Spiritual ancestry of God's people
1. Physical ancestry insufficient to be saved ... Ro 9:6–7
2. Requirements for becoming true children of Abraham
—We must be chosen by God ... Ro 9:10–13
—We must believe in Jesus ... Ro 4:11,16; Gal 3:7,26–29
—We must do God's will ... Jn 8:39–40
3. True children of Abraham
—Are heirs of God ... Ro 8:17; Gal 3:29
—Include both Jews and Gentiles ... Ro 4:16–17; Eph 3:6

ANDREW

—Brother of Simon Peter ... Mt 4:18
—Fisherman ... Mk 1:16–18
—Disciple of John the Baptist ... Jn 1:35–40
—Introduced Peter to Jesus ... Jn 1:41–42
—Became a disciple of Jesus ... Mt 4:18
—Introduced little boy to Jesus ... Jn 6:8
—Introduced Greeks to Jesus ... Jn 12:21–22
—Asked Jesus about destruction of temple ... Mk 13:3
—One of the apostles ... Ac 1:13

ANGEL

—Spiritual beings created by God
A. Their origin and nature
—They are spirits ... Heb 1:14
—They were created by God ... Ps 148:2,5; Col 1:16
—They were created early in creation ... Job 38:6–7
—They were created good ... Ge 1:31
—They are not to be worshiped ... Col 2:18; Rev 19:10
—They do not marry or die ... Lk 20:35–36
—Some angels rebelled against God ... 2Pe 2:4
B. Names and ranks of good angels
—Michael ... Da 12:1; Jude 9; Rev 12:7
—Gabriel ... Da 9:21; Lk 1:19,26
—Archangels ... 1Th 4:16
—Seraphs ... Isa 6:2
—Cherubim ... Eze 10:1–3
—Rulers and authorities ... Eph 3:10; Col 1:16
—Thrones and powers ... Col 1:16
—There are numerous angels ... Rev 5:11
C. Duties of good angels
1. General duties
—They revealed the law ... Ac 7:38; Gal 3:19; Heb 2:2
—They bring messages from God ... Zec 1:14–17; Ac 10:3–6
—They praise and worship God ... Heb 1:6; Rev 5:11–12
—They provide for God's people ... 1Ki 19:5–8; Mt 4:11; Heb 1:14
—They protect God's people ... Ps 91:11; Da 6:22; Ac 12:7–10
—Some serve as guardian angels ... Mt 18:10; Ac 12:15
—They give guidance to God's people ... Ac 8:26; Ac 27:23–24
—They interpret God's will ... Da 7:16; Zec 1:9,13–14
—They carry out God's will ... Nu 22:22; Ps 103:20–21; Mt 28:2
—They punish God's enemies ... 2Ki 19:35; Ac 12:23; Rev 14:17–16:21
2. Duties connected with Christ
—Gabriel announced conception to Mary ... Lk 1:26–38
—An angel announced conception to Joseph ... Mt 1:20–21
—An angel announced his birth ... Lk 2:9–12
—Angels sang at his birth ... Lk 2:13–14
—An angel warned Joseph to flee to Egypt ... Mt 2:13
—An angel told Joseph to return ... Mt 2:19–20
—Angels strengthened Christ ... Mt 4:11; Lk 22:43
—Angels were available to help him ... Mt 26:53
—An angel rolled away the stone ... Mt 28:2
—Angels announced his resurrection ... Mt 28:5–7; Lk 24:23; Jn 20:11–13
—Angels were present at his ascension ... Ac 1:11
—Angels will return with Christ ... Mt 25:31; 2Th 1:7
D. Evil angels
1. Satan is their leader ... Job 1:6; Zec 3:1; Mt 4:10
2. Duties
—They oppose good angels ... Rev 12:7–9
—They work through false teachers ... 2Th 2:9–10; 1Ti 4:1–2
—They try to separate believers from God ... Ro 8:38–39
—They oppose Christ and his church ... Rev 12:3–6,13–17
—They do evil to humans ... Job 2:6–8; Mt 13:38–39; Lk 13:11,16
—They tempt humans to sin ... Mt 4:3; 1Pe 5:8
—They accuse us before God ... Zec 3:1

ANGEL OF THE LORD

A. To whom did he appear?

- —To Hagar ... Ge 16:7; Ge 21:17
- —To Abraham ... Ge 22:11,15
- —To Jacob ... Ge 31:11–13
- —To Moses ... Ex 3:2
- —To the Israelites in the exodus ... Ex 14:19
- —To Balaam ... Nu 22:22–36
- —To Joshua ... Jdg 2:1,4
- —To Gideon ... Jdg 6:11
- —To Samson's parents ... Jdg 13:21–22
- —To David ... 1Ch 21:16
- —To Elijah ... 2Ki 1:3–6
- —To Daniel ... Da 6:22

B. What tasks did he perform?

- —Delivered messages from the Lord ... Ge 22:15–18
- —Protected God's people ... 2Ki 19:34–35
- —Redeemed God's people ... Isa 63:9
- —Punished God's people ... 2Sa 24:16–17
- —Destroyed God's enemies ... Ex 23:23

C. How can we identify him as God (Jesus)?

- —He uses "I" when he brings a message ... Ge 16:10; Ge 22:16–17; Ge 31:13; Ex 3:6; Jdg 6:14
- —He describes himself as holy ... Ex 3:2,5
- —He carries out God's judgment ... 2Sa 24:16; 2Ki 19:35
- —God's name is in him ... Ex 23:20–23
- —He takes on a human appearance ... Jos 5:13–15; Jdg 13:6,10,21

ANGER

A. Human anger

1. Expressed by such people as:
   - —Cain ... Ge 4:5–6
   - —Jacob ... Ge 30:2
   - —Moses ... Ex 11:8
   - —Saul ... 1Sa 20:30
   - —David ... 2Sa 6:8
   - —Naaman ... 2Ki 5:11
   - —Nehemiah ... Ne 5:6
   - —Jonah ... Jnh 4:1,9
2. Control of our anger
   - —We must refrain from anger ... Ps 37:8; Eph 4:31
   - —We must be slow to anger ... Jas 1:19–20
   - —We must keep our temper in check ... Pr 16:32
   - —In our anger we must not sin ... Ps 4:4; Eph 4:26–27
3. Anger puts us in danger of hell ... Mt 5:21–22
4. We must let God avenge sin ... Ps 94:1; Ro 12:19; 2Th 1:6–8

B. The anger of Jesus

- —At injustice ... Mk 3:5; Mk 10:14
- —At the misuse of God's house ... Jn 2:12–17
- —In the final judgment ... Rev 6:16–17

C. The anger of God

1. God's anger is righteous ... Ro 3:5–6; Rev 16:5–6
2. Reasons for his anger
   - —The worship of idols ... 1Ki 14:9,15,22; 2Ch 34:25
   - —Sin ... Dt 9:7; 2Ki 22:13; Ro 1:18
   - —Unbelief ... Ps 78:21–22; Jn 3:36
   - —Unjust treatment of others ... Isa 10:1–4; Am 2:6–7
   - —Refusal to repent ... Isa 9:13,17; Ro 2:5
3. Expressions of his anger
   - —In temporal judgments ... Nu 11:1,33; Isa 10:5; La 1:12
   - —In the day of the Lord ... Ps 110:5; Zep 1:15,18; Ro 2:5,8; Rev 11:18
4. God's control of his anger
   - —God is slow to anger ... Ex 34:6; Ps 103:8
   - —God's mercy overshadows his anger ... Ps 30:5; Isa 54:8; Hos 11:8–11
   - —God will turn away his anger ... Ps 78:38; Isa 48:9; Da 9:16
   - —Believers are spared from God's anger ... Ro 5:9; 1Th 1:10; 1Th 5:9

ANIMALS

A. Animals mentioned in the Bible

- —Antelope ... Dt 14:5
- —Ape ... 1Ki 10:22
- —Baboon ... 1Ki 10:22
- —Bear ... 1Sa 17:34–37
- —Behemoth ... Job 40:15–24
- —Camel ... Lev 11:4
- —Cattle (bull, cow, calf) ... 1Sa 6:7; Ps 68:30
- —Deer ... Ps 42:1
- —Dog ... Mt 15:26–27
- —Donkey ... Mt 21:2,5
- —Fish ... Jn 21:3–11
- —Fox ... Mt 8:20
- —Gazelle ... Dt 14:5
- —Goat ... Ge 30:35
- —Horse ... Ge 47:17
- —Hyena ... Isa 13:22
- —Hyrax ... Lev 11:5
- —Ibex ... Dt 14:5
- —Jackal ... Isa 13:21
- —Leopard ... Isa 11:6
- —Leviathan ... Job 41:1
- —Lion ... Ge 49:9
- —Mole ... Isa 2:20
- —Mule ... 2Sa 18:9
- —Ox ... Ex 22:1,4
- —Pig ... Mk 5:11–16
- —Rabbit ... Lev 11:6
- —Rat ... Isa 66:17
- —Sheep (ram, ewe, lamb) ... Ge 32:14; 2Sa 12:1–4
- —Weasel ... Lev 11:29
- —Wolf ... Isa 11:6

B. Animals used as symbols

1. Behemoth: symbolizes power ... Job 40:15–24
2. Deer
   - —Symbolizes the thirsty soul ... Ps 42:1
   - —Symbolizes the joy of the redeemed ... Isa 35:6; Hab 3:19
3. Dog
   - —Symbolizes God's judgment ... 1Ki 21:19,23–24; Rev 22:15
   - —Symbolizes a fool ... Pr 26:11
   - —Symbolizes an enemy ... Ps 22:16,20
4. Donkey: symbolizes gentleness ... Zec 9:9
5. Fish
   See FISH
6. Fox
   - —Symbolizes that which threatens us ... SS 2:15
   - —Symbolizes slyness ... Lk 13:32
7. Horse
   See HORSE

8. Lamb
   See LAMB
9. Lion
   See LION
10. Ox: symbolizes faithfulness . . . Isa 1:3
11. Wolf: symbolizes a false prophet . . . Mt 7:15; Ac 20:29

See also BIRDS; INSECTS; REPTILES

ANNA
—A prophetess from the tribe of Asher . . . Lk 2:36
—Elderly widow . . . Lk 2:36–37
—Witnessed to others about baby Jesus . . . Lk 2:28

ANNAS
—High priest when John the Baptist ministered . . . Lk 3:2
—Father-in-law of Caiaphas, the high priest . . . Jn 18:13
—Jesus on trial before him . . . Jn 18:13,19–23
—Sent Jesus to Caiaphas . . . Jn 18:24
—Peter and John on trial before him . . . Ac 4:5–7

ANOINTING
—Pouring oil on God's servants
A. Purposes of anointing with oil
   1. For beautifying oneself . . . Ru 3:3; Ps 104:15
   2. For healing . . . Lk 10:34; Jas 5:14
   3. For dedicating officials to God . . . Ex 29:7; 1Sa 10:1; 1Ki 19:16
   4. For dedicating things to God
      —Jacob's stone pillow . . . Ge 28:18
      —The tabernacle and its utensils . . . Ex 40:9–11
B. Which officials received an anointing?
   1. In the Old Testament
      a. Prophets . . . 1Ki 19:16; Ps 105:15
      b. Priests . . . Ex 29:1,7; Lev 8:12
      c. Kings
         —Specific examples . . . 1Sa 10:1; 1Sa 16:1,13; 1Ki 19:16
         —Kings called "the LORD's anointed" . . . 1Sa 12:3; 1Sa 26:9; 2Ch 6:42
   2. In the New Testament
      a. Jesus, anointed by the Holy Spirit
         —Prophesied . . . Ps 2:2; Isa 61:1; Da 9:25–26
         —Performed at his baptism . . . Mt 3:16; Jn 1:32–33
      b. Christians, anointed by the Holy Spirit . . . 2Co 1:21; 1Jn 2:20,27

ANTICHRIST
A. Anyone who opposes Christ
   —Called an antichrist . . . 1Jn 2:18,22; 1Jn 4:3; 2Jn 7
   —Called a false Christ . . . Mt 24:24; Mk 13:22
B. *The* antichrist
   1. Given the title "the antichrist" . . . 1Jn 2:18
   2. Symbols of the antichrist
      —Daniel's little horn . . . Da 7:8,24–26
      —The king who exalts himself . . . Da 11:36–45
      —The abomination that causes desolation . . . Mk 13:14
      —The man of lawlessness . . . 2Th 2:3–4,8–10
      —The beast . . . Rev 11:7; Rev 13:1,11
   3. Characteristics of the antichrist
      —He is controlled by Satan . . . 2Th 2:9; Rev 13:2
      —He opposes God . . . Da 7:25; Da 11:36; 2Th 2:4; Rev 13:6
      —He teaches false views of Christ . . . 1Jn 2:22; 1Jn 4:3; 2Jn 7
      —He lies and deceives humanity . . . 1Jn 2:22; 2Jn 7
      —He performs counterfeit miracles . . . 2Th 2:9; Rev 13:3; Rev 19:20
      —He persecutes Christians . . . Rev 13:7
      —He gains political control of the world . . . Da 7:25; Da 11:40–45; Rev 13:7
      —He gains economic control of the world . . . Rev 13:16–17
      —He gains religious control of the world . . . 2Th 2:4; Rev 13:11–14
   4. The end of the antichrist
      —He is now being restrained . . . 2Th 2:6–7
      —He will be destroyed at Christ's return . . . 2Th 2:8
      —He will be thrown into the lake of fire . . . Rev 19:20; Rev 20:10

ANTIOCH
A. The capital of Syria
   1. Important Christian events at Antioch
      —First Gentile church located there . . . Ac 11:19–21
      —Barnabas sent there . . . Ac 11:22–24
      —Paul brought there by Barnabas . . . Ac 11:25–26
      —Disciples first called Christians there . . . Ac 11:26
      —Agabus prophesied there . . . Ac 11:27
      —Peter and Paul had conflict there . . . Gal 2:11–14
      —Sent delegates to council in Jerusalem . . . Ac 15:1–3
      —Church heard report of the council . . . Ac 15:22–31
   2. Antioch as a missionary church
      —Church sent out Paul and Barnabas . . . Ac 13:1–3
      —Paul and Barnabas reported to them . . . Ac 14:26–27
      —Paul's second journey began from there . . . Ac 15:35–40
      —Paul returned there after second journey . . . Ac 18:22
      —Paul's third journey began from there . . . Ac 18:23
B. An important town in Pisidia
   —Paul preached the gospel there . . . Ac 13:14–48
   —Word spread from there throughout region . . . Ac 13:49
   —Antioch Jews ran Paul out of town . . . Ac 13:50–51
   —Paul made brief return visit . . . Ac 14:21–23
   —Paul recalled persecution that occurred there . . . 2Ti 3:11

ANXIETY
—The experience of worry and concern
A. The experience of anxiety
   1. Appropriate concern
      —For other family members . . . 1Sa 10:2; Lk 2:48
      —At the thought of having sinned . . . Ps 139:23–24
      —For not being able to understand a vision . . . Da 7:15
      —For the welfare of other Christians . . . 2Co 11:28–29; Php 2:20,26,28
   2. Inappropriate anxiety
      —For life's basic necessities . . . Ecc 2:22–23; Eze 4:16–17; Mt 6:25–34; Lk 12:22–31
      —For trivial, unnecessary things . . . Lk 10:41
      —For the cares of this life . . . Mk 4:18–19
   3. Anxiety weighs us down . . . Pr 12:25
B. The cure for anxiety
   —We must not be anxious . . . Ecc 11:10; Mt 6:31; 1Co 7:32
   —God promises to remove anxiety . . . Ps 94:19
   —God promises to take care of us . . . Mt 6:34; 1Pe 5:7
   —We must rely on Jesus . . . Lk 21:14–15

—We must pray .... Php 4:6
See also PROVIDENCE

APOLLOS
—Jewish Christian from Alexandria .... Ac 18:24–25
—Instructed by Aquila and Priscilla .... Ac 18:26
—Ministered at Corinth .... Ac 18:27–28; Ac 19:1; 1Co 3:4–9
—Urged to revisit Corinth 1Co 16:12
—Messenger for Paul to Titus .... Titus 3:13

APOSTASY
—Falling away from the truth
See FALLING AWAY

APOSTLE
—Someone sent out on an official commission
A. Related themes
PETER AND PAUL is a theme of Acts .... Ac 19:11
DEFENSE is a theme of Galatians .... Gal 1:10
SELF-DEFENSE is a theme of 2 Corinthians 2Co 12:19
B. Jesus was an apostle, sent out by God .... Heb 3:1
C. Apostles sent out by Jesus
1. The 12 disciples as apostles
—Commissioned before his resurrection .... Mt 10:5–10
—Commissioned after his resurrection .... Mt 28:19; Ac 1:8
2. Paul as an apostle
—His call from the risen Christ .... Ac 9:5–6; Ac 22:8–10,18; Ac 26:15–18
—His defense of his apostleship .... 1Co 9:1–2; 2Co 10:1–11:33; 2Co 12:11–13; Gal 1:1–2:10
—His calling as apostle to the Gentiles .... Ro 11:13; Ro 15:16; Gal 2:8–9
3. Others called apostles
—Barnabas, with Paul .... Ac 14:4
—James, the Lord's brother .... Gal 1:19
—Andronicus and Junias .... Ro 16:7
—Silas and Timothy, with Paul 1Th 2:6
D. The duties of Christ's apostles
—Apostleship is one of God's gifts .... 1Co 12:28; Eph 4:11
—Forming the foundation of the church .... Eph 2:20; Rev 21:14
—Witnessing about Christ .... Ac 1:8
—Teaching true doctrine .... Ac 2:42
—Ministering the word of God .... Ac 6:2,4
—Making important decisions for the church .... Ac 15:1–2; Gal 2:1–3,7–10
E. The signs of apostleship
—Having seen the risen Christ .... Ac 1:21–22; 1Co 9:1
—Performing signs, wonders and miracles 2Co 12:12
—Being persecuted for the Lord .... Ac 5:40–41; 2Co 11:22–33

AQUILA
—Husband of Priscilla; tentmakers .... Ac 18:1–3
—Invited Paul to live with them .... Ac 18:3
—Traveled with Paul to Ephesus .... Ac 18:18–19
—Instructed Apollos .... Ac 18:26
—Paul considered him a co-worker .... Ro 16:3
—Church met in their house .... Ro 16:4

ARAM, ARAMEANS
See DAMASCUS

ARK OF THE COVENANT LAW
A. Its construction
—Made of acacia wood, overlaid with gold .... Ex 25:10–11; Ex 37:1–2
—Had gold rings for poles .... Ex 25:12–15; Ex 37:3–5
—Its lid was the atonement cover .... Ex 25:17–21; Ex 37:6–9
B. Its contents
—A jar of manna .... Ex 16:32–34
—Aaron's staff that had budded .... Nu 17:10–11
—The Ten Commandments .... Dt 10:1–2; 1Ki 8:9
—All three mentioned together .... Heb 9:4
C. Its symbolism
—Symbolized God's presence among his people .... Ex 30:6
—Symbolized the power of God .... Nu 10:35–36; Ps 132:8
—Sprinkled blood symbolized forgiveness of sin .... Lev 16:15–16
D. Its history
1. During the time of Moses and Joshua
—Placed in the Most Holy Place of tabernacle .... Ex 26:34
—Went before the Israelites on journey .... Nu 10:33
—Instrumental in crossing the Jordan .... Jos 3:1–3,14–17
—Instrumental in the capture of Jericho .... Jos 6:4–11
—Joshua prayed before the ark after Ai .... Jos 7:6
—Present at covenant renewal at Mount Ebal .... Jos 8:30–33
2. During the time of the judges
—Placed at Shiloh during Eli's time 1Sa 3:3,21
—Taken by Israelites into battle 1Sa 4:3–5
—Captured by Philistines 1Sa 4:11,17
—Returned by Philistines 1Sa 5:1–6:16
—Desecrated at Beth Shemesh 1Sa 6:19–20
—Sent to Kiriath Jearim 1Sa 6:21–7:2
3. During the time of David and Solomon
—Uzzah touched the ark and was killed 2Sa 6:1–8; 1Ch 13:1–10
—Ark stationed at the house of Obed-Edom 2Sa 6:10–11; 1Ch 13:13–14
—David brought it to Jerusalem 2Sa 6:12–17; 1Ch 15:1–16:1
—Temporarily removed under Absalom 2Sa 15:24–29
—Placed in the Most Holy Place of the temple 1Ki 8:3–9; 2Ch 5:2–10

See also TABERNACLE

ARMAGEDDON
See MEGIDDO

ARTAXERXES
—Permitted Ezra and his group to go to Canaan .... Ezr 7:1,11–26
—Employed Nehemiah as cupbearer .... Ne 2:1
—Issued order to stop rebuilding Jerusalem .... Ezr 4:7–23
—Sent Nehemiah to rebuild walls of Jerusalem .... Ne 2:1–9
—Appointed Nehemiah as governor .... Ne 5:14

ASA
—Son of Abijah; king of Judah 1Ki 14:31; 1Ki 15:8–10
—A godly reformer 1Ki 15:11–12; 2Ch 15:1–19
—Removed grandmother as queen 1Ki 15:13
—Increased strength of Judah 2Ch 14:7–8
—Defeated Cushites 2Ch 14:9–15
—Waged war with Israel 1Ki 15:16–17
—Made alliance with Ben-Hadad 1Ki 15:18–21; 2Ch 16:2–6
—Hanani prophesied against him 2Ch 16:7–9
—Punished by God in his death 2Ch 16:11–14

ASAHEL
—Nephew of David 1Ch 2:16
—One of David's warriors 1Ch 11:26
—One of David's 12 commanders 1Ch 27:7
—Pursued Abner 2Sa 2:18–22
—Killed by Abner 2Sa 2:23
—Death avenged by Joab 2Sa 3:22–27

ASAPH
A. Father of Hezekiah's recorder .... 2Ki 18:18,37; Isa 36:3,22
B. A Levite musician 1Ch 15:19; 1Ch 16:4–7,37

—Called a seer — 2Ch 29:30
—His descendants were singers — 1Ch 25:1–2,6; Ezr 2:41; Ne 11:22–23
—Wrote various psalms — 2Ch 29:30; Ps 50; Ps 73–83

ASCENSION

—The return of Jesus to heaven

A. The event
—Prophesied in the Old Testament — Ps 24:7–11; Ps 68:18; Ps 110:1
—Prophesied by Jesus — Jn 7:33; Jn 13:1,3; Jn 20:17
—Recorded in the New Testament — Mk 16:19; Lk 24:51; Ac 1:9
—Occurred 40 days after the resurrection — Ac 1:3

B. Activities of the ascended Christ
—He sat at God's right hand — Ac 2:33; Ac 5:31; Heb 1:3
—He stood at God's right hand — Ac 7:55–56
—He brought his atoning blood to God — Heb 9:12
—He sent forth his Spirit — Jn 16:7; Ac 1:4–5; Ac 2:33
—He gave gifts to humans — Eph 4:8–10
—He is now enthroned in power — Eph 1:20–21; Php 2:9–11; 1Pe 3:22; Rev 1:5
—He is crowned with glory and honor — 1Ti 3:16; Heb 2:9
—He is praised by multitudes in heaven — Rev 5:6–14; Rev 7:9–12
—He is destroying God's enemies — 1Co 15:24–26; Heb 10:12–13
—He is interceding for us — Ro 8:34; Heb 7:25–26; 1Jn 2:1
—He is preparing a place for us — Jn 14:2–3
—He is preparing for us to reign with him — 2Ti 2:12; Rev 20:5–6
—He is planning his return — Jn 14:18,28; Ac 1:11

C. Activities of the ascended Christ on earth
—He identifies himself with believers — Mt 25:40; Jn 17:21–23; Ac 9:4–5
—He draws believers to himself — Eph 2:6; Col 3:1–4
—He is with Christians gathered in his name — Mt 18:20
—He is with us always — Mt 28:20
—He protects Christians — Ac 18:9–10
—He directs Christians — Ac 22:17–21

ASHER

A. Son of Jacob by Zilpah — Ge 35:26
—Name means "happy" — Ge 30:12–13
—Went to Egypt with family — Ge 46:8,17
—Father of five sons — Ge 46:17
—Blessed by Jacob — Ge 49:20

B. Tribe descended from Asher
—Blessed by Moses — Dt 33:24–25
—Numbered — Nu 1:40–41; Nu 26:44–47
—Allotted land in Canaan — Jos 19:24–31; Eze 48:2
—Failed to possess land — Jdg 1:31–32
—Failed to support Deborah — Jdg 5:17
—Supported Gideon — Jdg 6:35; Jdg 7:23
—Supported David — 1Ch 12:36
—Supported Hezekiah — 2Ch 30:10–11
—Anna from the tribe of Asher — Lk 2:36
—One of the tribes of the 144,000 — Rev 7:6

ASIA

—Area east of the Aegean Sea (present-day Turkey)

A. The Jews of Asia
—Were in Jerusalem at Pentecost — Ac 2:7–9
—Opposed Stephen — Ac 6:9
—Incited riot against Paul in Jerusalem — Ac 21:27–31

B. The church in Asia

1. Churches established there
—Ephesus — Eph 1:1; Rev 2:1
—Colossae — Col 1:1
—Laodicea — Col 4:16; Rev 3:14
—Troas — Ac 20:6–12
—Smyrna — Rev 2:8
—Pergamum — Rev 2:12
—Thyatira — Rev 2:18
—Sardis — Rev 3:1
—Philadelphia — Rev 3:7

2. Events
—Paul's first convert was Epenetus — Ro 16:5
—Paul ministered in Ephesus — Ac 19:8–10,22; Ac 20:17–18
—Gospel went through Asia from Ephesus — Ac 19:10,26
—Paul suffered greatly there — 2Co 1:8–9
—Paul addressed letters to them — Eph 1:1; Col 1:2; Col 4:16
—Peter addressed his letter to them — 1Pe 1:1
—Timothy ministered in Ephesus — 1Ti 1:3
—John wrote to seven churches there — Rev 1:4

ASSURANCE

—Being certain of our salvation

A. Of what can we be sure?
—Our calling and election — 2Pe 1:10
—God's abiding love — Ro 8:38–39
—Being God's children — Ro 8:16
—Our salvation at the last day — Php 1:6; 2Ti 1:12
—Our inheritance from God — Heb 6:11–12
—Our resurrection at the last day — Job 19:25–26
—Seeing our ascended Lord — 1Jn 3:2
—Receiving a crown of righteousness — 2Ti 4:8
—Having eternal life — 1Jn 5:13

B. How do we obtain assurance?
—By believing God's word — 1Jn 5:13
—By accepting God's promises — Jn 3:16,36; Jn 6:39–40; 1Jn 5:12–13

C. On what is our assurance founded?
—On God's choosing of us — Eph 1:4–8; 1Th 1:4
—On God's keeping us safe — Jn 6:39; Jn 10:28–30
—On God's powerful love — Ro 8:35–39

D. What assures us of our salvation?
—The Spirit living within us — Ro 8:14–16; Gal 4:6
—Our faith — Ac 13:48; Ro 3:22,30; Ro 10:9–10; Eph 2:8
—Our hope — Heb 6:11,18–19
—Our life of love and good works — Mt 7:20; Gal 5:19–24; 2Pe 1:5–8,10; 1Jn 3:10–14

E. Examples of those who experienced assurance
—David — Ps 23:6

—Old Testament saints ... Isa 32:17
—Paul ... 2Ti 1:12; 2Ti 4:7–8,18
—Christians in general ... 1Jn 2:12–14

F. Assurance is compatible with
—Doubt ... Mk 9:23–24
—Sin in our lives ... Gal 6:1; 1Jn 1:8–10
—Partial understanding of God's truth ... 1Co 13:8–12

ASSYRIANS

A. Their identity
—Descendants of Cush, grandson of Noah ... Ge 10:6,8–11
—Capital city is Nineveh ... Ge 10:11
See NINEVEH
—Located by the Euphrates River ... Isa 27:12–13; Jer 2:18

B. Kings of Assyria (in chronological order)
—Pul ... 2Ki 15:19
—Tiglath-Pileser ... 2Ki 15:29
—Shalmaneser ... 2Ki 17:3–4
—Sargon ... Isa 20:1
—Sennacherib ... 2Ki 18:13
—Esarhaddon ... 2Ki 19:37
—Ashurbanipal ... Ezr 4:10

C. Campaigns against God's people
1. Against the northern kingdom
—First invasion ... 2Ki 15:19
—Received tribute money and withdrew ... 2Ki 15:19–20
—Second invasion ... 2Ki 15:29
—Territories annexed and people deported ... 2Ki 15:29
—Hoshea refused to submit ... 2Ki 17:3–4
—Three-year siege of Samaria ... 2Ki 17:5; 2Ki 18:9
—Samaria captured and people deported ... 2Ki 17:6; 2Ki 18:10–11
—Other people settled in Samaria ... 2Ki 17:24
2. Against the southern kingdom
—King Ahaz allied with Assyria ... 2Ki 16:7–9; 2Ch 28:16–18
—Assyria did not help Ahaz ... 2Ch 28:19–21
—Hezekiah refused to pay tribute ... 2Ki 18:7
—Sennacherib attacked cities of Judah ... 2Ki 18:13
—Hezekiah paid tribute from temple riches ... 2Ki 18:14–16
—Sennacherib attacked Jerusalem ... 2Ki 18:17–19:13; 2Ch 32:9–19; Isa 36:1–37:13
—Hezekiah prayed for deliverance ... 2Ki 19:14–19; Isa 37:14–20
—Isaiah prophesied the fall of Assyria ... 2Ki 19:20–34; Isa 37:21–35
—The defeat of Assyria and Sennacherib ... 2Ki 19:35–36; 2Ch 32:20–21; Isa 37:36–38

D. Important data concerning them
1. Garden of Eden in vicinity of Ashur ... Ge 2:14
2. Country of Assyria was beautiful ... Eze 31:3–9
3. Character of the Assyrians
—A godless nation ... Isa 10:6
—A powerful nation ... 2Ki 19:11,17; Isa 28:2
—A proud nation ... 2Ki 19:23–24; Isa 10:12; Eze 31:3,10
—A cruel nation ... Na 3:1–4
4. God used Assyrians to punish Israelites ... 2Ki 17:7–17; Isa 7:17–25; Isa 10:5–6
5. Prophecies concerning them
—Assyrians to be destroyed ... Isa 10:5,12–19; Isa 30:31–33; Na 2:1–13; Zep 2:13–15
—Israelites to be called back from Assyria ... Isa 11:11–16; Isa 27:12–13; Hos 11:11; Mic 7:11–12; Zec 10:8–12
—Assyrians to worship the Lord someday ... Isa 19:23–25

ATHALIAH

—Daughter of Ahab ... 2Ki 8:26
—Wife of Jehoram and mother of Ahaziah ... 2Ki 8:18,26; 2Ch 22:2
—Made herself queen by killing Ahaziah's sons ... 2Ki 11:1–2; 2Ch 22:10–12
—Ruled for six years ... 2Ki 11:3
—Killed when Joash was made king ... 2Ki 11:4–16; 2Ch 23:1–15

ATHLETICS

A. References to athletic activities in the Bible
—Wrestling ... Ge 32:24–25
—Slinging ... Jdg 20:16
—Archery ... 1Sa 20:18–22, 35–40
—Running ... 2Sa 18:19–26
—Boxing ... 1Co 9:26
—Competing in the games ... 1Co 9:25

B. Athletics used in symbolic ways
1. Archery: Job felt like God's target ... Job 16:12–13
2. Ball-throwing: symbol of God's judgment ... Isa 22:17–18
3. Running races
—Running in the path of God's commands ... Ps 119:32
—Running the Christian race ... Heb 12:1–2
—Not running in vain ... Gal 2:2; Php 2:16
4. Wrestling: symbol of struggling with Satan ... Eph 6:12
5. The games
—The necessity of strict training ... 1Co 9:24–27
—Competing according to the rules ... 2Ti 2:5
6. The crown or prize awaiting believers ... 1Co 9:25; Php 3:13–14; 2Ti 2:5; 2Ti 4:8; 1Pe 5:4

ATONEMENT

—Procedure of reconciling sinners to God

A. Elements involved in atonement
—Sin of humanity ... Isa 6:7; Isa 27:9; Da 9:24; Jn 1:29
—Blood must be shed ... Lev 16:14,18; Heb 9:19–22
—Substitutionary sacrifice is offered ... Lev 4:13–20; Lev 5:5–10; Isa 53:4–7; 1Jn 2:2
—Guilt is transferred to the substitute ... Lev 1:3–4; Lev 16:21–22; 2Co 5:21
—Forgiveness is granted ... Lev 4:26,31,35; Ro 3:23–25

B. Old Testament Day of Atonement
—Description of the Day of Atonement ... Lev 16:2–34; Lev 23:26–32; Nu 29:7–11
—Involved only the high priest ... Heb 9:7
—Performed in the Most Holy Place ... Lev 16:2,16–20; Heb 9:8,25
—Done once a year ... Ex 30:10; Lev 16:34; Heb 9:7
—Year of Jubilee began on Day of Atonement ... Lev 25:9

C. Atonement accomplished by Christ
1. Symbolized in Old Testament sacrifices
—The Passover lamb ... Ex 12:1–7,12–13; 1Co 5:7

—A lamb that takes away sin ..... Isa 53:7
Jn 1:29,36
1Pe 1:18–19
Rev 5:6
—The Day of Atonement ..... Heb 9:7–14,23–28

2. Fulfilled in the New Testament
—Sacrifice of Christ atones for sin..... Ro 3:25
1Co 5:7
Heb 9:28
1Jn 2:2
1Jn 4:10
—Christ presented his blood to God..... Heb 9:12,14

3. The results of Christ's atoning blood
—Our sins are forgiven..... Eph 1:7
—We are purified from sin..... 1Jn 1:7
—We are freed from sin ..... Rev 1:5
—We are redeemed ..... Ro 3:24–25
1Pe 1:18
—We are saved ..... Ro 5:9
—We are reconciled with God..... Ro 5:10
Col 1:20
—We have peace with God ..... Col 1:20
—We are made holy..... Heb 13:12
—We are reconciled to other Christians..... Eph 2:14–17
—The power of the devil is destroyed..... Col 2:15
Heb 2:14

AUTHORITY

—The ability to exercise power over others

A. Related themes
1. AUTHORITY is a theme of:
—Matthew..... Mt 7:29
—John..... Jn 10:18
2. LEADERSHIP is a theme of:
—Ezra..... Ezr 7:10
—Nehemiah..... Ne 13:25
—1 Timothy..... 1Ti 4:16

B. Human authority
1. Given as a gift from God and Christ
—To humans for ruling creation ..... Ge 1:28
Ps 8:6–8
—To kings for ruling people..... Ps 72:1
Ro 13:1–5
—To prophets for speaking ..... Dt 18:18
—To disciples for driving out demons..... Mk 6:7,13
—To apostles for forgiving sins ..... Jn 20:22–23
—To apostles for founding the church ..... Mt 16:19
Mt 18:18
—To church leaders for building the church 2Co 10:8
2Co 13:10
Eph 4:11–13
Titus 2:15
—To saints for judging the world 1Co 6:2–3
2. Exercised by humans
—Often done by exerting power..... Mt 20:25
Mk 10:42
Lk 22:25
—Christian authority defined by service ..... Mt 20:26–28
Mk 10:43–45
Lk 22:26–27
See SERVANT
3. Misused by humans
—In ascribing power to ourselves, not God..... Dt 8:10–18
—In depending on ourselves, not God..... Ps 147:10–11
—In oppressing the poor..... Ps 10:2–11
—In exalting power rather than wisdom..... Ecc 9:12–18

C. Divine authority
1. Authority of God
—Power and authority ascribed to him..... 2Ch 20:6
Ps 66:3,5–7
Jude 25
—His authority may not be questioned..... Ro 9:20–21
—Even Satan under his control..... Job 1:6–12
Job 2:1–7
2. Authority of Jesus
a. While on earth
—To drive out evil spirits ..... Mk 1:34
—To preach the word ..... Mt 7:28–29
—To forgive sins ..... Mk 2:5–12
—To give eternal life..... Jn 17:2
—To control nature..... Mk 4:39–41
—To raise the dead..... Jn 10:17–18
Jn 11:23–27,38–44
—To judge ..... Jn 5:27–30
b. Now in heaven
—All authority given to him ..... Mt 28:18
Php 2:9–11
—Has authority at God's right hand..... Eph 1:20–23
Col 2:9–10
—Controls history..... Rev 5:1–5
—Is ruler of the kings of the earth ..... Rev 1:5
—Is King of kings and Lord of lords..... Rev 17:14
Rev 19:16

AWE

—Reverence for the Lord
See FEAR

BAASHA

—Killed Nadab to become king of Israel 1Ki 15:27–28
—Killed rest of Jeroboam's family..... 1Ki 15:29–30
—Fought against Asa of Judah 1Ki 15:16–22,32
—Evil reign for 24 years 1Ki 15:33–34
—Jehu prophesied against him..... 1Ki 16:1–4
—Family killed by Zimri 1Ki 16:9–13

BABYLON

A. Identity and early history of the city
—Descendants of Ham..... Ge 10:6,8–10
—City is built by Nimrod..... Ge 10:8–10
—Rebellion against God at the tower of Babel..... Ge 11:1–9

B. The nation of Babylon
1. Significant Babylonians
—Marduk-Baladan: paid visit to Hezekiah..... 2Ki 20:12–13
—Nebuchadnezzar 2Ki 24:1
See NEBUCHADNEZZAR
—Nebuzaradan: commander of army 2Ki 24:8
—Awel-Marduk: released Jehoiachin..... 2Ki 25:27
—Belshazzar: saw handwriting on the wall ..... Da 5:1
2. Chronological history
—Under the control of Assyria..... 2Ki 17:24
—Envoys visited Hezekiah 2Ki 20:12–18
—Invaded Judah during Jehoiakim's reign 2Ki 24:1–2
—Exiles deported with Jehoiachin 2Ki 24:10–16
—Nebuchadnezzar's dream..... Da 2:1–49
—Nebuchadnezzar's image and fiery furnace..... Da 3:1–30
—King Zedekiah's revolt..... 2Ch 36:13
—Nebuchadnezzar marched on Jerusalem ..... Jer 52:4–5
—Jerusalem totally destroyed..... 2Ki 25:4,8–10
Jer 52:12–14
—A second group deported..... 2Ki 25:11
2Ch 36:20
—Nebuchadnezzar's madness and restoration ..... Da 4:1–37
—A third group deported..... Jer 52:24–27
—King Belshazzar's banquet..... Da 5:1–4
—Medes took over Babylon..... Da 5:30–31
3. Jews in Babylon
—Three waves of exiles ..... Jer 52:28–30
—Daniel and friends in royal service ..... Da 1:1–21
—Ezekiel saw visions ..... Eze 1:1–28
—Jews encouraged to settle there ..... Jer 29:1–7
—Seventy years of exile..... Jer 25:11
2Ch 36:21
—Jews experienced grief..... Ps 137:1–6
—Jews allowed to return under Persians..... 2Ch 36:22–23
Ezr 1:1–4
4. Characteristics of the Babylonians
a. A powerful nation
—A naval power ..... Isa 43:14

—A military power … Jer 5:15–17; Jer 51:34
—A worldwide kingdom … Da 2:37–38; Da 4:22
—A glorious nation … Da 4:28–30,36
—A wealthy people … Jer 51:13

b. A wicked nation
—They trusted in wickedness … Isa 47:10
—They were idolatrous … Jer 50:38
—They engaged in sacrilegious feasting … Da 5:1–3
—They were cruel … Isa 14:4,16–17; Hab 1:6–7
—They showed arrogance against God … Isa 14:13–14

5. Prophecies concerning Babylon
—They will conquer the world … Jer 21:3–10; Jer 27:1–11; Eze 21:18–23; Eze 29:19
—They will be destroyed … Isa 13:1–14:23; Isa 14:3–22; Isa 21:1–10; Isa 47:1–15; Jer 50:1–51:58

C. New Testament references to Babylon
1. As a symbol of the Roman Empire … 1Pe 5:13
2. As a symbol of the power of the antichrist
—Inspires people to sin … Rev 14:8; Rev 18:2–5
—Persecutes the church … Rev 17:5–6; Rev 18:24
—Makes war with the Lamb … Rev 17:9–18
—Will be destroyed completely … Rev 18:2–10,16–24

BALAAM

A. Personal data
—Son of Beor … Nu 22:5
—Lived in Mesopotamia … Dt 23:4
—Considered a prophet … 2Pe 2:16
—Killed by Israelites … Nu 31:8; Jos 13:22

B. His history
—Asked by Balak to curse Israelites … Nu 22:4–8
—Commanded by God not to go … Nu 22:9–13
—Asked by Balak a second time … Nu 22:15–17
—Permitted to go … Nu 22:18–20
—Met by an angel on the way … Nu 22:21–35
—Uttered blessings instead of curses … Nu 23:1–24:10
—Prophesied about Christ … Nu 24:15–19
—Advised Balak to intermarry with Israelites … Nu 31:15–16
—Returned home … Nu 24:25

C. New Testament references
—Considered an example of greed … 2Pe 2:14–15; Jude 11
—Considered a teacher of immorality … Rev 2:14

BALAK

—Moabite king, frightened by Israelites … Nu 22:1–4
—Hired Balaam to curse Israelites … Nu 22:4–20; Jos 24:9
—Encouraged Moabites to marry Israelites … Rev 2:14

BANNER

—A flag or insignia

A. How banners were used
—To designate different families … Nu 2:2
—To rally troops … SS 6:4
—To send messages … Isa 13:2; Isa 18:3

B. The banner used as a symbol
—The Lord as our Banner … Ex 17:15
—Jesus Christ as a banner for all nations … Isa 11:10
—The banner of love … SS 2:4
—God rallies us to his banner … Ps 60:4
—God rallies all nations to his banner … Isa 11:12; Isa 49:22–23
—We lift up victory banners … Ps 20:5
—We raise a banner for the nations … Isa 62:10–11
—God rallies armies to use in judgment … Isa 5:26–29; Isa 13:2

BAPTISM

—The sacrament of initiation

A. Baptism of John the Baptist
—Where John baptized … Jn 1:28; Jn 3:23
—He baptized many people … Mt 3:5–6
—He baptized Jesus … Mt 3:13–15
—His baptism symbolized repentance … Mt 3:11
—His baptism meant to reveal Jesus … Jn 1:31
—His baptism looked ahead to Spirit baptism … Lk 3:16

B. Baptism by Jesus' disciples … Jn 3:22; Jn 4:1–2

C. Christian baptism
1. It was commanded by Jesus … Mt 28:19–20; Mk 16:16
2. It was done in the name
—Of the Father, the Son, the Holy Spirit … Mt 28:19
—Of Jesus Christ … Ac 2:38; Ac 10:48
—Of the Lord Jesus … Ac 19:5
3. It was typified in the Old Testament
—In the story of the flood … 1Pe 3:19–21
—In the rite of circumcision … Col 2:11–12
—In the crossing of the "Red Sea" … 1Co 10:2
4. Occurrences of Christian baptism
—3,000 on Pentecost … Ac 2:41
—New believers in Samaria … Ac 8:12
—Ethiopian eunuch … Ac 8:36–38
—Saul at his conversion … Ac 9:18
—Cornelius and his friends … Ac 10:48
—Lydia and her household … Ac 16:15
—Philippian jailer and his household … Ac 16:33
—New believers in Corinth … Ac 18:8
—Gaius, Crispus, household of Stephanas … 1Co 1:14–16
—New believers at Ephesus … Ac 19:1–7
5. Symbolism of Christian baptism
—Forgiveness of sins … Ac 2:38
—Washing away of sin … Ac 22:16
—Spiritual rebirth … Titus 3:5
—Salvation … 1Pe 3:21
—Dying with Christ … Ro 6:3–4; Col 2:12
—Spiritual circumcision … Col 2:11–12
—Inclusion in the body of Christ … 1Co 12:13
—Unity in the body of Christ … Eph 4:3–6
—Being clothed with Christ … Gal 3:27
6. Characteristics of Christian baptism
—Only one baptism … Eph 4:5
—Done with water … Ac 8:36–38; Ac 10:47
—Faith is essential … Mk 16:16; Ac 8:12; Ac 16:31–34
—Repentance is essential … Ac 2:38
—Linked with receiving the Holy Spirit … Ac 2:38; Ac 10:44–48; Ac 19:2–6
—Separated from receiving the Spirit … Ac 8:14–17
—Administered to households … Ac 16:15,33; 1Co 1:16

BAPTISM OF THE HOLY SPIRIT

A. Jesus was baptized with the Holy Spirit … Mt 3:16; Jn 1:32–33

B. Jesus baptized with the Holy Spirit
—Prophesied by John … Mt 3:11; Lk 3:16
—Prophesied by Jesus … Ac 1:5
—Fulfilled at Pentecost … Ac 2:1–4

C. Relationship to water baptism
—Water baptism linked with Spirit baptism ... Ac 2:38–39
Ac 9:17–18
Ac 10:44–48
Ac 19:1–6
—Water baptism separated from Spirit baptism ... Ac 8:12,14–17
—Born of water and the Spirit ... Jn 3:5
—Baptized by one Spirit into one body ... 1Co 12:13
—Washing of rebirth and renewal by Spirit ... Titus 3:5

BARABBAS
—Prisoner at the time of Jesus ... Mt 27:16
—Committed murder and insurrection ... Mk 15:7
Jn 18:40
—Received freedom in place of Jesus ... Mt 27:17–26
Ac 3:13–14

BARAK
—Warrior who fought with Deborah against Sisera ... Jdg 4:6–16
—Sang song with Deborah ... Jdg 5:1–31
—Considered an example of faith ... Heb 11:32

BARNABAS
A. Personal data
—Originally named Joseph ... Ac 4:36
—Full of the Holy Spirit and faith ... Ac 11:24
—Sold property, brought proceeds to the church ... Ac 4:37
—Considered a prophet and teacher ... Ac 13:1
—Considered an apostle ... Ac 14:14
B. Relationship with Paul
—Brought Paul to the apostles ... Ac 9:27
—Brought Paul to Antioch ... Ac 11:25–26
—Brought gift with Paul to Jerusalem ... Ac 11:28–29
—Accompanied Paul on missionary journey ... Ac 13–14
—Went to Jerusalem for conference ... Ac 15:1–2,12
Gal 2:1–9
—Conflict with Paul over John Mark ... Ac 15:36–40
—Conflict with Paul over eating with Gentiles ... Gal 2:11–13
—Co-worker with Paul ... 1Co 9:6
Col 4:10

BARTHOLOMEW
—Disciple of Jesus ... Mk 3:18
—One of the apostles ... Mt 10:3
Ac 1:13
—Probably also known as Nathanael ... Jn 1:45–49

BARUCH
—Son of Neriah ... Jer 32:12
—Jeremiah's secretary and friend ... Jer 32:12–16
Jer 36:4–32
—Forced to go to Egypt ... Jer 43:1–7
—Received comforting message from Jeremiah ... Jer 45:1–5

BARZILLAI
—Gileadite who aided David ... 2Sa 17:27–29
—Unable to go with David because of age ... 2Sa 19:31–39

BATHSHEBA
—Wife of Uriah ... 2Sa 11:3
—Committed adultery with David ... 2Sa 11:4
—Sent message she was pregnant ... 2Sa 11:5
—Became wife of David after Uriah was killed ... 2Sa 11:27
—First child died ... 2Sa 12:13–23
—Mother of Solomon ... 2Sa 12:24
—Influenced David to make Solomon king ... 1Ki 1:11–31
—Pleaded with Solomon for Adonijah ... 1Ki 2:13–25

BEERSHEBA
A. History of Beersheba
—Southernmost city in the land of Israel ... Jdg 20:1
—Hagar fled there from Sarah ... Ge 21:14–19
—Abraham made a treaty with Abimelek there ... Ge 21:22–31
—Abraham lived there a while ... Ge 22:19
—Isaac made a treaty with Abimelek there ... Ge 26:23–33
—Jacob stopped there on the way to Egypt ... Ge 46:1–5
—Allotted to tribe of Judah ... Jos 15:21,28
—Later allotted to tribe of Simeon ... Jos 19:1–2
—Samuel's sons served as judges there ... 1Sa 8:1–3
—Elijah escaped there from Jezebel ... 1Ki 19:3
—Became a center of idolatry ... 2Ki 23:8
Am 8:14
—Resettled after the exile ... Ne 11:27,30
B. Appearances of God there
—To Hagar, to give her water ... Ge 21:17–19
—To Isaac, to bless him ... Ge 26:23–25
—To Jacob, to reassure him ... Ge 46:1–4
—To Elijah, to strengthen him ... 1Ki 19:3–7

BELSHAZZAR
—King of Babylon ... Da 7:1
—Gave a huge feast ... Da 5:1–4
—Saw handwriting on the wall ... Da 5:5–29
—Killed by the Medes ... Da 5:30–31

BENEVOLENCE
See THE RICH AND THE POOR; STEWARDSHIP

BEN-HADAD
A. King of Damascus ... 1Ki 15:18
—Made treaty with Asa ... 1Ki 15:18–19
—Fought against Israelite cities ... 1Ki 15:20–21
B. Another king of Damascus ... 1Ki 20:1
—Fought against Ahab ... 1Ki 20:2–12
—Defeated by Ahab ... 1Ki 20:13–21
—Fought Israel again the next year ... 1Ki 20:26–28
—Again defeated by Ahab ... 1Ki 20:29–30
—Made peace with Israelites ... 1Ki 20:31–34
—Later besieged Samaria ... 2Ki 6:24
—Siege miraculously lifted ... 2Ki 7:5–7
—Killed by Hazael ... 2Ki 8:7–15
C. Another king of Damascus ... 2Ki 13:24
—Son of Hazael ... 2Ki 13:24
—Defeated by Jehoash three times ... 2Ki 13:25
—Amos prophesied against him ... Am 1:3–5

BENJAMIN
A. Twelfth son of Jacob, second of Rachel ... Ge 35:16–24
—Name means "son of my right hand" ... Ge 35:16–18
—Favored by Jacob ... Ge 42:4
—Accompanied brothers to Egypt ... Ge 43:1–15
—Royal cup found in his sack ... Ge 44:1–13
—Judah interceded for him ... Ge 44:18–34
—Moved to Egypt with his family ... Ge 46:8,19
—Father of ten sons ... Ge 46:21
—Blessed by Jacob ... Ge 49:27
B. Tribe descended from Benjamin
—Blessed by Moses ... Dt 33:12
—Numbered ... Nu 1:36–37
Nu 26:38–41
—Allotted land ... Jos 18:11–28
—Failed to possess land fully ... Jdg 1:21
—Nearly obliterated ... Jdg 20–21
—King Saul from this tribe ... 1Sa 10:20–24
—Sided with Ish-Bosheth after Saul's death ... 2Sa 2:8–11
—Turned to David ... 1Ch 12:23,29
—The apostle Paul was from this tribe ... Ro 11:1
Php 3:5
—One of the tribes of the 144,000 ... Rev 7:8

BETHANY
—A town on the Mount of Olives ... Lk 19:29
—Less than two miles from Jerusalem ... Jn 11:18
—The hometown of Mary, Martha and Lazarus ... Jn 11:1
—Jesus stayed there after Triumphal Entry ... Mk 11:11
—Jesus anointed by Mary there ... Mt 26:6–13
Mk 14:3–9
Jn 12:1–8
—Jesus ascended into heaven from there ... Lk 24:50–51

BETHEL
A. Identity of Bethel
—Originally called Luz ... Ge 28:19
—Close to Ai ... Jos 12:9
—On the border between Ephraim and Benjamin ... Jos 16:1–2
Jos 18:11–13
—Originally given to Benjamin ... Jos 18:21–22

—Later belonged to Ephraim ... Jdg 4:5
1Ch 7:20,28
—Southernmost city of northern kingdom ... 1Ki 12:26–29

B. History of Bethel
—Abram built an altar near there ... Ge 12:8
Ge 13:3
—Jacob had a dream there ... Ge 28:10–17
—Jacob returned there with his family ... Ge 35:1–7
—Ephraim attacked the city and took it ... Jdg 1:22–26
—Samuel served as judge there ... 1Sa 7:15–16
—Prophet spoke against Jeroboam there ... 1Ki 13:1–6
—Abijah captured it from Jeroboam ... 2Ch 13:19–20
—Youths mocked Elisha and were killed ... 2Ki 2:23–24
—Amos prophesied against Israel there ... Am 7:10–13
—Josiah destroyed Jeroboam's altars ... 2Ki 23:15
—Resettled after exile ... Ne 11:31

C. Religious importance of Bethel
—God appeared to Jacob there ... Ge 28:10–19
Ge 35:9–15
—God was "the God of Bethel" ... Ge 31:13
—People inquired of the Lord there ... Jdg 20:18
Jdg 21:2–3
—The ark was kept there for a while ... Jdg 20:26–27
—Jeroboam set up golden calf there ... 1Ki 12:28–32
—A company of prophets lived there ... 2Ki 2:2–3,23
—Became known for its idolatry ... Am 4:4
—Prophesied against because of idolatry ... Hos 10:15
Am 3:14
Am 5:5–6

BETHLEHEM

A. Identity of Bethlehem
—Originally called Ephrath ... Ge 35:19
—A city given to Judah ... Ru 1:1
—Known as "the town of David" ... Lk 2:4,11

B. Important events at Bethlehem
—Rachel buried there ... Ge 35:19–20
—Ibzan judged there ... Jdg 12:8–10
—Home of Elimelek and Naomi ... Ru 1:1,19–22
—Ruth married Boaz there ... Ru 4:11–13
—David anointed king there ... 1Sa 16:4–13
—Philistines controlled it for a while ... 2Sa 23:14–17
—Rehoboam fortified it ... 2Ch 11:5–6

C. Jesus and Bethlehem
—Micah prophesied Messiah to be born there ... Mic 5:2
Mt 2:3–6
Jn 7:42
—Jesus was born in Bethlehem ... Mt 2:1
Lk 2:1–7
—Herod killed babies there ... Mt 2:16–18

BETHSAIDA

—A town in Galilee ... Jn 12:21
—Three of the disciples came from there ... Jn 1:44
—Feeding of the 5,000 occurred there ... Lk 9:10–17
—Jesus healed a blind man there ... Mk 8:22–26
—Jesus denounced it for unbelief ... Mt 11:20–22
Lk 10:13–14

BEZALEL

—Craftsman filled with God's Spirit ... Ex 31:1–3
Ex 35:30–31
—Supervised building of the tabernacle ... Ex 31:4–11
Ex 36:1–5

BILDAD

—One of Job's friends who tried to comfort him ... Job 2:11–13
—His first speech ... Job 8:1–22
—His second speech ... Job 18:1–21
—His third speech ... Job 25:1–6
—Offered sacrifices to God after Job's restoration ... Job 42:7–9

BILHAH

—Servant of Rachel ... Ge 29:29
—Mother of Dan and Naphtali ... Ge 30:1–7
Ge 35:25
—Reuben slept with her ... Ge 35:22

BIRDS

A. Birds mentioned in the Bible
—Bat ... Lev 11:19
—Birds of prey ... Ge 15:11
—Carrion birds ... Eze 39:4
—Chicken ... Mt 23:37
—Cormorant ... Lev 11:17
—Dove ... SS 2:12,14
—Eagle ... Jer 49:16
—Falcon ... Dt 14:13
—Gull ... Lev 11:16
—Hawk ... Lev 11:16
—Heron ... Lev 11:19
—Hoopoe ... Lev 11:19
—Kite (various types) ... Lev 11:14
—Mourning dove ... Isa 38:14
—Osprey ... Lev 11:18
—Ostrich ... Job 39:13–18
—Owl (various types) ... Isa 34:11
—Partridge ... 1Sa 26:20
—Pigeon ... Lev 5:7,11
—Quail ... Nu 11:31–32
—Raven ... Ge 8:7
—Rooster ... Mt 26:74
—Sparrow ... Ps 84:3
—Stork ... Lev 11:19
—Swallow ... Pr 26:2
—Swift ... Jer 8:7
—Thrush ... Jer 8:7
—Vulture (various types) ... Lev 11:13

B. Birds used as symbols

1. The dove
—Symbolizes mourning ... Isa 38:14
Isa 59:11
—Symbolizes renewal ... Ge 8:10–12
—Symbolizes the Holy Spirit ... Mt 3:16
—Symbolizes innocence ... Mt 10:16

2. The eagle
—Symbolizes deliverance ... Ex 19:4
Rev 12:14
—Symbolizes power ... Jer 4:13
Eze 17:3,7
—Symbolizes youthfulness ... Ps 103:5
Isa 40:31

3. The sparrow
—Symbolizes God's protecting care ... Ps 84:3
Mt 10:29–31

BLASPHEMY

—Bringing reproach against God

A. How can one blaspheme God?
—By speaking against God ... Lev 24:11,16
Mt 26:64–65
Ac 6:11
—By speaking against God's word ... Ac 6:11
—By engaging in idolatry ... Ne 9:18,26
Eze 20:27–28
—By persecuting the church ... 1Ti 1:13
—By oppressing the poor ... Jas 2:2–7
—By bearing a sacrilegious name ... Rev 13:1

B. Regulations concerning blasphemy
—Prohibited by the law of God ... Ex 20:7
Ex 22:28
—Punishable by death ... Lev 24:13–16,23
Mt 26:65–66

C. Jesus is charged with blasphemy
—For claiming to forgive sins ... Mt 9:2–3
Mk 2:7
—For claiming to be Son of Man ... Mt 26:64–65
—For claiming to be God ... Jn 10:33

D. Blasphemy against Holy Spirit
—Linked with calling Jesus an agent of Satan ... Mt 12:24–27
Mk 3:22–26
—Considered an unforgivable sin ... Mt 12:31–32
Mk 3:29
Lk 12:10

BLESSING

A. Human blessings
1. Blessing sacred things
   - —Sacrifices … 1Sa 9:13
   - —The cup in the Lord's Supper … 1Co 10:16
2. Blessing other human beings
   - —A father blesses his sons … Ge 27:1–40; Ge 48:15–16
   - —A family blesses a daughter leaving … Ge 24:60
   - —Moses blesses the Israelites … Dt 33
   - —Leaders bless the people … Ex 39:43; Jos 22:6–7; 2Sa 6:18; 1Ki 8:14; 2Ch 31:8
   - —Priests bless the people … Nu 6:24–26; 1Sa 2:20; 2Ch 30:27
   - —A prophet blesses the people … Nu 23:11,25–26
   - —The people bless the king … 1Ki 8:66
   - —A blessing used as a greeting … Ru 2:4; 1Sa 15:13
   - —Children bless their mother … Pr 31:28
   - —The command to bless one's enemies … Lk 6:28; Ro 12:14

B. Divine blessings
1. What/whom does God bless?
   - —Nature … Ge 1:22
   - —The Sabbath … Ex 20:11
   - —The work of his people … Dt 28:8,12
   - —Humanity in general … Ge 1:28
   - —His covenant people … Ge 9:1; Ge 24:1; Dt 2:7
   - —God-fearing individuals … Ps 1:1–3; Pr 3:13; Pr 16:20
   - —Those who live by godly principles … Ps 41:1; Pr 14:21; Mt 5:3–11
   - —The home of the righteous … Pr 3:33
   - —Nations other than Israel … Ge 39:5; Isa 19:25; Jer 4:2
2. What are God's blessings?
   a. Material blessings given to us
   - —General statements … Dt 7:13–14; Dt 28:2–14
   - —Peace and prosperity … Eze 34:26
   - —Health, happiness and long life … Ps 21:3–5
   - —Children and a happy home … Ps 128:1–6
   - —Abundant crops and food … Ps 67:6–7; Mal 3:10–12; Ac 14:17
   - —Showers of blessing … Eze 34:26–30

   b. Spiritual blessings given to us
   - —General statements … Jn 1:16–17; 1Co 9:23; Eph 1:3
   - —God's favor and grace … Ps 5:12
   - —Forgiveness of sins … Ps 32:1–2; Ro 4:7–8
   - —Salvation … Ro 10:12–13
   - —Being part of God's people … Ro 15:27
   - —Eternal joy … Ps 21:6
   - —Spiritual strength and peace … Ps 29:11
   - —Having God as a shepherd … Ps 28:9

   c. The blessing of Abraham
   - —First mentioned to Abram … Ge 12:2–3
   - —Repeated to Abraham … Ge 22:17–18
   - —Repeated to Isaac … Ge 26:3–5
   - —Repeated to Jacob … Ge 28:13–15
   - —Repeated regarding David's line … Ps 72:17
   - —Fulfilled in Christ for the Jews … Ac 3:24–26
   - —Fulfilled in Christ for the Gentiles … Gal 3:8–9,14
3. Who are blessed by the Lord?
   - —Those who avoid sin … Ps 1:1
   - —Those who take refuge in the Lord … Ps 2:12
   - —Those whose sins are forgiven … Ps 32:1
   - —Those who trust in the Lord … Ps 40:4
   - —Those who show concern for the weak … Ps 41:1
   - —Those chosen by the Lord … Ps 65:4
   - —Those who dwell in God's house … Ps 84:4
   - —Those disciplined by the Lord … Ps 94:12
   - —Those who fear the Lord … Ps 112:1
   - —Those who walk according to God's law … Ps 119:1–2
   - —Those who find wisdom in the Lord … Pr 3:13
   - —Those who wait for the Lord … Isa 30:18
   - —Those who follow the way of Jesus … Mt 5:3–12; Lk 6:20–22
   - —Those who confess Jesus as God's Son … Mt 16:16–17
   - —Those who hear and obey God's word … Lk 11:28
   - —Those who persevere in their faith … Jas 1:12
   - —Those who die in the Lord … Rev 14:13
   - —Those invited to Christ's marriage feast … Rev 19:9

BLOOD

A. Blood referred to literally
   - —In a human being … 2Sa 20:12
   - —In an animal … Ge 9:4

B. Blood used as a symbol
1. Blood symbolizes life
   - —Abel's blood meant his life … Ge 4:10
   - —Eating blood means eating life … Dt 12:23
   - —"Shedding blood" means taking a life … Ge 9:5–6; Hab 2:8,17; Mt 27:24
   - —"Being innocent of blood" means not being responsible for physical death … Mt 27:24
   - —"Being innocent of blood" means not being responsible for spiritual death … Eze 3:17–19; Ac 18:6
2. Blood used in Old Testament sacrifices
   - —Examples … Lev 1:5,11; Lev 3:2,8,13; Lev 16:14–16
   - —Shed blood symbolized forgiveness … Lev 17:11; Heb 9:22
3. The blood shed by Christ
   a. What happened to it
   - —It flowed from the cross … Jn 19:34
   - —It was presented to God in heaven … Heb 9:12,24–28

   b. What it accomplishes
   - —Our forgiveness … Eph 1:7; Heb 9:22; Rev 1:5
   - —Our redemption … Ac 20:28; Heb 9:12; 1Pe 1:18–19
   - —Our atonement … Ro 3:25
   - —Our justification … Ro 5:9
   - —Our reconciliation … Eph 2:13–16
   - —Our cleansing … Heb 9:14; 1Jn 1:7; Rev 7:14
   - —Our holiness … Heb 10:29; Heb 13:12
   - —Our new life … Jn 6:53–56
   - —Establishment of the new covenant … Lk 22:20; 1Co 11:25
   - —Power over Satan … Rev 12:11

BOASTING

See PRIDE

BOAZ

- —Bethlehemite … Ru 2:1
- —Acted kindly to Ruth … Ru 2:8–16
- —Married Ruth … Ru 4:1–13
- —Became ancestor of David … Ru 4:18–22; 1Ch 2:12–15

—Became ancestor of Jesus . . . Mt 1:5–16; Lk 3:23–32

BODY

A. The human body

1. Refers to the physical body
   - —Originally fashioned by God . . . Ge 2:7,22
   - —Now formed in the womb . . . Ps 139:13,15–16; Isa 44:2
   - —Refers to one's outward appearance . . . Ge 25:25; SS 5:10–16
   - —We clothe the body . . . Mt 6:25
   - —Refers to the sexual side of humans . . . 1Co 7:4
   - —The body must be controlled . . . 1Th 4:4; Jas 3:2
   - —The body can be healthy . . . Pr 3:8
   - —The body can become ill . . . Ps 38:3,7
   - —The body can suffer . . . 1Pe 4:1
   - —The body remains behind at death . . . 1Sa 31:10; 1Ki 13:24–25
2. Refers to the whole human person
   - —It experiences life and peace . . . Pr 14:30
   - —It experiences freedom . . . Mk 5:29
   - —We can discipline it . . . 1Co 9:27
   - —We can love or hate it . . . Eph 5:29
   - —It can be washed by God . . . Heb 10:22
   - —It can yearn for God . . . Ps 63:1
   - —It can please God . . . Ro 12:1
   - —It can reveal the living Jesus . . . 2Co 4:10; Php 1:20
3. Effects of sin on the human body/person
   - —It becomes an instrument of sin . . . Ro 6:12–13,19; Ro 7:5
   - —It becomes subject to death . . . Ge 3:19; Ps 90:3–5; Ro 8:10
4. Effects of salvation on the human body/person
   - —It receives new life . . . Ro 8:11
   - —It becomes a member of Christ . . . 1Co 6:15
   - —It becomes a temple of the Spirit . . . 1Co 6:19
   - —It seeks to do God's will . . . Ro 6:13,19
   - —It must honor God . . . Ro 12:1; 1Co 5:20; Php 1:20
5. The future of the Christian's body
   - —Our bodies will be resurrected . . . Jn 5:28–29; Jn 11:23–24; 1Co 15:42–44
   - —Our bodies will be redeemed . . . Ro 8:23
   - —We will receive new bodies, like Jesus . . . 1Co 15:52–54; Php 3:21

B. The body of Christ

1. His physical body
   - —Jesus came in a human body . . . 1Ti 3:16; 1Jn 4:2–3
   - —Jesus was conceived by the Holy Spirit . . . Lk 1:35
   - —Jesus suffered in his body . . . 1Pe 4:1
   - —Jesus sacrificed himself in his body . . . Heb 10:10
   - —Jesus died in his body . . . Ro 7:4; 1Pe 3:18
   - —Jesus' body was buried . . . Mt 27:58–60; Jn 19:38–40
   - —Jesus' body was raised to life . . . Ac 2:31–32
   - —Jesus received a glorified body . . . Php 3:21
2. Spiritual significance of his body
   - a. His body symbolized by bread in the Lord's Supper . . . Mt 26:26; 1Co 10:16; 1Co 11:24
   - b. The church as the body of Christ
     - —Identified as such . . . Col 1:24
     - —Christ as the head of his body . . . Eph 1:22–23; Col 1:18
     - —Christ as Savior of his body . . . Eph 5:23
     - —Emphasis on one body . . . Ro 12:4–5; 1Co 10:16–17
     - —Emphasis on unity in the body . . . 1Co 12:25–26; Eph 2:14–16; Eph 4:3–4,12–13
     - —Each member in the body important . . . 1Co 12:14–24

BOLDNESS

See COURAGE

BOOK

A. In the Old Testament

1. Books of the law and prophecy
   - —The book(s) of God . . . Ex 32:32–33; Ps 139:16; Da 7:10
   - —The Book of the Covenant . . . Ex 24:7
   - —The Book of the Law . . . Dt 28:61; Ne 8:1,3,8,18
   - —The Book of Moses . . . Ezr 6:18
   - —The book of Jeremiah's prophecies . . . Jer 25:13; Jer 30:2–3
   - —The book of the vision of Nahum . . . Na 1:1
   - —The Book of Truth . . . Da 10:21
2. Books of history and poetry
   - —The Book of the Wars of the LORD . . . Nu 21:14
   - —The Book of Jashar . . . Jos 10:12–13
   - —The book of the annals of King David . . . 1Ch 27:24
   - —The book of the annals of Solomon . . . 1Ki 11:41
   - —The book of the annals of the kings . . . 1Ki 14:19,29
   - —The book of the Laments . . . 2Ch 35:25
   - —The book of the annals of Persian kings . . . Est 2:23
3. No end to the making of books . . . Ecc 12:12

B. In the New Testament

1. References to parts of the Old Testament
   - —The book of Moses . . . Mk 12:26
   - —The Book of the Law . . . Gal 3:10
   - —The book of the prophets . . . Ac 7:42
   - —The Book of Isaiah . . . Lk 3:4; Ac 8:28
   - —The Book of Psalms . . . Lk 20:42; Ac 1:20
2. References to parts of the New Testament
   - —The Gospel of Luke . . . Ac 1:1
   - —The Gospel of John . . . Jn 20:30
   - —The Revelation of John . . . Rev 22:7,18–19
3. God's special books
   - —The scroll of history . . . Rev 5:1–5
   - —The book of life . . . Php 4:3; Rev 3:5; Rev 21:27
   - —The books opened on the judgment day . . . Rev 20:12

BORN AGAIN

—Spiritual rebirth by the power of Jesus

A. Why is spiritual birth necessary?
   - —Because we are dead in sin . . . Eph 2:1,4–5; Col 2:13
   - —Because we need the Spirit . . . Jn 3:3–6

B. How does spiritual birth take place?
   - —By a decision of God . . . Jn 1:13
   - —By a decision of Jesus, the Son of God . . . Jn 5:21
   - —By an act of God through Christ . . . Col 2:13
   - —By the Holy Spirit . . . Jn 3:6; Titus 3:5
   - —Through the word of God . . . Jas 1:18; 1Pe 1:23
   - —Through believing in Jesus . . . 1Jn 5:1

C. What does spiritual birth result in?
   - —Salvation and new life . . . Titus 3:5
   - —Entrance into God's kingdom . . . Jn 3:3
   - —Being a new creation . . . 2Co 5:17; Eph 4:24
   - —Victory over a sinful life . . . Ro 6:4–7; 1Jn 3:9; 1Jn 5:4,18
   - —Ability to do what is right . . . 1Jn 2:29
   - —Ability to love one another . . . 1Jn 4:7
   - —Safety from the evil one . . . 1Jn 5:18

BREAD

A. Physical bread
  1. Bread as a food
    —Bread is eaten	Ge 14:18
      1Ki 17:6
      Mt 14:16–17
    —Bread stands for life's necessities	Dt 8:3
      Ps 37:25
      Pr 30:8
      Mt 6:11
  2. God's use of bread
    —God tested Israel by giving only manna	Dt 8:3
    —God tested Israel by a lack of bread	Nu 21:5
    —God punished Israel by cutting off bread	Lev 26:26
      La 1:11
B. Bread in Old Testament worship
  1. Used in fellowship offerings	Lev 7:11–13
  2. Used in Aaron's ordination	Lev 8:2,26,31–32
  3. The bread of the Presence
    —Placed in tabernacle	Ex 25:30
    —Placed in the temple	2Ch 4:19
    —12 loaves for 12 tribes	Lev 24:5–8
    —David was given this bread	1Sa 21:3–6
      Mt 12:3–4
  4. First bread each harvest offered to God	Nu 15:19–21
  5. The Festival of Unleavened Bread
    —A reminder of bread used in the exodus	Ex 12:8–20
    —Regulations given	Lev 23:6
      Dt 16:3–4
    —Celebrated in Israel's history	Jos 5:11
      2Ch 30:21–27
      2Ch 35:17–19
      Ezr 6:22
    —Celebrated at the time of Jesus	Mt 26:17
    —Celebrated in the early church	Ac 20:6
C. Bread related to Jesus
  1. Physical bread
    —Feeding of the 5,000	Mt 14:13–21
      Mk 6:35–44
      Lk 9:12–17
      Jn 6:5–13
    —Feeding of the 4,000	Mt 15:29–38
      Mk 8:1–9
    —A parable on bread	Lk 11:5–8
    —Jesus served bread in the upper room	Mt 26:26
  2. Bread used symbolically
    —Jesus as bread of life	Jn 6:35,41,48,51
    —"This [bread] is my body"	Mk 14:22
      Lk 22:19
      1Co 11:23–24
    —Participating in the body of Christ	1Co 10:16
    —Being one body in Christ	1Co 10:17

BROTHERS AND SISTERS

A. Natural use of brother and sister
  1. People with the same parents	Ge 4:2,8
    Ge 34:13–15
  2. People with the same father	Ge 20:12
    Ge 37:2,4,8
  3. Any relative
    —Members of the Israelite nation	Hos 2:1
    —People with same ancestors (Esau/Jacob)	Nu 20:14
B. Brothers and sisters of Jesus
  1. Names
    —James	Mt 13:55
      Gal 1:19
    —Joseph	Mt 13:55
    —Simon	Mt 13:55
    —Judas	Mt 13:55
      Jude 1
  2. Relationship to Jesus
    —Wanted to see Jesus	Mt 12:46–47
    —Gave advice to Jesus	Jn 7:3
    —Did not believe in Jesus	Jn 7:5
    —Later became disciples of Jesus	Ac 1:14
    —Went on missionary excursions	1Co 9:5
    —James became a leader of the church	Ac 15:13–21
      Gal 2:9
C. Spiritual use of brother and sister
  —Christ is our brother	Ro 8:29
    Heb 2:11
  —We are brothers and sisters of Christ	Mt 12:50
  —Christians are brothers and sisters of one another	Mt 23:8
    1Co 6:6
    Phm 16
  —Specific references to sisters	Ro 16:1
    Phm 2
    Jas 2:15
    2Jn 13
D. Living as Christian brothers and sisters
  —Be concerned about a brother or sister in need	Jas 2:15
    1Jn 3:17
  —Forgive each other	Mt 5:23–24
    Mt 18:15,21–22
  —Love each other	1Th 4:9–10
    Heb 13:1
  —Overlook social differences	Phm 15–16
    Gal 3:28
  —Discipline an errant brother or sister	2Th 3:6
  —Do not judge each other	Ro 14:10,13
    1Co 6:5–8
    Jas 4:11
  —Do not destroy each other	1Co 8:9–13

BUILDING

A. Building in a physical sense
  1. Things built to honor the Lord
    —Altars	Ge 12:8
      Ge 35:1
    —The tabernacle	Ex 35:8–38:20
    —The temple	1Ki 6:1–38
  2. Things built against God's will
    —The tower of Babel	Ge 11:4
    —Altars to pagan gods	Ex 32:5
      1Ki 12:26–31
B. Building in a spiritual sense
  1. Christians as builders
    —Of their own lives on Christ and his words	Mt 7:24–27
      1Co 3:12–15
      Col 2:7
    —Of themselves in the faith	Jude 20
    —Of the church into a unified body	Eph 2:21
      Eph 4:16
    —Of other Christians in love	Ro 15:2
      1Co 8:1
      1Th 5:11
  2. The Lord as a builder
    —Of Jerusalem	Ps 147:2
    —Of the house of David	2Sa 7:27
      1Ki 11:38
    —Of the nation of Judah	Jer 31:4
    —Of our homes	Ps 127:1
    —Of the church	Mt 16:18
    —Of a place in heaven for his people	Jn 14:1–2
      2Co 5:1
    —Of the new Jerusalem	Heb 11:10
    —Christ is the cornerstone	Ps 118:22–23
      1Pe 2:6

CAESAREA

—A seacoast city	Ac 9:30
  Ac 18:22
—Roman capital of Palestine	Ac 12:19–20
  Ac 23:23–24
—Philip's home and headquarters for preaching	Ac 8:40
  Ac 21:8
—Cornelius stationed there	Ac 10:1
—Peter preached to Cornelius there	Ac 10:23–48
—Paul imprisoned for two years there	Ac 24:1,27

C. Jesus denounced Capernaum for unbelief . . . Mt 11:23–24; Lk 10:15

CASTING LOTS

A. Occasions for casting lots
  1. Decisions of God's people through casting lots
    —Choosing a goat on Day of Atonement . . . Lev 16:8
    —Dividing Canaan for the tribes of Israel . . . Jos 18:6–10
    —Determining a guilty party . . . 1Sa 14:40–44
    —Assigning duties to priests and Levites . . . 1Ch 24:5,31; 1Ch 26:13–16; Lk 1:5–9
    —Deciding who would live in Jerusalem . . . Ne 11:1
    —Choosing a replacement for Judas . . . Ac 1:26
  2. Decisions by pagans through casting lots
    —Haman's choice of a day for killing Jews . . . Est 3:7
    —Detection of Jonah by sailors . . . Jnh 1:7
    —Owners of conquered Israelites . . . Joel 3:3; Ob 11; Na 3:10
    —Recipient of Jesus' garment . . . Mt 27:35
B. God controls the casting of lots . . . Pr 16:33
C. Urim and Thummim likely a form of casting lots . . . Ex 28:30; Lev 8:8; Nu 27:21; Dt 33:8; 1Sa 28:6

CEPHAS

See PETER

CHARIOT

A. Uses for the chariot
  1. For royalty to ride in . . . Ge 41:43; 1Ki 18:44
  2. For important officials to ride in . . . 2Ki 5:21; Ac 8:28–30
  3. For use in war
    —The Egyptians . . . Ex 14:7
    —The Canaanites . . . Jos 11:4,6,9
    —The Philistines . . . 1Sa 13:5
    —The Arameans . . . 1Ki 22:31–33
    —The Assyrians . . . 2Ki 19:23
    —The Israelites . . . 1Ch 18:4
    —The Cushites . . . 2Ch 14:9
    —The Babylonians . . . Eze 23:15,23–24
  4. For use in pagan worship . . . 2Ki 23:11
B. The chariot referred to symbolically
  —Elijah's ascension in a fiery chariot . . . 2Ki 2:11–12
  —The clouds are God's chariot . . . Ps 104:3
  —God's heavenly host are charioteers . . . 2Ki 6:15–17; Ps 68:17
  —God executes judgment by his chariots . . . Isa 66:15–16

CHASTISEMENT

See DISCIPLINE

CHILDREN

A. Proper opinion of children
  —A gift from God . . . Ge 4:1; Ge 33:5
  —A heritage from the Lord . . . Ps 127:3–5
  —A blessing from God . . . Lk 1:42
  —A crown to the aged . . . Pr 17:6
B. Familiar stories involving children
  —Abraham's willingness to sacrifice Isaac . . . Ge 22:1–19
  —The baby Moses . . . Ex 2:1–10
  —Jephthah's daughter . . . Jdg 11:29–40
  —The call of Samuel . . . 1Sa 3:1–18
  —David anointed king . . . 1Sa 16:1–13
  —David killed a lion and a bear . . . 1Sa 17:34–37
  —Elijah raised a dead boy . . . 1Ki 17:17–24
  —Elisha raised a dead boy . . . 2Ki 4:8–37
  —Joash became king at seven years . . . 2Ki 11:4–12,21; 2Ch 23:1–11; 2Ch 24:1
  —Josiah became king at eight years . . . 2Ki 22:1–2; 2Ch 34:1–2
  —Jesus raised a girl from the dead . . . Mt 9:22–25; Mk 5:35–43; Lk 8:49–56
  —Jesus raised a boy from the dead . . . Lk 7:11–15
  —Jesus used a boy's lunch to feed a crowd . . . Jn 6:1–13
  —Jesus called children to come to him . . . Mt 19:13–15; Mk 10:13–16; Lk 18:15–17
C. God's relationship to children
  1. Blesses barren women with children . . . Ps 113:9
    —Sarah . . . Ge 21:1–3
    —Rebekah . . . Ge 25:21–22
    —Rachel . . . Ge 30:1–2
    —Hannah . . . 1Sa 1:6–8
    —Elizabeth . . . Lk 1:7,24–25
  2. Forms children in the womb . . . Ps 139:13–16
  3. Knows children even before birth . . . Jer 1:5; Gal 1:15
  4. Includes children in his covenant . . . Ge 17:7; Ac 2:39
  5. Considers children of believers holy . . . 1Co 7:14
  6. Shows concern for orphans . . . Dt 10:18; Ps 10:14; Hos 14:3; Jas 1:27
D. Jesus and children
  1. His own childhood
    —His conception . . . Mt 1:18; Lk 1:26–38
    —His birth . . . Mt 1:25; Lk 2:1–7
    —His circumcision and dedication . . . Lk 2:21–38
    —His flight into Egypt . . . Mt 2:14–15
    —His visit to the temple at 12 years old . . . Lk 2:41–50
    —Summary of his boyhood . . . Lk 2:51–52
  2. His feelings about children
    —He wanted children to come to him . . . Mt 19:13–15; Mk 10:13–16; Lk 18:15–17
    —He used them to teach disciples humility . . . Mt 18:1–4; Mk 9:36–37; Lk 9:46–48
    —He used them in parables . . . Mt 11:16–17
    —He raised them from the dead . . . Mt 9:22–25; Mk 5:35–43; Lk 7:11–15; Lk 8:49–56
E. Relationship between parents and children
  1. Parents' duties to children
    —Give them names . . . Ge 21:3; Ge 29:31–30:24; Mt 1:25; Lk 1:59–63
    —Care for their physical needs . . . 1Sa 1:22–24
    —Educate them . . . Dt 6:6–7
    See EDUCATION
    —Discipline them . . . Pr 23:13–14
    See DISCIPLINE
    —Lay up inheritance for them . . . 2Co 12:14
  2. Children's duties to parents
    —Obey them . . . Pr 6:20; Eph 6:1; Col 3:20
    —Listen to and follow their instruction . . . Pr 1:8–9; Pr 3:1–2
    —Honor them . . . Ex 20:12; Lev 19:3
    —Respect them in their old age . . . Pr 23:22
    —Care for them . . . 1Ti 5:4
F. Symbolic use of "children"
  —Jesus' term for his disciples . . . Mk 10:24
  —A term for all believers . . . Ro 8:16–17
  See ADOPTION
  —An elderly pastor's term for his church . . . 1Jn 2:1,18

—Must be accompanied by heart circumcision........ Dt 10:16
Dt 30:6
Jer 4:4

C. Circumcision in the New Testament
1. Controversy in early church
—A circumcision group in the church............ Ac 11:2–3
Gal 2:12
Gal 6:12–13
Titus 1:10
—Discussed by leaders in Jerusalem .... Ac 15:1–22
Gal 2:4
—Decision: circumcision unnecessary .... Ac 15:6–29
Gal 2:1–3,15–16
2. Discussion in Paul's letters
—Physical circumcision means nothing........... 1Co 7:19
Gal 5:6
Col 3:11
—Circumcision not needed for salvation .... Ro 4:9–12
Gal 2:2–3
1Co 7:18
—True circumcision involves obedience........... Ro 2:25
—True circumcision is of the heart .... Ro 2:28–29
—True worshipers are true circumcision .... Php 3:3
—Christians are circumcised in baptism........... Col 2:11–12

CITY

A. Major cities mentioned in the Bible
—Antioch .... Ac 11:19–20
—Athens... Ac 17:15
—Babel/Babylon................................. Ge 11:9
Da 4:30
—Caesarea .... Ac 23:23
—Corinth .... Ac 18:1
—Damascus 2Sa 8:6
—Ephesus....................................... Ac 19:1
—Jericho.. Jos 6:1
—Jerusalem 2Sa 5:6–7
—Nineveh .... Jnh 1:2
—Philippi .... Ac 16:12
—Rome.. Ac 28:14
—Samaria 1Ki 16:24
—Sodom and Gomorrah.......................... Ge 18:20

B. Types of Israelite cities
—The capital city................................. 2Sa 5:6–9
1Ki 16:24
—Cities for defense............................... 2Ch 11:5–12
—Chariot cities 2Ch 1:14
—Cities for storage 2Ch 8:4,6
—Cities for the Levites .... Nu 35:1–5,7
—Cities of refuge................................. Nu 35:6–15
Dt 19:1–3
Jos 20:1–9

C. Critical importance of cities
1. Defense of cities
—Usually fortified with walls .... Nu 13:28
Dt 3:5
Jos 6:5
2Ch 11:5–13
—Besieged by armies.......................... 1Ki 20:1
2Ki 16:5
—Kingdom fell when the city was entered........ 2Ki 17:5–6
2Ki 25:1–7
2. Cities as centers for missions
a. Jonah sent to Nineveh .... Jnh 1:2
b. Disciples evangelized cities .... Mt 10:23
c. Paul preached in cities
—Antioch.................................. Ac 11:25–26
—Paphos on Cyprus .... Ac 13:6–12
—Antioch of Pisidia......................... Ac 13:14–49
—Philippi.................................. Ac 16:12–40
—Thessalonica............................. 1Th 1:7–10
—Corinth .... Ac 18:1–17
—Ephesus .... Ac 19:1–41

D. The city used as a symbol
—Of total rebellion against God .... Rev 18:1–24
See BABYLON
—Of the church and of heaven .... Heb 12:22–23
Rev 21:1–4
See JERUSALEM

CLEANNESS

A. The Old Testament regarding clean/unclean
1. How did one become unclean?
—By eating unclean foods...................... Lev 11:1–23
—Through childbirth .... Lev 12:1–8
—Through skin diseases........................ Lev 13:1–14:57
—Through discharges from the body .... Lev 15:1–33
—By touching a dead body .... Nu 5:2
—By worshiping false gods..................... Jer 13:25–27
Hos 8:5
—Through a life of sin......................... Isa 64:5–7
2. How could one become clean?
—By washing self and clothes................... Ex 19:10–14
Ex 30:18–21
Lev 22:6
—By certain sacrifices and ceremonies .... Lev 12:6–8
Lev 14:1–11
—By turning to the Lord........................ Ps 51:2,7
Isa 4:4
Isa 6:5–7

B. Inward cleansing from sin
1. The need for such cleansing .... Mt 23:25–28
2. God's promise for such cleansing .... Jer 33:8
Eze 36:25,33
3. The process of such cleansing
—The believer must ask for it .... Ps 51:2,7
1Jn 1:9
—It takes place in the heart..................... Ps 24:3–4
Mk 7:18–23
—It occurs through Christ's blood................ Heb 9:14
Heb 10:19–22
1Jn 1:7
—It occurs through the word of God .... Eph 5:25–27
4. The results of such cleansing
—It leads to a life of holiness................... 2Co 7:1
—It leads to a life of purity 1Jn 3:3
—It leads to a life of love 1Pe 1:22

CLOTHING

A. Purposes and uses of clothing
1. Clothing for natural uses
—To cover nakedness .... Ge 3:7,21
—To keep warm................................ Pr 31:21
—To trade in business.......................... Pr 31:24
Ac 16:14
2. Clothing for religious purposes
—To use in special service to God .... Ex 28:1–5
—To symbolize a message from God 1Ki 11:29–32
—To appoint a prophet as successor............. 1Ki 19:19
2Ki 2:13–14
3. Clothing used for display
—Special favor to a child .... Ge 37:3–4
—Honor to a citizen .... Est 6:11
—One's wealth................................ Mt 11:8
—One's power .... Ac 12:21
—One's position as ruler........................ Ge 41:42
—One's self-righteousness...................... Mt 23:5
—Mourning .... Ge 37:34
2Sa 3:31
Job 1:20
—Sorrow for sin............................... Ezr 9:3
—Shock .... Mk 14:63
Ac 14:14

B. Significant garments in the Bible
—Garments sewn by God for Adam and Eve.......... Ge 3:21
—The robe of Joseph from his father .... Ge 37:3–4
—The garments stolen by Achan.................... Jos 7:20–21
—The purple robe put on Jesus..................... Mk 15:17
—The seamless garment of Jesus at the cross......... Mt 27:35
Mk 15:24
Jn 19:23–24

C. Clothing used as a symbol
—Taking off a garment means putting off sin .... Eph 4:22
Col 3:9
—Putting on a garment means putting on Jesus ...... Ro 13:14
Gal 3:27
—Receiving a new garment symbolizes forgiveness ... Zec 3:3–5
Mt 22:11–13
Rev 3:5
—Being clothed with white robes in heaven .... Rev 7:9,13–14

COMFORT

—Consolation and strength in a time of need

A. Related theme
COMFORT is a theme of Nahum .... Na 2:2

B. People who need comfort
—Those grieving .... Ge 37:33–35
Job 2:11
Isa 61:2
Mt 5:4
—Those in a new country .... Ru 2:13
—Those facing troubles .... Ps 71:21
Isa 51:19
—Those downcast 2Co 7:6
—Those being punished for sin .... Isa 40:1
La 1:9,17
2Co 2:6–7

C. Sources of comfort
1. Human comfort given by
—Spouses .... Ge 24:67
2Sa 12:24
—Children .... Ge 37:33–35
—Friends .... Job 2:11–13
Jn 11:19
—Prophets .... Isa 40:1–2
1Co 14:3
—Preachers .... Isa 61:1–2
2Co 1:4–6
1Th 2:11–12
—Any Christian 2Co 2:6–7
Col 4:11
2. Divine comfort given through
—God .... Isa 51:3,12
Isa 57:18
Isa 66:13
Zec 1:17
—The God of all comfort .... Jer 8:18
2Co 1:3
—God's rod and staff .... Ps 23:4
—God's promises .... Ps 119:50,76
—Jesus Christ .... Jn 14:27
Jn 16:33
—Christ's love .... Php 2:1
—The Holy Spirit as Counselor (Advocate) .... Jn 14:16,26
Jn 16:7

COMPASSION

—Deep feeling of concern for suffering and needy people

A. Related themes
1. CONCERN is a theme of:
—Nehemiah .... Ne 2:2
—1 Thessalonians 1Th 2:17
2. SOCIAL CONCERN is a theme of:
—Deuteronomy .... Dt 26:12
—Luke .... Lk 7:22

B. Human compassion commanded
—In the Old Testament .... Mic 6:8
Zec 7:9
—In the New Testament .... Gal 6:2
Eph 4:32
Col 3:12
1Pe 3:8

C. The compassion of Christ
—To people without leaders .... Mt 9:36
Mk 6:34
—To sick people .... Mt 14:14
Mt 20:34
Mk 1:41
—To hungry people .... Mt 15:32
Mk 8:2
—To a grieving widow .... Lk 7:13
—To all of us in our weaknesses .... Heb 4:15

D. The compassion of God
1. A chief characteristic of God
—God is the God of compassion 2Co 1:3
—He is compassionate .... Ex 34:6
Ps 103:8
Jnh 4:2
—He is full of compassion .... Ps 116:5
Jas 5:11
—His compassions never fail .... La 3:22
2. His expressions of compassion
—To Adam and Eve when they sinned .... Ge 3:15
—To the Israelites in Egypt .... Ex 3:7
—To the Israelites in the desert .... Ne 9:17–21
—To the Israelites groaning under enemies .... Jdg 2:18
—To the Israelites in exile .... Isa 54:7–8
Jer 42:11–12
—To all of us as sinners .... Ps 51:1
Ps 103:8–12
Mic 7:19
—To foreigners and the oppressed .... Ex 22:27
Dt 10:18–19

See also MERCY

CONFESSION

A. Related theme
CONFESSION is a theme of Psalms .... Ps 51:2

B. Confession of sin before God
1. Examples of people confessing sin
—Aaron .... Nu 12:11
—David 2Sa 12:13
Ps 32:5
Ps 38:18
Ps 51:1–5
—Nehemiah .... Ne 1:6–7
—Isaiah .... Isa 6:5
—Peter .... Lk 5:8
—A tax collector .... Lk 18:13
2. Those who may confess sin
—Individual sinners .... Lev 5:5
Mt 6:12
—Priests on behalf of the people .... Lev 16:21
Ezr 9:5–10:1
—Prophets on behalf of the people .... Isa 6:5
Isa 59:12–15
Jer 14:7,20–21
Da 9:7–11
3. The results of confessing sin
—We receive God's mercy .... Pr 28:13
—We receive God's forgiveness .... Ps 32:5
1Jn 1:9
—We are justified .... Lk 18:13–14
—We receive healing .... Jas 5:16
—We become purified 1Jn 1:9

C. Confession of faith in Jesus Christ
1. Such confession is necessary to be saved .... Mt 10:32–33
Ro 10:9–10
2. Earliest confessions of faith
—"Jesus is Lord" .... Jn 20:28
Ro 10:9
1Co 12:3
Php 2:11
—"Jesus is the Messiah" .... Mt 16:16
Jn 20:31
Ac 17:2–3
1Jn 2:22
—"Jesus is the Son of God" .... Mt 16:16
Mt 27:54
Jn 20:31
1Jn 4:15

3. Other elements added to confessions
   - —Certain teachings about Christ ... 1Jn 4:2–3; 2Jn 7
   - —Trustworthy sayings ... 1Ti 1:15; 1Ti 4:9–10; 2Ti 2:11; Titus 3:8
4. Brief creeds in the New Testament ... 1Co 15:3–5; 1Ti 3:16; 2Ti 2:11–13; Titus 3:4–7

CONFIDENCE

See ASSURANCE

CONSCIENCE

—An inner voice defining right and wrong

A. Everyone has a conscience ... Ro 2:14–15

B. Our conscience and sin
- —It helps us do what is right ... Ro 2:15; 2Co 1:12
- —It accuses us of sin ... 2Sa 24:10; Ac 2:37; 1Co 8:7
- —It can be distorted ... Pr 30:20; Eph 4:19; 1Ti 4:2
- —A good conscience can be rejected ... 1Ti 1:19

C. Our conscience and Christ
- —It becomes cleansed through Christ ... Heb 9:14; Heb 10:19,22
- —It inspires us to love others ... 1Ti 1:5
- —It inspires us to obey God's law ... 1Jn 3:21–22
- —We must hold a clear conscience ... Ac 24:16; 1Ti 3:9; Heb 13:18

D. Our conscience and other Christians
- —A weak Christian has a weak conscience ... 1Co 8:7,10; 1Co 10:27–29
- —A weak Christian's faith can be destroyed ... Ro 14:14–15; 1Co 8:11
- —We must protect a weak Christian ... Ro 14:13,15,19–21; 1Co 8:9–13; 1Co 10:27–32
- —We must not judge another's conscience ... Ro 14:1–13; 1Co 10:29

CONTENTMENT

See COVETING

CONVERSION

See REPENTANCE

CORINTH

A. Events of the church in Corinth
- —Paul preached there for one and a half years ... Ac 18:1–11
- —Paul's trial before Gallio ... Ac 18:12–17
- —Apollos sent there ... Ac 18:27–19:1
- —First (lost) letter of Paul to them ... 1Co 5:9–10
- —Paul's second letter to them ... 1Co 1:1–2
- —Timothy sent there ... 1Co 4:17; 1Co 16:10–11
- —Paul's third (lost) letter to them ... 2Co 2:3–4; 2Co 7:8–12
- —Titus sent there ... 2Co 7:5–7
- —Paul's fourth letter to them ... 2Co 1:1
- —Titus sent there again ... 2Co 8:16–24
- —Paul's visit there for three months ... Ac 20:2–3
- —Paul's collection among them ... Ro 15:25–27; 1Co 16:1–4; 2Co 8:6–15; 2Co 9:1–15

B. Character of the church in Corinth
- —Most held to the teachings of Paul ... 1Co 11:2; 1Co 15:1–2
- —Disunified ... 1Co 1:11–12
- —Spiritually immature ... 1Co 3:1–2; 1Co 14:20
- —Proud; tolerated sinners ... 1Co 5:1–2
- —Lack of concern for weak Christians ... 1Co 8:9–13
- —Lack of love for each other ... 1Co 11:17–22
- —Trouble over speaking in tongues ... 1Co 14:1–20
- —Some denied the resurrection ... 1Co 15:12
- —Some challenged Paul's leadership ... 2Co 10:1–11; 2Co 11:13–21

CORNELIUS

- —Roman centurion who feared God ... Ac 10:1–2
- —Received vision from God ... Ac 10:3–8
- —Peter preached to him ... Ac 10:23–43
- —Received Holy Spirit ... Ac 10:44–46
- —Became a baptized Christian ... Ac 10:47–48

COUNSELOR

—One who gives advice and direction for life

A. Human counselors
1. A class of people called counselors ... Isa 3:3
2. Wise counsel
   - —Good counsel is necessary ... Pr 15:22; Pr 22:20–21
   - —Wisdom counsels us ... Pr 8:12–16
   - —God's law counsels us ... Ps 119:24
   - —David had wise counselors ... 1Ch 27:32–33
   - —Jeremiah was a good counselor ... Jer 38:14–27
3. Foolish counsel
   - —Wicked counselors must be rejected ... Job 21:16; Ps 1:1
   - —Rehoboam followed foolish counselors ... 1Ki 12:1–15
   - —The Babylonians had poor counselors ... Isa 47:13

B. God as counselor
- —The Lord as counselor ... Ps 16:7; Ps 73:24; Isa 28:29
- —Christ, the Wonderful Counselor ... Isa 9:6
- —The Holy Spirit as Counselor (Advocate) ... Isa 11:2; Jn 14:16,26; Jn 15:26; Jn 16:7

COURAGE

—The ability to face danger without fear

A. Remarkable stories of courage
- —Moses and Aaron confronting Pharaoh ... Ex 5:1–4; Ex 10:24–29
- —Ehud killing Eglon ... Jdg 3:15–30
- —Gideon against the Midianites ... Jdg 7:1–24
- —Jonathan against the Philistines ... 1Sa 14:1–14
- —David against Goliath ... 1Sa 17:26–50
- —Elijah on Mount Carmel ... 1Sa 18:1–40
- —Esther approaching King Xerxes ... Est 5:1–8
- —Daniel's three friends and the fiery furnace ... Da 3:1–30
- —Daniel and the lions' den ... Da 6:1–23
- —The apostles facing the Sanhedrin ... Ac 4:1–22; Ac 5:17–41
- —Saul (Paul) preaching in Damascus ... Ac 9:20–25
- —Paul heading to Jerusalem ... Ac 21:10–14

B. The command to be courageous
- —To the Israelites from Moses ... Dt 31:6
- —To the Israelites from Joshua ... Jos 10:25
- —To Joshua from Moses ... Dt 31:7,23
- —To Joshua from the Lord ... Jos 1:6–9,18
- —To Solomon from David ... 1Ch 22:13; 1Ch 28:20
- —To judges from King Jehoshaphat ... 2Ch 19:11
- —To the Israelites from Hezekiah ... 2Ch 32:7
- —To Peter from Jesus ... Mt 14:27
- —To the disciples from Jesus ... Mk 6:50
- —To Paul from the Lord ... Ac 23:11
- —To all of us ... 1Co 16:13; Heb 3:6

C. Aspects of courage
1. When do we need courage?
   - —As we face dangers and difficulties ... Jos 1:6–9; 1Co 16:13

—As we face the future .... Ro 8:37–39
2Co 5:1–7

2. Who is our source of courage?
—God .... Ge 26:24
Jos 1:9
Ps 18:29–50
Ps 46:1–2
—Christ .... Php 4:13
Col 1:11
Rev 1:17–18
—The Holy Spirit .... Ac 4:8–13

COVENANT

—An agreement established between two parties

A. Related themes
1. COVENANT is a theme of:
—Genesis .... Ge 17:4
—Exodus .... Ex 24:3
—2 Samuel 2Sa 23:5
2. RENEWAL is a theme of:
—Deuteronomy .... Dt 29:12
—Joshua .... Jos 24:25
—Malachi .... Mal 3:7

B. Covenants between humans
1. Examples of human covenants
—Between Isaac and Abimelek .... Ge 26:26–31
—Between Jacob and Laban .... Ge 31:43–54
—Between Joshua and the Gibeonites .... Jos 9:3–15
—Between David and Jonathan 1Sa 18:3
—Between David and Abner 2Sa 3:12–16
—Between Jehoiada and the guards 2Ki 11:4–12
—Between Joash and the people 2Ki 11:17
—Between Zedekiah and the people .... Jer 34:8–10
2. Elements in a covenant
—Promises 1Sa 20:14–17
—Stipulations 2Sa 3:13
—Oaths .... Ge 31:53
—Responsibilities 2Ki 12:8
—Witnesses .... Ge 31:45–48
1Sa 20:42
—Implied threats .... Ge 31:53

C. Covenants between God and humans
1. Examples of such covenants
—With Adam before the fall .... Ge 2:15–17
—With Adam after the fall .... Ge 3:14–19
—With Noah .... Ge 9:1–19
—With Abram .... Ge 12:1–3
—With Israel at Sinai .... Ex 19:5–8
—With Israel before entering the promised land ... Dt 29–30
—With Israel in the promised land .... Jos 24:1–27
—With David 2Sa 7:14–17
—With the returned exiles .... Ne 9:38–10:39
—Future covenant of peace .... Eze 34:25–31
—The new covenant .... Jer 31:33–34
2. The covenants with Adam
a. First covenant (before the fall)
—Requirement was obedience .... Ge 2:16–17
—Promise was life .... Ge 3:22
—Penalty was death .... Ge 2:17
—Adam and Eve disobeyed .... Ge 3:1–6
—God pronounced punishment .... Ge 3:14–19
—Christ perfectly obeyed God's will .... Jn 6:38
Ro 5:18–19
2Co 5:21
Heb 4:15
—Christ's death reversed Adam's .... Ro 5:15–19
b. Second covenant (after the fall)
—Conflict between Satan and humans .... Ge 3:15
—God promised Satan's defeat .... Ge 3:15
—Fulfilled in Satan's defeat by Christ .... Ro 16:20
Heb 2:14
1Jn 3:8
3. The covenant with Abraham
a. Where is it mentioned?
—First mentioned to Abram .... Ge 12:2–3
—Repeated to Abraham .... Ge 22:17–18
—Repeated to Isaac .... Ge 26:3–5
—Repeated to Jacob .... Ge 28:13–15
—Repeated to Moses .... Ex 6:2–4
—Celebrated by the psalmists .... Ps 105:7–11
—Acknowledged by the returned exiles .... Ne 9:7–8
b. What are its elements?
—Several promises .... Ge 12:2–3
—No conditions attached .... Ge 12:2–3
—Faith came later .... Ge 15:6
—Law of circumcision followed faith .... Ge 17:3–14
c. How was it fulfilled in Christ?
—John the Baptist began fulfillment .... Lk 1:72–75
—Peter preached its fulfillment .... Ac 3:25
—Its center is faith in Christ .... Gal 3:6–9
—The law follows faith .... Ro 4:9–13
4. The covenant of the law made at Mount Sinai
a. Where is it mentioned?
—First made at Mount Sinai .... Ex 19:3–6
—Confirmed by the Israelites .... Ex 24:1–8
—Renewed at the border of Canaan .... Dt 29
—Renewed at Mount Ebal .... Jos 8:30–35
—Renewed at Shechem .... Jos 24:1–27
—Rejected by the ten tribes 2Ki 17:7–20
—Renewed under Josiah 2Ch 34:29–33
—Broken by the nation of Judah .... Jer 31:32
—Renewed by the returned exiles .... Ne 9:38–10:39
b. What are its elements?
—Centered on the law of God .... Ex 34:27–28
Dt 4:13–14
—Required obedience .... Ex 24:7
Ex 34:10–11
Dt 29:9
—Linked with blessings and curses .... Dt 28
Jos 8:34–35
—Did not annul covenant with Abraham .... Gal 3:15–17
—Pointed out human sin .... Ro 3:20,23
Gal 3:19
—Increased sin .... Ro 5:20
—Prepared for the coming of Christ .... Gal 3:23–25
c. How was it fulfilled in Christ?
—He fulfilled the law .... Mt 5:17
—He perfectly obeyed the law .... Ro 5:18–19
2Co 5:21
Heb 4:15
—He died the death of a curse .... Gal 3:10–13
—His death removed the curse from us .... Gal 3:13–14
5. The covenant with David
a. Where is it mentioned?
—First promised to David 2Sa 7:4–17
—Celebrated by David 2Sa 23:5
—Mentioned to Solomon 1Ki 2:2–4
—Celebrated by Solomon 1Ki 8:22–26
—Mentioned to Jeroboam 1Ki 11:34–36
—Reaffirmed during Jehoram's reign 2Ki 8:19
—Celebrated by psalmists .... Ps 89:3
Ps 132:10–12
—Reaffirmed by Isaiah .... Isa 9:6–7
—Reaffirmed by Ezekiel .... Eze 37:24–25
b. What are its elements?
—Several promises 2Sa 7:9–16
—No conditions attached 2Sa 7:15–16
c. How was it fulfilled in Christ?
—Mentioned by Gabriel to Mary .... Lk 1:32–33
—Preached by Paul .... Ac 13:22–23,34
—Hinted at in book of Hebrews .... Heb 1:8
—Jesus is the Son of David .... Mt 1:1
Ro 1:3
—Jesus is a king who rules .... Jn 18:33–37
1Co 15:24–25
Rev 19:16
6. The new covenant
a. Where is it promised?
—Through Jeremiah .... Jer 31:33–34
Jer 32:38–40

—Through Ezekiel .... Eze 16:60–62
Eze 34:25–31
—Through Hosea .... Hos 2:18–20
b. What are its elements?
—Several promises .... Jer 31:33–34
—No conditions attached .... Jer 31:33–34
c. How was it fulfilled in Christ?
—Asserted by Christ in the upper room .... Lk 22:20
1Co 11:25
—Mentioned by Paul 2Co 3:6
—Explained in book of Hebrews .... Heb 8:6–13
Heb 9:15–28
Heb 10:11–18
Heb 12:22–24
7. God's relationship to his covenants
—He establishes his covenant .... Ge 6:18
Ge 17:7
Ex 6:4
Eze 16:60–62
—He is faithful to his covenant .... Dt 7:9
1Ki 8:23
Ne 9:32
Da 9:4
—He remembers his covenant .... Ex 2:24
Ps 105:8
Ps 111:5
Eze 16:60
Lk 1:72

COVETING

—The sinful desire for what belongs to someone else; greed
A. The command against coveting
—In the Old Testament .... Ex 20:17
Dt 5:21
Dt 7:25
—In the New Testament .... Ro 7:7–11
Eph 5:3
Col 3:5
B. Coveting often leads to other sins 1Ti 6:10
1Jn 2:15–16
—To deceit (Jacob) .... Ge 27:18–26
—To adultery (David) 2Sa 11:1–5
—To disobedience to God (Achan) .... Jos 7:20–21
—To hypocritical worship (Saul) 1Sa 15:9–23
—To murder (Ahab) 1Ki 21:1–14
—To theft (Gehazi) 2Ki 5:20–24
—To family disharmony .... Pr 15:27
—To lying (Ananias and Sapphira) .... Ac 5:1–10
C. Contentment as the answer to coveting
—The command to be content .... Lk 3:14
1Ti 6:8
Heb 13:5
—The experience of Paul .... Php 4:11–12

CREATION

A. Related theme
BEGINNINGS is a theme of Genesis .... Ge 1:1
B. The work of creation
—Accounts of creation .... Ge 1:1–2:3
Ge 2:4–24
Job 38:4–38
Ps 104:1–26
—Done out of nothing .... Heb 11:3
—Done in six days .... Ge 1:3–31
Ex 20:11
Ex 31:17
C. Creation as the work of God
—God as the creator .... Ge 1:1
Isa 44:24
Ac 4:24
—Accomplished through Christ .... Jn 1:3,10
Col 1:16
Heb 1:2
—The Holy Spirit involved in creation .... Job 33:4
Ps 104:30
D. Creation reveals God
—His glory .... Ps 19:1
—His power .... Isa 40:26,28
—His divine nature .... Ro 1:20
—His wisdom .... Ps 104:24
—His love .... Ps 33:5–6
E. Creation after Adam and Eve sinned
—Was cursed by God .... Ge 3:14,17–19
—Was subjected to frustration .... Ro 8:20
—Praises God .... Ps 145:10
Ps 148:1–5
Isa 55:12
—Eagerly awaits redemption .... Ro 8:19
—Will someday be liberated .... Ro 8:21
—Will someday be recreated .... Isa 65:17
2Pe 3:10–13
Rev 21:1
F. Humans commanded to rule creation .... Ge 1:26,28
Ps 8:6–8
Ps 115:16

CREED

See CONFESSION

CROSS

A. Jesus and the cross
1. What it involved
—The means to bring about Jesus' death .... Jn 19:17–18
Ac 5:30
—Was the death of a curse .... Gal 3:13
—Planned by God .... Lk 24:26–27
Ac 2:23
—Carried out by humans .... Ac 2:23
Ac 5:30
—Showed Jesus' obedience .... Php 2:8
2. What it accomplished
—Redeemed us from the curse of God .... Gal 3:10,13
—Took away our sins .... Col 2:13–14
1Pe 2:24
—Reconciled us with God .... Eph 2:16
Col 1:20
—Gave us eternal life .... Jn 3:14–15
—Brought about victory over Christ's enemies .... Col 2:15
B. The message of the cross
—Was preached by the apostles .... Ac 2:23
Ac 8:32–35
Ac 13:28–29
1Co 1:23
1Co 2:1–2
—Was a stumbling block to Jews 1Co 1:23
—Was foolishness to Gentiles 1Co 1:18,23
C. Believers and the cross
—They are crucified with Christ .... Gal 2:20
—Their sinful nature is put to death .... Ro 6:6
Gal 5:24
1Pe 2:24
—They are crucified to the world .... Gal 6:14
—They must carry their cross .... Mt 10:38

CROWN

A. Examples of those who wore a crown
—Priests .... Lev 8:9
Zec 6:9–11
—Kings 2Sa 12:30
SS 3:11
—Queens .... Est 1:11
Est 2:17
—Christ with a crown of thorns .... Mt 27:29
Jn 19:2,5
—Christ with a royal crown .... Rev 14:14
Rev 19:12
B. Crowns used as a symbol
1. In the present life
—God crowns humans with glory and honor .... Ps 8:5
—God crowns us with salvation .... Ps 149:4

CURSE, CURSING

CYRUS

DAMASCUS

DAN

DANCING

A. There is a time to dance — Ecc 3:4
B. Occasions for dancing
  1. Appropriate
    —To praise and worship God — Ex 15:20–21; Ps 68:24–25; Ps 149:3; Ps 150:4
    —To express human elation — 1Sa 18:6–7; 2Sa 6:16; Jer 31:4
  2. Inappropriate
    —In pagan worship — Ex 32:5–6,19; 1Ki 18:26–29; 1Co 10:7
    —Herodias before Herod — Mt 14:6
  3. Dancing ceases at a time of sorrow — La 5:15; Mt 11:17
C. God's blessing turns sorrow into dancing — Ps 30:11

DANIEL

A. Hebrew exiled to Babylon — Da 1:6
  —Educated in Babylonia — Da 1:3–5
  —Name changed to Belteshazzar — Da 1:7
  —Refused non-Jewish food — Da 1:8–21
  —Interpreted dreams of Nebuchadnezzar — Da 2:24–47; Da 4:4–27
  —Interpreted handwriting on the wall — Da 5:1–28
  —Survived the lions' den — Da 6:1–23
  —Recorded visions — Da 7:1–12:13
  —Jesus referred to his prophecy — Mt 24:15
B. Son of David and Abigail — 1Ch 3:1

DARIUS

A. King of the Medes; conquered Babylon — Da 5:31
  —Son of Xerxes — Da 9:1
B. A later king of Persia — Ezr 4:5; Hag 1:1,15
  —Asked to stop rebuilding of temple — Ezr 5:3–17
  —Allowed rebuilding of temple — Ezr 6:1–12

DARKNESS

A. Physical darkness
  —Created by God — Isa 45:7
  —Originally covered the earth — Ge 1:2
  —Separated from light — Ge 1:4
  —Called night — Ge 1:5
  —Comes when the sun sets — Ge 15:17
  —God can see things in the dark — Ps 139:11–12; Da 2:22
B. Darkness as a symbol
  1. For the mysteriousness of God — Ex 20:21; Ps 18:9; Ps 97:2
  2. For afflictions — Job 18:6,18; Isa 59:9; La 3:1–2
  3. For ignorance about God — Job 37:19; Isa 60:2; 1Jn 2:8
  4. For sin and evil
    —Sinful deeds are deeds of darkness — Ro 13:12; Eph 5:11
    —The way of the wicked is darkness — Pr 2:13; Pr 4:19; 1Th 5:4–5
    —Living in sin is walking in darkness — Jn 3:19; 1Jn 1:6; 1Jn 2:9,11
  5. For judgment from God — Joel 2:2; Am 5:18,20; Rev 16:10
  6. For the realm of Satan — Lk 22:53; Eph 6:12; Col 1:13
  7. For hell as a place of punishment — Mt 8:12; 2Pe 2:17; Jude 13
C. Antidotes to darkness as evil
  1. God
    —His first act was to dispel darkness — Ge 1:2–3
    —He surrounds himself with light — Ps 104:1–2; 1Ti 6:16
    —He is the God of light — 1Jn 1:5
  2. Jesus
    —Jesus came to dispel darkness — Jn 1:4–9; Jn 3:19–21; Jn 12:46
    —Jesus is the light of the world — Jn 8:12; Jn 9:5
  3. Heaven
    —God's light permeates heaven — Isa 60:19–20; Rev 21:23
    —Heaven has no night — Zec 14:7; Rev 22:5

See also LIGHT

DAVID

A. Related theme
  DAVID is a theme of 1 Chronicles — 1Ch 28:4
B. Personal data
  1. Ancestry
    —Son of Jesse — Ru 4:17–22; 1Ch 2:13–15
    —Youngest in the family — 1Sa 16:10–13
  2. Wives
    —Michal, daughter of Saul — 1Sa 18:2–27
    —Abigail, widow of Nabal — 1Sa 25:39–44
    —Bathsheba, widow of Uriah — 2Sa 11
    —Many wives and concubines — 2Sa 5:13–15
  3. Descendants
    —Solomon — 2Sa 12:24
    —Amnon — 2Sa 13:1
    —Absalom — 2Sa 13:1
    —Adonijah — 1Ki 1:5–6
    —Many sons — 2Sa 3:2–5; 1Ch 3:1–9
    —Jesus was the Son of David — Mt 1:1–17; Lk 3:31
  4. Occupations
    —A shepherd — 1Sa 16:11; 1Sa 17:20,34–37
    —A musician — 1Sa 16:14–23; 2Sa 23:1
    —A psalmist — 1Ch 16:7; Ps 3–34, etc.; Lk 20:42
    —A prophet — 2Sa 23:1–2; Ac 2:25–31
    —A king — 2Sa 5:3–4
C. David's life during Saul's reign
  1. His anointing as future king — 1Sa 16:1–13
  2. His work in Saul's service
    —Played music for Saul — 1Sa 16:14–23; 1Sa 18:10
    —Killed Goliath — 1Sa 17:4–51
    —Became a mighty warrior — 1Sa 18:2–7
  3. Saul's reaction to David
    —Was jealous of him — 1Sa 18:6–9,12,29
    —Tried to kill him — 1Sa 18:10–11; 1Sa 19:1–18
  4. David's flights
    —To Nob — 1Sa 21:1
    —To Gath — 1Sa 21:10
    —To the cave of Adullam — 1Sa 22:1
    —To Keilah — 1Sa 23:7
    —To desert strongholds — 1Sa 23:14–24
    —To the land of the Philistines — 1Sa 27:1–3
    —David spared Saul's life — 1Sa 24:1–21; 1Sa 26:1–25

5. His military victories
   —Killed 200 Philistines........................ 1Sa 18:24–27
   —Saved town of Keilah 1Sa 23:1–6
   —Defeated Amalekites........................ 1Sa 30:1–31
   —Not allowed to fight on side of Philistines....... 1Sa 29:1–11
6. His covenant with Jonathan 1Sa 18:1–4
   1Sa 20:16–17
   1Sa 23:15–18
7. His lament over Saul and Jonathan 2Sa 1:17–27

D. David's life as king
1. His fight to become king
   —Became king of Judah......................... 2Sa 2:1–11
   —Fought with Saul's supporters.................. 2Sa 2:8–4:12
   —Became king of all Israel...................... 2Sa 5:1–4
   1Ch 11:1–3
2. His military accomplishments
   —Conquered Jerusalem......................... 2Sa 5:6–10
   1Ch 11:4–9
   —Conquered Philistines........................ 2Sa 5:17–25
   2Sa 21:15–22
   1Ch 14:8–17
   —Conquered Ammonites........................ 2Sa 10:1–19
   1Ch 19:1–19
   —Conquered many others....................... 2Sa 8:1–14
   1Ch 18:1–13
   —Avenged the Gibeonites....................... 2Sa 21:1–14
   —Organized army and government............... 1Ch 27:1–34
   —Had many mighty men........................ 2Sa 23:8–39
   1Ch 11–12
   —Numbered his army, which angered the Lord 2Sa 24:1–17
   1Ch 21:1–19
3. His involvement in Israel's worship
   —Brought ark to Jerusalem...................... 2Sa 6:1–19
   —Planned the temple 1Ch 22:1–19
   1Ch 28:8–29:9
   —Organized Israel's worship.................... 1Ch 15:16–16:43
   —Organized priests and Levites.................. 1Ch 23:26
4. God's covenant with him 2Sa 7:1–17
   See COVENANT
5. David's sin and its consequences
   —His sin with Bathsheba........................ 2Sa 11:1–5
   —Attempt at cover-up......................... 2Sa 11:6–27
   —Sin exposed by Nathan....................... 2Sa 12:1–14
   —Death of his son............................ 2Sa 12:15–23
   —Absalom's revolt 2Sa 14:1–18:8
   —Death of Absalom 2Sa 18:9–18
   —David mourned Absalom's death................ 2Sa 18:33–19:4
   —Return to Jerusalem 2Sa 19:9–43
   —Sheba's revolt.............................. 2Sa 20:1–22
6. His last days
   —Abishag took care of him 1Ki 1:1–4
   —Appointed Solomon king...................... 1Ki 1:28–2:9
   —Gave charge to Solomon...................... 1Ki 2:1–9
   —His last words............................. 2Sa 23:1–7
   —His death 1Ki 2:10–12

E. His spiritual life
1. Positive qualities
   —Depended on the Lord 1Sa 17:45–47
   Ps 27:1–6
   —Trusted in the Lord.......................... Ps 25:1–5
   —Praised God 1Ch 16:7–10
   Ps 9:1–2
   —Was concerned about God's house 1Ch 17:1–2
   1Ch 22:5
   —Respected those in authority.................. 1Sa 24:5
   1Sa 26:9–11
   —Was faithful to his promises.................. 2Sa 9:1–13
   —Repented of his sin 2Sa 12:13
   Ps 32:3–5
2. Negative qualities
   —Took pride in his military power 2Sa 24:1–10
   —Committed adultery with Bathsheba............ 2Sa 11:1–5
   —Committed a murder indirectly................. 2Sa 11:14–17

F. New Testament significance
   —Jesus is David's Son .... Mt 1:1
   2Ti 2:8
   —Jesus is the Root of David...................... Rev 5:5
   Rev 22:16
   —Jesus sat on David's throne..................... Lk 1:30–33
   —David confessed Jesus to be Lord................. Mt 22:42–43
   —David was not a legalist .... Lk 6:1–5
   —David prophesied the resurrection .... Ac 2:25–31
   —David believed righteousness came through faith ... Ro 4:6–8
   —David was a hero of faith .... Heb 11:32–33
   —God spoke through David...................... Heb 4:7

DAY

A. Meanings of the word "day"
1. The period of light after the night
   —Light called "day" by God .... Ge 1:5
   —"Day and night"............................. Ge 8:22
   Est 4:16
   Jn 9:4–5
   —Divided into 12 hours .... Mt 20:1–12
   Jn 11:9
2. The time period of 24 hours...................... Ge 1:5,13,19
   Ge 8:4–5,13–14
   Ex 2:11,13
3. A synonym for "time"
   —The day of creation .... Dt 4:32
   —The day of the exodus........................ 1Ki 8:16
   —The day of the giving of the law .... Nu 15:23
   —A day of disaster .... Dt 32:35
   —To the present day.......................... Jos 4:9
   —The day of one's death .... Jdg 13:7
   —The day Jerusalem was built .... Jer 32:31
   —The day the temple was built.................. Hag 2:18
   —The day of salvation 2Co 6:2

B. The day of the Lord
1. In the Old Testament, it can refer to:
   —The time of God's judgment................... Joel 1:15
   Am 5:18
   Am 8:11–14
   Zep 1:14–17
   —The time of Israel's restoration................ Isa 10:20
   Isa 11:10–11
   Zec 9:16
   —The first coming of Christ .... Mal 3:1–3
   —The outpouring of the Spirit.................. Joel 2:28–31
   —The kingdom of Christ....................... Isa 4:2–6
   Mic 4:1–7
   —The end of the world........................ Isa 24:21–23
   Isa 27:12–13
   Zec 14:1–3
2. In the New Testament, it can refer to:
   —The day of the final battle .... Rev 16:14
   —The day of Christ's return .... Mk 13:24–27
   1Co 1:7–8
   2Co 1:14
   —The day of judgment......................... 1Co 3:12–15
   1Th 5:2–3
   2Pe 3:12
   —The day of God's wrath .... Ro 2:5–6
   —The day of blessing for Christians 1Co 1:8
   2Ti 4:8

DEACON

A. Often translated "servant" or "minister"
   —Used of Jesus .... Ro 15:8
   —Used of Paul and Apollos 1Co 3:5
   —Used of Timothy............................. 1Ti 4:6
   —Used of any follower of Christ .... Jn 12:26
B. An office in the New Testament church .... Php 1:1
   —Assistants to apostles........................ Ac 6:1–4
   —Qualifications given .... Ac 6:3
   1Ti 3:8–13
   —Possibly women were deaconesses............... Ro 16:1
   1Ti 3:11

DEATH

A. Physical death

1. Phrases used
   - —Dying .... Ge 5:5,8,11
   - —Returning to the dust .... Ge 3:19; Ecc 12:7
   - —Lying down in the dust .... Job 7:21
   - —Going to one's ancestors .... Ge 15:15
   - —Resting with one's ancestors .... Dt 31:16; 2Sa 7:12
   - —Being gathered to one's people .... Ge 25:8; Ge 49:29
   - —Breathing one's last .... Ge 35:29; Lk 23:46
   - —Going down to the grave .... Ge 37:35; 1Ki 2:6,9
   - —Falling asleep .... Jn 11:11; Ac 7:60
   - —Sleeping the last sleep .... Ps 76:5
   - —Being away from the body 2Co 5:8
   - —Departing .... Php 1:23; 2Ti 4:6; 2Pe 1:15
2. All human beings die .... Ecc 8:8; Heb 9:27
   - —First examples .... Ge 4:8; Ge 5:5–20,25–31
   - —Two exceptions: Enoch and Elijah .... Ge 5:21–24; 2Ki 2:11–12
3. Death came as a result of sin
   - —A result of Adam's sin .... Ge 2:17; Ro 5:12; 1Co 15:21–22
   - —The wages of sin for everyone .... Ro 6:23
4. Death was conquered by Christ
   - —He was raised from the dead .... Ro 6:9
   - —He holds the keys of death .... Rev 1:18
   - —He releases us from fear of death .... Heb 2:15
   - —He will destroy death completely 1Co 15:26,53–57
5. What is death for believers?
   - —Falling asleep in Christ 1Co 15:18; 1Th 4:14
   - —Gain .... Php 1:21
   - —Precious to God .... Ps 116:15; Rev 14:13
   - —The entrance into peace .... Isa 57:1–2
   - —The entrance into glory .... Ps 73:24
   - —Clothes us with our heavenly dwelling 2Co 5:4
   - —Prepares us to receive a crown 2Ti 4:8
6. What is death for the wicked?
   - —Without salvation .... Eze 3:19; Jn 8:21
   - —Without hope .... Job 8:13; Pr 11:7
   - —A judgment from God .... Nu 16:29–30; Lk 12:20
   - —The pathway to hell .... Lk 16:22–23; Ac 1:25
   - —Not pleasurable to God .... Eze 18:23,32
   - —Something for them to fear .... Job 27:19–21; Pr 10:24

B. Spiritual death

1. Its origin
   - —Came as a result of sin .... Ge 2:17; Ro 5:12; Ro 6:23
   - —Is part of the sinful human nature .... Ro 8:6
2. Who are spiritually dead?
   - —Everyone who does not have Christ .... Eph 2:1,5; Col 2:13; 1Jn 5:12
   - —Those seeking personal pleasure .... Eph 4:17–19; 1Ti 5:6
   - —Those not serving God by good works .... Heb 6:1; Heb 9:14; Rev 3:1–2
3. How can one overcome spiritual death?
   - —Through faith in Christ .... Eph 2:4–5; Eph 5:14; 1Jn 5:12
   - —By repenting and turning to God .... Lk 15:17–24; Rev 3:1–3

C. Eternal death

1. Phrases used to describe eternal death
   - —Eternal punishment .... Mt 25:46
   - —Hell .... Mt 5:29–30
   - —The eternal fire .... Mt 25:41
   - —The fiery lake of burning sulfur .... Rev 19:20
   - —The lake of fire .... Rev 20:15
   - —Shut out from God's presence 2Th 1:9
   - —The darkness outside .... Mt 25:30
   - —The blackest darkness .... Jude 13
   - —The second death .... Rev 20:6
   - —The coming wrath 1Th 1:10
2. What is its origin?
   - —Came as a result of sin .... Ge 2:17; Ro 5:12; Ro 6:23; Jas 1:15
   - —Symbolized by removal from Eden .... Ge 3:22–24
3. Who are subject to eternal death?
   - —The devil and his angels .... 2Pe 2:4; Rev 20:10
   - —The antichrist .... 2Th 2:8; Rev 19:20
   - —Those who worship the beast .... Rev 14:9–11
   - —Those who choose the broad road .... Mt 7:13
   - —Those who live a wicked life .... Ro 1:28–31
   - —Those who do not love the needy .... Mt 25:41–46
   - —Those who do not believe in Jesus .... Jn 3:36
   - —False teachers in the church 2Pe 2:1–17
   - —Godless, greedy people in the church .... Jude 4,8–13
4. Jesus conquered eternal death 1Co 15:20,54–57; 2Ti 1:10
5. Who will escape eternal death?
   - —Those who believe in Jesus .... Jn 3:16,18,36; Jn 11:25–26
   - —Those who are raised with Christ .... Ro 6:5–11
   - —Those who keep the word of God .... Jn 8:51
   - —Those who choose the narrow road .... Mt 7:14
   - —Those who are kind to the needy .... Mt 25:34–40
   - —Those who do not worship the beast .... Rev 20:4–6

DEBORAH

A. Rebekah's nurse .... Ge 35:8

B. A prophetess .... Jdg 4:4
   - —Judged Israel .... Jdg 4:5
   - —Fought Sisera's army with Barak .... Jdg 4:6–10,14–16
   - —Deborah's song of triumph .... Jdg 5:1–31

DEBT

—What is owed to another person

A. Financial debts

1. Regulated by Old Testament laws
   - —No interest to be charged .... Ex 22:25; Lev 25:36–37; Dt 15:8; Dt 23:19–20
   - —Security to be returned .... Ex 22:26–27; Dt 24:10–13
   - —The seventh year for canceling debts .... Dt 15:1–6
   - —The Year of Jubilee for canceling debts .... Lev 25:8–54
2. Examples of oppressed debtors
   - —Numerous people in David's time 1Sa 22:2
   - —A widow in Elisha's day 2Ki 4:1–7
   - —The poor in Amos's day .... Am 2:6–8
   - —Many Israelites in Nehemiah's day .... Ne 5:1–13

2. God's discipline of us
 —By instruction and warning .... Jer 7:27–28; Jer 17:23
 —By adversity and affliction .... Lev 26:23–26; Job 33:19; Ps 39:10–11; Jer 2:30

C. Motives of discipline
 —Love .... 2Sa 7:14–15; Pr 3:12; Heb 12:6; Rev 3:19
 —Desire for another's growth and improvement .... Job 5:17; Pr 25:12; Pr 29:15; Heb 12:10

D. Types of discipline
1. Self-discipline .... Ro 6:12–14; Ro 8:13; 1Co 9:26–27
2. Discipline in the home .... Pr 13:24; Pr 15:5; Pr 19:18
3. Mutual discipline
 —Between friends .... Pr 17:10; Pr 27:5–6; Pr 28:23
 —Among believers .... Lk 17:3; 1Th 5:11,14–15; 2Th 3:15
4. Church discipline
 a. Done through preaching the word .... 2Ti 3:16–17; 2Ti 4:2; Titus 2:15
 b. Done through direct measures
  —Rebuke sinners publicly .... 1Ti 5:20; Titus 1:13
  —Have nothing to do with sinners .... Ro 16:17; 1Co 5:9–11; 2Th 3:6,14; Titus 3:10
  —Remove sinners from the church 1Co 5:1–5,13; 1Ti 1:20

DIVORCE

—The breaking of the marital bond

A. Physical divorce
1. Divorce in the Old Testament
 —Not part of God's original plan .... Ge 2:24; Mt 19:8
 —Allowed and regulated .... Dt 22:13–19,28–29; Dt 24:1–4
 —Evidence of human stubbornness .... Mt 19:8
 —Priests not to marry divorcees .... Lev 21:7,14
 —Hated by God .... Mal 2:16
 —Defiled the land .... Jer 3:1–2
 —Required for those with idolatrous wives .... Ezr 10:2–17
2. Divorce in the New Testament
 —Marriage considered binding .... Mt 19:3–6; Ro 7:2–3
 —Permitted by Jesus for unfaithfulness .... Mt 5:31–33; Mt 19:9
 —Permitted by Paul in mixed marriages 1Co 7:12–15
 —Divorce was a pardonable sin .... Jn 4:17–18,39–42

B. Spiritual divorce
1. A result of sin and idolatry .... Isa 50:1; Jer 3:2
2. Northern kingdom (Israel): divorced by God .... Jer 3:8
3. Southern kingdom (Judah)
 —Equally as adulterous as Israel .... Jer 3:8–11
 —Temporary separation through the exile .... Isa 50:1; Isa 54:7
 —Taken back by God as spouse .... Isa 54:6–8; Isa 62:4–5

See also ADULTERY; MARRIAGE

DOCTRINE

—True teachings concerning faith and life

A. Related themes
1. DIRECTION is a theme of Proverbs .... Pr 3:5
2. DEFENSE is a theme of Colossians .... Col 2:8
3. DISCERNMENT is a theme of 2 John 2Jn 10
4. FALSE DOCTRINE is a theme of 1 Timothy 1Ti 1:3
5. FALSE TEACHERS is a theme of:
 —2 Peter 2Pe 2:1
 —Jude .... Jude 4

B. The importance of knowing doctrine
 —Stressed in the Old Testament .... Ps 78:1–8; Pr 7:1–5; Pr 13:14
 —Stressed in the New Testament .... 1Co 11:2; 2Th 2:15; 2Ti 1:13; Titus 1:9; Titus 2:1

See also CONFESSION; EDUCATION

C. Concern over false doctrine
1. The identity of false teachers
 —The teachers of the law .... Mt 23:2–4,16–22; Mk 12:38–40; Lk 20:46–47; 1Ti 1:6–7
 —Teachers of unsound doctrine .... 1Ti 4:1–3; 2Ti 4:3–4; Titus 1:9–11
 —Teachers who distort the truth .... Ac 20:29–30; 2Ti 2:17–18
 —Teachers who introduce heresies 2Pe 2:1; 2Jn 7
 —Teachers who cause divisions .... Ro 16:17; 1Ti 6:3–5
 —Teachers who promote immorality .... 2Ti 3:6–8; Rev 2:14,20
2. Commands concerning false teachers
 —Watch out for them .... Mk 12:38; Lk 20:46; Ac 20:31; 2Jn 8
 —Command them to stop teaching .... 1Ti 1:3–4; Titus 1:10–11,13–14
 —Withdraw from them .... Ro 16:17; 2Ti 2:16–18; 2Jn 10–11

DOEG

—An Edomite; Saul's head shepherd 1Sa 21:7
—Reported to Saul about priests of Nob 1Sa 22:9–10
—Killed the priests of Nob for Saul 1Sa 22:18–19
—David wrote a psalm about the incident .... Ps 52:1–9

DOG

See ANIMALS

DORCAS

—Disciple in Joppa who died .... Ac 9:36–37
—Raised to life by Peter .... Ac 9:38–41

DOUBT

—A questioning of one's faith

A. Examples of believers who doubted
 —Abram .... Ge 12:10–20; Ge 15:2–3; Ge 16:1–4; Ge 20:1–13
 —Moses .... Ex 33:15–19
 —Gideon .... Jdg 6:36–37,39
 —John the Baptist .... Mt 11:2–3
 —Peter .... Mt 14:28–31
 —Martha .... Jn 11:39
 —Some disciples .... Mt 28:17
 —Thomas .... Jn 20:24–25

B. Ending doubt
1. How doubts were ended
—Abram, by believing God's word ... Ge 15:6
—Moses, by seeing God's glory ... Ex 33:21–23
—Gideon, by throwing out the fleece ... Jdg 6:36–40
—John, by seeing Christ's miracles ... Mt 11:4–6
—Peter, by reaching out to Christ ... Mt 14:30–31
—Thomas, by seeing the risen Christ ... Jn 20:26–29
2. God wants us to overcome doubt ... Mk 11:22–24
Jas 1:6
Jude 22

DOVE
See BIRDS

DREAMS AND VISIONS
A. Dreams and visions in general
—Closely related ... Da 7:1–2
—Used by God for revelation ... Nu 12:6
—Authenticity must be tested ... Dt 13:1–5
—God alone can interpret dreams ... Ge 40:8
Ge 41:16
Da 2:27–28

B. Examples of dreams and visions used for revelation
1. Dreams
—Jacob ... Ge 28:12–16
—Joseph ... Ge 37:5–9
—Pharaoh, interpreted by Joseph ... Ge 41:1–36
—Solomon ... 1Ki 3:5
—Nebuchadnezzar, interpreted by Daniel ... Da 2:24–47
Da 4:4–27
—Joseph, husband of Mary ... Mt 1:20–21
2. Visions
—Abram ... Ge 15:1
—Jacob ... Ge 46:2
—Samuel ... 1Sa 3:10–15
—Various prophets ... Isa 1:1
Da 7:1
Ob 1
Mic 1:1
Na 1:1
—Cornelius ... Ac 10:3–6
—Peter ... Ac 10:9–17
—Paul ... Ac 18:9
C. Warnings against those who feign dreams ... Jer 23:25–28
Eze 13:3–9
Zec 10:2
Jude 8

DROUGHT
See HUNGER AND THIRST

DRUGS
See ALCOHOL

DRUNKENNESS
See ALCOHOL

DUST
A. Humans are creatures of dust
—Created from the dust of the ground ... Ge 2:7
Ecc 3:20
1Co 15:47
—Pictures human frailty ... Ps 103:14
—Will return to the dust ... Ge 3:19
Ps 104:29
Ecc 12:7
B. Dust used as a symbol
—Dust symbolizes a large number ... Ge 13:16
Nu 23:10
—Rain turned into dust as God's judgment ... Dt 28:24
—Dust on the head expresses grief ... Job 2:12
Isa 47:1
—Sitting in dust expresses repentance ... Jnh 3:6
—Lying in dust expresses humiliation ... Ps 44:25
Ps 113:7
—Lying down in dust means death ... Job 7:21
Ps 7:5
—Enemies licking the dust means defeat ... Ps 72:9
Mic 7:17
—Shaking dust off the feet means rejection ... Mt 10:14
Ac 13:51
—Throwing dust in the air expresses shock ... Ac 22:23

EAGLE
See BIRDS

EAR
A. The human ear
1. Uses for the human ear
—To hear ... 2Sa 7:22
—To acquire wisdom and knowledge ... Pr 2:2
Pr 18:15
—To wear earrings ... Ge 35:4
—To designate, by piercing, a permanent servant ... Ex 21:6
2. Types of human ears
—The ear eager to listen to Jesus ... Mt 11:15
—The ear eager to listen to the Spirit ... Rev 2:7,11,17,29
—The understanding ear ... Job 13:1
—The deaf ear ... Isa 43:8
—The closed ear ... Jer 6:10
—The uncircumcised ear ... Ac 7:51
—The ear itching to hear falsehood ... 2Ti 4:3
B. The ears of God
—His ears are attentive to our prayers ... Ps 34:15
1Pe 3:12
—His ears hear the cries of the oppressed ... Jas 5:4
—His ear is not dull ... Isa 59:1
—His ears hear insolence ... 2Ki 19:28
—He closes his ears to sinners ... Eze 8:18
—We can ask God to give ear to us ... Ps 5:1
Ps 17:1,6
Ps 130:2

EARTH
A. God and the earth
1. His actions regarding it
—He created it ... Ge 1:1
—He laid its foundations ... Heb 1:10
—He suspended it in space ... Job 26:7
—He called forth plants from it ... Ge 1:11
—He called forth animals from it ... Ge 1:24
—He made people from it ... Ge 2:7
—He filled it with his creatures ... Ps 104:24
—He holds it firmly ... Ps 75:3
—He governs it ... Job 34:12–15
—He will judge it ... Ps 96:13
See also CREATION; PROVIDENCE
2. His relationship to it
—He owns it ... Ps 24:1
1Co 10:26
—He is King over all of it ... Ps 47:2,7,9
—He loves it ... Ps 33:5
—His glory fills it ... Isa 6:3
—His knowledge will fill it ... Isa 11:9
Hab 2:14
—It is his footstool ... Isa 66:1
Mt 5:35
B. Humans and the earth
—Made from the earth ... Ge 2:7
1Co 15:47
—It is given to humans ... Ps 115:16
—Humans must fill and rule it ... Ge 1:28
Ge 9:7
Ps 8:6–8
—Believers shall inherit it ... Mt 5:5
Ro 4:13
C. The earth and sin
—Ground cursed after Adam's sin ... Ge 3:17–19
—Earth groans as a result of sin ... Ro 8:22
—Earth became the domain for Satan ... Rev 12:9
—Earth waits for redemption ... Ro 8:20–21
—God will someday make a new earth ... Isa 65:17
2Pe 3:13
Rev 21:1

EARTHQUAKE

—At the Lord's appearance to Elijah — 1Ki 19:11–12
—At the Lord's judgment of Jerusalem — Isa 29:5–6
—During the reign of Uzziah — Am 1:1; Zec 14:5
—After the death of Christ — Mt 27:54
—At the resurrection of Christ — Mt 28:2
—During Paul's imprisonment in Philippi — Ac 16:26
—As a sign of Christ's coming — Mt 24:4–8; Mk 13:3–8; Lk 21:7–11
—In the great tribulation — Rev 6:12; Rev 11:13
—In God's final judgment — Rev 16:17–18

EDOMITES

A. Their identity
—The descendants of Esau (Edom) — Ge 25:30; Ge 36:8–9
—Lived in hill country, southeast of Israel — Ge 36:9
—Country also called Mount Seir — Ge 32:3
—Territory bordered on Judah — Jos 15:21

B. Significant Edomites
—Numerous kings listed — Ge 36:31–39; 1Ch 1:43–50
—Doeg: head shepherd of King Saul — 1Sa 21:7; 1Sa 22:9,18–19
—Hadad: fought against Solomon — 1Ki 11:14–22

C. Their wars
—Defeated by King Saul — 1Sa 14:47
—Defeated by David — 2Sa 8:11–14; 1Ch 18:11–13
—Defeated Moab with Israel and Judah — 2Ki 3:1–27
—Allied with Moab against Jehoshaphat — 2Ch 20:1,10
—Their warriors killed by Moabites and Ammonites — 2Ch 20:22–24
—Defeated Jehoram of Judah — 2Ki 8:20–22; 2Ch 21:8–10
—Defeated by King Amaziah — 2Ki 14:7; 2Ch 25:10–12
—Defeated King Ahaz of Judah — 2Ch 28:17

D. Important data concerning them
—Refused passage to Israelites in desert — Nu 20:14–21
—Israelites passed around their country — Nu 21:4; Jdg 11:17–18
—Solomon intermarried with them — 1Ki 11:1
—Prophecies concerning their destruction — Isa 34:4–15; Jer 49:7–22; Eze 25:12–14; Eze 35:1–15; Am 1:11–12; Ob 1–21

EDUCATION

A. People as educators
1. Primary educators: parents
—A never-ending task — Dt 4:9; Dt 6:4–7; Pr 1:8; Pr 6:20
—Usually done by fathers — Ge 18:19; Ps 44:1; Eph 6:4
—Could be done by mothers — Pr 6:20; 2Ti 1:5; 2Ti 3:15
2. Officials authorized by a government — Ezr 7:6,10; 2Ch 17:7–9; Ne 8:7–8; Ac 7:22
3. Authorized religious officials — Mk 12:28; Jn 3:10; Ac 22:3
4. The apostles — Mt 28:20; Ac 2:42; Ac 4:2
5. People gifted by the Spirit — 1Co 12:28–29; Eph 4:11
6. Any mature Christian — Heb 5:11–14

B. The content of education
—The law of God — Dt 6:6–7; Dt 33:10
—The praiseworthy deeds of God — Ps 78:4–6
—The holy Scriptures — 2Ti 3:14–17
—General knowledge and wisdom — Da 1:17; Col 2:3

C. The foundation of education
—The fear of God — Ps 111:10; Pr 1:7; Pr 9:10
—Knowing the Lord Jesus Christ — 1Co 1:30; Col 2:3

D. Purpose of education
—To impart information — Ps 78:4–6
—To inspire trust and obedience — Ps 78:7–8; Pr 22:19
—To inspire wisdom — Pr 4:5–8
—To attain skill in holy living — Ge 18:19; Pr 1:2–4; 2Ti 3:17
—To prepare for adulthood — Pr 22:6

EGLON

A. City in Canaan — Jos 10:3
—Its king joined others against city of Gibeon — Jos 10:3–8
—Defeated by Joshua — Jos 10:9–14

B. King of Moab — Jdg 3:12–14
—Killed by Ehud — Jdg 3:16–23

EGYPT

A. Names and geography
1. Other terms for Egypt
—The land of Ham — Ps 105:23
—The land of slavery — Ex 20:2
—The South — Da 11:5
—Rahab — Isa 51:9–10
2. Areas of Egypt
—Upper and Lower Egypt — Isa 11:11
—The Nile River — Eze 29:3
—The land of Goshen — Ge 47:6
—Rameses, a district in Goshen — Ge 47:11
—Pithom and Rameses: built by Israelites — Ex 1:11
—Memphis, the capital city — Hos 9:6
—Thebes — Eze 30:14
—Tahpanhes, the city to which Jews fled — Jer 43:8; Jer 44:1

B. Important Egyptians
—Their kings were called pharaohs
See PHARAOH
—Hagar: servant of Sarai — Ge 16:1
—Potiphar: owner of Joseph — Ge 39:1
—Shishak: ransacked the temple — 1Ki 14:25–26

C. Interaction with God's people
1. During the time of the patriarchs
—Abram went to Egypt during famine — Ge 12:10–20
—Joseph sold there by merchants — Ge 37:28
—Joseph became governor of Egypt — Ge 41:33–45
—Joseph's brothers bought grain there — Ge 42:1–26; Ge 43:1–44:3
—Jacob and his sons moved there — Ge 46:1–47:12
2. At the time of the exodus
See EXODUS
3. During the time of the kings
—Solomon intermarried with them — 1Ki 3:1
—Solomon ruled territory to its border — 1Ki 4:21
—Solomon traded with them — 1Ki 10:28–29; 2Ch 1:16–17
—Enemies of Solomon fled there — 1Ki 11:14–18; 1Ki 11:40
—Gained victory over Rehoboam — 1Ki 14:25–26; 2Ch 12:1–12

ELIJAH

A. His life as a prophet of God
- —Predicted drought in Israel . . . 1Ki 17:1; Jas 5:17
- —Fed by ravens . . . 1Ki 17:2–6
- —Stayed with a widow in Zarephath . . . 1Ki 17:7–16
- —Raised the widow's dead son . . . 1Ki 17:17–24
- —Challenged Baal's prophets to a contest . . . 1Ki 18:19–26
- —Prayed for fire from heaven . . . 1Ki 18:30–39
- —Killed the prophets of Baal . . . 1Ki 18:40
- —Prayed for rain . . . 1Ki 18:41–45
- —Fled from Jezebel . . . 1Ki 19:1–3
- —Prayed that he might die . . . 1Ki 19:4–5
- —Strengthened by the Lord . . . 1Ki 19:6–18
- —Anointed Elisha as successor . . . 1Ki 19:19–21
- —Confronted Ahab after death of Naboth . . . 1Ki 21:17–29
- —Prophesied death of Azariah . . . 2Ki 1:3–17
- —Taken to heaven without dying . . . 2Ki 2:11–12

B. Later references
- —Malachi prophesied his return . . . Mal 4:5–6
- —John the Baptist likened to him . . . Mt 17:9–13; Mk 9:9–13
- —Jesus compared to him . . . Mt 16:14
- —Jesus compared his rejection to Elijah's . . . Lk 4:24–26
- —Appeared to Jesus in the transfiguration . . . Mt 17:1–8; Mk 9:1–8
- —Paul recalled a remnant in Elijah's day . . . Ro 11:2–5
- —His prayers are an example for us . . . Jas 5:17–18

ELIMELEK

- —Husband of Naomi . . . Ru 1:2
- —Fled to Moab during famine . . . Ru 1:1
- —Died in Moab . . . Ru 1:3

ELIPHAZ

A. Firstborn son of Esau . . . Ge 36:4,10

B. One of Job's friends who tried to comfort him . . . Job 2:11
- —His first speech . . . Job 4:1–5:27
- —His second speech . . . Job 15:1–35
- —His third speech . . . Job 22:1–30
- —Offered sacrifices to God after Job's restoration . . . Job 42:7–9

ELISHA

A. His association with Elijah
- —Anointed by Elijah as successor . . . 1Ki 19:16–21
- —Accompanied Elijah on his last day . . . 2Ki 2:1–8
- —Inherited Elijah's cloak . . . 2Ki 2:9–13
- —Divided the Jordan with Elijah's cloak . . . 2Ki 2:14

B. His ministry
- —Purified bad water . . . 2Ki 2:19–22
- —Pronounced a curse on mocking young men . . . 2Ki 2:23–25
- —Aided Israelites in the defeat of Moab . . . 2Ki 3:11–20
- —Increased widow's oil . . . 2Ki 4:1–7
- —Raised Shunammite's son . . . 2Ki 4:8–37
- —Purified food by a miracle . . . 2Ki 4:38–41
- —Fed a hundred men by a miracle . . . 2Ki 4:42–44
- —Healed Naaman's leprosy . . . 2Ki 5:1–19
- —Caused axhead to float . . . 2Ki 6:1–7
- —Captured Arameans . . . 2Ki 6:8–23
- —Advised king of Israel . . . 2Ki 6:24–8:6
- —Prophesied end to siege of Arameans . . . 2Ki 7:1–2
- —Prophesied Ben-Hadad's death . . . 2Ki 8:7–15
- —Anointed Jehu as king of Israel . . . 2Ki 9:1–3
- —Prophesied victory for Jehoash . . . 2Ki 13:14–17
- —His death . . . 2Ki 13:20

C. Later references
- —His dead body raised another one to life . . . 2Ki 13:20–21
- —Jesus compared his rejection to Elisha's . . . Lk 4:24,27

ELIZABETH

- —Wife of Zechariah; barren . . . Lk 1:5–7
- —Relative of the virgin Mary . . . Lk 1:36
- —Gave birth to John the Baptist . . . Lk 1:11–23,57–58
- —Visited by Mary . . . Lk 1:39–45

ELKANAH

- —Husband of Hannah and Peninnah . . . 1Sa 1:1–2
- —Worshiped every year at Shiloh . . . 1Sa 1:3–8
- —Father of Samuel . . . 1Sa 1:19–20

ENCOURAGEMENT

—Giving support and inspiration

A. Related theme

ENCOURAGEMENT is a theme of Zechariah . . . Zec 10:12

B. Human encouragement

1. Those who need encouragement
   - —Leaders . . . Dt 1:38; Dt 3:28
   - —The oppressed . . . Isa 1:17
   - —The persecuted . . . Ac 14:21–22; 1Th 3:1–3
   - —All Christians . . . Ac 20:1; Heb 3:13
2. Those who do the encouraging
   - —Kings . . . 2Sa 19:7; 2Ch 32:6–8
   - —Prophets . . . Ac 15:32
   - —Apostles . . . Ac 16:40; Ac 20:2; 1Th 2:11–12
   - —Church pastors . . . Col 4:7–8; 2Ti 4:2; Titus 2:15; 1Pe 5:12
   - —Specially gifted Christians . . . Ro 12:6,8
   - —All Christians to each other . . . Ro 1:12; 1Th 4:18; Heb 10:25

C. Divine encouragement
- —God encourages us . . . Ps 10:17; 2Th 2:16–17; Heb 6:17–18
- —Christ encourages us . . . Php 2:1; 2Th 2:16–17
- —The Holy Spirit encourages us . . . Ac 9:31
- —The Scriptures encourage us . . . Ro 15:4; Heb 12:5

ENEMY

A. Types of enemies
- —Pagan nations . . . Jos 5:13; 1Sa 4:3; Jer 12:7
- —Personal adversaries . . . 2Sa 4:8; 1Ki 21:20; Est 7:6; Pr 16:7
- —Spiritual forces . . . Eph 6:12; 1Pe 5:8
- —Death . . . 1Co 15:26

B. Reactions to one's enemies

1. In Israelite history
   - —Destroyed in war

     See WARFARE
   - —Occasionally treated kindly . . . 1Sa 26:7–12
2. In the psalms
   - —Prayers for deliverance from them . . . Ps 59:1; Ps 64:1–2; Ps 143:9
   - —Prayers for God to judge them . . . Ps 35:4–8,26; Ps 58:6–9; Ps 69:22–28; Ps 109:6–15
3. In the New Testament
   - —Jesus prayed for them . . . Lk 23:34
   - —Stephen prayed for them . . . Ac 7:60

C. Commands from God regarding enemies
- —Treat them with kindness . . . Pr 25:21–22; Ro 12:19–21
- —Pray for them . . . Mt 5:44
- —Love them . . . Mt 5:44; Lk 6:27,35

ENOCH

A. Son of Cain — Ge 4:17–18
B. Descendant of Seth — Ge 5:19–20
 —Walked with God — Ge 5:22–24
 —Taken by God to heaven without dying — Ge 5:24
 —An example of faith — Heb 11:5

ENVY

—Intense feeling of ill will or malice
A. In the Old Testament
 —Examples of envy — Ge 37:11; Nu 16:1–3; Ps 106:16–18
 —The command not to envy — Pr 3:31; Pr 23:17; Pr 24:1
B. In the New Testament
 —Examples of envy — Mt 27:18; Mk 15:10; Php 1:15,17
 —Negative effects of envy — Mk 7:20–23; Jas 3:14,16
 —A positive result from envy — Ro 11:13–14
 —Envy in a list of vices — Ro 1:29; Gal 5:21; 1Pe 2:1
 —Love does not envy — 1Co 13:4

EPHESUS

—Paul left Priscilla and Aquila there — Ac 18:19
—Apollos learned about Christ there — Ac 18:24–26
—Paul converted some disciples of John there — Ac 19:1–7
—Paul spent two years there — Ac 19:8–22
—Riot over Paul's evangelism there — Ac 19:23–41
—Paul wrote letter to the church there — Eph 1:1
—Timothy ministered there — 1Ti 1:3
—Tychicus ministered there — 2Ti 4:12
—Church there lost its first love — Rev 2:1–7

EPHRAIM

A. Second son of Joseph — Ge 41:52; Ge 46:20
 —Name means "twice fruitful" — Ge 41:52
 —Blessed by Jacob ahead of Manasseh — Ge 48:12–20
B. Tribe descended from Ephraim
 —Numbered — Nu 1:33; Nu 26:37
 —Blessed by Moses — Dt 33:17
 —Allotted land in Canaan — Jos 16:4–9; Eze 48:5
 —Failed to possess the land — Jos 16:10; Jdg 1:29
 —Quarreled with Gideon — Jdg 8:1–3
 —Quarreled with Jephthah — Jdg 12:1–6
 —Many joined kingdom of Judah during Asa's reform — 2Ch 15:8–9
C. A synonym for the northern kingdom — Isa 7:17; Hos 5:5

ESAU

A. His birth
 —Firstborn of Isaac — Ge 25:25
 —Twin with Jacob — Ge 25:26
 —Also called Edom — Ge 25:30
B. Significant events
 —Became a hunter — Ge 25:27
 —Sold his birthright — Ge 25:29–34
 —His blessing stolen by Jacob — Ge 27:1–40
 —Wanted to kill Jacob — Ge 27:41
 —Married pagan women — Ge 26:34; Ge 28:6–9
 —Reconciled to Jacob — Ge 33:1–17
 —With Jacob, buried Isaac — Ge 35:29
C. His descendants — Ge 36:1–43
 See EDOMITES
D. Later significance of Esau
 —Descendants to be obliterated — Ob 1–21; Jer 49:7–22
 —Jacob chosen over him — Mal 1:2–3
 —Demonstrates God's purpose of election — Ro 9:11–13
 —His rejection for not repenting — Heb 12:16–17

ESTHER

—Daughter of Abihail — Est 2:15
—Cousin of Mordecai — Est 2:7
—Chosen queen by Xerxes — Est 2:8–18
—Objected to appearing before Xerxes — Est 4:10–11
—Asked for a fast — Est 4:15–16
—Risked her life by approaching Xerxes — Est 5:1–2
—Foiled Haman's plan to kill Jews — Est 7:1–8
—Caused Haman's execution — Est 7:9–10
—Her plan preserved the Jews — Est 8:1–9:17
—Decreed celebration of Purim — Est 9:18–32

ETERNAL

—Without end in time
A. Eternity related to humans
 1. The human body does not live forever — Ecc 12:7
  See DEATH
 2. Eternal life for believers
  —Jesus came to give eternal life — Jn 11:25–26; 2Ti 1:10; 1Jn 5:11–12
  —We receive eternal life through faith — Jn 3:16,36; 1Jn 5:13
  —We receive eternal salvation through Christ — Heb 5:9; Heb 9:12
  —We have an eternal house in heaven — 2Co 5:1
  —We are called into God's eternal glory — 1Pe 5:10
  —We enter an eternal kingdom — 2Pe 1:11
  —We receive an eternal inheritance — Heb 9:15
 3. Eternal punishment for the wicked — Mt 25:46; 2Th 1:9; Rev 21:8
B. Eternity related to God
 1. His being and person
  —God is the eternal God — Dt 33:27
  —God is the eternal Rock — Isa 26:4
  —God is from everlasting to everlasting — Ps 90:2
  —God lives forever — Isa 57:15
  —God's name endures forever — Ps 135:13
  —God is not bound by time — Ps 90:4; 2Pe 3:8; Rev 1:8
 2. His attributes
  —He does not change — Ps 102:27; Mal 3:6; Heb 13:8
  —His love endures forever — 2Ch 7:3,6; Ps 136:1–26
  —His righteousness endures forever — Ps 111:3; 2Co 9:9
  —His faithfulness endures forever — Ps 100:5; Ps 117:2
  —His purpose for humanity is eternal — Eph 3:11
  —His power is eternal — Ro 1:20
 3. His kingdom
  —God is the eternal King — 1Ti 1:17
  —His kingdom is eternal — Ps 145:13; Da 4:3,34
  —Christ reigns forever and ever — Rev 11:15
 4. His everlasting covenant
  —With Abraham, Isaac, Jacob — Ge 17:7–8; 1Ch 16:17
  —With David — 2Sa 7:13–16; 2Sa 23:5
  —With us in the new covenant — Isa 55:3; Jer 32:40; Eze 37:26
 5. God's word is eternal — Ps 119:89; Isa 40:8; 1Pe 1:24–25

EUPHRATES

—One of the rivers of Eden. Ge 2:14
—Abraham came from beyond it. Jos 24:2–3
—Israel's borders to expand there. Ge 15:18; Dt 11:22–25
—Hittites controlled it. Jos 1:4
—David expanded kingdom to it. 2Sa 8:3; 1Ch 18:3
—Solomon's kingdom bordered on it. 1Ki 4:21; Ps 72:8
—Assyrians controlled it. 2Ki 23:29; Isa 8:7–8
—Babylon controlled it. 2Ki 24:1; Jer 46:2
—Christ's kingdom to reach to it. Zec 9:9–10
—Army of the final battle to come from there. Rev 9:14; Rev 16:12

EVANGELISM

See MISSION

EVE

A. Eve in the Old Testament
  1. Her history
    —Made in God's image. Ge 1:27; Ge 5:1–2
    —Made from Adam's rib. Ge 2:22
    —Became Adam's wife. Ge 2:23–24
    —Entered conversation with serpent. Ge 3:1–5
    —Ate forbidden fruit with Adam. Ge 3:6
    —Tried to hide from God. Ge 3:8
    —Blamed serpent for her sin. Ge 3:13
    —Received curse from God. Ge 3:16
    —Banished with Adam from Eden. Ge 3:23
    —Mother of Cain, Abel and Seth. Ge 4:1–2,25
  2. Her significance as mother of all humans. Ge 3:20
B. Eve in the New Testament
  —Significance of Eve being created after Adam. 1Co 11:8; 1Ti 2:13
  —Significance of Eve deceived by serpent. 2Co 11:3

EXAMPLE

A. Old Testament people as examples
  1. As warnings. 1Co 10:6–11; 2Ti 3:8
  2. As models for Christian behavior
    —Job in his perseverance. Jas 5:10–11
    —Elijah in his prayers. Jas 5:16–18
    —Numerous saints in their faith. Heb 11:4–40
B. Christ as an example
  —His humility. Php 2:5–8
  —His love. Jn 15:12–13; Eph 5:2
  —His service. Jn 13:14–15
  —His gentleness. Mt 11:29
  —His consideration of others. Ro 15:2–3
  —His grace of giving. 2Co 8:7–9
  —His forgiveness. Col 3:13
  —His purity. 1Jn 3:3
  —His unjust suffering. 1Pe 2:20–23
  —His obedience to the Father. Jn 15:10
  —His general walk of life. 1Jn 2:6
C. Paul as an example
  —Thessalonians followed his example. 1Th 1:6
  —Churches encouraged to imitate him. 1Co 4:16; 1Co 11:1; Php 3:17; 2Th 3:7,9
D. Christians as examples
  —The Thessalonians were examples. 1Th 1:7
  —Church leaders must be examples. 1Ti 4:12; Titus 2:7; 1Pe 5:3
  —We must all be examples. Mt 5:16; Php 2:14–15; 1Pe 2:12

EXHORTATION

See ENCOURAGEMENT

EXILE

—The captivity of the people of Judah by the Babylonians
A. Judah carried away into Babylon
  1. The story of the exile told. 2Ki 24:11–16; 2Ki 25:11
  2. Three waves of exiles. Jer 52:28–30
    —Daniel in the first. Da 1:1–6
    —Ezekiel in the second. Eze 1:1–3
    —Remainder of the people in the third. 2Ch 36:20
  3. Reasons for the exile
    —Because of the sins of Manasseh. 2Ki 21:10–15; Jer 15:1–4
    —Because of Judah's idolatry. Dt 28:45–52; Isa 40:2; Jer 5:7–17; Eze 6:1–8
    —Because Judah failed to heed prophets. 2Ch 36:15–20
  4. Lessons the Jews learned in the exile
    —That God was everywhere. Eze 11:16
    —That God was Redeemer. Isa 59:12–20
    —That God still loved them. Jer 30:10–11,18–22; Eze 34:20–31
    —That the Law was important. Ezr 7:10; Ne 8:1–9
B. The return from exile
  —Occurred after 70 years. Jer 25:11
  —God remembered his promises. Jer 29:10
  —God remembered his covenant. Eze 16:60
  —Cyrus decreed the Jews could return. 2Ch 36:23; Ezr 1:2–4
  —The Jews returned in two groups. Ezr 1:5–6; Ezr 7:1–9

EXODUS

—The escape of the Israelites from Egypt
A. Related themes
  FREEDOM is a theme of Exodus. Ex 6:6
  JOURNEY is a theme of Numbers. Nu 9:18
B. Jacob and his sons in Egypt
  —Moved to Egypt. Ge 46:1–27
  —Became slaves of the Egyptians. Ex 1:8–14
C. God's deliverance of his people from Egypt
  1. God's choosing of a deliverer
    —Moses preserved at birth. Ex 2:1–10
    —Moses called as deliverer. Ex 3:7–22
    —Aaron appointed to assist Moses. Ex 4:13–17,27–31
  2. The process of deliverance
    —Signs given to Moses. Ex 4:1–9
    —The first appearance before Pharaoh. Ex 5:1–5
    —The second appearance before Pharaoh. Ex 7:10–13
    —The first nine plagues. Ex 7:14–10:29
    —The preparation for the tenth plague. Ex 11:1–12:28
    —The slaying of the firstborn in Egypt. Ex 12:29–30
    —The escape from Egypt. Ex 12:31–39
    —The pursuit of the Israelites. Ex 14:5–9
    —The crossing of the "Red Sea". Ex 14:10–22,29
    —The drowning of the Egyptians. Ex 14:23–28
  3. God's motive in the exodus
    —Faithfulness to his promises. Ge 15:13–16; Dt 7:8–9
    —His love for his people. Dt 7:8–9; Hos 11:1
D. Israelite remembrance of the exodus
  —Sung after crossing the "Red Sea". Ex 15:1–21
  —Celebrated annually in the Passover. Ex 13:3–16
  —Recalled in the Ten Commandments. Ex 20:2; Dt 5:6
  —Celebrated by psalmists. Ps 66:5–6; Ps 78:12–14; Ps 105:26–39; Ps 106:8–12

—Taught by prophets .... Isa 43:16–21
Isa 63:11–14
Hos 12:9,13
Na 1:4

E. The exodus in the New Testament
—As an affirmation of God's power .... Ac 13:17
Ro 9:17
—As a picture of salvation in Christ 1Co 10:1–4
—As an example of God's care .... Jn 6:31–33
—As an example of human faith .... Heb 11:29
—As a warning against disobedience .... Heb 3:7–4:2
Jude 5

EYE

A. The human eye
1. The physical eyes
—Leah's weak eyes .... Ge 29:17
—Lovers' eyes .... SS 1:15
SS 7:4
—Cruelty in eyes being gouged out .... Jdg 16:21
2Ki 25:7
2. Figurative use of eyes
—Enlightened eyes symbolize knowledge .... Ps 19:8
Eph 1:18
—Opened eyes symbolize knowledge .... Ge 3:5,7
—Bright eyes symbolize well-being 1Sa 14:27
—Dim eyes symbolize grief .... Job 17:7
—Winking eyes express mockery .... Ps 35:19
—Winking eyes plot perversity .... Pr 16:30
—Dissatisfied eyes express greed .... Pr 27:20
—Closed eyes express spiritual blindness .... Isa 6:10
Mt 13:15
—Lustful eyes 1Jn 2:16
—Eyes full of adultery 2Pe 2:14
—Haughty eyes .... Ps 18:27
—A jealous eye 1Sa 18:9
B. The eye of God
—Symbolizes God's all-knowing nature .... Ps 139:16
Pr 15:3
—Symbolizes God's holiness .... Hab 1:13
—Symbolizes God watching over us .... Ezr 5:5
Ps 33:18
—Symbolizes Christ's control of history .... Rev 5:6

EZEKIEL

A. Family background and history
—A priest .... Eze 1:3
—Carried into exile .... Eze 1:1
—Called to be a prophet .... Eze 2:1–3:11
—Married; wife died .... Eze 24:18
B. His symbolic actions as a prophet
—City of Jerusalem on a clay tablet .... Eze 4:1–3
—Lying immobile for more than a year .... Eze 4:4–8
—Strange diet during the "siege" of Jerusalem .... Eze 4:9–17
—A strange haircut .... Eze 5:1–4
—Packing his belongings for exile .... Eze 12:1–16
—Shuddering while eating his food .... Eze 12:17–20
—Groaning in public .... Eze 20:6–7
—Not mourning when his wife died .... Eze 24:15–24
—A prophecy using sticks .... Eze 37:15–28
C. His parables as a prophet
—The parable of the useless vine .... Eze 15:1–8
—The parable of the wife turned prostitute .... Eze 16:1–63
—The parable of two eagles and a vine .... Eze 17:1–24
—The parable of the lion .... Eze 19:1–9
—The parable of the two adulterous sisters .... Eze 23:1–49

EZRA

—A priest .... Ezr 7:1–5
—A teacher of the Law .... Ezr 7:6–10
—Led exiles back to Jerusalem .... Ezr 8:15–36
—Concerned about intermarriage .... Ezr 9:1–4
—Prayed about intermarriage problem .... Ezr 9:5–15
—Corrected intermarriage problem .... Ezr 10:1–17
—Read Law at the Festival of Tabernacles .... Ne 8:1–8
—Participated in dedication of wall of Jerusalem .... Ne 12:31–36

FACE

A. The human face
1. Significance of the human face
—Seeing a face means meeting a person .... Ge 43:3,5
2Sa 14:28,32
—Talking face to face 2Jn 12
3Jn 14
—A radiant face means closeness to God .... Ex 34:29–30
—One can slap a face in anger 1Ki 22:24
—One can spit in a face in disgust .... Mt 26:67
2. Emotions expressed by the face
—The cheerful face .... Pr 15:13
—The face bowed down in respect .... Ge 48:12
1Sa 25:23
—The downcast face .... Ge 4:5–6
Lk 24:17
—The sad face .... Ne 2:3–4
—The face hidden in fear .... Ex 3:6
—The terrified face .... Da 5:6,9
—The face bowed down in grief .... Jos 7:10
—The face turned away in grief 2Ki 20:2
—The face turned away in shame .... Ezr 9:6
—The face covered with shame .... Ps 69:7
B. The face of God
—God's face synonymous with himself .... Hos 5:15
—God's glory seen in the face of Christ 2Co 4:6
—Seeing God face to face .... Ge 32:30
1Co 13:12
—Seeking God's face in prayer .... Ps 24:6
Ps 27:8
—God's face shining on us in blessing .... Nu 6:24–26
Ps 4:6
—God's face hidden from our sins .... Ps 51:9
—God's face hidden in judgment .... Dt 31:17–18
Ps 13:1–2
—God's face set against evildoers .... Lev 20:3,5
Ps 34:16
Eze 15:7
1Pe 3:12

FAITH

—Belief in a person or a teaching
A. Related themes
1. BELIEVE is a theme of John .... Jn 20:31
2. FAITH is a theme of:
—Galatians .... Gal 3:22
—James .... Jas 5:15
3. INDIVIDUALISM is a theme of Ezekiel .... Eze 18:4
B. What are the basic elements of faith?
1. Trust in God and commitment to Christ .... Ge 15:6
Pr 3:5
Ro 3:22
Heb 11:1
2. True knowledge of God and Christ
—Truths of the faith are important 1Ti 3:9
1Ti 4:1
—They must be based on God's word 2Ti 3:16
—They are worth fighting for .... Jude 3
C. What must we believe?
1. We must believe *in*:
—God .... Ex 14:31
Jn 14:1
—Christ .... Jn 2:11
Ac 16:31
—The name of the Son of God 1Jn 3:23
—The prophets .... Ex 14:31
2Ch 20:20
2. We must believe
a. What God has said
—The commandments of God .... Ps 119:66
—The writings of the Old Testament .... Lk 24:25
Jn 5:46–47
Ac 26:27
—The gospel .... Mk 1:15
1Co 15:1–2

—The holy Scriptures ... 2Ti 3:14–15
—The promises of God ... Ro 4:20–21
—Things God has said to us ... Ge 15:6
b. What God teaches about Jesus
—That Jesus is the Christ ... Jn 20:31; 1Jn 5:1
—That Jesus is God's Son ... 1Jn 5:5
—That Jesus was raised from the dead ... Ro 10:9
—Summary creed ... 1Co 15:3–11
See also CONFESSION; DOCTRINE

D. Where does faith come from?
—From God, as a gift ... Eph 2:8; Php 1:29
—From the Father and the Son ... Eph 6:23
—From the power of God in us ... 1Co 2:5
—From the Holy Spirit ... 1Co 12:9
—From hearing the gospel ... Jn 17:20; Ac 15:7; Ro 10:14,17
—From reading the Scriptures ... Jn 20:31; 1Jn 5:13

E. What happens when we believe?
—We receive forgiveness of sin ... Ac 10:43
—We are justified ... Ro 3:28; Gal 2:16
—We are saved ... Ac 16:30–31; Ro 10:9
—We receive eternal life ... Jn 3:14–16
—We become free from condemnation ... Jn 3:17
—We become free from spiritual death ... Jn 11:25–26
—We become God's children ... Jn 1:12; Gal 3:26
—We become children of light ... Jn 12:36
—We gain access to God ... Eph 3:12
—We enter God's rest ... Heb 4:3
—Our hearts are purified ... Ac 15:9
—We are sanctified ... Ac 26:18
—The word of God goes to work in us ... 1Th 2:13
—We receive peace with God ... Ro 5:1
—We experience joy ... Ac 16:34
—We gain security in God's power ... 1Pe 1:5

F. What must we do as believers?
—Live by faith ... 2Co 5:7; Gal 2:20
—Walk by faith ... Ro 4:12
—Face everything by faith ... Heb 11:33–39
—Remain true to the faith ... Ac 14:22
—Continue in the faith ... Col 1:23
—Stand firm in the faith ... 1Co 16:13; 1Pe 5:9
—Fight for the faith ... 1Ti 6:12; Jude 3
—Increase our faith ... Lk 17:5
—Grow in faith ... 2Th 1:3; Jude 20
—Please God by our faith ... Heb 11:6
—Combine faith with hope and love ... 1Co 13:2,13; Gal 5:6; 1Th 1:3
—Do everything by faith ... Ro 14:22–23
—Pray in faith ... Jas 1:5–6
—Tell others about our faith ... 2Co 4:13–14
—Demonstrate faith by good works ... Jas 2:14–26
—Overcome sin by our faith ... 1Jn 5:4–5
—Fight the devil by our faith ... Eph 6:16

G. Striking examples of faith
—Abraham ... Ro 4:1–3,9–21
—Numerous Old Testament people ... Heb 11:4–40
—Daniel's three friends ... Da 3:16–18
—Daniel ... Da 6:1–11
—A centurion ... Mt 8:5–10
—A sick woman ... Mt 9:20–22
—A Canaanite woman ... Mt 15:22–28
—Blind Bartimaeus ... Mk 10:46–52
—A sinful woman ... Lk 7:36–50
—Martha ... Jn 11:21–27
—Thomas ... Jn 20:24–29
—Philippian jailer ... Ac 16:29–34
—Lois, Eunice and Timothy ... 2Ti 1:5
—Paul ... 2Ti 1:12

FAITHFULNESS

—Remaining steadfast to one's commitments

A. Related themes
FAITHFULNESS is a theme of:
—Judges ... Jdg 2:18
—2 Kings ... 2Ki 8:19
—Lamentations ... La 3:23

B. Human faithfulness
1. Faithfulness is an aspect of the fruit of the Spirit ... Gal 5:22
2. Examples of those who were faithful
—Abraham ... Ne 9:8
—Moses ... Nu 12:7
—Hezekiah ... 2Ch 31:20
—The Zadokite priests ... Eze 48:11
—Timothy ... 1Co 4:17
—Epaphras ... Col 1:7
—Onesimus ... Col 4:9
—Silas ... 1Pe 5:12
3. We must be faithful
—In obeying God's commands ... Dt 11:13
—In our walk before God ... 1Ki 2:4
—In serving God ... 2Ch 19:9
—In our prayer life ... Ro 12:12
—In the use of our gifts ... 1Pe 4:10
—In persevering until death ... Rev 2:10
4. God's promises to those who are faithful
—He is faithful to them ... Ps 18:25
—His eyes are on them ... Ps 101:6
—He preserves them ... Ps 31:23
—He guards their lives ... Ps 97:10
—He protects them ... Pr 2:8
—He blesses them ... Dt 11:13–15
—He rewards them ... Mt 25:21–23
—He does not forsake them ... Ps 37:28
—He guarantees them life ... Eze 18:9

C. God's faithfulness
1. God is faithful in himself
—He is the faithful God ... Dt 7:9; Heb 10:23
—He abounds in faithfulness ... Ps 86:15
—His faithfulness is great ... La 3:23
—He will remain faithful ... 2Ti 2:13
2. God is faithful in his actions
—He is faithful in all he does ... Ps 33:4; Ps 111:7–8
—He is faithful to his covenant ... Ps 78:24–28
—He keeps all his promises ... Ge 21:1–2; 1Ki 8:20; Ac 13:23,32–33
—Christ fulfills all God's promises ... 2Co 1:18,20
3. God is faithful in his relationship to us
—In his love for us ... Ps 89:24; Ps 143:1
—In helping us ... 1Co 10:13
—In protecting us ... Ps 91:4; 2Th 3:3
—In forgiving us ... 1Jn 1:9
4. God's word is faithful ... 2Sa 7:28; Ps 19:7; Rev 21:5

FALLING AWAY

—Falling away from the faith, backsliding, apostasy

A. Falling away in the Old Testament
1. Examples
—At Mount Sinai ... Ex 32:1–35
—During the time of the judges ... Jdg 2:10–12
—In Israel ... 1Ki 16:30–33
—In Judah ... 2Ch 24:17–19
—A regular pattern ... Ps 106:6–47

2. Causes
—Mixed marriages ... Nu 25:1–3
Ne 13:26–27
—Poor examples of kings ... 1Ki 16:29–33
2Ki 21:1–11
3. Judgment for those who fall away ... Dt 13:13–18
2Ki 21:12–15

B. Falling away in the New Testament
1. Examples
—At the time of Jesus ... Jn 6:66
—In the early church ... 1Ti 1:19–20
2Ti 2:17–18
2Pe 2:20–21
—Future severe apostasy ... Mt 24:12
2Th 2:3
2Ti 3:1,5
2. Causes
—Influence of deceiving spirits ... 1Ti 4:1
—False teachers ... Ac 20:29–30
Rev 2:14–15
—Human desires ... 2Ti 4:3–4
—Love of world ... 2Ti 4:10
—Hardened hearts ... Ac 7:51–52
Ac 28:26–27
—Persecution ... Mt 24:9–10
—A time of testing ... Lk 8:13
3. Judgment for those who fell away
—Judgment from God ... Heb 10:26–31
Jude 11–15
—Removal from God's kingdom ... Rev 2:5
—Impossible to renew to repentance ... Heb 6:4–8
4. The antidote to falling away
—Heed the warning not to fall away ... Heb 3:12
2Pe 3:17
—Depend on God ... Ro 8:35–39
1Co 10:13
Jude 24
—Remain steadfast in faith ... Heb 6:11–12
Jude 20–21
—Continue reading God's word ... 2Ti 3:14–17
—Keep growing in Christian character ... 2Pe 1:5–10
—Associate with other believers ... Heb 3:13
Heb 10:24

FAMILY

A. Related theme
FAMILY is a theme of Ruth ... Ru 2:20
B. The establishment of the family
—Marriage begun in the Garden of Eden ... Ge 2:18–24
—The first children, given by God ... Ge 4:1–2
—The family built by God ... Ps 127:1–6
—The family blessed by God ... Ps 128:1–6
—The central unit in God's covenant ... Ge 17:7
Jos 24:15
C. Responsibilities in the family
1. The father as head
—Head of the family ... Ex 6:14
—Head of the wife ... Eph 5:23–24
—Must love his wife ... Eph 5:25–33
1Pe 3:7
—Must supervise religious observances ... Ge 35:1–7
Ex 12:3
1Sa 1:21
—Must supervise education of children ... Ps 44:1
Ps 78:3
Eph 6:4
—Must care for the children's needs ... 2Co 12:14
Col 3:21
2. The role of the mother
—Submissive to her husband ... Eph 5:24
1Pe 3:1–6
—Assist in training of children ... Pr 1:8
Pr 6:20
—Could take an important role in home ... 1Sa 1:9–28
Pr 31:10–31
2Ti 1:5
3. The place of children
—A blessing from the Lord ... Ps 127:3–5
—Must honor parents ... Ex 20:12
Lev 19:3
—Must obey parents ... Dt 21:18–21
Eph 6:1–3
Col 3:20
D. Things that disturb or destroy the family
—Jealousy and hatred ... Ge 4:3–8
—Lack of respect toward parents ... Ge 9:21–22
—Parents picking favorites ... Ge 25:27–28
—Rivalry and selfishness ... Ge 27:1–41
—Polygamy ... Ge 30:1–2
1Sa 1:1–6
—Lack of discipline ... 1Sa 2:22–25
—Lust and incest ... 2Sa 13:1–21
—Personal ambition ... Jdg 9:1–5
2Sa 15:1–17
—Mixed marriages ... Ne 13:23–27
—Materialism ... 1Ti 6:6–10
—False teaching ... Titus 1:10–11
E. New Testament teachings on the family
—Salvation took place in households ... Ac 16:15,31–34
Ac 18:8
1Co 1:16
1Co 16:15
—Children of believers are holy ... 1Co 7:14
—A well-ordered family is important ... 1Ti 3:4–5,12
Titus 1:6
—Care for members in the family circle ... 1Ti 5:4,8,16
F. The family used figuratively
—As a picture of the nation of Israel ... Ps 115:9–12
—As a picture of the church ... Gal 6:10
Eph 2:19
Heb 2:11
1Pe 4:17

See also CHILDREN; FATHER; MARRIAGE; MOTHER

FAMINE

See HUNGER AND THIRST

FASTING

—Voluntarily depriving oneself of food
A. In the Old Testament
1. Occasions for fasting
—To prepare to receive God's law ... Ex 34:28
Dt 9:9,18
—To prepare for the Day of Atonement ... Lev 16:29,31
—To show sorrow at time of death ... 1Sa 31:13
2Sa 1:12
—To show sorrow for sin ... 1Ki 21:27
Ne 9:1
Jnh 3:6–9
—To show humility ... Ps 35:13
—To pray in time of national need ... 2Ch 20:3
Ezr 8:21
Est 4:16
Joel 2:15–17
—To accompany deep personal prayer ... 2Sa 12:16,21
Ne 1:4
Da 9:3–4
2. Prophets criticized fasting as outward show ... Isa 58:3–7
Jer 14:12
Zec 7:4–10
B. In the New Testament
1. Occasions for fasting
—A regular pattern for many Jews ... Mt 9:14
Lk 2:37
Ac 23:12–14
—Paul after his conversion ... Ac 9:9
—To prepare for mission work ... Ac 13:2–3
Ac 14:23
—Not done by Jesus' disciples ... Mt 9:14
2. Jesus criticized fasting as outward show ... Mt 6:16–18
Lk 18:9–14

FATHER

A. Various meanings of father
- —Creator … Jas 1:17
- —Source or originator … Ge 4:20–21
- —Caretaker … Job 29:16
- —Counselor … Ge 45:8
- —A respected prophet … 2Ki 6:21
- —A respected priest … Jdg 17:10
- —One's male parent … Ge 4:18
- —One's grandfather … Ge 28:13
- —One's great-grandfather … 1Ki 15:11
- —One's ancestors in general … Jos 24:6; 2Ki 21:22

B. The father in the family
1. Duties of a father
   - —Supervise religious observances … Ge 35:1–7; Ex 12:3; 1Sa 1:21
   - —Responsible for education of children … Ge 18:19; Dt 4:9–10; Eph 6:5
   - —Responsible for discipline of children … Dt 8:4; Pr 3:11–12
   - —Care for his children's needs … 2Co 12:14; Col 3:21
   - —Give blessing to his children … Ge 27:27–29,39–40; Ge 49:1–28
2. Responsibility of children
   - —Respect their fathers … Ex 20:12; Lev 19:3
   - —Obey their fathers … Ex 20:12; Eph 6:1; Col 3:20

C. Spiritual use of father
- —Abraham as the father of believers … Ro 4:11,16–17; Gal 3:7
- —Paul as the father of his churches … 1Co 4:15; 1Th 2:11–12
- —God as Father of Jesus Christ … Jn 17:1,5; Eph 1:3
- —God as Father of everyone … Mal 2:10; Ac 17:28–29
- —God as Father of his chosen people … Isa 63:16; Jer 31:9
- —God as Father of believers in Jesus … Mt 6:9; Jn 1:12–13; Gal 1:1,4
- —Christians can call God "Abba" (Father) … Ro 8:15; Gal 4:6
- —The devil as father of the ungodly … Jn 8:44; 1Jn 3:10–12

FEAR

—One's apprehension in a frightening situation; reverence

A. Fear as being afraid
1. Why did people experience fear?
   - —Fear of seeing God … Ex 3:6
   - —Fear of a vision of angels … Mt 28:4; Lk 2:8–9
   - —Fear of the unknown … Lk 9:34,45
   - —Fear of punishment for sin … Ge 3:8–10; Ge 18:15; Ac 24:25
   - —Fear of danger … Ac 27:17,29
   - —Fear of being killed … Ge 26:7; 1Ki 19:3
   - —Fear of losing one's life … Jnh 1:5; Mt 14:30
   - —Fear of losing one's loved ones … Ge 31:31; Ge 42:4
   - —Fear of bringing unpleasant news … 1Sa 3:15; 2Sa 12:18
   - —Fear of an enemy … 1Sa 28:5; Jn 20:19
   - —Fear of a person in authority … Ne 2:2
   - —Fear of what another person might do … 1Sa 18:12,15
   - —Fear of what others might say … Gal 2:12
   - —Fear of the future … Ge 21:17
2. The command not to be afraid
   - —Given by God … Ge 21:17; Ge 26:24; Ac 18:9
   - —Given by Moses … Ex 14:13; Ex 20:20
   - —Given by Joshua … Jos 10:25
   - —Given by Samuel … 1Sa 12:20
   - —Given by Elijah … 1Ki 17:13
   - —Given by David … 1Ch 22:13
   - —Given by the prophet Jahaziel … 2Ch 20:15,17
   - —Given by Hezekiah … 2Ch 32:7
   - —Given by Isaiah … Isa 44:2,8
   - —Given by Jeremiah … Jer 42:11
   - —Given by Jesus … Mt 14:27; Mk 5:36; Lk 12:4,7,32; Jn 6:20
   - —Given by an angel … Lk 1:13,30; Lk 2:10; Ac 27:23–24
3. How to conquer fear
   - —By trusting in God … Ps 56:4,11
   - —By believing in Jesus … Mk 5:36
   - —By knowing God is with us … Ge 26:24; Dt 31:6,8; Ps 23:4; Isa 43:5
   - —By knowing Jesus is with us … Jn 6:20; Ac 18:9–10
   - —By knowing God is our Savior … Ps 27:1,3
   - —By knowing God is our refuge … Ps 46:1–2; Ps 91:1–6; Heb 13:6
   - —By knowing God will fight for us … Dt 3:22; Dt 20:3–4; 2Ch 20:15–17
   - —By obeying the Lord … 1Sa 12:20–21; 1Ch 22:12–13
4. Courage as the answer to fear

   See COURAGE

B. Fear as reverence for the Lord
1. The command to fear the Lord … Dt 6:13; Jos 24:14; 2Ch 19:7; Ps 33:8; Pr 3:7; Ecc 12:13
2. Examples of those who feared the Lord
   - —Noah … Heb 11:7
   - —Abraham … Ge 22:12
   - —Joseph … Ge 42:18
   - —Job … Job 1:1
   - —David … Ps 5:7
   - —Hezekiah … Jer 26:19
   - —Nehemiah … Ne 5:15
   - —The early church … Ac 9:31
3. Reasons for fearing the Lord
   - —His awesome power … Ex 20:18–20
   - —His glory … Lk 2:9
   - —His holiness … Rev 15:4
   - —His majesty … Ps 96:4–6
   - —His greatness … 1Sa 12:24
   - —His forgiveness … Ps 130:4
   - —His faithfulness … Ps 119:38
4. Benefits of fearing God
   - —A way to praise God … Ps 22:23
   - —A way to serve God … Ps 2:11
   - —A way to obey God … Ecc 12:13
   - —A way to fight evil … Pr 8:13; Pr 16:6
   - —A way to become wise … Ps 111:10; Pr 1:7

—A way to lengthen life . . . Pr 10:27
—God loves those who fear him . . . Ps 103:11,13,17
—God saves those who fear him . . . Ps 85:9
—God protects those who fear him . . . Ps 60:4; Pr 14:26–27
—God blesses those who fear him . . . Ps 115:12–13
—God provides for those who fear him . . . Ps 34:9; Ps 111:5

FEASTS AND FESTIVALS

A. Religious festivals
1. Commanded in the Old Testament
—Passover . . . Ex 12:1–14; Lev 23:5; Nu 9:1–14; Dt 16:1–7
—Unleavened Bread . . . Ex 12:15–20; Ex 13:3–10; Lev 23:6–8; Nu 28:17–25; Dt 16:3–4,8
—Firstfruits . . . Lev 23:9–14
—Weeks (Harvest, Pentecost) . . . Ex 23:16; Lev 23:15–21; Nu 28:26–31; Dt 16:9–12
—Trumpets . . . Lev 23:23–25; Nu 29:1–6
—Day of Atonement . . . Lev 16:1–34; Nu 29:7–11
—Tabernacles (Ingathering, Booths) . . . Ex 23:16; Lev 23:33–43; Nu 29:12–34; Dt 16:13–15
—Sacred assembly . . . Lev 23:36; Nu 29:35–38
—Purim . . . Est 9:27–28
2. Celebrations in the Old Testament
—Passover . . . Jos 5:10; 2Ki 23:21–23; 2Ch 30:1–20; 2Ch 35:1–17; Ezr 6:19–21
—Unleavened Bread . . . Jos 5:11; 2Ch 30:21–27; 2Ch 35:17–19; Ezr 6:22
—Day of Atonement . . . Ne 9:1–38
—Tabernacles (Booths) . . . Ezr 3:4; Ne 8:13–18
—Purim . . . Est 9:18–32
3. Celebrations in the New Testament
—Passover . . . Mt 26:1–2,17–29; Mk 14:12–25; Lk 22:7–38; Jn 2:13–25; Jn 11:55–56; Jn 13:1–30
—Unleavened Bread . . . Mt 26:17; Mk 14:1,12; Lk 22:1,7
—Weeks (Pentecost) . . . Ac 2:1–41
—Tabernacles (Booths) . . . Jn 7:2–36
—Sacred assembly . . . Jn 7:37–44
—Dedication (Hanukkah) . . . Jn 10:22–39
—The Lord's Supper . . . Mt 26:26–29; Mk 14:22–25; Lk 22:17–20; 1Co 11:17–26
4. Criticism when feasts and festivals became empty rituals
—In the Old Testament . . . Isa 1:14; Isa 5:12; Hos 2:11; Am 5:21–23
—In the New Testament . . . 2Pe 2:13; Jude 12

B. Non-religious occasions for feasting
—At weanings . . . Ge 21:8
—At the signing of a treaty . . . Ge 26:30
—At marriages . . . Ge 29:21–22; Jdg 14:10
—At a coronation . . . 1Ki 1:41
—At a family celebration . . . Lk 15:23

FELIX

—Governor of Judea . . . Ac 23:24
—Letter addressed to him . . . Ac 23:26–30
—Paul on trial before him . . . Ac 24:1–21
—Sought personal interview with Paul . . . Ac 24:24–26
—Kept Paul in prison to please the Jews . . . Ac 24:27
—Replaced by Festus . . . Ac 24:27

FELLOWSHIP

—A sharing together between persons
A. Human fellowship among God's people . . . Ge 2:18
1. Basis of such fellowship
—Fellowship with God . . . 1Jn 1:3,7
—The presence of Christ . . . Mt 18:20
—The word of God . . . Ac 2:42
2. The expression of such fellowship
—Prayed for by Christ . . . Jn 17:20–23
—Sung by the psalmists . . . Ps 133:1–2
—Demonstrated by mutual sharing . . . Ac 2:44–45; Ac 4:32–35
—Demonstrated by prayers for each other . . . Ac 1:14; Ac 4:24–31; Ro 15:30–32
—Symbolized in the Lord's Supper . . . Ac 2:46–47; 1Co 10:16–17
—Exercised among church leaders . . . Gal 2:9
3. "One another" commands
—Be devoted to one another . . . Ro 12:10
—Live in harmony with one another . . . Ro 12:16; 1Pe 3:8
—Accept one another . . . Ro 15:7
—Instruct one another . . . Ro 15:14
—Use your gifts for one another . . . 1Co 12:7; 1Pe 4:10
—Share with one another . . . 2Co 8:7,13–15
—Greet one another . . . 2Co 13:12
—Serve one another in love . . . Gal 5:13
—Carry one another's burdens . . . Gal 6:2
—Be kind to one another . . . Eph 4:32; 1Th 5:15
—Forgive one another . . . Eph 4:32
—Look to the interest of others . . . Php 2:3–4
—Bear with one another . . . Col 3:13
—Love one another . . . Col 3:14; 1Jn 4:11–12
—Admonish one another . . . Col 3:16
—Encourage one another . . . 1Th 5:11; Heb 10:25
—Build up one another . . . 1Th 5:11
—Live in peace with one another . . . 1Th 5:13
—Spur one another to good works . . . Heb 10:24
—Confess your sins to each other . . . Jas 5:16
—Pray for one another . . . Jas 5:16
—Be hospitable to one another . . . 1Pe 4:9
4. We may have no fellowship with the ungodly . . . 1Co 5:1–2; 2Co 6:14–16; Eph 5:5–7,11

B. Fellowship with God
1. Fellowship with the triune God
—With God the Father . . . 1Jn 1:3
—With God the Son . . . Jn 15:3–4; 1Co 1:9
—With God the Holy Spirit . . . 2Co 13:14; Php 2:1
2. Developing such fellowship
—By desiring it . . . Ps 42:1; Ps 63:1

—By believing in Jesus, God's Son . . . 1Jn 1:2–3
—By meditating on God's word. . . . Ps 1:2; Ps 119:10–15; 2Pe 1:4
—By praying to God . . . Mk 1:35; Lk 5:16
—By thinking wholesome thoughts. . . . Php 4:8–9
—By living a holy life . . . Ps 15:1–5; 2Co 6:14–18
—By participating in the Lord's Supper . . . 1Co 10:16; 1Co 11:23–26

3. Examples of such fellowship
—Enoch . . . Ge 5:22–24
—Noah . . . Ge 6:9
—Abraham. . . . Ge 18:17–19
—Jacob. . . . Ge 48:15
—Moses . . . Ex 33:1
—David. . . . Ps 23
—Jesus . . . Mt 26:39–42
—Paul. . . . Ac 22:17–21; 2Co 12:1–4

FESTUS

—Succeeded Felix as governor . . . Ac 24:27
—Visited Jerusalem authorities. . . . Ac 25:1–5
—Convened court to deal with Paul . . . Ac 25:6–12
—Paul appealed to Caesar before him . . . Ac 25:12
—Consulted Agrippa about Paul . . . Ac 25:13–22
—Arranged an audience for Agrippa with Paul. . . . Ac 25:23–26:29

FIRE

A. Human uses of fire
1. Domestic uses
—For cooking. . . . Isa 44:15–16; Jn 21:9
—For warmth . . . Isa 44:15–16; Mk 14:54
—For metalworking . . . Ex 32:24
2. Military uses
—For destroying a city . . . Jos 6:24; 1Sa 30:1; 2Ch 36:19
—For destroying crops . . . 2Sa 14:30
3. Religious uses
—For sacrifices. . . . Ge 8:20; Lev 1:9; Nu 18:17
—For burning incense . . . Ex 30:7–8; 1Ki 9:25; Lk 1:9
—For burning unclean substances . . . Lev 13:52,55
—Unholy fire could not be used . . . Lev 10:1–2

B. God's use of fire
1. God is a consuming fire . . . Dt 4:24; Heb 12:29
2. Positive uses of fire
a. To represent his presence
—To Moses in the burning bush . . . Ex 3:1–4
—To Israel in the pillar of fire. . . . Ex 13:21–22; Ex 14:24
—To Israel on Mount Sinai . . . Ex 19:18
—To Elijah going into heaven . . . 2Ki 2:11
—To the disciples on Pentecost . . . Ac 2:3
b. To burn sacrifices prepared for him. . . . Ge 15:17; 1Ki 18:38–39; 2Ch 7:1
c. To purify his people. . . . Isa 48:10; Mal 3:3
3. Negative uses of fire
—To express his wrath . . . Dt 32:22; Ps 89:46
—To judge sinners on earth. . . . Ge 19:24–25; Lev 10:2; Nu 11:1–2; 2Ki 1:10,12
—To punish eternally in hell . . . Mt 5:22; 2Th 1:7–8; Jas 3:6; Rev 18:17–18

FIRSTFRUITS

A. Firstfruits in the Old Testament
1. Firstfruits to be dedicated to God
—Firstborn son . . . Ex 13:1–2
—Firstborn of livestock. . . . Ex 13:1–2
—Firstfruits of the crops. . . . Ex 23:16; Lev 23:9
—Firstfruits of grain, wine, oil, wool . . . Dt 18:4; 2Ch 31:5
—Firstfruits of fruit trees . . . Lev 19:23–24
—Firstfruits of everything grown . . . Dt 26:2; Pr 3:9
2. Rules and regulations
a. General
—In the Law of Moses . . . Lev 2:11–16; Lev 23:9–14; Dt 26:1–15
—After the exile . . . Ne 10:35; Ne 12:44
—In the new temple. . . . Eze 44:30
b. Must be brought to the Lord's house . . . Ex 23:19; Ex 34:26
c. Must precede eating of harvested crops . . . Lev 23:14

B. Firstfruits as symbol in the New Testament
—Christ as the firstfruits of those raised . . . 1Co 15:20,23
—The Holy Spirit as our first blessing. . . . Ro 8:23
—The Holy Spirit as a guaranteed deposit. . . . 2Co 1:22; 2Co 5:5; Eph 1:14
—Early Christians as firstfruits of others . . . Jas 1:18

FISH

A. Fish in the Old Testament
—A food for humans. . . . Nu 11:5; Ne 13:16
—Humans given dominion over fish . . . Ge 1:26,28; Ps 8:6–8
—The great fish that swallowed Jonah . . . Jnh 1:17; Mt 12:40

B. Fish in the New Testament
1. Several disciples were fishermen . . . Mt 4:18–21; Jn 21:1–3
2. Miracles with fish
—Miraculous catch of fish . . . Lk 5:4–7; Jn 21:4–11
—Feeding the multitude with two fish . . . Mk 6:37–44; Jn 6:1–11
—Tax money in the mouth of a fish . . . Mt 17:24–27
3. Parable concerning fish and net . . . Mt 13:47–48

FLESH

—A willing instrument of sin. . . . Ro 7:5; Ro 8:5–8; Ro 13:14
—Describes the sinful nature. . . . Gal 5:13–24

FOLLY

A. Characteristics of the fool
—Begins with a denial of God. . . . Ps 14:1
—Does not trust in God . . . 2Ch 16:7–9
—Trusts in self. . . . Pr 28:26
—Has no desire to get wisdom . . . Pr 1:7,22; Pr 17:16
—Spurns discipline . . . Pr 15:5
—Finds pleasure in evil. . . . Pr 10:23; Titus 3:3
—Is rebellious . . . Ps 107:17
—Engages in senseless merriment. . . . Ecc 7:4–6
—Loves to quarrel. . . . Pr 20:3
—Does not control anger. . . . Pr 29:9,11
—Comes to ruin. . . . Pr 10:8,10,14

See also WISDOM

B. Special aspects of foolishness in the New Testament
- —The foolishness of preaching — 1Co 1:21–24
- —The foolishness of God is wiser than human wisdom — 1Co 1:25
- —Being fools for Christ's sake — 1Co 3:18; 1Co 4:10
- —Paul's speech of the fool — 2Co 11:16–12:13

FOOL

See FOLLY

FOOT

A. The human foot

1. Symbolic uses of the human foot
   - —Washing feet in ceremonial cleansing — Ex 30:17–21
   - —Washing feet as a sign of courtesy — Ge 18:4
   - —Washing feet as a sign of repentance — Lk 7:37–48
   - —Washing feet as a sign of servanthood — Jn 13:3–15
   - —Cutting off feet as a punishment — 2Sa 4:12
2. Metaphors concerning the foot
   - a. Dominion: everything under our feet — Ps 8:6
   - b. Security: feet on solid rock — Ps 40:2
   - c. Gratitude: falling down at one's feet — Lk 17:16
   - d. Victory
     - —Trampling underfoot — Mic 7:10
     - —Placing feet on the neck — Jos 10:24
     - —Enemies as one's footstool — Ps 110:1; Ac 2:35
   - e. Submission: falling down at one's feet — 1Sa 25:24; 2Sa 22:40; Rev 19:10
   - f. Rejection: shaking dust off one's feet — Mt 10:14; Ac 13:51
   - g. Sin
     - —Straying feet — Ps 44:18
     - —Stumbling feet — Ps 116:8
   - h. Miscellaneous
     - —Beautiful feet of gospel preachers — Isa 52:7; Ro 10:15
     - —God's word as a lamp to our feet — Ps 119:105

B. The feet of God
- —Bowing down at his feet in submission — Dt 33:3
- —The earth as God's footstool — Isa 66:1; Mt 5:35
- —The ark as God's footstool — 1Ch 28:2

FORBEARANCE

- —An attribute of God — Ro 2:4; Ro 3:25
- —An aspect of the fruit of the Spirit — Gal 5:22

See also PATIENCE

FOREIGNERS

See ALIEN

FORGET

A. Human forgetting

1. What we ought to forget
   - —Our troubles — Ge 41:51; Isa 65:16
   - —The trials of the past — Isa 43:18; Php 3:13
   - —Our sin and the shame it brings — Isa 54:4; Eze 39:26
2. What we ought not to forget
   - —The Lord — Dt 6:12; Isa 17:10; Jer 2:32
   - —God's mighty acts — Dt 4:9; Ps 78:7,11
   - —God's covenant with us — Dt 4:23,31; 2Ki 17:38
   - —God's law — Ps 119:61,83,109
   - —God's patience with us — 2Pe 3:9–10
   - —God's benefits to us — Ps 103:2
   - —The teachings of our parents — Pr 3:6; Pr 4:5

B. Divine forgetting

1. What God forgets
   - —The sins of those who repent — Isa 43:25; Jer 31:34; Heb 8:12
   - —Those who persistently refuse to believe — Jer 23:39–40
2. What God does not forget
   - —His people — Isa 44:21; Isa 49:21
   - —Our good deeds and love — Heb 6:10
   - —Even the smallest of his creatures — Lk 12:6
   - —The sins of those who refuse to repent — Am 8:7
3. Praying that God will not forget
   - —Us — Ps 13:1
   - —The helpless — Ps 10:12
   - —Those who are afflicted — Ps 74:19

See also REMEMBER

FORGIVENESS

—Pardon for human sins and shortcomings

A. Related theme

FORGIVENESS is a theme of Philemon — Phm 17

B. Human forgiveness of others

1. Examples
   - —Esau of his brother Jacob — Ge 33:4
   - —Joseph of his brothers — Ge 50:15–21
   - —The father of his wayward son — Lk 15:17–24
   - —Jesus of his enemies — Lk 23:34
   - —Stephen of his enemies — Ac 7:60
   - —Paul of those deserting him — 2Ti 4:16
2. Required of Christians — Mt 18:35; Lk 11:4; Eph 4:32; Col 3:13

C. God's forgiveness of us

1. Why does God forgive?
   - —Because of his compassion — Ex 34:6–7; Mic 7:19
   - —Because of his love — Ps 51:1
   - —Because of his grace — Ps 103:8
   - —Because of his mercy — Isa 55:7
2. How does God forgive?
   - —Always by shedding of blood — Heb 9:22
   - —Foreshadowed by Old Testament sacrifice — Lev 4:1–5:13
   - —Fulfilled by the blood of Christ — Col 1:14; Col 2:13–14; Heb 9:14,28
   - —Jesus can forgive sins — Mk 2:1–11
3. What happens to our sins?
   - —They go out of sight — Isa 38:17
   - —They go out of reach — Ps 103:12; Mic 7:19
   - —They go out of mind — Isa 43:25; Jer 31:34
   - —They go out of existence — Ps 51:1–2,7,9; Isa 44:22; Ac 3:19
4. How do we receive forgiveness?
   - —We must confess our sins — Ps 32:5; 1Jn 1:9
   - —We must repent of our sins — Ac 2:38; Ac 3:19
   - —We must believe in Christ — Lk 24:47; Ac 10:43; Ac 13:38

FORNICATION

See SEXUAL STANDARDS

FREEDOM

—Being liberated from bondage

A. Related themes

FREEDOM is a theme of:
- —Exodus — Ex 6:6
- —Galatians — Gal 5:13

—To build up the church ... 1Co 12:7; 1Co 14:3,5,12,26; 1Pe 4:10
—To demonstrate God's grace in us ... Ro 12:6
—To praise God ... 1Co 14:24–25; 1Pe 4:11

C. Gifts are subordinate to love
—The greatest way is the way of love ... 1Co 12:31–13:3
—Gifts will disappear ... 1Co 13:8–10
—Love will always remain ... 1Co 13:13

D. Warning against gifts that deceive
—False prophets can do wonders and signs ... Mt 24:24
—The antichrist will do counterfeit signs ... 2Th 2:9; Rev 13:13–14
—We must test the spirits ... 1Jn 4:1

GLORY

—The grandeur and majesty of God

A. Related theme
GLORY OF CHRIST is a theme of Colossians ... Col 1:27

B. God and his glory
1. Glory belongs to God ... 1Ch 29:11; Ps 29:1,3; Ps 96:7; Ro 11:36
2. God dwells in awesome majesty ... Job 37:22; Ps 93:1; Ps 145:5
3. God's name is glorious ... Dt 28:58; 1Ch 29:13; Ps 8:1; Ps 79:9
4. God reveals his glory
—In Jesus Christ ... Isa 40:5; Jn 1:14
—In the tent of meeting ... Ex 40:34–35
—In the temple ... 2Ch 5:14; Eze 10:4; Eze 43:5
—In his works ... Ps 19:1; Ps 111:3
—Through Moses ... Ex 34:29–35
—On Mount Sinai ... Ex 24:15–17
—To Isaiah ... Isa 6:3
—To his people through his redemption ... Isa 44:23; Isa 46:13
—To Ezekiel ... Eze 1:28
—To the shepherds of Bethlehem ... Lk 2:9
—To Stephen ... Ac 7:55
—To the whole world ... Ps 97:6; Isa 66:18; Hab 2:14

C. Jesus and his glory
1. He is the Lord of glory ... 1Co 2:8; Jas 2:1
2. He has God's glory
—Had glory from the beginning ... Jn 17:5
—Surpassed glory of the Old Testament ... 2Co 3:7–11
—Now exalted in glory ... 1Ti 3:16; Rev 5:12–13
—Will return in glory ... Mt 24:30; Mt 25:31
3. He revealed God's glory
—In human flesh ... Jn 1:14; Heb 1:3
—In his actions ... Jn 2:11; Jn 11:40–44
—In his transfiguration ... Lk 9:29–30; 2Pe 1:16–19
—In his death ... Jn 12:23–24
—In the resurrection ... Lk 24:26; Php 3:21

D. The Spirit and his glory
—Called the Spirit of glory ... 1Pe 4:14
—His ministry is glorious ... 2Co 3:8

E. Believers and the glory of God
1. The present
—We fall short of his glory ... Ro 3:23
—Christ came to bring us to glory ... Lk 2:29–32; Col 1:27
—We receive God's glory through Christ ... Jn 17:22; 2Co 4:6
—We receive the Spirit of glory ... 1Pe 4:14
—We must reflect his glory ... 1Co 10:31; 2Co 3:18
—We must pray that his glory will endure ... Ps 104:31
2. The future
—We will be brought into his glory ... Heb 2:10; Jude 24
—We will share in Christ's glory ... Ro 8:17–18; 1Pe 5:10
—Our new bodies will bear his glory ... 1Co 15:42–43; Php 3:21
—We will receive a crown of glory ... 1Pe 5:4

GOD

A. Related themes
1. GOD is a theme of:
—Genesis ... Ge 28:13
—Proverbs ... Pr 16:4
—Isaiah ... Isa 54:5
2. UNIVERSAL GOD is a theme of:
—Ruth ... Ru 1:16
—Ezekiel ... Eze 1:1
—Jonah ... Jnh 1:2

B. The being of God
See HOLY SPIRIT; JESUS CHRIST; TRINITY

C. Names of God
—God ... Ge 1:1
—LORD ... Ge 4:1,4
—LORD God ... Ge 2:4
—God Most High ... Ge 14:18–20
—The Sovereign LORD ... Ge 15:2
—God Almighty ... Ge 17:1
—The Eternal God ... Ge 21:33
—The God of Bethel ... Ge 31:13
—God of Abraham, Isaac, Jacob ... Ex 3:6
—I AM WHO I AM ... Ex 3:14
—The God of the Hebrews ... Ex 3:18
—Jealous ... Ex 34:14
—The God of Israel ... 1Sa 1:17
—God, the Rock ... 2Sa 22:47
—The LORD, the God of heaven ... Ezr 1:2
—The Mighty One, God, the LORD ... Ps 50:1
—God the King ... Ps 145:1
—The Holy One of Israel ... Isa 1:4
—The Mighty One of Israel ... Isa 1:24

D. Characteristics of God
1. Divine characteristics
—Holy ... Lev 11:44
—Eternal ... Ps 90:2
—Infinite ... 1Ki 8:27
—Immortal ... 1Ti 1:17
—Invisible ... Jn 1:18
—All-knowing ... Ps 147:5
—Everywhere present ... Ps 139:7–21
—All-powerful ... Isa 40:6–7
—Unchanging ... Mal 3:6
—Incomparable ... Isa 40:18,25
—Righteous ... Ps 145:17
—Perfect ... Mt 5:48
—Awesome and majestic ... Ex 15:11
—Gracious ... Ex 34:6
—Spirit ... Jn 4:24
2. Human characteristics ascribed to him
a. Physical characteristics
—Face of God ... Nu 6:25–26
See FACE
—Ears of God ... Ne 1:6
See EAR
—Eyes of God ... 2Ch 16:9
See EYE

—Nostrils of God … Ex 15:8
—Mouth of God … Dt 8:3
See MOUTH
—Voice of God … Ex 15:26
See VOICE
—Hands of God … Ezr 7:9
See HAND
—Fingers of God … Ps 8:3
—Arms of God … Dt 33:27
—Shoulders of God … Dt 33:12
—Back of God … Ex 33:21–22
—Feet of God … Ps 18:9
See FOOT

b. Physical actions
—God sits … Ps 102:12
—God stands … Ge 28:13
—God walks … Ge 3:8
—God comes down … Ge 11:5
—God goes up … Ge 17:22
—God marches … Zec 9:14
—God rides … Ps 68:33
—God soars … 2Sa 22:11
—God shoots arrows … 2Sa 22:15
—God reaches down … 2Sa 22:17
—God rests … Ge 2:2
—God sleeps … Ps 44:23

c. Emotional characteristics
—God loves … Ex 34:6; 1Jn 4:8–10
—God is compassionate … Ex 3:7
—God is patient … 2Pe 3:9
—God laughs … Ps 2:4
—God becomes angry … Dt 9:7
—God grieves … Ge 6:6
—God is jealous … Ex 34:14
—God fears … Dt 32:26–27
—God hates … Ps 5:5

E. Our response to God
—We should trust in him … Jn 14:1
See TRUST
—We should hope in him … Ps 131:3
See HOPE
—We should believe him … Ge 15:6
See FAITH
—We should fear him … Dt 6:13
See FEAR
—We should praise him … Ps 150:1–6
See PRAISE
—We should worship him … Ps 96:9
See WORSHIP
—We should stand in awe of him … Hab 3:2
—We should honor him … Pr 3:9
—We should glorify him … Ps 34:3
—We should thirst for him … Ps 42:2

GOLD

A. Uses for gold
1. In Israelite worship
—The tabernacle structure … Ex 26:29,32
—The tabernacle furniture … Ex 25:10–40; Ex 30:3–5
—Priestly garments … Ex 28:11–36
—The temple structure … 2Ch 3:4–6
—The temple furniture … 2Ch 4:7–8,20–22
2. In pagan worship
—The golden calf in the desert … Ex 32:1–4
—The golden calves of Jeroboam … 1Ki 12:26–30
—Other idols … Isa 2:20; Hos 8:4
3. For personal wealth … 2Ch 9:13; Ecc 2:8; Mt 10:9
4. For gifts … 2Ch 9:9; Ezr 2:69; Mt 2:11
5. For jewelry … Ge 24:22; Ex 32:2; Jdg 8:24,26
6. For royal display … 2Ch 9:15–16; Est 1:6–7

B. Value of gold for God's people
1. Positive: a blessing from God … Ge 13:2; Isa 60:6,17
2. Negative
—Spiritual values worth more than gold … Ps 19:10; Pr 3:13–14; 1Pe 1:7
—Gold valueless in redemption … 1Pe 1:18

C. Gold as a symbol
—For God's people surviving God's testing … Job 23:10
—For trustworthy spiritual values … 1Co 3:12–13; Rev 3:18
—For the new heaven … Rev 21:18,21

GOLIATH

—A Philistine giant … 1Sa 17:4–7
—Taunted the Israelite army … 1Sa 17:8–11
—David offered to fight him … 1Sa 17:32–37
—David killed him … 1Sa 17:48–51
—David obtained his sword … 1Sa 21:9

GOMORRAH

See SODOM AND GOMORRAH

GOSPEL

—The good news of salvation for humanity

A. Terms used to describe the gospel
—The gospel of God … Ro 1:1
—The good news of God's grace … Ac 20:24
—The gospel of God's Son … Ro 1:9
—The gospel of our Lord Jesus … 2Th 1:8
—The gospel of Christ … Ro 15:19
—The gospel that displays the glory of Christ … 2Co 4:4
—The good news about Jesus Christ … Mk 1:1
—The gospel of the kingdom … Mt 24:14
—The gospel of salvation … Eph 1:13
—The gospel of peace … Eph 6:15
—The eternal gospel … Rev 14:6

B. The gospel in the Old Testament
—First revealed to Adam and Eve … Ge 3:15
—Revealed to Abraham … Ge 12:2–3; Ge 18:18; Ge 22:18; Gal 3:8
—Revealed to Israel through prophets … Isa 40:9; Isa 52:7–10; Isa 61:6; Ro 1:1–2

C. The gospel in the New Testament
1. The proclaimers of the gospel
—The angel at Christ's birth … Lk 2:10
—John the Baptist … Lk 3:18
—Jesus Christ … Mk 1:14–15; Lk 4:43
—The 12 disciples … Lk 9:6
—The 12 apostles … Ac 5:42
—Peter and John … Ac 8:25; Ac 15:7
—Philip … Ac 8:12,40
—Paul … Ac 14:7; Ro 15:19
—Unnamed missionaries … 1Pe 1:12
—Our responsibility … Mt 24:14; Mt 28:19
2. The content of the gospel
—The basic story about Jesus … Mk 1:1; 1Co 15:1–8,11
—Jesus is the Christ … Ac 5:42
—Humans should repent … Mk 1:15
—Salvation is by faith in Jesus … Ro 1:16–17
—God gives us his grace … Ac 20:24
—Both Jew and Gentile can be saved … Eph 3:6–7

—Jesus will return as judge ..... Ro 2:16
—How believers should live ..... Php 1:27
3. The characteristics of the gospel
—It reveals the glory of Christ 2Co 4:4
—It is eternal ..... 1Pe 1:25; Rev 14:6
—It demonstrates God's power ..... Ro 1:16
—It calls us 2Th 2:14
—It saves us 1Co 15:2
—It gives us peace ..... Eph 6:15
—It gives us hope ..... Col 1:23
—It gives us life 2Ti 1:10
—It grows and bears fruit ..... Col 1:6
—It tolerates no rival ..... Gal 1:6–9
4. The response to the gospel
—We should believe it ..... Heb 4:2
—We should obey it ..... 2Co 9:13; 2Th 1:8; Heb 4:6
—We should not be ashamed of it ..... Ro 1:16
—We should live in line with its truth ..... Gal 2:14; Php 1:27
—We should serve it 2Co 8:18
—We should continue in it ..... Col 1:23
—We should promote it 1Co 9:16
—We should defend it ..... Php 1:7,16; Jude 3
—We should preach it ..... Mk 16:15; Ac 8:4; Ro 15:19–20; 1Co 9:16
—We may have to suffer for it 2Ti 1:8; 2Ti 2:8–9

GOVERNMENT

—The rule of humans by other humans

A. Phases of civil government among the Israelites/Jews
1. Rule by the fathers (patriarchs)
—Abram ..... Ge 14:13–16
—Isaac ..... Ge 26:26–32
—Jacob ..... Ge 34:5,30–31; Ge 46:5–27
2. Rule by God's chosen leaders
—Moses ..... Ex 3:7–12; Ex 18:13–26
—Moses and Aaron ..... Nu 17:1–13
—Joshua ..... Dt 31:1–8; Jos 1:1–11
3. Rule by God's chosen judges
See JUDGE, JUDGMENT
4. Rule through God's chosen kings
—Israel asked for a king 1Sa 8:4–22
—Israel's first king, Saul 1Sa 10:20–26
—David anointed as king 1Sa 16:1–13
—David's line to be the royal line 2Sa 7:8–16
See KING
5. Rule by foreign kings
—The Babylonians ..... 2Ch 36:15–21; Da 1:1–6
—The Persians ..... Ezr 1:1–4; Isa 44:28–45:6
—The Herods of Idumea ..... Mt 2:1–8,16–22
—The Romans ..... Mt 27:11–14; Jn 18:28–40

B. Principles of government
1. God and human government
—God is the real ruler ..... Dt 33:5; Jdg 8:23; 1Ch 29:23; Ps 29:10–11; Isa 33:22
—God rules through anointed servants ..... Ps 45:6–7; Isa 45:1
2. Humans in the government
—They derive authority from God ..... Da 4:17; Jn 19:11; Ro 13:1,4
—God's people may serve pagan governments ..... Ne 2:1–9; Ne 5:14–18; Est 8:1–2; Da 1:17–21

C. Our responsibility to government
—We must respect it 1Sa 14:6–7; 1Sa 26:7–11; 1Pe 2:17
—We must submit to it ..... Ro 13:1,5; Titus 3:1; 1Pe 2:13–14
—We must support it with taxes ..... Mt 22:15–21; Ro 13:6–7
—We must pray for it 1Ti 2:1–2
—Occasionally we may have to disobey it ..... Ac 5:29

GRACE

—God's free and undeserved favor

A. Related themes
GRACE is a theme of:
—Genesis ..... Ge 25:33
—Judges ..... Jdg 6:13
—Job ..... Job 42:10
—Jonah ..... Jnh 3:10
—Romans ..... Ro 11:6

B. Grace comes as a gift
—From God ..... Eph 2:8; 1Pe 5:10
—From the Father ..... Ps 84:11; Jas 1:17
—From Christ, the Son ..... Jn 1:17; 1Co 1:4
—From the Holy Spirit ..... Zec 12:10; Heb 10:29

C. How can we receive grace?
—We must accept Christ ..... Jn 1:14,16; 2Co 8:9; Eph 1:6–7
—We must be humble ..... Pr 3:34; Jas 4:6
—We cannot earn it by good works ..... Ro 11:6; 2Ti 1:9
—We cannot earn it by keeping the law ..... Ro 6:14; Gal 2:16

D. Examples of those who received grace
—Abraham ..... Gal 3:18
—Paul ..... Eph 3:2; 1Ti 1:12–16
—All believers ..... Eph 1:7–8

E. What happens to believers through grace?
—They are chosen ..... Ro 11:5
—They are called ..... Gal 1:15
—They believe ..... Ac 18:27
—They are justified ..... Ro 3:24; Titus 3:7
—They receive righteousness ..... Ro 5:17
—They are saved ..... Ac 15:11; Titus 2:11
—They are redeemed ..... Ro 3:24
—They are forgiven ..... Eph 1:7
—They receive many good things ..... Ro 8:32; Jas 1:17
—They receive spiritual gifts ..... Ro 12:6; Eph 4:7–12
—They receive encouragement 2Th 2:16
—They receive help in time of need ..... Heb 4:16
—They are able to bear up under suffering 2Co 12:9
—They have hope 2Th 2:16
—They are glorified in Christ 2Th 1:12

F. Relationship of believers to grace
—They are under grace ..... Ro 6:14
—They stand in grace ..... Ro 5:2
—They are what they are by grace 1Co 15:10
—They abound in grace 2Co 9:8; 1Ti 1:14
—They share in God's grace ..... Php 1:7

—Lack of doctrinal soundness . . . Eph 4:14
—Jealousy and quarreling . . . 1Co 3:1–3
—Living a life of evil . . . 1Co 14:20
—Inability to understand deeper truths . . . Heb 5:12–14

2. How does growth take place?
—By study of God's word . . . 1Pe 2:1–3
—By increasing our knowledge of God . . . Col 1:10
—By deepening our faith . . . Eph 4:13
—By showing love . . . Eph 4:15–16
—By developing Christian character . . . 2Pe 1:5–8

3. God wants us to grow and bear fruit . . . Ps 1:1–3; Ps 92:12–15; Jn 15:2,4–5,16

GUILT
—The condition of one who breaks the law

A. Guilt in the Old Testament
1. Standing guilty before God
—Because of deliberate sin . . . Lev 6:1–4
—Because of unintentional sin . . . Lev 5:2–4,14–17
—Guilty even before birth . . . Ps 51:5
—Dressed in dirty clothes . . . Isa 64:6; Zec 3:3–4
—God knows our guilt . . . Ps 69:5
—God does not leave guilt unpunished . . . Ex 34:7; Na 1:3

2. Feeling guilty because of sin . . . 2Sa 24:10; Ezr 9:5–7,15; Ps 38:4

3. Resolving guilt before God
—The call to acknowledge guilt . . . Jer 3:13; Hos 5:15
—The guilt offering . . . Lev 5:14–6:7; Lev 7:1–6
—Confession and forgiveness . . . Ps 32:5; Isa 6:5–7

B. Guilt in the New Testament
1. The reality of guilt
—Christ's coming convicts us of guilt . . . Jn 15:22,24
—The Spirit convicts us of guilt . . . Jn 16:7–8
—One sin makes us guilty of breaking the whole law . . . Jas 2:10
—All stand guilty before God . . . Ro 3:19,23
—All are guilty because of Adam's sin . . . Ro 5:12–14

2. The resolution of guilt
—We must confess our sins . . . 1Jn 1:9
—We must draw near to God in faith . . . Heb 10:22
—We become free of guilt through Christ . . . Ro 5:15–18

See also CONFESSION; FORGIVENESS; SIN

HAGAR
—Egyptian servant of Sarai . . . Ge 16:1
—Given to Abram to conceive a child . . . Ge 16:3
—Driven away by Sarai while pregnant . . . Ge 16:5–16
—Gave birth to Ishmael . . . Ge 25:12
—Driven away after birth of Isaac . . . Ge 21:9–21
—Story interpreted by Paul . . . Gal 4:21–31

HAGGAI
—A postexilic prophet . . . Ezr 5:1
—Encouraged rebuilding of temple . . . Ezr 6:14; Hag 1:12–13
—Warned God's people of dangers of selfishness . . . Hag 1:3–11

HAM
—Son of Noah . . . Ge 5:32; 1Ch 1:4
—Laughed at Noah's nakedness . . . Ge 9:20–27
—Father of Canaan . . . Ge 9:18; 1Ch 1:8–16

HAMAN
—Agagite noble honored by Xerxes . . . Est 3:1–2
—Angry when Mordecai would not bow down . . . Est 3:2–5
—Plotted to execute Jews . . . Est 3:6–15
—Set up pole upon which to impale Mordecai . . . Est 5:9–14
—Forced to honor Mordecai . . . Est 6:1–13
—Plot exposed by Esther . . . Est 7:1–8
—Impaled on his own pole . . . Est 7:9–10

HAND
A. The human hand
1. What the human hand does
—Works . . . Ps 90:17
—Holds . . . Rev 7:9
—Writes . . . Gal 6:11
—Touches . . . 1Jn 1:1
—Claps . . . Ps 47:1
—Fights . . . Ps 18:34
—Blesses . . . Lev 9:22
—Lifts up in prayer . . . 1Ti 2:8
—Lifts up in praise . . . Ps 134:2
—Takes oath before God . . . Ge 14:22

2. Significance of the right hand
—Place of honor . . . Ps 45:9
—Position of power . . . 1Ki 2:19
—Used to confirm an agreement . . . Gal 2:9

3. Laying on of hands
a. In the Old Testament
—Ordained Levites . . . Nu 8:10
—Ordained leaders . . . Nu 27:18,22–23
—Transferred guilt . . . Lev 16:20–21

b. In the New Testament
—Conferred healing . . . Mk 6:5; Lk 4:40; Ac 28:8
—Transferred the Holy Spirit . . . Ac 8:17; Ac 9:17; Ac 19:6
—Ordained missionaries . . . Ac 13:3
—Ordained church officers . . . Ac 6:6; 1Ti 4:14; 2Ti 1:6

B. The hand of God
1. What it does
—It saves us . . . Ex 6:1; Dt 5:15
—It guides us . . . Ezr 7:9
—It provides for us . . . Ps 104:28
—It protects us . . . Ps 139:10
—It receives our spirits . . . Ps 31:5
—It pleads with us . . . Isa 65:2
—It chastises us . . . Ps 32:4
—It punishes unbelievers . . . Ex 7:5

2. Significance of the right hand of God
—His hand of power . . . Ps 17:7; Ps 73:23; Ps 118:15–16
—Sitting at his right hand as ruler . . . Ps 110:1; Ac 2:33; Eph 1:20; Heb 1:3

HANNAH
—Wife of Elkanah . . . 1Sa 1:1–2
—Prayed to have a child . . . 1Sa 1:9–18
—Gave birth to Samuel . . . 1Sa 1:19–20
—Dedicated Samuel to the Lord's work . . . 1Sa 1:24–28
—Prayed at Samuel's dedication . . . 1Sa 2:1–10
—Blessed by Eli . . . 1Sa 2:18–20
—Gave birth to other children . . . 1Sa 2:21

HARAN/HARRAN
A. The father of Lot (Haran) . . . Ge 11:27
—Died in Ur . . . Ge 11:28

B. A city in Mesopotamia (Harran)
—Terah, Abram and Lot emigrated there . . . Ge 11:31; Ac 7:4
—Abram set out from there for Canaan . . . Ge 12:4
—Abraham sent there to find a wife for Isaac . . . Ge 24:1–4
—Jacob fled there . . . Ge 28:10
—Home of Laban, Leah and Rachel . . . Ge 29:4–6
—Jacob lived there 20 years . . . Ge 31:41
—Belonged to Assyrian Empire . . . 2Ki 19:12

HARVEST
A. The importance of harvests
1. Events were calculated by harvest times .... Ge 30:14; Jdg 15:1; Ru 1:22
2. Israelite festivals centered around harvest
—Festival of Firstfruits .... Lev 23:9–14
—Festival of Weeks .... Lev 23:15–21
—Festival of Tabernacles .... Lev 23:33–43
3. Provision made for the poor at harvesttime .... Lev 19:9–10; Dt 24:19–22; Ru 2:1–9

B. God's use of harvests
—Abundant harvest demonstrated his love .... Dt 8:7–9; Ps 23:1; Ps 144:12–15
—God chastised by means of crop failure and famine .... Isa 17:10–11; Joel 1:8–12; Hag 1:5–6

C. Harvesting used as a metaphor
1. To picture mission work
—Pray for workers in God's harvest .... Mt 9:37–38
—The fields ripe for harvest .... Jn 4:35–36
2. To picture God's judgment .... Isa 17:1–5; Jer 51:33
3. To picture the end of the world
—Gathering God's people .... Mt 13:24–30, 36–43
—Judging God's enemies .... Rev 14:14–19; Joel 3:12–13
4. The law of the harvest
—Reaping what we sow .... 2Co 9:6; Gal 6:7
—Sowing evil and reaping trouble .... Job 4:8; Pr 22:8; Hos 10:13
—Sowing good and reaping blessing .... Hos 10:12; Gal 6:8–9

HAZAEL
—A servant of King Ben-Hadad of Aram 2Ki 8:7–8
—Anointed by Elijah as king over Aram 1Ki 19:15
—Asked Elisha about Ben-Hadad 2Ki 8:8–9
—Murdered Ben-Hadad 2Ki 8:14–15
—Became king of Aram 2Ki 8:15
—Fought against Israel and Judah 2Ki 8:28; 2Ch 22:5–6
—Conquered part of Israel 2Ki 10:32–33; 2Ki 13:22
—Gained power over Joash 2Ki 12:17–18
—Succeeded by son Ben-Hadad 2Ki 13:24
—Judgment prophesied against him .... Am 1:3–5

HEAD
A. The human head
1. Literal use
—Hand put on the head in blessing .... Ge 48:14–18
—People were anointed on the head .... Ex 29:7; 1Sa 10:1
—Anointing head with oil meant blessings .... Ps 23:5
—Crowns were put on the head .... 1Ch 20:2; Est 2:17
—No razor on the head of a Nazirite .... Nu 6:5–6; Jdg 13:5
—Cutting off the head, a sign of victory 1Sa 17:51; 1Sa 31:9
—Woman's covered head showed submission 1Co 11:5,10
—A bowed head showed reverence .... Ge 24:26; Ge 43:28; Ex 4:31
—A bowed head showed grief .... Ps 35:14
—Dust on one's head showed sorrow 1Sa 4:12
—Pulling hair from the head showed sorrow .... Ezr 9:3
—Shaving hair from the head showed grief .... Job 1:20; Isa 15:2
—Ashes on one's head showed shame 2Sa 13:19
—Shaking the head showed disdain .... Job 16:4; Ps 22:7; Mt 27:39
2. Figurative use
—Blessings crown the head .... Pr 10:6
—Joy crowns the head .... Isa 35:10; Isa 51:11
—Blood on one's head meant guilt .... 2Sa 1:15–16; Eze 33:4
—Lifting up one's head meant pride .... Ps 83:2
—From head to foot meant the whole body .... Dt 28:35; Isa 1:6
—The Lord gives grace by lifting a head .... Ps 3:3; Ps 27:5–6
—Heaping coals of fire on the head .... Pr 25:22; Ro 12:20
—Jesus had nowhere to lay his head .... Mt 8:20

B. Head used in symbolic ways
1. Political leadership
—Heads as leaders of the clans of Israel .... Nu 1:16; Jos 14:1
—Heads as leaders of the tribes .... Nu 30:1
—Heads as leaders of families .... 2Ch 1:2; Ezr 2:68
—A head as the king of a country .... Isa 7:8–9
2. Husband as the head of his wife .... 1Co 11:3,8–10; Eph 5:23
3. Christ as the head
—Of all creation .... Eph 1:10
—Of every man 1Co 11:3
—Of the church .... Eph 5:23; Col 1:18; Col 2:19

HEALING
A. Roles in healing
1. God is the ultimate healer .... Dt 32:39; Ps 103:3; Jer 30:17
2. Human elements that play a role
—Faith .... Mt 13:58; Mk 5:34; Lk 18:42
—Prayer .... Jas 5:14–16
—Intercession .... Nu 12:10–15; 1Ki 13:6
—A cheerful heart .... Pr 17:22
—Positive words .... Pr 16:24

B. Physical healing of the body
1. Medical care used .... 2Ki 20:7; Lk 10:34–35; 1Ti 5:23
2. Miracles performed
—Directly by God .... Ge 20:17
—By prophets 1Ki 17:17–24; 2Ki 5:1–14
—By Jesus .... Mt 4:24
—By followers of Jesus .... Ac 5:15–16; Ac 28:8
—By agents of Satan .... 2Th 2:9; Rev 13:3
3. Spiritual gifts of miracles and healing 1Co 12:9–10,28

See also MIRACLE

C. Spiritual healing
—Received by the land 2Ch 7:13–14
—Received by people .... 2Ch 30:18–20; Hos 14:4; 1Pe 2:24
—Performed by Jesus with physical healing .... Mk 2:5–11

HEART
—The center of the human being
A. Basic concept of the heart
1. The wellspring of all life .... Pr 4:23; Lk 6:45

2. Combined with other basic human elements
   - —The heart and soul.......... Dt 6:5; 1Sa 14:7; Mt 22:37
   - —The heart and body.......... Ps 16:9
   - —The heart and mind.......... Ps 26:2; Mt 22:37; Rev 2:23
   - —The heart and spirit.......... Ps 51:10,17; Eze 18:31
   - —The heart and flesh.......... Ps 73:26; Ps 84:2
   - —The heart and thoughts.......... Ps 139:23
   - —The heart and understanding.......... Pr 3:5

B. What the heart controls

1. Human emotions
   - —The glad heart.......... Ex 4:14; Ac 2:26
   - —The singing heart.......... Eph 5:19
   - —The heart that loves.......... Dt 6:5; SS 3:1–3
   - —The heart that takes delight.......... Ecc 2:10; Jer 15:16
   - —The excited heart.......... Lk 24:32
   - —The courageous heart.......... 1Sa 10:26; Ps 27:14
   - —The heart that is encouraged.......... Col 2:2; 2Th 2:17
   - —The thankful heart.......... Col 3:16
   - —The repentant heart.......... Ps 51:17
   - —The humble heart.......... Mt 11:29
   - —The compassionate heart.......... Lk 7:13
   - —The anxious heart.......... Pr 12:25
   - —The discouraged heart.......... Jos 2:11
   - —The troubled heart.......... Jn 12:27
   - —The grieving heart.......... 1Sa 2:33; La 2:18
   - —The tormented heart.......... La 2:11
   - —The broken heart.......... Eze 21:6
   - —The heavy heart.......... Pr 25:20
   - —The anguished heart.......... Isa 65:14; Jer 4:19; Ro 9:2
   - —The fearful heart.......... Dt 28:67; Jos 5:1
   - —The angry heart.......... Ps 39:3; Pr 19:3
2. The human will
   - —To do according to one's heart.......... 1Sa 2:35; 1Ch 28:2
   - —To decide in the heart.......... 2Ch 6:7
   - —To devote the heart.......... 1Ch 22:19
   - —To direct the heart.......... 2Th 3:5
   - —To turn the heart.......... 1Ki 8:58; Ps 119:36
   - —To incline the heart.......... Dt 5:29
   - —To win over the heart.......... 2Sa 19:14
   - —To yield the heart.......... Jos 24:23
   - —To agree with one heart.......... Jer 32:39; Ac 4:32
   - —To be moved in the heart.......... Ex 35:21
   - —The purposes of the heart.......... Jer 23:20
   - —The motives of the heart.......... 1Co 4:5
   - —The desires of the heart.......... Ps 21:2; Ro 10:1
   - —The willing heart.......... 2Ch 29:31
   - —The unrepentant heart.......... Ro 2:5
   - —The hardened heart.......... Ex 4:21; Pr 28:14
3. The human intelligence
   - —To acknowledge in the heart.......... Dt 4:39
   - —To know in the heart.......... Dt 8:5
   - —To take something to heart.......... Ex 7:23; Ecc 7:2
   - —To fix words in the heart.......... Dt 11:18
   - —To lay up words in the heart.......... Job 22:22; Pr 4:21
   - —To search the heart.......... Ps 4:4
   - —To say in the heart.......... Ro 10:6
   - —To muse in the heart.......... Ps 77:6
   - —To ponder in the heart.......... Lk 2:19
   - —To think in the heart.......... Mk 2:8
   - —To understand in the heart.......... Pr 2:2
   - —To meditate in the heart.......... Ps 19:14
   - —To pray in the heart.......... Ge 24:45; 1Sa 1:13
   - —To believe in the heart.......... Ro 10:9
   - —To be wise in the heart.......... Pr 2:10; Pr 10:8
   - —To doubt in the heart.......... Mk 11:23
   - —To harbor deceit in the heart.......... Pr 26:24; Jer 17:9
   - —To devise evil in the heart.......... Ps 140:2
   - —The thoughts of the heart.......... Ge 6:5; Lk 2:35

C. Key elements in the human heart

1. Characteristics of the unregenerate heart
   - —Proud.......... Pr 18:12
   - —Foolish.......... Pr 12:23
   - —Deceitful.......... Jer 17:9
   - —Rebellious.......... Jer 5:23
   - —Perverse.......... Pr 11:20
   - —Evil.......... Ge 6:5
   - —Wicked.......... Pr 6:18
   - —Callous.......... Ps 119:70
   - —Malicious.......... Ps 28:3
   - —Hardened.......... Eph 4:18
   - —Darkened.......... Ro 1:21
   - —Deluded.......... Isa 44:20
   - —Unrepentant.......... Ro 2:5
   - —Unbelieving.......... Heb 3:12
   - —Gone astray.......... Ps 95:10
   - —Devoted to idols.......... Eze 11:21
   - —Filled with schemes to do wrong.......... Ecc 8:11
   - —Filled with madness.......... Ecc 9:3
   - —Far from God.......... Isa 29:13; Mk 7:6
2. What the regenerate heart does
   - —Cries out for the living God.......... Ps 84:2
   - —Seeks God.......... Ps 119:2,10
   - —Responds to God.......... 2Ki 22:19
   - —Trusts in the Lord.......... Pr 3:5
   - —Loves the Lord.......... Dt 6:5; Mt 22:37
   - —Praises the Lord.......... Ps 9:1
   - —Sings to the Lord.......... Ps 30:12
   - —Rejoices in the Lord.......... 1Sa 2:1
   - —Rejoices in salvation.......... Ps 13:5
   - —Is grateful to God.......... Col 3:16
   - —Obeys God's law.......... Ps 119:34,69,112; Eph 6:6
   - —Hides God's word within.......... Ps 119:11
   - —Is on fire for God's word.......... Jer 20:9
   - —Meditates on God and his word.......... Ps 19:14
   - —Is upright.......... Ps 7:10
   - —Speaks the truth.......... Ps 15:2
   - —Is steadfast and secure.......... Ps 57:7; Ps 112:7–8
   - —Is pure.......... Ps 24:4; Mt 5:8
   - —Is wise.......... Pr 10:8
   - —Is sincere.......... Ac 2:46; Heb 10:22
   - —Is unafraid and courageous.......... Ps 27:3,14
   - —Is contrite.......... Ps 51:17
   - —Is circumcised.......... Dt 10:16; Ro 2:29
   - —Walks blamelessly.......... Ps 101:2
   - —Loves others.......... 1Pe 1:22

D. God's relationship to the human heart
—He knows it. 1Sa 16:7
—He searches it. Ps 7:9; Jer 17:10
—He tests it. 1Ch 29:17; 1Th 2:4
—He influences it. Ezr 7:27
—He directs it. Pr 21:1
—He opens it. Ac 16:14
—He touches it. 1Sa 10:26
—He makes light shine in it. 2Co 4:6
—He cleanses it. Heb 10:22
—He writes his law on it. Jer 31:33
—He strengthens it. 1Th 3:13
—He keeps it loyal. 1Ch 29:18
—He gives a new heart. Ps 51:10; Eze 11:19

HEAVEN

A. What is heaven?
1. Part of God's creation. Ge 1:1
—A component of the universe. Ex 20:4; Php 2:10
—Where God placed sun, moon and stars. Ge 1:14–18; Dt 4:19
—Where precipitation comes from. Ge 8:2; Job 38:29; Isa 55:10
2. The place where God dwells
—His dwelling place. 1Ki 8:30; Mt 6:9
—His sanctuary. Ps 102:19
—Where his throne is. Ps 2:4; Isa 63:15
—Where Christ ascended. Lk 24:51; Heb 9:24

B. What does God do from heaven?
1. Actions in Bible history
—God talked to his people. Ge 22:11,15
—God made the Israelites hear him. Dt 4:36
—God heard his people when they prayed. Ne 9:27–28
—God sent bread. Ex 16:4,13–15; Ne 9:15
—God sent fire of judgment. 2Ki 1:12
—God sent fire for sacrifice. 1Ch 21:26
—God revealed mysteries. Da 2:18–19; Ac 10:10–16
2. Continuing actions
—God reigns. Ps 99:1–2
—God observes human actions. Ps 14:2; Ps 102:19
—God blesses his people. Dt 26:15
—God hears our prayers. 2Ch 6:21,23,25,27
—God saves us. Ps 57:3
—God sends his Holy Spirit. 1Pe 1:12
—God reveals his wrath. Ro 1:18
—Christ prepares a place for us. Jn 14:2–3
—Christ will return from heaven. 1Th 4:16

C. Our relationship to heaven
1. How can we enter heaven?
—We must be chosen and called. 2Pe 1:10–11
—We must be born again. Jn 3:5
—We must trust in God and in Jesus. Jn 14:1–2
—We must have our names recorded there. Lk 10:20
—We must be righteous. Mt 5:19–20
—We must live holy lives. Rev 22:14–15
—We must do the will of God. Mt 7:21
—We must be humble. Mt 18:3–4
—We must be poor in spirit. Mt 5:3
—We must overcome. Rev 2:7; Rev 21:7
—We must receive new bodies. 1Co 15:50–54
2. What should our attitude be toward heaven?
—We should lay up treasures there. Mt 6:20
—We should sacrifice everything for it. Mt 13:44–46
—We should long for it. 2Co 5:2
—We should eagerly look for it. 2Pe 3:13
—We should hope for it. Col 1:5
—In spirit we are already there. Eph 2:6; Php 3:20; Col 3:1

D. Aspects of the present heaven
1. Positive
—God dwells there. 1Ki 8:30
—Christ dwells there at God's right hand. Ac 7:55–56; Eph 1:20
—Christ intercedes for us there. Heb 9:24
—There is joy there. Lk 15:7,10
—There is comfort there. Lk 16:22–25
—Satan has been hurled down from there. Rev 12:7–9
2. Negative
—God reveals his wrath from there. 1Sa 2:10; Ro 1:18
—Powers of evil intrude there. Job 1:6–7; Eph 6:12; Rev 12:7
—Wars occur there. Rev 6:9–11
—Saints cry out from there. Rev 6:9–11
—Saints do not yet have new bodies. 1Co 15:48–54
—It must be destroyed and renewed. 2Pe 3:7,10,12–13; Rev 21:1

E. What the new heaven will be like
1. It will be free from:
—Death. Lk 20:35–36; Rev 21:4
—Pain, sorrow and crying. Isa 65:19–23; Rev 21:4
—Night. Rev 22:5
—Hunger and thirst. Rev 7:16
—The curse of God. Rev 22:3
—Wicked people. Rev 22:15
2. For believers, it will be:
—Eternal. 2Co 5:1
—A place of eternal light. Rev 22:5
—The home of righteousness. 2Pe 3:13
—The place of harmony and unity. Isa 65:25
—The place of eternal praise to God. Rev 7:15
—The place of exquisite beauty. Rev 21:10–21
—The place of purity. Rev 21:27
—The place of the tree of life. Rev 22:1–2

HEBRON

—A city, originally called Kiriath Arba. Jos 14:15
—Also called Mamre. Ge 23:19
—Abram built an altar and lived there. Ge 13:18
—Abraham and Sarah's burial plot located there. Ge 23:1–19
—Allied with other cities against Gibeonites. Jos 10:1–5
—Defeated by Joshua. Jos 10:6–26; Jos 11:21
—Given to Caleb. Jos 14:13–15; Jdg 1:9–10,20
—Later given to Kohathites. 1Ch 6:54–56
—David ruled from there for seven years. 2Sa 2:1–4; 1Ki 2:11
—Soldiers joined David there. 1Ch 12:23–40
—David anointed king of all Israel there. 2Sa 5:1–3; 1Ch 11:1–3
—Absalom crowned king there. 2Sa 15:7–10

HEIR

See INHERITANCE

HELL

A. A place of punishment
—For fallen angels. 2Pe 2:4
—For the devil and his angels. Mt 25:41
—For the beast and the false prophet. Rev 19:20
—For those who worship the beast. Rev 14:9–11
—For wicked humans. Rev 21:8
—For those who reject the gospel. Mt 10:11–15

B. Hints of hell in the Old Testament
—The wicked perish in death. Ps 49:10–15

—There will be judgment for the wicked ..... Job 24:21–24
—There will be eternal punishment ..... Isa 66:24; Da 12:2

C. Description of hell in the New Testament
—A place of separation from God 2Th 1:9
—The second death ..... Rev 21:8
—The place of condemnation ..... Mt 23:33
—The place of torment ..... Lk 16:23
—The place of weeping and the grinding of teeth ..... Mt 8:12; Mt 25:30
—The place where body and soul is destroyed ..... Mt 10:28
—Eternal punishment ..... Mt 25:46
—Everlasting destruction 2Th 1:9
—Everlasting chains ..... Jude 6
—Eternal fire ..... Mt 18:8; Jude 7
—The lake of fire ..... Rev 20:15
—The blackest darkness ..... Jude 13

HERESY

See DOCTRINE

HEROD

A. Herod the Great
—King of Judea at time of Jesus' birth ..... Mt 2:1; Lk 1:5
—Magi contacted him ..... Mt 2:1–8
—Ordered babies in Bethlehem killed ..... Mt 2:16

B. Herod Antipas
—Tetrarch of Galilee ..... Mt 14:1; Lk 3:1
—Beheaded John the Baptist ..... Mt 14:3–12
—Worried about Jesus ..... Lk 9:7–9
—Jesus called him a fox ..... Lk 13:31–32
—Participated in trial of Jesus ..... Lk 23:6–15

C. Herod Agrippa
—Persecuted the early church ..... Ac 12:1
—Killed James ..... Ac 12:2
—Arrested Peter ..... Ac 12:3–19
—Died a miserable death from God ..... Ac 12:19–23

HERODIAS

—Wife of Herod Antipas ..... Mt 14:3–4; Mk 6:17
—Told daughter to ask for John's severed head ..... Mt 14:6–11; Mk 6:21–27

HEZEKIAH

—King of Judah 2Ch 29:1
—Purified the temple 2Ch 29:3–19
—Restored proper sacrifices 2Ch 29:20–36
—Celebrated the Passover for two weeks 2Ch 30:1–27
—Cleansed land of idols 2Ch 31:1
—Organized priests and Levites 2Ch 31:2–19
—Collected Solomon's proverbs ..... Pr 25:1
—Sought the Lord for help against Assyria ..... 2Ch 32:1–20; Isa 36:1–37:20
—Witnessed the destruction of Sennacherib ..... 2Ch 32:21–23; Isa 37:36–37
—Had fatal illness 2Ki 20:1
—Illness healed by God through prayer ..... 2Ki 20:2–11; Isa 38:2–8
—Sang a song after his recovery ..... Isa 38:9–20
—Judged for sin of pride ..... 2Ki 20:12–21; Isa 39:1–8

HILKIAH

—High priest during time of Josiah 2Ki 22:4
—Reported his finding of the Book of the Law 2Ki 22:8; 2Ch 34:14–15
—Questioned Huldah about the Law 2Ki 22:14; 2Ch 34:22
—Ordered by Josiah to cleanse the temple 2Ki 23:4; 2Ch 34:9–11
—Became administrator of the temple 2Ch 35:8

HIRAM

—King of Tyre 2Sa 5:11
—Helped David build his palace 2Sa 5:11–12; 1Ch 14:1
—Helped Solomon build the temple 1Ki 5:1–12; 2Ch 2:3–18
—Scorned towns that Solomon gave him 1Ki 9:10–13
—Helped build Solomon's navy 1Ki 9:26–28; 2Ch 8:17–18
—Engaged in extensive trade 1Ki 10:11–12

HITTITES

A. Their identity
—Descendants of Canaan, grandson of Noah ..... Ge 10:6,15
—One of the seven Canaanite nations ..... Ex 33:2

B. Significant Hittites
—Ephron: sold Abraham a burial plot ..... Ge 23:10–20
—Judith and Basemath: wives of Esau ..... Ge 26:34
—Ahimelek: a soldier with David 1Sa 26:6
—Uriah: husband of Bathsheba 2Sa 11:3–24; 1Ki 15:5

C. Their wars
—Allied with others against Joshua ..... Jos 11:1–5
—Defeated by Joshua ..... Jos 12:7–8

D. Important data concerning them
—Controlled much land in Moses' time ..... Nu 13:27–29; Jos 1:4
—God promised their land to his people ..... Ex 3:8,17; Ex 34:11
—Israelites told to destroy them completely ..... Dt 7:1–6; Dt 20:17
—Israelites did not destroy them completely ..... Jdg 3:5
—Solomon traded with them 1Ki 10:29
—Many became Solomon's slaves 1Ki 9:20–21; 2Ch 8:7–8
—Intermarried with the Israelites ..... Jdg 3:5–6; 1Ki 11:1; Ezr 9:1–2

HOLINESS

—Being set apart from sin; purity

A. Related theme
HOLINESS is a theme of Leviticus ..... Lev 19:12

B. The holiness of God
1. In the Old Testament
—He is holy ..... Ps 99:3,5,9
—He is called the Holy One of Israel ..... 2Ki 19:22; Isa 30:11–12,15
—His Spirit is holy ..... Isa 63:10
—His name is holy ..... Ps 111:9
—His throne is holy ..... Ps 47:8
—He is majestic in holiness ..... Ex 15:11
—His holiness has splendor 1Ch 16:29
—He is surrounded by holiness ..... Isa 6:3
—He is unique in his holiness 1Sa 2:2
—He swears by his holiness ..... Am 4:2
—He will show himself holy ..... Isa 5:16
—His words are holy ..... Jer 23:9
—His arm is holy ..... Isa 52:10
2. In the New Testament
—The Father is holy ..... Mt 6:9; Jn 17:11
—The Son is holy ..... Lk 1:35; Ac 4:27,30
—The Spirit is holy ..... Ac 2:4; Ro 1:4

C. The holiness of God's people
1. Israel in the Old Testament
—They were holy to the Lord ..... Jer 2:3
—They were a holy people ..... Ex 19:6; Dt 7:6
—They formed a holy race ..... Ezr 9:2
—They were expected to be holy ..... Lev 11:44–45; Lev 19:12
—The priests were holy ..... Lev 21:5–6
2. Christians in the New Testament
—They are a holy people ..... Col 3:12; 1Pe 2:9

—They are a holy temple ... Eph 2:21
—They are sanctified (made holy) ... 1Co 6:11
—They are chosen to be holy ... Eph 1:4
—They are called to a holy life ... 1Th 4:7
—They must live holy lives ... Heb 12:14
1Pe 1:15–16
—They are to serve God in holiness ... Lk 1:74–75
—They must purify themselves in holiness ... 2Co 7:1
—They will be presented to God as holy ... Col 1:22

D. The holiness of special things
1. Referred to in the Old Testament
—The ground where one meets God ... Ex 3:4–5
—The Holy Place and the Most Holy Place ... Ex 26:33
—The altar in the tabernacle ... Ex 29:37
—The garments of the priests ... Ex 28:2–4
—The turban of the priest ... Ex 39:30–31
—The furnishings used by the priests ... Nu 4:15
—The guilt offering ... Lev 7:1
—Anything given to the Lord ... Lev 27:9,14,21,28
—The camp of the Israelites ... Dt 23:14
—The temple ... Hab 2:20
—The Sabbath ... Ex 16:23
—The Year of Jubilee ... Lev 25:12
—Mount Zion in Jerusalem ... Ps 2:6
Isa 27:13
—The city of Jerusalem ... Ne 11:1
2. Referred to in the New Testament
—The angels ... Ac 10:22
1Th 3:13
—The city of Jerusalem ... Mt 4:5
—The Scriptures ... Ro 1:2
2Ti 3:15
—The law of God ... Ro 7:12
—A Christian's faith ... Jude 20
—A Christian's hands in prayer ... 1Ti 2:8
—The kiss of greeting among Christians ... 1Co 16:20
1Th 5:26

See also SANCTIFICATION

HOLY SPIRIT

A. Related theme
HOLY SPIRIT is a theme of Acts ... Ac 13:2

B. The Spirit's divine nature
1. Called God ... Lk 1:32,35
Ac 5:3–4
2. United with the Father and Son ... Mt 28:19
2Co 13:14
3. Has characteristics of God
—Eternal ... Heb 9:14
—Everywhere present ... Ps 139:7–10
—All-knowing ... 1Co 2:10–11
—Has great power ... Ac 1:8
Ro 15:19
—Raised Christ from the dead ... 1Pe 3:18
—Performs miracles ... Mt 12:28
Ro 15:19
—Involved in creation ... Ge 1:2
—Gives spiritual life to us ... Jn 3:3–8

C. The Spirit as a person
—He teaches ... Jn 14:26
—He hears and speaks ... Jn 16:13
—He testifies about Christ ... Jn 15:26
—He encourages ... Ac 9:31
—He advocates ... Jn 14:16
—He convicts people of sin ... Jn 16:8
—He prays for us ... Ro 8:27
—He sends people out ... Ac 13:4
—He experiences grief ... Eph 4:30
—He can be resisted ... Ac 7:51
—He can be tested ... Ac 5:9

D. The Spirit's work
1. In the Old Testament
—Involved in creation ... Ge 1:2
—Gave life to God's creatures ... Ps 104:30
—Guided God's people ... Isa 63:11–13
—Instructed God's people ... Ne 9:20
—Led God's people in the right way ... Ps 143:10
—Inspired God's people to do right ... Ps 51:10–22
—Admonished God's people ... Ne 9:30
—Reacted to human evil ... Ge 6:3
—Gave artistic ability to individuals ... Ex 31:2–3
—Gave his power to Israel's leaders ... Jdg 6:34
1Sa 16:13
Zec 4:6
—Lived among God's people ... Hag 2:5
—Inspired the prophets ... Nu 11:29
Mic 3:8
Zec 7:12
2Pe 1:21
—Spoke through the psalmists ... 2Sa 23:2
Ac 1:16,20
Heb 3:7–11
—Old Testament prophecies on the Spirit ... Isa 11:1–3
Isa 32:15
Isa 42:1
Isa 44:3
Isa 61:1–3
Eze 39:29
Joel 2:28–32
2. In the life of Jesus Christ
—Jesus was conceived by the Spirit ... Lk 1:34–35
—He received the Spirit at his baptism ... Lk 3:21–22
—He was filled with the Spirit ... Lk 4:1
—He ministered in the power of the Spirit ... Mt 12:15–21
Lk 4:18–21
—He drove out demons by the Spirit ... Mt 12:28
—He offered himself to God through the Spirit ... Heb 9:14
—He was raised by the Spirit ... Ro 8:11
1Ti 3:16
1Pe 3:18
—He promised to send the Spirit ... Jn 15:26
—He sent the Spirit on Pentecost ... Ac 2:33
—The Spirit is the Spirit of Jesus ... Ac 16:7
Ro 8:28
Gal 4:6
3. In the church
—The Spirit came at Pentecost ... Ac 2:1–4
—He dwells in the church ... 1Co 3:16–17
Eph 2:22
—He appoints officers for the church ... Ac 20:28
—He directs decisions of the church ... Ac 15:28
—He chooses missionaries ... Ac 13:2
—He sends out missionaries ... Ac 13:4
—He directs the mission enterprise ... Ac 8:29,39
Ac 16:6–7
4. In individuals
—The Spirit dwells in us ... Jn 14:16–17
Ro 8:11
1Co 6:19
—He convicts us of sin ... Jn 16:7–11
—He gives us new life ... Jn 3:5–6
Titus 3:5
—He makes us realize God's love ... Ro 5:5
—He gives us power to witness ... Ac 1:8
Ac 6:9–10
—He teaches us what to say ... Lk 12:12
—He reveals God's secrets to us ... 1Co 2:10–16
—He brings Christ's presence to us ... Jn 14:16–18
—He keeps us in touch with God ... Ro 8:26
Jude 20
—He teaches us about Christ ... Jn 14:26
Jn 15:26
—He enables us to find the truth ... 1Jn 4:1–6
—He encourages us ... Ac 9:31
—He controls us ... Ro 8:9
—He gives us joy and peace ... Ro 14:17
—He draws us into fellowship ... 2Co 13:14
Php 2:1
—He enables us to live the Christian life ... Ro 8:5–9

—He works his fruit in us ... Gal 5:16–25
—He sanctifies us ... Ro 15:16; 2Th 2:13
—He gives us gifts ... 1Co 12:4–11
See GIFTS OF THE SPIRIT
—He gives us his sword to fight Satan ... Eph 6:17
—He prays for us in times of crisis ... Ro 8:26
—He will raise us from the dead ... Ro 8:11

E. The Spirit in our life
1. How to receive the Spirit
—We must repent of our sins ... Ac 2:37–38
—We must believe in Jesus ... Ac 11:15–17; Ro 8:9; Gal 3:2–3,14; Eph 1:13
—We must be baptized in Jesus' name ... Ac 2:38; Ac 19:1–6
—We must pray to receive him ... Lk 11:13; Ac 8:15
2. Being filled with the Holy Spirit
a. His filling is a gift for all believers
—Old Testament promise ... Joel 2:28–29
—New Testament fulfillment ... Ac 2:17–18
—New Testament promise to us ... Ac 2:38; Ro 8:9
b. Persons *filled* with the Holy Spirit
—Bezalel ... Ex 31:2–5
—Samson ... Jdg 14:19
—Saul ... 1Sa 10:10
—John the Baptist ... Lk 1:15
—Elizabeth ... Lk 1:47
—Zechariah ... Lk 1:67
—The disciples on Pentecost ... Ac 2:4
—Peter before the Jewish council ... Ac 4:8
—The early Christians at prayer ... Ac 4:31
—Paul in his preaching ... Ac 13:9
—New Christians ... Ac 13:52
c. Persons *full* of the Holy Spirit
—Jesus ... Lk 4:1
—The first deacons ... Ac 6:3
—Stephen ... Ac 6:5
—Barnabas ... Ac 11:24
d. The command to be filled with the Spirit
—To Paul at his conversion ... Ac 9:17
—To all Christians ... Eph 5:18
3. Being sealed with the Spirit ... 2Co 1:21–22; 2Co 5:5; Eph 1:13–14
4. Baptized with the Spirit
See BAPTISM OF THE SPIRIT

HOME
See FAMILY

HOMOSEXUALITY
See SEXUAL STANDARDS

HONESTY
See INTEGRITY

HOPE
—Certainty in the present and firm expectation for the future

A. Related themes
1. HOPE is a theme of:
—Isaiah ... Isa 9:7
—Jeremiah ... Jer 23:5
—Amos ... Am 9:11
—Micah ... Mic 4:1
—Zephaniah ... Zep 3:15
—Haggai ... Hag 2:7
—1 Thessalonians ... 1Th 1:10
—2 Thessalonians ... 2Th 2:3
—1 Peter ... 1Pe 1:3
—Revelation ... Rev 21:3
2. RESTORATION is a theme of:
—Ezekiel ... Eze 36:24
—Joel ... Joel 2:32

B. The nature of hope
1. Basic concept of hope
—It is linked with faith ... 1Co 13:13; Heb 11:1
—It is linked with trust ... Ps 33:20–21; Ro 15:13
—It is linked with expectation ... Ro 4:18–19; Titus 1:2
2. In whom/what do we hope?
—In God ... Ps 42:5,11; Ps 130:7; 1Ti 6:17
—In Jesus Christ ... Ro 15:12; 1Co 15:19; Eph 1:12; Php 2:19
—In the name of God ... Ps 52:9
—In the word of God ... Ps 119:74; Ps 130:5
—In the promises of God ... Ac 26:6
—In the resurrection of the dead ... Ac 23:6
3. For what do we hope?
—God's righteousness ... Gal 5:5
—Salvation ... Ro 8:24–25; 1Th 5:8
—God's saving arm ... Isa 51:5
—Liberation from bondage to decay ... Ro 8:20–21
—The resurrection ... Ac 2:26; Ac 26:7
—The glory of God ... Ro 5:2; 2Co 3:11–12
—Our glorious inheritance ... Eph 1:18; Col 1:5
—The appearance of Jesus Christ ... Titus 2:13; 1Jn 3:2–3
—A crown of righteousness ... 2Ti 4:8
—A crown of glory ... 1Pe 5:4
—A crown of life ... Rev 2:10
—Eternal life ... Titus 1:2; Titus 3:7

C. Jesus Christ and our hope
1. He is called our hope
—He is our hope ... 1Ti 1:1
—He is the hope of Israel ... Ac 28:20
—He is the hope of glory ... Col 1:27
2. He fulfilled the hope of the Old Testament
—Jesus confirms the promises of God ... Ac 26:6–7; Ro 15:8
—All promises of God fulfilled in him ... 2Co 1:20

D. Hope in the Christian life
1. The choice we face
—Hope in humans or in God ... Ps 33:16–19
—Hope in riches or in God ... 1Ti 6:17
—Without God, there is no hope ... Eph 2:12; 1Th 4:13
2. Attaining hope
—We are called to only one hope ... Eph 1:18; Eph 4:4
—We must set our hope fully on Jesus ... 1Pe 1:13
—We must believe the resurrection ... 1Pe 1:3
—We must abound in hope ... Ro 15:13; 1Co 13:13
—We must never lose our hope ... Ps 25:5
3. The benefits of hope
—Causes us to praise God ... Ps 71:14
—Causes us to rejoice ... Ro 5:2; Ro 12:12
—Renews our strength ... Isa 40:31
—Inspires us to a life of purity ... 1Jn 3:3
—Inspires us to persevere ... 1Th 1:3
—Cures the downcast soul ... Ps 42:5,11; La 3:20–21
—Will never disappoint us ... Isa 49:23; Ro 5:5
—Our hope is like a stabilizing anchor ... Heb 6:18–19
4. We should defend our hope ... 1Pe 3:15

HOPHNI

—Son of Eli; brother of Phinehas ... 1Sa 1:3
—A wicked priest ... 1Sa 2:12–17
—Scorned his father's rebuke ... 1Sa 2:22–25
—His death prophesied as a sign ... 1Sa 2:30–34
—Brought the ark into battle ... 1Sa 4:4
—Killed in the battle ... 1Sa 4:11,17

HOREB

See SINAI

HORSE

A. Literal uses of horses
  1. Military
    —Description of the war-horse ... Job 39:19–25
    —Pharaoh's horses ... Ex 14:9,23
    —Canaanite horses ... Jos 11:4
    —Solomon's horses ... 2Ch 1:14–16
    —Syrian horses ... 2Ki 6:14–15
  2. Non-military uses
    —Horses used to reinforce royal power ... 2Sa 15:1; 1Ki 1:5
    —Horse riding to honor a person ... Est 6:6–11
    —Horses as livestock ... Ge 47:17
    —Horses used in farm labor ... Isa 28:28
    —Horses used for transportation ... Isa 66:20
    —Horses used to bring messages ... Est 8:10
  3. Relying on horses
    —They cannot bring victory ... Ps 33:16–17
    —Trust in God instead of horses ... Ps 20:7; Isa 31:1

B. Figurative use of horses
  —Horses of fire carried Elijah to heaven ... 2Ki 2:11
  —God's people becoming like the proud horse ... Zec 10:3
  —God's angels using horses and chariots ... 2Ki 6:17
  —God's power symbolized in his horses ... Hab 3:8,15
  —The returning Lord riding a white horse ... Rev 19:11–13

HOSEA

—A prophet; son of Beeri ... Hos 1:1
—His wife pictured unfaithful Israel ... Hos 1:2–11
—Became reconciled with his wife ... Hos 3:1–3

HOSHEA

A. Original name of Joshua ... Nu 13:16
B. Last king of Israel ... 2Ki 17:1
  —Murdered Pekah to get throne ... 2Ki 15:30
  —Captured and deported by Assyria ... 2Ki 17:2–6

HOSPITALITY

See KINDNESS

HULDAH

—A prophetess ... 2Ki 22:14
—Visited by Hilkiah during Josiah's reign ... 2Ki 22:12–20; 2Ch 34:19–28

HUMILITY

—Lowliness; freedom from pride

A. Related theme
  HUMILITY is a theme of 1 Corinthians ... 1Co 1:29
B. What humility involves
  —A childlike attitude ... Mt 18:1–4
  —Repentance ... Isa 66:2; Lk 18:13–14
  —Submission before God ... 2Ch 34:27; Da 5:22–23
  —Seeking God's face in prayer ... 2Ch 7:14
  —Fasting ... Ezr 8:21; Ps 35:13
  —Following God's laws ... Jer 44:10; Zep 2:3
  —Working for justice and mercy ... Mic 6:6–8
  —Opposite of pride ... Pr 3:34; Da 4:37; 1Pe 5:5
C. Humility in our lives
  1. The command to be humble
    —We must humble ourselves ... Eph 4:2; 1Pe 5:6
    —We must walk humbly with God ... Mic 6:8
    —We must clothe ourselves with humility ... Col 3:12; 1Pe 5:5
    —We must value others above ourselves ... Php 2:3
    —We must avoid false humility ... Col 2:18,23
  2. The benefits of humility
    —God saves the humble ... Ps 18:27
    —God shows favor to the humble ... Pr 3:34; Isa 66:2; Jas 4:6
    —God lifts up/exalts the lowly ... Mt 23:12; Lk 1:52
    —God revives the lowly ... Isa 57:15
    —God honors the humble ... Pr 15:33; Pr 18:12
    —God rewards the humble ... Pr 22:4
    —God blesses the humble ... 2Ch 7:14
    —God guides and teaches the humble ... Ps 25:9
    —With humility comes wisdom ... Pr 11:2
D. Examples of humility
  1. The supreme example: Jesus Christ
    —In his coming to earth ... 2Co 8:9
    —In his lowliness ... Mt 11:29
    —In his life of service ... Lk 22:27
    —In his submission to God's will ... Jn 6:38
    —In his sufferings ... Isa 53:1–9
    —In his washing of the disciples' feet ... Jn 13:4–5
    —In his Triumphal Entry ... Mt 21:5,7
    —In his death on the cross ... Php 2:5–8
  2. Other examples
    —The Israelites in the desert ... Dt 8:3
    —Ahab ... 1Ki 21:29
    —Josiah ... 2Ki 22:19
    —Rehoboam and his people ... 2Ch 12:5–12
    —Job ... Job 42:2–6
    —Isaiah ... Isa 6:1–6
    —John the Baptist ... Jn 3:27–30
    —Peter ... Lk 5:8–9
    —Paul ... Ac 20:19

HUNGER AND THIRST

A. Examples of famines and droughts
  —Worldwide famine in Joseph's day ... Ge 41:53
  —Famine in Bethlehem ... Ru 1:1
  —Famine in David's time ... 2Sa 21:1
  —Drought and famine in Elijah's day ... 1Ki 17:1
  —Famine in Elisha's day ... 2Ki 6:25; 2Ki 8:1
  —Famine in Jerusalem ... 2Ki 25:3
  —Famine in Nehemiah's day ... Ne 5:3
  —Famine predicted by Agabus ... Ac 11:27–28
B. How times of hunger and thirst were used:
  1. By God
    —To fulfill his plan for his people ... Ge 15:13–14; Ge 41:56–42:3; Ge 46:3–4
    —To humble and teach the Israelites ... Ex 16:2–3; Dt 8:2–3
    —To get people to look to him for help ... Jdg 6:3–6; Ps 107:4–9
    —To punish stubborn disobedience ... Dt 28:47–48; Isa 65:11–13
    —To bring judgment on sinners ... Isa 9:18–21; Am 4:6,9
  2. By Jesus
    —To demonstrate his compassion ... Mk 6:34–44; Mk 8:1–9
    —To show he was bread from heaven ... Jn 6:33,48–51
  3. By the church
    —To show kindness to the needy ... Ac 11:28–30; 2Co 8:13–15
    —To show church unity ... Ro 15:25–27
C. Spiritual hunger and thirst
  1. The reality of such hunger and thirst
    —Physical bread cannot satisfy ... Dt 8:3; Mt 4:4
    —Prediction of a famine of God's word ... Am 8:11–12

2. Satisfying such hunger and thirst
   —God promises to satisfy. . . . . Isa 55:1–3; Mt 5:6
   —Jesus is the bread of life . . . . . Jn 6:35,48–58; 1Co 10:16
   —Jesus is the water of life . . . . . Jn 4:13–14; Jn 7:37–38

HUR
—A chief magistrate of the Israelites . . . . . Ex 24:14
—With Aaron, supported Moses' hand. . . . . Ex 17:10–12

HUSHAI
—Friend of David. 2Sa 15:37
—Conspired with David to outwit Absalom. 2Sa 15:32–37
—Foiled Absalom's revolt by giving poor advice 2Sa 16:15–17:16

HYPOCRISY
—Open display of religion without genuine commitment
A. Related theme
   HYPOCRISY is a theme of James . . . . . Jas 3:9
B. Description of hypocrisy
   —Displaying religion with no love for God . . . . . Isa 29:13; Mt 6:2–6,16–18; Mt 23:5–7
   —Claiming love for God, mistreating others . . . . . Mk 12:38–40; 1Jn 3:17; 1Jn 4:20
   —Not practicing what one preaches. . . . . Mt 23:3; Ro 2:17–24
   —Sticking only to the letter of the law. . . . . Mt 23:16–23; Lk 13:15–16
   —Criticizing another for one's own sins . . . . . Mt 7:3–5; Mk 7:6–13
   —Being outwardly beautiful but inwardly rotten. . . . . Mt 23:27–28
   —Having only an outward form of godliness 2Co 11:13–15; 2Ti 3:5
   —Lying to make oneself look good. . . . . Ac 5:1–10
C. God and human hypocrisy
   1. God's reaction to hypocrites
      —Is angry with them . . . . . Lk 13:14–15
      —Has no reward for them . . . . . Mt 6:2,5,16
      —Pronounces woe to them . . . . . Mt 23:13–16,23–29
      —Has punishment in store for them . . . . . Lk 20:46–47
      —Condemns them to hell . . . . . Mt 23:33
   2. God's will for his people
      —Wants us to avoid hypocrites. 2Ti 3:5
      —Warns us against hypocrisy 1Pe 2:1
      —Wants us to express our faith by works . . . . . Jas 2:14–17; 1Jn 3:17–19
      —Wants us to show genuine love. . . . . Ro 12:9; 1Pe 1:22
      —Wants us to exercise a sincere faith. 1Ti 1:5; 2Ti 1:5

ICHABOD
—Son born to Phinehas's wife after his death. 1Sa 4:19–22
—Name means "no glory" 1Sa 4:21

IDOLATRY
—The worship of false gods
A. Idols mentioned in the Bible
   —Adrammelek 2Ki 17:31
   —Anammelek 2Ki 17:31
   —Artemis. . . . . Ac 19:24,27–28
   —Asherah. 1Ki 14:15
   —Ashima 2Ki 17:30
   —Ashtoreth 1Sa 31:10
   —Baal. 1Ki 16:31–32
   —Baal-Berith. . . . . Jdg 8:33
   —Baal-Zebub. 2Ki 1:3
   —Bel. . . . . Isa 46:1
   —Chemosh. 1Ki 11:7,33
   —Dagon 1Sa 5:2–4
   —Golden calf. 1Ki 12:28
   —Hermes. . . . . Ac 14:12
   —Ishtar (Queen of Heaven) . . . . . Jer 7:18
   —Molek 1Ki 11:5,7
   —Marduk . . . . . Jer 50:2
   —Nergal 2Ki 17:30
   —Nebo . . . . . Isa 46:1
   —Nibhaz. 2Ki 17:31
   —Nisrok 2Ki 19:37
   —Rephan . . . . . Ac 7:43
   —Rimmon 2Ki 5:18
   —Sukkoth Benoth. 2Ki 17:30
   —Tammuz . . . . . Eze 8:14
   —Tartak 2Ki 17:31
   —Zeus. . . . . Ac 14:12
B. Principles concerning idols
   —They have no real existence 1Co 8:4
   —They cannot save. . . . . Ps 115:4–8; Ps 135:14–18; Isa 46:1–7; Da 5:23
   —The worship of idols is mocked . . . . . 1Ki 18:27; Isa 44:9–20; Jer 10:3–5
C. God's perspective concerning idolatry
   1. In the Old Testament
      —Israel may not worship idols . . . . . Ex 20:3–4; 2Ki 17:35; Ex 34:14,17
      —Israel must destroy idols in Canaan. . . . . Ex 23:24; Ex 34:13; Dt 7:5
   2. In the New Testament
      —Idolaters do not inherit the kingdom . . . . . 1Co 6:9–10; Gal 5:20–21
      —We must flee from idolatry 1Co 10:14; 1Jn 5:21
      —Greed condemned as idolatry . . . . . Col 3:5
      —Money considered a false god . . . . . Mt 6:24

IMAGE OF GOD
A. Humans created in God's image . . . . . Ge 1:26–27; Ge 5:1; 1Co 11:7
B. The image and humanity's fall into sin
   1. The image was lost
      —Sin pervades everyone . . . . . Ro 3:23; Ro 5:12–14
      —We need to be restored in God's image . . . . . Ro 8:29; Col 3:10
   2. The image was partially retained
      —All humans are in touch with God. . . . . Ac 17:27–28
      —God's image in us rules out murder. . . . . Ge 9:6
      —God's image in us rules out cursing. . . . . Jas 3:9
C. Christ and the image of God
   1. He bears God's perfect image
      —He is the image of God *par excellence* . . . . . 2Co 4:4; Col 1:15; Heb 1:3
      —We see God in Christ . . . . . Jn 1:18; Jn 12:45; Jn 14:9
   2. He works in fallen, but redeemed humans
      —To restore us to God's image. . . . . Ro 8:29; 2Co 3:18
      —To renew us in knowledge . . . . . Col 3:10
      —To renew us in righteousness. . . . . Eph 4:24
      —To renew us in holiness. . . . . Eph 4:24
      —Some day he will completely restore us. 1Co 15:49; 1Jn 3:2
D. Our responsibility as image-bearers of God
   —We must rule creation wisely. . . . . Ge 1:28; Ps 8:6–8
   —We may not worship images created by humans . . . . . Ex 20:4; Ac 17:29
   —We may not murder another person. . . . . Ge 9:6
   —We may not curse another person . . . . . Jas 3:9

INCARNATION

See JESUS CHRIST

INCENSE

A. Incense burned
  1. To pagan gods .... 1Ki 11:7–8; 2Ki 17:9–12; Jer 11:12
  2. To the Lord God
    a. Two incense offerings
      —Daily burning on altar of incense .... Ex 30:1–8; 2Ch 2:4
      —Incense on the Day of Atonement .... Lev 16:12–13; 1Ch 6:49
    b. Regulations concerning incense .... Ex 30:9,34–38; Lev 10:1–2; Nu 16:35–38
    c. Continued in the New Testament .... Lk 1:8–9
    d. Incense detestable if insincere .... Isa 1:13; Jer 6:20

B. Incense as symbolic of prayer .... Ps 141:2; Lk 1:10; Rev 5:8; Rev 8:3–4

INHERITANCE

A. Inheritance in the Old Testament
  1. Family inheritance
    —Firstborn son received birthright .... Ge 25:29–34; Dt 21:15–17
    —Firstborn son received double share .... Dt 21:17
    —If no sons, daughters inherit .... Nu 27:1–8
    —If no children, next of kin inherit .... Nu 27:9
    —Land had to stay within the tribe .... Nu 36:7; 1Ki 21:3
    —Each allotted land was an inheritance .... Nu 26:53,56
  2. Israel's inheritance
    —Canaan: the land of God's inheritance .... Dt 4:21; 1Ki 8:36; Ps 78:55
    —Promised to Abram .... Ge 12:7; Ge 15:18–21
    —Land divided as inheritance to Israelites .... Jos 11:23
    —To remain an heir required obedience .... Dt 4:25–27; 2Ki 21:12–15
    —Inheritance lost in the exile .... Ps 79:1–8
    —Inheritance regained in the return .... Ne 11:20; Isa 65:8–9; Eze 36:12
  3. Spiritualizing the inheritance
    —The Lord as the people's inheritance .... Ps 73:26; Ps 142:5
    —The people as the Lord's inheritance .... Dt 4:20; Isa 47:6
    —God's inheritance to include Gentiles .... Ps 2:8; Jer 10:16

B. Inheritance in the New Testament
  1. Jesus is the heir .... Heb 1:2
  2. We become heirs
    —When we become sons of God .... Gal 4:7
    —When we believe in Jesus .... Ro 4:13; Heb 6:12
    —When we receive God's grace .... Gal 3:18
    —We become co-heirs with Christ .... Ro 8:17
  3. What we are to inherit
    —The earth .... Mt 5:5
    —The kingdom of light .... Col 1:12
    —The kingdom of heaven .... Mt 25:34
    —The kingdom of God 1Co 6:9
    —Eternal life .... Mt 19:29; Titus 3:7
    —Everything .... Rev 21:7
  4. The nature of our inheritance
    —It is given by God and his word .... Ac 20:32
    —It is received as a reward .... Col 3:24
    —It is kept in heaven for us 1Pe 1:4
    —It is imperishable 1Co 15:50–53; 1Pe 1:4
    —It is eternal .... Heb 9:15
    —It is guaranteed by the Spirit .... Eph 1:13–14
    —It can be lost through disobedience .... Mt 25:41–46; Heb 4:6,11

INSECTS

A. Insects and other small creatures mentioned in the Bible
  —Ant .... Pr 6:6
  —Bee .... Jdg 14:8
  —Cricket .... Lev 11:22
  —Flea 1Sa 24:14
  —Fly .... Ex 8:21–24
  —Gadfly .... Jer 46:20
  —Gnat .... Ex 8:16–18
  —Grasshopper .... Ps 78:46
  —Hornet .... Jos 24:12
  —Katydid .... Lev 11:22
  —Leech .... Pr 30:15
  —Locust .... Joel 1:4
  —Maggot .... Ex 16:20,24
  —Moth .... Job 27:18
  —Scorpion .... Dt 8:15
  —Spider .... Job 8:14
  —Worm .... Jnh 4:7

B. God's use of insects
  —Some suitable for food, some not .... Lev 11:21–24
  —Sometimes used as a judgment .... Ex 8:16–32; Joel 1:2–12
  —Ants used to teach us lessons .... Pr 6:6–8
  —Moths used as a symbol of destruction .... Mt 6:19–20
  —Honey used as a symbol of God's blessing .... Dt 11:9

INSPIRATION OF SCRIPTURE

—The Bible as God's written word

A. Scripture is inspired by God
  1. Basic statement 2Ti 3:16; 2Pe 1:21
  2. Affirmations in the Old Testament
    —God put words in prophets' mouths .... Dt 18:18; Isa 51:16; Jer 1:9
    —The Spirit spoke through David 2Sa 23:2
    —"This is what the LORD says" .... Isa 43:1; Jer 6:16
    —"The word of the LORD came to ..." .... 1Ki 17:2; Eze 1:3
  3. Affirmations in the New Testament
    —David spoke by the Holy Spirit .... Mk 12:36; Ac 4:25
    —God speaks in the Old Testament .... Heb 4:3,7; Heb 8:8
    —The Spirit speaks in the Old Testament .... Ac 28:25; Heb 3:7
    —In the Old Testament, "It is written" .... Mt 4:4,6,10; 1Co 1:19,31
    —The Scriptures cannot be broken .... Jn 10:35
    —The Scriptures must be fulfilled .... Mt 5:18; Mt 24:35; Lk 24:44

B. Characteristics of the inspired word of God
  —Trustworthy .... 2Sa 7:28; Ps 111:7–8; Jn 17:17
  —Eternally fixed .... Ps 119:89; Isa 40:8
  —Unbreakable .... Mt 5:18; Jn 10:35
  —A sure guide for life .... Ps 119:105; 2Ti 3:16–17
  —Effective in its purposes .... Jer 23:29; Heb 4:12

C. How Bible writers received their material
—In various ways ... Heb 1:1
—By direct speech from God ... Ex 34:27–28; Nu 12:8; Jer 30:1–2
—By angels ... Zec 1:12–17; Ac 7:53
—By visions ... Ge 15:1; Mic 1:1
—By dreams... Da 7:1
See DREAMS AND VISIONS
—By an inner impulse from God... Jer 20:9; 2Pe 1:21
—By eyewitness accounts ... Lk 1:2; 1Jn 1:1–4
—By careful research ... Lk 1:3–4

INTEGRITY

—Honesty in life and adherence to moral principle

A. Examples of those showing integrity
—Job... Job 2:3
—David... 1Ch 28:17; Ps 78:72
—Financial officials of the temple ... 2Ki 12:9–15
—Hananiah ... Ne 7:2
—Jesus ... Mt 22:16

B. Expectation of living in integrity and honesty
—Linked with observing all God's commands... 1Ki 9:4
—Preferred above wealth ... Pr 28:6
—Expected of the upright ... Pr 11:3
—Expected of Christian leaders... Titus 2:7
—Required in business dealings... Lev 19:36; Dt 25:15; Pr 16:11

C. Blessings of living in integrity and honesty
—We please God ... 1Ch 29:17
—We gain a good reputation... Pr 16:13
—We receive God's protection... Pr 2:7
—We gain security for ourselves... Ps 25:21; Pr 10:9
—We gain security for future generations... 1Ki 9:4–5

See also TRUTH

INTERCESSION

—The prayer of one person for another

A. Related theme
INTERCESSION is a theme of Numbers ... Nu 14:19

B. Human intercession
1. Examples of intercession by officials
—By leaders... Ex 32:11–14; Nu 14:13–19; Jos 7:6–9
—By priests ... Lev 5:10; Lev 16:21; Ezr 9:5–15
—By prophets ... 1Sa 7:5–6; 1Ki 13:6; Da 9:3–19; Jas 5:17–18
—By kings ... 2Sa 24:17; 1Ki 8:33–51
—By apostles... Ac 8:15; Eph 3:14–19; Php 1:9–11; Col 1:9–12
—By elders... Jas 5:14

2. Examples of intercession by individuals
a. In the Old Testament
—Abraham for Lot ... Ge 18:23–32
—David for his sick child ... 2Sa 12:16
—David for Solomon... 1Ch 29:19
—Job for his children ... Job 1:5
—A psalmist for the people... Ps 20:1–5; Ps 25:22
—A psalmist for all nations ... Ps 67:3–5

b. In the New Testament
—Stephen for his persecutors... Ac 7:60
—Peter for Dorcas... Ac 9:40
—Paul for a sick man ... Ac 28:8
—Paul for Timothy ... 2Ti 1:3
—Paul for Philemon ... Phm 4
—Christians for their persecutors... Mt 5:44
—The church for Peter ... Ac 12:5,12
—The church for missionaries ... Mt 9:38; Ac 13:3; Heb 13:18
—The church for Paul ... Ro 15:31–32; Eph 6:19–20
—The church for each other... Jas 5:16
—The church for all people ... 1Ti 2:1–2

3. The purposes of human intercession
—For averting judgment ... Ge 18:23–32; Nu 14:13–19
—For escape from danger ... Ac 12:5,12; Ro 15:31
—For God's blessings ... Nu 6:24–26; 1Ki 18:41–45
—For the Holy Spirit's power... Ac 8:15–17; Eph 3:14–17
—For healing... 1Ki 17:20–21; Ac 28:8; Jas 5:14–16
—For forgiveness... Ezr 9:5–15; Ac 7:60
—For the ability to rule well ... 1Ch 29:19; 1Ti 2:2
—For Christian growth ... Php 1:9–11; Col 1:10–11
—For effective pastors ... 2Ti 1:3–7
—For effective mission work... Mt 9:38; Eph 6:19–20
—For the salvation of others ... Ro 10:1–4
—For others to praise God ... Ps 67:3–5

C. Divine intercession
1. The intercession of Christ
—For his followers ... Lk 22:32; Jn 14:16; Jn 17:6–26
—For his enemies ... Lk 23:34
—Continual intercession for us ... Ro 8:34; Heb 7:24; Heb 9:24; 1Jn 2:1

2. The Spirit as intercessor ... Ro 8:26–27

INTEREST

See DEBT

ISAAC

A. History of Isaac
—Promised son of Abraham and Sarah ... Ge 17:19; 1Ch 1:28
—His birth ... Ge 21:1–3
—His circumcision... Ge 21:4
—Party at his weaning... Ge 21:8–13
—Offered up by Abraham ... Ge 22:1–14; Heb 11:17–19
—Took Rebekah as wife ... Ge 24:1–67
—Inherited Abraham's estate ... Ge 25:5
—With Ishmael, buried Abraham ... Ge 25:7–11
—Fathered Esau and Jacob ... Ge 25:19–26; 1Ch 1:34
—Lied to Abimelek about Rebekah ... Ge 26:1–11
—Became very wealthy... Ge 26:12–13
—Made a covenant with Abimelek... Ge 26:14–31
—Tricked into blessing Jacob... Ge 27:1–40
—Sent Jacob away to find a wife ... Ge 28:1–5
—His death ... Ge 35:27–29

B. Significance of Isaac
—Perpetuated Abrahamic covenant... Ge 17:21; Ge 26:2–5

JAIR
—Judge from Gilead — Jdg 10:3–5

JAIRUS
—Synagogue ruler whose daughter Jesus raised — Mk 5:22–43; Lk 8:41–56

JAMES
A. A disciple of Jesus
- —Son of Zebedee and brother of John — Mt 4:21–22; Mk 3:17
- —Originally a fisherman — Mt 4:21
- —Wanted hostile Samaritans killed — Lk 9:52–55
- —Observed the transfiguration — Mt 17:1–13; Mk 9:1–13
- —Sought top place in Jesus' kingdom — Mk 10:35–45
- —Accompanied Jesus to Gethsemane — Mt 26:36–46
- —One of the apostles — Ac 1:13
- —Killed by Herod — Ac 12:2

B. Another disciple of Jesus
- —Son of Alphaeus — Mt 10:3; Mk 3:18
- —One of the apostles — Ac 1:13

C. Son of Joseph and Mary — Mt 13:55
- —A half brother of the Lord Jesus — Gal 1:19
- —Brother of Jude — Jude 1
- —Did not believe in Jesus — Jn 7:3–5
- —Met the risen Lord — 1Co 15:7
- —Stayed with believers before Pentecost — Ac 1:13
- —Became leader of the Jerusalem church — Ac 12:17; Gal 2:9,12
- —Proposed solution at the council in Jerusalem — Ac 15:12–21
- —Visited by Paul — Ac 21:18; Gal 1:19
- —Wrote the letter of James — Jas 1:1

JAPHETH
- —Son of Noah — Ge 5:32; 1Ch 1:4–5
- —With Shem, covered his father with a garment — Ge 9:23
- —Blessed by Noah — Ge 9:27
- —Sons listed — Ge 10:2–5

JEALOUSY
—An emotion expressing possessiveness; related to zeal

A. Jealousy as a positive emotion
1. In humans
   - —Jealous for the things of the Lord — Nu 25:11–13; 1Ki 19:10,14
   - —Jealous for faithfulness in marriage — Pr 6:34; SS 8:6
   - —Jealous for the purity of the church — 2Co 11:2
2. In God
   - —He is jealous for his people — Joel 2:18; Zec 1:14; Zec 8:2
   - —He jealously tolerates no rivals — Ex 20:5; Jos 24:19; 1Co 10:21–22
   - —Sin arouses him to jealousy — Ps 78:58; Na 1:2
   - —His name is Jealous — Ex 34:14

B. Jealousy as a negative emotion
1. Sins that it leads to
   - —To envy — Ge 37:11; Ps 106:16–18
   - —To discontent — Ge 30:1
   - —To quarreling — 1Co 3:3–4
   - —To verbal abuse — Ac 13:45
   - —To intense anger — Pr 27:4
   - —To persecution — Ac 5:17–18
2. The command to get rid of jealousy — Ro 13:13; 2Co 12:20; Gal 5:20

JECONIAH
See JEHOIACHIN

JEHOAHAZ
A. Son of Jehu; king of Israel — 2Ki 13:1–9

B. Son of Josiah; king of Judah — 2Ki 23:31–34; 2Ch 36:1–4

JEHOASH
A. A king of Judah
See JOASH

B. Son of Jehoahaz; king of Israel — 2Ki 13:10–11
- —Defeated Arameans three times — 2Ki 13:14–25
- —Defeated Amaziah, king of Judah — 2Ki 14:1–16; 2Ch 25:17–24

JEHOIACHIN
- —Son of Jehoiakim; king of Judah — 2Ki 24:8–9; 2Ch 36:8–9
- —Brought to Babylon by Nebuchadnezzar — 2Ki 24:10–15; 2Ch 36:10; Jer 24:1
- —Freed from prison in Babylon — 2Ki 25:27–30; Jer 52:31–34

JEHOIADA
- —A priest during Athaliah's reign — 2Ki 11:1–4
- —Son-in-law of King Jehoram — 2Ch 22:11
- —Helped hide Joash for six years in temple — 2Ch 22:11–12
- —Arranged for crowning of Joash as king — 2Ki 11:5–16; 2Ch 23:1–15
- —Decided to rid the land of idols — 2Ki 11:17–20; 2Ch 23:16–17
- —Managed the temple — 2Ch 23:18–21
- —Advised Joash — 2Ki 12:2; 2Ch 24:2
- —With Joash, repaired the temple — 2Ki 12:4–16; 2Ch 24:3–14
- —His death — 2Ch 24:15–16

JEHOIAKIM
- —Son of Josiah; king of Judah — 2Ki 23:34
- —Had conflict with Nebuchadnezzar — 2Ki 24:1–6; 2Ch 36:5–8
- —Killed the prophet Uriah — Jer 26:20–23
- —Burned scroll of Jeremiah's prophecies — Jer 36:16–26

JEHORAM
A. Son of Jehoshaphat; king of Judah — 2Ki 8:16–19; 2Ch 21:4–7
- —Warred against Edom — 2Ki 8:20–22
- —Prophesied against by Elijah — 2Ch 21:12–15
- —Warred against the Philistines — 2Ch 21:16–17
- —Killed by the Lord — 2Ch 21:18–19

B. A king of Israel
See JORAM

JEHOSHAPHAT
- —Son of Asa; king of Judah — 1Ki 22:41–44; 2Ch 17:1
- —Strengthened his kingdom — 2Ch 17:2–19
- —Joined with Ahab of Israel against Aram — 1Ki 22:1–33; 2Ch 18:1–32
- —Appointed judges — 2Ch 19:4–11
- —Joined with Joram of Israel against Moab — 2Ki 3:5–27
- —Miraculously delivered from Moab and Ammon — 2Ch 20:1–26
- —Prayed intensely to the Lord — 2Ch 20:5–12
- —Punished for alliance with Israel — 2Ch 20:35–37

JEHU
A. Prophet who spoke against Baasha — 1Ki 16:1–4,12

B. King of Israel — 2Ki 9:6
- —Elijah told to anoint him king — 1Ki 19:16
- —Anointed by servant of Elisha — 2Ki 9:1–13
- —Appointed to obliterate house of Ahab — 2Ki 9:6–10
- —Killed Joram and Ahaziah — 2Ki 9:14–29; 2Ch 22:7–9
- —Killed Jezebel — 2Ki 9:30–37
- —Killed relatives of Ahab — 2Ki 10:1–17
- —Killed ministers of Baal — 2Ki 10:18–29
- —His death — 2Ki 10:30–36

JEPHTHAH
—Judge from Gilead … Jdg 11:1–3
—Delivered Israel from Ammon … Jdg 11:4–33
—Made a rash vow affecting his daughter … Jdg 11:30–40
—Punished the Ephraimites … Jdg 12:1–6
—His death … Jdg 12:7

JEREMIAH
—Prophet to kingdom of Judah … Jer 1:1–3
—Called by the Lord … Jer 1:4–19
—Composed laments at Josiah's death … 2Ch 35:25
—His life threatened for continuing to prophesy … Jer 11:18–23; Jer 26:1–16
—Put in stocks … Jer 20:1–3
—Opposed by Hananiah … Jer 28:1–17
—Wrote scroll that was burned by king … Jer 36:1–26
—Rewrote the scroll … Jer 36:27–32
—Imprisoned; Zedekiah sought his advice … Jer 37:1–21
—Charged with treason and thrown into cistern … Jer 38:1–13
—Zedekiah sought his advice again … Jer 38:14–27
—Purchased field just before Jerusalem destroyed … Jer 32:1–15
—Taken with some of the people to Egypt … Jer 43:1–7

JERICHO
A. Identity
—Located in a valley … Dt 34:3
—Near the Jordan River … Nu 33:50
—Called "City of Palms" … Dt 34:3
B. History of the city
1. In the Old Testament
—Rahab lived there … Jos 2:1
—Israelites spied it out … Jos 2:1–21
—Israelites camped opposite it … Jos 3:16
—Israelites marched around it … Jos 6:1–15
—Its walls collapsed … Jos 6:20
—All except Rahab destroyed … Jos 6:21–25
—Joshua pronounced curse on rebuilding it … Jos 6:26
—Curse fulfilled when Hiel rebuilt it … 1Ki 16:34
—A company of prophets stationed there … 2Ki 2:5
—It was reinhabited … 2Ch 28:15; Ne 3:2
2. In the New Testament
—Good Samaritan headed toward it … Lk 10:30–35
—Jesus healed Bartimaeus there … Mk 10:46–52; Lk 18:35–43
—Jesus healed two blind men there … Mt 20:29–34
—Zacchaeus lived there … Lk 19:1–10

JEROBOAM
A. First king of the northern kingdom
—An official of king Solomon … 1Ki 11:26–28
—Ahijah prophesied he would be king … 1Ki 11:29–39
—Fled to Egypt … 1Ki 11:40
—Led rebellion against Rehoboam … 1Ki 12:18–19
—Became king of the northern kingdom … 1Ki 12:20
—Instituted idolatry … 1Ki 12:25–33
—Judged for idolatry … 1Ki 13:1–6; 1Ki 14:1–18
—His death … 1Ki 14:19–20
B. Son of Jehoash; king of Israel … 2Ki 14:23–29
—Denounced by Amos … Am 7:10–11

JERUB-BAAL
See GIDEON

JERUSALEM
A. Related theme
JERUSALEM is a theme of 2 Samuel … 2Sa 6:12
B. Important names for this city
—Salem … Ge 14:18; Ps 76:2
—The Jebusite city … Jos 18:28
—Jebus … 1Ch 11:4
—Jerusalem … 2Sa 5:6
—Zion … 2Sa 5:7; Ps 48:12
—The City of David … 2Sa 6:12,16; 1Ki 2:10
—The city of the Great King … Ps 48:2
—The city of God … Ps 46:4; Ps 87:3
—The City of the LORD … Isa 60:14
—The City of Righteousness … Isa 1:26
—The Faithful City … Zec 8:3
—The holy city … Ne 11:1,18; Isa 48:2
—THE LORD IS THERE … Eze 48:35
—Moriah … Ge 22:1–2; 2Ch 3:1
—Ariel … Isa 29:1
C. Significant historical events of Jerusalem
—Abraham's "sacrifice" of Isaac … Ge 22:1–18
—King of Jerusalem conquered by Joshua … Jos 10:1–14
—City given to the tribe of Benjamin … Jos 18:28
—Conquered by David; became his capital … 2Sa 5:6–10
—Temple built there … 2Ch 3:1
—Became capital of the southern kingdom … 1Ki 14:21
—Destroyed by Nebuchadnezzar … 2Ch 36:19
—The center of Jewish life after exile … Ezr 1:5; Mt 2:1,3
—Jesus entered it as king … Mt 21:9–10
—Jesus was crucified there … Lk 9:31; Lk 24:18
—Holy Spirit poured out there … Ac 2:1–5
—Gospel spread out from there … Lk 24:47; Ac 1:8
—First council of the church held there … Ac 15:1–2; Gal 2:1–5
—Jesus predicted its destruction … Lk 19:42–44; Lk 21:20–24
D. Spiritual significance of Jerusalem
—The city chosen by God … 1Ki 11:13
—The place where God put his Name … Dt 12:11; 1Ki 14:21
—The city that Jews prayed toward … 1Ki 8:44; Da 6:10
—The place from which God's word comes … Isa 2:3
—The place from which God rules … Ps 48:1–3,12–14; Ps 99:1–2
—The place from which the Messiah rules … Isa 9:6–7
—The site of history's final battle … Zec 14:1–5; Rev 20:7–10
—A symbol of the church … Gal 4:26; Heb 12:22
—Heaven as the new Jerusalem … Rev 3:12; Rev 21:2,10–27

JESSE
—Grandson of Boaz and Ruth; father of David … Ru 4:17–22
—Visited by Samuel … 1Sa 16:1–13
—Had eight sons … 1Sa 16:8–11; 1Sa 17:12
—Sent David to enter Saul's service … 1Sa 16:18–20
—Sent David to visit his brothers at battle … 1Sa 17:17–19

JESUS CHRIST
A. Related themes
1. SON OF GOD is a theme of Mark … Mk 14:61
2. JESUS = GOD/MAN is a theme of:
—John … Jn 1:1
—Hebrews … Heb 4:15
3. ACTION is a theme of Mark … Mk 1:41
B. His divine nature
1. Preexistence with God
—Asserted in the Old Testament … Isa 9:6–7; Mic 5:2
—Asserted in the New Testament … Jn 1:1; Php 2:6; Col 1:15–17; Rev 1:4,8
2. Divine names ascribed to him
—God … Jn 1:1; Heb 1:8; 1Jn 5:20
—God the One and Only … Jn 1:18

—God over all ..... Ro 9:5
—Immanuel ("God with us") ..... Isa 7:14; Mt 1:23
—Our God and Savior ..... Titus 2:13; 2Pe 1:1
—Lord ..... Ac 2:36; Ro 10:9; Php 2:11; Col 2:6
—Lord of all ..... Ac 10:36
—Lord and God ..... Jn 20:28
—Lord and Savior 2Pe 1:11; 2Pe 2:20; 2Pe 3:18
—Lord of glory 1Co 2:8
—Lord of lords ..... Rev 17:14; Rev 19:16
—Alpha and Omega ..... Rev 1:8; Rev 21:5–6
—The Living One ..... Rev 1:18
—The Holy One of God ..... Mk 1:24
—The Holy and Righteous One ..... Ac 3:14
—The "I am" ..... Jn 8:58

3. His relationship with the Father
—Equal with the Father ..... Jn 5:18; Jn 10:33; Php 2:6
—One with the Father ..... Jn 10:33; Jn 17:22

4. Divine qualities ascribed to him
—Has the fullness of God ..... Col 2:9
—Was involved in creation ..... Jn 1:3; Col 1:16; Heb 1:2
—Has the glory of God ..... Jn 1:14; Heb 1:3
—Preserves creation ..... Col 1:17; Heb 1:3
—Is present everywhere ..... Mt 28:20
—Is all-powerful ..... Mt 28:18; Php 3:21
—Knows everything ..... Jn 2:24–25; Jn 6:61,64
—Is unchanging ..... Heb 1:12; Heb 13:8
—Has the power to forgive sins ..... Mk 2:5–11; Lk 7:48
—Receives worship from people ..... Mt 2:11; Rev 5:11–14
—Receives worship from angels ..... Heb 1:6
—We must believe in him as we do in God ..... Jn 14:1; Ac 16:31–34

C. His human nature

1. Had a human genealogy ..... Mt 1:1–17; Lk 3:23–28

2. His birth and childhood
—Conceived in Mary's womb ..... Mt 1:20; Lk 1:26–37
—His human birth ..... Mt 1:25; Lk 2:1–7
—Circumcised on the eighth day ..... Lk 2:21
—Visited the temple as a boy ..... Lk 2:41–51
—Grew as anyone else does ..... Lk 2:52

3. His suffering, death and burial
—Bloody sweat in the garden ..... Lk 22:44
—Death on the cross ..... Mt 27:50; Jn 19:33; Php 2:7–8
—Blood and water flowed from his wound ..... Jn 19:34–35
—Body taken down from the cross ..... Lk 23:53
—Body prepared and laid in a tomb ..... Jn 19:39–41
—Burial clothes used ..... Jn 20:6–7

4. His resurrection and ascension
—His resurrection on Easter Sunday ..... Mt 28:1–15; Lk 24:1–8
—His appearances for 40 days ..... Lk 24:9–49; Jn 20:1–29; Ac 1:1–5
—His body still a human body ..... Lk 24:40–43; Jn 20:24–29
—His ascension into heaven ..... Lk 24:50–51; Ac 1:9–11

5. He had human characteristics
—Could be touched ..... Mk 5:27–32; Jn 20:27; 1Jn 1:1
—Became hungry ..... Mt 4:2; Mt 21:18
—Became thirsty ..... Jn 19:28
—Became tired ..... Jn 4:6
—Needed sleep ..... Mt 8:20; Mk 4:38
—Showed compassion ..... Mt 9:36; Mk 8:2
—Showed anger and indignation ..... Mk 10:14; Jn 2:13–16
—Wept ..... Lk 19:41; Jn 11:35

6. His human nature specifically mentioned
—He became flesh ..... Jn 1:14
—He shared our humanity ..... Heb 2:14
—He is like us in all things–except sin ..... Heb 2:17; Heb 4:15
—We must acknowledge that Jesus came in the flesh 1Jn 4:2; 2Jn 7

D. His most important names
—Jesus ("the LORD saves") ..... Mt 1:21
—Immanuel ..... Mt 1:23
—The Messiah ..... Mt 16:16; Ac 17:3
—The Son of God ..... Lk 1:35; Jn 20:31
—The Holy One of God ..... Mk 1:24
—The cornerstone ..... Mk 12:10
—The Word of God ..... Jn 1:1; Rev 19:13
—The Lamb of God ..... Jn 1:36
—The bridegroom of the church ..... Jn 3:29
—The Prophet ..... Jn 6:14
—The bread of life ..... Jn 6:48
—The light of the world ..... Jn 8:12
—The good shepherd ..... Jn 10:11; Heb 13:20; 1Pe 5:4
—The resurrection and the life ..... Jn 11:25
—The King of Israel ..... Jn 12:13
—The way, the truth, the life ..... Jn 14:6
—King of the Jews ..... Jn 19:19–21
—The author of life ..... Ac 3:15
—Prince and Savior ..... Ac 5:31
—Son of Man ..... Ac 7:56
—Judge of the living and the dead ..... Ac 10:42
—Lord ..... Ro 10:9; Php 2:11
—The Lord of glory 1Co 2:8
—Our Passover lamb 1Co 5:8
—The second Adam 1Co 15:45–47
—Husband of the church 2Co 11:2
—Head of the church ..... Col 1:18
—The mediator 1Ti 2:5
—The righteous Judge 2Ti 4:8
—Great high priest ..... Heb 4:14
—Alpha and Omega ..... Rev 1:8
—The Lion of the tribe of Judah ..... Rev 5:5
—Lord of lords ..... Rev 17:14
—The Root and Offspring of David ..... Rev 22:16
—The bright Morning Star ..... Rev 22:16

E. His work on earth and in heaven
1. His work on earth
—Did his Father's will ... Mt 26:39; Jn 4:34; Jn 6:38
—Fulfilled the Old Testament ... Mt 5:17
—Came to seek and save the lost ... Lk 19:10
—Came to give us eternal life ... Jn 10:10,28
—Gave his life as a ransom for many ... Mk 10:45
—Made an atoning sacrifice ... Ro 3:25; 1Jn 2:2
—Died for our sins ... 1Co 15:3; Gal 1:4; 1Pe 3:18
—Reconciled us to God ... 2Co 5:18–19; Eph 2:14–17
—Rose again for our justification ... Ro 4:25
—Destroyed the works of Satan ... Heb 2:14; 1Jn 3:8
2. His work as God's Anointed One
—Called God's anointed one ... Ac 4:26
—His anointing as Prophet ... Jn 6:14; Ac 3:21–23; Heb 1:1
—His anointing as Priest ... Heb 6:20; Heb 9:11–14,23–28
—His anointing as King ... Jn 12:13; Rev 19:13–16
3. His work as the exalted Lord in heaven
—Sent out the Spirit ... Jn 15:26; Ac 2:32–33
—Rules the world at God's right hand ... 1Co 15:25; Heb 1:3–4
—Rules the church at God's right hand ... Eph 1:20–22; Col 1:18
—Makes intercession for us ... Ro 8:34; Heb 7:25
—Will overcome all his enemies ... 1Co 15:26–28; Rev 17:14; Rev 19:11–21
—Will come again to take us to himself ... 1Th 5:16–17
—Will come again to judge humanity ... Ac 10:42; 2Co 5:10; 2Ti 4:1

See also TRINITY

JETHRO
—Father-in-law of Moses; priest of Midian ... Ex 3:1
—Also called Reuel ... Nu 10:29
—Owned flocks of sheep ... Ex 2:16–20
—Permitted Moses to return to Egypt from Midian ... Ex 4:18
—Brought wife and sons to Moses in desert ... Ex 18:1–7
—Acknowledged power of the Lord ... Ex 18:9–12
—Advised Moses to appoint judges for Israel ... Ex 18:13–27

JEW
A. Their identity
—Name given to God's people in Babylon ... Est 3:4–6; Est 8:9; Jer 32:12; Jer 44:1
—Jews returned to Jerusalem ... Ezr 5:1,5; Ne 4:1–2
—Jews lived all over the world ... Zec 8:23; Ac 24:5
B. The Jews in the New Testament
1. Their history
—Many opposed Jesus ... Jn 5:15–16; Jn 9:22
—They asked for Jesus' death ... Jn 19:4–12; 1Th 2:14–16
—First Christians were Jews ... Ac 2:5–14
—Jews continued to become believers ... Ac 14:1; Ac 17:4,12
—The Jews persecuted the apostles ... Ac 9:23; Ac 13:50; Ac 17:5–9,13
2. Paul and the Jews
—Paul was proud to be a Jew ... Php 3:4–5
—His message was to the Jew first ... Ac 13:46; Ro 1:16
—Jews were as sinful as Gentiles ... Ro 2:9–10
—Christ is Savior of Jew and Gentile ... Ro 10:12–13; 1Co 1:24
—True Jew is marked by inner regeneration ... Ro 2:28–29
—Paul's sorrow over Jews rejecting Jesus ... Ro 9:1–5
—Salvation of Gentiles would arouse Jews ... Ro 11:13–15

JEZEBEL
—Sidonian wife of Ahab ... 1Ki 16:31
—Promoted Baal worship ... 1Ki 16:32–33
—Killed prophets of the Lord ... 1Ki 18:4,13
—Opposed Elijah ... 1Ki 19:1–2
—Had Naboth killed ... 1Ki 21:1–15
—Death prophesied ... 1Ki 21:23
—Killed by Jehu ... 2Ki 9:30–37
—Became a symbol of wickedness ... Rev 2:20

JOAB
—Nephew of David ... 1Ch 2:16
—Commander of David's army ... 2Sa 8:16
—Defeated Ish-Bosheth and his army ... 2Sa 2:10–32
—Killed Abner ... 2Sa 3:22–27
—Captured the city of Jerusalem ... 1Ch 11:6
—Defeated Ammon ... 2Sa 10:7–19; 1Ch 19:8–19
—Put Uriah in front line of battle ... 2Sa 11:16–24
—Defeated Rabbah ... 1Ch 20:1–3
—Devised plan to reconcile David and Absalom ... 2Sa 14:1–24
—Killed Absalom ... 2Sa 18:9–15
—Rebuked David's grief over Absalom's death ... 2Sa 19:1–8
—Put down Sheba's revolt ... 2Sa 20:1–22
—Tried to convince David not to number his men ... 2Sa 24:1–4
—Numbered David's men ... 2Sa 24:9
—Supported Adonijah over Solomon ... 1Ki 1:7
—Killed under Solomon's orders ... 1Ki 2:28–34

JOASH
—Son of Ahaziah; king of Judah ... 2Ki 11:2
—Sheltered from Athaliah ... 2Ki 11:2–3; 2Ch 22:11–12
—Proclaimed king by Jehoiada at seven years of age ... 2Ki 11:4–12,21; 2Ch 23:1–11
—Repaired the temple ... 2Ki 12:1–16; 2Ch 24:1–14
—Gave temple objects to king of Aram ... 2Ki 12:17–18
—Later led the people into idolatry ... 2Ch 24:17–19
—Assassinated ... 2Ki 12:20; 2Ch 24:23–25

JOB
—A God-fearing man from Uz ... Job 1:1
—Very wealthy ... Job 1:1–3
—His righteousness tested by disaster ... Job 1:6–22
—His righteousness tested by affliction ... Job 2:7–8
—His three friends tried to comfort him ... Job 2:11–13
—Cursed the day of his birth ... Job 3:1–26
—Gave rebuttals to Eliphaz ... Job 6:1–7:21; Job 16:1–17:16; Job 23:1–24:25
—Gave rebuttals to Bildad ... Job 9:1–10:22; Job 19:1–29; Job 26:1–31:40
—Gave rebuttals to Zophar ... Job 12:1–13:28; Job 21:1–34
—Repented ... Job 42:1–6
—Prayed for his friends ... Job 42:10
—Was made prosperous again ... Job 42:10–17
—Considered an example of righteousness ... Eze 14:14,20
—Considered an example of perseverance ... Jas 5:11

JOCHEBED

—Mother of Moses and Aaron ... Ex 6:20; Nu 26:59
—Hid Moses from the Egyptians ... Ex 2:1–2
—Hid Moses among the reeds ... Ex 2:3–4
—Was asked to take care of Moses ... Ex 2:7–10
—Considered an example of faith ... Heb 11:23

JOHN

A. John the Baptist
—His birth announced to his father Zechariah ... Lk 1:11–20
—Mother Elizabeth conceived ... Lk 1:23–25
—His birth ... Lk 1:57–66
—Ministered in the Desert of Judea ... Mt 3:1–12; Mk 1:2–8
—Preached a baptism of repentance ... Lk 3:7–14; Ac 13:24; Ac 19:3–4
—Witnessed concerning Jesus ... Mt 3:11–12; Mk 1:7–8; Jn 1:29–36
—Said Jesus must become greater ... Jn 3:25–30
—Baptized Jesus ... Mt 3:13–17; Lk 3:21–22
—Expressed doubts about Jesus ... Mt 11:2–6; Lk 7:18–23
—Arrested by Herod ... Mt 4:12; Mk 1:14
—Beheaded by Herod ... Mt 14:1–12; Mk 6:14–29
—Fulfilled prophecy about Elijah ... Mt 11:7–19; Mk 9:11–13

B. A disciple of Jesus
1. Events during Jesus' lifetime
—Son of Zebedee and brother of James ... Mt 4:21–22; Mk 3:17
—Originally a fisherman ... Mt 4:21
—Uneducated ... Ac 4:13
—Wanted hostile Samaritans killed ... Lk 9:52–55
—Observed the transfiguration ... Mt 17:1–13; Mk 9:2–13
—Sought top place in Jesus' kingdom ... Mk 10:35–45
—With Peter, prepared for the Passover ... Lk 22:8
—Accompanied Jesus to Gethsemane ... Mt 26:36–45
—Was called the disciple whom Jesus loved ... Jn 13:23; Jn 19:26; Jn 20:2; Jn 21:7,20
—Jesus committed his mother to him ... Jn 19:26–27
—Ran to the tomb on Easter Sunday ... Jn 20:2–8
—Breakfast with Jesus after resurrection ... Jn 21:1–14
2. Events after Jesus' ascension
—One of the apostles ... Ac 1:13
—Healed a lame man with Peter ... Ac 3:1–8
—Arrested with Peter ... Ac 4:1–3
—Questioned before the Sanhedrin ... Ac 4:7–21
—Sent to new Christians in Samaria ... Ac 8:14–17
—Involved in the council at Jerusalem ... Gal 2:9
—Wrote letters as "the elder" ... 2Jn 1; 3Jn 1
—Exiled to Patmos ... Rev 1:9
—The prophet who wrote Revelation ... Rev 1:1–33; Rev 22:8

C. Cousin of Barnabas
See MARK

JONAH

—Prophet in the days of Jeroboam II ... 2Ki 14:25
—Called to preach to city of Nineveh ... Jnh 1:1–2
—Fled to Tarshish ... Jnh 1:3
—His flight caused a storm ... Jnh 1:4–12
—Thrown overboard ... Jnh 1:13–16
—Swallowed by fish ... Jnh 1:17
—Prayed while inside the fish ... Jnh 2:1–9
—Called a second time to preach to Nineveh ... Jnh 3:1–4
—Reproved by the Lord ... Jnh 4:1–11
—His life considered a sign of resurrection ... Mt 12:39–41; Lk 11:29–32

JONATHAN

—Oldest son of King Saul ... 1Sa 14:49
—Attacked Philistines ... 1Sa 13:3–4; 1Sa 14:1–14
—Ate honey in disobedience to Saul ... 1Sa 14:24–45
—Became David's best friend ... 1Sa 18:1
—Made covenant with David ... 1Sa 18:3–4; 1Sa 20:16–17; 1Sa 23:16–18
—Informed David of Saul's plans ... 1Sa 19:1–3
—Interceded for David ... 1Sa 19:4–6
—Warned David to flee ... 1Sa 20:18–42
—Killed in battle ... 1Sa 31:2

JORAM

A. Son of Ahab; king of Israel ... 2Ki 1:17; 2Ki 3:1–3
—Fought with Jehoshaphat against Moab ... 2Ki 3:4–27
—Wounded in battle against Hazael ... 2Ki 8:25–29; 2Ch 22:5–6
—Killed by Jehu ... 2Ki 9:14–26; 2Ch 22:7–8

B. King of Judah
See JEHORAM

JORDAN

—The river flowing from the Sea of Galilee to the Dead Sea

A. In the time of the patriarchs
—Well-watered plain where Lot settled ... Ge 13:10–11
—Jacob crossed it, going to Harran ... Ge 32:10
—Jacob's sons mourned Jacob's death there ... Ge 50:10–11

B. In the time of Moses and Joshua
—Israelites camped along it ... Nu 22:1
—A census taken there ... Nu 26:1–4
—Some Israelites given land east of the Jordan ... Nu 32:1–33; Nu 34:10–15
—Israelites crossed the Jordan ... Jos 3:1–17; Ps 114:3,5
—12 stones from the Jordan formed a memorial ... Jos 4:1–9
—Canaanites afraid because of the crossing ... Jos 5:1

C. In the time of the judges and kings
—Controlling the Jordan important in war ... Jdg 3:28; Jdg 7:24–25; Jdg 12:5–6
—David fled from Absalom across the Jordan ... 2Sa 17:21–22
—Elijah miraculously crossed the Jordan ... 2Ki 2:7–8
—Elisha miraculously crossed the Jordan ... 2Ki 2:13–14
—Naaman cured by washing in the Jordan ... 2Ki 5:9–14
—Axhead floated in the Jordan ... 2Ki 6:1–7

D. In the New Testament
—John the Baptist baptized there ... Mt 3:6; Mk 1:5; Lk 3:3
—Jesus was baptized in the Jordan ... Mt 3:13–17; Mk 1:9–11; Lk 3:21–22
—Jesus ministered across the Jordan ... Mt 19:1; Mk 10:1; Jn 10:40–42

JOSEPH

A. Son of Jacob by Rachel
1. His life in Canaan
—His birth ... Ge 30:24
—Name means "may he add" ... Ge 30:24
—Favored by Jacob, hated by brothers ... Ge 37:3–4
—His dreams ... Ge 37:5–11
—Sold by brothers to Midianites ... Ge 37:12–36
2. His life in Egypt
—Served under Potiphar ... Ge 39:1–19
—Put into prison ... Ge 39:20–23
—Interpreted dreams of Pharaoh's servants ... Ge 40:1–19

JOSHUA

JOSIAH

JOTHAM

JOY

—For victory over enemies ... 1Sa 18:6–7
2Ch 20:27–28
—For the return from exile ... Ps 126:1–3
Jer 31:10–13

2. In the New Testament
—For the birth of Jesus ... Mt 2:10
Lk 2:10,20
—For the resurrection of Jesus ... Mt 28:8
Lk 24:41,52
—For salvation ... Ac 13:48
1Pe 1:8–9
—For our names in the book of life ... Lk 10:20
—For miraculous healing ... Ac 8:7–8
—For privilege of preaching about Christ ... Php 1:18
—For one sinner who repents ... Lk 15:7,10
—For the wedding of the Lamb ... Rev 19:7

JUDAH

A. Son of Jacob by Leah ... Ge 35:23
1Ch 2:1
—Name means "praise" ... Ge 29:35
—Spoke against killing brother Joseph ... Ge 37:25–27
—Married a woman from Adullam ... Ge 38:1–5
—Engaged in illicit sex with Tamar ... Ge 38:12–24
—Fathered Perez and Zerah by Tamar ... Ge 38:27–30
—Promised to be security for Benjamin ... Ge 43:8–10
—Interceded for Benjamin before Joseph ... Ge 44:18–34
—Went to Egypt with family ... Ge 46:8,12
—Father of five sons ... Ge 46:12
—Blessed by Jacob ... Ge 49:8–12

B. Tribe descended from Judah
—Blessed by Moses ... Dt 33:7
—Numbered ... Nu 1:27
Nu 26:22
—Allotted land ... Jos 15
Eze 48:7
—Failed to fully possess the land ... Jos 15:63
Jdg 1:1–20
—David was from this tribe ... 1Ch 28:2–4
Mt 1:2–6
—David ruled this tribe first ... 2Sa 2:1–4
—Became the name for the southern kingdom ... 1Ki 12:21–22
1Ki 14:21–22
—Taken captive to Babylon ... 2Ki 24:1–16
—Returned from exile ... Ezr 1:1–5
—One of the tribes of the 144,000 ... Rev 7:5

JUDAS

A. Disciple of Jesus, called Iscariot ... Mt 10:4
Mk 3:19
—Criticized Mary for wastefulness ... Jn 12:4–5
—Treasurer of disciples; pilfered money ... Jn 12:6
—Satan entered into him ... Lk 22:3
Jn 13:27
—Agreed with Jews to betray Jesus ... Mt 26:14–16
Mk 14:10–11
—Identified as betrayer in upper room ... Mt 26:25
Jn 13:21–30
—Betrayed Jesus with a kiss ... Mt 26:47–49
Mk 14:43–45
Lk 22:47–48
—Returned money to the Jews ... Mt 27:3–5
—Committed suicide ... Mt 27:5
—Died a horrible death ... Ac 1:18–19
—Better not to have been born ... Mk 14:21
—Called a devil ... Jn 6:70–71
—Jesus said he was doomed to destruction ... Jn 17:12
—Replaced by Matthias ... Ac 1:15–26

B. Another disciple of Jesus; son of James ... Lk 6:16
Jn 14:22
—Probably also called Thaddaeus ... Mt 10:3
Mk 3:18
—One of the apostles ... Ac 1:13

C. Brother of Jesus and James ... Mt 13:55
Mk 6:3
—Also called Jude ... Jude 1

D. A Christian prophet ... Ac 15:22–32
—Also called Barsabbas ... Ac 15:22

JUDE

See JUDAS

JUDEA

A. A district governed by the Romans
—Located west of the Jordan River ... Mt 19:1
—Ruled by King Herod at birth of Jesus ... Mt 2:1–3
Lk 1:5
—Ruled by Herod's son Archelaus ... Mt 2:22
—Governed by Pilate ... Lk 3:1
—Ruled by Herod Agrippa ... Ac 12:1–3,19

B. Important towns in Judea
—Jerusalem ... Mt 2:1
Ac 26:20
—Bethlehem ... Mt 2:1
Lk 2:4
—Arimathea ... Lk 23:51

C. John the Baptist preached in Desert of Judea ... Mt 3:1

D. Jesus and Judea
—Born in Bethlehem of Judea ... Mt 2:1–6
—Preached in synagogues of Judea ... Lk 4:44
—Ministered in Judean countryside ... Jn 3:22
—News about Jesus spread throughout Judea ... Lk 7:17
Lk 23:5
—Many from Judea followed Jesus ... Mt 4:25
Mk 3:8
Lk 6:17
—Jesus crucified in Judea ... 1Th 2:14–15

E. The apostles and Judea
—Gospel was to spread throughout Judea ... Ac 1:8
—Residents of Judea present on Pentecost ... Ac 2:5–9
—Christians scattered throughout Judea ... Ac 8:1
—Famine aid for Christians in Judea ... Ac 11:29
Ro 15:25–26
—Christians there suffered persecution ... 1Th 2:14–16

JUDGE, JUDGMENT

A. Related themes
1. JUDGMENT is a theme of:
—Exodus ... Ex 34:7
—2 Kings ... 2Ki 17:22
—Isaiah ... Isa 65:6
—Jeremiah ... Jer 6:19
—Ezekiel ... Eze 24:21
—Hosea ... Hos 6:5
—Amos ... Am 6:8
—Obadiah ... Ob 18
—Micah ... Mic 1:6
—Nahum ... Na 3:7
—Zephaniah ... Zep 1:4
—Revelation ... Rev 16:5
2. DEVASTATION is a theme of Joel ... Joel 1:2

B. Judgment done by humans
1. Official judgment
a. In the political realm
—God raised up judges for his people ... Jdg 2:16
—Ehud as judge ... Jdg 3:12–30
—Deborah as judge ... Jdg 4:4–16
—Gideon as judge ... Jdg 6:11–8:32
—Jephthah as judge ... Jdg 10:6–12:7
—Samson as judge ... Jdg 13:1–16:31
—Eli as judge ... 1Sa 4:18
—Samuel as judge ... 1Sa 7:15–17
b. In the legal realm
—Judges set up by Moses ... Ex 18:13–26
Dt 16:18–20
—Approved transactions regarding Ruth ... Ru 4:1–12
—Judges set up by Jehoshaphat ... 2Ch 19:5–7
—Judges set up by Ezra ... Ezr 8:25–27
—Pilate was a judge ... Mt 27:19
Jn 19:13
—Paul on trial before Gallio ... Ac 18:12–16

—Paul on trial before Felix.................. Ac 24:1–23
—Paul on trial before Festus.................. Ac 25:6–12
—Lawsuits among believers.................. 1Co 6:1–8
—Lawsuits often instituted by the rich........ Jas 2:6–7

c. In the religious realm
—Sanhedrin against Jesus.................. Mt 26:57–66
—Sanhedrin against followers of Jesus........ Jn 9:22,28–34
—Sanhedrin against Christians.................. Ac 4:5–21
Ac 5:21–40
Ac 22:30–23:7
—Judgment done by the church.................. 1Co 5:1–5
1Ti 1:20
Titus 3:10–11

d. Standards for official judgment
—Two or three witnesses needed.................. Dt 19:15
Mt 26:60
—Must be impartial.................. Dt 1:17
Dt 16:19
Pr 24:23
—Must be fair and just.................. Dt 1:16
Dt 16:20
Isa 56:1
—Oath could be required.................. Ex 22:11
Heb 6:16
—Decisions made before witnesses.................. Ru 4:9–11
—Casting lots sometimes used.................. Pr 18:18

2. The judging attitude
—We must not judge others.................. Mt 7:1–5
Ro 14:1–4,13
1Co 4:5
1Co 10:29
Jas 4:11–12
—We must judge ourselves.................. Mt 7:3–5
Gal 6:1,4

3. Human participation in the final judgment........ Mt 19:28
Lk 22:30
1Co 6:2–3

C. Judgment done by God

1. God described as a judge
—God as judge of all the earth.................. Ge 18:26
Ps 94:2
—Christ as judge.................. Jn 5:22
Ac 10:42
2Ti 4:1
—His judgment is always right.................. Dt 32:4
Job 34:10
2Th 1:5

2. Temporal judgments

a. Examples of those whom God judged
—The world in the flood.................. Ge 7:17–23
—Sodom and Gomorrah.................. Ge 19:24–26
—The firstborn in Egypt.................. Ex 12:29–30
—Pharaoh and his army.................. Ex 14:23–28
—The Israelites in the desert.................. Nu 14:26–35
—Korah and his men.................. Nu 16:31–35
—The Israelites during the judges.................. Jdg 2:14–15
—Ahab and his family.................. 2Ki 9:6–10
—The city of Samaria.................. 2Ki 17:16–18
—The Jews in exile.................. 2Ki 24:1–4
—Proud Nebuchadnezzar.................. Da 4:29–33
—King Belshazzar.................. Da 5:25–30
—The city of Jerusalem.................. Lk 19:41–44
—King Herod.................. Ac 12:21–23
—The magician Elymas.................. Ac 13:9–11

b. Types of temporal judgments
—Drought.................. 1Ki 17:1
—Famine.................. La 2:11–12
—Fire from heaven.................. 2Ki 1:10,12
—Flood.................. Ge 7:17–23
—An invasion of locusts.................. Joel 1:2–7
—Earthquake.................. Isa 24:18–20
—Plague.................. 2Sa 24:15–16
—Blight and mildew.................. Am 4:9
—Severe storms.................. Jos 10:10–11
—Destruction of property.................. Eze 33:23–29
—Exile.................. 2Ch 36:20
—Famine of hearing God's word.................. Am 8:11
—Death.................. 2Ki 9:8–10,30–33

c. Purposes of temporal judgments
—To punish sin.................. Ge 6:5–7
Hos 5:1,8–11
—To reveal himself as God.................. Ex 9:14–16
Eze 5:13
—To purify his people.................. Mal 3:2–4
Jn 15:2
—To drive his people to repentance.................. Am 5:6,15
Lk 13:2–5

3. The final judgment

a. Names for the final judgment
—The day of judgment.................. 2Pe 2:9
—The day of the Lord.................. 1Th 5:2
—The day of God's wrath.................. Ro 2:5–6
—The great Day.................. Jude 6
—The Day.................. 1Co 3:13

b. The judges of the final judgment
—God as the judge.................. Ps 96:13
Ecc 3:17
—Administration given to Christ.................. Jn 5:22
Ac 10:42
Ro 2:16

c. Those who are to be judged
—The living and the dead.................. Ac 10:42
—All nations.................. Mt 25:31–32
—All people.................. 2Co 5:10
Heb 9:27
Rev 20:11–14

d. Time of the final judgment: unknown.................. Mt 24:36–42
Lk 12:40
1Th 5:1–3

e. The basis of the final judgment
—Our faith in Jesus.................. Jn 3:16–18
Jn 5:24–26
—Our sincere commitment to Jesus.................. Mt 7:22–23
—Our being heirs of God.................. Mt 25:34
—Our names being in the book of life.................. Rev 20:15
—Our adherence to God's law.................. Ro 2:12–16
Jas 2:12
—What we've done with God's gifts.................. Lk 12:48
—Our actions.................. Ecc 12:14
Mt 25:35–46
1Co 3:12–15
2Co 5:10
—Our words.................. Mt 12:36–37
Jas 3:1–2
—Our inner thoughts.................. 1Co 4:5
—Our perseverance to the end.................. Mt 24:13
—In God mercy triumphs over judgment.................. Jas 2:13

f. The results of the final judgment
—Unbelievers will be punished.................. Ro 2:5
2Th 1:8–9
Rev 20:15
—Believers will receive eternal life.................. Jn 3:16
1Jn 5:11–12
—Believers will receive salvation.................. Ro 13:11
Heb 9:27–28
—Believers will receive redemption.................. Lk 21:28
Eph 4:30
—Believers will receive a crown.................. 2Ti 4:8
Jas 1:12

g. Attitude toward the final judgment
—Be on your guard.................. Mk 13:23,33
—Be alert.................. 1Th 5:6
—Watch.................. Mt 25:13

JUSTICE

—Fairness in the treatment of others

A. Related themes
JUSTICE is a theme of Lamentations.................. La 4:13
SOCIAL JUSTICE is a theme of Amos.................. Am 5:24

B. Human justice
1. Israelites commanded to exercise justice . . . Ex 23:1–3,6; Lev 19:15; Dt 1:17; Dt 16:18–20
2. The prophets and justice
—They called the people to justice . . . Jer 22:3; Hos 12:6; Am 5:24; Mic 6:8
—They spoke against injustice . . . Isa 3:15; Am 2:6–8; Mic 3:1–3
3. Christians called to exercise justice . . . Mt 23:23; Col 4:1; Jas 2:1–4

C. The justice of God
1. God is just . . . 2Th 1:6
—His ways are just . . . Dt 32:4; Da 4:37; Rev 15:3
—He loves justice . . . Ps 11:7; Ps 33:5
—He does no wrong . . . Zep 3:5
—He judges justly . . . 1Pe 2:23; Rev 16:5,7
2. The nature of God's justice
—He is impartial . . . 2Ch 19:7; Job 34:19; Ro 2:11
—He champions victims of injustice . . . Ps 10:17–18; Ps 103:6
3. Expressions of God's justice
—Requires death for sin . . . Ge 2:17; Ro 6:23
—Is expressed in his forgiveness . . . 1Jn 1:9

See also RIGHTEOUSNESS

JUSTIFICATION

—Being declared right with God; acceptance by God

A. The basis of justification
—Christ as our righteousness . . . 1Co 1:30
—Christ's perfect obedience . . . Ro 5:19; 2Co 5:21; Heb 4:15; 1Pe 2:22
—Christ's death on the cross . . . Ro 3:24–25; Ro 5:9
—Christ's resurrection . . . Ro 4:25

B. The manner of justification
—We cannot earn it by obedience . . . Ro 3:28; Ro 9:31–32; Gal 2:16; Gal 3:11; Php 3:9
—We receive it as a gift of God's grace . . . Ro 3:24; Ro 4:16; Ro 5:15–17; Gal 2:21
—We receive it by repenting . . . Lk 18:13–14
—We receive it through faith . . . Ac 13:39; Ro 3:22,26–28; Ro 4:10–12; Gal 2:16; Gal 5:5; Php 3:9
—Faith must be a living faith . . . Jas 2:14–26

C. The results of justification
—We become children of Abraham . . . Ro 4:11–12,16–17; Gal 3:6–7
—We are redeemed . . . Ro 3:24
—We receive forgiveness of sins . . . Ac 13:38–39
—We receive the gift of eternal life . . . Ro 5:17–18; Ro 8:10; Titus 3:7
—We are saved from God's wrath . . . Ro 5:9
—We become free from condemnation . . . Ro 8:1,33–34
—We have peace with God . . . Ro 5:1
—We are blessed by God . . . Ro 4:6–9; Gal 3:9,14
—We are considered to have kept God's law . . . Ro 8:3–4; 2Co 5:21
—We become free from the law . . . Gal 5:1
—We share in Christ's sufferings . . . Php 3:10
—We go on to live a life of holiness . . . Ro 6:19,22; Gal 2:17–19
—We will someday be glorified . . . Ro 8:30

KADESH, KADESH BARNEA

—City bordering on Edom . . . Nu 20:14–16
—God appeared to Hagar near there . . . Ge 16:7–14
—Abraham lived near there . . . Ge 20:1
—Moses sent out spies from there . . . Nu 13:1–2,26; Dt 1:19–25; Jos 14:6–7
—Israelites rebelled against the Lord there . . . Nu 14:1–45; Dt 1:26–45; Dt 9:23–24
—Israelites camped there again for many days . . . Dt 1:46; Jdg 11:16–17
—Miriam died there . . . Nu 20:1
—Moses struck the rock there to get water . . . Nu 20:2–12
—Joshua conquered that area . . . Jos 10:41
—Became southernmost town of Judah . . . Jos 15:3; Eze 47:19

KETURAH

—Wife of Abraham after Sarah . . . Ge 25:1
—Also called Abraham's concubine . . . 1Ch 1:32
—Mother of six sons . . . Ge 25:2

KINDNESS

—A hospitable, friendly attitude toward others

A. Related theme
HOSPITALITY is a theme of 3 John . . . 3Jn 8

B. Human kindness
1. Expected of Christians
—Commanded . . . 2Co 6:6; Gal 5:22; Col 3:12; 2Pe 1:7
—One aspect of the fruit of the Spirit . . . Gal 5:22
2. Expressions of kindness
—Showing forgiveness . . . Ge 50:21
—Sparing someone's life . . . Jos 2:12–13
—Healing the sick . . . Ac 4:9
—Helping the needy . . . 2Sa 9:1–7; Pr 14:21,31; Pr 19:17
—Helping victims of injustice . . . Ge 40:14
—Helping strangers . . . Ac 28:2; Heb 13:1–2; 3Jn 5–8

C. Kindness of God
—In giving us salvation . . . Titus 3:4
—In being faithful to his promises . . . 1Ki 3:6
—In watching over us . . . Job 10:12
—In showing compassion to us . . . Isa 54:8
—In providing for needs . . . Ge 32:10; Ru 2:20; Hos 11:4; Ac 14:17
—In helping us in various life situations . . . Ge 39:21; Ezr 9:9

See also MERCY

KING

A. Related theme
KINGSHIP is a theme of 1 Samuel . . . 1Sa 11:15

B. Human kings
1. Examples of non-Israelite kings
—Four kings warring against five . . . Ge 14:8–11

—Melchizedek, king of Salem .... Ge 14:18
—List of the kings of Edom .... Ge 36:32–39
—Pharaoh, king of Egypt .... Ex 1:8,15–22
—Sihon and Og defeated .... Nu 21:21–35
—Various kings in Canaan defeated .... Jos 8:1–2; Jos 10:1–3,16–42; Jos 12
—David defeated various kings 2Sa 8:1–14
—The king of Assyria took Israel 2Ki 17:3–6
—King Nebuchadnezzar took Judah 2Ki 25:1–7
—King Cyrus allowed return to Judah .... Ezr 1:1–4
—Nehemiah served King Artaxerxes .... Ne 2:1
—Esther became wife of King Xerxes .... Est 2:1,17–18
—Caesar as king .... Jn 19:12,15
—The kings of the earth .... Ps 2:2; Ps 102:15; Ps 138:4

2. The kings of Israel and Judah
   a. The beginning of kingship
      —The people asked for a king 1Sa 8:4–5
      —Samuel warned them 1Sa 8:10–18
      —Saul anointed as first king 1Sa 10:20–24; 1Sa 11:14–15
   b. Kings of the united kingdom
      —Saul (42 years) 1Sa 13:1
      See SAUL
      —David (40 years) 1Ki 2:11
      See DAVID
      —Solomon (40 years) 1Ki 11:42
      See SOLOMON
   c. The kings of Israel (in chronological order)
      —Jeroboam (22 years) 1Ki 12:25–14:20
      —Nadab (2 years) 1Ki 15:25–31
      —Baasha (24 years) 1Ki 15:32–16:7
      —Elah (2 years) 1Ki 16:8–14
      —Zimri (7 days) 1Ki 16:15–20
      —Tibni (with Omri) 1Ki 16:21–22
      —Omri (12 years) 1Ki 16:23–28
      —Ahab (22 years) 1Ki 16:29–22:40; 2Ch 18:1–34
      —Ahaziah (2 years) 1Ki 22:51–53; 2Ki 1:1–18
      —Joram (12 years) 2Ki 3:1–8:15
      —Jehu (28 years) 2Ki 9:6–10:36
      —Jehoahaz (17 years) 2Ki 13:1–9
      —Jehoash (16 years) 2Ki 13:10–25
      —Jeroboam II (41 years) 2Ki 14:23–29
      —Zechariah (6 months) 2Ki 15:8–12
      —Shallum (1 month) 2Ki 15:13–15
      —Menahem (10 years) 2Ki 15:16–22
      —Pekahiah (2 years) 2Ki 15:23–26
      —Pekah (20 years) 2Ki 15:27–31
      —Hoshea (9 years) 2Ki 17:1–6
      See also entries for each of these kings
   d. The kings of Judah (in chronological order)
      —Rehoboam (17 years) 1Ki 12:1–24; 1Ki 14:21–31; 2Ch 10:1–12:16
      —Abijah (3 years) 1Ki 15:1–8; 2Ch 13:1–14:1
      —Asa (41 years) 1Ki 15:9–24; 2Ch 14:2–16:14
      —Jehoshaphat (25 years) 1Ki 22:41–50; 2Ch 17:1–21:3
      —Jehoram (8 years) 2Ki 8:16–24; 2Ch 21:4–20
      —Ahaziah (1 year) 2Ki 8:25–29; 2Ch 22:1–9
      —Athaliah (7 years) 2Ki 11:1–21; 2Ch 22:10–23:21
      —Joash (40 years) 2Ki 12:1–21; 2Ch 24:1–27
      —Amaziah (29 years) 2Ki 14:1–22; 2Ch 25:1–28
      —Azariah/Uzziah (52 years) 2Ki 15:1–7; 2Ch 26:1–23
      —Jotham (16 years) 2Ki 15:32–38; 2Ch 27:1–8
      —Ahaz (16 years) 2Ki 16:1–20; 2Ch 28:1–27
      —Hezekiah (29 years) .... 2Ki 18:1–20:21; 2Ch 29:1–32:33; Isa 36:1–39:8
      —Manasseh (55 years) 2Ki 21:1–18; 2Ch 33:1–20
      —Amon (2 years) 2Ki 21:19–26; 2Ch 33:21–25
      —Josiah (31 years) 2Ki 22:1–23:30; 2Ch 34:1–35:27
      —Jehoahaz (3 months) 2Ki 23:31–33; 2Ch 36:1–4
      —Jehoiakim (11 years) 2Ki 23:24–24:7; 2Ch 36:5–8
      —Jehoiachin (3 months) 2Ki 24:8–17; 2Ch 36:9–10
      —Zedekiah (11 years) 2Ki 24:18–25:26; 2Ch 36:11–21
      See also entries for each of these kings

C. God as a king
1. God called a king
   —The King of heaven .... Da 4:37
   —The King of glory .... Ps 24:10
   —The eternal, immortal, invisible King 1Ti 1:17
   —The great King .... Ps 47:2
   —He rules over all the earth .... 2Ch 20:6; Ps 99:1–2; Isa 52:7
   —He rules from his throne .... 1Ki 22:19; Ps 9:4,7–8; Isa 6:1–3

2. Christ is a king
   a. Prophesied in the Old Testament
      —The coming one will have a scepter .... Ge 49:10; Nu 24:17
      —He will rule on David's throne .... Ps 132:11–12; Isa 9:6–7; Jer 33:17
      —He will rule at God's right hand .... Ps 110:1
      —He will rule eternally .... Da 2:44–45
      —He will rule with authority .... Da 7:13–14
      —He will rule as a shepherd .... Isa 40:10–11; Eze 34:23–24; Mic 5:2–4
      —He will rule wisely .... Isa 52:13; Jer 23:5
      —He will rule with justice .... Isa 32:1; Jer 33:15–16
      —He will rule humbly .... Zec 9:9
      —He will function as a priest .... Ps 110:4; Zec 6:12–13
   b. Fulfilled in the New Testament
      —He is the King of the Jews .... Mt 2:2; Jn 19:19–21
      —He is the King of Israel .... Jn 1:49
      —He claimed kingship .... Mt 27:11; Jn 18:37
      —He entered Jerusalem as king .... Mt 21:1–9
      —He came to rule on David's throne .... Lk 1:32–33; Ac 2:29–33
      —He now rules at God's right hand .... Eph 1:20–23; Heb 1:3–8
      —He is ruling over his enemies 1Co 15:25–27
      —He will sit as a King who judges .... Mt 25:31–34

KINGDOM

—The rule of humans or God over others

A. Related themes
   KINGDOM is theme of:
   —2 Samuel 2Sa 5:12
   —1 Kings 1Ki 4:21

B. Human kingdoms
 1. General kingdoms of Bible history
  —Kingdom of Bashan .... Nu 32:33
  —Kingdom of the Amorites .... Nu 32:33
  —The Aramean kingdom 1Ch 18:6
  —The kingdom of Babylon .... Da 1:20
   Da 4:36
  —The kingdom of Media and Persia .... Est 1:2–4
   Da 5:28,30
  —Four kingdoms in Nebuchadnezzar's dream .... Da 2:36–43
  —All the kingdoms of the earth .... Dt 28:25
   2Ki 19:15,19
   Jer 15:4
   Mt 4:8
 2. The kingdom(s) of Israel and Judah
  —The kingdom taken away from Saul 1Sa 13:13–14
  —The kingdom united under David 2Sa 5:1–5,12
  —The kingdom expanded under David 2Sa 8:11–14
  —The kingdom given to Solomon 1Ki 1:28–40
  —The kingdom to be divided after Solomon 1Ki 11:9–13
  —The kingdom divided under Rehoboam 1Ki 12:16–24
  —The kingdom of Israel destroyed 2Ki 17:7–23
  —The kingdom of Judah destroyed 2Ki 25:1–21
C. Kingdom of God
 1. When and where is that kingdom?
  a. The kingdom is present in Jesus
   —John preached it was near .... Mt 3:2
   —Jesus preached it was near .... Mk 1:15
   —Jesus preached good news of the kingdom .... Mt 4:23
   —Some parables describe its life .... Mt 13:11–52
   —Jesus' miracles proved its presence .... Lk 7:18–22
   —Driving out demons proved it .... Lk 11:20
   —"The kingdom of God is in [our] midst" .... Lk 17:20–21
   —It comes through Jesus' death .... Lk 23:42–43
   —It comes through Jesus' resurrection 1Co 15:20–25
   —The apostles preached the kingdom .... Ac 8:12
    Ac 19:8
    Ac 28:23,28
   —Christ brings us into his kingdom .... Col 1:12–13
  b. The kingdom is yet to come
   —Jesus prayed, "Your kingdom come" .... Mt 6:10
   —Some parables describe it as future .... Mt 25:1–34
   —It comes with the return of Jesus 2Ti 4:1
   —It is something we will inherit .... Mt 25:34
    1Co 15:50
    Jas 2:5
   —It is a heavenly kingdom 2Ti 4:18
    Heb 12:26–28
   —It is a kingdom we will receive 2Pe 1:11
   —The millennial kingdom .... Rev 20:1–6
 2. How can we enter the kingdom?
  —By experiencing new birth .... Jn 3:3
  —By receiving it as a gift from Jesus .... Lk 22:29
  —By responding to God's call 1Th 2:12
  —By repenting of our sins .... Mk 1:15
  —By being redeemed through Christ .... Col 1:12–14
  —By accepting Christ's righteousness .... Mt 5:20
  —By following Jesus .... Mt 19:21–24
   Lk 9:61–62
  —By loving God .... Jas 2:5
  —By persevering in the faith .... Ac 14:22
   2Th 1:4–5
  —By doing the will of God .... Mt 7:21–23
 3. What is life in the kingdom like?
  —Described in the Sermon on the Mount .... Mt 5:1–7:27
  —Described in the Sermon on the Plain .... Lk 6:17–49
  —Described in many parables of Jesus .... Mt 13:11–52
   Mt 18:23–35
   Mt 20:1–16
   Mt 21:28–22:14
  —A life of childlike humility .... Mt 18:1–4
  —A life of joy and peace .... Ro 14:17
  —A life free from sin's control 1Co 6:9–11
   Gal 5:16–21
   Eph 5:3–5
  —A life of producing the fruit of the Spirit .... Gal 5:21–23
 4. How must we relate to the kingdom?
  —We must pray for it .... Mt 6:10
  —We must seek it first .... Mt 6:33
  —We must preach it .... Ac 8:22
   Ac 28:31
  —We must work for it .... Col 4:11
  —We may have to suffer for it .... Ac 14:22
   2Ti 4:16–18

KISS

A. Legitimate uses
 —To say hello .... Ge 29:13
  Ge 33:4
 —To say good-bye .... Ge 31:55
  Ru 1:9
  1Sa 20:41
 —To accompany a blessing .... Ge 27:26–27
 —To express deep affection 1Sa 20:41
 —To express sexual love .... SS 1:2
 —To express grief .... Ge 50:1
  Ac 20:37
 —To demonstrate forgiveness .... Ge 33:4
  Ge 45:15
  Lk 15:20
 —To show honor and respect 1Sa 10:1
  Lk 7:38
 —To express submission .... Ps 2:12
 —To show Christian love .... Ro 16:16
  1Pe 5:14
B. Pagan use: kissing idols 1Ki 19:18
  Job 31:26–27
  Hos 13:2
C. Hypocritical uses
 —Absalom trying to gain popularity 2Sa 15:5
 —Joab when he killed Amasa 2Sa 20:9
 —Judas when he betrayed Jesus .... Mt 26:48–49
  Mk 14:44–45
  Lk 22:47–48
 —A prostitute seducing a man .... Pr 7:13
 —Can be used by any enemy .... Pr 27:6

KNOWLEDGE

A. Related theme
 KNOWLEDGE is a theme of 2 Peter 2Pe 1:3
B. Human knowledge of God and his ways
 1. Source of our knowledge
  —God himself .... Pr 2:6
   Jer 9:23–24
  —Christ .... Col 2:3,8
  —The Holy Spirit 1Co 2:9–16
  —The world around us .... Ps 19:1
   Ro 1:19–20
  —God's word .... Pr 2:1–5
   Jn 17:17
   2Ti 3:15–16
  —God's mighty acts for his people .... Ex 6:6–7
   Eze 37:13–14
 2. Corruption of human knowledge of God
  —First sin: seeking knowledge apart from God .... Ge 3:4–7
  —Humans suppress the truth about God .... Ro 1:18
   2Ti 3:7
   Titus 1:16
  —Idolatry is evidence of this .... Ro 1:21–23
 3. Proper attitude to the knowledge of God
  —We must know God .... Jer 9:24
  —To know God is to do his will .... Jer 22:15–16
  —We must know Christ .... Php 3:8,10
  —We must pray for knowledge .... Ps 119:66
  —We must grow in knowledge .... Eph 4:13
   Heb 5:12–6:1
   2Pe 1:5–8
   2Pe 3:18
  —We must recognize its limitations 1Co 13:8–12
  —We must realize love surpasses it 1Co 8:1
   Eph 3:19

—We must not become proud of it ... 1Co 8:1
—We must not wander away from it ... 1Ti 6:20–21
4. Benefits of the knowledge of God
—Gives stability to life ... Pr 24:3–6
—Enables us to know the love of God ... 1Jn 3:1
—Enables us to fight sin and evil ... 2Pe 1:3–4
—Keeps us from destruction by God ... Hos 4:6
—Essential to eternal life ... Jn 17:3
C. Knowledge possessed by God
—God is all-knowing ... Ps 139:1–6
Isa 46:10
1Jn 3:20
—God's knowledge of us precedes our birth ... Ps 139:15–16
Jer 1:5
—God knows what is inside us ... 1Sa 16:7
Ps 44:21
—God knows our needs ... Ps 103:13–14
Mt 6:31–32
—Little things do not escape his notice ... Mt 10:29–30
—God cannot be taught by humans ... Job 21:22
Isa 40:12–14
—Jesus knew God's will for him ... Lk 18:31–33
Jn 13:1
—Jesus knows us completely ... Jn 2:25
Jn 4:16–18
Jn 6:64
—All knowledge is hidden in Christ ... Col 2:3

KORAH

—A descendant of Levi ... Ex 6:19,21,24
—Led a rebellion against Moses ... Nu 16:1–3
—Killed by the Lord for this rebellion ... Nu 16:4–35
—His descendants became temple gatekeepers ... 1Ch 9:17,19
1Ch 26:1
—His descendants became temple musicians ... 1Ch 6:31–32,37
2Ch 20:19
—Sons of Korah wrote various psalms ... Ps 44–49,85–88
—His rebellion illustrates God's judgment ... Jude 11

LABAN

—Son of Bethuel ... Ge 24:24
—Brother of Rebekah ... Ge 24:29
—Father of Leah and Rachel ... Ge 29:16
—Deceived Jacob into marrying Leah ... Ge 29:22–27
—Became Jacob's boss ... Ge 29:18–20
Ge 30:25–34
—Became jealous of Jacob's prosperity ... Ge 31:1–2
—Disinherited his daughters ... Ge 31:14–16
—Pursued the fleeing Jacob ... Ge 31:22–25
—Made a covenant with Jacob ... Ge 31:43–55

LAMB

A. Uses for lambs
—For food ... Dt 32:14
Am 6:4
—For clothing ... Pr 27:26
—For sealing a treaty ... Ge 21:27–31
—For the payment of tribute ... 2Ki 3:4
—For a sacrifice in place of Isaac ... Ge 22:8,13
—For a regular burnt offering ... Ex 29:38–42
—For offerings at special festivals ... Nu 28:27
Nu 29:2
—For the Passover ... Ex 12:3–6
Nu 28:16–19
B. The lamb as a symbol
—Of extraordinary joy ... Ps 114:1–4
—Of innocence ... 2Sa 12:1–4
—Of weak people ... Isa 40:11
Jn 21:15
—Of peace-loving missionaries ... Lk 10:3
—Of the age of peace ... Isa 11:6
Isa 65:25
C. Jesus as the Lamb of God
—Prophesied by Isaiah ... Isa 53:4–7
—Fulfilled in Jesus ... Ac 8:32–35
—Called the Lamb of God ... Jn 1:29,36
—Called the Passover lamb ... 1Co 5:7
—Shed his blood as a lamb without blemish ... 1Pe 1:19
—Receives praise as the slain Lamb ... Rev 5:6–13
Rev 7:9–11
—Celebrates with his 144,000 ... Rev 14:1–5
—Conquers the antichrist ... Rev 17:14
—Marries the church as a bride ... Rev 19:7,9
Rev 21:9

LANGUAGE

A. Languages mentioned in the Bible
—Hebrew ... Isa 36:11,13
—Babylonian ... Da 1:4
—Aramaic ... Ezr 4:7
—Ashdod ... Ne 13:23–24
—Lycaonian ... Ac 14:11
—Latin ... Jn 19:20
—Greek ... Ac 21:37
—Numerous languages ... Ge 10:5,20,31
Ac 2:5–11
B. Language barriers begun at Babel ... Ge 11:1–9
C. Language barriers removed
—At Pentecost ... Ac 2:4–11
—Through gift of tongues ... Ac 10:46
Ac 19:6
1Co 12:10,28–30
1Co 13:1
—Through the interpretation of tongues ... 1Co 12:10,30
1Co 14:5,13,27
—In heaven ... Rev 5:9
Rev 7:9

LAW

A. Related themes
LAW is a theme of:
—Leviticus ... Lev 7:37
—1 Chronicles ... 1Ch 22:12
—2 Chronicles ... 2Ch 8:13
B. Meanings of the word "law"
—A general principle ... Ro 7:23
—Rules of conduct in the conscience ... Ro 2:14
—Edicts made by human governments ... Da 6:12
—Rules revealed by God through Moses ... Ex 21:1
Ro 5:13
Ac 15:5
—The first five books of the Bible ... Gal 3:10
—The whole Old Testament ... Jn 15:25
1Co 14:21
C. The law of God
1. Characteristics
—True ... Ps 119:142,151
—Perfect ... Ps 19:7
Jas 1:25
—Trustworthy ... Ps 19:7
Ps 119:86,138
—Enduring ... Ps 119:91,160
Mt 5:18
—Right and righteous ... Ps 19:8
Ps 119:75,137
Ro 7:12
—Holy ... Ro 7:12
—Good ... Ro 7:12,16
1Ti 1:8
—Spiritual ... Ro 7:14
—Love is its summary ... Mt 22:37–40
Ro 13:8–10
Gal 5:14
2. Brief history of God's law revealed to Moses
—Spoken directly by God ... Ex 20:1,18–19
Dt 5:4,22
—Spoken by Moses to the Israelites ... Ex 20:22
—Written on tablets of stone ... Ex 24:12
Ex 31:18
—Tablets broken by Moses ... Ex 32:15–19

—Written on tablets a second time ... Ex 34:1–5,27–28
—Repeated in Deuteronomy ... Dt 4:44–46
—Placed in the ark of the covenant ... Dt 31:24–26
—Repeated by Joshua ... Jos 24:25–26
—Honored by David ... 1Ch 16:40
—Disobeyed by God's people ... 2Ki 17:12–20
—Taught by Jehoshaphat ... 2Ch 17:9; 2Ch 19:8
—Honored during Joash's reign ... 2Ch 23:18–19
—Honored during Hezekiah's reign ... 2Ch 31:3–4,21
—Rediscovered during Josiah's reign ... 2Ch 34:14–18
—Studied by Ezra ... Ezr 7:10
—Reintroduced by Ezra to the people ... Ne 8:1–18
—Read in the synagogues ... Ac 15:21
—Fulfilled by Jesus Christ ... Mt 5:17–18

3. Purpose of the law of God
—To show the way to life ... Lev 18:4–5; Dt 30:15–20; Gal 3:12
—To point out our sin ... Ro 3:20; Gal 3:19
—To increase sin ... Ro 5:20
—To show that we are under its curse ... Gal 3:10,13
—To lead us to Christ ... Gal 3:24

4. The Israelites and the law of God
—Must know it ... Ex 33:12–13
—Must fix it in their hearts ... Dt 11:18; Ps 119:11
—Must teach it ... Dt 4:9–10; Dt 11:19–21
—Must observe it ... Dt 4:1,6; Dt 29:9
—Must remember it ... Nu 15:38–40; Mal 4:4
—Must love it ... Ps 119:47,97
—Must delight in it ... Ps 1:2; Ps 112:1

5. Jesus Christ and the law of God
—Came to fulfill it ... Mt 5:17–18
—Born under it ... Gal 4:4
—Circumcised according to it ... Lk 2:21
—Consecrated according to it ... Lk 2:22–24
—Attended festivals prescribed in it ... Mk 14:12–16; Jn 2:23
—Perfectly obeyed it ... 2Co 5:21; Heb 4:15; 1Pe 2:22–23
—Completed what it pointed to ... Heb 8:5–6; Heb 9:11–15,23–28
—Bore its curse on the cross ... Gal 3:13
—Ended its burden ... Ro 7:4–6; Ro 10:1–5; Gal 3:24–25
—Gave us freedom from it ... Jn 8:31–36; Gal 5:1

6. Christians and the law of God
—Cannot keep it perfectly ... Ro 3:19–20,23; Ro 7:4–5
—Cannot be justified through it ... Ro 3:20,28; Gal 3:11
—Have met its requirements ... Ro 8:4
—Are free from its condemnation ... Ro 8:2
—Are free from its curse ... Gal 3:13–14
—Are free from its burden ... Gal 2:1–5; Gal 5:1
—Have it written on their hearts ... Heb 8:10–13
—Are under the law of Christ ... Jn 14:15; 1Co 9:21; Gal 6:2
—Must keep the law of love ... Jn 13:34–35; Ro 13:8–10; Gal 5:13–14; 1Jn 3:11–18
—Must keep the Ten Commandments ... Eph 6:2; Jas 2:8–11

7. The Spirit and the law
—Sets us free from it ... Ro 8:2,13; 2Co 3:17
—Enables us to keep its spirit ... Ro 7:6; 2Co 3:6; Gal 5:16–17,22–25

LAZARUS

A. Poor man in Jesus' parable ... Lk 16:19–31
B. Brother of Mary and Martha ... Jn 11:1
—Became sick and died ... Jn 11:2–15
—Raised from the dead ... Jn 11:38–44
—Present at a meal with Jesus ... Jn 12:2
—His resurrection caused a stir ... Jn 12:17–19

LEADER

A. Related themes
LEADERSHIP is a theme of:
—Ezra ... Ezr 7:10
—Nehemiah ... Ne 13:25
—1 Timothy ... 1Ti 4:6

B. Types of leaders
—Moses as God's chosen leader ... Nu 33:1; Mic 6:4
—Joshua as Moses' successor ... Dt 1:38; Jos 1:6
—Tribal leaders ... Nu 2:3,5,7,10; Nu 7:2
—Judges ... Jdg 4:4; Jdg 12:7–14
—Kings ... 1Sa 8:5–6,20; 1Ch 11:2; 2Ch 1:10
—Priests ... Ne 9:38
—The shepherds of Israel ... Jer 25:34–36
—Church officials ... Ac 15:22; Heb 13:7,17,24

C. Principles of leadership
1. Positive principles
—Depend on the Lord's strength ... Jos 1:6
—Obey the law of God ... Jos 1:7–8
—Use wisdom and knowledge from God ... 2Ch 1:10; Jer 3:15
—Exercise justice ... Mic 3:1–3
—Live an exemplary life ... 1Ti 4:12; 1Pe 5:3
—Serve the people selflessly ... Mt 20:26; Lk 22:26–27; 1Pe 5:2
—Govern diligently ... Ro 12:8

2. Negative principles
—Do not be rebellious against God ... Jer 2:8–9; Hos 9:15–17
—Do not lead the people astray ... Isa 3:12–15; Jer 23:30–32; 1Jn 3:7
—Do not be a poor example ... Ezr 9:1–2
—Do not exert power ... Mt 20:25–26; 1Pe 5:3
—Do not seek your own needs and wants first ... Eze 34:1–6; Am 5:11–13

See also KING; SHEPHERD

D. God as leader of his people
—God the Father as leader ... Ex 15:13; Dt 8:2,15; 2Ch 13:12; Ps 23:1–3; Ps 139:23–24
—Jesus the Son as leader ... Jn 10:2–3,10–14; Jn 13:12–15
—The Holy Spirit as leader ... Ro 8:14; Gal 5:18

LEAH

—Older daughter of Laban ... Ge 29:16
—First wife of Jacob ... Ge 29:22–27

—Not loved by Jacob — Ge 29:31
—Bore six sons and one daughter — Ge 29:31–35
Ge 30:17–21
Ge 35:23
—Buried with Abraham and Sarah — Ge 49:31

LEAVEN
See YEAST

LEBANON
A. Location of Lebanon
—Northeast part of the promised land — Dt 11:24
Jos 13:5–6
—Land of mountains and valleys — Jos 12:7
Jdg 3:3
—Contained Mount Hermon — Jos 11:17
B. Importance of Lebanon to Israelites
—Never totally occupied by Israelites — Jos 13:5–6
—Its wood used in the first temple — 1Ki 5:6–10
—Its wood used in Solomon's palace — 1Ki 7:2–3
—Its wood used in the second temple — Ezr 3:7
C. Lebanon used as a symbol
—Of the majesty of the Creator — Ps 104:16
—Of the power of the Creator — Ps 29:4–6
—Of the fruitfulness of God's people — Ps 72:16
Ps 92:12–14
—Of the new world of the redeemed — Isa 35:1–2
Isa 60:13
—Of one's beauty and majesty — SS 3:6–9
SS 5:15
—Of the importance of the royal house — Jer 22:6–7
—Of the arrogance of humanity — Isa 2:12–18

LEGALISM
See FREEDOM

LEISURE
See REST

LEVI, LEVITE
A. Son of Jacob by Leah — Ge 35:23
1Ch 2:1
—Name means "attached" — Ge 29:34
—With Simeon, avenged rape of sister Dinah — Ge 34:25–31
—Went to Egypt with family — Ge 46:8,11
—Father of three sons — Ge 46:11
—Blessed by Jacob — Ge 49:5–7
B. Tribe descended from Levi
1. History of the tribe
—Moses and Aaron from that tribe — Ex 2:1
—Tribe blessed by Moses — Dt 33:8–11
—Tribe chosen to serve as priests — Nu 3:1–4:49
—Made ceremonially clean — Nu 8:5–26
—Numbered — Nu 3:39
Nu 26:62
—Allotted cities, but not land — Nu 18:20,24
Nu 35:1–5
—Allotted land — Eze 48:8–22
—One of the tribes of the 144,000 — Rev 7:7
2. Duties
—Belonged to the Lord — Nu 3:11–13
—Were Israel's religious leaders — Dt 10:8
—Were in charge of the tabernacle — Nu 1:50–53
Nu 4:1–33
—Assisted Aaron — Nu 3:5–9
Nu 18:1–7
—Prepared the sacrifices — 2Ch 35:10–14
Ezr 6:19–21
—Gathered tithes and offerings — Nu 18:20–24
Dt 18:1–2
Ne 10:37–39
—Served as judges of the people — Dt 17:8–9
1Ch 23:3–4
1Ch 26:29
—Recited the curses of God — Dt 27:14–26
—Supervised the work of the temple — 1Ch 23:3–4,28–32
1Ch 26:20–28
—Instructed the people in the law — Ne 8:7–9
—Some were gatekeepers — 1Ch 23:3–5
1Ch 26:1–19
—Some were musicians — 1Ch 23:3–5
1Ch 25:1–31
Ne 12:24,27–43
C. One of Jesus' disciples
See MATTHEW

LIFE
A. Related themes
1. LIFE is a theme of:
—John — Jn 3:16
—1 John — 1Jn 5:20
2. LIFE'S PURPOSE is a theme of Ecclesiastes — Ecc 12:13
B. God and life
—God is a living God — Dt 5:26
Ps 42:2
1Th 1:9
—God has life in himself — Jn 5:26
—Jesus is the Living One — Rev 1:18
—Jesus is the life — Jn 11:25
Jn 14:6
1Jn 1:1–2
—Jesus has life in himself — Jn 1:4
—The Spirit of life — Ro 8:2
C. Physical life
1. Plant and animal life
—Created by God — Ge 1:11–12,20–25
Ps 104:24–25,30
—Preserved by God — Ps 104:21,24–28
Ps 145:15–16
Ps 147:8–9
2. Human life
—God is its source — Ge 2:7
Job 33:4
Isa 42:5
Ac 17:26,28
—God preserves it — Job 12:10
Ps 138:7
—God removes it as punishment for sin — Ge 3:19
Ro 5:12
—Human life should be reproduced — Ge 1:28
Ge 9:1,7
—Human life is fleeting and fragile — Job 20:4–11
Ps 90:3–10
Ps 103:14–16
—God's kingdom is more important — Mt 6:25–34
Mt 10:38–39
Jn 12:25
—Taking a human life is forbidden — Ge 9:5–6
Ex 20:13
Ro 13:9–10
D. Spiritual life
1. The source of spiritual life
—God, the Father — Eph 2:4–5
Col 2:13
—Jesus Christ, God's Son — Jn 1:4
Jn 10:10
Ac 3:15
—The Holy Spirit — Eze 37:14
Jn 3:5–6
Ro 8:2,11
—The word of God — Jas 1:18
1Pe 1:23
2. Phrases describing spiritual life
—Being born again — Jn 3:3–8
—Being crucified with Christ — Gal 2:20
Ro 6:8–10
—Being raised with Christ — Ro 6:4
Col 3:1–3
—Being a new creation — 2Co 5:17
—Walking/living by the Spirit — Gal 5:16,25
—Having names in the book of life — Lk 10:20
Php 4:3

—Already having eternal life ... Jn 3:36
Jn 6:47
1Jn 5:11–13
—Not being subject to the second death ... Rev 20:6

3. How to obtain spiritual life
—We must choose it ... Dt 30:19–20
—We must hear the word of God ... Ac 16:14
Ro 10:13–14
—We must be called by God ... 2Th 2:13–14
—We must repent of our sins ... Ac 2:38
—We must believe in Jesus ... Jn 3:15–16
Jn 20:31

4. Stages of spiritual life
—The time of birth ... Jn 3:3–8
1Pe 1:23
—Being infants in Christ ... 1Co 3:1
1Pe 2:2
—Growth must take place ... Eph 4:14–16
Col 1:10
1Pe 2:2
—Becoming mature Christians ... 1Co 2:6
Eph 4:13
Heb 5:14–6:1
Jas 1:4
—We must not slip back ... Php 3:13–16
Heb 5:12–14

See also GROWTH

E. Eternal life

1. How can we receive eternal life?
—By being appointed to it by God ... Ac 13:48
—By being called to it ... 1Ti 6:12
—By reading the Scriptures ... Jn 5:39
—By receiving it as a gift from God ... Ro 6:23
—By receiving it as a gift from Jesus ... Jn 5:40
Jn 10:28
—By taking hold of it ... 1Ti 6:12,19
—By realizing Jesus is eternal life ... 1Jn 1:2
1Jn 5:20
—By believing in Jesus ... Jn 3:15–16
—By trusting in Jesus ... Jn 14:1–3
—By drinking of Jesus as water of life ... Jn 4:13–14
—By eating of Jesus as bread of life ... Jn 6:48–51
—By eating of the tree of life ... Ge 3:22
Rev 2:7
—By dying with Christ ... 2Ti 2:11
—By knowing God ... Jn 17:3
—By being righteous ... Mt 25:46
—By obeying the commands of God ... Jn 12:50
—By pleasing the Spirit ... Gal 6:8

2. Eternal life begins now
—We have eternal life ... Jn 3:36
Jn 5:24
—We are already with Christ in heaven ... Eph 2:6
Col 3:3

3. Eternal life is still in the future
—We have been promised it ... 1Ti 4:8
—We have hope of it ... Titus 1:2
Titus 3:7
—We will rise again to receive it ... Jn 5:28–29
—We will receive it as a crown ... 1Pe 5:4
—We will inherit it ... Mt 19:29
—We will reap it ... Gal 6:8
—We will reign in it ... Ro 5:17
—Jesus will bring us to it ... Jude 21
—We will someday be in paradise ... Lk 23:43
Rev 2:7

LIGHT

A. God and light
—God is light ... 1Jn 1:5
—He created light ... Ge 1:3
Isa 45:7
—He is the Father of lights ... Jas 1:17
—He lives in light ... Ps 104:2
1Ti 6:16
—Jesus reflects the Father's light ... Heb 1:3
—Jesus is the light of the world ... Jn 1:9
Jn 8:12
Jn 9:5

B. God's word as a light
—God's word is a light ... Ps 119:105
Pr 6:23
2Pe 1:19
—God's word gives light ... Ps 119:130
—The gospel proclaims light ... Ac 26:18,23
2Co 4:4
—In God's light we see light ... Ps 19:8
Ps 36:9
—God's light guides us ... Ps 43:3
Isa 51:4

C. Believers and the light of God
—We are enlightened ... Heb 6:4
Heb 10:32
—We are children of the light ... 1Th 5:5
Mt 5:14
—We are called into God's light ... 1Pe 2:9
—We confess that the Lord is our light ... Ps 27:1
Mic 7:8–9
—We walk in the light ... Isa 2:5
1Jn 1:5,7
—Our path gets ever brighter ... Pr 4:18
—We put on the armor of light ... Ro 13:12
—We live as children of light ... Eph 5:8–11
—We must be light to the world ... Mt 5:14–16
Php 2:15
—We shall someday enter the kingdom of light ... Col 1:12–13
—We look for a new heaven of only light ... Isa 60:19
Rev 21:23
Rev 22:5
—We have no fellowship with darkness ... Lk 11:35
2Co 6:14
Eph 5:11

See DARKNESS

LION

A. Lion stories in the Bible
—Samson killed a lion ... Jdg 14:5–6
—David killed a lion ... 1Sa 17:34–35
—A lion killed a prophet ... 1Ki 13:24
1Ki 20:36
—Settlers in Samaria killed by lions ... 2Ki 17:25–26
—Daniel in the lions' den ... Da 6:16–24

B. The lion as a symbol

1. Characteristics that stand out
—Majestic ... Pr 30:29–30
—Fierce ... Am 3:8
—Stealthy ... Job 10:16
—Mean when hungry ... Ps 17:12

2. As a symbol of evil
—Of the devil ... 1Pe 5:8
—Of enemies attacking God's people ... Isa 5:29
—Of cruel rulers of the people ... Zep 3:3
—Of one's persecutors ... Ps 17:10–12
Ps 22:13,21
2Ti 4:17

3. As a symbol of God and good
—Of Christ, the triumphant Ruler ... Rev 5:5
—Of the protecting power of God ... Isa 31:4–5
—Of the anger of God against sin ... Hos 5:14
Hos 13:8
—Of the powerful Israelites ... Nu 24:9
—Of the tribe of Judah ... Ge 49:9
Mic 5:8
—Of the bravery of humans ... 2Sa 1:23
—Of the boldness of believers ... Pr 28:1
—Of the victory of believers ... Ps 91:13
—The lion lies peacefully with the lamb ... Isa 11:6–9
Isa 65:25

LORD

A. Human lords
—Used to refer to someone in authority .... Ge 44:16,18
2Sa 24:3
—Used as a title of respect .... Ge 23:15
Jdg 4:18
1Sa 1:15
B. God as the Lord
1. The God of Israel
—First revealed as LORD to Moses .... Ex 3:13–14
Ex 6:2–8
—Called the Lord of lords .... Dt 10:17
Ps 136:3
1Ti 6:15
—Reigns in majesty and strength .... Ps 93:1
Ps 96:6
—Expects trust and reverence as Lord .... Dt 28:58
Ps 96:4
Pt 3:5–6
2. Jesus as Lord
—The Lord Jesus Christ 2Co 13:14
2Th 1:2
—Our Lord Jesus Christ 1Th 5:9
Eph 6:24
—Jesus Christ our Lord 1Co 1:9
1Ti 1:2
—Designated Lord through his resurrection .... Ro 10:9
Php 2:8–11
—He is the Old Testament "LORD" .... Ac 2:21
Ro 10:13
2Ti 2:19
—He is Lord of all .... Ac 10:36
Ro 14:9
—He is the Lord of lords .... Rev 17:14
Rev 19:13–16
—He is the only Lord 1Co 8:6
Eph 4:5
3. Believers confess Jesus as Lord
—Confession of Thomas .... Jn 20:28
—Confession of early Christians .... Ac 2:36
1Co 1:2
1Co 12:3
Col 2:6
—Confession commanded of us .... Ro 10:9
Php 2:11

LORD'S SUPPER

—The sacramental meal of God's people
A. Titles for this feast
—The Lord's Supper 1Co 11:20
—The breaking of bread .... Ac 2:42
Ac 20:7
—Participation in body and blood of Christ 1Co 10:16
B. Celebration of this feast
—Commanded by Christ .... Lk 22:17–20
1Co 11:23–24
—Done frequently in the early church .... Ac 2:42,46–47
Ac 20:7,11
—Sometimes done in the wrong spirit 1Co 11:20–22
C. Purpose of this feast
—To remember the death of Christ .... Lk 22:19
1Co 11:24–25
—To symbolize Christ's body and blood .... Mt 26:26,28
Jn 6:51–56
1Co 10:16
—To participate in Christ's body and blood 1Co 10:16
—To proclaim the death of Christ 1Co 11:26
—To recall eating with the risen Lord .... Lk 24:30,35,41–43
Jn 21:13
Ac 1:4
—To introduce the new covenant .... Mt 26:28
1Co 11:25
—To have fellowship with one another .... Ac 2:42,46–47
1Co 10:16–17
—To anticipate Christ's return .... Mt 26:29
1Co 11:26

LOT

A. Nephew of Abram .... Ge 11:27
—Went with Abram to Canaan .... Ge 12:5
—Chose to live in Sodom .... Ge 13:5–12
—Rescued from four kings .... Ge 14:11–16
—Rescued from Sodom .... Ge 19:1–29
2Pe 2:7
—His wife killed while fleeing Sodom .... Ge 19:26
Lk 17:32
—Fathered Moab and Ammon by his daughters .... Ge 19:30–38
B. Casting the lot
See CASTING LOTS

LOVE

A. Related themes
LOVE is a theme of:
—Song of Songs .... SS 1:2
—Hosea .... Hos 2:23
—John .... Jn 15:9
—1 Corinthians 1Co 13:13
—1 John 1Jn 4:19
B. Human love
1. Love for God
a. Expressions of this love
—Expressed by the psalmist .... Ps 18:1
Ps 116:1
—Commanded in the Old Testament .... Dt 6:5
Ps 31:23
—The first and great commandment .... Mt 22:37–38
b. What we receive through this love
—God's love .... Ex 20:6
Ps 119:132
—God's protecting care .... Ps 91:14
Ps 145:20
Ro 8:28
—Blessing from God .... Dt 11:13–15
—A life of joy .... Ps 5:11
—Life in the promised land .... Ps 69:35–36
—The kingdom as inheritance .... Jas 2:5
—A crown of life .... Jas 1:12
c. What we do through this love
—Love others 1Jn 4:20–21
—Obey God's law .... Dt 13:3–4
1Jn 5:2–3
—Hate evil .... Ps 97:10
2. Love for Christ
a. Expressing this love
—Should be foremost in our lives .... Mt 10:37
—Should be a permanent love .... Eph 6:24
—Linked with faith in Christ 1Pe 1:8
—Linked with love for God .... Jn 8:42
1Jn 5:1
—Linked with obedience to God .... Jn 14:21,23
—Expressed by loving others .... Mt 25:40
b. Results of this love
—Results in God's love for us .... Jn 14:21
Jn 16:27
—Results in a call to care for the church .... Jn 21:15–17
—Lack of such love strongly rebuked 1Co 16:22
3. Love for other Christians
a. The command for such love
—Commanded by God 1Jn 4:21
2Jn 6
—Commanded by Jesus .... Jn 13:34–35
Jn 15:12,17
1Jn 3:11,23
—Commanded by Paul .... Ro 12:9–10
Gal 5:13
Eph 5:2
Php 2:2–4
Col 3:14
1Th 4:9–10
1Ti 1:5
—Commanded in Hebrews .... Heb 10:24
Heb 13:1

—Commanded by Peter 1Pe 1:22
1Pe 2:17
1Pe 4:8
2Pe 1:7
—Encouraged by John 1Jn 3:18
1Jn 4:7,11–12
2Jn 5
—We should pray for it to increase Php 1:9
1Th 3:12
b. Expressions of this love
—An aspect of the fruit of the Spirit Gal 5:22
Col 1:8
—Linked with faith and hope 1Co 13:13
Col 1:4–5
—Expresses itself in self-sacrifice Jn 15:13
1Co 13:4–7
—Involves concern for the weak Ro 14:1,13–16
—Involves caring for the needy 2Co 8:7–8
Phm 9–10
—No fear in such love 1Jn 4:18
c. Results of this love
—Demonstrates we are true disciples Jn 13:35
—Assures us of eternal life 1Jn 3:14–15
—Builds the church 1Co 8:1
Eph 4:15–16
4. Love for all humans
a. Love your neighbor as yourself
—Commanded in the Old Testament Lev 19:18
—Commanded by Jesus Mt 22:39
—Commanded by the apostles Ro 13:9
Gal 5:14
Jas 2:8
b. Love for strangers Lev 19:34
Dt 10:19
Heb 13:2
c. Do good to all humans Gal 6:10
d. Love even for enemies
—Commanded in the Old Testament Ex 23:4–5
Pr 25:21–22
—Commanded by Jesus Mt 5:43–45
—Commanded by Paul Ro 12:20–21
—Commanded by Peter 1Pe 3:9
5. The "song of love" 1Co 13
—Highest of all Christian virtues 1Co 13:13
—Everything valueless without it 1Co 13:1–3
—Central nature is selflessness 1Co 13:4–7
—Endures throughout eternity 1Co 13:8–13
C. Love of Christ
1. Love of Christ for the Father Jn 14:31
2. Love of Christ for his people
—His love for Mary, Martha, Lazarus Jn 11:3,5,36
—His love for his disciples Jn 13:1,34
Jn 15:9,12
—The disciple whom Jesus loved Jn 13:23
Jn 19:26
Jn 20:2
Jn 21:7,20
—His love for the church Eph 5:25
—His love expressed by his sacrifice Jn 15:13
Gal 2:20
Eph 5:2,25
3. Our relationship to this love
—We must realize how extensive it is Eph 3:17–19
—We must remain in it Jn 15:9–10
—Nothing can separate us from it Ro 8:35–37
—It motivates us to love others Jn 13:34
Jn 15:12
Eph 5:2
—It serves as a pattern for husbands Eph 5:25–28
—It motivates us to mission work 2Co 5:14
D. Love of God
1. God is love 1Jn 4:8,16
2. God loves the Son
—Prophesied in the Old Testament Isa 42:1
Mt 12:18
—Expressed at Jesus' baptism Mt 3:17
—Expressed at the transfiguration Mt 17:5
2Pe 1:17
—Acknowledged by Jesus Jn 5:20
Jn 10:17
Jn 15:9–10
Jn 17:23–24,26
3. God loves the sinful world
—His love for the world stated Jn 3:16
—His love in spite of sin Ro 5:8
Titus 3:3–4
—His love expressed in sending his Son Jn 3:16
1Jn 4:9–10
4. God expresses a special love for his people
—In his love for Jesus Jn 16:27
Jn 17:23
—In our election Eph 1:4
1Th 1:4
—In our being called Ro 1:7
Jude 1
—In our receiving his grace 2Th 2:16
—In our adoption 1Jn 3:1
—In our salvation 2Th 2:13
Titus 3:4–5
—In our redemption Dt 7:8
Isa 63:9
—In our forgiveness Isa 38:17
—In our being made alive with Christ Eph 2:4–5
—In our receiving the Holy Spirit Ro 5:5
—In our being disciplined Heb 12:5–7
—In our obedience 1Jn 2:5
—In our love for others 1Jn 3:17
1Jn 4:12
—In our receiving eternal life Jude 21
5. Our relationship to this love
—It is everlasting Jer 31:3
—We must be directed into it 2Th 3:5
—We must keep ourselves in it Jude 21
—Nothing can separate us from it Ro 8:35–39

LUKE

—The beloved doctor Col 4:14
—Co-worker with Paul 2Ti 4:11
Phm 24
—Likely a travel companion with Paul Ac 16:10–17
Ac 20:5–21:18
Ac 27:1–28:16

LUST

See SEXUAL STANDARDS

LYDIA

—Seller of cloth from Thyatira Ac 16:14
—Responded to Paul's preaching Ac 16:14
—Invited Paul to stay at her house in Philippi Ac 16:15
—Church met in her house Ac 16:40

LYING

—Misrepresenting or falsifying the truth
A. Perspectives on lying
—God does not lie Titus 1:2
—Denying that Jesus is the Christ is lying 1Jn 2:22
1Jn 5:10
—Hypocrites are liars Ps 62:4
1Jn 4:20
—The antichrist deceives humanity 2Th 2:9–10
—Satan is the father of lies Jn 8:44
Ac 13:10
—Lying will be exposed Pr 12:19
B. The prohibition against lying
—Ninth commandment prohibits lying Ex 20:16
Dt 5:20
—Other laws prohibit lying Lev 19:11
Eph 4:25
Col 3:9
—Lying is detestable to God Pr 6:16–17
—Pray to be kept from lying Pr 30:8

C. The punishment for lying
- —Severe punishment for false witnesses … Dt 19:16–19; Pr 19:5
- —God silences liars … Ps 63:11
- —God punishes liars … Ps 120:3–4
- —God destroys liars … Ps 5:6; Mic 6:12–13
- —God excludes liars from heaven … Rev 21:8,27

D. Examples of lying in the Bible
1. Sinful lying
   - —Satan in the Garden of Eden … Ge 3:4
   - —Cain to God … Ge 4:9
   - —Abram about Sarai … Ge 12:10–20
   - —Sarah to God … Ge 18:15
   - —Jacob to his father … Ge 27:14–25
   - —Joseph's brothers to Jacob … Ge 37:31–33
   - —Gibeonites to Joshua … Jos 9:1–13
   - —Saul to Samuel … 1Sa 15:1–3,13–22
   - —False witnesses about Naboth … 1Ki 21:11–12
   - —Lying prophets to Ahab … 1Ki 22:6,19–28
   - —Gehazi to Naaman … 2Ki 5:20–24
   - —False prophets to the people … Eze 13:1–9
   - —False witnesses about Jesus … Mt 26:59–62
   - —Peter about Jesus … Mt 26:69–74
   - —Ananias and Sapphira to God … Ac 5:1–10
2. Lying with God's approval
   - —Midwives lie to spare babies … Ex 1:15–21
   - —Rahab lies to save the spies … Jos 2:1–14
   - —Ehud deceives King Eglon … Jdg 3:15–18
   - —Jael deceives Sisera … Jdg 4:17–21; Jdg 5:24–27

See also HYPOCRISY; TRUTH

MACEDONIA

—A Roman province, north of Achaia (Greece)

A. Paul in the main cities of Macedonia
- —Paul's vision of man of Macedonia … Ac 16:9
- —Philippi … Ac 16:12–40
- —Thessalonica … Ac 17:1–9
- —Berea … Ac 17:10–15

See also PAUL

B. Christians in Macedonia
- —Suffered persecution … Ac 17:5–8,13; 1Th 1:6
- —Were dedicated believers … 1Th 1:7–10; 2Co 8:1,5
- —Were poor … 2Co 8:1–2
- —Gave generously to the poor … Ro 15:25–26; 2Co 8:2–4
- —Helped Paul financially … 2Co 11:7–9; Php 4:14–18

MACHPELAH

- —Cave purchased by Abraham from Ephron … Ge 23:7–18
- —Sarah buried there … Ge 23:19
- —Abraham buried there … Ge 25:9–10
- —Isaac, Rebekah and Leah buried there … Ge 49:29–31
- —Jacob buried there … Ge 50:12–13

MAGIC, WITCHCRAFT AND SORCERY

A. Terms used
- —Divination … Dt 18:10
- —Sorcery … Dt 18:10
- —Interpreting omens … Dt 18:10
- —Witchcraft … Dt 18:10
- —Casting spells … Dt 18:11
- —Mediums and spiritists … Dt 18:11
- —Consulting the dead … Dt 18:11
- —Magic … Eze 13:18,20

B. Purpose of magic and sorcery
- —To determine the future … Ge 44:15; 1Sa 28:5–7; Da 2:2,27
- —To control the future … Ge 30:14; Nu 23:23

C. Warnings against magic and sorcery
- —In the law … Ex 22:18; Lev 19:26,31; Lev 20:6,27; Dt 18:10–12,20–21
- —In the prophets … Isa 2:6; Isa 47:10–14; Jer 27:9; Mic 5:12; Mal 3:5
- —In the early church … Ac 8:9–24; Ac 13:6–12; Ac 16:16–18; Ac 19:13–19; Gal 5:20; Rev 21:8

MANASSEH

A. Firstborn of Joseph … Ge 41:51; Ge 46:20
- —Name means "forget" … Ge 41:51
- —Blessed by Jacob, but not as firstborn … Ge 48:12–20

B. Tribe descended from Manasseh
- —Blessed by Moses … Dt 33:17
- —Numbered … Nu 1:35; Nu 26:34
- —Allotted land east of the Jordan … Nu 32:33,39–42; Jos 13:8–33
- —Allotted land west of the Jordan … Jos 17:1–11; Eze 48:4
- —Failed to fully possess the land … Jos 17:12–13; Jdg 1:27
- —One of the tribes of the 144,000 … Rev 7:6

C. Son of Hezekiah; king of Judah … 2Ki 20:21; 2Ch 32:33
- —Judah's most wicked king … 2Ki 21:1–11; 2Ch 33:1–10
- —Captured by Assyrians … 2Ch 33:11
- —Repented of his sins … 2Ch 33:12–13
- —Began to clear land of idols … 2Ch 33:15–16
- —Judah exiled for his sins … 2Ki 21:10–15

MARK

- —Jewish name is John … Ac 12:25
- —A cousin of Barnabas … Col 4:10
- —A close friend of Peter … 1Pe 5:13
- —Believers gathered at his home to pray … Ac 12:12
- —Went to Antioch with Barnabas and Saul … Ac 12:25
- —Did mission work with Barnabas and Saul … Ac 13:4–5
- —Deserted Paul in Pamphylia … Ac 15:37–38
- —Returned with Barnabas to Cyprus … Ac 15:39
- —Later became fellow worker with Paul again … Phm 24; 2Ti 4:11

MARRIAGE

A. God and marriage
1. God honors marriage
   - —Established it in Garden of Eden … Ge 2:18,21–24
   - —Command repeated in New Testament … Mt 19:5; Eph 5:31
   - —Regulated it by Old Testament laws … Lev 20:10–21; Nu 36:1–12; Dt 25:5–10
   - —Jesus attended a wedding … Jn 2:1–2
   - —Marriage must be honored … Mal 2:15; Heb 13:4
2. Monogamy versus polygamy
   - —Ideal is monogamy … Ge 2:24; 1Ti 3:2,12
   - —Polygamy practiced in Old Testament … Ge 29:16–30; 1Sa 1:1–2; 1Sa 25:42–43; 1Ki 11:1–3
   - —Polygamy often caused friction … Ge 30:1; Lev 18:18; 1Sa 1:3–8

3. Adultery
   —In all cases forbidden .... Ex 20:14; Lev 18:20
   —Excludes one from the kingdom of God .... Gal 5:19–21; 1Co 6:9

   See ADULTERY
4. Marriage with unbelievers forbidden
   —In the Old Testament law .... Ex 34:15–16; Dt 7:3–4
   —By Old Testament examples .... Jdg 16:4–21; 1Ki 11:1–8; Ezr 9:1–5,10–15; Ne 13:23–27
   —In the New Testament 1Co 7:12–16; 2Co 6:14–18
5. Permanency of marriage
   —Marriage is union for life .... Mt 19:3–6,9; Ro 7:2–3; 1Co 7:39
   —God hates divorce .... Mal 2:16
   —Divorce allowed for hardness of heart .... Dt 24:1–4; Mt 19:7–8

   See DIVORCE

B. Being single and being married
1. Remaining single is an option
   —It is a gift from God 1Co 7:7–8
   —It is preferable in times of crisis 1Co 7:25–28
   —It frees one to serve God totally 1Co 7:32–35
2. Purposes of marriage
   —To inspire human happiness .... Ge 2:18
   —To express love intimately .... Pr 5:15–20; SS 2:3–7; SS 8:5–7
   —To have children .... Ge 1:27–28; Mal 2:15; 1Ti 5:14
   —To prevent immorality 1Co 7:2,8–9

C. Weddings in the Bible
—The wedding of Isaac .... Ge 24:62–67
—The weddings of Jacob .... Ge 29:21–28
—The wedding of Samson .... Jdg 14:10–19
—The wedding of a king .... Ps 45:1–17
—Jesus at a wedding in Cana .... Jn 2:1–11
—Wedding parables of Jesus .... Mt 22:1–14; Mt 25:1–13; Lk 14:8–11

D. Duties of marriage partners
—Husband to love and respect his wife .... Eph 5:25; Col 3:19; 1Pe 3:7
—Wife to submit to her husband .... Eph 5:22; Col 3:18; 1Pe 3:1
—Equal responsibility 1Co 7:1–5,32–35

E. Marriage as a symbol
—God as the husband of Israel .... Isa 54:5; Jer 3:14; Hos 2:16,19–20
—Christ as the bridegroom of the church .... Mk 2:19–20; Jn 3:29
—Christ as the husband of the church .... 2Co 11:2; Eph 5:22–32
—Church as the bride of Christ .... Eph 5:22–24; Rev 21:2,9–10
—Heaven begins with a wedding .... Mt 22:1–10; Mt 25:1–10; Rev 19:7,9

MARTHA
—Sister of Mary and Lazarus .... Lk 10:38–39; Jn 11:1
—Kept busy in the kitchen .... Lk 10:40
—Rebuked by Jesus .... Lk 10:41–42
—Went to meet Jesus after Lazarus died .... Jn 11:20
—Confessed the resurrection .... Jn 11:20–27
—Objected to opening Lazarus's tomb .... Jn 11:38–40

MARY
A. Mother of Jesus .... Mt 1:16
—Angel announced her pregnancy .... Lk 1:26–38
—Visited cousin Elizabeth .... Lk 1:39–40
—Sang a song .... Lk 1:46–55
—Her virgin birth announced to Joseph .... Mt 1:18–25
—Gave birth to Jesus in Bethlehem .... Lk 2:1–7
—Presented Jesus in the temple .... Lk 2:21–24
—Fled with Joseph and baby to Egypt .... Mt 2:13–15
—Returned and settled in Nazareth .... Mt 2:19–23
—With 12-year-old Jesus in temple .... Lk 2:41–52
—Had other children .... Mk 6:3
—Went to a wedding in Cana .... Jn 2:1–5
—Questioned Jesus' sanity .... Mk 3:21
—Observed Jesus' crucifixion .... Mt 27:55–56
—Entrusted to John at the cross .... Jn 19:25–27
—Among the disciples after ascension .... Ac 1:14

B. Mary Magdalene
—Former demoniac .... Lk 8:2
—Helped support Jesus' ministry .... Lk 8:1–3
—Present at the cross .... Mt 27:56; Mk 15:40
—Present at Jesus' burial .... Mt 27:61; Mk 15:47
—Went to the tomb early on Easter Sunday .... Mt 28:1
—Saw angel after the resurrection .... Mt 28:2–10; Mk 16:1–8
—Saw Jesus after the resurrection .... Mk 16:9; Jn 20:1–2,10–18

C. Sister of Martha and Lazarus
—Jesus visited them .... Lk 10:38–39
—Went to meet Jesus after Lazarus died .... Jn 11:28–32
—Listened to Jesus' teaching .... Lk 10:39
—Washed Jesus' feet .... Jn 11:2; Jn 12:1–8
—Commended by Jesus .... Mt 26:6–13; Lk 10:41–42

MATTHEW
—A disciple of Jesus .... Mt 10:3; Mk 3:18
—A tax collector, called by Jesus to follow him .... Mt 9:9
—Also called Levi .... Mk 2:14–17; Lk 5:27–32
—Held dinner for Jesus .... Mt 9:10–13
—One of the apostles .... Ac 1:13

MATTHIAS
—Apostle, chosen to replace Judas .... Ac 1:26

MEDES AND PERSIANS
A. Two related nations .... Est 1:14; Da 6:8,12,15; Da 8:20

B. Significance for God's people
—Northern kingdom deported there 2Ki 17:6; 2Ki 18:11
—Defeated Babylonians .... Isa 13:17; Jer 51:11,28; Da 5:28,30–31
—Allowed Jews to rebuild temple 2Ch 36:20–23

C. Kings of the Medes and Persians, in chronological order
—Darius the Mede .... Da 5:31
—Cyrus .... Ezr 1:1–2
—Darius the Persian .... Ezr 4:5,24
—Xerxes .... Est 1:1
—Artaxerxes .... Ezr 7:1; Ne 2:1

See entries for each individual king

MEDIATOR
—Someone who helps bring reconciliation between two parties

A. Related theme
MEDIATOR is a theme of Job .... Job 9:33

B. Human mediators at work
—Judah spoke to Joseph for Benjamin .... Ge 44:18–34

—Moses spoke to Pharaoh for the Israelites .... Ex 5:1–5
—Jonathan spoke to Saul for David 1Sa 19:1–7
—Abigail spoke to David for her husband 1Sa 25:14–35
—Esther spoke to the king for her people .... Est 7:1–6

C. Mediators between God and humans
1. The need for a mediator
—Israelites desired one at Mount Sinai .... Ex 20:18–19
—Job cried out for one .... Job 9:33
—Job knew one existed .... Job 16:19–21
—The task of a mediator .... 1Sa 2:25; Job 33:23–25; Gal 3:20

2. Human mediators between God and his people
—Moses .... Ex 32:7–14; Nu 14:11–20; Dt 5:5; Gal 3:19
—Prophets .... 1Ki 21:17–19; Jer 23:21–22; Da 9:3–19; Heb 1:1
—Priests .... Lev 16:20–21; Nu 6:22–27; Ezr 9:3–15
—Kings 1Ki 8:22–53; 1Ch 21:16–17

3. Jesus as mediator between us and God
a. Described as a mediator
—Our mediator with God .... Heb 8:6; Heb 9:15; Heb 12:24
—The only mediator needed 1Ti 2:5
b. His qualifications as a mediator
—He is fully God .... Jn 1:1; Heb 1:3; 1Jn 5:20
—He is fully human .... Jn 1:14; Php 2:6–8; Heb 2:14,17; 1Jn 4:2
c. His tasks as our mediator
—Isaiah prophesied Jesus' task .... Isa 53:3–12
—Reversed consequences of Adam's sin .... Ro 5:15–19; 1Co 15:21–22
—Reconciled us to God through death .... 2Co 5:18–21; Col 1:21–22
—Intercedes with God on our behalf .... Jn 17:6–26; Ro 8:34; Heb 7:25; 1Jn 2:1
—Brings messages from God to us .... Jn 12:49–50; Heb 1:1–2

MEDITATION

—Reflecting on God and his word

A. On what are we to meditate?
—On God .... Ps 63:6
—On God's law .... Ps 1:2; Ps 119:15,48,97
—On God's promises .... Ps 119:148
—On God's unfailing love .... Ps 48:9
—On God's works .... Ps 77:12; Ps 143:5; Ps 145:5

B. What does meditation accomplish?
—Gives us a sense of peace .... Php 4:6–9
—Develops close relationship with God .... Ps 63:6–8
—Prepares us for important decisions .... Lk 6:12–13
—Gives us strength for Christian living .... Ps 1:2–3; 2Co 12:7–9
—Helps give us direction for life .... Ac 22:17–21

C. When did people meditate?
—In the morning .... Ps 5:1–3; Mk 1:35
—All day long .... Ps 119:97
—Day and night .... Jos 1:8; Ps 1:2
—In the evening .... Ge 24:63
—Through the watches of the night .... Ps 119:148

D. Examples of those who meditated
—Isaac .... Ge 24:63
—Psalmists .... Ps 48:9; Ps 119:48,97,148; Ps 143:5
—Jesus .... Mt 14:23; Mk 1:35; Lk 5:16
—Jesus' followers .... Ac 9:11–12; Ac 10:2,9–16; Ac 22:17–18

MEEKNESS

—The quality of a gentle spirit

A. Human meekness
1. Meekness is required of us
—A Christian quality .... Col 3:12; 1Ti 6:11
—An aspect of the fruit of the Spirit .... Gal 5:22–23
—We must act with gentleness .... Eph 4:2; Php 4:5; 1Pe 3:15
2. Meekness is a powerful force
—A gentle tongue is persuasive .... Pr 25:15
—A gentle answer turns away anger .... Pr 15:1
—A gentle spirit wins people to Christ 1Pe 3:1–4
3. The meek are blessed .... Ps 37:11; Mt 5:5

See also HUMILITY

B. God's meekness
—The gentle whisper of God 1Ki 19:12
—The meekness and gentleness of Christ .... Zec 9:9; Mt 21:5; 2Co 10:1

MEGIDDO

—Its king defeated by Joshua .... Jos 12:21
—A city given to Manasseh .... Jos 17:11
—Manasseh did not conquer it .... Jdg 1:27
—Deborah and Barak fought there .... Jdg 5:19
—Solomon built it up 1Ki 9:15
—King Ahaziah died there 2Ki 9:27
—Josiah was killed there 2Ki 23:29–30; 2Ch 35:20–27
—Final battle at Armageddon ("hill of Megiddo") .... Rev 16:14–16

MELCHIZEDEK

—King of Salem; priest of God Most High .... Ge 14:18
—Blessed Abram .... Ge 14:19–20
—Called a high priest forever .... Ps 110:4
—His priesthood prophetic of Jesus .... Heb 5:6; Heb 6:20
—His priesthood explained .... Heb 7:1–28

MENAHEM

—King of Israel 2Ki 15:17–22
—Assassinated Shallum to become king 2Ki 15:14
—Extremely cruel 2Ki 15:16

MEPHIBOSHETH

—Son of Jonathan 2Sa 4:4
—Shown kindness by David 2Sa 9:1–13
—Accused by Ziba of siding with Absalom 2Sa 16:1–4
—Explained his story to David 2Sa 19:24–30
—Spared from death 2Sa 21:7

MERCY

—Underserved kindness and compassion

A. Human mercy
1. The command to be merciful
—Be merciful .... Lk 6:36; Ro 12:8; Jude 22

—Mercy is more important than sacrifice ... Hos 6:6; Mic 6:6–8; Mt 9:13
2. Expressions of human mercy
—Being forgiving ... Mt 18:23–35
—Being kind to the hurting ... Lk 10:30–37
—Being kind to the poor ... Lk 16:19–26
B. The mercy of God
1. A part of his nature
—God is merciful ... Dt 4:31; Ne 9:31; Lk 6:36
—God exercises mercy freely ... Ex 33:19; Ro 9:15–18
—Mercy triumphs over judgment ... Jas 2:13
2. Expressions of his mercy
—Forgiving our sins ... Ps 51:1–2; Da 9:9; 1Ti 1:13–16
—Saving us in Christ ... Eph 2:4–5; Titus 3:4–5; 1Pe 1:3–4
—Being faithful to his covenant ... Dt 4:31; Dt 13:17–18; Ne 9:31
—Receiving us back to himself ... Jer 3:12–13
—Healing us when ill ... Php 2:27
—Sparing his own from destruction ... Ge 19:16; Ps 116:1–6
—Keeping us safe from the enemy ... Ps 6:9–10; Ps 28:6–7
3. Praying for God's mercy
—"Have mercy" ... Ps 4:1; Ps 9:13
—"Hear my cry for mercy" ... Ps 28:2; Ps 86:6
—"Remember your great mercy" ... Ps 25:6
—"Have mercy on me, a sinner" ... Lk 18:13
—"Have mercy on us, Son of David" ... Mt 9:27; Mt 20:30–31

See also GRACE; COMPASSION

MESHACH

—Hebrew deported to Babylon ... Da 1:1–6
—Name changed from Mishael ... Da 1:7
—Refused to be defiled by food ... Da 1:8–20
—Appointed administrator over Babylon ... Da 2:49
—Refused to worship idols ... Da 3:1–12
—Saved from the fiery furnace ... Da 3:13–30

MESSIAH

See JESUS CHRIST

METHUSELAH

—Son of Enoch, father of Lamech ... Ge 5:21–27
—Lived 969 years ... Ge 5:27

MICAIAH

—Prophet of the Lord ... 1Ki 22:7–8
—Warned Ahab of disaster ... 1Ki 22:9–28; 2Ch 18:1–27

MICHAEL

—An archangel ... Jude 9
—Stood against the forces of evil ... Da 10:13,21
—Conducted war in heaven against Satan ... Rev 12:7

MICHAL

—Daughter of Saul ... 1Sa 14:49
—Became wife of David ... 1Sa 18:20–28
—Warned David of Saul's plot ... 1Sa 19:11–17
—Given by Saul to Paltiel ... 1Sa 25:44
—Retrieved by David ... 2Sa 3:13–16
—Criticized David for dancing before the ark ... 2Sa 6:16–23; 1Ch 15:29

MIDIANITES

A. Their identity
—Descendants of Abraham through Keturah ... Ge 25:1–4
—Very wealthy ... Jdg 8:24–26
B. Important Midianites
—Jethro: priest of Midian ... Ex 3:1
—Zipporah: Moses' wife ... Ex 2:21
—Kozbi: killed for marrying an Israelite ... Nu 25:14–15
—Oreb and Zeeb: kings killed by Gideon ... Jdg 7:25–26
—Zeba and Zalmunna: kings killed by Gideon ... Jdg 8:12,21
C. Their interactions with God's people
—Brought Joseph to Egypt ... Ge 37:36
—Allied with Moabites against Israelites ... Nu 22:4,7
—Intermarried with the Israelites ... Nu 25:6
—Were considered enemies of Israel ... Nu 25:16–18
—Defeated by Moses ... Nu 31:1–12
—Oppressed the Israelites ... Jdg 6:1–6
—Defeated by Gideon ... Jdg 7:1–25

MILK

A. Sources of milk
—Cattle ... Dt 32:14
—Cows ... 2Sa 17:29
—Goats ... Pr 27:27
—Mothers ... Isa 28:9
B. Importance of milk
1. As a staple food
—For infants ... Isa 28:9
—For adults ... Ge 18:8; Jdg 4:19
2. As a figure of speech
—A land flowing with milk and honey ... Ex 3:8,17; Nu 16:13–14; Dt 6:3
—A special blessing from God ... Isa 7:21–22
—A symbol of whiteness ... Ge 49:12
—A symbol of a lover's charms ... SS 4:11
—A symbol of spiritual blessings ... Isa 55:1; Joel 3:17–18
—A symbol of instruction for the immature ... 1Co 3:1–2; Heb 5:12–13
—A symbol of pure doctrine ... 1Pe 2:2

MIND

A. What does the mind do?
1. Involved with the human will
—Can be made up ... 2Co 2:1
—Can make decisions ... 1Ch 12:38
—Can make plans ... 2Sa 7:1–3
—Can be willing to do things ... 1Ch 28:9
—Can give guidance ... Ecc 2:3
—Can sing and pray ... 1Co 14:15
—Can vacillate (double-minded) ... Jas 1:8
—Can change ... 2Ki 24:1
—Can plot evil ... Ps 83:5
2. Involved with human intelligence
—Can be opened ... Lk 24:45
—Can think ... Ne 5:7
—Can seek knowledge ... 1Ki 10:1–2
—Can understand ... Da 5:12
—Can remember ... Ge 37:11
—Can be made dull ... 2Co 3:14
—Can be blinded ... 2Co 4:4
—Can be closed ... Isa 44:18
3. Involved with human emotions
—The troubled mind ... Ge 41:8
—A disturbed mind ... Da 7:15
—The anxious mind ... Dt 28:65
—The doubting mind ... Lk 24:38
4. A person can be out of his or her mind ... Mk 3:21; Mk 5:3–5,15; Ac 26:24; 2Co 5:13
B. The believer's mind
1. God and our minds
—God searches them ... Ps 7:9; Ps 26:2
—God tests them ... Jer 11:20
—God puts his law in them ... Jer 31:33; Heb 8:10

—God guards them ... Php 4:7
—Christ searches them ... Rev 2:23
—The Spirit shapes them ... Ro 8:5
—We have the mind of Christ ... 1Co 2:16
2. Our responsibility to our minds
—They must be made new ... Ro 12:2
Eph 4:23
—We must set them on things above ... Col 3:2
—We must prepare them to serve God ... 1Pe 1:13
—We must love God with all the mind ... Mt 22:37
Mk 12:30
Lk 10:27
—We must be of one mind as Christians ... Ac 4:32
1Co 1:10
2Co 13:11

MIRACLE

A. Related theme
MIRACLES is a theme of Exodus ... Ex 15:11
B. Words used to designate miracles
—Miracles ... Ex 7:9
Jn 7:21
—Signs ... Ex 4:8
Mt 12:38–39
—Wonders ... Dt 13:1–2
Jn 4:48
C. Purposes of miracles
1. In the Old Testament
—To demonstrate God is Lord ... Ex 9:14
1Ki 18:36–39
2Ki 5:8–15
—To designate God's messengers ... Ex 4:1–9
1Ki 17:17–24
2Ki 1:10,12
—To confirm one's faith ... Jdg 6:37–40
2Ki 2:13–14
—To deliver God's people ... Ex 14:21–30
Jos 10:12–14
—To care for God's people ... Ex 17:1–6
Nu 11:31–32
—To care for the needy ... 1Ki 17:10–16
2Ki 4:1–7
—To punish sinners ... Ge 19:24–26
Nu 16:28–35
2. In the life of Jesus
—To show compassion ... Mt 14:14
Mt 15:32
—To prove he was God ... Mk 2:8–12
Jn 20:30–31
—To prove he was the Messiah ... Mt 11:2–5
Jn 5:36
—To demonstrate the kingdom of God ... Lk 11:20
Jn 10:37–38
—To secure redemption of believers ... Ro 4:25
1Co 15:17–20
—Not to dazzle crowds ... Mt 16:1–4
Lk 23:8–9
3. In the early church
—To demonstrate Jesus is Savior and Lord ... Ac 4:8–12
Ac 14:3
—To lead people to faith ... Ac 13:12
Ac 9:42
—To advance the gospel ... Ac 12:1–11
Ac 16:16–18
—To show compassion ... Ac 9:32–41
Ac 20:9–10
—To judge sinners ... Ac 5:1–11
Ac 13:8–11
D. People who performed miracles
—Moses and Aaron ... Ex 7:8–21
Ps 105:26–27
—Joshua ... Jos 3:9–17
Jos 10:12–14
—A prophet of Judah ... 1Ki 13:4–6
—Elijah ... 1Ki 17:15–23
1Ki 18:30–38
—Elisha ... 2Ki 2:19–22
2Ki 4:1–7
—Isaiah ... 2Ki 20:7–11
—Daniel's three friends ... Da 3:19–27
—Daniel ... Da 6:16–24
—Jesus ... Mt 4:23–24
Jn 20:30–31
—The 72 sent out by Jesus ... Lk 10:9,17
—The apostles as a group ... Ac 2:43
Ac 5:12
—Peter ... Ac 3:1–7
Ac 5:15–16
—Stephen ... Ac 6:8
—Philip ... Ac 8:6–7,13
—Paul and Barnabas ... Ac 14:3
—Paul ... Ac 14:8–10
Ac 19:11–12
—One of the gifts given to the church ... 1Co 12:10,29
Gal 3:5
E. Miracles of Jesus
—Turned water into wine ... Jn 2:1–11
—Healed official's son at Capernaum ... Jn 4:43–65
—Drove out demon in Capernaum ... Mk 1:23–26
Lk 4:33–35
—Healed Peter's mother-in-law ... Mt 8:14–17
Mk 1:29–31
Lk 4:38–39
—Healed leper ... Mt 8:2–4
Mk 1:40–45
Lk 5:12–13
—Net full of fish ... Lk 5:4–11
—Healed paralyzed man ... Mt 9:1–8
Mk 2:1–12
Lk 5:18–25
—Healed crippled man ... Jn 5:1–9
—Healed shriveled hand ... Mt 12:10–13
Mk 3:1–5
Lk 6:6–10
—Healed centurion's servant ... Mt 8:5–13
Lk 7:1–10
—Raised widow's son ... Lk 7:11–17
—Drove out demon ... Mt 12:22–23
Lk 11:14
—Stilled a storm ... Mt 8:23–27
Mk 4:37–41
Lk 8:22–25
—Drove out demons in Gerasenes ... Mt 8:28–34
Mk 5:1–20
Lk 8:27–35
—Healed woman's bleeding and raised Jairus's daughter ... Mt 9:18–26
Mk 5:21–43
Lk 8:26–41
—Healed two blind men ... Mt 9:27–31
—Healed mute man ... Mt 9:32–33
—Fed the 5,000 ... Mt 14:15–21
Mk 6:35–44
Lk 9:12–17
Jn 6:5–13
—Walked on water ... Mt 14:25–33
Mk 6:48–52
Jn 6:19–21
—Healed Canaanite woman's daughter ... Mt 15:21–28
Mk 7:24–30
—Fed the 4,000 ... Mt 15:32–39
Mk 8:1–9
—Healed deaf man ... Mk 7:31–37
—Healed blind man at Bethsaida ... Mk 8:22–26
—Drove demon out of boy ... Mt 17:14–18
Mk 9:14–29
Lk 9:38–43
—Provided temple tax from fish's mouth ... Mt 17:24–27
—Healed ten lepers ... Lk 17:11–19
—Healed man born blind ... Jn 9:1–7

—Raised Lazarus ... Jn 11:1–44
—Healed crippled woman ... Lk 13:11–17
—Healed man with abnormal swelling of his body ... Lk 14:1–6
—Healed two blind men ... Mt 20:29–34; Mk 10:46–52; Lk 18:35–43
—Cursed a fig tree ... Mt 21:18–22; Mk 11:12–14
—Healed Malchus's ear ... Lk 22:50–51
—Helped disciples catch 153 fish ... Jn 21:1–14

F. Counterfeit miracles
—Performed by Egyptian magicians ... Ex 7:11,22
—Performed by Simon the sorcerer ... Ac 8:9–11
—Performed by false prophets ... Dt 13:1–3; Mt 24:24
—Performed by the antichrist ... 2Th 2:9; Rev 13:13; Rev 19:20

MIRIAM

—Sister of Moses and Aaron ... Nu 26:59
—Watched over baby Moses ... Ex 2:3–4
—Arranged for Moses' mother to care for Moses ... Ex 2:5–10
—Led dancing at "Red Sea" ... Ex 15:20–21
—Criticized Moses; struck with leprosy ... Nu 12:1–15
—Her death ... Nu 20:1

MISSION

—Being sent out on a task

A. Related themes
WORLDWIDE MISSION is a theme of:
—Matthew ... Mt 21:43
—Acts ... Ac 28:14
—Romans ... Ro 15:19

B. Examples of those sent by God on a mission
1. People
—Abram ... Ge 12:1–3
—Joseph ... Ge 45:5–7; Ps 105:17
—Moses ... Ex 3:10,14
—Moses and Aaron ... Ps 105:26
—Isaiah ... Isa 6:8
—Jeremiah ... Jer 26:16
—Ezekiel ... Eze 3:4–5
—Amos ... Am 7:14–15
—Jonah ... Jnh 1:1–2; Jnh 3:1–2
—Haggai ... Hag 1:12
—Zechariah ... Zec 2:9,11
—Prophets in general ... Jer 7:25; Jer 25:4; Zec 7:12
—John the Baptist ... Mal 3:1; Mk 1:2
—The 12 disciples ... Mt 10:1–10
—The 72 messengers ... Lk 10:1–7
—The apostles as missionaries ... Mt 28:19–20; Jn 17:18; Jn 20:21; Ac 13:4; Ac 22:21; Gal 1:1
2. Jesus, God's Son ... Lk 4:18–19; Jn 17:3; Gal 4:4–6
3. The Holy Spirit ... Jn 14:26; Jn 15:26
4. The angels
—To Abraham's servant ... Ge 24:7,40
—To the Israelites ... Ex 23:20–23
—To the inhabitants of Jerusalem ... 1Ch 21:15–18
—To God's people in general ... Ps 91:11
—To Daniel's three friends ... Da 3:28
—To Daniel ... Da 6:22
—To Mary ... Lk 1:26–38
—To Peter ... Ac 12:6–11
—To all of us ... Heb 1:14

C. For what purpose were they sent?
1. Jesus' unique mission
—To atone for sin ... Mk 10:45; Gal 4:4–5; 1Jn 4:9–10
—To preach and to heal ... Mt 9:35–36; Lk 4:18–21
2. Leaders, prophets and missionaries
—To lead God's people ... 1Sa 12:8
—To prepare the way before the Lord ... Mal 3:1; Mt 11:10
—To bring a message of redemption ... Isa 61:1; Jnh 1:1–2; Mk 3:14; Mt 28:19–20; Ro 10:13–15; 1Co 1:17
—To call the people to repent ... Jer 35:15; Jer 42:21
—To heal hurting people ... Isa 61:1–3; Mt 10:8
—To warn God's people ... Jer 26:15; Eze 3:18–21
—To pronounce judgment ... Jer 26:12; Eze 2:3–8; Mt 23:33–36
3. Angels
See ANGEL

MOABITES

A. Their identity
—Descendants of Moab, son of Lot ... Ge 19:37
—Related to Ammonites ... Ge 19:36–38
—Held land east of the Jordan ... Nu 33:48–49; Dt 2:9
—Served the god Chemosh ... 1Ki 11:7

B. Important Moabites
—Balak: hired Balaam to curse Israelites ... Nu 22:2–24:25
—Eglon: killed by Ehud ... Jdg 3:12,15–23
—Ruth: married Boaz ... Ru 1:22
See RUTH

C. Their wars against Israelites
—Allied with Midianites against Israel ... Nu 22:4,7
—Allied with Ammonites against Israel ... Jdg 3:12–13
—Defeated by Israelites under Ehud ... Jdg 3:28–30
—Defeated by King Saul ... 1Sa 14:47
—Defeated by David ... 2Sa 8:11–12; 1Ch 18:11
—Rebelled against Israel ... 2Ki 3:5
—Defeated by Joram and Jehoshaphat ... 2Ki 3:6–25
—Allied with Ammonites against Judah ... 2Ch 20:1
—They and Ammonites destroyed each other ... 2Ch 20:22–24
—Raided the land of Israel ... 2Ki 13:20
—Allied against Jehoiakim ... 2Ki 24:1–2

D. Important data concerning them
1. Before the time of the kings
—Intermarried with Israelites ... Nu 25:1–3
—Israelites did not pass through Moab ... Jdg 11:17–18
—Not allowed to join Israelites ... Dt 23:3; Ne 13:1–3
—Moses died on Mount Pisgah in Moab ... Dt 34:1–5
—Elimelek and Naomi lived there ... Ru 1:1–5
2. During the time of the kings
—David brought his parents there ... 1Sa 22:3–4
—Solomon intermarried with them ... 1Ki 11:1
—Israelites worshiped their gods ... 1Ki 11:7
—Paid tribute to Ahab ... 2Ki 3:4
3. Numerous Jews intermarried with them ... Ezr 9:1; Ne 13:23–27
4. Prophecies concerning their destruction ... Isa 15:1–16:14; Jer 48:1–47; Eze 25:8–11; Am 2:1–3; Zep 2:8–11

MONEY
See THE RICH AND THE POOR; STEWARDSHIP

MONTH
—12 time segments per year, based on the moon
—Aviv or Nisan, the first month ... Ex 13:4; Ne 2:1
—Ziv or Iyyar, the second month ... 1Ki 6:1
—Sivan, the third month ... Est 8:9
—Tammuz, the fourth month ... Jer 52:6
—Av, the fifth month ... Nu 33:38
—Elul, the sixth month ... Ne 6:15
—Ethanim or Tishri, the seventh month ... 1Ki 8:2
—Bul or Heshvan, the eighth month ... 1Ki 6:38
—Kislev, the ninth month ... Zec 7:1
—Tebeth, the tenth month ... Est 2:16
—Shebat, the eleventh month ... Zec 1:7
—Adar, the twelfth month ... Ezr 6:15

MOON
A. Data concerning the moon
—Created by God ... Ge 1:16; Ps 8:3
—Controlled by God ... Jos 10:12–13; Jer 31:35
—Governs the night ... Ge 1:16; Ps 136:9
—Marks off the seasons ... Ge 1:14; Ps 104:19
—New Moon feasts ... Nu 10:10; 1Sa 20:5,18,24; Am 8:5
—Involved in the blessing of productive land ... Dt 33:13–14
—Must praise God ... Ps 148:3
—Believed to cause mental illness ... Ps 121:6
—Worshiped by pagans ... 2Ki 23:5; Jer 8:2
—No moon needed in heaven ... Isa 60:19–20; Rev 21:23

B. The moon used in a symbolic way
—Of stability and endurance ... Ps 72:5,7
—Of judgment at the end of time ... Isa 13:10–11; Mt 24:29; Rev 6:12

MORDECAI
—Benjamite exile who brought up Esther ... Est 2:5–10
—Exposed plot to kill Xerxes ... Est 2:19–23
—Refused to honor Haman ... Est 3:1–6; Est 5:9–14
—Pole made to impale him ... Est 5:14
—Begged Esther to foil Haman's plot ... Est 4:1–17
—Haman forced to honor him ... Est 6:1–11
—Exalted by the king ... Est 8:1–2,15; Est 9:3–4
—With Esther, established Purim ... Est 9:18–32

MORIAH
—Region where Abraham went to "sacrifice" Isaac ... Ge 22:1–18
—Mountain on which temple was built ... 2Ch 3:1–2

MOSES
A. Family data
—Son of Amram and Jochebed ... Ex 6:20; 1Ch 6:3
—Tribe of Levi ... Ex 2:1
—Brother of Aaron ... Ex 4:14
—Name means "draw out" ... Ex 2:10
—Married Zipporah ... Ex 2:21
—Father of Gershom and Eliezer ... Ex 2:22; Ex 18:2–4

B. His history

1. His youth
—Hid by his parents for three months ... Ex 2:2; Heb 11:23
—Hid in a basket in the Nile ... Ex 2:3–4
—Discovered by Pharaoh's daughter ... Ex 2:5–9
—Brought up by Pharaoh's daughter ... Ex 2:10
—Killed an Egyptian ... Ex 2:11–12
—Fled to Midian ... Ex 2:13–15
—Became a shepherd ... Ex 3:1

2. Delivered Israel from Egypt
—Called by God ... Ex 3:2–4:17
—Explained his call to Israelites ... Ex 4:29–31
—Made demands to Pharaoh ... Ex 5:1–5
—The ten plagues ... Ex 7:14–11:9
—Arranged the Passover ... Ex 12:1–28
—Led Israelites out of Egypt ... Ex 12:29–42
—Led them to the border of the "Red Sea" ... Ex 13:17–14:4
—Led them across the "Red Sea" ... Ex 14:21–31
—Sang song of deliverance ... Ex 15:1–21

3. Led Israel to Mount Sinai
—Water at Marah and Elim ... Ex 15:22–27
—Asked God for food; received manna ... Ex 16:1–16
—Brought water from the rock ... Ex 17:1–7
—Raised hands to defeat Amalekites ... Ex 17:8–16
—Delegated judges ... Ex 18:13–27; Dt 1:9–18
—Received law at Mount Sinai ... Ex 19:3–25; Ex 24:12–18; Jn 1:17
—Announced law to Israel ... Ex 24:3–7
—Broke tablets because of golden calf ... Ex 32:19–20; Dt 9:7–17
—Received law a second time ... Ex 34:1–4,27–28
—Saw glory of the Lord ... Ex 33:18–23
—His face reflected glory of God ... Ex 34:29–35
—Supervised building of tabernacle ... Ex 35:4–36:7
—Set apart Aaron and priests ... Lev 8:1–9:24
—Numbered tribes ... Nu 1:1–4:49

4. From Sinai to the border of Canaan
—Left Sinai ... Nu 10:11–13
—Handled the people's complaints ... Nu 11:1–34
—Opposed by Aaron and Miriam ... Nu 12:1–15
—Sent spies into Canaan ... Nu 13:1–33
—Prayed for the rebellious people ... Nu 14:1–25
—Announced 40 years of wandering ... Nu 14:26–40
—Opposed by Korah ... Nu 16:1–50
—Struck rock; forbidden to enter Canaan ... Nu 20:1–13; Dt 1:37
—Put bronze snake on a pole for healing ... Nu 21:4–9; Jn 3:14
—Defeated kings in battle ... Nu 21:1–3,21–31
—Numbered tribes a second time ... Nu 26:1–65
—Designated Joshua as successor ... Nu 27:12–23; Dt 34:9
—Gave final address (Deuteronomy) ... Dt 1:5
—Sang a song ... Dt 31:30–32:43
—Blessed the 12 tribes ... Dt 33:1–29
—Saw the promised land ... Dt 34:1–4
—His death ... Dt 34:5–8

C. Titles ascribed to him
—The man of God ... Ezr 3:2
—God's chosen one ... Ps 106:23
—The servant of God ... 2Ch 24:6,9; Ps 105:26
—The lawgiver ... Jn 1:17
—Prophet of the Lord ... Dt 18:15,18
—Intimate friend of God ... Ex 33:11
—Leader of God's people ... Mic 6:4
—Shepherd of God's people ... Ps 77:20

D. Moses in the New Testament
—Appeared to Jesus at the transfiguration ... Mt 17:2–4
—Respected for giving the Law ... Mt 19:7–8; Jn 7:19,23
—Exemplified true faith ... Heb 11:24–28
—Foreshadowed Jesus as the Prophet ... Ac 3:21–23
—His writings prophetic of Jesus ... Jn 1:45
—His lifting up of snake pictured Jesus' death ... Jn 3:14–15
—Crossing the "Red Sea" pictured baptism ... 1Co 10:1–2
—His veil symbolized the old covenant ... 2Co 3:7–16

—His faithfulness foreshadowed that of Jesus .... Heb 3:1–6
—God, not Moses, gave manna..................... Jn 6:30–33

MOTHER

A. Motherhood in the Bible
1. The experience of motherhood
—It is a gift from God .... Ps 113:9
Ps 127:3
—It can be painful............................ Ge 3:16
Isa 13:8
Jn 16:21
—Infertility can cause frustration................ Ge 25:21
Ge 30:1
1Sa 1:1–20
2. Women saved through childbearing 1Ti 2:15
3. Significant experiences of motherhood
—Eve, the mother of the living.................. Ge 3:20
Ge 4:1–2,25
—Sarah..................................... Ge 21:1–5
—Rebekah.................................. Ge 25:21–26
—Leah .... Ge 29:31–35
Ge 30:17–21
—Rachel.................................... Ge 30:1–3,22–23
Ge 35:16–18
—Jochabed (Moses' mother).................... Ex 2:1–10
—Samson's mother............................ Jdg 13:1–24
—Ruth .... Ru 4:13–15
—Hannah.................................... 1Sa 1:1–20
—Bathsheba 2Sa 12:24–25
—Isaiah's wife .... Isa 8:3–4
—Hosea's wife............................... Hos 1:2–9
—Elizabeth.................................. Lk 1:24–25,39–44
—The virgin Mary .... Lk 1:26–38
Lk 2:4–7

B. The mother in the family
1. Duties of a mother to her children
—Loves them................................ 1Ki 3:26
Isa 49:15
—Comforts and cares for them .... Ru 4:16
Isa 66:13
1Th 2:13
—Protects them .... Ex 2:1–3
Heb 11:23
—With their husbands, educates them .... Pr 1:8
Pr 31:1,26
—Educates them alone, if necessary 2Ti 1:5
2Ti 3:15
—Watches over their affairs..................... Ge 27:5–17
1Ki 1:11–31
Pr 31:15,27
2. Responsibility of children to mothers
—Obey them .... Dt 21:18
Eph 6:1–2
—Respect them.............................. Ex 20:12
Lev 19:3
Pr 23:22
—Listen to them .... Pr 1:8
Pr 6:20

C. Mother used as a symbol
—God compared to a mother .... Isa 49:15
Isa 66:13
—The church as mother.......................... Isa 66:10–11
Gal 4:26

MOUNTAIN

A. Mountains mentioned in the Bible
—Mount Ararat.................................. Ge 8:4
—Mount Baalah .... Jos 15:11
—Mount Carmel 1Ki 18:19
—Mount Ebal................................... Dt 11:29
—Mount Ephron .... Jos 15:9
—Mount Gaash .... Jos 24:30
—Mount Gerizim................................. Dt 11:29
—Mount Gilboa.................................. 1Sa 31:1
—Mount Gilead.................................. Jdg 7:3
—Mount Halak .... Jos 11:17
—Mount Heres................................... Jdg 1:35
—Mount Hermon .... Dt 3:8
—Mount Hor .... Nu 20:22
—Mount Horeb .... Ex 33:6
—Mount Jearim.................................. Jos 15:10
—Mount Mizar................................... Ps 42:6
—Mount Moriah 2Ch 3:1
—Mount Nebo................................... Dt 32:49
—Mount of Olives .... Zec 14:4
See OLIVES, MOUNT OF
—Mount Paran .... Dt 33:2
—Mount Perazim .... Isa 28:21
—Mount Pisgah.................................. Jos 12:3
—Mount Samaria .... Am 4:1
—Mount Seir .... Dt 1:2
—Mount Shepher .... Nu 33:23
—Mount Sinai .... Ex 19:11
See SINAI
—Mount Sirion .... Dt 4:48
—Mount Tabor................................... Jdg 4:6
—Mount Zalmon.................................. Jdg 9:48
—Mount Zemaraim................................ 2Ch 13:4
—Mount Zion.................................... Ps 48:2
See ZION

B. Mountains used in illustrations
—Of God's creative power .... Am 4:13
—Of God's continuing power....................... Ps 65:5–7
—Of God's redemptive power .... Isa 40:4–5
—Of the power of God's judgment .... Rev 6:14–16
—Of God's righteousness .... Ps 36:6
—Of God's glory in the new age .... Isa 2:2–3
—Of prosperity for God's people .... Ps 72:3
Am 9:13
—Of the strength of human faith .... Mt 17:20–21
—Of the joy of the redeemed .... Isa 44:23

MOUTH

A. The human mouth
1. Appropriate functions of our mouths
—To praise God .... Ps 63:5
—To sing to the Lord........................... Ps 40:3
—To testify concerning God..................... Ps 89:1
—To confess Jesus as Lord .... Ro 10:9–10
—To reveal God's word .... Dt 18:18
—To reveal what is in the heart.................. Mt 12:34–35
—To speak words.............................. Ps 19:14
—To laugh with joy............................ Ps 126:2
—To eat...................................... 1Sa 14:26–27
—To drink.................................... Jdg 7:6
—To kiss .... SS 1:2
2. Responsibilities to our mouths
a. Negative
—Keep them from sin....................... Ecc 5:6
—Keep them from perversity .... Pr 4:24
—Keep them from flattery................... Pr 26:28
—Keep them from arrogance 1Sa 2:3
—Keep them from lies .... Rev 14:5
—Keep them from unwholesome talk......... Eph 4:29
—Keep them from cursing................... Jas 3:9–10
b. Positive
—Speak what is true and just .... Pr 8:7–8
—Speak what is wise .... Ps 37:30
—Guide them properly...................... Pr 16:23
—Guard them properly .... Pr 21:23

B. The mouth of God
—God created with his mouth...................... Ps 33:6
—God gave his law with his mouth .... Ps 119:13,72
—God gives promises with his mouth .... Isa 40:3–5
—God teaches with his mouth .... Dt 8:3
—God pronounces judgment with his mouth......... Isa 1:20
—God rejects by spitting us out of his mouth .... Rev 3:16
—God destroys with his mouth..................... Ps 18:8
—Jesus destroys with a sword in his mouth .... Rev 2:16
Rev 19:15

MURDER

—The deliberate killing of another human
A. The command against murder
—The sixth commandment .... Ex 20:13
Dt 5:17
Jas 2:10–11
—Anger as the root of murder .... Mt 5:21–22
—Hatred as the root of murder 1Jn 3:15
—Murder comes out of a sinful heart .... Mt 15:18–19
B. What happens after a murder
—One can be cursed by God .... Ge 4:11
—One can be excluded from heaven 1Jn 3:15
Rev 22:15
—One is subject to capital punishment .... Ge 9:5–6
Ex 21:12–14,23
—More than one witness required .... Nu 35:30
Dt 19:15
—Cities of refuge in Israel .... Nu 35:16–32
Dt 19:1–14
—Murderers can be forgiven .... Lk 23:34
Ac 7:60
C. Examples of murder in the Bible
—Cain killed Abel .... Ge 4:8
—Moses killed an Egyptian .... Ex 2:11–12
—Abimelek killed his brothers .... Jdg 9:5
—David killed Uriah 2Sa 12:9
—Absalom killed Ammon 2Sa 13:28–33
—Jezebel killed Naboth 1Ki 21:8–14
—Hazael killed Ben-Hadad 2Ki 8:14–15
—Athaliah killed the royal family 2Ki 11:1
—Herod killed the babies in Bethlehem .... Mt 2:16
—Herod killed John the Baptist .... Mt 14:6–11
—The Jews killed Jesus .... Ac 2:23
1Th 2:15
—The Jews killed Stephen .... Ac 7:57–60
—Herod killed James .... Ac 12:2

MUSIC AND SONG

A. Related theme
MUSIC is a theme of 2 Chronicles 2Ch 5:13
B. Musical instruments
1. Begun by Jubal .... Ge 4:21
2. Types of instruments in the Bible
—Bells .... Ex 28:33–35
—Castanets 2Sa 6:5
—Cymbals 2Sa 6:5
—Harp 1Ch 25:3
—Flute .... Da 3:5,7,10,15
—Horn .... Da 3:5,7,10,15
—Lyre 2Sa 6:5
—Pipe .... Da 3:5,10,15
—Sistrum 2Sa 6:5
—Timbrel 2Sa 6:5
—Trumpet .... Nu 10:2
—Zither .... Da 3:5,10,15
3. Used in Israelite worship
—Organized by David 1Ch 25:1,6
2Ch 7:6
—Mentioned in the psalms .... Ps 47:6
Ps 98:5–6
Ps 150:4–5
4. Used when Jesus returns 1Co 15:52
1Th 4:16
C. Songs
1. In the Old Testament
a. Occasions for singing
—In sacred processions 2Sa 6:5
1Ch 13:8
—At dedications 2Ch 5:12–13
Ezr 3:10–11
Ne 12:27–28,40
—On festival days 2Ch 30:21
—At coronations 2Ch 23:13
—To celebrate victories .... Ex 15:1–18
Nu 21:17
Jdg 5:1–31
b. The psalmist's intention to sing .... Ps 27:6
Ps 57:7,9
Ps 61:8
Ps 101:1
Ps 104:33
c. Instructions to sing .... Ps 30:4
Ps 68:32
Ps 98:1
Ps 149:1
d. All creation should sing .... Ps 148:1–12
Isa 44:23
Isa 49:13
2. In the New Testament
—Songs at the birth of Jesus .... Lk 1:46–55,68–79
Lk 2:14,29–32
—Songs in the worshiping church 1Co 14:15
Eph 5:19
Col 3:16
Jas 5:13
—Songs in heaven .... Rev 5:9–10,12–13
Rev 7:10,12,15–17
Rev 15:3–4
Rev 19:1–8

MYSTERY

—Secret truths revealed by God
A. Related theme
MYSTERY is a theme of Mark .... Mk 4:11
B. God and his secret truths
1. God discloses mysteries
—To his prophets .... Ge 40:8
Isa 48:6
Am 3:7
Da 2:18,27–28
Ro 16:25–26
—To his apostles .... Mk 4:10–12
Eph 3:4–5
Rev 1:19–20
2. Only believers understand mysteries .... Mk 4:10–12
1Co 2:6–11
2Co 4:3–6
C. Mysteries revealed to God's people
1. In the Old Testament
—Future events revealed to Joseph .... Ge 40:8–22
Ge 41:1–32
—Future events revealed to Daniel .... Da 2:24–47
Da 4:19–27
2. In the New Testament
—Basic teachings about Christ 1Ti 3:16
—Basic message of the gospel .... Col 4:3
—All wisdom hidden in Christ .... Col 2:2–3
—The nature of the kingdom of God .... Lk 8:10–15
—The union of Christ and his church .... Eph 5:29–32
—Christ's care for his church .... Rev 1:19–20
—What happens at Christ's return 1Co 15:51–52
—Inclusion of Gentiles in the kingdom .... Eph 3:6
Col 1:26
—Plan to reach the Jews with gospel .... Ro 11:25–26
D. Love is preferable to knowing mysteries 1Co 13:2

NAAMAN

—Aramean general afflicted with leprosy 2Ki 5:1
—Cured by Elisha 2Ki 5:2–14
—Took Israelite soil back to Damascus 2Ki 5:15–19
—His cure mentioned by Jesus .... Lk 4:27

NABAL

—Wealthy Carmelite; husband of Abigail 1Sa 25:1–3
—Name means "fool" 1Sa 25:25
—Refused to help David 1Sa 25:4–13
—Abigail pleaded for his life 1Sa 25:14–25
—His death 1Sa 25:36–38

NABOTH

—Owner of a vineyard in Jezreel 1Ki 21:1
—Refused to sell vineyard to King Ahab 1Ki 21:2–3
—Killed by Jezebel 1Ki 21:4–14

—Ahab's family destroyed for this . . . 1Ki 21:17–24
—Joram killed in Naboth's vineyard . . . 2Ki 9:21–26

NADAB

A. Firstborn of Aaron . . . Ex 6:23
—Went up Mount Sinai . . . Ex 24:1,9
—Consecrated as priest . . . Ex 28:1
—Killed for offering unauthorized fire . . . Lev 10:1–3; Nu 3:2–4
—Had no sons . . . 1Ch 24:2

B. Son of Jeroboam I; king of Israel . . . 1Ki 15:25
—Killed all his brothers . . . 1Ki 15:29
—Killed by Baasha . . . 1Ki 15:27–28

NAME

A. Human names

1. Giving a name implied authority . . . Ge 2:19; Ge 41:45; 2Ki 23:34; Da 1:7

2. Bible names could express
—The feelings of the mother at birth . . . Ge 4:1,25; Ge 29:31–35; Ge 30:4–24
—The feelings of the father at birth . . . Ge 35:16–18; Ge 41:51–52
—Circumstances of the child's conception . . . Ge 17:17,19; 1Sa 1:20
—Circumstances of the child's birth . . . Ge 25:24–26; Ge 38:27–30; Ex 2:10
—Historical situation at time of birth . . . 1Sa 4:19–22; Isa 8:1–4; Hos 1:6–9
—How a person's life would develop . . . Ge 3:20; Ge 27:36; 1Sa 25:25; 1Ch 22:9; Mt 1:21
—A name directly given by God . . . Lk 1:13,60

3. A name change meant a new role
—From Abram to Abraham . . . Ge 17:5–6
—From Sarai to Sarah . . . Ge 17:15–16
—From Jacob to Israel . . . Ge 32:28
—From Simon to Peter . . . Jn 1:42
—Promise of new names for us . . . Isa 62:2; Rev 2:17

4. The names of believers
—Are called Christians . . . Ac 11:26
—Are known by Christ . . . Jn 10:3–4
—Are acknowledged before the Father . . . Mt 10:32; Rev 3:5
—Are entered into the book of life . . . Lk 10:20; Php 4:3; Rev 20:15

B. The name of God and Christ

1. God's name describes him
—It is identical with himself . . . 2Sa 7:5,13; Ps 99:6
—It defines his nature . . . Isa 9:6
—It defines his power . . . Heb 1:4

2. God's name has power
—It delivers us . . . Ex 3:13–15
—It saves us . . . Ps 54:1; Mt 1:21,23; Ac 4:12
—It gives us life . . . Jn 20:31
—It justifies us . . . 1Co 6:11
—It sanctifies us . . . 1Co 6:11
—It protects us . . . Pr 18:10
—It helps us . . . Ps 116:3–4; Jn 14:13–14

3. Our attitude toward God's name
—Praise it . . . Ps 68:4; Ps 99:3
—Glorify it . . . Ps 86:12; Ps 105:3
—Exalt it . . . Ps 34:3
—Hallow it . . . Mt 6:9
—Rejoice in it . . . Ps 89:16
—Love it . . . Isa 56:6
—Give thanks to it . . . Ps 106:47
—Trust in it . . . Ps 33:21
—Hope in it . . . Ps 52:9
—Fear it . . . Ps 86:11; Isa 59:19
—Call on it . . . Ps 116:4,13,17; Joel 2:32
—Declare it . . . Ps 22:22
—Live to reflect it . . . Dt 28:9–10; Ro 2:21–24
—Don't misuse it . . . Ex 20:7; Mal 1:6

4. Our attitude toward Christ's name
—Bow before it . . . Php 2:10–11
—Believe in it . . . Jn 2:23; 1Jn 3:23
—Confess it . . . Ro 10:9; Heb 13:15
—Be baptized into it . . . Ac 10:48
—Call on it . . . 1Co 1:2
—Pray in it . . . Jn 14:13–14; Jn 16:23–24
—Give thanks in it . . . Eph 5:20
—Assemble in it . . . 1Co 5:4
—Preach it . . . Ac 8:12; Ac 9:27–28
—Live to reflect it . . . 2Th 1:12
—Do miracles in it . . . Mk 16:17; Ac 3:16; Ac 4:30
—May have to suffer for it . . . Ac 5:40–41; Ac 9:16; Rev 2:3

NAOMI

—Wife of Elimelek; mother-in-law of Ruth . . . Ru 1:2,4
—Left Bethlehem for Moab during famine . . . Ru 1:1
—Returned as a widow with Ruth . . . Ru 1:6–22
—Advised Ruth to seek marriage with Boaz . . . Ru 2:17–3:4
—Cared for Ruth's son Obed . . . Ru 4:13–17

NAPHTALI

A. Son of Jacob by Bilhah . . . Ge 35:25; 1Ch 2:2
—Name means "my struggle" . . . Ge 30:7–8
—Went to Egypt with family . . . Ge 46:8,24
—Father of four sons . . . Ge 46:24
—Blessed by Jacob . . . Ge 49:21

B. Tribe descended from Naphtali
—Blessed by Moses . . . Dt 33:23
—Numbered . . . Nu 1:43; Nu 26:50
—Allotted land . . . Jos 19:32–39; Eze 48:3
—Failed to fully possess the land . . . Jdg 1:33
—Supported Deborah . . . Jdg 4:10; Jdg 5:18
—Supported David . . . 1Ch 12:34
—One of the tribes of the 144,000 . . . Rev 7:6

NATHAN

—A prophet and chronicler . . . 1Ch 29:29; 2Ch 9:29
—Announced God's covenant with David . . . 2Sa 7:1–17; 1Ch 17:1–15
—Denounced David's sin with Bathsheba . . . 2Sa 12:1–15
—Revealed Adonijah's plot to David . . . 1Ki 1:10–27
—Participated in Solomon's coronation . . . 1Ki 1:28–40

NATHANAEL
—One of Jesus' disciples Jn 1:45–51
Jn 21:2
—Probably also called Bartholomew Mt 10:3
Ac 1:13

NATIONS
A. The origin of nations
—Came from one family Ac 17:26
—Began after the flood Ge 10:1–32
—God divided up the nations Dt 32:8
B. God's intentions for the nations
1. God is king over all nations 2Ch 20:6
Ps 47:2
Jer 10:7,10
2. God chose a special nation
—Began with God's choice of Abram Ge 12:2
—Israelites were a holy, chosen nation Ex 19:5–6
Am 3:1–2
—Israelites commanded to remain separate Ex 34:15–16
Dt 7:1–6
—God's choice intended to bless all nations Ge 12:3
Ge 18:18
Ge 22:18
3. God prophesied salvation for all nations Ps 22:27–28
Ps 67:2
Isa 45:22–23
Isa 52:10
Zec 8:20–23
4. The nations are called to salvation
—Called by Jonah in the Old Testament Jnh 3:1–10
—Gospel to be preached to all nations Mt 24:14
Mt 28:19
Mk 16:15
Lk 24:47
Ac 1:8
—Apostles preached to all nations Ac 2:5–14
Ac 10:34–35
Ro 1:16
Ro 15:8–12,19
—Church composed of all nations Eph 2:11–22
Rev 5:9
Rev 7:9

NATURE
See CREATION

NAZARETH
—A Galilean town Mt 4:13
—Had a poor reputation Jn 1:46
—Gabriel appeared to Mary there Lk 1:26–38
—Jesus grew up there Mt 2:23
Lk 2:39,51–52
—Jesus called "Jesus of Nazareth" Jn 18:5,7
Jn 19:19
Ac 2:22
—Jesus was rejected by the town Mt 13:54–58
Mk 6:1–6
Lk 4:16–30

NEBUCHADNEZZAR
—Babylonian king 2Ki 24:1
—Campaigned against Judah 2Ki 24:1–4,10–16
2Ch 36:6–10
—Destroyed Jerusalem and the temple 2Ki 25:1–17
2Ch 36:15–21
Jer 39:1–10
—Was kind to Jeremiah Jer 39:11–14
—Was impressed with Daniel and his friends Da 1:18–20
—Dreams interpreted by Daniel Da 2:14–47
Da 4:9–27
—Put Daniel's three friends in fiery furnace Da 3:1–27
—Lived seven years like an animal Da 4:28–33
—Worshiped God Da 3:28–29
Da 4:34–37

NECHO
See PHARAOH

NEEDY
See THE RICH AND THE POOR

NEHEMIAH
—Cupbearer for Artaxerxes Ne 1:11
—Became sad over condition of the exiles Ne 1:2–11
—Became governor of Jews Ne 8:9
—Inspected walls of Jerusalem Ne 2:11–20
—Rebuilt walls of Jerusalem Ne 3:1–4:23
Ne 6:15–19
—Showed concern for the poor Ne 5:1–13
—With Ezra, reestablished true worship Ne 8:1–12
—Signed a renewed covenant with the Lord Ne 9:38–10:1
—Dedicated walls of Jerusalem Ne 12:27–47
—Made a later visit to Jerusalem Ne 13:1–30

NEIGHBOR
—Anyone near you; any fellow human being
A. How not to treat your neighbors
—Do not give false testimony against them Ex 20:16
—Do not covet what is theirs Ex 20:17
—Do not deceive them Lev 6:2
—Do not rob them Lev 19:13
—Do not kill them Dt 22:26
—Do not plot harm against them Pr 3:29
—Do not despise them Pr 14:21
—Do not deceive them Pr 26:19
—Do not flatter them Pr 29:5
—Do not judge them Jas 4:12
—Do not commit adultery with neighbor's wife Lev 20:10
B. How to treat your neighbors
—Love them as yourself Lev 19:18
Mt 22:39
Ro 13:9
Jas 2:8
—Be kind to them Lk 10:29–37
—Speak the truth to them Eph 4:25

NICODEMUS
—Pharisee who visited Jesus at night Jn 3:1–21
—Argued for fair treatment of Jesus Jn 7:50–52
—With Joseph, prepared Jesus for burial Jn 19:38–42

NIGHT
See DARKNESS

NINEVEH
—A city founded by Nimrod Ge 10:11–12
—The capital of Assyria 2Ki 19:36
Isa 37:37
—Jonah told to preach against it Jnh 1:1–2
Jnh 3:1–3
—The people of Nineveh repented Jnh 3:5–10
—The people of Nineveh condemn unbelievers Mt 12:41
Lk 11:32
—Prophecies concerning its destruction Na 1:8–3:19
Zep 2:13–15

NOAH
—A righteous man Eze 14:14,20
—Called to build the ark Ge 6:11–22
—Entered the ark Ge 7:1–9
—Survived the flood Ge 8:15–19
—Worshiped the Lord after the flood Ge 8:20–22
—God made covenant with him Ge 9:1–17
—Became drunk Ge 9:18–23
—Blessed Shem and Japheth and cursed Canaan Ge 9:24–27

NUMBERS
A. Numbers used as a literary device
—In poetry Ps 62:11
Pr 6:16–19
Pr 30:15–29
—In prophecy Am 1:3–2:6
Mic 5:5
—In genealogies Mt 1:17

B. Numbers used in a symbolic fashion
 1. The number "one"
  —One God . . . . Dt 6:4; 1Co 8:6; Eph 4:6; Jas 2:19
  —One Lord . . . . 1Co 8:6; Eph 4:5
  —One Spirit . . . . 1Co 12:13; Eph 4:4
  —Father and Son are one . . . . Jn 10:30
  —One body . . . . Ro 12:4–5; Eph 4:4
  —One in Christ . . . . Jn 17:11,21; Gal 3:28; Eph 2:14–15
  —One hope . . . . Eph 4:4
  —One faith and one baptism . . . . Eph 4:5
  —One father of the human race, Adam . . . . Ac 17:26; Ro 5:12; 1Co 15:21–22
  —One flesh in marriage . . . . Ge 2:24; Eph 5:31
 2. The number "two"
  —Two ways to choose . . . . Jos 24:15; 1Ki 18:21; Mt 7:13–14
  —The two-edged sword . . . . Heb 4:12; Rev 1:16
  —Male and female . . . . Ge 1:27
  —Two by two into the ark . . . . Ge 7:8–9,15–16
  —Two tablets of the law . . . . Ex 32:15
  —Disciples sent out two by two . . . . Mk 6:7
  —Two witnesses . . . . Nu 35:30; Jn 8:17–18; 2Co 13:1
 3. The number "three"
  —Father, Son, Holy Spirit . . . . Mt 28:19; 2Co 13:14
  See TRINITY
  —Three annual festivals in Israel . . . . Ex 23:14–17
  —Threefold benediction by priests . . . . Nu 6:24–26
  —Job's three friends . . . . Job 2:11
  —Jonah's three days in the fish . . . . Jnh 1:17; Mt 12:40
  —Three temptations of Jesus . . . . Mt 4:3–10
  —Three prayers in Gethsemane . . . . Mt 26:39–44
  —Three denials of Peter . . . . Mt 26:34,69–75
  —Jesus' resurrection on the third day . . . . Mt 16:21; Lk 24:46; 1Co 15:4
  —Three questions for Peter . . . . Jn 21:15–17
  —Peter's three visions . . . . Ac 10:10–16
  —Faith, hope, love 1Co 13:13
 4. The number "four"
  —The four rivers in Eden . . . . Ge 2:10–14
  —The four winds . . . . Jer 49:36
  —The four corners of the earth . . . . Eze 7:2
  —Series of fours in Zechariah's visions . . . . Zec 1:8,18–21
  —Four creatures around God's throne . . . . Eze 1:4–14; Rev 4:6–8
  —Four kingdoms seen in a vision . . . . Da 2:36–43; Da 7:2–7,17
 5. The number "seven"
  —Creation in seven days . . . . Ge 1:1–2:3
  —The Sabbath on the seventh day . . . . Ex 20:8–11
  —The sabbath year . . . . Lev 25:1–7
  —The Year of Jubilee (seven sabbath years) . . . . Lev 25:8–12
  —Seven lamps on the lampstand . . . . Ex 25:37
  —Festival of Unleavened Bread for seven days . . . . Ex 34:18
  —Festival of Tabernacles for seven days . . . . Lev 23:34
  —Seven sprinklings for a cleansed leper . . . . Lev 14:7,16
  —Seven dippings for leper Naaman 2Ki 5:10,14
  —Seven days marching around Jericho . . . . Jos 6:1–16
  —Seven deacons . . . . Ac 6:3–5
  —Numerous series of sevens in Revelation . . . . Rev 1:12–20; Rev 5:1; Rev 8:1–2; Rev 15:1,6–8
 6. The number "ten"
  —Ten righteous men to save Sodom . . . . Ge 18:32
  —The ten plagues . . . . Ex 7:14–12:36
  —The Ten Commandments . . . . Ex 34:28
  —Ten testings of the Israelites . . . . Nu 14:22
  —The tithe (a tenth) . . . . Ge 14:20
  See TITHES AND OFFERINGS
  —Ten virgins in Jesus' parable . . . . Mt 25:1–13
  —Ten horns and crowns on a beast . . . . Rev 13:1
 7. The number "12"
  —12 sons of Jacob . . . . Ge 35:22–26
  —12 tribes . . . . Ex 24:4
  —12 stones from the Jordan . . . . Jos 4:9
  —12 stones in Elijah's altar 1Ki 18:31
  —12 disciples of Jesus . . . . Mt 10:1–5
  —12 hours of daylight . . . . Jn 11:9
  —A crown of 12 stars . . . . Rev 12:1
  —12 apostles . . . . Ac 1:26
  —Several 12s in the new Jerusalem . . . . Rev 21:12–14,21
 8. The number "40"
  —Rain for 40 days and nights . . . . Ge 7:12
  —Moses for 40 days on Mount Sinai . . . . Ex 24:18
  —40 years wandering in the desert . . . . Nu 14:33–34
  —Moses' life divided into three 40s . . . . Ac 7:23,30,36
  —David's reign of 40 years 1Ki 2:11
  —Solomon's reign of 40 years 1Ki 11:42
  —Elijah for 40 days on the mountain 1Ki 19:8
  —Jesus for 40 days in the desert . . . . Mt 4:2
  —Jesus ascended after 40 days . . . . Ac 1:3
 9. The number "70"
  —70 people came to Egypt . . . . Ge 46:27
  —70 elders in Israel . . . . Ex 24:1,9
  —70 years of exile . . . . Jer 25:11–12
  —70 "sevens" in Daniel's visions . . . . Da 9:20–27
  —Forgiving 77 times . . . . Mt 18:22
  —The sending of the 72 . . . . Lk 10:1,17
 10. "Thousands"
  —1,000 years (the millennium) . . . . Rev 20:1–7
  —A thousand years as one day . . . . Ps 90:4; 2Pe 3:8
  —3,000 converts on Pentecost . . . . Ac 2:41
  —Feeding the 4,000 . . . . Mt 15:29–38
  —Feeding the 5,000 . . . . Mt 14:13–21
  —7,000 not bowing to Baal . . . . 1Ki 19:18; Ro 11:4
  —Thousands who love and obey the Lord . . . . Ex 20:6
  —Thousands of thousands of chariots . . . . Ps 68:17
  —Thousands and thousands before God . . . . Da 7:10
  —Thousands and thousands praising God . . . . Heb 12:22; Rev 5:11
  —144,000 . . . . Rev 7:4–8; Rev 14:1–3
 11. Mysterious numbers
  —42 months . . . . Rev 11:2; Rev 13:5
  —1,260 days . . . . Rev 11:3; Rev 12:6
  —666 . . . . Rev 13:18

OATH

A. The human oath
 1. Expressions of the oath
  —"May God . . . judge between us" . . . . Ge 31:53
  —"As surely as the LORD lives" . . . . Ru 3:13
  —"May God deal with you . . . severely" 1Sa 3:17
  —"As surely as you live" 1Sa 17:55
  —"The LORD is witness between you and me" 1Sa 20:23,42
  —"I am telling the truth, I am not lying" 1Ti 2:7
  —"God . . . is my witness" . . . . Ro 1:9
  —"I speak the truth in Christ" . . . . Ro 9:1

2. Features of the oath
   a. Purposes
      —To settle an issue .... Ex 22:10–11
      —To confirm an agreement with someone .... Ge 31:45–54
      —To confirm a covenant with a people .... Jos 9:3–15
      —To confirm a covenant with God 2Ch 15:12–15
      —To ensure obedience to a master .... Ge 24:1–4
      —To ensure obedience to a king .... Ecc 8:2
      —To ensure obedience to the Lord .... Ne 10:29
   b. Other aspects of the oath
      —Must be fulfilled .... Nu 30:1–2
      —Could bind future generations .... Ge 50:24–25
      —Conditions sometimes attached .... Jos 2:12–21
      —Not necessary for Christians .... Mt 5:33–37; Jas 5:12
      —Christ responded to an oath .... Mt 26:63–64

C. God's oath
   1. Content of God's oaths
      —To give Canaan to Abraham's descendants .... Ge 22:15–18; Ge 50:24
      —To keep someone on David's throne 2Sa 7:10–16
      —To set up a priesthood like Melchizedek's .... Ps 110:4
   2. Character of God's oaths
      —He swears by himself .... Ge 22:16; Heb 6:13–15
      —God does not lie .... Nu 23:19; Heb 6:16–18
      —God fulfills his oaths .... Ps 105:42–43; Lk 1:69–75; Lk 1:32–33; Heb 6:19–7:22

See also CURSE; VOW

OBADIAH

A. Servant of King Ahab 1Ki 18:3
   —Sheltered 100 prophets from Jezebel 1Ki 18:4
   —Notified Ahab of Elijah's return 1Ki 18:7–16
B. Prophet against Edom .... Ob 1

OBEDIENCE

A. Related themes
   1. OBEDIENCE is a theme of:
      —1 Samuel 1Sa 12:14
      —2 Samuel 2Sa 12:10
      —1 Kings 1Ki 9:4
      —2 Kings 2Ki 22:19
      —Daniel .... Da 1:8
      —1 Corinthians 1Co 7:19
   2. TRUST AND OBEY is a theme of Joshua .... Jos 10:25
B. Obedience in the Old Testament
   1. Relationships of obedience
      —Israelites obey the Lord their God .... Ex 19:5; Dt 4:30
      —Israelites obey the law of God .... Ex 34:11; Dt 11:13,27,32
      —Citizens obey the king .... 1Ki 2:43; Ecc 8:2
      —Children obey parents .... Ex 20:12; Pr 1:8–9; Pr 6:20–21
   2. Rewards for obedience .... Ex 19:5–6; Dt 28:1–14; Jos 1:7–8
   3. Punishment for disobedience .... Dt 28:15–68; 1Sa 12:15; 2Ki 17:7–20; Jer 11:1–3
   4. Obedience more important than outward ritual .... 1Sa 15:22; Ps 40:6–8; Pr 21:3; Jer 7:22–23
C. Obedience in the New Testament
   1. Relationships of obedience
      —Christians obey God .... Heb 12:9; Jas 4:7; 1Jn 5:3
      —Christians obey Christ .... Jn 14:13,23; Ro 1:5; 1Co 9:21; Gal 6:2; Heb 5:9
      —Citizens obey government authorities .... Ro 13:1–5; 1Pe 2:13–14
      —Christians obey church leaders .... Heb 13:17
      —Servants obey masters .... Eph 6:5–8; Col 3:22
      —Children obey parents .... Eph 6:1; Col 3:20
   2. Obeying God precedes obeying humans .... Ac 4:19–20; Ac 5:29

OCCULT

See MAGIC, WITCHCRAFT AND SORCERY

OFFERINGS

See TITHES AND OFFERINGS

OG

—King of Bashan .... Nu 21:33; Dt 1:4
—Destroyed by the Israelites .... Nu 21:34–35; Dt 3:1–11
—Victory sung by the Israelites .... Ps 136:20

OLIVES, MOUNT OF

—A hill east of Jerusalem .... Eze 11:23; Zec 14:4
—David climbed it while fleeing from Absalom 2Sa 15:30
—Jesus often went there .... Lk 22:39; Jn 8:1
—"Triumphal" Entry began from there .... Mt 21:1–9; Mk 11:1–10; Lk 19:29–40
—Jesus predicted destruction of Jerusalem there .... Mt 24:3–34; Mk 13:3–31
—Gethsemane located there .... Mt 26:30,36; Mk 14:26,32
—Jesus ascended into heaven from there .... Ac 1:9–12

OMRI

—King of Israel 1Ki 16:21–28
—Father of Ahab 1Ki 16:28

ORDER

A. Related theme
   ORGANIZATION is a theme of Numbers .... Nu 2:34
   CHURCH ORDER is a theme of 1 Timothy 1Ti 3:15
B. Order needed among God's people
   —For the Israelites in the desert .... Nu 2:1–34
   —In Christian worship 1Co 14:40
   —In the Christian life .... Col 2:5
   —In presenting the truth about Christ .... Lk 1:3

See also CHURCH; DEACON; ELDER

ORPAH

—Moabitess; daughter-in-law of Naomi .... Ru 1:3–5
—Remained in Moab .... Ru 1:14

OTHNIEL

—Nephew of Caleb; married Caleb's daughter .... Jos 15:15–19; Jdg 1:12–15
—Became a judge .... Jdg 3:10
—Freed Israelites from Arameans .... Jdg 3:7–11

PAIN

—Various types of suffering experienced in our lives
A. Related themes
   1. SUFFERING is a theme of:
      —Job .... Job 2:13
      —Jeremiah .... Jer 15:18
      —Mark .... Mk 8:31
      —2 Corinthians 2Co 1:8
      —1 Peter 1Pe 4:12
   2. COMPLAINT is a theme of:
      —Psalms .... Ps 123:4
      —Habakkuk .... Hab 1:2

3. HARD TIMES is a theme of 2 Timothy 2Ti 1:8
4. UNJUST PERSECUTION is a theme of Acts........... Ac 12:2

B. Pain and suffering as a universal experience
1. In humans
—The righteous................................ Ps 22:1–2,12–18
—The wicked.................................. Pr 10:16
Pr 12:21
2. In creation as a whole........................... Ro 8:20–22

C. The problem of pain and suffering for God's people
1. Examples of those who experienced pain
—Joseph...................................... Ge 39:11–20
—The Israelites in Egypt......................... Ex 1:8–14
—The poor.................................... Ne 5:1–5
Am 2:6–7
—Job... Job 2:7–13
—David....................................... Ps 22:1–18
—Asaph...................................... Ps 73:2–14
—Daniel's three friends .... Da 3:13–23
—Daniel...................................... Da 6:16–17
—Peter and John............................... Ac 5:40–41
—Paul.. Ac 14:19
2Co 11:23–26
—The Hebrew Christians .... Heb 10:33–34
—Other Christians.............................. 1Th 2:14–15
1Pe 2:19–21
—Christians in Smyrna.......................... Rev 2:9–10
—Saints in John's vision......................... Rev 6:9–10
2. Christian attitude toward pain
—We must expect it............................ Mt 24:9
Jn 16:1–4,33
2Ti 3:12
—We may have to endure it 2Ti 2:3
2Ti 4:5
—We must realize not all are delivered .... Heb 11:35–38
—We must be patient in it....................... Ro 12:12
1Pe 2:20–21
—We can rejoice in it .... Ro 5:3
Col 1:24
Jas 1:2–3
1Pe 4:12–14
—We must overcome it .... Ro 8:35–37
Rev 2:10–11
—We must not become discouraged .... Eph 3:13
—We must not lose heart 2Co 4:7–10,16–17
1Th 3:3
—We do complain against it..................... Job 3:3–26
Ps 74:1,10–11
2Co 12:7–8
3. Why does God allow such pain?
—To punish sins................................ 2Sa 12:9–18
2Ch 33:10–11
—To test us.................................... Dt 8:2
Job 2:1–6
Isa 48:10
—To teach us his will........................... Ps 119:71,75
—To teach us patience .... Ro 5:3
Jas 1:3
—To humble us .... Dt 8:3
2Ch 7:13–14
—To discipline us in love .... Heb 12:4–11
—To drive us to repentance .... Jdg 6:1–6
Ps 107:4–6,10–13
Hos 5:15
—To get us to rely on his grace 2Co 12:7–10
—To purify us.................................. Zec 13:7–9
Mal 3:2–3
Jn 15:2
—To promote his glory.......................... Jn 9:1–3
—To further the gospel.......................... Ac 8:3–4
2Ti 4:16–17
4. How does God relate to pain?
—He is in control.............................. Job 1:6–12
Ro 8:38–39
—He causes good to triumph .... Ps 49:13–15
Ps 73:16–20
Ro 8:28
—He is a refuge for believers.................... Ps 16:1,8
Ps 46:1
Isa 25:4
—He shares our pain........................... Isa 53:2–4
Isa 63:9
—He walks with us through pain .... Ps 23:4
Ps 46:7,11
Isa 43:2
—He comforts us.............................. Isa 49:13
Zec 1:17
2Co 1:4–5
Mt 11:28–30
—He will terminate pain at Christ's return......... 2Th 1:4–7
Rev 21:1–4
5. How should believers relate to those in pain?
—We should pray for them .... Ac 12:5
Ro 15:30–31
2Co 1:10–11
Jas 5:13–16
—We should comfort them...................... Job 2:11–13
2Co 1:6–8
—We should share their burdens .... Job 30:25
Ro 12:15
Gal 6:2
Heb 13:3
—We should encourage them................... 1Th 5:11
—We should give them help.................... Isa 58:7
Lk 10:30–37
Php 4:14
1Jn 3:17–18

PARABLE

—Stories that illustrate spiritual truths

A. The purposes of parables
—To teach things to children....................... Ps 78:2–4
Pr 1:1–6
—To make an important point...................... Jdg 9:7–20
1Sa 12:1–7
—To give a prophetic message .... Isa 5:1–7
Eze 17:1–18
Hos 12:10
—To teach us about the kingdom................... Mk 4:2,10
—To obscure teaching from unbelievers .... Mt 13:11–15

B. Parables and fables in the Old Testament
—The fable of Jotham to Abimelek.................. Jdg 9:7–15
—The parable of Nathan to David................... 2Sa 12:1–6
—The fable of Jehoash to Amaziah.................. 2Ki 14:9
—The parable of Isaiah to the people................ Isa 5:1–7
—The parables of Ezekiel to the people .... Eze 17:1–8,22–24
Eze 20:45–49
Eze 24:1–5

C. Jesus' use of parables
—He used them regularly .... Mk 4:33–34
—He explained things to the disciples alone.......... Mt 13:10–13
Mk 4:3–8,14–20
Lk 8:9–10
—He taught about the kingdom of God.............. Mk 4:11,26,30–32

D. Parables of Jesus
—Lamp on a stand .... Mt 5:14–15
Mk 4:21–22
Lk 8:16
—Wise and foolish builders........................ Mt 7:24–27
Lk 6:47–49
—New cloth on an old garment .... Mt 9:16
Mk 2:21
Lk 5:36
—New wine in old wineskins .... Mt 9:17
Mk 2:22
Lk 5:37–38
—Sower .... Mt 13:3–23
Mk 4:3–25
Lk 8:5–15

—Growing seed ... Mk 4:25–29
—Wheat and weeds ... Mt 13:24–30,36–43
—Mustard seed ... Mt 13:31–32
Mk 4:30–32
Lk 13:18–19
—Yeast ... Mt 13:33
Lk 13:20–21
—Hidden treasure ... Mt 13:43
—Valuable pearl ... Mt 13:45–46
—Net ... Mt 13:47–51
—House owner ... Mt 13:52
—Good Samaritan ... Lk 10:25–37
—Wandering sheep ... Mt 18:10–14
Lk 15:3–7
—Lost coin ... Lk 15:8–10
—Lost son ... Lk 15:11–32
—Unmerciful servant ... Mt 18:15–35
—Shrewd manager ... Lk 16:1–9
—Rich man and Lazarus ... Lk 16:19–31
—Persistent widow ... Lk 18:1–8
—Pharisee and tax collector ... Lk 18:9–14
—Workers in the vineyard ... Mt 20:1–16
—Two sons ... Mt 21:28–32
—Tenants ... Mt 21:33–46
Mk 12:1–6
Lk 20:9–18
—Wedding banquet ... Mt 22:1–14
—Faithful servant ... Mt 24:45–51
Lk 12:42–48
—Ten virgins ... Mt 25:1–13
—Bags of gold/Ten minas ... Mt 25:14–30
Lk 19:12–27
—Sheep and goats ... Mt 25:31–46

PATIENCE

—Long-suffering, perseverance, forbearance
A. Human patience
1. The command to be patient
—Be patient ... Ro 12:12
1Th 5:14
Heb 12:1
Jas 5:7–8
—Bear with others' shortcomings ... Eph 4:2
Col 3:12–13
2. The manner of achieving patience
—By dependence on God ... Ro 15:5
Col 1:11
—Through hope in Christ ... 1Th 1:3
Jas 5:7
—As part of the fruit of the Spirit ... Gal 5:22
3. Examples of patience
—Abraham ... Heb 6:15
—Job ... Jas 5:11
—The prophets ... Jas 5:10
—Paul ... 2Ti 3:10
—John ... Rev 1:9
See also FORBEARANCE, PERSEVERANCE
B. Patience of God
1. Statements of God's patience
—God is slow to anger ... Ex 34:6
Nu 14:18
Ps 30:5
Ps 78:38
—Jesus is patient with us ... 1Ti 1:16
2. Purpose: to call humans to repentance ... Ro 2:4
2Pe 3:9,15
3. God's patience at time of Noah ... 1Pe 3:20

PAUL

A. Related themes
PETER AND PAUL is a theme of Acts ... Ac 19:11
MINISTRY is a theme of 2 Corinthians ... 2Co 4:1
DEFENSE is a theme of Galatians ... Gal 1:10
B. His background
—Originally called Saul ... Ac 13:9
—From Tarsus ... Ac 9:11
Ac 21:39
—From the tribe of Benjamin ... Php 3:5
—A Pharisee ... Php 3:5
—Educated by Gamaliel ... Ac 22:3
—Unmarried ... 1Co 7:8
C. His life as a persecutor of Christians
—Assisted in stoning of Stephen ... Ac 7:58
Ac 8:1
—Zealously persecuted church ... Ac 9:1
Gal 1:13–14
Php 3:6
—Cast vote against Christians ... Ac 26:9–10
—Went to Damascus to persecute ... Ac 9:2
Ac 22:4–5
—Converted on the way to Damascus ... Ac 9:3–19
Ac 22:6–21
Ac 26:12–18
D. His life as an apostle
1. From conversion to first missionary journey
—Called as missionary to Gentiles ... Ac 22:17–21
Ac 26:16–18
—Went to Arabia ... Gal 1:17
—Preached in Damascus; escaped in basket ... Ac 9:19–25
2Co 11:32–33
—Went to Jerusalem ... Ac 9:26–29
—Went to Tarsus ... Ac 9:30
—Brought to Antioch by Barnabas ... Ac 11:22–26
—Brought offering to Jerusalem ... Ac 11:29–30
—Returned to Antioch ... Ac 12:25
2. First missionary journey
—Called by God ... Ac 13:2–4
—Preached throughout Cyprus ... Ac 13:5–12
—Preached in Pisidian Antioch ... Ac 13:14–52
—Was persecuted in Iconium ... Ac 14:1–7
—Preached and stoned at Lystra ... Ac 14:8–20
—Preached at Derbe ... Ac 14:20–21
—Returned to Antioch ... Ac 14:21–28
3. The Jerusalem council
—Sent to Jerusalem ... Ac 15:1–4
Gal 2:1–2
—Discussed circumcision privately ... Gal 2:3–10
—Open meeting on circumcision issue ... Ac 15:5–22
—Letter drafted and sent with them ... Ac 15:23–31
—Friction developed with Peter ... Gal 2:11–14
4. Second missionary journey
—Split with Barnabas over John Mark ... Ac 15:36–41
—Took Silas along ... Ac 15:40
—Visited previous churches ... Ac 15:41
—Added Timothy to his group ... Ac 16:1–4
—At Troas, called to Macedonia ... Ac 16:6–10
—Preached to women at Philippi ... Ac 16:13–15
—Imprisoned and freed in Philippi ... Ac 16:16–40
—Ministered in Thessalonica ... Ac 17:1–9
—Ministered in Berea ... Ac 17:10–15
—Preached in Athens ... Ac 17:16–33
—Ministered in Corinth for 18 months ... Ac 18:1–11
—Attacked by Jews ... Ac 18:12–17
—Left Corinth and returned to Antioch ... Ac 18:18–22
5. Third missionary journey
—Arrived at Ephesus in Asia ... Ac 19:1
—Ministered for two years there ... Ac 19:2–22
—Suffered many hardships there ... 2Co 1:3–10
—Visited with leaders from Corinth ... 1Co 16:17–18
—Riot in Ephesus ... Ac 19:23–41
—Left for Macedonia ... Ac 20:1
—Met Titus in Macedonia ... 2Co 7:5–7
—Gathered money for Jerusalem ... 2Co 8:1–5
Ro 15:26
—Arrived in Greece ... Ac 20:2–3
—Gathered more money for Jerusalem ... Ro 15:26
—Left Greece for Jerusalem ... Ac 20:3–6
Ro 15:25
—Spoke all night at Troas ... Ac 20:7–12

—Said farewell to elders of Ephesus . . . Ac 20:17–38
—Sailed for Jerusalem . . . Ac 21:1–6
—Traveled to Jerusalem . . . Ac 21:7–17
—Reported to Jerusalem leaders . . . Ac 21:17–25

6. Paul's period of imprisonment
—Attacked and beaten by Jews from Asia . . . Ac 21:27–32
—Arrested by Roman commander . . . Ac 21:33–35
—Addressed the Jewish crowd . . . Ac 22:1–21
—Addressed Sanhedrin . . . Ac 23:1–11
—Transferred to Caesarea . . . Ac 23:12–35
—On trial before Felix . . . Ac 24:1–21
—Kept in prison in Caesarea . . . Ac 24:22–27
—On trial before Festus . . . Ac 25:1–12
—Appealed to Caesar . . . Ac 25:12
—Spoke before Agrippa . . . Ac 25:13–26:32
—Sailed for Rome; shipwrecked . . . Ac 27:1–44
—Stranded on island of Malta . . . Ac 28:1–10
—Arrived in Rome . . . Ac 28:11–16
—Preached to Jews of Rome . . . Ac 28:17–28
—Remained two years in Rome . . . Ac 28:30–31
—Freed after trial before emperor . . . 2Ti 4:16–17

7. Travels after release from imprisonment
—In Macedonia . . . 1Ti 1:3
—In Crete . . . Titus 1:5
—In Nicopolis . . . Titus 3:12
—In Miletus . . . 2Ti 4:20
—In Troas . . . 2Ti 4:13
—Imprisoned again . . . 2Ti 2:8–9
—Probably killed this time . . . 2Ti 4:6–8

E. Significant issues in Paul's letters
—His apostleship . . . 1Co 9:1–3
2Co 11:4–12:13
Gal 1:1–2:14
—Salvation possible only in the name of Jesus . . . Ro 3:21–26
Ro 5:1–2
Ro 10:3–13
2Co 5:18–21
Gal 3:10–14,24–29
Eph 2:1–22
Php 3:7–14
Col 1:13–23
1Ti 1:12–16
—Salvation through faith alone . . . Ro 3:21–5:1
Gal 2:15–21
Eph 2:8–9
Php 3:9
—Circumcision not necessary for salvation . . . Ro 4:9–12
Gal 2:3
Gal 5:1–6
Col 2:11–12
—Christian freedom . . . Ro 14:1–15:13
1Co 8:1–13
1Co 11:23–33
Gal 4:31–5:13
—Concern for the salvation of Jews . . . Ro 9:1–5
Ro 10:1–4
—Proper use of spiritual gifts . . . Ro 12:3–8
1Co 12:1–14:40
—Life led by the Spirit of God . . . Ro 8:1–17
Gal 5:16–26
—Proper order needed in the church . . . 1Co 11:17–34
1Co 14:26–40
1Ti 2:1–3:15
Titus 1:5–2:15

PEACE

—Wholeness and well-being in all areas of life

A. Basic meanings of peace

1. Peace ("Shalom") is a basic greeting
—Hello . . . Da 10:19
Jn 20:19
Gal 1:3
—Good-bye . . . 1Sa 25:35
2Sa 15:9
1Pe 5:14
3Jn 14

2. Peace in a political sense
—On the international scene . . . 1Sa 7:14
1Ki 4:24
Ac 24:2
—On the national scene . . . 2Sa 3:21–23
1Ki 22:44
2Ch 14:1

3. Peace in human relationships
—In relationships with others . . . Ro 12:18
Heb 12:14
1Pe 3:11
—Among the Israelite people . . . Ps 34:14
Ps 122:6–7
—In relationships in the church . . . Ac 9:31
Ro 14:19
2Co 13:11
Eph 2:14–17
—In relationships in the home . . . Ge 44:17
Pr 17:1
Pr 29:17
1Co 7:15

4. Personal sense of peace
—In relationship with oneself . . . Ps 4:8
Pr 14:30
2Co 2:13
—In relationship with God . . . Nu 6:26
Isa 26:3
Ro 5:1
Php 4:7–9
Col 1:20

B. The source of peace

1. It comes as a divine gift
—From God the Father . . . Ro 1:7
Ro 15:33
Php 4:7
—From the Lord Jesus Christ . . . Isa 9:6–7
Lk 2:14
Jn 14:27
Ro 1:7
Eph 2:14
2Th 3:16
—From the Holy Spirit . . . Ro 14:17
Gal 5:22
Eph 4:3
—God promises a covenant of peace . . . Isa 54:10
Eze 34:25
Eze 37:26
—We must pray to God for peace . . . Ps 122:6–7
Jer 29:7
1Ti 2:1

2. It comes through human effort
—We must let peace rule in us . . . Col 3:15
—We must live in peace . . . 2Co 13:11
1Th 5:13
—We must seek peace . . . Ps 34:14
1Pe 3:11
—We must try to live in peace . . . Ro 12:18
Ro 14:19
Heb 12:14
—We must pursue peace . . . Ps 34:14
2Ti 2:22
—We must obey God to receive peace . . . Lev 26:3,6

C. Jesus and our peace
—Prophesied to be the Prince of Peace . . . Isa 9:6
—Peace proclaimed at his birth . . . Lk 2:14
—Peace promised to his disciples . . . Jn 14:27
Jn 16:33
—Peace achieved on the cross . . . Isa 53:5
Col 1:20
—Began the good news of peace . . . Isa 52:7
Ac 10:36
—He is our peace . . . Eph 2:14
—Enables us to have peace with God . . . Ro 5:1
—Establishes peace within the church . . . Eph 2:15
—Guides us in the way of peace . . . Lk 1:79

—Blesses us with peace .... Nu 6:24–26; Ps 29:11; 1Co 1:3
—Enables us to die in peace .... Lk 2:29–31
The wicked and peace
—They proclaim a false peace .... Jer 6:14; Eze 13:10
—They do not know the way of peace .... Isa 59:8; Lk 19:42
—They hate peace .... Ps 120:6–7
—They have no peace .... Isa 48:18,22; Isa 57:21

PEKAH

—King of Israel 2Ki 15:27–31
—Assassinated Pekahiah to become king 2Ki 15:25
—Allied with Syria against Judah .... 2Ki 15:37; Isa 7:1–2
—Inflicted much destruction on Judah 2Ch 28:5–8
—Destruction of the alliance foretold .... Isa 7:3–9
—Failed in attempt to take Jerusalem 2Ki 16:5–6

PEKAHIAH

—King of Israel 2Ki 15:23–26
—Assassinated by Pekah, an officer 2Ki 15:25

PERFECTION

—Complete and without sin or error
A. Perfection as a human goal
1. The goal stated .... Mt 5:48; 2Co 13:9,11
2. Perfection possible only in the Lord
—Animal sacrifice cannot make us perfect .... Heb 10:1
—The law cannot make us perfect .... Ro 3:20; Heb 7:11,19
—God makes our way perfect 2Sa 22:33
—God's strength makes us perfect 2Co 12:7–10
—Jesus is the perfecter of our faith .... Heb 12:2
—Jesus makes us perfect by his sacrifice .... Heb 10:14
—The Spirit helps us attain perfection .... Gal 3:3
3. Perfection requires various human actions
—Learning God's wisdom .... Col 1:28
—Knowing God's word 2Ti 3:14–17
—Pressing forward in faith .... Php 3:12–14
—Self-sacrifice .... Mt 19:21
—Love .... Col 3:14
—Purifying ourselves 2Co 7:1
—Controlling what we say .... Jas 3:2
—Not being afraid 1Jn 4:18
4. Perfection attained only in the hereafter .... 1Co 13:8–10; Heb 12:22–23

See also HOLINESS; SANCTIFICATION
B. Perfection as the nature of God
1. God the Father
—He is perfect .... Mt 5:48
—His works are perfect .... Dt 32:4
—His way is perfect 2Sa 22:31
—His law is perfect .... Ps 19:7; Jas 1:25
—His will is perfect .... Ro 12:2
—He is perfect in knowledge .... Job 37:16
—He is perfect in faithfulness .... Isa 25:1
2. Christ the Son
—He is without sin .... 2Co 5:21; Heb 7:26; 1Jn 3:5
—He was made perfect through suffering .... Heb 2:10; Heb 5:8–9; Heb 7:28

PERSECUTION

—Oppression because of one's faith
A. Examples of persecution
1. The prophets
—Prophets in general .... 2Ch 36:15–16; Mt 5:12; Mt 23:31,37; Ac 7:52
—Elijah 1Ki 19:1–3
—Micaiah 1Ki 22:9–28
—Jeremiah .... Jer 26:1–19; Jer 37:11–38:13
—Uriah son of Shemaiah .... Jer 26:20–22
2. The apostles
—Persecution prophesied .... Mt 24:9; Jn 15:18–21; Jn 16:1–4
—The apostles as a group .... Ac 5:27,40
—James .... Ac 12:1–2
—Peter .... Ac 12:3–5
—Paul .... Ac 14:5–6,19–20; Ac 16:22–24; Ac 22:27–36; 2Co 11:23–26
—John .... Rev 1:9
3. Christians in general
—Stephen .... Ac 7:57–60
—Christians in Judea .... Ac 8:1–3; 1Th 2:14–15
—Christians outside Judea .... Ac 9:1–2; Ac 26:11
—Christians in Thessalonica 1Th 2:14–15
—Christians in Smyrna .... Rev 2:9–10
—To be expected for all 2Ti 3:12
B. Attitudes in relationship to persecution
—Commit yourself to God 1Pe 4:19
—Persevere under it .... Mk 13:13; Heb 10:32–36; Jas 1:12; Rev 2:10
—Rejoice in it .... Mt 5:12; Ac 5:41; Php 2:17; Col 1:24
—Flee from it .... Mt 10:23; Ac 14:6
—Do not be ashamed 1Pe 4:16
—Pray for persecutors .... Mt 5:44; Lk 23:34; Ac 7:60

PERSEVERANCE

—Remaining firm in our faith
A. Related themes
PERSEVERANCE is a theme of:
—2 Timothy 2Ti 2:3
—Hebrews .... Heb 10:36
B. God preserves us in our faith
—He draws us firmly to himself .... Jn 6:37
—He holds us in his hand .... Ps 37:24; Jn 10:27–29
—He keeps us in his love .... Ro 8:35–39
—He watches over us .... Ps 121:3–8; Ps 145:20
—He protects us from the evil one 2Th 3:3; 1Jn 5:18
—He keeps our commitment firm 1Co 1:8; 2Ti 1:12
—He will keep us until the final day .... Php 1:6; 1Pe 1:4–5
C. We must persevere in our faith
—The command to persevere .... Heb 10:35–36; Heb 12:2; Jas 1:12
—The command to use spiritual armor .... Eph 6:10–17; 1Th 5:8
—The warning not to turn away from God .... Heb 3:12; Heb 6:1–6; Heb 10:26–31; Rev 2:4–5
—The possibility of rejecting the faith .... 1Ti 1:19–20; 1Ti 6:20–21; 2Ti 2:17–18; Heb 3:16–18

PERSIA
See MEDES AND PERSIANS

PETER
A. Related theme
PETER AND PAUL is a theme of Acts . . . Ac 19:11
B. Background information
—Father's name was John . . . Jn 1:42
—Given name: Simon . . . Jn 1:42
—Brother of Andrew . . . Mt 10:2
—A native of Bethsaida . . . Jn 1:44
—Originally a fisherman . . . Lk 5:1–5
—Uneducated . . . Ac 4:13
—Married . . . Mk 1:30
1Co 9:5
C. Events during Jesus' public ministry
—Let Jesus use his boat to speak from . . . Lk 5:3
—Caught numerous fish at Jesus' command . . . Lk 5:5–7
—Given the name Cephas (Peter) . . . Mt 16:17–18
Jn 1:42
—Called by Jesus to fish for people . . . Mt 4:18–20
Mk 1:16–18
—Witnessed raising of Jairus's daughter . . . Mk 5:37–41
—Walked on water at Jesus' bidding . . . Mt 14:28–31
—Confessed Christ as Son of God . . . Mt 16:13–16
Mk 8:27–30
Lk 9:18–20
—Rebuked by Jesus . . . Mt 16:21–23
Mk 8:31–33
—Observed the transfiguration . . . Mt 17:1–8
Mk 9:2–8
—Caught fish that had coin in its mouth . . . Mt 17:24–27
—Inquired about limits of forgiveness . . . Mt 18:21
—Did not want Jesus to wash his feet . . . Jn 13:6–10
—Jesus prayed for him . . . Lk 22:31–32
—His denial of Jesus predicted . . . Mt 26:31–35
Mk 14:27–31
Lk 22:33–34
—Accompanied Jesus to Gethsemane . . . Mt 26:36–45
Mk 14:32–42
—Cut off ear of the high priest's servant . . . Jn 18:10–11
—Denied Jesus three times . . . Mt 26:69–75
Mk 14:66–72
Lk 22:54–62
Jn 18:15–18,25–27
D. Events between resurrection and Pentecost
—Ran to tomb on Easter Sunday . . . Lk 24:12
Jn 20:2–8
—Jesus appeared to him . . . Lk 24:33–34
1Co 15:5
—Decided to go fishing . . . Jn 21:3
—Had breakfast with Jesus . . . Jn 21:4–14
—Was asked three times, "Do you love me?" . . . Jn 21:15–17
—One of the apostles in upper room . . . Ac 1:13
—Suggested that Judas's vacancy be filled . . . Ac 1:15–22
E. Events after Pentecost
—Preached a sermon on Pentecost Sunday . . . Ac 2:14–36
—Called the people to repent . . . Ac 2:37–40
—With John, healed a lame man . . . Ac 3:1–8
—Preached in the temple . . . Ac 3:11–26
—Arrested with John . . . Ac 4:1–3
—Questioned before the Sanhedrin . . . Ac 4:7–21
Ac 5:27–32
—Spoke judgment against Ananias and Sapphira . . . Ac 5:1–10
—His shadow healed people . . . Ac 5:15–16
—Was sent to new Christians in Samaria . . . Ac 8:14–17
—Through a vision, was sent to Cornelius . . . Ac 10:9–48
—Explained how God was saving Gentiles . . . Ac 11:1–18
—Imprisoned by Herod . . . Ac 12:3–5
—Freed from prison by an angel . . . Ac 12:6–11
—Left Jerusalem . . . Ac 12:17
—Did missionary work among the Jews . . . 1Co 9:5
Gal 2:9
—Had conflict with Paul at Antioch . . . Gal 2:11–14
—Spoke at council in Jerusalem . . . Ac 15:7–11
F. His character and significance
1. Often spoke impulsively
—Asked to come to Jesus on the water . . . Mt 14:28
—Rebuked Jesus . . . Mt 16:22
—Said he was willing to die with Jesus . . . Lk 22:33
—Claimed he would never deny Jesus . . . Mt 26:33–35
—Did not want Jesus to wash his feet . . . Jn 13:6–9
2. A leader among the disciples
—His name always mentioned first . . . Mt 10:2
Mk 3:16
Lk 6:14
Ac 1:13
—Often the spokesman for the rest . . . Mt 16:16
Mt 26:33–35
Ac 2:14
Ac 4:29
3. One of the major leaders of the church
—Called "rock" by Jesus . . . Mt 16:18
—Led the church in Jerusalem . . . Ac 5:1–9
—Paul met specifically with him . . . Gal 1:18
—Spoke at Jerusalem council . . . Ac 15:7–11
—Called a "pillar" . . . Gal 2:9
—A party at Corinth called by his name . . . 1Co 1:12
—Wrote two letters . . . 1Pe 1:1
2Pe 1:1

PETITION
—Asking God for personal things in prayer
A. Why must we ask?
—God commands it . . . Mt 7:7–9
—We have needs . . . Php 4:19
—We follow the example of God's holy people . . . 1Ch 16:4
Da 6:11
Da 9:17–18
B. How must we ask?
—In faith . . . Mk 11:24
Jn 14:12–14
—With thanksgiving . . . Php 4:6
—In Jesus' name . . . Jn 14:6,13
Jn 15:16
Jn 16:23–24
Ro 5:2
—Without worry . . . Mt 6:25–34
Lk 12:22–31
C. For what may we ask?
—For daily bread . . . Mt 6:11
—For forgiveness . . . Da 9:19
Mt 6:12
—For freedom from temptation . . . Mt 6:13
—For the Holy Spirit . . . Lk 11:13
—For the ability to witness with boldness . . . Ac 4:29–30
—For safety in travel . . . Ezr 8:21–23
—For healing . . . Isa 38:2
Mk 1:40
—For a child . . . 1Sa 1:11
—For anything . . . Jn 14:14

PHARAOH
—The title given to the king of Egypt
A. Pharaohs mentioned in the Bible
1. The pharaoh at the time of Abram
—Sarai taken into his palace . . . Ge 12:14–15
—Diseases inflicted on his household . . . Ge 12:17
—Expelled Abram from Egypt . . . Ge 12:18–20
2. The pharaoh at the time of Joseph
—Put butler and baker in prison . . . Ge 40:1–4
—Had dreams, interpreted by Joseph . . . Ge 41:1–32
—Made Joseph second in command . . . Ge 41:37–43
—Gave Joseph a wife . . . Ge 41:44–45
—Invited Jacob to live in Egypt . . . Ge 45:16–20
—Greeted Jacob and his family . . . Ge 47:1–10
—Settled Jacob and family in Goshen . . . Ge 47:5–6
—Allowed Joseph to bury Jacob in Canaan . . . Ge 50:4–6
3. The pharaoh at the time of the exodus
a. Oppression of the Israelites
—Did not know about Joseph . . . Ex 1:8

—Turned the Israelites into slaves............ Ex 1:9–11
—Ordered the death of baby boys .... Ex 1:15–22
—Tried to kill Moses .... Ex 2:15
—Increased burden of slavery............... Ex 5:1–18

b. Interaction with Moses and Aaron
—First appearance before him .... Ex 5:1–5
—Second appearance, first miracles.......... Ex 7:10–21
—Asked for plagues to be stopped........... Ex 8:8,28
Ex 9:27–28
Ex 10:16–17
—Agreed to let Israelites worship............ Ex 8:25–29
Ex 9:27–28
Ex 10:8–10,24
—Hardened his heart........................ Ex 7:13,22
Ex 8:15,32
Ex 9:7,12,34–35
Ex 10:1,20,27

c. The exodus
—His firstborn son killed .... Ex 12:29–30
—Ordered Israelites to leave .... Ex 12:31–32
—Changed mind and pursued Israelites .... Ex 14:5–9
—Followed Israelites into the sea............ Ex 14:23–25
—Drowned................................. Ex 14:26–28
Ps 106:10–11

4. The pharaoh at the time of Solomon
—Alliance between him and Solomon........... 1Ki 3:1
—Solomon married his daughter................ 1Ki 3:1
1Ki 11:1
—Conquered Gezer and gave it to Solomon 1Ki 9:16

5. Shishak, at the end of Solomon's reign
—Befriended Hadad, adversary of Solomon....... 1Ki 11:14–22
—Befriended Jeroboam......................... 1Ki 11:40
—Attacked and defeated Rehoboam 1Ki 14:25–26
2Ch 12:1–11

6. The pharaoh in Hoshea's time
—Possibly called So 2Ki 17:4
—Hoshea made alliance with him 2Ki 17:4

7. The pharaoh in Hezekiah's time
—Made alliance with Hezekiah................. Isa 30:1–2
—Advanced against Sennacherib 2Ki 19:9
—A weak pharaoh............................ 2Ki 18:21
Isa 36:6
—Unable to save Judah .... Isa 30:3–5
Isa 31:1–3

8. Pharaoh Necho
—Allied with Assyria against Babylon 2Ki 23:29
2Ch 35:20
—Fought and defeated Josiah.................. 2Ki 23:29–30
2Ch 35:20–24
—Deposed Jehoahaz 2Ki 23:33
2Ch 36:3
—Made Jehoiakim king 2Ki 23:34–35
2Ch 36:4
—Defeated by the Babylonians.................. Jer 46:2

9. Hophra, at the time of the exile
—Zedekiah asked his help against Babylon........ Eze 17:15
—Marched against the Babylonians.............. Jer 37:5
—Deserted Zedekiah .... Jer 37:7
—His defeat to Nebuchadnezzar prophesied....... Jer 44:30
Eze 29:19–20

B. Prophecies against Pharaoh
—By Jeremiah .... Jer 44:30
Jer 46:14–19
—By Ezekiel .... Eze 29:1–5
Eze 32:1–15

PHARISEES

—A Jewish party, prominent at the time of Jesus

A. Major characteristics
—Political leaders of the Jews...................... Mt 27:62–64
—Members of the Sanhedrin (Jewish council) .... Ac 23:6
—Leaders of the synagogue .... Jn 9:13–16,22
—Official interpreters of the law.................... Mt 23:2
—Strict observers of the Law of Moses............... Mt 12:2,8–14
Mt 23:23
—Strict adherents of Jewish traditions .... Mk 7:2–3
Gal 1:14
—Believed circumcision was necessary .... Ac 15:5
—Believed in the resurrection and in angels.......... Ac 23:8
—Tried to remain separate from sinners .... Mt 9:11
—Promoted Judaism throughout the world .... Mt 23:15

B. Prominent Pharisees in the Bible
—Nicodemus.................................... Jn 3:1
—Gamaliel....................................... Ac 5:34
—Paul... Ac 23:6
Php 3:5

C. The Pharisees and Jesus
1. Regularly questioned and tested Jesus .... Lk 11:53–54
—About eating with sinners .... Mt 9:11
Mk 2:16
Lk 5:30
—About fasting................................ Mt 9:14
Mk 2:18
Lk 5:33
—About failing to keep the Sabbath .... Mt 12:2
Mk 2:24
Lk 6:2
—About not keeping traditions.................. Mt 15:1–2
Mk 7:5
—About marriage and divorce .... Mt 19:3
Mk 10:2
—About a woman caught in adultery .... Jn 8:1–6
—About paying taxes to Caesar.................. Mt 22:15–17
Mk 12:13–15
—About the most important commandment...... Mt 22:34–36
—About the kingdom of God.................... Lk 17:20–21
—About the validity of Jesus' testimony .... Jn 8:12–13
—About their own blindness.................... Jn 8:40
—Asked for a miraculous sign................... Mt 12:38
—Asked for a sign from heaven.................. Mt 16:1
Mk 8:11
2. Criticized Jesus
—Said he was controlled by a demon .... Mt 9:34
Mt 12:24
—Said he spoke blasphemy...................... Lk 5:21
—Said he failed to keep the Sabbath .... Lk 6:6–7
—Criticized his association with sinners .... Lk 7:36–39
Lk 15:1–2
—Criticized his acceptance of praise............. Lk 19:38–39
3. Desired to get rid of Jesus
—Tried to arrest him........................... Jn 7:32
Jn 18:1–3
—Sought to kill him .... Mt 12:14
Mk 3:6
Jn 11:46–50
—Asked for soldiers to guard the tomb .... Mt 27:62–64
4. Some secretly believed in Jesus .... Jn 12:42–43

D. Jesus criticized the Pharisees
—For their lack of true righteousness................ Mt 5:20
—For their questionable teachings.................. Mt 16:6,11–12
—For persecuting God's messengers .... Mt 21:33–46
Mt 23:33–36
—For failing to understand Scripture................ Mt 22:41–45
—For their hypocrisy.............................. Mt 23:1–32
Lk 11:37–44
Lk 18:9–14
—For their lack of concern for people................ Lk 14:1–14
—For their love of money.......................... Lk 16:14–15

PHILIP

A. Disciple of Jesus.................................. Mt 10:3
Mk 3:18
—Brought Nathanael to Jesus...................... Jn 1:44–46
—Jesus tested him at feeding of the 5,000 .... Jn 6:5–7
—Introduced Greeks to Jesus....................... Jn 12:20–22
—Wanted to see the Father .... Jn 14:8–9
—One of the apostles.............................. Ac 1:13

B. One of the seven deacons .... Ac 6:1–7
—Became an evangelist in Samaria.................. Ac 8:5–13
—Witnessed to and baptized Ethiopian eunuch....... Ac 8:26–39

—Continued preaching the gospel ... Ac 8:40
—Had four daughters who prophesied ... Ac 21:9

PHILISTINES

A. Their identity
—Descendants of Egypt, son of Ham ... Ge 10:6,13–14
—Came from Caphtor (Crete) ... Am 9:7
—Five main cities ... Jos 13:3
1Sa 6:17
—Advanced in culture and war techniques ... 1Sa 13:5–7,19–21
—Their land not fully taken over by Joshua ... Jos 13:2
Jdg 3:1–3

B. Prominent Philistines
—Abimelek: wanted Rebekah as wife ... Ge 26:1,7–11
—Delilah: Samson's lover and deceiver ... Jdg 16:4–20
—Goliath: giant killed by David ... 1Sa 17:4,41–49
—Achish: king of Gath, friend of David ... 1Sa 21:10–15
1Sa 27:1–7

C. Their wars
1. The period of the judges
a. Defeated by Shamgar ... Jdg 3:31
b. Fought Israel at time of Jephthah ... Jdg 10:7–9
c. Fought Israel at time of Samson ... Jdg 13:1,5
See SAMSON
d. Fought Israel at time of Samuel
—Captured the ark in battle ... 1Sa 4:1–11
—Returned the ark ... 1Sa 6:1–12
—Defeated by Samuel at Mizpah ... 1Sa 7:2–14
2. The period of the kings
a. During Saul's reign
—Attacked by Jonathan ... 1Sa 13:3–7
—Defeated by Jonathan and troops ... 1Sa 14:1–47
—Defeated after death of Goliath ... 1Sa 17:1–53
—200 killed by David ... 1Sa 18:24–27
—Defeated by David ... 1Sa 19:8
1Sa 23:1–5
—Attacked King Saul ... 1Sa 28:1,4–5
—Defeated Israelites; Saul died ... 1Sa 31:1–7
1Ch 10:1–7
b. During David's reign
—God promised to defeat them ... 2Sa 3:18
—David's victories over them ... 2Sa 5:17–25
2Sa 8:1
2Sa 21:15–22
1Ch 14:8–17
1Ch 18:1
1Ch 20:4–8
—Exploits of David's mighty men ... 2Sa 23:9–17
1Ch 11:12–19
c. Solomon ruled them ... 1Ki 4:21
2Ch 9:26
d. Jehoshaphat ruled them ... 2Ch 17:10–11
e. They defeated Jehoram ... 2Ch 21:16–17
f. Uzziah defeated them ... 2Ch 26:6–7
g. They defeated Ahaz ... 2Ch 28:18
h. Hezekiah defeated them ... 2Ki 18:8

D. Important data concerning them
—Isaac made treaty with Abimelek ... Ge 26:26–31
—David hid from Saul among them ... 1Sa 27:1–7
1Sa 29:1–11
—Prophecies against them ... Isa 14:28–32
Jer 47:1–7
Eze 25:15–17
Am 1:6–8
Zep 2:4–7
Zec 9:5–7
—Promise concerning their salvation ... Ps 87:4

PHINEHAS

A. Son of Eleazar and grandson of Aaron ... Ex 6:25
—Killed Zimri and Kozbi to end plague ... Nu 25:6–15
—Investigated an altar across the Jordan ... Jos 22:13–31
B. Son of Eli; brother of Hophni ... 1Sa 1:3
—A wicked priest ... 1Sa 2:12–17
—Scorned his father's rebuke ... 1Sa 2:22–25
—His death prophesied as a sign to Eli ... 1Sa 2:30–34
—Brought the ark into battle ... 1Sa 4:4
—Killed in the battle ... 1Sa 4:11,17

PHOEBE

—Christian from Cenchreae commended by Paul ... Ro 16:1–2

PIETY

See MEDITATION; SPIRITUALITY

PILATE

—Governor of Judea ... Jn 18:28–29
—Presided over Jesus' trial ... Mt 27:11–26
Mk 15:1–15
Lk 23:1–5,13–25
Jn 18:28–19:16
—Sent Jesus to Herod ... Lk 23:6–12
—Washed his hands as sign of innocence ... Mt 27:24–25
—Consented to Jesus' crucifixion ... Mt 27:15–26
Mk 15:6–15
—Gave body of Jesus to Joseph and Nicodemus ... Mt 27:57–60
Jn 19:38–42
—Authorized a guard at the tomb ... Mt 27:62–66
—His name forever associated with Jesus' death ... Ac 3:13
Ac 4:27
Ac 13:28
1Ti 6:13

PITY

See COMPASSION; MERCY

POTIPHAR

—Egyptian official who bought Joseph ... Ge 37:36
—Put Joseph in charge of his household ... Ge 39:1–6
—Sent Joseph to prison, unjustly ... Ge 39:7–20

POVERTY

See THE RICH AND THE POOR

POWER

See AUTHORITY

PRAISE

A. Related theme
PRAISE is a theme of Psalms ... Ps 150:6
B. Praising God is a command
1. Commanded throughout the Bible
—In the Mosaic law ... Dt 8:10
—In the Prophets ... 1Ch 29:20
Isa 61:11
Jer 20:13
Joel 2:26
—In the Psalms ... Ps 103:1
Ps 104:1
Ps 145–150
—In the New Testament ... Eph 1:3,6,12,14
1Pe 1:3,7
Rev 19:5
2. Praise is commanded of:
—God's people ... Ps 30:4
Ps 135:1–2,19–21
—Children ... Ps 8:2
Mt 21:16
—The nations ... Ps 67:3–5
Ps 117:1
Ro 15:11
—The angels ... Ps 103:20
Ps 148:2
—Everything that breathes ... Ps 150:6
—All creation ... Ps 98:8
Ps 148:3–12
Isa 44:23

C. Reasons for praise
—God's greatness ... Ps 145:3
—God's splendor and majesty ... Ps 96:4–6
—God's glory ... Ps 66:1–2
—God's holiness ... Ps 99:3
Isa 6:3
—God's love and faithfulness ... Ps 57:9–10
Ps 89:1–2

—God's acts of power ... Ps 150:2
—God's marvelous deeds ... Isa 25:1
—God's glorious grace ... Eph 1:6
—God's salvation ... Ps 106:1–5
Lk 1:68–75
Lk 2:14,20
—God's benefits to his people ... Ps 103:1–18
Ps 111:1–10
Isa 63:7
—God's deliverance of us ... Ps 40:1–3
Ps 124:6–8

D. Methods of praise
—By public worship ... Ps 100:4
—By singing ... Ps 146:1
Ps 147:1
—By musical instruments ... Ps 150:3–5
—By speaking ... Ps 51:15
Heb 13:15
—By dancing ... Ps 149:3
—By witnessing to unbelievers ... 1Pe 2:9

PRAYER

—Communication with God

A. Related themes
PRAYER is a theme of Luke ... Lk 11:1
PRAY AND WORK is a theme of Nehemiah ... Ne 4:9

B. What is prayer?
—Calling on the name of the Lord ... Ge 4:26
Ge 12:8
Zep 3:9
—Calling to God ... Ps 4:1,3
Ps 17:6
—Seeking God's face ... 2Ch 7:14
Ps 27:8
—Seeking the Lord ... Ps 34:4
Isa 55:6
—Crying out to God ... Ps 3:4
Ps 66:1
—Lifting up the soul to God ... Ps 25:1
Ps 86:4
—Lifting up one's hands to God ... Ps 28:2
Ps 141:2
—Approaching God's throne of grace ... Heb 4:16
—Drawing near to God ... Heb 10:22

C. To whom should we pray?
—To God ... 2Ch 20:5–6
Ezr 9:6
Ac 4:24
—To the Father ... Eph 1:17
Eph 3:14
Col 1:3
—To the Lord ... 2Ch 20:5–6
Ac 4:24
2Co 12:8
—To Jesus Christ ... Lk 23:42
Ac 7:59

D. What are the elements of prayer?
—Praise ... Ps 150
Mt 11:25–26
See PRAISE
—Thanksgiving ... Ps 136
Php 4:6
See THANKSGIVING
—Confession ... Ps 51
Mt 6:12
See CONFESSION
—Intercession ... Ps 122:6–9
Jn 17:6–26
See INTERCESSION
—Petition ... Ps 27:7–12
Mt 26:39,42
See PETITION

E. How should we pray?
1. Divine elements
—Through Jesus Christ ... Ro 1:8
—In the name of Jesus Christ ... Jn 14:13–14
Eph 5:20
—In the Holy Spirit ... Eph 6:18
Jude 20
2. Human elements
—In the fear of the Lord ... Ps 145:19
Pr 1:28–29
—In faith ... Mk 11:24
Jas 1:6
Jas 5:15
—In humility ... 2Ch 7:14
2Ch 33:12–13
—In repentance ... 2Ch 6:37
Ac 3:19
—With all our heart ... Dt 4:29
Jer 29:13
—With a heart free from sin ... Ps 66:18–19
Isa 1:15–16
Jn 9:31
—With a life free from selfishness ... Lk 18:9–14
Jas 4:3
—With a heart free from doubt ... Mt 21:21
Jas 1:5–7
—With a forgiving spirit ... Mt 6:14–15
Mk 11:25
—With confidence ... Eph 3:12
Heb 10:19,35
1Jn 3:21–22
—With persistence ... Lk 11:5–10
Lk 18:1–7
1Th 5:17
—With sincerity and simplicity ... Mt 6:5–8
Mk 12:38–40
—In accordance with God's will ... Mt 26:42
1Jn 5:14
—By accompanying prayer with obedience ... 1Jn 3:22

F. Does God answer the prayers of his people?
1. Remarkable answers to prayers
—Abraham's servant for a wife for Isaac ... Ge 24:12–27
—Moses for the defeat of Amalek ... Ex 17:8–13
—Gideon and his fleece ... Jdg 6:36–40
—Samson for strength ... Jdg 16:25–30
—Hannah for a child ... 1Sa 1:9–20
—Elijah for return to life of a dead boy ... 1Ki 17:19–23
—Elijah for fire from heaven ... 1Ki 18:30–38
—Elijah for rain ... 1Ki 18:41–45
Jas 5:17–18
—Elisha for return to life of a dead boy ... 2Ki 4:32–35
—Hezekiah for healing ... 2Ki 20:1–7
—Daniel for safety in the lions' den ... Da 6:10,16–22
—Zechariah for a child ... Lk 1:7,11–17
—The criminal on the cross for salvation ... Lk 23:42–43
—Early Christians for Peter in prison ... Ac 12:3–11
—Paul and Silas in prison ... Ac 16:25–26
2. God's promises to answer us
—In the Old Testament ... Ps 86:7
Isa 30:19
Isa 58:9
—In the words of Jesus ... Mt 7:7–11
Jn 14:13–14
—In New Testament letters ... Jas 1:5–8
1Jn 5:14–15
3. The basis of God's answers
—God's glory ... Nu 14:13–16
Jn 17:1–5
—God's grace ... Ex 32:31–32
Nu 14:17–19
Isa 30:19
2Co 12:8–9
—God's faithfulness to his word ... Ex 32:12–13
2Ch 20:7–9
4. The manner of God's answers
—Sometimes immediately ... Nu 14:20
1Ki 17:20–21
Lk 23:43
—Sometimes after a delay ... Lk 18:1–7

—Sometimes more than asked for ... 1Ki 18:24,36–38
Eph 3:20
—Sometimes different from the request ... 1Ki 19:1–9
2Co 12:7–9
—Sometimes "No" ... 2Sa 12:15–20
—God requires action on our part ... Ne 4:9

G. Various aspects of prayer
1. Postures of prayer
—Standing ... 1Ki 8:22
Ne 9:4–5
—Sitting ... 1Ch 17:16
Lk 10:13
—Kneeling ... Ezr 9:5
Da 6:10
Ac 20:36
—Bowing down ... Ex 34:8
Ps 5:7
Ps 95:6
—Lying on the ground ... 2Sa 12:16
Mt 26:39
—Lifting up hands ... Ps 28:2
Isa 1:15
1Ti 2:8
2. Manner of prayer
—Alone, silently ... 1Sa 1:18
—Alone, aloud ... Eze 11:13
—With two or three ... Mt 18:19
—In a larger group ... Ps 35:18
3. Time of prayer
—In the morning ... Ps 5:1–3
Mk 1:35
—In the evening ... Ge 24:63
—At fixed times ... Ps 55:17
Da 6:10
—Always ... Lk 18:1
Ro 1:10
1Th 5:17
4. Possible places of prayer
—In secret ... Mt 6:6
—In bed ... Ps 63:6
—In a family setting ... Ac 10:1–2
—Out in the open ... Ge 24:11–12
—In the battlefield ... Jos 10:12–13
—By the riverside ... Ac 16:13
—In the temple ... 2Ki 19:14
—In the church gathered together ... Ac 4:23–24,31
—Anywhere ... 1Ti 2:8

PREACHING

A. Preachers in the Bible
1. Old Testament saints who preached
—Noah ... 2Pe 2:5
—Jonah ... Jnh 1:2
Jnh 3:2
—Isaiah ... Isa 61:1
—Ezekiel ... Eze 21:2
—Amos ... Am 7:16
—Haggai and Zechariah ... Ezr 6:14
2. New Testament saints who preached
—John the Baptist ... Mt 3:1
—Jesus ... Mt 4:17
—Peter and John ... Ac 8:25
—Philip ... Ac 8:40
—Paul ... Ac 9:27
1Co 9:16
—Timothy ... 1Ti 4:13
—Numerous believers ... Ac 8:4
Ac 15:35
—All Christians ... Mt 28:19
Mk 16:15

B. The content of preaching
1. In the Old Testament
—A message of judgment ... Eze 20:46
Eze 21:2
Am 7:16
Jnh 3:4
—A message of hope ... Isa 40:1–2,9
Isa 52:7–10
Am 9:11–15
2. In the New Testament
—The good news of the kingdom ... Lk 9:2
Lk 16:16
Ac 20:25
—The good news of salvation ... 1Co 1:21
1Co 15:1–2
—The cross of Christ ... 1Co 2:1–2
—The resurrection of Christ ... Ac 17:18,31
1Co 15:12–14
—Jesus Christ is Lord ... 2Co 4:5
—Fulfillment of the Scriptures in Christ ... Ac 2:14–36
Ac 4:12–26
Ac 13:16–41
1Co 15:3–5
—The coming judgment ... Ac 10:42
Ac 17:31
—The call to repent and believe ... Mk 1:15
Ac 2:38
Ac 10:43
Ac 26:20

PREDESTINATION

See ELECTION; PROVIDENCE

PRIDE

A. Legitimate pride
1. Occasions for such pride
—Boasting in the Lord ... Ps 34:2
Ps 44:8
Jer 9:24
1Co 1:31
—Boasting in the cross of Christ ... Gal 6:14
—Boasting about God-fearing churches ... 2Co 1:14
2Co 7:4
Php 2:16
2. The glory of such pride
—Must be in God's grace ... 2Co 1:12
—Must be in Jesus Christ ... Ro 15:17–18
—Must be in the Holy Spirit ... Ro 15:18–19

B. Sinful pride
1. Characteristics of a proud person
—Tries to be like God ... Ge 3:5–6
—Thinks himself or herself better than others ... Lk 18:10–12
—Boasts about ancestry ... Lk 3:8
Jn 8:33
—Takes pride in the temple ... Jer 7:4
—Takes pride in self-accomplishment ... Isa 10:12–15
Eze 28:1–7
1Co 4:7
2. Notable examples
—Adam and Eve ... Ge 3:5–6
—David ... 1Ch 21:1–7
—Uzziah ... 2Ch 26:16
—Hezekiah ... 2Ch 32:25
—Nebuchadnezzar ... Da 4:30
—Herod ... Ac 12:21–23
3. Results of such pride
—Deceives the heart ... Jer 49:16
—Hardens the heart ... Da 5:20
—Produces quarrels ... Pr 13:10
—Brings disgrace ... Pr 11:2
—Leads to destruction ... Pr 16:18
—Brings opposition from God ... Pr 3:34
Jas 4:6
—Brings judgment from God ... Lev 26:18–20
Zep 2:10–11
Mal 4:1
4. Warnings against such pride ... Pr 8:13
Pr 16:5,18
Pr 21:4,24
Lk 18:9
Ro 12:16
1Jn 2:16

See also HUMILITY

PRIEST

A. Basic requirements for being priests
- —Must belong to the tribe of Levi .... Ex 29:9,44; Ezr 2:61–62
- —Had to follow special marriage laws .... Lev 21:7–9,13–15
- —Had to remain unshaven .... Lev 21:5–6
- —Had to honor proper procedures .... Lev 10:1–7
- —Non-priests punished for doing priestly work .... Nu 18:7; 1Sa 13:8–14; 2Ch 26:16–21

B. Basic tasks of the priests (including Levites)
- —Presented needs of the people to God .... Heb 5:1–3
- —Made atonement for sin .... Lev 16:1–22
- —Sprinkled blood of the sacrifices .... Lev 1:5,11; Lev 17:11
- —Offered sacrifices on the altar .... Lev 6:8–9
- —Kept fire burning on the altar .... Lev 6:13
- —Burned incense on the altar .... Ex 30:7–9; Lk 1:5–9
- —Took care of the sanctuary .... Nu 3:38
- —Responsible for the treasury 1Ch 26:20
- —Supervised the work of the temple 1Ch 23:4
- —Carried the ark .... Nu 4:15
- —Led the people in music .... Ne 12:27–43
- —Blessed the people .... Nu 6:23–27
- —Prayed for the people .... Lev 16:20–21; Ezr 9:5–15
- —Made diagnosis regarding leprosy .... Lev 13:1–8
- —Taught the law .... Ne 8:7–8; Mal 2:7
- —Made judgments according to the law .... Dt 21:5; 1Ch 23:4

C. Christ fulfilled the Old Testament priesthood
- —Compared to a high priest .... Heb 8:1–6
- —Sacrificed himself .... Heb 9:26,28; Heb 10:12; 1Jn 2:2
- —Brought his blood into heaven .... Heb 9:12
- —Justifies us .... Ro 3:24–28
- —Reconciles us to God 2Co 5:18–19
- —Continues to pray for us .... Ro 8:34; Heb 7:25; 1Jn 2:1

D. Priesthood of all believers
- —Believers are called a holy priesthood .... 1Pe 2:5,9; Rev 1:6
- —We can approach God directly through Christ .... Jn 14:6; Ro 5:2; Eph 2:18
- —We can confess sins directly to God .... Mt 6:12; Lk 18:13; Ac 2:37–38; Ac 17:30
- —Our lives must be spiritual sacrifices .... Ro 12:1; Heb 13:15–16; 1Pe 2:5

PRISCILLA

- —Wife of Aquila; tentmakers .... Ac 18:1–3
- —Invited Paul to live with them .... Ac 18:3
- —Traveled with Paul to Ephesus .... Ac 18:18–19
- —Instructed Apollos .... Ac 18:26
- —Paul considered her a co-worker .... Ro 16:3
- —Church met in their house .... Ro 16:4

PROMISE

—God's pledge for the future

A. Major promises of God

1. Concerning Christ
   - —Coming offspring of the woman .... Ge 3:15
   - —Abraham as a father of many .... Ge 12:1–3
   - —Scepter to come from Judah .... Ge 49:10
   - —Star to come from Jacob .... Nu 24:17
   - —Prophet like Moses .... Dt 18:15,18
   - —David's throne to be established forever 2Sa 7:16
   - —The virgin birth .... Isa 7:14
   - —The coming Prince of Peace .... Isa 9:6–7
   - —The suffering servant of God .... Isa 53:1–12
   - —The new covenant .... Jer 31:31–34
   - —The coming shepherd .... Eze 34:23
   - —The coming Holy Spirit .... Joel 2:28–32
   - —A king born in Bethlehem .... Mic 5:2–4
   - —Jesus riding into Jerusalem .... Zec 9:9
   - —The forerunner of the Messiah .... Mal 3:1
2. Concerning believers
   - —God will forgive sin 1Jn 1:9
   - —God will give us peace .... Ps 85:8
   - —God will bless us .... Ps 67:6–7
   - —God will lead us .... Ps 23:1–6
   - —God will never leave us .... Heb 13:5
   - —Jesus will never leave us .... Mt 28:20
   - —God will answer prayer 1Jn 5:14–15
   - —Jesus will answer prayer .... Jn 14:13–14
   - —God will help us overcome temptation 1Co 10:13
   - —God will protect us from Satan 2Th 3:3
   - —God will give us eternal life 1Jn 2:25
   - —God will give us the kingdom .... Jas 2:5
   - —God will make us his heirs .... Gal 3:29

B. God's attitude to his promises
- —Gives us many promises 2Pe 1:4
- —Confirms his promises by an oath .... Heb 6:13–20
- —Remembers his promises .... Ps 105:42
- —Keeps his promises .... Jos 23:15; Isa 38:7; Ac 13:23,32–33; 2Pe 3:9
- —Is faithful to his promises .... 1Th 5:24; Heb 10:23
- —Fulfills all his promises in Christ 2Co 1:18,20
- —God's promises never fail 1Ki 8:56

C. Believers and God's promises
- —We have them from God 2Co 7:1
- —We must believe them .... Ps 106:12,24; Ro 4:16–21
- —We must share in them .... Eph 3:6
- —We must rejoice in them .... Ps 119:162
- —We must meditate on them .... Ps 119:148
- —We must not fall short of them .... Heb 4:1

PROPHET

A. Related themes

1. PROPHETS is a theme of:
   - —1 Kings 1Ki 11:29
   - —2 Kings 2Ki 6:12
2. FULFILLMENT is a theme of:
   - —Matthew .... Mt 5:17
   - —Hebrews .... Heb 7:27

B. How did one become a prophet?
- —Called directly by God .... Isa 6:8; Jer 1:4–5; Am 7:14–15
- —Inspired by God to prophesy 1Sa 10:6,9–11; 1Sa 19:23–24
- —Appointed by another prophet 1Ki 19:19–21
- —Some joined the company of the prophets 2Ki 2:3,5,7; 2Ki 6:1–4

C. What did a prophet do?

1. Spoke messages from God to the people
   - —God commanded them to speak .... Dt 18:18; Jnh 3:2
   - —The Spirit moved them to speak 2Pe 1:21
   - —They said, "This is what the LORD says" .... Isa 44:6; Jer 6:16
2. Served as watchmen for the people .... Jer 6:16–17; Eze 3:16–21
3. Pointed out the sins of kings 2Sa 12:1–12; 1Ki 18:18–19
4. Pronounced judgment on the people .... 1Ki 21:20–24; Isa 2:6–21; Jer 4:5–18

5. Predicted the future 1Sa 9:9
—The near future 1Ki 17:1
Ac 11:28
—The distant future . . . . . Isa 65:17–25
Joel 2:28–32
Mic 5:2–5
Lk 24:25–27
6. Called the people to repentance 2Ki 17:13
Jer 18:11
Am 5:4–6,14–15
7. Gave hope to the people . . . . . Jer 23:3–8
Am 9:11–15
Zep 3:9–17
8. Interpreted dreams . . . . . Da 2:17–45
Da 3:9–28
9. Wrote down messages from God . . . . . Jer 30:2
Hab 2:2
Rev 1:11,19

D. Tests for determining the true prophet
—Does the prophecy come true? . . . . . Dt 18:21–22
Jer 28:1–17
—Does it correspond with God's word? . . . . . Dt 13:1–3
1Ki 22:17–28,37
1Jn 4:1–3
—Does the prophet live a God-fearing life? . . . . . Jer 23:9–18
2Pe 2:1–3,13–18

E. Responses to the prophets
1. Positive
—They were to be heeded . . . . . Dt 18:15
—They were to be trusted 2Ch 20:20
2. Negative
—They were often persecuted 2Ch 36:16
Ac 7:52
—They were sometimes put in prison 2Ch 18:25–26
Jer 37:15–16
—They were even killed 1Ki 19:10
Mt 21:35–36
1Th 2:15

F. Jesus Christ as God's final prophet
—He fulfilled God's promise of a prophet . . . . . Dt 18:15,18
Ac 3:21–23
Ac 7:37
—He fulfilled all Old Testament prophecies . . . . . Mt 5:17
2Co 1:20
1Pe 1:10–11
—He is called "the Prophet" . . . . . Jn 6:14–15
Jn 7:40
—He called himself a prophet . . . . . Mt 13:57
Lk 13:33
—He perfectly spoke God's word . . . . . Jn 7:16
Jn 12:49–50
Heb 1:1–2
—He is the Word of God in human flesh . . . . . Jn 1:14

G. Prophets in the New Testament church
1. Names
—Agabus . . . . . Ac 11:28
Ac 21:10
—Judas and Silas . . . . . Ac 15:32
—12 men in Ephesus . . . . . Ac 19:6
—Daughters of Philip . . . . . Ac 21:9
—Paul 1Co 13:2
1Th 4:13–17
—Peter 2Pe 3:10–13
—John . . . . . Rev 1:1
2. Prophecy as a gift of the Spirit
—Mentioned by Peter on Pentecost . . . . . Ac 2:17
—Mentioned by Paul 1Co 12:10
1Co 14:1
Eph 4:11
—Distinct from the gift of teaching . . . . . Ac 13:1
1Co 12:28
Eph 4:11
3. Function of prophets in the church
—Served as foundation of the church . . . . . Eph 2:20
—Their gift preferred to tongues 1Co 14:1–5
—Message must edify the church 1Co 14:4–5,12
—Message must reach unbelievers 1Co 14:23–25
—Message must be tested by other prophets 1Co 14:29–32
1Th 5:19–20
1Jn 4:1

PROVIDENCE

—God's care over creation and his control of history

A. Related themes
1. PROVIDENCE is a theme of:
—Numbers . . . . . Nu 21:3
—Ruth . . . . . Ru 4:14
—Ezra . . . . . Ezr 8:31
—Esther . . . . . Est 6:4
2. PLAN OF GOD is a theme of:
—Luke . . . . . Lk 16:16
—Ephesians . . . . . Eph 1:10
3. GOD'S CONTROL is a theme of:
—Jeremiah . . . . . Jer 10:10
—Daniel . . . . . Da 4:35
—Habakkuk . . . . . Hab 2:13
—Zechariah . . . . . Zec 12:1
4. GOD'S FREEDOM is a theme of Job . . . . . Job 40:8

B. God's care for his whole creation
1. Aspects of God's providence
—Cares for all his creatures . . . . . Ps 145:9
Mt 10:29
—Provides food for his creatures . . . . . Ps 104:14,27–28
Ps 145:16
Mt 6:26
—Preserves his creatures . . . . . Ne 9:6
Ps 36:6
—Determines the events of history . . . . . Ge 50:20
Ps 33:10–11
Ac 2:22–23
—Determines the ways of humans . . . . . Pr 16:1,9
Pr 19:21
—Controls everything that happens . . . . . Isa 40:22–26
Da 4:35
Ac 17:26
Eph 1:11
—Controls the weather . . . . . Ps 68:9
Mt 5:45
Ac 14:15–17
—Controls the smallest details . . . . . Mt 10:29–30
—Controls evil . . . . . Job 2:1–8
Isa 14:24–27
Isa 45:7
Am 3:6
2. Means of God's control
—By his powerful word . . . . . Ps 29:3–9
Heb 1:3
—By Jesus Christ . . . . . Col 1:17

C. God's special care for his own people
1. General statements . . . . . Ps 91:1–16
Isa 31:5
Ro 8:35–39
1Pe 3:12
2. Specific statements
—Opens hearts to believe the gospel . . . . . Lk 24:45
Ac 16:14
—Controls specific events . . . . . Ge 22:8,13–14
Ps 105:5–44
Ps 136:10–24
Isa 38:17
—Works for good of those who love him . . . . . Ge 50:20
Ro 8:28

D. Our response to God's providence
—Acknowledge it 1Sa 2:6–10
1Ch 29:11–12
—Rejoice in it . . . . . Ps 4:7–8
Ps 16:7–11
—Trust in it . . . . . Ps 13:6
Ps 28:7

—Humble ourselves in the face of it . . . Dt 8:2–3; Job 1:20–22; Job 42:1–6
—Do not worry about tomorrow . . . Mt 6:25–34; Mt 10:28–31

PUNISHMENT

—Penalty inflicted because of sin

A. Related theme
CYCLES is a theme of Judges . . . Jdg 10:6

B. Human punishment through law
1. Principles of punishment
—Power to punish given to government . . . Ro 13:4
—Eye for eye, tooth for tooth . . . Ex 21:23–25; Lev 24:19–20; Dt 19:21
—Restitution to be made . . . Ex 22:1–9; Nu 5:5–8
—Must be impartial . . . Lev 24:22; Dt 1:16–17
—Innocent must be acquitted . . . Dt 25:1
2. Methods of punishment
a. Non-capital punishments
—Fines . . . Ex 21:22; Am 2:8
—Confiscation of property . . . Ezr 7:26
—Beating . . . Dt 25:2–3; 2Co 11:23–25
—Gouging out eyes . . . Jdg 16:21
—Imprisonment . . . 1Ki 22:27; Ac 12:4
—Confinement in a dungeon . . . Jer 38:6
—Chains . . . 2Ki 23:33; Php 1:7,13
—Banishment . . . Ezr 7:26; Rev 1:9
—Excommunication from synagogue . . . Jn 9:22; Jn 16:2
b. Capital punishment
—Stoning . . . Dt 22:24; Ac 7:59
—Burning . . . Lev 20:14
—Killing by the sword . . . Ac 12:2
—Impaling on a pole . . . Est 7:9–10
—Crucifying . . . Mk 15:20,24
—Beheading . . . Ge 40:19
—Sawing in pieces . . . Heb 11:37
—Throwing to wild beasts . . . Da 6:16,24

C. God's punishment
1. Basic reasons for God's punishment
—Human sin . . . Am 1:3–2:16; Ro 6:23
—Idolatry . . . 2Ki 17:14–20; Jer 2:9–13
—Disobedience to God's law . . . Dt 28:15–68; Ne 9:26–27
2. Methods of God's punishments
a. Temporal
—Sickness . . . 2Ch 26:19–20
—Death of a loved one . . . 2Sa 12:14
—Drought . . . 1Ki 17:1
—Famine . . . La 2:11–12
—Violent storms . . . Jnh 1:4
—Plagues . . . Joel 1:2–11
—Defeat by foreign armies . . . Jdg 2:10–15
—Exile . . . 2Ch 36:15–20
b. Eternal punishment
See HELL

QUEEN

A. Queen of Sheba
—Came to visit Solomon . . . 1Ki 10:1–2; 2Ch 9:1
—Overwhelmed at Solomon's wisdom . . . 1Ki 10:3–9; 2Ch 9:2–8
—Gave Solomon many gifts . . . 1Ki 10:10; 2Ch 9:9
—Received gifts from Solomon . . . 1Ki 10:13; 2Ch 9:12
—Jesus used her as an example . . . Mt 12:42; Lk 11:31

B. Queen Athaliah
See ATHALIAH

C. Queen Vashti
See VASHTI

D. Queen Esther
See ESTHER

E. Queen of Heaven (goddess Ishtar) . . . Jer 7:18; Jer 44:17–19,25

F. Babylon pictured as a queen . . . Isa 47:5–8; Rev 18:7

RACHEL

—Younger daughter of Laban . . . Ge 29:16
—Second wife of Jacob . . . Ge 29:28
—Loved by Jacob more than Leah . . . Ge 29:30
—Bore two sons . . . Ge 30:22–24; Ge 35:16–18,24
—Stole Laban's gods . . . Ge 31:19,32–35
—Her death . . . Ge 35:19–20
—Prophecy concerning her . . . Jer 31:15
—Prophecy fulfilled at the birth of Jesus . . . Mt 2:16–18

RAHAB

—Prostitute at Jericho who hid spies . . . Jos 2:1–21
—Spared when Jericho was destroyed . . . Jos 6:22–25
—Mother of Boaz . . . Mt 1:5
—An example of true faith . . . Heb 11:31; Jas 2:25–26

RAIN

See WEATHER

RANSOM

See REDEMPTION

REBEKAH

—Sister of Laban . . . Ge 24:29
—Secured as bride for Isaac . . . Ge 24:34–61
—Mother of Esau and Jacob . . . Ge 25:19–26
—Abimelek discovered that she was Isaac's wife . . . Ge 26:1–11
—Helped Jacob deceitfully get Isaac's blessing . . . Ge 27:1–17
—Convinced Isaac that Jacob should leave . . . Ge 27:42–28:4
—Buried in cave of Machpelah . . . Ge 49:29–31

RECONCILIATION

—Establishing harmony between conflicting parties

A. The need for reconciliation
1. Between humans
—Adam and Eve argued in Eden . . . Ge 3:12–13
—Abram and Lot could not agree . . . Ge 13:5–11
—Sarai and Hagar could not get along . . . Ge 16:3–6
—Jacob fled from Esau . . . Ge 27:41–45
—There will always be conflicts . . . Mt 24:6
2. Between God and humans
—Adam and Eve hid from God . . . Ge 3:8
—Sinners are hostile to God . . . Ro 8:7; Col 1:21
—Sinners cannot stand in God's presence . . . Ps 5:5–6
—Isaiah fearful of God's presence . . . Isa 6:5
3. Between God and nature
—Nature cursed by God . . . Ge 3:14–18
—Nature groans because of sin . . . Ro 8:20,22

B. The process of reconciliation
1. Only God can reconcile us to himself
—God took the initiative . . . 2Co 5:18
—God reconciles sinners to himself . . . 2Co 5:19; Col 1:22
—He reconciles all things to himself . . . Eph 1:10; Col 1:20
2. Accomplished through the cross . . . Ro 5:10; 2Co 5:18–19; Col 1:22; Heb 2:17

3. Reconciliation among humans rooted in Christ
—Christ is our peace ... Eph 2:14–17
—We are one in Christ ... Jn 17:11,22–23
Gal 3:28
Col 3:11
—Harmony experienced in the early church ... Ac 2:44–45
Ac 4:32–35

C. Believers and reconciliation
1. Reconciliation with God
—We must be reconciled to God ... 2Co 5:20
—We must proclaim reconciliation ... 2Co 5:19–20
2. Reconciliation among believers
—Conflicts resolved in the early church ... Ac 15:1–29
Gal 2:1–10
—We may show no partiality in the church ... Jas 2:1–4,9
1Pe 1:17
—There may be no divisions in the church ... 1Co 1:10–13
1Co 11:18–22
—We must work for harmony in the church ... Gal 6:1–2
Eph 4:29–32
Php 2:1–5
—We must end personal conflicts ... Mt 5:23–24
Mt 18:15–16
1Co 6:1–8
Php 4:2–3

REDEMPTION

—Freedom obtained through a price paid

A. Related theme
REDEMPTION is a theme of Isaiah ... Isa 43:1

B. Redemption among humans
1. Redemption of an Israelite slave
—Slave could redeem himself ... Lev 25:49
—Slave could be redeemed by relatives ... Lev 25:48–49
—Slave released in Year of Jubilee ... Lev 25:54
2. Redemption of property
—A person could redeem his own land ... Lev 25:26–27
—A relative could redeem the land ... Lev 25:25,48–53
—Land returned in the Year of Jubilee ... Lev 25:28,39–43
—Land could be redeemed through marriage ... Ru 4:1–12

C. Redemption by God
1. Natural redemption for Israelites
—Israelites were slaves in Egypt ... Ge 15:13
Ex 1:11–14
Dt 5:15
—Israelites redeemed through the exodus ... Ex 6:6
2Sa 7:22–24
Ps 106:8–10
Mic 6:4
—Price paid was the destruction of Egypt ... Isa 43:3
—Judah redeemed from Babylon ... Isa 54:5–8
Jer 31:10–11
Mic 4:10
2. Spiritual redemption from sin
a. We need redemption
—We are all slaves to sin ... Jn 8:34
Ro 6:17
—Humans cannot redeem themselves ... Ps 49:7–8
b. God redeemed the Israelites ... Ps 130:8
Isa 44:21–22
Lk 1:68–71
c. Christ redeems us
—Redemption accomplished in Christ ... Ro 3:24
Col 1:13–14
—The ransom paid was his blood ... Eph 1:7
1Pe 1:19
Rev 5:9
—The ransom paid was his death ... Mk 10:45
Heb 9:15
1Ti 2:6
d. The purpose of redemption
—To justify us before God ... Ro 3:24
—To free us from wickedness ... Ro 6:7,22
Titus 2:14
—To free us from the law ... Gal 4:5
—To free us from the curse ... Gal 3:13
—To free us from an empty way of life ... 1Pe 1:18
e. The results of redemption
—We are forgiven ... Eph 1:7
Col 1:14
—We can now live free lives ... Gal 5:1,13
—We can now serve God ... 1Pe 2:16
—We await our final redemption ... Lk 21:27–28
Ro 8:23
Eph 1:14

REGENERATION

See BORN AGAIN

REHOBOAM

—Son of Solomon; king of Judah ... 1Ki 11:43
1Ch 3:10
—Had various wives ... 2Ch 11:18–21
—Was asked to lighten Israelite yoke ... 1Ki 12:1–4
2Ch 10:1–4
—Refused to ease the Israelites' burden ... 1Ki 12:5–15
2Ch 10:5–15
—Caused division in the kingdom ... 1Ki 12:16–24
2Ch 10:16–19
—Told not to fight to regain ten tribes ... 2Ch 11:1–4
—Built up defenses of Judah ... 2Ch 11:5–12
—Supported by Levites from Israel ... 2Ch 11:13–17
—Led Judah into idolatry ... 1Ki 14:21–24
2Ch 12:1,14
—Fought with Shishak of Egypt ... 1Ki 14:25–28
2Ch 12:2–11
—Humbled himself ... 2Ch 12:12
—His death ... 1Ki 14:31
2Ch 12:16

REJOICE

See JOY

REMEMBER

A. Human remembrance
1. Examples of what humans must remember
—The day of the exodus ... Ex 13:3
—The Sabbath day ... Ex 20:8
—God's care during 40 years in wilderness ... Dt 8:2
—Rebellion against God ... Dt 9:7
—The power of God ... Ne 4:14
—The miracles of God ... Ps 77:11
—The name of God ... Ps 119:55
—The Creator ... Ecc 12:1,6
—The body and blood of the Lord ... 1Co 11:24–25
—The poor ... Gal 2:10
—The stranger ... Heb 13:2
2. What do humans do when they remember?
—They celebrate the Passover ... Ex 13:3–10
—They keep the Sabbath holy ... Ex 20:8
—They trust God ... Dt 8:17–18
—They obey and serve God ... Dt 10:12–13
—They fight for the Lord ... Ne 4:14
—They meditate on God and his mighty acts ... Ps 77:11–20
—They keep God's law ... Ps 119:55
—They fear God and keep his commandments ... Ecc 12:13
—They celebrate the Lord's Supper ... 1Co 11:26–29
—They give on behalf of the poor ... Gal 2:10
—They show hospitality ... Heb 13:2

B. Divine remembrance
1. Examples of what/whom God remembers
—His covenant with Noah ... Ge 9:14–15
—His covenant with Abraham ... Ex 2:23–25
Ps 105:8
—His promises ... Ps 105:42
—His love and faithfulness ... Ps 98:3
—Noah ... Ge 8:1
—Abraham ... Ge 19:29
—Rachel ... Ge 30:22
—Hannah ... 1Sa 1:19–20
—The wickedness of his people ... Jer 14:10
Hos 8:13

2. What does God do when he remembers?
   - —He spares the world from a flood … Ge 9:14–15
   - —He rescues his people from Egypt … Ex 3:7–9; Ps 105:43–44
   - —He saves his people … Ps 98:3
   - —He dries up the earth … Ge 8:1
   - —He brings Lot out of Sodom … Ge 19:29
   - —He gives children to barren women … Ge 30:22–24; 1Sa 1:20
   - —He punishes sin … Jer 14:10; Hos 8:13

See also FORGET

REMNANT

—A small but faithful number of God's people preserved

A. Basis of God's promise to keep a remnant
- —The honor of his name … 1Sa 12:22
- —His promise to Abraham … Ge 17:7
- —His promise to David … 1Ki 6:13

B. God kept his promise to preserve a remnant
- —Remnant kept at the time of Elijah … 1Ki 19:18; Ro 11:4
- —A remnant of Israel joined with Judah … 2Ch 30:25; 2Ch 34:9; Isa 10:20–22; Ro 9:27–29
- —The entire nation of Judah was a remnant … 2Ki 17:18; Hos 1:7
- —Remnant preserved from Assyria … 2Ki 19:4,29–31; Mic 5:6–8
- —Remnant kept after Jerusalem was destroyed … 2Ch 36:20; Jer 40:11; Jer 42:2; Eze 11:13
- —Remnant returned from the exile … Ezr 9:8,13–15; Ne 1:2; Jer 23:3; Eze 34:12–14; Hag 1:12,14
- —Believing Jews were a remnant of Israel … Ro 11:5

C. God's promise to preserve the church
- —Promise of Jesus to Peter … Mt 16:18
- —Promise of Jesus for the end times … Mt 24:21–22
- —Remnant preserved in Thyatira … Rev 2:24–25
- —Remnant preserved in Sardis … Rev 3:4–5

REPENTANCE

—Sorrow for sin and turning to God

A. Related themes

REPENTANCE is a theme of:
- —Joel … Joel 2:13
- —Zechariah … Zec 1:3

B. The command to repent
- —God calls all people to repent … Jer 18:11; Eze 18:30–32; Ac 17:30; 2Pe 3:9
- —Christ calls people to repent … Mk 1:14–15; Lk 13:1–5; Rev 2:5,16; Rev 3:3
- —John the Baptist called people to repent … Mt 3:2
- —The apostles called people to repent … Mk 6:12; Ac 2:38; Ac 3:19–20; Ac 26:20
- —The call must go out today … Lk 24:46–48

C. Essential aspects of repentance
- —Acknowledging we are lost … Lk 15:3–7
- —Expressing sorrow for sin … Lk 5:32; Ac 2:37–38; Ac 8:22; 2Co 7:9–10
- —Returning to the Father … Lk 15:17–20
- —Believing in Jesus Christ … Mk 1:15; Ac 20:21; Rev 3:19–20
- —Doing good works … Jer 18:11–12; Mt 3:8; Ac 26:20; Rev 2:4–5

D. The results of repentance
- —Escape from disaster … Jer 18:7–8
- —Forgiveness … 1Ki 8:46–50; Ac 2:38
- —Salvation … 2Co 7:10
- —A new heart and spirit … Eze 18:30–31
- —A knowledge of the truth … 2Ti 2:25
- —Eternal life … Ac 11:18
- —Regret without repentance brings death … Mt 27:3–5; 2Co 7:10

REPTILES

A. Reptiles mentioned in the Bible
- —Adder … Isa 30:6
- —Chameleon … Lev 11:30
- —Cobra … Isa 11:8
- —Frog … Ex 8:2–13
- —Gecko … Lev 11:30
- —Lizard … Lev 11:29–30
- —Serpent … Job 26:13
- —Snake … Ps 58:4
- —Viper … Ac 28:3
- —Worm … Jnh 4:7

B. Serpents and snakes used symbolically
- —As a symbol of healing … Nu 21:8–9; Jn 3:14–15
- —As a symbol of shrewdness … Mt 10:16
- —As a symbol of alcohol's effects … Pr 23:31–32
- —As a symbol of hypocrites … Mt 23:23; Lk 3:7–8
- —As a symbol of evil people … Dt 32:33; Ps 140:1–3
- —As a symbol of God's judgment … Nu 21:6–7; Isa 14:28–29
- —As a symbol of Satan … Ge 3:1–5; Rev 12:9; Rev 20:2

REST

A. Types of rest
- —The Sabbath day … Ex 20:8–11
- —Sleep … Pr 3:23–24
- —Life in the land of Canaan … Jos 1:13
- —Absence of war … 1Ch 22:9
- —Getting away from trouble … Ps 55:6–8
- —Getting away from people … Mk 6:31
- —Death … 1Ki 2:10; 1Th 4:13,15
- —Heaven as the land of rest … Heb 4:8–11; Rev 14:13

B. The human need for rest
- —Because of six days of work … Ex 20:8–10
- —Because of fatigue … Mt 8:24; Mt 26:43
- —Because of overwork … Mk 6:30–31
- —Because of depression … 1Ki 19:3–6
- —Because of anxiety … Ecc 2:22–23; 2Co 2:13
- —Because of the storms of life … Job 3:20–26; Ps 55:4–8

C. The realization of true rest
- —Through trusting in God … Ps 37:3–7; Ps 91:1–2
- —Through resting in God … Ps 23:1–3; Ps 62:1,5
- —Through experiencing God's presence … Ex 33:14; Ps 31:19–20
- —Through coming to Jesus … Mt 11:28–29; Jn 16:33
- —Through the Spirit of God … Isa 63:14

RESURRECTION

—Resuscitation of a dead body

A. The resurrection of Christ

1. Prophecies of Christ's resurrection
   a. The Old Testament in general . . . Lk 24:25–26,44–46
   Jn 20:9
   1Co 15:4
   b. Specific prophecies in the Old Testament
   —David . . . Ps 16:3–11
   Ac 2:24–32
   —Isaiah . . . Isa 55:3
   Ac 13:34
   —Jonah . . . Jnh 1:17
   Mt 12:39–40
   c. Prophesied by Jesus before his death . . . Mk 8:31
   Mk 9:9,31
   Mk 10:33–34
   Jn 2:19–22
2. The event of Christ's resurrection . . . Mt 28:1–7
   Mk 16:1–8
   Lk 24:1–8
   Jn 20:1–8
3. The power used to raise Christ
   —The power of God . . . Ac 2:24
   Eph 1:19–20
   Col 2:12
   —Christ's own power . . . Jn 10:18
   —Jesus is *the* resurrection . . . Jn 11:25–26
   —The power of the Spirit . . . Ro 8:11
   1Pe 3:18
4. The nature of Christ's resurrected body
   a. The same body that died was raised . . . Lk 24:39–40
   Jn 20:27
   b. It was a physical body
   —He ate . . . Lk 24:41–43
   Jn 21:12–13
   Ac 10:40–41
   —He could be touched . . . Jn 20:27
   1Jn 1:1
   c. It was a glorified body . . . 1Co 15:42–44
   Php 3:21
   —He passed through locked doors . . . Jn 20:19,26
   —He ascended into heaven . . . Ac 1:9
5. The appearances of the risen Christ
   —To Mary Magdalene . . . Mk 16:9
   Jn 20:10–18
   —To several women . . . Mt 28:8–10
   —To Peter . . . Lk 24:34
   1Co 15:5
   —To two disciples going to Emmaus . . . Lk 24:13–31
   —To a group of disciples . . . Lk 24:36–44
   —To the disciples, minus Thomas . . . Jn 20:19–25
   —To the disciples, with Thomas . . . Jn 20:26–29
   1Co 15:5
   —To disciples at the Sea of Galilee . . . Jn 21:1–14
   —To the disciples in Galilee . . . Mt 28:16–20
   —To a group of more than 500 . . . 1Co 15:6
   —To James . . . 1Co 15:7
   —To all the apostles in Jerusalem . . . Ac 1:4–9
   1Co 15:7
   —To Paul . . . Ac 9:3–6
   1Co 15:8
   —Jesus gave many convincing proofs . . . Ac 1:3
6. The significance of Christ's resurrection
   —Declares his deity . . . Ro 1:4
   —Declares his lordship . . . Ro 10:9
   —Justifies us . . . Ro 4:25
   —Forgives us . . . 1Co 15:17
   —Saves us . . . Ro 10:9
   1Pe 3:21
   —Gives us living hope . . . 1Co 15:18–19
   1Pe 1:3
   —Gives us victory over death . . . Ro 6:9–11
   1Co 15:57
   —Guarantees our resurrection . . . 1Co 15:20,23
   Php 3:10–11
   —Guarantees the coming judgment . . . Ac 17:31
7. The proclamation of Christ's resurrection
   —Proclaimed by angels . . . Mt 28:5–7
   Lk 24:3–7
   —Acknowledged by Christ's enemies . . . Mt 28:11–15
   —Preached by Peter . . . Ac 2:24–32
   Ac 10:40–41
   —Preached by Paul . . . Ac 13:30–37
   Ac 17:31
   1Co 15:3–5

B. The resurrection of humans

1. Resurrection miracles
   a. In the Old Testament
   —By Elijah . . . 1Ki 17:17–23
   —By Elisha . . . 2Ki 4:19–37
   2Ki 13:21
   b. In the New Testament
   —By Jesus . . . Mk 5:38–42
   Lk 7:11–15
   Jn 11:38–44
   —At Jesus' death . . . Mt 27:52–53
   —By Peter . . . Ac 9:32–35
   —By Paul . . . Ac 20:9–10
   —In Hebrews . . . Heb 11:35
2. The resurrection at the last day
   a. Affirmed in the Old Testament . . . Job 19:26
   Ps 16:10
   Isa 26:19
   Da 12:2
   b. Affirmed in the New Testament
   —Believed by the Jews . . . Jn 11:24
   Ac 23:6
   Ac 24:15
   —Denied by the Sadducees . . . Mt 22:23
   Ac 23:7–8
   —Prophesied by Jesus . . . Mk 12:26–27
   Jn 5:28–29
   Jn 5:39,44
   —Proclaimed by the apostles . . . Ac 24:14–15
   Ro 2:7–8
   Ro 8:11
   1Co 15:50–57
   1Th 4:13–17
   Rev 20:4–5,12–13
3. The nature of the resurrection
   a. For believers
   —Have already risen to a new life . . . Ro 6:3–4
   Eph 2:6
   Col 2:12
   —Will rise first . . . 1Th 4:6
   Rev 20:4–5
   —Will receive bodies like Christ's . . . Php 3:21
   1Jn 3:2
   —Will receive imperishable bodies . . . 1Co 15:42
   —Will receive glorious bodies . . . 1Co 15:43
   —Will receive spiritual bodies . . . 1Co 15:44
   b. For unbelievers
   —Will go to everlasting contempt . . . Da 12:2
   —Will be condemned . . . Jn 5:28–29
   —Will be judged . . . Rev 20:14–15

REUBEN

A. Firstborn of Jacob by Leah . . . Ge 35:23
1Ch 2:1
—Name means "He has seen my misery" . . . Ge 29:32
—Slept with his father's concubine . . . Ge 35:22
Ge 49:4
—Attempted to rescue Joseph . . . Ge 37:21–30
—Went to Egypt with family . . . Ge 46:8–9
—Father of four sons . . . Ge 46:9
—Blessed by Jacob . . . Ge 49:3–4

B. Tribe descended from Reuben
—Blessed by Moses . . . Dt 33:6

—Numbered ... Nu 1:21
Nu 26:7
—Allotted land east of the Jordan ... Nu 32:1–33
Nu 34:14
—Allotted land west of the Jordan ... Eze 48:6
—Failed to help Deborah ... Jdg 5:15–16
—Supported David ... 1Ch 12:37
—One of the tribes of the 144,000 ... Rev 7:5

REVELATION

—God's disclosure of himself and his truth

A. God's revelation in nature
—It reveals God's glory ... Ps 19:1–6
—It reveals God's kindness ... Ac 14:17
—It proclaims his majesty ... Ps 8:1
—It proclaims his righteousness ... Ps 50:6
Ps 97:6
—It proclaims his eternal power ... Ro 1:19–20

B. God's special revelation to his people
1. Direct revelation
—By speaking ... Ge 17:1–2
Ex 33:11
Rev 1:10–11
—By dreams ... Ge 20:3
Nu 12:6
—By visions ... Ge 15:1
Job 33:14–15
2Co 12:1–4
2. Revelation in events of Bible history ... Dt 3:24
Eze 6:13–14
Eze 37:13–14
3. Revelation in his written word
—God revealed to prophets ... 2Ti 3:15–16
2Pe 1:21
—God revealed to apostles ... 1Co 2:10
2Co 12:7
2Pe 3:15
4. His key revelation is Jesus Christ
—Jesus reveals the Father ... Jn 1:18
Jn 14:9
Heb 1:1–2
—Jesus is the Word of God ... Jn 1:1,14
Rev 19:11–13

C. God's continuing revelation to the church
—Revelation is a gift of the Spirit ... 1Co 14:26
Eph 1:17
—Revelations must witness to Christ ... 1Co 12:3
—Revelations must be evaluated by the church ... 1Co 14:29–32

See also DREAMS AND VISIONS; WORD OF GOD

REWARD

—What God has in store for humans

A. In the Old Testament
1. Rewarded according to one's deeds
—Stated in the Mosaic law ... Lev 26:3–39
Dt 28:1–68
—Stated in the Psalms ... Ps 19:11
Ps 28:4
Ps 62:12
—Stated in Proverbs ... Pr 1:29–31
Pr 12:14
Pr 14:14
—Stated in the Prophets ... Isa 59:18
Isa 66:6
Jer 17:10
Jer 21:13–14
Eze 9:9–10
2. Cannot always be applied to this life ... Job 1:1–2:10
Job 9:21–22
Ps 73:1–14
Ecc 9:1–12
3. God does not treat us as our sin deserves ... Ezr 9:13
Job 33:26–28
Ps 103:8–10
4. God's final reward is in the world to come ... Ps 73:16–20
Ecc 12:13–14

B. In the New Testament
1. Whom does God reward with good?
—Those who receive God's grace ... Ro 6:23
Ro 11:6
—Those who believe in Jesus ... Jn 14:1–3
Ro 4:5,16
—Those who have an obedient faith ... Lk 14:12–14
1Co 3:8,12–14
Eph 6:8
Col 3:23–24
Jas 2:14–24
—Those persecuted for Jesus' sake ... Mt 5:11–12
2. Do we earn our reward?
—We *inherit* our reward ... Mt 25:34
Ac 20:32
Col 1:12
Rev 21:7
—Good works are not done for rewards ... Mt 6:1–6,16–18
Lk 17:7–10
3. What is our reward?
—A crown of righteousness ... 2Ti 4:8
—A crown of glory ... 1Pe 5:4
—A crown of life ... Jas 1:12
—A crown that lasts forever ... 1Co 9:25
—The kingdom prepared for us ... Mt 25:34
—A place in heaven ... Jn 14:2–3
2Co 5:1
2Ti 4:8
—Eternal life ... Ro 2:7
Gal 6:8
—Eternal glory ... 2Co 4:17
4. Judgment in store for the disobedient ... Ro 1:18
Ro 2:8–9
Rev 21:8
Rev 22:14–15

THE RICH AND THE POOR

A. Related themes
1. MONEY is a theme of 2 Corinthians ... 2Co 9:7
2. SOCIAL CONCERN is a theme of:
—Deuteronomy ... Dt 26:12
—Luke ... Lk 7:22

B. God is the source of all wealth
—He owns everything ... Ex 19:5
Ps 24:1
Hag 2:8
1Co 10:26
—He gives wealth ... Ge 26:12–13
Dt 8:16–18
1Co 4:7
—He decides who is rich or poor ... 1Sa 2:7
Pr 10:22
Pr 22:2

C. Riches
1. Examples of wealthy people
—Abraham ... Ge 24:34–35
—Isaac ... Ge 26:12–14
—Esau ... Ge 36:7
—Laban ... Ge 30:29–30
—Jacob ... Ge 30:43
—Nabal ... 1Sa 25:2–3
—David ... 2Sa 5:9–13
—Solomon ... 1Ki 10:14–29
—Jehoshaphat ... 2Ch 17:5
—Job ... Job 1:1–3
—Joseph of Arimathea ... Mt 27:57
2. Means of gaining wealth
—Prosperity as God's reward to righteous ... Ps 25:12–13
Ps 112:1–3
Pr 10:22
—The wicked can also be wealthy ... Job 21:7–13
Ps 73:3,12
Jer 12:1–2

- —Wealth gained by taking bribes. . . . Isa 1:23; Eze 22:12; Am 5:12
- —Wealth gained by usury and extortion. . . . Ne 5:1–7; Pr 28:8; Jer 22:17; Eze 22:12
- —Wealth gained by exploiting the poor . . . . Isa 3:14–15; Jer 2:34; Am 2:6–8; Jas 2:6

3. Reactions of the rich to their wealth
   - a. Unwholesome reactions
     - —Hoard it up for themselves. . . . Ecc 5:13; Lk 12:16–19; Jas 5:3
     - —Become greedy and fall into sin . . . . Pr 15:27; 1Ti 6:9–10
     - —Trust in it. . . . Job 31:24–28; Ps 49:5–6; Ps 52:7; 1Ti 6:17
     - —Become proud because of it. . . . Eze 28:5; Hos 12:8; Rev 3:17
     - —Reject God because of it. . . . Dt 8:12–14; Dt 32:15; Ne 9:25–26; Mt 19:16–22
   - b. Wholesome reactions
     - —Use it to help the poor . . . . Ne 5:14–19; Job 29:11–17; Lk 19:8–9; Ac 4:34–37; 2Co 8:1–4
     - —Use it to help bring about peace . . . . Ge 32:13–21; Ge 43:11–15; 1Sa 25:18–35; Pr 18:16
4. God's commands concerning wealth
   - —We must acknowledge God as the source . . . . Dt 8:18; 1Ch 29:12; Hos 2:8
   - —We must use wealth in God's service . . . . Ex 35:4–9; 1Ch 29:3; Mal 3:8–10
   - —We must help the poor. . . . Ps 82:3–4; Mt 19:16–21; Eph 4:28; 1Ti 6:18
   - —We must not store up treasures on earth. . . . Mt 6:19–21
   - —We should not trust in wealth. . . . Ps 62:10; 1Ti 6:17
   - —We should not be greedy . . . . Eph 5:3; Col 3:5; 1Pe 5:2
   - —We cannot serve both God and money. . . . Mt 6:24–25
5. Riches are considered
   - —Fleeting. . . . Pr 23:5; Pr 27:24
   - —Corruptible. . . . Mt 6:19; Jas 5:2–3
   - —Perishable. . . . 1Pe 1:18
   - —Uncertain 1Ti 6:17
   - —Unsatisfying. . . . Ecc 4:8; Ecc 5:10
   - —Deceitful. . . . Mt 13:22
   - —Spiritually dangerous . . . . Lk 18:18–25
6. Judgments often spoken against the rich
   - —In the Old Testament. . . . Isa 1:23–25; Jer 17:11; Am 4:1–3; Mic 2:1–5; Hab 2:6–8; Zec 7:8–14
   - —In the New Testament. . . . Lk 6:24–25; Lk 16:13–15; Ac 8:20–23; Jas 5:1–6; 2Pe 2:3,14–15
7. True riches are spiritual
   - —Having Jesus is worth everything . . . . Mt 13:44–47; Php 3:7–8; Heb 10:34
   - —Believing in Jesus brings true wealth. . . . 1Pe 1:7; Rev 3:17–18
   - —God's grace brings spiritual riches. . . . Eph 1:7,18; Eph 3:8,16; Col 1:27
   - —All things are ours in Christ 1Co 3:21–23
   - —We should store up treasures in heaven. . . . Mt 6:20; 1Ti 6:19

D. Poverty

1. Examples of poor people
   - —Lot. . . . Ge 19:23–30
   - —Naomi and Ruth . . . . Ru 1:20–2:2
   - —Widow of Zarephath 1Ki 17:10–12
   - —Jesus . . . . Mt 8:20; 2Co 8:9
   - —Lazarus . . . . Lk 16:20
   - —Paul (on occasion). . . . Php 4:12
2. Reasons for becoming poor
   - a. God's choice for us. . . . 1Sa 2:7
   - b. Exploitation by the rich . . . . Isa 3:14–15; Jer 2:34; Am 2:6–8; Mic 3:1–3; Jas 2:6
   - c. The result of
     - —Laziness . . . . Pr 6:9–11
     - —Haste. . . . Pr 21:5
     - —Alcohol . . . . Pr 23:21
     - —Greed . . . . Pr 22:16
3. Laws given to protect the poor
   - —There must be no poor . . . . Dt 15:4
   - —Poor must not be taken advantage of . . . . Ex 22:22–23
   - —The poor must be paid daily. . . . Dt 24:14–15
   - —Poor allowed to glean in fields . . . . Lev 19:10; Dt 24:19–21
   - —Laws regarding security on loans . . . . Dt 24:10–13
   - —No interest may be charged to the poor. . . . Ex 22:25; Lev 25:36
   - —The year for canceling debts . . . . Dt 15:1–11
   - —The Year of Jubilee. . . . Lev 25:5–55
   - —Equal justice for rich and poor. . . . Ex 23:2–3,6; Dt 1:17; Pr 31:9
4. Blessings for those who show kindness to the poor
   - —Their throne will be secure. . . . Ps 72:1–5; Pr 29:14
   - —Their righteousness endures forever. . . . Ps 112:9; Isa 58:6–8
   - —God will answer their prayers . . . . Isa 58:6–7,9
   - —They will be rewarded by God . . . . Pr 14:21; Pr 19:17; Pr 22:9; Pr 28:27
   - —They will have treasure in heaven. . . . Mt 19:21; Lk 12:33; Lk 19:8–9
5. God as the hope of the poor
   - —He is their refuge. . . . Ps 14:6; Isa 25:4
   - —He is their protector . . . . Ps 12:5
   - —He is their deliverer. . . . 1Sa 2:8; Ps 34:6; Ps 113:7
   - —He is their helper. . . . Ps 40:17; Ps 70:5; Isa 41:17

—He is their provider . . . Ps 132:15
Isa 61:1–3
Lk 4:18–19

RIGHTEOUSNESS

—The state of being perfect and without sin

A. Related theme
RIGHTEOUSNESS is a theme of Romans . . . Ro 1:17

B. The righteousness of humans

1. In themselves humans are unrighteous
—No one is righteous . . . Ps 14:1–3
Ps 53:1–3
Ro 3:10–12,23
—Our righteous acts are like filthy rags . . . Isa 64:6
—We deserve God's wrath . . . Ro 1:18
Eph 2:3

2. God gives us righteousness
a. Experienced in the Old Testament
—By Abram . . . Ge 15:6
—By David . . . Ps 32:1–2
Ps 103:17
—By Isaiah . . . Isa 45:8,24
Isa 46:13
Isa 61:10

b. Experienced by believers in Christ
—God declares us righteous . . . Ro 3:21–22
Ro 4:1–8
Gal 3:21–22
Php 3:8–9
—God credits us with Christ's righteousness . . . Ro 4:11,22–24
—His righteousness is a gift . . . Ro 5:17
—We become God's righteousness . . . 2Co 5:21

3. Believers are called "the righteous"
—In the Old Testament . . . Ps 1:5–6
Pr 10:3,6–7,20–21
Isa 26:7
Hos 14:9
—In the New Testament . . . Mt 25:37,46
Heb 12:23
Jas 5:16

4. Responsibilities regarding a righteous way of life
—Be instruments of righteousness . . . Ro 6:13
—Be slaves to righteousness . . . Ro 6:18–19
—Long for righteousness . . . Mt 5:6
—Perform righteousness . . . Am 5:24
Mt 5:20
—Pursue righteousness . . . Isa 51:1
1Ti 6:11
2Ti 2:22
—Put on righteousness . . . Eph 4:24
Eph 6:14
—Seek righteousness . . . Mt 6:33
—Bring forth fruits of righteousness . . . Hos 10:12
2Co 9:10
Heb 12:11
—Live for righteousness . . . 1Pe 2:24
—Do what is right . . . 1Jn 2:29
1Jn 3:7
—Shun wickedness . . . 2Co 6:14–15

5. God's word teaches how to be righteous . . . 2Ti 3:16–17

6. Our final righteousness
—Heaven is the home of righteousness . . . 2Pe 3:13
—We receive a crown of righteousness . . . 2Ti 4:8

See also JUSTIFICATION

C. The righteousness of God

1. God the Father
—God is righteous . . . Ps 7:9
Isa 45:21
Jer 12:1
Jn 17:25
—He always acts righteously . . . 1Sa 12:7
Ps 145:17
Jer 9:24
Mic 6:5
—He judges righteously . . . Ps 9:4
Ps 98:9
Jer 11:20
—His commandments are righteous . . . Ps 19:9
Ps 119:138,160
Ro 1:32
Ro 7:12
—His righteousness endures forever . . . Ps 111:3
Ps 112:3

2. Jesus is righteous
a. Old Testament prophecies
—His name is "The Lord Our Righteous Savior" . . . Jer 23:6
Jer 33:16
—He is the righteous servant . . . Isa 53:11
—He is the sun of righteousness . . . Mal 4:2
—He is clothed in righteousness . . . Isa 11:5
Isa 59:16–17
—He loves righteousness . . . Ps 45:7
—He judges in righteousness . . . Ps 72:2
Isa 11:4
—He reigns in righteousness . . . Isa 32:1
Zec 9:9

b. New Testament assertions
—He is the Righteous One . . . Ac 3:14
Ac 7:52
1Jn 2:1
—He fulfilled all righteousness . . . Mt 3:15
—He lived a righteous life . . . Ro 5:18
2Co 5:21
1Pe 3:18
—He is our righteousness . . . 1Co 1:30
—He loves righteousness . . . Heb 1:8–9
—He is the righteous Judge . . . 2Ti 4:8

3. Believers and God's righteousness
—They acknowledge it . . . Ezr 9:15
Da 9:7
—They see it . . . Mic 7:9
—They speak of it . . . Ps 35:28
—They proclaim it . . . Ps 22:31
Ps 71:15–16
—They sing of it . . . Ps 51:14
—They celebrate it . . . Ps 89:16
—They give thanks for it . . . Ps 7:17
—They are led in it . . . Ps 5:8
—They are upheld by it . . . Isa 41:10
—They pray for it . . . Ps 31:1
Ps 143:11

RIVER

A. Rivers and streams mentioned in the Bible
—Abana . . . 2Ki 5:12
—Ahava . . . Ezr 8:15,21
—Arnon . . . Nu 21:13,24
—Besor . . . 1Sa 30:9,21
—Egypt . . . Ge 15:18
—Euphrates . . . Dt 1:7
See EUPHRATES
—Gihon . . . 1Ki 1:33,38
—Gozan . . . 1Ch 5:26
—Jabbok . . . Ge 32:22
—Jordan . . . Ge 13:10
See JORDAN
—Kanah . . . Jos 16:8
—Kebar . . . Eze 10:15
—Kerith . . . 1Ki 17:3–5
—Kidron . . . Jn 18:1
—Kishon . . . Jdg 4:7,13
—Nile . . . Ge 41:1,3,17
—Pharpar . . . 2Ki 5:12
—Pishon . . . Ge 2:11
—Shihor . . . Jos 13:3
—Tigris . . . Ge 2:14
—Ulai . . . Da 8:2
—Zered . . . Dt 2:13–14

B. How were rivers and streams used?
1. Literally
—For drinking . . . 1Ki 17:3–4
—For bathing. . . . Ex 2:5
—For irrigation . . . Ge 2:10
—For transportation. . . . Isa 23:3
—For fishing . . . Lev 11:9–10
—For healing. . . . 2Ki 5:14
—For baptism . . . Mk 1:5
2. As a symbol
—Of an enemy's strength. . . . Ps 124:1–4
—Of God's judgment. . . . Ps 88:16–17
Isa 42:15
—Of God's blessings . . . Ps 36:8
Isa 41:17–18
—Of God's peace . . . Isa 48:18
Isa 66:12
—Of wisdom . . . Pr 18:4
—Of life in the Spirit. . . . Jn 7:38–39
—Of healing, life-giving power. . . . Eze 47:1–12
Rev 22:1–2

ROCK
A. Uses for rocks
—As a pillow . . . Ge 28:11
—As an altar . . . Jdg 6:20–21
—As a landmark . . . Jdg 15:8
—As a memorial . . . Jos 4:1–9
—As a habitat for animals . . . Ps 104:18
—As a hiding place. . . . 1Sa 13:6
—As a tomb. . . . Mt 27:60
—As a place from which water flowed. . . . Ex 17:6
Nu 20:8–11
B. The rock as a symbol
1. Of Simon, named Peter . . . Mt 16:18
Jn 1:42
2. Of the apostles as the church's foundation . . . Eph 2:20
Rev 21:14
3. Of Christ
—The rock in the wilderness . . . 1Co 10:4
—The foundation of the church. . . . 1Co 3:11
—The cornerstone of the church . . . Eph 2:20
1Pe 2:6
—A stone over which people stumble . . . Ro 9:33
1Pe 2:8
4. Of God who protects and saves. . . . Dt 32:4,15
Ps 18:2
Isa 26:4
Hab 1:12

ROME
—The capital city of the New Testament world
A. The government of Rome
—Ruled the world at the time of Christ . . . Lk 2:1
Jn 18:28
Ac 16:12
—Expelled Jews from the city. . . . Ac 18:2
—Gave privileges to Roman citizens. . . . Ac 16:37–38
Ac 22:25–29
B. Christianity and Rome
1. Jews from Rome in Jerusalem at Pentecost. . . . Ac 2:10
2. Paul and Rome
—Paul wrote to the church in Rome. . . . Ro 1:7
—Paul wanted to go to Rome . . . Ro 1:15
Ro 15:23–24
—Paul arrived in Rome as a prisoner . . . Ac 28:14–16
—Paul visited with Christians of Rome. . . . Ac 28:15
—Paul preached in Rome. . . . Ac 28:23–31
Php 1:12–13
—Paul was probably killed in Rome . . . 2Ti 4:6–8
3. Peter may have referred to Rome as Babylon . . . 1Pe 5:13

RUTH
—Moabitess; widowed daughter-in-law of Naomi . . . Ru 1:3–5
—Went with Naomi to Bethlehem . . . Ru 1:22
—Gleaned in field of Boaz . . . Ru 2:2–17
—Proposed marriage to Boaz . . . Ru 3:1–14
—Married Boaz . . . Ru 4:1–13
—Gave birth to Obed . . . Ru 4:13–17
—Ancestor of David. . . . Ru 4:17–22
—Ancestor of Jesus . . . Mt 1:5

SABBATH
—Seventh day of the week, the day of rest
A. The Sabbath in the Old Testament
1. The Sabbath day of rest
a. God rested on the Sabbath . . . Ge 2:2–3
b. Israel observed it before law was given. . . . Ex 16:23,25
c. Laws concerning the Sabbath
—The fourth commandment. . . . Ex 20:8–11
—No work to be done. . . . Ex 31:14–15
Ex 35:2–3
—A day of sacred assembly . . . Lev 23:2–3
—A day for special offerings . . . Nu 28:9–10
2. Purposes of the Sabbath
—To be a sign of the covenant. . . . Ex 31:16–17
Isa 56:6
Eze 20:12,20
—To honor God . . . Isa 58:13
—To worship God . . . Lev 23:3
—To remember God's salvation. . . . Dt 5:15
—To rest from work. . . . Dt 5:12–14
3. The sabbath year. . . . Lev 25:1–7
Eze 46:3
4. The Israelites and the Sabbath
—Disobeyed the Sabbath. . . . Jer 17:20–23
—Desecrated the Sabbath . . . Eze 20:21,24
Eze 22:8
Eze 23:38–39
—Couldn't wait for Sabbath to be over . . . Am 8:4–5
—Wanted to work on Sabbath . . . Ne 13:20–21
—Nehemiah reinstituted Sabbath laws. . . . Ne 13:15–22
B. In the New Testament
1. The Jews and the Sabbath
—Worshiped regularly on that day. . . . Lk 4:16,31
Ac 13:14–15
Ac 17:2
—Used it as a focal point for legalism . . . Mt 12:2,10
Lk 13:14
Jn 9:13–16
2. Jesus and the Sabbath
—Is Lord of the Sabbath. . . . Mt 12:8
Mk 2:28
—Tried to restore its proper spirit . . . Lk 13:10–16
Lk 14:1–6
Jn 5:16–18
—Taught Sabbath was for our good . . . Mk 2:27
3. Symbolism of the Sabbath
—Symbolizes the rest God wants for us. . . . Heb 4:3–4
—Symbolizes the eternal Sabbath . . . Heb 4:8–11
4. The day of worship in the early church
a. The Sabbath. . . . Ac 13:14
Ac 17:2
Ac 18:4
b. The first day of the week
—Christ's resurrection on that day . . . Lk 24:1–7
Jn 20:1,19
—Pentecost on that day. . . . Ac 2:1
—Worship on that day . . . Ac 20:7
—Offerings set aside on that day . . . 1Co 16:2
—John's vision on the Lord's Day. . . . Rev 1:10

SACRIFICE
A. Related theme
SACRIFICE is a theme of Philippians . . . Php 2:17
B. Sacrifices in the Old Testament
1. Persons performing them
—Cain and Abel. . . . Ge 4:3–5
—Noah . . . Ge 8:20–21
—Abram. . . . Ge 12:7–8
Ge 15:9–11

—Jacob ... Ge 31:54; Ge 46:1
—Job ... Job 1:5
—Regular duties of priests ... Lev 1:3–17

2. Types of sacrifices
   a. According to substances used
      —Various animal sacrifices ... Lev 1:2–17; Lev 3:1–4:35
      —Grain sacrifices ... Lev 2:1–16; Lev 6:14–23
   b. According to time performed
      —Daily sacrifices ... Ex 29:38–41; Nu 28:1–8
      —Weekly sacrifices ... Nu 28:9–10
      —Monthly sacrifices ... Nu 28:11–15
      —Annual sacrifices ... Nu 28:16–29:38
3. Purpose of sacrifices
   a. As cleansing for sin
      —Burnt offerings ... Lev 1:3–17
      —Sin offerings ... Lev 4:1–5:13
      —Guilt offerings ... Lev 5:14–6:7
   b. As thanksgiving to God
      —Grain offerings ... Lev 2:1–16
      —Fellowship offerings ... Lev 3:1–16
4. The insufficiency of sacrifices alone
   a. Had to be accompanied by
      —A true faith ... Heb 11:4
      —A humble heart ... Ps 51:17; Isa 66:2–3
      —A repentant heart ... Isa 1:11–16
      —A life of obedience ... 1Sa 15:22; Ps 40:6–8
      —A life of justice ... Mic 6:6–8
      —A desire to give one's best ... Mal 1:6–14
   b. Despised if offered by unjust people ... Isa 1:11–15; Am 5:21–24

C. Sacrifice in the New Testament
1. View of Old Testament sacrifices
   —They cannot take away sin ... Heb 9:9–10,23; Heb 10:1–4,11
   —They point to the sacrifice of Christ ... Heb 9:11–14,24–26
2. The sacrifice of Christ
   —He is the Lamb who was sacrificed ... Jn 1:29; 1Co 5:7; Rev 5:6
   —He is the atoning sacrifice ... Ro 3:25; Heb 7:27; Heb 9:28; 1Jn 4:10
3. Sacrifices expected of the Christian
   —Total commitment to Christ ... Mt 16:24–25
   See SELF-DENIAL
   —Lives of service to God ... Ro 12:1; 1Pe 2:5
   —Praising and confessing God ... Heb 13:15
   —Deeds of kindness ... Heb 13:16
   —Gifts of money for use in God's work ... Php 4:18

SADDUCEES

—A Jewish party, prominent at the time of Jesus

A. Major characteristics
   —Members of the Sanhedrin (Jewish council) ... Ac 23:6
   —Did not believe in the resurrection of the dead ... Mt 22:23; Ac 23:8

B. The Sadducees and Jesus
1. The Sadducees questioned and tested Jesus
   —About a sign from heaven ... Mt 16:1; Mk 8:11
   —About the resurrection of the dead ... Mt 22:23–27; Mk 12:18–23; Lk 20:27–33
2. Jesus criticized the Sadducees ... Mt 16:6,11–12

C. The Sadducees and the early church
   —Persecuted the church ... Ac 4:1–3; Ac 5:17–18
   —Put the apostles on trial ... Ac 5:21–32
   —Put Paul on trial ... Ac 22:30–23:6

SALOME

—The mother of James and John, sons of Zebedee ... Mt 27:56; Mk 15:40
—Wanted a high position for her sons ... Mt 20:20–23
—Watched Jesus die on the cross ... Mk 15:40
—Went to the empty tomb ... Mk 16:1

SALT

A. Uses for salt
   —For seasoning food ... Job 6:6
   —For seasoning sacrifices ... Lev 2:13; Eze 43:24
   —For ratifying a covenant ... Nu 18:19; 2Ch 13:5
   —For rubbing a newborn child ... Eze 16:4

B. Symbolism of salt
   —Symbol of judgment ... Ge 19:26; Jer 48:9
   —Symbol of permanency of covenant ... Nu 18:19
   —Symbol of preservation ... Mt 5:13
   —Symbol of peace ... Mk 9:50; Col 4:6

SALVATION

A. Related theme
   WORLDWIDE SAVIOR is a theme of Luke ... Lk 19:9

B. Definition of salvation
1. "Save" translated as "heal" ... Mk 10:52; Mk 6:56; Ac 14:9
2. "Save" as rescue from physical danger ... Da 6:27; Mt 8:25; Lk 23:39; Ac 27:20,31; Heb 5:7
3. "Save" as rescue from personal enemies ... Ps 18:3; Ps 59:2
4. "Save" as deliverance from political oppression
   —Salvation from Egypt ... Ex 14:13,30; Ps 106:8–11
   —Salvation from enemies invading Canaan ... Jdg 3:9,31; Jdg 8:22; 2Ki 14:27
5. "Save" as deliverance from sin
   a. In the Old Testament
      —Asking for salvation from sin ... Ps 39:8
      —Promise of salvation through Messiah ... Jer 23:5–6; Eze 37:23
   b. In the New Testament, it embraces
      —The past: "have been saved"/"saved" ... Eph 2:5,8; 2Ti 1:9; Titus 3:5
      —The present: "are being saved" ... 1Co 1:18; 2Co 2:15
      —The future: "will be saved" ... Ro 5:9–10; 1Pe 1:5

C. God as the source of salvation
1. Israel's God in the Old Testament
   a. He is called "Savior" ... 1Ch 16:35; Ps 25:5; Isa 43:11; Isa 45:15,21; Mic 7:7
   b. He is Israel's salvation ... Ex 15:1–2; Ps 27:1; Isa 12:2; Jnh 2:9
   c. He promised worldwide salvation ... Ps 67:2; Isa 49:6; Isa 52:10
2. Christ as Savior
   —Salvation is in his name alone ... Ac 4:12; Ac 10:43; Ro 10:13

—He is called Savior . . . Lk 2:11
Eph 5:23
Titus 1:4
—He saves his people from sin . . . Mt 1:21
Ac 5:31
Titus 2:13–14
—He saves the lost . . . Lk 15:3–10
Lk 19:10
—He saves the world . . . Jn 3:16–17
Jn 12:47
1Jn 4:14

D. The process of salvation
1. Salvation required the work of Christ
—His coming to this earth . . . 2Co 8:9
Php 2:6–8
—His death on the cross . . . Jn 3:14–15
1Co 1:18
1Co 15:2–3
—The shedding of his blood . . . 1Pe 1:18–19
Rev 5:9
—His resurrection from the dead . . . Ro 10:9
1Pe 1:3–5
—His ascension into heaven . . . Ac 5:31
2. Salvation comes as a gift from God
—A gift of his love . . . Ro 5:8–9
Titus 3:5
1Jn 4:9–10
—A gift of his grace . . . Eph 2:5,8
Titus 2:11
—A gift of his mercy . . . Titus 3:4–5
1Pe 1:3
3. Requirements for salvation
—Read the Scriptures . . . 2Ti 3:15
—Believe in Jesus Christ . . . Jn 3:16
Ac 16:30–31
Eph 2:8
—Repent of our sins . . . Isa 30:15
Ac 2:37–38
Ac 3:19
2Co 7:10
—Accept salvation as a free gift . . . Isa 55:1
Rev 21:6
—Realize we can do nothing to earn salvation . . . Eph 2:8–9
2Ti 1:9
Titus 3:5
—Give our all in response to salvation . . . Mt 13:44–46
Lk 14:33
Php 3:7–8

E. Our relationship to God's salvation
—We long for it . . . Ps 119:81,174
—We wait for it . . . La 3:26
—We hope for it . . . 1Th 5:8–9
—We pray for it . . . Ps 54:1
Ps 85:7
Jer 31:7
—We realize that it is *now* . . . 2Co 6:2
—We must count its cost . . . Lk 14:25–33
—We are clothed with it . . . 2Ch 6:41
Isa 61:10
—We rejoice in it . . . Ps 9:14
Isa 25:9
—We delight in it . . . Ps 35:9
—We love it . . . Ps 40:16
—We make it known . . . Ps 67:2
—We proclaim it . . . 1Ch 16:23
Ps 96:2
—We grow in it . . . 1Pe 2:2
—We work it out . . . Php 2:12

F. Pictures of salvation
—Horn of salvation . . . 2Sa 22:3
Ps 18:2
—Fortress of salvation . . . Ps 28:8
—Cup of salvation . . . Ps 116:13
—Wells of salvation . . . Isa 12:3
—Walls and ramparts of salvation . . . Isa 26:1
—A rich store of salvation . . . Isa 33:6
—Springs of salvation . . . Isa 45:8
—Helmet of salvation . . . Isa 59:17
Eph 6:17
—Garments of salvation . . . Isa 61:10
—Torch of salvation . . . Isa 62:1
—Gospel of salvation . . . Eph 1:13

SAMARIA

A. Identity of Samaria
—City built by Omri, king of Israel . . . 1Ki 16:23–24
—Became capital of northern kingdom . . . 1Ki 16:29,32
1Ki 21:18
—Became synonymous with the northern kingdom . . . 1Ki 21:1
Hos 7:1

B. History in the Old Testament
—Besieged by Ben-Hadad . . . 2Ki 6:24–25
—Besieged by Assyria . . . 2Ki 17:5
—City taken; people deported . . . 2Ki 17:6
2Ki 18:10–12
—City plundered . . . Isa 8:4
—Other people settled in the region . . . 2Ki 17:24
—Capital city of Trans-Euphrates province . . . Ezr 4:17
Ne 4:1–2

C. History in the New Testament
—Jesus visited it . . . Lk 17:11
Jn 4:4–6
—Gospel must be preached there . . . Ac 1:8
—Gospel spread there . . . Ac 8:1
—Philip preached there . . . Ac 8:5–7
—Holy Spirit was poured out there . . . Ac 8:14–17
—Simon the sorcerer lived there . . . Ac 8:9–13,18–24
—Paul traveled through there . . . Ac 15:3

SAMARITANS

A. In the Old Testament
—A mixed race resettled in Samaria . . . 2Ki 17:24
—Had a polytheistic religion . . . 2Ki 17:25–33
—Wanted to help rebuild the temple . . . Ezr 4:1–2
—Offer to rebuild the temple refused . . . Ezr 4:3
—Tried to frustrate rebuilding of the temple . . . Ezr 4:4–5,24
Ezr 5:3–17
—Tried to frustrate rebuilding of Jerusalem . . . Ezr 4:7–23
Ne 4:1–23
Ne 6:1–14

B. In the New Testament
—Jews and Samaritans did not associate . . . Jn 4:9
—Jesus told parable of Good Samaritan . . . Lk 10:30–35
—A Samaritan leper returned to thank Jesus . . . Lk 17:11–19
—A Samaritan town rejected Jesus . . . Lk 9:52–53
—James and John wanted to destroy the town . . . Lk 9:54–55
—Jesus talked with a Samaritan woman . . . Jn 4:7–26
—Many Samaritans believed in Jesus . . . Jn 4:39–42
Ac 8:5,12

SAMSON

A. History of his life
—Judge from the tribe of Dan . . . Jdg 13:2,24–25
—Birth promised . . . Jdg 13:2–14
—Married Philistine woman . . . Jdg 14:1–18
—Took revenge on Philistines . . . Jdg 15:1–20
—Betrayed by Delilah . . . Jdg 16:1–20
—Captured and eyes gouged out . . . Jdg 16:21–22
—His death . . . Jdg 16:23–31

B. Feats of strength
—Killed a lion . . . Jdg 14:6
—Killed 30 Philistines . . . Jdg 14:19
—Killed a thousand Philistines with jawbone . . . Jdg 15:13–17
—Carried off gates of Gaza . . . Jdg 16:3
—Pushed down temple of Dagon, at cost of his life . . . Jdg 16:25–30

C. An example of faith . . . Heb 11:32

SAMUEL

A. Early life
—Hannah prayed that God would give her a son . . . 1Sa 1:10–18

—Dedicated to God's service ... 1Sa 1:21–28
—Raised by Eli ... 1Sa 2:11,18–26
—Called by God to be a prophet ... 1Sa 3:1–20

B. His life as prophet and judge
—Judged Israel many years ... 1Sa 7:15–17
—Functioned as prophet ... 1Sa 9:9,19
—Led Israel to victory over Philistines ... 1Sa 7:2–14
—Israelites asked him to anoint a king ... 1Sa 8:1–22
—Anointed Saul as king ... 1Sa 10:1,17–24
Ac 13:20–21
—Gave farewell speech as Israel's leader ... 1Sa 12:1–25
—Rebuked Saul for offering a sacrifice ... 1Sa 13:8–14
—Rebuked Saul for disobedience ... 1Sa 15:12–23
—Announced God's rejection of Saul ... 1Sa 15:24–29
—Anointed David as king ... 1Sa 16:1–13
Ac 13:22
—David fled to him for protection ... 1Sa 19:18–24
—Wrote about the events of his day ... 1Ch 29:29
—His death ... 1Sa 25:1

C. Importance after his death
—Summoned by a medium to speak to Saul ... 1Sa 28:5–20
—Seen as a prophet who spoke of Jesus ... Ac 3:24
—Considered an example of faith ... Ps 99:6
Heb 11:32

SANBALLAT

—Chief political opponent of Nehemiah ... Ne 2:10
—Ridiculed rebuilding of Jerusalem ... Ne 2:19
Ne 4:1–2
—Opposed rebuilding of Jerusalem ... Ne 4:7–12
—Schemed to harm Nehemiah ... Ne 6:1–14
—His daughter married high priest's son ... Ne 13:28

SANCTIFICATION

—Being holy and becoming holy

A. Christians have been sanctified
—Sanctified in Christ ... 1Co 1:2
1Co 6:11
—Sanctified through Christ's blood ... Heb 10:29
—Sanctified by the Holy Spirit ... Ro 15:16
—Sanctified by faith ... Ac 26:18
—Christians are called God's holy people ... 1Co 1:2
2Co 1:1
Php 1:1

B. Christians are being sanctified ... Ac 20:32
—Through the word of God ... Jn 17:17–19
—Through the work of God ... 1Th 5:23
—Through the work of the Holy Spirit ... 2Th 2:13
1Pe 1:2
—Through resisting sin ... 1Th 4:3–7

See also HOLINESS

SANHEDRIN

—The Jewish political and religious council

A. Its structure
1. Members
—Elders, chief priests, teachers of law ... Mt 16:21
Mt 27:41
—Chief priests and Pharisees ... Jn 11:47
—Pharisees and Sadducees ... Ac 23:6
2. Led by high priest ... Mt 26:59,62–66

B. Meetings and decisions mentioned in the Bible
1. Concerning Jesus
—Decided that he should be put to death ... Jn 11:47–50
—Made agreement with Judas to betray him ... Mt 26:14–16
Mk 14:10–11
Lk 22:3–6
—Condemned him to death ... Mt 26:57–66
Mk 14:53–64
Jn 18:12–14,19–24
—Asked Pilate for a guard at the tomb ... Mt 27:62–65
2. Concerning the apostles
—Interviewed Peter and John ... Ac 4:5–17
—Ordered them not to preach about Jesus ... Ac 4:18–21
—Interviewed them a second time ... Ac 5:27–40
—Flogged the apostles ... Ac 5:40–41
—Brought Stephen before their assembly ... Ac 6:12–7:56
—Decided to kill Stephen ... Ac 7:57–58
—Voted to kill numerous believers ... Ac 26:10
—Authorized Saul to persecute believers in Damascus ... Ac 9:1–2
—Interviewed Paul in Jerusalem ... Ac 22:30–23:9
—Prosecuted Paul before Felix ... Ac 24:1–9
—Prosecuted Paul before Festus ... Ac 25:6–7

SAPPHIRA

—Wife of Ananias ... Ac 5:1
—Deceitfully kept back part of their money ... Ac 5:2
—Died for lying to God ... Ac 5:7–10

SARAH

A. Her life
—Original name: Sarai ... Ge 11:29
—Wife of Abram; barren ... Ge 11:29–30
—Went with Abram to Canaan ... Ge 12:4–5
—Thought by Pharaoh to be Abram's sister ... Ge 12:10–20
—Gave Hagar to Abram as concubine ... Ge 16:3
—Mistreated Hagar so that Hagar ran away ... Ge 16:4–6
—Name changed to Sarah ... Ge 17:15
—Birth of Isaac promised ... Ge 17:16–21
—Laughed about a possible pregnancy ... Ge 18:10–15
—Thought by Abimelek to be Abraham's sister ... Ge 20:1–18
—Isaac born ... Ge 21:1–7
—Wanted Abraham to send Hagar and Ishmael away ... Ge 21:8–21
—Her death and burial ... Ge 23:1–19

B. Significance of Sarah
—Mother of the Israelites ... Isa 51:2
—Birth of Isaac shows God's election ... Ro 9:6–9
—Sending Hagar away illustrates our freedom ... Gal 4:21–31
—An example of true faith with Abraham ... Heb 11:11–13
—An example of a submissive wife ... 1Pe 3:5–6

SATAN

—An angel who became the archenemy of God

A. Terms for Satan
—The accuser ... Zec 3:1
Rev 12:10
—The devil ... Mt 4:1
Rev 12:9
—The tempter ... Mt 4:3
1Th 3:5
—The evil one ... Mt 6:13
1Jn 2:13–14
—Beelzebub ... Mt 12:24
—Belial ... 2Co 6:15
—A murderer from the beginning ... Jn 8:44
—The father of lies ... Jn 8:44
—The prince of this world ... Jn 12:31
Jn 14:30
—The god of this age ... 2Co 4:4
—Ruler of the kingdom of the air ... Eph 2:2
—The angel of the Abyss ... Rev 9:11
—Abaddon or Apollyon ... Rev 9:11
—The ancient serpent ... Rev 12:9

B. Activities of Satan
1. Activities in the past
—Originally created as good ... Ge 1:31
—Led revolt of angels in heaven ... 2Pe 2:4
Rev 12:7–8
—Tempted Adam and Eve ... Ge 3:1–7
—Incited David to sin ... 1Ch 21:1–2
—Afflicted Job ... Job 1:6–19
Job 2:1–10
—Tempted Jesus ... Mt 4:1–11
—Involved in effort to put Jesus to death ... Lk 22:3
Jn 14:30–31
2. Activities in the present
—Rules a kingdom opposed to God ... Mt 12:25–26
Mt 25:41
—Controls the present sinful world ... 1Jn 5:19
Rev 12:9

—Afflicts people with illness .... Job 2:7
Lk 13:16
Ac 10:38
2Co 12:7
—Tempts believers to sin 1Ch 21:1
Mt 16:23
Ac 5:3
1Th 3:5
—Tries to keep people from true worship .... Mt 13:19
1Pe 5:8–9
—Thwarts the spread of the gospel .... Mt 13:19
2Co 4:3–4
1Th 2:18
—Wants people to worship him .... Mt 4:9
—Masquerades as an angel of light 2Co 11:14
—Uses many schemes 2Co 2:11
Eph 6:11
—Persecutes the church .... Rev 2:10
Rev 12:13–17
—Holds the power of death .... Heb 2:14–15

3. Future activities
—Will be bound in the millennium .... Rev 20:2–3
—Will be set free during the great tribulation .... Rev 20:7–9
—Will empower the antichrist 2Th 2:9
Rev 13:2–4

C. Victory over Satan
1. God has power over him .... Job 1:6–12
Job 2:1–6
Lk 22:31–32
2. Christ has disarmed him
—Prophesied in Eden .... Ge 3:15
—Christ came to destroy him 1Jn 3:8
—Demonstrated in Christ's victory over temptation .... Mt 4:1–11
—Demonstrated by driving out demons .... Lk 10:18
Lk 11:20
—The cross of Christ sealed his defeat .... Jn 12:31–33
Col 2:15
Rev 12:11
3. Believers must fight against him
—We must pray for deliverance .... Mt 6:13
—We must keep busy for the Lord 1Ti 5:13–15
—We must resist his temptations 1Co 7:5
Jas 4:7
—We must extinguish his flaming arrows by our faith .... Eph 6:16
—We must overcome him 1Jn 2:13
Rev 2:10–11
Rev 12:10–11
—Christ prays for the victory of our faith .... Lk 22:31–32
4. Final defeat of Satan
—Prophesied by Paul .... Ro 16:20
—Satan bound in the millennium .... Rev 20:2–3
—Final victory at Christ's return .... Mt 25:31,41
Rev 20:10,14

SAUL

A. First king of Israel
1. Family data and early life
—A member of the tribe of Benjamin 1Sa 9:1–2
—Son of Kish 1Sa 9:1–2
—His family 1Sa 14:49–50
1Ch 8:33
—Searched for his father's donkeys 1Sa 9:3–4
—Consulted Samuel 1Sa 9:5–20
—Anointed king by Samuel 1Sa 10:1
—Prophesied 1Sa 10:9–13
1Sa 19:23–24
—Chosen as king at Mizpah 1Sa 10:20–26
2. Early events as king
—Defeated Ammonites at Jabesh Gilead 1Sa 11:1–11
—Confirmed as king 1Sa 11:12–15
—Fought the Philistines 1Sa 13:1–7,16–22
—Did not wait for Samuel to offer sacrifice 1Sa 13:8–14
—Disobeyed God regarding Amalekites 1Sa 15:1–23
—Repented 1Sa 15:24–31
3. His interaction with David
—Employed David as musician 1Sa 16:14–23
—Approved David's offer to fight Goliath 1Sa 17:31–39
—Became jealous of David 1Sa 18:1–9
—Tried to kill David, who was playing music 1Sa 18:10–11
—Gave David his daughter Michal as wife 1Sa 18:20–28
—Again tried to kill David 1Sa 19:1–17
—Angry at Jonathan for befriending David 1Sa 20:26–34
—Pursued David; killed priests at Nob 1Sa 22:6–19
—Went to Keilah and Ziph 1Sa 23:7–28
—Spared by David in a cave at En Gedi 1Sa 24:1–21
—Spared by David while sleeping in camp 1Sa 26:1–25
4. Saul's death
—Sought Samuel's advice through a medium 1Sa 28:1–14
—Rebuked by Samuel's spirit 1Sa 28:15–20
—Wounded by Philistines; killed himself 1Sa 31:1–6
1Ch 10:1–6
—His death lamented by David 2Sa 1:17–27

B. One of Christ's apostles
See PAUL

SEA

A. Seas mentioned in the Bible
1. The Mediterranean Sea .... Ex 23:31
Nu 34:5
Nu 34:6–7
Dt 11:24
2. The "Red Sea" .... Ac 7:36
—The "Sea of Reeds" (NIV text note) .... Ex 10:19
—The Egyptian sea .... Isa 11:15
3. The Sea of Galilee .... Mt 4:18
Nu 34:11
—The Sea of Tiberias .... Jn 6:1
4. The Dead Sea .... Nu 34:3
Zec 14:8
—The Sea of the Arabah .... Dt 3:17
5. The Adriatic Sea .... Ac 27:27

B. The sea used as a symbol
1. Negative
—Of human sin and restlessness .... Ge 49:4
Isa 57:20
Eph 4:14
—Of human instability .... Jas 1:6
—Of the lifestyle of heretics .... Jude 13
—Of God's judgment .... Jer 49:23–24
La 2:13
—Of the abode of satanic powers .... Da 7:2–3
Rev 13:1
—No sea in heaven .... Rev 21:1
2. Positive
—Of the vast mysteries of God .... Job 11:7–9
—Of God's presence everywhere .... Ps 139:9
—Of the wide expanse of a kingdom .... Ps 72:8
—Of God's great forgiveness .... Mic 7:19
—Of God's promise of righteousness .... Isa 48:18
—Of the extension of the gospel .... Isa 11:9
Hab 2:14

See also WATER

SEAL

A. Literal uses of the seal
—A plate on the high priest's turban .... Ex 39:30–31
—An item for personal identification .... Ge 38:18,25
—A mark for identifying correspondence 1Ki 21:8
—A governmental mark warning people .... Mt 27:66
—A mark securing a title deed .... Jer 32:9–14

B. Figurative use of the seal
—Circumcision: a seal of the covenant .... Ro 4:11
—Zerubbabel: a seal of the coming Messiah .... Hag 2:23
—The Holy Spirit: a seal of salvation 2Co 1:22
Eph 1:14
Eph 4:30
—Christians: a seal of apostleship 1Co 9:2
—God's word: a seal for the church 2Ti 2:19
—The seven seals: Jesus' control of history .... Rev 5:1–6:17

—His death by murder .... 2Ki 19:37; 2Ch 32:21; Isa 37:38

SERVANT

A. Essential qualities of a servant
- —Must have only one master .... Lk 16:13
- —Must be submissive to a master's will .... Ps 123:2; Eph 6:5; 1Pe 2:18
- —Must be faithful to a master 1Co 4:2

B. Servants on a human level
1. Servants in the home
   - —Hagar .... Ge 16:1
   - —Abraham's servant (Eliezer) .... Ge 24:1–2
   - —Zilpah .... Ge 29:24
   - —Bilhah .... Ge 29:29
   - —Joseph .... Ge 39:1–4
2. Servants in the economic realm
   - —Laws concerning servants and slaves .... Ex 21:2–11; Lev 25:39–46
   - —Hired servants .... 2Ch 24:12; Mt 20:1–15; Lk 15:17–19
3. Servants on a political level
   - —Servants of a king 1Sa 16:16,18; 2Sa 12:18–19; 2Ki 9:28
   - —The king's children are called servants 2Sa 13:24; 1Ki 1:17
   - —The king as servant of the people 1Ki 12:7
   - —A king as servant to another king 2Ki 16:7; 2Ki 24:1

C. Believers as servants of one another
- —We are called to serve as Jesus did .... Jn 13:14–16; 1Pe 2:21
- —We are commanded to serve others .... Gal 5:13; Eph 5:21
- —Paul as a servant of others 1Co 9:19–23; 2Co 4:5

D. Servants of the Lord
1. Examples of servants of the Lord
   - —Abraham, Isaac and Jacob .... Ex 32:13
   - —Moses .... Nu 12:7
   - —Joshua .... Jdg 2:8
   - —Samson .... Jdg 15:18
   - —David 2Sa 7:5
   - —Elijah 1Ki 18:36
   - —The prophets .... 2Ki 9:7; Zec 1:6; Rev 10:7
   - —The apostles .... 1Co 4:1; 2Co 6:4; Php 1:1
   - —All Christians .... Ro 6:22; Eph 6:6; 1Pe 2:16
   - —The 144,000 .... Rev 7:4
2. Isaiah's servant songs .... Isa 42:1–4; Isa 49:1–6; Isa 50:4–9; Isa 52:13–53:12
3. Jesus as the servant of the Lord
   - —Fulfilled the servant songs of Isaiah .... Mt 12:17–21; Ac 8:32–35; 1Pe 2:22–25
   - —Took the nature of a servant .... Php 2:7
   - —Called himself a servant .... Mk 10:45; Lk 22:27
   - —Compared himself to a servant .... Lk 12:37
   - —Demonstrated servanthood by washing feet .... Jn 13:4–11
   - —Demonstrated servanthood by his cross .... Isa 53:4–6; Php 2:7–8
   - —Exalted as servant .... Isa 52:13

SETH

- —Third son of Adam and Eve .... Ge 4:25
- —Took the place of Abel .... Ge 4:25
- —Made in Adam's likeness .... Ge 5:3
- —His family .... Ge 5:6–8
- —An ancestor of Jesus .... Lk 3:38

SEXUAL STANDARDS

A. Sexual sins condemned in the Bible
- —Adultery .... Ex 20:14; Pr 5:1–23
- —Incest .... Lev 20:19–21
- —Sex with animals .... Lev 20:15–16
- —Loss of virginity before marriage .... Dt 22:20–21
- —Prostitution .... Dt 23:17–18; Pr 7:10–27
- —Homosexuality .... Ro 1:26–27; 1Co 6:9
- —Obscenity .... Eph 5:4
- —Lust .... Mt 5:27–28; 1Th 4:5

B. God's will regarding sexual standards
1. In negative terms
   - —Laws against illicit sexual behavior .... Ex 20:14; Lev 20:10–21; Dt 23:17–18
   - —The command to flee immorality .... 1Co 6:18; Eph 5:3; Col 3:5; 1Th 4:3
   - —Sexual sin excludes one from the kingdom .... 1Co 6:9–10; Gal 5:19–21; Eph 5:3–5; Rev 22:15
2. In positive terms
   - —Strive for purity 1Th 4:4,7; 1Pe 3:2
   - —Be faithful in marriage 1Co 7:2–4
   - —Exercise self-control .... 1Co 7:8–9; Gal 5:23; 1Th 4:4

See also MARRIAGE; ADULTERY; DIVORCE

SHADRACH

- —Hebrew deported to Babylon .... Da 1:6
- —Name changed from Hananiah .... Da 1:7
- —Refused to be defiled by food .... Da 1:8–20
- —Appointed administrator over Babylon .... Da 2:49
- —Refused to worship idols .... Da 3:1–18
- —Saved from fiery furnace .... Da 3:19–30

SHALLUM

- —King of Israel 2Ki 15:10–15
- —Assassinated by Menahem 2Ki 15:14

SHAME

A. Reasons for feeling ashamed
- —Being naked .... Ge 3:7; Eze 23:29
- —Experiencing defeat .... Ps 6:10; Isa 29:22–23
- —Being humiliated .... Eze 16:63; Zec 13:3–5; 1Co 1:27–29
- —Experiencing sin .... Ezr 9:6; Jer 22:22; 2Th 3:14
- —Being taunted by one's enemies .... Ps 44:15–16
- —Having an undisciplined child .... Pr 19:26
- —Falsely accusing someone .... Pr 25:8–10; 1Pe 3:16
- —Giving less than poorer people 2Co 9:3–4
- —Being inconsistent with one's principles .... Ezr 8:22

B. When the Christian need not be ashamed
- —When looking to the Lord .... Ps 34:5
- —When hoping in the Lord .... Ps 25:3

—When taking refuge in the Lord .... Ps 25:20
—When trusting in the Lord .... Ro 9:33; 1Pe 2:6
—When believing in Christ .... Mk 8:38; 2Ti 1:12
—When believing Christ and his word .... Mk 8:38; Lk 9:26
—When preaching the gospel .... Ro 1:16; 2Ti 1:8
—When suffering for Christ's sake 1Pe 4:16
—When obeying God's law .... Ps 119:5–6
—When doing one's best for the Lord 2Ti 2:15
—When the Lord returns 1Jn 2:28

SHAMGAR

—Judge; killed 600 Philistines .... Jdg 3:31

SHAPHAN

—Secretary during Josiah's reign 2Ki 22:3
—Supervised finances for temple repairs 2Ki 22:3–7; 2Ch 34:8–13,16–17
—Brought newly discovered Book of the Law to Josiah 2Ki 22:8–10; 2Ch 34:14–17
—Read the Book of the Law to Josiah 2Ki 22:10; 2Ch 34:18
—With others, visited prophetess Huldah 2Ki 22:14–20; 2Ch 34:20–28

SHECHEM

A. A man who raped Jacob's daughter Dinah .... Ge 34:1–4
—Agreed to circumcision and marriage .... Ge 34:11–24
—Killed by Simeon and Levi .... Ge 34:25–29

B. A city in Canaan
—The Lord appeared to Abram there .... Ge 12:6–7
—Jacob purchased land there .... Ge 33:18–19
—Pillaged by the sons of Jacob .... Ge 34:26–29
—Joseph went there to find his brothers .... Ge 37:14–17
—One of the cities of refuge .... Jos 20:7
—Joshua renewed the covenant there .... Jos 24:1–27
—Gideon's son Abimelek was crowned its king .... Jdg 9:1–6
—Civil war between Abimelek and Shechem .... Jdg 9:22–57
—Rehoboam was made king there 1Ki 12:1
—Jeroboam fortified it as his capital 1Ki 12:25
—In New Testament, Shechem is Sychar .... Jn 4:5

SHEEP

See LAMB

SHEM

—Son of Noah .... Ge 5:32; 1Ch 1:4
—With Japheth, covered his father with a garment .... Ge 9:23
—Blessed by Noah .... Ge 9:26
—Sons listed .... Ge 10:21–31
—Abram came from his line .... Ge 11:10–26

SHEOL

See GRAVE

SHEPHERD

A. Related theme
PASTORAL ADVICE is a theme of Titus .... Titus 3:8

B. The shepherd as an human occupation
1. Examples of shepherds .... Ge 4:2; Ge 29:9; 1Sa 16:11; Lk 2:8
2. Responsibilities of shepherds
—Find pasture for flocks .... Eze 34:2,13–14
—Provide water for flocks .... Ge 29:2–8; Ex 2:16
—Protect the flocks .... 1Sa 17:34–36; Lk 2:8
—Seek lost sheep .... Eze 34:16; Mt 18:10–13
—Care for injured sheep .... Mt 12:11
—Regularly account for the sheep .... Jn 10:2–5
—Know what happens to the sheep .... Ge 31:38–39
—Shear the sheep .... Ge 38:12; 1Sa 25:2,7

C. Figurative use of shepherd
1. Leaders of God's people as shepherds
a. Old Testament leaders
—Joshua .... Nu 27:15–18
—David .... 2Sa 5:2; Ps 78:70–72
—Cyrus .... Isa 44:28
—Selfish shepherds .... Isa 56:10–11; Jer 10:21; Eze 34:2–6; Zec 10:2–3
b. Church leaders .... Jn 21:15–17; Ac 20:28–31; 1Pe 5:2–3
2. God as a shepherd
—God is called a shepherd .... Ps 23:1; Ps 80:1
—We are his sheep .... Ps 95:7; Ps 100:3
—God acted as a shepherd in the exodus .... Ps 77:20; Ps 78:52; Isa 63:11
—God cares for us like a shepherd .... Isa 40:11; Eze 34:11–16; Mic 7:14
3. Jesus Christ as a shepherd
a. He is called a shepherd
—The good shepherd .... Jn 10:11,14
—The great Shepherd .... Heb 13:20
—The Chief Shepherd 1Pe 5:4
—The Shepherd and Overseer 1Pe 2:25
b. He acts as a shepherd
—Old Testament prophecies .... Isa 40:11; Eze 34:23; Mic 5:2–4; Zec 13:7
—He died for the sheep .... Jn 10:15
—He has compassion for the sheep .... Mt 9:36
—He knows his sheep .... Jn 10:3–4,14
—He searches for wandering sheep .... Mt 18:12–14; Lk 15:3–7
—He will judge like a shepherd .... Mt 25:32

SHILOH

—Located in Ephraim, near Bethel .... Jdg 21:19
—The first religious center in Canaan .... Jos 18:1; Jdg 18:31
—Joshua's political center .... Jos 21:1–2
—Joshua divided the land there .... Jos 18:9
—Benjamites seized women there .... Jdg 21:19–23
—Hannah asked for a son there 1Sa 1:3–18
—Eli and sons ministered there 1Sa 2:12–14
—God appeared to Samuel there 1Sa 3:21
—Ark taken into battle from there .... 1Sa 4:3–6; Ps 78:60–61
—Eli died there 1Sa 4:12–18
—Prophet Ahijah ministered there 1Ki 11:29; 1Ki 14:2
—City lay in ruins in Jeremiah's day .... Jer 7:12–14; Jer 26:9

SHIMEI

—A Benjamite who cursed David 2Sa 16:5–14
—Spared from execution 2Sa 19:16–23
—Killed on Solomon's orders 1Ki 2:8–9,36–46

SIDON

A. Identity and location
—A chief city of Phoenicia .... Isa 23:11–12
—A seacoast city .... Ac 27:3
—Often linked with Tyre .... Isa 23:1–2; Mt 15:21
—Sidonians were descendants of Ham .... Ge 10:6,15
—A peaceful, prosperous people .... Jdg 18:7

—Skillful in felling timber 1Ki 5:6
1Ch 22:4
Zec 9:2
—Served the goddess Ashtoreth 1Ki 11:5,33

B. Significance of Sidon
1. In the Old Testament
—Territory given to tribe of Asher . . . . . Jos 19:24,28
—Asher did not drive out its inhabitants . . . . . Jdg 1:31
—Cut timber for the temple 1Ki 5:6
—Solomon intermarried with them 1Ki 11:1
—Ahab married Jezebel, a Sidonian 1Ki 16:31
—Elijah stayed with a Sidonian widow 1Ki 17:9–16
—Prophecies against them . . . . . Isa 23:2,4,11–12
Eze 28:20–23
Joel 3:4–8
2. In the New Testament
—Jesus ministered there . . . . . Mt 15:21–28
Mk 7:24–30
—Paul spent a night there . . . . . Ac 27:3

SIDONIANS
See SIDON

SIGN
—An outward event with a spiritual significance

A. Miracles as signs
1. In the Old Testament
—Signs for Israel . . . . . Ex 4:29–31
Nu 14:11
—Signs for Pharaoh . . . . . Ex 10:1–2
—Signs for Gideon . . . . . Jdg 6:17–24,36–40
—Signs for Saul 1Sa 10:7,9
—A sign for Jeroboam 1Ki 13:3–5
—A sign for Ahaz . . . . . Isa 7:11–14
2. In the New Testament
—Jesus' miracles were signs . . . . . Jn 2:11,23
Jn 12:37
Jn 20:30
—The Jews wanted miraculous signs . . . . . Mt 12:38–40
Mt 16:1–4
Jn 2:18
1Co 1:22
—The apostles performed signs . . . . . Ac 4:16,30
Ac 8:6
Ac 14:3

B. Signs of the covenant
1. In the Old Testament
—The rainbow with Noah . . . . . Ge 9:12–16
—Circumcision with Abraham . . . . . Ge 17:11
Ro 4:11
—The blood of the Passover at the exodus . . . . . Ex 12:13
—The Sabbath at Mount Sinai . . . . . Ex 31:12–17
—The altar at the crossing of the Jordan . . . . . Jos 4:5–7
2. In the New Testament
—The water of baptism . . . . . Mt 28:19
1Pe 3:21
—Bread and wine of the Lord's Supper 1Co 11:23–26

C. Signs of the end times
1. Jesus is asked to reveal these signs . . . . . Mk 13:1–4
2. Listing of these signs
—Wars and rumors of wars . . . . . Mk 13:7–8
—Persecution of Christians . . . . . Mk 13:9
Jn 15:18–21
—False teachers and false messiahs . . . . . Mk 13:6,22
1Jn 2:18–19
—The worldwide spread of the gospel . . . . . Mt 24:14
Rev 7:9–10
—The antichrist 2Th 2:3–4,8
Rev 13:1–9
—The great tribulation . . . . . Mk 13:14–20
Rev 7:14
—Signs in the heavens . . . . . Lk 21:11,25

D. The purpose of signs
—To bring about faith in God . . . . . Nu 14:11
Jn 20:30
—To strengthen faith in God . . . . . Jos 24:16–17
Ro 4:11
—To confirm a message from God 2Ki 19:28–29
Lk 2:12,16–20
—To protect God's people from danger . . . . . Ex 12:13
—To bring to mind God's care and promises . . . . . Ge 9:12–16
Ex 13:7–9
1Co 11:23–26

SIHON
—King of the Amorites . . . . . Nu 21:21
Dt 1:4
—Marched out against Israelites . . . . . Nu 21:23
—Destroyed by Israelites . . . . . Nu 21:24–31
Dt 2:32–36
—Victory sung by the Israelites . . . . . Nu 21:27–30
Ps 136:19

SILAS
—A prophet of the early church . . . . . Ac 15:32
—Delegated to report on council in Jerusalem . . . . . Ac 15:22
—Traveled with Paul on second missionary journey . . . . . Ac 15:40
—With Paul in prison at Philippi . . . . . Ac 16:19–36
—With Paul in Thessalonica and Berea . . . . . Ac 17:1–10
—Stayed behind in Berea . . . . . Ac 17:14
—Came to Paul in Corinth . . . . . Ac 18:5
—Preached with Paul in Corinth 2Co 1:19
—Co-writer with Paul 1Th 1:1
2Th 1:1
—Co-writer with Peter 1Pe 5:12

SILVER
A. Uses for silver
1. In Israelite worship
—The tabernacle furniture . . . . . Ex 26:19–25
Ex 27:9–11,17
—Offerings . . . . . Nu 7:13,19,25
Ezr 1:4,6,9–11
—The temple building 1Ch 29:2–5
—The temple furniture 1Ch 28:14–17
2. In crafting idol gods . . . . . Isa 2:20
Hos 8:4
Ac 19:24
3. For personal wealth . . . . . Ge 13:2
Ecc 2:8
4. For gifts 1Ki 15:18–19
Ezr 2:69
5. For payment as money . . . . . Ge 42:25–27
Jdg 9:4
Mt 26:15
6. For jewelry . . . . . Ge 24:53
Eze 16:17
7. For royal display . . . . . Ge 44:2
Est 1:6–7

B. Value of silver for God's people
1. Positive: a blessing from God . . . . . Ge 13:2
Isa 60:9,17
2. Negative
—Wisdom worth more than silver . . . . . Job 28:12–15
Pr 3:13–14
Pr 16:16
—Silver valueless in redemption 1Pe 1:18

C. Silver as a symbol
—For saints surviving God's testing . . . . . Isa 48:10
Zec 13:9
—For God's dependable word . . . . . Ps 12:6
—For trustworthy spiritual values 1Co 3:12–13

SIMEON
A. Son of Jacob by Leah . . . . . Ge 35:23
1Ch 2:1
—Name means "one who hears" . . . . . Ge 29:33
—With Levi, avenged rape of Dinah . . . . . Ge 34:25–31
—Held hostage by Joseph in Egypt . . . . . Ge 42:24–43:23
—Went to Egypt with family . . . . . Ge 46:8,10
—Father of six sons . . . . . Ge 46:10
—Blessed by Jacob . . . . . Ge 49:5–7

—Visited by the queen of Sheba — 1Ki 10:1–13; 2Ch 9:1–12
—Had a glorious kingdom — 1Ki 10:14–29; 2Ch 9:13–28

C. His later life as king
—Wives turned his heart from God — 1Ki 11:1–13
—Hadad and Rezon rebelled against him — 1Ki 11:14–25
—Jeroboam rebelled against him — 1Ki 11:26–40
—His death — 1Ki 11:41–43; 2Ch 9:29–31

D. Solomon remembered after his death
—For his organization of temple service — 2Ch 35:3–4; Ne 12:45
—For marrying idolatrous wives — Ne 13:26
—For his splendor — Mt 6:29
—For his wisdom — Mt 12:42
—For his building of the temple — Ac 7:47

SON OF MAN

A. "Son of man" denotes someone merely human
—"Son of man" means "man" — Ps 80:17
—Ezekiel called "son of man" — Eze 2:1; Eze 3:1

B. Jesus as the Son of Man
—Prophesied in the Old Testament — Da 7:13–14
—Identified himself as such — Mk 2:10; Lk 7:34; Lk 9:58; Jn 9:35–37
—Died and rose again — Mk 8:31; Mk 9:31; Mk 10:33–34; Jn 3:14–15
—Is in heaven — Mt 26:64; Ac 7:56; Rev 1:13
—Will return — Mt 13:41; Mk 13:26; Mk 14:62
—We must feed on him — Jn 6:53

SONG

See MUSIC AND SONG

SORROW

See GRIEF

SOUL

—The non-physical element in humans

A. Defining the soul

1. Basic concepts
—Humans were created as whole people — Ge 2:7
—Soul referred to in the context of death — Mt 10:28; Rev 6:9

2. Soul often synonymous with:
—Spirit — Ecc 12:7; Lk 1:46–47
—Heart — Ps 19:7–8; Ps 84:2
—Life — Ps 26:9
—One's whole being — Ps 35:9–10

3. Sometimes soul appears distinct from:
—Heart — Dt 4:29; Dt 6:5
—Spirit — 1Th 5:23; Heb 4:12

B. What does the soul do?

1. Expresses human emotions
—Peace — Ps 23:2–3
—Refreshment — Ps 19:7
—Joy — Ps 35:9
—Courage — Jdg 5:21
—Support — 1Sa 14:7
—Grief — 1Sa 1:10,15; Job 30:25
—Sorrow — Mt 26:38
—Bitterness — Job 7:11
—Anguish — Ps 6:3
—Depression — Ps 42:5,11; La 3:20

2. Has spiritual desires
—Thirsts for God — Ps 42:1–2
—Yearns for God — Ps 84:2
—Seeks God — Dt 4:29; 2Ch 15:12
—Finds rest in God — Ps 62:1,5
—Turns to God — Dt 30:10; 1Ki 8:48
—Loves God — Dt 6:5; Dt 13:3
—Serves God — Dt 10:12; Jos 22:5
—Obeys God — Dt 30:2; 2Ki 23:3
—Praises God — Ps 103:1–2,22
—Cries out to God — Rev 6:9–10

C. What does God do for the soul?
—He saves the soul — 1Pe 1:9
—Gives hope as an anchor for the soul — Heb 6:19

SPIRIT

—An immaterial being

A. The human spirit

1. Defining the spirit
See SOUL

2. What does the spirit do?

a. Involved with the emotions
—The compelled spirit — Job 32:18–20
—The stirred-up spirit — 1Ch 5:26
—The revived spirit — Ge 45:27
—The stubborn spirit — Dt 2:30
—The bitter spirit — 1Sa 30:6
—The fainting spirit — Ps 142:3
—The broken spirit — Ps 51:17
—The troubled spirit — Jn 13:21
—The anguished spirit — Job 7:11
—The crushed spirit — Ps 34:18
—The provoked spirit — Ecc 7:9
—The haughty spirit — Pr 16:18
—The lowly spirit — Isa 57:15
—The contrite spirit — Isa 66:2
—The joyful spirit — Lk 1:47
—The gentle, quiet spirit — 1Pe 3:4

b. Involved with the will
—The spirit that follows God — Nu 14:24
—The spirit that follows itself — Eze 13:3
—The steadfast spirit — Ps 51:10
—The willing spirit — Ps 51:12
—The wayward spirit — Isa 29:24

c. Involved with the intellect
—The inquiring spirit — Ps 77:6
—The understanding spirit — Isa 29:24

3. What does God do for the spirit?
—He can stir it up — Hag 1:14
—He searches it — Pr 20:27
—He gives us a new one — Eze 36:26
—He gives it new birth — Jn 3:6
—He testifies with our spirit — Ro 8:16
—It returns to him — Ecc 12:7
—He receives it — Ps 31:5

B. The Holy Spirit
See HOLY SPIRIT

C. Spirit beings

1. God sends out spirits
—Angels are spirits he sends out — Heb 1:14
See ANGEL
—A reporting spirit sent to Sennacherib — Isa 37:7
—An evil spirit sent to Abimelek — Jdg 9:23
—An evil spirit sent to Saul — 1Sa 16:14–15,23
—A lying spirit sent to false prophets — 1Ki 22:19–23

2. Evil spirits
—Have influence over humans . . . 1Ti 4:1; Rev 16:13–14
—Were driven out by Jesus . . . Mt 8:16; Mk 1:23–27
—Were driven out by the apostles . . . Ac 5:16; Ac 16:16–18

SPIRITUALITY

See HOLINESS; MEDITATION

STARS

A. Data concerning the stars
—Created by God . . . Ge 1:16; Ps 8:3
—Controlled by God . . . Ps 147:4; Jer 31:35
—Show God's power . . . Isa 40:26
—Must praise God . . . Ps 148:3
—Were worshiped by pagans . . . 2Ki 21:3; Jer 19:13; Ac 7:43

B. Stars and constellations mentioned in the Bible
—The Bear . . . Job 9:9
—Orion . . . Job 9:9
—Pleiades . . . Am 5:8
—The star of Bethlehem . . . Mt 2:2,9

C. Stars used as symbols
—Of Jesus the Messiah . . . Nu 24:17; Rev 22:16
—Of an innumerable number . . . Ge 22:17; Ne 9:23
—Of Christians as witnesses . . . Php 2:15–16
—Of the saints in heaven . . . Da 12:3
—Of angels . . . Rev 1:16,20
—Of heretics . . . Jude 13
—Of judgment at the end of time . . . Isa 13:10–11; Mt 24:29; Rev 6:12

STEADFASTNESS

See PERSEVERANCE

STEALING

—Taking what belongs to someone else

A. The command against stealing
—The eighth commandment . . . Ex 20:15; Dt 5:19; Mt 19:17–18
—Fraud and dishonest weights outlawed . . . Lev 19:13; Pr 20:10,23
—Theft prohibited in Paul's writings . . . Ro 13:8–9; Eph 4:28
—Theft profanes the name of God . . . Lev 19:11–12; Jer 7:9–11
—Theft often accompanied by greed . . . Ps 62:10

B. The punishment for thieves
—Expected to make restitution . . . Ex 22:1–9; Nu 5:5–8
—Are subject to God's judgment . . . Hab 2:6
—Can be excluded from the kingdom of God . . . 1Co 6:9–10

C. Examples of stealing in the Bible
—Rachel and the household gods . . . Ge 31:19,30–32
—Achan and goods from Jericho . . . Jos 7:11
—Micah and 1,100 shekels of silver . . . Jdg 17:2
—Ahab and Naboth's vineyard . . . 1Ki 21:16,19

See also THE RICH AND THE POOR

D. Theft used as a metaphor
—For gaining admiration (stealing hearts) . . . 2Sa 15:6
—For withholding tithes (robbing God) . . . Mal 3:8–9
—For claiming to speak God's word (stealing words from others) . . . Jer 23:30
—For the unexpectedness of Christ's return . . . Lk 12:39–40; 1Th 5:2; 2Pe 3:10; Rev 3:3

STEPHEN

—One of the seven deacons . . . Ac 6:5
—Spoke eloquently . . . Ac 6:8–10
—Arrested by the Jews . . . Ac 6:11–15
—Gave powerful speech to the Sanhedrin . . . Ac 7:1–53
—Stoned to death . . . Ac 7:54–60; Ac 22:20

STEWARDSHIP

—How one handles what God has given

A. God's relationship to what we have
1. God owns everything . . . Ex 19:5; Ps 24:1; Hag 2:8
2. God is the source of everything
—All our wealth . . . Ge 26:12–13; 1Co 4:7
—Our personal talents . . . Ro 12:3,6; 1Co 12:7–11
—Our ability to work . . . Dt 8:17–18; Ecc 2:24–25
—Every moment of our lives . . . Ps 39:4–5; Mt 6:27
—Everything we have . . . Job 1:21; Jn 3:27

B. Our relationship to what we have
1. Our gifts and talents
—Must use them faithfully . . . Mt 25:14–27; 1Co 4:2
—Must be trustworthy with them . . . Lk 16:10–12
—Must use them for God's glory . . . 1Sa 17:45–46; Ro 14:7–8; 1Co 10:31; 1Pe 4:11
—Must use them to serve others . . . Ro 14:19; 1Co 12:7; 1Co 14:12; 1Pe 4:10
2. Our time
—Recognize the brevity of time . . . Job 7:7; Ps 89:47; Ecc 9:11–12
—Must be faithful in use of time . . . Ps 90:12,17; Eph 5:15–16
3. Our wealth and possessions
a. Basic attitude
—Must believe that God will provide . . . Mt 6:25–34; Php 4:19
—Cannot take credit for what we have . . . Da 4:28–35; 1Co 4:7
—Must be content with what we have . . . Php 4:11–12; 1Ti 6:6–8; Heb 13:5
b. Principles of giving to the Lord
—Giving should be proportionate . . . Pr 3:9; Mal 3:8–10; 1Co 16:1–2
—Giving should be willing . . . Ex 25:1–2; 1Ch 29:6–9; 2Co 8:1–5,11–12
—Giving should be spontaneous . . . 2Co 9:2–5
—Giving should be cheerful . . . 2Ch 24:10; 2Co 9:7
—Giving should be generous . . . 2Co 8:2; 2Co 9:5,11,13
c. Blessings await a giver
—On earth . . . Dt 15:4; Ac 20:35; 2Co 9:6,10
—In heaven . . . Mt 19:21; 1Ti 6:19

STRANGERS

See ALIEN

SUFFERING
See PAIN

SUN
A. Data concerning the sun
—Created by God ... Ge 1:16
Ps 74:16
—Governs the day ... Ge 1:16
Ps 136:8
—Controlled by God ... Jos 10:12–13
Ps 19:4–6
Jer 31:35
—Needed for crops ... Dt 33:13–14
—Needed for warmth ... Ps 19:6
—Must praise God ... Ps 148:3
—Can harm a person ... Ps 121:6
—Worshiped by pagans ... 2Ki 23:5,11
Jer 8:2
—No sun needed in heaven ... Isa 60:19–20
Rev 21:23
B. The sun used as a symbol
—Of God ... Ps 84:11
—Of God's glory ... Ps 19:1–6
—Of Christ ... Mal 4:2
—Of Christ's glory ... Mt 17:2
Ac 26:13–15
Rev 1:16
—Of the future glory of believers ... Mt 13:43
—Of stability and endurance ... Ps 72:5,17
—Of judgment at the end of time ... Isa 13:10–11
Mt 24:29
Rev 6:12

SWEARING
See CURSE

SYMPATHY
See COMPASSION

SYRIA, SYRIANS
See DAMASCUS

TABERNACLE
A. Related theme
TABERNACLE is a theme of Exodus ... Ex 40:34
B. Also called "the tent of meeting" ... Nu 4:25
Nu 9:17–18
C. The building of the tabernacle
1. Planning the tabernacle
—Extensive plans outlined by God ... Ex 25:8–30:38
—Based on pattern of heaven ... Heb 8:5
Heb 9:24
2. Building the tabernacle
—Material collected ... Ex 35:4–29
Ex 36:3–7
—Supervisors chosen ... Ex 35:30–36:2
—Work performed ... Ex 36:8–39:31
—Inspected by Moses ... Ex 39:32–43
—The completed tabernacle set up ... Ex 40:1–33
3. Structure of the tabernacle
a. Contents of the courtyard
—Its construction ... Ex 38:9–20
—Altar of burnt offering ... Ex 38:1–7
—Basin for washing ... Ex 38:8
b. Contents of the Holy Place
—Table for bread of the Presence ... Ex 25:23–30
—Golden lampstand ... Ex 37:17–24
—Altar of incense ... Ex 37:25–29
c. Contents of the Most Holy Place ... Ex 37:1–9
Heb 9:4
See ARK OF THE COVENANT LAW
d. Two parts separated by a curtain ... Ex 26:33
Heb 9:3
D. History of the tent of meeting
—God talked with Moses there ... Lev 1:1
Nu 7:89
—Aaron and his sons were consecrated there ... Ex 29:1–4,10–11
—Filled with God's glory at dedication ... Ex 40:34–35
—Covered by the cloud ... Nu 9:15–23
—Used in Israelite sacrifices ... Lev 1:3–5
Lev 3:2,8
—Placed in the center of the camp ... Nu 2:1–2,17
—Joshua was commissioned there ... Dt 31:14–15,23
—Set up at Shiloh in Canaan ... Jos 18:1
Jdg 18:31
1Sa 2:14,22
—Located at Nob during Saul's time ... 1Sa 21:1–6
—Located at Gibeon during David's time ... 1Ch 16:37–40
—Brought to Jerusalem during David's reign ... 1Ch 23:25–26,32
2Ch 1:4,13
—Solomon replaced it with the temple ... 2Ch 5:4–6
E. Symbolism of the tabernacle
1. Symbol of God's presence among the people ... Ex 25:8
Ex 29:43
Ex 40:34–35
2. Its contents symbolized Christ
—He made his dwelling ("tabernacle") among human beings ... Jn 1:14
—His death is the atoning sacrifice ... 1Jn 4:10
—His body is sacred bread ... Jn 6:27–59
—His body is the curtain ... Heb 10:20
—His blood washes and purifies us ... 1Jn 1:7

TAMAR
A. Wife of Judah's sons Er and Onan ... Ge 38:1–10
—Tricked Judah into fathering children ... Ge 38:11–26
—Gave birth to twins ... Ge 38:27–30
—An ancestor of Jesus ... Mt 1:3
B. Daughter of David, sister of Absalom ... 2Sa 13:1
—Raped by half brother Amnon ... 2Sa 13:2–21
—Rape avenged by Absalom ... 2Sa 13:23–33

TEACHING
See DOCTRINE; EDUCATION

TEMPLE
A. Related themes
1. TEMPLE is a theme of:
—1 Kings ... 1Ki 6:1
—2 Chronicles ... 2Ch 7:1
2. REBUILDING is a theme of Ezra ... Ezr 5:2
B. The first temple
1. Its construction
—The idea conceived by David ... 2Sa 7:1–2
—David not allowed to construct it ... 2Sa 7:4–13
—Planned by David ... 1Ch 28:11–19
—Gifts collected by David ... 1Ch 29:1–9
—Built by Solomon ... 2Ch 3:1–5:1
2. Its structure based on the tabernacle
—Contained the Most Holy Place ... 2Ch 3:8–14
—Its parts separated by a curtain ... 2Ch 3:14
Mt 27:51
3. Its history
—Ark brought into it ... 2Ch 5:2–10
—Filled with the glory of God ... 2Ch 5:13–14
2Ch 7:1–3
—Dedicated by Solomon ... 2Ch 6:1–13
2Ch 7:4–7
—Ransacked by Shishak of Egypt ... 2Ch 12:9
—Refurbished by Asa ... 2Ch 15:8,18
—Joash hidden there ... 2Ch 22:12
—Restored by Joash ... 2Ch 24:4–14
—Furnishings sent by Ahaz to Assyria ... 2Ch 28:21,24
—Purified by Hezekiah ... 2Ch 29:3–19
—Desecrated by Manasseh ... 2Ch 33:3–7
—Purified by Josiah ... 2Ch 34:8–11
—Ransacked by Nebuchadnezzar ... 2Ch 36:7
—Destroyed by Nebuchadnezzar ... 2Ch 36:18–19
C. The second temple
1. Its construction
—Cyrus ordered its rebuilding ... Ezr 1:1–4
—Rebuilding begun under Zerubbabel ... Ezr 3:7–13
—Opposition to its rebuilding ... Ezr 4:1–4

—Work resumed ... Ezr 5:1–2
—Completed ... Ezr 6:13–15
—Dedicated ... Ezr 6:16–18
—Repaired and beautified by Herod ... Jn 2:20
2. New Testament events in the temple
—Zechariah met by an angel there ... Lk 1:8–20
—Jesus presented there ... Lk 2:22,27
—Jesus there at 12 years old ... Lk 2:42–50
—Jesus taught there ... Mt 26:55
Mk 12:35
Jn 7:14,28
—Jesus drove out money changers ... Mt 21:12–13
Jn 2:14–17
—Curtain torn at Jesus' death ... Mt 27:51
—Early Christians worshiped there ... Ac 2:46
—Apostles taught there ... Ac 3:1–4:2
Ac 5:21,42
—Paul arrested there ... Ac 21:27–33
Ac 26:21
D. Prophecies regarding the temple
1. Temple should not give false sense of security
—Jeremiah ... Jer 7:2–8
—Micah ... Mic 3:9–12
—Stephen ... Ac 7:47–50
2. Predictions of its destruction
—The first temple ... Jer 7:14
Eze 24:20–21
—The second temple ... Mk 13:1–2
3. Prophets bemoaned its destruction ... Isa 64:10–11
La 1:9–10
4. Prophets stirred up the people to rebuild ... Ezr 5:1
Ezr 6:14
Hag 1:2–15
Zec 4:8–9
5. Predictions of its future glory ... Isa 60:7,13
Hag 2:3,7–9
6. Ezekiel's new temple ... Eze 40:1–43:27
Eze 47:1–12
7. The new Jerusalem has no temple ... Rev 21:22
E. Symbolism of the temple
1. Symbol in the Old Testament
—Of God dwelling with his people ... 2Ch 6:20,33
Ps 18:6
—Of God's favor to his people ... Ps 65:4
2. Symbol in the New Testament
—Jesus Christ as a temple ... Jn 2:19–22
—The church as a temple ... 1Co 3:16–17
2Co 6:16
Eph 2:21–22
Heb 3:6
—The human body as a temple ... 1Co 6:19

TEMPTATION

—Enticing one to sin against God
A. The source of temptation
1. God does not tempt us to sin ... Jas 1:13
2. Satan entices us to sin
—Adam and Eve ... Ge 3:1–4
—David ... 1Ch 21:1
—Job ... Job 1:6–12
—Jesus ... Mt 4:1–11
—Ananias and Sapphira ... Ac 5:1–3
3. Situations tempt us to sin
—Taking the easy way ... Mt 7:13–14
Mt 16:21–23
—The things of the world ... Mt 18:7–9
—Weakness of faith ... Lk 22:31–32
—Sexual desire ... 1Co 7:3–5
—Pride in one's own strength ... Gal 6:1
—Persecution ... 1Th 3:4–5
—Riches ... 1Ti 6:9
—Evil desires ... Jas 1:14–15
B. The fight against temptation
—We must beware of the devil's schemes ... 2Co 2:11
Eph 6:11
—We must watch out for temptation ... Mt 26:41
Lk 22:40,46
1Pe 5:8
—God helps us overcome temptation ... 1Co 10:13
—Christ helps us overcome temptation ... Heb 2:17–18
Heb 4:15–16
—We must pray for help against temptation ... Mt 6:13

TEN COMMANDMENTS

—Given by God from Mount Sinai ... Ex 20:1–17
Ex 34:28
Dt 5:7–21
—Written on stone tablets ... Ex 34:1
Dt 4:13
Dt 10:4
—Stored in the ark of the covenant law ... Dt 10:1–2
1Ki 8:9
—Summary of commandments is love ... Mt 22:37–40
Ro 13:9–10
—Ten individual commandments ... Ex 34:28
Dt 4:13

See ADULTERY; CHILDREN; COVETING; CURSE; IDOLATRY; LYING; MURDER; SABBATH; SEXUAL STANDARDS; STEALING; WORSHIP

TESTAMENT

See COVENANT

TESTING

A. Humans' testing
1. Testing God
a. Positive examples
—Gideon testing God's call ... Jdg 6:36–40
—Ahaz invited to test God ... Isa 7:10–12
—Israelites invited to test God ... Mal 3:10
b. Negative examples
—Grumbling over water ... Ex 17:1–2,7
Dt 33:8
Ps 95:9
—Grumbling over food ... Ps 78:17–18
Ps 106:14–15
—Many times of testing ... Nu 14:22
Ps 78:41
—Pharisees tested Jesus ... Mt 16:1
Mt 19:3
Mk 8:11
—Ananias and Sapphira test the Spirit ... Ac 5:1–10
c. The command not to test God ... Dt 6:16
Mt 4:7
1Co 10:9
2. The testing of ourselves
—The Teacher tests himself ... Ecc 2:1–11
—We must test our faith ... 2Co 13:5–7
—We must test our actions ... Gal 6:4
—We must test everything ... 1Th 5:21
—We must test the spirits ... 1Jn 4:1
B. God's testing of humans
1. God as a testing God
—God tests our hearts ... 1Ch 29:17
Pr 17:3
Jer 11:20
1Th 2:4
—His testing refines us ... Ps 66:10
Isa 48:10
Jer 9:7
—We may ask God to test us ... Ps 26:2
Ps 139:23
2. Examples of God's testing
—Abraham, with sacrifice of Isaac ... Ge 22:1
Heb 11:17
—The Israelites, with lack of water ... Ex 15:22–26
—The Israelites, with rules on manna ... Ex 16:4–5
Dt 8:2–3,16
—The Israelites, with thunder on Mount Sinai ... Ex 20:18–20
—The Israelites, with false prophets ... Dt 13:1–3
—The Israelites, with pagan nations ... Jdg 2:20–3:4
—Hezekiah, with envoys from Babylon ... 2Ch 32:31

3. Phrases used in God's timetable of history
 - —"The time has come" — Mk 1:15
 - —"When the set time had fully come" — Gal 4:4
 - —"The times of the Gentiles" — Lk 21:24
 - —"In the last days" — Ac 2:17; 2Ti 3:1
 - —"At the last day" — Jn 12:48

4. The end of time
 - —Time is moving toward final victory — Ac 1:6–7
 - —Time ends at Christ's return — Mt 16:27; Ac 1:11; 1Th 4:15–17
 - —Time ends with final judgment — Rev 20:11–15

B. Time as opportunity
 - —A time for everything — Ecc 3:1–8,17; Ecc 8:6
 - —Our times are in God's hands — Ps 31:15
 - —We must make proper use of time — Ps 90:12; 1Co 7:29–31; Eph 5:15; Col 4:5

TIMOTHY

A. Early life
 - —From Lystra — Ac 16:1–2
 - —From a mixed marriage; uncircumcised — Ac 16:1,3
 - —Brought up as a good Jewish boy — 2Ti 3:15
 - —Taught by mother and grandmother — 2Ti 1:5
 - —Became a believer through Paul — 1Co 4:17; 1Ti 1:1
 - —Circumcised by Paul — Ac 16:3
 - —A young man — 1Ti 4:12

B. His life as co-worker with Paul
 - —Went with Paul on second missionary journey — Ac 16:3–4
 - —Stayed in Berea with Silas — Ac 17:14
 - —Sent to Thessalonica — 1Th 3:2
 - —Came to Paul in Corinth — Ac 18:5; 1Th 3:6
 - —Sent to Macedonia — Ac 19:22
 - —Sent to settle problems at Corinth — 1Co 4:17; 1Co 16:10
 - —Accompanied Paul as he headed to Jerusalem — Ac 20:1–4
 - —Co-writer with Paul — 2Co 1:1; Col 1:1; 1Th 1:1
 - —Ministered to Paul in Philippi — Php 2:19–24
 - —Led church at Ephesus — 1Ti 1:3
 - —A pastor responsible for worship — 1Ti 2:1–10; 2Ti 4:2–5
 - —Spent some time in prison — Heb 13:23

C. His character
 - —A hard worker for the Lord — Php 2:19–24; 2Ti 2:15; 2Ti 4:5
 - —A good follower of Paul — 1Co 4:17; Php 2:22; 2Ti 1:13–14
 - —Somewhat timid — 2Ti 1:6–7
 - —Needed encouragement — 1Ti 4:11–16; 1Ti 6:11–14,20
 - —Tendency to get sick — 1Ti 5:23

TITHES AND OFFERINGS

A. Tithes

1. In the Old Testament
 - —Tithing commanded — Lev 27:30–33; Dt 12:6–7; 2Ch 31:4–8
 - —A tenth of everything required — Ge 14:20; Ge 28:22; Dt 14:23
 - —Tithes used to support Levites — Nu 18:21–24; Dt 14:22–27
 - —Israelites stopped tithing — Ne 13:10–12; Mal 3:8–10

2. In the New Testament
 - —Tithing became hypocritical — Mt 23:23; Lk 11:42
 - —Tithers were self-righteous — Lk 18:9–12

B. Offerings

1. In the Old Testament
 - a. The burnt offering — Lev 1:1–17; Lev 6:8–13; Lev 8:18–21
 - b. The grain offering — Lev 2:1–16; Lev 6:14–23
 - c. The fellowship offering — Lev 3:1–17; Lev 7:11–34
 - d. The sin offering — Lev 4:1–5:13; Lev 6:24–30; Lev 8:14–17
 - e. The guilt offering — Lev 5:14–6:7; Lev 7:1–6
 - f. Freewill offerings
   - —For the tabernacle — Ex 25:1–7; Ex 35:4–9,29
   - —For the first temple — 1Ch 29:6–9; 2Ch 24:8–11
   - —For the second temple — Ezr 2:68
   - —In the Festival of Weeks — Dt 16:10
   - —As one of the fellowship offerings — Lev 7:16
 - g. Offerings sometimes given hypocritically — Isa 1:11–13; Hag 2:14; Mal 1:6–14; Mal 3:8–9

2. Freewill offerings in the New Testament
 - —Given for the poor — Lk 19:8; Ac 11:28–30; Ro 15:25–27
 - —Given to support Paul — 2Co 11:8–9; Php 4:15–18

3. Principles of giving offerings
 - —Freely — Mt 10:8
 - —Joyfully — 2Co 9:7
 - —In proportion to income — Dt 16:17; Pr 3:9; 1Co 16:2
 - —Generously — Ps 37:26; 2Co 9:5–6; 1Ti 6:18

See also THE RICH AND THE POOR; SACRIFICE; STEWARDSHIP

TITUS

 - —A Christian led by Paul to the Lord — Titus 1:4
 - —Gentile co-worker of Paul — 2Co 8:23; Gal 2:1–3
 - —Sent to Corinth — 2Co 2:13; 2Co 8:6,16–18; 2Co 12:18
 - —Sent to Crete — Titus 1:4–5
 - —Sent to Dalmatia — 2Ti 4:10

TONGUES

See GIFTS OF THE SPIRIT; LANGUAGE

TRADITION

—Teachings and religious observances handed down

A. Teachings passed down
 - —By parents to children — Ps 78:3–6; Pr 1:7
 - —By the Jewish elders — Mk 7:3,5
 - —By the apostles — 1Co 11:2,23–26; 1Co 15:3–7; 2Th 2:15

B. Dangers of traditions
 - —Can obscure God's word — Mt 15:1–9; Mk 7:1–13
 - —Can misdirect a person's life — Mic 6:16; Gal 1:14

C. Reactions to traditions
 - —Consider bad ones to be rubbish — Php 3:4–8
 - —Hold fast to good ones — 1Co 15:1–5; 2Th 2:15

TREE

A. Kinds of trees mentioned in the Bible
—Acacia ... Ex 25:5
—Algum ... 2Ch 2:8
—Almond ... Ge 30:37
—Apple ... SS 2:3
—Broom ... 1Ki 19:4
—Cedar ... 1Ki 4:33
—Citron ... Rev 18:12
—Cypress ... Ge 6:14
—Ebony ... Eze 27:15
—Fig ... Mt 21:19
—Fir ... Isa 41:19
—Juniper ... Isa 41:19
—Myrtle ... Ne 8:15
—Nut ... SS 6:11
—Oak ... Ge 35:4
—Olive ... Jdg 9:8
—Palm ... Ex 15:27
—Pine ... Isa 44:14
—Plane ... Ge 30:37
—Pomegranate ... 1Sa 14:2
—Poplar ... Ps 137:2
—Sycamore ... Lk 19:4
—Tamarisk ... Ge 21:33
—Terebinth ... Hos 4:13
—Willow ... Eze 17:5

B. Trees used in a symbolic way
1. Significant trees
—The tree of the knowledge of good and evil ... Ge 2:17
—The tree of life ... Ge 3:22,24
Rev 22:2
2. Comparison to trees
—The righteous are like a tree ... Ps 1:3
Ps 92:12–15
Isa 61:3
—Wisdom is like a tree ... Pr 3:18
—The Branch is a symbol of Christ ... Isa 11:1
Jer 23:5–6
3. Illustrations connected with trees
—Parable of the trees and thornbush ... Jdg 9:7–20
—Parable of the coming new tree ... Eze 17:22–24
—Parable of the tree and its fruit ... Mt 7:17–19
—Parable of the mustard seed ... Mt 13:31–32
—Parable of the barren fig tree ... Lk 13:6–9
—Cursing of the fig tree ... Mk 11:12–14,20–21
—A lesson from the fig tree ... Mt 24:32–33
—Parable of the two olive trees ... Ro 11:17–24

TRIBULATION

See GREAT TRIBULATION; PAIN

TRINITY

—One God in three persons—Father, Son and Holy Spirit

A. There is only one God
—Expressed in the Old Testament ... Dt 4:35,39
Dt 6:4
Isa 45:21
—Expressed in the New Testament ... 1Co 8:5–6
Eph 4:6
1Ti 2:5
Jas 2:19

B. Hints of a plurality in God in the Old Testament
—God speaks of himself as "us" ... Ge 1:26–27
Ge 3:22
Ge 11:7
Isa 6:8
—Someone coming from God is God ... Isa 7:14
Isa 9:6
—The angel of the Lord speaks as God
See ANGEL OF THE LORD

C. The Son as God
See JESUS CHRIST

D. The Holy Spirit as God
See HOLY SPIRIT

E. Father, Son and Spirit together
—One name for the three ... Mt 28:19
—The three persons mentioned together ... Mt 3:16–17
Jn 15:26
Ro 5:5–6
Ro 8:11,16–17
1Co 12:4–6
2Co 13:14
Gal 4:4–6
Eph 4:4–6
1Th 1:2–5
2Th 2:13
Titus 3:4–6
1Pe 1:2
1Jn 4:2
Jude 20–21

F. Similar divine characteristics for all three
1. Holiness
—Of the Father ... Jn 17:11
—Of the Son ... 1Co 1:30
—Of the Spirit ... Ro 1:4
2. Eternity
—Of the Father ... 1Ti 1:17
—Of the Son ... Heb 1:2–3,8
—Of the Spirit ... Heb 9:14
3. All-knowing
—Of the Father ... Mt 6:8,32
—Of the Son ... Jn 2:24–25
—Of the Spirit ... 1Co 2:10–11
4. All-powerful
—Of the Father ... Ps 135:5–7
—Of the Son ... 1Co 15:24–27
—Of the Spirit ... Ro 15:13,19
5. Everywhere present
—Of the Father ... Jer 23:24
—Of the Son ... Mt 28:20
—Of the Spirit ... Ps 139:7–10

G. Similar divine activities for all three
1. Creating
—By the Father ... Ge 1:1
—By the Son ... Jn 1:3
—By the Spirit ... Ps 104:30
2. Giving of spiritual life
—By the Father ... Eph 2:4–5
—By the Son ... Jn 10:10
—By the Spirit ... Eze 37:14
3. Performing miracles
—By the Father ... 1Ki 18:38
—By the Son ... Mt 4:23–24
—By the Spirit ... Ro 15:19
4. Teaching
—By the Father ... Ps 71:17
Isa 48:17
—By the Son ... Jn 13:13
—By the Spirit ... Jn 14:26
5. Experiencing grief because of sin
—By the Father ... Ge 6:6
—By the Son ... Lk 19:41–44
—By the Spirit ... Eph 4:30

TRUST

—Confidence put in someone or something

A. Related themes
TRUST is a theme of Psalms ... Ps 62:5
TRUST AND OBEY is a theme of Joshua ... Jos 10:25

B. In whom/what must we trust?
—In God ... Ps 56:3–4,11
Ps 91:2
—In the Lord ... Ps 4:5
Pr 3:5
Na 1:7
Ac 14:23
—In Jesus Christ ... Jn 14:1
Ro 10:11
1Pe 2:6

—In the name of the Lord ... Ps 20:7
Isa 50:10
Zep 3:12
—In God's word ... Ps 119:42
—In God's unfailing love ... Ps 52:8

C. What are the results of trusting in God?
—We become righteous and just ... Ps 37:5–6
—We are saved ... Isa 25:9
—We are blessed ... Ps 40:4
—We experience joy ... Ps 33:21
—We are released from fear ... Ps 56:3–4
—We receive direction from the Lord ... Pr 3:5–6
—We stand firm ... Ps 20:7–8
—We prosper ... Pr 28:25
—God keeps us safe ... Jer 39:17–18
—God delivers us ... Ps 22:4
—God cares for us ... Na 1:7
—God surrounds us with his love ... Ps 32:10
—Jesus prepares a place for us ... Jn 14:1–2

D. In what ought we *not* trust?
—In idols ... 2Ki 17:14–15
Isa 42:17
Jer 13:25
—In other people ... Ps 118:8–9
Ps 146:3
Jer 17:5–7
—In ourselves ... Pr 28:26
—In fortified cities ... Jer 5:17
—In horses and chariots ... Ps 20:7
Isa 31:1–3
—In weapons ... Ps 44:6
—In riches ... Job 31:24–28
Ps 52:7
Lk 12:13–21
1Ti 6:17

TRUTH

—What is accurate and agrees with reality

A. Related theme
TRUTH is a theme of 1 John ... 1Jn 2:8

B. Of whom/what is truth characteristic?
1. God
—The Father ... Ps 31:5
Isa 65:16
—Jesus ... Jn 1:14
Jn 14:6
—The Spirit ... Jn 14:17
1Jn 5:6
2. God's revelation
—God's law ... Ps 119:43
—God's word ... 2Sa 7:28
Isa 45:19
Jn 17:17
—The testimony of Jesus ... Jn 8:45–46
Jn 18:37
—The word of the prophets ... 1Ki 18:24
1Ki 22:16
Jer 26:15
—The gospel proclaimed by the apostles ... 2Co 4:2
Gal 2:5,14
Eph 1:13
3. The church, the pillar of truth ... 1Ti 3:15

C. How must believers relate to the truth?
—Must know it ... Ps 51:6
1Ti 2:4
—Must come to a knowledge of it ... 2Ti 2:25
Titus 1:1
Heb 10:26
—Must seek it ... Jer 5:1
—Must choose it ... Ps 119:30
—Must buy it ... Pr 23:23
—Must believe it ... 2Th 2:13
—Must love it ... Zec 8:19
—Must walk in it ... Ps 26:3
3Jn 3–5
—Must live by it ... Jn 3:21
1Jn 1:6
—Must obey it ... Gal 5:7
—Must worship in it ... Jn 4:23–24
—Must speak it ... Ps 15:2
Zec 8:16
Eph 4:25

D. What does the truth do for us?
—Protects us ... Ps 40:11
—Guides us ... Ps 43:3
—Sets us free ... Jn 8:31–32
—Sanctifies us ... Jn 17:17,19
—Purifies us ... 1Pe 1:22

E. What do the wicked do with respect to truth?
—Reject it ... Isa 59:14–15
Ro 2:8
—Do not speak it ... Jer 9:5
—Distort it ... Ac 20:30
—Suppress it ... Ro 1:18
—Exchange it for a lie ... Ro 1:25
—Wander away from it ... 2Ti 2:18
—Oppose it ... 2Ti 3:8
—Turn away from it ... 2Ti 4:4

TYRE

A. Identity and location
—A merchant city ... Ne 13:16
—A seacoast city ... Lk 6:17
—Often linked with Sidon ... Isa 23:1–2
Mt 15:21
See SIDON

B. Significance of Tyre
1. In the Old Testament
—Territory given to tribe of Asher ... Jos 19:24,29
—King Hiram sent wood for David's palace ... 2Sa 5:11–12
1Ch 14:1–2
—King Hiram sent wood for the temple ... 1Ki 5:7–12
2Ch 2:11–16
—Huram of Tyre was a temple craftsman ... 1Ki 7:13–14
—Prophecies against them ... Isa 23:1–18
Eze 26:1–28:19
Joel 3:4–8
Am 1:9–10
2. In the New Testament
—Jesus ministered there ... Mt 15:21–28
Mk 7:24–30
—Paul spent seven days there ... Ac 21:3–6

UNION WITH CHRIST

A. Related theme
IN CHRIST is a theme of Ephesians ... Eph 2:6

B. Christians are:
—In Christ ... 1Th 2:14
—New creatures in Christ ... 2Co 5:17
—The faithful in Christ ... Eph 1:1

C. Our participation in events of Christ's life
—We suffer with him ... Ro 8:17
Php 3:10
1Pe 4:13
—We share in his broken body ... 1Co 10:16–17
—We share in his shed blood ... 1Co 10:16–17
—We are crucified with him ... Ro 6:6,8
Col 2:20
—We are buried with him ... Ro 6:4
Col 2:12
—We are raised with him ... Eph 2:6
Col 2:12
Col 3:1
—We sit at God's right hand with him ... Eph 2:6
Col 3:1
—We will return with him ... 1Th 4:14
—We will share in his glory ... Ro 8:17
—We will reign with him ... 2Ti 2:12

D. Our involvement in Christ
—We are chosen in him ... Eph 1:4,11

—We are justified in him Gal 2:17
—We who are in him are free from condemnation Ro 8:1
—We are baptized into him Gal 3:27; Col 2:11–13
—We are infants in him 1Co 3:1
—We are found in him Php 3:9
—We are one with him Jn 14:20; Jn 17:21,23; 1Co 6:17
—We must remain in him Jn 15:4–5,7
—We live in him 1Jn 3:24
—Our way of life is in him 1Co 4:17
—We grow in him Eph 4:16
—We pray in him Eph 2:18; Eph 3:12
—We are blessed in him Eph 1:3
—We are sanctified in him 1Co 1:2
—We fall asleep (die) in him 1Th 4:14,16; 1Co 15:18
—We will be made alive in him 1Co 15:22

E. Pictures of union with Christ
—Vine and branches Jn 15:1–7
—Foundation and building 1Co 3:10–11; Eph 2:20–21
—Head and members of the body Ro 12:4–5; 1Co 12:14–27
—Husband and wife Eph 5:23–32
—Shepherd and sheep Jn 10:11,14–16

UNITY

A. Related themes
UNITY is a theme of:
—Acts Ac 4:32
—1 Corinthians 1Co 12:13

B. Expressions of the unity of the church
—One nation and people 1Pe 2:9–10
—One body Ro 12:4–5; 1Co 12:13,27
—One family Eph 2:19
—One bride/spouse 2Co 11:2; Eph 5:23–30
—One temple 1Co 3:16–17
—One building with one foundation 1Co 3:9–11; Eph 2:20–21
—One spiritual house 1Pe 2:5
—One field/vineyard Jn 15:5; 1Co 3:9
—One flock Jn 10:16
—One city Heb 12:22–23

C. The basis of unity
—Christ's unity with the Father Jn 17:20–23
—Christ's death on the cross Eph 2:14–16
—Our unity with Christ Gal 3:26–28
—The one Holy Spirit Eph 4:3–4
—Our common faith and hope Eph 4:4–5,13

D. Demonstrations of unity
—The life of the early church Ac 2:42–47; Ac 4:32
—The Lord's Supper 1Co 10:16–17

E. Important elements of unity
—Unity is good and pleasant Ps 133:1
—Unity makes God's people fruitful Ps 133:3
—Unity is a challenge we must strive to achieve Eph 4:12–16; Php 1:27; Php 2:1–3; 1Th 5:13; 1Pe 3:8
—Unity requires that we love one another Eph 4:15–16
—Diversity in gifts is consistent with unity Ro 12:4–8; 1Co 12:7–30
—Diversity in thinking is consistent with unity Ro 14:1–6

F. Causes of disunity
—Quarreling Ac 15:36–39; 1Co 3:3
—Favoritism Jas 2:1–4
—Spiritual immaturity 1Co 1:10–12; 1Co 3:1–2
—Hypocrisy Gal 2:11–14; 1Pe 2:1

URIAH

—Hittite husband of Bathsheba 2Sa 11:2–3
—One of David's brave warriors 2Sa 23:39
—Devoted to duty 2Sa 11:8–13
—Killed on David's orders 2Sa 11:16–25

URIM AND THUMMIM

See CASTING LOTS

USURY

See DEBT

UZZIAH

—Son of Amaziah; king of Judah 2Ch 26:1–5
—Also called Azariah 2Ki 15:1
—An effective and powerful king 2Ch 26:6–15
—Became proud and unlawfully burnt incense 2Ch 26:16–19
—Punished with leprosy 2Ki 15:5; 2Ch 26:20–21

VASHTI

—Wife of Xerxes; queen of Persia Est 1:9
—Refused to display her beauty Est 1:10–12
—Deposed as queen Est 1:15–21
—Replaced by Esther Est 2:17

VICTORY

See WARFARE

VINEYARD

A. Significant vineyards in the Bible
—Noah's Ge 9:20
—Those in Canaan Nu 13:23–24; Dt 8:8
—Naboth's 1Ki 21:1–16
—Vineyards in Jesus' parables Mt 20:1–15; Mt 21:28–31, 33–40

B. Design and care of vineyards
1. The design
—Had protecting walls Nu 22:24; Pr 24:30–31
—Had a tower for watchmen Isa 5:1–2; Mt 21:33
—Had a winepress in it Isa 5:2; Mt 21:33

2. The care
—Clearing the field Isa 5:2
—Planting Ps 107:37; Ecc 2:4; Isa 5:2
—Cultivating Dt 28:39; Isa 7:25
—Pruning Lev 25:3; Jn 15:2
—Harvesting Lev 19:10; Jdg 9:27
—Treading the winepress Isa 16:10

C. Vineyards used as a symbol
1. A symbol of prosperity and security
—To sit in one's vineyard meant security 1Ki 4:25; Mic 4:4
—To eat from one's vineyard meant prosperity 2Ki 18:31; Ps 107:37–38; Isa 36:16

2. Spiritual symbols
—A symbol of the Israelite nation Ps 80:8–11; Isa 5:7; Jer 2:21; Hos 10:1
—A symbol of the followers of Jesus Jn 15:1–6
—A symbol of the kingdom of heaven Mt 20:1–15; Mt 21:28–33

VISION
See DREAMS AND VISIONS

VOICE
A. The human voice
1. Uses of the human voice
—Ordinary communication 1Sa 24:16
—Recognizing a person .... Ge 27:22; 1Sa 26:17; Ac 12:14
—Expressing unity (one voice) .... Ex 24:3
—Praying .... Ps 66:19
—Requesting a favor .... Lk 17:13
—Preaching .... Ac 2:14
2. Expressions of the human voice
—The praising voice .... 2Ch 20:19; Lk 17:15
—The shouting voice .... Isa 40:9
—The complaining voice .... Ps 64:1
—The weeping voice .... Jer 31:15–16
B. The voice of God
1. Expressions of God's voice
a. People called by his voice
—Moses .... Ex 3:4–6; Ac 7:31–32
—Samuel 1Sa 3:1–14
—Isaiah .... Isa 6:8–10
b. The power of his voice
—Accompanied by fire .... Dt 4:33
—Sounds like thunder .... 2Sa 22:14; Job 37:4–5; Ps 29:3–4
—Accomplishes great things .... Ps 29:5–9; Ps 46:6
—Can come as a gentle whisper 1Ki 19:12–13
c. Messages of his voice
—His law from Mount Sinai .... Dt 5:22–26
—Affirmation of Jesus as his Son .... Mt 3:17; Lk 9:35–36
—Glorification of Jesus .... Jn 12:28–30
2. The voice of Jesus
—Jesus proclaimed with a loud voice .... Jn 7:37–38
—Jesus cried out with a loud voice .... Mt 27:46,50
—His voice raised Lazarus .... Jn 11:43
—His voice called Paul to be an apostle .... Ac 9:4–6
—His voice revealed things to John .... Rev 1:10–13
—His voice calls his sheep .... Jn 10:16,27
—His voice will raise the dead .... Jn 5:25,28
3. Our response to God's voice
—We must recognize his voice .... Jn 10:3–5
—We must listen to his voice .... Ex 15:26; Dt 30:20
—We must obey his voice .... 1Sa 15:22; Hag 1:12

VOW
—A solemn promise made to God
A. Significant vows in the Bible
—Jacob's vow at Bethel .... Ge 28:20–22
—The Nazirite vow .... Nu 6:1–21
—Jephthah's vow .... Jdg 11:30–31
—Nazirite vow required for Samson .... Jdg 13:1–7
—Hannah's vow regarding Samuel 1Sa 1:11
—David's vow regarding a temple for the Lord .... Ps 132:1–5
—Paul's Nazirite vow .... Ac 18:18
B. The nature of the vow
—Often arose in times of distress .... Ge 28:20–22; Nu 21:1–2; Ps 66:13–14; Ps 116:7–14
—Made only to God .... Lev 27:2,9; Dt 23:21–23; Isa 19:21
—Was completely voluntary .... Dt 23:22; Ecc 5:5
—Had to be fulfilled .... Dt 23:21,23; Ecc 5:4,6
—Should not be made rashly .... Pr 20:25
—Rules for redeeming vows .... Lev 27:1–33
—Could be abused at times .... Mk 7:9–13

WALK OF LIFE
—The Christian way of life
A. Related themes
1. CHRISTIAN LIVING is a theme of:
—Romans .... Ro 12:1
—Ephesians .... Eph 4:1
—Philippians .... Php 1:27
—Colossians .... Col 3:12
—1 Thessalonians 1Th 4:1
—James .... Jas 1:27
—1 Peter 1Pe 5:6
2. RESPONSE is a theme of Deuteronomy .... Dt 13:4
3. ATTITUDE is a theme of Proverbs .... Pr 10:12
B. What the Christian walk is not
—Not walking according to the sinful nature .... Ro 8:4; Gal 5:16–21
—Not walking in the ways of evildoers .... 1Ki 15:26,34; Pr 4:14
—Not walking in dark ways .... Pr 2:13
—Not walking in darkness .... Jn 8:12; 1Jn 1:6; 1Jn 2:11
—Not walking in the counsel of the wicked .... Ps 1:1
—Not walking in pride .... Da 4:37; Mic 2:3
C. What the Christian walk is
—Walking with God .... Ps 56:13; Mic 6:8; Rev 3:4
—Walking in God's ways .... Dt 5:33; Dt 10:12; Jos 22:5
—Walking before God 1Ki 2:4; 2Ch 7:17
—Walking in truth .... Ps 26:3; 3Jn 3–4
—Walking in the light .... Ps 89:15; Isa 2:5; 1Jn 1:7
—Walking in the name of God .... Mic 4:5
—Walking in the fear of God .... Ne 5:9
—Walking in the law of God .... Ps 119:1
—Walking in love and obedience 2Jn 6
—Walking in the Spirit .... Ro 8:4
—Walking in the paths of the righteous .... Pr 2:20
—Walking as Jesus walked 1Jn 2:6
D. Examples of those who walked with God
—Enoch .... Ge 5:22–24
—Noah .... Ge 6:9
—Abraham .... Ge 24:40
—Isaac .... Ge 48:15
—Levi .... Mal 2:4–6
—Jotham 2Ch 27:6
—Hezekiah .... Isa 38:3
E. God's promise to walk with us .... Lev 26:12; 2Co 6:16

WARFARE
A. Related themes
1. CONFLICT is a theme of Revelation .... Rev 12:7
2. GOD'S HELP is a theme of 1 Samuel 1Sa 17:45
3. GOD'S INTERVENTION is a theme of 2 Chronicles 2Ch 20:17
4. DELIVERANCE is a theme of Esther .... Est 8:11
5. VICTORY is a theme of:
—Joshua .... Jos 21:43
—Daniel .... Da 6:27
6. CHRIST'S VICTORY is a theme of Revelation .... Rev 11:15
B. Physical Warfare
1. Wars in the Bible
a. First recorded war .... Ge 14:1–17

b. Israelite wars on the way to Canaan .... Ex 17:8–13; Nu 21:1–3,21–35

c. Wars of Joshua
—The battle against Jericho .... Jos 6:1–25
—The battle against Ai .... Jos 7:3–5; Jos 8:1–29
—The battle against five kings .... Jos 10:1–28
—The southern cities defeated .... Jos 10:29–43
—The northern cities defeated .... Jos 11:1–23

d. Wars in the period of the judges
—Deborah and Barak .... Jdg 4:12–23
—Gideon .... Jdg 7:1–25
—Jephthah .... Jdg 11:4–33
—During Eli's judgeship 1Sa 4:1–10; 1Sa 7:2–14

e. Wars during the time of Saul
—Saul rescued the city of Jabesh 1Sa 11:1–11
—Against the Philistines 1Sa 13:2–7; 1Sa 14:1–46; 1Sa 17:1–54; 1Sa 31:1–7
—Against the Amalekites 1Sa 15:4–9; 1Sa 30:1–20

f. Wars during the time of David
—Gained control of all Israel 2Sa 2:8–4:12
—Against the Philistines 2Sa 5:17–25; 2Sa 21:15–22
—Against the Ammonites 2Sa 10:1–14
—Against the Arameans 2Sa 10:15–19
—Civil war against Absalom 2Sa 15:1–18:18
—Summary of wars 2Sa 8:1–14

g. Wars of the northern kingdom
—Against the southern kingdom 1Ki 15:16–17,32; 2Ki 13:12; 2Ki 14:9–14; 2Ki 16:5–6
—Against the Philistines 1Ki 16:15–17
—Against the Arameans 1Ki 20:1–34; 1Ki 22:1–37; 2Ki 6:8–7:11; 2Ki 8:28–29; 2Ki 13:3–7
—Against Assyria 2Ki 15:19–20,29–30; 2Ki 16:7–10; 2Ki 17:1–6

h. Wars of the southern kingdom
—Against the Egyptians 1Ki 14:25–26
—Against the Edomites 2Ki 8:20–22; 2Ki 14:7
—Against the Ammonites and Moabites 2Ch 20:1–26
—Against Assyria 2Ch 32:1–22; 2Ch 33:10–11
—Against Babylon 2Ki 24:1–4,10–16; 2Ki 25:1–21

2. Victory for God's people

a. God is the source of victory .... Nu 21:3; Dt 20:1–4; Jos 11:7–8; 2Ch 20:15–17; Ps 18:29,34–43; Pr 21:31

b. Principles of victory
—Success when faithful to the Lord .... Jdg 7:1–25; 1Sa 17:41–50; 2Ch 20:20
—Defeat when unfaithful 2Ki 17:5–20; 2Ki 21:10–15

c. God controls foreign armies .... Isa 13:3–5; Jer 25:8–9; Eze 21:18–22

C. Spiritual warfare

1. God is at war with Satan
—At the time of Job .... Job 1:6–12; Job 26:6–13
—In the days of Israel .... Isa 27:1
—At the time of Christ .... Mt 4:1–11; Lk 10:18
—In heaven .... Rev 12:7–9

2. Christians are at war
—With the devil .... Ge 3:1–15; 2Co 2:11; 1Pe 5:8
—With the powers of darkness .... Eph 6:12
—With the world .... Jn 15:18–19; 1Jn 2:15–17
—With the old self .... Ro 6:6,12
—With the sinful nature .... Ro 8:5–9; Gal 5:16–25
—With sinful desires .... Ro 7:15–20; 1Pe 2:11
—With death .... 1Co 15:26; Heb 2:14–15

3. How Christians ought to fight
—By depending on God .... Ps 18:29,32; Ps 27:1–2
—By being dedicated to Jesus Christ 2Ti 2:4; 1Pe 5:10
—By standing firm in the Lord .... Eph 6:10–14
—By holding on to the faith 1Ti 1:18–19; 1Jn 5:4–5
—By laying hold of eternal life 1Ti 6:12
—By being good soldiers 2Ti 2:3
—By enduring hardship 2Ti 2:3
—By exercising self-denial 1Co 9:26–27
—By praying .... Eph 6:18
—By resisting the devil 1Pe 5:8–9

4. Protection provided by the Lord
—The full armor of God .... Eph 6:11,13
—The armor of light .... Ro 13:12
—God as our shield .... Ge 15:1; Dt 33:29; Ps 115:9–11
—The shield of faith .... Eph 6:16
—The belt of righteousness .... Isa 11:5
—The belt of truth .... Eph 6:14
—The breastplate of righteousness .... Isa 59:17; Eph 6:14
—The breastplate of faith and love 1Th 5:8
—Feet ready to run to bring the good news .... Isa 52:7; Eph 6:15
—The helmet of salvation .... Eph 6:17; 1Th 5:8
—The sword of the Spirit, the word of God .... Eph 6:17; Heb 4:12

5. Victory is certain

a. Accomplished by Christ
—On the cross .... Jn 12:31–33; Col 2:15; Heb 2:14
—In his ascension .... Eph 1:20–21; Php 2:9–11
—In his return .... 1Co 15:24–28; Rev 19:11–16

b. Our victory given through Christ
—God gives us the victory .... Ro 7:25; 1Co 15:55–57
—We can do all things in Christ .... Php 4:13
—God will crush Satan under our feet .... Ro 16:20

c. Victory over sin through the Spirit .... Ro 8:9–13; Gal 5:16–18

WATCHFULNESS

A. God watches over people
—His protective watch .... Ge 31:49; Ps 121:3–8; Isa 27:2–3; Jer 31:10
—His watch over good and evil .... Job 7:17–21; Job 13:27; Pr 15:3; Jer 31:28

B. God's people must be watchful
 1. What we must watch
  —Ourselves and our manner of life .... Dt 4:9; Dt 4:15; Ps 39:1; 1Ti 4:16
  —For false teachers.......................... Mk 13:5–6; Ac 20:28–31; Php 3:2–3; 2Jn 8
  —For those who divide the church............... Ro 16:17
  —For hypocrites .... Mk 12:38–40
  —For the second coming of Jesus................ Mt 25:13; 1Th 5:5–6; Rev 16:15
 2. How we must watch
  —With prayer .... Mk 14:38; Eph 6:18
  —With alertness.............................. Mk 13:33; 1Th 5:6
  —With care not to fall into temptation .... Mk 14:38; Gal 6:1
  —With care not to forget what God has done...... Dt 4:9
  —With hope.................................. Mic 7:7
  —With thankfulness........................... Col 4:2

WATER

A. Uses of water
 1. Water for washing
  a. Simple cleansing
   —Washing body .... Ru 3:3
   —Washing face............................ Ge 43:31
   —Washing feet .... Ge 18:4; 2Sa 11:8; Jn 13:4–5
  b. Ritual cleansing
   —Washing clothes at Mount Sinai .... Ex 19:10,14
   —Washing necessary for priests.............. Ex 30:17–21
   —Washing necessary for Levites.............. Nu 8:5–7
   —Washing parts of a sacrifice................ Lev 1:9,13
   —Washing after a skin disease .... Lev 14:8–9
   —Washing after uncleanness .... Lev 15:5–13,21–22; Nu 19:11–13
   —Various Jewish washing rituals............. Mt 23:25–26; Mk 7:3–4
 2. Water for drinking
  a. Water drunk by humans and animals .... Ge 24:11–19; Jdg 7:4–5; Mt 10:42
  b. God provided water for his people
   —Hagar .... Ge 21:15–19
   —The Israelites in the desert................. Ex 17:1–6; Nu 20:1–11; Ps 78:20
   —The Israelites in the time of Elisha........... 2Ki 3:15–20

B. God and water
 1. God is the source of living water.................. Ps 23:2; Isa 55:1; Jer 2:13
 2. Christ is the source of living water .... Jn 4:10–14; Jn 7:37–38; Rev 21:6; Rev 22:1–2
 3. Water used in judgment by God
  —The flood.................................. Ge 7:17–24; 1Pe 3:20
  —The destruction of the Egyptians............... Ex 14:26–30; Ps 106:9–11
  —The destruction of the Philistines .... Jer 47:2–5
  —The storm in the story of Jonah................ Jnh 1:3–15
  —Sea storms in general........................ Ps 107:23–30

C. Water used as a symbol
 1. As a symbol of evil people .... Ge 49:4; Isa 57:20; Jude 13
 2. As a symbol of personal affliction
  —Waters overwhelming someone............... Ps 42:7; Ps 69:1–2,14–15; Jer 49:23
  —God protects his people from the waters........ Ps 18:16–17; Ps 124:1–5; Isa 43:2
  —Heaven has no sea.......................... Rev 21:1
 3. As a symbol of cleansing from sin................. Isa 1:16; Eze 36:25; Eph 5:26; Heb 10:22
 4. As a cleansing symbol in baptism................. Ac 8:36; Ac 22:16; 1Pe 3:21
 5. As a symbol of the Holy Spirit .... Isa 44:3; Jn 7:38–39
 6. As a symbol of heavenly peace .... Isa 35:6–7; Isa 43:19–21; Jer 31:11–12; Zec 14:6–9; Rev 22:1–2

WEALTH

See THE RICH AND THE POOR

WEATHER

A. God and the weather
 1. God controls the weather
  —He sends sunshine........................... Ps 19:4–6; Mt 5:45
  —He sends rain and snow .... Job 5:10; Job 38:22–30; Ps 147:16–17
  —He sends wind .... Ex 10:13; Ps 78:26; Ps 147:18
  —He sends storms .... Ps 107:25–26; Jnh 1:4; Eze 13:13
 2. God uses weather elements
  a. To exhibit his power .... Ex 19:16
  b. To bless his people .... Dt 11:13–15; Ps 65:9–11; Ps 147:7–9
  c. To help his people in battle .... Jos 10:11–14; 1Sa 7:10; 2Sa 22:13–15
  d. To judge people
   —By withholding rain .... Lev 26:18–20; 1Ki 17:1; Am 4:7
   —By sending floods .... Ge 7:11–24; Isa 8:6–8; Na 1:8
   —By sending violent storms .... Ex 9:22–26; Ps 107:25–27; Na 1:3–4; Hag 2:17

B. Weather elements used as symbols
 1. The sun
  See SUN
 2. Clouds
  —God's presence among his people.............. Ex 13:21–22; Ps 104:3
  —The mystery of God.......................... Ps 97:2
  —Sin and forgiveness.......................... Isa 44:22
  —Departed Christians who surround us as witnesses .... Heb 12:1
  —God's judgment............................. Joel 2:2
  —An advancing army.......................... Jer 4:13
 3. Wind
  —God's presence around us..................... Ps 104:3
  —The Holy Spirit .... Jn 3:8; Ac 2:2

—Meaninglessness .... Ecc 1:6,14
—False teaching .... Eph 4:14
4. Gentle rain showers
—The word of God .... Isa 55:10–12
—God's blessings .... Eze 34:26
Hos 6:3
5. Snow
—Forgiveness .... Ps 51:7
Isa 1:18
—Leprosy .... Nu 12:10
—God's wonders .... Job 38:22
—Brightness .... Mt 28:3
—Glory of Christ .... Rev 1:14
6. Hail
—God's wonders .... Job 38:22
—God's power and majesty .... Ps 18:12
—God's judgment .... Rev 8:7
7. Thunder
—God's voice .... Ps 18:13
Ps 29:3–7
Ps 68:32–33
—God's majesty .... Rev 4:5
8. Lightning
—Christ's return .... Mt 24:27
Lk 17:24
—Satan's fall .... Lk 10:18
9. Violent storms, as God's final judgment .... Eze 38:22
Rev 11:19
Rev 16:18–21

See also HUNGER AND THIRST; WATER

WICKEDNESS

See SIN

WILL OF GOD

A. God's will: what God wants us to do
1. What does God's will include?
—His law in general .... Ro 2:18
1Pe 4:2–3
—His word in general .... Ac 20:27
—Doing what is good 1Pe 2:15
—Avoiding sexual immorality 1Th 4:3
—Giving thanks in all circumstances 1Th 5:18
2. How did Jesus relate to God's will?
—He came to do God's will .... Jn 4:34
Jn 6:38
Heb 10:5,7
—He was obedient to God's will .... Php 2:7–8
—He submitted to God's will for him .... Mt 26:39,42
3. How must we relate to God's will
—We must know his will .... Col 1:9
—We must understand his will .... Eph 5:17
—We must choose to do his will .... Jn 7:17
—We must do his will .... Ps 40:8
Ps 143:10
Mt 12:50
—We must approve his will by obedience .... Ro 12:2
—We must stand firm in his will .... Col 4:12
B. God's will: what God plans in history
1. Aspects of God's will
—God does whatever he pleases .... Ps 115:3
Ps 135:6
Da 4:35
Ro 9:18–21
—Everything occurs according to his will .... Eph 1:11
2. What can we know about God's plan?
a. His plan may be kept secret
—Hidden in the Old Testament .... Eph 1:9
Eph 3:4–5
—Hidden from learned people .... Mt 11:25–26
—Even now we may not understand it .... Ro 9:18–24
b. Some parts of his plan are revealed
—That salvation is in Christ .... Gal 1:4
—That God saves both Jew and Gentile .... Eph 3:6
—That everyone should be saved 1Ti 2:4
2Pe 3:9
—That all God's children come to him .... Mt 18:14
Jn 6:39–40
—That Paul was called as an apostle 1Co 1:1
3. God's will and human suffering
—His will may include suffering .... Job 1:6–22
1Pe 3:17
1Pe 4:19
—God works for his people's good .... Ge 50:20
Jer 29:11
Ro 8:28
See also PAIN
4. Our relationship to God's plan for us
—Pray that God's will be done .... Mt 6:10
—Pray that things happen by God's will .... Ac 18:21
Ro 15:31–32
1Co 16:7
Jas 4:13–15
—Submit to God's plan for us .... Ac 21:14

WIND

See WEATHER

WINE

See ALCOHOL

WISDOM

—Comprehensive knowledge that is put into practice
A. Related theme
WISDOM is a theme of Proverbs .... Pr 2:6
B. Human wisdom
1. Source of wisdom
—Received as a gift from God 1Ki 3:11–12
Pr 2:6
Ecc 2:26
Da 2:21
Jas 1:5
—Received as a gift from the Spirit 1Co 12:8
Eph 1:17
—Starts with the fear of the Lord .... Job 28:28
Ps 111:10
Pr 9:10
—Comes from listening to the wise .... Pr 1:2
Pr 4:1–11
Pr 13:20
—Comes from research and education .... Ecc 1:13,17
Ecc 7:25
—Comes from discipline .... Pr 29:15
—Comes from admonishing one another .... Col 3:16
2. Expressions of wisdom
—Serving as craftsman .... Ex 28:3
—Following God's law .... Dt 4:6
Hos 14:9
Mt 7:24–26
—Writing proverbs and songs 1Ki 4:29,32
—Studying God's creation 1Ki 4:29,33
—Administering justice 1Ki 3:16–28
1Ki 10:8–9
—Avoiding evil .... Pr 5:1–6
—Taking advice .... Pr 13:10
—Giving advice .... Da 1:20
—Interpreting visions and dreams .... Da 2:23,30
—Preparing for the future .... Mt 25:1–13
—Exercising patience .... Pr 19:11
—Living the Christian lifestyle .... Pr 2:20–21
Jas 3:17
—Defending the gospel .... Ac 6:3,10
3. Benefits of wisdom
—Makes us blessed .... Pr 3:13
—Leads to a long life .... Pr 3:16
—Preserves our lives .... Ecc 7:12
—Protects us .... Pr 4:6
—Exalts us .... Pr 4:8–9
—Brings us joy .... Pr 29:3
Pr 27:11
—Gives us strength .... Ecc 7:19
—Brings us healing .... Pr 12:18
—Saves us from evil ways .... Pr 2:12–19

C. Divine wisdom
  1. True wisdom centers in God
    —God has wisdom .... Job 12:13; Job 28:20–24; Da 2:20
    —Christ is the wisdom of God .... 1Co 1:24,30; Col 2:3
    —The Spirit is the Spirit of wisdom .... Isa 11:2; Eph 1:17
  2. The nature of God's wisdom
    —Profound .... Job 9:4
    —Precious .... Pr 8:18–19
    —Deep and rich .... Ro 11:33
    —Magnificent .... Isa 28:29
    —Manifold .... Eph 3:10
    —Unsurpassable .... Jer 10:7
  3. Activities of God's wisdom
    —Operative in creation .... Ps 104:24; Pr 3:19; Pr 8:22–31; Jer 10:12
    —Controls nature .... Job 26:12; Job 39:26
    —Controls history .... Isa 10:12–13
    —Counsels rulers .... Pr 8:14–16

WITCHCRAFT

See MAGIC, WITCHCRAFT AND SORCERY

WITNESS

—One who bears testimony to something or someone

A. Types of witnesses
  —God as a witness .... Ge 31:50; Jdg 11:10
  —People as witnesses .... Jos 24:22; Ru 4:9–11; Jer 32:12
  —Things as witnesses .... Dt 31:19–21; Jos 24:27; Isa 19:19–20

B. Legal witnesses
  —Two or three necessary to convict someone .... Dt 17:6; Mt 26:60–61; 2Co 13:1
  —No false testimony to be given .... Ex 20:16; Dt 19:16–18; Pr 24:28–29

C. Witnesses to God's truth and salvation
  —Israel as witnesses .... Isa 43:10–12; Isa 44:8
  —The prophets as witnesses .... Ac 10:43; Ac 26:22–23
  —John the Baptist as witness .... Jn 1:7,15,32–34; Jn 5:33–34
  —Jesus Christ as the faithful witness .... Jn 8:18; Jn 18:37; Rev 1:5–6
  —The Holy Spirit as witness .... Jn 15:26; Ac 5:30–32; Ro 8:16
  —Signs and wonders as witnesses .... Jn 2:11; Jn 20:30–31; Heb 2:3–4
  —Jesus' followers as witnesses .... Lk 1:2; Ac 1:8; Ac 3:15–16; Ac 5:30–32; Ac 10:41–42

WOMEN

A. Status of women
  1. In creation
    —Created in the image of God .... Ge 1:27
    —Equal responsibility and blessing .... Ge 1:26,28–30
    —Created as a companion for man .... Ge 2:18,20
    —Created second, from man .... Ge 2:21–22; 1Co 11:3,7–8,12
  2. In and after the fall
    —Eve was tempted and sinned first .... Ge 3:1–6; 2Co 11:3; 1Ti 2:14
    —Were subordinated to husbands .... Ge 3:16
    —Were considered weak and insecure .... Isa 19:16; Jer 50:37; 1Pe 3:7
  3. In the covenant of the Old Testament
    —Circumcision only for males .... Ge 17:10–14
    —Only males instructed to appear before the Lord .... Ex 23:17
    —Value of woman was less than that of a man .... Lev 27:1–8
    —Sons had priority over daughters .... Nu 36:1–9; Ps 127:3–4
    —Women served in the worship of God .... Ex 15:20; Ex 38:8; Ezr 2:65
    —Women also expected to keep the festivals .... Dt 16:9–15
  4. Jesus' attitude toward women
    —Healed women as well as men .... Mk 1:30–31; Mk 5:25–34; Lk 13:10–17
    —Used women as examples in parables .... Lk 13:20–21; Lk 15:8–10; Lk 17:35; Lk 18:1–8
    —Was supported by women .... Lk 8:1–3
    —Affirmed women eager to learn .... Lk 10:38–42; Jn 4:7–26
    —Praised a poor widow and her gift .... Lk 21:1–4
    —Praised Martha's confession .... Jn 11:24–27
    —Women were first witnesses to resurrection .... Mt 28:1–10; Mk 16:1–8; Lk 24:1–11; Jn 20:1–2,10–18
  5. In the redemption won by Christ
    —In Christ no male or female .... Gal 3:28
    —Salvation came through woman .... Gal 4:4–5
    —Woman saved through childbearing 1Ti 2:15
    —Spirit poured out on sons and daughters .... Joel 2:28–29; Ac 2:17–18
    —Women filled with the Holy Spirit .... Lk 1:41–45; Ac 2:1–4
    —Women and men both saved .... Ac 9:36–39; Ac 17:4,12
    —Women prayed and prophesied .... Ac 1:14; 1Co 11:5
    —Women were to be silent in the churches 1Co 14:33–35; 1Ti 2:11–12

B. Roles and occupations of women
  —Wife
  See MARRIAGE
  —Mother
  See MOTHER
  —Shepherdess .... Ge 29:6; Ex 2:16
  —Businesswoman .... Pr 31:13–19; Ac 16:14
  —Judge .... Jdg 4:4–5
  —Prophetess .... 2Ki 22:14–20; Ac 21:8–9
  —Teacher .... Ac 18:26
  —Workers in the church .... Ro 16:1–2; Php 4:2–3

C. Prominent women in the Bible
  —Abigail 1Sa 25:3
  —Anna .... Lk 2:36
  —Athaliah 2Ki 11:1
  —Bathsheba 2Sa 11:3
  —Deborah .... Jdg 4:4
  —Dorcas .... Ac 9:36
  —Elizabeth .... Lk 1:5
  —Esther .... Est 2:7
  —Eve .... Ge 3:20

—Hagar Ge 16:1
—Hannah 1Sa 1:2
—Huldah 2Ki 22:14
—Jael Jdg 4:17
—Jezebel 1Ki 16:31
—Leah Ge 29:16
—Lydia Ac 16:14
—Mary the mother of Jesus Lk 1:27
—Mary Magdalene Lk 8:2
—Mary and Martha Lk 10:38–39
—Miriam Ex 15:20
—Phoebe Ro 16:1
—Priscilla Ac 18:2
—Rachel Ge 29:16
—Rahab Jos 2:3
—Rebekah Ge 24:29
—Ruth Ru 1:4
—Salome Mk 15:40
—Sapphira Ac 5:1
—Sarah Ge 12:5
—Tamar Ge 38:6
See also entries for each of these women

WORD OF GOD

A. What is the word of God?
—The word God spoke in creation Ps 33:6–9
—The word God spoke to the prophets 1Ki 17:2,8; Jer 1:2,4,11–13; Eze 6:1–3
—The Old Testament revelation Jn 10:34–45
—The word spoken by Jesus Lk 5:1
—Jesus himself as the Word become flesh Jn 1:1,14
—The word spoken by the apostles Ac 13:44; 1Th 2:13; 1Pe 1:25
—Instructions given by pastors Gal 6:6; 2Ti 4:2

B. What power does the word of God have?
—The power to create Ps 33:6; Heb 11:3; 2Pe 3:5
—The power to sustain all of creation Ps 147:15–18; Heb 1:3
—The power to heal Ps 107:20; Mt 8:8
—The power to judge our hearts Heb 4:12
—The power to give us new birth Jas 1:18; 1Pe 1:23
—The power to lead us to faith Ro 10:17
—The power to save us 2Ti 3:15
—The power to make us holy Eph 5:26
—The power to fight against Satan Eph 6:17; Rev 19:13–15
—The power to destroy the world 2Pe 3:7

C. Characteristics of God's word
—It is reliable 2Sa 7:28
—It is true 1Ki 17:24; Jn 17:17
—It is flawless Pr 30:5
—It is alive and active Heb 4:12
—It is eternal Ps 119:89
—It will endure Isa 40:8; Mt 5:18; Mt 24:35
—It will not return empty Isa 55:11

D. Our reaction to the word of God
—We must hear it Isa 1:10; Jer 7:1–2
—We must understand it Mt 13:23
—We must accept it Mk 4:20; Ac 2:41; 1Th 2:13
—We must hide it in our hearts Ps 119:11
—We must retain it Lk 8:15
—We must let it dwell among us Col 3:16
—We must trust in it Ps 119:42
—We must hope in it Ps 119:74,81,114; Ps 130:5
—We must praise it Ps 56:4,10
—We must live according to it Ps 119:9
—We must obey it Ps 119:17,67; Jas 1:22–24
—We must handle it correctly 2Ti 2:15
—We must preach it Ac 8:4

E. Pictures used for the word of God
—Lamp and light Ps 119:105
—Rain producing fruit Isa 55:10–11
—Consuming fire Jer 5:14
—Destroying hammer Jer 23:29
—Seed Mk 4:14
—Sword Eph 6:17; Heb 4:12

F. Scripture as the word of God
See INSPIRATION OF SCRIPTURE

G. Jesus as the Word of God
—He is the Word of God Jn 1:1
—He is the creative Word Jn 1:3
—He is the Word become flesh Jn 1:14
—He is the Word of life 1Jn 1:2
—He is the victorious Word Rev 19:13–16

WORK

A. Related themes
PRAY AND WORK is a theme of Nehemiah Ne 4:9
DAILY WORK is a theme of 2 Thessalonians 2Th 3:6

B. The work of humans
1. Humans in general
a. Nature of work
—Required of Adam before the fall Ge 1:28; Ge 2:15,19–20
—Required of humans after the fall Ex 20:9; Eph 4:28; 1Th 4:11
—Became hard work Ge 3:17–19; Ecc 3:9–10
—Can seem meaningless Ecc 1:14; Ecc 2:11,17
b. God's relationship to human work
—He commands it Dt 5:13
—He expects it Ps 104:23
—He blesses honest toil Pr 14:23; Pr 27:23–27
—He speaks against laziness Pr 6:6–11; Pr 10:4–5
2. Daily work for Christians
—We must earn our daily bread 2Th 3:10
—We must pray for God to establish it Ps 90:17
—We must depend on God in it Ps 127:1–2; Isa 26:12
—We must bring glory to God's name through it 1Co 10:31; Col 3:17
—We must accompany it with prayer Ne 4:6–9
—Our work is not in vain 1Co 15:58

C. The work of God
1. Aspects of his work
—Created the world Ge 1:1–2:3; Ps 8:3
—Preserves the world Ps 36:6
—Governs the world Ac 17:26; Eph 1:11
—Redeems the world Jn 3:16–17; Jn 12:47
—Always at work in the world Jn 5:17
2. His works described as:
—Numerous Ps 104:24
—Great Ps 92:5
—Awesome Ps 66:5
—Marvelous Rev 15:3
—Wonderful Ps 139:14
—Faithful Ps 111:7

3. Our reaction to God's works
   - —We should see them ... Ps 46:8; Ps 66:5
   - —We should have regard for them ... Ps 28:5
   - —We should consider them ... Ps 8:3
   - —We should meditate on them ... Ps 77:12; Ps 143:5
   - —We should sing for joy at them ... Ps 92:4
   - —We should praise them ... Job 36:24
   - —We should tell others about them ... Ps 107:21–22; Ps 145:4–6

WORLD

A. Related themes
1. WORLDWIDE MISSION is a theme of:
   - —Matthew ... Mt 21:43
   - —Acts ... Ac 28:14
   - —Romans ... Ro 15:19
2. WORLDWIDE SAVIOR is a theme of Luke ... Lk 19:9

B. Meaning of the word "world"
- —The entire created universe ... Jer 10:12
- —All men and women on earth ... Ge 11:1,9; 1Sa 17:46; Isa 12:5; Jn 3:16
- —People opposed to God ... Jn 14:30–31; 1Jn 5:19
- —Natural life as opposed to spiritual life ... 1Co 7:33

C. God's relationship to the sinful world
1. God the Father
   - —He loves it ... Jn 3:16
   - —He sent Jesus to save it ... Jn 3:16–17; Jn 17:18,23
   - —He reconciled it through Christ ... 2Co 5:19
   - —He holds it accountable to him ... Ro 3:19
   - —He will judge it ... Ps 96:13; Ps 98:9
2. Jesus the Son
   - —He is its light ... Jn 3:19; Jn 8:12; Jn 9:5
   - —He takes away its sin ... Jn 1:29
   - —He is its Savior ... Lk 2:10–11; Jn 4:42; 1Ti 1:15; 1Jn 4:14
   - —He gives it life ... Jn 6:33,51
   - —He has overcome it ... Jn 16:33
   - —He will judge it ... Ac 17:31

D. Our relationship to the sinful world
1. How we relate to the world
   - —We are in it ... Jn 17:15; 2Co 10:3
   - —We are strangers in it ... 1Pe 2:11
   - —We are not of it ... Jn 15:19; Jn 17:14,16; Jas 4:4
   - —We may not adopt its standards ... Ro 12:2; Titus 2:12; Jas 1:27
   - —We must not love it ... 2Ti 4:10; 1Jn 2:15–16
   - —We must be crucified to it ... Ro 6:6; Gal 6:14
   - —We must overcome it ... Jn 16:33; 1Jn 5:4–5
   - —We must proclaim the gospel to it ... Mt 24:14; Mt 28:19; Mk 16:15
   - —We will judge it ... 1Co 6:2
2. How the world relates to us
   - —The world hates us ... Jn 15:18; Jn 17:14; 1Jn 3:13
   - —The world persecutes us ... Jn 15:20–21; 2Ti 3:12
   - —The world has false prophets ... 1Jn 4:1,3; 2Jn 7

WORSHIP

A. Related themes

WORSHIP is a theme of:
- —Leviticus ... Lev 23:2
- —1 Chronicles ... 1Ch 25:1

B. The call to worship
1. Commanded by God ... 2Ki 17:35–39; Ps 29:2; Ps 96:9
2. Affirmed by believers ... Ps 95:6; Ps 100:1–2; Ps 132:6–7; Heb 10:25

C. Examples of people at worship
1. The formal worship of God
   - —Cain and Abel ... Ge 4:3–4
   - —Noah ... Ge 8:20
   - —Abraham ... Ge 22:5
   - —Isaac ... Ge 26:23–25
   - —Jacob ... Ge 35:1–7
   - —The Israelites under Moses ... Ex 24:1–8
   - —The Israelites under David ... 1Ch 23:28–31
   - —Daniel ... Da 6:10
   - —The returned exiles ... Ezr 3:10–11; Ne 8:2–18
   - —Jesus ... Lk 4:15–27
   - —The apostles ... Ac 3:1
   - —The early church ... Ac 2:42,46–47; Ac 20:7–11
   - —The hosts of heaven ... Rev 5:8–14; Rev 7:9–17
2. The worship of Christ
   - —The Magi ... Mt 2:11
   - —Christ's disciples ... Mt 14:33; Mt 28:17; Lk 24:52
   - —A blind man who received his sight ... Jn 9:38
   - —The heavenly hosts ... Rev 5:8–14

D. The day for worship

See SABBATH

E. Characteristics of true worship
1. Principles to follow
   - —Worship God alone ... Ex 20:4–5; Ex 23:24–25; Mt 4:10
   - —Love God with all your heart ... Dt 6:4–6; Dt 10:12–13
   - —Be humble in heart ... Ps 51:17; Isa 66:2; Mic 6:6–8
   - —Depend on the Holy Spirit ... Jn 4:20–24; Php 3:3
   - —Formal ritual alone is insufficient ... Isa 1:11–15; Am 5:21–24
2. Specific elements in Christian worship
   - —Reading Scripture ... 1Ti 4:13
   - —Preaching ... Ac 20:7; 2Ti 4:2

     See PREACHING
   - —Praying ... 1Ti 2:1,8

     See PRAYER
   - —Singing ... Col 3:16

     See MUSIC AND SONG
   - —Giving an offering ... 1Co 16:1–2

     See TITHES AND OFFERINGS
   - —Exercising spiritual gifts ... 1Co 14:26–33

     See GIFTS OF THE SPIRIT
   - —Celebrating the sacraments ... Ac 2:41–42; 1Co 11:18–29

     See BAPTISM; LORD'S SUPPER

WRATH
See ANGER

XERXES
—King of Persia Est 1:1–2
—Deposed Queen Vashti Est 1:15–21
—Made Esther queen Est 2:17
—Signed edict to annihilate the Jews Est 3:12–15
—Received Esther without having summoned her Est 5:1–8
—Honored Mordecai Est 6:1–11
—Furious at Haman Est 7:1–8
—Impaled Haman on a pole Est 7:9–10
—Signed edict allowing Jews to defend themselves Est 8:3–14
—Exalted Mordecai Est 8:1–2,15; Est 9:4

YEAR OF JUBILEE
See THE RICH AND THE POOR; SLAVERY

YEAST
—A leavening substance for bread
A. Yeast and bread
—Allowed in some offerings Lev 7:13; Lev 23:17
—Not allowed in other offerings Ex 23:15–16; Lev 2:11; Dt 16:1–8
—The Festival of Unleavened Bread
See FESTIVALS
B. Yeast as a symbol
—A symbol of corruption and evil Mt 16:6,12; Gal 5:7–9; 1Co 5:6–8
—A symbol of the penetrating influence of the kingdom Mt 13:33; Lk 13:21

YOKE
A. Uses for the yoke
—To use on animals at work 1Ki 19:19–21
—To control slaves 1Ti 6:1
—To wear as a prophetic symbol Jer 27:2
B. The yoke as a symbol
1. Positive
—A symbol of service to God's law Jer 2:20
—A symbol of discipleship Mt 11:28–30
2. Negative
—A symbol of oppression 1Ki 12:4,9–11; Jer 28:10–14
—A symbol of bondage to sin La 1:14
—A symbol of legalism Ac 15:10; Gal 5:1
—A symbol of union with unbelievers 2Co 6:14

YOUTH
A. Characteristics of youth
—Strong Pr 20:29; Isa 40:30; 1Jn 2:14
—Devoted and zealous 1Ki 18:12; Jer 2:2; Gal 1:13–14
—Inexperienced 1Sa 17:33; 1Ch 22:5; Jer 1:6
—Sinful and foolish Job 13:26; 1Sa 2:17; 1Ki 12:8–15; Ps 25:7; 2Ti 2:22
—Lacking in knowledge and judgment Ge 37:2–11; Pr 1:4; Pr 7:7
B. Encouragement to youth
—To commit their lives to God Ps 119:9; Ecc 12:1; La 3:27
—To seek knowledge from God 1Ki 3:7–9
—To enjoy life Pr 5:18; Ecc 11:9
—To see visions and to prophesy Joel 2:28; Ac 2:17
—To exercise self-control Titus 2:6
C. Familiar stories involving youths
—Joseph sold into Egypt Ge 37:12–28
—Joseph serving faithfully in Egypt Ge 39:1–12
—Gideon called to be military leader Jdg 6:15–16
—David killing Goliath 1Sa 17:26–50
—Joash repairing the temple 2Ch 24:4–14
—Josiah purifying the land and the temple 2Ch 34:3–13
—Jeremiah called to serve as prophet Jer 1:4–19
—James and John following Jesus Mk 1:19–20
—Timothy accompanying Paul Ac 16:1–3
—Timothy serving as pastor 1Ti 4:12

ZACCHAEUS
—Tax collector Lk 19:1–2
—Climbed a tree to see Jesus Lk 19:3–4
—Welcomed Jesus into his house Lk 19:5–7
—Saved by Jesus Lk 19:8–9

ZADOK
—A priest in the time of David 2Sa 8:17
—Ministered in Hebron after Saul's death 1Ch 12:23–28
—Helped bring the ark to Jerusalem 1Ch 15:11–13
—Became David's priest 1Ch 16:39–40; 1Ch 24:6
—Loyal to David during Absalom's rebellion 2Sa 15:24–36; 2Sa 17:15,17–21
—Loyal to David during Adonijah's rebellion 1Ki 1:8
—Anointed Solomon king 1Ki 1:32–40
—Became Solomon's priest 1Ki 2:35; 1Ki 4:4; 1Ch 29:22

ZEAL
See JEALOUSY

ZEBULUN
A. Son of Jacob by Leah Ge 35:23; 1Ch 2:1
—Name means "honor" Ge 30:20
—Went to Egypt with family Ge 46:8,14
—Father of three sons Ge 46:14
—Blessed by Jacob Ge 49:13
B. Tribe descended from Zebulun
—Blessed by Moses Dt 33:18–19
—Numbered Nu 1:31; Nu 26:27
—Allotted land Jos 19:10–16; Eze 48:26
—Failed to fully possess the land Jdg 1:30
—Supported Deborah Jdg 4:6–10; Jdg 5:14,18
—Supported David 1Ch 12:33
—One of the tribes of the 144,000 Rev 7:8

ZECHARIAH
A. Son of Jeroboam II; king of Israel 2Ki 15:8–9
—Assassinated by Shallum 2Ki 15:10
B. A postexilic prophet
—Encouraged rebuilding of temple Ezr 5:1; Ezr 6:14
—Received various visions and prophecies Zec 1:1,7; Zec 7:1,8
C. Father of John the Baptist
—Took his turn as priest in temple Lk 1:5,8–10
—Received announcement of the birth of a son Lk 1:11–20
—Could not speak for nine months Lk 1:20–22
—Gave name "John" to his son Lk 1:59–63
—Praised God with a song Lk 1:64–79

ZEDEKIAH
A. A false prophet 1Ki 22:11; 2Ch 18:10

—Slapped true prophet Micaiah in the face 1Ki 22:24
2Ch 18:23
B. Son of Josiah 1Ch 3:15
—Also called Mattaniah 2Ki 24:17
—Made king of Judah by Nebuchadnezzar 2Ki 24:17–20
2Ch 36:10
—Asked Jeremiah to pray for Jerusalem .... Jer 37:3
—Consulted with Jeremiah .... Jer 38:14–27
—Rebelled against Nebuchadnezzar 2Ki 24:20
2Ch 36:13
—Jerusalem destroyed during his time 2Ki 25:1–17
2Ch 36:15–19
—Saw his sons killed .... Jer 39:5–6
—Blinded and taken to Babylon .... Jer 39:7

ZERUBBABEL

—Descendant of David 1Ch 3:19
Mt 1:3
—Led return of Jews from exile .... Ezr 2:2
Ne 7:7
—Restored worship in Judah .... Ezr 3:1–8
—Helped rebuild temple .... Ezr 3:8–13
Hag 1:1–12
Zec 4:1–9
—Handled opposition to rebuilding .... Ezr 4:1–5

ZILPAH

—Servant of Leah .... Ge 29:24
—Mother of Gad and Asher .... Ge 30:9–12
Ge 35:26

ZIMRI

—King of Israel 1Ki 16:9–20
—Gained throne by assassination 1Ki 16:9–10
—Committed suicide 1Ki 16:18

ZION

A. Zion as an earthly place
—The Jebusite city captured by David 2Sa 5:6–7
—The place where David built his palace 2Ch 5:2
—The temple of the Lord .... Ps 20:2
Isa 18:7
—The holy mountain of God in Jerusalem .... Ps 74:2
Joel 3:17,21
—The whole city of Jerusalem 2Ki 19:31
Ps 48:1–2
Isa 33:20
Am 1:2
—The whole nation of Judah .... Ps 78:68
Isa 51:16
B. Zion as a symbolic place
—The heavenly throne of God .... Ps 9:7,11
Mic 4:7
—The prophetic kingdom of Jesus .... Ps 2:6
Ps 110:2
Isa 28:16
Isa 59:20
—The heavenly Jerusalem .... Heb 12:22
—The place from which Christ rules .... Rev 14:1

ZIPPORAH

—Daughter of Reuel; wife of Moses .... Ex 2:18,21–22
—Moved with Moses back to Egypt .... Ex 4:20
—Had two sons .... Ex 18:2–4
—Circumcised her son .... Ex 4:24–26
—Visited Moses in the desert .... Ex 18:5–6

ZOPHAR

—One of Job's friends who tried to comfort him .... Job 2:11–13
—His first speech .... Job 11:1–20
—His second speech .... Job 20:1–29
—Offered sacrifices to God after Job's restoration .... Job 42:7–9

INDEX TO NOTES

All entries are words or concepts in the study notes, charts, essays and book introductions, not in the NIV text. For references to key words in the text, consult either the Index to Topics or the Concordance. For location of geographical names, check the Index to Maps (pp. 2510–2513).

A

B

C

D

E

F

H

I

J

K

L

M

N

O

P

Q

R

S

T

U

V

W

X

Y

Z

CONCORDANCE

The NIV Concordance, created by John R. Kohlenberger III, has been developed specifically for use with the New International Version (NIV). Like all concordances, it is a special index that contains an alphabetical listing of words used in the Bible text.

This concordance contains 4,795 word entries, with nearly 36,000 Scripture references. Each word entry is followed by significant Scripture references in which that particular word is found, as well as by a brief excerpt from the surrounding context. In the context, the entry word is abbreviated by its first letter in bold print. Other forms of the entry word and related words indexed in this concordance are in parentheses.

This concordance also contains 339 biographical entries for significant people in the Bible. The descriptive phrases replace the brief context surrounding each occurrence of the name. In those instances where more than one Bible character has the same name, that name is placed under one block entry, and each person is given a number (1), (2), etc.

Two entry words are marked with a dagger (†). LORD† and LORD'S† list occurrences of the proper name of God, *Yahweh,* spelled "LORD" and "LORD's" in the NIV. These entries are distinguished from LORD and LORD's, which list occurrences of the title "Lord" and "Lord's."

There are 1,312 entries that list every appearance of that word in the NIV. When this occurs, the entry is marked with an asterisk (*).

This concordance is a valuable tool for Bible study. While one of its key purposes is to help the reader find forgotten references to familiar verses, it can also be used to do word studies and to locate and trace biblical themes. Whenever you find a significant context, be sure to read at least the whole verse in the NIV to discover its fuller meaning in its larger context.

AARON

Genealogy of (Ex 6:16–20; Jos 21:4, 10; 1Ch 6:3–15).

Priesthood of (Ex 28:1; Nu 17; Heb 5:1–4; 7), garments (Ex 28; 39), consecration (Ex 29), ordination (Lev 8).

Spokesman for Moses (Ex 4:14–16, 27–31; 7:1–2). Supported Moses' hands in battle (Ex 17:8–13). Built golden calf (Ex 32; Dt 9:20). Talked against Moses (Nu 12). Priesthood opposed (Nu 16); staff budded (Nu 17). Forbidden to enter land (Nu 20:1–12). Death (Nu 20:22–29; 33:38–39).

ABADDON*

Rev 9: 11 whose name in Hebrew is **A**

ABANDON (ABANDONED)

Dt 4: 31 he will not **a** or destroy you
1Ki 6: 13 and will not **a** my people Israel."
Ne 9: 19 compassion you did not **a** them
9: 31 not put an end to them or **a** them,
Ps 16: 10 because you will not **a** me
Ac 2: 27 because you will not **a** me
1Ti 4: 1 in later times some will **a** the faith

ABANDONED (ABANDON)

Ge 24: 27 who has not **a** his kindness
2Co 4: 9 persecuted, but not **a**;

ABBA*

Mk 14: 36 "**A**, Father," he said,
Ro 8: 15 by him we cry, "**A**, Father."
Gal 4: 6 the Spirit who calls out, "**A**,

ABEDNEGO

Deported to Babylon with Daniel (Da 1:1–6). Name changed from Azariah (Da 1:7). Refused defilement by food (Da 1:8–20). Refused idol worship (Da 3:1–12); saved from furnace (Da 3:13–30).

ABEL

Second son of Adam (Ge 4:2). Offered proper sacrifice (Ge 4:4; Heb 11:4). Murdered by Cain (Ge 4:8; Mt 23:35; Lk 11:51; 1Jn 3:12).

ABHOR

Lev 26: 30 of your idols, and I will **a** you.
Ps 26: 5 I **a** the assembly of evildoers
139: 21 **a** those who are in rebellion against
Am 6: 8 "I **a** the pride of Jacob and detest
Ro 2: 22 You who **a** idols, do you rob

ABIATHAR

High priest in days of Saul and David (1Sa 22; 2Sa 15; 1Ki 1–2; Mk 2:26). Escaped Saul's slaughter of priests (1Sa 22:18–23). Supported David in Absalom's revolt (2Sa 15:24–29). Supported Adonijah (1Ki 1:7–42); deposed by Solomon (1Ki 2:22–35; cf. 1Sa 2:31–35).

ABIGAIL

1. Sister of David (1Ch 2:16–17).

2. Wife of Nabal (1Sa 25:30); pled for his life with David (1Sa 25:14–35). Became David's wife after Nabal's death (1Sa 25:36–42); bore him Kileab (2Sa 3:3) also known as Daniel (1Ch 3:1).

ABIHU

Son of Aaron (Ex 6:23; 24:1, 9); killed for offering unauthorized fire (Lev 10; Nu 3:2–4; 1Ch 24:1–2).

ABIJAH

1. Second son of Samuel (1Ch 6:28); a corrupt judge (1Sa 8:1–5).

2. An Aaronic priest (1Ch 24:10; Lk 1:5).

3. Son of Jeroboam I of Israel; died as prophesied by Ahijah (1Ki 14:1–18).

4. Son of Rehoboam; king of Judah who fought Jeroboam I attempting to reunite the kingdom (1Ki 14:31—15:8; 2Ch 12:16—14:1; Mt 1:7).

ABILITY (ABLE)

Ex 35: 34 tribe of Dan, the **a** to teach others.
Dt 8: 18 for it is he who gives you the **a**
Ezr 2: 69 According to their **a** they gave
Mt 25: 15 one bag, each according to his **a**.
2Co 1: 8 far beyond our **a** to endure,
8: 3 were able, and even beyond their **a**.

ABIMELEK

1. King of Gerar who took Abraham's wife Sarah, believing her to be his sister (Ge 20). Later made a covenant with Abraham (Ge 21:22–33).

2. King of Gerar who took Isaac's wife Rebekah, believing her to be his sister (Ge 26:1–11). Later made a covenant with Isaac (Ge 26:12–31).

3. Son of Gideon (Jdg 8:31). Attempted to make himself king (Jdg 9).

ABISHAG*

Shunammite virgin; attendant of David in his old age (1Ki 1:1–15; 2:17–22).

ABISHAI

Son of Zeruiah, David's sister (1Sa 26:6; 1Ch 2:16). One of David's chief warriors (1Ch 11:15–21): against Edom (1Ch 18:12–13), Ammon (2Sa 10), Absalom (2Sa 18), Sheba (2Sa 20). Wanted to kill Saul (1Sa 26), killed Abner (2Sa 2:18–27; 3:22–39), wanted to kill Shimei (2Sa 16:5–13; 19:16–23).

ABLE (ABILITY ENABLE ENABLED ENABLES ENABLING)
Nu 14: 16 'The LORD was not **a** to bring
1Ch 29: 14 that we should be **a** to give as
2Ch 2: 6 who is **a** to build a temple for him,
Pr 17: 16 they are not **a** to understand it?
Eze 7: 19 gold will not be **a** to deliver them
Da 3: 17 the God we serve is **a** to deliver us
4: 37 walk in pride he is **a** to humble.
Mt 9: 28 you believe that I am **a** to do this?"
Lk 13: 24 try to enter and will not be **a** to.
14: 30 to build and wasn't **a** to finish.'
21: 15 your adversaries will be **a** to resist
21: 36 pray that you may be **a** to escape
21: 36 you may be **a** to stand before
Ac 5: 39 will not be **a** to stop these men;
11: 29 as each one was **a**,
Ro 8: 39 will be **a** to separate us
14: 4 the Lord is **a** to make them stand.
16: 25 to him who is **a** to establish you
2Co 9: 8 God is **a** to bless you abundantly,
Eph 3: 20 him who is **a** to do immeasurably
6: 13 may be **a** to stand your ground,
1Ti 3: 2 respectable, hospitable, **a** to teach,
2Ti 1: 12 that he is **a** to guard what I have
2: 24 be kind to everyone, **a** to teach,
3: 15 which are **a** to make you wise
Heb 2: 18 he is **a** to help those who are being
7: 25 he is **a** to save completely
Jas 3: 2 **a** to keep their whole body in check.
Jude : 24 To him who is **a** to keep you
Rev 5: 5 He is **a** to open the scroll and its

ABNER
Cousin of Saul and commander of his army (1Sa 14:50; 17:55–57; 26). Made Ish-Bosheth king after Saul (2Sa 2:8–10), but later defected to David (2Sa 3:6–21). Killed Asahel (2Sa 2:18–32), for which he was killed by Joab and Abishai (2Sa 3:22–39).

ABOLISH* (ABOLISHED)
Da 11: 31 and will **a** the daily sacrifice.
Hos 2: 18 and battle I will **a** from the land,
Mt 5: 17 think that I have come to **a** the Law
5: 17 I have not come to **a** them

ABOLISHED* (ABOLISH)
Da 12: 11 time that the daily sacrifice is **a**
Gal 5: 11 the offense of the cross has been **a**.

ABOMINATION*
Da 9: 27 set up an **a** that causes desolation,
11: 31 set up the **a** that causes desolation.
12: 11 the **a** that causes desolation is set
Mt 24: 15 in the holy place 'the **a** that causes
Mk 13: 14 "When you see 'the **a** that causes

ABOUND (ABOUNDING ABOUNDS)
2Co 9: 8 you will **a** in every good work.
Php 1: 9 your love may **a** more and more

ABOUNDING* (ABOUND)
Ex 34: 6 to anger, **a** in love and faithfulness,
Nu 14: 18 **a** in love and forgiving sin
Dt 33: 23 "Naphtali is **a** with the favor
Ne 9: 17 slow to anger and **a** in love.
Ps 86: 5 **a** in love to all who call to you.
86: 15 to anger, **a** in love and faithfulness.
103: 8 gracious, slow to anger, **a** in love.
Joel 2: 13 slow to anger and **a** in love, and he
Jnh 4: 2 slow to anger and **a** in love, a God

ABOUNDS (ABOUND)
2Co 1: 5 also our comfort **a** through Christ.

ABRAHAM
Abram, son of Terah (Ge 11:26–27), husband of Sarah (Ge 11:29).
Covenant relation with the LORD (Ge 12:1–3; 13:14–17; 15; 17; 22:15–18; Ex 2:24; Ne 9:8; Ps 105; Mic 7:20; Lk 1:68–75; Ro 4; Heb 6:13–15).
Called from Ur, via Harran, to Canaan (Ge 12:1; Ac 7:2–4; Heb 11:8–10). Moved to Egypt, nearly lost Sarah to Pharoah (Ge 12:10–20). Divided the land with Lot; settled in Hebron (Ge 13). Saved Lot from four kings (Ge 14:1–16); blessed by Melchizedek (Ge 14:17–20; Heb 7:1–20). Declared righteous by faith (Ge 15:6; Ro 4:3; Gal 3:6–9). Fathered Ishmael by Hagar (Ge 16).
Name changed from Abram (Ge 17:5; Ne 9:7). Circumcised (Ge 17; Ro 4:9–12). Entertained three visitors (Ge 18); promised a son by Sarah (Ge 18:9–15; 17:16). Questioned destruction of Sodom and Gomorrah (Ge 18:16–33). Moved to Gerar; nearly lost Sarah to Abimelek (Ge 20). Fathered Isaac by Sarah (Ge 21:1–7; Ac 7:8; Heb 11:11–12); sent away Hagar and Ishmael (Ge 21:8–21; Gal 4:22–30). Covenant with Abimelek (Ge 21:22–32). Tested by offering Isaac (Ge 22; Heb 11:17–19; Jas 2:21–24). Sarah died; bought field of Ephron for burial (Ge 23). Secured wife for Isaac (Ge 24). Fathered children by Keturah (Ge 25:1–6; 1Ch 1:32–33). Death (Ge 25:7–11).
Called servant of God (Ge 26:24), friend of God (2Ch 20:7; Isa 41:8; Jas 2:23), prophet (Ge 20:7), father of Israel (Ex 3:15; Isa 51:2; Mt 3:9; Jn 8:39–58).

ABSALOM
Son of David by Maakah (2Sa 3:3; 1Ch 3:2). Killed Amnon for rape of his sister Tamar; banished by David (2Sa 13). Returned to Jerusalem; received by David (2Sa 14). Rebelled against David; siezed kingdom (2Sa 15–17). Killed (2Sa 18).

ABSENT
Col 2: 5 For though I am **a** from you

ABSOLUTE*
1Ti 5: 2 women as sisters, with **a** purity.

ABSTAIN (ABSTAINS)
Ex 19: 15 **A** from sexual relations."
Nu 6: 3 they must **a** from wine and other
Ac 15: 20 them to **a** from food polluted
1Pe 2: 11 and exiles, to **a** from sinful desires,

ABSTAINS* (ABSTAIN)
Ro 14: 6 and whoever **a** does so to the Lord

ABUNDANCE (ABUNDANT)
Ge 41: 29 great **a** are coming throughout
Job 36: 31 the nations and provides food in **a**.
Ps 66: 12 but you brought us to a place of **a**.
Ecc 5: 12 rich, their **a** permits them no sleep.
Isa 66: 11 and delight in her overflowing **a**."
Jer 2: 22 and use an **a** of cleansing powder,
Mt 13: 12 more, and they will have an **a**.
25: 29 more, and they will have an **a**.
Lk 12: 15 not consist in an **a** of possessions."
1Pe 1: 2 Grace and peace be yours in **a**.
2Pe 1: 2 yours in **a** through the knowledge
Jude : 2 peace and love be yours in **a**.

ABUNDANT (ABUNDANCE)
Dt 28: 11 will grant you **a** prosperity—
32: 2 grass, like **a** rain on tender plants.
Job 36: 28 and **a** showers fall on mankind.
Ps 68: 9 You gave **a** showers, O God;
78: 15 gave them water as **a** as the seas;
132: 15 I will bless her with **a** provisions;
145: 7 They celebrate your **a** goodness
Pr 12: 11 work their land will have **a** food,
28: 19 work their land will have **a** food,
Jer 33: 9 will tremble at the **a** prosperity
Ro 5: 17 who receive God's **a** provision

ABUSE (ABUSIVE)
2Pe 2: 10 afraid to heap **a** on celestial beings;
2: 11 do not heap **a** on such beings

ABUSIVE (ABUSE)
2Ti 3: 2 proud, **a**, disobedient to their

ABYSS*
Lk 8: 31 not to order them to go into the **A**.
Rev 9: 1 given the key to the shaft of the **A**.
9: 2 he opened the **A**, smoke rose
9: 2 darkened by the smoke from the **A**.
9: 11 king over them the angel of the **A**,
11: 7 up from the **A** will attack them,
17: 8 will come up out of the **A** and go
20: 1 having the key to the **A** and
20: 3 He threw him into the **A**,

ACCEPT (ACCEPTABLE ACCEPTANCE ACCEPTED ACCEPTS)
Ex 23: 8 not **a** a bribe, for a bribe blinds
Dt 16: 19 Do not **a** a bribe, for a bribe blinds
Job 42: 8 and I will **a** his prayer and not deal
Pr 10: 8 The wise in heart **a** commands,
19: 20 Listen to advice and **a** discipline,
Ro 15: 7 **A** one another, then, just as Christ
Jas 1: 21 humbly **a** the word planted in you,

ACCEPTABLE (ACCEPT)
Pr 21: 3 just is more **a** to the LORD than

ACCEPTANCE* (ACCEPT)
Ro 11: 15 what will their **a** be but life
1Ti 1: 15 saying that deserves full **a**:
4: 9 saying that deserves full **a**.

ACCEPTED (ACCEPT)
Ge 4: 7 do what is right, will you not be **a**?
Job 42: 9 and the LORD **a** Job's prayer.
Lk 4: 24 "no prophet is **a** in his hometown.
Gal 1: 9 you a gospel other than what you **a**,

ACCEPTS (ACCEPT)
Ps 6: 9 the LORD **a** my prayer.
Jn 13: 20 whoever **a** me **a** the one who sent

ACCESS*
Est 1: 14 who had special **a** to the king
Ro 5: 2 through whom we have gained **a**
Eph 2: 18 through him we both have **a**

ACCOMPANIED (ACCOMPANY)
1Co 10: 4 from the spiritual rock that **a** them,
Jas 2: 17 if it is not **a** by action, is dead.

ACCOMPANIES (ACCOMPANY)
2Co 9: 13 obedience that **a** your confession

ACCOMPANY (ACCOMPANIED ACCOMPANIES)
Dt 28: 2 **a** you if you obey the LORD your
Mk 16: 17 *signs will **a** those who believe:*

ACCOMPLISH
Ecc 2: 2 And what does pleasure **a**?"
Isa 44: 28 and will **a** all that I please;
55: 11 but will **a** what I desire and achieve

ACCORD
Nu 24: 13 not do anything of my own **a**,
Jn 10: 18 me, but I lay it down of my own **a**.

ACCOUNT (ACCOUNTABLE)
Ge 2: 4 This is the **a** of the heavens
5: 1 This is the written **a** of Adam's
6: 9 This is the **a** of Noah and his
10: 1 This is the **a** of Shem,
11: 10 This is the **a** of Shem's family line.
11: 27 This is the **a** of Terah's family line.
25: 12 This is the **a** of the family line
25: 19 This is the **a** of the family line
36: 1 This is the **a** of the family line
36: 9 This is the **a** of the family line
37: 2 This is the **a** of Jacob's family line.
Mt 12: 36 will have to give **a** on the day
Lk 16: 2 Give an **a** of your management,
Ro 14: 12 of us will give an **a** of ourselves
Heb 4: 13 of him to whom we must give **a**.

ACCOUNTABLE* (ACCOUNT)
Eze 3: 18 I will hold you **a** for their blood.
3: 20 I will hold you **a** for their blood.
33: 6 I will hold the watchman **a** for
33: 8 I will hold you **a** for their blood.
34: 10 and will hold them **a** for my flock.
Da 6: 2 The satraps were made **a** to them
Jnh 1: 14 Do not hold us **a** for killing
Ro 3: 19 and the whole world held **a** to God.

ACCURATE
Dt 25: 15 You must have **a** and honest
Pr 11: 1 but **a** weights find favor with him.

ACCURSED (CURSE)
2Pe 2: 14 are experts in greed—an **a** brood!

ACCUSATION (ACCUSE)
1Ti 5: 19 not entertain an **a** against an elder

ACCUSE (ACCUSATION ACCUSER ACCUSES ACCUSING)
Pr 3: 30 Do not **a** anyone for no reason—
Lk 3: 14 money and don't **a** people falsely—

ACCUSER* (ACCUSE)
Job 31: 35 let my **a** put his indictment
Ps 109: 6 let an **a** stand at his right hand.
Isa 50: 8 Who is my **a**? Let him confront
Jn 5: 45 Your **a** is Moses, on whom your
Rev 12: 10 the **a** of our brothers and sisters,

ACCUSES* (ACCUSE)
Job 40: 2 Let him who **a** God answer him!"
Isa 54: 17 will refute every tongue that **a** you.
Rev 12: 10 who **a** them before our God day

ACCUSING (ACCUSE)
Ro 2: 15 their thoughts sometimes **a** them

ACHAN*
Sin at Jericho caused defeat at Ai; stoned (Jos 7; 22:20; 1Ch 2:7 ["Achar"]).

ACHE*
Pr 14: 13 Even in laughter the heart may **a**,

ACHIEVE
Ps 45: 4 your right hand **a** awesome deeds.
Isa 55: 11 **a** the purpose for which I sent it.

ACHISH
King of Gath before whom David feigned insanity (1Sa 21:10–15). Later "ally" of David (2Sa 27–29).

ACKNOWLEDGE (ACKNOWLEDGED ACKNOWLEDGES)
Jer 3: 13 Only **a** your guilt—
Hos 6: 3 Let us **a** the LORD; let us press
Mt 10: 32 also **a** before my Father in heaven.
Lk 12: 8 also **a** before the angels of God.
Jn 12: 42 they would not openly **a** their faith
Ro 14: 11 every tongue will **a** God.'"
Php 2: 11 every tongue **a** that Jesus Christ is
1Th 5: 12 **a** those who work hard among you,
Heb 3: 1 whom we **a** as our apostle and high
1Jn 4: 3 spirit that does not **a** Jesus is not

ACKNOWLEDGED (ACKNOWLEDGE)
Lk 7: 29 words, **a** that God's way was right,

ACKNOWLEDGES* (ACKNOWLEDGE)
Ps 91: 14 will protect him, for he **a** my name.
Mt 10: 32 "Whoever **a** me before others,
Lk 12: 8 you, whoever publicly **a** me before
1Jn 2: 23 whoever **a** the Son has the Father
4: 2 Every spirit that **a** that Jesus Christ
4: 15 If anyone **a** that Jesus is the Son

ACQUIRES*
Pr 18: 15 of the discerning **a** knowledge,

ACQUIT (ACQUITTING)
Ex 23: 7 to death, for I will not **a** the guilty.

ACQUITTING* (ACQUIT)
Dt 25: 1 **a** the innocent and condemning
Pr 17: 15 **A** the guilty and condemning

ACT (ACTION ACTIONS ACTIVE ACTIVITY ACTS)
1Ki 2: 2 "So be strong, **a** like a man,
Ps 106: 3 Blessed are those who **a** justly,
119:126 It is time for you to **a**, LORD;

ACTION (ACT)
2Co 9: 2 has stirred most of them to **a**.
Jas 2: 17 if it is not accompanied by **a**,

ACTIONS (ACT)
Gal 6: 4 Each one should test their own **a**.
Titus 1: 16 God, but by their **a** they deny him.

ACTIVE* (ACT)
Heb 4: 12 For the word of God is alive and **a**.

ACTIVITY (ACT)
Ecc 3: 1 for every **a** under the heavens:
3: 17 for there will be a time for every **a**,

ACTS (ACT)
1Ch 16: 9 tell of all his wonderful **a**.
Ps 40: 9 I proclaim your saving **a** in the
71: 15 of your saving **a** all day long—
71: 16 come and proclaim your mighty **a**,
71: 24 tell of your righteous **a** all day long,
105: 2 tell of all his wonderful **a**.
106: 2 Who can proclaim the mighty **a**
145: 4 they tell of your mighty **a**.
145: 12 people may know of your mighty **a**
150: 2 Praise him for his **a** of power;
Isa 64: 6 all our righteous **a** are like filthy

ADAM
1. First man (Ge 1:26—2:25; Ro 5:14, 45; 1Ti 2:13). Sin of (Ge 3; Hos 6:7; Ro 5:12–21). Children of (Ge 4:1—5:5). Death of (Ge 5:5; Ro 5:12–21; 1Co 15:22).
2. City (Jos 3:16).

ADD (ADDED)
Dt 4: 2 Do not **a** to what I command you
12: 32 do not **a** to it or take away from it.
Pr 1: 5 wise listen and **a** to their learning,
9: 9 and they will **a** to their learning.
30: 6 Do not **a** to his words, or he will
Mt 6: 27 you by worrying **a** a single hour
Lk 12: 25 by worrying can **a** a single hour
Rev 22: 18 them, God will **a** to that person

ADDED (ADD)
Ecc 3: 14 nothing can be **a** to it and nothing
Ac 2: 47 the Lord **a** to their number daily
Gal 3: 19 It was **a** because of transgressions

ADDICTED*
Titus 2: 3 to be slanderers or **a** to much wine,

ADMINISTRATION*
Eph 3: 2 heard about the **a** of God's grace
3: 9 to everyone the **a** of this mystery,

ADMIRABLE*
Php 4: 8 whatever is lovely, whatever is **a**—

ADMONISH* (ADMONISHING)
Col 3: 16 and **a** one another with all wisdom
1Th 5: 12 for you in the Lord and who **a** you.

ADMONISHING* (ADMONISH)
Col 1: 28 **a** and teaching everyone with all

ADONIJAH
1. Son of David by Haggith (2Sa 3:4; 1Ch 3:2). Attempted to be king after David; killed by Solomon's order (1Ki 1–2).
2. Levite; teacher of the Law (2Ch 17:8).

ADOPTION*
Gal 4: 5 that we might receive **a** to sonship.
Eph 1: 5 he predestined us for **a** to sonship
Ro 8: 15 brought about your **a** to sonship.
8: 23 wait eagerly for our **a** to sonship,
9: 4 Theirs is the **a** to sonship;

ADORE*
SS 1: 4 How right they are to **a** you!

ADORN (ADORNMENT ADORNS)
1Pe 3: 5 hope in God used to **a** themselves.

ADORNMENT* (ADORN)
1Pe 3: 3 should not come from outward **a**,

ADORNS* (ADORN)
Ps 93: 5 holiness **a** your house for endless
Pr 15: 2 tongue of the wise **a** knowledge,
Isa 61: 10 as a bridegroom **a** his head like
61: 10 as a bride **a** herself with her jewels.

ADULTERER* (ADULTERY)
Lev 20: 10 both the **a** and the adulteress are
Job 24: 15 The eye of the **a** watches for dusk;
Heb 13: 4 for God will judge the **a** and all

ADULTERERS (ADULTERY)
1Co 6: 9 nor idolaters nor **a** nor men who

ADULTERESS (ADULTERY)
Hos 3: 1 loved by another man and is an **a**.

ADULTERIES (ADULTERY)
Jer 3: 8 sent her away because of all her **a**.

ADULTEROUS (ADULTERY)
Mk 8: 38 and my words in this **a** and sinful
Jas 4: 4 You **a** people, don't you know

ADULTERY (ADULTERER ADULTERERS ADULTERESS ADULTERIES ADULTEROUS)
Ex 20: 14 "You shall not commit **a**.
Dt 5: 18 "You shall not commit **a**.
Mt 5: 27 was said, 'You shall not commit **a**.'
5: 28 lustfully has already committed **a**
5: 32 makes her the victim of **a**,
5: 32 a divorced woman commits **a**.
15: 19 murder, **a**, sexual immorality, theft,
19: 9 another woman commits **a**."
19: 18 you shall not commit **a**, you shall
Mk 10: 11 woman commits **a** against her.
10: 12 another man, she commits **a**."
10: 19 you shall not commit **a**, you shall
Lk 16: 18 marries another woman commits **a**,
18: 20 'You shall not commit **a**, you shall
Jn 8: 4 *a woman caught in the act of* ***a***.
Rev 18: 3 of the earth committed **a** with her,

ADULTS*
1Co 14: 20 infants, but in your thinking be **a**.

ADVANCE (ADVANCED)
Ps 18: 29 your help I can **a** against a troop;
Php 1: 12 has actually served to **a** the gospel.

ADVANCED (ADVANCE)
Job 32: 7 **a** years should teach wisdom.'

ADVANTAGE
Ex 22: 22 "Do not take **a** of the widow
Dt 24: 14 Do not take **a** of a hired worker
Ro 3: 1 What **a**, then, is there in being
2Co 11: 20 or exploits you or takes **a** of you
1Th 4: 6 should wrong or take **a** of a brother

ADVERSITY*
Pr 17: 17 a brother is born for a time of **a**.
Isa 30: 20 the Lord gives you the bread of **a**

ADVICE (ADVISERS)
1Ki 12: 8 Rehoboam rejected the **a** the elders
12: 14 he followed the **a** of the young men
2Ch 10: 8 Rehoboam rejected the **a** the elders
Pr 12: 5 but the **a** of the wicked is deceitful.
12: 15 to them, but the wise listen to **a**.
19: 20 Listen to **a** and accept discipline,
20: 18 Plans are established by seeking **a**;
27: 9 springs from their heartfelt **a**.

ADVISERS (ADVICE)
Pr 11: 14 but victory is won through many **a**.

ADVOCATE*
Job 16: 19 is in heaven; my **a** is on high.
Jn 14: 16 he will give you another **a** to help
14: 26 But the **A**, the Holy Spirit,
15: 26 "When the **A** comes, whom I will
16: 7 away, the **A** will not come to you;
1Jn 2: 1 sin, we have an **a** with the Father—

AFFECTION
2Pe 1: 7 mutual **a**; and to mutual **a**, love.

AFFLICTED (AFFLICTION)
Job 2: 7 **a** Job with painful sores
36: 6 alive but gives the **a** their rights.
Ps 9: 12 does not ignore the cries of the **a**.
9: 18 the hope of the **a** will never perish.
73: 14 All day long I have been **a**,
119: 67 Before I was **a** I went astray,
119: 71 me to be **a** so that I might learn
119: 75 that in faithfulness you have **a** me.
Isa 49: 13 have compassion on his **a** ones.
53: 4 by God, stricken by him, and **a**.
53: 7 He was oppressed and **a**, yet he did
Na 1: 12 Although I have **a** you, Judah,

AFFLICTION (AFFLICTED AFFLICTIONS)
Dt 16: 3 the bread of **a**, because you left
Ps 107: 41 he lifted the needy out of their **a**
Isa 30: 20 of adversity and the water of **a**,
48: 10 have tested you in the furnace of **a**.
La 3: 33 For he does not willingly bring **a**
Ro 12: 12 patient in **a**, faithful in prayer.

AFFLICTIONS (AFFLICTION)
Col 1: 24 still lacking in regard to Christ's **a**,

AFRAID (FEAR)
Ge 3: 10 and I was **a** because I was naked;
26: 24 Do not be **a**, for I am with you;
Ex 2: 14 Then Moses was **a** and thought,
3: 6 because he was **a** to look at God.
Dt 1: 21 Do not be **a**; do not be
1: 29 be terrified; do not be **a** of them.
20: 1 than yours, do not be **a** of them,
20: 3 Do not be fainthearted or **a**;
2Ki 25: 24 "Do not be **a** of the Babylonian
1Ch 13: 12 David was **a** of God that day
Ps 27: 1 of my life—of whom shall I be **a**?
56: 3 I am **a**, I put my trust in you.
56: 4 in God I trust and am not **a**.
Pr 3: 24 you lie down, you will not be **a**;
Isa 10: 24 Zion, do not be **a** of the Assyrians,
12: 2 I will trust and not be **a**.
44: 8 Do not tremble, do not be **a**.
Jer 1: 8 Do not be **a** of them, for I am
Mt 8: 26 of little faith, why are you so **a**?"
10: 28 Do not be **a** of those who kill
10: 28 be **a** of the One who can destroy
10: 31 So don't be **a**; you are worth more
Mk 5: 36 said, Jesus told him, "Don't be **a**;
Lk 9: 34 and they were **a** as they entered
Jn 14: 27 hearts be troubled and do not be **a**.
Ac 27: 24 and said, 'Do not be **a**, Paul.
Heb 13: 6 Lord is my helper; I will not be **a**.

AGAG (AGAGITE)
King of Amalekites not killed by Saul (1Sa 15).

AGAGITE (AGAG)
Est 8: 3 to the evil plan of Haman the **A**,

AGED (AGES)
Job 12: 12 Is not wisdom found among the **a**?
Pr 17: 6 children are a crown to the **a**,
Pr 30: 17 that scorns an **a** mother, will be

AGES (AGED)
Pr 8: 23 I was formed long **a** ago, at the
Ro 16: 25 the mystery hidden for long **a** past,
Eph 2: 7 in the coming **a** he might show
3: 9 for **a** past was kept hidden in God,
Col 1: 26 that has been kept hidden for **a**

AGONY
Lk 16: 24 because I am in **a** in this fire.'
Rev 16: 10 People gnawed their tongues in **a**

AGREE (AGREEMENT AGREES)
Mt 18: 19 earth **a** about anything they ask for,
Ro 7: 16 want to do, I **a** that the law is good.

AGREEMENT (AGREE)
2Co 6: 16 What **a** is there between the temple

AGREES* (AGREE)
Ac 7: 42 This **a** with what is written
1Co 4: 17 Jesus, which **a** with what I teach

AGRIPPA*
Descendant of Herod; king before whom Paul pled his case in Caesarea (Ac 25:13—26:32).

AHAB
1. Son of Omri; king of Israel (1Ki 16:28—22:40), husband of Jezebel (1Ki 16:31). Promoted Baal worship (1Ki 16:31–33); opposed by Elijah (1Ki 17:1; 18; 21), a prophet (1Ki 20:35–43), Micaiah (1Ki 22:1–28). Defeated Ben-Hadad (1Ki 20). Killed for failing to kill Ben-Hadad and for murder of Naboth (1Ki 20:35—21:40).
2. A false prophet (Jer 29:21–22).

AHAZ
1. Son of Jotham; king of Judah, (2Ki 16; 2Ch 28). Idolatry of (2Ki 16:3–4, 10–18; 2Ch 28:1–4, 22–25). Defeated by Aram and Israel (2Ki 16:5–6; 2Ch 28:5–15). Sought help from Assyria rather than the LORD (2Ki 16:7–9; 2Ch 28:16–21; Isa 7).
2. Benjamite, descendant of Saul (1Ch 8:35–36).

AHAZIAH
1. Son of Ahab; king of Israel (1Ki 22:51–2Ki 1:18; 2Ch 20:35–37). Made an unsuccessful alliance with Jehoshaphat of Judah (2Ch 20:35–37). Died for seeking Baal rather than the LORD (2Ki 1).
2. Son of Jehoram; king of Judah (2Ki 8:25–29; 9:14–29), also called Jehoahaz (2Ch 21:17—22:9; 25:23). Killed by Jehu while visiting Joram (2Ki 9:14–29; 2Ch 22:1–9).

AHIJAH
1Sa 14: 18 Saul said to **A**, "Bring the ark
1Ki 14: 2 **A** the prophet is there—the one

AHIMELEK
1. Priest who helped David in his flight from Saul (1Sa 21–22).
2. One of David's warriors (1Sa 26:6).

AHITHOPHEL
One of David's counselors who sided with Absalom (2Sa 15:12, 31–37; 1Ch 27:33–34); committed suicide when his advice was ignored (2Sa 16:15—17:23).

AI
Jos 7: 4 they were routed by the men of **A**,
8: 28 So Joshua burned **A** and made it

AID
Isa 38: 14 Lord, come to my **a**!"
Php 4: 16 you sent me **a** more than once

AIM
1Co 7: 34 Her **a** is to be devoted to the Lord

AIR
1Co 9: 26 not fight like a boxer beating the **a**.
14: 9 You will just be speaking into the **a**.
Eph 2: 2 the ruler of the kingdom of the **a**,
1Th 4: 17 clouds to meet the Lord in the **a**.

ALABASTER*
Mt 26: 7 him with an **a** jar of very expensive
Mk 14: 3 a woman came with an **a** jar of
Lk 7: 37 so she came there with an **a** jar

ALARM (ALARMED)
2Co 7: 11 indignation, what **a**, what longing,

ALARMED (ALARM)
Mk 13: 7 and rumors of wars, do not be **a**.
2Th 2: 2 or **a** by the teaching allegedly

ALERT*
Jos 8: 4 far from it. All of you be on the **a**.
Ps 17: 11 me, with eyes **a**, to throw me
Isa 21: 7 on camels, let him be **a**, fully **a**."
Mk 13: 33 Be **a**! You do not know
Eph 6: 18 be **a** and always keep on praying
1Pe 1: 13 with minds that are **a** and fully
4: 7 Therefore be **a** and of sober mind
5: 8 Be **a** and of sober mind.

ALIENATED*
Job 19: 13 "He has **a** my family from me;
Gal 5: 4 the law have been **a** from Christ;
Col 1: 21 Once you were **a** from God

ALIVE (LIVE)
1Sa 2: 6 LORD brings death and makes **a**;
Lk 24: 23 vision of angels, who said he was **a**.
Ac 1: 3 convincing proofs that he was **a**.
Ro 6: 11 to sin but **a** to God in Christ Jesus.
1Co 15: 22 die, so in Christ all will be made **a**.
Eph 2: 5 made us **a** with Christ even
Heb 4: 12 the word of God is **a** and active.

ALMIGHTY (MIGHT)
Ge 17: 1 to him and said, "I am God **A**;
Ex 6: 3 to Isaac and to Jacob as God **A**,
Ru 1: 20 because the **A** has made my life
Job 11: 7 Can you probe the limits of the **A**?
33: 4 the breath of the **A** gives me life.
Ps 89: 8 Who is like you, LORD God **A**?
91: 1 will rest in the shadow of the **A**.
Isa 6: 3 "Holy, holy, holy is the LORD **A**;
45: 13 or reward, says the LORD **A**."
47: 4 the LORD **A** is his name—
48: 2 the LORD **A** is his name:
51: 15 the LORD **A** is his name.
54: 5 the LORD **A** is his name—
Am 5: 14 the LORD God **A** will be with you,
5: 15 the LORD God **A** will have mercy
Rev 4: 8 holy is the Lord God **A**,' who was,
19: 6 For our Lord God **A** reigns.

ALPHA*
Rev 1: 8 "I am the **A** and the Omega,"
21: 6 I am the **A** and the Omega,
22: 13 the **A** and the Omega, the First

ALTAR
Ge 8: 20 Noah built an **a** to the LORD and,
12: 7 So he built an **a** there
13: 18 There he built an **a** to the LORD.
22: 9 his son Isaac and laid him on the **a**,
26: 25 Isaac built an **a** there and called
35: 1 and build an **a** there to God,
Ex 17: 15 Moses built an **a** and called it
27: 1 "Build an **a** of acacia wood,
30: 1 "Make an **a** of acacia wood
37: 25 They made the **a** of incense
Dt 27: 5 Build there an **a** to the LORD your
Jos 8: 30 on Mount Ebal an **a** to the LORD,
22: 10 Manasseh built an imposing **a**
Jdg 6: 24 So Gideon built an **a** to the LORD
21: 4 the next day the people built an **a**
1Sa 7: 17 he built an **a** there to the LORD.
14: 35 Then Saul built an **a** to the LORD;
2Sa 24: 25 David built an **a** to the LORD
1Ki 12: 33 went up to the **a** to make offerings.
13: 2 he cried out against the **a**: "**A**, **a**!
16: 32 He set up an **a** for Baal
18: 30 he repaired the **a** of the LORD,
2Ki 16: 11 So Uriah the priest built an **a**
1Ch 21: 26 David built an **a** to the LORD
2Ch 4: 1 a bronze **a** twenty cubits long,
4: 19 the golden **a**; the tables
15: 8 He repaired the **a** of the LORD
32: 12 'You must worship before one **a**
33: 16 he restored the **a** of the LORD
Ezr 3: 2 began to build the **a** of the God
Isa 6: 6 had taken with tongs from the **a**.
Eze 40: 47 the **a** was in front of the temple.
Mt 5: 23 if you are offering your gift at the **a**
Ac 17: 23 worship, I even found an **a**
Heb 13: 10 We have an **a** from which those
Rev 6: 9 I saw under the **a** the souls of those

ALTER*
Ps 89: 34 or **a** what my lips have uttered.

ALWAYS
Dt 15: 11 There will **a** be poor people
Ps 16: 8 I keep my eyes **a** on the LORD.
51: 3 and my sin is **a** before me.
119: 98 Your commands are **a** with me
Pr 23: 7 person who is **a** thinking
Mt 26: 11 The poor you will **a** have with you, but you will not **a** have me.
28: 20 And surely I am with you **a**,
Mk 14: 7 The poor you will **a** have with you,
Jn 12: 8 You will **a** have the poor among
1Co 13: 7 It **a** protects, **a** trusts, **a** hopes,
Php 4: 4 Rejoice in the Lord **a**. I will say it
1Pe 3: 15 **A** be prepared to give an answer

AMALEKITES
Ex 17: 8 The **A** came and attacked
1Sa 15: 2 'I will punish the **A** for what they

AMASA
Nephew of David (1Ch 2:17). Commander of Absalom's forces (2Sa 17:24–27). Returned to David (2Sa 19:13). Killed by Joab (2Sa 20:4–13).

AMASSES*
Pr 28: 8 or profit from the poor **a** it for

AMAZED
Mt 7: 28 the crowds were **a** at his teaching,
Mk 6: 6 He was **a** at their lack of faith.
10: 24 The disciples were **a** at his words.
Ac 2: 7 Utterly **a**, they asked:
13: 12 for he was **a** at the teaching

AMAZIAH
1. Son of Joash; king of Judah (2Ki 14; 2Ch 25). Defeated Edom (2Ki 14:7; 2Ch 25:5–13); defeated by Israel for worshiping Edom's gods (2Ki 14:8–14; 2Ch 25:14–24).
2. Idolatrous priest who opposed Amos (Am 7:10–17).

AMBASSADOR* (AMBASSADORS)
Eph 6: 20 for which I am an **a** in chains.

AMBASSADORS (AMBASSADOR)
2Co 5: 20 We are therefore Christ's **a**,

AMBITION*
Ro 15: 20 It has always been my **a** to preach
2Co 12: 20 fits of rage, selfish **a**, slander,
Gal 5: 20 fits of rage, selfish **a**, dissensions,
Php 1: 17 preach Christ out of selfish **a**,
2: 3 Do nothing out of selfish **a** or vain
1Th 4: 11 make it your **a** to lead a quiet life:
Jas 3: 14 envy and selfish **a** in your hearts,
3: 16 where you have envy and selfish **a**,

AMENDS
Pr 14: 9 Fools mock at making **a** for sin,

AMNON
Firstborn of David (2Sa 3:2; 1Ch 3:1). Killed by Absalom for raping his sister Tamar (2Sa 13).

AMON
1. Son of Manasseh; king of Judah (2Ki 21:18–26; 1Ch 3:14; 2Ch 33:21–25).
2. Ruler of Samaria under Ahab (1Ki 22:26; 2Ch 18:25).

AMOS
1. Prophet from Tekoa (Am 1:1; 7:10–17).
2. Ancestor of Jesus (Lk 3:25).

ANAK (ANAKITES)
Nu 13: 28 even saw descendants of **A** there.

ANAKITES (ANAK)
Dt 1: 28 We even saw the **A** there.'"
2: 10 and numerous, and as tall as the **A**.
9: 2 "Who can stand up against the **A**?"

ANANIAS
1. Husband of Sapphira; died for lying to God (Ac 5:1–11).
2. Disciple who baptized Saul (Ac 9:10–19).
3. High priest at Paul's arrest (Ac 22:30—24:1).

ANCESTORS (ANCESTRY)
1Ki 19: 4 I am no better than my **a**."
Jn 4: 20 Our **a** worshiped on this mountain,
Heb 1: 1 to our **a** through the prophets
1Pe 1: 18 handed down to you from your **a**,

ANCESTRY (ANCESTORS)
Ro 9: 5 them is traced the human **a**

ANCHOR
Heb 6: 19 We have this hope as an **a**

ANCIENT
Da 7: 9 and the **A** of Days took his seat.
7: 13 He approached the **A** of Days
7: 22 until the **A** of Days came

ANDREW*
Apostle; brother of Simon Peter (Mt 4:18; 10:2; Mk 1:16–18, 29; 3:18; 13:3; Lk 6:14; Jn 1:35–44; 6:8–9; 12:22; Ac 1:13).

ANGEL (ANGELS ARCHANGEL)
Ge 16: 7 The **a** of the LORD found Hagar
22: 11 the **a** of the LORD called
Ex 23: 20 I am sending an **a** ahead of you
Nu 22: 23 the donkey saw the **a** of the LORD
Jdg 2: 1 The **a** of the LORD went
6: 22 I have seen the **a** of the LORD
13: 15 said to the **a** of the LORD,
2Sa 24: 16 When the **a** stretched out his hand
1Ki 19: 7 The **a** of the LORD came back
2Ki 19: 35 That night the **a** of the LORD went
Ps 34: 7 The **a** of the LORD encamps
Hos 12: 4 He struggled with the **a**
Mt 2: 13 **a** of the Lord appeared to Joseph
28: 2 for an **a** of the Lord came down
Lk 1: 26 God sent the **a** Gabriel to
2: 9 An **a** of the Lord appeared to them,
22: 43 An **a** from heaven appeared to him
Ac 6: 15 his face was like the face of an **a**.
12: 7 Suddenly an **a** of the Lord

2Co 11: 14 Satan himself masquerades as an **a**
Gal 1: 8 or an **a** from heaven should preach

ANGELS (ANGEL)
Ps 8: 5 made them a little lower than the **a**
91: 11 command his **a** concerning you
Mt 4: 6 command his **a** concerning you,
13: 39 of the age, and the harvesters are **a**.
13: 49 The **a** will come and separate
18: 10 that their **a** in heaven always see
25: 41 prepared for the devil and his **a**.
Lk 4: 10 command his **a** concerning you
20: 36 for they are like the **a**.
1Co 6: 3 you not know that we will judge **a**?
13: 1 in the tongues of men or of **a**,
Col 2: 18 the worship of **a** disqualify you.
Heb 1: 4 the **a** as the name he has inherited
1: 6 "Let all God's **a** worship him."
1: 7 "He makes his **a** spirits, and his
1: 14 Are not all **a** ministering spirits
2: 7 them a little lower than the **a**;
2: 9 who was made lower than the **a**
13: 2 hospitality to **a** without knowing it.
1Pe 1: 12 Even **a** long to look into these
2Pe 2: 4 if God did not spare **a** when they
Jude : 6 And the **a** who did not keep their

ANGER (ANGERED ANGRY)
Ex 15: 7 You unleashed your burning **a**;
22: 24 My **a** will be aroused, and I will kill
32: 10 that my **a** may burn against them
32: 11 "why should your **a** burn against
32: 12 Turn from your fierce **a**;
32: 19 his **a** burned and he threw
34: 6 slow to **a**, abounding in love
Lev 26: 28 my **a** I will be hostile toward you,
Nu 14: 18 'The LORD is slow to **a**,
25: 11 has turned my **a** away
32: 10 The LORD's **a** was aroused
32: 13 The LORD's **a** burned against
Dt 9: 19 I feared the **a** and wrath
29: 28 In furious **a** and in great wrath
Jdg 14: 19 Burning with **a**, he returned to his
2Sa 12: 5 burned with **a** against the man
2Ki 22: 13 Great is the LORD's **a** that burns
Ne 9: 17 slow to **a** and abounding in love.
Ps 30: 5 For his **a** lasts only a moment,
78: 38 Time after time he restrained his **a**
86: 15 slow to **a**, abounding in love
90: 7 We are consumed by your **a**
103: 8 slow to **a**, abounding in love.
Pr 15: 1 wrath, but a harsh word stirs up **a**.
30: 33 so stirring up **a** produces strife."
Jnh 4: 2 slow to **a** and abounding in love,
Eph 4: 26 "In your **a** do not sin": Do not let
Jas 1: 20 because human **a** does not produce

ANGERED (ANGER)
Pr 22: 24 do not associate with one easily **a**,
1Co 13: 5 it is not easily **a**, it keeps no record

ANGRY (ANGER)
Ps 2: 12 he will be **a** and your way will lead
95: 10 For forty years I was **a**
Pr 29: 22 An **a** person stirs up conflict,
Mt 5: 22 that anyone who is **a** with a brother
Jas 1: 19 to speak and slow to become **a**,

ANGUISH
Jer 4: 19 Oh, my **a**, my **a**! I writhe in pain.
Zep 1: 15 a day of distress and **a**, a day
Lk 21: 25 nations will be in **a** and perplexity
22: 44 And being in **a**, he prayed more
Ro 9: 2 and unceasing **a** in my heart.

ANIMALS
Ge 1: 24 the wild **a**, each according to its
7: 16 The **a** going in were male
Dt 14: 4 These are the **a** you may eat:
Job 12: 7 "But ask the **a**, and they will teach
Isa 43: 20 The wild **a** honor me, the jackals

ANNOUNCE (ANNOUNCED)
Mt 6: 2 needy, do not **a** it with trumpets,

ANNOUNCED (ANNOUNCE)
Isa 48: 5 before they happened I **a** them
Gal 3: 8 faith, and **a** the gospel in advance

ANNOYANCE*
Pr 12: 16 Fools show their **a** at once,

ANNUAL*
Ex 30: 10 This **a** atonement must be made
Jdg 21: 19 there is the **a** festival of the LORD
1Sa 1: 21 offer the **a** sacrifice to the LORD
2: 19 her husband to offer the **a** sacrifice.
20: 6 an **a** sacrifice is being made
2Ch 8: 13 Moons and the three **a** festivals—
Heb 10: 3 those sacrifices are an **a** reminder

ANOINT (ANOINTED ANOINTING)
Ex 30: 26 use it to **a** the tent of meeting,
30: 30 "**A** Aaron and his sons
1Sa 9: 16 **A** him ruler over my people Israel;
15: 1 to **a** you king over his people Israel;
2Ki 9: 3 I **a** you king over Israel.'
Ps 23: 5 You **a** my head with oil;
Da 9: 24 and to **a** the Most Holy Place.
Jas 5: 14 **a** them with oil in the name

ANOINTED (ANOINT)
1Ch 16: 22 "Do not touch my **a** ones;
Ps 105: 15 "Do not touch my **a** ones;
Isa 61: 1 because the LORD has **a** me
Da 9: 26 the **A** One will be put to death
Lk 4: 18 because he has **a** me to proclaim
Ac 10: 38 how God **a** Jesus of Nazareth

ANOINTING (ANOINT)
Lev 8: 12 He poured some of the **a** oil
1Ch 29: 22 **a** him before the LORD to be ruler
Ps 45: 7 your companions by **a** you
Heb 1: 9 your companions by **a** you
1Jn 2: 20 you have an **a** from the Holy One,
2: 27 as his **a** teaches you about all things

ANT* (ANTS)
Pr 6: 6 Go to the **a**, you sluggard;

ANTICHRIST* (ANTICHRISTS)
1Jn 2: 18 have heard that the **a** is coming,
2: 22 Such a person is the **a**—
4: 3 This is the spirit of the **a**, which
2Jn : 7 person is the deceiver and the **a**.

ANTICHRISTS* (ANTICHRIST)
1Jn 2: 18 even now many **a** have come.

ANTIOCH
Ac 11: 26 were called Christians first at **A**.

ANTS* (ANT)
Pr 30: 25 **A** are creatures of little strength,

ANXIETIES* (ANXIOUS)
Lk 21: 34 drunkenness and the **a** of life,

ANXIETY (ANXIOUS)
Pr 12: 25 **A** weighs down the heart, but
1Pe 5: 7 Cast all your **a** on him because he

ANXIOUS (ANXIETIES ANXIETY)
Php 4: 6 Do not be **a** about anything,

APOLLOS*
Christian from Alexandria, learned in the Scriptures; instructed by Aquila and Priscilla (Ac 18:24–28). Ministered at Corinth (Ac 19:1; 1Co 1:12; 3:4–22; 4:6; 16:42; Titus 3:13).

APOLLYON*
Rev 9: 11 Abaddon and in Greek is **A** (that

APOSTLE (APOSTLES APOSTLES')
Ro 11: 13 Inasmuch as I am the **a**
1Co 9: 1 Am I not an **a**? Have I not seen
2Co 12: 12 among you the marks of a true **a**,
Gal 2: 8 in Peter as an **a** to the circumcised,
2: 8 work in me as an **a** to the Gentiles.
1Ti 2: 7 was appointed a herald and an **a**—
2Ti 1: 11 a herald and an **a** and a teacher.
Heb 3: 1 whom we acknowledge as our **a**

APOSTLES (APOSTLE)
See also Andrew, Bartholomew, James, John, Judas, Matthew, Matthias, Nathanael, Paul, Peter, Philip, Simon, Thaddaeus, Thomas.
Lk 11: 49 'I will send them prophets and **a**,
Ac 1: 26 so he was added to the eleven **a**.
2: 43 and signs performed by the **a**.
1Co 12: 28 placed in the church first of all **a**,
15: 9 For I am the least of the **a** and do
2Co 11: 13 For such people are false **a**,
11: 13 masquerading as **a** of Christ.
Eph 2: 20 built on the foundation of the **a**
4: 11 So Christ himself gave the **a**,
Rev 21: 14 names of the twelve **a** of the Lamb.

APOSTLES' (APOSTLE)
Ac 5: 2 the rest and put it at the **a** feet.
8: 18 at the laying on of the **a** hands,

APPEAL
Ac 25: 11 me over to them. I **a** to Caesar!"
Phm : 9 yet I prefer to **a** to you on the basis

APPEAR (APPEARANCE APPEARANCES APPEARED APPEARING APPEARS)
Ge 1: 9 to one place, and let dry ground **a**."
Lev 16: 2 For I will **a** in the cloud over
Mt 24: 30 will **a** the sign of the Son of Man
Mk 13: 22 false prophets will **a** and perform
Lk 19: 11 of God was going to **a** at once.
2Co 5: 10 we must all **a** before the judgment
Col 3: 4 you also will **a** with him in glory.
Heb 9: 24 now to **a** for us in God's presence.
9: 28 and he will **a** a second time,

APPEARANCE (APPEAR)
1Sa 16: 7 People look at the outward **a**,
Isa 52: 14 his **a** was so disfigured beyond
53: 2 in his **a** that we should desire him.

APPEARANCES* (APPEAR)
Jn 7: 24 Stop judging by mere **a**, but instead
2Co 10: 7 You are judging by **a**. If anyone is

APPEARED (APPEAR)
Nu 14: 10 the glory of the LORD **a** at the tent
Mt 1: 20 an angel of the Lord **a** to him
Lk 2: 9 An angel of the Lord **a** to them,
1Co 15: 5 and that he **a** to Cephas,
Heb 9: 26 But he has **a** once for all

APPEARING (APPEAR)
1Ti 6: 14 blame until the **a** of our Lord Jesus
2Ti 1: 10 now been revealed through the **a**
4: 8 to all who have longed for his **a**.
Titus 2: 13 the **a** of the glory of our great God

APPEARS (APPEAR)
Mal 3: 2 Who can stand when he **a**?
Col 3: 4 who is your life, **a**, then you
1Pe 5: 4 And when the Chief Shepherd **a**,
1Jn 3: 2 But we know that when Christ **a**,

APPETITE
Pr 13: 2 but the unfaithful have an **a**
13: 4 A sluggard's **a** is never filled,
16: 26 The **a** of laborers works for them;
Ecc 6: 7 yet their **a** is never satisfied.
Jer 50: 19 their **a** will be satisfied on the hills

APPLES
Pr 25: 11 Like **a** of gold in settings of silver is

APPLY (APPLYING)
Pr 22: 17 **a** your heart to what I teach,
23: 12 **A** your heart to instruction and

APPLYING (APPLY)
Pr 2: 2 **a** your heart to understanding—

APPOINT (APPOINTED)
Ps 61: 7 **a** your love and faithfulness
1Th 5: 9 God did not **a** us to suffer wrath
Titus 1: 5 and **a** elders in every town, as I

APPOINTED (APPOINT)
Dt 1: 15 **a** them to have authority over you—
Da 11: 27 an end will still come at the **a** time.
Hab 2: 3 For the revelation awaits an **a** time;
Lk 1: 20 will come true at their **a** time."
Jn 15: 16 you and **a** you so that you might go
Ro 9: 9 "At the **a** time I will return,

APPROACH (APPROACHING)
Ex 24: 2 but Moses alone is to **a** the LORD;
Eph 3: 12 in him we may **a** God with freedom
Heb 4: 16 then **a** God's throne of grace

APPROACHING (APPROACH)
Heb 10: 25 all the more as you see the Day **a**.
1Jn 5: 14 is the confidence we have in **a** God:

APPROPRIATE
Ecc 5: 18 that it is **a** for a person to eat,
1Ti 2: 10 deeds, **a** for women who profess

APPROVAL (APPROVE)
Jdg 18: 6 Your journey has the LORD's **a**."
Jn 6: 27 the Father has placed his seal of **a**."
Ro 14: 18 to God and receives human **a**.
1Co 11: 19 to show which of you have God's **a**.
Gal 1: 10 trying to win the **a** of human beings,

APPROVE (APPROVAL APPROVED APPROVES)
Ro 2: 18 **a** of what is superior because you
12: 2 to test and **a** what God's will is—

APPROVED* (APPROVE)
2Co 10: 18 who commends himself who is **a**,
1Th 2: 4 we speak as those **a** by God to be
2Ti 2: 15 to present yourself to God as one **a**,

APPROVES* (APPROVE)
Ro 14: 22 not condemn himself by what he **a**.

APT*
Pr 15: 23 finds joy in giving an **a** reply—

AQUILA*
Husband of Priscilla; co-worker with Paul, instructor of Apollos (Ac 18; Ro 16:3; 1Co 16:19; 2Ti 4:19).

ARABIA
Gal 1: 17 before I was, but I went into **A**.
4: 25 Hagar stands for Mount Sinai in **A**

ARARAT
Ge 8: 4 to rest on the mountains of **A**.

ARAUNAH
2Sa 24: 16 threshing floor of **A** the Jebusite.

ARBITER*
Lk 12: 14 me a judge or an **a** between you?"

ARCHANGEL* (ANGEL)
1Th 4: 16 with the voice of the **a**
Jude : 9 But even the **a** Michael, when he

ARCHER
Pr 26: 10 Like an **a** who wounds at random

ARCHIPPUS*
Col 4: 17 Tell **A**: "See to it that you complete
Phm : 2 sister and **A** our fellow soldier—

ARCHITECT*
Heb 11: 10 whose **a** and builder is God.

AREOPAGUS*
Ac 17: 19 brought him to a meeting of the **A**,
17: 22 stood up in the meeting of the **A**
17: 34 a member of the **A**, also a woman

ARGUE (ARGUMENT ARGUMENTS)
Job 13: 3 and to **a** my case with God.
13: 8 Will you **a** the case for God?

ARGUMENT (ARGUE)
Heb 6: 16 is said and puts an end to all **a**.

ARGUMENTS (ARGUE)
Isa 41: 21 "Set forth your **a**," says Jacob's
Col 2: 4 deceive you by fine-sounding **a**.
2Ti 2: 23 to do with foolish and stupid **a**,
Titus 3: 9 and genealogies and **a** and quarrels

ARK
Ge 6: 14 So make yourself an **a** of cypress
Ex 25: 10 "Have them make an **a** of acacia
25: 21 and put in the **a** the tablets of
Dt 10: 5 put the tablets in the **a** I had made,
1Sa 4: 11 The **a** of God was captured,
7: 2 The **a** remained at Kiriath Jearim
2Sa 6: 17 They brought the **a** of the LORD
1Ki 8: 9 the **a** except the two stone tablets
1Ch 13: 9 out his hand to steady the **a**,
2Ch 35: 3 "Put the sacred **a** in the temple
Heb 9: 4 the gold-covered **a** of the covenant.
9: 4 This **a** contained the gold jar
11: 7 in holy fear built an **a** to save his
Rev 11: 19 within his temple was seen the **a**

ARM (ARMY)
Nu 11: 23 "Is the LORD's **a** too short?
Dt 4: 34 hand and an outstretched **a**,
7: 19 mighty hand and outstretched **a**,
Ps 44: 3 nor did their **a** bring them victory;
98: 1 his holy **a** have worked salvation
Jer 27: 5 outstretched **a** I made the earth
1Pe 4: 1 **a** yourselves also with the same

ARMAGEDDON*
Rev 16: 16 place that in Hebrew is called **A**.

ARMIES (ARMY)
1Sa 17: 26 he should defy the **a** of the living
Rev 19: 14 The **a** of heaven were following

ARMOR (ARMY)
1Ki 20: 11 his **a** should not boast like one who
Ps 35: 2 Take up shield and **a**;
Jer 46: 4 Polish your spears, put on your **a**!
Ro 13: 12 darkness and put on the **a** of light.
Eph 6: 11 Put on the full **a** of God, so that
6: 13 Therefore put on the full **a** of God,

ARMS (ARMY)
Dt 33: 27 underneath are the everlasting **a**.
Ps 18: 32 It is God who **a** me with strength
Pr 31: 17 her **a** are strong for her tasks.
31: 20 She opens her **a** to the poor
Isa 40: 11 He gathers the lambs in his **a**
Mk 10: 16 And he took the children in his **a**,
Heb 12: 12 strengthen your feeble **a** and weak

ARMY (ARM ARMIES ARMOR ARMS)
Ps 33: 16 king is saved by the size of his **a**;
Joel 2: 2 a large and mighty **a** comes,
2: 5 like a mighty **a** drawn up for battle.
2: 11 thunders at the head of his **a**;
Rev 19: 19 the rider on the horse and his **a**.

AROMA
Ge 8: 21 The LORD smelled the pleasing **a**
Ex 29: 18 a pleasing **a**, a food offering
Lev 3: 16 as a food offering, a pleasing **a**.
2Co 2: 14 us to spread the **a** of the knowledge
2: 15 the pleasing **a** of Christ among
2: 16 an **a** that brings that brings death; to the other, an **a** that brings life.

AROUSE (AROUSED)
Ro 11: 14 I may somehow **a** my own people

AROUSED (AROUSE)
Ps 78: 58 they **a** his jealousy with their idols.

ARRAYED*
Ps 110: 3 **A** in holy splendor, your young
Isa 61: 10 **a** me in a robe of his righteousness,

ARREST
Mt 10: 19 But when they **a** you, do not worry

ARROGANCE (ARROGANT)
1Sa 2: 3 or let your mouth speak such **a**,
Pr 8: 13 I hate pride and **a**, evil behavior
Mk 7: 22 lewdness, envy, slander, **a** and folly.
2Co 12: 20 slander, gossip, **a** and disorder.

ARROGANT (ARROGANCE)
Ps 5: 5 The **a** cannot stand in your
119: 78 May the **a** be put to shame
Pr 21: 24 The proud and **a** person—
Ro 1: 30 God-haters, insolent, **a** and
11: 20 Do not be **a**, but tremble.
1Ti 6: 17 this present world not to be **a** nor

ARROW (ARROWS)
Ps 91: 5 of night, nor the **a** that flies by day,
Pr 25: 18 or a sharp **a** is one who gives false

ARROWS (ARROW)
Ps 64: 3 and aim cruel words like deadly **a**.
64: 7 God will shoot them with his **a**;
127: 4 Like **a** in the hands of a warrior are
Pr 26: 18 Like a maniac shooting flaming **a**
Eph 6: 16 can extinguish all the flaming **a**

ARTAXERXES
King of Persia; allowed rebuilding of temple under Ezra (Ezr 4; 7), and of walls of Jerusalem under his cupbearer Nehemiah (Ne 2; 5:14; 13:6).

ARTEMIS
Ac 19: 28 "Great is **A** of the Ephesians!"

ASA
King of Judah (1Ki 15:8–24; 1Ch 3:10; 2Ch 14–16). Godly reformer (2Ch 15); in later years defeated Israel with help of Aram, not the LORD (1Ki 15:16–22; 2Ch 16).

ASAHEL
1. Nephew of David, one of his warriors (2Sa 23:24; 1Ch 2:16; 11:26; 27:7). Killed by Abner (2Sa 2); avenged by Joab (2Sa 3:22–39).
2. Levite; teacher (2Ch 17:8).

ASAPH
1. Recorder to Hezekiah (2Ki 18:18, 37; Isa 36:3, 22).
2. Levitical musician (1Ch 6:39; 15:17–19; 16:4–7, 37). Sons of (1Ch 25; 2Ch 5:12; 20:14; 29:13; 35:15; Ezr 2:41; 3:10; Ne 7:44; 11:17; 12:27–47). Psalms of (2Ch 29:30; Ps 50; 73–83).

ASCEND* (ASCENDED ASCENDING)
Dt 30: 12 "Who will **a** into heaven to get it
Ps 24: 3 Who may **a** the mountain
Isa 14: 13 your heart, "I will **a** to the heavens;
14: 14 will **a** above the tops of the clouds;
Jn 6: 62 of Man **a** to where he was before!
Ac 2: 34 For David did not **a** to heaven,
Ro 10: 6 heart, 'Who will **a** into heaven?'"

ASCENDED (ASCEND)
Ps 68: 18 When you **a** on high, you took
Eph 4: 8 "When he **a** on high, he took many

ASCENDING (ASCEND)
Ge 28: 12 and the angels of God were **a**
Jn 1: 51 angels of God **a** and descending

ASCRIBE*
1Ch 16: 28 **A** to the LORD, all you families
16: 28 **a** to the LORD glory and strength.
16: 29 **A** to the LORD the glory due his
Job 36: 3 I will **a** justice to my Maker.
Ps 29: 1 **A** to the LORD, you heavenly
29: 1 **a** to the LORD glory and strength.
29: 2 **A** to the LORD the glory due his
96: 7 **A** to the LORD, all you families
96: 7 **a** to the LORD glory and strength.
96: 8 **A** to the LORD the glory due his

ASHAMED (SHAME)
Mk 8: 38 If anyone is **a** of me and my words
8: 38 the Son of Man will be **a** of them
Lk 9: 26 Whoever is **a** of me and my words,
9: 26 the Son of Man will be **a** of them
Ro 1: 16 For I am not **a** of the gospel,
2Ti 1: 8 So do not be **a** of the testimony
2: 15 worker who does not need to be **a**

ASHER
Son of Jacob by Zilpah (Ge 30:13; 35:26; 46:17; Ex 1:4; 1Ch 2:2). Tribe of blessed (Ge 49:20; Dt 33:24–25), numbered (Nu 1:40–41; 26:44–47), allotted land (Jos 10:24–31; Eze 48:2), failed to fully possess (Jdg 1:31–32), failed to support Deborah (Jdg 5:17), supported Gideon (Jdg 6:35; 7:23) and David (1Ch 12:36), 12,000 from (Rev 7:6).

ASHERAH (ASHERAHS)
Ex 34: 13 stones and cut down their **A** poles.
1Ki 18: 19 the four hundred prophets of **A**,

ASHERAHS* (ASHERAH)
Jdg 3: 7 and served the Baals and the **A**.

ASHES
Job 42: 6 myself and repent in dust and **a**."
Mt 11: 21 long ago in sackcloth and **a**.

ASHTORETHS
Jdg 2: 13 him and served Baal and the **A**.
1Sa 7: 4 put away their Baals and **A**,

ASLEEP (SLEEP)
1Co 15: 18 who have fallen **a** in Christ are lost.

ASPIRES*
1Ti 3: 1 Whoever **a** to be an overseer

ASSEMBLY
Ps 1: 5 sinners in the **a** of the righteous.
35: 18 will give you thanks in the great **a**;
82: 1 God presides in the great **a**;
149: 1 praise in the **a** of his faithful

ASSIGNED
1Ki 7: 14 and did all the work **a** to him.
Mk 13: 34 each with their **a** task, and tells
1Co 3: 5 as the Lord has **a** to each his task.
7: 17 whatever situation the Lord has **a**
2Co 10: 13 of service God himself has **a** to us,

ASSOCIATE
Pr 22: 24 do not **a** with one easily angered,
Jn 4: 9 Jews do not **a** with Samaritans.)
Ac 10: 28 against our law for a Jew to **a**
Ro 12: 16 be willing to **a** with people of low
1Co 5: 9 in my letter not to **a** with sexually
5: 11 you must not **a** with anyone who
2Th 3: 14 Do not **a** with them, in order

ASSURANCE (ASSURED)
Heb 10: 22 and with the full **a** that faith brings,

ASSURED (ASSURANCE)
Col 4: 12 the will of God, mature and fully **a**.

ASTRAY
Ps 119: 67 Before I was afflicted I went **a**,
Pr 10: 17 ignores correction leads others **a**.
20: 1 whoever is led **a** by them is not
Isa 53: 6 have gone **a**, each of us has turned
Jer 50: 6 their shepherds have led them **a**
1Pe 2: 25 For "you were like sheep going **a**,"
1Jn 3: 7 do not let anyone lead you **a**.

ASTROLOGERS
Isa 47: 13 Let your **a** come forward,
Da 2: 2 **a** to tell him what he had dreamed.

ATE (EAT)
Ge 3: 6 wisdom, she took some and **a** it.
27: 25 Jacob brought it to him and he **a**;
2Sa 9: 11 So Mephibosheth **a** at David's table
Ps 78: 25 Human beings **a** the bread
Jer 15: 16 When your words came, I **a** them;
Eze 3: 3 So I **a** it, and it tasted as sweet as
Mt 14: 20 They all **a** and were satisfied,
15: 37 They all **a** and were satisfied.
Mk 6: 42 They all **a** and were satisfied,
Lk 9: 17 They all **a** and were satisfied,

ATHALIAH
Granddaughter of Omri; wife of Jehoram and mother of Ahaziah; encouraged their evil ways (2Ki 8:18, 27; 2Ch 22:2). At death of Ahaziah she made herself queen, killing all his sons but Joash (2Ki 11:1–3; 2Ch 22:10–12); killed six years later when Joash was revealed (2Ki 11:4–16; 2Ch 23:1–15).

ATHLETE*
2Ti 2: 5 competes as an **a** does not receive

ATONE* (ATONEMENT)
Ex 30: 15 to the LORD to **a** for your lives.
2Ch 29: 24 for a sin offering to **a** for all Israel,
Da 9: 24 an end to sin, to **a** for wickedness,

ATONED* (ATONEMENT)
Dt 21: 8 Then the bloodshed will be **a** for,
1Sa 3: 14 of Eli's house will never be **a**
Pr 16: 6 love and faithfulness sin is **a** for;
Isa 6: 7 is taken away and your sin **a** for."
22: 14 day this sin will not be **a** for,"
27: 9 will Jacob's guilt be **a** for, and this

ATONEMENT (ATONE ATONED)
Ex 25: 17 "Make an **a** cover of pure gold—
30: 10 Once a year Aaron shall make **a**
Lev 17: 11 blood that makes **a** for one's life.
23: 27 this seventh month is the Day of **A**.
Nu 25: 13 God and made **a** for the Israelites."
Ro 3: 25 presented Christ as a sacrifice of **a**,
Heb 2: 17 that he might make **a** for the sins

ATTACK
Ps 109: 3 they **a** me without cause.

ATTAINED
Php 3: 16 live up to what we have already **a**.
Heb 7: 11 could have been **a** through

ATTENTION (ATTENTIVE)
Pr 4: 1 pay **a** and gain understanding.
4: 20 My son, pay **a** to what I say;
5: 1 My son, pay **a** to my wisdom,
7: 24 listen to me; pay **a** to what I say.
21: 11 by paying **a** to the wise they get
22: 17 Pay **a** and turn your ear
Ecc 7: 21 Do not pay **a** to every word people
Isa 42: 20 many things, but you pay no **a**;
Titus 1: 14 and will pay no **a** to Jewish myths
Heb 2: 1 We must pay the most careful **a**,

ATTENTIVE (ATTENTION)
Ne 1: 11 your ear be **a** to the prayer of this
1Pe 3: 12 and his ears are **a** to their prayer,

ATTITUDE (ATTITUDES)
Eph 4: 23 made new in the **a** of your minds;
1Pe 4: 1 yourselves also with the same **a**,

ATTITUDES* (ATTITUDE)
Heb 4: 12 the thoughts and **a** of the heart.

ATTRACTIVE
Titus 2: 10 teaching about God our Savior **a**.

AUDIENCE
Pr 29: 26 Many seek an **a** with a ruler, but it

AUTHORITIES (AUTHORITY)
Ro 13: 1 be subject to the governing **a**,
13: 5 it is necessary to submit to the **a**,
13: 6 for the **a** are God's servants,
Eph 3: 10 and **a** in the heavenly realms,
6: 12 against the **a**, against the powers
Col 1: 16 thrones or powers or rulers or **a**;
2: 15 having disarmed the powers and **a**,
Titus 3: 1 to be subject to rulers and **a**,
1Pe 3: 22 **a** and powers in submission to

AUTHORITY (AUTHORITIES)
Mt 7: 29 he taught as one who had **a**,
9: 6 the Son of Man has **a** on earth
28: 18 "All **a** in heaven and on earth has
Mk 1: 22 he taught them as one who had **a**,
2: 10 the Son of Man has **a** on earth
Lk 4: 32 teaching, because his words had **a**.
5: 24 the Son of Man has **a** on earth
Jn 10: 18 I have **a** to lay it down and **a** to take
Ac 1: 7 the Father has set by his own **a**.
Ro 7: 1 the law has **a** over someone only as
13: 1 for there is no **a** except
13: 2 rebels against the **a** is rebelling
1Co 11: 10 ought to have **a** over her own head,
15: 24 all dominion, **a** and power.
1Ti 2: 2 for kings and all those in **a**, that we
2: 12 to teach or to assume **a** over a man;
Titus 2: 15 Encourage and rebuke with all **a**.
Heb 13: 17 your leaders and submit to their **a**,
1Pe 2: 13 the Lord's sake to every human **a**:

AUTUMN*
Dt 11: 14 its season, both **a** and spring rains,
Ps 84: 6 the **a** rains also cover it with pools.
Jer 5: 24 who gives **a** and spring rains
Joel 2: 23 has given you the **a** rains because
2: 23 showers, both **a** and spring rains,
Jas 5: 7 crop, patiently waiting for the **a**
Jude : 12 **a** trees, without fruit and uprooted

AVENGE (VENGEANCE)
Lev 26: 25 on you to **a** the breaking
Dt 32: 35 It is mine to **a**; I will repay.
32: 43 for he will **a** the blood of his
Ro 12: 19 "It is mine to **a**; I will repay,"
Heb 10: 30 him who said, "It is mine to **a**;
Rev 6: 10 of the earth and **a** our blood?"

AVENGER (VENGEANCE)
Nu 35: 27 the **a** of blood may kill the accused
Jos 20: 3 protection from the **a** of blood.
Ps 8: 2 to silence the foe and the **a**.

AVENGES (VENGEANCE)
Ps 94: 1 The LORD is a God who **a**. O God who **a**, shine forth.

AVENGING* (VENGEANCE)
1Sa 25: 26 and from **a** yourself with your own
25: 33 from **a** myself with my own hands.
Na 1: 2 The LORD is a jealous and **a** God;

AVOID (AVOIDED AVOIDS)
Pr 4: 15 **A** it, do not travel on it; turn from
15: 12 correction, so they **a** the wise.
20: 3 It is to one's honor to **a** strife,
20: 19 so **a** anyone who talks too much.
Ecc 7: 18 fears God will **a** all extremes.
1Th 4: 3 you should **a** sexual immorality;
2Ti 2: 16 **A** godless chatter, because those
Titus 3: 9 But **a** foolish controversies

AVOIDED* (AVOID)
Pr 16: 6 the fear of the LORD evil is **a**.

AVOIDS* (AVOID)
Pr 16: 17 The highway of the upright **a** evil;

AWAITS (WAIT)
Pr 15: 10 Stern discipline **a** anyone who
28: 22 are unaware that poverty **a** them.

AWAKE (WAKE)
Ps 17: 15 when I **a**, I will be satisfied
Pr 6: 22 when you **a**, they will speak to you.
1Th 5: 6 asleep, but let us be **a** and sober.

AWARD*
2Ti 4: 8 Judge, will **a** to me on that day—

AWARE
Ex 34: 29 he was not **a** that his face was
Mt 24: 50 him and at an hour he is not **a** of.
Lk 12: 46 him and at an hour he is not **a** of.

AWE* (AWESOME OVERAWED)
Jos 4: 14 they stood in **a** of him all the days
4: 14 as they had stood in **a** of Moses.
1Sa 12: 18 So all the people stood in **a**
1Ki 3: 28 they held the king in **a**, because
Job 25: 2 "Dominion and **a** belong to God;
Ps 65: 8 The whole earth is filled with **a**
119:120 I stand in **a** of your laws.
Isa 29: 23 will stand in **a** of the God of Israel.
Jer 2: 19 your God and have no **a** of me,"
33: 9 they will be in **a** and will tremble
Hab 3: 2 I stand in **a** of your deeds, LORD.
Mal 2: 5 me and stood in **a** of my name.
Mt 9: 8 saw this, they were filled with **a**;
Lk 1: 65 the neighbors were filled with **a**,
5: 26 They were filled with **a** and said,
7: 16 They were all filled with **a**
Ac 2: 43 Everyone was filled with **a**
Heb 12: 28 acceptably with reverence and **a**,

AWESOME* (AWE)
Ge 28: 17 and said, "How **a** is this place!
Ex 15: 11 majestic in holiness, **a** in glory,
34: 10 among will see how **a** is the work
Dt 4: 34 or by great and **a** deeds, like all
7: 21 is among you, is a great and **a** God.
10: 17 God, mighty and **a**, who shows no
10: 21 **a** wonders you saw with your own
28: 58 revere this glorious and **a** name—
34: 12 performed the **a** deeds that Moses
Jdg 13: 6 looked like an angel of God, very **a**.
2Sa 7: 23 **a** wonders by driving out nations
1Ch 17: 21 **a** wonders by driving out nations
Ne 1: 5 the great and **a** God, who keeps his
4: 14 who is great and **a**, and fight
9: 32 God, mighty and **a**, who keeps his
Job 10: 16 again display your **a** power against
37: 22 God comes in **a** majesty.
Ps 45: 4 your right hand achieve **a** deeds.
47: 2 For the LORD Most High is **a**,
65: 5 answer us with **a** and righteous
66: 3 to God, "How **a** are your deeds!
66: 5 has done, his **a** deeds for mankind!
68: 35 You, God, are **a** in your sanctuary;
89: 7 he is more **a** than all who surround
99: 3 praise your great and **a** name—
106: 22 Ham and **a** deeds by the Red Sea.
111: 9 holy and **a** is his name.
145: 6 tell of the power of your **a** works—
Isa 64: 3 you did **a** things that we did not
Eze 1: 18 Their rims were high and **a**, and all
1: 22 vault, sparkling like crystal, and **a**.
Da 2: 31 dazzling statue, **a** in appearance.
9: 4 the great and **a** God, who keeps his
Zep 2: 11 The LORD will be **a** to them

AX
Mt 3: 10 The **a** is already at the root
Lk 3: 9 The **a** is already at the root

BAAL
Jdg 6: 25 Tear down your father's altar to **B**
1Ki 16: 32 set up an altar for **B** in the temple
18: 25 Elijah said to the prophets of **B**,
19: 18 knees have not bowed down to **B**
2Ki 10: 28 So Jehu destroyed **B** worship
Jer 19: 5 in the fire as offerings to **B**—
Ro 11: 4 have not bowed the knee to **B**."

BAASHA
King of Israel (1Ki 15:16—16:7; 2Ch 16:1–6).

BABBLER* (BABBLING)
Ac 17: 18 "What is this **b** trying to say?"

BABBLING* (BABBLER)
Mt 6: 7 do not keep on **b** like pagans,

BABIES* (BABY)
Ge 25: 22 The **b** jostled each other within
Ex 2: 6 "This is one of the Hebrew **b**,"
Lk 18: 15 bringing **b** to Jesus for him to place
Ac 7: 19 their newborn **b** so that they would
1Pe 2: 2 Like newborn **b**, crave pure

BABY* (BABIES BABY'S)
Ex 1: 16 you see that the **b** is a boy, kill him;
2: 6 She opened it and saw the **b**.
2: 7 women to nurse the **b** for you?"
2: 9 "Take this **b** and nurse him for me,
2: 9 the woman took the **b** and nursed
1Ki 3: 17 I had a **b** while she was there
3: 18 was born, this woman also had a **b**.
3: 26 my lord, give her the living **b**!
3: 27 "Give the living **b** to the first
Isa 49: 15 "Can a mother forget the **b** at her
Lk 1: 41 greeting, the **b** leaped in her womb,
1: 44 the **b** in my womb leaped for joy.
1: 57 time for Elizabeth to have her **b**,
2: 6 the time came for the **b** to be born,
2: 12 You will find a **b** wrapped in cloths
2: 16 and the **b**, who was lying
Jn 16: 21 **b** is born she forgets the anguish

BABY'S* (BABY)
Ex 2: 8 the girl went and got the **b** mother.

BABYLON
Ps 137: 1 By the rivers of **B** we sat and wept
Jer 29: 10 seventy years are completed for **B**,
51: 37 **B** will be a heap of ruins, a haunt
Rev 14: 8 Fallen is **B** the Great,' which made
17: 5 on her forehead was a mystery: **B**

BACKS
2Pe 2: 21 their **b** on the sacred command

BACKSLIDING* (BACKSLIDINGS)
Jer 2: 19 your **b** will rebuke you.
3: 22 I will cure you of **b**."
15: 6 "You keep on **b**. So I will reach
Eze 37: 23 save them from all their sinful **b**,

BACKSLIDINGS* (BACKSLIDING)
Jer 5: 6 rebellion is great and their **b** many.

BALAAM
Prophet who attempted to curse Israel (Nu 22–24; Dt 23:4–5; 2Pe 2:15; Jude 11). Killed in Israel's vengeance on Midianites (Nu 31:8; Jos 13:22).

BALAK
Moabite king who hired Balaam to curse Israel (Nu 22–24; Jos 24:9).

BALM
Jer 8: 22 Is there no **b** in Gilead? Is there no

BANISH (BANISHED)
Jer 25: 10 will **b** from them the sounds of joy

BANISHED (BANISH)
Dt 30: 4 have been **b** to the most distant

BANNER
Ex 17: 15 and called it The LORD is my **B**.
SS 2: 4 hall, and let his **b** over me be love.
Isa 11: 10 of Jesse will stand as a **b**

BANQUET
SS 2: 4 Let him lead me to the **b** hall,
Lk 14: 13 But when you give a **b**,

BAPTISM* (BAPTIZE)
Mt 21: 25 John's **b**—where did it come from?
Mk 1: 4 preaching a **b** of repentance
10: 38 with the **b** I am baptized with?"
10: 39 with the **b** I am baptized with,
11: 30 John's **b**—was it from heaven,
Lk 3: 3 preaching a **b** of repentance
12: 50 But I have a **b** to undergo, and
20: 4 John's **b**—was it from heaven,
Ac 1: 22 beginning from John's **b** to the
10: 37 after the **b** that John preached—
13: 24 and **b** to all the people of Israel.
18: 25 though he knew only the **b** of John.
19: 3 "Then what **b** did you receive?"
19: 3 "John's **b**," they replied.
19: 4 "John's **b** was a **b** of repentance.
Ro 6: 4 with him through **b** into death
Eph 4: 5 one Lord, one faith, one **b**;
Col 2: 12 having been buried with him in **b**,
1Pe 3: 21 this water symbolizes **b** that now

BAPTIZE* (BAPTISM BAPTIZED BAPTIZING)
Mt 3: 11 "I **b** you with water for repentance.
3: 11 He will **b** you with the Holy Spirit
Mk 1: 8 I **b** you with water, but he will **b** you with the Holy Spirit
Lk 3: 16 them all, "I **b** you with water.
3: 16 He will **b** you with the Holy Spirit
Jn 1: 25 you **b** if you are not the Messiah,
1: 26 "I **b** with water," John replied,
1: 33 one who sent me to **b** with water
1: 33 remain is the one who will **b**
1Co 1: 14 that I did not **b** any of you except
1: 17 For Christ did not send me to **b**,

BAPTIZED* (BAPTIZE)
Mt 3: 6 they were **b** by him in the Jordan
3: 13 to the Jordan to be **b** by John.
3: 14 "I need to be **b** by you, and do you
3: 16 As soon as Jesus was **b**, he went
Mk 1: 5 they were **b** by him in the Jordan
1: 9 and was **b** by John in the Jordan.
10: 38 or be **b** with the baptism I am **b** with?"
10: 39 be **b** with the baptism I am **b** with,
16: 16 *believes and is* **b** *will be saved,*
Lk 3: 7 crowds coming out to be **b** by him,
3: 12 Even tax collectors came to be **b**.
3: 21 When all the people were being **b**, Jesus was **b** too.
7: 29 because they had been **b** by John.
7: 30 because they had not been **b**
Jn 3: 22 spent some time with them, and **b**.
3: 23 people were coming and being **b**.
4: 2 in fact it was not Jesus who **b**,
Ac 1: 5 For John **b** with water, but in a few days you will be **b**
2: 38 "Repent and be **b**, every one
2: 41 who accepted his message were **b**,
8: 12 they were **b**, both men and women.
8: 13 Simon himself believed and was **b**.
8: 16 had simply been **b** in the name
8: 36 stand in the way of my being **b**?"
8: 38 into the water and Philip **b** him.
9: 18 He got up and was **b**,
10: 47 the way of their being **b** with water.
10: 48 ordered that they be **b** in the name
11: 16 'John **b** with water, but you will be **b** with the Holy Spirit.'
16: 15 members of her household were **b**,
16: 33 he and all his household were **b**.
18: 8 heard Paul believed and were **b**.
19: 5 were **b** in the name of the Lord
22: 16 up, be **b** and wash your sins away,
Ro 6: 3 us who were **b** into Christ Jesus were **b** into his death?
1Co 1: 13 Were you **b** in the name of Paul?
1: 15 say that you were **b** in my name.
1: 16 also **b** the household of Stephanas;
1: 16 don't remember if I **b** anyone else.)
10: 2 They were all **b** into Moses
12: 13 we were all **b** by one Spirit so as
15: 29 those do who are **b** for the dead?
15: 29 at all, why are people **b** for them?
Gal 3: 27 of you who were **b** into Christ have

BAPTIZING* (BAPTIZE)
Mt 3: 7 coming to where he was **b**, he said
28: 19 **b** them in the name of the Father
Jn 1: 28 of the Jordan, where John was **b**.
1: 31 the reason I came **b** with water was
3: 23 also was **b** at Aenon near Salim,
3: 26 he is **b**, and everyone is going
4: 1 and **b** more disciples than John—
10: 40 the place where John had been **b**

BAR-JESUS*
Ac 13: 6 and false prophet named **B**,

BARABBAS
Mt 27: 26 Then he released **B** to them.

BARAK*
Judge who fought with Deborah against Canaanites (Jdg 4–5; 1Sa 12:11; Heb 11:32).

BARBARIAN*
Col 3: 11 circumcised or uncircumcised, **b**,

BARBS*
Nu 33: 55 remain will become **b** in your eyes

BARE
Hos 2: 3 make her as **b** as on the day she
Heb 4: 13 and laid **b** before the eyes of him

BARNABAS*
Disciple, originally Joseph (Ac 4:36), prophet (Ac 13:1), apostle (Ac 14:14). Brought Paul to apostles (Ac 9:27), Antioch (Ac 11:22–30; Gal 2:1–13), on the first missionary journey (Ac 13–14). Together at Jerusalem Council, they separated over John Mark (Ac 15). Later coworkers (1Co 9:6; Col 4:10).

BARREN
Isa 54: 1 "Sing, **b** woman, you who never
Gal 4: 27 "Be glad, **b** woman, you who never

BARTHOLOMEW*
Apostle (Mt 10:3; Mk 3:18; Lk 6:14; Ac 1:13). Possibly also known as Nathanael (Jn 1:45–49; 21:2).

BARUCH
Jeremiah's secretary (Jer 32:12–16; 36; 43:1–6; 45:1–2).

BARZILLAI
1. Gileadite who aided David during Absalom's revolt (2Sa 17:27; 19:31–39).
2. Son-in-law of 1. (Ezr 2:61; Ne 7:63).

BASHAN
Jos 22: 7 Moses had given land in **B**,
Ps 22: 12 strong bulls of **B** encircle me.

BASIN
Ex 30: 18 "Make a bronze **b**, with its bronze

BASKET
Ex 2: 3 she got a papyrus **b** for him
Ac 9: 25 him in a **b** through an opening
2Co 11: 33 was lowered in a **b** from a window

BATCH*
Ro 11: 16 is holy, then the whole **b** is holy;
1Co 5: 6 a little yeast leavens the whole **b**
5: 7 you may be a new unleavened **b**—
Gal 5: 9 yeast works through the whole **b**

BATH (BATHING)
Jn 13: 10 "Those who have had a **b** need

BATHING (BATH)
2Sa 11: 2 From the roof he saw a woman **b**.

BATHSHEBA*
Wife of Uriah who committed adultery with and became wife of David (2Sa 11), mother of Solomon (2Sa 12:24; 1Ki 1–2; 1Ch 3:5; Ps 51:T).

BATTLE (BATTLES)
1Sa 17: 47 for the **b** is the LORD's, and he
2Ch 20: 15 For the **b** is not yours, but God's.
Ps 24: 8 mighty, the LORD mighty in **b**.
Ecc 9: 11 to the swift or the **b** to the strong,
Isa 31: 4 come down to do **b** on Mount Zion
Eze 13: 5 will stand firm in the **b** on the day
Rev 16: 14 them for the **b** on the great day
20: 8 and to gather them for **b**.

BATTLES* (BATTLE)
1Sa 8: 20 go out before us and fight our **b**."
18: 17 and fight the **b** of the LORD."
25: 28 because you fight the LORD's **b**,
2Ch 32: 8 God to help us and to fight our **b**."

BEAR (BEARING BEARS BIRTH BIRTHRIGHT BORE BORN CHILDBEARING CHILDBIRTH FIRSTBORN NEWBORN REBIRTH)
Ge 4: 13 punishment is more than I can **b**.
Ps 38: 4 me like a burden too heavy to **b**.
Isa 11: 7 The cow will feed with the **b**,
53: 11 many, and he will **b** their iniquities.
Da 7: 5 beast, which looked like a **b**.
Mt 7: 18 A good tree cannot **b** bad fruit,
7: 18 and a bad tree cannot **b** good fruit.
Lk 21: 13 And so you will **b** testimony to me.
Jn 15: 2 branch that does **b** fruit he prunes
15: 8 that you **b** much fruit,
15: 16 so that you might go and **b** fruit—
Ro 7: 4 that we might **b** fruit for God.
15: 1 We who are strong ought to **b**
1Co 10: 13 tempted beyond what you can **b**.
Col 3: 13 **B** with each other and forgive one

BEARD
Lev 19: 27 head or clip off the edges of your **b**.
Isa 50: 6 to those who pulled out my **b**;

BEARING (BEAR)
Eph 4: 2 patient, **b** with one another in love.
Col 1: 10 **b** fruit in every good work,
Heb 13: 13 the camp, **b** the disgrace he bore.

BEARS (BEAR)
1Ki 8: 43 house I have built **b** your Name.
Ps 68: 19 Savior, who daily **b** our burdens.

BEAST (BEASTS)
Rev 13: 18 calculate the number of the **b**, for it
16: 2 people who had the mark of the **b**
19: 20 had received the mark of the **b**

BEASTS (BEAST)
Da 7: 3 Four great **b**, each different
1Co 15: 32 If I fought wild **b** in Ephesus

BEAT (BEATEN BEATING BEATINGS)
Isa 2: 4 They will **b** their swords
Joel 3: 10 **B** your plowshares into swords
Mic 4: 3 They will **b** their swords

BEATEN (BEAT)
Lk 12: 47 do what the master wants will be **b**
12: 48 deserving punishment will be **b**
2Co 11: 25 Three times I was **b** with rods,

BEATING (BEAT)
1Co 9: 26 I do not fight like a boxer **b** the air.
1Pe 2: 20 if you receive a **b** for doing wrong

BEATINGS (BEAT)
Pr 19: 29 and **b** for the backs of fools.

BEAUTIFUL* (BEAUTY)
Ge 6: 2 the daughters of humans were **b**,
12: 11 "I know what a **b** woman you are.
12: 14 saw that Sarai was a very **b** woman.
24: 16 The woman was very **b**, a virgin;
26: 7 of Rebekah, because she is **b**."
29: 17 had a lovely figure and was **b**.
49: 21 is a doe set free that bears **b** fawns.
Nu 24: 5 "How **b** are your tents, Jacob,
Dt 21: 11 among the captives a **b** woman
Jos 7: 21 I saw in the plunder a **b** robe
1Sa 25: 3 was an intelligent and **b** woman,
2Sa 11: 2 The woman was very **b**,
13: 1 the **b** sister of Absalom son
14: 27 Tamar, and she became a **b** woman
1Ki 1: 3 Israel for a **b** young woman
1: 4 The woman was very **b**;
Est 2: 2 search be made for **b** young virgins
2: 3 bring all these **b** young women
2: 7 had a lovely figure and was **b**.
Job 42: 15 there found women as **b** as Job's
Ps 48: 2 **B** in its loftiness, the joy
Pr 11: 22 snout is a **b** woman who shows no
24: 4 are filled with rare and **b** treasures.
Ecc 3: 11 He has made everything **b** in its
SS 1: 8 do not know, most **b** of women,
1: 10 Your cheeks are **b** with earrings,
1: 15 How **b** you are, my darling!
1: 15 Oh, how **b**! Your eyes are doves.
2: 10 my darling, my **b** one,
2: 13 my **b** one, come with me."
4: 1 How **b** you are, my darling!
4: 1 Oh, how **b**! Your eyes behind your
4: 7 You are altogether **b**, my darling;
5: 9 than others, most **b** of women?
6: 1 beloved gone, most **b** of women?
6: 4 You are as **b** as Tirzah, my darling,
7: 1 How **b** your sandaled feet,
7: 6 How **b** you are and how pleasing,
Isa 4: 2 the Branch of the LORD will be **b**
28: 5 a **b** wreath for the remnant of his
52: 7 How **b** on the mountains are the
Jer 3: 19 land, the most **b** inheritance of any
6: 2 Daughter Zion, so **b** and delicate.
11: 16 olive tree with fruit **b** in form.
46: 20 "Egypt is a **b** heifer, but a gadfly is
Eze 7: 20 They took pride in their **b** jewelry

Eze 16: 12 ears and a **b** crown on your head.
16: 13 You became very **b** and rose to be
20: 6 and honey, the most **b** of all lands.
20: 15 honey, the most **b** of all lands—
23: 42 sister and **b** crowns on their heads.
27: 24 they traded with you **b** garments,
31: 3 with **b** branches overshadowing
31: 9 made it **b** with abundant branches,
33: 32 who sings love songs with a **b** voice
Da 4: 12 Its leaves were **b**, its fruit abundant,
4: 21 with **b** leaves and abundant fruit,
8: 9 to the east and toward the **B** Land.
11: 16 will establish himself in the **B** Land
11: 41 He will also invade the **B** Land.
11: 45 the seas at the **b** holy mountain.
Zec 9: 17 How attractive and **b** they will be!
Mt 23: 27 which look **b** on the outside
26: 10 She has done a **b** thing to me.
Mk 14: 6 She has done a **b** thing to me.
Lk 21: 5 temple was adorned with **b** stones
Ac 3: 2 carried to the temple gate called **B**,
3: 10 begging at the temple gate called **B**,
Ro 10: 15 "How **b** are the feet of those who

BEAUTY* (BEAUTIFUL)
Est 1: 11 order to display her **b** to the people
2: 3 let **b** treatments be given to them.
2: 9 provided her with her **b** treatments
2: 12 months of **b** treatments prescribed
Ps 27: 4 to gaze on the **b** of the LORD
45: 11 the king be enthralled by your **b**;
50: 2 Zion, perfect in **b**, God shines
Pr 6: 25 not lust in your heart after her **b**
31: 30 is deceptive, and **b** is fleeting;
Isa 3: 24 instead of **b**, branding.
28: 1 his glorious **b**, set on the head
28: 4 his glorious **b**, set on the head
33: 17 Your eyes will see the king in his **b**
53: 2 He had no **b** or majesty to attract
61: 3 them a crown of **b** instead of ashes,
La 2: 15 that was called the perfection of **b**,
Eze 16: 14 the nations on account of your **b**,
16: 14 given you made your **b** perfect,
16: 15 you trusted in your **b** and used
16: 15 passed by and your **b** became his.
16: 16 to him, and he possessed your **b**.
16: 25 lofty shrines and degraded your **b**,
27: 3 say, Tyre, "I am perfect in **b**."
27: 4 your builders brought your **b**
27: 11 they brought your **b** to perfection.
28: 7 draw their swords against your **b**
28: 12 full of wisdom and perfect in **b**.
28: 17 proud on account of your **b**,
31: 7 It was majestic in **b**, with its
31: 8 garden of God could match its **b**.
Jas 1: 11 blossom falls and its **b** is destroyed.
1Pe 3: 3 Your **b** should not come
3: 4 unfading **b** of a gentle and quiet

BED (SICKBED)
Isa 28: 20 The **b** is too short to stretch out on,
Lk 11: 7 and my children and I are in **b**.
17: 34 night two people will be in one **b**;
Heb 13: 4 and the marriage **b** kept pure,

BEELZEBUL*
Mt 10: 25 of the house has been called **B**,
12: 24 said, "It is only by **B**, the prince
12: 27 And if I drive out demons by **B**,
Mk 3: 22 said, "He is possessed by **B**!
Lk 11: 15 said, "By **B**, the prince of demons,
11: 18 claim that I drive out demons by **B**.
11: 19 Now if I drive out demons by **B**,

BEER
Pr 20: 1 Wine is a mocker and **b** a brawler;

BEERSHEBA
Ge 21: 14 and wandered in the Desert of **B**.
Jdg 20: 1 all Israel from Dan to **B**
1Sa 3: 20 Dan to **B** recognized that Samuel
2Sa 3: 10 Israel and Judah from Dan to **B**."
17: 11 Let all Israel, from Dan to **B**—
24: 2 the tribes of Israel from Dan to **B**
24: 15 of the people from Dan to **B** died.
1Ki 4: 25 from Dan to **B**, lived in safety,
1Ch 21: 2 count the Israelites from **B** to Dan.
2Ch 30: 5 throughout Israel, from **B** to Dan,

BEGGING
Ps 37: 25 forsaken or their children **b** bread.
Ac 16: 9 of Macedonia standing and **b** him,

BEGINNING
Ge 1: 1 In the **b** God created the heavens
Ps 102: 25 In the **b** you laid the foundations
Ps 111: 10 of the LORD is the **b** of wisdom;
Pr 1: 7 the LORD is the **b** of knowledge,
4: 7 The **b** of wisdom is this:
9: 10 of the LORD is the **b** of wisdom,
Ecc 3: 11 fathom what God has done from **b**
Isa 40: 21 it not been told you from the **b**?
46: 10 I make known the end from the **b**,
Mt 24: 8 All these are the **b** of birth pains.
Lk 1: 3 investigated everything from the **b**,
Jn 1: 1 In the **b** was the Word,
1Jn 1: 1 That which was from the **b**,
Rev 21: 6 and the Omega, the **B** and the End.
22: 13 and the Last, the **B** and the End.

BEHAVE (BEHAVIOR)
Ro 13: 13 us **b** decently, as in the daytime,

BEHAVIOR (BEHAVE)
Pr 1: 3 receiving instruction in prudent **b**,
1Pe 3: 1 words by the **b** of their wives,
3: 16 maliciously against your good **b**

BEHEMOTH*
Job 40: 15 "Look at **B**, which I made along

BELIEVE (BELIEVED BELIEVER BELIEVERS BELIEVES BELIEVING)
Ex 4: 1 "What if they do not **b** me or listen
1Ki 10: 7 I did not **b** these things until I
2Ch 9: 6 But I did not **b** what they said until
Ps 78: 32 of his wonders, they did not **b**.
Pr 14: 15 The simple **b** anything,
Hab 1: 5 in your days that you would not **b**,
Mt 18: 6 those who **b** in me—
21: 22 If you **b**, you will receive whatever
27: 42 the cross, and we will **b** in him.
Mk 1: 15 Repent and **b** the good news!"
5: 36 told him, "Don't be afraid; just **b**."
9: 24 the boy's father exclaimed, "I do **b**;
9: 42 those who **b** in me—
11: 24 prayer, **b** that you have received it,
15: 32 the cross, that we may see and **b**."
16: 16 *does not **b** will be condemned.*
16: 17 *will accompany those who **b**:*
Lk 8: 12 that they may not **b** and be saved.
8: 13 They **b** for a while, but in the time
8: 50 just **b**, and she will be healed."
22: 67 "If I tell you, you will not **b** me,
24: 25 how slow to **b** all that the prophets
Jn 1: 7 so that through him all might **b**.
3: 18 does not **b** stands condemned
4: 42 "We no longer **b** just because
5: 38 for you do not **b** the one he sent.
5: 46 you would **b** me, for he wrote
6: 29 to **b** in the one he has sent."
6: 69 We have come to **b** and to know
7: 5 even his own brothers did not **b**
8: 24 if you do not **b** that I am he,
9: 35 "Do you **b** in the Son of Man?"
9: 36 "Tell me so that I may **b** in him."
9: 38 "Lord, I **b**," and he worshiped him.
10: 26 you do not **b** because you are not
10: 37 Do not **b** me unless I do the works
10: 38 even though you do not **b** me,
11: 27 "I **b** that you are the Messiah,
11: 40 "Did I not tell you that if you **b**,
12: 36 **B** in the light while you have the
12: 37 they still would not **b** in him.
12: 39 For this reason they could not **b**,
12: 44 in me does not **b** in me only,
13: 19 it does happen you will **b** that I am
14: 1 You **b** in God; **b** also in me.
14: 10 Don't you **b** that I am in the Father,
14: 11 **B** me when I say that I am
14: 11 or at least **b** on the evidence
16: 30 This makes us **b** that you came
16: 31 "Do you now **b**?" Jesus replied.
17: 21 the world may **b** that you have sent
19: 35 he testifies so that you also may **b**.
20: 27 into my side. Stop doubting and **b**."
20: 31 may **b** that Jesus is the Messiah,
Ac 16: 31 They replied, "**B** in the Lord Jesus,
19: 4 He told the people to **b** in the one
24: 14 I **b** everything that is in accordance
26: 27 Agrippa, do you **b** the prophets?
Ro 3: 22 faith in Jesus Christ to all who **b**.
4: 11 he is the father of all who **b**
10: 9 **b** in your heart that God raised
10: 10 For it is with your heart that you **b**
10: 14 how can they **b** in the one of whom
1Co 1: 21 was preached to save those who **b**.
Gal 3: 22 might be given to those who **b**.
Php 1: 29 of Christ not only to **b** in him,
1Th 4: 14 For we **b** that Jesus died and rose
2Th 2: 11 delusion so that they will **b** the lie
1Ti 4: 10 and especially of those who **b**.
Titus 1: 6 a man whose children **b** and are
Heb 11: 6 comes to him must **b** that he exists
Jas 1: 6 you ask, you must **b** and not doubt,
2: 19 You **b** that there is one God. Good! Even the demons **b** that—
1Pe 2: 7 Now to you who **b**, this stone is
1Jn 3: 23 to **b** in the name of his Son,
4: 1 Dear friends, do not **b** every spirit,
5: 13 things to you who **b** in the name

BELIEVED (BELIEVE)
Ge 15: 6 Abram **b** the LORD, and he
Ex 4: 31 and they **b**. And when they heard
Isa 53: 1 Who has **b** our message
Jnh 3: 5 The Ninevites **b** God. A fast was
Lk 1: 45 Blessed is she who has **b**
Jn 1: 12 those who **b** in his name, he gave
2: 11 and his disciples **b** in him.
2: 22 Then they **b** the scripture
3: 18 already because they have not **b**
5: 46 If you **b** Moses, you would believe
7: 31 Still, many in the crowd **b** in him.
7: 39 whom those who **b** in him were
8: 30 Even as he spoke, many **b** in him.
11: 45 had seen what Jesus did, **b** in him.
12: 38 who has **b** our message
20: 8 also went inside. He saw and **b**.
20: 29 you have seen me, you have **b**;
20: 29 who have not seen and yet have **b**."
Ac 13: 48 were appointed for eternal life **b**.
19: 2 the Holy Spirit when you **b**?"
Ro 4: 3 "Abraham **b** God, and it was
10: 14 call on the one they have not **b** in?
10: 16 "Lord, who has **b** our message?"
1Co 15: 2 Otherwise, you have **b** in vain.
Gal 3: 6 So also Abraham "**b** God, and it
2Th 2: 12 who have not **b** the truth
1Ti 3: 16 the nations, was **b** on in the world,
2Ti 1: 12 because I know whom I have **b**,
Jas 2: 23 that says, "Abraham **b** God, and it

BELIEVER* (BELIEVE)
1Ki 18: 3 (Obadiah was a devout **b**
Ac 16: 1 a **b** but whose father was a Greek.
16: 15 you consider me a **b** in the Lord,"
1Co 7: 12 brother has a wife who is not a **b**
7: 13 has a husband who is not a **b** and
7: 17 each person should live as a **b** in
2Co 6: 15 what does a **b** have in common
2Th 3: 15 warn them as you would a fellow **b**.
1Ti 5: 16 any woman who is a **b** has widows
2Th 3: 6 keep away from every **b** who is idle

BELIEVERS (BELIEVE)
Jn 4: 41 of his words many more became **b**.
Ac 1: 15 up among the **b** (a group numbering
2: 44 All the **b** were together and had
4: 32 All the **b** were one in heart
5: 12 all the **b** used to meet together
9: 41 Then he called for the **b**,
10: 45 The circumcised **b** who had come
11: 2 the circumcised **b** criticized him
15: 2 along with some other **b**, to go
15: 5 some of the **b** who belonged
15: 23 To the Gentile **b** in Antioch,
15: 32 to encourage and strengthen the **b**.
21: 25 As for the Gentile **b**, we have
1Co 6: 5 to judge a dispute between **b**?
14: 22 a sign, not for **b** but for unbelievers;
14: 22 is not for unbelievers but for **b**.
2Co 11: 26 and in danger from false **b**.
Gal 2: 4 because some false **b** had infiltrated
6: 10 those who belong to the family of **b**.
1Th 1: 7 a model to all the **b** in Macedonia
1Ti 4: 12 set an example for the **b** in speech,
6: 2 masters are dear to them as fellow **b**
Jas 2: 1 **b** in our glorious Lord Jesus Christ
1Pe 2: 17 love the family of **b**, fear God,
3Jn : 10 he even refuses to welcome other **b**.

BELIEVES* (BELIEVE)
Mk 9: 23 is possible for one who **b**."
11: 23 **b** that what they say will happen,
16: 16 *Whoever **b** and is baptized*
Jn 3: 15 everyone who **b** may have eternal
3: 16 whoever **b** in him shall not perish
3: 18 Whoever **b** in him is not
3: 36 Whoever **b** in the Son has eternal
5: 24 **b** him who sent me has eternal life
6: 35 and whoever **b** in me will never be
6: 40 and **b** in him shall have eternal life,

Jn 6: 47 you, the one who **b** has eternal life.
7: 38 Whoever **b** in me, as Scripture has
11: 25 The one who **b** in me will live,
12: 44 "Whoever **b** in me does not believe
12: 46 that no one who **b** in me should stay
14: 12 whoever **b** in me will do the works I
Ac 10: 43 that everyone who **b** in him receives
13: 39 him everyone who **b** is set free
Ro 1: 16 brings salvation to everyone who **b**:
9: 33 the one who **b** in him will never be
10: 4 righteousness for everyone who **b**.
10: 11 "Anyone who **b** in him will never
1Jn 5: 1 Everyone who **b** that Jesus is
5: 5 Only the one who **b** that Jesus is
5: 10 Whoever **b** in the Son of God

BELIEVING* (BELIEVE)
Jn 11: 26 whoever lives by **b** in me will never
12: 11 going over to Jesus and **b** in him.
20: 31 by **b** you may have life in his name.
Ac 9: 26 not **b** that he really was a disciple.
1Co 7: 14 sanctified through her **b** husband.
9: 5 have the right to take a **b** wife along
Gal 3: 2 of the law, or by **b** what you heard?
3: 5 law, or by your **b** what you heard?
1Ti 6: 2 Those who have **b** masters should

BELLY
Ge 3: 14 You will crawl on your **b** and you
Da 2: 32 of silver, its **b** and thighs of bronze,
Mt 12: 40 three nights in the **b** of a huge fish,

BELONG (BELONGS)
Ge 40: 8 "Do not interpretations **b** to God?
Lev 25: 55 for the Israelites **b** to me as servants.
Dt 10: 14 LORD your God **b** the heavens,
29: 29 The secret things **b** to the LORD
29: 29 but the things revealed **b** to us
Job 12: 13 "To God **b** wisdom and power;
12: 16 To him **b** strength and insight;
25: 2 "Dominion and awe **b** to God;
Ps 47: 9 for the kings of the earth **b** to God;
95: 4 and the mountain peaks **b** to him.
115: 16 The highest heavens **b**
Jer 5: 10 for these people do not **b**
Jn 8: 44 You **b** to your father, the devil,
15: 19 As it is, you do not **b** to the world,
Ro 1: 6 those Gentiles who are called to **b**
7: 4 that you might **b** to another, to him
8: 9 of Christ, they do not **b** to Christ.
14: 8 we live or die, we **b** to the Lord.
1Co 7: 39 wishes, but he must **b** to the Lord.
15: 23 when he comes, those who **b** to him.
Gal 3: 29 If you **b** to Christ, then you are
5: 24 Those who **b** to Christ Jesus have
1Th 5: 5 We do not **b** to the night
5: 8 But since we **b** to the day, let us be
1Jn 3: 19 how we know that we **b** to the truth

BELONGS (BELONG)
Lev 27: 30 from the trees, **b** to the LORD;
Dt 1: 17 of anyone, for judgment **b** to God.
Job 41: 11 Everything under heaven **b** to me.
Ps 22: 28 for dominion **b** to the LORD
89: 18 Indeed, our shield **b** to the LORD,
111: 10 To him **b** eternal praise.
Eze 18: 4 For everyone **b** to me, the parent as
Jn 8: 47 Whoever **b** to God hears what God
Ro 12: 5 and each member **b** to all the others.
Rev 7: 10 "Salvation **b** to our God, who sits

BELOVED* (LOVE)
Dt 33: 12 "Let the **b** of the LORD rest
SS 1: 13 My **b** is to me a sachet of myrrh
1: 14 My **b** is to me a cluster of henna
1: 16 How handsome you are, my **b**!
2: 3 the forest is my **b** among the young
2: 8 Listen! My **b**! Look!
2: 9 My **b** is like a gazelle or a young
2: 10 My **b** spoke and said to me, "Arise,
2: 16 My **b** is mine and I am his;
2: 17 my **b**, and be like a gazelle or like
4: 16 Let my **b** come into his garden
5: 2 My **b** is knocking: "Open to me,
5: 4 My **b** thrust his hand through
5: 5 I arose to open for my **b**, and my
5: 6 I opened for my **b**, but my **b** had
5: 8 if you find my **b**, what will you tell
5: 9 How is your **b** better than others,
5: 9 How is your **b** better than others,
5: 10 My **b** is radiant and ruddy,
5: 16 This is my **b**, this is my friend,
6: 1 Where has your **b** gone,
6: 1 Which way did your **b** turn,
SS 6: 2 My **b** has gone down to his garden,
6: 3 am my beloved's and my **b** is mine;
7: 9 May the wine go straight to my **b**,
7: 10 I belong to my **b**, and his desire is
7: 11 my **b**, let us go to the countryside,
7: 13 that I have stored up for you, my **b**.
8: 5 the wilderness leaning on her **b**?
8: 14 my **b**, and be like a gazelle or like
Jer 11: 15 "What is my **b** doing in my temple

BELOVED'S* (LOVE)
SS 6: 3 I am my **b** and my beloved is mine;

BELSHAZZAR
King of Babylon in days of Daniel (Da 5).

BELT
Ex 12: 11 with your cloak tucked into your **b**,
1Ki 18: 46 tucking his cloak into his **b**, he ran
2Ki 4: 29 "Tuck your cloak into your **b**,
9: 1 "Tuck your cloak into your **b**,
Isa 11: 5 Righteousness will be his **b**
Eph 6: 14 the **b** of truth buckled around your

BENEFICIAL* (BENEFIT)
1Co 6: 12 but not everything is **b**.
10: 23 but not everything is **b**.

BENEFIT (BENEFICIAL BENEFITS)
Job 22: 2 "Can a man be of **b** to God?
22: 2 Can even a wise person **b** him?
Isa 38: 17 my **b** that I suffered such anguish.
Ro 6: 22 the **b** you reap leads to holiness,
2Co 4: 15 All this is for your **b**,

BENEFITS (BENEFIT)
Ps 103: 2 my soul, and forget not all his **b**—
Jn 4: 38 and you have reaped the **b** of their

BENJAMIN
Twelfth son of Jacob by Rachel (Ge 35:16–24; 46:19–21; 1Ch 2:2). Jacob refused to send him to Egypt, but relented (Ge 42–45). Tribe of blessed (Ge 49:27; Dt 33:12), numbered (Nu 1:37; 26:41), allotted land (Jos 18:11–28; Eze 48:23), failed to fully possess (Jdg 1:21), nearly obliterated (Jdg 20–21), sided with Ish-Bosheth (2Sa 2), but turned to David (1Ch 12:2, 29). 12,000 from (Rev 7:8).

BEREAN*
Ac 17: 11 Now the **B** Jews were of more noble

BESTOWS
Ps 84: 11 the LORD **b** favor and honor;

BETHANY
Mk 11: 1 and **B** at the Mount of Olives,

BETHEL
Ge 28: 19 He called that place **B**,

BETHLEHEM
Ru 1: 19 went on until they came to **B**.
1Sa 16: 1 I am sending you to Jesse of **B**.
2Sa 23: 15 from the well near the gate of **B**!"
Mic 5: 2 "But you, **B** Ephrathah, though you
Mt 2: 1 After Jesus was born in **B** in Judea,
2: 6 "'But you, **B**, in the land

BETHPHAGE
Mt 21: 1 came to **B** on the Mount of Olives,

BETHSAIDA
Jn 12: 21 Philip, who was from **B** in Galilee,

BETRAY (BETRAYED BETRAYS)
Ps 89: 33 nor will I ever **b** my faithfulness.
Pr 25: 9 do not **b** another's confidence,
Mt 10: 21 "Brother will **b** brother to death,
26: 21 I tell you, one of you will **b** me."

BETRAYED (BETRAY)
Mt 27: 4 said, "for I have **b** innocent blood."

BETRAYS (BETRAY)
Pr 11: 13 A gossip **b** a confidence,
20: 19 A gossip **b** a confidence;

BEULAH*
Isa 62: 4 called Hephzibah, and your land **B**;

BEWITCHED*
Gal 3: 1 Who has **b** you? Before your very

BEZALEL
Judahite craftsman in charge of building the tabernacle (Ex 31:1–11; 35:30—39:31).

BIDDING*
Ps 103: 20 you mighty ones who do his **b**,
148: 8 clouds, stormy winds that do his **b**,

BILDAD
One of Job's friends (Job 8; 18; 25).

BILHAH
Servant of Rachel, mother of Jacob's sons Dan and Naphtali (Ge 30:1–7; 35:25; 46:23–25).

BIND (BINDS BOUND)
Dt 6: 8 and **b** them on your foreheads.
Pr 3: 3 **b** them around your neck,
6: 21 **B** them always on your heart;
7: 3 **B** them on your fingers;
Isa 61: 1 He has sent me to **b**
Mt 16: 19 whatever you **b** on earth will be

BINDS (BIND)
Ps 147: 3 and **b** up their wounds.
Isa 30: 26 when the LORD **b** up the bruises
Ro 7: 2 from the law that **b** her to him.

BIRD (BIRDS)
Pr 27: 8 Like a **b** that flees its nest is anyone
Ecc 10: 20 a **b** on the wing may report what

BIRDS (BIRD)
Mt 8: 20 "Foxes have dens and **b** have nests,
Lk 9: 58 "Foxes have dens and **b** have nests,

BIRTH (BEAR)
Dt 32: 18 forgot the God who gave you **b**.
Ps 51: 5 Surely I was sinful at **b**,
58: 3 Even from **b** the wicked go astray;
Isa 26: 18 in labor, but we gave **b** to wind.
Mt 1: 18 This is how the **b** of Jesus
24: 8 these are the beginning of **b** pains.
Jn 3: 6 Flesh gives **b** to flesh, but the Spirit gives **b** to spirit.
1Pe 1: 3 great mercy he has given us new **b**

BIRTHRIGHT (BEAR)
Ge 25: 34 and left. So Esau despised his **b**.

BITTEN
Nu 21: 8 anyone who is **b** can look at it

BITTER (BITTERNESS EMBITTER)
Ex 12: 8 along with **b** herbs, and bread
Pr 27: 7 hungry even what is **b** tastes sweet.

BITTERNESS (BITTER)
Pr 14: 10 Each heart knows its own **b**,
17: 25 and **b** to the mother who bore him.
Ro 3: 14 mouths are full of cursing and **b**."
Eph 4: 31 Get rid of all **b**, rage and anger,

BLACK
Zec 6: 6 the **b** horses is going toward
Rev 6: 5 and there before me was a **b** horse!

BLAMELESS* (BLAMELESSLY)
Ge 6: 9 **b** among the people of his time,
17: 1 walk before me faithfully and be **b**.
Dt 18: 13 You must be **b** before the LORD
2Sa 22: 24 I have been **b** before him and have
22: 26 to the **b** you show yourself **b**,
Job 1: 1 This man was **b** and upright;
1: 8 is **b** and upright, a man who fears
2: 3 is **b** and upright, a man who fears
4: 6 and your **b** ways your hope?
8: 20 God does not reject one who is **b**
9: 20 if I were **b**, it would pronounce me
9: 21 "Although I am **b**, I have no
9: 22 say, 'He destroys both the **b**
12: 4 though righteous and **b**!
22: 3 would he gain if your ways were **b**?
31: 6 and he will know that I am **b**—
Ps 15: 2 The one whose walk is **b**, who does
18: 23 I have been **b** before him and have
18: 25 to the **b** you show yourself **b**,
19: 13 Then I will be **b**, innocent of great
26: 1 me, LORD, for I have led a **b** life;
26: 11 I lead a **b** life; deliver me and be
37: 18 The **b** spend their days under
37: 37 Consider the **b**, observe the
50: 23 to the **b** I will show my salvation."
84: 11 from those whose walk is **b**.
101: 2 I will be careful to lead a **b** life—
101: 2 affairs of my house with a **b** heart.
101: 6 one whose walk is **b** will minister
119: 1 are those whose ways are **b**,
Pr 2: 7 is a shield to those whose walk is **b**,
2: 21 land, and the **b** will remain in it;
10: 29 of the LORD is a refuge for the **b**,
11: 5 of the **b** makes their paths straight,
11: 20 delights in those whose ways are **b**.
19: 1 the poor whose walk is **b** than
20: 7 The righteous lead **b** lives;
28: 6 poor whose walk is **b** than the rich
28: 10 trap, but the **b** will receive a good
28: 18 one whose walk is **b** is kept safe,
Eze 28: 15 You were **b** in your ways
1Co 1: 8 so that you will be **b** on the day
Eph 1: 4 world to be holy and **b** in his sight.

Eph 5: 27 any other blemish, but holy and **b**.
Php 1: 10 be pure and **b** for the day of Christ,
2: 15 that you may become **b** and pure,
1Th 2: 10 and **b** we were among you who
3: 13 your hearts so that you will be **b**
5: 23 body be kept **b** at the coming of
Titus 1: 6 An elder must be **b**, faithful to his
1: 7 God's household, he must be **b**—
Heb 7: 26 one who is holy, **b**, pure, set apart
2Pe 3: 14 spotless, **b** and at peace with him.
Rev 14: 5 found in their mouths; they are **b**.

BLAMELESSLY* (BLAMELESS)
Lk 1: 6 Lord's commands and decrees **b**.

BLASPHEME* (BLASPHEMED BLASPHEMER BLASPHEMES BLASPHEMIES BLASPHEMING BLASPHEMOUS BLASPHEMY)
Ex 22: 28 "Do not **b** God or curse the ruler
Lev 24: 16 when they **b** the Name they are
Ac 26: 11 and I tried to force them to **b**.
1Ti 1: 20 over to Satan to be taught not to **b**.
2Pe 2: 12 these people **b** in matters they do
Rev 13: 6 It opened its mouth to **b** God,

BLASPHEMED* (BLASPHEME)
Lev 24: 11 of the Israelite woman **b** the Name
1Sa 3: 13 his sons **b** God, and he failed
2Ki 19: 6 of the king of Assyria have **b** me.
19: 22 is it you have ridiculed and **b**?
Isa 37: 6 of the king of Assyria have **b** me.
37: 23 is it you have ridiculed and **b**?
52: 5 day long my name is constantly **b**.
Eze 20: 27 also your ancestors **b** me by being
Ac 19: 37 robbed temples nor **b** our goddess.
Ro 2: 24 "God's name is **b** among

BLASPHEMER* (BLASPHEME)
Lev 24: 14 "Take the **b** outside the camp.
24: 23 they took the **b** outside the camp
1Ti 1: 13 Even though I was once a **b**

BLASPHEMES* (BLASPHEME)
Lev 24: 16 anyone who **b** the name
Nu 15: 30 **b** the LORD and must be cut off
Mk 3: 29 whoever **b** against the Holy Spirit
Lk 12: 10 but anyone who **b** against the Holy

BLASPHEMIES* (BLASPHEME)
Ne 9: 18 or when they committed awful **b**.
9: 26 they committed awful **b**.
Rev 13: 5 mouth to utter proud words and **b**

BLASPHEMING* (BLASPHEME)
Mt 9: 3 to themselves, "This fellow is **b**!"
Mk 2: 7 He's **b**! Who can forgive sins
Jas 2: 7 the ones who are **b** the noble name

BLASPHEMOUS* (BLASPHEME)
Ac 6: 11 Stephen speak **b** words against
Rev 13: 1 horns, and on each head a **b** name.
17: 3 that was covered with **b** names

BLASPHEMY* (BLASPHEME)
Mt 12: 31 but **b** against the Spirit will not be
12: 31 but **b** against the Spirit will not be
26: 65 clothes and said, "He has spoken **b**!
26: 65 Look, now you have heard the **b**.
Mk 14: 64 "You have heard the **b**.
Lk 5: 21 "Who is this fellow who speaks **b**?
Jn 10: 33 replied, "but for **b**, because you,
10: 36 you accuse me of **b** because I said,

BLAST*
Ex 15: 8 By the **b** of your nostrils the waters
19: 13 sounds a long **b** may they approach
19: 16 and a very loud trumpet **b**.
Nu 10: 5 When a trumpet **b** is sounded,
10: 6 At the sounding of a second **b**,
10: 6 The **b** will be the signal for setting
10: 9 you, sound a **b** on the trumpets.
Jos 6: 5 you hear them sound a long **b**
6: 16 the priests sounded the trumpet **b**,
2Sa 22: 16 at the **b** of breath from his nostrils.
Job 4: 9 At the **b** of his anger they are no
39: 25 At the **b** of the trumpet it snorts,
Ps 18: 15 the **b** of breath from your nostrils.
98: 6 and the **b** of the ram's horn—
147: 17 Who can withstand his icy **b**?
Isa 27: 8 with his fierce **b** he drives her out,
Eze 22: 20 furnace to be melted with a fiery **b**,
Am 2: 2 war cries and the **b** of the trumpet.
Heb 12: 19 to a trumpet **b** or to such a voice

BLEATING*
1Sa 15: 14 then is this **b** of sheep in my ears?

BLEMISH* (BLEMISHES)
Lev 22: 21 it must be without defect or **b** to be
Nu 19: 2 you a red heifer without defect or **b**
2Sa 14: 25 of his foot there was no **b** in him.
Eph 5: 27 stain or wrinkle or any other **b**,
Col 1: 22 in his sight, without **b** and free
1Pe 1: 19 Christ, a lamb without **b** or defect.

BLEMISHES* (BLEMISH)
2Pe 2: 13 They are blots and **b**,
Jude : 12 These people are **b** at your love

BLESS (BLESSED BLESSES BLESSING BLESSINGS)
Ge 12: 3 I will **b** those who **b** you,
32: 26 not let you go unless you **b** me."
Dt 7: 13 He will love you and **b** you
33: 11 **B** all his skills, LORD, and be
Ps 72: 15 pray for him and **b** him all day
Ro 12: 14 **B** those who persecute you;

BLESSED (BLESS)
Ge 1: 22 God **b** them and said, "Be fruitful
2: 3 Then God **b** the seventh day
22: 18 all nations on earth will be **b**,
Nu 24: 9 "May those who bless you be **b**
1Ch 17: 27 LORD, have **b** it, and it will be **b**
Ps 1: 1 **B** is the one who does not walk
2: 12 **B** are all who take refuge in him.
32: 2 **B** is the one whose sin the LORD
33: 12 **B** is the nation whose God is
40: 4 **B** is the one who trusts
41: 1 **B** are those who have regard
84: 5 **B** are those whose strength is
89: 15 **B** are those who have learned
94: 12 **B** is the one you discipline, LORD,
106: 3 **B** are those who act justly,
112: 1 **B** are those who fear the LORD,
118: 26 **B** is he who comes in the name
119: 1 **B** are those whose ways are
119: 2 **B** are those who keep his statutes
127: 5 **B** is the man whose quiver is full
Pr 3: 13 **B** are those who find wisdom,
8: 34 **B** are those who listen to me,
28: 20 A faithful person will be richly **b**,
29: 18 **b** is the one who heeds wisdom's
31: 28 Her children arise and call her **b**;
Isa 30: 18 **B** are all who wait for him!
Mal 3: 12 all the nations will call you **b**,
3: 15 But now we call the arrogant **b**.
Mt 5: 3 "**B** are the poor in spirit, for theirs
5: 4 **B** are those who mourn, for they
5: 5 **B** are the meek, for they will
5: 6 **B** are those who hunger and thirst
5: 7 **B** are the merciful, for they will be
5: 8 **B** are the pure in heart, for they
5: 9 **B** are the peacemakers, for they
5: 10 **B** are those who are persecuted
5: 11 "**B** are you when people insult you,
Lk 1: 48 on all generations will call me **b**,
Jn 12: 13 "**B** is he who comes in the name
12: 13 "**B** is the king of Israel!"
Ac 20: 35 'It is more **b** to give than
Titus 2: 13 while we wait for the **b** hope—
Jas 1: 12 **B** is the one who perseveres under
Rev 1: 3 **B** is the one who reads aloud
1: 3 **b** are those who hear it and take
22: 7 **B** is the one who keeps the words
22: 14 "**B** are those who wash their robes,

BLESSES (BLESS)
Ps 29: 11 the LORD **b** his people with peace.
Ro 10: 12 all and richly **b** all who call on him,

BLESSING (BLESS)
Ge 27: 4 I may give you my **b** before I die."
Dt 23: 5 turned the curse into a **b** for you,
33: 1 This is the **b** that Moses the man
Pr 10: 22 The **b** of the LORD brings wealth,
Eze 34: 26 there will be showers of **b**.
Gal 4: 15 Where, then, is your **b** of me now?

BLESSINGS (BLESS)
Dt 11: 29 proclaim on Mount Gerizim the **b**,
Jos 8: 34 of the law—the **b** and the curses—
Pr 10: 6 **B** crown the head of the righteous,
Ro 15: 27 have shared in the Jews' spiritual **b**,
15: 27 share with them their material **b**.

BLIND (BLINDED)
Mt 15: 14 Leave them; they are **b** guides.
15: 14 If the **b** lead the **b**, both will fall
23: 16 "Woe to you, **b** guides! You say,
Mk 10: 46 were leaving the city, a **b** man,
Lk 6: 39 "Can the **b** lead the **b**?
Jn 9: 25 I do know. I was **b** but now I see!"

BLINDED (BLIND)
Jn 12: 40 "He has **b** their eyes and hardened
2Co 4: 4 god of this age has **b** the minds

BLOOD (BLOODSHED BLOODTHIRSTY)
Ge 4: 10 Your brother's **b** cries out to me
9: 6 "Whoever sheds human **b**, by humans shall their **b** be shed;
Ex 12: 13 when I see the **b**, I will pass over
24: 8 "This is the **b** of the covenant
Lev 16: 15 and take its **b** behind the curtain
17: 11 the life of a creature is in the **b**,
17: 11 it is the **b** that makes atonement
Dt 12: 23 be sure you do not eat the **b**, because the **b** is the life,
Ps 59: 2 me from those who are after my **b**.
72: 14 for precious is their **b** in his sight.
Pr 6: 17 hands that shed innocent **b**,
Isa 1: 11 I have no pleasure in the **b** of bulls
Mt 26: 28 This is my **b** of the covenant,
27: 24 "I am innocent of this man's **b**,"
Mk 14: 24 "This is my **b** of the covenant,
Lk 22: 44 his sweat was like drops of **b** falling
Jn 6: 53 of the Son of Man and drink his **b**,
Ac 15: 20 of strangled animals and from **b**.
20: 26 that I am innocent of the **b** of any
Ro 3: 25 through the shedding of his **b**—
5: 9 have now been justified by his **b**,
1Co 11: 25 cup is the new covenant in my **b**;
Eph 1: 7 we have redemption through his **b**,
2: 13 brought near by the **b** of Christ.
Col 1: 20 by making peace through his **b**,
Heb 9: 7 a year, and never without **b**,
9: 12 Place once for all by his own **b**,
9: 20 said, "This is the **b** of the covenant,
9: 22 everything be cleansed with **b**,
12: 24 speaks a better word than the **b**
1Pe 1: 19 but with the precious **b** of Christ,
1Jn 1: 7 and the **b** of Jesus, his Son,
Rev 1: 5 has freed us from our sins by his **b**,
5: 9 with your **b** you purchased for God
7: 14 them white in the **b** of the Lamb.
12: 11 over him by the **b** of the Lamb
19: 13 He is dressed in a robe dipped in **b**,

BLOODSHED (BLOOD)
Jer 48: 10 who keeps their sword from **b**!
Eze 35: 6 I will give you over to **b** and it
Hab 2: 12 to him who builds a city with **b**

BLOODTHIRSTY* (BLOOD)
Ps 5: 6 The **b** and deceitful you, LORD,
26: 9 my life with those who are **b**,
55: 23 the **b** and deceitful will not live
139: 19 Away from me, you who are **b**!
Pr 29: 10 The **b** hate a person of integrity

BLOSSOM
Isa 35: 1 the wilderness will rejoice and **b**.

BLOT (BLOTS)
Ex 32: 32 **b** me out of the book you have
Ps 51: 1 to your great compassion **b** out my
Rev 3: 5 I will never **b** out the name

BLOTS* (BLOT)
Isa 43: 25 "I, even I, am he who **b** out your
2Pe 2: 13 They are **b** and blemishes, reveling

BLOWN
Eph 4: 14 and **b** here and there by every wind
Jas 1: 6 the sea, **b** and tossed by the wind.
Jude : 12 without rain, **b** along by the wind;

BLUSH
Jer 6: 15 they do not even know how to **b**.

BOAST (BOASTING)
1Ki 20: 11 his armor should not **b** like one
Ps 44: 8 In God we make our **b** all day long,
Pr 27: 1 Do not **b** about tomorrow, for you
Isa 45: 25 and will make their **b** in him.
Jer 9: 23 or the strong **b** of their strength
9: 24 let the one who boasts **b** about this:
Ro 2: 17 if you rely on the law and **b** in God;
2: 23 You who **b** in the law, do you
5: 2 And we **b** in the hope of the glory
1Co 1: 31 "Let the one who boasts **b**
2Co 10: 17 "Let the one who boasts **b**
11: 30 If I must **b**, I will **b** of the things
Gal 6: 14 May I never **b** except in the cross
Eph 2: 9 not by works, so that no one can **b**.
Php 3: 3 by his Spirit, who **b** in Christ Jesus,
Jas 4: 16 is, you **b** in your arrogant schemes.

BOASTING (BOAST)
Php 1: 26 you again your **b** in Christ Jesus

BOAZ
Wealthy Bethlehemite who showed favor to Ruth (Ru 2), married her (Ru 4). Ancestor

of David (Ru 4:18–22; 1Ch 2:12–15), Jesus (Mt 1:5–16; Lk 3:23–32).

BODIES (BODY)
Isa 26: 19 will live, LORD; their **b** will rise—
Ro 12: 1 to offer your **b** as a living sacrifice,
1Co 6: 15 not know that your **b** are members
6: 19 not know that your **b** are temples
6: 20 Therefore honor God with your **b**.
Eph 5: 28 to love their wives as their own **b**.

BODILY (BODY)
Col 2: 9 of the Deity lives in **b** form,

BODY (BODIES BODILY EMBODIMENT)
Zec 13: 6 are these wounds on your **b**?'
Mt 10: 28 be afraid of those who kill the **b**
10: 28 can destroy both soul and **b** in hell.
26: 26 "Take and eat; this is my **b**."
Mk 14: 22 saying, "Take it; this is my **b**."
Lk 22: 19 "This is my **b** given for you;
Jn 13: 10 their whole **b** is clean.
Ro 12: 4 us has one **b** with many members,
1Co 11: 24 "This is my **b**, which is for you;
12: 12 but all its many parts form one **b**,
12: 13 by one Spirit so as to form one **b**—
12: 24 But God has put the **b** together,
15: 44 it is sown a natural **b**, it is raised a spiritual **b**.
Eph 1: 23 which is his **b**, the fullness of him
4: 25 for we are all members of one **b**.
5: 30 for we are members of his **b**.
Php 1: 20 Christ will be exalted in my **b**,
Col 1: 24 for the sake of his **b**, which is

BOLD (BOLDNESS)
Pr 21: 29 The wicked put up a **b** front,
28: 1 but the righteous are as **b** as a lion.

BOLDNESS* (BOLD)
Ac 4: 29 to speak your word with great **b**.
28: 31 with all **b** and without hindrance!

BONDAGE
Ezr 9: 9 God has not forsaken us in our **b**.

BONES
Ge 2: 23 "This is now bone of my **b**
Ps 22: 14 water, and all my **b** are out of joint.
22: 17 All my **b** are on display;
Eze 37: 1 middle of a valley; it was full of **b**.
Jn 19: 36 "Not one of his **b** will be broken,"

BOOK (BOOKS)
Ex 32: 33 against me I will blot out of my **b**.
Jos 1: 8 Keep this **B** of the Law always
2Ki 22: 8 "I have found the **B** of the Law
2Ch 34: 15 "I have found the **B** of the Law
Ne 8: 8 They read from the **B** of the Law
Ps 69: 28 they be blotted out of the **b** of life
Da 12: 1 name is found written in the **b**—
Jn 20: 30 which are not recorded in this **b**.
Php 4: 3 whose names are in the **b** of life.
Rev 3: 5 of that person from the **b** of life,
20: 12 Another **b** was opened, which is the **b** of life.
20: 15 written in the **b** of life was thrown
21: 27 are written in the Lamb's **b** of life.

BOOKS* (BOOK)
Ecc 12: 12 Of making many **b** there is no end,
Da 7: 10 was seated, and the **b** were opened.
Jn 21: 25 for the **b** that would be written.
Rev 20: 12 the throne, and **b** were opened.
20: 12 they had done as recorded in the **b**.

BORE (BEAR)
Isa 53: 4 up our pain and **b** our suffering,
53: 12 For he **b** the sin of many, and made
Mt 8: 17 our infirmities and **b** our diseases."
1Pe 2: 24 "He himself **b** our sins" in his body

BORN (BEAR)
Ecc 3: 2 a time to be **b** and a time to die,
Isa 9: 6 For to us a child is **b**, to us a son is
66: 8 Can a country be **b** in a day
Lk 2: 11 a Savior has been **b** to you;
Jn 3: 3 of God unless they are **b** again."
3: 4 into their mother's womb to be **b**!"
3: 5 of God unless they are **b** of water
3: 7 my saying, 'You must be **b** again.'
3: 8 it is with everyone **b** of the Spirit."
1Pe 1: 23 For you have been **b** again,
1Jn 3: 9 because they have been **b** of God.
4: 7 Everyone who loves has been **b**
5: 1 that Jesus is the Christ is **b** of God,
5: 4 everyone **b** of God overcomes
5: 18 anyone **b** of God does not continue
5: 18 the One who was **b** of God keeps

BORROWER
Pr 22: 7 and the **b** is slave to the lender.

BOTHER (BOTHERING)
Lk 11: 7 one inside answers, 'Don't **b** me.

BOTHERING (BOTHER)
Lk 18: 5 yet because this widow keeps **b** me,

BOUGHT (BUY)
Ac 20: 28 which he **b** with his own blood.
1Co 6: 20 you were **b** at a price.
7: 23 You were **b** at a price;
2Pe 2: 1 the sovereign Lord who **b** them—

BOUND (BIND)
Isa 56: 3 Let no foreigner who is **b**
Mt 16: 19 bind on earth will be **b** in heaven,
18: 18 bind on earth will be **b** in heaven,
Ro 7: 2 by law a married woman is **b** to her
1Co 7: 39 A woman is **b** to her husband as
Jude : 6 **b** with everlasting chains
Rev 20: 2 and **b** him for a thousand years.

BOUNDARY (BOUNDS)
Nu 34: 3 Your southern **b** will start in the
Pr 23: 10 Do not move an ancient **b** stone
Hos 5: 10 are like those who move **b** stones.

BOUNDLESS
Eph 3: 8 the Gentiles the **b** riches of Christ,

BOUNDS (BOUNDARY)
2Co 7: 4 all our troubles my joy knows no **b**.

BOUNTY*
Ge 49: 26 than the **b** of the age-old hills.
Dt 28: 12 storehouse of his **b**, to send rain
1Ki 10: 13 he had given her out of his royal **b**.
Ps 65: 11 You crown the year with your **b**,
68: 10 settled in it, and from your **b**, God,
Jer 31: 12 will rejoice in the **b** of the LORD—
31: 14 people will be filled with my **b**,"

BOW (BOWED BOWS)
Dt 5: 9 You shall not **b** down to them
1Ki 22: 34 But someone drew his **b** at random
Ps 5: 7 in reverence I **b** down toward your
44: 6 I put no trust in my **b**, my sword
95: 6 Come, let us **b** down in worship,
138: 2 I will **b** down toward your holy
Isa 44: 19 Shall I **b** down to a block
45: 23 Before me every knee will **b**;
Ro 14: 11 Lord, 'every knee will **b** before me;
Php 2: 10 name of Jesus every knee should **b**,

BOWED (BOW)
Ps 145: 14 fall and lifts up all who are **b** down.
146: 8 lifts up those who are **b** down,

BOWS (BOW)
Isa 44: 15 he makes an idol and **b** down to it.
44: 17 he **b** down to it and worships.

BOY (BOY'S BOYS)
Ge 21: 17 God heard the **b** crying,
22: 12 "Do not lay a hand on the **b**,"
Jdg 13: 5 by a razor because the **b** is to be
1Sa 2: 11 the **b** ministered before the LORD
3: 8 that the LORD was calling the **b**.
Isa 7: 16 for before the **b** knows enough
Mt 17: 18 it came out of the **b**, and he was
Lk 2: 43 home, the **b** Jesus stayed behind

BOY'S (BOY)
1Ki 17: 22 and the **b** life returned to him,
2Ki 4: 34 on him, the **b** body grew warm.

BOYS (BOY)
Ge 25: 24 there were twin **b** in her womb.
Ex 1: 18 Why have you let the **b** live?"

BRACE*
Job 38: 3 **B** yourself like a man; I will
40: 7 "**B** yourself like a man; I will
Na 2: 1 watch the road, **b** yourselves,

BRAG*
Am 4: 5 **b** about your freewill offerings—

BRANCH (BRANCHES)
Isa 4: 2 that day the **B** of the LORD will be
Jer 23: 5 raise up for David a righteous **B**,
33: 15 I will make a righteous **B** sprout
Zec 3: 8 going to bring my servant, the **B**.
6: 12 is the man whose name is the **B**,
Jn 15: 2 cuts off every **b** in me that bears

BRANCHES (BRANCH)
Jn 15: 5 "I am the vine; you are the **b**.
Ro 11: 21 if God did not spare the natural **b**,

BRAVE
2Sa 2: 7 then, be strong and **b**, for Saul your
13: 28 you this order? Be strong and **b**."

BREACH (BREAK)
Ps 106: 23 stood in the **b** before him to keep

BREACHING (BREAK)
Pr 17: 14 Starting a quarrel is like **b** a dam;

BREAD
Ex 12: 8 herbs, and **b** made without yeast.
23: 15 the Festival of Unleavened **B**;
25: 30 Put the **b** of the Presence on this
Dt 8: 3 that man does not live on **b** alone
Ps 78: 25 Human beings ate the **b** of angels;
Pr 30: 8 riches, but give me only my daily **b**.
Isa 55: 2 spend money on what is not **b**,
Mt 4: 3 God, tell these stones to become **b**."
4: 4 'Man shall not live on **b** alone,
6: 11 Give us today our daily **b**.
26: 26 Jesus took **b**, and when he had
Mk 14: 22 Jesus took **b**, and when he had
Lk 4: 3 God, tell this stone to become **b**."
4: 4 'Man shall not live on **b** alone.'"
9: 13 "We have only five loaves of **b**
11: 3 Give us each day our daily **b**.
22: 19 And he took **b**, gave thanks
Jn 6: 33 the **b** of God is the **b** that comes
6: 35 Jesus declared, "I am the **b** of life.
6: 41 "I am the **b** that came down
6: 48 I am the **b** of life.
6: 51 I am the living **b** that came down
6: 51 Whoever eats this **b** will live
6: 51 This **b** is my flesh, which I will
21: 13 took the **b** and gave it to them,
1Co 10: 16 And is not the **b** that we break
11: 23 the night he was betrayed, took **b**,
11: 26 For whenever you eat this **b**

BREAK (BREACH BREACHING BREAKERS BREAKING BREAKS BROKE BROKEN BROKENNESS)
Nu 30: 2 must not **b** his word but must do
Jdg 2: 1 'I will never **b** my covenant
Ps 2: 9 You will **b** them with a rod of iron;
Pr 25: 15 and a gentle tongue can **b** a bone.
Isa 42: 3 A bruised reed he will not **b**,
Mt 12: 20 A bruised reed he will not **b**,
Ac 20: 7 week we came together to **b** bread.
1Co 10: 16 the bread that we **b** a participation
Rev 5: 2 "Who is worthy to **b** the seals

BREAKERS* (BREAK)
Ps 42: 7 waves and **b** have swept over me.
93: 4 mightier than the **b** of the sea—
Jnh 2: 3 your waves and **b** swept over me.

BREAKING (BREAK)
Jos 9: 20 fall on us for **b** the oath we swore
Eze 16: 59 my oath by **b** the covenant.
17: 18 the oath by **b** the covenant.
Ac 2: 42 to the **b** of bread and to prayer.
Jas 2: 10 just one point is guilty of **b** all of it.

BREAKS (BREAK)
Jer 23: 29 "and like a hammer that **b** a rock
1Jn 3: 4 Everyone who sins **b** the law;

BREASTPIECE (BREASTPLATE)
Ex 28: 15 a **b** for making decisions—

BREASTPLATE* (BREASTPIECE)
2Ch 18: 33 hit the king of Israel between the **b**
Isa 59: 17 He put on righteousness as his **b**,
Eph 6: 14 the **b** of righteousness in place,
1Th 5: 8 putting on faith and love as a **b**,

BREASTS
La 4: 3 Even jackals offer their **b** to nurse

BREATH (BREATHED GOD-BREATHED)
Ge 2: 7 into his nostrils the **b** of life,

BREATHED (BREATH)
Ge 2: 7 **b** into his nostrils the breath of life,
Mk 15: 37 With a loud cry, Jesus **b** his last.
Jn 20: 22 with that he **b** on them and said,

BRIBE
Ex 23: 8 "Do not accept a **b**, for a **b** blinds
Dt 16: 19 Do not accept a **b**, for a **b** blinds
27: 25 "Cursed is anyone who accepts a **b**
Pr 6: 35 he will refuse a **b**, however great it

BRIDE
Isa 62: 5 as a bridegroom rejoices over his **b**,
Rev 19: 7 and his **b** has made herself ready.
21: 2 prepared as a **b** beautifully dressed
21: 9 I will show you the **b**, the wife
22: 17 The Spirit and the **b** say, "Come!"

BRIDEGROOM
Ps 19: 5 It is like a **b** coming out of his
Mt 25: 1 lamps and went out to meet the **b**.
25: 5 The **b** was a long time in coming,

BRIGHTENS* (BRIGHTNESS)
Pr 16: 15 When a king's face **b**, it means life;
Ecc 8: 1 A person's wisdom **b** their face

BRIGHTER (BRIGHTNESS)
Pr 4: 18 shining ever **b** till the full light

BRIGHTNESS* (BRIGHTENS BRIGHTER)
2Sa 22: 13 Out of the **b** of his presence bolts
23: 4 the **b** after rain that brings grass
Ps 18: 12 Out of the **b** of his presence clouds
Isa 59: 9 for **b**, but we walk in deep
60: 3 and kings to the **b** of your dawn.
60: 19 nor will the **b** of the moon shine
Da 12: 3 who are wise will shine like the **b**
Am 5: 20 pitch-dark, without a ray of **b**?

BRILLIANCE* (BRILLIANT)
Ac 22: 11 because the **b** of the light had
Rev 1: 16 was like the sun shining in all its **b**.
21: 11 **b** was like that of a very precious

BRILLIANT* (BRILLIANCE)
Ecc 9: 11 or wealth to the **b** or favor
Eze 1: 4 and surrounded by **b** light.
1: 27 and **b** light surrounded him.

BRITTLE*
Da 2: 42 will be partly strong and partly **b**.

BROAD
Mt 7: 13 gate and **b** is the road that leads

BROKE (BREAK)
Mt 26: 26 he **b** it and gave it to his disciples,
Mk 14: 22 he **b** it and gave it to his disciples,
Ac 2: 46 They **b** bread in their homes and
20: 11 he went upstairs again and **b** bread
1Co 11: 24 had given thanks, he **b** it and said,

BROKEN (BREAK)
1Sa 2: 10 who oppose the LORD will be **b**.
Ps 34: 20 bones, not one of them will be **b**.
51: 17 My sacrifice, O God, is a **b** spirit;
Ecc 4: 12 of three strands is not quickly **b**.
Lk 20: 18 on that stone will be **b** to pieces;
Jn 7: 23 that the law of Moses may not be **b**,
19: 36 "Not one of his bones will be **b**,"
Ro 11: 20 they were **b** off because of unbelief,

BROKENHEARTED* (HEART)
Ps 34: 18 The LORD is close to the **b**
109: 16 the poor and the needy and the **b**.
147: 3 He heals the **b** and binds up their
Isa 61: 1 He has sent me to bind up the **b**,

BROKENNESS* (BREAK)
Isa 65: 14 of heart and wail in **b** of spirit.

BRONZE
Ex 27: 2 piece, and overlay the altar with **b**.
30: 18 "Make a **b** basin, with its **b** stand,
Nu 21: 9 Moses made a **b** snake and put it
Da 2: 32 of silver, its belly and thighs of **b**,
10: 6 legs like the gleam of burnished **b**,
Rev 1: 15 His feet were like **b** glowing
2: 18 whose feet are like burnished **b**.

BROTHER (BROTHER'S BROTHERLY BROTHERS)
Pr 17: 17 a **b** is born for a time of adversity.
18: 24 a friend who sticks closer than a **b**.
Mt 18: 15 "If your **b** or sister sins,
Mk 3: 35 Whoever does God's will is my **b**
Lk 17: 3 "If your **b** or sister sins against you,
Ro 14: 13 obstacle in the way of a **b** or sister.
14: 15 If your **b** or sister is distressed
14: 21 anything else that will cause your **b**
1Co 7: 15 The **b** or the sister is not bound
8: 13 if what I eat causes my **b** or sister
Phm : 16 but better than a slave, as a dear **b**.
Jas 2: 15 Suppose a **b** or a sister is without
4: 11 Anyone who speaks against a **b**
1Jn 2: 9 but hates a **b** or sister is still
2: 10 who loves their **b** and sister lives
3: 10 does not love their **b** and sister.
3: 15 hates a **b** or sister is a murderer,
3: 17 sees a **b** or sister in need but has
4: 20 claims to love God yet hates a **b**
4: 20 For whoever does not love their **b**
5: 16 If you see any **b** or sister commit

BROTHER'S (BROTHER)
Ge 4: 9 "Am I my **b** keeper?"

BROTHERS (BROTHER)
Mt 12: 49 "Here are my mother and my **b**.
19: 29 everyone who has left houses or **b**
25: 40 did for one of the least of these **b**
Mk 3: 33 "Who are my mother and my **b**?"
10: 29 "no one who has left home or **b**
Lk 21: 16 even by parents, **b** and sisters,
22: 32 turned back, strengthen your **b**."
Jn 7: 5 For even his own **b** did not believe
1Th 4: 10 urge you, **b** and sisters, to do so
2Th 3: 6 we command you, **b** and sisters,
Heb 2: 11 Jesus is not ashamed to call them **b**
13: 1 Keep on loving one another as **b**
Rev 12: 10 the accuser of our **b** and sisters,

BROW
Ge 3: 19 your **b** you will eat your food until

BRUISED (BRUISES)
Isa 42: 3 A **b** reed he will not break,
Mt 12: 20 A **b** reed he will not break,

BRUISES* (BRUISED)
Pr 23: 29 Who has needless **b**? Who has
Isa 30: 26 LORD binds up the **b** of his people

BRUTAL (BRUTE)
2Ti 3: 3 without self-control, **b**, not lovers

BRUTE* (BRUTAL)
Ps 73: 22 I was a **b** beast before you.
Pr 30: 2 Surely I am only a **b**, not a man;

BUBBLING*
Isa 35: 7 pool, the thirsty ground **b** springs.

BUCKET*
Isa 40: 15 the nations are like a drop in a **b**;

BUCKLED*
Eph 6: 14 belt of truth **b** around your waist,

BUD (BUDDED)
Isa 27: 6 Israel will **b** and blossom and fill

BUDDED (BUD)
Heb 9: 4 Aaron's staff that had **b**,

BUILD (BUILDER BUILDERS BUILDING BUILDS BUILT REBUILD REBUILT)
2Sa 7: 5 Are you the one to **b** me a house
1Ki 6: 1 he began to **b** the temple
Ecc 3: 3 time to tear down and a time to **b**,
Mt 16: 18 on this rock I will **b** my church,
Ac 20: 32 which can **b** you up and give you
Ro 15: 2 for their good, to **b** them up.
1Co 3: 10 But each one should **b** with care.
14: 12 excel in those that **b** up the church.
1Th 5: 11 one another and **b** each other up,

BUILDER (BUILD)
Isa 62: 5 so will your **B** marry you;
1Co 3: 10 I laid a foundation as a wise **b**,
Heb 3: 3 just as the **b** of a house has greater
3: 4 but God is the **b** of everything.
11: 10 whose architect and **b** is God.

BUILDERS (BUILD)
Ps 118: 22 The stone the **b** rejected has
Mt 21: 42 "'The stone the **b** rejected has
Mk 12: 10 "'The stone the **b** rejected has
Lk 20: 17 "'The stone the **b** rejected has
Ac 4: 11 is "'the stone you **b** rejected,
1Pe 2: 7 "The stone the **b** rejected has

BUILDING (BUILD)
Ezr 3: 8 to supervise the **b** of the house
Ne 4: 17 who were **b** the wall.
Ro 15: 20 I would not be **b** on someone else's
1Co 3: 9 you are God's field, God's **b**.
2Co 5: 1 destroyed, we have a **b** from God,
10: 8 authority the Lord gave us for **b**
13: 10 the Lord gave me for **b** you up,
Eph 2: 21 him the whole **b** is joined together
4: 29 only what is helpful for **b** others
Jude : 20 by **b** yourselves up in your most

BUILDS (BUILD)
Ps 127: 1 Unless the LORD **b** the house,
Pr 14: 1 The wise woman **b** her house,
1Co 3: 12 If anyone **b** on this foundation
8: 1 puffs up while love **b** up.
Eph 4: 16 grows and **b** itself up in love,

BUILT (BUILD)
1Ki 6: 14 So Solomon **b** the temple
Mt 7: 24 is like a wise man who **b** his house
Lk 6: 49 is like a man who **b** a house
Ac 17: 24 live in temples **b** by human hands.
1Co 3: 14 If what has been **b** survives,
14: 26 so that the church may be **b** up.
2Co 5: 1 in heaven, not **b** by human hands.
Eph 2: 20 **b** on the foundation of the apostles
4: 12 that the body of Christ may be **b**
Col 2: 7 rooted and **b** up in him,
1Pe 2: 5 are being **b** into a spiritual house

BULL (BULLS)
Lev 4: 3 LORD a young **b** without defect as

BULLS (BULL)
1Ki 7: 25 The Sea stood on twelve **b**,
Heb 10: 4 It is impossible for the blood of **b**

BURDEN (BURDENED BURDENS BURDENSOME)
Ps 38: 4 overwhelmed me like a **b** too heavy
Ecc 1: 13 What a heavy **b** God has laid
Mt 11: 30 my yoke is easy and my **b** is light."
Ac 15: 28 to us not to **b** you with anything
2Co 11: 9 kept myself from being a **b** to you
12: 14 and I will not be a **b** to you,
1Th 2: 9 be a **b** to anyone while we preached
2Th 3: 8 so that we would not be a **b** to any
Heb 13: 17 joy, not a **b**, for that would be of no

BURDENED* (BURDEN)
Isa 43: 23 I have not **b** you with grain
43: 24 But you have **b** me with your sins
Mic 6: 3 How have I **b** you? Answer me.
Mt 11: 28 all you who are weary and **b**, and I
2Co 5: 4 we groan and are **b**, because we do
Gal 5: 1 do not let yourselves be **b** again
1Ti 5: 16 not let the church be **b** with them,

BURDENS (BURDEN)
Ps 68: 19 our Savior, who daily bears our **b**.
Lk 11: 46 down with **b** they can hardly carry,
Gal 6: 2 Carry each other's **b**, and in this

BURDENSOME (BURDEN)
1Jn 5: 3 And his commands are not **b**,

BURIED (BURY)
Ru 1: 17 die I will die, and there I will be **b**.
Ro 6: 4 We were therefore **b** with him
1Co 15: 4 that he was **b**, that he was raised
Col 2: 12 been **b** with him in baptism,

BURN (BURNING BURNT)
Dt 7: 5 poles and **b** their idols in the fire.
Ps 79: 5 long will your jealousy **b** like fire?
1Co 7: 9 to marry than to **b** with passion.

BURNING (BURN)
Ex 27: 20 so that the lamps may be kept **b**.
Lev 6: 9 the fire must be kept **b** on the altar.
Ps 18: 28 You, LORD, keep my lamp **b**;
Pr 25: 22 you will heap **b** coals on his head,
Ro 12: 20 you will heap **b** coals on his head."
Rev 19: 20 alive into the fiery lake of **b** sulfur.

BURNISHED*
1Ki 7: 45 of the LORD were of **b** bronze.
Eze 1: 7 of a calf and gleamed like **b** bronze.
Da 10: 6 and legs like the gleam of **b** bronze,
Rev 2: 18 and whose feet are like **b** bronze.

BURNT (BURN)
Ge 8: 20 he sacrificed **b** offerings on it.
22: 2 Sacrifice him there as a **b** offering
Ex 10: 25 **b** offerings to present to the LORD
18: 12 brought a **b** offering and other
40: 6 "Place the altar of **b** offering
Lev 1: 3 the offering is a **b** offering
Jos 8: 31 offered to the LORD **b** offerings
Jdg 6: 26 the second bull as a **b** offering."
13: 16 But if you prepare a **b** offering,
1Ki 3: 4 offered a thousand **b** offerings
9: 25 year Solomon sacrificed **b** offerings
10: 5 and the **b** offerings he made
Ezr 3: 2 Israel to sacrifice **b** offerings on it,
Eze 43: 18 for sacrificing **b** offerings

BURST
Ps 98: 4 **b** into jubilant song with music;
Isa 44: 23 **B** into song, you mountains,
49: 13 **b** into song, you mountains!
52: 9 **B** into songs of joy together,
54: 1 **b** into song, shout for joy, you who
55: 12 hills will **b** into song before you,

BURY (BURIED)
Mt 8: 22 and let the dead **b** their own dead."
Lk 9: 60 "Let the dead **b** their own dead,

BUSH
Ex 3: 2 in flames of fire from within a **b**.
3: 2 though the **b** was on fire it did not
Mk 12: 26 in the account of the burning **b**,
Lk 20: 37 in the account of the burning **b**,
Ac 7: 35 who appeared to him in the **b**.

BUSINESS
Ecc 4: 8 too is meaningless—a miserable **b**!
Da 8: 27 got up and went about the king's **b**.
1Co 5: 12 What **b** is it of mine to judge those
1Th 4: 11 You should mind your own **b**
Jas 1: 11 even while they go about their **b**.

BUSY*
1Ki 18: 27 deep in thought, or **b**, or traveling.
20: 40 While your servant was **b** here
Hag 1: 9 of you is **b** with your own house.
2Th 3: 11 are not **b**; they are busybodies.
Titus 2: 5 pure, to be **b** at home, to be kind,

BUSYBODIES*
2Th 3: 11 They are not busy; they are **b**.
1Ti 5: 13 but also **b** who talk nonsense,

BUY (BOUGHT BUYS)
Pr 23: 23 **B** the truth and do not sell it—
Isa 55: 1 have no money, come, **b** and eat!
Rev 13: 17 so that they could not **b** or sell

BUYS (BUY)
Pr 31: 16 She considers a field and **b** it;

BYWORD (WORD)
1Ki 9: 7 a **b** and an object of ridicule
Ps 44: 14 made us a **b** among the nations;
Joel 2: 17 of scorn, a **b** among the nations.

CAESAR
Mt 22: 21 give back to **C** what is Caesar's,

CAIN
Firstborn of Adam (Ge 4:1), murdered brother Abel (Ge 4:1–16; 1Jn 3:12).

CALAMITIES (CALAMITY)
Dt 31: 17 disasters and **c** will come on them,
31: 21 disasters and **c** come on them,

CALAMITY (CALAMITIES)
Pr 22: 8 Whoever sows injustice reaps **c**,

CALEB
Judahite who spied out Canaan (Nu 13:6); allowed to enter land because of faith (Nu 13:30–14:38; Dt 1:36). Possessed Hebron (Jos 14:6–15:19).

CALF
Ex 32: 4 into an idol cast in the shape of a **c**,
Pr 15: 17 love than a fattened **c** with hatred.
Lk 15: 23 Bring the fattened **c** and kill it.
Ac 7: 41 made an idol in the form of a **c**.

CALL (CALLED CALLING CALLS)
Ex 3: 15 the name you shall **c** me
1Ki 18: 24 you **c** on the name of your god,
18: 24 will **c** on the name of the LORD.
2Ki 5: 11 **c** on the name of the LORD his
Ps 116: 13 and **c** on the name of the LORD.
116: 17 and **c** on the name of the LORD.
145: 18 LORD is near to all who **c** on him,
Pr 31: 28 children arise and **c** her blessed;
Isa 5: 20 Woe to those who **c** evil good
55: 6 **c** on him while he is near.
65: 24 Before they **c** I will answer;
Jer 33: 3 '**C** to me and I will answer you
Zep 3: 9 all of them may **c** on the name
Zec 13: 9 They will **c** on my name and I will
Mt 9: 13 I have not come to **c** the righteous,
Mk 2: 17 I have not come to **c** the righteous,
Lk 5: 32 I have not come to **c** the righteous,
Ac 2: 39 all whom the Lord our God will **c**."
9: 14 to arrest all who **c** on your name."
9: 21 in Jerusalem among those who **c**
Ro 10: 12 richly blesses all who **c** on him,
11: 29 gifts and his **c** are irrevocable.
1Co 1: 2 all those everywhere who **c**
1Th 4: 7 For God did not **c** us to be impure,
2Ti 2: 22 with those who **c** on the Lord

CALLED (CALL)
Ge 2: 23 she shall be **c** 'woman,' for she was
12: 8 and **c** on the name of the LORD.
21: 33 and there he **c** on the name
26: 25 and **c** on the name of the LORD.
1Sa 3: 5 and said, "Here I am; you **c** me."
2Ch 7: 14 my people, who are **c** by my name,
Ps 34: 6 This poor man **c**, and the LORD
116: 4 I **c** on the name of the LORD:
Isa 56: 7 for my house will be **c** a house
La 3: 55 I **c** on your name, LORD,
Hos 11: 1 him, and out of Egypt I **c** my son.
Mt 1: 16 of Jesus who is **c** the Messiah.
2: 15 "Out of Egypt I **c** my son."
21: 13 "'My house will be **c** a house
Mk 11: 17 'My house will be **c** a house
Lk 1: 32 will be **c** the Son of the Most High.
1: 35 be born will be **c** the Son of God.
Ro 1: 1 **c** to be an apostle and set apart
1: 6 among those Gentiles who are **c**
1: 7 by God and **c** to be his holy people:
8: 28 who have been **c** according to his
Ro 8: 30 those he predestined, he also **c**;
those he **c**, he also justified;
1Co 1: 1 **c** to be an apostle of Christ Jesus
1: 2 Jesus and **c** to be his holy people,
1: 24 but to those whom God has **c**,
1: 26 of what you were when you were **c**.
7: 15 God has **c** us to live in peace.
7: 17 to them, just as God has **c** them.
Gal 1: 6 deserting the one who **c** you
1: 15 womb and **c** me by his grace,
5: 13 and sisters, were **c** to be free.
Eph 1: 18 the hope to which he has **c** you,
4: 4 just as you were **c** to one hope
Col 3: 15 of one body you were **c** to peace.
2Th 2: 14 **c** you to this through our gospel,
1Ti 6: 12 you were **c** when you made your
2Ti 1: 9 saved us and **c** us to a holy life—
Heb 9: 15 that those who are **c** may receive
1Pe 1: 15 But just as he who **c** you is holy,
2: 9 the praises of him who **c** you
3: 9 to this you were **c** so that you may
5: 10 who **c** you to his eternal glory
2Pe 1: 3 of him who **c** us by his own glory
Jude : 1 To those who have been **c**, who are

CALLING (CALL)
Isa 40: 3 A voice of one **c**:
Mt 3: 3 "A voice of one **c** in the wilderness,
Mk 1: 3 "a voice of one **c** in the wilderness,
10: 49 On your feet! He's **c** you."
Lk 3: 4 "A voice of one **c** in the wilderness,
Jn 1: 23 voice of one **c** in the wilderness,
Ac 22: 16 your sins away, **c** on his name.'
Eph 4: 1 worthy of the **c** you have received.
2Th 1: 11 may make you worthy of his **c**,
2Pe 1: 10 every effort to confirm your **c**

CALLOUS* (CALLOUSED)
Ps 17: 10 They close up their **c** hearts,
73: 7 From their **c** hearts comes iniquity;
119: 70 Their hearts are **c** and unfeeling,

CALLOUSED* (CALLOUS)
Isa 6: 10 Make the heart of this people **c**;
Mt 13: 15 this people's heart has become **c**;
Ac 28: 27 this people's heart has become **c**;

CALLS (CALL)
Ps 147: 4 the stars and **c** them each by name.
Isa 40: 26 and **c** forth each of them by name.
Joel 2: 32 everyone who **c** on the name
Mt 22: 43 by the Spirit, **c** him 'Lord'?
Jn 10: 3 He **c** his own sheep by name
Ac 2: 21 everyone who **c** on the name
Ro 10: 13 "Everyone who **c** on the name
1Th 2: 12 who **c** you into his kingdom
5: 24 The one who **c** you is faithful,

CALM (CALMS)
Ps 107: 30 They were glad when it grew **c**,
Pr 29: 11 but the wise bring **c** in the end.
Isa 7: 4 careful, keep **c** and don't be afraid.
Eze 16: 42 I will be **c** and no longer angry.

CALMS* (CALM)
Pr 15: 18 one who is patient **c** a quarrel.

CAMEL
Mt 19: 24 easier for a **c** to go through the eye
23: 24 strain out a gnat but swallow a **c**.
Mk 10: 25 easier for a **c** to go through the eye
Lk 18: 25 easier for a **c** to go through the eye

CAMP (ENCAMPS)
Heb 13: 13 go to him outside the **c**,

CANAAN (CANAANITE CANAANITES)
Ge 10: 15 **C** was the father of Sidon his
Lev 14: 34 "When you enter the land of **C**,
25: 38 of Egypt to give you the land of **C**
Nu 13: 2 some men to explore the land of **C**,
33: 51 'When you cross the Jordan into **C**,
Jdg 4: 2 into the hands of Jabin king of **C**,
1Ch 16: 18 **C** as the portion you will inherit."
Ps 105: 11 **C** as the portion you will inherit."
Ac 13: 19 he overthrew seven nations in **C**,

CANAANITE (CANAAN)
Ge 10: 18 Later the **C** clans scattered
28: 1 "Do not marry a **C** woman.
Jos 5: 1 the **C** kings along the coast heard
Jdg 1: 32 lived among the **C** inhabitants

CANAANITES (CANAAN)
Ex 33: 2 before you and drive out the **C**,

CANCEL (CANCELED)
Dt 15: 1 every seven years you must **c** debts.

CANCELED* (CANCEL)
Mt 18: 27 on him, **c** the debt and let him go.
18: 32 'I **c** all that debt of yours because
Col 2: 14 having **c** the charge of our legal

CANDLESTICKS See LAMPSTANDS

CANOPY*
2Sa 22: 12 made darkness his **c** around him—
2Ki 16: 18 He took away the Sabbath **c**
Ps 18: 11 his covering, his **c** around him—
Isa 4: 5 everything the glory will be a **c**.
40: 22 stretches out the heavens like a **c**,
Jer 43: 10 he will spread his royal **c**

CAPERNAUM
Mt 4: 13 he went and lived in **C**, which was
Jn 6: 59 teaching in the synagogue in **C**.

CAPITAL
Dt 21: 22 someone guilty of a **c** offense is put

CAPSTONE* (STONE)
Zec 4: 7 he will bring out the **c** to shouts
4: 10 rejoice when they see the chosen **c**

CAPTIVATE* (CAPTIVE)
Pr 6: 25 or let her **c** you with her eyes.

CAPTIVE (CAPTIVATE CAPTIVES CAPTIVITY CAPTURED)
Ac 8: 23 are full of bitterness and **c** to sin."
2Co 10: 5 we take **c** every thought to make it
Col 2: 8 no one takes you **c** through hollow
2Ti 2: 26 has taken them **c** to do his will.

CAPTIVES (CAPTIVE)
Ps 68: 18 on high, you took many **c**;
Isa 61: 1 to proclaim freedom for the **c**
Eph 4: 8 he took many **c** and gave gifts to

CAPTIVITY (CAPTIVE)
Dt 28: 41 them, because they will go into **c**.
2Ki 25: 21 So Judah went into **c**,
Jer 30: 3 Judah back from **c** and restore
52: 27 So Judah went into **c**,
Eze 29: 14 I will bring them back from **c**

CAPTURED (CAPTIVE)
1Sa 4: 11 The ark of God was **c**, and Eli's two
2Sa 5: 7 David **c** the fortress of Zion—
2Ki 17: 6 the king of Assyria **c** Samaria

CARCASS
Jdg 14: 9 taken the honey from the lion's **c**.
Mt 24: 28 Wherever there is a **c**,

CARE (CAREFUL CAREFULLY CARES CARING)
Ps 8: 4 human beings that you **c** for them?
43: 3 me your light and your faithful **c**,
65: 9 You **c** for the land and water it;
144: 3 human beings that you **c** for them,
Pr 12: 10 The righteous **c** for the needs
29: 7 The righteous **c** about justice
Mk 5: 26 suffered a great deal under the **c**
Lk 10: 34 him to an inn and took **c** of him.
18: 4 fear God or **c** what people think,
Jn 21: 16 Jesus said, "Take **c** of my sheep."
1Co 3: 10 But each one should build with **c**.
Eph 5: 29 but they feed and **c** for their body,
1Ti 3: 5 family, how can he take **c** of God's
6: 20 what has been entrusted to your **c**.
Heb 2: 6 a son of man that you **c** for him?
1Pe 5: 2 of God's flock that is under your **c**,

CAREFUL* (CARE)
Ge 31: 24 "Be **c** not to say anything to Jacob,
31: 29 'Be **c** not to say anything to Jacob,
Ex 19: 12 'Be **c** that you do not approach
23: 13 "Be **c** to do everything I have said
34: 12 Be **c** not to make a treaty with
34: 15 "Be **c** not to make a treaty
Lev 18: 4 laws and be **c** to follow my decrees.
25: 18 decrees and be **c** to obey my laws,
26: 3 and are **c** to obey my commands,
Dt 2: 4 will be afraid of you, but be very **c**.
4: 9 Only be **c**, and watch yourselves
4: 23 Be **c** not to forget the covenant
5: 32 So be **c** to do what the LORD your
6: 3 be **c** to obey so that it may go well
6: 12 be **c** that you do not forget
6: 25 we are **c** to obey all this law before
7: 12 laws and are **c** to follow them,
8: 1 Be **c** to follow every command
8: 11 Be **c** that you do not forget
11: 16 Be **c**, or you will be enticed to turn
12: 1 laws you must be **c** to follow
12: 13 Be **c** not to sacrifice your burnt
12: 19 Be **c** not to neglect the Levites as

Dt 12: 28 Be **c** to obey all these regulations I
12: 30 **c** not to be ensnared by inquiring
15: 5 are **c** to follow all these commands
15: 9 Be **c** not to harbor this wicked
17: 10 Be **c** to do everything they instruct
24: 8 be very **c** to do exactly as
Jos 1: 7 Be **c** to obey all the law my servant
1: 8 that you may be **c** to do everything
22: 5 very **c** to keep the commandment
23: 6 be **c** to obey all that is written
23: 11 So be very **c** to love the LORD
1Ki 8: 25 if only your descendants are **c** in all
2Ki 10: 31 Yet Jehu was not **c** to keep the law
17: 37 You must always be **c** to keep
21: 8 only they will be **c** to do everything
1Ch 22: 13 if you are **c** to observe the decrees
28: 8 Be **c** to follow all the commands
2Ch 6: 16 if only your descendants are **c** in all
33: 8 only they will be **c** to do everything
Ezr 4: 22 Be **c** not to neglect this matter.
Job 36: 18 Be **c** that no one entices you
Ps 45: 10 daughter, and pay **c** attention:
101: 2 I will be **c** to lead a blameless life—
Pr 4: 26 Give **c** thought to the paths for
13: 24 one who loves their children is **c**
21: 28 a **c** listener will testify successfully.
27: 23 give **c** attention to your herds;
Isa 7: 4 him, 'Be **c**, keep calm and don't be
Jer 17: 21 Be **c** not to carry a load
17: 24 But if you are **c** to obey me,
22: 4 For if you are **c** to carry out these
Eze 11: 20 decrees and be **c** to keep my laws.
18: 19 has been **c** to keep all my decrees,
20: 19 decrees and be **c** to keep my laws.
20: 21 they were not **c** to keep my laws,
36: 27 decrees and be **c** to keep my laws.
37: 24 laws and be **c** to keep my decrees.
Hag 1: 5 "Give **c** thought to your ways.
1: 7 "Give **c** thought to your ways.
2: 15 "'Now give **c** thought to this
2: 18 give **c** thought to the day
2: 18 temple was laid. Give **c** thought:
Mt 6: 1 "Be **c** not to practice your
16: 6 "Be **c**," Jesus said to them.
23: 3 So you must be **c** to do everything
Mk 8: 15 "Be **c**," Jesus warned them.
Lk 21: 34 "Be **c**, or your hearts will be
Ro 12: 17 Be **c** to do what is right in the eyes
1Co 8: 9 Be **c**, however, that the exercise
10: 12 firm, be **c** that you don't fall!
Eph 5: 15 Be very **c**, then, how you live—
2Ti 4: 2 great patience and **c** instruction.
Titus 3: 8 God may be **c** to devote themselves
Heb 2: 1 We must pay the most **c** attention,
4: 1 be **c** that none of you be found

CAREFULLY (CARE)
Pr 12: 26 righteous choose their friends **c**,
Mt 2: 8 "Go and search **c** for the child.

CARES* (CARE)
Dt 11: 12 a land the LORD your God **c** for;
Job 39: 16 **c** not that her labor was in vain,
Ps 55: 22 Cast your **c** on the LORD and he
142: 4 no one **c** for my life.
Ecc 5: 3 comes when there are many **c**,
Jer 12: 11 because there is no one who **c**.
30: 17 outcast, Zion for whom no one **c**.'
Na 1: 7 He **c** for those who trust in him,
Jn 10: 13 hand and **c** nothing for the sheep.
1Th 2: 7 Just as a nursing mother **c** for her
1Pe 5: 7 on him because he **c** for you.

CARING* (CARE)
1Ti 5: 4 practice by **c** for their own family

CAROUSING*
Lk 21: 34 will be weighed down with **c**,
Ro 13: 13 daytime, not in **c** and drunkenness,
1Pe 4: 3 orgies, **c** and detestable idolatry.

CARPENTER (CARPENTER'S)
Mk 6: 3 Isn't this the **c**? Isn't this Mary's

CARPENTER'S* (CARPENTER)
Mt 13: 55 "Isn't this the **c** son?

CARRIED (CARRY)
Ex 19: 4 and how I **c** you on eagles' wings
Dt 1: 31 how the LORD your God **c** you,
Isa 63: 9 up and **c** them all the days of old.
Heb 13: 9 Do not be **c** away by all kinds
2Pe 1: 21 God as they were **c** along
3: 17 you may not be **c** away by the error

CARRIES (CARRY)
Dt 32: 11 to catch them and **c** them aloft.
Isa 40: 11 arms and **c** them close to his heart;

CARRY (CARRIED CARRIES CARRYING)
Lev 16: 22 The goat will **c** on itself all their
26: 15 and fail to **c** out all my commands
Isa 46: 4 I have made you and I will **c** you;
Lk 14: 27 whoever does not **c** their cross
Gal 6: 2 **C** each other's burdens, and in this
6: 5 each one should **c** their own load.

CARRYING (CARRY)
Jn 19: 17 **C** his own cross, he went
1Jn 5: 2 God and **c** out his commands.

CARVED
Nu 33: 52 Destroy all their **c** images and their

CASE
Pr 22: 23 for the LORD will take up their **c**
23: 11 he will take up their **c** against you.

CAST (CASTING)
Lev 16: 8 He is to **c** lots for the two goats—
Ps 22: 18 them and **c** lots for my garment.
55: 22 **C** your cares on the LORD and he
Pr 16: 33 The lot is **c** into the lap, but its
Jn 19: 24 them and **c** lots for my garment."
1Pe 5: 7 **C** all your anxiety on him because

CASTING (CAST)
Pr 18: 18 **C** the lot settles disputes and keeps
Mt 27: 35 divided up his clothes by **c** lots.

CATCH (CATCHES CAUGHT)
Lk 5: 4 and let down the nets for a **c**."

CATCHES (CATCH)
Job 5: 13 He **c** the wise in their craftiness,
1Co 3: 19 "He **c** the wise in their craftiness";

CATTLE
Ps 50: 10 and the **c** on a thousand hills.

CAUGHT (CATCH)
Ge 22: 13 in a thicket he saw a ram **c** by its
2Co 12: 2 who fourteen years ago was **c** up
1Th 4: 17 are left will be **c** up together

CAUSE (CAUSES)
Ps 7: 16 The trouble they **c** recoils on them;
25: 3 who are treacherous without **c**.
Ps 82: 3 uphold the **c** of the poor
Pr 24: 28 against your neighbor without **c**—
Ecc 8: 3 Do not stand up for a bad **c**, for he
Mt 18: 7 the things that **c** people to stumble!
Ro 14: 21 that will **c** your brother or sister
1Co 10: 32 Do not **c** anyone to stumble,

CAUSES (CAUSE)
Isa 8: 14 he will be a stone that **c** people
Mt 5: 29 If your right eye **c** you to stumble,
5: 30 if your right hand **c** you to stumble,
18: 6 "If anyone **c** one of these little
18: 8 hand or your foot **c** you to stumble,
Ro 14: 20 eat anything that **c** someone else
1Co 8: 13 if what I eat **c** my brother or sister
1Pe 2: 8 "A stone that **c** people to stumble

CEASE
Ps 46: 9 He makes wars **c** to the ends

CELEBRATE*
Ex 10: 9 because we are to **c** a festival
12: 14 to come you shall **c** it as a festival
12: 17 "**C** the Festival of Unleavened
12: 17 **C** this day as a lasting ordinance
12: 47 community of Israel must **c** it.
12: 48 **c** the LORD's Passover must have
23: 14 times a year you are to **c** a festival
23: 15 "**C** the Festival of Unleavened
23: 16 "**C** the Festival of Harvest
23: 16 "**C** the Festival of Ingathering
34: 18 "**C** the Festival of Unleavened
34: 22 "**C** the Festival of Weeks
Lev 23: 39 **c** the festival to the LORD
23: 41 **C** this as a festival to the LORD
23: 41 **c** it in the seventh month.
Nu 9: 2 "Have the Israelites **c** the Passover
9: 3 **C** it at the appointed time,
9: 4 told the Israelites to **c** the Passover,
9: 6 of them could not **c** the Passover
9: 10 are still to **c** the LORD's Passover,
9: 12 When they **c** the Passover,
9: 13 on a journey fails to **c** the Passover,
9: 14 also to **c** the LORD's Passover
29: 12 **C** a festival to the LORD for seven
Dt 16: 1 **c** the Passover of the LORD your
16: 10 Then **c** the Festival of Weeks
16: 13 **C** the Festival of Tabernacles
16: 15 For seven days **c** the festival
Jdg 16: 23 to Dagon their god and to **c**,
2Sa 6: 21 I will **c** before the LORD.
2Ki 23: 21 "**C** the Passover to the LORD
2Ch 30: 1 and **c** the Passover to the LORD,
30: 2 decided to **c** the Passover
30: 3 They had not been able to **c** it
30: 5 and **c** the Passover to the LORD,
30: 13 in Jerusalem to **c** the Festival
30: 23 to **c** the festival seven more days;
Ne 8: 12 of food and to **c** with great joy,
12: 27 to **c** joyfully the dedication
Est 9: 21 them **c** annually the fourteenth
Ps 2: 11 fear and **c** his rule with trembling.
89: 16 they **c** your righteousness.
145: 7 They **c** your abundant goodness
Isa 30: 29 on the night you **c** a holy festival;
Hos 5: 7 they **c** their New Moon feasts,
Na 1: 15 **C** your festivals, Judah, and fulfill
Zec 14: 16 to **c** the Festival of Tabernacles.
14: 18 up to **c** the Festival of Tabernacles.
14: 19 up to **c** the Festival of Tabernacles.
Mt 26: 18 I am going to **c** the Passover
Lk 15: 23 and kill it. Let's have a feast and **c**.
15: 24 and is found.' So they began to **c**.
15: 29 me even a young goat so I could **c**
15: 32 But we had to **c** and be glad,
Rev 11: 10 will **c** by sending each other gifts,

CELESTIAL*
2Pe 2: 10 afraid to heap abuse on **c** beings;
Jude : 8 and heap abuse on **c** beings.

CENSER (CENSERS)
Lev 16: 12 is to take a **c** full of burning coals
Rev 8: 3 had a golden **c**, came and stood

CENSERS (CENSER)
Nu 16: 6 followers are to do this: Take **c**

CENTURION
Mt 8: 5 Capernaum, a **c** came to him,
27: 54 When the **c** and those with him
Mk 15: 39 And when the **c**, who stood there
Lk 7: 3 The **c** heard of Jesus and sent some
23: 47 The **c**, seeing what had happened,
Ac 10: 1 **c** in what was known as the Italian
27: 1 handed over to a **c** named Julius,

CEPHAS* (PETER)
Jn 1: 42 You will be called **C**" (which,
1Co 1: 12 another, "I follow **C**";
3: 22 Paul or Apollos or **C** or the world
9: 5 and the Lord's brothers and **C**?
Gal 2: 9 James, **C** and John, those esteemed

CEREMONIAL* (CEREMONY)
Lev 14: 2 at the time of their **c** cleansing,
15: 13 off seven days for his **c** cleansing;
Mk 7: 3 they give their hands a **c** washing,
Jn 2: 6 used by the Jews for **c** washing,
3: 25 Jew over the matter of **c** washing.
11: 55 for their **c** cleansing before
18: 28 to avoid **c** uncleanness they did not
Heb 9: 10 drink and various **c** washings—
13: 9 not by eating **c** foods, which is of

CEREMONIALLY* (CEREMONY)
Lev 4: 12 outside the camp to a place **c** clean,
5: 2 touch anything **c** unclean (whether
6: 11 the camp to a place that is **c** clean.
7: 19 touches anything **c** unclean must
7: 19 meat, anyone **c** clean may eat it.
10: 14 Eat them in a **c** clean place;
11: 4 it is **c** unclean for you.
12: 2 to a son will be **c** unclean for seven
12: 7 she will be **c** clean from her flow
13: 3 shall pronounce them **c** unclean.
14: 8 then they will be **c** clean.
15: 28 and after that she will be **c** clean.
15: 33 with a woman who is **c** unclean.
17: 15 they will be **c** unclean till evening;
21: 1 must not make himself **c** unclean
22: 3 of your descendants is **c** unclean
27: 11 they vowed is a **c** unclean animal—
Nu 5: 2 who is **c** unclean because of a dead
6: 7 not make themselves **c** unclean
8: 6 Israelites and make them **c** clean.
9: 6 day because they were **c** unclean
9: 13 if anyone who is **c** clean and not
18: 11 household who is **c** clean may eat
18: 13 household who is **c** clean may eat
19: 7 he will be **c** unclean till evening.
19: 9 in a **c** clean place outside the camp.
19: 18 a man who is **c** clean is to take
Dt 12: 15 Both the **c** unclean and the clean
12: 22 Both the **c** unclean and the clean
14: 7 they are **c** unclean for you.
15: 22 Both the **c** unclean and the clean

1Sa 20: 26 to David to make him **c** unclean—
2Ch 13: 11 the bread on the **c** clean table
30: 17 for all those who were not **c** clean
Ezr 6: 20 themselves and were all **c** clean.
Ne 12: 30 Levites had purified themselves **c**,
Isa 66: 20 of the LORD in **c** clean vessels.
Eze 22: 10 period, when they are **c** unclean.
Ac 24: 18 I was **c** clean when they found me
Heb 9: 13 those who are **c** unclean sanctify

CEREMONY* (CEREMONIAL CEREMONIALLY)
Ge 50: 11 Egyptians are holding a solemn **c**
Ex 12: 25 you as he promised, observe this **c**.
12: 26 'What does this **c** mean to you?'
13: 5 are to observe this **c** in this month:

CERTAINTY*
Lk 1: 4 you may know the **c** of the things
Jn 17: 8 They knew with **c** that I came

CERTIFICATE* (CERTIFIED)
Dt 24: 1 and he writes her a **c** of divorce,
24: 3 her and writes her a **c** of divorce,
Isa 50: 1 "Where is your mother's **c**
Jer 3: 8 I gave faithless Israel her **c**
Mt 5: 31 divorces his wife must give her a **c**
19: 7 a man give his wife a **c** of divorce
Mk 10: 4 a man to write a **c** of divorce

CERTIFIED* (CERTIFICATE)
Jn 3: 33 Whoever has accepted it has **c**

CHAFF
Ps 1: 4 They are like **c** that the wind blows
35: 5 May they be like **c** before the wind,
Da 2: 35 became like **c** on a threshing floor
Mt 3: 12 up the **c** with unquenchable fire."

CHAINED (CHAINS)
2Ti 2: 9 But God's word is not **c**.

CHAINS (CHAINED)
Eph 6: 20 for which I am an ambassador in **c**.
Col 4: 18 Remember my **c**. Grace be
2Ti 1: 16 me and was not ashamed of my **c**.
Jude : 6 with everlasting **c** for judgment

CHAMPION
1Sa 17: 4 A **c** named Goliath, who was from
Ps 19: 5 like a **c** rejoicing to run his course.

CHANCE
Ecc 9: 11 but time and **c** happen to them all.

CHANGE (CHANGED)
1Sa 15: 29 being, that he should **c** his mind."
Ps 110: 4 has sworn and will not **c** his mind:
Jer 7: 5 If you really **c** your ways and your
Mal 3: 6 "I the LORD do not **c**. So you,
Mt 18: 3 unless you **c** and become like little
Heb 7: 21 has sworn and will not **c** his mind:
Jas 1: 17 lights, who does not **c** like shifting

CHANGED (CHANGE)
1Sa 10: 6 will be **c** into a different person.
Hos 11: 8 My heart is **c** within me;
1Co 15: 51 not all sleep, but we will all be **c**—

CHARACTER*
Ru 3: 11 that you are a woman of noble **c**.
Pr 12: 4 of noble **c** is her husband's crown,
31: 10 A wife of noble **c** who can find?
Ac 17: 11 were of more noble **c** than those
Ro 5: 4 perseverance, **c**; and **c**, hope.
1Co 15: 33 "Bad company corrupts good **c**."

CHARGE (CHARGED CHARGES)
Job 34: 13 Who put him in **c** of the whole
Ro 8: 33 will bring any **c** against those
1Co 9: 18 the gospel I may offer it free of **c**,
2Co 11: 7 the gospel of God to you free of **c**?
2Ti 4: 1 and his kingdom, I give you this **c**:
Phm : 18 or owes you anything, **c** it to me.

CHARGED (CHARGE)
Ro 5: 13 sin is not **c** against anyone's

CHARGES (CHARGE)
Isa 50: 8 Who then will bring **c** against me?

CHARIOT (CHARIOTS)
2Ki 2: 11 suddenly a **c** of fire and horses
Ps 104: 3 makes the clouds his **c** and rides
Ac 8: 28 sitting in his **c** reading the Book

CHARIOTS (CHARIOT)
2Ki 6: 17 and **c** of fire all around Elisha.
Ps 20: 7 trust in **c** and some in horses,
68: 17 The **c** of God are tens of thousands

CHARM* (CHARMING)
Pr 17: 8 A bribe is seen as a **c** by the one
31: 30 **C** is deceptive, and beauty is

CHARMING* (CHARM)
Pr 26: 25 Though their speech is **c**, do not
SS 1: 16 Oh, how **c**! And our bed is verdant.

CHASE
Lev 26: 8 Five of you will **c** a hundred,
Pr 12: 11 who **c** fantasies have no sense.
28: 19 those who **c** fantasies will have

CHASTENS*
Heb 12: 6 and he **c** everyone he accepts as his

CHASM*
Lk 16: 26 you a great **c** has been set in place,

CHATTER* (CHATTERING)
1Ti 6: 20 Turn away from godless **c**
2Ti 2: 16 Avoid godless **c**, because those who

CHATTERING* (CHATTER)
Pr 10: 8 but a **c** fool comes to ruin.
10: 10 grief, and a **c** fool comes to ruin.

CHEAT* (CHEATED CHEATING)
Lev 6: 2 stolen, or if they **c** their neighbor,
Mal 1: 14 "Cursed is the **c** who has
1Co 6: 8 you yourselves **c** and do wrong,

CHEATED* (CHEAT)
Ge 31: 7 yet your father has **c** me
1Sa 12: 3 Whom have I **c**? Whom have I
12: 4 "You have not **c** or oppressed us,"
Lk 19: 8 if I have **c** anybody out of anything,
1Co 6: 7 Why not rather be **c**?

CHEATING* (CHEAT)
Am 8: 5 price and **c** with dishonest scales,

CHEEK (CHEEKS)
Mt 5: 39 anyone slaps you on the right **c**, turn to them the other **c** also.
Lk 6: 29 If someone slaps you on one **c**,

CHEEKS (CHEEK)
Isa 50: 6 my **c** to those who pulled out my

CHEERFUL* (CHEERS)
Pr 15: 13 A happy heart makes the face **c**,
15: 15 the **c** heart has a continual feast.
17: 22 A **c** heart is good medicine,
2Co 9: 7 for God loves a **c** giver.

CHEERS (CHEERFUL)
Pr 12: 25 the heart, but a kind word **c** it up.

CHEMOSH
2Ki 23: 13 for **C** the vile god of Moab,

CHERISHED (CHERISHES)
Ps 66: 18 If I had **c** sin in my heart,

CHERISHES* (CHERISHED)
Pr 19: 8 **c** understanding will soon prosper.

CHERUB (CHERUBIM)
Ex 25: 19 Make one **c** on one end
Eze 28: 14 You were anointed as a guardian **c**,

CHERUBIM (CHERUB)
Ge 3: 24 east side of the Garden of Eden **c**
1Sa 4: 4 who is enthroned between the **c**.
2Sa 6: 2 who is enthroned between the **c**
22: 11 He mounted the **c** and flew;
1Ki 6: 23 inner sanctuary he made a pair of **c**
2Ki 19: 15 enthroned between the **c**, you
1Ch 13: 6 who is enthroned between the **c**—
Ps 18: 10 He mounted the **c** and flew;
80: 1 who sit enthroned between the **c**,
99: 1 he sits enthroned between the **c**,
Isa 37: 16 enthroned between the **c**, you
Eze 10: 1 that was over the heads of the **c**.

CHEST
2Ki 12: 9 Jehoiada the priest took a **c**
Da 2: 32 pure gold, its **c** and arms of silver,
Rev 1: 13 with a golden sash around his **c**.

CHEWS
Lev 11: 3 a divided hoof and that **c** the cud.

CHIEF
1Pe 5: 4 And when the **C** Shepherd appears,

CHILD (CHILDBEARING CHILDBIRTH CHILDHOOD CHILDLESS CHILDREN GRANDCHILDREN)
Pr 22: 15 Folly is bound up in the heart of a **c**,
23: 13 Do not withhold discipline from a **c**;
29: 15 but a **c** left undisciplined disgraces
Isa 9: 6 For to us a **c** is born, to us a son is
11: 6 and a little **c** will lead them.
66: 13 As a mother comforts her **c**, so will
Eze 18: 20 The **c** will not share the guilt
Mt 18: 2 He called a little **c** to him,
Lk 1: 42 and blessed is the **c** you will bear!
1: 80 And the **c** grew and became strong
1Co 13: 11 When I was a **c**, I talked like a **c**,
1Jn 5: 1 loves the father loves his **c** as well.

CHILDBEARING (BEAR CHILD)
Ge 3: 16 make your pains in **c** very severe;
1Ti 2: 15 women will be saved through **c**—
Heb 11: 11 who was past **c** age, was enabled

CHILDBIRTH (BEAR CHILD)
Gal 4: 19 pains of **c** until Christ is formed

CHILDHOOD (CHILD)
1Co 13: 11 I put the ways of **c** behind me.

CHILDLESS (CHILD)
Ge 11: 30 Now Sarai was **c** because she was
29: 31 to conceive, but Rachel remained **c**.
Ps 113: 9 settles the **c** woman in her home

CHILDREN (CHILD)
Ex 20: 5 punishing the **c** for the sin
Dt 4: 9 Teach them to your **c** and to their **c**
6: 7 Impress them on your **c**.
11: 19 Teach them to your **c**,
14: 1 You are the **c** of the LORD your
24: 16 nor **c** put to death for their parents;
30: 19 life, so that you and your **c** may live
32: 46 you may command your **c** to obey
Job 1: 5 "Perhaps my **c** have sinned
Ps 8: 2 Through the praise of **c** and infants
17: 14 may their **c** gorge themselves on it,
78: 5 our ancestors to teach their **c**,
127: 3 **C** are a heritage from the LORD,
Pr 13: 24 spares the rod hates their **c**,
17: 6 parents are the pride of their **c**.
20: 7 blessed are their **c** after them.
20: 11 Even small **c** are known by their
22: 6 Start **c** off on the way they should
29: 17 Discipline your **c**, and they will
31: 28 Her **c** arise and call her blessed;
Isa 54: 13 All your **c** will be taught
Hos 1: 10 they will be called '**c** of the living
Joel 1: 3 Tell it to your **c**, and let your **c** tell it to their **c**,
Mal 4: 6 the hearts of the parents to their **c**,
4: 6 the hearts of the **c** to their parents;
Mt 5: 9 for they will be called **c** of God.
7: 11 how to give good gifts to your **c**,
11: 25 and revealed them to little **c**.
18: 3 change and become like little **c**,
19: 14 said, "Let the little **c** come to me,
21: 16 "'From the lips of **c** and infants
Mk 9: 37 these little **c** in my name welcomes
10: 14 them, "Let the little **c** come to me,
10: 16 And he took the **c** in his arms,
13: 12 **C** will rebel against their parents
Lk 6: 35 and you will be **c** of the Most High,
10: 21 and revealed them to little **c**.
18: 16 said, "Let the little **c** come to me,
Jn 1: 12 the right to become **c** of God—
12: 36 so that you may become **c** of light."
Ac 2: 39 your **c** and for all who are far off—
Ro 8: 14 the Spirit of God are the **c** of God.
8: 16 with our spirit that we are God's **c**.
9: 26 there they will be called '**c**
1Co 14: 20 and sisters, stop thinking like **c**.
2Co 12: 14 **c** should not have to save up for
Gal 3: 26 in Christ Jesus you are all **c** of God
Eph 6: 1 **C**, obey your parents in the Lord,
6: 4 Fathers, do not exasperate your **c**;
Col 3: 20 **C**, obey your parents in everything,
3: 21 do not embitter your **c**, or they will
1Th 2: 7 we were like young **c** among you.
2: 7 as a nursing mother cares for her **c**,
1Ti 3: 4 well and see that his **c** obey him,
3: 12 wife and must manage his **c** and
5: 10 such as bringing up **c**,
Heb 2: 13 am I, and the **c** God has given me."
12: 7 God is treating you as his **c**.
1Jn 3: 1 that we should be called **c** of God!

CHOKE
Mk 4: 19 things come in and **c** the word,

CHOOSE (CHOOSES CHOSE CHOSEN)
Dt 30: 19 Now **c** life, so that you and your
Jos 24: 15 **c** for yourselves this day whom you
Pr 8: 10 **C** my instruction instead of silver,
Jn 15: 16 You did not **c** me, but I chose you

CHOOSES (CHOOSE)
Mt 11: 27 to whom the Son **c** to reveal him.
Lk 10: 22 to whom the Son **c** to reveal him."
Jn 7: 17 who **c** to do the will of God

CHORAZIN
Mt 11: 21 "Woe to you, **C**! Woe to you,

CHOSE (CHOOSE)
Ge 13: 11 Lot c for himself the whole plain
Ps 33: 12 the people he c for his inheritance.
Jn 15: 16 but I c you and appointed you so
1Co 1: 27 But God c the foolish things
Eph 1: 4 For he c us in him before
2Th 2: 13 because God c you as firstfruits

CHOSEN (CHOOSE)
Isa 41: 8 whom I have c, you descendants
Mt 22: 14 many are invited, but few are c."
Lk 10: 42 Mary has c what is better, and it
23: 35 if he is God's Messiah, the C One."
Jn 1: 34 I testify that this is God's C One."
15: 19 but I have c you out of the world.
1Pe 1: 20 He was c before the creation
2: 9 But you are a c people, a royal

CHRIST (CHRIST'S CHRISTIAN CHRISTIANS)
Jn 1: 41 found the Messiah" (that is, the C).
Ac 9: 34 said to him, "Jesus C heals you.
Ro 1: 4 from the dead: Jesus C our Lord.
3: 22 faith in Jesus C to all who believe.
5: 1 God through our Lord Jesus C,
5: 6 powerless, C died for the ungodly.
5: 8 we were still sinners, C died for us.
5: 11 in God through our Lord Jesus C,
5: 17 life through the one man, Jesus C!
6: 4 just as C was raised from the dead
6: 9 we know that since C was raised
6: 23 is eternal life in C Jesus our Lord.
7: 4 to the law through the body of C,
8: 1 for those who are in C Jesus,
8: 9 does not have the Spirit of C, they do not belong to C.
8: 17 heirs of God and co-heirs with C,
8: 34 C Jesus who died—more than that,
8: 35 separate us from the love of C?
10: 4 C is the culmination of the law so
12: 5 so in C we, though many, form one
13: 14 yourselves with the Lord Jesus C,
14: 9 C died and returned to life so that
15: 3 even C did not please himself but,
15: 5 toward each other that C Jesus had,
15: 7 then, just as C accepted you,
16: 18 people are not serving our Lord C,
1Co 1: 2 to those sanctified in C Jesus
1: 7 for our Lord Jesus C to be revealed.
1: 13 Is C divided? Was Paul crucified
1: 17 For C did not send me to baptize,
1: 17 lest the cross of C be emptied of
1: 23 but we preach C crucified:
1: 30 of him that you are in C Jesus,
2: 2 while I was with you except Jesus C
3: 11 one already laid, which is Jesus C.
5: 7 For C, our Passover lamb, has been
6: 15 bodies are members of C himself?
8: 6 Jesus C, through whom all things
8: 12 conscience, you sin against C.
10: 4 them, and that rock was C.
10: 9 We should not test C, as some
11: 1 as I follow the example of C.
11: 3 that the head of every man is C,
11: 3 and the head of C is God.
12: 27 Now you are the body of C,
15: 3 C died for our sins according
15: 14 And if C has not been raised,
15: 22 die, so in C all will be made alive.
15: 57 victory through our Lord Jesus C.
2Co 1: 5 abundantly in the sufferings of C,
1: 5 our comfort abounds through C.
3: 3 show that you are a letter from C,
3: 14 because only in C is it taken away.
4: 4 gospel that displays the glory of C,
4: 5 but Jesus C as Lord, and ourselves
4: 6 glory displayed in the face of C.
5: 10 before the judgment seat of C,
5: 17 if anyone is in C, the new creation
6: 15 What harmony is there between C
10: 1 the humility and gentleness of C,
11: 2 to C, so that I might present you as
Gal 1: 7 trying to pervert the gospel of C.
2: 4 on the freedom we have in C Jesus
2: 16 of the law, but by faith in Jesus C
2: 16 we may be justified by faith in C
2: 17 that mean that C promotes sin?
2: 20 I have been crucified with C and I no longer live, but C lives in me.
2: 21 the law, C died for nothing!"
3: 13 C redeemed us from the curse
3: 16 meaning one person, who is C.
3: 26 So in C Jesus you are all children
4: 19 of childbirth until C is formed
Gal 5: 1 for freedom that C has set us free.
5: 4 law have been alienated from C;
5: 24 to C Jesus have crucified the flesh
6: 14 in the cross of our Lord Jesus C,
Eph 1: 3 with every spiritual blessing in C.
1: 10 in heaven and on earth under C.
1: 20 when he raised C from the dead
2: 5 made us alive with C even when
2: 10 created in C Jesus to do good
2: 12 time you were separate from C,
2: 20 with C Jesus himself as the chief
3: 8 Gentiles the boundless riches of C,
3: 17 so that C may dwell in your hearts
4: 7 has been given as C apportioned it.
4: 13 whole measure of the fullness of C.
4: 15 of him who is the head, that is, C.
4: 32 other, just as in C God forgave you.
5: 2 just as C loved us and gave himself
5: 21 one another out of reverence for C.
5: 23 head of the wife as C is the head
5: 25 just as C loved the church and gave
Php 1: 18 motives or true, C is preached.
1: 21 to live is C and to die is gain.
1: 23 I desire to depart and be with C,
1: 27 manner worthy of the gospel of C.
1: 29 on behalf of C not only to believe
2: 5 have the same mindset as C Jesus:
3: 7 now consider loss for the sake of C.
3: 10 I want to know C—yes, to know
3: 18 live as enemies of the cross of C.
4: 19 to the riches of his glory in C Jesus.
Col 1: 4 have heard of your faith in C Jesus
1: 27 which is C in you, the hope
1: 28 present everyone fully mature in C.
2: 2 the mystery of God, namely, C,
2: 6 as you received C Jesus as Lord,
2: 9 in C all the fullness of the Deity
2: 13 flesh, God made you alive with C.
2: 17 the reality, however, is found in C.
3: 1 you have been raised with C,
3: 1 hearts on things above, where C is,
3: 3 your life is now hidden with C
3: 15 Let the peace of C rule in your
1Th 5: 9 through our Lord Jesus C.
2Th 2: 1 the coming of our Lord Jesus C
2: 14 in the glory of our Lord Jesus C.
1Ti 1: 12 I thank C Jesus our Lord, who has
1: 15 C Jesus came into the world to save
1: 16 C Jesus might display his immense
2: 5 and mankind, the man C Jesus,
2Ti 1: 9 us in C Jesus before the beginning
1: 10 appearing of our Savior, C Jesus,
2: 1 in the grace that is in C Jesus.
2: 3 like a good soldier of C Jesus.
2: 8 Remember Jesus C,
2: 10 the salvation that is in C Jesus,
3: 12 life in C Jesus will be persecuted,
3: 15 salvation through faith in C Jesus.
4: 1 the presence of God and of C Jesus,
Titus 2: 13 our great God and Savior, Jesus C,
Heb 3: 6 C is faithful as the Son over God's
3: 14 We have come to share in C,
5: 5 C did not take on himself the glory
6: 1 the elementary teachings about C
9: 11 when C came as high priest
9: 14 will the blood of C, who through
9: 15 For this reason C is the mediator
9: 24 C did not enter a sanctuary made
9: 26 Otherwise C would have had
9: 28 so C was sacrificed once to take
10: 10 of the body of Jesus C once for all.
13: 8 Jesus C is the same yesterday
1Pe 1: 2 Spirit, to be obedient to Jesus C
1: 3 and Father of our Lord Jesus C!
1: 11 Spirit of C in them was pointing
1: 19 but with the precious blood of C,
2: 21 called, because C suffered for you,
3: 15 in your hearts revere C as Lord.
3: 18 For C also suffered once for sins,
3: 21 you by the resurrection of Jesus C,
4: 13 participate in the sufferings of C,
4: 14 insulted because of the name of C,
2Pe 1: 1 a servant and apostle of Jesus C,
1: 16 of our Lord Jesus C in power,
1Jn 2: 1 Jesus C, the Righteous One.
2: 22 whoever denies that Jesus is the C.
3: 16 Jesus C laid down his life for us.
3: 23 Jesus C, and to love one another as
4: 2 that Jesus C has come in the flesh
5: 1 believes that Jesus is the C is born
5: 20 is true by being in his Son Jesus C.
2Jn : 9 teaching of C does not have God;
Jude : 4 deny Jesus C our only Sovereign
Rev 1: 1 The revelation from Jesus C,
1: 5 and from Jesus C, who is
20: 4 reigned with C a thousand years.
20: 6 of C and will reign with him

CHRIST'S (CHRIST)
1Co 9: 21 God's law but am under C law),
2Co 2: 14 captives in C triumphal procession
5: 14 For C love compels us, because we
5: 20 We are therefore C ambassadors,
5: 20 We implore you on C behalf:
12: 9 so that C power may rest on me.
Col 1: 22 by C physical body through death

CHRISTIAN* (CHRIST)
Ac 26: 28 you can persuade me to be a C?"
1Pe 4: 16 if you suffer as a C, do not be

CHRISTIANS* (CHRIST)
Ac 11: 26 The disciples were called C first

CHURCH
Mt 16: 18 and on this rock I will build my c,
18: 17 refuse to listen, tell it to the c;
18: 17 they refuse to listen even to the c,
Ac 20: 28 Be shepherds of the c of God,
1Co 5: 12 mine to judge those outside the c?
14: 4 one who prophesies edifies the c.
14: 12 excel in those that build up the c.
14: 26 done so that the c may be built up.
15: 9 because I persecuted the c of God.
Gal 1: 13 how intensely I persecuted the c
Eph 5: 23 wife as Christ is the head of the c,
Col 1: 18 he is the head of the body, the c;
1: 24 the sake of his body, which is the c.

CHURNING
Pr 30: 33 For as c cream produces butter,

CIRCLE
Isa 40: 22 enthroned above the c of the earth,

CIRCUMCISE (CIRCUMCISED CIRCUMCISION)
Dt 10: 16 C your hearts, therefore, and do

CIRCUMCISED (CIRCUMCISE)
Ge 17: 10 Every male among you shall be c.
17: 12 who is eight days old must be c,
Jos 5: 3 c the Israelites at Gibeath
Gal 2: 8 in Peter as an apostle to the c,
5: 2 you that if you let yourselves be c,

CIRCUMCISION (CIRCUMCISE)
Ro 2: 25 C has value if you observe the law,
2: 29 and c is c of the heart, by the Spirit,
1Co 7: 19 C is nothing and uncircumcision is

CIRCUMSTANCES
Php 4: 11 to be content whatever the c.
1Th 5: 18 give thanks in all c; for this is God's

CITIES (CITY)
Lk 19: 17 small matter, take charge of ten c.'
19: 19 'You take charge of five c.'

CITIZENS (CITIZENSHIP)
Eph 2: 19 but fellow c with God's people

CITIZENSHIP* (CITIZENS)
Ac 22: 28 to pay a lot of money for my c."
Eph 2: 12 excluded from c in Israel
Php 3: 20 But our c is in heaven.

CITY (CITIES)
Ac 18: 10 I have many people in this c."
Heb 13: 14 here we do not have an enduring c,
Rev 21: 2 I saw the Holy C, the new

CIVILIAN*
2Ti 2: 4 a soldier gets entangled in c affairs,

CLAIM (CLAIMS RECLAIM)
Pr 25: 6 do not c a place among his great
1Jn 1: 6 If we c to have fellowship with him
1: 8 If we c to be without sin,
1: 10 If we c we have not sinned,

CLAIMS (CLAIM)
Jas 2: 14 if someone c to have faith but has
1Jn 2: 6 Whoever c to live in him must live
2: 9 Anyone who c to be in the light

CLANGING*
1Co 13: 1 a resounding gong or a c cymbal.

CLAP* (CLAPPED CLAPS)
Job 21: 5 c your hand over your mouth.
Ps 47: 1 C your hands, all you nations;
98: 8 Let the rivers c their hands,
Pr 30: 32 evil, c your hand over your mouth!
Isa 55: 12 trees of the field will c their hands.

La 2: 15 who pass your way **c** their hands
Na 3: 19 the news about you **c** their hands

CLAPPED* (CLAP)
2Ki 11: 12 and the people **c** their hands
Eze 25: 6 Because you have **c** your hands

CLAPS* (CLAP)
Job 27: 23 It **c** its hands in derision and hisses
34: 37 scornfully he **c** his hands among us

CLASSIFY*
2Co 10: 12 We do not dare to **c** or compare

CLAUDIUS
Ac 11: 28 happened during the reign of **C**.)
18: 2 because **C** had ordered all Jews

CLAY
Isa 45: 9 Does the **c** say to the potter,
64: 8 We are the **c**, you are the potter;
Jer 18: 6 "Like **c** in the hand of the potter,
La 4: 2 are now considered as pots of **c**,
Da 2: 33 of iron and partly of baked **c**.
Ro 9: 21 the same lump of **c** some pottery
2Co 4: 7 this treasure in jars of **c** to show
2Ti 2: 20 and silver, but also of wood and **c**;

CLEAN (CLEANNESS CLEANSE CLEANSED CLEANSING)
Ge 7: 2 pairs of every kind of **c** animal,
Lev 4: 12 the camp to a place ceremonially **c**,
16: 30 you will be **c** from all your sins.
Ps 24: 4 one who has **c** hands and a pure
51: 7 me with hyssop, and I will be **c**;
Pr 20: 9 I am **c** and without sin"?
Eze 36: 25 I will sprinkle **c** water on you, and you will be **c**;
Mt 8: 2 are willing, you can make me **c**."
12: 44 swept **c** and put in order.
23: 25 You **c** the outside of the cup
Mk 7: 19 this, Jesus declared all foods **c**.)
Jn 13: 10 you are **c**, though not every one
15: 3 You are already **c** because
Ac 10: 15 impure that God has made **c**."
Ro 14: 20 All food is **c**, but it is wrong

CLEANNESS (CLEAN)
2Sa 22: 25 according to my **c** in his sight.

CLEANSE (CLEAN)
Ps 51: 2 my iniquity and **c** me from my sin.
51: 7 **C** me with hyssop, and I will be
2Ti 2: 21 Those who **c** themselves
Heb 9: 14 **c** our consciences from acts
10: 22 having our hearts sprinkled to **c** us

CLEANSED (CLEAN)
Mt 11: 5 those who have leprosy are **c**,
Heb 9: 22 nearly everything be **c** with blood,
2Pe 1: 9 they have been **c** from their past

CLEANSING (CLEAN)
Eph 5: 26 **c** her by the washing with water
Heb 6: 2 instruction about **c** rites, the laying

CLEFT*
Ex 33: 22 I will put you in a **c** in the rock

CLEVER (CLEVERNESS)
Isa 5: 21 own eyes and **c** in their own sight.

CLEVERNESS (CLEVER)
Pr 23: 4 get rich; do not trust your own **c**.

CLING
Ps 63: 8 I **c** to you; your right hand upholds
Ro 12: 9 Hate what is evil; **c** to what is good.

CLOAK
Ex 12: 11 with your **c** tucked into your belt,
2Ki 4: 29 "Tuck your **c** into your belt,
9: 1 to him, "Tuck your **c** into your belt,

CLOSE (CLOSER)
2Ki 11: 8 Stay **c** to the king wherever he
Ps 34: 18 The LORD is **c**
148: 14 of Israel, the people **c** to his heart.
Pr 28: 27 but those who **c** their eyes to them
Isa 40: 11 and carries them **c** to his heart;
Jer 30: 21 near and he will come **c** to me—

CLOSER (CLOSE)
Ex 3: 5 "Do not come any **c**," God said.
Pr 18: 24 friend who sticks **c** than a brother.

CLOTHE (CLOTHED CLOTHES CLOTHING CLOTHS)
Ps 45: 3 **c** yourself with splendor
Isa 52: 1 Zion, **c** yourself with strength!
Ro 13: 14 **c** yourselves with the Lord Jesus
Col 3: 12 **c** yourselves with compassion,
1Pe 5: 5 **c** yourselves with humility toward

CLOTHED (CLOTHE)
Ps 30: 11 my sackcloth and **c** me with joy,
104: 1 you are **c** with splendor
Pr 31: 22 she is **c** in fine linen and purple.
31: 25 She is **c** with strength and dignity;
Isa 61: 10 For he has **c** me with garments
Lk 24: 49 the city until you have been **c**
Gal 3: 27 into Christ have **c** yourselves

CLOTHES (CLOTHE)
Dt 8: 4 Your **c** did not wear out and your
Mt 6: 25 food, and the body more than **c**?
6: 28 "And why do you worry about **c**?
27: 35 divided up his **c** by casting lots.
Jn 11: 44 "Take off the grave **c** and let him
19: 24 "They divided my **c** among them

CLOTHING (CLOTHE)
Dt 22: 5 A woman must not wear men's **c**,
22: 5 nor a man wear women's **c**,
Job 29: 14 I put on righteousness as my **c**;
Mt 7: 15 They come to you in sheep's **c**,
1Ti 6: 8 But if we have food and **c**, we will

CLOTHS (CLOTHE)
Lk 2: 12 You will find a baby wrapped in **c**

CLOUD (CLOUDS)
Ex 13: 21 them in a pillar of **c** to guide them
1Ki 18: 44 "A **c** as small as a man's hand is
Pr 16: 15 his favor is like a rain **c** in spring.
Isa 19: 1 the LORD rides on a swift **c** and is
Lk 21: 27 of Man coming in a **c** with power
Heb 12: 1 by such a great **c** of witnesses,
Rev 14: 14 seated on the **c** was one like a son

CLOUDS (CLOUD)
Dt 33: 26 you and on the **c** in his majesty.
Ps 68: 4 extol him who rides on the **c**;
104: 3 makes the **c** his chariot and rides
Pr 25: 14 Like **c** and wind without rain is one
Da 7: 13 man, coming with the **c** of heaven.
Mt 24: 30 of Man coming on the **c** of heaven,
26: 64 and coming on the **c** of heaven."
Mk 13: 26 Man coming in **c** with great power
1Th 4: 17 them in the **c** to meet the Lord
Rev 1: 7 he is coming with the **c**,"

CLUB
Pr 25: 18 a **c** or a sword or a sharp arrow

CO-HEIRS* (INHERIT)
Ro 8: 17 heirs of God and **c** with Christ,

CO-WORKERS (WORK)
Ro 16: 3 Priscilla and Aquila, my **c** in Christ
1Co 3: 9 For we are **c** in God's service;

COALS
Pr 25: 22 will heap burning **c** on his head,
Ro 12: 20 this, you will heap burning **c** on his

COARSE*
Eph 5: 4 foolish talk or **c** joking, which are

COAT
Mt 5: 40 shirt, hand over your **c** as well.

CODE*
Ro 2: 27 even though you have the written **c**
2: 29 by the Spirit, not by the written **c**.
7: 6 not in the old way of the written **c**.

COINS
Mt 18: 28 who owed him a hundred silver **c**.
Mk 12: 42 put in two very small copper **c**,
Lk 15: 8 suppose a woman has ten silver **c**

COLD
Pr 25: 25 Like **c** water to a weary soul is
Mt 10: 42 anyone gives even a cup of **c** water
24: 12 the love of most will grow **c**,

COLLECTION
1Co 16: 1 about the **c** for the Lord's people:

COLT
Zec 9: 9 on a **c**, the foal of a donkey.
Mt 21: 5 a donkey, and on a **c**, the foal

COMFORT* (COMFORTED COMFORTER COMFORTERS COMFORTING COMFORTS)
Ge 5: 29 said, "He will **c** us in the labor
37: 35 sons and daughters came to **c** him,
1Ch 7: 22 and his relatives came to **c** him.
Job 2: 11 sympathize with him and **c** him.
7: 13 When I think my bed will **c** me
16: 5 **c** from my lips would bring you
36: 16 to the **c** of your table laden
Ps 23: 4 your rod and your staff, they **c** me.
71: 21 my honor and **c** me once more.
119: 50 My **c** in my suffering is this:
119: 52 ancient laws, and I find **c** in them.
119: 76 May your unfailing love be my **c**,
119: 82 I say, "When will you **c** me?"
Isa 40: 1 **C**, **c** my people, says your God.
51: 3 The LORD will surely **c** Zion
51: 19 upon you—who can **c** you?—
57: 18 and restore **c** to Israel's mourners,
61: 2 of our God, to **c** all who mourn,
66: 13 comforts her child, so will I **c** you;
Jer 16: 7 offer food to **c** those who mourn
31: 13 I will give them **c** and joy instead
La 1: 2 her lovers there is no one to **c** her.
1: 9 there was none to **c** her.
1: 16 No one is near to **c** me, no one
1: 17 hands, but there is no one to **c** her.
1: 21 but there is no one to **c** me.
2: 13 that I may **c** you, Virgin Daughter
Eze 16: 54 all you have done in giving them **c**.
Na 3: 7 Where can I find anyone to **c** you?"
Zec 1: 17 the LORD will again **c** Zion
10: 2 that are false, they give **c** in vain.
Lk 6: 24 you have already received your **c**.
Jn 11: 19 Mary to **c** them in the loss of their
1Co 14: 3 strengthening, encouraging and **c**.
2Co 1: 3 of compassion and the God of all **c**,
1: 4 that we can **c** those in any trouble
1: 4 with the **c** we ourselves receive
1: 5 also our **c** abounds through Christ.
1: 6 it is for your **c** and salvation;
1: 6 it is for your **c**, which produces
1: 7 so also you share in our **c**.
2: 7 you ought to forgive and **c** him,
7: 7 also by the **c** you had given him.
Php 2: 1 Christ, if any **c** from his love, if any
Col 4: 11 and they have proved a **c** to me.

COMFORTED* (COMFORT)
Ge 24: 67 Isaac was **c** after his mother's
37: 35 him, but he refused to be **c**.
2Sa 12: 24 Then David **c** his wife Bathsheba,
Job 42: 11 They **c** and consoled him over all
Ps 77: 2 hands, and I would not be **c**.
86: 17 LORD, have helped me and **c** me.
Isa 12: 1 turned away and you have **c** me.
52: 9 for the LORD has **c** his people,
54: 11 lashed by storms and not **c**, I will
66: 13 and you will be **c** over Jerusalem."
Jer 31: 15 her children and refusing to be **c**,
Mt 2: 18 her children and refusing to be **c**,
5: 4 who mourn, for they will be **c**.
Lk 16: 25 but now he is **c** here and you are
Ac 20: 12 man home alive and were greatly **c**.
2Co 1: 6 if we are **c**, it is for your comfort,
7: 6 **c** us by the coming of Titus,

COMFORTER* (COMFORT)
Ecc 4: 1 and they have no **c**;
4: 1 and they have no **c**.
Jer 8: 18 You who are my **C** in sorrow,

COMFORTERS* (COMFORT)
Job 16: 2 you are miserable **c**, all of you!
Ps 69: 20 was none, for **c**, but I found none.

COMFORTING* (COMFORT)
Isa 66: 11 and be satisfied at her **c** breasts;
Zec 1: 13 **c** words to the angel who talked
Jn 11: 31 with Mary in the house, **c** her,
1Th 2: 12 **c** and urging you to live lives

COMFORTS* (COMFORT)
Job 29: 25 I was like one who **c** mourners.
Isa 49: 13 For the LORD **c** his people
51: 12 "I, even I, am he who **c** you.
66: 13 As a mother **c** her child, so will I
2Co 1: 4 who **c** us in all our troubles,
7: 6 But God, who **c** the downcast,

COMMAND (COMMANDED COMMANDING COMMANDMENT COMMANDMENTS COMMANDS)
Ex 7: 2 You are to say everything I **c** you,
Nu 14: 41 are you disobeying the LORD's **c**?
24: 13 to go beyond the **c** of the LORD—
Dt 4: 2 Do not add to what I **c** you and do
8: 1 to follow every **c** I am giving you
12: 32 See that you do all I **c** you;
15: 11 I **c** you to be openhanded
30: 16 For I **c** you today to love
32: 46 so that you may **c** your children
Ps 91: 11 he will **c** his angels concerning you
148: 5 for at his **c** they were created,
Pr 6: 23 For this **c** is a lamp, this teaching is
13: 13 whoever respects a **c** is rewarded.
Ecc 8: 2 Obey the king's **c**, I say,

Jer 1: 7 you to and say whatever I **c** you.
1: 17 and say to them whatever I **c** you.
7: 23 Walk in obedience to all I **c** you,
11: 4 me and do everything I **c** you,
26: 2 Tell them everything I **c** you;
Joel 2: 11 mighty is the army that obeys his **c**.
Mt 4: 6 "'He will **c** his angels concerning
15: 3 why do you break the **c** of God
Lk 4: 10 "'He will **c** his angels concerning
Jn 13: 34 "A new **c** I give you:
15: 12 My **c** is this: Love each other as I
15: 14 are my friends if you do what I **c**.
15: 17 This is my **c**: Love each other.
Ro 13: 9 are summed up in this one **c**:
1Co 14: 37 I am writing to you is the Lord's **c**.
Gal 5: 14 is fulfilled in keeping this one **c**:
1Ti 1: 5 The goal of this **c** is love,
1: 18 I am giving you this **c** in keeping
6: 14 keep this **c** without spot or blame
6: 17 **C** those who are rich in this
Heb 9: 19 Moses had proclaimed every **c**
11: 3 the universe was formed at God's **c**,
2Pe 2: 21 on the sacred **c** that was passed
3: 2 and the **c** given by our Lord
1Jn 2: 7 I am not writing you a new **c**
2: 7 This old **c** is the message you have
3: 23 And this is his **c**: to believe
4: 21 And he has given us this **c**:
2Jn : 6 his **c** is that you walk in love.

COMMANDED (COMMAND)
Ge 2: 16 And the LORD God **c** the man,
7: 5 Noah did all that the LORD **c** him.
50: 12 Jacob's sons did as he had **c** them:
Ex 7: 6 did just as the LORD **c** them.
19: 7 all the words the LORD had **c** him
Dt 4: 5 laws as the LORD my God **c** me,
6: 24 The LORD **c** us to obey all these
Jos 1: 9 Have I not **c** you? Be strong
1: 16 "Whatever you have **c** us we will
2Sa 5: 25 So David did as the LORD **c** him,
2Ki 17: 13 entire Law that I **c** your ancestors
21: 8 careful to do everything I **c** them
2Ch 33: 8 do everything I **c** them concerning
Ps 33: 9 came to be; he **c**, and it stood firm.
78: 5 which he **c** our ancestors to teach
Mt 28: 20 to obey everything I have **c** you.
1Co 9: 14 way, the Lord has **c** that those who
1Jn 3: 23 and to love one another as he **c** us.
2Jn : 4 in the truth, just as the Father **c** us.

COMMANDING (COMMAND)
2Ti 2: 4 rather tries to please his **c** officer.

COMMANDMENT* (COMMAND)
Jos 22: 5 be very careful to keep the **c**
Mt 22: 36 which is the greatest **c** in the Law?"
22: 38 This is the first and greatest **c**.
Mk 12: 31 There is no **c** greater than these."
Lk 23: 56 the Sabbath in obedience to the **c**.
Ro 7: 8 the opportunity afforded by the **c**,
7: 9 but when the **c** came, sin sprang
7: 10 that the very **c** that was intended
7: 11 and through the **c** put me to death.
7: 12 and the **c** is holy,
7: 13 that through the **c** sin might
Eph 6: 2 is the first **c** with a promise—

COMMANDMENTS* (COMMAND)
Ex 20: 6 those who love me and keep my **c**.
24: 12 the law and **c** I have written for
34: 28 words of the covenant—the Ten **C**.
Dt 4: 13 the Ten **C**, which he commanded
5: 10 those who love me and keep my **c**.
5: 22 These are the **c** the LORD
6: 6 These **c** that I give you today are
7: 9 those who love him and keep his **c**.
9: 10 On them were all the **c** the LORD
10: 4 Ten **C** he had proclaimed to you
Ne 1: 5 those who love him and keep his **c**,
Pr 19: 16 Whoever keeps **c** keeps their life,
Ecc 12: 13 Fear God and keep his **c**, for this is
Da 9: 4 those who love him and keep his **c**,
Mt 19: 17 you want to enter life, keep the **c**."
22: 40 the Prophets hang on these two **c**."
Mk 10: 19 You know the **c**: 'You shall not
12: 28 "Of all the **c**, which is the most
Lk 18: 20 You know the **c**: 'You shall not
Ro 13: 9 The **c**, "You shall not commit

COMMANDS (COMMAND)
Ex 25: 22 give you all my **c** for the Israelites.
34: 32 gave them all the **c** the LORD had
Lev 22: 31 "Keep my **c** and follow them.
Nu 15: 39 so you will remember all the **c**
Dt 7: 11 take care to follow the **c**,
11: 1 decrees, his laws and his **c** always.
11: 27 you obey the **c** of the LORD your
28: 1 carefully follow all his **c** I give you
30: 10 and keep his **c** and decrees that are
Jos 22: 5 to keep his **c**, to hold fast to him
1Ki 2: 3 keep his decrees and **c**, his laws
8: 58 obedience to him and keep the **c**,
8: 61 live by his decrees and obey his **c**,
1Ch 28: 7 is unswerving in carrying out my **c**
29: 19 devotion to keep your **c**,
2Ch 31: 21 in obedience to the law and the **c**,
Ps 78: 7 his deeds but would keep his **c**.
112: 1 who find great delight in his **c**.
119: 10 do not let me stray from your **c**.
119: 32 I run in the path of your **c**, for you
119: 35 Direct me in the path of your **c**,
119: 47 in your **c** because I love them.
119: 48 I reach out for your **c**, which I love,
119: 73 me understanding to learn your **c**.
119: 86 All your **c** are trustworthy;
119: 96 a limit, but your **c** are boundless.
119: 98 Your **c** are always with me
119:115 that I may keep the **c** of my God!
119:127 I love your **c** more than gold,
119:131 and pant, longing for your **c**.
119:143 but your **c** give me delight.
119:151 and all your **c** are true.
119:172 for all your **c** are righteous.
119:176 I have not forgotten your **c**.
Pr 2: 1 and store up my **c** within you,
3: 1 but keep my **c** in your heart,
10: 8 The wise in heart accept **c**,
Isa 48: 18 you had paid attention to my **c**,
Mt 5: 19 sets aside one of the least of these **c**
5: 19 teaches these **c** will be called great
Mk 7: 8 You have let go of the **c** of God
7: 9 way of setting aside the **c** of God
Lk 1: 6 God, observing all the Lord's **c**
Jn 14: 15 "If you love me, keep my **c**.
14: 21 Whoever has my **c** and keeps them
15: 10 just as I have kept my Father's **c**
Ac 17: 30 now he **c** all people everywhere
1Co 7: 19 Keeping God's **c** is what counts.
Eph 2: 15 aside in his flesh the law with its **c**
1Jn 2: 3 come to know him if we keep his **c**.
2: 4 but does not do what he **c** is a liar,
3: 22 because we keep his **c** and do what
3: 24 The one who keeps God's **c** lives
5: 2 loving God and carrying out his **c**.
5: 3 this is love for God: to keep his **c**.
5: 3 And his **c** are not burdensome,
2Jn : 6 that we walk in obedience to his **c**.
Rev 12: 17 those who keep God's **c** and hold
14: 12 the people of God who keep his **c**

COMMEMORATE
Ex 12: 14 "This is a day you are to **c**;

COMMEND* (COMMENDABLE COMMENDED COMMENDS)
Ecc 8: 15 So I **c** the enjoyment of life,
Ro 16: 1 I **c** to you our sister Phoebe,
2Co 3: 1 we beginning to **c** ourselves again?
4: 2 the truth plainly we **c** ourselves
5: 12 We are not trying to **c** ourselves
6: 4 God we **c** ourselves in every way:
10: 12 with some who **c** themselves.
1Pe 2: 14 wrong and to **c** those who do right.

COMMENDABLE* (COMMEND)
1Pe 2: 19 it is **c** if someone bears up under
2: 20 you endure it, this is **c** before God.

COMMENDED* (COMMEND)
Ne 11: 2 The people **c** all who volunteered
Job 29: 11 of me, and those who saw me **c** me,
Lk 16: 8 "The master **c** the dishonest
Ac 15: 40 **c** by the believers to the grace
Ro 13: 3 do what is right and you will be **c**.
2Co 12: 11 I ought to have been **c** by you, for I
Heb 11: 2 is what the ancients were **c** for.
11: 4 By faith he was **c** as righteous,
11: 5 he was **c** as one who pleased God.
11: 39 These were all **c** for their faith,

COMMENDS* (COMMEND)
Ps 145: 4 One generation **c** your works
2Co 10: 18 not the one who **c** himself who is
10: 18 but the one whom the Lord **c**.

COMMIT (COMMITS COMMITTED)
Ex 20: 14 "You shall not **c** adultery.
Dt 5: 18 "You shall not **c** adultery.
1Sa 7: 3 and **c** yourselves to the LORD
Ps 31: 5 Into your hands I **c** my spirit;
37: 5 **C** your way to the LORD;
Pr 16: 3 **C** to the LORD whatever you do,
Mt 5: 27 was said, 'You shall not **c** adultery.'
19: 18 you shall not **c** adultery, you shall
Mk 10: 19 you shall not **c** adultery, you shall
Lk 18: 20 'You shall not **c** adultery, you shall
23: 46 into your hands I **c** my spirit."
Ac 20: 32 "Now I **c** you to God
Ro 2: 22 should not **c** adultery, do you **c** adultery?
13: 9 "You shall not **c** adultery,"
1Co 10: 8 We should not **c** sexual immorality,
Jas 2: 11 "You shall not **c** adultery,"
1Pe 4: 19 to God's will should **c** themselves
Rev 2: 22 I will make those who **c** adultery

COMMITS* (COMMIT)
Lev 20: 10 man **c** adultery with another man's
Pr 6: 32 a man who **c** adultery has no sense;
29: 22 hot-tempered person **c** many sins.
Ecc 8: 12 a wicked person who **c** a hundred
Eze 18: 12 the poor and needy. He **c** robbery.
18: 14 who sees all the sins his father **c**,
18: 24 from their righteousness and **c** sin
18: 26 from their righteousness and **c** sin,
22: 11 you one man **c** a detestable offense
Mt 5: 32 a divorced woman **c** adultery.
19: 9 marries another woman **c** adultery."
Mk 10: 11 another woman **c** adultery against
10: 12 another man, she **c** adultery."
Lk 16: 18 marries another woman **c** adultery,
16: 18 a divorced woman **c** adultery.
1Co 6: 18 All other sins a person **c** are

COMMITTED (COMMIT)
Nu 5: 7 must confess the sin they have **c**.
1Ki 8: 61 may your hearts be fully **c**
15: 14 Asa's heart was fully **c**
2Ch 16: 9 those whose hearts are fully **c**
Mt 5: 28 lustfully has already **c** adultery
11: 27 "All things have been **c** to me
Lk 10: 22 "All things have been **c** to me
Ac 14: 23 and fasting, **c** them to the Lord,
14: 26 where they had been **c** to the grace
1Co 9: 17 I am simply discharging the trust **c**
2Co 5: 19 And he has **c** to us the message
1Pe 2: 22 "He **c** no sin, and no deceit was
Rev 17: 2 the kings of the earth **c** adultery,
18: 3 of the earth **c** adultery with her,
18: 9 the earth who **c** adultery with her

COMMON
Ge 11: 1 had one language and a **c** speech.
Lev 10: 10 between the holy and the **c**,
Pr 22: 2 Rich and poor have this in **c**:
29: 13 and the oppressor have this in **c**:
Ac 2: 44 together and had everything in **c**.
Ro 9: 21 purposes and some for **c** use?
1Co 10: 13 has overtaken you except what is **c**
2Co 6: 14 and wickedness have in **c**?
2Ti 2: 20 purposes and some for **c** use.

COMMUNITY
Pr 6: 19 who stirs up conflict in the **c**.

COMPANION (COMPANIONS)
Ps 55: 13 like myself, my **c**, my close friend,
55: 20 My **c** attacks his friends;
Pr 13: 20 wise, for a **c** of fools suffers harm.
28: 7 a **c** of gluttons disgraces his father.
29: 3 but a **c** of prostitutes squanders his
Rev 1: 9 your brother and **c** in the suffering

COMPANIONS (COMPANION)
Ps 45: 7 you above your **c** by anointing you
Heb 1: 9 you above your **c** by anointing you

COMPANY
Ps 14: 5 is present in the **c** of the righteous.
Pr 21: 16 comes to rest in the **c** of the dead.
24: 1 the wicked, do not desire their **c**;
Jer 15: 17 I never sat in the **c** of revelers,
1Co 15: 33 "Bad **c** corrupts good character."

COMPARE* (COMPARED COMPARING COMPARISON)
Job 28: 17 Neither gold nor crystal can **c**
28: 19 The topaz of Cush cannot **c** with it;
39: 13 they cannot **c** with the wings
Ps 40: 5 None can **c** with you; were I
86: 8 no deeds can **c** with yours.
89: 6 skies above can **c** with the LORD?
Pr 3: 15 nothing you desire can **c** with her.
8: 11 nothing you desire can **c** with her.
Isa 40: 18 With whom, then, will you **c** God?
40: 25 "To whom will you **c** me?
46: 5 "With whom will you **c** me

a 2: 13 With what can I **c** you,
ze 31: 8 nor could the plane trees **c** with its
)a 1: 13 **c** our appearance
Mt 11: 16 "To what can I **c** this generation?
k 7: 31 then, can I **c** the people of this
13: 18 of God like? What shall I **c** it to?
13: 20 shall I **c** the kingdom of God
2Co 10: 12 or **c** ourselves with some who
10: 12 and **c** themselves with themselves,

COMPARED* (COMPARE)
Jdg 8: 2 "What have I accomplished **c**
8: 3 What was I able to do **c** to you?"
sa 46: 5 you liken me that we may be **c**?
Eze 31: 2 "'Who can be **c** with you
31: 18 the trees of Eden can be **c** with you
Ro 5: 16 the gift of God be **c** with the result

COMPARING* (COMPARE)
Ro 8: 18 present sufferings are not worth **c**
2Co 8: 8 of your love by **c** it
Gal 6: 4 without **c** themselves to someone

COMPARISON* (COMPARE)
2Co 3: 10 was glorious has no glory now in **c**

COMPASSION* (COMPASSIONATE COMPASSIONS)
Ex 33: 19 I will have **c** on whom I will have **c**.
Dt 13: 17 you mercy, and will have **c** on you.
28: 54 man among you will have no **c**
30: 3 your fortunes and have **c** on you
2Ki 13: 23 had **c** and showed concern for
2Ch 30: 9 your children will be shown **c**
Ne 9: 19 your great **c** you did not abandon
9: 27 and in your great **c** you gave them
9: 28 in your **c** you delivered them time
Ps 51: 1 to your great **c** blot out my
77: 9 Has he in anger withheld his **c**?"
90: 13 will it be? Have **c** on your servants.
102: 13 You will arise and have **c** on Zion,
103: 4 pit and crowns you with love and **c**,
103: 13 As a father has **c** on his children,
103: 13 so the LORD has **c** on those who
116: 5 our God is full of **c**.
119: 77 Let your **c** come to me that I may
119:156 Your **c**, LORD, is great;
135: 14 and have **c** on his servants.
145: 9 he has **c** on all he has made.
Isa 13: 18 infants, nor will they look with **c**
14: 1 The LORD will have **c** on Jacob;
27: 11 so their Maker has no **c** on them,
30: 18 he will rise up to show you **c**.
49: 10 He who has **c** on them will guide
49: 13 will have **c** on his afflicted ones.
49: 15 and have no **c** on the child she has
51: 3 will look with **c** on all her ruins;
54: 7 with deep **c** I will bring you back.
54: 8 everlasting kindness I will have **c**
54: 10 says the LORD, who has **c** on you.
60: 10 you, in favor I will show you **c**.
63: 7 Israel, according to his **c** and many
63: 15 and **c** are withheld from us.
Jer 12: 15 I will again have **c** and will bring
13: 14 or **c** to keep me from destroying
21: 7 show them no mercy or pity or **c**.'
30: 18 tents and have **c** on his dwellings;
31: 20 I have great **c** for him,"
33: 26 fortunes and have **c** on them.'"
42: 12 I will show you **c** so that he will have **c** on you
La 3: 32 grief, he will show **c**, so great is his
Eze 9: 5 and kill, without showing pity or **c**.
16: 5 or had **c** enough to do any of these
39: 25 and will have **c** on all the people
Da 1: 9 to show favor and **c** to Daniel,
Hos 2: 19 and justice, in love and **c**.
11: 8 all my **c** is aroused.
13: 14 "I will have no **c**,
14: 3 for in you the fatherless find **c**."
Jnh 3: 9 with **c** turn from his fierce anger so
Mic 7: 19 You will again have **c** on us;
Zec 7: 9 show mercy and **c** to one another.
10: 6 I will restore them because I have **c**
Mal 3: 17 just as a father has **c** and spares his
Mt 9: 36 saw the crowds, he had **c** on them,
14: 14 he had **c** on them and healed their
15: 32 and said, "I have **c** for these people;
20: 34 Jesus had **c** on them and touched
Mk 6: 34 a large crowd, he had **c** on them,
8: 2 "I have **c** for these people;
Lk 15: 20 him and was filled with **c** for him;
Ro 9: 15 I will have **c** on whom I have **c**."
2Co 1: 3 the Father of **c** and the God of all
Php 2: 1 the Spirit, if any tenderness and **c**,
Col 3: 12 clothe yourselves with **c**, kindness,
Jas 5: 11 The Lord is full of **c** and mercy.

COMPASSIONATE* (COMPASSION)
Ex 22: 27 to me, I will hear, for I am **c**.
34: 6 LORD, the **c** and gracious God,
2Ch 30: 9 LORD your God is gracious and **c**.
Ne 9: 17 gracious and **c**, slow to anger
Ps 86: 15 Lord, are a **c** and gracious God,
103: 8 The LORD is **c** and gracious,
111: 4 the LORD is gracious and **c**.
112: 4 for those who are gracious and **c**
145: 8 The LORD is gracious and **c**,
La 4: 10 their own hands **c** women have
Joel 2: 13 for he is gracious and **c**,
Jnh 4: 2 that you are a gracious and **c** God,
Eph 4: 32 Be kind and **c** to one another,
1Pe 3: 8 love one another, be **c** and humble.

COMPASSIONS* (COMPASSION)
La 3: 22 not consumed, for his **c** never fail.

COMPELLED (COMPULSION)
Ac 20: 22 "And now, **c** by the Spirit, I am
1Co 9: 16 boast, since I am **c** to preach.

COMPELS (COMPULSION)
Job 32: 18 and the spirit within me **c** me;
2Co 5: 14 For Christ's love **c** us, because we

COMPETENCE* (COMPETENT)
2Co 3: 5 but our **c** comes from God.

COMPETENT* (COMPETENCE)
Ro 15: 14 and **c** to instruct one another.
1Co 6: 2 are you not **c** to judge trivial cases?
2Co 3: 5 Not that we are **c** in ourselves
3: 6 He has made us **c** as ministers

COMPETES*
1Co 9: 25 Everyone who **c** in the games goes
2Ti 2: 5 anyone who **c** as an athlete does

COMPLACENCY* (COMPLACENT)
Pr 1: 32 the **c** of fools will destroy them;
Eze 30: 9 ships to frighten Cush out of her **c**.

COMPLACENT* (COMPLACENCY)
Isa 32: 9 You women who are so **c**,
32: 11 Tremble, you **c** women;
Am 6: 1 Woe to you who are **c** in Zion,
Zep 1: 12 lamps and punish those who are **c**,

COMPLETE (COMPLETENESS)
Dt 16: 15 your hands, and your joy will be **c**.
Jn 3: 29 That joy is mine, and it is now **c**.
15: 11 in you and that your joy may be **c**.
16: 24 will receive, and your joy will be **c**.
17: 23 they may be brought to **c** unity.
Ac 20: 24 **c** the task the Lord Jesus has given
Php 2: 2 then make my joy **c** by being
Col 4: 17 it that you **c** the ministry you have
Jas 1: 4 so that you may be mature and **c**,
2: 22 faith was made **c** by what he did.
1Jn 1: 4 We write this to make our joy **c**.
2: 5 for God is truly made **c** in them.
4: 12 in us and his love is made **c** in us.
4: 17 is how love is made **c** among us so
2Jn : 12 to face, so that our joy may be **c**.

COMPLETENESS* (COMPLETE)
1Co 13: 10 but when **c** comes, what is in part

COMPLIMENTS*
Pr 23: 8 eaten and will have wasted your **c**.

COMPREHEND* (COMPREHENDED COMPREHENDS)
Ecc 8: 17 No one can **c** what goes on under
8: 17 they know, they cannot really **c** it.

COMPREHENDED* (COMPREHEND)
Job 38: 18 Have you **c** the vast expanses

COMPREHENDS* (COMPREHEND)
Job 28: 13 No mortal **c** its worth; it cannot be

COMPULSION (COMPELLED COMPELS)
2Co 9: 7 not reluctantly or under **c**, for God

CONCEAL (CONCEALED CONCEALS)
Ps 40: 10 I do not **c** your love and your
Pr 25: 2 It is the glory of God to **c** a matter;

CONCEALED (CONCEAL)
Jer 16: 17 me, nor is their sin **c** from my eyes.
Mt 10: 26 there is nothing **c** that will not be
Mk 4: 22 whatever is **c** is meant to be
Lk 8: 17 nothing **c** that will not be known
12: 2 There is nothing **c** that will not be

CONCEALS* (CONCEAL)
Pr 10: 11 mouth of the wicked **c** violence.
10: 18 Whoever **c** hatred with lying lips
28: 13 Whoever **c** their sins does not

CONCEIT* (CONCEITED)
Isa 16: 6 of her **c**, her pride and her
Jer 48: 29 her **c** and the haughtiness of her
Php 2: 3 out of selfish ambition or vain **c**.

CONCEITED* (CONCEIT)
1Sa 17: 28 I know how **c** you are and how
Ro 11: 25 sisters, so that you may not be **c**:
12: 16 of low position. Do not be **c**.
2Co 12: 7 order to keep me from becoming **c**,
Gal 5: 26 Let us not become **c**,
1Ti 3: 6 he may become **c** and fall under
6: 4 they are **c** and understand nothing.
2Ti 3: 4 rash, **c**, lovers of pleasure rather

CONCEIVE (CONCEIVED CONCEIVES)
Isa 7: 14 The virgin will **c** and give birth
Mt 1: 23 "The virgin will **c** and give birth
Lk 1: 7 Elizabeth was not able to **c**,

CONCEIVED (CONCEIVE)
Ps 51: 5 from the time my mother **c** me.
Mt 1: 20 because what is **c** in her is
1Co 2: 9 and what no human mind has **c**"—
Jas 1: 15 after desire has **c**, it gives birth

CONCEIVES* (CONCEIVE)
Ps 7: 14 is pregnant with evil **c** trouble

CONCERN* (CONCERNED)
Ge 39: 6 he did not **c** himself with anything
39: 8 "my master does not **c** himself
1Sa 23: 21 LORD bless you for your **c** for me.
2Ki 13: 23 showed **c** for them because of his
Job 9: 21 blameless, I have no **c** for myself;
19: 4 my error remains my **c** alone.
Ps 131: 1 I do not **c** myself with great matters
Pr 29: 7 but the wicked have no such **c**.
Eze 36: 21 I had **c** for my holy name,
Jnh 4: 11 I not have **c** for the great city
Ac 18: 17 and Gallio showed no **c** whatever.
1Co 7: 32 I would like you to be free from **c**.
12: 25 that its parts should have equal **c**
2Co 7: 7 deep sorrow, your ardent **c** for me,
7: 11 what **c**, what readiness to see
8: 16 of Titus the same **c** I have for you.
11: 28 of my **c** for all the churches.
Php 2: 20 who will show genuine **c** for your
4: 10 at last you renewed your **c** for me.

CONCERNED (CONCERN)
Ex 2: 25 Israelites and was **c** about them.
Ps 142: 4 my right hand; no one is **c** for me.
Jnh 4: 10 "You have been **c** about this plant,
1Co 7: 32 An unmarried man is **c**
9: 9 Is it about oxen that God is **c**?
Php 4: 10 Indeed, you were **c**, but you had no

CONCESSION*
1Co 7: 6 I say this as a **c**, not as a command.

CONDEMN* (CONDEMNATION CONDEMNED CONDEMNING CONDEMNS)
Job 9: 20 innocent, my mouth would **c** me;
34: 17 you **c** the just and mighty One?
34: 29 he remains silent, who can **c** him?
40: 8 Would you **c** me to justify yourself?
Ps 94: 21 and **c** the innocent to death.
109: 7 guilty, and may his prayers **c** him.
109: 31 from those who would **c** them.
Isa 50: 9 Who will **c** me? They will all wear
Mt 12: 41 with this generation and **c** it;
12: 42 with this generation and **c** it;
20: 18 of the law. They will **c** him to death
Mk 10: 33 They will **c** him to death and will
Lk 6: 37 Do not **c**, and you will not be
11: 31 of this generation and **c** them,
11: 32 with this generation and **c** it,
Jn 3: 17 Son into the world to **c** the world,
7: 51 "Does our law **c** a man without
8: 11 *"Then neither do I **c** you,"*
12: 48 words I have spoken will **c** them
Ro 2: 27 yet obeys the law will **c** you who,
14: 22 is the one who does not **c** himself
2Co 7: 3 I do not say this to **c** you;
1Jn 3: 20 If our hearts **c** us, we know that
3: 21 if our hearts do not **c** us, we have
Jude : 9 did not himself dare to **c** him

CONDEMNATION* (CONDEMN)
Eze 33: 12 former wickedness will not bring **c**.
Ro 3: 8 good may result"? Their **c** is just!
5: 16 followed one sin and brought **c**,
5: 18 just as one trespass resulted in **c**
8: 1 there is now no **c** for those who are

2Co 3: 9 that brought **c** was glorious,
2Pe 2: 3 Their **c** has long been hanging over
Jude : 4 individuals whose **c** was written

CONDEMNED* (CONDEMN)
Dt 13: 17 none of the **c** things are to be
Job 32: 3 to refute Job, and yet had **c** him.
Ps 34: 21 the foes of the righteous will be **c**.
34: 22 who takes refuge in him will be **c**.
37: 33 let them be **c** when brought to trial.
79: 11 your strong arm preserve those **c**
102: 20 and release those **c** to death."
Mt 12: 7 you would not have **c** the innocent.
12: 37 and by your words you will be **c**."
23: 33 How will you escape being **c**
27: 3 saw that Jesus was **c**, he was seized
Mk 14: 64 They all **c** him as worthy of death.
16: 16 *does not believe will be* **c**.
Lk 6: 37 condemn, and you will not be **c**.
Jn 3: 18 Whoever believes in him is not **c**,
3: 18 not believe stands **c** already
5: 29 done what is evil will rise to be **c**.
8: 10 *Has no one* **c** *you?"*
16: 11 prince of this world now stands **c**.
Ac 25: 15 against him and asked that he be **c**.
Ro 3: 7 glory, why am I still **c** as a sinner?"
8: 3 And so he **c** sin in the flesh,
14: 23 whoever has doubts is **c** if they eat,
1Co 4: 9 like those **c** to die in the arena.
11: 32 that we will not be finally **c**
Gal 2: 11 him to his face, because he stood **c**.
Col 2: 14 which stood against us and **c** us;
2Th 2: 12 all will be **c** who have not believed
Titus 2: 8 of speech that cannot be **c**,
Heb 11: 7 By his faith he **c** the world
Jas 5: 6 You have **c** and murdered
5: 12 Otherwise you will be **c**.
2Pe 2: 6 if he **c** the cities of Sodom
Rev 19: 2 He has **c** the great prostitute who

CONDEMNING* (CONDEMN)
Dt 25: 1 the innocent and **c** the guilty.
1Ki 8: 32 **c** the guilty by bringing down
2Ch 6: 23 **c** the guilty and bringing down
Pr 17: 15 the guilty and **c** the innocent—
Ac 13: 27 in **c** him they fulfilled the words
Ro 2: 1 you are **c** yourself, because you

CONDEMNS* (CONDEMN)
Job 15: 6 Your own mouth **c** you, not mine;
Pr 12: 2 but he **c** those who devise wicked
14: 34 a nation, but sin **c** any people.
Ro 8: 34 then is the one who **c**? No one.

CONDITION
Pr 27: 23 Be sure you know the **c** of your

CONDUCT (CONDUCTED)
Ps 112: 5 who **c** their affairs with justice.
Pr 20: 11 is their **c** really pure and upright?
21: 8 but the **c** of the innocent is upright.
Ecc 6: 8 how to **c** themselves before others?
Jer 4: 18 "Your own **c** and actions have
17: 10 each person according to their **c**,
Eze 7: 3 I will judge you according to your **c**
Php 1: 27 **c** yourselves in a manner worthy of
1Ti 3: 15 how people ought to **c** themselves
4: 12 believers in speech, in **c**, in love,

CONDUCTED* (CONDUCT)
2Co 1: 12 we have **c** ourselves in the world,

CONFESS* (CONFESSED CONFESSES CONFESSING CONFESSION)
Lev 5: 5 they must **c** in what way they have
16: 21 and **c** over it all the wickedness
26: 40 if they will **c** their sins and the sins
Nu 5: 7 **c** the sin they have committed.
Ne 1: 6 I **c** the sins we Israelites,
Ps 32: 5 "I will **c** my transgressions
38: 18 I **c** my iniquity; I am troubled by
Jn 1: 20 He did not fail to **c**, but confessed
Jas 5: 16 Therefore **c** your sins to each other
1Jn 1: 9 If we **c** our sins, he is faithful

CONFESSED* (CONFESS)
1Sa 7: 6 day they fasted and there they **c**,
Ne 9: 2 in their places and **c** their sins
Da 9: 4 to the LORD my God and **c**:
Jn 1: 20 confess, but **c** freely, "I am not
Ac 19: 18 and openly **c** what they had done.

CONFESSES* (CONFESS)
Pr 28: 13 **c** and renounces them finds mercy.
2Ti 2: 19 "Everyone who **c** the name

CONFESSING* (CONFESS)
Ezr 10: 1 While Ezra was praying and **c**,
Da 9: 20 **c** my sin and the sin of my people
Mt 3: 6 **C** their sins, they were baptized
Mk 1: 5 **C** their sins, they were baptized

CONFESSION* (CONFESS)
Ne 9: 3 and spent another quarter in **c**
2Co 9: 13 accompanies your **c** of the gospel
1Ti 6: 12 when you made your good **c**
6: 13 Pontius Pilate made the good **c**,

CONFIDENCE* (CONFIDENT)
Jdg 9: 26 and its citizens put their **c** in him.
2Ki 18: 19 are you basing this **c** of yours?
2Ch 32: 8 And the people gained **c** from what
32: 10 On what are you basing your **c**,
Job 4: 6 Should not your piety be your **c**
Ps 71: 5 LORD, my **c** since my youth.
Pr 3: 32 but takes the upright into his **c**.
11: 13 A gossip betrays a **c**,
20: 19 A gossip betrays a **c**;
25: 9 to court, do not betray another's **c**,
31: 11 Her husband has full **c** in her
Isa 32: 17 will be quietness and **c** forever.
36: 4 are you basing this **c** of yours?
Jer 17: 7 in the LORD, whose **c** is in him.
49: 31 ease, which lives in **c**,"
Eze 29: 16 will no longer be a source of **c**
Mic 7: 5 put no **c** in a friend.
2Co 2: 3 I had **c** in all of you, that you
3: 4 Such **c** we have through Christ
7: 16 I am glad I can have complete **c**
8: 22 so because of his great **c** in you.
Eph 3: 12 approach God with freedom and **c**.
Php 3: 3 and who put no **c** in the flesh—
3: 4 I myself have reasons for such **c**.
3: 4 have reasons to put **c** in the flesh,
2Th 3: 4 We have **c** in the Lord that you are
Heb 3: 6 if indeed we hold firmly to our **c**
4: 16 God's throne of grace with **c**,
10: 19 since we have **c** to enter the Most
10: 35 So do not throw away your **c**;
11: 1 Now faith is **c** in what we hope for
13: 6 So we say with **c**, "The Lord is my
13: 17 Have **c** in your leaders and submit
1Jn 3: 21 condemn us, we have **c** before God
4: 17 us so that we will have **c** on the day
5: 14 This is the **c** we have

CONFIDENT* (CONFIDENCE)
Job 6: 20 because they had been **c**;
Ps 27: 3 against me, even then I will be **c**.
27: 13 I remain **c** of this: I will see
Lk 18: 9 To some who were **c** of their own
2Co 1: 15 Because I was **c** of this, I wanted
5: 6 Therefore we are always **c**
5: 8 We are **c**, I say, and would prefer
9: 4 be ashamed of having been so **c**.
10: 7 If anyone is **c** that they belong
Gal 5: 10 I am **c** in the Lord that you will
Php 1: 6 being **c** of this, that he who began
1: 14 sisters have become **c** in the Lord
2: 24 I am **c** in the Lord that I myself will
Phm : 21 **C** of your obedience, I write to
1Jn 2: 28 that when he appears we may be **c**

CONFIDES*
Ps 25: 14 The LORD **c** in those who fear

CONFIRM
2Pe 1: 10 make every effort to **c** your calling

CONFLICT
Pr 6: 14 in his heart—he always stirs up **c**.
6: 19 who stirs up **c** in the community.
10: 12 Hatred stirs up **c**, but love covers
15: 18 A hot-tempered person stirs up **c**,
16: 28 A perverse person stirs up **c**,
28: 25 The greedy stir up **c**, but those who
29: 22 An angry person stirs up **c**, and a
Heb 10: 32 in a great **c** full of suffering.

CONFORM* (CONFORMED CONFORMITY CONFORMS)
Ro 12: 2 not **c** to the pattern of this world,
1Pe 1: 14 do not **c** to the evil desires you had

CONFORMED* (CONFORM)
Eze 5: 7 You have not even **c**
11: 12 but have **c** to the standards
Ac 26: 5 that I **c** to the strictest sect of our
Ro 8: 29 predestined to be **c** to the image

CONFORMITY* (CONFORM)
Eph 1: 11 everything in **c** with the purpose

CONFORMS* (CONFORM)
1Ti 1: 11 that **c** to the gospel concerning

CONQUEROR* (CONQUERORS)
Mic 1: 15 I will bring a **c** against you who live
Rev 6: 2 rode out as a **c** bent on conquest.

CONQUERORS* (CONQUEROR)
Ro 8: 37 are more than **c** through him who

CONSCIENCE* (CONSCIENCE-STRICKEN CONSCIENCES CONSCIENTIOUS)
Ge 20: 5 I have done this with a clear **c**
20: 6 I know you did this with a clear **c**,
1Sa 25: 31 have on his **c** the staggering burden
Job 27: 6 my **c** will not reproach me as long
Ac 23: 1 to God in all good **c** to this day."
24: 16 to keep my **c** clear before God
Ro 9: 1 my **c** confirms it through the Holy
13: 5 but also as a matter of **c**.
1Co 4: 4 My **c** is clear, but that does not
8: 7 a god, and since their **c** is weak,
8: 10 if someone with a weak **c** sees you,
8: 12 this way and wound their weak **c**,
10: 25 without raising questions of **c**,
10: 27 you without raising questions of **c**.
10: 28 who told you and for the sake of **c**.
10: 29 referring to the other person's **c**,
10: 29 being judged by another's **c**?
2Co 1: 12 Our **c** testifies that we have
4: 2 to everyone's **c** in the sight of God.
5: 11 and I hope it is also plain to your **c**.
1Ti 1: 5 and a good **c** and a sincere faith.
1: 19 holding on to faith and a good **c**,
3: 9 truths of the faith with a clear **c**.
2Ti 1: 3 with a clear **c**, as night and day I
Heb 9: 9 able to clear the **c** of the worshiper.
10: 22 to cleanse us from a guilty **c**
13: 18 We are sure that we have a clear **c**
1Pe 3: 16 keeping a clear **c**, so that those who
3: 21 the pledge of a clear **c** toward God.

CONSCIENCE-STRICKEN* (CONSCIENCE)
1Sa 24: 5 David was **c** for having cut off
2Sa 24: 10 David was **c** after he had counted

CONSCIENCES* (CONSCIENCE)
Ro 2: 15 hearts, their **c** also bearing witness,
1Ti 4: 2 whose **c** have been seared as
Titus 1: 15 their minds and **c** are corrupted.
Heb 9: 14 cleanse our **c** from acts that lead

CONSCIENTIOUS* (CONSCIENCE)
2Ch 29: 34 for the Levites had been more **c**

CONSCIOUS*
Ro 3: 20 through the law we become **c** of
1Pe 2: 19 unjust suffering because they are **c**

CONSECRATE (CONSECRATED)
Ex 13: 2 "**C** to me every firstborn male.
40: 9 **c** it and all its furnishings, and it
Lev 20: 7 "'**C** yourselves and be holy,
25: 10 **C** the fiftieth year and proclaim
1Ch 15: 12 fellow Levites are to **c** yourselves

CONSECRATED (CONSECRATE)
Ex 29: 43 and the place will be **c** by my glory.
Lev 8: 30 So he **c** Aaron and his garments
2Ch 7: 16 **c** this temple so that my Name may
Lk 2: 23 male is to be **c** to the Lord"),
1Ti 4: 5 because it is **c** by the word of God

CONSENT
1Co 7: 5 other except perhaps by mutual **c**

CONSIDER (CONSIDERATE CONSIDERED CONSIDERS)
1Sa 12: 24 **c** what great things he has done
16: 7 "Do not **c** his appearance or his
2Ch 19: 6 them, "**C** carefully what you do,
Job 37: 14 stop and **c** God's wonders.
Ps 8: 3 When I **c** your heavens, the work
77: 12 I will **c** all your works and meditate
143: 5 and **c** what your hands have done.
Pr 6: 6 **c** its ways and be wise!
20: 25 and only later to **c** one's vows.
Ecc 7: 13 **C** what God has done:
Lk 12: 24 **C** the ravens: They do not sow
12: 27 "**C** how the wild flowers grow.
Php 3: 8 I **c** everything a loss because
3: 8 I **c** them garbage, that I may gain
Heb 10: 24 And let us **c** how we may spur one
Jas 1: 2 **C** it pure joy, my brothers
1: 26 Those who **c** themselves religious

CONSIDERATE* (CONSIDER)
Titus 3: 2 to be peaceable and **c**, and always
Jas 3: 17 then peace-loving, **c**, submissive,
1Pe 2: 18 only to those who are good and **c**,
3: 7 the same way be **c** as you live

CONSIDERED (CONSIDER)
Job 1: 8 "Have you **c** my servant Job?
2: 3 "Have you **c** my servant Job?
Ps 44: 22 we are **c** as sheep to be slaughtered.
Isa 53: 4 yet we **c** him punished by God,
Ro 8: 36 all day long; we are **c** as sheep to be

CONSIDERS (CONSIDER)
Pr 31: 16 She **c** a field and buys it; out of her
Ro 14: 5 One person **c** one day more sacred
14: 5 another **c** every day alike.

CONSIST (CONSISTS)
Lk 12: 15 life does not **c** in an abundance

CONSISTS (CONSIST)
Eph 5: 9 fruit of the light **c** in all goodness,

CONSOLATION
Ps 94: 19 within me, your **c** brought me joy.

CONSPIRE
Ps 2: 1 Why do the nations **c**

CONSTANT
Dt 28: 66 You will live in **c** suspense,
Pr 19: 13 wife is like the **c** dripping of a leaky
Ac 27: 33 "you have been in **c** suspense
Heb 5: 14 by **c** use have trained themselves

CONSTRUCTIVE*
1Co 10: 23 but not everything is **c**.

CONSULT
Gal 1: 16 was not to **c** any human being.

CONSUME (CONSUMES CONSUMING)
Jn 2: 17 "Zeal for your house will **c** me."

CONSUMES (CONSUME)
Ps 69: 9 for zeal for your house **c** me,

CONSUMING (CONSUME)
Dt 4: 24 For the LORD your God is a **c** fire,
Heb 12: 29 for our "God is a **c** fire."

CONTAIN* (CONTAINED CONTAINS)
1Ki 8: 27 the highest heaven, cannot **c** you.
2Ch 2: 6 the highest heavens, cannot **c** him?
6: 18 the highest heavens, cannot **c** you.
Ecc 8: 8 has power over the wind to **c** it,
2Pe 3: 16 His letters **c** some things that are

CONTAINED (CONTAIN)
Heb 9: 4 This ark **c** the gold jar of manna,

CONTAINS (CONTAIN)
Pr 15: 6 of the righteous **c** great treasure,

CONTAMINATES*
2Co 7: 1 from everything that **c** body

CONTEMPLATE*
2Co 3: 18 unveiled faces **c** the Lord's glory,

CONTEMPT
Pr 14: 31 oppresses the poor shows **c** for
17: 5 Whoever mocks the poor shows **c**
18: 3 so does **c**, and with shame comes
Da 12: 2 others to shame and everlasting **c**.
Mal 1: 6 "It is you priests who show **c**
Ro 2: 4 do you show **c** for the riches of his
14: 3 treat with **c** the one who does not,
Gal 4: 14 did not treat me with **c** or scorn.
1Th 5: 20 Do not treat prophecies with **c**

CONTEND (CONTENDED CONTENDING CONTENTIOUS)
Ge 6: 3 "My Spirit will not **c** with humans
Ps 35: 1 **C**, LORD, with those who **c**
Isa 49: 25 I will **c** with those who **c** with you,
Jude : 3 urge you to **c** for the faith that was

CONTENDED (CONTEND)
Php 4: 3 these women since they have **c**

CONTENDING* (CONTEND)
Col 2: 1 to know how hard I am **c** for you

CONTENT* (CONTENTMENT)
Ge 25: 27 while Jacob was **c** to stay at home
Jos 7: 7 If only we had been **c** to stay
Ps 131: 2 like a weaned child I am **c**.
Pr 13: 25 The righteous eat to their hearts' **c**,
19: 23 then one rests **c**,
Ecc 4: 8 toil, yet his eyes were not **c** with his
Lk 3: 14 be **c** with your pay."
Php 4: 11 to be **c** whatever the circumstances.
4: 12 learned the secret of being **c** in any
1Ti 6: 8 clothing, we will be **c** with that.
Heb 13: 5 and be **c** with what you have,

CONTENTIOUS* (CONTEND)
1Co 11: 16 If anyone wants to be **c** about this,

CONTENTMENT* (CONTENT)
Job 36: 11 in prosperity and their years in **c**.
SS 8: 10 in his eyes like one bringing **c**.
1Ti 6: 6 But godliness with **c** is great gain.

CONTINUAL (CONTINUE)
Pr 15: 15 but the cheerful heart has a **c** feast.

CONTINUE (CONTINUAL CONTINUES CONTINUING)
1Ki 8: 23 servants who **c** wholeheartedly
2Ch 6: 14 servants who **c** wholeheartedly
Ps 36: 10 **C** your love to those who know
Ac 13: 43 them to **c** in the grace of God.
Ro 11: 22 that you **c** in his kindness.
Gal 3: 10 Cursed is everyone who does not **c**
Php 2: 12 **c** to work out your salvation
Col 1: 23 if you **c** in your faith,
2: 6 as Lord, **c** to live your lives in him,
1Ti 2: 15 if they **c** in faith, love and holiness
2Ti 3: 14 **c** in what you have learned and
1Jn 2: 28 dear children, **c** in him,
3: 9 who is born of God will **c** to sin,
5: 18 born of God does not **c** to sin;
2Jn : 9 not **c** in the teaching of Christ
Rev 22: 11 Let the one who does wrong **c** to
22: 11 let the one who does right **c** to do
22: 11 let the holy person **c** to be holy."

CONTINUES (CONTINUE)
Ps 100: 5 his faithfulness **c** through all
119: 90 Your faithfulness **c** through all
2Co 10: 15 is that, as your faith **c** to grow,
1Jn 3: 6 No one who **c** to sin has either seen

CONTINUING (CONTINUE)
Ro 13: 8 except the **c** debt to love one

CONTRIBUTION (CONTRIBUTIONS)
Ro 15: 26 to make a **c** for the poor among

CONTRIBUTIONS (CONTRIBUTION)
2Ch 24: 10 the people brought their **c** gladly,
31: 12 they faithfully brought in the **c**,

CONTRITE*
Ps 51: 17 a broken and **c** heart you, God,
Isa 57: 15 with the one who is **c** and lowly
57: 15 and to revive the heart of the **c**.
66: 2 who are humble and **c** in spirit,

CONTROL (CONTROLLED CONTROLS SELF-CONTROL SELF-CONTROLLED)
1Co 7: 9 But if they cannot **c** themselves,
7: 37 but has **c** over his own will,
1Th 4: 4 should learn to **c** your own body

CONTROLLED (CONTROL)
Ps 32: 9 understanding but must be **c** by bit

CONTROLS* (CONTROL)
Job 37: 15 you know how God **c** the clouds

CONTROVERSIES*
Ac 26: 3 with all the Jewish customs and **c**.
1Ti 6: 4 have an unhealthy interest in **c**
Titus 3: 9 But avoid foolish **c** and genealogies

CONVERSATION
Col 4: 6 Let your **c** be always full of grace,

CONVERT
1Ti 3: 6 He must not be a recent **c**, or he

CONVICT (CONVICTED CONVICTION)
Pr 24: 25 go well with those who **c** the guilty,
Jude : 15 to **c** all of them of all the ungodly

CONVICTED (CONVICT)
1Co 14: 24 they are **c** of sin and are brought

CONVICTION* (CONVICT)
1Th 1: 5 with the Holy Spirit and deep **c**.
Heb 3: 14 we hold our original **c** firmly

CONVINCED* (CONVINCING)
Ge 45: 28 And Israel said, "I'm **c**!
Lk 16: 31 they will not be **c** even if someone
Ac 19: 26 hear how this fellow Paul has **c**
26: 9 "I too was **c** that I ought to do all
26: 26 am **c** that none of this has escaped
28: 24 Some were **c** by what he said,
Ro 2: 19 if you are **c** that you are a guide
8: 38 I am **c** that neither death nor life,
14: 5 them should be fully **c** in their own
14: 14 I am **c**, being fully persuaded
15: 14 I myself am **c**, my brothers
2Co 5: 14 because we are **c** that one died
Php 1: 25 **C** of this, I know that I will remain,
2Ti 1: 12 am **c** that he is able to guard what I
3: 14 have learned and have become **c** of,
Heb 6: 9 we are **c** of better things in your

CONVINCING* (CONVINCED)
Ac 1: 3 and gave many **c** proofs that he was

COPIES (COPY)
Heb 9: 23 for the **c** of the heavenly things

COPY (COPIES)
Dt 17: 18 himself on a scroll a **c** of this law,
Heb 8: 5 They serve at a sanctuary that is a **c**
9: 24 that was only a **c** of the true one;

CORBAN*
Mk 7: 11 their father or mother is **C** (that is,

CORD (CORDS)
Jos 2: 18 you have tied this scarlet **c**
Ecc 4: 12 A **c** of three strands is not quickly

CORDS (CORD)
Pr 5: 22 the **c** of their sins hold them fast.
Isa 54: 2 lengthen your **c**, strengthen your
Hos 11: 4 I led them with **c** of human

CORINTH
Ac 18: 1 Paul left Athens and went to **C**.
1Co 1: 2 To the church of God in **C**,
2Co 1: 1 To the church of God in **C**,

CORNELIUS*
Roman to whom Peter preached; first Gentile Christian (Ac 10).

CORNER (CORNERS CORNERSTONE)
Ru 3: 9 "Spread the **c** of your garment over
Pr 21: 9 Better to live on a **c** of the roof
25: 24 Better to live on a **c** of the roof
Ac 26: 26 because it was not done in a **c**.

CORNERS (CORNER)
Mt 6: 5 on the street **c** to be seen by others.
22: 9 So go to the street **c** and invite

CORNERSTONE* (CORNER STONE)
Job 38: 6 its footings set, or who laid its **c**—
Ps 118: 22 builders rejected has become the **c**;
Isa 28: 16 a precious **c** for a sure foundation;
Jer 51: 26 rock will be taken from you for a **c**,
Zec 10: 4 From Judah will come the **c**,
Mt 21: 42 builders rejected has become the **c**;
Mk 12: 10 builders rejected has become the **c**;
Lk 20: 17 rejected has become the **c**'?
Ac 4: 11 rejected, which has become the **c**.'
Eph 2: 20 Christ Jesus himself as the chief **c**.
1Pe 2: 6 a chosen and precious **c**, and the
2: 7 rejected has become the **c**,"

CORRECT* (CORRECTED CORRECTING CORRECTION CORRECTS)
Job 6: 26 Do you mean to **c** what I say,
40: 2 contends with the Almighty **c** him?
2Ti 4: 2 **c**, rebuke and encourage—

CORRECTED* (CORRECT)
Pr 29: 19 Servants cannot be **c** by mere

CORRECTING* (CORRECT)
2Ti 3: 16 **c** and training in righteousness,

CORRECTION* (CORRECT)
Lev 26: 23 things you do not accept my **c**
Job 36: 10 He makes them listen to **c**
Pr 5: 12 How my heart spurned **c**!
6: 23 and **c** and instruction are the way
10: 17 but whoever ignores **c** leads others
12: 1 but whoever hates **c** is stupid.
13: 18 but whoever heeds **c** is honored.
15: 5 whoever heeds **c** shows prudence.
15: 10 the one who hates **c** will die.
15: 12 Mockers resent **c**, so they avoid
15: 31 Whoever heeds life-giving **c** will be
15: 32 who heeds **c** gains understanding.
Jer 2: 30 they did not respond to **c**.
5: 3 crushed them, but they refused **c**.
7: 28 LORD its God or responded to **c**.
Zep 3: 2 She obeys no one, she accepts no **c**.
3: 7 you will fear me and accept **c**!'

CORRECTS* (CORRECT)
Job 5: 17 "Blessed is the one whom God **c**;
Pr 9: 7 Whoever **c** a mocker invites insults

CORRUPT (CORRUPTED CORRUPTION CORRUPTS)
Ge 6: 11 Now the earth was **c** in God's sight
Ps 14: 1 They are **c**, their deeds are vile;
14: 3 turned away, all have become **c**;
Pr 4: 24 keep **c** talk far from your lips.
6: 12 who goes about with a **c** mouth,
19: 28 A **c** witness mocks at justice,

CORRUPTED (CORRUPT)
2Co 7: 2 wronged no one, we have **c** no one,
Titus 1: 15 their minds and consciences are **c**.

CORRUPTION (CORRUPT)
2Pe 1: 4 having escaped the **c** in the world
2: 20 have escaped the **c** of the world

CORRUPTS* (CORRUPT)
Ecc 7: 7 into a fool, and a bribe **c** the heart.
1Co 15: 33 "Bad company **c** good character."
Jas 3: 6 It **c** the whole body, sets the whole

COST (COSTS)
Nu 16: 38 who sinned at the **c** of their lives.
Pr 4: 7 Though it **c** all you have,
7: 23 little knowing it will **c** him his life.
Isa 55: 1 milk without money and without **c**.
Lk 14: 28 estimate the **c** to see if you have
Rev 21: 6 thirsty I will give water without **c**

COSTS (COST)
Pr 6: 31 though it **c** him all the wealth of

COUNCIL
Ps 89: 7 the **c** of the holy ones God is
107: 32 praise him in the **c** of the elders.

COUNSEL (COUNSELOR COUNSELS)
1Ki 22: 5 "First seek the **c** of the LORD."
2Ch 18: 4 "First seek the **c** of the LORD."
Ps 73: 24 You guide me with your **c**,
Pr 8: 14 **C** and sound judgment are mine;
15: 22 Plans fail for lack of **c**,
1Ti 5: 14 So I **c** younger widows to marry,
Rev 3: 18 I **c** you to buy from me gold

COUNSELOR (COUNSEL)
Isa 9: 6 And he will be called Wonderful **C**,
Ro 11: 34 Or who has been his **c**?"

COUNSELS* (COUNSEL)
Ps 16: 7 I will praise the LORD, who **c** me;

COUNT (COUNTED COUNTING COUNTS)
Eze 33: 12 former righteousness will **c**
Ro 4: 8 Lord will never **c** against them."
6: 11 **c** yourselves dead to sin but alive

COUNTED (COUNT)
Ac 5: 41 because they had been **c** worthy
2Th 1: 5 as a result you will be **c** worthy

COUNTERFEIT*
1Jn 2: 27 as that anointing is real, not **c**—

COUNTING (COUNT)
2Co 5: 19 not **c** people's sins against them.

COUNTRY
Pr 28: 2 When a **c** is rebellious, it has many
29: 4 By justice a king gives a **c** stability,
Isa 66: 8 Can a **c** be born in a day or
Lk 15: 13 had, set off for a distant **c** and there
Jn 4: 44 prophet has no honor in his own **c**.)
2Co 11: 26 in danger in the **c**, in danger at sea;
Heb 11: 14 are looking for a **c** of their own.

COUNTS (COUNT)
Jn 6: 63 the flesh **c** for nothing.
1Co 7: 19 God's commands is what **c**.
Gal 5: 6 that **c** is faith expressing itself
6: 15 what **c** is the new creation.

COURAGE* (COURAGEOUS)
Jos 2: 11 everyone's **c** failed because of you,
5: 1 they no longer had the **c** to face
2Sa 4: 1 he lost **c**, and all Israel became
7: 27 So your servant has found **c** to pray
1Ch 17: 25 So your servant has found **c** to pray
2Ch 15: 8 of Oded the prophet, he took **c**.
19: 11 Act with **c**, and may the LORD be
Ezr 7: 28 I took **c** and gathered leaders
10: 4 support you, so take **c** and do it."
Ps 107: 26 in their peril their **c** melted away.
Eze 22: 14 Will your **c** endure or your hands
Da 11: 25 and **c** against the king of the South.
Mt 14: 27 immediately said to them: "Take **c**!
Mk 6: 50 he spoke to them and said, "Take **c**!
Ac 4: 13 When they saw the **c** of Peter
23: 11 stood near Paul and said, "Take **c**!
27: 22 now I urge you to keep up your **c**,
27: 25 So keep up your **c**, men, for I have
Php 1: 20 will have sufficient **c** so that now as

COURAGEOUS* (COURAGE)
Dt 31: 6 Be strong and **c**. Do not be afraid
31: 7 "Be strong and **c**, for you must go
31: 23 "Be strong and **c**, for you will bring
Jos 1: 6 Be strong and **c**, because you will
1: 7 "Be strong and very **c**. Be careful
1: 9 Be strong and **c**. Do not be afraid;
1: 18 to death. Only be strong and **c**!"
10: 25 Be strong and **c**. This is what
1Ch 22: 13 Be strong and **c**. Do not be afraid
28: 20 "Be strong and **c**, and do the work.
2Ch 26: 17 eighty other **c** priests of the LORD
32: 7 "Be strong and **c**. Do not be afraid
1Co 16: 13 firm in the faith; be **c**; be strong.

COURSE
Ps 19: 5 a champion rejoicing to run his **c**.
Pr 2: 8 for he guards the **c** of the just
15: 21 understanding keeps a straight **c**.
16: 9 In their hearts humans plan their **c**,
17: 23 in secret to pervert the **c** of justice.
Jas 3: 6 sets the whole **c** of one's life on fire,

COURT (COURTS)
Pr 22: 22 and do not crush the needy in **c**,
25: 8 do not bring hastily to **c**, for what
Mt 5: 25 adversary who is taking you to **c**.
1Co 4: 3 judged by you or by any human **c**;
6: 6 one brother takes another to **c**—

COURTS (COURT)
Ps 84: 10 your **c** than a thousand elsewhere;
100: 4 thanksgiving and his **c** with praise;
Am 5: 15 maintain justice in the **c**.
Zec 8: 16 and sound judgment in your **c**;

COURTYARD
Ex 27: 9 "Make a **c** for the tabernacle.

COUSIN
Est 2: 7 Mordecai had a **c** named Hadassah
Col 4: 10 as does Mark, the **c** of Barnabas.

COVENANT (COVENANTS)
Ge 9: 9 "I now establish my **c** with you
17: 2 I will make my **c** between me
Ex 19: 5 if you obey me fully and keep my **c**,
24: 7 he took the Book of the **C** and read
Dt 4: 13 He declared to you his **c**, the Ten
29: 1 of the **c** the LORD commanded
Jdg 2: 1 'I will never break my **c** with you,
1Sa 23: 18 them made a **c** before the LORD.
1Ki 8: 21 which is the **c** of the LORD that he
8: 23 you who keep your **c** of love
2Ki 23: 2 all the words of the Book of the **C**,
1Ch 16: 15 He remembers his **c** forever,
2Ch 6: 14 you who keep your **c** of love
34: 30 all the words of the Book of the **C**,
Ne 1: 5 who keeps his **c** of love with those
Job 31: 1 "I made a **c** with my eyes not
Ps 105: 8 He remembers his **c** forever,
Pr 2: 17 ignored the **c** she made before God
Isa 42: 6 make you to be a **c** for the people
61: 8 make an everlasting **c** with them.
Jer 11: 2 "Listen to the terms of this **c**
31: 31 I will make a new **c** with the people
31: 32 It will not be like the **c** I made
31: 32 because they broke my **c**, though I
31: 33 "This is the **c** I will make
Eze 37: 26 will make a **c** of peace with them;
37: 26 it will be an everlasting **c**.
Da 9: 27 He will confirm a **c** with many
Hos 6: 7 at Adam, they have broken the **c**;
Mal 2: 14 the wife of your marriage **c**.
3: 1 the messenger of the **c**, whom you
Mt 26: 28 This is my blood of the **c**, which is
Mk 14: 24 "This is my blood of the **c**, which is
Lk 22: 20 "This cup is the new **c** in my blood,
1Co 11: 25 "This cup is the new **c** in my blood;
2Co 3: 6 as ministers of a new **c**—
Gal 4: 24 One **c** is from Mount Sinai
Heb 8: 6 since the new **c** is established
8: 8 I will make a new **c** with the people
9: 15 Christ is the mediator of a new **c**,
12: 24 to Jesus the mediator of a new **c**,

COVENANTS* (COVENANT)
Ro 9: 4 the **c**, the receiving of the law,
Gal 4: 24 The women represent two **c**.
Eph 2: 12 foreigners to the **c** of the promise,

COVER (COVER-UP COVERED COVERING COVERINGS COVERS)
Ex 25: 17 "Make an atonement **c** of pure
25: 21 Place the **c** on top of the ark and
33: 22 and **c** you with my hand until I
Lev 16: 2 of the atonement **c** on the ark,
16: 2 in the cloud over the atonement **c**.
Ps 32: 5 you and did not **c** up my iniquity.
91: 4 He will **c** you with his feathers,
Hos 10: 8 will say to the mountains, "**C** us!"
Lk 23: 30 and to the hills, "**C** us!"'
1Co 11: 6 if a woman does not **c** her head,
11: 6 shaved, then she should **c** her head.
11: 7 A man ought not to **c** his head,
Jas 5: 20 and **c** over a multitude of sins.

COVER-UP* (COVER)
1Pe 2: 16 do not use your freedom as a **c**

COVERED (COVER)
Ps 32: 1 are forgiven, whose sins are **c**.
85: 2 of your people and **c** all their sins.
Isa 6: 2 With two wings they **c** their faces,
51: 16 **c** you with the shadow of my hand
Ro 4: 7 are forgiven, whose sins are **c**.
1Co 11: 4 with his head **c** dishonors his head.

COVERING (COVER)
1Co 11: 15 For long hair is given to her as a **c**.

COVERINGS (COVER)
Ge 3: 7 and made **c** for themselves.
Pr 31: 22 She makes **c** for her bed;

COVERS (COVER)
Pr 10: 12 conflict, but love **c** over all wrongs.
17: 9 would foster love **c** over an offense,
2Co 3: 15 Moses is read, a veil **c** their hearts.
1Pe 4: 8 because love **c** over a multitude

COVET* (COVETED COVETING)
Ex 20: 17 "You shall not **c** your neighbor's
20: 17 You shall not **c** your neighbor's
34: 24 no one will **c** your land when you
Dt 5: 21 "You shall not **c** your neighbor's
7: 25 Do not **c** the silver and gold
Mic 2: 2 They **c** fields and seize them,
Ro 7: 7 had not said, "You shall not **c**."
13: 9 "You shall not **c**," and whatever
Jas 4: 2 You **c** but you cannot get what you

COVETED* (COVET)
Jos 7: 21 shekels, I **c** them and took them.
Ac 20: 33 I have not **c** anyone's silver or gold

COVETING*
Ro 7: 7 not have known what **c** really was
7: 8 produced in me every kind of **c**.

COWARDLY*
Rev 21: 8 But the **c**, the unbelieving, the vile,

COWS
Ge 41: 2 of the river there came up seven **c**,
1Sa 6: 7 with two **c** that have calved

CRAFTINESS* (CRAFTY)
Job 5: 13 He catches the wise in their **c**,
1Co 3: 19 "He catches the wise in their **c**";
Eph 4: 14 and **c** of people in their deceitful

CRAFTY* (CRAFTINESS)
Ge 3: 1 the serpent was more **c** than any
1Sa 23: 22 They tell me he is very **c**.
Job 5: 12 He thwarts the plans of the **c**,
15: 5 you adopt the tongue of the **c**.
Pr 7: 10 like a prostitute and with **c** intent.
2Co 12: 16 Yet, **c** fellow that I am, I caught you

CRAVE* (CRAVED CRAVES CRAVING CRAVINGS)
Nu 11: 4 with them began to **c** other food,
Dt 12: 20 you, and you **c** meat and say,
Pr 21: 10 The wicked **c** evil;
23: 3 not **c** his delicacies, for that food
23: 6 host, do not **c** his delicacies;
31: 4 drink wine, not for rulers to **c** beer,
Mic 7: 1 eat, none of the early figs that I **c**.
1Pe 2: 2 babies, **c** pure spiritual milk,

CRAVED* (CRAVE)
Nu 11: 34 the people who had **c** other food.
Ps 78: 18 test by demanding the food they **c**.
78: 29 he had given them what they **c**.
78: 30 they turned from what they **c**,

CRAVES* (CRAVES)
Pr 21: 26 All day long he **c** for more,

CRAVING* (CRAVE)
Job 20: 20 he will have no respite from his **c**;
Ps 106: 14 In the desert they gave in to their **c**;
Pr 10: 3 but he thwarts the **c** of the wicked.
21: 25 **c** of a sluggard will be the death
Jer 2: 24 desert, sniffing the wind in her **c**—

CRAVINGS* (CRAVE)
Ps 10: 3 He boasts about the **c** of his heart;
Eph 2: 3 gratifying the **c** of our flesh

CRAWL
Ge 3: 14 You will **c** on your belly and you

CREATE* (CREATED CREATES CREATING CREATION CREATOR)
Ps 51: 10 **C** in me a pure heart, O God,
Isa 4: 5 the LORD will **c** over all of Mount
45: 7 I form the light and **c** darkness,
45: 7 I bring prosperity and **c** disaster;
45: 18 he did not **c** it to be empty,
65: 17 I will **c** new heavens and a new
65: 18 and rejoice forever in what I will **c**,
65: 18 I will **c** Jerusalem to be a delight
Jer 31: 22 The LORD will **c** a new thing
Mal 2: 10 Did not one God **c** us? Why do we
Eph 2: 15 His purpose was to **c** in himself

CREATED* (CREATE)
Ge 1: 1 the beginning God **c** the heavens
1: 21 So God **c** the great creatures
1: 27 So God **c** mankind in his own
1: 27 in the image of God he **c** them; male and female he **c** them.
2: 4 and the earth when they were **c**,
5: 1 When God **c** mankind, he made
5: 2 He **c** them male and female
5: 2 "Mankind" when they were **c**.
6: 7 earth the human race I have **c**—
Dt 4: 32 the day God **c** human beings
Ps 89: 12 You **c** the north and the south;
89: 47 futility you have **c** all humanity!
102: 18 a people not yet **c** may praise
104: 30 they are **c**, and you renew the face
139: 13 For you **c** my inmost being;
148: 5 for at his command they were **c**,
Ecc 7: 29 God **c** mankind upright, but they
Isa 40: 26 to the heavens: Who **c** all these?
41: 20 that the Holy One of Israel has **c** it.
43: 1 he who **c** you, Jacob, he who
43: 7 my name, whom I **c** for my glory,
45: 8 I, the LORD, have **c** it.
45: 12 the earth and **c** mankind on it.
45: 18 he who **c** the heavens, he is God;
48: 7 They are **c** now, and not long ago;
54: 16 it is I who **c** the blacksmith who
54: 16 it is I who have **c** the destroyer
57: 16 the very people I have **c**.
Eze 21: 30 In the place where you were **c**,
28: 13 day you were **c** they were prepared.
28: 15 day you were **c** till wickedness was
Mk 13: 19 when God **c** the world, until now—
Ro 1: 25 and served **c** things rather than
1Co 11: 9 neither was man **c** for woman,
Eph 2: 10 **c** in Christ Jesus to do good works,
3: 9 hidden in God, who **c** all things.
4: 24 the new self, **c** to be like God in
Col 1: 16 For in him all things were **c**:
1: 16 all things have been **c** through him
1Ti 4: 3 which God **c** to be received
4: 4 For everything God **c** is good,
Heb 12: 27 that is, **c** things—so that what
Jas 1: 18 be a kind of firstfruits of all he **c**.
Rev 4: 11 for you **c** all things, and by your will they were **c**
10: 6 who **c** the heavens and all that is

CREATES* (CREATE)
Am 4: 13 the mountains, who **c** the wind,

CREATING* (CREATE)
Ge 2: 3 all the work of **c** that he had done.
Isa 57: 19 **c** praise on their lips.

CREATION* (CREATE)
Ps 96: 13 Let all **c** rejoice before the LORD,
Hab 2: 18 who makes it trusts in his own **c**;
Mt 13: 35 will utter things hidden since the **c**
25: 34 for you since the **c** of the world.
Mk 10: 6 of **c** God 'made them male
16: 15 *preach the gospel to all* **c**.
Jn 17: 24 because you loved me before the **c**
Ro 1: 20 For since the **c** of the world God's
8: 19 For the **c** waits in eager expectation
8: 20 For the **c** was subjected
8: 21 that the **c** itself will be liberated
8: 22 the whole **c** has been groaning as
8: 39 nor anything else in all **c**, will be
2Co 5: 17 is in Christ, the new **c** has come:
Gal 6: 15 what counts is the new **c**.
Eph 1: 4 us in him before the **c** of the world
Col 1: 15 God, the firstborn over all **c**.
Heb 4: 3 have been finished since the **c**
4: 13 Nothing in all **c** is hidden
9: 11 that is to say, is not a part of this **c**.
9: 26 suffer many times since the **c**
1Pe 1: 20 He was chosen before the **c**
2Pe 3: 4 as it has since the beginning of **c**."
Rev 3: 14 true witness, the ruler of God's **c**.
13: 8 was slain from the **c** of the world.
17: 8 book of life from the **c** of the world

CREATOR* (CREATE)
Ge 14: 19 Most High, **C** of heaven and earth.
14: 22 Most High, **C** of heaven and earth,
Dt 32: 6 your **C**, who made you and formed
Ecc 12: 1 Remember your **C** in the days
Isa 27: 11 and their **C** shows them no favor.
40: 28 God, the **C** of the ends of the earth.
42: 5 the **C** of the heavens, who stretches
43: 15 Holy One, Israel's **C**, your King."
Mt 19: 4 at the beginning the **C** 'made them
Ro 1: 25 created things rather than the **C**—
Col 3: 10 in knowledge in the image of its **C**.
1Pe 4: 19 themselves to their faithful **C**

CREATURE (CREATURES)
Lev 17: 11 For the life of a **c** is in the blood,
17: 14 the life of every **c** is its blood.
17: 14 must not eat the blood of any **c**,
Ps 136: 25 He gives food to every **c**.
Eze 1: 15 on the ground beside each **c** with
Rev 4: 7 The first living **c** was like a lion,

CREATURES (CREATURE)
Ge 6: 19 into the ark two of all living **c**,
8: 21 again will I destroy all living **c**, as I
Ps 104: 24 the earth is full of your **c**.
Eze 1: 5 was what looked like four living **c**.

CREDIT (CREDITED CREDITOR CREDITS)
Lk 6: 33 good to you, what **c** is that to you?
Ro 4: 24 whom God will **c** righteousness—
1Pe 2: 20 it to your **c** if you receive a beating

CREDITED (CREDIT)
Ge 15: 6 and he **c** it to him as righteousness.
Ps 106: 31 This was **c** to him as righteousness
Eze 18: 20 of the righteous will be **c** to them,
Ro 4: 3 it was **c** to him as righteousness."
4: 4 wages are not **c** as a gift but as
4: 5 their faith is **c** as righteousness.
4: 9 Abraham's faith was **c** to him as
4: 23 The words "it was **c** to him" were
Gal 3: 6 it was **c** to him as righteousness."
Php 4: 17 is that more be **c** to your account.
Jas 2: 23 it was **c** to him as righteousness,"

CREDITOR (CREDIT)
Dt 15: 2 Every **c** shall cancel any loan they

CREDITS* (CREDIT)
Ro 4: 6 whom God **c** righteousness apart

CRETANS (CRETE)
Titus 1: 12 "**C** are always liars, evil brutes,

CRETE (CRETANS)
Ac 27: 12 This was a harbor in **C**, facing both

CRIED (CRY)
Ex 2: 23 groaned in their slavery and **c** out,
14: 10 terrified and **c** out to the LORD.
Nu 20: 16 but when we **c** out to the LORD,
Jos 24: 7 But they **c** to the LORD for help,
Jdg 3: 9 But when they **c** out to the LORD,
3: 15 Again the Israelites **c**
4: 3 they **c** to the LORD for help.
6: 6 the Israelites that they **c**
10: 12 you and you **c** to me for help, did I
1Sa 7: 9 He **c** out to the LORD on Israel's
12: 8 they **c** to the LORD for help,
12: 10 They **c** out to the LORD and said,
Ps 18: 6 I **c** to my God for help.

CRIMINALS
Lk 23: 32 both **c**, were also led out with him

CRIMSON
Isa 1: 18 though they are red as **c**, they shall
63: 1 with his garments stained **c**?

CRIPPLED
Mk 9: 45 to enter life **c** than to have two feet

CRISIS*
1Co 7: 26 Because of the present **c**, I think

CRITICISM*
2Co 8: 20 want to avoid any **c** of the way we

CROOKED*
Dt 32: 5 are a warped and **c** generation.
Ps 125: 5 to **c** ways the LORD will banish
Pr 2: 15 whose paths are **c** and who are
8: 8 none of them is **c** or perverse.
10: 9 whoever takes **c** paths will be
Ecc 1: 15 What is **c** cannot be straightened;
7: 13 can straighten what he has made **c**?
Isa 59: 8 have turned them into **c** roads;
La 3: 9 he has made my paths **c**.
Lk 3: 5 The **c** roads shall become straight,
Php 2: 15 fault in a warped and **c** generation."

CROP (CROPS)
Mt 13: 8 good soil, where it produced a **c**—
21: 41 his share of the **c** at harvest time."

CROPS (CROP)
Pr 3: 9 with the firstfruits of all your **c**;
10: 5 He who gathers **c** in summer is
28: 3 like a driving rain that leaves no **c**.
2Ti 2: 6 the first to receive a share of the **c**.

CROSS (CROSSED CROSSING)
Dt 4: 21 swore that I would not **c** the Jordan
12: 10 But you will **c** the Jordan and settle
Mt 10: 38 Whoever does not take up their **c**
16: 24 and take up their **c** and follow me.
Mk 8: 34 and take up their **c** and follow me.
Lk 9: 23 take up their **c** daily and follow me.
14: 27 whoever does not carry their **c**
Jn 19: 17 Carrying his own **c**, he went
Ac 2: 23 to death by nailing him to the **c**.
5: 30 you killed by hanging him on a **c**.
1Co 1: 17 lest the **c** of Christ be emptied of
1: 18 the message of the **c** is foolishness
Gal 5: 11 offense of the **c** has been abolished.
6: 12 persecuted for the **c** of Christ.
6: 14 in the **c** of our Lord Jesus Christ,
Eph 2: 16 both of them to God through the **c**,
Php 2: 8 even death on a **c**!
3: 18 live as enemies of the **c** of Christ.
Col 1: 20 through his blood, shed on the **c**.
2: 14 taken it away, nailing it to the **c**.
2: 15 triumphing over them by the **c**.
Heb 12: 2 set before him he endured the **c**,
1Pe 2: 24 bore our sins" in his body on the **c**,

CROSSED (CROSS)
Jos 4: 7 When it **c** the Jordan, the waters
Jn 5: 24 but has **c** over from death to life.

CROSSING (CROSS)
Ge 48: 14 and **c** his arms, he put his left hand

CROSSROADS (ROAD)
Jer 6: 16 "Stand at the **c** and look;

CROUCHING
Ge 4: 7 what is right, sin is **c** at your door;

CROWD (CROWDS)
Ex 23: 2 pervert justice by siding with the **c**,

CROWDS (CROWD)
Mt 9: 36 When he saw the **c**, he had

CROWED (CROWS)
Mt 26: 74 Immediately a rooster **c**.

CROWN (CROWNED CROWNS)
Pr 4: 9 and present you with a glorious **c**."
10: 6 Blessings **c** the head
12: 4 noble character is her husband's **c**,
16: 31 Gray hair is a **c** of splendor;
17: 6 Children's children are a **c**
Isa 35: 10 everlasting joy will **c** their heads.
51: 11 everlasting joy will **c** their heads.
61: 3 on them a **c** of beauty instead
62: 3 You will be a **c** of splendor
Eze 16: 12 and a beautiful **c** on your head.
Zec 9: 16 in his land like jewels in a **c**.
Mt 27: 29 then twisted together a **c** of thorns
Mk 15: 17 then twisted together a **c** of thorns
Jn 19: 2 The soldiers twisted together a **c**
19: 5 came out wearing the **c** of thorns
1Co 9: 25 do it to get a **c** that will not last,
9: 25 to get a **c** that will last forever.
Php 4: 1 joy and **c**, stand firm in the Lord
1Th 2: 19 the **c** in which we will glory
2Ti 2: 5 not receive the victor's **c** except
4: 8 store for me the **c** of righteousness,
Jas 1: 12 that person will receive the **c** of life
1Pe 5: 4 you will receive the **c** of glory
Rev 2: 10 will give you life as your victor's **c**.
3: 11 so that no one will take your **c**.
14: 14 of man with a **c** of gold on his head

CROWNED* (CROWN)
Ps 8: 5 the angels and **c** them with glory
Pr 14: 18 the prudent are **c** with knowledge.
SS 3: 11 which his mother **c** him on the day
Heb 2: 7 you **c** them with glory and honor
2: 9 now **c** with glory and honor

CROWNS (CROWN)
Ps 103: 4 from the pit and **c** you with love
149: 4 he **c** the humble with victory.
Rev 4: 4 and had **c** of gold on their heads.
4: 10 They lay their **c** before the throne
12: 3 ten horns and seven **c** on its heads.
19: 12 fire, and on his head are many **c**.

CROWS (CROWED)
Mt 26: 34 night, before the rooster **c**, you will

CRUCIFIED* (CRUCIFY)
Mt 20: 19 to be mocked and flogged and **c**.
26: 2 Man will be handed over to be **c**."
27: 26 and handed him over to be **c**.
27: 35 When they had **c** him, they divided
27: 38 Two rebels were **c** with him,
27: 44 same way the rebels who were **c**
28: 5 are looking for Jesus, who was **c**.
Mk 15: 15 and handed him over to be **c**.

Mk 15: 24 And they **c** him. Dividing up his
15: 25 in the morning when they **c** him.
15: 27 They **c** two rebels with him,
15: 32 Those **c** with him also heaped
16: 6 for Jesus the Nazarene, who was **c**.
Lk 23: 23 insistently demanded that he be **c**,
23: 33 called the Skull, they **c** him there,
24: 7 be **c** and on the third day be raised
24: 20 to death, and they **c** him;
Jn 19: 16 handed him over to them to be **c**.
19: 18 There they **c** him, and with him
19: 20 where Jesus was **c** was near the city,
19: 23 When the soldiers **c** Jesus, they
19: 32 the first man who had been **c**
19: 41 At the place where Jesus was **c**,
Ac 2: 36 Jesus, whom you **c**, both Lord
4: 10 whom you **c** but whom God raised
Ro 6: 6 that our old self was **c** with him so
1Co 1: 13 Was Paul **c** for you?
1: 23 but we preach Christ **c**:
2: 2 you except Jesus Christ and him **c**.
2: 8 they would not have **c** the Lord
2Co 13: 4 to be sure, he was **c** in weakness,
Gal 2: 20 I have been **c** with Christ and I no
3: 1 Christ was clearly portrayed as **c**.
5: 24 have **c** the flesh with its passions
6: 14 which the world has been **c** to me,
Rev 11: 8 where also their Lord was **c**.

CRUCIFY* (CRUCIFIED CRUCIFYING)
Mt 23: 34 Some of them you will kill and **c**;
27: 22 They all answered, "**C** him!"
27: 23 shouted all the louder, "**C** him!"
27: 31 Then they led him away to **c** him.
Mk 15: 13 "**C** him!" they shouted.
15: 14 shouted all the louder, "**C** him!"
15: 20 Then they led him out to **c** him.
Lk 23: 21 kept shouting, "**C** him! **C** him!"
Jn 19: 6 saw him, they shouted, "**C**! **C**!"
19: 6 "You take him and **c** him.
19: 10 either to free you or to **c** you?"
19: 15 **C** him!" "Shall I **c** your king?"

CRUCIFYING* (CRUCIFY)
Heb 6: 6 their loss they are **c** the Son of God

CRUSH (CRUSHED)
Ge 3: 15 he will **c** your head, and you will
Isa 53: 10 it was the Lord's will to **c** him
Ro 16: 20 peace will soon **c** Satan under your

CRUSHED (CRUSH)
Ps 34: 18 and saves those who are **c** in spirit.
Pr 17: 22 but a **c** spirit dries up the bones.
18: 14 but a **c** spirit who can bear?
Isa 53: 5 he was **c** for our iniquities;
2Co 4: 8 pressed on every side, but not **c**;

CRY (CRIED)
Ex 2: 23 their **c** for help because of their
Ps 5: 2 Hear my **c** for help, my King
34: 15 and his ears are attentive to their **c**;
40: 1 he turned to me and heard my **c**.
130: 1 Out of the depths I **c** to you,
Pr 21: 13 their ears to the **c** of the poor will
La 2: 18 The hearts of the people **c**
Hab 2: 11 The stones of the wall will **c** out,
Lk 19: 40 keep quiet, the stones will **c** out."

CULMINATION
Ro 10: 4 Christ is the **c** of the law so

CUNNING
2Co 11: 3 was deceived by the serpent's **c**,
Eph 4: 14 by the **c** and craftiness of people

CUP
Ps 23: 5 my head with oil; my **c** overflows.
Isa 51: 22 that **c**, the goblet of my wrath,
Mt 10: 42 anyone gives even a **c** of cold water
20: 22 "Can you drink the **c** I am going
23: 25 You clean the outside of the **c**
23: 26 First clean the inside of the **c**
26: 27 Then he took a **c**, and when he had
26: 39 may this **c** be taken from me.
26: 42 for this **c** to be taken away unless I
Mk 9: 41 anyone who gives you a **c** of water
10: 38 "Can you drink the **c** I drink or be
10: 39 "You will drink the **c** I drink and
14: 23 Then he took a **c**, and when he had
14: 36 Take this **c** from me.
Lk 11: 39 Pharisees clean the outside of the **c**
22: 17 After taking the **c**, he gave thanks
22: 20 "This **c** is the new covenant in my
22: 42 are willing, take this **c** from me;
Jn 18: 11 Shall I not drink the **c** the Father
1Co 10: 16 Is not the **c** of thanksgiving
1Co 10: 21 You cannot drink the **c** of the Lord and the **c** of demons too;
11: 25 "This **c** is the new covenant in my

CUPBEARER
Ge 40: 1 the **c** and the baker of the king
Ne 1: 11 of this man." I was **c** to the king.

CURE (CURED)
Jer 17: 9 above all things and beyond **c**.
30: 15 wound, your pain that has no **c**?
Hos 5: 13 But he is not able to **c** you, not able
Lk 9: 1 out all demons and to **c** diseases,

CURED (CURE)
Lk 6: 18 troubled by impure spirits were **c**,

CURSE (ACCURSED CURSED CURSES CURSING)
Ge 4: 11 Now you are under a **c** and driven
8: 21 again will I **c** the ground because
12: 3 and whoever curses you I will **c**;
Dt 11: 26 you today a blessing and a **c**—
11: 28 the **c** if you disobey the commands
21: 23 is hung on a pole is under God's **c**.
23: 5 turned the **c** into a blessing for you,
Job 1: 11 he will surely **c** you to your face."
2: 5 he will surely **c** you to your face."
2: 9 **C** God and die!"
Ps 109: 28 While they **c**, may you bless;
Pr 3: 33 The Lord's **c** is on the house
Jer 42: 18 You will be a **c** and an object
Mal 2: 2 "I will send a **c** on you, and I will **c** your blessings.
Lk 6: 28 bless those who **c** you,
Ro 12: 14 bless and do not **c**.
Gal 1: 8 to you, let them be under God's **c**!
3: 10 the works of the law are under a **c**,
3: 13 redeemed us from the **c** of the law by becoming a **c** for us,
Jas 3: 9 and with it we **c** human beings,
Rev 22: 3 No longer will there be any **c**.

CURSED (CURSE)
Ge 3: 17 "**C** is the ground because of you;
Dt 27: 15 "**C** is anyone who makes an idol—
27: 16 "**C** is anyone who dishonors their
27: 17 "**C** is anyone who moves their
27: 18 "**C** is anyone who leads the blind
27: 19 "**C** is anyone who withholds justice
27: 20 "**C** is anyone who sleeps with his
27: 21 "**C** is anyone who has sexual
27: 22 "**C** is anyone who sleeps with his
27: 23 "**C** is anyone who sleeps with his
27: 24 "**C** is anyone who kills their
27: 25 "**C** is anyone who accepts a bribe
27: 26 "**C** is anyone who does not uphold
Pr 24: 24 be **c** by peoples and denounced
Jer 17: 5 "**C** is the one who trusts in man,
Mal 1: 14 "**C** is the cheat who has
Ro 9: 3 I could wish that I myself were **c**
1Co 12: 3 When we are **c**, we bless;
12: 3 "Jesus be **c**," and no one can say,
Gal 3: 10 "**C** is everyone who does not
3: 13 "**C** is everyone who is hung

CURSES (CURSE)
Ex 21: 17 "Anyone who **c** their father
Lev 20: 9 "'Anyone who **c** their father
Nu 5: 23 priest is to write these **c** on a scroll
Jos 8: 34 the blessings and the **c**—just as it is
Pr 20: 20 someone **c** their father or mother,
28: 27 their eyes to them receive many **c**.
Mt 15: 4 and 'Anyone who **c** their father
Mk 7: 10 and, 'Anyone who **c** their father

CURSING (CURSE)
Ps 109: 18 He wore **c** as his garment;
Ro 3: 14 "Their mouths are full of **c**
Jas 3: 10 the same mouth come praise and **c**.

CURTAIN
Ex 26: 31 "Make a **c** of blue,
26: 33 The **c** will separate the Holy Place
Mt 27: 51 that moment the **c** of the temple
Mk 15: 38 The **c** of the temple was torn in
Lk 23: 45 the **c** of the temple was torn in two.
Heb 6: 19 the inner sanctuary behind the **c**,
9: 3 Behind the second **c** was a room
10: 20 way opened for us through the **c**,

CUSTODY
Gal 3: 23 we were held in **c** under the law,

CUSTOM
Job 1: 5 This was Job's regular **c**.
Mk 10: 1 and as was his **c**, he taught them.
Lk 4: 16 into the synagogue, as was his **c**.
Ac 17: 2 As was his **c**, Paul went

CUT
Lev 19: 27 "'Do not **c** the hair at the sides
21: 5 of their beards or **c** their bodies.
1Ki 3: 25 "**C** the living child in two and give
Isa 51: 1 to the rock from which you were **c**
53: 8 For he was **c** off from the land
Da 2: 45 of the vision of the rock **c**
Mt 3: 10 produce good fruit will be **c** down
24: 22 "If those days had not been **c** short,
1Co 11: 6 for a woman to have her hair **c** off

CYMBAL* (CYMBALS)
1Co 13: 1 a resounding gong or a clanging **c**.

CYMBALS (CYMBAL)
1Ch 15: 16 lyres, harps and **c**.
2Ch 5: 12 dressed in fine linen and playing **c**,
Ps 150: 5 praise him with the clash of **c**,
150: 5 praise him with resounding **c**.

CYRUS
Persian king who allowed exiles to return (2Ch 36:22–Ezr 1:8), to rebuild temple (Ezr 5:13—6:14), as appointed by the Lord (Isa 44:28—45:13).

DAGON
Jdg 16: 23 a great sacrifice to **D** their god
1Sa 5: 2 Dagon's temple and set it beside **D**.

DAMASCUS
Ac 9: 3 As he neared **D** on his journey,

DAN
1. Son of Jacob by Bilhah (Ge 30:4–6; 35:25; 46:23). Tribe of blessed (Ge 49:16–17; Dt 33:22), numbered (Nu 1:39; 26:43), allotted land (Jos 19:40–48; Eze 48:1), failed to fully possess (Jdg 1:34–35), failed to support Deborah (Jdg 5:17), possessed Laish/Dan (Jdg 18).
2. Northernmost city in Israel (Ge 14:14; Jdg 18; 20:1).

DANCE (DANCED DANCING)
Ecc 3: 4 a time to mourn and a time to **d**,
Mt 11: 17 the pipe for you, and you did not **d**;

DANCED (DANCE)
Mk 6: 22 of Herodias came in and **d**,

DANCING (DANCE)
2Sa 6: 14 David was **d** before the Lord
Ps 30: 11 You turned my wailing into **d**;
149: 3 Let them praise his name with **d**

DANGER
Pr 22: 3 The prudent see **d** and take refuge,
27: 12 The prudent see **d** and take refuge,
Mt 5: 22 will be in **d** of the fire of hell.
Ro 8: 35 or nakedness or **d** or sword?
2Co 11: 26 bandits, in **d** from my fellow Jews,

DANIEL
1. Hebrew exile to Babylon, name changed to Belteshazzar (Da 1:6–7). Refused to eat unclean food (Da 1:8–21). Interpreted Nebuchadnezzar's dreams (Da 2; 4), writing on the wall (Da 5). Thrown into lion's den (Da 6). Visions of (Da 7–12).
2. Son of David (1Ch 3:1).

DARIUS
1. King of Persia (Ezr 4:5), allowed rebuilding of temple (Ezr 5–6).
2. Mede who conquered Babylon (Da 5:31).

DARK (DARKENED DARKENS DARKEST DARKNESS)
Ps 18: 9 **d** clouds were under his feet.
SS 1: 6 Do not stare at me because I am **d**,
Jn 12: 35 the **d** does not know where they
Ro 2: 19 a light for those who are in the **d**,
2Pe 1: 19 it, as to a light shining in a **d** place,

DARKENED (DARK)
Joel 2: 10 the sun and moon are **d**,
Mt 24: 29 of those days "'the sun will be **d**,
Ro 1: 21 and their foolish hearts were **d**.
Eph 4: 18 They are **d** in their understanding

DARKENS* (DARK)
Am 5: 8 into dawn and **d** day into night,

DARKEST* (DARK)
Ps 23: 4 though I walk through the **d** valley,
88: 6 in the lowest pit, in the **d** depths.

DARKNESS (DARK)
Ge 1: 2 **d** was over the surface of the deep,
1: 4 he separated the light from the **d**.
Ex 10: 22 total **d** covered all Egypt for three
20: 21 approached the thick **d** where God
2Sa 22: 29 the Lord turns my **d** into light.

Ps 18: 28 my God turns my **d** into light.
91: 6 the pestilence that stalks in the **d**,
112: 4 Even in **d** light dawns
139: 12 day, for **d** is as light to you.
Pr 4: 19 way of the wicked is like deep **d**;
Isa 5: 20 who put **d** for light and light for **d**,
42: 16 I will turn the **d** into light before
45: 7 I form the light and create **d**,
58: 10 then your light will rise in the **d**,
61: 1 release from **d** for the prisoners,
Joel 2: 31 The sun will be turned to **d**
Mt 4: 16 living in **d** have seen a great light;
6: 23 If then the light within you is **d**,
Lk 11: 34 your body also is full of **d**.
23: 44 **d** came over the whole land until
Jn 1: 5 The light shines in the **d**, and the **d**
3: 19 but people loved **d** instead of light
Ac 2: 20 The sun will be turned to **d**
2Co 4: 6 "Let light shine out of **d**," made his
6: 14 fellowship can light have with **d**?
Eph 5: 8 For you were once **d**, but now you
5: 11 to do with the fruitless deeds of **d**,
1Pe 2: 9 out of **d** into his wonderful light.
2Pe 2: 17 Blackest **d** is reserved for them.
1Jn 1: 5 in him there is no **d** at all.
2: 9 a brother or sister is still in the **d**.
Jude : 6 these he has kept in **d**,
: 13 whom blackest **d** has been reserved

DASH
Ps 2: 9 you will **d** them to pieces like

DAUGHTER (DAUGHTERS)
Ex 2: 10 she took him to Pharaoh's **d** and he
Jdg 11: 40 commemorate the **d** of Jephthah
Est 2: 7 had taken her as his own **d** when
Ps 9: 14 your praises in the gates of **D** Zion,
137: 8 **D** Babylon, doomed to destruction
Isa 62: 11 "Say to **D** Zion, 'See, your Savior
Zec 9: 9 Rejoice greatly, **D** Zion! Shout,
Mk 5: 34 He said to her, "**D**, your faith has
7: 29 the demon has left your **d**."

DAUGHTERS (DAUGHTER)
Ge 6: 2 the **d** of humans were beautiful,
19: 36 So both of Lot's **d** became pregnant
Nu 36: 10 So Zelophehad's **d** did as
Joel 2: 28 Your sons and **d** will prophesy,

DAVID
Son of Jesse (Ru 4:17–22; 1Ch 2:13–15), ancestor of Jesus (Mt 1:1–17; Lk 3:31). Wives and children (1Sa 18; 25:39–44; 2Sa 3:2–5; 5:13–16; 11:27; 1Ch 3:1–9).

Anointed king by Samuel (1Sa 16:1–13). Musician to Saul (1Sa 16:14–23; 18:10). Killed Goliath (1Sa 17). Relation with Jonathan (1Sa 18:1–4; 19–20; 23:16–18; 2Sa 1). Disfavor of Saul (1Sa 18:6—23:29). Spared Saul's life (1Sa 24; 26). Among Philistines (1Sa 21:10–14; 27–30). Lament for Saul and Jonathan (2Sa 1).

Anointed king of Judah (2Sa 2:1–11). Conflict with house of Saul (2Sa 2–4). Anointed king of Israel (2Sa 5:1–4; 1Ch 11:1–3). Conquered Jerusalem (2Sa 5:6–10; 1Ch 11:4–9). Brought ark to Jerusalem (2Sa 6; 1Ch 13; 15–16). The LORD promised eternal dynasty (2Sa 7; 1Ch 17; Ps 132). Showed kindness to Mephibosheth (2Sa 9). Adultery with Bathsheba, murder of Uriah (2Sa 11–12). Son Amnon raped daughter Tamar; killed by Absalom (2Sa 13). Absalom's revolt (2Sa 14–17); death (2Sa 18). Sheba's revolt (2Sa 20). Victories: Philistines (2Sa 5:17–25; 1Ch 14:8–17; 2Sa 21:15–22; 1Ch 20:4–8), Ammonites (2Sa 10; 1Ch 19), various (2Sa 8; 1Ch 18). Mighty men (2Sa 23:8–39; 1Ch 11–12). Punished for numbering army (2Sa 24; 1Ch 21). Appointed Solomon king (1Ki 1:28—2:9). Prepared for building of temple (1Ch 22–29). Last words (2Sa 23:1–7). Death (1Ki 2:10–12; 1Ch 29:28).

Psalmist (Mt 22:43–45), musician (Am 6:5), prophet (2Sa 23:2–7; Ac 1:16; 2:30).

Psalms of: 2 (Ac 4:25), 3–32, 34–41, 51–65, 68–70, 86, 95 (Heb 4:7), 101, 103, 108–110, 122, 124, 131, 133, 138–145.

DAWN (DAWNED DAWNS)
Ps 37: 6 righteous reward shine like the **d**,
Isa 14: 12 heaven, morning star, son of the **d**!
Am 4: 13 mankind, who turns **d** to darkness,
5: 8 who turns midnight into **d**

DAWNED (DAWN)
Isa 9: 2 land of deep darkness a light has **d**.
Mt 4: 16 the shadow of death a light has **d**."

DAWNS* (DAWN)
Ps 65: 8 where morning **d**, where evening
112: 4 in darkness light **d** for the upright,
Hos 10: 15 When that day **d**, the king of Israel
2Pe 1: 19 the day **d** and the morning star

DAY (DAYS)
Ge 1: 5 God called the light "**d**,"
1: 5 there was morning—the first **d**.
1: 8 there was morning—the second **d**.
1: 13 there was morning—the third **d**.
1: 19 there was morning—the fourth **d**.
1: 23 there was morning—the fifth **d**.
1: 31 there was morning—the sixth **d**.
2: 2 so on the seventh **d** he rested
8: 22 **d** and night will never cease."
Ex 16: 30 the people rested on the seventh **d**.
20: 8 "Remember the Sabbath **d**
Lev 16: 30 on this **d** atonement will be made
23: 28 Do not do any work on that **d**, because it is the **D** of Atonement,
Nu 14: 14 in a pillar of cloud by **d**
Jos 1: 8 meditate on it **d** and night,
2Ki 7: 9 This is a **d** of good news and we
25: 30 **D** by **d** the king gave Jehoiachin
1Ch 16: 23 proclaim his salvation **d** after **d**.
Ne 8: 18 **D** after **d**, from the first **d**
Ps 84: 10 Better is one **d** in your courts than
96: 2 proclaim his salvation **d** after **d**.
118: 24 The LORD has done it this very **d**;
Pr 27: 1 do not know what a **d** may bring.
Isa 13: 9 the **d** of the LORD is coming—
13: 9 a cruel **d**, with wrath and fierce
Jer 46: 10 But that **d** belongs to the Lord,
50: 31 "for your **d** has come, the time
Eze 30: 2 and say, "Alas for that **d**!"
Joel 1: 15 Alas for that **d**! For the **d**
2: 31 great and dreadful **d** of the LORD.
Am 3: 14 "On the **d** I punish Israel for her
5: 20 Will not the **d** of the LORD be
Ob : 15 "The **d** of the LORD is near for all
Zep 1: 14 The great **d** of the LORD is near—
Zec 2: 11 be joined with the LORD in that **d**
14: 1 A **d** of the LORD is coming,
14: 7 a unique **d**—a **d** known only
Mal 4: 5 dreadful **d** of the LORD comes.
Mt 24: 38 up to the **d** Noah entered the ark;
Lk 11: 3 Give us each **d** our daily bread.
17: 24 in his **d** will be like the lightning,
Ac 5: 42 **D** after **d**, in the temple courts
17: 11 examined the Scriptures every **d**
17: 17 as well as in the marketplace **d** by **d**
Ro 14: 5 considers one **d** more sacred
14: 5 another considers every **d** alike.
1Co 5: 5 may be saved on the **d** of the Lord.
2Co 4: 16 we are being renewed **d** by **d**.
11: 25 a night and a **d** in the open sea,
1Th 5: 2 the **d** of the Lord will come like
5: 4 that this **d** should surprise you like
2Th 2: 2 the **d** of the Lord has already come.
Heb 7: 27 need to offer sacrifices **d** after **d**,
2Pe 3: 8 the Lord a **d** is like a thousand
3: 8 and a thousand years are like a **d**.
3: 10 the **d** of the Lord will come like
Rev 6: 17 great **d** of their wrath has come,
16: 14 on the great **d** of God Almighty.

DAYS (DAY)
Dt 17: 19 he is to read it all the **d** of his life so
32: 7 Remember the **d** of old;
Ps 23: 6 love will follow me all the **d** of my
34: 12 and desires to see many good **d**,
39: 5 You have made my **d** a mere
90: 10 Our **d** may come to seventy years,
90: 12 Teach us to number our **d**, that we
128: 5 of Jerusalem all the **d** of your life.
Pr 31: 12 not harm, all the **d** of her life.
Ecc 9: 9 all the **d** of this meaningless life
12: 1 Creator in the **d** of your youth,
Isa 38: 20 stringed instruments all the **d** of
Da 7: 9 and the Ancient of **D** took his seat.
7: 13 He approached the Ancient of **D**
7: 22 until the Ancient of **D** came
Hos 3: 5 and to his blessings in the last **d**.
Joel 2: 29 I will pour out my Spirit in those **d**.
Mic 4: 1 In the last **d** the mountain
Lk 19: 43 The **d** will come upon you
Ac 2: 17 "'In the last **d**, God says, I will
2Ti 3: 1 will be terrible times in the last **d**.
Heb 1: 2 in these last **d** he has spoken to us
2Pe 3: 3 that in the last **d** scoffers will come,

DAZZLING*
Da 2: 31 an enormous, **d** statue,
Mk 9: 3 His clothes became **d** white,

DEACON* (DEACONS)
Ro 16: 1 a **d** of the church in Cenchreae.
1Ti 3: 12 A **d** must be faithful to his wife

DEACONS* (DEACON)
Php 1: 1 together with the overseers and **d**:
1Ti 3: 8 way, **d** are to be worthy of respect,
3: 10 against them, let them serve as **d**.

DEAD (DIE)
Lev 17: 15 who eats anything found **d** or torn
Dt 18: 11 or spiritist or who consults the **d**.
Job 26: 6 realm of the **d** is naked before God;
Ps 49: 15 me from the realm of the **d**;
Isa 8: 19 Why consult the **d** on behalf
Mt 8: 22 and let the **d** bury their own **d**."
28: 7 'He has risen from the **d** and is
Lk 15: 24 For this son of mine was **d** and is
24: 46 rise from the **d** on the third day,
Ac 2: 27 abandon me to the realm of the **d**,
Ro 6: 11 count yourselves **d** to sin but alive
1Co 15: 29 who are baptized for the **d**?
Eph 2: 1 you were **d** in your transgressions
1Th 4: 16 and the **d** in Christ will rise first.
Jas 2: 17 is not accompanied by action, is **d**.
2: 26 As the body without the spirit is **d**, so faith without deeds is **d**.
Rev 14: 13 Blessed are the **d** who die
20: 12 The **d** were judged according

DEAR* (DEARER)
2Sa 1: 26 you were very **d** to me.
Ps 102: 14 her stones are **d** to your servants;
Jer 31: 20 Is not Ephraim my **d** son, the child
Ac 15: 25 to you with our **d** friends Barnabas
Ro 12: 19 Do not take revenge, my **d** friends,
16: 5 Greet my **d** friend Epenetus,
16: 8 my **d** friend in the Lord.
16: 9 in Christ, and my **d** friend Stachys.
16: 12 Greet my **d** friend Persis,
1Co 4: 14 but to warn you as my **d** children.
10: 14 Therefore, my **d** friends,
15: 58 my **d** brothers and sisters,
2Co 7: 1 we have these promises, **d** friends,
12: 19 and everything we do, **d** friends,
Gal 4: 19 My **d** children, for whom I am
Eph 6: 21 the **d** brother and faithful servant
Php 2: 12 Therefore, my **d** friends, as you
4: 1 in the Lord in this way, **d** friends!
Col 1: 7 Epaphras, our **d** fellow servant,
4: 7 is a **d** brother, a faithful minister
4: 9 our faithful and **d** brother, who is
4: 14 Our **d** friend Luke, the doctor,
1Ti 6: 2 better because their masters are **d**
2Ti 1: 2 To Timothy, my **d** son:
Phm : 1 To Philemon our **d** friend
: 16 better than a slave, as a **d** brother.
: 16 He is very **d** to me but even dearer
Heb 6: 9 we speak like this, **d** friends,
Jas 1: 16 my **d** brothers and sisters.
1: 19 My **d** brothers and sisters, take
2: 5 Listen, my **d** brothers and sisters:
1Pe 2: 11 **D** friends, I urge you, as foreigners
4: 12 **D** friends, do not be surprised
2Pe 3: 1 **D** friends, this is now my second
3: 8 not forget this one thing, **d** friends:
3: 14 So then, **d** friends, since you are
3: 15 as our **d** brother Paul also wrote
3: 17 Therefore, **d** friends, since you
1Jn 2: 1 My **d** children, I write this to you
2: 7 **D** friends, I am not writing you
2: 12 I am writing to you, **d** children,
2: 14 I write to you, **d** children,
2: 18 **D** children, this is the last hour;
2: 28 And now, **d** children,
3: 2 **D** friends, now we are children
3: 7 **D** children, do not let anyone lead
3: 18 **D** children, let us not love
3: 21 **D** friends, if our hearts do not
4: 1 **D** friends, do not believe every
4: 4 You, **d** children, are from God
4: 7 **D** friends, let us love one another,
4: 11 **D** friends, since God so loved us,
5: 21 **D** children, keep yourselves
2Jn : 5 And now, **d** lady, I am not writing
3Jn : 1 To my **d** friend Gaius, whom I love
: 2 **D** friend, I pray that you may enjoy
: 5 **D** friend, you are faithful in what
: 11 **D** friend, do not imitate what is
Jude : 3 **D** friends, although I was very

Jude : 17 But, **d** friends, remember what
: 20 But you, **d** friends, by building

DEARER* (DEAR)
Phm : 16 very dear to me but even **d** to you,

DEATH (DIE)
Ex 21: 12 with a fatal blow is to be put to **d**.
Nu 35: 16 the murderer is to be put to **d**.
Dt 30: 19 I have set before you life and **d**,
Ru 1: 17 if even **d** separates you and me."
2Ki 4: 40 of God, there is **d** in the pot!"
Ps 44: 22 your sake we face **d** all day long;
89: 48 Who can live and not see **d**, or who
116: 15 of the LORD is the **d** of his faithful
Pr 8: 36 all who hate me love **d**."
11: 19 but whoever pursues evil finds **d**.
14: 12 right, but in the end it leads to **d**.
15: 11 **D** and Destruction lie open before
16: 25 right, but in the end it leads to **d**.
18: 21 tongue has the power of life and **d**,
19: 18 do not be a willing party to their **d**.
23: 14 with the rod and save them from **d**.
Ecc 7: 2 for **d** is the destiny of everyone;
Isa 25: 8 he will swallow up **d** forever.
53: 12 he poured out his life unto **d**,
Eze 18: 23 pleasure in the **d** of the wicked?
18: 32 no pleasure in the **d** of anyone,
33: 11 no pleasure in the **d** of the wicked,
Da 9: 26 the Anointed One will be put to **d**
Hos 13: 14 I will redeem them from **d**.
13: 14 Where, O **d**, are your plagues?
Jn 5: 24 but has crossed over from **d** to life.
Ro 4: 25 He was delivered over to **d** for our
5: 12 and **d** through sin, and in this way **d** came to all
5: 14 **d** reigned from the time of Adam
6: 3 Jesus were baptized into his **d**?
6: 23 For the wages of sin is **d**,
7: 24 from this body that is subject to **d**?
8: 13 Spirit you put to **d** the misdeeds
8: 36 your sake we face **d** all day long;
1Co 15: 21 For since **d** came through a man,
15: 26 last enemy to be destroyed is **d**.
15: 31 I face **d** every day—yes, just as
15: 55 "Where, O **d**, is your victory?
2Ti 1: 10 Jesus, who has destroyed **d** and has
Heb 2: 14 by his **d** he might break the power
1Jn 5: 16 a sin that does not lead to **d**,
5: 16 There is a sin that leads to **d**.
Rev 1: 18 I hold the keys of **d** and Hades.
2: 11 not be hurt at all by the second **d**.
20: 6 The second **d** has no power over
20: 14 Then **d** and Hades were thrown
20: 14 The lake of fire is the second **d**.
21: 4 There will be no more **d**'
21: 8 This is the second **d**."

DEBAUCHERY*
Ro 13: 13 not in sexual immorality and **d**,
2Co 12: 21 and **d** in which they have indulged.
Gal 5: 19 sexual immorality, impurity and **d**;
Eph 5: 18 drunk on wine, which leads to **d**.
1Pe 4: 3 living in **d**, lust, drunkenness,

DEBORAH*
1. Prophetess who led Israel to victory over Canaanites (Jdg 4–5).
2. Rebekah's nurse (Ge 35:8).

DEBT* (DEBTOR DEBTORS DEBTS INDEBTEDNESS)
Dt 15: 3 you must cancel any **d** your fellow
24: 6 as security for a **d**,
1Sa 22: 2 or in **d** or discontented gathered
Job 24: 9 infant of the poor is seized for a **d**.
Mt 18: 25 that he had be sold to repay the **d**.
18: 27 canceled the **d** and let him go.
18: 30 prison until he could pay the **d**.
18: 32 said, 'I canceled all that **d** of yours
Lk 7: 43 who had the bigger **d** forgiven."
Ro 13: 8 Let no **d** remain outstanding,
13: 8 the continuing **d** to love one

DEBTOR* (DEBT)
Isa 24: 2 as for lender, for **d** as for creditor.

DEBTORS* (DEBT)
Mt 6: 12 as we also have forgiven our **d**.
Lk 16: 5 called in each one of his master's **d**.

DEBTS* (DEBT)
Dt 15: 1 seven years you must cancel **d**.
15: 2 canceling **d** has been proclaimed.
15: 9 the year for canceling **d**, is near,"
31: 10 in the year for canceling **d**,
2Ki 4: 7 "Go, sell the oil and pay your **d**.
Ne 10: 31 the land and will cancel all **d**.
Pr 22: 26 in pledge or puts up security for **d**;
Mt 6: 12 And forgive us our **d**, as we
Lk 7: 42 back, so he forgave the **d** of both.

DECAY*
Ps 16: 10 will you let your faithful one see **d**.
49: 9 live on forever and not see **d**.
49: 14 Their forms will **d** in the grave,
55: 23 down the wicked into the pit of **d**;
Pr 12: 4 a disgraceful wife is like **d** in his
Isa 5: 24 so their roots will **d** and their
Hab 3: 16 **d** crept into my bones, and my legs
Ac 2: 27 will not let your holy one see **d**.
2: 31 of the dead, nor did his body see **d**.
13: 34 that he will never be subject to **d**.
13: 35 will not let your holy one see **d**.'
13: 37 raised from the dead did not see **d**.
Ro 8: 21 be liberated from its bondage to **d**

DECEIT (DECEIVE)
Isa 53: 9 nor was any **d** in his mouth.
Da 8: 25 He will cause **d** to prosper, and he
Mk 7: 22 greed, malice, **d**, lewdness, envy,
Jn 1: 47 an Israelite in whom there is no **d**."
Ac 13: 10 You are full of all kinds of **d**
Ro 1: 29 envy, murder, strife, **d** and malice.
3: 13 their tongues practice **d**."
1Pe 2: 1 yourselves of all malice and all **d**,
2: 22 and no **d** was found in his mouth."

DECEITFUL (DECEIVE)
Jer 17: 9 The heart is **d** above all things
Hos 10: 2 Their heart is **d**, and now they
Zep 3: 13 A **d** tongue will not be found
2Co 11: 13 are false apostles, **d** workers,
Eph 4: 14 of people in their **d** scheming.
4: 22 is being corrupted by its **d** desires;
1Pe 3: 10 evil and their lips from **d** speech.
Rev 21: 27 who does what is shameful or **d**,

DECEITFULNESS* (DECEIVE)
Mt 13: 22 the **d** of wealth choke the word,
Mk 4: 19 the **d** of wealth and the desires
Heb 3: 13 of you may be hardened by sin's **d**.

DECEIVE (DECEIT DECEITFUL DECEITFULNESS DECEIVED DECEIVER DECEIVERS DECEIVES DECEIVING DECEPTION DECEPTIVE)
Lev 19: 11 "'Do not **d** one another.
Pr 14: 5 An honest witness does not **d**,
Jer 37: 9 Do not **d** yourselves, thinking,
Zec 13: 4 garment of hair in order to **d**.
Mt 24: 5 am the Messiah,' and will **d** many.
24: 11 will appear and **d** many people.
24: 24 great signs and wonders to **d**,
Mk 13: 6 'I am he,' and will **d** many.
13: 22 perform signs and wonders to **d**,
Ro 16: 18 flattery they **d** the minds of naive
1Co 3: 18 Do not **d** yourselves. If any of you
Gal 6: 3 they are not, they **d** themselves.
Eph 5: 6 no one **d** you with empty words,
Col 2: 4 one may **d** you by fine-sounding
2Th 2: 3 Don't let anyone **d** you in any way,
Jas 1: 22 to the word, and so **d** yourselves.
Jas 1: 26 rein on their tongues **d** themselves,
1Jn 1: 8 we **d** ourselves and the truth is not
Rev 20: 8 to **d** the nations in the four corners

DECEIVED (DECEIVE)
Ge 3: 13 said, "The serpent **d** me, and I ate."
Lk 21: 8 "Watch out that you are not **d**.
1Co 6: 9 Do not be **d**: Neither the sexually
2Co 11: 3 just as Eve was **d** by the serpent's
Gal 6: 7 Do not be **d**: God cannot be
1Ti 2: 14 Adam was not the one **d**; it was the woman who was **d**
2Ti 3: 13 to worse, deceiving and being **d**.
Titus 3: 3 **d** and enslaved by all kinds
Jas 1: 16 Don't be **d**, my dear brothers
Rev 13: 14 it **d** the inhabitants of the earth.
20: 10 And the devil, who **d** them,

DECEIVER (DECEIVE)
Mt 27: 63 while he was still alive that **d** said,
2Jn : 7 Any such person is the **d**

DECEIVERS* (DECEIVE)
Job 11: 11 Surely he recognizes **d**; and when
Ps 49: 5 when wicked **d** surround me—
2Jn : 7 I say this because many **d**, who do

DECEIVES* (DECEIVE)
Pr 26: 19 is one who **d** their neighbor
Jer 9: 5 Friend **d** friend, and no one speaks
Mt 24: 4 "Watch out that no one **d** you.
Mk 13: 5 "Watch out that no one **d** you.
Jn 7: 12 replied, "No, he **d** the people."
2Th 2: 10 that wickedness **d** those who are

DECEIVING (DECEIVE)
Lev 6: 2 the LORD by **d** a neighbor
1Ki 22: 22 be a **d** spirit in the mouths of all
1Ti 4: 1 the faith and follow **d** spirits
2Ti 3: 13 to worse, **d** and being deceived.
Rev 20: 3 from **d** the nations anymore until

DECENCY* (DECENTLY)
1Ti 2: 9 modestly, with **d** and propriety,

DECENTLY* (DECENCY)
Ro 13: 13 Let us behave **d**, as in the daytime,

DECEPTION (DECEIVE)
Pr 14: 8 ways, but the folly of fools is **d**.
26: 26 malice may be concealed by **d**,
Mt 27: 64 This last **d** will be worse than
2Co 4: 2 we do not use **d**, nor do we distort
Titus 1: 10 full of meaningless talk and **d**,

DECEPTIVE (DECEIVE)
Pr 11: 18 A wicked person earns **d** wages,
31: 30 Charm is **d**, and beauty is fleeting;
Jer 7: 4 Do not trust in **d** words and say,
Col 2: 8 through hollow and **d** philosophy,

DECIDED (DECISION)
2Co 9: 7 you should give what you have **d**

DECISION (DECIDED)
Ex 28: 29 **d** as a continuing memorial before
Joel 3: 14 multitudes in the valley of **d**!

DECLARE (DECLARED DECLARING)
1Ch 16: 24 **D** his glory among the nations,
Ps 19: 1 The heavens **d** the glory of God;
96: 3 **D** his glory among the nations,
Isa 42: 9 taken place, and new things I **d**;
Ro 10: 9 If you **d** with your mouth, "Jesus is

DECLARED (DECLARE)
Mk 7: 19 saying this, Jesus **d** all foods clean.)
Ro 2: 13 the law who will be **d** righteous.
3: 20 no one will be **d** righteous

DECLARING (DECLARE)
Ps 71: 8 **d** your splendor all day long.
Ac 2: 11 hear them **d** the wonders of God

DECREE (DECREED DECREES)
1Ch 16: 17 He confirmed it to Jacob as a **d**,
Ps 2: 7 I will proclaim the LORD's **d**:
7: 6 Awake, my God; **d** justice.
81: 4 this is a **d** for Israel, an ordinance
148: 6 he issued a **d** that will never pass
Da 4: 24 and this is the **d** the Most High has
Lk 2: 1 days Caesar Augustus issued a **d**
Ro 1: 32 they know God's righteous **d**

DECREED (DECREE)
Ps 78: 5 He **d** statutes for Jacob
Jer 40: 2 LORD your God **d** this disaster
La 3: 37 it happen if the Lord has not **d** it?
Da 9: 24 "Seventy 'sevens' are **d** for your
9: 26 end, and desolations have been **d**.
Lk 22: 22 Son of Man will go as it has been **d**.

DECREES (DECREE)
Ge 26: 5 my **d** and my instructions."
Ex 15: 26 his commands and keep all his **d**,
18: 16 and inform them of God's **d**
18: 20 Teach them his **d** and instructions,
Lev 10: 11 Israelites all the **d** the LORD has
18: 4 laws and be careful to follow my **d**.
18: 5 Keep my **d** and laws, for the person
18: 26 you must keep my **d** and my laws.
Ps 119: 12 to you, LORD; teach me your **d**.
119: 16 I delight in your **d**; I will not
119: 48 that I may meditate on your **d**.
119:112 on keeping your **d** to the very end.

DEDICATE (DEDICATED DEDICATION REDEDICATE)
Pr 20: 25 It is a trap to **d** something rashly

DEDICATED (DEDICATE)
Lev 21: 12 it, because he has been **d**
Nu 18: 6 **d** to the LORD to do the work
1Ki 8: 63 all the Israelites **d** the temple
2Ch 29: 31 "You have now **d** yourselves
Ne 3: 1 They **d** it and set its doors in

DEDICATION (DEDICATE)
Nu 6: 2 a vow of **d** to the LORD as
6: 9 the hair that symbolizes their **d**,
6: 19 the hair that symbolizes their **d**,
Jn 10: 22 the Festival of **D** at Jerusalem.
1Ti 5: 11 sensual desires overcome their **d**

DEED (DEEDS)
Jer 32: 10 I signed and sealed the **d**, had it

Jer 32: 16 I had given the **d** of purchase
Col 3: 17 whether in word or **d**, do it all
2Th 2: 17 strengthen you in every good **d**

DEEDS (DEED)
Dt 3: 24 or on earth who can do the **d**
4: 34 or by great and awesome **d**, like all
34: 12 or performed the awesome **d**
1Sa 2: 3 knows, and by him **d** are weighed.
1Ch 16: 24 his marvelous **d** among all peoples.
Job 34: 25 Because he takes note of their **d**,
Ps 26: 7 and telling of all your wonderful **d**.
45: 4 right hand achieve awesome **d**.
65: 5 us with awesome and righteous **d**,
66: 3 to God, "How awesome are your **d**!
66: 5 done, his awesome **d** for mankind!
71: 17 day I declare your marvelous **d**.
72: 18 who alone does marvelous **d**.
73: 28 I will tell of all your **d**.
75: 1 people tell of your wonderful **d**.
77: 11 I will remember the **d**
77: 12 and meditate on all your mighty **d**."
78: 4 next generation the praiseworthy **d**
78: 7 would not forget his **d** but would
86: 8 no **d** can compare with yours.
86: 10 you are great and do marvelous **d**;
88: 12 or your righteous **d** in the land
90: 16 May your **d** be shown to your
92: 4 For you make me glad by your **d**,
96: 3 his marvelous **d** among all peoples.
107: 8 and his wonderful **d** for mankind,
107: 15 and his wonderful **d** for mankind,
107: 21 and his wonderful **d** for mankind.
107: 24 his wonderful **d** in the deep.
107: 31 and his wonderful **d** for mankind.
107: 43 ponder the loving **d** of the LORD.
111: 3 Glorious and majestic are his **d**,
145: 6 and I will proclaim your great **d**.
Jer 32: 19 conduct and as their **d** deserve.
Hab 3: 2 I stand in awe of your **d**, LORD.
Mt 5: 16 that they may see your good **d**
11: 19 wisdom is proved right by her **d**."
Lk 1: 51 He has performed mighty **d** with
23: 41 we are getting what our **d** deserve.
Ac 26: 20 their repentance by their **d**.
1Ti 6: 18 good, to be rich in good **d**,
Heb 10: 24 on toward love and good **d**,
Jas 2: 14 claims to have faith but has no **d**?
2: 18 Show me your faith without **d**, and I will show you my faith by my **d**.
2: 20 that faith without **d** is useless?
2: 26 is dead, so faith without **d** is dead.
1Pe 2: 12 they may see your good **d**
Rev 2: 19 I know your **d**, your love and faith,
2: 23 each of you according to your **d**.
3: 1 I know your **d**; you have
3: 2 I have found your **d** unfinished
3: 8 I know your **d**. See, I have placed
3: 15 I know your **d**, that you are neither
14: 13 labor, for their **d** will follow them."
15: 3 "Great and marvelous are your **d**,

DEEP (DEPTH DEPTHS)
Ge 1: 2 was over the surface of the **d**,
8: 2 Now the springs of the **d**
Job 34: 22 There is no **d** shadow, no utter
Ps 42: 7 **D** calls to **d** in the roar of your
Pr 25: 27 search out matters that are too **d**.
Lk 5: 4 "Put out into **d** water, and let down
1Co 2: 10 things, even the **d** things of God.
1Ti 3: 9 must keep hold of the **d** truths

DEER
Ps 42: 1 As the **d** pants for streams of water,

DEFAMED*
Isa 48: 11 How can I let myself be **d**?

DEFEATED
1Co 6: 7 have been completely **d** already.

DEFEND (DEFENDED DEFENDER DEFENDING DEFENDS DEFENSE)
Ps 72: 4 May he **d** the afflicted among
74: 22 Rise up, O God, and **d** your cause;
82: 2 "How long will you **d** the unjust
82: 3 **D** the weak and the fatherless;
119:154 **D** my cause and redeem me;
Pr 31: 9 **d** the rights of the poor and needy.
Isa 1: 17 seek justice. **D** the oppressed.
1: 23 They do not **d** the cause
Jer 5: 28 they do not **d** the just cause
50: 34 He will vigorously **d** their cause so

DEFENDED (DEFEND)
Jer 22: 16 He **d** the cause of the poor

DEFENDER (DEFEND)
Ex 22: 2 the **d** is not guilty of bloodshed;
Ps 68: 5 to the fatherless, a **d** of widows,
Pr 23: 11 for their **D** is strong; he will take

DEFENDING (DEFEND)
Ps 10: 18 **d** the fatherless and the oppressed,
Ro 2: 15 and at other times even **d** them.)
Php 1: 7 and, whether I am in chains or **d**

DEFENDS* (DEFEND)
Dt 10: 18 He **d** the cause of the fatherless
33: 7 With his own hands he **d** his cause.
Isa 51: 22 says, your God, who **d** his people:

DEFENSE (DEFEND)
Ex 15: 2 LORD is my strength and my **d**;
Ps 35: 23 Awake, and rise to my **d**!
Php 1: 16 am put here for the **d** of the gospel.

DEFERRED*
Pr 13: 12 Hope **d** makes the heart sick,

DEFIED
1Sa 17: 45 armies of Israel, whom you have **d**.
1Ki 13: 26 is the man of God who **d** the word

DEFILE (DEFILED)
Da 1: 8 Daniel resolved not to **d** himself
Mt 15: 11 someone's mouth does not **d** them,
Rev 14: 4 are those who did not **d** themselves

DEFILED (DEFILE)
Isa 24: 5 The earth is **d** by its people;

DEFRAUD
Lev 19: 13 "'Do not **d** or rob your neighbor.
Mk 10: 19 you shall not **d**, honor your father

DEITY*
Col 2: 9 Christ all the fullness of the **D** lives

DELAY
Ecc 5: 4 a vow to God, do not **d** to fulfill it.
Isa 48: 9 my own name's sake I **d** my wrath;
Heb 10: 37 coming will come and will not **d**."
Rev 10: 6 and said, "There will be no more **d**!

DELIBERATE*
Ac 2: 23 over to you by God's **d** plan

DELICACIES
Ps 141: 4 do not let me eat their **d**.
Pr 23: 3 Do not crave his **d**, for that food is
23: 6 host, do not crave his **d**;

DELICIOUS*
Pr 9: 17 food eaten in secret is **d**!"

DELIGHT* (DELIGHTED DELIGHTFUL DELIGHTING DELIGHTS)
Lev 26: 31 and I will take no **d** in the pleasing
Dt 30: 9 The LORD will again **d** in you
1Sa 2: 1 for I **d** in your deliverance.
15: 22 "Does the LORD **d** in burnt
Ne 1: 11 of your servants who **d** in revering
Job 22: 26 you will find **d** in the Almighty
27: 10 Will they find **d** in the Almighty?
Ps 1: 2 but whose **d** is in the law
16: 3 noble ones in whom is all my **d**."
35: 9 the LORD and **d** in his salvation.
35: 27 those who **d** in my vindication
37: 4 Take **d** in the LORD, and he will
43: 4 of God, to God, my joy and my **d**.
51: 16 You do not **d** in sacrifice, or I
51: 19 you will **d** in the sacrifices
62: 4 my lofty place; they take **d** in lies.
68: 30 Scatter the nations who **d** in war.
111: 2 are pondered by all who **d** in them.
112: 1 who find great **d** in his commands.
119: 16 I **d** in your decrees; I will not
119: 24 Your statutes are my **d**; they are my
119: 35 your commands, for there I find **d**.
119: 47 for I **d** in your commands because
119: 70 and unfeeling, but I **d** in your law.
119: 77 I may live, for your law is my **d**.
119: 92 If your law had not been my **d**,
119:143 but your commands give me **d**.
119:174 LORD, and your law gives me **d**.
147: 10 his **d** in the legs of the warrior;
149: 4 the LORD takes **d** in his people;
Pr 1: 22 How long will mockers **d**
2: 14 who **d** in doing wrong and rejoice
8: 30 I was filled with **d** day after day,
18: 2 but **d** in airing their own opinions.
23: 26 and let your eyes **d** in my ways,
Ecc 2: 10 My heart took **d** in all my labor,
SS 1: 4 We rejoice and **d** in you;
2: 3 I **d** to sit in his shade, and his fruit
Isa 11: 3 he will **d** in the fear of the LORD.
13: 17 for silver and have no **d** in gold.
Isa 32: 14 forever, the **d** of donkeys,
42: 1 my chosen one in whom I **d**;
55: 2 you will **d** in the richest of fare.
58: 13 if you call the Sabbath a **d**
61: 10 I **d** greatly in the LORD;
62: 4 for the LORD will take **d** in you,
65: 18 for I will create Jerusalem to be a **d**
65: 19 Jerusalem and take **d** in my people;
66: 3 and they **d** in their abominations;
66: 11 **d** in her overflowing abundance."
Jer 9: 24 earth, for in these I **d**,"
15: 16 they were my joy and my heart's **d**,
31: 20 dear son, the child in whom I **d**?
49: 25 abandoned, the town in which I **d**?
Eze 24: 16 away from you the **d** of your eyes.
24: 21 you take pride, the **d** of your eyes,
24: 25 joy and glory, the **d** of their eyes,
Hos 7: 3 "They **d** the king with their
Mic 1: 16 for the children in whom you **d**;
7: 18 angry forever but **d** to show mercy.
Zep 3: 17 He will take great **d** in you;
Mt 12: 18 the one I love, in whom I **d**;
Mk 12: 37 large crowd listened to him with **d**.
Lk 1: 14 He will be a joy and **d** to you,
Ro 7: 22 in my inner being I **d** in God's law;
1Co 13: 6 Love does not **d** in evil but rejoices
2Co 12: 10 for Christ's sake, I **d** in weaknesses,
Col 2: 5 and **d** to see how disciplined you

DELIGHTED (DELIGHT)
2Sa 22: 20 he rescued me because he **d** in me.
1Ki 10: 9 who has **d** in you and placed you
2Ch 9: 8 who has **d** in you and placed you
Ps 18: 19 he rescued me because he **d** in me.
Isa 5: 7 of Judah are the vines he **d** in.
Lk 13: 17 but the people were **d** with all

DELIGHTFUL* (DELIGHT)
Ps 16: 6 surely I have a **d** inheritance.
SS 1: 2 for your love is more **d** than wine.
4: 10 How **d** is your love, my sister,
Mal 3: 12 for yours will be a **d** land,"

DELIGHTING* (DELIGHT)
Pr 8: 31 his whole world and **d** in mankind.

DELIGHTS (DELIGHT)
Est 6: 6 for the man the king **d** to honor?"
Ps 22: 8 deliver him, since he **d** in him."
35: 27 who **d** in the well-being of his
36: 8 them drink from your river of **d**.
37: 23 the steps of the one who **d** in him;
147: 11 the LORD **d** in those who fear
Pr 3: 12 loves, as a father the son he **d** in.
10: 23 of understanding **d** in wisdom.
11: 20 but he **d** in those whose ways are
12: 22 **d** in people who are trustworthy.
14: 35 A king **d** in a wise servant,
29: 17 will bring you the **d** you desire.
Col 2: 18 Do not let anyone who **d** in false

DELILAH*
Woman who betrayed Samson (Jdg 16:4–22).

DELIVER (DELIVERANCE DELIVERED DELIVERER DELIVERS)
Dt 32: 39 and no one can **d** out of my hand.
Ps 22: 8 Let him **d** him, since he delights
72: 12 he will **d** the needy who cry out,
79: 9 **d** us and forgive our sins for your
109: 21 of the goodness of your love, **d** me.
119:170 **d** me according to your promise.
Isa 50: 2 Was my arm too short to **d** you?
Eze 7: 19 gold will not be able to **d** them
Da 3: 17 the God we serve is able to **d** us
Hos 13: 14 will **d** this people from the power
Mt 6: 13 but **d** us from the evil one.'
2Co 1: 10 hope that he will continue to **d** us,

DELIVERANCE (DELIVER)
1Sa 2: 1 my enemies, for I delight in your **d**.
Ps 3: 8 From the LORD comes **d**.
32: 7 and surround me with songs of **d**.
33: 17 A horse is a vain hope for **d**;
Ob : 17 But on Mount Zion will be **d**;

DELIVERED (DELIVER)
Job 33: 28 God has **d** me from going down
Ps 34: 4 he **d** me from all my fears.
71: 23 praise to you—I whom you have **d**.
107: 6 and he **d** them from their distress.
116: 8 LORD, have **d** me from death,
Da 7: 25 The holy people will be **d** into his
12: 1 written in the book—will be **d**.
Ro 4: 25 He was **d** over to death for our sins

DELIVERER* (DELIVER)
Jdg 3: 9 he raised up for them a **d**,

Jer 17: 10 according to what their deeds **d**."
21: 14 I will punish you as your deeds **d**,
32: 19 their conduct and as their deeds **d**.
49: 12 who do not **d** to drink the cup
La 3: 64 Pay them back what they **d**,
Eze 16: 59 I will deal with you as you **d**,
Zec 1: 6 us what our ways and practices **d**,
Mt 8: 8 I do not **d** to have you come under
22: 8 those I invited did not **d** to come.
Lk 7: 6 I do not **d** to have you come under
23: 15 he has done nothing to **d** death.
23: 41 we are getting what our deeds **d**.
Ro 1: 32 those who do such things **d** death,
1Co 15: 9 and do not even **d** to be called
16: 18 Such men **d** recognition.
2Co 11: 15 end will be what their actions **d**.
Rev 16: 6 them blood to drink as they **d**."

DESERVED* (DESERVE)
2Sa 19: 28 descendants **d** nothing
Ezr 9: 13 punished us less than our sins **d**
Job 33: 27 is right, but I did not get what I **d**.
Ac 23: 29 no charge against him that **d** death

DESERVES* (DESERVE)
Nu 35: 31 the life of a murderer, who **d** to die.
Dt 25: 2 If the guilty person **d** to be beaten,
25: 2 the number of lashes the crime **d**,
Jdg 9: 16 Have you treated him as he **d**?
Job 34: 11 on them what their conduct **d**.
Jer 51: 6 he will repay her what she **d**.
Lk 7: 4 "This man **d** to have you do this,
10: 7 for the worker **d** his wages.
Ac 26: 31 is not doing anything that **d** death
1Ti 1: 15 saying that **d** full acceptance:
4: 9 saying that **d** full acceptance.
5: 18 and "The worker **d** his wages."
Heb 10: 29 severely do you think someone **d**

DESIGNATED
Lk 6: 13 of them, whom he also **d** apostles:
Heb 5: 10 was **d** by God to be high priest

DESIRABLE* (DESIRE)
Ge 3: 6 and also **d** for gaining wisdom,
Pr 22: 1 name is more **d** than great riches;

DESIRE* (DESIRABLE DESIRED DESIRES)
Ge 3: 16 Your **d** will be for your husband,
Dt 5: 21 You shall not set your **d** on your
1Sa 9: 20 whom is all the **d** of Israel turned,
2Sa 19: 38 anything you **d** from me I will do
23: 5 salvation and grant me my every **d**.
2Ki 9: 15 "If you **d** to make me king,
1Ch 28: 9 and understands every **d** and every
2Ch 1: 11 "Since this is your heart's **d**
9: 8 and his **d** to uphold them forever,
Job 13: 3 But I **d** to speak to the Almighty
21: 14 We have no **d** to know your ways.
Ps 10: 17 LORD, hear the **d** of the afflicted;
20: 4 he give you the **d** of your heart
21: 2 You have granted him his heart's **d**
27: 12 turn me over to the **d** of my foes,
40: 6 and offering you did not **d**—
40: 8 I **d** to do your will, my God;
40: 14 may all who **d** my ruin be turned
41: 2 them over to the **d** of their foes.
70: 2 may all who **d** my ruin be turned
73: 25 earth has nothing I **d** besides you.
Pr 3: 15 nothing you **d** can compare
8: 11 and nothing you **d** can compare
10: 24 what the righteous **d** will be
11: 23 The **d** of the righteous ends only
12: 12 The wicked **d** the stronghold
19: 2 **D** without knowledge is not good
24: 1 wicked, do not **d** their company;
29: 17 will bring you the delights you **d**.
Ecc 6: 2 they lack nothing their hearts **d**,
12: 5 along and **d** no longer is stirred.
SS 6: 12 it, my **d** set me among the royal
7: 10 to my beloved, and his **d** is for me.
Isa 26: 8 and renown are the **d** of our hearts.
53: 2 appearance that we should **d** him.
55: 11 but will accomplish what I **d**
Eze 24: 25 their heart's **d**, and their sons
Hos 6: 6 For I **d** mercy, not sacrifice,
Mic 7: 3 the powerful dictate what they **d**—
Mal 3: 1 covenant, whom you **d**, will come,"
Mt 9: 13 'I **d** mercy, not sacrifice.'
12: 7 what these words mean, 'I **d** mercy,
Ro 7: 18 For I have the **d** to do what is good,
9: 16 depend on human **d** or effort,
10: 1 my heart's **d** and prayer to God
1Co 12: 31 Now eagerly **d** the greater gifts.
14: 1 and eagerly **d** gifts of the Spirit,
2Co 8: 10 give but also to have the **d** to do so.
8: 13 Our **d** is not that others might be
Php 1: 23 I **d** to depart and be with Christ,
4: 17 Not that I **d** your gifts; what I **d** is
2Th 1: 11 fruition your every **d** for goodness
Heb 10: 5 and offering you did not **d**,
10: 8 and sin offerings you did not **d**,
13: 18 **d** to live honorably in every way.
Jas 1: 14 dragged away by their own evil **d**
1: 15 after **d** has conceived, it gives birth
4: 2 You **d** but do not have, so you kill.
2Pe 2: 10 of those who follow the corrupt **d**

DESIRED (DESIRE)
Ps 51: 6 Yet you **d** faithfulness even
Hag 2: 7 what is **d** by all nations will come,
Lk 22: 15 them, "I have eagerly **d** to eat this

DESIRES* (DESIRE)
Ge 4: 7 it **d** to have you, but you must rule
41: 16 will give Pharaoh the answer he **d**."
2Sa 3: 21 rule over all that your heart **d**."
14: 14 But that is not what God **d**;
1Ki 11: 37 will rule over all that your heart **d**;
1Ch 29: 18 keep these **d** and thoughts
Job 17: 11 Yet the **d** of my heart
31: 16 "If I have denied the **d** of the poor
Ps 34: 12 life and **d** to see many good days,
37: 4 will give you the **d** of your heart.
103: 5 who satisfies your **d** with good
140: 8 Do not grant the wicked their **d**,
145: 16 satisfy the **d** of every living thing.
145: 19 He fulfills the **d** of those who fear
Pr 11: 6 the unfaithful are trapped by evil **d**.
13: 4 but the **d** of the diligent are fully
19: 22 What a person **d** is unfailing love;
SS 2: 7 arouse or awaken love until it so **d**.
3: 5 arouse or awaken love until it so **d**.
8: 4 arouse or awaken love until it so **d**.
Hab 2: 4 puffed up; his **d** are not upright—
Mk 4: 19 and the **d** for other things come
Jn 8: 44 want to carry out your father's **d**.
Ro 1: 24 over in the sinful **d** of their hearts
6: 12 body so that you obey its evil **d**.
8: 5 their minds set on what the flesh **d**;
8: 5 minds set on what the Spirit **d**.
13: 14 how to gratify the **d** of the flesh.
Gal 5: 16 and you will not gratify the **d**
5: 17 For the flesh **d** what is contrary
5: 24 the flesh with its passions and **d**.
Eph 2: 3 and following its **d** and thoughts.
4: 22 being corrupted by its deceitful **d**;
Col 3: 5 lust, evil **d** and greed, which is
1Ti 3: 1 to be an overseer **d** a noble task.
5: 11 when their sensual **d** overcome
6: 9 harmful **d** that plunge people
2Ti 2: 22 Flee the evil **d** of youth and pursue
3: 6 are swayed by all kinds of evil **d**,
4: 3 to suit their own **d**, they will gather
Jas 1: 20 the righteousness that God **d**.
4: 1 from your **d** that battle within you?
1Pe 1: 14 do not conform to the evil **d** you
2: 11 to abstain from sinful **d**,
4: 2 their earthly lives for evil human **d**,
2Pe 1: 4 in the world caused by evil **d**.
2: 18 to the lustful **d** of the flesh,
3: 3 and following their own evil **d**.
1Jn 2: 17 The world and its **d** pass away,
Jude : 16 they follow their own evil **d**;
: 18 will follow their own ungodly **d**."

DESOLATE (DESOLATION)
Isa 54: 1 the children of the **d** woman than
Gal 4: 27 the children of the **d** woman than

DESOLATION (DESOLATE)
Da 11: 31 up the abomination that causes **d**.
12: 11 abomination that causes **d** is set
Mt 24: 15 'the abomination that causes **d**,'

DESPAIR (DESPAIRED)
Isa 61: 3 of praise instead of a spirit of **d**.
2Co 4: 8 perplexed, but not in **d**;

DESPAIRED* (DESPAIR)
2Co 1: 8 to endure, so that we **d** of life itself.

DESPERATE*
2Sa 12: 18 He may do something **d**."
Job 6: 26 say, and treat my **d** words as wind?
Ps 60: 3 have shown your people **d** times;
79: 8 to meet us, for we are in **d** need.
142: 6 to my cry, for I am in **d** need;

DESPISE (DESPISED DESPISES)
2Sa 12: 9 Why did you **d** the word
Job 5: 17 so do not **d** the discipline
Job 42: 6 Therefore I **d** myself and repent
Ps 51: 17 contrite heart you, God, will not **d**.
102: 17 he will not **d** their plea.
Pr 1: 7 fools **d** wisdom and instruction.
3: 11 do not **d** the LORD's discipline,
6: 30 People do not **d** a thief if he steals
14: 21 It is a sin to **d** one's neighbor,
15: 32 disregard discipline **d** themselves,
23: 22 do not **d** your mother when she is
Jer 14: 21 the sake of your name do not **d** us;
Am 5: 21 "I hate, I **d** your religious festivals;
Zec 4: 10 "Who dares **d** the day of small
Mt 6: 24 devoted to the one and **d** the other.
18: 10 do not **d** one of these little ones.
Lk 16: 13 devoted to the one and **d** the other.
1Co 11: 22 Or do you **d** the church of God
Titus 2: 15 Do not let anyone **d** you.
2Pe 2: 10 desire of the flesh and **d** authority.

DESPISED (DESPISE)
Ge 25: 34 and left. So Esau **d** his birthright.
Ps 22: 6 by everyone, **d** by the people.
Pr 12: 8 and one with a warped mind is **d**.
Isa 53: 3 He was **d** and rejected by mankind,
1Co 1: 28 of this world and the **d** things—

DESPISES (DESPISE)
Job 36: 5 "God is mighty, but **d** no one;
Pr 15: 20 but a foolish man **d** his mother.

DESTINED (DESTINY)
Lk 2: 34 "This child is **d** to cause the falling
1Co 2: 7 God **d** for our glory before time
Col 2: 22 things that are all **d** to perish
1Th 3: 3 quite well that we are **d** for them.
Heb 9: 27 Just as people are **d** to die once,
1Pe 2: 8 which is also what they were **d** for.

DESTINY* (DESTINED PREDESTINED)
Job 8: 13 Such is the **d** of all who forget God;
Ps 73: 17 then I understood their final **d**.
Ecc 7: 2 for death is the **d** of everyone;
9: 2 All share a common **d**—
9: 3 The same **d** overtakes all.
Isa 65: 11 and fill bowls of mixed wine for **D**,
Php 3: 19 Their **d** is destruction, their god is

DESTITUTE
Ps 102: 17 will respond to the prayer of the **d**;
Pr 31: 8 for the rights of all who are **d**.
Heb 11: 37 in sheepskins and goatskins, **d**,

DESTROY (DESTROYED DESTROYING DESTROYS DESTRUCTION DESTRUCTIVE)
Ge 6: 17 to **d** all life under the heavens,
9: 11 will there be a flood to **d** the earth."
Pr 1: 32 complacency of fools will **d** them;
11: 9 the godless **d** their neighbors,
Mt 10: 28 of the One who can **d** both soul
Mk 14: 58 say, 'I will **d** this temple made
Lk 4: 34 Have you come to **d** us?
Jn 10: 10 comes only to steal and kill and **d**;
Ac 8: 3 But Saul began to **d** the church.
Rev 11: 18 destroying those who **d** the earth."

DESTROYED (DESTROY)
Dt 8: 19 you today that you will surely be **d**.
Job 19: 26 And after my skin has been **d**,
Pr 6: 15 he will suddenly be **d**—
11: 3 but the unfaithful are **d** by their
29: 1 many rebukes will suddenly be **d**—
Da 2: 44 up a kingdom that will never be **d**,
6: 26 his kingdom will not be **d**,
1Co 8: 11 died, is **d** by your knowledge.
15: 24 Father after he has **d** all dominion,
15: 26 The last enemy to be **d** is death.
2Co 4: 9 struck down, but not **d**.
5: 1 if the earthly tent we live in is **d**,
Gal 5: 15 out or you will be **d** by each other.
Eph 2: 14 groups one and has **d** the barrier,
2Ti 1: 10 who has **d** death and has brought
Heb 10: 39 those who shrink back and are **d**,
2Pe 2: 12 born only to be caught and **d**,
3: 10 the elements will be **d** by fire,
3: 11 Since everything will be **d** in this
Jude : 5 later **d** those who did not believe.
: 11 they have been **d** in Korah's

DESTROYING (DESTROY)
Jer 23: 1 "Woe to the shepherds who are **d**

DESTROYS (DESTROY)
Pr 6: 32 whoever does so **d** himself.
18: 9 his work is brother to one who **d**.
28: 24 wrong," is partner to one who **d**.
Ecc 9: 18 war, but one sinner **d** much good.
1Co 3: 17 If anyone **d** God's temple, God will

DESTRUCTION (DESTROY)
Nu 32: 15 you will be the cause of their **d**."
Ps 1: 6 the way of the wicked leads to **d**.
Pr 16: 18 Pride goes before **d**, a haughty
17: 19 builds a high gate invites **d**.
24: 22 for those two will send sudden **d**
Hos 13: 14 Where, O grave, is your **d**?
Mt 7: 13 broad is the road that leads to **d**,
Lk 6: 49 collapsed and its **d** was complete."
Jn 17: 12 lost except the one doomed to **d** so
Ro 9: 22 of his wrath—prepared for **d**?
1Co 5: 5 over to Satan for the **d** of the flesh,
Gal 6: 8 flesh, from the flesh will reap **d**;
Php 3: 19 Their destiny is **d**, their god is their
1Th 5: 3 **d** will come on them suddenly,
2Th 1: 9 will be punished with everlasting **d**
2: 3 is revealed, the man doomed to **d**.
1Ti 6: 9 that plunge people into ruin and **d**.
2Pe 2: 1 bringing swift **d** on themselves.
2: 3 and their **d** has not been sleeping.
3: 7 of judgment and **d** of the ungodly.
3: 12 bring about the **d** of the heavens
3: 16 other Scriptures, to their own **d**.
Rev 17: 8 up out of the Abyss and go to its **d**.
17: 11 to the seven and is going to his **d**.

DESTRUCTIVE (DESTROY)
2Pe 2: 1 will secretly introduce **d** heresies,

DETERMINED (DETERMINES)
Job 14: 5 A person's days are **d**;
Isa 14: 26 This is the plan **d** for the whole
Da 11: 36 what has been **d** must take place.

DETERMINES* (DETERMINED)
Ps 147: 4 He **d** the number of the stars
1Co 12: 11 them to each one, just as he **d**.

DETEST (DETESTABLE DETESTED DETESTS)
Dt 7: 26 Regard it as vile and utterly **d** it,
Ps 119:163 I hate and **d** falsehood
Pr 8: 7 is true, for my lips **d** wickedness.
13: 19 soul, but fools **d** turning from evil.
16: 12 Kings **d** wrongdoing, for a throne
24: 9 are sin, and people **d** a mocker.
29: 27 The righteous **d** the dishonest;
29: 27 the wicked **d** the upright.
Am 5: 10 and **d** the one who tells the truth.

DETESTABLE (DETEST)
Pr 6: 16 hates, seven that are **d** to him:
21: 27 The sacrifice of the wicked is **d**—
28: 9 even their prayers are **d**.
Isa 1: 13 Your incense is **d** to me.
41: 24 whoever chooses you is **d**.
44: 19 Shall I make a **d** thing from what is
Jer 44: 4 'Do not do this **d** thing that I hate!'
Eze 8: 13 doing things that are even more **d**."
Lk 16: 15 What people value highly is **d**
Titus 1: 16 They are **d**, disobedient and unfit
1Pe 4: 3 orgies, carousing and **d** idolatry.

DETESTED* (DETEST)
Zec 11: 8 The flock **d** me, and I grew weary

DETESTS* (DETEST)
Dt 22: 5 the LORD your God **d** anyone who
23: 18 the LORD your God **d** them both.
25: 16 the LORD your God **d** anyone who
Pr 3: 32 For the LORD **d** the perverse
11: 1 The LORD **d** dishonest scales,
11: 20 The LORD **d** those whose hearts
12: 22 The LORD **d** lying lips, but he
15: 8 The LORD **d** the sacrifice
15: 9 The LORD **d** the way
15: 26 The LORD **d** the thoughts
16: 5 The LORD **d** all the proud
17: 15 the LORD **d** them both.
20: 10 the LORD **d** them both.
20: 23 The LORD **d** differing weights,

DEVIATE*
2Ch 8: 15 They did not **d** from the king's

DEVICES
Ps 81: 12 hearts to follow their own **d**.

DEVIL* (DEVIL'S)
Mt 4: 1 wilderness to be tempted by the **d**.
4: 5 the **d** took him to the holy city
4: 8 the **d** took him to a very high
4: 11 Then the **d** left him, and angels
13: 39 the enemy who sows them is the **d**.
25: 41 the eternal fire prepared for the **d**
Lk 4: 2 forty days he was tempted by the **d**.
4: 3 The **d** said to him, "If you are
4: 5 The **d** led him up to a high place
4: 9 The **d** led him to Jerusalem and
4: 13 **d** had finished all this tempting,
8: 12 then the **d** comes and takes away
Jn 6: 70 Yet one of you is a **d**!"
8: 44 the **d**, and you want to carry
13: 2 the **d** had already prompted Judas,
Ac 10: 38 were under the power of the **d**,
13: 10 "You are a child of the **d**
Eph 4: 27 and do not give the **d** a foothold.
1Ti 3: 6 under the same judgment as the **d**.
2Ti 2: 26 and escape from the trap of the **d**,
Heb 2: 14 power of death—that is, the **d**—
Jas 4: 7 Resist the **d**, and he will flee
1Pe 5: 8 Your enemy the **d** prowls around
1Jn 3: 8 does what is sinful is of the **d**,
3: 8 because the **d** has been sinning
3: 10 and who the children of the **d** are:
Jude : 9 disputing with the **d** about the
Rev 2: 10 **d** will put some of you in prison
12: 9 that ancient serpent called the **d**,
12: 12 sea, because the **d** has gone down
20: 2 serpent, who is the **d**, or Satan,
20: 10 And the **d**, who deceived them,

DEVIL'S* (DEVIL)
Eph 6: 11 your stand against the **d** schemes.
1Ti 3: 7 into disgrace and into the **d** trap.
1Jn 3: 8 was to destroy the **d** work.

DEVIOUS*
2Sa 22: 27 to the **d** you show yourself shrewd.
Ps 18: 26 to the **d** you show yourself shrewd.
Pr 2: 15 and who are **d** in their ways.
14: 2 who despise him are **d** in their
21: 8 The way of the guilty is **d**,

DEVISED
2Pe 1: 16 we did not follow cleverly **d** stories

DEVOTE* (DEVOTED DEVOTING DEVOTION DEVOUT)
1Ch 22: 19 Now **d** your heart and soul
2Ch 31: 4 Levites so they could **d** themselves
Job 11: 13 "Yet if you **d** your heart to him
Jer 30: 21 who is he who will **d** himself to be
Mic 4: 13 You will **d** their ill-gotten gains
1Co 7: 5 you may **d** yourselves to prayer.
Col 4: 2 **D** yourselves to prayer,
1Ti 1: 4 or to **d** themselves to myths
4: 13 **d** yourself to the public reading
Titus 3: 8 may be careful to **d** themselves
3: 14 people must learn to **d** themselves

DEVOTED (DEVOTE)
1Ki 11: 4 and his heart was not fully **d**
Ezr 7: 10 For Ezra had **d** himself to the study
Mt 6: 24 or you will be **d** to the one
Mk 7: 11 is Corban (that is, **d** to God)—
Ac 2: 42 They **d** themselves to the apostles'
18: 5 Paul **d** himself exclusively
Ro 12: 10 Be **d** to one another in love.
1Co 7: 34 Her aim is to be **d** to the Lord
16: 15 and they have **d** themselves
2Co 7: 12 for yourselves how **d** to us you are.

DEVOTING* (DEVOTE)
1Ti 5: 10 **d** herself to all kinds of good deeds.

DEVOTION* (DEVOTE)
2Ki 20: 3 with wholehearted **d** and have
1Ch 28: 9 serve him with wholehearted **d**
29: 3 in my **d** to the temple of my God I
29: 19 son Solomon the wholehearted **d**
2Ch 32: 32 acts of **d** are written in the vision
35: 26 and his acts of **d** in accordance
Job 15: 4 piety and hinder **d** to God.
Isa 38: 3 wholehearted **d** and have done
Jer 2: 2 "'I remember the **d** of your
1Co 7: 35 way in undivided **d** to the Lord.
2Co 11: 3 your sincere and pure **d** to Christ.

DEVOUR (DEVOURED DEVOURS)
2Sa 2: 26 to Joab, "Must the sword **d** forever?
Mk 12: 40 They **d** widows' houses
Gal 5: 15 If you bite and **d** each other,
1Pe 5: 8 lion looking for someone to **d**.

DEVOURED (DEVOUR)
Jer 30: 16 all who devour you will be **d**;

DEVOURS (DEVOUR)
2Sa 11: 25 the sword **d** one as well as another.

DEVOUT* (DEVOTE)
1Ki 18: 3 (Obadiah was a **d** believer
Isa 57: 1 the **d** are taken away, and no one
Lk 2: 25 Simeon, who was righteous and **d**.
Ac 10: 2 He and all his family were **d**
10: 7 and a **d** soldier who was one of his
13: 43 **d** converts to Judaism followed
22: 12 He was a **d** observer of the law

DEW
Jdg 6: 37 If there is **d** only on the fleece

DICTATED
Jer 36: 4 while Jeremiah **d** all the words

DIE (DEAD DEATH DIED DIES DYING)
Ge 2: 17 eat from it you will certainly **d**."
3: 3 must not touch it, or you will **d**.'"
3: 4 "You will not certainly **d**,"
Ex 11: 5 Every firstborn son in Egypt will **d**,
Ru 1: 17 Where you **d** I will **d**, and there I
2Ki 14: 6 each will **d** for their own sin."
Job 2: 9 Curse God and **d**!"
Pr 5: 23 For lack of discipline they will **d**,
10: 21 many, but fools **d** for lack of sense.
11: 7 placed in mortals **d** with them;
15: 10 one who hates correction will **d**.
23: 13 them with the rod, they will not **d**.
Ecc 3: 2 a time to be born and a time to **d**,
Isa 22: 13 you say, "for tomorrow we **d**!"
66: 24 the worms that eat them will not **d**,
Jer 31: 30 everyone will **d** for their own sin;
Eze 3: 18 wicked person will **d** for their sin,
3: 19 ways, they will **d** for their sin;
3: 20 them, they will **d** for their sin.
18: 4 one who sins is the one who will **d**.
18: 20 who sins is the one who will **d**.
18: 31 Why will you **d**, people of Israel?
33: 8 wicked person will **d** for their sin,
Mt 26: 52 all who draw the sword will **d**
Mk 9: 48 worms that eat them do not **d**,
Jn 8: 21 for me, and you will **d** in your sin.
11: 25 will live, even though they **d**;
11: 26 by believing in me will never **d**.
Ro 5: 7 Very rarely will anyone **d**
14: 8 if we **d**, we **d** for the Lord.
1Co 15: 22 For as in Adam all **d**, so in Christ
15: 32 eat and drink, for tomorrow we **d**."
Php 1: 21 to live is Christ and to **d** is gain.
Heb 9: 27 as people are destined to **d** once,
1Pe 2: 24 so that we might **d** to sins and live
Rev 14: 13 Blessed are the dead who **d**

DIED (DIE)
1Ki 16: 18 palace on fire around him. So he **d**,
1Ch 1: 51 Hadad also **d**. The chiefs of Edom
10: 13 Saul **d** because he was unfaithful
Lk 16: 22 rich man also **d** and was buried.
Ro 5: 6 Christ **d** for the ungodly.
5: 8 were still sinners, Christ **d** for us.
6: 2 We are those who have **d** to sin;
6: 7 anyone who has **d** has been set free
6: 8 Now if we **d** with Christ, we believe
6: 10 The death he **d**, he **d** to sin once
14: 9 Christ **d** and returned to life so
14: 15 someone for whom Christ **d**.
1Co 8: 11 for whom Christ **d**, is destroyed
15: 3 that Christ **d** for our sins according
2Co 5: 14 we are convinced that one **d** for all, and therefore all **d**.
5: 15 he **d** for all, that those who live
Col 2: 20 Since you **d** with Christ
3: 3 For you **d**, and your life is now
1Th 4: 14 we believe that Jesus **d** and rose
5: 10 He **d** for us so that, whether we are
2Ti 2: 11 If we **d** with him, we will also live
Heb 9: 15 that he has **d** as a ransom to set
9: 17 force only when somebody has **d**;
Rev 2: 8 Last, who **d** and came to life again.

DIES (DIE)
Job 14: 14 If someone **d**, will they live again?
Pr 26: 20 without a gossip a quarrel **d** down.
Jn 12: 24 But if it **d**, it produces many seeds.
Ro 7: 2 if her husband **d**, she is released
14: 7 none of us **d** for ourselves alone.
1Co 7: 39 But if her husband **d**, she is free
15: 36 does not come to life unless it **d**.

DIFFERENCE* (DIFFERENT)
2Sa 19: 35 Can I tell the **d** between what is
2Ch 12: 8 learn the **d** between serving me
Eze 22: 26 there is no **d** between the unclean
44: 23 my people the **d** between the holy
Ro 3: 22 There is no **d** between Jew
10: 12 For there is no **d** between Jew
Gal 2: 6 whatever they were makes no **d**

DIFFERENCES* (DIFFERENT)
1Co 11: 19 there have to be **d** among you

DIFFERENT* (DIFFERENCE DIFFERENCES DIFFERING DIFFERS)
Lev 19: 19 "'Do not mate **d** kinds
Nu 14: 24 my servant Caleb has a **d** spirit

1Sa 10: 6 will be changed into a **d** person.
Est 1: 7 of gold, each one **d** from the other,
3: 8 Their customs are **d** from those
Eze 15: 2 how is the wood of a vine **d**
Da 7: 3 beasts, each **d** from the others,
7: 7 It was **d** from all the former beasts,
7: 19 which was **d** from all the others
7: 23 It will be **d** from all the other
7: 24 will arise, **d** from the earlier ones;
11: 29 this time the outcome will be **d**
Mk 16: 12 *Jesus appeared in a **d** form*
Ro 12: 6 We have **d** gifts,
1Co 4: 7 makes you **d** from anyone else?
12: 4 There are **d** kinds of gifts,
12: 5 There are **d** kinds of service,
12: 6 There are **d** kinds of working,
12: 10 to another speaking in **d** kinds
12: 28 and of **d** kinds of tongues.
2Co 11: 4 receive a **d** spirit from the Spirit
11: 4 or a **d** gospel from the one you
Gal 1: 6 and are turning to a **d** gospel—
4: 1 underage, he is no **d** from a slave,
Heb 7: 13 are said belonged to a **d** tribe,
Jas 2: 25 and sent them off in a **d** direction?

DIFFERING* (DIFFERENT)
Dt 25: 13 Do not have two **d** weights in your
25: 14 Do not have two **d** measures in
Pr 20: 10 **D** weights and **d** measures—
20: 23 The LORD detests **d** weights,

DIFFERS* (DIFFERENT)
1Co 15: 41 and star **d** from star in splendor.

DIFFICULT (DIFFICULTIES)
Ex 18: 22 but have them bring every **d** case
Dt 30: 11 commanding you today is not too **d**
2Ki 2: 10 "You have asked a **d** thing,"
Ac 15: 19 that we should not make it **d**

DIFFICULTIES* (DIFFICULT)
2Co 12: 10 in hardships, in persecutions, in **d**.

DIGNITY
Pr 31: 25 She is clothed with strength and **d**;

DIGS
Pr 26: 27 Whoever **d** a pit will fall into it;

DILIGENCE (DILIGENT)
Ezr 5: 8 work is being carried on with **d**
Heb 6: 11 show this same **d** to the very end,

DILIGENT* (DILIGENCE)
2Ch 24: 13 men in charge of the work were **d**,
Pr 10: 4 poverty, but **d** hands bring wealth.
12: 24 **D** hands will rule, but laziness ends
12: 27 **d** feed on the riches of the hunt.
13: 4 desires of the **d** are fully satisfied.
21: 5 The plans of the **d** lead to profit as
1Ti 4: 15 Be **d** in these matters;

DINAH*
Only daughter of Jacob, by Leah (Ge 30:21; 46:15). Raped by Shechem; avenged by Simeon and Levi (Ge 34).

DINE
Pr 23: 1 When you sit to **d** with a ruler,

DIOTREPHES*
3Jn : 9 but **D**, who loves to be first,

DIRECT (DIRECTED DIRECTIVES DIRECTS)
Ge 18: 19 so that he will **d** his children and
Ps 119: 35 **D** me in the path of your
119:133 **D** my footsteps according to your
Jer 10: 23 it is not for them to **d** their steps.
2Th 3: 5 May the Lord **d** your hearts
1Ti 5: 17 The elders who **d** the affairs

DIRECTED (DIRECT)
Ge 24: 51 master's son, as the LORD has **d**."
Nu 16: 40 as the LORD **d** him through
Dt 2: 1 Red Sea, as the LORD had **d** me.
6: 1 laws the LORD your God **d** me
Jos 11: 9 did to them as the LORD had **d**:
11: 23 just as the LORD had **d** Moses,
Pr 20: 24 A person's steps are **d**
Jer 13: 2 as the LORD **d**, and put it around
Ac 7: 44 It had been made as God **d** Moses,
Titus 1: 5 elders in every town, as I **d** you.

DIRECTIVES* (DIRECT)
1Co 11: 17 In the following **d** I have no praise

DIRECTS* (DIRECT)
Ps 42: 8 By day the LORD **d** his love,
Isa 48: 17 who **d** you in the way you should

DIRGE*
Mt 11: 17 we sang a **d**, and you did not
Lk 7: 32 we sang a **d**, and you did not cry.'

DISABLED*
2Sa 4: 4 to leave, he fell and became **d**.
Jn 5: 3 a great number of **d** people used
Heb 12: 13 so that the lame may not be **d**,

DISAGREEMENT*
Ac 15: 39 They had such a sharp **d** that they

DISAPPEAR (DISAPPEARED DISAPPEARS)
Mt 5: 18 until heaven and earth **d**,
5: 18 by any means **d** from the Law until
Lk 16: 17 earth to **d** than for the least stroke
Heb 8: 13 obsolete and outdated will soon **d**.
2Pe 3: 10 The heavens will **d** with a roar;

DISAPPEARED (DISAPPEAR)
1Ki 20: 40 busy here and there, the man **d**."

DISAPPEARS (DISAPPEAR)
1Co 13: 10 comes, what is in part **d**.

DISAPPROVE*
Pr 24: 18 the LORD will see and **d** and turn

DISARMED*
Col 2: 15 And having **d** the powers

DISASTER
Ex 32: 12 and do not bring **d** on your people.
Ps 57: 1 your wings until the **d** has passed.
Pr 1: 26 turn will laugh when **d** strikes you;
3: 25 Have no fear of sudden **d**
6: 15 Therefore **d** will overtake him
16: 4 even the wicked for a day of **d**.
17: 5 whoever gloats over **d** will not go
27: 10 house when **d** strikes you—
Isa 45: 7 I bring prosperity and create **d**;
Jer 17: 17 you are my refuge in the day of **d**.
Eze 7: 5 Unheard-of **d**! See, it comes!

DISCERN (DISCERNED DISCERNING DISCERNMENT)
Ps 19: 12 But who can **d** their own errors?
139: 3 You **d** my going out and my lying
Php 1: 10 you may be able to **d** what is best

DISCERNED* (DISCERN)
1Co 2: 14 because they are **d** only through

DISCERNING (DISCERN)
1Ki 3: 9 So give your servant a **d** heart
3: 12 I will give you a wise and **d** heart,
Pr 1: 5 and let the **d** get guidance—
8: 9 To the **d** all of them are right;
10: 13 is found on the lips of the **d**,
14: 6 knowledge comes easily to the **d**.
14: 33 reposes in the heart of the **d**
15: 14 The **d** heart seeks knowledge,
16: 21 The wise in heart are called **d**,
17: 10 A rebuke impresses a **d** person
17: 24 A **d** person keeps wisdom in view,
17: 28 and **d** if they hold their tongues.
18: 15 heart of the **d** acquires knowledge,
19: 25 rebuke the **d**, and they will gain
28: 7 A **d** son heeds instruction,
28: 11 and **d** sees how deluded they are.
1Co 11: 31 if we were more **d** with regard

DISCERNMENT (DISCERN)
Ps 119:125 give me **d** that I may understand

DISCHARGED (DISCHARGING)
Ecc 8: 8 As no one is **d** in time of war,

DISCHARGING* (DISCHARGED)
1Co 9: 17 I am simply **d** the trust committed

DISCIPLE (DISCIPLES DISCIPLES')
Mt 10: 42 of these little ones who is my **d**,
Mt 13: 52 of the law who has become a **d**
Lk 14: 26 such a person cannot be my **d**.
14: 27 and follow me cannot be my **d**.
Jn 13: 23 of them, the **d** whom Jesus loved,
19: 26 and the **d** whom he loved standing
21: 7 the **d** whom Jesus loved said
21: 20 that the **d** whom Jesus loved was

DISCIPLES (DISCIPLE)
Mt 10: 1 Jesus called his twelve **d** to him
26: 56 Then all the **d** deserted him
28: 19 go and make **d** of all nations,
Mk 3: 7 withdrew with his **d** to the lake,
16: 20 *Then the **d** went out and*
Lk 6: 13 he called his **d** to him and chose
14: 33 you have cannot be my **d**.
Jn 2: 11 and his **d** believed in him.
6: 66 time many of his **d** turned back
8: 31 my teaching, you are really my **d**.
12: 16 At first his **d** did not understand all
13: 35 will know that you are my **d**, if you
15: 8 showing yourselves to be my **d**.
20: 20 The **d** were overjoyed when they

Ac 6: 1 the number of **d** was increasing,
11: 26 The **d** were called Christians first
14: 22 strengthening the **d** and
18: 23 Phrygia, strengthening all the **d**.

DISCIPLES'* (DISCIPLE)
Jn 13: 5 basin and began to wash his **d** feet,

DISCIPLINE* (DISCIPLINED DISCIPLINES SELF-DISCIPLINE)
Dt 4: 36 made you hear his voice to **d** you.
11: 2 experienced the **d** of the LORD
21: 18 listen to them when they **d** him,
Job 5: 17 so do not despise the **d**
Ps 6: 1 your anger or **d** me in your wrath.
38: 1 your anger or **d** me in your wrath.
39: 11 rebuke and **d** anyone for their sin,
94: 12 Blessed is the one you **d**, LORD,
Pr 3: 11 do not despise the LORD's **d**,
5: 12 You will say, "How I hated **d**!
5: 23 For lack of **d** they will die,
10: 17 Whoever heeds **d** shows the way
12: 1 Whoever loves **d** loves knowledge,
13: 18 Whoever disregards **d** comes
13: 24 their children is careful to **d** them.
15: 5 A fool spurns a parent's **d**,
15: 10 Stern **d** awaits anyone who leaves
15: 32 disregard **d** despise themselves,
19: 18 **D** your children, for in that there is
19: 20 Listen to advice and accept **d**,
22: 15 the rod of **d** will drive it far away.
23: 13 Do not withhold **d** from a child;
29: 17 **D** your children, and they will give
Jer 10: 24 **D** me, LORD, but only in due
17: 23 would not listen or respond to **d**.
30: 11 I will **d** you but only in due
32: 33 would not listen or respond to **d**.
46: 28 I will **d** you but only in due
Hos 5: 2 I will **d** all of them.
1Co 4: 21 Shall I come to you with a rod of **d**,
Heb 12: 5 do not make light of the Lord's **d**,
12: 7 Endure hardship as **d**;
12: 8 and everyone undergoes **d**—
12: 11 No **d** seems pleasant at the time,
Rev 3: 19 Those whom I love I rebuke and **d**.

DISCIPLINED* (DISCIPLINE)
Isa 26: 16 when you **d** them, they could
Jer 31: 18 'You **d** me like an unruly calf, and I have been **d**.
1Co 11: 32 we are being **d** so that we will not
Col 2: 5 delight to see how **d** you are
Titus 1: 8 upright, holy and **d**.
Heb 12: 7 For what children are not **d** by
12: 8 If you are not **d**—
12: 9 all had human fathers who **d** us
12: 10 They **d** us for a little while as they

DISCIPLINES* (DISCIPLINE)
Dt 8: 5 as a man **d** his son, so the LORD your God **d** you.
Ps 94: 10 Does he who **d** nations not punish?
Pr 3: 12 because the LORD **d** those he
Heb 12: 6 the Lord **d** the one he loves,
12: 10 God **d** us for our good, in order

DISCLOSED
Lk 8: 17 nothing hidden that will not be **d**,
Col 1: 26 but is now **d** to the Lord's people.
Heb 9: 8 had not yet been **d** as long as

DISCORD
Gal 5: 20 hatred, **d**, jealousy, fits of rage,

DISCOURAGED* (DISCOURAGEMENT)
Nu 32: 9 they **d** the Israelites from entering
Dt 1: 21 Do not be afraid; do not be **d**."
31: 8 Do not be afraid; do not be **d**."
Jos 1: 9 do not be **d**, for the LORD your
8: 1 "Do not be afraid; do not be **d**.
10: 25 "Do not be afraid; do not be **d**.
1Ch 22: 13 Do not be afraid or **d**.
28: 20 Do not be afraid or **d**,
2Ch 20: 15 or **d** because of this vast army.
20: 17 Do not be afraid; do not be **d**.
32: 7 or **d** because of the king of Assyria
Job 4: 5 comes to you, and you are **d**;
Isa 42: 4 or be **d** till he establishes justice
Eph 3: 13 not to be **d** because of my
Col 3: 21 children, or they will become **d**.

DISCOURAGEMENT* (DISCOURAGED)
Ex 6: 9 not listen to him because of their **d**

DISCOVERED
2Ki 23: 24 that Hilkiah the priest had **d**

DISCREDIT* (DISCREDITED)
Ne 6: 13 give me a bad name to **d** me.
Job 40: 8 "Would you **d** my justice?

DISCREDITED (DISCREDIT)
2Co 6: 3 so that our ministry will not be **d**.

DISCRETION*
1Ch 22: 12 May the LORD give you **d**
Pr 1: 4 knowledge and **d** to the young—
2: 11 **D** will protect you,
3: 21 preserve sound judgment and **d**;
5: 2 that you may maintain **d** and your
8: 12 I possess knowledge and **d**.
11: 22 beautiful woman who shows no **d**.

DISCRIMINATE* (DISCRIMINATED)
Ac 15: 9 He did not **d** between us and them,

DISCRIMINATED* (DISCRIMINATE)
Jas 2: 4 have you not **d** among yourselves

DISEASE (DISEASES)
Nu 12: 10 saw that she had a defiling skin **d**,
Mt 4: 23 healing every **d** and sickness
9: 35 and healing every **d** and sickness.
10: 1 and to heal every **d** and sickness.

DISEASES (DISEASE)
Ps 103: 3 all your sins and heals all your **d**,
Mt 8: 17 up our infirmities and bore our **d**."
Mk 3: 10 those with **d** were pushing forward
Lk 9: 1 drive out all demons and to cure **d**,

DISFIGURE* (DISFIGURED)
Mt 6: 16 they **d** their faces to show others

DISFIGURED (DISFIGURE)
Isa 52: 14 his appearance was so **d** beyond

DISGRACE (DISGRACEFUL DISGRACES)
Ps 44: 15 I live in **d** all day long, and my face
52: 1 who are a **d** in the eyes of God?
74: 21 not let the oppressed retreat in **d**;
Pr 6: 33 Blows and **d** are his lot, and his
11: 2 then comes **d**, but with humility
19: 26 is a child who brings shame and **d**.
Mt 1: 19 not want to expose her to public **d**,
Ac 5: 41 of suffering **d** for the Name.
1Co 11: 6 if it is a **d** for a woman to have her
11: 14 man has long hair, it is a **d** to him,
1Ti 3: 7 so that he will not fall into **d**
Heb 6: 6 and subjecting him to public **d**.
11: 26 regarded **d** for the sake of Christ
13: 13 the camp, bearing the **d** he bore.

DISGRACEFUL* (DISGRACE)
Pr 10: 5 sleeps during harvest is a **d** son.
12: 4 a **d** wife is like decay in his bones.
17: 2 servant will rule over a **d** son
Hos 4: 7 glorious God for something **d**.
1Co 14: 35 for it is **d** for a woman to speak

DISGRACES (DISGRACE)
Pr 28: 7 companion of gluttons **d** his father.
29: 15 left undisciplined **d** its mother.

DISGUISE
Pr 26: 24 Enemies **d** themselves with their

DISH
Pr 19: 24 sluggard buries his hand in the **d**;
Mt 23: 25 clean the outside of the cup and **d**,

DISHEARTENED
1Th 5: 14 encourage the **d**, help the weak,

DISHONEST*
Ex 18: 21 trustworthy men who hate **d** gain
Lev 19: 35 "'Do not use **d** standards
1Sa 8: 3 They turned aside after **d** gain
Pr 11: 1 The LORD detests **d** scales,
13: 11 **D** money dwindles away,
20: 23 and **d** scales do not please him.
29: 27 The righteous detest the **d**;
Jer 22: 17 your heart are set only on **d** gain,
Eze 28: 18 **d** trade you have desecrated your
Hos 12: 7 The merchant uses **d** scales
Am 8: 5 price and cheating with **d** scales,
Mic 6: 11 I acquit someone with **d** scales,
Lk 16: 8 commended the **d** manager
16: 10 whoever is **d** with very little will also be **d** with much.
1Ti 3: 8 wine, and not pursuing **d** gain.
Titus 1: 7 not violent, not pursuing **d** gain.
1: 11 and that for the sake of **d** gain.
1Pe 5: 2 not pursuing **d** gain, but eager

DISHONOR* (DISHONORED DISHONORS)
Lev 18: 7 "'Do not **d** your father by having
18: 8 that would **d** your father.
18: 10 that would **d** you.
18: 14 "'Do not **d** your father's brother
18: 16 that would **d** your brother.
20: 19 for that would **d** a close relative;
Dt 22: 30 he must not **d** his father's bed.
Pr 30: 9 and so **d** the name of my God.
Jer 14: 21 do not **d** your glorious throne.
20: 11 their **d** will never be forgotten.
La 2: 2 princes down to the ground in **d**.
Eze 22: 10 are those who **d** their father's bed;
Jn 8: 49 I honor my Father and you **d** me.
Ro 2: 23 do you **d** God by breaking the law?
1Co 13: 5 It does not **d** others, it is not
15: 43 it is sown in **d**, it is raised in glory;
2Co 6: 8 through glory and **d**, bad report

DISHONORED* (DISHONOR)
Lev 20: 11 his father's wife, he has **d** his father.
20: 17 He has **d** his sister and will be held
20: 20 with his aunt, he has **d** his uncle.
20: 21 of impurity; he has **d** his brother.
Dt 21: 14 her as a slave, since you have **d** her.
Ezr 4: 14 not proper for us to see the king **d**,
1Co 4: 10 You are honored, we are **d**!
Jas 2: 6 But you have **d** the poor. Is it not

DISHONORS* (DISHONOR)
Dt 27: 16 is anyone who **d** their father
27: 20 wife, for he **d** his father's bed."
Job 20: 3 I hear a rebuke that **d** me, and my
Mic 7: 6 For a son **d** his father, a daughter
1Co 11: 4 with his head covered **d** his head.
11: 5 her head uncovered **d** her head—

DISILLUSIONMENT*
Ps 7: 14 trouble and gives birth to **d**.

DISMAYED
Isa 41: 10 do not be **d**, for I am your God.

DISOBEDIENCE* (DISOBEY)
Jos 22: 22 in rebellion or **d** to the LORD,
Jer 43: 7 So they entered Egypt in **d**
Ro 5: 19 as through the **d** of the one man
11: 30 mercy as a result of their **d**,
11: 32 has bound everyone over to **d** so
2Co 10: 6 be ready to punish every act of **d**,
Heb 2: 2 and **d** received its just punishment,
4: 6 did not go in because of their **d**,
4: 11 by following their example of **d**.

DISOBEDIENT* (DISOBEY)
Ne 9: 26 they were **d** and rebelled against
Lk 1: 17 and the **d** to the wisdom
Ac 26: 19 I was not **d** to the vision
Ro 10: 21 I have held out my hands to a **d**
11: 30 at one time **d** to God have now
11: 31 so they too have now become **d**
Eph 2: 2 is now at work in those who are **d**.
5: 6 wrath comes on those who are **d**.
5: 12 to mention what the **d** do in secret.
2Ti 3: 2 proud, abusive, **d** to their parents,
Titus 1: 6 to the charge of being wild and **d**.
1: 16 **d** and unfit for doing anything
3: 3 At one time we too were foolish, **d**,
Heb 11: 31 not killed with those who were **d**.
1Pe 3: 20 to those who were **d** long ago

DISOBEY* (DISOBEDIENCE DISOBEDIENT DISOBEYED DISOBEYING DISOBEYS)
Dt 11: 28 the curse if you **d** the commands
2Ch 24: 20 'Why do you **d** the LORD's
Est 3: 3 "Why do you **d** the king's
Jer 42: 13 and so **d** the LORD your God,
Ro 1: 30 of doing evil; they **d** their parents;
1Pe 2: 8 because they **d** the message—

DISOBEYED* (DISOBEY)
Nu 14: 22 in the wilderness but who **d** me
27: 14 Zin, both of you **d** my command
Jdg 2: 2 Yet you have **d** me. Why have you
Ne 9: 29 arrogant and **d** your commands.
Isa 24: 5 they have **d** the laws,
Jer 43: 4 and all the people **d** the LORD's
Lk 15: 29 for you and never **d** your orders.
Heb 3: 18 enter his rest if not to those who **d**?

DISOBEYING* (DISOBEY)
Nu 14: 41 said, "Why are you **d** the LORD's

DISOBEYS* (DISOBEY)
Eze 33: 12 'If someone who is righteous **d**,

DISORDER*
Job 10: 22 of utter darkness and **d**, where
1Co 14: 33 For God is not a God of **d**
2Co 12: 20 slander, gossip, arrogance and **d**.
Jas 3: 16 there you find **d** and every evil

DISOWN (DISOWNS)
Pr 30: 9 I may have too much and **d** you
Mt 10: 33 will **d** before my Father in heaven.
26: 35 to die with you, I will never **d** you."
2Ti 2: 12 If we **d** him, he will also **d** us;

DISOWNS (DISOWN)
Lk 12: 9 whoever **d** me before others will be

DISPENSATION See ADMINISTRATION, TRUST

DISPLACES*
Pr 30: 23 and a servant who **d** her mistress.

DISPLAY (DISPLAYED DISPLAYS)
Ps 22: 17 All my bones are on **d**;
Eze 39: 21 "I will **d** my glory among
Ro 9: 17 that I might **d** my power in you
1Co 4: 9 God has put us apostles on **d**
1Ti 1: 16 Christ Jesus might **d** his immense

DISPLAYED (DISPLAY)
Jn 9: 3 works of God might be **d** in him.

DISPLAYS (DISPLAY)
Isa 44: 23 Jacob, he **d** his glory in Israel.
2Th 2: 9 He will use all sorts of **d** of power

DISPLEASE (DISPLEASED)
1Th 2: 15 They **d** God and are hostile

DISPLEASED (DISPLEASE)
2Sa 11: 27 thing David had done **d** the LORD.

DISPUTABLE* (DISPUTE)
Ro 14: 1 without quarreling over **d** matters.

DISPUTE (DISPUTABLE DISPUTES DISPUTING)
Pr 17: 14 the matter before a **d** breaks out.
1Co 6: 1 If any of you has a **d** with another,

DISPUTES (DISPUTE)
Pr 18: 18 Casting the lot settles **d** and keeps

DISPUTING (DISPUTE)
1Ti 2: 8 up holy hands without anger or **d**.

DISQUALIFY* (DISQUALIFIED)
Col 2: 18 and the worship of angels **d** you.

DISQUALIFIED* (DISQUALIFY)
1Co 9: 27 I myself will not be **d** for the prize.

DISREGARD (DISREGARDS)
Pr 15: 32 Those who **d** discipline despise

DISREGARDS* (DISREGARD)
Pr 13: 18 Whoever **d** discipline comes

DISREPUTE*
2Pe 2: 2 will bring the way of truth into **d**.

DISRUPTING*
Titus 1: 11 they are **d** whole households

DISSENSION* (DISSENSIONS)
Ro 13: 13 debauchery, not in **d** and jealousy.

DISSENSIONS* (DISSENSION)
Gal 5: 20 of rage, selfish ambition, **d**,

DISTINGUISH (DISTINGUISHING)
1Ki 3: 9 and to **d** between right and wrong.
Heb 5: 14 have trained themselves to **d** good

DISTINGUISHING
1Co 12: 10 to another **d** between spirits,

DISTORT
Ac 20: 30 **d** the truth in order to draw away
2Co 4: 2 nor do we **d** the word of God.
2Pe 3: 16 ignorant and unstable people **d**,

DISTRACTED*
Lk 10: 40 Martha was **d** by all the

DISTRESS (DISTRESSED)
2Ch 15: 4 in their **d** they turned to the LORD,
Ps 18: 6 In my **d** I called to the LORD;
81: 7 In your **d** you called and I rescued
86: 7 When I am in **d**, I call to you,
116: 3 I was overcome by **d** and sorrow.
120: 1 I call on the LORD in my **d**,
Jnh 2: 2 "In my **d** I called to the LORD,
Mt 24: 21 For then there will be great **d**,
Jas 1: 27 and widows in their **d** and to keep

DISTRESSED (DISTRESS)
Ro 14: 15 sister is **d** because of what you eat,

DIVIDE (DIVIDED DIVIDING DIVISION DIVISIONS DIVISIVE)
Ps 22: 18 They **d** my clothes among them

DIVIDED (DIVIDE)
Mt 12: 25 "Every kingdom **d** against itself
Lk 23: 34 **d** up his clothes by casting lots.
1Co 1: 13 Is Christ **d**? Was Paul crucified

DIVIDING (DIVIDE)
Eph 2: 14 the barrier, the **d** wall of hostility,
Heb 4: 12 it penetrates even to **d** soul

DIVINATION
Lev 19: 26 "'Do not practice **d** or seek

DIVINE
Ro 1: 20 his eternal power and **d** nature—
2Co 10: 4 they have **d** power to demolish
2Pe 1: 4 may participate in the **d** nature,

DIVISION (DIVIDE)
Lk 12: 51 on earth? No, I tell you, but **d**.
1Co 12: 25 there should be no **d** in the body,

DIVISIONS (DIVIDE)
Ro 16: 17 to watch out for those who cause **d**
1Co 1: 10 and that there be no **d** among you,
11: 18 as a church, there are **d** among you,

DIVISIVE* (DIVIDE)
Titus 3: 10 Warn a **d** person once,

DIVORCE* (DIVORCED DIVORCES)
Dt 22: 19 he must not **d** her as long as he
22: 29 He can never **d** her as long as he
24: 1 and he writes her a certificate of **d**,
24: 3 and writes her a certificate of **d**,
Isa 50: 1 is your mother's certificate of **d**
Jer 3: 8 faithless Israel her certificate of **d**
Mt 1: 19 he had in mind to **d** her quietly.
5: 31 must give her a certificate of **d**.'
19: 3 for a man to **d** his wife for any
19: 7 man give his wife a certificate of **d**
19: 8 **d** your wives because your hearts
Mk 10: 2 it lawful for a man to **d** his wife?"
10: 4 a man to write a certificate of **d**
1Co 7: 11 a husband must not **d** his wife.
7: 12 to live with him, he must not **d** her.
7: 13 live with her, she must not **d** him.

DIVORCED* (DIVORCE)
Lev 21: 7 or **d** from their husbands,
21: 14 not marry a widow, a **d** woman,
22: 13 daughter becomes a widow or is **d**,
Nu 30: 9 or **d** woman will be binding on her.
Dt 24: 4 then her first husband, who **d** her,
1Ch 8: 8 after he had **d** his wives Hushim
Eze 44: 22 not marry widows or **d** women;
Mt 5: 32 who marries a **d** woman commits
Lk 16: 18 who marries a **d** woman commits

DIVORCES* (DIVORCE)
Jer 3: 1 "If a man **d** his wife and she leaves
Mal 2: 16 man who hates and **d** his wife,"
Mt 5: 31 'Anyone who **d** his wife must give
5: 32 tell you that anyone who **d** his wife,
19: 9 tell you that anyone who **d** his wife,
Mk 10: 11 "Anyone who **d** his wife
10: 12 if she **d** her husband and marries
Lk 16: 18 "Anyone who **d** his wife

DOCTOR
Mt 9: 12 "It is not the healthy who need a **d**,
Col 4: 14 Our dear friend Luke, the **d**,

DOCTRINE* (DOCTRINES)
1Ti 1: 10 else is contrary to the sound **d**
4: 16 Watch your life and **d** closely.
2Ti 4: 3 will not put up with sound **d**.
Titus 1: 9 can encourage others by sound **d**
2: 1 what is appropriate to sound **d**.

DOCTRINES* (DOCTRINE)
1Ti 1: 3 not to teach false **d** any longer

DOEG*
Edomite; Saul's head shepherd; responsible for murder of priests at Nob (1Sa 21:7; 22:6–23; Ps 52).

DOG (DOGS)
Pr 26: 11 As a **d** returns to its vomit, so fools
Ecc 9: 4 even a live **d** is better off than
2Pe 2: 22 "A **d** returns to its vomit," and,

DOGS (DOG)
Mt 7: 6 "Do not give **d** what is sacred;
15: 26 bread and toss it to the **d**."

DOMINION
Job 25: 2 "**D** and awe belong to God;
Ps 22: 28 for **d** belongs to the LORD and he

DONKEY
Nu 22: 30 The **d** said to Balaam, "Am I not
Zec 9: 9 lowly and riding on a **d**, on a colt,
Mt 21: 5 gentle and riding on a **d**,
2Pe 2: 16 rebuked for his wrongdoing by a **d**

DOOR (DOORS)
Job 31: 32 for my **d** was always open
Ps 141: 3 keep watch over the **d** of my lips.
Mt 6: 6 close the **d** and pray to your Father,
7: 7 and the **d** will be opened to you.
Ac 14: 27 how he had opened a **d** of faith
1Co 16: 9 because a great **d** for effective work
2Co 2: 12 the Lord had opened a **d** for me,
Rev 3: 20 I stand at the **d** and knock.

DOORFRAMES
Dt 6: 9 Write them on the **d** of your

DOORKEEPER
Ps 84: 10 I would rather be a **d** in the house

DOORS (DOOR)
Ps 24: 7 ancient **d**, that the King of glory

DORCAS
Ac 9: 36 Tabitha (in Greek her name is **D**);

DOUBLE
2Ki 2: 9 "Let me inherit a **d** portion of your
1Ti 5: 17 church well are worthy of **d** honor,

DOUBLE-EDGED (EDGE)
Heb 4: 12 Sharper than any **d** sword,
Rev 1: 16 of his mouth was a sharp, **d** sword.
2: 12 of him who has the sharp, **d** sword.

DOUBLE-MINDED* (MIND)
Ps 119:113 I hate **d** people, but I love your law.
Jas 1: 8 Such a person is **d** and unstable
4: 8 and purify your hearts, you **d**.

DOUBT (DOUBTING DOUBTS)
Mt 14: 31 faith," he said, "why did you **d**?"
21: 21 if you have faith and do not **d**,
Mk 11: 23 and does not **d** in their heart
Jas 1: 6 you must believe and not **d**,
Jude : 22 Be merciful to those who **d**;

DOUBTING* (DOUBT)
Jn 20: 27 it into my side. Stop **d** and believe."

DOUBTS* (DOUBT)
Lk 24: 38 and why do **d** rise in your minds?
Ro 14: 23 whoever has **d** is condemned if
Jas 1: 6 because the one who **d** is like

DOVE (DOVES)
Ge 8: 8 he sent out a **d** to see if the water
Mt 3: 16 Spirit of God descending like a **d**

DOVES (DOVE)
Lev 12: 8 she is to bring two **d** or two young
Mt 10: 16 as snakes and as innocent as **d**.
Lk 2: 24 "a pair of **d** or two young pigeons."

DOWNCAST
Ps 42: 5 Why, my soul, are you **d**?
2Co 7: 6 who comforts the **d**, comforted us

DOWNFALL
Hos 14: 1 Your sins have been your **d**!

DRAGON
Rev 12: 7 and his angels fought against the **d**,
13: 2 The **d** gave the beast his power
20: 2 He seized the **d**, that ancient

DRAW (DRAWING DRAWS)
Mt 26: 52 "for all who **d** the sword will die
Jn 12: 32 earth, will **d** all people to myself."
Heb 10: 22 let us **d** near to God with a sincere

DRAWING (DRAW)
Lk 21: 28 your redemption is **d** near."

DRAWS (DRAW)
Jn 6: 44 the Father who sent me **d** them,

DREAD (DREADFUL)
Ps 53: 5 overwhelmed with **d**, where there was nothing to **d**.

DREADFUL (DREAD)
Mt 24: 19 How **d** it will be in those days
Heb 10: 31 It is a **d** thing to fall into the hands

DREAM
Joel 2: 28 your old men will **d** dreams,
Ac 2: 17 your old men will **d** dreams.

DRESS
1Ti 2: 9 want the women to **d** modestly,

DRIFT
Heb 2: 1 heard, so that we do not **d** away.

DRINK (DRINKING DRINKS DRUNK DRUNKARD DRUNKARD'S DRUNKARDS DRUNKENNESS)
Ex 29: 40 of a hin of wine as a **d** offering.
Nu 6: 3 from wine or other fermented **d**.
6: 3 They must not **d** grape juice or eat
Jdg 7: 5 from those who kneel down to **d**."
2Sa 23: 15 someone would get me a **d** of water
Pr 5: 15 **D** water from your own cistern,
Mt 20: 22 "Can you **d** the cup I am going to **d**?"
26: 27 saying, "**D** from it, all of you.
Mk 16: 18 *when they **d** deadly poison,*
Lk 12: 19 eat, **d** and be merry."'
Jn 7: 37 who is thirsty come to me and **d**.
18: 11 Shall I not **d** the cup the Father has
1Co 10: 4 and drank the same spiritual **d**;
12: 13 were all given the one Spirit to **d**.
Php 2: 17 like a **d** offering on the sacrifice
2Ti 4: 6 being poured out like a **d** offering,
Rev 14: 10 too, will **d** the wine of God's fury,

DRINKING (DRINK)
Ro 14: 17 is not a matter of eating and **d**,

DRINKS (DRINK)
Isa 5: 22 wine and champions at mixing **d**,
Jn 4: 13 "Everyone who **d** this water will be
6: 54 and **d** my blood has eternal life,
1Co 11: 27 bread or **d** the cup of the Lord

DRIPPING
Pr 19: 13 wife is like the constant **d** of a leaky
27: 15 A quarrelsome wife is like the **d**

DRIVE (DRIVES)
Ex 23: 30 little I will **d** them out before you,
Nu 33: 52 **d** out all the inhabitants of the land
Jos 13: 13 But the Israelites did not **d**
23: 13 LORD your God will no longer **d**
Pr 22: 10 **D** out the mocker, and out goes
Mt 10: 1 them authority to **d** out impure
Jn 6: 37 comes to me I will never **d** away.

DRIVES (DRIVE)
Mt 12: 26 If Satan **d** out Satan, he is divided
1Jn 4: 18 But perfect love **d** out fear,

DROP (DROPS)
Pr 17: 14 so **d** the matter before a dispute
Isa 40: 15 Surely the nations are like a **d**

DROPS (DROP)
Lk 22: 44 his sweat was like **d** of blood falling

DROSS
Ps 119:119 of the earth you discard like **d**;
Pr 25: 4 Remove the **d** from the silver,
26: 23 silver **d** on earthenware are fervent

DROUGHT
Jer 17: 8 It has no worries in a year of **d**

DROWNED
Ex 15: 4 Pharaoh's officers are **d** in the Red
Mt 18: 6 to be **d** in the depths of the sea.
Heb 11: 29 tried to do so, they were **d**.

DROWSINESS*
Pr 23: 21 poor, and **d** clothes them in rags.

DRUNK (DRINK)
1Sa 1: 13 Eli thought she was **d**
Ac 2: 15 These people are not **d**, as you
Eph 5: 18 Do not get **d** on wine, which leads

DRUNKARD (DRINK)
Mt 11: 19 'Here is a glutton and a **d**, a friend
1Co 5: 11 or slanderer, a **d** or swindler.

DRUNKARD'S* (DRINK)
Pr 26: 9 thornbush in a **d** hand is a proverb

DRUNKARDS (DRINK)
Pr 23: 21 for **d** and gluttons become poor,
1Co 6: 10 the greedy nor **d** nor slanderers

DRUNKENNESS (DRINK)
Lk 21: 34 **d** and the anxieties of life,
Ro 13: 13 in carousing and **d**, not in sexual
Gal 5: 21 and envy; **d**, orgies, and the like.
1Ti 3: 3 not given to **d**, not violent
1Pe 4: 3 living in debauchery, lust, **d**, orgies,

DRY
Ge 1: 9 place, and let **d** ground appear."
Ex 14: 16 go through the sea on **d** ground.
Jos 3: 17 the Jordan and stood on **d** ground,
Isa 53: 2 and like a root out of **d** ground.
Eze 37: 4 bones and say to them, '**D** bones,

DUE
Pr 3: 27 good from those to whom it is **d**,

DULL
Isa 6: 10 make their ears **d** and close their
2Co 3: 14 But their minds were made **d**,

DUST
Ge 2: 7 a man from the **d** of the ground
3: 19 for **d** you are and to **d** you will
Job 42: 6 myself and repent in **d** and ashes."
Ps 22: 15 you lay me in the **d** of death.
103: 14 he remembers that we are **d**.
Ecc 3: 20 come from **d**, and to **d** all return.
Mt 10: 14 town and shake the **d** off your feet.
1Co 15: 47 first man was of the **d** of the earth;

DUTIES (DUTY)
2Ti 4: 5 all the **d** of your ministry.

DUTY (DUTIES)
Ecc 12: 13 for this is the **d** of all mankind.
Ac 23: 1 I have fulfilled my **d** to God in all
1Co 7: 3 husband should fulfill his marital **d**

DWELL (DWELLING DWELLINGS DWELLS DWELT)
Ex 25: 8 for me, and I will **d** among them.
2Sa 7: 5 one to build me a house to **d** in?
1Ki 8: 27 "But will God really **d** on earth?
Ps 23: 6 I will **d** in the house of the LORD
37: 3 **d** in the land and enjoy safe
61: 4 I long to **d** in your tent forever
Pr 8: 12 wisdom, **d** together with prudence;
Isa 33: 14 can **d** with everlasting burning?"
43: 18 do not **d** on the past.
Jn 5: 38 nor does his word **d** in you, for
Ro 7: 18 that good itself does not **d** in me,
Eph 3: 17 Christ may **d** in your hearts
Col 1: 19 to have all his fullness **d** in him,
3: 16 Christ **d** among you richly as you

DWELLING (DWELL)
Lev 26: 11 I will put my **d** place among you,
Dt 26: 15 your holy **d** place, and bless your
Ps 90: 1 been our **d** place throughout all
2Co 5: 2 instead with our heavenly **d**,
Eph 2: 22 built together to become a **d**

DWELLINGS (DWELL)
Lk 16: 9 will be welcomed into eternal **d**.

DWELLS (DWELL)
Ps 46: 4 holy place where the Most High **d**.
91: 1 Whoever **d** in the shelter
1Co 3: 16 that God's Spirit **d** in your midst?

DWELT (DWELL)
Dt 33: 16 of him who **d** in the burning bush.

DYING (DIE)
Ro 7: 6 now, by **d** to what once bound us,
2Co 6: 9 **d**, and yet we live on;

EAGER
Pr 31: 13 and flax and works with **e** hands.
Ro 8: 19 the creation waits in **e** expectation
1Co 14: 12 Since you are **e** for gifts
14: 39 sisters, be **e** to prophesy, and do
Titus 2: 14 his very own, **e** to do what is good.
1Pe 5: 2 dishonest gain, but **e** to serve;

EAGLE (EAGLE'S EAGLES)
Dt 32: 11 like an **e** that stirs up its nest
Eze 1: 10 each also had the face of an **e**.
Rev 4: 7 man, the fourth was like a flying **e**.
12: 14 given the two wings of a great **e**,

EAGLE'S (EAGLE)
Ps 103: 5 your youth is renewed like the **e**.

EAGLES (EAGLE)
Isa 40: 31 They will soar on wings like **e**;

EAR (EARS)
Ex 21: 6 and pierce his **e** with an awl.
Pr 2: 2 turning your **e** to wisdom
1Co 2: 9 eye has seen, what no **e** has heard,
12: 16 And if the **e** should say, "Because I

EARN (EARNINGS)
2Th 3: 12 down and **e** the food they eat.

EARNESTNESS
2Co 7: 11 what **e**, what eagerness to clear
8: 7 in complete **e** and in the love we

EARNINGS (EARN)
Pr 31: 16 out of her **e** she plants a vineyard.

EARRING (EARRINGS)
Pr 25: 12 Like an **e** of gold or an ornament

EARRINGS (EARRING)
Ex 32: 2 them, "Take off the gold **e** that

EARS (EAR)
Job 42: 5 My **e** had heard of you but now my
Ps 34: 15 and his **e** are attentive to their cry;
Pr 21: 13 Whoever shuts their **e** to the cry
26: 17 dog by the **e** is someone who
Isa 6: 10 make their **e** dull and close their
Mt 11: 15 Whoever has **e**, let them hear.
2Ti 4: 3 to say what their itching **e** want
1Pe 3: 12 his **e** are attentive to their prayer,
Rev 2: 7 Whoever has **e**, let them hear what

EARTH (EARTH'S EARTHLY)
Ge 1: 1 God created the heavens and the **e**.
1: 2 Now the **e** was formless and empty,
7: 24 The waters flooded the **e**
14: 19 High, Creator of heaven and **e**.
1Ki 8: 27 "But will God really dwell on **e**?
Job 26: 7 he suspends the **e** over nothing.
Ps 24: 1 The **e** is the LORD's,
46: 6 he lifts his voice, the **e** melts.
97: 5 before the Lord of all the **e**.
102: 25 you laid the foundations of the **e**,
108: 5 let your glory be over all the **e**.
Pr 8: 26 its fields or any of the dust of the **e**.
Isa 6: 3 the whole **e** is full of his glory."
24: 20 The **e** reels like a drunkard,
37: 16 You have made heaven and **e**.
40: 22 enthroned above the circle of the **e**,
51: 6 the **e** will wear out like a garment
54: 5 he is called the God of all the **e**.
55: 9 the heavens are higher than the **e**,
65: 17 create new heavens and a new **e**.
66: 1 throne, and the **e** is my footstool.
Jer 10: 10 When he is angry, the **e** trembles;
23: 24 "Do not I fill heaven and **e**?"
33: 25 the laws of heaven and **e**,
Hab 2: 20 let all the **e** be silent before him.
Zep 1: 18 sudden end of all who live on the **e**.
Mt 5: 5 meek, for they will inherit the **e**.
5: 35 or by the **e**, for it is his footstool;
6: 10 will be done, on **e** as it is in heaven.
16: 19 you bind on **e** will be bound
16: 19 you loose on **e** will be loosed
24: 35 Heaven and **e** will pass away,
28: 18 and on **e** has been given to me.
Lk 2: 14 on **e** peace to those on whom his
Jn 12: 32 when I am lifted up from the **e**,
Ac 4: 24 the heavens and the **e** and the sea,
7: 49 throne, and the **e** is my footstool.
1Co 10: 26 for, "The **e** is the Lord's,
Eph 3: 15 heaven and on **e** derives its name.
Php 2: 10 heaven and on **e** and under the **e**,
Heb 1: 10 you laid the foundations of the **e**,
2Pe 3: 13 to a new heaven and a new **e**,
Rev 8: 7 and it was hurled down on the **e**.
12: 12 But woe to the **e** and the sea,
20: 11 The **e** and the heavens fled from
21: 1 I saw "a new heaven and a new **e**,"
21: 1 and the first **e** had passed away,

EARTH'S (EARTH)
Job 38: 4 you when I laid the **e** foundation?

EARTHENWARE*
Pr 26: 23 of silver dross on **e** are fervent lips

EARTHLY (EARTH)
Ro 1: 3 as to his **e** life was a descendant
Eph 4: 9 descended to the lower, **e** regions?
Php 3: 19 Their mind is set on **e** things.
Col 3: 2 on things above, not on **e** things.
3: 5 whatever belongs to your **e** nature:

EARTHQUAKE (EARTHQUAKES)
Eze 38: 19 time there shall be a great **e**
Mt 28: 2 There was a violent **e**, for an angel
Rev 6: 12 There was a great **e**. The sun

EARTHQUAKES (EARTHQUAKE)
Mt 24: 7 be famines and **e** in various places.

EASE
Ru 2: 13 put me at **e** by speaking kindly
Pr 1: 33 will live in safety and be at **e**,

EASIER (EASY)
Lk 16: 17 It is **e** for heaven and earth
18: 25 it is **e** for a camel to go through

EAST
Ge 2: 8 God had planted a garden in the **e**,
Ps 103: 12 as far as the **e** is from the west,
Eze 43: 2 God of Israel coming from the **e**.
Mt 2: 1 Magi from the **e** came to Jerusalem

EASY (EASIER)
Mt 11: 30 For my yoke is **e** and my burden is

EAT (ATE EATEN EATER EATING EATS)
Ge 2: 16 "You are free to **e** from any tree
2: 17 you must not **e** from the tree
3: 19 you will **e** your food until you
Ex 12: 11 **E** it in haste; it is the LORD's
Lev 11: 2 land, these are the ones you may **e**:
17: 12 "None of you may **e** blood,
Dt 8: 16 He gave you manna to **e**
14: 4 These are the animals you may **e**:
Jdg 14: 14 "Out of the eater, something to **e**;
2Sa 9: 7 and you will always **e** at my table."
Pr 31: 27 does not **e** the bread of idleness.
Isa 55: 1 have no money, come, buy and **e**!
65: 25 the lion will **e** straw like the ox,
Eze 3: 1 "Son of man, **e** what is before you, **e** this scroll;
Mt 14: 16 You give them something to **e**."
15: 2 wash their hands before they **e**!"
26: 26 his disciples, saying, "Take and **e**;
Mk 14: 14 where I may **e** the Passover with
Lk 10: 8 welcomed, **e** what is offered to you.
12: 19 **e**, drink and be merry."'
12: 22 about your life, what you will **e**;
Jn 4: 32 "I have food to **e** that you know
6: 31 them bread from heaven to **e**.'"
6: 52 can this man give us his flesh to **e**?"
Ac 10: 13 him, "Get up, Peter. Kill and **e**."
Ro 14: 2 faith allows them to **e** anything,
14: 15 is distressed because of what you **e**,
14: 20 a person to **e** anything that causes
14: 21 It is better not to **e** meat or drink
14: 23 has doubts is condemned if they **e**,
1Co 5: 11 Do not even **e** with such people.
8: 13 if what I **e** causes my brother
10: 25 **E** anything sold in the meat market
10: 27 to go, **e** whatever is put before you
10: 31 So whether you **e** or drink
11: 26 For whenever you **e** this bread
2Th 3: 10 is unwilling to work shall not **e**."
Rev 2: 7 I will give the right to **e**
3: 20 come in and **e** with that person,

EATEN (EAT)
Ge 3: 11 Have you **e** from the tree that I
Ac 10: 14 "I have never **e** anything impure
Rev 10: 10 but when I had **e** it, my stomach

EATER (EAT)
Isa 55: 10 for the sower and bread for the **e**,

EATING (EAT)
Ex 34: 28 and forty nights without **e** bread
Ro 14: 15 Do not by your **e** destroy someone
14: 17 of God is not a matter of **e**
14: 23 because their **e** is not from faith;
1Co 8: 4 about **e** food sacrificed to idols:
8: 10 knowledge, **e** in an idol's temple,
Jude : 12 **e** with you without the slightest

EATS (EAT)
1Sa 14: 24 be anyone who **e** food before
Lk 15: 2 sinners and **e** with them."
Jn 6: 51 Whoever **e** this bread will live
6: 54 Whoever **e** my flesh and drinks my
Ro 14: 2 faith is weak, **e** only vegetables.
14: 3 one who **e** everything must not
Ro 14: 6 Whoever **e** meat does so to
1Co 11: 27 whoever **e** the bread or drinks

EBAL
Dt 11: 29 and on Mount **E** the curses.
Jos 8: 30 Joshua built on Mount **E** an altar

EBENEZER
1Sa 7: 12 He named it **E**, saying, "Thus far

EDEN
Ge 2: 8 planted a garden in the east, in **E**;
Eze 28: 13 You were in **E**, the garden of God;

EDGE (DOUBLE-EDGED)
Mt 9: 20 him and touched the **e** of his cloak.

EDICT
Heb 11: 23 they were not afraid of the king's **e**.

EDIFICATION* (EDIFIED EDIFIES)
Ro 14: 19 leads to peace and to mutual **e**.

EDIFIED* (EDIFICATION)
1Co 14: 5 so that the church may be **e**.
14: 17 well enough, but no one else is **e**.

EDIFIES* (EDIFICATION)
1Co 14: 4 speaks in a tongue **e** themselves,
14: 4 one who prophesies **e** the church.

EDOM
Ge 36: 1 the family line of Esau (that is, **E**).
Isa 63: 1 Who is this coming from **E**,
Ob : 1 Sovereign LORD says about **E**—

EDUCATED*
Ac 7: 22 Moses was **e** in all the wisdom

EFFECT* (EFFECTIVE)
Job 41: 26 The sword that reaches it has no **e**,
Isa 32: 17 its **e** will be quietness
Zep 2: 2 before the decree takes **e**
1Co 15: 10 his grace to me was not without **e**.
Eph 1: 10 be put into **e** when the times reach
Heb 9: 17 it never takes **e** while the one who
9: 18 was not put into **e** without blood.

EFFECTIVE* (EFFECT)
Phm : 6 in the faith may be **e** in deepening

1Co 16: 9 a great door for **e** work has opened
Jas 5: 16 righteous person is powerful and **e**.

EFFORT*
Ecc 2: 19 toil into which I have poured my **e**
Da 6: 14 every **e** until sundown to save
Lk 13: 24 "Make every **e** to enter through
Ro 9: 16 depend on human desire or **e**,
14: 19 Let us therefore make every **e** to do
Eph 4: 3 Make every **e** to keep the unity
1Th 2: 16 in their **e** to keep us from speaking
2: 17 intense longing we made every **e**
Heb 4: 11 make every **e** to enter that rest,
12: 14 Make every **e** to live in peace
2Pe 1: 5 make every **e** to add to your faith
1: 15 I will make every **e** to see
1: 10 make every **e** to confirm your
3: 14 make every **e** to be found spotless,

EGG*
Lk 11: 12 Or if he asks for an **e**, will give him

EGLON
1. Fat king of Moab killed by Ehud (Jdg 3:12–30).
2. City in Canaan (Jos 10).

EGYPT (EGYPTIANS)
Ge 12: 10 Abram went down to **E** to live
37: 28 Ishmaelites, who took him to **E**.
42: 3 went down to buy grain from **E**.
45: 20 the best of all **E** will be yours.'"
46: 6 and all his offspring went to **E**,
47: 27 Now the Israelites settled in **E**
Ex 3: 11 and bring the Israelites out of **E**?"
12: 40 people lived in **E** was 430 years.
12: 41 all the LORD's divisions left **E**.
32: 1 Moses who brought us up out of **E**,
Nu 11: 18 We were better off in **E**!"
14: 4 choose a leader and go back to **E**."
24: 8 "God brought them out of **E**;
Dt 6: 21 "We were slaves of Pharaoh in **E**,
6: 21 us out of **E** with a mighty hand.
1Ki 4: 30 greater than all the wisdom of **E**.
10: 28 horses were imported from **E**
11: 40 but Jeroboam fled to **E**, to Shishak
14: 25 king of **E** attacked Jerusalem.
2Ch 35: 20 Necho king of **E** went up to fight
36: 3 The king of **E** dethroned him
Isa 19: 23 there will be a highway from **E**
Hos 11: 1 him, and out of **E** I called my son.
Mt 2: 15 "Out of **E** I called my son."
Heb 11: 27 By faith he left **E**, not fearing
Rev 11: 8 figuratively called Sodom and **E**—

EGYPTIANS (EGYPT)
Nu 14: 13 "Then the **E** will hear about it!

EHUD
Left-handed judge who delivered Israel from Moabite king, Eglon (Jdg 3:12–30).

EKRON
1Sa 5: 10 So they sent the ark of God to **E**.

ELABORATE*
1Ti 2: 9 not with **e** hairstyles or gold
1Pe 3: 3 as **e** hairstyles and the wearing

ELAH
Son of Baasha; king of Israel (1Ki 16:6–14).

ELATION*
Pr 28: 12 righteous triumph, there is great **e**;

ELDER* (ELDERLY ELDERS)
Isa 3: 2 the prophet, the diviner and the **e**,
1Ti 5: 19 accusation against an **e** unless it is
Titus 1: 6 An **e** must be blameless,
1Pe 5: 1 I appeal as a fellow **e** and a witness
2Jn : 1 The **e**, To the lady chosen by God
3Jn : 1 The **e**, To my dear friend Gaius,

ELDERLY* (ELDER)
Lev 19: 32 show respect for the **e** and revere
2Ch 36: 17 young women, the **e** or the infirm.

ELDERS (ELDER)
1Ki 12: 8 rejected the advice the **e** gave him
Mt 15: 2 break the tradition of the **e**?
Mk 7: 3 holding to the tradition of the **e**.
7: 5 to the tradition of the **e** instead
Ac 11: 30 their gift to the **e** by Barnabas
14: 23 Barnabas appointed **e** for them
15: 2 apostles and **e** about this question.
15: 4 the church and the apostles and **e**,
15: 6 **e** met to consider this question.
15: 22 Then the apostles and **e**,
15: 23 The apostles and **e**, your brothers,
16: 4 and **e** in Jerusalem for the people
Ac 20: 17 to Ephesus for the **e** of the church.
21: 18 James, and all the **e** were present.
23: 14 the chief priests and the **e** and said,
24: 1 to Caesarea with some of the **e**
1Ti 4: 14 the body of **e** laid their hands
5: 17 The **e** who direct the affairs
Titus 1: 5 and appoint **e** in every town, as I
Jas 5: 14 Let them call the **e** of the church
1Pe 5: 1 To the **e** among you, I appeal as
Rev 4: 4 seated on them were twenty-four **e**.
4: 10 the twenty-four **e** fall down before

ELEAZAR
Third son of Aaron (Ex 6:23–25). Succeeded Aaron as high priest (Nu 20:26; Dt 10:6). Allotted land to tribes (Jos 14:1). Death (Jos 24:33).

ELECT* (ELECTION)
Mt 24: 22 the **e** those days will be shortened.
24: 24 to deceive, if possible, even the **e**.
24: 31 they will gather his **e** from the four
Mk 13: 20 But for the sake of the **e**, whom he
13: 22 to deceive, if possible, even the **e**.
13: 27 gather his **e** from the four winds,
Ro 11: 7 The **e** among them did,
1Ti 5: 21 and Christ Jesus and the **e** angels,
2Ti 2: 10 everything for the sake of the **e**,
Titus 1: 1 to further the faith of God's **e**
1Pe 1: 1 Christ, To God's **e**, exiles scattered

ELECTION* (ELECT)
Ro 9: 11 God's purpose in **e** might stand:
11: 28 but as far as **e** is concerned, they
2Pe 1: 10 to confirm your calling and **e**.

ELEMENTARY* (ELEMENTS)
Heb 5: 12 to teach you the **e** truths of God's
6: 1 let us move beyond the **e** teachings

ELEMENTS* (ELEMENTARY)
2Pe 3: 10 the **e** will be destroyed by fire,
3: 12 fire, and the **e** will melt in the heat.

ELEVATE*
2Co 11: 7 in order to **e** you by preaching

ELI
High priest in youth of Samuel (1Sa 1–4). Blessed Hannah (1Sa 1:12–18); raised Samuel (1Sa 2:11–26). Prophesied against because of wicked sons (1Sa 2:27–36). Death of Eli and sons (1Sa 4:11–22).
Mt 27: 46 in a loud voice, "*E, E*,

ELIHU
One of Job's friends (Job 32–37).

ELIJAH
Prophet; predicted famine in Israel (1Ki 17:1; Jas 5:17). Fed by ravens (1Ki 17:2–6). Raised Sidonian widow's son (1Ki 17:7–24). Defeated prophets of Baal at Carmel (1Ki 18:16–46). Ran from Jezebel (1Ki 19:1–9). Prophesied death of Azariah (2Ki 1). Succeeded by Elishah (1Ki 19:19–21; 2Ki 2:1–18). Taken to heaven in whirlwind (2Ki 2:11–12).
Return prophesied (Mal 4:5–6); equated with John the Baptist (Mt 17:9–13; Mk 9:9–13; Lk 1:17). Appeared with Moses in transfiguration of Jesus (Mt 17:1–8; Mk 9:1–8).

ELIMELEK
Ru 1: 3 Now **E**, Naomi's husband, died,

ELIPHAZ
1. Firstborn of Esau (Ge 36).
2. One of Job's friends (Job 4–5; 15; 22).

ELISHA
Prophet; successor of Elijah (1Ki 19:16–21); inherited his cloak (2Ki 2:1–18). Purified bad water (2Ki 2:19–22). Cursed young men (2Ki 2:23–25). Aided Israel's defeat of Moab (2Ki 3). Provided widow with oil (2Ki 4:1–7). Raised Shunammite woman's son (2Ki 4:8–37). Purified food (2Ki 4:38–41). Fed 100 men (2Ki 4:42–44). Healed Naaman's leprosy (2Ki 5). Made axhead float (2Ki 6:1–7). Captured Arameans (2Ki 6:8–23). Political adviser to Israel (2Ki 6:24—8:6; 9:1–3; 13:14–19), Damascus (2Ki 8:7–15). Death (2Ki 13:20).

ELIZABETH*
Mother of John the Baptist, relative of Mary (Lk 1:5–58).

ELKANAH
Husband of Hannah, father of Samuel (1Sa 1–2).

ELOI*
Mk 15: 34 in a loud voice, "*E, E*,

ELOQUENCE* (ELOQUENT)
1Co 1: 17 gospel—not with wisdom and **e**,
1Co 2: 1 I did not come with **e** or human

ELOQUENT* (ELOQUENCE)
Ex 4: 10 I have never been **e**,
Pr 17: 7 **E** lips are unsuited to a godless

ELYMAS
Ac 13: 8 **E** the sorcerer (for that is what his

EMBEDDED*
Ecc 12: 11 sayings like firmly **e** nails—

EMBERS
Pr 26: 21 As charcoal to **e** and as wood

EMBITTER* (BITTER)
Col 3: 21 Fathers, do not **e** your children,

EMBODIMENT* (BODY)
Ro 2: 20 have in the law the **e** of knowledge

EMPEROR
1Pe 2: 13 whether to the **e**, as the supreme
2: 17 of believers, fear God, honor the **e**.

EMPTIED (EMPTY)
1Co 1: 17 cross of Christ be **e** of its power.

EMPTY (EMPTIED)
Ge 1: 2 Now the earth was formless and **e**,
Job 26: 7 out the northern skies over **e** space;
Isa 45: 18 he did not create it to be **e**,
55: 11 It will not return to me **e**, but will
Jer 4: 23 earth, and it was formless and **e**;
Mt 12: 36 for every **e** word they have spoken.
Lk 1: 53 things but has sent the rich away **e**.
Eph 5: 6 no one deceive you with **e** words,
1Pe 1: 18 you were redeemed from the **e** way
2Pe 2: 18 For they mouth **e**, boastful words

ENABLE* (ABLE)
Lk 1: 74 to **e** us to serve him without fear
Ac 4: 29 **e** your servants to speak your word

ENABLED (ABLE)
Lev 26: 13 **e** you to walk with heads held high.
Ru 4: 13 her, the LORD **e** her to conceive,
Jn 6: 65 me unless the Father has **e** them."
Ac 2: 4 other tongues as the Spirit **e** them.
7: 10 and **e** him to gain the goodwill
Heb 11: 11 was **e** to bear children because she

ENABLES* (ABLE)
Hab 3: 19 he **e** me to tread on the heights.
Php 3: 21 by the power that **e** him to bring

ENABLING* (ABLE)
Ac 14: 3 grace by **e** them to perform signs

ENCAMPS* (CAMP)
Ps 34: 7 the LORD **e** around those who fear

ENCOURAGE* (ENCOURAGED ENCOURAGEMENT ENCOURAGES ENCOURAGING)
Dt 1: 38 **E** him, because he will lead Israel
3: 28 Joshua, and **e** and strengthen him,
2Sa 11: 25 and destroy it.' Say this to **e** Joab."
19: 7 Now go out and **e** your men.
Job 16: 5 But my mouth would **e** you;
Ps 10: 17 you **e** them, and you listen to their
64: 5 They **e** each other in evil plans,
Jer 29: 8 to the dreams you **e** them to have.
Ac 15: 32 said much to **e** and strengthen
Ro 12: 8 if it is to **e**, then give
2Co 13: 11 for full restoration, **e** one another,
Eph 6: 22 how we are, and that he may **e** you.
Col 4: 8 and that he may **e** your hearts.
1Th 3: 2 strengthen and **e** you in your faith,
4: 18 Therefore **e** one another with these
5: 11 Therefore **e** one another and build
5: 14 and disruptive, **e** the disheartened,
2Th 2: 17 **e** your hearts and strengthen you
2Ti 4: 2 correct, rebuke and **e**—
Titus 1: 9 he can **e** others by sound doctrine
2: 6 Similarly, **e** the young men to be
2: 15 **E** and rebuke with all authority.
Heb 3: 13 But **e** one another daily, as long as

ENCOURAGED* (ENCOURAGE)
Jdg 7: 11 you will be **e** to attack the camp."
20: 22 But the Israelites **e** one another
2Ch 22: 3 his mother **e** him to act wickedly.
32: 6 gate and **e** them with these words:
35: 2 and **e** them in the service
Eze 13: 22 and because you **e** the wicked not
Ac 9: 31 the Lord and **e** by the Holy Spirit,
11: 23 **e** them all to remain true to the
16: 40 brothers and sisters and **e** them.
18: 27 the brothers and sisters **e** him

Ac 27: 36 They were all **e** and ate some food
28: 15 Paul thanked God and was **e**.
Ro 1: 12 I may be mutually **e** by each other's
1Co 14: 31 everyone may be instructed and **e**.
2Co 7: 4 I am greatly **e**; in all our troubles
7: 13 By all this we are **e**. In addition
Col 2: 2 goal is that they may be **e** in heart
1Th 3: 7 persecution we were **e** about you
Heb 6: 18 hope set before us may be greatly **e**.

ENCOURAGEMENT* (ENCOURAGE)
Ac 4: 36 (which means "son of **e**"),
20: 2 speaking many words of **e**
Ro 12: 8 if it is to encourage, then give **e**;
15: 4 the **e** they provide we might have
15: 5 **e** give you the same attitude of
2Co 7: 13 In addition to our own **e**, we were
Php 2: 1 you have any **e** from being united
2Th 2: 16 by his grace gave us eternal **e**
Phm : 7 love has given me great joy and **e**,
Heb 12: 5 completely forgotten this word of **e**

ENCOURAGES* (ENCOURAGE)
Isa 41: 7 The metalworker **e** the goldsmith,

ENCOURAGING* (ENCOURAGE)
Ac 14: 22 **e** them to remain true to the faith.
15: 31 it and were glad for its **e** message.
20: 1 after **e** them, said goodbye and set
1Co 14: 3 their strengthening, **e** and comfort.
1Th 2: 12 **e**, comforting and urging you to
Heb 10: 25 habit of doing, but **e** one another—
1Pe 5: 12 **e** you and testifying that this is

ENCROACH
Pr 23: 10 or **e** on the fields of the fatherless,

END (ENDS)
Ps 119: 33 that I may follow it to the **e**.
119:112 keeping your decrees to the very **e**.
Pr 5: 4 but in the **e** she is bitter as gall,
5: 11 At the **e** of your life you will groan,
14: 12 right, but in the **e** it leads to death.
14: 13 ache, and rejoicing may **e** in grief.
16: 25 right, but in the **e** it leads to death.
19: 20 the **e** you will be counted among
20: 21 soon will not be blessed at the **e**.
23: 32 In the **e** it bites like a snake
25: 8 do in the **e** if your neighbor puts
28: 23 the **e** gain favor rather than one
Ecc 3: 11 God has done from beginning to **e**.
7: 8 The **e** of a matter is better than its
12: 12 making many books there is no **e**,
Eze 7: 2 to the land of Israel: "'The **e**!
Mt 10: 22 stands firm to the **e** will be saved.
24: 13 stands firm to the **e** will be saved.
24: 14 nations, and then the **e** will come.
Lk 21: 9 but the **e** will not come right away."
Jn 13: 1 the world, he loved them to the **e**.
1Co 15: 24 Then the **e** will come, when he
Rev 21: 6 Omega, the Beginning and the **E**.
22: 13 the Last, the Beginning and the **E**.

ENDS (END)
Ps 19: 4 their words to the **e** of the world.
Pr 20: 17 but one **e** up with a mouth full
Isa 49: 6 may reach to the **e** of the earth."
62: 11 proclamation to the **e** of the earth:
Ac 13: 47 salvation to the **e** of the earth.'"
Ro 10: 18 their words to the **e** of the world."

ENDURANCE* (ENDURE)
Ro 15: 4 so that through the **e** taught
15: 5 May the God who gives **e**
2Co 1: 6 you patient **e** of the same sufferings
6: 4 in great **e**; in troubles,
Col 1: 11 might so that you may have great **e**
1Th 1: 3 **e** inspired by hope in our Lord
1Ti 6: 11 faith, love, **e** and gentleness.
2Ti 3: 10 my purpose, faith, patience, love, **e**,
Titus 2: 2 and sound in faith, in love and in **e**.
Rev 1: 9 and patient **e** that are ours in Jesus,
13: 10 This calls for patient **e**
14: 12 This calls for patient **e** on the part

ENDURE (ENDURANCE ENDURED ENDURES ENDURING)
Ps 72: 17 May his name **e** forever;
Pr 12: 19 Truthful lips **e** forever, but a lying
27: 24 for riches do not **e** forever,
Ecc 3: 14 everything God does will **e** forever;
Isa 55: 13 sign, that will **e** forever."
Da 2: 44 to an end, but it will itself **e** forever.
Mal 3: 2 who can **e** the day of his coming?
1Co 4: 12 when we are persecuted, we **e** it;
10: 13 a way out so that you can **e** it.
2Co 1: 8 far beyond our ability to **e**,
2Ti 2: 10 Therefore I **e** everything
2: 12 if we **e**, we will also reign with him.
4: 5 head in all situations, **e** hardship,
Heb 12: 7 **E** hardship as discipline;
1Pe 2: 20 suffer for doing good and you **e** it,
Rev 3: 10 kept my command to **e** patiently,

ENDURED* (ENDURE)
Ps 123: 3 for we have **e** no end of contempt.
123: 4 We have **e** no end of ridicule
Ac 13: 18 forty years he **e** their conduct
2Ti 3: 11 and Lystra, the persecutions I **e**.
Heb 10: 32 when you **e** in a great conflict full
12: 2 joy set before him he **e** the cross,
12: 3 him who **e** such opposition
Rev 2: 3 and have **e** hardships for my name,

ENDURES (ENDURE)
Ps 102: 12 your renown **e** through all
112: 9 poor, their righteousness **e** forever;
136: 1 *His love **e** forever.*
Pr 12: 12 but the root of the righteous **e**.
Isa 40: 8 but the word of our God **e** forever."
Da 9: 15 yourself a name that **e** to this day,
2Co 9: 9 their righteousness **e** forever."
1Pe 1: 25 but the word of the Lord **e** forever."

ENDURING (ENDURE)
2Th 1: 4 persecutions and trials you are **e**.
1Pe 1: 23 the living and **e** word of God.

ENEMIES (ENEMY)
Ps 23: 5 before me in the presence of my **e**.
110: 1 until I make your **e** a footstool
Pr 16: 7 he causes their **e** to make peace
26: 24 **E** disguise themselves with their
29: 24 of thieves are their own **e**;
Isa 59: 18 so will he repay wrath to his **e**
Mic 7: 6 a man's **e** are the members of his
Mt 5: 44 love your **e** and pray for those who
10: 36 a man's **e** will be the members
Lk 6: 27 Love your **e**, do good to those who
6: 35 But love your **e**, do good to them,
20: 43 until I make your **e** a footstool
Ro 5: 10 if, while we were God's **e**, we were
1Co 15: 25 he has put all his **e** under his feet.
Php 3: 18 tears, many live as **e** of the cross
Heb 1: 13 until I make your **e** a footstool
10: 13 for his **e** to be made his footstool.

ENEMY (ENEMIES ENMITY)
Pr 24: 17 Do not gloat when your **e** falls;
25: 21 If your **e** is hungry, give him food
27: 6 trusted, but an **e** multiplies kisses.
Lk 10: 19 to overcome all the power of the **e**;
Ro 12: 20 "If your **e** is hungry, feed him;
1Co 15: 26 The last **e** to be destroyed is death.
1Ti 5: 14 and to give the **e** no opportunity
1Pe 5: 8 Your **e** the devil prowls around like

ENERGY*
Col 1: 29 the **e** Christ so powerfully works

ENGRAVED
Isa 49: 16 I have **e** you on the palms of my
2Co 3: 7 which was **e** in letters on stone,

ENHANCES*
Ro 3: 7 my falsehood **e** God's truthfulness

ENJOY (JOY)
Dt 6: 2 and so that you may **e** long life.
Est 5: 14 king to the banquet and **e** yourself."
Ps 37: 3 in the land and **e** safe pasture.
Pr 28: 16 ill-gotten gain will **e** a long reign.
Ecc 3: 22 for a person than to **e** their work,
Eph 6: 3 and that you may **e** long life
Heb 11: 25 than to **e** the fleeting pleasures
3Jn : 2 I pray that you may **e** good health

ENJOYMENT (JOY)
Ecc 4: 8 why am I depriving myself of **e**?"
1Ti 6: 17 us with everything for our **e**.

ENLARGE (ENLARGES)
2Co 9: 10 seed and will **e** the harvest of your

ENLARGES (ENLARGE)
Dt 33: 20 is he who **e** Gad's domain!

ENLIGHTENED* (LIGHT)
Eph 1: 18 eyes of your heart may be **e** in order
Heb 6: 4 for those who have once been **e**,

ENMITY (ENEMY)
Ge 3: 15 I will put **e** between you
Jas 4: 4 the world means **e** against God?

ENOCH
1. Son of Cain (Ge 4:17–18).
2. Descendant of Seth; walked with God and taken by him (Ge 5:18–24; Heb 11:5). Prophet (Jude 14).

ENSLAVED (SLAVE)
Gal 4: 9 to be **e** by them all over again?
Titus 3: 3 and **e** by all kinds of passions

ENSNARE (SNARE)
Pr 5: 22 evil deeds of the wicked **e** them;
Ecc 7: 26 her, but the sinner she will **e**.

ENSNARED* (SNARE)
Dt 7: 25 or you will be **e** by it, for it is
12: 30 be careful not to be **e** by inquiring
Ps 9: 16 the wicked are **e** by the work
Pr 6: 2 said, **e** by the words of your mouth.
22: 25 learn their ways and get yourself **e**.

ENTANGLED (ENTANGLES)
2Ti 2: 4 No one serving as a soldier gets **e**
2Pe 2: 20 Jesus Christ and are again **e** in it

ENTANGLES* (ENTANGLED)
Heb 12: 1 hinders and the sin that so easily **e**.

ENTER (ENTERED ENTERING ENTERS ENTRANCE)
Ps 95: 11 'They shall never **e** my rest.'"
100: 4 **E** his gates with thanksgiving
Pr 2: 10 For wisdom will **e** your heart,
Mt 5: 20 will certainly not **e** the kingdom
7: 13 "**E** through the narrow gate.
7: 21 will **e** the kingdom of heaven,
18: 3 you will never **e** the kingdom
18: 8 It is better for you to **e** life maimed
19: 17 If you want to **e** life,
19: 23 who is rich to **e** the kingdom
Mk 9: 43 you to **e** life maimed than with two
9: 45 you to **e** life crippled than to have
9: 47 for you to **e** the kingdom of God
10: 15 like a little child will never **e** it."
10: 23 the rich to **e** the kingdom of God!"
Lk 13: 24 to **e** through the narrow door,
18: 17 like a little child will never **e** it."
18: 24 the rich to **e** the kingdom of God!
Jn 3: 5 no one can **e** the kingdom of God
Heb 3: 11 'They shall never **e** my rest.'"
4: 11 make every effort to **e** that rest,

ENTERED (ENTER)
Ps 73: 17 till I **e** the sanctuary of God;
Eze 4: 14 impure meat has ever **e** my mouth."
Ac 11: 8 or unclean has ever **e** my mouth.'
Ro 5: 12 just as sin **e** the world through one
Heb 9: 12 he **e** the Most Holy Place once

ENTERING (ENTER)
Mt 21: 31 the prostitutes are **e** the kingdom
Lk 11: 52 have hindered those who were **e**."
Heb 4: 1 promise of **e** his rest still stands,

ENTERS (ENTER)
Mk 7: 18 that nothing that **e** a person
Jn 10: 2 The one who **e** by the gate is

ENTERTAIN* (ENTERTAINMENT)
Jdg 16: 25 "Bring out Samson to **e** us."
Mt 9: 4 "Why do you **e** evil thoughts
1Ti 5: 19 Do not **e** an accusation against

ENTERTAINMENT* (ENTERTAIN)
Da 6: 18 without any **e** being brought to

ENTHRALLED*
Ps 45: 11 Let the king be **e** by your beauty;

ENTHRONED* (THRONE)
1Sa 4: 4 who is **e** between the cherubim.
2Sa 6: 2 who is **e** between the cherubim
2Ki 19: 15 of Israel, **e** between the cherubim,
1Ch 13: 6 who is **e** between the cherubim—
Ps 2: 4 The One **e** in heaven laughs;
7: 7 while you sit **e** over them on high.
9: 4 sitting **e** as the righteous judge.
9: 11 praises of the LORD, **e** in Zion;
22: 3 Yet you are **e** as the Holy One;
29: 10 The LORD sits **e** over the flood;
29: 10 the LORD is **e** as King forever.
55: 19 God, who is **e** from of old,
61: 7 May he be **e** in God's presence
80: 1 You who sit **e** between
99: 1 he sits **e** between the cherubim,
102: 12 But you, LORD, sit **e** forever;
113: 5 God, the One who sits **e** on high,
123: 1 to you, to you who sit **e** in heaven.
132: 14 here I will sit **e**, for I have desired
Isa 14: 13 I will sit **e** on the mount
37: 16 of Israel, **e** between the cherubim,
40: 22 He sits **e** above the circle
52: 2 rise up, sit **e**, Jerusalem.
Rev 18: 7 heart she boasts, 'I sit **e** as queen.

ENTHRONES* (THRONE)
Job 36: 7 he **e** them with kings and exalts

ENTHUSIASM*
2Co 8: 17 he is coming to you with much **e**
9: 2 your **e** has stirred most of them

ENTICE (ENTICED ENTICES)
Pr 1: 10 if sinful men **e** you, do not give
2Pe 2: 18 they **e** people who are just escaping
Rev 2: 14 who taught Balak to **e** the Israelites

ENTICED (ENTICE)
Dt 4: 19 do not be **e** into bowing down
11: 16 or you will be **e** to turn away
2Ki 17: 21 Jeroboam **e** Israel away
Job 31: 9 my heart has been **e** by a woman,
31: 27 so that my heart was secretly **e**
Jas 1: 14 by their own evil desire and **e**.

ENTICES* (ENTICE)
Dt 13: 6 your closest friend secretly **e** you,
Job 36: 18 careful that no one **e** you by riches;
Pr 16: 29 A violent person **e** their neighbor

ENTIRE
Gal 5: 14 For the **e** law is fulfilled in keeping

ENTRANCE (ENTER)
Mt 27: 60 stone in front of the **e** to the tomb
Mk 15: 46 he rolled a stone against the **e**
16: 3 away from the **e** of the tomb?"
Jn 11: 38 cave with a stone laid across the **e**.
20: 1 had been removed from the **e**.

ENTRUST (TRUST)
Ps 143: 8 I should go, for to you I **e** my life.
Jn 2: 24 Jesus would not **e** himself to them,
2Ti 2: 2 many witnesses **e** to reliable people

ENTRUSTED (TRUST)
Jer 13: 20 is the flock that was **e** to you,
Jn 5: 22 but has **e** all judgment to the Son,
Ro 3: 2 the Jews have been **e** with the very
1Co 4: 1 as those **e** with the mysteries God
1Th 2: 4 by God to be **e** with the gospel.
1Ti 1: 11 the blessed God, which he **e** to me.
6: 20 guard what has been **e** to your care.
2Ti 1: 12 to guard what I have **e** to him until
1: 14 good deposit that was **e** to you—
Titus 1: 3 through the preaching **e** to me
1Pe 2: 23 he **e** himself to him who judges
5: 3 not lording it over those **e** to you,
Jude : 3 once for all **e** to God's holy people.

ENVIOUS (ENVY)
Dt 32: 21 I will make them **e** by those who
Pr 24: 19 of evildoers or be **e** of the wicked,
Ro 10: 19 "I will make you **e** by those who

ENVOY
Pr 13: 17 but a trustworthy **e** brings healing.

ENVY (ENVIOUS ENVYING)
Pr 3: 31 Do not **e** the violent or choose any
14: 30 to the body, but **e** rots the bones.
23: 17 Do not let your heart **e** sinners,
24: 1 Do not **e** the wicked, do not desire
Mk 7: 22 malice, deceit, lewdness, **e**, slander,
Ro 1: 29 They are full of **e**, murder, strife,
11: 14 arouse my own people to **e** and
1Co 13: 4 It does not **e**, it does not boast, it is
Gal 5: 21 and **e**; drunkenness, orgies,
Php 1: 15 that some preach Christ out of **e**
1Ti 6: 4 about words that result in **e**,
Titus 3: 3 We lived in malice and **e**,
Jas 3: 14 if you harbor bitter **e** and selfish
3: 16 For where you have **e** and selfish
1Pe 2: 1 hypocrisy, **e**, and slander of every

ENVYING* (ENVY)
Gal 5: 26 provoking and **e** each other.

EPHAH
Lev 19: 36 an honest **e** and an honest hin.
Eze 45: 10 use accurate scales, an accurate **e**

EPHESUS
Ac 18: 19 They arrived at **E**, where Paul left
19: 1 the interior and arrived at **E**.
Eph 1: 1 God, To God's holy people in **E**,
Rev 2: 1 the angel of the church in **E** write:

EPHRAIM
1. Second son of Joseph (Ge 41:52; 46:20). Blessed as firstborn by Jacob (Ge 48). Tribe of numbered (Nu 1:33; 26:37), blessed (Dt 33:17), allotted land (Jos 16:4–9; Eze 48:5), failed to fully possess (Jos 16:10; Jdg 1:29).
2. Synonymous with northern kingdom (Isa 7:17; Hos 5).

EQUAL (EQUALITY EQUITY)
Dt 33: 25 and your strength will **e** your days.
Isa 40: 25 Or who is my **e**?" says the Holy
46: 5 you compare me or count me **e**?
Da 1: 19 and he found none **e** to Daniel,
Jn 5: 18 Father, making himself **e** with God.
1Co 12: 25 its parts should have **e** concern
2Co 2: 16 And who is **e** to such a task?

EQUALITY* (EQUAL)
2Co 8: 13 pressed, but that there might be **e**.
8: 14 what you need. The goal is **e**,
Php 2: 6 God, did not consider **e** with God

EQUIP* (EQUIPPED)
Eph 4: 12 to **e** his people for works of service,
Heb 13: 21 **e** you with everything good

EQUIPPED (EQUIP)
2Ti 3: 17 God may be thoroughly **e** for every

EQUITY* (EQUAL)
Ps 9: 8 and judges the peoples with **e**.
58: 1 Do you judge people with **e**?
67: 4 for you rule the peoples with **e**
75: 2 it is I who judge with **e**.
96: 10 he will judge the peoples with **e**.
98: 9 and the peoples with **e**.
99: 4 you have established **e**; in Jacob

ERODES*
Job 14: 18 "But as a mountain **e** and crumbles

ERROR (ERRORS)
Ro 1: 27 the due penalty for their **e**.
Jas 5: 20 the **e** of their way will save them
2Pe 2: 18 escaping from those who live in **e**.

ERRORS* (ERROR)
Ps 19: 12 But who can discern their own **e**?

ESAU
Firstborn of Isaac, twin of Jacob (Ge 25:21–26). Also called Edom (Ge 25:30). Sold Jacob his birthright (Ge 25:29–34); lost blessing (Gen 27). Married Hittites (Ge 26:34), Ishmaelites (Ge 28:6–9). Reconciled to Jacob (Gen 33). Genealogy (Ge 36). The LORD chose Jacob over Esau (Mal 1:2–3), but gave Esau land (Dt 2:2–12). Descendants eventually obliterated (Ob 1–21; Jer 49:7–22).

ESCAPE (ESCAPED ESCAPING)
Ps 68: 20 the Sovereign LORD comes **e**
89: 48 who can **e** the power of the grave?
Pr 11: 9 knowledge the righteous **e**.
12: 13 talk, and so the innocent **e** trouble.
Ro 2: 3 think you will **e** God's judgment?
1Th 5: 3 woman, and they will not **e**.
2Ti 2: 26 and **e** from the trap of the devil,
Heb 2: 3 how shall we **e** if we ignore so great
12: 25 If they did not **e** when they refused

ESCAPED (ESCAPE)
2Pe 1: 4 **e** the corruption in the world
2: 20 If they have **e** the corruption

ESCAPING (ESCAPE)
1Co 3: 15 only as one **e** through the flames.
2Pe 2: 18 they entice people who are just **e**

ESTABLISH (ESTABLISHED ESTABLISHES)
Ge 6: 18 But I will **e** my covenant with you,
17: 21 my covenant I will **e** with Isaac,
2Sa 7: 11 the LORD himself will **e** a house
1Ki 9: 5 will **e** your royal throne over Israel
1Ch 28: 7 I will **e** his kingdom forever if he is
Ps 90: 17 **e** the work of our hands for us—
Pr 16: 3 you do, and he will **e** your plans.
Isa 26: 12 LORD, you **e** peace for us;
Ro 10: 3 of God and sought to **e** their own,
16: 25 Now to him who is able to **e** you
Heb 10: 9 sets aside the first to **e** the second.

ESTABLISHED (ESTABLISH)
Ge 9: 17 the covenant I have **e** between me
Ex 6: 4 **e** my covenant with them to give
Ps 8: 2 infants you have **e** a stronghold
111: 8 They are **e** for ever and ever,
Pr 16: 12 throne is **e** through righteousness.
20: 18 Plans are **e** by seeking advice;
Jer 33: 25 night and **e** the laws of heaven
Heb 8: 6 one, since the new covenant is **e**

ESTABLISHES (ESTABLISH)
Job 25: 2 he **e** order in the heights of heaven.
Pr 16: 9 course, but the LORD **e** their steps.
Isa 42: 4 or be discouraged till he **e** justice

ESTATE
Ps 136: 23 He remembered us in our low **e**

ESTEEM (ESTEEMED)
Isa 53: 3 and we held him in low **e**.
Gal 2: 6 those who were held in high **e**—

ESTEEMED (ESTEEM)
Pr 22: 1 to be **e** is better than silver or gold.

ESTHER
Jewess, originally named Hadassah, who lived in Persia; cousin of Mordecai (Est 2:7). Chosen queen of Xerxes (Est 2:8–18). Persuaded by Mordecai to foil Haman's plan to exterminate the Jews (Est 3–4). Revealed Haman's plans to Xerxes, resulting in Haman's death (Est 7), the Jews' preservation (Est 8–9), Mordecai's exaltation (Est 8:15; 9:4; 10). Decreed celebration of Purim (Est 9:18–32).

ETERNAL* (ETERNITY)
Ge 21: 33 the name of the LORD, the **E** God.
Dt 33: 27 The **e** God is your refuge,
1Ki 10: 9 of the LORD's **e** love for Israel,
Ps 16: 11 with **e** pleasures at your right hand.
111: 10 To him belongs **e** praise.
119: 89 Your word, LORD, is **e**;
119:160 all your righteous laws are **e**.
Ecc 12: 5 Then people go to their **e** home
Isa 26: 4 the LORD himself, is the Rock **e**.
47: 7 said, 'I am forever—the **e** queen!'
Jer 10: 10 he is the living God, the **e** King.
Da 4: 3 His kingdom is an **e** kingdom;
4: 34 His dominion is an **e** dominion;
Mt 18: 8 two feet and be thrown into **e** fire.
19: 16 good thing must I do to get **e** life?"
19: 29 as much and will inherit **e** life.
25: 41 the **e** fire prepared for the devil
25: 46 they will go away to **e** punishment,
25: 46 but the righteous to **e** life."
Mk 3: 29 they are guilty of an **e** sin."
10: 17 "what must I do to inherit **e** life?"
10: 30 and in the age to come **e** life.
Lk 10: 25 "what must I do to inherit **e** life?"
16: 9 will be welcomed into **e** dwellings.
18: 18 what must I do to inherit **e** life?"
18: 30 age, and in the age to come **e** life."
Jn 3: 15 who believes may have **e** life
3: 16 him shall not perish but have **e** life.
3: 36 believes in the Son has **e** life,
4: 14 of water welling up to **e** life."
4: 36 wage and harvests a crop for **e** life,
5: 24 believes him who sent me has **e** life
5: 39 think that in them you have **e** life.
6: 27 but for food that endures to **e** life,
6: 40 believes in him shall have **e** life,
6: 47 the one who believes has **e** life.
6: 54 and drinks my blood has **e** life,
6: 68 You have the words of **e** life.
10: 28 I give them **e** life, and they shall
12: 25 in this world will keep it for **e** life.
12: 50 that his command leads to **e** life.
17: 2 he might give **e** life to all those you
17: 3 Now this is **e** life: that they know
Ac 13: 46 yourselves worthy of **e** life,
13: 48 were appointed for **e** life believed.
Ro 1: 20 his **e** power and divine nature—
2: 7 and immortality, he will give **e** life.
5: 21 bring **e** life through Jesus Christ
6: 22 to holiness, and the result is **e** life.
6: 23 of God is **e** life in Christ Jesus our
16: 26 by the command of the **e** God,
2Co 4: 17 for us an **e** glory that far outweighs
4: 18 temporary, but what is unseen is **e**.
5: 1 from God, an **e** house in heaven,
Gal 6: 8 from the Spirit will reap **e** life.
Eph 3: 11 according to his **e** purpose that he
2Th 2: 16 his grace gave us **e** encouragement
1Ti 1: 16 believe in him and receive **e** life.
1: 17 Now to the King **e**, immortal,
6: 12 Take hold of the **e** life to which you
2Ti 2: 10 that is in Christ Jesus, with **e** glory.
Titus 1: 2 in the hope of **e** life, which God,
3: 7 heirs having the hope of **e** life.
Heb 5: 9 he became the source of **e** salvation
6: 2 of the dead, and **e** judgment.
9: 12 thus obtaining **e** redemption.
9: 14 who through the **e** Spirit offered
9: 15 receive the promised **e** inheritance
13: 20 of the **e** covenant brought back
1Pe 5: 10 who called you to his **e** glory
2Pe 1: 11 a rich welcome into the **e** kingdom
1Jn 1: 2 and we proclaim to you the **e** life,
2: 25 this is what he promised us—**e** life.
3: 15 no murderer has **e** life residing
5: 11 God has given us **e** life, and this life
5: 13 you may know that you have **e** life.

1Jn 5: 20 He is the true God and **e** life.
Jude : 7 suffer the punishment of **e** fire.
: 21 Jesus Christ to bring you to **e** life.
Rev 14: 6 he had the **e** gospel to proclaim

ETERNITY* (ETERNAL)
Ps 93: 2 you are from all **e**.
Ecc 3: 11 has also set **e** in the human heart;

ETHIOPIAN*
Jer 13: 23 Can an **E** change his skin
Ac 8: 27 on his way he met an **E** eunuch,

EUNUCH (EUNUCHS)
Ac 8: 27 on his way he met an Ethiopian **e**,

EUNUCHS (EUNUCH)
Isa 56: 4 "To the **e** who keep my Sabbaths,
Mt 19: 12 For there are **e** who were born
19: 12 choose to live like **e** for the sake

EUTYCHUS*
Ac 20: 9 was a young man named **E**,

EVANGELIST* (EVANGELISTS)
Ac 21: 8 stayed at the house of Philip the **e**,
2Ti 4: 5 do the work of an **e**, discharge all

EVANGELISTS* (EVANGELIST)
Eph 4: 11 the **e**, the pastors and teachers,

EVE*
Ge 3: 20 Adam named his wife **E**,
4: 1 Adam made love to his wife **E**,
2Co 11: 3 afraid that just as **E** was deceived
1Ti 2: 13 For Adam was formed first, then **E**.

EVEN-TEMPERED* (TEMPER)
Pr 17: 27 whoever has understanding is **e**.

EVENING
Ge 1: 5 And there was **e**, and there was

EVER (EVERLASTING FOREVER FOREVERMORE)
Ex 15: 18 "The LORD reigns for **e** and **e**."
Dt 8: 19 you **e** forget the LORD your God
1Ki 3: 12 like you, nor will there **e** be.
Job 4: 7 being innocent, has **e** perished?
Ps 5: 11 you be glad; let them **e** sing for joy.
10: 16 The LORD is King for **e** and **e**;
21: 4 length of days, for **e** and **e**.
25: 3 one who hopes in you will **e** be put
25: 15 My eyes are **e** on the LORD,
45: 6 O God, will last for **e** and **e**;
45: 17 will praise you for **e** and **e**.
48: 14 this God is our God for **e** and **e**;
52: 8 unfailing love for **e** and **e**.
61: 8 I will **e** sing in praise of your name
71: 6 I will **e** praise you.
84: 4 they are **e** praising you.
89: 33 nor will I **e** betray my faithfulness.
111: 8 They are established for **e** and **e**,
119: 44 always obey your law, for **e** and **e**.
132: 12 sit on your throne for **e** and **e**."
145: 1 praise your name for **e** and **e**.
145: 2 and extol your name for **e** and **e**.
145: 21 praise his holy name for **e** and **e**.
Pr 4: 18 shining **e** brighter till the full light
5: 19 may you **e** be intoxicated with her
Isa 66: 8 Who has **e** heard of such things?
Jer 7: 7 the land I gave your ancestors for **e**
25: 5 you and your ancestors for **e** and **e**.
31: 36 "will Israel **e** cease being a nation
Da 2: 20 "Praise be to the name of God for **e**
7: 18 possess it forever—yes, for **e** and **e**.'
12: 3 like the stars for **e** and **e**.
Mic 4: 5 the LORD our God for **e** and **e**.
Mt 13: 14 "'You will be **e** hearing but never
13: 14 you will be **e** seeing but never
Mk 4: 12 "'they may be **e** seeing but never
Jn 1: 18 No one has **e** seen God, but the
Gal 1: 5 to whom be glory for **e** and **e**.
Eph 3: 21 all generations, for **e** and **e**! Amen.
Php 4: 20 and Father be glory for **e** and **e**.
1Ti 1: 17 be honor and glory for **e** and **e**.
2Ti 4: 18 To him be glory for **e** and **e**. Amen.
Heb 1: 8 throne, O God, will last for **e** and **e**;
13: 21 to whom be glory for **e** and **e**.
1Pe 4: 11 glory and the power for **e** and **e**.
5: 11 To him be the power for **e** and **e**.
1Jn 4: 12 No one has **e** seen God; but if we
Rev 1: 6 be glory and power for **e** and **e**!
1: 18 now look, I am alive for **e** and **e**!
21: 27 Nothing impure will **e** enter it,
22: 5 And they will reign for **e** and **e**.

EVER-INCREASING* (INCREASE)
Ro 6: 19 to impurity and to **e** wickedness,
2Co 3: 18 into his image with **e** glory,

EVERLASTING (EVER)
Ge 9: 16 remember the **e** covenant between
17: 7 covenant as an **e** covenant between
17: 8 I will give as an **e** possession to you
17: 13 in your flesh is to be an **e** covenant.
17: 19 with him as an **e** covenant for his
48: 4 give this land as an **e** possession
Nu 18: 19 It is an **e** covenant of salt before
Dt 33: 15 and the fruitfulness of the **e** hills;
33: 27 and underneath are the **e** arms.
2Sa 23: 5 have made with me an **e** covenant,
1Ch 16: 17 a decree, to Israel as an **e** covenant:
16: 36 the God of Israel, from **e** to **e**.
29: 10 of our father Israel, from **e** to **e**.
Ezr 9: 12 your children as an **e** inheritance.'
Ne 9: 5 your God, who is from **e** to **e**."
Ps 41: 13 the God of Israel, from **e** to **e**.
52: 5 God will bring you down to **e** ruin:
74: 3 your steps toward these **e** ruins,
78: 66 he put them to **e** shame.
90: 2 world, from **e** to **e** you are God.
103: 17 But from **e** to **e** the LORD's love is
105: 10 a decree, to Israel as an **e** covenant:
106: 48 the God of Israel, from **e** to **e**.
119:142 Your righteousness is **e** and your
139: 24 and lead me in the way **e**.
145: 13 Your kingdom is an **e** kingdom,
Isa 9: 6 Mighty God, **E** Father,
24: 5 statutes and broken the **e** covenant.
30: 8 to come it may be an **e** witness.
33: 14 of us can dwell with **e** burning?"
35: 10 **e** joy will crown their heads.
40: 28 The LORD is the **e** God,
45: 17 by the LORD with an **e** salvation;
45: 17 to shame or disgraced, to ages **e**.
51: 11 **e** joy will crown their heads.
54: 8 **e** kindness I will have compassion
55: 3 I will make an **e** covenant with you,
55: 13 for an **e** sign, that will endure
56: 5 I will give them an **e** name that will
60: 15 I will make you the **e** pride
60: 19 for the LORD will be your **e** light,
60: 20 the LORD will be your **e** light,
61: 7 your land, and **e** joy will be yours.
61: 8 make an **e** covenant with them.
63: 12 them, to gain for himself **e** renown,
Jer 5: 22 the sea, an **e** barrier it cannot cross.
23: 40 I will bring on you **e** disgrace—
23: 40 I will bring on you **e** disgrace—
25: 9 of horror and scorn, and an **e** ruin.
31: 3 "I have loved you with an **e** love;
32: 40 I will make an **e** covenant
50: 5 to the LORD in an **e** covenant
Eze 16: 60 I will establish an **e** covenant
37: 26 it will be an **e** covenant.
Da 7: 14 His dominion is an **e** dominion
7: 27 His kingdom will be an **e** kingdom,
9: 24 to bring in **e** righteousness, to seal
12: 2 some to **e** life, others to shame and **e** contempt.
Mic 6: 2 you **e** foundations of the earth.
Hab 1: 12 LORD, are you not from **e**?
2Th 1: 9 will be punished with **e** destruction
Jude : 6 bound with **e** chains for judgment

EVER-PRESENT*
Ps 46: 1 and strength, an **e** help in trouble.

EVERYONE
Ps 11: 4 He observes **e** on earth;
Eze 18: 4 For **e** belongs to me, the parent as
Lk 6: 26 to you when **e** speaks well of you,
Jn 13: 35 By this **e** will know that you are my
1Ti 5: 20 sinning you are to reprove before **e**,

EVIDENCE (EVIDENT)
Jn 14: 11 on the **e** of the works themselves.
2Th 1: 5 All this is **e** that God's judgment is
Jas 2: 20 do you want **e** that faith without

EVIDENT (EVIDENCE)
Php 4: 5 Let your gentleness be **e** to all.

EVIL (EVILDOER EVILDOERS EVILS)
Ge 2: 9 of the knowledge of good and **e**.
3: 5 be like God, knowing good and **e**."
6: 5 heart was only **e** all the time.
Ex 32: 22 how prone these people are to **e**.
Jdg 2: 11 the Israelites did **e** in the eyes
3: 7 The Israelites did **e** in the eyes
3: 12 the Israelites did **e** in the eyes
4: 1 the Israelites did **e** in the eyes
6: 1 The Israelites did **e** in the eyes
10: 6 the Israelites did **e** in the eyes
13: 1 the Israelites did **e** in the eyes
1Ki 11: 6 So Solomon did **e** in the eyes
16: 25 But Omri did **e** in the eyes
2Ki 15: 24 Pekahiah did **e** in the eyes
Job 1: 1 he feared God and shunned **e**.
1: 8 a man who fears God and shuns **e**."
34: 10 Far be it from God to do **e**,
36: 21 Beware of turning to **e**, which you
Ps 5: 4 you, **e** people are not welcome.
23: 4 will fear no **e**, for you are with me;
34: 13 keep your tongue from **e** and your
34: 14 Turn from **e** and do good;
34: 16 LORD is against those who do **e**,
37: 1 not fret because of those who are **e**
37: 8 do not fret—it leads only to **e**.
37: 27 Turn from **e** and do good;
49: 5 should I fear when **e** days come,
51: 4 and done what is **e** in your sight;
97: 10 those who love the LORD hate **e**,
101: 4 have nothing to do with what is **e**.
141: 4 drawn to what is **e** so that I take
Pr 4: 27 or the left; keep your foot from **e**.
8: 13 To fear the LORD is to hate **e**;
11: 19 but whoever pursues **e** finds death.
11: 27 **e** comes to one who searches for it.
14: 16 wise fear the LORD and shun **e**,
17: 13 **E** will never leave the house of one who pays back **e** for good.
20: 30 Blows and wounds scrub away **e**,
26: 23 are fervent lips with an **e** heart.
Ecc 12: 14 thing, whether it is good or **e**.
Isa 5: 20 who call **e** good and good **e**,
13: 11 I will punish the world for its **e**,
Jer 4: 14 wash the **e** from your heart and be
18: 8 nation I warned repents of its **e**,
18: 11 So turn from your **e** ways, each one
Eze 33: 11 Turn from your **e** ways!
33: 13 will die for the **e** they have done.
33: 15 that give life, and do no **e**—
Am 5: 13 in such times, for the times are **e**.
Hab 1: 13 Your eyes are too pure to look on **e**;
Zec 8: 17 do not plot **e** against each other,
Mt 5: 45 He causes his sun to rise on the **e**
6: 13 but deliver us from the **e** one.'
7: 11 though you are **e**, know how to
12: 34 you who are **e** say anything good?
12: 35 an **e** man brings **e** things out of the **e** stored up
15: 19 out of the heart come **e** thoughts—
Mk 7: 21 heart, that **e** thoughts come—
Lk 6: 45 an **e** man brings **e** things out of the **e** stored up
11: 13 though you are **e**, know how to
Jn 3: 19 of light because their deeds were **e**.
3: 20 Everyone who does **e** hates
17: 15 you protect them from the **e** one.
Ro 1: 30 they invent ways of doing **e**;
2: 8 who reject the truth and follow **e**,
2: 9 for every human being who does **e**:
3: 8 "Let us do **e** that good may
6: 12 body so that you obey its **e** desires.
7: 19 do, but the **e** I do not want to do—
7: 21 do good, **e** is right there with me.
12: 9 Hate what is **e**; cling to what is
12: 17 Do not repay anyone **e** for **e**.
12: 21 Do not be overcome by **e**, but overcome **e** with good.
14: 16 know is good be spoken of as **e**.
16: 19 and innocent about what is **e**.
1Co 13: 6 Love does not delight in **e**
14: 20 In regard to **e** be infants, but in
Eph 5: 16 because the days are **e**.
6: 12 against the spiritual forces of **e**
6: 16 all the flaming arrows of the **e** one.
Col 3: 5 lust, **e** desires and greed, which is
1Th 5: 22 reject every kind of **e**.
2Th 3: 3 and protect you from the **e** one.
1Ti 6: 10 of money is a root of all kinds of **e**.
2Ti 2: 22 Flee the **e** desires of youth
3: 6 are swayed by all kinds of **e** desires,
Heb 5: 14 to distinguish good from **e**.
Jas 1: 13 For God cannot be tempted by **e**,
1: 21 filth and the **e** that is so prevalent
3: 6 a world of **e** among the parts
3: 8 It is a restless **e**, full of deadly
1Pe 2: 16 your freedom as a cover-up for **e**;
3: 9 Do not repay **e** with **e** or
3: 9 contrary, repay **e** with blessing,
3: 10 days must keep their tongue from **e**
3: 17 for doing good than for doing **e**.
1Jn 2: 13 you have overcome the **e** one.
2: 14 and you have overcome the **e** one.

1Jn 3: 12 Cain, who belonged to the **e** one
5: 18 and the **e** one cannot harm them.
5: 19 is under the control of the **e** one.
3Jn : 11 do not imitate what is **e** but what

EVILDOER* (EVIL)
2Sa 3: 39 the LORD repay the **e** according
Ps 10: 15 call the **e** to account for his
101: 8 I will cut off every **e** from the city
Pr 24: 20 for the **e** has no future hope,
Mal 4: 1 and every **e** will be stubble,

EVILDOERS (EVIL)
1Sa 24: 13 'From **e** come evil deeds,' so my
Job 8: 20 or strengthen the hands of **e**.
34: 8 He keeps company with **e**;
34: 22 utter darkness, where **e** can hide.
Ps 14: 4 Do all these **e** know nothing?
14: 6 You **e** frustrate the plans
26: 5 I abhor the assembly of **e** and
36: 12 See how the **e** lie fallen—
53: 4 Do all these **e** know nothing?
59: 2 Deliver me from **e** and save me
64: 2 of the wicked, from the plots of **e**.
92: 7 up like grass and all **e** flourish,
92: 9 all **e** will be scattered.
94: 4 all the **e** are full of boasting.
94: 16 will take a stand for me against **e**?
119:115 Away from me, you **e**, that I may
125: 5 the LORD will banish with the **e**.
141: 5 still be against the deeds of **e**.
141: 9 safe from the traps set by **e**,
Pr 21: 15 to the righteous but terror to **e**.
24: 19 Do not fret because of **e** or be
28: 5 **E** do not understand what is right,
29: 6 **E** are snared by their own sin,
Isa 1: 4 great, a brood of **e**, children given
31: 2 nation, against those who help **e**.
Jer 23: 14 They strengthen the hands of **e**,
Hos 10: 9 Will not war again overtake the **e**
Mal 3: 15 Certainly **e** prosper, and even
Mt 7: 23 Away from me, you **e**!'
Lk 13: 27 Away from me, all you **e**!'
18: 11 robbers, **e**, adulterers—
2Ti 3: 13 while **e** and impostors will go

EVILS* (EVIL)
Mk 7: 23 All these **e** come from inside

EWE
2Sa 12: 3 except one little **e** lamb he had

EXACT*
Ge 43: 21 us found his silver—the **e** weight—
Est 4: 7 including the **e** amount of money
Pr 22: 23 up their case and will **e** life for life.
Mt 2: 7 from them the **e** time the star had
Jn 4: 53 realized that this was the **e** time
Heb 1: 3 the **e** representation of his being,

EXALT* (EXALTED EXALTS)
Ex 15: 2 my father's God, and I will **e** him.
Jos 3: 7 "Today I will begin to **e** you
1Sa 2: 10 and **e** the horn of his anointed."
1Ch 25: 5 the promises of God to **e** him.
29: 12 power to **e** and give strength to all.
Job 19: 5 If indeed you would **e** yourselves
Ps 30: 1 I will **e** you, LORD, for you lifted
34: 3 let us **e** his name together.
35: 26 may all who **e** themselves over me
37: 34 He will **e** you to inherit the land;
38: 16 **e** themselves over me when my feet
75: 6 from the desert can **e** themselves.
89: 17 and by your favor you **e** our horn.
99: 5 **E** the LORD our God and worship
99: 9 **E** the LORD our God and worship
107: 32 Let them **e** him in the assembly
118: 28 you are my God, and I will **e** you.
145: 1 I will **e** you, my God the King;
Pr 4: 8 Cherish her, and she will **e** you;
25: 6 Do not **e** yourself in the king's
30: 32 "If you play the fool and **e** yourself,
Isa 24: 15 **e** the name of the LORD, the God
25: 1 I will **e** you and praise your name,
Eze 29: 15 will never again **e** itself
Da 4: 37 praise and **e** and glorify the King
11: 36 He will **e** and magnify himself
11: 37 but will **e** himself above them all.
Hos 11: 7 High, I will by no means **e** them.
Mt 23: 12 For those who **e** themselves will be
Lk 14: 11 all those who **e** themselves will be
Lk 18: 14 all those who **e** themselves will be
2Th 2: 4 will **e** himself over everything

EXALTED* (EXALT)
Ex 15: 1 to the LORD, for he is highly **e**.
Ex 15: 21 to the LORD, for he is highly **e**.
Nu 24: 7 their kingdom will be **e**.
Jos 4: 14 day the LORD **e** Joshua
2Sa 5: 12 had **e** his kingdom for the sake
22: 47 **E** be my God, the Rock, my Savior!
22: 49 You **e** me above my foes;
23: 1 of the man **e** by the Most High,
1Ch 14: 2 his kingdom had been highly **e**
17: 17 me as though I were the most **e**
29: 11 you are **e** as head over all.
29: 25 The LORD highly **e** Solomon
Ne 9: 5 and may it be **e** above all blessing
Job 24: 24 For a little while they are **e**,
36: 22 "God is **e** in his power. Who is
37: 23 beyond our reach and **e** in power;
Ps 18: 46 to my Rock! **E** be God my Savior!
18: 48 You **e** me above my foes;
21: 13 Be **e** in your strength, LORD;
27: 6 Then my head will be **e**
35: 27 "The LORD be **e**, who delights
46: 10 I will be **e** among the nations, I will
be **e** in the earth."
47: 9 belong to God; he is greatly **e**.
57: 5 Be **e**, O God, above the heavens;
57: 11 Be **e**, O God, above the heavens;
89: 13 hand is strong, your right hand **e**.
89: 24 my name his horn will be **e**.
89: 27 the most **e** of the kings of the earth.
89: 42 You have **e** the right hand of his
92: 8 But you, LORD, are forever **e**.
92: 10 You have **e** my horn like
97: 9 you are **e** far above all gods.
99: 2 he is **e** over all the nations.
108: 5 Be **e**, O God, above the heavens;
113: 4 The LORD is **e** over all
138: 2 you have so **e** your solemn decree
138: 6 Though the LORD is **e**, he looks
148: 13 the LORD, for his name alone is **e**;
Pr 11: 11 blessing of the upright a city is **e**,
Isa 2: 2 it will be **e** above the hills, and all
2: 11 the LORD alone will be **e**
2: 12 for all that is **e** (and they will be
2: 17 the LORD alone will be **e**
5: 16 the LORD Almighty will be **e**
6: 1 high and **e**, seated on a throne;
12: 4 and proclaim that his name is **e**.
33: 5 The LORD is **e**, for he dwells
33: 10 "Now will I be **e**; now will I be
52: 13 raised and lifted up and highly **e**.
57: 15 is what the high and **e** One says—
Jer 17: 12 throne, **e** from the beginning,
La 2: 17 you, he has **e** the horn of your foes.
Eze 21: 26 The lowly will be **e** and the **e** will be
brought low.
Hos 13: 1 he was **e** in Israel.
Mic 4: 1 it will be **e** above the hills,
6: 6 and bow down before the **e** God?
Mt 23: 12 who humble themselves will be **e**.
Lk 14: 11 who humble themselves will be **e**."
18: 14 who humble themselves will be **e**."
Ac 2: 33 **E** to the right hand of God, he has
5: 31 God **e** him to his own right hand
Php 1: 20 now as always Christ will be **e**
2: 9 Therefore God **e** him to the highest
Heb 7: 26 from sinners, **e** above the heavens.

EXALTS* (EXALT)
1Sa 2: 7 he humbles and he **e**.
Job 36: 7 with kings and **e** them forever.
Ps 75: 7 He brings one down, he **e** another.
Pr 14: 34 Righteousness **e** a nation, but sin

EXAMINE (EXAMINED EXAMINES)
Ps 11: 4 everyone on earth; his eyes **e** them.
17: 3 though you **e** me at night and test
26: 2 try me, **e** my heart and my mind;
Jer 17: 10 search the heart and **e** the mind,
20: 12 you who **e** the righteous and probe
La 3: 40 Let us **e** our ways and test them,
1Co 11: 28 to **e** themselves before they eat
2Co 13: 5 **E** yourselves to see whether you

EXAMINED (EXAMINE)
Job 13: 9 Would it turn out well if he **e** you?
Ac 17: 11 **e** the Scriptures every day to see

EXAMINES (EXAMINE)
Ps 11: 5 The LORD **e** the righteous,
Pr 5: 21 the LORD, and he **e** all your paths.

EXAMPLE* (EXAMPLES)
2Ki 14: 3 everything he followed the **e** of his
Ecc 9: 13 saw under the sun this **e** of wisdom
Eze 14: 8 and make them an **e** and a byword.
Jn 13: 15 I have set you an **e** that you should
Ro 6: 19 I am using an **e** from everyday life
7: 2 For **e**, by law a married woman is
1Co 11: 1 Follow my **e**, as I follow the **e** of
Christ.
Gal 3: 15 let me take an **e** from everyday life.
Eph 5: 1 Follow God's **e**, therefore, as dearly
Php 3: 17 Join together in following my **e**,
2Th 3: 7 how you ought to follow our **e**.
1Ti 1: 16 his immense patience as an **e**
4: 12 set an **e** for the believers in speech,
Titus 2: 7 everything set them an **e** by doing
Heb 4: 11 following their **e** of disobedience.
Jas 3: 4 Or take ships as an **e**.
5: 10 as an **e** of patience in the face
1Pe 2: 21 leaving you an **e**, that you should
2Pe 2: 6 made them an **e** of what is going
Jude : 7 They serve as an **e** of those who

EXAMPLES* (EXAMPLE)
1Co 10: 6 Now these things occurred as **e**
10: 11 things happened to them as **e**
1Pe 5: 3 to you, but being **e** to the flock.

EXASPERATE*
Eph 6: 4 Fathers, do not **e** your children;

EXCEL* (EXCELLENT)
Ge 49: 4 you will no longer **e**, for you went
1Co 14: 12 try to **e** in those that build
2Co 8: 7 But since you **e** in everything—
8: 7 also **e** in this grace of giving.

EXCELLENT (EXCEL)
1Co 12: 31 yet I will show you the most **e** way.
Php 4: 8 if anything is **e** or praiseworthy—
1Ti 3: 13 have served well gain an **e** standing
Titus 3: 8 These things are **e** and profitable

EXCESSIVE
2Co 2: 7 not be overwhelmed by **e** sorrow.

EXCHANGE (EXCHANGED)
Mt 16: 26 what can anyone give in **e** for their
Mk 8: 37 what can anyone give in **e** for their
2Co 6: 13 As a fair **e**—I speak as to my

EXCHANGED (EXCHANGE)
Ps 106: 20 They **e** their glorious God
Jer 2: 11 people have **e** their glorious God
Hos 4: 7 they **e** their glorious God
Ro 1: 23 **e** the glory of the immortal God
1: 25 **e** the truth about God for a lie,
1: 26 Even their women **e** natural sexual

EXCLAIM
Ps 35: 10 My whole being will **e**, "Who is

EXCUSE* (EXCUSES)
Lk 14: 18 I must go and see it. Please **e** me.'
14: 19 way to try them out. Please **e** me.'
Jn 15: 22 now they have no **e** for their sin.
Ro 1: 20 made, so that people are without **e**.
2: 1 have no **e**, you who pass judgment

EXCUSES* (EXCUSE)
Lk 14: 18 "But they all alike began to make **e**.

EXERTED*
Eph 1: 20 he **e** when he raised Christ

EXHORT* (EXHORTATION)
1Ti 5: 1 but **e** him as if he were your
father.

EXHORTATION (EXHORT)
Ac 13: 15 have a word of **e** for the people,

EXILE (EXILES)
2Ki 17: 23 their homeland into **e** in Assyria,
25: 11 into **e** the people who remained

EXILES (EXILE)
1Pe 2: 11 as foreigners and **e**, to abstain

EXISTS
Heb 2: 10 and through whom everything **e**,
11: 6 to him must believe that he **e**

EXPECT (EXPECTATION EXPECTED EXPECTING)
Mt 24: 44 at an hour when you do not **e** him.
Lk 12: 40 at an hour when you do not **e** him."
Php 1: 20 I eagerly **e** and hope that I will in

EXPECTATION (EXPECT)
Ro 8: 19 waits in eager **e** for the children
Heb 10: 27 but only a fearful **e** of judgment

EXPECTED (EXPECT)
Hag 1: 9 "You **e** much, but see, it turned

EXPECTING (EXPECT)
Lk 6: 35 to them without **e** to get anything

EXPEL* (EXPELLED)
1Co 5: 13 "**E** the wicked person from among

1t 13: 58 there because of their lack of **f**.
14: 31 "You of little **f**," he said, "why did
15: 28 to her, "Woman, you have great **f**!
16: 8 "You of little **f**, why are you talking
17: 20 "Because you have so little **f**.
17: 20 you have **f** as small as a mustard
21: 21 if you have **f** and do not doubt,
24: 10 many will turn away from the **f**
Λk 2: 5 When Jesus saw their **f**, he said
4: 40 Do you still have no **f**?"
5: 34 "Daughter, your **f** has healed you.
6: 6 He was amazed at their lack of **f**.
10: 52 said Jesus, "your **f** has healed you."
11: 22 "Have **f** in God," Jesus answered.
16: 14 *rebuked them for their lack of* **f**
k 5: 20 When Jesus saw their **f**, he said,
7: 9 I have not found such great **f** even
7: 50 the woman, "Your **f** has saved you;
8: 25 "Where is your **f**?" he asked his
8: 48 "Daughter, your **f** has healed you.
12: 28 will he clothe you—you of little **f**!
17: 5 said to the Lord, "Increase our **f**!"
17: 6 "If you have **f** as small as a mustard
17: 19 your **f** has made you well."
18: 8 comes, will he find **f** on the earth?"
18: 42 your **f** has healed you."
22: 32 Simon, that your **f** may not fail.
in 12: 42 not openly acknowledge their **f**
Ac 3: 16 By **f** in the name of Jesus, this man
3: 16 the **f** that comes through him
6: 5 a man full of **f** and of the Holy
6: 7 of priests became obedient to the **f**.
11: 24 full of the Holy Spirit and **f**,
13: 8 to turn the proconsul from the **f**.
14: 9 him, saw that he had **f** to be healed
14: 22 them to remain true to the **f**.
14: 27 how he had opened a door of **f**
15: 9 for he purified their hearts by **f**.
16: 5 were strengthened in the **f**
20: 21 and have **f** in our Lord Jesus.
24: 24 him as he spoke about **f** in Christ
26: 18 those who are sanctified by **f**
27: 25 men, for I have **f** in God that it will
Ro 1: 5 comes from **f** for his name's sake.
1: 8 because your **f** is being reported all
1: 12 encouraged by each other's **f**.
1: 17 righteousness that is by **f** from first
1: 17 "The righteous will live by **f**."
3: 22 righteousness is given through **f**
3: 25 of his blood—to be received by **f**.
3: 26 one who justifies those who have **f**
3: 27 because of the law that requires **f**.
3: 28 a person is justified by **f** apart
3: 30 will justify the circumcised by **f**
3: 30 uncircumcised through that same **f**.
3: 31 we, then, nullify the law by this **f**?
4: 5 their **f** is credited as righteousness.
4: 9 that Abraham's **f** was credited
4: 11 **f** while he was still uncircumcised.
4: 12 of the **f** that our father Abraham
4: 13 the righteousness that comes by **f**.
4: 14 **f** means nothing and the promise
4: 16 the promise comes by **f**, so that it
4: 16 those who have the **f** of Abraham.
4: 19 Without weakening in his **f**,
4: 20 was strengthened in his **f** and gave
5: 1 we have been justified through **f**,
5: 2 whom we have gained access by **f**
9: 30 it, a righteousness that is by **f**;
9: 32 Because they pursued it not by **f**
10: 6 the righteousness that is by **f** says:
10: 8 the message concerning **f** that we
10: 10 your mouth that you profess your **f**
10: 17 **f** comes from hearing the message,
11: 20 of unbelief, and you stand by **f**.
12: 3 with the **f** God has distributed
12: 6 prophesy in accordance with your **f**;
14: 1 Accept the one whose **f** is weak,
14: 2 One person's **f** allows them to eat
14: 2 but another, whose **f** is weak,
14: 23 because their eating is not from **f**;
14: 23 that does not come from **f** is sin.
16: 26 the obedience that comes from **f**—
1Co 2: 5 so that your **f** might not rest
7: 22 who was a slave when called to **f**
12: 9 to another **f** by the same Spirit,
13: 2 have a **f** that can move mountains,
13: 13 three remain: **f**, hope and love.
15: 14 is useless and so is your **f**.
15: 17 has not been raised, your **f** is futile;
16: 13 stand firm in the **f**; be courageous;
2Co 1: 24 Not that we lord it over your **f**,
1: 24 because it is by **f** you stand firm.
4: 13 Since we have that same spirit of **f**,
5: 7 For we live by **f**, not by sight.
8: 7 in **f**, in speech, in knowledge,
10: 15 is that, as your **f** continues to grow,
13: 5 to see whether you are in the **f**;
Gal 1: 23 now preaching the **f** he once tried
2: 16 the law, but by **f** in Jesus Christ.
2: 16 have put our **f** in Christ Jesus
2: 16 we may be justified by **f** in Christ
2: 20 body, I live by **f** in the Son of God,
3: 7 that those who have **f** are children
3: 8 would justify the Gentiles by **f**,
3: 9 who rely on **f** are blessed along with
Abraham, the man of **f**.
3: 11 "the righteous will live by **f**."
3: 12 The law is not based on **f**;
3: 14 by **f** we might receive the promise
3: 22 being given through **f** in Jesus
3: 23 Before the coming of this **f**,
3: 23 law, locked up until the **f** that was
3: 24 that we might be justified by **f**.
3: 25 Now that this **f** has come, we are
3: 26 are all children of God through **f**,
5: 5 eagerly await by **f** the righteousness
5: 6 counts is **f** expressing itself through
Eph 1: 15 heard about your **f** in the Lord
2: 8 you have been saved, through **f**—
3: 12 through **f** in him we may approach
3: 17 may dwell in your hearts through **f**.
4: 5 one Lord, one **f**, one baptism;
4: 13 until we all reach unity in the **f**
6: 16 take up the shield of **f**,
6: 23 love with **f** from God the Father
Php 1: 25 for your progress and joy in the **f**,
1: 27 as one for the **f** of the gospel
2: 17 and service coming from your **f**,
3: 9 that which is through **f** in Christ—
3: 9 comes from God on the basis of **f**.
Col 1: 4 have heard of your **f** in Christ Jesus
1: 5 the **f** and love that spring
1: 23 if you continue in your **f**,
2: 5 and how firm your **f** in Christ is.
2: 7 in the **f** as you were taught,
2: 12 him through your **f** in the working
1Th 1: 3 Father your work produced by **f**,
1: 8 your **f** in God has become known
3: 2 and encourage you in your **f**,
3: 5 I sent to find out about your **f**.
3: 6 brought good news about your **f**
3: 7 about you because of your **f**.
3: 10 supply what is lacking in your **f**.
5: 8 be sober, putting on **f** and love as
2Th 1: 3 because your **f** is growing more
1: 4 and **f** in all the persecutions
1: 11 your every deed prompted by **f**.
3: 2 evil people, for not everyone has **f**.
1Ti 1: 2 To Timothy my true son in the **f**:
1: 4 which is by **f**.
1: 5 a good conscience and a sincere **f**.
1: 14 along with the **f** and love that are
1: 19 holding on to **f** and a good
1: 19 shipwreck with regard to the **f**.
2: 15 if they continue in **f**,
3: 9 of the **f** with a clear conscience.
3: 13 assurance in their **f** in Christ Jesus.
4: 1 later times some will abandon the **f**
4: 6 nourished on the truths of the **f**
4: 12 conduct, in love, in **f** and in purity.
5: 8 has denied the **f** and is worse than
6: 10 have wandered from the **f**
6: 11 righteousness, godliness, **f**, love,
6: 12 Fight the good fight of the **f**.
6: 21 so doing have departed from the **f**.
2Ti 1: 5 I am reminded of your sincere **f**,
1: 13 with **f** and love in Christ Jesus.
2: 18 and they destroy the **f** of some.
2: 22 youth and pursue righteousness, **f**,
3: 8 who, as far as the **f** is concerned,
3: 10 way of life, my purpose, **f**, patience,
3: 15 salvation through **f** in Christ Jesus.
4: 7 finished the race, I have kept the **f**.
Titus 1: 1 to further the **f** of God's elect
1: 4 my true son in our common **f**:
1: 13 so that they will be sound in the **f**
2: 2 and sound in **f**, in love
3: 15 Greet those who love us in the **f**.
Phm : 5 and your **f** in the Lord Jesus.
: 6 with us in the **f** may be effective
Heb 4: 2 because they did not share the **f**
Heb 4: 14 us hold firmly to the **f** we profess.
6: 1 that lead to death, and of **f** in God,
6: 12 to imitate those who through **f**
10: 22 the full assurance that **f** brings,
10: 38 my righteous one will live by **f**.
10: 39 to those who have **f** and are saved.
11: 1 Now **f** is confidence in what we
11: 3 By **f** we understand that the
11: 4 **f** Abel brought God a better
11: 4 By **f** he was commended as
11: 4 And by **f** Abel still speaks,
11: 5 By **f** Enoch was taken from this
11: 6 without **f** it is impossible to please
11: 7 By **f** Noah, when warned
11: 7 By his **f** he condemned the world
11: 7 that is in keeping with **f**.
11: 8 By **f** Abraham, when called to go
11: 9 By **f** he made his home
11: 11 And by **f** even Sarah, who was past
11: 13 these people were still living by **f**
11: 17 By **f** Abraham, when God tested
11: 20 By **f** Isaac blessed Jacob and Esau
11: 21 By **f** Jacob, when he was dying,
11: 22 By **f** Joseph, when his end was
11: 23 By **f** Moses' parents hid him
11: 24 By **f** Moses, when he had grown
11: 27 By **f** he left Egypt, not fearing
11: 28 By **f** he kept the Passover
11: 29 **f** the people passed through the
11: 30 By **f** the walls of Jericho fell,
11: 31 By **f** the prostitute Rahab,
11: 33 through **f** conquered kingdoms,
11: 39 were all commended for their **f**,
12: 2 the pioneer and perfecter of **f**.
13: 7 their way of life and imitate their **f**.
Jas 1: 3 of your **f** produces perseverance.
2: 5 the eyes of the world to be rich in **f**
2: 14 if someone claims to have **f** but has
2: 14 Can such **f** save them?
2: 17 In the same way, **f** by itself, if
2: 18 But someone will say, "You have **f**;
2: 18 Show me your **f** without deeds,
2: 18 I will show you my **f** by my deeds.
2: 20 that **f** without deeds is useless?
2: 22 You see that his **f** and his actions
2: 22 his **f** was made complete by what
2: 24 by what they do and not by **f** alone.
2: 26 is dead, so **f** without deeds is dead.
5: 15 in **f** will make the sick person well;
1Pe 1: 5 through **f** are shielded by God's
1: 7 the proven genuineness of your **f**—
1: 9 receiving the end result of your **f**,
1: 21 and so your **f** and hope are in God.
5: 9 standing firm in the **f**, because you
2Pe 1: 1 have received a **f** as precious as
1: 5 effort to add to your **f** goodness;
1Jn 5: 4 overcome the world, even our **f**.
Jude : 3 contend for the **f** that was once
: 20 yourselves up in your most holy **f**
Rev 2: 13 You did not renounce your **f** in me,
2: 19 your love and **f**, your service

FAITHFUL (FAITH)
Nu 12: 7 he is **f** in all my house.
Dt 7: 9 he is the **f** God, keeping his
32: 4 A **f** God who does no wrong,
1Sa 2: 35 I will raise up for myself a **f** priest,
2Sa 20: 19 We are the peaceful and **f** in Israel.
22: 26 "To the **f** you show yourself **f**,
1Ki 3: 6 David, because he was **f** to you
2Ch 31: 18 For they were **f** in consecrating
31: 20 and **f** before the LORD his God.
Ne 9: 8 You found his heart **f** to you,
Ps 4: 3 LORD has set apart his **f** servant
12: 1 LORD, for no one is **f** anymore;
16: 10 will you let your **f** one see decay.
18: 25 To the **f** you show yourself **f**,
25: 10 and **f** toward those who keep
31: 5 deliver me, LORD, my **f** God.
31: 23 Love the LORD, all his **f** people!
33: 4 right and true; he is **f** in all he does.
37: 28 just and will not forsake his **f** ones.
78: 8 whose spirits were not **f** to him.
78: 37 they were not **f** to his covenant.
86: 2 Guard my life, for I am **f** to you;
89: 19 a vision, to your **f** people you said:
89: 24 My **f** love will be with him,
89: 37 the moon, the **f** witness in the sky."
97: 10 for he guards the lives of his **f** ones
101: 6 eyes will be on the **f** in the land,
111: 7 The works of his hands are **f**
145: 13 all he promises and **f** in all he does.

Ps 145: 17 in all his ways and **f** in all he does.
146: 6 he remains **f** forever.
Pr 2: 8 and protects the way of his **f** ones.
20: 6 love, but a **f** person who can find?
28: 20 A **f** person will be richly blessed,
31: 26 and **f** instruction is on her tongue.
Isa 1: 21 See how the **f** city has become
1: 26 City of Righteousness, the **F** City."
49: 7 who is **f**, the Holy One of Israel,
55: 3 you, my **f** love promised to David.
Jer 3: 12 for I am **f**,' declares the LORD,
42: 5 **f** witness against us if we do not act
Eze 43: 11 so that they may be **f** to its design
48: 11 who were **f** in serving me and did
Hos 11: 12 God, even against the **f** Holy One.
Zec 8: 3 Jerusalem will be called the **F** City,
8: 8 I will be **f** and righteous to them as
Mt 24: 45 then is the **f** and wise servant,
25: 21 'Well done, good and **f** servant!
25: 21 You have been **f** with a few things;
25: 23 'Well done, good and **f** servant!
25: 23 You have been **f** with a few things;
Lk 12: 42 then is the **f** and wise manager,
Ro 12: 12 patient in affliction, **f** in prayer.
1Co 1: 9 God is **f**, who has called you
4: 2 been given a trust must prove **f**.
4: 17 whom I love, who is **f** in the Lord.
10: 13 And God is **f**; he will not let you be
2Co 1: 18 But as surely as God is **f**,
Eph 1: 1 in Ephesus, the **f** in Christ Jesus:
6: 21 brother and **f** servant in the Lord,
Col 1: 2 the **f** brothers and sisters in Christ:
1: 7 who is a **f** minister of Christ on our
4: 7 a **f** minister and fellow servant
4: 9 Onesimus, our **f** and dear brother,
1Th 5: 24 The one who calls you is **f**, and he
2Th 3: 3 But the Lord is **f**, and he will
1Ti 2: 7 a true and **f** teacher of the Gentiles.
3: 2 to be above reproach, **f** to his wife,
3: 12 A deacon must be **f** to his wife
5: 9 sixty, has been **f** to her husband,
2Ti 2: 13 he remains **f**, for he cannot disown
Titus 1: 6 must be blameless, **f** to his wife,
Heb 2: 17 and **f** high priest in service to God,
3: 2 He was **f** to the one who appointed
3: 2 just as Moses was **f** in all God's
3: 5 "Moses was **f** as a servant in all
3: 6 Christ is **f** as the Son over God's
8: 9 because they did not remain **f** to
10: 23 profess, for he who promised is **f**.
11: 11 she considered him **f** who had
1Pe 4: 10 as **f** stewards of God's grace in its
4: 19 themselves to their **f** Creator
5: 12 whom I regard as a **f** brother,
1Jn 1: 9 he is **f** and just and will forgive us
3Jn : 5 you are **f** in what you are doing
Rev 1: 5 who is the **f** witness, the firstborn
2: 10 Be **f**, even to the point of death,
2: 13 the days of Antipas, my **f** witness,
3: 14 the Amen, the **f** and true witness,
14: 12 commands and remain **f** to Jesus.
17: 14 his called, chosen and **f** followers."
19: 11 whose rider is called **F** and True.

FAITHFULLY (FAITH)
Dt 11: 13 So if you **f** obey the commands I
Jos 2: 14 and **f** when the LORD gives us
1Sa 12: 24 and serve him **f** with all your heart;
1Ki 2: 4 if they walk **f** before me with all
2Ki 20: 3 how I have walked before you **f**
2Ch 19: 9 "You must serve **f**
31: 12 they **f** brought in the contributions,
31: 15 and Shekaniah assisted him **f**
32: 1 all that Hezekiah had so **f** done,
34: 12 The workers labored **f**. Over them
Ne 9: 33 you have acted **f**, while we acted
13: 14 what I have so **f** done for the house
Isa 38: 3 how I have walked before you **f**
Jer 23: 28 one who has my word speak it **f**.
Eze 18: 9 my decrees and **f** keeps my laws.

FAITHFULNESS* (FAITH)
Ge 24: 27 his kindness and **f** to my master.
24: 49 show kindness and **f** to my master,
32: 10 **f** you have shown your servant.
47: 29 you will show me kindness and **f**.
Ex 34: 6 to anger, abounding in love and **f**,
Jos 24: 14 the LORD and serve him with all **f**.
1Sa 26: 23 for their righteousness and **f**.
2Sa 2: 6 now show you kindness and **f**,
15: 20 LORD show you kindness and **f**."
Ps 26: 3 have lived in reliance on your **f**.
30: 9 Will it proclaim your **f**?
Ps 36: 5 to the heavens, your **f** to the skies.
40: 10 I speak of your **f** and your saving
40: 10 and your **f** from the great assembly.
40: 11 your love and **f** always protect me.
51: 6 you desired **f** even in the womb;
54: 5 in your **f** destroy them.
57: 3 God sends forth his love and his **f**.
57: 10 your **f** reaches to the skies.
61: 7 your love and **f** to protect him.
71: 22 praise you with the harp for your **f**,
85: 10 Love and **f** meet together;
85: 11 **F** springs forth from the earth,
86: 11 LORD, that I may rely on your **f**;
86: 15 to anger, abounding in love and **f**.
88: 11 in the grave, your **f** in Destruction?
89: 1 make your **f** known through all
89: 2 that you have established your **f**
89: 5 LORD, your **f** too, in the assembly
89: 8 mighty, and your **f** surrounds you.
89: 14 love and **f** go before you.
89: 33 him, nor will I ever betray my **f**.
89: 49 in your **f** you swore to David?
91: 4 his **f** will be your shield
92: 2 in the morning and your **f** at night,
96: 13 and the peoples in his **f**.
98: 3 his love and his **f** to Israel;
100: 5 his **f** continues through all
108: 4 your **f** reaches to the skies.
111: 8 ever, enacted in **f** and uprightness.
115: 1 glory, because of your love and **f**.
117: 2 the **f** of the LORD endures forever.
119: 30 I have chosen the way of **f**;
119: 75 and that in **f** you have afflicted me.
119: 90 Your **f** continues through all
138: 2 for your unfailing love and your **f**,
143: 1 in your **f** and righteousness come
Pr 3: 3 Let love and **f** never leave you;
14: 22 plan what is good find love and **f**.
16: 6 Through love and **f** sin is atoned
20: 28 Love and **f** keep a king safe;
Isa 11: 5 and **f** the sash around his waist.
16: 5 in **f** a man will sit on it—
25: 1 perfect **f** you have done wonderful
38: 18 to the pit cannot hope for your **f**.
38: 19 tell their children about your **f**.
40: 6 all their **f** is like the flowers
42: 3 In **f** he will bring forth justice;
61: 8 In my **f** I will reward my people
La 3: 23 new every morning; great is your **f**.
Hos 2: 20 I will betroth you in **f**, and you will
4: 1 "There is no **f**, no love,
Hab 2: 4 righteous person will live by his **f**—
Mt 23: 23 of the law—justice, mercy and **f**.
Ro 3: 3 their unfaithfulness nullify God's **f**?
Gal 5: 22 forbearance, kindness, goodness, **f**,
3Jn : 3 testified about your **f** to the truth,
Rev 13: 10 and **f** on the part of God's people.

FAITHLESS* (FAITH)
Ps 78: 57 ancestors they were disloyal and **f**,
101: 3 I hate what **f** people do; I will have
119:158 I look on the **f** with loathing,
Pr 14: 14 The **f** will be fully repaid for their
Jer 3: 6 you seen what **f** Israel has done?
3: 8 I gave **f** Israel her certificate
3: 11 "**F** Israel is more righteous than
3: 12 "'Return, **f** Israel,'
3: 14 "Return, **f** people,"
3: 22 "Return, **f** people; I will cure you
12: 1 Why do all the **f** live at ease?
2Ti 2: 13 if we are **f**, he remains faithful,

FALL (FALLEN FALLS)
Ps 37: 24 he will not **f**, for the LORD
69: 9 of those who insult you **f** on me.
145: 14 The LORD upholds all who **f**
Pr 11: 28 who trust in their riches will **f**,
Isa 40: 7 The grass withers and the flowers **f**,
Mt 7: 25 yet it did not **f**, because it had its
13: 21 of the word, they quickly **f** away.
Lk 10: 18 "I saw Satan **f** like lightning
11: 17 a house divided against itself will **f**.
23: 30 say to the mountains, "**F** on us!"
Jn 16: 1 you so that you will not **f** away.
Ro 3: 23 and **f** short of the glory of God,
14: 4 own master, servants stand or **f**.

FALLEN (FALL)
2Sa 1: 19 How the mighty have **f**!
Isa 14: 12 How you have **f** from heaven,
1Co 11: 30 and a number of you have **f** asleep.
15: 6 living, though some have **f** asleep.
15: 18 have **f** asleep in Christ are lost.
1Co 15: 20 of those who have **f** asleep.
Gal 5: 4 you have **f** away from grace.
1Th 4: 15 precede those who have **f** asleep.
Heb 6: 6 and who have **f** away, to be brought

FALLS (FALL)
Pr 11: 14 For lack of guidance a nation **f**,
24: 17 Do not gloat when your enemy **f**;
28: 14 whoever hardens their heart **f**
Mt 21: 44 Anyone who **f** on this stone will be
Jn 12: 24 a kernel of wheat **f** to the ground
Heb 12: 15 it that no one **f** short of the grace

FALSE (FALSEHOOD FALSELY)
Ex 20: 16 shall not give **f** testimony against
23: 1 "Do not spread **f** reports.
23: 7 Have nothing to do with a **f** charge
Dt 5: 20 shall not give **f** testimony against
Pr 12: 17 the truth, but a **f** witness tells lies.
13: 5 The righteous hate what is **f**,
14: 5 but a **f** witness pours out lies.
14: 25 lives, but a **f** witness is deceitful.
19: 5 A **f** witness will not go unpunished,
19: 9 A **f** witness will not go unpunished,
21: 28 A **f** witness will perish, but a
25: 18 one who gives **f** testimony against
Isa 44: 25 who foils the signs of **f** prophets
Jer 23: 16 they fill you with **f** hopes.
Mt 7: 15 "Watch out for **f** prophets.
15: 19 theft, **f** testimony, slander.
19: 18 steal, you shall not give **f** testimony,
24: 11 and many **f** prophets will appear
24: 24 For **f** messiahs and **f** prophets will
Mk 10: 19 you shall not give **f** testimony,
13: 22 For **f** messiahs and **f** prophets will
Lk 6: 26 ancestors treated the **f** prophets.
18: 20 steal, you shall not give **f** testimony,
1Co 15: 15 found to be **f** witnesses about God,
2Co 11: 13 For such people are **f** apostles,
11: 26 and in danger from **f** believers.
Gal 2: 4 arose because some **f** believers had
Php 1: 18 whether from **f** motives or true,
Col 2: 18 anyone who delights in **f** humility
2: 23 their **f** humility and their harsh
1Ti 1: 3 not to teach **f** doctrines any longer
2Pe 2: 1 also **f** prophets among the people,
2: 1 there will be **f** teachers among you.
1Jn 4: 1 because many **f** prophets have gone
Rev 16: 13 out of the mouth of the **f** prophet.
19: 20 the **f** prophet who had performed
20: 10 the **f** prophet had been thrown.

FALSEHOOD* (FALSE)
Job 21: 34 is left of your answers but **f**!"
31: 5 "If I have walked with **f** or my foot
Ps 52: 3 **f** rather than speaking the truth.
119:163 and detest **f** but I love your law.
Pr 30: 8 Keep **f** and lies far from me;
Isa 28: 15 our refuge and **f** our hiding place."
Ro 3: 7 my **f** enhances God's truthfulness
Eph 4: 25 each of you must put off **f**
1Jn 4: 6 Spirit of truth and the spirit of **f**.
Rev 22: 15 everyone who loves and practices **f**.

FALSELY (FALSE)
Lev 19: 12 "'Do not swear **f** by my name
Isa 59: 3 Your lips have spoken **f**, and your
Mt 5: 11 **f** say all kinds of evil against you
Lk 3: 14 money and don't accuse people **f**—
1Ti 6: 20 ideas of what is **f** called knowledge,

FALTER*
Pr 24: 10 If you **f** in a time of trouble,
Isa 42: 4 he will not **f** or be discouraged till

FAME
Jos 9: 9 of the **f** of the LORD your God.
Isa 66: 19 islands that have not heard of my **f**
Hab 3: 2 LORD, I have heard of your **f**;

FAMILIES (FAMILY)
Ps 68: 6 God sets the lonely in **f**, he leads

FAMILY (FAMILIES)
Pr 31: 15 she provides food for her **f**
Lk 9: 61 go back and say goodbye to my **f**."
12: 52 in one **f** divided against each other,
Ac 10: 2 He and all his **f** were devout
1Ti 3: 4 He must manage his own **f** well
3: 5 know how to manage his own **f**,
5: 4 practice by caring for their own **f**

FAMINE
Ge 12: 10 Now there was a **f** in the land,
26: 1 Now there was a **f** in the land—
41: 30 seven years of **f** will follow them.
Ru 1: 1 ruled, there was a **f** in the land.
1Ki 18: 2 Now the **f** was severe in Samaria,

Am 8: 11 I will send a **f** through the land—
8: 11 but a **f** of hearing the words
Ro 8: 35 or persecution or **f** or nakedness

FAN*
2Ti 1: 6 this reason I remind you to **f**

FANTASIES*
Ps 73: 20 Lord, you will despise them as **f**.
Pr 12: 11 those who chase **f** have no sense.
28: 19 who chase **f** will have their fill

FASHIONED
Ps 94: 9 Does he who **f** the ear not hear?

FAST (FASTING)
Dt 10: 20 Hold **f** to him and take your oaths
11: 22 to him and to hold **f** to him—
13: 4 serve him and hold **f** to him.
30: 20 to his voice, and hold **f** to him.
Jos 22: 5 to hold **f** to him and to serve him
23: 8 to hold **f** to the LORD your God,
2Ki 18: 6 He held **f** to the LORD and did not
Ps 119: 31 I hold **f** to your statutes, LORD;
139: 10 me, your right hand will hold me **f**.
Mt 6: 16 "When you **f**, do not look somber
1Pe 5: 12 the true grace of God. Stand **f** in it.

FASTING (FAST)
Ps 35: 13 and humbled myself with **f**.
Ac 13: 2 were worshiping the Lord and **f**,
14: 23 with prayer and **f**, committed them

FATAL
Ex 21: 12 who strikes a person with a **f** blow

FATHER (FATHER'S FATHERLESS FATHERS)
Ge 2: 24 That is why a man leaves his **f**
17: 4 You will be the **f** of many nations.
Ex 20: 12 "Honor your **f** and your mother,
21: 15 "Anyone who attacks their **f**
21: 17 "Anyone who curses their **f**
Lev 18: 7 "'Do not dishonor your **f**
19: 3 must respect your mother and **f**,
20: 9 "'Anyone who curses their **f**
Dt 1: 31 carried you, as a **f** carries his son,
5: 16 "Honor your **f** and your mother,
21: 18 son who does not obey his **f**
32: 6 Is he not your **F**, your Creator,
2Sa 7: 14 I will be his **f**, and he will be my
1Ch 17: 13 I will be his **f**, and he will be my
22: 10 will be my son, and I will be his **f**.
28: 6 to be my son, and I will be his **f**.
Job 38: 28 Does the rain have a **f**?
Ps 2: 7 today I have become your **f**.
27: 10 Though my **f** and mother forsake
68: 5 A **f** to the fatherless, a defender
89: 26 out to me, 'You are my **F**, my God,
103: 13 As a **f** has compassion on his
Pr 3: 12 loves, as a **f** the son he delights in.
10: 1 A wise son brings joy to his **f**,
17: 25 A foolish son brings grief to his **f**
23: 22 Listen to your **f**, who gave you life,
23: 24 The **f** of a righteous child has great
28: 7 of gluttons disgraces his **f**.
28: 24 Whoever robs their **f** or mother
29: 3 loves wisdom brings joy to his **f**,
Isa 9: 6 Everlasting **F**, Prince of Peace.
45: 10 Woe to the one who says to a **f**,
63: 16 our **F**, our Redeemer from of old
Jer 2: 27 wood, 'You are my **f**,' and to stone,
3: 19 I thought you would call me '**F**'
31: 9 because I am Israel's **f**,
Eze 18: 19 the son not share the guilt of his **f**?'
Mic 7: 6 a son dishonors his **f**, a daughter
Mal 1: 6 If I am a **f**, where is the honor due
2: 10 Do we not all have one **F**?
Mt 3: 9 'We have Abraham as our **f**.'
5: 16 deeds and glorify your **F** in heaven.
6: 9 "'Our **F** in heaven, hallowed be
6: 26 yet your heavenly **F** feeds them.
10: 37 "Anyone who loves their **f**
11: 27 one knows the Son except the **F**,
11: 27 no one knows the **F** except the Son
15: 4 said, 'Honor your **f** and mother'
15: 4 and 'Anyone who curses their **f**
18: 10 see the face of my **F** in heaven.
19: 5 this reason a man will leave his **f**
19: 19 honor your **f** and mother,' and 'love
19: 29 brothers or sisters or **f** or mother
23: 9 do not call anyone on earth '**f**,' for
you have one **F**,
Mk 7: 10 said, 'Honor your **f** and mother,'
Lk 9: 59 first let me go and bury my **f**."
12: 53 **f** against son and son against **f**,
14: 26 and does not hate **f** and mother,
Lk 18: 20 honor your **f** and mother.'"
23: 34 Jesus said, "**F**, forgive them,
Jn 3: 35 The **F** loves the Son and has placed
4: 21 you will worship the **F** neither
5: 17 "My **F** is always at his work to this
5: 18 he was even calling God his own **F**,
5: 20 For the **F** loves the Son and shows
6: 44 unless the **F** who sent me draws
6: 46 from God; only he has seen the **F**.
8: 19 "You do not know me or my **F**,"
8: 28 just what the **F** has taught me.
8: 41 "The only **F** we have is God
8: 42 "If God were your **F**, you would
8: 44 You belong to your **f**, the devil,
8: 44 he is a liar and the **f** of lies.
10: 17 The reason my **F** loves me is that I
10: 30 I and the **F** are one."
10: 38 that the **F** is in me, and I in the **F**."
14: 6 comes to the **F** except through me.
14: 9 who has seen me has seen the **F**.
14: 28 for the **F** is greater than I.
15: 9 "As the **F** has loved me, so have I
15: 23 hates me hates my **F** as well.
20: 17 I have not yet ascended to the **F**.
20: 17 ascending to my **F** and your **F**,
Ac 13: 33 today I have become your **f**.'
Ro 4: 11 he is the **f** of all who believe
4: 16 He is the **f** of us all.
8: 15 And by him we cry, *"Abba,* **F**."
1Co 4: 15 became your **f** through the gospel.
2Co 6: 18 And, "I will be a **F** to you, and you
Eph 5: 31 this reason a man will leave his **f**
6: 2 "Honor your **f** and mother"—
Php 2: 11 is Lord, to the glory of God the **F**.
Heb 1: 5 today I have become your **F**"?
12: 7 are not disciplined by their **f**?
1Jn 1: 3 our fellowship is with the **F**
2: 15 world, love for the **F** is not in them.
2: 22 denying the **F** and the Son.

FATHER'S (FATHER)
Pr 13: 1 A wise son heeds his **f** instruction,
19: 13 A foolish child is a **f** ruin,
Mt 16: 27 come in his **F** glory with his angels,
Lk 2: 49 know I had to be in my **F** house?"
Jn 2: 16 Stop turning my **F** house
10: 29 can snatch them out of my **F** hand.
14: 2 My **F** house has many rooms;
15: 8 This is to my **F** glory, that you bear

FATHERLESS (FATHER)
Ex 22: 22 advantage of the widow or the **f**.
Dt 10: 18 He defends the cause of the **f**
14: 29 the **f** and the widows who live
24: 17 the foreigner or the **f** of justice,
24: 19 the foreigner, the **f** and the widow,
26: 12 the foreigner, the **f** and the widow,
Ps 68: 5 A father to the **f**, a defender
82: 3 Defend the weak and the **f**;
Pr 23: 10 or encroach on the fields of the **f**,

FATHERS (FATHER)
Lk 11: 11 "Which of you **f**, if your son asks
1Co 4: 15 you do not have many **f**,
Eph 6: 4 **F**, do not exasperate your children;
Col 3: 21 **F**, do not embitter your children,
Heb 12: 9 all had human **f** who disciplined us

FATHOM* (FATHOMED)
Job 11: 7 "Can you **f** the mysteries of God?
Ps 145: 3 his greatness no one can **f**.
Ecc 3: 11 no one can **f** what God has done
Isa 40: 13 Who can **f** the Spirit of the LORD,
40: 28 his understanding no one can **f**.
1Co 13: 2 of prophecy and can **f** all mysteries

FATHOMED* (FATHOM)
Job 5: 9 performs wonders that cannot be **f**,
9: 10 performs wonders that cannot be **f**,

FATTENED
Pr 15: 17 with love than a **f** calf with hatred.
Lk 15: 23 Bring the **f** calf and kill it.

FAULT (FAULTS)
1Sa 29: 3 now, I have found no **f** in him."
Mt 18: 15 sins, go and point out their **f**,
Php 2: 15 of God without **f** in a warped
Jas 1: 5 generously to all without finding **f**,
Jude : 24 his glorious presence without **f**

FAULTFINDERS*
Jude : 16 These people are grumblers and **f**;

FAULTLESS*
Php 3: 6 righteousness based on the law, **f**.
Jas 1: 27 Father accepts as pure and **f** is this:

FAULTS* (FAULT)
Job 10: 6 that you must search out my **f**
Ps 19: 12 Forgive my hidden **f**.

FAVOR (FAVORITISM)
Ge 4: 4 The LORD looked with **f** on Abel
6: 8 But Noah found **f** in the eyes
Ex 33: 12 and you have found **f** with me.'
34: 9 "if I have found **f** in your eyes,
Lev 26: 9 "'I will look on you with **f**
Nu 11: 15 if I have found **f** in your eyes—
Jdg 6: 17 "If now I have found **f** in your eyes,
1Sa 2: 26 in stature and in **f** with the LORD
2Sa 2: 6 you the same **f** because you have
2Ki 13: 4 Jehoahaz sought the LORD's **f**,
2Ch 33: 12 In his distress he sought the **f**
Est 7: 3 "If I have found **f** with you,
Ps 90: 17 May the **f** of the Lord our God rest
Pr 3: 34 mockers but shows **f** to the humble
8: 35 life and receive **f** from the LORD.
10: 32 of the righteous know what finds **f**,
11: 1 accurate weights find **f** with him.
18: 22 and receives **f** from the LORD.
19: 6 Many curry **f** with a ruler,
Isa 61: 2 proclaim the year of the LORD's **f**
Zec 11: 7 called one **F** and the other Union,
Lk 1: 30 you have found **f** with God.
2: 14 to those on whom his **f** rests."
2: 52 and in **f** with God and man.
4: 19 proclaim the year of the Lord's **f**."
2Co 6: 2 "In the time of my **f** I heard you,
1Pe 5: 5 proud but shows **f** to the humble."

FAVORITISM* (FAVOR)
Ex 23: 3 do not show **f** to a poor person
Lev 19: 15 to the poor or **f** to the great,
Ac 10: 34 true it is that God does not show **f**
Ro 2: 11 For God does not show **f**.
Gal 2: 6 God does not show **f**—
Eph 6: 9 heaven, and there is no **f** with him.
Col 3: 25 for their wrongs, and there is no **f**.
1Ti 5: 21 and to do nothing out of **f**.
Jas 2: 1 Lord Jesus Christ must not show **f**.
2: 9 But if you show **f**, you sin and are

FEAR (AFRAID FEARED FEARS FRIGHTENED GOD-FEARING)
Dt 6: 13 **F** the LORD your God, serve him
10: 12 you but to **f** the LORD your God,
31: 12 learn to **f** the LORD your God
31: 13 to **f** the LORD your God as long as
Jos 4: 24 that you might always **f** the LORD
24: 14 "Now **f** the LORD and serve him
1Sa 12: 14 If you **f** the LORD and serve
12: 24 be sure to **f** the LORD and serve
2Sa 23: 3 when he rules in the **f** of God,
2Ch 19: 7 Now let the **f** of the LORD be
26: 5 instructed him in the **f** of God.
Job 1: 9 "Does Job **f** God for nothing?"
Ps 2: 11 Serve the LORD with **f**
19: 9 The **f** of the LORD is pure,
23: 4 the darkest valley, I will **f** no evil,
27: 1 and my salvation—whom shall I **f**?
33: 8 Let all the earth **f** the LORD;
34: 7 encamps around those who **f** him,
34: 9 **F** the LORD, you his holy people,
46: 2 Therefore we will not **f**,
86: 11 heart, that I may **f** your name.
90: 11 Your wrath is as great as the **f** that
91: 5 You will not **f** the terror of night,
111: 10 The **f** of the LORD is
112: 1 are those who **f** the LORD,
118: 4 Let those who **f** the LORD say:
128: 1 Blessed are all who **f** the LORD,
145: 19 the desires of those who **f** him;
147: 11 LORD delights in those who **f** him,
Pr 1: 7 The **f** of the LORD is
1: 33 and be at ease, without **f** of harm."
8: 13 To **f** the LORD is to hate evil;
9: 10 The **f** of the LORD is
10: 27 The **f** of the LORD adds length
14: 16 The wise **f** the LORD and shun
14: 27 The **f** of the LORD is a fountain
15: 33 instruction is to **f** the LORD,
16: 6 through the **f** of the LORD evil is
19: 23 The **f** of the LORD leads to life;
22: 4 Humility is the **f** of the LORD;
29: 25 **F** of man will prove to be a snare,
31: 21 she has no **f** for her household;
Ecc 3: 14 does it so that people will **f** him.
5: 7 Therefore **f** God.
8: 12 go better with those who **f** God,
12: 13 of the matter: **F** God and keep his

Isa 11: 3 will delight in the **f** of the LORD.
33: 6 the **f** of the LORD is the key to this
35: 4 fearful hearts, "Be strong, do not **f**;
41: 10 So do not **f**, for I am with you;
41: 13 and says to you, Do not **f**;
43: 1 "Do not **f**, for I have redeemed
51: 7 Do not **f** the reproach of mere
54: 14 you will have nothing to **f**.
Jer 10: 7 Who should not **f** you,
17: 8 It does not **f** when heat comes;
Lk 12: 5 show you whom you should **f**:
2Co 5: 11 we know what it is to **f** the Lord,
Php 2: 12 to work out your salvation with **f**
1Jn 4: 18 There is no **f** in love.
4: 18 But perfect love drives out **f**,
Jude : 23 others show mercy, mixed with **f**—
Rev 14: 7 voice, "**F** God and give him glory,

FEARED (FEAR)
Job 1: 1 he **f** God and shunned evil.
Ps 76: 7 It is you alone who are to be **f**.
Mal 3: 16 those who **f** the LORD talked

FEARS (FEAR)
Job 1: 8 a man who **f** God and shuns evil."
2: 3 a man who **f** God and shuns evil.
Ps 34: 4 he delivered me from all my **f**.
Pr 14: 26 Whoever **f** the LORD has a secure
31: 30 a woman who **f** the LORD is to be
2Co 7: 5 conflicts on the outside, **f** within.
1Jn 4: 18 The one who **f** is not made perfect

FEAST (FEASTING FEASTS)
Pr 15: 15 the cheerful heart has a continual **f**.
2Pe 2: 13 in their pleasures while they **f**

FEASTING (FEAST)
Pr 17: 1 and quiet than a house full of **f**,

FEASTS (FEAST)
Jude : 12 people are blemishes at your love **f**,

FEATHERS
Ps 91: 4 He will cover you with his **f**,

FEEBLE
Job 4: 3 you have strengthened **f** hands.
Isa 35: 3 Strengthen the **f** hands,
Heb 12: 12 strengthen your **f** arms and weak

FED (FEED)
Ps 105: 40 he **f** them well with the bread

FEED (FED FEEDS)
Jn 21: 15 Jesus said, "**F** my lambs."
21: 17 Jesus said, "**F** my sheep.
Ro 12: 20 "If your enemy is hungry, **f** him;
Jude : 12 shepherds who **f** only themselves.

FEEDS (FEED)
Pr 15: 14 but the mouth of a fool **f** on folly.
Mt 6: 26 yet your heavenly Father **f** them.
Jn 6: 57 so the one who **f** on me will live

FEEL
Jdg 16: 26 "Put me where I can **f** the pillars
Ps 115: 7 They have hands, but cannot **f**,

FEET (FOOT)
Ru 3: 8 there was a woman lying at his **f**!
Ps 8: 6 you put everything under their **f**:
22: 16 they pierce my hands and my **f**.
40: 2 he set my **f** on a rock and gave me
56: 13 death and my **f** from stumbling,
66: 9 lives and kept our **f** from slipping.
73: 2 as for me, my **f** had almost slipped;
110: 1 enemies a footstool for your **f**."
119:105 Your word is a lamp to my **f**
Pr 4: 26 thought to the paths for your **f**
Isa 52: 7 the mountains are the **f** of those
Da 2: 33 iron, its **f** partly of iron and partly
Na 1: 15 the **f** of one who brings good news,
Mt 10: 14 town and shake the dust off your **f**.
22: 44 put your enemies under your **f**."'
Lk 1: 79 death, to guide our **f** into the path
20: 43 enemies a footstool for your **f**."'
24: 39 Look at my hands and my **f**. It is I
Jn 13: 5 and began to wash his disciples' **f**,
13: 14 also should wash one another's **f**.
Ro 3: 15 "Their **f** are swift to shed blood;
10: 15 "How beautiful are the **f** of those
16: 20 will soon crush Satan under your **f**.
1Co 12: 21 And the head cannot say to the **f**,
15: 25 has put all his enemies under his **f**.
Eph 1: 22 God placed all things under his **f**
1Ti 5: 10 washing the **f** of the Lord's people,
Heb 1: 13 enemies a footstool for your **f**"?
2: 8 and put everything under their **f**."
12: 13 "Make level paths for your **f**,"
Rev 1: 15 His **f** were like bronze glowing

FELIX
Governor before whom Paul was tried (Ac 23:23—24:27).

FELLOWSHIP
Ex 20: 24 burnt offerings and **f** offerings,
Lev 3: 1 "'If your offering is a **f** offering,
1Co 1: 9 who has called you into **f** with his
5: 2 put out of your **f** the man who has
2Co 6: 14 **f** can light have with darkness?
13: 14 the **f** of the Holy Spirit be with you
Gal 2: 9 Barnabas the right hand of **f**
1Jn 1: 3 that you also may have **f** with us.
1: 3 And our **f** is with the Father
1: 6 If we claim to have **f** with him
1: 7 light, we have **f** with one another,

FEMALE
Ge 1: 27 male and **f** he created them.
5: 2 He created them male and **f**
Mt 19: 4 Creator 'made them male and **f**,'
Mk 10: 6 God 'made them male and **f**.'
Gal 3: 28 nor is there male and **f**, for you are

FEROCIOUS
Mt 7: 15 but inwardly they are **f** wolves.

FERTILE (FERTILIZE)
Isa 32: 15 and the desert becomes a **f** field,
Jer 2: 7 I brought you into a **f** land to eat

FERTILIZE* (FERTILE)
Lk 13: 8 year, and I'll dig around it and **f** it.

FERVOR*
Ac 18: 25 he spoke with great **f** and taught
Ro 12: 11 but keep your spiritual **f**,

FESTIVAL (FESTIVALS)
1Co 5: 8 Therefore let us keep the **F**,
Col 2: 16 or with regard to a religious **f**,

FESTIVALS (FESTIVALS)
Am 5: 21 "I hate, I despise your religious **f**;

FESTUS
Successor of Felix; sent Paul to Caesar (Ac 25–26).

FEVER
Job 30: 30 my body burns with **f**.
Mt 8: 14 lying in bed with a **f**.
Lk 4: 38 was suffering from a high **f**,
Jn 4: 52 in the afternoon, the **f** left him."
Ac 28: 8 suffering from **f** and dysentery.

FIDELITY*
Ro 1: 31 no understanding, no **f**, no love,
16: 10 **f** to Christ has stood the test.

FIELD (FIELDS)
Ge 4: 8 Abel, "Let's go out to the **f**."
Lev 19: 9 not reap to the very edges of your **f**
19: 19 "'Do not plant your **f** with two
Pr 31: 16 She considers a **f** and buys it;
Isa 40: 6 is like the flowers of the **f**.
Mt 6: 28 See how the flowers of the **f** grow.
6: 30 how God clothes the grass of the **f**,
13: 38 The **f** is the world, and the good
13: 44 is like treasure hidden in a **f**.
Lk 14: 18 'I have just bought a **f**, and I must
1Co 3: 9 you are God's **f**, God's building.
1Pe 1: 24 glory is like the flowers of the **f**;

FIELDS (FIELD)
Ru 2: 2 "Let me go to the **f** and pick
Lk 2: 8 shepherds living out in the **f**
Jn 4: 35 open your eyes and look at the **f**!

FIERY (FIRE)
1Pe 4: 12 do not be surprised at the **f** ordeal

FIG (FIGS SYCAMORE-FIG)
Ge 3: 7 so they sewed **f** leaves together
Jdg 9: 10 the trees said to the **f** tree,
1Ki 4: 25 vine and under their own **f** tree.
Pr 27: 18 one who guards a **f** tree will eat its
Mic 4: 4 vine and under their own **f** tree,
Zec 3: 10 to sit under your vine and **f** tree,'
Mt 21: 19 Seeing a **f** tree by the road, he went
Lk 13: 6 "A man had a **f** tree growing in his
Jas 3: 12 and sisters, can a **f** tree bear olives,
Rev 6: 13 as figs drop from a **f** tree

FIGHT (FIGHTING FIGHTS FOUGHT)
Ex 14: 14 The LORD will **f** for you;
Dt 1: 30 is going before you, will **f** for you,
3: 22 the LORD your God himself will **f**
1Sa 25: 28 because you **f** the LORD's battles,
Ne 4: 20 Our God will **f** for us!"
Ps 35: 1 **f** against those who **f** against me.
Jn 18: 36 my servants would **f** to prevent my
1Co 9: 26 I do not **f** like a boxer beating
2Co 10: 4 The weapons we **f** with are not
1Ti 1: 18 them you may **f** the battle well,
6: 12 **F** the good **f** of the faith.
2Ti 4: 7 I have fought the good **f**, I have

FIGHTING (FIGHT)
Jos 10: 14 Surely the LORD was **f** for Israel!

FIGHTS (FIGHT)
Jos 23: 10 because the LORD your God **f**
Jas 4: 1 What causes **f** and quarrels among

FIGS (FIG)
Lk 6: 44 People do not pick **f**
Jas 3: 12 bear olives, or a grapevine bear **f**?

FILL (FILLED FILLING FILLS FULL FULLNESS FULLY)
Ge 1: 28 **f** the earth and subdue it.
Ps 16: 11 you will **f** me with joy in your
81: 10 wide your mouth and I will **f** it.
Pr 28: 19 chase fantasies will have their **f**
Hag 2: 7 and I will **f** this house with glory,'
Jn 6: 26 you ate the loaves and had your **f**.
Ac 2: 28 you will **f** me with joy in your
Ro 15: 13 May the God of hope **f** you with all

FILLED (FILL)
Ex 31: 3 I have **f** him with the Spirit of God,
35: 31 he has **f** him with the Spirit of God,
Dt 34: 9 son of Nun was **f** with the spirit
1Ki 8: 10 Place, the cloud **f** the temple
8: 11 glory of the LORD **f** his temple.
2Ch 5: 14 the glory of the LORD **f** the temple
7: 1 glory of the LORD **f** the temple.
Ps 72: 19 may the whole earth be **f** with his
119: 64 The earth is **f** with your love,
Isa 6: 4 and the temple was **f** with smoke.
11: 9 for the earth will be **f**
Eze 10: 3 in, and a cloud **f** the inner court.
10: 4 The cloud **f** the temple,
43: 5 glory of the LORD **f** the temple.
Hab 2: 14 For the earth will be **f**
3: 3 heavens and his praise **f** the earth.
Mt 5: 6 for righteousness, for they will be **f**.
Lk 1: 15 he will be **f** with the Holy Spirit
1: 41 Elizabeth was **f** with the Holy Spirit
1: 67 His father Zechariah was **f**
2: 40 was **f** with wisdom, and the grace
Jn 12: 3 the house was **f** with the fragrance
Ac 2: 2 **f** the whole house where they were
2: 4 of them were **f** with the Holy Spirit
4: 8 Then Peter, **f** with the Holy Spirit,
4: 31 they were all **f** with the Holy Spirit
9: 17 and be **f** with the Holy Spirit."
13: 9 called Paul, **f** with the Holy Spirit,
Eph 5: 18 Instead, be **f** with the Spirit,
Php 1: 11 **f** with the fruit of righteousness
Rev 15: 8 the temple was **f** with smoke

FILLING (FILL)
Eze 44: 4 the glory of the LORD **f** the temple

FILLS (FILL)
Nu 14: 21 of the LORD **f** the whole earth,
Ps 107: 9 and **f** the hungry with good things.
Eph 1: 23 him who **f** everything in every way.

FILTH (FILTHY)
Isa 4: 4 The Lord will wash away the **f**
Jas 1: 21 get rid of all moral **f** and the evil

FILTHY (FILTH)
Isa 64: 6 all our righteous acts are like **f** rags;
Col 3: 8 and **f** language from your lips.

FINAL (FINALITY)
Ps 73: 17 then I understood their **f** destiny.

FINALITY* (FINAL)
Ro 9: 28 on earth with speed and **f**."

FINANCIAL*
1Ti 6: 5 that godliness is a means to **f** gain.

FIND (FINDS FOUND)
Nu 32: 23 be sure that your sin will **f** you out.
Dt 4: 29 you will **f** him if you seek him
1Sa 23: 16 and helped him **f** strength in God.
Job 23: 3 If only I knew where to **f** him;
Ps 62: 5 Yes, my soul, **f** rest in God;
91: 4 under his wings you will **f** refuge;
112: 1 LORD, who **f** great delight in his
Pr 3: 13 Blessed are those who **f** wisdom,
8: 17 me, and those who seek me **f** me.
8: 35 For those who **f** me **f** life
14: 22 those who plan what is good **f** love
20: 6 but a faithful person who can **f**?
24: 14 If you **f** it, there is a future hope

r 31: 10 wife of noble character who can **f**?
er 6: 16 and you will **f** rest for your souls.
29: 13 and **f** me when you seek me with
At 7: 7 seek and you will **f**;
11: 29 and you will **f** rest for your souls.
16: 25 loses their life for me will **f** it.
22: 9 invite to the banquet anyone you **f**.'
k 11: 9 seek and you will **f**;
18: 8 will he **f** faith on the earth?"
n 10: 9 come in and go out, and **f** pasture.

FINDS (FIND)
Ps 62: 1 Truly my soul **f** rest in God;
119:162 promise like one who **f** great spoil.
Pr 11: 27 Whoever seeks good **f** favor,
18: 22 He who **f** a wife **f** what is good
Mt 7: 8 the one who seeks **f**; and to the one
10: 39 Whoever **f** their life will lose it,
Lk 11: 10 the one who seeks **f**; and to the one
12: 37 whose master **f** them watching
12: 43 servant whom the master **f** doing
15: 4 go after the lost sheep until he **f** it?
15: 8 and search carefully until she **f** it?

FINE
Pr 17: 26 imposing a **f** on the innocent is not
Zec 3: 4 and I will put **f** garments on you."

FINE-SOUNDING* (SOUND)
Col 2: 4 may deceive you by **f** arguments.

FINGER
Ex 8: 19 to Pharaoh, "This is the **f** of God."
31: 18 of stone inscribed by the **f** of God.
Dt 9: 10 tablets inscribed by the **f** of God.
Lk 11: 20 I drive out demons by the **f** of God,
16: 24 to dip the tip of his **f** in water
Jn 8: 6 *write on the ground with his* **f**.
20: 25 and put my **f** where the nails were,

FINISH (FINISHED)
Jn 4: 34 who sent me and to **f** his work.
5: 36 that the Father has given me to **f**—
Ac 20: 24 my only aim is to **f** the race
2Co 8: 11 Now **f** the work, so that your eager
Gal 3: 3 are you now trying to **f** by means
Jas 1: 4 Let perseverance **f** its work so

FINISHED (FINISH)
Ge 2: 2 seventh day God had **f** the work he
Jn 19: 30 the drink, Jesus said, "It is **f**."
2Ti 4: 7 the good fight, I have **f** the race,

FIRE (FIERY)
Ex 3: 2 bush was on **f** it did not burn up.
13: 21 in a pillar of **f** to give them light,
Lev 6: 12 The **f** on the altar must be kept
9: 24 **F** came out from the presence
1Ki 18: 38 Then the **f** of the LORD fell
2Ki 2: 11 suddenly a chariot of **f** and horses
Isa 5: 24 as tongues of **f** lick up straw and as
30: 27 and his tongue is a consuming **f**.
Jer 23: 29 "Is not my word like **f**,"
Da 3: 25 four men walking around in the **f**,
Zec 3: 2 stick snatched from the **f**?"
Mal 3: 2 For he will be like a refiner's **f**
Mt 3: 11 you with the Holy Spirit and **f**.
3: 12 up the chaff with unquenchable **f**."
5: 22 will be in danger of the **f** of hell.
18: 8 feet and be thrown into eternal **f**.
25: 41 the eternal **f** prepared for the devil
Mk 9: 43 hell, where the **f** never goes out.
9: 48 not die, and the **f** is not quenched.'
9: 49 Everyone will be salted with **f**.
Lk 3: 16 you with the Holy Spirit and **f**.
12: 49 have come to bring **f** on the earth,
Ac 2: 3 to be tongues of **f** that separated
1Co 3: 13 It will be revealed with **f**, and the **f**
Heb 12: 29 for our "God is a consuming **f**."
Jas 3: 5 what a great forest is set on **f**
3: 6 The tongue also is a **f**, a world
3: 6 and is itself set on **f** by hell.
2Pe 3: 10 the elements will be destroyed by **f**,
Jude : 7 suffer the punishment of eternal **f**.
: 23 by snatching them from the **f**;
Rev 1: 14 and his eyes were like blazing **f**.
20: 14 The lake of **f** is the second death.

FIRM*
Ex 14: 13 Stand **f** and you will see
2Ch 20: 17 stand **f** and see the deliverance
Ezr 9: 8 giving us a **f** place in his sanctuary,
Job 11: 15 you will stand **f** and without fear.
36: 5 he is mighty, and **f** in his purpose.
41: 23 they are **f** and immovable.
Ps 19: 9 The decrees of the LORD are **f**,
20: 8 fall, but we rise up and stand **f**.
Ps 30: 7 made my royal mountain stand **f**;
33: 9 he commanded, and it stood **f**.
33: 11 plans of the LORD stand **f** forever,
37: 23 The LORD makes **f** the steps
40: 2 and gave me a **f** place to stand.
75: 3 quake, it is I who hold its pillars **f**.
89: 2 that your love stands **f** forever,
89: 4 and make your throne **f** through all
93: 1 world is established, **f** and secure.
93: 5 Your statutes, LORD, stand **f**;
119: 89 it stands **f** in the heavens.
Pr 10: 25 but the righteous stand **f** forever.
12: 7 the house of the righteous stands **f**.
Isa 7: 9 If you do not stand **f** in your faith,
22: 17 is about to take **f** hold of you
22: 23 drive him like a peg into a **f** place;
22: 25 into the **f** place will give way;
Eze 13: 5 so that it will stand **f** in the battle
Zec 8: 23 nations will take **f** hold of one Jew
Mt 10: 22 the one who stands **f** to the end
24: 13 the one who stands **f** to the end
Mk 13: 13 the one who stands **f** to the end
Lk 21: 19 Stand **f**, and you will win life.
1Co 1: 8 He will also keep you **f** to the end,
10: 12 if you think you are standing **f**,
15: 58 dear brothers and sisters, stand **f**.
16: 13 on your guard; stand **f** in the faith;
2Co 1: 7 And our hope for you is **f**,
1: 21 both us and you stand **f** in Christ.
1: 24 because it is by faith you stand **f**.
Gal 5: 1 Stand **f**, then, and do not let
Eph 6: 14 Stand **f** then, with the belt of truth
Php 1: 27 that you stand **f** in the one Spirit,
4: 1 stand **f** in the Lord in this way,
Col 1: 23 established and **f**, and do not move
2: 5 and how **f** your faith in Christ is.
4: 12 that you may stand **f** in all the will
1Th 3: 8 you are standing **f** in the Lord.
2Th 2: 15 stand **f** and hold fast to the
1Ti 6: 19 themselves as a **f** foundation
2Ti 2: 19 God's solid foundation stands **f**,
Heb 6: 19 anchor for the soul, **f** and secure.
Jas 5: 8 be patient and stand **f**,
1Pe 5: 9 Resist him, standing **f** in the faith,
5: 10 make you strong, **f** and steadfast.

FIRST
Ge 1: 5 and there was morning—the **f** day.
13: 4 and where he had **f** built an altar.
Ex 34: 19 "The **f** offspring of every womb
1Ki 22: 5 of Israel, "**F** seek the counsel
Pr 18: 17 a lawsuit the **f** to speak seems right,
Isa 44: 6 I am the **f** and I am the last;
48: 12 he; I am the **f** and I am the last.
Mt 5: 24 **F** go and be reconciled to them;
6: 33 But seek **f** his kingdom and his
7: 5 **f** take the plank out of your own
19: 30 But many who are **f** will be last,
20: 16 "So the last will be **f**, and the **f** will
20: 27 wants to be **f** must be your slave—
22: 38 This is the **f** and greatest
23: 26 **F** clean the inside of the cup
Mk 9: 35 wants to be **f** must be the very last,
10: 31 are **f** will be last, and the last **f**."
10: 44 wants to be **f** must be slave
13: 10 the gospel must **f** be preached to all
Lk 13: 30 who are last who will be **f**, and **f** who will be last."
Jn 8: 7 *without sin be the* **f** *to throw*
Ac 11: 26 disciples were called Christians **f**
Ro 1: 16 **f** to the Jew, then to the Gentile.
1: 17 that is by faith from **f** to last, just as
2: 9 **f** for the Jew, then for the Gentile;
2: 10 **f** for the Jew, then for the Gentile.
1Co 12: 28 in the church **f** of all apostles,
15: 45 "The **f** man Adam became a living
2Co 8: 5 They gave themselves **f** of all
Eph 6: 2 which is the **f** commandment
1Th 4: 16 and the dead in Christ will rise **f**.
1Ti 2: 13 For Adam was formed **f**, then Eve.
Heb 10: 9 He sets aside the **f** to establish
Jas 3: 17 comes from heaven is **f** of all pure;
1Jn 4: 19 We love because he **f** loved us.
3Jn : 9 who loves to be **f**, will not welcome
Rev 1: 17 I am the **F** and the Last.
2: 4 have forsaken the love you had at **f**.
22: 13 and the Omega, the **F** and the Last,

FIRSTBORN (BEAR)
Ex 11: 5 Every **f** son in Egypt will die,
34: 20 Redeem all your **f** sons. "No one
Ps 89: 27 And I will appoint him to be my **f**,
Lk 2: 7 and she gave birth to her **f**, a son.
Ro 8: 29 be the **f** among many brothers
Col 1: 15 God, the **f** over all creation.
1: 18 and the **f** from among the dead,
Heb 1: 6 God brings his **f** into the world,
12: 23 the church of the **f**, whose names
Rev 1: 5 witness, the **f** from the dead,

FIRSTFRUITS
Ex 23: 16 with the **f** of the crops you sow
23: 19 "Bring the best of the **f** of your soil
Ro 8: 23 who have the **f** of the Spirit,
1Co 15: 23 Christ, the **f**; then, when he comes,
Rev 14: 4 mankind and offered as **f** to God

FISH
Ge 1: 26 they may rule over the **f** in the sea
Jnh 1: 17 in the belly of the **f** three days
Mt 4: 19 I will send you out to **f** for people."
7: 10 Or if he asks for a **f**, will give him
12: 40 three nights in the belly of a huge **f**,
14: 17 five loaves of bread and two **f**,"
Mk 1: 17 I will send you out to **f** for people."
6: 38 out, they said, "Five—and two **f**."
Lk 5: 6 caught such a large number of **f**
5: 10 from now on you will **f** for people."
9: 13 five loaves of bread and two **f**—
Jn 6: 9 small barley loaves and two small **f**,
21: 5 "Friends, haven't you any **f**?"
21: 11 It was full of large **f**, 153, but even

FISHERMEN
Mk 1: 16 a net into the lake, for they were **f**.

FISHHOOK*
Job 41: 1 "Can you pull in Leviathan with a **f**

FISTS
Mt 26: 67 face and struck him with their **f**.

FIT (FITTING)
Jdg 17: 6 everyone did as they saw **f**.
21: 25 everyone did as they saw **f**.

FITTING* (FIT)
Ps 33: 1 it is **f** for the upright to praise him.
147: 1 how pleasant and **f** to praise him!
Pr 19: 10 It is not **f** for a fool to live
26: 1 in harvest, honor is not **f** for a fool.
1Co 14: 40 everything should be done in a **f**
Col 3: 18 your husbands, as is **f** in the Lord.
Heb 2: 10 to glory, it was **f** that God,

FIX* (FIXED FIXING)
Dt 11: 18 **F** these words of mine in your
Job 14: 3 Do you **f** your eye on them?
Pr 4: 25 **f** your gaze directly before you.
2Co 4: 18 So we **f** our eyes not on what is
Heb 3: 1 calling, **f** your thoughts on Jesus,

FIXED* (FIX)
2Ki 8: 11 him with a **f** gaze until Hazael was
Job 38: 10 when I **f** limits for it and set its
Ps 141: 8 But my eyes are **f** on you,
Pr 8: 28 **f** securely the fountains of the deep

FIXING* (FIX)
Heb 12: 2 **f** our eyes on Jesus, the pioneer

FLAME (FLAMES FLAMING)
2Ti 1: 6 you to fan into **f** the gift of God,

FLAMES (FLAME)
1Co 3: 15 only as one escaping through the **f**.

FLAMING (FLAME)
Eph 6: 16 you can extinguish all the **f** arrows

FLANK
Eze 34: 21 Because you shove with **f**

FLASH
1Co 15: 52 in a **f**, in the twinkling of an eye,

FLATTER* (FLATTERING FLATTERY)
Job 32: 21 no partiality, nor will I **f** anyone;
Ps 12: 2 they **f** with their lips but harbor
36: 2 their own eyes they **f** themselves
78: 36 would **f** him with their mouths,
Pr 29: 5 Those who **f** their neighbors are
Jude : 16 **f** others for their own advantage.

FLATTERING* (FLATTER)
Ps 12: 3 May the LORD silence all **f** lips
Pr 26: 28 it hurts, and a **f** mouth works ruin.
28: 23 than one who has a **f** tongue.
Eze 12: 24 or **f** divinations among the people

FLATTERY* (FLATTER)
Job 32: 22 for if I were skilled in **f**, my Maker
Da 11: 32 **f** he will corrupt those who have
Ro 16: 18 **f** they deceive the minds of naive
1Th 2: 5 You know we never used **f**, nor did

FLAWLESS*
2Sa 22: 31 The LORD's word is **f**;
Job 11: 4 'My beliefs are **f** and I am pure

Ps 12: 6 And the words of the LORD are **f**,
18: 30 The LORD's word is **f**;
Pr 30: 5 "Every word of God is **f**; he is
SS 5: 2 my darling, my dove, my **f** one.

FLEE
Ps 139: 7 Where can I **f** from your presence?
Pr 28: 1 The wicked **f** though no one
1Co 6: 18 **F** from sexual immorality.
10: 14 my dear friends, **f** from idolatry.
1Ti 6: 11 man of God, **f** from all this,
2Ti 2: 22 **F** the evil desires of youth
Jas 4: 7 the devil, and he will **f** from you.

FLEECE
Jdg 6: 37 If there is dew only on the **f** and

FLEETING*
Job 14: 2 like **f** shadows, they do not endure.
Ps 39: 4 let me know how **f** my life is.
89: 47 Remember how **f** is my life.
144: 4 their days are like a **f** shadow.
Pr 21: 6 made by a lying tongue is a **f** vapor
31: 30 is deceptive, and beauty is **f**;
Heb 11: 25 than to enjoy the **f** pleasures of sin.

FLESH
Ge 2: 23 bone of my bones and **f** of my **f**;
2: 24 to his wife, and they become one **f**.
2Ch 32: 8 With him is only the arm of **f**,
Job 19: 26 yet in my **f** I will see God;
Eze 11: 19 of stone and give them a heart of **f**.
36: 26 of stone and give you a heart of **f**.
Mt 19: 5 and the two will become one **f**'?
26: 41 spirit is willing, but the **f** is weak."
Mk 10: 8 and the two will become one **f**.'
Jn 1: 14 The Word became **f** and made his
6: 51 This bread is my **f**, which I will
Ro 8: 4 who do not live according to the **f**
8: 5 live according to the **f** have their minds set on what the **f** desires;
8: 7 governed by the **f** is hostile to God;
8: 8 realm of the **f** cannot please God.
8: 13 live according to the **f**, you will die;
13: 14 how to gratify the desires of the **f**.
1Co 5: 5 Satan for the destruction of the **f**,
6: 16 said, "The two will become one **f**."
15: 39 Not all **f** is the same:
Gal 3: 3 trying to finish by means of the **f**?
4: 23 was born according to the **f**,
4: 29 born according to the **f** persecuted
5: 13 use your freedom to indulge the **f**;
5: 16 will not gratify the desires of the **f**.
5: 19 The acts of the **f** are obvious:
5: 24 to Christ Jesus have crucified the **f**
6: 8 Whoever sows to please their **f**, from the **f** will reap destruction;
Eph 5: 31 and the two will become one **f**."
6: 12 For our struggle is not against **f**
Php 3: 2 evildoers, those mutilators of the **f**.
Col 2: 11 self ruled by the **f** was put off
2Pe 2: 18 to the lustful desires of the **f**,
1Jn 4: 2 that Jesus Christ has come in the **f**
Jude : 23 the clothing stained by corrupted **f**.

FLIGHT
Dt 32: 30 or two put ten thousand to **f**,

FLINT
Isa 50: 7 Therefore have I set my face like **f**,
Zec 7: 12 They made their hearts as hard as **f**

FLIRTING*
Isa 3: 16 necks, **f** with their eyes,

FLOCK (FLOCKS)
Ps 77: 20 You led your people like a **f**
78: 52 he brought his people out like a **f**;
95: 7 of his pasture, the **f** under his care.
Isa 40: 11 He tends his **f** like a shepherd:
Jer 10: 21 prosper and all their **f** is scattered.
23: 2 "Because you have scattered my **f**
31: 10 watch over his **f** like a shepherd.'
Eze 34: 2 not shepherds take care of the **f**?
Zec 11: 17 shepherd, who deserts the **f**!
Mt 26: 31 the sheep of the **f** will be scattered.'
Lk 12: 32 little **f**, for your Father has been
Jn 10: 16 and there shall be one **f** and one
Ac 20: 28 all the **f** of which the Holy Spirit
1Co 9: 7 Who tends a **f** and does not drink
1Pe 5: 2 of God's **f** that is under your care,
5: 3 to you, but being examples to the **f**.

FLOCKS (FLOCK)
Lk 2: 8 keeping watch over their **f** at night.

FLOG (FLOGGED FLOGGING)
Pr 19: 25 **F** a mocker, and the simple will
Ac 22: 25 **f** a Roman citizen who hasn't even

FLOGGED (FLOG)
Jn 19: 1 Pilate took Jesus and had him **f**.
Ac 5: 40 the apostles in and had them **f**.
16: 23 After they had been severely **f**,
2Co 11: 23 frequently, been **f** more severely,

FLOGGING (FLOG)
Heb 11: 36 Some faced jeers and **f**, and even

FLOOD (FLOODGATES)
Ge 7: 7 ark to escape the waters of the **f**.
Mal 2: 13 You **f** the LORD's altar with tears.
Mt 24: 38 For in the days before the **f**,
2Pe 2: 5 he brought the **f** on its ungodly

FLOODGATES (FLOOD)
Ge 7: 11 the **f** of the heavens were opened.
Mal 3: 10 will not throw open the **f** of heaven

FLOOR
Jas 2: 3 there" or "Sit on the **f** by my feet,"

FLOUR
Lev 2: 1 their offering is to be of the finest **f**.
Nu 7: 13 the finest **f** mixed with olive oil as
28: 9 of the finest **f** mixed with olive oil.

FLOURISH (FLOURISHING)
Ps 72: 7 In his days may the righteous **f**
92: 7 up like grass and all evildoers **f**,
92: 12 righteous will **f** like a palm tree,
Pr 14: 11 but the tent of the upright will **f**.
Ac 12: 24 of God continued to spread and **f**.

FLOURISHING (FLOURISH)
Ps 52: 8 am like an olive tree **f** in the house

FLOW (FLOWING FLOWS)
Nu 13: 27 and it does **f** with milk and honey!
Jn 7: 38 of living water will **f** from within

FLOWER (FLOWERS)
Ps 103: 15 they flourish like a **f** of the field;
Jas 1: 10 they will pass away like a wild **f**.

FLOWERS (FLOWER)
Job 14: 2 They spring up like **f** and wither
Ps 37: 20 the LORD's enemies are like the **f**
Isa 40: 6 all their faithfulness is like the **f**
40: 7 The grass withers and the **f** fall,
Lk 12: 27 "Consider how the wild **f** grow.
1Pe 1: 24 the grass withers and the **f** fall,

FLOWING (FLOW)
Ex 3: 8 a land **f** with milk and honey—
33: 3 Go up to the land **f** with milk
Nu 16: 14 brought us into a land **f** with milk
Jos 5: 6 us, a land **f** with milk and honey.
Ps 107: 33 **f** springs into thirsty ground,
107: 35 the parched ground into **f** springs;
Jer 32: 22 a land **f** with milk and honey.
Eze 20: 6 a land **f** with milk and honey,
Rev 22: 1 **f** from the throne of God

FLOWS (FLOW)
Pr 4: 23 for everything you do **f** from it.

FOAL*
Zec 9: 9 donkey, on a colt, the **f** of a donkey.
Mt 21: 5 and on a colt, the **f** of a donkey.'"

FOILS*
Ps 33: 10 The LORD **f** the plans
Isa 44: 25 who **f** the signs of false prophets

FOLD (FOLDING)
Ecc 4: 5 Fools **f** their hands and ruin

FOLDING* (FOLD)
Pr 6: 10 a little **f** of the hands to rest—
24: 33 a little **f** of the hands to rest—

FOLLOW (FOLLOWED FOLLOWING FOLLOWS)
Ex 23: 2 "Do not **f** the crowd in doing
Lev 18: 4 laws and be careful to **f** my decrees.
Dt 5: 1 Learn them and be sure to **f** them.
17: 19 **f** carefully all the words of this law
1Ki 11: 6 he did not **f** the LORD completely,
2Ch 34: 33 they did not fail to **f** the LORD,
Ps 23: 6 love will **f** me all the days of my
119:166 LORD, and I **f** your commands.
Mt 4: 19 "Come, **f** me," Jesus said, "and I
8: 19 I will **f** you wherever you go."
8: 22 But Jesus told him, "**F** me, and let
16: 24 and take up their cross and **f** me.
19: 27 "We have left everything to **f** you!
Lk 9: 23 take up their cross daily and **f** me.
9: 61 another said, "I will **f** you, Lord;
Jn 10: 4 his sheep **f** him because they know
10: 5 But they will never **f** a stranger;
10: 27 I know them, and they **f** me.
12: 26 Whoever serves me must **f** me;
21: 19 Then he said to him, "**F** me!"
1Co 1: 12 One of you says, "I **f** Paul";
1: 12 still another, "I **f** Christ."
11: 1 **F** my example, as I **f** the example
14: 1 **F** the way of love and eagerly desire
Eph 5: 1 **F** God's example, therefore,
1Pe 2: 21 that you should **f** in his steps.
Rev 14: 4 They **f** the Lamb wherever he goes.

FOLLOWED (FOLLOW)
Nu 32: 11 they have not **f** me wholeheartedly,
Dt 1: 36 his feet on, because he **f** the LORD
Jos 14: 14 ever since, because he **f** the LORD,
2Ch 10: 14 he **f** the advice of the young men
Mt 4: 20 once they left their nets and **f** him.
9: 9 and Matthew got up and **f** him.
26: 58 But Peter **f** him at a distance,
Lk 18: 43 he received his sight and **f** Jesus,

FOLLOWING (FOLLOW)
Ps 119: 14 in **f** your statutes as one rejoices
Php 3: 17 Join together in **f** my example,

FOLLOWS (FOLLOW)
Jn 8: 12 Whoever **f** me will never walk

FOLLY (FOOL)
Pr 14: 29 who is quick-tempered displays **f**.
19: 3 person's own **f** leads to their ruin,
Ecc 10: 1 so a little **f** outweighs wisdom
Mk 7: 22 envy, slander, arrogance and **f**.
2Ti 3: 9 their **f** will be clear to everyone.

FOOD (FOODS)
Ge 1: 30 I give every green plant for **f**."
Pr 12: 9 to be somebody and have no **f**.
12: 11 their land will have abundant **f**,
20: 13 awake and you will have **f** to spare.
20: 17 **F** gained by fraud tastes sweet,
21: 20 The wise store up choice **f** and
22: 9 for they share their **f** with the poor.
23: 3 delicacies, for that **f** is deceptive.
23: 6 Do not eat the **f** of a begrudging
25: 21 enemy is hungry, give him **f** to eat;
31: 14 ships, bringing her **f** from afar.
31: 15 she provides **f** for her family
Isa 58: 7 not to share your **f** with the hungry
Eze 18: 7 but gives his **f** to the hungry
Da 1: 8 to defile himself with the royal **f**
Mt 3: 4 His **f** was locusts and wild honey.
6: 25 Is not life more than **f**, and the
Jn 4: 32 "I have **f** to eat that you know
4: 34 "My **f**," said Jesus, "is to do
6: 27 Do not work for **f** that spoils,
6: 27 for **f** that endures to eternal life,
6: 55 For my flesh is real **f** and my blood
Ac 15: 20 to abstain from **f** polluted by idols,
1Co 8: 1 Now about **f** sacrificed to idols:
8: 8 **f** does not bring us near to God;
2Co 11: 27 and have often gone without **f**;
1Ti 6: 8 But if we have **f** and clothing,
Heb 5: 14 But solid **f** is for the mature,
Jas 2: 15 sister is without clothes and daily **f**.

FOODS (FOOD)
Mk 7: 19 this, Jesus declared all **f** clean.)

FOOL (FOLLY FOOL'S FOOLISH FOOLISHNESS FOOLS)
1Sa 25: 25 his name means **F**, and folly goes
Ps 14: 1 The **f** says in his heart, "There is
Pr 10: 10 and a chattering **f** comes to ruin.
10: 18 lying lips and spreads slander is a **f**.
14: 16 but a **f** is hotheaded and yet feels
15: 5 A **f** spurns a parent's discipline,
17: 12 of her cubs than a **f** bent on folly.
17: 21 a **f** for a child brings grief;
20: 3 but every **f** is quick to quarrel.
26: 4 not answer a **f** according to his
26: 5 Answer a **f** according to his folly,
26: 7 is a proverb in the mouth of a **f**.
26: 12 There is more hope for a **f** than
27: 22 Though you grind a **f** in a mortar,
29: 20 There is more hope for a **f** than
Mt 5: 22 And anyone who says, 'You **f**!'
Lk 12: 20 "But God said to him, 'You **f**!
2Co 11: 21 I am speaking as a **f**—I also dare

FOOL'S (FOOL)
Pr 12: 23 but a **f** heart blurts out folly.
14: 3 A **f** mouth lashes out with pride,

FOOLISH (FOOL)
Pr 10: 1 a **f** son brings grief to his mother.
14: 1 her own hands the **f** one tears hers
15: 20 but a **f** man despises his mother.
17: 25 A **f** son brings grief to his father

Pr 19: 13 A **f** child is a father's ruin,
Mt 7: 26 practice is like a **f** man who built
25: 2 Five of them were **f** and five were
Lk 11: 40 You **f** people! Did not the one who
24: 25 He said to them, "How **f** you are,
1Co 1: 20 Has not God made **f** the wisdom
1: 27 God chose the **f** things of the world
Gal 3: 1 You **f** Galatians!
Eph 5: 4 obscenity, **f** talk or coarse joking,
5: 17 Therefore do not be **f**,
Titus 3: 9 But avoid **f** controversies

FOOLISHNESS* (FOOL)
2Sa 15: 31 turn Ahithophel's counsel into **f**."
1Co 1: 18 of the cross is **f** to those who are
1: 21 God was pleased through the **f**
1: 23 block to Jews and **f** to Gentiles,
1: 25 the **f** of God is wiser than human
2: 14 Spirit of God but considers them **f**,
3: 19 of this world is **f** in God's sight.
2Co 11: 1 you will put up with me in a little **f**.

FOOLS (FOOL)
Pr 1: 7 but **f** despise wisdom
3: 35 inherit honor, but **f** get only shame.
12: 15 The way of **f** seems right to them,
12: 16 **F** show their annoyance at once,
13: 19 soul, but **f** detest turning from evil.
13: 20 for a companion of **f** suffers harm.
14: 9 **F** mock at making amends for sin,
14: 24 crown, but the folly of **f** yields folly.
17: 16 Why should **f** have money in hand
17: 28 Even **f** are thought wise if they
18: 2 **F** find no pleasure in
18: 7 The mouths of **f** are their undoing,
23: 9 Do not speak to **f**, for they will
24: 7 Wisdom is too high for **f**;
26: 11 to its vomit, so **f** repeat their folly.
28: 26 who trust in themselves are **f**,
29: 11 **F** give full vent to their rage,
Ecc 7: 5 than to listen to the song of **f**.
7: 6 the pot, so is the laughter of **f**.
10: 6 **F** are put in many high positions,
Mt 23: 17 You blind **f**! Which is greater:
Ro 1: 22 claimed to be wise, they became **f**
1Co 3: 18 you should become "**f**" so that you
4: 10 We are **f** for Christ, but you are so

FOOT (FEET FOOTHOLD)
Jos 1: 3 every place where you set your **f**,
Ps 121: 3 He will not let your **f** slip—
Pr 3: 23 safety, and your **f** will not stumble.
4: 27 or the left; keep your **f** from evil.
25: 17 Seldom set **f** in your neighbor's
Isa 1: 6 the sole of your **f** to the top of your
Mt 18: 8 or your **f** causes you to stumble,
Lk 4: 11 you will not strike your **f** against
1Co 12: 15 Now if the **f** should say, "Because I
Rev 10: 2 He planted his right **f** on the sea

FOOTHOLD* (FOOT)
Ps 69: 2 miry depths, where there is no **f**.
73: 2 I had nearly lost my **f**.
Eph 4: 27 and do not give the devil a **f**.

FOOTSTEPS (STEP)
Ps 119:133 Direct my **f** according to your

FOOTSTOOL
Ps 99: 5 our God and worship at his **f**;
110: 1 hand until I make your enemies a **f**
Isa 66: 1 is my throne, and the earth is my **f**.
Mt 5: 35 or by the earth, for it is his **f**;
Ac 7: 49 is my throne, and the earth is my **f**.
Heb 1: 13 hand until I make your enemies a **f**
10: 13 for his enemies to be made his **f**.

FORBEARANCE*
Ro 2: 4 of his kindness, **f** and patience,
3: 25 his **f** he had left the sins committed
Gal 5: 22 love, joy, peace, **f**, kindness,

FORBID
1Co 14: 39 and do not **f** speaking in tongues.
1Ti 4: 3 They **f** people to marry and order

FORCE (FORCED FORCEFUL FORCES FORCING)
Jn 6: 15 to come and make him king by **f**,
Ac 26: 11 and I tried to **f** them to blaspheme.
Gal 2: 14 that you **f** Gentiles to follow Jewish

FORCED (FORCE)
Mt 27: 32 and they **f** him to carry the cross.
Phm : 14 any favor you do would not seem **f**

FORCEFUL* (FORCE)
2Co 10: 10 "His letters are weighty and **f**,

FORCES (FORCE)
Mt 5: 41 If anyone **f** you to go one mile,
Eph 6: 12 against the spiritual **f** of evil

FORCING (FORCE)
Lk 16: 16 and everyone is **f** their way into it.

FOREHEAD (FOREHEADS)
Ex 13: 9 a reminder on your **f** that this law
13: 16 your **f** that the LORD brought us
1Sa 17: 49 and struck the Philistine on the **f**.

FOREHEADS (FOREHEAD)
Dt 6: 8 hands and bind them on your **f**.
Rev 9: 4 not have the seal of God on their **f**.
13: 16 on their right hands or on their **f**,
14: 1 Father's name written on their **f**.

FOREIGN (FOREIGNER FOREIGNERS)
Ge 35: 2 "Get rid of the **f** gods you have
2Ch 14: 3 He removed the **f** altars and the
33: 15 He got rid of the **f** gods
Isa 28: 11 with **f** lips and strange tongues

FOREIGNER (FOREIGN)
Ex 22: 21 "Do not mistreat or oppress a **f**,
Lev 24: 22 are to have the same law for the **f**
Ps 146: 9 The LORD watches over the **f**
Lk 17: 18 give praise to God except this **f**?"
1Co 14: 11 is saying, I am a **f** to the speaker,

FOREIGNERS (FOREIGN)
Ex 23: 9 know how it feels to be **f**,
1Co 14: 21 through the lips of **f** I will speak
Eph 2: 12 **f** to the covenants of the promise,
2: 19 you are no longer **f** and strangers,
1Pe 2: 11 urge you, as **f** and exiles, to abstain

FOREKNEW* (KNOW)
Ro 8: 29 those God **f** he also predestined
11: 2 not reject his people, whom he **f**.

FOREKNOWLEDGE* (KNOW)
Ac 2: 23 you by God's deliberate plan and **f**;
1Pe 1: 2 to the **f** of God the Father,

FORESAW*
Gal 3: 8 Scripture **f** that God would justify

FOREST
Jas 3: 5 Consider what a great **f** is set on

FOREVER (EVER)
Ge 3: 22 the tree of life and eat, and live **f**."
6: 3 will not contend with humans **f**,
Ex 3: 15 "This is my name **f**, the name you
2Sa 7: 26 so that your name will be great **f**.
1Ki 2: 33 there be the LORD's peace **f**."
9: 3 built, by putting my Name there **f**.
1Ch 16: 15 He remembers his covenant **f**,
16: 34 for he is good; his love endures **f**.
16: 41 LORD, "for his love endures **f**."
17: 24 and that your name will be great **f**.
2Ch 5: 13 "He is good; his love endures **f**."
20: 21 the LORD, for his love endures **f**."
Ps 9: 7 The LORD reigns **f**;
23: 6 dwell in the house of the LORD **f**.
28: 9 their shepherd and carry them **f**.
29: 10 the LORD is enthroned as King **f**.
33: 11 plans of the LORD stand firm **f**,
44: 8 and we will praise your name **f**.
61: 4 I long to dwell in your tent **f**
72: 19 Praise be to his glorious name **f**;
73: 26 of my heart and my portion **f**.
77: 8 Has his unfailing love vanished **f**?
79: 13 of your pasture, will praise you **f**;
81: 15 and their punishment would last **f**.
86: 12 I will glorify your name **f**.
89: 1 sing of the LORD's great love **f**;
92: 8 But you, LORD, are **f** exalted.
100: 5 is good and his love endures **f**;
102: 12 But you, LORD, sit enthroned **f**;
104: 31 the glory of the LORD endure **f**;
107: 1 for he is good; his love endures **f**.
110: 4 "You are a priest **f**, in the order
111: 3 and his righteousness endures **f**.
112: 6 they will be remembered **f**.
117: 2 of the LORD endures **f**.
118: 1 for he is good; his love endures **f**.
119:111 Your statutes are my heritage **f**;
119:152 that you established them to last **f**.
136: 1 *His love endures **f**.*
146: 6 he remains faithful **f**.
Pr 10: 25 but the righteous stand firm **f**.
27: 24 for riches do not endure **f**,
Isa 25: 8 he will swallow up death **f**.
26: 4 Trust in the LORD **f**,
32: 17 will be quietness and confidence **f**.
40: 8 the word of our God endures **f**."
Isa 51: 6 But my salvation will last **f**,
51: 8 But my righteousness will last **f**,
57: 15 he who lives **f**, whose name is holy:
59: 21 from this time on and **f**,"
Jer 33: 11 his love endures **f**."
Eze 37: 26 put my sanctuary among them **f**.
Da 2: 44 to an end, but it will itself endure **f**.
3: 9 "May the king live **f**!
Hab 3: 6 but he marches on **f**.
Jn 6: 51 Whoever eats this bread will live **f**.
14: 16 to help you and be with you **f**—
Ro 9: 5 who is God over all, **f** praised!
16: 27 God be glory **f** through Jesus
1Co 9: 25 do it to get a crown that will last **f**.
1Th 4: 17 And so we will be with the Lord **f**.
Heb 5: 6 "You are a priest **f**, in the order
7: 17 "You are a priest **f**, in the order
7: 24 but because Jesus lives **f**, he has
13: 8 same yesterday and today and **f**.
1Pe 1: 25 the word of the Lord endures **f**."
1Jn 2: 17 does the will of God lives **f**.
2Jn : 2 lives in us and will be with us **f**:

FOREVERMORE (EVER)
Ps 113: 2 LORD be praised, both now and **f**.

FORFEIT
Mk 8: 36 the whole world, yet **f** their soul?
Lk 9: 25 and yet lose or **f** their very self?

FORGAVE* (FORGIVE)
Ps 32: 5 And you **f** the guilt of my sin.
65: 3 by sins, you **f** our transgressions.
78: 38 he **f** their iniquities and did not
85: 2 You **f** the iniquity of your people
Lk 7: 42 him back, so he **f** the debts of both.
Eph 4: 32 other, just as in Christ God **f** you.
Col 2: 13 He **f** us all our sins,
3: 13 Forgive as the Lord **f** you.

FORGET (FORGETS FORGETTING FORGOT FORGOTTEN)
Dt 4: 23 Be careful not to **f** the covenant
6: 12 that you do not **f** the LORD,
2Ki 17: 38 Do not **f** the covenant I have made
Ps 9: 17 the dead, all the nations that **f** God.
10: 12 O God. Do not **f** the helpless.
50: 22 you who **f** God, or I will tear you
78: 7 in God and would not **f** his deeds
103: 2 my soul, and **f** not all his benefits—
119: 93 I will never **f** your precepts,
137: 5 If I **f** you, Jerusalem, may my right hand **f** its skill.
Pr 3: 1 My son, do not **f** my teaching,
4: 5 do not **f** my words or turn away
Isa 49: 15 "Can a mother **f** the baby at her
49: 15 may **f**, I will not **f** you!
51: 13 that you **f** the LORD your Maker,
Jer 2: 32 Does a young woman **f** her jewelry,
23: 39 I will surely **f** you and cast you
Heb 6: 10 will not **f** your work and the love
13: 2 Do not **f** to show hospitality
13: 16 And do not **f** to do good
2Pe 3: 8 But do not **f** this one thing,

FORGETS (FORGET)
Jn 16: 21 is born she **f** the anguish because
Jas 1: 24 immediately **f** what he looks like.

FORGETTING* (FORGET)
Php 3: 13 **F** what is behind and straining
Jas 1: 25 not **f** what they have heard,
2Pe 1: 9 **f** that they have been cleansed

FORGIVE* (FORGAVE FORGIVENESS FORGIVES FORGIVING)
Ge 50: 17 I ask you to **f** your brothers the sins
50: 17 please **f** the sins of the servants
Ex 10: 17 Now **f** my sin once more and pray
23: 21 he will not **f** your rebellion,
32: 32 But now, please **f** their sin—
34: 9 **f** our wickedness and our sin,
Nu 14: 19 great love, **f** the sin of these people,
Dt 29: 20 will never be willing to **f** them;
Jos 24: 19 He will not **f** your rebellion
1Sa 15: 25 **f** my sin and come back with me,
25: 28 "Please **f** your servant's
1Ki 8: 30 place, and when you hear, **f**.
8: 34 and **f** the sin of your people Israel
8: 36 and **f** the sin of your servants,
8: 39 **F** and act; deal with everyone
8: 50 **f** your people, who have sinned
8: 50 **f** all the offenses they have
2Ki 5: 18 may the LORD **f** your servant
5: 18 may the LORD **f** your servant
24: 4 and the LORD was not willing to **f**.

2Ch 6: 21 and when you hear, **f**.
6: 25 and **f** the sin of your people Israel
6: 27 and **f** the sin of your servants,
6: 30 **F**, and deal with everyone
6: 39 **f** your people, who have sinned
7: 14 and I will **f** their sin and will heal
Job 7: 21 pardon my offenses and **f** my sins?
Ps 19: 12 **F** my hidden faults.
25: 11 LORD, **f** my iniquity, though it is
79: 9 and **f** our sins for your name's sake.
Isa 2: 9 do not **f** them.
Jer 5: 1 seeks the truth, I will **f** this city.
5: 7 "Why should I **f** you?
18: 23 Do not **f** their crimes or blot
31: 34 "For I will **f** their wickedness
33: 8 and will **f** all their sins of rebellion
36: 3 then I will **f** their wickedness
50: 20 for I will **f** the remnant I spare.
Da 9: 19 Lord, **f**! Lord, hear and act!
Hos 1: 6 to Israel, that I should at all **f** them.
14: 2 "**F** all our sins and receive us
Am 7: 2 I cried out, "Sovereign LORD, **f**!
Mt 6: 12 And **f** us our debts, as we also have
6: 14 if you **f** other people when they sin
6: 14 heavenly Father will also **f** you.
6: 15 if you do not **f** others their sins,
6: 15 your Father will not **f** your sins.
9: 6 has authority on earth to **f** sins."
18: 21 many times shall I **f** my brother
18: 35 of you unless you **f** your brother
Mk 2: 7 Who can **f** sins but God alone?"
2: 10 has authority on earth to **f** sins."
11: 25 anything against anyone, **f** them,
11: 25 in heaven may **f** you your sins."
Lk 5: 21 Who can **f** sins but God alone?"
5: 24 has authority on earth to **f** sins."
6: 37 **F**, and you will be forgiven.
11: 4 **F** us our sins, for we also **f** everyone
17: 3 and if they repent, **f** them.
17: 4 saying 'I repent,' you must **f** them."
23: 34 "Father, **f** them, for they do not
Jn 20: 23 If you **f** anyone's sins, their sins
20: 23 if you do not **f** them, they are not
Ac 5: 31 to repentance and **f** their sins.
8: 22 that he may **f** you for having such
2Co 2: 7 you ought to **f** and comfort him,
2: 10 Anyone you **f**, I also **f**.
2: 10 if there was anything to **f**—
12: 13 a burden to you? **F** me this wrong!
Col 3: 13 and **f** one another if any of you
3: 13 **F** as the Lord forgave you.
Heb 8: 12 For I will **f** their wickedness
1Jn 1: 9 just and will **f** us our sins and

FORGIVENESS* (FORGIVE)
Ps 130: 4 But with you there is **f**, so that we
Mt 26: 28 out for many for the **f** of sins.
Mk 1: 4 of repentance for the **f** of sins.
Lk 1: 77 through the **f** of their sins,
3: 3 of repentance for the **f** of sins.
24: 47 for the **f** of sins will be preached
Ac 2: 38 Jesus Christ for the **f** of your sins.
10: 43 in him receives **f** of sins through
13: 38 that through Jesus the **f** of sins is
26: 18 so that they may receive **f** of sins
Eph 1: 7 through his blood, the **f** of sins,
Col 1: 14 we have redemption, the **f** of sins.
Heb 9: 22 the shedding of blood there is no **f**.

FORGIVES* (FORGIVE)
Ps 103: 3 who **f** all your sins and heals all
Mic 7: 18 **f** the transgression of the remnant
Lk 7: 49 "Who is this who even **f** sins?"

FORGIVING* (FORGIVE)
Ex 34: 7 **f** wickedness, rebellion and sin.
Nu 14: 18 abounding in love and **f** sin
Ne 9: 17 But you are a **f** God,
Ps 86: 5 Lord, are **f** and good,
99: 8 you were to Israel a **f** God,
Da 9: 9 Lord our God is merciful and **f**,
Eph 4: 32 to one another, **f** each other, just as

FORGOT (FORGET)
Dt 32: 18 you **f** the God who gave you birth.
Ps 78: 11 They **f** what he had done,
106: 13 But they soon **f** what he had done

FORGOTTEN (FORGET)
Job 11: 6 God has even **f** some of your sin.
Ps 44: 20 If we had **f** the name of our God
Isa 17: 10 You have **f** God your Savior;
Hos 8: 14 Israel has **f** their Maker and built
Lk 12: 6 Yet not one of them is **f** by God.

FORM (FORMED)
Isa 52: 14 and his **f** marred beyond human
2Ti 3: 5 having a **f** of godliness but denying

FORMED (FORM)
Ge 2: 7 the LORD God **f** a man
2: 19 Now the LORD God had **f**
Ps 103: 14 for he knows how we are **f**,
Pr 8: 23 I was **f** long ages ago, at the very
Ecc 11: 5 or how the body is **f** in a mother's
Isa 29: 16 Shall what is **f** say to the one who **f**
45: 18 be empty, but **f** it to be inhabited—
49: 5 he who **f** me in the womb to be his
Jer 1: 5 "Before I **f** you in the womb I knew
Ro 9: 20 is **f** say to the one who **f** it,
Gal 4: 19 childbirth until Christ is **f** in you,
1Ti 2: 13 For Adam was **f** first, then Eve.
Heb 11: 3 that the universe was **f** at God's
2Pe 3: 5 and the earth was **f** out of water

FORMLESS*
Ge 1: 2 Now the earth was **f** and empty,
Jer 4: 23 the earth, and it was **f** and empty;

FORSAKE (FORSAKEN)
Dt 31: 6 he will never leave you nor **f** you."
Jos 1: 5 I will never leave you nor **f** you.
24: 16 us to **f** the LORD to serve other
2Ch 15: 2 you, but if you **f** him, he will **f** you.
Ps 27: 10 my father and mother **f** me,
94: 14 he will never **f** his inheritance.
Isa 55: 7 Let the wicked **f** their ways
Heb 13: 5 will I leave you; never will I **f** you."

FORSAKEN (FORSAKE)
Ezr 9: 9 God has not **f** us in our bondage.
Ps 22: 1 God, my God, why have you **f** me?
37: 25 I have never seen the righteous **f**
Mt 27: 46 my God, why have you **f** me?").
Rev 2: 4 You have **f** the love you had at first.

FORTIFIED
Pr 18: 10 name of the LORD is a **f** tower;

FORTRESS
2Sa 22: 2 is my rock, my **f** and my deliverer;
Ps 18: 2 is my rock, my **f** and my deliverer;
31: 2 of refuge, a strong **f** to save me.
59: 16 you are my **f**, my refuge in times
71: 3 me, for you are my rock and my **f**.
Pr 14: 26 fears the LORD has a secure **f**,

FORTUNE-TELLING*
Ac 16: 16 deal of money for her owners by **f**.

FORTY
Ge 7: 4 will send rain on the earth for **f** days and **f** nights,
18: 29 "For the sake of **f**, I will not do it."
Ex 16: 35 The Israelites ate manna **f** years,
24: 18 he stayed on the mountain **f** days
Nu 14: 34 For **f** years—one year for each
Jos 14: 7 I was **f** years old when Moses
1Sa 4: 18 He had led Israel **f** years.
2Sa 5: 4 king, and he reigned **f** years.
1Ki 19: 8 he traveled **f** days and **f** nights until
2Ki 12: 1 he reigned in Jerusalem **f** years.
2Ch 9: 30 in Jerusalem over all Israel **f** years.
Eze 29: 12 cities will lie desolate **f** years
Jnh 3: 4 "**F** more days and Nineveh will be
Mt 4: 2 After fasting **f** days and **f** nights,

FOUGHT (FIGHT)
1Co 15: 32 If I **f** wild beasts in Ephesus with
2Ti 4: 7 I have **f** the good fight, I have

FOUND (FIND)
1Sa 9: 2 young man as could be **f** anywhere
2Ki 22: 8 "I have **f** the Book of the Law
1Ch 28: 9 If you seek him, he will be **f** by you;
2Ch 15: 15 God eagerly, and he was **f** by them.
Isa 55: 6 Seek the LORD while he may be **f**;
65: 1 I was **f** by those who did not seek
Da 5: 27 on the scales and **f** wanting.
Mt 1: 18 she was **f** to be pregnant through
Lk 15: 6 I have **f** my lost sheep.'
15: 9 I have **f** my lost coin.'
15: 24 is alive again; he was lost and is **f**.'
Ac 4: 12 Salvation is **f** in no one else,
Ro 10: 20 "I was **f** by those who did not seek
Jas 2: 8 If you really keep the royal law **f**
Rev 5: 4 no one was **f** who was worthy

FOUNDATION (FOUNDATIONS FOUNDED)
Isa 28: 16 a precious cornerstone for a sure **f**;
Mt 7: 25 fall, because it had its **f** on the rock.
Lk 14: 29 For if you lay the **f** and are not able
Ro 15: 20 be building on someone else's **f**.
1Co 3: 10 me, I laid a **f** as a wise builder,
1Co 3: 11 one can lay any **f** other than the
Eph 2: 20 built on the **f** of the apostles
1Ti 3: 15 God, the pillar and **f** of the truth.
2Ti 2: 19 God's solid **f** stands firm,
Heb 6: 1 not laying again the **f** of repentance

FOUNDATIONS (FOUNDATION)
Ps 102: 25 In the beginning you laid the **f**
Heb 1: 10 Lord, you laid the **f** of the earth,

FOUNDED (FOUNDATION)
Jer 10: 12 he **f** the world by his wisdom

FOUNTAIN
Ps 36: 9 For with you is the **f** of life;
Pr 14: 27 The fear of the LORD is a **f** of life,
18: 4 **f** of wisdom is a rushing stream.
Zec 13: 1 that day a **f** will be opened

FOX* (FOXES)
Ne 4: 3 a **f** climbing up on it would break
Lk 13: 32 "Go tell that **f**, 'I will keep

FOXES (FOX)
SS 2: 15 Catch for us the **f**, the little **f**
Mt 8: 20 "**F** have dens and birds have nests,

FRAGRANCE (FRAGRANT)
Ex 30: 38 like it to enjoy its **f** must be cut off
Jn 12: 3 was filled with the **f** of the perfume.

FRAGRANT (FRAGRANCE)
Eph 5: 2 himself up for us as a **f** offering
Php 4: 18 They are a **f** offering, an acceptable

FRANKINCENSE
Mt 2: 11 him with gifts of gold, **f** and myrrh.

FREE (FREED FREEDOM FREELY)
Ge 2: 16 "You are **f** to eat from any tree
Ps 146: 7 The LORD sets prisoners **f**,
Pr 6: 3 to **f** yourself, since you have fallen
Lk 4: 18 for the blind, to set the oppressed **f**,
Jn 8: 32 truth, and the truth will set you **f**."
8: 36 So if the Son sets you **f**, you will be **f** indeed.
Ro 6: 7 anyone who has died has been set **f**
6: 18 You have been set **f** from sin
8: 2 Spirit who gives life has set you **f**
1Co 7: 27 you **f** from such a commitment?
12: 13 Jews or Gentiles, slave or **f**—
Gal 3: 28 neither slave nor **f**, nor is there
5: 1 for freedom that Christ has set us **f**.
1Pe 2: 16 Live as **f** people, but do not use

FREED (FREE)
Ps 116: 16 you have **f** me from my chains.
Rev 1: 5 has **f** us from our sins by his blood,

FREEDOM (FREE)
Ps 119: 45 I will walk about in **f**, for I have
Isa 61: 1 to proclaim **f** for the captives
Lk 4: 18 me to proclaim **f** for the prisoners
Ro 8: 21 brought into the **f** and glory
1Co 7: 21 although if you can gain your **f**,
2Co 3: 17 the Spirit of the Lord is, there is **f**.
Gal 2: 4 spy on the **f** we have in Christ Jesus
5: 13 But do not use your **f** to indulge
Jas 1: 25 into the perfect law that gives **f**,
1Pe 2: 16 do not use your **f** as

FREELY (FREE)
Isa 55: 7 to our God, for he will **f** pardon.
Mt 10: 8 **F** you have received; **f** give.
Ro 3: 24 and all are justified **f** by his grace
Eph 1: 6 which he has **f** given us in the One

FRESH
Jas 3: 11 Can both **f** water and salt water

FRET*
Ps 37: 1 Do not **f** because of those who are
37: 7 do not **f** when people succeed
37: 8 do not **f**—it leads only to evil.
Pr 24: 19 Do not **f** because of evildoers or be

FRICTION*
1Ti 6: 5 constant **f** between people of

FRIEND (FRIENDS FRIENDSHIP)
Ex 33: 11 face to face, as one speaks to a **f**.
2Ch 20: 7 descendants of Abraham your **f**?
Pr 17: 17 A **f** loves at all times, and a brother
18: 24 there is a **f** who sticks closer than
27: 6 Wounds from a **f** can be trusted,
27: 10 Do not forsake your **f** or a **f** of your
Isa 41: 8 you descendants of Abraham my **f**,
Mt 11: 19 a **f** of tax collectors and sinners.'
Jn 19: 12 this man go, you are no **f** of Caesar.
Ro 16: 8 Ampliatus, my dear **f** in the Lord.
Jas 2: 23 and he was called God's **f**.
4: 4 to be a **f** of the world becomes

FRIENDS (FRIEND)
Pr 16: 28 and a gossip separates close **f**.
17: 9 repeats the matter separates close **f**.
18: 24 who has unreliable **f** soon comes
Zec 13: 6 I was given at the house of my **f**.'
Jn 15: 13 to lay down one's life for one's **f**.
15: 14 You are my **f** if you do what I

FRIENDSHIP (FRIEND)
Lk 11: 8 give you the bread because of **f**,
Jas 4: 4 don't you know that **f**

FRIGHTENED (FEAR)
Php 1: 28 without being **f** in any way by
1Pe 3: 14 not fear their threats; do not be **f**."

FROGS
Ex 8: 2 go, I will send a plague of **f** on your
Rev 16: 13 impure spirits that looked like **f**;

FROLIC
Mal 4: 2 go out and **f** like well-fed calves.

FRUIT (FRUITFUL)
Jdg 9: 11 'Should I give up my **f**, so good
Ps 1: 3 which yields its **f** in season
Pr 11: 30 The **f** of the righteous is a tree
12: 14 the **f** of their lips people are filled
27: 18 who guards a fig tree will eat its **f**,
Isa 11: 1 from his roots a Branch will bear **f**.
27: 6 and fill all the world with **f**.
32: 17 The **f** of that righteousness will be
Jer 17: 8 drought and never fails to bear **f**."
Hos 10: 12 reap the **f** of unfailing love,
14: 2 that we may offer the **f** of our lips.
Am 8: 1 a basket of ripe **f**.
Mt 3: 8 Produce **f** in keeping
3: 10 does not produce good **f** will be cut
7: 16 By their **f** you will recognize them.
7: 17 every good tree bears good **f**, but a bad tree bears bad **f**.
7: 20 by their **f** you will recognize them.
12: 33 a tree good and its **f** will be good,
12: 33 for a tree is recognized by its **f**.
Lk 3: 9 does not produce good **f** will be cut
6: 43 "No good tree bears bad **f**, nor does a bad tree bear good **f**.
13: 6 he went to look for **f** on it but did
Jn 15: 2 every branch in me that bears no **f**,
15: 2 branch that does bear **f** he prunes
15: 16 so that you might go and bear **f**—
Ro 7: 4 order that we might bear **f** for God.
Gal 5: 22 But the **f** of the Spirit is love, joy,
Php 1: 11 filled with the **f** of righteousness
Col 1: 10 bearing **f** in every good work,
Heb 13: 15 the **f** of lips that openly profess his
Jas 3: 17 full of mercy and good **f**,
Jude : 12 trees, without **f** and uprooted—
Rev 22: 2 bearing twelve crops of **f**,

FRUITFUL (FRUIT)
Ge 1: 22 "Be **f** and increase in number
9: 1 "Be **f** and increase in number
35: 11 be **f** and increase in number.
Ex 1: 7 the Israelites were exceedingly **f**;
Ps 128: 3 wife will be like a **f** vine within
Jn 15: 2 so that it will be even more **f**.
Php 1: 22 body, this will mean **f** labor for me.

FRUITLESS*
Eph 5: 11 to do with the **f** deeds of darkness,

FRUSTRATION
Ro 8: 20 For the creation was subjected to **f**,

FUEL
Isa 44: 19 to say, "Half of it I used for **f**;

FULFILL (FULFILLED FULFILLMENT FULFILLS)
Nu 23: 19 Does he promise and not **f**?
Ps 61: 8 name and **f** my vows day after day.
116: 14 I will **f** my vows to the LORD
Ecc 5: 5 vow than to make one and not **f** it.
Isa 46: 11 land, a man to **f** my purpose.
Jer 33: 14 I will **f** the good promise I made
Mt 1: 22 **f** what the Lord had said through
3: 15 us to do this to **f** all righteousness."
4: 14 **f** what was said through the
5: 17 to abolish them but to **f** them.
8: 17 to **f** what was spoken through
12: 17 to **f** what was spoken through
21: 4 to **f** what was spoken through
Jn 12: 38 This was to **f** the word of Isaiah
13: 18 this is to **f** this passage of Scripture:
15: 25 this is to **f** what is written in their
1Co 7: 3 The husband should **f** his marital

FULFILLED (FULFILL)
Jos 21: 45 to Israel failed; every one was **f**.
23: 14 Every promise has been **f**;
Pr 13: 12 sick, but a longing **f** is a tree of life.
13: 19 A longing **f** is sweet to the soul,
Mt 2: 15 so was **f** what the Lord had said
2: 17 the prophet Jeremiah was **f**:
2: 23 So was **f** what was said through
13: 14 In them is **f** the prophecy of Isaiah:
13: 35 So was **f** what was spoken through
26: 54 would the Scriptures be **f** that say it
26: 56 of the prophets might be **f**."
27: 9 by Jeremiah the prophet was **f**:
Mk 13: 4 sign that they are all about to be **f**?"
14: 49 But the Scriptures must be **f**."
Lk 4: 21 "Today this scripture is **f** in your
18: 31 about the Son of Man will be **f**.
24: 44 Everything must be **f** that is
Jn 18: 9 words he had spoken would be **f**:
19: 24 the scripture might be **f** that said,
19: 28 and so that Scripture would be **f**,
19: 36 so that the scripture would be **f**:
Ac 1: 16 the Scripture had to be **f**
Gal 5: 14 the entire law is **f** in keeping this
Ro 13: 8 whoever loves others has **f** the law.
Jas 2: 23 And the scripture was **f** that says,

FULFILLMENT (FULFILL)
Ro 13: 10 Therefore love is the **f** of the law.

FULFILLS (FULFILL)
Ps 145: 19 He **f** the desires of those who fear

FULL (FILL)
2Ch 24: 10 them into the chest until it was **f**.
Ps 127: 5 is the man whose quiver is **f**
Pr 27: 7 One who is **f** loathes honey
31: 11 Her husband has **f** confidence in
Isa 6: 3 the whole earth is **f** of his glory."
Mt 12: 34 speaks what the heart is **f** of.
Lk 4: 1 Jesus, **f** of the Holy Spirit,
6: 45 speaks what the heart is **f** of.
Jn 10: 10 may have life, and have it to the **f**.
Ac 6: 3 who are known to be **f** of the Spirit
6: 5 a man **f** of faith and of the Holy
7: 55 But Stephen, **f** of the Holy Spirit,
11: 24 man, **f** of the Holy Spirit and faith,
Ro 11: 12 riches will their **f** inclusion bring!
Eph 4: 19 of impurity, and they are **f** of greed.

FULL-GROWN* (GROW)
Jas 1: 15 sin, when it is **f**, gives birth to

FULLNESS* (FILL)
Dt 33: 16 its **f** and the favor of him who
Jn 1: 16 of his **f** we have all received grace
Eph 1: 23 the **f** of him who fills everything
3: 19 to the measure of all the **f** of God.
4: 13 whole measure of the **f** of Christ.
Col 1: 19 to have all his **f** dwell in him,
1: 25 to you the word of God in its **f**—
2: 9 in Christ all the **f** of the Deity lives
2: 10 Christ you have been brought to **f**.

FULLY (FILL)
1Ki 8: 61 may your hearts be **f** committed
2Ch 16: 9 whose hearts are **f** committed
Ps 119: 4 precepts that are to be **f** obeyed.
119:138 they are **f** trustworthy.
Pr 13: 4 of the diligent are **f** satisfied.
Lk 6: 40 everyone who is **f** trained will be
Ro 4: 21 being **f** persuaded that God had
14: 5 should be **f** convinced in their
1Co 13: 12 then I shall know **f**, even as I am **f**
15: 58 Always give yourselves **f**
2Ti 4: 17 the message might be **f** proclaimed

FURIOUS (FURY)
Dt 29: 28 In **f** anger and in great wrath
Jer 21: 5 mighty arm in **f** anger and in great
32: 37 where I banish them in my **f** anger

FURNACE
Isa 48: 10 tested you in the **f** of affliction.
Da 3: 6 be thrown into a blazing **f**."
Mt 13: 42 will throw them into the blazing **f**,

FURY (FURIOUS)
Isa 14: 6 in **f** subdued nations with
Am 1: 11 and his **f** flamed unchecked,
Rev 14: 10 too, will drink the wine of God's **f**,
16: 19 with the wine of the **f** of his wrath.
19: 15 the winepress of the **f** of the wrath

FUTILE (FUTILITY)
Mal 3: 14 have said, 'It is **f** to serve God.
1Co 3: 20 that the thoughts of the wise are **f**."

FUTILITY (FUTILE)
Eph 4: 17 do, in the **f** of their thinking.

FUTURE
Ps 37: 37 a **f** awaits those who seek peace.
Pr 23: 18 There is surely a **f** hope for you,
Ecc 7: 14 discover anything about their **f**.
8: 7 Since no one knows the **f**, who can
Jer 29: 11 you, plans to give you hope and a **f**.
Ro 8: 38 neither the present nor the **f**, nor
1Co 3: 22 or death or the present or the **f**—

GABRIEL*
Angel who interpreted Daniel's visions (Da 8:16–26; 9:20–27); announced births of John (Lk 1:11–20), Jesus (Lk 1:26–38).

GAD
1. Son of Jacob by Zilpah (Ge 30:9–11; 35:26; 1Ch 2:2). Tribe of blessed (Ge 49:19; Dt 33:20–21), numbered (Nu 1:25; 26:18), allotted land east of the Jordan (Nu 32; 34:14; Jos 18:7; 22), west (Eze 48:27–28), 12,000 from (Rev 7:5).
2. Prophet; seer of David (1Sa 22:5; 2Sa 24:11–19; 1Ch 29:29).

GAIN (GAINED GAINS)
Ex 14: 17 I will **g** glory through Pharaoh
Ps 60: 12 With God we will **g** the victory,
Pr 3: 13 those who **g** understanding,
4: 1 pay attention and **g** understanding.
8: 5 You who are simple, **g** prudence;
28: 16 who hates ill-gotten **g** will enjoy
28: 23 the end **g** favor rather than one
29: 23 low, but the lowly in spirit **g** honor.
Isa 63: 12 **g** for himself everlasting renown,
Da 2: 8 that you are trying to **g** time,
Mt 16: 26 for someone to **g** the whole world,
Mk 8: 36 for someone to **g** the whole world,
Lk 9: 25 for someone to **g** the whole world,
1Co 13: 3 but do not have love, I **g** nothing.
Php 1: 21 me, to live is Christ and to die is **g**.
3: 8 them garbage, that I may **g** Christ
1Ti 3: 13 have served well **g** an excellent
6: 5 godliness is a means to financial **g**.
6: 6 with contentment is great **g**.
1Pe 5: 2 not pursuing dishonest **g**, but eager

GAINED (GAIN)
Jer 32: 20 **g** the renown that is still yours.
Ro 5: 2 through whom we have **g** access

GAINS (GAIN)
Pr 11: 16 A kindhearted woman **g** honor,
15: 32 heeds correction **g** understanding.
Php 3: 7 But whatever were **g** to me I now

GALILEE
Isa 9: 1 in the future he will honor **G**
Mt 4: 15 the Jordan, **G** of the Gentiles—
26: 32 I will go ahead of you into **G**."
28: 10 Go and tell my brothers to go to **G**;

GALL
Mt 27: 34 Jesus wine to drink, mixed with **g**;

GALLIO
Ac 18: 12 While **G** was proconsul of Achaia,

GAMALIEL
Ac 5: 34 But a Pharisee named **G**, a teacher

GAMES*
1Co 9: 25 who competes in the **g** goes

GAP
Eze 22: 30 stand before me in the **g** on behalf

GARBAGE*
1Co 4: 13 the earth, the **g** of the world—
Php 3: 8 I consider them **g**, that I may gain

GARDEN (GARDENER)
Ge 2: 8 the LORD God had planted a **g**
2: 15 put him in the **G** of Eden to work it
SS 4: 12 You are a **g** locked up, my sister,
Isa 58: 11 You will be like a well-watered **g**,
Jer 31: 12 They will be like a well-watered **g**,
Eze 28: 13 You were in Eden, the **g** of God;
31: 9 the trees of Eden in the **g** of God.

GARDENER (GARDEN)
Jn 15: 1 true vine, and my Father is the **g**.
20: 15 Thinking he was the **g**, she said,

GARLAND*
Pr 1: 9 They are a **g** to grace your head
4: 9 She will give you a **g** to grace your

GARMENT (GARMENTS)
Ps 22: 18 among them and cast lots for my **g**.
102: 26 they will all wear out like a **g**.
Isa 50: 9 They will all wear out like a **g**;
51: 6 the earth will wear out like a **g**
61: 3 a **g** of praise instead of a spirit

Mt 9: 16 patch will pull away from the **g**,
Jn 19: 23 This **g** was seamless, woven in one
Heb 1: 11 they will all wear out like a **g**.

GARMENTS (GARMENT)
Ge 3: 21 The LORD God made **g** of skin
Ex 28: 2 Make sacred **g** for your brother
Lev 16: 23 take off the linen **g** he put on
16: 24 area and put on his regular **g**.
Isa 61: 10 For he has clothed me with **g**
63: 1 with his **g** stained crimson?
Joel 2: 13 Rend your heart and not your **g**.
Zec 3: 4 sin, and I will put fine **g** on you."

GATE (GATES)
Ps 118: 20 This is the **g** of the LORD through
Pr 31: 23 husband is respected at the city **g**,
31: 31 works bring her praise at the city **g**.
Mt 7: 13 "Enter through the narrow **g**.
7: 13 For wide is the **g** and broad is
Jn 10: 1 not enter the sheep pen by the **g**,
10: 2 who enters by the **g** is the shepherd
10: 7 I tell you, I am the **g** for the sheep.
10: 9 I am the **g**; whoever enters through
Heb 13: 12 suffered outside the city **g** to make
Rev 21: 21 each **g** made of a single pearl.

GATES (GATE)
Ps 24: 7 Lift up your heads, you **g**;
24: 9 Lift up your heads, you **g**;
100: 4 Enter his **g** with thanksgiving
118: 19 Open for me the **g** of the righteous;
Isa 60: 11 Your **g** will always stand open,
60: 18 walls Salvation and your **g** Praise.
62: 10 Pass through, pass through the **g**!
Mt 16: 18 **g** of Hades will not overcome it.
Rev 21: 12 high wall with twelve **g**, and with twelve angels at the **g**.
21: 25 On no day will its **g** ever be shut,
22: 14 may go through the **g** into the city.

GATH
1Sa 17: 23 the Philistine champion from **G**,
2Sa 1: 20 "Tell it not in **G**, proclaim it not
Mic 1: 10 Tell it not in **G**; weep not at all.

GATHER (GATHERED GATHERS)
Ps 106: 47 and **g** us from the nations, that we
Isa 11: 12 nations and **g** the exiles of Israel;
Jer 3: 17 all nations will **g** in Jerusalem
23: 3 "I myself will **g** the remnant of my
31: 10 who scattered Israel will **g** them
Zep 2: 1 **G** together, **g** yourselves together,
3: 20 At that time I will **g** you;
Zec 14: 2 I will **g** all the nations to Jerusalem
Mt 12: 30 and whoever does not **g** with me
13: 30 then **g** the wheat and bring it
23: 37 longed to **g** your children together,
24: 31 they will **g** his elect from the four
25: 26 **g** where I have not scattered seed?
Mk 13: 27 **g** his elect from the four winds,
Lk 3: 17 and to **g** the wheat into his barn,
11: 23 and whoever does not **g** with me
13: 34 longed to **g** your children together,

GATHERED (GATHER)
Ex 16: 18 the one who **g** much did not have
16: 18 Everyone had **g** just as much as
Pr 30: 4 Whose hands have **g** up the wind?
Mt 25: 32 the nations will be **g** before him,
2Co 8: 15 "The one who **g** much did not have
2Th 2: 1 Christ and our being **g** to him,
Rev 16: 16 they **g** the kings together

GATHERS (GATHER)
Ps 147: 2 he **g** the exiles of Israel.
Pr 10: 5 He who **g** crops in summer is
Isa 40: 11 He **g** the lambs in his arms
Mt 23: 37 as a hen **g** her chicks under her

GAVE (GIVE)
Ge 2: 20 So the man **g** names to all
3: 6 She also **g** some to her husband,
14: 20 Abram **g** him a tenth of everything.
28: 4 the land God **g** to Abraham."
35: 12 The land I **g** to Abraham and Isaac
39: 23 **g** him success in whatever he did.
47: 11 **g** them property in the best part
Ex 4: 11 him, "Who **g** human beings their
31: 18 he **g** him the two tablets
Dt 2: 12 the land the LORD **g** them as their
2: 36 The LORD our God **g** us all
3: 12 I **g** the Reubenites and the Gadites
3: 13 I **g** to the half-tribe of Manasseh.
3: 15 And I **g** Gilead to Makir.
3: 16 and the Gadites I **g** the territory
8: 16 He **g** you manna to eat
Dt 26: 9 us to this place and **g** us this land,
32: 8 the Most High **g** the nations their
Jos 11: 23 he **g** it as an inheritance to Israel
13: 14 tribe of Levi he **g** no inheritance,
14: 13 **g** him Hebron as his inheritance.
21: 44 The LORD **g** them rest on every
24: 13 So I **g** you a land on which you did
1Sa 27: 6 on that day Achish **g** him Ziklag,
2Sa 12: 8 I **g** your master's house to you,
1Ki 4: 29 God **g** Solomon wisdom and very
5: 12 The LORD **g** Solomon wisdom,
Ezr 2: 69 their ability they **g** to the treasury
Ne 9: 15 their hunger you **g** them bread
9: 20 You **g** your good Spirit to instruct
9: 22 "You **g** them kingdoms
9: 27 compassion you **g** them deliverers,
Job 1: 21 The LORD **g** and the LORD has
42: 10 and **g** him twice as much as he had
Ps 69: 21 and **g** me vinegar for my thirst.
135: 12 he **g** their land as an inheritance,
Ecc 12: 7 the spirit returns to God who **g** it.
Eze 3: 2 and he **g** me the scroll to eat.
Mt 1: 25 And he **g** him the name Jesus.
25: 35 and you **g** me something to eat,
25: 42 and you **g** me nothing to drink,
26: 26 he broke it and **g** it to his disciples,
27: 50 in a loud voice, he **g** up his spirit.
Mk 6: 7 and **g** them authority over impure
Jn 1: 12 he **g** the right to become children
3: 16 so loved the world that he **g** his
17: 4 finishing the work you **g** me to do.
17: 6 you to those whom you **g** me
19: 30 bowed his head and **g** up his spirit.
Ac 1: 3 **g** many convincing proofs that he
11: 17 if God **g** them the same gift he **g** us
Ro 1: 24 Therefore God **g** them over
1: 26 God **g** them over to shameful lusts.
1: 28 so God **g** them over to a depraved
8: 32 own Son, but **g** him up for us all—
2Co 5: 18 **g** us the ministry of reconciliation:
8: 3 they **g** as much as they were able,
8: 5 They **g** themselves first of all
Gal 1: 4 **g** himself for our sins to rescue
2: 20 loved me and **g** himself for me.
Eph 4: 8 captives and **g** gifts to his people."
5: 2 **g** himself up for us as a fragrant
5: 25 church and **g** himself up for her
2Th 2: 16 us and by his grace **g** us eternal
1Ti 2: 6 who **g** himself as a ransom for all
Titus 2: 14 who **g** himself for us to redeem us
1Jn 3: 24 We know it by the Spirit he **g** us.

GAZE
Ps 27: 4 to **g** on the beauty of the LORD
Pr 4: 25 fix your **g** directly before you.

GEDALIAH
Governor of Judah appointed by Nebuchadnezzar (2Ki 25:22–26; Jer 39–41).

GEHAZI*
Servant of Elisha (2Ki 4:12—5:27; 8:4–5).

GENEALOGIES
1Ti 1: 4 themselves to myths and endless **g**.
Titus 3: 9 avoid foolish controversies and **g**

GENERATION (GENERATIONS)
Ex 3: 15 name you shall call me from **g** to **g**.
Nu 32: 13 until the whole **g** of those who had
Dt 1: 35 this evil **g** shall see the good land
Jdg 2: 10 another **g** grew up who knew
Job 8: 8 "Ask the former **g** and find
Ps 24: 6 Such is the **g** of those who seek
48: 13 you may tell of them to the next **g**.
71: 18 I declare your power to the next **g**,
78: 4 will tell the next **g** the praiseworthy
102: 18 Let this be written for a future **g**,
112: 2 the **g** of the upright will be blessed.
145: 4 One **g** commends your works
La 5: 19 your throne endures from **g** to **g**.
Da 4: 3 his dominion endures from **g** to **g**.
4: 34 his kingdom endures from **g** to **g**.
Joel 1: 3 and their children to the next **g**.
Mt 12: 39 and adulterous **g** asks for a sign!
17: 17 "You unbelieving and perverse **g**,"
23: 36 tell you, all this will come on this **g**.
24: 34 this **g** will certainly not pass away
Mk 9: 19 "You unbelieving **g**,"
13: 30 this **g** will certainly not pass away
Lk 1: 50 to those who fear him, from **g** to **g**.
11: 29 Jesus said, "This is a wicked **g**.
11: 30 will the Son of Man be to this **g**.
11: 50 Therefore this **g** will be held
21: 32 this **g** will certainly not pass away
Ac 2: 40 yourselves from this corrupt **g**."
Php 2: 15 fault in a warped and crooked **g**."

GENERATIONS (GENERATION)
Ge 9: 12 you, a covenant for all **g** to come:
17: 7 after you for the **g** to come, to be
17: 9 after you for the **g** to come.
Ex 20: 6 a thousand **g** of those who love me
31: 13 me and you for the **g** to come,
Dt 7: 9 thousand **g** of those who love him
32: 7 consider the **g** long past.
1Ch 16: 15 promise he made, for a thousand **g**,
Ps 22: 30 future **g** will be told about the Lord
33: 11 purposes of his heart through all **g**.
45: 17 your memory through all **g**;
89: 1 faithfulness known through all **g**.
90: 1 dwelling place throughout all **g**.
100: 5 faithfulness continues through all **g**
102: 12 renown endures through all **g**.
105: 8 promise he made, for a thousand **g**,
119: 90 faithfulness continues through all **g**
135: 13 renown, LORD, through all **g**.
145: 13 dominion endures through all **g**.
146: 10 your God, O Zion, for all **g**.
Pr 27: 24 and a crown is not secure for all **g**.
Isa 41: 4 through, calling forth the **g**
51: 8 my salvation through all **g**."
Lk 1: 48 now on all **g** will call me blessed,
Eph 3: 5 other **g** as it has now been revealed
3: 21 in Christ Jesus throughout all **g**,
Col 1: 26 been kept hidden for ages and **g**,

GENEROSITY* (GENEROUS)
2Co 8: 2 poverty welled up in rich **g**.
9: 11 and through us your **g** will result
9: 13 for your **g** in sharing with them

GENEROUS* (GENEROSITY)
Ps 37: 26 They are always **g** and lend freely;
112: 5 Good will come to those who are **g**
Pr 11: 25 A **g** person will prosper;
22: 9 The **g** will themselves be blessed,
Mt 20: 15 are you envious because I am **g**?'
Lk 11: 41 be **g** to the poor, and everything
Ac 28: 7 showed us **g** hospitality for three
2Co 9: 5 for the **g** gift you had promised.
9: 5 Then it will be ready as a **g** gift,
9: 11 you can be **g** on every occasion,
1Ti 6: 18 and to be **g** and willing to share.

GENTILE (GENTILES)
Ac 21: 25 As for the **G** believers, we have
Ro 1: 16 first to the Jew, then to the **G**.
2: 9 first for the Jew, then for the **G**;
2: 10 first for the Jew, then for the **G**.
10: 12 no difference between Jew and **G**—
Gal 3: 28 There is neither Jew nor **G**,
Col 3: 11 Here there is no **G** or Jew,

GENTILES (GENTILE)
Isa 42: 6 for the people and a light for the **G**,
49: 6 also make you a light for the **G**,
Lk 2: 32 a light for revelation to the **G**,
21: 24 trampled on by the **G** until the times of the **G** are fulfilled.
Ac 9: 15 to proclaim my name to the **G**
10: 45 had been poured out even on **G**.
11: 18 to **G** God has granted repentance
13: 16 and you **G** who worship God,
13: 46 eternal life, we now turn to the **G**.
13: 47 have made you a light for the **G**,
14: 27 opened a door of faith to the **G**.
15: 14 a people for his name from the **G**.
18: 6 From now on I will go to the **G**."
22: 21 send you far away to the **G**.'"
26: 20 and then to the **G**, I preached
28: 28 salvation has been sent to the **G**,
Ro 2: 14 when **G**, who do not have the law,
3: 9 **G** alike are all under the power
3: 29 Is he not the God of **G** too?
9: 24 from the Jews but also from the **G**?
11: 11 to the **G** to make Israel envious.
11: 12 their loss means riches for the **G**,
11: 13 as I am the apostle to the **G**,
15: 9 that the **G** might glorify God for
15: 9 I will praise you among the **G**;
1Co 1: 23 block to Jews and foolishness to **G**,
Gal 1: 16 I might preach him among the **G**,
2: 2 gospel that I preach among the **G**.
2: 8 work in me as an apostle to the **G**.
2: 9 agreed that we should go to the **G**,
3: 8 God would justify the **G** by faith,
3: 14 to the **G** through Christ Jesus,
Eph 3: 6 the gospel the **G** are heirs together
3: 8 preach to the **G** the boundless

Col 1: 27 known among the **G** the glorious
1Ti 2: 7 a true and faithful teacher of the **G**.
2Ti 4: 17 and all the **G** might hear it.

GENTLE* (GENTLENESS)
Dt 28: 54 Even the most **g** and sensitive man
28: 56 The most **g** and sensitive woman
28: 56 and **g** that she would not venture
2Sa 18: 5 Be **g** with the young man Absalom
1Ki 19: 12 after the fire came a **g** whisper.
Job 41: 3 Will it speak to you with **g** words?
Pr 15: 1 A **g** answer turns away wrath,
25: 15 and a **g** tongue can break a bone.
Jer 11: 19 I had been like a **g** lamb led
Mt 11: 29 for I am **g** and humble in heart,
21: 5 to you, **g** and riding on a donkey,
Ac 27: 13 When a **g** south wind began
1Co 4: 21 I come in love and with a **g** spirit?
Eph 4: 2 Be completely humble and **g**;
1Ti 3: 3 not violent but **g**, not quarrelsome,
Titus 3: 2 always to be **g** toward everyone.
1Pe 3: 4 unfading beauty of a **g** and quiet

GENTLENESS* (GENTLE)
2Co 10: 1 By the humility and **g** of Christ,
Gal 5: 23 **g** and self-control.
Php 4: 5 Let your **g** be evident to all.
Col 3: 12 kindness, humility, **g** and patience.
1Ti 6: 11 faith, love, endurance and **g**.
1Pe 3: 15 But do this with **g** and respect,

GENUINE* (GENUINENESS)
2Co 6: 8 **g**, yet regarded as impostors;
Php 2: 20 who will show **g** concern for your

GENUINENESS* (GENUINE)
1Pe 1: 7 that the proven **g** of your faith—

GERIZIM
Dt 27: 12 on Mount **G** to bless the people:

GERSHOM
Ex 2: 22 and Moses named him **G**, saying,

GETHSEMANE*
Mt 26: 36 his disciples to a place called **G**,
Mk 14: 32 They went to a place called **G**,

GHOST See also SPIRIT
Lk 24: 39 a **g** does not have flesh and bones,

GIBEON
Jos 10: 12 "Sun, stand still over **G**, and you,

GIDEON*
Judge, also called Jerub-Baal; freed Israel from Midianites (Jdg 6–8; Heb 11:32). Given sign of fleece (Jdg 6:36–40).

GIFT (GIFTED GIFTS)
Pr 18: 16 A **g** opens the way and ushers
21: 14 A **g** given in secret soothes anger,
Ecc 3: 13 all their toil—this is the **g** of God.
Mt 5: 23 you are offering your **g** at the altar
Jn 4: 10 "If you knew the **g** of God and who
Ac 1: 4 wait for the **g** my Father promised,
2: 38 you will receive the **g** of the Holy
11: 17 gave them the same **g** he gave us
Ro 6: 23 the **g** of God is eternal life in Christ
12: 6 If your **g** is prophesying,
1Co 7: 7 of you has your own **g** from God;
7: 7 one has this **g**, another has that.
2Co 8: 12 the **g** is acceptable according
9: 15 be to God for his indescribable **g**!
Eph 2: 8 yourselves, it is the **g** of God—
1Ti 4: 14 Do not neglect your **g**, which was
2Ti 1: 6 you to fan into flame the **g** of God,
Heb 6: 4 who have tasted the heavenly **g**,
Jas 1: 17 good and perfect **g** is from above,
1Pe 3: 7 with you of the gracious **g** of life,
4: 10 you should use whatever **g** you
Rev 22: 17 the one who wishes take the free **g**

GIFTED* (GIFT)
1Co 14: 37 or otherwise **g** by the Spirit,

GIFTS (GIFT)
Ps 76: 11 all the neighboring lands bring **g**
112: 9 They have freely scattered their **g**
Pr 25: 14 is one who boasts of **g** never given.
Mt 2: 11 and presented him with **g** of gold,
7: 11 to give good **g** to your children,
7: 11 in heaven give good **g** to those who
Lk 11: 13 to give good **g** to your children,
Ac 10: 4 and **g** to the poor have come up as
Ro 11: 29 for God's **g** and his call are
12: 6 We have different **g**,
1Co 12: 1 Now about the **g** of the Spirit,
12: 4 There are different kinds of **g**,
12: 28 then **g** of healing, of helping,
1Co 12: 30 Do all have **g** of healing?
12: 31 Now eagerly desire the greater **g**.
14: 1 and eagerly desire **g** of the Spirit,
14: 12 Since you are eager for **g**
2Co 9: 9 "They have freely scattered their **g**
Eph 4: 8 captives and gave **g** to his people."
Heb 2: 4 by **g** of the Holy Spirit distributed
9: 9 indicating that the **g** and sacrifices

GILEAD
1Ch 27: 21 the half-tribe of Manasseh in **G**:
Jer 8: 22 Is there no balm in **G**? Is there no
46: 11 "Go up to **G** and get balm,

GILGAL
Jos 5: 9 So the place has been called **G**

GIRD*
Ps 45: 3 **G** your sword on your side,

GIRL
2Ki 5: 2 had taken captive a young **g**
Mk 5: 41 (which means "Little **g**, I say

GIVE (GAVE GIVEN GIVER GIVES GIVING LIFE-GIVING)
Ge 28: 4 he **g** you and your descendants
28: 22 that you **g** me I will **g** you a tenth."
Ex 20: 16 "You shall not **g** false testimony
30: 15 the poor are not to **g** less when you
Nu 6: 26 toward you and **g** you peace."'
Dt 5: 20 "You shall not **g** false testimony
15: 10 **G** generously to them and do so
15: 14 **G** to them as the LORD your God
1Sa 1: 11 I will **g** him to the LORD for all
1: 28 So now I **g** him to the LORD.
2Ch 15: 7 be strong and do not **g** up, for your
Pr 21: 26 the righteous **g** without sparing.
23: 26 **g** me your heart and let your eyes
25: 21 enemy is hungry, **g** him food to
25: 26 well are the righteous who **g** way
28: 27 Those who **g** to the poor will lack
30: 8 **g** me neither poverty nor riches,
30: 8 but **g** me only my daily bread.
Ecc 3: 6 a time to search and a time to **g** up,
Eze 36: 26 I will **g** you a new heart and put
Mt 6: 11 **G** us today our daily bread.
7: 11 your Father in heaven **g** good gifts
10: 8 Freely you have received; freely **g**.
16: 19 will **g** you the keys of the kingdom
22: 21 them, "So **g** back to Caesar what is
Mk 8: 37 what can anyone **g** in exchange
10: 19 you shall not **g** false testimony,
Lk 6: 38 **G**, and it will be given to you.
11: 3 **G** us each day our daily bread.
11: 13 Father in heaven **g** the Holy Spirit
14: 33 you who do not **g** up everything
Jn 10: 28 I **g** them eternal life, and they shall
13: 34 "A new command I **g** you:
14: 16 he will **g** you another advocate
14: 27 I leave with you; my peace I **g** you.
14: 27 do not **g** to you as the world gives.
17: 2 people that he might **g** eternal life
Ac 2: 45 possessions to **g** to anyone who
20: 35 'It is more blessed to **g** than
Ro 2: 7 immortality, he will **g** eternal life.
8: 32 him, graciously **g** us all things?
12: 8 if it is giving, then **g** generously;
13: 7 **G** to everyone what you owe them:
14: 12 then, each of us will **g** an account
1Co 13: 3 If I **g** all I possess to the poor and **g**
2Co 9: 7 have decided in your heart to **g**,
Gal 2: 5 We did not **g** in to them
6: 9 reap a harvest if we do not **g** up.
Rev 14: 7 voice, "Fear God and **g** him glory,
21: 6 thirsty I will **g** water without cost

GIVEN (GIVE)
Nu 8: 16 Israelites who are to be **g** wholly
Dt 26: 11 things the LORD your God has **g**
Job 3: 23 Why is life **g** to a man whose way
Ps 115: 16 but the earth he has **g** to mankind.
Isa 9: 6 us a son is **g**, and the government
Mt 6: 33 all these things will be **g** to you as
7: 7 "Ask and it will be **g** to you;
13: 12 Whoever has will be **g** more,
22: 30 people will neither marry nor be **g**
25: 29 For whoever has will be **g** more,
Lk 6: 38 Give, and it will be **g** to you.
8: 10 kingdom of God has been **g** to you,
11: 9 Ask and it will be **g** to you;
22: 19 saying, "This is my body **g** for you;
Jn 3: 27 can receive only what is **g** them
17: 24 glory you have **g** me because you
18: 11 the cup the Father has **g** me?"
Ac 5: 32 God has **g** to those who obey
7: 53 the law that was **g** through angels
20: 24 the task the Lord Jesus has **g** me—
Ro 5: 5 Holy Spirit, who has been **g** to us.
1Co 4: 2 those who have been **g** a trust must
11: 24 when he had **g** thanks, he broke
12: 13 and we were all **g** the one Spirit
2Co 5: 5 has **g** us the Spirit as a deposit,
Gal 3: 19 Why, then, was the law **g** at all?
3: 19 The law was **g** through angels
Eph 1: 6 he has freely **g** us in the One he
4: 7 of us grace has been **g** as Christ
1Ti 4: 14 which was **g** you through prophecy
1Jn 4: 13 he in us: He has **g** us of his Spirit.

GIVER* (GIVE)
Pr 18: 16 ushers the **g** into the presence
2Co 9: 7 for God loves a cheerful **g**.

GIVES (GIVE)
Job 35: 10 Maker, who **g** songs in the night,
Ps 119:130 unfolding of your words **g** light;
Pr 11: 24 One person **g** freely, yet gains even
14: 30 A heart at peace **g** life to the body,
15: 30 good news **g** health to the bones.
19: 6 is the friend of one who **g** gifts.
29: 4 justice a king **g** a country stability,
Isa 40: 29 He **g** strength to the weary
Hab 2: 15 him who **g** drink to his neighbors,
Mt 10: 42 anyone **g** even a cup of cold water
Jn 5: 21 raises the dead and **g** them life,
6: 63 The Spirit **g** life; the flesh counts
1Co 15: 57 He **g** us the victory through our
2Co 3: 6 the letter kills, but the Spirit **g** life.
1Th 4: 8 the very God who **g** you his Holy
Jas 1: 25 into the perfect law that **g** freedom,
4: 6 But he **g** us more grace. That is

GIVING (GIVE)
Ne 8: 8 **g** the meaning so that the people
Est 9: 19 a day for **g** presents to each other.
Ps 19: 8 are radiant, **g** light to the eyes.
Pr 15: 23 person finds joy in **g** an apt reply—
Mt 6: 4 so that your **g** may be in secret.
24: 38 marrying and **g** in marriage,
Ac 15: 8 accepted them by **g** the Holy Spirit
2Co 8: 7 you also excel in this grace of **g**.
Php 4: 15 shared with me in the matter of **g**
Heb 10: 25 not **g** up meeting together, as some

GLAD* (GLADDENS GLADNESS)
Ex 4: 14 you, and he will be **g** to see you.
Jos 22: 33 They were **g** to hear the report
Jdg 8: 25 "We'll be **g** to give them."
1Sa 19: 5 Israel, and you saw it and were **g**.
2Sa 1: 20 daughters of the Philistines be **g**,
1Ki 8: 66 **g** in heart for all the good things
1Ch 16: 31 heavens rejoice, let the earth be **g**;
2Ch 7: 10 **g** in heart for the good things
Ps 5: 11 let all who take refuge in you be **g**;
9: 2 I will be **g** and rejoice in you;
14: 7 let Jacob rejoice and Israel be **g**!
16: 9 Therefore my heart is **g** and my
21: 6 made him **g** with the joy of your
31: 7 I will be **g** and rejoice in your love,
32: 11 Rejoice in the LORD and be **g**,
40: 16 seek you rejoice and be **g** in you;
45: 8 music of the strings makes you **g**.
46: 4 whose streams make **g** the city
48: 11 of Judah are **g** because of your
53: 6 let Jacob rejoice and Israel be **g**!
58: 10 The righteous will be **g** when they
67: 4 May the nations be **g** and sing
68: 3 may the righteous be **g** and rejoice
69: 32 The poor will see and be **g**—
70: 4 seek you rejoice and be **g** in you;
90: 14 sing for joy and be **g** all our days.
90: 15 Make us **g** for as many days as you
92: 4 For you make me **g** by your deeds,
96: 11 heavens rejoice, let the earth be **g**;
97: 1 LORD reigns, let the earth be **g**;
97: 8 of Judah are **g** because of your
105: 38 Egypt was **g** when they left,
107: 30 They were **g** when it grew calm,
118: 24 let us rejoice today and be **g**.
149: 2 people of Zion be **g** in their King.
Pr 23: 15 then my heart will be **g** indeed;
29: 6 righteous shout for joy and are **g**.
Ecc 8: 15 sun than to eat and drink and be **g**.
Isa 25: 9 rejoice and be **g** in his salvation."
35: 1 and the parched land will be **g**;
65: 18 be **g** and rejoice forever in what I
66: 10 with Jerusalem and be **g** for her,
Jer 20: 15 who made him very **g**, saying,

Jer 31: 13 young women will dance and be **g**,
41: 13 who were with him, they were **g**.
50: 11 "Because you rejoice and are **g**,
La 4: 21 Rejoice and be **g**, Daughter Edom,
Joel 2: 21 land of Judah; be **g** and rejoice.
2: 23 Be **g**, people of Zion,
Hab 1: 15 and so he rejoices and is **g**.
Zep 3: 14 Be **g** and rejoice with all your heart
Zec 2: 10 "Shout and be **g**, Daughter Zion.
8: 19 will become joyful and **g** occasions
10: 7 their hearts will be **g** as with wine.
Mt 5: 12 Rejoice and be **g**, because great is
Lk 15: 32 But we had to celebrate and be **g**,
Jn 4: 36 and the reaper may be **g** together.
8: 56 he saw it and was **g**."
11: 15 your sake I am **g** I was not there,
14: 28 you would be **g** that I am going
Ac 2: 26 Therefore my heart is **g** and my
2: 46 and ate together with **g** and sincere
11: 23 he was **g** and encouraged them all
13: 48 they were **g** and honored the word
15: 3 news made all the believers very **g**.
15: 31 were **g** for its encouraging message.
1Co 16: 17 I was **g** when Stephanas,
2Co 2: 2 who is left to make me **g** but you
7: 16 I am **g** I can have complete
13: 9 We are **g** whenever we are weak
Gal 4: 27 "Be **g**, barren woman, you who
Php 2: 17 I am **g** and rejoice with all of you.
2: 18 So you too should be **g** and rejoice
2: 28 you see him again you may be **g**
Rev 19: 7 and be **g** and give him glory!

GLADDENS* (GLAD)
Ps 104: 15 wine that **g** human hearts,

GLADNESS* (GLAD)
2Ch 29: 30 So they sang praises with **g**
Est 8: 16 of happiness and joy, **g** and honor.
8: 17 was joy and **g** among the Jews,
Job 3: 22 who are filled with **g** and rejoice
Ps 35: 27 my vindication shout for joy and **g**;
45: 15 Led in with joy and **g**, they enter
51: 8 Let me hear joy and **g**; let the
65: 12 the hills are clothed with **g**.
100: 2 Worship the LORD with **g**;
Ecc 5: 20 God keeps them occupied with **g**
9: 7 eat your food with **g**, and drink
Isa 16: 10 **g** are taken away from the
35: 10 **G** and joy will overtake them,
51: 3 Joy and **g** will be found in her,
51: 11 **G** and joy will overtake them,
Jer 7: 34 an end to the sounds of joy and **g**
16: 9 an end to the sounds of joy and **g**
25: 10 from them the sounds of joy and **g**,
31: 13 I will turn their mourning into **g**;
33: 11 the sounds of joy and **g**, the voices
48: 33 and **g** are gone from the orchards
Joel 1: 16 and **g** from the house of our God?

GLEAM*
Da 10: 6 legs like the **g** of burnished bronze,

GLOAT (GLOATS)
Pr 24: 17 Do not **g** when your enemy falls;

GLOATS* (GLOAT)
Pr 17: 5 whoever **g** over disaster will not go

GLORIES* (GLORY)
1Pe 1: 11 and the **g** that would follow.

GLORIFIED* (GLORY)
Isa 66: 5 'Let the LORD be **g**, that we may
Da 4: 34 and **g** him who lives forever.
Jn 7: 39 since Jesus had not yet been **g**.
11: 4 God's Son may be **g** through it."
12: 16 after Jesus was **g** did they realize
12: 23 come for the Son of Man to be **g**.
12: 28 "I have **g** it, and will glorify it
13: 31 "Now the Son of Man is **g** and God is **g** in him.
13: 32 If God is **g** in him, God will glorify
Jn 14: 13 the Father may be **g** in the Son.
Ac 3: 13 our fathers, has **g** his servant Jesus.
Ro 1: 21 they neither **g** him as God nor gave
8: 30 those he justified, he also **g**.
2Th 1: 10 he comes to be **g** in his holy people
1: 12 of our Lord Jesus may be **g** in you,
1Pe 1: 21 him from the dead and **g** him,

GLORIFIES* (GLORY)
Lk 1: 46 "My soul **g** the Lord
Jn 8: 54 as your God, is the one who **g** me.

GLORIFY* (GLORY)
Ps 34: 3 **G** the LORD with me; let us exalt
63: 3 better than life, my lips will **g** you.
Ps 69: 30 song and **g** him with thanksgiving.
86: 12 I will **g** your name forever.
Isa 60: 13 and I will **g** the place for my feet.
Da 4: 37 and exalt and **g** the King of heaven,
Mt 5: 16 deeds and **g** your Father in heaven.
Jn 8: 54 "If I **g** myself, my glory means
12: 28 Father, **g** your name!" Then a voice
12: 28 glorified it, and will **g** it again."
13: 32 God will **g** the Son in himself, and will **g** him at once.
16: 14 He will **g** me because it is from me
17: 1 **G** your Son, that your Son may **g**
17: 5 **g** me in your presence
21: 19 death by which Peter would **g** God.
Ro 15: 6 one voice you may **g** the God
15: 9 the Gentiles might **g** God for his
1Pe 2: 12 and **g** God on the day he visits us.
Rev 16: 9 they refused to repent and **g** him.

GLORIFYING* (GLORY)
Lk 2: 20 **g** and praising God for all the

GLORIOUS* (GLORY)
Dt 28: 58 do not revere this **g** and awesome
33: 29 and helper and your **g** sword.
1Ch 29: 13 thanks, and praise your **g** name.
Ne 9: 5 "Blessed be your **g** name, and may
Ps 45: 13 All **g** is the princess within her
66: 2 of his name; make his praise **g**.
72: 19 Praise be to his **g** name forever;
87: 3 **G** things are said of you,
106: 20 They exchanged their **g** God
111: 3 **G** and majestic are his deeds,
145: 5 They speak of the **g** splendor
145: 12 the **g** splendor of your kingdom.
Pr 4: 9 and present you with a **g** crown."
Isa 3: 8 the LORD, defying his **g** presence.
4: 2 the LORD will be beautiful and **g**,
11: 10 him, and his resting place will be **g**.
12: 5 LORD, for he has done **g** things;
28: 1 to the fading flower, his **g** beauty,
28: 4 That fading flower, his **g** beauty,
28: 5 Almighty will be a **g** crown,
42: 21 to make his law great and **g**.
60: 7 altar, and I will adorn my **g** temple.
63: 12 who sent his **g** arm of power to be
63: 14 to make for yourself a **g** name.
63: 15 from your lofty throne, holy and **g**.
64: 11 Our holy and **g** temple, where our
Jer 2: 11 people have exchanged their **g** God
13: 18 for your **g** crowns will fall
14: 21 do not dishonor your **g** throne.
17: 12 A **g** throne,
48: 17 scepter, how broken the **g** staff!'
Hos 4: 7 they exchanged their **g** God
Zec 2: 8 the **G** One has sent me against
Mt 19: 28 Son of Man sits on his **g** throne,
25: 31 him, he will sit on his **g** throne.
Lk 9: 30 and Elijah, appeared in **g** splendor,
Ac 2: 20 of the great and **g** day of the Lord.
2Co 3: 8 of the Spirit be even more **g**?
3: 9 that brought condemnation was **g**, how much more **g** is the ministry
3: 10 For what was **g** has no glory now
Eph 1: 6 to the praise of his **g** grace,
1: 17 our Lord Jesus Christ, the **g** Father,
1: 18 the riches of his **g** inheritance in
3: 16 his **g** riches he may strengthen you
Php 3: 21 so that they will be like his **g** body.
Col 1: 11 power according to his **g** might so
1: 27 among the Gentiles the **g** riches
Jas 2: 1 in our **g** Lord Jesus Christ must not
1Pe 1: 8 with an inexpressible and **g** joy,
Jude : 24 you before his **g** presence without

GLORY (GLORIES GLORIFIED GLORIFIES GLORIFY GLORIFYING GLORIOUS)
Ex 14: 4 But I will gain **g** for myself through
14: 17 I will gain **g** through Pharaoh
15: 11 awesome in **g**, working wonders?
16: 10 and there was the **g** of the LORD
24: 16 and the **g** of the LORD settled
33: 18 said, "Now show me your **g**."
40: 34 and the **g** of the LORD filled
Nu 14: 21 and as surely as the **g** of the LORD
Dt 5: 24 LORD our God has shown us his **g**
Jos 7: 19 "My son, give **g** to the LORD,
1Sa 4: 21 "The **G** has departed from Israel"
1Ch 16: 10 **G** in his holy name; let the hearts
16: 24 Declare his **g** among the nations,
16: 28 ascribe to the LORD **g**
29: 11 power and the **g** and the majesty
Ps 8: 1 You have set your **g** in the heavens.
Ps 8: 5 crowned them with **g** and honor.
19: 1 The heavens declare the **g** of God;
24: 7 that the King of **g** may come in.
26: 8 live, the place where your **g** dwells.
29: 1 beings, ascribe to the LORD **g**
29: 9 And in his temple all cry, "**G**!"
34: 2 I will **g** in the LORD;
57: 5 let your **g** be over all the earth.
66: 2 Sing the **g** of his name;
72: 19 the whole earth be filled with his **g**.
96: 3 Declare his **g** among the nations,
102: 15 of the earth will revere your **g**.
108: 5 let your **g** be over all the earth.
149: 9 this is the **g** of all his faithful
Pr 19: 11 is to one's **g** to overlook an offense.
25: 2 It is the **g** of God to conceal
Isa 4: 5 over everything the **g** will be
6: 3 the whole earth is full of his **g**."
24: 16 "**G** to the Righteous One."
24: 23 and before its elders—with great **g**.
26: 15 You have gained **g** for yourself;
35: 2 they will see the **g** of the LORD,
40: 5 And the **g** of the LORD will be
42: 8 I will not yield my **g** to another
42: 12 Let them give **g** to the LORD
43: 7 whom I created for my **g**, whom I
44: 23 Jacob, he displays his **g** in Israel.
48: 11 I will not yield my **g** to another.
66: 18 and they will come and see my **g**.
66: 19 not heard of my fame or seen my **g**.
Eze 1: 28 the likeness of the **g** of the LORD.
10: 4 Then the **g** of the LORD rose
39: 13 and the day I display my **g** will be
43: 2 I saw the **g** of the God of Israel
43: 2 the land was radiant with his **g**.
44: 4 saw the **g** of the LORD filling
Hab 2: 14 of the **g** of the LORD as the waters
3: 3 His **g** covered the heavens and his
Zec 2: 5 LORD, 'and I will be its **g** within.'
Mt 16: 27 in his Father's **g** with his angels,
24: 30 of heaven, with power and great **g**.
25: 31 the Son of Man comes in his **g**,
Mk 8: 38 in his Father's **g** with the holy
13: 26 in clouds with great power and **g**.
Lk 2: 9 and the **g** of the Lord shone around
2: 14 "**G** to God in the highest heaven,
9: 26 of them when he comes in his **g**
9: 26 and in the **g** of the Father
9: 32 they saw his **g** and the two men
19: 38 in heaven and **g** in the highest!"
21: 27 in a cloud with power and great **g**.
24: 26 these things and then enter his **g**?"
Jn 1: 14 We have seen his **g**, the **g** of the
2: 11 through which he revealed his **g**;
5: 44 can you believe since you accept **g**
7: 18 own does so to gain personal **g**,
8: 50 I am not seeking **g** for myself;
8: 54 myself, my **g** means nothing.
11: 4 it is for God's **g** so that God's Son
11: 40 believe, you will see the **g** of God?"
12: 41 said this because he saw Jesus' **g**
15: 8 This is to my Father's **g**, that you
17: 4 I have brought you **g** on earth
17: 5 your presence with the **g** I had
17: 10 **g** has come to me through them.
17: 22 I have given them the **g** that you
17: 24 and to see my **g**, the **g** you have
Ac 7: 2 The God of **g** appeared to our
7: 55 up to heaven and saw the **g** of God,
Ro 1: 23 exchanged the **g** of the immortal
2: 7 persistence in doing good seek **g**,
2: 10 **g**, honor and peace for everyone
3: 7 truthfulness and so increases his **g**,
3: 23 and fall short of the **g** of God,
4: 20 in his faith and gave **g** to God,
8: 17 that we may also share in his **g**.
8: 18 with the **g** that will be revealed
8: 21 and **g** of the children of God.
9: 4 theirs the divine **g**, the covenants,
9: 23 to make the riches of his **g** known
9: 23 he prepared in advance for **g**—
11: 36 To him be the **g** forever! Amen.
15: 17 Therefore I **g** in Christ Jesus in my
16: 27 God be **g** forever through Jesus
1Co 2: 7 for our **g** before time began.
10: 31 do it all for the **g** of God.
11: 7 he is the image and **g** of God;
11: 7 but woman is the **g** of man.
11: 15 a woman has long hair, it is her **g**?
15: 43 sown in dishonor, it is raised in **g**;
2Co 1: 20 is spoken by us to the **g** of God.

2Co 3: 7 came with **g**, so that the Israelites
3: 7 the face of Moses because of its **g**,
3: 10 what was glorious has no **g** now
3: 10 comparison with the surpassing **g**.
3: 11 if what was transitory came with **g**,
3: 18 faces contemplate the Lord's **g**,
3: 18 his image with ever-increasing **g**,
4: 4 gospel that displays the **g** of Christ,
4: 6 the knowledge of God's **g** displayed
4: 15 to overflow to the **g** of God.
4: 17 us an eternal **g** that far outweighs
Gal 1: 5 to whom be **g** for ever and ever.
Eph 1: 12 might be for the praise of his **g**.
1: 14 to the praise of his **g**.
3: 13 for you, which are your **g**.
3: 21 to him be **g** in the church
Php 1: 11 to the **g** and praise of God.
2: 11 is Lord, to the **g** of God the Father.
4: 19 the riches of his **g** in Christ Jesus.
4: 20 To our God and Father be **g** for
Col 1: 27 is Christ in you, the hope of **g**.
3: 4 you also will appear with him in **g**.
1Th 2: 12 calls you into his kingdom and **g**.
2: 19 which we will **g** in the presence
2: 20 Indeed, you are our **g** and joy.
2Th 1: 9 Lord and from the **g** of his might
2: 14 in the **g** of our Lord Jesus Christ.
1Ti 1: 11 to the gospel concerning the **g**
1: 17 be honor and **g** for ever and ever.
3: 16 on in the world, was taken up in **g**.
2Ti 2: 10 is in Christ Jesus, with eternal **g**.
4: 18 To him be **g** for ever and ever.
Titus 2: 13 appearing of the **g** of our great God
Heb 1: 3 The Son is the radiance of God's **g**
2: 7 crowned them with **g** and honor
2: 9 now crowned with **g** and honor
2: 10 many sons and daughters to **g**,
5: 5 on himself the **g** of becoming a
9: 5 ark were the cherubim of the **G**,
13: 21 to whom be **g** for ever and ever.
1Pe 1: 7 **g** and honor when Jesus Christ is
1: 24 all their **g** is like the flowers
4: 11 To him be the **g** and the power
4: 13 overjoyed when his **g** is revealed.
4: 14 for the Spirit of **g** and of God rests
5: 1 will share in the **g** to be revealed:
5: 4 you will receive the crown of **g**
5: 10 you to his eternal **g** in Christ,
2Pe 1: 3 of him who called us by his own **g**
1: 17 and **g** from God the Father
1: 17 came to him from the Majestic **G**,
3: 18 To him be **g** both now and forever!
Jude : 25 to the only God our Savior be **g**,
Rev 1: 6 to him be **g** and power for ever
4: 9 the living creatures give **g**,
4: 11 to receive **g** and honor and power,
5: 12 and honor and **g** and praise!"
5: 13 praise and honor and **g** and power,
7: 12 Praise and **g** and wisdom and
11: 13 and gave **g** to the God of heaven.
14: 7 "Fear God and give him **g**,
15: 4 Lord, and bring **g** to your name?
15: 8 with smoke from the **g** of God
19: 1 Salvation and **g** and power belong
19: 7 rejoice and be glad and give him **g**!
21: 11 It shone with the **g** of God, and its
21: 23 for the **g** of God gives it light,
21: 26 The **g** and honor of the nations will

GLOWING
1Sa 16: 12 He was **g** with health and had a
Eze 8: 2 was as bright as **g** metal.
Rev 1: 15 His feet were like bronze **g**

GLUTTONS* (GLUTTONY)
Pr 23: 21 for drunkards and **g** become poor,
28: 7 of **g** disgraces his father.
Titus 1: 12 always liars, evil brutes, lazy **g**."

GLUTTONY* (GLUTTONS)
Pr 23: 2 to your throat if you are given to **g**.

GNASHING
Mt 8: 12 will be weeping and **g** of teeth."

GNAT* (GNATS)
Mt 23: 24 You strain out a **g** but swallow

GNATS (GNAT)
Ex 8: 16 of Egypt the dust will become **g**."

GOADS
Ecc 12: 11 The words of the wise are like **g**,
Ac 26: 14 hard for you to kick against the **g**.'

GOAL*
Lk 13: 32 on the third day I will reach my **g**.'
Ro 9: 31 have not attained their **g**.
2Co 5: 9 So we make it our **g** to please him,
8: 14 what you need. The **g** is equality,
Php 3: 12 or have already arrived at my **g**,
3: 14 on toward the **g** to win the prize
Col 2: 2 **g** is that they may be encouraged
1Ti 1: 5 The **g** of this command is love,

GOAT (GOATS SCAPEGOAT)
Ge 15: 9 "Bring me a heifer, a **g** and a ram,
30: 32 and every spotted or speckled **g**.
37: 31 slaughtered a **g** and dipped the
Ex 26: 7 "Make curtains of **g** hair
Lev 16: 9 shall bring the **g** whose lot falls
Nu 7: 16 one male **g** for a sin offering;
Isa 11: 6 leopard will lie down with the **g**,
Da 8: 5 a **g** with a prominent horn

GOATS (GOAT)
Nu 7: 17 five male **g** and five male lambs
Mt 25: 32 separates the sheep from the **g**.
Heb 10: 4 of bulls and **g** to take away sins.

GOD (GOD'S GODLINESS GODLY GODS)
Ge 1: 1 beginning **G** created the heavens
1: 2 of **G** was hovering over the waters.
1: 3 And **G** said, "Let there be light,"
1: 7 So **G** made the vault and separated
1: 9 And **G** said, "Let the water under
1: 11 Then **G** said, "Let the land produce
1: 20 And **G** said, "Let the water teem
1: 21 And **G** saw that it was good.
1: 25 And **G** saw that it was good.
1: 26 Then **G** said, "Let us make
1: 27 So **G** created mankind in his own
1: 27 in the image of **G** he created them;
1: 31 **G** saw all that he had made, and it
2: 3 Then **G** blessed the seventh day
2: 7 the LORD **G** formed a man
2: 8 Now the LORD **G** had planted
2: 18 The LORD **G** said, "It is not good
2: 22 the LORD **G** made a woman
3: 1 to the woman, "Did **G** really say,
3: 5 and you will be like **G**,
3: 8 of the LORD **G** as he was walking
3: 9 the LORD **G** called to the man,
3: 21 The LORD **G** made garments
3: 22 And the LORD **G** said, "The man
3: 23 So the LORD **G** banished him
5: 1 he made them in the likeness of **G**.
5: 22 walked faithfully with **G** 300 years
5: 24 Enoch walked faithfully with **G**;
6: 2 sons of **G** saw that the daughters
6: 9 and he walked faithfully with **G**.
6: 12 **G** saw how corrupt the earth had
8: 1 But **G** remembered Noah and all
9: 1 Then **G** blessed Noah and his sons,
9: 6 image of **G** has **G** made mankind.
9: 16 everlasting covenant between **G**
14: 18 He was priest of **G** Most High,
14: 19 be Abram by **G** Most High,
16: 13 "You are the **G** who sees me,"
17: 1 to him and said, "I am **G** Almighty;
17: 7 to be your **G** and the **G** of your
21: 4 him, as **G** commanded him.
21: 6 said, "**G** has brought me laughter,
21: 20 **G** was with the boy as he grew up.
21: 22 "**G** is with you in everything you
21: 33 name of the LORD, the Eternal **G**.
22: 1 Some time later **G** tested Abraham.
22: 8 "**G** himself will provide the lamb
22: 12 Now I know that you fear **G**,
25: 11 death, **G** blessed his son Isaac,
28: 12 the angels of **G** were ascending
28: 17 is none other than the house of **G**;
31: 42 But **G** has seen my hardship
31: 50 that **G** is a witness between you
32: 1 way, and the angels of **G** met him.
32: 28 because you have struggled with **G**
32: 30 "It is because I saw **G** face to face,
33: 11 for **G** has been gracious to me and
35: 1 and build an altar there to **G**,
35: 5 the terror of **G** fell on the towns
35: 10 **G** said to him, "Your name is
35: 11 And **G** said to him, "I am **G**
41: 51 said, "It is because **G** has made me
41: 52 said, "It is because **G** has made me
50: 20 me, but **G** intended it for good
50: 24 But **G** will surely come to your aid
Ex 2: 24 **G** heard their groaning and he
3: 5 "Do not come any closer," **G** said.
3: 6 he said, "I am the **G** of your father, the **G** of Abraham, the **G** of Isaac and the **G** of Jacob."
3: 6 because he was afraid to look at **G**.
3: 12 And **G** said, "I will be with you.
3: 14 **G** said to Moses, "I AM WHO I AM.
4: 27 he met Moses at the mountain of **G**
6: 7 know that I am the LORD your **G**,
8: 10 is no one like the LORD our **G**.
10: 16 sinned against the LORD your **G**
13: 18 So **G** led the people around
15: 2 He is my **G**, and I will praise him,
16: 12 that I am the LORD your **G**.'"
17: 9 with the staff of **G** in my hands."
18: 5 camped near the mountain of **G**.
19: 3 Then Moses went up to **G**,
20: 1 And **G** spoke all these words:
20: 2 "I am the LORD your **G**,
20: 5 the LORD your **G**, am a jealous **G**,
20: 7 the name of the LORD your **G**,
20: 10 is a sabbath to the LORD your **G**.
20: 12 the LORD your **G** is giving you.
20: 19 But do not have **G** speak to us or
20: 20 **G** has come to test you,
22: 20 any **g** other than the LORD must
22: 28 "Do not blaspheme **G** or curse
23: 19 to the house of the LORD your **G**.
31: 18 stone inscribed by the finger of **G**.
34: 6 the compassionate and gracious **G**,
34: 14 Do not worship any other **g**,
34: 14 name is Jealous, is a jealous **G**.
Lev 2: 13 the covenant of your **G** out of your
11: 44 I am the LORD your **G**;
18: 21 not profane the name of your **G**.
19: 2 I, the LORD your **G**, am holy.
20: 7 because I am the LORD your **G**.
21: 6 not profane the name of their **G**.
22: 33 you out of Egypt to be your **G**.
26: 12 walk among you and be your **G**,
Nu 15: 40 and will be consecrated to your **G**.
22: 18 the command of the LORD my **G**.
22: 38 I must speak only what **G** puts
23: 19 **G** is not human, that he should lie,
25: 13 was zealous for the honor of his **G**
Dt 1: 17 anyone, for judgment belongs to **G**.
1: 21 LORD, the **G** of your ancestors,
1: 30 The LORD your **G**, who is going
3: 22 the LORD your **G** himself will
3: 24 For what **g** is there in heaven
4: 24 the LORD your **G** is a consuming fire, a jealous **G**.
4: 29 there you seek the LORD your **G**,
4: 31 the LORD your **G** is a merciful **G**;
4: 39 day that the LORD is **G** in heaven
5: 9 the LORD your **G**, am a jealous **G**,
5: 11 the name of the LORD your **G**,
5: 12 the LORD your **G** has commanded
5: 14 is a sabbath to the LORD your **G**.
5: 15 the LORD your **G** brought you
5: 16 the LORD your **G** is giving you.
5: 24 a person can live even if **G** speaks
5: 26 voice of the living **G** speaking
6: 2 fear the LORD your **G** as long as
6: 4 The LORD our **G**, the LORD is
6: 5 Love the LORD your **G** with all
6: 13 Fear the LORD your **G**, serve him
6: 16 Do not put the LORD your **G**
7: 6 people holy to the LORD your **G**.
7: 6 The LORD your **G** has chosen you
7: 9 that the LORD your **G** is **G**;
7: 12 the LORD your **G** will keep his
7: 19 The LORD your **G** will do
7: 21 is a great and awesome **G**.
8: 5 the LORD your **G** disciplines you.
8: 11 do not forget the LORD your **G**,
8: 18 But remember the LORD your **G**,
9: 10 tablets inscribed by the finger of **G**.
10: 12 what does the LORD your **G** ask
10: 12 but to fear the LORD your **G**,
10: 12 serve the LORD your **G** with all
10: 14 To the LORD your **G** belong
10: 17 For the LORD your **G** is **G** of gods
10: 21 he is your **G**, who performed
11: 1 Love the LORD your **G** and keep
11: 13 to love the LORD your **G**
12: 12 rejoice before the LORD your **G**—
12: 28 in the eyes of the LORD your **G**.
13: 3 The LORD your **G** is testing you
13: 4 It is the LORD your **G** you must
15: 6 the LORD your **G** will bless you
15: 19 the LORD your **G** every firstborn

Dt 16: 11 rejoice before the LORD your **G**
16: 17 the LORD your **G** has blessed you.
18: 13 before the LORD your **G**.
18: 15 The LORD your **G** will raise
19: 9 to love the LORD your **G**
22: 5 the LORD your **G** detests anyone
23: 5 the LORD your **G** loves you.
23: 14 the LORD your **G** moves
23: 21 make a vow to the LORD your **G**,
25: 16 the LORD your **G** detests anyone
26: 5 declare before the LORD your **G**:
29: 13 he may be your **G** as he promised
29: 29 things belong to the LORD our **G**,
30: 2 return to the LORD your **G**
30: 4 the LORD your **G** will gather you
30: 6 The LORD your **G** will circumcise
30: 16 today to love the LORD your **G**,
30: 20 you may love the LORD your **G**,
31: 6 the LORD your **G** goes with you;
32: 3 Oh, praise the greatness of our **G**!
32: 4 A faithful **G** who does no wrong,
33: 27 The eternal **G** is your refuge,
Jos 1: 9 the LORD your **G** will be with you
14: 8 the LORD my **G** wholeheartedly.
14: 9 the LORD my **G** wholeheartedly.'
14: 14 the LORD, the **G** of Israel,
22: 5 to love the LORD your **G**, to walk
22: 22 "The Mighty One, **G**, the LORD!
22: 34 that the LORD is **G**.
23: 8 to hold fast to the LORD your **G**,
23: 11 careful to love the LORD your **G**.
23: 14 the LORD your **G** gave you has
23: 15 the LORD your **G** has promised
24: 19 He is a holy **G**; he is a jealous **G**.
24: 23 to the LORD, the **G** of Israel."
Jdg 5: 3 praise the LORD, the **G** of Israel,
16: 28 Please, **G**, strengthen me just once
Ru 1: 16 be my people and your **G** my **G**.
2: 12 by the LORD, the **G** of Israel,
1Sa 2: 2 there is no Rock like our **G**.
2: 3 for the LORD is a **G** who knows,
2: 25 **G** may mediate for the offender;
10: 26 men whose hearts **G** had touched.
12: 12 the LORD your **G** was your king.
16: 15 evil spirit from **G** is tormenting
17: 26 defy the armies of the living **G**?"
17: 36 defied the armies of the living **G**.
17: 45 the **G** of the armies of Israel,
17: 46 know that there is a **G** in Israel.
23: 16 and helped him find strength in **G**.
28: 15 me, and **G** has departed from me.
30: 6 found strength in the LORD his **G**.
2Sa 7: 22 and there is no **G** but you, as we
7: 23 one nation on earth that **G** went
14: 14 But that is not what **G** desires;
21: 14 **G** answered prayer in behalf
22: 3 my **G** is my rock, in whom I take
22: 31 "As for **G**, his way is perfect:
22: 32 For who is **G** besides the LORD?
22: 33 It is **G** who arms me with strength
22: 47 Exalted be my **G**, the Rock,
1Ki 2: 3 what the LORD your **G** requires:
4: 29 **G** gave Solomon wisdom and very
5: 5 for the Name of the LORD my **G**,
8: 23 there is no **G** like you in heaven
8: 27 "But will **G** really dwell on earth?
8: 60 may know that the LORD is **G**
8: 61 committed to the LORD our **G**,
10: 24 to hear the wisdom **G** had put in
15: 30 of the LORD, the **G** of Israel.
18: 21 If the LORD is **G**, follow him;
18: 36 today that you are **G** in Israel
18: 37 are **G**, and that you are turning
20: 28 Arameans think the LORD is a **g**
2Ki 5: 15 no **G** in all the world except
18: 5 in the LORD, the **G** of Israel.
19: 15 you alone are **G** over all
19: 19 that you alone, LORD, are **G**."
1Ch 12: 18 you, for your **G** will help you."
13: 2 if it is the will of the LORD our **G**,
16: 35 Cry out, "Save us, **G** our Savior;
17: 20 and there is no **G** but you, as we
17: 24 Almighty, the **G** over Israel,
21: 8 Then David said to **G**, "I have
22: 1 of the LORD **G** is to be here,
22: 19 the sanctuary of the LORD **G**,
28: 2 for the footstool of our **G**, and I
28: 9 acknowledge the **G** of your father,
28: 20 for the LORD **G**, my **G**,
29: 1 the one whom **G** has chosen,
29: 2 provided for the temple of my **G**—
1Ch 29: 3 and silver for the temple of my **G**,
29: 10 LORD, the **G** of our father Israel,
29: 13 Now, our **G**, we give you thanks,
29: 16 LORD our **G**, all this abundance
29: 17 my **G**, that you test the heart and
29: 18 the **G** of our fathers Abraham,
2Ch 2: 4 festivals of the LORD our **G**.
5: 14 the LORD filled the temple of **G**.
6: 4 be to the LORD, the **G** of Israel,
6: 14 there is no **G** like you in heaven
6: 18 will **G** really dwell on earth
10: 15 for this turn of events was from **G**,
13: 12 **G** is with us; he is our leader.
15: 3 time Israel was without the true **G**,
15: 12 LORD, the **G** of their ancestors,
15: 15 They sought **G** eagerly, and he was
18: 13 can tell him only what my **G** says."
19: 3 have set your heart on seeking **G**."
19: 7 with the LORD our **G** there is no
20: 6 "LORD, the **G** of our ancestors,
20: 20 Have faith in the LORD your **G**
25: 8 for **G** has the power to help
26: 5 He sought **G** during the days
26: 5 the LORD, **G** gave him success.
30: 9 for the LORD your **G** is gracious
30: 19 sets their heart on seeking **G**—
31: 21 he sought his **G** and worked
32: 31 **G** left him to test him and to know
33: 12 the favor of the LORD his **G**
34: 33 in Israel serve the LORD their **G**.
Ezr 6: 21 to seek the LORD, the **G** of Israel.
7: 18 accordance with the will of your **G**.
7: 23 for the temple of the **G** of heaven.
8: 22 "The gracious hand of our **G** is
8: 31 The hand of our **G** was on us,
9: 6 my **G**, to lift up my face to you,
9: 9 our **G** has not forsaken us in our
9: 13 our **G**, you have punished us less
9: 15 LORD, the **G** of Israel, you are
Ne 1: 5 "LORD, the **G** of heaven,
5: 9 fear of our **G** to avoid the reproach
5: 15 for **G** I did not act like that.
7: 2 feared **G** more than most people
8: 8 from the Book of the Law of **G**,
8: 18 from the Book of the Law of **G**.
9: 5 up and praise the LORD your **G**,
9: 17 But you are a forgiving **G**,
9: 31 you are a gracious and merciful **G**.
9: 32 "Now therefore, our **G**, the great **G**,
10: 29 through Moses the servant of **G**
10: 39 not neglect the house of our **G**."
12: 43 rejoicing because **G** had given
13: 11 is the house of **G** neglected?"
13: 26 was loved by his **G**, and **G** made
13: 31 Remember me with favor, my **G**.
Job 1: 1 he feared **G** and shunned evil.
1: 22 by charging **G** with wrongdoing.
2: 10 Shall we accept good from **G**,
4: 17 mortal be more righteous than **G**?
5: 17 is the one whom **G** corrects;
8: 3 Does **G** pervert justice?
8: 20 "Surely **G** does not reject one who
9: 2 prove their innocence before **G**?
11: 7 you fathom the mysteries of **G**?
12: 13 "To **G** belong wisdom and power;
16: 7 Surely, **G**, you have worn me out;
19: 26 yet in my flesh I will see **G**;
21: 19 '**G** stores up the punishment
21: 22 anyone teach knowledge to **G**,
22: 12 "Is not **G** in the heights of heaven?
22: 13 Yet you say, 'What does **G** know?
22: 21 "Submit to **G** and be at peace
25: 2 "Dominion and awe belong to **G**;
25: 4 a mortal be righteous before **G**?
26: 6 of the dead is naked before **G**;
30: 20 "I cry out to you, **G**, but you do not
31: 6 let **G** weigh me in honest scales
31: 14 will I do when **G** confronts me?
32: 13 let **G**, not a man, refute him.'
33: 14 For **G** does speak—now one way,
33: 26 that person can pray to **G** and find
34: 10 Far be it from **G** to do evil,
34: 12 that **G** would do wrong,
34: 23 **G** has no need to examine people
34: 33 Should **G** then reward you on your
36: 5 "**G** is mighty, but despises no one;
36: 26 How great is **G**—
37: 22 **G** comes in awesome majesty.
Ps 5: 4 you are not a **G** who is pleased
7: 11 **G** is a righteous judge, a **G** who
10: 14 But you, **G**, see the trouble
Ps 14: 5 for **G** is present in the company
18: 2 my **G** is my rock, in whom I take
18: 28 my **G** turns my darkness into light.
18: 30 As for **G**, his way is perfect:
18: 31 For who is **G** besides the LORD?
18: 31 who is the Rock except our **G**?
18: 32 It is **G** who arms me with strength
18: 46 Exalted be **G** my Savior!
19: 1 The heavens declare the glory of **G**;
22: 1 My **G**, my **G**, why have you
22: 10 womb you have been my **G**.
27: 9 me or forsake me, **G** my Savior.
29: 3 the **G** of glory thunders, the LORD
31: 5 deliver me, LORD, my faithful **G**.
31: 14 I say, "You are my **G**."
33: 12 the nation whose **G** is the LORD,
35: 24 your righteousness, LORD my **G**;
37: 31 law of their **G** is in their hearts;
40: 3 mouth, a hymn of praise to our **G**.
40: 8 I desire to do your will, my **G**;
42: 1 so my soul pants for you, my **G**.
42: 2 soul thirsts for **G**, for the living **G**.
42: 2 When can I go and meet with **G**?
42: 5 praise him, my Savior and my **G**.
42: 8 a prayer to the **G** of my life.
42: 11 Put your hope in **G**, for I will
43: 4 with the lyre, O **G**, my **G**.
44: 8 **G** we make our boast all day long,
45: 6 O **G**, will last for ever and ever;
45: 7 therefore **G**, your **G**, has set you
46: 1 **G** is our refuge and strength,
46: 5 **G** is within her, she will not fall;
46: 10 "Be still, and know that I am **G**;
47: 1 shout to **G** with cries of joy.
47: 6 Sing praises to **G**, sing praises;
47: 7 For **G** is the King of all the earth;
48: 9 **G**, we meditate on your unfailing
49: 7 or give to **G** a ransom for them—
50: 2 perfect in beauty, **G** shines forth.
50: 3 **G** comes and will not be silent;
51: 1 O **G**, according to your unfailing
51: 10 O **G**, and renew a steadfast spirit
51: 17 sacrifice, O **G**, is a broken spirit;
53: 2 **G** looks down from heaven on all
53: 2 who understand, any who seek **G**.
54: 4 Surely **G** is my help; the Lord is
55: 19 **G**, who is enthroned from of old,
55: 19 because they have no fear of **G**.
56: 4 In **G**, whose word I praise—in **G** I
56: 10 In **G**, whose word I praise,
56: 13 I may walk before **G** in the light
57: 3 **G** sends forth his love and his
57: 7 My heart, O **G**, is steadfast,
59: 17 you, **G**, are my fortress, my **G**
62: 1 Truly my soul finds rest in **G**;
62: 7 and my honor depend on **G**;
62: 8 hearts to him, for **G** is our refuge.
62: 11 "Power belongs to you, **G**,
63: 1 **G**, are my **G**, earnestly I seek
65: 5 and righteous deeds, **G** our Savior,
66: 1 Shout for joy to **G**, all the earth!
66: 3 Say to **G**, "How awesome are your
66: 5 Come and see what **G** has done,
66: 16 Come and hear, all you who fear **G**;
66: 20 Praise be to **G**, who has not
68: 4 Sing to **G**, sing in praise of his
68: 6 **G** sets the lonely in families,
68: 20 Our **G** is a **G** who saves;
68: 24 the procession of my **G** and King
68: 35 the **G** of Israel gives power
69: 5 You, **G**, know my folly; my guilt is
70: 1 Hasten, O **G**, to save me;
70: 5 come quickly to me, O **G**.
71: 17 my youth, **G**, you have taught
71: 18 my **G**, till I declare your power
71: 19 Who is like you, **G**?
71: 22 harp for your faithfulness, my **G**;
73: 17 till I entered the sanctuary of **G**;
73: 26 but **G** is the strength of my heart
76: 11 Make vows to the LORD your **G**
77: 13 What **g** is as great as our **G**?
77: 14 You are the **G** who performs
78: 19 They spoke against **G**;
79: 9 Help us, **G** our Savior, for the glory
81: 1 Sing for joy to **G** our strength;
82: 1 **G** presides in the great assembly;
84: 2 my flesh cry out for the living **G**.
84: 10 the house of my **G** than dwell
84: 11 For the LORD **G** is a sun
86: 12 you, Lord my **G**, with all my heart;
86: 15 a compassionate and gracious **G**,

Ps 87: 3 things are said of you, city of **G**:
89: 7 of the holy ones **G** is greatly feared;
90: 2 to everlasting you are **G**.
91: 2 fortress, my **G**, in whom I trust."
94: 22 and my **G** the rock in whom I take
95: 7 for he is our **G** and we are
99: 8 you were to Israel a forgiving **G**,
99: 9 for the LORD our **G** is holy.
100: 3 Know that the LORD is **G**.
108: 1 My heart, O **G**, is steadfast;
113: 5 Who is like the LORD our **G**,
115: 3 Our **G** is in heaven;
116: 5 our **G** is full of compassion.
123: 2 our eyes look to the LORD our **G**,
136: 2 Give thanks to the **G** of gods.
136: 26 Give thanks to the **G** of heaven.
139: 17 to me are your thoughts, **G**!
139: 23 Search me, **G**, and know my heart;
143: 10 to do your will, for you are my **G**;
144: 2 He is my loving **G** and my fortress,
147: 1 good it is to sing praises to our **G**,
Pr 3: 4 a good name in the sight of **G**
14: 31 is kind to the needy honors **G**.
25: 2 It is the glory of **G** to conceal
28: 14 one who always trembles before **G**,
30: 5 "Every word of **G** is flawless;
Ecc 2: 26 who pleases him, **G** gives wisdom,
3: 11 no one can fathom what **G** has
3: 13 their toil—this is the gift of **G**.
3: 14 that everything **G** does will endure
3: 14 **G** does it so that people will fear
5: 4 When you make a vow to **G**, do
5: 19 when **G** gives someone wealth
8: 12 go better with those who fear **G**,
11: 5 cannot understand the work of **G**,
12: 7 the spirit returns to **G** who gave it.
12: 13 of the matter: Fear **G** and keep his
Isa 5: 16 the holy **G** will be proved holy
9: 6 Mighty **G**, Everlasting Father,
12: 2 **G** is my salvation; I will trust
25: 9 they will say, "Surely this is our **G**;
28: 11 strange tongues **G** will speak to
29: 23 will stand in awe of the **G** of Israel.
30: 18 For the LORD is a **G** of justice.
35: 4 your **G** will come, he will come
37: 16 you alone are **G** over all
40: 1 comfort my people, says your **G**.
40: 3 in the desert a highway for our **G**.
40: 8 the word of our **G** endures forever."
40: 18 whom, then, will you compare **G**?
40: 28 The LORD is the everlasting **G**,
41: 10 not be dismayed, for I am your **G**.
41: 13 the LORD your **G** who takes hold
43: 10 Before me no **g** was formed,
44: 6 apart from me there is no **G**.
44: 15 also fashions a **g** and worships it;
45: 18 who created the heavens, he is **G**;
48: 17 "I am the LORD your **G**,
52: 7 who say to Zion, "Your **G** reigns!"
52: 12 the **G** of Israel will be your rear
55: 7 and to our **G**, for he will freely
57: 21 says my **G**, "for the wicked."
59: 2 have separated you from your **G**;
60: 19 and your **G** will be your glory.
61: 2 and the day of vengeance of our **G**,
61: 10 my soul rejoices in my **G**.
62: 5 so will your **G** rejoice over you.
Jer 7: 23 I will be your **G** and you will be my
10: 10 But the LORD is the true **G**;
10: 10 he is the living **G**, the eternal
10: 12 **G** made the earth by his power;
23: 23 "Am I only a **G** nearby,"
23: 36 distort the words of the living **G**,
31: 33 I will be their **G**, and they will be
32: 27 the LORD, the **G** of all mankind.
42: 6 we will obey the LORD our **G**,
51: 10 what the LORD our **G** has done.'
51: 56 the LORD is a **G** of retribution;
Eze 28: 13 You were in Eden, the garden of **G**;
34: 31 and I am your **G**,
Da 2: 28 there is a **G** in heaven who reveals
3: 17 the **G** we serve is able to deliver us
3: 29 for no other **g** can save in this
6: 16 "May your **G**, whom you serve
9: 4 the great and awesome **G**,
10: 12 to humble yourself before your **G**,
11: 36 magnify himself above every **g**
11: 36 things against the **G** of gods.
Hos 1: 9 my people, and I am not your **G**.
1: 10 be called 'children of the living **G**.'
4: 6 have ignored the law of your **G**,
Hos 6: 6 of **G** rather than burnt offerings.
9: 8 along with my **G**, is the watchman
12: 6 But you must return to your **G**;
Joel 2: 13 Return to the LORD your **G**, for he
2: 23 rejoice in the LORD your **G**, for he
Am 4: 12 Israel, prepare to meet your **G**."
4: 13 the LORD **G** Almighty is his
Jnh 1: 6 Get up and call on your **g**!
4: 2 a gracious and compassionate **G**,
Mic 6: 8 and to walk humbly with your **G**.
7: 7 **G** my Savior; my **G** will hear me.
7: 18 Who is a **G** like you, who pardons
Na 1: 2 is a jealous and avenging **G**;
Hab 3: 18 I will be joyful in **G** my Savior.
Zep 3: 17 The LORD your **G** is with you,
Zec 14: 5 Then the LORD my **G** will come,
Mal 2: 10 Did not one **G** create us?
2: 16 says the LORD, the **G** of Israel,
3: 8 "Will a mere mortal rob **G**?
Mt 1: 23 (which means "**G** with us").
4: 4 comes from the mouth of **G**.'"
4: 7 'Do not put the Lord your **G**
4: 10 'Worship the Lord your **G**,
5: 8 pure in heart, for they will see **G**.
6: 24 You cannot serve both **G**
19: 6 Therefore what **G** has joined
19: 26 but with **G** all things are possible."
22: 21 Caesar's, and to **G** what is God's."
22: 32 'I am the **G** of Abraham,
22: 32 He is not the **G** of the dead
22: 37 "'Love the Lord your **G** with all
27: 46 (which means "My **G**, my **G**,
Mk 2: 7 Who can forgive sins but **G** alone?"
7: 13 Thus you nullify the word of **G**
10: 6 of creation **G** 'made them male
10: 9 Therefore what **G** has joined
10: 18 "No one is good—except **G** alone.
10: 27 impossible, but not with **G**; all things are possible with **G**."
11: 22 "Have faith in **G**," Jesus answered.
12: 17 Caesar's and to **G** what is God's."
12: 29 The Lord our **G**, the Lord is one.
12: 30 Love the Lord your **G** with all your
15: 34 (which means "My **G**, my **G**,
16: 19 *sat at the right hand of* **G**.
Lk 1: 30 you have found favor with **G**.
1: 37 For no word from **G** will ever fail."
1: 47 my spirit rejoices in **G** my Savior,
2: 14 "Glory to **G** in the highest heaven,
2: 52 and in favor with **G** and man.
4: 8 'Worship the Lord your **G** and
5: 21 Who can forgive sins but **G** alone?"
8: 39 tell how much **G** has done for you."
10: 9 'The kingdom of **G** has come near
10: 27 "'Love the Lord your **G** with all
13: 18 "What is the kingdom of **G** like?
18: 19 "No one is good—except **G** alone.
18: 27 with man is possible with **G**."
20: 25 Caesar's, and to **G** what is God's."
20: 38 He is not the **G** of the dead,
22: 69 at the right hand of the mighty **G**."
Jn 1: 1 and the Word was with **G**, and the Word was **G**.
1: 18 No one has ever seen **G**, but the
1: 29 the Lamb of **G**, who takes away
3: 16 For **G** so loved the world that he
3: 34 the one whom **G** has sent speaks
3: 34 **G** gives the Spirit without limit.
4: 24 **G** is spirit, and his worshipers must
5: 44 glory that comes from the only **G**?
6: 29 answered, "The work of **G** is this:
7: 17 my teaching comes from **G**
8: 42 "If **G** were your Father, you would
8: 42 not come on my own; **G** sent me.
8: 47 belongs to **G** hears what **G** says.
11: 40 you will see the glory of **G**?"
13: 3 that he had come from **G** and was returning to **G**;
13: 31 glorified and **G** is glorified in him.
14: 1 You believe in **G**;
17: 3 the only true **G**, and Jesus Christ,
20: 17 Father, to my **G** and your **G**.'"
20: 28 said to him, "My Lord and my **G**!"
20: 31 the Son of **G**, and that by believing
Ac 2: 11 them declaring the wonders of **G**
2: 24 But **G** raised him from the dead,
2: 33 Exalted to the right hand of **G**,
2: 36 **G** has made this Jesus, whom you
3: 15 but **G** raised him from the dead.
3: 19 turn to **G**, so that your sins may
4: 31 and spoke the word of **G** boldly.
Ac 5: 4 lied just to human beings but to **G**."
5: 29 "We must obey **G** rather than
5: 31 **G** exalted him to his own right
5: 32 whom **G** has given to those who
7: 55 to heaven and saw the glory of **G**,
7: 55 standing at the right hand of **G**.
8: 21 your heart is not right before **G**.
11: 9 impure that **G** has made clean.'
12: 24 the word of **G** continued to spread
13: 32 What **G** promised our ancestors
15: 10 why do you try to test **G** by putting
17: 23 inscription: TO AN UNKNOWN **G**.
17: 30 In the past **G** overlooked such
20: 27 to you the whole will of **G**.
20: 32 "Now I commit you to **G**
24: 16 keep my conscience clear before **G**
Ro 1: 16 because it is the power of **G**
1: 17 righteousness of **G** is revealed—
1: 18 The wrath of **G** is being revealed
1: 24 Therefore **G** gave them over
1: 26 **G** gave them over to shameful
2: 11 For **G** does not show favoritism.
2: 16 **G** judges people's secrets through
3: 4 Let **G** be true, and every human
3: 19 world held accountable to **G**.
3: 23 and fall short of the glory of **G**,
3: 29 Or is **G** the **G** of Jews only?
3: 29 Is he not the **G** of Gentiles too?
4: 3 "Abraham believed **G**, and it was
4: 6 whom **G** credits righteousness
4: 17 the **G** who gives life to the dead
4: 24 whom **G** will credit righteousness
5: 1 **G** through our Lord Jesus Christ,
5: 8 **G** demonstrates his own love for us
6: 22 sin and have become slaves of **G**,
6: 23 the gift of **G** is eternal life in Christ
8: 7 by the flesh is hostile to **G**;
8: 17 heirs of **G** and co-heirs with Christ
8: 28 in all things **G** works for the good
9: 14 then shall we say? Is **G** unjust?
9: 18 Therefore **G** has mercy on whom
10: 9 in your heart that **G** raised him
11: 2 **G** did not reject his people,
11: 22 the kindness and sternness of **G**:
11: 32 For **G** has bound everyone over
13: 1 that which **G** has established.
14: 12 give an account of ourselves to **G**.
16: 20 The **G** of peace will soon crush
1Co 1: 18 being saved it is the power of **G**.
1: 20 not **G** made foolish the wisdom
1: 25 of **G** is wiser than human wisdom,
1: 25 **G** is stronger than human strength.
1: 27 **G** chose the foolish things
1: 27 **G** chose the weak things
2: 9 the things **G** has prepared for those
2: 11 the thoughts of **G** except the Spirit
3: 6 but **G** has been making it grow.
3: 17 temple, **G** will destroy that person;
6: 20 Therefore honor **G** with your
7: 7 of you has your own gift from **G**;
7: 15 **G** has called us to live in peace.
7: 20 they were in when **G** called them.
7: 24 they were in when **G** called them.
8: 3 whoever loves **G** is known by **G**.
8: 8 food does not bring us near to **G**;
10: 13 And **G** is faithful; he will not let
10: 31 you do, do it all for the glory of **G**.
12: 24 But **G** has put the body together,
14: 33 For **G** is not a **G** of disorder
15: 24 over the kingdom to **G** the Father
15: 28 him, so that **G** may be all in all.
15: 34 are some who are ignorant of **G**—
15: 57 But thanks be to **G**! He gives us
2Co 1: 9 not rely on ourselves but on **G**,
2: 14 But thanks be to **G**, who always
2: 15 we are to **G** the pleasing aroma
2: 17 we do not peddle the word of **G**
2: 17 sincerity, as those sent from **G**.
3: 5 our competence comes from **G**.
4: 2 nor do we distort the word of **G**.
4: 7 this all-surpassing power is from **G**
5: 5 us for this very purpose is **G**,
5: 19 that **G** was reconciling the world
5: 20 Be reconciled to **G**.
5: 21 **G** made him who had no sin to be
5: 21 become the righteousness of **G**.
6: 16 we are the temple of the living **G**.
6: 16 I will be their **G**, and they will
9: 7 for **G** loves a cheerful giver.
9: 8 **G** is able to bless you abundantly,
10: 13 of service **G** himself has assigned

Gal 2: 6 **G** does not show favoritism—
3: 5 does **G** give you his Spirit and
3: 6 So also Abraham "believed **G**,
3: 11 on the law is justified before **G**,
3: 26 are all children of **G** through faith,
6: 7 **G** cannot be mocked.
Eph 1: 22 **G** placed all things under his feet
2: 8 yourselves, it is the gift of **G**—
2: 10 **G** prepared in advance for us
2: 22 in which **G** lives by his Spirit.
4: 6 one **G** and Father of all, who is
4: 24 to be like **G** in true righteousness
6: 6 the will of **G** from your heart.
Php 2: 6 being in very nature **G**, did not consider equality with **G**
2: 9 Therefore **G** exalted him
2: 13 for it is **G** who works in you to will
4: 7 And the peace of **G**,
4: 19 And my **G** will meet all your needs
Col 1: 19 For **G** was pleased to have all his
2: 13 **G** made you alive with Christ.
1Th 2: 4 not trying to please people but **G**,
2: 13 also thank **G** continually because,
3: 9 How can we thank **G** enough
4: 7 For **G** did not call us to be impure,
4: 9 yourselves have been taught by **G**
5: 9 For **G** did not appoint us to suffer
1Ti 2: 5 For there is one **G** and one mediator between **G**
4: 4 For everything **G** created is good,
5: 4 for this is pleasing to **G**.
2Ti 1: 6 you to fan into flame the gift of **G**,
Titus 1: 2 life, which **G**, who does not lie,
2: 13 of the glory of our great **G**
Heb 1: 1 In the past **G** spoke to our
3: 4 but **G** is the builder of everything.
4: 4 the seventh day **G** rested from all
4: 12 For the word of **G** is alive
6: 10 **G** is not unjust; he will not forget
6: 18 it is impossible for **G** to lie,
7: 19 by which we draw near to **G**.
7: 25 those who come to **G** through him,
10: 22 let us draw near to **G** with a sincere
10: 31 fall into the hands of the living **G**.
11: 5 because **G** had taken him away."
11: 5 commended as one who pleased **G**.
11: 6 faith it is impossible to please **G**,
12: 7 **G** is treating you as his children.
12: 10 but **G** disciplines us for our good,
12: 29 for our "**G** is a consuming fire."
13: 15 us continually offer to **G** a sacrifice
Jas 1: 13 For **G** cannot be tempted by evil,
1: 27 that **G** our Father accepts as pure
2: 19 You believe that there is one **G**.
2: 23 "Abraham believed **G**, and it was
4: 4 the world becomes an enemy of **G**.
4: 6 "**G** opposes the proud but shows
4: 8 Come near to **G** and he will come
1Pe 1: 23 the living and enduring word of **G**.
2: 20 it, this is commendable before **G**.
3: 18 the unrighteous, to bring you to **G**.
4: 11 who speaks the very words of **G**.
5: 5 "**G** opposes the proud but shows
2Pe 1: 21 from **G** as they were carried along
2: 4 if **G** did not spare angels when they
1Jn 1: 5 him and declare to you: **G** is light;
2: 5 love for **G** is truly made complete
2: 17 does the will of **G** lives forever.
3: 1 we should be called children of **G**!
3: 9 one who is born of **G** will continue
3: 10 we know who the children of **G** are
3: 20 that **G** is greater than our hearts,
4: 7 another, for love comes from **G**.
4: 8 does not love does not know **G**, because **G** is love.
4: 9 This is how **G** showed his love
4: 11 Dear friends, since **G** so loved us,
4: 12 No one has ever seen **G**; but if we
4: 12 **G** lives in us and his love is made
4: 15 that Jesus is the Son of **G**, **G** lives in them and they in **G**.
4: 16 Whoever lives in love lives in **G**,
4: 20 claims to love **G** yet hates a brother
4: 21 Anyone who loves **G** must also
5: 2 by loving **G** and carrying out his
5: 3 In fact, this is love for **G**:
5: 4 born of **G** overcomes the world.
5: 10 believed the testimony **G** has given
5: 14 we have in approaching **G**:
5: 18 was born of **G** keeps them safe,
Rev 4: 8 holy is the Lord **G** Almighty,'
7: 12 strength be to our **G** for ever
7: 17 **G** will wipe away every tear
11: 16 seated on their thrones before **G**,
15: 3 are your deeds, Lord **G** Almighty.
17: 17 For **G** has put it into their hearts
19: 6 For our Lord **G** Almighty reigns.
21: 3 and **G** himself will be with them and be their **G**.

GOD-BREATHED* (BREATH)
2Ti 3: 16 All Scripture is **G** and is useful

GOD-FEARING* (FEAR)
Ac 2: 5 were staying in Jerusalem **G** Jews
10: 2 all his family were devout and **G**;
10: 22 He is a righteous and **G** man,
13: 26 of Abraham and you **G** Gentiles,
13: 50 leaders incited the **G** women
17: 4 as did a large number of **G** Greeks
17: 17 with both Jews and **G** Greeks,

GOD-HATERS* (HATE)
Ro 1: 30 slanderers, **G**, insolent,

GOD'S (GOD)
2Ch 20: 15 For the battle is not yours, but **G**.
Job 33: 6 I am the same as you in **G** sight;
37: 14 stop and consider **G** wonders.
Ps 52: 8 I trust in **G** unfailing love for ever
69: 30 I will praise **G** name in song
Mk 3: 35 Whoever does **G** will is my brother
Jn 10: 36 because I said, 'I am **G** Son'?
Ro 2: 3 think you will escape **G** judgment?
2: 4 that **G** kindness is intended
3: 3 nullify **G** faithfulness?
5: 5 because **G** love has been poured
7: 22 my inner being I delight in **G** law;
9: 16 desire or effort, but on **G** mercy.
11: 29 for **G** gifts and his call are
12: 2 test and approve what **G** will is—
13: 6 for the authorities are **G** servants,
1Co 7: 19 Keeping **G** commands is what
2Co 6: 2 now is the time of **G** favor, now is
Eph 1: 7 with the riches of **G** grace
5: 1 Follow **G** example, therefore,
1Th 4: 3 It is **G** will that you should be
5: 18 for this is **G** will for you in Christ
1Ti 6: 1 so that **G** name and our teaching
2Ti 2: 19 **G** solid foundation stands firm,
Titus 1: 7 an overseer manages **G** household,
Heb 1: 3 The Son is the radiance of **G** glory
9: 24 to appear for us in **G** presence.
11: 3 was formed at **G** command,
1Pe 2: 15 For it is **G** will that by doing good
3: 4 which is of great worth in **G** sight.

GODLESS
Job 20: 5 the joy of the **g** lasts but a moment.
1Ti 6: 20 Turn away from **g** chatter

GODLINESS (GOD)
1Ti 2: 2 quiet lives in all **g** and holiness.
3: 16 mystery from which true **g** springs
4: 8 value, but **g** has value for all things,
6: 5 and who think that **g** is a means
6: 6 **g** with contentment is great gain.
6: 11 and pursue righteousness, **g**, faith,
2Ti 3: 5 a form of **g** but denying its power.
2Pe 1: 6 and to perseverance, **g**;

GODLY (GOD)
2Co 7: 10 **G** sorrow brings repentance
11: 2 jealous for you with a **g** jealousy.
2Ti 3: 12 live a **g** life in Christ Jesus will be
2Pe 3: 11 You ought to live holy and **g** lives

GODS (GOD)
Ex 20: 3 shall have no other **g** before me.
Dt 5: 7 shall have no other **g** before me.
32: 17 They sacrificed to false **g**,
1Ch 16: 26 all the **g** of the nations are idols,
Ps 82: 6 "I said, 'You are "**g**"; you are
106: 37 sons and their daughters to false **g**.
Jn 10: 34 Law, 'I have said you are "**g**"'?
Ac 19: 26 He says that **g** made by human hands are no **g** at all.

GOG
Eze 38: 18 When **G** attacks the land of Israel,
Rev 20: 8 of the earth—**G** and Magog—

GOLD
1Ki 20: 3 'Your silver and **g** are mine,
Job 22: 25 then the Almighty will be your **g**,
23: 10 tested me, I will come forth as **g**.
28: 15 cannot be bought with the finest **g**,
31: 24 "If I have put my trust in **g** or said
Ps 19: 10 They are more precious than **g**,
119:127 more than **g**, more than pure **g**,
Pr 3: 14 and yields better returns than **g**.
22: 1 esteemed is better than silver or **g**.
Hag 2: 8 silver is mine and the **g** is mine,'
Mt 2: 11 and presented him with gifts of **g**,
Rev 3: 18 buy from me **g** refined in the fire,

GOLGOTHA*
Mt 27: 33 a place called **G** (which means
Mk 15: 22 to the place called **G** (which means
Jn 19: 17 (which in Aramaic is called **G**).

GOLIATH
Philistine giant killed by David (1Sa 17; 21:9).

GOMORRAH
Ge 19: 24 burning sulfur on Sodom and **G**—
Mt 10: 15 **G** on the day of judgment than
2Pe 2: 6 and **G** by burning them to ashes,
Jude : 7 Sodom and **G** and the surrounding

GOOD
Ge 1: 4 God saw that the light was **g**,
1: 10 And God saw that it was **g**.
1: 12 And God saw that it was **g**.
1: 18 And God saw that it was **g**.
1: 21 And God saw that it was **g**.
1: 25 And God saw that it was **g**.
1: 31 he had made, and it was very **g**.
2: 9 pleasing to the eye and **g** for food.
2: 9 the tree of the knowledge of **g**
2: 18 "It is not **g** for the man to be alone.
3: 22 like one of us, knowing **g** and evil.
50: 20 God intended it for **g** to
2Ch 7: 3 to the LORD, saying, "He is **g**;
31: 20 doing what was **g** and right
Job 2: 10 Shall we accept **g** from God,
Ps 14: 1 there is no one who does **g**.
34: 8 Taste and see that the LORD is **g**;
34: 14 Turn from evil and do **g**;
37: 3 Trust in the LORD and do **g**;
37: 27 Turn from evil and do **g**;
52: 9 in your name, for your name is **g**.
53: 3 there is no one who does **g**, not
84: 11 no **g** thing does he withhold
86: 5 are forgiving and **g**,
100: 5 For the LORD is **g** and his love
103: 5 your desires with **g** things so
112: 5 **G** will come to those who are
119: 68 You are **g**, and what you do is **g**;
133: 1 How **g** and pleasant it is
145: 9 The LORD is **g** to all;
147: 1 How **g** it is to sing praises to our
Pr 3: 4 and a **g** name in the sight of God
3: 27 Do not withhold **g** from those
11: 27 Whoever seeks **g** finds favor,
13: 21 are rewarded with **g** things.
13: 22 A **g** person leaves an inheritance
14: 22 those who plan what is **g** find love
15: 3 watch on the wicked and the **g**.
15: 23 and how **g** is a timely word!
15: 30 **g** news gives health to the bones.
17: 22 A cheerful heart is **g** medicine,
18: 22 He who finds a wife finds what is **g**
19: 2 Desire without knowledge is not **g**
22: 1 A **g** name is more desirable than
31: 12 She brings him **g**, not harm,
Ecc 12: 14 thing, whether it is **g** or evil.
Isa 5: 20 Woe to those who call evil **g** and **g**
40: 9 You who bring **g** news to Zion,
52: 7 the feet of those who bring **g** news,
61: 1 anointed me to proclaim **g** news
Jer 6: 16 ask where the **g** way is, and walk
13: 23 can you do **g** who are accustomed
Eze 34: 14 will lie down in **g** grazing land,
Mic 6: 8 shown you, O mortal, what is **g**.
Na 1: 15 the feet of one who brings **g** news,
Mt 5: 45 sun to rise on the evil and the **g**,
7: 11 heaven give **g** gifts to those who
7: 17 every **g** tree bears **g** fruit,
7: 18 and a bad tree cannot bear **g** fruit.
12: 35 A **g** man brings **g** things out of the **g** stored up
13: 8 Still other seed fell on **g** soil,
13: 24 is like a man who sowed **g** seed
13: 48 and collected the **g** fish in baskets,
19: 17 "There is only One who is **g**.
22: 10 the bad as well as the **g**,
25: 21 'Well done, **g** and faithful servant!
Mk 1: 15 Repent and believe the **g** news!"
3: 4 to do **g** or to do evil, to save life
4: 8 Still other seed fell on **g** soil.
8: 36 What **g** is it for someone to gain

Mk 10: 18 "No one is **g**—except God alone.
k 2: 10 I bring you **g** news that will cause
3: 9 does not produce **g** fruit will be cut
6: 27 do **g** to those who hate you,
6: 43 "No **g** tree bears bad fruit, nor
6: 45 A **g** man brings **g** things out of the **g** stored up
8: 8 Still other seed fell on **g** soil.
9: 25 What **g** is it for someone to gain
14: 34 "Salt is **g**, but if it loses its
18: 19 "No one is **g**—except God alone.
19: 17 "'Well done, my **g** servant!'
n 10: 11 "I am the **g** shepherd. The **g**
Ro 3: 12 there is no one who does **g**, not
7: 12 is holy, righteous and **g**.
7: 16 want to do, I agree that the law is **g**.
7: 18 I know that **g** itself does not dwell
8: 28 for the **g** of those who love him,
10: 15 feet of those who bring **g** news!"
12: 2 his **g**, pleasing and perfect will.
12: 9 Hate what is evil; cling to what is **g**.
13: 4 is God's servant for your **g**.
16: 19 you to be wise about what is **g**,
1Co 7: 1 "It is **g** for a man not to have sexual
10: 24 No one should seek their own **g**, but the **g** of others.
15: 33 company corrupts **g** character."
2Co 9: 8 you will abound in every **g** work.
Gal 4: 18 provided the purpose is **g**, and to
6: 9 us not become weary in doing **g**,
6: 10 let us do **g** to all people,
Eph 2: 10 in Christ Jesus to do **g** works,
6: 8 each one for whatever **g** they do,
Php 1: 6 he who began a **g** work in you will
Col 1: 10 bearing fruit in every **g** work,
1Th 5: 15 strive to do what is **g** for each other
5: 21 test them all; hold on to what is **g**,
2Th 3: 13 never tire of doing what is **g**.
1Ti 3: 7 have a **g** reputation with outsiders,
4: 4 For everything God created is **g**,
6: 12 Fight the **g** fight of the faith.
6: 18 Command them to do **g**, to be rich in **g** deeds,
2Ti 3: 17 equipped for every **g** work.
4: 7 I have fought the **g** fight, I have
Titus 1: 8 one who loves what is **g**, who is
2: 7 an example by doing what is **g**.
2: 14 his very own, eager to do what is **g**.
Heb 5: 14 to distinguish **g** from evil.
10: 24 on toward love and **g** deeds,
12: 10 but God disciplines us for our **g**,
13: 16 do not forget to do **g** and to share
Jas 4: 17 knows the **g** they ought to do
1Pe 2: 3 you have tasted that the Lord is **g**.
2: 12 Live such **g** lives among the pagans
2: 18 not only to those who are **g**
3: 17 to suffer for doing **g** than for doing

GOODS
Ecc 5: 11 As **g** increase, so do those who

GORGE
Pr 23: 20 wine or **g** themselves on meat,

GOSHEN
Ge 45: 10 You shall live in the region of **G**
Ex 8: 22 deal differently with the land of **G**,

GOSPEL
Mk 16: 15 *preach the g to all creation.*
Ac 14: 7 they continued to preach the **g**.
14: 21 They preached the **g** in that city
Ro 1: 16 For I am not ashamed of the **g**,
15: 16 duty of proclaiming the **g** of God,
15: 20 preach the **g** where Christ was not
1Co 1: 17 to baptize, but to preach the **g**—
9: 12 anything rather than hinder the **g**
9: 14 who preach the **g** should receive their living from the **g**.
9: 16 Woe to me if I do not preach the **g**!
15: 1 to remind you of the **g** I preached
15: 2 By this **g** you are saved, if you hold
2Co 4: 4 light of the **g** that displays the glory
9: 13 your confession of the **g** of Christ,
Gal 1: 7 trying to pervert the **g** of Christ.
Eph 6: 15 that comes from the **g** of peace.
Php 1: 27 a manner worthy of the **g** of Christ.
Col 1: 23 This is the **g** that you heard
1Th 2: 4 by God to be entrusted with the **g**.
2Th 1: 8 not obey the **g** of our Lord Jesus.
2Ti 1: 10 immortality to light through the **g**.
Rev 14: 6 he had the eternal **g** to proclaim

GOSSIP* (GOSSIPS)
Pr 11: 13 A **g** betrays a confidence, but a
16: 28 and a **g** separates close friends.
18: 8 of a **g** are like choice morsels;
20: 19 A **g** betrays a confidence;
26: 20 without a **g** a quarrel dies down.
26: 22 of a **g** are like choice morsels;
2Co 12: 20 slander, **g**, arrogance and disorder.

GOSSIPS* (GOSSIP)
Ro 1: 29 deceit and malice. They are **g**,

GOVERN (GOVERN GOVERNMENT)
Ge 1: 16 the greater light to **g** the day
Job 34: 17 Can someone who hates justice **g**?

GOVERNED (GOVERN)
Ro 8: 6 The mind **g** by the flesh is death,
8: 6 the mind **g** by the Spirit is life

GOVERNMENT (GOVERN)
Isa 9: 6 and the **g** will be on his shoulders.

GRACE* (GRACIOUS)
Ps 45: 2 lips have been anointed with **g**,
Pr 1: 9 They are a garland to **g** your head
3: 22 you, an ornament to **g** your neck.
4: 9 give you a garland to **g** your head
22: 11 speaks with **g** will have the king
Isa 26: 10 But when **g** is shown to the wicked,
Zec 12: 10 of Jerusalem a spirit of **g**
Lk 2: 40 and the **g** of God was on him.
Jn 1: 14 from the Father, full of **g** and truth.
1: 16 we have all received **g** in place of **g** already given.
1: 17 **g** and truth came through Jesus
Ac 4: 33 God's **g** was so powerfully at work
6: 8 a man full of God's **g** and power,
11: 23 saw what the **g** of God had done,
13: 43 them to continue in the **g** of God.
14: 3 message of his **g** by enabling them
14: 26 been committed to the **g** of God
15: 11 We believe it is through the **g** of
15: 40 the believers to the **g** of the Lord.
18: 27 to those who by **g** had believed.
20: 24 to the good news of God's **g**.
20: 32 to God and to the word of his **g**,
Ro 1: 5 Through him we received **g**
1: 7 **G** and peace to you from God our
3: 24 by his **g** through the redemption
4: 16 so that it may be by **g** and may be
5: 2 by faith into this **g** in which we
5: 15 how much more did God's **g**
5: 15 came by the **g** of the one man,
5: 17 God's abundant provision of **g**
5: 20 increased, **g** increased all the more,
5: 21 **g** might reign through
6: 1 on sinning so that **g** may increase?
6: 14 are not under the law, but under **g**.
6: 15 are not under the law but under **g**?
11: 5 there is a remnant chosen by **g**.
11: 6 if by **g**, then it cannot be based
11: 6 were, **g** would no longer be **g**.
12: 3 by the **g** given me I say to every
12: 6 according to the **g** given to each
15: 15 because of the **g** God gave me
16: 20 The **g** of our Lord Jesus be
1Co 1: 3 **G** and peace to you from God our
1: 4 you because of his **g** given you
3: 10 By the **g** God has given me, I laid
15: 10 by the **g** of God I am what I am,
15: 10 his **g** to me was not without effect.
15: 10 but the **g** of God that was with me.
16: 23 The **g** of the Lord Jesus be
2Co 1: 2 **G** and peace to you from God our
1: 12 on worldly wisdom but on God's **g**.
4: 15 so that the **g** that is reaching more
6: 1 you not to receive God's **g** in vain.
8: 1 about the **g** that God has given
8: 6 to completion this act of **g** on your
8: 7 you also excel in this **g** of giving.
8: 9 you know the **g** of our Lord Jesus
9: 14 surpassing **g** God has given you.
12: 9 to me, "My **g** is sufficient for you,
13: 14 May the **g** of the Lord Jesus Christ,
Gal 1: 3 **G** and peace to you from God our
1: 6 called you to live in the **g** of Christ
1: 15 womb and called me by his **g**,
2: 9 they recognized the **g** given to me.
2: 21 I do not set aside the **g** of God,
3: 18 God in his **g** gave it to Abraham
5: 4 you have fallen away from **g**.
6: 18 The **g** of our Lord Jesus Christ be
Eph 1: 2 **G** and peace to you from God our
1: 6 to the praise of his glorious **g**,
1: 7 with the riches of God's **g**
2: 5 it is by **g** you have been saved.
2: 7 the incomparable riches of his **g**,
2: 8 For it is by **g** you have been saved,
3: 2 of God's **g** that was given to me
3: 7 of God's **g** given me through
3: 8 Lord's people, this **g** was given me:
4: 7 of us **g** has been given as Christ
6: 24 **G** to all who love our Lord Jesus
Php 1: 2 **G** and peace to you from God our
1: 7 all of you share in God's **g** with me.
4: 23 The **g** of the Lord Jesus Christ be
Col 1: 2 **G** and peace to you from God our
1: 6 it and truly understood God's **g**.
4: 6 conversation be always full of **g**,
4: 18 **G** be with you.
1Th 1: 1 **G** and peace to you.
5: 28 The **g** of our Lord Jesus Christ be
2Th 1: 2 **G** and peace to you from God
1: 12 according to the **g** of our God
2: 16 **g** gave us eternal encouragement
3: 18 The **g** of our Lord Jesus Christ be
1Ti 1: 2 **G**, mercy and peace from God
1: 14 The **g** of our Lord was poured
6: 21 from the faith. **G** be with you all.
2Ti 1: 2 **G**, mercy and peace from God
1: 9 because of his own purpose and **g**.
1: 9 This **g** was given us in Christ Jesus
2: 1 be strong in the **g** that is in Christ
4: 22 with your spirit. **G** be with you all.
Titus 1: 4 **G** and peace from God the Father
2: 11 For the **g** of God has appeared
3: 7 having been justified by his **g**,
3: 15 us in the faith. **G** be with you all.
Phm : 3 **G** and peace to you from God our
: 25 The **g** of the Lord Jesus Christ be
Heb 2: 9 the **g** of God he might taste death
4: 16 approach God's throne of **g**
4: 16 **g** to help us in our time of need.
10: 29 who has insulted the Spirit of **g**?
12: 15 no one falls short of the **g** of God
13: 9 our hearts to be strengthened by **g**,
13: 25 **G** be with you all.
Jas 4: 6 But he gives us more **g**. That is why
1Pe 1: 2 **G** and peace be yours in
1: 10 spoke of the **g** that was to come
1: 13 set your hope on the **g** to be
4: 10 of God's **g** in its various forms.
5: 10 And the God of all **g**, who called
5: 12 that this is the true **g** of God.
2Pe 1: 2 **G** and peace be yours in
3: 18 grow in the **g** and knowledge of
2Jn : 3 **G**, mercy and peace from God
Jude : 4 who pervert the **g** of our God
Rev 1: 4 **G** and peace to you from him who
22: 21 The **g** of the Lord Jesus be

GRACIOUS (GRACE)
Ex 34: 6 the compassionate and **g** God,
Nu 6: 25 face shine on you and be **g** to you;
Ne 9: 17 God, **g** and compassionate,
Ps 67: 1 May God be **g** to us and bless us
Pr 16: 21 and **g** words promote instruction.
16: 24 **G** words are a honeycomb,
Isa 30: 18 the LORD longs to be **g** to you;

GRAIN
Lev 2: 1 anyone brings a **g** offering
Ecc 11: 1 Ship your **g** across the sea;
Lk 17: 35 women will be grinding **g** together;
1Co 9: 9 an ox while it is treading out the **g**."

GRANDCHILDREN (CHILD)
1Ti 5: 4 But if a widow has children or **g**,

GRANDMOTHER (MOTHER)
2Ti 1: 5 which first lived in your **g** Lois

GRANT (GRANTED)
Ps 20: 5 May the LORD **g** all your
51: 12 salvation and **g** me a willing spirit,

GRANTED (GRANT)
Pr 10: 24 what the righteous desire will be **g**.
Mt 15: 28 Your request is **g**."
Php 1: 29 For it has been **g** to you on behalf

GRAPES
Nu 13: 23 bearing a single cluster of **g**.
Jer 31: 29 'The parents have eaten sour **g**,
Eze 18: 2 "'The parents eat sour **g**,
Mt 7: 16 people pick **g** from thornbushes,
Rev 14: 18 earth's vine, because its **g** are ripe."

GRASS
Ps 103: 15 The life of mortals is like **g**,
Isa 40: 6 "All people are like **g**, and all their
Mt 6: 30 that is how God clothes the **g**
1Pe 1: 24 the **g** withers and the flowers fall,

GRASSHOPPERS
Nu 13: 33 We seemed like **g** in our own eyes,

GRATIFY* (GRATITUDE)
Ro 13: 14 how to **g** the desires of the flesh.
Gal 5: 16 and you will not **g** the desires

GRATITUDE (GRATIFY)
Col 3: 16 to God with **g** in your hearts.

GRAVE (GRAVES)
Nu 19: 16 who touches a human bone or a **g**,
Dt 34: 6 day no one knows where his **g** is.
Ps 5: 9 Their throat is an open **g**;
Pr 7: 27 Her house is a highway to the **g**,
Hos 13: 14 Where, O **g**, is your destruction?
Jn 11: 44 "Take off the **g** clothes and let him

GRAVES (GRAVE)
Eze 37: 12 I am going to open your **g** and
Jn 5: 28 are in their **g** will hear his voice
Ro 3: 13 "Their throats are open **g**;

GRAY
Pr 16: 31 **G** hair is a crown of splendor;
20: 29 **g** hair the splendor of the old.

GREAT (GREATER GREATEST GREATNESS)
Ge 12: 2 "I will make you into a **g** nation,
12: 2 I will make your name **g**, and you
Ex 32: 11 brought out of Egypt with **g** power
Nu 14: 19 In accordance with your **g** love,
Dt 4: 32 Has anything so **g** as this ever
10: 17 gods and Lord of lords, the **g** God,
29: 28 **g** wrath the LORD uprooted them
Jos 7: 9 will you do for your own **g** name?"
Jdg 16: 5 you the secret of his **g** strength
2Sa 7: 22 "How **g** you are,
22: 36 your help has made me **g**.
24: 14 of the LORD, for his mercy is **g**;
1Ch 17: 19 made known all these **g** promises.
Ps 18: 35 your help has made me **g**.
19: 11 in keeping them there is **g** reward.
40: 16 always say, "The LORD is **g**!"
47: 2 the **g** King over all the earth.
57: 10 For **g** is your love,
70: 4 always say, "The LORD is **g**!"
89: 1 sing of the LORD's **g** love forever;
103: 11 so **g** is his love for those who fear
108: 4 For **g** is your love, higher than
117: 2 For **g** is his love toward us,
119:165 **G** peace have those who love your
145: 3 **G** is the LORD and most worthy
Pr 22: 1 is more desirable than **g** riches;
23: 24 of a righteous child has **g** joy;
Isa 42: 21 his righteousness to make his law **g**
Jer 27: 5 With my **g** power and outstretched
32: 19 **g** are your purposes and mighty
La 3: 23 **g** is your faithfulness.
Da 9: 4 "Lord, the **g** and awesome God,
Joel 2: 11 The day of the LORD is **g**;
2: 20 Surely he has done **g** things!
Zep 1: 14 The **g** day of the LORD is near—
Mal 1: 11 name will be **g** among the nations,
4: 5 prophet Elijah to you before that **g**
Mt 20: 26 become **g** among you must be your
Mk 10: 43 become **g** among you must be your
Lk 6: 23 because **g** is your reward in heaven.
6: 35 Then your reward will be **g**, and
21: 27 in a cloud with power and **g** glory.
Eph 1: 19 his incomparably **g** power for us
2: 4 But because of his **g** love for us,
1Ti 6: 6 with contentment is **g** gain.
Titus 2: 13 of the glory of our **g** God
Heb 2: 3 if we ignore so **g** a salvation?
1Jn 3: 1 See what **g** love the Father has
Rev 6: 17 For the **g** day of their wrath has
20: 11 I saw a **g** white throne and him

GREATER (GREAT)
Mt 11: 11 has not risen anyone **g** than John
12: 6 something **g** than the temple is
12: 41 now something **g** than Jonah is
12: 42 now something **g** than Solomon is
Mk 12: 31 is no commandment **g** than these."
Jn 1: 50 You will see **g** things than that."
3: 30 He must become **g**; I must become
14: 12 will do even **g** things than these,
15: 13 **G** love has no one than this:
1Co 12: 31 Now eagerly desire the **g** gifts.
2Co 3: 11 how much **g** is the glory
Heb 3: 3 worthy of **g** honor than Moses,
7: 7 doubt the lesser is blessed by the **g**.
11: 26 as of **g** value than the treasures
1Jn 3: 20 know that God is **g** than our hearts
4: 4 is in you is **g** than the one who is

GREATEST (GREAT)
Mt 22: 38 is the first and **g** commandment.
23: 11 The **g** among you will be your
Lk 9: 48 least among you all who is the **g**."
1Co 13: 13 But the **g** of these is love.

GREATNESS* (GREAT)
Ex 15: 7 "In the **g** of your majesty you
Dt 3: 24 to show to your servant your **g**
32: 3 Oh, praise the **g** of our God!
1Ch 29: 11 the **g** and the power and the glory
2Ch 9: 6 not even half the **g** of your wisdom
Est 10: 2 a full account of the **g** of Mordecai,
Ps 145: 3 his **g** no one can fathom.
150: 2 praise him for his surpassing **g**.
Isa 9: 7 Of the **g** of his government and
63: 1 forward in the **g** of his strength?
Eze 38: 23 And so I will show my **g** and my
Da 4: 22 your **g** has grown until it reaches
5: 18 Nebuchadnezzar sovereignty and **g**
7: 27 **g** of all the kingdoms under heaven
Mic 5: 4 his **g** will reach to the ends
Lk 9: 43 were all amazed at the **g** of God.

GREED (GREEDY)
Lk 12: 15 your guard against all kinds of **g**;
Ro 1: 29 wickedness, evil, **g** and depravity.
Eph 5: 3 or of **g**, because these are improper
Col 3: 5 desires and **g**, which is idolatry.
2Pe 2: 14 they are experts in **g**—

GREEDY (GREED)
Pr 15: 27 The **g** bring ruin to their
1Co 6: 10 thieves nor the **g** nor drunkards
Eph 5: 5 No immoral, impure or **g** person—

GREEKS
1Co 1: 22 signs and **G** look for wisdom,

GREEN
Ps 23: 2 makes me lie down in **g** pastures,

GREW (GROW)
Lk 1: 80 the child **g** and became strong
2: 52 And Jesus **g** in wisdom and stature,
Ac 16: 5 in the faith and **g** daily in numbers.

GRIEF (GRIEFS GRIEVE GRIEVED)
Ps 10: 14 you consider their **g** and take it
Pr 10: 1 foolish son brings **g** to his mother.
14: 13 ache, and rejoicing may end in **g**.
17: 21 To have a fool for a child brings **g**;
Ecc 1: 18 the more knowledge, the more **g**.
La 3: 32 Though he brings **g**, he will show
Jn 16: 20 grieve, but your **g** will turn to joy.
1Pe 1: 6 have had to suffer **g** in all kinds

GRIEFS* (GRIEF)
1Ti 6: 10 pierced themselves with many **g**.

GRIEVANCE
Col 3: 13 of you has a **g** against someone.

GRIEVE (GRIEF)
Eph 4: 30 do not **g** the Holy Spirit of God,
1Th 4: 13 so that you do not **g** like the rest

GRIEVED (GRIEF)
Isa 63: 10 they rebelled and **g** his Holy Spirit.

GRINDING
Lk 17: 35 women will be **g** grain together;

GROAN (GROANING GROANS)
Ro 8: 23 **g** inwardly as we wait eagerly
2Co 5: 4 in this tent, we **g** and are burdened,

GROANING (GROAN)
Ex 2: 24 God heard their **g** and he
Eze 21: 7 they ask you, 'Why are you **g**?'
Ro 8: 22 the whole creation has been **g** as

GROANS (GROAN)
Ro 8: 26 for us through wordless **g**.

GROUND
Ge 1: 10 God called the dry **g** "land,"
3: 17 it,' "Cursed is the **g** because of you;
4: 10 blood cries out to me from the **g**.
Ex 3: 5 where you are standing is holy **g**."
15: 19 walked through the sea on dry **g**.
Isa 53: 2 shoot, and like a root out of dry **g**.
Mt 10: 29 to the **g** outside your Father's care.
25: 25 out and hid your gold in the **g**.
Jn 8: 6 *write on the **g** with his finger.*
Eph 6: 13 you may be able to stand your **g**,

GROW (FULL-GROWN GREW GROWING GROWS)
Pr 13: 11 money little by little makes it **g**.
20: 13 not love sleep or you will **g** poor;
Isa 40: 31 they will run and not **g** weary,
Mt 6: 28 See how the flowers of the field **g**.
1Co 3: 6 it, but God has been making it **g**.
2Pe 3: 18 But **g** in the grace and knowledge

GROWING (GROW)
Lk 13: 6 "A man had a fig tree **g** in his
Col 1: 6 and **g** throughout the whole world
1: 10 work, **g** in the knowledge of God,
2Th 1: 3 so, because your faith is **g** more

GROWS (GROW)
Eph 4: 16 **g** and builds itself up in love,
Col 2: 19 sinews, **g** as God causes it to grow.

GRUMBLE (GRUMBLED GRUMBLERS GRUMBLING)
1Co 10: 10 do not **g**, as some of them did—
Jas 5: 9 Don't **g** against one another,

GRUMBLED (GRUMBLE)
Ex 15: 24 So the people **g** against Moses,
Nu 14: 29 census and who has **g** against me.

GRUMBLERS* (GRUMBLE)
Jude : 16 people are **g** and faultfinders;

GRUMBLING (GRUMBLE)
Jn 6: 43 "Stop **g** among yourselves,"
Php 2: 14 everything without **g** or arguing,
1Pe 4: 9 to one another without **g**.

GUARANTEEING* (GUARANTOR)
2Co 1: 22 as a deposit, **g** what is to come.
5: 5 as a deposit, **g** what is to come.
Eph 1: 14 is a deposit **g** our inheritance until

GUARANTOR* (GUARANTEEING)
Heb 7: 22 Jesus has become the **g** of a better

GUARD (GUARDED GUARDIAN-REDEEMER GUARDIAN)
1Sa 2: 9 He will **g** the feet of his faithful
Ps 141: 3 Set a **g** over my mouth, LORD;
Pr 2: 11 you, and understanding will **g** you.
4: 13 let it go; **g** it well, for it is your life.
4: 23 Above all else, **g** your heart,
7: 2 **g** my teachings as the apple of your
13: 3 Those who **g** their lips preserve
21: 23 Those who **g** their mouths and
Isa 52: 12 God of Israel will be your rear **g**.
Mk 13: 33 Be on **g**! Be alert! You do not know
Lk 12: 1 "Be on your **g** against the yeast
12: 15 Be on your **g** against all kinds
Ac 20: 31 So be on your **g**!
1Co 16: 13 Be on your **g**; stand firm
Php 4: 7 will **g** your hearts and your minds
1Ti 6: 20 **g** what has been entrusted to your
2Ti 1: 14 **G** the good deposit that was

GUARDED (GUARD)
Eze 44: 15 and who **g** my sanctuary

GUARDIAN-REDEEMER (GUARD)
Ru 3: 9 since you are a **g** of our family."
4: 14 has not left you without a **g**.

GUARDIAN (GUARD)
Eze 28: 14 You were anointed as a **g** cherub,
Gal 3: 24 law was our **g** until Christ came

GUEST (GUEST)
Lk 2: 7 there was no **g** room available

GUIDANCE (GUIDE)
Pr 1: 5 and let the discerning get **g**—
11: 14 For lack of **g** a nation falls,
24: 6 Surely you need **g** to wage war,
1Co 12: 28 of **g**, and of different kinds

GUIDE (GUIDANCE GUIDED GUIDES)
Ex 13: 21 of cloud to **g** them on their way
15: 13 In your strength you will **g** them
Ne 9: 19 cloud did not fail to **g** them on
Ps 25: 5 **G** me in your truth and teach me,
48: 14 he will be our **g** even to the end.
67: 4 and **g** the nations of the earth.
73: 24 You **g** me with your counsel,
139: 10 even there your hand will **g** me,
Pr 6: 22 When you walk, they will **g** you;
Isa 58: 11 The LORD will **g** you always;
Jn 16: 13 he will **g** you into all the truth.

GUIDED (GUIDE)
Ps 107: 30 he **g** them to their desired haven.

GUIDES (GUIDE)
Ps 23: 3 He **g** me along the right paths
25: 9 He **g** the humble in what is right
Pr 11: 3 integrity of the upright **g** them,
Mt 23: 16 "Woe to you, blind **g**! You say,
23: 24 You blind **g**! You strain out a gnat

GUILT (GUILTY)
Lev 5: 15 It is a **g** offering.
Ps 32: 5 And you forgave the **g** of my sin.

Ps 38: 4 My **g** has overwhelmed me like
Isa 6: 7 your **g** is taken away and your sin
Jer 2: 22 stain of your **g** is still before me,"
Eze 18: 19 'Why does the son not share the **g**

GUILTY (GUILT)
Ex 23: 1 Do not help a **g** person by being
34: 7 does not leave the **g** unpunished;
Job 10: 2 Do not declare me **g**, but tell me
Mk 3: 29 they are **g** of an eternal sin."
Jn 8: 46 Can any of you prove me **g** of sin?
1Co 11: 27 in an unworthy manner will be **g**
Heb 10: 2 would no longer have felt **g** for
10: 22 to cleanse us from a **g** conscience
Jas 2: 10 at just one point is **g** of breaking all

GULLIBLE* (GULLIBLE)
2Ti 3: 6 and gain control over **g** women,

GULP*
Pr 21: 20 olive oil, but fools **g** theirs down.

HABAKKUK*
Prophet to Judah (Hab 1:1; 3:1).

HABIT
1Ti 5: 13 they get into the **h** of being idle
Heb 10: 25 as some are in the **h** of doing,

HADAD
Edomite adversary of Solomon (1Ki 11:14–25).

HADES*
Mt 11: 23 No, you will go down to **H**.
16: 18 the gates of **H** will not overcome it.
Lk 10: 15 No, you will go down to **H**.
16: 23 In **H**, where he was in torment,
Rev 1: 18 I hold the keys of death and **H**.
6: 8 **H** was following close behind him.
20: 13 and **H** gave up the dead that were
20: 14 **H** were thrown into the lake of fire.

HAGAR
Servant of Sarah, wife of Abraham, mother of Ishmael (Ge 16:1–6; 25:12). Driven away by Sarah while pregnant (Ge 16:5–16); after birth of Isaac (Ge 21:9–21; Gal 4:21–31).

HAGGAI*
Post-exilic prophet who encouraged re-building of the temple (Ezr 5:1; 6:14; Hag 1–2).

HAIL
Ex 9: 19 because the **h** will fall on every
Rev 8: 7 there came **h** and fire mixed

HAIR (HAIRS HAIRY)
Lev 19: 27 "'Do not cut the **h** at the sides
Nu 6: 5 they must let their **h** grow long.
2Sa 18: 9 Absalom's **h** got caught in the tree.
Pr 16: 31 Gray **h** is a crown of splendor;
20: 29 gray **h** the splendor of the old.
Lk 7: 44 tears and wiped them with her **h**.
21: 18 not a **h** of your head will perish.
Jn 11: 2 and wiped his feet with her **h**.)
12: 3 feet and wiped his feet with her **h**.
1Co 11: 6 might as well have her **h** cut off;
11: 14 teach you that if a man has long **h**,
11: 15 but that if a woman has long **h**,
Rev 1: 14 The **h** on his head was white like

HAIRS (HAIR)
Mt 10: 30 even the very **h** of your head are all
Lk 12: 7 the very **h** of your head are all

HAIRY (HAIR)
Ge 27: 11 brother Esau is a **h** man while I

HALF
Ex 30: 13 This **h** shekel is an offering
Jos 8: 33 **h** of them in front of Mount Ebal,
1Ki 3: 25 child in two and give **h** to one and **h** to the other."
10: 7 Indeed, not even **h** was told me;
Est 5: 3 Even up to **h** the kingdom, it will
Da 7: 25 for a time, times and **h** a time.
Mk 6: 23 give you, up to **h** my kingdom."

HALF-TRIBE (TRIBE)
Nu 32: 33 the **h** of Manasseh son of Joseph

HALL
Eze 41: 1 the man brought me to the main **h**

HALLELUJAH*
Rev 19: 1 multitude in heaven shouting: "**H**!
19: 3 And again they shouted: "**H**!
19: 4 And they cried: "Amen, **H**!"
19: 6 peals of thunder, shouting: "**H**!

HALLOWED* (HOLY)
Mt 6: 9 Father in heaven, **h** be your name,
Lk 11: 2 "'Father, **h** be your name,

HALT
Job 38: 11 here is where your proud waves **h**'?

HAM
Son of Noah (Ge 5:32; 1Ch 1:4), father of Canaan (Ge 9:18; 10:6–20; 1Ch 1:8–16). Saw Noah's nakedness (Ge 9:20–27).

HAMAN
Agagite nobleman honored by Xerxes (Est 3:1–2). Plotted to exterminate the Jews because of Mordecai (Est 3:3–15). Forced to honor Mordecai (Est 5–6). Plot exposed by Esther (Est 5:1–8; 7:1–8). Hanged (Est 7:9–10).

HAMPERED*
Pr 4: 12 you walk, your steps will not be **h**;

HAND (HANDED HANDFUL HANDIWORK HANDS OPENHANDED)
Ge 24: 2 had, "Put your **h** under my thigh.
47: 29 eyes, put your **h** under my thigh
Ex 13: 3 you out of it with a mighty **h**.
15: 6 Your right **h**, LORD, was majestic
33: 22 with my **h** until I have passed by.
Dt 12: 7 everything you have put your **h** to,
1Ki 8: 42 mighty **h** and your outstretched
13: 4 stretched out his **h** from the altar
1Ch 29: 14 you only what comes from your **h**.
29: 16 Holy Name comes from your **h**,
2Ch 6: 15 with your **h** you have fulfilled it—
Ne 4: 17 did their work with one **h**
Job 40: 4 I put my **h** over my mouth.
Ps 16: 8 With him at my right **h**, I will not
32: 4 and night your **h** was heavy on me;
37: 24 the LORD upholds him with his **h**.
44: 3 it was your right **h**, your arm,
45: 9 at your right **h** is the royal bride
63: 8 your right **h** upholds me.
75: 8 In the **h** of the LORD is a cup full
91: 7 ten thousand at your right **h**, but it
98: 1 his right **h** and his holy arm have
109: 31 stands at the right **h** of the needy,
110: 1 "Sit at my right **h** until I make your
137: 5 may my right **h** forget its skill.
139: 10 even there your **h** will guide me,
145: 16 You open your **h** and satisfy
Pr 27: 16 the wind or grasping oil with the **h**.
Ecc 9: 10 Whatever your **h** finds to do, do it
Isa 11: 8 child will put its **h** into the viper's
40: 12 the waters in the hollow of his **h**,
40: 12 his **h** marked off the heavens?
41: 13 God who takes hold of your right **h**
44: 5 still others will write on their **h**,
48: 13 my right **h** spread out the heavens;
64: 8 we are all the work of your **h**.
La 3: 3 has turned his **h** against me again
Da 10: 10 A **h** touched me and set me
Jnh 4: 11 who cannot tell their right **h**
Hab 3: 4 rays flashed from his **h**, where his
Mt 5: 30 And if your right **h** causes you
6: 3 not let your left **h** know what your right **h** is doing,
12: 10 a man with a shriveled **h** was there.
18: 8 If your **h** or your foot causes you
22: 44 my right **h** until I put your enemies
26: 64 at the right **h** of the Mighty One
Mk 3: 1 a man with a shriveled **h** was there.
9: 43 If your **h** causes you to stumble,
12: 36 my right **h** until I put your enemies
16: 19 *sat at the right **h** of God.*
Lk 6: 6 there whose right **h** was shriveled.
20: 42 said to my Lord: "Sit at my right **h**
22: 69 at the right **h** of the mighty God."
Jn 10: 28 one will snatch them out of my **h**.
20: 27 Reach out your **h** and put it into
Ac 7: 55 standing at the right **h** of God.
1Co 12: 15 say, "Because I am not a **h**, I do not
Heb 1: 13 "Sit at my right **h** until I make your

HANDED (HAND)
1Ti 1: 20 whom I have **h** over to Satan to be

HANDFUL (HAND)
Ecc 4: 6 Better one **h** with tranquillity than

HANDIWORK (HAND)
Eph 2: 10 For we are God's **h**,

HANDLE (HANDLES)
Col 2: 21 "Do not **h**! Do not taste!

HANDLES (HANDLE)
2Ti 2: 15 who correctly **h** the word of truth.

HANDS (HAND)
Ge 27: 22 Jacob, but the **h** are the **h** of Esau."
Ex 17: 11 As long as Moses held up his **h**,
29: 10 sons shall lay their **h** on its head.
Dt 6: 8 Tie them as symbols on your **h**
Jdg 7: 6 of them drank from cupped **h**,
2Ki 11: 12 and the people clapped their **h**
2Ch 6: 4 **h** has fulfilled what he promised
Ps 22: 16 they pierce my **h** and my feet.
24: 4 The one who has clean **h** and a
31: 5 Into your **h** I commit my spirit;
31: 15 My times are in your **h**;
47: 1 Clap your **h**, all you nations;
63: 4 in your name I will lift up my **h**.
Pr 10: 4 Lazy **h** make for poverty,
21: 25 him, because his **h** refuse to work.
31: 13 and flax and works with eager **h**.
31: 20 and extends her **h** to the needy.
Ecc 5: 15 toil that they can carry in their **h**.
10: 18 because of idle **h**, the house leaks.
Isa 35: 3 Strengthen the feeble **h**,
49: 16 you on the palms of my **h**;
55: 12 trees of the field will clap their **h**.
65: 2 out my **h** to an obstinate people,
La 3: 41 hearts and our **h** to God in heaven,
Lk 18: 15 for him to place his **h** on them.
23: 46 into your **h** I commit my spirit."
Ac 6: 6 prayed and laid their **h** on them.
8: 18 at the laying on of the apostles' **h**,
13: 3 they placed their **h** on them and
19: 6 When Paul placed his **h** on them,
28: 8 placed his **h** on him and healed
1Th 4: 11 business and work with your **h**,
1Ti 2: 8 lifting up holy **h** without anger
4: 14 body of elders laid their **h** on you.
5: 22 not be hasty in the laying on of **h**,
2Ti 1: 6 you through the laying on of my **h**.
Heb 6: 2 the laying on of **h**, the resurrection
Rev 13: 16 to receive a mark on their right **h**

HANDSOME*
Ge 39: 6 Now Joseph was well-built and **h**,
1Sa 9: 2 **h** a young man as could be found
16: 12 a fine appearance and **h** features.
17: 42 glowing with health and **h**, and he
2Sa 14: 25 for his **h** appearance as Absalom.
1Ki 1: 6 also very **h** and was born next
SS 1: 16 How **h** you are, my beloved!
Eze 23: 6 all of them **h** young men,
23: 12 horsemen, all **h** young men.
23: 23 Assyrians with them, **h** young men
Da 1: 4 men without any physical defect, **h**,
Zec 11: 13 **h** price at which they valued me!

HANG (HANGED HANGING HUNG)
Mt 22: 40 and the Prophets **h** on these two

HANGED* (HANG)
2Sa 17: 23 house in order and then **h** himself.
Mt 27: 5 Then he went away and **h** himself.

HANGING (HANG)
Ac 10: 39 They killed him by **h** him

HANNAH*
Wife of Elkanah, mother of Samuel (1Sa 1). Prayer at dedication of Samuel (1Sa 2:1–10). Blessed (1Sa 2:18–21).

HAPPIER* (HAPPY)
Ecc 4: 2 already died, are **h** than the living,
Mt 18: 13 he is **h** about that one sheep than
1Co 7: 40 she is **h** if she stays as she is—

HAPPINESS* (HAPPY)
Dt 24: 5 bring **h** to the wife he has married.
Est 8: 16 For the Jews it was a time of **h**
Job 7: 7 my eyes will never see **h** again.
Ecc 2: 26 knowledge and **h**, but to the sinner
Mt 25: 21 Come and share your master's **h**!'
25: 23 Come and share your master's **h**!'

HAPPY* (HAPPIER HAPPINESS)
Ge 30: 13 Then Leah said, "How **h** I am!
30: 13 The women will call me **h**."
1Ki 4: 20 ate, they drank and they were **h**.
10: 8 How **h** your people must be! How **h** your officials,
2Ch 9: 7 How **h** your people must be! How **h** your officials,
Est 5: 9 Haman went out that day **h**
Ps 68: 3 may they be **h** and joyful.
113: 9 home as a **h** mother of children.
137: 8 **h** is the one who repays you
137: 9 **H** is the one who seizes your
Pr 15: 13 A **h** heart makes the face cheerful,
Ecc 3: 12 better for people than to be **h**
5: 19 their lot and be **h** in their toil—
7: 14 When times are good, be **h**;
11: 9 young, be **h** while you are young,

Jnh 4: 6 Jonah was very **h** about the plant.
Zec 8: 19 occasions and **h** festivals for Judah.
1Co 7: 30 who are **h**, as if they were not;
2Co 7: 9 yet now I am **h**, not because you
7: 13 delighted to see how **h** Titus was,
Jas 5: 13 Is anyone **h**? Let them sing songs

HARD (HARDEN HARDENED HARDENING HARDENS HARDER HARDSHIP HARDSHIPS)
Ge 18: 14 Is anything too **h** for the LORD?
1Ki 10: 1 to test Solomon with **h** questions.
Pr 14: 23 All **h** work brings a profit, but
Jer 32: 17 Nothing is too **h** for you.
Zec 7: 12 They made their hearts as **h** as flint
Mt 19: 23 it is **h** for someone who is rich
Mk 10: 5 "It was because your hearts were **h**
Jn 6: 60 disciples said, "This is a **h** teaching.
Ac 20: 35 of **h** work we must help the weak,
26: 14 It is **h** for you to kick against
Ro 16: 12 those women who work **h**
16: 12 woman who has worked very **h**
1Co 4: 12 We work **h** with our own hands.
2Co 6: 5 in **h** work, sleepless nights
1Th 5: 12 those who work **h** among you,
Rev 2: 2 **h** work and your perseverance.

HARDEN (HARD)
Ex 4: 21 I will **h** his heart so that he will not
Ps 95: 8 "Do not **h** your hearts as you did
Ro 9: 18 he hardens whom he wants to **h**.
Heb 3: 8 do not **h** your hearts as you did

HARDENED (HARD)
Ex 10: 20 But the LORD **h** Pharaoh's heart,
Jn 12: 40 their eyes and **h** their hearts,

HARDENING* (HARD)
Ro 11: 25 Israel has experienced a **h** in part
Eph 4: 18 them due to the **h** of their hearts.

HARDENS* (HARD)
Pr 28: 14 but whoever **h** their heart falls
Ro 9: 18 he **h** whom he wants to harden.

HARDER (HARD)
1Co 15: 10 No, I worked **h** than all of them—
2Co 11: 23 I have worked much **h**,

HARDHEARTED* (HEART)
Dt 15: 7 do not be **h** or tightfisted toward

HARDSHIP (HARD)
Ro 8: 35 Shall trouble or **h** or persecution
1Co 13: 3 give over my body to **h** that I may
2Ti 4: 5 endure **h**, do the work
Heb 12: 7 Endure **h** as discipline;

HARDSHIPS (HARD)
Ac 14: 22 "We must go through many **h**
2Co 6: 4 in troubles, **h** and distresses;
12: 10 in insults, in **h**, in persecutions,
Rev 2: 3 and have endured **h** for my name,

HARM
1Ch 16: 22 do my prophets no **h**."
Ps 105: 15 do my prophets no **h**."
121: 6 the sun will not **h** you by day,
Pr 3: 29 not plot **h** against your neighbor,
8: 36 who fail to find me **h** themselves;
12: 21 No **h** overtakes the righteous,
31: 12 good, not **h**, all the days of her life.
Jer 10: 5 they can do no **h** nor can they do
29: 11 to prosper you and not to **h** you,
Ro 13: 10 Love does no **h** to a neighbor.
1Co 11: 17 meetings do more **h** than good.
1Jn 5: 18 and the evil one cannot **h** them.

HARMONY*
Zec 6: 13 there will be **h** between the two.'
Ro 12: 16 Live in **h** with one another.
2Co 6: 15 What **h** is there between Christ

HARP (HARPS)
Ps 33: 2 Praise the LORD with the **h**;
98: 5 music to the LORD with the **h**,
150: 3 praise him with the **h** and lyre,
Rev 5: 8 Each one had a **h** and they were

HARPS (HARP)
Ps 137: 2 on the poplars we hung our **h**,

HARSH
Pr 15: 1 wrath, but a **h** word stirs up anger.
Col 2: 23 and their **h** treatment of the body,
3: 19 wives and do not be **h** with them.
1Pe 2: 18 but also to those who are **h**.

HARVEST (HARVESTERS)
Ge 8: 22 seedtime and **h**, cold and heat,
Ex 23: 16 "Celebrate the Festival of **H**
Dt 16: 15 God will bless you in all your **h**
Pr 10: 5 sleeps during **h** is a disgraceful
Jer 8: 20 "The **h** is past, the summer has
Joel 3: 13 Swing the sickle, for the **h** is ripe.
Mt 9: 37 "The **h** is plentiful but the workers
Lk 10: 2 He told them, "The **h** is plentiful,
10: 2 send out workers into his **h** field.
Jn 4: 35 'It's still four months until **h**'?
4: 35 the fields! They are ripe for **h**.
1Co 9: 11 if we reap a material **h** from you?
2Co 9: 10 seed and will enlarge the **h** of your
Gal 6: 9 at the proper time we will reap a **h**
Heb 12: 11 it produces a **h** of righteousness
Jas 3: 18 in peace reap a **h** of righteousness.
Rev 14: 15 come, for the **h** of the earth is ripe."

HARVESTERS (HARVEST)
Ru 2: 3 and began to glean behind the **h**.

HASTE (HASTEN HASTY)
Ex 12: 11 Eat it in **h**; it is the LORD's
Pr 21: 5 lead to profit as surely as **h** leads
29: 20 you see someone who speaks in **h**?

HASTEN (HASTE)
Ps 70: 1 **H**, O God, to save me;
119: 60 I will **h** and not delay to obey your

HASTY* (HASTE)
Pr 19: 2 how much more will **h** feet miss
Ecc 5: 2 do not be **h** in your heart to utter
1Ti 5: 22 Do not be **h** in the laying

HATE (GOD-HATERS HATED HATES HATING HATRED)
Lev 19: 17 "'Do not **h** a fellow Israelite
Ps 5: 5 You **h** all who do wrong;
36: 2 too much to detect or **h** their sin.
45: 7 righteousness and **h** wickedness;
97: 10 those who love the LORD **h** evil,
119:104 therefore I **h** every wrong path.
119:163 I **h** and detest falsehood but I love
139: 21 Do I not **h** those who **h** you, LORD,
Pr 8: 13 To fear the LORD is to **h** evil; I **h**
9: 8 rebuke mockers or they will **h** you;
13: 5 The righteous **h** what is false,
25: 17 much of you, and they will **h** you.
29: 10 The bloodthirsty **h** a person
Ecc 3: 8 a time to love and a time to **h**,
Isa 61: 8 I **h** robbery and wrongdoing.
Eze 35: 6 Since you did not **h** bloodshed,
Am 5: 15 **H** evil, love good;
Mt 5: 43 your neighbor and **h** your enemy.'
Lk 6: 22 Blessed are you when people **h**
6: 27 do good to those who **h** you,
14: 26 and does not **h** father and mother,
Ro 12: 9 **H** what is evil; cling to what is

HATED (HATE)
Mal 1: 3 Esau I have **h**, and I have turned
Mt 10: 22 be **h** by everyone because of me,
Jn 15: 18 keep in mind that it **h** me first.
Ro 9: 13 "Jacob I loved, but Esau I **h**."
Eph 5: 29 all, no one ever **h** their own body,
Heb 1: 9 righteousness and **h** wickedness;

HATES (HATE)
Pr 6: 16 There are six things the LORD **h**,
13: 24 spares the rod **h** their children,
15: 27 but the one who **h** bribes will live.
26: 28 A lying tongue **h** those it hurts,
Mal 2: 16 "The man who **h** and divorces his
Jn 3: 20 Everyone who does evil **h** the light,
12: 25 while anyone who **h** their life in
1Jn 2: 9 to be in the light but **h** a brother
4: 20 claims to love God yet **h** a brother

HATING* (HATE)
Titus 3: 3 being hated and **h** one another.
Jude : 23 **h** even the clothing stained

HATRED (HATE)
Pr 10: 12 **H** stirs up conflict, but love covers
15: 17 love than a fattened calf with **h**.

HAUGHTY
Pr 6: 17 **h** eyes, a lying tongue,
16: 18 destruction, a **h** spirit before a fall.
18: 12 Before a downfall the heart is **h**,

HAVEN
Ps 107: 30 he guided them to their desired **h**.

HAY
1Co 3: 12 costly stones, wood, **h** or straw,

HEAD (HEADS HOTHEADED)
Ge 3: 15 he will crush your **h**, and you will
Nu 6: 5 no razor may be used on their **h**.
Jdg 16: 17 If my **h** were shaved, my strength
1Sa 9: 2 he was a **h** taller than anyone else.
Ps 23: 5 You anoint my **h** with oil;
133: 2 is like precious oil poured on the **h**,
Pr 10: 6 Blessings crown the **h**
25: 22 will heap burning coals on his **h**,
Isa 59: 17 the helmet of salvation on his **h**;
Eze 33: 4 their blood will be on their own **h**.
Mt 8: 20 of Man has no place to lay his **h**."
Jn 19: 2 crown of thorns and put it on his **h**
Ro 12: 20 will heap burning coals on his **h**."
1Co 11: 3 the **h** of every man is Christ,
11: 3 and the **h** of the woman is man,
11: 3 and the **h** of Christ is God.
11: 5 her **h** uncovered dishonors her **h**—
12: 21 And the **h** cannot say to the feet,
Eph 1: 22 him to be **h** over everything
5: 23 the husband is the **h** of the wife as Christ is the **h** of the church,
Col 1: 18 And he is the **h** of the body,
2Ti 4: 5 you, keep your **h** in all situations,
Rev 14: 14 man with a crown of gold on his **h**
19: 12 fire, and on his **h** are many crowns.

HEADS (HEAD)
Lev 26: 13 you to walk with **h** held high.
Ps 22: 7 they hurl insults, shaking their **h**.
24: 7 Lift up your **h**, you gates;
Isa 35: 10 everlasting joy will crown their **h**.
51: 11 everlasting joy will crown their **h**.
Mt 27: 39 insults at him, shaking their **h**
Lk 21: 28 stand up and lift up your **h**,
Ac 18: 6 "Your blood be on your own **h**!
Rev 4: 4 and had crowns of gold on their **h**.

HEAL* (HEALED HEALING HEALS)
Nu 12: 13 the LORD, "Please, God, **h** her!"
Dt 32: 39 I have wounded and I will **h**, and
2Ki 20: 5 and seen your tears; I will **h** you.
20: 8 the sign that the LORD will **h** me
2Ch 7: 14 their sin and will **h** their land.
Job 5: 18 he injures, but his hands also **h**.
Ps 6: 2 **h** me, LORD, for my bones are
41: 4 **h** me, for I have sinned against
Ecc 3: 3 a time to kill and a time to **h**,
Isa 19: 22 he will strike them and **h** them.
19: 22 respond to their pleas and **h** them.
57: 18 seen their ways, but I will **h** them;
57: 19 "And I will **h** them."
Jer 17: 14 **H** me, LORD, and I will be healed;
30: 17 you to health and **h** your wounds,'
33: 6 I will **h** my people and will let
La 2: 13 as deep as the sea. Who can **h** you?
Hos 5: 13 cure you, not able to **h** your sores.
6: 1 torn us to pieces but he will **h** us;
7: 1 whenever I would **h** Israel, the sins
14: 4 "I will **h** their waywardness
Na 3: 19 Nothing can **h** you; your wound is
Zec 11: 16 **h** the injured, or feed the healthy,
Mt 8: 7 to him, "Shall I come and **h** him?"
10: 1 to **h** every disease and sickness.
10: 8 **H** the sick, raise the dead,
12: 10 "Is it lawful to **h** on the Sabbath?"
13: 15 and turn, and I would **h** them.'
17: 16 but they could not **h** him."
Mk 3: 2 if he would **h** him on the Sabbath.
6: 5 on a few sick people and **h** them.
Lk 4: 23 'Physician, **h** yourself!'
5: 17 Lord was with Jesus to **h** the sick.
6: 7 see if he would **h** on the Sabbath.
7: 3 him to come and **h** his servant.
8: 43 years, but no one could **h** her.
9: 2 kingdom of God and to **h** the sick.
10: 9 **H** the sick who are there and tell
14: 3 "Is it lawful to **h** on the Sabbath
Jn 4: 47 begged him to come and **h** his son,
12: 40 and I would **h** them."
Ac 4: 30 Stretch out your hand to **h**
28: 27 and turn, and I would **h** them.'

HEALED* (HEAL)
Ge 20: 17 and God **h** Abimelek, his wife
Ex 21: 19 see that the victim is completely **h**.
Lev 13: 37 in it, the affected person is **h**.
14: 3 If they have been **h** of their defiling
Jos 5: 8 were in camp until they were **h**.
1Sa 6: 3 Then you will be **h**, and you will
2Ki 2: 21 'I have **h** this water.
2Ch 30: 20 heard Hezekiah and **h** the people.
Ps 30: 2 to you for help, and you **h** me.
107: 20 He sent out his word and **h** them;
Isa 6: 10 their hearts, and turn and be **h**."
53: 5 him, and by his wounds we are **h**.
Jer 14: 19 afflicted us so that we cannot be **h**?
17: 14 Heal me, LORD, and I will be **h**;

er 51: 8 for her pain; perhaps she can be **h**.
51: 9 "'We would have **h** Babylon, but she cannot be **h**;
Eze 30: 21 It has not been bound up to be **h**
34: 4 the weak or **h** the sick
Hos 11: 3 did not realize it was I who **h** them.
Mt 4: 24 and the paralyzed; and he **h** them.
8: 8 the word, and my servant will be **h**.
8: 13 his servant was **h** at that moment.
8: 16 with a word and **h** all the sick.
9: 21 I only touch his cloak, I will be **h**."
9: 22 he said, "your faith has **h** you."
9: 22 the woman was **h** at that moment.
12: 15 him, and he **h** all who were ill.
12: 22 and Jesus **h** him, so that he could
14: 14 on them and **h** their sick.
14: 36 and all who touched it were **h**.
15: 28 daughter was **h** at that moment.
15: 30 them at his feet; and he **h** them.
17: 18 boy, and he was **h** at that moment.
19: 2 followed him, and he **h** them there.
21: 14 him at the temple, and he **h** them.
Mk 1: 34 and Jesus **h** many who had various
3: 10 For he had **h** many, so that those
5: 23 hands on her so that she will be **h**
5: 28 I just touch his clothes, I will be **h**."
5: 34 "Daughter, your faith has **h** you.
6: 13 sick people with oil and **h** them.
6: 56 and all who touched it were **h**.
10: 52 said Jesus, "your faith has **h** you."
Lk 4: 40 his hands on each one, he **h** them.
5: 15 him and to be **h** of their sicknesses.
6: 18 him and to be **h** of their diseases.
7: 7 the word, and my servant will be **h**.
8: 47 and how she had been instantly **h**.
8: 48 "Daughter, your faith has **h** you.
8: 50 just believe, and she will be **h**."
9: 11 and **h** those who needed healing.
9: 42 **h** the boy and gave him back to his
13: 14 Indignant because Jesus had **h**
13: 14 So come and be **h** on those days,
14: 4 he **h** him and sent him on his way.
17: 15 when he saw he was **h**, came back,
18: 42 your faith has **h** you."
22: 51 touched the man's ear and **h** him.
Jn 5: 10 said to the man who had been **h**,
5: 13 The man who was **h** had no idea
Ac 3: 16 him that has completely **h** him,
4: 9 and are being asked how he was **h**,
4: 10 that this man stands before you **h**.
4: 14 who had been **h** standing there
4: 22 who was miraculously **h** was over
5: 16 spirits, and all of them were **h**.
8: 7 were paralyzed or lame were **h**.
14: 9 him, saw that he had faith to be **h**
28: 8 his hands on him and **h** him.
Heb 12: 13 may not be disabled, but rather **h**.
Jas 5: 16 each other so that you may be **h**.
1Pe 2: 24 "by his wounds you have been **h**."
Rev 13: 3 but the fatal wound had been **h**.
13: 12 whose fatal wound had been **h**.

HEALING* (HEAL)
2Ch 28: 15 food and drink, and **h** balm.
Pr 12: 18 but the tongue of the wise brings **h**.
13: 17 but a trustworthy envoy brings **h**.
16: 24 to the soul and **h** to the bones.
Isa 58: 8 and your **h** will quickly appear;
Jer 8: 15 for a time of **h** but there is only
8: 22 is there no **h** for the wound of my
14: 19 for a time of **h** but there is only
30: 12 is incurable, your injury beyond **h**.
30: 13 remedy for your sore, no **h** for you.
33: 6 I will bring health and **h** to it;
46: 11 there is no **h** for you.
Eze 47: 12 for food and their leaves for **h**."
Mal 4: 2 righteousness will rise with **h** in its
Mt 4: 23 and **h** every disease and sickness
9: 35 of the kingdom and **h** every disease
Lk 6: 19 coming from him and **h** them all.
9: 6 news and **h** people everywhere.
9: 11 and healed those who needed **h**.
13: 32 out demons and **h** people today
Jn 6: 2 he had performed by **h** the sick.
7: 23 me for **h** a man's whole body
Ac 10: 38 **h** all who were under the power
1Co 12: 9 to another gifts of **h** by that one
12: 28 miracles, then gifts of **h**, of helping,
12: 30 Do all have gifts of **h**? Do all speak
Rev 22: 2 the tree are for the **h** of the nations.

HEALS* (HEAL)
Ex 15: 26 for I am the LORD, who **h** you."
Lev 13: 18 has a boil on their skin and it **h**,
Ps 103: 3 your sins and **h** all your diseases,
147: 3 He **h** the brokenhearted and binds
Isa 30: 26 and **h** the wounds he inflicted.
Ac 9: 34 said to him, "Jesus Christ **h** you.

HEALTH* (HEALTHIER HEALTHY)
1Sa 16: 12 He was glowing with **h** and had
17: 42 glowing with **h** and handsome,
25: 6 Good **h** to you and your household
25: 6 And good **h** to all that is yours!
Ps 38: 3 wrath there is no **h** in my body;
38: 7 there is no **h** in my body.
Pr 3: 8 This will bring **h** to your body
4: 22 them and **h** to one's whole body.
15: 30 good news gives **h** to the bones.
Isa 38: 16 You restored me to **h** and let me
Jer 30: 17 I will restore you to **h** and heal
33: 6 I will bring **h** and healing to it;
3Jn : 2 I pray that you may enjoy good **h**

HEALTHIER* (HEALTH)
Da 1: 15 end of the ten days they looked **h**

HEALTHY* (HEALTH)
Ge 41: 5 Seven heads of grain, **h** and good,
41: 7 of grain swallowed up the seven **h**,
Ps 73: 4 their bodies are **h** and strong.
Zec 11: 16 or feed the **h**, but will eat the meat
Mt 6: 22 If your eyes are **h**, your whole body
9: 12 "It is not the **h** who need a doctor,
Mk 2: 17 "It is not the **h** who need a doctor,
Lk 5: 31 "It is not the **h** who need a doctor,
11: 34 When your eyes are **h**, your whole

HEAP
Pr 25: 22 you will **h** burning coals on his
Ro 12: 20 you will **h** burning coals on his

HEAR (HEARD HEARING HEARS)
Ex 15: 14 The nations will **h** and tremble;
22: 27 I will **h**, for I am compassionate.
Nu 14: 13 the Egyptians will **h** about it!
Dt 1: 16 time, "**H** the disputes between your
4: 36 heaven he made you **h** his voice
6: 4 **H**, O Israel: The LORD our God,
19: 20 The rest of the people will **h** of this
31: 13 law, must **h** it and learn to fear
Jos 7: 9 of the country will **h** about this
1Ki 8: 30 **H** from heaven, your dwelling
8: 30 and when you **h**, forgive.
2Ki 19: 16 Give ear, LORD, and **h**;
2Ch 7: 14 then I will **h** from heaven, and I
Job 31: 35 ("Oh, that I had someone to **h** me!
Ps 94: 9 he who fashioned the ear not **h**?
95: 7 if only you would **h** his voice,
Ecc 7: 21 or you may **h** your servant cursing
Isa 21: 3 I am staggered by what I **h**, I am
29: 18 day the deaf will **h** the words
30: 21 your ears will **h** a voice behind you,
51: 7 "**H** me, you who know what is
59: 1 to save, nor his ear too dull to **h**.
65: 24 they are still speaking I will **h**.
Jer 5: 21 see, who have ears but do not **h**:
Eze 33: 7 **h** the word I speak and give them
37: 4 bones, **h** the word of the LORD!
Mt 11: 5 the deaf **h**, the dead are raised,
11: 15 Whoever has ears, let them **h**.
13: 17 to **h** what you **h** but did not **h** it.
Mk 12: 29 Jesus, "is this: '**H**, O Israel:
Lk 7: 22 the deaf **h**, the dead are raised,
Jn 8: 47 The reason you do not **h** is that
Ac 13: 7 because he wanted to **h** the word
13: 44 whole city gathered to **h** the word
17: 32 "We want to **h** you again on this
Ro 2: 13 is not those who **h** the law who are
10: 14 how can they **h** without someone
2Ti 4: 3 what their itching ears want to **h**.
Heb 3: 7 "Today, if you **h** his voice,
Rev 1: 3 blessed are those who **h** it and take

HEARD (HEAR)
Ex 2: 24 God **h** their groaning and he
Dt 4: 32 has anything like it ever been **h** of?
2Sa 7: 22 as we have **h** with our own ears.
Job 42: 5 My ears had **h** of you but now my
Isa 40: 21 Have you not **h**? Has it not been
40: 28 Have you not **h**? The LORD is
66: 8 Who has ever **h** of such things?
Jer 18: 13 Who has ever **h** anything like this?
Da 10: 12 words were **h**, and I have come
12: 8 I **h**, but I did not understand.
Hab 3: 16 I **h** and my heart pounded, my lips
Mt 5: 21 "You have **h** that it was said
5: 27 "You have **h** that it was said,
Mt 5: 33 you have **h** that it was said
5: 38 "You have **h** that it was said,
5: 43 "You have **h** that it was said,
Lk 12: 3 the dark will be **h** in the daylight,
Jn 8: 26 what I have **h** from him I tell
Ac 2: 6 because each one **h** their own
1Co 2: 9 what no ear has **h**, and what no
2Co 12: 4 and **h** inexpressible things,
1Th 2: 13 which you **h** from us, you accepted
2Ti 1: 13 What you **h** from me, keep as
Jas 1: 25 not forgetting what they have **h**,
Rev 22: 8 am the one who **h** and saw these

HEARING (HEAR)
Isa 6: 9 "'Be ever **h**, but never
Mt 13: 14 "'You will be ever **h** but never
Mk 4: 12 ever **h** but never understanding;
Ac 28: 26 say, "You will be ever **h** but never
Ro 10: 17 faith comes from **h** the message,
1Co 12: 17 where would the sense of **h** be?

HEARS (HEAR)
Jn 5: 24 whoever **h** my word and believes
1Jn 5: 14 according to his will, he **h** us.
Rev 3: 20 If anyone **h** my voice and opens

HEART (BROKENHEARTED FAINTHEARTED HARDHEARTED HEART'S HEARTACHE HEARTS KINDHEARTED WHOLEHEARTED WHOLEHEARTEDLY)
Ge 6: 5 of the human **h** was only evil all
Ex 4: 21 I will harden his **h** so that he will
25: 2 everyone whose **h** prompts them
35: 21 and whose **h** moved them came
Lev 19: 17 not hate a fellow Israelite in your **h**.
Dt 4: 9 from your **h** as long as you live.
4: 29 him if you seek him with all your **h**
6: 5 LORD your God with all your **h**
10: 12 LORD your God with all your **h**
11: 13 and to serve him with all your **h**
13: 3 you love him with all your **h**
15: 10 and do so without a grudging **h**;
26: 16 observe them with all your **h**
29: 18 you today whose **h** turns away
30: 2 obey him with all your **h**
30: 6 you may love him with all your **h**
30: 10 LORD your God with all your **h**
Jos 22: 5 and to serve him with all your **h**
23: 14 You know with all your **h** and soul
1Sa 10: 9 God changed Saul's **h**, and all these
12: 20 serve the LORD with all your **h**.
12: 24 serve him faithfully with all your **h**;
13: 14 sought out a man after his own **h**
14: 7 I am with you **h** and soul."
16: 7 but the LORD looks at the **h**."
17: 32 "Let no one lose **h** on account
1Ki 2: 4 faithfully before me with all their **h**
3: 9 So give your servant a discerning **h**
3: 12 give you a wise and discerning **h**,
8: 48 turn back to you with all their **h**
9: 3 eyes and my **h** will always be there.
9: 4 me faithfully with integrity of **h**
10: 24 the wisdom God had put in his **h**.
11: 4 his wives turned his **h** after other
11: 4 his **h** was not fully devoted
14: 8 and followed me with all his **h**,
15: 14 Asa's **h** was fully committed
2Ki 22: 19 Because your **h** was responsive
23: 3 decrees with all his **h** and all his
1Ch 28: 9 for the LORD searches every **h**
2Ch 6: 38 turn back to you with all their **h**
7: 16 eyes and my **h** will always be there.
15: 12 ancestors, with all their **h** and soul.
15: 17 Asa's **h** was fully committed
17: 6 His **h** was devoted to the ways
22: 9 sought the LORD with all his **h**."
34: 31 decrees with all his **h** and all his
36: 13 hardened his **h** and would not turn
Ezr 1: 5 everyone whose **h** God had moved
Ne 4: 6 the people worked with all their **h**.
Job 19: 27 How my **h** yearns within me!
22: 22 and lay up his words in your **h**.
37: 1 "At this my **h** pounds and leaps
Ps 9: 1 to you, LORD, with all my **h**;
14: 1 says in his **h**, "There is no God."
16: 9 Therefore my **h** is glad and my
19: 14 this meditation of my **h** be pleasing
20: 4 he give you the desire of your **h**
24: 4 who has clean hands and a pure **h**,
26: 2 me, examine my **h** and my mind;
37: 4 will give you the desires of your **h**.
44: 21 since he knows the secrets of the **h**?
45: 1 My **h** is stirred by a noble theme as

Ps 51: 10 Create in me a pure **h**, O God,
51: 17 a broken and contrite **h** you, God,
53: 1 says in his **h**, "There is no God."
66: 18 If I had cherished sin in my **h**,
73: 1 Israel, to those who are pure in **h**.
73: 26 My flesh and my **h** may fail,
86: 11 give me an undivided **h**, that I may
90: 12 that we may gain a **h** of wisdom.
97: 11 and joy on the upright in **h**.
108: 1 My **h**, O God, is steadfast;
109: 22 and my **h** is wounded within me.
111: 1 LORD with all my **h** in the council
119: 2 and seek him with all their **h**—
119: 10 I seek you with all my **h**; do not let
119: 11 in my **h** that I might not sin against
119: 30 I have set my **h** on your laws.
119: 34 your law and obey it with all my **h**.
119: 36 Turn my **h** toward your statutes
119: 58 sought your face with all my **h**;
119: 69 I keep your precepts with all my **h**.
119:111 they are the joy of my **h**.
119:112 My **h** is set on keeping your
119:145 I call with all my **h**;
125: 4 to those who are upright in **h**.
138: 1 praise you, LORD, with all my **h**;
139: 23 Search me, God, and know my **h**;
Pr 2: 2 applying your **h** to understanding
3: 1 but keep my commands in your **h**,
3: 3 write them on the tablet of your **h**.
3: 5 Trust in the LORD with all your **h**
4: 4 hold of my words with all your **h**;
4: 21 sight, keep them within your **h**;
4: 23 guard your **h**, for everything you
6: 21 Bind them always on your **h**;
7: 3 write them on the tablet of your **h**.
10: 8 The wise in **h** accept commands,
13: 12 Hope deferred makes the **h** sick,
14: 13 Even in laughter the **h** may ache,
14: 30 A **h** at peace gives life to the body,
15: 13 A happy **h** makes the face cheerful,
15: 15 the cheerful **h** has a continual feast.
15: 28 The **h** of the righteous weighs its
15: 30 eyes brings joy to the **h**, and good
17: 22 A cheerful **h** is good medicine,
20: 9 can say, "I have kept my **h** pure;
22: 11 One who loves a pure **h** and who
22: 17 apply your **h** to what I teach,
22: 18 when you keep them in your **h**
23: 15 if your **h** is wise, then my **h** will be
23: 19 and set your **h** on the right path:
23: 26 give me your **h** and let your eyes
24: 17 stumble, do not let your **h** rejoice,
27: 19 the face, so one's life reflects the **h**.
Ecc 3: 11 also set eternity in the human **h**;
5: 2 your **h** to utter anything before God.
8: 5 the wise **h** will know the proper
11: 10 banish anxiety from your **h** and
SS 3: 1 I looked for the one my **h** loves;
4: 9 You have stolen my **h**, my sister,
5: 2 I slept but my **h** was awake. Listen!
5: 4 my **h** began to pound for him.
8: 6 Place me like a seal over your **h**,
Isa 6: 10 the **h** of this people calloused;
40: 11 and carries them close to his **h**;
51: 7 have taken my instruction to **h**:
57: 15 and to revive the **h** of the contrite.
66: 14 your **h** will rejoice and you will
Jer 3: 15 give you shepherds after my own **h**,
4: 14 wash the evil from your **h** and be
9: 26 of Israel is uncircumcised in **h**."
17: 9 The **h** is deceitful above all things
20: 9 his word is in my **h** like a fire, a fire
24: 7 I will give them a **h** to know me,
29: 13 when you seek me with all your **h**.
32: 39 I will give them singleness of **h**
32: 41 them in this land with all my **h**
51: 46 Do not lose **h** or be afraid
Eze 11: 19 I will give them an undivided **h**
11: 19 remove from them their **h** of stone
and give them a **h** of flesh.
18: 31 and get a new **h** and a new spirit.
36: 26 I will give you a new **h** and put
36: 26 remove from you your **h** of stone
and give you a **h** of flesh.
44: 7 foreigners uncircumcised in **h**
Joel 2: 12 "return to me with all your **h**,
2: 13 Rend your **h** and not your
Zep 3: 14 Be glad and rejoice with all your **h**,
Mt 5: 8 Blessed are the pure in **h**, for they
5: 28 adultery with her in his **h**.
6: 21 treasure is, there your **h** will be
Mt 11: 29 for I am gentle and humble in **h**,
12: 34 mouth speaks what the **h** is full of.
13: 15 For this people's **h** has become
15: 18 a person's mouth come from the **h**,
15: 19 out of the **h** come evil thoughts—
18: 35 your brother or sister from your **h**."
22: 37 the Lord your God with all your **h**
Mk 7: 21 out of a person's **h**, that evil
11: 23 and does not doubt in their **h**
12: 30 the Lord your God with all your **h**
12: 33 To love him with all your **h**, with
Lk 2: 19 and pondered them in her **h**.
2: 51 treasured all these things in her **h**.
6: 45 out of the good stored up in his **h**,
6: 45 mouth speaks what the **h** is full of.
8: 15 for those with a noble and good **h**,
10: 27 the Lord your God with all your **h**
12: 34 treasure is, there your **h** will be
Ac 1: 24 "Lord, you know everyone's **h**.
2: 37 they were cut to the **h** and said
4: 32 All the believers were one in **h**
8: 21 because your **h** is not right before
15: 8 who knows the **h**, showed that he
16: 14 The Lord opened her **h** to respond
28: 27 For this people's **h** has become
Ro 2: 29 is circumcision of the **h**,
6: 17 to obey from your **h** the pattern
10: 9 in your **h** that God raised him
10: 10 it is with your **h** that you believe
1Co 4: 5 will expose the motives of the **h**.
2Co 2: 4 anguish of **h** and with many tears,
4: 1 this ministry, we do not lose **h**.
4: 16 Therefore we do not lose **h**.
9: 7 you have decided in your **h** to give,
Eph 1: 18 eyes of your **h** may be enlightened
5: 19 music from your **h** to the Lord,
6: 5 and with sincerity of **h**, just as you
6: 6 doing the will of God from your **h**.
Php 1: 7 you, since I have you in my **h** and,
Col 2: 2 that they may be encouraged in **h**
3: 22 with sincerity of **h** and reverence
3: 23 you do, work at it with all your **h**,
1Ti 1: 5 which comes from a pure **h**
2Ti 2: 22 call on the Lord out of a pure **h**.
Phm : 12 who is my very **h**—back to you.
: 20 in the Lord; refresh my **h** in Christ.
Heb 4: 12 the thoughts and attitudes of the **h**.
1Pe 1: 22 one another deeply, from the **h**.

HEART'S* (HEART)
2Ch 1: 11 "Since this is your **h** desire and you
Ps 21: 2 You have granted him his **h** desire
Jer 15: 16 they were my joy and my **h** delight,
Eze 24: 25 delight of their eyes, their **h** desire,
Ro 10: 1 my **h** desire and prayer to God

HEARTACHE* (HEART)
Pr 15: 13 cheerful, but **h** crushes the spirit.

HEARTLESS*
La 4: 3 have become **h** like ostriches

HEARTS (HEART)
Lev 26: 41 their uncircumcised **h** are humbled
Dt 6: 6 give you today are to be on your **h**.
10: 16 Circumcise your **h**, therefore,
11: 18 Fix these words of mine in your **h**
30: 6 your God will circumcise your **h**
Jos 11: 20 himself who hardened their **h**
24: 23 you and yield your **h** to the LORD,
1Sa 7: 3 to the LORD with all your **h**,
10: 26 by valiant men whose **h** God had
2Sa 15: 6 so he stole the **h** of the people
1Ki 8: 39 do, since you know their **h** (for you
8: 61 may your **h** be fully committed
18: 37 you are turning their **h** back again."
1Ch 29: 18 and keep their **h** loyal to you.
2Ch 6: 30 do, since you know their **h** (for you
11: 16 Israel who set their **h** on seeking
29: 31 all whose **h** were willing brought
Ps 7: 9 God who probes minds and **h**.
33: 21 In him our **h** rejoice, for we trust
37: 31 The law of their God is in their **h**;
62: 8 pour out your **h** to him, for God is
95: 8 "Do not harden your **h** as you did
112: 7 their **h** are steadfast,
112: 8 Their **h** are secure, they will have
Pr 16: 23 The **h** of the wise make their
Isa 26: 8 and renown are the desire of our **h**.
29: 13 lips, but their **h** are far from me.
35: 4 say to those with fearful **h**,
63: 17 harden our **h** so we do not revere
65: 14 will sing out of the joy of their **h**,
Jer 4: 4 circumcise your **h**, you people
Jer 12: 2 on their lips but far from their **h**.
17: 1 on the tablets of their **h**
31: 33 their minds and write it on their **h**.
Mal 4: 6 He will turn the **h** of the parents
4: 6 **h** of the children to their parents;
Mt 15: 8 lips, but their **h** are far from me.
Mk 6: 52 their **h** were hardened.
7: 6 lips, but their **h** are far from me.
Lk 1: 17 to turn the **h** of the parents to their
16: 15 of others, but God knows your **h**.
24: 32 "Were not our **h** burning within us
Jn 5: 42 not have the love of God in your **h**.
14: 1 "Do not let your **h** be troubled.
14: 27 Do not let your **h** be troubled and
Ac 7: 51 Your **h** and ears are still
11: 23 true to the Lord with all their **h**.
15: 9 for he purified their **h** by faith.
28: 27 understand with their **h** and turn,
Ro 1: 21 and their foolish **h** were darkened.
2: 15 of the law are written on their **h**,
5: 5 into our **h** through the Holy Spirit,
8: 27 searches our **h** knows the mind
1Co 14: 25 the secrets of their **h** are laid bare.
2Co 1: 22 put his Spirit in our **h** as a deposit,
3: 2 written on our **h**, known and read
3: 3 of stone but on tablets of human **h**.
4: 6 shine in our **h** to give us the light
6: 11 and opened wide our **h** to you.
6: 13 open wide your **h** also.
7: 2 Make room for us in your **h**.
Gal 4: 6 the Spirit of his Son into our **h**,
Eph 3: 17 may dwell in your **h** through faith.
Php 4: 7 will guard your **h** and your minds
Col 3: 1 Christ, set your **h** on things above,
3: 15 the peace of Christ rule in your **h**,
3: 16 to God with gratitude in your **h**.
1Th 2: 4 people but God, who tests our **h**.
3: 13 May he strengthen your **h** so
2Th 2: 17 encourage your **h** and strengthen
Phm : 7 have refreshed the **h** of the Lord's
Heb 3: 8 do not harden your **h** as you did
8: 10 minds and write them on their **h**.
10: 16 I will put my laws in their **h**, and I
10: 22 having our **h** sprinkled to cleanse
Jas 4: 8 you sinners, and purify your **h**,
2Pe 1: 19 the morning star rises in your **h**.
1Jn 3: 20 If our **h** condemn us, we know that
God is greater than our **h**,

HEAT
2Pe 3: 12 and the elements will melt in the **h**.

HEAVEN (HEAVENLY HEAVENS HEAVENWARD)
Ge 14: 19 Most High, Creator of **h** and earth.
28: 12 with its top reaching to **h**,
Ex 16: 4 "I will rain down bread from **h**
20: 22 that I have spoken to you from **h**:
Dt 26: 15 Look down from **h**, your holy
30: 12 It is not up in **h**, so that you have
1Ki 8: 27 even the highest **h**, cannot contain
8: 30 Hear from **h**, your dwelling place,
22: 19 multitudes of **h** standing around
2Ki 2: 1 take Elijah up to **h** in a whirlwind,
19: 15 You have made **h** and earth.
2Ch 7: 14 then I will hear from **h**, and I will
Isa 14: 12 How you have fallen from **h**,
66: 1 "**H** is my throne, and the earth is
Da 7: 13 man, coming with the clouds of **h**.
Mt 3: 2 the kingdom of **h** has come near."
3: 16 At that moment **h** was opened,
4: 17 the kingdom of **h** has come near."
5: 12 because great is your reward in **h**,
5: 19 be called least in the kingdom of **h**,
5: 19 called great in the kingdom of **h**.
6: 9 "'Our Father in **h**, hallowed be
6: 10 will be done, on earth as it is in **h**.
6: 20 up for yourselves treasures in **h**,
7: 21 the will of my Father who is in **h**.
16: 19 you the keys of the kingdom of **h**;
18: 3 will never enter the kingdom of **h**.
18: 18 bind on earth will be bound in **h**,
18: 18 loose on earth will be loosed in **h**.
19: 14 the kingdom of **h** belongs to such
19: 21 and you will have treasure in **h**.
19: 23 is rich to enter the kingdom of **h**.
23: 13 the kingdom of **h** in people's faces.
24: 35 **H** and earth will pass away, but my
24: 30 the sign of the Son of Man in **h**.
26: 64 and coming on the clouds of **h**."
28: 18 "All authority in **h** and on earth has
Mk 1: 10 he saw **h** being torn open
10: 21 and you will have treasure in **h**.

Mk 13: 31 **H** and earth will pass away, but my
14: 62 and coming on the clouds of **h**."
16: 19 *he was taken up into h*
Lk 3: 21 as he was praying, **h** was opened
10: 18 Satan fall like lightning from **h**.
10: 20 that your names are written in **h**."
12: 33 a treasure in **h** that will never fail,
15: 7 **h** over one sinner who repents
18: 22 and you will have treasure in **h**.
21: 33 **H** and earth will pass away, but my
24: 51 left them and was taken up into **h**.
Jn 3: 13 gone into **h** except the one who came from **h**—
6: 38 I have come down from **h** not to
12: 28 Then a voice came from **h**, "I have
Ac 1: 11 has been taken from you into **h**,
7: 49 "'**H** is my throne, and the earth is
7: 55 looked up to **h** and saw the glory
9: 3 a light from **h** flashed around him.
26: 19 disobedient to the vision from **h**.
Ro 10: 6 heart, 'Who will ascend into **h**?'"
1Co 15: 47 the earth; the second man is of **h**.
2Co 5: 1 an eternal house in **h**, not built
12: 2 ago was caught up to the third **h**.
Eph 1: 10 to bring unity to all things in **h**
Php 2: 10 in **h** and on earth and under
3: 20 But our citizenship is in **h**.
Col 1: 16 things in **h** and on earth,
4: 1 that you also have a Master in **h**.
1Th 1: 10 and to wait for his Son from **h**,
4: 16 himself will come down from **h**,
Heb 1: 3 the right hand of the Majesty in **h**.
4: 14 priest who has ascended into **h**,
8: 5 a copy and shadow of what is in **h**.
9: 24 he entered **h** itself, now to appear
12: 23 whose names are written in **h**.
1Pe 1: 4 inheritance is kept in **h** for you,
3: 22 who has gone into **h** and is at God's
2Pe 3: 13 we are looking forward to a new **h**
Rev 5: 13 I heard every creature in **h**
11: 19 God's temple in **h** was opened,
12: 7 Then war broke out in **h**.
15: 5 I looked, and I saw in **h** the temple
19: 1 of a great multitude in **h** shouting:
19: 11 I saw **h** standing open and there
21: 1 I saw "a new **h** and a new earth,"
21: 10 coming down out of **h** from God.

HEAVENLY (HEAVEN)
2Co 5: 2 instead with our **h** dwelling,
Eph 1: 3 who has blessed us in the **h** realms
1: 20 at his right hand in the **h** realms,
2Ti 4: 18 bring me safely to his **h** kingdom.
Heb 12: 22 of the living God, the **h** Jerusalem.

HEAVENS (HEAVEN)
Ge 1: 1 In the beginning God created the **h**
11: 4 with a tower that reaches to the **h**,
Dt 33: 26 who rides across the **h** to help you
1Ki 8: 27 The **h**, even the highest heaven,
2Ch 2: 6 since the **h**, even the highest **h**,
Ezr 9: 6 and our guilt has reached to the **h**.
Ne 9: 6 You made the **h**, even the highest **h**,
Job 11: 8 They are higher than the **h** above—
38: 33 Do you know the laws of the **h**?
Ps 8: 3 When I consider your **h**, the work
19: 1 The **h** declare the glory of God;
33: 6 of the LORD the **h** were made,
57: 5 Be exalted, O God, above the **h**;
71: 19 righteousness, God, reaches to the **h**,
102: 25 the **h** are the work of your hands.
103: 11 high as the **h** are above the earth,
108: 4 is your love, higher than the **h**;
115: 16 The highest **h** belong
119: 89 it stands firm in the **h**.
135: 6 him, in the **h** and on the earth,
139: 8 If I go up to the **h**, you are there;
148: 1 Praise the LORD from the **h**;
Isa 24: 4 the **h** languish with the earth.
40: 26 Lift up your eyes and look to the **h**:
45: 8 "You **h** above, rain down my
51: 6 the **h** will vanish like smoke,
55: 9 "As the **h** are higher than the earth,
65: 17 will create new **h** and a new earth.
Jer 31: 37 if the **h** above can be measured
32: 17 you have made the **h** and the earth
Eze 1: 1 **h** were opened and I saw visions
Da 12: 3 shine like the brightness of the **h**,
Joel 2: 30 I will show wonders in the **h**
Mt 24: 31 from one end of the **h** to the other.
Mk 13: 27 of the earth to the ends of the **h**.
Eph 4: 10 ascended higher than all the **h**,
Heb 7: 26 from sinners, exalted above the **h**.
2Pe 3: 5 God's word the **h** came into being
3: 10 The **h** will disappear with a roar;
Rev 20: 11 and the **h** fled from his presence,

HEAVENWARD* (HEAVEN)
Php 3: 14 God has called me **h** in Christ

HEAVIER (HEAVY)
Pr 27: 3 a fool's provocation is **h** than both.

HEAVY (HEAVIER)
1Ki 12: 4 "Your father put a **h** yoke on us,
Ecc 1: 13 What a **h** burden God has laid
Isa 47: 6 on the aged you laid a very **h** yoke.
Mt 23: 4 They tie up **h**, cumbersome loads

HEBREW (HEBREWS)
Ge 14: 13 and reported this to Abram the **H**.
2Ki 18: 26 speak to us in **H** in the hearing
Php 3: 5 tribe of Benjamin, a **H** of Hebrews;

HEBREWS (HEBREW)
Ex 9: 1 the LORD, the God of the **H**, says:
2Co 11: 22 Are they **H**? So am I.

HEBRON
Ge 13: 18 near the great trees of Mamre at **H**,
23: 2 (that is, **H**) in the land of Canaan,
Jos 14: 13 and gave him **H** as his inheritance.
20: 7 is, **H**) in the hill country of Judah.
21: 13 Aaron the priest they gave **H**
2Sa 2: 11 in **H** over Judah was seven years

HEDGE
Job 1: 10 "Have you not put a **h** around him

HEED (HEEDS)
Ecc 7: 5 It is better to **h** the rebuke of a wise

HEEDS (HEED)
Pr 10: 17 Whoever **h** discipline shows
13: 1 A wise son **h** his father's
13: 18 whoever **h** correction is honored.
15: 5 but whoever **h** correction shows
15: 31 Whoever **h** life-giving correction
15: 32 but the one who **h** correction gains

HEEL
Ge 3: 15 head, and you will strike his **h**."
25: 26 with his hand grasping Esau's **h**;

HEIGHT (HIGH)
1Sa 17: 4 His **h** was six cubits and a span.

HEIR (INHERIT)
Gal 4: 7 child, God has made you also an **h**.
Heb 1: 2 whom he appointed **h** of all things,

HEIRS (INHERIT)
Ro 8: 17 then we are **h**—**h** of God
Gal 3: 29 and **h** according to the promise.
Eph 3: 6 gospel the Gentiles are **h** together
1Pe 3: 7 as **h** with you of the gracious gift

HELD (HOLD)
Ex 17: 11 As long as Moses **h** up his hands,
Dt 4: 4 you who **h** fast to the LORD your
2Ki 18: 6 He **h** fast to the LORD and did not
SS 3: 4 I **h** him and would not let him go
Isa 65: 2 All day long I have **h** out my hands
Ro 10: 21 says, "All day long I have **h** out my
Col 2: 19 and **h** together by its ligaments

HELL*
Mt 5: 22 will be in danger of the fire of **h**.
5: 29 whole body to be thrown into **h**.
5: 30 for your whole body to go into **h**.
10: 28 destroy both soul and body in **h**.
18: 9 and be thrown into the fire of **h**.
23: 15 as much a child of **h** as you are.
23: 33 you escape being condemned to **h**?
Mk 9: 43 than with two hands to go into **h**,
9: 45 two feet and be thrown into **h**.
9: 47 two eyes and be thrown into **h**,
Lk 12: 5 has authority to throw you into **h**.
Jas 3: 6 on fire, and is itself set on fire by **h**.
2Pe 2: 4 but sent them to **h**, putting them

HELMET
Isa 59: 17 and the **h** of salvation on his head;
Eph 6: 17 Take the **h** of salvation
1Th 5: 8 and the hope of salvation as a **h**.

HELP (HELPED HELPER HELPFUL HELPING HELPLESS HELPS)
Ex 23: 5 be sure you **h** them with it.
Lev 25: 35 **h** them as you would a foreigner
Dt 33: 26 rides across the heavens to **h** you
2Sa 22: 36 your **h** has made me great.
2Ch 16: 12 in his illness he did not seek **h**
Ps 18: 6 I cried to my God for **h**.
30: 2 called to you for **h**, and you healed
33: 20 he is our **h** and our shield.
40: 10 faithfulness and your saving **h**.
40: 16 long for your saving **h** always say,
46: 1 an ever-present **h** in trouble.
70: 4 long for your saving **h** always say,
72: 12 the afflicted who have no one to **h**.
79: 9 **H** us, God our Savior, for the glory
108: 12 enemy, for human **h** is worthless.
115: 9 he is their **h** and shield.
121: 1 where does my **h** come from?
Ecc 4: 10 falls and has no one to **h** them up.
Isa 41: 10 I will strengthen you and **h** you;
Jnh 2: 2 the realm of the dead I called for **h**,
Mk 9: 24 **h** me overcome my unbelief!"
Lk 11: 46 will not lift one finger to **h** them.
Ac 16: 9 over to Macedonia and **h** us."
18: 27 he was a great **h** to those who
20: 35 of hard work we must **h** the weak,
2Co 9: 2 For I know your eagerness to **h**,
1Ti 5: 16 the church can **h** those widows

HELPED (HELP)
1Sa 7: 12 "Thus far the LORD has **h** us."
Ac 26: 22 But God has **h** me to this very day;

HELPER (HELP)
Ge 2: 18 I will make a **h** suitable for him."
Ps 10: 14 you are the **h** of the fatherless.
Heb 13: 6 confidence, "The Lord is my **h**;

HELPFUL (HELP)
Eph 4: 29 only what is **h** for building others

HELPING (HELP)
Ac 9: 36 always doing good and **h** the poor.
1Co 12: 28 gifts of healing, of **h**, of guidance,
1Ti 5: 10 **h** those in trouble and devoting

HELPLESS (HELP)
Ps 10: 12 hand, O God. Do not forget the **h**.
Mt 9: 36 because they were harassed and **h**,

HELPS (HELP)
Ro 8: 26 the Spirit **h** us in our weakness.

HEN*
Zec 6: 14 **H** son of Zephaniah as a memorial
Mt 23: 37 as a **h** gathers her chicks under her
Lk 13: 34 as a **h** gathers her chicks under her

HERALD
1Ti 2: 7 this purpose I was appointed a **h**
2Ti 1: 11 of this gospel I was appointed a **h**

HERBS
Ex 12: 8 along with bitter **h**, and bread

HERITAGE (INHERIT)
Ps 61: 5 you have given me the **h** of those
119:111 Your statutes are my **h** forever;
127: 3 Children are a **h** from the LORD,

HERO
2Sa 23: 1 of Jacob, the **h** of Israel's songs:

HEROD
1. King of Judea who tried to kill Jesus (Mt 2; Lk 1:5).
2. Son of 1. Tetrarch of Galilee who arrested and beheaded John the Baptist (Mt 14:1–12; Mk 6:14–29; Lk 3:1, 19–20; 9:7–9); tried Jesus (Lk 23:6–15).
3. Grandson of 1. King of Judea who killed James (Ac 12:2); arrested Peter (Ac 12:3–19). Death (Ac 12:19–23).

HERODIAS
Wife of Herod the tetrarch who persuaded her daughter to ask for John the Baptist's head (Mt 14:1–12; Mk 6:14–29).

HEWN*
Isa 51: 1 the quarry from which you were **h**;

HEZEKIAH
King of Judah. Restored the temple and worship (2Ch 29–31). Sought the Lord for help against Assyria (2Ki 18–19; 2Ch 32:1–23; Isa 36–37). Illness healed (2Ki 20:1–11; 2Ch 32:24–26; Isa 38). Judged for showing Babylonians his treasures (2Ki 20:12–21; 2Ch 32:31; Isa 39).

HID (HIDE)
Ge 3: 8 they **h** from the LORD God among
Ex 2: 2 child, she **h** him for three months.
Jos 6: 17 because she **h** the spies we sent.
1Ki 18: 13 I **h** a hundred of the LORD's
2Ch 22: 11 she **h** the child from Athaliah so
Isa 54: 8 In a surge of anger I **h** my face
Mt 13: 44 a man found it, he **h** it again,
25: 25 out and **h** your gold in the ground.
Heb 11: 23 By faith Moses' parents **h** him for

HIDDEN (HIDE)
1Sa 10: 22 "Yes, he has **h** himself among
Job 28: 11 rivers and bring **h** things to light.
Ps 19: 12 Forgive my **h** faults.
119: 11 I have **h** your word in my heart
Pr 2: 4 and search for it as for **h** treasure,
27: 5 Better is open rebuke than **h** love.
Isa 59: 2 your sins have **h** his face from you,
Da 2: 22 He reveals deep and **h** things;
Mt 5: 14 A town built on a hill cannot be **h**.
10: 26 or **h** that will not be made known.
11: 25 because you have **h** these things
13: 35 utter things **h** since the creation
13: 44 heaven is like treasure **h** in a field.
Mk 4: 22 For whatever is **h** is meant to be
Ro 16: 25 of the mystery **h** for long ages past,
1Co 2: 7 a mystery that has been **h**
Eph 3: 9 for ages past was kept **h** in God,
Col 1: 26 that has been kept **h** for ages
2: 3 in whom are **h** all the treasures
3: 3 and your life is now **h** with Christ

HIDE (HID HIDDEN HIDING)
Dt 31: 17 I will **h** my face from them,
Ps 17: 8 **h** me in the shadow of your wings
27: 5 he will **h** me in the shelter of his
143: 9 LORD, for I **h** myself in you.
Isa 53: 3 whom people **h** their faces he was

HIDING (HIDE)
Ps 32: 7 You are my **h** place;
Pr 28: 12 rise to power, people go into **h**.

HIGH (HEIGHT)
Ge 14: 18 He was priest of God Most **H**,
14: 22 God Most **H**, Creator of heaven
Ps 21: 7 the Most **H** he will not be shaken.
82: 6 you are all sons of the Most **H**.'
Isa 14: 14 will make myself like the Most **H**."
Da 4: 17 the Most **H** is sovereign over all
Mk 5: 7 me, Jesus, Son of the Most **H** God?
Heb 7: 1 Salem and priest of God Most **H**.

HIGHWAY
Isa 40: 3 in the desert a **h** for our God.

HILL (HILLS)
Isa 40: 4 every mountain and **h** made low;
Mt 5: 14 town built on a **h** cannot be hidden
Lk 3: 5 every mountain and **h** made low.

HILLS (HILL)
1Ki 20: 23 him, "Their gods are gods of the **h**.
Ps 50: 10 and the cattle on a thousand **h**.
Hos 10: 8 and to the **h**, "Fall on us!"
Lk 23: 30 and to the **h**, "Cover us!"'
Rev 17: 9 The seven heads are seven **h**

HINDER (HINDERED HINDERS)
1Sa 14: 6 Nothing can **h** the LORD
Mt 19: 14 do not **h** them, for the kingdom
1Co 9: 12 anything rather than **h** the gospel
1Pe 3: 7 so that nothing will **h** your prayers.

HINDERED (HINDER)
Lk 11: 52 and you have **h** those who were

HINDERS* (HINDER)
Heb 12: 1 let us throw off everything that **h**

HINT*
Eph 5: 3 you there must not be even a **h**

HIP
Ge 32: 32 of Jacob's **h** was touched near

HIRAM
King of Tyre; helped David build his palace (2Sa 5:11–12; 1Ch 14:1); helped Solomon build the temple (1Ki 5; 2Ch 2) and his navy (1Ki 9:10–27; 2Ch 8).

HIRED
Lk 15: 15 and **h** himself out to a citizen
Jn 10: 12 The **h** hand is not the shepherd

HOARDED* (HOARDS)
Ecc 5: 13 wealth **h** to the harm of its owners,
Isa 23: 18 they will not be stored up or **h**.
Jas 5: 3 You have **h** wealth in the last days.

HOARDS* (HOARDED)
Pr 11: 26 People curse the one who **h** grain,

HOLD (HELD HOLDING)
Ex 20: 7 LORD will not **h** anyone guiltless
Lev 19: 13 "'Do not **h** back the wages
Dt 5: 11 LORD will not **h** anyone guiltless
11: 22 to him and to **h** fast to him—
13: 4 serve him and **h** fast to him.
30: 20 to his voice, and **h** fast to him.
Jos 22: 5 to **h** fast to him and to serve him
2Ki 4: 16 "you will **h** a son in your arms."
Ps 18: 16 from on high and took **h** of me;
73: 23 you **h** me by my right hand.
Pr 4: 4 "Take **h** of my words with all your
10: 19 but the prudent **h** their tongues.
17: 28 discerning if they **h** their tongues.
Isa 41: 13 the LORD your God who takes **h**
54: 2 tent curtains wide, do not **h** back;
Eze 3: 18 I will **h** you accountable for their
3: 20 I will **h** you accountable for their
33: 6 I will **h** the watchman accountable
Zec 8: 23 nations will take firm **h** of one Jew
Mk 11: 25 if you **h** anything against anyone,
Jn 20: 17 Jesus said, "Do not **h** on to me,
Php 2: 16 as you **h** firmly to the word of life.
3: 12 I press on to take **h** of that
Col 1: 17 and in him all things **h** together.
1Th 5: 21 test them all; **h** on to what is good,
1Ti 6: 12 Take **h** of the eternal life
Heb 10: 23 Let us **h** unswervingly to the hope

HOLDING (HOLD)
Jer 15: 6 I am tired of **h** back.

HOLES
Hag 1: 6 to put them in a purse with **h** in it."

HOLINESS* (HOLY)
Ex 15: 11 majestic in **h**, awesome in glory,
Dt 32: 51 you did not uphold my **h** among
1Ch 16: 29 the LORD in the splendor of his **h**.
2Ch 20: 21 the splendor of his **h** as they went
Ps 29: 2 the LORD in the splendor of his **h**.
89: 35 for all, I have sworn by my **h**—
93: 5 **h** adorns your house for endless
96: 9 the LORD in the splendor of his **h**;
Isa 29: 23 they will acknowledge the **h**
35: 8 it will be called the Way of **H**;
Eze 36: 23 I will show the **h** of my great name,
38: 23 I will show my greatness and my **h**,
Am 4: 2 LORD has sworn by his **h**:
Lk 1: 75 in **h** and righteousness before him
Ro 1: 4 Spirit of **h** was appointed the Son
6: 19 to righteousness leading to **h**.
6: 22 the benefit you reap leads to **h**,
1Co 1: 30 righteousness, **h** and redemption.
2Co 7: 1 perfecting **h** out of reverence
Eph 4: 24 God in true righteousness and **h**.
1Ti 2: 2 quiet lives in all godliness and **h**.
2: 15 in faith, love and **h** with propriety.
Heb 12: 10 in order that we may share in his **h**.
12: 14 without **h** no one will see the Lord.

HOLY (HALLOWED HOLINESS)
Ge 2: 3 the seventh day and made it **h**,
Ex 3: 5 you are standing is **h** ground."
16: 23 rest, a **h** sabbath to the LORD.
19: 6 kingdom of priests and a **h** nation.'
20: 8 the Sabbath day by keeping it **h**.
26: 33 curtain will separate the **H** Place from the Most **H** Place.
28: 36 on a seal: **H** TO THE LORD.
29: 37 Then the altar will be most **h**, and whatever touches it will be **h**.
30: 10 It is most **h** to the LORD."
30: 29 whatever touches them will be **h**.
31: 13 I am the LORD, who makes you **h**.
40: 9 all its furnishings, and it will be **h**.
Lev 10: 3 approach me I will be proved **h**;
10: 10 you can distinguish between the **h**
11: 44 and be **h**, because I am **h**.
11: 45 therefore be **h**, because I am **h**.
19: 2 'Be **h** because I, the LORD your God, am **h**.
19: 8 they have desecrated what is **h**
19: 24 fourth year all its fruit will be **h**,
20: 3 and profaned my **h** name.
20: 7 yourselves and be **h**, because I am
20: 8 I am the LORD, who makes you **h**.
20: 26 You are to be **h** to me because I,
21: 6 They must be **h** to their God
21: 8 Consider them **h**, because I the LORD am **h**—
22: 9 am the LORD, who makes them **h**.
22: 32 Do not profane my **h** name, for I
22: 32 I am the LORD, who made you **h**
25: 12 a jubilee and is to be **h** for you;
27: 9 given to the LORD becomes **h**.
Nu 4: 15 they must not touch the **h** things
6: 5 They must be **h** until the period
20: 12 to honor me as **h** in the sight
20: 13 he was proved **h** among them.
Dt 5: 12 the Sabbath day by keeping it **h**,
23: 14 Your camp must be **h**, so that he
Dt 26: 15 heaven, your **h** dwelling place,
33: 2 myriads of **h** ones from the south,
Jos 5: 15 place where you are standing is **h**."
24: 19 He is a **h** God; he is a jealous God.
1Sa 2: 2 "There is no one **h** like the LORD;
6: 20 of the LORD, this **h** God?
21: 5 The men's bodies are **h** even
2Ki 4: 9 often comes our way is a **h** man
1Ch 16: 10 Glory in his **h** name; let the hearts
16: 35 may give thanks to your **h** name,
29: 3 I have provided for this **h** temple:
2Ch 30: 27 heaven, his **h** dwelling place.
Ezr 9: 2 have mingled the **h** race
Ne 11: 1 to live in Jerusalem, the **h** city,
Job 6: 10 denied the words of the **H** One.
Ps 2: 6 my king on Zion, my **h** mountain."
11: 4 The LORD is in his **h** temple;
16: 3 the **h** people who are in the land,
22: 3 you are enthroned as the **H** One;
24: 3 Who may stand in his **h** place?
30: 4 praise his **h** name.
77: 13 Your ways, God, are **h**. What god is
78: 54 them to the border of his **h** land,
99: 3 great and awesome name—he is **h**.
99: 5 worship at his footstool; he is **h**.
99: 9 for the LORD our God is **h**.
105: 3 Glory in his **h** name; let the hearts
111: 9 **h** and awesome is his name.
Pr 9: 10 of the **H** One is understanding.
Isa 5: 16 the **h** God will be proved **h** by his
6: 3 "**H**, **h**, **h** is the LORD Almighty;
8: 13 is the one you are to regard as **h**,
29: 23 hands, they will keep my name **h**;
40: 25 who is my equal?" says the **H** One.
43: 3 your God, the **H** One of Israel,
54: 5 the **H** One of Israel is your
57: 15 "I live in a high and **h** place,
58: 13 and the LORD's **h** day honorable,
Jer 17: 22 but keep the Sabbath day **h**, as I
Eze 20: 41 I will be proved **h** through you
22: 26 to my law and profane my **h** things;
28: 22 and within you am proved to be **h**.
28: 25 I will be proved **h** through them
36: 20 nations they profaned my **h** name,
38: 16 I am proved **h** through you before
44: 23 the difference between the **h**
Da 9: 24 and to anoint the Most **H** Place.
Hab 2: 20 The LORD is in his **h** temple;
Zec 14: 5 come, and all the **h** ones with him.
14: 20 On that day **H** TO THE LORD
Mt 24: 15 in the **h** place 'the abomination
Mk 1: 24 who you are—the **H** One of God!"
Lk 1: 35 "The **H** Spirit will come on you,
1: 35 So the **h** one to be born will be
1: 49 great things for me—**h** is his name.
4: 34 who you are—the **H** One of God!"
Jn 6: 69 that you are the **H** One of God."
Ac 2: 27 will not let your **h** one see decay.
13: 35 will not let your **h** one see decay.'
Ro 1: 2 his prophets in the **H** Scriptures
7: 12 law is **h**, and the commandment
11: 16 is **h**, then the whole batch is **h**;
12: 1 sacrifice, **h** and pleasing to God—
1Co 1: 2 Jesus and called to be his **h** people,
7: 14 be unclean, but as it is, they are **h**.
Eph 1: 4 the creation of the world to be **h**
2: 21 to become a **h** temple in the Lord.
3: 5 by the Spirit to God's **h** apostles
5: 26 to make her **h**, cleansing her
Col 1: 22 death to present you **h** in his sight,
1Th 2: 10 of how **h**, righteous and blameless
3: 13 Jesus comes with all his **h** ones.
4: 7 us to be impure, but to live a **h** life.
2Th 1: 10 to be glorified in his **h** people
1Ti 2: 8 lifting up **h** hands without anger
2Ti 1: 9 saved us and called us to a **h** life—
2: 21 made **h**, useful to the Master
3: 15 you have known the **H** Scriptures,
Titus 1: 8 upright, **h** and disciplined.
Heb 2: 11 Both the one who makes people **h**
7: 26 one who is **h**, blameless, pure,
10: 10 we have been made **h** through
10: 14 those who are being made **h**.
10: 19 the Most **H** Place by the blood
12: 14 peace with everyone and to be **h**;
13: 12 make the people **h** through his
1Pe 1: 15 as he who called you is **h**, so be **h** in all you do;
1: 16 "Be **h**, because I am **h**."
2: 5 house to be a **h** priesthood,
2: 9 a royal priesthood, a **h** nation,

1Pe 3: 5 this is the way the **h** women
2Pe 3: 11 You ought to live **h** and godly lives
Jude : 14 upon thousands of his **h** ones
Rev 3: 7 are the words of him who is **h**
4: 8 "'**H**, **h**, **h** is the Lord God
15: 4 For you alone are **h**. All nations
20: 6 **h** are those who share in the first
22: 11 let the **h** person continue to be **h**."

HOME (HOMES)
Dt 6: 7 Talk about them when you sit at **h**
11: 19 about them when you sit at **h**
20: 5 Let him go **h**, or he may die in
24: 5 one year he is to be free to stay at **h**
Ru 1: 11 said, "Return **h**, my daughters.
2Sa 7: 10 that they can have a **h** of their own
1Ch 16: 43 David returned **h** to bless his
Ps 84: 3 Even the sparrow has found a **h**,
113: 9 woman in her **h** as a happy mother
Pr 3: 33 he blesses the **h** of the righteous.
27: 8 its nest is anyone who flees from **h**.
Ecc 12: 5 people go to their eternal **h**
Eze 36: 8 Israel, for they will soon come **h**.
Mt 1: 24 him and took Mary **h** as his wife.
Mk 10: 29 "no one who has left **h** or brothers
Lk 10: 38 named Martha opened her **h**
Jn 14: 23 them and make our **h** with them.
19: 27 on, this disciple took her into his **h**.
Ac 16: 15 baptized, she invited us to her **h**.
Titus 2: 5 pure, to be busy at **h**, to be kind,

HOMELESS*
1Co 4: 11 we are brutally treated, we are **h**.

HOMES (HOME)
Ne 4: 14 daughters, your wives and your **h**."
Isa 32: 18 in secure **h**, in undisturbed places
Mic 2: 2 They defraud people of their **h**,
Mk 10: 30 **h**, brothers, sisters, mothers,
1Ti 5: 14 to manage their **h** and to give

HOMETOWN
Mt 13: 54 to his **h**, he began teaching
Lk 4: 24 "no prophet is accepted in his **h**.

HOMOSEXUALITY*
1Ti 1: 10 for those practicing **h**, for slave

HONEST (HONESTY)
Lev 19: 36 Use **h** scales and **h** weights, an **h** ephah and an **h** hin.
Dt 25: 15 must have accurate and **h** weights
2Ki 22: 7 to them, because they are **h** in their
Job 31: 6 let God weigh me in **h** scales and
Pr 12: 17 An **h** witness tells the truth,
14: 5 An **h** witness does not deceive,
17: 26 to flog **h** officials is not right.
22: 21 teaching you to be **h** and to speak

HONESTY (HONEST)
2Ki 12: 15 they acted with complete **h**.

HONEY (HONEYCOMB)
Ex 3: 8 a land flowing with milk and **h**—
Jdg 14: 8 saw a swarm of bees and some **h**.
1Sa 14: 26 woods, they saw the **h** oozing out;
Ps 19: 10 they are sweeter than **h**, than **h**
119:103 taste, sweeter than **h** to my mouth!
Pr 24: 14 also that wisdom is like **h** for you:
25: 16 If you find **h**, eat just enough—
SS 4: 11 milk and **h** are under your tongue.
Isa 7: 15 **h** when he knows enough to reject
Eze 3: 3 it tasted as sweet as **h** in my mouth.
Mt 3: 4 His food was locusts and wild **h**.
Rev 10: 9 mouth it will be as sweet as **h**.'"

HONEYCOMB (HONEY)
Ps 19: 10 honey, than honey from the **h**.
SS 4: 11 Your lips drop sweetness as the **h**,
5: 1 I have eaten my **h** and my honey;

HONOR (HONORABLE HONORABLY HONORED HONORS)
Ex 20: 12 "**H** your father and your mother,
Nu 20: 12 in me enough to **h** me as holy
25: 13 he was zealous for the **h** of his God
Dt 5: 16 "**H** your father and your mother,
Jdg 4: 9 are taking, the **h** will not be yours,
1Sa 2: 8 and has them inherit a throne of **h**.
2: 30 Those who **h** me I will **h**, but those
1Ch 29: 12 Wealth and **h** come from you;
2Ch 1: 11 possessions or **h**, nor for the death
18: 1 had great wealth and **h**,
Ezr 10: 11 Now **h** the LORD, the God of your
Est 6: 6 the man the king delights to **h**?"
Ps 8: 5 crowned them with glory and **h**.
45: 11 **h** him, for he is your lord.
84: 11 the LORD bestows favor and **h**;
Pr 3: 9 **H** the LORD with your wealth,
3: 35 The wise inherit **h**, but fools get
11: 16 A kindhearted woman gains **h**,
15: 33 and humility comes before **h**.
18: 12 but humility comes before **h**.
20: 3 It is to one's **h** to avoid strife,
31: 31 **H** her for all that her hands have
Isa 29: 13 mouth and **h** me with their lips,
Jer 33: 9 **h** before all nations on earth
Mt 13: 57 "A prophet is not without **h** except
15: 4 '**H** your father and mother'
15: 8 "'These people **h** me with their
19: 19 **h** your father and mother,' and
23: 6 they love the place of **h** at banquets
Mk 6: 4 "A prophet is not without **h** except
Lk 14: 8 do not take the place of **h**,
Jn 5: 23 all may **h** the Son just as they **h**
12: 26 My Father will **h** the one who
Ro 12: 10 **H** one another above yourselves.
1Co 6: 20 Therefore **h** God with your bodies.
Eph 6: 2 "**H** your father and mother"—
1Ti 5: 17 church well are worthy of double **h**,
Heb 2: 7 crowned them with glory and **h**
Rev 4: 9 **h** and thanks to him who sits

HONORABLE (HONOR)
1Th 4: 4 body in a way that is holy and **h**,

HONORABLY (HONOR)
Heb 13: 18 and desire to live **h** in every way.

HONORED (HONOR)
Ps 12: 8 what is vile is **h** by the human race.
Pr 13: 18 but whoever heeds correction is **h**.
Da 4: 34 I **h** and glorified him who lives
1Co 12: 26 if one part is **h**, every part rejoices
Heb 13: 4 Marriage should be **h** by all,

HONORS (HONOR)
Ps 15: 4 but **h** those who fear the LORD;
Pr 14: 31 is kind to the needy **h** God.
3Jn : 6 their way in a manner that **h** God.

HOOF
Ex 10: 26 not a **h** is to be left behind.

HOOKS
Isa 2: 4 and their spears into pruning **h**.
Joel 3: 10 and your pruning **h** into spears.
Mic 4: 3 and their spears into pruning **h**.

HOPE (HOPES)
Job 13: 15 he slay me, yet will I **h** in him;
Ps 33: 17 A horse is a vain **h** for deliverance;
33: 18 on those whose **h** is in his unfailing
42: 5 Put your **h** in God, for I will yet
62: 5 rest in God; my **h** comes from him.
119: 74 for I have put my **h** in your word.
130: 5 waits, and in his word I put my **h**.
130: 7 Israel, put your **h** in the LORD,
146: 5 whose **h** is in the LORD their God.
147: 11 put their **h** in his unfailing love.
Pr 13: 12 **H** deferred makes the heart sick,
23: 18 There is surely a future **h** for you,
23: 18 and your **h** will not be cut off.
Isa 40: 31 but those who **h** in the LORD will
Jer 29: 11 plans to give you **h** and a future.
La 3: 21 call to mind and therefore I have **h**:
Zec 9: 12 to your fortress, you prisoners of **h**;
Ro 5: 4 and character, **h**.
8: 20 of the one who subjected it, in **h**
8: 24 But **h** that is seen is no **h** at all.
8: 25 if we **h** for what we do not yet have,
12: 12 Be joyful in **h**, patient in affliction,
15: 4 they provide we might have **h**.
15: 13 May the God of **h** fill you with all
1Co 13: 13 three remain: faith, **h** and love.
15: 19 for this life we have **h** in Christ,
Eph 2: 12 without **h** and without God
Col 1: 27 is Christ in you, the **h** of glory.
1Th 1: 3 your endurance inspired by **h** in
5: 8 and the **h** of salvation as a helmet.
1Ti 4: 10 because we have put our **h**
6: 17 nor to put their **h** in wealth,
Titus 1: 2 in the **h** of eternal life, which God,
2: 13 while we wait for the blessed **h**—
Heb 6: 19 We have this **h** as an anchor
10: 23 unswervingly to the **h** we profess,
11: 1 faith is confidence in what we **h**
1Jn 3: 3 All who have this **h** in him purify

HOPES (HOPE)
Ps 25: 3 No one who **h** in you will ever be
1Co 13: 7 trusts, always **h**, always perseveres.

HORN (HORNS)
Ex 19: 13 the ram's **h** sounds a long blast
27: 2 Make a **h** at each of the four
Da 7: 8 This **h** had eyes like the eyes

HORNS (HORN)
Da 7: 24 The ten **h** are ten kings who will
Rev 5: 6 The Lamb had seven **h** and seven
12: 3 ten **h** and seven crowns on its
13: 1 It had ten **h** and seven heads,
17: 3 and had seven heads and ten **h**.

HORRIBLE (HORROR)
Jer 5: 30 "A **h** and shocking thing has

HORROR (HORRIBLE)
Jer 2: 12 and shudder with great **h**,"

HORSE
Ps 147: 10 is not in the strength of the **h**,
Pr 26: 3 A whip for the **h**, a bridle
Zec 1: 8 me was a man mounted on a red **h**.
Rev 6: 2 and there before me was a white **h**!
6: 4 another **h** came out, a fiery red
6: 5 and there before me was a black **h**!
6: 8 and there before me was a pale **h**!
19: 11 and there before me was a white **h**,

HOSANNA
Mt 21: 9 shouted, "**H** to the Son of David!"
21: 9 "**H** in the highest heaven!"
Mk 11: 9 those who followed shouted, "**H**!"
Jn 12: 13 out to meet him, shouting, "**H**!"

HOSEA*
Prophet whose wife and family pictured the unfaithfulness of Israel (Hos 1–3; Ro 9:25).

HOSHEA (JOSHUA)
1. Original name of Joshua (Nu 13:16).
2. Last king of Israel (2Ki 15:30; 17:1–6).

HOSPITABLE* (HOSPITALITY)
1Ti 3: 2 respectable, **h**, able to teach,
Titus 1: 8 he must be **h**, one who loves what

HOSPITALITY* (HOSPITABLE)
Ac 28: 7 showed us generous **h** for three
Ro 12: 13 people who are in need. Practice **h**.
16: 23 whose **h** I and the whole church
1Ti 5: 10 showing **h**, washing the feet
Heb 13: 2 not forget to show **h** to strangers,
13: 2 **h** to angels without knowing it.
1Pe 4: 9 Offer **h** to one another without
3Jn : 8 to show **h** to such people so that

HOSTILE (HOSTILITY)
Ro 8: 7 governed by the flesh is **h** to God;

HOSTILITY (HOSTILE)
Eph 2: 14 the barrier, the dividing wall of **h**,
2: 16 by which he put to death their **h**.

HOT
1Ti 4: 2 have been seared as with a **h** iron.
Rev 3: 15 that you are neither cold nor **h**.

HOT-TEMPERED* (TEMPER)
Pr 15: 18 A **h** person stirs up conflict,
19: 19 A **h** person must pay the penalty;
22: 24 not make friends with a **h** person,
29: 22 and a **h** person commits many sins.

HOTHEADED* (HEAD)
Pr 14: 16 but a fool is **h** and yet feels secure.

HOUR
Ecc 9: 12 one knows when their **h** will come:
Mt 6: 27 add a single **h** to your life?
Lk 12: 40 an **h** when you do not expect him."
Jn 2: 4 "My **h** has not yet come."
12: 23 "The **h** has come for the Son
12: 27 'Father, save me from this **h**'?
12: 27 this very reason I came to this **h**.
17: 1 "Father, the **h** has come.

HOUSE (HOUSEHOLD HOUSEHOLDS HOUSES STOREHOUSE)
Ex 12: 22 the door of your **h** until morning.
20: 17 shall not covet your neighbor's **h**.
Nu 12: 7 he is faithful in all my **h**.
Dt 5: 21 your desire on your neighbor's **h**
2Sa 7: 2 living in a **h** of cedar, while the ark
7: 11 LORD himself will establish a **h**
1Ch 17: 23 and his **h** be established forever.
Ne 10: 39 "We will not neglect the **h** of our
Ps 23: 6 in the **h** of the LORD forever.
27: 4 in the **h** of the LORD all the days
69: 9 for zeal for your **h** consumes me,
84: 10 in the **h** of my God than dwell
122: 1 "Let us go to the **h** of the LORD."
127: 1 Unless the LORD builds the **h**,
Pr 7: 27 Her **h** is a highway to the grave,
21: 9 of the roof than share a **h**
Isa 56: 7 for my **h** will be called a **h** of prayer

Jer 7: 11 Has this **h**, which bears my Name,
18: 2 "Go down to the potter's **h**,
Joel 3: 18 will flow out of the LORD's **h**
Hab 2: 9 who builds his **h** by unjust gain,
Zec 13: 6 I was given at the **h** of my friends.'
Mt 7: 24 is like a wise man who built his **h**
10: 11 and stay at their **h** until you leave.
12: 29 can anyone enter a strong man's **h**
21: 13 "'My **h** will be called a **h**
Mk 3: 25 If a **h** is divided against itself,
11: 17 'My **h** will be called a **h** of prayer
Lk 6: 48 They are like a man building a **h**,
10: 7 Do not move around from **h** to **h**.
11: 17 a **h** divided against itself will fall.
11: 24 it says, 'I will return to the **h** I left.'
15: 8 sweep the **h** and search carefully
19: 9 salvation has come to this **h**,
Jn 2: 16 Stop turning my Father's **h**
2: 17 for your **h** will consume me."
12: 3 the **h** was filled with the fragrance
14: 2 My Father's **h** has many rooms;
Ac 20: 20 you publicly and from **h** to **h**.
Ro 16: 5 the church that meets at their **h**.
Heb 3: 3 of a **h** has greater honor than the **h**
1Pe 2: 5 spiritual **h** to be a holy priesthood,

HOUSEHOLD (HOUSE)
Ex 12: 3 lamb for his family, one for each **h**.
Jos 24: 15 But as for me and my **h**, we will
Pr 31: 21 it snows, she has no fear for her **h**;
31: 27 watches over the affairs of her **h**
Mic 7: 6 are the members of his own **h**.
Mt 10: 36 will be the members of his own **h**.'
12: 25 or **h** divided against itself will not
Ac 16: 31 will be saved—you and your **h**."
16: 33 he and all his **h** were baptized.
16: 34 in God—he and his whole **h**.
Eph 2: 19 people and also members of his **h**,
1Ti 3: 12 manage his children and his **h** well.
3: 15 to conduct themselves in God's **h**,
5: 8 and especially for their own **h**,

HOUSEHOLDS (HOUSE)
Pr 15: 27 The greedy bring ruin to their **h**,
Titus 1: 11 they are disrupting whole **h**

HOUSES (HOUSE)
Ex 12: 27 who passed over the **h**
Mt 19: 29 who has left **h** or brothers

HOVERING* (HOVERS)
Ge 1: 2 Spirit of God was **h** over the waters
Isa 31: 5 Like birds **h** overhead, the LORD

HOVERS* (HOVERING)
Dt 32: 11 up its nest and **h** over its young,

HULDAH*
Prophetess inquired by Hilkiah for Josiah (2Ki 22; 2Ch 34:14–28).

HUMAN (HUMANITY HUMANKIND HUMANS MAN)
Ge 6: 6 he had made **h** beings on the earth,
6: 7 earth the **h** race I have created—
9: 6 "Whoever sheds **h** blood,
Lev 24: 17 who takes the life of a **h** being is
1Sa 15: 29 for he is not a **h** being, that he
2Ki 19: 18 and stone, fashioned by **h** hands.
2Ch 32: 19 of the world—the work of **h** hands.
Ps 8: 4 **h** beings that you care for them?
144: 3 what are **h** beings that you care
Isa 52: 14 form marred beyond **h** likeness—
Mk 7: 7 their teachings are merely **h** rules.'
Jn 8: 15 You judge by **h** standards;
Ac 5: 29 obey God rather than **h** beings!
Ro 9: 5 them is traced the **h** ancestry
1Co 1: 25 of God is wiser than **h** wisdom,
1: 25 God is stronger than **h** strength.
1: 26 of you were wise by **h** standards;
2: 5 faith might not rest on **h** wisdom,
2: 13 in words taught us by **h** wisdom
3: 21 no more boasting about **h** leaders!
2Co 3: 3 of stone but on tablets of **h** hearts.
Gal 1: 10 to win the approval of **h** beings,
1Th 2: 13 you accepted it not as a **h** word,
Heb 9: 11 that is not made with **h** hands,
9: 24 a sanctuary made with **h** hands
2Pe 1: 21 never had its origin in the **h** will,

HUMANITY* (HUMAN)
Eph 2: 15 create in himself one new **h**
Heb 2: 14 he too shared in their **h** so

HUMANS (HUMAN)
Ge 6: 3 will not contend with **h** forever,
1Co 3: 3 Are you not acting like mere **h**?

HUMBLE (HUMBLED HUMBLES HUMILIATE HUMILIATED HUMILIATING HUMILITY)
Nu 12: 3 (Now Moses was a very **h** man,
2Ch 7: 14 **h** themselves and pray and seek
Ps 18: 27 You save the **h** but bring low those
25: 9 He guides the **h** in what is right
149: 4 he crowns the **h** with victory.
Pr 3: 34 favor to the **h** and oppressed.
Isa 66: 2 those who are **h** and contrite
Mt 11: 29 for I am gentle and **h** in heart,
23: 12 and those who **h** themselves will be
Lk 14: 11 and those who **h** themselves will be
18: 14 and those who **h** themselves will be
Eph 4: 2 Be completely **h** and gentle;
Jas 4: 6 proud but shows favor to the **h**."
4: 10 **H** yourselves before the Lord,
1Pe 5: 5 proud but shows favor to the **h**."
5: 6 **H** yourselves, therefore,

HUMBLED (HUMBLE)
Mt 23: 12 who exalt themselves will be **h**,
Lk 14: 11 who exalt themselves will be **h**,
Php 2: 8 he **h** himself by becoming obedient

HUMBLES* (HUMBLE)
1Sa 2: 7 he **h** and he exalts.
Isa 26: 5 He **h** those who dwell on high,

HUMILIATE* (HUMBLE)
Pr 25: 7 for him to **h** you before his nobles.

HUMILIATED (HUMBLE)
Jer 31: 19 **h** because I bore the disgrace of my
Lk 14: 9 Then, **h**, you will have to take

HUMILIATING* (HUMBLE)
1Co 11: 22 God by **h** those who have nothing?

HUMILITY* (HUMBLE)
Ps 45: 4 in the cause of truth, **h** and justice;
Pr 11: 2 but with **h** comes wisdom.
15: 33 LORD, and **h** comes before honor.
18: 12 haughty, but **h** comes before honor.
22: 4 **H** is the fear of the LORD;
Zep 2: 3 Seek righteousness, seek **h**;
Ac 20: 19 I served the Lord with great **h**
2Co 10: 1 By the **h** and gentleness of Christ,
Php 2: 3 in **h** value others above yourselves,
Col 2: 18 let anyone who delights in false **h**
2: 23 their false **h** and their harsh
3: 12 kindness, **h**,
Jas 3: 13 deeds done in the **h** that comes
1Pe 5: 5 with **h** toward one another,

HUNG (HANG)
Dt 21: 23 because anyone who is **h** on a pole
Mt 18: 6 a large millstone **h** around their
Lk 19: 48 because all the people **h** on his
Gal 3: 13 "Cursed is everyone who is **h**

HUNGER (HUNGRY)
Ne 9: 15 In their **h** you gave them bread
Pr 6: 30 to satisfy his **h** when he is starving.
Mt 5: 6 Blessed are those who **h** and thirst
Lk 6: 21 Blessed are you who **h** now, for you
2Co 6: 5 hard work, sleepless nights and **h**;
11: 27 I have known **h** and thirst and have
Rev 7: 16 'Never again will they **h**;

HUNGRY (HUNGER)
Job 24: 10 carry the sheaves, but still go **h**.
Ps 107: 9 and fills the **h** with good things.
146: 7 oppressed and gives food to the **h**.
Pr 19: 15 deep sleep, and the shiftless go **h**.
25: 21 If your enemy is **h**, give him food
27: 7 to the **h** even what is bitter tastes
Isa 58: 7 it not to share your food with the **h**
58: 10 spend yourselves in behalf of the **h**
Eze 18: 7 gives his food to the **h** and
18: 16 gives his food to the **h** and
Mt 15: 32 I do not want to send them away **h**,
25: 35 For I was **h** and you gave me
25: 42 For I was **h** and you gave me
Lk 1: 53 has filled the **h** with good things
Jn 6: 35 comes to me will never go **h**,
Ro 12: 20 "If your enemy is **h**, feed him;
1Co 4: 11 To this very hour we go **h**
Php 4: 12 whether well fed or **h**,

HUR
Ex 17: 12 Aaron and **H** held his hands up—

HURL
Mic 7: 19 **h** all our iniquities into the depths

HURT (HURTS)
Ecc 8: 9 lords it over others to his own **h**.
Mk 16: 18 *it will not* **h** *them at all;*
Rev 2: 11 one who is victorious will not be **h**

HURTS* (HURT)
Ps 15: 4 who keeps an oath even when it **h**,
Pr 26: 28 A lying tongue hates those it **h**,

HUSBAND (HUSBAND'S HUSBANDS)
Pr 31: 11 Her **h** has full confidence in her
31: 23 Her **h** is respected at the city gate,
31: 28 her **h** also, and he praises her:
Isa 54: 5 For your Maker is your **h**—
Jer 3: 14 the LORD, "for I am your **h**.
3: 20 like a woman unfaithful to her **h**,
Jn 4: 17 "I have no **h**," she replied.
Ro 7: 2 bound to her **h** as long as he is
7: 2 but if her **h** dies, she is released
1Co 7: 2 and each woman with her own **h**.
7: 3 The **h** should fulfill his marital
7: 3 and likewise the wife to her **h**.
7: 4 her own body but yields it to her **h**.
7: 4 the **h** does not have authority over
7: 10 wife must not separate from her **h**.
7: 11 or else be reconciled to her **h**.
7: 11 a **h** must not divorce his wife.
7: 13 And if a woman has a **h** who is not
7: 14 sanctified through her believing **h**.
7: 39 bound to her **h** as long as he lives.
7: 39 But if her **h** dies, she is free
2Co 11: 2 I promised you to one **h**, to Christ,
Gal 4: 27 woman than of her who has a **h**."
Eph 5: 23 For the **h** is the head of the wife as
5: 33 and the wife must respect her **h**.
1Ti 5: 9 sixty, has been faithful to her **h**,

HUSBANDMAN See GARDENER

HUSBAND'S (HUSBAND)
Dt 25: 5 Her **h** brother shall take her
Pr 12: 4 of noble character is her **h** crown,

HUSBANDS (HUSBAND)
Eph 5: 22 yourselves to your own **h** as you do
5: 25 **H**, love your wives, just as Christ
5: 28 **h** ought to love their wives as their
Col 3: 18 submit yourselves to your **h**, as is
3: 19 **H**, love your wives and do not be
Titus 2: 4 the younger women to love their **h**
2: 5 and to be subject to their **h**,
1Pe 3: 1 yourselves to your own **h** so that,
3: 7 **H**, in the same way be considerate

HUSHAI
Wise man of David who frustrated Ahithophel's advice and foiled Absalom's revolt (2Sa 15:32–37; 16:15—17:16; 1Ch 27:33).

HYMN* (HYMNS)
Ps 40: 3 mouth, a **h** of praise to our God.
Mt 26: 30 When they had sung a **h**, they went
Mk 14: 26 When they had sung a **h**, they went
1Co 14: 26 each of you has a **h**, or a word

HYMNS* (HYMN)
Ac 16: 25 were praying and singing **h** to God,
Eph 5: 19 to one another with psalms, **h**,
Col 3: 16 with all wisdom through psalms, **h**,

HYPOCRISY* (HYPOCRITE HYPOCRITES HYPOCRITICAL)
Mt 23: 28 on the inside you are full of **h**
Mk 12: 15 But Jesus knew their **h**.
Lk 12: 1 yeast of the Pharisees, which is **h**.
Gal 2: 13 The other Jews joined him in his **h**,
2: 13 by their **h** even Barnabas was led
1Pe 2: 1 of all malice and all deceit, **h**, envy,

HYPOCRITE* (HYPOCRISY)
Mt 7: 5 You **h**, first take the plank
Lk 6: 42 You **h**, first take the plank

HYPOCRITES* (HYPOCRISY)
Ps 26: 4 deceitful, nor do I associate with **h**.
Mt 6: 2 as the **h** do in the synagogues
6: 5 do not be like the **h**, for they love
6: 16 do not look somber as the **h** do,
15: 7 You **h**! Isaiah was right when he
22: 18 "You **h**, why are you trying to trap
23: 13 of the law and Pharisees, you **h**!
23: 15 of the law and Pharisees, you **h**!
23: 23 of the law and Pharisees, you **h**!
23: 25 of the law and Pharisees, you **h**!
23: 27 of the law and Pharisees, you **h**!
23: 29 of the law and Pharisees, you **h**!
24: 51 and assign him a place with the **h**,
Mk 7: 6 when he prophesied about you **h**;
Lk 12: 56 **H**! You know how to interpret
13: 15 The Lord answered him, "You **h**!

HYPOCRITICAL* (HYPOCRISY)
1Ti 4: 2 teachings come through **h** liars,

HYSSOP
Ex 12: 22 Take a bunch of **h**, dip it
Ps 51: 7 Cleanse me with **h**, and I will be
Jn 19: 29 sponge on a stalk of the **h** plant,

ICHABOD*
1Sa 4: 21 She named the boy **I**, saying,

IDLE* (IDLENESS IDLERS)
Dt 32: 47 They are not just **i** words for you—
Job 11: 3 Will your **i** talk reduce others
Ecc 10: 18 because of **i** hands, the house leaks.
11: 6 at evening let your hands not be **i**,
Isa 58: 13 as you please or speaking **i** words,
Col 2: 18 with **i** notions by their unspiritual
1Th 5: 14 those who are **i** and disruptive,
2Th 3: 6 away from every believer who is **i**
3: 7 We were not **i** when we were
3: 11 We hear that some among you are **i**
1Ti 5: 13 they get into the habit of being **i**

IDLENESS* (IDLE)
Pr 31: 27 and does not eat the bread of **i**.

IDLERS* (IDLE)
1Ti 5: 13 And not only do they become **i**,

IDOL (IDOLATER IDOLATERS IDOLATRY IDOLS)
Ex 32: 4 made it into an **i** cast in the shape
Dt 27: 15 is anyone who makes an **i**—
Isa 40: 19 As for an **i**, a metalworker casts it,
41: 7 other nails down the **i** so it will not
44: 15 he makes an **i** and bows down to it.
44: 17 From the rest he makes a god, his **i**;
Hab 2: 18 "Of what value is an **i** carved
1Co 8: 4 We know that "An **i** is nothing

IDOLATER* (IDOL)
1Co 5: 11 or greedy, an **i** or slanderer,
Eph 5: 5 such a person is an **i**—

IDOLATERS (IDOL)
1Co 5: 10 or the greedy and swindlers, or **i**.
6: 9 immoral nor **i** nor adulterers nor

IDOLATRY (IDOL)
1Sa 15: 23 and arrogance like the evil of **i**.
1Co 10: 14 my dear friends, flee from **i**.
Gal 5: 20 **i** and witchcraft;
Col 3: 5 evil desires and greed, which is **i**.
1Pe 4: 3 orgies, carousing and detestable **i**.

IDOLS (IDOL)
Ex 34: 17 "Do not make any **i**.
Dt 32: 16 angered him with their detestable **i**.
Ps 78: 58 aroused his jealousy with their **i**.
Isa 44: 9 All who make **i** are nothing,
Eze 23: 39 sacrificed their children to their **i**,
Mic 5: 13 I will destroy your **i** and your
Ac 15: 20 to abstain from food polluted by **i**,
21: 25 abstain from food sacrificed to **i**,
1Co 8: 1 Now about food sacrificed to **i**:
1Jn 5: 21 children, keep yourselves from **i**.
Rev 2: 14 so that they ate food sacrificed to **i**

IGNORANT (IGNORE)
1Co 15: 34 there are some who are **i** of God—
Heb 5: 2 to deal gently with those who are **i**
1Pe 2: 15 good you should silence the **i** talk
2Pe 3: 16 **i** and unstable people distort,

IGNORE (IGNORANT IGNORED IGNORES)
Dt 22: 1 not **i** it but be sure to take it back
Ps 9: 12 he does not **i** the cries
Heb 2: 3 escape if we **i** so great a salvation?

IGNORED (IGNORE)
Hos 4: 6 because you have **i** the law of your
1Co 14: 38 this, they will themselves be **i**.

IGNORES* (IGNORE)
Pr 10: 17 whoever **i** correction leads others
1Co 14: 38 But if anyone **i** this, they will

ILL (ILLNESS)
Mt 4: 24 to him all who were **i** with various

ILL-GOTTEN
Pr 1: 19 the paths of all who go after **i** gain;
10: 2 **I** treasures have no lasting value,

ILLNESS (ILL)
2Ki 8: 9 ask, 'Will I recover from this **i**?'"
2Ch 16: 12 even in his **i** he did not seek help
Ps 41: 3 restores them from their bed of **i**.
Isa 38: 9 Hezekiah king of Judah after his **i**

ILLUMINATED*
Eph 5: 13 that is **i** becomes a light.
Rev 18: 1 and the earth was **i** by his splendor.

IMAGE (IMAGES)
Ge 1: 26 "Let us make mankind in our **i**,
Ge 1: 27 God created mankind in his own **i**, in the **i** of God
9: 6 for in the **i** of God has God made
Ex 20: 4 make for yourself an **i** in the form
Isa 40: 18 To what **i** will you liken him?
Da 3: 1 King Nebuchadnezzar made an **i**
Lk 20: 24 Whose **i** and inscription are on it?"
Ro 8: 29 to be conformed to the **i** of his Son,
1Co 11: 7 since he is the **i** and glory of God;
2Co 3: 18 his **i** with ever-increasing glory,
4: 4 of Christ, who is the **i** of God.
Col 1: 15 The Son is the **i** of the invisible
3: 10 in knowledge in the **i** of its Creator.
Rev 13: 14 set up an **i** in honor of the beast

IMAGES (IMAGE)
Ps 97: 7 who worship **i** are put to shame,
Jer 10: 14 The **i** he makes are a fraud;
Ro 1: 23 the immortal God for **i** made to

IMAGINATION (IMAGINE)
Eze 13: 2 who prophesy out of their own **i**:

IMAGINE (IMAGINATION)
Eph 3: 20 more than all we ask or **i**,

IMITATE* (IMITATORS)
Dt 18: 9 not learn to **i** the detestable ways
Eze 23: 48 may take warning and not **i** you.
1Co 4: 16 Therefore I urge you to **i** me.
2Th 3: 9 ourselves as a model for you to **i**.
Heb 6: 12 but to **i** those who through faith
13: 7 of their way of life and **i** their faith.
3Jn : 11 do not **i** what is evil but what is

IMITATORS* (IMITATE)
1Th 1: 6 became **i** of us and of the Lord,
2: 14 became **i** of God's churches

IMMANUEL*
Isa 7: 14 birth to a son, and will call him **I**.
8: 8 cover the breadth of your land, **I**!"
Mt 1: 23 they will call him **I**" (which means

IMMENSE
1Ti 1: 16 might display his **i** patience as

IMMORAL* (IMMORALITY)
1Co 5: 9 associate with sexually **i** people—
5: 10 the people of this world who are **i**,
5: 11 or sister but is sexually **i** or greedy,
6: 9 Neither the sexually **i** nor idolaters
Eph 5: 5 No **i**, impure or greedy person—
1Ti 1: 10 for the sexually **i**, for those
Heb 12: 16 See that no one is sexually **i**, or is
13: 4 the adulterer and all the sexually **i**.
Rev 21: 8 the sexually **i**, those who practice
22: 15 arts, the sexually **i**, the murderers,

IMMORALITY* (IMMORAL)
Nu 25: 1 in sexual **i** with Moabite women,
Jer 3: 9 Because Israel's **i** mattered so little
Mt 5: 32 except for sexual **i**, makes her
15: 19 adultery, sexual **i**, theft,
19: 9 except for sexual **i**, and marries
Mk 7: 21 sexual **i**, theft, murder,
Ac 15: 20 from sexual **i**, from the meat
15: 29 animals and from sexual **i**.
21: 25 animals and from sexual **i**."
Ro 13: 13 not in sexual **i** and debauchery,
1Co 5: 1 that there is sexual **i** among you,
6: 13 is not meant for sexual **i**
6: 18 Flee from sexual **i**. All other sins
7: 2 But since sexual **i** is occurring,
10: 8 We should not commit sexual **i**,
Gal 5: 19 sexual **i**, impurity and debauchery;
Eph 5: 3 must not be even a hint of sexual **i**,
Col 3: 5 sexual **i**, impurity, lust, evil desires
1Th 4: 3 that you should avoid sexual **i**;
Jude : 4 of our God into a license for **i**
: 7 gave themselves up to sexual **i**
Rev 2: 14 to idols and committed sexual **i**.
2: 20 misleads my servants into sexual **i**
2: 21 given her time to repent of her **i**,
9: 21 arts, their sexual **i** or their thefts.

IMMORTAL* (IMMORTALITY)
Ro 1: 23 exchanged the glory of the **i** God
1Ti 1: 17 Now to the King eternal, **i**,
6: 16 who alone is **i** and who lives

IMMORTALITY* (IMMORTAL)
Pr 12: 28 there is life; along that path is **i**.
Ro 2: 7 and **i**, he will give eternal life.
1Co 15: 53 and the mortal with **i**.
15: 54 and the mortal with **i**,
2Ti 1: 10 and **i** to light through the gospel.

IMPART
Pr 29: 15 A rod and a reprimand **i** wisdom,

IMPARTIAL*
Jas 3: 17 and good fruit, **i** and sincere.

IMPERISHABLE
1Co 15: 42 is sown is perishable, it is raised **i**;
15: 50 does the perishable inherit the **i**.
1Pe 1: 23 seed, but of **i**, through the living

IMPLORE*
2Co 5: 20 We **i** you on Christ's behalf:

IMPORTANCE* (IMPORTANT)
1Co 15: 3 I passed on to you as of first **i**:

IMPORTANT (IMPORTANCE)
Mt 23: 23 have neglected the more **i** matters
Mk 12: 29 "The most **i** one," answered Jesus,
12: 33 as yourself is more **i** than all burnt
Php 1: 18 The **i** thing is that in every way,

IMPOSSIBLE
Mt 17: 20 Nothing will be **i** for you."
19: 26 "With man this is **i**, but with God
Mk 10: 27 "With man this is **i**, but not
Lk 18: 27 "What is **i** with man is possible
Ac 2: 24 because it was **i** for death to keep
Heb 6: 4 It is **i** for those who have once been
6: 18 in which it is **i** for God to lie,
10: 4 It is **i** for the blood of bulls
11: 6 without faith it is **i** to please God,

IMPOSTORS
2Ti 3: 13 and **i** will go from bad to worse,

IMPRESS* (IMPRESSES)
Dt 6: 7 **I** them on your children.

IMPRESSES* (IMPRESS)
Pr 17: 10 A rebuke **i** a discerning person more

IMPRISONED (PRISON)
1Pe 3: 19 made proclamation to the **i** spirits—

IMPRISONMENT (PRISON)
Heb 11: 36 flogging, and even chains and **i**.

IMPROPER*
Eph 5: 3 because these are **i** for God's holy

IMPURE (IMPURITY)
Mt 12: 43 "When an **i** spirit comes out of a
Ac 10: 15 "Do not call anything **i** that God
Eph 5: 5 No immoral, **i** or greedy person—
1Th 2: 3 not spring from error or **i** motives,
4: 7 For God did not call us to be **i**,
Rev 21: 27 Nothing **i** will ever enter it, nor

IMPURITY (IMPURE)
Ro 1: 24 hearts to sexual **i** for the degrading
Gal 5: 19 immorality, **i** and debauchery;
Eph 4: 19 so as to indulge in every kind of **i**,
5: 3 or of any kind of **i**, or of greed,
Col 3: 5 sexual immorality, **i**, lust,

INCENSE
Ex 30: 1 altar of acacia wood for burning **i**.
40: 5 Place the gold altar of **i** in front
Ps 141: 2 my prayer be set before you like **i**;
Heb 9: 4 which had the golden altar of **i**
Rev 5: 8 were holding golden bowls full of **i**,
8: 4 The smoke of the **i**,

INCLINATION* (INCLINES)
Ge 6: 5 that every **i** of the thoughts
8: 21 every **i** of the human heart is evil

INCLINES* (INCLINATION)
Ecc 10: 2 The heart of the wise **i** to the right,

INCOME
Ecc 5: 10 is never satisfied with their **i**.
1Co 16: 2 of money in keeping with your **i**,

INCOMPARABLE*
Eph 2: 7 ages he might show the **i** riches

INCREASE (EVER-INCREASING INCREASED INCREASING)
Ge 1: 22 "Be fruitful and **i** in number and
8: 17 be fruitful and **i** in number on it."
Ps 62: 10 though your riches **i**, do not set
Pr 22: 16 oppresses the poor to **i** his wealth
Mt 24: 12 Because of the **i** of wickedness,
Lk 17: 5 said to the Lord, "**I** our faith!"
Ro 5: 20 in so that the trespass might **i**.
1Th 3: 12 May the Lord make your love **i**

INCREASED (INCREASE)
Ac 6: 7 of disciples in Jerusalem **i** rapidly,
9: 31 by the Holy Spirit, it **i** in numbers.
Ro 5: 20 where sin **i**, grace **i** all the more,

INCREASING (INCREASE)
Ac 6: 1 the number of disciples was **i**,
2Th 1: 3 all of you have for one another is **i**.
2Pe 1: 8 these qualities in **i** measure,

INCREDIBLE*
Ac 26: 8 you consider it **i** that God raises

INDEBTEDNESS* (DEBT)
Col 2: 14 canceled the charge of our legal **i**,

INDEPENDENT*
1Co 11: 11 in the Lord woman is not **i** of man, nor is man **i** of woman.

INDESCRIBABLE*
2Co 9: 15 Thanks be to God for his **i** gift!

INDESTRUCTIBLE*
Heb 7: 16 the basis of the power of an **i** life.

INDIGNANT
Mk 1: 41 Jesus was **i**. He reached out his
10: 14 When Jesus saw this, he was **i**.

INDISPENSABLE*
1Co 12: 22 body that seem to be weaker are **i**,

INEFFECTIVE*
2Pe 1: 8 they will keep you from being **i**

INEXPRESSIBLE*
2Co 12: 4 up to paradise and heard **i** things,
1Pe 1: 8 are filled with an **i** and glorious joy,

INFANCY* (INFANTS)
2Ti 3: 15 from **i** you have known the Holy

INFANTS (INFANCY)
Ps 8: 2 **i** you have established a stronghold
Mt 21: 16 the lips of children and **i** you, Lord,
1Co 3: 1 are still worldly—mere **i** in Christ.
14: 20 In regard to evil be **i**, but in your
Eph 4: 14 Then we will no longer be **i**,

INFIRMITIES*
Mt 8: 17 "He took up our **i** and bore our

INFLAMED
Ro 1: 27 were **i** with lust for one another.

INFLUENTIAL*
1Co 1: 26 not many were **i**; not many were

INHABITANTS (INHABITED)
Nu 33: 55 do not drive out the **i** of the land,
Rev 8: 13 Woe to the **i** of the earth,

INHABITED (INHABITANTS)
Isa 45: 18 to be empty, but formed it to be **i**—

INHERIT (CO-HEIRS HEIR HEIRS HERITAGE INHERITANCE)
Dt 1: 38 because he will lead Israel to **i** it.
Jos 1: 6 these people to **i** the land I swore
Ps 37: 11 the meek will **i** the land and enjoy
37: 29 The righteous will **i** the land
Zec 2: 12 The Lord will **i** Judah as his
Mt 5: 5 the meek, for they will **i** the earth.
19: 29 as much and will **i** eternal life.
Mk 10: 17 "what must I do to **i** eternal life?"
Lk 10: 25 "what must I do to **i** eternal life?"
18: 18 what must I do to **i** eternal life?"
1Co 6: 9 wrongdoers will not **i** the kingdom
15: 50 cannot **i** the kingdom of God,
Rev 21: 7 who are victorious will **i** all this,

INHERITANCE (INHERIT)
Lev 20: 24 I will give it to you as an **i**, a land
Dt 4: 20 to be the people of his **i**, as you
10: 9 the Lord is their **i**, as the Lord
Jos 14: 3 the Levites an **i** among the rest,
Ps 16: 6 surely I have a delightful **i**.
33: 12 the people he chose for his **i**.
136: 21 and gave their land as an **i**,
Pr 13: 22 A good person leaves an **i** for their
Mt 25: 34 take your **i**, the kingdom prepared
Eph 1: 14 deposit guaranteeing our **i** until
5: 5 has any **i** in the kingdom of Christ
Col 1: 12 share in the **i** of his holy people
3: 24 you will receive an **i** from the Lord
Heb 9: 15 receive the promised eternal **i**—
1Pe 1: 4 into an **i** that can never perish,
1: 4 This **i** is kept in heaven for you,

INIQUITIES (INIQUITY)
Ps 78: 38 he forgave their **i** and did not
103: 10 or repay us according to our **i**.
Isa 53: 5 he was crushed for our **i**;
53: 11 many, and he will bear their **i**.
59: 2 your **i** have separated you from
Mic 7: 19 hurl all our **i** into the depths

INIQUITY (INIQUITIES)
Ps 25: 11 forgive my **i**, though it is great.
32: 5 to you and did not cover up my **i**.
51: 2 Wash away all my **i** and cleanse me
51: 9 from my sins and blot out all my **i**.
Isa 53: 6 has laid on him the **i** of us all.

INJURED
Eze 34: 16 I will bind up the **i** and strengthen
Zec 11: 16 or heal the **i**, or feed the healthy,

INJUSTICE
2Ch 19: 7 the Lord our God there is no **i**

INK
2Co 3: 3 not with **i** but with the Spirit

INN*
Lk 10: 34 brought him to an **i** and took care

INNOCENT
Ex 23: 7 do not put an **i** or honest person
Dt 25: 1 acquitting the **i** and condemning
Pr 6: 17 tongue, hands that shed **i** blood,
17: 26 a fine on the **i** is not good,
Joel 3: 21 I leave their **i** blood unavenged?
Mt 10: 16 shrewd as snakes and as **i** as doves.
27: 4 said, "for I have betrayed **i** blood."
27: 24 "I am **i** of this man's blood,"
Ac 18: 6 be on your own heads! I am **i** of it.
20: 26 you today that I am **i** of the blood
Ro 16: 19 is good, and **i** about what is evil.
1Co 4: 4 clear, but that does not make me **i**.

INQUIRE
Isa 8: 19 should not a people **i** of their God?

INSCRIPTION
Mt 22: 20 image is this? And whose **i**?"
2Ti 2: 19 stands firm, sealed with this **i**:

INSIGHT
1Ki 4: 29 Solomon wisdom and very great **i**,
Ps 119: 99 I have more **i** than all my teachers,
Pr 5: 1 turn your ear to my words of **i**,
7: 4 and to **i**, "You are my relative."
16: 16 gold, to get **i** rather than silver!
20: 5 but one who has **i** draws them out.
21: 30 no **i**, no plan that can succeed
23: 23 wisdom, instruction and **i** as well.
Php 1: 9 more in knowledge and depth of **i**,
2Ti 2: 7 Lord will give you **i** into all this.

INSOLENT
Pr 29: 21 from youth will turn out to be **i**.
Ro 1: 30 **i**, arrogant and boastful;

INSPIRED*
2Sa 23: 1 "The **i** utterance of David son of
Pr 30: 1 Agur son of Jakeh—an **i** utterance.
31: 1 Lemuel—an **i** utterance his mother
Hos 9: 7 a fool, the **i** person a maniac.
1Th 1: 3 your endurance **i** by hope in our

INSTALLED
Ps 2: 6 "I have **i** my king on Zion, my holy

INSTINCT* (INSTINCTS)
2Pe 2: 12 creatures of **i**, born only to be
Jude : 10 things they do understand by **i**—

INSTINCTS* (INSTINCT)
Jude : 19 who follow mere natural **i** and do

INSTITUTED
Ro 13: 2 is rebelling against what God has **i**,

INSTRUCT (INSTRUCTED INSTRUCTION INSTRUCTIONS INSTRUCTOR)
Dt 17: 10 to do everything they **i** you to do.
Ps 32: 8 I will **i** you and teach you
105: 22 to **i** his princes as he pleased
Pr 4: 11 I **i** you in the way of wisdom
9: 9 **I** the wise and they will be wiser
Ro 15: 14 and competent to **i** one another.
1Co 2: 16 mind of the Lord so as to **i** him?"
14: 19 **i** others than ten thousand words

INSTRUCTED (INSTRUCT)
2Ch 26: 5 who **i** him in the fear of God.
Isa 50: 4 my ear to listen like one being **i**.
1Co 14: 31 in turn so that everyone may be **i**
2Ti 2: 25 Opponents must be gently **i**,

INSTRUCTION (INSTRUCT)
Pr 1: 2 for gaining wisdom and **i**;
1: 3 for receiving **i** in prudent behavior,
1: 7 but fools despise wisdom and **i**.
1: 8 your father's **i** and do not forsake
4: 1 Listen, my sons, to a father's **i**;
4: 13 Hold on to **i**, do not let it go;
6: 23 correction and **i** are the way to life,
8: 10 Choose my **i** instead of silver,
8: 33 Listen to my **i** and be wise;
13: 1 A wise son heeds his father's **i**,
13: 13 Whoever scorns **i** will pay for it,
15: 33 Wisdom's **i** is to fear the Lord,
16: 20 Whoever gives heed to **i** prospers,
16: 21 and gracious words promote **i**.
Pr 23: 12 Apply your heart to **i** and your ears
23: 23 wisdom, **i** and insight as well.
28: 9 If anyone turns a deaf ear to my **i**,
29: 18 is the one who heeds wisdom's **i**.
Isa 8: 20 Consult God's **i** and the testimony
1Co 14: 6 or prophecy or word of **i**?
14: 26 hymn, or a word of **i**, a revelation,
Eph 6: 4 in the training and **i** of the Lord.
1Th 4: 8 who rejects this **i** does not reject
2Th 3: 14 anyone who does not obey our **i**
1Ti 6: 3 sound **i** of our Lord Jesus Christ
2Ti 4: 2 with great patience and careful **i**.

INSTRUCTIONS (INSTRUCT)
1Ti 3: 14 I am writing you these **i** so that,

INSTRUCTOR (INSTRUCT)
Mt 23: 10 for you have one **I**, the Messiah.
Gal 6: 6 share all good things with their **i**.

INSTRUMENT* (INSTRUMENTS)
Eze 33: 32 beautiful voice and plays an **i** well,
Ac 9: 15 man is my chosen **i** to proclaim
Ro 6: 13 to sin as an **i** of wickedness,
6: 13 to him as an **i** of righteousness.

INSTRUMENTS (INSTRUMENT)
2Ch 23: 13 their **i** were leading the praises.
2Ti 2: 21 from the latter will be **i** for special

INSULT (INSULTED INSULTS)
Pr 12: 16 but the prudent overlook an **i**.
Mt 5: 11 are you when people **i** you,
Lk 6: 22 when they exclude you and **i** you
1Pe 3: 9 not repay evil with evil or **i** with **i**.

INSULTED (INSULT)
Heb 10: 29 and who has **i** the Spirit of grace?
1Pe 4: 14 If you are **i** because of the name

INSULTS (INSULT)
Ps 22: 7 they hurl **i**, shaking their heads.
69: 9 the **i** of those who insult you fall
Pr 9: 7 corrects a mocker invites **i**;
22: 10 quarrels and **i** are ended.
Mk 15: 29 who passed by hurled **i** at him,
Jn 9: 28 Then they hurled **i** at him and said,
Ro 15: 3 "The **i** of those who insult you
2Co 12: 10 in weaknesses, in **i**, in hardships,
1Pe 2: 23 When they hurled their **i** at him,

INTEGRITY*
Dt 9: 5 your **i** that you are going in to take
1Ki 9: 4 walk before me faithfully with **i**
1Ch 29: 17 the heart and are pleased with **i**.
Ne 7: 2 he was a man of **i** and feared God
Job 2: 3 And he still maintains his **i**,
2: 9 "Are you still maintaining your **i**?
6: 29 reconsider, for my **i** is at stake.
27: 5 till I die, I will not deny my **i**.
Ps 7: 8 according to my **i**, O Most High.
25: 21 May **i** and uprightness protect me,
41: 12 Because of my **i** you uphold me
78: 72 David shepherded them with **i**
Pr 10: 9 Whoever walks in **i** walks securely,
11: 3 The **i** of the upright guides them,
13: 6 guards the person of **i**,
29: 10 The bloodthirsty hate a person of **i**
Isa 45: 23 mouth has uttered in all **i** a word
59: 4 no one pleads a case with **i**.
Mt 22: 16 "we know that you are a man of **i**
Mk 12: 14 we know that you are a man of **i**.
2Co 1: 12 you, with **i** and godly sincerity.
Titus 2: 7 In your teaching show **i**,

INTELLIGENCE (INTELLIGENT)
Isa 29: 14 the **i** of the intelligent will vanish."
1Co 1: 19 the **i** of the intelligent I will

INTELLIGENT (INTELLIGENCE)
Isa 29: 14 intelligence of the **i** will vanish."

INTELLIGIBLE*
1Co 14: 9 Unless you speak **i** words with
14: 19 I would rather speak five **i** words

INTENDED
Ge 50: 20 You **i** to harm me, but God **i** it

INTENSE
1Th 2: 17 our **i** longing we made every effort
Rev 16: 9 They were seared by the **i** heat

INTERCEDE (INTERCEDES INTERCEDING INTERCESSION INTERCESSOR)
1Sa 2: 25 sins against the Lord, who will **i**
Heb 7: 25 him, because he always lives to **i**

INTERCEDES* (INTERCEDE)
Ro 8: 26 the Spirit himself **i** for us through
8: 27 Spirit, because the Spirit **i** for God's

INTERCEDING* (INTERCEDE)
Ro 8: 34 hand of God and is also **i** for us.

INTERCESSION* (INTERCEDE)
Isa 53: 12 and made **i** for the transgressors.
1Ti 2: 1 **i** and thanksgiving be made for all

INTERCESSOR* (INTERCEDE)
Job 16: 20 My **i** is my friend as my eyes pour

INTEREST (INTERESTS)
Lev 25: 36 Do not take **i** or any profit
Dt 23: 20 You may charge a foreigner **i**,
Ps 15: 5 lends money to the poor without **i**;
Ne 5: 10 But let us stop charging **i**!
Mt 25: 27 would have received it back with **i**.

INTERESTS (INTEREST)
1Co 7: 34 and his **i** are divided.
Php 2: 4 each of you to the **i** of the others.
2: 21 everyone looks out for their own **i**,

INTERFERE*
2Sa 19: 22 What right do you have to **i**?
Ezr 6: 7 Do not **i** with the work on this

INTERMARRY (MARRY)
Dt 7: 3 Do not **i** with them. Do not give
Ezr 9: 14 **i** with the peoples who commit

INTERPRET (INTERPRETATION INTERPRETER INTERPRETS)
Ge 41: 15 a dream, and no one can **i** it.
Mt 16: 3 cannot **i** the signs of the times.
1Co 12: 30 Do all speak in tongues? Do all **i**?
14: 13 pray that they may **i** what they say.
14: 27 one at a time, and someone must **i**.

INTERPRETATION (INTERPRET)
1Co 12: 10 to still another the **i** of tongues.
14: 26 a revelation, a tongue or an **i**.
2Pe 1: 20 by the prophet's own **i** of things.

INTERPRETER* (INTERPRET)
Ge 42: 23 them, since he was using an **i**.
1Co 14: 28 If there is no **i**, the speaker should

INTERPRETS (INTERPRET)
1Co 14: 5 someone **i**, so that the church

INTERVENED
Ac 15: 14 to us how God first **i** to choose

INTOXICATED
Pr 5: 19 may you ever be **i** with her love.
5: 20 son, be **i** with another man's wife?

INVADED
2Ki 17: 5 king of Assyria **i** the entire land,
24: 1 king of Babylon **i** the land,

INVENT*
Ro 1: 30 they **i** ways of doing evil;

INVESTIGATED
Lk 1: 3 I myself have carefully **i** everything

INVISIBLE*
Ro 1: 20 of the world God's **i** qualities—
Col 1: 15 The Son is the image of the **i** God,
1: 16 visible and **i**, whether thrones
1Ti 1: 17 eternal, immortal, **i**, the only God,
Heb 11: 27 because he saw him who is **i**.

INVITE (INVITED INVITES)
Pr 18: 6 strife, and their mouths **i** a beating.
Mt 22: 9 **i** to the banquet anyone you find.'
25: 38 we see you a stranger and **i** you in,
Lk 14: 12 or dinner, do not **i** your friends,
14: 13 you give a banquet, **i** the poor,

INVITED (INVITE)
Zep 1: 7 he has consecrated those he has **i**.
Mt 22: 14 "For many are **i**, but few are
25: 35 I was a stranger and you **i** me in,
Lk 14: 10 But when you are **i**, take the lowest
Rev 19: 9 Blessed are those who are **i**

INVITES (INVITE)
1Co 10: 27 If an unbeliever **i** you to a meal

IRON
2Ki 6: 6 threw it there, and made the **i** float.
Ps 2: 9 You will break them with a rod of **i**;
Pr 27: 17 As **i** sharpens **i**, so one person
Da 2: 33 its legs of **i**, its feet partly of **i**
1Ti 4: 2 have been seared as with a hot **i**.
Rev 2: 27 'will rule them with an **i** scepter
12: 5 all the nations with an **i** scepter."
19: 15 will rule them with an **i** scepter."

IRRELIGIOUS*
1Ti 1: 9 the unholy and **i**, for those who kill

IRREVOCABLE*
Ro 11: 29 for God's gifts and his call are **i**.

ISAAC
Son of Abraham by Sarah (Ge 17:19; 21:1–7; 1Ch 1:28). Abrahamic covenant perpetuated through (Ge 17:21; 26:2–5). Offered up by Abraham (Ge 22; Heb 11:17–19). Rebekah taken as wife (Ge 24). Inherited Abraham's estate (Ge 25:5). Fathered Esau and Jacob (Ge 25:19–26; 1Ch 1:34). Nearly lost Rebekah to Abimelek (Ge 26:1–11). Covenant with Abimelek (Ge 26:12–31). Tricked into blessing Jacob (Ge 27). Death (Ge 35:27–29). Father of Israel (Ex 3:6; Dt 29:13; Ro 9:10).

ISAIAH
Prophet to Judah (Isa 1:1). Called by the LORD (Isa 6). Announced judgment to Ahaz (Isa 7), deliverance from Assyria to Hezekiah (2Ki 19; Isa 36–37), deliverance from death to Hezekiah (2Ki 20:1–11; Isa 38). Chronicler of Judah's history (2Ch 26:22; 32:32).

ISH-BOSHETH*
Son of Saul who attempted to succeed him as king (2Sa 2:8—4:12; 1Ch 8:33).

ISHMAEL
Son of Abraham by Hagar (Ge 16; 1Ch 1:28). Blessed, but not son of covenant (Ge 17:18–21; Gal 4:21–31). Sent away by Sarah (Ge 21:8–21). Children (Ge 25:12–18; 1Ch 1:29–31). Death (Ge 25:17).

ISLAND
Rev 1: 9 was on the **i** of Patmos because
16: 20 Every **i** fled away

ISRAEL (ISRAEL'S ISRAELITE ISRAELITES)
1. Name given to Jacob (see JACOB).
2. Corporate name of Jacob's descendants; often specifically northern kingdom.
Ex 28: 11 the sons of **I** on the two stones
28: 29 of the sons of **I** over his heart
Nu 24: 17 a scepter will rise out of **I**.
Dt 6: 4 Hear, O **I**: The LORD our God,
10: 12 And now, **I**, what does the LORD
Jos 4: 22 them, '**I** crossed the Jordan on dry
Jdg 17: 6 In those days **I** had no king;
Ru 2: 12 the God of **I**, under whose wings
1Sa 3: 20 And all **I** from Dan to Beersheba
4: 21 "The Glory has departed from **I**"—
14: 23 So on that day the LORD saved **I**,
15: 26 has rejected you as king over **I**!"
17: 46 will know that there is a God in **I**.
18: 16 But all **I** and Judah loved David,
2Sa 5: 2 'You will shepherd my people **I**,
5: 3 they anointed David king over **I**.
14: 25 all **I** there was not a man so highly
1Ki 1: 35 I have appointed him ruler over **I**
10: 9 of the LORD's eternal love for **I**,
12: 1 all **I** had gone there to make him
18: 17 "Is that you, you troubler of **I**?"
19: 18 Yet I reserve seven thousand in **I**—
2Ki 5: 8 know that there is a prophet in **I**."
1Ch 17: 22 made your people **I** your very own
21: 1 Satan rose up against **I** and incited
29: 25 Solomon in the sight of all **I**
2Ch 9: 8 the love of your God for **I** and his
Ps 73: 1 Surely God is good to **I**, to those
81: 8 if you would only listen to me, **I**!
98: 3 his love and his faithfulness to **I**;
99: 8 you were to **I** a forgiving God,
Isa 11: 12 nations and gather the exiles of **I**;
27: 6 **I** will bud and blossom and fill all
44: 21 Jacob, for you, **I**, are my servant.
46: 13 salvation to Zion, my splendor to **I**.
Jer 2: 3 **I** was holy to the LORD,
23: 6 be saved and **I** will live in safety.
31: 2 I will come to give rest to **I**."
31: 10 'He who scattered **I** will gather
31: 31 new covenant with the people of **I**
33: 17 a man to sit on the throne of **I**,
Eze 3: 17 a watchman for the people of **I**;
33: 7 a watchman for the people of **I**;
34: 2 against the shepherds of **I**;
37: 28 that I the LORD make **I** holy,
39: 23 that the people of **I** went into exile
Da 9: 20 the sin of my people **I** and making
Hos 11: 1 "When **I** was a child, I loved him,
Am 4: 12 this is what I will do to you, **I**,
7: 11 and **I** will surely go into exile,
8: 2 "The time is ripe for my people **I**;
9: 14 I will bring my people **I** back
Mic 5: 2 one who will be ruler over **I**,
Zec 11: 14 family bond between Judah and **I**.
Mal 1: 5 even beyond the borders of **I**!'
Mt 2: 6 who will shepherd my people **I**.'"
10: 6 Go rather to the lost sheep of **I**.
15: 24 sent only to the lost sheep of **I**."
Mk 12: 29 'Hear, O **I**: The Lord our God,
Lk 22: 30 judging the twelve tribes of **I**.
Ac 1: 6 going to restore the kingdom to **I**?"
9: 15 their kings and to the people of **I**.
Ro 9: 4 the people of **I**. Theirs is
9: 6 all who are descended from **I** are **I**.
9: 31 but the people of **I**, who pursued
11: 7 of **I** sought so earnestly they did
11: 26 and in this way all **I** will be saved.
Gal 6: 16 follow this rule—to the **I** of God.
Eph 2: 12 excluded from citizenship in **I**
3: 6 Gentiles are heirs together with **I**,
Heb 8: 8 new covenant with the people of **I**
Rev 7: 4 144,000 from all the tribes of **I**.
21: 12 the names of the twelve tribes of **I**.

ISRAEL'S (ISRAEL)
Jdg 10: 16 he could bear **I** misery no longer.
2Sa 23: 1 God of Jacob, the hero of **I** songs:
Isa 44: 6 **I** King and Redeemer, the LORD
Jer 3: 9 Because **I** immorality mattered so
31: 9 because I am **I** father, and Ephraim
Jn 3: 10 "You are **I** teacher," said Jesus,

ISRAELITE (ISRAEL)
Ex 16: 1 The whole **I** community set
35: 29 All the **I** men and women who
Nu 8: 16 offspring from every **I** woman.
20: 1 the whole **I** community arrived
20: 22 The whole **I** community set
Jn 1: 47 "Here truly is an **I** in whom there
Ro 11: 1 I am an **I** myself, a descendant

ISRAELITES (ISRAEL)
Ex 1: 7 but the **I** were exceedingly fruitful;
2: 23 The **I** groaned in their slavery
3: 9 the cry of the **I** has reached me,
12: 35 The **I** did as Moses instructed
12: 37 The **I** journeyed from Rameses
14: 22 the **I** went through the sea on dry
16: 12 have heard the grumbling of the **I**.
16: 35 The **I** ate manna forty years,
24: 17 To the **I** the glory of the LORD
28: 30 for the **I** over his heart before
29: 45 I will dwell among the **I** and be
31: 16 The **I** are to observe the Sabbath,
33: 5 "Tell the **I**, 'You are a stiff-necked
39: 42 The **I** had done all the work just as
Lev 22: 32 be acknowledged as holy by the **I**.
25: 46 rule over your fellow **I** ruthlessly.
25: 55 for the **I** belong to me as servants.
Nu 2: 32 These are the **I**, counted according
6: 23 'This is how you are to bless the **I**.
9: 2 "Have the **I** celebrate the Passover
9: 17 the cloud settled, the **I** encamped.
10: 12 **I** set out from the Desert of Sinai
14: 2 All the **I** grumbled against Moses
20: 12 me as holy in the sight of the **I**,
21: 6 bit the people and many **I** died.
26: 65 had told those **I** they would surely
27: 12 and see the land I have given the **I**.
33: 3 The **I** set out from Rameses
35: 10 "Speak to the **I** and say to them:
Dt 33: 1 on the **I** before his death.
Jos 1: 2 about to give to them—to the **I**.
5: 6 The **I** had moved
7: 1 the **I** were unfaithful in regard
8: 32 in the presence of the **I**,
18: 1 whole assembly of the **I** gathered
21: 3 the **I** gave the Levites the following
22: 9 of Manasseh left the **I** at Shiloh
Jdg 2: 11 Then the **I** did evil in the eyes
3: 12 Again the **I** did evil in the eyes
4: 1 Again the **I** did evil in the eyes
6: 1 The **I** did evil in the eyes
10: 6 because the **I** forsook the LORD
13: 1 Again the **I** did evil in the eyes
1Sa 17: 2 Saul and the **I** assembled
1Ki 8: 63 all the **I** dedicated the temple
9: 22 did not make slaves of any of the **I**;
12: 17 as for the **I** who were living
2Ki 17: 24 towns of Samaria to replace the **I**.
1Ch 9: 2 in their own towns were some **I**,
10: 1 the **I** fled before them, and many
11: 4 all the **I** marched to Jerusalem
2Ch 7: 6 and all the **I** were standing.
Ne 1: 6 I confess the sins we **I**,
Jer 16: 14 who brought the **I** up out of Egypt,'
Hos 1: 10 "Yet the **I** will be like the sand
3: 1 Love her as the LORD loves the **I**,

Am 4: 5 you **I**, for this is what you love
Mic 5: 3 of his brothers return to join the **I**.
Ro 9: 27 number of the **I** be like the sand
10: 1 to God for the **I** is that they may be
10: 16 all the **I** accepted the good news.
2Co 11: 22 So am I. Are they **I**? So am I.

ISSACHAR

Son of Jacob by Leah (Ge 30:18; 35:23; 1Ch 2:1). Tribe of blessed (Ge 49:14–15; Dt 33:18–19), numbered (Nu 1:29; 26:25), allotted land (Jos 19:17–23; Eze 48:25), assisted Deborah (Jdg 5:15), 12,000 from (Rev 7:7).

ITALY

Ac 27: 1 decided that we would sail for **I**,
Heb 13: 24 from **I** send you their greetings.

ITCHING*

2Ti 4: 3 say what their **i** ears want to hear.

ITHAMAR

Son of Aaron (Ex 6:23; 1Ch 6:3). Duties at tabernacle (Ex 38:21; Nu 4:21–33; 7:8).

ITTAI

2Sa 15: 19 The king said to **I** the Gittite,

IVORY

1Ki 10: 22 silver and **i**, and apes and baboons.
22: 39 palace he built and adorned with **i**,

JABBOK

Ge 32: 22 sons and crossed the ford of the **J**.
Dt 3: 16 the border) and out to the **J** River,

JABESH (JABESH GILEAD)

1Sa 31: 12 wall of Beth Shan and went to **J**,
1Ch 10: 12 bones under the great tree in **J**,

JABESH GILEAD (JABESH)

Jdg 21: 8 none of the people of **J** were there.
1Sa 11: 1 Ammonite went up and besieged **J**.
2Sa 2: 4 men from **J** who had buried Saul,

JACOB

Second son of Isaac, twin of Esau (Ge 25:21–26; 1Ch 1:34). Bought Esau's birthright (Ge 25:29–34); tricked Isaac into blessing him (Ge 27:1–37). Fled to Harran (Ge 28:1–5). Abrahamic covenant perpetuated through (Ge 28:13–15; Mal 1:2). Vision at Bethel (Ge 28:10–22). Served Laban for Rachel and Leah (Ge 29:1–30). Children (Ge 29:31—30:24; 35:16–26; 1Ch 2–9). Flocks increased (Ge 30:25–43). Returned to Canaan (Ge 31). Wrestled with God; name changed to Israel (Ge 32:22–32). Reconciled to Esau (Ge 33). Returned to Bethel (Ge 35:1–15). Favored Joseph (Ge 37:3). Sent sons to Egypt during famine (Ge 42–43). Settled in Egypt (Ge 46). Blessed Ephraim and Manasseh (Ge 48). Blessed sons (Ge 49:1–28; Heb 11:21). Death (Ge 49:29–33). Burial (Ge 50:1–14).

JAEL*

Woman who killed Canaanite general, Sisera (Jdg 4:17–22; 5:24–27).

JAIR

Judge from Gilead (Jdg 10:3–5).

JAIRUS*

Synagogue ruler whose daughter Jesus raised (Mk 5:22–43; Lk 8:41–56).

JAMES

1. Apostle; brother of John (Mt 4:21–22; 10:2; Mk 3:17; Lk 5:1–10). At transfiguration (Mt 17:1–13; Mk 9:1–13; Lk 9:28–36). Killed by Herod (Ac 12:2).

2. Apostle; son of Alphaeus (Mt 10:3; Mk 3:18; Lk 6:15).

3. Brother of Jesus (Mt 13:55; Mk 6:3; Lk 24:10; Gal 1:19) and Judas (Jude 1). With believers before Pentecost (Ac 1:13). Leader of church at Jerusalem (Ac 12:17; 15; 21:18; Gal 2:9, 12). Author of epistle (Jas 1:1).

JAPHETH

Son of Noah (Ge 5:32; 1Ch 1:4–5). Blessed (Ge 9:18–28). Sons of (Ge 10:2–5).

JAR (JARS)

Ge 24: 14 'Please let down your **j** that I may
1Ki 17: 14 'The **j** of flour will not be used
Jer 19: 1 "Go and buy a clay **j** from a potter.
Lk 8: 16 hides it in a clay **j** or puts it under

JARS (JAR)

Jn 2: 6 Nearby stood six stone water **j**,
2Co 4: 7 we have this treasure in **j** of clay

JASPER

Ex 28: 20 row shall be topaz, onyx and **j**.
Eze 28: 13 topaz, onyx and **j**, lapis lazuli,
Rev 4: 3 sat there had the appearance of **j**
21: 19 The first foundation was **j**,

JAVELIN

1Sa 17: 45 me with sword and spear and **j**,

JAWBONE

Jdg 15: 15 Finding a fresh **j** of a donkey,

JEALOUS (JEALOUSLY JEALOUSY)

Ex 20: 5 am a **j** God, punishing the children
34: 14 whose name is **J**, is a **j** God.
Dt 4: 24 God is a consuming fire, a **j** God.
6: 15 is a **j** God and his anger will burn
32: 21 They made me **j** by what is no god
Jos 24: 19 He is a holy God; he is a **j** God.
Eze 16: 38 vengeance of my wrath and **j** anger.
16: 42 **j** anger will turn away from you;
23: 25 I will direct my **j** anger against you,
36: 6 in my **j** wrath because you have
Joel 2: 18 Then the LORD was **j** for his land
Na 1: 2 The LORD is a **j** and avenging
Zep 3: 8 consumed by the fire of my **j** anger.
Zec 1: 14 'I am very **j** for Jerusalem and Zion
8: 2 "I am very **j** for Zion;
2Co 11: 2 am **j** for you with a godly jealousy.

JEALOUSLY* (JEALOUS)

Jas 4: 5 says without reason that he **j** longs

JEALOUSY (JEALOUS)

Ps 79: 5 How long will your **j** burn like fire?
Pr 6: 34 For **j** arouses a husband's fury,
27: 4 but who can stand before **j**?
SS 8: 6 death, its **j** unyielding as the grave.
Zep 1: 18 fire of his **j** the whole earth will be
Zec 8: 2 I am burning with **j** for her."
Ro 13: 13 not in dissension and **j**.
1Co 3: 3 For since there is **j** and quarreling
10: 22 we trying to arouse the Lord's **j**?
2Co 11: 2 I am jealous for you with a godly **j**.
12: 20 I fear that there may be discord, **j**,
Gal 5: 20 hatred, discord, **j**, fits of rage,

JEERS*

Heb 11: 36 Some faced **j** and flogging,

JEHOAHAZ

1. Son of Jehu; king of Israel (2Ki 13:1–9).

2. Son of Josiah; king of Judah (2Ki 23:31–34; 2Ch 36:1–4).

JEHOASH

1. See JOASH.

2. Son of Jehoahaz; king of Israel. Defeat of Aram prophesied by Elisha (2Ki 13:10–25). Defeated Amaziah in Jerusalem (2Ki 14:1–16; 2Ch 25:17–24).

JEHOIACHIN

Son of Jehoiakim; king of Judah exiled by Nebuchadnezzar (2Ki 24:8–17; 2Ch 36:8–10; Jer 22:24–30; 24:1). Raised from prisoner status (2Ki 25:27–30; Jer 52:31–34).

JEHOIADA

Priest who sheltered Joash from Athaliah (2Ki 11–12; 2Ch 22:11—24:16).

JEHOIAKIM

Son of Josiah; made king of Judah by Pharaoh Necho (2Ki 23:34—24:6; 2Ch 36:4–8; Jer 22:18–23). Burned scroll of Jeremiah's prophecies (Jer 36).

JEHORAM

1. Son of Jehoshaphat; king of Judah (2Ki 8:16–24). Prophesied against by Elijah; killed by the LORD (2Ch 21).

2. See JORAM.

JEHOSHAPHAT

Son of Asa; king of Judah. Strengthened his kingdom (2Ch 17). Joined with Ahab against Aram (2Ki 22; 2Ch 18). Established judges (2Ch 19). Joined with Joram against Moab (2Ki 3; 2Ch 20).

JEHU

1. Prophet against Baasha (2Ki 16:1–7).

2. King of Israel. Anointed by Elijah to obliterate house of Ahab (1Ki 19:16–17); anointed by servant of Elisha (2Ki 9:1–13). Killed Joram and Ahaziah (2Ki 9:14–29; 2Ch 22:7–9), Jezebel (2Ki 9:30–37), relatives of Ahab (2Ki 10:1–17), ministers of Baal (2Ki 10:18–29). Death (2Ki 10:30–36).

JEPHTHAH

Judge from Gilead who delivered Israel from Ammon (Jdg 10:6—12:7). Made rash vow concerning his daughter (Jdg 11:30–40).

JEREMIAH

Prophet to Judah (Jer 1:1–3). Called by the LORD (Jer 1). Put in stocks (Jer 20:1–3). Threatened for prophesying (Jer 11:18–23; 26). Opposed by Hananiah (Jer 28). Scroll burned (Jer 36). Imprisoned (Jer 37). Thrown into cistern (Jer 38). Forced to Egypt with those fleeing Babylonians (Jer 43).

JERICHO

Nu 22: 1 along the Jordan across from **J**.
Jos 3: 16 the people crossed over opposite **J**.
5: 10 camped at Gilgal on the plains of **J**,
Lk 10: 30 going down from Jerusalem to **J**,
Heb 11: 30 By faith the walls of **J** fell,

JEROBOAM

1. Official of Solomon; rebelled to become first king of Israel (1Ki 11:26–40; 12:1–20; 2Ch 10). Idolatry (1Ki 12:25–33); judgment for (1Ki 13–14; 2Ch 13).

2. Son of Jehoash; king of Israel (1Ki 14:23–29).

JERUSALEM

Jos 10: 1 Now Adoni-Zedek king of **J** heard
15: 8 slope of the Jebusite city (that is, **J**).
Jdg 1: 8 The men of Judah attacked **J**
1Sa 17: 54 Philistine's head and brought it to **J**
2Sa 5: 5 in **J** he reigned over all Israel
5: 6 his men marched to **J** to attack
9: 13 And Mephibosheth lived in **J**,
11: 1 But David remained in **J**.
15: 29 took the ark of God back to **J**
24: 16 stretched out his hand to destroy **J**,
1Ki 3: 1 the LORD, and the wall around **J**.
9: 15 terraces, the wall of **J**, and Hazor,
9: 19 whatever he desired to build in **J**,
10: 26 cities and also with him in **J**.
10: 27 silver as common in **J** as stones,
11: 7 On a hill east of **J**, Solomon built
11: 13 my servant and for the sake of **J**,
11: 36 always have a lamp before me in **J**,
11: 42 in **J** over all Israel forty years.
12: 27 at the temple of the LORD in **J**,
14: 21 he reigned seventeen years in **J**,
14: 25 Shishak king of Egypt attacked **J**.
15: 2 and he reigned in **J** three years.
15: 10 and he reigned in **J** forty-one years.
22: 42 he reigned in **J** twenty-five years.
2Ki 8: 17 and he reigned in **J** eight years.
8: 26 king, and he reigned in **J** one year.
12: 1 and he reigned in **J** forty years.
12: 17 Then he turned to attack **J**.
14: 2 he reigned in **J** twenty-nine years.
14: 13 broke down the wall of **J**
15: 2 he reigned in **J** fifty-two years.
15: 33 and he reigned in **J** sixteen years.
16: 2 and he reigned in **J** sixteen years.
16: 5 Israel marched up to fight against **J**
18: 2 he reigned in **J** twenty-nine years.
18: 17 They came up to **J** and stopped
19: 31 For out of **J** will come a remnant,
21: 1 and he reigned in **J** fifty-five years.
21: 12 going to bring such disaster on **J**
21: 19 king, and he reigned in **J** two years.
22: 1 he reigned in **J** thirty-one years.
23: 27 I will reject **J**, the city I chose,
23: 31 and he reigned in **J** three months.
23: 36 and he reigned in **J** eleven years.
24: 8 and he reigned in **J** three months.
24: 10 king of Babylon advanced on **J**
24: 14 He carried all **J** into exile:
24: 18 and he reigned in **J** eleven years.
24: 20 anger that all this happened to **J**
25: 1 Babylon marched against **J** with his
25: 9 royal palace and all the houses of **J**.
1Ch 11: 4 all the Israelites marched to **J**
21: 16 sword in his hand extended over **J**.
2Ch 1: 4 he had pitched a tent for it in **J**.
3: 1 the LORD in **J** on Mount Moriah,
6: 6 now I have chosen **J** for my Name
9: 1 she came to **J** to test him with hard
20: 15 and all who live in Judah and **J**!
20: 27 Judah and **J** returned joyfully to **J**,
29: 8 LORD has fallen on Judah and **J**;
36: 19 and broke down the wall of **J**;
Ezr 1: 2 a temple for him at **J** in Judah.
2: 1 to Babylon (they returned to **J**
3: 1 assembled together as one in **J**.
4: 12 up to us from you have gone to **J**

Ezr 4: 24 of God in **J** came to a standstill
6: 12 or to destroy this temple in **J**.
7: 8 Ezra arrived in **J** in the fifth month
9: 9 a wall of protection in Judah and **J**.
10: 7 **J** for all the exiles to assemble in **J**.
Ne 1: 2 survived the exile, and also about **J**.
1: 3 The wall of **J** is broken down,
2: 11 I went to **J**, and after staying there
2: 17 let us rebuild the wall of **J**,
2: 20 you have no share in **J** or any claim
3: 8 They restored **J** as far as the Broad
4: 8 fight against **J** and stir up trouble
11: 1 leaders of the people settled in **J**.
12: 27 At the dedication of the wall of **J**,
12: 43 in **J** could be heard far away.
Ps 51: 18 Zion, to build up the walls of **J**.
79: 1 they have reduced **J** to rubble.
122: 2 feet are standing in your gates, **J**.
122: 3 **J** is built like a city that is closely
122: 6 Pray for the peace of **J**:
125: 2 As the mountains surround **J**,
128: 5 see the prosperity of **J** all the days
137: 5 If I forget you, **J**, may my right
147: 2 The LORD builds up **J**;
147: 12 Extol the LORD, **J**;
SS 6: 4 as lovely as **J**, as majestic as troops
Isa 1: 1 and **J** that Isaiah son of Amoz saw
2: 1 Amoz saw concerning Judah and **J**:
3: 1 is about to take from **J** and Judah
3: 8 **J** staggers, Judah is falling;
4: 3 are recorded among the living in **J**.
8: 14 for the people of **J** he will be a trap
27: 13 LORD on the holy mountain in **J**.
31: 5 the LORD Almighty will shield **J**;
33: 20 your eyes will see **J**, a peaceful
40: 2 Speak tenderly to **J**, and proclaim
40: 9 You who bring good news to **J**,
52: 1 on your garments of splendor, **J**,
52: 2 rise up, sit enthroned, **J**.
62: 6 posted watchmen on your walls, **J**;
62: 7 give him no rest till he establishes **J**
65: 18 for I will create **J** to be a delight
Jer 2: 2 and proclaim in the hearing of **J**:
3: 17 time they will call **J** The Throne
4: 5 in Judah and proclaim in **J** and say:
4: 14 **J**, wash the evil from your heart
5: 1 "Go up and down the streets of **J**,
6: 6 and build siege ramps against **J**.
8: 5 Why does **J** always turn away?
9: 11 "I will make **J** a heap of ruins,
13: 27 Woe to you, **J**! How long will you
23: 14 the people of **J** are like Gomorrah."
24: 1 carried into exile from **J** to Babylon
26: 18 **J** will become a heap of rubble,
32: 2 of Babylon was then besieging **J**,
33: 10 the streets of **J** that are deserted,
39: 1 Babylon marched against **J** with his
51: 50 a distant land, and call to mind **J**."
52: 14 broke down all the walls around **J**.
La 1: 7 and wandering **J** remembers all
Eze 14: 21 I send against **J** my four dreadful
16: 2 man, confront **J** with her detestable
Da 6: 10 the windows opened toward **J**.
9: 2 of **J** would last seventy years.
9: 12 done like what has been done to **J**.
9: 25 rebuild **J** until the Anointed One,
Joel 3: 1 restore the fortunes of Judah and **J**,
3: 16 from Zion and thunder from **J**;
3: 17 **J** will be holy; never again will
Am 2: 5 will consume the fortresses of **J**."
Ob : 11 entered his gates and cast lots for **J**,
Mic 1: 5 is Judah's high place? Is it not **J**?
4: 2 the word of the LORD from **J**.
Zep 3: 16 On that day they will say to **J**,
Zec 1: 14 'I am very jealous for **J** and Zion,
1: 17 comfort Zion and choose **J**.'"
2: 2 me, "To measure **J**, to find out how
2: 4 man, '**J** will be a city without walls
8: 3 **J** will be called the Faithful City,
8: 8 I will bring them back to live in **J**;
8: 15 determined to do good again to **J**
8: 22 powerful nations will come to **J**
9: 9 Shout, Daughter **J**! See, your king
9: 10 Ephraim and the warhorses from **J**,
12: 3 I will make **J** an immovable rock
12: 10 the inhabitants of **J** a spirit of grace
14: 2 I will gather all the nations to **J**
14: 8 living water will flow out from **J**,
14: 16 nations that have attacked **J** will go
Mt 16: 21 to his disciples that he must go to **J**
20: 18 "We are going up to **J**, and the Son
21: 10 When Jesus entered **J**, the whole
23: 37 "**J**, **J**, you who kill the prophets
Mk 10: 33 "We are going up to **J**," he said,
Lk 2: 22 Mary took him to **J** to present him
2: 41 Every year Jesus' parents went to **J**
2: 43 the boy Jesus stayed behind in **J**,
4: 9 The devil led him to **J** and had him
9: 31 about to bring to fulfillment at **J**.
9: 51 Jesus resolutely set out for **J**.
13: 34 "**J**, **J**, you who kill the prophets
18: 31 them, "We are going up to **J**,
19: 41 As he approached **J** and saw
21: 20 "When you see **J** being surrounded
21: 24 **J** will be trampled
24: 47 name to all nations, beginning at **J**.
Jn 4: 20 where we must worship is in **J**."
Ac 1: 4 "Do not leave **J**, but wait
1: 8 and you will be my witnesses in **J**,
6: 7 of disciples in **J** increased rapidly,
20: 22 I am going to **J**, not knowing what
23: 11 As you have testified about me in **J**,
Ro 15: 19 So from **J** all the way around
Gal 4: 25 to the present city of **J**,
4: 26 But the **J** that is above is free,
Heb 12: 22 of the living God, the heavenly **J**.
Rev 3: 12 the new **J**, which is coming down
21: 2 the new **J**, coming down
21: 10 and showed me the Holy City, **J**,

JESSE

Father of David (Ru 4:17–22; 1Sa 16; 1Ch 2:12–17).

JESUS

LIFE: Genealogy (Mt 1:1–17; Lk 3:21–37). Birth announced (Mt 1:18–25; Lk 1:26–45). Birth (Mt 2:1–12; Lk 2:1–40). Escape to Egypt (Mt 2:13–23). As a boy in the temple (Lk 2:41–52). Baptism (Mt 3:13–17; Mk 1:9–11; Lk 3:21–22; Jn 1:32–34). Temptation (Mt 4:1–11; Mk 1:12–13; Lk 4:1–13). Ministry in Galilee (Mt 4:12—18:35; Mk 1:14—9:50; Lk 4:14—13:9; Jn 1:35—2:11; 4; 6), Transfiguration (Mt 17:1–8; Mk 9:2–8; Lk 9:28–36), on the way to Jerusalem (Mt 19–20; Mk 10; Lk 13:10—19:27), in Jerusalem (Mt 21–25; Mk 11–13; Lk 19:28—21:38; Jn 2:12—3:36; 5; 7–12). Last supper (Mt 26:17–35; Mk 14:12–31; Lk 22:1–38; Jn 13–17). Arrest and trial (Mt 26:36—27:31; Mk 14:43—15:20; Lk 22:39—23:25; Jn 18:1—19:16). Crucifixion (Mt 27:32–66; Mk 15:21–47; Lk 23:26–55; Jn 19:28–42). Resurrection and appearances (Mt 28; Mk 16; Lk 24; Jn 20–21; Ac 1:1–11; 7:56; 9:3–6; 1Co 15:1–8; Rev 1:1–20).

MIRACLES. Healings: official's son (Jn 4:43–54), demoniac in Capernaum (Mk 1:23–26; Lk 4:33–35), Peter's mother-in-law (Mt 8:14–17; Mk 1:29–31; Lk 4:38–39), leper (Mt 8:2–4; Mk 1:40–45; Lk 5:12–16), paralytic (Mt 9:1–8; Mk 2:1–12; Lk 5:17–26), cripple (Jn 5:1–9), shriveled hand (Mt 12:10–13; Mk 3:1–5; Lk 6:6–11), centurion's servant (Mt 8:5–13; Lk 7:1–10), widow's son raised (Lk 7:11–17), demoniac (Mt 12:22–23; Lk 11:14), Gerasenes demoniacs (Mt 8:28–34; Mk 5:1–20; Lk 8:26–39), woman's bleeding and Jairus's daughter (Mt 9:18–26; Mk 5:21–43; Lk 8:40–56), blind man (Mt 9:27–31), mute man (Mt 9:32–33), Canaanite woman's daughter (Mt 15:21–28; Mk 7:24–30), deaf man (Mk 7:31–37), blind man (Mk 8:22–26), demoniac boy (Mt 17:14–18; Mk 9:14–29; Lk 9:37–43), ten lepers (Lk 17:11–19), man born blind (Jn 9:1–7), Lazarus raised (Jn 11), crippled woman (Lk 13:11–17), man with abnormal swelling (Lk 14:1–6), two blind men (Mt 20:29–34; Mk 10:46–52; Lk 18:35–43), Malchus's ear (Lk 22:50–51). Other miracles: water to wine (Jn 2:1–11), catch of fish (Lk 5:1–11), storm stilled (Mt 8:23–27; Mk 4:37–41; Lk 8:22–25), 5,000 fed (Mt 14:15–21; Mk 6:35–44; Lk 9:10–17; Jn 6:1–14), walking on water (Mt 14:25–33; Mk 6:48–52; Jn 6:15–21), 4,000 fed (Mt 15:32–39; Mk 8:1–9), money from fish (Mt 17:24–27), fig tree cursed (Mt 21:18–22; Mk 11:12–14), catch of fish (Jn 21:1–14).

MAJOR TEACHING: Sermon on the Mount/Plain (Mt 5–7; Lk 6:17–49), to Nicodemus (Jn 3), to Samaritan woman (Jn 4), Bread of Life (Jn 6:22–59), at Festival of Tabernacles (Jn 7–8), woes to Pharisees (Mt 23; Lk 11:37–54), Good Shepherd (Jn 10:1–18), Olivet Discourse (Mt 24–25; Mk 13; Lk 21:5–36), Upper Room Discourse (Jn 13–16).

PARABLES: Sower (Mt 13:3–23; Mk 4:3–25; Lk 8:5–18), seed's growth (Mk 4:26–29), wheat and weeds (Mt 13:24–30, 36–43), mustard seed (Mt 13:31–32; Mk 4:30–32), yeast (Mt 13:33; Lk 13:20–21), hidden treasure (Mt 13:44), valuable pearl (Mt 13:45–46), net (Mt 13:47–51), house owner (Mt 13:52), good Samaritan (Lk 10:25–37), unmerciful servant (Mt 18:15–35), lost sheep (Mt 18:10–14; Lk 15:4–7), lost coin (Lk 15:8–10), lost son (Lk 15:11–32), shrewd manager (Lk 16:1–13), rich man and Lazarus (Lk 16:19–31), persistent widow (Lk 18:1–8), Pharisee and tax collector (Lk 18:9–14), payment of workers (Mt 20:1–16), tenants and the vineyard (Mt 21:28–46; Mk 12:1–12; Lk 20:9–19), wedding banquet (Mt 22:1–14), faithful servant (Mt 24:45–51), ten virgins (Mt 25:1–13), bags of gold/ten minas (Mt 25:1–30; Lk 19:12–27).

DISCIPLES see APOSTLES. Call of (Jn 1:35–51; Mt 4:18–22; 9:9; Mk 1:16–20; 2:13–14; Lk 5:1–11, 27–28). Named apostles (Mk 3:13–19; Lk 6:12–16). Twelve sent out (Mt 10; Mk 6:7–11; Lk 9:1–5). Seventy-two sent out (Lk 10:1–24). Defection of (Jn 6:60–71; Mt 26:56; Mk 14:50–52). Final commission (Mt 28:16–20; Jn 21:15–23; Ac 1:3–8).

Ac 2: 32 God has raised this **J** to life, and we
9: 5 Saul asked. "I am **J**, whom you are
9: 34 said to him, "**J** Christ heals you.
15: 11 of our Lord **J** that we are saved,
16: 31 "Believe in the Lord **J**, and you will
20: 24 the task the Lord **J** has given me—
Ro 3: 24 redemption that came by Christ **J**.
5: 17 life through the one man, **J** Christ!
8: 1 for those who are in Christ **J**,
1Co 1: 7 our Lord **J** Christ to be revealed.
2: 2 I was with you except **J** Christ
6: 11 in the name of the Lord **J** Christ
8: 6 and there is but one Lord, **J** Christ,
12: 3 Spirit of God says, "**J** be cursed,"
12: 3 and no one can say, "**J** is Lord,"
2Co 4: 5 but **J** Christ as Lord, and ourselves
13: 5 Do you not realize that Christ **J** is
Gal 2: 16 the law, but by faith in **J** Christ.
3: 28 for you are all one in Christ **J**.
5: 6 in Christ **J** neither circumcision
6: 17 I bear on my body the marks of **J**.
Eph 1: 5 to sonship through **J** Christ,
2: 10 in Christ **J** to do good works,
2: 20 with Christ **J** himself as the chief
Php 1: 6 until the day of Christ **J**.
2: 5 have the same mindset as Christ **J**:
2: 10 name of **J** every knee should bow,
Col 3: 17 do it all in the name of the Lord **J**,
1Th 1: 10 **J**, who rescues us from the coming
4: 14 with **J** those who have fallen asleep
5: 23 at the coming of our Lord **J** Christ.
2Th 1: 7 happen when the Lord **J** is revealed
2: 1 the coming of our Lord **J** Christ
1Ti 1: 15 **J** came into the world to save
2Ti 1: 10 Christ **J**, who has destroyed death
2: 3 like a good soldier of Christ **J**.
3: 12 life in Christ **J** will be persecuted,
Titus 2: 13 our great God and Savior, **J** Christ,
Heb 2: 9 But we do see **J**, who was made
2: 11 So **J** is not ashamed to call them
3: 1 fix your thoughts on **J**, whom we
3: 3 **J** has been found worthy of greater
4: 14 into heaven, **J** the Son of God,
6: 20 our forerunner, **J**, has entered
7: 22 **J** has become the guarantor
7: 24 but because **J** lives forever, he has
8: 6 the ministry **J** has received is as
12: 2 fixing our eyes on **J**, the pioneer
12: 24 **J** the mediator of a new covenant,
1Pe 1: 3 the resurrection of **J** Christ
2Pe 1: 16 of our Lord **J** Christ in power,
1Jn 1: 7 and the blood of **J**, his Son,
2: 1 **J** Christ, the Righteous One.
2: 6 to live in him must live as **J** did.
4: 15 acknowledges that **J** is the Son
Rev 1: 1 The revelation from **J** Christ,
22: 16 "I, **J**, have sent my angel to give
22: 20 Amen. Come, Lord **J**.

JETHRO

Father-in-law and adviser of Moses (Ex 3:1; 18). Also known as Reuel (Ex 2:18).

JEW (JEWS JEWS' JUDAISM)

Est 2: 5 the citadel of Susa a **J** of the tribe
Zec 8: 23 take firm hold of one **J** by the hem
Ac 21: 39 "I am a **J**, from Tarsus in Cilicia,

Ro 1: 16 first to the **J**, then to the Gentile.
2: 28 A person is not a **J** who is one only
10: 12 there is no difference between **J**
1Co 9: 20 To the Jews I became like a **J**,
Gal 2: 14 all, "You are a **J**, yet you live like
3: 28 There is neither **J** nor Gentile,
Col 3: 11 Here there is no Gentile or **J**,

JEWEL* (JEWELRY JEWELS)
Pr 20: 15 that speak knowledge are a rare **j**.
SS 4: 9 eyes, with one **j** of your necklace.
Isa 13: 19 Babylon, the **j** of kingdoms,
Rev 21: 11 was like that of a very precious **j**,

JEWELRY (JEWEL)
Ex 35: 22 and brought gold **j** of all kinds:
Jer 2: 32 Does a young woman forget her **j**,
Eze 16: 11 I adorned you with **j**: I put
1Pe 3: 3 wearing of gold **j** or fine clothes.

JEWELS (JEWEL)
Isa 54: 12 your gates of sparkling **j**, and all
61: 10 as a bride adorns herself with her **j**.
Zec 9: 16 in his land like **j** in a crown.

JEWS (JEW)
Ne 4: 1 He ridiculed the **J**,
Est 3: 13 kill and annihilate all the **J**—
4: 14 deliverance for the **J** will arise
Mt 2: 2 who has been born king of the **J**?
27: 11 him, "Are you the king of the **J**?"
Jn 4: 9 (For **J** do not associate
4: 22 know, for salvation is from the **J**.
19: 3 saying, "Hail, king of the **J**!"
Ac 20: 21 I have declared to both **J**
Ro 3: 29 Or is God the God of **J** only?
9: 24 not only from the **J**
1Co 1: 22 **J** demand signs and Greeks look
9: 20 To the **J** I became like a Jew, to win the **J**.
12: 13 whether **J** or Gentiles,
2Co 11: 26 in danger from my fellow **J**,
Rev 2: 9 slander of those who say they are **J**
3: 9 claim to be **J** though they are not,

JEWS'* (JEW)
Ro 15: 27 shared in the **J** spiritual blessings,

JEZEBEL
Sidonian wife of Ahab (1Ki 16:31). Promoted Baal worship (1Ki 16:32–33). Killed prophets of the LORD (1Ki 18:4, 13). Opposed Elijah (1Ki 19:1–2). Had Naboth killed (1Ki 21). Death prophesied (1Ki 21:17–24). Killed by Jehu (2Ki 9:30–37).

JEZREEL
2Ki 9: 36 **J** dogs will devour Jezebel's flesh.
10: 7 baskets and sent them to Jehu in **J**.
Hos 1: 4 "Call him **J**, because I will soon

JOAB
Nephew of David (1Ch 2:16). Commander of his army (2Sa 8:16). Victorious over Ammon (2Sa 10; 1Ch 19), Rabbah (2Sa 11; 1Ch 20), Jerusalem (1Ch 11:6), Absalom (2Sa 18), Sheba (2Sa 20). Killed Abner (2Sa 3:22–39), Amasa (2Sa 20:1–13). Numbered David's army (2Sa 24; 1Ch 21). Sided with Adonijah (1Ki 1:17, 19). Killed by Benaiah (1Ki 2:5–6, 28–35).

JOASH
Son of Ahaziah; king of Judah. Sheltered from Athaliah by Jehoiada (2Ki 11; 2Ch 22:10—23:21). Repaired temple (2Ki 12; 2Ch 24).

JOB
Wealthy man from Uz; feared God (Job 1:1–5). Righteousness tested by disaster (Job 1:6–22), personal affliction (Job 2). Maintained innocence in debate with three friends (Job 3–31), Elihu (Job 32–37). Rebuked by the LORD (Job 38–41). Vindicated and restored to greater stature by the LORD (Job 42). Example of righteousness (Eze 14:14, 20).

JOCHEBED*
Mother of Moses and Aaron (Ex 6:20; Nu 26:59).

JOEL
Prophet (Joel 1:1; Ac 2:16).

JOHN
1. Son of Zechariah and Elizabeth (Lk 1). Called the Baptist (Mt 3:1–12; Mk 1:2–8). Witness to Jesus (Mt 3:11–12; Mk 1:7–8; Lk 3:15–18; Jn 1:6–35; 3:27–30; 5:33–36). Doubts about Jesus (Mt 11:2–6; Lk 7:18–23). Arrest (Mt 4:12; Mk 1:14). Execution (Mt 14:1–12; Mk 6:14–29; Lk 9:7–9). Ministry compared to Elijah (Mt 11:7–19; Mk 9:11–13; Lk 7:24–35).
2. Apostle; brother of James (Mt 4:21–22; 10:2; Mk 3:17; Lk 5:1–10). At transfiguration (Mt 17:1–13; Mk 9:1–13; Lk 9:28–36). Desire to be greatest (Mk 10:35–45). Leader of church at Jerusalem (Ac 4:1–3; Gal 2:9). Elder who wrote epistles (2Jn 1; 3Jn 1). Prophet who wrote Revelation (Rev 1:1; 22:8).
3. Cousin of Barnabas, co-worker with Paul, (Ac 12:12—13:13; 15:37), see MARK.

JOIN (JOINED JOINS)
Ne 10: 29 these now **j** their fellow Israelites
Pr 23: 20 not **j** those who drink too much
24: 21 do not **j** with rebellious officials,
Jer 3: 18 people of Judah will **j** the people
Eze 37: 17 **J** them together into one stick so
Da 11: 34 who are not sincere will **j** them.
Ro 15: 30 to **j** me in my struggle by praying
2Ti 1: 8 **j** with me in suffering
2: 3 **J** with me in suffering, like a good
1Pe 4: 4 you do not **j** them in their reckless,

JOINED (JOIN)
Zec 2: 11 "Many nations will be **j**
Mt 19: 6 Therefore what God has **j** together,
Mk 10: 9 Therefore what God has **j** together,
Ac 1: 14 They all **j** together constantly
Eph 2: 21 the whole building is **j** together
4: 16 body, **j** and held together by every

JOINS (JOIN)
1Co 16: 16 to everyone who **j** in the work

JOINT (JOINTS)
Ps 22: 14 water, and all my bones are out of **j**.

JOINTS* (JOINT)
Heb 4: 12 soul and spirit, **j** and marrow;

JOKING*
Ge 19: 14 his sons-in-law thought he was **j**.
Pr 26: 19 neighbor and says, "I was only **j**!"
Eph 5: 4 foolish talk or coarse **j**, which are

JONAH
Prophet in days of Jeroboam II (2Ki 14:25). Called to Nineveh; fled to Tarshish (Jnh 1:1–3). Cause of storm; thrown into sea (Jnh 1:4–16). Swallowed by fish (Jnh 1:17). Prayer (Jnh 2). Preached to Nineveh (Jnh 3). Attitude reproved by the LORD (Jnh 4). Sign of (Mt 12:39–41; Lk 11:29–32).

JONATHAN
Son of Saul (1Sa 13:16; 1Ch 8:33). Valiant warrior (1Sa 13–14). Relation to David (1Sa 18:1–4; 19:20; 23:16–18). Killed at Gilboa (1Sa 31). Mourned by David (2Sa 1).

JOPPA
Ezr 3: 7 logs by sea from Lebanon to **J**,
Jnh 1: 3 went down to **J**, where he found
Ac 9: 43 Peter stayed in **J** for some time

JORAM
1. Son of Ahab; king of Israel. Fought with Jehoshaphat against Moab (2Ki 3). Killed with Ahaziah by Jehu (2Ki 8:25–29; 9:14–26; 2Ch 22:5–9).
2. See JEHORAM.

JORDAN
Ge 13: 10 **J** toward Zoar was well watered,
Nu 22: 1 and camped along the **J** across
34: 12 boundary will go down along the **J**
Dt 3: 27 you are not going to cross this **J**.
Jos 1: 2 cross the **J** River into the land I am
3: 11 all the earth will go into the **J**
3: 17 stopped in the middle of the **J**
4: 22 'Israel crossed the **J** on dry ground.'
2Ki 2: 7 and Elisha had stopped at the **J**.
2: 13 and stood on the bank of the **J**.
5: 10 wash yourself seven times in the **J**,
6: 4 They went to the **J** and began to
Ps 114: 3 looked and fled, the **J** turned back;
Isa 9: 1 the Way of the Sea, beyond the **J**—
Jer 12: 5 manage in the thickets by the **J**?
Mt 3: 6 baptized by him in the **J** River.
4: 15 the Sea, beyond the **J**,
Mk 1: 9 and was baptized by John in the **J**.

JOSEPH
1. Son of Jacob by Rachel (Ge 30:24; 1Ch 2:2). Favored by Jacob, hated by brothers (Ge 37:3–4). Dreams (Ge 37:5–11). Sold by brothers (Ge 37:12–36). Served Potiphar; imprisoned by false accusation (Ge 39). Interpreted dreams of Pharaoh's servants (Ge 40), of Pharaoh (Ge 41:4–40). Made greatest in Egypt (Ge 41:41–57). Sold grain to brothers (Ge 42–45). Brought Jacob and sons to Egypt (Ge 46–47). Sons Ephraim and Manasseh blessed (Ge 48). Blessed (Ge 49:22–26; Dt 33:13–17). Death (Ge 50:22–26; Ex 13:19; Heb 11:22). 12,000 from (Rev 7:8).
2. Husband of Mary, mother of Jesus (Mt 1:16–24; 2:13–19; Lk 1:27; 2; Jn 1:45).
3. Disciple from Arimathea, who gave his tomb for Jesus' burial (Mt 27:57–61; Mk 15:43–47; Lk 23:50–53).
4. Original name of Barnabas (Ac 4:36).

JOSHUA (HOSHEA)
1. Son of Nun; name changed from Hoshea (Nu 13:8, 16; 1Ch 7:27). Fought Amalekites under Moses (Ex 17:9–14). Servant of Moses on Sinai (Ex 24:13; 32:17). Spied Canaan (Nu 13). With Caleb, allowed to enter land (Nu 14:6, 30). Succeeded Moses (Dt 1:38; 31:1–8; 34:9).
Charged Israel to conquer Canaan (Jos 1). Crossed Jordan (Jos 3–4). Circumcised sons of wilderness wanderings (Jos 5). Conquered Jericho (Jos 6), Ai (Jos 7–8), five kings at Gibeon (Jos 10:1–28), southern Canaan (Jos 10:29–43), northern Canaan (Jos 11–12). Defeated at Ai (Jos 7). Deceived by Gibeonites (Jos 9). Renewed covenant (Jos 8:30–35; 24:1–27). Divided land among tribes (Jos 13–22). Last words (Jos 23). Death (Jos 24:28–31).
2. High priest during rebuilding of temple (Hag 1–2; Zec 3:1–9; 6:11).

JOSIAH
Son of Amon; king of Judah (2Ki 21:26; 1Ch 3:14). Prophesied (1Ki 13:2). Book of Law discovered during his reign (2Ki 22; 2Ch 34:14–31). Reforms (2Ki 23:1–25; 2Ch 34:1–13; 35:1–19). Killed by Pharaoh Necho (2Ki 23:29–30; 2Ch 35:20–27).

JOTHAM
1. Son of Gideon (Jdg 9).
2. Son of Azariah (Uzziah); king of Judah (2Ki 15:32–38; 2Ch 26:21—27:9).

JOURNEY
Dt 1: 33 who went ahead of you on your **j**,
2: 7 watched over your **j** through this
Jdg 18: 6 Your **j** has the LORD's approval."
Ezr 8: 21 ask him for a safe **j** for us and our
Isa 35: 8 The unclean will not **j** on it;
Mt 25: 14 it will be like a man going on a **j**,
Ro 15: 24 have you assist me on my **j** there,

JOY* (ENJOY ENJOYMENT JOYFUL JOYOUS OVERJOYED REJOICE REJOICES REJOICING)
Ge 31: 27 so I could send you away with **j**
Lev 9: 24 saw it, they shouted for **j** and fell
Dt 16: 15 hands, and your **j** will be complete.
Jdg 9: 19 may Abimelek be your **j**, and may
1Ch 12: 40 and sheep, for there was **j** in Israel.
16: 27 and **j** are in his dwelling place.
16: 33 them sing for **j** before the LORD,
29: 17 **j** how willingly your people who
29: 22 drank with great **j** in the presence
2Ch 30: 26 There was great **j** in Jerusalem,
Ezr 3: 12 while many others shouted for **j**.
3: 13 of the shouts of **j** from the sound
6: 16 of the house of God with **j**.
6: 22 they celebrated with **j** the Festival
6: 22 the LORD had filled them with **j**
Ne 8: 10 for the **j** of the LORD is your
8: 12 food and to celebrate with great **j**,
8: 17 And their **j** was very great.
12: 43 God had given them great **j**.
Est 8: 16 it was a time of happiness and **j**,
8: 17 there was **j** and gladness among
9: 17 and made it a day of feasting and **j**.
9: 18 and made it a day of feasting and **j**.
9: 19 of the month of Adar as a day of **j**
9: 22 their sorrow was turned into **j**
9: 22 the days as days of feasting and **j**
Job 3: 7 may no shout of **j** be heard in it.
6: 10 my **j** in unrelenting pain—that I
8: 21 and your lips with shouts of **j**.
9: 25 fly away without a glimpse of **j**.
10: 20 from me so I can have a moment's **j**
20: 5 brief, the **j** of the godless lasts
33: 26 will see God's face and shout for **j**;
38: 7 and all the angels shouted for **j**?
Ps 4: 7 Fill my heart with **j** when their
5: 11 be glad; let them ever sing for **j**.

Ps 16: 11 you will fill me with **j** in your
19: 8 are right, giving **j** to the heart.
20: 5 we shout for **j** over your victory
21: 1 How great is his **j** in the victories
21: 6 glad with the **j** of your presence.
27: 6 tent I will sacrifice with shouts of **j**;
28: 7 My heart leaps for **j**, and with my
30: 11 sackcloth and clothed me with **j**,
33: 3 play skillfully, and shout for **j**.
35: 27 in my vindication shout for **j**
42: 4 of the Mighty One with shouts of **j**
43: 4 God, to God, my **j** and my delight.
45: 7 by anointing you with the oil of **j**.
45: 15 Led in with **j** and gladness,
47: 1 shout to God with cries of **j**.
47: 5 God has ascended amid shouts of **j**,
48: 2 loftiness, the **j** of the whole earth,
51: 8 Let me hear **j** and gladness;
51: 12 to me the **j** of your salvation
65: 8 fades, you call forth songs of **j**.
65: 13 they shout for **j** and sing.
66: 1 Shout for **j** to God, all the earth!
67: 4 the nations be glad and sing for **j**,
71: 23 My lips will shout for **j** when I sing
81: 1 Sing for **j** to God our strength;
86: 4 Bring **j** to your servant, Lord, for I
89: 12 Hermon sing for **j** at your name.
90: 14 that we may sing for **j** and be glad
92: 4 I sing for **j** at what your hands have
94: 19 me, your consolation brought me **j**.
95: 1 let us sing for **j** to the LORD;
96: 12 all the trees of the forest sing for **j**.
97: 11 and **j** on the upright in heart.
98: 4 Shout for **j** to the LORD,
98: 6 shout for **j** before the LORD,
98: 8 the mountains sing together for **j**;
100: 1 Shout for **j** to the LORD,
105: 43 his chosen ones with shouts of **j**;
106: 5 I may share in the **j** of your nation
107: 22 tell of his works with songs of **j**.
118: 15 Shouts of **j** and victory resound
119:111 they are the **j** of my heart.
126: 2 our tongues with songs of **j**.
126: 3 and we are filled with **j**.
126: 5 with tears will reap with songs of **j**.
126: 6 to sow, will return with songs of **j**,
132: 9 your faithful people sing for **j**."
132: 16 faithful people will ever sing for **j**.
137: 3 tormentors demanded songs of **j**;
137: 6 consider Jerusalem my highest **j**.
149: 5 and sing for **j** on their beds.
Pr 10: 1 A wise son brings **j** to his father,
10: 28 The prospect of the righteous is **j**,
11: 10 wicked perish, there are shouts of **j**.
12: 20 those who promote peace have **j**.
14: 10 and no one else can share its **j**.
15: 20 A wise son brings **j** to his father,
15: 21 Folly brings **j** to one who has no
15: 23 A person finds **j** in giving an apt
15: 30 in a messenger's eyes brings **j**
17: 21 there is no **j** for the parent
21: 15 brings **j** to the righteous but terror
23: 24 of a righteous child has great **j**;
27: 9 and incense bring **j** to the heart,
27: 11 my son, and bring **j** to my heart;
29: 3 A man who loves wisdom brings **j**
29: 6 but the righteous shout for **j** and
Ecc 8: 15 **j** will accompany them in their toil
11: 9 let your heart give you **j** in the days
Isa 9: 3 the nation and increased their **j**;
12: 3 With **j** you will draw water
12: 6 Shout aloud and sing for **j**,
16: 9 shouts of **j** over your ripened fruit
16: 10 **J** and gladness are taken away
22: 13 But see, there is **j** and revelry,
24: 11 all **j** turns to gloom, all joyful
24: 14 raise their voices, they shout for **j**;
26: 19 the dust wake up and shout for **j**—
35: 2 will rejoice greatly and shout for **j**.
35: 6 and the mute tongue shout for **j**.
35: 10 everlasting **j** will crown their heads
35: 10 Gladness and **j** will overtake them,
42: 11 Let the people of Sela sing for **j**;
44: 23 Sing for **j**, you heavens,
48: 20 Announce this with shouts of **j**
49: 13 Shout for **j**, you heavens;
51: 3 **J** and gladness will be found in her,
51: 11 everlasting **j** will crown their heads
51: 11 Gladness and **j** will overtake them,
52: 8 together they shout for **j**.
52: 9 Burst into songs of **j** together,
Isa 54: 1 shout for **j**, you who were never
55: 12 You will go out in **j** and be led
56: 7 give them **j** in my house of prayer.
58: 14 you will find your **j** in the LORD,
60: 5 heart will throb and swell with **j**;
60: 15 pride and the **j** of all generations.
61: 3 the oil of **j** instead of mourning,
61: 7 and everlasting **j** will be yours.
65: 14 will sing out of the **j** of their hearts,
65: 18 to be a delight and its people a **j**.
66: 5 glorified, that we may see your **j**!'
Jer 7: 34 will bring an end to the sounds of **j**
15: 16 they were my **j** and my heart's
16: 9 will bring an end to the sounds of **j**
25: 10 banish from them the sounds of **j**
31: 7 "Sing with **j** for Jacob;
31: 12 shout for **j** on the heights of Zion;
31: 13 comfort and **j** instead of sorrow.
33: 9 this city will bring me renown, **j**,
33: 11 the sounds of **j** and gladness,
48: 33 **J** and gladness are gone
48: 33 one treads them with shouts of **j**.
48: 33 shouts, they are not shouts of **j**.
51: 48 them will shout for **j** over Babylon,
La 2: 15 of beauty, the **j** of the whole earth?"
5: 15 **J** is gone from our hearts;
Eze 7: 7 is panic, not **j**, on the mountains.
24: 25 their stronghold, their **j** and glory,
Joel 1: 12 Surely the people's **j** is withered
1: 16 **j** and gladness from the house of
Mt 13: 20 word and at once receives it with **j**.
13: 44 in his **j** went and sold all he had
28: 8 afraid yet filled with **j**, and ran
Mk 4: 16 word and at once receive it with **j**.
Lk 1: 14 He will be a **j** and delight to you,
1: 44 the baby in my womb leaped for **j**.
1: 58 great mercy, and they shared her **j**.
2: 10 will cause great **j** for all the people.
6: 23 "Rejoice in that day and leap for **j**,
8: 13 ones who receive the word with **j**
10: 17 The seventy-two returned with **j**
10: 21 full of **j** through the Holy Spirit,
24: 41 still did not believe it because of **j**
24: 52 returned to Jerusalem with great **j**.
Jn 3: 29 and is full of **j** when he hears
3: 29 That **j** is mine, and it is now
15: 11 told you this so that my **j** may be
15: 11 and that your **j** may be complete.
16: 20 grieve, but your grief will turn to **j**.
16: 21 because of her **j** that a child is born
16: 22 and no one will take away your **j**.
16: 24 and your **j** will be complete.
17: 13 full measure of my **j** within them.
Ac 2: 28 you will fill me with **j** in your
8: 8 So there was great **j** in that city.
13: 52 the disciples were filled with **j**
14: 17 of food and fills your hearts with **j**."
16: 34 filled with **j** because he had come
Ro 14: 17 peace and **j** in the Holy Spirit,
15: 13 the God of hope fill you with all **j**
15: 32 so that I may come to you with **j**,
2Co 1: 24 but we work with you for your **j**,
2: 3 you, that you would all share my **j**.
7: 4 troubles my **j** knows no bounds.
7: 7 so that my **j** was greater than ever.
8: 2 trial, their overflowing **j** and their
Gal 4: 27 shout for **j** and cry aloud, you who
5: 22 But the fruit of the Spirit is love, **j**,
Php 1: 4 for all of you, I always pray with **j**
1: 25 for your progress and **j** in the faith,
2: 2 then make my **j** complete by being
2: 29 him in the Lord with great **j**,
4: 1 love and long for, my **j** and crown,
1Th 1: 6 severe suffering with the **j** given
2: 19 our **j**, or the crown in which we
2: 20 Indeed, you are our glory and **j**.
3: 9 in return for all the **j** we have
2Ti 1: 4 you, so that I may be filled with **j**.
Phm : 7 Your love has given me great **j**
Heb 1: 9 by anointing you with the oil of **j**."
12: 2 the **j** set before him he endured
13: 17 this so that their work will be a **j**,
Jas 1: 2 Consider it pure **j**, my brothers
4: 9 to mourning and your **j** to gloom.
1Pe 1: 8 an inexpressible and glorious **j**,
1Jn 1: 4 write this to make our **j** complete.
2Jn : 4 It has given me great **j** to find some
: 12 face, so that our **j** may be complete.
3Jn : 3 It gave me great **j** when some
: 4 I have no greater **j** than to hear
Jude : 24 without fault and with great **j**—

JOYFUL* (JOY)
Dt 16: 14 Be **j** at your festival—
1Sa 18: 6 with **j** songs and with timbrels
1Ki 8: 66 **j** and glad in heart for all the good
1Ch 15: 16 to make a **j** sound with musical
2Ch 7: 10 **j** and glad in heart for the good
Ps 68: 3 may they be happy and **j**.
100: 2 come before him with **j** songs.
Pr 23: 25 may she who gave you birth be **j**!
Ecc 9: 7 and drink your wine with a **j** heart,
Isa 24: 8 The **j** timbrels are stilled,
24: 8 has stopped, the **j** harp is silent.
24: 11 all **j** sounds are banished from the
Jer 31: 4 and go out to dance with the **j**.
Hab 3: 18 I will be **j** in God my Savior.
Zec 8: 19 tenth months will become **j** and
10: 7 Their children will see it and be **j**;
Ro 12: 12 Be **j** in hope, patient in affliction,
Col 1: 12 and giving **j** thanks to the Father,
Heb 12: 22 thousands of angels in **j** assembly,

JOYOUS* (JOY)
Est 8: 15 the city of Susa held a **j** celebration.

JUBILANT
Ps 96: 12 Let the fields be **j**, and everything
98: 4 earth, burst into **j** song with music;

JUBILEE
Lev 25: 11 fiftieth year shall be a **j** for you;

JUDAH (JUDEA)
1. Son of Jacob by Leah (Ge 29:35; 35:23; 1Ch 2:1). Did not want to kill Joseph (Ge 37:26–27). Among Canaanites, fathered Perez by Tamar (Ge 38). Tribe of blessed as ruling tribe (Ge 49:8–12; Dt 33:7), numbered (Nu 1:27; 26:22), allotted land (Jos 15; Eze 48:7), failed to fully possess (Jos 15:63; Jdg 1:1–20).
2. Name used for people and land of southern kingdom.
Ru 1: 7 take them back to the land of **J**.
2Sa 2: 4 David king over the tribe of **J**.
Isa 1: 1 The vision concerning **J**
3: 8 Jerusalem staggers, **J** is falling;
Jer 13: 19 All **J** will be carried into exile,
30: 3 Israel and **J** back from captivity
Hos 1: 7 Yet I will show love to **J**; and I will
Zec 10: 4 From **J** will come the cornerstone,
Mt 2: 6 least among the rulers of **J**;
Heb 7: 14 that our Lord descended from **J**,
8: 8 of Israel and with the people of **J**.
Rev 5: 5 the Lion of the tribe of **J**, the Root

JUDAISM (JEW)
Ac 13: 43 devout converts to **J** followed Paul
Gal 1: 13 of my previous way of life in **J**,
1: 14 I was advancing in **J** beyond many

JUDAS
1. Apostle; son of James (Lk 6:16; Jn 14:22; Ac 1:13). Probably also called Thaddaeus (Mt 10:3; Mk 3:18).
2. Brother of James and Jesus (Mt 13:55; Mk 6:3), also called Jude (Jude 1).
3. Christian prophet (Ac 15:22–32).
4. Apostle, also called Iscariot, who betrayed Jesus (Mt 10:4; 26:14–56; Mk 3:19; 14:10–50; Lk 6:16; 22:3–53; Jn 6:71; 12:4; 13:2–30; 18:2–11). Suicide of (Mt 27:3–5; Ac 1:16–25).

JUDEA (JUDAH)
Mt 2: 1 Jesus was born in Bethlehem in **J**,
24: 16 let those who are in **J** flee
Lk 3: 1 Pontius Pilate was governor of **J**,
Ac 1: 8 and in all **J** and Samaria,
9: 31 Then the church throughout **J**,
1Th 2: 14 imitators of God's churches in **J**,

JUDGE (JUDGED JUDGES JUDGING JUDGMENT JUDGMENTS)
Ge 16: 5 May the LORD **j** between you
18: 25 Will not the **J** of all the earth do
Lev 19: 15 great, but **j** your neighbor fairly.
Dt 1: 16 between your people and **j** fairly,
17: 12 who shows contempt for the **j**
Jdg 2: 18 the LORD raised up a **j** for them,
2: 18 he was with the **j** and saved them
1Sa 2: 10 the LORD will **j** the ends
3: 13 I would **j** his family forever
24: 12 May the LORD **j** between you
1Ki 8: 32 **J** between your servants,
1Ch 16: 33 LORD, for he comes to **j** the earth.
2Ch 6: 23 **J** between your servants,
19: 7 **J** carefully, for with the LORD our
Job 9: 15 only plead with my **J** for mercy.

Ps 7: 8 Let the LORD **j** the peoples.
7: 11 God is a righteous **j**, a God who
9: 4 enthroned as the righteous **j**.
51: 4 verdict and justified when you **j**.
75: 2 it is I who **j** with equity.
76: 9 rose up to **j**, to save all the afflicted
82: 8 up, O God, **j** the earth, for all
94: 2 Rise up, **J** of the earth; pay back
96: 10 he will **j** the peoples with equity.
96: 13 he comes, he comes to **j** the earth.
96: 13 will **j** the world in righteousness
98: 9 LORD, for he comes to **j** the earth.
98: 9 will **j** the world in righteousness
110: 6 He will **j** the nations,
Pr 31: 9 Speak up and **j** fairly;
Isa 2: 4 He will **j** between the nations
3: 13 he rises to **j** the people.
11: 3 He will not **j** by what he sees
33: 22 For the LORD is our **j**, the LORD
Jer 11: 20 who **j** righteously and test the heart
Eze 7: 3 I will **j** you according to your
7: 27 their own standards I will **j** them.
18: 30 I will **j** each of you according
20: 36 Egypt, so I will **j** you,
22: 2 Will you **j** this city of bloodshed?
34: 17 I will **j** between one sheep
Joel 3: 12 there I will sit to **j** all the nations
Mic 3: 11 Her leaders **j** for a bribe, her priests
4: 3 He will **j** between many peoples
Mt 7: 1 "Do not **j**, or you too will be
Lk 6: 37 "Do not **j**, and you will not be
18: 2 there was a **j** who neither feared
Jn 5: 27 authority to **j** because he is the Son
5: 30 I **j** only as I hear, and my judgment
7: 24 but instead **j** correctly."
8: 16 But if I do **j**, my decisions are true,
12: 47 For I did not come to **j** the world,
12: 48 There is a **j** for the one who rejects
Ac 10: 42 the one whom God appointed as **j**
17: 31 set a day when he will **j** the world
Ro 3: 6 so, how could God **j** the world?
14: 10 do you **j** your brother or sister?
1Co 4: 3 indeed, I do not even **j** myself.
4: 5 Therefore **j** nothing before
6: 2 Lord's people will **j** the world?
6: 2 not competent to **j** trivial cases?
Col 2: 16 Therefore do not let anyone **j** you
2Ti 4: 1 who will **j** the living and the dead,
4: 8 the righteous **J**, will award to me
Heb 10: 30 "The Lord will **j** his people."
12: 23 You have come to God, the **J** of all,
13: 4 for God will **j** the adulterer and all
Jas 4: 12 There is only one Lawgiver and **J**,
4: 12 who are you to **j** your neighbor?
1Pe 4: 5 to him who is ready to **j** the living
Rev 20: 4 who had been given authority to **j**.

JUDGED (JUDGE)
Mt 7: 1 "Do not judge, or you too will be **j**.
Jn 5: 24 will not be **j** but has crossed over
1Co 4: 3 I care very little if I am **j** by you
10: 29 For why is my freedom being **j**
Jas 3: 1 who teach will be **j** more strictly.
Rev 20: 12 The dead were **j** according to what

JUDGES (JUDGE)
Jdg 2: 16 Then the LORD raised up **j**,
Job 9: 24 of the wicked, he blindfolds its **j**.
Ps 9: 8 and **j** the peoples with equity.
58: 11 there is a God who **j** the earth."
75: 7 It is God who **j**: He brings one
Pr 29: 14 If a king **j** the poor with fairness,
Jn 5: 22 Moreover, the Father **j** no one,
Ro 2: 16 **j** people's secrets through Jesus
1Co 4: 4 It is the Lord who **j** me.
Heb 4: 12 it **j** the thoughts and attitudes
1Pe 1: 17 a Father who **j** each person's work
2: 23 himself to him who **j** justly.
Rev 19: 11 With justice he **j** and wages war.

JUDGING (JUDGE)
Pr 24: 23 To show partiality in **j** is not good:
Isa 16: 5 one who in **j** seeks justice
Mt 19: 28 **j** the twelve tribes of Israel.
Jn 7: 24 Stop **j** by mere appearances,
2Co 10: 7 You are **j** by appearances.

JUDGMENT (JUDGE)
Nu 33: 4 the LORD had brought **j** on their
Dt 1: 17 of anyone, for **j** belongs to God.
32: 41 sword and my hand grasps it in **j**,
1Sa 25: 33 May you be blessed for your good **j**
Ps 1: 5 the wicked will not stand in the **j**,
9: 7 he has established his throne for **j**.
Ps 76: 8 From heaven you pronounced **j**,
82: 1 he renders **j** among the "gods":
119: 66 Teach me knowledge and good **j**,
143: 2 Do not bring your servant into **j**,
Pr 3: 21 preserve sound **j** and discretion;
8: 14 Counsel and sound **j** are mine;
18: 1 against all sound **j** starts quarrels.
Ecc 12: 14 God will bring every deed into **j**,
Isa 3: 14 enters into **j** against the elders
28: 6 of justice to the one who sits in **j**,
53: 8 and **j** he was taken away.
66: 16 his sword the LORD will execute **j**
Jer 2: 35 I will pass **j** on you because you
25: 31 he will bring **j** on all mankind
51: 18 their **j** comes, they will perish.
Eze 11: 10 and I will execute **j** on you
Da 7: 22 pronounced **j** in favor of the holy
Am 7: 4 Sovereign LORD was calling for **j**
Zec 8: 16 true and sound **j** in your courts;
Mt 5: 21 who murders will be subject to **j**.'
5: 22 brother or sister will be subject to **j**.
10: 15 Gomorrah on the day of **j** than
11: 24 on the day of **j** than for you."
12: 36 the day of **j** for every empty word
12: 41 up at the **j** with this generation
Jn 5: 22 but has entrusted all **j** to the Son,
5: 30 and my **j** is just, for I seek not
8: 26 "I have much to say in **j** of you.
9: 39 "For **j** I have come into this world,
12: 31 Now is the time for **j** on this world;
16: 8 about sin and righteousness and **j**:
16: 11 and about **j**, because the prince
Ac 24: 25 self-control and the **j** to come,
Ro 2: 1 you who pass **j** do the same
2: 2 God's **j** against those who do such
5: 16 The **j** followed one sin and brought
12: 3 think of yourself with sober **j**,
14: 10 will all stand before God's **j** seat.
14: 13 Therefore let us stop passing **j**
1Co 7: 40 In my **j**, she is happier if she stays
11: 29 eat and drink **j** on themselves.
14: 24 sin and are brought under **j** by all,
2Co 5: 10 we must all appear before the **j** seat
2Th 1: 5 is evidence that God's **j** is right,
1Ti 3: 6 fall under the same **j** as the devil.
5: 12 Thus they bring **j** on themselves,
Heb 6: 2 of the dead, and eternal **j**.
9: 27 to die once, and after that to face **j**,
10: 27 only a fearful expectation of **j**
Jas 2: 13 Mercy triumphs over **j**.
4: 11 not keeping it, but sitting in **j** on it.
1Pe 4: 17 For it is time for **j** to begin
2Pe 2: 9 for punishment on the day of **j**.
3: 7 fire, being kept for the day of **j**
1Jn 4: 17 have confidence on the day of **j**:
Jude : 6 everlasting chains for **j** on the great
Rev 14: 7 because the hour of his **j** has come.

JUDGMENTS (JUDGE)
Jer 1: 16 will pronounce my **j** on my people
Da 9: 11 and sworn **j** written in the Law
Hos 6: 5 then my **j** go forth like the sun.
Ro 11: 33 How unsearchable his **j**, and his
1Co 2: 15 the Spirit makes **j** about all things,
2: 15 is not subject to merely human **j**,
Rev 16: 7 Almighty, true and just are your **j**."

JUG
1Sa 26: 12 spear and water **j** near Saul's head,
1Ki 17: 12 in a jar and a little olive oil in a **j**.

JUST (JUSTICE JUSTIFICATION JUSTIFIED JUSTIFIES JUSTIFY JUSTIFYING JUSTLY)
Ge 18: 19 by doing what is right and **j**,
Dt 2: 12 place, **j** as Israel did in the land
6: 3 milk and honey, **j** as the LORD,
27: 3 milk and honey, **j** as the LORD,
30: 9 **j** as he delighted in your ancestors,
32: 4 are perfect, and all his ways are **j**.
32: 4 does no wrong, upright and **j** is he.
32: 47 They are not **j** idle words for you—
32: 50 **j** as your brother Aaron died
2Sa 8: 15 doing what was **j** and right for all
1Ch 18: 14 doing what was **j** and right for all
2Ch 12: 6 and said, "The LORD is **j**."
Ne 9: 13 and laws that are **j** and right,
Job 34: 17 you condemn the **j** and mighty
35: 2 "Do you think this is **j**? You say,
Ps 37: 28 For the LORD loves the **j** and will
37: 30 and their tongues speak what is **j**.
99: 4 in Jacob you have done what is **j**
111: 7 of his hands are faithful and **j**;
119:121 have done what is righteous and **j**;
Pr 1: 3 doing what is right and **j** and fair;
2: 8 for he guards the course of the **j**
2: 9 will understand what is right and **j**
8: 8 All the words of my mouth are **j**;
8: 15 and rulers issue decrees that are **j**;
12: 5 The plans of the righteous are **j**,
21: 3 **j** is more acceptable to the LORD
Isa 32: 7 when the plea of the needy is **j**.
58: 2 They ask me for **j** decisions
Jer 4: 2 **j** and righteous way you swear,
22: 3 Do what is **j** and right.
22: 15 He did what was right and **j**, so all
23: 5 do what is **j** and right in the land.
33: 15 he will do what is **j** and right
Eze 18: 5 a righteous man who does what is **j**
18: 19 Since the son has done what is **j**
18: 21 and does what is **j** and right,
18: 25 say, 'The way of the Lord is not **j**.'
18: 27 and does what is **j** and right,
18: 29 say, 'The way of the Lord is not **j**.'
33: 14 sin and do what is **j** and right—
33: 16 They have done what is **j** and right;
33: 17 'The way of the Lord is not **j**.' But it is their way that is not **j**.
33: 19 and does what is **j** and right,
33: 20 say, 'The way of the Lord is not **j**.'
45: 9 and do what is **j** and right.
Da 4: 37 does is right and all his ways are **j**.
Jn 5: 30 my judgment is **j**, for I seek not
Ro 3: 8 Their condemnation is **j**!
3: 26 time, so as to be **j** and the one who
2Th 1: 6 God is **j**: He will pay back trouble
Heb 2: 2 received its **j** punishment,
1Jn 1: 9 he is faithful and **j** and will forgive
Rev 15: 3 **J** and true are your ways,
16: 5 "You are **j** in these judgments,
16: 7 true and **j** are your judgments."
19: 2 for true and **j** are his judgments.

JUSTICE* (JUST)
Ge 49: 16 "Dan will provide **j** for his people
Ex 23: 2 do not pervert **j** by siding
23: 6 "Do not deny **j** to your poor people
Lev 19: 15 "'Do not pervert **j**; do not show
Dt 16: 19 Do not pervert **j** or show partiality.
16: 20 Follow **j** and **j** alone, so that you
24: 17 the foreigner or the fatherless of **j**,
27: 19 "Cursed is anyone who withholds **j**
1Sa 8: 3 accepted bribes and perverted **j**.
2Sa 15: 4 and I would see that they receive **j**."
15: 6 who came to the king asking for **j**,
1Ki 3: 11 for discernment in administering **j**,
3: 28 wisdom from God to administer **j**.
7: 7 hall, the Hall of **J**, where he was
10: 9 he has made you king to maintain **j**
2Ch 9: 8 to maintain **j** and righteousness."
Ezr 7: 25 to administer **j** to all the people
Est 1: 13 experts in matters of law and **j**,
Job 8: 3 Does God pervert **j**?
9: 19 And if it is a matter of **j**, who can
19: 7 though I call for help, there is no **j**.
27: 2 has denied me **j**, the Almighty,
29: 14 **j** was my robe and my turban.
31: 13 "If I have denied **j** to any of my
34: 5 am innocent, but God denies me **j**.
34: 12 that the Almighty would pervert **j**.
34: 17 Can someone who hates **j** govern?
36: 3 I will ascribe **j** to my Maker.
36: 17 and **j** have taken hold of you.
37: 23 in his **j** and great righteousness,
40: 8 "Would you discredit my **j**?
Ps 7: 6 Awake, my God; decree **j**.
9: 16 LORD is known by his acts of **j**;
11: 7 the LORD is righteous, he loves **j**;
33: 5 LORD loves righteousness and **j**;
36: 6 your **j** like the great deep.
45: 4 the cause of truth, humility and **j**;
45: 6 a scepter of **j** will be the scepter
50: 6 righteousness, for he is a God of **j**.
72: 1 Endow the king with your **j**,
72: 2 your afflicted ones with **j**.
89: 14 **j** are the foundation of your throne
97: 2 **j** are the foundation of his throne.
99: 4 The King is mighty, he loves **j**—
101: 1 I will sing of your love and **j**;
103: 6 and **j** for all the oppressed.
112: 5 who conduct their affairs with **j**.
140: 12 the LORD secures **j** for the poor
Pr 8: 20 righteousness, along the paths of **j**,
16: 10 and his mouth does not betray **j**.
17: 23 in secret to pervert the course of **j**.
18: 5 and so deprive the innocent of **j**.

Pr 19: 28 A corrupt witness mocks at **j**,
21: 15 When **j** is done, it brings joy
29: 4 By **j** a king gives a country stability,
29: 7 The righteous care about **j**
29: 26 is from the LORD that one gets **j**.
Ecc 3: 16 was there, in the place of **j**—
5: 8 a district, and **j** and rights denied,
Isa 1: 17 Learn to do right; seek **j**.
1: 21 She once was full of **j**;
1: 27 Zion will be delivered with **j**,
5: 7 And he looked for **j**, but saw
5: 16 Almighty will be exalted by his **j**,
5: 23 a bribe, but deny **j** to the innocent.
9: 7 and upholding it with **j**
10: 2 withhold **j** from the oppressed of
11: 4 with **j** he will give decisions
16: 5 one who in judging seeks **j**
28: 6 He will be a spirit of **j** to the one
28: 17 I will make **j** the measuring line
29: 21 deprive the innocent of **j**.
30: 18 For the LORD is a God of **j**.
32: 1 and rulers will rule with **j**.
32: 16 The LORD's **j** will dwell
33: 5 he will fill Zion with his **j**
42: 1 and he will bring **j** to the nations.
42: 3 In faithfulness he will bring forth **j**;
42: 4 be discouraged till he establishes **j**
51: 4 my **j** will become a light
51: 5 my arm will bring **j** to the nations.
56: 1 "Maintain **j** and do what is right,
59: 4 No one calls for **j**; no one pleads
59: 8 there is no **j** in their paths.
59: 9 So **j** is far from us,
59: 11 We look for **j**, but find none;
59: 14 So **j** is driven back,
59: 15 was displeased that there was no **j**.
61: 8 "For I, the LORD, love **j**;
Jer 5: 28 have no limit; they do not seek **j**.
9: 24 **j** and righteousness on earth,
12: 1 would speak with you about your **j**:
21: 12 "'Administer **j** every morning;
La 3: 36 to deprive them of **j**—would not
Eze 22: 29 the foreigner, denying them **j**.
34: 16 I will shepherd the flock with **j**.
Hos 2: 19 betroth you in righteousness and **j**,
12: 6 maintain love and **j**, and wait
Am 2: 7 and deny **j** to the oppressed.
5: 7 There are those who turn **j**
5: 10 who hate the one who upholds **j** in
5: 12 deprive the poor of **j** in the courts.
5: 15 maintain **j** in the courts.
5: 24 But let **j** roll on like a river,
6: 12 But you have turned **j** into poison
Mic 3: 1 Should you not embrace **j**,
3: 8 and with **j** and might, to declare
3: 9 who despise **j** and distort all that is
Hab 1: 4 is paralyzed, and **j** never prevails.
1: 4 the righteous, so that **j** is perverted.
Zep 3: 5 by morning he dispenses his **j**,
Zec 7: 9 'Administer true **j**; show mercy
Mal 2: 17 them" or "Where is the God of **j**?"
3: 5 the foreigners among you of **j**,
Mt 12: 18 he will proclaim **j** to the nations.
12: 20 out, till he has brought **j** through
23: 23 **j**, mercy and faithfulness.
Lk 11: 42 you neglect **j** and the love of God.
18: 3 'Grant me **j** against my adversary.'
18: 5 I will see that she gets **j**, so that she
18: 7 will not God bring about **j** for his
18: 8 you, he will see that they get **j**,
Ac 8: 33 humiliation he was deprived of **j**.
17: 31 he will judge the world with **j**
28: 4 the goddess **J** has not allowed him
2Co 7: 11 what readiness to see **j** done.
Heb 1: 8 a scepter of **j** will be the scepter
11: 33 administered **j**, and gained what
Rev 19: 11 With **j** he judges and wages war.

JUSTIFICATION* (JUST)
Eze 16: 52 you have furnished some **j** for your
Ac 13: 39 sin, a **j** you were not able to obtain
Ro 4: 25 sins and was raised to life for our **j**.
5: 16 many trespasses and brought **j**.
5: 18 one righteous act resulted in **j**

JUSTIFIED* (JUST)
Ps 51: 4 your verdict and **j** when you judge.
Lk 18: 14 the other, went home **j** before God.
Ro 3: 24 all are **j** freely by his grace through
3: 28 that a person is **j** by faith apart
4: 2 in fact, Abraham was **j** by works,
5: 1 since we have been **j** through faith,
5: 9 Since we have now been **j** by his
Ro 8: 30 those he called, he also **j**; those he **j**, he also glorified.
10: 10 heart that you believe and are **j**,
1Co 6: 11 you were **j** in the name of the Lord
Gal 2: 16 that a person is not **j** by the works
2: 16 Jesus that we may be **j** by faith
2: 16 works of the law no one will be **j**.
2: 17 seeking to be **j** in Christ, we Jews
3: 11 relies on the law is **j** before God,
3: 24 came that we might be **j** by faith.
5: 4 be **j** by the law have been alienated
Titus 3: 7 so that, having been **j** by his grace,

JUSTIFIES* (JUST)
Ro 3: 26 the one who **j** those who have faith
4: 5 but trusts God who **j** the ungodly,
8: 33 God has chosen? It is God who **j**.

JUSTIFY* (JUST)
Est 7: 4 such distress would **j** disturbing
Job 40: 8 you condemn me to **j** yourself?
Isa 53: 11 my righteous servant will **j** many,
Lk 10: 29 But he wanted to **j** himself, so he
16: 15 "You are the ones who **j** yourselves
Ro 3: 30 who will **j** the circumcised by faith
Gal 3: 8 that God would **j** the Gentiles

JUSTIFYING* (JUST)
Job 32: 2 Job for **j** himself rather than God.

JUSTLY* (JUST)
Ps 58: 1 Do you rulers indeed speak **j**?
106: 3 Blessed are those who act **j**,
Jer 7: 5 actions and deal with each other **j**,
Mic 6: 8 To act **j** and to love mercy
Lk 23: 41 We are punished **j**, for we are
1Pe 2: 23 himself to him who judges **j**.

KADESH (KADESH BARNEA)
Nu 20: 1 Desert of Zin, and they stayed at **K**.
Dt 1: 46 so you stayed in **K** many days—

KADESH BARNEA (KADESH)
Nu 32: 8 I sent them from **K** to look over

KEBAR
Eze 1: 1 among the exiles by the **K** River,

KEDORLAOMER
Ge 14: 17 Abram returned from defeating **K**

KEEP (KEEPER KEEPING KEEPS KEPT)
Ge 31: 49 "May the LORD **k** watch between
Ex 15: 26 commands and **k** all his decrees,
20: 6 love me and **k** my commandments.
Lev 15: 31 "'You must **k** the Israelites
Nu 6: 24 LORD bless you and **k** you;
Dt 4: 2 **k** the commands of the LORD your
6: 17 Be sure to **k** the commands
7: 9 love him and **k** his commandments.
7: 12 your God will **k** his covenant
11: 1 your God and **k** his requirements,
13: 4 **K** his commands and obey him;
30: 10 your God and **k** his commands
30: 16 and to **k** his commands,
Jos 22: 5 careful to **k** the commandment
1Ki 8: 58 to him and **k** the commands,
2Ki 17: 19 Judah did not **k** the commands
23: 3 the LORD and **k** his commands,
1Ch 29: 18 and **k** their hearts loyal to you.
2Ch 6: 14 you who **k** your covenant of love
34: 31 the LORD and **k** his commands,
Ne 1: 5 love him and **k** his commandments,
Job 14: 16 my steps but not **k** track of my sin.
Ps 18: 28 You, LORD, **k** my lamp burning;
19: 13 **K** your servant also from willful
78: 10 they did not **k** God's covenant
119: 2 Blessed are those who **k** his statutes
121: 7 The LORD will **k** you from all
141: 3 **k** watch over the door of my lips.
Pr 4: 21 sight, **k** them within your heart;
4: 24 **K** your mouth free of perversity;
12: 23 The prudent **k** their knowledge
17: 28 are thought wise if they **k** silent,
30: 8 **K** falsehood and lies far from me;
Ecc 3: 6 up, a time to **k** and a time to throw
12: 13 Fear God and **k** his commandments,
Isa 26: 3 You will **k** in perfect peace those
42: 6 I will **k** you and will make you to
46: 8 "Remember this, **k** it in mind,
58: 13 "If you **k** your feet from breaking
Jer 16: 11 forsook me and did not **k** my law.
Eze 20: 19 and be careful to **k** my laws.
Da 9: 4 love him and **k** his commandments,
Am 5: 13 Therefore the prudent **k** quiet
Mt 10: 10 staff, for the worker is worth his **k**.
19: 17 enter life, **k** the commandments."
Lk 12: 35 service and **k** your lamps burning,
Lk 17: 33 tries to **k** their life will lose it,
Jn 10: 24 saying, "How long will you **k** us
12: 25 this world will **k** it for eternal life.
14: 15 "If you love me, **k** my commands.
15: 10 If you **k** my commands, you will
Ac 2: 24 for death to **k** its hold on him.
18: 9 **k** on speaking, do not be silent.
Ro 7: 19 not want to do—this I **k** on doing.
12: 11 but **k** your spiritual fervor,
14: 22 these things **k** between yourself
16: 17 **K** away from them.
1Co 1: 8 He will also **k** you firm to the end,
2Co 12: 7 in order to **k** me from becoming
Gal 5: 25 let us **k** in step with the Spirit.
Eph 4: 3 Make every effort to **k** the unity
2Th 3: 6 to **k** away from every believer who
1Ti 5: 22 the sins of others. **K** yourself pure.
2Ti 4: 5 you, **k** your head in all situations,
Heb 9: 20 God has commanded you to **k**."
13: 5 **K** your lives free from the love
Jas 1: 26 yet do not **k** a tight rein on their
2: 8 If you really **k** the royal law found
3: 2 to **k** their whole body in check.
2Pe 1: 8 they will **k** you from being
1Jn 5: 3 love for God: to **k** his commands.
Jude : 21 **k** yourselves in God's love as you
: 24 To him who is able to **k** you
Rev 3: 10 **k** you from the hour of trial that is
12: 17 those who **k** God's commands
14: 12 of God who **k** his commands
22: 9 with all who **k** the words of this

KEEPER (KEEP)
Ge 4: 9 "Am I my brother's **k**?"

KEEPING (KEEP)
Ex 20: 8 the Sabbath day by **k** it holy.
Dt 5: 12 the Sabbath day by **k** it holy,
13: 18 your God by **k** all his commands
Ps 19: 11 in **k** them there is great reward.
119:112 My heart is set on **k** your decrees
Pr 15: 3 **k** watch on the wicked and the good.
Mt 3: 8 Produce fruit in **k** with repentance.
Lk 2: 8 **k** watch over their flocks at night.
1Co 7: 19 **K** God's commands is what counts.
Jas 4: 11 law, you are not **k** it, but sitting
1Pe 3: 16 **k** a clear conscience, so that those
2Pe 3: 9 Lord is not slow in **k** his promise,

KEEPS (KEEP)
Ne 1: 5 who **k** his covenant of love
Ps 15: 4 who **k** an oath even when it hurts,
Pr 15: 21 has understanding **k** a straight
19: 16 Whoever **k** commandments **k** their life,
Isa 56: 2 **k** their hands from doing any evil."
Da 9: 4 who **k** his covenant of love
Jn 7: 19 Yet not one of you **k** the law.
14: 21 **k** them is the one who loves me.
1Co 13: 5 angered, it **k** no record of wrongs.
Jas 2: 10 For whoever **k** the whole law
1Jn 3: 24 The one who **k** God's commands
Rev 22: 7 Blessed is the one who **k** the words

KEILAH
1Sa 23: 13 that David had escaped from **K**,

KEPT (KEEP)
Ex 12: 42 Because the LORD **k** vigil
Dt 7: 8 and **k** the oath he swore to your
2Ki 18: 6 he **k** the commands the LORD had
Ne 9: 8 You have **k** your promise because
Ps 130: 3 LORD, **k** a record of sins, Lord,
Isa 38: 17 In your love you **k** me from the pit
Mt 19: 20 "All these I have **k**," the young
Jn 15: 10 as I have **k** my Father's commands
2Co 11: 9 have **k** myself from being a burden
2Ti 4: 7 finished the race, I have **k** the faith.
1Pe 1: 4 This inheritance is **k** in heaven

KERNEL*
Mk 4: 28 head, then the full **k** in the head.
Jn 12: 24 you, unless a **k** of wheat falls

KEY (KEYS)
Isa 33: 6 the LORD is the **k** to this treasure.
Rev 20: 1 having the **k** to the Abyss

KEYS* (KEY)
Mt 16: 19 will give you the **k** of the kingdom
Rev 1: 18 And I hold the **k** of death

KICK*
Ac 26: 14 hard for you to **k** against the goads.'

KILL (KILLED KILLS)
Ecc 3: 3 a time to **k** and a time to heal,

Mt 10: 28 those who **k** the body but cannot **k** the soul.
17: 23 They will **k** him, and on the third
Mk 9: 31 will **k** him, and after three days
10: 34 spit on him, flog him and **k** him.

KILLED (KILL)
Ge 4: 8 his brother Abel and **k** him.
Ex 2: 12 he **k** the Egyptian and hid him
13: 15 the LORD **k** the firstborn of both
Nu 35: 11 who has **k** someone accidentally
1Sa 17: 50 down the Philistine and **k** him.
Ne 9: 26 They **k** your prophets, who had
Hos 6: 5 I **k** you with the words of my
Lk 11: 48 they **k** the prophets, and you build
Ac 3: 15 You **k** the author of life, but God

KILLS (KILL)
Lev 24: 21 whoever **k** a human being is to be
2Co 3: 6 the letter **k**, but the Spirit gives

KIND (KINDNESS KINDNESSES KINDS)
Ge 1: 24 animals, each according to its **k**."
2Ch 10: 7 "If you will be **k** to these people
Pr 11: 17 who are **k** benefit themselves,
12: 25 the heart, but a **k** word cheers it up.
14: 21 blessed is the one who is **k**
14: 31 whoever is **k** to the needy honors
19: 17 Whoever is **k** to the poor lends
Da 4: 27 by being **k** to the oppressed.
Lk 6: 35 because he is **k** to the ungrateful
1Co 13: 4 Love is patient, love is **k**.
15: 35 what **k** of body will they come?"
Eph 4: 32 Be **k** and compassionate to one
2Ti 2: 24 but must be **k** to everyone,
Titus 2: 5 to be **k**, and to be subject to their

KINDHEARTED* (HEART)
Pr 11: 16 A **k** woman gains honor,

KINDNESS (KIND)
Ge 24: 12 show **k** to my master Abraham.
32: 10 I am unworthy of all the **k**
39: 21 he showed him **k** and granted him
Ru 2: 20 "He has not stopped showing his **k**
2Sa 9: 3 to whom I can show God's **k**?"
22: 51 he shows unfailing **k** to his
Job 6: 14 "Anyone who withholds **k**
Ps 141: 5 that is a **k**; let him rebuke me—
Isa 54: 8 with everlasting **k** I will have
Jer 9: 24 who exercises **k**,
31: 3 I have drawn you with unfailing **k**.
Hos 11: 4 I led them with cords of human **k**,
Ac 14: 17 He has shown **k** by giving you rain
Ro 11: 22 but **k** to you, provided that you continue in his **k**.
2Co 6: 6 understanding, patience and **k**;
Gal 5: 22 peace, forbearance, **k**, goodness,
Eph 2: 7 expressed in his **k** to us in Christ
Col 3: 12 yourselves with compassion, **k**,
Titus 3: 4 But when the **k** and love of God

KINDNESSES* (KIND)
Ps 106: 7 did not remember your many **k**,
Isa 63: 7 I will tell of the **k** of the LORD,
63: 7 to his compassion and many **k**.

KINDS (KIND)
Ge 1: 12 bearing seed according to their **k**
1Co 12: 4 There are different **k** of gifts,
1Ti 6: 10 of money is a root of all **k** of evil.
1Pe 1: 6 had to suffer grief in all **k** of trials.

KING (KING'S KINGDOM KINGDOMS KINGS)

1. Kings of Judah and Israel: see Saul, David, Solomon.

2. Kings of Judah: see Rehoboam, Abijah, Asa, Jehoshaphat, Jehoram, Ahaziah, Athaliah (Queen), Joash, Amaziah, Azariah (Uzziah), Jotham, Ahaz, Hezekiah, Manasseh, Amon, Josiah, Jehoahaz, Jehoiakim, Jehoiachin, Zedekiah.

3. Kings of Israel: see Jeroboam I, Nadab, Baasha, Elah, Zimri, Tibni, Omri, Ahab, Ahaziah, Joram, Jehu, Jehoahaz, Jehoash, Jeroboam II, Zechariah, Shallum, Menahem, Pekah, Pekahiah, Hoshea.

Ex 1: 8 Then a new **k**, to whom Joseph
Dt 17: 14 "Let us set a **k** over us like all
Jdg 17: 6 In those days Israel had no **k**;
1Sa 8: 5 now appoint a **k** to lead us, such as
11: 15 made Saul **k** in the presence
12: 12 we want a **k** to rule over us'—
12: 12 the LORD your God was your **k**.
2Sa 2: 4 anointed David **k** over the tribe
1Ki 1: 30 Solomon your son shall be **k**
Ps 2: 6 "I have installed my **k** on Zion,
24: 7 that the **K** of glory may come in.
44: 4 You are my **K** and my God,
47: 7 For God is the **K** of all the earth;
Isa 32: 1 a **k** will reign in righteousness
Jer 30: 9 their God and David their **k**,
Hos 3: 5 their God and David their **k**.
Mic 2: 13 Their **K** will pass through before
Zec 9: 9 See, your **k** comes to you,
Mt 2: 2 is the one who has been born **k**
27: 11 him, "Are you the **k** of the Jews?"
Lk 19: 38 "Blessed is the **k** who comes
23: 3 Jesus, "Are you the **k** of the Jews?"
23: 38 THIS IS THE **K** OF THE
Jn 1: 49 you are the **k** of Israel."
12: 13 "Blessed is the **k** of Israel!"
Ac 17: 7 saying that there is another **k**,
1Ti 1: 17 Now to the **K** eternal, immortal,
6: 15 the **K** of kings and Lord of lords,
Heb 7: 1 This Melchizedek was **k** of Salem
Rev 15: 3 are your ways, **K** of the nations.
17: 14 is Lord of lords and **K** of kings—
19: 16 this name written: **K** OF KINGS

KING'S (KING)
Pr 21: 1 the LORD's hand the **k** heart is
Ecc 8: 3 in a hurry to leave the **k** presence.

KINGDOM (KING)
Ex 19: 6 you will be for me a **k** of priests
Dt 17: 18 When he takes the throne of his **k**,
2Sa 7: 12 blood, and I will establish his **k**.
1Ki 11: 31 'See, I am going to tear the **k**
1Ch 17: 11 own sons, and I will establish his **k**.
29: 11 Yours, LORD, is the **k**;
Ps 45: 6 justice will be the scepter of your **k**.
103: 19 in heaven, and his **k** rules over all.
145: 11 They tell of the glory of your **k**
Eze 29: 14 There they will be a lowly **k**.
Da 2: 39 "After you, another **k** will arise,
4: 3 His **k** is an eternal **k**;
7: 27 His **k** will be an everlasting **k**,
Ob : 21 And the **k** will be the LORD's.
Mt 3: 2 for the **k** of heaven has come near."
4: 17 for the **k** of heaven has come near."
4: 23 the good news of the **k**,
5: 3 spirit, for theirs is the **k** of heaven.
5: 10 for theirs is the **k** of heaven.
5: 19 be called least in the **k** of heaven,
5: 19 be called great in the **k** of heaven.
5: 20 you will certainly not enter the **k**
6: 10 your **k** come, your will be done,
6: 33 But seek first his **k** and his
7: 21 Lord,' will enter the **k** of heaven,
8: 11 Isaac and Jacob in the **k** of heaven.
8: 12 of the **k** will be thrown outside,
9: 35 the good news of the **k**
10: 7 'The **k** of heaven has come near.'
11: 11 the **k** of heaven is greater than he.
11: 12 the **k** of heaven has been subjected
12: 25 "Every **k** divided against itself will
12: 26 How then can his **k** stand?
12: 28 the **k** of God has come upon you.
13: 11 of the **k** of heaven has been given
13: 19 hears the message about the **k**
13: 24 "The **k** of heaven is like a man who
13: 31 "The **k** of heaven is like a mustard
13: 33 "The **k** of heaven is like yeast
13: 38 seed stands for the people of the **k**.
13: 41 of his **k** everything that causes sin
13: 43 like the sun in the **k** of their Father.
13: 44 "The **k** of heaven is like treasure
13: 45 the **k** of heaven is like a merchant
13: 47 the **k** of heaven is like a net that
13: 52 in the **k** of heaven is like the owner
16: 19 you the keys of the **k** of heaven;
16: 28 the Son of Man coming in his **k**."
18: 1 is the greatest in the **k** of heaven?"
18: 3 will never enter the **k** of heaven.
18: 4 is the greatest in the **k** of heaven.
18: 23 the **k** of heaven is like a king who
19: 12 for the sake of the **k** of heaven.
19: 14 for the **k** of heaven belongs to such
19: 23 is rich to enter the **k** of heaven.
19: 24 who is rich to enter the **k** of God."
20: 1 the **k** of heaven is like a landowner
20: 21 the other at your left in your **k**."
21: 31 the prostitutes are entering the **k**
21: 43 the **k** of God will be taken away
22: 2 "The **k** of heaven is like a king who
23: 13 shut the door of the **k** of heaven
24: 7 rise against nation, and **k** against **k**.
24: 14 gospel of the **k** will be preached
25: 1 the **k** of heaven will be like ten
Mt 25: 34 the **k** prepared for you since
26: 29 it new with you in my Father's **k**."
Mk 1: 15 "The **k** of God has come near.
3: 24 If a **k** is divided against itself, that **k**
4: 11 of the **k** of God has been given
4: 26 "This is what the **k** of God is like.
4: 30 "What shall we say the **k** of God is
6: 23 I will give you, up to half my **k**."
9: 1 see that the **k** of God has come
9: 47 you to enter the **k** of God with one
10: 14 for the **k** of God belongs to such as
10: 15 anyone who will not receive the **k**
10: 23 for the rich to enter the **k** of God!"
10: 24 hard it is to enter the **k** of God!
10: 25 who is rich to enter the **k** of God."
11: 10 "Blessed is the coming **k** of our
12: 34 are not far from the **k** of God."
13: 8 rise against nation, and **k** against **k**.
14: 25 I drink it new in the **k** of God."
15: 43 himself waiting for the **k** of God,
Lk 1: 33 his **k** will never end."
4: 43 the good news of the **k** of God
6: 20 are poor, for yours is the **k** of God.
7: 28 in the **k** of God is greater than he."
8: 1 the good news of the **k** of God.
8: 10 of the **k** of God has been given
9: 2 them out to proclaim the **k** of God
9: 11 spoke to them about the **k** of God,
9: 27 taste death before they see the **k**
9: 60 you go and proclaim the **k** of God."
9: 62 is fit for service in the **k** of God."
10: 9 'The **k** of God has come near
10: 11 The **k** of God has come near.'
11: 2 be your name, your **k** come.
11: 17 "Any **k** divided against itself will
11: 18 himself, how can his **k** stand?
11: 20 the **k** of God has come upon you.
12: 31 But seek his **k**, and these things
12: 32 has been pleased to give you the **k**.
13: 18 asked, "What is the **k** of God like?
13: 20 What shall I compare the **k** of God
13: 28 all the prophets in the **k** of God,
13: 29 places at the feast in the **k** of God.
14: 15 eat at the feast in the **k** of God."
16: 16 of the **k** of God is being preached,
17: 20 when the **k** of God would come,
17: 20 the **k** of God is not something
17: 21 is,' because the **k** of God is in your
18: 16 for the **k** of God belongs to such as
18: 17 anyone who will not receive the **k**
18: 24 for the rich to enter the **k** of God!
18: 25 who is rich to enter the **k** of God."
18: 29 for the sake of the **k** of God
19: 11 that the **k** of God was going
21: 10 rise against nation, and **k** against **k**.
21: 31 you know that the **k** of God is near.
22: 16 it finds fulfillment in the **k** of God."
22: 18 the vine until the **k** of God comes."
22: 29 And I confer on you a **k**, just as my
22: 30 drink at my table in my **k** and sit
23: 42 me when you come into your **k**."
23: 51 was waiting for the **k** of God.
Jn 3: 3 no one can see the **k** of God unless
3: 5 no one can enter the **k** of God
18: 36 said, "My **k** is not of this world.
Ac 1: 3 days and spoke about the **k** of God.
1: 6 going to restore the **k** to Israel?"
8: 12 the good news of the **k** of God
14: 22 hardships to enter the **k** of God,"
19: 8 persuasively about the **k** of God.
20: 25 preaching the **k** will ever see me
28: 23 explaining about the **k** of God,
28: 31 He proclaimed the **k** of God
Ro 14: 17 For the **k** of God is not a matter
1Co 4: 20 For the **k** of God is not a matter
6: 9 wrongdoers will not inherit the **k**
6: 10 nor swindlers will inherit the **k**
15: 24 when he hands over the **k** to God
15: 50 blood cannot inherit the **k** of God,
Gal 5: 21 live like this will not inherit the **k**
Eph 2: 2 and of the ruler of the **k** of the air,
5: 5 any inheritance in the **k** of Christ
Col 1: 12 of his holy people in the **k** of light.
1: 13 us into the **k** of the Son he loves,
4: 11 my co-workers for the **k** of God,
1Th 2: 12 who calls you into his **k** and glory.
2Th 1: 5 be counted worthy of the **k** of God,
2Ti 4: 1 in view of his appearing and his **k**,
4: 18 bring me safely to his heavenly **k**.
Heb 1: 8 justice will be the scepter of your **k**.
12: 28 since we are receiving a **k**

Jas 2: 5 inherit the **k** he promised those
2Pe 1: 11 into the eternal **k** of our Lord
Rev 1: 6 has made us to be a **k** and priests
1: 9 companion in the suffering and **k**
5: 10 You have made them to be a **k**
11: 15 the world has become the **k** of our
12: 10 the power and the **k** of our God,
16: 10 its **k** was plunged into darkness.
17: 12 who have not yet received a **k**,

KINGDOMS (KING)
2Ki 19: 15 you alone are God over all the **k**
19: 19 all the **k** of the earth may know
2Ch 20: 6 You rule over all the **k**
Ps 68: 32 Sing to God, you **k** of the earth,
Isa 37: 16 you alone are God over all the **k**
37: 20 all the **k** of the earth may know
Eze 29: 15 It will be the lowliest of **k** and will
37: 22 nations or be divided into two **k**.
Da 4: 17 Most High is sovereign over all **k**
Zep 3: 8 to gather the **k** and to pour out my

KINGS (KING)
Ps 2: 2 The **k** of the earth rise
47: 9 the **k** of the earth belong to God;
68: 29 at Jerusalem **k** will bring you gifts.
72: 11 May all **k** bow down to him and all
110: 5 he will crush **k** on the day of his
149: 8 to bind their **k** with fetters,
Pr 16: 12 **K** detest wrongdoing, for a throne
Isa 24: 21 and the **k** on the earth below.
52: 15 **k** will shut their mouths because
60: 11 their **k** led in triumphal procession.
Da 2: 21 he deposes **k** and raises up others.
7: 17 'The four great beasts are four **k**
7: 24 ten horns are ten **k** who will come
Lk 21: 12 you will be brought before **k**
1Ti 2: 2 for **k** and all those in authority,
6: 15 the King of **k** and Lord of lords,
Rev 1: 5 and the ruler of the **k** of the earth.
17: 14 he is Lord of lords and King of **k**—
19: 16 this name written: KING OF **K**

KISS (KISSED KISSES)
Ps 2: 12 **K** his son, or he will be angry
Pr 24: 26 An honest answer is like a **k**
SS 1: 2 Let him **k** me with the kisses of his
8: 1 I would **k** you, and no one would
Lk 22: 48 the Son of Man with a **k**?"
Ro 16: 16 Greet one another with a holy **k**.
1Co 16: 20 Greet one another with a holy **k**.
2Co 13: 12 Greet one another with a holy **k**.
1Th 5: 26 all God's people with a holy **k**.
1Pe 5: 14 Greet one another with a **k** of love.

KISSED (KISS)
Mk 14: 45 Judas said, "Rabbi!" and **k** him.
Lk 7: 38 hair, **k** them and poured perfume

KISSES* (KISS)
Pr 27: 6 trusted, but an enemy multiplies **k**.
SS 1: 2 kiss me with the **k** of his mouth—

KNEE (KNEES)
Isa 45: 23 Before me every **k** will bow;
Ro 14: 11 Lord, 'every **k** will bow before me;
Php 2: 10 name of Jesus every **k** should bow,

KNEEL (KNELT)
Est 3: 2 Mordecai would not **k** down or pay
Ps 95: 6 let us **k** before the LORD our
Eph 3: 14 this reason I **k** before the Father,

KNEES (KNEE)
1Ki 19: 18 all whose **k** have not bowed down
Isa 35: 3 hands, steady the **k** that give way;
Da 6: 10 times a day he got down on his **k**
Lk 5: 8 saw this, he fell at Jesus' **k** and said,
Heb 12: 12 your feeble arms and weak **k**.

KNELT* (KNEEL)
2Ch 6: 13 **k** down before the whole assembly
7: 3 they **k** on the pavement with their
29: 29 everyone present with him **k** down
Est 3: 2 officials at the king's gate **k** down
Mt 8: 2 leprosy came and **k** before him
9: 18 leader came and **k** before him
15: 25 woman came and **k** before him.
17: 14 approached Jesus and **k** before him
27: 29 Then they **k** in front of him
Lk 22: 41 beyond them, **k** down and prayed,
Ac 20: 36 he **k** down with all of them
21: 5 there on the beach we **k** to pray.

KNEW (KNOW)
2Ch 33: 13 Manasseh **k** that the LORD is God.
Job 23: 3 If only I **k** where to find him;
Pr 24: 12 say, "But we **k** nothing about this,"
Jer 1: 5 I formed you in the womb I **k** you,
Jnh 4: 2 I **k** that you are a gracious
Mt 7: 23 tell them plainly, 'I never **k** you.
12: 25 Jesus **k** their thoughts and said
Jn 2: 24 to them, for he **k** all people.

KNIFE
Ge 22: 10 hand and took the **k** to slay his son.
Pr 23: 2 put a **k** to your throat if you are

KNOCK* (KNOCKS)
Mt 7: 7 **k** and the door will be opened
Lk 11: 9 **k** and the door will be opened
Rev 3: 20 I stand at the door and **k**.

KNOCKS (KNOCK)
Mt 7: 8 and to the one who **k**, the door will
Lk 11: 10 and to the one who **k**, the door will

KNOW (FOREKNEW FOREKNOWLEDGE KNEW KNOWING KNOWLEDGE KNOWN KNOWS)
Ge 22: 12 Now I **k** that you fear God,
Ex 6: 7 you will **k** that I am the LORD
14: 4 the Egyptians will **k** that I am
33: 13 teach me your ways so I may **k** you
Dt 7: 9 **K** therefore that the LORD your
18: 21 "How can we **k** when a message
Jos 4: 24 of the earth might **k** that the hand
23: 14 You **k** with all your heart and soul
1Sa 17: 46 the whole world will **k** that there is
1Ki 8: 39 you alone **k** every human heart),
Job 11: 6 **K** this: God has even forgotten
19: 25 I **k** that my redeemer lives,
42: 3 things too wonderful for me to **k**.
Ps 9: 10 Those who **k** your name trust
46: 10 says, "Be still, and **k** that I am God;
73: 11 Does the Most High **k** anything?"
100: 3 **K** that the LORD is God. It is he
139: 1 me, LORD, and you **k** me.
139: 23 Search me, God, and **k** my heart;
145: 12 all people may **k** of your mighty
Pr 27: 1 you do not **k** what a day may bring.
30: 4 the name of his son? Surely you **k**!
Ecc 8: 5 wise heart will **k** the proper time
8: 17 Even if the wise claim they **k**,
Isa 29: 15 think, "Who sees us? Who will **k**?"
29: 16 say to the potter, "You **k** nothing"?
40: 21 Do you not **k**? Have you not heard?
Jer 6: 15 they do not even **k** how to blush.
9: 24 have the understanding to **k** me,
22: 16 Is that not what it means to **k** me?"
24: 7 I will give them a heart to **k** me,
31: 34 say to one another, '**K** the LORD,'
31: 34 because they will all **k** me,
33: 3 unsearchable things you do not **k**.'
Eze 2: 5 they will **k** that a prophet has been
6: 10 they will **k** that I am the LORD;
Da 11: 32 but the people who **k** their God
Mt 6: 3 let your left hand **k** what your right
7: 11 **k** how to give good gifts to your
9: 6 want you to **k** that the Son of Man
22: 29 you do not **k** the Scriptures
24: 42 because you do not **k** on what day
26: 74 to them, "I don't **k** the man!"
Mk 12: 24 you do not **k** the Scriptures
Lk 1: 4 so that you may **k** the certainty
11: 13 **k** how to give good gifts to your
12: 48 the one who does not **k** and does
13: 25 'I don't **k** you or where you come
21: 31 you **k** that the kingdom of God is
23: 34 they do not **k** what they are doing."
Jn 1: 26 stands one you do not **k**.
3: 11 we speak of what we **k**, and we
4: 22 worship what you do not **k**; we worship what we do **k**,
4: 42 and we **k** that this man really is
6: 69 to **k** that you are the Holy One
7: 28 you **k** me, and you **k** where I
8: 14 valid, for I **k** where I came
8: 19 "You do not **k** me or my Father,"
8: 32 Then you will **k** the truth,
9: 25 One thing I do **k**. I was blind
10: 4 him because they **k** his voice.
10: 14 I **k** my sheep and my sheep **k** me—
10: 27 I **k** them, and they follow me.
12: 35 the dark does not **k** where they are
13: 17 Now that you **k** these things,
13: 35 this everyone will **k** that you are
14: 7 If you really **k** me, you will **k** my
14: 17 But you **k** him, for he lives with
15: 21 they do not **k** the one who sent me.
16: 30 we can see that you **k** all things
17: 3 that they **k** you, the only true God,
Jn 17: 23 the world will **k** that you sent me
21: 15 he said, "you **k** that I love you."
21: 24 We **k** that his testimony is true.
Ac 1: 7 "It is not for you to **k** the times
1: 24 "Lord, you **k** everyone's heart.
Ro 3: 17 the way of peace they do not **k**."
6: 3 don't you **k** that all of us who were
6: 6 we **k** that our old self was crucified
6: 16 Don't you **k** that when you offer
7: 14 We **k** that the law is spiritual;
7: 18 I **k** that good itself does not dwell
8: 22 We **k** that the whole creation has
8: 26 We do not **k** what we ought to pray
8: 28 we **k** that in all things God works
1Co 1: 21 through its wisdom did not **k** him,
2: 2 I resolved to **k** nothing while I was
3: 16 Don't you **k** that you yourselves are
5: 6 Don't you **k** that a little yeast
6: 2 do you not **k** that the Lord's people
6: 15 Do you not **k** that your bodies are
6: 16 Do you not **k** that he who unites
6: 19 Do you not **k** that your bodies are
7: 16 How do you **k**, wife, whether you
7: 16 Or, how do you **k**, husband,
8: 2 think they **k** something do not
9: 13 Don't you **k** that those who serve
9: 24 Do you not **k** that in a race all
13: 9 For we **k** in part and we prophesy
13: 12 Now I **k** in part; then I shall **k** fully,
14: 16 since they do not **k** what you are
15: 58 because you **k** that your labor
2Co 5: 1 For we **k** that if the earthly tent we
5: 11 we **k** what it is to fear the Lord,
8: 9 For you **k** the grace of our Lord
Gal 1: 11 want you to **k**, brothers and sisters,
2: 16 **k** that a person is not justified
Eph 1: 17 so that you may **k** him better.
1: 18 in order that you may **k** the hope
6: 8 because you **k** that the Lord will
6: 9 since you **k** that he who is both
Php 3: 10 I want to **k** Christ—yes, to **k**
4: 12 I **k** what it is to be in need, and I **k**
Col 2: 2 order that they may **k** the mystery
4: 1 because you **k** that you also have
4: 6 may **k** how to answer everyone.
1Th 3: 3 For you **k** quite well that we are
5: 2 for you **k** very well that the day
2Th 1: 8 punish those who do not **k** God
1Ti 1: 7 they do not **k** what they are talking
3: 5 anyone does not **k** how to manage
3: 15 you will **k** how people ought
2Ti 1: 12 because I **k** whom I have believed,
2: 23 because you **k** they produce
3: 14 because you **k** those from whom
Heb 8: 11 say to one another, '**K** the Lord,'
8: 11 because they will all **k** me,
11: 8 though he did not **k** where he was
Jas 1: 3 because you **k** that the testing
3: 1 because you **k** that we who teach
4: 4 don't you **k** that friendship
4: 14 do not even **k** what will happen
1Pe 1: 18 For you **k** that it was not
2Pe 1: 12 even though you **k** them and are
1Jn 2: 3 We **k** that we have come to **k** him
2: 4 Whoever says, "I **k** him," but does
2: 5 This is how we **k** we are in him:
2: 11 do not **k** where they are going,
2: 20 One, and all of you **k** the truth.
2: 29 If you **k** that he is righteous, you **k**
3: 1 reason the world does not **k** us is that it did not **k** him.
3: 2 But we **k** that when Christ appears,
3: 10 This is how we **k** who the children
3: 14 We **k** that we have passed
3: 16 This is how we **k** what love is:
3: 19 This is how we **k** that we belong
3: 24 this is how we **k** that he lives in us:
3: 24 We **k** it by the Spirit he gave us.
4: 8 does not love does not **k** God,
4: 13 This is how we **k** that we live in
4: 16 so we **k** and rely on the love God
5: 2 This is how we **k** that we love
5: 13 may **k** that you have eternal life.
5: 15 And if we **k** that he hears us—
5: 18 We **k** that anyone born of God
5: 20 so that we may **k** him who is true.
Rev 2: 2 I **k** your deeds, your hard work
2: 9 I **k** your afflictions and your
2: 19 I **k** your deeds, your love and faith,
3: 3 you will not **k** at what time I will
3: 15 I **k** your deeds, that you are neither

KNOWING (KNOW)
Ge 3: 5 will be like God, **k** good and evil."
3: 22 like one of us, **k** good and evil.
Jn 19: 28 **k** that everything had now been
Php 3: 8 worth of **k** Christ Jesus my Lord,
Phm : 21 **k** that you will do even more than I
Heb 13: 2 hospitality to angels without **k** it.

KNOWLEDGE (KNOW)
Ge 2: 9 the tree of the **k** of good and evil.
2: 17 eat from the tree of the **k** of good
2Ch 1: 10 Give me wisdom and **k**, that I may
Job 21: 22 "Can anyone teach **k** to God,
38: 2 my plans with words without **k**?
42: 3 that obscures my plans without **k**?'
Ps 19: 2 night after night they reveal **k**.
94: 10 he who teaches mankind lack **k**?
119: 66 Teach me **k** and good judgment,
139: 6 Such **k** is too wonderful for me,
Pr 1: 4 **k** and discretion to the young—
1: 7 of the LORD is the beginning of **k**,
2: 5 the LORD and find the **k** of God.
2: 6 from his mouth come **k**
2: 10 and **k** will be pleasant to your soul.
3: 20 by his **k** the watery depths were
8: 10 of silver, **k** rather than choice gold,
8: 12 I possess **k** and discretion.
9: 10 **k** of the Holy One is understanding
10: 14 The wise store up **k**, but the mouth
12: 1 Whoever loves discipline loves **k**,
12: 23 The prudent keep their **k**
13: 16 All who are prudent act with **k**,
14: 6 **k** comes easily to the discerning.
15: 7 The lips of the wise spread **k**,
15: 14 The discerning heart seeks **k**,
17: 27 The one who has **k** uses words
18: 15 heart of the discerning acquires **k**,
19: 2 Desire without **k** is not good—
19: 25 discerning, and they will gain **k**.
20: 15 lips that speak **k** are a rare jewel.
23: 12 and your ears to words of **k**.
24: 4 through **k** its rooms are filled
Ecc 7: 12 but the advantage of **k** is this:
Isa 11: 2 the Spirit of the **k** and fear
11: 9 the **k** of the LORD as the waters
40: 14 Who was it that taught him **k**,
Jer 3: 15 heart, who will lead you with **k**
Hos 4: 6 are destroyed from lack of **k**.
Hab 2: 14 will be filled with the **k** of the glory
Mal 2: 7 lips of a priest ought to preserve **k**,
Mt 13: 11 "Because the **k** of the secrets
Lk 8: 10 He said, "The **k** of the secrets
11: 52 you have taken away the key to **k**.
Ac 18: 24 a thorough **k** of the Scriptures.
Ro 1: 28 worthwhile to retain the **k** of God,
10: 2 but their zeal is not based on **k**.
11: 33 riches of the wisdom and **k** of God!
1Co 8: 1 But **k** puffs up while love builds up.
8: 11 Christ died, is destroyed by your **k**.
12: 8 to another a message of **k** by means
13: 2 can fathom all mysteries and all **k**,
13: 8 where there is **k**, it will pass away.
2Co 2: 14 aroma of the **k** of him everywhere.
4: 6 of the **k** of God's glory displayed
8: 7 in **k**, in complete earnestness
11: 6 as a speaker, but I do have **k**.
Eph 3: 19 know this love that surpasses **k**—
4: 13 and in the **k** of the Son of God
Php 1: 9 and more in **k** and depth of insight,
Col 1: 9 with the **k** of his will through all
1: 10 work, growing in the **k** of God,
2: 3 all the treasures of wisdom and **k**.
3: 10 is being renewed in **k** in the image
1Ti 2: 4 and to come to a **k** of the truth.
6: 20 ideas of what is falsely called **k**,
Titus 1: 1 and their **k** of the truth that leads
Heb 10: 26 we have received the **k** of the truth,
2Pe 1: 5 and to goodness, **k**;
3: 18 in the grace and **k** of our Lord

KNOWN (KNOW)
Ex 6: 3 I did not make myself fully **k**
Ps 16: 11 You make **k** to me the path of life;
89: 1 make your faithfulness **k** through
98: 2 LORD has made his salvation **k**
105: 1 make **k** among the nations what he
119:168 for all my ways are **k** to you.
Pr 20: 11 Even small children are **k** by their
Isa 12: 4 make **k** among the nations what he
46: 10 I make **k** the end
61: 9 descendants will be **k** among
Eze 38: 23 I will make myself **k** in the sight
39: 7 "'I will make **k** my holy name
Mt 10: 26 or hidden that will not be made **k**.
24: 43 of the house had **k** at what time
Lk 19: 42 had only **k** on this day what would
Jn 15: 15 my Father I have made **k** to you.
16: 14 he will receive what he will make **k**
17: 26 I have made you **k** to them,
Ac 2: 28 You have made **k** to me the paths
Ro 1: 19 since what may be **k** about God is
3: 21 of God has been made **k**,
9: 22 his wrath and make his power **k**,
11: 34 "Who has **k** the mind of the Lord?
15: 20 the gospel where Christ was not **k**,
16: 26 and made **k** through the prophetic
1Co 2: 16 "Who has **k** the mind of the Lord
8: 3 whoever loves God is **k** by God.
13: 12 know fully, even as I am fully **k**.
2Co 3: 2 our hearts, **k** and read by everyone.
Gal 4: 9 or rather are **k** by God—how is it
Eph 3: 5 which was not made **k** to people
6: 19 I will fearlessly make **k** the mystery
2Ti 3: 15 from infancy you have **k** the Holy
2Pe 2: 21 than to have **k** it and then to turn

KNOWS (KNOW)
1Sa 2: 3 for the LORD is a God who **k**,
Est 4: 14 who **k** but that you have come
Job 23: 10 But he **k** the way that I take;
Ps 44: 21 since he **k** the secrets of the heart?
94: 11 The LORD **k** all human plans; he **k**
103: 14 for he **k** how we are formed,
Ecc 8: 7 Since no one **k** the future, who can
9: 12 one **k** when their hour will come:
Mt 6: 8 Father **k** what you need before
11: 27 one **k** the Son except the Father,
11: 27 no one **k** the Father except the Son
24: 36 about that day or hour no one **k**,
Lk 12: 47 "The servant who **k** the master's
16: 15 of others, but God **k** your hearts.
Ac 15: 8 God, who **k** the heart,
Ro 8: 27 searches our hearts **k** the mind
1Co 2: 11 who **k** a person's thoughts except
2Ti 2: 19 "The Lord **k** those who are his,"
Jas 4: 17 **k** the good they ought to do
1Jn 4: 6 and whoever **k** God listens to us;
4: 7 has been born of God and **k** God.

KOHATHITE (KOHATHITES)
Nu 3: 29 The **K** clans were to camp

KOHATHITES (KOHATHITE)
Nu 3: 28 The **K** were responsible for the
4: 15 The **K** are to carry those things

KORAH
Levite who led rebellion against Moses and Aaron (Nu 16; Jude 11).

LABAN
Brother of Rebekah (Ge 24:29), father of Rachel and Leah (Ge 29:16). Received Abraham's servant (Ge 24:29–51). Provided daughters as wives for Jacob in exchange for Jacob's service (Ge 29:1–30). Provided flocks for Jacob's service (Ge 30:25–43). After Jacob's departure, pursued and covenanted with him (Ge 31).

LABOR (LABORING)
Ex 1: 11 to oppress them with forced **l**,
20: 9 Six days you shall **l** and do all your
Dt 5: 13 Six days you shall **l** and do all your
Ps 127: 1 the house, the builders **l** in vain.
128: 2 You will eat the fruit of your **l**;
Pr 12: 24 rule, but laziness ends in forced **l**.
Isa 54: 1 for joy, you who were never in **l**;
55: 2 your **l** on what does not satisfy?
Mt 6: 28 They do not **l** or spin.
Jn 4: 38 have reaped the benefits of their **l**."
1Co 3: 8 rewarded according to their own **l**.
15: 58 know that your **l** in the Lord is not
Gal 4: 27 cry aloud, you who were never in **l**;
Php 2: 16 that I did not run or **l** in vain.
Rev 14: 13 "they will rest from their **l**, for their

LABORING* (LABOR)
2Th 3: 8 **l** and toiling so that we would not

LACK (LACKED LACKING LACKS)
Ps 34: 9 for those who fear him **l** nothing.
Pr 5: 23 For **l** of discipline they will die,
10: 21 many, but fools die for **l** of sense.
11: 14 For **l** of guidance a nation falls,
15: 22 Plans fail for **l** of counsel,
28: 27 who give to the poor will **l** nothing,
Mk 6: 6 He was amazed at their **l** of faith.
16: 14 *rebuked them for their **l** of faith*
1Co 1: 7 you do not **l** any spiritual gift
7: 5 because of your **l** of self-control.
Col 2: 23 but they **l** any value in restraining

LACKED (LACK)
Dt 2: 7 you, and you have not **l** anything.
Ne 9: 21 they **l** nothing, their clothes did
1Co 12: 24 greater honor to the parts that **l** it,

LACKING (LACK)
Ro 12: 11 Never be **l** in zeal, but keep your
Jas 1: 4 and complete, not **l** anything.

LACKS (LACK)
Pr 25: 28 is a person who **l** self-control.
31: 11 in her and **l** nothing of value.
Eze 34: 8 because my flock **l** a shepherd
Jas 1: 5 If any of you **l** wisdom, you should

LAID (LAY)
Isa 53: 6 and the LORD has **l** on him
Mk 6: 29 took his body and **l** it in a tomb.
Lk 6: 48 deep and **l** the foundation on rock.
Ac 6: 6 prayed and **l** their hands on them.
1Co 3: 11 other than the one already **l**,
1Ti 4: 14 the body of elders **l** their hands
1Jn 3: 16 Jesus Christ **l** down his life for us.

LAKE
Mt 8: 24 a furious storm came up on the **l**,
14: 25 went out to them, walking on the **l**.
Mk 4: 1 Again Jesus began to teach by the **l**.
Lk 8: 33 down the steep bank into the **l**
Jn 6: 25 him on the other side of the **l**,
Rev 19: 20 into the fiery **l** of burning sulfur.
20: 14 were thrown into the **l** of fire.
20: 14 The **l** of fire is the second death.

LAMB (LAMB'S LAMBS)
Ge 22: 8 "God himself will provide the **l**
Ex 12: 21 and slaughter the Passover **l**.
Nu 9: 11 They are to eat the **l**,
2Sa 12: 4 he took the ewe **l** that belonged
Isa 11: 6 The wolf will live with the **l**,
53: 7 he was led like a **l** to the slaughter,
Mk 14: 12 to sacrifice the Passover **l**,
Jn 1: 29 "Look, the **L** of God, who takes
Ac 8: 32 as a **l** before its shearer is silent,
1Co 5: 7 our Passover **l**, has been sacrificed.
1Pe 1: 19 a **l** without blemish or defect.
Rev 5: 6 The **L** had seven horns and seven
5: 12 "Worthy is the **L**, who was slain,
7: 14 them white in the blood of the **L**.
14: 4 They follow the **L** wherever he
15: 3 God's servant Moses and of the **L**:
17: 14 They will wage war against the **L**, but the **L** will triumph
19: 9 to the wedding supper of the **L**!"
21: 23 gives it light, and the **L** is its lamp.

LAMB'S* (LAMB)
Rev 13: 8 been written in the **L** book of life,
21: 27 names are written in the **L** book

LAMBS (LAMB)
Lk 10: 3 you out like **l** among wolves.
Jn 21: 15 Jesus said, "Feed my **l**."

LAME
2Sa 9: 3 he is **l** in both feet."
Isa 33: 23 even the **l** will carry off plunder.
35: 6 Then will the **l** leap like a deer,
Mt 11: 5 The blind receive sight, the **l** walk,
15: 31 the **l** walking and the blind seeing.
Lk 14: 21 the crippled, the blind and the **l**.'

LAMENT
2Sa 1: 17 took up this **l** concerning Saul
Eze 19: 1 a **l** concerning the princes

LAMP (LAMPS LAMPSTAND LAMPSTANDS)
2Sa 22: 29 You, LORD, are my **l**;
Ps 18: 28 You, LORD, keep my **l** burning;
119:105 Your word is a **l** to my feet
132: 17 set up a **l** for my anointed one.
Pr 6: 23 For this command is a **l**,
20: 27 The human spirit is the **l**
31: 18 and her **l** does not go out at night.
Mt 6: 22 "The eye is the **l** of the body.
Lk 8: 16 "No one lights a **l** and hides it
Rev 21: 23 gives it light, and the Lamb is its **l**.
22: 5 They will not need the light of a **l**

LAMPS (LAMP)
Mt 25: 1 be like ten virgins who took their **l**
Lk 12: 35 service and keep your **l** burning,
Rev 4: 5 of the throne, seven **l** were blazing.

LAMPSTAND (LAMP)
Ex 25: 31 "Make a **l** of pure gold.
Zec 4: 2 "I see a solid gold **l** with a bowl
4: 11 on the right and the left of the **l**?"

Heb 9: 2 In its first room were the **l**
Rev 2: 5 and remove your **l** from its place.

LAMPSTANDS (LAMP)
2Ch 4: 7 He made ten gold **l** according
Rev 1: 12 when I turned I saw seven golden **l**,
1: 20 the seven **l** are the seven churches.

LAND (LANDS)
Ge 1: 10 God called the dry ground "**l**,"
1: 11 said, "Let the **l** produce vegetation:
1: 24 "Let the **l** produce living creatures
12: 1 household to the **l** I will show you.
12: 7 your offspring I will give this **l**."
13: 15 All the **l** that you see I will give
15: 18 "To your descendants I give this **l**,
50: 24 this **l** to the **l** he promised on oath
Ex 3: 8 a **l** flowing with milk and honey—
6: 8 I will bring you to the **l** I swore
33: 3 Go up to the **l** flowing with milk
Lev 25: 23 you reside in my **l** as foreigners
Nu 14: 8 he will lead us into that **l**,
35: 33 not pollute the **l** where you are.
35: 33 Bloodshed pollutes the **l**,
Dt 1: 8 See, I have given you this **l**.
8: 7 God is bringing you into a good **l**
11: 10 is not like the **l** of Egypt,
28: 21 you from the **l** you are entering
29: 19 on the watered **l** as well as the dry.
34: 1 Lord showed him the whole **l**—
Jos 13: 2 "This is the **l** that remains:
14: 4 Levites received no share of the **l**
14: 9 me, 'The **l** on which your feet have
2Sa 21: 14 answered prayer in behalf of the **l**.
2Ki 17: 5 of Assyria invaded the entire **l**,
24: 1 king of Babylon invaded the **l**,
25: 21 into captivity, away from her **l**.
2Ch 7: 14 their sin and will heal their **l**.
7: 20 then I will uproot Israel from my **l**,
36: 21 The **l** enjoyed its sabbath rests;
Ezr 9: 11 entering to possess is a **l** polluted
Ne 9: 36 the **l** you gave our ancestors so
Ps 37: 11 meek will inherit the **l** and enjoy
37: 29 The righteous will inherit the **l**
136: 21 and gave their **l** as an inheritance,
142: 5 my portion in the **l** of the living."
Pr 2: 21 For the upright will live in the **l**,
12: 11 work their **l** will have abundant
Isa 6: 13 seed will be the stump in the **l**."
53: 8 was cut off from the **l** of the living;
Jer 2: 7 came and defiled my **l** and made
Eze 36: 24 bring you back into your own **l**.

LANDS (LAND)
Ps 111: 6 giving them the **l** of other nations.
Eze 20: 6 honey, the most beautiful of all **l**.
Zec 10: 9 in distant **l** they will remember me.

LANGUAGE (LANGUAGES)
Ge 11: 1 Now the whole world had one **l**
11: 9 there the Lord confused the **l**
Jn 8: 44 speaks his native **l**, for he is a liar
Ac 2: 6 Sheard their own **l** being spoken.
Col 3: 8 slander, and filthy **l** from your lips.
Rev 5: 9 God persons from every tribe and **l**
7: 9 people and **l**, standing before
14: 6 to every nation, tribe, **l** and people.

LANGUAGES (LANGUAGE)
Isa 66: 18 the people of all nations and **l**,
Zec 8: 23 "In those days ten people from all **l**

LAODICEA
Rev 3: 14 the angel of the church in **L** write:

LAP
Jdg 7: 5 "Separate those who **l** the water

LASHES
Pr 17: 10 more than a hundred **l** a fool.
2Co 11: 24 the Jews the forty **l** minus one.

LAST (LASTING LASTS LATTER)
Ex 14: 24 During the **l** watch of the night
2Sa 23: 1 These are the **l** words of David:
Isa 2: 2 In the **l** days the mountain
41: 4 the first of them and with the **l**—
44: 6 I am the first and I am the **l**;
48: 12 I am the first and I am the **l**.
Hos 3: 5 and to his blessings in the **l** days.
Mic 4: 1 In the **l** days the mountain
Mt 19: 30 are first will be **l**, and many who are **l** will be first.
20: 8 beginning with the **l** ones hired
21: 37 **L** of all, he sent his son to them.
Mk 9: 35 wants to be first must be the very **l**,
10: 31 But many who are first will be **l**,
15: 37 a loud cry, Jesus breathed his **l**.
Jn 6: 40 I will raise them up at the **l** day."
15: 16 fruit that will **l**—and so
Ac 2: 17 "'In the **l** days, God says, I will
Ro 1: 17 is by faith from first to **l**, just as
1Co 15: 26 The **l** enemy to be destroyed is
15: 52 of an eye, at the **l** trumpet.
2Ti 3: 1 will be terrible times in the **l** days.
2Pe 3: 3 in the **l** days scoffers will come,
Jude : 18 "In the **l** times there will be scoffers
Rev 1: 17 I am the First and the **L**.
22: 13 the First and the **L**, the Beginning

LASTING (LAST)
Ex 12: 14 to the Lord—a **l** ordinance.
Lev 24: 8 of the Israelites, as a **l** covenant.
Nu 25: 13 have a covenant of a **l** priesthood,
Heb 10: 34 had better and **l** possessions.

LASTS (LAST)
Ps 30: 5 For his anger **l** only a moment, but his favor **l** a lifetime;
2Co 3: 11 greater is the glory of that which **l**!

LATTER (LAST)
Job 42: 12 The Lord blessed the **l** part
Mt 23: 23 You should have practiced the **l**,
Php 1: 16 The **l** do so out of love,

LAUGH (LAUGHED LAUGHS LAUGHTER)
Ps 59: 8 But you **l** at them, Lord;
Pr 31: 25 she can **l** at the days to come.
Ecc 3: 4 a time to weep and a time to **l**,
Lk 6: 21 you who weep now, for you will **l**.
6: 25 Woe to you who **l** now, for you will

LAUGHED (LAUGH)
Ge 17: 17 **l** and said to himself, "Will a son
18: 12 So Sarah **l** to herself as she thought,

LAUGHS (LAUGH)
Ps 2: 4 The One enthroned in heaven **l**;
37: 13 but the Lord **l** at the wicked, for he

LAUGHTER (LAUGH)
Ge 21: 6 said, "God has brought me **l**,
Ps 126: 2 Our mouths were filled with **l**,
Pr 14: 13 Even in **l** the heart may ache,
Jas 4: 9 Change your **l** to mourning and

LAVISHED
Eph 1: 8 that he **l** on us. With all wisdom
1Jn 3: 1 See what great love the Father has **l**

LAW (LAWFUL LAWGIVER LAWS)
Ex 31: 18 the two tablets of the covenant **l**,
Lev 24: 22 to have the same **l** for the foreigner
Nu 6: 13 "'Now this is the **l** of the Nazirite
Dt 1: 5 Moses began to expound this **l**,
6: 25 to obey all this **l** before the Lord
27: 26 of this **l** by carrying them out."
31: 11 you shall read this **l** before them
31: 26 "Take this Book of the **L** and place
Jos 1: 7 to obey all the **l** my servant Moses
1: 8 Keep this Book of the **L** always
22: 5 the **l** that Moses the servant
2Ki 22: 8 the Book of the **L** in the temple
2Ch 6: 16 walk before me according to my **l**,
17: 9 the Book of the **L** of the Lord;
34: 14 the Book of the **L** of the Lord
Ezr 7: 6 well versed in the **L** of Moses,
Ne 8: 2 the priest brought the **L** before
8: 8 from the Book of the **L** of God,
Ps 1: 2 delight is in the **l** of the Lord,
19: 7 The **l** of the Lord is perfect,
37: 31 The **l** of their God is in their hearts
40: 8 your **l** is within my heart."
119: 18 may see wonderful things in your **l**.
119: 70 unfeeling, but I delight in your **l**.
119: 72 The **l** from your mouth is more
119: 77 I may live, for your **l** is my delight.
119: 97 Oh, how I love your **l**! I meditate
119:163 detest falsehood but I love your **l**.
119:165 peace have those who love your **l**,
Isa 2: 3 The **l** will go out from Zion,
42: 21 righteousness to make his **l** great
Jer 2: 8 deal with the **l** did not know me;
8: 8 for we have the **l** of the Lord,"
31: 33 "I will put my **l** in their minds
Mic 4: 2 The **l** will go out from Zion,
Hab 1: 7 they are a **l** to themselves
Zec 7: 12 would not listen to the **l**
Mt 5: 17 that I have come to abolish the **L**
7: 12 you, for this sums up the **L**
22: 36 greatest commandment in the **L**?"
22: 40 All the **L** and the Prophets hang
23: 23 more important matters of the **l**—
Lk 11: 52 "Woe to you experts in the **l**,
16: 17 of a pen to drop out of the **L**.
Lk 24: 44 about me in the **L** of Moses,
Jn 1: 17 For the **l** was given through Moses;
Ac 13: 39 able to obtain under the **l** of Moses.
Ro 2: 12 sin apart from the **l** will also perish apart from the **l**,
2: 12 under the **l** will be judged by the **l**.
2: 15 requirements of the **l** are written
2: 20 you have in the **l** the embodiment
2: 25 has value if you observe the **l**,
3: 19 it says to those who are under the **l**,
3: 20 through the **l** we become conscious
3: 21 apart from the **l** the righteousness
3: 28 faith apart from the works of the **l**.
3: 31 nullify the **l** by this faith?
3: 31 Not at all! Rather, we uphold the **l**.
4: 13 It was not through the **l**
4: 15 because the **l** brings wrath.
4: 16 not only to those who are of the **l**
5: 13 account where there is no **l**.
5: 20 The **l** was brought in so
6: 14 because you are not under the **l**,
6: 15 sin because we are not under the **l**
7: 1 the **l** has authority over someone
7: 4 died to the **l** through the body
7: 5 passions aroused by the **l** were
7: 6 we have been released from the **l** so
7: 7 Is the **l** sinful? Certainly not!
7: 8 For apart from the **l**, sin was dead.
7: 12 So then, the **l** is holy,
7: 14 We know that the **l** is spiritual;
7: 22 my inner being I delight in God's **l**;
7: 25 in my mind am a slave to God's **l**,
8: 2 has set you free from the **l** of sin
8: 3 For what the **l** was powerless to do
8: 4 of the **l** might be fully met in us,
8: 7 it does not submit to God's **l**,
9: 4 the receiving of the **l**, the temple
9: 31 who pursued the **l** as the way
10: 4 Christ is the culmination of the **l**
13: 8 loves others has fulfilled the **l**.
13: 10 love is the fulfillment of the **l**.
1Co 9: 9 For it is written in the **L** of Moses:
9: 20 those under the **l** I became like one
9: 21 I am not free from God's **l** but am under Christ's **l**),
15: 56 is sin, and the power of sin is the **l**.
Gal 2: 16 not justified by the works of the **l**,
2: 19 "For through the **l** I died to the **l** so
3: 2 the Spirit by the works of the **l**,
3: 5 among you by the works of the **l**,
3: 10 works of the **l** are under a curse,
3: 11 on the **l** is justified before God,
3: 13 curse of the **l** by becoming a curse
3: 17 The **l**, introduced 430 years later,
3: 19 The **l** was given through angels
3: 21 Is the **l**, therefore, opposed
3: 23 were held in custody under the **l**,
3: 24 So the **l** was our guardian until
4: 21 you who want to be under the **l**,
5: 3 he is obligated to obey the whole **l**.
5: 4 by the **l** have been alienated
5: 14 For the entire **l** is fulfilled
5: 18 the Spirit, you are not under the **l**.
6: 2 in this way you will fulfill the **l**
Eph 2: 15 his flesh the **l** with its commands
Php 3: 6 as for righteousness based on the **l**,
3: 9 of my own that comes from the **l**,
1Ti 1: 8 We know that the **l** is good if one
Heb 7: 12 the **l** must be changed also.
7: 19 (for the **l** made nothing perfect),
10: 1 The **l** is only a shadow of the good
Jas 1: 25 the perfect **l** that gives freedom,
2: 8 you really keep the royal **l** found
2: 10 For whoever keeps the whole **l**
4: 11 When you judge the **l**, you are not
1Jn 3: 4 Everyone who sins breaks the **l**;

LAWFUL (LAW)
Mt 12: 12 Therefore it is **l** to do good

LAWGIVER* (LAW)
Isa 33: 22 the Lord is our **l**, the Lord is
Jas 4: 12 There is only one **L** and Judge,

LAWLESS (LAWLESSNESS)
2Th 2: 8 then the **l** one will be revealed,
Heb 10: 17 **l** acts I will remember no more."

LAWLESSNESS* (LAWLESS)
2Th 2: 3 occurs and the man of **l** is revealed,
2: 7 the secret power of **l** is already
1Jn 3: 4 sins breaks the law; in fact, sin is **l**.

LAWS (LAW)
Ex 21: 1 "These are the **l** you are to set

Lev 25: 18 and be careful to obey my l,
Dt 4: 1 and I l am about to teach you.
30: 16 keep his commands, decrees and l;
Ps 119: 30 I have set my heart on your l.
119: 43 for I have put my hope in your l.
119:120 fear of you; I stand in awe of your l.
119:164 I praise you for your righteous l.
119:175 and may your l sustain me.
Eze 36: 27 and be careful to keep my l.
Heb 8: 10 I will put my l in their minds
10: 16 I will put my l in their hearts, and I

LAWSUIT (LAWSUIT)
Pr 18: 17 In a l the first to speak seems right,

LAWSUITS (LAWSUITS)
Hos 10: 4 l spring up like poisonous weeds
1Co 6: 7 you have l among you means you

LAY (LAID LAYING LAYS)
Ex 29: 10 his sons shall l their hands on its
Lev 1: 4 You are to l your hand on the head
4: 15 the community are to l their hands
Nu 8: 10 the Israelites are to l their hands
27: 18 and l your hand on him.
1Sa 26: 9 Who can l a hand on the LORD's
Job 1: 12 the man himself do not l a finger."
22: 22 and l up his words in your heart.
Ecc 10: 4 calmness can l great offenses
Isa 28: 16 "See, I l a stone in Zion, a tested
Mt 8: 20 of Man has no place to l his head."
28: 6 Come and see the place where he l.
Mk 6: 5 except l his hands on a few sick
Lk 9: 58 of Man has no place to l his head."
Jn 10: 15 and I l down my life for the sheep.
10: 18 I have authority to l it down
15: 13 to l down one's life for one's
Ac 8: 19 whom I l my hands may receive
Ro 9: 33 I l in Zion a stone that causes
1Co 3: 11 no one can l any foundation other
1Pe 2: 6 "See, I l a stone in Zion, a chosen
1Jn 3: 16 we ought to l down our lives for
Rev 4: 10 They l their crowns before

LAYING* (LAY)
2Ch 32: 9 and all his forces were l siege
Job 34: 30 ruling, from l snares for the people.
Lk 4: 40 and l his hands on each one,
Ac 8: 18 the Spirit was given at the l
1Ti 5: 22 not be hasty in the l on of hands,
2Ti 1: 6 is in you through the l on of my
Heb 6: 1 not l again the foundation
6: 2 cleansing rites, the l on of hands,

LAYS (LAY)
Jn 10: 11 The good shepherd l down his life

LAZARUS
1. Poor man in Jesus' parable (Lk 16:19–31).
2. Brother of Mary and Martha whom Jesus raised from the dead (Jn 11:1—12:19).

LAZINESS* (LAZY)
Pr 12: 24 will rule, but l ends in forced labor.
19: 15 L brings on deep sleep,
Ecc 10: 18 Through l, the rafters sag;

LAZY* (LAZINESS)
Ex 5: 8 They are l; that is why they are
5: 17 "L, that's what you are—l!
Pr 10: 4 L hands make for poverty,
12: 27 The l do not roast any game,
26: 15 he is too l to bring it back to his
Mt 25: 26 replied, 'You wicked, l servant!
Titus 1: 12 always liars, evil brutes, l gluttons."
Heb 6: 12 We do not want you to become l,

LEAD (LEADER LEADERS LEADERSHIP LEADS LED)
Ex 15: 13 love you will l the people you have
Nu 14: 8 with us, he will l us into that land,
Dt 31: 2 and I am no longer able to l you.
Jos 1: 6 because you will l these people
1Sa 8: 5 now appoint a king to l us, such as
2Ch 1: 10 that I may l this people, for who is
Ps 27: 11 l me in a straight path because
43: 3 your faithful care, let them l me;
61: 2 l me to the rock that is higher than
139: 24 and l me in the way everlasting.
143: 10 may your good Spirit l me on level
Pr 4: 11 and l you along straight paths.
20: 7 The righteous l blameless lives;
Ecc 5: 6 Do not let your mouth l you
Isa 11: 6 and a little child will l them.
49: 10 and l them beside springs of water.
Da 12: 3 those who l many to righteousness,
Mt 6: 13 And l us not into temptation,
15: 14 If the blind l the blind, both will
Lk 11: 4 And l us not into temptation.'"
Ro 12: 8 if it is to l, do it diligently; if it is
1Th 4: 11 it your ambition to l a quiet life:
1Jn 3: 7 do not let anyone l you astray.
Rev 7: 17 'he will l them to springs of living

LEADER (LEAD)
1Sa 7: 6 Now Samuel was serving as l
7: 15 continued as Israel's l all the days
12: 2 Now you have a king as your l.

LEADERS (LEAD)
Heb 13: 7 Remember your l, who spoke
13: 17 Have confidence in your l

LEADERSHIP* (LEAD)
Nu 27: 18 a man in whom is the spirit of l,
33: 1 by divisions under the l of Moses
Ps 109: 8 may another take his place of l.
Ac 1: 20 another take his place of l.'

LEADS (LEAD)
Dt 27: 18 is anyone who l the blind astray
Ps 23: 2 he l me beside quiet waters,
37: 8 do not fret—it l only to evil.
68: 6 he l out the prisoners with singing;
Pr 2: 18 Surely her house l down to death
10: 17 ignores correction l others astray.
14: 23 but mere talk l only to poverty.
16: 25 right, but in the end it l to death.
19: 23 The fear of the LORD l to life;
21: 5 as surely as haste l to poverty.
Isa 40: 11 he gently l those that have young.
Mt 7: 13 gate and broad is the road that l
Jn 10: 3 sheep by name and l them out.
Ro 6: 16 slaves to sin, which l to death,
6: 22 the benefit you reap l to holiness,
14: 19 every effort to do what l to peace
2Co 2: 14 God, who always l us as captives
7: 10 sorrow brings repentance that l
Titus 1: 1 of the truth that l to godliness—

LEAH
Wife of Jacob (Ge 29:16–30); bore six sons and one daughter (Ge 29:31—30:21; 34:1; 35:23).

LEAN (LEANED)
Pr 3: 5 l not on your own understanding;

LEANED (LEAN)
Ge 47: 31 Israel worshiped as he l on the top
Jn 21: 20 one who had l back against Jesus
Heb 11: 21 worshiped as he l on the top of his

LEAP (LEAPED LEAPS)
Isa 35: 6 Then will the lame l like a deer,
Lk 6: 23 "Rejoice in that day and l for joy,

LEAPED (LEAP)
Lk 1: 41 greeting, the baby l in her womb,

LEAPS (LEAP)
Ps 28: 7 My heart l for joy, and with my

LEARN (LEARNED LEARNING)
Dt 4: 10 they may l to revere me as long as
5: 1 L them and be sure to follow them.
31: 12 and l to fear the LORD your God
Ps 119: 7 heart as I l your righteous laws.
Isa 1: 17 L to do right; seek justice.
26: 9 of the world l righteousness.
Mt 11: 29 my yoke upon you and l from me,
Jn 14: 31 that the world may l that I love
1Th 4: 4 you should l to control your own
1Ti 2: 11 A woman should l in quietness
5: 4 should l first of all to put their

LEARNED (LEARN)
Ps 119:152 Long ago I l from your statutes
Mt 11: 25 these things from the wise and l,
Jn 6: 45 and l from him comes to me.
Php 4: 9 Whatever you have l or received
4: 11 I have l to be content whatever
2Ti 3: 14 continue in what you have l
Heb 5: 8 he was, he l obedience from what

LEARNING (LEARN)
Pr 1: 5 the wise listen and add to their l,
9: 9 and they will add to their l.
Isa 44: 25 who overthrows the l of the wise
Jn 7: 15 man get such l without having
2Ti 3: 7 always l but never able to come

LEATHER
Nu 4: 6 cover the curtain with a durable l,
2Ki 1: 8 and had a l belt around his waist."
Mt 3: 4 he had a l belt around his waist.

LEAVES
Ge 3: 7 so they sewed fig l together
Eze 47: 12 Their l will not wither, nor will
47: 12 for food and their l for healing."
Rev 22: 2 l of the tree are for the healing

LEBANON
Dt 11: 24 will extend from the desert to L,
1Ki 4: 33 from the cedar of L to the hyssop

LED (LEAD)
Ex 3: 1 he l the flock to the far side
Dt 8: 2 the LORD your God l you all
1Ki 11: 3 and his wives l him astray.
2Ch 26: 16 his pride l to his downfall.
Ne 13: 26 even he was l into sin by foreign
Ps 78: 52 he l them like sheep through
Pr 7: 21 persuasive words she l him astray;
20: 1 whoever is l astray by them is not
Isa 53: 7 he was l like a lamb
Jer 11: 19 I had been like a gentle lamb l
Am 2: 10 I l you forty years in the wilderness
Mt 4: 1 Jesus was l by the Spirit
27: 31 they l him away to crucify him.
Lk 4: 1 and was l by the Spirit
Ac 8: 32 "He was l like a sheep
Ro 8: 14 For those who are l by the Spirit
2Co 7: 9 but because your sorrow l you
Gal 5: 18 But if you are l by the Spirit,

LEEKS*
Nu 11: 5 melons, l, onions and garlic.

LEFT
Dt 28: 14 to the right or to the l,
Jos 1: 7 turn from it to the right or to the l,
23: 6 aside to the right or to the l.
2Ki 22: 2 aside to the right or to the l.
Pr 4: 27 Do not turn to the right or the l;
Isa 30: 21 you turn to the right or to the l,
Mt 6: 3 do not let your l hand know what
25: 33 on his right and the goats on his l.

LEGAL
Col 2: 14 the charge of our l indebtedness,

LEGION
Mk 5: 9 "My name is L," he replied,

LEGITIMATE*
Heb 12: 8 then you are not l, not true sons

LEND (LENDER LENDS MONEYLENDER)
Ex 22: 25 "If you l money to one of my
Lev 25: 37 You must not l them money
Dt 15: 8 freely l them whatever they need.
Ps 37: 26 are always generous and l freely;
112: 5 who are generous and l freely,
Eze 18: 8 He does not l to them at interest
Lk 6: 34 Even sinners l to sinners,

LENDER* (LEND)
Pr 22: 7 and the borrower is slave to the l.
Isa 24: 2 for borrower as for l, for debtor as

LENDS (LEND)
Ps 15: 5 who l money to the poor without
Pr 19: 17 is kind to the poor l to the LORD,

LENGTH (LONG)
Pr 10: 27 fear of the LORD adds l to life,

LENGTHY* (LONG)
Mk 12: 40 and for a show make l prayers.
Lk 20: 47 and for a show make l prayers.

LEOPARD
Isa 11: 6 the l will lie down with the goat,
Da 7: 6 beast, one that looked like a l.
Rev 13: 2 The beast I saw resembled a l,

LEPROSY (LEPROUS)
2Ki 5: 1 was a valiant soldier, but he had l.
7: 3 Now there were four men with l
2Ch 26: 21 King Uzziah had l until the day he
Mt 11: 5 those who have l are cleansed,
Lk 17: 12 ten men who had l met him.

LEPROUS (LEPROSY)
Ex 4: 6 he took it out, the skin was l—

LETTER (LETTERS)
Mt 5: 18 not the smallest l, not the least
2Co 3: 2 You yourselves are our l,
3: 6 not of the l but of the Spirit; for the l kills,
2Th 3: 14 not obey our instruction in this l.

LETTERS (LETTER)
2Co 3: 7 which was engraved in l on stone,
10: 10 "His l are weighty and forceful,
2Pe 3: 16 His l contain some things that are

LEVEL
Ps 143: 10 good Spirit lead me on l ground.
Isa 26: 7 The path of the righteous is l;
40: 4 the rough ground shall become l,

Jer 31: 9 l path where they will not stumble,
Heb 12: 13 "Make l paths for your feet,"

LEVI (LEVITE LEVITES LEVITICAL)

1. Son of Jacob by Leah (Ge 29:34; 46:11; 1Ch 2:1). With Simeon avenged rape of Dinah (Ge 34). Tribe of blessed (Ge 49:5–7; Dt 33:8–11), chosen as priests (Nu 3–4), numbered (Nu 3:39; 26:62), allotted cities, but not land (Nu 18; 35; Dt 10:9; Jos 13:14; 21), land (Eze 48:8–22), 12,000 from (Rev 7:7).

2. See MATTHEW.

LEVIATHAN

Job 41: 1 "Can you pull in L with a fishhook
Ps 74: 14 you who crushed the heads of L
Isa 27: 1 L the gliding serpent, L the coiling

LEVITE (LEVI)

Dt 26: 12 tithe, you shall give it to the L,
Jdg 19: 1 a L who lived in a remote area

LEVITES (LEVI)

Nu 1: 53 The L are to be responsible
3: 12 The L are mine,
8: 6 "Take the L from among all
18: 21 "I give to the L all the tithes
35: 7 must give the L forty-eight towns,
2Ch 31: 2 to their duties as priests or L—
Mal 3: 3 will purify the L and refine them

LEVITICAL (LEVI)

Heb 7: 11 attained through the L priesthood

LEVY

Am 5: 11 You l a straw tax on the poor

LEWDNESS

Mk 7: 22 malice, deceit, l, envy, slander,

LIAR* (LIE)

Dt 19: 18 and if the witness proves to be a l,
Job 34: 6 I am right, I am considered a l;
Ps 116: 11 my alarm I said, "Everyone is a l."
Pr 17: 4 a l pays attention to a destructive
19: 22 better to be poor than a l.
30: 6 will rebuke you and prove you a l.
Mic 2: 11 If a l and deceiver comes and says,
Jn 8: 44 for he is a l and the father of lies.
8: 55 I would be a l like you, but I do
Ro 3: 4 be true, and every human being a l.
1Jn 1: 10 we make him out to be a l and his
2: 4 not do what he commands is a l,
2: 22 Who is the l? It is whoever denies
4: 20 yet hates a brother or sister is a l.
5: 10 God has made him out to be a l,

LIARS* (LIE)

Ps 63: 11 the mouths of l will be silenced.
Isa 57: 4 brood of rebels, the offspring of l?
Mic 6: 12 your inhabitants are l and their
1Ti 1: 10 for slave traders and l
4: 2 come through hypocritical l,
Titus 1: 12 "Cretans are always l, evil brutes,
Rev 3: 9 Jews though they are not, but are l
21: 8 magic arts, the idolaters and all l—

LIBERATED*

Ro 8: 21 the creation itself will be l from its

LICENSE*

Jude : 4 of our God into a l for immorality

LICK

Ps 72: 9 him and his enemies l the dust.
Isa 49: 23 they will l the dust at your feet.
Mic 7: 17 They will l dust like a snake,

LIE (LIAR LIARS LIED LIES LYING)

Lev 6: 3 find lost property and l about it,
19: 11 "'Do not l. "'Do not deceive
Nu 23: 19 he should l, not a human being,
Dt 6: 7 when you l down and when you
25: 2 the judge shall make them l down
1Sa 15: 29 is the Glory of Israel does not l
Ps 4: 8 In peace I will l down and sleep,
23: 2 He makes me l down in green
89: 35 and I will not l to David—
Pr 3: 24 when you l down, your sleep will
Isa 11: 6 the leopard will l down
28: 15 for we have made a l our refuge
Jer 9: 5 have taught their tongues to l;
23: 14 They commit adultery and live a l.
Eze 13: 6 are false and their divinations a l.
34: 14 There they will l down in good
Ro 1: 25 the truth about God for a l,
Col 3: 9 Do not l to each other, since you
2Th 2: 9 signs and wonders that serve the l,
2: 11 so that they will believe the l
Titus 1: 2 who does not l, promised before
Heb 6: 18 which it is impossible for God to l,
1Jn 2: 21 because no l comes from the truth.
Rev 14: 5 No l was found in their mouths;

LIED (LIE)

Ac 5: 4 have not l just to human beings

LIES (LIE)

Ps 5: 6 you destroy those who tell l.
5: 9 with their tongues they tell l.
10: 7 His mouth is full of l and threats;
12: 2 Everyone l to their neighbor;
34: 13 evil and your lips from telling l.
58: 3 they are wayward, spreading l.
144: 8 whose mouths are full of l,
Pr 6: 19 a false witness who pours out l
12: 17 the truth, but a false witness tells l.
19: 5 pours out l will not go free.
19: 9 whoever pours out l will perish.
29: 12 If a ruler listens to l, all his officials
30: 8 Keep falsehood and l far from me;
Jer 5: 31 prophets prophesy l, the priests
9: 3 their tongue like a bow, to shoot l;
14: 14 "The prophets are prophesying l
Hos 11: 12 has surrounded me with l,
Jn 8: 44 he is a liar and the father of l.

LIFE (LIVE)

Ge 1: 30 that has the breath of l in it—
2: 7 into his nostrils the breath of l,
2: 9 of the garden were the tree of l
6: 17 to destroy all l under the heavens,
9: 5 for the l of another human being.
9: 11 Never again will all l be destroyed
Ex 21: 6 Then he will be his servant for l.
21: 23 you are to take l for l,
23: 26 I will give you a full l span.
Lev 17: 14 the l of every creature is its
24: 17 "'Anyone who takes the l
24: 18 make restitution—l for l.
Nu 35: 31 a ransom for the l of a murderer,
Dt 4: 42 one of these cities and save their l.
12: 23 because the blood is the l,
12: 23 must not eat the l with the meat.
19: 21 l for l, eye for eye, tooth for
30: 15 See, I set before you today l
30: 19 Now choose l, so that you and your
30: 20 For the LORD is your l, and he
32: 39 I put to death and I bring to l,
32: 47 words for you—they are your l.
1Sa 19: 5 He took his l in his hands when he
Job 2: 6 but you must spare his l."
33: 4 breath of the Almighty gives me l.
33: 30 the light of l may shine on them.
Ps 16: 11 make known to me the path of l;
17: 14 world whose reward is in this l.
23: 6 will follow me all the days of my l,
27: 1 LORD is the stronghold of my l—
34: 12 Whoever of you loves l and desires
36: 9 For with you is the fountain of l;
39: 4 let me know how fleeting my l is.
49: 7 No one can redeem the l of
49: 8 the ransom for a l is costly,
63: 3 Because your love is better than l,
69: 28 they be blotted out of the book of l
91: 16 With long l I will satisfy him
103: 15 The l of mortals is like grass,
104: 33 I will sing to the LORD all my l;
119: 25 preserve my l according to your
Pr 1: 19 it takes away the l of those who get
3: 2 will prolong your l many years
3: 18 She is a tree of l to those who take
6: 23 and instruction are the way to l,
6: 26 man's wife preys on your very l.
7: 23 little knowing it will cost him his l.
8: 35 For those who find me find l
10: 11 of the righteous is a fountain of l,
10: 27 fear of the LORD adds length to l,
11: 30 fruit of the righteous is a tree of l,
13: 12 but a longing fulfilled is a tree of l.
13: 14 of the wise is a fountain of l,
14: 27 of the LORD is a fountain of l,
15: 4 The soothing tongue is a tree of l,
16: 22 Prudence is a fountain of l
19: 23 The fear of the LORD leads to l;
21: 21 righteousness and love finds l,
22: 5 who would preserve their l stay far
22: 23 up their case and will exact l for l.
Isa 53: 10 the LORD makes his l an offering
53: 11 he will see the light of l and be
53: 12 he poured out his l unto death,
La 3: 58 up my case; you redeemed my l.
Eze 18: 27 and right, they will save their l.
Eze 37: 5 enter you, and you will come to l.
Da 12: 2 some to everlasting l,
Jnh 2: 6 God, brought my l up from the pit.
Mal 2: 5 him, a covenant of l and peace,
Mt 6: 25 do not worry about your l,
6: 25 Is not l more than food,
7: 14 narrow the road that leads to l,
10: 39 Whoever finds their l will lose it,
10: 39 whoever loses their l for my sake
16: 21 and on the third day be raised to l.
16: 25 wants to save their l will lose it,
16: 25 but whoever loses their l for me
18: 8 is better for you to enter l maimed
19: 16 thing must I do to get eternal l?"
19: 29 as much and will inherit eternal l.
20: 28 to give his l as a ransom for many."
25: 46 but the righteous to eternal l."
Mk 8: 35 wants to save their l will lose it,
8: 35 but whoever loses their l for me
9: 43 to enter l maimed than with two
10: 17 must I do to inherit eternal l?"
10: 30 and in the age to come eternal l.
10: 45 to give his l as a ransom for many."
Lk 6: 9 do evil, to save l or to destroy it?"
9: 22 and on the third day be raised to l."
9: 24 wants to save their l will lose it,
9: 24 but whoever loses their l for me
12: 15 l does not consist in an abundance
12: 22 not worry about your l, what you
12: 25 can add a single hour to your l?
14: 26 yes, even their own l—
17: 33 tries to keep their l will lose it,
17: 33 whoever loses their l will preserve
21: 19 Stand firm, and you will win l.
Jn 1: 4 In him was l, and that l was the light
3: 15 who believes may have eternal l
3: 36 believes in the Son has eternal l,
4: 14 of water welling up to eternal l."
5: 21 even so the Son gives l to whom he
5: 24 has crossed over from death to l.
5: 26 For as the Father has l in himself,
5: 39 that in them you have eternal l.
5: 40 you refuse to come to me to have l.
6: 27 for food that endures to eternal l,
6: 33 heaven and gives l to the world."
6: 35 Jesus declared, "I am the bread of l.
6: 40 believes in him shall have eternal l,
6: 47 the one who believes has eternal l.
6: 48 I am the bread of l.
6: 51 I will give for the l of the world."
6: 53 his blood, you have no l in you.
6: 63 The Spirit gives l; the flesh
6: 68 You have the words of eternal l.
8: 12 but will have the light of l."
10: 10 I have come that they may have l,
10: 15 and I lay down my l for the sheep.
10: 17 loves me is that I lay down my l—
10: 28 I give them eternal l, and they shall
11: 25 "I am the resurrection and the l.
12: 25 who loves their l will lose it,
12: 25 will keep it for eternal l.
12: 50 his command leads to eternal l.
13: 37 I will lay down my l for you."
14: 6 am the way and the truth and the l.
15: 13 lay down one's l for one's friends.
17: 2 he might give eternal l to all those
17: 3 this is eternal l: that they know
20: 31 by believing you may have l in his
Ac 2: 32 God has raised this Jesus to l,
3: 15 You killed the author of l, but God
11: 18 granted repentance that leads to l."
13: 48 appointed for eternal l believed.
Ro 2: 7 immortality, he will give eternal l.
4: 25 was raised to l for our justification.
5: 10 shall we be saved through his l!
5: 18 in justification and l for all people.
5: 21 bring eternal l through Jesus Christ
6: 4 the Father, we too may live a new l.
6: 13 have been brought from death to l;
6: 22 holiness, and the result is eternal l.
6: 23 God is eternal l in Christ Jesus our
8: 6 the mind governed by the Spirit is l
8: 11 give l to your mortal bodies
8: 38 convinced that neither death nor l,
1Co 15: 19 If only for this l we have hope
15: 36 does not come to l unless it dies.
2Co 2: 16 to the other, an aroma that brings l.
3: 6 the letter kills, but the Spirit gives l.
4: 10 so that the l of Jesus may also be
5: 4 mortal may be swallowed up by l.
Gal 2: 20 The l I now live in the body, I live

LISTENING (LISTEN)
1Sa 3: 9 LORD, for your servant is **l**.'"
Pr 18: 13 To answer before **l**—that is folly
Lk 10: 39 at the Lord's feet **l** to what he said.

LISTENS (LISTEN)
Lk 10: 16 "Whoever **l** to you **l** to me;
1Jn 4: 6 and whoever knows God **l** to us;

LIVE (ALIVE LIFE LIFE-GIVING LIFETIME LIVES LIVING)
Ge 3: 22 tree of life and eat, and **l** forever."
Ex 20: 12 that you may **l** long in the land
33: 20 face, for no one may see me and **l**."
Nu 21: 8 who is bitten can look at it and **l**."
Dt 5: 24 a person can **l** even if God speaks
6: 2 LORD your God as long as you **l**
8: 3 that man does not **l** on bread alone
Job 14: 14 If someone dies, will they **l** again?
Ps 15: 1 may **l** on your holy mountain?
24: 1 in it, the world, and all who **l** in it;
26: 8 I love the house where you **l**,
119:175 Let me **l** that I may praise you,
Pr 21: 9 Better to **l** on a corner of the roof
21: 19 Better to **l** in a desert than
Ecc 9: 4 a **l** dog is better off than a dead
Isa 26: 19 But your dead will **l**, LORD;
55: 3 come to me; listen, that you may **l**.
Eze 17: 19 As surely as I **l**, I will repay him
20: 11 the person who obeys them will **l**.
37: 3 "Son of man, can these bones **l**?"
Am 5: 6 Seek the LORD and **l**, or he will
Hab 2: 4 the righteous person will **l** by his
Zec 2: 11 I will **l** among you and you will
Mt 4: 4 'Man shall not **l** on bread alone,
Lk 4: 4 'Man shall not **l** on bread
Jn 14: 19 Because I **l**, you also will **l**.
Ac 17: 24 not **l** in temples built by human
17: 28 'For in him we **l** and move and
Ro 1: 17 "The righteous will **l** by faith."
2Co 5: 7 For we **l** by faith, not by sight.
6: 16 "I will **l** with them and walk among
Gal 2: 20 with Christ and I no longer **l**,
3: 11 because "the righteous will **l**
5: 25 Since we **l** by the Spirit, let us keep
Eph 4: 17 must no longer **l** as the Gentiles
Php 1: 21 me, to **l** is Christ and to die is gain.
Col 1: 10 so that you may **l** a life worthy
1Th 4: 1 we instructed you how to **l** in order
5: 13 **L** in peace with each other.
1Ti 2: 2 that we may **l** peaceful and quiet
2Ti 3: 12 who wants to **l** a godly life
Titus 2: 12 and to **l** self-controlled,
Heb 10: 38 my righteous one will **l** by faith.
12: 14 Make every effort to **l** in peace
1Pe 1: 17 **l** out your time as foreigners here

LIVES (LIVE)
Ge 45: 7 save your **l** by a great deliverance.
Job 19: 25 I know that my redeemer **l**,
Pr 11: 30 and the one who is wise saves **l**.
13: 3 guard their lips preserve their **l**,
Isa 57: 15 he who **l** forever, whose name is
Jer 10: 23 that people's **l** are not their own;
Da 3: 28 to give up their **l** rather than serve
Jn 14: 17 he **l** with you and will be in you.
Ro 6: 10 but the life he **l**, he **l** to God.
8: 9 if indeed the Spirit of God **l** in you.
14: 7 none of us **l** for ourselves alone,
Gal 2: 20 I no longer live, but Christ **l** in me.
1Th 2: 8 the gospel of God but our **l** as well.
1Ti 2: 2 peaceful and quiet **l** in all godliness
Titus 2: 12 and godly **l** in this present age,
Heb 7: 24 but because Jesus **l** forever, he has
13: 5 Keep your **l** free from the love
1Pe 3: 2 the purity and reverence of your **l**.
4: 2 rest of their earthly **l** for evil
2Pe 3: 11 You ought to live holy and godly **l**
1Jn 3: 16 to lay down our **l** for our brothers
4: 16 Whoever **l** in love **l** in God,

LIVING (LIVE)
Ge 2: 7 life, and the man became a **l** being.
1Sa 17: 26 defy the armies of the **l** God?"
Isa 53: 8 was cut off from the land of the **l**;
Jer 2: 13 the spring of **l** water, and have dug
Eze 1: 5 what looked like four **l** creatures.
Zec 14: 8 On that day **l** water will flow
Mt 22: 32 the God of the dead but of the **l**."
Jn 4: 10 he would have given you **l** water."
6: 51 I am the **l** bread that came down
7: 38 said, rivers of **l** water will flow
Ro 8: 11 Jesus from the dead is **l** in you,
Ro 12: 1 to offer your bodies as a **l** sacrifice,
1Co 9: 14 the gospel should receive their **l**
Heb 10: 20 and **l** way opened for us through
10: 31 to fall into the hands of the **l** God.
1Pe 1: 23 through the **l** and enduring word
Rev 1: 18 I am the **L** One; I was dead,
4: 6 were four **l** creatures, and they
7: 17 will lead them to springs of **l** water.'

LOAD (LOADS)
Gal 6: 5 each one should carry their own **l**.

LOADS (LOAD)
Mt 23: 4 cumbersome **l** and put them

LOAF (LOAVES)
Hos 7: 8 Ephraim is a flat **l** not turned over.
1Co 10: 17 one body, for we all share the one **l**.

LOAVES (LOAF)
Mk 6: 41 he gave thanks and broke the **l**.
8: 6 When he had taken the seven **l**
Lk 11: 5 'Friend, lend me three **l** of bread;

LOCKED
Jn 20: 26 Though the doors were **l**,
Gal 3: 22 Scripture has **l** up everything
3: 23 **l** up until the faith that was to

LOCUSTS
Ex 10: 4 I will bring **l** into your country
Joel 2: 25 for the years the **l** have eaten—
Mt 3: 4 His food was **l** and wild honey.
Rev 9: 3 of the smoke **l** came down

LOFTY
Ps 139: 6 for me, too **l** for me to attain.

LONELY
Ps 68: 6 God sets the **l** in families, he leads
Lk 5: 16 Jesus often withdrew to **l** places

LONG (LENGTH LENGTHY LONGED LONGING LONGINGS LONGS)
Ex 17: 11 As **l** as Moses held up his hands,
Nu 6: 5 they must let their hair grow **l**.
1Ki 18: 21 "How **l** will you waver between
Ps 40: 16 may those who **l** for your saving
70: 4 may those who **l** for your saving
119: 97 I meditate on it all day **l**.
119:174 I **l** for your salvation, LORD,
Hos 7: 13 I **l** to redeem them but they speak
Am 5: 18 Woe to you who **l** for the day
Mt 25: 5 The bridegroom was a **l** time
Jn 9: 4 As **l** as it is day, we must do
1Co 11: 14 teach you that if a man has **l** hair,
Eph 3: 18 to grasp how wide and **l** and high
Php 1: 8 God can testify how I **l** for all
1Pe 1: 12 Even angels **l** to look into these

LONGED (LONG)
Mt 13: 17 righteous people **l** to see what you
23: 37 how often I have **l** to gather your
Lk 13: 34 how often I have **l** to gather your
2Ti 4: 8 to all who have **l** for his appearing.

LONGING* (LONG)
Dt 28: 65 eyes weary with **l**, and a despairing
Job 7: 2 Like a slave **l** for the evening
Ps 119: 20 My soul is consumed with **l** for
119: 81 My soul faints with **l** for your
119:131 and pant, **l** for your commands.
Pr 13: 12 sick, but a **l** fulfilled is a tree of life.
13: 19 A **l** fulfilled is sweet to the soul,
Eze 23: 27 will not look on these things with **l**
Lk 16: 21 and **l** to eat what fell from the rich
Ro 15: 23 since I have been **l** for many years
2Co 5: 2 **l** to be clothed instead with our
7: 7 He told us about your **l** for me,
7: 11 what alarm, what **l**, what concern,
1Th 2: 17 our intense **l** we made every effort
Heb 11: 16 they were **l** for a better country—

LONGINGS* (LONG)
Ps 38: 9 All my **l** lie open before you, Lord;
112: 10 the **l** of the wicked will come

LONGS* (LONG)
Ps 63: 1 for you, my whole being **l** for you,
Isa 26: 9 in the morning my spirit **l** for you.
30: 18 Yet the LORD **l** to be gracious
Php 2: 26 For he **l** for all of you and is
Jas 4: 5 he jealously **l** for the spirit he has

LOOK (LOOKED LOOKING LOOKS)
Ge 19: 17 Don't **l** back, and don't stop
Ex 3: 6 because he was afraid to **l** at God.
Nu 21: 8 anyone who is bitten can **l** at it
32: 8 Kadesh Barnea to **l** over the land.
1Sa 16: 7 The LORD does not **l** at the things people **l** at.
Job 31: 1 my eyes not to **l** lustfully at a young
Ps 34: 5 Those who **l** to him are radiant;
105: 4 **L** to the LORD and his strength;
113: 6 who stoops down to **l**
123: 2 so our eyes **l** to the LORD our
Pr 1: 28 they will **l** for me but will not find
4: 25 Let your eyes **l** straight ahead;
Isa 17: 7 day people will **l** to their Maker
31: 1 do not **l** to the Holy One of Israel,
40: 26 up your eyes and **l** to the heavens:
60: 5 Then you will **l** and be radiant,
Jer 3: 3 Yet you have the brazen **l**
6: 16 "Stand at the crossroads and **l**;
Eze 34: 11 for my sheep and **l** after them.
34: 12 them, so will I **l** after my sheep.
Hab 1: 13 Your eyes are too pure to **l** on evil;
Zec 12: 10 They will **l** on me, the one they
Mt 18: 12 go to **l** for the one that wandered
23: 27 which **l** beautiful on the outside
Mk 13: 21 the Messiah!' or, '**L**, there he is!'
Lk 6: 41 "Why do you **l** at the speck
24: 39 **L** at my hands and my feet. It is I
Jn 1: 36 by, he said, "**L**, the Lamb of God!"
4: 35 open your eyes and **l** at the fields!
19: 37 "They will **l** on the one they have
1Ti 4: 12 Don't let anyone **l** down on you
Jas 1: 27 to **l** after orphans and widows
1Pe 1: 12 Even angels long to **l** into these
2Pe 3: 12 as you **l** forward to the day of God

LOOKED (LOOK)
Ge 19: 26 But Lot's wife **l** back, and she
Ex 2: 25 So God **l** on the Israelites and was
1Sa 6: 19 to death because they **l** into the ark
SS 3: 1 I **l** for him but did not find him.
Eze 22: 30 "I **l** for someone among them who
34: 6 and no one searched or **l** for them.
44: 4 I **l** and saw the glory of the LORD
Da 7: 9 "As I **l**, "thrones were set in place,
10: 5 I **l** up and there before me was
Hab 3: 6 he **l**, and made the nations tremble.
Mt 25: 36 I was sick and you **l** after me, I was
Lk 18: 9 and **l** down on everyone else,
22: 61 Lord turned and **l** straight at Peter.
1Jn 1: 1 which we have **l** at and our hands

LOOKING (LOOK)
Ps 69: 3 My eyes fail, **l** for my God.
119: 82 My eyes fail, **l** for your promise;
119:123 My eyes fail, **l** for your salvation,
Mk 16: 6 "You are **l** for Jesus the Nazarene,
Php 2: 4 not **l** to your own interests but each
1Th 2: 6 We were not **l** for praise
2Pe 3: 13 his promise we are **l** forward
Rev 5: 6 a Lamb, **l** as if it had been slain,

LOOKS (LOOK)
1Sa 16: 7 but the LORD **l** at the heart."
Ezr 8: 22 God is on everyone who **l** to him,
Ps 104: 32 he who **l** at the earth, and it
138: 6 is exalted, he **l** kindly on the lowly;
Mt 5: 28 anyone who **l** at a woman lustfully
16: 4 adulterous generation **l** for a sign,
Lk 9: 62 and **l** back is fit for service
Jn 6: 40 is that everyone who **l** to the Son
12: 45 The one who **l** at me is seeing
Php 2: 21 For everyone **l** out for their own
Jas 1: 25 whoever **l** intently into the perfect

LOOSE
Isa 33: 23 Your rigging hangs **l**: The mast is
Mt 16: 19 and whatever you **l** on earth will be
18: 18 and whatever you **l** on earth will be

LORD (LORD'S LORDED LORDING)
Ge 18: 27 been so bold as to speak to the **L**,
Ex 15: 17 the sanctuary, **L**, your hands
Nu 16: 13 now you also want to **l** it over us!
Dt 10: 17 God is God of gods and **L** of lords,
Jos 3: 13 the **L** of all the earth—
1Ki 3: 10 The **L** was pleased that Solomon
Ne 4: 14 Remember the **L**, who is great
Job 28: 28 human race, "The fear of the **L**—
Ps 37: 13 but the **L** laughs at the wicked,
38: 22 to help me, my **L** and my Savior.
54: 4 the **L** is the one who sustains me.
62: 12 and with you, **L**, is unfailing love";
69: 6 **L**, the LORD Almighty, may those
86: 5 You, **L**, are forgiving and good,
86: 8 the gods there is none like you, **L**;
89: 49 **L**, where is your former great love,
110: 1 The LORD says to my **L**:
110: 5 The **L** is at your right hand;
130: 3 kept a record of sins, **L**, who could
135: 5 that our **L** is greater than all gods.

Ps 136: 3 Give thanks to the **L** of lords:
147: 5 Great is our **L** and mighty in
Isa 6: 1 died, I saw the **L**, high and exalted,
Da 2: 47 the God of gods and the **L** of kings
9: 4 "**L**, the great and awesome God,
9: 7 "**L**, you are righteous, but this day
9: 9 The **L** our God is merciful
9: 19 **L**, listen! **L**, forgive! **L**, hear and act!
Mt 3: 3 'Prepare the way for the **L**,
4: 7 'Do not put the **L** your God
4: 10 'Worship the **L** your God, and
7: 21 "Not everyone who says to me, '**L**,
9: 38 Ask the **L** of the harvest, therefore,
12: 8 Son of Man is **L** of the Sabbath."
20: 25 rulers of the Gentiles **l** it over them
21: 9 who comes in the name of the **L**!"
22: 37 "'Love the **L** your God with all
22: 44 "'The **L** said to my **L**: "Sit at my
23: 39 comes in the name of the **L**.'"
Mk 1: 3 'Prepare the way for the **L**,
12: 11 the **L** has done this, and it is
12: 29 The **L** our God, the **L** is one.
12: 30 Love the **L** your God with all your
Lk 2: 9 angel of the **L** appeared to them,
6: 5 Son of Man is **L** of the Sabbath."
6: 46 "Why do you call me, '**L**, **L**,'
10: 27 "'Love the **L** your God with all
11: 1 one of his disciples said to him, "**L**,
24: 34 The **L** has risen and has appeared
Jn 1: 23 straight the way for the **L**.'"
Ac 2: 21 on the name of the **L** will be saved.'
2: 25 "'I saw the **L** always before me.
2: 34 yet he said, "'The **L** said to my **L**:
8: 16 baptized in the name of the **L**
9: 5 "Who are you, **L**?" Saul asked.
10: 36 Jesus Christ, who is **L** of all.
11: 23 true to the **L** with all their hearts.
16: 31 "Believe in the **L** Jesus, and you
Ro 4: 24 him who raised Jesus our **L**
5: 11 in God through our **L** Jesus Christ,
6: 23 is eternal life in Christ Jesus our **L**.
8: 39 of God that is in Christ Jesus our **L**.
10: 9 "Jesus is **L**," and believe in your
10: 13 the name of the **L** will be saved."
10: 16 For Isaiah says, "**L**, who has
11: 34 has known the mind of the **L**?
12: 11 your spiritual fervor, serving the **L**.
13: 14 yourselves with the **L** Jesus Christ,
14: 4 the **L** is able to make them stand.
14: 8 live or die, we belong to the **L**.
1Co 1: 31 the one who boasts boast in the **L**."
3: 5 as the **L** has assigned to each his
4: 5 wait until the **L** comes.
6: 13 sexual immorality but for the **L**,
6: 14 his power God raised the **L**
7: 32 how he can please the **L**.
7: 34 to be devoted to the **L** in both body
7: 35 in undivided devotion to the **L**.
7: 39 but he must belong to the **L**.
8: 6 and there is but one **L**, Jesus Christ,
11: 23 The **L** Jesus, on the night he was
12: 3 "Jesus is **L**," except by the Holy
15: 57 victory through our **L** Jesus Christ.
15: 58 your labor in the **L** is not in vain.
16: 22 let that person be cursed! Come, **L**!
2Co 1: 24 Not that we **l** it over your faith,
2: 12 that the **L** had opened a door
3: 17 Now the **L** is the Spirit,
4: 5 but Jesus Christ as **L**,
5: 6 the body we are away from the **L**.
8: 5 gave themselves first of all to the **L**,
8: 21 not only in the eyes of the **L**
10: 17 the one who boasts boast in the **L**."
10: 18 the one whom the **L** commends.
13: 10 the authority the **L** gave me
Gal 6: 14 in the cross of our **L** Jesus Christ,
Eph 4: 5 one **L**, one faith, one baptism;
5: 8 but now you are light in the **L**.
5: 10 and find out what pleases the **L**.
5: 19 music from your heart to the **L**,
5: 22 own husbands as you do to the **L**.
6: 1 obey your parents in the **L**, for this
6: 7 as if you were serving the **L**,
6: 8 that the **L** will reward each one
6: 10 strong in the **L** and in his mighty
Php 2: 11 acknowledge that Jesus Christ is **L**,
3: 1 and sisters, rejoice in the **L**!
3: 8 of knowing Christ Jesus my **L**,
4: 1 stand firm in the **L** in this way,
4: 4 Rejoice in the **L** always. I will say it
4: 5 be evident to all. The **L** is near.
Col 1: 10 you may live a life worthy of the **L**
2: 6 as you received Christ Jesus as **L**,
3: 13 Forgive as the **L** forgave you.
3: 17 do it all in the name of the **L** Jesus,
3: 18 husbands, as is fitting in the **L**.
3: 20 everything, for this pleases the **L**.
3: 23 working for the **L**, not for human
3: 24 inheritance from the **L** as a reward.
3: 24 It is the **L** Christ you are serving.
4: 17 you have received in the **L**."
1Th 3: 8 you are standing firm in the **L**.
3: 12 May the **L** make your love increase
4: 1 urge you in the **L** Jesus to do this
4: 6 The **L** will punish all those who
4: 15 are left until the coming of the **L**,
5: 2 day of the **L** will come like a thief
5: 23 at the coming of our **L** Jesus Christ.
2Th 1: 7 when the **L** Jesus is revealed
1: 12 of our **L** Jesus may be glorified
2: 1 the coming of our **L** Jesus Christ
2: 8 whom the **L** Jesus will overthrow
3: 3 But the **L** is faithful, and he will
3: 5 May the **L** direct your hearts
1Ti 6: 15 the King of kings and **L** of lords,
2Ti 1: 8 of the testimony about our **L**
2: 19 "The **L** knows those who are his,"
4: 8 which the **L**, the righteous Judge,
4: 17 the **L** stood at my side and gave
Heb 1: 10 "In the beginning, **L**, you laid
10: 30 "The **L** will judge his people."
12: 14 holiness no one will see the **L**.
13: 6 confidence, "The **L** is my helper;
Jas 1: 12 of life that the **L** has promised
3: 9 With the tongue we praise our **L**
4: 10 Humble yourselves before the **L**,
5: 11 The **L** is full of compassion
1Pe 1: 25 the word of the **L** endures forever."
2: 3 you have tasted that the **L** is good.
3: 12 **L** is against those who do evil."
3: 15 in your hearts revere Christ as **L**.
2Pe 1: 11 into the eternal kingdom of our **L**
1: 16 the coming of our **L** Jesus Christ
2: 1 sovereign **L** who bought them—
2: 9 then the **L** knows how to rescue
3: 9 The **L** is not slow in keeping his
3: 18 and knowledge of our **L** and Savior
Jude : 14 the **L** is coming with thousands
Rev 4: 8 holy is the **L** God Almighty,'
4: 11 "You are worthy, our **L** and God,
11: 15 has become the kingdom of our **L**
17: 14 triumph over them because he is **L**
19: 16 KING OF KINGS AND **L** OF LORDS.
22: 5 for the **L** God will give them light.
22: 20 Amen. Come, **L** Jesus.

LORD'S (LORD)
Lk 1: 38 "I am the **L** servant,"
Ac 11: 21 The **L** hand was with them,
21: 14 up and said, "The **L** will be done."
Ro 12: 13 Share with the **L** people who are
1Co 7: 32 is concerned about the **L** affairs—
10: 26 "The earth is the **L**, and everything
11: 26 you proclaim the **L** death until he
2Co 3: 18 faces contemplate the **L** glory,
Eph 5: 17 but understand what the **L** will is.
2Ti 2: 24 And the **L** servant must not be
Heb 12: 5 not make light of the **L** discipline,
Jas 4: 15 "If it is the **L** will, we will live
5: 8 firm, because the **L** coming is near.
1Pe 2: 13 Submit yourselves for the **L** sake

LORDED (LORD)
Ne 5: 15 assistants also **l** it over the people.

LORDING (LORD)
1Pe 5: 3 not **l** it over those entrusted to you,

LORD† (LORD'S†)
Ge 2: 4 when the **L** God made the earth
2: 7 the **L** God formed a man
2: 22 the **L** God made a woman
3: 21 The **L** God made garments of skin
3: 23 So the **L** God banished him
4: 4 The **L** looked with favor on Abel
4: 26 began to call on the name of the **L**.
6: 7 So the **L** said, "I will wipe
7: 16 Then the **L** shut him in.
9: 26 "Praise be to the **L**, the God
11: 9 because there the **L** confused
12: 1 The **L** had said to Abram,
15: 6 Abram believed the **L**, and he
15: 18 that day the **L** made a covenant
17: 1 the **L** appeared to him and said,
18: 1 The **L** appeared to Abraham near
Ge 18: 14 Is anything too hard for the **L**?
18: 19 way of the **L** by doing what is right
21: 1 Now the **L** was gracious to Sarah as
22: 14 that place The **L** Will Provide.
24: 1 the **L** had blessed him in every
26: 2 The **L** appeared to Isaac and said,
28: 13 There above it stood the **L**, and he
31: 49 "May the **L** keep watch between
39: 2 The **L** was with Joseph so that he
39: 21 the **L** was with him; he showed
Ex 3: 2 There the angel of the **L** appeared
4: 11 them blind? Is it not I, the **L**?
4: 31 heard that the **L** was concerned
6: 2 also said to Moses, "I am the **L**.
9: 12 But the **L** hardened Pharaoh's heart
12: 27 the Passover sacrifice to the **L**,
12: 43 The **L** said to Moses and Aaron,
13: 9 the **L** brought you out of Egypt
13: 21 By day the **L** went ahead of them
14: 13 deliverance the **L** will bring you
14: 30 That day the **L** saved Israel
15: 3 The **L** is a warrior; the **L** is his
15: 11 among the gods is like you, **L**?
15: 26 for I am the **L**, who heals you."
16: 12 know that I am the **L** your God.'"
16: 23 rest, a holy sabbath to the **L**.
17: 15 and called it The **L** is my Banner.
19: 8 will do everything the **L** has said."
19: 20 The **L** descended to the top
20: 2 "I am the **L** your God, who
20: 5 for I, the **L** your God, am a jealous
20: 7 misuse the name of the **L** your God
20: 10 day is a sabbath to the **L** your God.
20: 11 in six days the **L** made the heavens
20: 11 the **L** blessed the Sabbath
20: 12 the land the **L** your God is giving
23: 25 Worship the **L** your God, and his
24: 3 "Everything the **L** has said we will
24: 12 The **L** said to Moses,
24: 16 the glory of the **L** settled on Mount
25: 1 The **L** said to Moses,
28: 36 on it as on a seal: HOLY TO THE **L**.
30: 11 Then the **L** said to Moses,
31: 13 so you may know that I am the **L**,
31: 18 When the **L** finished speaking
33: 11 The **L** would speak to Moses face
33: 19 my name, the **L**, in your presence.
34: 1 The **L** said to Moses,
34: 6 proclaiming, "The **L**, the **L**,
34: 10 work that I, the **L**, will do for you.
34: 29 because he had spoken with the **L**.
40: 34 glory of the **L** filled the tabernacle.
40: 38 of the **L** was over the tabernacle
Lev 8: 36 did everything the **L** commanded
9: 23 the glory of the **L** appeared to all
10: 2 them, and they died before the **L**.
19: 2 'Be holy because I, the **L** your God,
20: 8 I am the **L**, who makes you holy.
20: 26 to me because I, the **L**, am holy,
23: 40 rejoice before the **L** your God
Nu 6: 24 "'"The **L** bless you and keep
8: 5 The **L** said to Moses:
11: 1 fire from the **L** burned among
14: 18 'The **L** is slow to anger,
14: 21 glory of the **L** fills the whole earth,
21: 6 the **L** sent venomous snakes among
22: 31 Then the **L** opened Balaam's eyes,
23: 12 "Must I not speak what the **L** puts
30: 2 When a man makes a vow to the **L**
32: 12 followed the **L** wholeheartedly.'
Dt 1: 21 take possession of it as the **L**,
2: 7 forty years the **L** your God has
4: 29 there you seek the **L** your God,
5: 6 am the **L** your God, who brought
5: 9 for I, the **L** your God, am a jealous
6: 4 The **L** our God, the **L** is one.
6: 5 Love the **L** your God with all your
6: 16 Do not put the **L** your God
6: 25 all this law before the **L** our God,
7: 1 When the **L** your God brings you
7: 6 The **L** your God has chosen you
7: 8 it was because the **L** loved you
7: 9 that the **L** your God is God; he is
7: 12 then the **L** your God will keep his
8: 5 so the **L** your God disciplines you.
9: 10 The **L** gave me two stone tablets
10: 12 but to fear the **L** your God,
10: 12 serve the **L** your God with all
10: 14 **L** your God belong the heavens,
10: 17 For the **L** your God is God of gods
10: 20 Fear the **L** your God and serve

Dt 10: 22 now the **L** your God has made you
11: 1 Love the **L** your God and keep his
11: 13 to love the **L** your God and to serve
16: 1 the Passover of the **L** your God,
17: 15 you a king the **L** your God chooses.
28: 1 If you fully obey the **L** your God
28: 15 if you do not obey the **L** your God
29: 1 covenant the **L** commanded Moses
29: 29 things belong to the **L** our God,
30: 4 there the **L** your God will gather
30: 6 The **L** your God will circumcise
30: 10 if you obey the **L** your God
30: 16 today to love the **L** your God,
30: 16 the **L** your God will bless you
30: 20 you may love the **L** your God,
30: 20 For the **L** is your life,
31: 6 for the **L** your God goes with you;
34: 5 the servant of the **L** died there
Jos 10: 14 the **L** was fighting for Israel!
22: 5 to love the **L** your God, to walk
23: 11 careful to love the **L** your God.
24: 15 household, we will serve the **L**."
24: 18 We too will serve the **L**, because
Jdg 2: 12 They forsook the **L**, the God of
Ru 1: 8 May the **L** show you kindness,
4: 13 her, the **L** enabled her to conceive,
1Sa 1: 11 give him to the **L** for all the days
1: 15 I was pouring out my soul to the **L**.
1: 28 So now I give him to the **L**.
2: 2 "There is no one holy like the **L**;
2: 25 but if anyone sins against the **L**,
2: 26 favor with the **L** and with people.
3: 9 say, 'Speak, **L**, for your servant is
3: 19 The **L** was with Samuel as he grew
7: 12 "Thus far the **L** has helped us."
9: 17 sight of Saul, the **L** said to him,
11: 15 fellowship offerings before the **L**,
12: 18 Then Samuel called on the **L**,
12: 18 the people stood in awe of the **L**
12: 22 his great name the **L** will not reject
12: 24 be sure to fear the **L** and serve him
13: 14 the **L** has sought out a man after
14: 6 Nothing can hinder the **L**
15: 22 as much as in obeying the **L**?
16: 13 the Spirit of the **L** came powerfully
17: 45 you in the name of the **L** Almighty,
2Sa 6: 14 David was dancing before the **L**
7: 22 "How great you are, Sovereign **L**!
8: 6 The **L** gave David victory wherever
12: 7 This is what the **L**, the God
22: 2 "The **L** is my rock, my fortress
22: 29 You, **L**, are my lamp; the **L** turns
1Ki 1: 30 day what I swore to you by the **L**,
2: 3 and observe what the **L** your God
3: 7 "Now, **L** my God, you have made
5: 5 for the Name of the **L** my God,
5: 12 The **L** gave Solomon wisdom,
8: 11 the glory of the **L** filled his temple.
8: 23 "**L**, the God of Israel, there is no
8: 61 fully committed to the **L** our God,
9: 3 The **L** said to him: "I have heard
10: 9 Praise be to the **L** your God,
15: 14 fully committed to the **L** all his life.
18: 21 If the **L** is God, follow him;
18: 36 "**L**, the God of Abraham,
18: 39 **L**—he is God! The **L**—he is God!"
21: 23 also concerning Jezebel the **L** says:
2Ki 13: 23 But the **L** was gracious to them
17: 18 So the **L** was very angry with Israel
18: 5 Hezekiah trusted in the **L**, the God
19: 1 and went into the temple of the **L**.
20: 11 the **L** made the shadow go back
21: 12 Therefore this is what the **L**,
22: 2 what was right in the eyes of the **L**
22: 8 of the Law in the temple of the **L**."
23: 3 to follow the **L** and keep his
23: 21 the Passover to the **L** your God, as
23: 25 who turned to the **L** as he did—
24: 2 The **L** sent Babylonian, Aramean,
24: 4 the **L** was not willing to forgive.
1Ch 10: 13 he did not keep the word of the **L**
11: 3 as the **L** had promised through
11: 9 because the **L** Almighty was
13: 6 up from there the ark of God the **L**,
16: 8 Give praise to the **L**, proclaim his
16: 11 Look to the **L** and his strength;
16: 14 He is the **L** our God;
16: 23 Sing to the **L**, all the earth;
17: 1 covenant of the **L** is under a tent."
21: 24 not take for the **L** what is yours,
22: 5 be built for the **L** should be of great

1Ch 22: 11 build the house of the **L** your God,
22: 13 and laws that the **L** gave Moses
22: 16 the work, and the **L** be with you."
22: 19 build the sanctuary of the **L** God,
25: 7 and skilled in music for the **L**—
28: 9 for the **L** searches every heart
28: 20 the temple of the **L** is finished.
29: 1 is not for man but for the **L** God.
29: 11 Yours, **L**, is the kingdom;
29: 18 **L**, the God of our fathers Abraham,
29: 25 The **L** highly exalted Solomon
2Ch 1: 1 for the **L** his God was with him
5: 13 the temple of the **L** was filled
5: 14 the glory of the **L** filled the temple
6: 16 "Now, **L**, the God of Israel,
6: 41 "Now arise, **L** God, and come
6: 42 **L** God, do not reject your anointed
7: 1 the glory of the **L** filled the temple.
7: 12 the **L** appeared to him at night
7: 21 'Why has the **L** done such a thing
9: 8 king to rule for the **L** your God.
13: 12 do not fight against the **L**, the God
14: 2 right in the eyes of the **L** his God.
15: 14 to the **L** with loud acclamation,
16: 9 the **L** range throughout the earth
17: 9 them the Book of the Law of the **L**;
18: 13 "As surely as the **L** lives, I can tell
19: 6 for mere mortals but for the **L**,
19: 9 wholeheartedly in the fear of the **L**.
20: 15 This is what the **L** says to you:
20: 20 Have faith in the **L** your God
26: 5 As long as he sought the **L**,
26: 16 was unfaithful to the **L** his God,
29: 30 to praise the **L** with the words
30: 9 for the **L** your God is gracious
31: 20 and faithful before the **L** his God.
32: 8 with us is the **L** our God to help us
34: 14 taken into the temple of the **L**,
34: 31 covenant in the presence of the **L**—
Ezr 3: 10 foundation of the temple of the **L**,
7: 6 the hand of the **L** his God was
7: 10 observance of the Law of the **L**,
9: 5 hands spread out to the **L** my God
9: 8 the **L** our God has been gracious
9: 15 **L**, the God of Israel, you are
Ne 1: 5 "**L**, the God of heaven, the great
8: 1 which the **L** had commanded
9: 6 You alone are the **L**. You made
Job 1: 6 to present themselves before the **L**,
1: 21 The **L** gave and the **L** has taken
1: 21 may the name of the **L** be praised."
38: 1 the **L** spoke to Job out of the storm.
42: 9 what the **L** told them; and the **L**
42: 12 **L** blessed the latter part of Job's
Ps 1: 2 whose delight is in the law of the **L**,
1: 6 For the **L** watches over the way
4: 6 Many, **L**, are asking, "Who will
4: 8 for you alone, **L**, make me dwell
5: 3 In the morning, **L**, you hear my
6: 1 **L**, do not rebuke me in your anger
8: 1 **L**, our Lord, how majestic is your
9: 9 The **L** is a refuge for the oppressed,
9: 19 Arise, **L**, do not let mortals
10: 16 The **L** is King for ever and ever;
12: 6 the words of the **L** are flawless,
16: 5 **L**, you alone are my portion and
16: 8 I keep my eyes always on the **L**.
18: 1 I love you, **L**, my strength.
18: 6 In my distress I called to the **L**;
19: 7 The law of the **L** is perfect,
19: 14 heart be pleasing in your sight, **L**,
20: 5 May the **L** grant all your requests.
20: 7 trust in the name of the **L** our God.
22: 8 they say, "let the **L** rescue him.
23: 1 The **L** is my shepherd, I lack
23: 6 dwell in the house of the **L** forever.
24: 3 may ascend the mountain of the **L**?
24: 8 The **L** strong and mighty, the **L**
25: 10 All the ways of the **L** are loving
27: 1 The **L** is the stronghold of my life
27: 4 to gaze on the beauty of the **L**
27: 6 will sing and make music to the **L**.
29: 1 Ascribe to the **L**, you heavenly
29: 4 The voice of the **L** is powerful;
30: 4 Sing the praises of the **L**, you his
31: 5 deliver me, **L**, my faithful God.
32: 2 one whose sin the **L** does not count
33: 1 Sing joyfully to the **L**,
33: 6 of the **L** the heavens were made,
33: 12 is the nation whose God is the **L**,
33: 18 the eyes of the **L** are on those who

Ps 34: 1 I will extol the **L** at all times;
34: 3 Glorify the **L** with me; let us exalt
34: 4 sought the **L**, and he answered me;
34: 7 the **L** encamps around those who
34: 8 Taste and see that the **L** is good;
34: 9 Fear the **L**, you his holy people,
34: 15 The eyes of the **L** are
34: 18 The **L** is close to the brokenhearted
37: 4 Take delight in the **L**, and he will
37: 5 Commit your way to the **L**;
39: 4 "Show me, **L**, my life's end
40: 1 I waited patiently for the **L**;
40: 5 Many, **L** my God, are the wonders
46: 8 Come and see what the **L** has done,
47: 2 For the **L** Most High is awesome,
48: 1 Great is the **L**, and most worthy
50: 1 the **L**, speaks and summons
55: 22 Cast your cares on the **L** and he
59: 8 But you laugh at them, **L**;
68: 4 his name is the **L**.
68: 18 that you, **L** God, might dwell there.
68: 20 from the Sovereign **L** comes escape
69: 31 This will please the **L** more than
70: 4 help always say, "The **L** is great!"
72: 18 Praise be to the **L** God, the God
75: 8 In the hand of the **L** is a cup full
78: 4 the praiseworthy deeds of the **L**,
84: 8 Hear my prayer, **L** God Almighty;
84: 11 the **L** God is a sun and shield;
85: 7 Show us your unfailing love, **L**,
86: 11 Teach me your way, **L**, that I may
87: 2 The **L** loves the gates of Zion more
89: 5 heavens praise your wonders, **L**,
89: 8 Who is like you, **L** God Almighty?
91: 2 I will say of the **L**, "He is my
92: 1 It is good to praise the **L** and make
92: 4 make me glad by your deeds, **L**;
92: 13 planted in the house of the **L**,
93: 1 The **L** reigns, he is robed in
93: 5 Your statutes, **L**, stand firm;
94: 1 The **L** is a God who avenges.
94: 12 Blessed is the one you discipline, **L**,
94: 18 your unfailing love, **L**,
95: 1 Come, let us sing for joy to the **L**;
95: 3 the **L** is the great God, the great
95: 6 kneel before the **L** our Maker;
96: 1 Sing to the **L** a new song;
96: 5 idols, but the **L** made the heavens.
96: 8 to the **L** the glory due his name;
96: 9 Worship the **L** in the splendor of
96: 13 Let all creation rejoice before the **L**,
97: 1 The **L** reigns, let the earth be glad;
97: 9 For you, **L**, are the Most High over
98: 1 Sing to the **L** a new song, for he has
98: 2 The **L** has made his salvation
98: 4 Shout for joy to the **L**, all the earth,
99: 1 The **L** reigns, let the nations
99: 2 Great is the **L** in Zion; he is exalted
99: 5 Exalt the **L** our God and worship
100: 1 Shout for joy to the **L**, all the earth.
100: 2 Worship the **L** with gladness;
100: 3 Know that the **L** is God. It is he
100: 5 For the **L** is good and his love
101: 1 to you, **L**, I will sing praise.
102: 12 But you, **L**, sit enthroned forever;
103: 1 Praise the **L**, my soul; all my
103: 8 The **L** is compassionate
103: 19 The **L** has established his throne
104: 1 Praise the **L**, my soul. **L** my God,
104: 24 How many are your works, **L**!
104: 33 I will sing to the **L** all my life;
105: 4 Look to the **L** and his strength;
105: 7 He is the **L** our God;
106: 2 proclaim the mighty acts of the **L**
107: 1 thanks to the **L**, for he is good;
107: 8 thanks to the **L** for his unfailing
107: 21 thanks to the **L** for his unfailing
107: 43 ponder the loving deeds of the **L**.
108: 3 I will praise you, **L**,
109: 26 Help me, **L** my God;
110: 1 The **L** says to my lord: "Sit at my
110: 4 The **L** has sworn and will not
111: 2 Great are the works of the **L**;
111: 4 the **L** is gracious
111: 10 The fear of the **L** is the beginning
112: 1 Blessed are those who fear the **L**,
113: 1 praise the name of the **L**.
113: 2 Let the name of the **L** be praised,
113: 4 The **L** is exalted over all the
113: 5 Who is like the **L** our God, the One
115: 1 Not to us, **L**, not to us but to your

Ps 116: 12 return to the **L** for all his goodness
116: 15 the sight of the **L** is the death of his
117: 1 Praise the **L**, all you nations;
118: 1 thanks to the **L**, for he is good;
118: 5 hard pressed, I cried to the **L**;
118: 8 to take refuge in the **L** than to trust
118: 18 The **L** has chastened me severely,
118: 23 the **L** has done this, and it is
118: 24 The **L** has done it this very day;
118: 26 who comes in the name of the **L**.
119: 1 walk according to the law of the **L**.
119: 64 earth is filled with your love, **L**;
119: 89 Your word, **L**, is eternal;
119:126 It is time for you to act, **L**;
119:159 preserve my life, **L**, in accordance
120: 1 I call on the **L** in my distress,
121: 2 My help comes from the **L**,
121: 5 The **L** watches over you—the **L** is your shade
121: 8 the **L** will watch over your coming
122: 1 "Let us go to the house of the **L**."
123: 2 our eyes look to the **L** our God,
124: 1 If the **L** had not been on our side—
124: 8 Our help is in the name of the **L**,
125: 2 so the **L** surrounds his people
126: 3 The **L** has done great things for us,
126: 4 Restore our fortunes, **L**,
127: 1 Unless the **L** builds the house,
127: 3 Children are a heritage from the **L**,
128: 1 Blessed are all who fear the **L**,
130: 1 Out of the depths I cry to you, **L**;
130: 3 If you, **L**, kept a record of sins,
130: 5 I wait for the **L**,
131: 3 Israel, put your hope in the **L**
132: 1 **L**, remember David and all his
132: 13 For the **L** has chosen Zion,
133: 3 there the **L** bestows his blessing,
134: 3 May the **L** bless you from Zion,
135: 4 For the **L** has chosen Jacob
135: 6 The **L** does whatever pleases him,
136: 1 Give thanks to the **L**,
137: 4 How can we sing the songs of the **L**
138: 1 I will praise you, **L**, with all
138: 8 The **L** will vindicate me;
139: 1 You have searched me, **L**,
140: 1 Rescue me, **L**, from evildoers;
141: 1 I call to you, **L**, come quickly
141: 3 Set a guard over my mouth, **L**;
142: 5 I cry to you, **L**; I say,
143: 9 Rescue me from my enemies, **L**,
144: 3 **L**, what are human beings that you
145: 3 Great is the **L** and most worthy
145: 8 **L** is gracious and compassionate,
145: 9 The **L** is good to all;
145: 17 The **L** is righteous in all his ways
145: 18 The **L** is near to all who call
146: 5 whose hope is in the **L** their God.
146: 7 The **L** sets prisoners free,
147: 2 The **L** builds up Jerusalem;
147: 7 Sing to the **L** with grateful praise;
147: 11 **L** delights in those who fear him,
147: 12 Extol the **L**, Jerusalem;
148: 1 Praise the **L** from the heavens;
148: 7 Praise the **L** from the earth,
149: 4 **L** takes delight in his people;
150: 1 Praise the **L**. Praise God
150: 6 that has breath praise the **L**.
Pr 1: 7 The fear of the **L** is the beginning
1: 29 and did not choose to fear the **L**.
2: 5 will understand the fear of the **L**
2: 6 For the **L** gives wisdom;
3: 5 Trust in the **L** with all your heart
3: 7 fear the **L** and shun evil.
3: 9 Honor the **L** with your wealth,
3: 12 because the **L** disciplines those he
3: 19 By wisdom the **L** laid the earth's
5: 21 your ways are in full view of the **L**,
6: 16 There are six things the **L** hates,
8: 13 To fear the **L** is to hate evil;
9: 10 The fear of the **L** is the beginning
10: 27 fear of the **L** adds length to life,
11: 1 The **L** detests dishonest scales,
12: 22 The **L** detests lying lips, but he
14: 2 fears the **L** walks uprightly,
14: 26 Whoever fears the **L** has a secure
14: 27 The fear of the **L** is a fountain
15: 3 The eyes of the **L** are everywhere,
15: 16 the fear of the **L** than great wealth
15: 33 instruction is to fear the **L**,
16: 2 but motives are weighed by the **L**.
16: 3 Commit to the **L** whatever you do,
Pr 16: 4 The **L** works out everything to its
16: 5 The **L** detests all the proud of heart
16: 9 but the **L** establishes their steps.
16: 33 but its every decision is from the **L**.
18: 10 name of the **L** is a fortified tower;
18: 22 and receives favor from the **L**.
19: 14 but a prudent wife is from the **L**.
19: 17 is kind to the poor lends to the **L**,
19: 23 The fear of the **L** leads to life;
20: 10 the **L** detests them both.
21: 2 right, but the **L** weighs the heart.
21: 3 acceptable to the **L** than sacrifice.
21: 30 plan that can succeed against the **L**.
21: 31 battle, but victory rests with the **L**.
22: 2 The **L** is the Maker of them all.
22: 23 for the **L** will take up their case
23: 17 be zealous for the fear of the **L**.
24: 18 or the **L** will see and disapprove
24: 21 Fear the **L** and the king, my son,
25: 22 head, and the **L** will reward you.
29: 26 is from the **L** that one gets justice.
30: 7 "Two things I ask of you, **L**;
31: 30 a woman who fears the **L** is to be
Isa 2: 3 the word of the **L** from Jerusalem.
2: 10 from the fearful presence of the **L**
3: 17 the **L** will make their scalps bald."
4: 2 Branch of the **L** will be beautiful
5: 16 the **L** Almighty will be exalted
6: 3 holy, holy is the **L** Almighty;
9: 7 of the **L** Almighty will accomplish
11: 2 Spirit of the **L** will rest on him—
11: 9 of the **L** as the waters cover the sea.
12: 2 The **L**, the **L** himself, is my strength
18: 7 of the Name of the **L** Almighty.
24: 1 the **L** is going to lay waste the earth
25: 1 **L**, you are my God; I will exalt you
25: 6 this mountain the **L** Almighty will
25: 8 The Sovereign **L** will wipe away
26: 4 the **L** himself, is the Rock
26: 8 Yes, **L**, walking in the way of your
26: 13 **L** our God, other lords besides you
26: 21 the **L** is coming out of his dwelling
27: 1 the **L** will punish with his sword—
27: 12 that day the **L** will thresh
28: 5 In that day the **L** Almighty will be
29: 6 the **L** Almighty will come
29: 15 to hide their plans from the **L**,
30: 18 For the **L** is a God of justice.
30: 26 when the **L** binds up the bruises
30: 27 the Name of the **L** comes from afar,
30: 30 The **L** will cause people to hear his
33: 2 **L**, be gracious to us; we long
33: 6 the fear of the **L** is the key to
33: 22 our lawgiver, the **L** is our king;
34: 2 The **L** is angry with all nations;
35: 2 they will see the glory of the **L**,
35: 10 those the **L** has rescued will return.
38: 7 **L** will do what he has promised:
40: 3 prepare the way for the **L**;
40: 5 glory of the **L** will be revealed,
40: 7 because the breath of the **L** blows
40: 10 the Sovereign **L** comes with power,
40: 14 Whom did the **L** consult
40: 28 The **L** is the everlasting God,
40: 31 in the **L** will renew their strength.
41: 14 declares the **L**, your Redeemer,
41: 20 the hand of the **L** has done this,
42: 6 "I, the **L**, have called you
42: 8 "I am the **L**; that is my name!
42: 13 The **L** will march out like
42: 21 It pleased the **L** for the sake of his
43: 3 For I am the **L** your God, the Holy
43: 11 am the **L**, and apart from me there
44: 6 and Redeemer, the **L** Almighty:
44: 24 the **L**, the Maker of all things,
45: 5 I am the **L**, and there is no other;
45: 7 I, the **L**, do all these things.
45: 21 Was it not I, the **L**?
48: 17 the **L** your God, who teaches
50: 4 The Sovereign **L** has given me
50: 10 Who among you fears the **L**
51: 1 righteousness and who seek the **L**:
51: 11 the **L** has rescued will return.
51: 15 the **L** Almighty is his name.
53: 1 has the arm of the **L** been revealed?
53: 6 the **L** has laid on him the iniquity
53: 10 the will of the **L** will prosper
54: 5 the **L** Almighty is his name—
55: 6 Seek the **L** while he may be found;
55: 7 Let them turn to the **L**, and he
56: 6 to love the name of the **L**,
Isa 58: 8 of the **L** will be your rear guard.
58: 11 The **L** will guide you always;
59: 1 the arm of the **L** is not too short
60: 1 the glory of the **L** rises upon you.
60: 16 know that I, the **L**, am your Savior,
60: 20 the **L** will be your everlasting light,
61: 1 because the **L** has anointed me
61: 3 a planting of the **L** for the display
61: 10 I delight greatly in the **L**;
61: 11 grow, so the Sovereign **L** will make
62: 4 for the **L** will take delight in you,
63: 7 tell of the kindnesses of the **L**,
64: 8 Yet you, **L**, are our Father.
66: 15 See, the **L** is coming with fire,
Jer 1: 9 Then the **L** reached out his hand
2: 19 when you forsake the **L** your God
3: 25 have not obeyed the **L** our God."
4: 4 Circumcise yourselves to the **L**,
8: 7 know the requirements of the **L**.
9: 24 these I delight," declares the **L**.
10: 6 No one is like you, **L**; you are great,
10: 10 But the **L** is the true God; he is
12: 1 You are always righteous, **L**, when I
14: 7 us, do something, **L**, for the sake
14: 20 acknowledge our wickedness, **L**,
16: 15 said, 'As surely as the **L** lives,
16: 19 **L**, my strength and my fortress,
17: 7 is the one who trusts in the **L**,
17: 10 "I the **L** search the heart
20: 11 But the **L** is with me like a mighty
23: 6 The **L** Our Righteous Savior.
24: 7 heart to know me, that I am the **L**.
28: 9 as one truly sent by the **L** only if
31: 11 For the **L** will deliver Jacob
31: 22 The **L** will create a new thing
31: 34 'Know the **L**,' because they will
32: 27 "I am the **L**, the God of all
33: 16 The **L** Our Righteous Savior.'
36: 6 the **L** that you wrote as I dictated.
40: 3 now the **L** has brought it about;
42: 3 the **L** your God will tell us where
42: 4 pray to the **L** your God as you have
42: 6 we will obey the **L** our God,
50: 4 in tears to seek the **L** their God.
51: 10 "'The **L** has vindicated us;
51: 56 For the **L** is a God of retribution;
La 3: 24 to myself, "The **L** is my portion;
3: 25 The **L** is good to those whose hope
3: 40 them, and let us return to the **L**.
Eze 1: 3 the hand of the **L** was on him.
1: 28 the likeness of the glory of the **L**.
4: 14 I said, "Not so, Sovereign **L**!
10: 4 the glory of the **L** rose
15: 7 you will know that I am the **L**.
30: 3 is near, the day of the **L** is near—
36: 23 nations will know that I am the **L**,
37: 4 'Dry bones, hear the word of the **L**!
43: 4 the **L** entered the temple through
44: 4 the glory of the **L** filling the temple
Da 9: 2 the word of the **L** given to Jeremiah
Hos 1: 7 but I, the **L** their God, will save
2: 20 and you will acknowledge the **L**.
3: 1 as the **L** loves the Israelites,
3: 5 They will come trembling to the **L**
6: 1 "Come, let us return to the **L**.
6: 3 Let us acknowledge the **L**;
10: 12 for it is time to seek the **L**, until he
12: 5 the **L** God Almighty, the **L** is his
14: 1 Return, Israel, to the **L** your God.
Joel 1: 1 The word of the **L** that came to Joel
1: 15 For the day of the **L** is near;
2: 1 for the day of the **L** is coming.
2: 11 The day of the **L** is great;
2: 13 Return to the **L** your God, for he is
2: 23 rejoice in the **L** your God, for he
2: 31 the great and dreadful day of the **L**.
2: 32 on the name of the **L** will be saved;
2: 32 the survivors whom the **L** calls.
3: 14 day of the **L** is near in the valley
3: 16 The **L** will roar from Zion
Am 4: 13 the **L** God Almighty is his name.
5: 6 Seek the **L** and live, or he will
5: 15 Perhaps the **L** God Almighty will
5: 18 who long for the day of the **L**!
7: 15 But the **L** took me from tending
8: 12 searching for the word of the **L**,
9: 5 The Lord, the **L** Almighty—
Ob : 15 "The day of the **L** is near for all
Jnh 1: 3 But Jonah ran away from the **L**
1: 4 the **L** sent a great wind on the sea,
1: 17 Now the **L** provided a huge fish

Jnh 2: 9 'Salvation comes from the **L**.'"
4: 2 He prayed to the **L**, "Isn't this
4: 6 the **L** God provided a leafy plant
Mic 1: 1 The word of the **L** that came
4: 2 the word of the **L** from Jerusalem.
5: 4 his flock in the strength of the **L**,
6: 2 the **L** has a case against his people;
6: 8 what does the **L** require of you?
7: 7 I watch in hope for the **L**, I wait
Na 1: 2 The **L** is a jealous and avenging
1: 3 The **L** is slow to anger but great
Hab 2: 14 the **L** as the waters cover the sea.
2: 20 The **L** is in his holy temple;
3: 2 **L**, I have heard of your fame;
Zep 1: 1 The word of the **L** that came
1: 7 Be silent before the Sovereign **L**,
3: 17 The **L** your God is with you,
Hag 1: 1 of the **L** came through the prophet
1: 8 in it and be honored," says the **L**.
Zec 1: 1 the word of the **L** came
1: 17 and the **L** will again comfort Zion
3: 1 standing before the angel of the **L**,
4: 6 by my Spirit,' says the **L** Almighty.
6: 12 and build the temple of the **L**.
8: 21 'Let us go at once to entreat the **L**
9: 16 **L** their God will save his people
14: 5 Then the **L** my God will come,
14: 9 On that day there will be one **L**,
14: 16 worship the King, the **L** Almighty,
Mal 1: 1 of the **L** to Israel through Malachi.
3: 6 "I the **L** do not change. So you,
4: 5 and dreadful day of the **L** comes.

LORD'S† (LORD†)
Ex 4: 14 the **L** anger burned against Moses
12: 11 Eat it in haste; it is the **L** Passover.
34: 34 he entered the **L** presence to speak
Lev 23: 4 These are the **L** appointed festivals,
Nu 9: 23 At the **L** command they encamped,
14: 41 you disobeying the **L** command?
32: 13 The **L** anger burned against Israel
Dt 6: 18 is right and good in the **L** sight,
10: 13 to observe the **L** commands and
32: 9 For the **L** portion is his people,
Jos 21: 45 Not one of all the **L** good promises
1Sa 24: 10 lord, because he is the **L** anointed.'
2Sa 22: 31 is perfect: The **L** word is flawless;
1Ki 10: 9 of the **L** eternal love for Israel,
Ps 18: 30 is perfect: The **L** word is flawless;
24: 1 The earth is the **L**, and everything
32: 10 the **L** unfailing love surrounds the
89: 1 will sing of the **L** great love forever;
103: 17 **L** love is with those who fear him,
118: 15 "The **L** right hand has done mighty
Pr 3: 11 do not despise the **L** discipline,
19: 21 but it is the **L** purpose that prevails.
Isa 24: 14 west they acclaim the **L** majesty.
30: 9 to listen to the **L** instruction.
49: 4 Yet what is due me is in the **L** hand,
53: 10 Yet it was the **L** will to crush him
55: 13 This will be for the LORD's **r**,
61: 2 to proclaim the year of the **L** favor
62: 3 a crown of splendor in the **L** hand,
Jer 25: 17 So I took the cup from the **L** hand
48: 10 who is lax in doing the **L** work!
51: 7 was a gold cup in the **L** hand;
La 3: 22 Because of the **L** great love we are
Eze 7: 19 them in the day of the **L** wrath.
Joel 3: 18 A fountain will flow out of the **L**
Ob : 21 And the kingdom will be the **L**.
Mic 4: 1 the **L** temple will be established as
6: 2 you mountains, the **L** accusation;
Hab 2: 16 The cup from the **L** right hand is
Zep 2: 3 sheltered on the day of the **L** anger.

LOSE (LOSES LOSS LOST)
1Sa 17: 32 "Let no one **l** heart on account
Isa 7: 4 Do not **l** heart because of these two
Mt 10: 39 Whoever finds their life will **l** it,
Lk 9: 25 and yet **l** or forfeit their very self?
Jn 6: 39 that I shall **l** none of all those he
2Co 4: 1 this ministry, we do not **l** heart.
4: 16 Therefore we do not **l** heart.
Heb 12: 3 will not grow weary and **l** heart.
12: 5 not **l** heart when he rebukes you,
2Jn : 8 you do not **l** what we have worked

LOSES (LOSE)
Mt 5: 13 But if the salt **l** its saltiness,
Lk 15: 4 a hundred sheep and **l** one of them.
15: 8 has ten silver coins and **l** one.

LOSS (LOSE)
Ro 11: 12 **l** means riches for the Gentiles,
1Co 3: 15 the builder will suffer **l** but yet will
Php 3: 8 I consider everything a **l** because

LOST (LOSE)
Ps 73: 2 I had nearly **l** my foothold.
Jer 50: 6 "My people have been **l** sheep;
Eze 34: 4 the strays or searched for the **l**.
34: 16 I will search for the **l** and bring
Lk 15: 4 after the **l** sheep until he finds it?
15: 6 I have found my **l** sheep.'
15: 9 I have found my **l** coin.'
15: 24 he was **l** and is found.'
19: 10 came to seek and to save the **l**."
Php 3: 8 for whose sake I have **l** all things.

LOT (LOTS)
Nephew of Abraham (Ge 11:27; 12:5). Chose to live in Sodom (Ge 13). Rescued from four kings (Ge 14). Rescued from Sodom (Ge 19:1–29; 2Pe 2:7). Fathered Moab and Ammon by his daughters (Ge 19:30–38).
Est 3: 7 the **l**) was cast in the presence
9: 24 the **l**) for their ruin and
Pr 16: 33 The **l** is cast into the lap, but its
18: 18 Casting the **l** settles disputes
Ecc 3: 22 their work, because that is their **l**.
Ac 1: 26 cast lots, and the **l** fell to Matthias;

LOTS (LOT)
Jos 18: 10 then cast **l** for them in Shiloh
Ps 22: 18 them and cast **l** for my garment.
Joel 3: 3 They cast **l** for my people
Ob : 11 his gates and cast **l** for Jerusalem,
Mt 27: 35 divided up his clothes by casting **l**.
Ac 1: 26 Then they cast **l**, and the lot fell

LOVE* (BELOVED BELOVED'S LOVED LOVELY LOVER LOVERS LOVES LOVING)
Ge 4: 1 Adam made **l** to his wife Eve,
4: 17 Cain made **l** to his wife, and she
4: 25 Adam made **l** to his wife again,
20: 13 'This is how you can show your **l**
22: 2 son, your only son, whom you **l**—
29: 18 Jacob was in **l** with Rachel and
29: 20 days to him because of his **l** for her.
29: 21 and I want to make **l** to her."
29: 23 to Jacob, and Jacob made **l** to her.
29: 30 Jacob made **l** to Rachel also, and
29: 30 his **l** for Rachel was greater than his **l** for Leah.
29: 32 Surely my husband will **l** me now."
38: 2 He married her and made **l** to her;
Ex 15: 13 In your unfailing **l** you will lead
20: 6 showing **l** to a thousand generations of those who **l** me
21: 5 'I **l** my master and my wife
34: 6 abounding in **l** and faithfulness,
34: 7 maintaining **l** to thousands,
Lev 19: 18 but **l** your neighbor as yourself.
19: 34 **L** them as yourself, for you were
Nu 14: 18 abounding in **l** and forgiving sin
14: 19 In accordance with your great **l**,
Dt 5: 10 showing **l** to a thousand generations of those who **l** me
6: 5 **L** the LORD your God with all
7: 9 God, keeping his covenant of **l**
7: 9 generations of those who **l** him
7: 12 God will keep his covenant of **l**
7: 13 He will **l** you and bless you
10: 12 to **l** him, to serve the LORD your
10: 19 are to **l** those who are foreigners,
11: 1 **L** the LORD your God and keep
11: 13 to **l** the LORD your God
11: 22 to **l** the LORD your God, to walk
13: 3 whether you **l** him with all your
13: 6 or the wife you **l**, or your closest
19: 9 to **l** the LORD your God
21: 15 is the son of the wife he does not **l**,
21: 16 the son of the wife he does not **l**.
30: 6 you may **l** him with all your heart
30: 16 today to **l** the LORD your God,
30: 20 you may **l** the LORD your God,
33: 3 Surely it is you who **l** the people;
Jos 22: 5 to **l** the LORD your God, to walk
23: 11 careful to **l** the LORD your God.
Jdg 5: 31 may all who **l** you be like the sun
14: 16 You don't really **l** me.
16: 4 he fell in **l** with a woman
16: 15 "How can you say, 'I **l** you,'
Ru 4: 13 When he made **l** to her, the LORD
1Sa 1: 19 Elkanah made **l** to his wife Hannah
18: 20 Saul's daughter Michal was in **l**
18: 22 you, and his attendants all **l** you;
20: 17 reaffirm his oath out of **l** for him,
2Sa 1: 26 Your **l** for me was wonderful,
7: 15 my **l** will never be taken away
11: 11 and drink and make **l** to my wife?
12: 24 he went to her and made **l** to her.
13: 1 son of David fell in **l** with Tamar,
13: 4 said to him, "I'm in **l** with Tamar,
16: 17 "So this is the **l** you show your
19: 6 You **l** those who hate you and hate those who **l** you.
1Ki 3: 3 Solomon showed his **l**
3: 26 deeply moved out of **l** for her son
8: 23 you who keep your covenant of **l**
10: 9 of the LORD's eternal **l** for Israel,
11: 2 Solomon held fast to them in **l**.
1Ch 2: 21 He made **l** to her, and she bore him
7: 23 Then he made **l** to his wife again,
16: 34 he is good; his **l** endures forever.
16: 41 "for his **l** endures forever."
17: 13 I will never take my **l** away
2Ch 5: 13 his **l** endures forever."
6: 14 you who keep your covenant of **l**
6: 42 Remember the great **l** promised
7: 3 his **l** endures forever."
7: 6 saying, "His **l** endures forever."
9: 8 Because of the **l** of your God
19: 2 and **l** those who hate the LORD?
20: 21 LORD, for his **l** endures forever."
Ezr 3: 11 his **l** toward Israel endures forever."
Ne 1: 5 who keeps his covenant of **l** with those who **l** him
9: 17 slow to anger and abounding in **l**.
9: 32 who keeps his covenant of **l**, do not
13: 22 to me according to your great **l**.
Job 15: 34 the tents of those who **l** bribes.
19: 19 those I **l** have turned against me.
37: 13 to water his earth and show his **l**.
Ps 4: 2 How long will you **l** delusions
5: 7 by your great **l**, can come into your
5: 11 those who **l** your name may rejoice
6: 4 me because of your unfailing **l**.
11: 5 those who **l** violence, he hates
13: 5 But I trust in your unfailing **l**;
17: 7 me the wonders of your great **l**,
18: 1 I **l** you, LORD, my strength.
18: 50 shows unfailing **l** to his anointed,
21: 7 through the unfailing **l** of the Most
23: 6 **l** will follow me all the days of my
25: 6 your great mercy and **l**, for they are
25: 7 according to your **l** remember me,
26: 3 been mindful of your unfailing **l**
26: 8 I **l** the house where you live,
31: 7 I will be glad and rejoice in your **l**,
31: 16 save me in your unfailing **l**.
31: 21 me the wonders of his **l** when I was
31: 23 **L** the LORD, all his faithful
32: 10 LORD's unfailing **l** surrounds
33: 5 the earth is full of his unfailing **l**.
33: 18 whose hope is in his unfailing **l**,
33: 22 May your unfailing **l** be with us,
36: 5 Your **l**, LORD,
36: 7 How priceless is your unfailing **l**,
36: 10 Continue your **l** to those who
40: 10 I do not conceal your **l** and your
40: 11 may your **l** and faithfulness always
42: 8 By day the LORD directs his **l**,
44: 26 us because of your unfailing **l**.
45: 7 You **l** righteousness and hate
48: 9 we meditate on your unfailing **l**.
51: 1 God, according to your unfailing **l**;
52: 3 You **l** evil rather than good,
52: 4 You **l** every harmful word,
52: 8 I trust in God's unfailing **l** for ever
57: 3 God sends forth his **l** and his
57: 10 For great is your **l**,
59: 16 in the morning I will sing of your **l**;
60: 5 that those you **l** may be delivered.
61: 7 appoint your **l** and faithfulness
62: 12 and with you, Lord, is unfailing **l**";
63: 3 Because your **l** is better than life,
66: 20 prayer or withheld his **l** from me!
69: 13 in your great **l**, O God, answer me
69: 16 out of the goodness of your **l**;
69: 36 those who **l** his name will dwell
77: 8 his unfailing **l** vanished forever?
85: 7 Show us your unfailing **l**, LORD,
85: 10 **L** and faithfulness meet together;
86: 5 abounding in **l** to all who call
86: 13 For great is your **l** toward me;
86: 15 abounding in **l** and faithfulness.
88: 11 Is your **l** declared in the grave,
89: 1 sing of the LORD's great **l** forever;

Ps 89: 2 that your **l** stands firm forever,
89: 14 **l** and faithfulness go before you.
89: 24 My faithful **l** will be with him,
89: 28 I will maintain my **l** to him forever,
89: 33 but I will not take my **l** from him,
89: 49 where is your former great **l**,
90: 14 the morning with your unfailing **l**,
92: 2 proclaiming your **l** in the morning
94: 18 slipping," your unfailing **l**, LORD,
97: 10 Let those who **l** the LORD hate
98: 3 He has remembered his **l** and his
100: 5 is good and his **l** endures forever;
101: 1 I will sing of your **l** and justice;
103: 4 crowns you with **l** and compassion,
103: 8 slow to anger, abounding in **l**.
103: 11 so great is his **l** for those who fear
103: 17 to everlasting the LORD's **l** is
106: 1 for he is good; his **l** endures forever.
106: 45 and out of his great **l** he relented.
107: 1 he is good; his **l** endures forever.
107: 8 to the LORD for his unfailing **l**
107: 15 to the LORD for his unfailing **l**
107: 21 to the LORD for his unfailing **l**
107: 31 to the LORD for his unfailing **l**
108: 4 For great is your **l**, higher than
108: 6 that those you **l** may be delivered.
109: 21 out of the goodness of your **l**,
109: 26 me according to your unfailing **l**.
115: 1 because of your **l** and faithfulness.
116: 1 I **l** the LORD, for he heard my
117: 2 For great is his **l** toward us,
118: 1 he is good; his **l** endures forever.
118: 2 "His **l** endures forever."
118: 3 "His **l** endures forever."
118: 4 "His **l** endures forever."
118: 29 he is good; his **l** endures forever.
119: 41 May your unfailing **l** come to me,
119: 47 your commands because I **l** them.
119: 48 which I **l**, that I may meditate
119: 64 The earth is filled with your **l**,
119: 76 May your unfailing **l** be my
119: 88 In your unfailing **l** preserve my life,
119: 97 Oh, how I **l** your law! I meditate
119:113 people, but I **l** your law.
119:119 therefore I **l** your statutes.
119:124 your servant according to your **l**
119:127 Because I **l** your commands more
119:132 do to those who **l** your name.
119:149 voice in accordance with your **l**;
119:159 See how I **l** your precepts;
119:159 LORD, in accordance with your **l**.
119:163 detest falsehood but I **l** your law.
119:165 peace have those who **l** your law,
119:167 your statutes, for I **l** them greatly.
122: 6 "May those who **l** you be secure.
130: 7 for with the LORD is unfailing **l**
136: 1 *His **l** endures forever.*
136: 2 *His **l** endures forever.*
136: 3 *His **l** endures forever.*
136: 4 *His **l** endures forever.*
136: 5 *His **l** endures forever.*
136: 6 *His **l** endures forever.*
136: 7 *His **l** endures forever.*
136: 8 *His **l** endures forever.*
136: 9 *His **l** endures forever.*
136: 10 *His **l** endures forever.*
136: 11 *His **l** endures forever.*
136: 12 *His **l** endures forever.*
136: 13 *His **l** endures forever.*
136: 14 *His **l** endures forever.*
136: 15 *His **l** endures forever.*
136: 16 *His **l** endures forever.*
136: 17 *His **l** endures forever.*
136: 18 *His **l** endures forever.*
136: 19 *His **l** endures forever.*
136: 20 *His **l** endures forever.*
136: 21 *His **l** endures forever.*
136: 22 *His **l** endures forever.*
136: 23 *His **l** endures forever.*
136: 24 *His **l** endures forever.*
136: 25 *His **l** endures forever.*
136: 26 *His **l** endures forever.*
138: 2 your name for your unfailing **l**
138: 8 your **l**, LORD, endures forever—
143: 8 bring me word of your unfailing **l**,
143: 12 In your unfailing **l**, silence my
145: 8 slow to anger and rich in **l**.
145: 20 watches over all who **l** him,
147: 11 their hope in his unfailing **l**.
Pr 1: 22 who are simple **l** your simple ways?
3: 3 Let **l** and faithfulness never leave

Pr 4: 6 **l** her, and she will watch over you.
5: 19 you ever be intoxicated with her **l**.
7: 18 let's drink deeply of **l** till morning;
7: 18 let's enjoy ourselves with **l**!
8: 17 I **l** those who **l** me, and those who
8: 21 rich inheritance on those who **l** me
8: 36 all who hate me **l** death."
9: 8 rebuke the wise and they will **l** you.
10: 12 but **l** covers over all wrongs.
14: 22 those who plan what is good find **l**
15: 17 with **l** than a fattened calf
16: 6 Through **l** and faithfulness sin is
17: 9 Whoever would foster **l** covers
18: 21 and those who **l** it will eat its fruit.
19: 22 a person desires is unfailing **l**;
20: 6 Many claim to have unfailing **l**,
20: 13 Do not **l** sleep or you will grow
20: 28 **L** and faithfulness keep a king safe;
20: 28 through **l** his throne is made
21: 21 righteousness and **l** finds life,
27: 5 is open rebuke than hidden **l**.
Ecc 3: 8 a time to **l** and a time to hate,
9: 1 no one knows whether **l** or hate
9: 6 Their **l**, their hate and their
9: 9 whom you **l**, all the days of this
SS 1: 2 your **l** is more delightful than wine.
1: 3 wonder the young women **l** you!
1: 4 will praise your **l** more than wine.
1: 7 you whom I **l**, where you graze
2: 4 and let his banner over me be **l**.
2: 5 with apples, for I am faint with **l**.
2: 7 or awaken **l** until it so desires.
3: 5 or awaken **l** until it so desires.
3: 10 purple, its interior inlaid with **l**.
4: 10 How delightful is your **l**, my sister,
4: 10 more pleasing is your **l** than wine,
5: 1 drink your fill of **l**.
5: 8 Tell him I am faint with **l**.
7: 6 pleasing, my **l**, with your delights!
7: 12 there I will give you my **l**.
8: 4 or awaken **l** until it so desires.
8: 6 for **l** is as strong as death,
8: 7 Many waters cannot quench **l**;
8: 7 the wealth of one's house for **l**,
Isa 1: 23 they all **l** bribes and chase
8: 3 Then I made **l** to the prophetess,
5: 1 sing for the one I **l** a song about his
16: 5 In **l** a throne will be established;
38: 17 In your **l** you kept me from the pit
43: 4 and because I **l** you, I will give
54: 10 yet my unfailing **l** for you will not
55: 3 my faithful **l** promised to David.
56: 6 to him, to **l** the name of the LORD,
56: 10 around and dream, they **l** to sleep.
57: 8 a pact with those whose beds you **l**,
61: 8 "For I, the LORD, **l** justice;
63: 9 In his **l** and mercy he redeemed
66: 10 be glad for her, all you who **l** her;
Jer 2: 25 I **l** foreign gods, and I must go
2: 33 How skilled you are at pursuing **l**!
5: 31 and my people **l** it this way.
12: 7 I will give the one I **l** into the hands
14: 10 "They greatly **l** to wander;
16: 5 my **l** and my pity from this people,"
31: 3 loved you with an everlasting **l**;
32: 18 You show **l** to thousands but bring
33: 11 his **l** endures forever."
La 3: 22 of the LORD's great **l** we are not
3: 32 so great is his unfailing **l**.
Eze 16: 8 saw that you were old enough for **l**,
23: 17 to the bed of **l**, and in their lust
33: 31 Their mouths speak of **l**, but their
33: 32 more than one who sings **l** songs
Da 9: 4 who keeps his covenant of **l** with those who **l** him
Hos 1: 6 for I will no longer show **l** to Israel,
1: 7 Yet I will show **l** to Judah;
2: 4 will not show my **l** to her children,
2: 19 and justice, in **l** and compassion.
2: 23 I will show my **l** to the one I called
3: 1 show your **l** to your wife again,
3: 1 **L** her as the LORD loves
3: 1 and **l** the sacred raisin cakes."
4: 1 no **l**, no acknowledgment of God
4: 18 their rulers dearly **l** shameful ways.
6: 4 Your **l** is like the morning mist,
9: 1 you **l** the wages of a prostitute
9: 15 I will no longer **l** them;
10: 12 reap the fruit of unfailing **l**,
11: 4 of human kindness, with ties of **l**.
12: 6 maintain **l** and justice, and wait

Hos 14: 4 waywardness and **l** them freely,
Joel 2: 13 slow to anger and abounding in **l**,
Am 4: 5 for this is what you **l** to do,"
5: 15 Hate evil, **l** good; maintain justice
Jnh 2: 8 turn away from God's **l** for them.
4: 2 slow to anger and abounding in **l**,
Mic 3: 2 you who hate good and **l** evil;
6: 8 to **l** mercy and to walk humbly
7: 20 and show **l** to Abraham, as you
Zep 3: 17 his **l** he will no longer rebuke you,
Zec 8: 17 other, and do not **l** to swear falsely.
8: 19 Therefore **l** truth and peace."
Mt 3: 17 said, "This is my Son, whom I **l**;
5: 43 said, '**L** your neighbor and hate
5: 44 **l** your enemies and pray for those
5: 46 If you **l** those who **l** you,
6: 5 for they **l** to pray standing
6: 24 will hate the one and **l** the other,
12: 18 the one I **l**, in whom I delight;
17: 5 said, "This is my Son, whom I **l**;
19: 19 '**l** your neighbor as yourself.'"
22: 37 "'**L** the Lord your God with all
22: 39 '**L** your neighbor as yourself.'
23: 6 they **l** the place of honor at
23: 7 they **l** to be greeted with respect
24: 12 the **l** of most will grow cold,
Mk 1: 11 "You are my Son, whom I **l**;
9: 7 "This is my Son, whom I **l**.
12: 30 **L** the Lord your God with all your
12: 31 '**L** your neighbor as yourself.'
12: 33 To **l** him with all your heart,
12: 33 **l** your neighbor as yourself is more
Lk 3: 22 "You are my Son, whom I **l**;
6: 27 **L** your enemies, do good to those
6: 32 "If you **l** those who **l** you,
6: 32 Even sinners **l** those who **l** them.
6: 35 But **l** your enemies, do good
7: 42 which of them will **l** him more?"
7: 47 as her great **l** has shown.
10: 27 "'**L** the Lord your God with all
10: 27 '**L** your neighbor as yourself.'"
11: 42 neglect justice and the **l** of God.
11: 43 because you **l** the most important
16: 13 will hate the one and **l** the other,
20: 13 I will send my son, whom I **l**;
20: 46 **l** to be greeted with respect
Jn 5: 42 that you do not have the **l** of God
8: 42 you would **l** me, for I have come
11: 3 Jesus, "Lord, the one you **l** is sick."
13: 34 I give you: **L** one another.
13: 34 so you must **l** one another.
13: 35 my disciples, if you **l** one another."
14: 15 "If you **l** me, keep my commands.
14: 21 I too will **l** them and show myself
14: 23 My Father will **l** them, and we will
14: 24 Anyone who does not **l** me will not
14: 31 world may learn that I **l** the Father
15: 9 I loved you. Now remain in my **l**.
15: 10 you will remain in my **l**, just as
15: 10 commands and remain in his **l**.
15: 12 **L** each other as I have loved you.
15: 13 Greater **l** has no one than this:
15: 17 This is my command: **L** each other.
15: 19 world, it would **l** you as its own.
17: 26 that the **l** you have for me may
21: 15 do you **l** me more than these?"
21: 15 he said, "you know that I **l** you."
21: 16 son of John, do you **l** me?"
21: 16 Lord, you know that I **l** you."
21: 17 son of John, do you **l** me?"
21: 17 the third time, "Do you **l** me?"
21: 17 you know that I **l** you."
Ro 1: 31 no fidelity, no **l**, no mercy.
5: 5 because God's **l** has been poured
5: 8 God demonstrates his own **l** for us
8: 28 for the good of those who **l** him,
8: 35 separate us from the **l** of Christ?
8: 39 separate us from the **l** of God that
12: 9 **L** must be sincere. Hate what is evil
12: 10 Be devoted to one another in **l**.
13: 8 continuing debt to **l** one another,
13: 9 "**L** your neighbor as yourself."
13: 10 **L** does no harm to a neighbor.
13: 10 Therefore **l** is the fulfillment
14: 15 eat, you are no longer acting in **l**.
15: 30 Christ and by the **l** of the Spirit,
1Co 2: 9 prepared for those who **l** him—
4: 17 my son whom I **l**, who is faithful
4: 21 shall I come in **l** and with a gentle
8: 1 puffs up while **l** builds up.
13: 1 but do not have **l**, I am only

1Co 13: 2 but do not have **l**, I am nothing.
13: 3 but do not have **l**, I gain nothing.
13: 4 **L** is patient, **l** is kind. It does not
13: 6 **L** does not delight in evil
13: 8 **L** never fails. But where there are
13: 13 three remain: faith, hope and **l**.
13: 13 But the greatest of these is **l**.
14: 1 Follow the way of **l** and eagerly
16: 14 Do everything in **l**.
16: 22 If anyone does not **l** the Lord,
16: 24 My **l** to all of you in Christ Jesus.
2Co 2: 4 know the depth of my **l** for you.
2: 8 to reaffirm your **l** for him.
5: 14 For Christ's **l** compels us,
6: 6 in the Holy Spirit and in sincere **l**;
8: 7 in the **l** we have kindled in you—
8: 8 sincerity of your **l** by comparing it
8: 24 show these men the proof of your **l**
11: 11 Because I do not **l** you?
12: 15 If I **l** you more, will you **l** me less?
13: 11 the God of **l** and peace will be
13: 14 the **l** of God, and the fellowship
Gal 5: 6 is faith expressing itself through **l**.
5: 13 serve one another humbly in **l**.
5: 14 "**L** your neighbor as yourself."
5: 22 But the fruit of the Spirit is **l**, joy,
Eph 1: 4 holy and blameless in his sight. In **l**
1: 15 and your **l** for all God's people,
2: 4 But because of his great **l** for us,
3: 17 being rooted and established in **l**,
3: 18 high and deep is the **l** of Christ,
3: 19 and to know this **l** that surpasses
4: 2 bearing with one another in **l**.
4: 15 speaking the truth in **l**, we will
4: 16 grows and builds itself up in **l**,
5: 2 and walk in the way of **l**, just as
5: 25 Husbands, **l** your wives, just as
5: 28 to **l** their wives as their own bodies.
5: 33 must **l** his wife as he loves himself,
6: 23 **l** with faith from God the Father
6: 24 to all who **l** our Lord Jesus Christ
with an undying **l**.
Php 1: 9 that your **l** may abound more
1: 16 The latter do so out of **l**,
2: 1 if any comfort from his **l**, if any
2: 2 having the same **l**, being one
4: 1 sisters, you whom I **l** and long for,
Col 1: 4 and of the **l** you have for all God's
1: 5 **l** that spring from the hope stored
1: 8 also told us of your **l** in the Spirit.
2: 2 in heart and united in **l**,
3: 14 And over all these virtues put on **l**,
3: 19 **l** your wives and do not be harsh
1Th 1: 3 your labor prompted by **l**, and your
3: 6 good news about your faith and **l**.
3: 12 May the Lord make your **l** increase
4: 9 your **l** for one another we do not
4: 9 taught by God to **l** each other.
4: 10 in fact, you do **l** all of God's family
5: 8 on faith and **l** as a breastplate,
5: 13 in the highest regard in **l** because
2Th 1: 3 **l** all of you have for one another
2: 10 because they refused to **l** the truth
3: 5 Lord direct your hearts into God's **l**
1Ti 1: 5 The goal of this command is **l**,
1: 14 faith and **l** that are in Christ Jesus.
2: 15 faith, **l** and holiness with propriety.
4: 12 conduct, in **l**, in faith and in purity.
6: 10 For the **l** of money is a root of all
6: 11 faith, **l**, endurance and gentleness.
2Ti 1: 7 us power, **l** and self-discipline.
1: 13 with faith and **l** in Christ Jesus.
2: 22 faith, **l** and peace, along with those
3: 3 without **l**, unforgiving, slanderous,
3: 10 faith, patience, **l**, endurance,
Titus 2: 2 in faith, in **l** and in endurance.
2: 4 women to **l** their husbands
3: 4 and **l** of God our Savior appeared,
3: 15 Greet those who **l** us in the faith.
Phm : 5 about your **l** for all his holy people
: 7 Your **l** has given me great joy
: 9 to appeal to you on the basis of **l**.
Heb 6: 10 the **l** you have shown him as you
10: 24 may spur one another on toward **l**
13: 5 your lives free from the **l** of money
Jas 1: 12 has promised to those who **l** him.
2: 5 he promised those who **l** him?
2: 8 "**L** your neighbor as yourself,"
1Pe 1: 8 you have not seen him, you **l** him;
1: 22 you have sincere **l** for each other,
1: 22 you have sincere **l** for each other,
1Pe 2: 17 everyone, **l** the family of believers,
3: 8 be sympathetic, **l** one another,
3: 10 For, "Whoever would **l** life and see
4: 8 Above all, **l** each other deeply,
4: 8 because **l** covers over a multitude
5: 14 Greet one another with a kiss of **l**.
2Pe 1: 7 and to mutual affection, **l**.
1: 17 saying, "This is my Son, whom I **l**;
1Jn 2: 5 **l** for God is truly made complete
2: 15 Do not **l** the world or anything
2: 15 **l** for the Father is not in them.
3: 1 See what great **l** the Father has
3: 10 who does not **l** their brother
3: 11 We should **l** one another.
3: 14 life, because we **l** each other.
3: 14 Anyone who does not **l** remains
3: 16 This is how we know what **l** is:
3: 17 them, how can the **l** of God be
3: 18 let us not **l** with words or speech
3: 23 **l** one another as he commanded
4: 7 Dear friends, let us **l** one another,
for **l** comes from God.
4: 8 Whoever does not **l** does not know
God, because God is **l**.
4: 9 is how God showed his **l** among us:
4: 10 This is **l**: not that we loved God,
4: 11 us, we also ought to **l** one another.
4: 12 but if we **l** one another, God
4: 12 and his **l** is made complete in us.
4: 16 and rely on the **l** God has for us.
4: 16 God is **l**. Whoever lives in **l**
4: 17 This is how **l** is made complete
4: 18 There is no fear in **l**. But perfect **l**
4: 18 fears is not made perfect in **l**.
4: 19 We **l** because he first loved us.
4: 20 claims to **l** God yet hates a brother
4: 20 whoever does not **l** their brother
4: 20 they have seen, cannot **l** God,
4: 21 loves God must also **l** their brother
5: 2 we know that we **l** the children
5: 3 this is **l** for God: to keep his
2Jn : 1 whom I **l** in the truth—
: 3 Son, will be with us in truth and **l**.
: 5 I ask that we **l** one another.
: 6 And this is **l**: that we walk
: 6 command is that you walk in **l**.
3Jn : 1 friend Gaius, whom I **l** in the truth.
: 6 have told the church about your **l**.
Jude : 2 peace and **l** be yours in abundance.
: 12 are blemishes at your **l** feasts,
: 21 yourselves in God's **l** as you wait
Rev 2: 4 You have forsaken the **l** you had
2: 19 know your deeds, your **l** and faith,
3: 19 Those whom I **l** I rebuke
12: 11 they did not **l** their lives so much

LOVED* (LOVE)
Ge 24: 67 she became his wife, and he **l** her;
25: 28 **l** Esau, but Rebekah **l** Jacob.
29: 31 the LORD saw that Leah was not **l**,
29: 33 the LORD heard that I am not **l**,
34: 3 he **l** the young woman and spoke
37: 3 Now Israel **l** Joseph more than any
37: 4 that their father **l** him more than
Dt 4: 37 Because he **l** your ancestors
7: 8 it was because the LORD **l** you
10: 15 on your ancestors and **l** them,
1Sa 1: 5 a double portion because he **l** her,
18: 1 David, and he **l** him as himself.
18: 3 David because he **l** him as
himself.
18: 16 But all Israel and Judah **l** David,
18: 28 that his daughter Michal **l** David,
20: 17 because he **l** him as he **l** himself.
2Sa 1: 23 in life they were **l** and admired,
12: 24 The LORD **l** him;
12: 25 and because the LORD **l** him,
13: 15 hated her more than he had **l** her.
1Ki 11: 1 **l** many foreign women besides
2Ch 11: 21 Rehoboam **l** Maakah daughter
26: 10 in the fertile lands, for he **l** the soil.
Ne 13: 26 He was **l** by his God, and God
Ps 44: 3 light of your face, for you **l** them.
47: 4 us, the pride of Jacob, whom he **l**.
78: 68 of Judah, Mount Zion, which he **l**.
109: 17 He **l** to pronounce a curse—
Isa 5: 1 My **l** one had a vineyard on a
Jer 2: 2 youth, how as a bride you **l** me
8: 2 which they have **l** and served
31: 3 "I have **l** you with an everlasting
Eze 16: 37 those you **l** as well as those you
Hos 1: 6 (which means "not **l**"),
Hos 2: 1 and of your sisters, 'My **l** one.'
2: 23 to the one I called 'Not my **l** one.'
3: 1 though she is **l** by another man
9: 10 became as vile as the thing they **l**.
11: 1 "When Israel was a child, I **l** him,
Mal 1: 2 "I have **l** you," says the LORD.
1: 2 "But you ask, 'How have you **l** us?'
1: 2 "Yet I have **l** Jacob,
Mk 10: 21 Jesus looked at him and **l** him.
12: 6 one left to send, a son, whom he **l**.
Lk 16: 14 The Pharisees, who **l** money,
Jn 3: 16 For God so **l** the world that he gave
3: 19 people **l** darkness instead of light
11: 5 Now Jesus **l** Martha and her sister
11: 36 the Jews said, "See how he **l** him!"
12: 43 for they **l** human praise more than
13: 1 Having **l** his own who were
13: 1 he **l** them to the end.
13: 23 the disciple whom Jesus **l**,
13: 34 As I have **l** you, so you must love
14: 21 The one who loves me will be **l**
14: 28 If you **l** me, you would be glad
15: 9 "As the Father has **l** me, so have
I **l** you.
15: 12 Love each other as I have **l** you.
16: 27 loves you because you have **l** me
17: 23 have **l** them even as you have **l** me.
17: 24 me because you **l** me before
19: 26 disciple whom he **l** standing
20: 2 disciple, the one Jesus **l**, and said,
21: 7 the disciple whom Jesus **l** said
21: 20 whom Jesus **l** was following them.
Ro 1: 7 To all in Rome who are **l** by God
8: 37 conquerors through him who **l** us.
9: 13 "Jacob I **l**, but Esau I hated."
9: 25 I will call her 'my **l** one' who is not
my **l** one,"
11: 28 they are **l** on account
Gal 2: 20 who **l** me and gave himself for me.
Eph 5: 1 therefore, as dearly **l** children
5: 2 just as Christ **l** us and gave himself
5: 25 just as Christ **l** the church and gave
Col 3: 12 holy and dearly **l**, clothe yourselves
1Th 1: 4 brothers and sisters **l** by God,
2: 8 Because we **l** you so much, we were
2Th 2: 13 brothers and sisters **l** by the Lord,
2: 16 who **l** us and by his grace gave us
2Ti 4: 10 for Demas, because he **l** this world,
Heb 1: 9 You have **l** righteousness and hated
2Pe 2: 15 who **l** the wages of wickedness.
1Jn 4: 10 not that we **l** God, but that he **l** us
4: 11 since God so **l** us, we also ought
4: 19 We love because he first **l** us.
Jude : 1 who are **l** in God the Father
Rev 3: 9 and acknowledge that I have **l** you.

LOVELY* (LOVE)
Ge 29: 17 but Rachel had a **l** figure and was
Est 1: 11 and nobles, for she was **l** to look at.
2: 7 had a **l** figure and was beautiful.
Ps 84: 1 How **l** is your dwelling place,
SS 1: 5 am I, yet **l**, daughters of Jerusalem,
2: 14 voice is sweet, and your face is **l**.
4: 3 a scarlet ribbon; your mouth is **l**.
5: 16 sweetness itself; he is altogether **l**.
6: 4 my darling, as **l** as Jerusalem,
Am 8: 13 "In that day "the **l** young women
Php 4: 8 is pure, whatever is **l**, whatever is

LOVER* (LOVE)
Isa 47: 8 listen, you **l** of pleasure,
1Ti 3: 3 not quarrelsome, not a **l** of money.

LOVERS* (LOVE)
Jer 3: 1 lived as a prostitute with many **l**—
3: 2 the roadside you sat waiting for **l**,
4: 30 Your **l** despise you; they want to
La 1: 2 Among all her **l** there is no one
Eze 16: 33 gifts, but you give gifts to all your **l**,
16: 36 in your promiscuity with your **l**,
16: 37 I am going to gather all your **l**,
16: 39 you into the hands of your **l**,
16: 41 and you will no longer pay your **l**.
23: 5 and she lusted after her **l**,
23: 9 her into the hands of her **l**,
23: 20 There she lusted after her **l**,
23: 22 I will stir up your **l** against you,
Hos 2: 5 'I will go after my **l**, who give me
2: 7 She will chase after her **l** but not
2: 10 lewdness before the eyes of her **l**;
2: 12 she said were her pay from her **l**;
2: 13 and went after her **l**, but me she
8: 9 Ephraim has sold herself to **l**.

2Ti 3: 2 will be **l** of themselves, **l** of money,
3: 3 brutal, not **l** of the good,
3: 4 **l** of pleasure rather than **l** of God—

LOVES* (LOVE)
Ge 44: 20 sons left, and his father **l** him.'
Dt 10: 18 **l** the foreigner residing among you,
15: 16 because he **l** you and your family
21: 15 and he **l** one but not the other,
21: 16 son of the wife he **l** in preference
23: 5 the LORD your God **l** you.
28: 54 or the wife he **l** or his surviving
28: 56 will begrudge the husband she **l**
33: 12 one the LORD **l** rests between his
Ru 4: 15 who **l** you and who is better to you
2Ch 2: 11 "Because the LORD **l** his people,
Ps 11: 7 LORD is righteous, he **l** justice;
33: 5 The LORD **l** righteousness
34: 12 Whoever of you **l** life and desires
37: 28 For the LORD **l** the just and will
87: 2 The LORD **l** the gates of Zion
91: 14 "Because he **l** me,"
99: 4 The King is mighty, he **l** justice—
119:140 tested, and your servant **l** them.
127: 2 he grants sleep to those he **l**.
146: 8 the LORD **l** the righteous.
Pr 3: 12 the LORD disciplines those he **l**,
12: 1 Whoever **l** discipline **l** knowledge,
13: 24 but the one who **l** their children is
15: 9 wicked, but he **l** those who pursue
17: 17 A friend **l** at all times, and a
17: 19 Whoever **l** a quarrel **l** sin;
19: 8 The one who gets wisdom **l** life;
21: 17 Whoever **l** pleasure will become
21: 17 whoever **l** wine and olive oil will
22: 11 One who **l** a pure heart and who
29: 3 A man who **l** wisdom brings joy
Ecc 5: 10 **l** money never has enough;
5: 10 whoever **l** wealth is never
SS 3: 1 I looked for the one my heart **l**;
3: 2 will search for the one my heart **l**.
3: 3 you seen the one my heart **l**?"
3: 4 when I found the one my heart **l**.
Hos 3: 1 her as the LORD **l** the Israelites,
10: 11 Ephraim is a trained heifer that **l**
12: 7 dishonest scales and **l** to defraud.
Mal 2: 11 the sanctuary the LORD **l**
Mt 10: 37 "Anyone who **l** their father
10: 37 who **l** their son or daughter
Lk 7: 5 he **l** our nation and has built
7: 47 has been forgiven little **l** little."
Jn 3: 35 The Father **l** the Son and has
5: 20 For the Father **l** the Son and shows
10: 17 The reason my Father **l** me is that I
12: 25 Anyone who **l** their life will lose it,
14: 21 keeps them is the one who **l** me.
14: 21 The one who **l** me will be loved
14: 23 "Anyone who **l** me will obey my
16: 27 the Father himself **l** you because
Ro 13: 8 for whoever **l** others has fulfilled
1Co 8: 3 whoever **l** God is known by God.
2Co 9: 7 for God **l** a cheerful giver.
Eph 1: 6 has freely given us in the One he **l**.
5: 28 He who **l** his wife **l** himself.
5: 33 must love his wife as he **l** himself,
Col 1: 13 into the kingdom of the Son he **l**,
Titus 1: 8 hospitable, one who **l** what is good,
Heb 12: 6 the Lord disciplines the one he **l**,
1Jn 2: 10 Anyone who **l** their brother
2: 15 If anyone **l** the world, love for
4: 7 Everyone who **l** has been born
4: 21 Anyone who **l** God must also love
5: 1 who **l** the father **l** his child
3Jn : 9 but Diotrephes, who **l** to be first,
Rev 1: 5 To him who **l** us and has freed us
20: 9 camp of God's people, the city he **l**.
22: 15 and everyone who **l** and practices

LOVING* (LOVE)
Ps 25: 10 All the ways of the LORD are **l**
32: 8 I will counsel you with my **l** eye
107: 43 ponder the **l** deeds of the LORD.
144: 2 He is my **l** God and my fortress,
Pr 5: 19 A **l** doe, a graceful deer—
Heb 13: 1 Keep on **l** one another as brothers
1Jn 5: 2 by **l** God and carrying out his

LOW (LOWER LOWLY)
Ps 116: 6 when I was brought **l**, he saved me.

LOWER (LOW)
Ps 8: 5 made them a little **l** than the angels
2Co 11: 7 it a sin for me to **l** myself in order
Heb 2: 7 them a little **l** than the angels;

LOWING
1Sa 15: 14 What is this **l** of cattle that I hear?"

LOWLY (LOW)
Job 5: 11 The **l** he sets on high, and those
Ps 138: 6 is exalted, he looks kindly on the **l**;
Pr 29: 23 low, but the **l** in spirit gain honor.
Isa 57: 15 one who is contrite and **l** in spirit,
57: 15 to revive the spirit of the **l**
Eze 21: 26 The **l** will be exalted and the
Zec 9: 9 **l** and riding on a donkey,
Mt 18: 4 takes the **l** position of this child is
1Co 1: 28 God chose the **l** things of this

LOYAL (LOYALTY)
1Ch 29: 18 and keep their hearts **l** to you.
Ps 78: 8 whose hearts were not **l** to God,

LOYALTY (LOYAL)
Jdg 8: 35 failed to show any **l** to the family

LUKE*
Co-worker with Paul (Col 4:14; 2Ti 4:11; Phm 24).

LUKEWARM*
Rev 3: 16 So, because you are **l**—

LUST (LUSTED LUSTS)
Pr 6: 25 Do not **l** in your heart after her
Eze 20: 30 did and **l** after their vile images?
Col 3: 5 impurity, **l**, evil desires and greed,
1Th 4: 5 not in passionate **l** like the pagans,
1Pe 4: 3 living in debauchery, **l**,
1Jn 2: 16 the **l** of the flesh, the **l** of the eyes,

LUSTED (LUST)
Eze 23: 5 and she **l** after her lovers,

LUSTS* (LUST)
Nu 15: 39 after the **l** of your own hearts
Ro 1: 26 God gave them over to shameful **l**.

LUXURY
Jas 5: 5 You have lived on earth in **l**

LYDIA'S*
Ac 16: 40 they went to **L** house, where they

LYING (LIE)
Pr 6: 17 haughty eyes, a **l** tongue,
12: 22 The LORD detests **l** lips, but he
21: 6 by a **l** tongue is a fleeting vapor
26: 28 A **l** tongue hates those it hurts,

LYRE (LYRE)
1Sa 16: 23 David would take up his **l** and play.

MACEDONIA
Ac 16: 9 a vision of a man of **M** standing

MAD
Dt 28: 34 sights you see will drive you **m**.

MADE (MAKE)
Ge 1: 7 So God **m** the vault and separated
1: 16 God **m** two great lights—
1: 16 He also **m** the stars.
1: 25 God **m** the wild animals according
1: 31 God saw all that he had **m**, and it
2: 22 the LORD God **m** a woman
6: 6 that he had **m** human beings
9: 6 of God has God **m** mankind.
15: 18 day the LORD **m** a covenant
Ex 20: 11 six days the LORD **m** the heavens
20: 11 the Sabbath day and **m** it holy.
24: 8 that the LORD has **m** with you
32: 4 **m** it into an idol cast in the shape
Lev 16: 34 Atonement is to be **m** once a year
Dt 32: 6 who **m** you and formed you?
Jos 24: 25 that day Joshua **m** a covenant
2Ki 19: 15 You have **m** heaven and earth.
2Ch 2: 12 of Israel, who **m** heaven and earth!
Ne 9: 6 You **m** the heavens,
9: 10 You **m** a name for yourself,
Ps 33: 6 of the LORD the heavens were **m**,
95: 5 for he **m** it, and his hands formed
96: 5 but the LORD **m** the heavens.
100: 3 It is he who **m** us, and we are his;
136: 7 who **m** the great lights—
139: 14 I am fearfully and wonderfully **m**;
Ecc 3: 11 He has **m** everything beautiful in
Isa 43: 7 my glory, whom I formed and **m**."
45: 12 It is I who **m** the earth and created
45: 18 he who fashioned and **m** the earth,
66: 2 not my hand **m** all these things,
Jer 10: 12 But God **m** the earth by his power;
27: 5 outstretched arm I **m** the earth
32: 17 you have **m** the heavens
33: 2 LORD says, he who **m** the earth,
51: 15 "He **m** the earth by his power;
Eze 3: 17 I have **m** you a watchman
33: 7 I have **m** you a watchman
Am 5: 8 He who **m** the Pleiades and Orion,
Jnh 1: 9 who **m** the sea and the dry land."
Mk 2: 27 "The Sabbath was **m** for man,
Jn 1: 3 Through him all things were **m**;
Ac 17: 24 "The God who **m** the world
Heb 1: 2 whom also he **m** the universe.
Jas 3: 9 who have been **m** in God's likeness.
Rev 14: 7 Worship him who **m** the heavens,

MAGDALENE
Lk 8: 2 Mary (called **M**) from whom seven

MAGI
Mt 2: 1 **M** from the east came to Jerusalem

MAGIC (MAGICIANS)
Eze 13: 20 I am against your **m** charms
Rev 21: 8 those who practice **m** arts,
22: 15 dogs, those who practice **m** arts,

MAGICIANS (MAGIC)
Ex 7: 11 the Egyptian **m** also did the same
Da 2: 2 So the king summoned the **m**,

MAGNIFICENCE* (MAGNIFICENT)
1Ch 22: 5 for the LORD should be of great **m**

MAGNIFICENT (MAGNIFICENCE)
1Ki 8: 13 I have indeed built a **m** temple
Isa 28: 29 is wonderful, whose wisdom is **m**.
Mk 13: 1 What **m** buildings!"

MAGOG
Eze 38: 2 of the land of **M**, the chief prince
39: 6 I will send fire on **M** and on those
Rev 20: 8 Gog and **M**—and to gather them

MAIMED
Mt 18: 8 It is better for you to enter life **m**

MAINTAIN (MAINTAINING)
Hos 12: 6 **m** love and justice, and wait
Am 5: 15 **m** justice in the courts.
Ro 3: 28 For we **m** that a person is justified

MAINTAINING (MAINTAIN)
Ex 34: 7 **m** love to thousands, and forgiving

MAJESTIC* (MAJESTY)
Ex 15: 6 hand, LORD, was **m** in power.
15: 11 **m** in holiness, awesome in glory,
Job 37: 4 he thunders with his **m** voice.
Ps 8: 1 **m** is your name in all the earth!
8: 9 **m** is your name in all the earth!
29: 4 the voice of the LORD is **m**.
68: 15 Mount Bashan, **m** mountain,
76: 4 more **m** than mountains rich
111: 3 Glorious and **m** are his deeds,
SS 6: 4 as **m** as troops with banners.
6: 10 sun, **m** as the stars in procession?
Isa 30: 30 cause people to hear his **m** voice
Eze 31: 7 It was **m** in beauty, with its
2Pe 1: 17 came to him from the **M** Glory,

MAJESTY (MAJESTIC)
Ex 15: 7 your **m** you threw down those who
Dt 5: 24 has shown us his glory and his **m**,
11: 2 his **m**, his mighty hand,
33: 17 In **m** he is like a firstborn bull;
33: 26 you and on the clouds in his **m**.
1Ch 16: 27 Splendor and **m** are before him;
29: 11 glory and the **m** and the splendor,
Est 1: 4 the splendor and glory of his **m**.
7: 3 you, Your **M**, and if it pleases you,
Job 37: 22 God comes in awesome **m**.
40: 10 clothe yourself in honor and **m**.
Ps 21: 5 bestowed on him splendor and **m**.
45: 3 yourself with splendor and **m**.
45: 4 In your **m** ride forth victoriously
68: 34 of God, whose **m** is over Israel,
93: 1 LORD reigns, he is robed in **m**;
96: 6 Splendor and **m** are before him;
104: 1 are clothed with splendor and **m**.
145: 5 the glorious splendor of your **m**—
Isa 2: 10 LORD and the splendor of his **m**!
2: 19 LORD and the splendor of his **m**,
2: 21 LORD and the splendor of his **m**,
24: 14 west they acclaim the LORD's **m**.
26: 10 do not regard the **m** of the LORD.
53: 2 beauty or **m** to attract us to him,
Eze 31: 2 can be compared with you in **m**?
31: 18 with you in splendor and **m**?
Da 4: 30 power and for the glory of my **m**?"
Mic 5: 4 in the **m** of the name of the LORD
Zec 6: 13 he will be clothed with **m** and will
Ac 19: 27 will be robbed of her divine **m**."
25: 26 to write to His **M** about him.
Heb 1: 3 the right hand of the **M** in heaven.
8: 1 of the throne of the **M** in heaven,

2Pe 1: 16 but we were eyewitnesses of his **m**.
Jude : 25 only God our Savior be glory, **m**,

MAKE (MADE MAKER MAKERS MAKES MAKING)
Ge 1: 26 "Let us **m** mankind in our image,
2: 18 I will **m** a helper suitable for him."
6: 14 So **m** yourself an ark of cypress
12: 2 "I will **m** you into a great nation,
Ex 22: 3 steals must certainly **m** restitution,
25: 9 **M** this tabernacle and all its
25: 40 See that you **m** them according
Nu 6: 25 the LORD **m** his face shine on you
2Sa 7: 9 Now I will **m** your name great,
Job 7: 17 is mankind that you **m** so much
Ps 4: 8 LORD, **m** me dwell in safety.
20: 4 heart and **m** all your plans succeed.
108: 1 sing and **m** music with all my soul.
110: 1 right hand until I **m** your enemies
119:165 and nothing can **m** them stumble.
Pr 3: 6 and he will **m** your paths straight.
16: 23 the wise **m** their mouths prudent,
Isa 14: 14 I will **m** myself like the Most
29: 16 formed it, "You did not **m** me"?
55: 3 I will **m** an everlasting covenant
61: 8 and **m** an everlasting covenant
Jer 31: 31 "when I will **m** a new covenant
Eze 37: 26 I will **m** a covenant of peace
Mt 3: 3 Lord, **m** straight paths for him.'"
28: 19 go and **m** disciples of all nations,
Lk 13: 24 "**M** every effort to enter through
Ro 14: 19 Let us therefore **m** every effort to
2Co 5: 9 So we **m** it our goal to please him,
Eph 4: 3 **M** every effort to keep the unity
Col 4: 5 **m** the most of every opportunity.
1Th 4: 11 **m** it your ambition to lead a quiet
2Th 1: 11 our God may **m** you worthy of his
Heb 4: 11 **m** every effort to enter that rest,
8: 5 it that you **m** everything according
12: 14 **M** every effort to live in peace
2Pe 1: 5 **m** every effort to add to your faith
3: 14 **m** every effort to be found spotless,

MAKER* (MAKE)
Job 4: 17 man be more pure than his **M**?
9: 9 He is the **M** of the Bear and Orion,
32: 22 my **M** would soon take me away.
35: 10 'Where is God my **M**, who gives
36: 3 I will ascribe justice to my **M**.
40: 19 yet its **M** can approach it with his
Ps 95: 6 us kneel before the LORD our **M**;
115: 15 LORD, the **M** of heaven and earth.
121: 2 LORD, the **M** of heaven and earth.
124: 8 LORD, the **M** of heaven and earth.
134: 3 he who is the **M** of heaven
146: 6 He is the **M** of heaven and earth,
149: 2 Let Israel rejoice in their **M**;
Pr 14: 31 poor shows contempt for their **M**,
17: 5 poor shows contempt for their **M**;
22: 2 The LORD is the **M** of them all.
Ecc 11: 5 work of God, the **M** of all things.
Isa 17: 7 that day people will look to their **M**
27: 11 so their **M** has no compassion
44: 24 I am the LORD, the **M** of all things,
45: 9 to those who quarrel with their **M**,
45: 11 the Holy One of Israel, and its **M**:
51: 13 that you forget the LORD your **M**,
54: 5 For your **M** is your husband—
Jer 10: 16 these, for he is the **M** of all things,
51: 19 these, for he is the **M** of all things,
Hos 8: 14 Israel has forgotten their **M**

MAKERS* (MAKE)
Isa 45: 16 All the **m** of idols will be put

MAKES (MAKE)
Ps 23: 2 **m** me lie down in green pastures,
Pr 13: 12 Hope deferred **m** the heart sick,
1Co 3: 7 but only God, who **m** things grow.

MAKING (MAKE)
Ps 19: 7 are trustworthy, **m** wise the simple.
Ecc 12: 12 Of **m** many books there is no end,
Jn 5: 18 Father, **m** himself equal with God.
1Co 3: 6 it, but God has been **m** it grow.
Eph 5: 16 **m** the most of every opportunity,

MALACHI*
Mal 1: 1 of the LORD to Israel through **M**.

MALE
Ge 1: 27 **m** and female he created them.
Ex 13: 2 to me every firstborn **m**.
Nu 8: 16 the first **m** offspring from every
Mt 19: 4 the Creator 'made them **m**
Gal 3: 28 nor free, nor is there **m** and female,

MALICE (MALICIOUS)
Mk 7: 22 greed, **m**, deceit, lewdness,
Ro 1: 29 envy, murder, strife, deceit and **m**.
1Co 5: 8 with the old bread leavened with **m**
Eph 4: 31 along with every form of **m**.
Col 3: 8 anger, rage, **m**, slander, and filthy
1Pe 2: 1 rid yourselves of all **m** and all

MALICIOUS (MALICE)
1Ti 3: 11 not **m** talkers but temperate
6: 4 envy, strife, **m** talk, evil suspicions

MALIGN
Titus 2: 5 no one will **m** the word of God.

MAN (HUMAN MANKIND MEN WOMAN WOMEN)
Ge 2: 7 the LORD God formed a **m**
2: 7 and the **m** became a living being.
2: 8 there he put the **m** he had formed.
2: 15 The LORD God took the **m**
2: 18 is not good for the **m** to be alone.
2: 20 So the **m** gave names to all
2: 23 The **m** said, "This is now bone
2: 23 for she was taken out of **m**."
3: 9 the LORD God called to the **m**,
3: 22 "The **m** has now become like one
4: 1 LORD I have brought forth a **m**."
Dt 8: 3 **m** does not live on bread alone
1Sa 13: 14 sought out a **m** after his own heart
Ps 127: 5 Blessed is the **m** whose quiver is
Pr 30: 19 way of a **m** with a young woman.
Isa 53: 3 by mankind, a **m** of suffering,
Jer 17: 5 "Cursed is the one who trusts in **m**,
Mt 4: 4 '**M** shall not live on bread alone,
19: 5 this reason a **m** will leave his father
Lk 4: 4 '**M** shall not live on bread alone.'"
Ro 5: 12 entered the world through one **m**,
1Co 7: 1 "It is good for a **m** not to have
7: 2 **m** should have sexual relations
11: 3 the head of every **m** is Christ,
11: 3 and the head of the woman is **m**,
13: 11 When I became a **m**, I put the ways
15: 21 For since death came through a **m**,
15: 47 The first **m** was of the dust
15: 47 the second **m** is of heaven.
2Co 12: 2 I know a **m** in Christ who fourteen
Eph 5: 31 this reason a **m** will leave his father
Php 2: 8 being found in appearance as a **m**,
1Ti 2: 12 or to assume authority over a **m**;
Heb 2: 6 a son of **m** that you care for him?

MANAGE* (MANAGER MANAGES)
Jer 12: 5 how will you **m** in the thickets
1Ti 3: 4 He must **m** his own family well
3: 5 not know how to **m** his own family,
3: 12 to his wife and must **m** his children
5: 14 to **m** their homes and to give

MANAGER (MANAGE)
Lk 12: 42 then is the faithful and wise **m**,
16: 1 a rich man whose **m** was accused

MANAGES* (MANAGE)
Titus 1: 7 an overseer **m** God's household,

MANASSEH
1. Firstborn of Joseph (Ge 41:51; 46:20). Blessed by Jacob but not firstborn (Ge 48). Tribe of blessed (Dt 33:17), numbered (Nu 1:35; 26:34), half allotted land east of Jordan (Nu 32; Jos 13:8–33), half west (Jos 17; Eze 48:4), failed to fully possess (Jos 17:12–13; Jdg 1:27), 12,000 from (Rev 7:6).
2. Son of Hezekiah; king of Judah (2Ki 21:1–18; 2Ch 33:1–20). Judah exiled for his detestable sins (2Ki 21:10–15). Repentance (2Ch 33:12–19).

MANDRAKES
Ge 30: 14 give me some of your son's **m**."

MANGER
Lk 2: 12 in cloths and lying in a **m**."

MANIFESTATION*
1Co 12: 7 one the **m** of the Spirit is given

MANKIND (MAN)
Ge 1: 26 said, "Let us make **m** in our image,
Ps 8: 4 what is **m** that you are mindful of
33: 13 LORD looks down and sees all **m**;
Pr 8: 31 whole world and delighting in **m**.
Ecc 7: 29 God created **m** upright, but they
Isa 45: 12 the earth and created **m** on it.
Jer 32: 27 "I am the LORD, the God of all **m**.
Zec 2: 13 Be still before the LORD, all **m**,
Jn 1: 4 that life was the light of all **m**.
Heb 2: 6 "What is **m** that you are mindful of
1Ti 2: 5 one mediator between God and **m**,

MANNA
Ex 16: 31 people of Israel called the bread **m**.
Dt 8: 16 He gave you **m** to eat
Jn 6: 49 Your ancestors ate the **m**
Rev 2: 17 I will give some of the hidden **m**.

MANNER
1Co 11: 27 in an unworthy **m** will be guilty
Php 1: 27 conduct yourselves in a **m** worthy

MANSIONS*
Ps 49: 14 grave, far from their princely **m**.
Isa 5: 9 the fine **m** left without occupants.
Am 3: 15 and the **m** will be demolished,"
5: 11 though you have built stone **m**,

MARCH
Jos 6: 4 day, **m** around the city seven times,
Isa 42: 13 The LORD will **m** out like

MARITAL* (MARRY)
Ex 21: 10 of her food, clothing and **m** rights.
1Co 7: 3 husband should fulfill his **m** duty

MARK (MARKED MARKS)
Cousin of Barnabas (Col 4:10; 2Ti 4:11; Phm 24; 1Pe 5:13), see JOHN.
Ge 4: 15 the LORD put a **m** on Cain so
Rev 13: 16 to receive a **m** on their right hands

MARKED (MARK)
Ac 17: 26 he **m** out their appointed times

MARKET (MARKETPLACE MARKETPLACES)
Jn 2: 16 my Father's house into a **m**!"

MARKETPLACE (MARKET)
Lk 7: 32 are like children sitting in the **m**

MARKETPLACES (MARKET)
Mt 23: 7 to be greeted with respect in the **m**

MARKS (MARK)
Jn 20: 25 "Unless I see the nail **m** in his
Gal 6: 17 I bear on my body the **m** of Jesus.

MARRED
Isa 52: 14 and his form **m** beyond human

MARRIAGE (MARRY)
Mt 22: 30 neither marry nor be given in **m**;
24: 38 marrying and giving in **m**,
Heb 13: 4 **M** should be honored by all,
13: 4 and the **m** bed kept pure,

MARRIED (MARRY)
Dt 24: 5 happiness to the wife he has **m**.
Ezr 10: 10 you have **m** foreign women,
Pr 30: 23 contemptible woman who gets **m**,
Mt 1: 18 was pledged to be **m** to Joseph,
Mk 12: 23 be, since the seven were **m** to her?"
Ro 7: 2 by law a **m** woman is bound to her
1Co 7: 33 But a **m** man is concerned
7: 36 is not sinning. They should get **m**.

MARRIES (MARRY)
Mt 5: 32 anyone who **m** a divorced woman
19: 9 and **m** another woman commits
Lk 16: 18 the man who **m** a divorced woman

MARROW
Heb 4: 12 soul and spirit, joints and **m**;

MARRY (INTERMARRY MARITAL MARRIAGE MARRIED MARRIES)
Dt 25: 5 brother shall take her and **m** her
Mt 22: 30 people will neither **m** nor be given
1Co 7: 9 they should **m**, for it is better to **m**
7: 28 But if you do **m**, you have not
1Ti 4: 3 They forbid people to **m** and order
5: 14 So I counsel younger widows to **m**,

MARTHA*
Sister of Mary and Lazarus (Lk 10:38–42; Jn 11; 12:2).

MARVELED* (MARVELOUS)
Lk 2: 33 mother **m** at what was said
2Th 1: 10 to be **m** at among all those who

MARVELING* (MARVELOUS)
Lk 9: 43 While everyone was **m** at all

MARVELOUS* (MARVELED MARVELING)
1Ch 16: 24 his **m** deeds among all peoples.
Job 37: 5 God's voice thunders in **m** ways;
Ps 71: 17 to this day I declare your **m** deeds.
72: 18 of Israel, who alone does **m** deeds.
86: 10 For you are great and do **m** deeds;
96: 3 his **m** deeds among all peoples.
98: 1 song, for he has done **m** things;
118: 23 done this, and it is **m** in our eyes.
Zec 8: 6 "It may seem **m** to the remnant
8: 6 time, but will it seem **m** to me?"
Mt 21: 42 done this, and it is **m** in our eyes'?

Mk 12: 11 done this, and it is **m** in our eyes'?"
Rev 15: 1 heaven another great and **m** sign:
15: 3 "Great and **m** are your deeds,

MARY

1. Mother of Jesus (Mt 1:16–25; Lk 1:27–56; 2:1–40). With Jesus at temple (Lk 2:41–52), at wedding in Cana (Jn 2:1–5), questioning his sanity (Mk 3:21), at the cross (Jn 19:25–27). Among disciples after Jesus' ascension (Ac 1:14).

2. Magdalene; former demoniac (Lk 8:2). Helped support Jesus' ministry (Lk 8:1–3). At the cross (Mt 27:56; Mk 15:40; Jn 19:25), burial (Mt 27:61; Mk 15:47). Saw angel after resurrection (Mt 28:1–10; Mk 16:1–9; Lk 24:1–12); also saw Jesus (Jn 20:1–18).

3. Sister of Martha and Lazarus (Jn 11). Washed Jesus' feet (Jn 12:1–8).

MASQUERADES*
2Co 11: 14 for Satan himself **m** as an angel

MASTER (MASTER'S MASTERED MASTERS MASTERY)
Pr 25: 13 he refreshes the spirit of his **m**.
Hos 2: 16 you will no longer call me 'my **m**.'
Mal 1: 6 If I am a **m**, where is the respect
Mt 10: 24 teacher, nor a servant above his **m**.
24: 46 servant whose **m** finds him doing
25: 21 "His **m** replied, 'Well done,
25: 23 "His **m** replied, 'Well done,
Ro 6: 14 For sin shall no longer be your **m**,
14: 4 To their own **m**, servants stand
Col 4: 1 that you also have a **M** in heaven.
2Ti 2: 21 useful to the **M** and prepared to do

MASTER'S (MASTER)
Mt 25: 21 and share your **m** happiness!'

MASTERED* (MASTER)
1Co 6: 12 but I will not be **m** by anything.
2Pe 2: 19 are slaves to whatever has **m** them."

MASTERS (MASTER)
Mt 6: 24 "No one can serve two **m**.
Lk 16: 13 "No one can serve two **m**.
Eph 6: 5 obey your earthly **m** with respect
6: 9 **m**, treat your slaves in the same
Col 3: 22 obey your earthly **m** in everything;
4: 1 **M**, provide your slaves with what is
1Ti 6: 1 should consider their **m** worthy
6: 2 who have believing **m** should not
Titus 2: 9 be subject to their **m** in everything,
1Pe 2: 18 God submit yourselves to your **m**,

MASTERY* (MASTER)
Ro 6: 9 death no longer has **m** over him.

MAT
Mk 2: 9 'Get up, take your **m** and walk'?
Ac 9: 34 Get up and roll up your **m**."

MATCHED*
2Co 8: 11 do it may be **m** by your completion

MATTHEW*

Apostle; former tax collector (Mt 9:9–13; 10:3; Mk 3:18; Lk 6:15; Ac 1:13). Also called Levi (Mk 2:14–17; Lk 5:27–32).

MATTHIAS
Ac 1: 26 they cast lots, and the lot fell to **M**;

MATURE* (MATURITY)
Lk 8: 14 and pleasures, and they do not **m**.
1Co 2: 6 message of wisdom among the **m**,
Eph 4: 13 of the Son of God and become **m**,
4: 15 in every respect the **m** body of him
Php 3: 15 who are **m** should take such a view
Col 1: 28 we may present everyone fully **m**
4: 12 will of God, **m** and fully assured.
Heb 5: 14 But solid food is for the **m**,
Jas 1: 4 its work so that you may be **m**

MATURITY* (MATURE)
Heb 6: 1 Christ and be taken forward to **m**,

MEAL
1Co 10: 27 If an unbeliever invites you to a **m**
Heb 12: 16 single **m** sold his inheritance rights

MEANING
Ne 8: 8 and giving the **m** so that the people

MEANINGLESS
Ecc 1: 2 "**M**! **M**!" says the Teacher.
1Ti 1: 6 these and have turned to **m** talk.

MEANS
1Co 9: 22 all possible **m** I might save some.

MEASURE (MEASURED MEASURES)
Jer 10: 24 me, LORD, but only in due **m**—
30: 11 discipline you but only in due **m**;
46: 28 discipline you but only in due **m**;
Eze 45: 3 **m** off a section 25,000 cubits long
Zec 2: 2 "To **m** Jerusalem, to find out how
Lk 6: 38 For with the **m** you use, it will be
Eph 3: 19 be filled to the **m** of all the fullness
4: 13 to the whole **m** of the fullness
Rev 11: 1 "Go and **m** the temple of God

MEASURED (MEASURE)
Isa 40: 12 has **m** the waters in the hollow
Jer 31: 37 if the heavens above can be **m**

MEASURES (MEASURE)
Dt 25: 14 Do not have two differing **m** in
Pr 20: 10 Differing weights and differing **m**

MEAT
Pr 23: 20 wine or gorge themselves on **m**,
Ro 14: 6 eats **m** does so to the Lord,
14: 21 It is better not to eat **m** or drink
1Co 8: 13 I will never eat **m** again, so that I
10: 25 sold in the **m** market without

MEDDLER*
1Pe 4: 15 kind of criminal, or even as a **m**.

MEDIATE* (MEDIATOR)
1Sa 2: 25 God may **m** for the offender;
Job 9: 33 If only there were someone to **m**

MEDIATOR* (MEDIATE)
Gal 3: 19 angels and entrusted to a **m**.
3: 20 A **m**, however, implies more than
1Ti 2: 5 one God and one **m** between God
Heb 8: 6 which he is **m** is superior to the old
9: 15 this reason Christ is the **m** of a new
12: 24 to Jesus the **m** of a new covenant,

MEDICINE*
Pr 17: 22 A cheerful heart is good **m**,

MEDITATE* (MEDITATED MEDITATES MEDITATION)
Ge 24: 63 out to the field one evening to **m**,
Jos 1: 8 **m** on it day and night, so that you
Ps 48: 9 God, we **m** on your unfailing love.
77: 3 I **m**, and my spirit grew faint.
77: 6 My heart **m** and my spirit asked:
77: 12 and **m** on all your mighty deeds."
119: 15 I **m** on your precepts and consider
119: 23 servant will **m** on your decrees.
119: 27 I may **m** on your wonderful deeds.
119: 48 love, that I may **m** on your decrees.
119: 78 but I will **m** on your precepts.
119: 97 I **m** on it all day long.
119: 99 teachers, for I **m** on your statutes.
119:148 that I may **m** on your promises.
143: 5 I **m** on all your works
145: 5 I will **m** on your wonderful works.

MEDITATED* (MEDITATE)
Ps 39: 3 While I **m**, the fire burned;

MEDITATES* (MEDITATE)
Ps 1: 2 and who **m** on his law day

MEDITATION* (MEDITATE)
Ps 19: 14 this **m** of my heart be pleasing
49: 3 the **m** of my heart will give you
104: 34 May my **m** be pleasing to him, as I

MEDIUM
Lev 20: 27 or woman who is a **m** or spiritist

MEEK*
Ps 37: 11 But the **m** will inherit the land
Zep 3: 12 I will leave within you the **m**
Mt 5: 5 Blessed are the **m**, for they will

MEET (MEETING MEETINGS MEETS)
Ps 42: 2 When can I go and **m** with God?
85: 10 Love and faithfulness **m** together;
Am 4: 12 Israel, prepare to **m** your God."
1Co 11: 34 you **m** together it may not result
1Th 4: 17 the clouds to **m** the Lord in the air.

MEETING (MEET)
Ex 40: 34 the cloud covered the tent of **m**,
Heb 10: 25 not giving up **m** together, as some

MEETINGS* (MEET)
1Co 11: 17 your **m** do more harm than good.

MEETS (MEET)
Heb 7: 26 a high priest truly **m** our need—

MELCHIZEDEK
Ge 14: 18 **M** king of Salem brought out bread
Ps 110: 4 a priest forever, in the order of **M**."
Heb 7: 11 one in the order of **M**,

MELT (MELTS)
Dt 1: 28 brothers have made our hearts **m**
2Pe 3: 12 the elements will **m** in the heat.

MELTS (MELT)
Am 9: 5 he touches the earth and it **m**,

MEMBER (MEMBERS)
Ro 12: 5 each **m** belongs to all the others.

MEMBERS (MEMBER)
Mic 7: 6 a man's enemies are the **m** of his
Mt 10: 36 man's enemies will be the **m** of his
Ro 12: 4 of us has one body with many **m**,
12: 4 these **m** do not all have the same
1Co 6: 15 bodies are **m** of Christ himself?
Eph 3: 6 Israel, **m** together of one body,
4: 25 for we are all **m** of one body.
5: 30 for we are **m** of his body.
Col 3: 15 since as **m** of one body you were

MEMORABLE* (MEMORY)
Eze 39: 13 I display my glory will be a **m** day

MEMORIES* (MEMORY)
1Th 3: 6 you always have pleasant **m** of us

MEMORY (MEMORABLE MEMORIES)
Mt 26: 13 done will also be told, in **m** of her."

MEN (MAN)
Ge 6: 4 the heroes of old, **m** of renown.
Ro 1: 27 **M** committed shameful acts with other **m**,
1Co 13: 1 in the tongues of **m** or of angels,
16: 18 Such **m** deserve recognition.
Gal 1: 1 Paul, an apostle—sent not from **m**
1Ti 5: 1 Treat younger **m** as brothers,
Heb 7: 28 the law appoints as high priests **m**

MENAHEM*

King of Israel (2Ki 15:17–23).

MENE
Da 5: 25 inscription that was written: M, M,

MEPHIBOSHETH

Son of Jonathan shown kindness by David (2Sa 4:4; 9; 21:7). Accused of siding with Absalom (2Sa 16:1–4; 19:24–30).

MERCHANT
Pr 31: 14 She is like the **m** ships, bringing
Mt 13: 45 heaven is like a **m** looking for fine

MERCIFUL (MERCY)
Dt 4: 31 the LORD your God is a **m** God;
Ne 9: 31 for you are a gracious and **m** God.
Ps 77: 9 Has God forgotten to be **m**?
78: 38 Yet he was **m**; he forgave their
Da 9: 9 The Lord our God is **m**
Mt 5: 7 Blessed are the **m**, for they will be
Lk 1: 54 Israel, remembering to be **m**
6: 36 Be **m**, just as your Father is **m**.
Heb 2: 17 in order that he might become a **m**
Jas 2: 13 to anyone who has not been **m**.
Jude : 22 Be **m** to those who doubt;

MERCY (MERCIFUL)
Ex 33: 19 have **m** on whom I will have **m**,
2Sa 24: 14 of the LORD, for his **m** is great;
1Ch 21: 13 the LORD, for his **m** is very great;
Ne 9: 31 great **m** you did not put an end
Ps 25: 6 LORD, your great **m** and love,
28: 6 for he has heard my cry for **m**.
57: 1 Have **m** on me, my God, have **m**
Pr 28: 13 and renounces them finds **m**.
Isa 63: 9 his love and **m** he redeemed them;
Da 9: 18 but because of your great **m**.
Hos 6: 6 For I desire **m**, not sacrifice,
Am 5: 15 LORD God Almighty will have **m**
Mic 6: 8 to love **m** and to walk humbly
7: 18 forever but delight to show **m**.
Hab 3: 2 in wrath remember **m**.
Zec 7: 9 show **m** and compassion to one
Mt 5: 7 merciful, for they will be shown **m**.
9: 13 'I desire **m**, not sacrifice.'
12: 7 mean, 'I desire **m**, not sacrifice,'
18: 33 Shouldn't you have had **m** on your
23: 23 justice, **m** and faithfulness.
Lk 1: 50 His **m** extends to those who fear
Ro 1: 31 no fidelity, no love, no **m**.
9: 15 "I will have **m** on whom I have **m**,
9: 18 God has **m** on whom he wants to have **m**,
11: 32 so that he may have **m** on them all.
12: 1 in view of God's **m**, to offer your
12: 8 if it is to show **m**, do it cheerfully.
Eph 2: 4 love for us, God, who is rich in **m**,
1Ti 1: 13 I was shown **m** because I acted
1: 16 very reason I was shown **m** so
Titus 3: 5 we had done, but because of his **m**.
Heb 4: 16 so that we may receive **m** and find
Jas 2: 13 **M** triumphs over judgment.

Jas 3: 17 full of **m** and good fruit,
5: 11 Lord is full of compassion and **m**.
1Pe 1: 3 In his great **m** he has given us new
2: 10 once you had not received **m**, but now you have received **m**.
Jude : 23 to others show **m**, mixed with fear

MERRY
Lk 12: 19 eat, drink and be **m**."'

MESHACH
Hebrew exiled to Babylon; name changed from Mishael (Da 1:6–7). Refused defilement by food (Da 1:8–20). Refused to worship idol (Da 3:1–18); saved from furnace (Da 3:19–30).

MESSAGE (MESSENGER)
Isa 53: 1 Who has believed our **m**
Jn 12: 38 who has believed our **m**
Ac 10: 36 You know the **m** God sent
17: 11 for they received the **m** with great
Ro 10: 16 "Lord, who has believed our **m**?"
10: 17 faith comes from hearing the **m**,
1Co 1: 18 the **m** of the cross is foolishness
2: 4 My **m** and my preaching were not
2Co 5: 19 to us the **m** of reconciliation.
Col 3: 16 Let the **m** of Christ dwell among
2Th 3: 1 that the **m** of the Lord may spread
Titus 1: 9 to the trustworthy **m** as it has been
Heb 4: 2 the **m** they heard was of no value
1Pe 2: 8 because they disobey the **m**—
2Pe 1: 19 have the prophetic **m** as something

MESSENGER (MESSAGE)
Pr 25: 13 at harvest time is a trustworthy **m**
Mal 3: 1 "I will send my **m**, who will
Mt 11: 10 "'I will send my **m** ahead of you,
2Co 12: 7 a thorn in my flesh, a **m** of Satan,

MESSIAH (MESSIAHS)
Mt 1: 16 of Jesus who is called the **M**.
16: 16 "You are the **M**, the Son
22: 42 "What do you think about the **M**?
Mk 1: 1 the good news about Jesus the **M**,
8: 29 Peter answered, "You are the **M**."
14: 61 him, "Are you the **M**, the Son
Lk 9: 20 Peter answered, "God's **M**."
Jn 1: 41 "We have found the **M**" (that is,
4: 25 that **M**" (called Christ) "is coming.
20: 31 may believe that Jesus is the **M**,
Ac 2: 36 you crucified, both Lord and **M**."
5: 42 the good news that Jesus is the **M**.
9: 22 by proving that Jesus is the **M**.
17: 3 proving that the **M** had to suffer
18: 28 the Scriptures that Jesus was the **M**.
26: 23 that the **M** would suffer and,
Ro 9: 5 the human ancestry of the **M**,
Rev 11: 15 kingdom of our Lord and of his **M**,

MESSIAHS* (MESSIAH)
Mt 24: 24 For false **m** and false prophets will
Mk 13: 22 For false **m** and false prophets will

METHUSELAH
Ge 5: 27 **M** lived a total of 969 years,

MICAH
1. Idolater from Ephraim (Jdg 17–18).
2. Prophet from Moresheth (Jer 26:18–19; Mic 1:1).

MICAIAH
Prophet of the LORD who spoke against Ahab (1Ki 22:1–28; 2Ch 18:1–27).

MICHAEL
Archangel (Jude 9); warrior in angelic realm, protector of Israel (Da 10:13, 21; 12:1; Rev 12:7).

MICHAL
Daughter of Saul, wife of David (1Sa 14:49; 18:20–28). Warned David of Saul's plot (1Sa 19). Saul gave her to Paltiel (1Sa 25:44); David retrieved her (2Sa 3:13–16). Criticized David for dancing before the ark (2Sa 6:16–23); 1Ch 15:29).

MIDIAN
Ex 2: 15 Pharaoh and went to live in **M**,
Jdg 7: 2 cannot deliver **M** into their hands,

MIDWIVES
Ex 1: 17 The **m**, however, feared God

MIGHT (ALMIGHTY MIGHTIER MIGHTY)
Jdg 16: 30 Then he pushed with all his **m**,
2Sa 6: 5 with all their **m** before the LORD,
6: 14 before the LORD with all his **m**,
2Ch 20: 6 Power and **m** are in your hand,
Ps 21: 13 we will sing and praise your **m**.
54: 1 vindicate me by your **m**.
Isa 11: 2 the Spirit of counsel and of **m**,
63: 15 Where are your zeal and your **m**?
Mic 3: 8 and with justice and **m**, to declare
Zec 4: 6 'Not by **m** nor by power, but by my
Col 1: 11 glorious **m** so that you may have
1Ti 6: 16 To him be honor and **m** forever.

MIGHTIER* (MIGHT)
Ps 93: 4 **M** than the thunder of the great
93: 4 **m** than the breakers of the sea—

MIGHTY (MIGHT)
Ge 49: 24 of the hand of the **M** One of Jacob,
Ex 6: 1 of my **m** hand he will let them go;
13: 3 you out of it with a **m** hand.
Dt 5: 15 you out of there with a **m** hand
7: 8 he brought you out with a **m** hand
10: 17 the great God, **m** and awesome,
34: 12 one has ever shown the **m** power
2Sa 1: 19 How the **m** have fallen!
23: 8 the names of David's **m** warriors:
Ne 9: 32 the great God, **m** and awesome,
Job 36: 5 "God is **m**, but despises no one;
Ps 24: 8 and **m**, the LORD **m** in battle.
45: 3 sword on your side, you **m** one;
50: 1 The **M** One, God, the LORD,
62: 7 he is my **m** rock, my refuge.
68: 11 women who proclaim it are a **m**
68: 33 who thunders with **m** voice.
71: 16 come and proclaim your **m** acts,
77: 12 and meditate on all your **m** deeds."
77: 15 your **m** arm you redeemed your
89: 8 are **m**, and your faithfulness
93: 4 the LORD on high is **m**.
99: 4 The King is **m**, he loves justice—
110: 2 LORD will extend your **m** scepter
118: 15 right hand has done **m** things!
136: 12 a **m** hand and outstretched arm;
145: 4 they tell of your **m** acts.
145: 12 people may know of your **m** acts
147: 5 Great is our Lord and **m** in power;
SS 8: 6 like blazing fire, like a **m** flame.
Isa 9: 6 Wonderful Counselor, **M** God,
60: 16 Redeemer, the **M** One of Jacob.
63: 1 I, proclaiming victory, **m** to save."
Jer 10: 6 and your name is **m** in power.
20: 11 LORD is with me like a **m** warrior;
32: 18 Great and **m** God, whose name is
32: 19 purposes and **m** are your deeds.
Eze 20: 33 I will reign over you with a **m** hand
Zep 3: 17 you, the **M** Warrior who saves.
Mt 26: 64 at the right hand of the **M** One
Eph 1: 19 is the same as the **m** strength
6: 10 in the Lord and in his **m** power.
1Pe 5: 6 under God's **m** hand, that he may

MILE*
Mt 5: 41 If anyone forces you to go one **m**,

MILK
Ex 3: 8 a land flowing with **m** and honey—
23: 19 a young goat in its mother's **m**.
Isa 55: 1 buy wine and **m** without money
1Co 3: 2 I gave you **m**, not solid food,
Heb 5: 12 You need **m**, not solid food!
1Pe 2: 2 crave pure spiritual **m**, so that by it

MILLSTONE (STONE)
Lk 17: 2 with a **m** tied around their neck

MIND (DOUBLE-MINDED LIKE-MINDED MINDFUL MINDS MINDSET)
Nu 23: 19 being, that he should change his **m**.
Dt 28: 65 LORD will give you an anxious **m**,
1Sa 15: 29 does not lie or change his **m**;
1Ch 28: 9 devotion and with a willing **m**,
2Ch 30: 12 to give them unity of **m** to carry
Ps 26: 2 me, examine my heart and my **m**;
110: 4 sworn and will not change his **m**:
Jer 17: 10 the heart and examine the **m**,
Da 7: 4 the **m** of a human was given to it.
Mt 22: 37 all your soul and with all your **m**.'
Mk 12: 30 with all your **m** and with all your
Lk 10: 27 your strength and with all your **m**';
Ac 4: 32 believers were one in heart and **m**.
Ro 1: 28 gave them over to a depraved **m**,
7: 25 then, I myself in my **m** am a slave
8: 6 The **m** governed by the flesh is
8: 6 the **m** governed by the Spirit is
8: 7 The **m** governed by the flesh is
12: 2 by the renewing of your **m**.
14: 13 make up your **m** not to put any
15: 6 so that with one **m** and one voice
1Co 1: 10 that you be perfectly united in **m**
2: 9 what no human **m** has conceived"
14: 14 spirit prays, but my **m** is unfruitful.
2Co 13: 11 another, be of one **m**, live in peace.
Php 2: 2 being one in spirit and of one **m**.
3: 19 Their **m** is set on earthly things.
4: 2 to be of the same **m** in the Lord.
Col 2: 18 idle notions by their unspiritual **m**.
1Th 4: 11 You should **m** your own business
Heb 7: 21 sworn and will not change his **m**:
1Pe 4: 7 of sober **m** so that you may pray.

MINDFUL* (MIND)
Ps 8: 4 is mankind that you are **m** of them,
26: 3 for I have always been **m** of your
Lk 1: 48 he has been **m** of the humble state
Heb 2: 6 is mankind that you are **m** of them,

MINDS (MIND)
Dt 11: 18 of mine in your hearts and **m**;
Ps 7: 9 the righteous God who probes **m**
Isa 26: 3 peace those whose **m** are steadfast,
Jer 31: 33 "I will put my law in their **m**
Lk 24: 38 and why do doubts rise in your **m**?
24: 45 he opened their **m** so they could
Ro 8: 5 the flesh have their **m** set on what
8: 5 the Spirit have their **m** set on what
2Co 4: 4 god of this age has blinded the **m**
Eph 4: 23 new in the attitude of your **m**;
Col 3: 2 Set your **m** on things above,
Heb 8: 10 I will put my laws in their **m**
10: 16 and I will write them on their **m**."
1Pe 1: 13 **m** that are alert and fully sober,
Rev 2: 23 am he who searches hearts and **m**,

MINDSET* (MIND)
Php 2: 5 have the same **m** as Christ Jesus:

MINISTER (MINISTERING MINISTERS MINISTRY)
Ps 101: 6 one whose walk is blameless will **m**
1Ti 4: 6 you will be a good **m** of Christ

MINISTERING (MINISTER)
Heb 1: 14 Are not all angels **m** spirits sent

MINISTERS (MINISTER)
2Co 3: 6 He has made us competent as **m**

MINISTRY (MINISTER)
Ac 6: 4 to prayer and the **m** of the word."
Ro 11: 13 the Gentiles, I take pride in my **m**
2Co 4: 1 God's mercy we have this **m**, we do
5: 18 gave us the **m** of reconciliation:
6: 3 that our **m** will not be discredited.
2Ti 4: 5 discharge all the duties of your **m**.
Heb 8: 6 in fact the **m** Jesus has received is

MIRACLE* (MIRACLES MIRACULOUS)
Ex 7: 9 'Perform a **m**,' then say to Aaron,
Mk 9: 39 no one who does a **m** in my name
Jn 7: 21 them, "I did one **m**, and you are all

MIRACLES* (MIRACLE)
1Ch 16: 12 done, his **m**, and the judgments he
Ne 9: 17 to remember the **m** you performed
Job 5: 9 **m** that cannot be counted.
9: 10 **m** that cannot be counted.
Ps 77: 11 will remember your **m** of long ago.
77: 14 You are the God who performs **m**;
78: 12 He did **m** in the sight of their
105: 5 done, his **m**, and the judgments he
106: 7 they gave no thought to your **m**;
106: 22 **m** in the land of Ham and
Mt 7: 22 in your name perform many **m**?'
11: 20 most of his **m** had been performed,
11: 21 the **m** that were performed in you
11: 23 the **m** that were performed in you
13: 58 did not do many **m** there because
Mk 6: 2 What are these remarkable **m** he is
6: 5 He could not do any **m** there,
Lk 10: 13 the **m** that were performed in you
19: 37 voices for all the **m** they had seen:
Ac 2: 22 accredited by God to you by **m**,
8: 13 by the great signs and **m** he saw.
19: 11 did extraordinary **m** through Paul,
1Co 12: 28 then **m**, then gifts of healing,
12: 29 Are all teachers? Do all work **m**?
2Co 12: 12 including signs, wonders and **m**.
Gal 3: 5 work **m** among you by the works
Heb 2: 4 wonders and various **m**, and by

MIRACULOUS (MIRACLE)
Mt 13: 54 this wisdom and these **m** powers?"
1Co 12: 10 to another **m** powers, to another

MIRE
Ps 40: 2 slimy pit, out of the mud and **m**;
Isa 57: 20 whose waves cast up **m** and mud.

MIRIAM
Sister of Moses and Aaron (Nu 26:59). Led dancing at "Red Sea" (Ex 15:20–21). Struck with leprosy for criticizing Moses (Nu 12). Death (Nu 20:1).

MIRROR*
Job 37: 18 skies, hard as a **m** of cast bronze?
1Co 13: 12 we see only a reflection as in a **m**;
Jas 1: 23 who looks at his face in a **m**

MISDEEDS*
Ps 99: 8 though you punished their **m**.
Ro 8: 13 you put to death the **m** of the body,

MISERY
Ex 3: 7 "I have indeed seen the **m** of my
Jdg 10: 16 he could bear Israel's **m** no longer.
Hos 5: 15 in their **m** they will earnestly seek
Ro 3: 16 ruin and **m** mark their ways,
Jas 5: 1 because of the **m** that is coming

MISFORTUNE
Ob : 12 your brother in the day of his **m**,

MISLEAD (MISLED)
Pr 24: 28 would you use your lips to **m**?
Isa 47: 10 knowledge **m** you when you say

MISLED (MISLEAD)
1Co 15: 33 Do not be **m**:

MISS
Pr 19: 2 more will hasty feet **m** the way!

MIST
Hos 6: 4 Your love is like the morning **m**,
Jas 4: 14 You are a **m** that appears for a little

MISTREAT (MISTREATED)
Ex 22: 21 "Do not **m** or oppress a foreigner,
Eze 22: 29 and needy and **m** the foreigner,
Lk 6: 28 you, pray for those who **m** you.

MISTREATED (MISTREAT)
Eze 22: 7 the foreigner and **m** the fatherless
Heb 11: 25 He chose to be **m** along
11: 37 destitute, persecuted and **m**—
13: 3 and those who are **m** as if you

MISUSE* (MISUSES)
Ex 20: 7 "You shall not **m** the name
Dt 5: 11 "You shall not **m** the name
Ps 139: 20 your adversaries **m** your name.

MISUSES* (MISUSE)
Ex 20: 7 anyone guiltless who **m** his name.
Dt 5: 11 anyone guiltless who **m** his name.

MIXED (MIXING)
Da 2: 41 even as you saw iron **m** with clay.

MIXING (MIXED)
Isa 5: 22 wine and champions at **m** drinks,

MOAB
Ge 19: 37 had a son, and she named him **M**;
Dt 34: 6 He buried him in **M**, in the valley
Ru 1: 1 for a while in the country of **M**.
1: 22 returned from **M** accompanied
Isa 15: 1 A prophecy against **M**: Ar in **M**
Jer 48: 16 "The fall of **M** is at hand;
Am 2: 1 "For three sins of **M**, even for four,

MOAN
Ps 90: 9 we finish our years with a **m**.

MOCK (MOCKED MOCKER MOCKERS MOCKING MOCKS)
Ps 22: 7 All who see me **m** me;
119: 51 The arrogant **m** me unmercifully,
Pr 1: 26 I will **m** when calamity overtakes
14: 9 Fools **m** at making amends for sin,
Mk 10: 34 who will **m** him and spit on him,

MOCKED (MOCK)
Ps 89: 51 have **m**, with which they have **m**
Mt 27: 29 knelt in front of him and **m** him.
27: 41 of the law and the elders **m** him.
Gal 6: 7 not be deceived: God cannot be **m**.

MOCKER (MOCK)
Pr 9: 7 corrects a **m** invites insults;
9: 12 you are a **m**, you alone will suffer.
20: 1 Wine is a **m** and beer a brawler;
22: 10 Drive out the **m**, and out goes

MOCKERS (MOCK)
Ps 1: 1 take or sit in the company of **m**,
Pr 29: 8 **M** stir up a city, but the wise turn

MOCKING (MOCK)
Isa 50: 6 I did not hide my face from **m**

MOCKS (MOCK)
Pr 17: 5 Whoever **m** the poor shows
30: 17 "The eye that **m** a father,

MODEL*
Php 3: 17 and just as you have us as a **m**,
1Th 1: 7 And so you became a **m** to all
2Th 3: 9 to offer ourselves as a **m** for you

MODESTY*
1Co 12: 23 are treated with special **m**,

MOLDED*
Job 10: 9 Remember that you **m** me like clay.

MOLDY
Jos 9: 5 their food supply was dry and **m**.

MOLEK
Lev 20: 2 any of his children to **M** is to be
1Ki 11: 33 and **M** the god of the Ammonites,

MOMENT (MOMENTARY)
Job 20: 5 the joy of the godless lasts but a **m**.
Ps 2: 12 for his wrath can flare up in a **m**.
30: 5 For his anger lasts only a **m**, but his
Pr 12: 19 but a lying tongue lasts only a **m**.
Isa 54: 7 "For a brief **m** I abandoned you,
66: 8 a nation be brought forth in a **m**?
Gal 2: 5 We did not give in to them for a **m**,

MOMENTARY* (MOMENT)
2Co 4: 17 **m** troubles are achieving for us

MONEY
Pr 13: 11 Dishonest **m** dwindles away,
Ecc 5: 10 loves **m** never has enough;
Isa 55: 1 and you who have no **m**, come,
Mt 6: 24 You cannot serve both God and **m**.
27: 5 So Judas threw the **m**
Lk 3: 14 "Don't extort **m** and don't accuse
9: 3 bag, no bread, no **m**, no extra shirt.
16: 13 cannot serve both God and **m**."
Ac 5: 2 kept back part of the **m** for himself,
1Co 16: 2 you should set aside a sum of **m**
1Ti 3: 3 not quarrelsome, not a lover of **m**.
6: 10 the love of **m** is a root of all kinds
2Ti 3: 2 themselves, lovers of **m**, boastful,
Heb 13: 5 your lives free from the love of **m**

MONEYLENDER* (LEND)
Lk 7: 41 people owed money to a certain **m**.

MONTH (MONTHS)
Ex 12: 2 "This **m** is to be for you the first **m**,
Eze 47: 12 Every **m** they will bear fruit,
Rev 22: 2 of fruit, yielding its fruit every **m**.

MONTHS (MONTH)
Gal 4: 10 are observing special days and **m**
Rev 11: 2 trample on the holy city for 42 **m**.
13: 5 its authority for forty-two **m**.

MOON
Jos 10: 13 and the **m** stopped, till the nation
Ps 8: 3 your fingers, the **m** and the stars,
74: 16 you established the sun and **m**.
89: 37 be established forever like the **m**,
104: 19 made the **m** to mark the seasons,
121: 6 you by day, nor the **m** by night.
136: 9 **m** and stars to govern the night;
148: 3 Praise him, sun and **m**;
SS 6: 10 fair as the **m**, bright as the sun,
Joel 2: 31 the **m** to blood before the coming
Hab 3: 11 **m** stood still in the heavens
Mt 24: 29 and the **m** will not give its light;
Ac 2: 20 the **m** to blood before the coming
1Co 15: 41 **m** another and the stars another;
Col 2: 16 a New **M** celebration or a Sabbath
Rev 6: 12 the whole **m** turned blood red,
21: 23 the sun or the **m** to shine on it,

MORAL*
Jas 1: 21 get rid of all **m** filth and the evil

MORDECAI
Benjamite exile who raised Esther (Est 2:5–15). Exposed plot to kill Xerxes (Est 2:19–23). Refused to honor Haman (Est 3:1–6; 5:9–14). Charged Esther to foil Haman's plot against the Jews (Est 4). Xerxes forced Haman to honor Mordecai (Est 6). Mordecai exalted (Est 8–10). Established Purim (Est 9:18–32).

MORIAH*
Ge 22: 2 Isaac—and go to the region of **M**.
2Ch 3: 1 LORD in Jerusalem on Mount **M**,

MORNING
Ge 1: 5 was evening, and there was **m**—
Dt 28: 67 In the **m** you will say, "If only
2Sa 23: 4 he is like the light of **m** at sunrise
Ps 5: 3 In the **m**, LORD, you hear my
Pr 4: 18 of the righteous is like the **m** sun,
27: 14 their neighbor early in the **m**,
Isa 14: 12 have fallen from heaven, **m** star,
La 3: 23 They are new every **m**; great is
2Pe 1: 19 and the **m** star rises in your hearts.
Rev 2: 28 I will also give that one the **m** star.
22: 16 of David, and the bright **M** Star."

MORTAL (MORTALS)
Ge 6: 3 humans forever, for they are **m**;
Job 10: 4 Do you see as a **m** sees?
Ps 9: 20 the nations know they are only **m**.
Ro 8: 11 give life to your **m** bodies because
1Co 15: 53 and the **m** with immortality.
2Co 5: 4 that what is **m** may be swallowed

MORTALS (MORTAL)
Job 14: 1 "**M**, born of woman, are of few
Ps 103: 15 The life of **m** is like grass,

MOSES
Levite; brother of Aaron (Ex 6:20; 1Ch 6:3). Put in basket into Nile; discovered and raised by Pharaoh's daughter (Ex 2:1–10). Fled to Midian after killing Egyptian (Ex 2:11–15). Married to Zipporah, fathered Gershom (Ex 2:16–22).

Called by the LORD to deliver Israel (Ex 3–4). Pharaoh's resistance (Ex 5). Ten plagues (Ex 7–11). Passover and Exodus (Ex 12–13). Led Israel through "Red Sea" (Ex 14). Song of deliverance (Ex 15:1–21). Brought water from rock (Ex 17:1–7). Raised hands to defeat Amalekites (Ex 17:8–16). Delegated judges (Ex 18; Dt 1:9–18).

Received Law at Sinai (Ex 19–23; 25–31; Jn 1:17). Announced Law to Israel (Ex 19:7–8; 24; 35). Broke tablets because of golden calf (Ex 32; Dt 9). Saw glory of the Lord (Ex 33–34). Supervised building of tabernacle (Ex 36–40). Set apart Aaron and priests (Lev 8–9). Numbered tribes (Nu 1–4; 26). Opposed by Aaron and Miriam (Nu 12). Sent spies into Canaan (Nu 13). Announced forty years of wandering for failure to enter land (Nu 14). Opposed by Korah (Nu 16). Forbidden to enter land for striking rock (Nu 20:1–13; Dt 1:37). Lifted bronze snake for healing (Nu 21:4–9; Jn 3:14). Final address to Israel (Dt 1–33). Succeeded by Joshua (Nu 27:12–23; Dt 34). Death (Dt 34:5–12).

"Law of Moses" (1Ki 2:3; Ezr 3:2; Mk 12:26; Lk 24:44). "Book of Moses" (2Ch 25:12; Ne 13:1). "Song of Moses" (Ex 15:1–21; Rev 15:3). "Prayer of Moses" (Ps 90).

MOTHS
Mt 6: 19 where **m** and vermin destroy,

MOTHER (GRANDMOTHER MOTHER-IN-LAW MOTHER'S)
Ge 2: 24 why a man leaves his father and **m**
3: 20 because she would become the **m**
Ex 20: 12 "Honor your father and your **m**,
Lev 20: 9 they have cursed their father or **m**,
Dt 5: 16 "Honor your father and your **m**,
21: 18 does not obey his father and **m**
27: 16 who dishonors their father or **m**."
Jdg 5: 7 arose, until I arose, a **m** in Israel.
1Sa 2: 19 Each year his **m** made him a little
Ps 113: 9 her home as a happy **m** of children.
Pr 10: 1 a foolish son brings grief to his **m**.
23: 22 do not despise your **m** when she is
23: 25 May your father and **m** rejoice;
29: 15 left undisciplined disgraces its **m**.
30: 17 that scorns an aged **m**, will be
31: 1 utterance his **m** taught him.
Isa 49: 15 "Can a **m** forget the baby at her
66: 13 As a **m** comforts her child, so will I
Jer 20: 17 with my **m** as my grave, her womb
Mic 7: 6 a daughter rises up against her **m**,
Mt 10: 35 father, a daughter against her **m**,
10: 37 or **m** more than me is not worthy
12: 48 "Who is my **m**, and who are my
15: 4 said, 'Honor your father and **m**'
19: 5 a man will leave his father and **m**
19: 19 honor your father and **m**,' and 'love
Mk 7: 10 'Honor your father and **m**,' and,
10: 19 honor your father and **m**.'"
Lk 11: 27 "Blessed is the **m** who gave you
12: 53 **m** against daughter and daughter
18: 20 honor your father and **m**.'"
Jn 19: 27 to the disciple, "Here is your **m**."
Gal 4: 26 is above is free, and she is our **m**.
Eph 5: 31 a man will leave his father and **m**
6: 2 "Honor your father and **m**"—
1Th 2: 7 Just as a nursing **m** cares for her
2Ti 1: 5 Lois and in your **m** Eunice and,

MOTHER-IN-LAW (MOTHER)
Ru 2: 19 Ruth told her **m** about the one
Mt 10: 35 a daughter-in-law against her **m**—

MOTHER'S (MOTHER)
Job 1: 21 "Naked I came from my **m** womb,
Pr 1: 8 do not forsake your **m** teaching.
Ecc 5: 15 comes naked from their **m** womb,
11: 5 the body is formed in a **m** womb,
Jn 3: 4 a second time into their **m** womb

MOTIVES*
Pr 16: 2 but **m** are weighed by the LORD.
1Co 4: 5 and will expose the **m** of the heart.
Php 1: 18 way, whether from false **m** or true,
1Th 2: 3 not spring from error or impure **m**,
Jas 4: 3 because you ask with wrong **m**,

MOUNT (MOUNTAIN MOUNTAINS MOUNTAINTOPS)
Ps 89: 9 its waves **m** up, you still them.
Isa 14: 13 the utmost heights of **M** Zaphon.
Eze 28: 14 You were on the holy **m** of God;
Zec 14: 4 **M** of Olives will be split in two

MOUNTAIN (MOUNT)
Ge 22: 14 "On the **m** of the LORD it will be
Ex 24: 18 he stayed on the **m** forty days
Dt 5: 4 to face out of the fire on the **m**.
Job 14: 18 "But as a **m** erodes and crumbles
Ps 24: 3 Who may ascend the **m**
48: 1 in the city of our God, his holy **m**.
Isa 40: 4 up, every **m** and hill made low;
Mic 4: 2 let us go up to the **m** of the LORD,
Mt 4: 8 devil took him to a very high **m**
17: 20 you can say to this **m**,
Mk 9: 2 him and led them up a high **m**,
Lk 3: 5 every **m** and hill made low.
Jn 4: 21 the Father neither on this **m** nor
2Pe 1: 18 we were with him on the sacred **m**.

MOUNTAINS (MOUNT)
Ps 36: 6 righteousness is like the highest **m**,
46: 2 the **m** fall into the heart of the sea,
90: 2 Before the **m** were born or you
121: 1 I lift up my eyes to the **m**—
Isa 52: 7 beautiful on the **m** are the feet
54: 10 Though the **m** be shaken
55: 12 the **m** and hills will burst into song
Eze 34: 6 My sheep wandered over all the **m**
Mt 24: 16 who are in Judea flee to the **m**.
Lk 23: 30 Then "'they will say to the **m**,
1Co 13: 2 if I have a faith that can move **m**,
Rev 6: 16 They called to the **m** and the rocks,

MOUNTAINTOPS (MOUNT)
Isa 42: 11 let them shout from the **m**.

MOURN (MOURNING MOURNS)
Ecc 3: 4 a time to **m** and a time to dance,
Isa 61: 2 of our God, to comfort all who **m**,
Mt 5: 4 Blessed are those who **m**, for they
Ro 12: 15 **m** with those who **m**.

MOURNING (MOURN)
Isa 61: 3 the oil of joy instead of **m**,
Jer 31: 13 I will turn their **m** into gladness;
Rev 21: 4 There will be no more death' or **m**

MOURNS (MOURN)
Zec 12: 10 for him as one **m** for an only child,

MOUTH (MOUTHS)
Nu 22: 38 only what God puts in my **m**."
Dt 8: 3 comes from the **m** of the LORD.
18: 18 and I will put my words in his **m**.
30: 14 it is in your **m** and in your heart so
2Ki 4: 34 the bed and lay on the boy, **m** to **m**,
Ps 10: 7 His **m** is full of lies and threats;
17: 3 my **m** has not transgressed.
19: 14 May these words of my **m** and this
40: 3 put a new song in my **m**, a hymn
71: 8 My **m** is filled with your praise,
119:103 taste, sweeter than honey to my **m**!
141: 3 Set a guard over my **m**, LORD;
Pr 2: 6 from his **m** come knowledge
4: 24 Keep your **m** free of perversity;
10: 11 but the **m** of the wicked conceals
10: 31 the **m** of the righteous comes
26: 28 and a flattering **m** works ruin.
27: 2 praise you, and not your own **m**;
Ecc 5: 2 Do not be quick with your **m**, do
SS 1: 2 kiss me with the kisses of his **m**—
5: 16 His **m** is sweetness itself;
Isa 29: 13 come near to me with their **m**
40: 5 the **m** of the LORD has spoken."
45: 23 my **m** has uttered in all integrity
51: 16 I have put my words in your **m**
Isa 53: 7 silent, so he did not open his **m**.
55: 11 my word that goes out from my **m**:
59: 21 I have put in your **m** will always be
Eze 3: 2 So I opened my **m**, and he gave me
Mal 2: 7 seek instruction from his **m**.
Mt 4: 4 that comes from the **m** of God.'"
12: 34 the **m** speaks what the heart is full
15: 11 someone's **m** does not defile them,
15: 18 a person's **m** come from the heart,
Lk 6: 45 the **m** speaks what the heart is full
Ro 10: 9 If you declare with your **m**,
1Pe 2: 22 and no deceit was found in his **m**."
Rev 1: 16 coming out of his **m** was a sharp,
2: 16 them with the sword of my **m**.
3: 16 I am about to spit you out of my **m**.
19: 15 out of his **m** is a sharp sword

MOUTHS (MOUTH)
Ps 37: 30 The **m** of the righteous utter
78: 36 would flatter him with their **m**,
Pr 16: 23 of the wise make their **m** prudent,
Eze 33: 31 Their **m** speak of love, but their
Ro 3: 14 "Their **m** are full of cursing
Eph 4: 29 talk come out of your **m**, but only
Jas 3: 3 we put bits into the **m** of horses

MOVE (MOVED MOVES)
Dt 19: 14 not **m** your neighbor's boundary
Pr 23: 10 not **m** an ancient boundary stone
Ac 17: 28 'For in him we live and **m** and have
1Co 13: 2 have a faith that can **m** mountains,
15: 58 Let nothing **m** you.
Col 1: 23 do not **m** from the hope held

MOVED (MOVE)
Ex 35: 21 and whose heart **m** them came
1Ki 3: 26 whose son was alive was deeply **m**
2Ch 36: 22 the LORD **m** the heart of Cyrus
Ezr 1: 5 everyone whose heart God had **m**
Jn 11: 33 he was deeply **m** in spirit

MOVES (MOVE)
Dt 23: 14 For the LORD your God **m**

MUD (MUDDIED)
Ps 40: 2 slimy pit, out of the **m** and mire;
Isa 57: 20 whose waves cast up mire and **m**.
Jn 9: 6 made some **m** with the saliva,
2Pe 2: 22 returns to her wallowing in the **m**."

MUDDIED (MUD)
Pr 25: 26 Like a **m** spring or a polluted well
Eze 32: 13 man or **m** by the hooves of cattle.

MULBERRY*
Lk 17: 6 seed, you can say to this **m** tree,

MULTITUDE (MULTITUDES)
Isa 31: 1 who trust in the **m** of their chariots
Jas 5: 20 death and cover over a **m** of sins.
1Pe 4: 8 because love covers over a **m**
Rev 7: 9 there before me was a great **m**
19: 1 of a great **m** in heaven shouting:

MULTITUDES (MULTITUDE)
Ne 9: 6 and the **m** of heaven worship you.
Da 12: 2 **M** who sleep in the dust of the
Joel 3: 14 **M**, **m** in the valley of decision!

MURDER (MURDERED MURDERER MURDERERS)
Ex 20: 13 "You shall not **m**.
Dt 5: 17 "You shall not **m**.
Pr 28: 17 the guilt of **m** will seek refuge
Mt 5: 21 'You shall not **m**, and anyone who
15: 19 **m**, adultery, sexual immorality,
Ro 1: 29 They are full of envy, **m**, strife,
13: 9 "You shall not **m**,"
Jas 2: 11 also said, "You shall not **m**."

MURDERED (MURDER)
Mt 23: 31 of those who **m** the prophets.
Ac 7: 52 you have betrayed and **m** him—
1Jn 3: 12 to the evil one and **m** his brother.

MURDERER (MURDER)
Nu 35: 16 the **m** is to be put to death.
Jn 8: 44 He was a **m** from the beginning,
1Jn 3: 15 hates a brother or sister is a **m**,
3: 15 no **m** has eternal life residing

MURDERERS (MURDER)
1Ti 1: 9 kill their fathers or mothers, for **m**,
Rev 21: 8 vile, the **m**, the sexually immoral,
22: 15 the **m**, the idolaters and everyone

MUSIC (MUSICAL MUSICIAN MUSICIANS)
Ge 31: 27 and singing to the **m** of timbrels
1Ch 6: 31 charge of the **m** in the house
6: 32 with **m** before the tabernacle,
25: 6 their father for the **m** of the temple
1Ch 25: 7 and skilled in **m** for the LORD—
Ne 12: 27 and with the **m** of cymbals,
Job 21: 12 They sing to the **m** of timbrel
Ps 27: 6 sing and make **m** to the LORD.
33: 2 make **m** to him on the ten-stringed
45: 8 ivory the **m** of the strings makes
57: 7 I will sing and make **m**.
81: 2 Begin the **m**, strike the timbrel,
87: 7 As they make **m** they will sing,
92: 1 LORD and make **m** to your name,
92: 3 to the **m** of the ten-stringed lyre
95: 2 and extol him with **m** and song.
98: 4 burst into jubilant song with **m**;
98: 5 make **m** to the LORD
108: 1 sing and make **m** with all my soul.
144: 9 the ten-stringed lyre I will make **m**
147: 7 make **m** to our God on the harp.
149: 3 and make **m** to him with timbrel
Isa 30: 32 club will be to the **m** of timbrels
La 5: 14 young men have stopped their **m**.
Eze 26: 13 the **m** of your harps will be heard
Da 3: 5 pipe and all kinds of **m**, you must
3: 7 lyre, harp and all kinds of **m**,
3: 10 all kinds of **m** must fall down
3: 15 pipe and all kinds of **m**, if you are
Am 5: 23 not listen to the **m** of your harps.
Hab 3: 19 For the director of **m**.
Lk 15: 25 house, he heard **m** and dancing.
Eph 5: 19 **m** from your heart to the Lord,
Rev 18: 22 The **m** of harpists and musicians,

MUSICAL* (MUSIC)
1Ch 15: 16 a joyful sound with **m** instruments:
23: 5 the **m** instruments I have provided
2Ch 7: 6 with the LORD's **m** instruments,
34: 12 skilled in playing **m** instruments—
Ne 12: 36 with **m** instruments prescribed
Am 6: 5 and improvise on **m** instruments.

MUSICIAN* (MUSIC)
1Ch 6: 33 Heman, the **m**, the son of Joel,

MUSICIANS (MUSIC)
1Ki 10: 12 to make harps and lyres for the **m**.
1Ch 9: 33 Those who were **m**, heads of Levite
15: 19 The **m** Heman, Asaph and Ethan
2Ch 5: 12 All the Levites who were **m**—
9: 11 to make harps and lyres for the **m**.
35: 15 The **m**, the descendants of Asaph,
Ps 68: 25 are the singers, after them the **m**;
Rev 18: 22 The music of harpists and **m**,

MUSTARD
Mt 13: 31 of heaven is like a **m** seed,
17: 20 you have faith as small as a **m** seed,
Mk 4: 31 It is like a **m** seed, which is

MUSTER
Pr 24: 5 have knowledge **m** their strength.

MUTILATORS*
Php 3: 2 evildoers, those **m** of the flesh.

MUTUAL* (MUTUALLY)
Ro 14: 19 leads to peace and to **m** edification.
1Co 7: 5 other except perhaps by **m** consent
2Pe 1: 7 and to godliness, **m** affection; and
to **m** affection, love.

MUTUALLY* (MUTUAL)
Ro 1: 12 I may be **m** encouraged by each

MUZZLE*
Dt 25: 4 Do not **m** an ox while it is treading
Ps 39: 1 I will put a **m** on my mouth while
1Co 9: 9 Do not **m** an ox while it is treading
1Ti 5: 18 Do not **m** an ox while it is treading

MYRRH
Ps 45: 8 All your robes are fragrant with **m**
SS 1: 13 of **m** resting between my breasts.
Mt 2: 11 gifts of gold, frankincense and **m**.
Mk 15: 23 offered him wine mixed with **m**,
Jn 19: 39 brought a mixture of **m** and aloes,
Rev 18: 13 of incense, **m** and frankincense,

MYSTERIES* (MYSTERY)
Job 11: 7 "Can you fathom the **m** of God?
Da 2: 28 is a God in heaven who reveals **m**.
2: 29 of **m** showed you what is going
2: 47 Lord of kings and a revealer of **m**,
1Co 4: 1 with the **m** God has revealed.
13: 2 fathom all **m** and all knowledge,
14: 2 they utter **m** by the Spirit.

MYSTERY* (MYSTERIES)
Da 2: 18 God of heaven concerning this **m**,
2: 19 During the night the **m** was
2: 27 the king the **m** he has asked about,
2: 30 this **m** has been revealed to me,

Da 2: 47 for you were able to reveal this **m**."
4: 9 and no **m** is too difficult for you.
Ro 11: 25 want you to be ignorant of this **m**,
16: 25 the revelation of the **m** hidden
1Co 2: 7 a **m** that has been hidden
15: 51 Listen, I tell you a **m**: We will not
Eph 1: 9 to us the **m** of his will according
3: 3 that is, the **m** made known to me
3: 4 my insight into the **m** of Christ,
3: 6 This **m** is that through the gospel
3: 9 the administration of this **m**,
5: 32 This is a profound **m**—but I am
6: 19 I will fearlessly make known the **m**
Col 1: 26 the **m** that has been kept hidden
1: 27 the glorious riches of this **m**,
2: 2 that they may know the **m** of God,
4: 3 we may proclaim the **m** of Christ,
1Ti 3: 16 the **m** from which true godliness
Rev 1: 20 The **m** of the seven stars that you
10: 7 the **m** of God will be accomplished,
17: 5 written on her forehead was a **m**:
17: 7 explain to you the **m** of the woman

MYTHS*
1Ti 1: 4 or to devote themselves to **m**
4: 7 Have nothing to do with godless **m**
2Ti 4: 4 from the truth and turn aside to **m**.
Titus 1: 14 will pay no attention to Jewish **m**

NAAMAN
Aramean general whose leprosy was cleansed by Elisha (2Ki 5).

NABAL
Wealthy Carmelite the LORD killed for refusing to help David (1Sa 25). David married Abigail, his widow (1Sa 25:39–42).

NABOTH*
Jezreelite killed by Jezebel for his vineyard (1Ki 21). Ahab's family destroyed for this (1Ki 21:17–24; 2Ki 9:21–37).

NADAB
1. Firstborn of Aaron (Ex 6:23); killed with Abihu for offering unauthorized fire (Lev 10; Nu 3:4).
2. Son of Jeroboam I; king of Israel (1Ki 15:25–32).

NAGGING
Pr 21: 19 with a quarrelsome and **n** wife.

NAHUM
Prophet against Nineveh (Na 1:1).

NAIL* (NAILING)
Jn 20: 25 "Unless I see the **n** marks in his

NAILING* (NAIL)
Ac 2: 23 him to death by **n** him to the cross.
Col 2: 14 has taken it away, **n** it to the cross.

NAIVE*
Ro 16: 18 they deceive the minds of **n** people.

NAKED
Ge 2: 25 Adam and his wife were both **n**,
Job 1: 21 "**N** I came from my mother's womb, and **n** I will depart.
Isa 58: 7 you see the **n**, to clothe them,
2Co 5: 3 are clothed, we will not be found **n**.

NAME (NAMED NAMES)
Ge 2: 19 man to see what he would **n** them;
4: 26 to call on the **n** of the LORD.
11: 4 we may make a **n** for ourselves;
12: 2 I will make your **n** great, and you
32: 29 Jacob said, "Please tell me your **n**."
Ex 3: 15 "This is my **n** forever, the **n** you
20: 7 "You shall not misuse the **n**
34: 14 for the LORD, whose **n** is Jealous,
Lev 24: 11 Israelite woman blasphemed the **N**
Dt 5: 11 "You shall not misuse the **n**
12: 11 choose as a dwelling for his **N**—
18: 5 minister in the LORD's **n** always.
25: 6 carry on the **n** of the dead brother
28: 58 this glorious and awesome **n**—
Jos 7: 9 and wipe out our **n** from the earth.
Jdg 13: 17 "What is your **n**, so that we may
1Sa 12: 22 of his great **n** the LORD will not
2Sa 6: 2 which is called by the **N**, the **n**
7: 9 Now I will make your **n** great,
1Ki 5: 5 will build the temple for my **N**.'
8: 29 you said, 'My **N** shall be there,'
1Ch 17: 8 I will make your **n** like the names
2Ch 7: 14 people, who are called by my **n**,
Ne 9: 10 You made a **n** for yourself,
Ps 8: 1 how majestic is your **n** in all
9: 10 Those who know your **n** trust
Ps 20: 7 in the **n** of the LORD our God.
29: 2 to the LORD the glory due his **n**;
34: 3 let us exalt his **n** together.
44: 20 we had forgotten the **n** of our God
66: 2 Sing the glory of his **n**;
68: 4 his **n** is the LORD.
79: 9 our Savior, for the glory of your **n**;
96: 8 to the LORD the glory due his **n**;
103: 1 my inmost being, praise his holy **n**.
115: 1 not to us but to your **n** be the glory,
138: 2 praise your **n** for your unfailing
145: 1 I will praise your **n** for ever
147: 4 the stars and calls them each by **n**.
Pr 3: 4 and a good **n** in the sight of God
10: 7 The **n** of the righteous is used
10: 7 but the **n** of the wicked will rot.
18: 10 The **n** of the LORD is a fortified
22: 1 A good **n** is more desirable than
30: 4 What is his **n**, and what is the **n**
Ecc 7: 1 A good **n** is better than fine
SS 1: 3 your **n** is like perfume poured out.
Isa 12: 4 and proclaim that his **n** is exalted.
26: 8 your **n** and renown are the desire
40: 26 and calls forth each of them by **n**.
42: 8 "I am the LORD; that is my **n**!
56: 5 I will give them an everlasting **n**
57: 15 who lives forever, whose **n** is holy:
63: 14 to make for yourself a glorious **n**.
Jer 14: 7 LORD, for the sake of your **n**.
15: 16 for I bear your **n**, LORD God
Eze 20: 9 But for the sake of my **n**, I brought
20: 14 of my **n** I did what would keep it
20: 22 of my **n** I did what would keep it
Da 12: 1 everyone whose **n** is found written
Hos 12: 5 God Almighty, the LORD is his **n**!
Joel 2: 32 the **n** of the LORD will be saved;
Mic 5: 4 of the **n** of the LORD his God.
Zep 3: 9 may call on the **n** of the LORD
Zec 6: 12 is the man whose **n** is the Branch,
14: 9 one LORD, and his **n** the only **n**.
Mal 1: 6 who show contempt for my **n**.
Mt 1: 21 you are to give him the **n** Jesus,
6: 9 in heaven, hallowed be your **n**,
18: 20 where two or three gather in my **n**,
24: 5 For many will come in my **n**,
28: 19 baptizing them in the **n** of the
Mk 9: 41 water in my **n** because you belong
Lk 11: 2 hallowed be your **n**, your kingdom
Jn 10: 3 He calls his own sheep by **n**
14: 13 I will do whatever you ask in my **n**,
16: 24 not asked for anything in my **n**.
Ac 2: 21 on the **n** of the Lord will be saved.'
4: 12 is no other **n** under heaven given
Ro 10: 13 on the **n** of the Lord will be saved."
Php 2: 9 gave him the **n** that is above every **n**,
2: 10 at the **n** of Jesus every knee should
Col 3: 17 do it all in the **n** of the Lord Jesus,
Heb 1: 4 the angels as the **n** he has inherited
Jas 5: 14 them with oil in the **n** of the Lord.
1Jn 5: 13 you who believe in the **n** of the Son
Rev 2: 17 stone with a new **n** written on it,
3: 5 I will never blot out the **n** of that
3: 12 write on them the **n** of my God
3: 12 and the **n** of the city of my God,
3: 12 I will also write on them my new **n**.
19: 13 and his **n** is the Word of God.
20: 15 Anyone whose **n** was not found

NAMED (NAME)
Ge 5: 2 And he **n** them "Mankind" when

NAMES (NAME)
Ex 28: 9 engrave on them the **n** of the sons
Lk 10: 20 but rejoice that your **n** are written
Php 4: 3 whose **n** are in the book of life.
Heb 12: 23 whose **n** are written in heaven.
Rev 21: 27 only those whose **n** are written

NAOMI
Wife of Elimelek, mother-in-law of Ruth (Ru 1:2, 4). Left Bethlehem for Moab during famine (Ru 1:1). Returned a widow, with Ruth (Ru 1:6–22). Advised Ruth to seek marriage with Boaz (Ru 2:17—3:4). Cared for Ruth's son Obed (Ru 4:13–17).

NAPHTALI
Son of Jacob by Bilhah (Ge 30:8; 35:25; 1Ch 2:2). Tribe of blessed (Ge 49:21; Dt 33:23), numbered (Nu 1:43; 26:50), allotted land (Jos 19:32–39; Eze 48:3), failed to fully possess (Jdg 1:33), supported Deborah (Jdg 4:10; 5:18), David (1Ch 12:34), 12,000 from (Rev 7:6).

NARROW
Mt 7: 13 "Enter through the **n** gate.
7: 14 and **n** the road that leads to life,

NATHAN
Prophet and chronicler of Israel's history (1Ch 29:29; 2Ch 9:29). Announced the Davidic covenant (2Sa 7; 1Ch 17). Denounced David's sin with Bathsheba (2Sa 12). Supported Solomon (1Ki 1).

NATHANAEL*
Apostle (Jn 1:45–49; 21:2). Probably also called Bartholomew (Mt 10:3).

NATION (NATIONS)
Ge 12: 2 "I will make you into a great **n**,
Ex 19: 6 a kingdom of priests and a holy **n**.'
Dt 4: 7 What other **n** is so great as to have
Jos 5: 8 the whole **n** had been circumcised,
2Sa 7: 23 the one **n** on earth that God went
Ps 33: 12 Blessed is the **n** whose God is
Pr 11: 14 For lack of guidance a **n** falls,
14: 34 Righteousness exalts a **n**, but sin
Isa 2: 4 **N** will not take up sword against **n**,
26: 2 that the righteous **n** may enter,
60: 12 For the **n** or kingdom that will not
65: 1 a **n** that did not call on my name,
66: 8 a **n** be brought forth in a moment?
Mic 4: 3 **N** will not take up sword against **n**,
Mt 24: 7 **N** will rise against **n**, and kingdom
Mk 13: 8 **N** will rise against **n**, and kingdom
1Pe 2: 9 a holy **n**, God's special possession,
Rev 5: 9 and language and people and **n**.
7: 9 could count, from every **n**, tribe,
14: 6 to every **n**, tribe,

NATIONS (NATION)
Ge 17: 4 You will be the father of many **n**.
18: 18 and all **n** on earth will be blessed
Ex 19: 5 of all **n** you will be my treasured
Lev 20: 26 apart from the **n** to be my own.
Dt 7: 1 seven **n** larger and stronger than
15: 6 You will rule over many **n** but none
Jdg 3: 1 These are the **n** the LORD left
2Ch 20: 6 rule over all the kingdoms of the **n**.
Ne 1: 8 I will scatter you among the **n**,
Ps 2: 1 Why do the **n** conspire
2: 8 I will make the **n** your inheritance,
9: 5 You have rebuked the **n**
22: 28 the LORD and he rules over the **n**.
46: 10 I will be exalted among the **n**, I will
47: 8 God reigns over the **n**; God is
66: 7 his power, his eyes watch the **n**—
67: 2 earth, your salvation among all **n**.
68: 30 Scatter the **n** who delight in war.
72: 17 all **n** will be blessed through him,
96: 3 Declare his glory among the **n**,
99: 2 he is exalted over all the **n**.
106: 35 mingled with the **n** and adopted
110: 6 He will judge the **n**,
113: 4 LORD is exalted over all the **n**,
Isa 2: 2 the hills, and all **n** will stream to it.
11: 10 the **n** will rally to him, and his
12: 4 known among the **n** what he has
40: 15 Surely the **n** are like a drop
42: 1 and he will bring justice to the **n**.
49: 22 I will beckon to the **n**, I will lift
51: 4 justice will become a light to the **n**.
52: 15 so he will sprinkle many **n**,
56: 7 called a house of prayer for all **n**."
60: 3 **N** will come to your light,
66: 18 and gather the people of all **n**
Jer 1: 5 you as a prophet to the **n**."
3: 17 and all **n** will gather in Jerusalem
31: 10 the word of the LORD, you **n**;
33: 9 honor before all **n** on earth that
46: 28 completely destroy all the **n** among
Eze 22: 4 you an object of scorn to the **n**
34: 13 I will bring them out from the **n**
36: 23 Then the **n** will know that I am
37: 22 they will never again be two **n** or
39: 21 will display my glory among the **n**,
Hos 7: 8 "Ephraim mixes with the **n**;
Joel 2: 17 of scorn, a byword among the **n**.
3: 2 scattered my people among the **n**
Am 9: 12 and all the **n** that bear my name,"
Zep 3: 8 I have decided to assemble the **n**,
Hag 2: 7 what is desired by all **n** will come,
Zec 8: 13 have been a curse among the **n**,
8: 23 **n** will take firm hold of one Jew
9: 10 He will proclaim peace to the **n**.
14: 2 I will gather all the **n** to Jerusalem
Mt 12: 18 he will proclaim justice to the **n**.

Mt 24: 9 you will be hated by all **n** because
24: 14 whole world as a testimony to all **n**,
25: 32 All the **n** will be gathered before
28: 19 go and make disciples of all **n**,
Mk 11: 17 called a house of prayer for all **n**'?
Ac 4: 25 "'Why do the **n** rage
Ro 15: 12 who will arise to rule over the **n**;
Gal 3: 8 "All **n** will be blessed through
1Ti 3: 16 was preached among the **n**,
Rev 15: 3 true are your ways, King of the **n**.
15: 4 All **n** will come and worship before
21: 24 The **n** will walk by its light,
22: 2 the tree are for the healing of the **n**.

NATURAL (NATURE)
1Co 15: 44 it is sown a **n** body, it is raised

NATURE (NATURAL)
Ro 1: 20 his eternal power and divine **n**—
7: 18 dwell in me, that is, in my sinful **n**.
Php 2: 6 Who, being in very **n** God, did not
Col 3: 5 whatever belongs to your earthly **n**:
2Pe 1: 4 may participate in the divine **n**,

NAZARENE* (NAZARETH)
Mt 2: 23 that he would be called a **N**.
Mk 14: 67 "You also were with that **N**,
16: 6 "You are looking for Jesus the **N**,
Ac 24: 5 He is a ringleader of the **N** sect

NAZARETH (NAZARENE)
Mt 4: 13 Leaving **N**, he went and lived
Lk 4: 16 He went to **N**, where he had been
Jn 1: 46 "**N**! Can anything good come

NAZIRITE
Nu 6: 2 of dedication to the LORD as a **N**,
Jdg 13: 7 because the boy will be a **N** of God

NEBO
Dt 34: 1 Moses climbed Mount **N**

NEBUCHADNEZZAR
Babylonian king. Subdued and exiled Judah (2Ki 24–25; 2Ch 36; Jer 39). Dreams interpreted by Daniel (Da 2; 4). Worshiped God (Da 3:28–29; 4:34–37).

NECESSARY*
Ac 1: 21 Therefore it is **n** to choose one
Ro 13: 5 it is **n** to submit to the authorities,
2Co 9: 5 I thought it **n** to urge the brothers
Php 1: 24 it is more **n** for you that I remain
2: 25 I think it is **n** to send back to you
Heb 8: 3 and so it was **n** for this one
9: 16 it is **n** to prove the death of the one
9: 23 It was **n**, then, for the copies
10: 18 sacrifice for sin is no longer **n**.

NECHO
Pharaoh who killed Josiah (2Ki 23:29–30; 2Ch 35:20–22), deposed Jehoahaz (2Ki 23:33–35; 2Ch 36:3–4).

NECK (STIFF-NECKED)
Pr 3: 22 an ornament to grace your **n**.
6: 21 fasten them around your **n**.
Mt 18: 6 millstone hung around their **n**

NEED (NEEDS NEEDY)
1Ki 8: 59 Israel according to each day's **n**,
Ps 79: 8 meet us, for we are in desperate **n**.
142: 6 to my cry, for I am in desperate **n**;
Mt 6: 8 knows what you **n** before you ask
Lk 15: 14 country, and he began to be in **n**.
Ac 2: 45 to give to anyone who had **n**.
Ro 12: 13 the Lord's people who are in **n**.
1Co 12: 21 say to the hand, "I don't **n** you!"
Eph 4: 28 something to share with those in **n**.
1Ti 5: 3 those widows who are really in **n**.
Heb 4: 16 grace to help us in our time of **n**.
1Jn 3: 17 sister in **n** but has no pity on them,

NEEDLE
Mt 19: 24 to go through the eye of a **n** than

NEEDS (NEED)
Isa 58: 11 he will satisfy your **n**
Php 2: 25 you sent to take care of my **n**.
4: 19 God will meet all your **n** according
Jas 2: 16 nothing about their physical **n**,

NEEDY (NEED)
Dt 15: 11 who are poor and **n** in your land.
1Sa 2: 8 and lifts the **n** from the ash heap;
Ps 35: 10 and **n** from those who rob them."
69: 33 The LORD hears the **n** and does
72: 12 he will deliver the **n** who cry out,
140: 12 and upholds the cause of the **n**.
Pr 14: 21 is the one who is kind to the **n**.
14: 31 is kind to the **n** honors God.
Pr 22: 22 and do not crush the **n** in court,
31: 9 the rights of the poor and **n**.
31: 20 and extends her hands to the **n**.
Mt 6: 2 "So when you give to the **n**, do not

NEGLECT* (NEGLECTED)
Dt 12: 19 to **n** the Levites as long as you live
14: 27 do not **n** the Levites living in your
Ezr 4: 22 Be careful not to **n** this matter.
Ne 10: 39 "We will not **n** the house of our
Est 6: 10 Do not **n** anything you have
Ps 119: 16 I will not **n** your word.
SS 1: 6 my own vineyard I had to **n**.
Lk 11: 42 but you **n** justice and the love
Ac 6: 2 for us to **n** the ministry of the word
1Ti 4: 14 not **n** your gift, which was given

NEGLECTED (NEGLECT)
Mt 23: 23 But you have **n** the more important

NEHEMIAH
Cupbearer of Artaxerxes (Ne 2:1); governor of Israel (Ne 8:9). Returned to Jerusalem to rebuild walls (Ne 2–6). With Ezra, reestablished worship (Ne 8). Prayer confessing nation's sin (Ne 9). Dedicated wall (Ne 12).

NEIGHBOR (NEIGHBOR'S NEIGHBORS)
Ex 20: 16 give false testimony against your **n**.
20: 17 anything that belongs to your **n**."
Lev 19: 13 "'Do not defraud or rob your **n**.
19: 17 Rebuke your **n** frankly so you will
19: 18 people, but love your **n** as yourself.
Ps 15: 3 who does no wrong to a **n**,
88: 18 have taken from me friend and **n**—
Pr 3: 29 Do not plot harm against your **n**,
11: 12 derides their **n** has no sense,
14: 21 It is a sin to despise one's **n**,
16: 29 A violent person entices their **n**
24: 28 against your **n** without cause—
25: 18 gives false testimony against a **n**.
27: 10 better a **n** nearby than a relative far
27: 14 anyone loudly blesses their **n** early
Jer 31: 34 No longer will they teach their **n**,
Mt 5: 43 'Love your **n** and hate your enemy.'
19: 19 and 'love your **n** as yourself.'"
Mk 12: 31 'Love your **n** as yourself.'
Lk 10: 27 and, 'Love your **n** as yourself.'"
10: 29 asked Jesus, "And who is my **n**?"
Ro 13: 9 "Love your **n** as yourself."
13: 10 Love does no harm to a **n**.
Gal 5: 14 "Love your **n** as yourself."
Eph 4: 25 and speak truthfully to your **n**,
Heb 8: 11 No longer will they teach their **n**,
Jas 2: 8 "Love your **n** as yourself,"

NEIGHBOR'S (NEIGHBOR)
Ex 20: 17 "You shall not covet your **n** house.
Dt 5: 21 "You shall not covet your **n** wife.
19: 14 not move your **n** boundary stone
27: 17 moves their **n** boundary stone."
Pr 25: 17 Seldom set foot in your **n** house—

NEIGHBORS (NEIGHBOR)
Pr 29: 5 who flatter their **n** are spreading
Ro 15: 2 of us should please our **n** for their

NESTS
Mt 8: 20 "Foxes have dens and birds have **n**,

NET (NETS)
Pr 1: 17 spread a **n** where every bird can
Hab 1: 15 he catches them in his **n**,
Mt 13: 47 heaven is like a **n** that was let down
Jn 21: 6 unable to haul the **n** in because

NETS (NET)
Ps 141: 10 the wicked fall into their own **n**,
Mt 4: 20 At once they left their **n**
Lk 5: 4 and let down the **n** for a catch."

NEVER-FAILING*
Am 5: 24 river, righteousness like a **n** stream!

NEW
Ps 40: 3 He put a **n** song in my mouth,
98: 1 Sing to the LORD a **n** song, for he
Ecc 1: 9 there is nothing **n** under the sun.
Isa 42: 9 taken place, and **n** things I declare;
62: 2 you will be called by a **n** name
65: 17 I will create **n** heavens and a **n**
66: 22 "As the **n** heavens and the **n** earth
Jer 31: 31 I will make a **n** covenant
La 3: 23 They are **n** every morning;
Eze 11: 19 heart and put a **n** spirit in them;
18: 31 and get a **n** heart and a **n** spirit.
36: 26 will give you a **n** heart and put a **n**
Zep 3: 5 and every **n** day he does not fail,
Mt 9: 17 pour **n** wine into **n** wineskins,
Mk 16: 17 *they will speak in **n** tongues;*
Lk 5: 39 drinking old wine wants the **n**,
22: 20 "This cup is the **n** covenant in my
Jn 13: 34 "A **n** command I give you:
Ac 5: 20 tell the people all about this **n** life."
Ro 6: 4 the Father, we too may live a **n** life.
1Co 5: 7 may be a **n** unleavened batch—
11: 25 "This cup is the **n** covenant in my
2Co 3: 6 as ministers of a **n** covenant—
5: 17 in Christ, the **n** creation has come:
5: 17 The old has gone, the **n** is here!
Gal 6: 15 what counts is the **n** creation.
Eph 4: 23 be made **n** in the attitude of your
4: 24 and to put on the **n** self,
Col 3: 10 and have put on the **n** self, which is
Heb 8: 8 I will make a **n** covenant
9: 15 is the mediator of a **n** covenant,
10: 20 a **n** and living way opened for us
12: 24 Jesus the mediator of a **n** covenant,
1Pe 1: 3 great mercy he has given us **n** birth
2Pe 3: 13 looking forward to a **n** heaven and a **n** earth,
1Jn 2: 8 Yet I am writing you a **n** command;
Rev 2: 17 white stone with a **n** name written
3: 12 city of my God, the **n** Jerusalem,
3: 12 will also write on them my **n** name.
21: 1 I saw "a **n** heaven and a **n** earth,"

NEWBORN (BEAR)
1Pe 2: 2 Like **n** babies, crave pure spiritual

NEWS
2Ki 7: 9 This is a day of good **n** and we are
Ps 112: 7 They will have no fear of bad **n**;
Pr 15: 30 good **n** gives health to the bones.
25: 25 to a weary soul is good **n**
Isa 40: 9 You who bring good **n** to Zion,
52: 7 the feet of those who bring good **n**,
61: 1 me to proclaim good **n** to the poor.
Na 1: 15 the feet of one who brings good **n**,
Mt 4: 23 proclaiming the good **n**
9: 35 proclaiming the good **n**
11: 5 and the good **n** is proclaimed
Mk 1: 15 Repent and believe the good **n**!"
Lk 1: 19 to you and to tell you this good **n**.
2: 10 I bring you good **n** that will cause
3: 18 proclaimed the good **n** to them.
4: 43 "I must proclaim the good **n**
8: 1 proclaiming the good **n**
16: 16 the good **n** of the kingdom of God
Ac 5: 42 proclaiming the good **n** that Jesus
10: 36 announcing the good **n** of peace
17: 18 Paul was preaching the good **n**
Ro 10: 15 feet of those who bring good **n**!"

NICODEMUS*
Pharisee who visited Jesus at night (Jn 3). Argued fair treatment of Jesus (Jn 7:50–52). With Joseph, prepared Jesus for burial (Jn 19:38–42).

NIGHT (NIGHTS)
Ge 1: 5 and the darkness he called "**n**."
1: 16 the lesser light to govern the **n**.
Ex 13: 21 by **n** in a pillar of fire to give
14: 24 of the **n** the LORD looked down
Dt 28: 66 filled with dread both **n** and day,
Jos 1: 8 meditate on it day and **n**, so that
Job 35: 10 Maker, who gives songs in the **n**,
Ps 1: 2 meditates on his law day and **n**.
19: 2 **n** after **n** they reveal knowledge.
42: 8 his love, at **n** his song is with me—
63: 6 you through the watches of the **n**.
77: 6 I remembered my songs in the **n**.
90: 4 gone by, or like a watch in the **n**.
91: 5 You will not fear the terror of **n**,
119:148 open through the watches of the **n**,
121: 6 by day, nor the moon by **n**.
136: 9 moon and stars to govern the **n**;
Pr 31: 15 She gets up while it is still **n**;
31: 18 and her lamp does not go out at **n**.
Isa 21: 11 "Watchman, what is left of the **n**?
58: 10 and your **n** will become like
Jer 33: 20 day and my covenant with the **n**,
Zec 14: 7 no distinction between day and **n**.
Lk 2: 8 watch over their flocks at **n**.
6: 12 and spent the **n** praying to God.
Jn 3: 2 He came to Jesus at **n** and said,
9: 4 **N** is coming, when no one can
1Th 5: 2 Lord will come like a thief in the **n**.
5: 5 We do not belong to the **n**
Rev 21: 25 shut, for there will be no **n** there.

NIGHTS (NIGHT)
Jnh 1: 17 of the fish three days and three **n**.

Mt 4: 2 After fasting forty days and forty **n**,
12: 40 three **n** in the belly of a huge fish,
12: 40 three **n** in the heart of the earth.
2Co 6: 5 hard work, sleepless **n** and hunger;

NIMROD
Ge 10: 9 "Like **N**, a mighty hunter before

NINEVEH
Jnh 1: 2 "Go to the great city of **N**
Na 1: 1 A prophecy concerning **N**.
Mt 12: 41 The men of **N** will stand

NOAH
Righteous man (Eze 14:14, 20) called to build ark (Ge 6–8; Heb 11:7; 1Pe 3:20; 2Pe 2:5). God's covenant with (Ge 9:1–17). Drunkenness of (Ge 9:18–23). Blessed sons, cursed Canaan (Ge 9:24–27).

NOBLE
Ru 3: 11 you are a woman of **n** character.
Ps 16: 3 "They are the **n** ones in whom is
45: 1 by a **n** theme as I recite my verses
Pr 12: 4 **n** character is her husband's crown,
31: 10 wife of **n** character who can find?
31: 29 "Many women do **n** things, but
Isa 32: 8 But the **n** make **n** plans, and by **n**
Lk 8: 15 good soil stands for those with a **n**
Php 4: 8 whatever is **n**, whatever is right,

NOSTRILS
Ge 2: 7 into his **n** the breath of life,
Ex 15: 8 blast of your **n** the waters piled up.
Ps 18: 15 at the blast of breath from your **n**.

NOTE
Ac 4: 13 they took **n** that these men had

NOTHING
2Sa 24: 24 burnt offerings that cost me **n**."
Ne 9: 21 they lacked **n**, their clothes did not
Ps 73: 25 earth has **n** I desire besides you.
Jer 32: 17 **N** is too hard for you.
Jn 15: 5 apart from me you can do **n**.
Ro 14: 14 Jesus, that **n** is unclean in itself.

NOURISH
Pr 10: 21 The lips of the righteous **n** many,

NULLIFY
Mt 15: 6 Thus you **n** the word of God
Ro 3: 31 we, then, **n** the law by this faith?

OATH
Ex 33: 1 go up to the land I promised on **o**
Nu 30: 2 takes an **o** to obligate himself
Dt 6: 18 land the LORD promised on **o**
7: 8 and kept the **o** he swore to your
29: 12 you this day and sealing with an **o**,
Ps 95: 11 So I declared on **o** in my anger,
119:106 I have taken an **o** and confirmed it,
132: 11 The LORD swore an **o** to David, a sure **o** he will not revoke:
Ecc 8: 2 because you took an **o** before God.
Mt 5: 33 'Do not break your **o**, but fulfill
Heb 7: 20 became priests without any **o**,

OBADIAH
1. Believer who sheltered 100 prophets from Jezebel (1Ki 18:1–16).
2. Prophet against Edom (Ob 1).

OBEDIENCE (OBEY)
Ge 49: 10 the **o** of the nations shall be his.
Dt 10: 12 to walk in **o** to him, to love him,
26: 17 and that you will walk in **o** to him,
30: 16 to walk in **o** to him, and to keep his
Jos 22: 5 to walk in **o** to him, to keep his
1Ch 21: 19 So David went up in **o** to the word
2Ch 31: 21 of God's temple and in **o** to the law
Lk 23: 56 rested on the Sabbath in **o**
Ac 21: 24 you yourself are living in **o**
Ro 1: 5 all the Gentiles to the **o** that comes
5: 19 through the **o** of the one man
6: 16 to death, or to **o**, which leads
16: 19 Everyone has heard about your **o**,
16: 26 might come to the **o** that comes
2Co 9: 13 God for the **o** that accompanies
10: 6 once your **o** is complete.
Phm : 21 Confident of your **o**, I write to you,
Heb 5: 8 he learned **o** from what he suffered
2Jn : 6 that we walk in **o** to his commands.

OBEDIENT* (OBEY)
Dt 30: 17 heart turns away and you are not **o**,
Jdg 2: 17 been **o** to the LORD's commands.
Isa 1: 19 If you are willing and **o**, you will
Lk 2: 51 with them and was **o** to them.
Ac 6: 7 of priests became **o** to the faith.
Ro 6: 16 yourselves to someone as **o** slaves,
2Co 2: 9 the test and be **o** in everything.
7: 15 he remembers that you were all **o**,
10: 5 thought to make it **o** to Christ.
Php 2: 8 himself by becoming **o** to death—
Titus 3: 1 to be **o**, to be ready to do whatever
1Pe 1: 2 be **o** to Jesus Christ and sprinkled
1: 14 As **o** children, do not conform

OBEY (OBEDIENCE OBEDIENT OBEYED OBEYING OBEYS)
Ex 12: 24 "**O** these instructions as a lasting
19: 5 Now if you **o** me fully and keep my
24: 7 the LORD has said; we will **o**."
Lev 18: 4 You must **o** my laws and be careful
25: 18 and be careful to **o** my laws,
Nu 15: 40 remember to **o** all my commands
Dt 5: 27 We will listen and **o**."
6: 3 be careful to **o** so that it may go
6: 24 commanded us to **o** all these
11: 13 faithfully **o** the commands I am
12: 28 **o** all these regulations I am giving
13: 4 Keep his commands and **o** him;
21: 18 son who does not **o** his father
28: 1 If you fully **o** the LORD your God
28: 15 you do not **o** the LORD your God
30: 2 God and **o** him with all your heart
30: 10 if you **o** the LORD your God
30: 14 and in your heart so you may **o** it.
32: 46 to **o** carefully all the words
Jos 1: 7 **o** all the law my servant Moses
24: 24 the LORD our God and **o** him."
1Sa 15: 22 To **o** is better than sacrifice,
1Ki 8: 61 his decrees and **o** his commands,
2Ki 17: 13 I commanded your ancestors to **o**
2Ch 34: 31 and to **o** the words of the covenant
Ps 103: 18 and remember to **o** his precepts.
103: 20 do his bidding, who **o** his word.
119: 17 I live, that I may **o** your word.
119: 34 your law and **o** it with all my heart.
119: 57 I have promised to **o** your words.
119: 67 went astray, but now I **o** your word.
119:100 the elders, for I **o** your precepts.
119:129 therefore I **o** them.
119:167 I **o** your statutes, for I love them
Pr 5: 13 I would not **o** my teachers or turn
Jer 7: 23 **O** me, and I will be your God
11: 4 I said, '**O** me and do everything I
11: 7 again and again, saying, "**O** me."
42: 6 we will **o** the LORD our God,
Mt 8: 27 the winds and the waves **o** him!"
28: 20 to **o** everything I have commanded
Lk 11: 28 hear the word of God and **o** it."
Jn 14: 23 who loves me will **o** my teaching.
14: 24 not love me will not **o** my teaching.
Ac 5: 29 must **o** God rather than human
5: 32 has given to those who **o** him."
Ro 2: 13 it is those who **o** the law who will
6: 12 body so that you **o** its evil desires.
6: 16 you are slaves of the one you **o**—
6: 17 have come to **o** from your heart
15: 18 in leading the Gentiles to **o** God
Gal 5: 3 he is obligated to **o** the whole law.
Eph 6: 1 **o** your parents in the Lord, for this
6: 5 **o** your earthly masters with respect
6: 5 just as you would **o** Christ.
Col 3: 20 **o** your parents in everything,
3: 22 Slaves, **o** your earthly masters
2Th 3: 14 who does not **o** our instruction
1Ti 3: 4 and see that his children **o** him,
Heb 5: 9 eternal salvation for all who **o** him
1Pe 4: 17 for those who do not **o** the gospel

OBEYED (OBEY)
Ge 22: 18 blessed, because you have **o** me."
Jos 1: 17 Just as we fully **o** Moses, so we will
Ps 119: 4 precepts that are to be fully **o**.
Da 9: 10 we have not **o** the LORD our God
Jnh 3: 3 Jonah **o** the word of the LORD
Mic 5: 15 on the nations that have not **o** me."
Jn 15: 20 If they **o** my teaching, they will
17: 6 to me and they have **o** your word.
Ac 7: 53 through angels but have not **o** it."
Php 2: 12 friends, as you have always **o**—
Heb 11: 8 as his inheritance, **o** and went,
1Pe 3: 6 who **o** Abraham and called him

OBEYING (OBEY)
1Sa 15: 22 as much as in **o** the LORD?
Ps 119: 5 were steadfast in **o** your decrees!
Gal 5: 7 you to keep you from **o** the truth?
1Pe 1: 22 purified yourselves by **o** the truth

OBEYS (OBEY)
Lev 18: 5 for the person who **o** them will live
Eze 20: 11 the person who **o** them will live.
Jn 8: 51 whoever **o** my word will never see
Ro 2: 27 yet **o** the law will condemn you
1Jn 2: 5 But if anyone **o** his word,

OBLIGATED (OBLIGATION)
Ro 1: 14 I am **o** both to Greeks
Gal 5: 3 that he is **o** to obey the whole law.

OBLIGATION (OBLIGATED)
Ro 8: 12 brothers and sisters, we have an **o**

OBSCENITY*
Eph 5: 4 Nor should there be **o**, foolish talk

OBSCURES*
Job 38: 2 "Who is this that **o** my plans
42: 3 **o** my plans without knowledge?'

OBSERVE
Ex 31: 13 'You must **o** my Sabbaths.
Lev 25: 2 the land itself must **o** a sabbath
Dt 4: 6 **O** them carefully, for this will show
5: 12 "**O** the Sabbath day by keeping it
8: 6 **O** the commands of the LORD
11: 22 you carefully **o** all these commands
26: 16 carefully **o** them with all your heart
Ps 37: 37 the blameless, **o** the upright;

OBSOLETE*
Heb 8: 13 "new," he has made the first one **o**;

OBSTACLE* (OBSTACLES)
Ro 14: 13 block or **o** in the way of a brother

OBSTACLES (OBSTACLE)
Ro 16: 17 put **o** in your way that are contrary

OBSTINATE
Isa 65: 2 held out my hands to an **o** people,
Ro 10: 21 to a disobedient and **o** people."

OBTAIN (OBTAINED OBTAINING)
Pr 12: 2 Good people **o** favor
Ro 11: 7 sought so earnestly they did not **o**.
2Ti 2: 10 they too may **o** the salvation that is

OBTAINED (OBTAIN)
Ro 9: 30 not pursue righteousness, have **o** it,
Php 3: 12 Not that I have already **o** all this,

OBTAINING* (OBTAIN)
Heb 9: 12 blood, thus **o** eternal redemption.

OBVIOUS*
Mt 6: 18 so that it will not be **o** to others
Gal 5: 19 The acts of the flesh are **o**:
1Ti 5: 24 The sins of some are **o**,
5: 25 good deeds are **o**, and even those
5: 25 are not **o** cannot remain hidden

OCCASIONS
Eph 6: 18 the Spirit on all **o** with all kinds

OFFENSE (OFFENSES OFFENSIVE)
Pr 17: 9 would foster love covers over an **o**,
19: 11 it is to one's glory to overlook an **o**.
Gal 5: 11 In that case the **o** of the cross has

OFFENSES (OFFENSE)
Ecc 10: 4 calmness can lay great **o** to rest.
Isa 44: 22 swept away your **o** like a cloud,
59: 12 For our **o** are many in your sight,
Eze 18: 30 Turn away from all your **o**;
33: 10 "Our **o** and sins weigh us down,

OFFENSIVE (OFFENSE)
Ps 139: 24 See if there is any **o** way in me,

OFFER (OFFERED OFFERING OFFERINGS OFFERS)
Ps 4: 5 **O** the sacrifices of the righteous
Ro 6: 13 not **o** any part of yourself to sin
6: 13 rather **o** yourselves to God as those
12: 1 **o** your bodies as a living sacrifice,
Heb 9: 25 he enter heaven to **o** himself again
13: 15 let us continually **o** to God

OFFERED (OFFER)
Isa 50: 6 I **o** my back to those who beat me,
1Co 9: 13 share in what is **o** on the altar?
10: 20 of pagans are **o** to demons,
Heb 7: 27 sins once for all when he **o** himself.
9: 14 Spirit **o** himself unblemished
11: 17 tested him, **o** Isaac as a sacrifice.
Jas 5: 15 the prayer **o** in faith will make

OFFERING (OFFER)
Ge 4: 3 of the soil as an **o** to the LORD.
22: 2 Sacrifice him there as a burnt **o**
22: 8 provide the lamb for the burnt **o**,
Ex 29: 24 before the LORD as a wave **o**.
29: 40 of a hin of wine as a drink **o**.

Lev 1: 3 "'If the **o** is a burnt **o**
2: 4 you bring a grain **o** baked
3: 1 "'If your **o** is a fellowship **o**,
4: 3 young bull without defect as a sin **o**
5: 15 the sanctuary shekel. It is a guilt **o**.
7: 37 are the regulations for the burnt **o**,
the grain **o**, the sin **o**,
9: 24 consumed the burnt **o** and the fat
22: 18 to fulfill a vow or as a freewill **o**,
22: 21 a special vow or as a freewill **o**,
1Sa 13: 9 And Saul offered up the burnt **o**.
1Ch 21: 26 heaven on the altar of burnt **o**.
2Ch 7: 1 and consumed the burnt **o**
Ps 40: 6 Sacrifice and **o** you did not desire
116: 17 I will sacrifice a thank **o** to you
Isa 53: 10 the LORD makes his life an **o**
Mt 5: 23 if you are **o** your gift at the altar
Ro 8: 3 likeness of sinful flesh to be a sin **o**.
Eph 5: 2 himself up for us as a fragrant **o**
Php 2: 17 out like a drink **o** on the sacrifice
4: 18 are a fragrant **o**, an acceptable
2Ti 4: 6 being poured out like a drink **o**,
Heb 10: 5 "Sacrifice and **o** you did not desire,
11: 4 God a better **o** than Cain did.
1Pe 2: 5 **o** spiritual sacrifices acceptable

OFFERINGS (OFFER)
1Sa 15: 22 the LORD delight in burnt **o**
2Ch 35: 7 lambs and goats for the Passover **o**,
Isa 1: 13 Stop bringing meaningless **o**!
Hos 6: 6 of God rather than burnt **o**.
Mal 3: 8 we robbing you?' "In tithes and **o**.
Mk 12: 33 is more important than all burnt **o**
Heb 10: 8 "Sacrifices and **o**, burnt **o** and sin **o**

OFFERS (OFFER)
Heb 10: 11 and again he **o** the same sacrifices,

OFFICER (OFFICIALS)
2Ti 2: 4 tries to please his commanding **o**.

OFFICIALS (OFFICER)
Ex 5: 21 his **o** and have put a sword in their
Pr 17: 26 surely to flog honest **o** is not right.
29: 12 to lies, all his **o** become wicked.

OFFSPRING
Ge 3: 15 and between your **o** and hers;
12: 7 "To your **o** I will give this land."
13: 16 I will make your **o** like the dust
26: 4 through your **o** all nations on earth
28: 14 be blessed through you and your **o**.
Ex 13: 2 The first **o** of every womb among
Ru 4: 12 Through the **o** the LORD gives
Isa 44: 3 I will pour out my Spirit on your **o**,
53: 10 he will see his **o** and prolong his
Ac 3: 25 'Through your **o** all peoples
17: 28 own poets have said, 'We are his **o**.'
17: 29 "Therefore since we are God's **o**,
Ro 4: 18 said to him, "So shall your **o** be."
9: 8 who are regarded as Abraham's **o**.

OG
Nu 21: 33 and **O** king of Bashan and his
Ps 136: 20 and **O** king of Bashan—

OIL
Ex 29: 7 Take the anointing **o** and anoint
30: 25 It will be the sacred anointing **o**.
Dt 14: 23 grain, new wine and olive **o**,
1Sa 10: 1 Samuel took a flask of olive **o**
16: 13 So Samuel took the horn of **o**
1Ki 17: 16 up and the jug of **o** did not run dry,
2Ki 4: 6 Then the **o** stopped flowing.
Ps 23: 5 You anoint my head with **o**;
45: 7 by anointing you with the **o** of joy.
104: 15 hearts, **o** to make their faces shine,
133: 2 It is like precious **o** poured
Pr 21: 17 wine and olive **o** will never be rich.
Isa 1: 6 bandaged or soothed with olive **o**.
61: 3 the **o** of joy instead of mourning,
Mt 25: 3 but did not take any **o** with them.
Heb 1: 9 by anointing you with the **o** of joy."

OLIVE (OLIVES)
Ge 8: 11 beak was a freshly plucked **o** leaf!
Jdg 9: 8 They said to the **o** tree, 'Be our
Jer 11: 16 LORD called you a thriving **o** tree
Zec 4: 3 Also there are two **o** trees by it,
Ro 11: 17 though a wild **o** shoot, have been
11: 24 grafted into a cultivated **o** tree,
11: 24 be grafted into their own **o** tree!
Rev 11: 4 They are "the two **o** trees"

OLIVES (OLIVE)
Zec 14: 4 the Mount of **O** will be split in two
Mt 24: 3 was sitting on the Mount of **O**,
Jas 3: 12 can a fig tree bear **o**, or a grapevine

OMEGA*
Rev 1: 8 "I am the Alpha and the **O**,"
21: 6 I am the Alpha and the **O**,
22: 13 I am the Alpha and the **O**, the First

OMENS
Lev 19: 26 not practice divination or seek **o**.

OMIT*
Jer 26: 2 I command you; do not **o** a word.

OMRI
King of Israel (1Ki 16:21–26).

ONESIMUS*
Col 4: 9 He is coming with **O**, our faithful
Phm : 10 that I appeal to you for my son **O**,

ONESIPHORUS*
2Ti 1: 16 show mercy to the household of **O**,
4: 19 Aquila and the household of **O**.

ONIONS*
Nu 11: 5 melons, leeks, **o** and garlic.

ONYX
Ex 28: 9 "Take two **o** stones and engrave
28: 20 row shall be topaz, **o** and jasper.

OPEN (OPENED)
Ps 78: 2 I will **o** my mouth with a parable;

OPENED (OPEN)
Ps 40: 6 but my ears you have **o**—

OPENHANDED* (HAND OPEN)
Dt 15: 8 be **o** and freely lend them whatever
15: 11 be **o** toward your fellow Israelites

OPINIONS*
1Ki 18: 21 will you waver between two **o**?
Pr 18: 2 but delight in airing their own **o**.

OPPONENTS (OPPOSE)
Pr 18: 18 disputes and keeps strong **o** apart.
2Ti 2: 25 **O** must be gently instructed,

OPPORTUNE (OPPORTUNITY)
Lk 4: 13 he left him until an **o** time.

OPPORTUNITY* (OPPORTUNE)
Jdg 9: 33 seize the **o** to attack them."
1Sa 18: 21 "Now you have a second **o**
Jer 46: 17 a loud noise; he has missed his **o**.'
Mt 26: 16 watched for an **o** to hand him over.
Mk 14: 11 watched for an **o** to hand him over.
Lk 22: 6 for an **o** to hand Jesus over
Ac 25: 16 have had an **o** to defend themselves
27: 13 began to blow, they saw their **o**;
Ro 7: 8 sin, seizing the **o** afforded
7: 11 sin, seizing the **o** afforded
1Co 16: 12 but he will go when he has the **o**.
2Co 5: 12 are giving you an **o** to take pride
11: 12 under those who want an **o** to be
Gal 6: 10 as we have **o**, let us do good to all
Eph 5: 16 making the most of every **o**,
Php 4: 10 but you had no **o** to show it.
Col 4: 5 make the most of every **o**.
1Ti 5: 14 to give the enemy no **o** for slander.
Heb 11: 15 they would have had **o** to return.

OPPOSE (OPPONENTS OPPOSED OPPOSES OPPOSING OPPOSITION)
Ex 23: 22 and will **o** those who **o** you.
1Sa 2: 10 those who **o** the LORD will be
Job 23: 13 stands alone, and who can **o** him?
Titus 1: 9 doctrine and refute those who **o** it.
2: 8 those who **o** you may be ashamed

OPPOSED (OPPOSE)
Gal 2: 11 to Antioch, I **o** him to his face,
3: 21 **o** to the promises of God?

OPPOSES (OPPOSE)
Jas 4: 6 "God **o** the proud but shows favor
1Pe 5: 5 "God **o** the proud but shows favor

OPPOSING (OPPOSE)
1Ti 6: 20 the **o** ideas of what is falsely called

OPPOSITION (OPPOSE)
Heb 12: 3 Consider him who endured such **o**

OPPRESS (OPPRESSED OPPRESSES OPPRESSION OPPRESSOR)
Ex 1: 11 slave masters over them to **o** them
22: 21 "Do not mistreat or **o** a foreigner,
Isa 3: 5 People will **o** each other—
Eze 22: 29 they **o** the poor and needy
Da 7: 25 Most High and **o** his holy people
Am 5: 12 are those who **o** the innocent
Zec 7: 10 Do not **o** the widow
Mal 3: 5 wages, who **o** the widows

OPPRESSED (OPPRESS)
Jdg 2: 18 their groaning under those who **o**

Ps 9: 9 The LORD is a refuge for the **o**,
82: 3 the cause of the poor and the **o**.
146: 7 He upholds the cause of the **o**
Pr 16: 19 along with the **o** than to share
31: 5 and deprive all the **o** of their rights.
Isa 1: 17 Defend the **o**. Take up the cause
53: 7 He was **o** and afflicted, yet he did
58: 10 and satisfy the needs of the **o**,
Zec 10: 2 the people wander like sheep **o**
Lk 4: 18 sight for the blind, to set the **o** free,

OPPRESSES* (OPPRESS)
Pr 14: 31 Whoever **o** the poor shows
22: 16 **o** the poor to increase his wealth
28: 3 A ruler who **o** the poor is like
Eze 18: 12 He **o** the poor and needy.

OPPRESSION (OPPRESS)
Ps 72: 14 He will rescue them from **o**
119:134 Redeem me from human **o**, that I
Isa 53: 8 By **o** and judgment he was taken
58: 9 "If you do away with the yoke of **o**,

OPPRESSOR (OPPRESS)
Ps 72: 4 of the needy; may he crush the **o**.
Isa 51: 13 For where is the wrath of the **o**?

ORDAINED
Ps 111: 9 he **o** his covenant forever—
139: 16 all the days **o** for me were written
Eze 28: 14 a guardian cherub, for so I **o** you.
Hab 1: 12 my Rock, have **o** them to punish.

ORDEAL*
1Pe 4: 12 at the fiery **o** that has come on you

ORDER (ORDERLY ORDERS)
Nu 9: 23 They obeyed the LORD's **o**,
Ps 110: 4 forever, in the **o** of Melchizedek."
Heb 5: 10 high priest in the **o** of Melchizedek.
9: 10 until the time of the new **o**.
Rev 21: 4 for the old **o** of things has passed

ORDERLY* (ORDER)
Lk 1: 3 I too decided to write an **o** account
1Co 14: 40 be done in a fitting and **o** way.

ORDERS (ORDER)
Mk 1: 27 He even gives **o** to impure spirits
3: 12 But he gave them strict **o** not to tell
9: 9 Jesus gave them **o** not to tell

ORDINARY
Ac 4: 13 that they were unschooled, **o** men,

ORGIES*
Gal 5: 21 drunkenness, **o**, and the like.
1Pe 4: 3 lust, drunkenness, **o**,

ORIGIN (ORIGINATE ORIGINS)
2Pe 1: 21 For prophecy never had its **o**

ORIGINATE* (ORIGIN)
1Co 14: 36 did the word of God **o** with you?

ORIGINS* (ORIGIN)
Mic 5: 2 Israel, whose **o** are from of old,

ORNAMENT*
Pr 3: 22 for you, an **o** to grace your neck.
25: 12 an **o** of fine gold is the rebuke

ORNATE
Ge 37: 3 and he made an **o** robe for him.

ORPHANS*
Jn 14: 18 I will not leave you as **o**;
Jas 1: 27 to look after **o** and widows in

OTHERWISE
1Ti 6: 3 If anyone teaches **o** and does not

OTHNIEL
Nephew of Caleb (Jos 15:15–19; Jdg 1:12–15). Judge who freed Israel from Aram (Jdg 3:7–11).

OUTCOME
Heb 13: 7 Consider the **o** of their way of life
1Pe 4: 17 what will the **o** be for those who do

OUTNUMBER
Ps 139: 18 they would **o** the grains of sand—

OUTSIDERS*
Col 4: 5 wise in the way you act toward **o**;
1Th 4: 12 daily life may win the respect of **o**
1Ti 3: 7 also have a good reputation with **o**,

OUTSTANDING
SS 5: 10 and ruddy, **o** among ten thousand.
Ro 13: 8 Let no debt remain **o**,

OUTSTRETCHED
Ex 6: 6 I will redeem you with an **o** arm
Dt 4: 34 by a mighty hand and an **o** arm,
5: 15 with a mighty hand and an **o** arm.

1Ki 8: 42 mighty hand and your **o** arm—
Ps 136: 12 with a mighty hand and **o** arm;
Jer 27: 5 power and **o** arm I made the earth
32: 17 by your great power and **o** arm.
Eze 20: 33 with a mighty hand and an **o** arm

OUTWEIGHS (WEIGH)
2Co 4: 17 an eternal glory that far **o** them all.

OUTWIT*
2Co 2: 11 in order that Satan might not **o** us.

OVERAWED* (AWE)
Ps 49: 16 not be **o** when others grow rich,

OVERBEARING*
Titus 1: 7 not **o**, not quick-tempered, not

OVERCOME (OVERCOMES)
Mt 16: 18 and the gates of Hades will not **o** it.
Mk 9: 24 help me **o** my unbelief!"
Lk 10: 19 to **o** all the power of the enemy;
Jn 1: 5 and the darkness has not **o** it.
16: 33 But take heart! I have **o** the world."
Ro 12: 21 Do not be **o** by evil, but **o** evil
2Pe 2: 20 are again entangled in it and are **o**,
1Jn 2: 13 because you have **o** the evil one.
4: 4 are from God and have **o** them,
5: 4 is the victory that has **o** the world,

OVERCOMES* (OVERCOME)
1Jn 5: 4 everyone born of God **o** the world.
5: 5 Who is it that **o** the world?

OVERFLOW (OVERFLOWING OVERFLOWS)
Ps 65: 11 and your carts **o** with abundance.
119:171 May my lips **o** with praise, for you
La 1: 16 I weep and my eyes **o** with tears.
Ro 5: 15 man, Jesus Christ, **o** to the many!
15: 13 so that you may **o** with hope
2Co 4: 15 may cause thanksgiving to **o**
1Th 3: 12 love increase and **o** for each other

OVERFLOWING (OVERFLOW)
Pr 3: 10 then your barns will be filled to **o**,
8: 24 were no springs **o** with water;
2Co 8: 2 trial, their **o** joy and their extreme
9: 12 **o** in many expressions of thanks
Col 2: 7 taught, and **o** with thankfulness.

OVERFLOWS* (OVERFLOW)
Ps 23: 5 anoint my head with oil; my cup **o**.

OVERJOYED* (JOY)
Da 6: 23 The king was **o** and gave orders
Mt 2: 10 they saw the star, they were **o**.
Jn 20: 20 The disciples were **o** when they
Ac 12: 14 she was so **o** she ran back without
1Pe 4: 13 that you may be **o** when his glory

OVERLOOK
Pr 19: 11 it is to one's glory to **o** an offense.

OVERSEER (OVERSEERS)
Pr 6: 7 has no commander, no **o** or ruler,
1Ti 3: 1 to be an **o** desires a noble task.
3: 2 Now the **o** is to be above reproach,
Titus 1: 7 Since an **o** manages God's
1Pe 2: 25 the Shepherd and **O** of your souls.

OVERSEERS (OVERSEER)
Ac 20: 28 the Holy Spirit has made you **o**.
Php 1: 1 together with the **o** and deacons:

OVERSHADOW* (OVERSHADOWING)
1Ch 28: 18 **o** the ark of the covenant of the
Lk 1: 35 power of the Most High will **o** you.

OVERSHADOWING (OVERSHADOW)
Ex 25: 20 upward, **o** the cover with them.
Heb 9: 5 the Glory, **o** the atonement cover.

OVERTAKES
Pr 12: 21 No harm **o** the righteous,

OVERTHROW (OVERTHROWS)
2Th 2: 8 whom the Lord Jesus will **o**

OVERTHROWS (OVERTHROW)
Pr 13: 6 but wickedness **o** the sinner.
Isa 44: 25 who **o** the learning of the wise

OVERWHELMED (OVERWHELMING)
2Sa 22: 5 the torrents of destruction **o** me.
1Ki 10: 5 temple of the LORD, she was **o**.
Ps 38: 4 My guilt has **o** me like a burden
65: 3 When we were **o** by sins,
Mt 26: 38 "My soul is **o** with sorrow
Mk 7: 37 People were **o** with amazement.
9: 15 they were **o** with wonder and ran
2Co 2: 7 so that he will not be **o** by excessive

OVERWHELMING (OVERWHELMED)
Pr 27: 4 Anger is cruel and fury **o**, but who
Isa 10: 22 has been decreed, **o** and righteous.
28: 15 When an **o** scourge sweeps by,

OWE
Ro 13: 7 Give to everyone what you **o** them: If you **o** taxes, pay taxes;
Phm : 19 that you **o** me your very self.

OWNER'S (OWNERSHIP)
Isa 1: 3 the donkey its **o** manger, but Israel

OWNERSHIP* (OWNER'S)
2Co 1: 22 set his seal of **o** on us, and put his

OX (OXEN)
Dt 25: 4 Do not muzzle an **o** while it is
Isa 11: 7 the lion will eat straw like the **o**.
Eze 1: 10 and on the left the face of an **o**;
Lk 13: 15 of you on the Sabbath untie your **o**
1Co 9: 9 "Do not muzzle an **o** while it is
1Ti 5: 18 "Do not muzzle an **o** while it is
Rev 4: 7 the second was like an **o**, the third

OXEN (OX)
1Ki 19: 20 then left his **o** and ran after Elijah.
Lk 14: 19 'I have just bought five yoke of **o**,

PAGAN (PAGANS)
Isa 2: 6 Philistines and embrace **p** customs.
Mt 18: 17 treat them as you would a **p** or a
Lk 12: 30 For the **p** world runs after all such

PAGANS* (PAGAN)
Mt 5: 47 Do not even **p** do that?
6: 7 do not keep on babbling like **p**,
6: 32 For the **p** run after all these things,
1Co 5: 1 a kind that even **p** do not tolerate:
10: 20 but the sacrifices of **p** are offered
12: 2 You know that when you were **p**,
1Th 4: 5 not in passionate lust like the **p**,
1Pe 2: 12 such good lives among the **p** that,
4: 3 past doing what **p** choose to do—
3Jn : 7 out, receiving no help from the **p**.

PAID (PAY)
Isa 40: 2 that her sin has been **p** for, that she
Zec 11: 12 So they **p** me thirty pieces of silver.

PAIN (PAINFUL PAINS)
Job 6: 10 my joy in unrelenting **p**—that I
33: 19 on a bed of **p** with constant distress
Isa 53: 4 Surely he took up our **p** and bore
Jer 4: 19 I writhe in **p**. Oh, the agony of my
15: 18 Why is my **p** unending and my
Mt 4: 24 those suffering severe **p**,
Jn 16: 21 to a child has **p** because her time
1Pe 2: 19 up under the **p** of unjust suffering
Rev 21: 4 death' or mourning or crying or **p**,

PAINFUL (PAIN)
Ge 3: 16 with **p** labor you will give birth
Ge 3: 17 through **p** toil you will eat food
5: 29 **p** toil of our hands caused
Job 6: 25 How **p** are honest words!
Eze 28: 24 neighbors who are **p** briers
2Co 2: 1 I would not make another **p** visit
Heb 12: 11 seems pleasant at the time, but **p**.

PAINS (PAIN)
Ge 3: 16 "I will make your **p** in childbearing
Mt 24: 8 these are the beginning of birth **p**.
Ro 8: 22 as in the **p** of childbirth right
Gal 4: 19 in the **p** of childbirth until Christ is
1Th 5: 3 as labor **p** on a pregnant woman,

PAIRS
Ge 7: 8 **P** of clean and unclean animals,

PALACE (PALACES)
Jer 22: 6 LORD says about the **p** of the king
22: 13 "Woe to him who builds his **p**

PALACES (PALACE)
Mt 11: 8 wear fine clothes are in kings' **p**.
Lk 7: 25 and indulge in luxury are in **p**.

PALE
Isa 29: 22 no longer will their faces grow **p**.
Jer 30: 6 labor, every face turned deathly **p**?
Da 10: 8 my face turned deathly **p** and I was
Rev 6: 8 and there before me was a **p** horse!

PALM (PALMS)
Jn 12: 13 They took **p** branches and went
Rev 7: 9 were holding **p** branches in their

PALMS (PALM)
Isa 49: 16 engraved you on the **p** of my hands

PAMPERED*
Pr 29: 21 A servant **p** from youth will turn

PANIC
Dt 20: 3 do not **p** or be terrified by them.
1Sa 14: 15 It was a **p** sent by God.
Isa 28: 16 on it will never be stricken with **p**.
Eze 7: 7 There is **p**, not joy,
Zec 14: 13 by the LORD with great **p**.

PANTS*
Ps 42: 1 As the deer **p** for streams of water, so my soul **p** for you,

PARABLE (PARABLES)
Ps 78: 2 I will open my mouth with a **p**;

PARABLES (PARABLE)
See also JESUS: PARABLES
Mt 13: 35 "I will open my mouth in **p**, I will
Lk 8: 10 but to others I speak in **p**, so that,

PARADISE*
Lk 23: 43 today you will be with me in **p**."
2Co 12: 4 was caught up to **p** and heard
Rev 2: 7 of life, which is in the **p** of God.

PARALYZED
Mt 9: 2 men brought to him a **p** man,
Mk 2: 3 bringing to him a **p** man,
Ac 9: 33 was **p** and had been bedridden

PARCHED
Ps 143: 6 I thirst for you like a **p** land.

PARCHMENTS*
2Ti 4: 13 and my scrolls, especially the **p**.

PARDON (PARDONED PARDONS)
2Ch 30: 18 LORD, who is good, **p** everyone
Job 7: 21 Why do you not **p** my offenses
Isa 55: 7 and to our God, for he will freely **p**.

PARDONED* (PARDON)
Nu 14: 19 just as you have **p** them

PARDONS* (PARDON)
Mic 7: 18 like you, who **p** sin and forgives

PARENT (PARENTS PARENT'S)
Pr 17: 21 is no joy for the **p** of a godless fool.

PARENT'S* (PARENT)
Pr 15: 5 A fool spurns a **p** discipline,

PARENTS (PARENT)
Ex 20: 5 for the sin of the **p** to the third
Pr 17: 6 **p** are the pride of their children.
19: 14 and wealth are inherited from **p**,
Jer 31: 29 say, 'The **p** have eaten sour grapes,
Mal 4: 6 hearts of the **p** to their children,
Mt 10: 21 children will rebel against their **p**
Lk 1: 17 the hearts of the **p** to their children
18: 29 sisters or **p** or children for the sake
21: 16 You will be betrayed even by **p**,
Jn 9: 3 this man nor his **p** sinned,"
Ro 1: 30 of doing evil; they disobey their **p**;
2Co 12: 14 not have to save up for their **p**, but **p** for their children.
Eph 6: 1 Children, obey your **p** in the Lord,
Col 3: 20 Children, obey your **p** in
1Ti 5: 4 family and so repaying their **p**
2Ti 3: 2 disobedient to their **p**, ungrateful,

PART
1Co 13: 10 comes, what is in **p** disappears.

PARTIAL* (PARTIALITY)
Pr 18: 5 It is not good to be **p** to the wicked

PARTIALITY (PARTIAL)
Lev 19: 15 do not show **p** to the poor
Dt 1: 17 Do not show **p** in judging;
10: 17 who shows no **p** and accepts no
16: 19 Do not pervert justice or show **p**.
2Ch 19: 7 our God there is no injustice or **p**
Job 32: 21 I will show no **p**, nor will I flatter
34: 19 who shows no **p** to princes and
Pr 24: 23 To show **p** in judging is not good:
Mal 2: 9 but have shown **p** in matters
Lk 20: 21 that you do not show **p** but teach
1Ti 5: 21 keep these instructions without **p**,

PARTICIPANTS* (PARTICIPATE)
1Co 10: 20 not want you to be **p** with demons.

PARTICIPATE (PARTICIPANTS PARTICIPATION)
1Pe 4: 13 But rejoice inasmuch as you **p**
2Pe 1: 4 that through them you may **p**

PARTICIPATION (PARTICIPATE)
1Co 10: 16 bread that we break a **p** in the body
Php 3: 10 and **p** in his sufferings,

PARTNER (PARTNERS PARTNERSHIP)
Pr 2: 17 who has left the **p** of her youth
Mal 2: 14 though she is your **p**, the wife
1Pe 3: 7 them with respect as the weaker **p**

PARTNERS (PARTNER)
Eph 5: 7 Therefore do not be **p** with them.

PARTNERSHIP* (PARTNER)
Php 1: 5 because of your **p** in the gospel
Phm : 6 I pray that your **p** with us

PASS (PASSED PASSER-BY PASSING)
Ex 12: 13 I see the blood, I will **p** over you.
33: 19 "I will cause all my goodness to **p**
1Ki 9: 8 All who **p** by will be appalled
19: 11 for the LORD is about to **p** by."
Ps 90: 10 for they quickly **p**, and we fly away.
105: 19 till what he foretold came to **p**,
Isa 31: 5 it, he will '**p** over' it and will rescue
43: 2 When you **p** through the waters,
62: 10 **P** through, **p** through the gates!
Jer 22: 8 many nations will **p** by this city
La 1: 12 nothing to you, all you who **p** by?
Da 7: 14 dominion that will not **p** away,
Am 5: 17 for I will **p** through your midst,"
Mt 24: 34 certainly not **p** away until all
24: 35 Heaven and earth will **p** away,
24: 35 but my words will never **p** away.
Mk 13: 31 Heaven and earth will **p** away,
Lk 21: 33 but my words will never **p** away.
1Co 13: 8 there is knowledge, it will **p** away.
Jas 1: 10 since they will **p** away like a wild
1Jn 2: 17 The world and its desires **p** away,

PASSED (PASS)
Ge 15: 17 appeared and **p** between the pieces.
Ex 33: 22 with my hand until I have **p** by.
2Ch 21: 20 He **p** away, to no one's regret,
Ps 57: 1 your wings until the disaster has **p**.
Lk 10: 32 saw him, **p** by on the other side.
1Co 15: 3 For what I received I **p** on to you as
Heb 11: 29 faith the people **p** through the Red

PASSER-BY* (PASS)
Pr 26: 10 is one who hires a fool or any **p**.

PASSING (PASS)
1Co 7: 31 world in its present form is **p** away.
2Co 3: 13 seeing the end of what was **p** away.
1Jn 2: 8 because the darkness is **p**

PASSION* (PASSIONATE PASSIONS)
Ps 11: 5 love violence, he hates with a **p**.
Hos 7: 6 Their **p** smolders all night;
1Co 7: 9 to marry than to burn with **p**.

PASSIONATE* (PASSION)
1Th 4: 5 not in **p** lust like the pagans, who

PASSIONS* (PASSION)
Ro 7: 5 the sinful **p** aroused by the law
1Co 7: 36 and if his **p** are too strong
Gal 5: 24 have crucified the flesh with its **p**
Titus 2: 12 to ungodliness and worldly **p**,
3: 3 and enslaved by all kinds of **p**

PASSOVER
Ex 12: 11 Eat it in haste; it is the LORD's **P**.
Nu 9: 2 "Have the Israelites celebrate the **P**
Dt 16: 1 celebrate the **P** of the LORD your
Jos 5: 10 the Israelites celebrated the **P**.
2Ki 23: 21 "Celebrate the **P** to the LORD
Ezr 6: 19 month, the exiles celebrated the **P**.
Mk 14: 12 preparations for you to eat the **P**?"
Lk 22: 1 called the **P**, was approaching,
1Co 5: 7 For Christ, our **P** lamb, has been
Heb 11: 28 By faith he kept the **P**

PAST
Isa 43: 18 do not dwell on the **p**.
65: 16 For the **p** troubles will be forgotten
Ro 15: 4 was written in the **p** was written
16: 25 the mystery hidden for long ages **p**,
Eph 3: 9 for ages **p** was kept hidden in God,
Heb 1: 1 In the **p** God spoke to our

PASTORS*
Eph 4: 11 the evangelists, the **p** and teachers,

PASTURE (PASTURES)
Ps 37: 3 dwell in the land and enjoy safe **p**.
95: 7 God and we are the people of his **p**,
100: 3 are his people, the sheep of his **p**.
Jer 50: 7 their verdant **p**, the LORD,
Eze 34: 13 I will **p** them on the mountains
Jn 10: 9 come in and go out, and find **p**.

PASTURES (PASTURE)
Ps 23: 2 He makes me lie down in green **p**,

PATCH
Mt 9: 16 "No one sews a **p** of unshrunk

PATH (PATHS)
Job 16: 22 years will pass before I take the **p**
Ps 16: 11 make known to me the **p** of life;
27: 11 me in a straight **p** because of my
119: 9 person stay on the **p** of purity?
119: 32 I run in the **p** of your commands,
119:105 to my feet and a light for my **p**.
Pr 2: 9 and just and fair—every good **p**.
12: 28 along that **p** is immortality.
15: 10 awaits anyone who leaves the **p**;
15: 19 the **p** of the upright is a highway.
15: 24 The **p** of life leads upward
21: 16 strays from the **p** of prudence
Isa 26: 7 The **p** of the righteous is level;
Jer 31: 9 on a level **p** where they will not
Mt 13: 4 some fell along the **p**, and the birds
Lk 1: 79 guide our feet into the **p** of peace."
2Co 6: 3 no stumbling block in anyone's **p**,

PATHS (PATH)
Ps 23: 3 He guides me along the right **p**
25: 4 ways, LORD, teach me your **p**.
Pr 1: 19 Such are the **p** of all who go
2: 13 who have left the straight **p** to walk
3: 6 and he will make your **p** straight.
4: 11 and lead you along straight **p**.
4: 26 thought to the **p** for your feet
5: 21 and he examines all your **p**.
8: 20 along the **p** of justice,
22: 5 In the **p** of the wicked are snares
Isa 2: 3 so that we may walk in his **p**."
Jer 6: 16 ask for the ancient **p**, ask where
Mic 4: 2 so that we may walk in his **p**."
Mt 3: 3 Lord, make straight **p** for him.'"
Ac 2: 28 made known to me the **p** of life;
Ro 11: 33 and his **p** beyond tracing out!
Heb 12: 13 "Make level **p** for your feet,"

PATIENCE* (PATIENT)
Pr 19: 11 A person's wisdom yields **p**; it is
25: 15 Through **p** a ruler can be
Ecc 7: 8 and **p** is better than pride.
Isa 7: 13 not enough to try the **p** of humans?
7: 13 Will you try the **p** of my God also?
Ro 2: 4 forbearance and **p**, not realizing
9: 22 bore with great **p** the objects of his
2Co 6: 6 understanding, **p** and kindness;
Col 1: 11 may have great endurance and **p**,
3: 12 humility, gentleness and **p**.
1Ti 1: 16 might display his immense **p** as
2Ti 3: 10 of life, my purpose, faith, **p**, love,
4: 2 great **p** and careful instruction.
Heb 6: 12 **p** inherit what has been promised.
Jas 5: 10 as an example of **p** in the face
2Pe 3: 15 that our Lord's **p** means salvation,

PATIENT* (PATIENCE PATIENTLY)
Ne 9: 30 many years you were **p** with them.
Job 6: 11 What prospects, that I should be **p**?
Pr 14: 29 Whoever is **p** has great
15: 18 the one who is **p** calms a quarrel.
16: 32 Better a **p** person than a warrior,
Mt 18: 26 'Be **p** with me,' he begged, 'and I
18: 29 and begged him, 'Be **p** with me,
Ro 12: 12 Be joyful in hope, **p** in affliction,
1Co 13: 4 Love is **p**, love is kind. It does not
2Co 1: 6 produces in you **p** endurance
Eph 4: 2 be **p**, bearing with one another
1Th 5: 14 help the weak, be **p** with everyone.
Jas 5: 7 Be **p**, then, brothers and sisters,
5: 8 You too, be **p** and stand firm,
2Pe 3: 9 Instead he is **p** with you,
Rev 1: 9 **p** endurance that are ours in Jesus,
13: 10 This calls for **p** endurance
14: 12 This calls for **p** endurance

PATIENTLY* (PATIENT)
Ps 37: 7 the LORD and wait **p** for him;
40: 1 I waited **p** for the LORD;
Isa 38: 13 I waited **p** till dawn, but like a lion
Hab 3: 16 Yet I will wait **p** for the day
Ac 26: 3 I beg you to listen to me **p**.
Ro 8: 25 we do not yet have, we wait for it **p**.
Heb 6: 15 And so after waiting **p**,
1Pe 3: 20 ago when God waited **p** in the days
Jas 5: 7 **p** waiting for the autumn and
Rev 3: 10 kept my command to endure **p**,

PATTERN
Ex 25: 40 according to the **p** shown you
Ro 5: 14 who is a **p** of the one to come.
12: 2 not conform to the **p** of this world,
2Ti 1: 13 keep as the **p** of sound teaching,
Heb 8: 5 according to the **p** shown you

PAUL
Also called Saul (Ac 13:9). Pharisee from Tarsus (Ac 9:11; Php 3:5). Apostle (Gal 1). At stoning of Stephen (Ac 8:1). Persecuted church (Ac 9:1–2; Gal 1:13). Vision of Jesus on road to Damascus (Ac 9:4–9; 26:12–18). In Arabia (Gal 1:17). Preached in Damascus; escaped death through the wall in a basket (Ac 9:19–25). In Jerusalem; sent back to Tarsus (Ac 9:26–30).

Brought to Antioch by Barnabas (Ac 11:22–26). First missionary journey to Cyprus and Galatia (Ac 13–14). Stoned at Lystra (Ac 14:19–20). At Jerusalem council (Ac 15). Split with Barnabas over Mark (Ac 15:36–41).

Second missionary journey with Silas (Ac 16–20). Called to Macedonia (Ac 16:6–10). Freed from prison in Philippi (Ac 16:16–40). In Thessalonica (Ac 17:1–9). Speech in Athens (Ac 17:16–33). In Corinth (Ac 18). In Ephesus (Ac 19). Return to Jerusalem (Ac 20). Farewell to Ephesian elders (Ac 20:13–38). Arrival in Jerusalem (Ac 21:1–26). Arrested (Ac 21:27–36). Addressed crowds (Ac 22), Sanhedrin (Ac 23:1–11). Transferred to Caesarea (Ac 23:12–35). Trial before Felix (Ac 24), Festus (Ac 25:1–12). Before Agrippa (Ac 25:13—26:32). Voyage to Rome; shipwreck (Ac 27). Arrival in Rome (Ac 28).

Epistles: Romans, 1 and 2 Corinthians, Galatians, Ephesians, Philippians, Colossians, 1 and 2 Thessalonians, 1 and 2 Timothy, Titus, Philemon.

PAVEMENT
Jn 19: 13 at a place known as the Stone **P**

PAY (PAID PAYMENT PAYS REPAID REPAY REPAYING)
Lev 26: 43 They will **p** for their sins because
Dt 7: 12 If you **p** attention to these laws
Pr 4: 1 **p** attention and gain understanding
4: 20 My son, **p** attention to what I say;
5: 1 My son, **p** attention to my wisdom,
6: 31 must **p** sevenfold, though it costs
19: 19 person must **p** the penalty;
22: 17 **P** attention and turn your ear
24: 29 I'll **p** them back for what they did."
Eze 40: 4 **p** attention to everything I am
Zec 11: 12 "If you think it best, give me my **p**;
Mt 20: 2 He agreed to **p** them a denarius
22: 16 because you **p** no attention to who
22: 17 Is it right to **p** the imperial tax
Lk 3: 14 be content with your **p**."
19: 8 I will **p** back four times
Ro 13: 6 This is also why you **p** taxes,
2Pe 1: 19 you will do well to **p** attention to it,

PAYMENT (PAY)
Ps 49: 8 a life is costly, no **p** is ever enough
Php 4: 18 I have received full **p** and have

PAYS (PAY)
Pr 17: 13 the house of one who **p** back evil
1Th 5: 15 sure that nobody **p** back wrong

PEACE (PEACEABLE PEACEFUL PEACEMAKERS)
Lev 26: 6 "'I will grant **p** in the land,
Nu 6: 26 toward you and give you **p**."'
25: 12 him I am making my covenant of **p**
Dt 20: 10 a city, make its people an offer of **p**.
Jdg 3: 11 So the land had **p** for forty years,
3: 30 and the land had **p** for eighty years.
5: 31 Then the land had **p** forty years.
6: 24 there and called it The LORD Is **P**.
8: 28 lifetime, the land had **p** forty years.
1Sa 7: 14 And there was **p** between Israel
2Sa 10: 19 they made **p** with the Israelites
1Ki 2: 33 there be the LORD's **p** forever."
22: 44 also at **p** with the king of Israel.
2Ki 9: 17 and ask, 'Do you come in **p**?'"
1Ch 19: 19 they made **p** with David and
22: 9 have a son who will be a man of **p**
2Ch 14: 1 his days the country was at **p** for
20: 30 kingdom of Jehoshaphat was at **p**,
Job 3: 26 I have no **p**, no quietness; I have no
22: 21 to God and be at **p** with him;
Ps 29: 11 LORD blesses his people with **p**.
34: 14 and do good; seek **p** and pursue it.
37: 11 land and enjoy **p** and prosperity.
37: 37 a future awaits those who seek **p**.
85: 10 and **p** kiss each other.
119:165 Great **p** have those who love your
120: 7 I am for **p**; but when I speak,
122: 6 Pray for the **p** of Jerusalem:
147: 14 He grants **p** to your borders
Pr 12: 20 but those who promote **p** have joy.
14: 30 A heart at **p** gives life to the body,
16: 7 enemies to make **p** with them.
17: 1 Better a dry crust with **p** and quiet
Ecc 3: 8 a time for war and a time for **p**.
Isa 9: 6 Everlasting Father, Prince of **P**.

Isa 14: 7 All the lands are at rest and at **p**;
26: 3 in perfect **p** those whose minds are
32: 17 of that righteousness will be **p**;
48: 18 **p** would have been like a river,
48: 22 "There is no **p**," says the LORD,
52: 7 who proclaim **p**, who bring good
53: 5 that brought us **p** was on him,
54: 10 nor my covenant of **p** be removed,"
55: 12 go out in joy and be led forth in **p**;
57: 2 who walk uprightly enter into **p**;
57: 19 **P**, **p**, to those far and near,"
57: 21 "There is no **p**," says my God,
59: 8 who walks along them will know **p**.
Jer 6: 14 '**P**, **p**,' they say, when there is no **p**.
8: 11 "**P**, **p**," they say, when there is no
30: 10 Jacob will again have **p**
46: 27 Jacob will again have **p**
Eze 13: 10 saying, "**P**," when there is no **p**,
34: 25 "'I will make a covenant of **p**
37: 26 I will make a covenant of **p**
Mic 5: 5 will be our **p** when the Assyrians
Zec 8: 19 Therefore love truth and **p**."
9: 10 He will proclaim **p** to the nations.
Mal 2: 5 a covenant of life and **p**,
2: 6 He walked with me in **p**
Mt 10: 34 have come to bring **p** to the earth.
10: 34 I did not come to bring **p**,
Mk 9: 50 and be at **p** with each other."
Lk 1: 79 guide our feet into the path of **p**."
2: 14 and on earth **p** to those on whom
10: 6 If someone who promotes **p** is there, your **p** will rest on them;
19: 38 "**P** in heaven and glory
Jn 14: 27 **P** I leave with you; my **p** I give you.
16: 33 so that in me you may have **p**.
Ro 1: 7 and **p** to you from God our Father
2: 10 and **p** for everyone who does good:
5: 1 we have **p** with God through our
8: 6 governed by the Spirit is life and **p**.
12: 18 on you, live at **p** with everyone.
14: 19 every effort to do what leads to **p**
1Co 7: 15 God has called us to live in **p**.
14: 33 is not a God of disorder but of **p**—
2Co 13: 11 be of one mind, live in **p**.
13: 11 God of love and **p** will be with you.
Gal 5: 22 Spirit is love, joy, **p**, forbearance,
Eph 2: 14 For he himself is our **p**, who has
2: 15 out of the two, thus making **p**,
2: 17 preached **p** to you who were far
6: 15 that comes from the gospel of **p**.
Php 4: 7 the **p** of God, which transcends
Col 1: 20 by making **p** through his blood,
3: 15 Let the **p** of Christ rule in your
3: 15 of one body you were called to **p**.
1Th 5: 3 people are saying, "**P** and safety,"
5: 13 Live in **p** with each other.
5: 23 the God of **p**, sanctify you through
2Th 3: 16 the Lord of **p** himself give you **p**
2Ti 2: 22 love and **p**, along with those who
Heb 7: 2 of Salem" means "king of **p**."
12: 11 **p** for those who have been trained
12: 14 effort to live in **p** with everyone
13: 20 Now may the God of **p**,
1Pe 3: 11 they must seek **p** and pursue it.
2Pe 3: 14 blameless and at **p** with him.
Rev 6: 4 power to take **p** from the earth

PEACEABLE* (PEACE)
Titus 3: 2 no one, to be **p** and considerate,

PEACEFUL (PEACE)
1Ti 2: 2 that we may live **p** and quiet lives

PEACE-LOVING*
Jas 3: 17 then **p**, considerate, submissive,

PEACEMAKERS* (PEACE)
Mt 5: 9 Blessed are the **p**, for they will be
Jas 3: 18 **P** who sow in peace reap a harvest

PEARL* (PEARLS)
Rev 21: 21 each gate made of a single **p**.

PEARLS (PEARL)
Mt 7: 6 do not throw your **p** to pigs.
13: 45 like a merchant looking for fine **p**.
1Ti 2: 9 or gold or **p** or expensive clothes,
Rev 21: 21 The twelve gates were twelve **p**,

PEDDLE*
2Co 2: 17 we do not **p** the word of God

PEG
Jdg 4: 21 She drove the **p** through his temple

PEKAH
King of Israel (2Ki 15:25–31; Isa 7:1).

PEKAHIAH*
Son of Menahem; king of Israel (2Ki 15:22–26).

PEN
Ps 45: 1 my tongue is the **p** of a skillful
Mt 5: 18 not the least stroke of a **p**,
Jn 10: 1 who does not enter the sheep **p**

PENETRATES*
Heb 4: 12 **p** even to dividing soul and spirit,

PENNIES* (PENNY)
Lk 12: 6 not five sparrows sold for two **p**?

PENNY* (PENNIES)
Mt 5: 26 out until you have paid the last **p**.
10: 29 Are not two sparrows sold for a **p**?
Lk 12: 59 out until you have paid the last **p**."

PENTECOST*
Ac 2: 1 When the day of **P** came, they were
20: 16 if possible, by the day of **P**.
1Co 16: 8 I will stay on at Ephesus until **P**,

PEOPLE (PEOPLE'S PEOPLES)
Ge 11: 6 said, "If as one **p** speaking the same
Ex 5: 1 'Let my **p** go, so that they may hold
6: 7 I will take you as my own **p**, and I
8: 23 make a distinction between my **p** and your **p**.
15: 13 will lead the **p** you have redeemed.
19: 8 The **p** all responded together,
24: 3 told the **p** all the LORD's words
32: 1 When the **p** saw that Moses was so
32: 9 "and they are a stiff-necked **p**.
33: 13 that this nation is your **p**."
Lev 9: 7 atonement for yourself and the **p**;
16: 24 for himself and for the **p**.
26: 12 be your God, and you will be my **p**.
Nu 11: 11 the burden of all these **p** on me?
14: 11 "How long will these **p** treat me
14: 19 forgive the sin of these **p**, just as
22: 5 "A **p** has come out of Egypt;
Dt 4: 6 is a wise and understanding **p**."
4: 20 be the **p** of his inheritance, as you
5: 28 "I have heard what this **p** said
7: 6 you are a **p** holy to the LORD your
26: 18 declared this day that you are his **p**,
31: 7 must go with this **p** into the land
31: 16 and these **p** will soon prostitute
32: 9 For the LORD's portion is his **p**,
32: 43 atonement for his land and **p**.
33: 29 like you, a **p** saved by the LORD?
Jos 1: 6 because you will lead these **p**
24: 24 And the **p** said to Joshua, "We will
Jdg 2: 7 The **p** served the LORD
Ru 1: 16 Your **p** will be my **p** and your God
1Sa 8: 7 to all that the **p** are saying to you;
12: 22 the LORD will not reject his **p**,
16: 7 **P** look at the outward appearance,
2Sa 5: 2 'You will shepherd my **p** Israel,
7: 10 Wicked **p** will not oppress them
1Ki 3: 8 a great **p**, too numerous to count
8: 30 of your **p** Israel when they pray
8: 56 to his **p** Israel just as he promised.
18: 39 When all the **p** saw this, they fell
2Ki 23: 3 all the **p** pledged themselves
1Ch 17: 21 And who is like your **p** Israel—
17: 21 out to redeem a **p** for himself,
29: 17 how willingly your **p** who are here
2Ch 2: 11 "Because the LORD loves his **p**,
7: 5 and all the **p** dedicated the temple
7: 14 if my **p**, who are called by my
30: 6 "**P** of Israel, return to the LORD,
36: 16 LORD was aroused against his **p**
Ezr 2: 1 these are the **p** of the province
3: 1 the **p** assembled together as one
Ne 1: 10 They are your servants and your **p**,
4: 6 the **p** worked with all their heart.
8: 1 all the **p** came together as one
Est 3: 6 a way to destroy all Mordecai's **p**,
Job 12: 2 you are the only **p** who matter,
Ps 29: 11 The LORD gives strength to his **p**;
30: 4 of the LORD, you his faithful **p**;
31: 23 Love the LORD, all his faithful **p**!
33: 12 the **p** he chose for his inheritance.
50: 4 the earth, that he may judge his **p**:
53: 6 When God restores his **p**, let Jacob
81: 13 "If my **p** would only listen to me,
94: 14 For the LORD will not reject his **p**;
95: 7 and we are the **p** of his pasture,
95: 10 said, 'They are a **p** whose hearts go
125: 2 LORD surrounds his **p** both now
133: 1 it is when God's **p** live together
Ps 135: 14 For the LORD will vindicate his **p**
144: 15 blessed is the **p** whose God is
149: 1 in the assembly of his faithful **p**.
149: 5 Let his faithful **p** rejoice in this
Pr 14: 34 a nation, but sin condemns any **p**.
29: 2 the righteous thrive, the **p** rejoice;
29: 18 is no revelation, **p** cast off restraint;
Isa 1: 3 know, my **p** do not understand."
1: 4 nation, a **p** whose guilt is great,
5: 13 Therefore my **p** will go into exile
6: 10 Make the heart of this **p** calloused;
9: 2 The **p** walking in darkness have
11: 12 he will assemble the scattered **p**
19: 25 "Blessed be Egypt my **p**,
29: 13 "These **p** come near to me
40: 1 comfort my **p**, says your God.
40: 5 and all **p** will see it together.
40: 7 Surely the **p** are grass.
42: 6 you to be a covenant for the **p**
49: 13 For the LORD comforts his **p**
51: 4 "Listen to me, my **p**; hear me,
52: 6 Therefore my **p** will know my
53: 8 of my **p** he was punished.
60: 21 Then all your **p** will be righteous
62: 12 They will be called the Holy **P**,
65: 23 for they will be a **p** blessed
Jer 2: 11 **p** have exchanged their glorious
2: 13 "My **p** have committed two sins:
2: 32 Yet my **p** have forgotten me,
4: 22 "My **p** are fools; they do not know
5: 14 and these **p** the wood it consumes.
5: 31 and my **p** love it this way.
7: 16 not pray for this **p** nor offer any
7: 23 be your God and you will be my **p**.
18: 15 Yet my **p** have forgotten me;
30: 3 'when I will bring my **p** Israel
Eze 13: 23 I will save my **p** from your hands.
36: 8 branches and fruit for my **p** Israel,
36: 28 you will be my **p**, and I will be your
36: 38 cities be filled with flocks of **p**.
37: 11 these bones are the **p** of Israel.
37: 13 you, my **p**, will know that I am
38: 14 day, when my **p** Israel are living
39: 7 my holy name among my **p** Israel.
Da 7: 18 But the holy **p** of the Most High
7: 27 to the holy **p** of the Most High.
8: 24 those who are mighty, the holy **p**.
9: 19 city and your **p** bear your Name."
9: 24 'sevens' are decreed for your **p**
9: 26 The **p** of the ruler who will come
10: 14 will happen to your **p** in the future,
11: 32 but the **p** who know their God will
12: 1 great prince who protects your **p**,
Hos 1: 10 'You are not my **p**,' they will be
2: 23 say to those called 'Not my **p**,' 'You are my **p**';
4: 14 a **p** without understanding will
Joel 2: 18 for his land and took pity on his **p**.
3: 16 LORD will be a refuge for his **p**,
Am 9: 14 I will bring my **p** Israel back
Mic 6: 2 the LORD has a case against his **p**;
7: 14 Shepherd your **p** with your staff,
Hag 1: 12 And the **p** feared the LORD.
Zec 2: 11 in that day and will become my **p**.
8: 7 "I will save my **p**
13: 9 'They are my **p**,' and they will say,
Mt 4: 19 I will send you out to fish for **p**."
23: 5 "Everything they do is done for **p**
Mk 5: 19 "Go home to your own **p** and tell
7: 6 "'These **p** honor me with their
8: 27 asked them, "Who do **p** say I am?"
Lk 1: 17 to make ready a **p** prepared
1: 68 because he has come to his **p**
2: 10 will cause great joy for all the **p**.
3: 6 all **p** will see God's salvation.'"
6: 22 Blessed are you when **p** hate you,
21: 23 the land and wrath against this **p**.
Jn 2: 24 himself to them, for he knew all **p**.
3: 19 **p** loved darkness instead of light
11: 50 one man die for the **p** than
12: 32 earth, will draw all **p** to myself."
18: 14 be good if one man died for the **p**.
Ac 15: 14 to choose a **p** for his name
18: 10 because I have many **p** in this city."
Ro 1: 18 godlessness and wickedness of **p**,
5: 12 and in this way death came to all **p**,
8: 27 for God's **p** in accordance
9: 3 from Christ for the sake of my **p**,
9: 25 call them 'my **p**' who are not my **p**;
11: 1 I ask then: Did God reject his **p**?
15: 10 you Gentiles, with his **p**."

1Co 6: 2 the Lord's **p** will judge the world?
9: 22 I have become all things to all **p** so
2Co 6: 16 their God, and they will be my **p**."
Eph 1: 15 Jesus and your love for all God's **p**,
1: 18 glorious inheritance in his holy **p**,
4: 8 captives and gave gifts to his **p**."
5: 3 are improper for God's holy **p**.
6: 18 keep on praying for all the Lord's **p**.
1Th 5: 26 Greet all God's **p** with a holy kiss.
1Ti 2: 4 who wants all **p** to be saved
2: 6 gave himself as a ransom for all **p**.
4: 10 God, who is the Savior of all **p**,
2Ti 2: 2 entrust to reliable **p** who will also
Titus 2: 11 that offers salvation to all **p**.
2: 14 himself a **p** that are his very own,
Phm : 7 refreshed the hearts of the Lord's **p**.
Heb 2: 17 atonement for the sins of the **p**.
4: 9 a Sabbath-rest for the **p** of God;
5: 1 priest is selected from among the **p**
5: 3 sins, as well as for the sins of the **p**.
9: 27 Just as **p** are destined to die once,
10: 30 again, "The Lord will judge his **p**."
11: 25 with the **p** of God rather than
13: 12 make the **p** holy through his own
1Pe 2: 9 But you are a chosen **p**, a royal
2: 10 Once you were not a **p**, but now you are the **p** of God;
2Pe 2: 1 also false prophets among the **p**,
3: 11 what kind of **p** ought you to be?
Rev 5: 8 which are the prayers of God's **p**.
18: 4 my **p**,' so that you will not share
19: 8 the righteous acts of God's holy **p**.)
21: 3 dwelling place is now among the **p**,
21: 3 They will be his **p**, and God

PEOPLE'S (PEOPLE)
Isa 25: 8 he will remove his **p** disgrace
Jer 10: 23 that **p** lives are not their own;

PEOPLES (PEOPLE)
Ge 17: 16 kings of **p** will come from her."
25: 23 and two **p** from within you will be
27: 29 serve you and **p** bow down to you.
28: 3 you become a community of **p**.
48: 4 I will make you a community of **p**,
Dt 14: 2 of all the **p** on the face of the earth,
28: 10 all the **p** on earth will see that you
32: 8 up boundaries for the **p** according
Jos 4: 24 all the **p** of the earth might know
1Ki 8: 43 all the **p** of the earth may know
2Ch 7: 20 an object of ridicule among all **p**.
Ps 9: 8 and judges the **p** with equity.
67: 5 may all the **p** praise you.
87: 6 will write in the register of the **p**:
96: 10 he will judge the **p** with equity.
Isa 2: 4 and will settle disputes for many **p**.
17: 12 Woe to the **p** who roar—
25: 6 a feast of rich food for all **p**,
34: 1 pay attention, you **p**!
55: 4 I have made him a witness to the **p**,
Jer 10: 3 the practices of the **p** are worthless;
Da 7: 14 **p** of every language worshiped him
Mic 4: 1 the hills, and **p** will stream to it.
4: 3 He will judge between many **p**
5: 7 the midst of many **p** like dew
Zep 3: 9 Then I will purify the lips of the **p**,
3: 20 praise among all the **p** of the earth
Zec 8: 20 "Many **p** and the inhabitants
12: 2 all the surrounding **p** reeling.
Rev 10: 11 prophesy again about many **p**,
17: 15 prostitute sits, are **p**, multitudes,

PEOR
Nu 25: 3 yoked themselves to the Baal of **P**.
Dt 4: 3 who followed the Baal of **P**,

PERCEIVE (PERCEIVING)
Ps 139: 2 you **p** my thoughts from afar.
Pr 24: 12 not he who weighs the heart **p** it?

PERCEIVING* (PERCEIVE)
Isa 6: 9 be ever seeing, but never **p**.'
Mt 13: 14 you will be ever seeing but never **p**.
Mk 4: 12 may be ever seeing but never **p**,
Ac 28: 26 will be ever seeing but never **p**."

PERFECT* (PERFECTER PERFECTING PERFECTION)
Dt 32: 4 his works are **p**, and all his ways
2Sa 22: 31 "As for God, his way is **p**:
Job 36: 4 one who has **p** knowledge is
37: 16 of him who has **p** knowledge?
Ps 18: 30 As for God, his way is **p**:
19: 7 The law of the LORD is **p**,
50: 2 Zion, **p** in beauty, God shines
64: 6 say, "We have devised a **p** plan!"
SS 6: 9 but my dove, my **p** one, is unique,
Isa 25: 1 for in **p** faithfulness you have done
26: 3 in **p** peace those whose minds are
Eze 16: 14 had given you made your beauty **p**,
27: 3 say, Tyre, "I am **p** in beauty."
28: 12 full of wisdom and **p** in beauty.
Mt 5: 48 Be **p**, therefore, as your heavenly Father is **p**.
19: 21 answered, "If you want to be **p**, go,
Ro 12: 2 his good, pleasing and **p** will.
2Co 12: 9 my power is made **p** in weakness."
Col 3: 14 binds them all together in **p** unity.
Heb 2: 10 of their salvation **p** through what
5: 9 made **p**, he became the source
7: 19 (for the law made nothing **p**),
7: 28 Son, who has been made **p** forever.
9: 11 more **p** tabernacle that is not made
10: 1 make **p** those who draw near
10: 14 he has made **p** forever those who
11: 40 with us would they be made **p**.
12: 23 the spirits of the righteous made **p**,
Jas 1: 17 good and **p** gift is from above,
1: 25 looks intently into the **p** law
3: 2 never at fault in what they say is **p**,
1Jn 4: 18 But **p** love drives out fear,
4: 18 The one who fears is not made **p**

PERFECTER* (PERFECT)
Heb 12: 2 on Jesus, the pioneer and **p** of faith.

PERFECTING* (PERFECT)
2Co 7: 1 **p** holiness out of reverence for God

PERFECTION* (PERFECT)
Ps 119: 96 To all **p** I see a limit, but your
La 2: 15 city that was called the **p** of beauty,
Eze 27: 4 builders brought your beauty to **p**.
27: 11 they brought your beauty to **p**.
28: 12 "'You were the seal of **p**,
43: 10 Let them consider its **p**,
Heb 7: 11 **p** could have been attained

PERFORM (PERFORMED PERFORMS)
Ex 3: 20 wonders that I will **p** among them.
2Sa 7: 23 to **p** great and awesome wonders
Jn 3: 2 For no one could **p** the signs you

PERFORMED (PERFORM)
Mt 11: 21 that were **p** in you had been **p**
Jn 10: 41 "Though John never **p** a sign,

PERFORMS (PERFORM)
Ps 77: 14 You are the God who **p** miracles;

PERFUME
Ecc 7: 1 A good name is better than fine **p**,
SS 1: 3 your name is like **p** poured out.
Mk 14: 3 jar and poured the **p** on his head.

PERIL
2Co 1: 10 delivered us from such a deadly **p**,

PERISH (PERISHABLE PERISHED PERISHES PERISHING)
Ge 6: 17 in it. Everything on earth will **p**.
Est 4: 16 is against the law. And if I **p**, I **p**."
Ps 37: 20 But the wicked will **p**:
73: 27 Those who are far from you will **p**;
102: 26 They will **p**, but you remain;
Pr 11: 10 the wicked **p**, there are shouts
19: 9 and whoever pours out lies will **p**.
21: 28 A false witness will **p**, but a careful
28: 28 but when the wicked **p**,
Isa 1: 28 who forsake the LORD will **p**.
29: 14 the wisdom of the wise will **p**,
60: 12 that will not serve you will **p**;
Zec 11: 9 the dying die, and the perishing **p**.
Mt 18: 14 any of these little ones should **p**.
Lk 13: 3 you repent, you too will all **p**.
13: 5 you repent, you too will all **p**."
21: 18 But not a hair of your head will **p**.
Jn 3: 16 believes in him shall not **p**
10: 28 eternal life, and they shall never **p**;
Ro 2: 12 law will also **p** apart from the law,
Col 2: 22 that are all destined to **p** with use,
2Th 2: 10 They **p** because they refused to
Heb 1: 11 They will **p**, but you remain;
1Pe 1: 4 an inheritance that can never **p**,
2Pe 3: 9 you, not wanting anyone to **p**,

PERISHABLE (PERISH)
1Co 15: 42 The body that is sown is **p**, it is
1Pe 1: 18 was not with **p** things such as silver
1: 23 not of **p** seed, but of imperishable,

PERISHED (PERISH)
Ps 119: 92 I would have **p** in my affliction.

PERISHES (PERISH)
Job 8: 13 so **p** the hope of the godless.
1Pe 1: 7 which **p** even though refined

PERISHING (PERISH)
1Co 1: 18 is foolishness to those who are **p**,
2Co 2: 15 being saved and those who are **p**.
4: 3 it is veiled to those who are **p**.

PERJURERS* (PERJURY)
Mal 3: 5 adulterers and **p**, against those who
1Ti 1: 10 for slave traders and liars and **p**—

PERJURY* (PERJURERS)
Jer 7: 9 commit adultery and **p**, burn

PERMANENT
Heb 7: 24 lives forever, he has a **p** priesthood.

PERMIT (PERMITTED)
Hos 5: 4 "Their deeds do not **p** them
1Ti 2: 12 I do not **p** a woman to teach

PERMITTED (PERMIT)
Mt 19: 8 "Moses **p** you to divorce your
2Co 12: 4 things that no one is **p** to tell.

PERSECUTE (PERSECUTED PERSECUTION PERSECUTIONS)
Mt 5: 11 **p** you and falsely say all kinds
5: 44 and pray for those who **p** you,
Jn 15: 20 persecuted me, they will **p** you
Ac 9: 4 "Saul, Saul, why do you **p** me?"
Ro 12: 14 Bless those who **p** you; bless and

PERSECUTED (PERSECUTE)
Ps 119: 86 me, for I am being **p** without cause.
Mt 5: 10 Blessed are those who are **p**
5: 12 same way they **p** the prophets who
Jn 15: 20 If they **p** me, they will persecute
1Co 4: 12 when we are **p**, we endure it;
15: 9 because I **p** the church of God.
2Co 4: 9 **p**, but not abandoned;
1Th 3: 4 telling you that we would be **p**.
2Ti 3: 12 godly life in Christ Jesus will be **p**,
Heb 11: 37 destitute, **p** and mistreated—

PERSECUTION (PERSECUTE)
Mt 13: 21 or **p** comes because of the word,
Ro 8: 35 trouble or hardship or **p** or famine

PERSECUTIONS* (PERSECUTE)
Mk 10: 30 along with **p**—and in the age
2Co 12: 10 in hardships, in **p**, in difficulties.
2Th 1: 4 faith in all the **p** and trials you are
2Ti 3: 11 **p**, sufferings—what kinds of things
3: 11 and Lystra, the **p** I endured.

PERSEVERANCE* (PERSEVERE)
Ro 5: 3 we know that suffering produces **p**;
5: 4 **p**, character; and character, hope.
2Th 1: 4 churches we boast about your **p**
3: 5 into God's love and Christ's **p**.
Heb 12: 1 let us run with **p** the race marked
Jas 1: 3 testing of your faith produces **p**.
1: 4 Let **p** finish its work so that you
5: 11 You have heard of Job's **p** and have
2Pe 1: 6 and to self-control, **p**; and to **p**,
Rev 2: 2 deeds, your hard work and your **p**.
2: 19 your service and **p**, and that you

PERSEVERE* (PERSEVERANCE PERSEVERED PERSEVERES PERSEVERING)
1Ti 4: 16 **P** in them, because if you do,
Heb 10: 36 You need to **p** so that when you

PERSEVERED* (PERSEVERE)
2Co 12: 12 I **p** in demonstrating among you
Heb 11: 27 he **p** because he saw him who is
Jas 5: 11 count as blessed those who have **p**.
Rev 2: 3 You have **p** and have endured

PERSEVERES* (PERSEVERE)
1Co 13: 7 trusts, always hopes, always **p**.
Jas 1: 12 one who **p** under trial because,

PERSEVERING* (PERSEVERE)
Lk 8: 15 retain it, and by **p** produce a crop.

PERSIANS
Da 6: 15 law of the Medes and **P** no decree

PERSISTENCE*
Ro 2: 7 those who by **p** in doing good seek

PERSUADE (PERSUADED PERSUASIVE)
Ac 18: 4 trying to **p** Jews and Greeks.
28: 23 the Prophets he tried to **p** them
2Co 5: 11 to fear the Lord, we try to **p** others.

PERSUADED (PERSUADE)
Ro 4: 21 being fully **p** that God had power

PERSUASIVE (PERSUADE)
1Co 2: 4 were not with wise and **p** words,

PERVERSION* (PERVERT)
Lev 18: 23 sexual relations with it; that is a **p**.
20: 12 What they have done is a **p**;
Jude : 7 up to sexual immorality and **p**.

PERVERT (PERVERSION PERVERTED)
Ex 23: 2 do not **p** justice by siding
Dt 16: 19 Do not **p** justice or show partiality.
Job 34: 12 that the Almighty would **p** justice.
Pr 17: 23 in secret to **p** the course of justice.
Gal 1: 7 are trying to **p** the gospel of Christ.

PERVERTED (PERVERT)
1Sa 8: 3 and accepted bribes and **p** justice.

PESTILENCE (PESTILENCES)
Ps 91: 6 the **p** that stalks in the darkness,

PESTILENCES* (PESTILENCE)
Lk 21: 11 famines and **p** in various places,

PETER
Apostle, brother of Andrew, also called Simon (Mt 10:2; Mk 3:16; Lk 6:14; Ac 1:13), and Cephas (Jn 1:42). Confession of Christ (Mt 16:13–20; Mk 8:27–30; Lk 9:18–27). At transfiguration (Mt 17:1–8; Mk 9:2–8; Lk 9:28–36; 2Pe 1:16–18). Caught fish with coin (Mt 17:24–27). Disowning of Jesus predicted (Mt 26:31–35; Mk 14:27–31; Lk 22:31–34; Jn 13:31–38). Disowned Jesus (Mt 26:69–75; Mk 14:66–72; Lk 22:54–62; Jn 18:15–27). Commissioned by Jesus to shepherd his flock (Jn 21:15–23).

Speech at Pentecost (Ac 2). Healed beggar (Ac 3:1–10). Speech at temple (Ac 3:11–26), before Sanhedrin (Ac 4:1–22). In Samaria (Ac 8:14–25). Sent by vision to Cornelius (Ac 10). Announced salvation of Gentiles in Jerusalem (Ac 11; 15). Freed from prison (Ac 12). Inconsistency at Antioch (Gal 2:11–21). At Jerusalem council (Ac 15).

Epistles: 1 and 2 Peter.

PETITION (PETITIONS)
Php 4: 6 by prayer and **p**, with thanksgiving,

PETITIONS (PETITION)
Heb 5: 7 up prayers and **p** with fervent cries

PHANTOM*
Ps 39: 6 goes around like a mere **p**;

PHARAOH (PHARAOH'S)
Ge 12: 15 they praised her to **P**, and she was
41: 14 So **P** sent for Joseph, and he was
Ex 14: 4 gain glory for myself through **P**
14: 17 I will gain glory through **P** and all

PHARAOH'S (PHARAOH)
Ex 7: 3 But I will harden **P** heart,

PHARISEE (PHARISEES)
Jn 3: 1 Now there was a **P**, a man named
Ac 23: 6 am a **P**, descended from Pharisees.
Php 3: 5 in regard to the law, a **P**;

PHARISEES (PHARISEE)
Mt 5: 20 surpasses that of the **P**
16: 6 guard against the yeast of the **P**
23: 13 you, teachers of the law and **P**,

PHILADELPHIA
Rev 3: 7 the angel of the church in **P** write:

PHILEMON*
Phm : 1 To **P** our dear friend and fellow

PHILIP
1. Apostle (Mt 10:3; Mk 3:18; Lk 6:14; Jn 1:43–48; 14:8; Ac 1:13).
2. Deacon (Ac 6:1–7); evangelist in Samaria (Ac 8:4–25), to Ethiopian (Ac 8:26–40).

PHILIPPI
Ac 16: 12 From there we traveled to **P**,
Php 1: 1 holy people in Christ Jesus at **P**,

PHILISTINE (PHILISTINES)
Jos 13: 3 held by the five **P** rulers in Gaza,
1Sa 14: 1 let's go over to the **P** outpost
17: 26 Who is this uncircumcised **P** that
17: 37 rescue me from the hand of this **P**."

PHILISTINES (PHILISTINE)
Jdg 10: 7 sold them into the hands of the **P**
13: 1 the hands of the **P** for forty years.
16: 5 The rulers of the **P** went to her
1Sa 4: 1 went out to fight against the **P**.
5: 8 together all the rulers of the **P**
13: 23 Now a detachment of **P** had gone
17: 1 Now the **P** gathered their forces
23: 1 the **P** are fighting against Keilah
27: 1 do is to escape to the land of the **P**.
31: 1 Now the **P** fought against Israel;
2Sa 5: 17 When the **P** heard that David had
8: 1 David defeated the **P** and subdued
21: 15 with his men to fight against the **P**,
2Ki 18: 8 he defeated the **P**, as far as Gaza
Am 1: 8 till the last of the **P** are dead,"

PHILOSOPHER* (PHILOSOPHY)
1Co 1: 20 Where is the **p** of this age?

PHILOSOPHY* (PHILOSOPHER)
Col 2: 8 through hollow and deceptive **p**,

PHINEHAS
Nu 25: 7 When **P** son of Eleazar, the son
Ps 106: 30 But **P** stood up and intervened,

PHOEBE*
Ro 16: 1 I commend to you our sister **P**,

PHYLACTERIES*
Mt 23: 5 They make their **p** wide

PHYSICAL*
Da 1: 4 young men without any **p** defect,
Ro 2: 28 merely outward and **p**.
9: 8 not the children by **p** descent who
Col 1: 22 by Christ's **p** body through death
1Ti 4: 8 For **p** training is of some value,
Jas 2: 16 does nothing about their **p** needs,

PICK (PICKED)
Mk 16: 18 *they will* **p** *up snakes with their*

PICKED (PICK)
Lk 14: 7 noticed how the guests **p** the places
Jn 5: 9 he **p** up his mat and walked.

PIECE (PIECES)
Jn 19: 23 in one **p** from top to bottom.

PIECES (PIECE)
Ge 15: 17 and passed between the **p**.
Jer 34: 18 two and then walked between its **p**.
Zec 11: 12 So they paid me thirty **p** of silver.
Mt 14: 20 of broken **p** that were left over.

PIERCE (PIERCED)
Ex 21: 6 doorpost and **p** his ear with an awl.
Ps 22: 16 they **p** my hands and my feet.
Pr 12: 18 words of the reckless **p** like swords,
Lk 2: 35 a sword will **p** your own soul too."

PIERCED (PIERCE)
Isa 53: 5 he was **p** for our transgressions,
Zec 12: 10 the one they have **p**, and they will
Jn 19: 37 will look on the one they have **p**."
Rev 1: 7 see him, even those who **p** him";

PIG'S* (PIGS)
Pr 11: 22 in a **p** snout is a beautiful woman
Isa 66: 3 is like one who presents **p** blood,

PIGEONS
Lev 5: 11 afford two doves or two young **p**,
Lk 2: 24 "a pair of doves or two young **p**."

PIGS (PIG'S)
Mt 7: 6 do not throw your pearls to **p**.
Mk 5: 11 A large herd of **p** was feeding

PILATE
Governor of Judea. Questioned Jesus (Mt 27:1–26; Mk 15:15; Lk 22:66—23:25; Jn 18:28—19:16); sent him to Herod (Lk 23:6–12); consented to his crucifixion when crowds chose Barabbas (Mt 27:15–26; Mk 15:6–15; Lk 23:13–25; Jn 19:1–10).

PILLAR (PILLARS)
Ge 19: 26 back, and she became a **p** of salt.
Ex 13: 21 in a **p** of cloud to guide them
13: 21 by night in a **p** of fire to give
1Ti 3: 15 the **p** and foundation of the truth.
Rev 3: 12 who is victorious I will make a **p**

PILLARS (PILLAR)
Gal 2: 9 those esteemed as **p**, gave me

PIPE
Ps 150: 4 praise him with the strings and **p**,
Mt 11: 17 "'We played the **p** for you,
1Co 14: 7 sounds, such as the **p** or harp,

PISGAH
Dt 3: 27 Go up to the top of **P** and look

PIT
Ps 7: 15 out falls into the **p** they have made.
40: 2 He lifted me out of the slimy **p**,
103: 4 who redeems your life from the **p**
Pr 23: 27 an adulterous woman is a deep **p**,
26: 27 Whoever digs a **p** will fall into it;
Isa 24: 17 Terror and **p** and snare await you,
38: 17 kept me from the **p** of destruction;
Mt 15: 14 the blind, both will fall into a **p**."

PITCH
Ge 6: 14 it and coat it with **p** inside and out.
Ex 2: 3 him and coated it with tar and **p**.

PITIED* (PITY)
1Co 15: 19 we are of all people most to be **p**.

PITY (PITIED)
Ps 72: 13 He will take **p** on the weak
Ecc 4: 10 But **p** anyone who falls and has no
Lk 10: 33 he saw him, he took **p** on him.

PLAGUE (PLAGUED PLAGUES)
2Ch 6: 28 famine or **p** comes to the land,
Ps 91: 6 nor the **p** that destroys at midday.

PLAGUED* (PLAGUE)
Ps 73: 5 they are not **p** by human ills.

PLAGUES (PLAGUE)
Hos 13: 14 Where, O death, are your **p**?
Rev 21: 9 bowls full of the seven last **p** came
22: 18 the **p** described in this scroll.

PLAIN
Isa 40: 4 level, the rugged places a **p**.
Ro 1: 19 be known about God is **p** to them,

PLAN (PLANNED PLANS)
Ex 26: 30 according to the **p** shown you
Pr 14: 22 those who **p** what is good find love
21: 30 no **p** that can succeed against
Isa 28: 29 Almighty, whose **p** is wonderful,
Am 3: 7 nothing without revealing his **p**
Eph 1: 11 to the **p** of him who works

PLANK
Mt 7: 3 attention to the **p** in your own eye?
Lk 6: 41 attention to the **p** in your own eye?

PLANNED (PLAN)
Ps 17: 3 you will find that I have **p** no evil;
40: 5 have done, the things you **p** for us.
Isa 14: 24 "Surely, as I have **p**, so it will be,
23: 9 The LORD Almighty **p** it, to bring
46: 11 what I have **p**, that I will do.
Heb 11: 40 since God had **p** something better

PLANS (PLAN)
Job 38: 2 obscures my **p** with words without
42: 3 obscures my **p** without knowledge?
Ps 20: 4 heart and make all your **p** succeed.
33: 11 But the **p** of the LORD stand firm
94: 11 The LORD knows all human **p**;
107: 11 despised the **p** of the Most High.
Pr 15: 22 **P** fail for lack of counsel,
16: 3 do, and he will establish your **p**.
19: 21 Many are the **p** in a person's heart,
20: 18 **P** are established by seeking advice;
Isa 29: 15 to hide their **p** from the LORD,
30: 1 those who carry out **p** that are not
32: 8 But the noble make noble **p**,
2Co 1: 17 I make my **p** in a worldly manner

PLANT (PLANTED PLANTING PLANTS)
Jnh 4: 6 the LORD God provided a leafy **p**
Am 9: 15 I will **p** Israel in their own land,
Mt 15: 13 "Every **p** that my heavenly Father

PLANTED (PLANT)
Ge 2: 8 the LORD God had **p** a garden
Ps 1: 3 person is like a tree **p** by streams
Jer 17: 8 They will be like a tree **p**
Mt 15: 13 Father has not **p** will be pulled
21: 33 was a landowner who **p** a vineyard.
1Co 3: 6 I **p** the seed, Apollos watered it,
Jas 1: 21 humbly accept the word **p** in you,

PLANTING (PLANT)
Isa 61: 3 a **p** of the LORD for the display

PLANTS (PLANT)
Pr 31: 16 of her earnings she **p** a vineyard.
1Co 3: 7 neither the one who **p** nor the one
9: 7 Who **p** a vineyard and does not eat

PLATTER
Mk 6: 25 head of John the Baptist on a **p**."

PLAY (PLAYED)
1Sa 16: 23 would take up his lyre and **p**.
Isa 11: 8 The infant will **p** near the cobra's

PLAYED (PLAY)
Lk 7: 32 "'We **p** the pipe for you, and you
1Co 14: 7 what tune is being **p** unless there is

PLEA (PLEAD PLEADED PLEADS)
1Ki 8: 28 prayer and his **p** for mercy,
Ps 102: 17 he will not despise their **p**.
La 3: 56 You heard my **p**: "Do not close

PLEAD (PLEA)
Isa 1: 17 **p** the case of the widow.
Mal 1: 9 **p** with God to be gracious to us.

PLEADED (PLEA)
2Co 12: 8 Three times I **p** with the Lord
PLEADS (PLEA)
Job 16: 21 of a man he **p** with God as one **p**
PLEASANT (PLEASE)
Ge 49: 15 resting place and how **p** is his land,
Ps 16: 6 lines have fallen for me in **p** places;
133: 1 and **p** it is when God's people live
135: 3 praise to his name, for that is **p**.
147: 1 how **p** and fitting to praise him!
Pr 2: 10 knowledge will be **p** to your soul.
3: 17 Her ways are **p** ways, and all her
Isa 30: 10 Tell us **p** things, prophesy illusions.
Jer 3: 19 my children and give you a **p** land,
1Th 3: 6 you always have **p** memories of us
Heb 12: 11 No discipline seems **p** at the time,
PLEASANTNESS* (PLEASE)
Pr 27: 9 the **p** of a friend springs from their
PLEASE (PLEASANT PLEASANTNESS PLEASED PLEASES PLEASING PLEASURE PLEASURES)
Ps 69: 31 This will **p** the LORD more than
Pr 20: 23 and dishonest scales do not **p** him.
21: 1 he channels toward all who **p** him.
Isa 46: 10 will stand, and I will do all that I **p**.'
Jer 6: 20 your sacrifices do not **p** me."
27: 5 on it, and I give it to anyone I **p**.
Jn 5: 30 for I seek not to **p** myself but him
Ro 8: 8 realm of the flesh cannot **p** God.
15: 1 of the weak and not to **p** ourselves.
15: 2 Each of us should **p** our neighbors
1Co 7: 32 how he can **p** the Lord.
10: 33 even as I try to **p** everyone in every
2Co 5: 9 So we make it our goal to **p** him,
Gal 1: 10 Or am I trying to **p** people?
6: 8 Whoever sows to **p** their flesh,
6: 8 whoever sows to **p** the Spirit,
Col 1: 10 the Lord and **p** him in every way:
1Th 2: 4 We are not trying to **p** people
4: 1 you how to live in order to **p** God,
2Ti 2: 4 tries to **p** his commanding officer.
Titus 2: 9 to try to **p** them, not to talk back
Heb 11: 6 faith it is impossible to **p** God,
PLEASED (PLEASE)
Dt 28: 63 Just as it **p** the LORD to make you
Jdg 18: 20 The priest was very **p**. He took
1Sa 12: 22 because the LORD was **p** to make
1Ki 3: 10 The Lord was **p** that Solomon had
1Ch 29: 17 the heart and are **p** with integrity.
Ps 5: 4 For you are not a God who is **p**
Mic 6: 7 Will the LORD be **p**
Mal 1: 10 I am not **p** with you,"
Mt 3: 17 with him I am well **p**."
17: 5 whom I love; with him I am well **p**.
Mk 1: 11 with you I am well **p**."
Lk 3: 22 with you I am well **p**."
10: 21 this is what you were **p** to do.
1Co 1: 21 God was **p** through the foolishness
Col 1: 19 God was **p** to have all his fullness
Heb 10: 6 and sin offerings you were not **p**.
10: 8 desire, nor were you **p** with them"
11: 5 commended as one who **p** God.
13: 16 for with such sacrifices God is **p**.
2Pe 1: 17 with him I am well **p**."
PLEASES (PLEASE)
Job 23: 13 He does whatever he **p**.
Ps 115: 3 he does whatever **p** him.
135: 6 The LORD does whatever **p** him,
Pr 15: 8 the prayer of the upright **p** him.
Ecc 2: 26 To the person who **p** him, God
7: 26 The man who **p** God will escape
Da 4: 35 He does as he **p** with the powers
Jn 3: 8 The wind blows wherever it **p**.
8: 29 alone, for I always do what **p** him."
Eph 5: 10 and find out what **p** the Lord.
Col 3: 20 in everything, for this **p** the Lord.
1Ti 2: 3 is good, and **p** God our Savior,
1Jn 3: 22 his commands and do what **p** him.
PLEASING (PLEASE)
Ge 2: 9 trees that were **p** to the eye
Lev 1: 9 offering, an aroma **p** to the LORD.
Ps 19: 14 of my heart be **p** in your sight,
104: 34 May my meditation be **p** to him,
SS 1: 3 **P** is the fragrance of your perfumes
4: 10 How much more **p** is your love
7: 6 How beautiful you are and how **p**,
Ro 12: 1 living sacrifice, holy and **p** to God
14: 18 Christ in this way is **p** to God
Php 4: 18 an acceptable sacrifice, **p** to God.
1Ti 5: 4 grandparents, for this is **p** to God.
Heb 13: 21 he work in us what is **p** to him,
PLEASURE (PLEASE)
Ps 51: 16 do not take **p** in burnt offerings.
147: 10 His **p** is not in the strength
Pr 10: 23 A fool finds **p** in wicked schemes,
16: 7 the LORD takes **p** in anyone's
18: 2 Fools find no **p** in understanding
21: 17 loves **p** will become poor;
Isa 1: 11 I have no **p** in the blood of bulls
Jer 6: 10 they find no **p** in it.
Eze 18: 23 Do I take any **p** in the death
18: 32 For I take no **p** in the death
33: 11 I take no **p** in the death
Eph 1: 5 in accordance with his **p** and will—
1: 9 of his will according to his good **p**,
1Ti 5: 6 for **p** is dead even while she lives.
2Ti 3: 4 lovers of **p** rather than lovers
Heb 10: 38 I take no **p** in the one who shrinks
2Pe 2: 13 Their idea of **p** is to carouse
PLEASURES* (PLEASE)
Ps 16: 11 with eternal **p** at your right hand.
Lk 8: 14 riches and **p**, and they do not
Titus 3: 3 by all kinds of passions and **p**.
Heb 11: 25 than to enjoy the fleeting **p** of sin.
Jas 4: 3 may spend what you get on your **p**.
2Pe 2: 13 reveling in their **p** while they feast
PLEDGE (PLEDGED)
Dt 24: 17 take the cloak of the widow as a **p**.
1Pe 3: 21 the **p** of a clear conscience toward
PLEDGED (PLEDGE)
1Co 7: 27 you **p** to a woman? Do not seek
PLEIADES
Job 38: 31 "Can you bind the chains of the **P**?
Am 5: 8 He who made the **P** and Orion,
PLENTIFUL (PLENTY)
Mt 9: 37 "The harvest is **p** but the workers
Lk 10: 2 "The harvest is **p**, but the workers
PLENTY (PLENTIFUL)
2Co 8: 14 the present time your **p** will supply
Php 4: 12 whether living in **p** or in want.
PLOT (PLOTS)
Est 2: 22 Mordecai found out about the **p**
Ps 2: 1 conspire and the peoples **p** in vain?
Pr 3: 29 Do not **p** harm against your
Zec 8: 17 do not **p** evil against each other,
Ac 4: 25 rage and the peoples **p** in vain?
PLOTS (PLOT)
Pr 6: 14 **p** evil with deceit in his heart—
PLOW (PLOWSHARES)
1Sa 13: 20 Philistines to have their **p** points,
Lk 9: 62 "No one who puts a hand to the **p**
PLOWSHARES* (PLOW)
Isa 2: 4 They will beat their swords into **p**
Joel 3: 10 Beat your **p** into swords and your
Mic 4: 3 They will beat their swords into **p**
PLUCK
Mk 9: 47 eye causes you to stumble, **p** it out.
PLUNDER (PLUNDERED)
Ex 3: 22 And so you will **p** the Egyptians."
Est 3: 13 of Adar, and to **p** their goods.
8: 11 to **p** the property of their enemies.
9: 10 did not lay their hands on the **p**.
Isa 3: 14 the **p** from the poor is in your
PLUNDERED (PLUNDER)
Ps 12: 5 "Because the poor are **p**
Eze 34: 8 so has been **p** and has become food
PLUNGE
1Ti 6: 9 harmful desires that **p** people
PODS
Lk 15: 16 the **p** that the pigs were eating,
POINT
Mt 4: 5 on the highest **p** of the temple.
26: 38 with sorrow to the **p** of death.
Jas 2: 10 yet stumbles at just one **p** is guilty
Rev 2: 10 even to the **p** of death, and I will
POISON
Ps 140: 3 the **p** of vipers is on their lips.
Mk 16: 18 *and when they drink deadly* **p**,
Ro 3: 13 "The **p** of vipers is on their lips."
Jas 3: 8 It is a restless evil, full of deadly **p**.
POLE (POLES)
Nu 21: 8 "Make a snake and put it up on a **p**;
Dt 16: 21 any wooden Asherah **p** beside
21: 23 hung on a **p** is under God's curse.
Est 7: 10 impaled Haman on the **p** he had
Gal 3: 13 is everyone who is hung on a **p**."
POLES (POLE)
Ex 25: 13 Then make **p** of acacia wood
POLISHED
Isa 49: 2 he made me into a **p** arrow
POLLUTE* (POLLUTED POLLUTES)
Nu 35: 33 "'Do not **p** the land where you
Jude : 8 these ungodly people **p** their own
POLLUTED* (POLLUTE)
Ezr 9: 11 is a land **p** by the corruption
Pr 25: 26 a **p** well are the righteous who give
Ac 15: 20 to abstain from food **p** by idols,
Jas 1: 27 oneself from being **p** by the world.
POLLUTES* (POLLUTE)
Nu 35: 33 Bloodshed **p** the land,
PONDER (PONDERED)
Ps 64: 9 of God and **p** what he has done.
107: 43 **p** the loving deeds of the LORD.
119: 95 me, but I will **p** your statutes.
PONDERED (PONDER)
Ps 111: 2 they are **p** by all who delight
Lk 2: 19 things and **p** them in her heart.
POOR (POVERTY)
Lev 19: 10 Leave them for the **p**
23: 22 Leave them for the **p**
27: 8 anyone making the vow is too **p**
Dt 15: 4 need be no **p** people among you,
15: 7 If anyone is **p** among your fellow
15: 11 There will always be **p** people
24: 12 If the neighbor is **p**, do not go
24: 14 of a hired worker who is **p**
Job 5: 16 So the **p** have hope, and injustice
24: 4 and force all the **p** of the land
Ps 14: 6 frustrate the plans of the **p**,
34: 6 This **p** man called, and the LORD
35: 10 You rescue the **p** from those too
40: 17 But as for me, I am **p** and needy;
68: 10 God, you provided for the **p**.
82: 3 uphold the cause of the **p**
112: 9 freely scattered their gifts to the **p**,
113: 7 He raises the **p** from the dust
140: 12 the LORD secures justice for the **p**
Pr 13: 7 another pretends to be **p**, yet has
14: 20 The **p** are shunned even by their
14: 31 oppresses the **p** shows contempt
17: 5 mocks the **p** shows contempt
19: 1 Better the **p** whose walk is
19: 17 Whoever is kind to the **p** lends
19: 22 better to be **p** than a liar.
20: 13 not love sleep or you will grow **p**;
21: 13 their ears to the cry of the **p** will
21: 17 loves pleasure will become **p**;
22: 2 Rich and **p** have this in common:
22: 9 they share their food with the **p**.
22: 22 not exploit the **p** because they are **p**
28: 6 Better the **p** whose walk is
28: 27 who give to the **p** will lack nothing,
29: 7 care about justice for the **p**,
31: 9 the rights of the **p** and needy.
31: 20 She opens her arms to the **p**
Ecc 4: 13 Better a **p** but wise youth than
Isa 3: 14 the plunder from the **p** is in your
10: 2 to deprive the **p** of their rights
14: 30 poorest of the **p** will find pasture,
25: 4 You have been a refuge for the **p**,
32: 7 schemes to destroy the **p** with lies,
61: 1 to proclaim good news to the **p**.
Jer 22: 16 He defended the cause of the **p**
Eze 18: 12 He oppresses the **p** and needy.
Am 2: 7 on the heads of the **p** as on the dust
4: 1 you women who oppress the **p**
5: 11 You levy a straw tax on the **p**
Zec 7: 10 fatherless, the foreigner or the **p**.
Mt 5: 3 "Blessed are the **p** in spirit,
11: 5 good news is proclaimed to the **p**.
19: 21 your possessions and give to the **p**,
26: 11 The **p** you will always have
Mk 12: 42 a **p** widow came and put in two
14: 7 The **p** you will always have
Lk 4: 18 to proclaim good news to the **p**.
6: 20 "Blessed are you who are **p**,
11: 41 generous to the **p**, and everything
14: 13 banquet, invite the **p**, the crippled,
21: 2 also saw a **p** widow put in two very
Jn 12: 8 will always have the **p** among you,
Ac 9: 36 doing good and helping the **p**.
10: 4 and gifts to the **p** have come up as
24: 17 to bring my people gifts for the **p**

Ro 15: 26 for the **p** among the Lord's people
1Co 13: 3 If I give all I possess to the **p**
2Co 6: 10 **p**, yet making many rich;
8: 9 yet for your sake he became **p**,
Gal 2: 10 continue to remember the **p**,
Jas 2: 2 and a **p** man in filthy old clothes
2: 5 not God chosen those who are **p**
2: 6 But you have dishonored the **p**.

POPULATION*
Pr 14: 28 A large **p** is a king's glory,

PORTION
Nu 18: 29 present as the LORD's **p** the best
Dt 32: 9 For the LORD's **p** is his people,
1Sa 1: 5 gave a double **p** because he loved
2Ki 2: 9 "Let me inherit a double **p** of your
Ps 73: 26 of my heart and my **p** forever.
119: 57 You are my **p**, LORD;
Isa 53: 12 I will give him a **p** among the great,
Jer 10: 16 He who is the **P** of Jacob is not like
La 3: 24 to myself, "The LORD is my **p**;
Zec 2: 12 LORD will inherit Judah as his **p**

PORTRAYED
Gal 3: 1 Christ was clearly **p** as crucified.

POSITION (POSITIONS)
Ro 12: 16 to associate with people of low **p**.
Jas 1: 9 ought to take pride in their high **p**.
2Pe 3: 17 lawless and fall from your secure **p**.

POSITIONS (POSITION)
2Ch 20: 17 Take up your **p**; stand firm and see
Jude : 6 the angels who did not keep their **p**

POSSESS (POSSESSED POSSESSING POSSESSION POSSESSIONS)
Nu 33: 53 for I have given you the land to **p**.
Dt 4: 14 you are crossing the Jordan to **p**.
Pr 8: 12 I **p** knowledge and discretion.

POSSESSED (POSSESS)
Jn 10: 21 the sayings of a man **p** by a demon.

POSSESSING* (POSSESS)
2Co 6: 10 nothing, and yet **p** everything.

POSSESSION (POSSESS)
Ge 15: 7 give you this land to take **p** of it."
Ex 6: 8 I will give it to you as a **p**. I am
19: 5 nations you will be my treasured **p**.
Nu 13: 30 go up and take **p** of the land,
Dt 7: 6 to be his people, his treasured **p**.
Jos 1: 11 take **p** of the land the LORD your
Ps 2: 8 the ends of the earth your **p**.
135: 4 own, Israel to be his treasured **p**.
Eph 1: 14 of those who are God's **p**—
1Pe 2: 9 God's special **p**, that you may

POSSESSIONS (POSSESS)
Mt 19: 21 go, sell your **p** and give to the poor,
Lk 11: 21 his own house, his **p** are safe.
12: 15 not consist in an abundance of **p**."
19: 8 now I give half of my **p** to the poor,
Ac 4: 32 that any of their **p** was their own,
2Co 12: 14 because what I want is not your **p**
Heb 10: 34 yourselves had better and lasting **p**.
1Jn 3: 17 If anyone has material **p** and sees

POSSIBLE
Mt 19: 26 but with God all things are **p**."
26: 39 if it is **p**, may this cup be taken
Mk 9: 23 "Everything is **p** for one who
10: 27 all things are **p** with God."
14: 35 if **p** the hour might pass from him.
Ro 12: 18 If it is **p**, as far as it depends on
1Co 6: 5 Is it **p** that there is nobody among
9: 19 to everyone, to win as many as **p**.
9: 22 by all **p** means I might save some.

POT (POTSHERDS POTTER POTTER'S POTTERY)
2Ki 4: 40 of God, there is death in the **p**!"
Jer 18: 4 the potter formed it into another **p**,

POTIPHAR*
Egyptian who bought Joseph (Ge 37:36), set him over his house (Ge 39:1–6), sent him to prison (Ge 39:7–30).

POTSHERDS (POT)
Isa 45: 9 but **p** among the **p** on the ground.

POTTER (POT)
Isa 29: 16 Can the pot say to the **p**,
45: 9 Does the clay say to the **p**,
64: 8 We are the clay, you are the **p**;
Jer 18: 6 with you, Israel, as this **p** does?"
Zec 11: 13 said to me, "Throw it to the **p**"—
Ro 9: 21 Does not the **p** have the right

POTTER'S (POT)
Mt 27: 7 to buy the **p** field as a burial place

POTTERY (POT)
Ro 9: 21 of clay some **p** for special purposes

POUR (POURED POURS)
Ps 62: 8 **p** out your hearts to him, for God
Isa 44: 3 I will **p** out my Spirit on your
Eze 20: 8 So I said I would **p** out my wrath
39: 29 for I will **p** out my Spirit
Joel 2: 28 I will **p** out my Spirit on all people.
Zec 12: 10 I will **p** out on the house of David
Mal 3: 10 **p** out so much blessing that there
Ac 2: 17 I will **p** out my Spirit on all people.

POURED (POUR)
Ps 22: 14 I am **p** out like water, and all my
Isa 32: 15 till the Spirit is **p** on us
Mt 26: 28 which is **p** out for many
Lk 22: 20 my blood, which is **p** out for you.
Ac 2: 33 and has **p** out what you now see
10: 45 the Holy Spirit had been **p** out
Ro 5: 5 because God's love has been **p**
Php 2: 17 if I am being **p** out like a drink
2Ti 4: 6 am already being **p** out like a drink
Titus 3: 6 whom he **p** out on us generously
Rev 16: 2 and **p** out his bowl on the land,

POURS (POUR)
Lk 5: 37 And no one **p** new wine into old

POVERTY* (POOR)
Dt 28: 48 in nakedness and dire **p**, you will
1Sa 2: 7 The LORD sends **p** and wealth;
Pr 6: 11 and **p** will come on you like a thief
10: 4 Lazy hands make for **p**, but diligent
10: 15 city, but **p** is the ruin of the poor.
11: 24 withholds unduly, but comes to **p**.
13: 18 disregards discipline comes to **p**
14: 23 but mere talk leads only to **p**.
21: 5 profit as surely as haste leads to **p**.
22: 16 gifts to the rich—both come to **p**.
24: 34 and **p** will come on you like a thief
28: 19 fantasies will have their fill of **p**.
28: 22 are unaware that **p** awaits them.
30: 8 give me neither **p** nor riches,
31: 7 forget their **p** and remember their
Ecc 4: 14 born in **p** within his kingdom.
Mk 12: 44 she, out of her **p**, put in everything
Lk 21: 4 she out of her **p** put in all she had
2Co 8: 2 their extreme **p** welled up in rich
8: 9 you through his **p** might become
Rev 2: 9 I know your afflictions and your **p**

POWER (POWERFUL POWERFULLY POWERS)
Ex 15: 6 hand, LORD, was majestic in **p**.
32: 11 brought out of Egypt with great **p**
Dt 8: 17 "My **p** and the strength of my
34: 12 one has ever shown the mighty **p**
1Ch 29: 11 greatness and the **p** and the glory
2Ch 20: 6 **P** and might are in your hand,
32: 7 for there is a greater **p** with us than
Job 9: 4 wisdom is profound, his **p** is vast.
36: 22 "God is exalted in his **p**. Who is
37: 23 beyond our reach and exalted in **p**;
Ps 20: 6 the victorious **p** of his right hand.
62: 11 "**P** belongs to you, God,
63: 2 and beheld your **p** and your glory.
66: 3 great is your **p** that your enemies
68: 34 Proclaim the **p** of God,
77: 14 you display your **p** among
89: 13 Your arm is endowed with **p**;
145: 6 of the **p** of your awesome works—
147: 5 Great is our Lord and mighty in **p**;
150: 2 Praise him for his acts of **p**;
Pr 3: 27 it is due, when it is in your **p** to act.
18: 21 The tongue has the **p** of life
24: 5 The wise prevail through great **p**,
Isa 40: 10 Sovereign LORD comes with **p**,
40: 26 Because of his great **p** and mighty
63: 12 who sent his glorious arm of **p** to
Jer 10: 6 and your name is mighty in **p**.
10: 12 But God made the earth by his **p**;
27: 5 With my great **p** and outstretched
32: 17 and the earth by your great **p**
Hos 13: 14 this people from the **p** of the grave;
Na 1: 3 is slow to anger but great in **p**;
Zec 4: 6 'Not by might nor by **p**, but by my
Mt 22: 29 the Scriptures or the **p** of God.
24: 30 of heaven, with **p** and great glory.
Lk 1: 35 and the **p** of the Most High will
4: 14 to Galilee in the **p** of the Spirit,
9: 1 he gave them **p** and authority
Lk 10: 19 to overcome all the **p** of the enemy;
24: 49 until you have been clothed with **p**
Ac 1: 8 you will receive **p** when the Holy
4: 28 They did what your **p** and will had
4: 33 With great **p** the apostles
10: 38 with the Holy Spirit and **p**,
26: 18 and from the **p** of Satan to God,
Ro 1: 16 because it is the **p** of God
1: 20 his eternal **p** and divine nature—
4: 21 that God had **p** to do what he had
9: 17 that I might display my **p** in you
15: 13 hope by the **p** of the Holy Spirit.
15: 19 through the **p** of the Spirit of God.
1Co 1: 17 cross of Christ be emptied of its **p**.
1: 18 us who are being saved it is the **p**
2: 4 a demonstration of the Spirit's **p**,
6: 14 By his **p** God raised the Lord
15: 24 all dominion, authority and **p**.
15: 56 is sin, and the **p** of sin is the law.
2Co 4: 7 this all-surpassing **p** is from God
6: 7 speech and in the **p** of God;
10: 4 they have divine **p** to demolish
12: 9 for you, for my **p** is made perfect
13: 4 yet by God's **p** we will live
Eph 1: 19 his incomparably great **p** for us
3: 16 you with **p** through his Spirit
3: 20 according to his **p** that is at work
6: 10 in the Lord and in his mighty **p**.
Php 3: 10 to know the **p** of his resurrection
3: 21 by the **p** that enables him to bring
Col 1: 11 strengthened with all **p** according
2: 10 He is the head over every **p**
1Th 1: 5 simply with words but also with **p**,
2Ti 1: 7 us timid, but gives us **p**,
3: 5 form of godliness but denying its **p**
Heb 2: 14 by his death he might break the **p** of him who holds the **p** of death—
7: 16 of the **p** of an indestructible life.
1Pe 1: 5 by God's **p** until the coming
2Pe 1: 3 divine **p** has given us everything
Jude : 25 majesty, **p** and authority,
Rev 4: 11 to receive glory and honor and **p**,
5: 12 receive **p** and wealth and wisdom
11: 17 you have taken your great **p**
19: 1 glory and **p** belong to our God,
20: 6 second death has no **p** over them,

POWERFUL (POWER)
2Ch 27: 6 Jotham grew **p** because he walked
Est 9: 4 and he became more and more **p**.
Ps 29: 4 The voice of the LORD is **p**;
Zec 8: 22 **p** nations will come to Jerusalem
Mk 1: 7 me comes the one more **p** than I,
Lk 24: 19 **p** in word and deed before God
2Th 1: 7 in blazing fire with his **p** angels.
Heb 1: 3 sustaining all things by his **p** word.
Jas 5: 16 prayer of a righteous person is **p**

POWERFULLY (POWER)
1Sa 10: 6 Spirit of the LORD will come **p**
10: 10 Spirit of God came **p** upon him,
11: 6 Spirit of God came **p** upon him,
16: 13 of the LORD came **p** upon David.

POWERLESS
Ro 5: 6 when we were still **p**, Christ died
8: 3 what the law was **p** to do because it

POWERS (POWER)
Da 4: 35 as he pleases with the **p** of heaven
Ro 8: 38 present nor the future, nor any **p**,
1Co 12: 10 to another miraculous **p**,
Eph 6: 12 against the **p** of this dark world
Col 1: 16 whether thrones or **p** or rulers
2: 15 And having disarmed the **p**
Heb 6: 5 of God and the **p** of the coming age
1Pe 3: 22 and **p** in submission to him.

PRACTICE (PRACTICED PRACTICES)
Lev 19: 26 "'Do not **p** divination or seek
Ps 119: 56 This has been my **p**: I obey your
Eze 33: 31 but they do not put them into **p**.
Mt 7: 24 **p** is like a wise man who built his
23: 3 for they do not **p** what they preach.
Lk 8: 21 hear God's word and put it into **p**."
Ro 12: 13 who are in need. **P** hospitality.
Php 4: 9 me, or seen in me—put it into **p**.
1Ti 5: 4 put their religion into **p** by caring

PRACTICED (PRACTICE)
Mt 23: 23 You should have **p** the latter,

PRACTICES (PRACTICE)
Ps 101: 7 No one who **p** deceit will dwell
Mt 5: 19 but whoever **p** and teaches these
Col 3: 9 taken off your old self with its **p**

PRAISE (PRAISED PRAISES PRAISEWORTHY PRAISING)
Ex 15: 2 and I will **p** him, my father's God,
Dt 10: 21 is the one you **p**; he is your God,
26: 19 declared that he will set you in **p**,
32: 3 Oh, **p** the greatness of our God!
Ru 4: 14 "**P** be to the LORD, who this day
2Sa 22: 4 who is worthy of **p**, and have been
22: 47 **P** be to my Rock!
1Ki 8: 33 to you and give **p** to your name,
8: 35 this place and give **p** to your name
1Ch 16: 8 Give **p** to the LORD, proclaim his
16: 25 the LORD and most worthy of **p**;
16: 35 holy name, and glory in your **p**."
23: 5 four thousand are to **p** the LORD
29: 10 saying, "**P** be to you, LORD,
2Ch 5: 13 joined in unison to give **p**
6: 24 turn back and give **p** to your name,
6: 26 this place and give **p** to your name
20: 21 to **p** him for the splendor of his
29: 30 ordered the Levites to **p** the LORD
Ezr 3: 10 took their places to **p** the LORD,
Ne 9: 5 be exalted above all blessing and **p**.
Ps 8: 2 Through the **p** of children
16: 7 I will **p** the LORD, who counsels
26: 7 proclaiming aloud your **p**
28: 7 for joy, and with my song I **p** him.
30: 4 faithful people; **p** his holy name.
30: 12 my God, I will **p** you forever.
33: 1 it is fitting for the upright to **p** him.
34: 1 his **p** will always be on my lips.
40: 3 mouth, a hymn of **p** to our God.
42: 5 for I will yet **p** him, my Savior
43: 5 for I will yet **p** him, my Savior
45: 17 therefore the nations will **p** you
47: 7 sing to him a psalm of **p**.
48: 1 and most worthy of **p**, in the city
51: 15 and my mouth will declare your **p**.
56: 4 In God, whose word I **p**—in God I
57: 9 I will **p** you, Lord,
63: 4 I will **p** you as long as I live,
65: 1 **P** awaits you, our God, in Zion;
66: 2 of his name; make his **p** glorious.
66: 8 let the sound of his **p** be heard;
68: 19 **P** be to the Lord, to God our Savior
68: 26 **P** God in the great congregation;
69: 30 I will **p** God's name in song
69: 34 Let heaven and earth **p** him,
71: 8 My mouth is filled with your **p**,
71: 14 I will **p** you more and more.
71: 22 I will **p** you with the harp fo
74: 21 the poor and needy **p** your name.
75: 1 We **p** you, God, we **p** you, for
86: 12 I will **p** you, Lord my God, with all
89: 5 The heavens **p** your wonders,
92: 1 It is good to **p** the LORD and make
96: 2 Sing to the LORD, **p** his name;
100: 4 thanksgiving and his courts with **p**;
101: 1 to you, LORD, I will sing **p**.
102: 18 not yet created may **p** the LORD:
103: 1 **P** the LORD, my soul;
103: 20 **P** the LORD, you his angels,
104: 1 **P** the LORD, my soul.
105: 2 Sing to him, sing **p** to him;
106: 1 **P** the LORD. Give thanks
108: 3 I will **p** you, LORD,
111: 1 **P** the LORD. I will extol
113: 1 **P** the LORD. **P** the LORD,
117: 1 **P** the LORD, all you nations;
118: 28 You are my God, and I will **p** you;
119:175 Let me live that I may **p** you,
135: 1 **P** the LORD. **P** the name of the LORD; **p** him,
135: 20 you who fear him, **p** the LORD.
138: 1 I will **p** you, LORD, with all
139: 14 I **p** you because I am fearfully
144: 1 **P** be to the LORD my Rock,
145: 3 the LORD and most worthy of **p**;
145: 10 All your works **p** you, LORD;
145: 21 every creature **p** his holy name
146: 1 **P** the LORD. **P** the LORD,
147: 1 **P** the LORD. How good it is
148: 1 **P** the LORD. **P** the LORD
148: 13 Let them **p** the name of the LORD,
149: 1 **P** the LORD. Sing to the LORD
149: 6 the **p** of God be in their mouths
149: 9 his faithful people. **P** the LORD.
150: 2 **p** him for his surpassing greatness.
150: 6 everything that has breath **p** the LORD. **P** the LORD.
Pr 27: 2 Let someone else **p** you, and not
Pr 27: 21 but people are tested by their **p**.
31: 31 let her works bring her **p** at the city
SS 1: 4 will **p** your love more than wine.
Isa 12: 1 "I will **p** you, LORD.
42: 10 his **p** from the ends of the earth,
61: 3 a garment of **p** instead of a spirit
Jer 33: 9 **p** and honor before all nations
Da 2: 20 "**P** be to the name of God for ever
4: 37 **p** and exalt and glorify the King
Mt 21: 16 Lord, have called forth your **p**'?"
Lk 19: 37 disciples began joyfully to **p** God
Jn 12: 43 for they loved human **p** more than **p** from God.
Ro 2: 29 Such a person's **p** is not from other
15: 7 you, in order to bring **p** to God.
2Co 1: 3 **P** be to the God and Father of our
Eph 1: 3 **P** be to the God and Father of our
1: 6 to the **p** of his glorious grace,
1: 12 might be for the **p** of his glory.
1: 14 to the **p** of his glory.
1Th 2: 6 We were not looking for **p**
Heb 13: 15 offer to God a sacrifice of **p**—
Jas 3: 9 With the tongue we **p** our Lord
5: 13 Let them sing songs of **p**.
Rev 5: 13 and to the Lamb be **p** and honor
7: 12 **P** and glory and wisdom and

PRAISED (PRAISE)
1Ch 29: 10 David **p** the LORD in the presence
Ne 8: 6 Ezra **p** the LORD, the great God;
Job 1: 21 may the name of the LORD be **p**."
Ps 113: 2 Let the name of the LORD be **p**,
Pr 31: 30 who fears the LORD is to be **p**.
Isa 63: 7 the deeds for which he is to be **p**,
Da 2: 19 Then Daniel **p** the God of heaven
4: 34 Then I **p** the Most High;
Lk 18: 43 the people saw it, they also **p** God.
23: 47 had happened, **p** God and said,
Ro 9: 5 who is God over all, forever **p**!
Gal 1: 24 And they **p** God because of me.
1Pe 4: 11 may be **p** through Jesus Christ.

PRAISES (PRAISE)
2Sa 22: 50 I will sing the **p** of your name.
Ps 18: 49 I will sing the **p** of your name.
47: 6 Sing **p** to God, sing **p**; sing **p** to our King, sing **p**.
147: 1 good it is to sing **p** to our God,
Pr 31: 28 her husband also, and he **p** her:
Ro 15: 9 I will sing the **p** of your name."
1Pe 2: 9 you may declare the **p** of him who

PRAISEWORTHY* (PRAISE)
Ps 78: 4 tell the next generation the **p** deeds
Php 4: 8 if anything is excellent or **p**—

PRAISING (PRAISE)
Lk 2: 13 with the angel, **p** God and saying,
2: 20 **p** God for all the things they had
Ac 2: 47 **p** God and enjoying the favor of all
10: 46 speaking in tongues and **p** God.
1Co 14: 16 when you are **p** God in the Spirit,

PRAY (PRAYED PRAYER PRAYERS PRAYING PRAYS)
Dt 4: 7 our God is near us whenever we **p**
1Sa 12: 23 the LORD by failing to **p** for you.
1Ki 8: 30 when they **p** toward this place.
2Ch 7: 14 will humble themselves and **p**
Ezr 6: 10 and **p** for the well-being of the king
Job 42: 8 My servant Job will **p** for you,
Ps 5: 2 King and my God, for to you I **p**.
32: 6 Therefore let all the faithful **p**
122: 6 **P** for the peace of Jerusalem:
Jer 29: 7 **P** to the LORD for it, because if it
29: 12 call on me and come and **p** to me,
42: 3 **P** that the LORD your God will
Mt 5: 44 and **p** for those who persecute you,
6: 5 "And when you **p**, do not be like
6: 9 "This, then, is how you should **p**:
14: 23 on a mountainside by himself to **p**.
19: 13 his hands on them and **p** for them.
26: 36 here while I go over there and **p**."
Lk 6: 28 you, **p** for those who mistreat you.
11: 1 teach us to **p**, just as John taught
18: 1 them that they should always **p**
22: 40 them, "**P** that you will not fall
Jn 17: 20 I **p** also for those who will believe
Ro 8: 26 not know what we ought to **p** for,
1Co 14: 13 in a tongue should **p** that they may
Eph 1: 18 I **p** that the eyes of your heart may
3: 16 I **p** that out of his glorious riches
6: 18 **p** in the Spirit on all occasions
Col 4: 3 And **p** for us, too, that God may
1Th 5: 17 **p** continually,
2Th 1: 11 in mind, we constantly **p** for you,
1Ti 2: 8 I want the men everywhere to **p**,
Jas 5: 13 Let them **p**. Is anyone happy?
5: 16 **p** for each other so that you may be
1Pe 4: 7 of sober mind so that you may **p**.

PRAYED (PRAY)
1Sa 1: 27 I **p** for this child, and the LORD
1Ki 18: 36 Elijah stepped forward and **p**:
19: 4 under it and **p** that he might die.
2Ki 6: 17 And Elisha **p**, "Open his eyes,
2Ch 30: 18 But Hezekiah **p** for them, saying,
Ne 4: 9 But we **p** to our God and posted
Job 42: 10 After Job had **p** for his friends,
Da 6: 10 he got down on his knees and **p**,
9: 4 I **p** to the LORD my God
Jnh 2: 1 From inside the fish Jonah **p**
Mt 26: 39 with his face to the ground and **p**,
Mk 1: 35 off to a solitary place, where he **p**.
14: 35 **p** that if possible the hour might
Lk 22: 41 beyond them, knelt down and **p**,
Jn 17: 1 he looked toward heaven and **p**:
Ac 4: 31 After they **p**, the place where they
6: 6 **p** and laid their hands on them.
8: 15 they **p** for the new believers there
13: 3 So after they had fasted and **p**,

PRAYER (PRAY)
2Ch 30: 27 for their **p** reached heaven, his holy
Ezr 8: 23 about this, and he answered our **p**.
Ps 4: 1 have mercy on me and hear my **p**.
6: 9 the LORD accepts my **p**.
17: 1 Hear my **p**—it does not rise
17: 6 turn your ear to me and hear my **p**.
65: 2 You who answer **p**, to you all
66: 19 surely listened and has heard my **p**.
66: 20 God, who has not rejected my **p**
86: 6 Hear my **p**, LORD; listen to my
Pr 15: 8 the **p** of the upright pleases him.
15: 29 but he hears the **p** of the righteous.
Isa 56: 7 house will be called a house of **p**
Mt 21: 13 house will be called a house of **p**,'
21: 22 receive whatever you ask for in **p**."
Mk 9: 29 kind can come out only by **p**."
11: 24 whatever you ask for in **p**,
Jn 17: 15 My **p** is not that you take them
Ac 1: 14 all joined together constantly in **p**,
2: 42 to the breaking of bread and to **p**.
6: 4 will give our attention to **p**
10: 31 God has heard your **p**
16: 13 we expected to find a place of **p**.
Ro 12: 12 patient in affliction, faithful in **p**.
1Co 7: 5 you may devote yourselves to **p**.
2Co 13: 9 and our **p** is that you may be fully
Php 1: 9 And this is my **p**: that your love
4: 6 every situation, by **p** and petition,
Col 4: 2 Devote yourselves to **p**,
1Ti 4: 5 by the word of God and **p**.
Jas 5: 15 the **p** offered in faith will make
1Pe 3: 12 and his ears are attentive to their **p**,

PRAYERS (PRAY)
1Ch 5: 20 He answered their **p**, because they
Isa 1: 15 even when you offer many **p**, I am
Mk 12: 40 and for a show make lengthy **p**.
2Co 1: 11 as you help us by your **p**.
Eph 6: 18 on all occasions with all kinds of **p**
1Ti 2: 1 that petitions, **p**,
1Pe 3: 7 so that nothing will hinder your **p**.
Rev 5: 8 which are the **p** of God's people.
8: 3 with the **p** of all God's people,

PRAYING (PRAY)
Ge 24: 45 "Before I finished **p** in my heart,
1Sa 1: 12 As she kept on **p** to the LORD,
Mk 11: 25 And when you stand **p**, if you hold
Lk 3: 21 And as he was **p**, heaven was
6: 12 pray, and spent the night **p** to God.
9: 29 As he was **p**, the appearance of his
Jn 17: 9 I am not **p** for the world,
Ac 9: 11 Tarsus named Saul, for he is **p**.
16: 25 Silas were **p** and singing hymns
Ro 15: 30 join me in my struggle by **p** to God
Eph 6: 18 always keep on **p** for all the Lord's
Jude : 20 holy faith and **p** in the Holy Spirit,

PRAYS (PRAY)
1Co 14: 14 tongue, my spirit **p**, but my mind is

PREACH (PREACHED PREACHING)
Mt 23: 3 they do not practice what they **p**.
Mk 16: 15 *and **p** the gospel to all creation.*
Ac 9: 20 At once he began to **p**
16: 10 God had called us to **p** the gospel
Ro 1: 15 is why I am so eager to **p** the gospel

Ro 10: 15 how can anyone **p** unless they are
15: 20 to **p** the gospel where Christ was
1Co 1: 17 to baptize, but to **p** the gospel—
1: 23 but we **p** Christ crucified:
9: 14 that those who **p** the gospel should
9: 16 boast, since I am compelled to **p**.
9: 16 Woe to me if I do not **p** the gospel!
2Co 4: 5 For what we **p** is not ourselves,
10: 16 so that we can **p** the gospel
Gal 1: 8 heaven should **p** a gospel other
2Ti 4: 2 **P** the word; be prepared in season

PREACHED (PREACH)
Mt 24: 14 the kingdom will be **p** in the whole
Mk 6: 12 and **p** that people should repent.
13: 10 the gospel must first be **p** to all
14: 9 the gospel is **p** throughout
Ac 8: 4 who had been scattered **p** the word
1Co 9: 27 so that after I have **p** to others,
15: 1 remind you of the gospel I **p** to you
2Co 11: 4 a Jesus other than the Jesus we **p**,
Gal 1: 8 a gospel other than the one we **p**
Eph 2: 17 **p** peace to you who were far away
Php 1: 18 false motives or true, Christ is **p**.
1Ti 3: 16 angels, was **p** among the nations,
1Pe 1: 25 this is the word that was **p** to you.

PREACHING (PREACH)
Ac 18: 5 devoted himself exclusively to **p**,
Ro 10: 14 can they hear without someone **p**
1Co 2: 4 and my **p** were not with wise
9: 18 in **p** the gospel I may offer it free
Gal 1: 9 anybody is **p** to you a gospel other
1Ti 4: 13 of Scripture, to **p** and to teaching.
5: 17 especially those whose work is **p**

PRECEDE*
1Th 4: 15 will certainly not **p** those who have

PRECEPTS*
Dt 33: 10 He teaches your **p** to Jacob and
Ps 19: 8 The **p** of the LORD are right,
103: 18 and remember to obey his **p**.
105: 45 that they might keep his **p**
111: 7 all his **p** are trustworthy.
111: 10 all who follow his **p** have good
119: 4 You have laid down **p** that are to be
119: 15 I meditate on your **p** and consider
119: 27 to understand the way of your **p**,
119: 40 How I long for your **p**!
119: 45 for I have sought out your **p**.
119: 56 been my practice: I obey your **p**.
119: 63 fear you, to all who follow your **p**.
119: 69 I keep your **p** with all my heart.
119: 78 but I will meditate on your **p**.
119: 87 but I have not forsaken your **p**.
119: 93 I will never forget your **p**,
119: 94 I have sought out your **p**.
119:100 than the elders, for I obey your **p**.
119:104 I gain understanding from your **p**;
119:110 but I have not strayed from your **p**.
119:128 because I consider all your **p** right,
119:134 oppression, that I may obey your **p**.
119:141 despised, I do not forget your **p**.
119:159 See how I love your **p**;
119:168 I obey your **p** and your statutes,
119:173 help me, for I have chosen your **p**.

PRECIOUS
Ps 19: 10 They are more **p** than gold,
72: 14 for **p** is their blood in his sight.
116: 15 **P** in the sight of the LORD is
119: 72 your mouth is more **p** to me than
139: 17 How **p** to me are your thoughts,
Pr 8: 11 for wisdom is more **p** than rubies,
Isa 28: 16 stone, a **p** cornerstone for a sure
1Pe 1: 19 but with the **p** blood of Christ,
2: 4 but chosen by God and **p** to him—
2: 6 a chosen and **p** cornerstone,
2Pe 1: 1 have received a faith as **p** as ours:
1: 4 us his very great and **p** promises,

PREDESTINED* (DESTINY)
Ro 8: 29 **p** to be conformed to the image
8: 30 And those he **p**, he also called;
Eph 1: 5 he **p** us for adoption to sonship
1: 11 been **p** according to the plan

PREDICTED (PREDICTION)
1Sa 28: 17 has done what he **p** through me.
Ac 7: 52 killed those who **p** the coming
1Pe 1: 11 pointing when he **p** the sufferings

PREDICTION* (PREDICTED PREDICTIONS)
Jer 28: 9 LORD only if his **p** comes true."

PREDICTIONS (PREDICTION)
Isa 44: 26 and fulfills the **p** of his messengers,

PREGNANT
Ex 21: 22 hit a **p** woman and she gives birth
Mt 24: 19 will be in those days for **p** women
1Th 5: 3 as labor pains on a **p** woman,

PREPARE (PREPARED)
Ps 23: 5 You **p** a table before me
Isa 25: 6 the LORD Almighty will **p** a feast
40: 3 "In the wilderness **p** the way
Am 4: 12 to you, Israel, **p** to meet your God."
Mal 3: 1 who will **p** the way before me.
Mt 3: 3 wilderness, '**P** the way for the Lord,
Jn 14: 2 that I am going there to **p** a place

PREPARED (PREPARE)
Ex 23: 20 to bring you to the place I have **p**.
Mt 25: 34 the kingdom **p** for you since
Ro 9: 22 of his wrath—**p** for destruction?
1Co 2: 9 the things God has **p** for those who
Eph 2: 10 which God **p** in advance for us
2Ti 2: 21 Master and **p** to do any good work.
4: 2 be **p** in season and out of season;
1Pe 3: 15 Always be **p** to give an answer

PRESCRIBED
Ezr 7: 23 Whatever the God of heaven has **p**,

PRESENCE (PRESENT)
Ex 25: 30 Put the bread of the **P** on this table
33: 14 replied, "My **P** will go with you,
Nu 4: 7 "Over the table of the **P** they are
1Sa 6: 20 can stand in the **p** of the LORD,
21: 6 of the **P** that had been removed
2Sa 22: 13 of the brightness of his **p** bolts
2Ki 17: 23 LORD removed them from his **p**,
23: 27 also from my **p** as I removed Israel,
Ezr 9: 15 not one of us can stand in your **p**."
Ps 16: 11 you will fill me with joy in your **p**,
21: 6 him glad with the joy of your **p**.
23: 5 before me in the **p** of my enemies.
31: 20 the shelter of your **p** you hide them
41: 12 me and set me in your **p** forever.
51: 11 not cast me from your **p** or take
52: 9 in the **p** of your faithful people.
89: 15 who walk in the light of your **p**,
90: 8 secret sins in the light of your **p**.
114: 7 at the **p** of the Lord, at the **p**
139: 7 Where can I flee from your **p**?
Isa 26: 17 pain, so were we in your **p**, LORD.
Jer 5: 22 "Should you not tremble in my **p**?
Eze 38: 20 of the earth will tremble at my **p**.
Hos 6: 2 us, that we may live in his **p**.
Na 1: 5 The earth trembles at his **p**,
Mal 3: 16 his **p** concerning those who feared
Ac 2: 28 you will fill me with joy in your **p**.'
1Th 3: 9 we have in the **p** of our God
3: 13 holy in the **p** of our God and
2Th 1: 9 shut out from the **p** of the Lord
Heb 9: 24 now to appear for us in God's **p**.
1Jn 3: 19 we set our hearts at rest in his **p**:
Jude : 24 before his glorious **p** without fault

PRESENT (PRESENCE)
1Co 3: 22 or death or the **p** or the future—
7: 26 Because of the **p** crisis, I think
2Co 11: 2 that I might **p** you as a pure virgin
Eph 5: 27 and to **p** her to himself as a radiant
1Ti 4: 8 holding promise for both the **p** life
2Ti 2: 15 Do your best to **p** yourself to God
Jude : 24 **p** you before his glorious presence

PRESERVE (PRESERVES)
Pr 19: 16 who would **p** their life stay far
Lk 17: 33 whoever loses their life will **p** it.

PRESERVES (PRESERVE)
Ps 119: 50 Your promise **p** my life.

PRESS (PRESSED PRESSURE)
Php 3: 12 I **p** on to take hold
3: 14 I **p** on toward the goal to win

PRESSED (PRESS)
Ps 118: 5 When hard **p**, I cried to the LORD;
Lk 6: 38 A good measure, **p** down,

PRESSURE (PRESS)
2Co 1: 8 We were under great **p**, far beyond
11: 28 I face daily the **p** of my concern

PRETENDED
1Sa 21: 13 So he **p** to be insane in their

PREVAILS
1Sa 2: 9 "It is not by strength that one **p**;
Pr 19: 21 it is the LORD's purpose that **p**.

PRICE (PRICELESS)
Job 28: 18 the **p** of wisdom is beyond rubies.
1Co 6: 20 you were bought at a **p**.
7: 23 You were bought at a **p**;

PRICELESS* (PRICE)
Ps 36: 7 How **p** is your unfailing love,

PRIDE (PROUD)
Pr 8: 13 I hate **p** and arrogance,
11: 2 When **p** comes, then comes
13: 10 there is **p**, but wisdom is found
16: 18 **P** goes before destruction,
29: 23 **P** brings a person low, but the
Isa 25: 11 will bring down their **p** despite
Da 4: 37 those who walk in **p** he is able
Am 8: 7 sworn by himself, the **P** of Jacob:
2Co 5: 12 an opportunity to take **p** in us,
7: 4 I take great **p** in you.
8: 24 and the reason for our **p** in you,
Gal 6: 4 can take **p** in themselves alone,
Jas 1: 9 to take **p** in their high position.

PRIEST (PRIESTHOOD PRIESTLY PRIESTS)
Ge 14: 18 He was **p** of God Most High,
Nu 5: 10 what they give to the **p** will belong
2Ch 13: 9 seven rams may become a **p** of
Ps 110: 4 "You are a **p** forever, in the order
Heb 2: 17 faithful high **p** in service to God,
3: 1 as our apostle and high **p**.
4: 14 a great high **p** who has ascended
4: 15 do not have a high **p** who is unable
5: 6 "You are a **p** forever, in the order
6: 20 He has become a high **p** forever,
7: 3 Son of God, he remains a **p** forever.
7: 15 **p** like Melchizedek appears,
7: 26 Such a high **p** truly meets our need
8: 1 We do have such a high **p**, who sat
10: 11 Day after day every **p** stands
13: 11 The high **p** carries the blood

PRIESTHOOD (PRIEST)
Heb 7: 24 lives forever, he has a permanent **p**.
1Pe 2: 5 a spiritual house to be a holy **p**,
2: 9 people, a royal **p**, a holy nation,

PRIESTLY (PRIEST)
Ro 15: 16 He gave me the **p** duty

PRIESTS (PRIEST)
Ex 19: 6 you will be for me a kingdom of **p**
Lev 21: 1 "Speak to the **p**, the sons of Aaron,
Eze 42: 13 where the **p** who approach
46: 2 The **p** are to sacrifice his burnt
Mal 1: 6 "It is you **p** who show contempt
Rev 5: 10 a kingdom and **p** to serve our God,
20: 6 but they will be **p** of God

PRIME
Isa 38: 10 the **p** of my life must I go through

PRINCE (PRINCES PRINCESS)
Isa 9: 6 Everlasting Father, **P** of Peace.
Eze 34: 24 David will be **p** among them.
37: 25 my servant will be their **p** forever.
Da 8: 25 and take his stand against the **P**
Jn 12: 31 now the **p** of this world will be
Ac 5: 31 him to his own right hand as **P**

PRINCES (PRINCE)
Ps 118: 9 in the LORD than to trust in **p**.
148: 11 you **p** and all rulers on earth,
Isa 40: 23 He brings **p** to naught and reduces

PRINCESS* (PRINCE)
Ps 45: 13 All glorious is the **p** within her

PRISCILLA*
Wife of Aquila; co-worker with Paul (Ac 18; Ro 16:3; 1Co 16:19; 2Ti 4:19); instructor of Apollos (Ac 18:24–28).

PRISON (IMPRISONED IMPRISONMENT PRISONER PRISONERS)
Ps 66: 11 You brought us into **p** and laid
142: 7 Set me free from my **p**, that I may
Isa 42: 7 blind, to free captives from **p**
Mt 25: 36 I was in **p** and you came to visit
2Co 11: 23 been in **p** more frequently,
Heb 13: 3 remember those in **p** as if you were together with them in **p**,
Rev 20: 7 Satan will be released from his **p**

PRISONER (PRISON)
Ro 7: 23 making me a **p** of the law of sin
Eph 3: 1 the **p** of Christ Jesus for the sake

PRISONERS (PRISON)
Ps 68: 6 he leads out the **p** with singing;
79: 11 groans of the **p** come before you;
107: 10 **p** suffering in iron chains,
146: 7 The LORD sets **p** free,
Zec 9: 12 to your fortress, you **p** of hope;
Lk 4: 18 me to proclaim freedom for the **p**

PRIVILEGE*
2Co 8: 4 for the **p** of sharing in this service

PRIZE*
1Co 9: 24 run, but only one gets the **p**?
9: 24 Run in such a way as to get the **p**.
9: 27 will not be disqualified for the **p**.
Php 3: 14 on toward the goal to win the **p**

PROBE (PROBES)
Job 11: 7 Can you **p** the limits
Ps 17: 3 Though you **p** my heart, though

PROBES* (PROBE)
Ps 7: 9 the righteous God who **p** minds

PROCEDURE
Ecc 8: 6 proper time and **p** for every matter,

PROCESSION
Ps 68: 24 Your **p**, God, has come into view,
118: 27 join in the festal **p** up to the horns
1Co 4: 9 on display at the end of the **p**,
2Co 2: 14 as captives in Christ's triumphal **p**

PROCLAIM (PROCLAIMED PROCLAIMING PROCLAIMS PROCLAMATION)
Ex 33: 19 and I will **p** my name, the LORD,
Lev 25: 10 **p** liberty throughout the land to all
Dt 30: 12 and **p** it to us so we may obey it?"
2Sa 1: 20 **p** it not in the streets of Ashkelon,
1Ch 16: 8 praise to the LORD, **p** his name;
16: 23 **p** his salvation day after day.
Ne 8: 15 and that they should **p** this word
Ps 2: 7 I will **p** the LORD's decree:
9: 11 **p** among the nations what he has
19: 1 the skies **p** the work of his hands.
22: 31 They will **p** his righteousness,
40: 9 I **p** your saving acts in the great
50: 6 the heavens **p** his righteousness,
64: 9 they will **p** the works of God
68: 11 the women who **p** it are a mighty
68: 34 **P** the power of God, whose majesty
71: 16 I will come and **p** your mighty acts,
71: 16 I will **p** your righteous deeds,
79: 13 to generation we will **p** your praise.
96: 2 **p** his salvation day after day.
97: 6 The heavens **p** his righteousness,
105: 1 praise to the LORD, **p** his name;
106: 2 Who can **p** the mighty acts
118: 17 will **p** what the LORD has done.
145: 6 and I will **p** your great deeds.
Isa 12: 4 praise to the LORD, **p** his name;
12: 4 and **p** that his name is exalted.
42: 12 and **p** his praise in the islands.
52: 7 bring good news, who **p** peace,
61: 1 has anointed me to **p** good news
61: 1 to **p** freedom for the captives
66: 19 They will **p** my glory among
Jer 7: 2 house and there **p** this message:
50: 2 and **p** among the nations,
Hos 5: 9 tribes of Israel I **p** what is certain.
Zec 9: 10 He will **p** peace to the nations.
Mt 10: 7 As you go, **p** this message:
10: 27 in your ear, **p** from the roofs.
12: 18 and he will **p** justice to the nations.
Lk 4: 18 he has anointed me to **p** good news
4: 18 He has sent me to **p** freedom
9: 60 you go and **p** the kingdom of God."
Ac 17: 23 this is what I am going to **p** to you.
20: 27 I have not hesitated to **p** to you
Ro 10: 8 concerning faith that we **p**:
1Co 11: 26 cup, you **p** the Lord's death until he
Col 1: 28 He is the one we **p**,
4: 4 Pray that I may **p** it clearly, as I
1Jn 1: 1 this we **p** concerning the Word

PROCLAIMED (PROCLAIM)
Ex 9: 16 name might be **p** in all the earth.
34: 5 there with him and **p** his name,
Ac 28: 31 He **p** the kingdom of God
Ro 15: 19 I have fully **p** the gospel of Christ.
Col 1: 23 has been **p** to every creature under
2Ti 4: 17 me the message might be fully **p**

PROCLAIMING (PROCLAIM)
Ps 26: 7 **p** aloud your praise and telling of
92: 2 **p** your love in the morning and
92: 15 **p**, "The LORD is upright;
Lk 9: 6 **p** the good news and healing
Ac 5: 42 **p** the good news that Jesus is

PROCLAIMS (PROCLAIM)
Dt 18: 22 If what a prophet **p** in the name

PROCLAMATION (PROCLAIM)
Isa 62: 11 The LORD has made **p** to the ends
1Pe 3: 19 made **p** to the imprisoned spirits—

PRODUCE (PRODUCES)
Mt 3: 8 **P** fruit in keeping with repentance.
3: 10 does not **p** good fruit will be cut

PRODUCES (PRODUCE)
Pr 30: 33 so stirring up anger **p** strife."
Ro 5: 3 that suffering **p** perseverance;
Heb 12: 11 it **p** a harvest of righteousness

PROFANE (PROFANED)
Lev 19: 12 and so **p** the name of your God.
22: 32 Do not **p** my holy name, for I must
Mal 2: 10 Why do we **p** the covenant of our

PROFANED (PROFANE)
Eze 36: 20 the nations they **p** my holy name,

PROFESS*
Ro 10: 10 your mouth that you **p** your faith
1Ti 2: 10 for women who **p** to worship God.
Heb 4: 14 let us hold firmly to the faith we **p**.
10: 23 unswervingly to the hope we **p**,
13: 15 fruit of lips that openly **p** his name.

PROFIT (PROFITABLE)
Pr 14: 23 All hard work brings a **p**, but mere
21: 5 lead to **p** as surely as haste leads
Isa 44: 10 casts an idol, which can **p** nothing?
Eze 18: 8 at interest or take a **p** from them.
2Co 2: 17 not peddle the word of God for **p**.

PROFITABLE* (PROFIT)
Pr 3: 14 for she is more **p** than silver
31: 18 She sees that her trading is **p**,
Titus 3: 8 are excellent and **p** for everyone.

PROFOUND
Job 9: 4 His wisdom is **p**, his power is vast.
Ps 92: 5 LORD, how **p** your thoughts!
Eph 5: 32 This is a **p** mystery—but I am

PROGRESS
Php 1: 25 continue with all of you for your **p**
1Ti 4: 15 so that everyone may see your **p**.

PROLONG*
Dt 5: 33 **p** your days in the land that you
Ps 85: 5 Will you **p** your anger through all
Pr 3: 2 for they will **p** your life many years
Isa 53: 10 see his offspring and **p** his days,
La 4: 22 he will not **p** your exile.

PROMISE (PROMISED PROMISES)
Nu 23: 19 Does he **p** and not fulfill?
Jos 23: 14 Every **p** has been fulfilled;
2Sa 7: 25 keep forever the **p** you have made
1Ki 8: 20 LORD has kept the **p** he made:
8: 24 You have kept your **p** to your
Ne 5: 13 anyone who does not keep this **p**.
9: 8 have kept your **p** because you are
Ps 77: 8 Has his **p** failed for all time?
119: 41 salvation, according to your **p**;
119: 50 Your **p** preserves my life.
119: 58 to me according to your **p**.
119:162 in your **p** like one who finds great
Pr 11: 7 all the **p** of their power comes
Ac 2: 39 The **p** is for you and your children
Ro 4: 13 his offspring received the **p** that he
4: 20 through unbelief regarding the **p**
Gal 3: 14 faith we might receive the **p**
Eph 2: 12 foreigners to the covenants of the **p**
1Ti 4: 8 holding **p** for both the present life
Heb 6: 13 God made his **p** to Abraham,
11: 11 him faithful who had made the **p**.
2Pe 3: 9 Lord is not slow in keeping his **p**,
3: 13 with his **p** we are looking forward

PROMISED (PROMISE)
Ge 21: 1 did for Sarah what he had **p**.
24: 7 spoke to me and **p** me on oath,
Ex 3: 17 I have **p** to bring you up out of
Nu 10: 29 for the LORD has **p** good things
Dt 15: 6 God will bless you as he has **p**,
26: 18 his treasured possession as he **p**,
2Sa 7: 28 and you have **p** these good things
1Ki 9: 5 as I **p** David your father when I
2Ch 6: 15 with your mouth you have **p**
Ps 119: 57 I have **p** to obey your words.
Lk 24: 49 to send you what my Father has **p**;
Ac 1: 4 but wait for the gift my Father **p**,
13: 32 What God **p** our ancestors
Ro 4: 21 had power to do what he had **p**.
Titus 1: 2 lie, **p** before the beginning of time,
Heb 10: 23 we profess, for he who **p** is faithful.
10: 36 you will receive what he has **p**.
Jas 1: 12 the Lord has **p** to those who love
2: 5 the kingdom he **p** those who love
2Pe 3: 4 say, "Where is this 'coming' he **p**?
1Jn 2: 25 And this is what he **p** us—

PROMISES (PROMISE)
Jos 21: 45 of all the LORD's good **p** to Israel
23: 14 all the good **p** the LORD your God
1Ki 8: 56 all the good **p** he gave through his
1Ch 17: 19 and made known all these great **p**.
Ps 85: 8 **p** peace to his people, his faithful
106: 12 they believed his **p** and sang his
119:140 **p** have been thoroughly tested,
119:148 that I may meditate on your **p**.
145: 13 LORD is trustworthy in all he **p**
Ro 9: 4 law, the temple worship and the **p**.
2Co 1: 20 matter how many **p** God has made,
7: 1 since we have these **p**, dear friends,
Heb 8: 6 covenant is established on better **p**.
2Pe 1: 4 us his very great and precious **p**,

PROMOTE
Pr 12: 20 but those who **p** peace have joy.
16: 21 and gracious words **p** instruction.
1Ti 1: 4 Such things **p** controversial

PROMPTED
1Th 1: 3 by faith, your labor **p** by love,
2Th 1: 11 and your every deed **p** by faith.

PRONOUNCE (PRONOUNCED)
1Ch 23: 13 to **p** blessings in his name forever.

PRONOUNCED (PRONOUNCE)
1Ch 16: 12 miracles, and the judgments he **p**,

PROOF (PROVE)
Ac 17: 31 He has given **p** of this to everyone
2Co 8: 24 Therefore show these men the **p**

PROPER
Ps 104: 27 give them their food at the **p** time.
145: 15 give them their food at the **p** time.
Ecc 8: 5 the wise heart will know the **p** time
Mt 24: 45 give them their food at the **p** time?
1Co 11: 13 Is it **p** for a woman to pray to God
Gal 6: 9 at the **p** time we will reap a harvest
1Ti 2: 6 been witnessed to at the **p** time.
1Pe 2: 17 Show **p** respect to everyone,

PROPERTY
Heb 10: 34 the confiscation of your **p**,

PROPHECIES (PROPHESY)
1Co 13: 8 But where there are **p**, they will
1Th 5: 20 Do not treat **p** with contempt

PROPHECY (PROPHESY)
Da 9: 24 seal up vision and **p** and to anoint
1Co 12: 10 powers, to another **p**, to another
13: 2 If I have the gift of **p** and can
14: 1 gifts of the Spirit, especially **p**.
14: 6 or knowledge or **p** or word
14: 22 **p**, however, is not for unbelievers
2Pe 1: 20 that no **p** of Scripture came
Rev 22: 18 the words of the **p** of this scroll:

PROPHESIED (PROPHESY)
Nu 11: 25 the Spirit rested on them, they **p**—
1Sa 19: 24 and he too **p** in Samuel's presence.
Jn 11: 51 that year he **p** that Jesus would die
Ac 19: 6 and they spoke in tongues and **p**.
21: 9 four unmarried daughters who **p**.

PROPHESIES (PROPHESY)
Jer 28: 9 But the prophet who **p** peace will
Eze 12: 27 and he **p** about the distant future.'
1Co 11: 4 **p** with his head covered dishonors
14: 3 the one who **p** speaks to people for

PROPHESY (PROPHECIES PROPHECY PROPHESIED PROPHESIES PROPHESYING PROPHET PROPHET'S PROPHETESS PROPHETIC PROPHETS)
1Sa 10: 6 you, and you will **p** with them;
Eze 13: 2 **p** against the prophets of Israel
13: 17 daughters of your people who **p**
34: 2 **p** against the shepherds of Israel;
37: 4 "**P** to these bones and say to them,
Joel 2: 28 Your sons and daughters will **p**,
Mt 7: 22 did we not **p** in your name
Ac 2: 17 Your sons and daughters will **p**,
1Co 13: 9 we know in part and we **p** in part,
14: 39 be eager to **p**, and do not forbid
Rev 11: 3 and they will **p** for 1,260 days,

PROPHESYING (PROPHESY)
1Ch 25: 1 and Jeduthun for the ministry of **p**,
Ro 12: 6 If your gift is **p**, then prophesy

PROPHET (PROPHESY)
Ex 7: 1 your brother Aaron will be your **p**.
15: 20 Then Miriam the **p**, Aaron's sister,
Nu 12: 6 "When there is a **p** among you, I,
Dt 13: 1 If a **p**, or one who foretells
18: 18 for them a **p** like you from among

Dt 18: 22 That **p** has spoken presumptuously,
Jdg 4: 4 Deborah, a **p**, the wife of
1Sa 3: 20 Samuel was attested as a **p**
9: 9 because the **p** of today used to be
1Ki 1: 8 Nathan the **p**, Shimei and Rei
18: 36 the **p** Elijah stepped forward
2Ki 5: 8 know that there is a **p** in Israel."
6: 12 "but Elisha, the **p** who is in Israel,
20: 1 The **p** Isaiah son of Amoz went
2Ch 35: 18 since the days of the **p** Samuel;
36: 12 himself before Jeremiah the **p**,
Ezr 5: 1 Haggai the **p** and Zechariah the **p**,
Eze 2: 5 that a **p** has been among them.
33: 33 that a **p** has been among them."
Hos 9: 7 so great, the **p** is considered a fool,
Am 7: 14 was neither a **p** nor the son of a **p**,
Hab 1: 1 that Habakkuk the **p** received.
Hag 1: 1 LORD came through the **p** Haggai
Zec 1: 1 came to the **p** Zechariah son
13: 4 that day every **p** will be ashamed
Mal 4: 5 "See, I will send the **p** Elijah to you
Mt 10: 41 Whoever welcomes a **p** as a **p** will
11: 9 A **p**? Yes, I tell you, and more than a **p**.
12: 39 it except the sign of the **p** Jonah.
Lk 1: 76 will be called a **p** of the Most High;
2: 36 There was also a **p**, Anna,
4: 24 "no **p** is accepted in his hometown.
7: 16 "A great **p** has appeared among
24: 19 "He was a **p**, powerful in word
Jn 1: 21 "Are you the **P**?"
Ac 7: 37 for you a **p** like me from your own
21: 10 a **p** named Agabus came down
1Co 14: 37 If anyone thinks they are a **p** or
Rev 16: 13 out of the mouth of the false **p**.

PROPHET'S (PROPHESY)
2Pe 1: 20 about by the **p** own interpretation

PROPHETESS* (PROPHESY)
Isa 8: 3 Then I made love to the **p**, and she

PROPHETIC (PROPHET)
2Pe 1: 19 have the **p** message as something

PROPHETS (PROPHESY)
Nu 11: 29 that all the LORD's people were **p**
1Sa 10: 11 Is Saul also among the **p**?"
28: 6 him by dreams or Urim or **p**.
1Ki 19: 10 put your **p** to death with the sword.
1Ch 16: 22 do my **p** no harm."
Ps 105: 15 do my **p** no harm."
Jer 23: 9 Concerning the **p**: My heart is
23: 30 "I am against the **p** who steal
Eze 13: 2 prophesy against the **p** of Israel
Mt 5: 17 come to abolish the Law or the **P**;
7: 12 for this sums up the Law and the **P**.
7: 15 "Watch out for false **p**.
22: 40 Law and the **P** hang on these two
23: 37 you who kill the **p** and stone those
24: 24 messiahs and false **p** will appear
26: 56 of the **p** might be fulfilled."
Lk 10: 24 I tell you that many **p** and kings
11: 49 'I will send them **p** and apostles,
24: 25 believe all that the **p** have spoken!
24: 44 of Moses, the **P** and the Psalms."
Ac 3: 24 all the **p** who have spoken have
10: 43 All the **p** testify about him
13: 1 the church at Antioch there were **p**
26: 22 saying nothing beyond what the **p**
28: 23 from the **P** he tried to persuade
Ro 1: 2 beforehand through his **p**
3: 21 to which the Law and the **P** testify.
11: 3 they have killed your **p** and torn
1Co 12: 28 apostles, second **p**, third teachers,
12: 29 Are all **p**? Are all teachers?
14: 32 The spirits of **p** are subject to the control of **p**.
Eph 2: 20 foundation of the apostles and **p**,
3: 5 Spirit to God's holy apostles and **p**.
4: 11 the apostles, the **p**, the evangelists,
Heb 1: 1 our ancestors through the **p** at
1Pe 1: 10 the **p**, who spoke of the grace
2Pe 3: 2 spoken in the past by the holy **p**
1Jn 4: 1 because many false **p** have gone
Rev 11: 10 because these two **p** had tormented
18: 20 Rejoice, apostles and **p**!

PROPORTION
Dt 16: 10 giving a freewill offering in **p**
16: 17 must bring a gift in **p** to the way

PROPRIETY*
1Ti 2: 9 with decency and **p**,
2: 15 in faith, love and holiness with **p**.

PROSPECT*
Pr 10: 28 The **p** of the righteous is joy,

PROSPER (PROSPERED PROSPERITY PROSPEROUS PROSPERS)
Dt 5: 33 you, so that you may live and **p**
28: 63 pleased the LORD to make you **p**
29: 9 you may **p** in everything you do.
1Ki 2: 3 this so that you may **p** in all you do
Ezr 6: 14 **p** under the preaching of Haggai
Pr 11: 10 When the righteous **p**, the city
11: 25 A generous person will **p**;
17: 20 whose heart is corrupt does not **p**;
19: 8 understanding will soon **p**.
28: 13 conceals their sins does not **p**,
28: 25 who trust in the LORD will **p**.
Isa 53: 10 of the LORD will **p** in his hand.
Jer 12: 1 Why does the way of the wicked **p**?

PROSPERED (PROSPER)
Ge 39: 2 was with Joseph so that he **p**,
2Ch 14: 7 on every side." So they built and **p**.
31: 21 And so he **p**.

PROSPERITY (PROSPER)
Dt 28: 11 LORD will grant you abundant **p**—
30: 15 I set before you today life and **p**,
Job 36: 11 spend the rest of their days in **p**
Ps 73: 3 when I saw the **p** of the wicked.
122: 9 LORD our God, I will seek your **p**.
128: 2 blessings and **p** will be yours.
Pr 3: 2 years and bring you peace and **p**.
21: 21 and love finds life, **p** and honor.
Isa 45: 7 I bring **p** and create disaster;

PROSPEROUS (PROSPER)
Dt 30: 9 your God will make you most **p**
Jos 1: 8 Then you will be **p** and successful.

PROSPERS (PROSPER)
Ps 1: 3 whatever they do **p**.
Pr 16: 20 gives heed to instruction **p**,

PROSTITUTE (PROSTITUTES PROSTITUTION)
Lev 20: 6 and spiritists to **p** themselves
Nu 15: 39 not **p** yourselves by chasing
Jos 2: 1 the house of a **p** named Rahab
Pr 6: 26 For a **p** can be had for a loaf
7: 10 dressed like a **p** and with crafty
Eze 16: 15 and used your fame to become a **p**.
23: 7 She gave herself as a **p** to all
Hos 3: 3 you must not be a **p** or be intimate
1Co 6: 15 of Christ and unite them with a **p**?
6: 16 who unites himself with a **p** is one
Rev 17: 1 you the punishment of the great **p**,

PROSTITUTES (PROSTITUTE)
Pr 29: 3 of **p** squanders his wealth.
Mt 21: 31 the **p** are entering the kingdom
Lk 15: 30 your property with **p** comes home,

PROSTITUTION (PROSTITUTE)
Eze 16: 16 where you carried on your **p**.
23: 3 engaging in **p** from their youth.
Hos 4: 10 they will engage in **p** but not

PROSTRATE
Dt 9: 18 again I fell **p** before the LORD
1Ki 18: 39 saw this, they fell **p** and cried,

PROTECT (PROTECTED PROTECTION PROTECTS)
Dt 23: 14 moves about in your camp to **p**
Ps 25: 21 integrity and uprightness **p** me,
32: 7 you will **p** me from trouble
40: 11 love and faithfulness always **p** me.
91: 14 I will **p** him, for he acknowledges
140: 1 **p** me from the violent,
Pr 2: 11 Discretion will **p** you,
4: 6 wisdom, and she will **p** you;
Jn 17: 11 **p** them by the power of your name,
17: 15 that you **p** them from the evil one.
2Th 3: 3 you and **p** you from the evil one.

PROTECTED (PROTECT)
Jos 24: 17 He **p** us on our entire journey
1Sa 30: 23 He has **p** us and delivered into our
Jn 17: 12 I **p** them and kept them safe

PROTECTION (PROTECT)
Ezr 9: 9 he has given us a wall of **p** in Judah
Ps 5: 11 Spread your **p** over them, that

PROTECTS (PROTECT)
Ps 41: 2 The LORD **p** and preserves them—
116: 6 The LORD **p** the unwary;
Pr 2: 8 **p** the way of his faithful ones.
27: 18 whoever **p** their master will be
1Co 13: 7 It always **p**, always trusts,

PROUD (PRIDE)
Ps 31: 23 him, but the **p** he pays back in full.
101: 5 has haughty eyes and a **p** heart,
Pr 3: 34 He mocks **p** mockers but shows
16: 5 The LORD detests all the **p**
16: 19 than to share plunder with the **p**.
21: 4 Haughty eyes and a **p** heart—
Isa 2: 12 has a day in store for all the **p**
Ro 12: 16 Do not be **p**, but be willing
1Co 13: 4 envy, it does not boast, it is not **p**.
2Ti 3: 2 of money, boastful, **p**, abusive,
Jas 4: 6 "God opposes the **p** but shows
1Pe 5: 5 "God opposes the **p** but shows

PROVE (PROOF PROVED PROVEN PROVING)
Pr 29: 25 Fear of man will **p** to be a snare,
Jn 8: 46 Can any of you **p** me guilty of sin?
16: 8 he will **p** the world to be
1Co 4: 2 been given a trust must **p** faithful.

PROVED (PROVE)
Isa 5: 16 the holy God will be **p** holy by his
Eze 28: 25 I will be **p** holy through them
Mt 11: 19 wisdom is **p** right by her deeds."
Ro 3: 4 may be **p** right when you speak

PROVEN* (PROVE)
1Pe 1: 7 the **p** genuineness of your faith—

PROVIDE (PROVIDED PROVIDES PROVISION)
Ge 22: 8 "God himself will **p** the lamb
22: 14 that place The LORD Will **P**.
Isa 43: 20 because I **p** water in the wilderness
61: 3 and **p** for those who grieve in Zion
1Co 10: 13 **p** a way out so that you can endure
1Ti 5: 8 Anyone who does not **p** for their
Titus 3: 14 in order to **p** for urgent needs

PROVIDED (PROVIDE)
Ps 68: 10 bounty, God, you **p** for the poor.
111: 9 He **p** redemption for his people;
Jnh 1: 17 Now the LORD **p** a huge fish
4: 6 the LORD God **p** a leafy plant
4: 7 dawn the next day God **p** a worm,
4: 8 rose, God **p** a scorching east wind,
Gal 4: 18 be zealous, **p** the purpose is good,
Heb 1: 3 he had **p** purification for sins,

PROVIDES (PROVIDE)
Ps 111: 5 He **p** food for those who fear him;
Pr 31: 15 she **p** food for her family
Eze 18: 7 and **p** clothing for the naked.
1Ti 6: 17 who richly **p** us with everything
1Pe 4: 11 do so with the strength God **p**,

PROVING* (PROVE)
Ac 9: 22 in Damascus by **p** that Jesus is
17: 3 **p** that the Messiah had to suffer
18: 28 **p** from the Scriptures that Jesus

PROVISION (PROVIDE)
Ro 5: 17 who receive God's abundant **p**

PROVOKED
Ecc 7: 9 Do not be quickly **p** in your spirit,
Jer 32: 32 Judah have **p** me by all the evil

PROWLS
1Pe 5: 8 enemy the devil **p** around like

PRUDENCE* (PRUDENT)
Pr 1: 4 giving **p** to those who are simple,
8: 5 You who are simple, gain **p**;
8: 12 "I, wisdom, dwell together with **p**;
12: 8 is praised according to their **p**,
15: 5 whoever heeds correction shows **p**.
16: 22 **P** is a fountain of life to the
19: 25 and the simple will learn **p**;
21: 16 from the path of **p** comes to rest

PRUDENT (PRUDENCE)
Pr 1: 3 receiving instruction in **p** behavior,
12: 16 once, but the **p** overlook an insult.
12: 23 The **p** keep their knowledge
13: 16 All who are **p** act with knowledge,
14: 8 The wisdom of the **p** is to give
14: 15 the **p** give thought to their steps.
14: 18 the **p** are crowned with knowledge.
19: 14 but a **p** wife is from the LORD.
22: 3 The **p** see danger and take refuge,
27: 12 The **p** see danger and take refuge,
Jer 49: 7 Has counsel perished from the **p**?
Am 5: 13 Therefore the **p** keep quiet in such

PRUNES* (PRUNING)
Jn 15: 2 does bear fruit he **p** so that it will

PRUNING (PRUNES)
Isa 2: 4 and their spears into **p** hooks.
Joel 3: 10 and your **p** hooks into spears.

PSALMS
Eph 5: 19 speaking to one another with **p**,
Col 3: 16 with all wisdom through **p**,

PUBERTY*
Eze 16: 7 grew and developed and entered **p**.

PUBLICLY
Ac 20: 20 have taught you **p** and from house

PUFFS*
1Co 8: 1 knowledge **p** up while love builds

PUNISH (PUNISHED PUNISHMENT)
Ge 15: 14 But I will **p** the nation they serve
Ex 32: 34 when the time comes for me to **p**,
Pr 23: 13 if you **p** them with the rod, they
Isa 13: 11 I will **p** the world for its evil,
Jer 2: 19 Your wickedness will **p** you;
21: 14 I will **p** you as your deeds deserve,
Zep 1: 12 and **p** those who are complacent,
Ac 7: 7 But I will **p** the nation they serve as
2Th 1: 8 He will **p** those who do not know
1Pe 2: 14 by him to **p** those who do wrong

PUNISHED (PUNISH)
Ezr 9: 13 you have **p** us less than our sins
Ps 99: 8 God, though you **p** their misdeeds.
Isa 53: 8 of my people he was **p**.
La 3: 39 should the living complain when **p**
Mk 12: 40 men will be **p** most severely."
Lk 23: 41 We are **p** justly, for we are getting
2Th 1: 9 They will be **p** with everlasting
Heb 10: 29 to be **p** who has trampled the Son

PUNISHMENT (PUNISH)
Isa 53: 5 the **p** that brought us peace was
Jer 4: 18 This is your **p**. How bitter it is!
Mt 25: 46 they will go away to eternal **p**,
Lk 12: 48 and does things deserving **p** will be
21: 22 this is the time of **p** in fulfillment
Ro 13: 4 wrath to bring **p** on the wrongdoer.
Heb 2: 2 disobedience received its just **p**,
2Pe 2: 9 to hold the unrighteous for **p**

PURCHASED
Ps 74: 2 the nation you **p** long ago,
Rev 5: 9 your blood you **p** for God persons

PURE (PURIFICATION PURIFIED PURIFIES PURIFY PURITY)
2Sa 22: 27 to the **p** you show yourself **p**,
2Ki 2: 22 the water has remained **p** to this
Job 14: 4 Who can bring what is **p**
Ps 19: 9 The fear of the LORD is **p**,
24: 4 who has clean hands and a **p** heart,
51: 10 Create in me a **p** heart, O God,
Pr 15: 26 gracious words are **p** in his sight.
20: 9 can say, "I have kept my heart **p**;
Isa 52: 11 Come out from it and be **p**, you
Hab 1: 13 Your eyes are too **p** to look on evil;
Mt 5: 8 Blessed are the **p** in heart, for they
2Co 11: 2 I might present you as a **p** virgin
Php 4: 8 whatever is **p**, whatever is lovely,
1Ti 1: 5 which comes from a **p** heart
5: 22 the sins of others. Keep yourself **p**.
2Ti 2: 22 call on the Lord out of a **p** heart.
Titus 1: 15 To the **p**, all things are **p**,
2: 5 to be self-controlled and **p**, to be
Heb 7: 26 **p**, set apart from sinners,
13: 4 all, and the marriage bed kept **p**,
Jas 1: 27 that God our Father accepts as **p**
3: 17 comes from heaven is first of all **p**;
1Jn 3: 3 purify themselves, just as he is **p**.

PURGE
Pr 20: 30 and beatings **p** the inmost being.

PURIFICATION (PURE)
Heb 1: 3 After he had provided **p** for sins,

PURIFIED (PURE)
Ac 15: 9 them, for he **p** their hearts by faith.
1Pe 1: 22 you have **p** yourselves by obeying

PURIFIES* (PURE)
1Jn 1: 7 of Jesus, his Son, **p** us from all sin.

PURIFY (PURE)
Nu 19: 12 They must **p** themselves
2Co 7: 1 let us **p** ourselves from everything
Titus 2: 14 to **p** for himself a people that are
Jas 4: 8 you sinners, and **p** your hearts,
1Jn 1: 9 and **p** us from all unrighteousness.
3: 3 this hope in him **p** themselves,

PURIM
Est 9: 26 these days were called **P**,

PURITY* (PURE)
Ps 119: 9 person stay on the path of **p**?
Hos 8: 5 long will they be incapable of **p**?
2Co 6: 6 in **p**, understanding,
1Ti 4: 12 conduct, in love, in faith and in **p**.
5: 2 women as sisters, with absolute **p**.
1Pe 3: 2 when they see the **p** and reverence

PURPLE
Pr 31: 22 she is clothed in fine linen and **p**.
Mk 15: 17 They put a **p** robe on him,

PURPOSE (PURPOSED PURPOSES)
Ex 9: 16 I have raised you up for this very **p**,
Job 36: 5 he is mighty, and firm in his **p**.
42: 2 no **p** of yours can be thwarted.
Pr 19: 21 it is the LORD's **p** that prevails.
Isa 46: 10 I say, 'My **p** will stand, and I will
55: 11 achieve the **p** for which I sent it.
Ro 8: 28 been called according to his **p**.
9: 11 God's **p** in election might stand:
9: 17 "I raised you up for this very **p**,
1Co 3: 8 the one who waters have one **p**,
2Co 5: 5 fashioned us for this very **p** is God,
Gal 4: 18 be zealous, provided the **p** is good,
Eph 1: 11 conformity with the **p** of his will,
3: 11 his eternal **p** that he accomplished
Php 2: 13 to act in order to fulfill his good **p**.
2Ti 1: 9 because of his own **p** and grace.

PURPOSED (PURPOSE)
Isa 14: 24 and as I have **p**, so it will happen.
14: 27 For the LORD Almighty has **p**,
Eph 1: 9 pleasure, which he **p** in Christ,

PURPOSES (PURPOSE)
Ps 33: 10 he thwarts the **p** of the peoples.
Jer 23: 20 until he fully accomplishes the **p**
32: 19 great are your **p** and mighty are

PURSE (PURSES)
Hag 1: 6 to put them in a **p** with holes in it."
Lk 10: 4 Do not take a **p** or bag or sandals;
22: 36 "But now if you have a **p**, take it,

PURSES (PURSE)
Lk 12: 33 Provide **p** for yourselves that will

PURSUE (PURSUES)
Ps 34: 14 and do good; seek peace and **p** it.
Pr 15: 9 loves those who **p** righteousness.
Ro 9: 30 who did not **p** righteousness,
1Ti 6: 11 and **p** righteousness, godliness,
2Ti 2: 22 of youth and **p** righteousness, faith,
1Pe 3: 11 they must seek peace and **p** it.

PURSUES (PURSUE)
Pr 21: 21 Whoever **p** righteousness and love
28: 1 The wicked flee though no one **p**,

QUAIL
Ex 16: 13 That evening **q** came and covered
Nu 11: 31 and drove **q** in from the sea.

QUALITIES* (QUALITY)
Da 6: 3 by his exceptional **q** that the king
Ro 1: 20 of the world God's invisible **q**—
2Pe 1: 8 if you possess these **q** in increasing

QUALITY (QUALITIES)
1Co 3: 13 and the fire will test the **q** of each

QUARREL (QUARRELING QUARRELS QUARRELSOME)
Pr 15: 18 the one who is patient calms a **q**.
17: 14 Starting a **q** is like breaching a dam
17: 19 Whoever loves a **q** loves sin;
20: 3 strife, but every fool is quick to **q**.
26: 17 who rushes into a **q** not their own.
26: 20 without a gossip a **q** dies down.
Isa 45: 9 to those who **q** with their Maker,
Jas 4: 2 what you want, so you **q** and fight.

QUARRELING (QUARREL)
1Co 3: 3 there is jealousy and **q** among you,
2Ti 2: 14 Warn them before God against **q**

QUARRELS (QUARREL)
2Ti 2: 23 because you know they produce **q**.
Jas 4: 1 causes fights and **q** among you?

QUARRELSOME (QUARREL)
Pr 19: 13 **q** wife is like the constant dripping
21: 9 than share a house with a **q** wife.
26: 21 so is a **q** person for kindling strife.
1Ti 3: 3 gentle, not **q**, not a lover of money.
2Ti 2: 24 the Lord's servant must not be **q**

QUEEN
1Ki 10: 1 When the **q** of Sheba heard
2Ch 9: 1 When the **q** of Sheba heard
Mt 12: 42 The **Q** of the South will rise

QUENCH (QUENCHED)
SS 8: 7 Many waters cannot **q** love;
1Th 5: 19 Do not **q** the Spirit.

QUENCHED (QUENCH)
Isa 66: 24 fire that burns them will not be **q**,
Mk 9: 48 do not die, and the fire is not **q**.'

QUICK-TEMPERED* (TEMPER)
Pr 14: 17 A **q** person does foolish things,
14: 29 but one who is **q** displays folly.
Titus 1: 7 not **q**, not given to drunkenness,

QUIET (QUIETNESS)
Ps 23: 2 he leads me beside **q** waters,
Pr 17: 1 and **q** than a house full of feasting,
Ecc 9: 17 The **q** words of the wise are more
Am 5: 13 Therefore the prudent keep **q**
Lk 19: 40 "if they keep **q**, the stones will cry
1Th 4: 11 it your ambition to lead a **q** life:
1Ti 2: 2 peaceful and **q** lives in all godliness
1Ti 2: 12 over a man; she must be **q**.
1Pe 3: 4 beauty of a gentle and **q** spirit,

QUIETNESS* (QUIET)
Job 3: 26 I have no peace, no **q**; I have no
Isa 30: 15 in **q** and trust is your strength,
32: 17 its effect will be **q** and confidence
1Ti 2: 11 A woman should learn in **q** and

QUIVER
Ps 127: 5 Blessed is the man whose **q** is full

RACE
Ecc 9: 11 The **r** is not to the swift or the
Ac 20: 24 my only aim is to finish the **r**
1Co 9: 24 that in a **r** all the runners run,
Gal 2: 2 had not been running my **r** in vain.
5: 7 You were running a good **r**.
2Ti 4: 7 I have finished the **r**, I have kept
Heb 12: 1 with perseverance the **r** marked

RACHEL
Daughter of Laban (Ge 29:16); wife of Jacob (Ge 29:28); bore two sons (Ge 30:22–24; 35:16–24; 46:19). Stole Laban's gods (Ge 31:19, 32–35). Death (Ge 35:19–20).

RADIANCE (RADIANT)
Eze 1: 28 rainy day, so was the **r** around him.
Heb 1: 3 The Son is the **r** of God's glory

RADIANT (RADIANCE)
Ex 34: 29 that his face was **r** because he had
Ps 34: 5 Those who look to him are **r**;
76: 4 You are **r** with light, more majestic
132: 18 will be adorned with a **r** crown."
SS 5: 10 My beloved is **r** and ruddy,
Isa 60: 5 Then you will look and be **r**,
Eph 5: 27 her to himself as a **r** church,

RAGE
Pr 29: 11 Fools give full vent to their **r**,
Ac 4: 25 "'Why do the nations **r**
Col 3: 8 anger, **r**, malice, slander, and filthy

RAGS
Isa 64: 6 our righteous acts are like filthy **r**;

RAHAB
Prostitute of Jericho who hid Israelite spies (Jos 2; 6:22–25; Heb 11:31; Jas 2:25). Mother of Boaz (Mt 1:5).

RAIN (RAINBOW)
Ge 7: 4 from now I will send **r** on the earth
1Ki 17: 1 there will be neither dew nor **r**
18: 1 and I will send **r** on the land."
Mt 5: 45 and sends **r** on the righteous
Jas 5: 17 earnestly that it would not **r**,
Jude : 12 They are clouds without **r**,

RAINBOW (RAIN)
Ge 9: 13 I have set my **r** in the clouds, and it
Eze 1: 28 Like the appearance of a **r** in the
Rev 4: 3 A **r** that shone like an emerald

RAISE (RISE)
Jn 6: 39 me, but **r** them up at the last day.
1Co 15: 15 he did not **r** him if in fact the dead

RAISED (RISE)
Ps 89: 19 I have **r** up a young man
Isa 52: 13 he will be **r** and lifted up and
Mt 17: 23 the third day he will be **r** to life."
Lk 7: 22 the dead are **r**, and the good news
Ac 2: 24 But God **r** him from the dead,
Ro 4: 25 was **r** to life for our justification.
6: 4 just as Christ was **r** from the dead
8: 11 he who **r** Christ from the dead will
10: 9 your heart that God **r** him
1Co 15: 4 he was **r** on the third day according
15: 20 Christ has indeed been **r**

RALLY*
Isa 11: 10 the nations will **r** to him, and his

RAM (RAMS)
Ge 22: 13 in a thicket he saw a **r** caught
Ex 25: 5 **r** skins dyed red and another type
Da 8: 3 there before me was a **r** with two

RAMPART*
Ps 91: 4 will be your shield and **r**.

RAMS (RAM)
1Sa 15: 22 to heed is better than the fat of **r**.
Mic 6: 7 be pleased with thousands of **r**,

RAN (RUN)
Jnh 1: 3 But Jonah **r** away from the LORD

RANSOM
Mt 20: 28 to give his life as a **r** for many."
Mk 10: 45 to give his life as a **r** for many."
1Ti 2: 6 who gave himself as a **r** for all
Heb 9: 15 he has died as a **r** to set them free

RARE
Pr 20: 15 that speak knowledge are a **r** jewel.

RAVEN (RAVENS)
Ge 8: 7 and sent out a **r**, and it kept flying
Job 38: 41 food for the **r** when its young cry

RAVENS (RAVEN)
1Ki 17: 6 The **r** brought him bread and meat
Ps 147: 9 and for the young **r** when they call.
Lk 12: 24 Consider the **r**: They do not sow

RAYS
Mal 4: 2 will rise with healing in its **r**.

READ (READING READS)
Dt 17: 19 he is to **r** it all the days of his life so
Jos 8: 34 Joshua **r** all the words of the law—
2Ki 23: 2 He **r** in their hearing all the words
Ne 8: 8 They **r** from the Book of the Law
Jer 36: 6 **r** to the people from the scroll
2Co 3: 2 hearts, known and **r** by everyone.

READING (READ)
1Ti 4: 13 to the public **r** of Scripture,

READS (READ)
Rev 1: 3 is the one who **r** aloud the words

REAFFIRM
2Co 2: 8 therefore, to **r** your love for him.

REAL* (REALITIES REALITY)
Jn 6: 55 For my flesh is **r** food and my blood is **r** drink.
1Jn 2: 27 all things and as that anointing is **r**,

REALITIES* (REAL)
1Co 2: 13 the Spirit, explaining spiritual **r**
Heb 10: 1 not the **r** themselves.

REALITY* (REAL)
Col 2: 17 the **r**, however, is found in Christ.

REALMS
Eph 1: 3 the heavenly **r** with every spiritual
2: 6 in the heavenly **r** in Christ Jesus,

REAP (REAPER REAPS)
Job 4: 8 evil and those who sow trouble **r** it.
Ps 126: 5 sow with tears will **r** with songs
Hos 8: 7 sow the wind and **r** the whirlwind.
10: 12 **r** the fruit of unfailing love,
Jn 4: 38 to **r** what you have not worked for.
Ro 6: 22 the benefit you **r** leads to holiness,
2Co 9: 6 sparingly will also **r** sparingly,
9: 6 generously will also **r** generously.
Gal 6: 8 from the flesh will **r** destruction;
6: 8 from the Spirit will **r** eternal life.

REAPER (REAP)
Jn 4: 36 and the **r** may be glad together.

REAPS (REAP)
Pr 11: 18 who sows righteousness **r** a sure
22: 8 Whoever sows injustice **r** calamity,
Gal 6: 7 A man **r** what he sows.

REASON (REASONED)
Mt 19: 5 this **r** a man will leave his father
Jn 12: 27 it was for this very **r** I came to this
15: 25 'They hated me without **r**.'
1Pe 3: 15 asks you to give the **r** for the hope
2Pe 1: 5 For this very **r**, make every effort

REASONED (REASON)
1Co 13: 11 thought like a child, I **r** like a child.

REBEKAH
Sister of Laban, secured as bride for Isaac (Ge 24). Mother of Esau and Jacob (Ge 25:19–26). Taken by Abimelek as sister of Isaac; returned (Ge 26:1–11). Encouraged Jacob to trick Isaac out of blessing (Ge 27:1–17).

REBEL (REBELLED REBELLION REBELS)
Nu 14: 9 Only do not **r** against the LORD.
1Sa 12: 14 do not **r** against his commands,
Mt 10: 21 children will **r** against their parents

REBELLED (REBEL)
Ps 78: 56 test and **r** against the Most High;
Isa 63: 10 Yet they **r** and grieved his Holy

REBELLION (REBEL)
Ex 34: 7 forgiving wickedness, **r** and sin.
Nu 14: 18 in love and forgiving sin and **r**.
1Sa 15: 23 For **r** is like the sin of divination,
2Th 2: 3 will not come until the **r** occurs

REBELS (REBEL)
Mk 15: 27 They crucified two **r** with him,
Ro 13: 2 whoever **r** against the authority is
1Ti 1: 9 but for lawbreakers and **r**,

REBIRTH* (BEAR)
Titus 3: 5 saved us through the washing of **r**

REBUILD (BUILD)
Ezr 5: 2 set to work to **r** the house of God
Ne 2: 17 let us **r** the wall of Jerusalem,
Ps 102: 16 For the LORD will **r** Zion
Da 9: 25 **r** Jerusalem until the Anointed
Am 9: 14 "They will **r** the ruined cities
Ac 15: 16 return and **r** David's fallen tent.

REBUILT (BUILD)
Zec 1: 16 and there my house will be **r**.

REBUKE (REBUKED REBUKES REBUKING)
Lev 19: 17 **R** your neighbor frankly so you
Ps 141: 5 let him **r** me—that is oil on my
Pr 3: 11 discipline, and do not resent his **r**,
9: 8 **r** the wise and they will love you.
17: 10 A **r** impresses a discerning person
19: 25 **r** the discerning, and they will gain
25: 12 of fine gold is the **r** of a wise judge
27: 5 Better is open **r** than hidden love.
30: 6 he will **r** you and prove you a liar.
Ecc 7: 5 to heed the **r** of a wise person than
Isa 54: 9 with you, never to **r** you again.
Jer 2: 19 your backsliding will **r** you.
Zep 3: 17 in his love he will no longer **r** you,
Lk 17: 3 or sister sins against you, **r** them;
1Ti 5: 1 Do not **r** an older man harshly,
2Ti 4: 2 correct, **r** and encourage—
Titus 1: 13 Therefore **r** them sharply,
2: 15 Encourage and **r** with all authority.
Rev 3: 19 Those whom I love I **r**

REBUKED (REBUKE)
Mk 16: 14 *he **r** them for their lack of faith*

REBUKES (REBUKE)
Job 22: 4 "Is it for your piety that he **r** you
Pr 28: 23 Whoever **r** a person will in the end
29: 1 many **r** will suddenly be destroyed
Heb 12: 5 do not lose heart when he **r** you,

REBUKING (REBUKE)
2Ti 3: 16 and is useful for teaching, **r**,

RECALLING
1Ti 1: 18 by **r** them you may fight the battle

RECEIVE (RECEIVED RECEIVES RECEIVING)
Mt 10: 41 a prophet will **r** a prophet's reward,
10: 41 righteous person will **r** a righteous
Mk 10: 15 anyone who will not **r** the kingdom
Jn 1: 12 Yet to all who did **r** him, to those
20: 22 them and said, "**R** the Holy Spirit.
Ac 1: 8 you will **r** power when the Holy
2: 38 will **r** the gift of the Holy Spirit.
19: 2 "Did you **r** the Holy Spirit
20: 35 more blessed to give than to **r**.'"
1Co 9: 14 the gospel should **r** their living
2Co 1: 4 the comfort we ourselves **r**
6: 17 no unclean thing, and I will **r** you."
1Ti 1: 16 believe in him and **r** eternal life.
Jas 1: 7 should not expect to **r** anything
2Pe 1: 11 you will **r** a rich welcome
1Jn 3: 22 and **r** from him anything we ask,
Rev 4: 11 to **r** glory and honor and power,
5: 12 to **r** power and wealth and wisdom

RECEIVED (RECEIVE)
Mt 6: 2 they have **r** their reward in full.
10: 8 Freely you have **r**; freely give.
Mk 11: 24 believe that you have **r** it, and it
Jn 1: 16 of his fullness we have all **r** grace
Ac 8: 17 them, and they **r** the Holy Spirit.
10: 47 They have **r** the Holy Spirit just as
Ro 8: 15 The Spirit you **r** does not make you
1Co 11: 23 For I **r** from the Lord what I
Col 2: 6 just as you **r** Christ Jesus as Lord,
1Pe 4: 10 should use whatever gift you have **r**

RECEIVES (RECEIVE)
Pr 18: 22 good and **r** favor from the LORD.
Mt 7: 8 For everyone who asks **r**;
Ac 10: 43 who believes in him **r** forgiveness

RECEIVING (RECEIVE)
Pr 1: 3 for **r** instruction in prudent

RECITE
Ps 45: 1 a noble theme as I **r** my verses

RECKLESS
Pr 12: 18 words of the **r** pierce like swords,
1Pe 4: 4 you do not join them in their **r**,

RECKONING
Isa 10: 3 What will you do on the day of **r**,
Hos 9: 7 coming, the days of **r** are at hand.

RECLAIM* (CLAIM)
Isa 11: 11 time to **r** the surviving remnant

RECOGNITION (RECOGNIZE)
1Co 16: 18 yours also. Such men deserve **r**.
1Ti 5: 3 Give proper **r** to those widows who

RECOGNIZE (RECOGNITION RECOGNIZED)
Mt 7: 16 By their fruit you will **r** them.
1Jn 4: 2 This is how you can **r** the Spirit
4: 6 This is how we **r** the Spirit of truth

RECOGNIZED (RECOGNIZE)
Mt 12: 33 be bad, for a tree is **r** by its fruit.
Ro 7: 13 in order that sin might be **r** as sin,

RECOMPENSE*
Isa 40: 10 him, and his **r** accompanies him.
62: 11 and his **r** accompanies him.'"

RECONCILE* (RECONCILED RECONCILIATION RECONCILING)
Ac 7: 26 He tried to **r** them by saying, 'Men,
Eph 2: 16 and in one body to **r** both of them
Col 1: 20 and through him to **r** to himself all

RECONCILED* (RECONCILE)
Mt 5: 24 First go and be **r** to them;
Lk 12: 58 try hard to be **r** on the way, or your
Ro 5: 10 were **r** to him through the death
5: 10 having been **r**, shall we be saved
1Co 7: 11 or else be **r** to her husband.
2Co 5: 18 who **r** us to himself through Christ
5: 20 you on Christ's behalf: Be **r** to God.
Col 1: 22 But now he has **r** you by Christ's

RECONCILIATION* (RECONCILE)
Ro 5: 11 whom we have now received **r**.
11: 15 For if their rejection brought **r**
2Co 5: 18 and gave us the ministry of **r**:
5: 19 committed to us the message of **r**.

RECONCILING* (RECONCILE)
2Co 5: 19 God was **r** the world to himself

RECORD (RECORDED)
Ps 130: 3 you, LORD, kept a **r** of sins, Lord,
Hos 13: 12 is stored up, his sins are kept on **r**.
1Co 13: 5 angered, it keeps no **r** of wrongs.

RECORDED (RECORD)
Job 19: 23 that my words were **r**, that they
Jn 20: 30 which are not **r** in this book.

RECOUNT*
Ps 119: 13 With my lips I **r** all the laws
Jer 23: 28 the prophet who has a dream **r** the

RED
Ex 15: 4 officers are drowned in the **R** Sea.
Ps 106: 9 He rebuked the **R** Sea, and it dried
Pr 23: 31 Do not gaze at wine when it is **r**,
Isa 1: 18 though they are **r** as crimson,

REDEDICATE* (DEDICATE)
Nu 6: 12 They must **r** themselves

REDEEM (REDEEMED REDEEMER REDEEMS REDEMPTION)
Ex 6: 6 I will **r** you with an outstretched
2Sa 7: 23 out to **r** as a people for himself,
Ps 49: 7 No one can **r** the life of another
49: 15 God will **r** me from the realm
130: 8 He himself will **r** Israel from all
Hos 13: 14 I will **r** them from death.
Gal 4: 5 to **r** those under the law, that we
Titus 2: 14 for us to **r** us from all wickedness

REDEEMED (REDEEM)
Ps 107: 2 Let the **r** of the LORD tell their
Isa 35: 9 But only the **r** will walk there,
63: 9 In his love and mercy he **r** them;
Gal 3: 13 **r** us from the curse of the law
1Pe 1: 18 you were **r** from the empty way

REDEEMER (REDEEM)
Job 19: 25 I know that my **r** lives,

Ps 19: 14 sight, LORD, my Rock and my **R**.
Isa 44: 6 Israel's King and **R**, the LORD
48: 17 your **R**, the Holy One of Israel:
59: 20 "The **R** will come to Zion, to those

REDEEMS* (REDEEM)
Ps 103: 4 who **r** your life from the pit

REDEMPTION (REDEEM)
Ps 130: 7 love and with him is full **r**.
Lk 21: 28 because your **r** is drawing near."
Ro 3: 24 by his grace through the **r** that
8: 23 to sonship, the **r** of our bodies.
1Co 1: 30 our righteousness, holiness and **r**.
Eph 1: 7 him we have **r** through his blood,
1: 14 our inheritance until the **r** of those
4: 30 you were sealed for the day of **r**.
Col 1: 14 in whom we have **r**, the forgiveness
Heb 9: 12 blood, thus obtaining eternal **r**.

REED
Isa 42: 3 A bruised **r** he will not break,
Mt 12: 20 A bruised **r** he will not break,

REFINE*
Jer 9: 7 "See, I will **r** and test them,
Zec 13: 9 I will **r** them like silver and test
Mal 3: 3 the Levites and **r** them like gold

REFLECTS*
Pr 27: 19 As water **r** the face, so one's life **r**

REFRESH (REFRESHED REFRESHES REFRESHING)
Phm : 20 in the Lord; **r** my heart in Christ.

REFRESHED (REFRESH)
Pr 11: 25 whoever refreshes others will be **r**.

REFRESHES (REFRESH)
Ps 23: 3 he **r** my soul. He guides me along

REFRESHING* (REFRESH)
Ps 19: 7 of the LORD is perfect, **r** the soul.
Ac 3: 19 of **r** may come from the Lord,

REFUGE
Nu 35: 11 some towns to be your cities of **r**,
Dt 33: 27 The eternal God is your **r**,
Jos 20: 2 to designate the cities of **r**,
Ru 2: 12 wings you have come to take **r**."
2Sa 22: 3 stronghold, my **r** and my savior—
22: 31 he shields all who take **r** in him.
Ps 2: 12 Blessed are all who take **r** in him.
5: 11 let all who take **r** in you be glad;
9: 9 The LORD is a **r**
16: 1 safe, my God, for in you I take **r**.
17: 7 your right hand those who take **r**
18: 2 in whom I take **r**, my shield
31: 2 be my rock of **r**, a strong fortress
34: 8 blessed is the one who takes **r**
36: 7 People take **r** in the shadow of your
46: 1 God is our **r** and strength,
62: 8 hearts to him, for God is our **r**.
71: 1 In you, LORD, I have taken **r**;
91: 2 "He is my **r** and my fortress,
144: 2 in whom I take **r**, who subdues
Pr 14: 26 and for their children it will be a **r**.
30: 5 a shield to those who take **r** in him.
Na 1: 7 is good, a **r** in times of trouble.

REFUSE (REFUSED)
Jn 5: 40 you **r** to come to me to have life.

REFUSED (REFUSE)
2Th 2: 10 They perish because they **r** to love
Rev 16: 9 they **r** to repent and glorify him.

REGARD (REGARDS)
1Th 5: 13 in the highest **r** in love because

REGARDS (REGARD)
Ro 14: 14 if anyone **r** something as unclean,

REGRET
2Co 7: 10 leads to salvation and leaves no **r**,

REHOBOAM
Son of Solomon (1Ki 11:43; 1Ch 3:10). Harsh treatment of subjects caused divided kingdom (1Ki 12:1–24; 14:21–31; 2Ch 10–12).

REIGN (REIGNED REIGNS)
Ps 68: 16 mountain where God chooses to **r**,
Isa 9: 7 He will **r** on David's throne
24: 23 for the LORD Almighty will **r**
32: 1 a king will **r** in righteousness
Jer 23: 5 a King who will **r** wisely and do
Eze 20: 33 will **r** over you with a mighty hand
Lk 1: 33 he will **r** over Jacob's descendants
Ro 6: 12 Therefore do not let sin **r** in your
1Co 4: 8 You have begun to **r**—
4: 8 that we also might **r** with you!
15: 25 For he must **r** until he has put all
2Ti 2: 12 we endure, we will also **r** with him.
Rev 11: 15 and he will **r** for ever and ever."
20: 6 **r** with him for a thousand years.
22: 5 And they will **r** for ever and ever.

REIGNED (REIGN)
Ro 5: 21 so that, just as sin **r** in death,
Rev 20: 4 and **r** with Christ a thousand years.

REIGNS (REIGN)
Ex 15: 18 "The LORD **r** for ever and ever."
Ps 9: 7 The LORD **r** forever;
47: 8 God **r** over the nations;
93: 1 The LORD **r**, he is robed
96: 10 the nations, "The LORD **r**."
97: 1 The LORD **r**, let the earth be glad;
99: 1 The LORD **r**, let the nations
146: 10 The LORD **r** forever, your God,
Isa 52: 7 who say to Zion, "Your God **r**!"
Rev 19: 6 For our Lord God Almighty **r**.

REIN
Jas 1: 26 yet do not keep a tight **r** on their

REJECT (REJECTED REJECTION REJECTS)
Ps 94: 14 the LORD will not **r** his people;
Ro 11: 1 I ask then: Did God **r** his people?
1Th 5: 22 **r** every kind of evil.

REJECTED (REJECT)
1Sa 8: 7 but they have **r** me as their king.
1Ki 19: 10 Israelites have **r** your covenant,
2Ki 17: 15 They **r** his decrees and the
Ps 66: 20 to God, who has not **r** my prayer
118: 22 stone the builders **r** has become
Isa 5: 24 for they have **r** the law
41: 9 chosen you and have not **r** you.
53: 3 was despised and **r** by mankind,
Jer 8: 9 Since they have **r** the word
Mt 21: 42 stone the builders **r** has become
1Ti 4: 4 nothing is to be **r** if it is received
1Pe 2: 4 **r** by humans but chosen by God
2: 7 stone the builders **r** has become

REJECTION* (REJECT)
Ro 11: 15 if their **r** brought reconciliation

REJECTS (REJECT)
Lk 10: 16 whoever **r** me **r** him who sent me."
Jn 3: 36 whoever **r** the Son will not see life,
1Th 4: 8 anyone who **r** this instruction does

REJOICE (JOY)
Dt 12: 7 shall **r** in everything you have put
1Ch 16: 10 of those who seek the LORD **r**.
16: 31 Let the heavens **r**, let the earth be
Ps 5: 11 those who love your name may **r**
9: 14 Zion, and there **r** in your salvation.
34: 2 let the afflicted hear and **r**.
63: 11 But the king will **r** in God;
66: 6 come, let us **r** in him.
68: 3 be glad and **r** before God;
105: 3 of those who seek the LORD **r**.
118: 24 let us **r** today and be glad.
119: 14 I **r** in following your statutes as one
119:162 I **r** in your promise like one who
149: 2 Let Israel **r** in their Maker;
Pr 5: 18 you **r** in the wife of your youth.
23: 25 May your father and mother **r**;
24: 17 stumble, do not let your heart **r**,
Isa 9: 3 as warriors **r** when dividing
35: 1 the wilderness will **r** and blossom.
61: 7 of disgrace you will **r** in your
62: 5 bride, so will your God **r** over you.
Jer 31: 12 they will **r** in the bounty
Zep 3: 17 but will **r** over you with singing."
Zec 9: 9 **R** greatly, Daughter Zion!
Lk 6: 23 "**R** in that day and leap for joy,
10: 20 but **r** that your names are written
15: 6 together and says, '**R** with me;
15: 9 together and says, '**R** with me;
Ro 12: 15 **R** with those who **r**;
16: 19 obedience, so I **r** because of you;
Php 2: 17 I am glad and **r** with all of you.
3: 1 brothers and sisters, **r** in the Lord!
4: 4 **R** in the Lord always. I will say it again: **R**!
1Th 5: 16 **R** always,
1Pe 4: 13 **r** inasmuch as you participate
Rev 19: 7 Let us **r** and be glad and give him

REJOICES (JOY)
Ps 13: 5 my heart **r** in your salvation.
16: 9 my heart is glad and my tongue **r**;
Pr 23: 24 a man who fathers a wise son **r**
Isa 61: 10 my soul **r** in my God.
62: 5 as a bridegroom **r** over his bride,
Lk 1: 47 and my spirit **r** in God my Savior,
Ac 2: 26 my heart is glad and my tongue **r**;
1Co 12: 26 is honored, every part **r** with it.
13: 6 delight in evil but **r** with the truth.

REJOICING (JOY)
2Sa 6: 12 to the City of David with **r**.
Ne 12: 43 The sound of **r** in Jerusalem could
Ps 30: 5 night, but **r** comes in the morning.
Pr 14: 13 may ache, and **r** may end in grief.
Lk 15: 7 the same way there will be more **r**
Ac 5: 41 **r** because they had been counted
2Co 6: 10 sorrowful, yet always **r**;

RELATE*
Ps 71: 15 I know not how to **r** them all.

RELATIONS
Lev 18: 22 "'Do not have sexual **r**
1Co 7: 1 to have sexual **r** with a woman."

RELATIVE (RELATIVES)
Pr 27: 10 neighbor nearby than a **r** far away.

RELATIVES (RELATIVE)
Pr 19: 7 The poor are shunned by all their **r**
Mk 6: 4 among his **r** and in his own home."
Lk 21: 16 brothers and sisters, **r** and friends,
1Ti 5: 8 who does not provide for their **r**,

RELEASE (RELEASED)
Isa 61: 1 **r** from darkness for the prisoners,

RELEASED (RELEASE)
Ro 7: 6 we have been **r** from the law so
1Co 7: 27 Do not seek to be **r**. Are you free
Rev 20: 7 Satan will be **r** from his prison

RELENT (RELENTED RELENTS)
Dt 32: 36 **r** concerning his servants when he
Am 1: 3 even for four, I will not **r**.

RELENTED (RELENT)
Ex 32: 14 the LORD **r** and did not bring
2Sa 24: 16 the LORD **r** concerning the disaster
Jdg 2: 18 for the LORD **r** because of their
Ps 106: 45 and out of his great love he **r**.
Jnh 3: 10 he **r** and did not bring on them

RELENTS* (RELENT)
Joel 2: 13 and he **r** from sending calamity.
Jnh 4: 2 God who **r** from sending calamity.

RELIABLE (RELY)
2Ti 2: 2 entrust to **r** people who will also be
2Pe 1: 19 message as something completely **r**

RELIANCE* (RELY)
Ps 26: 3 have lived in **r** on your faithfulness.
Pr 25: 19 a lame foot is **r** on the unfaithful

RELIED (RELY)
2Ch 13: 18 were victorious because they **r**
16: 8 Yet when you **r** on the LORD,
Ps 71: 6 From birth I have **r** on you;

RELIEF
Job 35: 9 they plead for **r** from the arm
Ps 94: 13 you grant them **r** from days
143: 1 and righteousness come to my **r**.
La 3: 49 will flow unceasingly, without **r**,
3: 56 not close your ears to my cry for **r**."
2Th 1: 7 and give **r** to you who are troubled,

RELIES* (RELY)
Isa 28: 16 the one who **r** on it will never be
Gal 3: 11 no one who **r** on the law is justified

RELIGION* (RELIGIOUS)
Ac 25: 19 dispute with him about their own **r**
26: 5 to the strictest sect of our **r**,
1Ti 5: 4 of all to put their **r** into practice
Jas 1: 26 and their **r** is worthless.
1: 27 **R** that God our Father accepts as

RELIGIOUS (RELIGION)
Jas 1: 26 Those who consider themselves **r**

RELY (RELIABLE RELIANCE RELIED RELIES)
Ps 59: 10 my God on whom I can **r**.
59: 17 fortress, my God on whom I can **r**.
Isa 50: 10 of the LORD and **r** on their God.
Eze 33: 26 You **r** on your sword, you do
2Co 1: 9 that we might not **r** on ourselves
Gal 3: 10 For all who **r** on the works
1Jn 4: 16 and **r** on the love God has for us.

REMAIN (REMAINS)
Nu 33: 55 you allow to **r** will become barbs
Ps 102: 27 But you **r** the same, and your years
Jn 1: 32 heaven as a dove and **r** on him.
15: 4 **R** in me, as I also **r** in you.
15: 4 by itself; it must **r** in the vine.
15: 7 If you **r** in me and my words **r**
15: 9 have I loved you. Now **r** in my love.

Ro 13: 8 Let no debt **r** outstanding,
1Co 13: 13 And now these three **r**:
Heb 1: 11 They will perish, but you **r**;
1Jn 2: 27 just as it has taught you, **r** in him.

REMAINS (REMAIN)
Ps 146: 6 he **r** faithful forever.
2Ti 2: 13 if we are faithless, he **r** faithful,
Heb 7: 3 Son of God, he **r** a priest forever.

REMEDY
Isa 3: 7 day he will cry out, "I have no **r**.

REMEMBER (REMEMBERED REMEMBERS REMEMBRANCE)
Ge 9: 15 I will **r** my covenant between me
Ex 20: 8 "**R** the Sabbath day by keeping it
33: 13 **R** that this nation is your people."
Dt 5: 15 **R** that you were slaves in Egypt
1Ch 16: 12 **R** the wonders he has done,
Job 36: 24 **R** to extol his work, which people
Ps 25: 6 **R**, LORD, your great mercy
63: 6 On my bed I **r** you; I think of you
74: 2 **R** the nation you purchased long
77: 11 I will **r** your miracles of long ago.
Ecc 12: 1 **R** your Creator in the days of your
Isa 46: 8 "**R** this, keep it in mind, take it
Jer 31: 34 and will **r** their sins no more."
Hab 3: 2 in wrath **r** mercy.
Lk 1: 72 and to **r** his holy covenant,
Gal 2: 10 we should continue to **r** the poor,
Php 1: 3 I thank my God every time I **r** you.
2Ti 2: 8 **R** Jesus Christ, raised from the
Heb 8: 12 and will **r** their sins no more."

REMEMBERED (REMEMBER)
Ex 2: 24 he **r** his covenant with Abraham,
Ps 98: 3 He has **r** his love and his
106: 45 for their sake he **r** his covenant
111: 4 He has caused his wonders to be **r**;
136: 23 He **r** us in our low estate
Isa 65: 17 The former things will not be **r**,
Eze 18: 22 committed will be **r** against them.
33: 13 that person has done will be **r**;

REMEMBERS (REMEMBER)
Ps 103: 14 are formed, he **r** that we are dust.
111: 5 he **r** his covenant forever.
Isa 43: 25 own sake, and **r** your sins no more.

REMEMBRANCE (REMEMBER)
Lk 22: 19 given for you; do this in **r** of me."
1Co 11: 24 is for you; do this in **r** of me."
11: 25 whenever you drink it, in **r** of me."

REMIND
Jn 14: 26 will **r** you of everything I have said
2Pe 1: 12 So I will always **r** you of these

REMNANT
Ezr 9: 8 has been gracious in leaving us a **r**
Isa 11: 11 the surviving **r** of his people
Jer 23: 3 "I myself will gather the **r** of my
Zec 8: 12 inheritance to the **r** of this people.
Ro 11: 5 the present time there is a **r** chosen

REMOVED
Ps 30: 11 you **r** my sackcloth and clothed me
103: 12 so far has he **r** our transgressions
Jn 20: 1 that the stone had been **r**

REND*
Isa 64: 1 you would **r** the heavens and come
Joel 2: 13 **R** your heart and not your

RENEW (RENEWAL RENEWED RENEWING)
Ps 51: 10 and **r** a steadfast spirit within me.
Isa 40: 31 in the LORD will **r** their strength.

RENEWAL (RENEW)
Isa 57: 10 You found **r** of your strength,
Titus 3: 5 of rebirth and **r** by the Holy Spirit,

RENEWED (RENEW)
Ps 103: 5 that your youth is **r** like the eagle's.
2Co 4: 16 yet inwardly we are being **r** day

RENEWING* (RENEW)
Ro 12: 2 transformed by the **r** of your mind.

RENOUNCE (RENOUNCED RENOUNCES)
Da 4: 27 **R** your sins by doing what is right,

RENOUNCED (RENOUNCE)
2Co 4: 2 we have **r** secret and shameful

RENOUNCES* (RENOUNCE)
Pr 28: 13 confesses and **r** them finds mercy.

RENOWN*
Ge 6: 4 were the heroes of old, men of **r**.
Ps 102: 12 your **r** endures through all
135: 13 endures forever, your **r**, LORD,
Isa 26: 8 and **r** are the desire of our hearts.

Isa 55: 13 This will be for the LORD's **r**,
63: 12 to gain for himself everlasting **r**,
Jer 13: 11 'to be my people for my **r**
32: 20 have gained the **r** that is still yours.
33: 9 Then this city will bring me **r**, joy,
49: 25 the city of **r** not been abandoned,
Eze 26: 17 of **r**, peopled by men of the sea!

REPAID (PAY)
Lk 6: 34 to sinners, expecting to be **r** in full.
14: 14 you will be **r** at the resurrection
Col 3: 25 Anyone who does wrong will be **r**

REPAY (PAY)
Dt 7: 10 those who hate him he will **r** to
32: 35 It is mine to avenge; I will **r**.
Ru 2: 12 May the LORD **r** you for what you
Ps 103: 10 or **r** us according to our iniquities.
Jer 25: 14 I will **r** them according to their
Ro 12: 17 Do not **r** anyone evil for evil.
12: 19 I will **r**," says the Lord.
1Pe 3: 9 Do not **r** evil with evil or insult
3: 9 contrary, **r** evil with blessing,

REPAYING (PAY)
1Ti 5: 4 own family and so **r** their parents

REPEATED
Heb 10: 1 the same sacrifices **r** endlessly year

REPENT (REPENTANCE REPENTED REPENTS)
1Ki 8: 47 **r** and plead with you in the land
Job 36: 10 commands them to **r** of their evil.
42: 6 I despise myself and **r** in dust
Jer 15: 19 "If you **r**, I will restore you that you
Eze 18: 30 declares the Sovereign LORD. **R**!
18: 32 the Sovereign LORD. **R** and live!
Mt 3: 2 and saying, "**R**, for the kingdom
4: 17 time on Jesus began to preach, "**R**,
Mk 6: 12 and preached that people should **r**.
Lk 13: 3 But unless you **r**, you too will all
17: 3 and if they **r**, forgive them.
Ac 2: 38 Peter replied, "**R** and be baptized,
3: 19 **R**, then, and turn to God,
17: 30 all people everywhere to **r**.
26: 20 I preached that they should **r**
Rev 2: 5 If you do not **r**, I will come to

REPENTANCE (REPENT)
Isa 30: 15 "In **r** and rest is your salvation,
Mt 3: 8 Produce fruit in keeping with **r**.
Mk 1: 4 preaching a baptism of **r**
Lk 3: 8 Produce fruit in keeping with **r**.
5: 32 call the righteous, but sinners to **r**."
24: 47 **r** for the forgiveness of sins will be
Ac 20: 21 that they must turn to God in **r**
26: 20 demonstrate their **r** by their deeds.
Ro 2: 4 is intended to lead you to **r**?
2Co 7: 10 Godly sorrow brings **r** that leads
2Pe 3: 9 perish, but everyone to come to **r**.

REPENTED (REPENT)
Mt 11: 21 they would have **r** long ago

REPENTS (REPENT)
Lk 15: 7 over one sinner who **r** than over
15: 10 of God over one sinner who **r**."

REPORTS
Ex 23: 1 "Do not spread false **r**. Do not help

REPOSES*
Pr 14: 33 Wisdom **r** in the heart

REPRESENTATION*
Heb 1: 3 glory and the exact **r** of his being,

REPRIMAND
Pr 29: 15 A rod and a **r** impart wisdom,

REPROACH
Job 27: 6 conscience will not **r** me as long
Isa 51: 7 Do not fear the **r** of mere mortals
1Ti 3: 2 Now the overseer is to be above **r**,

REPROVE*
1Ti 5: 20 you are to **r** before everyone,

REPUTATION
1Ti 3: 7 also have a good **r** with outsiders,

REQUESTS
Ps 20: 5 May the LORD grant all your **r**.
Php 4: 6 present your **r** to God.

REQUIRE (REQUIRED REQUIRES)
Mic 6: 8 what does the LORD **r** of you?

REQUIRED (REQUIRE)
1Co 4: 2 Now it is **r** that those who have

REQUIRES (REQUIRE)
1Ki 2: 3 what the LORD your God **r**:

Ro 3: 27 because of the law that **r** faith.
Heb 9: 22 the law **r** that nearly everything

RESCUE (RESCUED RESCUES)
Ps 22: 8 they say, "let the LORD **r** him.
31: 2 ear to me, come quickly to my **r**;
34: 22 The LORD will **r** his servants;
44: 26 **r** us because of your unfailing
69: 14 **R** me from the mire, do not let me
91: 14 says the LORD, "I will **r** him;
143: 9 **R** me from my enemies, LORD,
Da 6: 20 been able to **r** you from the lions?"
Ro 7: 24 Who will **r** me from this body
Gal 1: 4 sins to **r** us from the present evil
2Pe 2: 9 the Lord knows how to **r** the godly

RESCUED (RESCUE)
Ps 18: 17 He **r** me from my powerful enemy,
Pr 11: 8 The righteous person is **r**
Isa 35: 10 those the LORD has **r** will return.
Col 1: 13 For he has **r** us from the dominion

RESCUES (RESCUE)
Da 6: 27 He **r** and he saves;
1Th 1: 10 who **r** us from the coming wrath.

RESENT* (RESENTFUL)
Pr 3: 11 discipline, and do not **r** his rebuke,
15: 12 Mockers **r** correction, so they

RESENTFUL* (RESENT)
2Ti 2: 24 to everyone, able to teach, not **r**.

RESERVE (RESERVED)
1Ki 19: 18 Yet I **r** seven thousand in Israel—

RESERVED (RESERVE)
Ro 11: 4 "I have **r** for myself seven thousand

RESIST (RESISTED)
Da 11: 32 know their God will firmly **r** him.
Mt 5: 39 I tell you, do not **r** an evil person.
Lk 21: 15 of your adversaries will be able to **r**
Ro 9: 19 For who is able to **r** his will?"
Jas 4: 7 **R** the devil, and he will flee
1Pe 5: 9 **R** him, standing firm in the faith,

RESISTED (RESIST)
Job 9: 4 Who has **r** him and come

RESOLVED
Da 1: 8 Daniel **r** not to defile himself
1Co 2: 2 For I **r** to know nothing while I

RESOUNDING*
2Ch 30: 21 day with **r** instruments dedicated
Ps 150: 5 cymbals, praise him with **r** cymbals.
1Co 13: 1 I am only a **r** gong or a clanging

RESPECT (RESPECTABLE RESPECTED RESPECTS)
Lev 19: 3 of you must **r** your mother
19: 32 show **r** for the elderly and revere
Mal 1: 6 a master, where is the **r** due me?"
Eph 5: 33 and the wife must **r** her husband.
6: 5 obey your earthly masters with **r**
1Th 4: 12 that your daily life may win the **r**
1Ti 3: 4 do so in a manner worthy of full **r**.
3: 8 way, deacons are to be worthy of **r**,
3: 11 the women are to be worthy of **r**,
6: 1 their masters worthy of full **r**,
Titus 2: 2 worthy of **r**, self-controlled,
1Pe 2: 17 Show proper **r** to everyone,
3: 7 them with **r** as the weaker partner
3: 15 But do this with gentleness and **r**,

RESPECTABLE* (RESPECT)
1Ti 3: 2 self-controlled, **r**, hospitable,

RESPECTED (RESPECT)
Pr 31: 23 Her husband is **r** at the city gate,

RESPECTS (RESPECT)
Pr 13: 13 whoever **r** a command is rewarded.

RESPOND
Ps 102: 17 He will **r** to the prayer
Hos 2: 21 "In that day I will **r**,"

RESPONSIBLE
Nu 1: 53 The Levites are to be **r** for the care
1Co 7: 24 each person, as **r** to God,

REST (RESTED RESTING RESTS SABBATH-REST)
Ex 31: 15 seventh day is a day of sabbath **r**,
33: 14 go with you, and I will give you **r**."
Lev 25: 5 The land is to have a year of **r**.
Dt 31: 16 "You are going to **r** with your
Jos 14: 15 Then the land had **r** from war.
21: 44 The LORD gave them **r** on every
1Ki 5: 4 the LORD my God has given me **r**
1Ch 22: 9 who will be a man of peace and **r**,
Job 3: 17 and there the weary are at **r**.

Ps 16: 9 my body also will **r** secure,
62: 1 Truly my soul finds **r** in God;
62: 5 Yes, my soul, find **r** in God;
90: 17 favor of the Lord our God **r** on us;
91: 1 the Most High will **r** in the shadow
95: 11 'They shall never enter my **r**.'"
Pr 6: 10 a little folding of the hands to **r**—
Isa 11: 2 Spirit of the LORD will **r** on him—
30: 15 repentance and **r** is your salvation,
32: 18 homes, in undisturbed places of **r**.
57: 20 which cannot **r**, whose waves cast
Jer 6: 16 and you will find **r** for your souls.
47: 6 of the LORD, how long till you **r**?
Mt 11: 28 burdened, and I will give you **r**.
2Co 12: 9 that Christ's power may **r** on me.
Heb 3: 11 'They shall never enter my **r**.'"
4: 3 we who have believed enter that **r**,
4: 10 for anyone who enters God's **r**
Rev 14: 13 "they will **r** from their labor,

RESTED (REST)
Ge 2: 2 on the seventh day he **r** from all his
Heb 4: 4 the seventh day God **r** from all his

RESTING (REST)
Isa 11: 10 and his **r** place will be glorious.

RESTITUTION
Ex 22: 3 who steals must certainly make **r**,
Lev 6: 5 must make **r** in full, add a fifth
Nu 5: 8 the **r** belongs to the LORD

RESTORATION (RESTORE)
2Co 13: 11 Strive for full **r**, encourage one

RESTORE (RESTORATION RESTORED)
Ps 51: 12 **R** to me the joy of your salvation
80: 3 **R** us, O God; make your face shine
126: 4 **R** our fortunes, LORD,
Jer 31: 18 **R** me, and I will return, because
La 5: 21 **R** us to yourself, LORD, that we
Da 9: 25 the time the word goes out to **r**
Na 2: 2 The LORD will **r** the splendor
Gal 6: 1 by the Spirit should **r** that person
1Pe 5: 10 will himself **r** you and make you

RESTORED (RESTORE)
Job 42: 10 the LORD **r** his fortunes and gave
2Co 13: 9 prayer is that you may be fully **r**.

RESTRAINED (RESTRAINT)
Ps 78: 38 Time after time he **r** his anger

RESTRAINING (RESTRAINT)
Pr 27: 16 **r** her is like **r** the wind or grasping
Col 2: 23 any value in **r** sensual indulgence.

RESTRAINT (RESTRAINED RESTRAINING)
Pr 17: 27 has knowledge uses words with **r**,
29: 18 is no revelation, people cast off **r**;

RESTS (REST)
Dt 33: 12 one the LORD loves **r** between his
Pr 19: 23 then one **r** content,
Lk 2: 14 to those on whom his favor **r**."

RESULT (RESULTS)
Ro 6: 22 to holiness, and the **r** is eternal life.
11: 31 too may now receive mercy as a **r**
2Co 3: 3 from Christ, the **r** of our ministry,
2Th 1: 5 as a **r** you will be counted worthy
1Pe 1: 7 may **r** in praise, glory and honor
1Pe 1: 9 you are receiving the end **r** of your

RESULTS* (RESULT)
1Th 2: 1 our visit to you was not without **r**.

RESURRECTION*
Mt 22: 23 who say there is no **r**, came to him
22: 28 at the **r**, whose wife will she be
22: 30 the **r** people will neither marry nor
22: 31 But about the **r** of the dead—
27: 53 came out of the tombs after Jesus' **r**
Mk 12: 18 who say there is no **r**, came to him
12: 23 At the **r** whose wife will she be,
Lk 14: 14 be repaid at the **r** of the righteous."
20: 27 who say there is no **r**, came to Jesus
20: 33 at the **r** whose wife will she be,
20: 35 in the **r** from the dead will neither
20: 36 since they are children of the **r**.
Jn 11: 24 rise again in the **r** at the last day."
11: 25 said to her, "I am the **r** and the life.
Ac 1: 22 become a witness with us of his **r**."
2: 31 he spoke of the **r** of the Messiah,
4: 2 in Jesus the **r** of the dead.
4: 33 to testify to the **r** of the Lord Jesus.
17: 18 good news about Jesus and the **r**.
17: 32 they heard about the **r** of the dead,
23: 6 of the hope of the **r** of the dead."
23: 8 Sadducees say that there is no **r**,
24: 15 that there will be a **r** of both
Ac 24: 21 'It is concerning the **r** of the dead
Ro 1: 4 in power by his **r** from the dead:
6: 5 be united with him in a **r** like his.
1Co 15: 12 say that there is no **r** of the dead?
15: 13 If there is no **r** of the dead, then
15: 21 the **r** of the dead comes also
15: 29 Now if there is no **r**, what will
15: 42 So will it be with the **r** of the dead.
Php 3: 10 yes, to know the power of his **r**
3: 11 attaining to the **r** from the dead.
2Ti 2: 18 that the **r** has already taken place,
Heb 6: 2 on of hands, the **r** of the dead,
11: 35 they might gain an even better **r**.
1Pe 1: 3 a living hope through the **r** of Jesus
3: 21 It saves you by the **r** of Jesus Christ,
Rev 20: 5 This is the first **r**.
20: 6 are those who share in the first **r**.

RETALIATE*
1Pe 2: 23 their insults at him, he did not **r**;

RETRIBUTION
Ps 69: 22 may it become **r** and a trap.
Jer 51: 56 For the LORD is a God of **r**;
Ro 11: 9 a stumbling block and a **r** for them.

RETURN (RETURNED RETURNS)
Ge 3: 19 you are and to dust you will **r**."
2Sa 12: 23 to him, but he will not **r** to me."
2Ch 30: 9 If you **r** to the LORD, then your
Ne 1: 9 but if you **r** to me and obey my
Job 10: 21 before I go to the place of no **r**,
16: 22 pass before I take the path of no **r**.
22: 23 If you **r** to the Almighty, you will
Ps 80: 14 **R** to us, God Almighty!
116: 12 What shall I **r** to the LORD for all
126: 6 to sow, will **r** with songs of joy,
Isa 10: 21 A remnant will **r**, a remnant
35: 10 the LORD has rescued will **r**.
55: 11 It will not **r** to me empty, but will
Jer 24: 7 for they will **r** to me with all their
31: 8 a great throng will **r**.
31: 22 the woman will **r** to the man."
La 3: 40 them, and let us **r** to the LORD.
Hos 6: 1 "Come, let us **r** to the LORD.
12: 6 But you must **r** to your God;
14: 1 **R**, Israel, to the LORD your God.
Joel 2: 12 "**r** to me with all your heart,
Zec 1: 3 '**R** to me,' declares the LORD
1: 3 'and I will **r** to you,'
10: 9 will survive, and they will **r**.

RETURNED (RETURN)
Ps 35: 13 my prayers **r** to me unanswered,
Am 4: 6 town, yet you have not **r** to me,"
1Pe 2: 25 now you have **r** to the Shepherd

RETURNS (RETURN)
Pr 3: 14 silver and yields better **r** than gold.
Isa 52: 8 When the LORD **r** to Zion,
Mt 24: 46 finds him doing so when he **r**.

REUBEN
Firstborn of Jacob by Leah (Ge 29:32; 46:8; 1Ch 2:1). Attempted to rescue Joseph (Ge 37:21–30). Lost birthright for sleeping with Bilhah (Ge 35:22; 49:4). Tribe of blessed (Ge 49:3–4; Dt 33:6), numbered (Nu 1:21; 26:7), allotted land east of Jordan (Nu 32; 34:14; Jos 13:15), west (Eze 48:6), failed to help Deborah (Jdg 5:15–16), supported David (1Ch 12:37), 12,000 from (Rev 7:5).

REVEAL (REVEALED REVEALS REVELATION REVELATIONS)
Mt 11: 27 to whom the Son chooses to **r** him.
Gal 1: 16 to **r** his Son in me so that I might

REVEALED (REVEAL)
Dt 29: 29 but the things **r** belong to us
Isa 40: 5 the glory of the LORD will be **r**,
43: 12 I have **r** and saved and proclaimed
53: 1 has the arm of the LORD been **r**?
65: 1 "I **r** myself to those who did not
Mt 11: 25 and **r** them to little children.
Jn 12: 38 has the arm of the Lord been **r**?"
17: 6 "I have **r** you to those whom you
Ro 1: 17 the righteousness of God is **r**—
8: 18 with the glory that will be **r** in us.
10: 20 I **r** myself to those who did not ask
16: 26 now **r** and made known through
1Co 2: 10 these are the things God has **r** to us
2Th 1: 7 the Lord Jesus is **r** from heaven
2: 3 and the man of lawlessness is **r**,
1Pe 1: 7 and honor when Jesus Christ is **r**.
1: 20 was **r** in these last times for your
4: 13 be overjoyed when his glory is **r**.

REVEALS* (REVEAL)
Nu 23: 3 Whatever he **r** to me I will tell
Job 12: 22 He **r** the deep things of darkness
Da 2: 22 He **r** deep and hidden things;
2: 28 a God in heaven who **r** mysteries.
Am 4: 13 who **r** his thoughts to mankind,

REVELATION* (REVEAL)
2Sa 7: 17 David all the words of this entire **r**.
1Ch 17: 15 David all the words of this entire **r**.
Pr 29: 18 Where there is no **r**, people cast off
Da 10: 1 a **r** was given to Daniel (who was
Hab 2: 2 "Write down the **r** and make it
2: 3 For the **r** awaits an appointed time;
Lk 2: 32 a light for **r** to the Gentiles,
Ro 16: 25 with the **r** of the mystery hidden
1Co 14: 6 to you, unless I bring you some **r**
14: 26 a **r**, a tongue or an interpretation.
14: 30 And if a **r** comes to someone who
Gal 1: 12 I received it by **r** from Jesus Christ.
2: 2 I went in response to a **r** and,
Eph 1: 17 you the Spirit of wisdom and **r**,
3: 3 mystery made known to me by **r**,
Rev 1: 1 The **r** from Jesus Christ, which

REVELATIONS* (REVEAL)
2Co 12: 1 on to visions and **r** from the Lord.
12: 7 of these surpassingly great **r**.

REVELED* (REVELRY)
Ne 9: 25 they **r** in your great goodness.
Ac 7: 41 **r** in what their own hands had

REVELRY (REVELED)
Ex 32: 6 drink and got up to indulge in **r**.
1Co 10: 7 drink and got up to indulge in **r**."

REVENGE (VENGEANCE)
Lev 19: 18 "'Do not seek **r** or bear a grudge
Ro 12: 19 Do not take **r**, my dear friends,

REVERE* (REVERENCE REVERENT REVERING)
Lev 19: 32 for the elderly and **r** your God.
Dt 4: 10 learn to **r** me as long as they live
13: 4 must follow, and him you must **r**.
14: 23 to **r** the LORD your God always.
17: 19 may learn to **r** the LORD his God
28: 58 book, and do not **r** this glorious
Job 37: 24 Therefore, people **r** him, for does
Ps 22: 23 **R** him, all you descendants
33: 8 all the people of the world **r** him.
102: 15 kings of the earth will **r** your glory.
Isa 25: 3 cities of ruthless nations will **r** you.
59: 19 of the sun, they will **r** his glory.
63: 17 our hearts so we do not **r** you?
Hos 10: 3 because we did not **r** the LORD.
Mal 4: 2 for you who **r** my name, the sun
1Pe 3: 15 But in your hearts **r** Christ as Lord.
Rev 11: 18 and your people who **r** your name,

REVERENCE (REVERE)
Lev 19: 30 and have **r** for my sanctuary.
Ne 5: 15 of **r** for God I did not act like that.
Ps 5: 7 in **r** I bow down toward your holy
Da 6: 26 must fear and **r** the God of Daniel.
2Co 7: 1 holiness out of **r** for God.
Eph 5: 21 to one another out of **r** for Christ.
Col 3: 22 of heart and **r** for the Lord.
1Pe 3: 2 see the purity and **r** of your lives.

REVERENT* (REVERE)
Ecc 8: 12 fear God, who are **r** before him.
Titus 2: 3 women to be **r** in the way they live,
Heb 5: 7 heard because of his **r** submission.
1Pe 1: 17 time as foreigners here in **r** fear.
2: 18 in **r** fear of God submit yourselves

REVERING* (REVERE)
Dt 8: 6 in obedience to him and **r** him.
Ne 1: 11 who delight in **r** your name.

REVERSE*
Isa 43: 13 When I act, who can **r** it?"

REVIVE*
Ps 80: 18 **r** us, and we will call on your name
85: 6 Will you not **r** us again, that your
Isa 57: 15 to **r** the spirit of the lowly and to **r** the heart of the contrite.
Hos 6: 2 After two days he will **r** us;

REVOKED
Isa 45: 23 integrity a word that will not be **r**:

REWARD (REWARDED REWARDING REWARDS)
Ge 15: 1 am your shield, your very great **r**."
1Sa 24: 19 May the LORD **r** you well
Ps 19: 11 in keeping them there is great **r**.

Ps 62: 12 "You **r** everyone according to what
127: 3 the LORD, offspring a **r** from him.
Pr 9: 12 are wise, your wisdom will **r** you;
11: 18 sows righteousness reaps a sure **r**.
12: 14 work of their hands brings them **r**.
19: 17 he will **r** them for what they have
25: 22 head, and the LORD will **r** you.
Isa 40: 10 See, his **r** is with him, and his
49: 4 hand, and my **r** is with my God."
61: 8 my faithfulness I will **r** my people
62: 11 See, his **r** is with him, and his
Jer 17: 10 to **r** each person according to their
32: 19 you **r** each person according to
Mt 5: 12 because great is your **r** in heaven,
6: 1 will have no **r** from your Father
6: 5 they have received their **r** in full.
10: 41 prophet will receive a prophet's **r**,
10: 41 will receive a righteous person's **r**.
16: 27 he will **r** each person according
Lk 6: 23 because great is your **r** in heaven.
6: 35 Then your **r** will be great, and you
1Co 3: 14 the builder will receive a **r**.
Eph 6: 8 that the Lord will **r** each one
Col 3: 24 inheritance from the Lord as a **r**.
Heb 11: 26 he was looking ahead to his **r**.
Rev 22: 12 My **r** is with me, and I will give

REWARDED (REWARD)
Ru 2: 12 May you be richly **r** by the LORD,
2Sa 22: 21 cleanness of my hands he has **r** me.
2Ch 15: 7 give up, for your work will be **r**."
Ps 18: 24 The LORD has **r** me according
Pr 13: 13 whoever respects a command is **r**.
13: 21 righteous are **r** with good things.
14: 14 ways, and the good **r** for theirs.
Jer 31: 16 for your work will be **r**,"
1Co 3: 8 and they will each be **r** according
Heb 10: 35 it will be richly **r**.
2Jn : 8 for, but that you may be **r** fully.

REWARDING* (REWARD)
Rev 11: 18 for **r** your servants the prophets

REWARDS (REWARD)
1Sa 26: 23 The LORD **r** everyone for their
Heb 11: 6 he **r** those who earnestly seek him.

RIBS
Ge 2: 21 he took one of the man's **r**

RICH (RICHES RICHEST)
Job 34: 19 does not favor the **r** over the poor,
Ps 49: 16 be overawed when others grow **r**,
145: 8 slow to anger and **r** in love.
Pr 21: 17 wine and olive oil will never be **r**.
22: 2 **R** and poor have this in common:
23: 4 Do not wear yourself out to get **r**;
28: 6 blameless than the **r** whose ways
28: 20 to get **r** will not go unpunished.
28: 22 The stingy are eager to get **r** and
Ecc 5: 12 but as for the **r**, their abundance
Isa 33: 6 a **r** store of salvation and wisdom
53: 9 and with the **r** in his death,
Jer 9: 23 or the **r** boast of their riches,
Mt 19: 23 for someone who is **r** to enter
Lk 1: 53 but has sent the **r** away empty.
6: 24 "But woe to you who are **r**, for you
12: 21 but is not **r** toward God."
16: 1 There was a **r** man whose manager
21: 1 he saw the **r** putting their gifts
2Co 6: 10 poor, yet making many **r**;
8: 2 poverty welled up in **r** generosity.
8: 9 that though he was **r**, yet for your
Eph 2: 4 love for us, God, who is **r** in mercy,
1Ti 6: 9 Those who want to get **r** fall
6: 17 Command those who are **r** in this
6: 18 to be **r** in good deeds, and to be
Jas 1: 10 But the **r** should take pride in their
2: 5 eyes of the world to be **r** in faith
5: 1 Now listen, you **r** people,
Rev 2: 9 and your poverty—yet you are **r**!
3: 18 in the fire, so you can become **r**;

RICHES (RICH)
Job 36: 18 that no one entices you by **r**;
Ps 49: 6 wealth and boast of their great **r**?
62: 10 though your **r** increase, do not set
119: 14 statutes as one rejoices in great **r**.
Pr 3: 16 in her left hand are **r** and honor.
11: 28 Those who trust in their **r** will fall,
22: 1 is more desirable than great **r**;
22: 4 its wages are **r** and honor and life.
27: 24 for **r** do not endure forever,
30: 8 give me neither poverty nor **r**,
Isa 10: 3 Where will you leave your **r**?
60: 5 you the **r** of the nations will come.
Jer 9: 23 strength or the rich boast of their **r**,
Lk 8: 14 by life's worries, **r** and pleasures,
Ro 9: 23 to make the **r** of his glory known
11: 33 the depth of the **r** of the wisdom
Eph 2: 7 he might show the incomparable **r**
3: 8 to the Gentiles the boundless **r**
Col 1: 27 among the Gentiles the glorious **r**
2: 2 may have the full **r** of complete

RICHEST (RICH)
Isa 55: 2 and you will delight in the **r** of fare.

RID
Ge 21: 10 "Get **r** of that slave woman and her
1Co 5: 7 Get **r** of the old yeast, so that you
Gal 4: 30 "Get **r** of the slave woman and her

RIDE (RIDER RIDING)
Ps 45: 4 In your majesty **r** forth victoriously

RIDER (RIDE)
Rev 6: 2 Its **r** held a bow, and he was given
19: 11 whose **r** is called Faithful and True.

RIDING (RIDE)
Zec 9: 9 lowly and **r** on a donkey, on a colt,
Mt 21: 5 gentle and **r** on a donkey,

RIGGING
Isa 33: 23 Your **r** hangs loose: The mast is not

RIGHT (RIGHTS)
Ge 4: 7 If you do what is **r**, will you not be
18: 19 of the LORD by doing what is **r**
18: 25 not the Judge of all the earth do **r**?"
48: 13 on his **r** toward Israel's left hand
Ex 15: 6 Your **r** hand, LORD, was majestic
15: 26 God and do what is **r** in his eyes,
Dt 5: 32 do not turn aside to the **r**
6: 18 Do what is **r** and good
13: 18 and doing what is **r** in his eyes.
Jos 1: 7 do not turn from it to the **r**
1Sa 12: 23 you the way that is good and **r**.
1Ki 3: 9 distinguish between **r** and wrong.
15: 5 David had done what was **r**
2Ki 7: 9 other, "What we're doing is not **r**.
Ne 9: 13 and laws that are just and **r**,
Ps 16: 8 With him at my **r** hand, I will not
16: 11 eternal pleasures at your **r** hand.
17: 7 your **r** hand those who take refuge
18: 35 and your **r** hand sustains me;
19: 8 The precepts of the LORD are **r**,
23: 3 He guides me along the **r** paths
25: 9 He guides the humble in what is **r**
33: 4 For the word of the LORD is **r**
44: 3 it was your **r** hand, your arm,
45: 4 let your **r** hand achieve awesome
51: 4 so you are **r** in your verdict
63: 8 your **r** hand upholds me.
73: 23 you hold me by my **r** hand.
91: 7 ten thousand at your **r** hand, but it
98: 1 his **r** hand and his holy arm have
106: 3 act justly, who always do what is **r**.
110: 1 "Sit at my **r** hand until I make your
118: 15 "The LORD's **r** hand has done
137: 5 may my **r** hand forget its skill.
139: 10 me, your **r** hand will hold me fast.
Pr 1: 3 doing what is **r** and just and fair;
4: 27 Do not turn to the **r** or the left;
14: 12 There is a way that appears to be **r**,
16: 13 value the one who speaks what is **r**.
18: 17 a lawsuit the first to speak seems **r**,
28: 5 do not understand what is **r**,
Ecc 7: 20 no one who does what is **r**
SS 1: 4 How **r** they are to adore you!
Isa 1: 17 Learn to do **r**; seek justice.
7: 15 reject the wrong and choose the **r**,
30: 10 us no more visions of what is **r**!
30: 21 Whether you turn to the **r**
41: 10 you with my righteous **r** hand.
41: 13 God who takes hold of your **r** hand
48: 13 my **r** hand spread out the heavens;
64: 5 the help of those who gladly do **r**,
Jer 23: 5 do what is just and **r** in the land.
Eze 18: 5 man who does what is just and **r**.
18: 21 decrees and does what is just and **r**,
33: 14 their sin and do what is just and **r**
Hos 14: 9 The ways of the LORD are **r**;
Mt 5: 29 If your **r** eye causes you to stumble,
6: 3 know what your **r** hand is doing,
22: 44 my **r** hand until I put your enemies
25: 33 He will put the sheep on his **r**
Jn 1: 12 he gave the **r** to become children
Ac 2: 34 said to my Lord: "Sit at my **r** hand
7: 55 standing at the **r** hand of God.
Ro 3: 4 that you may be proved **r** when
8: 34 is at the **r** hand of God and is
9: 21 Does not the potter have the **r**
12: 17 careful to do what is **r** in the eyes
1Co 6: 12 "I have the **r** to do anything,"
9: 4 Don't we have the **r** to food
10: 23 "I have the **r** to do anything,"
2Co 8: 21 we are taking pains to do what is **r**,
Eph 1: 20 and seated him at his **r** hand
6: 1 parents in the Lord, for this is **r**.
Php 4: 8 whatever is **r**, whatever is pure,
Heb 1: 3 he sat down at the **r** hand
Jas 2: 8 as yourself," you are doing **r**.
1Pe 3: 14 if you should suffer for what is **r**,
1Jn 2: 29 who does what is **r** has been born
Rev 2: 7 I will give the **r** to eat from the tree
3: 21 I will give the **r** to sit with me
22: 11 let the one who does **r** continue

RIGHTEOUS (RIGHTEOUSLY RIGHTEOUSNESS)
Ge 6: 9 Noah was a **r** man,
18: 23 "Will you sweep away the **r**
Nu 23: 10 Let me die the death of the **r**,
Ne 9: 8 your promise because you are **r**.
9: 33 to us, you have remained **r**;
Job 36: 7 He does not take his eyes off the **r**;
Ps 1: 5 sinners in the assembly of the **r**.
5: 12 Surely, LORD, you bless the **r**;
9: 4 sitting enthroned as the **r** judge.
11: 7 For the LORD is **r**, he loves
15: 2 who does what is **r**, who speaks
34: 15 eyes of the LORD are on the **r**,
37: 6 will make your **r** reward shine like
37: 16 that the **r** have than the wealth
37: 21 repay, but the **r** give generously;
37: 25 yet I have never seen the **r** forsaken
37: 30 The mouths of the **r** utter wisdom,
55: 22 he will never let the **r** be shaken.
64: 10 The **r** will rejoice in the LORD
65: 5 us with awesome and **r** deeds,
68: 3 But may the **r** be glad and rejoice
71: 15 My mouth will tell of your **r** deeds,
112: 4 gracious and compassionate and **r**.
118: 19 Open for me the gates of the **r**;
118: 20 through which the **r** may enter.
119: 7 upright heart as I learn your **r** laws.
119:137 You are **r**, LORD, and your laws
119:144 Your statutes are always **r**;
140: 13 the **r** will praise your name,
143: 2 no one living is **r** before you.
145: 17 The LORD is **r** in all his ways
Pr 3: 33 but he blesses the home of the **r**.
4: 18 of the **r** is like the morning sun,
10: 7 The name of the **r** is used
10: 11 The mouth of the **r** is a fountain
10: 16 The wages of the **r** is life,
10: 20 The tongue of the **r** is choice silver,
10: 24 what the **r** desire will be granted.
10: 28 The prospect of the **r** is joy,
10: 32 lips of the **r** know what finds favor,
11: 23 The desire of the **r** ends only
11: 30 The fruit of the **r** is a tree of life,
12: 10 The **r** care for the needs of their
12: 21 No harm overtakes the **r**,
13: 9 The light of the **r** shines brightly,
15: 28 heart of the **r** weighs its answers,
15: 29 but he hears the prayer of the **r**.
18: 10 the **r** run to it and are safe.
20: 7 The **r** lead blameless lives;
21: 15 it brings joy to the **r** but terror
23: 24 father of a **r** child has great joy;
28: 1 but the **r** are as bold as a lion.
29: 6 but the **r** shout for joy and are glad.
29: 7 The **r** care about justice
29: 27 The **r** detest the dishonest;
Ecc 7: 20 there is no one on earth who is **r**,
Isa 5: 16 will be proved holy by his **r** acts.
26: 7 The path of the **r** is level;
41: 10 uphold you with my **r** right hand.
45: 21 from me, a **r** God and a Savior;
53: 11 by his knowledge my **r** servant will
64: 6 all our **r** acts are like filthy rags;
Jer 23: 5 I will raise up for David a **r** Branch,
23: 6 The LORD Our **R** Savior.
Eze 3: 20 when a **r** person turns from their
18: 5 "Suppose there is a **r** man who
18: 20 of the **r** will be credited to them,
33: 12 'If someone who is **r** disobeys,
Da 9: 18 requests of you because we are **r**,
Hab 2: 4 but the **r** person will live by his
Zec 9: 9 comes to you, **r** and victorious,

Mal 3: 18 see the distinction between the **r**
Mt 5: 45 and sends rain on the **r**
9: 13 For I have not come to call the **r**,
10: 41 will receive a **r** person's reward.
13: 43 the **r** will shine like the sun
13: 49 and separate the wicked from the **r**
25: 37 "Then the **r** will answer him, 'Lord,
25: 46 but the **r** to eternal life."
Ac 24: 15 will be a resurrection of both the **r**
Ro 1: 17 "The **r** will live by faith."
2: 5 his **r** judgment will be revealed.
2: 13 the law who will be declared **r**.
3: 10 "There is no one **r**, not even one;
3: 20 Therefore no one will be declared **r**
5: 18 one **r** act resulted in justification
5: 19 one man the many will be made **r**.
Gal 3: 11 because "the **r** will live by faith."
1Ti 1: 9 that the law is made not for the **r**
2Ti 4: 8 which the Lord, the **r** Judge,
Titus 3: 5 because of **r** things we had done,
Heb 10: 38 "But my **r** one will live by faith.
Jas 2: 24 is considered **r** by what they do
5: 16 prayer of a **r** person is powerful
1Pe 3: 12 the eyes of the Lord are on the **r**
3: 18 for sins, the **r** for the unrighteous,
4: 18 "If it is hard for the **r** to be saved,
1Jn 2: 1 Jesus Christ, the **R** One.
3: 7 The one who does what is right is **r**, just as he is **r**.
Rev 19: 8 (Fine linen stands for the **r** acts

RIGHTEOUSLY* (RIGHTEOUS)
Isa 33: 15 Those who walk **r** and speak what
Jer 11: 20 who judge **r** and test the heart

RIGHTEOUSNESS (RIGHTEOUS)
Ge 15: 6 and he credited it to him as **r**.
Dt 9: 4 of this land because of my **r**."
1Sa 26: 23 rewards everyone for their **r**
1Ki 10: 9 you king to maintain justice and **r**."
Job 37: 23 in his justice and great **r**, he does
Ps 7: 17 to the LORD because of his **r**;
9: 8 He rules the world in **r** and judges
33: 5 The LORD loves **r** and justice;
35: 28 My tongue will proclaim your **r**,
36: 6 Your **r** is like the highest
45: 7 You love **r** and hate wickedness;
48: 10 your right hand is filled with **r**.
71: 2 In your **r**, rescue me and deliver
71: 19 Your **r**, God,
85: 10 **r** and peace kiss each other.
89: 14 **R** and justice are the foundation
96: 13 He will judge the world in **r**
98: 9 He will judge the world in **r**
103: 6 The LORD works **r** and justice
103: 17 his **r** with their children's children
106: 31 to him as **r** for endless generations
111: 3 deeds, and his **r** endures forever.
132: 9 your priests be clothed with your **r**;
145: 7 and joyfully sing of your **r**.
Pr 11: 5 The **r** of the blameless makes their
11: 18 the one who sows **r** reaps a sure
13: 6 **R** guards the person of integrity,
14: 34 **R** exalts a nation, but sin
16: 8 Better a little with **r** than much
16: 12 a throne is established through **r**.
16: 31 it is attained in the way of **r**.
21: 21 Whoever pursues **r** and love finds
Isa 9: 7 with justice and **r** from that time
11: 4 but with **r** he will judge the needy,
16: 5 justice and speeds the cause of **r**.
26: 9 the people of the world learn **r**.
32: 17 The fruit of that **r** will be peace;
42: 6 the LORD, have called you in **r**;
42: 21 sake of his **r** to make his law great
45: 8 heavens above, rain down my **r**;
51: 1 you who pursue **r** and who seek
51: 6 last forever, my **r** will never fail.
51: 8 But my **r** will last forever,
58: 8 then your **r** will go before you,
59: 17 He put on **r** as his breastplate,
61: 10 and arrayed me in a robe of his **r**,
Jer 9: 24 justice and **r** on earth, for in these I
Eze 3: 20 righteous person turns from their **r**
14: 20 save only themselves by their **r**.
18: 20 The **r** of the righteous will be
33: 12 that person's former **r** will count
Da 9: 24 to bring in everlasting **r**, to seal
12: 3 and those who lead many to **r**,
Hos 10: 12 Sow **r** for yourselves, reap the fruit
Am 5: 24 river, **r** like a never-failing stream!
Mic 7: 9 out into the light; I will see his **r**.
Zep 2: 3 Seek **r**, seek humility;
Mal 4: 2 the sun of **r** will rise with healing
Mt 5: 6 those who hunger and thirst for **r**,
5: 10 who are persecuted because of **r**,
5: 20 you that unless your **r** surpasses
6: 1 not to practice your **r** in front
6: 33 seek first his kingdom and his **r**,
Jn 16: 8 to be in the wrong about sin and **r**
Ac 24: 25 As Paul talked about **r**,
Ro 1: 17 gospel the **r** of God is revealed—
3: 5 brings out God's **r** more clearly,
3: 22 This **r** is given through faith
3: 25 He did this to demonstrate his **r**,
3: 26 he did it to demonstrate his **r** at
4: 3 and it was credited to him as **r**."
4: 5 ungodly, their faith is credited as **r**.
4: 6 to whom God credits **r** apart
4: 9 faith was credited to him as **r**.
4: 13 through the **r** that comes by faith.
4: 22 why "it was credited to him as **r**."
6: 13 to him as an instrument of **r**.
6: 16 or to obedience, which leads to **r**?
6: 18 sin and have become slaves to **r**.
6: 19 yourselves as slaves to **r** leading
8: 10 the Spirit gives life because of **r**.
9: 30 obtained it, a **r** that is by faith;
10: 3 they did not submit to God's **r**.
14: 17 but of **r**, peace and joy in the Holy
1Co 1: 30 is, our **r**, holiness and redemption.
2Co 3: 9 is the ministry that brings **r**!
5: 21 we might become the **r** of God.
6: 7 with weapons of **r** in the right hand
6: 14 For what do **r** and wickedness have
9: 9 their **r** endures forever."
Gal 2: 21 **r** could be gained through the law,
3: 6 and it was credited to him as **r**."
3: 21 **r** would certainly have come
Eph 4: 24 created to be like God in true **r**
5: 9 in all goodness, **r** and truth)
6: 14 with the breastplate of **r** in place,
Php 1: 11 the fruit of **r** that comes through
3: 6 for **r** based on the law, faultless.
3: 9 the **r** that comes from God
1Ti 6: 11 all this, and pursue **r**, godliness,
2Ti 2: 22 evil desires of youth and pursue **r**,
3: 16 correcting and training in **r**,
4: 8 is in store for me the crown of **r**,
Heb 5: 13 with the teaching about **r**.
7: 2 Melchizedek means "king of **r**";
11: 7 and became heir of the **r** that is
12: 11 it produces a harvest of **r** and peace
Jas 2: 23 and it was credited to him as **r**,"
3: 18 sow in peace reap a harvest of **r**.
1Pe 2: 24 we might die to sins and live for **r**;
2Pe 2: 21 not to have known the way of **r**,
3: 13 and a new earth, where **r** dwells.

RIGHTS (RIGHT)
Pr 31: 8 for the **r** of all who are destitute.
Isa 10: 2 to deprive the poor of their **r**
La 3: 35 deny people their **r** before the Most
1Co 9: 18 so not make full use of my **r** as

RING
Pr 11: 22 Like a gold **r** in a pig's snout is
Lk 15: 22 Put a **r** on his finger and sandals

RIOTS
2Co 6: 5 in beatings, imprisonments and **r**;

RIPE
Joel 3: 13 the sickle, for the harvest is **r**.
Am 8: 1 a basket of **r** fruit.
Jn 4: 35 at the fields! They are **r** for harvest.
Rev 14: 15 for the harvest of the earth is **r**."

RISE (RAISE RAISED RISEN ROSE)
Nu 24: 17 a scepter will **r** out of Israel.
Isa 26: 19 their bodies will **r**—let those who
Mal 4: 2 of righteousness will **r** with healing
Mt 27: 63 'After three days I will **r** again.'
Mk 8: 31 killed and after three days **r** again.
Lk 18: 33 On the third day he will **r** again."
Jn 5: 29 who have done what is good will **r**
5: 29 who have done what is evil will **r**
20: 9 that Jesus had to **r** from the dead.)
Ac 17: 3 had to suffer and **r** from the dead.
1Th 4: 16 and the dead in Christ will **r** first.

RISEN (RISE)
Mt 28: 6 is not here; he has **r**, just as he said.
Mk 16: 6 He has **r**! He is not here.
Lk 24: 34 The Lord has **r** and has appeared

RIVER (RIVERS)
Ps 46: 4 There is a **r** whose streams make
Isa 66: 12 "I will extend peace to her like a **r**,
Eze 47: 12 will grow on both banks of the **r**.
Rev 22: 1 the angel showed me the **r**

RIVERS (RIVER)
Ps 137: 1 By the **r** of Babylon we sat
Jn 7: 38 **r** of living water will flow

ROAD (CROSSROADS ROADS)
Mt 7: 13 gate and broad is the **r** that leads

ROADS (ROAD)
Lk 3: 5 The crooked **r** shall become

ROARING
1Pe 5: 8 prowls around like a **r** lion looking

ROB (ROBBERS ROBBERY ROBS)
Mal 3: 8 "Will a mere mortal **r** God?

ROBBERS (ROB)
Jer 7: 11 Name, become a den of **r** to you?
Lk 19: 46 you have made it 'a den of **r**.'"
Jn 10: 8 come before me are thieves and **r**,

ROBBERY (ROB)
Isa 61: 8 I hate **r** and wrongdoing.

ROBE (ROBED ROBES)
Ge 37: 3 and he made an ornate **r** for him.
Isa 6: 1 the train of his **r** filled the temple.
61: 10 me in a **r** of his righteousness,
Rev 6: 11 each of them was given a white **r**,

ROBED (ROBE)
Ps 93: 1 the LORD is **r** in majesty
Isa 63: 1 Who is this, **r** in splendor,

ROBES (ROBE)
Ps 45: 8 All your **r** are fragrant with myrrh
Rev 7: 13 asked me, "These in white **r**—

ROBS* (ROB)
Pr 19: 26 Whoever **r** their father and drives
28: 24 Whoever **r** their father or mother

ROCK
Ge 49: 24 of the Shepherd, the **R** of Israel,
Ex 17: 6 Strike the **r**, and water will come
Nu 20: 8 Speak to that **r** before their eyes
Dt 32: 4 He is the **R**, his works are perfect,
32: 13 him with honey from the **r**,
2Sa 22: 2 "The LORD is my **r**, my fortress
Ps 18: 2 The LORD is my **r**, my fortress
19: 14 LORD, my **R** and my Redeemer.
40: 2 he set my feet on a **r** and gave me
61: 2 me to the **r** that is higher than I.
92: 15 he is my **R**, and there is no
Isa 26: 4 LORD himself, is the **R** eternal.
51: 1 Look to the **r** from which you were
Da 2: 34 you were watching, a **r** was cut out,
Mt 7: 24 man who built his house on the **r**.
16: 18 on this **r** I will build my church,
Ro 9: 33 and a **r** that makes them fall,
1Co 10: 4 them, and that **r** was Christ.
1Pe 2: 8 and a **r** that makes them fall."

ROD (RODS)
2Sa 7: 14 I will punish him with a **r** wielded
Ps 2: 9 will break them with a **r** of iron;
23: 4 your **r** and your staff, they comfort
Pr 13: 24 Whoever spares the **r** hates their
22: 15 the **r** of discipline will drive it far
23: 13 if you punish them with the **r**,
29: 15 A **r** and a reprimand impart
Isa 11: 4 the earth with the **r** of his mouth;

RODS (ROD)
2Co 11: 25 Three times I was beaten with **r**,

ROLL (ROLLED)
Mk 16: 3 "Who will **r** the stone away

ROLLED (ROLL)
Lk 24: 2 They found the stone **r** away

ROMAN
Ac 16: 37 even though we are **R** citizens,
22: 25 to flog a **R** citizen who hasn't even

ROOF (ROOFS)
Pr 21: 9 a corner of the **r** than share a house

ROOFS
Mt 10: 27 in your ear, proclaim from the **r**.

ROOM (ROOMS)
Mt 6: 6 go into your **r**, close the door
Mk 14: 15 He will show you a large **r** upstairs,
Lk 2: 7 there was no guest **r** available
Jn 8: 37 you have no **r** for my word.
21: 25 the whole world would not have **r**
2Co 7: 2 Make **r** for us in your hearts.

ROOMS (ROOM)
Ge 6: 14 ark of cypress wood; make **r** in it
Jn 14: 2 My Father's house has many **r**;

Ps 23: 3 the right paths for his name's **s**.
44: 22 your **s** we face death all day long;
106: 8 Yet he saved them for his name's **s**,
Isa 42: 21 for the **s** of his righteousness
43: 25 for my own **s**, and remembers your
48: 9 my own name's **s** I delay my wrath;
48: 11 For my own **s**, for my own **s**, I do
Jer 14: 7 LORD, for the **s** of your name.
14: 21 the **s** of your name do not despise
Eze 20: 9 But for the **s** of my name, I brought
20: 14 the **s** of my name I did what would
20: 22 the **s** of my name I did what would
36: 22 but for the **s** of my holy name,
Da 9: 17 For your **s**, Lord, look with favor
Mt 10: 39 loses their life for my **s** will find
19: 29 my **s** will receive a hundred times
1Co 9: 23 I do all this for the **s** of the gospel,
2Co 8: 9 yet for your **s** he became poor,
12: 10 is why, for Christ's **s**, I delight
Php 3: 7 consider loss for the **s** of Christ.
Heb 11: 26 disgrace for the **s** of Christ as
1Pe 2: 13 for the Lord's **s** to every human
3Jn : 7 It was for the **s** of the Name

SALEM
Ge 14: 18 Melchizedek king of **S** brought
Heb 7: 2 "king of **S**" means "king of peace."

SALT
Ge 19: 26 back, and she became a pillar of **s**.
Nu 18: 19 covenant of **s** before the LORD
Mt 5: 13 "You are the **s** of the earth.
5: 13 But if the **s** loses its saltiness,
Col 4: 6 seasoned with **s**, so that you may
Jas 3: 11 **s** water flow from the same spring?

SALVATION* (SAVE)
Ex 15: 2 he has become my **s**.
2Sa 22: 3 my shield and the horn of my **s**.
23: 5 he would not bring to fruition my **s**
1Ch 16: 23 proclaim his **s** day after day.
2Ch 6: 41 clothed with **s**, may your faithful
Ps 9: 14 Zion, and there rejoice in your **s**.
13: 5 my heart rejoices in your **s**.
14: 7 that **s** for Israel would come
18: 2 my shield and the horn of my **s**,
27: 1 The LORD is my light and my **s**—
28: 8 a fortress of **s** for his anointed one.
35: 3 Say to me, "I am your **s**."
35: 9 in the LORD and delight in his **s**.
37: 39 The **s** of the righteous comes
50: 23 to the blameless I will show my **s**."
51: 12 Restore to me the joy of your **s**
53: 6 that **s** for Israel would come
62: 1 rest in God; my **s** comes from him.
62: 2 Truly he is my rock and my **s**;
62: 6 Truly he is my rock and my **s**;
62: 7 **s** and my honor depend on God;
67: 2 on earth, your **s** among all nations.
69: 13 God, answer me with your sure **s**.
69: 27 do not let them share in your **s**.
69: 29 may your **s**, God, protect me.
74: 12 he brings **s** on the earth.
85: 7 love, LORD, and grant us your **s**.
85: 9 Surely his **s** is near those who fear
91: 16 satisfy him and show him my **s**."
95: 1 shout aloud to the Rock of our **s**.
96: 2 proclaim his **s** day after day.
98: 1 holy arm have worked **s** for him.
98: 2 The LORD has made his **s** known
98: 3 of the earth have seen the **s** of our
116: 13 I will lift up the cup of **s** and call
118: 14 he has become my **s**.
118: 21 you have become my **s**.
119: 41 your **s**, according to your promise;
119: 81 soul faints with longing for your **s**,
119:123 looking for your **s**, looking for your
119:155 **S** is far from the wicked, for they
119:166 I wait for your **s**, LORD, and I
119:174 I long for your **s**, LORD, and your
132: 16 I will clothe her priests with **s**,
Isa 12: 2 Surely God is my **s**; I will trust
12: 2 he has become my **s**."
12: 3 will draw water from the wells of **s**.
25: 9 let us rejoice and be glad in his **s**."
26: 1 God makes **s** its walls and
26: 18 We have not brought **s** to the earth,
30: 15 "In repentance and rest is your **s**,
33: 2 morning, our **s** in time of distress.
33: 6 a rich store of **s** and wisdom
45: 8 earth open wide, let **s** spring up,
45: 17 the LORD with an everlasting **s**;
46: 13 and my **s** will not be delayed.
46: 13 I will grant **s** to Zion, my splendor
Isa 49: 6 that my **s** may reach to the ends
49: 8 and in the day of **s** I will help you;
51: 5 near speedily, my **s** is on the way,
51: 6 But my **s** will last forever,
51: 8 my **s** through all generations."
52: 7 who proclaim **s**, who say to Zion,
52: 10 the earth will see the **s** of our God.
56: 1 for my **s** is close at hand and my
59: 16 so his own arm achieved **s** for him,
59: 17 and the helmet of **s** on his head;
60: 18 you will call your walls **S** and your
61: 10 has clothed me with garments of **s**
62: 1 the dawn, her **s** like a blazing torch.
63: 5 so my own arm achieved **s** for me,
Jer 3: 23 in the LORD our God is the **s**
La 3: 26 wait quietly for the **s** of the LORD.
Jnh 2: 9 '**S** comes from the LORD.'"
Lk 1: 69 He has raised up a horn of **s** for us
1: 71 **s** from our enemies
1: 77 of **s** through the forgiveness of
2: 30 For my eyes have seen your **s**,
3: 6 all people will see God's **s**.'"
19: 9 "Today **s** has come to this house,
Jn 4: 22 we do know, for **s** is from the Jews.
Ac 4: 12 **S** is found in no one else, for there
13: 26 this message of **s** has been sent.
13: 47 that you may bring **s** to the ends
28: 28 know that God's **s** has been sent
Ro 1: 16 brings **s** to everyone who believes:
11: 11 **s** has come to the Gentiles to make
13: 11 because our **s** is nearer now than
2Co 1: 6 it is for your comfort and **s**;
6: 2 and in the day of **s** I helped you."
6: 2 God's favor, now is the day of **s**.
7: 10 brings repentance that leads to **s**
Eph 1: 13 of truth, the gospel of your **s**.
6: 17 Take the helmet of **s** and the sword
Php 2: 12 to work out your **s** with fear
1Th 5: 8 and the hope of **s** as a helmet.
5: 9 to receive **s** through our Lord Jesus
2Ti 2: 10 they too may obtain the **s** that is
3: 15 make you wise for **s** through faith
Titus 2: 11 appeared that offers **s** to all people.
Heb 1: 14 to serve those who will inherit **s**?
2: 3 we escape if we ignore so great a **s**?
2: 3 This **s**, which was first announced
2: 10 of their **s** perfect through what he
5: 9 of eternal **s** for all who obey him
6: 9 the things that have to do with **s**.
9: 28 to bring **s** to those who are waiting
1Pe 1: 5 the coming of the **s** that is ready
1: 9 of your faith, the **s** of your souls.
1: 10 Concerning this **s**, the prophets,
2: 2 by it you may grow up in your **s**,
2Pe 3: 15 that our Lord's patience means **s**,
Jude : 3 write to you about the **s** we share,
Rev 7: 10 "**S** belongs to our God, who sits
12: 10 "Now have come the **s**
19: 1 **S** and glory and power belong to

SAMARIA (SAMARITAN)
1Ki 16: 24 bought the hill of **S** from Shemer
2Ki 17: 6 the king of Assyria captured **S**
Jn 4: 4 Now he had to go through **S**.
4: 5 came to a town in **S** called Sychar,

SAMARITAN (SAMARIA)
Lk 10: 33 But a **S**, as he traveled, came where
17: 16 and thanked him—and he was a **S**.
Jn 4: 7 When a **S** woman came to draw
Ac 8: 25 the gospel in many **S** villages.

SAMSON
Danite judge. Birth promised (Jdg 13). Married to Philistine, but wife given away (Jdg 14). Vengeance on Philistines (Jdg 15). Betrayed by Delilah (Jdg 16:1–22). Death (Jdg 16:23–31). Feats of strength: killed lion (Jdg 14:6), 30 Philistines (Jdg 14:19), 1,000 Philistines with jawbone (Jdg 15:13–17), carried off gates of Gaza (Jdg 16:3), pushed down temple of Dagon (Jdg 16:25–30).

SAMUEL
Ephraimite judge and prophet (Heb 11:32). Birth prayed for (1Sa 1:10–18). Dedicated to temple by Hannah (1Sa 1:21–28). Raised by Eli (1Sa 2:11, 18–26). Called as prophet (1Sa 3). Led Israel to victory over Philistines (1Sa 7). Asked by Israel for a king (1Sa 8). Anointed Saul as king (1Sa 9–10). Farewell speech (1Sa 12). Rebuked Saul for sacrifice (1Sa 13). Announced rejection of Saul (1Sa 15). Anointed David as king (1Sa 16). Protected David from Saul (1Sa 19:18–24). Death (1Sa 25:1). Returned from dead to condemn Saul (1Sa 28).

SANBALLAT
Led opposition to Nehemiah's rebuilding of Jerusalem (Ne 2:10, 19; 4; 6).

SANCTIFIED* (SANCTIFY)
Jn 17: 19 that they too may be truly **s**.
Ac 20: 32 among all those who are **s**.
26: 18 a place among those who are **s**
Ro 15: 16 to God, **s** by the Holy Spirit.
1Co 1: 2 to those **s** in Christ Jesus and called
6: 11 you were **s**, you were justified
7: 14 husband has been **s** through his
7: 14 wife has been **s** through her
1Th 4: 3 It is God's will that you should be **s**:
Heb 10: 29 blood of the covenant that **s** them,

SANCTIFY* (SANCTIFIED SANCTIFYING)
Jn 17: 17 **S** them by the truth; your word is
17: 19 For them I **s** myself, that they too
1Th 5: 23 peace, **s** you through and through.
Heb 9: 13 are ceremonially unclean **s** them so

SANCTIFYING* (SANCTIFY)
2Th 2: 13 be saved through the **s** work
1Pe 1: 2 through the **s** work of the Spirit,

SANCTUARY
Ex 25: 8 "Then have them make a **s** for me,
Lev 10: 13 Eat it in the **s** area, because it is
19: 30 and have reverence for my **s**.
Ps 63: 2 I have seen you in the **s** and beheld
68: 24 of my God and King into the **s**.
68: 35 You, God, are awesome in your **s**;
73: 17 till I entered the **s** of God;
102: 19 looked down from his **s** on high,
134: 2 Lift up your hands in the **s**
150: 1 Praise God in his **s**; praise him
Eze 37: 26 will put my **s** among them forever.
Da 9: 26 will destroy the city and the **s**.
Heb 6: 19 the inner **s** behind the curtain,
8: 2 and who serves in the **s**, the true
8: 5 They serve at a **s** that is a copy
9: 24 Christ did not enter a **s** made

SAND
Ge 22: 17 sky and as the **s** on the seashore.
Mt 7: 26 man who built his house on **s**.

SANDAL (SANDALS)
Ru 4: 7 one party took off his **s** and gave it

SANDALS (SANDAL)
Ex 3: 5 "Take off your **s**, for the place
Dt 25: 9 take off one of his **s**, spit in his face
Jos 5: 15 "Take off your **s**, for the place
Mt 3: 11 whose **s** I am not worthy to carry.

SANG (SING)
Ex 15: 1 and the Israelites **s** this song
15: 21 Miriam **s** to them:
Nu 21: 17 Then Israel **s** this song:
Jdg 5: 1 Barak son of Abinoam **s** this song:
1Sa 18: 7 As they danced, they **s**:
2Sa 22: 1 David **s** to the LORD the words
2Ch 5: 13 in praise to the LORD and **s**:
29: 30 So they **s** praises with gladness
Ezr 3: 11 thanksgiving they **s** to the LORD:
Job 38: 7 while the morning stars **s** together
Ps 106: 12 his promises and **s** his praise.
Rev 5: 9 And they **s** a new song, saying:
14: 3 **s** a new song before the throne
15: 3 **s** the song of God's servant Moses

SAP
Ro 11: 17 nourishing **s** from the olive root,

SAPPHIRA*
Ac 5: 1 together with his wife **S**, also sold

SARAH
Wife of Abraham, originally named Sarai; barren (Ge 11:29–31; 1Pe 3:6). Taken by Pharaoh as Abraham's sister; returned (Ge 12:10–20). Gave Hagar to Abraham; sent her away in pregnancy (Ge 16). Name changed; Isaac promised (Ge 17:15–21; 18:10–15; Heb 11:11). Taken by Abimelek as Abraham's sister; returned (Ge 20). Isaac born; Hagar and Ishmael sent away (Ge 21:1–21; Gal 4:21–31). Death (Ge 23).

SARDIS
Rev 3: 1 the angel of the church in **S** write:

SASH (SASHES)
Rev 1: 13 with a golden **s** around his chest.

SASHES (SASH)
Rev 15: 6 wore golden **s** around their chests.

SAT (SIT)
Ps 137: 1 By the rivers of Babylon we **s**
Mk 16: 19 *he **s** at the right hand of God.*
Lk 10: 39 who **s** at the Lord's feet listening
Heb 1: 3 he **s** down at the right hand
8: 1 who **s** down at the right hand
10: 12 **s** down at the right hand of God,
12: 2 and **s** down at the right hand

SATAN
Job 1: 6 and **S** also came with them.
Zec 3: 2 The LORD said to **S**, "The LORD rebuke you, **S**!
Mt 12: 26 If **S** drives out **S**, he is divided
16: 23 said to Peter, "Get behind me, **S**!
Mk 4: 15 **S** comes and takes away the word
Lk 10: 18 "I saw **S** fall like lightning
22: 3 Then **S** entered Judas,
Ro 16: 20 will soon crush **S** under your feet.
1Co 5: 5 hand this man over to **S**
2Co 11: 14 **S** himself masquerades as an angel
12: 7 a messenger of **S**, to torment me.
1Ti 1: 20 I have handed over to **S** to be
Rev 12: 9 or **S**, who leads the whole world
20: 2 **S**, and bound him for a thousand
20: 7 **S** will be released from his prison

SATISFIED (SATISFY)
Ps 17: 15 will be **s** with seeing your likeness.
22: 26 The poor will eat and be **s**;
63: 5 I will be fully **s** as with the richest
104: 28 hand, they are **s** with good things.
Pr 13: 4 desires of the diligent are fully **s**.
30: 15 are three things that are never **s**,
Ecc 5: 10 whoever loves wealth is never **s**
Isa 53: 11 he will see the light of life and be **s**;
Mt 14: 20 They all ate and were **s**,
Lk 6: 21 who hunger now, for you will be **s**.

SATISFIES* (SATISFY)
Ps 103: 5 **s** your desires with good things
107: 9 for he **s** the thirsty and fills
147: 14 and **s** you with the finest of wheat.

SATISFY (SATISFIED SATISFIES)
Ps 90: 14 **S** us in the morning with your
145: 16 **s** the desires of every living thing.
Pr 5: 19 may her breasts **s** you always,
Isa 55: 2 and your labor on what does not **s**?
58: 10 and **s** the needs of the oppressed,

SAUL
1. Benjamite; anointed by Samuel as first king of Israel (1Sa 9–10). Defeated Ammonites (1Sa 11). Rebuked for offering sacrifice (1Sa 13:1–15). Defeated Philistines (1Sa 14). Rejected as king for failing to annihilate Amalekites (1Sa 15). Soothed from evil spirit by David (1Sa 16:14–23). Sent David against Goliath (1Sa 17). Jealousy and attempted murder of David (1Sa 18:1–11). Gave David Michal as wife (1Sa 18:12–30). Second attempt to kill David (1Sa 19). Anger at Jonathan (1Sa 20:26–34). Pursued David: killed priests at Nob (1Sa 22), went to Keilah and Ziph (1Sa 23), life spared by David at En Gedi (1Sa 24) and in his tent (1Sa 26). Rebuked by Samuel's spirit for consulting witch at Endor (1Sa 28). Wounded by Philistines; took his own life (1Sa 31; 1Ch 10). Lamented by David (2Sa 1:17–27). Children (1Sa 14:49–51; 1Ch 8).
2. See PAUL

SAVAGE
Ac 20: 29 **s** wolves will come in among you

SAVE (SAFE SAFETY SALVATION SAVED SAVES SAVIOR)
Ge 45: 5 because it was to **s** lives that God
1Ch 16: 35 Cry out, "**S** us, God our Savior;
Job 40: 14 your own right hand can **s** you.
Ps 17: 7 who **s** by your right hand those
18: 27 You **s** the humble but bring low
28: 9 **S** your people and bless your
31: 16 **s** me in your unfailing love.
69: 35 for God will **s** Zion and rebuild
71: 2 turn your ear to me and **s** me.
72: 13 needy and **s** the needy from death.
91: 3 Surely he will **s** you
109: 31 to **s** their lives from those who
146: 3 in human beings, who cannot **s**.
Pr 2: 16 Wisdom will **s** you
Isa 35: 4 retribution he will come to **s** you."
38: 20 The LORD will **s** me, and we will
46: 7 cannot **s** them from their troubles.
59: 1 of the LORD is not too short to **s**,
63: 1 proclaiming victory, mighty to **s**."
Jer 17: 14 **s** me and I will be saved, for you
Eze 3: 18 evil ways in order to **s** their life,
14: 14 it, they could **s** only themselves
34: 22 I will **s** my flock, and they will no
Hos 1: 7 the LORD their God, will **s** them."
Zep 1: 18 nor their gold will be able to **s**
Zec 8: 7 "I will **s** my people
Mt 1: 21 because he will **s** his people
16: 25 wants to **s** their life will lose it,
Lk 19: 10 came to seek and to **s** the lost."
Jn 3: 17 but to **s** the world through him.
12: 47 judge the world, but to **s** the world.
Ro 11: 14 people to envy and **s** some of them.
1Co 7: 16 whether you will **s** your husband?
7: 16 whether you will **s** your wife?
1Ti 1: 15 came into the world to **s** sinners—
Heb 7: 25 to **s** completely those who come
Jas 5: 20 of their way will **s** them from death
Jude : 23 **s** others by snatching them

SAVED (SAVE)
Ps 22: 5 To you they cried out and were **s**;
33: 16 No king is **s** by the size of his army;
34: 6 he **s** him out of all his troubles.
106: 21 They forgot the God who **s** them,
116: 6 when I was brought low, he **s** me.
Isa 25: 9 we trusted in him, and he **s** us.
45: 22 "Turn to me and be **s**, all you ends
64: 5 How then can we be **s**?
Jer 4: 14 the evil from your heart and be **s**.
8: 20 has ended, and we are not **s**."
Eze 3: 19 but you will have **s** yourself.
33: 5 they would have **s** themselves.
Joel 2: 32 the name of the LORD will be **s**;
Mt 10: 22 stands firm to the end will be **s**.
24: 13 stands firm to the end will be **s**.
Mk 13: 13 stands firm to the end will be **s**.
16: 16 *believes and is baptized will be **s**,*
Jn 10: 9 enters through me will be **s**.
Ac 2: 21 on the name of the Lord will be **s**.'
2: 47 daily those who were being **s**.
4: 12 mankind by which we must be **s**."
15: 11 of our Lord Jesus that we are **s**,
16: 30 "Sirs, what must I do to be **s**?"
Ro 5: 9 how much more shall we be **s**
9: 27 the sea, only the remnant will be **s**.
10: 1 the Israelites is that they may be **s**.
10: 9 him from the dead, you will be **s**.
10: 13 on the name of the Lord will be **s**."
11: 26 and in this way all Israel will be **s**.
1Co 1: 18 us who are being **s** it is the power
3: 15 will suffer loss but yet will be **s**—
5: 5 that his spirit may be **s** on the day
10: 33 of many, so that they may be **s**.
15: 2 By this gospel you are **s**, if you hold
Eph 2: 5 it is by grace you have been **s**.
2: 8 For it is by grace you have been **s**,
2Th 2: 13 be **s** through the sanctifying work
1Ti 2: 4 who wants all people to be **s**
2: 15 will be **s** through childbearing—
2Ti 1: 9 He has **s** us and called us to a holy
Titus 3: 5 He **s** us through the washing
Heb 10: 39 to those who have faith and are **s**.

SAVES (SAVE)
Ps 7: 10 High, who **s** the upright in heart.
68: 20 Our God is a God who **s**;
145: 19 he hears their cry and **s** them.
Pr 11: 30 the one who is wise **s** lives.
Zep 3: 17 you, the Mighty Warrior who **s**.
1Pe 3: 21 **s** you by the resurrection of Jesus

SAVIOR* (SAVE)
Dt 32: 15 them and rejected the Rock their **S**.
2Sa 22: 3 stronghold, my refuge and my **s**—
22: 47 be my God, the Rock, my **S**!
1Ch 16: 35 Cry out, "Save us, God our **S**;
Ps 18: 46 to my Rock! Exalted be God my **S**!
24: 5 and vindication from God their **S**.
25: 5 you are God my **S**, and my hope
27: 9 reject me or forsake me, God my **S**.
38: 22 to help me, my Lord and my **S**.
42: 5 yet praise him, my **S** and my God.
42: 11 yet praise him, my **S** and my God.
43: 5 yet praise him, my **S** and my God.
51: 14 you who are God my **S**, and my
65: 5 God our **S**, the hope of all the ends
68: 19 to God our **S**, who daily bears our
79: 9 us, God our **S**, for the glory of your
85: 4 God our **S**, and put away your
89: 26 Father, my God, the Rock my **S**.'
Isa 17: 10 You have forgotten God your **S**;
19: 20 he will send them a **s** and defender,
43: 3 the Holy One of Israel, your **S**;
43: 11 and apart from me there is no **s**.
45: 15 himself, the God and **S** of Israel.
45: 21 from me, a righteous God and a **S**;
49: 26 am your **S**, your Redeemer,
60: 16 am your **S**, your Redeemer,
62: 11 Daughter Zion, 'See, your **S** comes!
63: 8 and so he became their **S**.
Jer 14: 8 of Israel, its **S** in times of distress,
23: 6 The LORD Our Righteous **S**.
33: 16 The LORD Our Righteous **S**.'
Hos 13: 4 no God but me, no **S** except me.
Mic 7: 7 the LORD, I wait for God my **S**;
Hab 3: 18 I will be joyful in God my **S**.
Lk 1: 47 and my spirit rejoices in God my **S**,
2: 11 town of David a **S** has been born
Jn 4: 42 that this man really is the **S**
Ac 5: 31 and **S** that he might bring Israel
13: 23 has brought to Israel the **S** Jesus,
Eph 5: 23 his body, of which he is the **S**.
Php 3: 20 we eagerly await a **S** from there,
1Ti 1: 1 by the command of God our **S**
2: 3 is good, and pleases God our **S**,
4: 10 God, who is the **S** of all people,
2Ti 1: 10 through the appearing of our **S**,
Titus 1: 3 me by the command of God our **S**,
1: 4 the Father and Christ Jesus our **S**.
2: 10 about God our **S** attractive.
2: 13 the glory of our great God and **S**,
3: 4 and love of God our **S** appeared,
3: 6 through Jesus Christ our **S**,
2Pe 1: 1 **S** Jesus Christ have received a faith
1: 11 of our Lord and **S** Jesus Christ.
2: 20 our Lord and **S** Jesus Christ and
3: 2 Lord and **S** through your apostles.
3: 18 of our Lord and **S** Jesus Christ.
1Jn 4: 14 his Son to be the **S** of the world.
Jude : 25 to the only God our **S** be glory,

SCALE (SCALES)
Ps 18: 29 with my God I can **s** a wall.

SCALES (SCALE)
Lev 11: 9 may eat any that have fins and **s**.
19: 36 Use honest **s** and honest weights,
Pr 11: 1 The LORD detests dishonest **s**,
Da 5: 27 You have been weighed on the **s**
Rev 6: 5 Its rider was holding a pair of **s**

SCAPEGOAT (GOAT)
Lev 16: 10 it into the wilderness as a **s**.

SCARECROW*
Jer 10: 5 Like a **s** in a cucumber field,

SCARLET
Jos 2: 21 she tied the **s** cord in the window.
Isa 1: 18 "Though your sins are like **s**,
Mt 27: 28 him and put a **s** robe on him,

SCATTER (SCATTERED SCATTERS)
Dt 4: 27 The LORD will **s** you among
Ne 1: 8 I will **s** you among the nations,
Jer 9: 16 I will **s** them among nations
30: 11 the nations among which I **s** you,
Zec 10: 9 I **s** them among the peoples,

SCATTERED (SCATTER)
Isa 11: 12 he will assemble the **s** people
Jer 31: 10 'He who **s** Israel will gather them
Zec 2: 6 "for I have **s** you to the four winds
13: 7 and the sheep will be **s**, and I will
Mt 26: 31 and the sheep of the flock will be **s**.'
Jn 11: 52 but also for the **s** children of God,
Ac 8: 4 who had been **s** preached the word
Jas 1: 1 To the twelve tribes **s** among
1Pe 1: 1 exiles **s** throughout the provinces

SCATTERS (SCATTER)
Mt 12: 30 does not gather with me **s**.

SCEPTER
Ge 49: 10 The **s** will not depart from Judah,
Nu 24: 17 a **s** will rise out of Israel.
Ps 45: 6 a **s** of justice will be the **s** of your
Heb 1: 8 a **s** of justice will be the **s** of your
Rev 2: 27 one 'will rule them with an iron **s**
12: 5 rule all the nations with an iron **s**."
19: 15 "He will rule them with an iron **s**."

SCHEMES
Pr 6: 18 a heart that devises wicked **s**,
10: 23 A fool finds pleasure in wicked **s**,
12: 2 those who devise wicked **s**.
14: 17 the one who devises evil **s** is hated.
24: 9 The **s** of folly are sin, and people
2Co 2: 11 For we are not unaware of his **s**.
Eph 6: 11 your stand against the devil's **s**.

SCOFFERS
2Pe 3: 3 that in the last days **s** will come,

SCORN (SCORNED SCORNING SCORNS)
Ps 69: 7 For I endure **s** for your sake,
69: 20 **S** has broken my heart and has left
89: 41 he has become the **s** of his
109: 25 I am an object of **s** to my accusers;
119: 22 Remove from me their **s**
Mic 6: 16 you will bear the **s** of the nations."

SCORNED (SCORN)
Ps 22: 6 and not a man, **s** by everyone,

SCORNING* (SCORN)
Heb 12: 2 he endured the cross, **s** its shame,

SCORNS* (SCORN)
Pr 13: 13 Whoever **s** instruction will pay
30: 17 that **s** an aged mother, will be

SCORPION
Lk 11: 12 asks for an egg, will give him a **s**?
Rev 9: 5 of the sting of a **s** when it strikes.

SCOUNDRELS
1Sa 2: 12 Eli's sons were **s**; they had no

SCRIPTURE (SCRIPTURES)
Jn 2: 22 they believed the **s** and the words
7: 42 Does not **S** say that the Messiah
10: 35 and **S** cannot be set aside—
Ac 8: 32 of **S** the eunuch was reading:
1Ti 4: 13 yourself to the public reading of **S**,
2Ti 3: 16 All **S** is God-breathed and is useful
2Pe 1: 20 that no prophecy of **S** came

SCRIPTURES (SCRIPTURE)
Mt 22: 29 because you do not know the **S**
Lk 24: 27 in all the **S** concerning himself.
24: 45 so they could understand the **S**.
Jn 5: 39 You study the **S** diligently because
Ac 17: 11 examined the **S** every day to see
2Ti 3: 15 you have known the Holy **S**,
2Pe 3: 16 as they do the other **S**, to their own

SCROLL
Ps 40: 7 it is written about me in the **s**.
Isa 34: 4 and the heavens rolled up like a **s**;
Eze 3: 1 eat what is before you, eat this **s**;
Heb 10: 7 it is written about me in the **s**—
Rev 6: 14 receded like a **s** being rolled up,
10: 8 the **s** that lies open in the hand
22: 18 the words of the prophecy of this **s**:

SCRUB*
Pr 20: 30 Blows and wounds **s** away evil,

SCUM
1Co 4: 13 We have become the **s** of the earth,

SEA (SEASHORE)
Ex 14: 16 the Israelites can go through the **s**
Dt 30: 13 Nor is it beyond the **s**, so that you
1Ki 7: 23 He made the **S** of cast metal,
Job 11: 9 the earth and wider than the **s**.
Ps 93: 4 mightier than the breakers of the **s**
95: 5 The **s** is his, for he made it, and his
Ecc 1: 7 All streams flow into the **s**, yet the **s** is never full.
11: 1 Ship your grain across the **s**;
Isa 57: 20 the wicked are like the tossing **s**,
Jnh 1: 4 LORD sent a great wind on the **s**,
Mic 7: 19 iniquities into the depths of the **s**.
Hab 2: 14 LORD as the waters cover the **s**.
Zec 9: 10 His rule will extend from **s** to **s**
Mt 18: 6 be drowned in the depths of the **s**.
1Co 10: 1 that they all passed through the **s**.
Jas 1: 6 who doubts is like a wave of the **s**,
Jude : 13 They are wild waves of the **s**,
Rev 10: 2 He planted his right foot on the **s**
13: 1 I saw a beast coming out of the **s**.
20: 13 The **s** gave up the dead that were
21: 1 and there was no longer any **s**.

SEAL (SEALED SEALS)
Ps 40: 9 I do not **s** my lips, LORD, as you
SS 8: 6 Place me like a **s** over your heart,
Eze 28: 12 "'You were the **s** of perfection,
Da 12: 4 **s** the words of the scroll until
Jn 6: 27 God the Father has placed his **s**
1Co 9: 2 For you are the **s** of my apostleship
2Co 1: 22 set his **s** of ownership on us,
Eph 1: 13 you were marked in him with a **s**,
Rev 6: 3 the Lamb opened the second **s**,
6: 5 the Lamb opened the third **s**,
6: 7 the Lamb opened the fourth **s**,
6: 9 When he opened the fifth **s**, I saw
6: 12 I watched as he opened the sixth **s**.
8: 1 When he opened the seventh **s**,
9: 4 people who did not have the **s**
22: 10 me, "Do not **s** up the words

SEALED (SEAL)
Eph 4: 30 with whom you were **s** for the day
2Ti 2: 19 stands firm, **s** with this inscription:
Rev 5: 1 both sides and **s** with seven seals.

SEALS (SEAL)
Rev 5: 2 "Who is worthy to break the **s**
6: 1 opened the first of the seven **s**.

SEAMLESS*
Jn 19: 23 This garment was **s**, woven in one

SEARCH (SEARCHED SEARCHES SEARCHING)
Ps 4: 4 beds, **s** your hearts and be silent.
139: 23 **S** me, God, and know my heart;
Pr 2: 4 and **s** for it as for hidden treasure,
25: 2 to **s** out a matter is the glory
25: 27 nor is it honorable to **s** out matters
SS 3: 2 I will **s** for the one my heart loves.
Jer 17: 10 "I the LORD **s** the heart
Eze 34: 11 I myself will **s** for my sheep
34: 16 I will **s** for the lost and bring back
Lk 15: 8 and **s** carefully until she finds it?

SEARCHED (SEARCH)
Ps 139: 1 You have **s** me, LORD, and you
Ecc 12: 10 The Teacher **s** to find just the right
1Pe 1: 10 **s** intently and with the greatest care

SEARCHES* (SEARCH)
1Ch 28: 9 for the LORD **s** every heart
Job 39: 8 pasture and **s** for any green thing.
Pr 11: 27 evil comes to one who **s** for it.
Ro 8: 27 who **s** our hearts knows the mind
1Co 2: 10 The Spirit **s** all things, even the
Rev 2: 23 know that I am he who **s** hearts

SEARCHING (SEARCH)
Jdg 5: 15 Reuben there was much **s** of heart.
Am 8: 12 east, **s** for the word of the LORD,

SEARED
1Ti 4: 2 whose consciences have been **s** as

SEASHORE (SEA)
Jos 11: 4 as numerous as the sand on the **s**.
1Ki 4: 29 as measureless as the sand on the **s**.

SEASON (SEASONED SEASONS)
Lev 26: 4 I will send you rain in its **s**,
Ps 1: 3 which yields its fruit in **s** and
2Ti 4: 2 be prepared in **s** and out of **s**;

SEASONED* (SEASON)
Col 4: 6 be always full of grace, **s** with salt,

SEASONS (SEASON)
Gal 4: 10 days and months and **s** and years!

SEAT (SEATED SEATS)
Pr 31: 23 he takes his **s** among the elders
Da 7: 9 and the Ancient of Days took his **s**.
Lk 14: 9 to you, 'Give this person your **s**.'
2Co 5: 10 all appear before the judgment **s**

SEATED (SEAT)
Ps 47: 8 God is **s** on his holy throne.
Isa 6: 1 high and exalted, **s** on a throne;
Lk 22: 69 of Man will be **s** at the right hand
Eph 1: 20 and **s** him at his right hand
2: 6 and **s** us with him in the heavenly
Col 3: 1 is, **s** at the right hand of God.
Rev 14: 14 **s** on the cloud was one like a son
20: 11 throne and him who was **s** on it.

SEATS (SEAT)
Lk 11: 43 you love the most important **s**

SECLUSION*
Lk 1: 24 and for five months remained in **s**.

SECRET (SECRETLY SECRETS)
Dt 29: 29 The **s** things belong to the LORD
Jdg 16: 6 "Tell me the **s** of your great
Ps 90: 8 you, our **s** sins in the light of your
139: 15 when I was made in the **s** place,
Pr 11: 13 but a trustworthy person keeps a **s**.
21: 14 A gift given in **s** soothes anger,
Jer 23: 24 Who can hide in **s** places so that I
Mt 6: 4 so that your giving may be in **s**.
6: 18 who sees what is done in **s**,
Mk 4: 11 "The **s** of the kingdom of God has
2Co 4: 2 we have renounced **s** and shameful
Eph 5: 12 what the disobedient do in **s**.
Php 4: 12 have learned the **s** of being content

SECRETLY (SECRET)
2Pe 2: 1 They will **s** introduce destructive
Jude : 4 long ago have **s** slipped in among

SECRETS (SECRET)
Ps 44: 21 since he knows the **s** of the heart?
Ro 2: 16 judges people's **s** through Jesus
1Co 14: 25 as the **s** of their hearts are laid bare.
Rev 2: 24 learned Satan's so-called deep **s**,

SECURE (SECURITY)
Dt 33: 12 beloved of the LORD rest **s** in him,
2Sa 22: 33 with strength and keeps my way **s**.
Ps 16: 5 and my cup; you make my lot **s**.
16: 9 my body also will rest **s**,
18: 32 with strength and keeps my way **s**.
93: 1 the world is established, firm and **s**.
112: 8 Their hearts are **s**, they will have
Pr 14: 26 fears the LORD has a **s** fortress,
Heb 6: 19 an anchor for the soul, firm and **s**.
2Pe 3: 17 and fall from your **s** position.

SECURITY (SECURE)
Job 31: 24 or said to pure gold, 'You are my **s**,'

SEED (SEEDS SEEDTIME)
Ge 1: 11 the land that bear fruit with **s** in it,
Isa 55: 10 so that it yields **s** for the sower
Mt 13: 3 "A farmer went out to sow his **s**.
13: 31 of heaven is like a mustard **s**,
17: 20 have faith as small as a mustard **s**,
Lk 8: 11 The **s** is the word of God.
1Co 3: 6 I planted the **s**, Apollos watered it,
2Co 9: 10 he who supplies **s** to the sower
Gal 3: 29 you are Abraham's **s**, and heirs
1Pe 1: 23 again, not of perishable **s**,
1Jn 3: 9 because God's **s** remains in them;

SEEDS (SEED)
Jn 12: 24 But if it dies, it produces many **s**.
Gal 3: 16 Scripture does not say "and to **s**,"

SEEDTIME* (SEED)
Ge 8: 22 as the earth endures, **s** and harvest,

SEEK (SEEKING SEEKS SELF-SEEKING SOUGHT)
Lev 19: 18 "'Do not **s** revenge or bear
Dt 4: 29 there you **s** the LORD your God,
4: 29 you will find him if you **s** him
1Ki 22: 5 of Israel, "First **s** the counsel
1Ch 28: 9 If you **s** him, he will be found
2Ch 7: 14 pray and **s** my face and turn
15: 2 If you **s** him, he will be found
Ps 34: 10 but those who **s** the LORD lack no
105: 3 of those who **s** the LORD rejoice.
105: 4 and his strength; **s** his face always.
119: 2 and **s** him with all their heart—
119: 10 I **s** you with all my heart; do not let
119:176 **S** your servant, for I have not
Pr 8: 17 me, and those who **s** me find me.
18: 15 for the ears of the wise **s** it out.
28: 5 those who **s** the LORD understand
Isa 55: 6 **S** the LORD while he may be
65: 1 found by those who did not **s** me.
Jer 29: 13 You will **s** me and find me
Hos 10: 12 for it is time to **s** the LORD,
Am 5: 4 says to Israel: "**S** me and live;
Zep 2: 3 **S** the LORD, all you humble
2: 3 **S** righteousness, **s** humility;
Mt 6: 33 But **s** first his kingdom and his
7: 7 given to you; **s** and you will find;
Lk 12: 31 But **s** his kingdom, and these
19: 10 For the Son of Man came to **s**
Jn 5: 30 for I **s** not to please myself but him
5: 44 do not **s** the glory that comes
Ro 10: 20 found by those who did not **s** me;
1Co 7: 27 Do not **s** to be released.
10: 24 No one should **s** their own good,
Heb 11: 6 rewards those who earnestly **s** him.
1Pe 3: 11 they must **s** peace and pursue it.

SEEKING (SEEK)
2Ch 30: 19 who sets their heart on **s** God—
Pr 20: 18 Plans are established by **s** advice;
Mal 3: 1 the Lord you are **s** will come to his
Jn 8: 50 I am not **s** glory for myself;
1Co 10: 33 For I am not **s** my own good

SEEKS (SEEK)
Pr 11: 27 Whoever **s** good finds favor,
Mt 7: 8 the one who **s** finds; and to the one
Jn 4: 23 the kind of worshipers the Father **s**.
Ro 3: 11 there is no one who **s** God.

SEER
1Sa 9: 9 of today used to be called a **s**.)

SELF-CONTROL* (CONTROL)
Pr 16: 32 with **s** than one who takes a city.
25: 28 through is a person who lacks **s**.
Ac 24: 25 **s** and the judgment to come,

1Co 7: 5 you because of your lack of **s**.
Gal 5: 23 gentleness and **s**.
2Ti 3: 3 slanderous, without **s**, brutal,
2Pe 1: 6 to knowledge, **s**; and to **s**, perseverance;

SELF-CONTROLLED* (CONTROL)
1Ti 3: 2 his wife, temperate, **s**, respectable,
Titus 1: 8 what is good, who is **s**, upright,
2: 2 worthy of respect, **s**, and sound
2: 5 to be **s** and pure, to be busy
2: 6 encourage the young men to be **s**.
2: 12 to live **s**, upright and godly lives

SELF-DENIAL* (SELF-DENIAL)
Ps 132: 1 remember David and all his **s**.

SELF-DISCIPLINE* (DISCIPLINE)
2Ti 1: 7 but gives us power, love and **s**.

SELF-INDULGENCE*
Mt 23: 25 inside they are full of greed and **s**.
Jas 5: 5 have lived on earth in luxury and **s**.

SELF-SEEKING* (SEEK)
Ro 2: 8 for those who are **s** and who reject
1Co 13: 5 it is not **s**, it is not easily angered,

SELFISH*
Ps 119: 36 statutes and not toward **s** gain.
Pr 18: 1 unfriendly person pursues **s** ends
2Co 12: 20 **s** ambition, slander, gossip,
Gal 5: 20 fits of rage, **s** ambition, dissensions,
Php 1: 17 preach Christ out of **s** ambition,
2: 3 Do nothing out of **s** ambition
Jas 3: 14 envy and **s** ambition in your hearts,
3: 16 you have envy and **s** ambition,

SELL (SELLING SELLS SOLD)
Ge 25: 31 "First **s** me your birthright."
Mk 10: 21 **s** everything you have and give
Rev 13: 17 buy or **s** unless they had the mark,

SELLING (SELL)
Lk 17: 28 buying and **s**, planting and

SELLS (SELL)
Pr 31: 24 makes linen garments and **s** them,

SEND (SENDING SENDS SENT)
Ps 43: 3 **S** me your light and your faithful
Isa 6: 8 And I said, "Here am I. **S** me!"
Mal 3: 1 "I will **s** my messenger, who will
Mt 9: 38 to **s** out workers into his harvest
24: 31 And he will **s** his angels with a loud
Mk 1: 2 "I will **s** my messenger ahead
1: 17 I will **s** you out to fish for people."
6: 7 he began to **s** them out two by two
Lk 20: 13 I will **s** my son, whom I love;
Jn 3: 17 God did not **s** his Son into the
16: 7 but if I go, I will **s** him to you.
1Co 1: 17 For Christ did not **s** me to baptize,

SENDING (SEND)
Mt 10: 16 "I am **s** you out like sheep among
Jn 20: 21 the Father has sent me, I am **s** you."
Ro 8: 3 God did by **s** his own Son

SENDS (SEND)
Ps 57: 3 He **s** from heaven and saves me,

SENNACHERIB
Assyrian king whose siege of Jerusalem was overthrown by the LORD following prayer of Hezekiah and Isaiah (2Ki 18:13—19:37; 2Ch 32:1-21; Isa 36-37).

SENSE (SENSES)
Pr 6: 32 who commits adultery has no **s**;
10: 21 many, but fools die for lack of **s**.
11: 12 derides their neighbor has no **s**,
12: 11 who chase fantasies have no **s**.
15: 21 brings joy to one who has no **s**,
17: 18 One who has no **s** shakes hands
24: 30 vineyard of someone who has no **s**;

SENSES* (SENSE)
Lk 15: 17 "When he came to his **s**, he said,
1Co 15: 34 Come back to your **s** as you ought,
2Ti 2: 26 that they will come to their **s**

SENSITIVITY*
Eph 4: 19 Having lost all **s**, they have given

SENSUAL* (SENSUALITY)
Col 2: 23 value in restraining **s** indulgence.
1Ti 5: 11 when their **s** desires overcome

SENSUALITY* (SENSUAL)
Eph 4: 19 given themselves over to **s** so as

SENT (SEND)
Ex 3: 14 'I AM has **s** me to you.'"
Isa 55: 11 achieve the purpose for which I **s**
61: 1 He has **s** me to bind
Jer 28: 9 will be recognized as one truly **s**
Mt 10: 40 me welcomes the one who **s** me.
Lk 4: 18 He has **s** me to proclaim freedom
9: 2 and he **s** them out to proclaim
10: 16 rejects me rejects him who **s** me."
Jn 1: 6 There was a man **s** from God
4: 34 "is to do the will of him who **s** me
5: 24 believes him who **s** me has eternal
8: 16 I stand with the Father, who **s** me.
9: 4 do the works of him who **s** me.
16: 5 now I am going to him who **s** me.
17: 3 and Jesus Christ, whom you have **s**.
17: 18 As you **s** me into the world, I have **s** them
20: 21 As the Father has **s** me, I am
Ro 10: 15 anyone preach unless they are **s**?
Gal 4: 4 had fully come, God **s** his Son,
1Jn 4: 10 **s** his Son as an atoning sacrifice

SENTENCE
2Co 1: 9 we felt we had received the **s**

SEPARATE (SEPARATED SEPARATES)
Mt 19: 6 has joined together, let no one **s**."
Ro 8: 35 Who shall **s** us from the love
1Co 7: 10 A wife must not **s** from her
2Co 6: 17 "Come out from them and be **s**,
Eph 2: 12 that time you were **s** from Christ,

SEPARATED (SEPARATE)
Isa 59: 2 your iniquities have **s** you from
Eph 4: 18 **s** from the life of God because

SEPARATES* (SEPARATE)
Ru 1: 17 if even death **s** you and me."
Pr 16: 28 and a gossip **s** close friends.
17: 9 repeats the matter **s** close friends.
Mt 25: 32 another as a shepherd **s** the sheep

SERAPHIM*
Isa 6: 2 Above him were **s**, each with six
6: 6 of the **s** flew to me with a live coal

SERIOUSNESS*
Titus 2: 7 In your teaching show integrity,

SERPENT (SERPENT'S)
Ge 3: 1 the **s** was more crafty than any
Isa 27: 1 Leviathan the gliding **s**,
Rev 12: 9 that ancient **s** called the devil,
20: 2 that ancient **s**, who is the devil,

SERPENT'S (SERPENT)
2Co 11: 3 Eve was deceived by the **s** cunning,

SERVANT (SERVANTS)
Ex 14: 31 trust in him and in Moses his **s**.
21: 2 "If you buy a Hebrew **s**, he is
1Sa 3: 10 "Speak, for your **s** is listening."
2Sa 7: 19 the future of the house of your **s**—
1Ki 20: 40 While your **s** was busy here
Job 1: 8 "Have you considered my **s** Job?
Ps 19: 11 By them your **s** is warned;
19: 13 Keep your **s** also from willful sins;
31: 16 Let your face shine on your **s**;
89: 3 one, I have sworn to David my **s**,
Pr 14: 35 A king delights in a wise **s**,
17: 2 A prudent **s** will rule over
Isa 41: 8 Israel, my **s**, Jacob, whom I have
49: 3 said to me, "You are my **s**, Israel,
53: 11 my righteous **s** will justify many,
Zec 3: 8 I am going to bring my **s**,
Mt 8: 13 his **s** was healed at that moment.
20: 26 great among you must be your **s**,
24: 45 then is the faithful and wise **s**,
25: 21 'Well done, good and faithful **s**!
Lk 1: 38 "I am the Lord's **s**,"
Jn 12: 26 and where I am, my **s** also will be.
Ro 1: 1 Paul, a **s** of Christ Jesus, called
13: 4 authority is God's **s** for your good.
Php 2: 7 by taking the very nature of a **s**,
Col 1: 23 of which I, Paul, have become a **s**.
2Ti 2: 24 And the Lord's **s** must not be
3: 17 the **s** of God may be thoroughly

SERVANTS (SERVANT)
Lev 25: 55 the Israelites belong to me as **s**.
1Sa 2: 9 guard the feet of his faithful **s**,
2Ki 17: 13 to you through my **s** the prophets."
Ezr 5: 11 "We are the **s** of the God of heaven
Ps 34: 22 The LORD will rescue his **s**;
103: 21 hosts, you his **s** who do his will.
104: 4 his messengers, flames of fire his **s**.
Pr 31: 15 and portions for her female **s**.
Isa 44: 26 who carries out the words of his **s**
65: 8 so will I do in behalf of my **s**;
65: 13 my **s** will rejoice, but you will be
Lk 17: 10 do, should say, 'We are unworthy **s**;
Jn 15: 15 I no longer call you **s**,
Ro 13: 6 for the authorities are God's **s**,
1Co 3: 5 Only **s**, through whom you came
Heb 1: 7 spirits, and his **s** flames of fire."

SERVE (SERVED SERVES SERVICE SERVING)
Dt 10: 12 to **s** the LORD your God with all
11: 13 and to **s** him with all your heart
13: 4 **s** him and hold fast to him.
28: 47 you did not **s** the LORD your God
Jos 22: 5 and to **s** him with all your heart
24: 15 household, we will **s** the LORD."
24: 18 We too will **s** the LORD,
1Sa 7: 3 to the LORD and **s** him only,
12: 20 **s** the LORD with all your heart.
12: 24 **s** him faithfully with all your heart;
2Ch 19: 9 "You must **s** faithfully
Job 36: 11 If they obey and **s** him, they will
Ps 2: 11 **S** the LORD with fear
Da 3: 17 the God we **s** is able to deliver us
Mt 4: 10 Lord your God, and **s** him only.'"
6: 24 "No one can **s** two masters.
6: 24 You cannot **s** both God and money.
20: 28 but to **s**, and to give his life as
Ro 12: 7 if it is serving, then **s**; if it is
Gal 5: 13 **s** one another humbly in love.
Eph 6: 7 **S** wholeheartedly, as if you were
1Ti 6: 2 they should **s** them even better
Heb 9: 14 so that we may **s** the living God!
1Pe 4: 10 gift you have received to **s** others,
5: 2 dishonest gain, but eager to **s**;
Rev 5: 10 kingdom and priests to **s** our God,

SERVED (SERVE)
Mt 20: 28 Son of Man did not come to be **s**,
Jn 12: 2 Martha **s**, while Lazarus was
Ac 17: 25 And he is not **s** by human hands,
Ro 1: 25 and **s** created things rather than
1Ti 3: 13 Those who have **s** well gain

SERVES (SERVE)
Lk 22: 26 one who rules like the one who **s**.
22: 27 But I am among you as one who **s**.
Jn 12: 26 Whoever **s** me must follow me;
12: 26 will honor the one who **s** me.
Ro 14: 18 because anyone who **s** Christ in
1Pe 4: 11 If anyone **s**, they should do so

SERVICE (SERVE)
Lk 9: 62 and looks back is fit for **s**
12: 35 "Be dressed ready for **s** and keep
Ro 15: 17 in Christ Jesus in my **s** to God.
1Co 12: 5 There are different kinds of **s**,
16: 15 to the **s** of the Lord's people.
2Co 9: 12 This **s** that you perform is not only
Eph 4: 12 to equip his people for works of **s**,
Rev 2: 19 and faith, your **s** and perseverance,

SERVING (SERVE)
Jos 24: 15 if **s** the LORD seems undesirable
2Ch 12: 8 learn the difference between **s** me
Pr 15: 17 Better a small **s** of vegetables
Ro 12: 7 if it is **s**, then serve;
12: 11 your spiritual fervor, **s** the Lord.
16: 18 people are not **s** our Lord Christ,
Eph 6: 7 as if you were **s** the Lord,
Col 3: 24 It is the Lord Christ you are **s**.
2Ti 2: 4 No one **s** as a soldier gets entangled

SETH
Ge 4: 25 birth to a son and named him **S**,

SETTLE
Isa 1: 18 "Come now, let us **s** the matter,"
Mt 5: 25 "**S** matters quickly with your
2Th 3: 12 in the Lord Jesus Christ to **s** down

SEVEN (SEVENS SEVENTH)
Ge 7: 2 Take with you **s** pairs of every kind
Jos 6: 4 march around the city **s** times,
1Ki 19: 18 Yet I reserve **s** thousand in Israel—
Pr 6: 16 hates, **s** that are detestable to him:
24: 16 though the righteous fall **s** times,
Isa 4: 1 that day **s** women will take hold
Da 9: 25 comes, there will be **s** 'sevens,'
Mt 18: 21 sins against me? Up to **s** times?"
Lk 11: 26 takes **s** other spirits more wicked
Ro 11: 4 for myself **s** thousand who have
Rev 1: 4 To the **s** churches in the province
1: 4 from the **s** spirits before his throne,
6: 1 opened the first of the **s** seals.
8: 2 I saw the **s** angels who stand before
8: 2 and **s** trumpets were given to them.
10: 4 And when the **s** thunders spoke,
15: 7 to the **s** angels **s** golden bowls filled

SEVENS* (SEVEN)
Da 9: 24 "Seventy 's' are decreed for your
9: 25 will be seven 's,' and sixty-two 's.'
9: 26 the sixty-two 's,' the Anointed

SEVENTH (SEVEN)
Ge 2: 2 **s** day God had finished the work
2: 2 so on the **s** day he rested from all
Ex 20: 10 the **s** day is a sabbath to the LORD
23: 11 during the **s** year let the land lie
23: 12 but on the **s** day do not work,
Heb 4: 4 "On the **s** day God rested from all

SEVERE
Ge 3: 16 your pains in childbearing very **s**;
2Co 8: 2 In the midst of a very **s** trial,
1Th 1: 6 midst of **s** suffering with the joy

SEWED (SEWS)
Ge 3: 7 so they **s** fig leaves together

SEWS (SEWED)
Mt 9: 16 "No one **s** a patch of unshrunk

SEX* (SEXUAL SEXUALLY)
Ge 19: 5 so that we can have **s** with them."
Jdg 19: 22 so we can have **s** with him."
1Co 6: 9 nor men who have **s** with men

SEXUAL (SEX)
Ex 22: 19 "Anyone who has **s** relations
Lev 18: 6 close relative to have **s** relations.
18: 7 your father by having **s** relations
18: 20 "'Do not have **s** relations
Mt 15: 19 adultery, **s** immorality, theft,
Ac 15: 20 from **s** immorality, from the meat
1Co 5: 1 there is **s** immorality among you,
6: 13 is not meant for **s** immorality
6: 18 Flee from **s** immorality.
10: 8 should not commit **s** immorality,
2Co 12: 21 **s** sin and debauchery in which they
Gal 5: 19 **s** immorality,
Eph 5: 3 not be even a hint of **s** immorality,
Col 3: 5 **s** immorality, impurity, lust,
1Th 4: 3 that you should avoid **s** immorality;

SEXUALLY (SEX)
1Co 5: 9 to associate with **s** immoral people
6: 9 the **s** immoral nor idolaters
6: 18 but whoever sins **s**, sins against
Heb 12: 16 See that no one is **s** immoral, or is
13: 4 the adulterer and all the **s** immoral.
Rev 21: 8 the murderers, the **s** immoral,

SHADE
Ps 121: 5 the LORD is your **s** at your right
Isa 25: 4 the storm and a **s** from the heat.

SHADOW
Ps 17: 8 hide me in the **s** of your wings
36: 7 take refuge in the **s** of your wings.
91: 1 will rest in the **s** of the Almighty.
Isa 51: 16 covered you with the **s** of my hand
Col 2: 17 These are a **s** of the things that
Heb 8: 5 a copy and **s** of what is in heaven.
10: 1 The law is only a **s** of the good

SHADRACH
Hebrew exiled to Babylon; name changed from Hananiah (Da 1:6–7). Refused defilement by food (Da 1:8–20). Refused to worship idol (Da 3:1–18); saved from furnace (Da 3:19–30).

SHAKE (SHAKEN SHAKING)
Ps 10: 6 himself, "Nothing will ever **s** me."
64: 8 all who see them will **s** their heads
99: 1 the cherubim, let the earth **s**.
Hag 2: 6 I will once more **s** the heavens
Heb 12: 26 "Once more I will **s** not only

SHAKEN (SHAKE)
Ps 16: 8 at my right hand, I will not be **s**.
30: 6 I said, "I will never be **s**."
55: 22 he will never let the righteous be **s**.
62: 2 he is my fortress, I will never be **s**.
112: 6 the righteous will never be **s**;
Isa 54: 10 you will not be **s** nor my covenant
Mt 24: 29 and the heavenly bodies will be **s**.'
Lk 6: 38 down, **s** together and running over,
Ac 2: 25 is at my right hand, I will not be **s**.
Heb 12: 27 that what cannot be **s** may remain.

SHAKING* (SHAKE)
Ps 22: 7 they hurl insults, **s** their heads.
Mt 27: 39 hurled insults at him, **s** their heads
Mk 15: 29 at him, **s** their heads and saying,

SHALLUM
King of Israel (2Ki 15:10–16).

SHAME (ASHAMED SHAMED SHAMEFUL)
Ps 22: 5 they trusted and were not put to **s**.
25: 3 hopes in you will ever be put to **s**,
34: 5 faces are never covered with **s**.
69: 6 seek you not be put to **s** because
Pr 13: 18 discipline comes to poverty and **s**,
18: 13 that is folly and **s**.
Jer 8: 9 The wise will be put to **s**;
8: 12 No, they have no **s** at all;
Ro 5: 5 And hope does not put us to **s**,
9: 33 in him will never be put to **s**."
10: 11 in him will never be put to **s**."
1Co 1: 27 things of the world to **s** the wise;
Heb 12: 2 scorning its **s**, and sat down

SHAMED (SHAME)
Jer 10: 14 every goldsmith is **s** by his idols.
Joel 2: 26 never again will my people be **s**.

SHAMEFUL (SHAME)
Ro 1: 27 Men committed **s** acts with other
2Co 4: 2 have renounced secret and **s** ways;
Rev 21: 27 nor will anyone who does what is **s**

SHAMGAR*
Judge; killed 600 Philistines (Jdg 3:31; 5:6).

SHAPE (SHAPES SHAPING)
Job 38: 14 The earth takes **s** like clay under

SHAPES (SHAPE)
Isa 44: 10 Who **s** a god and casts an idol,

SHAPING* (SHAPE)
Jer 18: 4 pot, **s** it as seemed best to him.

SHARE (SHARED SHARERS SHARING)
Ge 21: 10 that woman's son will never **s**
Lev 19: 17 neighbor frankly so you will not **s**
Dt 10: 9 That is why the Levites have no **s**
1Sa 30: 24 to the battle. All will **s** alike."
Pr 22: 9 they **s** their food with the poor.
Eze 18: 20 The child will not **s** the guilt
18: 20 nor will the parent **s** the guilt
Mt 25: 21 and **s** your master's happiness!'
Lk 3: 11 who has two shirts should **s**
Ro 8: 17 if indeed we **s** in his sufferings
8: 17 that we may also **s** in his glory.
12: 13 **S** with the Lord's people who are
1Co 10: 17 body, for we all **s** the one loaf.
2Co 1: 7 just as you **s** in our sufferings,
1: 7 so also you **s** in our comfort.
Gal 4: 30 the slave woman's son will never **s**
6: 6 the word should **s** all good things
Eph 4: 28 they may have something to **s**
Col 1: 12 who has qualified you to **s**
2Th 2: 14 that you might **s** in the glory of our
1Ti 5: 22 and do not **s** in the sins of others.
6: 18 to be generous and willing to **s**.
2Ti 2: 6 the first to receive a **s** of the crops.
Heb 12: 10 order that we may **s** in his holiness.
13: 16 to do good and to **s** with others,
Rev 22: 19 that person any **s** in the tree of life

SHARED (SHARE)
Ps 41: 9 I trusted, one who **s** my bread,
Jn 13: 18 'He who **s** my bread has turned
Ac 4: 32 but they **s** everything they had.
Heb 2: 14 he too **s** in their humanity so

SHARERS* (SHARE)
Eph 3: 6 **s** together in the promise in Christ

SHARING (SHARE)
1Co 9: 10 so in the hope of **s** in the harvest.
2Co 9: 13 for your generosity in **s** with them
Php 2: 1 if any common **s** in the Spirit,

SHARON
SS 2: 1 I am a rose of **S**, a lily

SHARP (SHARPENED SHARPENS SHARPER)
Pr 5: 4 as gall, **s** as a double-edged sword.
Isa 5: 28 Their arrows are **s**, all their bows
Rev 1: 16 coming out of his mouth was a **s**,
19: 15 out of his mouth is a **s** sword

SHARPENED (SHARP)
Eze 21: 9 sword, a sword, **s** and polished—

SHARPENS* (SHARP)
Pr 27: 17 As iron **s** iron, so one person **s** another.

SHARPER* (SHARP)
Heb 4: 12 **S** than any double-edged sword,

SHATTER (SHATTERED SHATTERS)
Jer 51: 20 with you I **s** nations, with you I

SHATTERED (SHATTER)
Job 16: 12 All was well with me, but he **s** me;
17: 11 days have passed, my plans are **s**.
Ecc 12: 6 before the pitcher is **s** at the spring,

SHATTERS (SHATTER)
Ps 46: 9 He breaks the bow and **s** the spear;

SHAVED
Jdg 16: 17 If my head were **s**, my strength
1Co 11: 5 it is the same as having her head **s**.

SHEAF (SHEAVES)
Lev 23: 11 wave the **s** before the LORD so it

SHEARER* (SHEARERS)
Ac 8: 32 and as a lamb before its **s** is silent,

SHEARERS (SHEARER)
Isa 53: 7 and as a sheep before its **s** is silent,

SHEAVES (SHEAF)
Ge 37: 7 while your **s** gathered around mine
Ps 126: 6 songs of joy, carrying **s** with them.

SHEBA
1. Benjamite who rebelled against David (2Sa 20).
2. See QUEEN.

SHECHEM
1. Raped Jacob's daughter Dinah; killed by Simeon and Levi (Ge 34).
2. City where Joshua renewed the covenant (Jos 24).

SHED (SHEDDING SHEDS)
Ge 9: 6 by humans shall their blood be **s**;
Pr 6: 17 hands that **s** innocent blood,
Ro 3: 15 "Their feet are swift to **s** blood;
Col 1: 20 through his blood, **s** on the cross.

SHEDDING (SHED)
Heb 9: 22 without the **s** of blood there is no

SHEDS (SHED)
Ge 9: 6 "Whoever **s** human blood,
Pr 20: 27 of the LORD that **s** light on one's

SHEEP (SHEEP'S SHEEPSKINS)
Nu 27: 17 not be like **s** without a shepherd."
Dt 17: 1 an ox or a **s** that has any defect
1Sa 15: 14 is this bleating of **s** in my ears?
Ps 44: 22 we are considered as **s** to be
78: 52 he led them like **s** through
100: 3 are his people, the **s** of his pasture.
119:176 I have strayed like a lost **s**.
SS 4: 2 teeth are like a flock of **s** just shorn,
Isa 53: 6 We all, like **s**, have gone astray,
53: 7 as a **s** before its shearers is silent,
Jer 50: 6 "My people have been lost **s**;
Eze 34: 11 I myself will search for my **s**
Zec 13: 7 and the **s** will be scattered, and I
Mt 9: 36 helpless, like **s** without a shepherd.
10: 16 you out like **s** among wolves.
12: 11 "If any of you has a **s** and it falls
18: 13 one **s** than about the ninety-nine
25: 32 as a shepherd separates the **s**
Jn 10: 1 who does not enter the **s** pen
10: 3 He calls his own **s** by name
10: 7 I tell you, I am the gate for the **s**.
10: 15 and I lay down my life for the **s**.
10: 27 My **s** listen to my voice;
21: 17 Jesus said, "Feed my **s**.
1Pe 2: 25 For "you were like **s** going astray,"

SHEEP'S* (SHEEP)
Mt 7: 15 They come to you in **s** clothing,

SHEEPSKINS* (SHEEP)
Heb 11: 37 went about in **s** and goatskins,

SHEKEL
Ex 30: 13 This half **s** is an offering

SHELTER
Ps 27: 5 hide me in the **s** of his sacred tent
31: 20 In the **s** of your presence you hide
55: 8 I would hurry to my place of **s**,
61: 4 take refuge in the **s** of your wings.
91: 1 in the **s** of the Most High will rest
Ecc 7: 12 Wisdom is a **s** as money is a **s**,
Isa 4: 6 It will be a **s** and shade
25: 4 a **s** from the storm and a shade
32: 2 Each one will be like a **s**
58: 7 provide the poor wanderer with **s**

SHEM
Son of Noah (Ge 5:32; 6:10). Blessed (Ge 9:26). Descendants (Ge 10:21–31; 11:10–32).

SHEPHERD (SHEPHERDS)
Ge 48: 15 God who has been my **s** all my life
49: 24 because of the **S**, the Rock of Israel,
Nu 27: 17 will not be like sheep without a **s**."
2Sa 7: 7 commanded to **s** my people Israel,
1Ki 22: 17 on the hills like sheep without a **s**,
Ps 23: 1 The LORD is my **s**, I lack nothing.
28: 9 be their **s** and carry them forever.
80: 1 Hear us, **S** of Israel, you who lead

Isa 40: 11 He tends his flock like a **s**:
Jer 31: 10 will watch over his flock like a **s**.'
Eze 34: 5 scattered because there was no **s**,
34: 12 As a **s** looks after his scattered
Zec 11: 4 "**S** the flock marked for slaughter.
11: 9 and said, "I will not be your **s**.
11: 17 "Woe to the worthless **s**,
13: 7 "Strike the **s**, and the sheep will
Mt 2: 6 come a ruler who will **s** my people
9: 36 helpless, like sheep without a **s**.
26: 31 will strike the **s**, and the sheep
Jn 10: 11 "I am the good **s**. The good **s** lays
10: 14 "I am the good **s**; I know my sheep
10: 16 there shall be one flock and one **s**.
Heb 13: 20 Jesus, that great **S** of the sheep,
1Pe 5: 4 And when the Chief **S** appears,
Rev 7: 17 center of the throne will be their **s**;

SHEPHERDS (SHEPHERD)
Jer 23: 1 "Woe to the **s** who are destroying
50: 6 their **s** have led them astray
Eze 34: 2 prophesy against the **s** of Israel;
Lk 2: 8 there were **s** living out in the fields
Ac 20: 28 Be **s** of the church of God, which
1Pe 5: 2 Be **s** of God's flock that is under
Jude : 12 **s** who feed only themselves.

SHIBBOLETH*
Jdg 12: 6 they said, "All right, say '**S**.'"

SHIELD (SHIELDED SHIELDS)
Ge 15: 1 I am your **s**, your very great
2Sa 22: 3 my **s** and the horn of my salvation.
22: 36 You make your saving help my **s**;
Ps 3: 3 you, LORD, are a **s** around me,
5: 12 them with your favor as with a **s**.
7: 10 My **s** is God Most High, who saves
18: 2 my **s** and the horn of my salvation,
28: 7 LORD is my strength and my **s**;
33: 20 he is our help and our **s**.
84: 11 For the LORD God is a sun and **s**;
91: 4 his faithfulness will be your **s**
115: 9 he is their help and **s**.
119:114 You are my refuge and my **s**;
144: 2 my **s**, in whom I take refuge,
Pr 2: 7 he is a **s** to those whose walk is
30: 5 he is a **s** to those who take refuge
Eph 6: 16 take up the **s** of faith,

SHIELDED (SHIELD)
1Pe 1: 5 who through faith are **s** by God's

SHIELDS (SHIELD)
Dt 33: 12 for he **s** him all day long,

SHIFTLESS*
Pr 19: 15 on deep sleep, and the **s** go hungry.

SHIMEI
Cursed David (2Sa 16:5–14); spared (2Sa 19:16–23). Killed by Solomon (1Ki 2:8–9, 36–46).

SHINE (SHINES SHINING SHONE)
Nu 6: 25 the LORD make his face **s** on you
Job 33: 30 that the light of life may **s** on them.
Ps 4: 6 Let the light of your face **s** on us.
37: 6 your righteous reward **s** like
67: 1 bless us and make his face **s** on us
80: 1 between the cherubim, **s** forth
118: 27 and he has made his light **s** on us.
Isa 60: 1 "Arise, **s**, for your light has come,
Da 12: 3 are wise will **s** like the brightness
Mt 5: 16 let your light **s** before others,
13: 43 the righteous will **s** like the sun
2Co 4: 6 made his light **s** in our hearts
Eph 5: 14 the dead, and Christ will **s** on you."
Php 2: 15 you will **s** among them like stars

SHINES (SHINE)
Ps 50: 2 perfect in beauty, God **s** forth.
Pr 13: 9 light of the righteous **s** brightly,
Jn 1: 5 The light **s** in the darkness,

SHINING (SHINE)
Pr 4: 18 **s** ever brighter till the full light
2Pe 1: 19 as to a light **s** in a dark place,
Rev 1: 16 His face was like the sun **s** in all its

SHIP (SHIPS SHIPWRECK SHIPWRECKS)
Ecc 11: 1 **S** your grain across the sea;

SHIPS (SHIP)
Pr 31: 14 She is like the merchant **s**,

SHIPWRECK (SHIP)
1Ti 1: 19 so have suffered **s** with regard

SHIPWRECKED* (SHIP)
2Co 11: 25 three times I was **s**, I spent a night

SHIRT (SHIRTS)
Lk 6: 29 do not withhold your **s** from them.

SHIRTS* (SHIRT)
Lk 3: 11 who has two **s** should share

SHISHAK
1Ki 14: 25 **S** king of Egypt attacked Jerusalem.
2Ch 12: 2 **S** king of Egypt attacked Jerusalem

SHOCKING*
Jer 5: 30 **s** thing has happened in the land:

SHONE (SHINE)
Mt 17: 2 His face **s** like the sun, and his
Lk 2: 9 glory of the Lord **s** around them,
Rev 21: 11 It **s** with the glory of God, and its

SHOOT
Isa 53: 2 grew up before him like a tender **s**,
Ro 11: 17 though a wild olive **s**, have been

SHORE
Lk 5: 3 asked him to put out a little from **s**.

SHORT (SHORTENED)
Nu 11: 23 Moses, "Is the LORD's arm too **s**?
Isa 50: 2 Was my arm too **s** to deliver you?
59: 1 of the LORD is not too **s** to save,
Mt 24: 22 "If those days had not been cut **s**,
Ro 3: 23 and fall **s** of the glory of God,
1Co 7: 29 and sisters, is that the time is **s**.
Heb 4: 1 you be found to have fallen **s** of it.
Rev 20: 3 he must be set free for a **s** time.

SHORTENED (SHORT)
Mt 24: 22 of the elect those days will be **s**.

SHOULDER (SHOULDERS)
Zep 3: 9 of the LORD and serve him **s** to **s**.

SHOULDERS (SHOULDER)
Dt 33: 12 LORD loves rests between his **s**."
Isa 9: 6 the government will be on his **s**.
Lk 15: 5 finds it, he joyfully puts it on his **s**

SHOUT (SHOUTED)
Ps 47: 1 **s** to God with cries of joy.
66: 1 **S** for joy to God, all the earth!
95: 1 let us **s** aloud to the Rock of our
98: 4 **S** for joy to the LORD,
100: 1 **S** for joy to the LORD,
Isa 12: 6 **S** aloud and sing for joy,
26: 19 in the dust wake up and **s** for joy—
35: 6 deer, and the mute tongue **s** for joy.
40: 9 lift up your voice with a **s**, lift it up,
42: 2 He will not **s** or cry out, or raise his
44: 23 **s** aloud, you earth beneath.
54: 1 burst into song, **s** for joy, you who
Zec 9: 9 **S**, Daughter Jerusalem!

SHOUTED (SHOUT)
Job 38: 7 and all the angels **s** for joy?

SHOW (SHOWED SHOWN SHOWS)
Ex 18: 20 and **s** them the way they are to live
33: 18 said, "Now **s** me your glory."
2Sa 22: 26 the faithful you **s** yourself faithful,
Ps 17: 7 **S** me the wonders of your great
25: 4 **S** me your ways, LORD, teach me
39: 4 "**S** me, LORD, my life's end
85: 7 **S** us your unfailing love, LORD,
143: 8 **S** me the way I should go, for to
SS 2: 14 the mountainside, **s** me your face,
Isa 30: 18 he will rise up to **s** you compassion.
Joel 2: 30 I will **s** wonders in the heavens
Zec 7: 9 **s** mercy and compassion to one
Ac 2: 19 I will **s** wonders in the heavens
10: 34 it is that God does not **s** favoritism
1Co 12: 31 yet I will **s** you the most excellent
Eph 2: 7 ages he might **s** the incomparable
Titus 2: 7 In your teaching **s** integrity,
Jas 2: 18 **S** me your faith without deeds,
2: 18 I will **s** you my faith by my deeds.
Jude : 23 to others **s** mercy, mixed with fear

SHOWED (SHOW)
1Ki 3: 3 Solomon **s** his love for the LORD
Lk 24: 40 this, he **s** them his hands and feet.
Ac 28: 7 **s** us generous hospitality for three
1Jn 4: 9 This is how God **s** his love among

SHOWERS
Eze 34: 26 there will be **s** of blessing.
Hos 10: 12 and **s** his righteousness on you.

SHOWN (SHOW)
Heb 13: 2 some people have **s** hospitality

SHOWS (SHOW)
Pr 3: 34 mockers but **s** favor to the humble
1Pe 5: 5 proud but **s** favor to the humble."

SHREWD
2Sa 22: 27 to the devious you show yourself **s**.
Mt 10: 16 Therefore be as **s** as snakes and as

SHRINK* (SHRINKS)
Heb 10: 39 do not belong to those who **s** back
Rev 12: 11 lives so much as to **s** from death.

SHRINKS* (SHRINK)
Heb 10: 38 no pleasure in the one who **s** back."

SHRIVEL
Isa 64: 6 we all **s** up like a leaf, and like

SHUDDER
Eze 32: 10 and their kings will **s** with horror

SHUHITE
Job 2: 11 Bildad the **S** and Zophar

SHUN* (SHUNS)
Job 28: 28 and to **s** evil is understanding."
Pr 3: 7 fear the LORD and **s** evil.
Pr 14: 16 wise fear the LORD and **s** evil,

SHUNS (SHUN)
Job 1: 8 a man who fears God and **s** evil."

SHUT
Ge 7: 16 Then the LORD **s** him in.
Isa 22: 22 what he opens no one can **s**,
60: 11 they will never be **s**, day or night,
Da 6: 22 and he **s** the mouths of the lions.
Heb 11: 33 who **s** the mouths of lions,
Rev 3: 7 What he opens no one can **s**,
21: 25 On no day will its gates ever be **s**,

SICK (SICKNESS)
Pr 13: 12 Hope deferred makes the heart **s**,
Eze 34: 4 healed the **s** or bound up the
Mt 9: 12 who need a doctor, but the **s**.
10: 8 Heal the **s**, raise the dead,
25: 36 I was **s** and you looked after me,
1Co 11: 30 many among you are weak and **s**,
Jas 5: 14 Is anyone among you **s**?

SICKBED* (BED)
Ps 41: 3 LORD sustains them on their **s**

SICKLE
Joel 3: 13 Swing the **s**, for the harvest is ripe.
Rev 14: 14 his head and a sharp **s** in his hand.

SICKNESS (SICK)
Mt 4: 23 disease and **s** among the people.

SIDE (SIDES)
Ps 91: 7 A thousand may fall at your **s**,
124: 1 the LORD had not been on our **s**—
Pr 3: 26 for the LORD will be at your **s**
Jn 18: 37 Everyone on the **s** of truth listens
20: 20 he showed them his hands and **s**.
2Ti 4: 17 the Lord stood at my **s** and gave
Heb 10: 33 at other times you stood **s** by **s**

SIDES (SIDE)
Nu 33: 55 in your eyes and thorns in your **s**.

SIFT*
Lk 22: 31 Satan has asked to **s** all of you as

SIGHING
Isa 35: 10 and sorrow and **s** will flee away.

SIGHT
Ps 51: 4 and done what is evil in your **s**;
90: 4 years in your **s** are like a day
116: 15 in the **s** of the LORD is the death
Pr 3: 4 a good name in the **s** of God
Mt 11: 5 The blind receive **s**, the lame walk,
1Co 3: 19 this world is foolishness in God's **s**.
2Co 5: 7 For we live by faith, not by **s**.
1Pe 3: 4 which is of great worth in God's **s**.

SIGN (SIGNS)
Ge 9: 12 "This is the **s** of the covenant I am
17: 11 and it will be the **s** of the covenant
Isa 7: 14 the Lord himself will give you a **s**:
55: 13 an everlasting **s**, that will endure
Eze 20: 12 my Sabbaths as a **s** between us,
Mt 12: 38 we want to see a **s** from you."
12: 39 adulterous generation asks for a **s**!
24: 3 what will be the **s** of your coming
24: 30 will appear the **s** of the Son of Man
Lk 2: 12 This will be a **s** to you:
11: 29 It asks for a **s**, but none will be
23: 8 see him perform a **s** of some sort.
Ac 4: 16 they have performed a notable **s**,
Ro 4: 11 he received circumcision as a **s**,
1Co 14: 22 are a **s**, not for believers

SIGNS (SIGN)
Ge 1: 14 let them serve as **s** to mark sacred
Ps 78: 43 the day he displayed his **s** in Egypt,
105: 27 They performed his **s** among them,

Da 6: 27 he performs **s** and wonders
Mt 24: 24 and perform great **s** and wonders
Mk 16: 17 *these **s** will accompany those who*
Jn 2: 11 of Galilee was the first of the **s**
2: 23 saw the **s** he was performing
3: 2 could perform the **s** you are doing
7: 31 he perform more **s** than this man?"
9: 16 can a sinner perform such **s**?"
12: 37 Jesus had performed so many **s**
20: 30 Jesus performed many other **s**
Ac 2: 19 above and **s** on the earth below,
1Co 1: 22 Jews demand **s** and Greeks look
2Co 12: 12 including **s**, wonders and miracles.
2Th 2: 9 of displays of power through **s**

SIHON
Nu 21: 21 to say to **S** king of the Amorites:
Ps 136: 19 **S** king of the Amorites

SILAS*
Prophet (Ac 15:22–32); co-worker with Paul on second missionary journey (Ac 16–18; 2Co 1:19). Co-writer with Paul (1Th 1:1; 2Th 1:1); Peter (1Pe 5:12).

SILENCE (SILENCED SILENT)
1Pe 2: 15 good you should **s** the ignorant
Rev 8: 1 there was **s** in heaven for about half

SILENCED (SILENCE)
Ro 3: 19 so that every mouth may be **s**
Titus 1: 11 They must be **s**, because they are

SILENT (SILENCE)
Est 4: 14 For if you remain **s** at this time,
Ps 30: 12 may sing your praises and not be **s**.
32: 3 When I kept **s**, my bones wasted
39: 2 So I remained utterly **s**, not even
Pr 17: 28 are thought wise if they keep **s**,
Ecc 3: 7 a time to be **s** and a time to speak,
Isa 53: 7 as a sheep before its shearers is **s**,
62: 1 For Zion's sake I will not keep **s**,
Hab 2: 20 let all the earth be **s** before him.
Ac 8: 32 as a lamb before its shearer is **s**,
1Co 14: 34 Women should remain **s**

SILVER
Ps 12: 6 like **s** purified in a crucible,
66: 10 tested us; you refined us like **s**.
Pr 2: 4 if you look for it as for **s** and search
3: 14 for she is more profitable than **s**
8: 10 my instruction instead of **s**,
22: 1 to be esteemed is better than **s**
25: 4 Remove the dross from the **s**,
25: 11 of **s** is a ruling rightly given.
Isa 48: 10 I have refined you, though not as **s**;
Eze 22: 18 They are but the dross of **s**.
Da 2: 32 its chest and arms of **s**, its belly
Hag 2: 8 'The **s** is mine and the gold is
Zec 13: 9 I will refine them like **s** and test
Mt 26: 15 out for him thirty pieces of **s**.
Ac 3: 6 Peter said, "**S** or gold I do not have,
1Co 3: 12 on this foundation using gold, **s**,
1Pe 1: 18 with perishable things such as **s**

SILVERSMITH
Ac 19: 24 A **s** named Demetrius, who made

SIMEON
Son of Jacob by Leah (Ge 29:33; 35:23; 1Ch 2:1). With Levi killed Shechem for rape of Dinah (Ge 34:25–29). Held hostage by Joseph in Egypt (Ge 42:24—43:23). Tribe of blessed (Ge 49:5–7), numbered (Nu 1:23; 26:14), allotted land (Jos 19:1–9; Eze 48:24), 12,000 from (Rev 7:7).

SIMON
1. See PETER.
2. Apostle, called the Zealot (Mt 10:4; Mk 3:18; Lk 6:15; Ac 1:13).
3. Samaritan sorcerer (Ac 8:9–24).

SIMPLE
Ps 19: 7 are trustworthy, making wise the **s**.
119:130 it gives understanding to the **s**.
Pr 8: 5 You who are **s**, gain prudence;
14: 15 The **s** believe anything,

SIN (SINFUL SINNED SINNER SINNERS SINNING SINS)
Ge 4: 7 right, **s** is crouching at your door;
Ex 32: 32 But now, please forgive their **s**—
Nu 5: 7 and must confess the **s** they have
32: 23 sure that your **s** will find you out.
Dt 24: 16 each will die for their own **s**.
1Sa 12: 23 that I should **s** against the LORD
15: 23 rebellion is like the **s** of divination,
1Ki 8: 46 there is no one who does not **s**—
2Ki 14: 6 each will die for their own **s**."
2Ch 7: 14 I will forgive their **s** and will heal
Job 1: 22 Job did not **s** by charging God
Ps 4: 4 Tremble and do not **s**; when you
32: 2 is the one whose **s** the LORD does
32: 5 And you forgave the guilt of my **s**.
36: 2 too much to detect or hate their **s**.
38: 18 I am troubled by my **s**.
39: 1 ways and keep my tongue from **s**;
51: 2 iniquity and cleanse me from my **s**.
66: 18 If I had cherished **s** in my heart,
119: 11 that I might not **s** against you.
119:133 to your word; let no **s** rule over me.
Pr 10: 19 **S** is not ended by multiplying
14: 9 mock at making amends for **s**,
14: 21 It is a **s** to despise one's neighbor,
16: 6 and faithfulness **s** is atoned for;
17: 19 Whoever loves a quarrel loves **s**;
20: 9 I am clean and without **s**"?
Isa 3: 9 they parade their **s** like Sodom;
6: 7 taken away and your **s** atoned for."
64: 5 we continued to **s** against them,
Jer 31: 30 everyone will die for their own **s**;
Eze 3: 18 wicked person will die for their **s**,
18: 26 their righteousness and commits **s**,
Am 4: 4 "Go to Bethel and **s**; go to Gilgal
Mic 6: 7 of my body for the **s** of my soul?
7: 18 you, who pardons **s** and forgives
Zec 3: 4 I have taken away your **s**, and I will
Mk 3: 29 they are guilty of an eternal **s**."
Jn 1: 29 who takes away the **s** of the world!
8: 7 *without **s** be the first to throw*
8: 34 everyone who sins is a slave to **s**.
8: 46 any of you prove me guilty of **s**?
Ro 2: 12 All who **s** apart from the law will
5: 12 just as **s** entered the world through
5: 20 But where **s** increased,
6: 2 We are those who have died to **s**;
6: 11 count yourselves dead to **s** but alive
6: 14 **s** shall no longer be your master,
6: 23 For the wages of **s** is death,
7: 7 not have known what **s** was had it
7: 25 sinful nature a slave to the law of **s**.
14: 23 that does not come from faith is **s**.
1Co 8: 12 conscience, you **s** against Christ.
14: 24 they are convicted of **s** and are
15: 56 The sting of death is **s**, and the power of **s** is the law.
2Co 5: 21 God made him who had no **s** to be **s** for us,
Gal 6: 1 if someone is caught in a **s**, you
Heb 4: 15 just as we are—yet he did not **s**.
9: 26 to do away with **s** by the sacrifice
11: 25 to enjoy the fleeting pleasures of **s**.
12: 1 and the **s** that so easily entangles.
Jas 1: 15 has conceived, it gives birth to **s**;
4: 17 and doesn't do it, it is **s** for them.
1Pe 2: 22 "He committed no **s**, and no deceit
1Jn 1: 7 his Son, purifies us from all **s**.
1: 8 If we claim to be without **s**,
2: 1 to you so that you will not **s**.
2: 1 But if anybody does **s**, we have
3: 4 in fact, **s** is lawlessness.
3: 5 away our sins. And in him is no **s**.
3: 6 continues to **s** has either seen him
3: 9 is born of God will continue to **s**,
5: 16 commit a **s** that does not lead
5: 16 There is a **s** that leads to death.
5: 17 wrongdoing is **s**, and there is **s**
5: 18 of God does not continue to **s**;

SINAI
Ex 19: 20 descended to the top of Mount **S**
31: 18 speaking to Moses on Mount **S**,
Ps 68: 17 the Lord has come from **S** into his

SINCERE* (SINCERITY)
Da 11: 34 many who are not **s** will join them.
Lk 20: 20 sent spies, who pretended to be **s**.
Ac 2: 46 ate together with glad and **s** hearts,
Ro 12: 9 Love must be **s**. Hate what is evil;
2Co 6: 6 in the Holy Spirit and in **s** love;
11: 3 somehow be led astray from your **s**
1Ti 1: 5 a good conscience and a **s** faith.
3: 8 are to be worthy of respect, **s**,
2Ti 1: 5 I am reminded of your **s** faith,
Heb 10: 22 us draw near to God with a **s** heart
Jas 3: 17 and good fruit, impartial and **s**.
1Pe 1: 22 that you have **s** love for each other,

SINCERITY* (SINCERE)
1Co 5: 8 with the unleavened bread of **s**
2Co 1: 12 you, with integrity and godly **s**.
2: 17 Christ we speak before God with **s**,
2Co 8: 8 I want to test the **s** of your love
Eph 6: 5 fear, and with **s** of heart, just as you
Col 3: 22 but with **s** of heart and reverence

SINFUL (SIN)
Ps 51: 5 Surely I was **s** at birth,
Pr 1: 10 if **s** men entice you, do not give
Lk 5: 8 from me, Lord; I am a **s** man!"
Ro 7: 5 the **s** passions aroused by the law
7: 18 dwell in me, that is, in my **s** nature.
7: 25 in my **s** nature a slave to the law
8: 3 in the likeness of **s** flesh to be a sin
Heb 3: 12 sisters, that none of you has a **s**,
1Pe 2: 11 to abstain from **s** desires,
1Jn 3: 8 The one who does what is **s** is

SINFUL NATURE see FLESH

SING (SANG SINGING SINGS SONG SONGS SUNG)
Ex 15: 1 "I will **s** to the LORD, for he is
Jdg 5: 3 I, even I, will **s** to the LORD;
Ps 5: 11 you be glad; let them ever **s** for joy.
13: 6 I will **s** the LORD's praise, for he
30: 4 **S** the praises of the LORD, you his
33: 1 **S** joyfully to the LORD,
47: 6 **S** praises to God, **s** praises;
57: 7 I will **s** and make music.
59: 16 But I will **s** of your strength,
63: 7 I **s** in the shadow of your wings.
66: 2 **S** the glory of his name;
89: 1 I will **s** of the LORD's great love
95: 1 let us **s** for joy to the LORD;
96: 1 **S** to the LORD a new song;
98: 1 **S** to the LORD a new song, for he
101: 1 I will **s** of your love and justice;
108: 1 I will **s** and make music with all my
137: 3 "**S** us one of the songs of Zion!"
147: 1 How good it is to **s** praises to our
149: 1 **S** to the LORD a new song,
Isa 54: 1 "**S**, barren woman, you who never
1Co 14: 15 I will **s** with my spirit, but I will
Eph 5: 19 **S** and make music from your heart
Jas 5: 13 Let them **s** songs of praise.

SINGING (SING)
Ps 63: 5 **s** lips my mouth will praise you.
68: 6 he leads out the prisoners with **s**;
98: 5 with the harp and the sound of **s**,
Isa 35: 10 They will enter Zion with **s**;
Zep 3: 17 but will rejoice over you with **s**."
Ac 16: 25 were praying and **s** hymns to God,
Col 3: 16 **s** to God with gratitude in your

SINGLE
Ex 23: 29 will not drive them out in a **s** year,
Mt 6: 27 worrying add a **s** hour to your life?

SINGS (SING)
Eze 33: 32 more than one who **s** love songs

SINNED (SIN)
Lev 5: 5 confess in what way they have **s**.
1Sa 15: 24 Saul said to Samuel, "I have **s**.
2Sa 12: 13 "I have **s** against the LORD."
24: 10 "I have **s** greatly in what I have
2Ch 6: 37 'We have **s**, we have done wrong
Job 1: 5 "Perhaps my children have **s**
33: 27 'I have **s**, I have perverted what is
Ps 51: 4 have I **s** and done what is evil
Jer 2: 35 you because you say, 'I have not **s**.'
14: 20 we have indeed **s** against you.
Da 9: 5 we have **s** and done wrong.
Mic 7: 9 Because I have **s** against him, I will
Mt 27: 4 "I have **s**," he said, "for I have
Lk 15: 18 I have **s** against heaven and against
Ro 3: 23 for all have **s** and fall short
5: 12 came to all people, because all **s**—
2Pe 2: 4 did not spare angels when they **s**,
1Jn 1: 10 If we claim we have not **s**, we make

SINNER (SIN)
Ecc 9: 18 war, but one **s** destroys much good.
Lk 15: 7 heaven over one **s** who repents
18: 13 said, 'God, have mercy on me, a **s**.'
Jas 5: 20 Whoever turns a **s** from the error
1Pe 4: 18 become of the ungodly and the **s**?"

SINNERS (SIN)
Ps 1: 1 stand in the way that **s** take or sit
37: 38 But all **s** will be destroyed;
Pr 23: 17 Do not let your heart envy **s**,
Mt 9: 13 come to call the righteous, but **s**."
Ro 5: 8 While we were still **s**, Christ died
Gal 2: 17 find ourselves also among the **s**,
1Ti 1: 15 came into the world to save **s**—
Heb 7: 26 set apart from **s**,

SINNING (SIN)
Ex 20: 20 be with you to keep you from **s**."
1Co 15: 34 senses as you ought, and stop **s**;
1Ti 5: 20 those elders who are **s** you are
Heb 10: 26 If we deliberately keep on **s** after
1Jn 3: 6 one who lives in him keeps on **s**.
3: 9 they cannot go on **s**, because they

SINS (SIN)
Lev 5: 1 "'If anyone **s** because they do not
16: 30 you will be clean from all your **s**.
26: 40 if they will confess their **s** and the **s**
Nu 15: 30 "'But anyone who **s** defiantly,
1Sa 2: 25 but if anyone **s** against the LORD,
Ezr 9: 6 because our **s** are higher than our
9: 13 us less than our **s** deserved
Ne 9: 2 confessed their **s** and the **s** of their
Ps 19: 13 your servant also from willful **s**;
32: 1 are forgiven, whose **s** are covered.
51: 9 Hide your face from my **s** and blot
79: 9 forgive our **s** for your name's sake.
85: 2 your people and covered all their **s**.
103: 3 forgives all your **s** and heals all
103: 10 does not treat us as our **s** deserve
130: 3 LORD, kept a record of **s**, Lord,
Pr 5: 22 the cords of their **s** hold them fast.
28: 13 Whoever conceals their **s** does not
29: 22 person commits many **s**.
Ecc 7: 20 who does what is right and never **s**.
Isa 1: 18 "Though your **s** are like scarlet,
38: 17 put all my **s** behind your back.
43: 25 and remembers your **s** no more.
59: 2 your **s** have hidden his face
64: 6 like the wind our **s** sweep us away.
Jer 31: 34 will remember their **s** no more."
La 3: 39 when punished for their **s**?
Eze 18: 4 The one who **s** is the one who will
33: 10 offenses and **s** weigh us down,
36: 33 day I cleanse you from all your **s**,
Hos 14: 1 Your **s** have been your downfall!
Mt 1: 21 will save his people from their **s**."
6: 15 your Father will not forgive your **s**.
9: 6 has authority on earth to forgive **s**."
18: 15 "If your brother or sister **s**,
26: 28 for many for the forgiveness of **s**.
Lk 5: 24 has authority on earth to forgive **s**."
11: 4 Forgive us our **s**, for we also forgive
17: 3 your brother or sister **s** against you,
Jn 8: 24 you will indeed die in your **s**."
20: 23 If you forgive anyone's **s**, their **s** are
Ac 2: 38 Christ for the forgiveness of your **s**.
3: 19 so that your **s** may be wiped out,
10: 43 forgiveness of **s** through his name."
22: 16 be baptized and wash your **s** away,
26: 18 they may receive forgiveness of **s**
Ro 4: 7 are forgiven, whose **s** are covered.
4: 25 delivered over to death for our **s**
1Co 15: 3 Christ died for our **s** according
2Co 5: 19 counting people's **s** against them.
Gal 1: 4 gave himself for our **s** to rescue us
Eph 2: 1 dead in your transgressions and **s**,
Col 2: 13 When you were dead in your **s**
2: 13 He forgave us all our **s**,
1Ti 5: 22 and do not share in the **s** of others.
Heb 1: 3 he had provided purification for **s**,
2: 17 atonement for the **s** of the people.
7: 27 sacrificed for their **s** once for all
8: 12 will remember their **s** no more."
9: 28 once to take away the **s** of many;
10: 4 of bulls and goats to take away **s**.
10: 12 for all time one sacrifice for **s**,
10: 26 the truth, no sacrifice for **s** is left,
Jas 5: 16 Therefore confess your **s** to each
5: 20 and cover over a multitude of **s**.
1Pe 2: 24 "He himself bore our **s**" in his
3: 18 For Christ also suffered once for **s**,
4: 8 love covers over a multitude of **s**.
1Jn 1: 9 If we confess our **s**, he is faithful
2: 2 is the atoning sacrifice for our **s**,
3: 5 so that he might take away our **s**.
4: 10 as an atoning sacrifice for our **s**.
Rev 1: 5 freed us from our **s** by his blood,

SISERA
Jdg 4: 2 **S**, the commander of his army,
5: 26 She struck **S**, she crushed his head,

SISTER (SISTERS)
Lev 18: 9 have sexual relations with your **s**,
Mk 3: 35 does God's will is my brother and **s**
1Co 7: 15 or the **s** is not bound in such
2Jn : 13 The children of your **s**, who is

SISTERS (SISTER)
Mt 13: 56 Aren't all his **s** with us?
19: 29 left houses or brothers or **s** or
Jn 11: 3 So the **s** sent word to Jesus, "Lord,
1Ti 5: 2 and younger women as **s**,

SIT (SAT SITS SITTING)
Dt 6: 7 about them when you **s** at home
1Ki 8: 25 have a successor to **s** before me
Ps 1: 1 or **s** in the company of mockers,
26: 5 and refuse to **s** with the wicked.
80: 1 You who **s** enthroned between
110: 1 "**S** at my right hand until I make
139: 2 know when I **s** and when I rise;
SS 2: 3 I delight to **s** in his shade, and his
Isa 16: 5 in faithfulness a man will **s** on it—
Mic 4: 4 Everyone will **s** under their own
Mt 20: 23 but to **s** at my right or left is not
22: 44 "**S** at my right hand until I put
Lk 22: 30 in my kingdom and **s** on thrones,
Heb 1: 13 "**S** at my right hand until I make
Rev 3: 21 I will give the right to **s** with me

SITS (SIT)
Ps 99: 1 he **s** enthroned between
Isa 40: 22 He **s** enthroned above the circle
Mt 19: 28 Son of Man **s** on his glorious
Rev 4: 9 thanks to him who **s** on the throne

SITTING (SIT)
Est 2: 19 Mordecai was **s** at the king's gate.
Mt 26: 64 the Son of Man **s** at the right hand
Rev 4: 2 in heaven with someone **s** on it.

SITUATION (SITUATIONS)
1Co 7: 24 should remain in the **s** they were
Php 4: 12 being content in any and every **s**,

SITUATIONS* (SITUATION)
2Ti 4: 5 you, keep your head in all **s**,

SKIES (SKY)
Ps 19: 1 the **s** proclaim the work of his
108: 4 your faithfulness reaches to the **s**.

SKILL (SKILLED SKILLFUL)
Ps 137: 5 may my right hand forget its **s**.
Ecc 10: 10 is needed, but **s** will bring success.

SKILLED (SKILL)
Pr 22: 29 Do you see someone **s** in their

SKILLFUL (SKILL)
Ps 45: 1 my tongue is the pen of a **s** writer.
78: 72 with **s** hands he led them.

SKIN (SKINS)
Job 19: 20 escaped only by the **s** of my teeth.
19: 26 And after my **s** has been destroyed,
Jer 13: 23 Can an Ethiopian change his **s**

SKINS (SKIN)
Ex 25: 5 ram **s** dyed red and another type
Lk 5: 37 the new wine will burst the **s**;

SKULL
Mt 27: 33 (which means "the place of the **s**").

SKY (SKIES)
Ge 1: 8 God called the vault "**s**."
Pr 30: 19 the way of an eagle in the **s**,
Isa 34: 4 the stars in the **s** will be dissolved
Jer 33: 22 me as countless as the stars in the **s**
Mt 24: 29 the stars will fall from the **s**,
Php 2: 15 among them like stars in the **s**

SLACK*
Pr 18: 9 One who is **s** in his work is brother

SLAIN (SLAY)
1Sa 18: 7 "Saul has **s** his thousands,
Eze 37: 9 winds and breathe into these **s**,
Rev 5: 6 looking as if it had been **s**,
5: 12 who was **s**, to receive power
6: 9 those who had been **s** because

SLANDER (SLANDERED SLANDERER SLANDERERS SLANDEROUS)
Lev 19: 16 spreading **s** among your people.
Ps 15: 3 whose tongue utters no **s**, who
Pr 10: 18 lying lips and spreads **s** is a fool.
Mk 3: 28 their sins and every **s** they utter,
2Co 12: 20 of rage, selfish ambition, **s**, gossip,
Eph 4: 31 brawling and **s**, along with every
1Ti 5: 14 the enemy no opportunity for **s**.
Titus 3: 2 to **s** no one, to be peaceable
1Pe 3: 16 may be ashamed of their **s**.

SLANDERED (SLANDER)
1Co 4: 13 when we are **s**, we answer kindly.

SLANDERER* (SLANDER)
Jer 9: 4 is a deceiver, and every friend a **s**.
1Co 5: 11 immoral or greedy, an idolater or **s**,

SLANDERERS (SLANDER)
Ro 1: 30 **s**, God-haters, insolent,
1Co 6: 10 nor drunkards nor **s** nor swindlers
Titus 2: 3 live, not to be **s** or addicted to much

SLANDEROUS* (SLANDER)
2Ti 3: 3 unforgiving, **s**, without self-control

SLAPS
Mt 5: 39 If anyone **s** you on the right cheek,

SLAUGHTER (SLAUGHTERED)
Isa 53: 7 he was led like a lamb to the **s**,
Jer 11: 19 been like a gentle lamb led to the **s**;
Ac 8: 32 "He was led like a sheep to the **s**,

SLAUGHTERED (SLAUGHTER)
Ps 44: 22 we are considered as sheep to be **s**.
Ro 8: 36 we are considered as sheep to be **s**."

SLAVE (ENSLAVED SLAVERY SLAVES)
Ge 21: 10 "Get rid of that **s** woman and her
Pr 22: 7 and the borrower is **s** to the lender.
Mal 1: 6 his father, and a **s** his master.
Mt 20: 27 wants to be first must be your **s**—
Jn 8: 34 everyone who sins is a **s** to sin.
Ro 7: 14 I am unspiritual, sold as a **s** to sin.
1Co 7: 21 Were you a **s** when you were
12: 13 whether Jews or Gentiles, **s** or free
Gal 3: 28 Jew nor Gentile, neither **s** nor free,
4: 30 "Get rid of the **s** woman and her
4: 7 no longer a **s**, but God's child;
Col 3: 11 **s** or free, but Christ is all,
1Ti 1: 10 for **s** traders and liars and perjurers
Phm : 16 no longer as a **s**, but better than a **s**,

SLAVERY (SLAVE)
Ex 2: 23 The Israelites groaned in their **s**
Gal 4: 3 in **s** under the elemental spiritual
1Ti 6: 1 of **s** should consider their masters

SLAVES (SLAVE)
Ps 123: 2 As the eyes of **s** look to the hand
Ecc 10: 7 I have seen **s** on horseback,
10: 7 while princes go on foot like **s**.
Ro 6: 6 we should no longer be **s** to sin—
6: 16 whether you are **s** to sin,
6: 19 so now offer yourselves as **s**
6: 22 sin and have become **s** of God,
Gal 2: 4 in Christ Jesus and to make us **s**.
4: 8 you were **s** to those who by nature
Eph 6: 5 **S**, obey your earthly masters
Col 3: 22 **S**, obey your earthly masters
4: 1 provide your **s** with what is right
Titus 2: 9 Teach **s** to be subject to their
2Pe 2: 19 for "people are **s** to whatever has

SLAY (SLAIN)
Job 13: 15 Though he **s** me, yet will I hope

SLEEP (ASLEEP SLEEPER SLEEPING SLEEPS)
Ge 2: 21 the man to fall into a deep **s**;
15: 12 Abram fell into a deep **s**,
28: 11 under his head and lay down to **s**.
Ps 4: 8 In peace I will lie down and **s**,
121: 4 Israel will neither slumber nor **s**.
127: 2 for he grants **s** to those he loves.
Pr 6: 9 When will you get up from your **s**?
Ecc 5: 12 The **s** of a laborer is sweet,
1Co 15: 51 We will not all **s**, but we will all be
1Th 4: 13 about those who **s** in death,
5: 7 For those who **s**, **s** at night,

SLEEPER* (SLEEP)
Eph 5: 14 "Wake up, **s**, rise from the dead,

SLEEPING (SLEEP)
Mk 13: 36 do not let him find you **s**.

SLEEPLESS*
2Co 6: 5 in hard work, **s** nights and hunger;

SLEEPS (SLEEP)
Pr 10: 5 son, but he who **s** during harvest is

SLIMY*
Ps 40: 2 He lifted me out of the **s** pit,

SLING
1Sa 17: 50 over the Philistine with a **s**

SLIP (SLIPPING)
Ps 121: 3 He will not let your foot **s**—

SLIPPING (SLIP)
Ps 66: 9 our lives and kept our feet from **s**.

SLOW
Ex 34: 6 and gracious God, **s** to anger,
Jas 1: 19 **s** to speak and **s** to become angry,
2Pe 3: 9 The Lord is not **s** in keeping his

SLUGGARD (SLUGGARD'S SLUGGARDS)
Pr 6: 6 Go to the ant, you **s**;
26: 15 A **s** buries his hand in the dish;

SLUGGARD'S* (SLUGGARD'S)
Pr 13: 4 A **s** appetite is never filled,

SLUGGARDS (SLUGGARD)
Pr 20: 4 **S** do not plow in season;

SLUMBER
Ps 121: 3 he who watches over you will not **s**;
Pr 6: 10 little **s**, a little folding of the hands
Ro 13: 11 for you to wake up from your **s**,

SLUR*
Ps 15: 3 neighbor, and casts no **s** on others;

SMELL
Ecc 10: 1 As dead flies give perfume a bad **s**,

SMOKE
Ex 19: 18 Mount Sinai was covered with **s**,
Ps 104: 32 touches the mountains, and they **s**.
Isa 6: 4 and the temple was filled with **s**.
Joel 2: 30 blood and fire and billows of **s**.
Ac 2: 19 blood and fire and billows of **s**.
Rev 15: 8 the temple was filled with **s**

SMYRNA
Rev 2: 8 the angel of the church in **S** write:

SNAKE (SNAKES)
Nu 21: 8 "Make a **s** and put it up on a pole;
Pr 23: 32 In the end it bites like a **s**
Jn 3: 14 lifted up the **s** in the wilderness,

SNAKES (SNAKE)
Mt 10: 16 Therefore be as shrewd as **s** and as
Mk 16: 18 *they will pick up* **s** *with their*

SNARE (ENSNARE ENSNARED SNARED)
Dt 7: 16 gods, for that will be a **s** to you.
Ps 69: 22 table set before them become a **s**;
91: 3 he will save you from the fowler's **s**
Pr 29: 25 Fear of man will prove to be a **s**,
Ro 11: 9 "May their table become a **s**

SNARED (SNARE)
Pr 3: 26 will keep your foot from being **s**.

SNATCH (SNATCHING)
Jn 10: 28 no one will **s** them out of my hand.

SNATCHING* (SNATCH)
Jude : 23 save others by **s** them from the fire;

SNEER
Ps 35: 21 They **s** at me and say, "Aha! Aha!

SNOUT*
Pr 11: 22 a pig's **s** is a beautiful woman who

SNOW
Ps 51: 7 me, and I will be whiter than **s**.
Isa 1: 18 scarlet, they shall be as white as **s**;

SNUFF (SNUFFED)
Isa 42: 3 smoldering wick he will not **s** out.
Mt 12: 20 smoldering wick he will not **s** out,

SNUFFED (SNUFF)
Pr 13: 9 but the lamp of the wicked is **s** out.

SOAP
Mal 3: 2 a refiner's fire or a launderer's **s**.

SOAR (SOARED)
Isa 40: 31 They will **s** on wings like eagles;

SOARED (SOAR)
2Sa 22: 11 he **s** on the wings of the wind.

SOBER*
1Sa 25: 37 Nabal was **s**, his wife told him
Ro 12: 3 think of yourself with **s** judgment,
1Th 5: 6 asleep, but let us be awake and **s**.
5: 8 be **s**, putting on faith and love
1Pe 1: 13 minds that are alert and fully **s**,
4: 7 of **s** mind so that you may pray.
5: 8 Be alert and of **s** mind.

SODOM
Ge 13: 12 plain and pitched his tents near **S**.
19: 24 rained down burning sulfur on **S**
Isa 1: 9 we would have become like **S**,
Lk 10: 12 that day for **S** than for that town.
Ro 9: 29 we would have become like **S**,
Rev 11: 8 which is figuratively called **S**

SOIL
Ge 4: 2 kept flocks, and Cain worked the **s**.
Mt 13: 23 the seed falling on good **s** refers

SOLD (SELL)
1Ki 21: 25 who **s** himself to do evil in the eyes
Mt 10: 29 not two sparrows **s** for a penny?
13: 44 in his joy went and **s** all he had
Ro 7: 14 I am unspiritual, **s** as a slave to sin.

SOLDIER
1Co 9: 7 Who serves as a **s** at his own
2Ti 2: 3 like a good **s** of Christ Jesus.

SOLE
Dt 28: 65 resting place for the **s** of your foot.
Isa 1: 6 From the **s** of your foot to the top

SOLID
2Ti 2: 19 God's **s** foundation stands firm,
Heb 5: 12 You need milk, not **s** food!

SOLOMON
Son of David by Bathsheba; king of Judah (2Sa 12:24; 1Ch 3:5, 10). Appointed king by David (1Ki 1); adversaries Adonijah, Joab, Shimei killed by Benaiah (1Ki 2). Asked for wisdom (1Ki 3; 2Ch 1). Judged between two prostitutes (1Ki 3:16–28). Built temple (1Ki 5–7; 2Ch 2–5); prayer of dedication (1Ki 8; 2Ch 6). Visited by Queen of Sheba (1Ki 10; 2Ch 9). Wives turned his heart from God (1Ki 11:1–13). Jeroboam rebelled against (1Ki 11:26–40). Death (1Ki 11:41–43; 2Ch 9:29–31).
Proverbs of (1Ki 4:32; Pr 1:1; 10:1; 25:1); psalms of (Ps 72; 127); song of (SS 1:1).

SON (SONS SONSHIP)
Ge 17: 19 your wife Sarah will bear you a **s**,
21: 10 rid of that slave woman and her **s**,
22: 2 said, "Take your **s**, your only **s**,
Ex 11: 5 Every firstborn **s** in Egypt will die,
Dt 1: 31 as a father carries his **s**, all the way
6: 20 your **s** asks you, "What is the
8: 5 that as a man disciplines his **s**,
21: 18 rebellious **s** who does not obey his
2Sa 7: 14 be his father, and he will be my **s**.
1Ki 3: 20 and put her dead **s** by my breast.
Ps 2: 7 He said to me, "You are my **s**;
2: 12 Kiss his **s**, or he will be angry
Pr 3: 12 as a father the **s** he delights in.
6: 20 My **s**, keep your father's command
Pr 10: 1 A wise **s** brings joy to his father, but a foolish **s** brings grief
Isa 7: 14 will conceive and give birth to a **s**,
Da 3: 25 and the fourth looks like a **s**
7: 13 there before me was one like a **s**
Hos 11: 1 and out of Egypt I called my **s**.
Am 7: 14 a prophet nor the **s** of a prophet,
Mt 1: 1 Jesus the Messiah the **s** of David, the **s** of Abraham:
1: 21 She will give birth to a **s**,
2: 15 "Out of Egypt I called my **s**."
3: 17 said, "This is my **S**, whom I love;
4: 3 "If you are the **S** of God, tell these
8: 20 the **S** of Man has no place to lay his
11: 27 one knows the **S** except the Father,
11: 27 whom the **S** chooses to reveal him.
12: 8 For the **S** of Man is Lord
12: 32 who speaks a word against the **S**
12: 40 so the **S** of Man will be three days
13: 41 The **S** of Man will send out his
13: 55 "Isn't this the carpenter's **s**?
14: 33 "Truly you are the **S** of God."
16: 16 Messiah, the **S** of the living God."
16: 27 For the **S** of Man is going to come
17: 5 said, "This is my **S**, whom I love;
19: 28 when the **S** of Man sits on his
20: 18 the **S** of Man will be delivered over
20: 28 just as the **S** of Man did not come
21: 9 "Hosanna to the **S** of David!"
22: 42 the Messiah? Whose **s** is he?"
22: 42 "The **s** of David," they replied.
24: 27 will be the coming of the **S** of Man.
24: 30 appear the sign of the **S** of Man
24: 44 because the **S** of Man will come
25: 31 "When the **S** of Man comes in his
26: 63 you are the Messiah, the **S** of God."
27: 54 "Surely he was the **S** of God!"
28: 19 and of the **S** and of the Holy Spirit,
Mk 1: 11 "You are my **S**, whom I love;
2: 28 So the **S** of Man is Lord even
8: 38 the **S** of Man will be ashamed
9: 7 "This is my **S**, whom I love.
10: 45 even the **S** of Man did not come
13: 32 nor the **S**, but only the Father.
14: 62 you will see the **S** of Man sitting
Lk 1: 32 and will be called the **S** of the Most
2: 7 she gave birth to her firstborn, a **s**.
3: 22 "You are my **S**, whom I love;
9: 35 saying, "This is my **S**, whom I have
9: 58 the **S** of Man has no place to lay his
12: 8 the **S** of Man will also acknowledge
15: 20 he ran to his **s**, threw his arms
18: 8 when the **S** of Man comes, will he
18: 31 about the **S** of Man will be fulfilled.
19: 10 For the **S** of Man came to seek
Jn 3: 14 so the **S** of Man must be lifted up,
3: 16 that he gave his one and only **S**,
Jn 3: 36 believes in the **S** has eternal life,
5: 19 the **S** can do nothing by himself;
6: 40 is that everyone who looks to the **S**
11: 4 God's **S** may be glorified through
17: 1 Glorify your **S**, that your **S** may
Ac 7: 56 the **S** of Man standing at the right
13: 33 "'You are my **s**; today I have
Ro 1: 4 was appointed the **S** of God
5: 10 to him through the death of his **S**,
8: 3 sending his own **S** in the likeness
8: 29 conformed to the image of his **S**,
8: 32 He who did not spare his own **S**,
1Co 15: 28 the **S** himself will be made subject
Gal 2: 20 I live by faith in the **S** of God,
4: 4 God sent his **S**, born of a woman,
4: 30 rid of the slave woman and her **s**,
1Th 1: 10 and to wait for his **S** from heaven,
Heb 1: 2 days he has spoken to us by his **S**,
1: 5 did God ever say, "You are my **S**;
4: 14 into heaven, Jesus the **S** of God,
5: 5 God said to him, "You are my **S**;
7: 28 appointed the **S**, who has been
10: 29 punished who has trampled the **S**
12: 6 everyone he accepts as his **s**."
2Pe 1: 17 saying, "This is my **S**, whom I love;
1Jn 1: 3 is with the Father and with his **S**,
1: 7 Jesus, his **S**, purifies us from all sin.
2: 23 who denies the **S** has the Father;
2: 23 acknowledges the **S** has the Father
3: 8 The reason the **S** of God appeared
4: 9 only **S** into the world that we might
4: 14 the Father has sent his **S** to be
5: 5 believes that Jesus is the **S** of God.
5: 11 eternal life, and this life is in his **S**.
Rev 1: 13 lampstands was someone like a **s**
14: 14 the cloud was one like a **s** of man

SONG (SING)
Ps 40: 3 He put a new **s** in my mouth,
69: 30 I will praise God's name in **s**
96: 1 Sing to the LORD a new **s**;
98: 4 burst into jubilant **s** with music;
119: 54 theme of my **s** wherever I lodge.
149: 1 Sing to the LORD a new **s**,
Isa 49: 13 burst into **s**, you mountains!
55: 12 hills will burst into **s** before you,
Rev 5: 9 And they sang a new **s**, saying:
15: 3 sang the **s** of God's servant Moses

SONGS (SING)
2Sa 23: 1 God of Jacob, the hero of Israel's **s**:
Job 35: 10 Maker, who gives **s** in the night,
Ps 100: 2 come before him with joyful **s**.
126: 6 to sow, will return with **s** of joy,
137: 3 "Sing us one of the **s** of Zion!"
Eph 5: 19 hymns, and **s** from the Spirit.
Jas 5: 13 Let them sing **s** of praise.

SONS (SON)
Ge 6: 2 the **s** of God saw that the daughters
10: 20 These are the **s** of Ham by their
Ru 4: 15 who is better to you than seven **s**,
Ps 132: 12 their **s** will sit on your throne
Joel 2: 28 **s** and daughters will prophesy,
2Co 6: 18 you will be my **s** and daughters,
Gal 4: 6 Because you are his **s**, God sent

SONSHIP* (SON)
Ro 8: 15 brought about your adoption to **s**.
8: 23 wait eagerly for our adoption to **s**,
9: 4 Israel. Theirs is the adoption to **s**;
Gal 4: 5 we might receive adoption to **s**.
Eph 1: 5 adoption to **s** through Jesus Christ,

SOOTHING
Pr 15: 4 The **s** tongue is a tree of life,

SORROW
Ps 6: 7 My eyes grow weak with **s**;
116: 3 I was overcome by distress and **s**.
Isa 60: 20 light, and your days of **s** will end.
Jer 31: 12 garden, and they will **s** no more.
Ro 9: 2 I have great **s** and unceasing
2Co 7: 10 Godly **s** brings repentance that
7: 10 regret, but worldly **s** brings death.

SOUGHT (SEEK)
2Ch 26: 5 He **s** God during the days
31: 21 he **s** his God and worked
Ps 34: 4 I **s** the LORD, and he answered
119: 58 have **s** your face with all my heart;

SOUL (SOULS)
Dt 6: 5 with all your **s** and with all your
10: 12 all your heart and with all your **s**,
30: 6 all your heart and with all your **s**,
Jos 22: 5 all your heart and with all your **s**."

2Ki 23: 25 and with all his **s** and with all his
Ps 23: 3 he refreshes my **s**. He guides me
42: 1 of water, so my **s** pants for you,
42: 11 Why, my **s**, are you downcast?
62: 5 Yes, my **s**, find rest in God;
103: 1 Praise the LORD, my **s**;
Pr 13: 19 A longing fulfilled is sweet to the **s**,
16: 24 sweet to the **s** and healing
La 3: 20 and my **s** is downcast within me.
Mt 10: 28 kill the body but cannot kill the **s**.
16: 26 the whole world, yet forfeit their **s**?
16: 26 give in exchange for their **s**?
22: 37 with all your **s** and with all your
Jn 12: 27 "Now my **s** is troubled, and what
Heb 4: 12 it penetrates even to dividing **s**
3Jn : 2 even as your **s** is getting along well.

SOULS (SOUL)
Jer 6: 16 it, and you will find rest for your **s**.
Mt 11: 29 and you will find rest for your **s**.

SOUND (FINE-SOUNDING)
Ge 3: 8 his wife heard the **s** of the LORD
Pr 3: 21 preserve **s** judgment and discretion
Eze 3: 12 me a loud rumbling **s** as the glory
Jn 3: 8 You hear its **s**, but you cannot tell
Ac 2: 2 Suddenly a **s** like the blowing
1Co 14: 8 the trumpet does not **s** a clear call,
15: 52 For the trumpet will **s**, the dead
1Ti 1: 10 else is contrary to the **s** doctrine
2Ti 4: 3 will not put up with **s** doctrine.
Titus 1: 9 can encourage others by **s** doctrine
2: 1 what is appropriate to **s** doctrine.

SOUR
Eze 18: 2 "'The parents eat **s** grapes,

SOURCE
Heb 5: 9 became the **s** of eternal salvation

SOVEREIGN (SOVEREIGNTY)
Ge 15: 2 But Abram said, "**S** LORD,
2Sa 7: 18 "Who am I, **S** LORD, and what is
Ps 71: 16 your mighty acts, **S** LORD;
Isa 25: 8 The **S** LORD will wipe away
40: 10 the **S** LORD comes with power,
50: 4 The **S** LORD has given me
61: 1 The Spirit of the **S** LORD is
61: 11 to grow, so the **S** LORD will make
Jer 32: 17 "Ah, **S** LORD, you have made
Eze 12: 28 'This is what the **S** LORD says:
Da 4: 25 Most High is **s** over all kingdoms
2Pe 2: 1 even denying the **s** Lord who
Jude : 4 deny Jesus Christ our only **S**

SOVEREIGNTY (SOVEREIGN)
Da 7: 27 Then the **s**, power and greatness

SOW (SOWER SOWN SOWS)
Job 4: 8 and those who **s** trouble reap it.
Ps 126: 5 Those who **s** with tears will reap
Hos 8: 7 "They **s** the wind and reap
10: 12 **S** righteousness for yourselves,
Mt 6: 26 they do not **s** or reap or store away
13: 3 "A farmer went out to **s** his seed.
1Co 15: 36 What you **s** does not come to life
Jas 3: 18 Peacemakers who **s** in peace reap
2Pe 2: 22 "A **s** that is washed returns to her

SOWER (SOW)
Isa 55: 10 so that it yields seed for the **s**
Mt 13: 18 to what the parable of the **s** means:
Jn 4: 36 so that the **s** and the reaper may be
2Co 9: 10 Now he who supplies seed to the **s**

SOWN (SOW)
Mt 13: 8 sixty or thirty times what was **s**.
Mk 4: 15 along the path, where the word is **s**.
1Co 15: 42 The body that is **s** is perishable,

SOWS (SOW)
Pr 11: 18 the one who **s** righteousness reaps
22: 8 Whoever **s** injustice reaps calamity,
2Co 9: 6 Whoever **s** sparingly will also reap
9: 6 and whoever **s** generously will
Gal 6: 7 A man reaps what he **s**.

SPARE (SPARES SPARING)
Est 7: 3 And **s** my people—this is my
Ro 8: 32 He who did not **s** his own Son,
11: 21 God did not **s** the natural branches,
he will not **s** you either.
2Pe 2: 4 if God did not **s** angels when they
2: 5 if he did not **s** the ancient world

SPARES (SPARE)
Pr 13: 24 Whoever **s** the rod hates their

SPARING (SPARE)
Pr 21: 26 but the righteous give without **s**.

SPARKLE*
Zec 9: 16 They will **s** in his land like jewels

SPARROW (SPARROWS)
Ps 84: 3 Even the **s** has found a home,

SPARROWS (SPARROW)
Mt 10: 29 Are not two **s** sold for a penny?

SPEAR (SPEARS)
1Sa 19: 10 to pin him to the wall with his **s**,
Ps 46: 9 breaks the bow and shatters the **s**;

SPEARS (SPEAR)
Isa 2: 4 and their **s** into pruning hooks.
Joel 3: 10 and your pruning hooks into **s**.
Mic 4: 3 and their **s** into pruning hooks.

SPECIAL
Jas 2: 3 If you show **s** attention to the man

SPECK
Mt 7: 3 do you look at the **s** of sawdust

SPECTACLE
1Co 4: 9 We have been made a **s** to the
Col 2: 15 he made a public **s** of them,

SPEECH
Ps 19: 3 They have no **s**, they use no words;
2Co 8: 7 in faith, in **s**, in knowledge,
1Ti 4: 12 an example for the believers in **s**,
1Jn 3: 18 let us not love with words or **s** but

SPEND (SPENT)
Pr 31: 3 Do not **s** your strength on women,
Isa 55: 2 Why **s** money on what is not bread,
2Co 12: 15 So I will very gladly **s** for you

SPENT (SPEND)
Mk 5: 26 doctors and had **s** all she had,
Lk 6: 12 and **s** the night praying to God.
15: 14 After he had **s** everything, there

SPIN
Mt 6: 28 They do not labor or **s**.

SPIRIT (SPIRIT'S SPIRIT-TAUGHT SPIRITS SPIRITUAL)
Ge 1: 2 the **S** of God was hovering over
6: 3 said, "My **S** will not contend
Ex 31: 3 I have filled him with the **S** of God,
Nu 11: 25 power of the **S** that was on him
Dt 34: 9 the **s** of wisdom because Moses
Jdg 6: 34 Then the **S** of the LORD came
11: 29 Then the **S** of the LORD came
13: 25 the **S** of the LORD began to stir
1Sa 10: 10 the **S** of God came powerfully
16: 13 day on the **S** of the LORD came
16: 14 Saul, and an evil **s** from the LORD
2Sa 23: 2 "The **S** of the LORD spoke
2Ki 2: 9 inherit a double portion of your **s**,"
Ne 9: 20 You gave your good **S** to instruct
9: 30 By your **S** you warned them
Job 33: 4 The **S** of God has made me;
Ps 31: 5 Into your hands I commit my **s**;
34: 18 saves those who are crushed in **s**.
51: 10 and renew a steadfast **s** within me.
51: 11 or take your Holy **S** from me.
51: 17 My sacrifice, O God, is a broken **s**;
106: 33 they rebelled against the **S** of God,
139: 7 Where can I go from your **S**?
143: 10 may your good **S** lead me on level
Isa 11: 2 The **S** of the LORD will rest
30: 1 but not by my **S**, heaping sin
32: 15 till the **S** is poured on us
44: 3 pour out my **S** on your offspring,
57: 15 to revive the **s** of the lowly
61: 1 The **S** of the Sovereign LORD is
63: 10 rebelled and grieved his Holy **S**.
Eze 11: 19 heart and put a new **s** in them;
13: 3 prophets who follow their own **s**
36: 26 a new heart and put a new **s** in you;
Da 4: 8 the **s** of the holy gods is in him.)
Joel 2: 28 I will pour out my **S** on all people.
Zec 4: 6 but by my **S**,' says the LORD
Mt 1: 18 to be pregnant through the Holy **S**.
3: 11 He will baptize you with the Holy **S**
3: 16 saw the **S** of God descending like
4: 1 led by the **S** into the wilderness
5: 3 "Blessed are the poor in **s**, for
10: 20 but the **S** of your Father speaking
12: 31 blasphemy against the **S** will not be
26: 41 The **s** is willing, but the flesh is
28: 19 and of the Son and of the Holy **S**,
Mk 1: 8 will baptize you with the Holy **S**."
Lk 1: 35 "The Holy **S** will come on you,
1: 80 child grew and became strong in **s**;
3: 16 He will baptize you with the Holy **S**
4: 18 "The **S** of the Lord is on me,
Lk 11: 13 in heaven give the Holy **S** to those
23: 46 into your hands I commit my **s**."
Jn 1: 33 who will baptize with the Holy **S**.'
3: 5 they are born of water and the **S**.
4: 24 God is **s**, and his worshipers must
worship in the **S**
6: 63 The **S** gives life; the flesh counts
7: 39 that time the **S** had not been given,
14: 26 the Holy **S**, whom the Father will
16: 13 But when he, the **S** of truth, comes,
20: 22 and said, "Receive the Holy **S**.
Ac 1: 5 will be baptized with the Holy **S**."
1: 8 when the Holy **S** comes on you;
2: 4 other tongues as the **S** enabled
2: 17 I will pour out my **S** on all people.
2: 38 will receive the gift of the Holy **S**.
4: 31 they were all filled with the Holy **S**
5: 3 that you have lied to the Holy **S**
6: 3 who are known to be full of the **S**
8: 15 that they might receive the Holy **S**,
9: 17 and be filled with the Holy **S**."
11: 16 will be baptized with the Holy **S**.'
13: 2 the Holy **S** said, "Set apart for me
19: 2 even heard that there is a Holy **S**."
Ro 1: 9 in my **s** in preaching the gospel
8: 4 to the flesh but according to the **S**.
8: 5 minds set on what the **S** desires.
8: 9 if indeed the **S** of God lives in you.
8: 13 but if by the **S** you put to death
8: 16 The **S** himself testifies with our **s**
8: 23 who have the firstfruits of the **S**,
8: 26 the **S** helps us in our weakness.
8: 26 the **S** himself intercedes for us
1Co 2: 10 God has revealed to us by his **S**.
2: 10 The **S** searches all things,
2: 14 without the **S** does not accept
2: 14 are discerned only through the **S**.
3: 1 as people who live by the **S** but
5: 3 present, I am with you in **s**.
6: 19 bodies are temples of the Holy **S**,
12: 1 Now about the gifts of the **S**,
12: 13 we were all baptized by one **S** so as
12: 13 and we were all given the one **S**
14: 1 and eagerly desire gifts of the **S**,
2Co 1: 22 put his **S** in our hearts as a deposit,
3: 3 but with the **S** of the living God,
3: 6 letter kills, but the **S** gives life.
3: 17 Now the Lord is the **S**, and where
5: 5 who has given us the **S** as a deposit,
7: 1 that contaminates body and **s**,
Gal 3: 2 Did you receive the **S** by the works
5: 16 say, walk by the **S**, and you will not
5: 22 But the fruit of the **S** is love, joy,
5: 25 Since we live by the **S**, let us keep
6: 1 who live by the **S** should restore
6: 8 whoever sows to please the **S**,
Eph 1: 13 with a seal, the promised Holy **S**,
2: 22 in which God lives by his **S**.
4: 4 There is one body and one **S**, just
4: 30 do not grieve the Holy **S** of God,
5: 18 Instead, be filled with the **S**,
5: 19 hymns, and songs from the **S**.
6: 17 of salvation and the sword of the **S**,
Php 2: 2 being one in **s** and of one mind.
1Th 5: 19 Do not quench the **S**.
5: 23 May your whole **s**, soul and body
2Th 2: 13 the sanctifying work of the **S**
1Ti 3: 16 was vindicated by the **S**, was seen
2Ti 1: 7 the **S** God gave us does not make
Heb 2: 4 of the Holy **S** distributed according
4: 12 even to dividing soul and **s**,
10: 29 who has insulted the **S** of grace?
1Pe 3: 4 beauty of a gentle and quiet **s**,
2Pe 1: 21 were carried along by the Holy **S**.
1Jn 3: 24 We know it by the **S** he gave us.
4: 1 do not believe every **s**, but test
4: 13 he in us: He has given us of his **S**.
Jude : 20 faith and praying in the Holy **S**,
Rev 2: 7 let them hear what the **S** says

SPIRIT'S* (SPIRIT)
1Co 2: 4 a demonstration of the **S** power,

SPIRIT-TAUGHT* (SPIRIT TEACH)
1Co 2: 13 spiritual realities with **S** words.

SPIRITS (SPIRIT)
1Co 12: 10 another distinguishing between **s**,
14: 32 The **s** of prophets are subject
Heb 1: 7 "He makes his angels **s**, and his
1Jn 4: 1 but test the **s** to see whether they

SPIRITUAL (SPIRIT)
Ro 12: 11 but keep your **s** fervor,

1Co 2: 13 the Spirit, explaining **s** realities
15: 44 a natural body, it is raised a **s** body.
Eph 1: 3 realms with every **s** blessing
6: 12 against the **s** forces of evil
1Pe 2: 2 crave pure **s** milk, so that by it you
2: 5 are being built into a **s** house to be

SPIT
Mt 27: 30 They **s** on him, and took the staff
Rev 3: 16 I am about to **s** you out of my

SPLENDOR
1Ch 16: 29 the LORD in the **s** of his holiness.
29: 11 glory and the majesty and the **s**,
Job 37: 22 of the north he comes in golden **s**;
Ps 29: 2 the LORD in the **s** of his holiness.
45: 3 clothe yourself with **s** and majesty.
96: 6 **S** and majesty are before him;
96: 9 the LORD in the **s** of his holiness;
104: 1 you are clothed with **s** and majesty.
110: 3 Arrayed in holy **s**, your young men
145: 5 of the glorious **s** of your majesty—
145: 12 the glorious **s** of your kingdom.
148: 13 his **s** is above the earth
Pr 16: 31 Gray hair is a crown of **s**;
20: 29 strength, gray hair the **s** of the old.
Isa 55: 5 for he has endowed you with **s**."
60: 21 my hands, for the display of my **s**.
61: 3 the LORD for the display of his **s**.
63: 1 robed in **s**, striding forward
Hab 3: 4 His **s** was like the sunrise;
Mt 6: 29 in all his **s** was dressed like one
Lk 9: 30 and Elijah, appeared in glorious **s**,
2Th 2: 8 and destroy by the **s** of his coming.

SPOIL (SPOILS)
Ps 119:162 promise like one who finds great **s**.

SPOILS (SPOIL)
Isa 53: 12 he will divide the **s** with the strong,
Jn 6: 27 Do not work for food that **s**,

SPOTLESS
2Pe 3: 14 make every effort to be found **s**,

SPOTS (SPOTTED)
Jer 13: 23 change his skin or a leopard its **s**?

SPOTTED (SPOTS)
Ge 30: 32 them every speckled or **s** sheep,

SPREAD (SPREADING SPREADS)
Ps 78: 19 "Can God really **s** a table
Ac 6: 7 So the word of God **s**.
12: 24 the word of God continued to **s**
13: 49 of the Lord **s** through the whole
19: 20 way the word of the Lord **s** widely
2Th 3: 1 message of the Lord may **s** rapidly

SPREADING (SPREAD)
Pr 29: 5 flatter their neighbors are **s** nets
1Th 3: 2 in God's service in **s** the gospel

SPREADS (SPREAD)
Pr 10: 18 lying lips and **s** slander is a fool.

SPRING (SPRINGS)
Jer 2: 13 forsaken me, the **s** of living water,
Jn 4: 14 in them a **s** of water welling
Jas 3: 12 can a salt **s** produce fresh water.

SPRINGS (SPRING)
2Pe 2: 17 These people are **s** without water

SPRINKLE (SPRINKLED)
Lev 16: 14 with his finger **s** it on the front

SPRINKLED (SPRINKLE)
Heb 10: 22 having our hearts **s** to cleanse us
1Pe 1: 2 Jesus Christ and **s** with his blood:

SPROUT
Pr 23: 5 for they will surely **s** wings and fly
Jer 33: 15 I will make a righteous Branch **s**

SPUR*
Heb 10: 24 consider how we may **s** one

SPURNS*
Pr 15: 5 A fool **s** a parent's discipline,

SPY
Gal 2: 4 had infiltrated our ranks to **s**

SQUANDERED (SQUANDERS)
Lk 15: 13 there **s** his wealth in wild living.

SQUANDERS* (SQUANDERED)
Pr 29: 3 of prostitutes **s** his wealth.

SQUARE
Rev 21: 16 The city was laid out like a **s**,

STABILITY*
Pr 29: 4 By justice a king gives a country **s**,

STAFF
Ge 49: 10 nor the ruler's **s** from between his
Ex 7: 12 Aaron's **s** swallowed up their staffs.
Nu 17: 6 and Aaron's **s** was among them.
Ps 23: 4 your rod and your **s**, they comfort

STAIN (STAINED)
Eph 5: 27 without **s** or wrinkle or any other

STAINED (STAIN)
Isa 63: 1 with his garments **s** crimson?

STAKES
Isa 54: 2 your cords, strengthen your **s**.

STAND (STANDING STANDS STOOD)
Ex 14: 13 **S** firm and you will see
Lev 19: 32 "'**S** up in the presence
Jos 10: 12 "Sun, **s** still over Gibeon, and you,
2Ch 20: 17 **s** firm and see the deliverance
Job 19: 25 in the end he will **s** on the earth.
Ps 1: 1 or **s** in the way that sinners take
1: 5 Therefore the wicked will not **s**
24: 3 Who may **s** in his holy place?
33: 11 plans of the LORD **s** firm forever,
40: 2 rock and gave me a firm place to **s**.
76: 7 Who can **s** before you when you
93: 5 Your statutes, LORD, **s** firm;
119:120 fear of you; I **s** in awe of your laws.
130: 3 of sins, Lord, who could **s**?
Isa 7: 9 If you do not **s** firm in your faith,
29: 23 will **s** in awe of the God of Israel.
Eze 22: 30 **s** before me in the gap on behalf
Hab 3: 2 I **s** in awe of your deeds, LORD.
Zec 14: 4 day his feet will **s** on the Mount
Mal 3: 2 Who can **s** when he appears?
Mt 12: 25 divided against itself will not **s**.
Lk 21: 19 **S** firm, and you will win life.
Ac 11: 17 think that I could **s** in God's way?"
Ro 14: 4 their own master, servants **s** or fall.
14: 4 for the Lord is able to make them **s**.
14: 10 we will all **s** before God's judgment
1Co 15: 58 dear brothers and sisters, **s** firm.
16: 13 on your guard; **s** firm in the faith;
Gal 5: 1 **S** firm, then, and do not let
Eph 6: 14 **S** firm then, with the belt of truth
2Th 2: 15 **s** firm and hold fast to the
Jas 5: 8 be patient and **s** firm,
Rev 3: 20 I **s** at the door and knock.

STANDING (STAND)
Ex 3: 5 where you are **s** is holy ground."
Jos 5: 15 the place where you are **s** is holy."
Ru 2: 1 side, a man of **s** from the clan
4: 11 May you have **s** in Ephrathah
1Ti 3: 13 have served well gain an excellent **s**
1Pe 5: 9 Resist him, **s** firm in the faith,

STANDS (STAND)
Ps 89: 2 that your love **s** firm forever,
119: 89 it **s** firm in the heavens.
Pr 12: 7 the house of the righteous **s** firm.
Mt 10: 22 the one who **s** firm to the end will
2Ti 2: 19 God's solid foundation **s** firm,

STAR (STARS)
Nu 24: 17 A **s** will come out of Jacob;
Isa 14: 12 morning **s**, son of the dawn!
Mt 2: 2 We saw his **s** when it rose and have
2Pe 1: 19 the morning **s** rises in your hearts.
Rev 2: 28 also give that one the morning **s**.
22: 16 David, and the bright Morning **S**."

STARS (STAR)
Ge 1: 16 He also made the **s**.
Job 38: 7 while the morning **s** sang together
Da 12: 3 like the **s** for ever and ever.
Php 2: 15 you will shine among them like **s**

STATURE
1Sa 2: 26 boy Samuel continued to grow in **s**
Lk 2: 52 And Jesus grew in wisdom and **s**,

STATUTES
Ps 19: 7 The **s** of the LORD are
93: 5 Your **s**, LORD, stand firm;
119: 2 Blessed are those who keep his **s**
119: 14 in following your **s** as one rejoices
119: 24 Your **s** are my delight; they are my
119: 36 Turn my heart toward your **s**
119: 99 teachers, for I meditate on your **s**.
119:111 Your **s** are my heritage forever;
119:125 that I may understand your **s**.
119:129 Your **s** are wonderful;
119:138 The **s** you have laid down are
119:152 your **s** that you established them
119:167 I obey your **s**, for I love them

STEADFAST*
Ps 51: 10 and renew a **s** spirit within me.
57: 7 My heart, O God, is **s**, my heart is **s**;
108: 1 My heart, O God, is **s**; I will sing
112: 7 their hearts are **s**,
119: 5 my ways were **s** in obeying your
Pr 4: 26 your feet and be **s** in all your ways.
Isa 26: 3 peace those whose minds are **s**,
1Pe 5: 10 and make you strong, firm and **s**.

STEADY
Isa 35: 3 hands, **s** the knees that give way;

STEAL (STOLEN)
Ex 20: 15 "You shall not **s**.
Lev 19: 11 "'Do not **s**."'Do not lie.
Dt 5: 19 "You shall not **s**.
Mt 19: 18 you shall not **s**, you shall not give
Ro 13: 9 "You shall not **s**," "You shall not
Eph 4: 28 has been stealing must **s** no longer,

STEP (FOOTSTEPS STEPS)
Job 34: 21 he sees their every **s**.
Ps 1: 1 is the one who does not walk in **s**
Gal 5: 25 let us keep in **s** with the Spirit.

STEPHEN*
Early church leader (Ac 6:5). Arrested (Ac 6:8–15). Speech to Sanhedrin (Ac 7). Stoned (Ac 7:54–60; 8:2; 11:19; 22:20).

STEPS (STEP)
Ps 37: 23 The LORD makes firm the **s**
Pr 14: 15 the prudent give thought to their **s**.
16: 9 but the LORD establishes their **s**.
20: 24 A person's **s** are directed
Jer 10: 23 it is not for them to direct their **s**.
1Pe 2: 21 that you should follow in his **s**.

STERN (STERNNESS)
Pr 15: 10 **S** discipline awaits anyone who

STERNNESS* (STERN)
Ro 11: 22 the kindness and **s** of God:
11: 22 **s** to those who fell, but kindness

STICKS
Pr 18: 24 there is a friend who **s** closer than

STIFF-NECKED (NECK)
Ex 34: 9 Although this is a **s** people,
Pr 29: 1 Whoever remains **s** after many

STILL
Jos 10: 13 So the sun stood **s**, and the moon
Ps 37: 7 Be **s** before the LORD and wait
46: 10 "Be **s**, and know that I am God;
89: 9 its waves mount up, you **s** them.
Zec 2: 13 Be **s** before the LORD,
Mk 4: 39 Be **s**!" Then the wind died down

STIMULATE*
2Pe 3: 1 of them as reminders to **s** you

STING
1Co 15: 55 Where, O death, is your **s**?"

STINGY*
Pr 28: 22 The **s** are eager to get rich and are

STIR (STIRRED STIRS)
Pr 28: 25 The greedy **s** up conflict, but those

STIRRED (STIR)
Ps 45: 1 My heart is **s** by a noble theme as I

STIRS (STIR)
Pr 6: 19 a person who **s** up conflict
10: 12 Hatred **s** up conflict, but love
15: 1 but a harsh word **s** up anger.
Pr 15: 18 A hot-tempered person **s** up
16: 28 A perverse person **s** up conflict,
29: 22 An angry person **s** up conflict,

STOLEN (STEAL)
Lev 6: 4 they must return what they have **s**
SS 4: 9 You have **s** my heart, my sister,

STOMACH
1Co 6: 13 "Food for the **s** and the **s** for food,
Php 3: 19 their god is their **s**, and their glory

STONE (CAPSTONE CORNERSTONE MILLSTONE STONES STONING)
Ex 24: 4 up twelve **s** pillars representing
28: 10 six names on one **s**
34: 1 out two **s** tablets like the first ones,
Dt 4: 13 then wrote them on two **s** tablets.
19: 14 your neighbor's boundary **s** set
1Sa 17: 50 the Philistine with a sling and a **s**;
Ps 91: 12 will not strike your foot against a **s**.
118: 22 The **s** the builders rejected has
Pr 22: 28 not move an ancient boundary **s**
Isa 8: 14 and Judah he will be a **s** that causes

Isa 28: 16 "See, I lay a **s** in Zion, a tested **s**,
Eze 11: 19 remove from them their heart of **s**
36: 26 remove from you your heart of **s**
Mt 7: 9 asks for bread, will give him a **s**?
21: 42 "'The **s** the builders rejected has
24: 2 you, not one **s** here will be left
Mk 16: 3 "Who will roll the **s** away
Lk 4: 3 God, tell this **s** to become bread."
Jn 8: 7 *first to throw a s at her."*
Ac 4: 11 Jesus is "'the **s** you builders
Ro 9: 32 stumbled over the stumbling **s**.
2Co 3: 3 not on tablets of **s** but on tablets
1Pe 2: 6 "See, I lay a **s** in Zion, a chosen
Rev 2: 17 person a white **s** with a new name

STONES (STONE)
Ex 28: 21 There are to be twelve **s**,
Jos 4: 3 take up twelve **s** from the middle
1Sa 17: 40 hand, chose five smooth **s**
Mt 3: 9 these **s** God can raise up children
1Co 3: 12 silver, costly **s**, wood, hay or straw,
2Co 11: 25 once I was pelted with **s**,
1Pe 2: 5 like living **s**, are being built

STONING (STONE)
Heb 11: 37 They were put to death by **s**;

STOOD (STAND)
Jos 10: 13 So the sun **s** still, and the moon
Lk 22: 28 You are those who have **s** by me
2Ti 4: 17 But the Lord **s** at my side and gave
Jas 1: 12 trial because, having **s** the test,

STOOPS
Ps 113: 6 who **s** down to look on the heavens

STOP (STOPPED)
Job 37: 14 **s** and consider God's wonders.
Isa 1: 13 **S** bringing meaningless offerings!
1: 16 out of my sight; **s** doing wrong.
2: 22 **S** trusting in mere humans,
Jer 32: 40 I will never **s** doing good to them,
Mk 9: 39 "Do not **s** him," Jesus said.
Jn 6: 43 "**S** grumbling among yourselves,"
7: 24 **S** judging by mere appearances,
20: 27 **S** doubting and believe."
Ro 14: 13 let us **s** passing judgment
1Co 14: 20 sisters, **s** thinking like children.

STOPPED (STOP)
Jos 3: 17 of the LORD **s** in the middle

STORE (STORED)
Pr 2: 1 **s** up my commands within you,
7: 1 **s** up my commands within you.
10: 14 The wise **s** up knowledge,
Isa 33: 6 a rich **s** of salvation and wisdom
Mt 6: 19 "Do not **s** up for yourselves
6: 26 not sow or reap or **s** away in barns,
2Ti 4: 8 Now there is in **s** for me the crown

STORED (STORE)
Lk 6: 45 out of the good **s** up in his heart,
6: 45 out of the evil **s** up in his heart.
Col 1: 5 spring from the hope **s** up for you

STOREHOUSE (HOUSE)
Mal 3: 10 Bring the whole tithe into the **s**,

STORIES*
2Pe 1: 16 we did not follow cleverly devised **s**
2: 3 will exploit you with fabricated **s**.

STORM
Job 38: 1 LORD spoke to Job out of the **s**.
Ps 107: 29 He stilled the **s** to a whisper;
Lk 8: 24 the **s** subsided, and all was calm.

STRAIGHT
Ps 27: 11 lead me in a **s** path because of my
107: 7 He led them by a **s** way to a city
Pr 2: 13 who have left the **s** paths to walk
3: 6 and he will make your paths **s**.
4: 11 and lead you along **s** paths.
4: 25 Let your eyes look **s** ahead;
11: 5 the blameless makes their paths **s**,
15: 21 understanding keeps a **s** course.
Isa 40: 3 make **s** in the desert a highway
Mt 3: 3 the Lord, make **s** paths for him.'"
Jn 1: 23 'Make **s** the way for the Lord.'"
2Pe 2: 15 They have left the **s** way

STRAIN (STRAINING)
Mt 23: 24 You **s** out a gnat but swallow

STRAINING (STRAIN)
Php 3: 13 behind and **s** toward what is ahead,

STRANGE (STRANGER STRANGERS)
Isa 28: 11 and **s** tongues God will speak to
Eze 3: 5 of obscure speech and **s** language,

STRANGER (STRANGE)
Ps 119: 19 I am a **s** on earth; do not hide your
Mt 25: 35 I was a **s** and you invited me in,
Jn 10: 5 But they will never follow a **s**;

STRANGERS (STRANGE)
Heb 13: 2 not forget to show hospitality to **s**,

STRAPS
Mk 1: 7 **s** of whose sandals I am not worthy

STRAW
Isa 11: 7 and the lion will eat **s** like the ox.
1Co 3: 12 silver, costly stones, wood, hay or **s**,

STRAYED (STRAYS)
Ps 119:176 I have **s** like a lost sheep.
Jer 31: 19 After I **s**, I repented; after I came

STRAYS (STRAYED)
Pr 21: 16 Whoever **s** from the path
Eze 34: 16 for the lost and bring back the **s**.

STREAM (STREAMS)
Am 5: 24 righteousness like a never-failing **s**!

STREAMS (STREAM)
Ps 1: 3 person is like a tree planted by **s**
46: 4 a river whose **s** make glad the city
Ecc 1: 7 All **s** flow into the sea, yet the sea

STREET
Mt 6: 5 and on the **s** corners to be seen
22: 9 So go to the **s** corners and invite
Rev 21: 21 The great **s** of the city was of gold,

STRENGTH (STRONG)
Ex 15: 2 "The LORD is my **s** and my
Dt 4: 37 by his Presence and his great **s**,
6: 5 all your soul and with all your **s**.
Jdg 16: 15 told me the secret of your great **s**."
2Sa 22: 33 It is God who arms me with **s**
2Ki 23: 25 with all his soul and with all his **s**,
1Ch 16: 11 Look to the LORD and his **s**;
16: 28 ascribe to the LORD glory and **s**.
29: 12 power to exalt and give **s** to all.
Ne 8: 10 the joy of the LORD is your **s**."
Ps 18: 1 I love you, LORD, my **s**.
21: 13 Be exalted in your **s**, LORD;
28: 7 The LORD is my **s** and my shield;
29: 11 The LORD gives **s** to his people;
33: 16 no warrior escapes by his great **s**.
46: 1 God is our refuge and **s**,
59: 17 You are my **s**, I sing praise to you;
65: 6 having armed yourself with **s**,
73: 26 but God is the **s** of my heart and
84: 5 Blessed are those whose **s** is in you,
96: 7 ascribe to the LORD glory and **s**.
105: 4 Look to the LORD and his **s**;
118: 14 The LORD is my **s** and my
147: 10 pleasure is not in the **s** of the horse,
Pr 24: 5 have knowledge muster their **s**.
30: 25 Ants are creatures of little **s**,
Isa 12: 2 himself, is my **s** and my defense;
31: 1 in the great **s** of their horsemen,
40: 26 of his great power and mighty **s**,
40: 31 in the LORD will renew their **s**.
63: 1 forward in the greatness of his **s**?
Jer 9: 23 strong boast of their **s** or the rich
Mic 5: 4 his flock in the **s** of the LORD,
Hab 3: 19 The Sovereign LORD is my **s**;
Mk 12: 30 all your mind and with all your **s**.'
1Co 1: 25 of God is stronger than human **s**.
Eph 1: 19 power is the same as the mighty **s**
Php 4: 13 this through him who gives me **s**.
Heb 11: 34 whose weakness was turned to **s**;
1Pe 4: 11 do so with the **s** God provides,

STRENGTHEN (STRONG)
2Ch 16: 9 to **s** those whose hearts are fully
Ps 119: 28 **s** me according to your word.
Isa 35: 3 **S** the feeble hands, steady the
41: 10 I will **s** you and help you;
Lk 22: 32 have turned back, **s** your brothers."
Eph 3: 16 of his glorious riches he may **s** you
1Th 3: 13 May he **s** your hearts so that you
2Th 2: 17 and **s** you in every good deed
Heb 12: 12 **s** your feeble arms and weak knees.

STRENGTHENED (STRONG)
Col 1: 11 being **s** with all power according
Heb 13: 9 for our hearts to be **s** by grace,

STRENUOUSLY*
Col 1: 29 To this end I **s** contend with all

STRETCHES
Ps 104: 2 he **s** out the heavens like a tent

STRICKEN (STRIKE)
Isa 53: 4 him punished by God, **s** by him,

STRICT
1Co 9: 25 in the games goes into **s** training.

STRIFE (STRIVE)
Pr 13: 10 Where there is **s**, there is pride,
17: 1 than a house full of feasting, with **s**.
20: 3 It is to one's honor to avoid **s**,
22: 10 out the mocker, and out goes **s**;
30: 33 so stirring up anger produces **s**."
1Ti 6: 4 about words that result in envy, **s**,

STRIKE (STROKE)
Ge 3: 15 your head, and you will **s** his heel."
Zec 13: 7 "**S** the shepherd, and the sheep will
Mt 4: 6 you will not **s** your foot against
26: 31 "'I will **s** the shepherd,
1Co 9: 27 I **s** a blow to my body and make it

STRIPS
Jn 20: 5 in at the **s** of linen lying there

STRIVE* (STRIFE STRIVING)
Ac 24: 16 So I **s** always to keep my
2Co 13: 11 **S** for full restoration, encourage
1Th 5: 15 always **s** to do what is good for
1Ti 4: 10 That is why we labor and **s**,

STRIVING (STRIVE)
Php 1: 27 **s** together as one for the faith

STROKE (STRIKE)
Mt 5: 18 letter, not the least **s** of a pen,

STRONG (STRENGTH STRENGTHEN STRENGTHENED STRONGER)
Dt 3: 24 your greatness and your **s** hand.
31: 6 Be **s** and courageous. Do not be
Jos 1: 6 Be **s** and courageous, because you
Jdg 5: 21 March on, my soul; be **s**!
2Sa 10: 12 Be **s**, and let us fight bravely for
1Ki 2: 2 "So be **s**, act like a man,
1Ch 28: 20 his son, "Be **s** and courageous,
2Ch 32: 7 "Be **s** and courageous. Do not be
Ps 24: 8 The LORD **s** and mighty,
31: 2 of refuge, a **s** fortress to save me.
Pr 31: 17 her arms are **s** for her tasks.
Ecc 9: 11 to the swift or the battle to the **s**,
SS 8: 6 for love is as **s** as death, its jealousy
Isa 35: 4 fearful hearts, "Be **s**, do not fear;
53: 12 he will divide the spoils with the **s**,
Jer 9: 23 or the **s** boast of their strength
50: 34 Yet their Redeemer is **s**;
Hag 2: 4 Be **s**, all you people of the land,'
Mt 12: 29 can anyone enter a **s** man's house
Lk 2: 40 And the child grew and became **s**;
Ro 15: 1 We who are **s** ought to bear
1Co 1: 27 things of the world to shame the **s**.
16: 13 in the faith; be courageous; be **s**.
2Co 12: 10 For when I am weak, then I am **s**.
Eph 6: 10 be **s** in the Lord and in his mighty
2Ti 2: 1 be **s** in the grace that is in Christ
1Pe 5: 10 restore you and make you **s**,

STRONGER (STRONG)
Dt 4: 38 you nations greater and **s** than you
1Co 1: 25 of God is **s** than human strength.

STRONGHOLD (STRONGHOLDS)
2Sa 22: 3 He is my **s**, my refuge and my
Ps 9: 9 oppressed, a **s** in times of trouble.
18: 2 and the horn of my salvation, my **s**.
27: 1 The LORD is the **s** of my life—
144: 2 my fortress, my **s** and my deliverer,

STRONGHOLDS (STRONGHOLD)
Zep 3: 6 their **s** are demolished.
2Co 10: 4 have divine power to demolish **s**.

STRUGGLE (STRUGGLED)
Ro 15: 30 join me in my **s** by praying to God
Eph 6: 12 For our **s** is not against flesh
Heb 12: 4 In your **s** against sin, you have not

STRUGGLED (STRUGGLE)
Ge 32: 28 because you have **s** with God

STUDENT (STUDY)
Lk 6: 40 The **s** is not above the teacher,

STUDY* (STUDENT)
Ezr 7: 10 Ezra had devoted himself to the **s**
Ecc 1: 13 I applied my mind to **s**
12: 12 end, and much **s** wearies the body.
Jn 5: 39 You **s** the Scriptures diligently

STUMBLE (STUMBLES STUMBLING)
Ps 37: 24 though he may **s**, he will not fall,
119:165 and nothing can make them **s**.
Pr 3: 23 in safety, and your foot will not **s**.
24: 17 when they **s**, do not let your heart
Isa 8: 14 be a stone that causes people to **s**
Jer 13: 16 before your feet **s** on the darkening

SWALLOW (SWALLOWED)
Isa 25: 8 he will **s** up death forever.
Jnh 1: 17 provided a huge fish to **s** Jonah,
Mt 23: 24 You strain out a gnat but **s** a camel.

SWALLOWED (SWALLOW)
1Co 15: 54 "Death has been **s** up in victory."
2Co 5: 4 so that what is mortal may be **s**

SWAYED
Mt 11: 7 A reed **s** by the wind?
22: 16 You aren't **s** by others, because you
2Ti 3: 6 are **s** by all kinds of evil desires,

SWEAR (SWORE SWORN)
Lev 19: 12 "'Do not **s** falsely by my name
Ps 24: 4 trust in an idol or **s** by a false god.
Isa 45: 23 by me every tongue will **s**.
Mt 5: 34 I tell you, do not **s** an oath at all:
Jas 5: 12 my brothers and sisters, do not **s**—

SWEAT*
Ge 3: 19 the **s** of your brow you will eat
Lk 22: 44 his **s** was like drops of blood falling

SWEET (SWEETER SWEETNESS)
Job 20: 12 "Though evil is **s** in his mouth
Ps 119:103 How **s** are your words to my taste,
Pr 9: 17 "Stolen water is **s**; food eaten
13: 19 A longing fulfilled is **s** to the soul,
16: 24 **s** to the soul and healing
20: 17 Food gained by fraud tastes **s**,
Ecc 5: 12 The sleep of a laborer is **s**,
Isa 5: 20 who put bitter for **s** and **s** for bitter.
Eze 3: 3 tasted as **s** as honey in my mouth.
Rev 10: 10 tasted as **s** as honey in my mouth,

SWEETER (SWEET)
Ps 19: 10 they are **s** than honey, than honey
119:103 taste, **s** than honey to my mouth!

SWEETNESS* (SWEET)
SS 4: 11 Your lips drop **s** as the honeycomb,
5: 16 His mouth is **s** itself;

SWEPT
Mt 12: 44 **s** clean and put in order.

SWIFT
Pr 1: 16 into evil, they are **s** to shed blood.
Ecc 9: 11 The race is not to the **s** or the battle
Isa 59: 7 they are **s** to shed innocent blood.
Ro 3: 15 "Their feet are **s** to shed blood;
2Pe 2: 1 bringing **s** destruction

SWINDLER* (SWINDLERS)
1Co 5: 11 or slanderer, a drunkard or **s**.

SWINDLERS* (SWINDLER)
1Co 5: 10 or the greedy and **s**, or idolaters.
6: 10 nor slanderers nor **s** will inherit

SWORD (SWORDS)
Ge 3: 24 and a flaming **s** flashing back
Dt 32: 41 when I sharpen my flashing **s**
Jos 5: 13 of him with a drawn **s** in his hand.
1Sa 17: 45 "You come against me with **s**
17: 47 here will know that it is not by **s**
31: 4 Saul took his own **s** and fell on it.
2Sa 12: 10 the **s** will never depart from your
Ps 44: 6 my **s** does not bring me victory;
45: 3 Gird your **s** on your side,
Isa 2: 4 will not take up **s** against nation,
Mic 4: 3 will not take up **s** against nation,
Mt 10: 34 not come to bring peace, but a **s**.
26: 52 all who draw the **s** will die by the **s**.
Lk 2: 35 a **s** will pierce your own soul too."
Ro 13: 4 for rulers do not bear the **s** for no
Eph 6: 17 of salvation and the **s** of the Spirit,
Heb 4: 12 Sharper than any double-edged **s**,
Rev 1: 16 was a sharp, double-edged **s**.
19: 15 of his mouth is a sharp **s**

SWORDS (SWORD)
Ps 64: 3 They sharpen their tongues like **s**
Pr 12: 18 words of the reckless pierce like **s**,
Isa 2: 4 They will beat their **s**
Joel 3: 10 Beat your plowshares into **s**

SWORE (SWEAR)
Heb 6: 13 him to swear by, he **s** by himself,

SWORN (SWEAR)
Ps 110: 4 The LORD has **s** and will not
Eze 20: 42 the land I had **s** with uplifted hand
Heb 7: 21 "The Lord has **s** and will not

SYCAMORE-FIG (FIG)
Am 7: 14 and I also took care of **s** trees.
Lk 19: 4 and climbed a **s** tree to see him,

SYMBOLIZES*
Nu 6: 9 the hair that **s** their dedication,
6: 18 off the hair that **s** their dedication.
6: 19 off the hair that **s** their dedication,
1Pe 3: 21 this water **s** baptism that now saves

SYMPATHETIC* (SYMPATHY)
1Pe 3: 8 like-minded, be **s**, love one another

SYMPATHY (SYMPATHETIC)
Ps 69: 20 I looked for **s**, but there was none,

SYNAGOGUE
Lk 4: 16 the Sabbath day he went into the **s**,
Ac 17: 2 Paul went into the **s**, and on three

TABERNACLE (TABERNACLES)
Ex 40: 34 the glory of the LORD filled the **t**.
Heb 8: 2 the true **t** set up by the Lord,
9: 11 more perfect **t** that is not made
9: 21 sprinkled with the blood both the **t**
Rev 15: 5 that is, the **t** of the covenant law—

TABERNACLES (TABERNACLE)
Lev 23: 34 the LORD's Festival of **T** begins,
Dt 16: 16 of Weeks and the Festival of **T**.
Zec 14: 16 and to celebrate the Festival of **T**.

TABLE (TABLES)
Ex 25: 23 "Make a **t** of acacia wood—
Ps 23: 5 You prepare a **t** before me

TABLES (TABLE)
Jn 2: 15 changers and overturned their **t**.
Ac 6: 2 word of God in order to wait on **t**.

TABLET (TABLETS)
Pr 3: 3 write them on the **t** of your heart.
7: 3 write them on the **t** of your heart.
Isa 30: 8 Go now, write it on a **t** for them,
Lk 1: 63 He asked for a writing **t**, and

TABLETS (TABLET)
Ex 31: 18 Mount Sinai, he gave him the two **t**
31: 18 **t** of stone inscribed by the finger
Dt 10: 5 put the **t** in the ark I had made,
2Co 3: 3 not on **t** of stone but on **t** of human

TAKE (TAKEN TAKES TAKING TOOK)
Ge 15: 7 give you this land to **t** possession
22: 17 Your descendants will **t** possession
Ex 3: 5 "**T** off your sandals, for the place
21: 23 injury, you are to **t** life for life,
22: 22 "Do not **t** advantage of the widow
Lev 10: 17 to you to **t** away the guilt
25: 14 do not **t** advantage of each other.
Nu 13: 30 go up and **t** possession of the land,
Dt 1: 8 **t** possession of the land the LORD
12: 32 do not add to it or **t** away from it.
31: 26 "**T** this Book of the Law and place
1Sa 8: 11 He will **t** your sons and make them
1Ch 17: 13 I will never **t** my love away
Job 23: 10 But he knows the way that I **t**;
Ps 2: 12 Blessed are all who **t** refuge in him.
25: 18 my distress and **t** away all my sins.
27: 14 be strong and **t** heart and wait
31: 24 Be strong and **t** heart, all you who
36: 7 People **t** refuge in the shadow
49: 17 for they will **t** nothing with them
51: 11 or **t** your Holy Spirit from me.
73: 24 afterward you will **t** me into glory.
118: 8 It is better to **t** refuge in the LORD
Pr 22: 23 for the LORD will **t** up their case
25: 9 If you **t** your neighbor to court,
Isa 62: 4 for the LORD will **t** delight in you,
Eze 3: 10 **t** to heart all the words I speak
33: 11 I **t** no pleasure in the death
Mt 10: 38 Whoever does not **t** up their cross
11: 29 **T** my yoke upon you and learn
16: 24 themselves and **t** up their cross
26: 26 to his disciples, saying, "**T** and eat;
Mk 14: 36 **T** this cup from me.
1Ti 6: 12 **T** hold of the eternal life

TAKEN (TAKE)
Ge 2: 23 for she was **t** out of man."
Lev 6: 4 they have stolen or **t** by extortion,
Nu 8: 16 I have **t** them as my own in place
19: 3 it is to be **t** outside the camp
Ecc 3: 14 added to it and nothing **t** from it.
Isa 6: 7 your guilt is **t** away and your sin
Zec 3: 4 "See, I have **t** away your sin, and I
Mt 13: 12 even what they have will be **t**
24: 40 one will be **t** and the other left.
26: 39 may this cup be **t** from me.
Mk 16: 19 *he was **t** up into heaven*
Ac 1: 9 he was **t** up before their very eyes,
1Ti 3: 16 on in the world, was **t** up in glory.

TAKES (TAKE)
1Ki 20: 11 not boast like one who **t** it off.'"
Ps 34: 8 blessed is the one who **t** refuge
Lk 6: 30 if anyone **t** what belongs to you,
Jn 1: 29 who **t** away the sin of the world!
10: 18 No one **t** it from me, but I lay it
Rev 22: 19 if anyone **t** words away from this

TAKING (TAKE)
Php 2: 7 made himself nothing by **t** the very

TALES*
1Ti 4: 7 godless myths and old wives' **t**;

TALL
1Ch 11: 23 an Egyptian who was five cubits **t**.

TAMAR
1. Wife of Judah's sons Er and Onan (Ge 38:1–10). Tricked Judah into fathering children when he refused her his third son (Ge 38:11–30).
2. Daughter of David, raped by Amnon (2Sa 13).

TAME* (TAMED)
Jas 3: 8 no human being can **t** the tongue.

TAMED* (TAME)
Jas 3: 7 creatures are being **t** and have been **t** by mankind,

TARSHISH
Jnh 1: 3 and sailed for **T** to flee

TARSUS
Ac 9: 11 ask for a man from **T** named Saul,

TASK (TASKS)
1Ch 29: 1 The **t** is great, because this palatial
Mk 13: 34 each with their assigned **t**, and tells
Ac 20: 24 complete the **t** the Lord Jesus has
1Co 3: 5 the Lord has assigned to each his **t**.
2Co 2: 16 And who is equal to such a **t**?
1Ti 3: 1 to be an overseer desires a noble **t**.

TASKS (TASK)
Pr 31: 17 her arms are strong for her **t**.

TASTE (TASTED TASTY)
Ps 34: 8 **T** and see that the LORD is good;
119:103 How sweet are your words to my **t**,
Pr 24: 13 from the comb is sweet to your **t**.
SS 2: 3 and his fruit is sweet to my **t**.
Col 2: 21 Do not **t**! Do not touch!"?
Heb 2: 9 God he might **t** death for everyone.

TASTED (TASTE)
Eze 3: 3 it **t** as sweet as honey in my mouth.
1Pe 2: 3 you have **t** that the Lord is good.
Rev 10: 10 It **t** as sweet as honey in my mouth,

TASTY (TASTE)
Ge 27: 4 Prepare me the kind of **t** food I like

TATTOO*
Lev 19: 28 dead or put **t** marks on yourselves.

TAUGHT (TEACH)
2Ki 17: 28 **t** them how to worship the LORD.
2Ch 17: 9 They **t** throughout Judah,
Ps 119:102 laws, for you yourself have **t** me.
Pr 4: 4 Then he **t** me, and he said to me,
31: 1 utterance his mother **t** him.
Isa 29: 13 human rules they have been **t**.
Mt 7: 29 because he **t** as one who had
Ac 20: 20 to you but have **t** you publicly
1Co 2: 13 but in words **t** by the Spirit,
Gal 1: 12 it from any man, nor was I **t** it;
1Ti 1: 20 to Satan to be **t** not to blaspheme.
1Jn 2: 27 just as it has **t** you, remain in him.

TAX (TAXES)
Mt 11: 19 a friend of **t** collectors and sinners.'
17: 24 your teacher pay the temple **t**?"
22: 17 to pay the imperial **t** to Caesar

TAXES (TAX)
Ro 13: 7 you owe them: If you owe **t**, pay **t**;

TEACH (SPIRIT-TAUGHT TAUGHT TEACHER TEACHERS TEACHES TEACHING TEACHINGS)
Ex 4: 12 speak and will **t** you what to say."
18: 20 **T** them his decrees and
33: 13 **t** me your ways so I may know you
Lev 10: 11 and so you can **t** the Israelites all
Dt 4: 9 **T** them to your children and to
6: 1 your God directed me to **t** you
8: 3 to **t** you that man does not live
11: 19 **T** them to your children,
1Sa 12: 23 I will **t** you the way that is good
1Ki 8: 36 **T** them the right way to live,
Job 12: 7 and they will **t** you, or the birds
Ps 32: 8 **t** you in the way you should go;
34: 11 I will **t** you the fear of the LORD.
51: 13 I will **t** transgressors your ways,

Ps 78: 5 our ancestors to **t** their children,
90: 12 **T** us to number our days, that we
119: 33 **T** me, LORD, the way of your
143: 10 **T** me to do your will, for you are
Pr 9: 9 **t** the righteous and they will add
Jer 31: 34 longer will they **t** their neighbor,
Mic 4: 2 He will **t** us his ways, so that we
Lk 11: 1 "Lord, **t** us to pray, just as John
12: 12 for the Holy Spirit will **t** you
Jn 14: 26 **t** you all things and will remind
Ro 2: 21 then, who **t** others, do you not **t**
15: 4 in the past was written to **t** us,
1Ti 2: 12 I do not permit a woman to **t**
3: 2 respectable, hospitable, able to **t**,
2Ti 2: 2 will also be qualified to **t** others.
2: 24 to everyone, able to **t**, not resentful.
Titus 2: 1 **t** what is appropriate to sound
2: 15 then, are the things you should **t**.
Heb 8: 11 longer will they **t** their neighbor,
Jas 3: 1 that we who **t** will be judged more
1Jn 2: 27 you do not need anyone to **t** you.

TEACHER (TEACH)
Ecc 1: 1 The words of the **T**, son of David,
Mt 10: 24 "The student is not above the **t**,
13: 52 "Therefore every **t** of the law who
23: 8 for you have one **T**, and you are all
Lk 6: 40 The student is not above the **t**,
Jn 3: 2 that you are a **t** who has come
13: 14 Lord and **T**, have washed your
1Co 1: 20 Where is the **t** of the law?

TEACHERS (TEACH)
Ps 119: 99 I have more insight than all my **t**,
Pr 5: 13 I would not obey my **t** or turn my
Lk 20: 46 "Beware of the **t** of the law.
1Co 12: 28 prophets, third **t**, then miracles,
Eph 4: 11 the evangelists, the pastors and **t**,
2Ti 4: 3 around them a great number of **t**
Heb 5: 12 by this time you ought to be **t**,
Jas 3: 1 Not many of you should become **t**,
2Pe 2: 1 as there will be false **t** among you.

TEACHES (TEACH)
Ps 25: 9 in what is right and **t** them his way.
94: 10 Does he who **t** mankind lack
Isa 48: 17 who **t** you what is best for you,
Mt 5: 19 and **t** these commands will be
1Ti 6: 3 If anyone **t** otherwise and does not
Titus 2: 12 It **t** us to say "No" to ungodliness
1Jn 2: 27 But as his anointing **t** you about all

TEACHING (TEACH)
Ezr 7: 10 to **t** its decrees and laws in Israel.
Pr 1: 8 and do not forsake your mother's **t**.
3: 1 son, do not forget my **t**, but keep
6: 23 command is a lamp, this **t** is a light,
Mt 28: 20 **t** them to obey everything I have
Lk 4: 15 He was **t** in their synagogues,
Jn 7: 17 out whether my **t** comes from God
8: 31 "If you hold to my **t**, you are really
14: 23 who loves me will obey my **t**.
Ac 2: 42 themselves to the apostles' **t**
Ro 12: 7 if it is **t**, then teach;
Eph 4: 14 there by every wind of **t**
2Th 3: 6 live according to the **t** you received
1Ti 4: 13 of Scripture, to preaching and to **t**.
5: 17 whose work is preaching and **t**.
6: 3 Lord Jesus Christ and to godly **t**,
2Ti 3: 16 is God-breathed and is useful for **t**,
Titus 1: 11 by **t** things they ought not to teach
2: 7 In your **t** show integrity,
Heb 5: 13 with the **t** about righteousness.
2Jn : 9 in the **t** has both the Father

TEACHINGS (TEACH)
Pr 7: 2 my **t** as the apple of your eye.
2Th 2: 15 hold fast to the **t** we passed
Heb 6: 1 us move beyond the elementary **t**

TEAR (TEARS)
Rev 7: 17 God will wipe away every **t**
21: 4 'He will wipe every **t** from their

TEARING
2Co 10: 8 you up rather than **t** you down,

TEARS (TEAR)
Ps 126: 5 Those who sow with **t** will reap
Isa 25: 8 LORD will wipe away the **t**
Jer 31: 16 weeping and your eyes from **t**,
50: 4 Judah together will go in **t** to seek
Lk 7: 38 she began to wet his feet with her **t**.
2Co 2: 4 anguish of heart and with many **t**,
Php 3: 18 and now tell you again even with **t**,

TEETH (TOOTH)
Job 19: 20 escaped only by the skin of my **t**.
Ps 35: 16 they gnashed their **t** at me.
Jer 31: 29 and the children's **t** are set on edge.'
Mt 8: 12 will be weeping and gnashing of **t**."

TEMPER* (EVEN-TEMPERED HOT-TEMPERED QUICK-TEMPERED)
1Sa 20: 7 if he loses his **t**, you can be sure

TEMPERANCE See SELF-CONTROL

TEMPERATE*
1Ti 3: 2 reproach, faithful to his wife, **t**,
3: 11 not malicious talkers but **t**
Titus 2: 2 Teach the older men to be **t**,

TEMPEST
Ps 50: 3 him, and around him a **t** rages.
55: 8 shelter, far from the **t** and storm."

TEMPLE (TEMPLES)
1Ki 6: 1 began to build the **t** of the LORD.
6: 38 the **t** was finished in all its details
8: 10 the cloud filled the **t** of the LORD.
8: 27 How much less this **t** I have built!
2Ch 36: 19 They set fire to God's **t** and broke
36: 23 appointed me to build a **t** for him
Ezr 6: 14 finished building the **t** according
Ps 27: 4 the LORD and to seek him in his **t**.
Isa 6: 1 the train of his robe filled the **t**.
Eze 10: 4 moved to the threshold of the **t**.
43: 4 LORD entered the **t** through
Hab 2: 20 The LORD is in his holy **t**;
Mt 12: 6 greater than the **t** is here.
26: 61 'I am able to destroy the **t** of God
27: 51 the curtain of the **t** was torn
Lk 21: 5 about how the **t** was adorned
Jn 2: 14 the **t** courts he found people selling
1Co 3: 16 that you yourselves are God's **t**
2Co 6: 16 For we are the **t** of the living God.
Rev 21: 22 Almighty and the Lamb are its **t**.

TEMPLES (TEMPLE)
Ac 17: 24 does not live in **t** built by human
1Co 6: 19 your bodies are **t** of the Holy Spirit,

TEMPORARY
2Co 4: 18 since what is seen is **t**, but what is

TEMPT* (TEMPTATION TEMPTED TEMPTER TEMPTING)
1Co 7: 5 Satan will not **t** you because of
Jas 1: 13 by evil, nor does he **t** anyone;

TEMPTATION* (TEMPT)
Mt 6: 13 lead us not into **t**, but deliver us
26: 41 pray so that you will not fall into **t**.
Mk 14: 38 pray so that you will not fall into **t**.
Lk 11: 4 And lead us not into **t**.'"
22: 40 "Pray that you will not fall into **t**."
22: 46 pray so that you will not fall into **t**."
1Co 10: 13 No **t** has overtaken you except
1Ti 6: 9 who want to get rich fall into **t**

TEMPTED* (TEMPT)
Mt 4: 1 the wilderness to be **t** by the devil.
Mk 1: 13 forty days, being **t** by Satan.
Lk 4: 2 for forty days he was **t** by the devil.
1Co 10: 13 not let you be **t** beyond what you
10: 13 But when you are **t**, he will
Gal 6: 1 yourselves, or you also may be **t**.
1Th 3: 5 in some way the tempter had **t** you
Heb 2: 18 he himself suffered when he was **t**,
2: 18 able to help those who are being **t**.
4: 15 but we have one who has been **t**
Jas 1: 13 When **t**, no one should say, "God
1: 13 For God cannot be **t** by evil,
1: 14 but each person is **t** when they are

TEMPTER* (TEMPT)
Mt 4: 3 The **t** came to him and said, "If you
1Th 3: 5 in some way the **t** had tempted you

TEMPTING* (TEMPT)
Lk 4: 13 the devil had finished all this **t**,
Jas 1: 13 no one should say, "God is **t** me."

TEN (TENTH TITHE TITHES)
Ex 34: 28 the **T** Commandments.
Lev 26: 8 of you will chase **t** thousand,
Dt 4: 13 covenant, the **T** Commandments,
10: 4 the **T** Commandments he had
Ps 91: 7 side, **t** thousand at your right hand,
Da 7: 24 The **t** horns are **t** kings who will
Mt 25: 1 will be like **t** virgins who took their
25: 28 give it to the one who has **t** bags.
Lk 15: 8 suppose a woman has **t** silver coins
Rev 12: 3 with seven heads and **t** horns

TENANTS
Mt 21: 34 servants to the **t** to collect his fruit.

TEND
Jer 23: 2 to the shepherds who **t** my people:
Eze 34: 14 I will **t** them in a good pasture,

TENDERNESS*
Isa 63: 15 **t** and compassion are withheld
Php 2: 1 the Spirit, if any **t** and compassion,

TENT (TENTMAKER TENTS)
Ex 27: 21 In the **t** of meeting,
40: 2 up the tabernacle, the **t** of meeting,
Isa 54: 2 "Enlarge the place of your **t**,
2Co 5: 1 that if the earthly **t** we live in is
2Pe 1: 13 long as I live in the **t** of this body,

TENTH (TEN)
Ge 14: 20 Abram gave him a **t** of everything.
Nu 18: 26 you must present a **t** of that tithe as
Dt 14: 22 Be sure to set aside a **t** of all
1Sa 8: 15 He will take a **t** of your grain
Lk 11: 42 because you give God a **t** of your
18: 12 a week and give a **t** of all I get.'
Heb 7: 4 patriarch Abraham gave him a **t**

TENTMAKER* (TENT)
Ac 18: 3 because he was a **t** as they were,

TENTS (TENT)
Ge 13: 12 and pitched his **t** near Sodom.
Ps 84: 10 than dwell in the **t** of the wicked.

TERAH
Ge 11: 31 **T** took his son Abram, his

TERRIBLE (TERROR)
2Ti 3: 1 There will be **t** times in the last

TERRIFIED (TERROR)
Dt 7: 21 Do not be **t** by them, for the LORD
20: 3 do not panic or be **t** by them.
Ps 90: 7 anger and **t** by your indignation.
Mt 14: 26 walking on the lake, they were **t**.
17: 6 they fell facedown to the ground, **t**.
27: 54 they were **t**, and exclaimed,
Mk 4: 41 They were **t** and asked each other,

TERRIFYING (TERROR)
Heb 12: 21 The sight was so **t** that Moses said,

TERRITORY
2Co 10: 16 already done in someone else's **t**.

TERROR (TERRIBLE TERRIFIED TERRIFYING)
Dt 2: 25 very day I will begin to put the **t**
28: 67 of the **t** that will fill your hearts
Job 9: 34 his **t** would frighten me no more.
Ps 91: 5 You will not fear the **t** of night,
Pr 21: 15 to the righteous but **t** to evildoers.
Isa 13: 8 **T** will seize them, pain and anguish
24: 17 **T** and pit and snare await you,
51: 13 live in constant **t** every day because
54: 14 **T** will be far removed; it will not
Lk 21: 26 People will faint from **t**,
Ro 13: 3 rulers hold no **t** for those who do

TEST (TESTED TESTING TESTS)
Dt 6: 16 your God to the **t** as you did
Jdg 3: 1 to **t** all those Israelites who had not
1Ki 10: 1 she came to **t** Solomon with hard
1Ch 29: 17 that you **t** the heart and are pleased
Ps 26: 2 **T** me, LORD, and try me,
78: 18 to the **t** by demanding the food
106: 14 wilderness they put God to the **t**.
139: 23 **t** me and know my anxious
Jer 11: 20 judge righteously and **t** the heart
Lk 4: 12 put the Lord your God to the **t**.'"
Ac 5: 9 could you conspire to **t** the Spirit
Ro 12: 2 you will be able to **t** and approve
1Co 3: 13 the fire will **t** the quality of each
10: 9 We should not **t** Christ, as some
2Co 13: 5 you are in the faith; **t** yourselves.
1Th 5: 21 but **t** them all; hold on to what is
Jas 1: 12 having stood the **t**, that person will
1Pe 4: 12 that has come on you to **t** you,
1Jn 4: 1 **t** the spirits to see whether they are

TESTED (TEST)
Ge 22: 1 Some time later God **t** Abraham.
Job 23: 10 when he has **t** me, I will come forth
34: 36 that Job might be **t** to the utmost
Ps 66: 10 For you, God, **t** us; you refined us
Pr 27: 21 but people are **t** by their praise.
Isa 28: 16 I lay a stone in Zion, a **t** stone,
48: 10 I have **t** you in the furnace
1Ti 3: 10 They must first be **t**;
Heb 11: 17 when God **t** him, offered Isaac as

TESTIFIES (TESTIFY)
Jn 5: 32 There is another who **t** in my favor,
Ro 8: 16 The Spirit himself **t** with our spirit

TESTIFY (TESTIFIES TESTIMONY)
Pr 24: 28 Do not **t** against your neighbor
Jn 1: 7 came as a witness to **t** concerning
1: 34 I **t** that this is God's Chosen One."
5: 39 These are the very Scriptures that **t**
7: 7 hates me because I **t** that its works
15: 26 the Father—he will **t** about me.
Ac 4: 33 power the apostles continued to **t**
10: 43 All the prophets **t** about him
1Jn 4: 14 **t** that the Father has sent his Son
5: 7 For there are three that **t**:

TESTIMONY (TESTIFY)
Ex 20: 16 shall not give false **t** against your
Nu 35: 30 only on the **t** of witnesses.
Dt 19: 18 a liar, giving false **t** against a fellow
Isa 8: 20 instruction and the **t** of warning.
Mt 15: 19 immorality, theft, false **t**, slander.
24: 14 whole world as a **t** to all nations,
Lk 18: 20 you shall not give false **t**,
Jn 2: 25 He did not need any **t**
21: 24 We know that his **t** is true.
2Ti 1: 8 be ashamed of the **t** about our Lord
1Jn 5: 9 We accept human **t**, but God's **t** is
Rev 12: 11 Lamb and by the word of their **t**;

TESTING (TEST)
Lk 8: 13 but in the time of **t** they fall away.
Heb 3: 8 rebellion, during the time of **t**
Jas 1: 3 that the **t** of your faith produces

TESTS (TEST)
Pr 17: 3 for gold, but the LORD **t** the heart.
1Th 2: 4 people but God, who **t** our hearts.

THADDAEUS*
Apostle (Mt 10:3; Mk 3:18); probably also known as Judas son of James (Lk 6:16; Ac 1:13).

THANK (THANKFUL THANKFULNESS THANKS THANKSGIVING)
Php 1: 3 I **t** my God every time I remember
1Th 3: 9 How can we **t** God enough for you

THANKFUL* (THANK)
Col 3: 15 you were called to peace. And be **t**.
4: 2 to prayer, being watchful and **t**.
Heb 12: 28 let us be **t**, and so worship God

THANKFULNESS* (THANK)
Lev 7: 12 they offer it as an expression of **t**,
1Co 10: 30 If I take part in the meal with **t**,
Col 2: 7 taught, and overflowing with **t**.

THANKS (THANK)
Ne 12: 31 assigned two large choirs to give **t**.
Ps 7: 17 will give **t** to the LORD because
9: 1 give **t** to you, LORD, with all
35: 18 I will give you **t** in the great
100: 4 give **t** to him and praise his name.
107: 1 Give **t** to the LORD, for he is
136: 1 Give **t** to the LORD, for he is
Ro 1: 21 glorified him as God nor gave **t**
1Co 11: 24 when he had given **t**, he broke it
15: 57 But **t** be to God! He gives us
2Co 2: 14 But **t** be to God, who always leads
9: 15 **T** be to God for his indescribable
1Th 5: 18 give **t** in all circumstances;
Rev 4: 9 and **t** to him who sits on the throne

THANKSGIVING (THANK)
Ps 95: 2 Let us come before him with **t**
100: 4 Enter his gates with **t** and his
1Co 10: 16 Is not the cup of **t** for which we
Php 4: 6 **t**, present your requests to God.
1Ti 4: 3 to be received with **t** by those who

THEFT (THIEF)
Mt 15: 19 adultery, sexual immorality, **t**,

THEFTS* (THIEF)
Rev 9: 21 their sexual immorality or their **t**.

THEME*
Ps 22: 25 From you comes the **t** of my praise
45: 1 by a noble **t** as I recite my verses
119: 54 Your decrees are the **t** of my song

THIEF (THEFT THEFTS THIEVES)
Pr 6: 30 do not despise a **t** if he steals
Lk 12: 39 at what hour the **t** was coming,
1Th 5: 2 of the Lord will come like a **t**
1Pe 4: 15 it should not be as a murderer or **t**
Rev 16: 15 "Look, I come like a **t**!

THIEVES (THIEF)
Mt 6: 19 and where **t** break in and steal.
Jn 10: 8 All who have come before me are **t**
1Co 6: 10 nor **t** nor the greedy nor drunkards

THINK (THINKING THOUGHT THOUGHTS)
Ps 63: 6 I **t** of you through the watches
Isa 44: 19 No one stops to **t**, no one has
Mt 22: 42 "What do you **t** about the Messiah?
Ro 12: 3 Do not **t** of yourself more highly
Php 4: 8 **t** about such things.

THINKING (THINK)
Pr 23: 7 of person who is always **t**
1Co 14: 20 be infants, but in your **t** be adults.
2Pe 3: 1 to stimulate you to wholesome **t**.

THIRST (THIRSTS THIRSTY)
Ps 69: 21 food and gave me vinegar for my **t**.
Mt 5: 6 hunger and **t** for righteousness,
Jn 4: 14 the water I give them will never **t**.
2Co 11: 27 I have known hunger and **t** and
Rev 7: 16 never again will they **t**.

THIRSTS* (THIRST)
Ps 42: 2 My soul **t** for God, for the living

THIRSTY (THIRST)
Ps 107: 9 for he satisfies the **t** and fills
Pr 25: 21 if he is **t**, give him water to drink.
Isa 55: 1 all you who are **t**,
Mt 25: 35 I was **t** and you gave me something
Jn 7: 37 "Let anyone who is **t** come to me
Ro 12: 20 if he is **t**, give him something
Rev 21: 6 the **t** I will give water without cost
22: 17 Let the one who is **t** come;

THOMAS*
Apostle (Mt 10:3; Mk 3:18; Lk 6:15; Jn 11:16; 14:5; 21:2; Ac 1:13). Doubted resurrection (Jn 20:24–28).

THORN (THORNBUSHES THORNS)
2Co 12: 7 I was given a **t** in my flesh,

THORNBUSHES (THORN)
Lk 6: 44 People do not pick figs from **t**,

THORNS (THORN)
Ge 3: 18 It will produce **t** and thistles for
Nu 33: 55 in your eyes and **t** in your sides.
Mt 13: 7 seed fell among **t**, which grew
27: 29 twisted together a crown of **t** and
Heb 6: 8 land that produces **t** and thistles is

THOUGHT (THINK)
1Ch 28: 9 every desire and every **t**.
Pr 4: 26 Give careful **t** to the paths for your
14: 15 the prudent give **t** to their steps.
21: 29 but the upright give **t** to their ways.
1Co 13: 11 I talked like a child, I **t** like a child,

THOUGHTS (THINK)
Ps 139: 23 test me and know my anxious **t**.
Isa 55: 8 "For my **t** are not your **t**,
Mt 15: 19 For out of the heart come evil **t**—
1Co 2: 11 knows a person's **t** except their own
Heb 4: 12 it judges the **t** and attitudes

THREATENED
Isa 38: 14 I am being **t**; Lord, come to my

THREE
Ge 6: 10 Noah had **t** sons: Shem,
Ex 23: 14 "**T** times a year you are to celebrate
Dt 19: 15 the testimony of two or **t** witnesses.
2Sa 23: 8 a Tahkemonite, was chief of the **T**;
Pr 30: 15 "There are **t** things that are never
30: 18 "There are **t** things that are too
30: 21 "Under **t** things the earth trembles,
30: 29 "There are **t** things that are stately
Ecc 4: 12 of **t** strands is not quickly broken.
Da 3: 24 "Weren't there **t** men that we tied
Am 1: 3 "For **t** sins of Damascus,
Jnh 1: 17 was in the belly of the fish **t** days
Mt 12: 40 as Jonah was **t** days and **t** nights
12: 40 so the Son of Man will be **t** days
17: 4 If you wish, I will put up **t** shelters
18: 20 where two or **t** gather in my name,
26: 34 you will disown me **t** times."
26: 75 you will disown me **t** times."
27: 63 said, 'After **t** days I will rise again.'
Mk 8: 31 be killed and after **t** days rise again.
9: 5 Let us put up **t** shelters—
14: 30 yourself will disown me **t** times."
Jn 2: 19 and I will raise it again in **t** days."
1Co 13: 13 And now these **t** remain:
14: 27 or at the most **t**—should speak,
2Co 13: 1 testimony of two or **t** witnesses."
1Jn 5: 7 For there are **t** that testify:

THRESHES* (THRESHING)
1Co 9: 10 whoever plows and **t** should be

THRESHING (THRESHES)
Ru 3: 6 So she went down to the **t** floor
2Sa 24: 18 altar to the LORD on the **t** floor
Lk 3: 17 in his hand to clear his **t** floor

THREW (THROW)
Da 6: 16 and **t** him into the lions' den.
Jnh 1: 15 took Jonah and **t** him overboard,

THRIVE
Pr 29: 2 When the righteous **t**, the people

THROAT (THROATS)
Ps 5: 9 Their **t** is an open grave;
Pr 23: 2 put a knife to your **t** if you are

THROATS (THROAT)
Ro 3: 13 "Their **t** are open graves;

THROB*
Isa 60: 5 your heart will **t** and swell with joy;

THRONE (ENTHRONED ENTHRONES THRONES)
2Sa 7: 16 your **t** will be established
1Ch 17: 12 and I will establish his **t** forever.
Ps 11: 4 the LORD is on his heavenly **t**.
45: 6 Your **t**, O God, will last for ever
47: 8 God is seated on his holy **t**.
89: 14 justice are the foundation of your **t**;
Isa 6: 1 high and exalted, seated on a **t**;
66: 1 "Heaven is my **t**, and the earth is
Eze 28: 2 I sit on the **t** of a god in the heart
Da 7: 9 His **t** was flaming with fire, and its
Mt 19: 28 Son of Man sits on his glorious **t**,
Ac 7: 49 "'Heaven is my **t**, and the earth is
Heb 1: 8 the Son he says, "Your **t**, O God,
4: 16 then approach God's **t** of grace
12: 2 at the right hand of the **t** of God.
Rev 3: 21 the right to sit with me on my **t**,
3: 21 sat down with my Father on his **t**.
4: 2 there before me was a **t** in heaven
4: 10 They lay their crowns before the **t**
20: 11 I saw a great white **t** and him who
22: 3 The **t** of God and of the Lamb will

THRONES (THRONE)
Mt 19: 28 me will also sit on twelve **t**,
Rev 4: 4 throne were twenty-four other **t**,

THROW (THREW)
Jn 8: 7 *the first to **t** a stone at her."*
Heb 10: 35 So do not **t** away your confidence;
12: 1 let us **t** off everything that hinders

THUNDER (THUNDERS)
Ps 93: 4 Mightier than the **t** of the great
Mk 3: 17 which means "sons of **t**"),

THUNDERS (THUNDER)
Job 37: 5 God's voice **t** in marvelous ways;
Ps 29: 3 the God of glory **t**, the LORD **t**
Rev 10: 3 the voices of the seven **t** spoke.

THWART* (THWARTED)
Isa 14: 27 has purposed, and who can **t** him?

THWARTED (THWART)
Job 42: 2 no purpose of yours can be **t**.

THYATIRA
Rev 2: 18 the angel of the church in **T** write:

TIBNI
King of Israel (1Ki 16:21–22).

TIDINGS*
Isa 52: 7 who bring good **t**, who proclaim

TIES
Hos 11: 4 of human kindness, with **t** of love.
Mt 12: 29 unless he first **t** up the strong man?

TIGHT*
Jas 1: 26 yet do not keep a **t** rein on their

TIGHTFISTED*
Dt 15: 7 not be hardhearted or **t** toward

TIMBREL
Ps 150: 4 praise him with **t** and dancing,

TIME (TIMES)
Est 4: 14 royal position for such a **t** as this?"
Ecc 3: 1 There is a **t** for everything,
8: 5 wise heart will know the proper **t**
Da 7: 25 hands for a **t**, times and half a **t**.
12: 7 be for a **t**, times and half a **t**.
Hos 10: 12 for it is **t** to seek the LORD,
Ro 9: 9 "At the appointed **t** I will return,
13: 11 this, understanding the present **t**:
1Co 7: 29 and sisters, is that the **t** is short.
2Co 6: 2 you, now is the **t** of God's favor,
2Ti 1: 9 Jesus before the beginning of **t**,
Titus 1: 2 before the beginning of **t**,
Heb 9: 28 and he will appear a second **t**,
10: 12 had offered for all **t** one sacrifice
1Pe 4: 17 For it is **t** for judgment to begin

TIMES (TIME)
Ps 9: 9 a stronghold in **t** of trouble.
31: 15 My **t** are in your hands;
62: 8 Trust in him at all **t**, you people;
Pr 17: 17 A friend loves at all **t**, and
Isa 46: 10 ancient **t**, what is still to come.
Am 5: 13 in such **t**, for the **t** are evil.
Mt 16: 3 cannot interpret the signs of the **t**.
18: 21 how many **t** shall I forgive my
18: 21 sins against me? Up to seven **t**?"
Ac 1: 7 "It is not for you to know the **t**
Rev 12: 14 for a time, **t** and half a time,

TIMID
2Ti 1: 7 God gave us does not make us **t**,

TIMOTHY
Believer from Lystra (Ac 16:1). Joined Paul on second missionary journey (Ac 16–20). Sent to settle problems at Corinth (1Co 4:17; 16:10). Led church at Ephesus (1Ti 1:3). Co-writer with Paul (1Th 1:1; 2Th 1:1; Phm 1).

TIP
Job 33: 2 words are on the **t** of my tongue.

TIRE (TIRED)
2Th 3: 13 never **t** of doing what is good.

TIRED (TIRE)
Ex 17: 12 When Moses' hands grew **t**,
Isa 40: 28 He will not grow **t** or weary, and

TITHE (TEN)
Lev 27: 30 "'A **t** of everything
Dt 12: 17 your own towns the **t** of your grain
Mal 3: 10 Bring the whole **t**

TITHES (TEN)
Nu 18: 21 the Levites all the **t** in Israel as
Mal 3: 8 "In **t** and offerings.

TITUS*
Gentile co-worker of Paul (Gal 2:1–3; 2Ti 4:10); sent to Corinth (2Co 2:13; 7–8; 12:18), Crete (Titus 1:4–5).

TODAY
Ps 2: 7 **t** I have become your father.
95: 7 **T**, if only you would hear his voice,
Mt 6: 11 Give us **t** our daily bread.
Lk 2: 11 **T** in the town of David a Savior has
23: 43 **t** you will be with me in paradise."
Ac 13: 33 **t** I have become your father.'
Heb 1: 5 **t** I have become your Father"?
3: 7 "**T**, if you hear his voice,
3: 13 as long as it is called "**T**,"
5: 5 **t** I have become your Father."
13: 8 Christ is the same yesterday and **t**

TOIL (TOILED TOILING)
Ge 3: 17 through painful **t** you will eat food
Ecc 5: 19 their lot and be happy in their **t**—

TOILED (TOIL)
2Co 11: 27 I have labored and **t** and have often

TOILING (TOIL)
2Th 3: 8 **t** so that we would not be a burden

TOLERATE
Hab 1: 13 you cannot **t** wrongdoing.
Rev 2: 2 that you cannot **t** wicked people,

TOMB
Mt 27: 65 make the **t** as secure as you know
Lk 24: 2 the stone rolled away from the **t**,

TOMORROW
Pr 27: 1 Do not boast about **t**, for you do
Isa 22: 13 drink," you say, "for **t** we die!"
Mt 6: 34 Therefore do not worry about **t**, for **t** will worry
1Co 15: 32 "Let us eat and drink, for **t** we die."
Jas 4: 13 "Today or **t** we will go to this

TONGUE (TONGUES)
Ex 4: 10 I am slow of speech and **t**."
Job 33: 2 my words are on the tip of my **t**.
Ps 34: 13 keep your **t** from evil and your lips
39: 1 my ways and keep my **t** from sin;
51: 14 Savior, and my **t** will sing of your
52: 4 harmful word, you deceitful **t**!
71: 24 My **t** will tell of your righteous acts
119:172 May my **t** sing of your word, for all
137: 6 my **t** cling to the roof of my mouth
139: 4 Before a word is on my **t** you,
Pr 6: 17 a lying **t**, hands that shed innocent
12: 18 but the **t** of the wise brings healing.
15: 4 The soothing **t** is a tree of life,
17: 20 one whose **t** is perverse falls
25: 15 and a gentle **t** can break a bone.
26: 28 A lying **t** hates those it hurts,
28: 23 than one who has a flattering **t**.
31: 26 and faithful instruction is on her **t**.
SS 4: 11 milk and honey are under your **t**.
Isa 32: 4 and the stammering **t** will be fluent
45: 23 by me every **t** will swear.
50: 4 has given me a well-instructed **t**,
59: 3 and your **t** mutters wicked things.
Lk 16: 24 his finger in water and cool my **t**,
Ro 14: 11 every **t** will acknowledge God.'"
1Co 14: 2 who speaks in a **t** does not speak
14: 4 speaks in a **t** edifies themselves,
14: 9 intelligible words with your **t**,
14: 13 one who speaks in a **t** should pray
14: 19 than ten thousand words in a **t**.
14: 26 revelation, a **t** or an interpretation.
14: 27 If anyone speaks in a **t**, two—
Php 2: 11 and every **t** acknowledge that Jesus
Jas 3: 5 the **t** is a small part of the body,
3: 8 no human being can tame the **t**.

TONGUES (TONGUE)
Ps 5: 9 with their **t** they tell lies.
12: 4 who say, "By our **t** we will prevail;
37: 30 and their **t** speak what is just.
126: 2 laughter, our **t** with songs of joy.
Pr 10: 19 words, but the prudent hold their **t**.
21: 23 and their **t** keep themselves
Isa 28: 11 strange **t** God will speak to this
Jer 23: 31 the prophets who wag their own **t**
Mk 16: 17 *they will speak in new **t**;*
Ac 2: 3 saw what seemed to be **t** of fire
2: 4 other **t** as the Spirit enabled them.
10: 46 For they heard them speaking in **t**
19: 6 they spoke in **t** and prophesied.
Ro 3: 13 their **t** practice deceit."
1Co 12: 10 speaking in different kinds of **t**,
12: 10 another the interpretation of **t**.
12: 28 and of different kinds of **t**.
12: 30 Do all speak in **t**? Do all interpret?
13: 1 If I speak in the **t** of men
13: 8 where there are **t**, they will be
14: 5 than the one who speaks in **t**,
14: 18 I speak in **t** more than all of you.
14: 21 "With other **t** and through the lips
14: 39 and do not forbid speaking in **t**.
Jas 1: 26 rein on their **t** deceive themselves,

TOOK (TAKE)
Ps 68: 18 on high, you **t** many captives;
Isa 53: 4 Surely he **t** up our pain and bore
Mt 8: 17 "He **t** up our infirmities and bore
26: 26 they were eating, Jesus **t** bread,
26: 27 Then he **t** a cup, and when he had
1Co 11: 23 the night he was betrayed, **t** bread,
11: 25 after supper he **t** the cup, saying,
Eph 4: 8 he **t** many captives and gave gifts
Php 3: 12 which Christ Jesus **t** hold of me.

TOOTH (TEETH)
Ex 21: 24 eye for eye, **t** for **t**, hand for hand,
Mt 5: 38 was said, 'Eye for eye, and **t** for **t**.'

TOP
Dt 28: 13 you will always be at the **t**,
Isa 1: 6 foot to the **t** of your head there is
Mt 27: 51 was torn in two from **t** to bottom.

TORMENT (TORMENTED TORMENTORS)
Lk 16: 28 not also come to this place of **t**.'
2Co 12: 7 a messenger of Satan, to **t** me.

TORMENTED (TORMENT)
Rev 20: 10 They will be **t** day and night

TORMENTORS (TORMENT)
Ps 137: 3 our **t** demanded songs of joy;

TORN
Gal 4: 15 you would have **t** out your eyes
Php 1: 23 I am **t** between the two: I desire

TORTURED*
Mt 18: 34 him over to the jailers to be **t**,
Heb 11: 35 There were others who were **t**,

TOSSED (TOSSING)
Eph 4: 14 **t** back and forth by the waves,
Jas 1: 6 the sea, blown and **t** by the wind.

TOSSING (TOSSED)
Isa 57: 20 But the wicked are like the **t** sea,

TOUCH (TOUCHED TOUCHES)
Ge 3: 3 and you must not **t** it, or you will
Ex 19: 12 the mountain or **t** the foot of it.
Ps 105: 15 "Do not **t** my anointed ones;
Mt 9: 21 "If I only **t** his cloak, I will be
Lk 24: 39 **T** me and see; a ghost does not
2Co 6: 17 **T** no unclean thing, and I will
Col 2: 21 Do not taste! Do not **t**!"?

TOUCHED (TOUCH)
1Sa 10: 26 men whose hearts God had **t**.
Isa 6: 7 With it he **t** my mouth and said,
Mt 14: 36 cloak, and all who **t** it were healed.
Lk 8: 45 "Who **t** me?" Jesus asked.
1Jn 1: 1 looked at and our hands have **t**—

TOUCHES (TOUCH)
Ex 19: 12 Whoever **t** the mountain is to be
Zec 2: 8 for whoever **t** you **t** the apple of his

TOWER
Ge 11: 4 a **t** that reaches to the heavens,
Pr 18: 10 name of the LORD is a fortified **t**;

TOWN (TOWNS)
Mt 2: 23 and lived in a **t** called Nazareth.
5: 14 **t** built on a hill cannot be hidden.
13: 57 without honor except in his own **t**

TOWNS (TOWN)
Nu 35: 2 to give the Levites **t** to live in
35: 15 These six **t** will be a place of refuge
Jer 11: 13 have as many gods as you have **t**;
Mt 9: 35 Jesus went through all the **t**

TRACING*
Ro 11: 33 and his paths beyond **t** out!

TRACK
Job 14: 16 my steps but not keep **t** of my sin.

TRADERS (TRADING)
1Ti 1: 10 for slave **t** and liars and perjurers—

TRADING (TRADERS)
1Ki 10: 22 The king had a fleet of **t** ships at
Pr 31: 18 She sees that her **t** is profitable,

TRADITION (TRADITIONS)
Mt 15: 2 "Why do your disciples break the **t**
15: 6 word of God for the sake of your **t**.
Mk 7: 13 your **t** that you have handed down.
Col 2: 8 which depends on human **t**

TRADITIONS (TRADITION)
Mk 7: 8 and are holding on to human **t**."
Gal 1: 14 zealous for the **t** of my fathers.

TRAIL
1Ti 5: 24 the sins of others **t** behind them.

TRAIN* (TRAINED TRAINING)
Isa 2: 4 nor will they **t** for war anymore.
6: 1 the **t** of his robe filled the temple.
Mic 4: 3 nor will they **t** for war anymore.
1Ti 4: 7 rather, **t** yourself to be godly.

TRAINED (TRAIN)
Lk 6: 40 everyone who is fully **t** will be like
Ac 22: 3 was thoroughly **t** in the law of our
Heb 5: 14 by constant use have **t** themselves
12: 11 for those who have been **t** by it.

TRAINING* (TRAIN)
1Co 9: 25 in the games goes into strict **t**.
Eph 6: 4 instead, bring them up in the **t**
1Ti 4: 8 For physical **t** is of some value,
2Ti 3: 16 correcting and **t** in righteousness,

TRAITOR (TRAITORS)
Lk 6: 16 and Judas Iscariot, who became a **t**.
Jn 18: 5 Judas the **t** was standing there

TRAITORS (TRAITOR)
Ps 59: 5 show no mercy to wicked **t**.

TRAMPLE (TRAMPLED)
Joel 3: 13 Come, **t** the grapes,
Am 2: 7 They **t** on the heads of the poor as
8: 4 you who **t** the needy and do away
Mt 7: 6 they may **t** them under their feet,
Lk 10: 19 I have given you authority to **t**

TRAMPLED (TRAMPLE)
Isa 63: 6 I **t** the nations in my anger;
Lk 21: 24 Jerusalem will be **t**
Heb 10: 29 to be punished who has **t** the Son
Rev 14: 20 They were **t** in the winepress

TRANCE*
Ac 10: 10 was being prepared, he fell into a **t**.
11: 5 praying, and in a **t** I saw a vision.
22: 17 praying at the temple, I fell into a **t**

TRANQUILLITY*
Ecc 4: 6 handful with **t** than two handfuls

TRANSACTIONS*
Ru 4: 7 method of legalizing **t** in Israel.)

TRANSCENDS*
Php 4: 7 God, which **t** all understanding,

TRANSFIGURED*
Mt 17: 2 There he was **t** before them.
Mk 9: 2 There he was **t** before them.

TRANSFORM* (TRANSFORMED)
Php 3: 21 will **t** our lowly bodies so that they

TRANSFORMED (TRANSFORM)
Ro 12: 2 be **t** by the renewing of your mind.
2Co 3: 18 are being **t** into his image

TRANSGRESSED* (TRANSGRESSION)
Ps 17: 3 my mouth has not **t**.
Da 9: 11 All Israel has **t** your law and turned

TRANSGRESSION* (TRANSGRESSED TRANSGRESSIONS TRANSGRESSORS)
Ps 19: 13 be blameless, innocent of great **t**.
Isa 53: 8 **t** of my people he was punished.
Da 9: 24 and your holy city to finish **t**,
Mic 1: 5 All this is because of Jacob's **t**,
1: 5 What is Jacob's **t**? Is it not Samaria?
3: 8 to declare to Jacob his **t**, to Israel
6: 7 Shall I offer my firstborn for my **t**,
7: 18 forgives the **t** of the remnant of his
Ro 4: 15 where there is no law there is no **t**.
11: 11 because of their **t**, salvation has
11: 12 their **t** means riches for the world,

TRANSGRESSIONS* (TRANSGRESSION)
Ps 32: 1 is the one whose **t** are forgiven,
32: 5 I said, "I will confess my **t**
39: 8 Save me from all my **t**; do not
51: 1 great compassion blot out my **t**.
51: 3 For I know my **t**, and my sin is
65: 3 by sins, you forgave our **t**.
103: 12 far has he removed our **t** from us.
Isa 43: 25 am he who blots out your **t**, for my
50: 1 your **t** your mother was sent away.
53: 5 But he was pierced for our **t**,
Mic 1: 13 the **t** of Israel were found in you.
Ro 4: 7 are those whose **t** are forgiven,
Gal 3: 19 added because of **t** until the Seed
Eph 2: 1 you were dead in your **t** and sins,
2: 5 even when we were dead in **t**—

TRANSGRESSORS* (TRANSGRESSION)
Ps 51: 13 Then I will teach **t** your ways,
Isa 53: 12 and was numbered with the **t**.
53: 12 and made intercession for the **t**.
Lk 22: 37 'And he was numbered with the **t**';

TRANSITORY*
2Co 3: 7 of its glory, **t** though it was,
3: 11 And if what was **t** came with glory,

TRAP (TRAPPED TRAPS)
Ps 69: 22 may it become retribution and a **t**.
Pr 20: 25 is a **t** to dedicate something rashly
28: 10 evil path will fall into their own **t**,
Isa 8: 14 people of Jerusalem he will be a **t**
Mt 22: 15 laid plans to **t** him in his words.
Lk 21: 34 will close on you suddenly like a **t**.
Ro 11: 9 their table become a snare and a **t**,
1Ti 3: 7 into disgrace and into the devil's **t**.
6: 9 and a **t** and into many foolish
2Ti 2: 26 and escape from the **t** of the devil,

TRAPPED (TRAP)
Pr 6: 2 you have been **t** by what you said,
12: 13 Evildoers are **t** by their sinful talk,

TRAPS (TRAP)
Jos 23: 13 will become snares and **t** for you,
La 4: 20 life breath, was caught in their **t**.

TRAVEL (TRAVELER)
Pr 4: 15 Avoid it, do not **t** on it; turn from it
Mt 23: 15 You **t** over land and sea to win

TRAVELER (TRAVEL)
Job 31: 32 my door was always open to the **t**
Jer 14: 8 like a **t** who stays only a night?

TREACHEROUS (TREACHERY)
Ps 25: 3 on those who are **t** without cause.
Zep 3: 4 unprincipled; they are **t** people.
2Ti 3: 4 **t**, rash, conceited, lovers of

TREACHERY (TREACHEROUS)
Isa 59: 13 rebellion and **t** against the LORD,

TREAD (TREADING TREADS)
Ps 91: 13 will **t** on the lion and the cobra;

TREADING (TREAD)
Dt 25: 4 Do not muzzle an ox while it is **t**
1Co 9: 9 "Do not muzzle an ox while it is **t**
1Ti 5: 18 "Do not muzzle an ox while it is **t**

TREADS (TREAD)
Rev 19: 15 He **t** the winepress of the fury

TREASURE (TREASURED TREASURES TREASURY)
Pr 2: 4 and search for it as for hidden **t**,
Isa 33: 6 of the LORD is the key to this **t**.
Mt 6: 21 where your **t** is, there your heart
13: 44 of heaven is like **t** hidden in a field.
Lk 12: 33 a **t** in heaven that will never fail,
2Co 4: 7 But we have this **t** in jars of clay
1Ti 6: 19 In this way they will lay up **t**

TREASURED* (TREASURE)
Ex 19: 5 you will be my **t** possession.
Dt 7: 6 to be his people, his **t** possession.
14: 2 chosen you to be his **t** possession.
26: 18 his **t** possession as he promised,
Job 23: 12 I have **t** the words of his mouth
Ps 135: 4 own, Israel to be his **t** possession.
Isa 64: 11 fire, and all that we **t** lies in ruins.
Mal 3: 17 "they will be my **t** possession.
Lk 2: 19 But Mary **t** up all these things
2: 51 his mother **t** all these things in her

TREASURES (TREASURE)
1Ch 29: 3 my God I now give my personal **t**
Pr 10: 2 Ill-gotten **t** have no lasting value,
Mt 6: 19 store up for yourselves **t** on earth,
13: 52 his storeroom new **t** as well as old."
Col 2: 3 in whom are hidden all the **t**
Heb 11: 26 of greater value than the **t** of Egypt,

TREASURY (TREASURE)
Mk 12: 43 more into the **t** than all the others.

TREAT (TREATED TREATING TREATMENT)
Lev 22: 2 sons to **t** with respect the sacred
Ps 103: 10 he does not **t** us as our sins deserve
Mt 18: 17 **t** them as you would a pagan
18: 35 how my heavenly Father will **t** each
Eph 6: 9 **t** your slaves in the same way.
1Th 5: 20 Do not **t** prophecies with contempt
1Ti 5: 1 **T** younger men as brothers,
1Pe 3: 7 **t** them with respect as the weaker

TREATED (TREAT)
Lev 19: 34 you must be **t** as your native-born.
25: 40 They are to be **t** as hired workers
1Sa 24: 17 "You have **t** me well, but I have **t**
Heb 10: 29 who has **t** as an unholy thing

TREATING (TREAT)
Ge 18: 25 **t** the righteous and the wicked
Heb 12: 7 God is **t** you as his children.

TREATMENT (TREAT)
Col 2: 23 and their harsh **t** of the body,

TREATY
Ex 34: 12 not to make a **t** with those who live
Dt 7: 2 Make no **t** with them, and show
23: 6 Do not seek a **t** of friendship

TREE (TREES)
Ge 2: 9 of the garden were the **t** of life
2: 9 the **t** of the knowledge of good
2Sa 18: 9 Absalom's hair got caught in the **t**.
1Ki 14: 23 hill and under every spreading **t**.
Ps 1: 3 is like a **t** planted by streams
52: 8 I am like an olive **t** flourishing
92: 12 will flourish like a palm **t**,
Pr 3: 18 She is a **t** of life to those who take
11: 30 fruit of the righteous is a **t** of life,
27: 18 who guards a fig **t** will eat its fruit,
Isa 65: 22 For as the days of a **t**, so will be
Jer 17: 8 They will be like a **t** planted
Eze 17: 24 I the LORD bring down the tall **t**
17: 24 and make the dry **t** flourish.
Da 4: 10 and there before me stood a **t**
Mic 4: 4 vine and under their own fig **t**,
Zec 3: 10 to sit under your vine and fig **t**,'
Mt 3: 10 every **t** that does not produce good
12: 33 "Make a **t** good and its fruit will be
12: 33 for a **t** is recognized by its fruit.
Lk 19: 4 climbed a sycamore-fig **t** to see
Ro 11: 24 an olive **t** that is wild by nature,
11: 24 be grafted into their own olive **t**!
Jas 3: 12 sisters, can a fig **t** bear olives,
Rev 2: 7 the right to eat from the **t** of life,
22: 2 side of the river stood the **t** of life,
22: 2 leaves of the **t** are for the healing
22: 14 may have the right to the **t** of life
22: 19 person any share in the **t** of life

TREES (TREE)
Jdg 9: 8 One day the **t** went out to anoint
Ps 96: 12 let all the **t** of the forest sing for joy.
Isa 55: 12 all the **t** of the field will clap their
Mt 3: 10 ax is already at the root of the **t**,
Mk 8: 24 they look like **t** walking around."
Jude : 12 autumn **t**, without fruit

TREMBLE (TREMBLED TREMBLES TREMBLING)
Ex 15: 14 The nations will hear and **t**;
1Ch 16: 30 **T** before him, all the earth!
Ps 114: 7 **T**, earth, at the presence of the
Isa 66: 2 in spirit, and who **t** at my word.
Jer 5: 22 "Should you not **t** in my presence?
Eze 38: 20 of the earth will **t** at my presence.
Joel 2: 1 Let all who live in the land **t**,
Hab 3: 6 he looked, and made the nations **t**.
Ro 11: 20 Do not be arrogant, but **t**.

TREMBLED (TREMBLE)
Ex 19: 16 Everyone in the camp **t**.
20: 18 in smoke, they **t** with fear.
2Sa 22: 8 they **t** because he was angry.
Ac 7: 32 Moses **t** with fear and did not dare

TREMBLES (TREMBLE)
Ps 97: 4 up the world; the earth sees and **t**.
104: 32 it **t**, who touches the mountains,
Jer 10: 10 When he is angry, the earth **t**;
Na 1: 5 The earth **t** at his presence,

TREMBLING (TREMBLE)
Ps 2: 11 fear and celebrate his rule with **t**.
Da 10: 10 me and set me **t** on my hands
Php 2: 12 out your salvation with fear and **t**,
Heb 12: 21 that Moses said, "I am **t** with fear."

TRESPASS* (TRESPASSES)
Ro 5: 15 But the gift is not like the **t**.
5: 15 many died by the **t** of the one man,
5: 17 if, by the **t** of the one man,
5: 18 just as one **t** resulted
5: 20 in so that the **t** might increase.

TRESPASSES* (TRESPASS)
Ro 5: 16 but the gift followed many **t**

TRIAL (TRIALS)
Ps 37: 33 be condemned when brought to **t**.
Mal 3: 5 "So I will come to put you on **t**.
Mk 13: 11 you are arrested and brought to **t**,
2Co 8: 2 In the midst of a very severe **t**,
Jas 1: 12 who perseveres under **t** because,
Rev 3: 10 you from the hour of **t** that is going

TRIALS* (TRIAL)
Dt 7: 19 saw with your own eyes the great **t**,
29: 3 own eyes you saw those great **t**,
Lk 22: 28 who have stood by me in my **t**.
1Th 3: 3 one would be unsettled by these **t**.
2Th 1: 4 and **t** you are enduring.
Jas 1: 2 whenever you face **t** of many kinds,
1Pe 1: 6 had to suffer grief in all kinds of **t**.
2Pe 2: 9 how to rescue the godly from **t**

TRIBE (HALF-TRIBE TRIBES)
Heb 7: 13 that **t** has ever served at the altar.
Rev 5: 5 the Lion of the **t** of Judah, the Root
5: 9 for God persons from every **t**
11: 9 days some from every people, **t**,
14: 6 to every nation, **t**,

TRIBES (TRIBE)
Ge 49: 28 All these are the twelve **t** of Israel,
Mt 19: 28 judging the twelve **t** of Israel.

TRIBULATION*
Rev 7: 14 who have come out of the great **t**;

TRICKERY*
Ac 13: 10 are full of all kinds of deceit and **t**.
2Co 12: 16 fellow that I am, I caught you by **t**!

TRIED (TRY)
Ps 73: 16 When I **t** to understand all this,
95: 9 they **t** me, though they had seen
Heb 3: 9 your ancestors tested and **t** me,

TRIES (TRY)
Lk 17: 33 Whoever **t** to keep their life will

TRIMMED
Mt 25: 7 virgins woke up and **t** their lamps.

TRIUMPH (TRIUMPHAL TRIUMPHED TRIUMPHING TRIUMPHS)
Ps 25: 2 nor let my enemies **t** over me.
54: 7 and my eyes have looked in **t** on
112: 8 the end they will look in **t** on their
118: 7 I look in **t** on my enemies.
Pr 28: 12 When the righteous **t**, there is great
Isa 42: 13 cry and will **t** over his enemies.
Rev 17: 14 the Lamb will **t** over them because

TRIUMPHAL* (TRIUMPH)
Isa 60: 11 their kings led in **t** procession.
2Co 2: 14 as captives in Christ's **t** procession

TRIUMPHED (TRIUMPH)
Rev 5: 5 of Judah, the Root of David, has **t**.
12: 11 They **t** over him by the blood

TRIUMPHING* (TRIUMPH)
Col 2: 15 of them, **t** over them by the cross.

TRIUMPHS* (TRIUMPH)
Jas 2: 13 Mercy **t** over judgment.

TROUBLE (TROUBLED TROUBLES TROUBLEMAKER)
Ge 41: 51 God has made me forget all my **t**
Jos 7: 25 The LORD will bring **t** on you
Job 2: 10 accept good from God, and not **t**?"
5: 7 to **t** as surely as sparks fly upward.
14: 1 are of few days and full of **t**.
42: 11 him over all the **t** the LORD had
Ps 7: 14 is pregnant with evil conceives **t**
7: 16 The **t** they cause recoils on them;
9: 9 a stronghold in times of **t**.
10: 14 you, God, see the **t** of the afflicted;
22: 11 for **t** is near and there is no one
27: 5 the day of **t** he will keep me safe
32: 7 you will protect me from **t**
37: 39 he is their stronghold in time of **t**.
41: 1 LORD delivers them in times of **t**.
46: 1 strength, an ever-present help in **t**.
50: 15 and call on me in the day of **t**;
59: 16 fortress, my refuge in times of **t**.
66: 14 my mouth spoke when I was in **t**.
91: 15 will be with him in **t**, I will deliver
107: 6 cried out to the LORD in their **t**,
107: 13 they cried to the LORD in their **t**,
119:143 **T** and distress have come upon me,
138: 7 Though I walk in the midst of **t**,
143: 11 righteousness, bring me out of **t**.
Pr 11: 8 righteous person is rescued from **t**,
12: 13 talk, and so the innocent escape **t**.
12: 21 but the wicked have their fill of **t**.
19: 23 one rests content, untouched by **t**.
24: 10 If you falter in a time of **t**,
25: 19 on the unfaithful in a time of **t**.
28: 14 hardens their heart falls into **t**.
Jer 30: 7 It will be a time of **t** for Jacob,
Na 1: 7 is good, a refuge in times of **t**.
Zep 1: 15 and anguish, a day of **t** and ruin,
Mt 6: 34 Each day has enough **t** of its own.
13: 21 When **t** or persecution comes
Jn 16: 33 In this world you will have **t**.
Ro 8: 35 Shall **t** or hardship or persecution
2Co 1: 4 any **t** with the comfort we
2Th 1: 6 He will pay back **t** to those who **t**
Jas 5: 13 Is anyone among you in **t**?

TROUBLED (TROUBLE)
Ge 6: 6 earth, and his heart was deeply **t**.
Ps 38: 18 I am **t** by my sin.
Mk 14: 33 to be deeply distressed and **t**.
Jn 14: 1 "Do not let your hearts be **t**.
14: 27 Do not let your hearts be **t** and do
2Th 1: 7 and give relief to you who are **t**,

TROUBLEMAKER (TROUBLE)
Pr 6: 12 A **t** and a villain, who goes about

TROUBLES (TROUBLE)
Ps 34: 6 he saved him out of all his **t**.
34: 17 he delivers them from all their **t**.
34: 19 righteous person may have many **t**,
40: 12 **t** without number surround me;
54: 7 have delivered me from all my **t**,
1Co 7: 28 those who marry will face many **t**
2Co 1: 4 who comforts us in all our **t**,
4: 17 momentary **t** are achieving for us
6: 4 in **t**, hardships and distresses;
7: 4 all our **t** my joy knows no bounds.
Php 4: 14 it was good of you to share in my **t**.

TRUE (TRULY TRUTH)
Nu 11: 23 not what I say will come **t** for you."
12: 7 this is not **t** of my servant Moses;
Dt 18: 22 does not take place or come **t**,
1Sa 9: 6 and everything he says comes **t**.
1Ki 10: 6 and your wisdom is **t**.
2Ch 6: 17 your servant David come **t**.
15: 3 time Israel was without the **t** God,
Ps 33: 4 word of the LORD is right and **t**;
119:142 is everlasting and your law is **t**.
119:151 and all your commands are **t**.
119:160 All your words are **t**;
Pr 8: 7 My mouth speaks what is **t**, for my
Isa 65: 16 land will swear by the one **t** God.
Jer 10: 10 But the LORD is the **t** God;
28: 9 only if his prediction comes **t**."
Eze 33: 33 "When all this comes **t**—
Lk 16: 11 who will trust you with **t** riches?
Jn 1: 9 The **t** light that gives light
4: 23 the **t** worshipers will worship
6: 32 Father who gives you the **t** bread
7: 28 authority, but he who sent me is **t**.
15: 1 "I am the **t** vine, and my Father is
Jn 17: 3 the only **t** God, and Jesus Christ,
19: 35 testimony, and his testimony is **t**.
21: 24 We know that his testimony is **t**.
Ac 10: 34 "I now realize how **t** it is that God
11: 23 them all to remain **t** to the Lord
14: 22 them to remain **t** to the faith.
17: 11 day to see if what Paul said was **t**.
Ro 3: 4 Let God be **t**, and every human
12: 1 this is your **t** and proper worship.
Php 4: 8 whatever is **t**, whatever is noble,
Col 1: 5 have already heard in the **t** message
Titus 1: 13 This saying is **t**. Therefore rebuke
1Jn 2: 8 and the **t** light is already shining.
5: 20 so that we may know him who is **t**.
5: 20 He is the **t** God and eternal life.
Rev 19: 9 "These are the **t** words of God."
22: 6 These words are trustworthy and **t**.

TRULY (TRUE)
Mt 5: 18 For **t** I tell you, until heaven
5: 26 **T** I tell you, you will not get
6: 2 **T** I tell you, they have received
6: 5 **T** I tell you, they have received
6: 16 **T** I tell you, they have received
8: 10 those following him, "**T** I tell you,
10: 15 **T** I tell you, it will be more
10: 23 **T** I tell you, you will not finish
10: 42 who is my disciple, **t** I tell you,
11: 11 **T** I tell you, among those born
13: 17 For **t** I tell you, many prophets
16: 28 "**T** I tell you, some who are
17: 20 **T** I tell you, if you have faith as
18: 3 "**T** I tell you, unless you change
18: 13 And if he finds it, **t** I tell you, he is
18: 18 "**T** I tell you, whatever you bind
19: 23 said to his disciples, "**T** I tell you,
19: 28 Jesus said to them, "**T** I tell you,
21: 21 Jesus replied, "**T** I tell you, if you
21: 31 Jesus said to them, "**T** I tell you,
23: 36 **T** I tell you, all this will come
24: 2 "**T** I tell you, not one stone here
24: 34 **T** I tell you, this generation will
24: 47 **T** I tell you, he will put him
25: 12 "But he replied, '**T** I tell you,
25: 40 "The King will reply, '**T** I tell you,
25: 45 "He will reply, '**T** I tell you,
26: 13 **T** I tell you, wherever this gospel is
26: 21 he said, "**T** I tell you, one of you
26: 34 "**T** I tell you," Jesus answered,
Mk 3: 28 **T** I tell you, people can be forgiven
8: 12 **T** I tell you, no sign will be given
9: 1 And he said to them, "**T** I tell you,
9: 41 **T** I tell you, anyone who gives you
10: 15 **T** I tell you, anyone who will not
10: 29 "**T** I tell you," Jesus replied,
11: 23 "**T** I tell you, if anyone says to this
12: 43 Jesus said, "**T** I tell you, this poor
13: 30 **T** I tell you, this generation will
14: 9 **T** I tell you, wherever the gospel is
14: 18 he said, "**T** I tell you, one of you
14: 25 "**T** I tell you, I will not drink again
14: 30 "**T** I tell you," Jesus answered,
Lk 4: 24 "**T** I tell you," he continued,
9: 27 "**T** I tell you, some who are
12: 37 **T** I tell you, he will dress himself
12: 44 **T** I tell you, he will put him
18: 17 **T** I tell you, anyone who will not
18: 29 "**T** I tell you," Jesus said to them,
21: 3 "**T** I tell you," he said, "this poor
21: 32 **T** I tell you, this generation will
23: 43 Jesus answered him, "**T** I tell you,
Jn 1: 51 He then added, "Very **t** I tell you,
3: 3 Jesus replied, "Very **t** I tell you,
3: 5 Jesus answered, "Very **t** I tell you,
3: 11 Very **t** I tell you, we speak of what
5: 19 "Very **t** I tell you, the Son can do
5: 24 "Very **t** I tell you, whoever hears
5: 25 Very **t** I tell you, a time is coming
6: 26 Jesus answered, "Very **t** I tell you,
6: 32 said to them, "Very **t** I tell you, it is
6: 47 Very **t** I tell you, the one who
6: 53 said to them, "Very **t** I tell you,
8: 34 Jesus replied, "Very **t** I tell you,
8: 51 Very **t** I tell you, whoever obeys my
8: 58 "Very **t** I tell you," Jesus answered,
10: 1 "Very **t** I tell you Pharisees,
10: 7 Jesus said again, "Very **t** I tell you,
12: 24 Very **t** I tell you, unless a kernel
13: 16 Very **t** I tell you, no servant is
13: 20 Very **t** I tell you, whoever accepts
13: 21 and testified, "Very **t** I tell you,
13: 38 Very **t** I tell you, before the rooster
Jn 14: 12 Very **t** I tell you, whoever believes
16: 7 But very **t** I tell you, it is for your
16: 20 Very **t** I tell you, you will weep
16: 23 Very **t** I tell you, my Father will
21: 18 Very **t** I tell you, when you were
Col 1: 6 it and **t** understood God's grace.

TRUMPET (TRUMPETS)
Isa 27: 13 in that day a great **t** will sound.
Eze 33: 5 Since they heard the sound of the **t**
Zec 9: 14 Sovereign LORD will sound the **t**;
Mt 24: 31 send his angels with a loud **t** call,
1Co 14: 8 if the **t** does not sound a clear call,
15: 52 twinkling of an eye, at the last **t**.
1Th 4: 16 and with the **t** call of God,
Rev 8: 7 The first angel sounded his **t**,

TRUMPETS (TRUMPET)
Jdg 7: 19 blew their **t** and broke the jars
Rev 8: 2 and seven **t** were given to them.

TRUST (ENTRUST ENTRUSTED TRUSTED TRUSTFULLY TRUSTING TRUSTS TRUSTWORTHY)
Ex 14: 31 the LORD and put their **t** in him
19: 9 and will always put their **t** in you."
Nu 20: 12 "Because you did not **t** in me
Dt 1: 32 you did not **t** in the LORD your
9: 23 You did not **t** him or obey him.
28: 52 walls in which you **t** fall down.
Jdg 11: 20 did not **t** Israel to pass through his
2Ki 17: 14 who did not **t** in the LORD their
18: 30 not let Hezekiah persuade you to **t**
1Ch 9: 22 to their positions of **t** by David
Job 4: 18 If God places no **t** in his servants,
8: 14 What they **t** in is fragile;
15: 15 If God places no **t** in his holy ones,
31: 24 "If I have put my **t** in gold or said
39: 12 Can you **t** it to haul in your grain
Ps 4: 5 the righteous and **t** in the LORD.
9: 10 Those who know your name **t**
13: 5 But I **t** in your unfailing love;
20: 7 Some **t** in chariots and some
20: 7 we **t** in the name of the LORD our
22: 9 you made me **t** in you, even at
22: 4 In you our ancestors put their **t**;
25: 2 I **t** in you; do not let me be put
31: 6 as for me, I **t** in the LORD.
31: 14 But I **t** in you, LORD; I say,
33: 21 rejoice, for we **t** in his holy name.
37: 3 **T** in the LORD and do good;
37: 5 **t** in him and he will do this:
40: 3 the LORD and put their **t** in him.
44: 6 I put no **t** in my bow, my sword
49: 6 those who **t** in their wealth
49: 13 fate of those who **t** in themselves,
52: 8 I **t** in God's unfailing love for ever
55: 23 But as for me, I **t** in you.
56: 3 I am afraid, I put my **t** in you.
56: 4 in God I **t** and am not afraid.
56: 11 in God I **t** and am not afraid.
62: 8 **T** in him at all times, you people;
62: 10 Do not **t** in extortion or put vain
78: 7 they would put their **t** in God
78: 22 in God or **t** in his deliverance.
91: 2 my fortress, my God, in whom I **t**."
115: 8 and so will all who **t** in them.
115: 9 All you Israelites, **t** in the LORD—
115: 10 House of Aaron, **t** in the LORD—
115: 11 who fear him, **t** in the LORD—
118: 8 in the LORD than to **t** in humans.
118: 9 in the LORD than to **t** in princes.
119: 42 taunts me, for I **t** in your word.
125: 1 Those who **t** in the LORD are like
135: 18 and so will all who **t** in them.
143: 8 love, for I have put my **t** in you.
146: 3 Do not put your **t** in princes,
Pr 3: 5 **T** in the LORD with all your heart
11: 28 who **t** in their riches will fall,
21: 22 the stronghold in which they **t**.
22: 19 So that your **t** may be
28: 25 but those who **t** in the LORD will
28: 26 Those who **t** in themselves are
Isa 8: 17 I will put my **t** in him.
12: 2 I will **t** and not be afraid.
26: 3 are steadfast, because they **t** in you.
26: 4 **T** in the LORD forever,
30: 15 in quietness and **t** is your strength,
31: 1 who **t** in the multitude of their
36: 15 not let Hezekiah persuade you to **t**
42: 17 But those who **t** in idols, who say
50: 10 **t** in the name of the LORD
Jer 2: 37 the LORD has rejected those you **t**;

Jer 5: 17 the fortified cities in which you **t**.
7: 4 not **t** in deceptive words and say,
7: 14 temple you **t** in, the place I gave
9: 4 do not **t** anyone in your clan.
12: 6 Do not **t** them, though they speak
28: 15 you have persuaded this nation to **t**
39: 18 with your life, because you **t** in me,
48: 7 Since you **t** in your deeds
49: 4 you **t** in your riches and say,
Eze 33: 13 then they **t** in their righteousness
Mic 7: 5 Do not **t** a neighbor;
Na 1: 7 He cares for those who **t** in him,
Zep 3: 2 She does not **t** in the LORD,
3: 12 remnant of Israel will **t** in the name
Lk 16: 11 who will **t** you with true riches?
Ac 14: 23 in whom they had put their **t**.
Ro 15: 13 all joy and peace as you **t** in him,
1Co 4: 2 been given a **t** must prove faithful.
9: 17 discharging the **t** committed
2Co 13: 6 I **t** that you will discover that we
Heb 2: 13 again, "I will put my **t** in him."

TRUSTED* (TRUST)
1Sa 27: 12 Achish **t** David and said to himself,
2Ki 18: 5 Hezekiah **t** in the LORD, the God
1Ch 5: 20 prayers, because they **t** in him.
Job 12: 20 He silences the lips of **t** advisers
Ps 5: 9 a word from their mouth can be **t**;
22: 4 they **t** and you delivered them.
22: 5 in you they **t** and were not put
26: 1 I have **t** in the LORD and have not
41: 9 someone I **t**, one who shared my
52: 7 stronghold but **t** in his great wealth
116: 10 I **t** in the LORD when I said,
Pr 27: 6 Wounds from a friend can be **t**,
Isa 20: 5 Those who **t** in Cush and boasted
25: 9 we **t** in him, and he saved us.
25: 9 This is the LORD, we **t** in him;
47: 10 You have **t** in your wickedness
Jer 13: 25 forgotten me and **t** in false gods.
38: 22 those **t** friends of yours.
48: 13 ashamed when they **t** in Bethel.
Eze 16: 15 "'But you **t** in your beauty
Da 3: 28 They **t** in him and defied the king's
6: 23 him, because he had **t** in his God.
Lk 11: 22 away the armor in which the man **t**
16: 10 "Whoever can be **t** with very little
can also be **t** with much,
Ac 12: 20 a **t** personal servant of the king,
Titus 2: 10 but to show that they can be fully **t**,
3: 8 those who have **t** in God may be

TRUSTFULLY* (TRUST)
Pr 3: 29 neighbor, who lives **t** near you.

TRUSTING* (TRUST)
Job 15: 31 himself by **t** what is worthless,
Ps 112: 7 hearts are steadfast, **t** in the LORD.
Isa 2: 22 Stop **t** in mere humans, who have
Jer 7: 8 you are **t** in deceptive words that

TRUSTS* (TRUST)
Ps 21: 7 For the king **t** in the LORD;
22: 8 "He **t** in the LORD," they say,
28: 7 heart **t** in him, and he helps me.
32: 10 love surrounds the one who **t**
40: 4 Blessed is the one who **t**
84: 12 blessed is the one who **t** in you.
86: 2 save your servant who **t** in you.
Pr 16: 20 and blessed is the one who **t**
29: 25 whoever **t** in the LORD is kept
Jer 17: 5 "Cursed is the one who **t** in man,
17: 7 "But blessed is the one who **t**
Hab 2: 18 the one who makes it **t** in his own
Mt 27: 43 He **t** in God. Let God rescue him
Ro 4: 5 **t** God who justifies the ungodly,
1Co 13: 7 protects, always **t**, always hopes,
1Pe 2: 6 the one who **t** in him will never be

TRUSTWORTHY* (TRUST)
Ex 18: 21 **t** men who hate dishonest gain—
2Sa 7: 28 Your covenant is **t**, and you have
Ne 13: 13 because they were considered **t**.
Ps 19: 7 The statutes of the LORD are **t**,
111: 7 all his precepts are **t**.
119: 86 All your commands are **t**;
119:138 are righteous; they are fully **t**.
145: 13 The LORD is **t** in all he promises
Pr 8: 6 Listen, for I have **t** things to say;
11: 13 but a **t** person keeps a secret.
12: 22 but he delights in people who are **t**.
13: 17 but a **t** envoy brings healing.
25: 13 harvest time is a **t** messenger
Da 2: 45 is true and its interpretation is **t**."
6: 4 he was **t** and neither corrupt
Lk 16: 11 if you have not been **t** in handling
16: 12 you have not been **t** with someone
19: 17 'Because you have been **t** in a very
Jn 8: 26 But he who sent me is **t**, and what I
1Co 7: 25 one who by the Lord's mercy is **t**.
1Ti 1: 12 that he considered me **t**,
1: 15 Here is a **t** saying that deserves full
3: 1 Here is a **t** saying:
3: 11 but temperate and **t** in everything.
4: 9 This is a **t** saying that deserves full
2Ti 2: 11 Here is a **t** saying: If we died
Titus 1: 9 the **t** message as it has been taught,
3: 8 This is a **t** saying. And I want you
Rev 21: 5 for these words are **t** and true."
22: 6 to me, "These words are **t** and true.

TRUTH* (TRUE TRUTHFUL TRUTHFULNESS TRUTHS)
Ge 42: 16 tested to see if you are telling the **t**.
1Ki 17: 24 LORD from your mouth is the **t**."
22: 16 the **t** in the name of the LORD?"
2Ch 18: 15 the **t** in the name of the LORD?"
Job 42: 7 have not spoken the **t** about me,
42: 8 have not spoken the **t** about me,
Ps 15: 2 who speaks the **t** from their heart;
25: 5 Guide me in your **t** and teach me,
45: 4 forth victoriously in the cause of **t**,
52: 3 rather than speaking the **t**.
119: 43 Never take your word of **t** from my
145: 18 on him, to all who call on him in **t**.
Pr 12: 17 An honest witness tells the **t**,
22: 21 to be honest and to speak the **t**,
23: 23 Buy the **t** and do not sell it—
Isa 45: 19 I, the LORD, speak the **t**;
48: 1 but not in **t** or righteousness—
59: 14 **t** has stumbled in the streets,
59: 15 **T** is nowhere to be found,
Jer 5: 1 who deals honestly and seeks the **t**,
5: 3 do not your eyes look for **t**?
7: 28 **T** has perished; it has vanished
9: 3 it is not by **t** that they triumph
9: 5 friend, and no one speaks the **t**.
26: 15 in **t** the LORD has sent me to you
Da 8: 12 and **t** was thrown to the ground.
9: 13 sins and giving attention to your **t**.
10: 21 what is written in the Book of **T**.
11: 2 "Now then, I tell you the **t**:
Am 5: 10 and detest the one who tells the **t**.
Zec 8: 16 Speak the **t** to each other, and
8: 19 Therefore love **t** and peace."
Mt 22: 16 of God in accordance with the **t**.
Mk 5: 33 with fear, told him the whole **t**.
12: 14 of God in accordance with the **t**.
Lk 20: 21 of God in accordance with the **t**.
Jn 1: 14 from the Father, full of grace and **t**.
1: 17 and **t** came through Jesus Christ.
3: 21 whoever lives by the **t** comes
4: 23 the Father in the Spirit and in **t**,
4: 24 worship in the Spirit and in **t**."
5: 33 John and he has testified to the **t**.
7: 18 the one who sent him is a man of **t**;
8: 32 Then you will know the **t**, and the **t**
8: 40 a man who has told you the **t** that I
8: 44 not holding to the **t**, for there is no **t**
in him.
8: 45 Yet because I tell the **t**, you do not
8: 46 If I am telling the **t**, why don't you
9: 24 glory to God by telling the **t**,"
14: 6 am the way and the **t** and the life.
14: 17 the Spirit of **t**. The world cannot
15: 26 the Spirit of **t** who goes
16: 13 when he, the Spirit of **t**, comes,
16: 13 he will guide you into all the **t**.
17: 17 Sanctify them by the **t**; your word
is **t**.
18: 23 But if I spoke the **t**, why did you
18: 37 into the world is to testify to the **t**.
18: 37 on the side of **t** listens to me."
18: 38 "What is **t**?" retorted Pilate.
19: 35 He knows that he tells the **t**, and he
Ac 20: 30 distort the **t** in order to draw away
21: 24 everyone will know there is no **t**
21: 34 could not get at the **t** because
24: 8 learn the **t** about all these charges
28: 25 "The Holy Spirit spoke the **t**
Ro 1: 18 people, who suppress the **t** by their
1: 25 They exchanged the **t** about God
2: 2 who do such things is based on **t**.
2: 8 who reject the **t** and follow evil,
2: 20 embodiment of knowledge and **t**—
9: 1 I speak the **t** in Christ—I am not
15: 8 of the Jews on behalf of God's **t**,
1Co 5: 8 bread of sincerity and **t**.
13: 6 in evil but rejoices with the **t**.
2Co 4: 2 by setting forth the **t** plainly we
11: 10 As surely as the **t** of Christ is in me,
12: 6 because I would be speaking the **t**.
13: 8 we cannot do anything against the **t**,
but only for the **t**.
Gal 2: 5 so that the **t** of the gospel might be
2: 14 in line with the **t** of the gospel,
4: 16 your enemy by telling you the **t**?
5: 7 to keep you from obeying the **t**?
Eph 1: 13 when you heard the message of **t**,
4: 15 Instead, speaking the **t** in love,
4: 21 in accordance with the **t** that is
5: 9 all goodness, righteousness and **t**)
6: 14 belt of **t** buckled around your waist
2Th 2: 10 because they refused to love the **t**
2: 12 who have not believed the **t**
2: 13 Spirit and through belief in the **t**.
1Ti 2: 4 to come to a knowledge of the **t**.
2: 7 I am telling the **t**, I am not lying—
3: 15 the pillar and foundation of the **t**.
4: 3 who believe and who know the **t**.
6: 5 who have been robbed of the **t**
2Ti 2: 15 correctly handles the word of **t**.
2: 18 who have departed from the **t**.
2: 25 them to a knowledge of the **t**,
3: 7 to come to a knowledge of the **t**.
3: 8 so also these teachers oppose the **t**.
4: 4 will turn their ears away from the **t**
Titus 1: 1 their knowledge of the **t** that leads
1: 14 of those who reject the **t**.
Heb 10: 26 received the knowledge of the **t**,
Jas 1: 18 give us birth through the word of **t**,
3: 14 do not boast about it or deny the **t**.
5: 19 of you should wander from the **t**
1Pe 1: 22 by obeying the **t** so that you have
2Pe 1: 12 established in the **t** you now have.
2: 2 and will bring the way of **t**
1Jn 1: 6 we lie and do not live out the **t**.
1: 8 ourselves and the **t** is not in us.
2: 4 liar, and the **t** is not in that person.
2: 8 its **t** is seen in him and in you,
2: 20 One, and all of you know the **t**.
2: 21 because you do not know the **t**,
2: 21 because no lie comes from the **t**.
3: 18 or speech but with actions and in **t**.
3: 19 we know that we belong to the **t**
4: 6 is how we recognize the Spirit of **t**
5: 6 testifies, because the Spirit is the **t**.
2Jn : 1 children, whom I love in the **t**—
: 1 but also all who know the **t**—
: 2 because of the **t**, which lives in us
: 3 Son, will be with us in **t** and love.
: 4 of your children walking in the **t**,
3Jn : 1 friend Gaius, whom I love in the **t**.
: 3 about your faithfulness to the **t**,
: 4 my children are walking in the **t**.
: 8 we may work together for the **t**.
: 12 and even by the **t** itself.

TRUTHFUL* (TRUTH)
Pr 12: 19 **T** lips endure forever, but a lying
14: 25 A **t** witness saves lives, but a false
22: 21 you bring back **t** reports to those
Jer 4: 2 and if in a **t**, just and righteous
way
Jn 3: 33 it has certified that God is **t**.
2Co 6: 7 **t** speech and in the power of God;

TRUTHFULNESS* (TRUTH)
Ro 3: 7 "If my falsehood enhances God's **t**

TRUTHS* (TRUTH)
1Ti 3: 9 keep hold of the deep **t** of the faith
4: 6 nourished on the **t** of the faith
Heb 5: 12 teach you the elementary **t** of God's

TRY (TRIED TRIES TRYING)
Ps 26: 2 and **t** me, examine my heart and
Isa 7: 13 Will you **t** the patience of my God
Lk 12: 58 **t** hard to be reconciled on the way,
13: 24 will **t** to enter and will not be able
1Co 10: 33 even as I **t** to please everyone
14: 12 **t** to excel in those that build
2Co 5: 11 the Lord, we **t** to persuade others.
Titus 2: 9 in everything, to **t** to please them,

TRYING (TRY)
2Co 5: 12 We are not **t** to commend ourselves
Gal 1: 10 Or am I **t** to please people? If I
1Th 2: 4 We are not **t** to please people
1Pe 1: 11 **t** to find out the time
1Jn 2: 26 those who are **t** to lead you astray.

Col 2: 2 have the full riches of complete **u**,
1Jn 5: 20 God has come and has given us **u**,

UNDERSTANDS (UNDERSTAND)
1Ch 28: 9 every heart and **u** every desire
Mt 13: 23 who hears the word and **u** it.
Ro 3: 11 there is no one who **u**; there is no

UNDERSTOOD (UNDERSTAND)
Ne 8: 8 the people **u** what was being read.
8: 12 because they now **u** the words
Ps 73: 17 then I **u** their final destiny.
Isa 40: 21 Have you not **u** since the earth was
Ro 1: 20 being **u** from what has been made,

UNDESIRABLE*
Jos 24: 15 serving the LORD seems **u** to you,

UNDIVIDED*
1Ch 12: 33 to help David with **u** loyalty—
Ps 86: 11 give me an **u** heart, that I may fear
Eze 11: 19 I will give them an **u** heart and put
1Co 7: 35 in a right way in **u** devotion

UNDOING
Pr 18: 7 The mouths of fools are their **u**,

UNDYING*
Eph 6: 24 Lord Jesus Christ with an **u** love.

UNENDING
Ps 21: 6 you have granted him **u** blessings

UNEQUALED*
Mt 24: 21 **u** from the beginning of the world
Mk 13: 19 of distress **u** from the beginning,

UNFADING*
1Pe 3: 4 the **u** beauty of a gentle and quiet

UNFAILING
Ex 15: 13 **u** love you will lead the people
1Sa 20: 14 But show me **u** kindness like
2Sa 22: 51 shows **u** kindness to his anointed,
Ps 6: 4 save me because of your **u** love.
13: 5 But I trust in your **u** love;
18: 50 he shows **u** love to his anointed,
21: 7 the **u** love of the Most High
26: 3 always been mindful of your **u** love
31: 16 save me in your **u** love.
32: 10 the LORD's **u** love surrounds
33: 5 the earth is full of his **u** love.
33: 18 those whose hope is in his **u** love,
33: 22 May your **u** love be with us,
36: 7 How priceless is your **u** love,
44: 26 rescue us because of your **u** love.
48: 9 God, we meditate on your **u** love.
51: 1 O God, according to your **u** love;
52: 8 I trust in God's **u** love for ever
77: 8 Has his **u** love vanished forever?
85: 7 Show us your **u** love, LORD,
90: 14 in the morning with your **u** love,
107: 8 thanks to the LORD for his **u** love
107: 15 thanks to the LORD for his **u** love
107: 21 thanks to the LORD for his **u** love
107: 31 thanks to the LORD for his **u** love
119: 41 May your **u** love come to me,
119: 76 May your **u** love be my comfort,
130: 7 for with the LORD is **u** love
143: 8 bring me word of your **u** love, for I
143: 12 In your **u** love, silence my enemies;
147: 11 who put their hope in his **u** love.
Pr 19: 22 What a person desires is **u** love;
20: 6 Many claim to have **u** love,
Isa 54: 10 yet my **u** love for you will not be
La 3: 32 compassion, so great is his **u** love.
Hos 10: 12 reap the fruit of **u** love, and break

UNFAITHFUL (UNFAITHFULNESS)
Lev 6: 2 is **u** to the LORD by deceiving
Nu 5: 6 and so is **u** to the LORD is guilty
1Ch 10: 13 Saul died because he was **u**
Pr 11: 6 the **u** are trapped by evil desires.
13: 2 the **u** have an appetite for violence.
13: 15 but the way of the **u** leads to their
22: 12 he frustrates the words of the **u**.
23: 28 and multiplies the **u** among men.
25: 19 foot is reliance on the **u** in a time
Jer 3: 20 Israel, have been **u** to me,"
Mal 2: 10 by being **u** to one another?
2: 11 Judah has been **u**. A detestable
2: 14 You have been **u** to her, though she
2: 15 and do not be **u** to the wife of your
2: 16 be on your guard, and do not be **u**.
Ro 3: 3 What if some were **u**?

UNFAITHFULNESS (UNFAITHFUL)
1Ch 9: 1 to Babylon because of their **u**.
Ro 3: 3 Will their **u** nullify God's

UNFIT*
Titus 1: 16 and **u** for doing anything good.

UNFOLDING*
Ps 119:130 The **u** of your words gives light;

UNFORGIVING*
2Ti 3: 3 without love, **u**, slanderous,

UNFRIENDLY*
Pr 18: 1 An **u** person pursues selfish ends

UNFRUITFUL
1Co 14: 14 my spirit prays, but my mind is **u**.

UNGODLINESS (UNGODLY)
Titus 2: 12 It teaches us to say "No" to **u**

UNGODLY (UNGODLINESS)
Ro 4: 5 but trusts God who justifies the **u**,
5: 6 powerless, Christ died for the **u**.
1Ti 1: 9 and rebels, the **u** and sinful,
2Ti 2: 16 in it will become more and more **u**.
2Pe 2: 6 of what is going to happen to the **u**;
Jude : 15 all the defiant words **u** sinners have

UNGRATEFUL*
Lk 6: 35 because he is kind to the **u**
2Ti 3: 2 disobedient to their parents, **u**,

UNHOLY*
1Ti 1: 9 and sinful, the **u** and irreligious,
2Ti 3: 2 to their parents, ungrateful, **u**,
Heb 10: 29 has treated as an **u** thing the blood

UNINTENTIONALLY
Lev 4: 2 'When anyone sins **u** and does
Nu 15: 22 you as a community **u** fail to keep
Dt 4: 42 had **u** killed a neighbor without

UNITE (UNITED UNITY)
1Co 6: 15 and **u** them with a prostitute?

UNITED (UNITE)
Ge 2: 24 and mother and is **u** to his wife,
Mt 19: 5 and mother and be **u** to his wife,
Ro 6: 5 be **u** with him in a resurrection
Eph 5: 31 and mother and be **u** to his wife,
Php 2: 1 from being **u** with Christ, if any
Col 2: 2 encouraged in heart and **u** in love,

UNITY* (UNITE)
2Ch 30: 12 the people to give them **u** of mind
Ps 133: 1 God's people live together in **u**!
Jn 17: 23 may be brought to complete **u**.
Eph 1: 10 to bring **u** to all things in heaven
4: 3 keep the **u** of the Spirit through
4: 13 until we all reach **u** in the faith
Col 3: 14 them all together in perfect **u**.

UNIVERSE*
1Co 4: 9 made a spectacle to the whole **u**,
Eph 4: 10 in order to fill the whole **u**.)
Heb 1: 2 through whom also he made the **u**.
11: 3 understand that the **u** was formed

UNJUST
Ro 3: 5 God is **u** in bringing his wrath
9: 14 shall we say? Is God **u**? Not at all!
1Pe 2: 19 pain of **u** suffering because they

UNKNOWN
Ac 17: 23 with this inscription: TO AN **U** GOD.

UNLEAVENED
Ex 12: 17 "Celebrate the Festival of **U** Bread,
Dt 16: 16 at the Festival of **U** Bread,

UNMARRIED
1Co 7: 8 good for them to stay **u**, as I do.
7: 32 An **u** man is concerned

UNPLOWED
Ex 23: 11 the seventh year let the land lie **u**
Hos 10: 12 love, and break up your **u** ground;

UNPRODUCTIVE
Titus 3: 14 urgent needs and not live **u** lives.
2Pe 1: 8 **u** in your knowledge of our Lord

UNPROFITABLE
Titus 3: 9 because these are **u** and useless.

UNPUNISHED
Ex 34: 7 Yet he does not leave the guilty **u**;
Pr 6: 29 no one who touches her will go **u**.
11: 21 The wicked will not go **u**, but those
19: 5 A false witness will not go **u**,

UNQUENCHABLE
Lk 3: 17 will burn up the chaff with **u** fire."

UNREASONING*
2Pe 2: 12 They are like **u** animals,

UNREPENTANT*
Ro 2: 5 stubbornness and your **u** heart,

UNRIGHTEOUS*
Isa 55: 7 ways and the **u** their thoughts.
Zep 3: 5 not fail, yet the **u** know no shame.
Mt 5: 45 rain on the righteous and the **u**.
1Pe 3: 18 righteous for the **u**, to bring you
2Pe 2: 9 to hold the **u** for punishment

UNSEARCHABLE
Ro 11: 33 How **u** his judgments, and his

UNSEEN*
Mt 6: 6 and pray to your Father, who is **u**.
6: 18 but only to your Father, who is **u**;
2Co 4: 18 but on what is **u**, since what is seen
4: 18 temporary, but what is **u** is eternal.

UNSETTLED*
1Th 3: 3 no one would be **u** by these trials.
2Th 2: 2 not to become easily **u** or alarmed

UNSHRUNK
Mt 9: 16 "No one sews a patch of **u** cloth

UNSPIRITUAL*
Ro 7: 14 but I am **u**, sold as a slave to sin.
Col 2: 18 with idle notions by their **u** mind.
Jas 3: 15 down from heaven but is earthly, **u**,

UNSTABLE*
Jas 1: 8 double-minded and **u** in all they
2Pe 2: 14 they seduce the **u**; they are experts
3: 16 ignorant and **u** people distort,

UNTHINKABLE*
Job 34: 12 It is **u** that God would do wrong,

UNTIE
Mk 1: 7 not worthy to stoop down and **u**.
Lk 13: 15 of you on the Sabbath **u** your ox

UNTRAINED*
2Co 11: 6 I may indeed be **u** as a speaker,

UNVEILED*
2Co 3: 18 with **u** faces contemplate the Lord's

UNWARY*
Ps 116: 6 The LORD protects the **u**;

UNWHOLESOME*
Eph 4: 29 Do not let any **u** talk come

UNWISE
Eph 5: 15 how you live—not as **u** but as wise,

UNWORTHY*
Ge 32: 10 I am **u** of all the kindness
Job 40: 4 "I am **u**—how can I reply to you?
Lk 17: 10 do, should say, 'We are **u** servants;
1Co 11: 27 Lord in an **u** manner will be guilty

UPHOLD (UPHOLDS)
Ps 82: 3 **u** the cause of the poor
Isa 41: 10 I will **u** you with my righteous
Ro 3: 31 Not at all! Rather, we **u** the law.

UPHOLDS* (UPHOLD)
Ps 37: 17 but the LORD **u** the righteous.
37: 24 for the LORD **u** him with his hand.
63: 8 cling to you; your right hand **u** me.
140: 12 poor and **u** the cause of the needy.
145: 14 The LORD **u** all who fall and lifts
146: 7 He **u** the cause of the oppressed
Am 5: 10 hate the one who **u** justice in court
Mic 7: 9 he pleads my case and **u** my cause.

UPRIGHT (UPRIGHTLY)
Dt 32: 4 does no wrong, **u** and just is he.
Job 1: 1 This man was blameless and **u**;
Ps 7: 10 High, who saves the **u** in heart.
11: 7 the **u** will see his face.
25: 8 Good and **u** is the LORD;
33: 1 it is fitting for the **u** to praise him.
64: 10 all the **u** in heart will glory in him!
92: 15 proclaiming, "The LORD is **u**;
97: 11 righteous and joy on the **u** in heart.
119: 7 an **u** heart as I learn your righteous
Pr 2: 7 He holds success in store for the **u**,
3: 32 but takes the **u** into his confidence.
8: 9 they are **u** to those who have found
15: 8 but the prayer of the **u** pleases him.
21: 29 the **u** give thought to their ways.
Isa 26: 7 you, the **U** One, make the way
Titus 1: 8 who is self-controlled, **u**,
2: 12 **u** and godly lives in this present

UPRIGHTLY* (UPRIGHT)
Pr 14: 2 Whoever fears the LORD walks **u**,
Isa 57: 2 who walk **u** enter into peace;

UPROOTED
Dt 28: 63 You will be **u** from the land you are
Jer 31: 40 The city will never again be **u**
Jude : 12 autumn trees, without fruit and **u**

UPSET
Lk 10: 41 worried and **u** about many things,

URGE
Titus 2: 4 they can **u** the younger women

URIAH
Hittite husband of Bathsheba, killed by David's order (2Sa 11).

USEFUL
Eph 4: 28 doing something **u** with their own
2Ti 2: 21 **u** to the Master and prepared to do
3: 16 is God-breathed and is **u** for
Phm : 11 now he has become **u** both to you

USELESS
1Co 15: 14 our preaching is **u** and so is your
Titus 3: 9 these are unprofitable and **u**.
Phm : 11 Formerly he was **u** to you, but now
Heb 7: 18 set aside because it was weak and **u**
Jas 2: 20 that faith without deeds is **u**?

UTMOST
Job 34: 36 the **u** for answering like a wicked

UTTER
Mt 13: 35 I will **u** things hidden since
1Co 14: 2 they **u** mysteries by the Spirit.

UZZIAH
Son of Amaziah; king of Judah also known as Azariah (2Ki 15:1–7; 1Ch 6:24; 2Ch 26). Struck with leprosy because of pride (2Ch 26:16–23).

VAIN
Ps 33: 17 A horse is a **v** hope for deliverance;
73: 13 in **v** I have kept my heart pure
127: 1 the house, the builders labor in **v**.
Isa 65: 23 They will not labor in **v**, nor will
1Co 15: 2 Otherwise, you have believed in **v**.
15: 58 your labor in the Lord is not in **v**.
2Co 6: 1 you not to receive God's grace in **v**.
Gal 2: 2 had not been running my race in **v**.

VALIANT
1Sa 10: 26 by **v** men whose hearts God had

VALID
Jn 8: 14 my testimony is **v**, for I know

VALLEY (VALLEYS)
Ps 23: 4 I walk through the darkest **v**,
Isa 40: 4 Every **v** shall be raised up,
Joel 3: 14 multitudes in the **v** of decision!

VALLEYS (VALLEY)
SS 2: 1 am a rose of Sharon, a lily of the **v**.

VALUABLE (VALUE)
Lk 12: 24 how much more **v** you are than

VALUE (VALUABLE)
Lev 27: 3 the **v** of a male between the ages
Pr 16: 13 they **v** the one who speaks what is
31: 11 in her and lacks nothing of **v**.
Mt 13: 46 When he found one of great **v**,
Lk 16: 15 What people **v** highly is detestable
1Ti 4: 8 physical training is of some **v**, but godliness has **v** for all things,
Php 2: 3 Rather, in humility **v** others
Heb 11: 26 as of greater **v** than the treasures

VANISHES
Jas 4: 14 for a little while and then **v**.

VASHTI*
Queen of Persia replaced by Esther (Est 1–2).

VAST
Ge 2: 1 were completed in all their **v** array.
Dt 1: 19 of the Amorites through all that **v**
8: 15 He led you through the **v**
Ps 139: 17 How **v** is the sum of them!

VAULT
Ge 1: 7 So God made the **v** and separated
1: 8 God called the **v** "sky."

VEGETABLES
Pr 15: 17 a small serving of **v** with love
Ro 14: 2 whose faith is weak, eats only **v**.

VEIL
Ex 34: 33 to them, he put a **v** over his face.
2Co 3: 14 to this day the same **v** remains

VENGEANCE (AVENGE AVENGER AVENGES AVENGING REVENGE)
Nu 31: 3 carry out the LORD's **v** on them.
Isa 34: 8 For the LORD has a day of **v**,
Na 1: 2 The LORD takes **v** on his foes

VERDICT
Ps 51: 4 so you are right in your **v**
Jn 3: 19 This is the **v**: Light has come

VICTOR'S* (VICTORY)
2Ti 2: 5 not receive the **v** crown except
Rev 2: 10 give you life as your **v** crown.

VICTORIES* (VICTORY)
Jdg 5: 11 They recite the **v** of the LORD,
5: 11 the **v** of his villagers in Israel.
2Sa 22: 51 "He gives his king great **v**;
Ps 18: 50 He gives his king great **v**;
21: 1 great is his joy in the **v** you give!
21: 5 Through the **v** you gave, his glory
44: 4 my God, who decrees **v** for Jacob.

VICTORIOUS (VICTORY)
Zec 9: 9 comes to you, righteous and **v**,
Rev 2: 7 To the one who is **v**, I will give
2: 11 The one who is **v** will not be hurt
2: 17 To the one who is **v**, I will give
2: 26 To the one who is **v** and does my
3: 5 The one who is **v** will, like them,
3: 12 The one who is **v** I will make
3: 21 To the one who is **v**, I will give
3: 21 just as I was **v** and sat down
21: 7 who are **v** will inherit all this,

VICTORIOUSLY* (VICTORY)
Ps 45: 4 In your majesty ride forth **v**

VICTORY (VICTOR'S VICTORIES VICTORIOUS VICTORIOUSLY)
2Sa 8: 6 LORD gave David **v** wherever he
Ps 20: 5 May we shout for joy over your **v**
44: 6 my sword does not bring me **v**;
60: 12 With God we will gain the **v**, and
129: 2 have not gained the **v** over me.
Ps 149: 4 he crowns the humble with **v**.
Pr 11: 14 **v** is won through many advisers.
Isa 63: 1 I, proclaiming **v**, mighty to save."
1Co 15: 54 has been swallowed up in **v**."
15: 57 He gives us the **v** through our Lord
1Jn 5: 4 This is the **v** that has overcome

VIEW
Pr 5: 21 ways are in full **v** of the LORD,
2Ti 4: 1 and in **v** of his appearing and his

VILE
Ps 12: 8 is **v** is honored by the human race.

VILLAGE
Mk 6: 6 Jesus went around teaching from **v** to **v**.

VINDICATE (VINDICATED VINDICATES VINDICATION)
Dt 32: 36 The LORD will **v** his people
Ps 138: 8 The LORD will **v** me;

VINDICATED (VINDICATE)
Job 13: 18 my case, I know I will be **v**.
Ps 17: 15 I will be **v** and will see your face;
1Ti 3: 16 in the flesh, was **v** by the Spirit,

VINDICATES (VINDICATE)
Ps 57: 2 Most High, to God, who **v** me.
Isa 50: 8 He who **v** me is near.

VINDICATION (VINDICATE)
Ps 24: 5 and **v** from God their Savior.
37: 6 dawn, your **v** like the noonday sun.

VINE (VINEYARD)
Ps 128: 3 like a fruitful **v** within your house;
Isa 36: 16 you will eat fruit from your own **v**
Jn 15: 1 "I am the true **v**, and my Father is

VINEGAR
Pr 10: 26 As **v** to the teeth and smoke
Mk 15: 36 filled a sponge with wine **v**, put it

VINEYARD (VINE)
1Ki 21: 1 The **v** was in Jezreel,
Pr 31: 16 out of her earnings she plants a **v**.
SS 1: 6 my own **v** I had to neglect.
Isa 5: 1 the one I love a song about his **v**:
1Co 9: 7 Who plants a **v** and does not eat its

VIOLATION
Heb 2: 2 every **v** and disobedience received

VIOLENCE (VIOLENT)
Ge 6: 11 in God's sight and was full of **v**.
Isa 53: 9 though he had done no **v**, nor was
60: 18 No longer will **v** be heard in your
Eze 45: 9 Give up your **v** and oppression
Joel 3: 19 because of **v** done to the people
Jnh 3: 8 give up their evil ways and their **v**.

VIOLENT (VIOLENCE)
Eze 18: 10 "Suppose he has a **v** son, who sheds
Mt 11: 12 and **v** people have been raiding it.
1Ti 1: 13 and a persecutor and a **v** man,
3: 3 to drunkenness, not **v** but gentle,
Titus 1: 7 not **v**, not pursuing dishonest gain.

VIPERS
Ps 140: 3 the poison of **v** is on their lips.
Lk 3: 7 baptized by him, "You brood of **v**!
Ro 3: 13 "The poison of **v** is on their lips."

VIRGIN (VIRGINS)
Dt 22: 15 at the gate proof that she was a **v**.
Isa 7: 14 The **v** will conceive and give birth
Mt 1: 23 "The **v** will conceive and give birth
Lk 1: 34 asked the angel, "since I am a **v**?"
2Co 11: 2 I might present you as a pure **v**

VIRGINS (VIRGIN)
Mt 25: 1 will be like ten **v** who took their
1Co 7: 25 Now about **v**: I have no command

VIRTUES*
Col 3: 14 And over all these **v** put on love,

VISIBLE
Eph 5: 13 exposed by the light becomes **v**—
Col 1: 16 and on earth, **v** and invisible,

VISION (VISIONS)
Da 9: 24 to seal up **v** and prophecy
Ac 26: 19 disobedient to the **v** from heaven.

VISIONS (VISION)
Nu 12: 6 reveal myself to them in **v**, I speak
Joel 2: 28 dreams, your young men will see **v**.
Ac 2: 17 your young men will see **v**,

VOICE
Dt 30: 20 listen to his **v**, and hold fast to him.
Job 40: 9 and can your **v** thunder like his?
Ps 19: 4 Yet their **v** goes out into all
29: 3 The **v** of the LORD is over
95: 7 if only you would hear his **v**,
Pr 8: 1 not understanding raise her **v**?
Isa 30: 21 your ears will hear a **v** behind you,
40: 3 A **v** of one calling:
Mk 1: 3 "a **v** of one calling
Jn 5: 28 are in their graves will hear his **v**
10: 3 him, and the sheep listen to his **v**.
Ro 10: 18 "Their **v** has gone out into all
15: 6 and one **v** you may glorify the God
Heb 3: 7 "Today, if you hear his **v**,
Rev 3: 20 If anyone hears my **v** and opens

VOLUNTARY*
Phm : 14 not seem forced but would be **v**.

VOMIT
Lev 18: 28 it will **v** you out as it vomited
Pr 26: 11 As a dog returns to its **v**, so fools
2Pe 2: 22 "A dog returns to its **v**," and,

VOW (VOWS)
Nu 6: 2 woman wants to make a special **v**,
30: 2 a man makes a **v** to the LORD
Jdg 11: 30 Jephthah made a **v** to the LORD:

VOWS (VOW)
Ps 116: 14 I will fulfill my **v** to the LORD
Pr 20: 25 and only later to consider one's **v**.

VULTURES
Mt 24: 28 is a carcass, there the **v** will gather.

WAGE (WAGES WAGING)
2Co 10: 3 we do not **w** war as the world does.

WAGES (WAGE)
Mal 3: 5 who defraud laborers of their **w**,
Lk 10: 7 you, for the worker deserves his **w**.
Ro 4: 4 **w** are not credited as a gift but as
6: 23 the **w** of sin is death, but the gift
1Ti 5: 18 and "The worker deserves his **w**."

WAGING (WAGE)
Ro 7: 23 **w** war against the law of my mind

WAILING
Ps 30: 11 You turned my **w** into dancing;

WAIST
2Ki 1: 8 had a leather belt around his **w**."
Mt 3: 4 he had a leather belt around his **w**.

WAIT (AWAITS WAITED WAITING WAITS)
Ps 27: 14 **W** for the LORD; be strong
130: 5 I **w** for the LORD, my whole being
Isa 30: 18 Blessed are all who **w** for him!
Ac 1: 4 **w** for the gift my Father promised,
Ro 8: 23 groan inwardly as we **w** eagerly
1Th 1: 10 and to **w** for his Son from heaven,
Titus 2: 13 while we **w** for the blessed hope—

WAITED (WAIT)
Ps 40: 1 I **w** patiently for the LORD;

WAITING (WAIT)
Heb 9: 28 to those who are **w** for him.

WAITS (WAIT)
Ro 8: 19 the creation **w** in eager expectation

WAKE (AWAKE WAKENS)
Eph 5: 14 "**W** up, sleeper, rise from the dead,

WAKENS* (WAKE)
Isa 50: 4 He **w** me morning by morning,
50: 4 He **w** me morning by morning,

WALK (WALKED WALKING WALKS)
Lev 26: 12 I will **w** among you and be your
Dt 5: 33 **W** in obedience to all
6: 7 and when you **w** along the road,
10: 12 God, to **w** in obedience to him,
11: 19 and when you **w** along the road,
11: 22 to **w** in obedience to him and
26: 17 you will **w** in obedience to him,
Jos 22: 5 God, to **w** in obedience to him,
Ps 1: 1 Blessed is the one who does not **w**
15: 2 The one whose **w** is blameless,
23: 4 though I **w** through the darkest
84: 11 from those whose **w** is blameless.
89: 15 **w** in the light of your presence,
119: 45 I will **w** about in freedom, for I
Pr 4: 12 When you **w**, your steps will not be
6: 22 When you **w**, they will guide you;
13: 20 **W** with the wise and become wise,
Isa 2: 3 so that we may **w** in his paths."
2: 5 let us **w** in the light of the LORD.
30: 21 saying, "This is the way; **w** in it."
33: 15 who **w** righteously and speak
40: 31 weary, they will **w** and not be faint.
57: 2 Those who **w** uprightly enter
Jer 6: 16 and **w** in it, and you will find rest
Da 4: 37 those who **w** in pride he is able
Am 3: 3 Do two **w** together unless they
Mic 4: 5 but we will **w** in the name
6: 8 and to **w** humbly with your God.
Mk 2: 9 say, 'Get up, take your mat and **w**'?
Jn 8: 12 Whoever follows me will never **w**
1Jn 1: 6 him and yet **w** in the darkness,
1: 7 But if we **w** in the light, as he is
2Jn : 6 his command is that you **w** in love.

WALKED (WALK)
Ge 5: 24 Enoch **w** faithfully with God;
Jos 14: 9 your feet have **w** will be your
Mt 14: 29 **w** on the water and came toward

WALKING (WALK)
1Ki 3: 3 the LORD by **w** according
Da 3: 25 see four men **w** around in the fire,
2Jn : 4 of your children **w** in the truth,

WALKS (WALK)
Pr 10: 9 Whoever **w** in integrity **w** securely,
Jn 11: 9 Anyone who **w** in the daytime will

WALL (WALLS)
Jos 6: 20 gave a loud shout, the **w** collapsed;
Ne 2: 17 let us rebuild the **w** of Jerusalem,
Eph 2: 14 barrier, the dividing **w** of hostility,
Rev 21: 12 a great, high **w** with twelve gates,

WALLOWING
2Pe 2: 22 returns to her **w** in the mud."

WALLS (WALL)
Isa 58: 12 be called Repairer of Broken **W**,
60: 18 you will call your **w** Salvation
Heb 11: 30 By faith the **w** of Jericho fell,

WANDER (WANDERED)
Nu 32: 13 he made them **w** in the wilderness
Jas 5: 19 one of you should **w** from the truth

WANDERED (WANDER)
Eze 34: 6 My sheep **w** over all the mountains
Mt 18: 12 go to look for the one that **w** off?
1Ti 6: 10 have **w** from the faith and pierced

WANT (WANTED WANTING WANTS)
1Sa 8: 19 they said. "We **w** a king over us.
Mt 19: 21 "If you **w** to be perfect, go,
Lk 19: 14 say, 'We don't **w** this man to be our
Ro 7: 15 For what I **w** to do I do not do,
13: 3 Do you **w** to be free from fear
2Co 12: 14 you, because what I **w** is not your
Php 3: 10 I **w** to know Christ—yes, to know

WANTED (WANT)
1Co 12: 18 of them, just as he **w** them to be.
Heb 6: 17 Because God **w** to make

WANTING (WANT)
Da 5: 27 weighed on the scales and found **w**.
2Pe 3: 9 with you, not **w** anyone to perish,

WANTS (WANT)
Mt 5: 42 from the one who **w** to borrow
20: 26 whoever **w** to become great among
Mk 8: 35 For whoever **w** to save their life
10: 43 whoever **w** to become great among

Ro 9: 18 on whom he **w** to have mercy,
9: 18 he hardens whom he **w** to harden.
1Ti 2: 4 who **w** all people to be saved
1Pe 5: 2 are willing, as God **w** you to be;

WAR (WARRIOR WARS)
Jos 11: 23 Then the land had rest from **w**.
1Sa 15: 18 wage **w** against them until you
Ps 68: 30 the nations who delight in **w**.
120: 7 but when I speak, they are for **w**.
144: 1 who trains my hands for **w**,
Isa 2: 4 nor will they train for **w** anymore.
Da 9: 26 **W** will continue until the end,
Ro 7: 23 me, waging **w** against the law of my
2Co 10: 3 we do not wage **w** as the world
1Pe 2: 11 which wage **w** against your soul.
Rev 12: 7 Then **w** broke out in heaven.
19: 11 justice he judges and wages **w**.

WARN* (WARNED WARNING WARNINGS)
Ex 19: 21 **w** the people so they do not force
Nu 24: 14 let me **w** you of what this people
1Sa 8: 9 but **w** them solemnly and let them
1Ki 2: 42 swear by the LORD and **w** you,
2Ch 19: 10 are to **w** them not to sin against
Ps 81: 8 me, my people, and I will **w** you—
Jer 42: 19 Be sure of this: I **w** you today
Eze 3: 18 you do not **w** them or speak
3: 19 if you do **w** the wicked person
3: 20 Since you did not **w** them, they will
3: 21 if you do **w** the righteous person
33: 3 blows the trumpet to **w** the people,
33: 6 blow the trumpet to **w** the people
33: 9 if you do **w** the wicked person
Lk 16: 28 Let him **w** them, so that they will
Ac 4: 17 must **w** them to speak no longer
1Co 4: 14 but to **w** you as my dear children.
Gal 5: 21 I **w** you, as I did before, that those
1Th 5: 14 **w** those who are idle and
2Th 3: 15 but **w** them as you would a fellow
2Ti 2: 14 **W** them before God against
Titus 3: 10 **W** a divisive person once,
Rev 22: 18 I **w** everyone who hears the words

WARNED (WARN)
2Ki 17: 13 The LORD **w** Israel and Judah
Ps 19: 11 By them your servant is **w**;
Jer 22: 21 I **w** you when you felt secure,
Mt 3: 7 **w** you to flee from the coming
1Th 4: 6 as we told you and **w** you before.
Heb 11: 7 when **w** about things not yet seen,
12: 25 they refused him who **w** them

WARNING (WARN)
Jer 6: 8 Take **w**, Jerusalem, or I will turn
1Ti 5: 20 so that the others may take **w**.

WARNINGS (WARN)
1Co 10: 11 and were written down as **w** for us,

WARRIOR (WAR)
Ex 15: 3 The LORD is a **w**; the LORD is
1Ch 28: 3 because you are a **w** and have shed
Pr 16: 32 Better a patient person than a **w**,

WARS (WAR)
Ps 46: 9 He makes **w** cease to the ends
Mt 24: 6 will hear of **w** and rumors of **w**,

WASH (WASHED WASHING)
Ps 51: 7 **w** me, and I will be whiter than
Jer 4: 14 **w** the evil from your heart and be
Jn 13: 5 and began to **w** his disciples' feet,
Ac 22: 16 be baptized and **w** your sins away,
Jas 4: 8 **W** your hands, you sinners,
Rev 22: 14 are those who **w** their robes,

WASHED (WASH)
Ps 73: 13 have **w** my hands in innocence.
1Co 6: 11 But you were **w**, you were
Heb 10: 22 and having our bodies **w** with pure
2Pe 2: 22 and, "A sow that is **w** returns to her
Rev 7: 14 they have **w** their robes and made

WASHING (WASH)
Eph 5: 26 the **w** with water through the word,
1Ti 5: 10 **w** the feet of the Lord's people,
Titus 3: 5 saved us through the **w** of rebirth

WASTED (WASTING)
Jn 6: 12 are left over. Let nothing be **w**."

WASTING (WASTED)
2Co 4: 16 Though outwardly we are **w** away,

WATCH (WATCHES WATCHING WATCHMAN)
Ge 31: 49 the LORD keep **w** between you
Ps 90: 4 gone by, or like a **w** in the night.
141: 3 keep **w** over the door of my lips.
Pr 4: 6 love her, and she will **w** over you.
6: 22 you sleep, they will **w** over you;
Jer 31: 10 them and will **w** over his flock like
Mic 7: 7 for me, I **w** in hope for the LORD,
Mt 24: 42 "Therefore keep **w**, because you do
26: 41 "**W** and pray so that you will not
Mk 13: 35 "Therefore keep **w** because you do
Lk 2: 8 keeping **w** over their flocks at night
1Ti 4: 16 **W** your life and doctrine closely.
Heb 13: 17 because they keep **w** over you as

WATCHES* (WATCH)
Nu 19: 5 While he **w**, the heifer is to be
Job 24: 15 eye of the adulterer **w** for dusk;
Ps 1: 6 For the LORD **w** over the way
33: 14 his dwelling place he **w** all who live
63: 6 of you through the **w** of the night.
119:148 My eyes stay open through the **w**
121: 3 who **w** over you will not slumber;
121: 4 he who **w** over Israel will neither
121: 5 The LORD **w** over you—
127: 1 Unless the LORD **w** over the city,
145: 20 LORD **w** over all who love him,
146: 9 The LORD **w** over the foreigner
Pr 31: 27 She **w** over the affairs of her
Ecc 11: 4 Whoever **w** the wind will not plant
La 2: 19 night, as the **w** of the night begin;
4: 16 he no longer **w** over them.

WATCHING (WATCH)
Lk 12: 37 whose master finds them **w** when
1Pe 5: 2 is under your care, **w** over them—

WATCHMAN (WATCH)
Eze 3: 17 I have made you a **w** for the people
33: 6 but I will hold the **w** accountable

WATER (WATERED WATERING WATERS WELL-WATERED)
Ex 7: 20 all the **w** was changed into blood.
17: 1 but there was no **w** for the people
Nu 20: 2 Now there was no **w**
Ps 1: 3 like a tree planted by streams of **w**,
22: 14 I am poured out like **w**, and all my
42: 1 As the deer pants for streams of **w**,
Pr 25: 21 if he is thirsty, give him **w** to drink.
Isa 12: 3 joy you will draw **w** from the wells
30: 20 of adversity and the **w** of affliction,
32: 2 like streams of **w** in the desert
49: 10 and lead them beside springs of **w**.
Jer 2: 13 spring of living **w**, and have dug
2: 13 broken cisterns that cannot hold **w**.
17: 8 a tree planted by the **w** that sends
31: 9 will lead them beside streams of **w**
Eze 36: 25 I will sprinkle clean **w** on you,
Zec 14: 8 On that day living **w** will flow
Mt 14: 29 walked on the **w** and came toward
Mk 9: 41 anyone who gives you a cup of **w**
Lk 5: 4 "Put out into deep **w**, and let down
Jn 3: 5 of God unless they are born of **w**
4: 10 he would have given you living **w**."
7: 38 rivers of living **w** will flow
Eph 5: 26 washing with **w** through the word,
Heb 10: 22 our bodies washed with pure **w**.
1Pe 3: 21 this **w** symbolizes baptism that
2Pe 2: 17 These people are springs without **w**
1Jn 5: 6 He did not come by **w** only, but by **w** and blood.
5: 8 the Spirit, the **w** and the blood;
Rev 7: 17 lead them to springs of living **w**.'
21: 6 thirsty I will give **w** without cost

WATERED (WATER)
1Co 3: 6 I planted the seed, Apollos **w** it,

WATERING (WATER)
Isa 55: 10 not return to it without **w** the earth

WATERS (WATER)
Ps 23: 2 he leads me beside quiet **w**,
SS 8: 7 Many **w** cannot quench love;
Isa 11: 9 the LORD as the **w** cover the sea.
43: 2 When you pass through the **w**,
55: 1 you who are thirsty, come to the **w**;
58: 11 like a spring whose **w** never fail.
Hab 2: 14 the LORD as the **w** cover the sea.
1Co 3: 7 nor the one who **w** is anything,

WAVE (WAVES)
Lev 23: 11 **w** the sheaf before the LORD so it
Jas 1: 6 the one who doubts is like a **w**

WAVER*
1Ki 18: 21 "How long will you **w** between two
Ro 4: 20 Yet he did not **w** through unbelief

WAVES (WAVE)
Isa 57: 20 whose **w** cast up mire and mud.
Mt 8: 27 the winds and the **w** obey him!"
Eph 4: 14 tossed back and forth by the **w**,

WAY (WAYS)
Ex 13: 21 of cloud to guide them on their **w**
18: 20 show them the **w** they are to live
Dt 1: 33 to show you the **w** you should go.
32: 6 Is this the **w** you repay the LORD,
1Sa 12: 23 I will teach you the **w** that is good
2Sa 22: 31 "As for God, his **w** is perfect:
1Ki 8: 23 wholeheartedly in your **w**.
8: 36 Teach them the right **w** to live,
Job 23: 10 But he knows the **w** that I take;
Ps 1: 1 stand in the **w** that sinners take or
32: 8 teach you in the **w** you should go;
37: 5 Commit your **w** to the LORD;
86: 11 Teach me your **w**, LORD, that I
139: 24 and lead me in the **w** everlasting.
Pr 4: 11 I instruct you in the **w** of wisdom
12: 15 The **w** of fools seems right to them,
14: 12 is a **w** that appears to be right,
16: 7 takes pleasure in anyone's **w**,
19: 2 more will hasty feet miss the **w**!
22: 6 off on the **w** they should go,
30: 19 and the **w** of a man with a young
Isa 30: 21 behind you, saying, "This is the **w**;
35: 8 it will be called the **W** of Holiness;
40: 3 the wilderness prepare the **w**
48: 17 directs you in the **w** you should go.
53: 6 of us has turned to our own **w**;
Jer 5: 31 and my people love it this **w**.
Mal 3: 1 who will prepare the **w** before me.
Mt 3: 3 'Prepare the **w** for the Lord,
Lk 7: 27 will prepare your **w** before you.'
Jn 14: 6 "I am the **w** and the truth
Ac 1: 11 the same **w** you have seen him go
9: 2 any there who belonged to the **W**,
24: 14 ancestors as a follower of the **W**,
1Co 10: 13 provide a **w** out so that you can
12: 31 will show you the most excellent **w**.
14: 1 Follow the **w** of love and eagerly
Col 1: 10 Lord and please him in every **w**:
Titus 2: 10 every **w** they will make the
Heb 4: 15 who has been tempted in every **w**,
9: 8 the **w** into the Most Holy Place had
10: 20 living **w** opened for us through
13: 18 desire to live honorably in every **w**.

WAYS (WAY)
Ex 33: 13 teach me your **w** so I may know
Dt 32: 4 are perfect, and all his **w** are just.
2Ch 11: 17 years, following the **w** of David
Job 34: 21 "His eyes are on the **w** of mortals;
Ps 25: 4 Show me your **w**, LORD, teach me
25: 10 All the **w** of the LORD are loving
37: 7 when people succeed in their **w**,
51: 13 I will teach transgressors your **w**,
77: 13 Your **w**, God, are holy. What god is
119: 59 I have considered my **w** and have
139: 3 you are familiar with all my **w**.
145: 17 The LORD is righteous in all his **w**
Pr 3: 6 in all your **w** submit to him, and he
4: 26 feet and be steadfast in all your **w**.
5: 21 For your **w** are in full view
16: 2 All a person's **w** seem pure to them,
16: 17 who guard their **w** preserve their
Isa 2: 3 He will teach us his **w**, so that we
55: 7 Let the wicked forsake their **w**
55: 8 neither are your **w** my **w**,"
Eze 28: 15 in your **w** from the day you were
33: 8 out to dissuade them from their **w**,
Hos 14: 9 The **w** of the LORD are right;
Ro 1: 30 they invent **w** of doing evil;
Jas 3: 2 We all stumble in many **w**.

WAYWARD
Pr 6: 24 the smooth talk of a **w** woman.

WEAK (WEAKER WEAKNESS WEAKNESSES)
Ps 41: 1 those who have regard for the **w**;
72: 13 He will take pity on the **w**
82: 3 Defend the **w** and the fatherless;
Eze 34: 4 You have not strengthened the **w**
Mt 26: 41 spirit is willing, but the flesh is **w**."
Ac 20: 35 of hard work we must help the **w**,
Ro 14: 1 Accept the one whose faith is **w**,
15: 1 to bear with the failings of the **w**
1Co 1: 27 God chose the **w** things of the
8: 9 a stumbling block to the **w**.
9: 22 To the **w** I became **w**, to win the **w**.
11: 30 is why many among you are **w**
2Co 12: 10 For when I am **w**, then I am strong.
1Th 5: 14 help the **w**, be patient
Heb 12: 12 your feeble arms and **w** knees.

WEAKER* (WEAK)
2Sa 3: 1 the house of Saul grew **w** and **w**.
1Co 12: 22 seem to be **w** are indispensable,
1Pe 3: 7 them with respect as the **w** partner

WEAKNESS* (WEAK)
La 1: 6 **w** they have fled before the pursuer
Ro 8: 26 way, the Spirit helps us in our **w**.
1Co 1: 25 **w** of God is stronger than human
2: 3 I came to you in **w** with great fear
15: 43 is sown in **w**, it is raised in power;
2Co 11: 30 boast of the things that show my **w**.
12: 9 my power is made perfect in **w**."
13: 4 he was crucified in **w**, yet he lives
Heb 5: 2 since he himself is subject to **w**.
7: 28 as high priests men in all their **w**;
11: 34 whose **w** was turned to strength;

WEAKNESSES* (WEAK)
2Co 12: 5 about myself, except about my **w**.
12: 9 all the more gladly about my **w**,
12: 10 sake, I delight in **w**, in insults,
Heb 4: 15 is unable to empathize with our **w**,

WEALTH
Dt 8: 18 gives you the ability to produce **w**,
2Ch 1: 11 and you have not asked for **w**,
Ps 39: 6 up **w** without knowing whose it
49: 12 despite their **w**, do not endure;
Pr 3: 9 Honor the LORD with your **w**,
10: 4 but diligent hands bring **w**.
11: 4 **W** is worthless in the day of wrath,
13: 7 to be poor, yet has great **w**.
15: 16 of the LORD than great **w**
Ecc 5: 10 whoever loves **w** is never satisfied
5: 13 **w** hoarded to the harm of its
SS 8: 7 to give all the **w** of one's house
Mt 13: 22 deceitfulness of **w** choke the word,
Mk 10: 22 away sad, because he had great **w**.
12: 44 They all gave out of their **w**;
Lk 15: 13 and there squandered his **w** in wild
1Ti 6: 17 nor to put their hope in **w**,
Jas 5: 2 Your **w** has rotted, and moths have
5: 3 You have hoarded **w** in the last

WEAPON (WEAPONS)
Ne 4: 17 one hand and held a **w** in the other,

WEAPONS (WEAPON)
Ecc 9: 18 Wisdom is better than **w** of war,
2Co 6: 7 **w** of righteousness in the right
10: 4 The **w** we fight with are not the **w**

WEAR (WEARING)
Dt 8: 4 Your clothes did not **w** out and
22: 5 woman must not **w** men's clothing,
22: 5 nor a man **w** women's clothing,
Ps 102: 26 they will all **w** out like a garment.
Pr 23: 4 Do not **w** yourself out to get rich;
Isa 51: 6 the earth will **w** out like a garment
Heb 1: 11 they will all **w** out like a garment.
Rev 3: 18 and white clothes to **w**, so you can

WEARIES (WEARY)
Ecc 12: 12 end, and much study **w** the body.

WEARING (WEAR)
Jn 19: 5 Jesus came out **w** the crown
Jas 2: 3 attention to the man **w** fine clothes
1Pe 3: 3 hairstyles and the **w** of gold jewelry
Rev 7: 9 They were **w** white robes and were

WEARY (WEARIES)
Isa 40: 28 He will not grow tired or **w**, and
40: 31 they will run and not grow **w**,
50: 4 know the word that sustains the **w**.
Mt 11: 28 all you who are **w** and burdened,
Gal 6: 9 us not become **w** in doing good,
Heb 12: 3 that you will not grow **w** and lose
Rev 2: 3 my name, and have not grown **w**.

WEDDING
Mt 22: 11 who was not wearing **w** clothes.
Rev 19: 7 For the **w** of the Lamb has come,

WEEDS
Mt 13: 25 and sowed **w** among the wheat,

WEEK
Mt 28: 1 at dawn on the first day of the **w**,
1Co 16: 2 On the first day of every **w**,

WEEP (WEEPING WEPT)
Ecc 3: 4 a time to **w** and a time to laugh,
Lk 6: 21 Blessed are you who **w** now,
23: 28 of Jerusalem, do not **w** for me;

WEEPING (WEEP)
Ps 30: 5 **w** may stay for the night,
126: 6 Those who go out **w**, carrying seed
Jer 31: 15 mourning and great **w**, Rachel **w**
Mt 2: 18 Rachel **w** for her children
8: 12 where there will be **w** and gnashing

WEIGH (OUTWEIGHS WEIGHED WEIGHS WEIGHTIER WEIGHTS)
1Co 14: 29 the others should **w** carefully what

WEIGHED (WEIGH)
Job 28: 15 nor can its price be **w** out in silver.
Da 5: 27 You have been **w** on the scales
Lk 21: 34 or your hearts will be **w** down

WEIGHS (WEIGH)
Pr 12: 25 Anxiety **w** down the heart,
15: 28 of the righteous **w** its answers,
21: 2 right, but the LORD **w** the heart.
24: 12 not he who **w** the heart perceive it?

WEIGHTIER* (WEIGH)
Jn 5: 36 "I have testimony **w** than

WEIGHTS (WEIGH)
Lev 19: 36 Use honest scales and honest **w**,
Dt 25: 13 Do not have two differing **w** in
Pr 11: 1 but accurate **w** find favor with him.

WELCOME (WELCOMES)
Mk 9: 37 welcomes me does not **w** me
2Pe 1: 11 you will receive a rich **w**

WELCOMES (WELCOME)
Mt 10: 40 "Anyone who **w** you **w** me,
18: 5 whoever **w** one such child in my name **w** me.
2Jn : 11 Anyone who **w** them shares in

WELL (WELLED WELLING WELLS)
Jer 32: 39 that all will then go **w** for them
Mt 15: 31 the crippled made **w**, the lame
Lk 14: 5 falls into a **w** on the Sabbath day,
17: 19 your faith has made you **w**."
Jas 5: 15 faith will make the sick person **w**;

WELL-WATERED (WATER)
Isa 58: 11 You will be like a **w** garden,

WELLED* (WELL)
2Co 8: 2 their extreme poverty **w** up in rich

WELLING* (WELL)
Jn 4: 14 in them a spring of water **w**

WELLS (WELL)
Isa 12: 3 draw water from the **w** of salvation.

WEPT (WEEP)
Ps 137: 1 and **w** when we remembered Zion.
Lk 22: 62 And he went outside and **w** bitterly.
Jn 11: 35 Jesus **w**.

WEST
Ps 103: 12 as far as the east is from the **w**,
107: 3 from east and **w**, from north

WHEAT
Mt 3: 12 gathering his **w** into the barn
13: 25 and sowed weeds among the **w**,
Lk 22: 31 has asked to sift all of you as **w**.
Jn 12: 24 you, unless a kernel of **w** falls

WHEELS
Eze 1: 16 appearance and structure of the **w**:

WHIRLWIND (WIND)
2Ki 2: 1 to take Elijah up to heaven in a **w**,
Hos 8: 7 sow the wind and reap the **w**.
Na 1: 3 His way is in the **w** and the storm,

WHISPER (WHISPERED)
1Ki 19: 12 And after the fire came a gentle **w**.
Job 26: 14 how faint the **w** we hear of him!
Ps 107: 29 He stilled the storm to a **w**;

WHISPERED (WHISPER)
Mt 10: 27 what is **w** in your ear,

WHITE (WHITER)
Isa 1: 18 scarlet, they shall be as **w** as snow;
Da 7: 9 His clothing was as **w** as snow;
7: 9 hair of his head was **w** like wool.
Mt 28: 3 and his clothes were **w** as snow.
Rev 1: 14 hair on his head was **w** like wool,
3: 4 dressed in **w**, for they are worthy.
6: 2 and there before me was a **w** horse!
7: 13 asked me, "These in **w** robes—
19: 11 and there before me was a **w** horse,
20: 11 I saw a great **w** throne and him

WHITER (WHITE)
Ps 51: 7 me, and I will be **w** than snow.

WHOLE
Ge 1: 29 plant on the face of the **w** earth
2: 6 the **w** surface of the ground.
11: 1 Now the **w** world had one language
Ex 12: 47 The **w** community of Israel must
19: 5 Although the **w** earth is mine,
Lev 16: 17 and the **w** community of Israel.
Nu 14: 21 of the LORD fills the **w** earth,
32: 13 until the **w** generation of those
Dt 13: 16 all its plunder as a **w** burnt offering
19: 8 gives you the **w** land he promised
Jos 2: 3 have come to spy out the **w** land."

1Sa 1: 28 For his **w** life he will be given over
17: 46 the **w** world will know that there is
1Ki 10: 24 The **w** world sought audience
2Ki 21: 8 keep the **w** Law that my servant
Ps 72: 19 may the **w** earth be filled with his
Pr 4: 22 them and health to one's **w** body.
8: 31 rejoicing in his **w** world
Isa 1: 5 Your **w** head is injured, your **w** heart afflicted.
6: 3 the **w** earth is full of his glory."
14: 26 plan determined for the **w** world;
Eze 34: 6 were scattered over the **w** earth,
Da 2: 35 mountain and filled the **w** earth.
Zep 1: 18 of his jealousy the **w** earth will be
Zec 14: 9 will be king over the **w** earth.
Mal 3: 10 Bring the **w** tithe
Mt 5: 29 your body than for your **w** body
6: 22 your **w** body will be full of light.
16: 26 for someone to gain the **w** world,
24: 14 in the **w** world as a testimony to all
Lk 21: 35 who live on the face of the **w** earth.
Jn 12: 19 Look how the **w** world has gone
13: 10 their **w** body is clean.
21: 25 even the **w** world would not have
Ac 17: 26 they should inhabit the **w** earth;
20: 27 proclaim to you the **w** will of God.
Ro 3: 19 and the **w** world held accountable
8: 22 the **w** creation has been groaning
1Co 4: 9 made a spectacle to the **w** universe,
12: 17 If the **w** body were an eye,
Gal 5: 3 he is obligated to obey the **w** law.
Eph 4: 10 in order to fill the **w** universe.)
4: 13 attaining to the **w** measure
1Th 5: 23 May your **w** spirit, soul and body
Jas 2: 10 For whoever keeps the **w** law
1Jn 2: 2 but also for the sins of the **w** world.
Rev 3: 10 to come on the **w** world to test

WHOLEHEARTED* (HEART)
2Ki 20: 3 with **w** devotion and have done
1Ch 28: 9 serve him with **w** devotion
29: 19 my son Solomon the **w** devotion
Isa 38: 3 with **w** devotion and have done

WHOLEHEARTEDLY* (HEART)
Nu 14: 24 a different spirit and follows me **w**,
32: 11 they have not followed me **w**,
32: 12 for they followed the LORD **w**.'
Dt 1: 36 he followed the LORD **w**."
Jos 14: 8 followed the LORD my God **w**.
14: 9 followed the LORD my God **w**.'
14: 14 the LORD, the God of Israel, **w**.
1Ki 8: 23 your servants who continue **w**
1Ch 29: 9 given freely and **w** to the LORD.
2Ch 6: 14 your servants who continue **w**
15: 15 oath because they had sworn it **w**.
19: 9 and **w** in the fear of the LORD.
25: 2 the eyes of the LORD, but not **w**.
31: 21 he sought his God and worked **w**.
Ps 119: 80 May I **w** follow your decrees,
Eph 6: 7 Serve **w**, as if you were serving

WHOLESOME*
2Pe 3: 1 to stimulate you to **w** thinking.

WICK
Isa 42: 3 a smoldering **w** he will not snuff
Mt 12: 20 a smoldering **w** he will not snuff

WICKED (WICKEDNESS)
Ge 13: 13 Now the people of Sodom were **w**
39: 9 could I do such a **w** thing and sin
Nu 14: 35 things to this whole **w** community,
Dt 15: 9 not to harbor this **w** thought:
Jdg 19: 22 some of the **w** men of the city
1Sa 15: 18 completely destroy those **w** people,
25: 17 He is such a **w** man that no one can
2Sa 13: 12 Don't do this **w** thing.
2Ki 17: 11 They did **w** things that aroused
2Ch 7: 14 face and turn from their **w** ways,
19: 2 "Should you help the **w** and love
Ne 13: 17 "What is this **w** thing you are
Ps 1: 1 does not walk in step with the **w**
1: 5 Therefore the **w** will not stand
7: 9 to an end the violence of the **w**
10: 13 Why does the **w** man revile God?
11: 5 but the **w**, those who love violence,
26: 5 and refuse to sit with the **w**.
32: 10 Many are the woes of the **w**,
36: 1 concerning the sinfulness of the **w**:
37: 13 but the Lord laughs at the **w**, for he
49: 5 when **w** deceivers surround me—
50: 16 But to the **w** person, God says:
58: 3 Even from birth the **w** go astray;
73: 3 when I saw the prosperity of the **w**.
82: 2 and show partiality to the **w**?
Ps 112: 10 The **w** will see and be vexed,
119: 61 Though the **w** bind me with ropes,
119:155 Salvation is far from the **w**,
140: 8 Do not grant the **w** their desires,
141: 10 Let the **w** fall into their own nets,
146: 9 he frustrates the ways of the **w**.
Pr 2: 12 save you from the ways of **w** men,
4: 14 not set foot on the path of the **w**
6: 18 a heart that devises **w** schemes,
9: 7 rebukes the **w** incurs abuse.
10: 20 the heart of the **w** is of little value.
10: 23 A fool finds pleasure in **w** schemes,
10: 28 hopes of the **w** come to nothing.
11: 5 but the **w** are brought down by
11: 10 when the **w** perish, there are shouts
11: 21 The **w** will not go unpunished,
12: 5 but the advice of the **w** is deceitful.
12: 10 the kindest acts of the **w** are cruel.
14: 19 the **w** at the gates of the righteous.
15: 3 keeping watch on the **w**
15: 26 detests the thoughts of the **w**,
21: 10 The **w** crave evil;
21: 29 The **w** put up a bold front,
28: 1 The **w** flee though no one pursues,
28: 4 forsake instruction praise the **w**,
29: 7 but the **w** have no such concern.
29: 16 When the **w** thrive, so does sin,
29: 27 the **w** detest the upright.
Isa 11: 4 breath of his lips he will slay the **w**.
13: 11 for its evil, the **w** for their sins.
26: 10 But when grace is shown to the **w**,
48: 22 says the LORD, "for the **w**."
53: 9 was assigned a grave with the **w**,
55: 7 Let the **w** forsake their ways
57: 20 But the **w** are like the tossing sea,
Jer 35: 15 of you must turn from your **w** ways
Eze 3: 18 that **w** person will die for their sin,
13: 22 because you encouraged the **w** not
14: 7 put a **w** stumbling block before
18: 21 if a **w** person turns away from all
18: 23 any pleasure in the death of the **w**?
21: 25 profane and **w** prince of Israel,
33: 8 that **w** person will die for their sin,
33: 11 no pleasure in the death of the **w**,
33: 14 And if I say to a **w** person,
33: 19 if a **w** person turns away from their
Da 12: 10 but the **w** will continue to be **w**.
Mt 12: 39 "A **w** and adulterous generation
12: 45 other spirits more **w** than itself,
12: 45 it will be with this **w** generation."
Lk 6: 35 he is kind to the ungrateful and **w**.
Ac 2: 23 with the help of **w** men, put him
1Co 5: 13 "Expel the **w** person from among
Rev 2: 2 that you cannot tolerate **w** people,

WICKEDNESS (WICKED)
Ge 6: 5 The LORD saw how great the **w**
Ex 34: 7 and forgiving **w**, rebellion and sin.
Lev 16: 21 and confess over it all the **w**
19: 29 prostitution and be filled with **w**.
Dt 9: 4 account of the **w** of these nations
Ps 45: 7 You love righteousness and hate **w**;
92: 15 Rock, and there is no **w** in him."
Pr 13: 6 but **w** overthrows the sinner.
Jer 3: 2 land with your prostitution and **w**.
8: 6 None of them repent of their **w**,
14: 20 We acknowledge our **w**, LORD,
Eze 18: 20 the **w** of the wicked will be charged
28: 15 you were created till **w** was found
33: 19 person turns away from their **w**
Da 4: 27 and your **w** by being kind
9: 24 end to sin, to atone for **w**, to bring
Jnh 1: 2 because its **w** has come up before
Mt 24: 12 Because of the increase of **w**,
Lk 11: 39 inside you are full of greed and **w**.
Ac 1: 18 the payment he received for his **w**,
Ro 1: 18 who suppress the truth by their **w**,
1Co 5: 8 bread leavened with malice and **w**,
2Co 6: 14 and **w** have in common?
2Ti 2: 19 the Lord must turn away from **w**."
Titus 2: 14 for us to redeem us from all **w**
Heb 1: 9 loved righteousness and hated **w**;
8: 12 For I will forgive their **w** and will
2Pe 2: 15 of Bezer, who loved the wages of **w**.

WIDE
Ps 81: 10 Open **w** your mouth and I will fill
Isa 54: 2 stretch your tent curtains **w**, do not
Mt 7: 13 For **w** is the gate and broad is
2Co 6: 13 open **w** your hearts also.
Eph 3: 18 to grasp how **w** and long and high

WIDOW (WIDOWS)
Ex 22: 22 "Do not take advantage of the **w**
Dt 10: 18 cause of the fatherless and the **w**,
Ps 146: 9 sustains the fatherless and the **w**,
Isa 1: 17 plead the case of the **w**.
Lk 21: 2 saw a poor **w** put in two very small
1Ti 5: 4 a **w** has children or grandchildren,

WIDOWS (WIDOW)
Ps 68: 5 a defender of **w**, is God in his holy
Ac 6: 1 Jews because their **w** were being
1Co 7: 8 to the unmarried and the **w** I say:
1Ti 5: 3 to those **w** who are really in need.
Jas 1: 27 orphans and **w** in their distress

WIFE (WIVES WIVES')
Ge 2: 24 and mother and is united to his **w**,
19: 26 But Lot's **w** looked back, and she
24: 67 So she became his **w**, and he loved
Ex 20: 17 shall not covet your neighbor's **w**,
Lev 20: 10 adultery with another man's **w**—
Dt 5: 21 shall not covet your neighbor's **w**.
22: 13 If a man takes a **w** and,
24: 5 happiness to the **w** he has married.
Ru 4: 13 took Ruth and she became his **w**.
Pr 5: 18 you rejoice in the **w** of your youth.
12: 4 A **w** of noble character is her
18: 22 who finds a **w** finds what is good
19: 13 quarrelsome **w** is like the constant
31: 10 A **w** of noble character who can
Hos 1: 2 for like an adulterous **w** this land is
Mal 2: 14 the **w** of your marriage covenant.
Mt 1: 20 to take Mary home as your **w**,
19: 3 for a man to divorce his **w** for any
Lk 17: 32 Remember Lot's **w**!
18: 29 "no one who has left home or **w**
1Co 7: 2 sexual relations with his own **w**,
7: 33 how he can please his **w**—
Eph 5: 23 head of the **w** as Christ is the head
5: 33 must love his **w** as he loves himself,
5: 33 the **w** must respect her husband.
1Ti 3: 2 faithful to his **w**, temperate,
Rev 21: 9 you the bride, the **w** of the Lamb."

WILD
Ge 1: 25 God made the **w** animals
8: 1 all the **w** animals and the livestock
Lk 15: 13 squandered his wealth in **w** living.
Ro 11: 17 and you, though a **w** olive shoot,

WILDERNESS
Nu 32: 13 them wander in the **w** forty years,
Dt 8: 16 He gave you manna to eat in the **w**,
29: 5 years that I led you through the **w**,
Ne 9: 19 did not abandon them in the **w**.
Ps 78: 19 God really spread a table in the **w**?
78: 52 led them like sheep through the **w**.
Isa 43: 20 because I provide water in the **w**
Mk 1: 3 "a voice of one calling in the **w**,
1: 13 and he was in the **w** forty days,
Rev 12: 6 fled into the **w** to a place prepared

WILL (WILLFUL WILLING WILLINGNESS)
Ps 40: 8 I desire to do your **w**, my God;
143: 10 Teach me to do your **w**, for you are
Isa 53: 10 Yet it was the LORD's **w** to crush
53: 10 the **w** of the LORD **w** prosper
Mt 6: 10 kingdom come, your **w** be done,
7: 21 only the one who does the **w** of my
10: 29 Yet not one of them **w** fall
12: 50 whoever does the **w** of my Father
26: 39 Yet not as I **w**, but as you **w**."
26: 42 I drink it, may your **w** be done."
Jn 6: 38 down from heaven not to do my **w**
6: 38 to do the **w** of him who sent me.
7: 17 chooses to do the **w** of God **w** find
Ac 20: 27 to you the whole **w** of God.
Ro 12: 2 test and approve what God's **w** is—
12: 2 his good, pleasing and perfect **w**.
1Co 7: 37 but has control over his own **w**,
Eph 5: 17 understand what the Lord's **w** is.
Php 2: 13 for it is God who works in you to **w**
1Th 4: 3 It is God's **w** that you should be
5: 18 for this is God's **w** for you in Christ
2Ti 2: 26 has taken them captive to do his **w**.
Heb 2: 4 distributed according to his **w**.
9: 16 In the case of a **w**, it is necessary
10: 7 I have come to do your **w**,
13: 21 everything good for doing his **w**,
Jas 4: 15 "If it is the Lord's **w**, we **w** live
1Pe 3: 17 if it is God's **w**, to suffer for doing
4: 2 but rather for the **w** of God.
2Pe 1: 21 had its origin in the human **w**,
1Jn 5: 14 ask anything according to his **w**,
Rev 4: 11 by your **w** they were created

WILLFUL (WILL)
Ps 19: 13 your servant also from **w** sins;

WILLING (WILL)
1Ch 28: 9 devotion and with a **w** mind,
29: 5 who is **w** to consecrate themselves
Ps 51: 12 salvation and grant me a **w** spirit,
Da 3: 28 were **w** to give up their lives rather
Mt 18: 14 Father in heaven is not **w** that any
23: 37 her wings, and you were not **w**.
26: 41 The spirit is **w**, but the flesh is
1Ti 6: 18 and to be generous and **w** to share.
1Pe 5: 2 but because you are **w**, as God

WILLINGNESS* (WILL)
2Co 8: 11 so that your eager **w** to do it may
8: 12 For if the **w** is there, the gift is

WIN (WON)
Lk 21: 19 Stand firm, and you will **w** life.
1Co 9: 19 everyone, to **w** as many as possible.
Php 3: 14 on toward the goal to **w** the prize
1Th 4: 12 your daily life may **w** the respect

WIND (WHIRLWIND WINDS)
Ps 1: 4 like chaff that the **w** blows away.
Ecc 2: 11 meaningless, a chasing after the **w**;
Hos 8: 7 "They sow the **w** and reap
Mk 4: 41 Even the **w** and the waves obey
Jn 3: 8 The **w** blows wherever it pleases.
Eph 4: 14 there by every **w** of teaching
Jas 1: 6 the sea, blown and tossed by the **w**.

WINDOW
Jos 2: 21 she tied the scarlet cord in the **w**.
Ac 20: 9 in a **w** was a young man named
2Co 11: 33 in a basket from a **w** in the wall

WINDS (WIND)
Ps 104: 4 He makes **w** his messengers,
Mt 24: 31 gather his elect from the four **w**,

WINE
Ps 104: 15 **w** that gladdens human hearts,
Pr 20: 1 **W** is a mocker and beer a brawler;
23: 20 join those who drink too much **w**
23: 31 Do not gaze at **w** when it is red,
31: 6 **w** for those who are in anguish!
SS 1: 2 love is more delightful than **w**.
Isa 28: 7 stagger from **w** and reel from beer:
55: 1 buy **w** and milk without money
Mt 9: 17 Neither do people pour new **w**
Lk 23: 36 They offered him **w** vinegar
Jn 2: 9 water that had been turned into **w**
Ro 14: 21 drink **w** or to do anything else
Eph 5: 18 Do not get drunk on **w**, which
1Ti 5: 23 and use a little **w** because of your
Rev 16: 19 the cup filled with the **w** of the fury

WINEPRESS
Isa 63: 2 like those of one treading the **w**?
Rev 19: 15 He treads the **w** of the fury

WINESKINS
Mt 9: 17 people pour new wine into old **w**.
9: 17 they pour new wine into new **w**,

WINGS
Ex 19: 4 how I carried you on eagles' **w**
Ru 2: 12 under whose **w** you have come
Ps 17: 8 hide me in the shadow of your **w**
91: 4 under his **w** you will find refuge;
Isa 6: 2 were seraphim, each with six **w**:
40: 31 They will soar on **w** like eagles;
Eze 1: 6 of them had four faces and four **w**.
Zec 5: 9 women, with the wind in their **w**!
Lk 13: 34 gathers her chicks under her **w**,
Rev 4: 8 the four living creatures had six **w**

WINTER
Mk 13: 18 that this will not take place in **w**,

WIPE (WIPED)
Isa 25: 8 Sovereign LORD will **w** away
Rev 7: 17 God will **w** away every tear
21: 4 'He will **w** every tear from their

WIPED (WIPE)
Lk 7: 38 Then she **w** them with her hair,
Ac 3: 19 so that your sins may be **w** out,

WISDOM (WISE)
Ge 3: 6 and also desirable for gaining **w**,
1Ki 4: 29 God gave Solomon **w** and very
2Ch 1: 10 Give me **w** and knowledge, that I
Ps 51: 6 taught me **w** in that secret place.
111: 10 the LORD is the beginning of **w**;
Pr 2: 6 For the LORD gives **w**;
3: 13 Blessed are those who find **w**,
4: 7 The beginning of **w** is this: Get **w**.
8: 11 for **w** is more precious than rubies,
11: 2 but with humility comes **w**.
13: 10 **w** is found in those who take
23: 23 **w**, instruction and insight as well.
29: 3 A man who loves **w** brings joy
29: 15 A rod and a reprimand impart **w**,
31: 26 She speaks with **w**, and faithful
Isa 11: 2 rest on him—the Spirit of **w**
28: 29 whose **w** is magnificent.
Jer 10: 12 he founded the world by his **w**
Mic 6: 9 and to fear your name is **w**—
Mt 11: 19 **w** is proved right by her deeds."
Lk 2: 52 And Jesus grew in **w** and stature,
Ac 6: 3 to be full of the Spirit and **w**.
Ro 11: 33 the depth of the riches of the **w**
1Co 1: 17 not with **w** and eloquence,
1: 30 has become for us **w** from God—
12: 8 through the Spirit a message of **w**,
Eph 1: 17 may give you the Spirit of **w**
Col 2: 3 are hidden all the treasures of **w**
2: 23 indeed have an appearance of **w**,
Jas 1: 5 If any of you lacks **w**, you should
3: 13 in the humility that comes from **w**.
Rev 5: 12 and wealth and **w** and strength

WISE (WISDOM WISER)
1Ki 3: 12 I will give you a **w** and discerning
Job 5: 13 He catches the **w** in their craftiness,
Ps 19: 7 trustworthy, making **w** the simple.
Pr 3: 7 Do not be **w** in your own eyes;
9: 8 rebuke the **w** and they will love
9: 9 Instruct the **w** and they will be
10: 1 A **w** son brings joy to his father,
11: 30 and the one who is **w** saves lives.
13: 1 A **w** son heeds his father's
13: 20 Walk with the **w** and become **w**,
16: 23 the **w** make their mouths prudent,
17: 28 Even fools are thought **w** if they
Ecc 9: 17 The quiet words of the **w** are more
Jer 9: 23 "Let not the **w** boast of their
Eze 28: 6 think you are **w**, as **w** as a god,
Da 2: 21 He gives wisdom to the **w**
12: 3 Those who are **w** will shine like
Mt 11: 25 hidden these things from the **w**
25: 2 them were foolish and five were **w**.
1Co 1: 19 will destroy the wisdom of the **w**;
1: 27 things of the world to shame the **w**;
3: 10 I laid a foundation as a **w** builder,
3: 19 "He catches the **w** in their
Eph 5: 15 not as unwise but as **w**,
2Ti 3: 15 make you **w** for salvation through
Jas 3: 13 Who is **w** and understanding

WISER (WISE)
Pr 9: 9 the wise and they will be **w** still;
1Co 1: 25 of God is **w** than human wisdom,

WISH (WISHES)
Jn 15: 7 ask whatever you **w**, and it will be
Ro 9: 3 I could **w** that I myself were cursed
Rev 3: 15 I **w** you were either one or the

WISHES (WISH)
Rev 22: 17 let the one who **w** take the free gift

WITCHCRAFT
Dt 18: 10 interprets omens, engages in **w**,
Gal 5: 20 idolatry and **w**;

WITHDREW
Lk 5: 16 But Jesus often **w** to lonely places

WITHER (WITHERS)
Ps 1: 3 season and whose leaf does not **w**
37: 19 In times of disaster they will not **w**;

WITHERS (WITHER)
Isa 40: 7 The grass **w** and the flowers fall,
1Pe 1: 24 the grass **w** and the flowers fall,

WITHHELD (WITHHOLD)
Ge 22: 12 because you have not **w** from me

WITHHOLD (WITHHELD WITHHOLDS)
Ps 84: 11 no good thing does he **w** from
Pr 23: 13 Do not **w** discipline from a child;

WITHHOLDS (WITHHOLD)
Dt 27: 19 "Cursed is anyone who **w** justice

WITNESS (EYEWITNESSES WITNESSES)
Pr 12: 17 An honest **w** tells the truth,
19: 9 A false **w** will not go unpunished,
Jn 1: 8 he came only as a **w** to the light.

WITNESSES (WITNESS)
Dt 19: 15 by the testimony of two or three **w**.
Mt 18: 16 by the testimony of two or three **w**.'
Ac 1: 8 and you will be my **w** in Jerusalem,

WIVES (WIFE)
Eph 5: 22 **W**, submit yourselves to your own
5: 25 love your **w**, just as Christ loved
1Pe 3: 1 **W**, in the same way submit

WIVES'* (WIFE)
1Ti 4: 7 with godless myths and old **w** tales;

WOE
Isa 6: 5 "**W** to me!" I cried. "I am ruined!
Eze 34: 2 **W** to you shepherds of Israel who
Mt 18: 7 **w** to the person through whom
23: 13 "**W** to you, teachers of the law
Jude : 11 **W** to them! They have taken

WOLF (WOLVES)
Isa 65: 25 The **w** and the lamb will feed

WOLVES (WOLF)
Mt 10: 16 you out like sheep among **w**.

WOMAN (MAN)
Ge 2: 22 the LORD God made a **w**
2: 23 she shall be called '**w**,' for she was
3: 6 When the **w** saw that the fruit
3: 12 "The **w** you put here with me—
3: 15 put enmity between you and the **w**,
3: 16 To the **w** he said, "I will make your
12: 11 "I know what a beautiful **w** you are.
20: 3 because of the **w** you have taken;
24: 5 if the **w** is unwilling to come
Ge 24: 16 The **w** was very beautiful, a virgin;
Ex 2: 1 tribe of Levi married a Levite **w**,
3: 22 Every **w** is to ask her neighbor
21: 10 If he marries another **w**, he must
21: 22 hit a pregnant **w** and she gives
Lev 12: 2 'A **w** who becomes pregnant
15: 19 "'When a **w** has her regular flow
15: 25 "'When a **w** has a discharge
18: 17 have sexual relations with both a **w**
20: 13 with a man as one does with a **w**,
Nu 5: 29 of jealousy when a **w** goes astray
30: 3 "When a young **w** still living in her
30: 9 divorced **w** will be binding on her.
30: 10 "If a **w** living with her husband
Dt 20: 7 Has anyone become pledged to a **w**
21: 11 among the captives a beautiful **w**
22: 5 A **w** must not wear men's clothing,
Jdg 4: 9 Sisera into the hands of a **w**."
13: 6 Then the **w** went to her husband
14: 2 "I have seen a Philistine **w**
16: 4 love with a **w** in the Valley of Sorek
20: 4 the husband of the murdered **w**,
Ru 3: 11 that you are a **w** of noble character.
1Sa 1: 15 "I am a **w** who is deeply troubled.
25: 3 was an intelligent and beautiful **w**,
28: 7 "Find me a **w** who is a medium,
2Sa 11: 2 From the roof he saw a **w** bathing.
13: 17 "Get this **w** out of my sight and
14: 2 had a wise **w** brought from there.
20: 16 a wise **w** called from the city,
1Ki 3: 18 was born, this **w** also had a baby.
17: 24 Then the **w** said to Elijah, "Now I
2Ki 4: 8 And a well-to-do **w** was there,
8: 1 to the **w** whose son he had restored
9: 34 "Take care of that cursed **w**,"
Job 14: 1 born of **w**, are of few days and full
Pr 11: 16 A kindhearted **w** gains honor,
11: 22 snout is a beautiful **w** who shows
14: 1 The wise **w** builds her house,
23: 27 for an adulterous **w** is a deep pit,
30: 19 the way of a man with a young **w**.
30: 23 contemptible **w** who gets married,
31: 30 a **w** who fears the LORD is to be
Isa 54: 1 barren **w**, you who never bore
62: 5 a young man marries a young **w**,
Jer 2: 32 Does a young **w** forget her jewelry,
Mt 5: 28 a **w** lustfully has already committed
9: 20 then a **w** who had been subject
15: 28 Then Jesus said to her, "**W**,
26: 7 a **w** came to him with an alabaster
Mk 5: 25 a **w** was there who had been
7: 25 him, a **w** whose little daughter was
Lk 7: 39 him and what kind of **w** she is—
10: 38 a village where a **w** named Martha
13: 12 her forward and said to her, "**W**,
15: 8 suppose a **w** has ten silver coins
Jn 2: 4 "**W**, why do you involve me?"
4: 7 a Samaritan **w** came to draw water,
8: 3 *brought in a **w** caught in adultery.*
19: 26 he said to her, "**W**, here is your
20: 15 He asked her, "**W**, why are you
Ac 9: 40 Turning toward the dead **w**, he
16: 14 of those listening was a **w**
Ro 7: 2 by law a married **w** is bound to her
1Co 7: 2 and each **w** with her own husband.
7: 34 An unmarried **w** or virgin is
7: 39 A **w** is bound to her husband as
11: 3 and the head of the **w** is man,

1Co 11: 7 but **w** is the glory of man.
11: 13 Is it proper for a **w** to pray to God
Gal 4: 4 born of a **w**, born under the law,
4: 31 we are not children of the slave **w**, but of the free **w**.
1Ti 2: 11 A **w** should learn in quietness
5: 16 any **w** who is a believer has widows
Rev 2: 20 You tolerate that **w** Jezebel,
12: 1 a **w** clothed with the sun,
12: 13 he pursued the **w** who had given
17: 3 There I saw a **w** sitting on a scarlet

WOMEN (MAN)
SS 1: 3 No wonder the young **w** love you!
Mt 11: 11 among those born of **w** there has
28: 5 The angel said to the **w**, "Do not be
Mk 15: 41 In Galilee these **w** had followed
Lk 1: 42 "Blessed are you among **w**,
8: 2 some **w** who had been cured of evil
23: 27 him, including **w** who mourned
24: 11 But they did not believe the **w**,
Ac 1: 14 along with the **w** and Mary
16: 13 to the **w** who had gathered there.
17: 4 and quite a few prominent **w**.
Ro 1: 26 Even their **w** exchanged natural
1Co 14: 34 **W** should remain silent
Php 4: 3 help these **w** since they have
1Ti 2: 9 I also want the **w** to dress modestly,
5: 2 older **w** as mothers, and younger **w**
Titus 2: 3 teach the older **w** to be reverent
2: 4 can urge the younger **w** to love
Heb 11: 35 **W** received back their dead,
1Pe 3: 5 is the way the holy **w** of the past

WOMB
Job 1: 21 I came from my mother's **w**,
Ps 139: 13 knit me together in my mother's **w**.
Pr 31: 2 Listen, son of my **w**!
Jer 1: 5 I formed you in the **w** I knew you,
Lk 1: 44 the baby in my **w** leaped for joy.
Jn 3: 4 into their mother's **w** to be born!"

WON (WIN)
1Pe 3: 1 they may be **w** over without words

WONDER (WONDERFUL WONDERS)
Dt 13: 1 and announces to you a sign or **w**,
SS 1: 3 No **w** the young women love you!

WONDERFUL* (WONDER)
2Sa 1: 26 Your love for me was **w**, more **w** than that of women.
1Ch 16: 9 praise to him; tell of all his **w** acts.
Job 42: 3 things too **w** for me to know.
Ps 9: 1 I will tell of all your **w** deeds.
26: 7 and telling of all your **w** deeds.
75: 1 people tell of your **w** deeds.
105: 2 praise to him; tell of all his **w** acts.
107: 8 love and his **w** deeds for mankind,
107: 15 love and his **w** deeds for mankind,
107: 21 love and his **w** deeds for mankind.
107: 24 LORD, his **w** deeds in the deep.
107: 31 love and his **w** deeds for mankind.
119: 18 that I may see **w** things in your law.
119: 27 I may meditate on your **w** deeds.
119:129 statutes are **w**; therefore I obey
131: 1 matters or things too **w** for me.
139: 6 Such knowledge is too **w** for me,
139: 14 your works are **w**, I know that
145: 5 I will meditate on your **w** works.
Isa 9: 6 he will be called **W** Counselor,
25: 1 you have done **w** things,
28: 29 whose plan is **w**, whose wisdom is
Mt 21: 15 of the law saw the **w** things he did
Lk 13: 17 with all the **w** things he was doing.
1Pe 2: 9 out of darkness into his **w** light.

WONDERS (WONDER)
Ex 3: 20 all the **w** that I will perform among
Dt 10: 21 awesome **w** you saw with your own
2Sa 7: 23 awesome **w** by driving out nations
Job 37: 14 stop and consider God's **w**.
Ps 17: 7 Show me the **w** of your great love,
31: 21 for he showed me the **w** of his love
89: 5 The heavens praise your **w**,
Joel 2: 30 I will show **w** in the heavens
Mt 24: 24 great signs and **w** to deceive,
Mk 13: 22 perform signs and **w** to deceive,
Jn 4: 48 you people see signs and **w**,"
Ac 2: 11 we hear them declaring the **w**
2: 19 I will show **w** in the heavens
2: 43 was filled with awe at the many **w**
5: 12 signs and **w** among the people.
Ro 15: 19 by the power of signs and **w**,
2Co 12: 12 including signs, **w** and miracles.
2Th 2: 9 signs and **w** that serve the lie,
Heb 2: 4 it by signs, **w** and various miracles,

WOOD
Isa 44: 19 Shall I bow down to a block of **w**?"
1Co 3: 12 costly stones, **w**, hay or straw,

WOOL
Pr 31: 13 She selects **w** and flax and works
Isa 1: 18 as crimson, they shall be like **w**.
Da 7: 9 hair of his head was white like **w**.
Rev 1: 14 hair on his head was white like **w**,

WORD (BYWORD WORDLESS WORDS)
Nu 30: 2 must not break his **w** but must do
Dt 8: 3 but on every **w** that comes
2Sa 22: 31 The LORD's **w** is flawless;
Ps 56: 4 In God, whose **w** I praise—in God
119: 9 By living according to your **w**.
119: 11 I have hidden your **w** in my heart
119:105 Your **w** is a lamp to my feet
Pr 12: 25 the heart, but a kind **w** cheers it up.
15: 1 wrath, but a harsh **w** stirs up anger.
30: 5 "Every **w** of God is flawless; he is
Isa 55: 11 so is my **w** that goes out from my
Jer 23: 29 "Is not my **w** like fire,"
Mt 4: 4 but on every **w** that comes
12: 36 every empty **w** they have spoken.
15: 6 Thus you nullify the **w** of God
Mk 4: 14 The farmer sows the **w**.
Jn 1: 1 In the beginning was the **W**,
1: 14 The **W** became flesh and made his
17: 17 them by the truth; your **w** is truth.
Ac 6: 4 prayer and the ministry of the **w**."
2Co 2: 17 we do not peddle the **w** of God
4: 2 nor do we distort the **w** of God.
Eph 6: 17 of the Spirit, which is the **w** of God.
Php 2: 16 as you hold firmly to the **w** of life.
2Ti 2: 15 and who correctly handles the **w**
Heb 4: 12 the **w** of God is alive and active.
Jas 1: 22 Do not merely listen to the **w**,

WORDLESS* (WORD)
Ro 8: 26 intercedes for us through **w** groans.

WORDS (WORD)
Dt 11: 18 Fix these **w** of mine in your hearts
Ps 12: 6 the **w** of the LORD are flawless,
19: 3 have no speech, they use no **w**;
119:103 How sweet are your **w** to my taste,
119:130 unfolding of your **w** gives light;
119:160 All your **w** are true;
Pr 2: 1 if you accept my **w** and store up my
10: 19 Sin is not ended by multiplying **w**,
16: 24 Gracious **w** are a honeycomb,
30: 6 Do not add to his **w**, or he will
Ecc 12: 11 The **w** of the wise are like goads,
Jer 15: 16 When your **w** came, I ate them;
Mt 24: 35 but my **w** will never pass away.
Lk 6: 47 and hears my **w** and puts them
Jn 6: 68 You have the **w** of eternal life.
15: 7 in me and my **w** remain in you,
1Co 2: 13 but in **w** taught by the Spirit,
2: 13 realities with Spirit-taught **w**.
14: 19 rather speak five intelligible **w**
Rev 22: 19 if anyone takes **w** away from this

WORK (CO-WORKERS WORKED WORKER WORKERS WORKING WORKS)
Ge 2: 2 God had finished the **w** he had
2: 2 day he rested from all his **w**.
Ex 23: 12 but on the seventh day do not **w**,
Nu 8: 11 be ready to do the **w** of the LORD.
Dt 5: 14 On it you shall not do any **w**,
Ps 19: 1 the skies proclaim the **w** of his
Jer 48: 10 who is lax in doing the LORD's **w**!
Jn 6: 27 Do not **w** for food that spoils,
9: 4 is coming, when no one can **w**.
Ac 13: 2 and Saul for the **w** to which I have
1Co 3: 13 test the quality of each person's **w**.
4: 12 We **w** hard with our own hands.
Eph 4: 16 up in love, as each part does its **w**.
Php 1: 6 he who began a good **w** in you will
2: 12 continue to **w** out your salvation
Col 3: 23 you do, **w** at it with all your heart,
1Th 4: 11 business and **w** with your hands,
5: 12 those who **w** hard among you,
2Th 3: 10 is unwilling to **w** shall not eat."
2Ti 3: 17 equipped for every good **w**.
Heb 6: 10 he will not forget your **w**
2Jn : 11 them shares in their wicked **w**.
3Jn : 8 we may **w** together for the truth.

WORKED (WORK)
1Co 15: 10 No, I **w** harder than all of them—
2Th 3: 8 the contrary, we **w** night and day,

WORKER (WORK)
Lk 10: 7 for the **w** deserves his wages.
1Ti 5: 18 and "The **w** deserves his wages."
2Ti 2: 15 a **w** who does not need to be

WORKERS (WORK)
Mt 9: 37 is plentiful but the **w** are few.
20: 1 morning to hire **w** for his vineyard.

WORKING (WORK)
Col 3: 23 all your heart, as **w** for the Lord,

WORKS (WORK)
Ps 145: 6 of the power of your awesome **w**—
Pr 8: 22 me forth as the first of his **w**,
31: 31 her **w** bring her praise at the city
Jn 7: 3 there may see the **w** you do.
10: 25 The **w** I do in my Father's name
10: 32 "I have shown you many good **w**
10: 38 believe the **w**, that you may know
14: 11 the evidence of the **w** themselves.
Ro 4: 2 Abraham was justified by **w**,
8: 28 in all things God **w** for the good
Eph 2: 9 not by **w**, so that no one can boast.
4: 12 to equip his people for **w** of service,

WORLD (WORLDLY)
Ps 9: 8 He rules the **w** in righteousness
50: 12 for the **w** is mine, and all that is
90: 2 or you brought forth the whole **w**,
96: 13 will judge the **w** in righteousness
Pr 8: 23 beginning, when the **w** came to be.
Isa 13: 11 I will punish the **w** for its evil,
Mt 5: 14 "You are the light of the **w**.
16: 26 for someone to gain the whole **w**,
Mk 16: 15 *"Go into all the **w** and preach*
Jn 1: 29 who takes away the sin of the **w**!
3: 16 God so loved the **w** that he gave his
8: 12 he said, "I am the light of the **w**.
15: 19 I have chosen you out of the **w**. That is why the **w** hates you.
16: 33 In this **w** you will have trouble.
16: 33 I have overcome the **w**."
17: 5 I had with you before the **w** began.
17: 14 word and the **w** has hated them,
17: 14 not of the **w** any more than I am
18: 36 said, "My kingdom is not of this **w**.
Ac 17: 24 "The God who made the **w**
Ro 3: 19 and the whole **w** held accountable
10: 18 their words to the ends of the **w**."
1Co 1: 27 things of the **w** to shame the wise;
3: 19 the wisdom of this **w** is foolishness
6: 2 the Lord's people will judge the **w**?
2Co 5: 19 that God was reconciling the **w**
10: 3 we do not wage war as the **w** does.
1Ti 6: 7 For we brought nothing into the **w**,
Heb 11: 38 the **w** was not worthy of them.
Jas 2: 5 the eyes of the **w** to be rich in faith
4: 4 the **w** means enmity against God?
1Pe 1: 20 before the creation of the **w**,
1Jn 2: 2 also for the sins of the whole **w**.
2: 15 Do not love the **w** or anything
5: 4 victory that has overcome the **w**,
Rev 13: 8 slain from the creation of the **w**.

WORLDLY (WORLD)
1Co 3: 1 Spirit but as people who are still **w**
Titus 2: 12 to ungodliness and **w** passions,

WORM (WORMS)
Ps 22: 6 I am a **w** and not a man, scorned
Jnh 4: 7 the next day God provided a **w**,

WORMS (WORM)
Isa 66: 24 the **w** that eat them will not die,
Mk 9: 48 "'the **w** that eat them do not

WORRY (WORRYING)
Mt 6: 25 I tell you, do not **w** about your life,
10: 19 do not **w** about what to say or how

WORRYING (WORRY)
Mt 6: 27 you by **w** add a single hour to your

WORSHIP (WORSHIPED WORSHIPS)
Jos 22: 27 that we will **w** the LORD at his
2Ki 17: 36 arm, is the one you must **w**.
1Ch 16: 29 **W** the LORD in the splendor of his
Ps 95: 6 let us bow down in **w**, let us kneel
100: 2 **W** the LORD with gladness;
Zec 14: 17 go up to Jerusalem to **w** the King,
Mt 2: 2 it rose and have come to **w** him."
4: 9 "if you will bow down and **w** me."
Jn 4: 24 his worshipers must **w** in the Spirit
Ro 12: 1 this is your true and proper **w**.
Heb 10: 1 perfect those who draw near to **w**.

WORSHIPED (WORSHIP)
2Ch 29: 30 gladness and bowed down and **w**.
Mt 28: 9 to him, clasped his feet and **w** him.

WORSHIPS (WORSHIP)
Isa 44: 15 But he also fashions a god and **w** it;

WORTH (WORTHY)
Job 28: 13 No mortal comprehends its **w**;
Pr 31: 10 She is **w** far more than rubies.
Mt 10: 31 you are **w** more than many
Ro 8: 18 sufferings are not **w** comparing
Php 3: 8 surpassing **w** of knowing Christ
1Pe 1: 7 of greater **w** than gold,
3: 4 which is of great **w** in God's sight.

WORTHLESS
Pr 11: 4 Wealth is **w** in the day of wrath,
Jas 1: 26 themselves, and their religion is **w**.

WORTHY (WORTH)
1Ch 16: 25 is the LORD and most **w** of praise;
Mt 10: 37 or mother more than me is not **w**
Lk 15: 19 I am no longer **w** to be called your
Eph 4: 1 live a life **w** of the calling you have
Php 1: 27 in a manner **w** of the gospel
Col 1: 10 you may live a life **w** of the Lord
1Ti 3: 8 way, deacons are to be **w** of respect,
Heb 3: 3 Jesus has been found **w** of greater
Rev 5: 2 "Who is **w** to break the seals

WOUND (WOUNDS)
1Co 8: 12 way and **w** their weak conscience,

WOUNDS (WOUND)
Pr 27: 6 **W** from a friend can be trusted,
Isa 53: 5 him, and by his **w** we are healed.
Zec 13: 6 'What are these **w** on your body?'
1Pe 2: 24 "by his **w** you have been healed."

WRAPS
Ps 104: 2 The LORD **w** himself in light as

WRATH
2Ch 36: 16 at his prophets until the **w**
Ps 2: 5 anger and terrifies them in his **w**,
76: 10 survivors of your **w** are restrained.
Pr 15: 1 A gentle answer turns away **w**,
Isa 13: 13 at the **w** of the LORD Almighty,
51: 17 of the LORD the cup of his **w**,
Jer 25: 15 cup filled with the wine of my **w**
Eze 5: 13 my **w** against them will subside,
20: 8 I would pour out my **w** on them
Na 1: 2 vengeance and is filled with **w**.
1: 2 vents his **w** against his enemies.
Zep 1: 15 That day will be a day of **w**—
Jn 3: 36 life, for God's **w** remains on them.
Ro 1: 18 The **w** of God is being revealed
2: 5 are storing up **w** against yourself
5: 9 saved from God's **w** through him!
9: 22 great patience the objects of his **w**
1Th 5: 9 God did not appoint us to suffer **w**
Rev 6: 16 and from the **w** of the Lamb!
19: 15 the fury of the **w** of God Almighty.

WRESTLED
Ge 32: 24 a man **w** with him till daybreak.

WRITE (WRITER WRITING WRITTEN WROTE)
Dt 6: 9 **W** them on the doorframes of your
10: 2 I will **w** on the tablets the words
Pr 7: 3 **w** them on the tablet of your heart.
Jer 31: 33 minds and **w** it on their hearts.
Heb 8: 10 minds and **w** them on their hearts.
Rev 3: 12 will also **w** on them my new name.

WRITER* (WRITE)
Ps 45: 1 tongue is the pen of a skillful **w**.

WRITING (WRITE)
1Co 14: 37 what I am **w** to you is the Lord's

WRITTEN (WRITE)
Dt 28: 58 which are **w** in this book, and do
Jos 1: 8 be careful to do everything **w** in it.
23: 6 obey all that is **w** in the Book
Ps 40: 7 it is **w** about me in the scroll.
Da 12: 1 everyone whose name is found **w**
Mal 3: 16 remembrance was **w** in his
Lk 10: 20 that your names are **w** in heaven."
24: 44 must be fulfilled that is **w** about me
Jn 20: 31 these are **w** that you may believe
21: 25 for the books that would be **w**.
Ro 2: 15 of the law are **w** on their hearts,
1Co 4: 6 "Do not go beyond what is **w**."
10: 11 were **w** down as warnings for us,
2Co 3: 3 **w** not with ink but with the Spirit
Heb 10: 7 it is **w** about me in the scroll—
Heb 12: 23 whose names are **w** in heaven.
Rev 21: 27 only those whose names are **w**

WRONG (WRONGDOERS WRONGDOING WRONGED WRONGS)
Ex 23: 2 not follow the crowd in doing **w**.
Nu 5: 7 for the **w** they have done,
Dt 32: 4 A faithful God who does no **w**,
Job 34: 12 unthinkable that God would do **w**,
Ps 5: 5 You hate all who do **w**;
1Th 5: 15 that nobody pays back **w** for **w**,

WRONGDOERS* (WRONG)
Ps 37: 28 **W** will be completely destroyed;
1Co 6: 9 that **w** will not inherit the kingdom

WRONGDOING (WRONG)
Job 1: 22 not sin by charging God with **w**.
1Jn 5: 17 All **w** is sin, and there is sin

WRONGED (WRONG)
Pr 18: 19 A brother **w** is more unyielding
1Co 6: 7 Why not rather be **w**?

WRONGS (WRONG)
Pr 10: 12 conflict, but love covers over all **w**.
1Co 13: 5 angered, it keeps no record of **w**.

WROTE (WRITE)
Ex 34: 28 he **w** on the tablets the words
Jn 5: 46 believe me, for he **w** about me.
8: 8 *and **w** on the ground.*

XERXES
King of Persia, husband of Esther. Deposed Vashti; replaced her with Esther (Est 1–2). Sealed Haman's edict to annihilate the Jews (Est 3). Received Esther without having called her (Est 5:1–8). Honored Mordecai (Est 6). Hanged Haman (Est 7). Issued edict allowing Jews to defend themselves (Est 8). Exalted Mordecai (Est 8:1–2, 15; 9:4; 10).

YEAR (YEARS)
Ex 34: 23 Three times a **y** all your men are
Lev 16: 34 to be made once a **y** for all the sins
25: 4 in the seventh **y** the land is to have a **y** of sabbath rest,
25: 11 The fiftieth **y** shall be a jubilee
Heb 10: 1 same sacrifices repeated endlessly **y**

YEARS (YEAR)
Ge 1: 14 mark sacred times, and days and **y**,
Ex 12: 40 people lived in Egypt was 430 **y**.
16: 35 The Israelites ate manna forty **y**,
Job 36: 26 number of his **y** is past finding out.
Ps 90: 4 A thousand **y** in your sight are like
90: 10 Our days may come to seventy **y**,
Pr 3: 2 they will prolong your life many **y**
Lk 3: 23 Jesus himself was about thirty **y** old
2Pe 3: 8 the Lord a day is like a thousand **y**, and a thousand **y** are like a day.
Rev 20: 2 and bound him for a thousand **y**.

YEAST
Ex 12: 15 are to eat bread made without **y**.
Mt 16: 6 on your guard against the **y**
1Co 5: 6 a little **y** leavens the whole batch

YESTERDAY
Heb 13: 8 Christ is the same **y** and today

YIELD
Isa 42: 8 I will not **y** my glory to another

YOKE (YOKED)
1Ki 12: 4 "Your father put a heavy **y** on us,
Mt 11: 29 Take my **y** upon you and learn
Gal 5: 1 be burdened again by a **y** of slavery.

YOKED (YOKE)
2Co 6: 14 Do not be **y** together

YOUNG (YOUNGER YOUTH)
2Ch 10: 14 he followed the advice of the **y** men
Ps 37: 25 I was **y** and now I am old, yet I
119: 9 can a **y** person stay on the path
Pr 20: 29 glory of **y** men is their strength,
Isa 40: 11 he gently leads those that have **y**.
Joel 2: 28 your **y** men will see visions.
Ac 2: 17 your **y** men will see visions,
7: 58 at the feet of a **y** man named Saul.
1Ti 4: 12 down on you because you are **y**,
Titus 2: 6 encourage the **y** men to be
1Jn 2: 13 I am writing to you, **y** men,

YOUNGER (YOUNG)
1Ti 5: 1 Treat **y** men as brothers,
Titus 2: 4 they can urge the **y** women to love
1Pe 5: 5 you who are **y**, submit yourselves

YOUTH (YOUNG)
Ps 103: 5 your **y** is renewed like the eagle's.
Ecc 12: 1 your Creator in the days of your **y**,
2Ti 2: 22 Flee the evil desires of **y** and

ZACCHAEUS
Lk 19: 2 A man was there by the name of **Z**;

ZEAL (ZEALOUS)
Ps 69: 9 for **z** for your house consumes me,
Isa 59: 17 wrapped himself in **z** as in a cloak.
Jn 2: 17 "**Z** for your house will consume
Ro 10: 2 their **z** is not based on knowledge.
12: 11 Never be lacking in **z**, but keep

ZEALOUS (ZEAL)
Nu 25: 13 because he was **z** for the honor
Pr 23: 17 but always be **z** for the fear
Eze 39: 25 and I will be **z** for my holy name.
Gal 4: 18 It is fine to be **z**,

ZEBULUN
Son of Jacob by Leah (Ge 30:20; 35:23; 1Ch 2:1). Tribe of blessed (Ge 49:13; Dt 33:18–19), numbered (Nu 1:31; 26:27), allotted land (Jos 19:10–16; Eze 48:26), failed to fully possess (Jdg 1:30), supported Deborah (Jdg 4:6–10; 5:14, 18), David (1Ch 12:33), 12,000 from (Rev 7:8).

ZECHARIAH
1. Son of Jeroboam II; king of Israel (2Ki 15:8–12).
2. Post-exilic prophet who encouraged rebuilding of temple (Ezr 5:1; 6:14; Zec 1:1).
3. Father of John the Baptist (Lk 1:13; 3:2).

ZEDEKIAH
1. False prophet (1Ki 22:11–24; 2Ch 18:10–23).
2. Mattaniah, son of Josiah (1Ch 3:15), made king of Judah by Nebuchadnezzar (2Ki 24:17—25:7; 2Ch 36:10–14; Jer 37–39; 52:1–11).

ZEPHANIAH
Prophet; descendant of Hezekiah (Zep 1:1).

ZERUBBABEL
Descendant of David (1Ch 3:19; Mt 1:3). Led return from exile (Ezr 2:2; Ne 7:7). Governor of Israel; helped rebuild altar and temple (Ezr 3; Hag 1–2; Zec 4).

ZILPAH
Servant of Leah, mother of Jacob's sons Gad and Asher (Ge 30:9–12; 35:26, 46:16–18).

ZIMRI
King of Israel (1Ki 16:9–20).

ZION
2Sa 5: 7 David captured the fortress of **Z**—
Ps 2: 6 "I have installed my king on **Z**,
9: 11 of the LORD, enthroned in **Z**;
74: 2 Mount **Z**, where you dwelt.
87: 2 **Z** more than all the other dwellings
102: 13 arise and have compassion on **Z**,
137: 3 "Sing us one of the songs of **Z**!"
Isa 2: 3 The law will go out from **Z**,
28: 16 I lay a stone in **Z**, a tested stone,
51: 11 They will enter **Z** with singing;
52: 8 When the LORD returns to **Z**,
Jer 50: 5 will ask the way to **Z** and turn
Joel 3: 21 The LORD dwells in **Z**!
Am 6: 1 to you who are complacent in **Z**,
Mic 4: 2 The law will go out from **Z**,
Zec 9: 9 Rejoice greatly, Daughter **Z**!
Ro 9: 33 I lay in **Z** a stone that causes people
11: 26 "The deliverer will come from **Z**;
Heb 12: 22 But you have come to Mount **Z**,
Rev 14: 1 standing on Mount **Z**, and with

ZIPPORAH*
Daughter of Reuel; wife of Moses (Ex 2:21–22; 4:20–26; 18:1–6).

ZOPHAR*
One of Job's friends (Job 2:11; 11; 20; 42:9).

INDEX TO MAPS

The Index to Maps will lead you to place-names found on the color maps on pp. 2515 – 2530 at the end of this study Bible. References are to the map number and the margin markings.

Map 1: **WORLD OF THE PATRIARCHS**

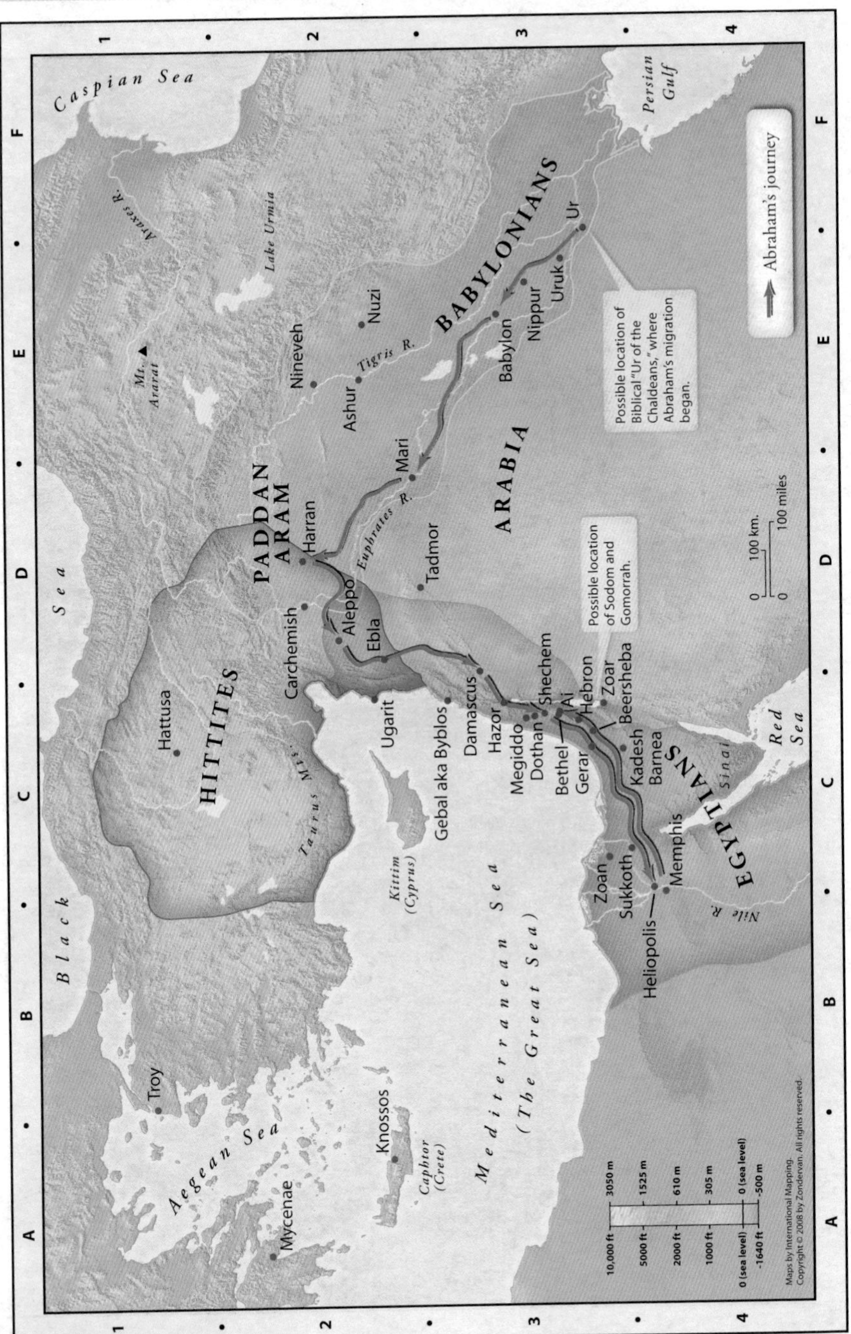
Caspian Sea
Black Sea
Aegean Sea
Mediterranean Sea
(The Great Sea)
Persian Gulf
Red Sea
Lake Urmia
Araxes R.
Tigris R.
Euphrates R.
Nile R.
Mt. Ararat
Taurus Mts.
Sinai
HITTITES
PADDAN ARAM
BABYLONIANS
ARABIA
EGYPTIANS
Troy
Mycenae
Knossos
Caphtor (Crete)
Kittim (Cyprus)
Hattusa
Carchemish
Harran
Aleppo
Ebla
Ugarit
Tadmor
Mari
Nineveh
Ashur
Nuzi
Babylon
Nippur
Uruk
Ur
Gebal aka Byblos
Damascus
Hazor
Megiddo
Dothan
Shechem
Bethel
Ai
Hebron
Gerar
Zoar
Beersheba
Kadesh Barnea
Zoan
Sukkoth
Heliopolis
Memphis
Possible location of Biblical "Ur of the Chaldeans," where Abraham's migration began.
Possible location of Sodom and Gomorrah.
Abraham's journey
0 100 km.
0 100 miles
10,000 ft 3050 m
5000 ft 1525 m
2000 ft 610 m
1000 ft 305 m
0 (sea level) 0 (sea level)
-1640 ft -500 m
A B C D E F
1 2 3 4

Map 2: **HOLY LAND AND SINAI**

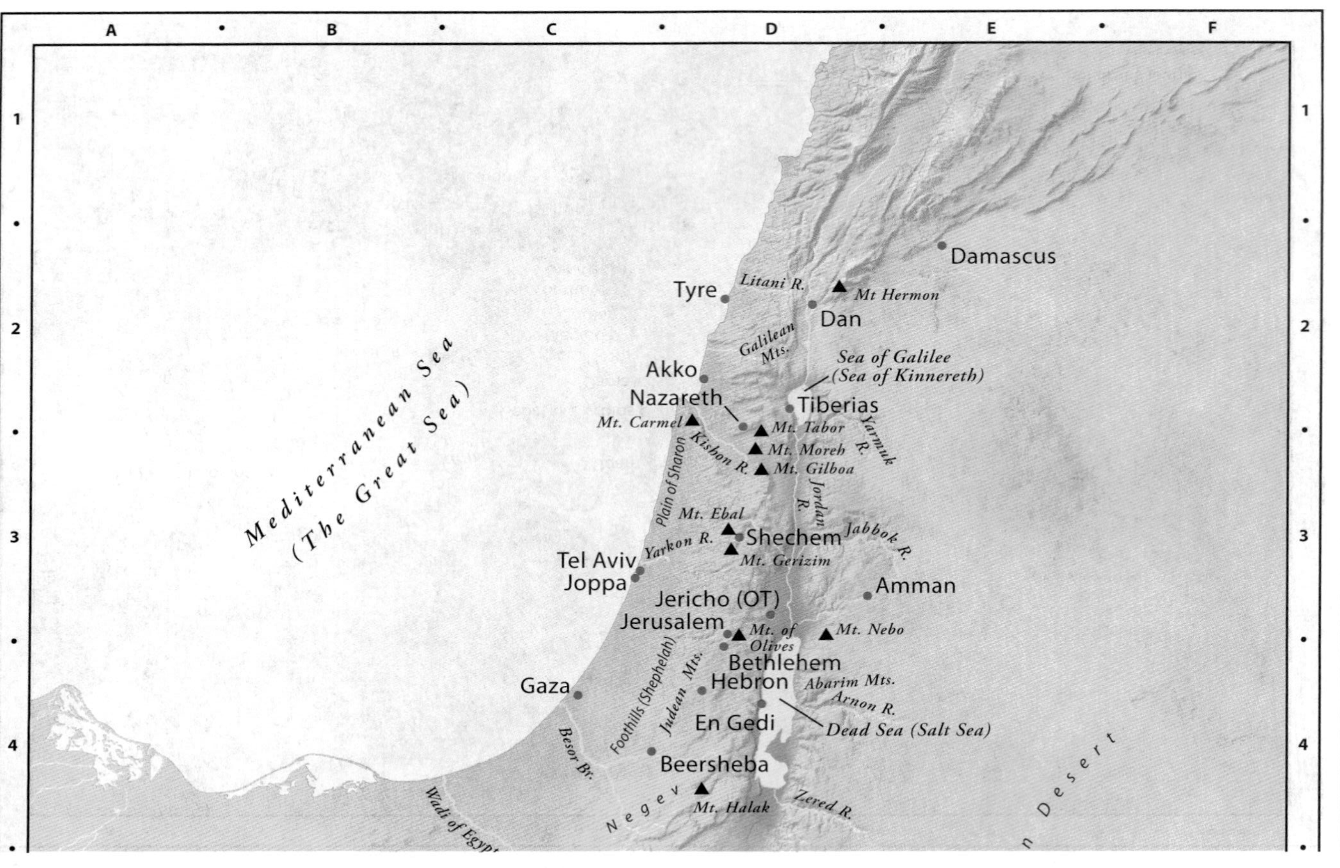

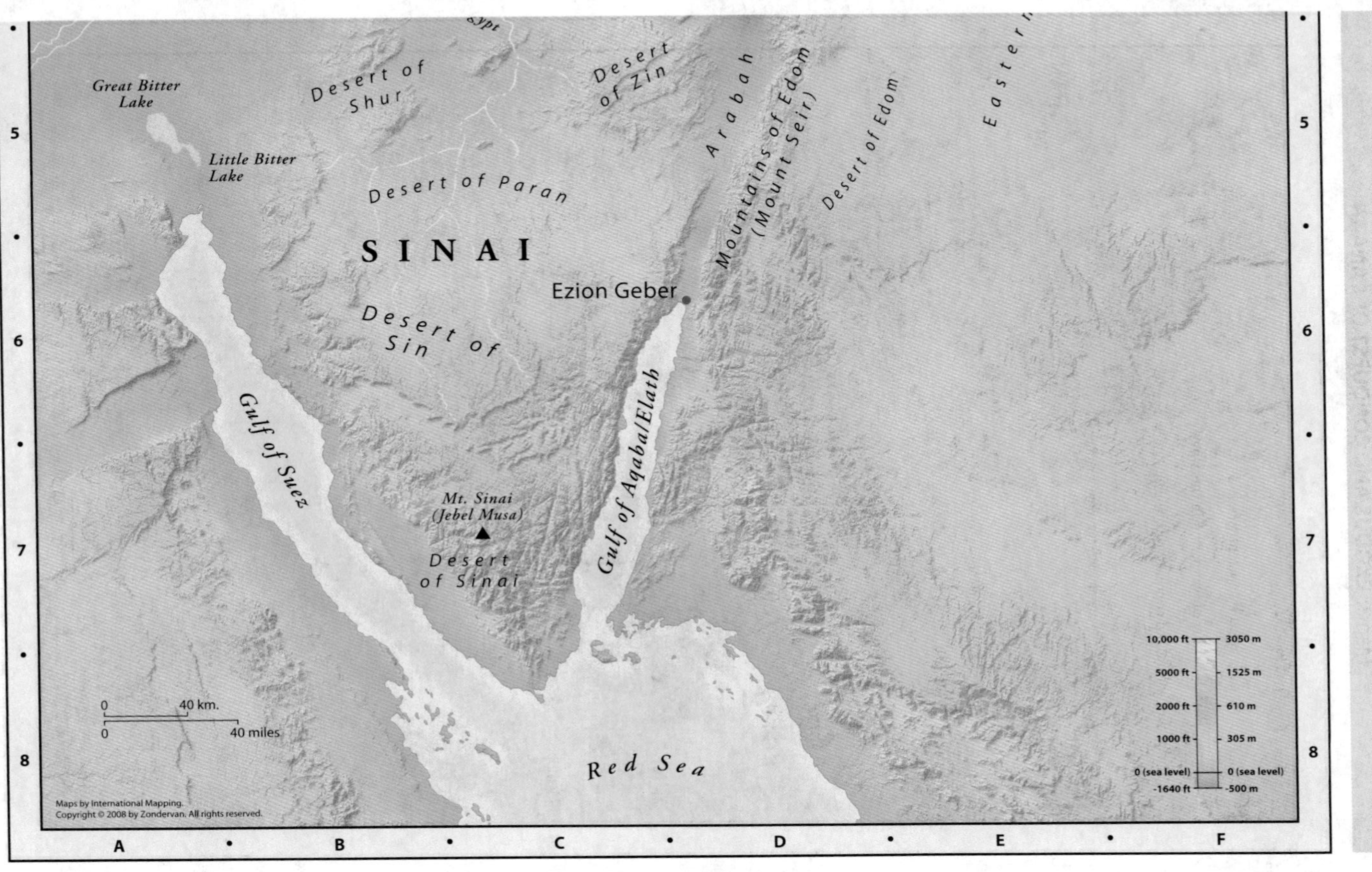
Great Bitter Lake
Little Bitter Lake
Desert of Shur
Desert of Zin
Desert of Paran
SINAI
Desert of Sin
Ezion Geber
Arabah
Mountains of Edom (Mount Seir)
Desert of Edom
Gulf of Suez
Gulf of Aqaba/Elath
Mt. Sinai (Jebel Musa)
Desert of Sinai
Red Sea
0 40 km.
0 40 miles
10,000 ft 3050 m
5000 ft 1525 m
2000 ft 610 m
1000 ft 305 m
0 (sea level) 0 (sea level)
-1640 ft -500 m
A B C D E F
5 6 7 8
Maps by International Mapping.
Copyright © 2008 by Zondervan. All rights reserved.

Map 3: EXODUS AND CONQUEST OF CANAAN

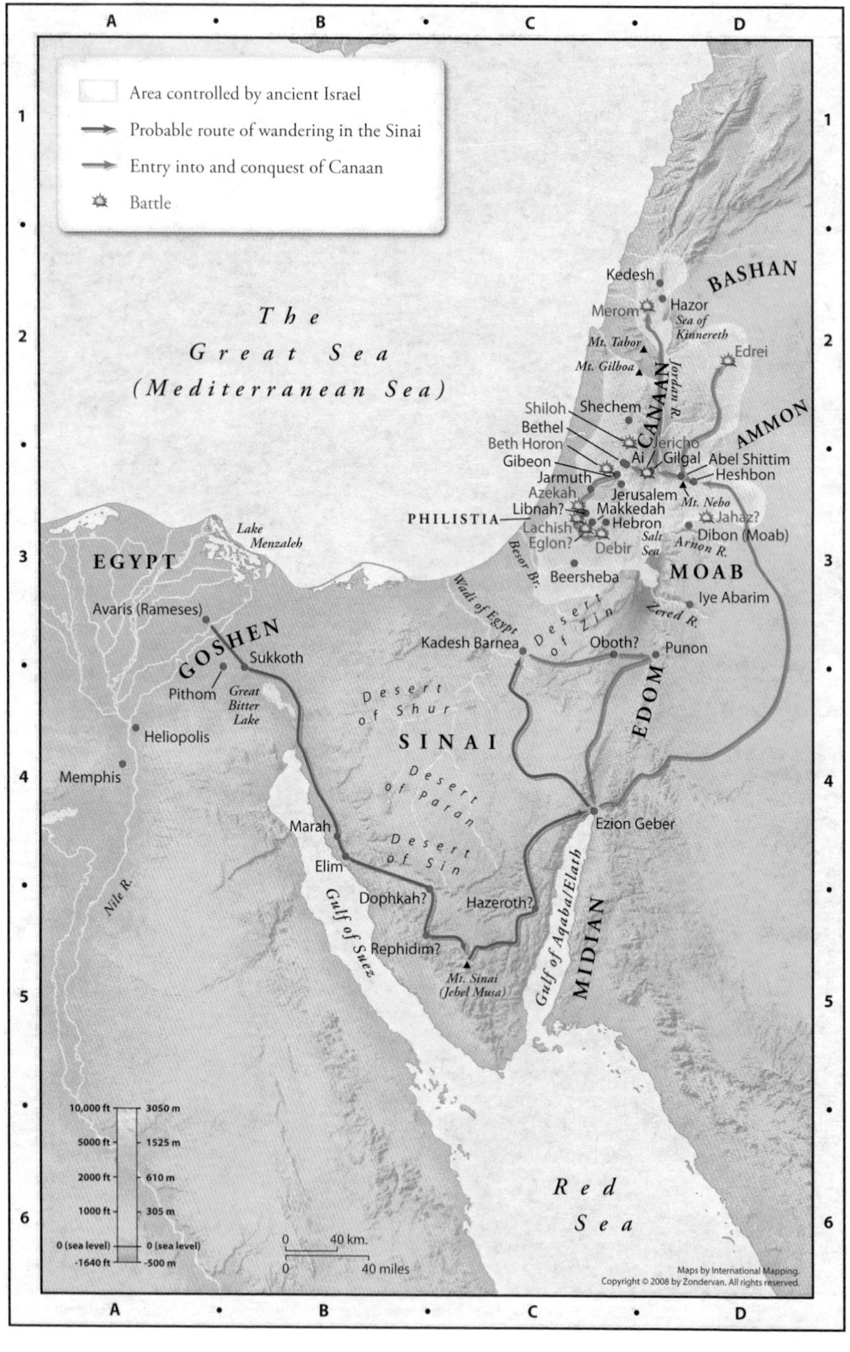
A
B
C
D
1
2
3
4
5
6
Area controlled by ancient Israel
Probable route of wandering in the Sinai
Entry into and conquest of Canaan
Battle
The Great Sea (Mediterranean Sea)
Kedesh
BASHAN
Merom
Hazor
Sea of Kinnereth
Mt. Tabor
Mt. Gilboa
Edrei
Jordan R.
CANAAN
Shiloh
Shechem
Bethel
Beth Horon
Gibeon
Jericho
Ai
Gilgal
AMMON
Abel Shittim
Heshbon
Jarmuth
Azekah
Jerusalem
Mt. Nebo
Libnah?
Makkedah
PHILISTIA
Lachish
Hebron
Jahaz?
Eglon?
Debir
Salt Sea
Arnon R.
Dibon (Moab)
Lake Menzaleh
EGYPT
Besor Br.
Beersheba
MOAB
Wadi of Egypt
Desert of Zin
Zered R.
Iye Abarim
Avaris (Rameses)
GOSHEN
Sukkoth
Kadesh Barnea
Oboth?
Punon
Pithom
Great Bitter Lake
Desert of Shur
EDOM
Heliopolis
SINAI
Memphis
Desert of Paran
Ezion Geber
Marah
Desert of Sin
Elim
Gulf of Aqaba/Elath
Nile R.
Dophkah?
Hazeroth?
MIDIAN
Gulf of Suez
Rephidim?
Mt. Sinai (Jebel Musa)
10,000 ft
3050 m
5000 ft
1525 m
2000 ft
610 m
1000 ft
305 m
0 (sea level)
0 (sea level)
-1640 ft
-500 m
0
40 km.
0
40 miles
Red Sea

Map 4: **LAND OF THE TWELVE TRIBES**

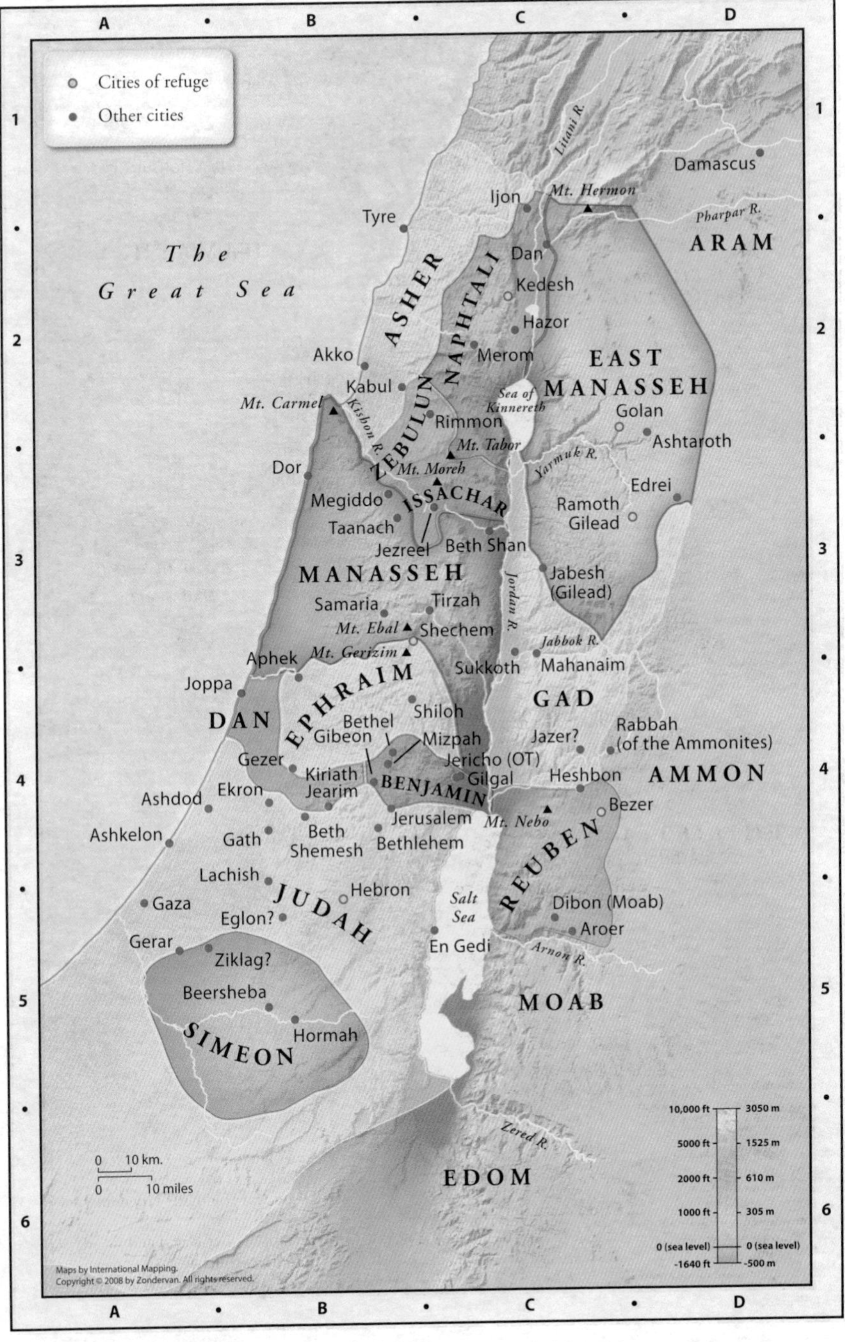

Map 5: **KINGDOM OF DAVID AND SOLOMON**

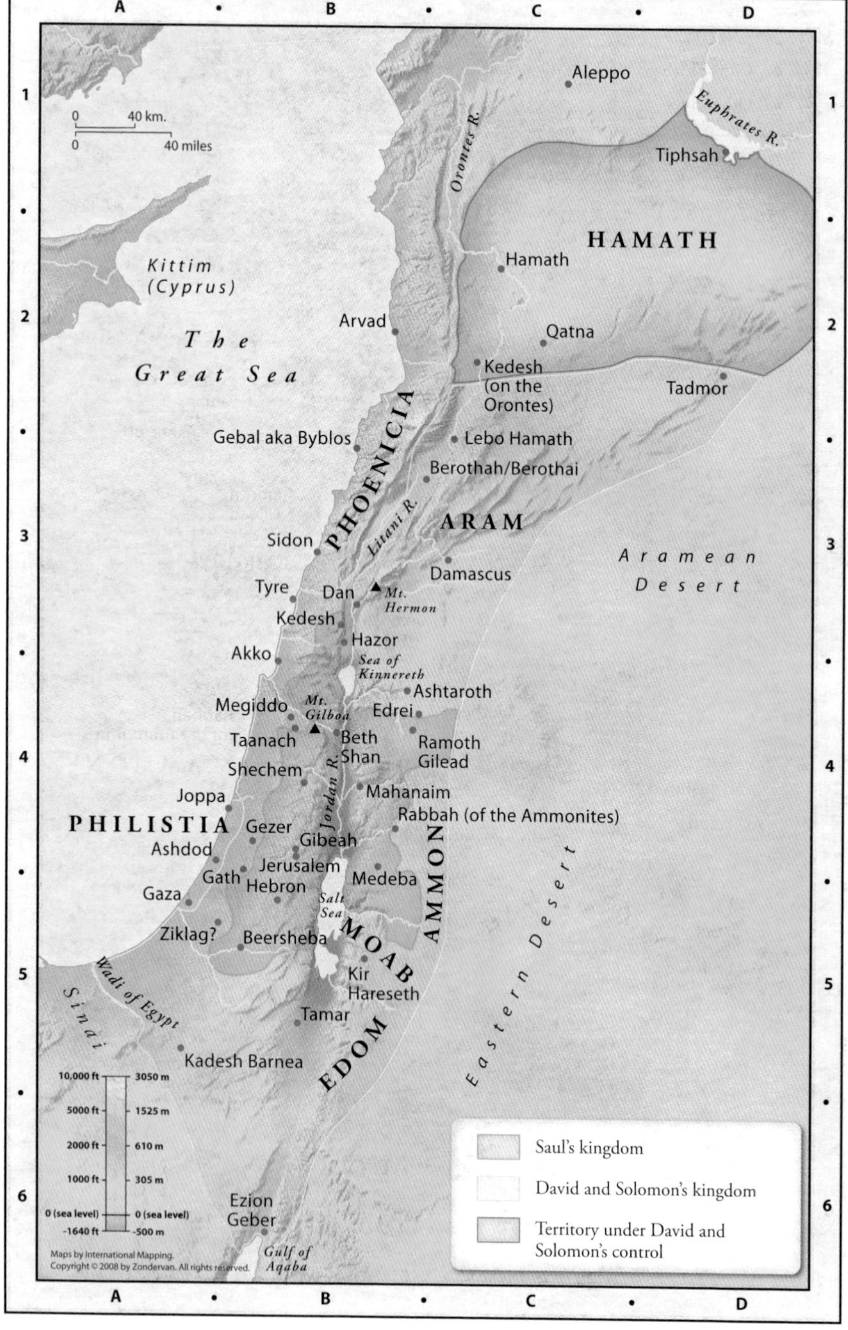
A
B
C
D
1
2
3
4
5
6
0 40 km.
0 40 miles
Aleppo
Euphrates R.
Tiphsah
Orontes R.
HAMATH
Hamath
Kittim
(Cyprus)
Arvad
Qatna
The
Great Sea
Kedesh
(on the
Orontes)
Tadmor
Gebal aka Byblos
Lebo Hamath
PHOENICIA
Berothah/Berothai
Litani R.
ARAM
Sidon
Damascus
Aramean
Desert
Tyre
Dan
Mt.
Hermon
Kedesh
Hazor
Akko
Sea of
Kinnereth
Ashtaroth
Megiddo
Mt.
Gilboa
Edrei
Taanach
Beth
Shan
Ramoth
Gilead
Shechem
Jordan R.
Mahanaim
Joppa
Rabbah (of the Ammonites)
PHILISTIA
Gezer
Gibeah
Ashdod
Jerusalem
Gath
Hebron
Medeba
Gaza
Salt
Sea
AMMON
Eastern Desert
Ziklag?
Beersheba
MOAB
Wadi of Egypt
Kir
Hareseth
Sinai
Tamar
EDOM
Kadesh Barnea
10,000 ft 3050 m
5000 ft 1525 m
2000 ft 610 m
1000 ft 305 m
0 (sea level) 0 (sea level)
-1640 ft -500 m
Ezion
Geber
Gulf of
Aqaba
Saul's kingdom
David and Solomon's kingdom
Territory under David and
Solomon's control
Maps by International Mapping.
Copyright © 2008 by Zondervan. All rights reserved.

Map 6: **KINGDOMS OF ISRAEL AND JUDAH**

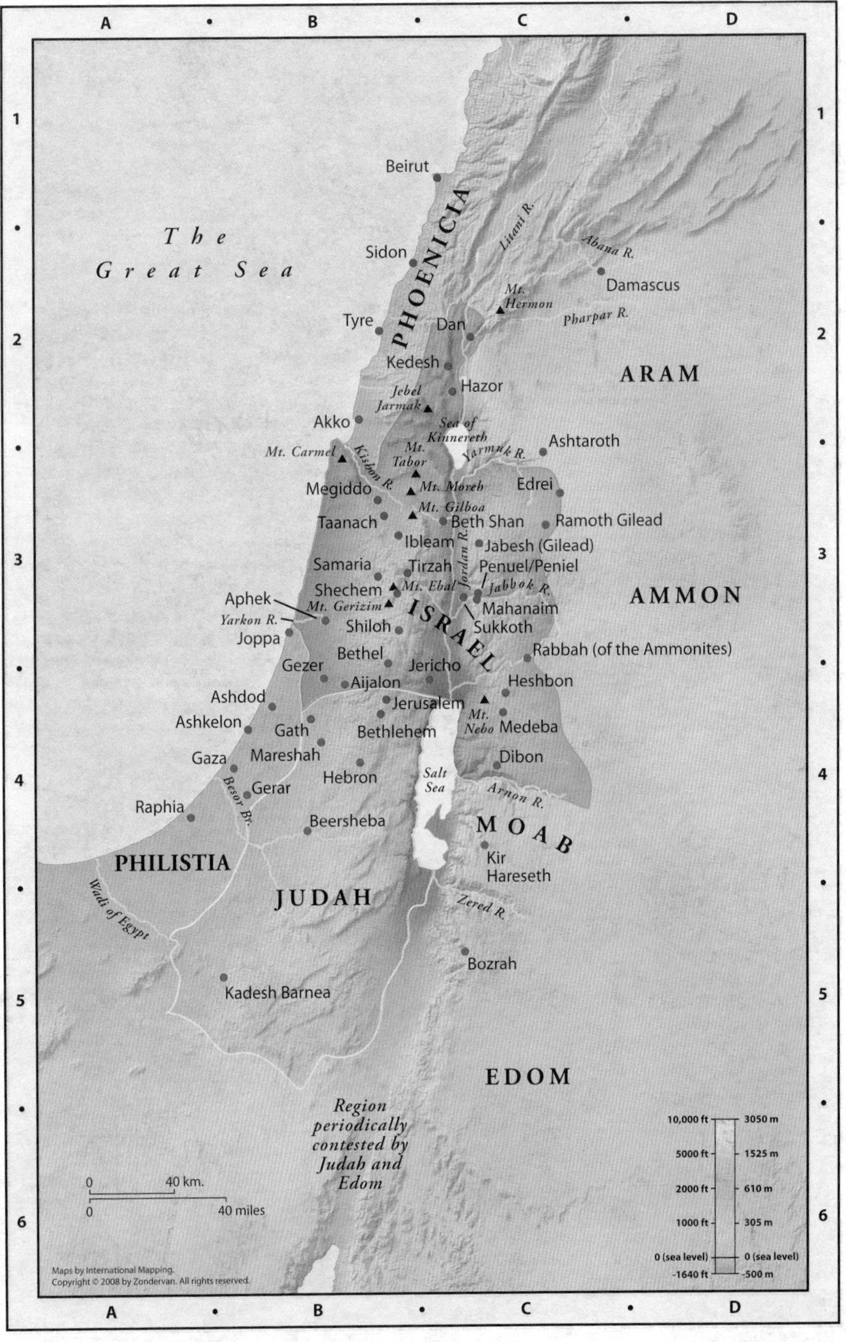
A
B
C
D
1
2
3
4
5
6
The Great Sea
Beirut
PHOENICIA
Litani R.
Abana R.
Sidon
Damascus
Mt. Hermon
Pharpar R.
Tyre
Dan
Kedesh
ARAM
Hazor
Jebel Jarmak
Akko
Sea of Kinnereth
Ashtaroth
Mt. Carmel
Kishon R.
Mt. Tabor
Yarmuk R.
Megiddo
Mt. Moreh
Edrei
Mt. Gilboa
Taanach
Beth Shan
Ramoth Gilead
Ibleam
Jordan R.
Jabesh (Gilead)
Samaria
Tirzah
Penuel/Peniel
Shechem
Mt. Ebal
Jabbok R.
AMMON
Aphek
Mt. Gerizim
ISRAEL
Mahanaim
Yarkon R.
Shiloh
Sukkoth
Joppa
Bethel
Rabbah (of the Ammonites)
Gezer
Jericho
Aijalon
Heshbon
Ashdod
Jerusalem
Mt. Nebo
Ashkelon
Gath
Bethlehem
Medeba
Gaza
Mareshah
Dibon
Hebron
Salt Sea
Gerar
Besor Br.
Arnon R.
Raphia
Beersheba
MOAB
Kir Hareseth
PHILISTIA
Wadi of Egypt
JUDAH
Zered R.
Bozrah
Kadesh Barnea
EDOM
Region periodically contested by Judah and Edom
0
40 km.
0
40 miles
10,000 ft
3050 m
5000 ft
1525 m
2000 ft
610 m
1000 ft
305 m
0 (sea level)
0 (sea level)
-1640 ft
-500 m
Maps by International Mapping.

Map 7: **PROPHETS IN ISRAEL AND JUDAH**

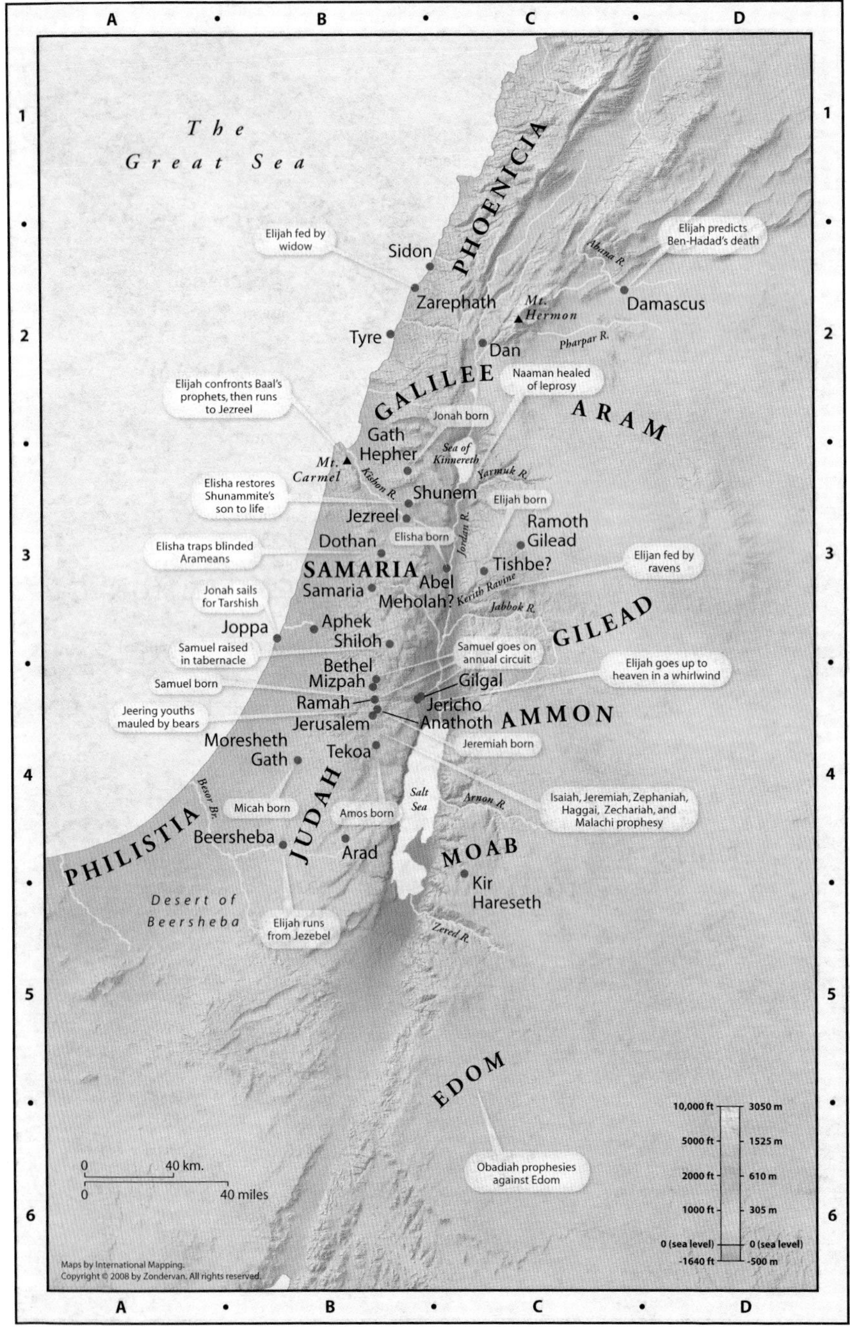
A
B
C
D
1
2
3
4
5
6
The Great Sea
PHOENICIA
Elijah fed by widow
Sidon
Zarephath
Tyre
Elijah predicts Ben-Hadad's death
Abana R.
Mt. Hermon
Damascus
Dan
Pharpar R.
Elijah confronts Baal's prophets, then runs to Jezreel
GALILEE
Naaman healed of leprosy
ARAM
Jonah born
Gath Hepher
Sea of Kinnereth
Mt. Carmel
Kishon R.
Yarmuk R.
Elisha restores Shunammite's son to life
Shunem
Elijah born
Jezreel
Ramoth Gilead
Elisha traps blinded Arameans
Dothan
Elisha born
Jordan R.
Tishbe?
Elijah fed by ravens
SAMARIA
Abel Meholah?
Kerith Ravine
Samaria
Jonah sails for Tarshish
Jabbok R.
Joppa
Aphek
Shiloh
Samuel raised in tabernacle
Samuel goes on annual circuit
GILEAD
Elijah goes up to heaven in a whirlwind
Bethel
Mizpah
Gilgal
Samuel born
Ramah
Jericho
Jeering youths mauled by bears
Anathoth
Jerusalem
AMMON
Moresheth Gath
Tekoa
Jeremiah born
Besor Br.
Salt Sea
Arnon R.
Isaiah, Jeremiah, Zephaniah, Haggai, Zechariah, and Malachi prophesy
Micah born
Amos born
JUDAH
PHILISTIA
Beersheba
Arad
MOAB
Kir Hareseth
Desert of Beersheba
Elijah runs from Jezebel
Zered R.
EDOM
Obadiah prophesies against Edom
0 40 km.
0 40 miles
10,000 ft 3050 m
5000 ft 1525 m
2000 ft 610 m
1000 ft 305 m
0 (sea level) 0 (sea level)
-1640 ft -500 m

Map 8: ASSYRIAN AND BABYLONIAN EMPIRES

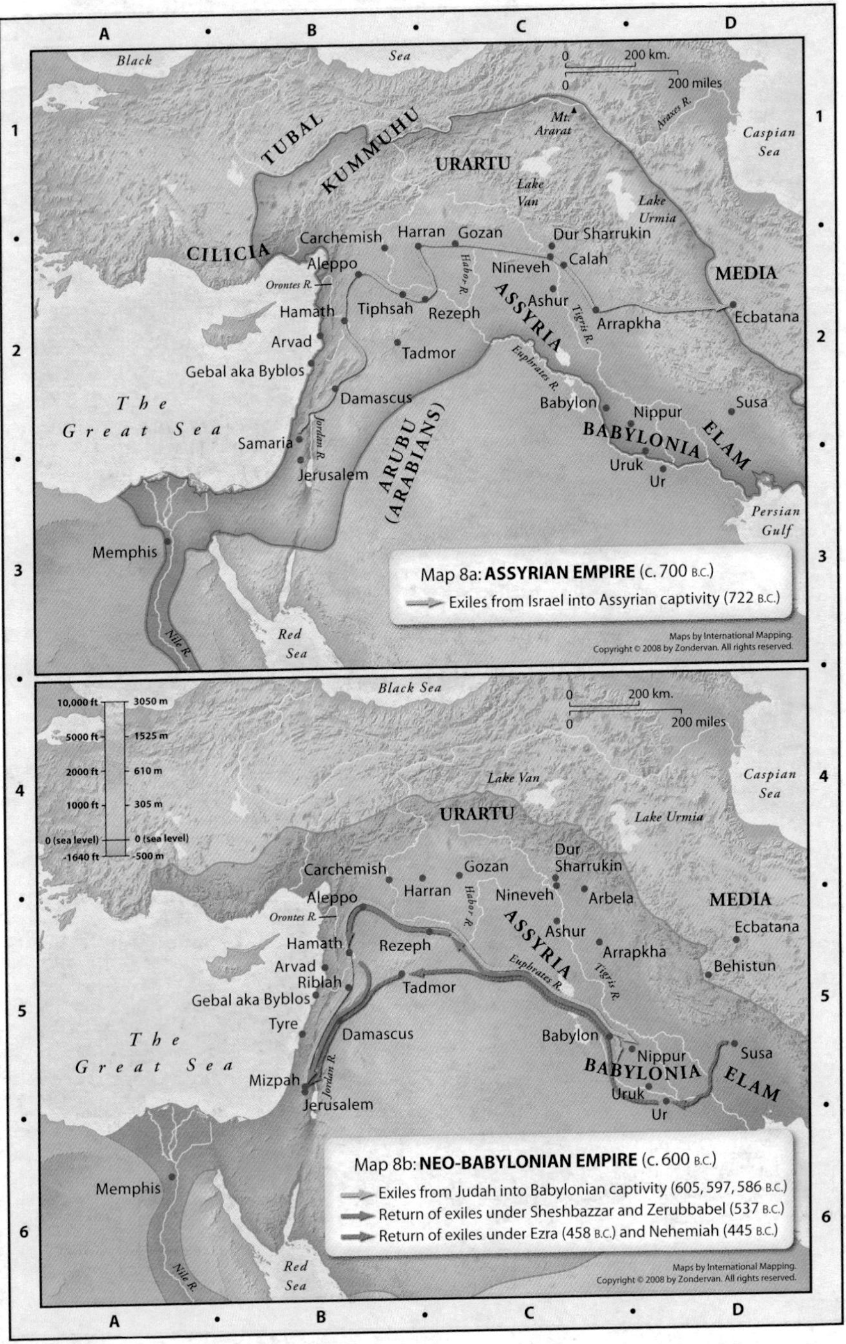

Map 9: **HOLY LAND IN THE TIME OF JESUS**

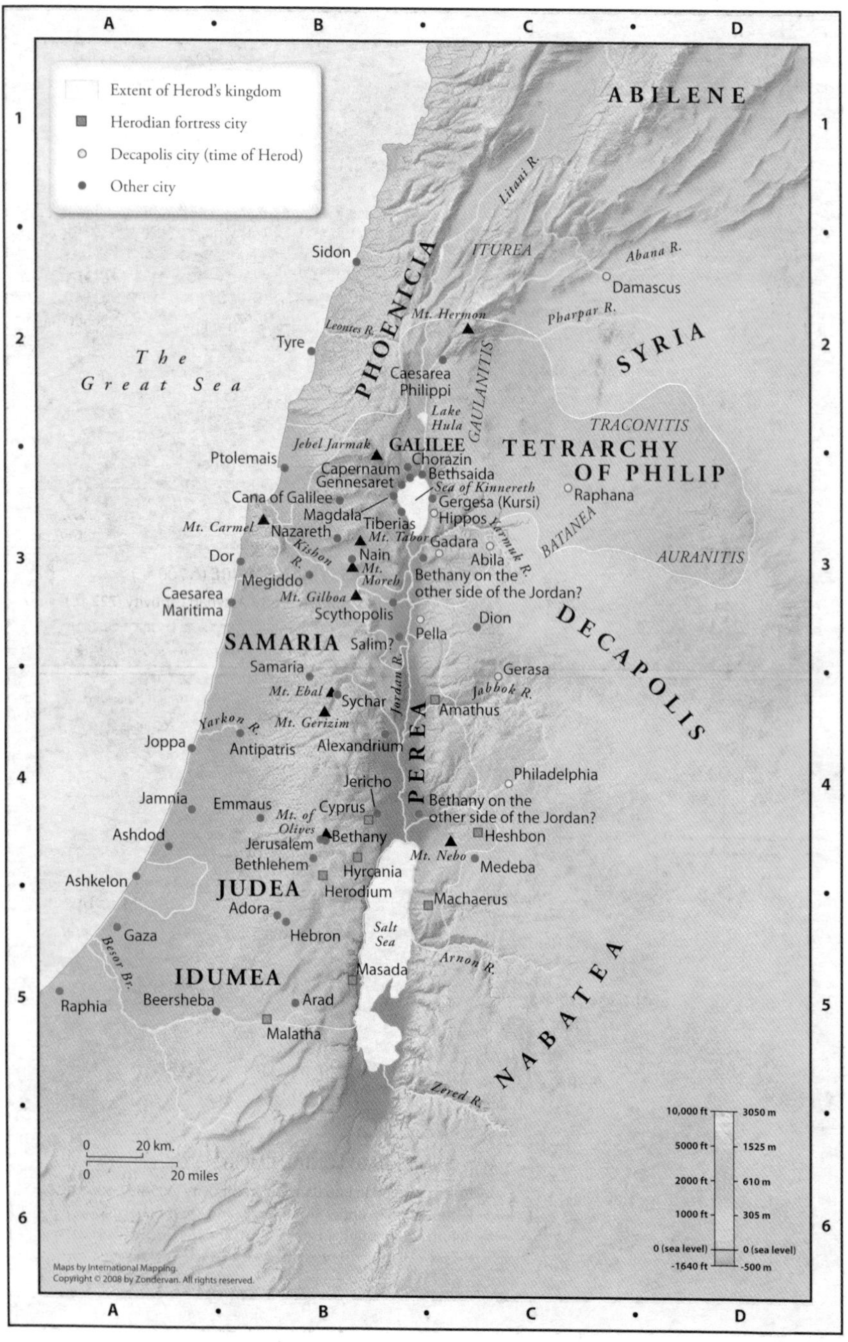

A
B
C
D
1
2
3
4
5
6
Extent of Herod's kingdom
Herodian fortress city
Decapolis city (time of Herod)
Other city
ABILENE
Litani R.
ITUREA
Abana R.
Damascus
Sidon
PHOENICIA
Mt. Hermon
Pharpar R.
Leontes R.
Tyre
SYRIA
The Great Sea
Caesarea Philippi
GAULANITIS
Lake Hula
TRACONITIS
Jebel Jarmak
GALILEE
TETRARCHY OF PHILIP
Ptolemais
Chorazin
Capernaum
Bethsaida
Gennesaret
Sea of Kinnereth
Raphana
Cana of Galilee
Gergesa (Kursi)
Magdala
Tiberias
Hippos
Mt. Carmel
Nazareth
Mt. Tabor
BATANEA
Yarmuk R.
Kishon R.
Gadara
Dor
Nain
Abila
AURANITIS
Mt. Moreh
Megiddo
Bethany on the other side of the Jordan?
Caesarea Maritima
Mt. Gilboa
Scythopolis
Dion
DECAPOLIS
Pella
SAMARIA
Salim?
Samaria
Gerasa
Jordan R.
Jabbok R.
Mt. Ebal
Sychar
Amathus
Yarkon R.
Mt. Gerizim
Joppa
Antipatris
Alexandrium
PEREA
Philadelphia
Jericho
Jamnia
Emmaus
Cyprus
Bethany on the other side of the Jordan?
Mt. of Olives
Ashdod
Bethany
Heshbon
Jerusalem
Mt. Nebo
Bethlehem
Medeba
Hyrcania
Ashkelon
JUDEA
Herodium
Machaerus
Adora
Salt Sea
Gaza
Hebron
Besor Br.
Arnon R.
Masada
IDUMEA
NABATEA
Raphia
Beersheba
Arad
Malatha
Zered R.
0 20 km.
0 20 miles
10,000 ft 3050 m
5000 ft 1525 m
2000 ft 610 m
1000 ft 305 m
0 (sea level) 0 (sea level)
-1640 ft -500 m
Maps by International Mapping.
Copyright © 2008 by Zondervan. All rights reserved.

Map 10: **JERUSALEM IN THE TIME OF JESUS**

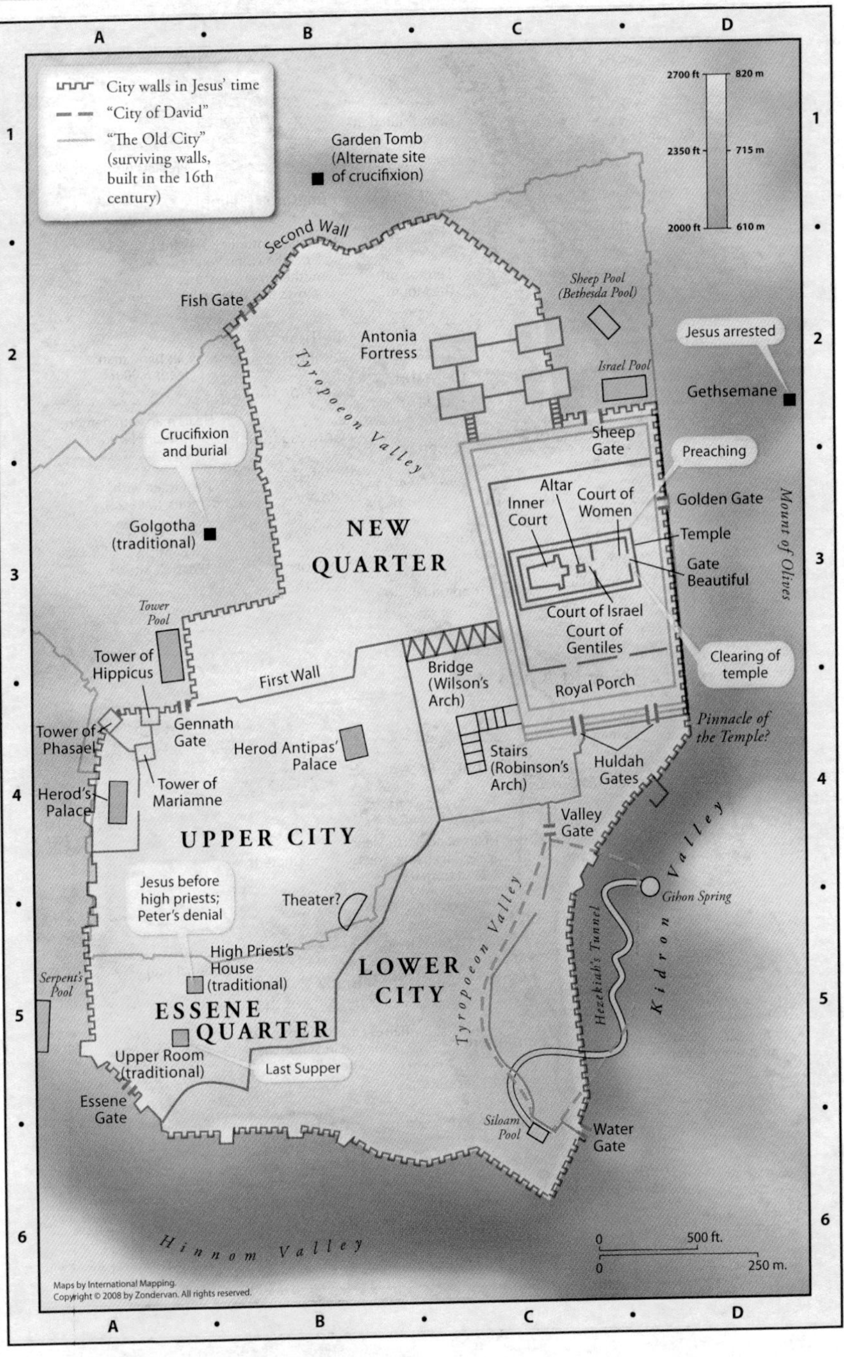
A
B
C
D
1
2
3
4
5
6
City walls in Jesus' time
"City of David"
"The Old City" (surviving walls, built in the 16th century)
Garden Tomb (Alternate site of crucifixion)
2700 ft
820 m
2350 ft
715 m
2000 ft
610 m
Second Wall
Fish Gate
Sheep Pool (Bethesda Pool)
Antonia Fortress
Jesus arrested
Israel Pool
Gethsemane
Tyropoeon Valley
Crucifixion and burial
Sheep Gate
Preaching
Altar
Inner Court
Court of Women
Golden Gate
Mount of Olives
Golgotha (traditional)
NEW QUARTER
Temple
Gate Beautiful
Court of Israel
Court of Gentiles
Tower Pool
Tower of Hippicus
Clearing of temple
First Wall
Bridge (Wilson's Arch)
Royal Porch
Pinnacle of the Temple?
Tower of Phasael
Gennath Gate
Herod Antipas' Palace
Stairs (Robinson's Arch)
Huldah Gates
Herod's Palace
Tower of Mariamne
Valley Gate
UPPER CITY
Kidron Valley
Jesus before high priests; Peter's denial
Theater?
Gihon Spring
Tyropoeon Valley
Hezekiah's Tunnel
High Priest's House (traditional)
LOWER CITY
Serpent's Pool
ESSENE QUARTER
Upper Room (traditional)
Last Supper
Essene Gate
Siloam Pool
Water Gate
Hinnom Valley
0
500 ft.
0
250 m.
Maps by International Mapping.

Map 11: **JESUS' MINISTRY**

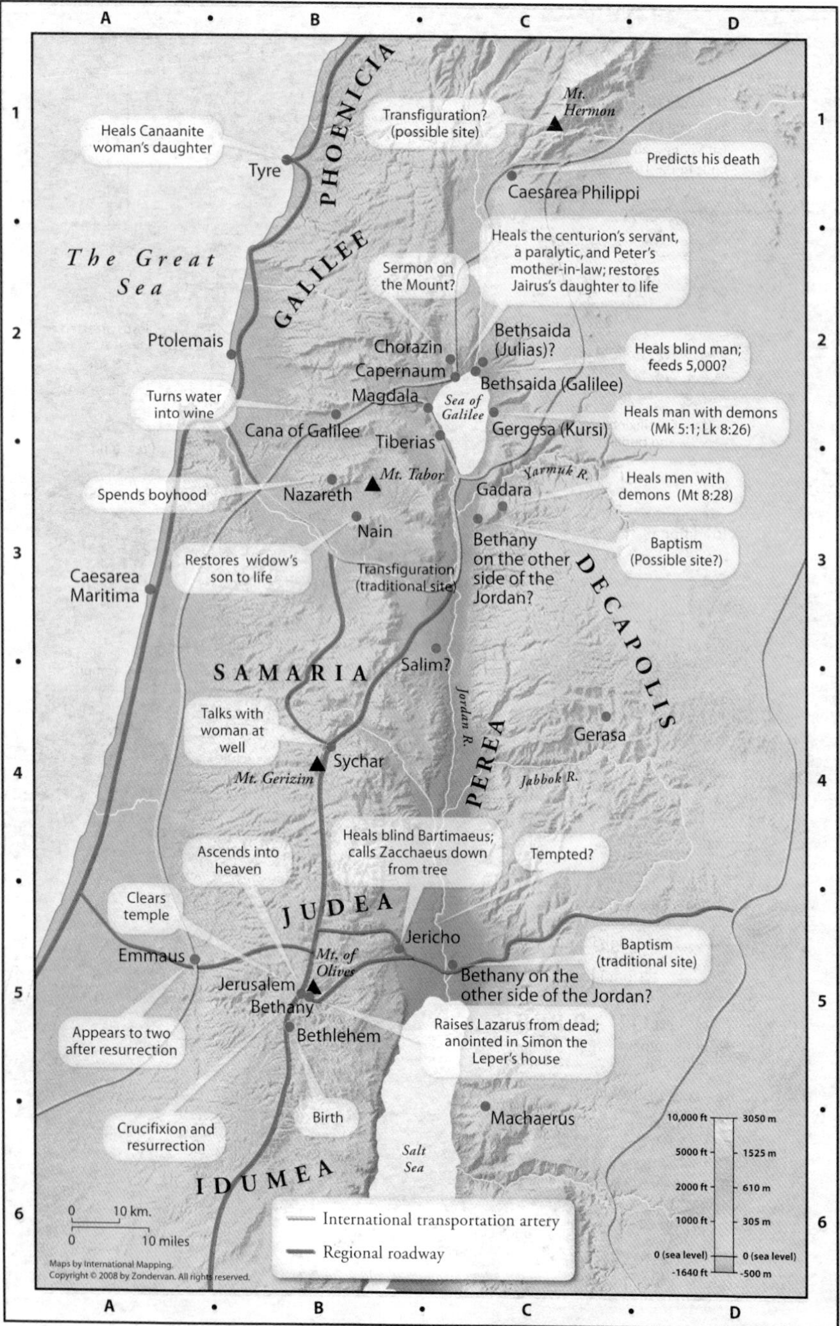

A
B
C
D
1
2
3
4
5
6
PHOENICIA
Mt. Hermon
Transfiguration? (possible site)
Heals Canaanite woman's daughter
Tyre
Predicts his death
Caesarea Philippi
The Great Sea
GALILEE
Heals the centurion's servant, a paralytic, and Peter's mother-in-law; restores Jairus's daughter to life
Sermon on the Mount?
Ptolemais
Chorazin
Capernaum
Bethsaida (Julias)?
Heals blind man; feeds 5,000?
Bethsaida (Galilee)
Turns water into wine
Magdala
Sea of Galilee
Heals man with demons (Mk 5:1; Lk 8:26)
Cana of Galilee
Tiberias
Gergesa (Kursi)
Mt. Tabor
Yarmuk R.
Spends boyhood
Nazareth
Gadara
Heals men with demons (Mt 8:28)
Nain
Bethany on the other side of the Jordan?
Baptism (Possible site?)
Restores widow's son to life
Transfiguration (traditional site)
Caesarea Maritima
DECAPOLIS
SAMARIA
Salim?
Jordan R.
Talks with woman at well
Gerasa
Sychar
PEREA
Mt. Gerizim
Jabbok R.
Ascends into heaven
Heals blind Bartimaeus; calls Zacchaeus down from tree
Tempted?
Clears temple
JUDEA
Jericho
Emmaus
Mt. of Olives
Baptism (traditional site)
Jerusalem
Bethany
Bethany on the other side of the Jordan?
Appears to two after resurrection
Bethlehem
Raises Lazarus from dead; anointed in Simon the Leper's house
Birth
Machaerus
Crucifixion and resurrection
Salt Sea
IDUMEA
0 10 km.
0 10 miles
International transportation artery
Regional roadway
10,000 ft 3050 m
5000 ft 1525 m
2000 ft 610 m
1000 ft 305 m
0 (sea level) 0 (sea level)
-1640 ft -500 m

Maps by International Mapping.

Map 12: **APOSTLES' EARLY TRAVELS**

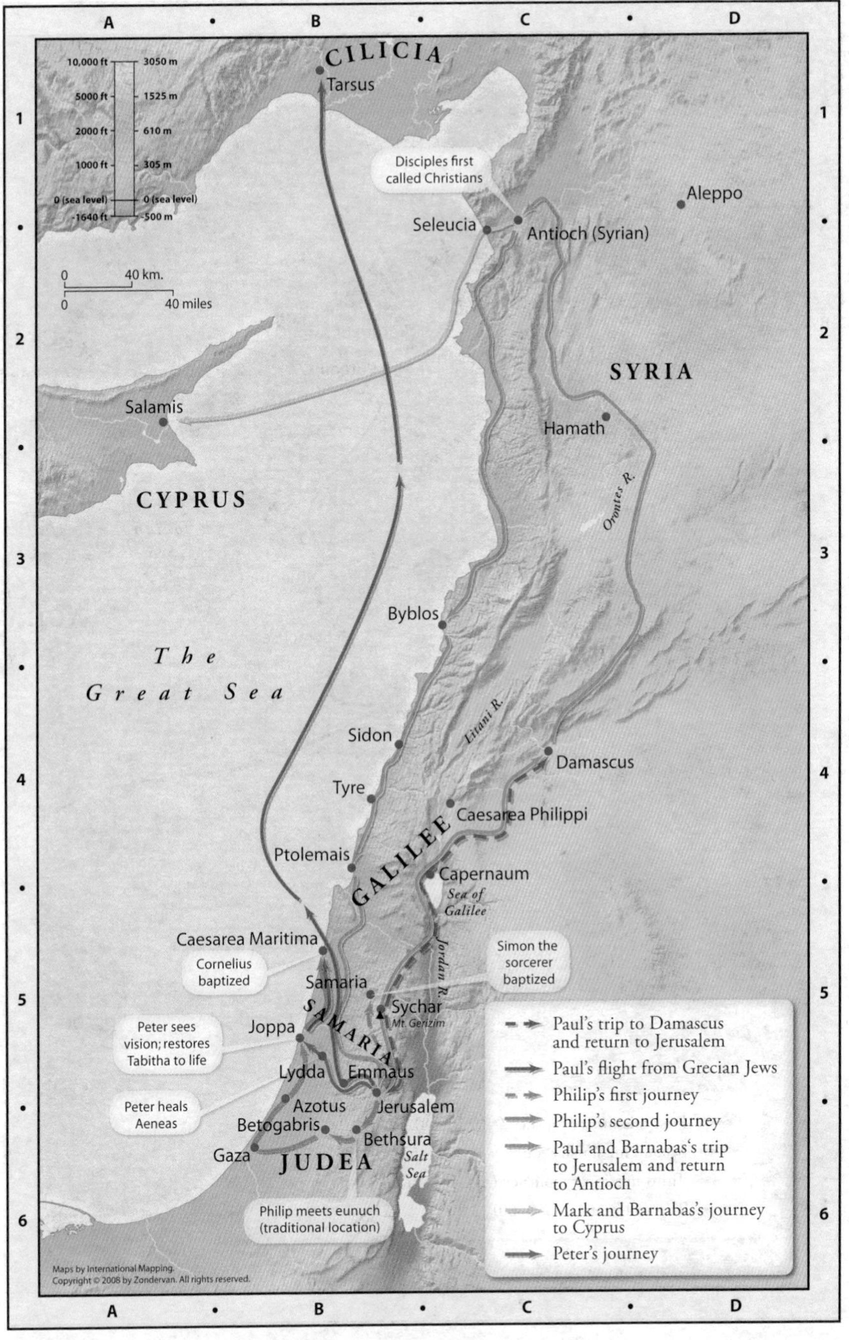

A • B • C • D
1
2
3
4
5
6
10,000 ft 3050 m
5000 ft 1525 m
2000 ft 610 m
1000 ft 305 m
0 (sea level) 0 (sea level)
-1640 ft -500 m
0 40 km.
0 40 miles
CILICIA
Tarsus
Disciples first called Christians
Aleppo
Seleucia
Antioch (Syrian)
SYRIA
Salamis
Hamath
CYPRUS
Orontes R.
Byblos
The Great Sea
Litani R.
Sidon
Damascus
Tyre
Caesarea Philippi
GALILEE
Ptolemais
Capernaum
Sea of Galilee
Caesarea Maritima
Cornelius baptized
Jordan R.
Simon the sorcerer baptized
Samaria
SAMARIA
Sychar
Mt. Gerizim
Peter sees vision; restores Tabitha to life
Joppa
Lydda
Emmaus
Peter heals Aeneas
Azotus
Jerusalem
Betogabris
Bethsura
Gaza
JUDEA
Salt Sea
Philip meets eunuch (traditional location)
Paul's trip to Damascus and return to Jerusalem
Paul's flight from Grecian Jews
Philip's first journey
Philip's second journey
Paul and Barnabas's trip to Jerusalem and return to Antioch
Mark and Barnabas's journey to Cyprus
Peter's journey

Map 13: **PAUL'S MISSIONARY JOURNEYS**

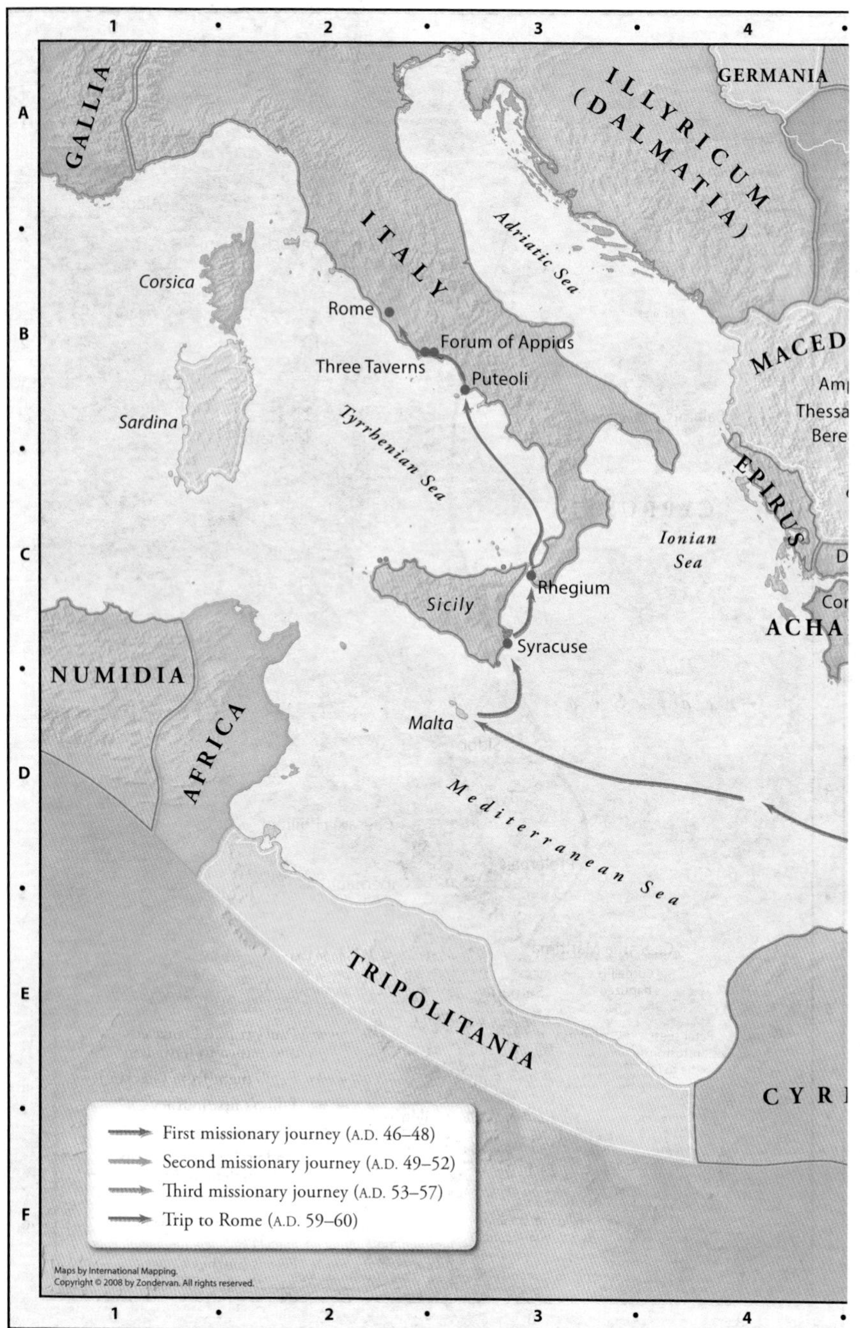

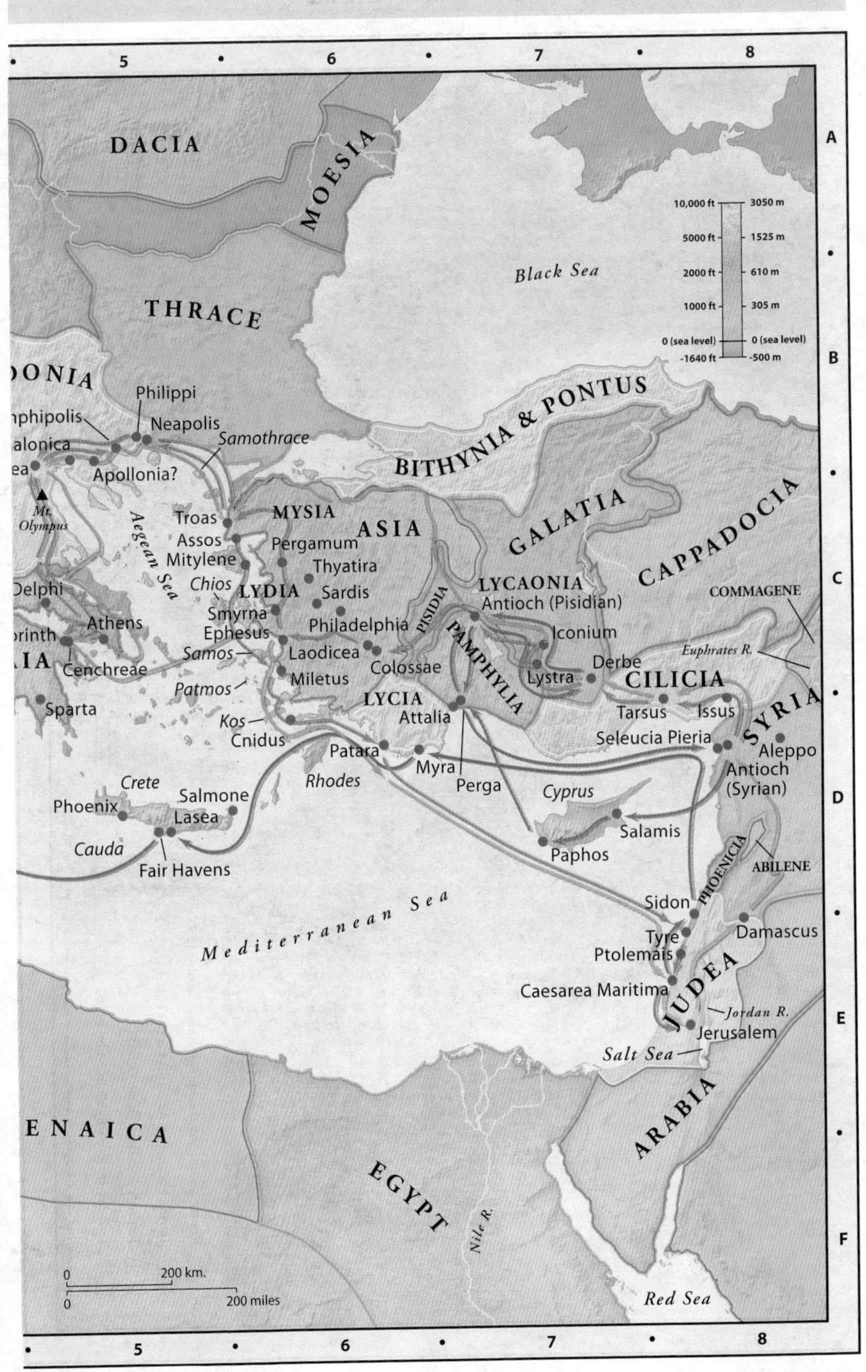
5
6
7
8
A
B
C
D
E
F
DACIA
MOESIA
THRACE
Black Sea
10,000 ft
3050 m
5000 ft
1525 m
2000 ft
610 m
1000 ft
305 m
0 (sea level)
0 (sea level)
-1640 ft
-500 m
BITHYNIA & PONTUS
GALATIA
CAPPADOCIA
Philippi
Neapolis
Samothrace
Apollonia?
Mt. Olympus
Aegean Sea
Troas
MYSIA
ASIA
Assos
Pergamum
Mitylene
Thyatira
Chios
LYDIA
Sardis
Delphi
Smyrna
Philadelphia
Athens
Ephesus
Samos
Laodicea
Colossae
Cenchreae
Miletus
Patmos
Sparta
Kos
Cnidus
LYCIA
Attalia
Patara
Myra
Perga
Rhodes
Crete
Phoenix
Salmone
Lasea
Cauda
Fair Havens
PISIDIA
PAMPHYLIA
LYCAONIA
Antioch (Pisidian)
Iconium
Lystra
Derbe
CILICIA
Tarsus
Issus
COMMAGENE
Euphrates R.
SYRIA
Seleucia Pieria
Aleppo
Antioch (Syrian)
Cyprus
Salamis
Paphos
PHOENICIA
ABILENE
Sidon
Tyre
Ptolemais
Damascus
Caesarea Maritima
JUDEA
Jordan R.
Jerusalem
Salt Sea
Mediterranean Sea
ENAICA
EGYPT
Nile R.
ARABIA
Red Sea
0
200 km.
0
200 miles

Map 14: **ROMAN EMPIRE**

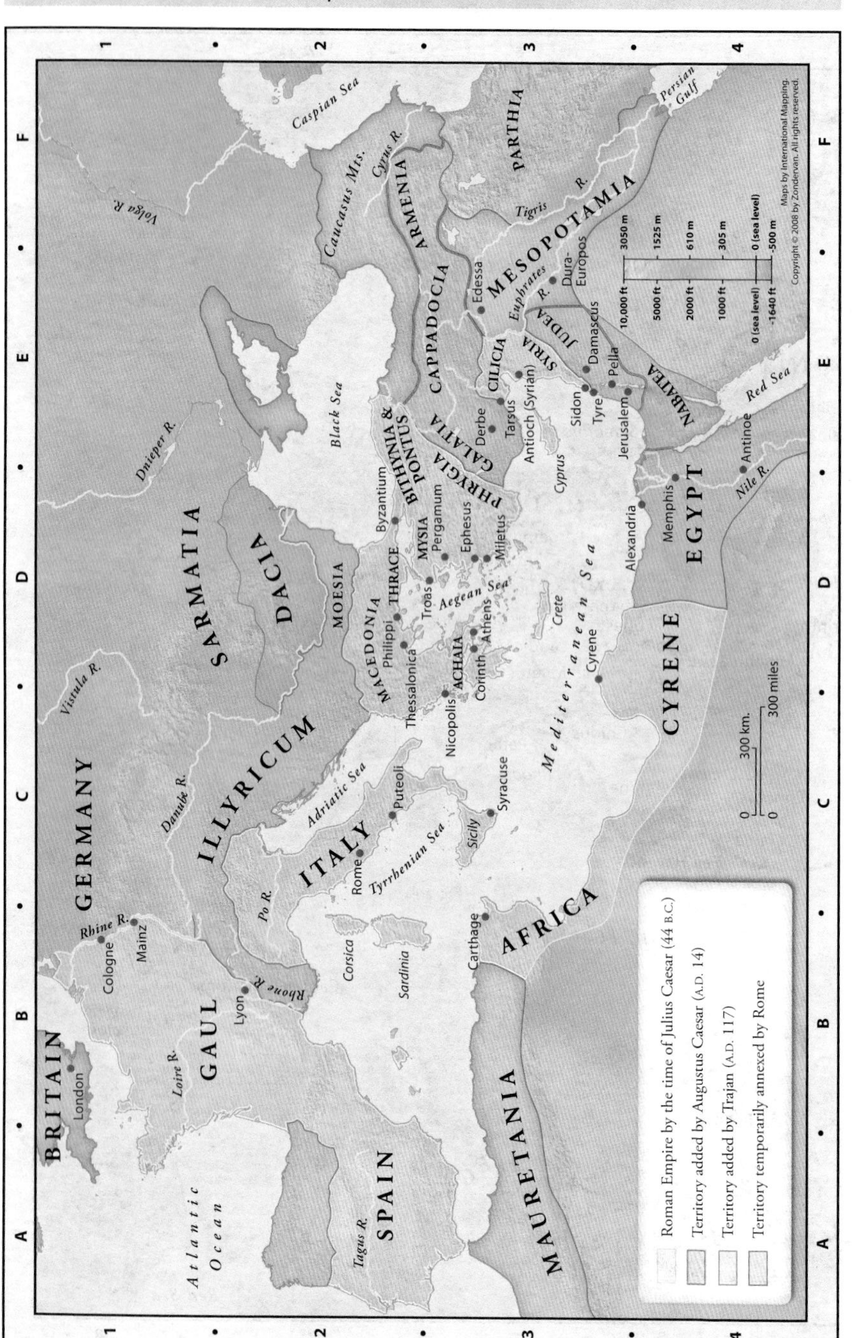